Pronunciation Table

Consonants 子音/輔音

K.K.	IPA	KEY WORD 範例
p	p	**p**en
b	b	**b**ack
t	t	**t**en
d	d	**d**ay
k	k	**k**ey
g	ɡ	**g**et
f	f	**f**at
v	v	**v**iew
θ	θ	**th**ing
ð	ð	**th**en
s	s	**s**oon
z	z	**z**ero
ʃ	ʃ	**sh**ip
ʒ	ʒ	plea**s**ure
h	h	**h**ot
x	x	lo**ch**
tʃ	tʃ	**ch**eer
dʒ	dʒ	**j**ump
m	m	su**m**
n	n	su**n**
ŋ	ŋ	su**ng**
w	w	**w**et
l	l	**l**et
r	r	**r**ed
j	j	**y**et

	K.K.	IPA	KEY WORD 範例
short 短音	ɪ	ɪ	b**i**t
	ɛ	e	b**e**d
	æ	æ	c**a**t
	ɑ	ɒ	p**o**t
	ʌ	ʌ	b**u**t
	ʊ	ʊ	p**u**t
	ə	ə	**a**bout
	ɪ	i	happ**y**
	ʊ	u	act**u**ality
long 長音	i	iː	sh**ee**p
	ɑ	ɑː	f**a**ther
	ɔ	ɔː	f**our**
	u	uː	b**oo**t
	ɝ	ɜː	b**ir**d
diphthongs 雙母音	e	eɪ	m**a**k**e**
	aɪ	aɪ	l**ie**
	ɔɪ	ɔɪ	b**oy**
	o	əʊ	n**o**t**e**
	aʊ	aʊ	n**ow**
	ɪr	ɪə	r**ear**
	ɛr	eə	h**air**
	ʊr	ʊə	s**ure**
	uə	uə	act**ual**
	jɚ	iə	pecul**iar**

Special signs 特別符號

;	此符號之左邊為 K.K. 音標 *，右邊為 IPA 音標 * *。K.K. 音標所標示的是美國音; IPA 音標所標示的是英國音。
/ˋ/, /ˈ/	表示主重音。
/ˏ/, /ˌ/	表示次重音。
/◂/	表示重音轉移。
/ᵻ/	表示有些人以 /ɪ/ 發音，有些人以 /ə/ 發音。
/ᵿ/	表示有些人以 /ʊ/ 發音, 有些人以 /ə/ 發音。
/*ə*/	表示 /ə/ 可發音可不發音。

* K.K. 音標是由美國兩位語言學家 John S. Kenyon 和 Thomas A. Knott 共同研究出來的，故取二人姓氏第一個字母而簡稱為 K.K. 音標。其特點是按照一般的美國讀法標音。

* * 本辭典所用的 IPA 音標是英國 Jones 音標的最新修訂形式。

關於讀音的更多信息, 參見第 xxvi 頁

當代高級辭典

(英英・英漢雙解)

LONGMAN DICTIONARY
of
Contemporary English

(English-Chinese)

This edition is published under the imprint of Longman, which is an imprint of Pearson Education Group.

Published by
Pearson Education Asia Limited
18/F Cornwall House, Taikoo Place, 979 King's Road
Quarry Bay, Hong Kong
Tel: 3181 0000
Fax: 2565 7440
E-mail: info@ilongman.com
Website: http://www.ilongman.com

培生教育出版亞洲有限公司
香港鰂魚涌英皇道 979 號太古坊康和大廈十八樓
電話：3181 0000
圖文傳真：2565 7440
電子郵遞：info@ilongman.com
網址：http://www.ilongman.com

First published 2004
Third impression 2005
二○○四年初版
二○○五年第三次印刷

ISBN 962 00 5271 4

Produced by Pearson Education Asia Ltd., Hong Kong

CTPSC/03

The publisher's policy is to use **paper manufactured from sustainable forests**

當代高級辭典

(英英・英漢雙解)

LONGMAN DICTIONARY of Contemporary English

(English-Chinese)

第三版
Third Edition

英漢雙解版工作人員名單

出版人 Publishers
- 吳天祝 T C Goh
- 李朋義 Li Pengyi

主審 Chief Reviser
- 汪榕培 Wang Rongpei

審訂 Revisers
- 區　鉷 Ou Hong
- 楊枕旦 Yang Zhendan
- 陳德彰 Chen Dezhang
- 夏祖煃 Xia Zukui

翻譯 Translators
- 王立弟 Wang Lidi
- 王峻岩 Wang Junyan
- 王逢鑫 Wang Fengxin
- 李紅梅 Li Hongmei
- 李景峯 Li Jingfeng
- 楊信彰 Yang Xinzhang
- 楊鎮明 Yang Zhenming
- 吳建平 Wu Jianping
- 宋志平 Song Zhiping
- 張顯奎 Zhang Xiankui
- 陳永培 Chen Yongpei
- 陳　凱 Chen Kai
- 柯克爾 Ke Ke'er
- 龔少瑜 Gong Shaoyu
- 常晨光 Chang Chenguang
- 梁衛紅 Liang Weihong
- 韓　紅 Han Hong
- 蔡關平 Cai Guanping
- 霍慶文 Huo Qingwen
- 戴瑞亮 Dai Ruiliang
- 楊枕旦（新詞） Yang Zhendan

	培生教育出版亞洲有限公司	外語教學與研究出版社
策劃編輯 Managing Editors	黃子昭 T C Wong	許海峯 Xu Haifeng
責任編輯 Executive Editors	陳麗敏 Lilian Chan；譚乃英 Tam Laying；謝福榮 Floyd Xie	楊鎮明 Yang Zhenming
編校人員 Editors and Proofreaders	余　遠 Brenda Yu；黃奇芳 Alice Wong；張康樂 Allan Chang；趙嘉文 Aman Chiu；管燕紅 Laura Guan；朱建中 Jackson Zhu；梁　路 John Liang；馮　奕 Fellow Feng；張瑾之 Kitty Zhang；勵　嘉 Lian Li	王　瑩 Wang Ying；車雲峯 Che Yunfeng；任玲娟 Ren Lingjuan；許海峯 Xu Haifeng；李　雲 Li Yun；張紅岩 Zhang Hongyan；沈中鋒 Shen Zhongfeng；羅來鷗 Luo Lai'ou；周子平 Zhou Ziping；周渝毅 Zhou Yuyi；周懿行 Zhou Yixing；趙岩華 Zhao Yanhua；徐　寧 Xu Ning；董燕萍 Dong Yanping
封面設計 Graphic Designers	梁若基 Timothy Leung	牛茜茜 Niu Qianqian
排版人員 Pagemaking	楊笑芬 Iris Yeung；王　瑩 Annie Wang；姚　琍 Judy Yao；趙平聲 Adam Zhao；張　慧 Amy Zhang；唐麗佳 Gail Tang	
新詞光碟製作人員 CD-ROM Production	周淑明 Christine Chow；容嘉敏 Gemma Yung；石礦明 Richard Shi；尹亞林 Yin Ya Lin；鄢　威 Lake Yan；夏靄瑩 Amy Xia；劉　柳 Liu Liu；李偉文 Li Wei Wen；崔玲美 Eolande Cui；盧劍飛 Lu Jian Fei	

The publishers and editorial team wish to thank the many people who have contributed advice to the making of the dictionary, in particular the Linglex Dictionary and Corpus Advisory Committee 本辭典英文版的出版者和編輯人員謹向曾為本辭典的編纂提供寶貴建議的多位人士致謝，特別向 Linglex 辭典與語料庫顧問委員會以下人士致謝:

Lord Quirk (Chair 主席)

Professor Douglas Biber, Rod Bolitho, Professor Gillian Brown, Professor David Crystal, Professor Geoffrey Leech, Dr Paul Meara, Philip Scholfield, Professor Peter Trudgill, Katie Wales, Professor John Wells

and also to Professor Yoshihiko Ikegami and the many teachers and students throughout the world who have given us feedback and advice, and helped in the piloting of the dictionary. 還要感謝 Yoshihiko Ikegami 教授以及世界各地的許多教師和學生，他們曾給我們反饋和建議，並在本辭典創意方面給予幫助。

Director
Della Summers

Editorial Director
Adam Gadsby

Associate Lexicographer
Sue Engineer

Usage Notes
Phil Scholfield, Ingrid Freebairn

Senior Editor (American English)
Wendalyn Nichols

Lexicographers (American English)
Karen Cleveland Marwick, Elaine McGregor, Karen Stern

Corpus development and computational analysis
Steve Crowdy, Denise Denney, Keith Mardell, Duncan Pettigrew

Frequency analysis and graphs
Nick Ham, Brigitta Mittmann, Sylvia Shaw, Dewayne Crawford, Adrienne Gavin

Computational Linguist
Adam Kilgarriff

Project Manager
Alan Savill

Production
Clive McKeough

Production Editors
Sarah Gumbrell, Alison Steadman, Benjamin White

Administrative Assistants
Brenda Francis, Helen Spencer, Jane Whittle

Managing Editor
Michael Rundell

Developmental Lexicographer
Nick Ham

Senior Editors (British English)
Chris Fox, Patrick Gillard, Ted Jackson, Stella O'Shea

Lexicographers (British English)
Peter Blanchard, Pat Bulhosen, Emma Campbell, Jane Hansell, Lucy Hollingworth, Jill Leatherbarrow, Joanna Leigh, Sophie Leighton, Helen McClelland, Glennis Pye, Sylvia Shaw, Laura Wedgeworth and Evadne Adrian-Vallance, Andrew Delahunty, Sheila Dignen, Gilian Lazar, Fiona McIntosh, Carole Owen, Elaine Pollard, Valerie Smith, Penny Stock

Pronunciation Editor
Dinah Jackson

Defining Vocabulary Research
Patrick Snellings

Design
Jenny Fleet, Martin Raynor, Kathy Baxendale, Ken Brooks

Illustrators
Dave Bowyer, Colin Brown, David Browne, Andrew Clark, Bob Corley, Paul B Davies, Diane Fawsett, Sian Francis, Bob Harvey, Jason Horley, Bill Le Fever, Andrew Riley, Andy Walker, Ross Watton, Kevin White

Keyboarders
Pauline Savill, Michelle Kemp

Contents

目　　錄

Language Notes 語言提示

Appendices 附錄

To Our Readers

致 讀 者

我們作為辭典的編輯人員，經常給人們問到以下的問題：辭典為甚麼要出新版？新版辭典中大部分的收詞還不是與舊的版本相同的嗎？這豈不是一項十分簡單容易的工作？對，如果我們只是把舊版所收的詞彙搬字過紙，只是簡單地更正幾個手民之誤，這確實是十分簡單容易的工作。但是，一本辭典作為大眾學習語文的圭臬及了解世界文化的工具，為讀者提供語文上的指引，其編輯及製作必須力求完美，去蕪存菁。

我們相隔一段時間便出版新一版的辭典，當然不是搬字過紙那麼簡單。《朗文當代高級辭典》（英英．英漢雙解）（第三版）面世，距離一九九七年出版的第二版，不經不覺已有七個年頭。在這七年中，人類的各個方面也有長足的進展，亦發生了很多以往沒有出現的事故。語言作為文化的載體，必然反映了這些事物，而辭典作為語言的書面記錄，也需要進行相應的編修工作。《朗文當代高級辭典》（英英．英漢雙解）（第三版）的面世正是見證了這七年來整個世界的變化，尤其是英語世界的變化。

由於科技發達，社會的發展，新事物層出不窮，對舊事物也可能有新的認識、新的理解，因此每年在各個領域，如政治（Blairism 貝理雅主義）、經濟（bancassurance 銀行保險業）、科技（bluetooth 藍芽技術）、醫學（biopharmaceutical 生物製藥）、運動（boogie board 臥式短衝浪板）、日常用品（lippy 口紅）等，亦不斷湧現新的詞語。按一些研究統計，每年產生的新詞由幾千至幾萬不等，這要視乎對新詞的界定、收集等各方面的標準而定。基本上，語言是活的，每天也在變化，只不過語言中某些層面的變化比較緩慢，例如句法方面，而另一些層面則比較容易察覺，例如新詞方面。此外，舊有的詞語也並非如一般人所想的一成不變，也會出現舊詞新用的情況，即是一些舊有的詞語有新的用法，例如"ill"一詞，一般解作"不健康的"、"有害的"的意思，現在也出現了新的用法，解作"很棒的"。如果一本辭典沒有系統地收編這些新詞、新的用法，讀者在查考這些詞彙時便得空手而回，那本辭典也就是沒有盡其補苴罅漏的功能。當然，修訂舊版中的錯漏及不足之處也是編製新版時的重要工作之一，這是不可或缺的。

《朗文當代高級辭典》（英英．英漢雙解）（第三版）收錄了 80,000 條詞目，提供了 200 項用法說明，詳細講解詞語間的細微區別和正確用法，加上 20 頁語言提示介紹語用學的知識，讓讀者不單知道個別詞彙本身的意義，還能夠根據不同語境選擇恰當的用語來遣詞造句。此外，本辭典更附有 24 頁全彩色插頁，讓讀者可以更具體地了解各種表物詞彙。新增的 IELTS（國際英語水平測試）常考詞彙表更加能夠協助將會參加這一考試的讀者作好準備。

隨著資訊科技的發展，現今可以利用以往沒有的媒體形式，以更生動、更美觀和更有效的方式，向讀者提供詞彙訊息，就正如《朗文當代高級辭典》（英英．英漢雙解）（第三版）免費附送新詞電腦光碟，內有釋義、英美讀音、圖片及短片，以嶄新的方式為讀者提供新詞的資料，這是舊版《朗文當代高級辭典》所無可媲美的。

正如上文所說，我們在編製《朗文當代高級辭典》(英英 · 英漢雙解)(第三版) 時均是根據嚴謹的編纂準則，悉力以赴，力求本辭典的各個方面準確無誤。雖然如此，在編製過程中難免有所錯漏，希望各讀者鑒諒，並提出批評及建議，我們必定會虛心接納，這是編製辭書的從業員應有的態度，也是提升素質的不二法門，從而讓我們這部辭書能夠盡善盡美，為更多讀者帶來裨益。

最後，謹向參與辭典編輯工作的所有人員致衷心感謝，當中包括譯者、編審、編輯、美術、排版、校對、光盤製作人員等等，沒有他們的努力，《朗文當代高級辭典》(英英 · 英漢雙解)(第三版)不可能如期出版，他們日以繼夜地工作，其熱誠實在令人感動。

培生教育出版亞洲有限公司
辭典部
2004年5月

Preface 1

序 言 一

我喜歡《朗文當代高級英語辭典》，早在 1983 年我的《實用英語詞彙學》中就把它的 1978 年版列入向學生推薦的兩部辭典之一 。二十多年過去了,《朗文當代高級英語辭典》1987 年出了第二版，1995 年出了第三版，2003 年出了第四版，這部辭典也在與時俱進 。所以，當外研社前年要我擔當這部辭典雙解版的主審工作時，我正好剛剛退休，時間比較充裕了，於是就欣然接受了這項工作 。

我之所以把《朗文當代高級英語辭典》列入向學生推薦的辭典，主要因為它特別適合學生的需要: 收詞量適中（80,000 詞），釋義用詞簡單（2,000 定義詞），標注了詞的使用頻率（1,000、2,000、3,000 常用詞），大量搭配和取自語料庫的例句，標明詞的正式程度、口語詞還是筆語詞、美國用語還是英國英語等，再加上用法説明、詞語辨析、口筆語使用頻率對比、精美的插圖等等，確實使這部辭典不僅是一般意義上的語言工具書，而且是外國學生學習英語的良師益友 。2001 年出版的第三版增補本又加上了 64 頁新詞語，更是學習、研究和使用新詞語的好幫手 。

《朗文當代高級英語辭典》的這些優點使它成為一部世界知名的優秀辭典，但是要給中國學生使用，畢竟還缺少詞語的漢語對應詞，有些例句偏難而不容易理解，給讀者帶來一定的不便 。例如，broccoli 的英語釋義是 a green vegetable that has short branch-like stems，中國學生看了這個定義之後可能還是沒有明白，有了漢語定義“西蘭花菜”再看一看插圖就甚麼問題都解決了 。又如，在 buck the trend 這一搭配後面有這樣的例句: The growth of the company has bucked the current recessionary trend in the industry，例句中的某些單詞讀者可能不認識，有了漢語翻譯“公司的發展頂住了該行業目前衰退的趨勢”，讀者在準確理解英語句子的同時可能還學到了新的英語單詞 。

《朗文當代高級辭典》（英英 / 英漢雙解）的出版，解決了中國學習者在使用中會遇到的上述難題，彌補了僅使用英英版的不足，其學習功效也遠遠超過一般的漢英辭典，從而成為中國各種程度英語學習者的最佳選擇 。

有些英語學習者希望有一種速成的方法，能夠“三個月説一口流利的英語”、“一個月突破英語難關”（均為廣告用語），其實，這樣的速成途徑是沒有的 。學習英語是一個循序漸進的過程，需要日積月累的努力，而一部好的學習辭典就是不離左右、百問不煩的好教員，有《朗文當代高級辭典》（英英 / 英漢雙解）在身邊，掌握它的特點，學習英語的速度就會明顯加快; 入門以後，今後也會常看常新 。我自己現在也要經常查辭典 。

我希望這部辭典能給英語學習者帶來好處 。

主審

汪榕培

蘇州大學教授、博士生導師

2004 年 3 月 14 日於蘇州幽蘭齋

Preface 2

序 言 二

我一輩子離不開辭典。

在我女兒三歲的時候，看到我動輒搬動掀動厚厚的辭典查看，便問她的母親，"這是甚麼書，爸爸老是看不完？"

答:"辭典。"

問:"甚麼是辭典？"

答:"你爸爸有不認識的字，就從上面查。"

女兒大為驚奇，她叫道:"原來爸爸不認識的字有這麼多！"

是的，女兒説得對，我就是有那麼多不認識的字。我沒有受過正規的高等教育，各式辭典就是我的 college。我沒有讀過英語系，各種英漢、漢英、雙解、專業辭典、大詞典就是我的 English Department。我缺少格物致知的功夫，各種辭典和擴大了的辭典——百科全書就是我的 professor 和 director。

不知道算不算有點忘恩負義或者過河拆橋，用多了辭典，也發現了一些遺憾。多數辭典顯得老氣，解釋千篇一律，跟不上活鮮鮮的生活。重要的、常用的與多用的詞與生僻的、正在沒落和淘汰的詞混在一起，而新崛起、新引進的詞則更難在辭典中找到説明解釋。

這時候我得到了有關《朗文當代高級辭典》(第三版) 出版的喜訊。這一版辭典用雙色印刷，排版清晰易讀。內容全面更新，加了不少新詞新義。這個辭書還經過統計從眾多的單詞中找出了最常用的 1000 個、2000 個、3000 個英語單詞，並指出它們是經常用於書面或口語。這些資料對於有志於學習英語但是基礎與成效都不佳的人如鄙人者，實在是太方便，太管用了。

這一版辭典還提供了頻率表，例如它告訴讀者，像"absolutely"這個詞，一般人每説一百萬個單詞就會使用 180 次左右，絕了，你在別的辭書裡很難得到這樣的資料。

這一版辭典的解釋相對來説是簡單明瞭的，編纂者説，用來解釋詞義的詞，只有 2000 個常用詞彙，深入淺出，這當然是辭書最最實用之處。除了詞義之外，這一版辭典還提供了多種用法説明與語言提示。以 day 一詞為例，它是包括幼稚園的孩子都知道的一個詞。但看了《朗文當代高級辭典》(第三版)，你才恍然於它可以當 24 小時這樣的一段時間講，可以當白天講，可以當將來、過去、人的一生或物的壽命、工作、每天、現在、壞事發生、好事發生、快樂、成功 (出名)、口語片語和其他意思。而所舉的用 day 詞的例句並不罕見，並不牽強，你 (指我這樣的低水準讀者) 讀了這些例句，不但弄懂了 day 的用法，而且如聞英語説話者的談話，如讀淺顯明白的英語讀物，與中文"天"、

"日"、"日子"等詞比較，從中甚至學到一點英語文化和比較語言學。比如中文說"總有一天"或者"等到了這一天"或者"再沒有這一天啦"，這與辭書上的英語例句"sb's day will come"和"have had your day"相比，令查辭典者感到多麼親切雀躍！這是多麼給人以知識而且令人感到滿足的呀。

對於正在急起直追的國人來說，學習英語的重要性自不待言。有一本好辭典對於學習重要性又是不需說的。我只說一句，祖國內地有人耽憂學好了英語忽略了母語，我想這是極低層次的問題，對於多數觀念正常和有志有智的人來說，雙語、多語的基礎是母語，雙語、多語的素養應該是有助於學好用好母語。內地的同胞特別是青年人，大可以放膽放心地學好英語，為社會，為中華民族也為人類做出更多的有益的事。

王蒙
中國著名作家
文化部原部長
全國政治協商會議常務委員

Preface 3

序 言 三

市面上的辭典種類繁多,適合不同使用者的需求。但要成為一本為市場廣泛接受的辭典,的確是非常不容易做到的事情。辭典必須整體地符合學術上及市場上的要求,才會得到大家的認同及採用。我嘗試從這兩方面看看《朗文當代高級辭典》的表現。

學術上的要求有三方面。

(一)收詞廣泛

英漢辭典收詞數目由六萬至四、五十萬詞條不等,完全視乎辭典服務的對象而定。通常由中國學者編纂作一般用途的英漢辭典是介乎二十萬至五十萬條目,由英語辭典雙語化的外語學習辭典則在六萬與八萬條目之間。《朗文當代高級辭典》有八萬詞目,收詞方面是全面而適合,尤其是新詞的收錄更加別出心裁,另出電腦光碟,有讀音、插圖、錄像配合,令到印刷辭典與社會流行用語的節拍一致,這是非常重要的補足部分。而以圖標說明書面語及口語的常用程度更是值得推薦的特色,使用者要特別留意這些常用條目的意義及用法,避免使用時出現錯誤。辭典對於這些常用詞目一般篇幅都較大,可以從中得到不少語法信息。

(二)釋義詳盡

釋義包括兩方面: 文字解釋及圖片說明。辭典義項豐富,全部以二千個英文單字作為釋義用詞,簡單明瞭。圖片則產生強烈的視覺認知效果,對於普通名詞與文化詞目的了解更加直接了當。釋義在雙語化辭典的要求當然是要翻譯準確、流暢、地道。《朗文當代高級辭典》在這幾方面都做得非常出色。辭典字義及例句的翻譯有其獨特的地方,在語境不足夠的情況下,偶爾有些妙譯是神來之筆,可遇但不可以常求。辭典例句的翻譯最可行的辦法是在很少上下文的短句中細味其意思,然後作出準確、適當而具有示範作用的翻譯。

(三)用法說明

這是學習語言很重要的部分。我們一般將辭典分為 passive dictionary 與 active dictionary。前者着重詞彙的了解,後者着重詞彙的運用。《朗文當代高級辭典》是兩者俱備的辭典,釋義譯義力求準確易明,用法則以語言提示及用法說明講解詞義區別及正確用法。這些都是語言學習辭典不可或缺的部分。

市場上的要求則有二方面。

(一)出版權威

朗文出版社一七二四年在倫敦創立,今年剛好是二百八十年。這家著名出版社在一七五五年出版了全球第一本英文字典,明年將是二百五十年紀念。在英語辭典出版方面,朗文比世界上任何一家出版社都要早。這二百多年累積的編纂經驗是非常珍貴的。朗文在一九八八年將英文版的 Longman Dictionary of Contemporary English 雙語化,出版該社第一本雙語辭典《朗文當代英漢雙解辭典》，至今已有十六年。有二百多年的歷史作為後盾，經十多年的時間去更新完善，《朗文當代高級辭典》今日在市場上得到的權威地位是實至名歸的。

（二）時代語言

對大部分辭典使用者來說，辭典一定要照顧到時代的需要。權威的出版社固然重要，但如果收錄的詞彙重古輕今，例句與時代脱節，對學習現代英語、真實英語、英美英語作用不大。《朗文當代高級辭典》是根據大型的朗文語料庫及英國國家語料庫，從數以億計的當代常用書面語及口語細心挑選最適合的八萬詞條，並加入流行新詞，這代表時代語言，代表現在通行英語，是今日學習英語人士最需要掌握的語言，亦是辭典最需要提供的資訊。

陳善偉
香港中文大學翻譯系系主任
及翻譯系教授

Preface 4

序 言 四

十八世紀的英國文豪約翰生 (Samuel Johnson) 曾經說過:「編辭典算得是於人無害的苦差事。」此言帶幾分自謙、自嘲，也不無一點自慰，因為他自己獨力編寫的《英語詞典》(A Dictionary of the English Language)，僅例句一項就蒐羅了約十萬名句，不愧是英文辭典的扛鼎之作。他又認為:「辭典就像手錶; 即使最壞的也聊勝於無，而最好的也不能指望它完全正確。」

約翰生博士說得沒錯。再好的辭典也只能教人不犯錯，少犯錯，充其量只能教人寫出通順暢達的文章，卻無法提供文采與妙思。傑出的作家或學者，當然不能只靠一部好辭典。但是反過來說，再傑出的作家或學者也不敢自誇，他可以完全不靠辭典。我寫作中文與英文，已逾半世紀之久，可稱「資深」，也薄有虛名，但每成一文，仍不免再三翻核辭典，以求心安。

辭典可稱「案頭老師」，不但隨時可以請教，而且幾乎有問必答。讀者要把英文學通，必須勤翻辭典，最好是翻破幾本。一般人學英文，每從單字入手，而且以為單字記得越多越好。其實徒記單字而不會活用，反而會消化不良。例如 rainbow 或 strawberry 之類的單純名詞，當然多記一個是一個; 可是像 come 一類的常用動詞，定義既多，和其他字眼的搭配 (collocation) 亦多，如果只記得單字本身，其實無法左右逢源，用處有限。come 一字的搭配，所謂 phrasal verb (片語動詞)，就包括常用的 come across，come by，come down，come off，come on，come out，come up，come upon 等等; 如果都不會用，或者只是一知半解，就不能自命已經掌握 come 一字的全貌。

《朗文當代高級辭典》告訴我們，字的本身是靜態的，但與其他的字發生關係，就有了動態。例如發音、詞類、定義，都是一個字的靜態; 但是把它與其他的字搭配，甚至用在實際的句子裡，就有了動態。靜態可謂字的「生理」，動態可謂字的「生態」。《朗文當代高級辭典》在字詞的搭配與例句上，舉證豐富，把常用字的生態分得非常清楚。例如 *Only 7 people attended the meeting./Please let us know if you are unable to attend.* 這兩句例證就説明了，attend 作動詞用，可以「及物」，也可以「不及物」。至於 attend 之後加上 school 而不帶冠詞，意為「上學」，就成了一個習用的片語。

七年前我曾為《朗文當代高級辭典》英英 · 英漢雙解版的初版寫過序言。二○○四年新出的這第三版加了不少新項目，例如三千個常用單詞在書面語及口語中使用的頻率，對於以漢語為母語的讀者就十分有用。

冷戰結束以來，英文漸已成為世界語: 十三億的中國人與一億多的俄羅斯人都在學英文，數量之多，遠超過了英、美、加拿大、澳洲、紐西蘭的母語人口。但在另一方面，近日學起中文來的外國人，也已增至三千萬人。所以這部英漢雙解的朗文辭典，不但造福全球華人，而且可以反過來用，同樣有益於英語世界的中文讀者。

余光中
著名詩人，散文家
台灣中山大學外文系教授
2004年3月於高雄中山大學

Preface 5

序言五

實用第一

從英語辭典的編纂史看，如果說19世紀大眾的心理是將辭典看作語言規範的神聖權威，那麼到了20世紀辭典編纂者自己就在編纂觀念上發生了重大的變化，用“實用”的標準取代了“純正”的標準。法蘭西學院編纂的辭典在規範法語方面的力度大概是最大的，但是人們對它的評價毀譽參半。辭典編纂的這種觀念轉變與語法書編寫的觀念轉變是一致的，但要比後者晚一些。（見《哥倫比亞百科大辭典》2001年第6版“辭典”條）“純語主義”（purism）或“純語主義者”（purist）這樣的名稱在今天是多少帶有貶義色彩的。（見 David Crystal 編《語言學和語音學辭典》1997年第4版）

《朗文當代英語辭典》充分體現了“實用第一”的原則。首先，這部辭典用來釋義的英語詞彙限於2000個左右的基礎常用詞彙，這就給英語學習者帶來極大的自信和方便，因為不少英語學習者害怕或不願意查辭典的原因就是釋義艱深，不容易讀懂。編纂者顯然對詞義有敏銳和深入的語義分析，然後用淺顯準確的文字表達出來，像 marital status 條的釋義就是最好的例子。釋義的好壞高低也許是評價一部辭典的最重要的標準。

新版《朗文當代英語辭典》的另一個特色是收詞廣泛。它收錄純粹口頭使用的詞彙，其來源是根據錄音轉寫的自然口語的材料。它們完全是老百姓在日常生活中口頭使用的，不僅不見於一般的書面文字，也不見於電台電視的廣播節目。這種口頭詞彙在“純語主義者”看來也許是“不規範”的，如 better 一詞的多種口頭用法，但卻是一部實用辭典應該收錄的。第3版增補本還增補了64頁的新詞新義，其中有不少也是這種口頭詞彙。收詞廣度也是評價一部辭典的一條重要標準。

這部辭典還有一個特色是提供了可靠的詞彙使用頻率的信息。一個語詞或一個義項是常用的還是罕見的，常用的程度如何，這也是英語學習者最關心的問題。一般的反映當代語言實際使用情況的辭典，在詞項或義項的排列上總是依照當今使用頻率的高低，而不是依照它們歷史上出現的先後，這部辭典自然也遵循這一規則，而且還用統計圖表表明同義詞或近義詞的頻率比較，例如，在日常生活中 let 比 permit 更常用。此外辭典還特別標注出3000個最常用的詞彙。

現在這部辭典的第3版增補本又有了英漢雙解本，這對我國廣大的英語學習者來說是一件好事。它的編纂觀念和編纂方式對我國當代漢語辭典的編纂也提供了有益的啟示。

沈家煊

中國社會科學院語言研究所所長

2004年3月9日

Preface 6

序　言　六

在《朗文當代英語辭典》的序言中，夸克教授 (Prof. Randolph Quirk) 指出這本詞典的兩大特點: 一是收詞廣泛，涵蓋了現代生活的各個方面，詞典本版 (即第三版) 要比第二版多收詞語近五分之一; 二是釋文精確，是經過多名英美詞典編纂學家通過語文分析的努力結果。

《朗文當代英語辭典》除了以上兩大優點外，還有不少其他優越之處。我認為對讀者 (特別是中國讀者)，還應該指出這本詞典特別注重詞彙的用法，並且舉了大量的例證。記得有位英國學者曾說過: "一個單詞的意義要看它在語言中是如何運用的。" ("The meaning of a word is its use in the language.") 單個的詞很難確切理解它的意義。舉個具體的例子"chair"來說，一般懂點英語的人都知道是"椅子"的意思。但是如果我們說: "chair a meeting"，那麼這個"chair"就變成"主持 (會議)"了。也許有人會說"chair"原為名詞，現在變成動詞了，所以意思上發生了變化。那麼"hold the chair of philosophy at a university"呢？這裡的"chair"的意義變成"教授"了。又如"take the chair" (擔任會議主席)；"leave the chair" (宣告會議結束)；"Chair! Chair!" (表示對會議混亂的不滿)。由此可見，詞彙的意義要在它運用中理解和掌握。《朗文當代英語辭典》特別注意詞彙的慣用法 (usage)，就是這個道理。

談到詞的用法，我想在這裡特別強調一下搭配 (collocation) 的問題。英語裡的搭配對於學習英語的外國 (族) 人來說，不易掌握，就是對於有相當英語水平的從事把本國 (族) 語譯成英語的譯者也是如此。英國翻譯家紐馬克 (Peter Newmark) 說過: 把本族語譯成外語的人"每次出 '毛病' 不在語法方面，他的語法可能比一個受過教育的本族人還要 '好些'；也不在詞彙方面，也許他掌握的詞彙比本族人還要多些。他的 '毛病' 出在搭配上，他的搭配無法令人接受，難以成立。" ("He will be 'caught' every time not by his grammar, which is probably suspiciously 'better' than an educated native's, not by his vocabulary, which may well be wider, but by his unacceptable or improbable collocations.") *

《朗文當代英語辭典》內的常用搭配均用粗體字標明。例如詞彙 determination 下就有 dogged determination (=very strong determination); 而在詞條 grim 下第三義項有 grim determination (=serious determination in spite of difficulties or dangers)。一般中國學生會用 strong or great determination，但是不大會用 dogged or grim determination一類形容詞 + 名詞的搭配。再如 imagination，與之搭配的動詞詞典內註明用 catch or capture (sb's imagination)，這個詞可以搭配的動詞不多，除以上兩個動詞外，還有 seize, grip 等幾個。如果用別的動詞，一不小心就會在搭配上犯錯誤，變成中式英語。又如 glance (一瞥)，常用的搭配動詞是 give, take, shoot or throw a glance。如果用短語 at a glance，與之搭配的動詞有 know, see, tell, realize 等。

以上扼要說明本詞典的特點之一，即突出英語的搭配問題。相信這對中國讀者，特別是希望能在口筆頭運用英語的讀者，一定會很有幫助的。

程鎮球
外交部資深翻譯專家，曾參加
《香港特別行政區基本法》英文本
定稿工作，2001 年被授予
資深外事翻譯家稱號

* P. Newmark, Approaches to Translation, 1981, P. 180

Preface 7

序 言 七

朗文當代英語辭典（第三版增補本）的英英 · 英漢雙解版，即將由外語教學與研究出版社出版，以饗我國讀者。這是一件大好事。

朗文當代英語辭典（以後簡稱為LDOCE）是一本英語界享譽甚高的辭典，值得向我國英語學習者和使用者推薦。辭典的優點是有目共睹的，它體積不大，但容量豐富，收錄了80,000個詞條，而且十分注意英語學習者的需要，在釋義和舉例，習慣用法的解釋和説明方面，要言不煩。在辭典的編排上又很生動活潑，方便查閱。更重要的是，這也是一本頗具原創性的辭典，值得辭典編纂學者認真研究和借鑑的一本辭典。顧名思義，辭典是編纂出來的，而辭典所收集的詞語是人民羣眾在使用過程中創造的，不可能有甚麼"創造發明"。我所指的原創性是指辭典編纂中所使用的以語料庫為基礎的思路、方法和工具。

首先，朗文出版社（現在已重組為培生教育出版公司）開發了一個4000多萬詞語的朗文英語口語和書面語語料庫（Longman Spoken and Written English Corpus），LDOCE基本上是根據這個語料庫所收集的信息來編纂的，參加語料庫的建設和統計運算的專家有10人之多。語料庫對辭典編纂有很大的幫助，例如牛津英語大辭典就利用語料庫收集了不少例句。但是LDOCE是比較廣泛地利用所開發的語料庫，體現在如下的幾個方面:

1. 按語料庫的頻率所提供的信息來排列每個詞語的義項和搭配的先後，使用最多的排在最前。例如great這個多義詞，一般的辭典的第一個義項是"大的、巨大的"，而LDOCE根據語料庫的頻率排列，它的第一個義項卻是"very good"。

2. 標注出最常用的3000詞。這個工作始自Thorndike的初級英語辭典。但是Thorndike根據的是手工收集的語料，而朗文根據的是其自身建立的大型語料庫，而且使用了計算機來進行排列，比較準確。這個語料庫收集了口語和書面語，所以LDOCE能夠分別標明屬於口語和書面語的常用3000詞。例如possibly在口語裡屬於第1個1000詞，而在書面語裡，卻屬於第2個1000詞。poster在口語裡屬於第3個1000詞，但在書面語裡卻不屬於最常用的3000詞。

3. LDOCE是一本英語學習辭典，辭典使用的定義詞都是英語學習者看得懂的。不少英語學習辭典都是這樣做的，但LDOCE卻是通過計算機在語料庫認真檢查，保證定義詞屬於最常用的2000詞，而且還在200多個學生做過檢測，了解他們確實看懂定義，而且能正確翻譯成他們的母語。試比較LDOCE和另一本英語學習辭典對accursed的定義:

LDOCE: **1** [only before noun] *formal* very annoying and causing you a lot of trouble **2** *old use* someone who is accursed has had a CURSE[2] (2) put on them

另一本學習辭典: under a curse; detestable; hateful.

4. 有些常用的動詞詞組也用圖表示其頻率，如 begin to do sth 佔 40%，begin 單獨用佔 23% 左右，begin with 約佔 15%，begin sth 佔 10%，begin doing sth 佔 7% 左右， begin by doing sth 和其他各約佔 2–3%。

5. 使用同樣的語料庫的資源，朗文還出版了《朗文英語口語和筆語語法》(Longman Grammar of Spoken and Written English) 兩者互相補充使用，相得益彰 。

其次，作為一本學習辭典，LDOCE 是對用戶十分友好的 。 辭典收集的是詞，對語法本來是無須解釋的，但是詞本身也有語法問題，故有人提出詞彙語法 (lexico-grammar) 的概念 。LDOCE 對詞類、屈折變化、名詞、動詞、形容詞、副詞的有關語法均有所說明，例如 carpet 可作及物動詞用，但不能用作被動語態，故只能說 carpeted with glass/flowers 。又如副詞 happily 除了一般的副詞用法 (in a happy way) 外，還有另一個修飾句子的功能，表示"fortunately"的意思，而且專門注明[sentence adverb] 。 英語習慣用法很多，不易掌握，辭典還專門建立一些"路標"幫助學習者快速檢索 。 辭典還十分注意英美英語在用法上的一些區別，從釋義到插圖都有所說明 。

LDOCE 在我國要發行英英 · 英漢雙解版，這也是有益於中國英語學習者的一件大好事 。 我希望雙解版能夠保持和發揮原版的優點，而且在釋義上有所探索 。 例如原版的特點是用簡單的英語來進行釋義，雙解版應該怎樣處理？ 是把簡單的英語譯成簡單的漢語？ 還是譯成對應的漢語？ 各有優缺點 。 這需要徵詢中國英語學習者的意見 。 如果能夠根據中國人學習英語的特點和問題，有所說明，就更有針對性了 。

桂詩春
廣東外語外貿大學英語教授
博士生導師
2004 年 3 月16 日

Preface 8

序 言 八

學習英語，特別是從事翻譯或英語寫作，須臾離不開英漢、漢英和英英詞典，所謂詞典是良師益友、終身伴侶的說法，皆源於此。

唯其如此，選擇好一兩本權威的、適合於自己水平的詞典，至關緊要，甚至成了一門學問。

毫無疑問，在英語國家中，英國編寫和出版的詞典首屈一指。而朗文，又是英國英語詞典的四家大出版公司之一，與牛津、柯林斯與麥克米倫並駕齊驅。過去，英國出版的詞典找不到美國英語的詞彙和詞義，現在大多數英國詞典都囊括這些詞義和用法，並以Am符號標出。LDOCE也不例外。

手頭的這本詞典有幾大特色：

一，詞彙量大，用法現代，而且附了五十五頁的新詞。

二，英文詞義解釋通俗易懂，局限於兩千基本詞彙。

我一向主張，學英語學到了一定程度，就要使用英英詞典，看英語解釋，逐步習慣用英語思維，這是擺脫僅用中文思維的最好辦法。現在LDOCE又有了中文解釋，使用時可先看英文解釋，實在看不懂或有疑問時再借用中文拐棍，而不要直接進入中文部分。這種辦法能使雙解詞典充分發揮作用，避免中文部分取代英文部分。當然，有些詞，如花草鳥獸等動植物，還是要看中文解釋，甚至要靠圖解。

三，多義詞處理得當。

大家知道，多義詞是英語的一大特點，越是普通的詞，其含義越多。人們初學英語時，往往會忽略它的這一特點，因而犯"只知其一，不知其二"的錯誤。目前市場上有些小詞典尤其是電子詞典，它們提供的含義有限，更助長這種錯誤傾向。LDOCE注意了這個英語語言現象，在多義詞和複合詞方面下功夫，不僅對每個字的不同意思設有單獨詞條，而且在同一詞條內還介紹了不同用法。下面試以 school 一字為例加以說明。LDOCE羅列了school的七種不同意思和它的十五個複合字。又如top這樣常見的字，僅僅作為動詞和名詞，配以不同的介詞，就有許多不同的意思。LDOCE對top這個字的解釋，名詞就有二十七條，形容詞八條，動詞十條，複合詞三十一條。那麼，會不會出現另一種傾向，即失之於過繁，讓人無法或只有費力才能找到自己所需要的解釋呢？LDOCE是根據不同詞義在報刊和書籍中出現的頻率來排列先後次序的。這一做法很科學，至少我個人在使用時感到它既合理又便捷。

四，例句源於現實生活，通俗易懂，頗有參考價值。

學好英語，要掌握相當大的詞彙量，不僅要看懂，還要能夠使用，即要有“both passive and active command”。這對非“native English speaker”的人來説，十分困難。有的字經常是一看就懂，一用就錯，不是介詞錯了，就是搭配不對。所以，參考詞典的例句有百利而無一害。

我們説詞典是終身伴侶，這不等於終身使用同一本詞典。定期替換詞典，這不是喜新厭舊。我們處於知識爆炸時代，不僅新詞與日俱增，而且舊詞還會出現新意。何況我們自己的水平也會有所提高，對詞典會有更高的要求。同時詞典也在不斷改進。所以説，我們對詞典的需求是經久不衰的，但對某一本具體的詞典來説，儘管使用起來得心應手，到了某個階段就需要淘汰，不能抱殘守缺。思想要與時俱進，設備要不斷更新，此之謂也。

林戊蓀
中國翻譯工作者協會常務副會長
國家高級翻譯職稱評委會主任
《中國翻譯》雜誌主編
2004年3月

英文版序

衡量一部辭典的質量和成就，有兩個關鍵方面，即：

• 收詞範圍

• 釋義

就收詞範圍而言，一部辭典需要給予讀者信心，便必須收錄了他們需要理解和使用的詞彙。收詞範圍反映出眾多英語國家及眾多主題領域中所出現的最新材料。主題領域不僅必須包括技術和學術方面，還必須涵蓋體育、休閒和社交活動各項，而來源不僅包括書面材料及當代的電子文本，而且也須兼顧日常生活中無所不在的口頭語言。

電腦化的語料素材的出現，使我們能夠大大擴闊了收詞範圍。Della Summers 領導的小組在發展這些語料和將這些語料用於辭典編纂方面一直處於領先地位。尤其是 Summers 女士參與策劃了英語口語語料庫，並首次應用於這部新版的《朗文當代英語辭典》中。由於收詞範圍有了新的創意，新版的《朗文當代英語辭典》比前一版內容擴充了約五分之一。

我指出的第二個關鍵方面是釋義。釋義的中心是語義分析，辭典編纂者確保每個單詞在當代使用中的所有主要義項都經過仔細研究，如同外科醫生的手術刀那樣銳利而精心。然後向本辭典使用者解釋清楚每個義項的含義。那麼如何在應享盛名、而且現在更進一步精益求精和不斷改進的《朗文當代英語辭典》釋義詞彙範圍內作出更好的解釋呢？由於每個釋義都用大約兩千個基本和人們熟悉的詞彙表達，因此所有的學習者 —— 即使是那些僅僅粗通英語的人 —— 都能夠輕而易舉地理解本辭典成千上萬條詞目的全部意義。

以 marital status（婚姻狀況）為例：這個相當誇張而帶有官腔的片語現被直截了當地釋義為“用於官方表格，詢問某人是否已婚”。

這些釋義用的詞彙不僅對《朗文當代英語辭典》使用者有價值，對辭典編纂者自身也是一次有意義的檢查，他們必須在這個範圍內盡可能將語義分析清楚，確保做到不遺漏詞義的任何方面，更不能含混或模糊不清。

但是收詞範圍和釋義還不足以使負責《朗文當代英語辭典》的辭典編纂者感到滿意。他們首先要想到，使用該辭典的是英語學習者，這些學習者身處許許多多的國家，有着各式各樣的興趣和不同的語言需求，包括文體學和語用學方面的指導。以 marital status 為例可以看出本辭典如何滿足這些需求。其釋義告訴學習者，這是一個官員們使用的正式的書面語 —— 從而學習者得到沒有言明的提醒：他們不應向晚會上遇到的人詢問對方的“婚姻狀況”！

上述例子還説明了這部新的《朗文當代英語辭典》的另一個顯著特徵 。不能把語言看作是僅僅包含大量的稱為“詞”的互不相關的單位 。事實上，一個詞往往總是與另外一個或更多的詞一起構成一個詞彙單元，而正是這種詞彙單元才具有意義 。一個這樣的單元是“What's the meaning of *this*?”（這是甚麼意思？）它説明“意義”本身的意思與我在本序中所用的有些不同。我們應該注意，用作一個詞彙單元時，這一問句是有一定前提的: 其一，這不是書面語，而是口語（並且通常是在憤怒時説出來的）; 其二，this 所指的決不是一個不熟悉的單詞，而是一個不能接受的情況 。

一篇序當然不足以逐一説明一部著作所有的特點，所以我只得割愛，不再一一贅述《朗文當代英語辭典》如何傑出地滿足了學習者的各種需求 。有一點要提一下，就是語法資料，例如，本辭典不僅是“解碼”（解釋使用者在聽到或讀到的語料中感到模糊不清的東西），而且是“編碼”的工具，因此學習者可以從中學會如何自行以動詞 to like 的情態和體組成以下句子: “I would have liked to have had this dictionary when I was a student”（我是學生的時候，曾想有這本辭典）。

RANDOLPH QUIRK
（QUIRK 勳爵、教授、不列顛學院院士）

Introduction

英文版導言

歡迎再次使用修訂一新的第三版《朗文當代英語辭典》。現在我們增加了一個新詞附錄。學生和英語教師都想及時地了解英語中的最新詞彙。近年來來自互聯網、科學、商業以及青年文化用語的新詞急劇增加。牛津大學的吉恩·艾奇遜為新詞附錄作了富有教益的導言（見新詞部分）。

所有詞目現在都以彩色標出，從而從視覺上使本辭典更易於查詢。

快速查詢與彩色詞目 —— 我們創造了指示標記這個概念，運用詞語或者片語來將較長條目的各個義項區分開來，從而提供了一個視覺索引，幫助使用者盡快地查找到自己所需要的義項。我們認為學生們不必在一大堆無關的詞義中艱難跋涉，因此所有的釋義均按使用頻率順序排列。換言之，最常用的詞義最先顯示。新採用的彩色詞目將幫助你更為輕鬆地查到自己想要查找的單詞。

英語口語 ——《朗文當代英語辭典》比任何其他英語教學類辭典都更為重視英語口語的重要性。為此，在聖巴巴拉加利福尼亞大學的幫助之下，我們建起了一個美國英語口語語料庫。該語料庫與英國國家語料庫中的口語部分一同使用，對自然的英語口語進行分析。所有的錄音都源自自然的話語，而不是源自廣播或電視節目，也不是源自以任何方式事先寫好的發言。這一做法對 mean 或 better 之類的一些常用詞的釋義面有着深刻的影響。本辭典對口語語料庫中特別常用的釋義均以 *spoken*【口】予以標注。

使用頻率 —— 許多使用者來信稱辭典中對 3,000 個在口語及書面語中最常用詞彙的標注非常有用。本辭典中的使用頻率圖表告訴使用者像 decide 之類的詞語有哪些句構是最常用的，let 比較為正式的 permit 究竟更常用到甚麼程度等等。如果沒有朗文語料庫網絡 —— 電腦化的數據庫中擁有 3.3 億個詞語，既涵蓋了英國英語，也涵蓋了美國英語 —— 中的真實語料，所有這些都將是無源之水，無本之木。我們一貫堅持的原則是，辭典編纂者所使用的語料庫務必要盡可能地具有"代表性"，即語料庫應該代表語言的廣大範圍，作為使用頻率信息的來源務必具有可靠性。

片語與搭配 —— 學習英語固定片語的重要性在英語教學中正日益獲得認同，因此在本辭典中，grim determination 和 invade somebody's privacy 之類的搭配，以及 bear with me, been there 和 done that 之類的片語均以粗體顯示。要重申的是，由於利用了朗文語料庫網絡，本辭典所涉及的語料整理工作才能做到如此精確。

我們希望本辭典能夠如人們所願的那樣清新現代，從而滿足 21 世紀學習者的需要。我們歡迎來自本辭典使用者的任何評論和建議。

請不吝賜教。我們對你對我們的工作的建議和支持深表感謝！

Della Summers
辭典部董事

Adam Gadsby
編輯部董事

Explanatory Chart

圖 示

ar·du·ous /ˋɑrdʒʊəs; ˈɑːdjuəs/ *adj* involving a lot of strength and effort 費力的, 艱巨的: *an arduous journey through the mountains* 艱難的山區旅行 —**arduously** *adv* —**arduousness** *n* [U]

讀音用國際音標標註。(前為美式 K.K. 音標, 後為英式 IPA 音標)。

am·ber /ˋæmbɚ; ˈæmbə/ *n* [U] **1** a yellowish brown colour 琥珀色 **2** a yellowish brown substance used to make jewellery 琥珀 —**amber** *adj*

詞類 —— 動詞、名詞、形容詞、介詞等等 —— 均用斜體標出。

a·bode[1] /əˋbod; əˈbəʊd/ *n* [C] *formal or humorous* someone's home【正式或幽默】住所: *Welcome to my humble abode.* 歡迎光臨寒舍。| **of no fixed abode** (=having no permanent home) 居無定所

abode[2] the past tense of ABIDE

拼寫相同但屬於不同詞類的詞彙當作同形詞處理, 分列詞條。

an·nu·al[1] /ˋænjuəl; ˈænjuəl/ *adj* **1** happening once a year 一年一度的, 每年的: *an annual conference* 年會 **2** based on or calculated over a period of one year 按年度計算的: *Steel output reached an annual figure of one million tons.* 鋼的年產量達到 100 萬噸。—**annually** *adv*

如果一個詞有一個以上意義, 每項詞義均用黑體數字標出。

ar·dour *BrE*【英】, **ardor** *AmE*【美】/ˋardɚ; ˈɑːdə/ *n* [U] **1** very strong positive feelings 激情, 熱誠: *They sang with real ardour.* 他們唱得很有激情。**2** *literary* strong feelings of love【文】熾熱的愛情

如果一個詞可以用兩種不同方法拼寫, 兩種拼法均列出。

a·bra·sive[1] /əˋbresɪv; əˈbreɪsɪv/ *adj* **1** seeming rude or unkind in the way you behave towards people because you say what you think very directly 生硬的; 粗魯的: *a rather abrasive manner* 相當粗魯的舉止

詞義均用 2,000 個朗文釋義詞彙解釋, 語言簡潔易明。

ar·cher /ˋartʃɚ; ˈɑːtʃə/ *n* [C] someone who shoots ARROWS (1) from a BOW[3] (1) 射箭運動員; 弓箭手

不在釋義詞彙範圍內的詞均用小號的大寫字母列出。

an·noy·ing /əˋnɔɪɪŋ; əˈnɔɪ-ɪŋ/ *adj* making you feel slightly angry 令人心煩的: *an annoying habit of interrupting* 打斷他人講話的令人惱火的習慣 | *The annoying thing is he's usually right.* 令人氣惱的是, 他通常都是對的。| **it's annoying that** *It's annoying that we didn't know about this before.* 令人惱火的是, 我們事先並不知道。—**annoyingly** *adv*: *annoyingly small portions* 量少得讓人惱火

有用的、自然的例子均以源自朗文語料庫網絡的資料為根據。

am·biv·a·lent /æmˋbɪvələnt; æmˈbɪvələnt/ *adj* not sure whether you want or like something or not (心情) 矛盾的: *Her feelings about getting married are distinctly ambivalent.* 她顯然對是否要結婚感到矛盾。—**ambivalence** *n* [U] —**ambivalently** *adv*

根據原詞詞義可以理解其詞義的派生詞列於原詞之後。

ad·here /ədˋhɪr; ədˈhɪə/ *v formal* [I+**to**] to stick firmly to something【正式】黏附, 附着

adhere to sth *phr v* [T] *formal* to continue to behave according to a particular rule, agreement, or belief【正式】堅持; 信守: *adhere to your principles* 堅持原則 | *adhere to the regulations* 遵守規定

片語[短語]動詞直接在其主要動詞的詞條後列出。

after ef·fect /ˈ·· ·ˌ·/ *n* [C usually plural 一般用複數] an unpleasant effect that remains for a long time after the condition or event that caused it 後效; 後作用; 副作用; 後遺效應: *the after-effects of his illness* 他這種病的後遺症

複合詞作為詞目列出, 標有重音符號。

au·ber·gine /ˋobɚˌʒin; ˈəʊbəʒiːn/ *n* [C,U] *BrE* a large dark purple vegetable【英】茄子; EGGPLANT *AmE*【美】—see picture on page A9 參見 A9 頁圖

英國英語和美國英語的詞均列出。

abandon[2] *n* [U] **with gay/wild abandon** in a careless or uncontrolled way without thinking or caring about what you are doing 盡情; 放縱: *The kids hurled pieces of wood on the fire with gay abandon.* 孩子們盡情地把木塊往火上扔。

片語[短語]與習語均列出, 並附其意義。

at·trib·u·ta·ble /əˋtrɪbjutəbḷ; əˈtrɪbjʊtəbəl/ *adj* [not before noun 不用於名詞前] likely to be caused by something 可歸因於…的: **[+to]** *Death was attributable to gunshot wounds.* 死因可能是槍傷。

ab·hor /əbˋhɔr; əbˈhɔː/ *v* **abhorred, abhorring** [T not in progressive 不用進行式] *formal* to hate a kind of behaviour or way of thinking, especially because you think it is morally wrong【正式】厭惡, 憎惡: *Some genuinely abhorred slavery, others were simply convinced by the economic arguments against it.* 有些人真正厭惡奴隸制, 而另一些人只是出於經濟上的理由才反對奴隸制的。

an·noyed /əˋnɔɪd; əˈnɔɪd/ *adj* slightly angry 感到煩惱[困擾]的: *I'll be annoyed if we don't finish by eight.* 如果我們到8點還未完成, 我會很懊惱。| **[+with]** *She was annoyed with Duncan for forgetting to phone.* 鄧肯忘了打電話使她氣惱。| **[+about/by]** *He was annoyed by her apparent indifference.* 她看起來很冷淡, 這讓他很氣惱。| **be annoyed that** *Mr Davies was annoyed that the books were missing.* 書本不見了, 戴維斯先生很懊惱。

ar·gu·ment /ˋɑrgjəmənt; ˈɑːgjʊmənt/ *n* **1** [C] a situation in which two or more people disagree, often angrily 爭論, 爭辯, 爭吵: **[+with]** *an argument with my husband* 跟我丈夫爭吵 | **[+about/over]** *The argument seemed to be about who was going to take the cat to the vet.* 爭論似乎是關於由誰帶貓去看獸醫。| **have an argument** *They were having an argument about the children.* 他們為孩子的事爭吵。| **get into an argument** *I got into an argument with the other driver.* 我和另一位司機吵了起來。| **win/lose an argument** *He lost his argument with the doctor.* 他說不過醫生。| **heated argument** (=very angry argument) 激烈的爭論

ab·sorb /əbˋsɔrb; əbˈsɔːb/ *v* [T]
1 ►LIQUID 液體◄ if something absorbs a liquid, it takes the liquid into itself from the surface or space around it 吸收〔液體〕: *Plants absorb nutrients from the soil.* 植物從土壤中吸收養分。
2 ►INFORMATION 信息◄ to read or hear a large amount of new information and understand it 理解, 掌握: *I haven't really had time to absorb everything that he said.* 我還沒有時間弄懂他說的一切。
3 ►INTEREST 興趣◄ to interest someone very much 吸引〔某人〕, 使專心: **be absorbed in** *Judith lay on the settee, absorbed in her book.* 朱迪思躺在沙發椅上, 專心致志地看書。| **absorb sb's attention** *The video was totally absorbing the children's attention.* 錄像完全吸引了孩子們的注意力。

ap·pend /əˋpɛnd; əˈpend/ *v* [T+to] *formal* to add something to a piece of writing【正式】附加, 增補

ante- /æntɪ; æntɪ/ *prefix* before 在…以前: *to antedate* (=be earlier than something) 先於, 早於 | *ante-natal* (=before birth) 出生前的 —compare 比較 ANTI-, POST-, PRE-

an·te¹ /ˋæntɪ; ˈænti/ *n* **up/raise the ante** to increase your demands or try to get more things from a situation, even though this involves more risks 加賭注 —see also 另見 PENNY ANTE

a·rise /əˋraɪz; əˈraɪz/ *v past tense* **arose** /əˋroz; əˈrəʊz/ *past participle* **arisen** /əˋrɪzṇ; əˈrɪzən/ [I]

語法信息置於例子前的方括號內，或用黑體字標示。

經常一起使用的單詞用粗體字標出，並附實例或解釋 。

較長詞條裡的指示標記幫助你找到所需要的詞義 。

某單詞用於何種情景及詞源方面的信息均用斜體字標出 。

“互見”標籤提示你參見其他單詞、片語[短語]、圖畫及用法說明 。

不規則動詞的各種形式及不規則名詞的複數形式均列出 。

Guide to the Dictionary

本辭典使用方法簡介

Contents 目錄

1 How to find the word you are looking for 如何查出你要尋找的詞

本辭典的詞彙按字母順序排列。

1.1 Compound words 複合詞

複合詞由兩個或兩個以上的詞組成，具有固定形式和特殊意義，例如 front man（發言人）和 front line（前線）。這些複合詞多數作為獨立的詞目列出（參見第1.6節片語[短語]與習語）。複合詞像普通單詞一樣按字母順序排列，其兩個部分之間的空間或連字符均不計算在內。

front·al
frontal sys·tem
front-and-center
front bench
front·bench·er
front door
fron·tier

1.2 Phrasal verbs 片語[短語]動詞

多個單詞組成的動詞，例如 give up 或 put off，按字母順序直接列在其主要動詞的詞條後。例如：

face² *v* [T]
  face sb ↔ **down**
  face up to
  face sb **with**
face card

1.3 Derived words without definition 不附釋義的派生詞

有些單詞通過添加後綴派生而成，故無需釋義。例如 gracefully 和 gracefulness 均派生自 graceful，而其意義即由原主要單詞意義加上後綴意義組合而成。這些派生詞在其源詞的詞條末尾列出。

grace·ful /ˈgresfəl; ˈgreɪsfəl/ *adj* **1** moving in a smooth and attractive way, or having an attractive shape〔動作，線條〕優美的，雅緻的：*a slim graceful figure* 修長的優美身材 **2** behaving in a polite and pleasant way 優雅得體的，體面的：*a graceful apology* 得體的道歉 — **gracefully** *adv*: *When I am no longer needed, I shall retire gracefully.* 當不再需要我的時候，我將體面地退休。—**gracefulness** *n* [U]

在此例中，gracefully 意為'以優美的方式'或'得體地'，而 gracefulness 意為'優美'或'得體'。

1.4 Homographs 同形異義詞

同形異義詞是指拼寫相同，但在其他方面有差異的單詞，這些單詞在辭典裡以獨立的詞條列出。在本辭典中，不同詞類的單詞作同形異義詞處理。

face¹ /fes; feɪs/ *n* [C]
1 ►FRONT OF YOUR HEAD 頭部的正面◄ the front part of the head from the chin to the forehead 臉，面部：*She has such a pretty face.* 她有那麼美的一張臉。| *Bob's face was covered in cuts and bruises.* 鮑勃的臉上滿是劃痕與擦傷。| **a sea of faces** (=a lot of faces seen together) 許許多多的臉 *The Principal looked down from the platform at the sea of faces below.* 校長從講台上看着下面數不清的臉。—see picture at 參見 HEAD¹ 圖
face² *v* [T]
1 ►DIFFICULT SITUATION 困難的局面◄ if you face a difficult situation or if it faces you, you must deal with it 面臨，面對：*The President faces the difficult task of putting the economy back on its feet.* 總統面對着恢復經濟的艱巨任務。| *McManus is facing the biggest challenge of his career.* 麥克馬納斯正面臨着畢生事業中的最大挑戰。| **be faced with/by** *I was faced with the awful job of breaking the news to the girl's family.* 我面臨着向女孩的家人報告這一消息的可怕任務。

同形異義詞排列順序取決於其常用程度。face 用作名詞的頻率比用作動詞為多，因此名詞 face 的詞條列在前面。

詞類和拼寫相同、而讀音不同的單詞，以分開的詞目列出。例如名詞 row (=a line 排，行) 和 row (=an argument 爭吵) 因為讀音不同，而分列為不同詞目。

如果兩個單詞拼寫形式相同，而其中一個以大寫字母開頭，並具有完全不同的意義，例如形容詞 catholic 和 Catholic，也分列為不同詞目。

某個名詞的複數形式具有獨自的意義時，通常當作該名詞的一個義項列出：

blue² *n* **1** [C,U] the colour that is blue 藍色：*the rich greens and blues of the tapestry* 掛毯濃豔的藍綠色調 | *She nearly always dresses in blue.* 她幾乎總穿藍色衣服。**2 blues** [plural] a slow sad style of music that came from the southern US 勃魯斯音樂〔起源於美國南方的一種緩慢、憂鬱的樂曲〕：*a blues singer* 勃魯斯歌手 — see also 另見 RHYTHM AND BLUES **3 the blues** [plural] *informal* feelings of sadness【非正式】憂鬱，沮喪：*Don't be surprised if you get the blues for a while after your baby is born.* 如果你在生完孩子後出現暫時的憂鬱，你不必感到驚訝。

但如果某個單詞的複數形式比其單數形式重要，而且有多層意義時，則作為獨立的詞目列出。因此，goods 作為一個詞條，與名詞 good 分列。

1.5 Other types of headwords 其他類型的詞目

縮略語及 dis- 一類的前綴或 -able 一類的後綴均作為詞目獨立列出。

不同的拼寫形式會放在詞目後，也會作為詞目另條列出，並指引你查找主要詞條。

in·quire, enquire /ɪnˋkwaɪr; ɪnˈkwaɪə/ *v* [I,T] **1** to ask someone for information 詢問，打聽：*"Are you getting married?" the television interviewer inquired.* "你準備結婚了嗎?"電視採訪記者問道。
en·quire /ɪnˋkwaɪr; ɪnˈkwaɪə/ *v* [I,T] *especially BrE*【尤英】another spelling of INQUIRE inquire 的另一種拼法

單詞的不規則屈折變化形式在其主要形式的詞條下列出，並作為獨立的詞目列出，引導你查找主要詞條。

have¹ /v, əv, həv; v, əv, həv; *strong* 強讀 hæv; hæv/ *auxiliary verb past tense* **had** /d, əd, həd; d, əd, həd; *strong* 強讀 hæd; hæd/ *third person singular present tense* **has** /əz, həz; z, əz, həz; *strong* 強讀 hæz; hæz/ *negative short forms* 否定縮略式= **haven't** /ˋhævn̩t; ˈhævənt/, **hadn't** /ˋhædn̩t; ˈhædnt/, **hasn't** /ˋhæzn̩t; ˈhæzənt/
had /əd, həd; d; əd, həd; *strong* 強讀 hæd; hæd/ **1** the past tense and past participle of HAVE

1.6 Phrases and idioms 片語[短語]與習語

有些單詞經常用於特定的片語[短語]裡，而本辭典的一個重要特色是將這些片語[短語]作為獨立的義項處理。例如：

face¹ /fes; feɪs/ *n* [C]

17 sb's face doesn't fit used to say that someone is not the right kind of person for a particular group, organization etc 某人不適合〔某個羣體、組織等〕
18 put a brave face (on) to make an effort to behave in a happy cheerful way when you are upset or disappointed〔雖然煩惱、失望等但〕裝作若無其事的樣子: *He was shattered, though he put on a brave face.* 他大為震驚, 儘管他裝作若無其事的樣子。
19 set your face against *especially BrE* to be very determined that something should not happen【尤英】沉下臉反對, 堅決反對

有些複合詞因為是習語, 也按此處理。如 big deal 作為 big 的一個詞義來處理。

片語[短語]與習語通常在該片語[短語]或習語的第一個主要單詞下列出(即不列在 the, to, something 或 be 這類詞下), 所以 have egg on your face 的釋義列在 egg 下, 而不在 face 下。但在 face 條下查找, 也會在該詞條末尾找到這個片語[短語]的相互參照説明, 告訴你在何處找到其釋義。

face¹ /fes; feɪs/ *n* [C]
—see also 另見 **have egg on your face** (EGG¹ (4)), **fly in the face of** (FLY¹ (28))

2. Understanding meaning 理解詞義

2.1 Words with more than one meaning 多義詞

一個單詞具有一個以上詞義時, 每項詞義都有一個編號, 並根據對我們的口語和書面語語料的分析, 最常用的詞義列在最前。

a·chieve·ment /əˋtʃivmənt; əˈtʃiːvmənt/ *n* **1** [C] something important that you succeed in doing by your own efforts 成績, 成就: *Winning three gold medals is a remarkable achievement.* 贏得三枚金牌是個了不起的成績。| **no mean achievement/quite an achievement** (=a very impressive achievement) 了不起的成績 **2** [U] the act of achieving something 實現; 完成; 達到: *the achievement of economic stability* 經濟穩定的實現 | **sense of achievement** (=a feeling of pride when you succeed in doing something difficult) 成就感 *You get a wonderful sense of achievement when you reach the top.* 當你到達最高處時, 你會有一種奇妙的成就感。

本辭典根據對大量的口頭英語和書面英語語料的分析, 標出單詞或片語[短語]的使用頻率, 並標示其在每個義項中的使用頻率。

片語[短語]如包含該單詞並具有獨特意義, 則作為獨立的義項列出, 並按其使用頻率順序排列。例如:

look·out /ˈlʊkˌaʊt; ˈlʊk-aʊt/ *n*
1 be on the lookout for to watch a place or situation continuously in order to find something you want or to be ready for problems or opportunities 監視, 留神觀察: *Police were on the lookout for anyone behaving suspiciously.* 警察隨時注意可疑的人。| *We're always on the lookout for new business opportunities.* 我們隨時留意新的商業機會。
2 keep a lookout to keep watching carefully for something or someone, especially for danger 密切注視〔尤指危險〕: **keep a sharp/special lookout** *When you're driving keep a sharp lookout for cyclists.* 駕駛時要特別注意騎腳踏車的人。
3 ►PERSON 人◄ [C] someone whose duty is to watch carefully for something, especially danger 監視者, 守望者: *A lookout reported an enemy plane approaching.* 監視哨報告説一架敵機正在飛近。
4 ►PLACE 地方◄ [C] a place for a lookout to watch from 哨所, 瞭望台: *a coastguard lookout on the clifftop* 海邊懸崖頂上的哨所
5 it's your/their own lookout *BrE spoken* used to say that what someone has chosen to do is their own problem or risk, and no one else's【英口】那是你們/他們自己的事〔與別人不相干〕: *If he wants to ruin his health with all these drugs, that's his own lookout.* 如果他要用所有這些毒品毀掉自己的健康, 那是他自己的事。
6 be a poor/bad lookout for sb *BrE spoken* used to say that something bad or unsatisfactory is likely to happen【英口】對某人不是件好事, 事情不妙: *It'll be a poor lookout for James if she finds that letter.* 如果她發現那封信, 詹姆斯就慘了。

這表示 lookout 的最常見用法是用於片語[短語] be on the lookout for 之中 。

2.2 Definitions 釋義

本辭典的所有釋義均用由大約 2,000 個常用詞構成的“朗文釋義詞彙”寫成, 文字清晰簡潔。這些釋義所用的詞彙列於本辭典末尾的附錄 8, 該處準確地説明了如何使用這些單詞。

2.3 Examples 例子

本辭典大部分釋義後均列有例子, 説明該詞用法。

例子有的是片語[短語], 有的是完整的句子, 均用斜體字標示:

clear instructions 清楚的指示 | *You must never do that again. Is that clear?* 不許你再那樣做, 明白嗎? |

本辭典的所有例子均以“朗文語料庫網絡”的口語和書面語語料內容為基礎。有些例子直接選自語料庫; 有些例子略有改動, 去掉了艱深的詞; 有些例子專門為該詞條編寫。不管甚麼情況, 例子均為精心挑選的, 有助於説明該單詞或片語[短語]的一般用法。

例子還可以用來説明該單詞的語法, 以及示範該單詞如何與其他詞語一起使用 (即詞語搭配) 。

be clear on *The rules are quite clear on the point.* 在這點上各項規定都明白易懂。| **clear to sb** *Is all this clear to you?* 你全都明白了嗎?

2.4 Collocations 詞語搭配

本辭典的一個重要目的是清楚地説明一個單詞的搭配, 即與該單詞經常而典型地一起使用的其他詞語。詞語搭配用藍色字標示出, 其後括號裡有簡短的釋義或例子, 或兩者都有。

make yourself clear (=express something well) 表達清楚 *To make yourself clear without using facial expressions can be very difficult.* 很難不藉助面部表情而清楚地表達自己。| **get sth clear** *Let's get one thing clear; you have my whole-hearted support.* 你要明白一件事, 我全力支持你。

這些詞語搭配按使用頻率順序列出, 最重要的搭配列在最前面。

2.5 Finding the meaning you want – Signposts 查出你需要的詞義 —— 指示標記

在有多項釋義的詞條裡, 我們加上了“指示標記”, 以有助

於快速查出需要的合適釋義。這些指示標記在釋義前用大寫字母標出，並且只用“朗文釋義詞彙”中的單詞編寫。

bridge¹ /brɪdʒ; brɪdʒ/ *n* [C]
1 ►OVER A RIVER/ROAD ETC 在河/路等的上方◄ a structure built over a river, road etc, that allows people or vehicles to cross from one side to the other 橋，橋梁
2 ►CONNECTION 連接◄ something that provides a connection between two things; LINK² (1)〔事物之間的〕橋梁，紐帶，聯繫: *The training programme is seen as a bridge between school and work.* 該培訓計劃被視為學校與工作之間的橋梁。
3 ►SHIP 船◄ the raised part of a ship from which the officers control it 船橋，艦橋，駕駛台
4 ►CARD GAME 紙牌戲◄ [U] a card game for four players who play in pairs 橋牌
5 the bridge of your nose the bony upper part of your nose between your eyes 鼻梁
6 ►PAIR OF GLASSES 眼鏡◄ the part of a pair of glasses that rests on the bridge of your nose〔眼鏡的〕鼻梁架 —see picture at 參見 GLASS¹ 圖
7 ►MUSICAL INSTRUMENT 樂器◄ a small piece of wood under the strings of a VIOLIN or GUITAR, used to keep them in position〔弦樂器的〕弦柱，弦馬，琴馬
8 ►FOR TEETH 用於牙齒的◄ a small piece of metal for keeping false teeth in place〔假牙上的〕齒橋 —see also 另見 **build bridges** (BUILD¹ (7)), **burn your bridges** (BURN¹ (22)), **cross that bridge when you come to it** (CROSS¹ (8)), **be (all) water under the bridge** (WATER¹ (7))

指示標記為單詞或片語[短語]，可以引導你查到合適的詞義。它可能是一個同義詞、一個簡短的釋義，或一個動詞的典型主語或受詞[賓語]。

2.6 Long entries with menus 附項目單的長詞條

在一些較長的詞條裡，緊密相關的詞義列在一起或成為一個段落。而詞條開頭的項目單列出各分段標題，便於找到所需詞義的部分。這些詞義均另起一行開始，為方便查找，往往還有指示標記。請看單詞 run 和 way 的分段方式作為參考。

2.7 Showing words with similar and opposite meanings 標示詞義相似和相反的單詞

有時，標出同義詞，即與該詞具有相同意義或幾乎相同意義的單詞是很有用的。同義詞在釋義之後列出，例如:

im·ma·te·ri·al /ˌɪməˋtɪrɪəl; ˌɪməˈtɪəriəl◄/ *adj* **1** not important in a particular situation; IRRELEVANT 無關緊要的；不相關的: *The causes of the problem are immaterial now – we need solutions.* 問題的原因現在已無關緊要，我們需要的是解決方法。**2** *formal* not having a real physical form【正式】非實體的，無形的

具有相似意義或相似形式的單詞標有 ‘compare’（比較）提示，也列出有用的反義詞。

i·ma·gi·na·ry /ɪˋmædʒəˌnɛrɪ; ɪˈmædʒɪ̣nəri/ *adj* not real, but produced from pictures or ideas in your mind 想像的，虛構的: *All the characters in this book are imaginary.* 本書人物純屬虛構。—compare 比較 IMAGINATIVE

im·mod·est /ɪˋmɑdɪst; ɪˈmɒdɪ̣st/ *adj* **1** having a very high opinion of yourself and your abilities, and not embarrassed about telling people how clever you are etc 驕傲的，不謙虛的 —opposite 反義詞 MODEST (1) **2** *old-fashioned* behaviour or clothes that are immodest may embarrass or offend people because they do not follow the usual social rules concerning sexual behaviour【過時】不端莊的，不正派的；下流的，有傷風化的 —**immodestly** *adv* —**immodesty** *n* [U]

3 Frequency 使用頻率

你已看到本辭典是按使用頻率排列的。一個單詞的使用頻率最高的意義首先列出，而同形異義詞也按照使用頻率順序標出。一個單詞的每一義項，說明語法和詞語搭配的例子，也均按使用頻率順序排列。我們對使用頻率的所有判斷是根據對語料庫資料的分析得出來的。這種組織編排原則提供了英語的重要信息，而且有助於學生學習。

對有些重要的單詞，圖表提供關於使用頻率的進一步信息。一些圖表說明某個單詞在英語口語中比在書面語中使用頻繁得多，而另一些圖表則比較具有相同意義的單詞，說明哪個單詞在書面語中使用得多，哪個單詞在口語中使用得多。還有些圖表說明某個單詞在其每項最常用的搭配或語法句型中的使用頻率，另外一些圖表則簡要說明了英國英語與美國英語的差異。

本辭典還對朗文所能得到的所有語料庫資料用電腦進行了分析，在這一基礎上說明哪些單詞是使用得最頻繁的詞彙。符號 S1、S2 和 S3 分別表示一個單詞屬於英語口語中前一千、前兩千和前三千個使用得最頻繁的詞彙。符號 W1、W2 和 W3 則相應表示一個單詞屬於英語書面語中前一千、前兩千和前三千個使用得最頻繁的詞彙。單詞的標記是 S1，S2 還是 W1，W2 等，乃根據其在美國英語與英國英語中的使用頻率而綜合計算出來的。

4 Grammar 語法

本辭典包含大量有關各單詞的語法資料，包括每個詞目所屬的詞類 —— 名詞、動詞、形容詞或某個其他類別的詞，以及詞彙屈折變化的資料 —— 即過去時態、複數、比較級以及其他形式的變化。此外，還有對詞彙的句法的完整解釋 —— 該單詞與其他單詞結合而組成的各種句型。

4.1 Word classes 詞類

詞類（或‘詞性’）是這樣標示的:

il·lo·gi·cal /ɪˋlɑdʒɪkl; ɪˈlɒdʒɪkəl/ *adj* **1** not sensible or reasonable 不合情理的，悖理的: *erratic and illogical behaviour* 古怪、乖戾的行為 —opposite 反義詞 LOGICAL (1) **2** not based on the principles of LOGIC 不合邏輯的: *an illogical conclusion* 荒謬的結論 —**illogically** /-klɪ; -kli/ *adv* —**illogicality** /ɪˌlɑdʒɪˋkælətɪ; ɪˌlɒdʒɪˈkælɪ̣ti/ *n* [U]

這意味着 illogical 是形容詞。其派生形式也標示了詞類: illogically 是副詞，而 illogicality 是名詞。

本辭典所使用的詞類為:

word class 詞類	**example** 例子
adj (adjective) 形容詞	a **fast** car, **straight** lines, **amazing** speed, **frequent** trains
adv (adverb) 副詞	smiling **happily**, put it **away**, **frankly**, I'm not bothered
auxiliary verb 助動詞	be, have
conjunction 連詞	and, but

determiner 限定詞	this, which
interjection 感嘆詞	damn, wow
modal verb 情態動詞	must, can, should
n (noun) 名詞	car, rabbit, president, dignity, excuse
number 數詞	five, ninth
phr v (phrasal verb) 片語[短語]動詞	put off, shut up, take over
predeterminer 前置限定詞	all, both
prefix 前綴	dis-, centi-
prep (preposition) 介詞	in, after, to
pron (pronoun) 代(名)詞	he, theirs, us
quantifier 數量詞	many, several
suffix 後綴	-ity, -ness
v (verb) 動詞	go, send, indicate

4.2 Inflections 屈折變化

屈折變化是單詞根據其在句子裡的語法作用而產生的形式變化。大部分單詞的屈折變化是有規律可循的。例如: 大部分名詞加 -s 或 -es 構成複數形式, 大部分動詞加 -ed 構成過去時形式。除非有可能引起混淆, 或規則變化的發音有難度, 本辭典一般不列出這些規則的屈折變化形式。

不規則的屈折變化形式則一律列出, 直接放在詞類後面, 用藍色字標出, 例如:

cri·sis /ˋkraɪsɪs; ˈkraɪsəs/ *n plural* **crises** /-siz; -siːz/ [C, U]
eat /it; iːt/ *v past tense* **ate** /et; eɪt/ *past participle* **eaten** /ˋitn̩; ˈiːtn/
good[1] /gud; gʊd/ *adj comparative* 比較級 **better** /ˋbɛtɚ; ˈbetə/ *superlative* 最高級 **best** /bɛst; best/

不規則屈折變化形式還按本身的字母順序作為詞目列出, 引導你去查找主詞:

ate /et; eɪt/ the past tense of EAT

列出的屈折變化還包括:

在過去式和 -ing 形式中需雙寫字母的動詞:

hug[1] /hʌg; hʌg/ *v* **hugged, hugging** [T]

以 -y 結尾的動詞:

car·ry[1] /ˋkærɪ; ˈkæri/ *v* **carried, carrying**

以 -y 結尾的形容詞:

dirt·y[1] /ˋdɝtɪ; ˈdɜːti/ *adj* **dirtier, dirtiest**

本辭典後從 C10 頁開始, 有不規則動詞表列出所有不規則變化的動詞。

4.3 Syntax – verbs 句法——動詞

動詞的基本用法在方括號內說明:

代號 [I] (不及物) 和 [T] (及物) 表示該動詞有受詞[賓語]還是沒有受詞[賓語]。

hard·en /ˋhɑrdn̩; ˈhɑːdn/ *v* **1** [I,T] to become firm or stiff, or to make something firm or stiff (使) 變硬; (使) 堅固; (使) 硬化: *Make sure you give the paint enough time to dry and harden.* 你一定要讓油漆有足夠的時間乾透和變硬。**2** [I] to become more strict and determined and less sympathetic 變得更堅定; 變得冷酷無情: *Opposition to the military regime has hardened since the massacres.* 大屠殺後, 反對軍政府的力量更加強硬了。| *a hardening of attitudes* 態度變得強硬 | *His face hardened.* 他的臉沉了下來。—compare 比較 SOFTEN (4) **3** [T] if an experience hardens someone, it makes them stronger and more able to deal with difficult or unpleasant situations 使變得堅強, 使更有忍耐力

代號 [linking verb 連繫動詞] 的意思是該動詞表示其前後的事物是同樣的事, 或是對前面事物的描述。

look[1] /luk; lʊk/ *v*
3 ►SEEM 看似◄ [linking verb 連繫動詞] to seem to be something, especially by having a particular appearance 看上去, 看起來: *How do I look in this dress?* 我穿這件連衣裙看起來怎樣? | **look like** *The intruder was holding what looked like a shotgun.* 闖入者手裡握着看似獵槍一樣的東西。| **look as if** *You look as if you haven't slept all night.* 你看上去似乎整夜沒有睡覺。
be[2] *v* **1** [linking verb 連繫動詞] used to show that someone or something is the same as the subject〔表示某人或某事與主語相同〕: *It's me.* 是我。| *Lack of money is our biggest problem.* 缺錢是我們最大的問題。| *If I were you, I shouldn't do it.* 如果我是你, 我就不會這樣做。

方括號也可能包含該動詞用法的限制, 包括 [not in progressive 不用進行式]:

pre·fer /prɪˋfɝ; prɪˈfɜː/ *v* **preferred, preferring** [T not in progressive 不用進行式] **1** to like someone or something more than someone or something else 更喜歡:

[I always+adv/prep]:

am·ble /ˋæmbl̩; ˈæmbəl/ *v* [I always+adv/prep] to walk in a slow relaxed way 漫步: **[+along/across etc]** *The old man came out and ambled over for a chat.* 老人出來, 從容地走過去聊天。—**amble** *n* [singular]

不可以只說 he ambled, 需加上 along 或 towards me 一類的詞或片語[短語]。

[usually in passive 一般用被動態]:

carpet[2] *v* [T] **1** [usually in passive 一般用被動態] to cover a floor with carpet 在…上鋪地毯: *a carpeted corridor* 鋪有地毯的走廊 **2** *informal especially BrE* to blame someone for something they have done; REPRIMAND【非正式, 尤英】斥責, 責備, 責罵 **3 carpeted with grass/flowers etc** *literary* covered with a thick layer of grass etc【文】覆蓋着一層厚厚的草/花等

[not in passive 不用被動態]:

concern[2] *v* [T] **1** if an activity, situation, rule etc concerns you, it affects you or involves you〔活動、情

況、規則等〕對…有影響; 與…相關: *The tax changes will concern large corporations rather than small businesses.* 稅收上的變化影響到的是大公司而不是小企業。**2** [not in passive 不用被動態] to make someone feel worried or upset 使憂慮, 使擔心: *The fact that she spends so much time on her own really concerns me.* 她很多時間都是一人獨處, 這真讓我擔心。**3** [not in passive 不用被動態] if a story, book, report etc concerns someone or something, it is about them〔故事、書、報告等〕與…有關, 關於: *This article concerns a man who was wrongly imprisoned.* 這篇文章寫的是一個被冤枉而入獄的人。**4 concern yourself with/about sth** to become involved in something because you are interested in it or because it worries you 關心, 擔心: *More and more people are concerning themselves with environmental problems.* 越來越多的人關心起環境問題。**5 to whom it may concern** an expression written at the beginning of a formal letter when you do not know the name of the person you want to communicate with〔寫信時的〕敬啟者 —see also 另見 CONCERNED

如果提供的基本信息適用於單詞的所有意義, 該信息會列在詞目後; 如果該信息只適用於單詞的某個義項, 則該信息會列在該義項的序號之後。

動詞其他用法的信息會在例子中顯示出來。典型的結構用藍色字表示, 後接例子。

4 decide in favour of/decide against a) to choose or not choose someone or something 選擇/不選擇〔某人或某物〕: *After long discussion they decided in favour of the younger candidate.* 經過長時間的討論, 他們決定選那個年輕些的候選人。**b)** if a judge or JURY (1) decides in favour of someone or against someone, they say in court that someone is guilty or not guilty 作出有利於/不利於〔某人的〕裁決: *The jury decided in favour of the plaintiff.* 陪審團作出了有利於原告的裁決。

這些例子按使用頻率順序列出, 將最常用的結構列在最前面。

4.4 Phrasal verbs 片語[短語]動詞

對於片語[短語]動詞而言, 其介詞是否既可以放在受詞[賓語]前面, 也可以放在其後, 或者只能放在受詞[賓語]前面或後面, 是非常重要的。這一點在本辭典裡用雙向箭頭表示。

hand² *v* [T]

hand sth ↔ **out** *phr v* [T] **1** to give something to each member of a group of people; DISTRIBUTE 分發, 散發: Could you start handing these books out. 請你把這些書分發出去吧。**2 hand out advice** to give advice, even if people do not want to hear it 出主意 —see also 另見 HANDOUT

hammer out sth *phr v* [T] to decide on an agreement, contract, etc after a lot of discussion and disagreement〔經詳細的討論及爭議後〕得出〔協議、解決辦法等〕: *The UN is trying to force the warring factions to get together and hammer out a solution.* 聯合國正在試圖拉攏各敵對派系一起尋求解決問題的方案。

這詞條表示你可以說 hand the books out, 或者說 hand out the books, 但是說 hammer an agreement out 則是不正確的。

4.5 Syntax – nouns 句法 —— 名詞

方括號內提供的語法信息, 表示名詞或其某個義項是可數的 (如 a pen, three pens), 或是不可數的 (如 honour, daylight)。

hab·i·ta·tion /ˌhæbəˋteʃən; ˌhæbə̇ˈteɪʃən/ *n formal*【正式】**1 unfit for human habitation** a building that is unfit for human habitation is not safe or healthy for people to live in 不適合人類居住, 不適宜住人 **2** [U] the act of living in a place 居住: *There was no sign of habita-tion as far as the eye could see.* 放眼望去, 看不到有人居住的跡象。**3** [C] a house or place to live in 住宅, 住處

hes·i·ta·tion /ˌhɛzəˋteʃən; ˌhezə̇ˈteɪʃən/ *n* [C,U] the action of hesitating 躊躇, 猶豫, 遲疑 (不決): *After some hesitation one of them began to speak.* 猶豫了一會兒之後, 其中的一個人開口了。| **have no hesitation in** *I would have no hesitation in declining the post.* 我會毫不猶豫地拒絕這個職位。| **after/without a moment's hesitation** *Without a moment's hesitation she kissed him.* 她毫不猶豫地親吻了他。

如果某個名詞或其某個義項總是單數, 或總是複數, 也在方括號內標明。

hard right /,· ˈ·◂/ *n* [singular] the part of a political party that believes strongly in RIGHT WING political ideas 強硬右派

high heels /,· ˈ·/ *n* [plural] women's shoes with high heels 高跟鞋 —**high-heeled** *adj* —see picture on page A17 參見 A17 頁圖

如果名詞後通常跟某個介詞或某幾個介詞, 這在說明該名詞的例子前用藍色字表示。某個名詞後的典型結構也在例子前用藍色字表示出來。

hope² *n* [U]

5 ►CHANCE 機會◄ [C,U] a chance of succeeding or of something good happening 機會, 可能性: **[+of]** *There was no hope of escape.* 沒有逃脫的希望了。| **hope that** *There is some hope that we'll find a solution to our problems.* 我們還有一點希望找到解決問題的方法。

4.6 Syntax – adjectives and adverbs 句法 —— 形容詞與副詞

形容詞或副詞用法的信息在方括號內說明, 包括:

[only before noun 僅用於名詞前]:

ac·tu·al /ˈæktʃuəl; ˈæktʃuəl/ *adj* [only before noun 僅用於名詞前] **1** real, especially as compared with what is believed, expected or intended 實際的, 現實的: *a big difference between the opinion polls and the actual election results* 民意測驗和實際選舉結果的巨大差異 | *I'm not joking. Those were his actual words.* 我不是開玩笑, 那都是他的原話。| **in actual fact** (=really) 實際上 *In actual fact, there is not much evidence to support these allegations.* 事實上, 沒有多少證據支持這些指控。

[only after noun 僅用於名詞後]:

ga·lore /gəˈlɔː/ *adj* [only after noun 僅用於名詞後] in large amounts or numbers 大量的, 許多的: *There are bargains galore in the sales this year.* 今年的大減價期間有許多便宜貨。

[not before noun 不用於名詞前]:

ad·vi·sab·le /ədˋvaɪzəbḷ; ədˈvaɪzəbəl/ *adj* [not before noun 不用於名詞前] something that is advisable should be done in order to avoid problems or risks 可取的; 明智的: *For heavy smokers, regular medical checks are advisable.* 抽煙很多的人最好定期進行健康檢查。| **it is advisable to do sth** *It is advisable to disconnect the computer before you open it up.* 拆開電腦之前, 最好先切斷電源。—**advisability** /ədˌvaɪzəˋbɪlətɪ; ədˌvaɪzəˈbɪlə̇ti/ *n* [U] [no comparative 無比較級]:

ef·fec·tive /əˋfɛktɪv; ɪˈfektɪv/ *adj* **1** producing the result that was wanted or intended 產生預期效果的; 有效的: *The ads were simple, but remarkably effective.* 這些廣告很簡單, 但效果出奇地好。**2** impressive or interesting enough to be noticed 引人注意的; 醒目的: *an effective use of colour* 使用引人注目的顏色 **3** [no comparative 無比較級] if a law, agreement, or system becomes effective, it officially starts〔法律、協議或制度等〕生效的: *The cut in interest rates is effective from Monday.* 從星期一起利率下調正式生效。**4** [no comparative 無比較級] real rather than what is officially intended or generally believed 實際的, 事實上的: *The rebels are in effective control of the city.* 反叛者實際上已控制了城市。—**effectiveness** *n* [U]

[+adj/adv]:

in·creas·ing·ly /ɪnˋkrisɪŋlɪ; ɪnˈkriːsɪŋli/ *adv* more and more all the time [+adj/adv] 不斷增加地, 越來越多地: *The classes at the college have become increasingly full over the past five years.* 在過去的五年中, 這所學院的各班級越來越滿。[sentence adverb 句子副詞]: *Increasingly, it is the industrial power of Japan and South East Asia that dominates world markets.* 主宰世界市場的是日本和東南亞的工業實力 —— 這一情況日益明顯。

[sentence adverb 句子副詞]:

hap·pi·ly /ˋhæpɪlɪ; ˈhæpˌli/ *adv* **1** in a happy way 高興地, 快樂地: *a happily married couple* 一對幸福的夫婦 **2** [sentence adverb 句子副詞] fortunately 幸運地: *Happily, his injuries were not serious.* 幸好, 他的傷並不嚴重。**3** very willingly 很樂意地: *I'd happily go for you.* 我很樂意為你去一趟。

[sentence adverb 句子副詞] 這一語法信息表示 happily 在這個義項上用以修飾全句。

某個形容詞後的介詞或結構在例子前用藍色字表示出來。

hope·ful¹ /ˋhopfəl; ˈhəʊpfəl/ *adj* **1** believing that what you hope for is likely to happen 抱有希望的, 抱樂觀態度的: **[+about]** *Everyone's feeling pretty hopeful about the future.* 人人都對未來充滿希望。| **hopeful that** *We're hopeful that the team will be fit for next Saturday's game.* 我們有信心球隊能以良好的狀態參加下星期六的比賽。| **be hopeful of doing sth** *BrE*【英】*The police are hopeful of finding more clues to the murder.* 警方有望找到更多有關這宗謀殺案的線索。

4.7 Very infrequent words 極不常用的單詞

對學生很可能不需要使用的極不常用的單詞, 只列出基本的語法信息, 不再舉例。

5. Information on register and usage 語域和用法方面的信息

5.1 indicating register 表示語域

有些單詞和義項後提供了它們很可能用於何種情景的信息。這種信息在詞目後或在義項序號後, 用斜體標出。

clobber² *n* [U] *informal especially BrE* someone's possessions, especially their clothes【非正式, 尤英】隨身帶的東西; 衣物: *Don't forget all your clobber if you're staying the night.* 如果在外面過夜, 別忘了帶衣服。| **fishing/swimming/football clobber etc** (=clothes and equipment needed for a particular activity) 漁具/泳衣/足球衣物

ab·ne·ga·tion /ˌæbnɪˋgeʃən; ˌæbnˌˈgeɪʃən/ *n* [U] *formal* the act of not allowing yourself to have or do something that you want【正式】自制, 克己

a·blu·tions /əbˋljuʃənz; əˈbluːʃənz/ *n* [plural] *formal or humorous* the things that you do to make yourself clean, such as washing yourself, cleaning your teeth etc【正式或幽默】沐浴; 漱洗

【俚】(俚語) 或【諱】(諱忌語), 而尤其是諱忌語, 表示即使在非正式場合也需謹慎使用。

【文】(文學用語)、【詩】(詩歌用語)、【術語】(技術用語)、【舊】(老式用語) 或【過時】(過時用語) 表示人們在講話或寫作中不常用。

5.2 Spoken words and phrases 口語單詞與片語[短語]

【口】(口語) 標誌表示片語[短語]典型地用於講話而不用於書面。

24 that's life *spoken* used when you are disappointed or upset that something has happened but realize that you must accept it【口】生活就是這樣〔表示無奈地接受令人失望或生氣之事〕: *Oh well, that's life!* 算了, 生活就是這樣!

由於朗文語料庫網絡中既有口語語料, 又有書面語語料, 所以我們能夠提供大量這類信息。有些重要單詞有圖表來説明其在口頭英語中的使用頻率比在書面英語中高多少。某些這樣的單詞, 例如 mean, 有特設的“口語片語[短語]”方框或段落加以説明。

5.3 Usage notes 用法説明

本辭典有英語特殊用法方面的説明。這些用法説明列在有關的主要單詞的詞條後面。該項用法説明涉及的其他單詞在各自詞條下有相互參照的指示。

6. Pronunciation 發音

每個單詞後用美式K.K. 音標和國際音標 (IPA) 標注發音, 兩種音標用分號 (;) 隔開。K.K. 音標列在前面; 國際音標列在後面。所用符號列在本辭典的發音表中。可替代的音標在逗號之後列出。如果該音標只有部分不同, 則只標出不同的部分, 用連字符標出其在單詞中的位置。

a·ber·rant /æbˋɛrənt; ˈæbərənt/ *adj formal* not usual or normal【正式】異常的; 脱離常規的: *aberrant behaviour* 異常行為

ab·duct /æbˋdʌkt; əbˈdʌkt/ *v* [T] to take someone away by force; KIDNAP 劫持, 綁架; 誘拐: *Police suspect she was abducted late last night.* 警方懷疑她昨天深夜被綁架了。—**abductor** *n* [C] —**abduction** /æbˋdʌkʃən; əbˈdʌkʃən/ *n* [C,U]

由某個單詞有規則地派生而成, 並列在該單詞後不附釋義的大多數單詞, 其發音即為其主詞加上後綴。在這種情況下不標注音標。其他情況下的派生詞則注有音標。

6.1 Compound words 複合詞

帶空格或連字符的複合詞, 一般不標注完整的音標。這是因為其中每個單詞都有自己的詞條, 詞條處都標注了音標。但這類複合詞都標有重音模式, 音節用圓點隔開, 標在上方和下方的重音符號分別表示主重音和次重音。重音模式與完整的音標標法相同。

aircraft car·ri·er /'·· ,···/ *n* [C] a type of ship that has a large flat surface that planes fly from 航空母艦

有些複合詞（如 plate glass）或一些單詞（如 independent），如果直接用在名詞前時（如 plate glass window 或 independent observer），則只有一個主重音（重音模式中第一個位置）。在這種情況下，表示重音轉移的符號 /◂/ 會標在複合詞的重音模式後面:

plate glass /,· '·◂/ *n* [U] big pieces of glass made in large thick sheets for use especially in shop windows 〔尤用於商店櫥窗的〕厚玻璃板, 平板玻璃

或在單詞的音標後面:

in·de·pen·dent /ˌɪndɪˈpɛndənt; ˌɪndʒˈpendənt◂/ *adj*

7. British and American English 英國英語與美國英語

參與本辭典編纂工作的詞條撰稿人有英國人也有美國人，因此本辭典收錄了大量的英國英語與美國英語。釋義正文是用英國英語寫的，但實例有英國英語也有美國英語。單詞的英國英語形式和美國英語形式在發音和拼寫方面的差異都列出標明。僅出現在英國英語的單詞、單詞的義項、語法結構、片語[短語]和詞語搭配標有 *BrE*【英】，而僅存在於美國英語的上述內容則標有 *AmE*【美】。更常用於英國英語的標有 *especially BrE*【尤英】，而更常用於美國英語的標有 *especially AmE*【尤美】。

7.1 Pronunciation and spelling differences 發音與拼寫的差異

英國英語和美國英語中拼寫不同的單詞，兩種拼寫方式均列出並注音。

cen·tre[1] *BrE*【英】, **center** *AmE*【美】/ˈsɛntɚ; ˈsentə/ *n* **1 ▶MIDDLE** 中間◀ [C] the middle of a space, area, or object, especially the exact middle〔空間、地域或物體的〕(正) 中間, 中心 (點): *Draw a line through the centre of the circle.* 劃一條線通過那個圓形的中心。| *Tony only likes chocolates with soft centres.* 東尼只愛吃夾心巧克力。| **[+of]** *There was an enormous oak table in the center of the room.* 房間中央有一張巨大的橡木桌子。

cen·ter /ˈsɛntɚ; ˈsentə/ *n v* the American spelling of CENTRE centre的美式拼法

如果某詞在英國英語或美國英語中有時拼寫方式不同於主詞，該拼寫方式列在"also 又作"之後。

jail[1] also 又作 **gaol** *BrE*【英】/dʒel; dʒeɪl/ *n* [C,U] a place where criminals are kept as part of their punishment, or where people who have been charged with a crime are kept before they are judged in a law court; PRISON (1) 監獄

有些動詞在英國英語中其過去式與 -ing 形式末字母要雙寫，而在美國英語中卻不需要。這時兩種拼寫均列出並標明:

label[2] *v* **labelled, labelling** *BrE*【英】, **labeled, labeling** *AmE*【美】[T]

7.2 Words and meanings – British and American differences 單詞與詞義 —— 英國英語和美國英語的差異

有時，英國英語和美國英語使用完全不同的單詞來表示相同的事物。在這種情況下，英國英語單詞的詞條釋義後面標出其美國英語的同義詞，反之亦然。

el·e·va·tor /ˈɛlə,vetɚ; ˈelɪ̈veɪtə/ *n* [C] **1** *AmE* a machine that takes people and goods from one level to another in a building【美】電梯; LIFT[2] (1) *BrE*【英】**2** a machine with a moving belt and containers, used for lifting grain and liquids, or for taking things off ships 〔運送糧食、液體或卸船的〕升降機, 起卸機

有時，一個英國英語的單詞在美國英語中沒有對等詞，或者該對等詞很少使用。這樣的單詞僅標上【英】或【美】:

airing cup·board /'·· ,··/ *n* [C] *BrE* a warm cupboard in a house where sheets and clean clothes are kept【英】〔儲存被單、衣服的〕烘櫃

air·head /ˈɛr,hɛd; ˈeəhed/ *n* [C] *slang especially AmE* someone who is stupid【俚, 尤美】傻瓜, 笨蛋

如果單詞的某義項僅存在於英國英語或美國英語，會於該義項序號後加以標明:

home·ly /ˈhomlɪ; ˈhəʊmli/ *adj* **1** *BrE* simple and ordinary in a way that makes you feel comfortable【英】樸實無華的; 家常的: *The cottage had a warm, homely feel.* 那間小屋給人一種温暖而隨和的感覺。**2** *AmE* people or faces that are homely are unattractive or ugly【美】相貌平庸的; 醜陋的: *I've never seen such a homely dog in my life!* 我這輩子從未見過如此難看的狗!

7.3 Differences in grammar 語法差異

有些單詞僅在英國英語或美國英語後跟某個特定的介詞或結構，這些差異均予標明。

一種差異是: 像 government 或 class 這類集合名詞在英國英語裡可以用複數動詞，但在美國英語裡卻不行。對於這類重要的單詞，這種差異均給以説明並標示出來:

gov·ern·ment /ˈgʌvɚnmənt; ˈgʌvəmənt/ *n* **1** also 又作 **Government** [C] the group of people who govern a country or state 政府: *The new military government does not have popular support.* 新上台的軍人政府沒有得到廣泛的支持。| [also+plural verb *BrE* 英] *The Government are planning further cuts in public spending.* 政府正計劃進一步削減公共支出。

7.4 Differences in phrases and collocations 片語[短語]與詞語搭配的差異

英國英語與美國英語的一個重要差異是兩者各有豐富的習語。有些單詞在這兩種英語之一有典型的搭配，而在另一種英語中卻沒有。僅在英國英語或美國英語中出現的片語[短語]和搭配均標示如下。

jack[2] *v*

jack sb **around** *phr v* [T] *AmE slang* to waste someone's time by deliberately making things difficult for them【美俚】故意刁難〔某人〕以浪費其時間: *Stop jacking me around and make up your mind!* 別浪費我時間了, 立定主意吧!

jack sth ↔ **in** *phr v* [T] *BrE informal* to stop doing something【英, 非正式】停止做: *I'd love to jack in my job and go live in the Bahamas.* 我會樂於辭去這份工作, 去巴哈馬居住。

本辭典所使用的符號説明

1. 本辭典英語原文所使用的各種符號可以參見辭典的 Explanatory Chart (圖示) 或 Grammar Codes (語法代號表); 如涉及語音的符號, 請參見 Pronunciation Table (發音表)。

2. 本辭典的中文譯文也使用了幾種不同的符號, 它們的形式和所表示的含義如下:

   (1) 魚尾括號【 】: 用於標示原文的説明性略語之中譯, 如: *derog*【貶】等。詳情請參見 Short Forms and Labels (縮略語和説明性略語)。

   (2) 六角括號〔 〕: 表示 ① 括號內為解釋性、限定性的文字;
   ② 某些動詞的受詞 [賓語] 的位置, 例如: **bale²** to tie something such as paper or hay into a large block 把〔紙、乾草等〕綁成一大捆

   (3) 三角括號〈 〉: 用於舉例, 如: **obeisance** 敬禮〈如鞠躬〉。

   (4) 圓括號 ( ): 表示 ① 括號內文字可省略;
   ② 括號內文字有及無兩種情況兼有。

   (5) 方括號 [ ]: 表示和括號前面的文字可相互替代, 例如: **aerogramme** 航空郵簡 [箋]。

   (6) 等號 =: 表示 ① 詞目與等號後的詞同義;
   ② 詞目的詳細釋義可參見等號後的詞的釋義。

The Dictionary

A,a

A, a /e; eɪ/ *plural* **A's, a's** *n* [C] the first letter of the English alphabet 英語字母表的第一個字母

1 1 **a** /ə; ə; *strong* 強讀 e; eɪ/ also 又作 **an** *indefinite article, determiner* **1** used before a noun that names something or someone that has not been mentioned before, or that the person you are talking to does not know about〔用於未曾提及或事先不知道的人或物名稱前〕: *Do you have a car?* 你有(小轎)車嗎? | *There's a spider in the bath.* 浴缸裡有隻蜘蛛。—compare 比較 THE **2 a)** used before a noun that is one of a particular group or class of people or things〔用於某個特定羣體、階層的人或事物前〕: *I want to train to be a teacher.* 我想接受培訓成為一名老師。**b)** used before someone's family name to show that they belong to that family〔用於某人的姓前表明其屬於這個家庭〕: *Only a Peterson would drive a car like that!* 只有彼得森家的人才會那樣開車! **3 a)** one 一(個): *a thousand pounds* 一千英鎊 | *a dozen eggs* 一打雞蛋 **b) a lot/a few/a little/a great deal etc** used before certain words that express an amount of something 許多/幾個/少許/大量等: *There were a lot of people at the party.* 晚會上有很多人。| *A few weeks from now I'll be in Venice.* 幾週以後我會在威尼斯。**4 twice a week/£5 a day etc** two times each week, £5 each day etc; per 每週兩次/每天五英鎊等: *I get paid once a month.* 我的工資一個月發一次。| *The eggs cost $2 a dozen.* 雞蛋兩元一打。**5** used before a noun to mean all things of that type〔用於名詞前代表一類〕: *A square has four sides.* (=all squares have four sides) 正方形有四條邊。**6** used before two nouns that are mentioned together so often that they are thought of as one thing〔用於兩個經常被一起提及因此被看作是一個物體的名詞前〕: *a cup and saucer* 一副杯碟 | *Does everyone have a knife and fork?* 每個人都有刀叉嗎? **7 a)** used before singular nouns, especially words for actions, meaning one example of that action〔用於單數名詞, 尤其是表示動作的名詞前〕: *Take a look at this.* 看看這個。| *It needs a good clean.* 這需要好好清潔一下。**b)** used before the -ing form of verbs when they are used as nouns〔用於帶 -ing 的動名詞之前〕: *a crashing of gears* 齒輪相撞 **c)** used before an UNCOUNTABLE noun when other information about the noun is added by an adjective or phrase〔用於由一個形容詞或片語在不可數名詞前作補充說明時〕: *Candidates must have a good knowledge of chemistry.* 候選人必須精通化學。| *a beauty that became legendary* 成為傳奇的美人 **8** used before an UNCOUNTABLE noun to mean a type of it 一種〔用於不可數名詞前表示種類〕: *a particularly fine Stilton cheese* 一種優質斯提爾頓乳酪 **9** used before the name of a painter or artist etc meaning a particular painting, sculpture etc by that person〔用於畫家或藝術家的名字前表示其繪畫或雕塑作品〕: *an early Rembrandt* 倫勃朗的一幅早期作品 **10** used before a name to mean having the same qualities as that person or thing〔用於某人或某物的名字前指與其具有同樣特性的人或物〕: *She was hailed as a new Marilyn Monroe.* 她被稱為又一個瑪麗蓮·夢露。**11 a)** used before someone's name when you do not know who they are 某一; 一位〔用於一個你不認識的人名前〕: *There is a Mr Tom Wilkins on the phone for you.* 一個叫湯姆·威爾金斯的人打電話找你。| **a certain** *A certain Lisa Blair wishes to speak to you.* 某位叫莉莎·布萊爾的人想和你說話。**b)** used before names of days, events in the year etc to mean a particular one〔用於日期、事件名稱前指某個特定的日子或事件〕: *I can't remember a Christmas like it.* 我想不起有過像這樣的聖誕節。**12** used after such, what, rather and (formal) many to emphasize what you are saying〔置於 such、what、rather 和(正式) many 後表示強調〕: *What a day! I was late for work and my car broke down.* 多麼糟糕的一天! 我上班遲到了, 車子也壞了。| *She had spent many a night* (=many nights) *waiting for him to come home.* 多少個晚上她都在等他回家。

A¹ /e; eɪ/ *n* **1** also 又作 **a** [C,U] the sixth note in the musical SCALE¹ (8) of C major or the musical KEY² (4) based on this note A 音〔C 大調音階中的第六個音〕 **2** [C] the highest mark that a student can get in an examination or for a piece of work A 級, 甲級, 甲等〔表示學業成績優秀〕: *I got an A in French.* 法語我得了個 A。**3 an A student** *AmE* someone who regularly gets the best marks possible for their work in school or college【美】優等生 **4 from A to B** from one place to another 從一地到另一地: *Hiring a car was the best way to get us from A to B.* 租車是我們從一地到另一地的最好方法。**5 from A to Z** describing, including, or knowing everything about a subject 從頭到尾〔表示描述、涵蓋或了解一個科目的全部內容〕: *the history of 20th century art from A to Z* 20 世紀的藝術通史 **6 A3/A4** standard sizes of paper in the European Union A3/A4 紙〔歐盟紙張標準規格〕 **7** [U] a common type of blood A 型〔一種常見血型〕

A² the written abbreviation of 縮寫= AMP

a-¹ /ə; ə/ *prefix* **1** in a particular condition or way 處於某種狀況; 以某種方式: *alive* (=living) 活(着)的 | *aloud* 大聲地 | *with nerves all atingle* (=tingling) 全身神經都發痛 **2** *old use* in, to, at, or on something【舊】在某物內[邊, 上]: *abed* (=in bed) 在牀上 | *afar* (=far away) 在遠處

a-² /e, æ, ə; eɪ, æ, ə/ *prefix* showing an opposite or the absence of something; not; without 與…相反; 缺乏…; 不; 沒有: *amoral* (=not moral) 非道德的 | *atypically* (=not typically) 非[不]典型地

A-1 /ˌe ˈwʌn; ˌeɪ ˈwʌn/ *adj old-fashioned* very good or completely healthy【過時】一流的, 極好的; 完全健康的: *Everything about the resort was A-1.* 這個度假勝地的所有設施都是一流的。

AA /e ˈe; eɪ ˈeɪ/ *n* [C] Associate of Arts; a two-year college degree in the US 副文學士〔美國大學的一種兩年制學位〕

aard·vark /ˈɑrdˌvɑrk; ˈɑːdvɑːk/ *n* [C] a large animal from southern Africa that has a very long nose and eats small insects 土豚

AB /ˌe ˈbi; ˌeɪ ˈbiː/ *n* **1** [U] a common type of blood AB 型〔一種常見血型〕 **2** [C] *AmE* Bachelor of Arts; a university degree in an arts (ART¹ (5)) subject that you get after studying for three or four years【美】文學士

a·back /əˈbæk; əˈbæk/ *adv* **be taken aback** to be very surprised or shocked by something 吃了一驚: *For a moment, I was completely taken aback by her request.* 好一會兒, 我對她的要求感到十分震驚。

ab·a·cus /ˈæbəkəs; ˈæbəkəs/ *n* [C] a wooden frame with small balls used for counting (COUNT¹ (2)) 算盤

ab·a·lo·ne /ˌæbəˈlonɪ; ˌæbəˈləʊni/ *n* [C,U] a kind of SHELLFISH which is used as food and whose shell contains MOTHER-OF-PEARL 鮑魚

a·ban·don¹ /əˈbændən; əˈbændən/ *v* [T] **1** to leave someone, especially someone you are responsible for 拋棄, 遺棄〔某人〕: *children abandoned by their parents* 被父母遺棄的孩子 **2** to go away from a place, vehicle etc, permanently, especially because the situation makes it impossible for you to stay 離棄, 逃離〔某地方或交通工具等〕: *We had to abandon the car and walk the rest* 3

of the way. 我們只好棄車，剩下的路走着去。| *Fearing further attacks, most of the population had abandoned the city.* 由於害怕遭受更多的襲擊，大多數市民已逃離該城市。**3** to stop doing something because there are too many problems and it is impossible to continue 放棄，中止：*The game had to be abandoned due to bad weather.* 由於天氣不好，比賽不得不中止。**4** to decide that you no longer believe in a particular idea or principle 放棄〔信仰或原則〕：*They were accused of abandoning their socialist principles.* 他們被指責放棄了社會主義原則。| **abandon hope (of doing sth)** *Imogen had abandoned all hope of ever seeing her brother again.* 伊莫金已經放棄了再次見到哥哥的全部希望。**5 abandon yourself to** *literary* to feel an emotion so strongly that you let it control you completely【文】沉湎於，放縱〔感情〕**6 abandon ship** to leave a ship because it is sinking〔由於船在下沉而〕棄船（逃生）—**abandonment** *n* [U]

abandon² *n* [U] **with gay/wild abandon** in a careless or uncontrolled way without thinking or caring about what you are doing 盡情；放縱：*The kids hurled pieces of wood on the fire with gay abandon.* 孩子們盡情地把木塊往火上扔。

a·ban·doned /əˋbændənd; əˈbændənd/ *adj* **1** an abandoned building, car, boat etc has been left completely by the people who owned it and is no longer used 廢棄的 **2** someone who is abandoned has been left completely alone by the person who was looking after them 被遺棄的 **3** *literary* behaving in a wild and uncontrolled way【文】無約束的，無度的，放蕩的

a·base /əˋbes; əˈbeɪs/ *v* **abase yourself** to behave in a way that shows you accept that someone has complete power over you 貶低自己，卑躬屈膝 —**abasement** *n* [U]

a·bashed /əˋbæʃt; əˈbæʃt/ *adj* [not before noun 不用於名詞前] embarrassed or ashamed because you have done something wrong or stupid 羞愧的，窘迫的，尷尬的：*She looked rather abashed.* 她看起來很羞愧。

a·bate /əˋbet; əˈbeɪt/ *v* [I,T] *formal* to become less strong or decrease, or to make something do this【正式】使減少，使減輕，使緩解：*We waited for the storm to abate.* 我們等風暴減弱。—**abatement** *n* [U]

ab·at·toir /ˌæbəˋtwɑr; ˈæbətwɑː/ *n* [C] *BrE* a place where animals are killed for their meat; SLAUGHTERHOUSE【英】屠宰場

ab·bess /ˋæbɪs; ˈæbɪ̈s/ *n* [C] a woman who is in charge of a CONVENT (=religious institution for women) 女修道院院長

ab·bey /ˋæbɪ; ˈæbi/ *n* [C] a large church, especially one with buildings next to it where MONK*s* and NUN*s* live or used to live 大修道院，大寺院

ab·bot /ˋæbət; ˈæbət/ *n* [C] a man who is in charge of a MONASTERY (=place where a group of MONK*s* live) 男修道院院長；大寺院男住持

abbr. also 又作 **abbrev.** the written abbreviation of 縮寫= ABBREVIATION

ab·bre·vi·ate /əˋbrivɪˌet; əˈbriːvieɪt/ *v* [T] to make a word or expression shorter by missing out letters or using only the first letter of each word 省略，縮略，縮寫：**be abbreviated to** *'Information technology' is usually abbreviated to 'IT'.* information technology（資訊技術）常被縮略為 IT。—**abbreviated** *adj*

ab·bre·vi·at·ed /əˋbrivɪˌetɪd; əˈbriːvietɪ̈d/ *adj* made shorter by missing out letters or missing out parts of a story, statement etc 縮寫的，縮略的：*Orders were passed to the commander at the front in an abbreviated form.* 命令以縮略的形式傳達給前線指揮員。

ab·bre·vi·a·tion /əˌbrivɪˋeʃən; əˌbriːviˈeɪʃən/ *n* **1** [C] a short form of a word or expression 縮寫，縮略語：*'Dr.' is the written abbreviation of 'Doctor'.* Dr. 是 Doctor 的縮寫形式。**2** [U] the act of abbreviating something 節略，縮寫

ABC¹ /ˌe bi ˋsi; ˌeɪ biː ˈsiː/ *n* also 又作 **ABCs** *AmE*【美】**1** [singular] the letters of the English alphabet as taught to children〔教兒童的〕英語字母（表）**2 the ABC of** the basic facts about a particular subject 基本知識，基礎知識

ABC² *n* [singular,U] American Broadcasting Corporation; one of the national television companies in the US 美國廣播公司

ab·di·cate /ˋæbdəˌket; ˈæbdɪkeɪt/ *v* [I,T] **1** to give up the position of being king or queen 放棄〔王位〕，退（位），讓（位）**2 abdicate responsibility** *formal* to refuse to accept responsibility for something any longer【正式】放棄責任 —**abdication** /ˌæbdəˋkeʃən; ˌæbdɪ̈ˈkeɪʃən/ *n* [C,U]

ab·do·men /æbˋdomən; ˈæbdəmən/ *n* [C] **1** the part of your body between your chest and legs which contains your stomach 腹（部）**2** the end part of an insect's body, joined to the THORAX〔昆蟲的〕腹 —**abdominal** /æbˋdɑmənḷ; æbˈdɒmɪ̈nəl/ *adj*: *acute abdominal pains* 急性腹痛

ab·duct /əbˋdʌkt; əbˈdʌkt/ *v* [T] to take someone away by force; KIDNAP 劫持，綁架；誘拐：*Police suspect she was abducted late last night.* 警方懷疑她昨天深夜被綁架了。—**abductor** *n* [C] —**abduction** /æbˋdʌkʃən; əbˈdʌkʃən/ *n* [C,U]

a·bed /əˋbɛd; əˈbed/ *adj* [not before noun 不用於名詞前] *old-fashioned* in bed【過時】在牀上的

a·ber·rant /æbˋɛrənt; ˈæbərənt/ *adj formal* not usual or normal【正式】異常的；脱離常規的：*aberrant behaviour* 異常行為

ab·er·ra·tion /ˌæbəˋreʃən; ˌæbəˈreɪʃən/ *n* [C,U] an action or event that is different from what usually happens or what someone usually does 偏離；異常：*a temporary aberration in US foreign policy* 美國外交政策短暫的異常變化 | *a mental aberration* 精神失常

a·bet /əˋbɛt; əˈbet/ *v* **abetted, abetting** [T] to help someone do something wrong or illegal 教唆，慫恿，唆使；夥同〔作案〕—see also 另見 **aid and abet** (AID² (2))

a·bey·ance /əˋbeəns; əˈbeɪəns/ *n* **in abeyance** something such as a custom, rule, or system that is in abeyance is not being used at the present time 擱置；中止；暫緩：**fall into abeyance** (=no longer be used) 暫時停用；暫時中止

ab·hor /əbˋhɔr; əbˈhɔː/ *v* **abhorred, abhorring** [T not in progressive 不用進行式] *formal* to hate a kind of behaviour or way of thinking, especially because you think it is morally wrong【正式】厭惡，憎惡：*Some genuinely abhorred slavery, others were simply convinced by the economic arguments against it.* 有些人真正厭惡奴隸制，而另一些人只是出於經濟上的理由才反對奴隸制的。

ab·hor·rence /əbˋhɔrəns; əbˈhɒrəns/ *n* [U] *formal* a deep feeling of hatred towards something【正式】痛恨

ab·hor·rent /əbˋhɔrənt; əbˈhɒrənt/ *adj formal* something that is abhorrent is completely unacceptable because it seems morally wrong; REPUGNANT【正式】可恨的，令人憎惡的：[+to] *The practice of killing animals for food is utterly abhorrent to me.* 我對將動物殺死作為盤中餐的做法非常痛恨。

a·bide /əˋbaɪd; əˈbaɪd/ *v* **1 can't abide** to dislike something or someone very much because you think they are very annoying 不能容忍［忍受］：*I can't abide that man – he's so self-satisfied.* 我受不了那個人，他太自滿了。**2** *past tense* also 過去式又作 **abode** /əˋbod; əˈbəʊd/ [I always+ adv/prep] *old-fashioned* to live somewhere【過時】居住

abide by sth *phr v* [T] to accept and obey a decision, rule, agreement etc, even though you may not agree with it 遵守〔法律〕；信守〔協議等〕：*You have to abide by the referee's decision.* 你必須服從裁判的決定。

a·bid·ing /əˋbaɪdɪŋ; əˈbaɪdɪŋ/ *adj* an abiding feeling or belief continues for a long time and is not likely to change〔情感或信仰〕永久的，持久的

a·bil·i·ty /əˋbɪlətɪ; əˈbɪlɪ̈ti/ *n plural* **abilities** [C,U] **1** something that you are able to do, especially because you have a particular mental or physical skill 能力；技

能; 本領: **ability to do sth** *Our ability to think and speak separates us from other mammals.* 思維和說話的能力使我們有別於其他哺乳動物。| **have the ability to do sth** (=be able to do something, especially something that most people, machines etc cannot do) 有能力做某事〔尤指大部分人、機器等做不了的事〕*These creatures have the ability to withstand very low temperatures.* 這些動物具有忍受極低氣温的能力。| **of great/exceptional etc ability** (=very good at something) 特別擅長… *a player of great ability* 非常有才華的球員 | *No one doubts her abilities as a manager.* 沒有人懷疑她當經理的能力。**2** someone's, especially a student's, level of intelligence or skill, especially in school or college work 智能, 智力: *There are children of all abilities in my class.* 我班上的學生智力水平各有不同。| **high/low/average ability** (=having a high, low etc level of intelligence or skill) 高/低/平均智力[技能] | **mixed ability class** (=a class of students with different levels of intelligence) 智力水平有差異的班級 **3 to the best of your ability** to do something as well as you can 竭盡全力

-ability /əˋbɪlətɪ; əˈbɪlɪ̣ti/ also 又作 **-ibility** *suffix* makes nouns from adjectives ending in -ABLE and -IBLE〔將以 -able 和 -ible 結尾的形容詞轉化為名詞的詞尾〕: *manageability* 可處理(性) | *suitability* 適合(性)

ab·ject /ˋæbdʒɛkt; ˈæbdʒekt/ *adj* **1 abject poverty/misery/failure etc** the state of being extremely poor, unhappy, unsuccessful etc 赤貧/慘痛/慘敗等 **2** an abject action or expression shows that you feel very ashamed 自卑的, 卑躬屈膝的: *an abject apology* 低聲下氣的道歉 —**abjectly** *adv* —**abjection** /æbˋdʒɛkʃən; æbˈdʒekʃən/ *n* [U]

ab·jure /əbˋdʒur; əbˈdʒʊə/ *v* [T] *formal* to state publicly that you will give up a particular belief or way of behaving; RENOUNCE (2)【正式】公開宣布放棄〔某信念、做法〕—**abjuration** /ˌæbdʒuˋreʃən; ˌæbdʒʊ̣ˈreɪʃən/ *n* [U]

a·blaze /əˋblez; əˈbleɪz/ *adj* **1 be ablaze** to be burning with a lot of flames, often causing serious damage 熊熊燃燒, 着火: *Within minutes the whole house was ablaze.* 幾分鐘內, 整座房子就成了一片火海。| **set sth ablaze** (=make something burn a lot) 點燃[放火燒]某物 *A tanker was set ablaze in the gunboat attack.* 油輪遭到砲艇攻擊起火了。**2** filled with a lot of bright light or colour 明亮的, 燈火輝煌的: *a passing pleasure-boat, with all its lights ablaze* 一艘駛過的遊船上燈火輝煌 | **[+with]** *Her yard was ablaze with summer flowers.* 她的院子裡夏季的鮮花五彩繽紛。**3 ablaze with anger/enthusiasm/excitement etc** very angry, excited etc about something 非常生氣/熱情/激動等 —see also 另見 BLAZE

1 1 **a·ble** /ˋebḷ; ˈeɪbəl/ *adj* **1 be able to do sth a)** to have the skill, strength, knowledge etc to do something 有能力做某事, 會做某事: *I've always wanted to be able to speak Japanese.* 我一直想(學)會講日語。**b)** to be able to do something because the situation makes it possible for you to do it 可以去做某事: *Despite his enormous workload the President still seems able to find time to go fishing.* 儘管工作擔子很重, 總統似乎還能找到時間去釣魚。| *I haven't been able to read that report yet.* 我到現在還未能看那份報告。—see 見 CAN[1] (USAGE) **2** clever or good at doing something, especially at doing an important job; COMPETENT (1) 熟練的; 勝任的, 稱職的: *one of my more able students* 我班上能力比較強的學生之一

-able /əbḷ; əbəl/ also 又作 **-ible** *suffix* [in adjectives 構成形容詞] **1** that you can do something to 可以…的: *washable* (=it can be washed) 可洗的 | *unbreakable* (=it cannot be broken) 不會破的, 不易打碎的 | *loveable* (=easy to love) 可愛的 **2** having a particular quality or condition 具有…性質的; 處於…狀態的: *knowledgeable* (=knowing a lot) 博學的 | *comfortable* 舒適的 —**-ably, -ibly** [in adverbs 構成副詞]: *unbelievably* 令人難以置信地

able-bod·ied /ˌ.. ˋ..◂/ *adj* physically strong and healthy, especially when compared with someone who is DISABLED 體格健全的, 強壯的: *Every able-bodied man had to fight for his country.* 每一個體格健全的人都必須為祖國而戰鬥。

able sea·man /ˌ.. ˋ../ *n* [C] a low rank in the navy, or someone who has this rank 一等水兵 —see table on page C6 參見 C6 頁附錄

a·blu·tions /əbˋluʃənz; əˈbluːʃənz/ *n* [plural] *formal or humorous* the things that you do to make yourself clean, such as washing yourself, cleaning your teeth etc【正式或幽默】沐浴; 漱洗

a·bly /ˋeblɪ; ˈeɪbli/ *adv* cleverly, skilfully, or well 能幹地; 巧妙地: *ably assisted by her team of researchers* 得到她研究小組人員的大力幫助

ab·ne·ga·tion /ˌæbnɪˋgeʃən; ˌæbnɪ̣ˈgeɪʃən/ *n* [U] *formal* the act of not allowing yourself to have or do something that you want【正式】自制, 克己

ab·norm·al /æbˋnɔrmḷ; æbˈnɔːməl/ *adj* very different from usual in a way that seems strange, worrying, wrong, or dangerous 不正常的, 反常的; 變態的: *abnormal behaviour* 異常行為 | *an abnormal level of cholesterol* 膽固醇水平異常 | **abnormal for sb to do sth** *My parents thought it was abnormal for a boy to be interested in ballet.* 我父母認為一個男孩子對芭蕾舞感興趣不正常。

ab·nor·mal·ity /ˌæbnɔrˋmælətɪ; ˌæbnɔːˈmælɪ̣ti/ *n* [C, U] an abnormal feature or characteristic, especially something that is wrong with part of someone's body 變異, 變態: *tests that can detect genetic abnormalities in the foetus* 檢查胎兒遺傳變異的試驗

ab·nor·mal·ly /æbˋnɔrməlɪ; æbˈnɔːməli/ *adv* **1 abnormally high/low/slow etc** unusually high, low etc, especially in a way that could cause problems 異常地高/低/慢等: *an abnormally high pulse rate* 異常快的脈搏跳動 **2** in an unusual and often worrying or dangerous way 異常地〔常指令人擔心或危險的行事方式〕

ab·o /ˋæbo; ˈæbəʊ/ *n* [C] *taboo* an offensive word for an Australian ABORIGINE【諱】土佬〔對澳洲土著人的蔑稱〕

a·board[1] /əˋbɔrd; əˈbɔːd/ *prep* on or onto a ship, plane, or train 上船[飛機, 火車]; 在船[飛機, 火車]上: **go aboard** *They finally went aboard the plane.* 他們終於登上了飛機。

aboard[2] *adv* **1** on or onto a ship, plane, or train 在船[飛機, 火車]上; 上船[飛機, 火車]: *The plane crashed killing all 200 people aboard.* 飛機失事, 機上 200 人全部遇難。| *The boat swayed as he stepped aboard.* 他上船時, 船晃了起來。**2 All aboard!** *spoken* used to tell passengers of a ship, bus, or train that they must get on because it will leave soon【口】請大家上船[上公共汽車, 上火車]!

a·bode[1] /əˋbod; əˈbəʊd/ *n* [C] *formal or humorous* someone's home【正式或幽默】住所: *Welcome to my humble abode.* 歡迎光臨寒舍。| **of no fixed abode** (=having no permanent home) 居無定所

abode[2] the past tense of ABIDE

a·bol·ish /əˋbɑlɪʃ; əˈbɒlɪʃ/ *v* [T] to officially end a law, system etc, especially one that has existed for a long time 廢除, 取消: *Slavery was abolished in America in the 19th century.* 美國於 19 世紀廢除了奴隸制。—**abolition** /ˌæbəˋlɪʃən; ˌæbəˈlɪʃən/ *n* [U]: *calls for the abolition of the monarchy* 廢除君主制的呼聲

ab·o·li·tion·ist /ˌæbəˋlɪʃənɪst; ˌæbəˈlɪʃənɪ̣st/ *n* [C] someone who wants to end a system or law 廢除主義者

A-bomb /ˋe ˌbɑm; ˈeɪ bɒm/ *n* [C] *old-fashioned* an ATOM BOMB【過時】原子彈

a·bom·i·na·ble /əˋbɑmɪnəbḷ; əˈbɒmɪnəbəl/ *adj* extremely unpleasant or of very bad quality 令人討厭的, 可惡的; 極差的 —**abominably** *adv*: *Mavis behaved abominably.* 梅維斯表現太差了。

abominable snow·man /.ˌ.... ˋ../ *n* [C] a large creature like a human that is supposed to live in the Himalayas; a YETI〔據傳生活在喜馬拉雅山一帶的〕雪人

A

a·bom·i·nate /əˋbɑmə͵net; əˈbɒmɪ̇neɪt/ *v* [T not in progressive 不用進行式] *formal* to hate something very much; ABHOR【正式】憎恨, 厭惡

a·bom·i·na·tion /ə͵bɑməˋneʃən; ə͵bɒmɪ̇ˈneɪʃən/ *n* **1** [C] someone or something that is extremely offensive or unacceptable 令人厭惡的人[事物]: *They considered homosexuality as an abomination.* 他們對同性戀深惡痛絕。**2** [U+**of**] *formal* great hatred【正式】痛恨

ab·o·rig·i·nal[1] /͵æbəˋrɪdʒənl; ͵æbəˈrɪdʒɪ̇nəl◂/ *adj* **1** *formal* connected with the people or animals that have existed in a place or country from the earliest times; INDIGENOUS【正式】土著的; 土生的 **2** connected with the Australian aborigines 澳洲土著(居民)的

aboriginal[2] *n* [C] an aborigine 土著居民; 土人

ab·o·rig·i·ne /͵æbəˋrɪdʒənɪ; ͵æbəˈrɪdʒɪ̇ni/ *n* [C] a member of the group of people who have lived in Australia from the earliest times (澳洲)土著居民

a·bort /əˋbɔrt; əˈbɔːt/ *v* **1** [T] to stop an activity because it would be difficult or dangerous to continue it 使〔活動〕中止, 夭折: *The shuttle developed a computer problem and the mission had to be aborted.* 太空穿梭機因電腦出現故障, 飛行任務不得不中止。**2** [T] to deliberately cause a baby to be born too soon so that it cannot live, often because the baby or the mother has medical problems 使〔胎兒〕流產; 墮胎: *Doctors decided to abort the pregnancy.* 醫生決定進行人工流產。**3** [I,T] if a woman aborts or aborts her baby, the baby is born too early and is dead when it is born 流產; 小產

a·bor·tion /əˋbɔrʃən; əˈbɔːʃən/ *n* [C,U] a medical operation in which a baby's development inside a woman is stopped so that it is not born alive 人工流產; 墮胎: **have an abortion** *an unmarried mother who had an abortion when she was 16* 16歲時做過人工流產的未婚母親 | *anti-abortion campaigners* 參與反墮胎運動的人

a·bor·tion·ist /əˋbɔrʃənɪst; əˈbɔːʃənɪ̇st/ *n* [C] someone who does abortions illegally 非法為人墮胎者

a·bor·tive /əˋbɔrtɪv; əˈbɔːtɪv/ *adj* an abortive action is not successful 流產的, 夭折的: *an abortive military coup* 未遂的軍事政變 | **abortive attempt/effort** *an abortive attempt to reform local government* 落空了的改革地方政府的計劃

a·bound /əˋbaund; əˈbaʊnd/ *v* [I] to exist in very large numbers or quantities 大量存在; 充滿: *Rumours abound as to the reasons for his resignation.* 有關他辭職的原因有各種各樣的謠傳。| *Examples of this abound in her book.* 這樣的例子在她書中不勝枚舉。

abound with/in sth *phr v* [T] if a place, situation etc abounds with something it contains a very large number or quantity of that thing 盛產, 富於

1 1 **a·bout**[1] /əˋbaut; əˈbaʊt/ *prep* **1** on or dealing with a particular subject 關於: *a book about politics* 有關政治的書 | *She said something about leaving town.* 她說到關於離開城鎮的事。| **all about** (=all the details of a particular subject) 關於…的全部內容 *Naturally, my mother wanted to know all about it.* 當然, 我母親想知道事情的全部。**2** in many different directions within a particular place, or in different parts of a place 到處: *We spent the whole afternoon walking about town.* 我們整個下午在城裡四處走。| *Books were scattered about the room.* 書本散布在房間裡。—see also 另見 ROUND (USAGE) —see picture on page A1 參見A1頁圖 **3** in the nature or character of a person or thing 性格上; 特點上: *There's something really odd about Liza.* 麗莎的為人真有點怪。| *What I like about the movie is the dialogue.* 這部電影, 我喜歡的是其對白。**4 what about/how about** *spoken*【口】**a)** used to ask for news or information about someone or something …怎麼樣〔用以打聽消息〕: *What about Jack? We can't just leave him here.* 傑克怎麼辦? 我們不能把他丟在這裡不管。**b)** used to make a suggestion …怎麼樣; …好嗎〔用以提建議〕: *How about a salad for lunch?* 中午飯吃沙拉怎麼樣? **5** *spoken* used to introduce a subject that you want to talk about【口】〔用來引出一個話題〕有關: *About that car of yours. How much are you selling it for?* 關於你那輛汽車, 你想賣多少錢? | **it's about** *It's about Tommy, doctor. He's been sick again.* 醫生, 是有關湯米的, 他又病了。**6 do sth about** to do something to solve a problem or stop a bad situation 想辦法做…, 解決…問題: *What can be done about the rising levels of pollution?* 該怎樣解決污染加劇問題? **7** if an organization, a job, an activity etc is about something, that is its basic purpose 宗旨是…; 關於: *Basically, the job's all about helping people get the benefits they are entitled to.* 基本上, 這項工作的宗旨是幫助人們得到他們應得的利益。**8 be quick about it** *spoken* used to tell someone to do something quickly【口】快點兒: *Get me a drink and be quick about it.* 給我拿點喝的, 快點兒。**9 while you're about it** *spoken* used to tell someone to do something while they are doing something else because it would be easier to do both at the same time【口】順便: *Clean up while I'm away and you might as well do the attic while you're about it.* 我不在時, 你徹底清掃一下, 順便打掃一下閣樓。**10 about your person** *formal* if you hide something about your person, you hide it in your clothes【正式】在身上, 在衣服裡: *He had concealed the weapon somewhere about his person.* 他把武器藏在身上某個地方了。**11** *literary* surrounding a person or thing【文】圍繞〔某人或某事〕: *Jo sensed fear and jealousy all about her.* 喬能覺察到她既恐懼又妒嫉。

about[2] *adv* **1** more or less a particular number or amount; approximately (APPROXIMATE[1]) 大約, 大概: *I live about 10 miles away.* 我住的地方離這裡十英里左右。| **round about** (=used when guessing an exact number or amount) 大概 *We left the restaurant at round about 10.30.* 我們大概是在十點半離開餐廳的。—see graph at 參見 APPROXIMATE[1] 圖表 **2** in many different directions within a place or in different parts of a place 到處: *Cushions were scattered about on the chairs.* 好幾個墊子散放在幾張椅子上。**3** near to you or in the same place as you 在附近, 在…周圍: *Is Derrick about? There's a phone call for him.* 德里克在附近嗎? 有電話找他。| *Quick! Let's go while there's no-one about.* 快點兒! 我們趁附近沒有人趕緊走。**4 there's a lot of sth about/there's not much of sth about** *especially spoken* used to say that something is very common, or that not much of it exists or is available【尤口】某物很普遍/不常見: *I hope she hasn't caught that flu bug. There's a lot of it about at the moment.* 我希望她沒感染流感病毒, 目前這種病毒到處都有。**5** *informal* almost【非正式】幾乎: *The food's about ready.* 食物就要(準備)好了。—see also 另見 **just about** (JUST[1] (8)) **6 that's about it/all** *informal* used to tell someone that you have told them everything you know【非正式】該說的都說了, 這就是全部: *He was a quiet chap, married with kids. That's about it really.* 他話不多, 已婚, 有孩子。大概就是這樣。**7** in the opposite direction that you were facing before (轉向)相反方向: *He quickly turned about.* 他很快轉過身。—see also 另見 ROUND[3] (USAGE) 1 1

about[3] *adj* **1 be about to do sth** if someone is about to do something or if something is about to happen, they will do it or it will happen very soon 即將[馬上]做某事: *Sit down everyone. The film's about to start.* 大家坐下, 電影馬上要開始了。**2 not be about to do sth** *informal* used to emphasize that you have no intention of doing something【非正式】不打算做某事: *I've never smoked in my life and I'm not about to start now.* 我從未抽過煙, 現在也不打算抽。—see also 另見 **be up and about** (UP[3] (6))

about-face /·,· ˈ·/ *n* [C usually singular 一般用單數] a complete change in the way someone thinks or behaves〔思想、行為的〕大轉變: **do an about-face** *The administration seems to have done a complete about-face on gun-control.* 政府對槍支管制(的態度)似乎來

了個一百八十度大轉變。

about-turn /ˌ· ˈ·/ *n* [C usually singular 一般用單數] *BrE* an about-face【英】大轉變

above 在…上方

The picture is above the fireplace/over the fireplace.
畫掛在壁爐上方。

The girl jumped over the wall. 那女孩跳過了牆。

The man put his hand over the boy's mouth.
那男子用手捂住了男孩的嘴。

2 1 **a·bove¹** /əˋbʌv; əˈbʌv/ *prep* **1** in a higher position than something 在…上方: *Our office is above the hairdresser's.* 我們的辦公室在理髮店上面。| *Raise your arms above your head.* 把雙臂舉過頭。—see also 另見 OVER¹ —opposite 反義詞 BELOW¹ (1) **2** more than a particular number, amount, or level 高於, 超出: *500 feet above sea level* 海拔500英尺 | *Tonight temperatures should be above freezing.* 今晚的溫度將會在零度以上。—opposite 反義詞 BELOW¹ (2) **3** to a greater degree than someone or something else 高於, 大於: *The management has always valued hard work above good ideas.* 管理層總是認為努力工作比提好建議重要。| **above and beyond** (=to a much greater degree) 遠不止 *bravery above and beyond the call of duty* 超越職責要求的勇敢精神 **4** higher in rank, power, or authority〔權力〕大於;〔地位〕高於: *A captain is above a lieutenant.* 上尉的軍銜比中尉高。—opposite 反義詞 BELOW¹ (3) **5** louder or having a higher PITCH than other sounds〔聲音〕比…高: *You can always hear her voice above everybody else's.* 你總會聽到她的嗓門壓過其他所有的人。**6 be above (doing) sth** to consider yourself so important that you do not have to do all the things that everyone else has to do 不屑於(做)某事: *She seems to think she's above doing any housework.* 她好像認為做家務有損自己的身分。| *politicians who think they are above the law* 認為自己可以凌駕於法律之上的政客 **7 above suspicion/reproach/criticism etc** so good that no one can question or criticize you 不會遭到懷疑/責難/批評等 **8 above all (else)** used to emphasize that something is more important than the other things you have already mentioned 尤其是, 最重要的是: *Max is fair, hardworking, and above all honest.* 馬克斯公正、勤勞, 最重要的是誠實。**9 get above yourself** to think you are better or more important than you really are 自高自大, 自命不凡 —see also 另見 **over and above** (OVER¹ (13))

2 1 **above²** *adv* **1** in a higher place than something else 在上面: *I heard a strange noise coming from the room above.* 我聽到樓上房間裡傳來奇怪的聲音。**2** more than a particular number, amount, or level 超過〔某數字、數量或水平〕: *Children aged 10 and above are not allowed in the learner pool.* 十歲及十歲以上的孩子不得在練習池裡游泳。**3** higher in rank, power, or authority〔官銜、權勢〕在上, 以上: *officers of the rank of Major and above* 少校及少校以上軍銜的軍官 **4** *formal* used in a book, article etc to describe someone or something mentioned earlier in the same piece of writing【正式】上述, 上文: *See above.* 見上文。| *Write to the address given above for further information.* 詳情請致函上述地址查詢。—opposite 反義詞 BELOW²

> **USAGE NOTE 用法說明: ABOVE**
> FORMALITY 正式程度
> **Above** meaning 'mentioned earlier' is only used in technical or official writing. In everyday writing you are more likely to put 表示"上述"意思時, above只用於專業性的或正式的文體。日常寫作中常用: *As I said earlier...* (=*...stated above*) 正如我在前面提到的… | *The facts discussed before...* (=*...discussed above*) 前面討論的事實… | *Please contact me at the address I have given you* (=*...at the above address*). 請按我給你的地址和我聯繫。| *from the last few paragraphs* (=*from the above paragraphs*) 從上面的幾段中

above³ *adj* **1** [only before noun 僅用於名詞前] used in a book, article etc to describe someone or something mentioned earlier in the same piece of writing 上述的: *For the above reasons, the management has no choice but to close the factory.* 基於上述原因, 資方別無選擇, 只好關閉工廠。**2 the above** *formal* [singular or plural] the person or thing mentioned before in the same piece of writing【正式】上面提到的人[事]: *The above is the profit before tax.* 上面提到的是稅前利潤。| *All the above are asked to attend tomorrow's meeting.* 以上各位請全部出席明天的會議。 3

above board /ˌ· ˈ·◂/ *adj* [not before noun 不用於名詞前] honest and legal 光明正大的: **open and above board** *The deal was completely open and above board.* 這筆交易完全是光明正大的。

above-men·tioned /ˌ·· ˈ··◂/ *adj* **1** [only before noun 僅用於名詞前] *formal* mentioned on a previous page or higher up on the same page【正式】上面的, 上述的 **2 the above-mentioned** people whose names have already been mentioned in a book, document etc 上面提到的人 —compare 比較 UNDERMENTIONED

ab·ra·ca·dab·ra /ˌæbrəkəˋdæbrə; ˌæbrəkəˈdæbrə/ *interjection* a word you say when you do a magic trick, which is supposed to make it successful〔魔術表演施行法術時所唸的〕咒語

a·brade /əˋbred; əˈbreɪd/ *v* [I,T] *technical* to rub something so hard that the surface becomes damaged【術語】磨損

a·bra·sion /əˋbreʒən; əˈbreɪʒən/ *n technical*【術語】**1** [C] an area, especially on the surface of your skin, that has been damaged or injured by being rubbed too hard 磨損處, 磨傷處: *minor abrasions* 少許磨損 **2** [U] the process of rubbing a surface very hard so that it becomes damaged or disappears 磨損(的過程), 磨蝕

a·bra·sive¹ /əˋbresɪv; əˈbreɪsɪv/ *adj* **1** seeming rude or unkind in the way you behave towards people because you say what you think very directly 生硬的; 粗魯的: *a rather abrasive manner* 相當粗魯的舉止 **2** having a rough surface, especially one that can be used to clean other surfaces by rubbing〔尤指可用於擦洗的東西表面〕粗糙的 —**abrasively** *adv*

abrasive² *n* [C usually plural 一般用複數] a substance with a rough surface that you use for cleaning other things by rubbing 磨料

abreast 並肩, 並排

They cycled three abreast. 他們三個人並排騎車。

a·breast /əˋbrɛst; əˈbrest/ *adv* **1 walk/ride etc abreast** to walk, ride etc next to each other 並肩走/並排騎等: **two/three/four abreast etc** (=with two or more people next to each other) 二/三/四人等並排 **2 keep abreast of** to make sure that you know all the most recent facts or information about a particular subject or situation 了解…的最新情況: *Henry tries to keep abreast of the latest developments in computing.* 亨利設法掌握計算技術的最新發展。

a·bridged /əˋbrɪdʒd; əˈbrɪdʒd/ *adj* an abridged book, play etc has been made shorter but keeps its basic structure and meaning 刪節的, 節略的, 壓縮的 —**abridge** *v* [T] —**abridgement** *n* [C,U]

2 3 **a·broad** /əˋbrɔd; əˈbrɔːd/ *adv* **1** in or to a foreign country 在國外; 到國外: *I've never lived abroad before.* 我以前從未在國外生活過。| **go abroad** *She often goes abroad on business.* 她經常出國公幹。**2** *formal* if a feeling, piece of news etc is abroad, a lot of people feel it or know about it【正式】廣泛流傳: *commercial secrets which we did not want to be spread abroad* 我們不想傳出去的商業祕密 **3** *old use* outdoors【舊】在戶外, 室外

ab·ro·gate /ˋæbrəˌget; ˈæbrəgeɪt/ *v* [T] *formal* to officially end a law, legal agreement, practice etc【正式】取消, 廢除: *Both governments voted to abrogate the treaty.* 兩國政府均投票廢除了這項條約。—**abrogation** /ˌæbrəˋgeʃən; ˌæbrəˈgeɪʃən/ *n* [C,U]

a·brupt /əˋbrʌpt; əˈbrʌpt/ *adj* **1** sudden and unexpected 突然的, 出其不意的: *an abrupt change of plan* 計劃的突然改變 | **abrupt halt** *The bus came to an abrupt halt.* 公共汽車突然停了下來。**2** seeming rude and unfriendly, especially because you do not waste time in friendly conversation; BRUSQUE 唐突的; 魯莽的, 莽撞的: *Sorry, I didn't mean to be so abrupt.* 對不起, 我不是故意這樣無禮的。—**abruptly** *adv* —**abruptness** *n* [U]

ABS /ˌe bi ˋɛs; ˌeɪ biː ˈes/ *n* [U] the abbreviation of 縮寫= ANTI-LOCK BRAKING SYSTEM

ab·scess /ˋæbˌsɛs; ˈæbses/ *n* [C] a painful swollen part of your skin or inside your body that has become infected and is full of a yellowish liquid 膿腫

ab·scond /æbˋskɑnd; əbˈskɒnd/ *v* [I] **1** to suddenly leave the place where you work after having stolen money from it〔攜款〕潛逃: **[+with]** *The chief accountant had absconded with all the money.* 總會計師攜帶所有的錢款潛逃了。**2** to escape from a place where you are being kept for doing something wrong 逃走, 逃匿: *Several boys have absconded from the detention centre.* 幾個男孩子從拘留所逃走了。

ab·seil /ˋæbsel; ˈæbseɪl/ *v* **[I+down]** *BrE* to go down a cliff or a rock by sliding down a rope and touching the cliff or rock with your feet【英】〔用繩索〕下降; RAPPEL *AmE*【美】

3 2 **ab·sence** /ˋæbsn̩s; ˈæbsəns/ *n* **1** [C,U] the fact that someone is not in the place where people expect them to be 不在, 缺席: **in/during sb's absence** (=while they are away) 某人不在的時候 *Ms Leighton will be in charge during my absence.* 我不在時, 由萊頓女士負責。**2** [U] the lack of something or the fact that it dose not exist 缺乏, 沒有: **[+of]** *a complete absence of any kind of planning* 毫無計劃 | **in the absence of** (=because something is missing or not available) 由於缺乏 *In the absence of any evidence, the police had to let Myers go.* 由於缺乏證據, 警察只好把邁爾斯放了。**3 absence makes the heart grow fonder** used to say that being away from someone makes you like them more 人不見, 心更念; 久別情更深 —see also 另見 **leave of absence** (LEAVE[2] (3)), **conspicuous by your absence** (CONSPICUOUS (3))

ab·sent[1] /ˋæbsn̩t; ˈæbsənt/ *adj* **1** not at work, school, a meeting etc, because you are sick or decide not to go 不在的, 缺席的: **[+from]** *students who are regularly absent from school* 經常缺課的學生 **2 absent look/expression etc** a look etc that shows you are not paying attention to or thinking about what is happening 心不在焉的樣子/表情等 —see also 另見 ABSENTLY **3** *formal* if something is absent, it is missing or it is not in the place where it is expected to be【正式】缺乏的, 不在場的: **[+from]** *What was absent from the discussion was any kind of direction or purpose.* 這場討論沒有任何方向或目的。

ab·sent[2] /æbˋsɛnt; əbˈsent/ *v* [T] **absent yourself (from)** *formal* to not go to a place or take part in an event where people expect you to be【正式】缺席; 置身於…之外

ab·sen·tee /ˌæbsn̩ˋti; ˌæbsənˈtiː◂/ *n* [C] someone who should be in a place or at an event but is not there 缺席者

absentee bal·lot /ˌ··· ˈ··/ *n* [C] *AmE* a process by which people can vote before an election because they will be away during the election【美】缺席投票〔因投票人在選舉期間不在而可提前投票的程序〕

ab·sen·tee·is·m /ˌæbsn̩ˋtiɪzəm; ˌæbsənˈtiːɪzəm/ *n* [U] regular absence from work or school without a good reason 經常曠工[缺課]

absentee land·lord /ˌ··· ˈ··/ *n* [C] someone who lives a long way away from a house or apartment which they rent to other people, and who rarely or never visits it〔住在很遠處、很少或從不到訪出租房產的〕在外房東, 在外地主

absentee vote /ˌ··· ˈ·/ *n* [C] *AmE* a vote which you send by post in an election because you cannot be in the place where you usually vote【美】缺席選票〔投票人在選舉期間不能到場而通過郵寄方式投的票〕; POSTAL VOTE *BrE*【英】

ab·sen·ti·a /æbˋsɛntɪə; æbˈsentiə/ *n* **in absentia** *formal* when you are not at a court or an official meeting where a decision is made about you【正式】在〔當事人〕缺席的情況下: *They were sentenced in absentia.* 他們在缺席的情況下被判刑。

ab·sent·ly /ˋæbsn̩tlɪ; ˈæbsəntli/ *adv* in a way that shows that you are not paying attention to or thinking about what is happening 心不在焉地: *Laura gazed absently out of the window.* 勞拉出神地看着窗外。

absent-mind·ed /ˌ·· ˈ··◂/ *adj* likely to forget things, especially because you are thinking about something else 心不在焉的, 茫然的: *She's getting very absent-minded.* 她變得心神恍惚。—**absent-mindedly** *adv* —**absent-mindedness** *n* [U]

ab·sinth, absinthe /ˋæbsɪnθ; ˈæbsɪnθ/ *n* [U] a bitter green very strong alcoholic drink 苦艾酒

ab·so·lute /ˋæbsəˌlut; ˈæbsəluːt/ *adj* **1** [only before noun 僅用於名詞前] *especially spoken* used to emphasize your opinion about something or someone, especially when you think they are very bad, stupid, unsuccessful etc【尤口】純粹的; 絕對的: **absolute disgrace/disaster/chaos etc** *The house looked an absolute shambles.* 屋子裡顯得凌亂不堪。| *I think it's an absolute disgrace the way* *they treat that child.* 我認為他們這樣對待那個孩子絕對不光彩。| **an absolute genius/fool/idiot etc** *How did you do that? You're an absolute genius.* 你是怎麼做的？你絕對是個天才。| **absolute nonsense/rubbish** (=used to say that you think that what someone is saying is completely stupid) 一派胡言 **2** absolute silence, freedom, loyalty etc is the state of being completely silent, free etc 完全的；絕對的：*I have absolute confidence in her.* 我對她絕對有信心。**3** absolute power or authority is complete and unlimited〔權力或權威〕絕對的，無限的：**absolute ruler/monarch** (=a ruler with unlimited power) 專制統治者／君主 **4** definite and not likely to change 確定的；不會更改的：*I can't give you any absolute guarantees about your safety.* 我不能絕對保證你的安全。**5 in absolute terms** measured by itself, not in comparison with other things 從絕對意義上說：*In absolute terms wages have risen, but not in comparison with the cost of living.* 從絕對意義上說，工資是提高了，但同生活費用相比較就不能這樣說了。

1 3 **ab·so·lute·ly** /ˋæbsəˌlutlɪ; ˈæbsəluːtli/ *adv* **1** *especially spoken* completely and in every way【尤口】完全地；絕對地：[+adj/adv] *He's an absolutely brilliant singer.* 他絕對是個出色的歌唱家。| *You can trust her absolutely!* 你可以完全信任她！| *You look absolutely fantastic in that dress.* 你穿那條裙子簡直美極了。| **absolutely no/nothing** (=none or nothing at all) 一點兒沒有 *He has absolutely no experience of marketing.* 他毫無銷售經驗。| *The burglars took absolutely everything.* 竊賊把所有的東西全拿走了。**2 absolutely!** *spoken* used to say that you completely agree with someone【口】正是！當然!：*Oh yes, absolutely. I think it's a great idea.* 噢，對，我看這絕對是個好主意。**3 absolutely not!** *spoken* used when saying strongly that someone must not do something or when strongly disagreeing with someone【口】絕對不行！當然不會！：*"Do you let your kids travel alone at night?" "Absolutely not!"* "你讓孩子晚上單獨外出嗎？""當然不會！"

Frequencies of the adverb **absolutely** in spoken and written English 副詞 absolutely 在英語口語和書面語中的使用頻率

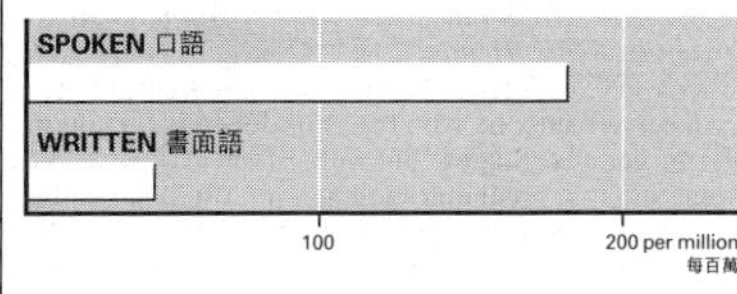

Based on the British National Corpus and the Longman Lancaster Corpus
據英國國家語料庫和朗文蘭卡斯特語料庫

This graph shows that the adverb **absolutely** is much more common in spoken English than in written English. This is because it is used to emphasize adjectives like **brilliant**, **stupid**, **fantastic** etc in spoken English. 本圖表顯示，副詞absolutely在英語口語中的使用頻率遠遠高於書面語，因為它在口語中用來強調 brilliant，stupid，fantastic 等一類的形容詞。

absolute ze·ro /ˌ··· ˈ··/ *n* [singular] the lowest temperature that is believed to be possible 絕對零度

ab·so·lu·tion /ˌæbsəˋluʃən; ˌæbsəˈluːʃən/ *n* [U] a process in the Christian religion by which someone is forgiven for the things they have done wrong〔基督教中的〕赦罪；寬恕

ab·so·lut·is·m /ˋæbsəlutˌɪzəm; ˈæbsəluːtɪzəm/ *n* [U] a political system in which one ruler has complete power and authority 專制主義（制度），獨裁政治

ab·solve /əbˋzɑlv; əbˈzɒlv/ *v* [T] *formal*【正式】**1** to say publicly that someone is not guilty or responsible for something 宣布…無罪；免除…〔責任等〕：**absolve sb from/of sth** *They were absolved of all responsibility for the accident.* 他們被免除對這起意外事故的一切責任。**2** [often passive 常用被動態] to forgive someone for something they have done wrong 饒恕

absorb 吸收

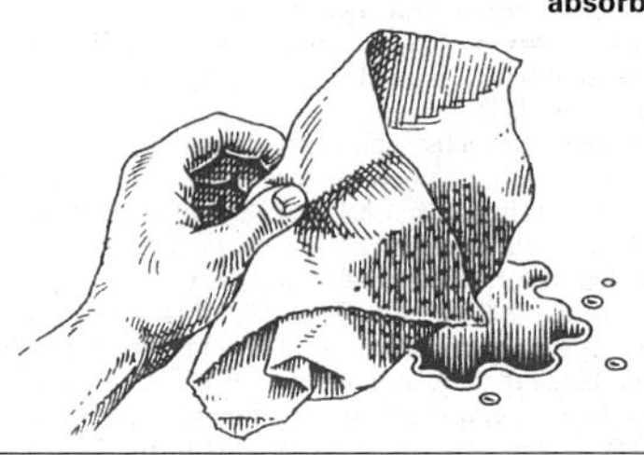

ab·sorb /əbˋsɔrb; əbˈsɔːb/ *v* [T] 3

1 ▶LIQUID 液體◀ if something absorbs a liquid, it takes the liquid into itself from the surface or space around it 吸收〔液體〕：*Plants absorb nutrients from the soil.* 植物從土壤中吸收養分。

2 ▶INFORMATION 信息◀ to read or hear a large amount of new information and understand it 理解，掌握：*I haven't really had time to absorb everything that he said.* 我還真沒有時間弄懂他說的一切。

3 ▶INTEREST 興趣◀ to interest someone very much 吸引〔某人〕，使專心：**be absorbed in** *Judith lay on the settee, absorbed in her book.* 朱迪思躺在沙發椅上專心致志地看書。| **absorb sb's attention** *The video was totally absorbing the children's attention.* 錄像完全吸引了孩子們的注意力。

4 ▶BECOME PART OF 成為…的一部分◀ to make a smaller country, company, or group of people become part of your country, company, or group 併入；吞併：*The US was able to absorb thousands of new immigrants.* 美國能吸引成千上萬的新移民。| **be absorbed into** *More and more newspapers are being absorbed into the Murdoch empire.* 越來越多的報紙被併入梅鐸的新聞帝國。

5 ▶MONEY/TIME ETC 金錢/時間等◀ if something absorbs money, time etc it uses a lot of it 消耗，花去：*Defence spending absorbs almost 20% of the country's wealth.* 國防開支消耗了這個國家差不多 20% 的財富。

6 ▶FORCE 力◀ to reduce the effect of a sudden violent movement 消減，緩衝：*The solid walls absorbed much of the impact of the explosion.* 這些堅固的牆大大減小了爆炸的衝擊力。

7 ▶LIGHT/HEAT/ENERGY 光/熱/能◀ if a substance or object absorbs light, heat, or energy, it keeps it and does not REFLECT it (=send it back) 吸收：*Black objects absorb heat more.* 黑色的物體吸熱多。

ab·sor·bent /əbˋsɔrbənt; əbˈsɔːbənt/ *adj* able to take in liquids easily 有吸水性的：*absorbent material* 吸水性材料

ab·sorb·ing /əbˋsɔrbɪŋ; əbˈsɔːbɪŋ/ *adj* enjoyable and interesting and holding your attention for a long time 十分吸引人的，引人入勝的：*an absorbing documentary about China* 一部引人入勝的關於中國的記錄片

ab·sorp·tion /əbˋsɔrpʃən; əbˈsɔːpʃən/ *n* [U] **1** [+with/in] the fact of being very interested in something 專注 **2** a process in which a material or object takes in liquid, gas, or heat 吸收 **3** a process in which a country or organization makes a smaller country, organization or group of people become part of itself 合併，併入

ab·stain /əbˋsten; əbˈsteɪn/ *v* [I] **1** to not vote either for or against something in an election 棄權，不投票 **2** *formal* to not do something, especially something enjoyable, because you think it is bad for your health or morally wrong【正式】戒除；迴避：[+from] *Pilots must abstain from alcohol for 24 hours before flying.* 飛行員在飛機

起飛前24小時必須禁酒。—**abstainer** *n* [C]

ab·ste·mi·ous /əb`stimɪəs; əb'sti:miəs/ *adj formal or humorous* careful not to have too much food, drink etc【正式或幽默】節儉的; 有節制的, 克制的 —**abstemiously** *adv* —**abstemiousness** *n* [U]

ab·sten·tion /əb`stɛnʃən; əb'stenʃən/ *n* [C,U] a vote in an election which is neither for nor against something or someone 棄權票

ab·sti·nence /`æbstənəns; 'æbstɪnəns/ *n* [U] the practice of not doing something you enjoy, especially not drinking alcohol 禁慾;〔尤指〕戒酒 —**abstinent** *adj*

ab·stract[1] /`æbstrækt; 'æbstrækt/ *adj* **1** based on general ideas or principles rather than specific examples or real events 純理論上的, 純概念的: **abstract thought/reasoning** (=thought about complicated ideas rather than about things that are around you) 抽象思維/推理 *a machine that is capable of abstract thought* 能進行抽象思維的機器 **2** existing only as an idea or quality rather than as something real that you can see or touch 抽象的: *Beauty is an abstract concept.* 美是一種抽象的概念。—compare 比較 CONCRETE[1] (2) **3** abstract paintings, designs etc consist of shapes and patterns that do not look like real people or things〔藝術〕抽象派的 —compare 比較 FIGURATIVE (2) —see also 另見 ABSTRACT NOUN

abstract[2] *n* [C] **1 in the abstract** considered in a general way rather than being based on specific details and examples 抽象地, 從理論上說: *Talking about bringing up children in the abstract just isn't enough.* 僅僅從理論上談論培養孩子是不夠的。**2** a short written statement of the most important ideas in a speech, article etc 摘要, 梗概 **3** a painting, design etc which contains shapes or images that do not look like real things or people 抽象派作品

ab·stract[3] /æb`strækt; əb'strækt/ *v* [T] **1** to use information from a speech, article etc in a shorter piece of writing that contains the most important ideas 作摘要, 節錄 **2** *formal* to remove something from somewhere or from a place【正式】轉移開

ab·stract·ed /æb`stræktɪd; əb'stræktɪd/ *adj* not noticing anything around you because you are thinking carefully about something else 心不在焉的, 出神的 —**abstractedly** *adv*

ab·strac·tion /æb`strækʃən; əb'strækʃən/ *n* **1** [C] a general idea about a type of situation, thing, or person, rather than a specific example from real life 抽象概念: *talking in abstractions* 抽象地談論 **2** [U] a state in which you do not notice what is happening around you because you are thinking carefully about something else 心不在焉, 出神

abstract noun /,·· '·/ *n* [C] a noun that names a feeling, quality, or state rather than an object, animal, or person 抽象名詞: *'Hunger' and 'beauty' are abstract nouns.* hunger (飢餓) 和 beauty (美麗) 是抽象名詞。

ab·struse /əb`strus; əb'stru:s/ *adj formal* difficult to understand in a way that seems unnecessarily complicated【正式】深奧的, 高深的 —**abstrusely** *adv* —**abstruseness** *n* [U]

ab·surd /əb`sɝd; əb'sɜ:d/ *adj* completely stupid or unreasonable; RIDICULOUS 荒謬的, 荒唐的, 愚蠢的: *Don't be absurd!* 別那麼荒唐! | *It seems quite absurd to expect anyone to drive for 3 hours just for a 20 minute meeting.* 指望一個人開3小時車去參加一個20分鐘的會議, 看來頗為荒唐。—**absurdity** *n* [C,U]

ab·surd·ly /əb`sɝdlɪ; əb'sɜ:dli/ *adv* **absurdly cheap/difficult/easy etc** so cheap, difficult etc that it seems surprising, unusual, or even funny 出奇地便宜/難/容易等: *Prices on the island seem absurdly low to Western tourists.* 在西方遊客看來, 這個島上的物價便宜得驚人。

a·bun·dance /ə`bʌndəns; ə'bʌndəns/ *n* [singular, U] a large quantity of something 充裕, 豐富: **an abundance of** *an abundance of wavy red hair* 一頭濃密的紅鬈髮 | **in abundance** *Wild flowers grow in abundance on the hillsides.* 山坡上長滿了野花。

a·bun·dant /ə`bʌndənt; ə'bʌndənt/ *adj* existing or available in large quantities so that there is more than enough; PLENTIFUL 豐富的, 充裕的: *abundant supplies* 充足的供應

a·bun·dant·ly /ə`bʌndəntlɪ; ə'bʌndəntli/ *adv* **1** in large quantities 大量地: *a force of Marines, abundantly equipped with anti-aircraft guns* 裝備大量防空砲的海軍陸戰隊 | *Melons grow abundantly in this region.* 這個地區盛產甜瓜。**2 abundantly clear** very easy to understand so that anyone should be able to realize it 顯而易見: *It's abundantly clear what the outcome will be.* 結果會怎樣已非常清楚。| **make sth abundantly clear** (=say something very clearly) 清楚地表達 *Caroline made it abundantly clear that she didn't want Chuck around.* 卡羅琳清楚地表明她不想查克在身邊。

a·buse[1] /ə`bjus; ə'bju:s/ *n* **1** [C,U] the use of something in a way that it should not be used 濫用: **[+of]** *government officials' abuse of power* 政府官員濫用職權 | **open to abuse** (=able or likely to be used in the wrong way) 易被濫用 *The city's metro system is open to abuse by fare dodgers.* 該市的地鐵系統很容易讓逃票者有機可乘。| **alcohol/drug/solvent abuse** (=the practice of drinking too much or taking illegal drugs) 酗酒/濫用毒品/濫用溶劑 *The fraud department only deals with the worst abuse.* 反詐騙部門只處理那些最嚴重的違紀問題。**2** [U] rude or offensive things that someone says to someone else 辱罵, 謾罵: *I don't see why I should put up with this kind of abuse from anyone.* 我不明白我為甚麼要忍受有人這樣辱罵我。| **a stream/torrent of abuse** (=a series of rude or angry words) 一連串的粗話[氣話] | **shout/scream/hurl abuse at** *The driver leaned out of his window and started hurling abuse at me.* 司機把頭探出窗外開始罵我。| **a term of abuse** (=a word or phrase used to insult someone) 罵人話 **3** [U] cruel or violent treatment, often involving forced sexual activity, of someone that you are responsible for or should look after 虐待: *child abuse* 虐待兒童 | *sexual abuse* 性虐待

a·buse[2] /ə`bjuz; ə'bju:z/ *v* [T] **1** to deliberately use something such as power or authority, for the wrong purpose 濫用〔職權〕: *Williams abused his position as Mayor to give jobs to his friends.* 威廉姆斯濫用自己市長的權力, 把許多職務給了朋友。| **abuse sb's trust/confidence etc** (=deceive someone who trusts or depends on you in order to get advantages for yourself) 背信棄義 **2** to treat someone in a cruel and violent way, often sexually, especially someone that you should look after 虐待: *People who were abused as children often turn into child-abusers themselves.* 孩提時代遭受虐待的人往往會變成虐童者。**3** to say rude or offensive things to someone 謾罵, 辱罵 **4** to treat something so badly that you start to destroy it 傷害; 摧殘: *Richards abused his body for years with heroin and cocaine.* 理查茲多年來吸食海洛因和可卡因, 身體每況愈下。**5 abuse yourself** to MASTURBATE 手淫

a·bu·sive /ə`bjusɪv; ə'bju:sɪv/ *adj* very rude and using offensive language, especially because you are angry 罵人的, 謾罵的: **get/become abusive** *She got quite abusive on the phone.* 她在電話裡發了火。—**abusively** *adv* —**abusiveness** *n* [U]

a·but /ə`bʌt; ə'bʌt/ also 又作 **abut on** *v* [T] *technical* if one piece of land or a building abuts another it is next to it or touches one side of it【術語】鄰接, 毗連

a·bys·mal /ə`bɪzml̩; ə'bɪzməl/ *adj* very bad; TERRIBLE (3) 極壞的: *the Labour Party's abysmal performance in the last election* 工黨在上次選舉中非常糟糕的表現 —**abysmally** *adv*: *Educational standards were abysmally low.* 教育水平低極了。

a·byss /ə`bɪs; ə'bɪs/ *n* [C] *literary*【文】**1** a deep empty space, seen from a high point such as a mountain 深淵: *The ocean floor drops away into a dark abyss.* 海底陡

然下斜形成深深的暗溝。**2** a very dangerous or frightening situation 危險[可怕]的局面: *the abyss of a nuclear war* 核戰爭的深淵 **3** a great difference which separates two people or groups 鴻溝: *the abyss between rich and poor* 貧富之間的天壤之別

AC 1 the written abbreviation of 縮寫= ALTERNATING CURRENT —compare 比較 DC (1) **2** the written abbreviation of 縮寫= AIR-CONDITIONING —see also 另見 AC/DC

a/c *BrE*【英】the written abbreviation of 縮寫= ACCOUNT[1] (2)

a·ca·cia /əˋkeʃə; əˈkeɪʃə/ *n* [C] a tree with small yellow or white flowers that grows in warm countries 金合歡屬植物〔尤指阿拉伯膠樹〕

ac·a·de·mi·a /ˌækəˋdimɪə; ˌækəˈdiːmiə/ *n* [U] the area of activity and work connected with education in colleges and universities 學術界

2 **ac·a·dem·ic**[1] /ˌækəˋdɛmɪk; ˌækəˈdemɪk◂/ *adj* **1** [usually before noun 一般用於名詞前] connected with education, especially at college or university level 學術的: *She loved the city, with its academic atmosphere.* 她喜歡這城市，喜歡其學術氛圍。| *academic books* 學術類書籍 | *a program designed to raise academic standards* 旨在提高學術水平的計劃 **2** [usually before noun 一般用於名詞前] concerned with studying from books, as opposed to practical work 學術上的; 理論上的 **3** something that is academic is not important because it cannot happen or have any effect; THEORETICAL 不合實際的, 理論的: **purely academic** *The question of where we go on holiday is purely academic since we don't have any money.* 我們去哪個地方度假這個問題完全不切實際, 因為我們根本沒有錢。**4** good at studying and getting good results at school or university 學業(成績)優秀的: *He's a popular child, but not very academic.* 他是個受人喜歡的孩子, 但學習成績不太好。—**academically** /-kḷɪ; -kli/ *adv*

academic[2] *n* [C] a teacher in a college or university 大學教師

a·cad·e·mi·cian /əˌkædəˋmɪʃən; əˌkædəˈmɪʃən/ *n* [C] a member of an academy 學會會員; 院士

academic year /ˌ···· ˈ·/ *n* [C] *especially BrE* the period of the year during which there are school or university classes; school year (SCHOOL[1])【尤英】學年

a·cad·e·my /əˋkædəmɪ; əˈkædəmi/ *n* [C] **1** an important official organization consisting of people interested in the development of literature, art, science etc 研究院; 學會: *the American Academy of Arts and Letters* 美國藝術和文學學會 **2** a college where students are taught a particular subject or skill 專科學院: *a military academy* 軍事學院 | *the Academy of Music* 音樂學院 **3** a school in Scotland for children between 11 and 16〔蘇格蘭11到16歲孩子上的〕文法學校

a cap·pel·la /ˌɑ kəˋpɛlə; ˌæ kæˈpelə/ *adj, adv* sung without any musical instruments 清唱的[地], 無樂器伴奏的[地]

acc. the written abbreviation of 縮寫= ACCOUNT[1]

ac·cede /əkˋsid; əkˈsiːd/ *v*

accede to sth *phr v* [T] *formal*【正式】**1** to agree to a demand, proposal etc, especially after first disagreeing with it〔最初不同意而後來〕同意, 答應: *The government would not accede to public pressure.* 政府不會屈從於公眾的壓力。**2** to achieve a position of power or authority 繼任, 就職, 即位

ac·cel·e·ran·do /ækˌsɛləˋrændo; ækˌseləˈrændəʊ/ *adj, adv music* getting gradually faster【音樂】漸快的[地]

ac·cel·e·rate /əkˋsɛləˌret; əkˈseləreɪt/ *v* **1** [I] if a vehicle or someone who is driving it accelerates, it starts to go faster 加快, 加速: *The Ferrari Mondial can accelerate from 0 to 60 mph in 6.3 seconds.* 法拉利蒙迪爾型汽車能在6.3秒內從每小時0英里加速到每小時60英里。**2** [I,T] if a process accelerates or if something accelerates it, it happens faster than usual or sooner than you expect (使)加快; (使)提前: *measures to accelerate the rate of economic growth* 加快經濟增長速度的措施 —opposite 反義詞 DECELERATE

ac·cel·e·ra·tion /əkˌsɛləˋreʃən; əkˌseləˈreɪʃən/ *n* **1** [U] the rate at which a car or other vehicle can go faster 加速: *The latest model has excellent acceleration.* 最新型號加速性能良好。**2** [singular, U] a process in which something happens more and more quickly 加快(的過程): *an acceleration in the decline of the coal industry* 煤炭工業加速衰退 **3** [U] *technical* the rate at which the speed of an object increases【術語】加速度, 速率

ac·cel·e·ra·tor /əkˋsɛləˌretə; əkˈseləreɪtə/ *n* [C] **1** the part of a vehicle, especially a car, that you press to make it go faster 加速器; 油門; GAS PEDAL *AmE*【美】—see picture on page A2 參見A2頁圖 **2** *technical* a large machine used to make extremely small pieces of matter move at extremely high speeds【術語】粒子加速器

ac·cent[1] /ˋæksɛnt; ˈæksənt/ *n* [C] **1** the way someone pronounces the words of a language, showing which country or which part of a country they come from 口音: *Alex spoke Portuguese with a Brazilian accent.* 亞歷克斯講葡萄牙語帶有巴西口音。| **strong/broad accent** *a broad Irish accent* 濃重的愛爾蘭口音 —compare 比較 DIALECT **2 the accent is on** if the accent is on a particular quality, feeling etc, that quality or feeling is emphasized 着眼點在…上, 強調: *We put the accent on team work at this club rather than individual skills.* 在這個俱樂部, 我們強調團隊精神而不是個人技能。**3** the part of a word that you should emphasize when you say it 重音: [+on] *In the word 'corset' the accent is on the first syllable.* corset一詞的重音在第一個音節上。—see also 另見 STRESS[1] (4) **4** a written mark used above certain letters in some languages to show how to pronounce that letter 重音符號: *an acute accent* 銳重音符號

ac·cent[2] /ˋæksɛnt; əkˈsent/ *v* [T] to emphasize a part of something, especially part of a word in speech 重讀

ac·cen·ted /ˋæksɛntɪd; əkˈsentɪ̣d/ *adj* **heavily accented** words or speech that are heavily accented are spoken with a very strong accent 帶有濃重口音的

ac·cen·tu·ate /əkˋsɛntʃuˌet; əkˈsentʃueɪt/ *v* [T] to emphasize something, especially the difference between two conditions or situations 使突出; 強調, 着重指出 —**accentuation** /əkˌsɛntʃuˋeʃən; əkˌsentʃuˈeɪʃən/ *n* [C,U]

ac·cept /əkˋsɛpt; əkˈsept/ *v* 1 1

1 ▶GIFT/OFFER/INVITATION 禮物/提議/邀請◀ [I,T] to take something that someone offers you, or to agree to do something that someone asked you to do 接受; 同意做〔某事〕: *Please accept this small gift.* 請收下這份小禮物。| *I've decided to accept the job.* 我決定接受這份工作。| *Are you going to accept their invitation?* 你會接受他們的邀請嗎? | *We've invited her here to give a talk, and she's accepted.* 我們邀請她到這裡演講, 她同意了。| **accept sth from sb** *He is charged with accepting bribes from local companies.* 他被指控接受當地公司賄賂。| **accept a challenge** (=agree to do something difficult) 接受挑戰 —see 見 REFUSE[1] (USAGE)

2 ▶PLAN/SUGGESTION/ADVICE 計劃/建議/忠告◀ [T] to decide to do what someone advises or suggests you should do 採納: *I wish I'd accepted your advice and kept my money in the bank.* 要是當初我接受了你的建議, 把錢存到銀行裡就好了。

3 ▶IDEA/STATEMENT/EXPLANATION 想法/聲明/解釋◀ [T] to agree that what someone says is right or true 接受, 同意: *She managed to persuade the jury to accept her version of events.* 她設法讓陪審團接受了她對事件的說法。| **accept that** *I'm willing to accept that some mistakes have been made.* 我願意承認出了一些差錯。

4 ▶SITUATION/PROBLEM ETC 情況/問題等◀ [T] to decide that there is nothing you can do to change a difficult and unpleasant situation or fact and continue with your normal life 認可, 承認: *There's nothing we can do about it so we'll just have to accept it.* 我們對此沒有辦法, 只好認同。| **accept the fact that** *I found it hard to*

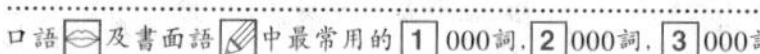

accept the fact that she's gone. 我難以接受她已經不在了的這個事實。

5 ►THINK SB/STH GOOD ENOUGH 認為某人/某物夠好◄ [T] to decide that someone has the necessary skill or intelligence for a particular job, course etc or that a piece of work is good enough 認為…符合要求, 採用: **accept sb/sth for** *My story's been accepted for the school magazine.* 校刊同意採用我的小說。

6 ►BECOME PART OF 成為…的部分◄ [T] to allow someone to become part of a group, society, or organization and to treat them in the same way as the other members 接納: *The children gradually began to accept her as one of the family.* 孩子們逐漸接納她為家中一員。| **accept sb into** *It often takes years for immigrants to be accepted into the host community.* 移民經常需要幾年的時間才會被當地社區所接納。

7 accept blame/responsibility to admit that you were responsible for something bad that happened 接受指責/承擔責任: *The ship's owners are refusing to accept any responsibility for the accident.* 船主拒絕對事故承擔任何責任。

8 accept sb's apology to say that you are no longer angry with someone after they have said they were sorry about something they have done 接受某人的道歉

9 ►MONEY 錢◄ [T] to allow customers to use a particular kind of money to pay for things 接受〔某種付款方式〕: *We don't accept travelers' checks.* 我們不接受旅行支票。

3 3 **ac·cep·ta·ble** /əkˋsɛptəbḷ; əkˈseptəbəl/ *adj* **1** good enough to be used for a particular purpose or to be considered satisfactory 合意的, 令人滿意的: *a cheap and acceptable substitute for rubber* 價廉物美的橡膠代用品 | **[+to]** *The dispute was settled in a way that was acceptable to both sides.* 爭端以雙方都能接受的方式解決了。**2** acceptable behaviour is considered to be morally or socially good enough〔行為〕可接受的: *Smoking is no longer considered socially acceptable by many people.* 許多人不再認為吸煙是可接受的社會行為。| **acceptable for sb to do sth** *I just don't think it's acceptable for children to interrupt all the time.* 我只是認為, 孩子總是打斷別人的話是不可接受的。| **acceptable level/amount** (=neither too high nor too low) 可接受的程度/量 *They talk about 'acceptable levels of unemployment'.* 他們談論關於"可接受的失業水平"。—**acceptably** *adv* —**acceptability** /əkˌsɛptəˋbɪlətɪ; əkˌseptəˈbɪlɪ̵ti/ *n* [U]

3 **ac·cept·ance** /əkˋsɛptəns; əkˈseptəns/ *n* **1** [U] official agreement to take something that you have been offered 正式接受; 認可: **[+of]** *Russia's acceptance of economic aid from Western countries* 俄羅斯接受西方國家的經濟援助 | **a letter of acceptance** (=a letter you write in which you agree to accept a job, an opportunity to study somewhere etc) 同意書,〔接受工作、學習機會等的〕答覆信 **2** [singular, U] the act of agreeing that an idea, statement, explanation etc is right or true 贊同, 贊成: **gain/find acceptance** (=become accepted) 被接受 *Feminist ideas have now found widespread acceptance.* 女權主義思想現已被人們廣泛接受。**3** [U] the ability to accept an unpleasant situation which cannot be changed, without getting angry or upset about it 承受(能力) **4** [singular, U] the process of allowing someone to become part of a group or a society and of treating them in the same way as the other members 接納(過程): *Acceptance by their peer group is important to most youngsters.* 被同輩所接納, 對大多數年輕人來說是很重要的。

3 1 **ac·cess¹** /ˈæksɛs; ˈækses/ *n* [U] **1** the way by which you can enter a building or reach a place 入口; 進入: *Access is by means of a small door on the right.* 可通過右邊的小門進入。| **[+to]** *Access to the restrooms is through the foyer.* 去洗手間要穿過門廳。**2** how easy or difficult it is for people to enter a public building or to reach a place 途徑: **[+for]** *We're trying to improve access for disabled visitors.* 我們正在設法使殘疾訪客能更容易進入。| **have easy/good access to** (=be able to reach another place easily) 容易接近 *The house is in a central location with good access to the shops.* 這幢房子在中心地段, 離商店比較近。**3** the right to enter a place 進入權; 使用權: **have access to** *The public don't have access to the site.* 公眾無權進入此地。**4 have access to** to have the right to see official documents, especially secret documents 有權接觸〔機密等〕: *Access to the papers is restricted to Defense Department personnel only.* 只有國防部人員才可以接觸這些文件。**5** the legal right to see and spend time with your children, a prisoner, an official etc 探視權: *My ex-husband has access to the children once a week.* 我的前夫有權每週探望孩子一次。**6 have access to a phone/a computer etc** to have a telephone, computer etc near you which you can use 附近有電話/電腦等可供使用 **7 gain/get access (to)** to succeed in entering a place or in seeing someone or something 到達〔某地〕; 見到〔某人或某物〕: *The police managed to gain access through an upstairs window.* 警察設法通過樓上的一扇窗戶進入了屋子。

access² *v* [T] to find information, especially on a computer 存取〔尤指電腦數據〕

ac·ces·si·ble /əkˋsɛsəbḷ; əkˈsesɪ̵bəl/ *adj* **1** easy to reach or get into 易到達的; 易進入的: *The cove is only accessible by boat.* 小海灣只有小船才能進入。—opposite 反義詞 INACCESSIBLE **2** easy to obtain or use 易得到的; 易使用的: **easily/readily accessible** *Storing customer details on computer makes them readily accessible.* 把顧客的詳細資料儲存到電腦裡可方便查找。**3** someone who is accessible is easy to meet and talk to, even if they are very important or powerful 易接近的, 隨和的, 平易近人的: *I think that you'll find she's very accessible.* 我想你會發現她十分平易近人。**4** easy to understand and enjoy 易懂的: *Buchan succeeds in making a difficult subject accessible to the reader.* 巴肯成功地把一個很難的題目變得為讀者易於理解。—**accessibly** *adv* —**accessibility** /əkˌsɛsəˋbɪlətɪ; əkˌsesɪ̵ˈbɪlɪ̵ti/ *n* [U]

ac·ces·sion /ækˋsɛʃən; əkˈseʃən/ *n formal*【正式】**1** [U] a process in which someone becomes king, queen, president etc 就職, 即位: **accession to the throne** (=the act of becoming king or queen) 登基 —compare 比較 SUCCESSION **2** [U+to] the act of agreeing to a demand 同意〔要求〕**3** [C,U] an object or work of art that is added to a collection, especially in a MUSEUM〔尤指博物館的〕新增的藏品

ac·ces·so·ry /əkˋsɛsərɪ; əkˈsesəri/ *n* [C usually plural 一般用複數] **1** something that you add to a machine, tool, car etc so that it can do other things, or in order to make it look attractive 附件, 附屬品: *Accessories include a CD player and alloy wheels.* 附件包括雷射唱機和合金車輪。**2** [C] something such as a bag, belt, jewellery etc that you wear or carry because it is attractive 裝飾物; 小配件〈如手袋、皮帶、珠寶等〉: *fashion accessories* 時尚飾品 **3** [C] *law* someone who helps a criminal, especially by helping them hide from the police【法律】同謀, 幫兇, 從犯: **[+to]** *an accessory to murder* 謀殺案的同謀 | **an accessory before/after the fact** (=someone who helps a criminal before or after the crime) 事前/事後從犯

access time /ˈ·· ˌ·/ *n* [C,U] *technical* the time taken by a computer to find and use a piece of information in its memory【術語】〔電腦的〕存取時間

ac·ci·dent /ˈæksədənt; ˈæksɪ̵dənt/ *n* [C] **1 by accident** in a way that is not planned or intended 偶然, 意外地: *I met her quite by accident.* 我遇見她頗為偶然。**2** a situation in which someone is injured or something is damaged without anyone intending them to be 事故, 意外事件: **have an accident** *Ken's had an accident at work and he's had to go to hospital.* 肯在工作中出了事故, 不得不去醫院。| **climbing/skiing/riding etc accident** *Five people have been killed in a climbing accident in Nepal.* 五個人在尼泊爾登山時遇難。**3** a crash involving cars, trains, planes etc 失事; 車禍: **car/automobile/traffic accident** *Her father's been involved in an automobile accident.* 他父親捲入一起車禍。| **bad/serious/nasty accident** *A serious accident is blocking the southbound side of the M1.* 一起嚴重的交通事故阻塞了一號高速公路向南行駛的一側。**4** something that happens without anyone planning or intending it 意外: *I'm really sorry about your camera – it was an accident.* 真對不起, 把你的照相機弄壞了 —— 這純屬意外。| **a happy accident** (=a lucky or pleasant event or situation which happens without anyone planning it) 好運氣, 僥倖 | **a chapter of accidents** (=a series of unfortunate events that happen without anyone planning them) 一連串意外事故 | **an accident of birth/nature/history etc** (=an event or situation that happens without anyone planning it) 出生/性質/歷史等的偶然性 **5 accidents will happen** *spoken* used to comfort someone who feels responsible for something bad that has happened【口】天意注定, 在所難免 **6 have an accident** if a child has an accident, he or she URINATEs by mistake〔小孩〕尿褲子; 尿牀

ac·ci·den·tal /ˌæksəˋdɛntḷ; ˌæksəˈdentl◂/ *adj* happening without being planned or intended 偶然的, 意外的: *an accidental discharge of toxic waste* 有毒廢料的意外泄漏

accidental death /ˌ···· ˈ·/ *n* [U] *law* an expression used by a British court when it has decided that someone's death was caused by an accident【法律】意外死亡〔英國法庭用語〕

ac·ci·den·tal·ly /ˌæksəˋdɛntḷɪ; ˌæksəˈdentl-i/ *adv* **1** without intending to 無意地: *I accidentally locked myself out of the house.* 我無意間把自己鎖在了門外。**2 accidentally on purpose** *humorous* used to say that someone did something deliberately although they pretend they did not【幽默】明明故意卻裝出無心的樣子; 故意地: *I think John lost his homework accidentally on purpose.* 約翰說他的作業不小心丟了, 我看是故意的。

accident prone /ˈ···· ·/ *adj* tending to get injured or break things easily 易遭遇意外的, 易惹事故的

ac·claim[1] /əˋklem; əˈkleɪm/ *v* [T] **1** to praise someone or something publicly 為…喝采, 稱讚; 推崇: *His last play was acclaimed by the critics as a masterpiece.* 他的最後一部戲劇被評論家讚譽為一部傑作。**2 acclaim sb king/queen/leader etc** *formal* to announce publicly that you accept someone as your king, queen etc【正式】擁戴某人為國王/女王/領袖等

acclaim[2] *n* [U] praise for a person or their achievements 表揚, 讚賞: **win acclaim** *Gail's artwork has won her international acclaim.* 蓋爾的藝術作品為她(自己)贏得了國際聲譽。

ac·claimed /əˋklemd; əˈkleɪmd/ *adj* publicly praised by a lot of people 廣受歡迎的, 備受推崇的: **highly/widely/universally acclaimed** *Spielberg's highly acclaimed movie, Schindler's List* 史匹堡備受好評的電影《舒特拉的名單》| **critically acclaimed** (=praised by people who are paid to give their opinion on art, music etc) 得到評論家好評的 *a critically acclaimed novel* 得到評論家好評的一部小說

ac·cla·ma·tion /ˌækləˋmeʃən; ˌækləˈmeɪʃən/ *n* [C,U] *formal* a loud expression of approval or welcome【正式】歡呼, 喝采

ac·cli·ma·tize also 又作 **-ise** *BrE*【英】/əˋklaɪməˌtaɪz; əˈklaɪmətaɪz/ also 又作 **acclimate** /ˋækləˌmet; əˈklaɪmət/ *AmE*【美】*v* [I,T] to become used to a new place, situation or type of weather, or to make someone become used to it (使) 適應: **get acclimatized** *It usually takes a while to get acclimatized to living in a new place.* 通常需要一段時間才能適應在一個新地方生活。—**acclimatization** /əˌklaɪmətəˋzeʃən; əˌklaɪmətaɪˈzeɪʃən/ *n* [U]

ac·co·lade /ˌækəˋled; ˈækəleɪd/ *n* [C] praise for someone who is greatly admired or a prize given to them for their work 嘉獎, 讚揚: *She received a 'Grammy Award', the highest accolade in the music business.* 她獲得了音樂界的最高榮譽"格林美獎"。

ac·com·mo·date /əˋkɑməˌdet; əˈkɒmədeɪt/ *v* **1** [T] to have or provide enough space for a particular number of people or things 容納: *The hall can only accommodate 200 people.* 這個大廳只能容納200人。| *building bigger and bigger highways to accommodate more cars* 修建更寬更廣的公路以容納更多的車輛 **2** [T] to give someone a place to stay, live, or work 為…提供住處[工作場所] **3** [T] to accept someone's opinions and try to do what they want, especially when their opinions or needs are different from yours 迎合; 遷就: *We've made every effort to accommodate your point of view.* 我們已經盡力遷就你們的觀點。**4** [I+to, T] *formal* to get used to a new situation or make yourself do this【正式】(使) 適應; (使) 順應 **5** [T] *formal* to give someone more time to pay you money that they owe you because they have financial problems【正式】寬限; 通融

ac·com·mo·dat·ing /əˋkɑməˌdetɪŋ; əˈkɒmədeɪtɪŋ/ *adj* helpful and willing to do what someone else wants 隨和的, 樂於助人的

ac·com·mo·da·tion /əˌkɑməˋdeʃən; əˌkɒməˈdeɪʃən/ 2 2 *n* **1** [U] a place for someone to stay, live, or work in 住處; 工作場所: *rented accommodation* 租用的房屋 **2 accommodations** [plural] *AmE formal* the rooms, food, services etc that are provided in a hotel or on a train, boat etc【美, 正式】〔酒店、火車、船等提供的〕住宿膳食服務 **3** [singular,U] *formal* a way of ending an argument which aims to satisfy both sides【正式】和解: **reach an accommodation** *We reached an accommodation between both parties.* 我們雙方達成了和解。

ac·com·pa·ni·ment /əˋkʌmpənɪmənt; əˈkʌmpənimənt/ *n* **1** [C,U] music played at the same time as a song or a tune played on another instrument 伴奏: *She starts by singing 'Amazing Grace' with a simple guitar accompaniment.* 她以結他伴奏演唱《奇妙的恩典》作開場。**2** [C] something that is provided or used with something else 伴隨物; 配料: *White wine makes an excellent accompaniment to fish.* 白葡萄酒是吃魚時最佳的佐餐酒。**3** [C] *formal* something that happens or exists at the same time as something else【正式】伴隨物, 附屬物: *The job losses are an inevitable accompaniment of this reorganization.* 職位減少是這次重組的必然產物。**4 to the accompaniment of** while another musical instrument is being played or another sound can be heard 在…伴奏下: *singing to the accompaniment of a piano* 在鋼琴伴奏下演唱 | *She left the stage to the accompaniment of loud cheers.* 她在一片歡呼聲中離開了舞台。

ac·com·pa·nist /əˋkʌmpənɪst; əˈkʌmpənəst/ *n* [C] someone who plays a musical instrument while another person sings or plays the main tune 伴奏者

ac·com·pa·ny /əˋkʌmpənɪ; əˈkʌmpəni/ *v* [T] **1** to go 2 somewhere with someone, especially in order to look after them 陪伴, 陪同: *Children under 14 must be accompanied by an adult.* 14歲以下兒童必須有成人陪同。**2** to play a musical instrument while someone sings a song or plays the main tune 為…伴奏 **3** [usually singular 一般用單數] to happen or exist at the same time as something else 伴隨 **4** if a book, document etc accompanies something, it explains what it is about or how it works 附有, 帶有, 配有: *Please see accompanying booklet for instructions.* 說明請參閱所附的小冊子。

ac·com·plice /əˋkɑmplɪs; əˈkʌmpləs/ *n* [C] a person who helps someone such as a criminal to do something wrong 幫兇, 同謀者, 共犯

ac·com·plish /əˋkɑmplɪʃ; əˈkʌmplɪʃ/ *v* [T] to succeed in doing something, especially after trying very hard; achieve 完成〔任務等〕, 取得〔成功〕: *We have accomplished all we set out to do.* 所有計劃要做的事情, 我們都已完成。

ac·com·plished /əˋkɑmplɪʃt; əˈkʌmplɪʃt/ *adj* an accomplished writer, painter, singer etc is vey skilful 有才華的; 有 (藝術) 造詣的

A

ac·com·plish·ment /əˋkɑmplɪʃmənt; əˈkʌmplɪʃmənt/ *n* **1** [C] something successful or impressive that is achieved after a lot of effort and hard work; achievement 成就, 成績: *This huge increase in growth would be an impressive accomplishment in any economy.* 這麼巨大的增長在任何經濟體制下, 都是了不起的成就。**2** [C] an ability to do something well; skill 才能, 才藝: *Playing the piano is one of her many accomplishments.* 彈鋼琴是她眾多才能中的一種。**3** [U] skill in doing something 技能: *a high level of accomplishment* 高水平技能 **4** [U] the act of finishing or achieving something good 成就; 完成, 實現

ac·cord¹ /əˋkɔrd; əˈkɔːd/ *n* **1 of your own accord** without being asked or forced to do something 出於自願, 主動地: *It's better that she comes of her own accord.* 她自己主動來更好。**2** [U] *formal* a situation in which two people, ideas, or statements agree with each other【正式】相符合, 一致: **be in accord with** *These results are in accord with earlier research.* 這些結果和以前的研究一致。| **in total/perfect accord** *For once the President and myself were in total accord.* 就這一次, 總統和我意見完全一致。| **speak with one accord** (=if two or more people speak with one accord they show total agreement with each other by what they say) 完全一致地說; 異口同聲 **3** [C] a formal agreement between countries or groups 正式協議: *the Helsinki accord on human rights* 赫爾辛基人權協定 **4 with one accord** *formal* if two or more people do something with one accord they do it together【正式】一致地: *With one accord they rushed down to the lake.* 他們不約而同向湖邊衝去。

accord² *v formal*【正式】**1** [T] to give someone or something special attention or treatment 給予〔關照〕: **accord sth to** *The Japanese accord a special reverence to trees and rivers.* 日本人特別珍愛樹木和河流。**2 accord with** to match or agree with something 符合, 一致

ac·cord·ance /əˋkɔrdn̩s; əˈkɔːdəns/ *n* **in accordance with** *formal* according to a rule, system etc【正式】按照, 依照: *accounts prepared in accordance with the Companies Act 1985* 按照1985年《公司法》準備的賬目 | **in accordance with sb's wishes** *He was buried in his home town, in accordance with his wishes.* 根據他生前意願, 他被葬在故鄉。

ac·cord·ing as /əˋkɔrdɪŋ æz; əˈkɔːdɪŋ æz/ *conjunction BrE formal* depending on whether【英, 正式】根據; 取決於

ac·cord·ing·ly /əˋkɔrdɪŋlɪ; əˈkɔːdɪŋli/ *adv* **1** in a way that is suitable for a particular situation or based on what someone has done or said 相應地: *I told them what changes I wanted made and they acted accordingly.* 我告訴他們我希望甚麼地方需要修改, 他們就照我的意見去做。**2** [sentence adverb 句子副詞] as a result of something; therefore 因此, 從而: *The budget for health care has been cut by 10%. Accordingly, some hospitals may be forced to close.* 保健方面的預算削減了10%。因此, 一些醫院可能會被迫關閉。

S2 W1 **according to** /·ˈ·· ·/ **1** as shown by something or said by someone 據…所說〔所示〕: *According to George, she's a great player.* 據喬治說, 她是一個優秀的演員。| *According to our records payment of $56 is now overdue.* 根據我們的記錄, 有56元的款項逾期未付。**2** in a way that agrees with 隨…而定: *We are paid according to how much work we do.* 我們的工資隨工作量而定。

ac·cor·di·on¹ /əˋkɔrdɪən; əˈkɔːdiən/ *n* [C] a musical instrument that you pull in and out to produce sounds while pushing buttons on one side to produce different notes 手風琴

accordion² *adj* [only before noun 僅用於名詞前] having many folds like an accordion〔如手風琴般〕可摺疊的: *an accordion file* 摺疊式文件夾

ac·cost /əˋkɔst; əˈkɒst/ *v* [T] to go towards someone you do not know and speak to them in an unpleasant or threatening way 走上前去跟…唐突地說話, 與…搭訕: *On the station she was accosted by a man asking for money.* 在車站, 一個男人走到她跟前硬向她要錢。

ac·count¹ /əˋkaunt; əˈkaʊnt/ *n* S2 W1

1 ►DESCRIPTION 描述◄ [C] **a)** a written or spoken description which gives details of an event 報道, 敍述, 描寫: *There were several different accounts of the story in the newspapers.* 報紙上對此事有不同的說法。| **give an account** *David gave us a vivid account of his trip to Rio.* 大衛向我們生動地講述了他去里約熱內盧旅行的情況。| **blow-by-blow account** (=a description of the details of all an event in the order that they happened) 詳細報道 | **eyewitness account** (=a description of events by someone who saw them) 目擊者的敍述 *an eyewitness account of the robbery* 目擊者對搶劫案的敍述 | **firsthand account** (=a description of events by someone who saw or took part in them) 第一手的敍述 *her fascinating firsthand account of the Chinese Cultural Revolution* 她對親身經歷的中國文化大革命令人難以忘懷的敍述 **b)** a detailed scientific description of a process which explains how it happens and what makes it possible 詳盡的科學描述: *Chomsky's account of how children learn their first language* 喬姆斯基關於兒童如何學習第一語言的科學描述

2 ►AT A BANK 在銀行◄ written abbreviation 縮寫為 **a/c** [C] an arrangement that you have with a bank to pay in or take out money 賬戶: *My salary is paid directly into my bank account.* 我的工資直接存入我的銀行賬戶。| **joint account** (=one that is shared by two people) 共用賬戶 —see also 另見 BANK ACCOUNT, CHECKING ACCOUNT, CURRENT ACCOUNT, DEPOSIT ACCOUNT, PROFIT AND LOSS ACCOUNT, SAVINGS ACCOUNT

3 take account of sth/take sth into account to consider or include particular facts or details when making a decision or judgment about something 把…考慮在內: *These figures do not take account of changes in the rate of inflation.* 這些數字沒有考慮到通貨膨脹率的變化。

4 on account of because of something else, especially because of a problem or difficulty 因為, 由於: *He can't run very fast on account of his asthma.* 由於患有哮喘, 他不能跑得很快。

5 accounts a) [plural] an exact record of the money that a company has received and the money it has spent 賬目: *The accounts for last year showed a profit of $2 million.* 去年的賬目顯示利潤為200萬美元。**b)** [U] a department in a company that is responsible for keeping these records 會計部: *Eileen works in accounts.* 艾琳在會計部工作。

6 on account if you buy goods on account, you take them away with you and pay for them later 賒賬

7 ►WITH A SHOP 與商店◄ [C] an arrangement that you have with a shop which allows you to buy goods and pay for them later; CREDIT ACCOUNT 賒購賬: *Can you charge this to my account please?* 你能把這錢記在我的〔賒購〕賬上嗎?

8 ►BILL 賬單◄ [C] a statement of money that you owe for things you have bought from a shop; bill 賬單: **pay/settle your account** (=pay what you owe) 付賬/結賬 *Accounts must be settled within 30 days.* 30天以內必須結賬。

9 ►ARRANGEMENT TO SELL GOODS 售貨安排◄ [C] an arrangement to sell goods and services to another company over a period of time〔給予售貨安排和服務的〕客戶: *Our Sales Manager has secured several big accounts recently.* 我們的銷售部經理最近得到了好幾家大客戶。

10 by/from all accounts according to what a lot of people say 根據各方面所說: *It's a very exciting film by all accounts.* 人人都說這是一部很精彩的電影。

11 on my/his etc account if you do something on someone's account, you do it because you think they want you to 為了我/他等的緣故: *Please don't leave on my account.* 看在我的情面上, 請不要離開。

12 on your own account by yourself or for yourself 靠自己; 為自己: *Carrie decided to do a little research on her own account.* 嘉莉決定自己做點研究。
13 on no account/not on any account used when saying that someone must not, for whatever reason, do something 決不: *On no account must you tell him about our plans.* 你決不能把我們的計劃告訴他。
14 by your own account according to what you have said, especially when you have admitted doing something wrong 據某人自己所說: *By his own account he was driving too fast.* 他自己也認為開車開得太快。
15 on that account/on this account concerning a particular situation 考慮到那種/這種情況: *There needn't be any more worries on that account.* 考慮到那種情況, 就不必擔心了。
16 give a good/poor account of yourself to do something or perform very well or very badly 表現好/表現差: *Kevin gave a good account of himself in today's game.* 凱文在今天的比賽中表現出色。
17 bring/call sb to account *formal* to force someone who is responsible for a mistake or a crime to explain publicly why they did it and punish them for it if necessary【正式】責令某人對…作出解釋: *The people responsible for the accident have never been brought to account.* 要對這起事故負責任的人至今仍逍遙法外。
18 put/turn sth to good account *formal* to use something for a good purpose【正式】充分利用某物: *Perhaps she could put some of her talents to good account by helping us.* 透過幫助我們, 也許她能把自己的某些才能充分發揮出來。
19 of no account/of little account *formal* not important【正式】不重要, 沒關係: *Don't worry about what he said, it's of no account.* 不必擔心他說的話, 那是無關緊要的。
20 of some account *formal* quite important【正式】相當重要

2 **account²** *v* [T]
account for sth *phr v* [T] **1** to be the reason why something happens 是…的原因: *Recent pressure at work may account for his behavior.* 他的行為也許應歸因於他最近的工作壓力。**2** to give a satisfactory explanation of why something has happened or why you did something 對…作出〔滿意的〕解釋: *How do you account for the sudden disappearance of the murder weapon?* 你如何解釋兇器突然消失? **3** to make up a particular amount or part of something 佔…〔比例〕: *Imports from Japan accounted for 40% of the total.* 進口的日本貨佔進口總量的40%。**4** to say where all the members of a group of people or things are, especially because you are worried that some of them may be lost 說明…在何處: *Is everyone accounted for?* 是不是所有人都有下落了? **5 there's no accounting for taste** *informal* used when you find it difficult to understand why someone likes something or wants to do something【非正式】人各有所好

ac·coun·ta·ble /ə`kaʊntəbḷ; ə'kaʊntəbəl/ *adj* [not before noun 不用於名詞前] responsible for the effects of your actions and willing to explain or be criticized for them 負有責任的: [+for] *Managers must be accountable for their decisions.* 經理必須對自己作出的決定負責。| **hold sb accountable for sth** (=consider someone responsible) 認為某人應對某事負責 *Should teachers be held accountable for their students' examination results?* 教師是否應對學生的考試成績負責? | **accountable to** *The bank was effectively accountable to nobody, and could do whatever it liked.* 這家銀行事實上不曾對任何人負責, 它想做甚麼就做甚麼。—**accountability** /ə͵kaʊntə`bɪlətɪ; ə͵kaʊntə'bɪlᵊti/ *n* [U]: *demands for greater police accountability* 要求警察負起更大的責任

ac·coun·tan·cy /ə`kaʊntənsɪ; ə'kaʊntənsi/ *n* [U] *especially BrE* the profession or work of keeping or checking financial accounts【尤英】會計行業[工作]

3 **ac·coun·tant** /ə`kaʊntənt; ə'kaʊntənt/ *n* [C] someone whose job is to keep and check financial accounts 會計師; 會計員

ac·coun·ting /ə`kaʊntɪŋ; ə'kaʊntɪŋ/ *n* [U] accountancy 會計行業[工作]

ac·cou·tre·ments /ə`kutəmənts; ə'ku:trᵊmənts/ also 又作 **accouterments** /ə`kutəmənts; ə'ku:təmənts/ *AmE*【美】*n* [plural] *formal or humorous* things that you use or carry when doing a particular activity【正式或幽默】裝備, 配備

ac·cred·i·ta·tion /ə͵krɛdɪ`teʃən; ə͵kredᵊ'teɪʃən/ *n* [U] official approval for a person or organization 正式認可, 授權, 委託

ac·cred·it·ed /ə`krɛdɪtɪd; ə'kredᵊtᵊd/ *adj* **1** having official approval to do something 得到授權的: *an accredited journalist* 有許可證的記者 **2 be accredited to** if a government official is accredited to another country, they are sent to that country to officially represent their government there〔作為本國政府代表〕被委派往〔他國〕**3** officially accepted as being of a satisfactory standard 經鑑定合格的: *an accredited language school* (經鑑定) 合格 [認可] 的語言學校

ac·cre·tion /ə`kriʃən; ə'kri:ʃən/ *n* **1** [C,U] *technical* a layer of a substance which slowly forms on something【術語】增加物; 積成物; 附着物 **2** [U] *formal* a gradual process by which new things are added and something gradually changes or gets bigger【正式】增加, 增大

ac·crue /ə`kru; ə'kru:/ *v* [I,T] *formal*【正式】**1** if advantages accrue to you, you get those advantages over a period of time〔利益、好處等〕產生, 形成: *tax benefits that accrue to investors* 給投資者帶來的稅收利益 **2** if money accrues or is accrued, it gradually increases over a period of time 增加, 增多: *The accrued interest will be paid annually.* 累積利息將逐年支付。

acct the written abbreviation for 縮寫= ACCOUNT

ac·cu·mu·late /ə`kjumjə͵let; ə'kju:mjᵊleɪt/ *v* **1** [T] to gradually get more and more money, possessions, knowledge etc over a period of time 積累, 積聚: *He accumulated a fortune through property speculation.* 他透過房產投機買賣積累了財富。**2** [I] to gradually increase in numbers or amount until there is a large quantity in one place 大量聚積: *Leaves had accumulated around the fallen trunks.* 樹葉大量聚積在倒地的樹幹周圍。—**accumulation** /ə͵kjumjə`leʃən; ə͵kju:mjᵊ'leɪʃən/ *n* [C,U]: *the accumulation of data* 資料的收集

ac·cu·mu·la·tive /ə`kjumjə͵letɪv; ə'kju:mjᵊlətɪv/ *adj* gradually increasing in amount or degree over a period of time; CUMULATIVE 累積的, 逐漸增加的 —**accumulatively** *adv*

ac·cu·mu·la·tor /ə`kjumjə͵letɚ; ə'kju:mjᵊleɪtə/ *n* [C] **1** *technical* a part of a computer that stores numbers【術語】〔電腦的〕累加器 **2** *especially BrE* a kind of BATTERY (1) which can take in new supplies of electricity so that it has enough power to keep working【尤英】蓄電池 **3** a system of betting (BET¹ (1)) on the results of a series of horse races, by which any money you win from a race is bet on the next race 累積賭注

ac·cu·ra·cy /`ækjərəsɪ; 'ækjᵊrəsi/ *n* [U] **1** the ability to do something in an exact way without making a mistake 準確度, 精確性 **2** the quality of being correct or true 準確(性): *I wasn't convinced about the accuracy of the report.* 我並不確信這個報告的準確性。

ac·cu·rate /`ækjərɪt; 'ækjᵊrət/ *adj* **1** accurate information, reports, descriptions etc are correct because all the details are true〔資料、報道、描述等〕準確的: *She was able to give the police an accurate description of her attacker.* 她能把襲擊者的情況向警方作出準確的描述。| *a fairly accurate assessment of the situation* 對形勢相當準確的評價 **2** an accurate measurement, calculation, record etc has been done in a careful and exact way and is completely correct〔測量、計算、記錄等〕精確的, 無差錯的 **3** a machine that is accurate is able to do something in an exact way without making a mistake〔儀器〕 2 3

精密的: *The cutter is accurate to within 1/2 a millimetre.* 切割器的精密度在½毫米以內。**4** an accurate shot, throw etc succeeds in hitting or reaching the thing that it is intended to hit〔射擊、投擲等〕準確的: *a devastatingly accurate shot by the Brazilian captain* 巴西隊隊長極其精準的一記射門 —**accurately** *adv*: *It's impossible to predict the weather accurately.* 要準確地預報天氣是不可能的。

ac·curs·ed /əˋkɝsɪd; əˈkɜːsɨ̞d/ *adj* **1** [only before noun 僅用於名詞前] *formal* very annoying and causing you a lot of trouble【正式】可惡的, 可憎的 **2** *old use* someone who is accursed has had a CURSE² (2) put on them【舊】被詛咒的

ac·cu·sa·tion /ˌækjəˋzeʃən; ˌækjʊˈzeɪʃən/ *n* [C] a statement saying that someone is guilty of a crime or of doing something wrong 控告, 告發; 指控: *There isn't a word of truth in your accusations.* 你的指控沒有一句是事實。| [+of] *accusations of corruption* 對貪污的指控 | **make an accusation against** *Several serious accusations have been made against the former state governor.* 對前任州長提出了幾項嚴重指控。| **face an accusation** (=be accused of something) 面臨指控 *The school is facing accusations of racism.* 這所學校面臨存在種族主義的指控。| **wild/unfounded accusation** (=one that is completely untrue) 胡亂指控, 誣告

ac·cu·sa·tive /əˋkjuzətɪv; əˈkjuːzətɪv/ *n* [C] *technical* a form of a noun in languages such as Latin or German, which shows that the noun is the DIRECT OBJECT of a verb【術語】〔拉丁文、德文等的〕受格, 賓格 —**accusative** *adj*

ac·cu·sa·to·ry /əˋkjuzəˌtorɪ; əˈkjuːzətəri/ *adj formal* an accusatory remark, look etc from someone shows that they think you have done something wrong【正式】指控的; 指責的

3 **ac·cuse** /əˋkjuz; əˈkjuːz/ *v* [T] to say that someone is guilty of a crime or of doing something bad 指責; 控告: **accuse sb of (doing) sth** *Are you accusing me of lying?* 你是在指責我說謊嗎? | *He's accused of murder.* 他被控謀殺。| **stand accused of** (=be officially accused of a serious offence) 正式被指控 *Local officials stand accused of gross mismanagement.* 當地官員被控嚴重瀆職。—**accuser** *n* [C]

ac·cused /əˋkjuzd; əˈkjuːzd/ *n* **the accused** [singular or plural] the person or group of people who have been officially accused of a crime or offence in a court of law 被告

ac·cus·ing /əˋkjuzɪŋ; əˈkjuːzɪŋ/ *adj* an accusing look from someone shows that they think that you have done something wrong 非難的, 譴責的 —**accusingly** *adv*

ac·cus·tom /əˋkʌstəm; əˈkʌstəm/ *v* [T] to make yourself or another person become used to a situation or place 使…習慣於: **accustom yourself to** *It took a while for me to accustom myself to all the new rules and regulations.* 我花了一段時間才逐漸適應了所有新的規章制度。

ac·cus·tomed /əˋkʌstəmd; əˈkʌstəmd/ *adj* **1 be accustomed to (doing) sth** to be used to something 習慣於(做)某事: *He was accustomed to a life of luxury.* 他習慣了奢華的生活。| *I'm not accustomed to getting up so early.* 我不習慣這麼早起牀。| **get/grow/become accustomed to** *Her eyes quickly became accustomed to the dark.* 她的眼睛很快適應了黑暗。**2** [only before noun 僅用於名詞前] *formal* usual【正式】慣常的, 通常的: *her accustomed seat at the head of the table* 桌子上首她常坐的位置

AC/DC /ˌ· ·ˋ· ·/ *adj slang* sexually attracted to people of both sexes【俚】雙性戀的

ace¹ /es; eɪs/ *n* [C] **1** a playing card with a single spot on it, which usually has the highest value in a game〔撲克牌中的〕A 牌, 幺點牌: *the ace of hearts* 紅桃 A **2 have an ace up your sleeve** to have a secret advantage which could help you to win or be successful 手中有王牌, 有獲勝的絕招 **3 hold all the aces** to have all the advantages in a situation so that you are sure to win 佔絕對優勢 **4 be/come within an ace of** to very nearly succeed in doing something 僅差一點兒: *She came within an ace of getting the job as Export Manager.* 她差一點就當上出口部經理。**5** a first shot in tennis or volleyball which is hit so well that your opponent cannot reach the ball and you win the point〔網球或排球〕得分的發球 **6** someone who is extremely skilful at doing something 一流高手, 能手: *a World War II flying ace* 第二次世界大戰中的王牌飛行員 | *an ace at chess* 下棋高手 **7 ace in the hole** *AmE informal* something that you keep secretly to use when you need it【美, 非正式】備用的祕密武器: *That fifty dollars is my ace in the hole.* 那五十元是我應急備用的錢。

ace² *adj* **1 ace pilot/player/skier etc** someone who is a very skilful pilot, player etc 一流的飛行員/運動員/滑雪者等: *ace footballer Diego Maradona* 一流的足球運動員迭戈·馬勒當拿 **2** *BrE slang* very good【英俚】棒極了: *The party was ace.* 晚會棒極了。

ace³ *v* [T] **1** *AmE informal* to do very well in an examination, a piece of written work etc【美, 非正式】考得好, 寫得好: *I think I aced the History test.* 我覺得我歷史考得很好。**2** to hit your first shot in tennis or volleyball so well that your opponent cannot reach the ball〔網球或排球〕發球得分

a·cer·bic /əˋsɝbɪk; əˈsɜːbɪk/ *adj* criticizing someone or something in a clever but rather cruel way 尖刻的, 辛辣的: *acerbic wit* 尖刻挖苦的言辭 —**acerbity** *n* [U]

ac·e·tate /ˋæsəˌtet; ˈæsɨ̞teɪt/ *n* [U] **1** a chemical made from acetic acid 醋酸鹽 **2** a smooth artificial cloth used to make clothes 醋酸纖維製品

a·ce·tic ac·id /əˌsitɪk ˋæsɪd; əˌsiːtɪk ˈæsɨ̞d/ *n* [U] the acid in VINEGAR 醋酸

a·cet·y·lene /əˋsɛtḷˌin; əˈsetɨ̞liːn/ *n* [U] a gas which burns with a bright flame and is used in equipment for cutting and joining pieces of metal 乙炔, 電石氣 —see also 另見 OXYACETYLENE

ache¹ /ek; eɪk/ *v* [I] **1** if part of your body aches, you feel a continuous, but not very sharp pain there〔隱隱地、持續地〕作痛: *The noise of the traffic made my head ache.* 車輛的噪聲使我感到頭痛。| *an aching back* 後背疼痛 **2 ache to do sth/for sth** to want to do or have something very much 渴望做某事/擁有某物: *I was aching to tell him the good news.* 我急不可待地想把好消息告訴他。

ache² *n* [C] **1** a continuous pain that is not sharp, for example the pain you feel after you have used part of your body too much 疼痛: *After three days the ache in his legs had almost gone.* 三天後, 他的腿幾乎不痛了。| *backache* 後背痛 | **dull ache** (=an annoying ache that is not very painful) 隱隱作痛 *My hand started to hurt with a sort of dull ache.* 我的手開始有些隱隱作痛。| **aches and pains** (=many small pains which you feel at the same time) 渾身疼痛 *Apart from the usual aches and pains, she felt all right.* 除了幾處經常性的疼痛以外, 她感到身體尚可。**2** a strong feeling of wanting something 渴望 —**achy** *adj*: *My arm feels all achy.* 我的胳膊很痛。

a·chieve /əˋtʃiv; əˈtʃiːv/ *v* **1** [T] to succeed in doing something good or getting the result you wanted, after trying hard for a long time 實現; 取得; 達到: *Women have yet to achieve full equality in the workplace.* 在工作領域, 婦女還沒有取得完全平等的地位。| *Britain has achieved the highest rate of economic growth in Europe this year.* 英國今年實現了歐洲最高的經濟增長率。| *On the test drive Segrave achieved speeds of over 200 mph.* 在試車時, 西格雷夫的車速達到每小時二百多英里。**2** [I] to be successful in a particular kind of job or activity 獲得成功: *We want all our students to achieve within their chosen profession.* 我們希望所有的學生在自己選擇的專業領域內都能有所成就。—**achievable** *adj* —see 見 OBTAIN (USAGE)

a·chieve·ment /əˋtʃivmənt; əˈtʃiːvmənt/ *n* **1** [C] something important that you succeed in doing by your own

efforts 成績, 成就: *Winning three gold medals is a remarkable achievement.* 贏得三枚金牌是個了不起的成績。| **no mean achievement/quite an achievement** (=a very impressive achievement) 了不起的成績 **2** [U] the act of achieving something 實現; 完成; 達到: *the achievement of economic stability* 經濟穩定的實現 | **sense of achievement** (=a feeling of pride when you succeed in doing something difficult) 成就感 *You get a wonderful sense of achievement when you reach the top.* 當你到達最高處時, 你會有一種絕妙的成就感。

a·chiev·er /ə`tʃivɚ; ə'tʃiːvə/ *n* [C] someone who is successful because they are determined and work hard 成功人士

A·chil·les' heel /ə,kɪliz `hil; ə,kɪliːz 'hiːl/ *n* [C] a weak part of something, especially of someone's character, which is easy for other people to attack 致命的弱點, 致命傷: *I think Frank's vanity is his Achilles' heel.* 我認為虛榮心是弗蘭克最大的弱點。

Achilles ten·don /ə,kɪliz `tɛndən; ə,kɪliːz 'tendən/ *n* [C] the part of your body that connects the muscles in the back of your foot with the muscles of your lower leg 跟腱

a·choo /ə`tʃu; ə'tʃuː/ *n* [C] a word used to represent the sound you make when you SNEEZE 阿嚏〔打噴嚏的聲音〕

2 **ac·id**[1] /`æsɪd; 'æsɪ̈d/ *n* **1** [C,U] a substance that forms a chemical SALT[1] (4) when combined with an ALKALI. Strong acids can burn holes in material or damage your skin〔化學中的〕酸: *sulphuric acid* 硫酸 **2** [U] *slang* the drug LSD【俚】迷幻藥〔麥角酸二乙胺〕

acid[2] *adj* **1** having a very sour taste 酸(味)的: *The wine had a very acid taste.* 這種葡萄酒味道很酸。**2 acid remark/comment/tone etc** an acid remark etc uses humour in an unkind way to criticize someone 尖酸刻薄的語言/評論/口吻等 **3 the acid test** a way of finding out whether something is as good as people say it is, whether it works, or whether it is true 決定性試驗, 嚴峻的考驗: *The acid test will come when the car goes on sale in the US.* 這種汽車在美國出售才是真正的考驗來臨的時候。**4** *technical* an acid soil does not contain enough LIME[1] (3)【術語】〔土壤〕酸性的 —**acidly** *adv* —**acidity** /ə`sɪdətɪ; ə'sɪdɪ̈ti/ *n* [U]

acid house /'‥ ·/ *n* [U] a kind of dance music that is played loudly using electronic instruments 迷幻豪斯音樂〔一種用電子樂器彈奏的快速舞蹈音樂〕

a·cid·ic /ə`sɪdɪk; ə'sɪdɪk/ *adj* **1** very sour 很酸的: *It tastes a bit acidic.* 這東西有點酸。**2** containing acid 含酸的, 酸性的

a·cid·i·fy /ə`sɪdəfaɪ; ə'sɪdɪ̈faɪ/ *v* [I,T] *technical* to become an acid or make something become an acid【術語】(使)變酸, (使)酸化

acid rain /,‥ '·/ *n* [U] rain that contains harmful acid which can damage the environment and is caused by smoke from factories 酸雨

3
3 **ac·knowl·edge** /ək`nɑlɪdʒ; ək'nɒlɪdʒ/ *v* [T]
1 ►ADMIT 承認◄ to admit or accept that something is true or that a situation exists 承認; 供認: *a broadcast message acknowledging their responsibility for the bombing* 他們承認對這起爆炸負責任的廣播消息 | **acknowledge that** *By November 1914 the government was forced to acknowledge that its policy had failed.* 直到1914年11月, 政府被迫承認他們的政策失敗了。| *It is now generally acknowledged that he was innocent.* 現在大家普遍認為他是無辜的。
2 be acknowledged as to be thought of as being very important or very good by a large number of people 被公認為是…: *Lasalle is widely acknowledged as the world's greatest living authority on Impressionist painting.* 拉薩爾被公認為是當今在世的關於印象派畫作的最偉大權威。
3 ►ACCEPT SB'S AUTHORITY 承認某人的權威◄ to officially accept that a government, court, leader etc has legal or official authority 承認〔政府、法庭、領袖等〕的合法性: *Both defendants refused to acknowledge the authority of the court.* 兩名被告都拒絕承認法庭有權審判他們。| **acknowledge sb as** *The people acknowledged Mandela as their leader.* 人民公認曼德拉為他們的領袖。
4 ►LETTER/MESSAGE ETC 信/口信等◄ to tell someone that you have received their message, letter, package etc 確認〔收悉〕: **acknowledge receipt of** *Please acknowledge receipt of this document by signing the enclosed form.* 請在附表中簽收這份文件。
5 ►SHOW THANKS FOR 表示感謝◄ to publicly announce that you are grateful for the help that someone has given you〔公開〕表示感謝: *The author wishes to acknowledge the assistance of the Defense Department.* 作者希望對國防部的協助表示感謝。
6 ►SHOW YOU NOTICE SB 表明注意到某人◄ to show someone that you have seen them or heard what they have said 打招呼, 理會: *Tina was so rude, she didn't even acknowledge my presence.* 蒂娜真沒禮貌, 見到我連個招呼也沒打。

ac·knowl·edge·ment, acknowledgment /ək`nɑlɪdʒmənt; ək'nɒlɪdʒmənt/ *n* **1** [C,U] the act of admitting or accepting that something is true 承認: *We have yet to hear any acknowledgement from them that a problem exists.* 我們尚未聽到他們承認有問題。**2** [C,U] the act of publicly thanking someone for something they have done 感謝: **in acknowledgement of** *a special award in acknowledgement of all his hard work* 為表彰他的辛勤工作的特別獎 **3** [C,U] a letter written to tell someone that you have received their letter, message etc 收悉通知; 回執 **4 acknowledgements** [plural] a short piece of writing at the beginning or end of a book in which the writer thanks all the people who have helped him or her〔作者的〕致謝

ac·me /`ækmɪ; 'ækmi/ *n* **the acme of** *formal* the best and highest level of something【正式】…的頂峯, …的極度: *the acme of perfection* 盡善盡美

ac·ne /`æknɪ; 'ækni/ *n* [U] a skin problem which causes a lot of small raised spots on the face and neck 痤瘡, 粉刺

ac·o·lyte /`ækəlaɪt; 'ækəlaɪt/ *n* [C] **1** *formal* someone who serves a leader or believes in their ideas【正式】侍者, 助手; 追隨者 **2** someone who helps a priest at a religious ceremony 侍僧, 輔祭〔教士的助手〕

a·corn /`e,kɔrn; 'eɪkɔːn/ *n* [C] the nut of the OAK tree 橡實

acorn 橡實

a·cous·tic /ə`kustɪk; ə'kuːstɪk/ *adj* **1** concerned with sound and the way people hear things 聲音的; 聽覺的 **2** an acoustic GUITAR or other musical instrument does not have its sound made louder electronically 原聲的, 不加電子設備傳聲的 —**acoustically** /-klɪ; -kli/ *adv*

a·cous·tics /ə`kustɪks; ə'kuːstɪks/ *n* [plural] **1** the qualities of a room, such as its shape and size, which affect the way sound is heard in it 音響效果: *The hall has excellent acoustics.* 禮堂的音響效果很好。**2** the scientific study of sound 聲學

ac·quaint /ə`kwent; ə'kweɪnt/ *v* [T] **1 be acquainted (with sb)** to know someone, especially because you have met once or twice before 認識(某人): *I am acquainted with him, but only on a professional basis.* 我認識他, 不過只是工作上的接觸。| **get/become acquainted** (=start to know someone that you have just met) 相識 *I'll leave you two alone for a while so that you can get better acquainted.* 我讓你們兩人單獨相處一會, 你們可以好好認識一下。**2 be acquainted with sth** *formal* to know about something, because you have seen it, read it, used it etc【正式】認識某物; 了解某事: *I'm not really acquainted with the southern part of the island.* 我不太了解這個島南部的情況。| **be fully acquainted with sth** *All our employees are fully acquainted with safety precautions.* 我們所有的雇員都十分熟悉安全措施。**3**

A

acquaint yourself with sth *formal* to deliberately find out about something【正式】了解某事, 查明某事: *She always took the trouble to acquaint herself with the students' interests.* 她總是不辭辛苦地去了解學生們的興趣。 **4 acquaint sb with sth** *formal* to give someone information about something【正式】把某事告訴某人: *My assistant should be able to acquaint you with all the details.* 我的助手會把所有的細節告訴你。

ac·quaint·ance /əˋkwentəns; əˈkweɪntəns/ *n* **1** [C] someone you know, but who is not a close friend 相識的人; 泛泛之交 **2 make sb's acquaintance** *formal* to meet someone for the first time【正式】結識某人: *I'm pleased to make your acquaintance.* 我非常高興結識你。 **3 of your acquaintance** *formal* a person of your acquaintance is someone that you know【正式】你認識的〔人〕: *a certain lawyer of my acquaintance* 我所認識的某個律師 **4** [U] *formal* knowledge or experience of a particular subject【正式】所知; 了解: **have a passing/nodding acquaintance with** (=have only slight knowledge or experience of something) 對…一知半解 *I must admit I have only a passing acquaintance with his books.* 我必須承認我對他的書只是一知半解。 **5 on further/closer acquaintance** *formal* when you start to know someone or something better【正式】進一步了解

ac·quaint·ance·ship /əˋkwentənsʃɪp; əˈkweɪntənsʃɪp/ *n* [U] *formal*【正式】**1** your experience or knowledge of a subject 所知; 了解 **2** the fact of knowing someone socially 相識

ac·qui·esce /ˌækwɪˋɛs; ˌækwiˈes/ *v* [I] *formal* to unwillingly agree to do what someone wants, or to let them do what they want, without arguing or complaining【正式】默許, 默認; 勉強同意: **[+in/to]** *The book accuses him of silently acquiescing in the Nazis' persecution of the Jews.* 這本書指控他默許納粹迫害猶太人。

ac·qui·es·cent /ækwɪˋɛsn̩t; ˌækwiˈesənt◂/ *adj formal* too ready to agree with someone or do what they want, without arguing or complaining【正式】默認的; 順從的 —**acquiescence** *n* [U] —**acquiescently** *adv*

2 **ac·quire** /əˋkwaɪr; əˈkwaɪə/ *v* [T] **1** *formal* to buy or obtain something, especially something expensive or difficult to get【正式】購得, 得到〔尤指昂貴的或難以得到的東西〕: *The museum has managed to acquire an important work by Dali.* 博物館設法弄到了〔西班牙超現實主義畫家〕達里的一幅重要作品。 **2** to learn or develop knowledge, skills etc by your own efforts, or to become well-known because of your abilities 掌握, 獲得〔知識、技能等〕: *I look on it as an opportunity to acquire fresh skills.* 我把這當作是一次學習新技能的機會。| *The team has acquired a fearsome reputation.* 這支隊伍贏得了令人生畏的名聲。 **3 acquire a taste for** to begin to like something 慢慢喜歡上: *This beer isn't bad. I'm beginning to acquire a taste for it.* 這啤酒不錯。我開始慢慢愛喝了。 **4 be an acquired taste** something that people only begin to like after they have tried it a few times 是後來喜歡上的東西 **5** *humorous* to get something by dishonest means【幽默】以不正當的方式獲得[佔有]

3 **ac·qui·si·tion** /ˌækwəˋzɪʃən; ˌækwɨ̍ˈzɪʃən/ *n* **1** [U] the act of getting new knowledge, skills etc〔新知識、新技能等的〕習得, 得到: *second language acquisition* 第二語言習得 **2** [U] the act of getting land, power, money etc〔土地、權力、錢等的〕獲得, 得到: *the acquisition of new territory* 新領土的獲得 **3** [C] *formal* something that you have bought or obtained, especially a valuable object【正式】獲得物〔尤指珍貴物品〕: *The National Gallery's latest acquisition is a painting by Goya.* 國家美術館最新得到的收藏品是〔西班牙宮廷畫家〕戈雅的一幅繪畫作品。

ac·quis·i·tive /əˋkwɪzətɪv; əˈkwɪzɨ̍tɪv/ *adj formal* showing too much desire to get new possessions【正式】貪得無厭的

ac·quit /əˋkwɪt; əˈkwɪt/ *v* **acquitted, acquitting 1** [T usually passive 一般用被動態] to give a decision in a court of law that someone is not guilty of a crime 宣判…無罪: *All the defendants were acquitted.* 所有的被告都被宣判無罪。| **acquit sb of sth** *She was acquitted of murder.* 她被宣判謀殺罪不成立。 **2 acquit yourself well/honourably** to do something well, especially something difficult that you do for the first time in front of other people 表現很好/表現得體

ac·quit·tal /əˋkwɪtl̩; əˈkwɪtl/ *n* [C,U] an official statement in a court of law that someone is not guilty 無罪判決, (被) 宣判無罪

a·cre /ˋekɚ; ˈeɪkə/ *n* [C] **1** a unit for measuring area, equal to 4047 square metres 英畝: *They own 200 acres of farmland.* 他們擁有200英畝農田。| *a 200-acre wood* 一片面積為200英畝的樹林 —see table on page C3 參見C3頁附錄 **2 acres of space/room** *BrE informal* a large amount of space【英, 非正式】很大面積

a·cre·age /ˋekərɪdʒ; ˈeɪkərɪdʒ/ *n* [U] the area of a piece of land measured in acres 英畝數; 以英畝計算的面積

ac·rid /ˋækrɪd; ˈækrɨ̍d/ *adj* **1** an acrid smell or taste is strong and unpleasant and stings your nose or throat 辛辣的, 刺激性的: *a cloud of acrid smoke* 一團刺鼻的煙霧 **2** *formal* an acrid comment, discussion etc is very critical or angry【正式】刻薄的, 尖酸的

ac·ri·mo·ni·ous /ˌækrəˋmonɪəs; ˌækrɨ̍ˈməʊniəs◂/ *adj formal* an acrimonious meeting, argument etc is full of angry comments because people feel very strongly about something【正式】激烈的, 唇槍舌劍的: *The meeting ended in an acrimonious dispute.* 會議不歡而散。—**acrimoniously** *adv* —**acrimoniousness** *n* [U]

ac·ri·mo·ny /ˋækrəˌmonɪ; ˈækrɨ̍məni/ *n* [U] *formal* anger and unpleasantness【正式】尖刻, 刻薄

ac·ro·bat /ˋækrəˌbæt; ˈækrəbæt/ *n* [C] someone who entertains people by doing difficult physical actions such as walking on their hands or balancing on a high rope, especially at a CIRCUS (1) 雜技演員

ac·ro·bat·ic /ˌækrəˋbætɪk; ˌækrəˈbætɪk◂/ *adj* acrobatic movements involve moving your body in a very skilful way, for example by jumping through the air or balancing on a rope 雜技(似)的: *amazing acrobatic feats* 令人稱奇的雜技技藝 —**acrobatically** /-kl̩ɪ; -kli/ *adv*

ac·ro·bat·ics /ˌækrəˋbætɪks; ˌækrəˈbætɪks/ *n* [plural] acrobatic movements 雜技(表演)

ac·ro·nym /ˋækrənɪm; ˈækrənɪm/ *n* [C] a word made up from the first letters of the name of something such as an organization. For example NATO is an acronym for the North Atlantic Treaty Organization. 首字母縮略詞〔比如NATO (北約) 由North Atlantic Treaty Organization的首字母縮略而成〕

a·cross¹ /əˋkrɔs; əˈkrɒs/ *prep* **1** going, looking etc from one side of a space, area, or line to the other side 橫過, 穿過: *flying across the Atlantic* 飛越大西洋 | *We gazed across the valley.* 我們注視山谷的對面。| *Would you like me to help you across the road?* (=help you to cross it) 要我幫你過馬路嗎? —see picture on page A1 參見A1頁圖 **2** reaching or spreading from one side of an area to the other 從一邊到另一邊: *a deep crack across the ceiling* 天花板上從一端到另一端的深縫 | *the only bridge across the river* 跨越這條河的唯一一座橋 | *Slowly a smile spread across her face.* 慢慢地她的臉上露出了微笑。| *Do you think this shirt is too tight across the shoulders?* 你覺得這襯衫的肩部是不是太緊了? | **right across** *The damn fool has parked right across the entrance to the driveway.* 這傻瓜把車正好停在了車道的入口。 **3** on or towards the opposite side of something 在對面; 向對面: *My best friend lives across the road.* 我最好的朋友住在馬路對面。| *Jim yelled across the street to his son.* 吉姆向街對面的兒子喊叫。| **just across** *He knew that just across the border lay freedom.* 他知道只要過了邊界線就自由了。| **across sth from** *Across the street from where we're standing, you can see the old churchyard.* 從我們現在站的地方穿過大街, 你就會看到舊教堂墓地。 **4** in every part of a country, organization etc 在全部…, 在整個…: *a TV series that became popular across five continents* 在五大洲廣受歡迎的電視系列片 | **right across** *Teachers are expected to teach a range of subjects right across the curriculum.* 教師應該能講授整個課程中的多個學科。

across² *adv* **1** from one side of something to the other 從一邊到另一邊: *There isn't a bridge. We'll have to swim across.* 沒有橋, 我們只好游過去。| *We'd got halfway across before Philip realized he'd left his money at home.* 我們都過了一半了, 菲利浦才意識到他把錢忘在家裡了。**2** if you go, look, shout etc across to someone, you go, look or shout across an area to the place where they are 朝向〔對面〕: *There's Brendan. Why don't you go across and say hello?* 那是布倫丹。你為甚麼不走過去打個招呼? | *I'm just taking this food across to Sarah. Won't be long.* 我正把這食品拿過去給薩拉。要不了多久。| **across to/at** *The referee looked across at his linesman before awarding the penalty.* 裁判先朝巡邊員那邊看了一下, 然後判罰球。**3 10 feet/10 miles etc across** if something is 10 feet etc across, that is how wide it is 十英尺 / 十英里寬: *At its widest point the river is 2 km across.* 這條河的最寬處為兩公里。**4 across from** opposite something or someone 在…對面: *a woman sitting across from me on the train* 火車上坐在我對面的女人

a·cross-the-board /ˌ· · ˈ·◂/ *adj* affecting everyone or everything in a situation or organization 全面的, 包括一切的: *an across-the-board pay increase* 全面的加薪 —across-the-board *adv*

a·cros·tic /əˈkrɔstɪk; əˈkrɒstɪk/ *n* [C] a poem or piece of writing in which the first or last letter of each line can be read downwards to spell a word 離合詩〔幾行詩句第一個詞的首字母或最後一個詞的尾字母能組合成詞或片語的一種詩體〕

a·cryl·ic /əˈkrɪlɪk; əˈkrɪlɪk/ *adj* acrylic paints or cloth are made from a chemical substance 丙烯酸的

a·cryl·ics /əˈkrɪlɪks; əˈkrɪlɪks/ *n* [plural] acrylic paints 丙烯酸塗料

act¹ /ækt; ækt/ *n* [C]
1 ▶ACTION 行為◀ [C] a particular kind of action 行為, 行動, 動作, 舉動: *a criminal act* 犯罪行為 | **act of kindness/revenge/courage etc** *The Bishop condemned the attack as an act of mindless violence.* 主教譴責襲擊事件是愚蠢的暴力行為。| *a supreme act of heroism* 高尚的英雄主義行為 | **the sexual act** (=the act of having sex) 性行為
2 be in the act of doing sth to be doing something at a particular moment, especially something that you should not do 正在做某事〔尤指壞事〕: **catch sb in the act (of doing sth)** *The photo shows her in the act of raising her gun to fire.* 照片上她舉起槍正要射擊。| *The thief was caught in the act.* 小偷作案時當場被捕。
3 ▶LAW 法律◀ [C] a law that has been officially accepted by Parliament or Congress〔正式通過的〕法令, 法案: *the 1991 Prevention of Terrorism Act* 1991 年《防止恐怖主義法案》| *an act of Congress* 國會的一項法令
4 ▶PRETENDING 假裝◀ [singular] insincere behaviour in which you pretend to have a particular kind of feeling 裝模作樣, 裝腔作勢: *A lot of people think Betty's very kind and caring, but it's all just a big act.* 很多人都認為貝蒂既善良又關心人, 其實那都是故意裝出來的。| **put on an act** (=pretend to have a particular feeling) 裝模作樣, 做戲 *He isn't really ill – he's just putting on an act.* 他並沒有真生病, 只不過是在裝模作樣。
5 get your act together *informal* to do something in a more organized way or use your abilities more effectively【非正式】更有條理些, 加把勁: *She could be an excellent photographer, if only she got her act together a bit more.* 如果她做事能更有條理一點, 她可以成為一名優秀的攝影家。
6 get in on the act *informal* to take part in an activity that someone else has started, especially in order to get a share of the advantages for yourself【非正式】〔為得到好處而〕插手, 參加
7 ▶PLAY 話劇◀ [C] one of the main parts into which a stage play, OPERA etc is divided〔戲劇、歌劇等的〕一幕: *Hamlet eventually kills the king in Act 5.* 在第五幕中, 哈姆雷特終於把國王殺死了。| *Everything is resolved in the final act.* 在最後一幕, 一切都得以解決。
8 ▶PERFORMANCE 演出◀ [C] one of the several short performances in a theatre or CIRCUS (1) show〔戲劇、馬戲的〕一段表演; 節目: *They used to do a comedy act together.* 他們過去常常合作表演喜劇。
9 ▶PERFORMER 演員◀ [C] a performer, singer, group of musicians etc 演出者: *top-selling British act 'The Happy Mondays'* 最熱門的英國組合"快樂的星期一"
10 act of God an event that is caused by natural forces, such as a storm, flood, or fire, which you cannot prevent or control 天災, 自然災害, 不可抗力
11 act of worship an occasion when people pray together and show their respect for God 拜祭; 祈禱
12 balancing/juggling act the action of doing several different kinds of work at the same time 保持平衡行動〔指同時做幾件事或兼顧好幾方面的工作〕—see also 另見 **clean up your act** (CLEAN²)

act² *v*
1 ▶DO SOMETHING 做某事◀ a) [I] to do something to deal with an urgent problem, especially by using your official power or authority〔尤指運用職權或權威〕採取行動: *The UN Security Council must act to end the war in Bosnia.* 聯合國安理會必須採取行動結束波斯尼亞的戰爭。**b)** [I always+adv/prep] to do something in a particular way or for a particular reason 行動, 表現: *The killer claims he was acting in self-defence.* 殺人者聲稱他那樣做是出於自衛。| *I acted more out of compassion than anything else.* 我這樣做更多地是出於同情。| **act in good faith** (=do something honestly without intending to deceive anyone) 誠實做事 *The shop manager says they acted in good faith and that they didn't know the camera was damaged.* 商店經理說他們誠實經營, 並不知道照相機是壞的。| **act on (sb's) advice/orders/suggestion etc** (=do what someone has advised, ordered etc) 按照(某人的) 意見 / 命令 / 建議等辦事 *Acting on a friend's advice, he bought $50,000 of shares in a television company.* 他按照朋友的意見, 買了一家電視公司的五萬美元的股票。| **act on information** (=do something because of information you have received) 根據了解到的信息採取行動 *The police were acting on information from a member of the public.* 警察正在根據一位市民提供的消息採取行動。
2 ▶BEHAVE 表現◀ [I always+adv/prep] to behave in a particular way 舉動; 表現: **act strangely/stupidly/correctly etc** *Henry's been acting very strangely recently.* 亨利近來行為異常。| *The teacher acted perfectly correctly under the circumstances.* 老師在那種情況下這樣做完全正確。| **act like/act as if** *If you act like a child, you're going to be treated like a child.* 如果你的表現像個孩子, 人們就會像對待孩子那樣對待你。| *He acted as if he'd never seen me before.* 他表現得好像以前從來就沒有見過我似的。| **act your age** *spoken* (=used to tell someone to be sensible and stop behaving like a child)【口】別要孩子氣了 | **act the fool** (=behave in a stupid and annoying way) 做蠢事 *Stop acting the fool, will you!* 別再做蠢事了, 行嗎!
3 ▶HAVE AN EFFECT 起作用◀ a) to have a particular effect or use 起作用: [+as] *The sugar in the fruit acts as a preservative.* 水果中的糖分起着防腐劑的作用。| [+on] *Antibiotics act on the bacteria that cause the disease.* 抗生素對致病細菌發生作用。**b)** to start to have an effect 顯效, 生效: *It takes a couple of minutes for the drug to act.* 這種藥顯效需要幾分鐘時間。
4 ▶PRETEND 假裝◀ [I,T] to pretend to have particular feelings, qualities etc 裝腔作勢: **act innocent/stupid/hurt etc** *She suddenly started acting all upset so that the others would feel sorry for her.* 她突然開始裝出傷

心的樣子以引起其他人的同情。| **act the fool/hero etc** *Whenever they're in public he always acts the loving husband.* 每次他們出現在公共場合，他總是表現得像個體貼的丈夫。| **act as if/act like** *They were all trying to act as if nothing had happened.* 他們都設法擺出若無其事的樣子。

5 ►PLAY/FILM ETC 戲劇/電影等◄ [I,T] to perform in a play or film 演出: *I first started acting when I was 12 years old.* 我12歲時第一次演出。| **act a part/role etc** *Who acted the part of Miss Ceeley?* 誰扮演茜莉小姐這一角色？| **well/badly acted** (=performed well or badly) 演得好/差 *I thought the play was extremely well acted.* 我認為這齣戲演得精彩極了。

6 ►LAWYER ETC 律師等◄ **act for sb/act on sb's behalf** to represent someone, especially in a court of law or by doing business for them 代表某人，代理: *I'm acting on behalf of my client, Mr Harding.* 我代表我的當事人哈丁先生。

7 ►DO THE JOB OF 擔任工作◄ **act as** to do a particular job for a short time, for example while the usual person is absent〔暫時性地〕代理〔某人的工作〕: *Mrs Odell is on holiday, and I'm acting as her replacement till she gets back.* 奧德爾夫人在休假，在她回來以前，我暫時接替她的工作。| *My brother speaks French – he will act as interpreter.* 我弟弟說法語，他將充當翻譯。—see also 另見 ACTING[1]

act sth ↔ **out** *phr v* [T] **1** if a group of people act out an event, they show how it happened by pretending to be the people who were involved in it 演出來 **2** to express your feelings about something through your behaviour or actions, especially when you have been feeling angry or nervous 表現出來: *Teenagers can act out their anxieties in various aggressive ways.* 青少年會以各種激進的方式宣泄他們的焦慮。

act up *phr v* [I] *informal*【非正式】**1** if children act up, they behave badly 調皮，搗亂 **2** if a machine or part of your body acts up, it does not work properly 運轉不正常，出毛病: *The photocopier has started acting up again.* 影印機又開始出毛病了。

act·ing[1] /ˈæktɪŋ; ˈæktɪŋ/ *adj* **acting manager/head teacher/director etc** someone who does an important job while the usual person is not there, or until a new person is chosen for the job 代經理/校長/董事長等

acting[2] *n* [U] the job or skill of performing in plays, films etc 表演；演技

ac·tion /ˈækʃən; ˈækʃən/ *n*

1 ►DOING THINGS 做某事◄ [U] the process of doing in order to deal with a problem or difficult situation 行動，活動；動作: *The union is urging strike action.* 工會敦促採取罷工行動。| *We need more action, and less talk!* 我們需要更多的行動，少一點空談！| **take action** *The police took firm action to deal with the riots.* 警方採取果斷的行動對付騷亂。| **go/spring into action** (=immediately begin doing something with a lot of energy) 採取緊急行動 *As soon as the SOS call was received, the rescue services sprang into action.* 一接到呼救信號，救援中心立即採取行動。| **course of action** (=a series of actions done in order to deal with something) 一連串的行動 *One possible course of action would be to raise taxes on alcohol and tobacco.* 一連串可能採取的行動是提高酒類和煙草的稅率。

2 ►SOMETHING DONE 所做的事◄ [C] something that someone does 行為，作為: *The child could not be held responsible for his actions.* 不能要求這個小孩對自己的行為負責。| *His prompt action probably saved my life.* 也許是他敏捷的行動救了我的命。

3 in action if you see someone or something in action you see them doing the job or activity that they are trained or designed to do 在運轉，在工作，在活動: *exciting photos of ski jumpers in action* 跳台滑雪者跳下時的精彩照片 | *I'd like to see the new computer system in action.* 我想看看運行着的新電腦系統。

4 put/call/bring sth into action to begin to use a plan or idea that you have, and to make it work 使…投入運作，啟動

5 be out of action if something or someone is out of action, they are broken or injured, so that they cannot move or work 失靈，發生故障: *My car's out of action at the moment, so I have to go by bus.* 我的汽車現在出了故障，所以我只好乘公共汽車去。| **put sth/sb out of action** *The torn ligaments in his knee put him out of action for the rest of the season.* 他膝蓋的韌帶撕裂使他在餘下的賽季裡無法參加比賽。

6 ►COURT 法庭◄ [C] the process of taking a case or a claim against someone to a court of law 訴訟: *They began an action to repossess the house.* 他們提起訴訟要求收回這座房子。| **legal/civil/libel etc action** *The European Commission is threatening legal action against Britain and France to protect the environment.* 歐洲委員會威脅說要對英法兩國提起訴訟以保護環境。| **bring an action (against)** *They will bring an action against him if he doesn't repay the loan.* 如果他不還貸款，他們會起訴他。

7 ►FIGHTING 戰鬥◄ [C,U] fighting or a battle during a war 戰鬥(行動): *When the action ended there were terrible losses on both sides.* 戰鬥結束時，雙方都損失慘重。| **in/into action** *The navy was sent into action.* 海軍被派往參加戰鬥。| **killed/wounded/missing in action** *Their son was reported missing in action.* 據報道，他們的兒子在戰鬥中失蹤。

8 ►EXCITING EVENTS 刺激的事◄ *informal* exciting and important things that are happening【非正式】(令人激動的) 事物；(重要的) 活動: *I was looking for some action in this hick town.* 我在這鄉鎮裡尋找一些刺激。| **where (all) the action is** *This is the design studio – where the action is.* 這是設計室——最熱鬧的地方。

9 ►STORY 故事◄ **the action** the things that happen in a play or book 情節，故事: *The action of 'Hamlet' takes place in Denmark.*《哈姆雷特》的故事發生在丹麥。

10 ►BODY MOVEMENT 身體動作◄ [C,U] a movement of the body, especially a particular type of movement 動作: *the action of the heart* 心臟的活動 | *the horse's trotting action* 馬的小跑

11 ►MACHINERY 機械◄ [singular] the movement of the parts of a clock, gun, piano etc 部件(的活動性能): *The action of this piano is rather stiff.* 這架鋼琴的機械部件有些不靈活了。

12 ►EFFECT 作用◄ [U] the way in which something such as a chemical or process has an effect on something else〔化學製品或過程等〕作用: *The rock had been worn away by the action of the falling water.* 石頭因落水作用而磨損。

13 action group/committee/project etc a group formed to do something specific, especially to change a social or political situation 行動小組/委員會/計劃等: *the Child Poverty Action Group* 兒童貧困行動小組

14 a piece of the action *informal* a share of something, such as profits, a business etc【非正式】〔利潤、生意等的〕一份

15 actions speak louder than words used to say that you are judged by what you do, rather than by what you say you will do 行動勝於言辭

16 ►FILMS 電影◄ **action!** used by film DIRECTORs to tell the actors and other film workers to begin filming 開拍！〔電影導演下令開始拍攝時說的話〕

ac·tio·na·ble /ˈækʃənəbl; ˈækʃənəbəl/ *adj* **1** [not before noun 不用於名詞前] if something you say or do is actionable, it is so serious or damaging that a claim could be made against you in a court of law because of it 可控訴的，可起訴的: *His allegations are actionable in my view.* 我認為對他的指控可以提出起訴。**2** [usually before noun 一般用於名詞前] an actionable plan, piece of information etc is one that can be done or used〔計劃、信息等〕可行的，可用的

action-packed /ˌ.. ˈ..◂/ *adj* an action-packed story or film contains a lot of exciting events 情節錯綜複雜的; 刺激的

action re·play /ˌ.. ˈ.../ *n* [C] *BrE* an important or exciting moment in a sports game on television that is shown again immediately after it happens; INSTANT REPLAY【英】即時重播, 精彩回放〈如電視中體育比賽的精彩瞬間〉

action sta·tions /ˈ.. ˌ../ *interjection* used to order soldiers etc to go to their positions ready for battle 各就各位〔用以對士兵等下命令〕

ac·tiv·ate /ˈæktəˌvet; ˈæktɪ̵veɪt/ *v* [T] **1** to make something, especially an electrical system, start working 起動, 開動, 使活動: *The lock is activated by a magnetic key.* 這個鎖用磁性鑰匙開。**2** *technical* to make a chemical action or natural process happen【術語】〔化學〕激活, 使活化: *The manufacture of chlorophyll is activated by sunlight.* 葉綠素的製造依靠陽光的照射。**3** *technical* to make something RADIOACTIVE【術語】使產生放射性 —**activation** /ˌæktəˈveʃən; ˌæktɪ̵ˈveɪʃən/ *n* [U]

2 2 **ac·tive**[1] /ˈæktɪv; ˈæktɪv/ *adj*

1 ▶DOING THINGS 做事◀ always doing things or ready to do things, especially physical activities 愛運動的; 愛活動的: *We had an active holiday, sailing, swimming and water skiing.* 我們在運動中度過假期, 駕駛帆船、游泳、滑水。| *She may be over 80, but she's still very active!* 她可能已經80多歲了, 但仍然十分喜愛活動!

2 ▶IN AN ORGANIZATION 在組織中◀ involved in an organization, activity etc and always busy doing things to help it 積極的, 活躍的: **active member** *an active member of the local Historical Society* 當地歷史學會的積極分子 | **be active in (doing) sth** *He's very active in local politics.* 他積極參加當地的政治活動。| *She's been active in raising money for the new church buildings.* 她積極為興建新教堂的大樓籌款。

3 active efforts/discussions etc efforts, attempts etc to do something, solve a problem etc, that are made with continuous energy and determination 積極的努力/討論等: *Active efforts are being made to reach a settlement.* 正在作出積極的努力以解決問題。

4 ▶ELECTRICAL SYSTEM 電力系統◀ *technical* operating in the way it is supposed to【術語】在活動中的, 起作用的: *The alarm becomes active when the switch is turned on.* 一按開關, 警報器就啟動了。

5 ▶MILITARY 軍事的◀ a) on active service a soldier etc who is on active service is fighting in a war 戰時服役 **b) on active duty** *AmE* employed by the army etc, as opposed to being in the reserves (RESERVE[2] (6))【美】服現役

6 ▶VOLCANO 火山◀ likely to explode and pour out fire 活的, 還會爆發的

7 ▶GRAMMAR 語法◀ *technical* if a verb or sentence is active, the person or thing doing the action is the SUBJECT[1] (5). In 'The boy kicked the ball', the verb 'kick' is active.【術語】主動的〈在 The boy kicked the ball 一句中, kick 是主動動詞〉—compare 比較 PASSIVE[1] (2)

8 ▶CHEMICAL 化學的◀ *technical* producing a reaction in a substance or with another chemical【術語】活性的 —**actively** *adv*: *The two sides are actively engaged in discussions.* 雙方積極參與討論。

active[2] *n* **the active/the active voice** *technical* the active form of a verb【術語】〔動詞的〕主動語態 —compare 比較 PASSIVE[2]

3 **ac·tiv·ist** /ˈæktɪvɪst; ˈæktɪ̵vɪ̵st/ *n* [C] someone who works hard to achieve social or political change, especially as an active member of a political organization 積極分子; 活動家: *Greenpeace activists* 綠色和平組織的積極分子

1 1 **ac·tiv·i·ty** /ækˈtɪvətɪ; ækˈtɪvɪ̵ti/ *n* **1** [U] a situation in which a lot of things are happening or people are doing things, moving around etc 活躍, 熱鬧: *I missed the noise and activity of the city.* 我懷念城市的喧鬧和忙碌。| *a huge amount of media activity during the elections* 大選期間頻繁的傳媒活動 —opposite 反義詞 INACTIVITY **2** [C] something that you do for interest or pleasure or because you want to achieve something 活動: *leisure activities* 娛樂活動 | *There'll be plenty of activities laid on for the kids.* 將為孩子們安排許多活動。| *terrorist activities* 恐怖主義活動

ac·tor /ˈæktɚ; ˈæktə/ *n* [C] someone who performs in a play, film, or television programme 演員 3

ac·tress /ˈæktrɪs; ˈæktrɪ̵s/ *n* [C] a woman who performs in a play, film, or television programme 女演員

ac·tu·al /ˈæktʃuəl; ˈæktʃuəl/ *adj* [only before noun 僅用於名詞前] **1** real, especially as compared with what is believed, expected or intended 實際的, 現實的: *a big difference between the opinion polls and the actual election results* 民意測驗和實際選舉結果的巨大差異 | *I'm not joking. Those were his actual words.* 我不是開玩笑, 那都是他的原話。| **in actual fact** (=really) 實際上 *In actual fact, there is not much evidence to support these allegations.* 事實上, 沒有多少證據支持這些指控。**2 the actual** used to introduce the main part of what you are describing 事實上: *The programme starts at 8.00 but the actual film doesn't start until 8.30.* 節目八點開始, 但實際上電影到八點半才放映。 1 2

ac·tu·al·i·ty /ˌæktʃuˈælətɪ; ˌæktʃuˈælɪ̵ti/ *n* **1** [C usually plural 一般用複數] something that is real; a fact 事實, 真實的情況: *the grim actualities of prison life* 監獄生活的嚴酷現實 **2** [U] *formal* the state of being real; EXISTENCE (1)【正式】現實(性) **3 in actuality** *formal* really【正式】真正地

ac·tu·al·ly /ˈæktʃuəlɪ; ˈæktʃuəli/ *adv* **1** [sentence adverb 句子副詞] *spoken* used when you are giving an opinion or adding new information to what you have just said【口】實際上, 其實〔用於說明個人觀點或補充新的資料〕: *I've known Barbara for years. Since we were babies, actually.* 我認識芭芭拉已多年了, 實際上我們從小就認識。| *I do actually think that things have improved.* 其實我的確認為情況有所好轉。| *We had quite a good time, actually.* 事實上, 我們玩得很愉快。| *Well actually you still owe me $200.* 實際上你還欠我200元。**2** used when you are telling or asking someone what the real and exact truth of a situation is, as opposed to what people may imagine 實際上, 事實上: *He may look young but he's actually 45.* 他可能看起來年輕, 但實際上已經45歲了。| *Disappointed? No, actually I'm rather glad.* 失望? 不, 實際上我相當高興。| *Unemployment has actually fallen for the past two months.* 近兩個月來, 失業人數實際上有所減少。| *Did he actually attack you, or just threaten you?* 他是真的攻擊你了, 還是只是威脅你? 1 1

Frequencies of the adverb **actually** in spoken and written English 副詞 actually 在英語口語和書面語中的使用頻率

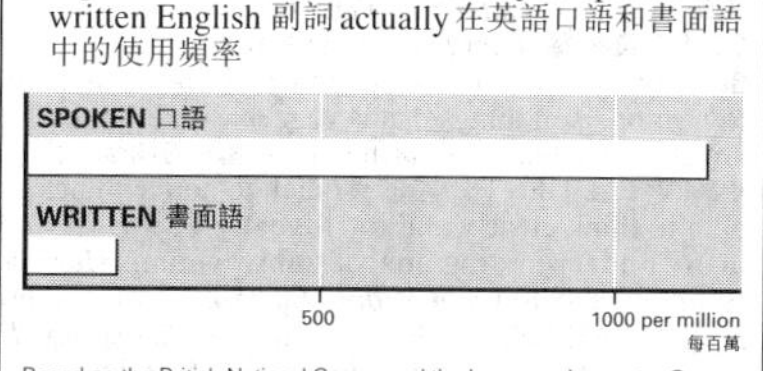

Based on the British National Corpus and the Longman Lancaster Corpus
據英國國家語料庫和朗文蘭卡斯特語料庫

This graph shows that the adverb **actually** is much more common in spoken English than in written English. 本圖表顯示, 副詞 actually 在英語口語中的使用頻率遠遠高於書面語。

USAGE NOTE 用法說明: ACTUALLY
WORD CHOICE 詞語辨析: **actually, currently, at present**

A

Actually (and **actual**) does not mean 'at the present time' in English. actually (和 actual) 在英語中並不是"現今"的意思。Compare **currently** and **at present** 比較 currently 和 at present: *"Have you ever met Simon?" "I actually met him two years ago."* (=in fact) "你見過西蒙嗎?" "事實上我兩年前見過他。" | *"Is the company doing well?" "Yes. It's currently doing very well/It's doing very well at present."* "公司現在情況好吧?" "是的。公司目前情況良好。"

In conversation, especially in British English, **actually** can be used to make what you are saying softer, especially if you are correcting someone, disagreeing, or complaining. 在會話中, 特別是英國英語, actually 可使語氣更緩和, 尤其是在糾正某人的觀點, 表示不同意或抱怨時: *"Great! I love French coffee!" "Er, it's German actually."* "太好了! 我喜歡法國咖啡!" "呃, 這其實是德國咖啡。" But it can be used with the opposite effect. 但也可起相反作用: *I didn't ask your opinion, actually.* 實際上, 我並沒有問你的意見。

ac·tu·a·ry /ˋæktʃʊˌɛrɪ; ˈæktʃuəri/ *n* [C] someone who advises insurance companies on how much to charge for insurance, after calculating the various risks 保險公司計算師, 精算師

ac·tu·ate /ˋæktʃʊˌet; ˈæktʃueɪt/ *v* [T] **1 be actuated by** *formal* to behave in a particular way because of a feeling or a quality in your character【正式】為...所驅使: *Iago was actuated by malice.* 伊阿古受到惡念的驅使。**2** *technical* to make a piece of machinery or electrical equipment start to operate【術語】驅動

a·cu·i·ty /əˋkjuətɪ; əˈkjuːəti/ *n* [U] *formal* the ability to think, see, or hear quickly and clearly【正式】靈敏, 敏銳, 銳利: *mental acuity* 思維敏捷

ac·u·men /əˋkjumən; ˈækjəmən/ *n* [U] the ability to think quickly and make good judgements 敏銳, 聰明, 機智: **business/political/financial etc acumen** *The firm's success is due to the director's ingenuity and business acumen.* 公司的成功歸功於董事的足智多謀和商業頭腦。

ac·u·pres·sure /ˋækjʊˌprɛʃɚ; ˈækjəˌpreʃə/ *n* [U] a method of stopping pain and curing disease by pressing on particular areas of the body 指壓(療法)

ac·u·punc·ture /ˋækjʊˌpʌŋktʃɚ; ˈækjəˌpʌŋktʃə/ *n* [U] a method of stopping pain and curing disease by putting special needles into particular parts of the body 針灸, 針刺(療法)

a·cute /əˋkjut; əˈkjuːt/ *adj*

1 ►SITUATION/FEELING ETC 情況/感覺等◄ very serious or severe 嚴重的: *an acute shortage of water* 嚴重缺水 | *acute embarrassment* 極其尷尬

2 ►PAIN 疼痛◄ very severe and sharp 劇烈的

3 acute hearing/acute sense of smell etc an ability to hear or smell things that is very sensitive, so that you are able to notice small differences 靈敏的聽覺/嗅覺等

4 ►INTELLIGENT 聰穎的◄ quick to notice things and able to think clearly and intelligently 敏銳的, 機敏的: **acute understanding/analysis/observations** *Her book is an acute analysis of Middle Eastern history.* 她的書是對中東歷史的精闢分析。| **acute observer** *De Tocqueville was an acute observer of American ways.* 德托克維爾是美國生活方式的敏銳觀察家。

5 ►MEDICAL 醫療的◄ *technical* an acute illness or disease quickly becomes dangerous【術語】急性的: *acute tuberculosis* 急性肺結核 —compare 比較 CHRONIC (1)

6 ►MATHEMATICS 數學◄ *technical* an acute angle is one that is less than 90°【術語】銳角的 —see picture at 參見 ANGLE[1] 圖

7 ►PRONUNCIATION MARK 發音符號◄ an acute ACCENT (=a mark used to show pronunciation) is the small mark put over a letter, such as é in French 發銳音的, 標有尖音符號 ˊ 的〈如法語 é〉—compare 比較 GRAVE[3], CIRCUMFLEX —**acuteness** *n* [U]

a·cute·ly /əˋkjutlɪ; əˈkjuːtli/ *adv* very strongly or painfully 嚴重地, 深切地; 痛苦地: *acutely embarrassed* 異常尷尬 | **acutely aware/conscious** *The president is acutely conscious of the need for more doctors and nurses.* 總統敏銳地意識到需要更多的醫生和護士。

AD /ˌe ˋdi; ˌeɪ ˈdiː◂/ Anno Domini; used to show that a date is a particular number of years after the birth of Christ 公元: *What will world population be by 2020 AD?* 到公元 2020 年, 世界人口將達到多少? | *in the first century AD* 公元一世紀 —compare 比較 BC

ad /æd; æd/ *n* [C] *informal* an advertisement【非正式】廣告 —see also 另見 CLASSIFIED AD

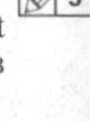

ad·age /ˋædɪdʒ; ˈædɪdʒ/ *n* [C] a well-known phrase that says something wise about human experience; PROVERB 格言, 諺語

a·da·gio /əˋdadʒo; əˈdɑːdʒəʊ/ *n* [C] a piece of music to be played or sung slowly 緩慢的音樂, 慢板 —**adagio** *adj, adv*

Ad·am /ˋædəm; ˈædəm/ *n* **not know someone from Adam** *informal* to not know someone at all【非正式】根本不認識某人

ad·a·mant /ˋædəˌmænt; ˈædəmənt/ *adj formal* determined not to change your opinion, decision, etc【正式】固執的, 堅強不屈的: *We tried to negotiate, but they were adamant.* 我們設法談判, 但他們很固執。| **adamant that** *Melinda was adamant that she would not travel with us.* 梅琳達堅持不和我們一起旅行。—**adamantly** *adv*

Ad·am's ap·ple /ˌ·· ˈ··/ *n* [C] the part at the front of your neck that sticks out slightly and moves when you talk or swallow 喉結, 喉核 —see picture at 參見 HEAD[1] 圖

a·dapt /əˋdæpt; əˈdæpt/ *v* **1** [I,T] to gradually change your behaviour and attitudes so that you get used to a new situation and can deal with it successfully (使)適應, (使)適合: **[+to]** *The children are finding it hard to adapt to their new school.* 孩子們發覺很難適應新學校。| *plants that have adapted themselves to desert conditions* 已適應沙漠環境的植物 **2** [T] to change something so that it can be used in a different way or for a different purpose 改造, 改裝: *The car's fuel system was adapted to take unleaded gas.* 汽車的燃油系統經改裝可使用無鉛汽油。| **[+for]** *The materials can be adapted for use with older children.* 這些材料改一下可給大一點的孩子用。**3 be well adapted to** to be particularly suitable for something 特別適應: *Alpine flowers which are well adapted to the harsh Swiss winters* 特別適應瑞士冬天的嚴寒氣候的高山花卉 **4** [T] to change a book or play so that it can be made into a film, television programme etc 改編 —compare 比較 ADJUST

a·dap·ta·ble /əˋdæptəbl; əˈdæptəbəl/ *adj* able to change so as to be suitable or successful in new and different situations 能適應的, 適應性很強的: *I'm sure she'll cope with the changes very well – she's very adaptable.* 我相信她會很妥善地應付這些變化——她的適應能力很強。| *The American constitution has proved adaptable in changing political conditions.* 事實證明, 美國憲法能適應日益變化的政治形勢。—**adaptability** /əˌdæptəˋbɪlətɪ; əˌdæptəˈbɪləti/ *n* [U]

ad·ap·ta·tion /ˌædæpˋteʃən; ˌædæpˈteɪʃən/ *n* **1** [C] a film or play that was first written in a different form, for example as a book 改編 **2** [U] the process by which something changes or is changed so that it can be used in a different way or in different conditions 改造; 適應: *adaptation to the environment* 適應環境

a·dapt·er, adaptor /əˋdæptɚ; əˈdæptə/ *n* [C] **1** something used to connect two pieces of equipment, especially when they are of different sizes 轉接器, 適配器 **2** *BrE* a special type of PLUG[1] (1) that makes it possible to connect more than one piece of equipment to the electricity supply【英】多頭插頭

ADC /ˌe di ˋsi; ˌeɪ diː ˈsiː/ the abbreviation of 縮寫= AIDE-DE-CAMP

add /æd; æd/ *v*
1 ▶PUT WITH 和...放到一起◀ [T] to put something with something else or with a group of other things 添加: **add sth to sth** *Do you want to add your name to the list?* 你想把你的名字加到名單裡嗎? | *I gave him a rare Swedish stamp to add to his collection.* 我給了他一張珍貴的瑞典郵票, 添加到他的收藏品中。
2 ▶COUNTING 計算◀ [I,T] to put two or more numbers together in order to calculate the total 相加, 求和: *Add 6 and 6 to make 12.* 6加6得12。| **add sth to** *Added to what we've already saved, it gives us $550.* 和我們省下的錢加在一起, 一共是550元。—compare 比較 SUBTRACT —see picture at 參見 MATHEMATICS 圖
3 ▶INCREASE 增加◀ [I,T] to increase the amount or cost of something by putting something more with it 增加: **add sth to** *The sales tax adds 15% to the price of clothes.* 銷售稅使服裝的價格增加了15%。| **[+to]** *Conforming to the new regulations will add to the cost of the project.* 遵照新的條例將增加該項目的成本。
4 ▶SAY 說◀ [T] to say something more that is related to what has been said already 補充, 繼續說: *That's all I have to say. Is there anything you'd like to add, David?* 我要說的就是這些。戴維, 你還有甚麼要補充的嗎? | *"And I don't care what you think," she added defiantly.* "我不在乎你怎麼想。" 她不服氣地補充道。| **add that** *Casey added that everything he had told us was, of course, top-secret.* 凱西補充說, 他告訴我們的話當然全部是絕密的。| **I might add** *spoken* (=used when adding something, especially to complain) 【口】而且 *The bus was two hours late, and, I might add, they tried to charge my children the full adult fares.* 公共汽車晚了兩小時, 而且, 他們還要我的孩子買全額成人票。
5 ▶COOKING 烹飪◀ [T] to mix one food with another while cooking 加入: *Cream the butter and sugar, then add the eggs.* 把黃油和糖攪成奶油狀, 然後加雞蛋。
6 ▶GIVE A QUALITY 給以某種性質◀ [T] to give a particular quality to an event, place, situation etc 增添: *Fine champagne always adds glamour to an occasion.* 上等的香檳酒總能為一場盛會增加點氣氛。
7 added to this/if you add to this used to introduce another fact, especially one that makes a situation seem even worse 再考慮到這一點: *If you add to this the young age of the victims, it makes the crime unforgivable.* 如果再考慮到受害者年紀那麼輕, 罪行就更加不可饒恕了。
8 add insult to injury to make a situation even more upsetting for someone, when they have already been badly or unfairly treated 既傷害又侮辱; 雪上加霜
9 add fuel to the fire/flames to make a bad situation even worse, especially by making someone more angry 火上加油

add sth ↔ **in** *phr v* [T] to include something with something else 加進, 包括: *By the time we added in the cost of the drinks the bill was over £100.* 我們再加上酒水的開銷, 賬單超過100英鎊。

add sth ↔ **on** *phr v* [T] **1** to make a building larger by building another room 加蓋, 加建: *They added on a bedroom at the back.* 他們在後面加蓋了一間臥室。**2** to increase the amount or cost of something by putting something more with it 附加, 增加〔...的量或費用〕: *Labor costs could add on a further 25%.* 算上勞動力成本, 費用可能還要增加25%。| **[+to]** *Service is added on to the bill.* 賬單中包含服務費。

add to sth *phr v* [T] to make something such as a feeling or quality stronger and more noticeable 增加, 使更加: *Our explanation seemed only to add to his bewilderment.* 我們的解釋似乎只有使他更困惑。| *a certain diffidence which added to his charm* 使他更具魅力的某種謙恭

add up *phr v* **1** [I,T **add** sth ↔ **up**] to calculate the total of several numbers 把...加起來: *Add your scores up and we'll see who won.* 把你的得分加起來, 我們就可以看出誰贏了。**2 not add up** if a set of facts does not add up, it does not provide a reasonable explanation for something 不合情理, 說不通: *He had been arrested for murder, but the evidence just didn't add up.* 他因謀殺罪被捕, 但那些證據並不合情理。**3** [I not in progressive 不用進行式] *informal* to increase by small amounts until there is a large total 【非正式】積少成多: *There are five of us using the phone so it soon adds up.* 我們五個人用電話, 所以不久就打得很多了。

add up to *phr v* [T not in progressive 不用進行式] to have a particular result 總的來講; 等於說: *With a meal included in the cost of the ticket, it all adds up to a really good evening's entertainment.* 入場券的費用裡還包括一頓飯, 總體來說, 這個晚上的招待真算是不錯了。

ad·ded /ˈædɪd; ˈædʒd/ *adj* in addition to what is usual or expected 額外的, 附加的, 增添的: *a breakfast cereal with added vitamins* 添加維生素的早餐麥片 | **added advantage/benefit/precaution etc** (=that makes something better) 額外的優勢/益處/預防措施等 *She had a deadbolt fitted as an added precaution.* 她叫人安裝了一把嵌鎖作為附加的預防措施。| **added difficulty/problem/complication** (=that makes something worse) 增加的難度/問題/複雜性

ad·den·dum /əˈdɛndəm; əˈdendəm/ *n plural* **addenda** /-də; -də/ [C] *technical* something that is added to the end of a speech or book, usually to give more information 【術語】補充; 補遺; 補編; 附錄

ad·der /ˈædɚ; ˈædə/ *n* [C] **1** a small poisonous snake living in northern Europe and northern Asia〔北歐和北亞生長的〕蝰蛇 **2** one of several types of snake living in North America〔北美生長的〕乳蛇

ad·dict /ˈædɪkt; ˈædɪkt/ *n* [C] **1** someone who is unable to stop taking drugs 吸毒上癮的人: *treatment centers for addicts* 戒毒中心 | **drug/heroin/morphine etc addict** *Many heroin addicts have contracted AIDS.* 許多有海洛因癮的人感染了愛滋病。**2** someone who spends too much time doing something they like 對...着迷的人: *a television addict* 電視迷

ad·dic·ted /əˈdɪktɪd; əˈdɪktʃd/ *adj* [not before noun 不用於名詞前] **1** unable to stop taking a harmful substance, especially a drug 有癮的, 上癮的: **[+to]** *He is seriously addicted to these tranquillizers.* 他對這些鎮靜劑已嚴重地上癮。**2** liking to do or have something so much you do not want to stop 對...痴迷的, 沉迷的: **[+to]** *kids addicted to computer games* 沉迷於電腦遊戲的孩子

ad·dic·tion /əˈdɪkʃən; əˈdɪkʃən/ *n* [C,U] the need to have something regularly because you are addicted to it 成癮; 癖好: *drug addiction* 毒癮 | **[+to]** *a program to deal with addiction to alcohol* 解決酗酒成癮問題的計劃

ad·dic·tive /əˈdɪktɪv; əˈdɪktɪv/ *adj* **1** a drug that is addictive makes you unable to stop taking it 使人成癮的, 上癮的: **highly addictive** *Crack is a potent, highly addictive form of cocaine.* 強效可卡因是很易使人上癮的烈性可卡因。**2** an activity that is addictive is one that you want to keep doing, especially because you enjoy it so much 使人着迷的, 使人沉溺於...的: *I took up skiing a couple of years ago and I find it quite addictive.* 我幾年前開始練滑雪, 我發覺這項運動挺令人着迷。

ad·di·tion /əˈdɪʃən; əˈdɪʃən/ *n* **1 in addition** used when adding another fact to what has already been mentioned 除此之外, 另外: *The hotel itself can accommodate 80 guests and, in addition, there are several self-catering apartments.* 旅館本身能容納80位客人, 除此之外, 還有幾個可供自己做飯的套房。| **in addition to** *He's now running his own research company – that's in addition to his job at the university.* 除了他在大學的工作以外, 他現在還經營自己的研究公司。**2** [U] the act of adding something to something else 增添, 添加: **[+of]** *The addition of networking facilities will greatly enhance the system.* 網絡設備的增加將會大大增強系統的性能。**3** [C] something that is added to something else, often in order to improve it 增加, 增強: **[+to]** *A bottle of wine would make a pleasant addition to the meal.* 一瓶葡萄酒將為這頓飯增色不少。**4** [U] the process of adding numbers 

or amounts to make a total 加法 —compare 比較 SUBTRACTION **5** [C] *AmE* a room or a part of a building that is added to the main building【美】〔主建築物的〕擴建部分: *They built a big addition at the back of their house.* 他們在房子後面又加蓋了一間很大的房子。

ad·di·tion·al /ə`dɪʃənl; ə'dɪʃənəl/ *adj* more than what was agreed or expected 追加的, 附加的, 另外的: *An additional charge is made on baggage over the weight allowance.* 行李超重要額外收費。

ad·di·tion·al·ly /ə`dɪʃənlɪ; ə'dɪʃənəli/ *adv* in addition; also 除此之外, 也: [sentence adverb 句子副詞] *A new contract had been agreed. Additionally, staff were offered a bonus scheme.* 一份新合同已經簽訂。除此之外, 還有一個給員工發獎金的方案。

ad·di·tive /`ædətɪv; 'ædʒtɪv/ *n* [C] a substance, especially a chemical, that is added to something such as food, to preserve it, give it colour, improve it etc 添加劑, 添加物: *Foods sold under this label are guaranteed free from additives.* 貼有這個標籤的食品保證不含添加劑。| *lead additives in petrol* 汽油中的鉛添加劑

ad·dle /`ædl; 'ædl/ *v* [T] to make someone confused and unable to think properly 使混亂, 使糊塗: **addle sb's brains** *All that drink has addled his brains!* 全是那些酒使他昏頭昏腦!

ad·dled /`ædld; 'ædld/ *adj* **1** an egg that is addled is no longer good to eat〔蛋〕變質的 **2** confused and unable to think properly 糊塗的, 頭腦混亂的

add-on /`·.·/ *n* [C] a piece of equipment that can be connected to a computer, such as a MODEM, to make the computer more useful〔電腦的〕附加設備; 附件 —compare 比較 PERIPHERAL[2]

ad·dress¹ /ə`drɛs; ə'dres/ *n* **1** [C] the number of the building and the name of the street and town etc where someone lives or works, especially when written on a letter or package 地址: *I wrote the wrong address on the envelope.* 我在信封上寫錯了地址。| **change of address** *Please notify us of any change of address.* 地址如有變更, 請通知我們。**2** [C] a formal speech made to a group of people who have come especially to listen to it 講話, 演說 **3** [C] a number that shows where a piece of information is stored in a computer's memory〔電腦的〕位址, 地址 **4 form/style/mode of address** the correct title or name that you use for someone when you are speaking to them 稱呼方式／風格／語氣

ad·dress² /ə`drɛs; ə'dres/ *v* [T] **1** to write on an envelope, package etc the name and address of the person you are sending it to 在〔信封、包裹等〕上寫姓名和地址: *If you address the letter, I'll mail it for you.* 如果你在信上寫上地址, 我就替你寄出去。| **address sth to sb** *The letter is addressed to you, not me.* 這封信是寫給你的, 不是給我的。**2** *formal* to speak directly to someone【正式】向...講話: *She turned to address the man on her left.* 她轉過頭對左邊的人說話。| **address sth to** *You will have to address your complaints to the Head Office.* 你有投訴就得向總部反映。**3 address a meeting/crowd/conference etc** to make a speech to a large group of people 在會上／對人羣／在大會上等發表演說: *The meeting was addressed by Senator Howard.* 會上由霍華德參議員作演講。**4** to use a particular title or name when speaking or writing to someone 稱呼: **address sb as** *The president should be addressed as 'Mr President'.* 對總統的稱呼應該是"總統先生"。**5** *formal* to discuss, think about, or do something about a particular problem or question, especially with the aim of solving a problem【正式】探討〔如何處理問題〕: *The article addresses the problems of diseases connected with malnutrition.* 這篇文章主要探討與營養不良有關的疾病。| **address yourself to** *Marlowe now addressed himself to the task of searching the room.* 馬洛現在忙於搜尋房間。

ad·dress·ee /͵ædrɛs`i; ͵ædre'siː/ *n* [C] the person a letter, package etc is addressed to 收信人, 收件人

ad·duce /ə`dus; ə'djuːs/ *v* [T] *formal* to mention a fact or reason in order to prove, explain, or support what you are claiming is true【正式】舉證, 引證

-ade /ed; eɪd/ *suffix* [in U nouns 構成不可數名詞] a drink made from a particular fruit〔指用某種水果製成的〕飲料, 果汁: *orangeade* (=drink made from orange juice) 橙汁

ad·e·noids /`ædn͵ɔɪdz; 'ædɪnɔɪdz/ *n* [plural] the small soft pieces of flesh at the back of your throat that sometimes have to be removed because they become swollen 腺樣增殖體 —**adenoidal** /͵ædn`ɔɪdl; ͵ædʒ'nɔɪdl◂/ *adj*

ad·ept¹ /ə`dɛpt; 'ædept/ *adj* good at doing something that needs care and skill 內行的, 熟練的: [+at/in] *Melissa soon became adept at predicting his moods.* 很快梅莉莎就善於預測他的情緒。—**adeptly** *adv*

ad·ept² /`ædɛpt; 'ædept/ *n* [C] someone who is good at doing something 內行, 能手

ad·e·quate /`ædəkwɪt; 'ædɪkwʒt/ *adj* **1** an adequate amount is enough for a particular purpose 適當的, 足夠的, 充分的: *The research cannot be completed without adequate funding.* 沒有足夠的資金, 這項研究就無法完成。| [+for] *Are the parking facilities adequate for fifty cars?* 停車設施能停放得下五十輛車嗎? **2** good enough in quality for a particular purpose or activity 可以勝任的: *Without the proper resources the department cannot do an adequate job.* 沒有適當的財力, 該部門就無法做好工作。| **adequate to do sth** *His explanation did not seem adequate to account for what had happened.* 他的解釋似乎不足以說明事情發生的緣由。**3** fairly good but not excellent 差強人意的, 過得去的: *Her performance was adequate but lacked originality.* 她的表演還過得去, 但缺乏獨創性。—**adequately** *adv*: *She wasn't adequately insured.* 她買的保險不夠。—**adequacy** *n* [U]

USAGE NOTE 用法說明: ADEQUATE

WORD CHOICE 詞語辨析: **adequate, sufficient, enough, good enough, satisfactory, (will) do**

Adequate and **sufficient** are both more formal than **enough**, but all three can be used to talk about quantity. adequate 和 sufficient 比 enough 更正式, 但這三個詞都可以指數量: *Will you have enough/sufficient/adequate money for the trip?* 你有足夠的錢去旅行嗎? However, **adequate** often sounds a little negative, suggesting that the amount is only just enough. 然而, adequate 通常帶有一點否定含義, 表明只是剛好足夠: *The water supply here is adequate/sufficient.* 這裡的供水還足夠。

If you want to say that the quality of something is enough, you use **good enough** or **satisfactory**. 如果想表示某物質量好, 用 good enough 或 satisfactory: *"I'm afraid your work isn't good enough/satisfactory."* "恐怕你的工作做得不夠好／令人滿意。" **Satisfactory** is a more formal word. satisfactory 較為正式。

Adequate can be used to talk about both quality and quantity together, especially with uncountable nouns. For example, if you ask: *Is the food adequate?* you might be asking whether there is enough in amount or whether it is good enough. However, with a plural countable noun the quality meaning is more likely. adequate 既可以指質量又可以指數量, 尤用於形容不可數名詞。例如, 如果你問: Is the food adequate? 問的可以是份量足不足, 也可以是質量好不好。然而, 如果跟可數名詞, 多指質量: *adequate resources/training/support etc* 足夠好的資源／充分的訓練／充分的支持等

In spoken English people often use **do** (but not in progressive forms) to talk about something being enough in either of these ways. 在英語口語中, 人們經常用 do (不用進行式) 來表達"足夠"之意: *"Do you have enough money?" "It should do."* (=it should be enough) "你錢夠嗎?" "應該夠。" | *It's not much but it'll have to do.* 不太多, 但只好如此了。

ad·here /əd`hɪr; əd'hɪə/ *v formal* [I+to] to stick firmly to something【正式】黏附, 附着
adhere to sth *phr v* [T] *formal* to continue to behave according to a particular rule, agreement, or belief【正式】堅持; 信守: *adhere to your principles* 堅持原則 | *adhere to the regulations* 遵守規定

ad·her·ence /əd`hɪrəns; əd'hɪərəns/ *n* [U] the act of behaving according to a particular rule or belief, or supporting a particular idea, even in difficult situations 堅持; 信守, 信奉: [+to] *strict adherence to the traditional caste system* 嚴格遵守傳統的種姓制度

ad·her·ent /əd`hɪrənt; əd'hɪərənt/ *n* [C] someone who supports a particular idea, plan, political party etc 信徒; 擁護者; 追隨者

ad·he·sion /əd`hiʒən; əd'hiːʒən/ *n* **1** [U] the state of one thing sticking to another 黏附, 黏合, 膠着 **2** [C] *technical* a piece of TISSUE (=flesh) that has grown around a small injury or diseased area【術語】〔身體內組織的〕黏連

ad·he·sive[1] /əd`hisɪv; əd'hiːsɪv/ *n* [C] a substance such as glue that can be used to make two things stick together 膠布; 膠黏劑

adhesive[2] *adj* adhesive material sticks to surfaces 黏着的, 有黏性的: *adhesive tape* 膠布, 膠帶

ad hoc /`æd `hɑk; ˌæd 'hɒk/ *adj* [usually before noun 一般用於名詞前] *Latin* done or arranged only when the situation makes it necessary, and without any previous planning【拉丁】特別 [專門] 安排的: *An ad hoc committee has been set up to deal with the problem.* 成立了一個專門委員會來處理這個問題。| **on an ad hoc basis** *Decisions were made on an ad hoc basis.* 決定是在事先未計劃的情況下作出的。—**ad hoc** *adv*

a·dieu /ə`du; ə'djuː/ *n plural* **adieux** /ə`duz; ə'djuːz/ *or* **adieus** [C] *literary* an act of saying goodbye【文】道別; 一路平安: **bid sb adieu** *He bid her a fond adieu.* 他深情地向她道別。—**adieu** *interjection*

ad in·fi·ni·tum /`æd ˌɪnfə`naɪtəm; ˌæd ɪnfɪ̵'naɪtəm/ *adv Latin* continuing or repeated without ever ending【拉丁】無限地, 無止境地

ad·i·os /ˌædɪ`os; ˌædi'əʊs/ *interjection Spanish* goodbye【西】再見

ad·i·pose /`ædəˌpos; 'ædɪ̵pəʊs/ *adj technical* consisting of or containing animal fat【術語】含動物脂肪質的, 脂肪多的: *adipose tissue* 脂肪組織

adj the written abbreviation for 縮寫= ADJECTIVE

ad·ja·cent /ə`dʒesn̩t; ə'dʒeɪsənt/ *adj* something that is adjacent to something else, especially a room, building, or area, is next to it 鄰近的, 毗連的: [+to] *The fire started in the building adjacent to the library.* 首先起火的是與圖書館毗連的一座建築物。

ad·jec·ti·val /ˌædʒɪk`taɪvl; ˌædʒɪ̵k'taɪvəl◂/ *adj* **adjectival phrase/clause etc** *technical* a phrase etc that is used as an adjective or that consists of adjectives. For example, 'fully furnished' is an adjectival phrase.【術語】形容詞片[短]語/子[從]句等〈例如, fully furnished就是一個形容詞片語〉—**adjectivally** *adv*

ad·jec·tive /`ædʒɪktɪv; 'ædʒɪ̵ktɪv/ *n* [C] a word that describes a noun or PRONOUN, such as 'black' in the sentence 'She wore a black hat.' or 'happy' in the sentence 'I'll try to make you happy.' 形容詞〔修飾名詞或代(名)詞〕—compare 比較 ADVERB

ad·join /ə`dʒɔɪn; ə'dʒɔɪn/ *v* [T] if a room, building, or piece of land adjoins another one, it is next to it and joined to it 貼近, 毗鄰: *The kitchen adjoins the sitting room.* 廚房緊挨着客廳。—**adjoining** *adj*: *adjoining rooms* 相鄰的房間

ad·journ /ə`dʒɝn; ə'dʒɜːn/ *v* **1** [I,T] if a meeting or law court adjourns, or if the person in charge adjourns it, it finishes or stops for a short time (使)〔會議、審訊〕暫停: *The chairman has the power to adjourn the meeting at any time.* 主席有隨時暫停會議的權力。| [+for/until] *The trial was adjourned for two weeks.* 審訊延期兩個星期。| *Can I suggest we adjourn for lunch now?* 我建議我們現在暫停會議去吃中午飯, 好嗎? **2 adjourn to** *humorous* to finish an activity and go somewhere【幽默】轉移到…, 移席到: *After the match we adjourned to the pub.* 比賽後我們轉移到酒館。—**adjournment** *n* [C,U]

ad·judge /ə`dʒʌdʒ; ə'dʒʌdʒ/ *v* [T] *formal* to make a judgement about something or someone【正式】宣判, 判決, 裁決: *Any foodstuffs adjudged unacceptable must be disposed of.* 所有被判定為不合格的食品都必須處理掉。

ad·ju·di·cate /ə`dʒudɪˌket; ə'dʒuːdɪkeɪt/ *v* **1** [I,T] to officially decide who is right in an argument between two groups or organizations 裁定, 評定, 評審: [+on/in] *An independent expert was called in to adjudicate.* 邀請了一位與各當事人無關的專家擔任評判。| *adjudicate a claim* 裁定要求 (的合理性) **2** [I] to be the judge in a competition 擔任裁判: *He adjudicated at all the regional music competitions.* 他在所有地方音樂比賽中擔任評判。—**adjudicator** *n* [C] —**adjudication** /əˌdʒudɪ`keʃən; əˌdʒuːdɪ'keɪʃən/ *n* [U]

ad·junct /`ædʒʌŋkt; 'ædʒʌŋkt/ *n* [C] **1** [+to] something that is added or joined to something but is not part of it 附件, 附屬物 **2** *technical* an ADVERBIAL word or phrase that adds meaning to another part of a sentence, such as 'on Sunday' in 'They arrived on Sunday.'【術語】修飾語, 附加語〈如 They arrived on Sunday 中的 on Sunday〉

ad·jure /ə`dʒʊr; ə'dʒʊə/ *v* [T] *formal* to try very hard to persuade someone to do something【正式】懇求, 祈求: *Gwendolyn adjured him to be truthful.* 格温德琳懇求他講出真相。

ad·just /ə`dʒʌst; ə'dʒʌst/ *v* **1** [T] to make small changes to something, especially to its position, in order to improve it, make it more effective etc 調整, 調節: *Check and adjust the brakes regularly.* 定期檢查和調節剎車裝置。**2** [I,T] to gradually get used to a new situation by making small changes to the way you do things 適應; 使適合: [+to] *Adjusting to the tropical heat was more difficult than they had expected.* 適應熱帶的炎熱氣候比他們預料的難得多。| *They'll soon settle in – kids are very good at adjusting.* 他們很快就會安頓下來, 孩子們很會適應環境。—see also 另見 WELL-ADJUSTED W3

ad·just·a·ble /ə`dʒʌstəbl̩; ə'dʒʌstəbəl/ *adj* something that is adjustable can be changed in shape, size, or position to make it suitable for a particular person or purpose 可調節的, 可校準的: *an adjustable desk lamp* 可調節的枱燈

ad·just·ment /ə`dʒʌstmənt; ə'dʒʌstmənt/ *n* [C,U] **1** a small change made to something, such as a machine, a system, or the way something looks 調整, 調節, 校正: **make adjustments** *We've had to make some adjustments to our original calculations.* 我們不得不對我們最初的計算作一些調整。| **slight/minor adjustments** (=small changes) 輕微/細微的調整 **2** a change that someone makes to the way they behave or think〔心態、行為等方面的〕調整: *the adjustments required of someone moving to a foreign country* 移居外國者必須作出的調整

ad·ju·tant /`ædʒətənt; 'ædʒʊ̵tənt/ *n* [C] an army officer responsible for office work〔陸軍中的〕副官

ad-lib /æd `lɪb; ˌæd 'lɪb/ *v* **ad-libbed, ad-libbing** [I,T] to say something in a speech, a performance of a play etc without preparing or planning it 即興表演; 即興演講: *She forgot her lines and had to ad-lib the rest of the scene.* 她忘記了台詞, 只好臨時編出餘下的場面。—**ad-lib** *n* [C] —**ad-lib** /ˌ· '·◂/ *adj, adv*

ad·man /`ædˌmæn; 'ædmæn/ *n plural* **admen** /-ˌmɛn; -men/ [C] *informal* someone who works in advertising【非正式】廣告員; 廣告製作人

ad·min /`ædmɪn; 'ædmɪn/ *n* [U] *informal especially BrE* ADMINISTRATION (2)【非正式, 尤英】行政部門: *She works in admin.* 她在行政部門工作。

ad·min·is·ter /əd`mɪnəstɚ; əd'mɪnɪ̵stə/ *v* [T] **1** to manage and organize the affairs of a company, government etc 管理, 治理: *the bureaucrats who administer welfare programs* 管理福利計劃的官員 | *The Navajo administer their own territory within the United States.* 在美國, 納瓦霍印第安人管理他們自己的領土。**2** to organize the way a test or punishment is given, or the way laws are used 執行, 實施: *the courts administering justice* 主持正義的法庭 | *The test was administered fairly and impartially.* 考試舉辦得公平、公正。**3** *formal* to give someone a medicine or drug to take【正式】給予, 用〔藥等〕

2 2 **ad·min·is·tra·tion** /əd͵mɪnəˋstreʃən; ədˌmɪnɪˈstreɪʃən/ *n* **1** [U] all the activities that are involved in managing and organizing the affairs of a company, institution etc 管理; 經營: *We're looking for someone with experience in administration.* 我們正在尋求一個有管理經驗的人。| *They spend too much on administration and not enough on doctors and nurses.* 他們在管理上花費太多, 但對醫護人員的資金卻投入不足。**2 the administration** the people who manage a company, institution etc 管理者; 經營者; 管理部門, 行政部門: *the college administration* 學院行政部門 **3** [C usually singular 一般用單數] the government of a country at a particular time 政府: *the Kennedy Administration* 甘迺迪政府 | *The problem has been ignored by successive administrations.* 連續幾屆政府都忽略了這個問題。**4** [U] the act of administering a test, law etc 執行, 施行: *the administration of justice* 司法, 執法

3 **ad·min·is·tra·tive** /ədˋmɪnə͵stretɪv; ədˈmɪnɪstrətɪv/ *adj* connected with the work of managing or organizing a company, institution etc 行政的; 管理的: *The job is mainly administrative.* 這項工作主要是行政性的。| *administrative duties* 管理職責 —**administratively** *adv*

ad·min·is·tra·tor /ədˋmɪnə͵stretɚ; ədˈmɪnɪstreɪtə/ *n* [C] someone whose job is connected with the management and organization of a company, institution etc 管理人; 行政官員; 主管

ad·mi·ra·ble /ˋædmərəbl; ˈædmərəbəl/ *adj* something that is admirable has many good qualities that you respect and admire 令人欽佩的, 極其出色的: *an admirable achievement* 令人欽佩的成就 —**admirably** *adv*

ad·mi·ral /ˋædmərəl; ˈædmərəl/ *n* [C] a high rank in the British or US navy, or someone who has this rank 海軍將官; 海軍上將; 艦隊司令 —see table on page C6 參見C6頁附錄

Ad·mi·ral·ty /ˋædmərəltɪ; ˈædmərəlti/ *n* **the Admiralty** the government department that controls the British navy (英國) 海軍部

ad·mi·ra·tion /͵ædməˋreʃən; ˌædməˈreɪʃən/ *n* [U] a feeling of admiring something or someone 敬佩, 欽佩, 羨慕: *Daniel gazed at her in admiration.* 丹尼爾用敬佩的目光注視着她。| **[+for]** *Tippett later developed a deep admiration for Wagner.* 蒂皮特後來對瓦格納表示出深深的敬佩。

3 **ad·mire** /ədˋmaɪr; ədˈmaɪə/ *v* [T not in progressive 不用進行式] **1** to have a very high opinion of someone because of a quality they have or because of something they have done 欽佩, 讚美, 羨慕: *I really admire the way she brings up those kids all on her own.* 我確實佩服她全靠自己一個人把那些孩子撫養大。| **admire sb for sth** *Lewis was admired for his work on medieval literature.* 劉易斯因其對中世紀文學的研究而受人仰慕。**2** to look at something and think how beautiful or impressive it is 欣賞, 觀賞: *We stopped half way up the hill to admire the view.* 我們上山中途停下來觀賞風景。**3 admire sb from afar** to be attracted to someone but without telling them how you feel 暗自仰慕: *Mary was still a good looking woman and Sid had admired her from afar for a long time.* 瑪麗風采依舊, 錫德對她仰慕已久。—**admiring** *adj* —**admiringly** *adv*

ad·mir·er /ədˋmaɪrɚ; ədˈmaɪərə/ *n* [C] **1** a man who is attracted to a particular woman〔女人的〕愛慕者: *a beautiful woman with many admirers* 有許多仰慕者的漂亮女子 | *a secret admirer* 暗戀者 **2 be an admirer of** to admire someone, especially a famous person, or their work 仰慕...: *The painter Turner was a great admirer of Byron.* 畫家透納是拜倫的忠實崇拜者。

ad·mis·si·ble /ədˋmɪsəbl; ədˈmɪsɪbəl/ *adj* admissible reasons, facts etc are acceptable or allowed, especially in a court of law 可採納的, 可接受的: *admissible evidence* 可採納的證據 —opposite 反義詞 INADMISSIBLE —**admissibility** /əd͵mɪsəˋbɪlətɪ; ədˌmɪsɪˈbɪlɪti/ *n* [U]

ad·mis·sion /ədˋmɪʃən; ədˈmɪʃən/ *n* **1** [C] a statement in which you admit that something is true or that you have done something wrong 承認; 供認: **admission that** *The Senator's admission that he had lied to Congress shocked many Americans.* 參議員承認他向國會說謊, 令許多美國人深感震驚。| **admission of guilt/failure/defeat etc** *The court may interpret your silence as an admission of guilt.* 法庭也許會將你的緘默作為認罪的表示。| **by/on your own admission** *By his own admission, he is a complete womanizer.* 他自己承認是個好色之徒。**2** [U] permission given to someone to enter or become a member of a school, club, building etc 允許進入 [加入]: **[+to]** *seeking admission to a prestigious university* 設法進入有名望的大學 | **gain admission** *Women gained admission to the club only recently.* 直到最近婦女才獲准加入這個俱樂部。**3 admissions** [plural] the process of allowing people to enter a university, institution, hospital etc, or the number of people who can enter 錄取〔允許進入〕的過程[人數]: *Doctors are reporting a steep rise in admissions.* 醫生報告住院病人的數量在急劇增加。| **admissions policy/procedures/officer etc** *This particular college has a very selective admissions policy.* 這所專門學院有一個十分嚴格的錄取政策。**4** [U] the cost of entrance to a concert, sports event etc 入場費: *The cost includes free admission to the casinos.* 費用包括賭場免費入場。| *Admission: £3.50.* 入場費: 3.50 英鎊。**5** [U] permission to enter a place〔進入某地的〕許可: *No admission after 10pm.* 晚上十點以後不准進入。

USAGE NOTE 用法說明: ADMISSION

WORD CHOICE 詞語辨析: **admission, admittance, admissions**

Admission is the usual word. **Admittance** is more formal and only used in the meaning 'permission to go in a building, park etc', usually given by someone in authority. On a notice you might see admission 是一個常用詞。admittance 比較正式, 只用於"允許進入建築物、公園等", 通常需要授權。告示上可見到: *Private Road: No Admittance.* 私人馬路, 禁止駛入。

Admissions is the word used by official organizations about the number of people entering a university, school, hospital etc. admissions 用於官方機構, 如大學、學校錄取多少人或醫院可接納多少病人住院等: *the admissions officer/policy/procedure* 負責錄取工作的官員/錄取政策/錄取程序 | *We have a lot of emergency admissions.* 我們收了許多急診住院病人。

ad·mit /ədˋmɪt; ədˈmɪt/ *v* **admitted, admitting** [T] **1** to accept and agree unwillingly that something is true or that someone else is right 承認, 贊同: *"I was really scared," Jenny admitted.* "我真害怕。"珍妮承認道。| **admit (that)** *You may not like her, but you have to admit that she's good at her job.* 你也許不喜歡她, 但你必須承認她勝任工作。| **I must admit** *spoken* (=when you are admitting something you are embarrassed about)【口】我得承認 *I must admit I didn't actually do anything to help her.* 我必須承認實際上我並沒有幫她忙。| **come on, admit it!** *spoken* (=used to try to make someone admit something)【口】快, 說老實話! *Come on, admit it! You were out with Keith last night?* 快坦白! 你昨晚和基思一起出去了吧? | **freely/openly admit** (=admit without being ashamed) 坦白, 公開承認 *Phillips openly admits to being selfish.* 菲力普斯坦白承認自己很自私。**2** also 又作 **admit to** to say that you have done something wrong, especially something criminal; CONFESS (1) 承認〔做錯了事, 犯了罪〕: **admit (to) doing sth** *A quarter of all workers admit to taking time off when they are not ill.* 四分之一的工人承認他們沒病的時候休過假。| **admit (to) sth** *After questioning he admitted to the murder.* 經過盤問後他承認自己是兇手。**3** to allow someone or something to enter a public place to watch a game, performance etc 允許…進入: **admit sb to/into** *Only ticket-holders will be admitted into the stadium.* 只有持票者才可進入體育場。**4** to allow someone to join an organization, club etc 允許加入, 接納: **admit sb to/into** *The UK was admitted to the EEC in 1973.* 英國於 1973 年獲准加入歐共體。**5 be admitted to hospital** *BrE* 【英】**/to the hospital** *AmE* 【美】 to be taken to a hospital because you are ill 被送進醫院: *He was admitted to the hospital Tuesday morning with stomach pains.* 他於星期二上午因胃痛被送進醫院。**6 admit defeat** to stop trying to do something because you realise you cannot succeed 〔中途〕承認失敗, 認輸: *Sean kept running, refusing to admit defeat.* 肖恩繼續跑, 不甘認輸。**7 an admitted alcoholic/atheist etc** someone who has admitted that they are an ALCOHOLIC, etc 自認的酒鬼/無神論者等

admit of sth *phr v* [T] *formal* if a situation admits of a particular explanation, that explanation can be accepted as possible 【正式】容許有: *The facts admit of no other explanation.* 事實毋容置疑。

ad·mit·tance /əd`mɪtn̩s; əd'mɪtəns/ *n* [U] *formal* permission to enter a place 【正式】進入權: **gain admittance** (=get admittance) 獲准進入 *Gaining admittance to his private club was no easy matter.* 獲准進入他的私人俱樂部不是一件容易事。—compare 比較 ADMISSION (5)

ad·mit·ted·ly /əd`mɪtɪdlɪ; əd'mɪtɨdli/ *adv* [sentence adverb 句子副詞] used when you are admitting that something is true 誠然, 確實地; 不可否認地: *The technique is painful, admittedly, but it benefits the patient greatly.* 應該承認, 採用這種技術會有點痛, 但對病人十分有益。| *This has led to financial losses, though admittedly on a fairly small scale.* 這已造成了財政損失, 儘管不可否認損失規模比較小。

ad·mix·ture /æd`mɪkstʃɚ; əd'mɪkstʃə/ *n* [C+of] *technical* a substance that is added to another substance in a mixture 【術語】攙和劑, 混合物, 合劑

ad·mon·ish /əd`mɑnɪʃ; əd'mɒnɪʃ/ *v* [T] *formal* to tell or warn someone severely that they have done something wrong 【正式】(嚴正) 警告, 告誡: *The witness was admonished for failing to answer the question.* 證人因未能回答問題而受到警告。—**admonishment** *n* [C]

ad·mo·ni·tion /ˌædmə`nɪʃən; ˌædmə'nɪʃən/ *n* [C,U] *formal* a warning or expression of disapproval about someone's behaviour 【正式】警告, 告誡 —**admonitory** *adj formal* 【正式】: *an admonitory glance* 告誡的目光

ad nau·se·am /`æd `nɔzɪˌæm; ˌæd 'nɔːziəm/ *adv* if you say or do something ad nauseam, you say or do it so often that it becomes annoying for other people 令人厭煩地: *Look, we've been over this ad nauseam – I think we should move on to the next item.* 看, 這個問題我們都已經說膩了, 我看我們還是進入下一項吧。

a·do /ə`du; ə'duː/ *n* [U] **without more/further ado** without delaying or wasting any time 不再延誤, 不再費時間: *So without further ado, I'll now ask Mr Davis to open the debate.* 不再多說了, 現在我請戴維斯先生宣布辯論開始。

a·do·be /ə`dobɪ; ə'dəʊbi/ *n* **1** [U] earth and STRAW (1) that are made into bricks for building houses 土坯, 泥磚 **2** [C] a house made using adobe 土坯房子

ad·o·les·cence /ˌædl̩`ɛsn̩s; ˌædə'lesəns/ *n* [U] the time, usually between the ages of 12 to 18, when a young person is developing into an adult 青春期

ad·o·les·cent /ˌædl̩`ɛsn̩t; ˌædə'lesənt◂/ *n* [C] a young person who is developing into an adult 青少年, 青春期的少男少女 —see picture at 參見 CHILD 圖

a·dopt /ə`dɑpt; ə'dɒpt/ *v* [T] [S2] [W2]

1 ►CHILD 孩子◄ to legally make another person's child part of your family so that he or she becomes one of your own children 收養, 領養: *My mother was adopted when she was four.* 我母親四歲時被人領養。—compare 比較 FOSTER[1] (1)

2 adopt an approach/strategy/policy to start to use a particular method or plan for dealing with something 採用某方法/戰略/政策: *The courts have been asked to adopt a more flexible approach to young offenders.* 要求法庭對年輕罪犯採用較靈活的處理方法。

3 ►STYLE/MANNER 風格/方式◄ to use a particular style of speaking, writing, or behaving, especially one that you do not usually use 採取, 採用: *"I can't say I blame him," Victor replied, adopting a more conciliatory tone.* "我不是說我要責備他。" 維克托回答道, 語氣緩和了一些。| *Papers like this tend to adopt a very simple writing style.* 這樣的論文往往採用十分樸實的寫作風格。

4 ►ACCEPT A SUGGESTION 接受建議◄ to formally approve a proposal, especially by voting 〔尤指通過表決〕正式批准; 認可; 接受: *They were trying to persuade the UN to adopt an aggressively anti-American resolution.* 他們竭力說服聯合國批准一個強烈反美的決議。

5 adopt a name/country to choose it to be your own 選定姓名/國家: *Italy is my adopted country.* 意大利是我選定的國家。

6 ►ELECTION 選舉◄ *BrE* to officially choose someone to represent a political party in an election 【英】提名…為候選人

a·dopt·ed /ə`dɑptɪd; ə'dɒptɨd/ *adj* **1** an adopted child has been legally made part of a family that he or she was not born into 領養的, 過繼的: *his adopted son* 他的養子 **2** your adopted country is one that you have chosen to live in permanently 〔國家〕被選擇居住的

a·dop·tion /ə`dɑpʃən; ə'dɒpʃən/ *n* **1** [C,U] the act or process of adopting a child 收養, 領養 **2** [U] the act of deciding to use a particular plan, method, way of speaking etc 採用, 採納 **3** [U] *BrE* the choice of a particular person to represent a political party in an election 【英】提名某人為候選人

a·dop·tive /ə`dɑptɪv; ə'dɒptɪv/ *adj* an adoptive parent is one who has adopted a child 收養 (孩子) 的

a·dor·a·ble /ə`dorəbl̩; ə'dɔːrəbəl/ *adj* someone or something that is adorable is so attractive that it fills you with feelings of love 值得愛慕的; 可愛的: *Oh what an adorable little baby!* 啊! 多麼可愛的小寶寶!

ad·o·ra·tion /ˌædə`reʃən; ˌædə'reɪʃən/ *n* [U] **1** great love and admiration 敬慕, 愛慕: *the look of adoration in his eyes* 他愛慕的眼神 **2** *literary* religious worship 【文】宗教崇拜

a·dore /ə`dor; ə'dɔː/ *v* [T not in progressive 不用進行式] **1** to love someone very much and feel very proud of them 敬慕, 愛慕: *Betty adores her grandchildren.* 貝蒂寵愛孫子孫女。**2** *informal* to like something very much 【非正式】非常喜歡: *I absolutely adore chocolate.* 我極喜歡巧克力。| *Don't you just adore these cookies?* 你難道不喜歡這些餅乾嗎?

a·dorn /ə`dɔrn; ə'dɔːn/ *v* [T] *formal* to decorate something 【正式】裝飾: *church walls adorned with religious paintings* 用宗教繪畫作品裝飾的教堂牆壁

a·dorn·ment /ə`dɔrnmənt; ə'dɔːnmənt/ *n* **1** [C] something that you use to decorate something 裝飾品 **2** [U] the act of adorning something 裝飾

a·dren·a·lin /æd`rɛnlɪn; ə'drenəl-ɨn/ *n* [U] **1** a chemical produced by your body when you are afraid, angry, or excited, which makes your heart beat faster so that you can move quickly 腎上腺素 **2 get the adrenalin**

going to make you feel nervously excited and full of energy 突然緊張、興奮起來

a·drift /əˋdrɪft; əˈdrɪft/ *adj, adv* **1** a boat that is adrift is not fastened to anything or controlled by anyone 漂浮着（的）; 漂流着（的） **2** someone who is adrift is confused about what to do in their life 漫無目標的[地] **3 come adrift** to become separated from something that fastens 散開; 脱落: *Her hair was forever coming adrift from the pins and combs she used to keep it in place.* 她的頭髮總是從固定頭髮的髮夾或梳子中散開來。

a·droit /əˋdrɔɪt; əˈdrɔɪt/ *adj* clever and skilful, especially in the way you use words and arguments 機敏的, 靈巧的;〔尤指〕口齒伶俐的: *an adroit negotiator* 精明的談判家 —**adroitly** *adv* —**adroitness** *n* [U]

a·du·ki bean /əˋdukɪ bin; əˈdu:ki bi:n/ *n* [C] a brown and red bean that is used in Chinese and Japanese cooking 赤豆, 小豆 —see picture on page A9 參見 A9 頁圖

ad·u·la·tion /ˌædʒəˋleʃən; ˌædʒʊˈleɪʃən/ *n* [U] praise and admiration for someone that is more than they really deserve 恭維, 奉承, 諂媚: *basking in the adulation of his fans* 沉浸於他的崇拜者的恭維之中 —**adulatory** /ˋædʒələˌtorɪ; ˌædʒʊˈleɪtəri/ *adj*

2 2 **ad·ult¹** /ˋædʌlt; ˈædʌlt/ *n* **1** a fully-grown person or animal 發育成熟的人或動物: *Some children find it difficult to talk to adults.* 一些孩子發覺與成年人很難談得來。**2** someone who is old enough to be considered legally responsible, and can for example vote in elections and get married without their parents' permission〔法律上的〕成年人

3 **adult²** *adj* **1** [only before noun 僅用於名詞前] fully grown or developed 發育成熟的, 成年的: *an adult lion* 成年的獅子 | **adult life** (= the part of your life when you are an adult) 成年的生活 **2** typical of an adult's behaviour or of the things adults do（適合）成年人的; 老成的, 成熟的: *dealing with problems in an adult way* 以老成持重的方式處理問題 **3 adult movie/magazine etc** a film etc that is about sex, shows sexual acts etc 成人電影/雜誌等

adult ed·u·ca·tion /ˌ‥ ‥ˈ‥/ *n* [U] education provided for adults outside the formal educational system, usually by means of classes that are held in the evening 成人教育

a·dul·ter·ate /əˋdʌltəˌret; əˈdʌltəreɪt/ *v* [T] to make food or drink less pure by adding another substance of lower quality to it 攙雜; 攙假 —see also 另見 UNADULTERATED —**adulteration** /əˌdʌltəˋreʃən; əˌdʌltəˈreɪʃən/ *n* [U]

a·dul·ter·er /əˋdʌltərə; əˈdʌltərə/ *n* [C] *old-fashioned* someone who is married and has sex with someone who is not their wife or husband【過時】姦夫; 淫婦; 通姦者

a·dul·ter·ess /əˋdʌltərɪs; əˈdʌltərɪs/ *n* [C] *old-fashioned* a married woman who has sex with a man who is not her husband【過時】姦婦, 淫婦

a·dul·ter·y /əˋdʌltərɪ; əˈdʌltəri/ *n* [U] sex between someone who is married and someone who is not their wife or husband 通姦, 私通: **commit adultery** *She had committed adultery on several occasions.* 她好幾次與人私通。—**adulterous** *adj*

ad·ult·hood /ˋædʌlthud; ˈædʌlthʊd/ *n* [U] the time when you are an adult 成年（時期）

ad·um·brate /ædˋʌmbret; ˈædʌmbreɪt/ *v* [T] *formal* to suggest or describe something in an incomplete way【正式】隱約預示, 暗示 —**adumbration** /ˌædʌmˋbreʃən; ˌædʌmˈbreɪʃən/ *n* [U]

adv the written abbreviation of 縮寫= ADVERB

3 2 **ad·vance¹** /ədˋvæns; ədˈvɑ:ns/ *n*

1 in advance before something happens or is expected to happen 預先, 提前: *I should warn you in advance, we may be delayed.* 我該預先提醒你, 我們也許會被耽擱。| **six months/a year in advance** *Rent is payable three months in advance.* 租金提前三個月支付。| **[+of]** *Could you distribute copies well in advance of the meeting?* 你能否在會前分發好材料？

2 ►DEVELOPMENT/IMPROVEMENT 發展/改進◄ [C] a change, discovery, or INVENTION that brings progress 進步, 進展: *His book argues that there have been major advances for women since 1945.* 他的書認為婦女的狀況自從 1945 年以來有了很大的改善。| **[+in]** *Recent advances in biotechnology have raised moral questions.* 生物技術近期的發展引出了道德問題。

3 ►FORWARD MOVEMENT 向前的移動◄ [C] forward movement or progress 前進: *the army's advance* 部隊向前推進

4 ►MONEY 金錢◄ [C usually singular 一般用單數] money paid to someone before the usual time 預付款

5 advances [plural] an attempt to start a friendly or sexual relationship with someone〔對異性的〕挑逗, 勾引: **make advances** *She accused her boss of making advances to her.* 她指控老闆對她圖謀不軌。

6 ►INCREASE 增加◄ [C] *technical* an increase in the price or value of something【術語】上漲, 攀升: *a further big advance in the price of gold* 黃金價格的又一輪暴漲

advance² *v*

1 ►MOVE 運動◄ [I] to move forward, especially in a slow and determined way〔尤指緩慢而堅定地〕前進, 推進: **advance on** (=move forward in order to attack) 向…推進 *Troops advanced on the rebel stronghold.* 軍隊向反叛者的據點推進。| **[+across/through/towards]** *The army slowly advanced across the frozen tundra.* 部隊緩緩地穿越凍土帶。

2 ►DEVELOP 發展◄ [I] if something such as technical or scientific knowledge advances, it develops and improves 進展: *Our understanding of human genetics has advanced considerably.* 我們對人類遺傳學的理解有了很大進展。

3 advance a plan/idea/proposal etc *formal* to suggest a plan etc so that other people can consider it【正式】提出計劃/看法/建議等: *A similar plan was advanced by the British delegation.* 英國代表團提出了一項類似的計劃。

4 ►MONEY 金錢◄ [T] to give someone money before they have earned it 預支: **advance sb sth** *Will they advance you some money until you get your first paycheck?* 在你拿到第一次工資以前, 他們是否會預支你一些錢？

5 advance a cause/your interests/your career etc to do something that will help you achieve advantage of success 拓展事業/興趣/職業生涯等

6 ►PRICE 價格◄ [I] *technical* if the price or value of something advances, it increases in amount【術語】〔價格、價值〕上漲: *Oil shares advanced today in heavy trading.* 在今天的大量交易中, 石油股價格上漲了。

7 ►CHANGE TIME 改變時間◄ [T] *formal* to change the time when an event should happen to an earlier time or date【正式】提前: *The time of the meeting has been advanced to ten o'clock.* 會議的時間提前到十時。

8 ►FILM/CLOCK 電影/鐘錶◄ [T] *formal* if you advance a film, clock etc, you make it go forward【正式】進〔片〕; 往前撥〔鐘錶〕—see also 另見 ADVANCING

advance³ *adj* **1 advance planning/warning/booking etc** planning etc that is done before an event 預先的計劃/警告/訂票[訂座]等: *We received no advance warning of the storm.* 我們沒有收到風暴的預先警報。**2 advance party/team** a group of people who go first to a place where something will happen to prepare for it〔提前到某地為活動做準備的〕先行組

ad·vanced /ədˋvænst; ədˈvɑ:nst/ *adj* **1** using the most modern ideas, equipment, and methods 高級的, 先進的: *advanced weapon systems* 先進的武器裝備 | *high levels of unemployment in the advanced capitalist economies* 發達資本主義經濟中的高失業率 —see 見 HIGH¹ (USAGE) **2** studying or dealing with a school subject at a difficult level 高深的, 高級的: *advanced learners of English* 高級程度的英語學習者 | *advanced physics* 高

A

等物理（學） **3** having reached a late point in time or development 晚期的: *By this time, the disease was too far advanced to be treated.* 這時，病已發展到晚期，無法醫治了。

Advanced lev·el /ˌ·ˈ· ˌ··/ *n* [C,U] *formal* A LEVEL【正式】高級程度考試

ad·vance·ment /ədˋvænsmənt; ədˈvɑːnsmənt/ *n* [C,U] *formal* progress or development in your job, level of knowledge etc【正式】進步；進展: *career advancement* 事業進展 | *advancements in science* 科學進步

ad·vanc·ing /ədˋvænsɪŋ; ədˈvɑːnsɪŋ/ *adj* **1** moving forward, especially in order to attack 前進的，向前推進的: *advancing Serbian forces* 向前推進的塞爾維亞部隊 **2 advancing years/age** the fact of growing older 年老，年事已高: *Blake had grown much quieter and more serious – another sign of his advancing years.* 布萊克變得越來越安靜，越來越嚴肅 —— 這是上了年紀的另一個跡象。

1 **ad·van·tage** /ədˋvæntɪdʒ; ədˈvɑːntɪdʒ/ *n*
1 **1 ▶THAT HELPS YOU** 有利於你的◀ [C,U] something that helps you to be better or more successful than others 有利條件，優勢: **[+of]** *the advantages of a university education* 大學教育的優勢 | **have an advantage (over)** *For certain types of work wood has advantages over plastic.* 對於某些製品來講，木頭要強於塑料。| **give sb an advantage** *New tax regulations had given them an advantage over their commercial rivals.* 新稅收法規使他們比其商業競爭對手更具優勢。| **big/great/definite advantage** *Her previous experience gives her a big advantage over the other applicants.* 她以前的經歷使她比其他申請者有更多的優勢。| **unfair advantage** *Government subsidies give these industries an unfair advantage.* 政府補助金使這些行業有着不公平的優勢。| **be to your advantage** (=give you an advantage) 對你有利 | **be at an advantage** (=have an advantage) 佔優勢 *Candidates with computer skills will be at an advantage.* 具有電腦技能的候選者會有優勢。| **gain/seek advantage** (=get or try to get something that will help you against your opponents) 得到／謀求優勢 *seeking political advantage by exploiting this sensitive issue* 利用這個敏感的問題謀求政治優勢

2 take advantage of sb to treat someone unfairly to get what you want, especially someone who is generous or easily persuaded〔不公正地〕利用某人，佔某人的便宜: *Don't lend them the car – they're taking advantage of you!* 不要把車借給他們 —— 他們在利用你！

3 take advantage of sth to use a particular situation to do or get what you want〔巧妙地〕利用某物: *I took advantage of the good weather to paint the shed.* 我趁天氣好給棚屋刷上油漆。

4 ▶STH GOOD 好事物◀ [C,U] a good or useful quality or condition that something has 好處，優點，利益: *one of the many advantages of living in the city* 住在城市的諸多好處之一 | *Is there really any advantage in getting there early?* 早到那兒真的有甚麼好處嗎？| **have the advantage of** *For children of this age, cereals have the advantage of being rich in iron.* 麥片含豐富鐵質，對這個年齡的孩子有好處。

5 to good advantage in a way that shows the best features of someone or something 表現出優點地，有利地

6 ▶TENNIS 網球◀ **advantage X** used to show that the person named has won the point after DEUCE X佔先，X領先一分〔終局前平分後先得一分〕: *Advantage Agassi.* 阿加西領先一分。

ad·van·ta·geous /ˌædvənˋtedʒəs; ˌædvənˈteɪdʒəs/ *adj* helpful and likely to make you successful 有利的，有益的: **[+to]** *terms advantageous to foreign companies* 對外國公司有利的條款 —**advantageously** *adv*

Ad·vent /ˋædvɛnt; ˈædvent/ *n* [singular] the period of four weeks before Christmas in the Christian religion〔基督教的〕降臨節〔聖誕節前的四個星期〕

advent *n* **the advent of** the time when something first begins to be widely used …的出現，來臨: *the advent of the motor car* 汽車的出現

ad·ven·ti·tious /ˌædvɛnˋtɪʃəs; ˌædvənˈtɪʃəs◂/ *adj formal* happening by chance; unexpected【正式】偶然的 —**adventitiously** *adj*

ad·ven·ture /ədˋvɛntʃɚ; ədˈventʃə/ *n* [C,U] an exciting experience in which dangerous or unusual things happen 冒險（經歷）: *a young man looking for adventure* 尋求冒險的青年人 | *Ahab's adventures at sea* 亞哈海上歷險記

adventure play·ground /ˌ·ˌ·· ˈ··/ *n* [C] *BrE* an area of ground for children to play on, with exciting equipment and structures for climbing on【英】歷險樂園〔提供富有刺激性的設施及裝置供兒童攀爬玩樂的場所〕

ad·ven·tur·er /ədˋvɛntʃərɚ; ədˈventʃərə/ *n* [C] **1** someone who enjoys adventure 冒險家: *an adventurer traveling the world* 周遊世界的冒險家 **2** *old-fashioned* someone who tries to become rich or socially important using dishonest or immoral methods【過時】投機分子；為求名利不擇手段的人

ad·ven·tur·ous /ədˋvɛntʃərəs; ədˈventʃərəs/ *adj* **1** also 又作 **adventuresome** *AmE*【美】eager to go to new places and do exciting or dangerous things 喜歡冒險的，有冒險精神的: *an adventurous expedition up the Amazon* 向亞馬遜河上游的冒險遠征 **2** not afraid of taking risks or trying new things 敢作敢為的；大膽創新的: *Andy isn't a very adventurous cook.* 安迪不是一個大膽創新的廚師。—**adventurously** *adv*

ad·verb /ˋædvɝb; ˈædvɜːb/ *n* [C] a word or group of words that describes or adds to the meaning of a verb, an adjective, another adverb, or a whole sentence, such as 'slowly' in 'He ran slowly.', 'very' in 'It's very hot.', or 'naturally' in 'Naturally, we want you to come.' 副詞〈如 He ran slowly 中的 slowly，It's very hot 中的 very，或 Naturally, we want you to come 中的 naturally〉— compare 比較 ADJECTIVE

ad·ver·bi·al¹ /ədˋvɝbɪəl; ədˈvɜːbiəl/ *adj* used as an adverb 副詞的，狀語的: *an adverbial phrase* 副詞片語

adverbial² *n* [C] *technical* a word or phrase used as an adverb【術語】副詞語，狀語

ad·ver·sa·ri·al /ˌædvɚˋsɛrɪəl; ˌædvɜːˈseəriəl◂/ *adj* an adversarial system, especially in politics and the law, is one in which two sides oppose and attack each other 對手的: *the adversarial nature of two-party politics* 兩黨政治的敵對本質

ad·ver·sa·ry /ˋædvɚˌsɛrɪ; ˈædvəsəri/ *n* [C] *formal* a country or person you are fighting or competing against; opponent【正式】對手，敵手

ad·verse /ədˋvɝs; ˈædvɜːs/ *adj* **1** not favourable 不利的；反對的；相反的: *an adverse report* 不利的報道 | *adverse publicity* 起反作用的宣傳 **2 adverse conditions/effects etc** conditions etc that make it difficult for something to happen or exist 不利的情況／影響等: *We had to abandon the climb because of adverse weather conditions.* 由於天氣十分惡劣，我們不得不放棄這次登山。—**adversely** *adv*

ad·ver·si·ty /ədˋvɝsətɪ; ədˈvɜːsəti/ *n* [U] a situation in which you have a lot of problems that seem to be caused by bad luck 逆境，不幸，厄運: *to keep the family together in times of adversity* 處在逆境時讓家人團結在一起

ad·vert¹ /ˋædvɝt; ˈædvɜːt/ *n* [C] *BrE* an advertisement【英】廣告

ad·vert² /ədˋvɝt; ədˈvɜːt/ *v*
advert to sth *phr v* [T] *formal* to mention something【正式】提及

ad·ver·tise /ˋædvɚˌtaɪz; ˈædvətaɪz/ *v* **1** [I,T] to tell people publicly about a product or service in order to persuade them to buy it（為…）做廣告（宣傳）: *Have you tried that new shampoo they've been advertising on TV?* 你試過用他們一直在電視上做廣告的那種新洗髮液嗎？ **2** [I,T] to make an announcement, for example in a newspaper or on a POSTER, that a job is available, an event is

going to happen etc 登廣告招聘; 做廣告宣傳〔某一活動等〕: *a big poster advertising a U2 concert* 一張〔愛爾蘭搖滾樂組合〕U2 音樂會的大型海報 | **[+for]** *I see they're advertising for a new Sales Director.* 我看到他們登廣告招聘新的銷售部主管。**3** [T] to show or tell something about yourself that it would be better to keep secret 宣揚〔不宜公開的事〕: *Don't advertise the fact that you're looking for another job.* 不要對外宣揚你正在另找工作的事。—**advertiser** *n* [C]

3 **ad·ver·tise·ment** /ˌædvɚˋtaɪzmənt; ədˈvɜːtɪ̵smənt/ *n* [C] **1** a picture, set of words, a film etc that is used to advertise a product or service〔宣傳產品或服務的〕廣告: *an advertisement for a free day of skiing in Vermont* 去佛蒙特州免費滑雪一天的廣告 **2** a statement in a newspaper that a job is available, an event is going to happen etc〔招聘、活動等的〕廣告 **3 be an advertisement for** to show the advantages of something 宣揚…的優點: *He's not a very good advertisement for private education.* 他不是非常理想的私立教育形象代言人。

3 **ad·ver·tis·ing** /ˈædvɚˌtaɪzɪŋ; ˈædvətaɪzɪŋ/ *n* [U] the activity or business of advertising things on television, in newspapers etc 廣告(業): *advertising aimed at 18-25 year olds* 針對18歲到25歲年輕人的廣告 | *a career in advertising* 廣告業生涯

advertising a·gen·cy /ˈ···· ˌ···/ *n* [C] a company that designs and makes advertisements for other companies 廣告公司, 廣告代理

1 1 **ad·vice** /ədˋvaɪs; ədˈvaɪs/ *n* [U] an opinion you give someone about what they should do 意見; 忠告, 勸告; 建議: **[+on/about]** *There's lots of advice in the book on baby care.* 這本書中有許多嬰兒護理方面的建議。| **give advice** *Can you give me some advice about buying a house?* 關於買房子一事, 你能不能給我一點意見? | **legal/medical/professional advice etc** (=advice from someone with special knowledge) 法律/醫療/職業等方面的建議 *If I were you, I'd get some legal advice.* 如果我是你, 我會諮詢一些法律方面的意見。| **ask sb's advice** *I want to ask your advice about where to stay in Taipei.* 我想徵求你的意見, 到台北住在哪裡好。| **follow/take sb's advice** (=do what they advise you) 聽從/採納某人的意見 *I followed my father's advice and sold the car.* 我遵照父親的意見把車賣了。| *Take my advice and study something practical.* 聽我的忠告, 學點實用的東西。| **a word/piece of advice** (=some advice) 一點建議 *Let me give you a piece of advice. Wear a blue or grey suit to the interview.* 讓我給你一點建議。穿藍色或灰色套裝去參加面試。| **on sb's advice** (=because they advised you) 根據某人的建議 *On my doctor's advice, I'm taking early retirement.* 根據醫生的意見, 我要提前退休。

This graph shows some of the words most commonly used with the noun **advice**. 本圖表所示為含有名詞advice的一些最常用詞組。

Based on the British National Corpus and the Longman Lancaster Corpus
據英國國家語料庫和朗文蘭卡斯特語料庫

advice col·umn /ˈ·· ˌ··/ *n* [C] *especially AmE* part of a newspaper or magazine in which someone gives advice to readers about their personal problems【尤美】〔報刊或雜誌上的〕諮詢欄; AGONY COLUMN *BrE*【英】—**advice columnist** *n* [C]

ad·vi·sab·le /ədˋvaɪzəbl; ədˈvaɪzəbəl/ *adj* [not before noun 不用於名詞前] something that is advisable should be done in order to avoid problems or risks 可取的; 明智的: *For heavy smokers, regular medical checks are advisable.* 抽煙很多的人最好定期進行健康檢查。| **it is advisable to do sth** *It is advisable to disconnect the computer before you open it up.* 拆開電腦之前, 最好先切斷電源。—**advisability** /ədˌvaɪzəˋbɪlətɪ; ədˌvaɪzəˈbɪlɪ̵ti/ *n* [U]

ad·vise /ədˋvaɪz; ədˈvaɪz/ *v* **1** [I,T] to tell someone what you think they should do, especially when you know more than they do about something 勸告, 忠告; 提供意見: **advise sb to do sth** *Passengers are advised not to leave their bags unattended.* 建議乘客看管好自己的提包。| **advise sb against doing sth** *I'd advise you against saying anything to the press.* 我勸你甚麼都不要對新聞界講。| **strongly advise** *You are strongly advised to take out medical insurance when visiting China.* 極力建議你到中國遊覽時購買醫療保險。| **advise caution/patience/restraint etc** (=advise people to be careful, patient etc) 建議〔人們〕小心/有耐心/克制等 *The makers advise extreme caution when handling this material.* 製造商建議處理這種材料時要格外小心。**2** [I,T] to be employed to give advice on a subject about which you have special knowledge or skill (向…) 提供〔專業的〕建議[諮詢]: **advise on sth** *She's been asked to advise on training the new team.* 她被請求為訓練新隊伍提供建議。| **advise sb on sth** *He advises us on tax matters.* 他就稅收問題向我們提供諮詢。**3** [T] *formal* to inform someone about something【正式】通知: **advise sb of sth** *We'll advise you of any changes in the delivery dates.* 發送日期有任何改變, 我們都會通知你。| **keep sb advised** (=continue to inform someone) 讓某人了解變化的情況 *Keep us advised of the developments.* 請隨時告訴我們進展情況。**4 you would be well/ill advised to do sth** used to tell someone that it is wise or unwise to do something 建議你最好做/不做某事…: *You would be well advised to stay in bed and rest.* 你最好臥牀休息。 

ad·vis·ed·ly /ədˋvaɪzɪdlɪ; ədˈvaɪzɪ̵dli/ *adv* after careful thought; deliberately 深思熟慮地; 有意地: *He behaved like a dictator, and I use the term advisedly.* 他的所作所為就像個獨裁者, 我用這個詞是經過認真考慮的。

ad·vis·er also 又作 **advisor** *AmE*【美】/ədˋvaɪzɚ; ədˈvaɪzə/ *n* [C] someone whose job is to give advice because they know a lot about a subject, especially in business, law, or politics 顧問: *an independent financial adviser* 獨立的金融顧問

ad·vi·so·ry /ədˋvaɪzərɪ; ədˈvaɪzəri/ *adj* having the purpose of giving advice 提供意見[諮詢]的: **advisory committee/body** *the Environmental Protection Advisory Committee* 環境保護顧問委員會 | **advisory role/capacity** *employed in a purely advisory role* 純粹以顧問身分受聘

ad·vo·ca·cy /ˋædvəkəsɪ; ˈædvəkəsi/ *n* [U] public support for a course of action or way of doing things 支持, 擁護, 提倡

ad·vo·cate¹ /ˋædvəket; ˈædvəkeɪt/ *v* [T] to publicly support a particular way of doing things 主張, 擁護, 鼓吹: *Extremists were openly advocating violence.* 極端主義者公開鼓吹使用暴力。

ad·vo·cate² /ˋædvəkɪt; ˈædvəkɪ̵t/ *n* [C] **1** someone who publicly supports a particular way of doing things 提倡者, 擁護者, 鼓吹者: **be an advocate of** *She's a passionate advocate of natural childbirth.* 她竭力主張自然分娩。**2** a lawyer who speaks in a court of law, especially in Scotland〔尤指蘇格蘭的〕律師 —see also 另見 **play/be the devil's advocate** (DEVIL (4))

adze also 又作 **adz** *AmE*【美】/ædz; ædz/ *n* [C] a sharp tool with the blade at a right angle to the handle, used to shape pieces of wood 手斧, 錛子

ae·gis /ˈidʒɪs; ˈiːdʒ$\frac{1}{2}$s/ *n* **under the aegis of** *formal* with the protection or support of a person or organization【正式】在…的支持〔保護〕下: *a refugee camp operating under the aegis of the UN* 在聯合國保護下的難民營

ae·on also 又作 **eon** *AmE*【美】/ˈiən; ˈiːən/ *n* [C] an extremely long period of time 極長的時期, 萬古

aer·ate /ˈeəˌret; ˈeəreɪt/ *v* [T] *technical* to put a gas or air into a liquid under pressure【術語】充氣於〔…液體〕中 —**aeration** /ˌeəˈreʃən; eəˈreɪʃən/ *n* [U]

aer·i·al[1] /ˈɛrɪəl; ˈeəriəl/ *adj* **1** from a plane 空中的, 來自飛機的: *an aerial attack* 空襲 | *aerial photographs* 在空中拍攝的照片 **2** in or moving through the air 空氣中的

aerial[2] *n* [C] a piece of equipment for receiving or sending radio or television signals, usually consisting of a piece of metal or wire〔無線電、電視的〕天線; ANTENNA (2) *AmE*【美】—see picture on page A2 參見 A2 頁圖

aero- /ɛro; eərəʊ/ *prefix* concerning the air or aircraft 空氣(的); 航空(的): *aerodynamics* (=science of movement through air) 空氣動力學 | *an aeroengine* 飛機引擎

aer·o·bat·ics /ˌɛrəˈbætɪks; ˌeərəˈbætɪks/ *n* [plural] tricks done in a plane that involve making difficult or dangerous movements in the air 特技飛行, 航空表演

ae·ro·bic /ɛˈrobɪk; eəˈrəʊbɪk/ *adj* **1** *technical* using oxygen【術語】需氧的 **2 aerobic exercise** a type of exercise intended to strengthen the heart and lungs 有氧健身運動: *Examples of aerobic exercise are running, cycling, and swimming.* 有氧健身運動的項目有跑步、騎車和游泳。

aer·o·bics /ɛˈrobɪks; eəˈrəʊbɪks/ *n* [U] a very active type of physical exercise done to music, usually in a class 增氧健身操

aer·o·drome /ˈɛrəˌdrom; ˈeərədrəʊm/ *n* [C] *old-fashioned BrE* a place that small planes fly from【過時, 英】小型機場

aer·o·dy·nam·ic /ˌɛrodaɪˈnæmɪk; ˌeərəʊdaɪˈnæmɪk◂/ *adj* **1** an aerodynamic car, design etc uses the principles of aerodynamics to achieve high speed or low use of petrol 流線型的 **2** *technical* related to or involving aerodynamics【術語】空氣動力學的: *aerodynamic efficiency* 空氣動力效率 —**aerodynamically** /-klɪ; -kli/ *adv*

aer·o·dy·nam·ics /ˌɛrodaɪˈnæmɪks; ˌeərəʊdaɪˈnæmɪks/ *n* [U] **1** the scientific study of how objects move through the air 空氣動力學 **2** the qualities needed for something to move through the air, especially smoothly and quickly 空氣動力特性

aer·o·gramme /ˈɛrəˌgræm; ˈeərəgræm/ *n* [C] a very light letter you send by AIRMAIL 航空郵簡〔箋〕; AIRLETTER *BrE*【英】

aer·o·nau·tics /ˌɛrəˈnɔtɪks; ˌeərəˈnɔːtɪks/ *n* [U] the science of designing and flying planes 航空學〔術〕—**aeronautic** *adj* —**aeronautical** *adj*

aer·o·plane /ˈɛrəˌplen; ˈeərəpleɪn/ *n* [C] *BrE* a flying vehicle with wings and at least one engine; AIRPLANE *AmE*【美】; plane【英】飛機 —see picture at 參見 AIRCRAFT 圖

aer·o·sol /ˈɛrəˌsɑl; ˈeərəsɒl/ *n* [U] a small metal container from which a liquid such as paint can be forced at high pressure 小型噴霧器 —see picture at 參見 SPRAY[1] 圖

aer·o·space[1] /ˈɛroˌspes; ˈeərəʊspeɪs/ *adj* involving the designing and building of aircraft and space vehicles 航空和航天的: *the aerospace industry* 宇航工業

aerospace[2] *n* [U] the industry that designs and builds aircraft and space vehicles 航空與航天工業, 宇航工業

aes·thete *especially BrE*【尤英】also 又作 **esthete** *AmE*【美】/ˈɛsθit; ˈiːsθiːt/ *n* [C] someone who loves and understands beautiful things, such as art and music 審美家

aes·thet·ic *especially BrE*【尤英】also 又作 **esthetic** *AmE*【美】/ɛsˈθɛtɪk; iːsˈθetɪk/ *adj* **1** connected with beauty and the study of beauty 美學的: *From an esthetic point of view, it's a nice design.* 從美學角度看, 這是個很不錯的設計。| *a work of great aesthetic appeal* 非常有美學感染力的作品 **2** designed in a beautiful way 有美感的; 有審美能力的: *The building is aesthetic, but not very practical to heat.* 這幢建築物外型美觀, 但隔熱功能不太好。—**aesthetically** /-klɪ; -kli/ *adj*: *aesthetically pleasing* 給人以美感的

aes·thet·ics *especially BrE*【尤英】also 又作 **esthetics** *AmE*【美】/ɛsˈθɛtɪks; iːsˈθetɪks/ *n* [U] the study of beauty, especially beauty in art〔尤指藝術方面的〕(審)美學

ae·ther /ˈiθɚ; ˈiːθə/ *n* [U] an old spelling of ETHER (=the air or sky) 蒼穹, 蒼天〔ether 的舊式拼法〕

ae·ti·ol·o·gy *BrE*【英】, **etiology** *AmE*【美】/ˌitɪˈɑlədʒɪ; ˌiːtiˈɒlədʒi/ *n* [U] the study of what causes disease 病因學; 病原學

a·far /əˈfɑr; əˈfɑː/ *adv* **from afar** *literary* from a long distance away【文】遙遠地; 在遠處: *I saw him from afar.* 我在遠處看到他。

af·fa·ble /ˈæfəbl̩; ˈæfəbəl/ *adj* friendly and easy to talk to 友善的; 和藹可親的; 容易交談的: *an affable guy* 平易近人的人 —**affably** *adv* —**affability** /ˌæfəˈbɪlətɪ; ˌæfəˈbɪl$\frac{1}{2}$ti/ *n* [U]

af·fair /əˈfɛr; əˈfeə/ *n* [C] S2 W1

1 affairs [plural] **a)** public or political events and activities 事情, 事務: *world affairs* 世界大事 | *They were accused of interfering in China's internal affairs.* 他們被指責干涉中國的內政。| *the exclusion of women from public affairs* 拒絕婦女參與公共事務 | **foreign affairs** (=political events in other countries) 外交事務 *a foreign affairs correspondent for the CNN* 美國有線新聞網的外事記者 **b)** things connected with your personal life, your financial situation etc (個人的)事: *I am not prepared to discuss my financial affairs with the press.* 我不打算向新聞界談論我的財務問題。—see also 另見 **state of affairs** (STATE[1] (8))

2 ▶EVENT 事件◀ an event or set of related events, especially one that is impressive or shocking 事件: *the Watergate affair* 水門事件 | *The dinner was an elegant affair.* 這頓飯很講究。

3 ▶RELATIONSHIP 關係◀ a secret sexual relationship between two people, when at least one of them is married to someone else〔非配偶的〕曖昧關係, 私通: **have an affair (with)** *He had an affair with his boss that lasted six years.* 他和他的老闆的曖昧關係持續了六年。—see also 另見 LOVE AFFAIR

4 ▶THING 事物◀ *informal* an object, machine etc of a particular kind【非正式】東西: *The computer was one of those little portable affairs.* 那台電腦是便於攜帶的那一種。

5 be sb's affair if something is your affair, it only concerns you and you do not want anyone else to get involved in it 是某人自己的事: *What I do in my time is my affair and nobody else's.* 我在自己的時間裡做甚麼是我自己的事, 與別人無關。

af·fect /əˈfɛkt; əˈfekt/ *v* [T] S1 W1 **1** to do something that produces an effect or change in someone or something 影響: *How will the tax affect people on low incomes?* 這項稅收會如何影響低收入人士? | *a disease that affects the central nervous system* 影響中樞神經系統的疾病 | *emergency relief for the areas affected by the hurricane* 對遭受颶風影響的地區的緊急救助 **2** [usually passive 一般用被動態] to make someone feel strong emotions 使某人產生強烈的感情, 使感動: *We were all deeply affected by the news of her death.* 她去世的消息使我們都深感悲痛。**3** *formal* to pretend to have a particular feeling, way of speaking etc【正式】故作姿態, 假裝: *Simon affected boredom to make me think he didn't care.* 西蒙假裝厭煩, 讓我以為他(對這件事)不在乎。| *to affect a foreign accent* 裝外國口音

A

USAGE NOTE 用法說明: AFFECT
WORD CHOICE 詞語辨析: **affect, effect**
Affect is the usual verb and **effect** is the usual noun. affect 通常為動詞, 而 effect 通常為名詞: *How do you think the changes will affect (v) you?* (NOT 不用 affect on/to/in you) 你認為這些變化會如何影響你? *What effect (n) do you think the changes will have on you?* 你認為這些變化會給你帶來甚麼樣的影響? The verb **effect** is fairly formal and is only used in particular meanings, for example, you might **effect** changes or a plan of action (=make them happen). It does not mean the same as **affect**. 動詞 effect 相當正式, 只用於表示某種特定的意思, 如造成改變、形成計劃等, 和 affect 的意思不一樣。

af·fec·ta·tion /ˌæfɛkˋteʃən; ˌæfekˈteɪʃən/ *n* [C,U] behaviour that is not sincere or natural 裝模作樣, 矯揉造作: *Those beatnik clothes of his are just an affectation.* 他那些"反傳統一代"式的衣服顯得很不自然。

af·fect·ed /əˋfɛktɪd; əˈfektɨd/ *adj* not sincere or natural 做作的, 不自然的: *that stupid affected laugh of hers* 她那愚蠢而又做作的大笑

af·fect·ing /əˋfɛktɪŋ; əˈfektɪŋ/ *adj formal* producing strong emotions of sadness, pity etc【正式】使人感動的: *a deeply affecting story* 感人至深的故事

af·fec·tion /əˋfɛkʃən; əˈfekʃən/ *n* [C,U] a gentle feeling of love and caring 感情; 慈愛; 摯愛: [+for] *Bart felt a great affection for the old man.* 巴特對這位老人有很深的感情。| **show affection** *Their mother never shows them much affection.* 他們的母親對他們從來沒有表現出多少的母愛。

af·fec·tion·ate /əˋfɛkʃənɪt; əˈfekʃənɨt/ *adj* showing in a gentle way that you love someone 親切的, 有感情的: *an affectionate hug* 親切的擁抱 | *a very affectionate child* 很有感情的孩子 —**affectionately** *adv*

af·fi·anced /əˋfaɪənst; əˈfaɪənst/ *adj old use* ENGAGED (1)【舊】已訂婚的

af·fi·da·vit /ˌæfəˋdevɪt; ˌæfɨˈdeɪvɨt/ *n* [C] *law* a written statement made under OATH (=after promising to tell the truth), for use as proof in a court of law【法律】〔法庭上作證用的書面〕宣誓書, 書面證詞

af·fil·i·ate¹ /əˋfɪlɪˌet; əˈfɪlieɪt/ *v* **1 be affiliated with/to** if a group or organization is affiliated to a larger one, it is connected with it or controlled by it 附屬於: *a TV station affiliated to CBS* 附屬於哥倫比亞廣播公司的電視台 **2 affiliate yourself to** to join or become connected with a larger group or organization 加入, 加盟, 併入

af·fil·i·ate² /əˋfɪlɪət; əˈfɪliɨt/ *n* [C] a small company, organization etc that is connected with or controlled by a larger one 支會; 分社; 子公司; 附屬機構

af·fil·i·a·tion /əˌfɪlɪˋeʃən; əˌfɪliˈeɪʃən/ *n* [C,U] **1** the fact of being involved with or a member of a political or religious organization 聯繫, 從屬關係: *What are her political affiliations?* 她屬於甚麼政治派系? **2** the act of a smaller group or organization joining a larger one 併入, 加盟, 加入

af·fin·i·ty /əˋfɪnətɪ; əˈfɪnɨti/ *n* **1** [singular] a strong feeling that you like and understand someone because you share the same ideas or interests 情投意合; 喜好: [+for/between/with] *I felt an immediate affinity for them.* 我馬上就對他們有了好感。**2** [C,U] a close connection between two things because of qualities or features that they share 類同; 密切關係: [+with/between] *There is a remarkable affinity between Christian and Chinese concepts of the spirit.* 基督教關於靈魂的概念和中國人的看法非常相似。

af·firm /əˋfɝm; əˈfɜːm/ *v* **1** [T] *formal* to state publicly that something is true【正式】斷言, 申明, 確認: *The general affirmed rumors of an attack.* 將軍證實了襲擊的傳聞。**2** [T] *formal* to strengthen a feeling, belief, or idea【正式】肯定, 強化〔感覺、信念等〕: *By submitting to male values, they symbolically affirm male superiority.* 通過承認男性價值觀, 他們象徵性地加強了男子的優越感。**3** [T] *technical* to promise to tell the truth in a court of law, but without mentioning God in the promise【術語】鄭重聲明, 〔不經宣誓而〕承認, 確認 —**affirmation** /ˌæfɚˋmeʃən; ˌæfəˈmeɪʃən/ *n* [C,U]

af·fir·ma·tive /əˋfɝmətɪv; əˈfɜːmətɪv/ *adj* **1 answer/reply in the affirmative** to say 'yes' 肯定地回答 —opposite 反義詞 NEGATIVE¹ (3) **2** *formal* a word, sign etc that means 'yes'【正式】〔話或符號〕表示同意的: *an affirmative nod* 點頭表示同意 —**affirmatively** *adv*

affirmative ac·tion /·,··· '··/ *n* [U] the practice of choosing people for a job or education course who are usually treated unfairly because of their race, sex etc〔鼓勵聘用或錄取女性、少數族裔等的〕積極行動, 反歧視行動; POSITIVE DISCRIMINATION *BrE*【英】: *an affirmative action employer* 採取積極行動的雇主

af·fix¹ /əˋfɪks; əˈfɪks/ *v* [T+to] *formal* to fasten or stick something to something else【正式】使固定; 黏上, 貼上

af·fix² /ˋæfɪks; ˈæfɪks/ *n* [C] *technical* a group of letters added to the beginning or end of a word to change its meaning or use, such as 'untie', 'misunderstand', 'kindness', or 'quickly'【術語】詞綴 —compare 比較 PREFIX¹ (1), SUFFIX

af·flict /əˋflɪkt; əˈflɪkt/ *v* [T often passive 常用被動態] *formal* to make someone suffer or experience serious problems【正式】使受痛苦, 折磨: **be afflicted with/by** *a country afflicted by famine* 飽受饑荒困擾的國家

af·flic·tion /əˋflɪkʃən; əˈflɪkʃən/ *n* [C,U] *formal* something, usually a medical condition, that causes pain or unhappiness【正式】痛苦, 苦惱, 折磨: *the afflictions of old age* 老年時的各種苦楚

af·flu·ent /ˋæfluənt; ˈæfluənt/ *adj* having plenty of money, so that you can afford to buy expensive things, live in a nice house etc 富裕的, 富足的: *affluent suburbs with large houses and treelined streets* 房子寬敞、街道綠樹成蔭的富裕郊區 —**affluence** *n* [U]

af·ford /əˋford; əˈfɔːd/ *v* [T] **1 can afford a)** to have enough money to buy or pay for something 買得起, 付得起錢: *Only the bigger clubs can afford the enormous fees that these players demand.* 只有較大的俱樂部才能支付得起這些運動員要的高價。| **afford to do sth** *We can't afford to go on vacation this year.* 今年我們沒錢去度假。**b)** to have enough time to do something 有足夠的時間〔做某事〕: *Helena doesn't feel she can afford any more time away from work.* 海倫娜認為她不能從工作中抽出更多的時間。**c)** to be able to do something without causing serious problems for yourself 承擔得起; 有能力做: **afford to do sth** *We simply can't afford to offend such an important customer.* 惹怒這樣一位重要客戶, 我們可擔當不起。**2** *formal* to provide something or allow something to happen【正式】提供, 給予: *The window affords a beautiful view out over the city.* 窗外可以看到城市的美麗景色。—**affordable** *adj*

af·for·es·ta·tion /əˌfɔrəsˋteʃən; əˌfɒrɨˈsteɪʃən/ *n* [U] *technical* the act of planting trees in order to make a forest【術語】植樹造林 —opposite 反義詞 DEFORESTATION —**afforest** /əˋfɔrɪst; əˈfɒrɨst/ *v* [T]

af·fray /əˋfre; əˈfreɪ/ *n* [C] *law* a noisy fight or quarrel in a public place【法律】在公共場所打架, 滋事

af·fri·cate /ˋæfrɪkɪt; ˈæfrɪkɨt/ *n* [C] *technical* a CONSONANT sound consisting of a PLOSIVE such as /t/ or /d/ that is immediately followed by a FRICATIVE pronounced in the same part of the mouth, such as /ʃ/ or /ʒ/. The word 'church', for example, contains the affricate /tʃ/.【術語】破擦音〔爆破音如 /t/ 或 /d/ 和摩擦音如 /ʃ/ 或 /ʒ/ 的組合, 例如"church"這個詞含有破擦音 /tʃ/〕

af·front¹ /əˋfrʌnt; əˈfrʌnt/ *v* [T usually passive 一般用被動態] to offend or insult someone, especially by not showing respect 當眾侮辱; 冒犯

affront² *n* [C usually singular 一般用單數] a remark or action that offends or insults someone 侮辱; 冒犯的言

行: [+to] *an affront to his pride* 對他自尊心的公然傷害

Af·ghan /ˋæfgæn; ˈæfgæn/ *n* [C] **1** someone who comes from Afghanistan 阿富汗人 **2** a warm cover for a bed made of wool knitted (KNIT[1] (1)) in colourful patterns 阿富汗毛毯 **3** also 又作 **Afghan hound** a tall thin dog with a pointed nose and very long silky hair 阿富汗獵犬 —**Afghan** *adj* —see picture at 參見 DOG[1] 圖

a·fi·cio·na·do /əˏfɪsjəˋnɑdo; əˌfɪʃəˈnɑːdəʊ/ *n* [C] someone who is very interested in a particular activity or subject and knows a lot about it …迷; 狂熱愛好者: *a film aficionado* 電影迷

a·field /əˋfild; əˈfiːld/ *adv* **far afield** far away, especially from home 遠離〔家鄉等〕; 到[在]遠方: *Don't go too far afield or you'll get lost.* 不要走得太遠, 要不然你會迷路的。

a·fire /əˋfaɪr; əˈfaɪə/ *adj, adv* [not before noun 不用於名詞前] *literary*【文】**1** burning 着火(的), 燃燒着(的): *The oil tanker was afire.* 油箱起火了。**2** filled with strong emotions or excitement 熱情的, 充滿激情的: [+with] *afire with patriotism* 充滿愛國主義的熱情

a·flame /əˋflem; əˈfleɪm/ *adj* [not before noun 不用於名詞前] *literary*【文】**1** burning 着火的, 燃燒着的 **2** very bright with colour or light 明亮的: [+with] *trees aflame with autumn leaves* 有火紅秋葉的樹木 **3** filled with strong emotions or excitement 熱情洋溢的 —**aflame** *adv*

AFL-CIO /ˌe ɛf ˌɛl si aɪ ˋo; ˌeɪ ef ˌel siː aɪ ˈəʊ/ *n* [singular] the American Federation of Labor and Congress of Industrial Organizations; an association of American TRADE UNIONS, which has a lot of influence in the US 勞聯一產聯〔全稱為美國勞工聯合會暨產業聯合會, 是全美最大、最有影響力的一個工會組織〕

a·float /əˋflot; əˈfləʊt/ *adj* [not before noun 不用於名詞前] **1** floating on water 漂浮的: *Help me get the boat afloat.* 幫我把那隻小船弄下水。**2** having enough money to operate or stay out of debt 不欠債的; 經濟上周轉得開的: *The company was just barely afloat.* 這家公司僅僅是勉強不欠債。**3** *literary* on a ship【文】在船上的 —**afloat** *adv*

a·foot /əˋfʊt; əˈfʊt/ *adj* [not before noun 不用於名詞前] **1** being planned or happening 醞釀中的; 進行中的: *There were plans afoot for a second attack.* 正在策劃第二次進攻。**2** *old use* moving, especially walking【舊】行動的;〔尤指〕步行的 —**afoot** *adv*

a·fore·said /əˋfɔrˏsɛd; əˈfɔːsed/ also 又作 **a·fore·men·tioned** /əˋforˋmɛnʃənd; əˈfɔːmenʃənd/ *adj* [only before noun 僅用於名詞前] *law* mentioned before in an earlier part of a document, article, book etc【法律】上述的, 前述的: *The property belongs to the aforesaid Ms Jones.* 這財產屬於前面提到的瓊斯女士。—**aforesaid** *n* [singular or plural]: *The aforesaid were present at the meeting.* 上述人員出席了會議。

a·fore·thought /əˋfɔrˏθɔt; əˈfɔːθɔːt/ *adj* —see 見 **with malice aforethought** (MALICE (2))

a·foul /əˋfaul; əˈfaʊl/ *adv* **run/fall afoul of** *formal especially AmE* to cause problems by doing something that is against the rules or that goes against people's beliefs【正式, 尤美】和…發生衝突; 和…抵觸: *run afoul of the school authorities* 同校方發生衝突

1 2 **a·fraid** /əˋfred; əˈfreɪd/ *adj* [not before noun 不用於名詞前] **1 I'm afraid** *spoken* used to politely tell someone something that may annoy them, upset them or disappoint them【口】恐怕: *That's the most we can offer you, I'm afraid.* 恐怕這是我們能提供的最高價。| [+(that)] *I'm afraid you've been given the wrong address.* 恐怕給你的地址不對。| *Excuse me, but I'm afraid this is a non-smoking area.* 對不起, 這裡不允許吸煙。| **I'm afraid so** (=yes) 恐怕是的 *"Is she really very ill?" "I'm afraid so."* "她真的病得很厲害嗎?" "恐怕是的。" | **I'm afraid not** (=no) 恐怕不是 *No, I'm afraid not, but we do have some tickets for tomorrow.* 對不起, 恐怕沒有了, 但我們還有一些明天的票。**2** unwilling to do something because you are worried about what will happen if you do it 不敢[害怕]〔做某事〕的: [+of] *I didn't tell her because I was afraid of upsetting her.* 我沒有把事情告訴她, 因為怕她不高興。| [+(that)] *I didn't say anything because I was afraid the other kids would laugh at me.* 我甚麼都沒說, 因為我怕其他孩子嘲笑我。**3** very frightened or worried about something 害怕的, 恐懼的, 擔心的: *The poor little thing looked so afraid.* 可憐的小傢伙看來很害怕。| **be afraid** *I could see in his eyes that he was afraid.* 從他的眼神裡, 我能看出他感到害怕。| [+of] *Don't be afraid of the dog – he's quite harmless.* 不要怕這隻狗, 牠不咬人。| **afraid to do sth** *Don't be afraid to ask for help.* 不要怕求人幫忙。| **be afraid of doing sth** *Luke is afraid of going to bed in the dark.* 盧克害怕摸黑睡覺。| **be afraid for** *They've been laying people off, and Charlie is afraid for his job.* 他們一直在裁員, 所以查理很擔心自己的工作。**4 afraid of your own shadow** easily frightened or always nervous 膽小怕事; 疑神疑鬼, 草木皆兵

This graph shows how common different grammar patterns of the adjective **afraid** are. 本圖表所示為形容詞 afraid 構成的不同語法模式的使用頻率。

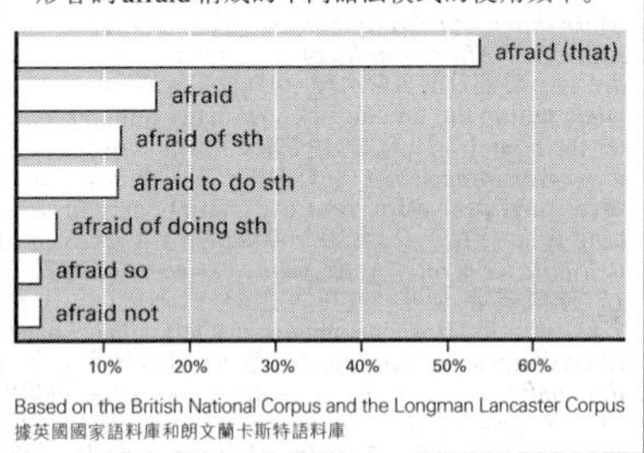

Based on the British National Corpus and the Longman Lancaster Corpus
據英國國家語料庫和朗文蘭卡斯特語料庫

a·fresh /əˋfrɛʃ; əˈfreʃ/ *adv formal* if you do something afresh, you do it again from the beginning【正式】再, 重新: **start afresh** *He moved to America to start his life afresh.* 他移居美國開始新生活。

Af·ri·can[1] /ˋæfrɪkən; ˈæfrɪkən/ *adj* from or connected with Africa 非洲的; 非洲人的

African[2] *n* [C] someone from Africa 非洲人

African A·mer·i·can /ˌ··· ·ˈ···/ *n* [C] *AmE* an American whose family originally came from Africa, especially as slaves【美】〔尤指作為奴隸的〕非洲裔美國人, 美國黑人 —see 見 NEGRO (USAGE)

Af·ri·kaans /ˌæfrɪˋkɑns; ˌæfrɪˈkɑːns/ *n* [U] a language of South Africa that is similar to Dutch 南非荷蘭語

Af·ri·ka·ner /ˌæfrɪˋkɑnɚ; ˌæfrɪˈkɑːnə/ *n* [C] a South African whose family came from the Dutch people who settled there in the 1600s 南非白人〔母語為南非荷蘭語的南非人, 尤指 17 世紀荷蘭移民的後裔〕

Af·ro /ˋæfro; ˈæfrəʊ/ *n* [C] a hair style popular with black people in the 1970s in which the hair is cut into a round shape 非洲式(蓬鬆)髮型, 埃弗羅髮式〔20 世紀 70 年代在黑人中流行的呈圓形的蓬鬆髮型〕

Afro- /æfro; æfrəʊ/ *prefix* **1** of Africa; African 非洲的: *an Afro-American* (=a black American person) 美國黑人, 非洲裔美國人 **2** African and 非洲及…的: *Afro-Asian* (=of both Africa and Asia) 亞非的

aft /æft; ɑːft/ *adj, adv technical* in or towards the back part of a boat【術語】在船尾(的); 向船尾(的) —opposite 反義詞 FORE[2]

after- /æftɚ; ɑːftə/ *prefix* coming or happening afterwards 在…以後(的): *aftercare* (=care given afterwards) 病後的調養 | *after-sales service* 售後服務

af·ter[1] /ˋæftɚ; ˈɑːftə/ *prep* **1** when a particular time or event has happened or is finished 在…後: *After the war many soldiers stayed in France.* 戰後, 許多士兵留在法國。| *I go swimming every day after work.* 每天下班後,  1 1

我都去游泳。| *It's on after the 9 o'clock news.* 在九點鐘新聞以後播出。| *Do you believe in life after death?* 你相信死後會有來世嗎? | **2 days/3 weeks etc after sth** *A few months after his birth we discovered that our son was deaf.* 兒子出生幾個月後, 我們發現他耳聾。| **the day/week/year after sth** *We leave the day after tomorrow.* 我們後天離開。| **soon/not long/shortly after sth** *Not long after the wedding his wife got ill.* 結婚不久, 他的妻子就病了。| **straight after sth** (=immediately after) 在某事之後立即 *Come home straight after the performance.* 演出結束後馬上就回家。| **come after sth** (=happen after something) 發生在...之後 *The first bomb attack came after midnight.* 第一次轟炸襲擊是在午夜之後。—see 見 SINCE³ (USAGE) **2** following someone or something else in a list, series, piece of writing, line of people etc 排在...之後: *Whose name is after yours on the roll?* 在點名冊上, 誰的名字排在你的後面? | *The date should be written after the address.* 日期應寫在地址之後。—see picture on page A1 參見A1頁圖 **3** when a particular amount of time has passed 〔一段時間〕以後: *After 10 minutes remove the cake from the oven.* 十分鐘以後, 把蛋糕從烤爐中取出。| *After a while things started to improve.* 過了一段時間, 情況開始好轉。| *After months of argument they decided to divorce.* 幾個月的爭吵之後, 他們決定離婚。**4** *AmE* used when telling the time to say how many minutes it is after the hour 【美】〔幾點〕過〔幾分〕: *The movie starts at a quarter after seven.* 電影七點一刻開始放映。**5 day after day/year after year etc** continuously for a very long time 日復一日/年復一年等: *He's worked in that hell-hole week after week, year after year, since he was 18.* 18歲開始, 他就一直在那地獄般的地方工作, 日復一日, 年復一年。**6** when someone has left a place, has finished doing something etc 在〔離開某地或做完某事〕後: *Remember to close the door after you.* 請記住隨手關門。| *I spend all day cleaning up after the kids.* 我整天跟在孩子後面收拾。**7 go/run/chase etc after sb** to follow someone in order to catch them 追趕某人: *Go after him and apologize.* 追上去向他道歉。**8** because of something or as a result of something 由於; 既然: *I'm not surprised he walked out, after the way she treated him.* 她那樣對待他, 所以我對他的出走並不感到驚奇。| *After your letter, I didn't think I'd ever see you again.* 由於你的這封信, 我想我再也不會見你了。**9** in spite of something 儘管, 雖然: *After all my hard work she still says it isn't neat enough.* 儘管我下了很大功夫, 她還是說不夠整潔。**10 call/shout/gaze etc after sb** to speak to or look towards someone as they move away from you 某人走開時叫/喊/凝視: *"You have a nice day, now!" she called after us.* "祝你們過得愉快!"我們走時她說。**11 be after sb/sth a)** to be looking for someone or something 尋找某人/某物: *Police are after a short man with a tattoo on his cheek.* 警察正在追捕一個臉上有刺青的矮個子男人。| *"Were you after anything in particular?" "No, we're just looking."* "有甚麼特別想要的嗎?" "不, 我們只是隨便看看。" **b)** *informal* to want to have something that belongs to someone else 【非正式】想佔有某物: *I think Chris is after my job.* 我想克里斯想要搶我的飯碗。**12 one after another/one after the other** if a series of events, actions etc happen one after another, each one happens soon after the previous one 一個接一個: *Ever since we moved into this house it's been one problem after another.* 自從我們搬進這房子, 問題就接連出現了。**13 after all a)** used to say that something is true or is a fact, in spite of another fact or situation 終究: *He wrote to say they couldn't give me a job after all.* 他寫信說他們終究還是不能給我一份工作。**b)** used to say that something should be remembered or considered, because it helps to explain why something else is true or is a fact 畢竟: *I don't know why you're so concerned, it isn't your problem after all.* 我不明白你為甚麼這樣擔心, 這畢竟不是你的問題。**14** used when listing or naming things, to mean that you have not included a particular thing because that is the first or best one 僅次於: *After dancing, going to the movies is my favorite weekend activity.* 除了跳舞, 看電影是我最喜歡的週末活動。**15** *especially BrE* given the same name as someone else, especially an older member of your family 【尤英】以...命名: *His name is Alessandro, after his grand-father.* 他的名字叫亞歷山德羅, 是以他祖父的名字命名的。**16** *formal* in the same style as a particular painter, musician etc 【正式】具有...風格的, 模仿...: *a painting after Rembrandt* 模仿倫勃朗風格的繪畫作品 **17 after you** *spoken* 【口】**a)** used to say politely that someone else can use or do something before you do 你先請: *"Do you need the copier?" "After you."* "你要用複印機嗎?" "你先用吧。" **b) after you with** used to ask someone if you can have or use something after they have finished 在〔某人〕之後〔用某物〕: *After you with that knife, please.* 請你用完刀子後給我。—see also 另見 **a man/woman after my own heart** (HEART), **take after** (TAKE¹)

USAGE NOTE 用法說明: AFTER

WORD CHOICE 詞語辨析: **after (prep), in, after (adv), afterwards, later**

You use **after** (*prep*) to talk about something that happens at the end of a period of time that is different from something that happens within that period. 介詞 after 用以表示在某段時間以後而不是該段時間內發生的事情: *After a few days I felt much better* (=not until a few days had passed). 幾天以後, 我感到好多了。You use **in** to talk about something that will happen before a period of time has finished. in 表示某一段時間結束之前將會發生的事: *You'll feel better in a few days* (=by the time a few days has passed). 過幾天你會感到好一些。

After (*prep*) is more often used to talk about events in the past, and **in** about the future. 介詞 after 常用於指過去, 而 in 則指將來: *She left after an hour* (=after an hour had passed). 她在一小時後離開了。| *She'll be leaving in an hour* (=after an hour has passed). 她將在一小時以後離開。

After (*adv*) with the meaning 'afterwards' usually follows another time adverb. 副詞 after 在表示"後來"的意義時常跟在另一個時間副詞之後: *We arrived just/soon/shortly after.* 我們隨後不久就到了。With words that show a length of time, **afterwards** or **later** is more usual. 在與表示一段時間的詞連用時, 多用 afterwards 和 later: *She arrived three days afterwards/later* (NOT usually 一般不用 *three days after,* though you could say 但是可以用 *after that*). 她於三天之後到達。

If you want to use a word with this meaning on its own, you would usually use **afterwards**. 如果想用一個單詞表示"隨後"之意, 通常用 afterwards: *We went swimming and walked home afterwards.* 我們去游泳, 然後步行回家。However, in informal British spoken English people sometimes say **after**. 然而, 在非正式的英國口語中, 有時也用 after: *We went swimming and walked home after.* 我們去游泳, 然後步行回家。You would not usually begin a sentence with **after**, though. 但 after 一般不用於句首: *Afterwards/After that, we left* (NOT 不用 *After, we left*). 後來, 我們就離開了。

after² *conjunction* when a particular time or event has happened or is finished 在...以後: *After you'd called the police, what did you do?* 報警之後, 你做了些甚麼? | *He changed his name after he left Germany.* 他離開德國以後把名字改了。| **two days/three weeks etc after** *Ten years after I bought the painting I discovered it was fake.* 我買了這幅畫十年以後, 才發現它是贋品。| **shortly/soon/not long after** *Shortly after the eggs have hatched,* *the mother goes off in search of food.* 雞蛋剛剛孵化完，雞媽媽就去找食物了。

after³ *adv* after something that has already been mentioned; afterwards 然後, 隨後: *What are you doing after? Do you want to go for a drink?* 然後你要幹甚麼? 想不想出去喝點東西? | **come after** (=happen after something else has happened) 在…後又發生 *Having lost the final pages, we can only guess at what might come after.* 最後幾頁沒有了, 我們只能猜想後來會怎麼樣。| **the day/the year etc after** *Once you've purchased the washing machine we guarantee it for up to 5 years after.* 你一經購買洗衣機, 我們會保用達五年。| **shortly/soon/not long after** *Not long after, I heard that Mike had been killed in the war.* 沒過多久, 我聽說邁克陣亡了。

after⁴ *adj* **1 in after years** *literary* in the years after the time that has been mentioned【文】在以後的幾年裡 **2** *technical* in the back part of a boat or an aircraft【術語】〔船、飛機〕後部的: *the after deck* 後甲板

af·ter·birth /ˋæftɚˌbɝθ; ˈɑːftəbɜːθ/ *n* [U] the substance that comes out of female humans or animals just after they have had a baby 胞衣, 胎盤和胎膜

af·ter·care /ˋæftɚˌkɛr; ˈɑːftəkeə/ *n* [U] *BrE* care or treatment given to someone after they have been in hospital【英】〔病人出院後的〕病後調養

after-ef·fect /ˈ·· ·ˌ·/ *n* [C usually plural 一般用複數] an unpleasant effect that remains for a long time after the condition or event that caused it 後效; 後作用; 副作用; 後遺效應: *the after-effects of his illness* 他這種病的後遺症

af·ter·glow /ˋæftɚˌglo; ˈɑːftəgləʊ/ *n* [C usually singular 一般用單數] **1** a pleasant feeling that remains after a happy experience〔歡樂後的〕餘味, 事後愉快的回憶; 餘韻: *the afterglow of the party* 對晚會的愉快回憶 **2** the light that remains in the western sky after the sun goes down 晚霞, 餘輝

af·ter·life /ˋæftɚˌlaɪf; ˈɑːftəlaɪf/ *n* [singular] the life that some people believe people have after death 來世, 來生

af·ter·math /ˋæftɚˌmæθ; ˈɑːftəmæθ/ *n* [singular] the period of time after something such as a war, storm, or accident when people are still dealing with the results 後果, 餘殃, 餘波: *the danger of disease in the aftermath of the earthquake* 地震後引發疫病的危險

1 2 **af·ter·noon** /ˌæftɚˋnun; ˌɑːftəˈnuːn◂/ *n* [C,U] **1** the period of time between midday and sunset or at the end of the day's work 下午, 午後: *We went swimming on Tuesday afternoon.* 星期二下午我們去游泳了。| *Harry went to sleep in the afternoon.* 午後哈里去睡覺了。| *Do you want to go shopping tomorrow afternoon?* 明天下午你想去購物嗎? | *tickets for the afternoon performance* 午後演出的票子 | **this afternoon** (=today in the afternoon) 今天下午 *Could you babysit for a few hours this afternoon?* 今天下午你能抽出幾小時來代我們照看孩子嗎? **2 afternoons** *especially AmE* during the afternoon each day【尤美】(每天) 下午: *She only works afternoons.* 她只在下午工作。—compare 比較 EVENING

af·ters /ˋæftɚz; ˈɑːftəz/ *n* [plural] *BrE informal* the part of a meal that comes after the main dish; DESSERT【英, 非正式】餐後的甜食

af·ter·shave /ˋæftɚʃev; ˈɑːftəʃeɪv/ *n* [C,U] a liquid with a pleasant smell that a man puts on his face after he shaves (SHAVE¹ (1))〔剃鬚後用的〕潤膚液

af·ter·taste /ˋæftɚˌtest; ˈɑːftəteɪst/ *n* [C usually singular 一般用單數] a taste that stays in your mouth after you have eaten or drunk something〔飲食後口中的〕餘味: *The wine leaves a strong aftertaste.* 這種葡萄酒飲後會留下濃烈的餘香。

af·ter·thought /ˋæftɚˌθɔt; ˈɑːftəθɔːt/ *n* [C] **1 as an afterthought** thought of and mentioned after you have finished talking about a particular subject 事後的想法: *He added as an afterthought, "Bring Melanie too."* 他想了想補充道, "把梅拉尼也帶來。" **2** something added later, especially something that was not part of the original plan〔尤指原計劃所沒有的〕後加的東西: *The tiles looked out of place, as if they had been an after-thought.* 這些瓷磚看起來不倫不類, 好像是後加上的。

af·ter·wards /ˋæftɚwɚdz; ˈɑːftəwədz/ *adv* also 又作 **afterward** *AmE*【美】after an event or time that has already been mentioned 隨後, 以後, 後來: *The ceremony lasts half an hour and afterward there's a meal.* 儀式持續了半個小時, 然後是進餐時間。| **2 days/3 weeks etc afterwards** *My parents met during the war but didn't marry till five years afterwards.* 我父母在戰爭期間相識, 但他們五年之後才結婚。—see 見 AFTER¹ (USAGE) 2 3

a·gain /əˋgɛn; əˈgen/ *adv* **1** if something happens again, or someone does something again, it happens or they do it one more time 又, 再一次: *Can you say that again? I didn't hear you.* 你能再說一遍嗎? 我沒聽見。| *I'll never go there again.* 我再也不去那兒了。| *I'm sorry, Mr Khan's line is busy. Can you try again later?* 對不起, 卡恩先生的電話佔線。你能不能過一會兒再打來? | **once again** (=again, usually for at least the third time) 再次, 再三〔通常三次以上〕*Once again the Allies marched in and pushed back the enemy troops.* 盟軍再次進攻, 擊退了敵軍。| **yet again** (=again, after happening many times before)〔多次以後〕再次 *Can you believe it! He told that story about his teeth yet again.* 你能信嗎? 他又一次講起他的牙齒的事。**2** back to the same state or situation that you were in before 還原, 復原: *His parents stayed and nursed him back to health again.* 他的父母留了下來, 一直護理到他康復。| *It's great to have you home again.* 你又回家了, 真是太好了。**3 all over again** if you do something all over again, you repeat it from the beginning 重新做起, 從頭再來: *There's no tape in the machine. We'll have to start the interview all over again.* 機器裡沒有放磁帶, 採訪只好從頭再來。**4 as much/as many/the same again** the same number or amount added to what there already is 同樣再來一遍: *What a fantastic lunch. I could eat the same again.* 好棒的午餐呀! 再有這麼多我也能吃得下。| *I thought my job was good until I heard Bernard earns twice as much again.* 要不是聽說伯納德掙的錢是我的兩倍, 我還一直以為我的工作不錯。**5** used when giving a fact or opinion that either explains something you have just said, or is very different from it 而, 另一方面, 再者: *And again, while the accident was not your fault, the damage must be paid for somehow.* 再者, 雖然事故不是你的過錯, 但損失總得賠償。| **then/there again** *spoken*【口】*Carol's always had nice clothes but then again she earns a lot.* 卡羅爾總有漂亮的衣服穿, 可話又說回來了, 她掙的錢也多。**6 again and again/time and (time) again/over and over again** very often 一再, 屢次: *I've told you again and again, don't play soccer near the windows.* 我再三地告訴你們不要在窗子附近踢足球。**7** *spoken* used when you want someone to repeat information that they have already given you【口】再(說): *What did you say your name was again?* 請再說一遍你叫甚麼名字? —see also 另見 **now and again** (NOW¹ (6)) 1 1

a·gainst /əˋgɛnst; əˈgenst/ *prep* **1** opposed to or disagreeing with an idea, belief, proposal etc 反對: *votes for and against the motion* 該項動議的贊成票和反對票 | *It's against my principles to borrow money.* 借錢不符合我的原則。| *Several members spoke against the proposal.* 有幾個成員發言反對這個建議。| **be against sth** *I'm against all forms of hunting.* 我反對任何形式的捕獵。| **against sb's wishes** (=when you know someone does not want something to happen) 違背某人的願望 *They got married against her wishes.* 他們是在她極不情願的情況下結婚的。| **against sb's will** (=when someone is forced to do something) 違背某人的意志 *She has been kept in the house against her will.* 她被迫關在屋子裡。| **against the law** (=illegal) 違法 —see graph at 參見 OPPOSED 圖表 **2** fighting or competing with another person, team, country etc 和…交戰[競爭, 比賽]: *He was injured in the game against the Cowboys.* 他在與牛仔隊的比賽 1 1

中受了傷。| *We'll be competing against some of the best companies in Europe.* 我們要和歐洲一些一流的公司競爭。| *the fight against terrorism* 反恐怖主義的鬥爭 **3** in a way that has an unfavourable effect on someone or causes them disadvantage 對〔某人〕不利; 造成劣勢: *discrimination against women* 對婦女的歧視 | *Your lack of experience could count against you.* 缺乏經驗對你會是個不利因素。| *The planning regulations tend to work against smaller companies.* 計劃中的規章制度可能會對小公司不利。**4** touching, hitting, or rubbing another surface 碰, 撞: *The rain drummed against the window.* 雨點打在窗上。| *I like it when the cat rubs its head against my legs.* 我喜歡貓用頭在我的腿上蹭來蹭去。| *The car skidded and we could hear the crunch of metal against metal.* 汽車打滑了, 我們能聽見金屬相碰的嘎吱嘎吱聲。—see picture on page A1 參見A1頁圖 **5** next to and touching an upright surface, especially for support 倚着, 靠着: *There was a ladder propped up against the wall.* 一把梯子靠着牆。| *The younger policeman was leaning against the bureau with his arms folded.* 那位較年輕的警官兩臂交叉地倚靠在大辦公桌旁。**6** in the opposite direction to 逆向: *sailing against the wind* 逆風航行 | *swimming against the current* 逆流游泳 **7** seen or shown with something else behind or as a background 以…為背景; 對照; 襯托: *He caught a glimpse of a man silhouetted against a dimly lit background.* 他瞥見在燈光微弱的背景中有一個男人的側影。| *knowing what colours look good against your skin* 知道甚麼顏色能把你的膚色襯得好看 **8** used to describe something in relation to other events that are happening at the same time 在…情況下; 在…背景下: *The reforms were introduced against a background of social unrest.* 改革是在社會動蕩的背景下開始的。**9** in comparison with 與…相比: *Only 3% of blacks were registered voters against 97% of the white residents.* 相比之下登記選民中黑人只佔3%, 而白人卻有97%。| *She checked the contents of the box against the list.* 她將箱子中的東西和清單相對照。**10** providing protection from harm or damage 防…, 抗…: *insurance against accident and sickness* 意外事故和疾病保險 | *This spray can be used against weevil and other crop pests.* 這種噴霧殺蟲劑可用於防治象鼻蟲和其他農作物害蟲。**11 be/come up against sth** to have to deal with a difficult opponent or problem 必須面對〔難應付的對手或問題〕: *You see, this is what we're up against – the suppliers just aren't reliable.* 你瞧, 這就是我們遇到的難題, 供應商根本不可靠。**12 have sth against sb/sth** to dislike or disapprove of someone or something 不喜歡[不贊成]某人/某事: *It's not that I have anything against babies. I just don't feel very comfortable with them.* 我並不是不喜歡嬰兒, 只是覺得跟他們在一起不太舒服。

a·gape /ə'gep; ə'geɪp/ *adj* with your mouth wide open, especially because you are surprised or shocked〔驚得〕大張着嘴的: *Vince watched, his mouth agape in horror.* 文斯在一旁看着, 嚇得目瞪口呆。

ag·ate /'ægɪt; 'ægɮt/ *n* [C] a hard stone with bands of different colours, used in jewellery 瑪瑙

-age /ɪdʒ; ɪdʒ/ *suffix* [in nouns 構成名詞] **1** the action or result of doing something〔做某事〕的動作或其結果: *Buy a larger size to allow for shrinkage.* (=getting smaller) 由於會縮水, 要買大些的。| *several breakages* (=things broken) 幾件破損的東西 **2** the cost of doing something〔做某事〕的費用: *Postage is extra.* 郵資另付。**3** a particular state or rank …身分[地位]: *a peerage* (=noble rank) 貴族爵位

S1 W1 **age**[1] /edʒ; eɪdʒ/ *n*

1 ►HOW OLD 多大◄ [C,U] the number of years someone has lived or something has existed 年齡; 存在時間: *Francis is the same age as me.* 弗朗西斯和我同齡。| *The boys were six years apart in age.* 男孩們的年齡相差六歲。| *There were dozens of kids there, all different ages.* 那兒有幾十個孩子, 年齡都不同。| **at the age of** (=when someone is a particular age) 在…年紀時 *Marco won the Grand Prix at the age of 19.* 馬爾科19歲就取得了國際汽車大獎賽的勝利。| **4/15 etc years of age** *formal* (=4, 15 etc years old)【正式】4歲/15歲等 *The missing girl is 19 years of age.* 失蹤的女孩19歲。| **at age 57/4/18 etc** *AmE* (=when someone is 57 etc years old)【美】57歲/4歲/18歲等時 *Saul entered Yale at age 14.* 索爾14歲考上了耶魯大學。| **at an early age** (=very young) 很年輕時 *girls who become mothers at a very early age* 年紀很小就做了母親的女孩 | **act your age** (=behave in a way that is suitable to how old you are) 行為舉止與年齡相稱 | **sb's age** (=how old someone is) 某人的年齡 *When you get to my age, it's quite difficult getting up stairs.* 當你到了我的年齡, 上樓就有點費勁了。| **for his/her age** (=compared with others of the same age) 以他/她的年齡來說 *She's very tall for her age, isn't she?* 以她的年齡來說, 她很高, 對吧? | **certain age** *Kids get to a certain age and say, right, that's it, and they just go.* 孩子們到了一定年齡, 對了, 是這樣, 他們就要離開父母了。

2 ►LEGAL AGE 法定年齡◄ [U] the age when you are legally old enough to do something 法定年齡: *What's the minimum age for getting a driver's license?* 取得駕駛執照的最小年齡是多少? | **under age** (=too young) 太小, 太年輕 *You're not allowed to be drinking, you're under age.* 你年紀太小, 不可以喝酒。| **over age** (=too old) 超齡 *Dan's over age, so the army won't accept him.* 丹已經超齡, 所以部隊不會接收他。

3 ►PERIOD OF LIFE 人生中的階段◄ [C,U] one of the particular periods of someone's life 人生的某個階段: *women of childbearing age* 育齡婦女 | *Phil's coming up to 13 – rather a difficult age.* 菲爾快13歲了 —— 相當麻煩的一個年紀。—see also 另見 OLD AGE, MIDDLE AGE, TEENAGE

4 ►BEING OLD 老了◄ [U] the state or fact of being old 年老; 時間久: *The newspapers were brown with age.* 時間太久了, 報紙都發黃了。| *Age had given his face a sort of crumpled look.* 歲月在他的臉上刻上了皺紋。

5 ►PERIOD OF HISTORY 歷史階段◄ [C usually singular 一般用單數] a particular period of history 時代, 世紀: *the last Ice Age* 最後一次冰河時期 | *We are living in the computer age.* 我們生活在電腦時代。—see also 另見 GOLDEN AGE, **in this day and age** (DAY (29))

6 come of age a) reach the age when you are legally considered to be a responsible adult 到達法定年齡; 成年 **b)** if something comes of age, it reaches a stage of development at which people accept it as being important, valuable etc 到達成熟時期: *It was during this period that the movies really came of age as a creative art form.* 正是在這個時期, 電影才真正進入了成熟期, 成為一種具有創造性的藝術形式。

7 ages [plural] also 又作 **an age** *informal, especially BrE* a long time【非正式, 尤英】長時間: *It'll be ages before we're ready to go.* 我們得要很久以後才能準備好走。| **for ages** *Simon! I haven't seen you for ages!* 西蒙, 我已經好久沒有見到你了! | **it's (been) ages since** *It's ages since we've played that game.* 我們已經好久沒有玩過那種遊戲了。| **take ages** *It takes ages to make that recipe.* 按那種烹調方法需要很長時間。

age[2] *v present participle* **ageing** *or* **aging 1** [I,T] to start looking older or to make someone look older, especially because they have suffered a lot (使) 變老: *Myra's recent illness has aged her considerably.* 邁拉最近的病使她蒼老了很多。**2** [I] to become older 老化, 陳舊: *The buildings are ageing, and some are unsafe.* 這些建築已很陳舊, 有些還不安全。**3** [I] to improve and develop in quality and taste, over a period of time (使) 成熟[味道變醇厚]: *a wine that has aged well* 陳年老酒

age brack·et /'· ,··/ *n* [C] the people between two particular ages, considered as a group〔介於兩個年齡之間的〕年齡段, 年齡組: *single people in the 40-50 age bracket* 40至50歲年齡段的獨身人士

3 **aged¹** /edʒd; eɪdʒd/ *adj* **aged 5/30/25 etc** 5, 30 etc years old 5歲/30歲/25歲等: *The course is open to children aged 12 and over.* 本課程是為12歲及以上的兒童而設。| **[+between]** *The police are looking for a man aged between 30 and 35.* 警察正在尋找一個年齡介於30到35歲之間的男子。

a·ged² /ˋedʒɪd; ˈeɪdʒɨd/ *adj* **1** very old 年老的: *my aged parents* 我年邁的父母 **2 the aged** old people 老年人: *plans to help the aged and infirm* 幫助年老體弱者的計劃

age dis·crim·i·na·tion /ˈ· ···,··/ *n* [U] *AmE* unfair treatment of people because they are old【美】〔對老年人的〕年齡歧視; AGEISM *BrE*【英】

age group /ˈ· ·/ *n* [C] all the people between two particular ages, considered as a group 年齡組, 年齡羣: *a book written for children in the 12-14 age group* 為12到14歲年齡組的兒童寫的書

age·ing¹ *BrE*【英】usually 一般作 **aging** *AmE*【美】/ˋedʒɪŋ; ˈeɪdʒɪŋ/ *adj* [only before noun 僅用於名詞前] becoming old, and usually less useful, attractive, suitable etc 變老的; 陳舊的: *aging movie stars* 上了年紀的電影明星 | *an ageing population* 老齡化人口

ageing² *BrE*【英】usually 一般作 **aging** *AmE*【美】*n* [U] the process of getting old 老化: *airlines with ageing fleets* 機羣老化的航空公司 | *products that claim to halt the ageing process* 宣稱能阻止老化的產品

age·is·m also 又作 **agism** /ˋedʒɪzəm; ˈeɪdʒɪzəm/ *n* [U] *BrE* unfair treatment of people because they are old【英】〔對老年人的〕年齡歧視; AGE DISCRIMINATION *AmE*【美】—**ageist** *adj* —**ageist** *n* [C]

age·less /ˋedʒlɪs; ˈeɪdʒləs/ *adj* **1** never looking old or old-fashioned 永不衰老的; 不過時的: *Good clothes should be ageless.* 好衣服應該總不過時。**2** continuing forever 永恆的: *the ageless fascination of the sea* 大海的永恆魅力 —**agelessness** *n* [U]

age lim·it /ˈ· ,··/ *n* [C] the youngest or oldest age at which you are allowed to do something 年齡限制: *The age limit at the new nightclub is 21.* 新夜總會的年齡限制是21歲。

2
1 **a·gen·cy** /ˋedʒənsɪ; ˈeɪdʒənsi/ *n* [C] **1** a business that provides information about other businesses and their products, or that provides a particular service 代辦處, 代理處, 經銷處, 中介處; 經紀業務: *I got this job through an employment agency.* 我是通過職業介紹所找到這份工作的。—see also 另見 DATING AGENCY, NEWS AGENCY **2** an organization or department, especially within a government, that does a specific job〔尤指政府內的〕局; 部; 處: *a UN agency responsible for helping refugees* 聯合國難民事務處 **3 by/through the agency of** being done with or as the result of someone's help 由於…的作用; 在〔某人〕的斡旋下

3 **a·gen·da** /əˋdʒɛndə; əˈdʒendə/ *n* [C] **1** a list of the subjects to be discussed at a meeting〔會議的〕議程: **on the agenda** *the first item on the agenda* 第一項議程 **2 be on the agenda** if something is on the agenda, you are planning to do something about it〔事項〕待辦; 待討論: **be on top of the agenda/be high on the agenda** (=be very important to do) 最重要的待辦事項 *Health care was on top of President Clinton's agenda.* 衛生保健是克林頓總統最急需解決的問題。**3** subjects that everyone has heard of and is talking about 話題, 議題: *Environmental issues are racing up the political agenda.* 環境問題正在迅速成為政治議題。—see also 另見 HIDDEN AGENDA

3
2 **a·gent** /ˋedʒənt; ˈeɪdʒənt/ *n* [C]
1 ►BUSINESS 商業◄ a person or company that represents another person or company in business, in their legal problems etc 代理人, 代理商; 經紀: *Our agent in Rio deals with all our Brazilian business.* 我們在里約熱內盧的業務代表處理我們在巴西的全部業務。| **[+for]** *We're acting as agents for Mr Watson.* 我們是沃森先生的代理人。—see also 另見 ESTATE AGENT, REAL ESTATE AGENT, LAND AGENT
2 ►ARTIST/ACTOR 藝術家/演員◄ someone who is paid by actors, musicians etc to find work for them 經理人, 經紀人: *My agent has an exciting new script for me to look at.* 我的經理人有一個精彩的新劇本要我看。
3 ►GOVERNMENT AGENT 政府特工人員◄ someone who works for a government or police department in order to get secret information about another country or organization; SPY 特工人員, 情報員, 間諜: *a Soviet agent in Czechoslovakia* 在捷克斯洛伐克的蘇聯間諜 —see also 另見 SECRET AGENT, DOUBLE AGENT
4 ►CHEMICAL 化學◄ *technical* a chemical or substance that makes other substances change【術語】作用劑: *Soap is a cleansing agent.* 肥皂是一種清潔劑。
5 ►FORCE 力◄ someone or something that affects or changes a situation 原動力, 動因: **agent for/of change** *Technological advances are the chief agents of change.* 技術進步是變革的主要原動力。

a·gent pro·voc·a·teur /,ɑʒɑn pro,vɑkəˋtɝ; ,æʒɒn prɒvɒkəˈtɜː/ *n* [C] *French* someone who is employed to encourage people who are working against a government to do something illegal so that they are caught【法】臥底密探, 坐探

age of con·sent /,· · ·ˈ·/ *n* [C] the age when someone can legally get married or have a sexual relationship 婚姻合法年齡,〔少女對性行為可以自主的〕同意年齡, 合法年齡

age-old /,· ˈ·◂/ *adj* having existed for a very long time 古老的; 存在已久的: *age-old customs* 古老習俗 | *It's nothing new. It's an age-old problem.* 這不是甚麼新鮮事。這個問題由來已久。

ag·glom·er·ate /əˋglɑmərɪt; əˈglɒmərɨt/ *n* [singular, U] *technical* a type of rock formed from pieces of material from a VOLCANO that have melted together【術語】〔火山爆發後形成的〕集塊岩

ag·glom·e·ra·tion /ə,glɑməˋreʃən; ə,glɒməˈreɪʃən/ *n* [C,U] a large collection of things that do not seem to belong together 堆積, 聚集: *an agglomeration of facts* 事實成堆 —**agglomerate** /əˋglɑmə,ret; əˈglɒməreɪt/ *v* —**agglomerate** /-rɪt; -rɨt/ *adj*

ag·glu·ti·na·tion /ə,glutnˋeʃən; ə,gluːtɨˈneɪʃən/ *n* [U] *technical*【術語】**1** the state of being stuck together 黏結; 凝集; 膠合 **2** the process of making new words by combining two or more words, such as combining 'ship' and 'yard' to make 'shipyard' 黏着法〔構詞法, 如ship和yard合成shipyard〕

ag·gran·dize·ment also 又作 **-isement** *BrE*【英】/əˋgrændɪzmənt; əˈgrændɨzmənt/ *n* [U] a word meaning an increase in power, size, or importance, used especially when you disapprove of this increase 擴大, 提高: *a war fought for national aggrandizement* 為擴張國家勢力而發動的戰爭 | *He did it for his own personal aggrandizement.* 他這樣做是為了擴大自己的個人權力。

ag·gra·vate /ˋægrə,vet; ˈægrəveɪt/ *v* [T] **1** to make a bad situation worse 使…加重, 使…惡化: *Their debt problem was aggravated by a rise in interest rates.* 由於利率上調, 他們的債務問題更加嚴重。**2** *informal* to make someone angry or annoyed【非正式】惹怒, 激怒: *Stop aggravating the cat!* 不要再惹那隻貓了! —**aggravating** *adj* —**aggravatingly** *adv* —**aggravation** /,ægrəˋveʃən; ,ægrəˈveɪʃən/ *n* [C,U]

ag·gre·gate¹ /ˋægrɪgɪt; ˈægrɪgɨt/ *n* [C] **1** the total after a lot of different parts or figures have been added together 總數, 合計: *Society is not just an aggregate of individuals.* 社會不只是每一個個體的總和。| **on aggregate** *BrE* (=when the points are added together)【英】總分 *Manchester United won 2-1 on aggregate.* 曼聯隊以二比一的總分獲勝。| **in (the) aggregate** (=as a group or in total) 作為總體 **2** [singular,U] *technical* sand or small stones that are used in making CONCRETE² 【術語】粒料, 混凝料

aggregate² *adj* [only before noun 僅用於名詞前]

technical being the total amount of something, especially money【術語】〔尤指錢〕總計的: *aggregate income and investment* 總收入和投資

ag·gre·gate³ /ˈægrɪˌget; ˈægrɪgeɪt/ *v* **1** [linking verb 連繫動詞] to be a particular amount when added together 總計達到, 合計為: **aggregate £100/20 etc** *Sheila's earnings from all sources aggregated £100,000.* 希拉的所有收入總計達十萬英鎊。**2** [I,T usually passive 一般用被動態] to put things together in a group to form a total; ASSEMBLE 使聚集, 收集: *We made estimates using the aggregated data.* 我們用所收集的數據進行評估。

ag·gres·sion /əˈgrɛʃən; əˈgreʃən/ *n* [U] **1** angry or threatening behaviour or feelings that often result in fighting 攻擊性行為; 敵對行為 [心理]: *Television violence can encourage aggression in children.* 電視暴力會助長孩子們的攻擊性行為。**2** the act of attacking a country, especially when that country has not attacked first 挑釁; 侵犯; 侵略: *territorial aggression* 領土侵略 | **act of aggression** *an unprovoked act of aggression on a peaceful nation* 對一個和平國家的無故侵犯

3 **ag·gres·sive** /əˈgrɛsɪv; əˈgresɪv/ *adj* **1** behaving in an angry, threatening way, as if you want to fight or attack someone 好鬥的, 挑釁性的: *The men were drunk, aggressive and looking for a fight.* 那些人喝醉了, 一副挑釁的架勢, 想找人打架。**2** someone who is aggressive is very determined to succeed or get what they want 有進取心的, 有衝勁的; 執着的: *A successful businessman has to be aggressive.* 成功的實業家要有股衝勁。**3** an aggressive action or plan is intended to achieve the right result 雄心勃勃的: *an aggressive marketing campaign* 雄心勃勃的營銷計劃 —**aggressively** *adv* —**aggressiveness** *n* [U]

ag·gres·sor /əˈgrɛsɚ; əˈgresə/ *n* [C] a person or country that begins a fight or war with another person or country 挑釁者; 攻擊者; 侵略者

ag·grieved /əˈgrivd; əˈgriːvd/ *adj* **1** feeling or showing anger and unhappiness because you think you have been unfairly treated 憤憤不平的; 感到委屈的; 憤恨的: *an aggrieved tone of voice* 委屈的口吻 **2** *law* having suffered as a result of the illegal actions of someone else【法律】受到損害的, 受害方的: **the aggrieved party** (=the person who has suffered) 受害方

ag·gro /ˈægro; ˈægrəʊ/ *n* [U] *BrE informal*【英, 非正式】**1** aggressive behaviour and fighting, especially between young men〔尤指年輕人的〕鬥毆, 打羣架; 糾紛 **2** problems or difficulties that annoy you 煩惱: *We had so much aggro with our insurance claim.* 我們在保險索賠上遇到了很大麻煩。

a·ghast /əˈgæst; əˈgɑːst/ *adj* [not before noun 不用於名詞前] feeling or looking shocked by something you have seen or just found out 大為震驚的, 嚇呆了的: **[+at]** *I was aghast at the violence I was witnessing.* 我被眼前的暴力場面嚇呆了。

a·gile /ˈædʒəl; ˈædʒaɪl/ *adj* **1** able to move quickly and easily〔動作〕敏捷的, 靈活的: *Andy climbed the tree, agile as a monkey.* 安迪像猴子一樣敏捷地爬上了樹。**2 agile mind** the ability to think very quickly and intelligently 敏捷的思維, 機敏的頭腦

ag·ing /ˈedʒɪŋ; ˈeɪdʒɪŋ/ an American spelling of AGEING ageing 的美式拼法

ag·is·m /ˈedʒɪzəm; ˈeɪdʒɪzəm/ an American spelling of AGEISM ageism 的美式拼法

a·gi·tate /ˈædʒəˌtet; ˈædʒɪ̈teɪt/ *v* **1** [I] to argue strongly in public for something you want, especially a political or social change 煽動, 鼓動; 宣傳: **[+for/against]** *unions agitating for higher pay* 工會鼓動要求增加工資 **2** [T] to shake or mix a liquid quickly 攪動; 搖動, 快速混合〔液體〕**3** [T] *formal* to make someone feel anxious, upset, and nervous【正式】使〔某人〕焦慮不安

a·gi·ta·ted /ˈædʒəˌtetɪd; ˈædʒɪ̈teɪtɪ̈d/ *adj* so nervous or upset that you are unable to keep still or think calmly 緊張不安的, 焦慮的: *An agitated waiter rushed up to apologize for the delay.* 緊張不安的侍應生趕快過去為遲了上菜而道歉。| *She got rather agitated.* 她變得頗有點緊張不安。

a·gi·ta·tion /ˌædʒəˈteʃən; ˌædʒɪ̈ˈteɪʃən/ *n* **1** [U] feeling of being so anxious, nervous, or upset that you cannot think calmly 焦慮, 緊張不安: *Perry's agitation was so great he could hardly speak.* 佩里極度焦慮, 幾乎說不出話來。**2** [C,U] a public argument or action for social or political change 煽動, 鼓動: **[+for/against]** *agitation for civil rights* 鼓動爭取民權 **3** [U] the act of shaking or mixing a liquid〔液體的〕攪動; 搖動, 混合

a·gi·ta·tor /ˈædʒəˌtetɚ; ˈædʒɪ̈teɪtə/ *n* [C] **1** someone who encourages people to work towards changing something in society 鼓動者, 煽動者: *a political agitator* 政治鼓動者 **2** a machine used to shake or mix liquids 攪拌器

a·git·prop /ˈædʒɪtˌprɑp; ˌædʒɪ̈tˈprɒp/ *n* [U] music, literature, or art that tried to persuade people that SOCIALIST ideas were good 宣傳鼓動〔尤指文藝作品〕: *1970s radical agitprop* 20 世紀 70 年代激進的宣傳鼓動

a·glow /əˈglo; əˈgləʊ/ *adj* **1** *literary* bright and shining with warmth, light, or colour【文】發(紅)光的: *The morning sun set the sky aglow.* 晨曦染紅了天空。**2** if someone's face or expression is aglow, they seem happy and excited 容光煥發的,〔興奮得〕面色發紅的: **[+with]** *Linda's face was aglow with happiness.* 琳達臉上洋溢着幸福的表情。

AGM /ˌe dʒi ˈɛm; ˌeɪ dʒiː ˈem/ *n* [C] *BrE* annual general meeting; a meeting held once a year by a club, business, or organization, for the members to discuss the previous year's business, elect officials etc【英】年會; ANNUAL MEETING *AmE*【美】

ag·nos·tic /ægˈnɑstɪk; ægˈnɒstɪk/ *n* [C] someone who believes that people cannot know whether God exists or not 不可知論者 —compare 比較 **atheist** (ATHEISM) —**agnostic** *adj* —**agnosticism** /-təˌsɪzəm; -tɪ̈sɪzəm/ *n* [U]

ago 以前的

I went to Tokyo six weeks ago. 我六週前曾去東京。 NOW 現在

I went to Tokyo for three weeks. 我去了東京三週。 NOW 現在

a·go /əˈgo; əˈgəʊ/ *adj* used to show how far back in the past something happened 以往的, 以前的: **5 minutes/an hour/20 years ago** *Michael left the office about half an hour ago.* 邁克爾大約半小時前離開了辦公室。| **long ago/a long time ago** *I met Aunt Hetty once, a very long time ago.* 我很久以前見過赫蒂姨媽一次。| **a minute/moment ago** *I had my keys a minute ago, and now I can't find them.* 剛才我的鑰匙還在, 現在卻找不到了。| **a little/short while ago** *Tom got a letter from him just a little while ago.* 湯姆剛在不久之前收到過他寄來的一封信。| **some time ago** (=a fairly long time ago) 有些時候了 *They moved to a new house some time ago, a couple of years I think.* 他們搬進新居已有些日子了, 我想大概兩三年吧。—compare 比較 FOR¹ (8), SINCE

a·gog /əˈgɑg; əˈgɒg/ *adj* [not before noun 不用於名詞前] very interested, excited, and surprised, especially at something you are experiencing for the first time 因期待已久而極度興奮的; 急切的, 渴望的: **(be all) agog (at)** *We were all agog at the sights of New York.* 看到紐約的景色, 我們都興奮不已。

ag·o·nize also 又作 **-ise** *BrE*【英】/ˈægəˌnaɪz; ˈægənaɪz/ *v* [I] to think about a difficult decision very carefully and with a lot of effort 焦慮, 憂愁, 苦惱: **[+over/about]**

There's no point in agonizing over which route to take. 沒有必要為走哪條路線而苦惱。—**agonizing** *n* [U]: *This time there was none of the agonizing and guilt that had accompanied her earlier decision.* 這次沒有像以往要她做出決定時的苦惱和內疚。

ag·o·nized also 又作 **-ised** *BrE*【英】/ˈægəˌnaɪzd; ˈægənaɪzd/ *adj* expressing very severe pain 痛苦的: *the agonized moans of wounded soldiers* 受傷士兵痛苦的呻吟聲

ag·o·niz·ing also 又作 **-ising** *BrE*【英】/ˈægəˌnaɪzɪŋ; ˈægənaɪzɪŋ/ *adj* extremely painful or difficult 令人痛苦的, 折磨人的: *agonizing pain* 難忍的疼痛 —**agonizingly** *adv*

ag·o·ny /ˈægənɪ; ˈægəni/ *n* [C,U] **1** very severe pain 極大的痛苦: *the agony of arthritis* 關節炎的劇烈疼痛 | **be in agony** *The poor guy was in agony.* 那可憐的傢伙十分痛苦。| **be agony** *spoken*【口】*It was agony having my wisdom teeth out.* 拔掉智慧齒令我很痛。**2** a very sad, difficult, or unpleasant situation 痛楚, 苦難: *It was agony not knowing if she would live.* 不知道她能不能活下來, 令人感到痛苦。 —see also 另見 **pile on the agony** (PILE[2]), **prolong the agony** (PROLONG (2))

agony aunt /ˈ··· ˌ·/ *n* [C] *BrE* someone who writes an agony column【英】知心阿姨〔"為讀者解憂"專欄女撰稿人〕

agony col·umn /ˈ··· ˌ··/ *n* [C] *BrE* a part of a newspaper or magazine in which someone gives advice to readers about their personal problems【英】〔報刊上〕"為讀者解憂"專欄; ADVICE COLUMN *AmE*【美】

ag·o·ra·pho·bi·a /ˌægərəˈfobɪə; ˌægərəˈfəʊbiə/ *n* [U] *technical* the fear of crowds and open spaces【術語】曠野[廣場]恐怖(症) —compare 比較 CLAUSTROPHOBIA

ag·o·ra·pho·bic /ˌægərəˈfobɪk; ˌægərəˈfəʊbɪk◂/ *n* [C] someone who suffers from agoraphobia 曠野[廣場]恐怖症患者 —**agoraphobic** *adj*

a·grar·i·an /əˈgrɛrɪən; əˈgreəriən/ *adj* concerning farming or farmers 土地的; 農業的: *an agrarian revolution in 17th century England* 英國17世紀的土地革命 | *a split between industrial and agrarian interests* 工業和農業利益的分歧

1 **a·gree** /əˈgri; əˈgriː/ *v*
1 **1 ▶SAME OPINION** 同樣看法◀ [I,T not in progressive 不用進行式] to have the same opinion about something as someone else 同意, 意見一致: [+with] *Mr Larsen seems to think it's too risky and I agree with him.* 拉森先生似乎認為太危險, 我同意他的看法。| **agree** *Teenagers and their parents rarely agree.* 十幾歲的孩子跟父母意見很少一致。| [+that] *Most scientists agree that global warming is a serious problem.* 大多數科學家都認為全球氣候變暖是個嚴重的問題。| [+on/about] *They belong to the same party, but they don't agree on everything.* 他們屬於同一個黨派, 但並不是在所有事情上都一致。| **I quite agree** *BrE spoken* (=I agree competely)【英口】我很同意 *"It's ridiculous." "Yes, I quite agree."* "這很荒謬。" "一點沒錯。" | **I couldn't agree more** *spoken* (=I agree completely)【口】我完全同意 —opposite 反義詞 DISAGREE (1) —see 見 REFUSE[1]

2 ▶DECIDE TOGETHER 共同決定◀ [I,T not in progressive 不用進行式] to make a decision with someone after a discussion with them 達成一致; 商定: **agree to do sth** *We agreed to meet up later and talk things over.* 我們同意稍後見面商量一些事情。| **agree that** *It was agreed that Mr. Rollins would sign the contract May 1st.* 約定了羅林斯先生於5月1日在合同上簽字。| [+on] *They managed to agree on a date for the wedding.* 他們總算商定了婚期。| [+to] *We voted to agree to the latest pay offer.* 我們投票贊同最後提出的工資方案。| **agree a price/plan/strategy etc** *We agreed a price and the car was mine.* 我們商定了價格, 車就歸我了。| *I think the committee will agree the changes soon.* 我認為委員會將很快就這些改動達成一致意見。

3 ▶SAY YES 給予肯定答覆◀ [I,T not in progressive 不用進行式] to say yes to an idea, plan, suggestion etc 贊成, 贊同; 答應: *I suggested we go somewhere for the weekend and she agreed at once.* 我提議我們去某個地方度週末, 她立即表示贊同。| **agree to do sth** *Why don't we agree right now to use recycled paper?* 為甚麼我們不馬上贊同使用再生紙呢?

4 ▶BE THE SAME 同樣◀ [I not in progressive 不用進行式] if two pieces of information agree with each other, they are the same 與…一致, 與…符合: [+with] *Your story doesn't agree with what the police have told us.* 你的敘述和警察告訴我們的不一樣。

5 agree to differ to accept that you do not have the same opinions as someone else and agree not to argue about it 同意各自保留不同意見

agree with *phr v* [T not in passive 不用被動態] **1** to believe that a decision, action, or suggestion is correct or right 贊成, 同意: *I don't agree with any form of terrorism.* 我不贊成任何形式的恐怖主義。**2 not agree with you** if a type of food does not agree with you, it makes you feel ill〔某種食物〕不對胃口, 吃了不舒服 **3** if an adjective, verb etc agrees with a word, it matches that word by being plural if the subject is plural etc〔語法上〕呼應, 與…一致

This graph shows how common different grammar patterns of the verb **agree** are in spoken and written English. 本圖表所示為動詞 agree 構成的不同語法模式在英語口語和書面語中的使用頻率。

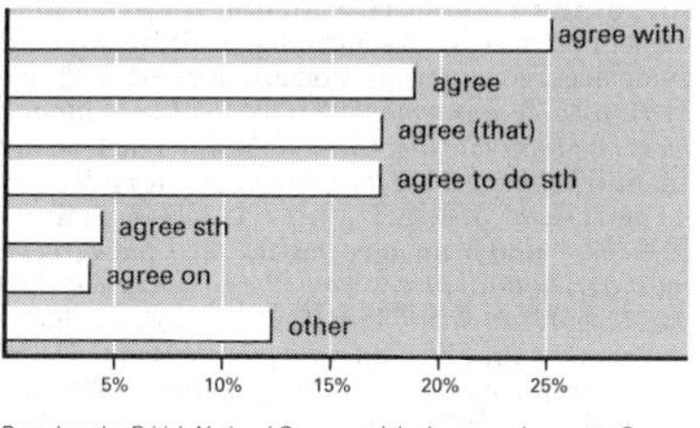

Based on the British National Corpus and the Longman Lancaster Corpus
據英國國家語料庫和朗文蘭卡斯特語料庫

USAGE NOTE 用法說明: AGREE

GRAMMAR 語法

If you have the same opinion as someone else you **agree with** them. You can also **agree with** (=approve of) their attitude, ideas, plans, rules etc, or an activity or principle that you approve of. 如果表示和某人的觀點一致, 用 agree with。agree with 也可以表示同意某人的態度、看法、計劃、規則等, 或是贊成一項活動或原則: *Do you agree with corporal punishment?* 你贊成體罰嗎?

You **agree** with people **about** or **on** other matters. 在某事上同意某人用 agree about 或 on: *I agree (with you) about Mark/on astrology/about this issue* (NOT 不用 *I agree this issue*). 我同意你關於馬克/占星術/這個問題的看法。

If you and others decide on or arrange to do something after discussing it, you **agree on** it. 經過討論然後達成一致去做某事用 agree on: *We finally agreed on a plan/a date/a solution/a deal.* 最後, 我們就某計劃/日期/解決辦法/貿易協議達成了一致。More formally you could also say 較正式時也可以說: *We agreed a plan/a date/a solution/a deal.*

If you accept something, especially something that was not your idea and perhaps you do not like, you **agree to** it. 接受了別人的看法, 但或許你並不樂意時說 agree to: *She agreed to the plan/the date/the solution/the deal* (NOT 不用 *She agreed the plan*

etc). 她接受了這個計劃/日期/解決辦法/貿易協議。You can also **agree to do** something 你也可以用 agree to do 來表示同意做某事: *They agreed to wait* (NOT 不用 *They accepted to wait*). 他們同意等待。

a·gree·a·ble /ə`griəbl; əˈgriːəbəl/ *adj* **1** pleasant or acceptable 宜人的; 可以接受的: *an agreeable spot for a picnic* 宜人的野餐地點 **2** someone who is agreeable is very nice and is liked by other people 令人愉快的, 受人喜歡的: *an agreeable young man* 叫人喜歡的年輕人 **3 be agreeable to sth** *formal* to be willing to do something or willing to allow something to be done【正式】欣然同意某事: *Are you sure Branson's agreeable to the idea?* 你肯定布蘭森同意這個想法嗎?

a·gree·a·bly /ə`griəblɪ; əˈgriːəbli/ *adv* intended to be pleasant or nice 愉快地: *He smiled agreeably.* 他愉快地笑了。

a·greed /ə`grid; əˈgriːd/ *adj* [only before noun 僅用於名詞前] **1** an agreed plan, price, arrangement etc is one that people have discussed and accepted 通過的, 一致同意的: *Reform had not yet been achieved, but it remained the party's agreed priority.* 改革尚未完成, 但它仍是這個黨一致同意的首要任務。**2 be agreed** if people are agreed, they have discussed something and agree about what to do 達成一致: **[+on]** *All parties are now agreed on the plan.* 所有黨派現在都一致同意這個計劃。

S1 W1 **a·gree·ment** /ə`grimənt; əˈgriːmənt/ *n* **1** [C] an arrangement or promise to do something, made by two or more companies, governments, organizations etc 協議, 協定, 合約: *a trade agreement* 貿易協定 | **[+on]** *an agreement on arms reduction* 削減武器協議 | **reach an agreement** *What happens if the warring parties fail to reach an agreement?* 交戰雙方如果沒有達成協議, 將會發生甚麼事情? | **under an agreement** *Under the agreement, most agricultural prices would be frozen or cut.* 根據協議, 大部分農產品的價格會被凍結或降低。| **have an agreement that** *We had an agreement that Ms Holst would keep me informed of any changes.* 我們有個協議, 如果有任何變化, 霍爾斯特女士都會通知我。**2** [U] a situation in which people have the same opinion as each other 一致(的意見), 相合: **[+that]** *There is agreement among doctors that pregnant women should not smoke.* 醫生們一致認為, 孕婦不應吸煙。| **[+on]** *Is there agreement on how much aid will be sent?* 應給予多少援助, 意見是否一致? | **be in agreement** *A decision will not be made until everyone is in agreement.* 直到所有人都同意才能作決定。**3** [C] an official document that people sign to show that they have agreed to something 協議書: *Please read the agreement and sign it.* 請看一下協議書, 然後在上面簽字。

ag·ri·busi·ness /`ægrɪˌbɪznɪs; ˈægrɪˌbɪznɪ̣s/ *n* [C,U] the production and sale of farm products, or a company involved in this 農業綜合經營(公司)

W2 **ag·ri·cul·ture** /`ægrɪˌkʌltʃɚ; ˈægrɪˌkʌltʃə/ *n* [U] the practice or science of farming 農業; 農學 —compare 比較 HORTICULTURE —**agricultural** /ˌægrɪ`kʌltʃərəl; ˌægrɪˈkʌltʃərəl◂/ *adj* —**agriculturalist** *n* [C]

agro- /ægro; ægrəʊ/ *prefix* also 又作 **agri-** /ægrɪ; ægrɪ/ concerning farming 農業(的), 與農業有關的: *agrobiology* 農業生物學 | *agribusiness* 農業綜合經營

a·ground /ə`graund; əˈgraʊnd/ *adv* **run/go aground** if a ship runs aground, it becomes stuck in a place where the water is not deep enough (船)擱淺

a·gue /`egju; ˈeɪgjuː/ *n* [C,U] *old-fashioned* a fever that makes you shake and feel cold【過時】(瘧疾的)瘧狀發熱, 寒顫

ah /ɑ; ɑː/ *interjection* used to show your surprise, anger, pain, happiness, agreement etc 啊(表示驚奇、憤怒、痛苦、喜悅、同意等): *Ah! There you are!* 啊! 你在這裡呀!

a·ha /ɑ`hɑ; ɑːˈhɑː/ *interjection* used to show that you understand or realize something 啊(表示明白、意識到某事): *Aha! So you planned all this, did you?* 啊! 原來這一切都是你事先計劃好的, 對吧? —see also 另見 HA¹

S2 W2 **a·head** /ə`hɛd; əˈhed/ *adv*

1 ►IN FRONT OF 在前面◄ in front of someone or something by a short distance 在前面: *He kept his gaze fixed on the car ahead.* 他一直注視着前面的那輛汽車。| **[+of]** *Tim pointed to a tree ahead of them.* 蒂姆指着他們前面的一棵樹。| **up ahead** *We could see the lights of Las Vegas up ahead.* 我們能看見正前方拉斯維加斯的燈光。

2 ►FORWARD 向前◄ if someone or something moves, looks ahead etc, they move or look towards a place in front of them 向前: *The ship forged ahead through the thin ice.* 那艘船衝破薄冰全速前進。| **straight ahead** *He's just staring straight ahead in a complete daze.* 他直視前方, 神情非常茫然。

3 ►BEFORE SB ELSE 在其他人之前◄ arriving, waiting, finishing etc before other people (比…)更早; (比…)更靠前: **[+of]** *There were four people ahead of me at the doctor's.* 在診所裡, 有四個人排在我前面。

4 ►BEFORE AN EVENT 在某事件之前◄ *AmE* before an event happens【美】事前: *You can prepare these salads ahead.* 你可以提前準備這些沙拉。| **ahead of time** *Can you tell me ahead of time if you're coming?* 如果你要來, 能不能事先告訴我?

5 ►FUTURE 未來◄ in the future 將來, 今後: *Rest now because you have a long journey ahead of you.* 現在休息一下, 因為你接下來還有很長的一段旅程。| **lie ahead** *We should try to predict the type of problems that may lie ahead.* 我們應設法預測一下擺在我們面前的會是何種問題。| **the years/days/months etc ahead** *The decisions you make in the days ahead are going to affect your whole future.* 今後幾天你所作的決定會影響你的整個未來。| **plan ahead** (=plan for the future) 提前計劃妥當

6 ahead of time/schedule etc earlier than planned or arranged 提前: *We might finish the project ahead of schedule.* 我們也許會比原計劃提前完成這個項目。

7 ►WINNING 獲勝◄ winning in a competition or election (在比賽或選舉中)領先: *Milligan's three-pointer puts them ahead by one.* 米利根的三分球使他們領先一分。

8 go ahead *spoken* used to tell someone they can do something【口】進行吧, 幹吧: *"Can I have the sports section?" "Yeah, go ahead, I've read it."* "我可以看看體育版嗎?" "當然, 拿去吧, 我已經讀過了。"

9 ►ADVANCED 先進的◄ ideas, achievements etc that are ahead of others, have made more progress or are more developed 先進的; 超越別人的; 勝過: *VEMCO was years ahead of us in their research.* VEMCO 公司在他們的研究方面超前了我們好多年。| **be ahead of its time** (=so new that people do not understand or like it) 走在時代之前 *Her educational theories were way ahead of their time.* 她的教育理論在他們所處的時代是超前的。

10 get ahead to make progress and be successful in your job, education etc 取得進步, 獲得成功: *Getting ahead at work is the most important thing to her at the moment.* 目前, 對她來說在工作上獲得成功是最重要的。

11 go ahead (with sth) to start doing something 着手做, 開始做: *Frank'll be late but we'll go ahead with the meeting anyway.* 弗蘭克會晚些時候到, 不過, 我們還是先開會。—see also 另見 GO-AHEAD

12 get/keep ahead (of the game) *AmE informal* to get into or be in a position where you are in control of something, so that it is easier to deal with【美, 非正式】成功; 領先, 超越: *I find it hard to keep ahead of the housework.* 我發覺要做好家務也不容易。

a·hem /m`hm; m'hm; *spelling pronunciation* 根據拼寫的讀音 ə`hɛm; əˈhem/ *interjection* a sound you make to attract someone's attention when you want to speak to them, warn them etc 啊哼(用於引起注意、發出警告等)

-aholic /əhɔlɪk; ; əhɒlɪk/ *suffix* [in nouns and adjectives 構成名詞和形容詞] *informal* someone who cannot stop doing something or using something【非正式】對…痴迷的（人），沉緬於…的（人）: *a workaholic* (=who loves working and cannot stop) 工作狂 | *a chocaholic* (=who loves chocolate) 嗜好巧克力的人

a·hoy /əˋhɔɪ; əˈhɔɪ/ *interjection* used by SAILORs to get someone's attention or greet them 啊嗨〔船員打招呼的喊聲〕: **ship ahoy!** (=used to say that a ship is approaching) 啊嗨，有船！

AI /ˌe ˋaɪ; ˌeɪ ˈaɪ/ *n* [U] the abbreviation of 縮寫 = ARTIFICIAL INTELLIGENCE

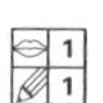

aid¹ /ed; eɪd/ *n* **1** [U] help, such as money or food, given by an organization to a country or to people who are in a difficult situation 援助，救助: *Aid is not getting through to the refugees.* 救濟品送不到難民手中。| **in aid of** (=in order to help) 用來幫助 *We're collecting money in aid of cancer research.* 我們正籌集資金以資助癌症研究。| **legal aid** (=free legal services) 法律援助 **2** help or advice given to someone who needs it 幫助: **come/go to sb's aid** (=help someone) 幫助某人 *I didn't speak any French, but a nice man came to my aid and told me where to go.* 我不會說法語，不過一個好心人幫了我的忙，告訴我怎麼走。**3** [C] something such as a machine or tool that helps someone do something 輔助性工具: *A video is a useful aid in the classroom.* 錄像在課堂教學中是有用的輔助教具。| **with the aid of** *He was able to prove the existence of the supergun with the aid of a photograph.* 藉助於一張照片，他能證明"超級大砲"的存在。**4 what's this in aid of?** *BrE spoken* used to ask what something is used for or why someone is doing something【英口】這有甚麼用途？這樣做是甚麼用意？: *What's this meeting tomorrow in aid of, then?* 那麼，明天的這個會有甚麼意義？**5** an American spelling of AIDE aide 的美式拼法 —see also 另見 FIRST AID

aid² *v* [T] *formal*【正式】**1** to help someone or something by making their situation or what they are doing easier 幫助，援助: *an index to aid the reader* 幫助讀者的索引 | **aid sb in/with sth** *The local community aided us in our investigation.* 當地社區協助我們調查。—see 見 HELP¹ (USAGE) **2 aid and abet** *law* to help someone do something illegal【法律】協助和教唆，夥同…作案，與…同謀

aide also 又作 **aid** *AmE*【美】/ed; eɪd/ *n* [C] someone whose job is to help someone in an important job, especially a politician〔尤指政治家的〕助手，助理

aide-de-camp /ˋed də ˋkæmp; ˌeɪd də ˈkɑːmp/ *n plural* **aides-de-camp** (same pronunciation 讀音相同) [C] a military officer who helps an officer of a higher rank to do his duties 副官，隨從武官

AIDS /edz; eɪdz/ *n* [U] Acquired Immune Deficiency Syndrome; a very serious disease caused by a VIRUS (1) that stops your body from defending itself against infections 愛滋病，艾滋病，後天免疫力缺乏症，獲得性免疫缺損綜合症

aid work·er /ˈ· ˌ··/ *n* [C] someone working for an international organization who brings food and other supplies to people in danger from war, famine etc 援助人員，救援人員: *UN aid workers in former Yugoslavia* 在前南斯拉夫的聯合國救援人員

ail /el; eɪl/ *v* **1** [T] *formal* to cause difficulties for someone or something【正式】使痛苦；使苦惱 **2** [I,T] *old-fashioned* to be ill, or to make someone feel ill or unhappy【過時】(使) 得病；(使) 難受[痛苦]

ai·ling /ˋelɪŋ; ˈeɪlɪŋ/ *adj* **1** an ailing company or ECONOMY¹ (1) is having a lot of problems and is not successful 不景氣的，狀況不佳的: *Vice-Chairman John Smith, who transformed GM's ailing European operations in the 80s* 扭轉了80年代通用汽車公司在歐洲不景氣局面的副主席約翰·史密斯 **2** *formal* ill【正式】生病的: *aged or ailing parents* 年老或有病的父母

ail·ment /ˋelmənt; ˈeɪlmənt/ *n* [C] an illness that is not very serious 疾病，小病

aim¹ /em; eɪm/ *n* **1** [C] what you are hoping to achieve by a plan, action, or activity 目標，目的，意圖: **[+of]** *The main aim of the course is to improve students' communication skills.* 這門課程的主要目的是提高學生的溝通技巧。| **with the aim of doing sth** *Research is being done with the specific aim of monitoring customer trends.* 做這個研究的特定目的是了解客戶的動向。**2 take aim** to point a gun or weapon at someone or something you want to shoot 瞄準: **[+at]** *Alan took aim at the tiger.* 艾倫瞄準了老虎。**3 sb's aim** someone's ability to hit what they are aiming at when they throw or shoot something 某人擊中目標的能力: *Val's aim was very good.* 瓦爾瞄得很準。 S2 W2

aim² *v* **1** [I,T] to choose the place, person etc that you want to hit and carefully point your gun, object etc towards them 瞄準，對準: *Denver aimed his gun but did not shoot.* 丹佛用槍瞄準了目標，但沒有開槍。| **[+at/for]** *The pitcher aimed at the upper half of the strike zone.* 投手把目標對準擊球區的上半區。**2** [I] to try or intend to achieve something 致力於，打算: **[+at/for]** *It's important that you should have some sort of a goal to aim for.* 有一個為之奮鬥的目標是很重要的。| **aim to do sth** *I'm aiming to lose 4kg before the summer holidays.* 我的目標是暑假前減掉四公斤體重。**3 aim sth at sb** to make something in such a way that a particular person or group of people will like it 使某物針對某人: *The program is aimed at a teenage audience.* 這個節目的對象是十幾歲的觀眾。 S2 W2

aim·less /ˋemlɪs; ˈeɪmləs/ *adj* without a clear purpose or reason 無目的 [目標] 的: *drifting through life in a rather aimless fashion* 過着毫無目標的漂泊生活 —**aimlessly** *adv* —**aimlessness** *n* [U]

ain't /ent; eɪnt/ *spoken* a short form of 'am not', 'is not', 'are not', 'has not', or 'have not', that many people think is incorrect【口】不〔一種不規範的否定縮寫形式〕

air¹ /ɛr; eə/ *n* S1 W1

1 ►GAS 氣體◄ [U] the mixture of gases that we breathe and that surrounds the Earth 空氣: *air pollution* 空氣污染 | *There was a strong smell of burning in the air.* 空氣中有一股濃烈的焚燒東西的味道。| **fresh air** (=clean air) 新鮮空氣 *Let's go out and get some fresh air.* 讓我們出去呼吸些新鮮空氣。—see also 另見 **a breath of fresh air** (BREATH (2))

2 ►SPACE ABOVE/BELOW 上／下方的空間◄ the space above the ground or around things 空中，天空: **through/into etc the air** *He fell 2000 metres through the air without a parachute.* 他在沒有降落傘的情況下在空中下降了2000米。

3 ►PLANES/FLYING 飛機／飛行◄ a) by air travelling by or using a plane 乘飛機: *It's actually less expensive to go by air to San Francisco.* 乘飛機去三藩市實際上更省錢。**b) air travel/crash/industry etc** involving or connected with planes and flying 乘飛機旅行／飛機失事／航空業等: *the victims of Britain's worst air disaster* 英國最嚴重空難的死難者

4 ►APPEARANCE 外表◄ if something or someone has an air of confidence, mystery etc, they seem confident, mysterious etc 神態；樣子；風度；氣氛: *She set about her task with an air of quiet confidence.* 她帶着悠然自信的風度開始了自己的工作。

5 it's up in the air *spoken* used to say that something has not been decided yet【口】懸着的，未定的

6 be on/off (the) air to be broadcasting on the radio or television at the present moment, or to stop broadcasting 正在廣播／停止廣播: *We'll be on air in about 3 minutes.* 大約三分鐘後我們開始廣播。

7 airs [plural] a way of behaving in which someone tries to make themselves seem more important than they are 裝腔作勢，擺架子: **put on airs/give yourself airs** *Trudy is always putting on airs and pretending she's posh.* 特魯迪總是擺架子，裝高貴。| **airs and graces** *Tristan, with his fancy education and his airs and graces* 擺出受

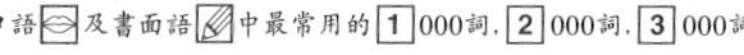

A

aircraft 飛機

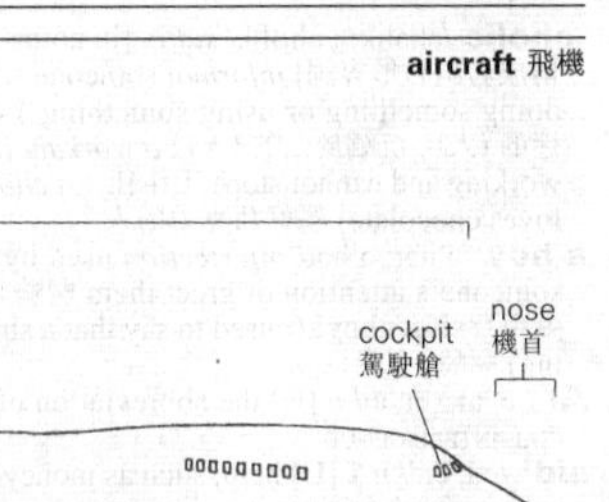

過昂貴的教育、裝腔作勢的特里斯坦

8 in the air if a particular emotion is in the air, a lot of people seem to feel it at the same time 流傳開的: *a sense of excitement in the air* 到處充滿了興奮的感覺

9 ►MUSIC 音樂◄ [C] a name given to a piece of music that means 'tune' 曲調, 旋律 —see also 另見 **hot air** (HOT¹ (28)), ON-AIR, **clear the air** (CLEAR² (13)), **thin air** (THIN¹ (15)), **walk on air** (WALK¹ (13))

air² *v*

1 ►CLOTHES 衣服◄ [I,T] also 又作 **air sth ↔ out** *AmE*【美】to put a piece of clothing in a place that is warm or has a lot of air, so that it smells clean (把…) 晾乾: *I've left my sweater on the washing-line to air.* 我已把毛線衫晾在衣繩上。

2 ►ROOM 房間◄ [I,T] also 又作 **air sth ↔ out** *AmE*【美】to let fresh air into a room, especially one that has been closed for a long time (使…) 通風

3 ►TV/RADIO 電視/無線電◄ [T] to broadcast a programme on television or radio 廣播, 播放

4 air your views/opinions etc to say publicly what you think about something important 發表觀點/看法等

5 air your grievances to tell other people about things that you think are unfair 發牢騷, 訴苦 —see also 另見 AIRING

air·bag /ˈɛr,bæg; ˈeəbæg/ *n* [C] a bag in a car that fills with air to protect the driver or passenger in an accident〔汽車的〕安全氣囊

air·base /ˈɛr,bes; ˈeəbeɪs/ *n* [C] a place where military aircraft begin and end their flights 空軍基地

air·bed /ˈɛr,bɛd; ˈeəbed/ *n* [C] a long rubber or plastic bag that you fill with air and lie on 充氣牀墊 —see picture at 參見 BED¹ 圖

air·borne /ˈɛr,bɔrn; ˈeəbɔːn/ *adj* **1** a plane that is airborne is in the air 在空中的, 在飛行中的 **2** airborne soldiers are trained to fight in areas that they get to by jumping out of a plane〔士兵〕空降作戰的

air·bus /ˈɛr,bʌs; ˈeəbʌs/ *n* [C] *trademark* a large plane that carries a lot of people for short distances【商標】空中巴士,〔短程飛行的〕大型客機

air chief mar·shal /,· · ˈ··◂/ *n* [C] a high rank in the British air force, or someone who has this rank〔英國的〕空軍上將 —see table on page C7 參見 C7 頁附錄

air com·mo·dore /,· ˈ···◂/ *n* [C] a high rank in the British air force, or someone who has this rank〔英國的〕空軍准將 —see table on page C7 參見 C7 頁附錄

air con·di·tion·ing /ˈ· ·,··/ *n* [C,U] a system that makes the air in buildings, rooms etc colder, or the machine that does this 空(氣)調(節)系統 —**air-conditioned** *adj*: *Our offices are fully air-conditioned.* 我們的辦公室都裝有空調。—**air conditioner** *n* [C]

air·craft /ˈɛr,kræft; ˈeəkrɑːft/ *n plural* **aircraft** [C] a plane or other vehicle that can fly 飛機; 飛行器, 航空器 —see also 另見 LIGHT AIRCRAFT

aircraft car·ri·er /ˈ·· ,···/ *n* [C] a type of ship that has a large flat surface that planes fly from 航空母艦

air·craft·man /ˈɛr,kræftmən; ˈeəkrɑːftmən/ *n* [C] a low rank in the British air force, or someone who has this rank〔英國〕空軍士兵 —see table on page C7 參見 C7 頁附錄

air·crew /ˈɛr,kru; ˈeəkruː/ *n* [C] the pilot and the people who are responsible for flying a plane and looking after the passengers 機組(全體人員), 空勤人員

air·fare /ˈɛr,fɛr; ˈeəfeə/ *n* [C] the price of a journey by plane 飛機票價

air·field /ˈɛr,fild; ˈeəfiːld/ *n* [C] a place where planes can fly from, especially one used by military planes〔尤指軍用的〕機場

air force /ˈ· ·/ *n* [C] the military organization of a country that uses planes to fight 空軍 —compare 比較 ARMY, NAVY

air fresh·en·er /ˈ· ,···/ *n* [C,U] a substance used to make the air in a room smell pleasant 空氣清新劑

air·gun /ˈɛr,gʌn; ˈeəgʌn/ *n* [C] *BrE* a gun that uses air pressure to fire a small round bullet【英】氣槍; BB GUN *AmE*【美】

air·head /ˈɛr,hɛd; ˈeəhed/ *n* [C] *slang especially AmE* someone who is stupid【俚, 尤美】傻瓜, 笨蛋

air host·ess /ˈ· ,··/ *n* [C] *BrE* a woman who serves food and drink to passengers on a plane【英】空中小姐, 飛機女服務員

air·i·ly /ˈɛrəlɪ; ˈeərɪ̈li/ *adv* without being serious or concerned 輕鬆地; 輕率地; 輕浮地: *"I don't really care," he replied airily.* "我不太在意。"他漫不經心地回答。

air·ing /ˈɛrɪŋ; ˈeərɪŋ/ *n* [singular] an occasion when an opinion, idea etc is discussed 公開發表: **give/get an airing** *The question will get a thorough airing at the next meeting.* 這個問題在下次會議上要徹底地公開討論一下。

airing cup·board /ˈ·· ,··/ *n* [C] *BrE* a warm cupboard in a house where sheets and clean clothes are kept【英】〔儲存被單、衣服的〕烘櫃

air·lane /ˈɛr,len; ˈeəleɪn/ *n* [C] a path through the air that is regularly used by planes 空中航線[航道]

air·less /ˈɛrlɪs; ˈeələs/ *adj* not having enough air or having air that does not move, so that it seems difficult to breathe 空氣不足的; 空氣不流通的: *The evening was muggy and airless.* 那天晚上天氣悶熱, 空氣不流通。

air·let·ter /ˈɛr,lɛtɚ; ˈeə,letə/ *n* [C] *BrE* a very light letter that you can send by AIRMAIL; AEROGRAMME【英】

航空信, 航空郵箋

air·lift /ˋɛr,lɪft; ˈeə,lɪft/ *n* [C] an act of taking people or things to an area by plane, when it is difficult or dangerous to use roads〔人員或物資的〕大規模空運; 空中補給: *airlifts of food supplies to famine areas* 給鬧饑荒地區空運食品 —**airlift** *v* [T]

2 3 **air·line** /ˋɛr,laɪn; ˈeəlaɪn/ *n* [C] a business that runs a regular service to take passengers and goods to different places by plane 航空公司

air·lin·er /ˋɛr,laɪnɚ; ˈeə,laɪnə/ *n* [C] *old-fashioned* a large passenger plane【過時】大型客機, 班機

air lock /ˈ· ·/ *n* [C] **1** a small room used for moving between two places that do not have the same air pressure, such as in a space vehicle or a vehicle under water 氣壓閘艙, 密封艙 **2** a BUBBLE[1] (1) in a pipe that stops liquid flowing through it 氣泡, 氣塞, 氣栓

air·mail /ˋɛr,mel; ˈeəmeɪl/ *n* [U] letters etc that are sent somewhere using a plane, or the system of doing this 航空郵件: *Send the letter by airmail.* 這封信用航空郵寄。

air·man /ˋɛrmən; ˈeəmən/ *n* [C] *plural* **airmen** /-mən; -mən/ a low rank in the US Air Force, or someone who has this rank〔美國〕空軍士兵 —see table on page C7 參見C7頁附錄

air·plane /ˋɛr,plen; ˈeəpleɪn/ *n* [C] *especially AmE* a flying vehicle that has one or more engines【尤美】飛機; AEROPLANE *BrE*【英】—see picture at 參見 AIRCRAFT 圖

air·pock·et /ˋɛr,pɑkɪt; ˈeə,pɒkɪ̵t/ *n* [C] a current of air that moves downwards and that makes a plane suddenly drop down〔會使飛機突然下降的〕氣穴, 氣阱

2 3 **air·port** /ˋɛr,pɔrt; ˈeəpɔːt/ *n* [C] a place where planes begin and stop flying, that has buildings for passengers to wait in 航空站 [港], 機場

air pump /ˈ· ·/ *n* [C] a piece of equipment used to blow air into something 氣泵

air raid /ˈ· ·/ *n* [C] an attack in which a lot of bombs are dropped on a place by planes 空襲

air ri·fle /ˈ· ,··/ *n* [C] a type of AIRGUN 氣步槍

air·ship /ˋɛr,ʃɪp; ˈeə,ʃɪp/ *n* [C] a large aircraft that has no wings, is filled with gas to make it float, and has an engine 飛船, 飛艇

air·sick /ˋɛr,sɪk; ˈeə,sɪk/ *adj* feeling sick because of the movement of a plane 暈機的 —**airsickness** *n* [U]

air·space /ˋɛr,spes; ˈeəspeɪs/ *n* [U] the sky above a particular country, that is thought of as being controlled by that country〔某個國家的〕領空: *The planes had entered Israeli airspace without permission.* 飛機未經允許進入了以色列領空。

air·speed /ˋɛr,spid; ˈeəspiːd/ *n* [singular,U] the speed at which a plane travels 飛行速度, 空速

air strike /ˈ· ·/ *n* [C] an attack in which a military aircraft drops bombs or shoots guns at a place 空(中)襲(擊)

air·strip /ˋɛr,strɪp; ˈeə,strɪp/ *n* [C] a long narrow piece of land that has been cleared so that planes can fly from it 臨時(飛機)跑道, 簡易機場

air terminal /ˈ· ,···/ *n* [C] **1** a place in a city from where passengers catch buses to the AIRPORT 航空終點站〔旅客乘車往返機場的市內集散處〕 **2** a large building at an AIRPORT where passengers wait to get on planes〔旅客候機的〕機場大廈, 候機大樓

air·tight /ˋɛrˋtaɪt; ˈeətaɪt/ *adj* not allowing air to get in or out 氣封的, 密封的: *airtight containers* 密封容器

air time /ˈ· ·/ *n* [U] the amount of time or the number of times that a radio or television station allows a particular song, advertisement etc to be broadcast 播放時段, 廣播時間: *smaller political parties trying to buy more air time* 設法買到更多廣播時間的小政黨

air-to-air /,· · ˈ·◂/ *adj* **air-to-air missile** a weapon that one plane shoots at another plane as they are flying 空對空導彈

air traf·fic con·trol·ler /,· ˈ·· ·,··/ *n* [C] someone at an airport who gives instructions to pilots by radio 空中交通指揮員 [調度員] —**air traffic control** *n* [U]

air vice-mar·shal /,· · ˈ··◂/ *n* [C] a high rank in the British Air Force, or someone who has this rank〔英國〕空軍少將 —see table on page C7 參見C7頁附錄

air·waves /ˋɛr,wevz; ˈeəweɪvz/ *n* [plural] *old-fashioned*【過時】**the airwaves** radio broadcasts 無線電波; 廣播: **on the airwaves** (=on the radio) 在廣播

air·way /ˋɛr,we; ˈeəweɪ/ *n* [C] **1** *technical* the passage in your throat that you breathe through【術語】〔喉嚨的〕氣道 **2** an area of the sky that is regularly used by planes 航線: *one of the world's busiest airways* 世界上最繁忙的航線之一

air·wor·thy /ˋɛr,wɝðɪ; ˈeə,wɜːði/ *adj* a plane that is airworthy is safe enough to fly〔飛機〕適於航行的 —**airworthiness** *n* [U]

air·y /ˋɛrɪ; ˈeəri/ *adj* **1** an airy room or building has plenty of fresh air because it is large or has lots of windows 通風的: *an airy first floor restaurant with sea views* 能看到海景、通風良好的一樓餐廳 **2** cheerful and confident, even when you should be serious or concerned about something 快活的, 無憂無慮的; 漫不經心的: *He dismissed her concerns with an airy wave of the hand.* 他漫不經心地揮一下手, 並不理會她的擔心。

airy fai·ry /,·· ˈ··◂/ *adj BrE* not very clear or practical; VAGUE【英】模糊的; 空洞的, 不切實際的: *airy fairy ideas* 不切實際的想法

aisle /aɪl; aɪl/ *n* [C] **1** a long passage between rows of seats, shelves, etc in a building or a plane 通道, 過道 —see picture at 參見 THEATRE 圖 **2** a narrow passage at the side of a church that is separated from the central part by a row of pillars (PILLAR (1))〔教堂兩邊以一排柱子同中殿隔開的〕側廊, 側堂, 耳堂 **3 go/walk down the aisle** *informal* to get married【非正式】步入教堂, 結婚 —see also 另見 **be rolling in the aisles** (ROLL[1] (18))

aitch /etʃ; eɪtʃ/ *n* [C] **1** the letter 'h' written as a word 字母h **2 drop your aitches** to fail to pronounce the letter 'h' at the beginning of a word 沒發詞首的h音

a·jar /əˋdʒɑr; əˈdʒɑː/ *adj* [not before noun 不用於名詞前] a door that is ajar is slightly open (門)半開着的 —see picture at 參見 OPEN[1] 圖

ak·a /ˋækə; ˈækə/ the abbreviation of 縮寫= 'also known as', used when giving someone's real name together with a different name they are known by 又名, 亦稱: *John Phillips, aka The Mississippi Mauler* 約翰·菲力浦斯, 又名"密西西比鐵拳"

a·kim·bo /əˋkɪmbo; əˈkɪmbəʊ/ *adj* **(with) arms akimbo** with your hands on your hips (HIP[1] (1)) so that your elbows point outwards 兩手叉腰的: *He stood with arms akimbo, glaring at the intruders.* 他兩手叉腰地站着, 怒視着闖進來的人。—see picture at 參見 ARM 圖

a·kin /əˋkɪn; əˈkɪn/ *adj* **akin to** very similar to something 與…相似的, 類似的: *The language is closely akin to Arabic.* 這種語言和阿拉伯語非常相近。

-al /əl; əl/ *suffix* also 又作 **-ial** **1** [in nouns and adjectives 構成名詞和形容詞] of or concerning something …的, 與…有關的: *coastal waters* (=near the coast) 近海水域 | *political* 政治的 **2** [in nouns 構成名詞] the action of doing something …的動作: *her arrival* (=arriving) 她的到達 | *a refusal* 拒絕

à la /ˋɑ lə; ˈæ lə/ *prep* in the style of 按照…的方式, 仿照…: *detective stories à la Agatha Christie* 仿照阿嘉莎·克莉絲蒂風格寫的偵探小說

al·a·bas·ter /ˋælə,bæstɚ; ˈæləbɑːstə/ *n* [U] a white stone, used for making STATUES or decorative objects 雪花石膏: *an alabaster vase* 雪花石膏(做的)花瓶

à la carte /,ɑ lə ˋkɑrt; ,æ lə ˈkɑːt/ *adj, adv* if food in a restaurant is à la carte, each dish has a separate price 照菜單點菜的[地]: *an à la carte menu* 點菜單

a·lack /əˋlæk; əˈlæk/ *interjection old use* used to express sorrow【舊】嗚呼〔表示哀傷〕

a·lac·ri·ty /əˋlækrətɪ; əˈlækrɪ̵ti/ *n* [U] quickness and eagerness 敏捷; 欣然: *They accepted our offer with alacrity.*

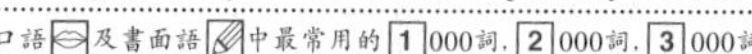

他們欣然接受了我們的建議。

à la mode /ˌɑ lə ˋmod; ˌæ lə ˈməʊd/ *adj, adv* **1** *old-fashioned* according to the latest fashion【過時】時髦的[地] **2** *AmE* served with ICE CREAM【美】加冰淇淋(的): *apple pie à la mode* 加冰淇淋的蘋果餡餅

alarms 警報裝置

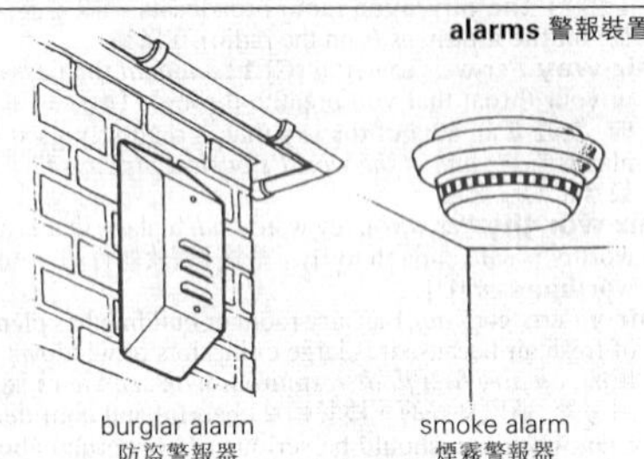

2 **a·larm¹** /əˋlɑrm; əˈlɑːm/ *n* **1** [U] a feeling of fear or anxiety because something dangerous might happen 驚恐, 驚慌: *I turned in alarm as the wind blew the door open.* 風把門吹開了, 我驚慌地轉過身去。**2** [C] something such as a bell or a light that warns people of danger 警報器: *a fire alarm* 火警裝置 | *Something has set the car alarm off.* 甚麼東西觸發了汽車警報器。**3 sound/raise the alarm** to warn everyone about something bad or dangerous that is already happening 發出警報: **[+about]** *The Red Cross has sounded the alarm about the threat of famine.* 紅十字會已發出了饑荒威脅的警報。**4** an alarm clock 鬧鐘 —see also 另見 **false alarm**

alarm² *v* [T] to make people very worried about a possible danger 使恐慌[不安, 焦慮]: *Her high temperature alarmed the doctors.* 她體溫很高, 使醫生感到不安。

alarm clock /·ˈ· ·/ *n* [C] a clock that will make a noise at a particular time to wake you up 鬧鐘: *The alarm clock went off at six.* 鬧鐘六點鐘響了。

a·larmed /əˋlɑrmd; əˈlɑːmd/ *adj* **1** frightened and worried 恐慌的, 擔憂的: *There's no need to look so alarmed!* 不必顯得這樣恐慌! | **[+by/at/over]** *Prison authorities have become increasingly alarmed by the number of prisoners trying to escape.* 試圖越獄的囚犯的人數之多令監獄方面越來越憂慮。**2** protected by an alarm system 裝有警報系統的

a·larm·ing /əˋlɑrmɪŋ; əˈlɑːmɪŋ/ *adj* worrying and frightening 令人擔憂的, 令人恐慌的: *an alarming increase in violent crime* 暴力犯罪案的驚人增長 | **at an alarming rate** (=happening so quickly that it makes people worried) 以驚人的速度 *The rainforest is disappearing at an alarming rate.* 熱帶雨林正在以驚人的速度消失。—**alarmingly** *adv*

a·larm·ist /əˋlɑrmɪst; əˈlɑːmɪst/ *adj* making people unnecessarily worried about dangers that do not exist 驚慌失措的, 大驚小怪的: *an alarmist report on population growth* 危言聳聽的人口增長報告 —**alarmist** *n* [C]

a·las¹ /əˋlæs; əˈlæs/ *adv* [sentence adverb 句子副詞] *formal* unfortunately【正式】不幸的是: *There is, alas, no short way to success.* 不幸的是, 成功沒有捷徑。

alas² *interjection old use* used to express sadness, shame, or fear【舊】唉; 哎呀〔表示悲傷、羞愧或恐懼〕

al·ba·tross /ˋælbəˌtrɔs; ˈælbətrɒs/ *n* [C] **1** a very large white sea bird 信天翁(鳥) **2 an albatross (around your neck)** something you have done that causes problems for you and prevents you from succeeding 無法擺脫的苦惱; 障礙: *His friendship with the gangster, Jimmy Hoffa, had become an albatross around his neck.* 他與匪徒吉米·霍法的交情成了他的包袱。

al·be·it /ɔlˋbiɪt; ɔːlˈbiːɪt/ *conjunction* even though, used to add information or details that are different from what you have already said 雖然, 儘管: *It was a small, albeit very important, mistake.* 這個錯誤雖小, 但很嚴重。

al·bi·no /ælˋbaɪno; ælˈbiːnəʊ/ *n* [C] a person or animal with an unusual GENETIC condition, light coloured eyes and very white hair and skin 患白化病的人或動物

al·bum /ˋælbəm; ˈælbəm/ *n* [C] **1** a book in which you put photographs, stamps etc〔收集相片、郵票等的〕簿冊: *a wedding album* 結婚相冊 **2** a record that has about 20 to 25 minutes music on each side 密紋唱片 3

al·bu·men /ælˋbjumən; ˈælbjʊmɪn/ *n* [U] *technical* the white or colourless part of the inside of an egg【術語】蛋白, 蛋清

al·che·my /ˋælkəmɪ; ˈælkəmi/ *n* [U] **1** a science studied in the Middle Ages that involved trying to change ordinary metals into gold 煉金術, 煉丹術 **2** *literary* magic【文】魔法, 法術: *By what alchemy did he manage to get elected?* 他用甚麼魔法當選的? —**alchemist** *n* [C]

al·co·hol /ˋælkəˌhɔl; ˈælkəhɒl/ *n* **1** [U] drinks such as beer or wine that contain a substance that can make you drunk 含酒精的飲品, 酒 **2** [C,U] a chemical substance, that can be used for medical or industrial purposes to clean things 酒精, 乙醇 3

al·co·hol·ic¹ /ˌælkəˋhɔlɪk; ˌælkəˈhɒlɪk◂/ *adj* **1** connected with alcohol or containing alcohol (含)酒精的: *alcoholic beverages* 酒精飲料 **2** caused by drinking alcohol 由酗酒引起的: *an alcoholic stupor* 醉得不省人事 —**alcoholically** /-klɪ; -kli/ *adv*

alcoholic² *n* [C] someone who regularly drinks too much alcohol and has difficulty stopping 酗酒者, 嗜酒成癮者

al·co·hol·is·m /ˋælkəhɔlˌɪzəm; ˈælkəhɒlɪzəm/ *n* [U] the medical condition of being an alcoholic 酒精中毒

al·cove /ˋælkov; ˈælkəʊv/ *n* [C] a place in the wall of a room that is built further back than the rest of the wall 凹室; 壁龕: *The bookcase just fits into the alcove in the living room.* 書櫥放在起居室的凹處正合適。

al den·te /æl ˋdɛntɪ; æl ˈdenti/ *adj* food, especially PASTA that is al dente is still firm after it has been cooked〔尤指麵食〕烹調得不太爛的, 耐嚼的

al·der·man /ˋɔldɚmən; ˈɔːldəmən/ *n* [C] **1** a member of a town or city council in the US〔美國城鎮的〕市參議員 **2** an important member of a town council in Britain in the past〔舊時英國市、鎮的〕參事

ale /el; eɪl/ *n* [U] **1** a type of beer made from MALT¹ (3) 高酒精度啤酒, 麥酒 **2** *old-fashioned* beer【過時】啤酒 —see also 另見 LIGHT ALE

al·eck /ˋælɪk; ˈælɪk/ *n* —see 見 SMART ALECK

ale·house /ˋelˌhaus; ˈeɪlhaʊs/ *n* [C] *old-fashioned* a place where people drank beer【過時】啤酒館, 酒館

a·lert¹ /əˋlɝt; əˈlɜːt/ *adj* **1** always watching and ready to notice anything strange or unusual 警惕的, 警覺的 **2** able to think quickly and clearly 機警的, 機敏的: *Despite her years, she still has a lively and alert mind.* 儘管她年紀很大, 她的思維仍然活躍、敏捷。| *Please remain alert and report any unattended luggage to the authorities.* 請保持警覺, 發現無人看管的行李請向當局報告。**3 be alert to** to realize that you must be careful about something or that something is dangerous 對...保持警惕, 對...警覺: *Tourists need to be alert to the dangers of travelling in the north of the country.* 遊客到該國北部旅遊必須對可能出現的危險保持警惕。

alert² *v* [T] **1** to officially warn someone of something, especially something dangerous, so that they can be ready to deal with it 使...警覺; 向...發出警報: *Alert air traffic control and tell them one engine isn't working.* 向空中交通管理發出警報, 告訴他們一個發動機失靈。| **[+that]** *Police have been alerted that a second prisoner has escaped.* 警察已經接到警報, 又有一個犯人逃走了。**2** to make someone notice something important or dangerous 提醒, 讓〔某人〕對...引起重視: **alert sb to sth** *Montessori alerted teachers to the importance of observing children at play.* 蒙特梭利提醒教師們, 孩子玩耍時注意觀察是很重要的。

alert[3] *n* **1** a warning to be ready for possible danger 警報: *a full-scale flood alert* 最高級別的防洪警報 —see also 另見 RED ALERT **2 be on the alert** to be ready to notice and deal with a situation or problem 保持戒備(狀態): *Be on the alert for pickpockets in the crowds.* 人多擁擠時要時刻提防扒手。| **be on full alert** (=completely ready to deal with a dangerous situation) 保持高度戒備狀態 *police on full alert against terrorist attacks* 保持高度戒備狀態以防範恐怖襲擊的警察

A lev·el /ˋe ˌlɛvl̩; ˈeɪ ˌlevəl/ *n* [C] an examination in a particular subject taken in schools in England and Wales, usually at the age of 18〔英格蘭和威爾斯中學生通常在18歲參加的某個科目的〕高級程度考試

al·fal·fa /ælˋfælfə; ælˈfælfə/ *n* [U] a plant grown especially in the US to feed farm animals 紫花苜蓿

alfalfa sprout /·ˈ·· ·/ *n* [C] a young alfalfa plant, eaten raw in SALADS 苜蓿苗〔可生食〕

al·fres·co /ælˋfrɛsko; ælˈfreskəʊ/ *adj, adv* in the open air 露天(的), 在戶外(的): *an alfresco meal* 野餐 | *We dined alfresco, on a balcony overlooking the sea.* 我們在陽台上吃飯, 從那裡可以眺望大海。

al·gae /ˋældʒi; ˈældʒiː/ *n* [U] a very simple plant without stems or leaves that grows in or near water 藻類(植物)

al·ge·bra /ˋældʒəbrə; ˈældʒɪ̈brə/ *n* [U] a type of mathematics that uses letters and other signs to represent numbers and values 代數 —**algebraic** /ˌældʒəˋbre·ɪk; ˌældʒɪ̈ˈbreɪ-ɪk◂/ *adj* —**algebraically** /-kl̩ɪ; -kli/ *adv*

al·go·rith·m /ˋælgəˌrɪðəm; ˈælgərɪðəm/ *n* [C] *technical* a set of instructions for solving a mathematical problem, making a computer program etc that are followed in a fixed order【術語】演算法, 計算程序

a·li·as[1] /ˋeliəs; ˈeɪliəs/ *prep* used when giving someone's real name together with another name they use 又名, 化名: *Velma Johnson, alias Annie Jones* 維爾瑪·約翰遜, 又名安妮·瓊斯

alias[2] *n* [C] a false name, usually used by a criminal〔通常指罪犯用的〕假名, 化名

al·i·bi /ˋæləˌbaɪ; ˈælɪ̈baɪ/ *n* [C] **1** someone or something that proves that someone was not in the area where a crime happened and therefore could not have done it (證明)某人不在犯罪現場的證人[證據]: *I've got an alibi for Tuesday night.* 我有星期二晚上不在現場的證據。**2** an excuse for something you have failed to do or done wrong 藉口; 託辭

a·li·en[1] /ˋeliən; ˈeɪliən/ *adj* **1** belonging to another country or race; FOREIGN (1) 外國的; 異族的: *an alien culture* 異域文化 **2** very different from what you are used to; strange 截然不同的; 非常怪異的: [+**to**] *a way of life that is totally alien to us* 和我們截然不同的生活方式 **3** [only before noun 僅用於名詞前] connected with creatures from another world 外星人的: *alien life-forms* 外星球的生命形式

alien[2] *n* [C] **1** *technical* someone who lives or works in your country, but who comes from another country【術語】外僑, 僑民: *illegal aliens entering the country* 非法僑民入境 **2** a creature from another world 外星人: *a film about aliens from Mars* 一部關於火星人的電影

a·li·en·ate /ˋelɪənˌet; ˈeɪliəneɪt/ *v* [T] **1** to do something that makes someone unfriendly or unwilling to support you 離間, 使疏遠[不和]: *The latest tax proposals will alienate many voters.* 最新的稅收建議會使很多選民不投我們的票。**2** *law* to give the legal right to a particular piece of land, property etc to someone else【法律】轉讓, 讓渡〔土地、財產等〕

a·li·en·a·ted /ˋelɪənetɪd; ˈeɪliəneɪtɪ̈d/ *adj* feeling separated from society or the group of people around you, and often unhappy 被疏遠的, 疏離於…的: [+**from**] *the psychological effects of being alienated from normal school life* 遠離正常學校生活產生的心理影響

a·li·en·a·tion /ˌelɪənˋeʃən; ˌeɪliəˈneɪʃən/ *n* [U] **1** the feeling of not being part of society or a group 疏離感: *the sense of alienation felt by many black people in our culture* 許多黑人在我們的文化中感受到的一種疏離感 **2** separation from a person who you used to be friendly with 離間, 疏遠

a·light[1] /əˋlaɪt; əˈlaɪt/ *adj* [not before noun 不用於名詞前] **1** burning 燃燒的: **set sth alight** *Several cars were set alight by rioters.* 好幾輛車被暴徒燒着了。**2** someone whose face or eyes are alight is excited and happy 喜悦的 **3** bright with light or colour 亮着的; 閃亮的

alight[2] *v* [I] *formal*【正式】**1** if a bird or insect alights on something, it stops flying to stand on something〔鳥、蟲等〕飛落, 下來 **2** to step out of a vehicle after a journey 從〔交通工具〕上下來

a·lign /əˋlaɪn; əˈlaɪn/ *v* [T] **1 align yourself with** to decide to publicly support a political group or country 與…保持一致; 與…結盟: *Church leaders have aligned themselves with the opposition.* 教會領袖和反對派達成了一致。| **be aligned with** *a country politically aligned with the West* 政治上與西方結盟的國家 **2** to arrange things so that they form a line or are parallel to each other 使排成一直線

a·lign·ment /əˋlaɪnmənt; əˈlaɪnmənt/ *n* **1** [U] the state of being arranged in a line with or parallel to something 排列成行; 排成直線: *the correct alignment of spine and pelvis* 脊柱和骨盆正確的直線排列 **2** [C,U] if countries or groups form an alignment, they support each other 聯盟, 結盟

a·like[1] /əˋlaɪk; əˈlaɪk/ *adj* [not before noun 不用於名詞前] very similar 相同的, 相像的: *My mother and I are alike in many ways.* 我和母親在許多方面很相似。

alike[2] *adv* **1** in a similar way 相似地, 相同地: *The twins were dressed alike.* 這對雙胞胎穿得一樣。**2** equally 同樣地, 一樣地: *I enjoyed being on this course – I learned a lot from teachers and students alike.* 我喜歡上這門課 —— 我從老師和學生身上都學到了很多知識。

al·i·men·ta·ry ca·nal /ˌæləmɛntərɪ kəˋnæl; ˌælɪ̈mentəri kəˈnæl/ *n* [C] the tube in your body that takes food through your body from your mouth to your ANUS 消化道

al·i·mo·ny /ˋæləˌmonɪ; ˈælɪ̈məni/ *n* [U] money that a court orders someone to pay regularly to their former wife or husband after their marriage has ended〔法院判定離婚一方須向另一方定期支付的〕贍養費

a·lit /əˋlɪt; əˈlɪt/ the past tense and past participle of ALIGHT[2]

a·live /əˋlaɪv; əˈlaɪv/ *adj* [not before noun 不用於名詞前] 2 3

1 ►NOT DEAD 沒有死◄ still living and not dead 活(着)的: *It was a really bad accident – they're lucky to be alive.* 這是一宗十分嚴重的意外 —— 他們能活着實屬幸運。| *None of my grandparents are alive now.* 我的祖父母和外祖父母都已去世了。| **stay alive** (=continue to live) 活下去 *They managed to stay alive by eating berries and roots.* 他們靠吃漿果和草根設法活了下來。| **keep sb alive** *He's being kept alive on a life-support machine.* 他在靠生命維持機維持生命。

2 ►CHEERFUL 高興的◄ active and happy; feel alive 活躍的, 充滿活力的: *It was the kind of morning when you wake up and feel really alive.* 這是一個醒來覺得充滿活力的早晨。

3 ►STILL EXISTING 仍存在的◄ continuing to exist 仍然存在的: *Ancient traditions are still very much alive in rural areas.* 不少古老的傳統在農村仍然存在。| **keep sth alive** *fighting to keep our academic institutions alive* 為保存我們的學術機構而鬥爭

4 come alive a) if a situation or event comes alive it becomes interesting and seems real 變得逼真, 變得有生氣: *For me the play only came alive in the final act.* 在我看來, 這齣戲在最後一幕才真正有點意思。**b)** if someone comes alive they start to be happy and interested in what is happening 活躍起來: *It was as if she came alive when she sat down at the piano.* 她一坐在鋼琴旁, 就好像充滿了生氣。**c)** if a town or city etc comes alive it becomes busy 變得生氣勃勃; 變得繁忙: *seaside resorts that come alive in the summer* 夏季變得繁忙的海濱度假勝地

5 bring sth alive to make something interesting 使…變得有生氣: *Plays need the sound of human voices to*

bring them alive. 戲劇需要有說話的聲音才有生氣。 **6 be alive and well a)** to be healthy and enjoy life 健康愉快的 **b)** *informal humorous* to be popular and successful【非正式, 幽默】流行, 成功: *The mini skirt is alive and well in Paris this year.* 迷你裙今年在巴黎很流行。 **7 be alive and kicking** to be very healthy and active 精神飽滿; 活躍: *"How's your father nowadays?" "Oh, still alive and kicking."* "你父親現在怎麼樣?" "哦, 身體很好呢。" **8 be alive to** to realize that something is happening and that it is important 意識到, 注意到: *The company is alive to the threat posed by foreign imports.* 這家公司清楚地意識到外來進口商品所造成的威脅。 **9 be alive with** to be full of people, animals, or things that are moving 充滿, 到處都是〔活物〕: *a tree trunk alive with ants* 爬滿螞蟻的樹幹 —see also 另見 **skin sb alive** (SKIN² (3))

al·ka·li /ˈælkəˌlaɪ; ˈælkəlaɪ/ *n* [C,U] a substance that forms a chemical salt when combined with an acid 鹼

al·ka·line /ˈælkəˌlaɪn; ˈælkəlaɪn/ *adj* containing an alkali 含鹼的, 鹼性的

all- /ɔl; ɔːl/ *prefix* **1** consisting or made only of one kind of thing 純, 全, 單一種類的: *an all-male club* 男性俱樂部 | *an all-wool dress* 純羊毛連衣裙 **2** for the whole of something 整個的, 全部的: *All-India Railways* 全印度鐵路公司 | *an all-night party* (=lasting all night) 通宵晚會 | *an all-night cafe* (=staying open all night) 通宵營業的咖啡館

all¹ /ɔl; ɔːl/ *determiner, predeterminer* **1** the complete amount or quantity of; the whole of 全部: *I've got all day tomorrow to do it.* 明天我有一整天做這件事。| *He had worked all his life in the mine.* 他在礦場工作了一輩子。| *Have you done all your homework?* 你所有的作業都做完了嗎? | *She didn't say a single word all the way back home.* 回家路上, 她一句話也沒說。| **all the time** (=very often, especially in a way that is annoying) 老是, 總是 *It rained all the time we were on holiday!* 我們放假的時候總下雨! **2** every one of 每一個, 所有的: *Someone's taken all my books!* 誰把我的書都拿走了! | *Will all the girls please stand over here.* 女孩子都請站到這邊來。| **all kinds of** *The course attracts all kinds of people.* 這門課程吸引了各種各樣的人。| *All these questions must be answered.* 所有這些問題都必須回答。| **you all/they all/it all etc** *They all passed the exam.* 他們考試全都及格了。**3** the greatest possible amount of 盡可能的: *With all due respect, I really cannot agree with your last statement.* 儘管我十分尊敬你, 恕我不同意你最後的陳述。**4 of all people/things/places etc** used to show surprise when mentioning a particular person, thing, or place 在所有的人/事/地方之中等唯獨…: *Of course you shouldn't have done it – you of all people should know that!* 當然你本不應該做這件事。別人可以不知道, 可你應該知道! **5 all innocence/smiles etc** used to emphasize that someone or something has a particular quality of appearance 一臉無辜的樣子/滿臉笑容等: *Elsie was all smiles when I saw her again the next morning.* 我第二天早晨再見到艾爾西的時候, 她一臉笑容。**6 for all...** in spite of a particular fact, quality, or situation 儘管: *For all her rudeness, she's actually quite a kind-hearted old soul.* 儘管她粗魯, 實際上是個熱心腸的老人。**7 go all out/make an all-out effort** to do everything you can to succeed 全力以赴, 竭盡全力: *We're all out to win the cup this year.* 我們今年要全力以赴贏得獎盃。

all² *adv* **1** [always+adj/adv/prep] **all alone/new/dark etc** 獨自一人/全新/漆黑一片等: *You shouldn't be sitting here by yourself, all alone.* 你不應該一個人孤零零地坐在這兒。| *I'm all confused now!* 我現在全給搞糊塗了! | *The room suddenly went all dark.* 房間裡突然一片漆黑。| **all for/all in favour of** (=used to say that you strongly support or agree with something) 完全贊成 *One minute he's all for all Labour policy, the next minute he's knocking it.* 他一會兒完全贊同工黨的政策, 一會兒又對其橫加指責。**2 one, four, ten all** used when giving the score of a game in which both sides have scored the same 一平, 四平, 十平 **3 not all that** *spoken* not very【口】不太: *It doesn't sound all that good, does it?* 這聽起來不太好, 是吧? | *I don't think it matters all that much.* 我認為這關係不大。**4 all along** *informal* all the time from the beginning while something was happening【非正式】一直, 自始至終: *I knew all along that this relationship wouldn't last.* 我自始至終都知道這種關係不會長久。| *Maybe this is what they were trying to achieve all along.* 也許這就是他們一直想要實現的目標。**5 all at once a)** happening all together at the same time 同時: *Obviously they can't do everything all at once.* 顯然, 他們不能同時做所有的事。**b)** suddenly and unexpectedly 突然, 出其不意地: *All at once, I knew there was something wrong.* 突然間, 我知道出了差錯。**6 all over a)** everywhere on an object or surface 遍佈表面的: *There were bits of paper all over the floor.* 地板上到處都是碎紙。| *He has cuts all over his legs.* 他的腿上到處是傷口。**b)** everywhere in a place 處處, 到處: *Antique clocks from all over the world are on display.* 來自世界各地的古玩鐘錶正在展出。| *People came from all over the country.* 人們來自全國各地。| *They're putting up new offices all over the place.* 他們正在各地設立新的辦事處。**c)** finished 結束: *I saw my old girlfriend the other day, but that's all over now.* (=our relationship is finished) 前幾天, 我見到了我以前的女朋友, 但現在都過去了。**7 that's sb all over** *spoken* that is typical of him or her【口】某人就是這樣, 那是典型某人: *He was late of course, but that's Tim all over!* 當然他又遲到了, 蒂姆就是這樣的! **8 all the easier/healthier/more effectively etc** used to emphasize how much easier, etc something is than it would normally have been 更加容易/健康/有效等: *Their success is all the more pleasing when you consider the effort they've made.* 考慮到他們付出的努力, 他們的成功就更令人高興。| *The job was made all the easier by having the proper tools.* 有了合適的工具, 工作就容易多了。**9 all the same** *spoken* in spite of something that you have just mentioned【口】(雖然…) 還是, 仍然: *We realised that the children would have to leave home, but all the same it was difficult when they went.* 我們意識到孩子們必須離開家, 但不管怎麼說, 他們真的離開時, 我們還是不太好受。**10 it's all the same to me** used to say that you do not mind what decision is made, that you would be pleased with any choice or that you do not really care 對我無所謂, 沒區別: *You can choose what we do, it's all the same to me.* 你可以選擇我們做甚麼, 對我來說都一樣。**11 all but** almost completely 幾乎, 差不多: *Their screams of excitement all but drowned out the music.* 他們激動的尖叫聲幾乎淹沒了音樂聲。**12 all too** much more than is desirable 極; 甚: *All too often it's the mother who gets blamed for her children's behaviour.* 孩子做錯了事, 受責備的卻往往是母親。**13 all told** counting or including everyone; all together 總計, 合計: *There were seventeen of us at the meeting, all told.* 我們總共有十七人參加會議。**14 it's all up (with)** *informal* used to say that it is impossible for someone to continue doing something, especially when they have been involved in criminal activities【非正式】全完了, 完蛋了 **15 (not) all there** *informal* someone who is not all there cannot think in a clear normal way and seems slightly crazy【非正式】神志(不)正常, 頭腦(不)清醒: *I don't think he's quite all there.* 我認為他腦子有些不正常。

all³ *pron* **1** every one or every part of something 每個人; 每樣東西; 全部: *I ate the whole packet, all of them!* 我把一整袋全吃了! | *That's all I know about it.* 那是我所知道的全部。| *Not all the children were vaccinated.* 並不是所有的孩子都注射了疫苗。| *I've heard it all before.* 這件事我以前全都聽過。**2** used to emphasize the most basic or necessary facts or details about a situation 一

切，全部：*All you need is a hammer and some nails.* 你需要的不過是一把錘子和一些釘子。| *All I'm asking for is a little respect.* 我要的不過是一點尊重而已。**3 for all sb knows/cares etc a)** used to say that something could happen, especially something very unpleasant or serious, and someone would not know or care about it 某人才不知道/才不在乎呢等：*The old woman could have been lying dead in the house for all her family cared.* 這位老人可能已經死在這幢房子裡，可是她家裡的人都不在乎。**4 and all a)** the whole thing; including everything or everybody mentioned 全部；包括所有：*They ate the whole fish; bones, tail, head, and all.* 他們把整條魚都吃掉了，骨頭、魚尾、魚頭等通通吃掉了。**b)** *spoken* an expression meaning as well, used to emphasize what you have just said【口】也，而且〔表示強調〕：*And you can take that smelly coat out of here and all!* 你也可以把那件有味的大衣拿走！| *"Look, it's snowing!" "Oh, it is and all!"* "看，下雪了！""啊，還真下了！" **5 it costs all of 50p/took all of 20 minutes etc** *spoken* used to emphasize or express how large or small an amount actually is【口】足足花了50便士/20分鐘等 **6 it was all I could do to...** used to say that you only just succeeded in doing something 我能做的也就是…：*It was all I could do to stop them hitting each other!* 我所能做的也只是阻止他們打架而已！**7 (not) at all** used in questions and negative statements to emphasize what you are saying 無論如何（都不），一點（都不）：*They've done nothing at all to try and put the problem right.* 他們根本沒有採取任何行動去解決問題。| *They obviously weren't at all happy.* 顯然，他們一點兒都不高興。| *Does he get no pension at all?* 他一點兒養老金也沒有拿到嗎？| *Do you know anything about it at all?* 這件事難道你一點都不知道嗎？| *He's not looking at all well.* (=he looks ill) 他看上去氣色不很好。| *"Do you mind if I stay for a bit longer?" "Not at all!"* (=certainly not, please do) "你介不介意我在這兒多留一會？""當然不（介意）！" **8 all in all** considering every part of a situation 一般來說，總的說來：*All in all, it's been a pretty bad year for John Major.* 總的說來，對約翰·梅傑來講這是糟糕的一年。**9 it's all or nothing a)** used to say that unless something is done completely or done in the exact way that you want, something else will happen, especially something unpleasant 要麼全部，要麼一點兒也沒有：*It was all or nothing for Susan; either the company offered her a pay rise or she would leave.* 對蘇珊而言，只有兩個可能，要麼公司給她加薪，要麼她離開。**b)** used to say that someone is using all their effort and energy in order to try and do something 竭盡全力 —see also 另見 **all and sundry** (SUNDRY (1)), EACH, EVERY

all[4] *n* **do/give your all** *literary* to do everything possible to try and achieve something【文】竭盡全力，全力以赴：*The coach expects everyone to give their all in every game.* 教練希望所有隊員在每場比賽中都全力以赴。

Al·lah /ˋælə; ˈælə/ *n* the Muslim name for God 真主，安拉〔穆斯林對其所信仰的神的稱呼〕

all-A·mer·i·can /ˌ· ·ˋ···◂/ *adj* **1** having qualities that are considered to be typically American and that American people admire, such as being healthy and working hard 純粹[典型]美國式的：*an all-American family, cheerful and friendly* 一個典型的美國式家庭，歡樂而溫馨 **2** belonging to a group of players who have been chosen as the best in their sport at American universities 全美最佳的〔代表美國大學生最高體育水平〕：*an all-American player out of UCLA* 從美國洛杉磯加州大學選出的全美最佳球員

all-a·round /ˌ· ·ˋ·/ *adj* [only before noun 僅用於名詞前] *AmE* good at doing many different things, especially at many different sports【美】〔體育運動〕全能的；ALL-ROUND[1] *BrE*【英】：*an all-around athlete* 全能運動員

al·lay /əˋle; əˈleɪ/ *v* [T] *formal*【正式】**allay fear/concern/suspicion etc** to make someone feel less afraid, worried etc 減輕恐懼/擔憂/疑慮等：*His reassurances did little to allay their fears for Robert's safety.* 他的安慰沒有起多大作用，他們仍舊十分擔心羅伯特的安全。

all clear /ˌ· ˋ·/ *n* **the all clear a)** official permission to begin doing something 批准，放行：*We've got the all clear from the board for the new project.* 這個新項目我們已經得到董事會的批准。**b)** a signal such as a loud whistle that tells you that a dangerous situation has ended 解除警報的信號：**give/sound the all clear** *The drone of the bombers faded, and the all clear was sounded.* 轟炸機的轟鳴聲逐漸減弱，警報解除的信號響了起來。

all-com·ers /ˌ· ˋ··/ *n* [plural] anyone who wants to take part in a competition whatever their age or experience 所有參與競爭的人，所有參賽者：*The marathon is open to all-comers.* 馬拉松比賽誰都可以報名參加。

al·le·ga·tion /ˌæləˋgeʃən; ˌælɪˈgeɪʃən/ *n* [C] a statement that has not been proved that someone has done something wrong or illegal 指控；宣稱：**[+of]** *allegations of fraud* 有欺詐行為的指控 | **allegation that** *allegations that the election had been fixed* 選舉結果已經內定的說法

al·lege /əˋlɛdʒ; əˈledʒ/ *v* [T] to say that something is true or that someone has done something wrong even though this has not been proved〔在未證實的情況下〕硬說，宣稱，聲稱；指控：**allege (that)** *It was alleged that policemen had accepted bribes.* 有人聲稱警察收受了賄賂。| **be alleged to be/do sth** *The new missiles are alleged to be capable of travelling enormous distances.* 據稱這種新式導彈可以發射到很遠的距離。

al·leged /əˋlɛdʒd; əˈledʒd/ *adj* [only before noun 僅用於名詞前] an alleged fact, quality etc is supposed to be true although there is no proof that it actually is 未有證據而被指稱的，涉嫌的：*reports of alleged police brutality* 關於警察涉嫌有野蠻行為的報道

allegedly /əˋlɛdʒɪdlɪ; əˈledʒɪdli/ *adv* [sentence adverb 句子副詞] used when reporting something that other people say is true, although there is no proof 據說：*He was allegedly caught shop-lifting in his local supermarket.* 據說，他在當地的超級市場行竊時被抓住。

al·le·giance /əˋlidʒəns; əˈliːdʒəns/ *n* [C,U] loyalty to a leader, country, belief etc〔對領袖、國家、信念等的〕忠誠，效忠：**[+to]** *allegiance to the king* 效忠國王 | **proclaim/pledge allegiance** *I pledge allegiance to the flag of the United States of America.* 我發誓效忠美國國旗。| **switch allegiance** (=start to support a different person, group etc) 轉而投靠，轉而擁戴

al·le·go·ry /ˋæləˌgorɪ; ˈæləgəri/ *n* [C,U] a story, painting etc in which the events and characters represent ideas or teach a moral lesson 寓言，諷喻 —**allegorical** /ˌæləˋgɔrɪkḷ; ˌæləˈgɒrɪkəl/ *adj* —**allegorically** *adv*

al·leg·ro /əˋlegro; əˈlegrəʊ/ *n* [C] a piece of music played or sung quickly〔樂曲的〕快板 —**allegro** *adj, adv*

al·le·lu·ia /ˌæləˋlujə; ˌæləˈluːjə◂/ *interjection* HALLELUJAH 哈利路亞〔猶太教和基督教對上帝的讚美詞〕

all-em·brac·ing /ˌ· ·ˋ··◂/ *adj* including everyone or everything 總括的；包羅萬象的：*an all-embracing vision of the cosmos* 宇宙總觀

Al·len key /ˋælən ki; ˈælən kiː/ *n* [C] *BrE* a small tool you use to turn an Allen screw (=a type of screw with a hole that has six sides)【英】艾倫內六角螺絲扳手

Allen wrench /ˋælən rɛntʃ; ˈælən rentʃ/ *n* [C] *AmE* an Allen key【美】艾倫內六角螺絲扳手

al·ler·gic /əˋlɝdʒɪk; əˈlɜːdʒɪk/ *adj* **1** having an allergy 過敏的：**be allergic to sth** *I'm allergic to penicillin.* 我對青黴素過敏。**2 allergic reaction/rash** an illness or a red painful area on your skin that some people get because of an allergy 過敏反應；過敏性皮疹 **3 allergic to sth** *informal* always trying to avoid an activity or thing that you do not like【非正式】不喜歡某事，對某事反感：*I think he's allergic to work!* 我看他討厭工作！

al·ler·gy /ˋælɚdʒɪ; ˈælədʒi/ *n* [C,U] a medical condition in which you become ill or in which your skin becomes red and painful because you have eaten certain foods, touched certain things etc 過敏性反應，過敏症：*Do you*

A

suffer from any allergies? 你對甚麼過敏嗎? | **[+to]** *an allergy to cat fur* 對貓毛過敏

al·le·vi·ate /əˋlivɪ,et; əˈliːvieɪt/ *v* [T] to make something less painful or difficult 減輕, 緩和〔痛苦或困難〕: *a medicine to alleviate cold symptoms* 減輕傷風症狀的藥 | *measures to alleviate poverty* 脫貧措施 —**alleviation** /ə,livɪˋeʃən; ə,liːviˈeɪʃən/ *n* [U]

al·ley /ˋælɪ; ˈæli/ *n* [C] **1** a narrow street between or behind buildings 小巷, 胡同 **2 right up/down sb's alley** *AmE* very suitable for someone【美】正合某人的胃口; 非常適合某人: *The job sounds right up your alley.* 這項工作聽上去正合你的胃口。—see also 另見 BLIND ALLEY, BOWLING ALLEY

alley cat /ˈ·· ·/ *n* [C] a cat that lives on the streets and does not belong to anyone 流浪貓, 野貓

al·ley·way /ˋælɪ,we; ˈæliwei/ *n* [C] an ALLEY (1) 小巷, 胡同

all-fired /,· ˈ·◂/ *adv AmE informal* a word meaning completely that you use before describing a quality that you think is extreme【美, 非正式】極度, 完全: *If he weren't so all-fired sure of himself, I'd like him better.* 如果他不是那麼過於自信, 我會更喜歡他。

all fours —see 見 **on all fours** (FOUR (4))

all go /,· ˈ·/ *adj* **it's all go** *spoken* used to say that a situation is very busy and full of activity【口】忙碌: *It was all go in the office as the deadline approached.* 由於最後期限日益臨近, 辦公室裡一片忙碌。

3 **al·li·ance** /əˋlaɪəns; əˈlaɪəns/ *n* [C] **1** an arrangement in which two or more countries, groups etc agree to work together in order to try to change or achieve something 聯盟, 同盟: **[+between]** *the alliance between students and factory workers in the 1960s* 20世紀60年代學生與工人之間的聯盟 | **[+with]** *Britain's military alliance with her NATO partners* 英國與其北約夥伴的軍事聯盟 | **enter into/form an alliance** (=agree to work together) 結盟 *The two countries entered into a defensive alliance.* 兩國訂立了防禦聯盟。**2** a group that is formed when two or more countries, groups etc work together 同盟 **3 in alliance (with)** if two groups, countries etc are in alliance, they work together to achieve something or protect one another 與…聯盟[結盟]: *Relief workers in alliance with local charities are trying to help the famine victims.* 救濟人員與當地慈善機構聯合起來正在設法幫助那些饑民。**4** *formal* close relationship, especially a marriage, between people【正式】〔家族間的〕親密關係;〔尤指〕聯姻 —see also 另見 **unholy alliance** (UNHOLY (3))

al·lied /ˋælaɪd; ˈælaɪd/ *adj* **1 Allied** belonging to or connected with the countries that fought together against Germany in the First or Second World War, or against Iraq in the Gulf War 結盟的, 同盟的〈如在第一、第二次世界大戰中共同反對德國, 或在海灣戰爭中共同反對伊拉克的結盟國家〉: *an Allied bombing raid* 聯合空襲 | *the Allied forces* 盟軍 **2 allied industries/organizations/trades etc** connected with each other because of being similar or dependent on each other; RELATED 相關的工業/組織/貿易等: *Agriculture and allied industries provided the state's main source of revenue.* 農業和相關產業構成了該國收入的主要來源。**3 (be) allied to/with** connected with 與…有關聯: *Cultural anthropology is closely allied to the field of social psychology.* 文化人類學與社會心理學領域有着緊密聯繫。**4** joined by common political, military, or economic aims〔政治、軍事或經濟〕目標一致的: *their allied effort to convince others of the danger of nuclear power* 他們為使他人認識核能危險而作出的共同努力

Al·lies /ˋælaɪz; ˈælaɪz/ *n* **the Allies** [plural] **a)** the countries, including Britain, the US, and the USSR, that fought together during the Second World War〔第二次世界大戰期間的〕同盟國〔包括英、美、蘇〕**b)** the countries, including Britain, the US, and France, that fought together during the First World War〔第一次世界大戰期間的〕協約國〔包括英、美、法〕**c)** the countries that fought together against Iraq in the Gulf War in the early 1990s〔20世紀90年代初海灣戰爭中共同反對伊拉克的〕聯合國多國部隊

al·li·ga·tor /ˋælə,getə; ˈæləgeɪtə/ *n* **1** [C] a large animal with a long mouth and sharp teeth that lives in the hot wet parts of the US and China 短吻鱷 **2** [U] the skin of this animal used as leather 短吻鱷皮革: *alligator shoes* 鱷魚皮鞋

all-in /,· ˈ·◂/ *adj* extremely tired 極度疲勞: *You look all-in. Are you o.k.?* 你看起來非常疲勞。你沒事吧?

all in *adv* **£5000/$100 all in** if you buy or sell something for a particular price all in, that price includes all services, parts etc 全部在內共5000英鎊/100美元

all-in·clu·sive /,· ·ˈ··◂/ *adj* including everything 全部包括的: *an all-inclusive price* 包含全部費用的價格

al·lit·er·a·tion /ə,lɪtəˋreʃən; ə,lɪtəˈreɪʃən/ *n* [U] the use of words that begin with the same sound in order to make a special effect, especially in poetry 頭韻(法)〔用起頭音相同的幾個詞來製造一種特別的效果, 尤用於詩歌〕

all-night·er /,· ˈ··/ *n* [C] *AmE informal* an occasion when you spend the whole night studying or doing written work in university【美, 非正式】〔在大學〕通宵學習

al·lo·cate /ˋælə,ket; ˈæləkeɪt/ *v* [T] to decide officially that a particular amount of money, time etc or something such as a house or job etc should be used for a particular purpose 分配, 配給: **allocate sb sth** *The duty officer allocated us a cabin for the night.* 值班軍官分配一間小屋給我們過夜。| **allocate sth for sth** *one million dollars allocated for disaster relief* 撥出一百萬美元用於救災 | **allocate sth to** *You need to decide how much time to allocate to each exam question.* 你需要確定每一道試題花多長時間。

al·lo·ca·tion /,æləˋkeʃən; ,æləˈkeɪʃən/ *n* **1** [C] the amount or share of something that has been allocated to a person or organization 配給物; 配給量, 份額 **2** [U] the decision to allocate something 撥給; 分配, 配給

al·lot /əˋlɑt; əˈlɒt/ *v* **allotted, allotting** [T] to decide officially to give something to someone or use something for a particular purpose 分配; 撥出: **allot sth to** *You may find it useful to allot 20 minutes each day to this task.* 你會發現每天拿出20分鐘時間做這項工作很有用。| **allot sb sth** *The boys were allotted a room each for studying.* 男孩們每人分到一個房間用於學習。

al·lot·ment /əˋlɑtmənt; əˈlɒtmənt/ *n* **1** [C,U] an amount or share of something such as money or time that is given to someone or something, or the process of doing this 分配物[額], 份額; 分配: *The budget allotment for each district is prepared at the provincial headquarters.* 各區的預算份額由各省總部分配。| **[+of]** *the allotment of funds to schools* 撥給學校的資金 **2** [C] a small area of land for growing vegetables that people who live in towns in Britain can rent〔在英國租給城鎮居民的〕小塊菜地

al·lot·ted /əˋlɑtɪd; əˈlɒtɪd/ *adj* **allotted money/time/resources etc** allotted money etc has been officially given to someone for a particular purpose 分配到的錢/時間/資源等: *The department has spent its allotted budget.* 這個部門已經花完了所分配的預算經費。| **in the allotted time** *I didn't finish the test in the allotted time.* 我沒有在規定時間內答完試卷。

all-out /,· ˈ·◂/ *adj* [only before noun 僅用於名詞前] an all-out effort or attack involves a lot of energy, determination, or anger 全力以赴的, 竭盡全力的: *fears of an all-out war* 對一場惡戰的恐懼 —**all out** *adv*: *Canada will have to go all out on the ice if they want to win.* 如果加拿大隊想贏, 就必須在冰上竭盡全力。

al·low /əˋlaʊ; əˈlaʊ/ *v* [T] **1** to let someone do or have something, or let something happen 允許, 容許, 准許: **allow sb to do sth** *The committee allowed the oil company to build a refinery on the island.* 委員會准許該石油公司在島上建一個煉油廠。| **allow sb sth** *We allow passengers one item of hand luggage each.* 我們允許每位乘客帶一件手提行李。| **allow sb in/out/up etc** *I don't* *allow the cat in the bedroom.* 我不允許貓進入臥室。| **be allowed** (=if something is allowed, it is permitted) 獲准 *"Can I smoke?" "I'm sorry, it's not allowed."* "我可以吸煙嗎?" "對不起, 不可以。" | *Abortions were allowed only for reasons of health.* 只有出於健康原因才允許墮胎。| **allow swimming/smoking/talking etc** *We do not allow eating in the classrooms.* 我們不允許在教室裡吃東西。| **be allowed (to do sth)** (=you are permitted to do something) 獲准做某事 *I wasn't allowed to stay out after 11 o'clock.* 我不可以在11點以後還不回家。—see graph at 參見 PERMIT[1] 圖表 **2** to be sure that you have enough time, money, food etc available for a particular purpose 〔為某種目的〕給予〔足夠的時間/金錢等〕: *We allowed ourselves plenty of time to get to the airport.* 我們給自己留出了足夠的時間去機場。**3** to make it possible for something to happen or for someone to do something, especially something helpful or useful 使有可能: **allow sb to do sth** *A 24-hour ceasefire allowed the two armies to bury their dead.* 24小時的停火協定使交戰雙方得以埋葬陣亡士兵。| **allowed sb sth** *The new seatbelt allows the driver greater freedom of movement.* 這種新式安全帶使司機活動更自如。**4** to accept or agree that something is correct or permitted by the rules or the law 認可; 被〔規定或法律〕視為正確[正當]: *The judge allowed the evidence.* 法官認可了這些證據。**5 allow that** *formal* to admit that something is true 【正式】承認: *I allow that there may have been a mistake.* 我承認可能有錯誤。**6 allow me!** *spoken* used as a polite way of offering to help someone do something 【口】讓我來幫你!: *"Allow me," the waiter said, helping her with her coat.* "讓我來幫你。" 服務員一邊說, 一邊幫她拿外衣。

allow for sb/sth *phr v* [T] to consider all the possible facts, problems, costs etc involved in a plan or situation and make sure that you can deal successfully with them 考慮, 顧及: *Allowing for inflation, the cost of the project is $2 million.* 考慮到通貨膨脹因素, 這個項目的費用為200萬美元。

allow of sth *phr v* [T] *formal* to show that something exists or is possible 【正式】容許有...的可能: *The facts allow of only one interpretation.* 這些事實只可能有一種解釋。—see graphs at 參見 FORBID, LET, PERMIT[1] 圖表

al·low·a·ble /ə'lauəbḷ; ə'lauəbəl/ *adj* **1** acceptable according to the rules 可允許的; 可承認的: *the maximum allowable dosage* 可允許的最大劑量 **2** allowable costs are costs that you do not pay tax on 可扣除的, 〔費用〕免稅的: *allowable deductions such as alimony and business expenses* 免稅的扣除額, 如贍養費和業務開銷

2 3 **al·low·ance** /ə'lauəns; ə'lauəns/ *n* [C] **1** an amount of money that you are given regularly or for a special reason 〔定期或出於特殊原因而給予的〕津貼, 補助: *His father gave him an allowance of £1000 a year.* 他父親每年給他1000英鎊的生活費。| **travel/clothing/housing allowance etc** (=money given officially to spend on travel etc) 旅行/服裝/住房等津貼 *Jo's salary includes a monthly clothing allowance.* 喬的薪水裡包括每月的服裝津貼。**2** an amount of something that it is acceptable or safe 允許量, 限額: *What's your daily calorie allowance?* 你的每天熱量攝入量最多是多少? | *The baggage allowance is 75 pounds per person.* 每個人准許帶75磅重的行李。**3** an amount of money that you can earn without paying tax on it 〔收入的〕免稅額: *In 1978 allowances amounted to $7,200 for a family of four.* 1978年, 一個四口之家的收入免稅額是7,200美元。**4** *especially AmE* a small amount of money that a parent regularly gives to a child 【尤美】零用錢; POCKET MONEY (1) *BrE* 【英】 **5 make allowances** to let someone behave in a way you would not normally approve of, because you know there are special reasons for their behaviour 體諒, 顧及: [+for] *Dad is under a lot of pressure, so we have to make allowances for him.* 爸爸承受着很大的壓力, 我們必須體諒他。**6 make (an) allowance for** to consider something when making a decision 考慮到: **make no allowance for** *My brother made no allowance for my shorter legs, and I had to run to keep up.* 我哥哥也不考慮我的腿比較短, 我得跑步才能跟上他。

al·loy[1] /'ælɔɪ; 'ælɔɪ/ *n* [C,U] a metal that consists of two or more metals mixed together 合金: *Brass is an alloy of copper and zinc.* 黃銅是銅和鋅的合金。

al·loy[2] /ə'lɔɪ; ə'lɔɪ/ *v* [T] **1** [+with] *technical* to mix one metal with another 【術語】將〔兩種金屬〕鑄成合金 **2** *literary* to lower the value or quality of something by mixing it with something else 【文】〔通過摻雜而〕使...降低價值[變壞]

all-pow·er·ful /,· '···◂/ *adj* having complete power or control 有無上權力的, 全能的, 無所不能的: *the all-powerful Senate Foreign Relations Committee* 擁有無上權力的參議院對外關係委員會

all-pur·pose /'· ,··/ *adj* [only before noun 僅用於名詞前] able to be used in any situation 通用的, 有多種用途的: *an all-purpose cleaner* 萬能清潔劑

all right[1] *adj, adv* [not before noun 不用於名詞前] *spoken* 【口】 1 2

1 ▶SATISFACTORY 令人滿意的◀ satisfactory or acceptable but not excellent 還算可以(的), 比較滿意的[地]: *"What's the food like?" "Well, it's all right I suppose, but the place on Melrose Avenue is better."* "食物味道怎麼樣?" "嗯, 我認為還可以, 不過麥爾羅斯大街的那家更好。" | *"How's school going, Steve?" "Oh, all right, I guess."* "史蒂夫, 學校情況怎麼樣?" "噢, 我想還不錯。"

2 ▶UNHARMED/WITHOUT PROBLEMS 未受傷害/無問題◀ not hurt, not upset, or not having any problems 安全的[地], 健康的[地], 安然無恙的[地]: *Katie looked really unhappy – I'd better go and make sure she's all right.* 凱蒂看起來很不高興, 我最好去看看, 確保她沒甚麼事。| **be getting on all right** (=not have any problems or difficulties) 進展順利, 無麻煩事 *The kids seem to be getting on all right at school.* 孩子們在學校似乎一切都順利。

3 go all right to happen without any problems 一切順利, 平安: *Did everything go all right with your test?* 你考試一切都順利吧?

4 be doing all right to be successful in your job, life etc 一切都不錯: *She's doing all right – she's got a job with Microsoft.* 她現在一切順利, 在微軟公司找到了工作。

5 ▶SUITABLE 合適的◀ used when saying whether something is suitable or at a good time 合適的: *I'd really like to see you – would Thursday morning be all right?* 我很想見你 —— 星期四上午行嗎?

6 it's all right used to make someone feel less afraid or worried 別怕, 沒事: *It's all right, Mommy's here.* 別怕, 媽媽在這兒。

7 it's all right/that's all right a) used as a reply when someone thanks you 別客氣: *"Thanks for all your help!" "That's all right – it was nothing really."* "謝謝你的幫助!" "不必客氣 —— 這不算甚麼。" **b)** used to tell someone that you are not angry when they say they are sorry for something 沒關係: *"Sorry I'm late." "That's all right."* "對不起, 我遲到了。" "沒關係。"

8 is it all right if/would it be all right if used when asking if you can do something 〔做某事〕可以嗎: *Is it all right if I close the window? It's getting cold in here.* 我可以把窗子關上嗎? 這裡有點冷。

9 it's/that's all right by me used to agree with someone's suggestion 我認為可以〔指同意某人的建議〕: *"Do you think we could finish early today?" "That's all right by me."* "你認為我們今天能早些完成嗎?" "我看可以。"

10 it's all right for you/her etc used to say that someone else does not have the same problems and difficulties that you have 你/她等沒有同樣問題[困難]: *It's all right for you – you don't have to work with her every day. She's driving me crazy.* 你是沒事兒 —— 你不必整天和她在一起工作。她簡直逼得我發瘋了。

11 ►CHECK UNDERSTANDING 檢查理解程度◄ [sentence adverb 句子副詞] used to check that someone has understood what you said, or to show that you have understood 明白(嗎): *I'll leave the key with the neighbours, all right?* 我把鑰匙放在鄰居家裡, 明白嗎? | *"Connect the positive first and then the negative." "Oh I see, all right."* "先接正極, 然後接負極。" "哦, 我明白了。"
12 ►GREETINGS 招呼◄ *especially BrE* used when greeting someone and asking about their health, what has happened to them recently etc【尤英】安好, 好嗎: *Hi, Stuart – you all right?* 嘿, 斯圖爾特 —— 你好嗎? | *"How are you John?" "Oh, all right – mustn't grumble!"* "約翰, 你好嗎?" "啊, 好的, 還不錯。"
13 she's/he's all right *BrE* used when you like someone【英】她/他挺好的: *"She's not bad our boss, is she?" "No, she's all right."* "她是個不錯的老闆, 對嗎?" "對, 她挺好的。"
14 ►CERTAINLY 當然◄ used to admit that something is true, especially when saying that you also think that something else is not 確實: *Wayne's experienced enough all right, but I don't know if he's right for this particular job.* 韋恩的確有豐富經驗, 但我不知道他是否適合這項特殊工作。—see also 另見 **a bit of all right** (BIT¹ (20))

all right² *interjection*
1 ►YES 是◄ **a)** used when agreeing with someone's suggestion or agreeing to do something 好的, 好吧〔用於同意某人的建議或做某事〕: *"Why don't we go to a movie?" "All right. Do you want to stop at Gino's for a pizza first?"* "我們為甚麼不去看電影呢?" "好吧。你要不要先到季諾餐廳買塊比薩餅?" **b)** used when agreeing to do something or to allow something, even though you do not want to 可以〔用於勉強同意或允許某事〕: *"Can I play with my new computer game?" "Oh all right then – so long as you don't make too much noise."* "我可以玩玩新電腦遊戲嗎?" "可以 —— 只要你不弄出太多的噪音。"
2 ►ANNOYED 感到惱了◄ **a)** used when saying that you have heard and understood what someone has said, especially when you are annoyed 得了, 行了〔尤用於不耐煩時〕: *"The train leaves at 5.30." "All right! I'm just coming!"* "火車五點半開。" "知道了! 我就來!" **b)** used when asking what has happened or what someone means, especially in an angry or threatening way 好了〔尤用於憤怒或威嚇時〕: *All right, what have you two been doing with that knife?* 好了, 你們倆到底在用那把刀幹甚麼?
3 ►INTRODUCE/CHANGE SUBJECT 介紹/改變話題◄ used to introduce a new subject or activity 好了: *All right, folks, I'd like to introduce our first speaker this evening.* 好了, 各位, 我想介紹一下今晚的第一位演講者。

all-round¹ /ˈ· ·/ *adj* [only before noun 僅用於名詞前] *BrE* good at doing many different things, especially at many different sports【英】才能多方面的, 〔尤指體育〕全能的; ALL-AROUND *AmE*【美】: *an all-round athlete* 全能運動員

all-round² /ˌ· ˈ·/ *adv BrE informal* used to say that you are thinking about someone or something generally rather than about particular details【英, 非正式】從各方面來看; 總的說來: *All-round it's not a bad car.* 總的來看, 這輛車不錯。

all-round·er /ˌ· ˈ··/ *n* [C] *BrE* someone who is good at many different things【英】多才多藝的人; 多面手; 全能運動員

all-seat·er sta·di·um /ˌ· ·· ˈ···/ *n* [C] *BrE* a stadium where sports are played and there are seats for everyone who is watching【英】全座位體育場

all-sing·ing, all-danc·ing /ˌ· ˈ··, ˈ··/ *adj* [only before noun 僅用於名詞前] *BrE humorous* an all-singing, all-dancing machine or system is able to do many different things because it is technically advanced【英, 幽默】〔機器或系統〕無所不能的, 多功能的

all·spice /ˈɔlˌspaɪs; ˈɔːlspaɪs/ *n* [U] a powder used in cooking to give food a special taste, made from the fruit of a tropical American tree 多香果粉〔一種用於烹調的香料〕

all-star /ˈ· ·/ *adj* [only before noun 僅用於名詞前] including many famous actors or sports players 明星薈萃的: *an all-star cast* 明星薈萃的陣容

all-ter·rain bi·cy·cle /ˌ· ·· ˈ···/ *n* [C] a MOUNTAIN BIKE 越野單車, 山地腳踏[自行]車

all-ter·rain ve·hi·cle /ˌ· ·· ˈ···/ *n* [C] a motor vehicle with three or four wheels that you can drive on rough ground 適應各種地形的車輛, 越野車

all-time /ˈ· ·/ *adj* **1 all-time high/low/best etc** the highest, lowest etc level there has ever been 前所未有[空前]的高/低/好等: *The price of wheat reached an all-time low of 42 cents in 1932.* 1932年小麥的價格降到了前所未有的低價 —— 42美分。**2 all-time record/classic etc** the best ever known 已知最好的紀錄/經典等: *He's one of pro football's all-time great receivers.* 他是職業橄欖球迄今最好的直傳球接手之一。

al·lude /əˈlud; əˈluːd/ *v*
allude to sb/sth *phr v* [T] *formal* to mention something or someone indirectly【正式】影射, 暗指: *The character's evil nature is constantly alluded to throughout the play.* 在整齣戲劇中, 該角色的邪惡本性不斷地被間接提到。

al·lure¹ /əˈlʊr; əˈljʊə/ *n* [singular,U] a mysterious, exciting, or desirable quality that is very attractive 誘惑, 魅力, 吸引力: *Even in her fifties she had lost none of her seductive allure.* 她雖年逾五十, 魅力卻絲毫未減。| *the allure of foreign travel* 出國旅行的誘惑

allure² *v* [T] to attract someone, especially because of an exciting or desirable quality 吸引, 誘惑 —**allurement** *n* [C]

al·lur·ing /əˈlʊrɪŋ; əˈljʊərɪŋ/ *adj* attractive or desirable 誘人的, 迷人的, 吸引人的: *a low, alluring voice* 低沉而迷人的嗓音

al·lu·sion /əˈluʒən; əˈluːʒən/ *n* [C,U] something that is said or written that brings attention to a particular subject in a way that is not direct 暗示, 暗指, 間接提到; 典故: [+to] *Eliot's poetry is full of allusions to other works of literature.* 艾略特的詩歌中有許多其他文學作品的典故。—**allusive** /-sɪv; -sɪv/ *adj* —**allusively** *adv*

al·lu·vi·al /əˈluvɪəl; əˈluːviəl/ *adj* made of soil left by rivers, lakes, floods etc 沖積的, 淤積的: *an alluvial plain* 沖積平原

al·lu·vi·um /əˈluvɪəm; əˈluːviəm/ *n* [C,U] *technical* soil left by rivers, lakes, floods etc【術語】沖積層; 沖積土

al·ly¹ /ˈælaɪ; ˈælaɪ/ *n* [C] **1** a country that makes an agreement to help or support another country, especially in a war 同盟國: *a meeting of the European allies* 歐洲諸盟國會議 —see also 另見 ALLIES **2** someone who helps and supports you in difficult situations 盟友, 支持者: *Thatcher and Reagan were close allies.* 戴卓爾和列根是親密的盟友。

al·ly² /əˈlaɪ; əˈlaɪ/ *v* [I,T] to join with other people or countries to help and support each other 結盟, 聯手: **ally yourself to/with** *They allied themselves to the other western states after the war.* 戰後他們與其他西方國家結盟。

al·ma ma·ter /ˈɑlmə ˈmɑtɚ; ˌælmə ˈmeɪtə/ *n* [singular] **1** the school, college, or university that you used to attend 母校 **2** *AmE* the song of a particular school, college, or university【美】校歌

al·ma·nac /ˈɔlməˌnæk; ˈɔːlmənæk/ *n* [C] **1** a book that gives information about the movements of the sun and moon, the times of the TIDES etc for each day of a particular year 天文年曆, 曆書 **2** a book gives information about what happened in a particular subject or activity in a particular year 年鑑: *a football almanac* 足球年鑑

al·might·y /ɔlˈmaɪtɪ; ɔːlˈmaɪti/ *adj* **1 Almighty God/Father** an expression used to talk about God when you want to emphasize his power 全能的上帝/天父 **2 the Almighty** God (全能的) 上帝[主] **3 God/Christ Almighty** an expression used when you are angry or upset that some people consider offensive 天啊: *God Almighty, what on earth will they do next?* 天啊, 他們接

下來究竟要幹甚麼? **4 almighty din/crash/row** *informal* a very loud noise, argument etc【非正式】巨大的嘈雜聲/碰撞聲/爭吵聲: *There was an almighty bang in the garden and the shed went up in flames.* 花園裡傳來一聲巨響, 棚屋化為一片火海。

al·mond /ˈɑmənd; ˈɑːmənd/ *n* [C] a flat pale nut with a slightly sweet taste, or the tree that produces these nuts 杏仁, 扁桃仁; 杏樹, 扁桃樹

al·mo·ner /ˈælmənɚ; ˈɑːmənə/ *n* [C] an official in a British hospital in former times who helped people who were ill with their financial and social problems〔英國舊時幫助病人的〕醫院社會工作者

1 1 **al·most** /ˈɔlˌmost; ˈɔːlməʊst/ *adv* very nearly but not completely 幾乎, 差不多, 差一點, 將近: *We've almost finished.* 我們差不多幹完了。| *We stayed there for almost a week.* 我們在那裡逗留了將近一星期。| **almost every** *They sold almost everything.* 他們幾乎賣掉了所有的東西。| **almost all** *Almost all the children here speak two languages.* 這兒的孩子差不多都會講兩種語言。| *an almost impossible task* 一項幾乎無法完成的任務 | *wines which are almost as expensive as champagne* 同香檳酒差不多一樣貴的葡萄酒 | **almost certainly** *The cause is almost certainly a virus.* 幾乎可以肯定病因是一種病毒。

USAGE NOTE 用法說明: ALMOST

WORD CHOICE 詞語辨析: **almost, nearly, hardly, scarcely, very, extremely**

Both **almost** and **nearly** can be used before words like *all, every,* and *everybody.* almost 和 nearly 都可用於 all, every 和 everybody 等詞前: *Almost/nearly all (of) my friends came to the party* (NOT 不用 *Almost of my friends came...* or 或 *Almost my friends came...*). 差不多我所有的朋友都來參加聚會了。

Both can also be used before negative verbs 兩個詞都可用於否定動詞前: *I almost/nearly didn't get up in time.* 我差點沒及時起牀。However, you do not use **not** with *hardly* or *scarcely.* 但 hardly 和 scarcely 不與 not 連用: *There was scarcely enough time to take a shower.* 幾乎沒有時間淋浴了。

Almost (NOT **nearly**) can be used before *any* and negative words like *no, nobody, never,* and *nothing.* almost 可用於 any 和否定詞 no, nobody, never 和 nothing 之前, 但 nearly 不可以: *Almost no one came to the party* (NOT 不用 *Nearly no one...*). 幾乎沒有人來參加晚會。| *You can find the meaning of almost any word here.* 在這裡你幾乎可以查到任何單詞的意思。However, it is more usual to use **hardly** or **scarcely** with *any, anybody, ever* etc than **almost** with *no, nobody, never* etc: For example, you are more likely to hear 但是 hardly 或 scarcely 與 any, anybody, ever 連用, 與 almost 和 no, nobody, never 連用比起來, 前者更常用些。例如, 你會較多聽到人們說: *Hardly anybody came to the party.* 幾乎沒甚麼人來參加晚會。而不是: *Almost no one came to the party.*

You can use *not* before **nearly**, but not usually before **almost**. nearly 前可加 not, 但 almost 前一般不加 not: *She's not nearly as pretty as her sister* (NOT 不用 *She's not almost as pretty...*). 她不如她姐姐漂亮。

Both **nearly** and **almost** can be used with adjectives that have an extreme meaning. nearly 和 almost 都可與有極端含義的形容詞連用: *nearly/almost perfect/frozen/dead/impossible* 幾近完美/凍結/死去/不可能。However, they are not usually used with other, less extreme, adjectives. In these cases you are more likely to use **very** or **extremely**. 然而, 它們通常不與沒有極端含義的形容詞連用, 在這類情況下, 多用 very 和 extremely: *The schools are extremely good there* (NOT 不用 *nearly good*). 那兒的學校特別好。| *The coast was very rocky* (NOT 不用 *almost rocky*). 這兒的海岸岩石極多。**Nearly** is more commonly used in British English, while **almost** is more common in American English. 英國英語裡多用 nearly, 而美國英語多用 almost。

alms /ɑmz; ɑːmz/ *n* [plural] *old-fashioned* money, food, clothes etc that are given to poor people【過時】施捨物, 救濟品[金]

alms-house /ˈ· ·/ *n* [C] a place where poor people could live without paying rent in former times 貧民所, 救濟院

a·loe /ˈælo; ˈæləʊ/ *n* **1** [U] the wood of an Indian tree that smells sweet 沉香木 **2 aloes** [plural] the juices of the leaves of the aloe plant used for making medicine 蘆薈(汁)

a·loft /əˈlɔft; əˈlɒft/ *adv formal* high up in the air【正式】在高處, 在空中: *a flag flying aloft* 高高飄揚的旗幟

a·lo·ha /əˈlohɑ; əˈləʊhə/ *interjection* used as a greeting or to say goodbye in Hawaii 喂; 再見〔表示問候或告別的夏威夷語〕

a·lone¹ /əˈlon; əˈləʊn/ *adj* **1** [not before noun 不用於名詞前] without any other people 單獨的, 獨自的: *She lives alone.* 她獨居。| **alone together** (=if two people are alone together there is no one else in the place where they are)〔兩人〕單獨在一起 *Suddenly they found themselves alone together in the room.* 突然, 他們發現屋子裡只剩他們兩個人。**2** without any friends or people who you know 孤獨的, 無伴的: **all alone** (=completely alone) 孤零零的, 獨自 *It was scary being all alone in a strange city.* 獨自一人身處陌生的城市真令人害怕。**3** [not before noun 不用於名詞前] feeling very unhappy and lonely 孤單的, 寂寞的: *He felt terribly alone when June left.* 瓊走後, 他感到非常孤獨。**4 you alone know/have/can do sth** used to say that you are the only person who knows or can do something 只有自己知道/有/能做某事: *Julie alone knew the terrible truth.* 只有朱莉一個人知道可怕的事實真相。| *Of all the applicants, she alone had the right qualifications.* 在所有的申請人中, 只有她符合條件。**5** used to emphasize that one particular thing is very important or has a great effect in a situation 僅僅…就, 只有: *The price alone was enough to put me off the idea.* 單看價格就讓我打消了這個念頭。**6 be alone in (doing) sth** be the only person to do something 是唯一做某事的人: *You're not alone in feeling upset by all this, believe me.* 相信我, 不是只有你一個人因為這一切感到不安。 2 1

Frequencies of **alone, on your/her own** and **by yourself** in spoken and written English 在英語口語和書面語中 alone, on your/her own 和 by yourself 的使用頻率

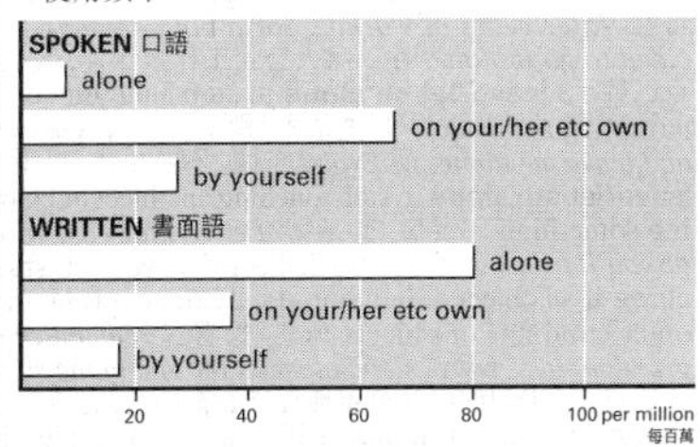

Based on the British National Corpus and the Longman Lancaster Corpus 據英國國家語料庫和朗文蘭卡斯特語料庫

In spoken English it is more usual to say **on your own** or **by yourself** rather than **alone**. In written or more formal English **alone** is more common. 英語口語中較常說的是 on your own 或 by yourself, 而不是 alone, 而在書面語或較正式的英語裡則是 alone 更常用。

USAGE NOTE 用法說明: ALONE

WORD CHOICE 詞語辨析: **alone, on your own, by yourself, lonely, lonesome, lone, solitary**

If you are **alone**, or less formally, **on your own/by yourself** that just means that no one else is with you, and is neither good nor bad. alone 或不大正式的 on your own/by yourself 都可表示"沒別人和你在一起", 既無褒意, 也無貶意: *I just wanted to stay at home alone/by myself.* 我只想一個人待在家裡。With verbs of action, **on your own** and **by yourself** often suggest that no one is helping you. 與動作動詞連用時, on your own 和 by yourself 表示沒有人幫忙: *I want to swim alone* (=with no one else there). 我想一個人游泳〔沒有旁人在〕。| *I want to swim on my own/by myself* (=either with nobody else there or with other people there but not helping). 我想自己一個人游泳〔意為沒有別人在或有別人在也不用幫忙〕。

If you are **lonely** or **lonesome** (*AmE*) you are unhappy because you are alone. lonely 或 lonesome (美) 表示"孤獨"和"寂寞"之意: *I feel lonely living away from home.* 離家在外我感到孤獨。| *a lonely old man* 孤獨的老人。Places etc can be **lonely** or **lonesome** if they make people feel lonely. lonely 或 lonesome 也可用來修飾地點, 表示"讓人感到寂寞的": *a lonesome little town on the prairie* 草原上一個人跡罕至的小鎮。Things that you do can also be **lonely**. lonely 也可形容事物: *a lonely journey/job/life etc* 孤單的旅程/寂寞的工作/孤寂的生活等。**Lonely** is never an adverb but **alone** often is. lonely 不作副詞用, 但 alone 常用作副詞: *She travelled alone*(NOT 不用 *lonely*). 她獨自旅行。

A **lone** or **solitary** person or thing is simply the only one in a place, and therefore might seem a little lonely. lone 或 solitary 修飾人或物表示此人或此物是某個地點唯一的一個, 因此會顯得寂寞: *a lone figure in the middle of the square* (=it is the only one there) 廣場中心孤零零的一個人像。In spoken English, you are more likely to talk about 英國口語中往往可以這樣說: *a figure on its own in the middle of the square* 廣場中心孤零零的一個人像。Sometimes **solitary** can suggest that you choose to be alone. 有時 solitary 可指喜歡獨處的: *She is a very solitary person.* 她是一個喜歡獨處的人。

alone² *adv* **1** if you do something difficult alone you do it on your own 單獨地, 獨自地: *Brian was left to put up the tent alone.* 剩下布萊恩一個人獨自搭帳篷。**2 go it alone** to start working or living on your own, especially after working or living with other people 單獨行動, 獨自幹: *After years of working for a big company I decided to go it alone.* 在一家大公司工作多年後, 我決定自己幹。**3 leave/let sb alone** to stop annoying or interrupting someone 不打擾某人, 別干涉某人: *Go away and leave me alone, will you?* 走開, 不要煩我, 好嗎? **4 leave/let sth alone** to stop touching an object or changing something 不要碰/動某物: *Leave that vase alone or you'll break it!* 不要動那花瓶, 小心打破它! **5 stand alone** if an object or building stands alone it is not near other buildings or objects 孤立, 獨處: *I remember my grandparent's house stood alone at the end of the street.* 我記得祖父[母]的房子孤單地佇立在街的盡頭。

1 1 **a·long¹** /əˋlɔŋ; əˈlɒŋ/ *adv* **1** if someone or something moves along, they move forward 向前: *I was driving along, thinking about Christmas.* 我一邊開車, 一邊想着聖誕節。| *He showed me the notes he had made as we went along.* 我們往前走着, 他把他的筆記拿給我看。**2 go/come/be along** to go or come to the place where something is happening, someone is waiting etc 前去/跟來/一起: *We're having a few drinks in the bar – you're welcome to come along.* 我們在酒吧裡喝幾杯, 歡迎你也一起來。| **be along in a minute** (=arrive soon) 馬上到 *There should be another bus along in a minute.* 另一輛公共汽車馬上會來。**3 go/come/tag along** to go or come with someone somewhere 一起去/來/跟隨着: *"I'm just out for a walk." "Is it alright if Sharon and I come along too?"* "我想出去走走。" "我和莎倫跟你一起去好嗎?" **4 take/bring sb along** to take or bring someone with you somewhere 帶某人一起去/來: *Mandy had brought some of her art-school friends along.* 曼迪帶了幾個她藝校的朋友來。**5 come/go/get along** to improve, develop, or make progress in a particular way 進展, 發展; 進步: **come along fine/nicely/well etc** *"How's she doing after her operation?" "Oh, she's coming along fine."* "她做完手術後怎麼樣?" "噢, 她情況良好。" | *How are things coming along at work?* 工作情況進展如何? **6 along with** together with 與...一起: *Robertson was murdered along with three RUC men near Armagh.* 羅伯遜和三個北愛爾蘭皇家警察在阿爾馬附近被殺害。

a·long² *prep* **1** if someone or something moves or looks along something, they move or look from one end of it to the other 沿着: *We're driving along Follyfoot Road.* 我們沿着福萊福特路行駛。| *The conductor came hurrying along the corridor.* 列車員沿着通道急匆匆地走過來。| *She glanced anxiously along the line of faces.* 她不安地掃視着這一排面孔。**2** something that is along something else goes down its whole length 沿着...的邊緣, 沿着...之傍: *They've put up a fence along Church Lane.* 他們沿着教堂路搭起了籬笆。| *a big crate with some strips of wood along the top* 頂端四週有一些木條的大貨箱 | *We found brambles and wild strawberries growing along the disused railway.* 我們發現廢棄的鐵路兩旁長滿了黑莓和野草莓。**3** if something is along a passage, wall etc, you can find it at some point there or it has been placed there 在沿...的某處: **just along** (=a short distance from a particular place) 在不遠處 *The bathroom is just along the corridor from my room.* 浴室就在離我房間不遠的走廊上。| *a waiting room with a bench along one wall* 靠牆有一條長櫈的候診[車]室

a·long·side /əˋlɔŋˋsaɪd; əˌlɒŋˈsaɪd/ *adv, prep* **1** next to or along the side of something 靠着, 沿...一側: *boats moored alongside each other* 並排停泊在一起的船隻 — see picture on page A1 參見 A1 頁圖 **2** if different types of things, ideas etc are used or exist alongside each other, they are used together or exist at the same time 並存的, 在一起的: *The teacher advised us to use these two course books alongside each other.* 老師建議我們同時用這兩本教科書。

a·loof /əˋluf; əˈluːf/ *adj* deliberately staying away from or not talking to other people, especially because you think you are better than they are 冷漠的; 疏遠的: **remain/keep/hold yourself aloof** *She preferred to remain distant and aloof.* 她喜歡離羣索居。—**aloofly** *adv* —**aloofness** *n* [U]

a·loud /əˋlaud; əˈlaʊd/ *adv* **1** if you say something aloud you say it in your normal voice 出聲地: *Joanne, would you read the poem aloud for us?* 喬安妮, 給我們朗讀一下這首詩好嗎? **2** in a loud voice 大聲地, 高聲地: *The pain made him cry aloud.* 他痛得大叫。

al·pac·a /ælˋpækə; ælˈpækə/ *n* **1** [C] an animal from Peru that looks like a LLAMA〔祕魯產的〕羊駝 **2** [U] the cloth made from the wool of an alpaca 羊駝呢絨

al·pha /ˋælfə; ˈælfə/ *n* [C usually singular 一般用單數] **1** the first letter of the Greek alphabet 希臘字母表中的第一個字母 **2 the alpha and omega a)** the beginning and the end of something 首尾, 始終 **b)** used to say that something is the best or most important kind of something 最好 [最優秀] 的東西; 最重要的部分

al·pha·bet /ˋælfəˌbɛt; ˈælfəbet/ *n* [C] a set of letters, arranged in a particular order, used in writing language 字母表: *the Cyrillic alphabet* 西里爾字母表

al·pha·bet·i·cal /ˌælfəˋbɛtɪkḷ; ˌælfəˈbetɪkəl◂/ also 又作

al·pha·bet·ic /ˌælfəˋbɛtɪk; ˌælfəˈbetɪk◂/ *adj* relating to the alphabet 字母表的; 按照字母順序的: **in alphabetical order** *The dictionary is arranged in alphabetical order.* 這本詞典是按字母順序編排的。—**alphabetically** /-klɪ; -kli/ *adv* —see graph at 參見 ORDER[1] 圖表

al·pha·nu·mer·ic /ˌælfənuˋmɛrɪk; ˌælfənjuːˈmerɪk◂/ *adj* using letters and numbers 字母數字(混合)的; 文數(式)的: *an alphanumeric code* 字母數字(混合)代碼

al·pine /ˋælpaɪn; ˈælpaɪn/ *adj* **1** related to the Alps 阿爾卑斯山脈的; 高山的 **2** alpine plants grow near the top of a mountain where trees cannot grow〔植物〕高山生長的

1 **al·read·y** /ɔlˋrɛdɪ; ɔːlˈredi/ *adv* **1** by or before now, or
1 before a particular time 已經〔表示在此之前或某個特定時間之前〕: *The design of the new house is similar to those that have already been built.* 新房子的設計與已建好的那些很類似。| *as I have already mentioned* 正如我已經提到的 **2** used to say that something has been done before and does not need to be done again 已做過: *She asked me to read this chapter, but I've already done it.* 她要我讀一下這一章, 但我已經讀過了。| *"Do you want a coffee?" "No, I've already got one thanks."* "要來杯咖啡嗎?" "不, 謝謝, 我已經有一杯了。" **3** used to say that something has happened too soon or before the expected time 比預期早: *Are you leaving already?* 你這麼早就要走嗎? | *I've forgotten already!* 我竟然已經忘了! | *Is it 5 o'clock already?* 現在已經五點了嗎? **4** used to say that a situation, especially a bad one, now exists and it might get worse, greater, etc 已經〔表示某種情況(尤指不好的情況)已經存在, 而且可能會進一步惡化〕: *The building's already costing us far too much money as it is.* 事實上, 這幢樓已經花費我們太多的錢。—see 見 JUST (USAGE), STILL (USAGE)

al·right /ˌɔlˋraɪt; ˌɔːlˈraɪt/ *adj, adv* another spelling of ALL RIGHT that many people think is incorrect〔all right 的另一種拼法, 但許多人認為是錯的〕

Al·sa·tian /ælˋseʃən; ælˈseɪʃən/ *n* [C] *especially BrE* a large dog used especially by police or to guard houses【尤英】阿爾薩斯狼狗, 德國牧羊犬; GERMAN SHEPHERD *especially AmE*【尤美】—see picture at 參見 DOG[1] 圖

1 **al·so** /ˋɔlso; ˈɔːlsəʊ/ *adv* **1** in addition to something else
1 you have mentioned; as well as 而且, 除此之外, 還: *She owns several houses in Leeds and also has business interests in Manchester.* 她不但在利茲擁有幾座房產, 在曼徹斯特還持有商業股權。| *I'll take the car because it's a long walk from the station; also the forecast is for rain.* 我會坐汽車, 因為從火車站要走很遠的路, 而且天氣預報說有雨。| *We can supply samples and there are other laboratories that can be consulted also.* 我們可以提供樣品, 並且還有其他實驗室可供諮詢。| **not only... but also...** *The report has not only attracted much attention but also some sharp criticism.* 報告不僅吸引了很多關注, 也惹來了一些尖銳的批評。**2** used when saying that the same thing is true about another person or thing 也, 同樣: *My girlfriend was also called Helen.* 我的女朋友也叫海倫。—see 見 MOREOVER (USAGE)

USAGE NOTE 用法說明: ALSO

WORD CHOICE 詞語辨析: **also, too, as well, either, neither**

When you want to say that something exists or happens in addition to something else, **too** and **as well** are more common than **also** in informal and spoken English. In a scientific report you might see 在非正式場合或口語中, 補充說明某物也存在或某事也發生時, 一般用 too 和 as well, 而不用 also。在科學報告中也許可以看到: *The acid also reacts with the coating.* 酸也與塗層產生反應。Or it can be used as part of a more formal request. also 也可用於比較正式的要求: *Could you also type this please?* 你能把這個也打一下嗎? In spoken English, **as well** is very common. 在英語口語中, as well 較常用: *Can you come too/as well?* 你也能來嗎? | *I was so busy I missed lunch and dinner as well.* 我太忙了, 錯過午餐又誤了晚餐。

If the verb is negative, you use **either**. 如動詞是否定形式, 用 either: *"I don't like grammar." "I don't like it either."* "我不喜歡語法。" "我也不喜歡。" (NOT *I don't like it too* or *I don't also like it,* though *I also don't like it* is possible, but more formal).〔不用 I don't like it too 或 I don't also like it, 但可以說 I also don't like it, 不過比較正式〕In informal English people usually say **not ... either** rather than **neither** 在非正式文體中, 人們一般用 not ... either 而不用 neither: *She won't come with me or with Grandpa either.* 她既不肯和我一起來, 也不肯和爺爺一起來。(If here you said: *She will neither come with me nor with Grandpa,* it would sound very formal and unnatural.)〔如果說: She will neither come with me nor with Grandpa, 聽起來太正式, 不自然。〕

GRAMMAR 語法

Also usually comes after the first auxiliary or modal verb and before the main verb. also 一般用在第一個助動詞或情態動詞之後, 在主要動詞之前: *The school also has a gymnasium* (NOT usually 一般不用 *The school has also a gymnasium*). 這所學校也有個體育館。| *He can also sing a little* (NOT usually 一般不用 *... also can*). 他也會唱一點兒。| *Many were bringing up children and also working.* 許多人既要撫養孩子又要工作。

Also usually follows the verb *to be* where it is used alone as a main verb. 動詞 to be 單獨作為主要動詞用時, also 通常跟在其後: *Osaka is also worth a visit.* 大阪也值得一遊。**Also** is not usual at the end of a sentence, where **too** and **as well** are common. 句末一般不用 also, 而用 too 和 as well。

also-ran /ˈ·· ·/ *n* [C] someone who has failed to win a competition or election〔比賽或選舉的〕失敗者, 落選者

al·tar /ˋɔltɚ; ˈɔːltə/ *n* [C] **1** a table or raised surface that is the centre of many religious ceremonies, especially in Christianity〔尤指基督教教堂中的〕祭壇, 聖臺: *the candles on the altar* 聖臺上的蠟燭 **2** the part of a church, often at the front, where the priest or minister stands〔牧師站立的〕講壇

altar boy /ˈ·· ·/ *n* [C] a boy who helps a Catholic priest during the church service 祭壇助手

al·tar·piece /ˋɔltɚˌpis; ˈɔːltəpiːs/ *n* [C] a painting or SCULPTURE (2) behind an altar 在祭壇後的繪畫或雕刻

al·ter /ˋɔltɚ; ˈɔːltə/ *v* **1** [I,T] to change or make someone 3
or something change 使變化, 改變: *Her face hadn't altered much over the years.* 過了這麼多年, 她的容貌並 3
沒有多大改變。| **alter sth** *Nothing can alter the fact that the refugees are our responsibility.* 沒有任何事情可以改變難民是我們的責任這個事實。**2** [T] to make a piece of clothing longer, wider etc 使改動, 更改〔把衣服加長、加寬等〕: *You'll have to have the dress altered for the wedding.* 你得請人把裙子改一下, 好在婚禮時穿。**3** [T] *AmE* to take away the sexual organs of a male cat or dog【美】閹割〔貓或狗〕

al·ter·a·tion /ˌɔltəˋreʃən; ˌɔːltəˈreɪʃən/ *n* [C] a small change that makes someone or something slightly different 變動, 改動: *Have you noticed any alteration in the patient's behaviour?* 你注意到病人的行為有甚麼變化嗎? | **to make alterations** *I'm having alterations made to the suit.* 我要請人把我的套裝改一下。| **minor alterations** *Your paper is fine except for some minor alterations I've suggested.* 除了我建議的少許改動以外, 你的論文寫得不錯。

al·ter·ca·tion /ˌɔltɚˋkeʃən; ˌɔːltəˈkeɪʃən/ *n* [C,U] *formal* a short but usually noisy argument【正式】爭辯, 爭吵, 吵嚷

al·ter e·go /ˋæltɚ ˋigo; ˌæltər ˈiːgəʊ/ *n* [C] **1** another

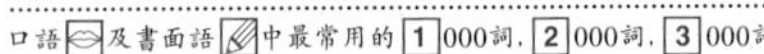

part of your character that is very different from your usual character, or a person in a film, book etc who shows part of the director or writer's character 個性的另一面；化身〔電影和書中反映出導演或作者某些性格特點的人物〕: *Mickey Mouse was Walt Disney's alter ego.* 米奇老鼠反映了華特·迪士尼性格的另一面。**2** someone who you trust who thinks about things in the same way as you do 至交, 知己, 密友

al·ter·nate¹ /ˋɔltɚˏnɪt; ɔːlˈtɜːnə̩t/ *adj* [usually before noun 一般用於名詞前] **1** two alternate actions, situations, or states happen one after the other in a repeated pattern 輪流的, 交替的: *walls painted with alternate strips of yellow and green* 塗有黃綠相間彩條的牆壁 | *alternate rain and sunshine* 時雨時晴 **2** *especially AmE* used instead of the one that was intended to be used; ALTERNATIVE¹ (1)【尤美】可替代的, 供選擇的: *We have to have an alternate plan in case it rains.* 我們必須有一個替代計劃, 以防下雨。**3** happening or doing something on one of every two days 間隔的: *He works alternate days.* 他隔天工作。| **alternate Mondays/weekends etc** *She visits her parents on alternate weekends.* 她隔個週末去看望父母。

al·ter·nate² /ˋɔltɚˏnet; ˈɔːltəneɪt/ *v* [I,T] if two things alternate or you alternate them, they happen one after the other in a repeated pattern (使) 輪流, 交替: **[+between]** *Her emotions alternated between outrage and sympathy.* 她時而表現出憤怒, 時而又流露出同情。| **alternate sth with sth** *We tried to alternate periods of work with sleep.* 我們盡量讓工作和睡覺交替進行。—**alternation** /ˏɔltɚˋneʃən; ˏɔːltəˈneɪʃən/ *n* [C,U]

al·ter·nat·ing cur·rent /ˏ····ˈ··/ *n* [U] a flow of electricity that regularly changes direction at a very fast rate 交流電 —compare 比較 DIRECT CURRENT

2 2 **al·ter·na·tive¹** /ɔlˋtɝnətɪv; ɔːlˈtɜːnətɪv/ *adj* **1** [only before noun 僅用於名詞前] an alternative idea, plan etc is one that can be used instead of another one 可替代的; 另外的; 兩者擇一的: *There doesn't seem to be an alternative option.* 似乎沒有另一個選擇。**2** [only before noun 僅用於名詞前] an alternative system or solution is considered less damaging or more effective than the old one 可取代〔舊有〕的: *alternative sources of energy* 替代能源 —see also 另見 ALTERNATIVE MEDICINE **3** not based on or believing in the established social or moral standards 另類的, 非正統的: *an alternative lifestyle* 另類的生活方式 | *alternative theatre* 非正統戲劇 —**alternatively** *adv*: *We could walk or alternatively we could go in Ted's car.* 我們可以走路去, 也可以搭特德的車去。

2 3 **alternative²** *n* [C] something that you can choose to do or use instead of something else 可供選擇的事物: *Check out the alternatives before deciding whether to go to a nearby college.* 在決定是否去一所附近的大學以前, 最好查一下有沒有其他可以選擇的學校。| **[+to]** *a viable alternative to the present system of welfare benefits* 可代替現有福利體制的一個切實可行的方案 | **have no alternative** (=used to say that you feel you must do something) 別無選擇 *I had no alternative but to report him to the police.* 除了向警察舉報他, 我別無選擇。| **there's no alternative** *I'm sorry, there's no alternative but to sell the car.* 對不起, 我別無選擇, 只好賣汽車。

alternative medi·cine /ˏ·ˏ···ˈ··/ *n* [U] one of the ways of treating illnesses that is not based on Western scientific methods 非傳統醫學, 非正統療法: *Homeopathy is a popular form of alternative medicine.* 順勢療法是一種流行的非正統療法。

al·ter·na·tor /ˋɔltɚˏnetɚ; ˈɔːltəneɪtə/ *n* [C] an electric GENERATOR for producing ALTERNATING CURRENT 交流發電機 —see picture at 參見 ENGINE 圖

1 1 **al·though** /ɔlˋðo; ɔːlˈðəʊ/ *conj* **1** in spite of the fact that; THOUGH (1) 雖然, 儘管: *Although she joined the company only a year ago, she's already been promoted twice.* 雖然她一年前才加入公司, 但是已經兩次升職。| *Although the car is old it still runs well.* 雖然車很舊, 但跑起來仍然不錯。**2** but; HOWEVER 但是, 然而: *I don't really enjoy sports, although I did watch the game.* 實際上我不太喜歡體育, 但我的確看過這場比賽。| *I can see his point, although, I have to say, I think he's wrong.* 我能理解他的觀點, 但我必須說, 我認為他的觀點是錯誤的。

al·ti·me·ter /ælˋtɪmətɚ; ˈæltɪˏmiːtə/ *n* [C] an instrument used in aircraft that tells you how high you are 高度計[表]

al·ti·tude /ˋæltəˏtud; ˈæltə̩tjuːd/ *n* **1** [C] the height of an object or place above the sea 海拔, 高度: *The plane was flying at an altitude of 30,000 feet.* 這架飛機在三萬英尺的高空飛行。**2 high/low altitudes** a high or low level above the sea 海拔高/低的地方: *At high altitudes it is difficult to get enough oxygen.* 在海拔很高的地方很難得到足夠的氧氣。—compare 比較 ELEVATION¹ (1)

al·to /ˋælto; ˈæltəʊ/ *n* [C] **1** a woman with a low singing voice 女低音（歌手）**2** [singular] the part of a piece of music that this person sings 中音部

al·to·geth·er¹ /ˏɔltəˋgɛðɚ; ˏɔːltəˈgeðə◂/ *adv* **1** a word meaning completely or thoroughly that is used to emphasize what you are saying 全然, 完全〔用於強調所說的內容〕: *It seems to have vanished altogether.* 它似乎完全消失了。| *Eventually they chose an altogether different design.* 最終他們選擇了一款截然不同的設計。| *How this is to be achieved is altogether a different matter.* 怎樣完成這個目標完全是另一回事。| **not altogether** *I'm not altogether sure if I'd want you as a wife!* 我沒有十足把握自己會選你做妻子! | *He did not altogether understand.* 他不完全理解。**2** used to make a final statement about several things you have just said 總的說來, 總而言之: *The hotel was nice; the weather was hot; the beaches were beautiful. Altogether I'd say it was a great vacation.* 賓館很舒適, 天氣很暖和, 海灘很美麗。總的來講, 我得說這個假期很愉快。**3** used when you are stating a total amount 總計: *There were five people altogether.* 總共有五個人。| *How much do I owe you altogether?* 我總共欠你多少錢?

altogether² *n* **in the altogether** *BrE* without any clothes on; NUDE【英】赤身露體

al·tru·is·m /ˋæltruˏɪzəm; ˈæltru-ɪzəm/ *n* [U] the practice of thinking of the needs and desires of other people instead of your own 利他主義, 無私 —**altruist** *n* [C]

al·tru·is·tic /ˏæltruˋɪstɪk; ˏæltruˈɪstɪk◂/ *adj* altruistic behaviour shows that you care about others more than you care for yourself 利他主義的, 關心他人勝過自己的: *Were his motives completely altruistic?* 他的動機是完全無私的嗎? —**altruistically** /-klɪ; -kli/ *adv*

al·um /ˋæləm; ˈæləm/ *n* [C+of] *AmE spoken* a former student of a school, college, university etc【美口】校友

al·u·min·i·um /ˏæljəˋmɪnɪəm; ˏæljʊˈmɪniəm◂/ *BrE*【英】**a·lu·min·um** *AmE*【美】/əˋlumɪnəm; əˈluːmə̩nəm/ *n* [U] a silver-white metal that is an ELEMENT (=simple substance) and is light and easily made into different shapes 鋁

aluminium foil /ˏ·····ˈ·/ *n* [U] a very thin sheet of shiny metal that you wrap around food to protect it; TINFOIL〔用於包食物的〕鋁箔, 錫箔紙

a·lum·na /əˋlʌmnə; əˈlʌmnə/ *n plural* **alumnae** /-ni; -niː/ [C] *formal especially AmE* a woman who is a former student of a school, college, or university【正式, 尤美】女校友

a·lum·ni /əˋlʌmnaɪ; əˈlʌmnaɪ/ *n* [plural] *AmE* the former students of a school, college, or university【美】校友: *Berkeley alumni* 伯克利大學的校友 | *the alumni association* 校友會

a·lum·nus /əˋlʌmnəs; əˈlʌmnəs/ *n* [C] *formal especially AmE* a former student of a school, college, or university【正式, 尤美】校友

al·ve·o·lar /ælˋviəlɚ; ˏælviˈəʊlə◂/ *n* [C] *technical* a CONSONANT sound such as t or d made by putting the end of the tongue at the top of the mouth behind the upper front teeth【術語】齒齦音〈如 t 或 d 等輔音〉—**alveolar** *adj*

A

al·ways /ˋɔlwez; ˈɔːlwɨz/ *adv* **1** all the time, at all times, on every occasion 總是, 每次都: *Always lock your bicycle to something secure.* 每次都把腳踏車鎖在某個固定物體上。| *Tea is always served at 5 o'clock.* 茶點總是五點鐘提供的。| *She had always assumed that Gabriel was a girl's name.* 她一直認為加布里埃爾是個女孩名字。| *Anne had always been pretty.* 安妮過去總是漂漂亮亮的。| *He wasn't always a butler.* (=he had other jobs at other times in his life) 他並不一直是當管家的。—see picture at 參見 FREQUENCY 圖 **2** for as long as you can remember or for a very long time 一直, 長久以來: *I've always wanted to go to Paris.* 我一直都想去巴黎。**3** if you say that you will always do something, you mean that you will do it forever 永遠: *I'll always remember that day.* 我會永遠記住那一天。| *He said he would love me always.* 他說他會永遠愛我。**4** if someone is always doing something, or if something always happens, it happens often, especially in an annoying way 沒完沒了地, 老是: *That wretched car is always breaking down!* 那輛破汽車老是拋錨! | *She's always flirting with him.* 她老是跟他調情。**5 you could always.../there is always...** *spoken* used to make a polite suggestion【口】你隨時可以...: *You could always try ringing her again.* 你可以隨時試着再給她打個電話。| *If you can't get it locally, there's always mail order.* 如果你在當地買不到, 總可以郵購。

USAGE NOTE 用法說明: ALWAYS

GRAMMAR 語法

Always usually comes after the first auxiliary or modal verb and before the main verb. always 通常放在第一個助動詞或情態動詞之後、主要動詞之前: *He always wanted/had a room of his own* (NOT 不用 *He had/wanted always a room of his own*). 他一直想要/有一間屬於自己的房間。| *He had always lived there* (*had* is auxiliary here). 他一直住在那兒〔had 在這裡是助動詞〕。| *You should always be careful walking alone at night* (NOT usually 一般不用 *should be always careful*). 晚上一個人走路你時時都要小心。

Always usually follows the verb *to be* where it is used alone as a main verb. 動詞 to be 單獨作為主要動詞用時, always 通常放在其後: *I am always hungry* (NOT 不用 *I always am hungry*). 我老覺得餓。

SPELLING 拼法

Remember it is **always** 記住其拼法是 always (NOT 不是 *allways* or 或 *all ways*).

AM /ˋe ˋɛm; ˌeɪ ˈem/ *n* [U] amplitude modulation; a system for broadcasting radio programmes that is not as clear as FM〔廣播〕調幅

am¹ /əm; m; *strong* 強讀 æm; æm/ *v* the first person singular of the present tense of the verb to BE〔動詞 be 的第一人稱單數現在式〕

am², AM /ˋe ˋɛm; ˌeɪ ˈem/ ante meridiem; used when talking about times that are after MIDNIGHT but before MIDDAY 午前, 上午: *I start work at 9 am.* 我上午九時開始工作。—see also 另見 PM

a·mal·gam /əˋmælgəm; əˈmælgəm/ *n* **1** [C] *formal* a mixture or combination of different things or substances【正式】混合物: [+of] *Her work is a strange amalgam of different musical styles.* 她的作品是各種音樂風格的奇特混合。**2** [C,U] *technical* a mixture of metals, used to fill holes in teeth【術語】〔補牙用的〕汞合金; 汞齊

a·mal·gam·ate /əˋmælgəˌmet; əˈmælgəmeɪt/ *v* [I+with,T] if two businesses or groups amalgamate, or if one business or group amalgamates with another, they join to form a bigger organization (使)〔公司或集團等〕聯合, (使)合併 —**amalgamation** /əˌmælgəˋmeʃən; əˌmælgəˈmeɪʃən/ *n* [C,U]

a·man·u·en·sis /əˌmænjuˋɛnsɪs; əˌmænjuˈensɨs/ *n* [C] *formal* someone whose job is to write down what someone else says or copy what they have written【正式】記錄員, 謄寫員, 文書

a·mass /əˋmæs; əˈmæs/ *v* [T] to gradually collect a large amount of money, knowledge, or information 積聚, 積累, 大量收集: *For twenty-five years Darwin amassed evidence to support his theories.* 達爾文用了二十五年時間收集大量的證據來支持自己的理論。

am·a·teur¹ /ˋæməˌtʃur; ˈæmətə/ *adj* **1** not doing something as your job, but only for pleasure or interest 業餘(愛好)的, 非職業的: *an amateur golfer* 業餘高爾夫球員 | *an amateur orchestra* 業餘管弦樂隊 **2** amateurish 外行的, 生手的

amateur² *n* [C] someone who does an activity for pleasure or interest, not as a job 業餘愛好者: *a gifted amateur* 有才華的業餘愛好者 —compare 比較 PROFESSIONAL² (1)

amateur dra·mat·ics /ˌ... ·ˋ··/ *n* [U] *BrE* the activity of producing or acting in plays by people who do it for pleasure and not as a job【英】業餘演劇活動; 業餘戲劇表演

am·a·teur·ish /ˌæməˋtɝɪʃ; ˈæmətərɪʃ/ *adj* not skilfully done or made 不熟練的, 外行的: *His paintings are amateurish.* 他的繪畫作品還不成熟。—**amateurishly** *adv* —**amateurishness** *n* [U]

am·a·teur·is·m /ˋæməˌtʃurɪzəm; ˈæmətərɨzəm/ *n* [U] the belief that enjoying a sport or other activity is more important than earning money from it 業餘愛好主義〔認為享受體育運動或其他活動的樂趣比從中掙錢更為重要〕

am·a·to·ry /ˋæməˌtɔrɪ; ˈæmətəri/ *adj literary* expressing sexual or romantic love【文】愛情的; 色情的

a·maze /əˋmez; əˈmeɪz/ *v* [T] to make someone very surprised 使大為驚奇, 使驚愕: *Dave amazed his friends by suddenly getting married.* 戴夫突然間結婚, 令朋友們非常吃驚。| *Their loyalty never ceases to amaze me.* 他們的忠誠一直令我驚嘆。

a·mazed /əˋmezd; əˈmeɪzd/ *adj* **be amazed** extremely surprised 感到驚奇, 驚訝: [+(that)] *I'm amazed you've never heard of Jeremy Bentham.* 你居然從未聽說過邊沁〔英國 19 世紀功利主義哲學家〕, 真讓我吃驚。| [+at] *We were amazed at his rapid recovery.* 我們對他這麼快就康復感到驚奇。| **amazed to see/hear/find etc** *Visitors are often amazed to discover how little the town has changed.* 旅遊者經常會驚奇地發現這個小城幾乎沒有甚麼變化。

a·maze·ment /əˋmezmənt; əˈmeɪzmənt/ *n* [U] a feeling of great surprise 吃驚, 驚奇: **in amazement** *Ralph gasped in amazement.* 拉爾夫吃驚得倒抽了一口氣。| **to my amazement** *To my amazement she came up and shook my hand.* 她竟然走過來和我握手, 令我吃了一驚。

a·maz·ing /əˋmezɪŋ; əˈmeɪzɪŋ/ *adj* **1** extremely good, especially in a surprising and unexpected way 驚人的; 了不起的: *He's an amazing player to watch.* 看他比賽那才叫精彩呢。| *an amazing bargain* 令人驚喜的廉價貨 **2** so surprising that it is hard to believe 令人驚訝的, 讓人難以相信的: *amazing stories of strange happenings during Geller's performances* 有關蓋勒表演中出現各種怪事的令人稱奇的傳說 —**amazingly** *adv*: *an amazingly generous offer* 極慷慨的出價

am·a·zon /ˋæməˌzɑn; ˈæməzən/ *n* [C] a tall strong woman 高大而強壯的女人; 悍婦 —**amazonian** /ˌæməˋzonɪən; ˌæməˈzəʊniən◂/ *adj*

am·bas·sa·dor /æmˋbæsədɚ; æmˈbæsədə/ *n* [C] an important official who represents his or her government in a foreign country 大使 —**ambassadorial** /æmˌbæsəˋdɔrɪəl; æmˌbæsəˈdɔːriəl/ *adj* —**ambassadorship** /æmˋbæsədɚˌʃɪp; æmˈbæsədəʃɪp/ *n* [C,U]

am·bas·sa·dress /æmˋbæsədrɪs; æmˈbæsədrɨs/ *n* [C] the wife of an ambassador 大使夫人

am·ber /ˋæmbɚ; ˈæmbə/ *n* [U] **1** a yellowish brown colour 琥珀色 **2** a yellowish brown substance used to make jewellery 琥珀 —**amber** *adj*

A

ambi- /æmbɪ; æmbɪ/ *prefix* both; double 兩個, 雙: *ambidextrous* (=using both hands equally well) 雙手都很靈巧的

am·bi·ance /ˋæmbɪəns; ˈæmbiəns/ *n* [singular,U] another spelling of AMBIENCE ambience 的另一種拼法

am·bi·dex·trous /ˏæmbəˋdɛkstrəs; ˌæmbɪˈdekstrəs◂/ *adj* able to use either hand with equal skill 雙手都能靈巧運用的

am·bi·ence /ˋæmbɪəns; ˈæmbiəns/ *n* [singular,U] the way a place makes you feel 氣氛, 情調, 環境: *a restaurant with a friendly ambience* 氣氛宜人的餐廳

am·bi·ent /ˋæmbɪənt; ˈæmbiənt/ *adj technical*【術語】 **ambient temperature/pressure** the temperature etc of the surrounding area 周圍的溫度/壓力

ambient music /ˏ‥ ˈ‥/ *n* [U] slow electronic music that you listen to when you want to relax 環境音樂

am·big·u·ous /æmˋbɪgjuəs; æmˈbɪgjuəs/ *adj* **1** having more than one meaning, so that it is not clear which is intended 歧義的; 含糊的, 不明確的: *an ambiguous sentence* 歧義句 **2** difficult to understand 難以理解的: *His role in the affair is ambiguous.* 他在事件中的角色並不明確。—**ambiguously** *adv* —**ambiguity** /ˏæmbɪˋgjuətɪ; ˌæmbɪ̥ˈgjuːɪ̥ti/ *n* [C,U]: *Her speech was full of ambiguities and contradictions.* 她的講話含糊其辭, 自相矛盾。

am·bit /ˋæmbɪt; ˈæmbɪ̥t/ *n* [singular] *formal* the range or limit of something【正式】界限, 範圍: *within the ambit of the law* 在法律允許的範圍內

am·bi·tion /æmˋbɪʃən; æmˈbɪʃən/ *n* **1** [U] determination to be successful, rich, powerful etc 抱負, 雄心; 野心: *Your problem is you have no ambition.* 你的問題在於胸無大志。**2** [C] a strong desire to achieve something 願望, 志向: *My ambition is to become a pilot.* 我的願望是當一名飛行員。

am·bi·tious /æmˋbɪʃəs; æmˈbɪʃəs/ *adj* **1** determined to be successful, rich, powerful etc 有抱負的, 有雄心大志的; 野心勃勃的: *an ambitious and hard-working junior manager* 雄心勃勃、工作勤奮的初級(部門)經理 | **be ambitious for sb** (=want them to be very successful) 希望某人成功 *Mothers are often highly ambitious for their children.* 做母親的往往都希望孩子事業有成。**2** an ambitious plan, idea etc shows a desire to do something good but difficult 雄心勃勃的, 需要極大努力或才幹才能完成的: *one of the most ambitious engineering projects of modern times* 現代難度最大的工程項目之一 —**ambitiously** *adv* —**ambitiousness** *n* [U]

am·biv·a·lent /æmˋbɪvələnt; æmˈbɪvələnt/ *adj* not sure whether you want or like something or not〔心情〕矛盾的: *Her feelings about getting married are distinctly ambivalent.* 她顯然對是否要結婚感到矛盾。—**ambivalence** *n* [U] —**ambivalently** *adv*

am·ble /ˋæmbḷ; ˈæmbəl/ *v* [I always+adv/prep] to walk in a slow relaxed way 漫步: [**+along/across etc**] *The old man came out and ambled over for a chat.* 老人出來了, 從容地走過去聊天。—**amble** *n* [singular]

am·bro·si·a /æmˋbroʒə; æmˈbrəʊziə/ *n* [U] food or drink that tastes or smells extremely good 珍饈美味

3 **am·bu·lance** /ˋæmbjələns; ˈæmbjɪ̥ləns/ *n* [C] a special vehicle used for taking people who are ill or injured to hospital 救護車

am·bu·lance·man /ˋæmbjələnsˏmæn; ˈæmjɪ̥lənsmæn/ *n plural* **ambulancemen** /-ˏmɛn; -men/ [C] *BrE* a man whose job is to drive an ambulance or look after the person being taken to hospital【英】救護車男司機; 男救護員

am·bu·lance·wom·an /ˋæmbjələnsˏwumən; ˈæmjɪ̥lənsˌwʊmən/ *n plural* **ambulancewomen** /-ˏwɪmɪn; -ˌwɪmɪn/ [C] *BrE* a woman whose job is to drive an ambulance or look after the person being taken to hospital【英】救護車女司機, 女救護員

am·bush¹ /ˋæmbuʃ; ˈæmbʊʃ/ *n* [C] a sudden attack by people who have been waiting and hiding, or the place where this happens 伏擊, 埋伏; 埋伏地點: **wait/lie in ambush** (=wait to ambush someone) 埋伏着等待襲擊某人 *Armed police lay in ambush behind the hedge.* 武裝警察埋伏在樹籬後面。

ambush² *v* [T] to attack someone from a place where you have been hiding 伏擊, 埋伏突襲

a·me·ba /əˋmibə; əˈmiːbə/ *n* [C] an American spelling of AMOEBA amoeba 的美式拼法

a·me·bic /əˋmibɪk; əˈmiːbɪk/ *adj* an American spelling of AMOEBIC amoebic 的美式拼法

a·me·li·o·rate /əˋmiljəˏret; əˈmiːliəreɪt/ *v* [T] *formal* to make something better【正式】使改善, 改進: *measures to ameliorate working conditions* 改善工作條件的舉措 —**amelioration** /əˏmiljəˋreʃən; əˌmiːliəˈreɪʃən/ *n* [U]

a·men /ˋɑˋmɛn; ɑːˈmen/ *interjection* **1** **Amen** used at the end of a prayer 阿門〔祈禱結束語, 意思是"誠心所願"〕: *Blessed be the Lord, Amen!* 感謝主, 阿門! **2** used to show that you agree or approve 同意, 贊成: *"I think we can close the meeting now." "Amen to that."* "我認為我們現在可以散會了。" "同意。"

a·men·a·ble /əˋminəbḷ; əˈmiːnəbəl/ *adj* willing to listen or to do something 易接受指導[影響]的, 順從的: [**+to**] *I'm sure they'll be amenable to rational argument.* 我確信他們是會接受合理論據的。

a·mend /əˋmɛnd; əˈmend/ *v* [T] to make small changes or improvements to a law or document 修改, 修訂〔法律或文件〕 

a·mend·ment /əˋmɛndmənt; əˈmendmənt/ *n* **1** [C,U] a written change or improvement to a law or document, or the process of doing this 修訂, 修正: [**+to**] *an amendment to the resolution* 對決議的修訂 | **table an amendment** (=say officially that you want to discuss an amendment) 提交修正案 **2** [C] one of the rights on the list of rights included in the US Constitution〔美國憲法的〕修正案

a·mends /əˋmɛndz; əˈmendz/ *n* **make amends** to say you are sorry for the harm you have caused and try to make things better 賠不是, 道歉; 補償; 補救

a·me·ni·ty /əˋmɛnətɪ; əˈmiːnɪ̥ti/ *n* [C usually plural 一般用複數] something such as a piece of equipment, shop, or park that makes it easier to live somewhere 便利設施; 娛樂[消遣]場所: *a town with all the amenities of a larger city* 擁有大城市所有便利設施的小城鎮 | **basic amenity** *simple huts with only the most basic amenities* 只具備最簡陋設施的小屋

Am·er·a·sian /ˏæməˋreʒən; ˌæməˈreɪʒən◂/ *n* [C] a word meaning someone who has one American parent and one Asian parent 美亞混血兒 —compare 比較 ASIAN-AMERICAN

A·mer·i·can¹ /əˋmɛrɪkən; əˈmerɪ̥kən/ *adj* **1** from or connected with the US 美國的: *American forces landed on the island at dawn.* 美國的軍隊拂曉時在島上登陸。| *the American writer William Boroughs* 美國作家威廉·伯勒斯 **2** *especially technical* connected with the CONTINENTS of North and South America【尤術語】美洲的: *a species found only in American rivers, especially in Brazil* 一種僅產於美洲尤其是巴西河流的物種

American² *n* [C] someone from the US 美國人

American foot·ball /ˏ‥ ˈ‥/ *n* [U] *BrE* a game played by two teams of eleven players, who carry, throw, or kick an OVAL (=egg shaped) ball【英】美式足球, 橄欖球; FOOTBALL (2) *AmE*【美】—see picture on page A22 參見 A22 頁圖

American In·di·an /ˏ‥ ˈ‥‥/ *n* [C] another name for a NATIVE AMERICAN (=someone from one of the first groups of people who lived in America) used especially about people from South America and sometimes considered offensive 美洲印第安人

A·mer·i·can·is·m /əˋmɛrəkənˏɪzəm; əˈmerɪ̥kənɪzəm/ *n* [C] a word, phrase, or sound that is typical of the English language as it is used in the US 美國英語, 美洲英語

A·mer·i·can·ize also 又作 **-ise** *BrE*【英】/əˋmɛrəkənˏaɪz; əˈmerɪkənaɪz/ *v* [T] to make something American

in character, for example a way of speaking or writing, or the way something is organized 使美國化 —**Americanization** *n* [U]: *Opponents of the burger bar said they were resisting the Americanization of our culture.* 漢堡包快餐店的競爭對手說他們正抵制我們的文化趨向美國化。

am·e·thyst /ˋæməθɪst; ˈæmɪ̈θɪ̈st/ *n* **1** [C] a valuable purple stone used in jewellery 紫水晶, 紫石英 **2** [U] a light purple colour 紫水晶色, 紫色 —**amethyst** *adj*

a·mi·a·ble /ˋemɪəbl̩; ˈeɪmiəbəl/ *adj* friendly and likeable 和藹可親的, 友好的, 親切的: *The driver was an amiable young man.* 司機是位和藹可親的年輕人。—**amiably** *adv* —**amiability** /ˌemɪəˋbɪlətɪ; ˌeɪmiəˈbɪlɪ̈ti/ *n* [U]

am·i·ca·ble /ˋæmɪkəbl̩; ˈæmɪkəbəl/ *adj* an amicable agreement, relationship etc is one in which people feel friendly towards each other and do not want to quarrel 友好的, 和睦的: *an amicable settlement that was acceptable to both sides* 雙方都能接受的友好協議 —**amicably** *adv* —**amicability** /ˌæmɪkəˋbɪlətɪ; ˌæmɪkəˈbɪlɪ̈ti/ *n* [U]

a·mid /əˋmɪd; əˈmɪd/ also 又作 **amidst** *prep* **1** happening while noisy, busy, or confused events are also happening 在…中間, 在…當中: *The dollar has fallen in value amid rumors of weakness in the US economy.* 在美國經濟不景氣的傳言聲中, 美元幣值下跌了。**2** *especially literary* among or surrounded by【尤文】在…之中; 被…所環繞: *Old gabled houses peeped out from amid the trees.* 樹叢中隱約露出一些有山形牆的老房子。

a·mid·ships /əˋmɪdˌʃɪps; əˈmɪdˌʃɪps/ *adv* in the middle part of a ship 在船中部

a·midst /əˋmɪdst; əˈmɪdst/ *prep* amid 在…當中, 在…中間

a·mi·no ac·id /əˌmino ˋæsɪd; əˌmiːnəʊ ˈæsɪ̈d/ *n* [C] one of the substances that combine to form PROTEINS 氨基酸

a·miss[1] /əˋmɪs; əˈmɪs/ *adv* **1 sth would not come/go amiss** *informal* used to say that something would be suitable or useful in a situation【非正式】某物很合適[有用]: *A cup of tea wouldn't go amiss.* 喝杯茶挺好。**2 take sth amiss** to feel upset or offended about something that someone has said or done 見怪, 對某事生氣

amiss[2] *adj* **be amiss** if something is amiss, there is a problem 有問題: *Elsa continued as if nothing was amiss.* 埃爾莎繼續下去, 就好像一切都正常。

am·i·ty /ˋæmətɪ; ˈæmɪ̈ti/ *n* [U] *formal* friendship, especially between countries【正式】〔尤指兩國之間的〕友好, 和睦: *a spirit of perfect amity* 精誠合作的精神

am·me·ter /ˋæmˌmitɚ; ˈæmɪtə/ *n* [C] a piece of equipment used to measure the strength of an electric current 安培計, 電表

am·mo /ˋæmo; ˈæməʊ/ *n* [U] *informal* ammunition【非正式】彈藥

am·mo·ni·a /əˋmonɪə; əˈməʊniə/ *n* [U] a poisonous gas or clear liquid with a strong smell 氨, 阿摩尼亞

am·mu·ni·tion /ˌæmjəˋnɪʃən; ˌæmjʊ̈ˈnɪʃən/ *n* [U] **1** bullets, shells (SHELL[1] (2)) etc that are fired from guns 彈藥 **2** information that you can use to criticize someone or win an argument against them〔攻擊他人的〕砲彈, 證據: *The oil spill was to give environmentalists powerful new ammunition against the oil companies.* 石油泄漏給環境保護主義者提供了新的強力砲彈來攻擊石油公司。

am·ne·si·a /æmˋniʒə; æmˈniːziə/ *n* [U] the medical condition of not being able to remember anything 記憶喪失, 健忘(症) —**amnesiac** /-ʒɪæk; -ziæk/ *adj* —**amnesiac** *n* [C]

am·nes·ty /ˋæmnəstɪ; ˈæmnəsti/ *n* [C] **1** an official order by a government that allows political prisoners to go free 赦免, 大赦: *an amnesty for all former terrorists* 對前恐怖分子的大赦 **2** a period of time when you can admit to doing something illegal without being punished 赦免期限〔自首可以免受處罰的期限〕: *an amnesty on illegal handguns* 非法持有槍枝的赦免期限

am·ni·o·cen·te·sis /ˌæmnɪosɛnˋtisɪs; ˌæmniəʊsenˈtiːsɪ̈s/ *n* [U] a test to see if an unborn baby has any diseases or other problems, done by taking liquid from the mother's WOMB 羊膜穿刺術〔抽取孕婦子宮羊水以檢查胎兒是否患病等的方法〕

a·moe·ba also 又作 **ameba** *AmE*【美】/əˋmibə; əˈmiːbə/ *n plural* **amoebas** or **amoebae** /-bi; -biː/ [C] a very small creature that has only one cell 變形蟲, 阿米巴

a·moe·bic also 又作 **amebic** *AmE*【美】/əˋmibɪk; əˈmiːbɪk/ *adj* connected with amoebas 變形蟲的, 阿米巴的

a·mok /əˋmɑk; əˈmɒk/ also 又作 **amuck** *adv* **run amok** to suddenly behave in a very violent and uncontrolled way 狂亂, 發狂: *'Gunman runs amok in Shopping Mall'* "持槍歹徒大鬧購物中心"

a·mong /əˋmʌŋ; əˈmʌŋ/ also 又作 **a·mongst** /əˋmʌŋst; əˈmʌŋst/ *prep* **1** in the middle of 在…當中, 為…所圍繞: *The girl quickly disappeared among the crowd.* 女孩很快消失在人羣中。| *I could hear voices coming from somewhere among the bushes.* 我能聽到灌木叢中某個地方傳來的聲音。—see picture on page A1 參見A1頁圖 —see 見 BETWEEN[1] (USAGE) **2 among friends/strangers** with people who are your friends or who you do not know 在朋友/陌生人中間: *Jim relaxed, knowing he was among friends.* 吉姆知道自己是在朋友中間, 就放鬆多了。**3** through or between 穿過; 在…中間: *We walked among the chestnut woods on the mountain slopes.* 我們在山坡上的板栗樹林裡穿行。| *She began rummaging among the books on her desk.* 她開始在桌上的書堆中翻找。**4** used to say that something such as a feeling or disease affects many people in a particular group, or that many people in a group have the same opinion 在…羣體中: *There is widespread concern among scientists about the long-term consequences of storing nuclear waste underground.* 在地下埋藏核廢料的長期後果在科學家中間引起了廣泛的關注。| *7,000 job losses among railway workers* 鐵路工人中7,000人失業 **5** used when talking about a particular person or thing in a group of people or things 在…(人員)中, 是…之一: *She was the eldest among them.* 她是他們當中年紀最大的。| *Innocent civilians were among the casualties.* 死傷者中有無辜平民。| *My grandfather had among his possessions a portrait by Matisse.* 我祖父有一幅〔法國畫家〕馬蒂斯畫的肖像畫。**6 among other** used to say that you are only mentioning one or two people or things out of a much larger group〔指在眾多人或物中只提到一兩個〕其中; 包括: **among other things** *At the meeting they discussed, among other things, recent events in Eastern Europe.* 在會議上除了其他議題外, 他們討論了東歐最近發生的事件。**7** if something is divided or shared among a group of people, each is given a part of it 在…之間分配 **8 talk/quarrel among yourselves** to talk or quarrel with other people 相互談話/爭吵: *Talk among yourselves for a while. I'll be ready soon.* 你們先談一會兒, 我馬上就準備好。

a·mor·al /eˋmɔrəl; eɪˈmɒrəl/ *adj* having no moral standards at all 毫無道德觀念的; 沒有道德的: *a completely amoral person* 毫無道德觀念的人 —**amorality** /ˌeməˋrælɪtɪ; ˌeɪmɒˈrælɪ̈ti/ *n* [U]

am·o·rous /ˋæmərəs; ˈæmərəs/ *adj* involving or expressing sexual love 求愛的; 色情的: *She resisted his amorous advances.* 她拒絕了他試圖跟她發生性關係的種種表示。—**amorously** *adv* —**amorousness** *n* [U]

a·mor·phous /əˋmɔrfəs; əˈmɔːfəs/ *adj formal* having no definite shape or features【正式】無固定形狀的, 不定形的: *an amorphous mass of twisted metal* 一堆扭曲變形的金屬 —**amorphously** *adv* —**amorphousness** *n* [U]

a·mor·tize also 又作 **-ise** *BrE*【英】/ˋæmɚˌtaɪz; əˈmɔːtaɪz/ *v* [T] *technical* to pay a debt by making regular payments【術語】分期償還〔債務〕—**amortizable** *adj*

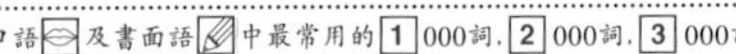

—**amortization** /ˌæmɚtəˈzeʃən; æˌmɔːtaɪˈzeɪʃən/ *n* [C, U]

a·mount¹ /əˈmaʊnt; əˈmaʊnt/ *n* [C,U] **1** a quantity of something such as time, money, or a substance 總數, 數量, 總額: **[+of]** *a considerable amount of money* 相當數額的錢 | **a small/large etc amount** *It's best to cook vegetables in a small amount of water.* 燒蔬菜時最好少放些水。**2** the level or degree to which a feeling, quality etc is present〔感情、質量等的〕程度: **[+of]** *Her case has attracted an enormous amount of public sympathy.* 她的情況得到了無數公眾的同情。| **a certain/fair amount of** (=a fairly high level of something) 相當多的 *Dina encountered a fair amount of envy among her colleagues.* 黛娜遭到了不少同事的妒嫉。**3 no amount of sth will do sth** used to say that something has no effect 毫無結果, 毫無影響: *No amount of persuasion could make her change her mind.* 怎麼勸她也無法讓她改變主意。| **any amount of sth** *BrE* (=a lot of)【英】很多 *The school has any amount of resources and equipment.* 這所學校財力雄厚, 設備齊全。

USAGE NOTE 用法說明: AMOUNT
GRAMMAR 語法
Amount is usually used with uncountable nouns, and some people think this is the only correct use. amount 一般和不可數名詞連用, 一些人認為這是唯一正確的用法: *a large amount of money/food/electricity/hard work* 大量的錢/食物/電/艱苦工作 (Note that you do not usually say a **high** or **big** amount 注意一般不用 high 或 big 修飾 amount)。With plural countable nouns it is best to use **number**. 修飾複數可數名詞最好用 number: *a large number of mistakes/people* 許多錯誤/人
However, people often use **amount** with plural countable nouns when what they are talking about is thought of as a group. 但是 amount 也經常和可數名詞的複數連用, 但意指整體概念: *We didn't expect such a large amount of people.* 我們沒有料到會有這麼多人。| *an enormous amount of problems* 一大堆問題

amount² *v*
amount to sth *phr v* [T not in progressive 不用進行式] **1** if figures, sums etc amount to a particular total, they equal that total when they are added together〔數量上〕達到, 總計: *Time lost through illness amounted to 1,357 working days.* 因疾病而損失的時間總計達到 1,357 個工作日。**2** if an attitude, remark, situation etc amounts to something, it has the same effect 等於, 意味着: *The court's decision amounts to a not guilty verdict.* 法庭的裁決等於宣判無罪。**3 not amount to much/anything/a great deal etc** to not seem important, valuable or successful 沒多大了不起[價值, 成功等]: *Her academic achievements don't amount to much.* 她在學術上的成就似乎沒有多大價值。

a·mour /əˈmʊr; əˈmʊə/ *n* [C] *literary* a sexual relationship, especially a secret one【文】偷情, 不正當的男女關係

am·our prop·re /ˌæmur ˈprɔprə; ˌæmʊə ˈprɒprə/ *n* [U] *literary* the quality of feeling respect for yourself【文】自尊心

amp /æmp; æmp/ *n* [C] **1** also 又作 **ampere** a unit for measuring electric current 安培〔電流單位〕: *a 3 amp fuse* 三安培的保險絲 **2** *informal* an AMPLIFIER【非正式】放大器, 擴音器, 揚聲器

am·per·age /ˈæmpərɪdʒ; ˈæmpərɪdʒ/ *n* [singular,U] *technical* the strength of an electrical current measured in amps【術語】安培數, 電流強度

am·pere /ˈæmpɪr; ˈæmpeə/ *n* [C] an AMP 安培

am·per·sand /ˈæmpɚsˌænd; ˈæmpəsænd/ *n* [C] the sign '&' that means 'and' 表示 and 之符號〔寫作 &〕: *Mills & Boon* 米爾斯和布恩〔出版公司名〕

am·phet·a·mine /æmˈfɛtəˌmin; æmˈfetəmiːn/ *n* [C,U] a drug that gives you a feeling of excitement and a lot of energy 苯丙胺, 安非他明〔一種興奮劑〕

am·phib·i·an /æmˈfɪbɪən; æmˈfɪbiən/ *n* [C] an animal that can live on both land and water 水陸兩棲動物

am·phib·i·ous /æmˈfɪbɪəs; æmˈfɪbiəs/ *adj* **1** able to live on both land and water 水陸兩棲的 **2 amphibious vehicle** a vehicle that is able to move on land and water 水陸兩用車輛 **3 amphibious operation/force/assault** an amphibious operation etc involves ships and land vehicles 水陸兩棲行動/部隊/攻擊

am·phi·thea·tre *especially BrE*【尤英】, **amphitheater** *AmE*【美】/ˈæmfəˌθɪətɚ; ˈæmfɪ̵ˌθɪətə/ *n* [C] a large circular building without a roof and with many rows of seats 圓形露天劇場 [競技場]

am·pho·ra /ˈæmfərə; ˈæmfərə/ *n* [C] a tall clay container for oil or wine, used in ancient times〔古代盛油或酒的〕雙耳陶罐

am·ple /ˈæmpl; ˈæmpəl/ *adj* **1** more than enough 充足的, 充裕的: *There's ample storage space in the new house.* 新房子有充足的貯藏空間。| **ample time/evidence/opportunity etc** *You will have ample opportunity to state your case later.* 以後你會有充分的機會陳述你的案子。**2 ample bosom/figure/torso etc** large in a way that is attractive or pleasant 寬闊的胸膛/豐滿的體形/魁梧的身材等 —**amply** *adv*: *Recent US history has amply demonstrated the risks of foreign intervention.* 最近的美國近代歷史已經充分證明了外國干預的危險。

am·pli·fi·er /ˈæmpləˌfaɪɚ; ˈæmplɪ̵faɪə/ *n* [C] a piece of electrical equipment that makes sound louder; AMP (2) 放大器, 擴音器, 揚聲器

am·pli·fy /ˈæmpləˌfaɪ; ˈæmplɪ̵faɪ/ *v* [T] **1** to make a sound louder, especially musical sound 放大〔聲音, 尤指音樂聲〕: *an amplified guitar* 帶有擴音設備的電結他 **2** *formal* to explain something that you have said by giving more information about it【正式】詳述, (進一步) 闡述: *Would you care to amplify that remark?* 請你把意見詳述一下好嗎? **3** *formal* to emphasize the importance of something【正式】強調〔重要性〕: *Successive reports amplified the case for privatisation.* 一個又一個的報告都強調了私有化很重要。—**amplification** /æmpləfəˈkeʃən; ˌæmplɪ̵fɪ̵ˈkeɪʃən/ *n* [U]

am·pli·tude /ˈæmpləˌtud; ˈæmplɪ̵tjuːd/ *n* [U] *technical* the distance between the middle and the top or bottom of a WAVE² (4) such as a SOUND WAVE【術語】振幅; 波幅; 幅度

am·poule *especially BrE*【尤英】also 又作 **ampule** *AmE*【美】/ˈæmpul; ˈæmpuːl/ *n* [C] a small container for medicine that will be put into someone with a special needle 安瓿〔裝注射液的小瓶〕

am·pu·tate /ˈæmpjuˌtet; ˈæmpjʊ̈teɪt/ *v* [I,T] to cut off someone's arm, leg, finger etc during a medical operation 切除, 截肢: *Two of her toes were amputated because of frostbite.* 由於凍傷, 她的兩個腳趾不得不截掉了。—**amputation** /ˌæmpjuˈteʃən; ˌæmpjʊ̈ˈteɪʃən/ *n* [C,U]

am·pu·tee /ˌæmpjuˈti; ˌæmpjʊ̈ˈtiː/ *n* [C] someone who has had an arm or a leg amputated 被截肢者

a·muck /əˈmʌk; əˈmʌk/ *adv* AMOK 狂亂, 發狂

am·u·let /ˈæmjəlɪt; ˈæmjʊ̈lət/ *n* [C] a small piece of jewellery worn to protect against bad luck, disease etc〔隨身佩戴的〕護身符, 驅邪物

a·muse /əˈmjuz; əˈmjuːz/ *v* [T] **1** to make someone laugh or smile 使開心, 逗笑: *What amused me most was the thought of Martin in a dress.* 想到馬丁穿着連衣裙我就覺得很好笑。**2** to make someone spend time in an enjoyable way without getting bored 給…提供娛樂 [消遣]: *Doing jigsaws would amuse Amy for hours on end.* 艾米會連續幾個小時津津有味地玩拼圖玩具。| **amuse yourself** *The kids amused themselves playing hide-and-seek.* 孩子們玩捉迷藏。

a·mused /əˈmjuzd; əˈmjuːzd/ *adj* **1** someone who is amused by something thinks it is funny so that they smile or laugh 被逗樂的, 感到有意思的: [+at/by] *Clare was highly amused by the little boy's antics.* 克萊爾被小男孩可笑的動作逗得很開心。| *He won't be very amused when he finds out what's happened to his garden.* 等他發現花園裡發生的情況時, 他就沒甚麼可樂的了。| *James watched the proceedings with an amused grin.* 詹姆士開心的笑着, 注視着事件的過程。**2 keep sb amused** to entertain or interest someone for a long time so that they do not get bored 使某人保持快樂的狀態: *If you could just keep them amused while I do the shopping!* 我購物的時候, 你要是能讓他們開開心心的就好了!

a·muse·ment /ə`mjuzmənt; əˈmjuːzmənt/ *n* **1** [U] the feeling you have when you think something is funny 開心, 愉悦, 樂趣: *Tom's tricks were a source of endless amusement to the other boys.* 湯姆的小戲法給其他孩子帶來無盡的樂趣。| **to sb's amusement** (=in a way that makes someone laugh or smile) 令某人發笑 *To everyone's amusement he turned up for work in a straw hat and jeans.* 可笑的是, 他戴着草帽, 穿着牛仔褲來上班。**2 amusements** [plural] special things such as machines or games that are intended to entertain people 娛樂設施; 娛樂活動: *The kids can ride on the amusements.* 那些娛樂設施可供孩子們騎在上面。**3** [U] the process of getting or providing pleasure and enjoyment 娛樂

amusement ar·cade /-ˈ·· ·,·/ *n* [C] *BrE* a place where you play games on machines by putting coins into them【英】〔有電子遊戲機等娛樂設施的〕遊樂場; 遊戲機室; VIDEO ARCADE *AmE*【美】

amusement park /-ˈ·· ,·/ *n* [C] a large park with many special machines that you can ride on, such as ROLLER-COASTERs and MERRY-GO-ROUNDs 遊樂場

a·mus·ing /ə`mjuzɪŋ; əˈmjuːzɪŋ/ *adj* funny and entertaining 引人發笑的, 好笑的, 有趣的: *I don't find his jokes at all amusing.* 我不覺得他的笑話有甚麼好笑。| **highly/vastly amusing** (=very funny) 特別有趣的 *a highly amusing film* 特別有趣的電影 —**amusingly** *adv*

1 **an** /ən; ən; *strong* 強讀 æn; æn/ *indefinite article, determiner*
1 [used when the following word begins with a vowel sound 同 a, 用於以母音開頭的單詞前] a 一個, 一隻, 一種等: *an orange* 一個橘子 | *an X-ray* 一次 X 光檢查 | *such an old house* 這樣一所舊房子 —see also 另見 A

an- /ən, æn; ən, æn/ *prefix* **1** the form used for A-[2] before a vowel sound〔用於以母音開頭的詞前, 相當於 a-[2]〕**2** not; without 無, 沒有: *anarchy* (=without government) 無政府狀態 | *anoxia* (=condition caused by lack of oxygen) 缺氧

-an /ən; ən/ *suffix* also 又作 **-ean, -ian 1** [in adjectives and nouns 構成形容詞和名詞] someone or something of, from, or connected with a particular thing, place, or person …地方的 (人或物); 與…有關的 (人或物): *an American* (=person from America) 美國人 | *the pre-Tolstoyan novel* 托爾斯泰之前的小説 **2** [in nouns 構成名詞] someone skilled in or studying a particular subject 精通 [研究]…的人: *a historian* (=someone who studies history) 歷史學家

-ana /ænə; ɑːnə/ *suffix* [in nouns 構成名詞] another form of the suffix -IANA …的匯編; …收藏品〔後綴 -iana 的另一種形式〕: *Americana* 美國史料 [文物]

an·a·bol·ic ste·roid /,ænəbɑlɪk `stɪrɔɪd; ,ænəbɒlɪk ˈstɪərɔɪd/ *n* [C] a drug that makes muscles grow quickly, sometimes used illegally by people in sport 促蛋白合成類固醇

a·nach·ro·nis·m /ə`nækrə,nɪzəm; əˈnækrənɪzəm/ *n* [C] **1** someone or something that seems to belong to the past, not the present 時代錯誤; 不合時代的人 [事物]: *The monarchy is something of an anachronism these days.* 如今君主制是一種不合時代的制度。**2** something in a play, film etc that seems wrong because it is being shown in the wrong period of time〔戲劇、電影等中的〕年代誤植 —**anachronistic** /ə,nækrə`nɪstɪk; ə,nækrəˈnɪstɪk◂/ *adj* —**anachronistically** /-klɪ; -kli/ *adv*

an·a·con·da /,ænə`kɑndə; ,ænəˈkɒndə/ *n* [C] a large South American snake 水蟒, 森蚺〔產於南美的一種大蟒蛇〕

a·nae·mi·a *especially BrE*【尤英】, **anemia** *AmE*【美】/ə`nimɪə; əˈniːmiə/ *n* [U] a medical condition in which there are too few red cells in your blood 貧血症

a·nae·mic *especially BrE*【尤英】, **anemic** *AmE*【美】/ə`nimɪk; əˈniːmɪk/ *adj* **1** suffering from anaemia 貧血的, 患貧血症的 **2** seeming weak and uninteresting 沒有活力的, 無精打采的: *an anaemic performance of King Lear*《李爾王》中有氣無力的表演 —**anaemically** /-klɪ; -kli/ *adv*

an·ae·ro·bic /,ænə`robɪk; ,ænəˈrəʊbɪk◂/ *adj technical* not needing oxygen in order to live【術語】厭氧的

an·aes·the·si·a *especially BrE*【尤英】, **anesthesia** *AmE*【美】/,ænəs`θiʒə; ,ænɪ̆sˈθiːziə/ *n* [U] **1** the use of anaesthetics in medicine 麻醉術 **2** the state of being unable to feel pain 感覺缺失, 麻木; 麻醉狀態

an·aes·thet·ic *especially BrE*【尤英】, **anesthetic** *AmE*【美】/,ænəs`θɛtɪk; ,ænɪ̆sˈθetɪk◂/ *n* [C,U] a drug that stops you feeling pain 麻醉劑: **under anaesthetic** (=using an anaesthetic) 在麻醉狀態下 *Wisdom teeth are usually removed under anaesthetic.* 拔除智齒通常要施麻醉劑。| **local anaesthetic/general anaesthetic** (=affecting a small part of your body/all of your body) 局部麻醉/全身麻醉

a·naes·the·tist *especially BrE*【尤英】, **anesthetist** *AmE*【美】/ə`nɛsθətɪst; əˈniːsθɪ̆tɪst/ *n* [C] a doctor or nurse who has been specially trained to give people anaesthetics 麻醉師

a·naes·the·tize also 又作 **-ise** *BrE*【英】, **anesthetize** *AmE*【美】/ə`nɛsθə,taɪz; əˈniːsθɪ̆taɪz/ *v* [T] to give someone an anaesthetic so that they do not feel pain 使麻醉, 給…施行麻醉

an·a·gram /`ænə,græm; ˈænəgræm/ *n* [C] a word or phrase that is made by changing the order of the letters in another word or phrase 變位詞 (組)〔改變某個詞或片語的字母順序後構成的新詞或片語〕: *'Silent' is an anagram of 'listen'.* silent 是 listen 的變位詞。

a·nal /`enl; ˈeɪnl/ *adj* **1** connected with the ANUS 肛門的 **2** showing too much concern with small details, especially in a way that annoys other people 吹毛求疵的: *Don't be so anal.* 不要這麼吹毛求疵。

an·al·ge·si·a /,ænæl`dʒiʒə; ,ænəlˈdʒiːziə/ *n* [U] *technical* the condition of being unable to feel pain while conscious【術語】痛覺缺失, 無痛覺

an·al·ge·sic /,ænæl`dʒizɪk; ,ænəlˈdʒiːzɪk◂/ *n* [C] *technical* a drug that reduces pain【術語】止痛劑, 鎮痛藥: *Aspirin is a mild analgesic.* 阿士匹靈是一種温和的鎮痛藥。—**analgesic** *adj*

a·nal·o·gous /ə`næləgəs; əˈnæləgəs/ *adj formal* similar to another situation or thing so that a comparison can be made【正式】相似的, 類似的: [**+to/with**] *Scharf's findings are analogous with our own.* 沙夫的發現和我們的類似。

an·a·logue /`ænl,ɔg; ˈænəlɒg/ *n* [C] **1 analogue clock/watch** a clock or watch that uses moving hands, not changing numbers 模擬指針式時鐘/錶 **2** *formal* something that is similar to something else in some way【正式】相似物, 類似物

analogue com·put·er /,··· ·ˈ··/ *n* [C] a computer that calculates things by measuring changing quantities such as of VOLTAGE rather than using a BINARY system of counting 模擬電腦, 類比電腦 —compare 比較 DIGITAL COMPUTER

a·nal·o·gy /ə`nælədʒɪ; əˈnælədʒi/ *n* [C,U] a comparison between two situations, processes etc that seem similar, or the process of making this comparison 類推, 類比, 比擬: **drawing/draw an analogy** (=make a comparison) 作比較 *analogies between human and animal behaviour* 人和動物行為的比較 | **by analogy (with)** (=using an analogy) 用類比法 *Dr Wood explained the* *movement of light by analogy with the movement of water.* 伍德博士用水的運動作比擬來解釋光的運動。

3 **an·a·lyse** *BrE*【英】, **analyze** *AmE*【美】/ˈænḷˌaɪz; ˈænəl-aɪz/ *v* [T] **1** to examine or think about something carefully, in order to understand it 分析: *A computer analyses the photographs sent by the satellite.* 電腦分析衛星發回的照片。| *analyse the text in detail* 詳細分析課文 **2** to examine someone's mental or emotional problems by using analysis (ANALYSIS (3)); PSYCHOANALYSE 對…進行精神分析

3 1 **a·nal·y·sis** /əˈnæləsɪs; əˈnælɪ̈sɪ̈s/ *n plural* **analyses** /-ˌsiz; -siːz/ **1** [C,U] a careful examination of something in order to understand it better 分析: *a detailed analysis of the week's news* 一週新聞的詳細分析 **2** [C,U] a careful examination of a substance to see what it is made of〔成分〕分析: *Forensic experts are doing analyses of the samples.* 法醫專家正在對樣本進行分析。**3** [U] a process in which a doctor makes someone talk about their past experiences, relationships etc in order to help them with mental or emotional problems; PSYCHOANALYSIS 精神分析 **4 in the final/last analysis** used when giving the most basic or important facts about a situation 最終, 歸根結底: *In the final analysis, profit is the motive.* 歸根結底, 利潤是動力。

an·a·lyst /ˈænḷɪst; ˈænəl-ɪ̈st/ *n* [C] **1** someone who makes a careful examination of events or materials in order to make judgments about them 分析者, 化驗員: *a food analyst* 食品化驗員 **2** a doctor who helps people who have mental or emotional problems by making them talk about their experiences and relationships 精神分析專家, 心理 (分析) 醫生 —see also 另見 SYSTEMS ANALYST

an·a·lyt·ic /ˌænḷˈɪtɪk; ˌænəlˈɪtɪk◂/ also 又作 **an·a·lyt·i·cal** /-tɪkḷ; -tɪkəl/ *adj* using methods that help you examine things carefully, especially by separating them into their different parts 分析的, (擅) 用分析方法的: *an analytic approach* 分析法

an·a·lyze /ˈænḷˌaɪz; ˈænəl-aɪz/ *v* [T] the American spelling of ANALYSE analyse 的美式拼法

an·a·paest *BrE*【英】, **anapest** *AmE*【美】/ˈænəˌpɛst; ˈænəpest/ *n* [C] *technical* part of a line of poetry consisting of two short sounds then one long one【術語】〔詩歌的〕抑抑揚格〔前兩拍短後一拍長〕—**anapaestic** /ˌænəˈpɛstɪk; ˌænəˈpiːstɪk◂/ *adj*

an·ar·chic /ænˈɑrkɪk; æˈnɑːkɪk/ *adj* lacking any rules or order, or not following the moral rules of society 無政府的; 無秩序的, 混亂的: *a lawless, anarchic city* 一個沒有法律的、失控的城市 | *Orton's anarchic sense of humour* 奧頓的不着邊際的幽默感

an·ar·chis·m /ˈænəˌkɪzəm; ˈænəkɪzəm/ *n* [U] the political belief that there should be no government and that ordinary people should work together to improve society 無政府主義

an·ar·chist /ˈænəkɪst; ˈænəkɪ̈st/ *n* [C] someone who believes that governments, laws etc are not necessary 無政府主義者 —**anarchistic** /ˌænəˈkɪstɪk; ˌænəˈkɪstɪk◂/ *adj* —**anarchistically** /-klɪ; -kli/ *adv*

an·ar·chy /ˈænəkɪ; ˈænəki/ *n* [U] a situation in which there is no effective government in a country or no order in an organization or situation 無政府狀態; 混亂狀態: *a state of complete anarchy* 完全的無政府狀態

a·nath·e·ma /əˈnæθəmə; əˈnæθɪ̈mə/ *n* [singular,U] something that is completely the opposite of what you believe in 令人極其討厭的事: [+to] *The idea of full-blown majority rule was anathema to many Afrikaners.* 全面的多數裁定原則的主張令許多南非白人極為反感。

an·a·tom·i·cal /ˌænəˈtɑmɪkḷ; ˌænəˈtɒmɪkəl◂/ *adj* connected with the structure of human or animal bodies 解剖 (學) 的: *an anatomical examination* 解剖檢查 —**anatomically** /-klɪ; -kli/ *adv*

a·nat·o·my /əˈnætəmɪ; əˈnætəmi/ *n* **1** [U] the scientific study of the structure of human or animal bodies 解剖 (學) **2** [C usually singular 一般用單數] the structure of body, or of a part of a body〔動、植物的〕解剖構造: *the anatomy of the nervous system* 神經系統的解剖構造 **3** *often humorous* your body【常幽默】身體: *a part of his anatomy that I'd rather not mention* 我不願提及的他身體的一部分 **4** [C,U] the process of cutting a body into pieces to study its different parts; DISSECTION 解剖 —**anatomist** *n* [C]

-ance /əns; əns/ *suffix*, **-ence** [in nouns 構成名詞] the action, state, or quality of doing something or of being something …的動作, …的狀態, …的性質: *his sudden appearance* (=he appeared suddenly) 他的突然出現 | *her brilliance* (=she is BRILLIANT) 她的聰穎

an·ces·tor /ˈænsɛstɚ; ˈænsəstə/ *n* [C] **1** a member of your family who lived a long time ago 祖先, 祖宗: *My ancestors were French.* 我的祖先是法國人。**2** the form in which a modern machine, vehicle etc first existed〔現代機器、車輛等的〕原型: *Babbage's invention was the ancestor of the modern computer.* 巴比奇的發明是現代電腦的原型。—compare 比較 DESCENDANT —**ancestral** /ænˈsɛstrəl; ænˈsestrəl/ *adj*: *the family's ancestral home* 這個家庭的祖居

an·ces·try /ˈænsɛstrɪ; ˈænsəstri/ *n* [C usually singular 一般用單數, U] the members of your family who lived a long time ago 祖先; 世系: **of French/Scottish etc ancestry** (=having ancestors who were French, Scottish etc) 有法蘭西/蘇格蘭等血統的

an·chor¹ /ˈæŋkɚ; ˈæŋkə/ *n* [C] **1** a piece of heavy metal that is lowered to the bottom of the sea, lake etc to prevent a ship or boat moving 錨: **weigh anchor** (=lift the anchor so that a ship can start moving) 起錨 | **drop/cast anchor** *We dropped anchor a few yards off-shore.* 我們在離岸幾碼遠的地方拋錨停航。**2** someone or something that provides a feeling of support and safety 可以依靠的人[物]; 精神支柱; 靠山 **3** *AmE* someone who reads the news on TV and introduces news reports【美】〔電視〕新聞節目主持人; NEWS-READER *BrE*【英】

anchor² *v*

1 ▶BOAT 船◀ [I,T] to lower the anchor on a ship or boat to hold it in one place 拋錨, 停船: *Three tankers were anchored in the harbor.* 三艘油輪停泊在港灣。

2 ▶FASTEN 使固定◀ [T usually passive 一般用被動態] to fasten something firmly so that it cannot move 使穩固, 固定: *The panel was firmly anchored by two large bolts.* 嵌板由兩個大螺栓牢牢固定着。

3 be anchored in to be strongly connected with a particular system, way of life etc 扎根於〔某種體系、生活方式等〕: *laws anchored in patriarchal society* 植根於父權制社會的法律

4 ▶SUPPORT 支持◀ [T] to provide a feeling of support or safety for someone 支持, 保護: *Her life was anchored by her religion.* 她對宗教的信仰給她的生活帶來了安全感。

5 ▶TV NEWS 電視新聞◀ [T] *AmE* to be the person who reads the news and introduces reports on TV【美】主持〔電視新聞節目〕: *Connie Chung anchors the 6 o'clock news.* 康妮·鍾主持6點鐘的新聞節目。

an·chor·age /ˈæŋkərɪdʒ; ˈæŋkərɪdʒ/ *n* **1** [C] a place where ships can anchor 泊處, 錨地 **2** [C,U] a place where something can be firmly fastened 可固定某物的地方: *Dig deep holes to get good anchorage for your new shrubs.* 坑挖得深一點讓新栽的灌木能固定住。

an·cho·rite /ˈæŋkəˌraɪt; ˈæŋkəraɪt/ *n* [C] *literary* someone who lives alone for religious reasons; HERMIT【文】隱士, 隱居修道者

an·chor·man /ˈæŋkɚˌmæn; ˈæŋkəmæn/ *n plural* **anchormen** /-ˌmɛn; -men/ [C] *AmE* a male anchorperson【美】男 (新聞) 主持人

an·chor·per·son /ˈæŋkɚˌpɝsn; ˈæŋkəˌpɜːsən/ *n* [C] *AmE* someone who reads the news on TV and introduces reports【美】(新聞) 主持人

an·chor·wom·an /ˈæŋkɚˌwʊmən; ˈæŋkəˌwʊmən/ *plural* **anchorwomen** /-ˌwɪmɪn; -ˌwɪmɪn/ *n* [C] *AmE* a

A

female anchorperson【美】女(新聞)主持人

an·cho·vy /ˋæn,tʃovɪ; ˈæntʃəvi/ *n* [C,U] a very small fish that tastes strongly of salt 鯷魚

2 **an·cient**¹ /ˋenʃənt; ˈeɪnʃənt/ *adj* **1** belonging to a time long ago 古代的: *the ancient civilizations of Asia* 亞洲的古代文明 **2** having existed for a very long time 古老的, 年代久遠的: *an ancient walled city* 有城牆的古城 **3** *usually humorous* very old【一般幽默】老掉牙的, 老的: *That photo makes me look ancient!* 那張照片顯得我很老!

ancient² *n* **the ancients** *old use* people who lived long ago, especially the Greeks and Romans【舊】古人〔尤指古希臘及古羅馬人〕: *The ancients believed that the sun and moon were planets.* 古人認為太陽和月亮都是行星。

an·cil·la·ry /ˋænsə,lɛrɪ; ænˈsɪləri/ *adj* **1 ancillary workers/staff etc** workers who provide additional help and services for the people who do the main work in hospitals, schools etc〔醫院、學校等的〕勤雜人員 **2** connected with or supporting something else, but less important than it 相關的; 輔助的, 附屬的, 次要的: *Agreement was reached on a number of ancillary matters.* 就一些相關問題達成了一致。

-ancy /ənsɪ; ənsi/ *suffix*, **-ency** [in nouns 構成名詞] the state or quality of doing something or of being something …的狀態, …的性質: *expectancy* (=state of expecting) 期待, 期望 | *hesitancy* 猶豫 | *complacency* (=being COMPLACENT) 自滿, 自鳴得意

1 1 **and** /ənd; ənd; *strong* 強讀 ænd; ænd/ *conj* **1** used to join two words, parts of sentences, etc 和, 及, 與, 又, 並〔連接詞與詞、句子成分間用的連詞〕: *Do you want a pen and a bit of paper?* 你要筆和紙嗎? | *The film starred Jack Lemmon and Shirley MacClaine.* 這齣電影由積·林蒙和莎莉·麥蓮主演。| *We've dealt with items one, two, and eleven.* 我們已經處理了第一項、第二項和第十一項。| *We'll have to reduce costs and borrow more money.* 我們必須降低費用, 再借些錢。| *You need to know what rights you have and how to use them.* 你需要知道你有哪些權利, 以及怎樣使用這些權利。**2** then; afterwards 然後, 其後: *Have your lunch and get a bath.* 先吃午飯, 然後去洗澡。| *She picked up the kitten and put it in the box.* 她抱起小貓放在盒子裡。| *He knocked on the door and went in.* 他敲敲門走了進去。| **wait and see** *You'll have to wait and see what happens.* 會發生甚麼事情, 你們只好等等看。**3** used to say that something is caused by something else〔用於表示結果〕: *I missed supper and I'm starving!* 我沒吃晚飯, 所以現在餓極了! | *She took some medicine and was sick.* 她服了些藥, 反而覺得不舒服。**4** used when adding numbers 加: *Six and four is ten.* 六加四等於十。**5 come and…/go and…/try and… etc** *especially BrE* used instead of 'to'【尤英】〔用於代替 to〕: *Shall we go and have a cup of coffee?* 我們出去喝杯咖啡好嗎? | *I'll see if I can try and persuade her to come.* 我看看我能不能設法說服她來。**6** *spoken* used to introduce a statement, comment, question etc【口】〔用於引出一個話題〕: *And now I'd like to introduce our next speaker, Mrs Thompson.* 現在我想介紹下一位發言人湯普森夫人。| *"We're trying to sort out our next holiday." "And where's the favourite place?" "Oh, America."* "我們正在選擇下一個度假地。" "哪裡最理想?" "啊, 美國。" **7** used between repeated words to emphasize what you are saying 越來越…, 一連, 許多〔用於連接重複的詞〕: *More and more people are losing their jobs.* 越來越多的人失業。| *We waited for hours and hours!* 我們一直等了好幾個小時! | *That was years and years ago.* 那是多少年以前的事了。| *We ran and ran.* 我們跑了又跑。**8 nice and…/good and…** used to emphasize how nice or good something is 很: *I like my tea nice and hot.* 我很喜歡熱茶。**9 a hundred and four/three thousand, five hundred and seventy six etc** used after the word 'hundred' and before the numbers 1 to 99 when saying numbers〔用於 hundred 之後, 以及 1 至 99 諸數目之前〕**10 three and three quarters, nineteen and a half etc** used after the whole number and before the FRACTION (2) when saying numbers〔用於整數和分數之間〕: *in about two and a half month's time* 大約兩個半月以後 | *five and a quarter percent* 百分之五點二五 **11** used in descriptions of food and drink to mean served with 和, 加〔用於描述食物或飲料〕: *Do you want some fish and chips?* 你想要些魚和薯條嗎? | *I'll have a gin and tonic.* 我要一杯加奎寧水的杜松子酒。| **bread and butter** (=bread with butter spread on it) 塗黃油的麵包 **2 there are experts and experts/computers and computers etc** used to say that some are much better than others 專家跟專家/電腦跟電腦大不一樣 **13 and?** *spoken* used when you want someone to add something to what they have just said【口】那麼? 還有?: *"I'm sorry." "And?" "And I promise it won't happen again."* "對不起。" "還有呢?" "我保證這樣的事再也不會發生了。"

An·dan·te /ænˋdæntɪ; ænˈdænti/ *n* [C] a piece of music played or sung at a speed that is neither very fast nor very slow〔樂曲的〕行板

andante *adj* played or sung at a speed that is neither very fast nor very slow 行板的; 徐緩的 —**andante** *adv*

an·di·ron /ˋænd,aɪɚn; ˈændaɪən/ *n* [C] one of a pair of iron objects that holds wood in a FIREPLACE〔壁爐的〕柴架

-andr- /ændr; ændr/ *prefix technical* concerning males or men【術語】雄性的; 男性的; 男子的: *androgynous plants* (=plants which are both male and female) 雌雄同株的植物 | *polyandry* (=having more than one husband at the same time) 一妻多夫制

an·drog·y·nous /ænˋdrɑdʒənəs; ænˈdrɒdʒɪnəs/ *adj* **1** having both male and female parts 雌雄同體的; 雌雄同株的 **2** someone who is androgynous looks both female and male 雙性的, 兼性的: *Bowie had a kind of androgynous sex appeal.* 鮑伊對男女都有一種吸引力。

an·droid /ˋændrɔɪd; ˈændrɔɪd/ *n* [C] a ROBOT that looks completely human〔似人的〕機器人

an·ec·dot·al /,ænɪkˋdotl̩; ,ænɪkˈdəʊtl◂/ *adj* consisting of short stories based on someone's personal experience 軼事的, 趣聞的: *Tom gave an anecdotal account of his recent trip to Morocco.* 湯姆敘述了他最近摩洛哥之行的趣聞。| *His findings are based on anecdotal evidence rather than serious research.* 他的發現是基於一些趣聞軼事的證據, 而不是認真的研究。

an·ec·dote /ˋænɪk,dot; ˈænɪkdəʊt/ *n* [C] a short story based on your personal experience〔基於個人經歷的〕趣聞, 軼事

a·ne·mi·a /əˋnimɪə; əˈniːmiə/ *n* [U] the usual American spelling of ANAEMIA anaemia 的一般美式拼法

a·ne·mic /əˋnimɪk; əˈniːmɪk/ *adj* the usual American spelling of ANAEMIC anaemic 的一般美式拼法

a·nem·o·ne /əˋnɛmə,ni; əˈneməni/ *n* [C] a plant with red, white, or blue flowers 銀蓮花

an·es·the·si·a /,ænəsˋθiʒə; ,ænɪ̈sˈθiːziə/ *n* [U] the usual American spelling of ANAESTHESIA anaesthesia 的一般美式拼法

an·es·the·si·ol·o·gist /,ænəs,θizɪˋɑlədʒɪst; ,ænəsθiːziˈɒlədʒɪ̈st/ *n* [C] *AmE* a doctor who gives ANAESTHETICS to a patient【美】麻醉師

an·es·thet·ic /,ænəsˋθɛtɪk; ,ænəsˈθetɪk◂/ *n* [C,U] the usual American spelling of ANAESTHETIC anaesthetic 的一般美式拼法

a·nes·the·tist /əˋnɛsθətɪst; əˈniːsθɪ̈tɪ̈st/ *n* [C] the usual American spelling of ANAESTHETIST anaesthetist 的一般美式拼法

a·nes·the·tize /əˋnɛsθə,taɪz; əˈniːsθɪ̈taɪz/ *v* [T] the usual American spelling of ANAESTHETISE anaesthetise 的一般美式拼法

a·new /əˋnu; əˈnjuː/ *adv literary*【文】**1 start life anew** to begin a different job, start to live in a different place etc, especially after a difficult period in your life〔尤指困難時期後〕開始新生活: *She resolved to start life anew*

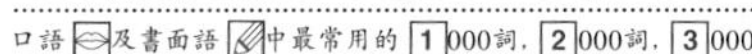

A

in Ireland. 她決心在愛爾蘭開始新的生活。**2** if you do something anew, you start doing it again 重新, 再

an·gel /ˋendʒəl; ˈeɪndʒəl/ *n* [C] **1** a spirit who lives with God in heaven, often shown as a person dressed in white with wings 天使 **2** someone who is very kind, very good, or very beautiful 仁慈而美麗的人, 安琪兒: *That little girl of theirs is an angel.* 他們的小女兒是個小天使。| **be an angel** *spoken* (=used to ask someone to do something for you) 【口】行行好, 做做好事 *Be an angel and get me my glasses, will you?* 幫幫忙, 把我的眼鏡拿過來好嗎? | **you're an angel** *spoken* (=used to tell someone that you are grateful to them) 【口】你真好 *Thanks for mailing those letters, you're an angel.* 謝謝你幫我寄了那些信, 你真好。| **sb's no angel** (=used to say that someone behaves very badly) 某人的表現差 *Sam was no angel at school, believe me.* 相信我, 薩姆在學校表現很差。**3** a way of speaking to a child or woman you love 乖乖, 寶貝兒: *How are you angel?* 你怎麼樣, 寶貝兒? **4** *informal* someone who supports a play, film, music group etc by giving money 【非正式】〔尤指戲劇、電影、樂隊等的〕贊助人 —see also 另見 GUARDIAN ANGEL

angel dust /ˋ·· ·/ *n* [U] *slang* PCP (=a drug) 【俚】天使塵〔一種麻醉致幻劑, 即苯環己哌啶〕

an·gel·ic /ænˋdʒɛlɪk; ænˈdʒelɪk/ *adj* **1** looking good, kind, and gentle or behaving in this way 天使般的: *She had an angelic smile, but a dreadful temper.* 她笑起來像個天使, 但發起脾氣來很可怕。**2** connected with angels 天使的 —**angelically** /-kḷɪ; -kli/ *adv*

an·gel·i·ca /ænˋdʒɛlɪkə; ænˈdʒelɪkə/ *n* [U] a plant that smells sweet and is used in cooking 白芷〔一種帶香味的植物, 用於烹調〕

3 **an·ger¹** /ˋæŋgɚ; ˈæŋgə/ *n* [U] a strong feeling of wanting to harm, hurt or criticize someone because they have done something unfair, cruel, offensive etc 憤怒, 怒火, 怒氣: *Paul's face was filled with anger and resentment.* 保羅一臉憤怒和不滿。| **do sth in anger** (=do it because you have very strong feelings) 生氣地做某事 *Her mother hardly ever shouted at her in anger.* 她的母親幾乎從來不怒氣沖沖地對她喊叫。

anger² *v* [T often passive 常用被動態] to make someone angry 使生氣, 激怒: *What angered me most was his total lack of remorse.* 最使我生氣的是他居然一點悔意都沒有。

an·gi·na /ænˋdʒaɪnə; ænˈdʒaɪnə/ *n* [U] a medical condition in which you have bad pains in your chest because your heart is weak 心絞痛

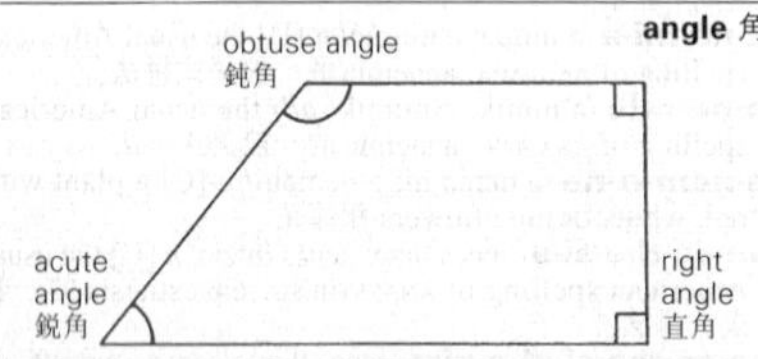

3
3 **an·gle¹** /ˋæŋgḷ; ˈæŋgəl/ *n* [C] **1** the space between two straight lines or surfaces that touch or cross each other, measured in degrees 角: *an angle of 45°* 45 度角 —see also 另見 RIGHT ANGLE **2** a position from which you look at something or photograph it 視角, 角度: *This drawing of the monastery was done from an unusual angle.* 這幅畫是以獨特的視角來描繪寺院的。**3** a way of considering a problem or situation 〔看問題的〕角度: *We need to look at the issue from a different angle.* 我們需要從一個不同的角度來看這個問題。**4 at an angle** leaning to one side and not straight or upright 歪着的: *The portrait was hanging at an angle.* 這幅畫像掛歪了。**5** the shape formed when two lines or surfaces join 〔兩條線或兩個平面相交的〕夾角, 邊角: *My head struck the angle of the shelf.* 我的頭碰在書架的角上。

angle² *v* [I,T] **1** if you angle something in a particular direction or if it angles in that direction, it is not upright or facing straight ahead (使) 按照某一角度轉動[移動]: *a mirror angled to reflect light from a window* 為反射窗外的光線而擺成某一角度的鏡子 **2** [T] to describe something unfairly by emphasizing some features but not others 帶成見地描述, 偏向: *a report which was angled in favour of the government* 偏向政府的報告

angle for sth *phr v* [T] to try to get something by making suggestions and remarks instead of asking directly 〔以暗示等方法〕獵取, 謀取: *She was angling for an invitation to that party.* 她拐彎抹角地想要弄到那個晚會的請柬。

an·gle·poise lamp /ˌæŋgḷpɔɪz ˋlæmp; ˌæŋgəlpɔɪz ˈlæmp/ *n* [C] *BrE trademark* a type of lamp that can be moved into different positions 【英, 商標】〔能旋轉至不同方位的〕活動(枱) 燈 —see picture at 參見 LIGHT¹ 圖

an·gler /ˋæŋglɚ; ˈæŋglə/ *n* [C] someone who catches fish as a sport 垂釣者 —compare 比較 FISHERMAN

An·gli·can /ˋæŋglɪkən; ˈæŋglɪkən/ *n* [C] a Christian who is a member of the Church of England 英國聖公會教徒 —**Anglican** *adj* —**Anglicanism** *n* [U]

an·gli·cis·m /ˋæŋgləˌsɪzəm; ˈæŋgləsɪzəm/ *n* [C] an English word or expression that is used in another language 〔其他語言中的〕英語詞語; 典型的英國說法

an·gli·cize also 又作 **-ise** *BrE* 【英】 /ˋæŋgləˌsaɪz; ˈæŋgləsaɪz/ *v* [T] to make something or someone more English 使英語化; 使英國化

an·gling /ˋæŋglɪŋ; ˈæŋglɪŋ/ *n* [U] **1** the sport of catching fish 垂釣運動; 釣魚 **2 go angling** to catch fish as a sport 去垂釣[釣魚]

Anglo-, anglo- /æŋglo; æŋgləʊ/ *prefix* **1** of England or Britain 英格蘭的; 英國的: *an anglophile* (=someone who loves Britain) 親英者, 崇英者 **2** English or British and 英格蘭[英國] 和…的: *an Anglo-Scottish family* 英裔蘇格蘭人家庭 | *an improvement in Anglo-American relations* 英美關係的改善

Anglo-A·mer·i·can¹ /ˌ·· ·ˋ···◂/ *adj* between or involving both Britain and the US 英美的: *Anglo-American relations* 英美關係

Anglo-American² *n* [C] an American whose family come from Britain 英裔美國人

An·glo-Cath·o·lic /ˌ·· ˋ···◂/ *n* [C] a Christian who is a member of the part of the Church of England that is similar to the Roman Catholic Church 〔與羅馬天主教相近的〕英國國教高教會派教徒 —**Anglo-Catholic** *adj* —**Anglo-Catholicism** /ˌ·· ·ˋ····/ *n* [U]

Anglo-In·di·an /ˌ·· ˋ···◂/ *n* [C] **1** someone whose family is partly British and partly Indian 英印混血兒 **2** *old use* a British person who was born or lives in India 【舊】出生或居住在印度的英國人 —**Anglo-Indian** *adj*

an·glo·phile /ˋæŋgloˌfaɪl; ˈæŋgləʊfaɪl/ *n* [C] someone who is not British but likes anything British 親英者, 崇英者 —**anglophilia** /ˌæŋgloˋfɪlɪə; ˌæŋgləʊˈfɪliə/ *n* [U]

an·glo·phobe /ˋæŋgloˌfob; ˈæŋgləʊfəʊb/ *n* [C] someone who dislikes anything British 仇英者 —**anglophobia** /ˌæŋgloˋfobɪə; ˌæŋgləʊˈfəʊbiə/ *n* [U]

an·glo·phone /ˋæŋgloˌfon; ˈæŋgləʊfəʊn/ *adj* anglophone populations or countries have English as one of their languages 〔人口或國家〕講英語的 —**anglophone** *n* [C]

Anglo-Sax·on /ˋæŋglo ˋsæksṇ; ˌæŋgləʊ ˈsæksən◂/ *n* **1** [C] a member of the people who lived in England from about 600 AD 盎格魯撒克遜人 **2** [U] the language of the Anglo-Saxons 盎格魯撒克遜語 **3** [C] *often humorous* an English person 【常幽默】英國人 —**Anglo-Saxon** *adj*

an·go·ra /ænˋgɔrə; æŋˈgɔːrə/ *n* **1** [U] wool or thread made from the fur of an angora goat or rabbit 用安哥拉羊毛[兔毛]製成的織物[毛線] **2** [C] a type of goat, rabbit, or cat with very long soft hair or fur 〔一種有柔軟長毛的〕安哥拉羊; 安哥拉兔; 安哥拉貓

an·gos·tur·a /ˌæŋgəsˋturə; ˌæŋgəˈstjʊərə◂/ *n* [U] a slightly bitter liquid used for adding taste to alcoholic drinks〔可增加酒香的〕安哥斯圖拉苦味液

3 3 **an·gry** /ˋæŋgrɪ; ˈæŋgri/ *adj* **1** feeling strong emotions which make you want to shout at someone or hurt them because they have behaved in an unfair, cruel, offensive etc way, or because you think that a situation is unfair, unacceptable etc 發怒的, 生氣的, 氣憤的: *I was very angry when I heard what happened.* 聽到所發生的事情我很氣憤。| **angry person/look etc** *an angry letter* 充滿憤怒的信 | *There were angry scenes when the police broke up the demonstration.* 警察驅散示威者時出現了憤怒的場面。| **[+with/at]** *She was so angry with him that she threatened to throw him out of the house.* 她很生他的氣, 威脅說要把他扔出屋去。| **[+about/over]** *Parents are justifiably angry about the decision to close the school.* 家長們對於關閉學校的決定表示氣憤是情有可原的。| **make sb angry** *It makes me really angry when I hear people talk about 'humane killing'.* 聽到人們談論甚麼"人道的殺戮"時, 我真的很氣憤。**2 angry with/at yourself** feeling strongly that you wish you had done something or had not done something 生自己的氣: *David was angry with himself for letting the others see his true feelings.* 戴維恨自己讓別人看出了他的真實感受。**3** *literary* an angry sky or cloud looks dark and stormy【文】黑壓壓的, 雨快來臨的 **4** *literary* an angry wound etc is painful and red and looks infected【文】〔傷口〕腫痛發炎的, 感染的 —**angrily** *adv*: *"The stupid young fool," he said angrily.* "這個愚蠢的年輕人。" 他生氣地說。

This graph shows how common different grammar patterns of the adjective **angry** are. 本圖表所示為形容詞 angry 構成的不同語法模式的使用頻率。

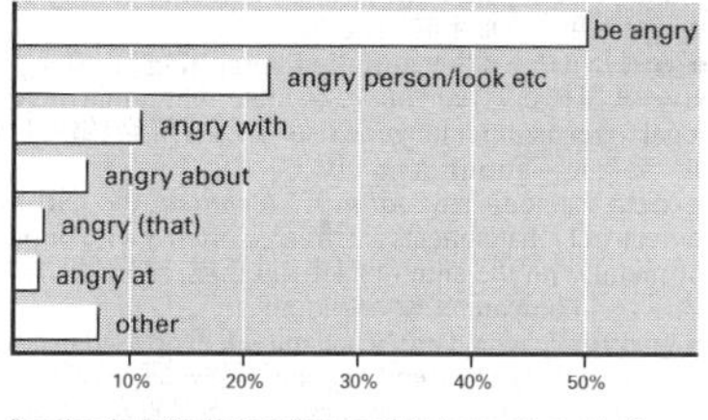

Based on the British National Corpus and the Longman Lancaster Corpus
據英國國家語料庫和朗文蘭卡斯特語料庫

angst /æŋst; æŋst/ *n* [U] strong feelings of anxiety and unhappiness because you are worried about your life, your future, or what you should do in a particular situation 焦慮不安, 煩惱: *love letters full of angst* 充滿焦慮的情書

an·guish /ˋæŋgwɪʃ; ˈæŋgwɪʃ/ *n* [U] mental or physical suffering caused by extreme pain or worry〔精神或身體上的〕極度痛苦: *the anguish of not knowing what had happened to her* 由於不知道她發生了甚麼事而痛苦不已 —**anguished** *adj*: *anguished cries for help* 痛苦的呼救聲

an·gu·lar /ˋæŋgjələ; ˈæŋgjə̇lə/ *adj* **1** thin and not having much flesh on your bones 瘦骨嶙峋的: *a tall, angular young man* 又高又瘦的年輕男子 **2** having sharp and definite corners 有尖角的: *an angular room* 有尖角的房間 **3** [only before noun 僅用於名詞前] having or forming an angle 有角的, 成角的

1 1 **an·i·mal¹** /ˋænəml̩; ˈænə̇məl/ *n* [C] **1** a living creature such as a dog or cat, that is not an insect, plant, fish, or person〔除昆蟲、植物、魚類或人類以外的生物〕動物, 獸類: *farm animals* 牲畜, 牲口 | **animal welfare/rights etc** *campaigning for animal rights* (保護) 動物權利運動 | **animal products/protein/fats etc** (=things that are made or come from animals) 動物產品/蛋白/脂肪等 **2** any living creature that is not a plant, including people 動物〔包括人〕: *Man is a highly intelligent animal.* 人是一種高智慧動物。**3** *informal* someone who behaves in a cruel, violent, or very rude way【非正式】畜牲, 兇殘野蠻的人: *These football hooligans are just animals.* 這些足球流氓簡直是畜牲。**4 a very/completely different animal** *informal* something that is very different from the thing you have mentioned【非正式】非常不同/截然不同的事 **5 a political/social animal etc** *informal* someone who is interested in politics, in meeting other people etc【非正式】善於搞政治/社交等的人

animal² *adj* [only before noun 僅用於名詞前] **animal urges/instincts etc** human feelings, desires etc that are connected with sex, food, and other basic needs 獸慾/動物本能等

animal hus·band·ry /ˌ··· ˈ···/ *n* [U] farming that involves keeping animals and producing milk, meat etc 畜牧業

animal rights /ˌ··· ˈ·/ *n* [U] the idea that people should treat animals well, and especially not use them in tests to develop medicines or other products 動物權利〔指人們應善待動物, 尤其不要把牠們用作試驗品來研製藥物或其他產品〕: **animal rights protestor/campaigner** (=someone who tries to stop cruelty to animals) 動物權利保護者/活動家

an·i·mate¹ /ˋænəmɪt; ˈænə̇mə̇t/ *adj* living 有生命的, 活的: *animate beings* 生物 —opposite 反義詞 INANIMATE

an·i·mate² /ˋænəˌmet; ˈænə̇meɪt/ *v* [T] to give life or energy to something 賦予…以生命; 使有生氣; 激勵: *Laughter animated his face for a moment.* 笑使他臉上一時增添了生氣。

an·i·ma·ted /ˋænəˌmetɪd; ˈænə̇meɪtə̇d/ *adj* **1** showing a lot of interest and energy 生氣勃勃的, 活躍的, 栩栩如生的: *An animated discussion ensued.* 接着進行了一場熱烈的討論。**2 animated cartoon/film/programme** a film made by photographing a series of pictures, clay models etc 動畫片/電影/節目 —**animatedly** *adv*

an·i·ma·tion /ˌænəˋmeʃən; ˌænə̇ˈmeɪʃən/ *n* [U] **1** the process of making animated films 動畫片的製作 **2** liveliness and excitement 興奮; 生氣; 活躍: *They were talking with animation.* 他們談得興趣盎然。

an·i·ma·tor /ˋænɪˌmetə; ˈænə̇meɪtə/ *n* [C] someone who makes animated films 動畫片製作人

an·i·mis·m /ˋænəˌmɪzəm; ˈænə̇mɪzəm/ *n* [U] a religion in which animals and plants are believed to have spirits 泛靈論, 萬物有靈論

an·i·mos·i·ty /ˌænəˋmɑsətɪ; ˌænə̇ˈmɒsə̇ti/ *n* [C,U] strong dislike or hatred; HOSTILITY 憎惡, 仇恨, 敵意: *There is no personal animosity between the party leaders.* 該黨領導人之間並沒有個人恩怨。

an·i·mus /ˋænɪməs; ˈænə̇məs/ *n* [singluar,U] *formal* a feeling of strong dislike or hatred; HOSTILITY【正式】憎惡, 仇恨, 敵意

an·i·seed /ˋænɪˌsid; ˈænə̇siːd/ *n* [U] the seeds of a plant used in alcoholic drinks and in sweets〔用於酒精飲料和糖果的〕洋茴香籽

an·kle /ˋæŋkl̩; ˈæŋkəl/ *n* [C] **1** the joint between your foot and your leg 腳踝 —see picture at 參見 FOOT¹ 圖 **2 ankle socks/boots** socks or boots that only come up to your ankle〔僅到腳踝的〕短襪/短靴

an·klet /ˋæŋklɪt; ˈæŋklə̇t/ *n* [C] a ring or BRACELET worn around your ankle 踝飾, 腳鐲

an·nals /ˋænl̩z; ˈænlz/ *n* [plural] **1** an official record of events or activities 年鑑, 年報, 編年史: *the Annals of the Zoological Society* 動物學學會年報 **2 in the annals of history/British politics etc** in the whole history of something 在整個歷史/英國政治史上: *one of the most disgraceful episodes in the annals of British politics* 英國政治史上最丟臉的事件之一

an·neal /əˋnil; əˈniːl/ *v* [T] to make metal or glass hard by heating it and then slowly letting it get cold 使…退

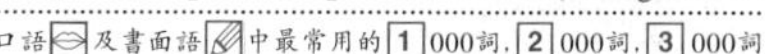

火，韌煉〔把金屬或玻璃加熱後緩緩冷卻使之堅硬〕

an·nex /ə`nɛks; ə'neks/ *v* [T] to take control of a country or area next to your own, especially by using force〔尤指透過使用武力〕併吞，兼併，霸佔〔國家或領土〕—**annexation** /ˌænɛks`eʃən; ˌænek'seɪʃən/ *n* [C,U]

an·nexe *BrE*【英】, **annex** *especially AmE*【尤美】/`ænɛks; 'æneks/ *n* [C] a separate building that has been added to a larger one 附屬建築，附加建築

an·ni·hi·late /ə`naɪəˌlet; ə'naɪəleɪt/ *v* [T] **1** to destroy something or someone completely 徹底毀滅，消滅: *stockpiles of weapons that could annihilate mankind* 貯藏大量能夠摧毀人類的武器 **2** to defeat someone easily and completely in a game, competition, or election〔遊戲、比賽或選舉中〕徹底戰勝: *Tyson annihilated his opponent in the first round.* 泰森在第一個回合就輕取對手。—**annihilation** /əˌnaɪə`leʃən; əˌnaɪə'leɪʃən/ *n* [U]

an·ni·ver·sa·ry /ˌænə`vɝsərɪ; ˌænɪ'vɜːsəri/ *n* [C] a date on which something special or important happened in a previous year 週年紀念(日): *our twentieth wedding anniversary* 我們結婚二十週年紀念日

An·no Dom·i·ni /`æno `dɑməˌnaɪ; ˌænəʊ 'dɒmɪnaɪ/ *formal* AD【正式】公元

an·no·tate /`ænəˌtet; 'ænəteɪt/ *v* [T] to add short notes to a book or piece of writing to explain parts of it 給…作註釋，註解: *an annotated edition of 'Othello'*《奧賽羅》的註釋本 —**annotation** /ˌænə`teʃən; ˌænə'teɪʃən/ *n* [C,U]

2 1 **an·nounce** /ə`naʊns; ə'naʊns/ *v* [T] **1** to officially tell people about a decision or something that will happen 宣布，通告，公布於眾: *They announced their engagement in 'The Times'.* 他們在《泰晤士報》上宣布了訂婚的消息。| **announce (that)** *A government spokesman announced that the hostages had been released.* 政府發言人宣布人質已經被釋放。**2** to say something in a loud or angry way 大聲宣布: **announce (that)** *Winston suddenly announced that he was leaving.* 溫斯頓突然宣布他要離開。| **announce a visitor/guest** (=say their name loudly, especially at a special event, so other people will know they have arrived) 通報客人的到來 **3** to give information to people using a LOUDSPEAKER or MICROPHONE, especially at an airport or railway station〔尤指在機場或火車站〕廣播: *announcing the arrival of Flight 207 from Minneapolis* 廣播報告來自明尼阿波利斯的 207 次航班到達 **4** to introduce a programme on television or radio〔在電視或電台〕主持〔節目〕

3 3 **an·nounce·ment** /ə`naʊnsmənt; ə'naʊnsmənt/ *n* **1** [C] an important or official statement〔重要或正式的〕通告，宣告，告示，聲明: **[+about]** *an important announcement about tax increases* 關於增加稅收的重要公告 | **announcement that** *We were shocked by the announcement that the mayor was resigning.* 我們對市長要辭職的聲明感到震驚。| **make an announcement** *Silence please, Mr Dacre has an announcement to make.* 請安靜，戴克先生有事要宣布。**2** [singular] the act of telling people something important is going to happen 發表，宣布，宣告: *the announcement of the general strike* 宣布總罷工 **3** [C] a small advertisement or statement in a newspaper〔報紙上的〕廣告，啟事: **birth/wedding/death announcement** *The wedding announcement appeared on the 16th of June.* 結婚啟事是6月16日發布的。

an·nounc·er /ə`naʊnsɚ; ə'naʊnsə/ *n* [C] someone who reads news or information on the television or radio〔電視或電台的〕廣播員，播音員，節目主持人

3 **an·noy** /ə`nɔɪ; ə'nɔɪ/ *v* [T] to make someone feel slightly angry and unhappy about something 使煩惱，煩擾，打攪: *The way Tina orders us around really annoys me.* 蒂娜把我們差來遣去的做法真使我惱火。| *It annoyed him that the model didn't fit together properly.* 使他懊惱的是這個型號安裝不上。

an·noy·ance /ə`nɔɪəns; ə'nɔɪəns/ *n* **1** [U] a feeling of slight anger 煩惱，氣惱: *A look of annoyance crossed her face.* 她一臉煩惱。| **to your annoyance** *To his annoyance, he discovered they hadn't waited.* 他發現他們沒有等他，因而感到很氣惱。**2** [C] something that makes you slightly angry 令人略感煩惱的事物: *Alan found the constant noise of the traffic an annoyance.* 不停的交通噪音讓艾倫覺得心煩。

an·noyed /ə`nɔɪd; ə'nɔɪd/ *adj* slightly angry 略感煩惱[生氣]的: *I'll be annoyed if we don't finish by eight.* 如果我們八時還未完成，我會很懊惱。| **[+with]** *She was annoyed with Duncan for forgetting to phone.* 鄧肯忘了打電話使她氣惱。| **[+about/by]** *He was annoyed by her apparent indifference.* 她看起來很冷淡，這讓他很惱火。| **be annoyed that** *Mr Davies was annoyed that the books were missing.* 那些書不見了，戴維斯先生很懊惱。

an·noy·ing /ə`nɔɪ-ɪŋ; ə'nɔɪ-ɪŋ/ *adj* making you feel slightly angry 令人略感心煩的: *an annoying habit of interrupting* 打斷他人講話的令人惱火的習慣 | *The annoying thing is he's usually right.* 令人氣惱的是，他通常都是對的。| **it's annoying that** *It's annoying that we didn't know about this before.* 令人惱火的是，我們事先並不知道。—**annoyingly** *adv*: *annoyingly small portions* 量少得讓人惱火

an·nu·al¹ /`ænjuəl; 'ænjuəl/ *adj* **1** happening once a year 一年一度的，每年的: *an annual conference* 年會 **2** based on or calculated over a period of one year 按年度計算的: *Steel output reached an annual figure of one million tons.* 鋼的年產量達到一百萬噸。—**annually** *adv* 2 2

annual² *n* [C] **1** a plant that lives for one year or season 一年生植物；一季生植物 —compare 比較 BIENNIAL (2), BIANNUAL **2** a book, especially for children, that is produced once a year with the same title but different stories, pictures etc 年刊，年報，年鑑〔尤指兒童年冊〕

annual meet·ing /ˌ⋯ `⋯/ *n* [C] a meeting held once a year by a club, business, or organization 年會；AGM *BrE*【英】

an·nu·i·ty /ə`nuətɪ; ə'njuːɪti/ *n* [C] a fixed amount of money that is paid each year to someone, usually until they die 年金；(每年的)養老金

an·nul /ə`nʌl; ə'nʌl/ *v* **annulled, annulling** [T often passive 常用被動態] *technical* to state that a marriage or legal agreement no longer exists【術語】解除〔婚約〕；廢止〔契約〕—**annulment** *n* [C,U]

an·ode /`ænod; 'ænəʊd/ *n* [C] *technical* the part of a BATTERY (1) that collects ELECTRONS, often a wire or piece of metal with the sign (+)【術語】正極，陽極〔用"+"號表示〕—compare 比較 CATHODE

an·o·dyne¹ /`ænəˌdaɪn; 'ænədaɪn/ *adj* expressed in a way that is unlikely to offend anyone 不惹人的，不冒犯他人的: *anodyne topics of conversation* 不冒犯人的話題

anodyne² *n* [C] **1** *technical* a medicine that reduces pain【術語】鎮痛藥 **2** *formal* an activity or thing that comforts people【正式】給人以安慰的事物

a·noint /ə`nɔɪnt; ə'nɔɪnt/ *v* [T] to put oil or water on someone's head or body during a religious ceremony【正式】〔宗教儀式中〕塗油[水]於〔人頭或身上〕—**anointment** *n* [C,U]

a·nom·a·lous /ə`nɑmələs; ə'nɒmələs/ *adj* different from what you expected to find 異常的，反常的；不規則的；畸形的: *clearly an anomalous result* 明顯反常的結果 —**anomalously** *adv*

a·nom·a·ly /ə`nɑməlɪ; ə'nɒməli/ *n* [C,U] *formal* a strange and unusual feature of a situation or process that often makes it unsatisfactory or unfair, or an example of this【正式】異常現象，反常現象；畸形: *various anomalies in the tax system* 稅制上的各種反常現象 | *a genetic anomaly* 遺傳變異

a·non¹ /ə`nɑn; ə'nɒn/ *adv literary* soon【文】不久，未幾: *See you anon.* 一會兒見。—see also 另見 **ever and anon** (EVER (9))

anon² written abbreviation of 縮寫= anonymous

an·o·nym·i·ty /ˌænə`nɪmətɪ; ˌænə'nɪmɪti/ *n* [U] **1** the state of not letting your name be known 匿名，不公開姓名: *Every step will be taken to preserve your anonymity.* 將採取各種措施不公開你的姓名。**2** the state of not

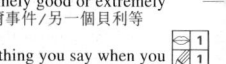

having any unusual or interesting features 平淡無奇, 無個性特徵: *the drab anonymity of the city* 城市的單調乏味、平淡無奇 **3** the state of not showing who is involved in something 無署名; 作者不明: *the anonymity of a typed envelope* 不具名打印的信封

a·non·y·mous /ə`nɑnəməs; əˈnɒnɪməs/ *adj* **1** unknown by name 無名的, 不署名的: *The benefactor wishes to remain anonymous.* 捐助者希望不留姓名。**2** done, sent, or given by someone who does not want their name to be known 匿名的, 不知姓名的: *an anonymous donation of £5,000* 一位不具名人士捐贈的 5,000 英鎊 | **anonymous phone call/letter etc** (=often unpleasant or containing threats) 匿名電話/信等 **3** without any interesting features or qualities 無特色的: *grey, anonymous housing estates* 灰色的、毫無特色的住宅區 —**anonymously** *adv*

a·noph·e·les /ə`nɑfə,liz; əˈnɒfɪliːz/ *n* [C] a kind of MOSQUITO, especially the kind that spreads MALARIA 瘧蚊

an·o·rak /`ænə,ræk; ˈænəræk/ *n* [C] *especially BrE* a short coat with a HOOD (1) that keeps out the wind and rain【尤英】帶風帽的夾克 [短風雨衣] —see picture at 參見 COAT¹ 圖

an·o·rex·i·a /,ænə`rɛksɪə; ,ænəˈreksiə◂/ also 又作 **anorexia ner·vo·sa** /-nɚ`vosə; -nɜːˈvəʊsə/ *n* [U] a mental illness that makes people, especially young women, stop eating 食慾缺乏, 厭食 (症)

an·o·rex·ic /,ænə`rɛksɪk; ,ænəˈreksɪk◂/ *adj* suffering from or connected with anorexia 厭食的 —**anorexic** *n* [C]

an·oth·er /ə`nʌðɚ; əˈnʌðə/ *determiner, pron* **1** used to refer to one more person or thing of the same kind〔同類的〕另一個: *Can you pass me another mug?* 你能再遞給我一個大杯嗎? | *I'm going to have another beer.* 我要再喝一杯啤酒。| *When you've eaten that, you can have another one.* 吃完那個以後, 你還可以再吃一個。| *"I can't find that pencil you've just given me." "Don't worry, here's another."* "我找不到你剛才給我的鉛筆。" "不要緊, 這兒還有一支。" | **[+of]** *Is this another of your schemes to make money?* 這是你另一個賺錢的方案嗎? | **yet another** *He has to go to yet another meeting.* (=he has already been to several) 他還得出席另一個會。| **from one...to another** *We seem to struggle from one crisis to another.* 我們好像在跟一個又一個危機鬥爭。| **one after another** (=used to talk about a series of similar things or events) 一個接一個 *Small businesses have been collapsing one after another.* 小型企業紛紛倒閉。**2** a different person or thing or some other kind of person or thing〔不同類的〕另外一個; 其他一種: *If that doesn't work, you'll have to find another way of solving the problem.* 如果那個方法不行, 你得找另外一種方法去解決問題。| *You can press enter to select this value or type another choice (such as N).* 你可以按輸入鍵選擇這個數值, 或者輸入另一個選項 (比如 N) 。| *We'll talk about that another time.* 那一點我們下次再談。| **another of** *Another of the speakers suggested abandoning the project altogether.* 另一個發言人建議放棄整個項目。| **...or another** (=used when you cannot be specific about what kind of things or people you mean) ... 或另一種 *All the kids in this class have learning difficulties of one sort or another.* 這個班上所有的孩子在學習中都有這樣或那樣的困難。| **that is another matter/thing altogether** *You can try it, but whether it will work is another thing altogether.* (=it is likely that it will not work) 你可以試一下, 但行不行完全是另一回事。**3** in addition to a particular amount, distance, period of time etc; FURTHER 再一, 又〔指數量、距離、時間等〕: *Let the soup simmer for another 10 minutes.* 讓湯再燉十分鐘。| *I let out another 50 feet of rope.* 我又放出 50 英尺繩子。| *A room with a sea view will cost another £7.* 窗外有海景的房間另加收七英鎊。**4 one another** used after a verb to show that two or more people or things do the same thing to each other〔用於動詞之後〕互相: *They seem to love one another very much.* 他們似乎彼此愛得很深。**5 another Chernobyl/another Pele etc** used when talking about a situation or person that reminds you of another famous situation or person, especially because they have extremely good or extremely bad qualities 又一個切爾諾貝爾事件/另一個貝利等

an·swer¹ /`ænsɚ; ˈɑːnsə/ *n*

1 ►REPLY 答覆◄ [C,U] something you say when you reply to a question that someone has asked you 回答, 答覆: *I asked Janine what she thought, but I'm still waiting for her answer.* 我問過雅尼納怎麼想, 可現在仍然在等她的答覆。| **give (sb) an answer** *You don't have to give them an answer straight away.* 你不必馬上就給他們答覆。| **the answer is yes/no!** *spoken*【口】*If it's money you're after again, the answer is no!* 如果你想要的又是錢, 那麼回答是沒有! | **in answer to** *In answer to your question, I think you can go.* 我來回答你的問題, 我想你可以走了。

2 ►TEST/COMPETITION ETC 測驗/比賽等◄ [C] something that you write or say in reply to a question in a test, exercise, competition etc 答案: *What was the answer to question 4?* 第四題的答案是甚麼?

3 ►INVITATION/LETTER ETC 請柬/信等◄ [C] a written reply to a letter, invitation, advertisement etc〔信、請柬、廣告等的〕回函: *Did you ever get an answer to your letter?* 你收到回信了嗎?

4 ►PROBLEM 問題◄ [C] a way of dealing with a problem 解決辦法: *There are no easy answers to today's environmental problems.* 當今的環境問題, 沒有容易的解決辦法。| **be the answer to sb's problems/worries etc** *If he could get a job it'd be the answer to all his worries.* 如果他能找到一份工作, 他所有的煩惱就會煙消雲散了。

5 not get an answer to not get a reply when you telephone someone or call at their house〔電話〕無應答: *I tried calling him all day but couldn't get an answer.* 我試着給他打了一天電話, 但無人應答。

6 sb's answer to someone or something that is considered to be just as good as a more famous person or thing〔與出名之人或物〕極為相似的人[物]: *Britain's answer to the Eiffel Tower* (簡直是) 英國的埃菲爾鐵塔

answer² *v*

1 ►REPLY 答覆◄ a) [I,T] to say something to someone as a reply when they have asked you a question, made a suggestion etc 回答, 答覆: *I had to answer lots of questions about my childhood.* 我必須回答許多關於我童年的問題。| **answer (that)** *When questioned, Hughes answered that he knew nothing about the robbery.* 問到休斯時, 他回答說對這宗搶劫案一無所知。| **answer sb** *How much was it? Come on, answer me.* 多少錢? 快點告訴我。| *Julie stared at him for a long time before answering.* 朱莉盯着他看了好久才回答。**b)** [T] to deal with someone's question in a satisfactory way 解答: *You still haven't answered my question.* 你還沒有解答我的問題。

2 answer criticism/charges/accusations etc to explain why you did something when people are criticizing you 就批評/指控/譴責等作出解釋: *How do you answer the criticism that your government has done nothing to help the homeless?* 有人批評你們的政府沒有採取任何行動幫助無家可歸者, 你怎樣解釋?

3 ►TEST 測試◄ [I,T] to write or say the answer to a question in a test, exercise, competition etc 答 (題) : *Answer as many questions as possible in the time provided.* 在規定的時間內盡量多答題。

4 answer the phone/door/a call to pick up the telephone when it rings or go to the door when someone calls 接電話/應門

5 ►LETTER 信◄ [T] to send a reply to a letter, advertisement etc 回信: *Simon got the job by answering an advertisement in the newspaper.* 西蒙通過應徵報紙上的一則廣告找到了工作。

6 ►DO STH AS A REACTION 作出反應◄ [I,T] to do something as a reaction to criticism or attack 以…行動回應: *The US answered by bombing North Vietnam.* 美國以轟炸北越作為回應。
7 ►DEAL WITH A PROBLEM 處理問題◄ [T] to be a way of dealing with or solving a problem 解決: *"You can borrow my car if you like." "Well, that answers one problem."* "如果你願意，可以借我的車。" "啊，這下解決問題了。"
8 answer a description if someone answers a description, they match that description 與描述的相符合: *A man answering the police's description was seen entering the building.* 有人看到一個和警方提供的相貌特徵相符的人進了樓。
9 answer a need to provide something that is needed 滿足需要

answer back *phr v* [I,T] to reply in a rude way to someone that you are supposed to obey 回嘴，反駁: **answer sb back** *Don't answer me back young man!* 年輕人，別跟我頂嘴！

answer for sth *phr v* [T] **1** to explain to people in authority why you did something wrong or why something happened, and be punished if necessary 對…負責: *The teachers must answer for their students' disgusting behaviour on the school trip.* 教師應對學生在學校旅行活動期間的不良行為負責。**2 have a lot to answer for** *informal* to be responsible for causing a lot of trouble【非正式】對許多問題負有責任: *That young man's got an awful lot to answer for.* 那個年輕人在許多事情上應承擔責任。**3 I can answer for him/her etc** *spoken* used to say that someone will definitely do something【口】我可以擔保某人〔一定會做某事〕: *I'm sure John will help us – I can't really answer for the others.* 我確信約翰會幫我們，但別人我就保證不了。

answer to sb/sth *phr v* [T] **1** to give an explanation to someone, especially about something that you have done wrong 對…負責，作出解釋〔尤指錯事〕: *Phipps answers to me and me alone.* 菲普斯只對我一個人負責。**2 answer to the name of a)** if a pet answers to a particular name, it comes when you call that name 對（叫…名）有反應: *Their dog answers to the name of Fido.* 他們的狗一聽到喊"菲多"這個名字就有反應。**b)** to be called a particular name 名叫，叫作: *George was over six feet tall, but he answered to the name of 'Shorty'.* 喬治身高有六英尺多，但外號卻叫"矮子"。

USAGE NOTE 用法說明: ANSWER

WORD CHOICE 詞語辨析: **answer, reply, respond, give an answer, get back to**

Answer is the usual verb you use to talk about answering questions. **Reply** is used especially when you mention the actual words that were said. 回答問題一般用 answer。提到回答的原話時往往用 reply: *I was so nervous I couldn't reply/answer.* 我太緊張，沒能回答問題。| *"Not in the least," he replied.* "一點也不。"他回答道。

Respond is more formal and less common and often suggests that a criticism is being replied to. respond 較正式，因而不常用，經常暗指對批評作出反應: *So far, the travel agent hasn't responded to our complaint.* 到目前為止，旅行社對我們的投訴尚未作出反應。

If you give someone a piece of information they have asked for, such as a decision you have made, you **give them an answer**. 如果你提供別人想要的信息，比如說你所作的決定，可說 give them an answer: *If we offer you the job, when could you give us an answer?* 如果我們給你這份工作，你甚麼時候能給我們一個答覆？

If you think you can answer someone later but not at once, you say you will **get back to them**. 如果你認為你可以稍後而不是馬上答覆某人，可說 get back to them: *Sorry, I'll need to think about that and get back to you.* 對不起，我需要考慮一下，然後再答覆你。

GRAMMAR 語法

You **answer** (*v*) a question, advertisement etc, not *to/at* it. Normally you **answer** a person too. If you **answer to** someone, they are the person directly responsible for you in an organization, at work etc, and you have to explain to them if anything goes wrong or if you are not doing something properly. 回答問題、應徵廣告等，用 answer 直接加受詞，不用 to 或 at。通常 answer 的受詞也可以是人。answer to 意為在工作單位或某機構中向某人負責，如有問題或者你做錯甚麼事情，就必須對他們作出解釋。

You give the **answer** (*n*) **to** a question or criticism, not *of* it. You get an **answer** (*n*) **from** someone, not *of* them. give the answer to 後可以接問題或批評，不用 of。得到某人的答覆說 get an answer from，不用 of。

an·swer·a·ble /ˋænsərəbḷ; ˈɑːnsərəbəl/ *adj* **1 be answerable to** to have to explain your actions to someone in authority 須向…說明理由；向…承擔責任: *I am answerable to the government for any decisions I make.* 我作出任何決定都要向政府負責。**2** a question that is answerable can be answered 可答覆的；可駁斥的

answering ma·chine /ˈ··· ·,·/ also 又作 **answerphone** *BrE*【英】*n* [C] a machine that records your telephone calls when you cannot answer them 錄音電話機，電話答錄機

ant /ænt; ænt/ *n* [C] **1** a small insect that lives in large groups 螞蟻 **2 have ants in your pants** *spoken* to be unable to sit or stand still【口】坐立不安

-ant /ənt; ənt/, **-ent** *suffix* [in nouns and adjectives 構成名詞和形容詞] someone or something that does something 做…的人；用作…的東西；處於…的狀態: *a servant* (=someone who serves others) 僕人 | *disinfectant* (=substance for killing germs) 消毒劑，殺菌劑 | *expectant* (=expecting) 期待的 | *pleasant* (=pleasing) 令人愉快的

an·tag·o·nis·m /ænˋtægə,nɪzəm; ænˈtægənɪzəm/ *n* [U] **1** hatred between people or groups of people〔人或團體之間的〕對抗，敵對: *the great antagonism between Futurists and Cubists* 未來派和立體派之間的強烈對抗 **2** opposition to an idea, plan etc〔對主張、計劃等的〕反對，對立: [+to/towards] *his obvious antagonism towards the press* 他對新聞界所持的明顯對立態度

an·tag·o·nist /ænˋtægə,nɪst; ænˈtægənɪst/ *n* [C] your opponent in a competition, battle, quarrel etc 對立[對抗]者；對手，敵手 —compare 比較 PROTAGONIST

an·tag·o·nis·tic /æn,tægəˋnɪstɪk; ən,tægəˈnɪstɪk◄/ **1** unfriendly; wanting to argue or disagree 對抗的，敵對的: *an antagonistic attitude* 對抗態度 **2** opposed to an idea or group 反對的: **[+to/towards]** *antagonistic to new ideas* 反對新觀點 —**antagonistically** /-klɪ; -kli/ *adv*

an·tag·o·nize also 又作 **-ise** *BrE*【英】/ænˋtægə,naɪz; ænˈtægənaɪz/ *v* [T] to annoy someone very much by doing something that they do not like 引起…敵對[對抗]: *Do not do anything to antagonize your customers.* 不要做任何得罪顧客的事情。

An·tarc·tic /æntˋɑrktɪk; ænˈtɑːktɪk/ *n* [singular] the very cold most southern part of the world 南極；南極地區

An·tarc·tic Cir·cle /·,·· ˈ··/ *n* [singular] an imaginary line drawn around the world at a certain distance from the most southern point (the South Pole) 南極圈 —compare 比較 ARCTIC CIRCLE —see picture at 參見 EARTH[1] 圖

ante- /æntɪ; ænti/ *prefix* before 在…以前: *to antedate* (=be earlier than something) 先於，早於 | *antenatal* (=before birth) 出生前的 —compare 比較 ANTI-, POST-, PRE-

an·te[1] /ˋæntɪ; ˈænti/ *n* **up/raise the ante** to increase your demands or try to get more things from a situation, even though this involves more risks 加賭注 —see also 另見 PENNY ANTE

ante[2] *v*

ante up *phr v past tense* **anted** or **anteed, anteing** [I, T **ante up** sth] *AmE* to pay an amount of money, especially in a game of chance【美】付賬〔尤指賭資〕

ant·eat·er /ˋænt͵itɚ; ˈænt͵iːtə/ *n* [C] an animal that has a very long nose and eats small insects 食蟻獸

an·te·ced·ent /͵æntəˋsidn̩t; ͵æntɪ̵ˈsiːdənt/ *n* [C] **1** *formal* an event, organization, or thing that is similar to the one you have mentioned but existed eariler【正式】先例: *historical antecedents* 歷史上的先例 **2 antecedents** [plural] *formal* the people in your family who lived a long time ago; ANCESTOR*s*【正式】祖先 **3** *technical* a word, phrase, or sentence that is represented by another word, for example a PRONOUN【術語】先行詞, 前述詞 —**antecedent** *adj*

an·te·cham·ber /ˋæntɪ͵tʃembɚ; ˈæntɪ͵tʃeɪmbə/ *n* [C] a small room connected to a larger room〔連接較大房間的〕前廳, 外室

an·te·date /ˋæntɪ͵det; ˈæntɪdeɪt/ *v* [T] *formal* to come from an earlier time in history than something else【正式】比…早, 先於, 早於: *It antedates the palace at Nineveh.* 這比〔伊拉克〕尼尼微的宮殿還要古老。

an·te·di·lu·vi·an /͵æntɪdɪˋluvɪən; ͵æntɪdɪ̵ˈluːviən◂/ *adj humorous* very old-fashioned; OUTDATED【幽默】老式的, 陳舊的, 過時的: *antediluvian ideas about women* 關於女性的陳舊觀念

an·te·lope /ˋæntl̩͵op; ˈæntɪ̵ləʊp/ *n* [C] an animal with long horns that can run very fast and is very graceful 羚羊

an·te·na·tal /͵æntɪˋnetl̩; ͵æntɪˈneɪtl◂/ *adj BrE* connected with the medical care given to women who are going to have a baby【英】產前的; PRENATAL *AmE*【美】: *antenatal clinic* 產前診所 —compare 比較 POSTNATAL

an·ten·na /ænˋtɛnə; ænˈtenə/ *n* [C] **1** *plural* **antennae** /-ni; -niː/ one of two long thin parts on an insect's head, that it uses to feel things 觸角; 觸鬚 **2** *plural* **antennas** *especially AmE* a wire, ROD (1) etc used for receiving radio and television signals【尤美】天線; AERIAL[2] *BrE*【英】—see picture on page A2 參見A2頁圖

an·ter·i·or /ænˋtɪrɪɚ; ænˈtɪəriə/ *adj* [no comparative 無比較級] **1** *technical* at or towards the front【術語】(在)前面的; 向前的: *anterior vertebrae* 前椎 **2** *formal* happening or existing before something else【正式】較…早的, …之前的, 先前的

an·te·room /ˋæntɪ͵rum; ˈæntɪrʊm/ *n* [C] a small room that is connected to a larger room, especially where people wait to go into the larger room〔通往較大房間的〕前室; 接待室

an·them /ˋænθəm; ˈænθəm/ *n* [C] **1** a formal or religious song 聖歌, 讚美詩 —see also 另見 NATIONAL ANTHEM **2** a song that a particular group of people consider to be very important〔某個羣體認為非常重要的〕歌曲: *The Rolling Stones' 'Satisfaction' became an anthem for a generation.* "滾石"樂隊的《滿足》成了一代人傳唱的歌曲。

an·ther /ˋænθɚ; ˈænθə/ *n* [C] *technical* the part of a male flower which contains POLLEN【術語】〔雄蕊的〕花葯, 花粉囊

ant·hill /ˋænt͵hɪl; ˈænt͵hɪl/ *n* [C] a place where ANT*s* live 蟻丘, 蟻塚

an·thol·o·gy /ænˋθɑlədʒɪ; ænˈθɒlədʒi/ *n* [C] a set of stories, poems, songs etc by different people collected together in one book〔故事、詩、歌曲等的〕選集: *an anthology of American literature* 美國文學選集 —**anthologist** *n* [C]

an·thra·cite /ˋænθrə͵saɪt; ˈænθrəsaɪt/ *n* [U] a very hard type of coal that burns slowly and produces a lot of heat 無煙煤

an·thrax /ˋænθræks; ˈænθræks/ *n* [U] a serious disease of cattle and sheep 炭疽病

anthropo- /ænθrəpə; ænθrəpə/ *prefix technical* like or concerning human beings【術語】人的, 人類的: *anthropomorphic* (=having human form or qualities) 被賦予人性的, 擬人的

an·thro·poid /ˋænθrə͵pɔɪd; ˈænθrəpɔɪd/ *adj* an anthropoid animal is very like a human〔動物〕似人的, 類人的 —**anthropoid** *n* [C]

an·thro·pol·o·gy /͵ænθrəˋpɑlədʒɪ; ͵ænθrəˈpɒlədʒi/ *n* [U] the scientific study of people, their societies, CULTURE*s* etc 人類學 —compare 比較 ETHNOLOGY, SOCIOLOGY —**anthropologist** *n* [C] —**anthropological** /͵ænθrəpəˋlɑdʒɪkl̩; ͵ænθrəpəˈlɒdʒɪkəl◂/ *adj*

an·thro·po·mor·phis·m /͵ænθrəpəˋmɔrfɪzəm; ͵ænθrəpəˈmɔːfɪzəm/ *n* [U] **1** the belief that animals or objects have the same feelings and qualities as humans 擬人論, 擬人觀 **2** *technical* the belief that God can appear in a human or animal form【術語】神與人或動物同形[同性]論 —**anthropomorphic** *adj*

anti- /æntɪ; æntɪ/ *prefix* **1** opposed to; against 反對: *anti-nuclear* (=opposing the use of atomic weapons and power) 反對使用核武器[核能]的 | *anti-American* 反美的 **2** the opposite of something 相反物, 對立面: *anticlimax* (=an unexciting ending instead of the expected CLIMAX[1] (1)) 突降法 | *antimatter* (=material completely opposite in kind to the ordinary material in the universe) 反物質 **3** acting to prevent something 防(止): *antifreeze* (=a liquid added to prevent freezing) 防凍劑 | *antiseptic* (=to stop bacteria) 抗菌的, 防腐的 —compare 比較 ANTE-, PRO-

an·ti·air·craft /͵æntɪˋɛr͵kræft; ͵æntiˈeəkrɑːft/ *adj* [only before noun 僅用於名詞前] antiaircraft weapons are used against enemy aircraft 防空的: *antiaircraft missiles* 防空導彈

an·ti·bi·ot·ic /͵æntɪbaɪˋɑtɪk; ͵æntɪbaɪˈɒtɪk◂/ *n* [C usually plural 一般用複數] a drug that is used to kill BACTERIA and cure infections 抗生素, 抗菌素

an·ti·bod·y /ˋæntɪ͵bɑdɪ; ˈæntɪ͵bɒdi/ *n* [C] a substance produced by your body to fight disease 抗體

an·tic·i·pate /ænˋtɪsə͵pet; ænˈtɪsɪ̵peɪt/ *v* [T] **1** to expect that something will happen and be ready for it 預期, 預料: *Organisers are anticipating a large crowd at the carnival.* 組織者預計狂歡節時人會很多。| **anticipate that** *It is anticipated that next year interest rates will fall.* 人們預計明年的利率會下調。| **anticipate doing sth** *I didn't anticipate having to do the cooking myself!* 我沒有預料到要自己做飯! **2** to think about something that is going to happen, especially something pleasant 期待〔尤指好事〕: *Daniel was eagerly anticipating her arrival.* 丹尼爾熱切地期待着她的到來。**3** to do something before someone else 先於…之前(做): *Copernicus anticipated in part the discoveries of the 17th and 18th centuries.* 17和18世紀的發現中有一部分哥白尼已經發現。**4** *formal* to use or consider something before you should【正式】預先考慮; 提前使用 —**anticipatory** /ænˋtɪsəpə͵torɪ; æn͵tɪsɪ̵ˈpeɪtəri/ *adj* 3

an·tic·i·pa·tion /æn͵tɪsəˋpeʃən; æn͵tɪsɪ̵ˈpeɪʃən/ *n* [U] the act of expecting something to happen 預期, 預料, 期望: *They waited, filled with nervous anticipation.* 他們等待着, 充滿不安的期盼。| **in anticipation of** *The workers have called off their strike in anticipation of a pay offer.* 工人們預料能夠得到工錢, 便取消了罷工。

an·ti·cler·i·cal /͵æntɪˋklɛrɪkl̩; ͵æntiˈklerɪkəl◂/ *adj* being opposed to priests having any political power or influence 反對教權的 —**anticlericalism** *n* [U]

an·ti·cli·max /͵æntɪˋklaɪmæks; ͵æntɪˈklaɪmæks/ *n* [C, U] a situation or event that does not seem exciting because it happens after something that was much better 突降; 令人突然泄氣之事: *Going back to work after a month travelling in China was bound to be an anticlimax.* 到中國旅行了一個月後回來工作肯定令人掃興。

an·ti·clock·wise /ˌæntɪˋklɑkwaɪz; ˌæntɪˈklɒkwaɪz◂/ *adv, adj BrE* moving in the opposite direction to the hands of a clock【英】逆時針方向地 [的]; COUNTERCLOCKWISE *AmE*【美】: *Turn the lid anticlockwise.* 往逆時針方向轉動這個蓋子。—opposite 反義詞 CLOCKWISE

an·tics /ˋæntɪks; ˈæntɪks/ *n* [plural] behaviour that seems strange, funny, silly, or annoying 古怪而可笑的舉動: *The public quickly grew tired of McEnroe's antics on court.* 公眾很快對麥肯羅在球場上的可笑舉動感到厭倦了。

an·ti·cy·clone /ˌæntɪˋsaɪklon; ˌæntɪˈsaɪkləʊn/ *n* [C] an area of high air pressure that causes calm weather in the place it is moving over 反氣旋, 高氣壓 —see also 另見 CYCLONE

an·ti·de·pres·sant /ˌæntɪdɪˋprɛsənt; ˌæntidɪˈpresənt/ *n* [C,U] a drug used to treat DEPRESSION (=a mental illness that makes people very unhappy) 抗抑鬱藥

an·ti·dote /ˋæntɪˌdot; ˈæntɪdəʊt/ *n* [C] **1** a substance that stops the effects of a poison 解毒劑: [+to] *There is no known antidote to a bite from this snake.* 尚沒有能治這種蛇毒的解藥。**2** something that makes an unpleasant situation better 緩解之物: *laughter, the antidote to stress* 大笑, 舒緩壓力的良藥

an·ti·freeze /ˌæntɪˋfriz; ˈæntɪfriːz/ *n* [U] a substance that is put in the water in car engines to stop it from freezing 防凍劑, 抗凝劑

an·ti·gen /ˋæntədʒən; ˈæntɪdʒən/ *n* [C] *technical* a substance that makes the body produce antibodies (ANTIBODY)【術語】抗原

an·ti·her·o /ˌæntɪˋhɪro; ˈæntɪˌhɪərəʊ/ *n* [C] a main character in a book, play, or film who is an ordinary or unpleasant person and lacks the qualities that you expect a hero to have〔書、戲劇或電影中的〕非正統主角,〔缺乏英雄品格的〕反英雄

an·ti·his·ta·mine /ˌæntɪˋhɪstəmin; ˌæntɪˈhɪstəmiːn/ *n* [C,U] a drug that is used to treat an ALLERGY (=an unpleasant reaction to particular foods, substances etc)〔治療過敏症的〕抗組 (織) 胺劑

an·ti·knock /ˌæntɪˋnɑk; ˌæntɪˈnɒk/ *n* [U] a chemical substance that is put in petrol to make car engines operate more smoothly〔加於汽油中使汽車運行更順暢的〕抗震劑, 抗爆劑

anti-lock brak·ing sys·tem /ˌ·· ·ˈ·· ˌ··/ *n* [U] a piece of equipment that makes a vehicle easier to control when you have to stop very suddenly 防鎖死剎車裝置

an·ti·ma·cas·sar /ˌæntɪməˋkæsɚ; ˌæntɪməˈkæsə/ *n* [C] a piece of decorated cloth that is put on the back of a chair to protect it 椅背套

an·ti·mat·ter /ˋæntɪˌmætɚ; ˈæntiˌmætə/ *n* [U] a form of MATTER (30) (=substance which the things in the universe are made of) consisting of antiparticles〔由反粒子構成的〕反物質

an·ti·par·ti·cle /ˋæntɪˌpɑrtɪkḷ; ˈæntiˌpɑːtɪkəl/ *n* [C] a very small part of an atom that has the opposite electrical charge to the one usually found in atoms 反粒子

an·ti·pas·to /ˌæntɪˋpɑsto; ˈæntipæstəʊ/ *n* [U] an Italian dish consisting of cold food that you eat before the main part of a meal 意大利式餐前小吃

an·ti·pa·thet·ic /ænˌtɪpəˋθɛtɪk; ˌæntɪpəˈθetɪk◂/ *adj* [+to] *formal* having a very strong feeling of disliking or opposing someone or something【正式】厭惡的, 反感的

an·tip·a·thy /ænˋtɪpəθɪ; ænˈtɪpəθi/ *n* [U+to/towards] *formal* strong dislike or opposition towards someone or something【正式】反感, 厭惡: *a strong personal antipathy towards Nixon* 個人對尼克遜的強烈反感

anti-per·son·nel /ˌ·· ··ˈ·/ *adj* an anti-personnel weapon is designed to hurt people rather than damage buildings, vehicles etc〔武器〕用於殺人的, 殺傷性的

anti-per·spi·rant /ˌ·· ˈ···/ *n* [U] a substance that prevents you sweating (SWEAT[1] (1)) 止汗劑

An·tip·o·des /ænˋtɪpəˌdiz; ænˈtɪpədiːz/ *n* **the Antipodes** *often humorous* Australia and New Zealand【常幽默】澳大利亞和紐西蘭 —**Antipodean** /ænˌtɪpəˋdiən; ænˌtɪpəˈdiːən/ *adj*: *antipodean culture* 澳紐文化

an·ti·quar·i·an /ˌæntɪˋkwɛrɪən; ˌæntɪ̵ˈkweəriən◂/ *adj* [only before noun 僅用於名詞前] an antiquarian bookshop sells old books 經營古書的; 古文物的; 研究 [收藏, 出售] 古文物的

an·ti·quat·ed /ˋæntəˌkwetɪd; ˈæntɪ̵kweɪtɪ̵d/ *adj* old-fashioned and not suitable for modern needs or conditions; OUTDATED (1) 過時的, 陳舊的, 老式的: *antiquated laws* 過時的法律

an·tique[1] /ænˋtik; ænˈtiːk/ *adj* **1** antique furniture, jewellery etc is old and often valuable 古時製造的, 古董的: *an antique rosewood desk* 古董紅木書桌 **2** *formal* connected with ancient times, especially ancient Rome or Greece【正式】古代的〔尤指古羅馬或古希臘的〕

antique[2] *n* [C] a piece of furniture, jewellery etc that was made a very long time ago and is therefore valuable 古董, 古玩, 古物: *The palace is full of priceless antiques.* 宮殿裡到處都是無價的古玩。| *an antique dealer* 古玩商

an·tiq·ui·ty /ænˋtɪkwətɪ; ænˈtɪkwɪ̵ti/ *n* **1** [U] ancient times 古代: *a tradition that stretches back into antiquity* 可追溯到遠古時代的傳統 **2** [U] the state of being very old 年代久遠: *a building of great antiquity* 很古老的建築物 **3** [C usually plural 一般用複數] a building or object made in ancient times 古蹟, 古物, 古建築: *a collection of Roman antiquities* 一批古羅馬文物

an·tir·rhi·num /ˌæntɪˋraɪnəm; ˌæntɪ̵ˈraɪnəm/ *n* [C] a garden plant with white, red, or yellow flowers; a SNAPDRAGON 金魚草

anti-Se·mite /ˌæntɪ ˋsɛmaɪt; ˌænti ˈsiːmaɪt/ *n* [C] someone who hates Jewish people 反猶太主義者 —**anti-Semitic** /ˌæntɪ səˋmɪtɪk; ˌænti sɪ̵ˈmɪtɪk◂/ *adj*

anti-Sem·i·tis·m /ˌæntɪ ˋsɛməˌtɪzəm; æntɪ ˈsemɪ̵tɪzəm/ *n* [U] hatred of Jewish people 反猶太主義

an·ti·sep·tic[1] /ˌæntəˋsɛptɪk; ˌæntɪ̵ˈseptɪk◂/ *n* [C] a chemical substance that helps stop a wound becoming infected 防腐劑, 殺菌劑, 消毒劑

antiseptic[2] *adj* **1** helping to prevent infection 抗菌的; 抗感染的: *antiseptic cream* 抗感染藥膏 **2** lacking emotion, interest, or excitement 缺乏感情的, 沒有情趣的: *dreary antiseptic prose* 乏味、沒意思的散文

anti-so·cial /ˌ·· ˈ··◂/ *adj* **1** unwilling to meet people and talk to them, especially in a way that seems unfriendly or rude 不喜歡社交的, 不合羣的: *a child who was aggressive and anti-social* 一個好鬥又孤僻的孩子 **2** an activity that is anti-social does not give you the chance to meet other people 沒有社交機會的, 結交不到人的: *The job's OK, but I have to work very anti-social hours.* 這份工作可以, 但我必須犧牲社交活動的時間來工作。**3** anti-social behaviour shows a lack of concern for other people 反社會的; 不考慮他人利益的: *Smoking cigarettes in public is increasingly considered anti-social.* 在公共場所吸煙越來越被看作是妨害公眾利益的。

anti-tank /ˌ·· ˈ·◂/ *adj* an anti-tank weapon is designed to destroy enemy tanks (TANK[1] (3))〔武器〕反坦克的

an·tith·e·sis /ænˋtɪθəsɪs; ænˈtɪθɪ̵sɪ̵s/ *n* [C usually singular 一般用單數] *formal* the exact opposite of something【正式】正相反, 相對; 對立面: *Connie's political views are the complete antithesis of mine.* 康妮的政治觀點和我的正相反。

an·ti·thet·i·cal /ˌæntɪˋθɛtɪkḷ; ˌæntɪ̵ˈθetɪkəl/ also 又作 **an·ti·thet·ic** /-ˋθɛtɪk; -ˈθetɪk◂/ *adj formal* exactly opposite to something【正式】正相反的; 對立的: [+to] *completely antithetical to democratic ideals* 和民主理想完全背道而馳的

an·ti·tox·in /ˌæntɪˋtɑksɪn; ˌæntiˈtɒksɪ̵n/ *n* a substance produced by your body or put in a medicine to stop the effects of a poison 抗毒素

anti trust law /ˌ·· ˈ· ˌ·/ *n* [C,U] *technical* an American law intended to prevent companies unfairly controlling prices【術語】〔美國〕反托拉斯法; 反壟斷法

ant·ler /ˋæntlɚ; ˈæntlə/ *n* [C] one of the two horns of a male DEER 鹿角

an·to·nym /ˈæntəˌnɪm; ˈæntənɪm/ *n* [C] a word that means the opposite to another word 反義詞: *'Good' is the antonym of 'bad'.* good是bad的反義詞。—compare 比較 SYNONYM —**antonymous** /ænˋtɑnɪməs; ænˈtɒnɪ̩məs/ *adj*

a·nus /ˋenəs; ˈeɪnəs/ *n* [C usually singular 一般用單數] the hole in your body through which solid waste leaves your BOWEL*s* 肛門 —see picture at 參見 DIGESTIVE SYSTEM 圖

an·vil /ˋænvɪl; ˈænvɪ̩l/ *n* [C] a heavy iron block on which pieces of metal are shaped using a hammer 鐵砧

3 3 **anx·i·e·ty** /æŋˋzaɪətɪ; æŋˈzaɪəti/ *n* **1** [C,U] the feeling of being very worried about something that may happen or may have happened, so that you think about it all the time 焦慮, 不安, 擔心: [+about/over] *anxiety among staff about job losses* 職員對失業的擔心 | *an anxiety attack* 突然間的焦慮 **2** [C] something that makes you worry 使人焦慮的事情: *the anxieties of parenthood* 父母們擔心的事 **3** [U] a feeling of wanting to do something very much but being worried that you will not succeed 渴望: **anxiety to do sth** *a natural anxiety to please one's parents* 渴望討好父母的自然心情

3 3 **anx·ious** /ˋæŋkʃəs; ˈæŋkʃəs/ *adj* **1** very worried about something that may happen or may have happened so that you think about it all the time 焦慮的, 不安的, 擔心的: [+about] *Helen is anxious about travelling on her own.* 海倫對自己一個人出門旅行感到擔心。| *"Feeling scared, Joe?" "No, just a little anxious."* "感到害怕嗎, 喬?" "不, 只是有點焦慮。" | **anxious look/expression etc** *an anxious glance at the fuel gauge* 焦慮地看一眼燃料表 | **anxious that** *anxious that it might be cancer* 擔心或許是癌症 **2** an anxious time or situation is one in which you feel nervous or worried〔時間或形勢〕緊張的, 使人焦慮的: *an anxious couple of weeks waiting for the test results* 等待考試成績那令人焦急的幾週時間 **3** feeling strongly that you want to do something or want something to happen 渴望…的, 急切希望…的: **anxious to do sth** *Peggy is anxious to show that she can cope with extra responsibility.* 佩吉急切地想表明她能承擔一些分外的事。—**anxiously** *adv*: *waiting anxiously by the phone* 在電話旁焦急地等待 —see 見 NERVOUS (USAGE)

1 1 **an·y¹** /ˋɛnɪ; ˈeni/ *determiner, pron* **1** used to refer to each one or all members of a group, saying it does not matter which 任何一個; 無論哪個: *Any child who attempts to escape is beaten.* 凡試圖逃走的孩子都要挨揍。| *You can obtain a valuation from any accredited insurance valuer.* 你可以請任何一家官方認可的保險評估公司進行估價。| *Any plan chosen should take these factors into account.* 所有入選方案都必須考慮這些因素。| *before you sign any written agreement* 在你簽訂任何書面協議以前 | *These tiles are an ideal choice for any bathroom setting.* 這些瓷磚是所有浴室裝修的理想選擇。| **any of** *before touching the computer or any of its parts* 在觸摸電腦或其任何部件之前 | *Do any of you remember?* 你們當中有誰記得嗎? | **any other** *Are there any other comments?* 還有其他評論嗎? **2** used especially in questions or as part of a negative statement to mean some or even the smallest amount 一點, 一些, 少許: *Few of the students had any knowledge of classical music.* 很少有學生具備古典音樂方面的一些知識。| *I didn't pay any attention to what he said.* 我一點兒也沒注意他說甚麼。| *She promised not to take any chances.* 她答應不會再冒任何風險。| *He had no friends and didn't deserve any.* 他沒有朋友, 也不配有朋友。| **I haven't any idea** (=I do not know at all) 我一點頭緒都沒有 | **any of** *I don't understand what any of this stuff means.* 我一點兒也不知道這東西是幹甚麼用的。| **any use** *I tried, but it wasn't any use.* (=it was not successful) 我試了, 但一點兒用也沒有。| **if any** *I don't suppose there will be more than a dozen left, if any.* (=it is likely that there will be none at all) 我認為即使還有的話也不過十幾個。| **in any way** *He was not in any way upset by his wife's decision.* 他絲毫也沒有因妻子的決定而感到不高興。| *If I can help you in any way, let me know.* 如果我在任何方面能幫上你甚麼忙, 請告訴我。**3** as much as possible; all 盡可能多的, 所有的: *They're going to need any help they can get.* 能得到的幫助他們都需要。**4 in any case/at any rate a)** no matter what may happen; at least 無論如何: *There was nothing else to be done. At any rate, I had learnt something.* 沒有甚麼別的可做了。但無論如何, 我還是了解到了一些情況。**b)** besides; also 此外, 也, 還: *In any case, he was a rude old man.* 此外, 他還是個粗魯的老人。**5 just any** used to refer to something that is ordinary and not special 普通的: *You can't wear just any old clothes to that sort of place, you have to dress up.* 去那種場合, 你可不能穿普普通通的舊衣服, 你得穿戴整齊。**6 any old how** in any way 用任何方式: *Just pack them in any old how.* 只要把它們裝進去就行。

any² *adv* **1** used especially in negative statements to mean in the least; at all 絲毫, 一點〔尤用於否定句〕: *It can't make it any worse, can it?* 不可能更糟了, 對嗎? | *I'm not any better than you.* 我一點兒也不比你好。| *I can't walk any further.* 我再也走不動了。| *The boy could not stand it any longer.* 那個男孩再也忍受不住了。**2** *AmE spoken* used to mean 'at all' at the end of a sentence【美口】根本〔用於句末〕: *We tried talking to him but that didn't help any.* 我們盡力說服他, 但一點兒用處也沒有。—compare 比較 EITHER, NEITHER 2

an·y·bod·y /ˋɛnɪˌbɑdɪ; ˈeniˌbɒdi/ *pron* any person or all people; anyone 任何人, 無論誰 1 3

an·y·how /ˋɛnɪˌhaʊ; ˈenihaʊ/ *adv* **1** [sentence adverb 句子副詞] *especially spoken* used to say that someone does something or something happens in spite of something else【尤口】無論如何, 不管怎樣: *It was felt that the scandal would damage her reputation but the press reported it anyhow.* 大家認為醜聞會敗壞她的名聲, 但不管怎樣, 新聞界還是報道了。**2** in a careless or untidy way 隨便地; 雜亂無章地: *The cupboard would hardly close, with all the shoes thrown in anyhow.* 鞋櫃亂塞了許多鞋, 幾乎關不上了。| **any old how** (=in a very careless way) 雜亂無章地 *The books were arranged any old how on the shelves.* 書隨便地亂放在書架上。**3** [sentence adverb 句子副詞] *especially spoken* used to add information that limits what has been mentioned before, makes it seem less important etc【尤口】反正, 好歹: *I've never been to a circus, not recently anyhow.* 我沒有看過馬戲, 反正最近是沒看過。**4** [sentence adverb 句子副詞] *especially spoken*【尤口】**a)** used when you want to return to the main subject of the conversation 不管怎樣〔用於交談中希望回到主題時〕: *So anyhow, as I was saying, when I arrived Tom was already there.* 不管怎樣, 正如我所說, 我到的時候湯姆已經在那兒了。**b)** used when you have not included some details in a story and you are saying what the final result was 結果: *Anyhow, when the doctor came he said there was nothing wrong with me.* 結果, 醫生來了卻說我甚麼病也沒有。**5** *AmE spoken* used to mean 'anyway' in spoken American English【美口】不管怎樣, 反正, 總之: *Martin's not feeling too well but he's going to come over anyhow.* 馬丁感到不太舒服, 但他無論如何要來。| *Anyhow the car finally came out of the garage in a worse state than when it went in.* 總之, 汽車最終從修車廠開出來時比進去時的狀況還要差。| *Anyhow, what difference does it make what I think?* 然而, 我怎麼看又有甚麼區別呢? | *Why are you calling anyhow?* 你打電話來到底幹甚麼? —see also 另見 ANYWAY 3

anymore /ˌɛnɪˋmɔr; ˌeniˈmɔː/ *adv* **not...anymore** not any longer 不再: *Nick doesn't live here anymore.* 尼克已不住在這裡了。| *They used to laugh at Sheila. Not anymore.* 他們過去常嘲笑希拉, 現在不再這樣了。

an·y·one /ˋɛnɪˌwʌn; ˈeniwʌn/ *pron* **1** any person in a group or in the world, when it is not important to say exactly who 任何人: *Anyone can cook risotto – it's easy!* 誰都會做肉汁燴飯, 這很容易。| *He's cleverer than* 

anyone I know. 他比我認識的任何人都聰明。| **anyone tall/rich etc** *Anyone stupid enough to believe that deserves everything they get!* 不管誰愚蠢到相信那一點都是咎由自取！| **anyone else** (=a different person) 其他人 *Anyone else would have been too embarrassed, but he walked right up and asked for her autograph.* 換了別人都會感到難為情，他卻偏偏走過去請她簽名留念。**2** used in questions and negatives to mean a person 有人，任何人〔用於疑問句或否定句〕: *Is anyone listening to me?* 有人在聽我講話嗎？| *If anyone sees Lisa, ask her to call me.* 如果有誰看見莉莎，請她打電話給我。| **anyone interesting/rich etc** *Anyone new coming to tonight's meeting?* 有哪位是今晚第一次來開會？| **anyone else** (=a different person) 其他人 *Do you know anyone else who wants a ticket?* 你知道還有誰要票嗎？—see also 另見 EVERYONE, SOMEONE

an·y·place /ˈɛnɪˌples; ˈenipleɪs/ *adv AmE* anywhere【美】無論何處，隨便哪裡: *It's funny, I've never felt anyplace was home before I came to Connecticut.* 說來有趣，只有我來康涅狄格州以後才覺得是到了家。

1 1 **an·y·thing** /ˈɛnɪˌθɪŋ; ˈeniθɪŋ/ *pron* **1** any thing, event, situation etc, when it does not matter exactly which 任何事物，無論何事: *Anything will do to wedge the door open.* 任何東西都可以，只要把門楔住讓它開着就行了。| *If you believe that, you'll believe anything!* 這樣的事你都相信，那你甚麼事都會相信了！| *OK, you can borrow the car – anything for a quiet life.* 好吧，你可以借車，只要能過上安寧的生活就甚麼都行。| **anything red/cheap etc** *She'll buy anything reduced in a sale.* 只要是減價的東西，她甚麼都買。| **anything else** (=any different thing) 別的甚麼（東西）*It's got to be Dior – anything else just isn't good enough.* 必須是迪奧牌的，別的牌子都不行。**2** used in questions, negatives, and statements expressing possibility to mean 'nothing' or 'something' 任何事物〔用於疑問句或否定句〕: *You can't believe anything she says.* 你不能相信她說的任何話。| *Have you heard anything about the new Garrison Keillor book?* 你有聽說過有關加里森·凱勒那本新書的事嗎？| **anything to say/to do etc** *It was a great health farm but there wasn't really anything to do in the evenings.* 這是一個非常好的健身農莊，只是晚上沒有甚麼事情可做。| **anything new/stupid etc** *We've almost sealed the deal, so don't do anything stupid.* 我們差不多已敲定了這樁交易，所以不要做任何傻事了。| **anything else** (=any other thing, event etc) 別的東西〔事情等〕*Would you like anything else to eat?* 你還要吃點兒別的東西嗎？**3 anything but clear/happy etc** used to emphasize that someone or something is not clear, happy etc 根本不清楚／不開心等: *The bridge is anything but safe.* 這道橋一點兒也不安全。| *We'd been warned he was a frail, withdrawn man but when I met him he was anything but.* 有人提醒我們他是一個脆弱內向的人，可當我見到他時，發現他根本不是那樣的人。—see also 另見 SOME

Frequencies of the word **anything** in spoken and written English 單詞anything在英語口語和書面語中的使用頻率

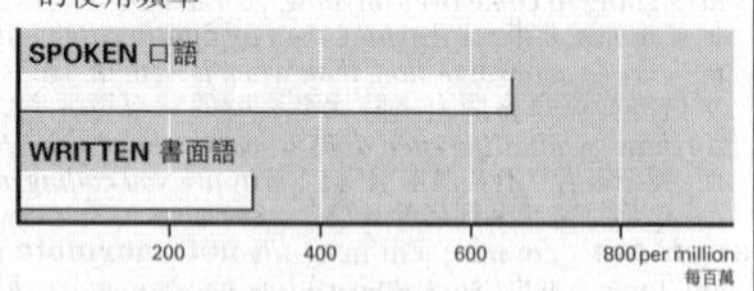

Based on the British National Corpus and the Longman Lancaster Corpus
據英國國家語料庫和朗文蘭卡斯特語料庫

This graph shows that the word **anything** is more common in spoken English than in written English. This is because it is used a lot in questions, and is used in some common spoken phrases. 本圖表顯示單詞anything在英語口語中比在書面語中常用，因為該詞經常用於疑問句中，而且口語中一些常用片語也是由anything構成的。

4 anything like similar in any way to something or someone else 像…，類似…: *Does she look anything like her mother?* 她長得像她母親嗎？**5 not anything like/near** *spoken* used to emphasize that someone or something is not in a particular condition or state【口】一點也不（像）: *We don't have anything like enough money to buy a new car.* 我們根本沒有足夠的錢買輛新汽車。**6 as easy/fast etc as anything** extremely easy, fast etc 非常容易／快速等: *It was a long lecture and as boring as anything.* 這是一個冗長的講座，非常乏味。**7 or anything** or something that is similar 或相似的另一件事物: *Would you like a gin and tonic or anything?* 你要加奎寧水的杜松子酒還是別的甚麼？**8 for anything** if you will not do something for anything, you will definitely not do it 決不，怎麼也不: *After what happened last time, I wouldn't work for them again for anything.* 自從上次發生的事情以後，我怎麼也不會再為他們工作了。**9 like anything** if you do something like anything, you do it a lot or to a great degree 非常，極其: *Tom only left last week and I already miss him like anything.* 湯姆上週才離開，我已經非常想念他。**10 anything you say** used to tell someone you agree with what they suggest when actually you do not 怎麼樣都行，好吧: *"You ought to keep the flat more tidy." "Anything you say."* "你應該讓公寓更加整潔。" "好吧。"

an·y·way /ˈɛnɪˌwe; ˈeniweɪ/ *adv* [sentence adverb 句子副詞] **1** used to say that someone does something or that something happens in spite of a problem 無論如何，不管怎樣: *He said he didn't know much about computers but that he'd try and help us anyway.* 他說他不太懂電腦，不過，他說無論如何也會設法幫助我們。 1 2

Frequencies of the adverb **anyway** in spoken and written English 副詞anyway在英語口語和書面語中的使用頻率

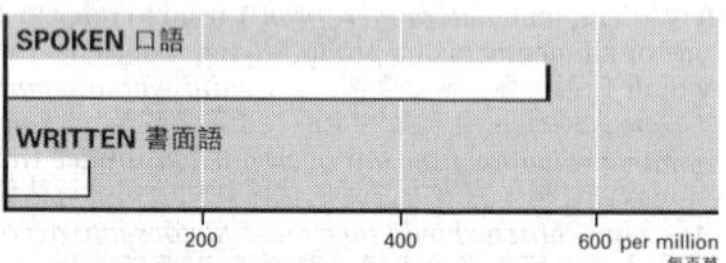

Based on the British National Corpus and the Longman Lancaster Corpus
據英國國家語料庫和朗文蘭卡斯特語料庫

This graph shows that the adverb **anyway** is much more common in spoken English than in written English. This is because it has some special uses in spoken English. 本圖表顯示，副詞anyway在口語中比在書面語中要常用得多，因為它在英語口語中有一些特殊的用法。

2 used when you are changing the subject of a conversation or returning to a previous subject 對了，好吧〔用於改變話題或轉到前一個話題上〕: *Anyway, what was I saying?* 對了，我剛才在說甚麼？**3** used when you want to finish saying something or continue without all the details 總之: *Anyway, I must be going now.* 總之，我現在得走了。| *Anyway, after three months at the clinic, she'd made a full recovery.* 總之，在診所治了三個月，她完全康復了。**4** used to add some extra information, an opinion or a question to something that you have just said 話又說回來，反正，然而: *Sam didn't get the job; but he's not worried because it didn't pay well anyway.* 薩姆沒

有得到那份工作, 但他並沒有擔心, 反正報酬也不算高。| *It was nice of you to offer anyway.* 話又說回來, 你主動提出總是件好事。**5** used to find out the real reason for something 究竟, 到底: *So anyway, what were you doing in the park at two in the morning?* 那麼, 你凌晨兩點在公園裡究竟在做甚麼? | *Why did he visit Alan anyway?* 那他到底為甚麼去艾倫那裡?

1 3 **an·y·where** /ˈɛnɪˌhwɛr; ˈeniweə/ also 又作 **anyplace** *AmE*【美】*adv* **1** in or to any place 無論何處, 隨便哪裡: *Sit anywhere, there are plenty of seats.* 隨便坐吧, 有的是座位。| *Tropical fruit used to be hard to find in Britain but now you can buy it anywhere.* 以前在英國很難看到熱帶水果, 不過現在到處都能買到。| **[+in]** *Apparently that restaurant does the best curry anywhere in London.* 顯然, 那家餐廳做的咖喱食品在倫敦是最好的。| **anywhere else** (=in or to a different place) 別的任何地方 *Anywhere else you'd have to pay airport tax but not when you visit this Pacific island.* 其他任何地方你都得付機場税, 但到這個太平洋島嶼旅遊就不用付。**2** used in questions, negatives, and statements expressing possibility to mean 'somewhere' or 'nowhere' 某個地方; 任何地方〔都不〕〔用於表示可能性的疑問句、否定句或陳述句〕: *I can't find it anywhere. Are you sure you left it here?* 我哪裡也找不到。你肯定是放這兒了嗎? | *Do they need anywhere to stay for the night?* 他們需要找個地方過夜嗎? | *Would you like a ride anywhere?* 你想騎車到甚麼地方玩玩嗎? | **anywhere interesting/cheap etc** *Did you go anywhere exotic on vacation this year?* 你今年假期有沒有去甚麼有異國情調的地方? | **anywhere else** *The photos are great – have you been anywhere else in Mexico?* 這些照片太漂亮了, 你有去墨西哥其他地方嗎? **3 not anywhere near a)** used to emphasize that someone or something is not near to another person or thing 老遠〔用於強調相隔的距離〕: *What do you mean it was my fault? My car wasn't anywhere near yours.* 你説是我的過錯到底是甚麼意思? 我的車離你的車老遠呢。**b)** used to emphasize that someone or something is not in a particular condition or state 差挺多, 差挺遠〔用於強調某人或某物不處於某種狀況或狀態〕: *The money doesn't come anywhere near compensating for what those people suffered.* 這些錢離補償那些人的損失還差很遠。**4 anywhere between one and ten/anywhere from one to ten etc** used to mean any age, number, amount etc between one and ten when it is difficult to know exactly which age, number etc 從一到十(任何一個), 在一到十之間等: *She was one of those women who could be anywhere between forty five and sixty years of age.* 她是那些介乎四十五到六十歲之間的婦女之一。**5 it won't get you anywhere** used to tell someone that they will not be able to change a situation 不會有甚麼改觀, 沒甚麼用處: *You can try writing to complain, but I don't think it will get you anywhere.* 你可以試試寫投訴信, 但我認為沒甚麼用。**6 not getting/going anywhere** not successful or not having plans for the future 沒甚麼成就[發展]: *Terry's a nice enough lad but he's not going anywhere.* 特里是一個很好的小伙子, 但沒甚麼發展。—see 見 PLACE[1] (USAGE)

AOB /ˌe o ˋbi; ˌeɪ əʊ ˈbiː/ *BrE* the abbreviation of 縮寫= 'any other business'; things that have not yet been discussed in the main part of a meeting【英】〔會議主要議題以外的〕任何其他事務

a·or·ta /eˋɔrtə; eɪˈɔːtə/ *n* [C] the largest ARTERY (=tube for carrying blood) in the body, taking blood from the heart 主動脈, 大動脈

a·pace /əˋpes; əˈpeɪs/ *adv literary* quickly【文】飛快地, 急速地: *Multimedia developments continue apace.* 多媒體技術在飛速發展。

3 1 **a·part** /əˋpɑrt; əˈpɑːt/ *adv, adj*
1 ▶DISTANCE 距離◀ if things are apart, they have an amount of space between them 分開, 相距, 相隔: *Joel stood apart from the group, frowning.* 喬爾皺着眉頭, 獨自站在一邊。| **two miles/six feet etc apart** *The two villages are 6 kilometres apart.* 兩村之間相距六公里。
2 ▶TIME 時間◀ **two hours/six weeks etc apart** if things are a particular time apart, they have that much time between them 相隔兩小時/六週等: *Our birthdays are exactly a month apart.* 我們倆的生日正好相差一個月。
3 ▶SEPARATE 分開◀ **a)** if you keep, pull, force etc two things apart, you separate them〔把...〕分開: *I try to keep my work and private life as far apart as possible.* 我設法把工作和私生活盡可能分開。| *The two boys started fighting so we had to pull them apart.* 兩個男孩打起架來, 我們不得不把他們拉開。**b)** if you take or pull something apart, or something comes or falls apart, it is separated into many different parts 拆開; 散開: *The mechanics took the engine apart.* 機械師把發動機拆開了。| *The chair fell apart in my hands.* 椅子在我手上散了架。
4 ▶SOMEWHERE ELSE 別處◀ in a different place from someone else 與〔某人〕分開在別處: *You never see the twins apart.* 你從未看見這對雙胞胎分開過。| *My wife and I are living apart at the moment.* 目前我和妻子分開住。
5 ▶RELATIONSHIP 關係◀ **a) be worlds/poles apart** if people, beliefs, or ideas are worlds or poles apart, they are completely different from each other 完全不同, 截然相反 **b) grow/drift apart** if people or groups grow apart, their relationship slowly ends 逐漸疏遠: *Sadly, the family has grown apart since Auntie Barbara died.* 不幸的是, 自從芭芭拉姑母去世後, 這家人之間就慢慢疏遠了。
6 ▶CONDITION 情況◀ if something is coming apart or falling apart etc, it is in a very bad condition 破碎(的), 破裂(的): *I must get some new trousers; these are all coming apart.* 我得買些新褲子, 這些都破了。| *Well, the relationship's fallen apart, to be honest.* 好吧, 説實話, 關係已經破裂。
7 joking apart used to say that you want to consider something seriously 説正經的: *Joking apart, we must do something about that hole.* 説正經的, 我們確實應採取措施補補那個洞。
8 quite apart from without even considering 撇開...來説, 不考慮...: *Quite apart from the cost, there's the question of your health to be considered.* 且不説開銷, 你的健康問題總應該考慮吧。
9 apart from also 又作 **aside from** *especially AmE*【尤美】**a)** used to introduce one small point which makes a statement not completely true 除了, 只是: *This essay's good apart from a couple of spelling mistakes.* 除了有些拼寫錯誤, 這篇文章寫得不錯。**b)** except for 除...以外: *Apart from the occasional visit, what does Alan do for his kids?* 艾倫除了偶爾去探望一下, 還為孩子們做些甚麼?

a·part·heid /əˋpɑrthet; əˈpɑːtheɪt/ *n* [U] the former South African political and social system in which only white people had full political rights and people of other races, especially black people, were forced to go to separate schools, live in separate areas etc〔舊時南非的〕種族隔離制度

a·part·ment /əˋpɑrtmənt; əˈpɑːtmənt/ *n* [C] **1** *especially AmE* a set of rooms within a large building, usually on one level, where someone lives【尤美】〔一般在同一樓層的〕一套住房, 公寓套間; FLAT[2] (1) *BrE*【英】: *How many bedrooms do you have in your new apartment?* 你的新房子有幾個臥室? **2** [usually plural 一般用複數] a large room with expensive furniture, decorations etc, used especially by an important person such as a president, prince etc〔大而豪華的〕套間: *the presidential apartments* 總統套間 —see graph at 參見 FLAT[2] 圖表 

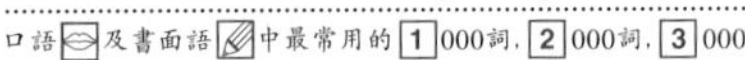

A

apartment block /ˈ·· ·/ *n* [C] *AmE* a large group of buildings containing many apartments【美】公寓樓羣 —see picture on page A4 參見 A4 頁圖

apartment build·ing /ˈ·· ˌ··/ also 又作 **apartment house** /ˈ·· ·/ *n* [C] *AmE* a large building containing many apartments【美】公寓大樓

ap·a·thet·ic /ˌæpəˋθɛtɪk; ˌæpəˈθetɪk◂/ *adj* not excited about something and not caring whether it happens, or not interested in anything and unwilling to make an effort to change and improve things 無興趣的; 無感情的; 冷淡的; 無動於衷的: *an apathetic electorate* 態度冷淡的選民 —**apathetically** /-klɪ; -kli/ *adv*

ap·a·thy /ˋæpəθɪ; ˈæpəθi/ *n* [U] the feeling of not being interested or not caring, either about a particular thing or about life 漠然, 冷淡; 無興趣; 無動於衷: *apathy among the public* 公眾的冷淡態度

ape¹ /ep; eɪp/ *n* [C] **1** a large monkey without a tail, or with a very short tail, such as a GORILLA or a CHIMPANZEE 猿 **2** an insulting word for a man who behaves in a stupid or annoying way 傻瓜, 笨蛋: *Push off you big ape.* 滾開, 你這個大笨蛋。**3 go ape** *slang* to suddenly become very angry or excited【俚】突然發怒[激動]

ape² *v* [T] to copy someone's behaviour, especially in a silly or unkind way〔尤指愚蠢或惡意地〕模仿

a·per·i·tif /əˌpɛrəˋtif; əˌperɪˈtiːf/ *n* [C] an alcoholic drink that is drunk before a meal 飯前酒, 開胃酒

ap·er·ture /ˋæpɚtʃɚ; ˈæpətʃə/ *n* [C] **1** the hole at the front of a camera or TELESCOPE¹, which can be changed to let more or less light in〔照相機的〕光圈, 孔徑 **2** *technical* a small hole or space in something which is used for a particular purpose【術語】孔, 縫隙: *an inspection aperture* 檢查孔

ape·shit /ˋepˌʃɪt; ˈeɪpʃɪt/ *adj* **go apeshit** *slang* to suddenly become very angry or excited【俚】勃然大怒

a·pex /ˋepɛks; ˈeɪpeks/ *n* [C] **1** *technical* the top or highest part of something【術語】頂點, 最高點: *the apex of the triangle* 三角形的頂點 **2** *formal* the most successful part【正式】頂峯: *the apex of his career* 他事業的頂峯

a·phid /ˋefɪd; ˈeɪfɪd/ *n* [C] a type of very small insect that drinks the juices of plants 蚜蟲

aph·o·ris·m /ˋæfəˌrɪzəm; ˈæfərɪzəm/ *n* [C] a short wise phrase 格言, 警句 —**aphoristic** /ˌæfəˋrɪstɪk; ˌæfəˈrɪstɪk◂/ *adj*

aph·ro·dis·i·ac /ˌæfrəˋdɪzɪˌæk; ˌæfrəˈdɪziæk◂/ *n* [C] a food, drink, or drug that makes you want to have sex 催情劑, 春藥 —**aphrodisiac** *adj*: *the aphrodisiac properties of the fruit* 這種水果能激發性慾的特性

a·pi·a·ry /ˋepɪˌɛrɪ; ˈeɪpiəri/ *n* [C] a place where BEE*s* are kept 養蜂場; 蜂房

a·piece /əˋpis; əˈpiːs/ *adv* [only after number or noun 僅用於數詞或名詞後] costing or having a particular amount each 每個, 每人, 每件: **ten pence/fifteen dollars etc apiece** *The tomato plants cost 60p apiece.* 番茄苗每株60便士。| **three pages/a ticket etc apiece** (=having three pages etc each) 每個人三頁/一張票等 *We shared the gold out equally – three bags apiece.* 我們平分了這些金子, 每人三袋。

a·plen·ty /əˋplɛntɪ; əˈplenti/ *adj* [only after noun 僅用於名詞後] *old use* in large amounts or numbers, especially more than you need【舊】豐富的, 大量的, 很多的〔尤指超過需要的〕: *There was food aplenty.* 有很多食物。

a·plomb /əˋplɑm; əˈplɒm/ *n* [U] **with aplomb** in a confident and skilful way, especially when you have to deal with difficult problems or a difficult situation 鎮靜地, 沉着地, 泰然自若地: *Ms Sharpe handled their hostile questions with great aplomb.* 夏普女士非常沉着地應付他們挑釁性的問題。

a·poc·a·lypse /əˋpɑkəˌlɪps; əˈpɒkəlɪps/ *n* [C] **1 the apocalypse** the destruction and end of the world 世界末日 **2** a dangerous, frightening, and very serious situation causing death, harm, or destruction 大災難: *3000 died in the apocalypse of the earthquake.* 有3000人死於這場大地震。

a·poc·a·lyp·tic /əˌpɑkəˋlɪptɪk; əˌpɒkəˈlɪptɪk◂/ *adj* **1** warning people about terrible events that will happen in the future 預言將有大災難的: *Orwell's apocalyptic vision of the future* 奧威爾對未來的災難性預言 **2** connected with the final destruction and end of the world 世界末日的

a·poc·ry·phal /əˋpɑkrəfəl; əˈpɒkrɪfəl/ *adj* an apocryphal story about a famous person or event is well-known but probably not ture 可疑的, 杜撰的: *Washington's apocryphal phrase: "Father, I cannot tell a lie."* 傳說中華盛頓講過的一句話: "父親, 我不會說謊。"

ap·o·gee /ˋæpəˌdʒi; ˈæpədʒiː/ *n* [C] **1** *formal* the most successful part of something【正式】〔權力或成就的〕頂峯: *the apogee of his political career* 他政治生涯的頂峯 **2** *technical* the point where an object travelling through space is farthest from the earth【術語】遠地點〔太空中物體運行軌道上離地球最遠之點〕—compare 比較 PERIGEE

a·po·lit·i·cal /ˌepəˋlɪtɪkḷ; ˌeɪpəˈlɪtɪkəl◂/ *adj* not having any interest in or connection with politics 非政治的; 不關心政治的

a·pol·o·get·ic /əˌpɑləˋdʒɛtɪk; əˌpɒləˈdʒetɪk◂/ *adj* showing or saying that you are sorry that something has happened, especially because you feel guilty or embarrassed about it 道歉的, 抱歉的: *The restaurant manager was very apologetic and said we could have our meal for free.* 飯店經理深表歉意, 並說我們這頓飯可以免費。| *an apologetic letter* 致歉信 —**apologetically** /-klɪ; -kli/ *adv*: *"I know," she said apologetically.* "我知道。"她抱歉地說。

ap·o·lo·gi·a /ˌæpəˋlodʒɪə; ˌæpəˈləʊdʒiə/ *n* [C+**for**] *formal* a statement in which you defend an idea that you believe in【正式】辯解, 辯護

a·pol·o·gist /əˋpɑlədʒɪst; əˈpɒlədʒɪst/ *n* [C] someone who tries to defend and explain an idea or system 辯護者, 辯解者: *one of Stalin's western apologists* 史太林的西方辯解者之一

a·pol·o·gize also 又作 **-ise** *BrE*【英】/əˋpɑləˌdʒaɪz; əˈpɒlədʒaɪz/ *v* [I] to tell someone that you are sorry that you have done something wrong 道歉, 謝罪: *That was an awful thing to say, I think you should apologize.* 那是很難聽的話, 我想你該道歉。| [+**for**] *I must apologise for the delay in replying to your letter.* 未能及時覆信, 我必須向你道歉。| **apologize to** *The US has apologized to Britain for the accident.* 美國已就這次意外事故向英國致歉。| **apologize profusely** (=apologize a lot) 非常抱歉 *She apologized profusely for being late.* 她非常抱歉自己來遲了。

a·pol·o·gy /əˋpɑlədʒɪ; əˈpɒlədʒi/ *n* [C] **1** something that you say or write to show that you are sorry for doing something wrong 道歉, 認錯: *Your behaviour was outrageous. I demand an apology!* 你的行為太蠻橫了, 我要求你道歉! | **accept sb's apology** (=forgive them after they have apologized) 接受某人的道歉 *Please accept our sincere apologies.* 請接受我們真誠的道歉。| **owe sb an apology** (=to have done something bad or unfair to someone) 應向某人道歉 *I owe you an apology for what I said last night – I'm really sorry.* 真對不起, 我該為昨晚說的向你道歉。| **make an apology** *The paper was forced to make a grovelling apology.* 報紙被迫作出卑躬的道歉。**2** *literary* a statement in which you defend something you believe in after it has been criticized by other people【文】辯解, 辯護 **3 an apology for** *humorous* a very bad example of something【幽默】權充...的東西; 勉強代用的東西: *an apology for a human being* 不像話的人

ap·o·plec·tic /ˌæpəˋplɛktɪk; ˌæpəˈplektɪk◂/ *adj* **1** *informal* so angry or excited that your face becomes red【非正式】氣得[激動得]臉發紅的: *The colonel was apoplectic with rage.* 上校勃然大怒。**2** connected with apoplexy 中風的

A

ap·o·plex·y /ˋæpəˌplɛksɪ; ˈæpəpleksi/ *n* [U] *old-fashioned* an illness caused by a problem in your brain which can damage your ability to move, feel, or think; STROKE¹ (1) 【過時】中風

a·pos·ta·sy /əˋpɑstəsɪ; əˈpɒstəsi/ *n* [U] *formal* the act of changing your beliefs so that you stop supporting a religion, political party etc【正式】叛教; 脫黨; 變節

a·pos·tate /əˋpɑstet; əˈpɒsteɪt/ *n* [C] *formal* someone who has stopped believing in and supporting their old religion or political party【正式】叛教者; 脫黨者; 變節者

a pos·ter·i·o·ri /ˋe pɑsˌtɪrɪˋoraɪ; ˌeɪ pɒsteriˈɔːraɪ/ *adj Latin formal* using facts or results to form a judgment about what must have happened before【拉丁, 正式】由事實或結果推斷出原因的, 歸納的 —compare 比較 A PRIORI

a·pos·tle /əˋpɑsḷ; əˈpɒsəl/ *n* [C] **1** one of the 12 people chosen by Christ to teach and spread the Christian religion 基督的十二使徒之一, 使徒 **2** *formal* someone who believes strongly in a new idea and tries to persuade other people【正式】倡導者, 先驅: **[+of]** *an apostle of revolutionary ideals* 革命理想的先驅

ap·o·stol·ic /ˌæpəsˋtɑlɪk; ˌæpəˈstɒlɪk◂/ *adj* **1** connected with the POPE (=leader of the Catholic church)（天主教）教宗的, 教皇的 **2** connected with one of Christ's 12 apostles（基督之）使徒的

a·pos·tro·phe /əˋpɑstrəfɪ; əˈpɒstrəfi/ *n* [C] **a)** the sign (') used in writing to show that numbers or letters have been left out, as in 'don't' (=do not) and '86 (=1986) 表示省略的撇號（'）〈如 don't 表示 do not, '86 表示 1986〉 **b)** the same sign used before 's' to show that something belongs to someone or something, or is connected with them, as in 'John's book', or 'Charles' mother', or 'Nixon's last year as president' 表示所有格的撇號（'）〈如 John's book, Charles' mother 或 Nixon's last year as president〉 **c)** used before 's' to show the plural of letters and numbers as in 'Your r's look like v's.' 用於 s 前表示字母和數字的複數〈如在 Your r's look like v's. 中〉

a·poth·e·ca·ry /əˋpɑθəˌkɛrɪ; əˈpɒθəkəri/ *n* [C] someone who mixed and sold medicines in former times〔舊時的〕藥劑師

a·poth·e·o·sis /əˌpɑθɪˋosɪs; əˌpɒθiˈəʊsəs/ *n plural* **apotheoses** /-siz; -siːz/ [C usually singular 一般用單數] *formal*【正式】**1** the best and most perfect example of something 典範, 最完美的榜樣: **[+of]** *the apotheosis of French 16th century art* 16世紀法國藝術的典範 **2** the state of getting to the highest level of something such as honour, importance etc〔榮譽、重要性等的〕極點, 頂峯

ap·pal *BrE*【英】, **appall** *AmE*【美】/əˋpɔl; əˈpɔːl/ *v* [T] to shock someone by being very bad or unpleasant 使驚駭; 使充滿恐懼: *The whole idea of killing animals for fur appals me.* 殺死動物取其毛皮的想法令我不寒而慄。

ap·palled /əˋpɔld; əˈpɔːld/ *adj* very shocked by something very bad or unpleasant 對...深表震驚的, 驚恐萬分的: **[+by/at]** *Rescue workers were appalled at what they saw.* 營救人員對看到的情況深感震驚。

ap·pal·ling /əˋpɔlɪŋ; əˈpɔːlɪŋ/ *adj* **1** so bad or unpleasant that you are shocked 駭人聽聞的; 令人震驚的; 可怕的: *We heard the appalling news about the earthquake.* 聽到有關地震的消息我們十分震驚。**2** very bad 極壞的, 糟透的: *Morrison's last album was absolutely appalling.* 莫里森的上一張唱片簡直糟透了。—**appallingly** *adv*: *You've behaved appallingly.* 你的表現太差了。| *appallingly bad taste* 極糟糕的味道

ap·pa·loo·sa /ˌæpəˋlusə; ˌæpəˈluːsə/ *n* [C] *AmE* a kind of horse that is pale coloured with dark spots【美】阿帕盧薩馬〔一種皮毛色淺、帶深色斑點的馬〕

ap·par·at·chik /ˌɑpəˋrɑtʃɪk; ˌɑːpəˈrɑːtʃɪk/ *n* [C] an official working for a government or other organization who obeys orders without thinking〔盲從的〕黨政工作人員

ap·pa·ra·tus /ˌæpəˋrætəs; ˌæpəˈreɪtəs/ *n plural* **apparatuses** or **apparatus** [C,U] **1** tools and machines used especially for scientific, medical, and technical purposes 設備, 儀器, 裝置, 器械, 用具: *the apparatus shown in the diagram* 圖表中顯示的器材 | *The astronauts have special breathing apparatus.* 宇航員有特殊的呼吸裝置。**2** a system or process for doing something 機制: *the apparatus for settling industrial disputes* 解決勞資糾紛的機制

ap·par·el¹ /əˋpærəl; əˈpærəl/ *n* [U] **1** *formal* clothes, especially clothes worn on a special occasion【正式】〔尤指華麗的〕服裝, 盛裝: *the Queen's ceremonial apparel* 女王的禮服 **2 ladies'/men's/children's apparel** *especially AmE* a word for clothes, often used in shops【尤美】女服/男服/兒童服裝〔商店用語〕

apparel² *v* [T+in] *old use* to dress someone, especially in special clothes【舊】為...穿衣; 〔尤指〕盛裝

ap·par·ent /əˋpærənt; əˈpærənt/ *adj* **1** easily noticed or understood 顯而易見的; 明白的: **[+to]** *Her anxiety was apparent to everyone.* 大家都看得出她的焦慮。| **it became apparent that** *It soon became apparent that our opponents were too strong for us.* 很快就看出, 我們的對手太強。| **for no apparent reason** (=without a clear reason) 沒明確的理由 *Suddenly, for no apparent reason, he walked away.* 他沒甚麼明確的理由就突然走了。**2** seeming to have a particular quality, feeling, or attitude 顯得...的, 表面上的: *I was shocked by Joe's apparent lack of concern for his child.* 喬表現出對孩子的漠不關心使我很震驚。

ap·par·ent·ly /əˋpærəntlɪ; əˈpærəntli/ *adv* **1** [sentence adverb 句子副詞] based on what you have heard is true, although you are not completely sure about it 看來, 似乎: *Apparently they've run out of tickets for the concert.* 看來, 他們賣光了音樂會的票。| *I wasn't there, but apparently it was a good party.* 我當時不在, 但據我所知, 那聚會搞得不錯。**2** according to the way someone looks or a situation appears, although you cannot be sure 顯然: *She managed to climb out of the car, apparently unhurt.* 她設法爬出了車外, 顯然沒有受傷。—compare 比較 EVIDENTLY, OBVIOUSLY

ap·pa·ri·tion /ˌæpəˋrɪʃən; ˌæpəˈrɪʃən/ *n* [C] something that you imagine you can see, especially the spirit of a dead person 幽靈, 鬼魂: *a ghostly apparition* 鬼魂

ap·peal¹ /əˋpil; əˈpiːl/ *n* **1** [C] an urgent request for something important such as money or help, especially to help someone in a bad situation 懇求; 呼籲: **[+for]** *The United Nations' appeal for a ceasefire has been largely ignored by both sides.* 總的來說, 雙方對聯合國關於停火的呼籲不予理會。| **appeal to sb to do sth** *an appeal to parents to supervise their children* 對家長監護好孩子的呼籲 | **make/launch an appeal** *In 1988 Bob Geldorf launched an urgent appeal for the famine victims.* 1988年, 鮑勃·吉爾多夫發出了援助饑民的緊急呼籲。**2** [U] a quality that makes you like someone or something, be interested in them, or want them 感染力, 吸引力: *Much of Corfu's appeal lies in its lively night life.* 科孚的魅力在於其多姿多采的夜生活。| **[+for]** *The film has great appeal for young audiences.* 這部電影對年輕觀眾有很大的吸引力。| **popular/wide appeal** (=liked by many people) 吸引眾人的感染力 *CD-ROMs now have wider popular appeal.* 現在越來越多的人喜歡用唯讀光碟。| **sex appeal** (=the quality of being sexually attractive) 性感 *Marilyn Monroe had amazing sex appeal.* 瑪麗蓮·夢露非常性感迷人。**3** [C,U] a formal request to a court or to someone in authority asking for a decision to be changed 上訴: **[+to]** *an appeal to the European court of Human Rights* 向歐洲人權法庭提出的上訴 —see also 另見 COURT OF APPEAL

appeal² *v* **1** [I] to make a serious public request for help, money, information etc 懇請, 懇求; 呼籲: **appeal (to sb) for sth** *The police are appealing to the public for information about the crime.* 警方呼籲公眾提供有關這宗罪

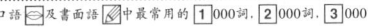

案的資料。| *The Bosnian government appealed for help from Western countries.* 波斯尼亞政府呼籲西方國家給予幫助。| **appeal to sb to do sth** *She appealed to the kidnappers to release her son.* 她哀求綁架者釋放她的兒子。**2 appeal to sb** if someone or something appeals to you, they seem attractive and interesting 吸引某人: *Does the idea of working abroad appeal to you?* 你對出國工作的主意感興趣嗎? | *The magazine is intended to appeal to working women in their 20s and 30s.* 這本雜誌的讀者對象是二十幾歲到三十幾歲的職業女性。**3** [I, T] to make a formal request to a court or someone in authority asking for a decision to be changed (提出)上訴: *If you are not satisfied, you can appeal.* 如果你不滿意, 可以上訴。**4 appeal to sb's better nature/sense of honour/sense of justice etc** to try to persuade someone to do something by reminding them that it is a good, honourable etc thing to do 呼喚某人的良知/榮譽感/正義感等

Appeal Court /ˈ·ˌ· ·/ *n* [singular] the COURT OF APPEAL 上訴法院

ap·peal·ing /əˋpilɪŋ; əˈpiːlɪŋ/ *adj* **1** attractive or interesting 有吸引力的; 有趣的: **find sb/sth appealing** *I find the idea of $100,000 dollars a year very appealing.* 我認為每年 10 萬美元很誘人。| *She does look rather appealing in that dress.* 她穿上那件衣服看起來頗有吸引力。**2 appealing look/voice etc** a look etc that shows that someone wants help or sympathy 求助的目光/語氣等: *I said I didn't know anything about computers and gave him an appealing look.* 我說我對電腦一無所知, 求助地看了他一眼。—**appealingly** *adv*

1 1 **ap·pear** /əˋpɪr; əˈpɪə/ *v*

1 ▶SEEM 似乎◀ [linking verb 連繫動詞, not in progressive 不用進行式] a word used especially in formal or written English meaning to seem 似乎, 好像, 看來〔尤用於正式場合或書面語中〕: **appear upset/calm etc** *Roger appeared very upset.* 羅傑看起來很不高興。| *The city appeared calm after the previous night's fighting.* 經過前一晚的戰鬥, 城市似乎很平靜。| **appear to be** *There appeared to be no significant difference between the two groups in the test.* 這兩組在測試中似乎沒有明顯的差異。| **appear to do sth** *The man appeared to have had a heart attack.* 那個人好像心臟病發作了。| **it appears that** *It appears that there has been a change in the plans.* 計劃好像作了修改。| **what appears to be** (=something that looks like) 看起來像... *Police have found what appear to be human remains.* 警方已經發現看起來像人的屍體的東西。| **make it appear that** *She put the gun next to the body, to make it appear that the victim had shot himself.* 她把槍放在屍體旁邊, 使受害者看起來像是自殺的樣子。| **so it would appear** (=used to say that it seems likely that something is true, although you are not completely sure) 看起來是這樣 *"The boys are completely innocent?" "So it would appear from the press reports."* "這些孩子完全是無辜的?" "從新聞報道看好像是的。"

2 ▶START TO BE SEEN 出現◀ [I] to start to be seen or to suddenly be seen 出現; 呈現: *An image appeared on the screen.* 屏幕上出現了一個影像。| *Two faces appeared at our window.* 我們窗前出現了兩張面孔。| **[+from]** *The manager hardly ever appeared from his office.* 經理很少走出他的辦公室。| **appear out of nowhere** (=suddenly appear in a way that is very surprising) 突然冒出來 *I don't know what caused the marks – they just seemed to appear out of nowhere.* 我不知道這些痕跡是怎麼來的 —— 好像是突然從甚麼地方冒出來似的。| **appear overnight** (=appear very quickly or suddenly) 一夜之間出現 *Software development is a fast-moving business – firms appear and disappear virtually overnight.* 軟件開發是瞬息萬變的產業, 一夜之間會有許多公司出現, 也會有許多公司消失。

3 ▶FILM/TV PROGRAMME ETC 電影/電視節目等◀ [I] to take part in a film, play, concert, television programme etc 參加演出, 露面, 亮相: **[+in/on]** *Roseanne Barr has appeared on the show several times.* 羅絲安妮·巴爾已經幾次登台演出。| **[+at]** *Vanessa Redgrave is currently appearing at the Theatre Royal, Drury Lane.* 瓦妮莎·雷德格雷夫目前正在德魯里街的皇家劇院演出。

4 ▶BE WRITTEN/SHOWN 寫出/顯出◀ [I] to be written or shown on a list, in a book or newspaper, in a document etc 刊登; 發表; 被寫進: *Her name appears at the front of the book.* 書的封面上印着她的名字。| *The story appeared in all the national newspapers.* 這篇報道刊載在所有的全國性報紙上。

5 ▶PRODUCT/BOOK 產品/書◀ [I] if a product or book appears, it becomes available to be bought for the first time 初次上市: *When the book finally appeared on the shelves it was a huge success.* 這本書終於上架開售, 大獲成功。

6 ▶STH NEW/DIFFERENT 新的/不同的事物◀ [I] if something new or surprising appears, it happens or exists for the first time 首次出現, 登場: *Several new-punk bands have recently appeared on the music scene.* 近來在樂壇出現了幾支新龐克樂隊。

7 ▶LAW COURT 法庭◀ [I] to be present in a court of law for a TRIAL[1] (1) that you are involved in 出庭: *Smith was ordered to appear in court to face charges on the 15th.* 史密斯接到指令在 15 日出庭面對指控。| **[+on behalf of/for]** *Sir Nicholas Gammon QC appeared on behalf of the defendant.* 女王法律顧問尼古拉斯·甘蒙爵士代表被告出庭。

8 ▶COMMITTEE/INQUIRY 委員會/詢問◀ appear before/in front of sth to answer questions by members of an official group who are trying to find out about something 到場〔回答問題〕: *The Senator appeared before the Ways and Means Committee.* 這位參議員出席回答眾議院歲入委員會的問題。

9 ▶ARRIVE 到達◀ [I] to arrive, especially when people are not expecting you to〔意外地〕到場: *Karen appeared at about 9 o'clock.* 卡倫大約九時到場的。

ap·pear·ance /əˋpɪrəns; əˈpɪərəns/ *n*

1 ▶WAY SB/STH LOOKS 外貌◀ [C,U] the way someone or something looks to other people 外表; 外觀: *You mustn't worry about your appearance – you look fine.* 你不用擔心自己的外表, 你看起來很好。| *They've changed the whole appearance of the building.* 他們改變了建築物的整個外觀。| **judge by appearances** (=judge someone or something by the way they look) 以貌取人 *It's usually best not to judge by appearances.* 最好不要以貌取人。| **have all the appearances of** (=have all the qualities or features that are typical of something) 具備...所有的特徵 *The case had all the appearances of a straightforward murder.* 從各方面看, 這個案件都像一宗簡單的謀殺。| **to/by all appearances** (=based on the way someone or something seems to most people) 從各方面看 *He was, to all appearances, a respectable, successful businessman.* 從各方面看, 他是個受人尊敬的成功商人。| **contrary to/against (all) appearances** (=in spite of the way they appear) 跟外表相反 *Contrary to appearances, she's actually quite funny when you get to know her.* 和外表相反, 當你了解她以後會發現她實際上很風趣。| **give/create the appearance of** (=seem) 給人以...的印象 *Nigel gives the appearance of being confident, but he isn't really.* 奈傑爾看起來很自信, 但實際上他並不是這樣。

2 ▶STH NEW 新事物◀ [singular] the point at which something new begins to exist or starts being used 出現, 呈現: **[+of]** *the appearance of the first mammals* 第一批哺乳動物的出現 | *the appearance of buds on the trees* 樹上露出了新芽

3 ▶ARRIVAL 到達◀ [C usually singular 一般用單數] the unexpected or sudden arrival of someone or something〔出其不意的〕到來, 出現: **[+of]** *The shouting suddenly stopped with the appearance of Peter's father.* 彼得的父親一出現, 叫喊聲突然停止了。

4 ▶PLAY/FILM/CONCERT ETC 戲劇/電影/音樂會等◀ [C] the act of taking part in a film, play, concert etc 登台, 表演: **make an appearance** *He made his first appearance on stage in a Broadway review.* 他第一次在百老匯的時事諷刺劇中露面。| *the band's only European appearance this year* 這個樂隊今年唯一一次在歐洲的演出
5 keep up appearances to continue to wear good clothes and behave as though you have plenty of money even though you no longer do 維持面子; 裝門面
6 for appearances' sake/for the sake of appearances if you do something for appearances' sake, you are trying to make people think you are still happy, successful etc 為了面子關係
7 put in an appearance/make an appearance to go to an event for a short time, because you think you should 露一下面: *At least Marc managed to put in an appearance at the party.* 至少, 馬克終於想辦法在聚會上露了一面。
8 ▶LAW COURT/MEETING 法庭/會議◀ [C] the act of being present at a court of law or official meeting 出庭; 出席: **make an appearance** *He made a brief appearance in court.* 他出庭作簡短的應訊。

ap·pease /ə`piz; ə'pi:z/ *v* [T] to make someone less angry or stop them from attacking you by giving them what they want 平息; 安撫; 緩解; 姑息

ap·pease·ment /ə`pizmənt; ə'pi:zmənt/ *n* [C,U] the act of trying to persuade someone not to attack you or to make them less angry by giving them what they want 緩和, 平息, 撫慰: *Chamberlain's policy of appeasement towards Hitler in the 30s* 張伯倫在 30 年代對希特拉所採取的綏靖政策

ap·pel·late court /ə,pɛlət `kɔrt; ə,pelət 'kɔ:t/ *n* [C] a court in which people appeal (APPEAL[1] (3)) against decisions made in other courts of law 上訴法院

ap·pel·la·tion /,æpə`leʃən; ,æpə'leɪʃən/ *n* [C] *literary* a name or title【文】名稱, 稱號

ap·pend /ə`pɛnd; ə'pend/ *v* [T+**to**] *formal* to add something to a piece of writing【正式】附加, 增補

ap·pend·age /ə`pɛndɪdʒ; ə'pendɪdʒ/ *n* [C] **1** something that is connected to a larger or more important thing 附加物, 附屬物 **2** *formal* an arm, leg or other body part【正式】附肢〔指臂、腿或身體其他部位〕

ap·pen·dec·to·my /,æpən`dɛktəmɪ; ,æpən'dektəmi/ *n* [C,U] a medical operation in which your APPENDIX (1) is removed 闌尾[盲腸] 切除術

ap·pen·di·ci·tis /ə,pɛndə`saɪtɪs; ə,pendə'saɪtəs/ *n* [U] an illness in which your APPENDIX (1) swells and causes pain 闌尾炎, 盲腸炎

ap·pen·dix /ə`pɛndɪks; ə'pendɪks/ *n plural* **appendixes** *or* **appendices** /-dɪsiz; -dəsi:z/ [C] **1** a small organ near your BOWEL (2) which has little or no use 闌尾: **have your appendix out** (=have it removed) 切除闌尾 —see picture at 參見 DIGESTIVE SYSTEM 圖 **2** a part at the end of a book containing additional information〔書末的〕附錄

ap·per·tain /,æpə`ten; ,æpə'teɪn/ *v formal*【正式】
appertain to sth *phr v* [T not in passive 不用被動態] to belong to or concern something 屬於…; 和…有關聯

ap·pe·tite /`æpə,taɪt; 'æpətaɪt/ *n* **1** [U] a desire for food 胃口, 食慾: *a healthy appetite* 好的胃口 | **lose your appetite** *She has completely lost her appetite since the operation.* 自手術以後, 她完全沒有食慾。| **have a huge/big/voracious appetite** (=have the ability to eat a lot of food) 胃口好, 食慾佳 | **spoil/ruin your appetite** (=eat before a meal and then not want to eat at the meal) 倒胃口, 影響食慾 *Don't eat that cake now, you'll spoil your appetite.* 現在不要吃那塊蛋糕, 會影響食慾的。| **give sb an appetite** (=make them want to eat) 使某人有食慾 *All that walking has given me a big appetite.* 走了那麼多路, 我胃口好極了。**2** [C] a desire or liking for a particular activity 慾望; 喜愛: [+**for**] *Paul has no appetite for hard work.* 保羅不喜歡賣力氣。| **sexual appetite** *an insatiable sexual appetite* 無法滿足的性慾 —see also 另見 **whet sb's appetite** (WHET (1))

ap·pe·tiz·er also 又作 **appetiser** *BrE*【英】/`æpə,taɪzə; 'æpətaɪzə/ *n* [C] a small dish at the beginning of a meal〔餐前的〕開胃小吃

ap·pe·tiz·ing also 又作 **appetising** *BrE*【英】/`æpə,taɪzɪŋ; 'æpətaɪzɪŋ/ *adj* food that is appetizing smells or looks very good 增進食慾的, 開胃的: *an appetizing aroma* 令人垂涎的香味 —**appetizingly** *adv*

ap·plaud /ə`plɔd; ə'plɔ:d/ *v* [I,T] **1** to hit your open hands together to show that you have enjoyed a play, concert, speaker etc; CLAP[1] (1, 2a)（為…）鼓掌 **2** to express strong approval of an idea, plan etc 稱讚, 讚許: *We applaud the decision to go ahead with the new building.* 我們贊成着手建造新大樓的決定。

ap·plause /ə`plɔz; ə'plɔ:z/ *n* [U] the sound of many people hitting their hands together and shouting, to show that they have enjoyed something 鼓掌, 掌聲: **thunderous applause** (=very loud) 雷鳴般的掌聲 | **a round of applause** (=a short period of applause) 一陣掌聲 *Let's have a round of applause for our speakers today.* 讓我們鼓掌歡迎今天的各位演講者。

ap·ple /`æpl; 'æpəl/ *n* [C,U] **1** a hard round fruit that has red, light green, or yellow skin and is white inside 蘋果: *apple pie* 蘋果餡餅 —see picture on page A8 參見 A8 頁圖 **2 be the apple of sb's eye** to be loved very much by someone 是某人心愛的人[掌上明珠]: *Ben was always the apple of his father's eye.* 本一直是父親疼愛的人。**3 bob/dunk/dip for apples** to play a game in which you must use your teeth to pick up apples floating in water 咬蘋果〔指用牙齒叼起浮在水上的蘋果的一種遊戲〕—see also 另見 **upset the apple cart** (UPSET[1] (5)), **a rotten apple** (ROTTEN[1] (5)) 2 3

ap·ple·jack /`æpl,dʒæk; 'æpəldʒæk/ *n* [U] *AmE* a very strong alcoholic drink made from apples【美】(烈性) 蘋果酒, 蘋果白蘭地

apple pie bed /,·· · '·/ *n* [C] *BrE* a trick you do to someone's bed in which you fold the sheets in a particular way so that they cannot get into it【英】蘋果餡餅式牀〔把被單捲起來, 使人無法睡進去的一種惡作劇〕—see also 另見 SHORT-SHEET

apple-pie or·der /,·· · '··/ *n* [U] **be in apple-pie order** to be in perfect order or perfectly arranged 整齊, 井然有序: *His tools are always in apple-pie order.* 他的工具總是擺放得整整齊齊。

apple pol·ish·er /'·· ,···/ *n* [C] *AmE spoken* someone who tries to gain something, become popular etc by praising or helping someone else without being sincere【美口】馬屁精

apple sauce /,·· '·/ *n* [U] a food made from crushed cooked apples 蘋果醬

ap·pli·ance /ə`plaɪəns; ə'plaɪəns/ *n* [C] a piece of electrical equipment such as a COOKER (1) or WASHING MACHINE, used in people's homes 家用電器; 設備, 工具: *labour-saving domestic appliances* 節省人力的家用電器 —see 見 MACHINE[1] (USAGE)

ap·plic·a·ble /`æplɪkəbl; ə'plɪkəbəl/ *adj* affecting or connected with a particular person, group, or situation 適合的, 適用的; 生效的: *Please give details about your mortgage, if applicable.* 如適用, 請說明你抵押貸款的有關詳細情況。| [+**to**] *Few of these laws are applicable to UK citizens while they are abroad.* 這些法律中幾乎沒有適用於在國外的英國公民的。—**applicability** /,æplɪkə`bɪlətɪ; ə,plɪkə'bɪləti/ *n* [U]

ap·pli·cant /`æpləkənt; 'æplɪkənt/ *n* [C] someone who has formally asked, usually in writing, for a job, university place etc 申請人

ap·pli·ca·tion /,æplə`keʃən; ,æplɪ'keɪʃən/ *n*

1 ▶WRITTEN REQUEST 書面要求◀ [C,U] a formal, usually written, request for something such as a job, place at university, or permission to do something 申請 (書):

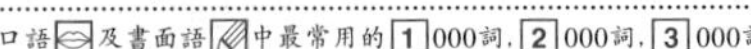
口語 及書面語 中最常用的 1 000詞, 2 000詞, 3 000詞

Developers have filed a planning application. 開發商正式提交了開發計劃申請書。| **[+for]** *There were more than 300 applications for the six jobs.* 有三百多人申請這六份工作。| **job/membership application** *We received hundreds of job applications.* 我們收到了幾百份工作申請。| **application form** (=the paper on which you write your details) 申請表 | **on application (to)** (=when you make an application) (向...) 申請 *Details will be sent on application.* 提出申請後將寄送詳細資料。
2 ►PRACTICAL USE 實用◄ [C,U] practical purpose for which a machine, idea etc can be used, or the act of using it for this 用途, 實際應用: *A micro computer has a wide range of applications for businesses.* 微(型)電腦在商業方面用途很廣。| **[+of/to/in]** *the application of this theory to actual economic practice* 這一理論在經濟實踐中的應用
3 ►PAINT/LIQUID 油漆/液體◄ [C,U] the act of putting something such as paint, liquid, medicine etc onto a surface 塗敷; 敷用: **[+of]** *The application of fertilizer increased the size of the plants.* 施肥使植株生長。
4 ►EFFORT 努力◄ [U] attention or effort over a long period of time 專心, 努力: *Making your new business successful requires luck, patience, and application.* 新的生意要想做好, 你需要運氣、耐心和努力。
5 ►COMPUTERS 電腦◄ a piece of SOFTWARE 應用軟件: *The top software application last year was Microsoft Office.* 去年最流行的應用軟件是微軟辦公系列。
6 ►RELATION TO STH 與某物的關係◄ [U] the way in which something can affect or be used on something else 適用: **[+to]** *That rule has no application to this case.* 那條規則不適用於這種情況。

ap·plied /əˋplaɪd; əˈplaɪd/ *adj* [usually before noun 一般用於名詞前] **applied science/physics/linguistics etc** science etc that has a practical use 應用科學/物理/語言學等 —compare 比較 PURE (10) —opposite 反義詞 THEORETICAL (1)

ap·pli·qué /ˌæplɪˋke; əˈpliːkeɪ/ *n* [C,U] the process of sewing decorative pieces of material onto a piece of clothing, or the pieces themselves 縫飾, 補花, 貼花 —**appliqué** *v* [T]

ap·ply /əˋplaɪ; əˈplaɪ/ *v*
1 ►REQUEST PERMISSION/A JOB 請求准許/求職◄ [I] to make a formal, usually written request for something such as a job, place in university, or permission to do something 申請: **[+to]** *I applied to four universities and was accepted by all of them.* 我向四所大學提出了申請, 都被接受了。| **[+for]** *Fletcher applied for the post of Eliot's secretary.* 弗萊徹申請艾略特的祕書這一職位。
2 ►USE STH 使用某物◄ [T] to use something such as a method, idea, or law in a particular situation, activity, or process 使用, 應用, 運用: *In some cases tribunals fail to apply the law properly.* 在有些案件中, 法庭沒有正確運用此法律。| **apply sth to** *New technology is being applied to almost every industrial process.* 新技術正被應用到幾乎所有工業流程。
3 ►AFFECT STH 影響某事物◄ [I,T not in progressive 不用進行式] to have an effect on or to concern a person, group, or situation 適用於〔某人、某種情況〕; 有效: **[+to]** *The questions on this part of the form only apply to married men.* 表中這部分的問題只適用於已婚男士。| *Many of the restrictions no longer apply.* 許多限制已不再有效。
4 apply yourself to work hard with a lot of attention for a long time 致力於, 專心於: *Stephen would do very well if only he applied himself.* 只要專心致志, 斯蒂芬會做得很好的。
5 ►MAKE STH WORK 使某物起作用◄ [T] to do something in order to make something such as a piece of equipment operate 使...起作用: *apply the brakes* 踩剎車 | *The crystal vibrates when a small electric current is applied to it.* 一點電流就能使水晶振動起來。
6 ►SPREAD PAINT/LIQUID ETC 塗油漆/液體等◄ [T] to put or spread something such as paint, liquid, or medicine onto a surface 塗, 敷: *Apply the cream evenly over the skin.* 將雪花膏均勻地塗在皮膚表面。
7 apply force/pressure to push on something 用力/施壓
8 ►USE A WORD 用某詞◄ [T] to use a particular word or name to describe something or someone 使用〔某個單詞或名稱〕: *The term 'mat' can be applied to any small rug.* mat 一詞可指各種小地毯。

ap·point /əˋpɔɪnt; əˈpɔɪnt/ *v* [T] **1** to choose someone for a position or a job 任命; 委派: *They appointed a new teacher at the school.* 他們給學校委派了一名新老師。| **appoint (sb) as sth** *O'Connell was appointed as Chairman of the Council.* 奧康奈爾被任命為委員會主席。| *The School Board have appointed her Superintendent of the city's schools.* 地方教育委員會任命她為該市所有學校的督學。| **appoint sb to sth** *He's been appointed to the State Supreme Court in California.* 他被派到加利福尼亞州最高法院任職。| **appoint sb to do sth** *She's been appointed to catalog the new books in the library.* 她被派到圖書館為新書登記分類。**2** *formal* to arrange or decide a time or place for something to happen【正式】約定, 指定, 確定〔時間、地點〕: *The committee appointed a day in June for celebrations.* 委員會指定六月的一天進行慶祝。| **the appointed time** (=the time that has been arranged) 約定的時間 *We met him at the appointed time outside the courtroom.* 我們按約定時間在法庭外見到了他。—**appointee** /əˌpɔɪnˋti; əˌpɔɪnˈtiː/ *n* [C]: *a presidential appointee* 總統任命的人 —see also 另見 SELF-APPOINTED, WELL-APPOINTED —see 見 HIRE[1] (USAGE)

ap·point·ment /əˋpɔɪntmənt; əˈpɔɪntmənt/ *n* **1** [C] an arrangement for a meeting at an agreed time and place, for some special purpose 約定, 預約: *a hospital appointment* 看病預約 | *a five o'clock appointment* 5 點鐘的約會 | **[+with]** *an appointment with the doctor at 10.30* 與醫生約定在 10 點 30 分看病 | **appointment to do sth** *I have an appointment to see the manager.* 我約好了見經理。| **make an appointment** *Phone his secretary and make an appointment.* 打電話給他的祕書約定時間。| **keep an appointment** (=be present at an appointment as arranged) 守約 *If you fail to keep the dentist's appointment you'll have to pay for it.* 如果你和牙醫約好時間但到時不去, 你得付錢。**2** [C,U] the choosing of someone for a position or job 任命, 委任: **[+as/to/of]** *His appointment as head of department has caused a lot of friction.* 任命他為部門經理引起了很多意見衝突。| **appointments column** *BrE* (=the part of a newspaper where jobs are advertised)【英】〔報紙上的〕招聘廣告欄 **3 by appointment** if you do something by appointment, you have to arrange it before you do it 按約定, 按事先確定的時間: *The Director sees students by appointment only.* 系主任只按約定的時間見學生。**4** [C] a job or position, usually involving some responsibility 委任的工作[職位]: *He was told he'd got the appointment yesterday morning.* 昨天上午他被告知得到了那個職位。**5 by appointment to the Queen** a phrase that can be used by a business that sells goods or services to the Queen 經女王御准〔可向王室出售商品或提供服務〕

ap·por·tion /əˋpɔrʃən; əˈpɔːʃən/ *v* [T] to decide how something should be shared between various people 分配, 分攤: **[+among/between]** *apportioning available funds among the different schools in the district* 在區內的各所學校分配可用的資金 | **apportion blame/praise etc** (=say who deserves to be blamed or praised) 分清責任/表揚等 *It's not easy to apportion blame when a marriage breaks up.* 婚姻破裂時, 很難分清夫妻倆的(過失)責任。—**apportionment** *n* [C,U]

ap·po·site /ˋæpəzɪt; ˈæpəzɪ̵t/ *adj formal* suitable to what is happening or being discussed【正式】適當的, 恰當的, 貼切的: *brief but apposite remarks* 簡短而恰到好處的言辭 —**appositely** *adv* —**appositeness** *n* [U]

ap·po·si·tion /ˌæpəˋzɪʃən; ˌæpəˈzɪʃən/ *n* [U] an arrange-

ment in grammar in which one simple sentence contains two or more noun phrases that are used in the same way and describe the same thing. For example, in the sentence 'The defendant, a woman of thirty, denies kicking the policeman' the two phrases 'the defendant' and 'a woman of thirty' are in apposition.〔語法〕同位, 同格〈如 The defendant, a woman of thirty, denies kicking the policeman (被告, 一位三十歲的婦女, 否認踢了警察) 一句中,"the defendant"和"a woman of thirty"是同位關係〉

ap·prais·al /ə`prezḷ; əˈpreɪzəl/ *n* [C,U] a statement or opinion judging the worth, value, or condition of something 評價; 估計; 鑑定: **[+of]** *What's your appraisal of the situation?* 你對局勢如何評價? | *an annual appraisal of employees' work* 對雇員工作的年度評估

ap·praise /ə`prez; əˈpreɪz/ *v* [T] to officially judge how successful, effective, or valuable someone or something is; EVALUATE 評定; 鑑定; 估價: *A dealer came to appraise the furniture.* 一個商人來對家具作了估價。

ap·pre·cia·ble /ə`priʃəbḷ; əˈpriːʃəbəl/ *adj* large enough to be noticed or considered important 明顯的, 可覺察到的; 值得重視的: *There's no appreciable change in the patient's condition.* 病人狀況沒有明顯改變。—**appreciably** *adv*: *The two plans are not appreciably different.* 這兩個計劃沒有明顯區別。

ap·pre·ci·ate /ə`priʃɪˌet; əˈpriːʃieɪt/ *v* **1** [T] to understand how good or useful someone or something is 欣賞; 賞識; 鑑賞: *Her abilities are not fully appreciated by her employer.* 她的才幹還沒有得到雇主的充分賞識。**2** [T] to be grateful for something that someone has done 感激: *I appreciated his help when we moved.* 我很感激他在我們搬家時給予的幫助。| **I would appreciate it if** (=please do what I ask) 如果你…, 我將不勝感激 *I would appreciate it if you would turn the music down.* 如果你把音樂關小一些, 我將不勝感激。**3** [T not in progressive 不用進行式] to understand how serious a situation or problem is or what someone's feelings are 完全理解, 明白: *I don't think you appreciate the difficulties his absence will cause.* 我認為你不完全了解他的缺席會造成甚麼樣的困難。**4** [I] to gradually become more valuable over a period of time 增值: *Most investments are expected to appreciate at a steady rate.* 人們盼望大多數投資會平穩增值。—opposite 反義詞 DEPRECIATE (1)

ap·pre·ci·a·tion /əˌpriʃɪ`eʃən; əˌpriːʃiˈeɪʃən/ *n* **1** [U] pleasure you feel when you realize something is good, useful, or well done 欣賞; 賞識; 鑑賞 **2 show sb your appreciation** to show someone that you are grateful for something they have done 對某人表達感激之情: *To show our appreciation for all your hard work, we'd like to give you a bonus.* 為了對你辛勤工作表示感謝, 我們要給你發獎金。**3** [C,U] an understanding of the importance or meaning of something 理解, 明白: **[+of]** *a realistic appreciation of the situation* 對局勢實事求是的理解 **4** [singular,U] a rise in value, especially of land or possessions〔尤指土地或財產的〕增值: *an appreciation of 50% in property values* 資產增值50%

ap·pre·cia·tive /ə`priʃɪˌetɪv; əˈpriːʃətɪv/ *adj* feeling or showing admiration or thanks 有欣賞力的; 感激的: *an appreciative audience* 有欣賞能力的觀眾 | **[+of]** *The visitors were appreciative of all the kindness they'd received.* 來訪者對他們受到的熱情接待表示感謝。—**appreciatively** *adv*

ap·pre·hend /ˌæprɪ`hɛnd; ˌæprɪˈhend/ *v* [T] **1** *formal* if a criminal is apprehended, they are found and taken away by the police; ARREST¹ (1)【正式】逮捕, 拘押 **2** *old use* to understand something【舊】了解, 明白

ap·pre·hen·sion /ˌæprɪ`hɛnʃən; ˌæprɪˈhenʃən/ *n* **1** [C,U] anxiety about the future, especially the worry that you will have to deal with something unpleasant or bad〔對未來的〕憂慮, 擔心: *a natural apprehension about being in hospital* 對住院自然會有的憂慮 **2** [U] the act of apprehending someone; ARREST² 逮捕, 拘押 **3** [U] *old use* understanding【舊】理解: *our apprehension of the nature of God* 我們對上帝之道的理解

ap·pre·hen·sive /ˌæprɪ`hɛnsɪv; ˌæprɪˈhensɪv◂/ *adj* worried or nervous about something that you are going to do, or about the future〔對將做的事或對未來〕恐懼的; 焦慮的: **[+about/for]** *feeling a little apprehensive about the treatment* 對治療感到有些恐懼 —**apprehensively** *adv*: *I waited apprehensively for his reply.* 我焦急地等待着他的答覆。

ap·pren·tice¹ /ə`prɛntɪs; əˈprentʃs/ *n* [C] someone who agrees to work for an employer for a fixed period of time in order to learn a particular skill or job 學徒, 徒弟: *She works in the hairdresser's as an apprentice.* 她在一家美髮店當學徒。| *an apprentice electrician* 電工學徒

apprentice² *v* [T usually passive 一般用被動態] to make someone an apprentice 使〔某人〕當學徒: **apprentice sb to** *He's apprenticed to a plumber.* 他跟一位管子工當學徒。

ap·pren·tice·ship /ə`prɛntɪsˌʃɪp; əˈprentʃsʃɪp/ *n* [C,U] the job of being an apprentice, or the period of time in which you are an apprentice 學徒身分; 學徒年限: *He's serving an apprenticeship as a printer.* 他現在是一名印刷工學徒。| *a five-year apprenticeship* 五年學徒期

ap·prise /ə`praɪz; əˈpraɪz/ *v* **[T+of]** *formal* to inform or tell someone about something【正式】通知; 告訴: *I write to apprise you of the latest situation.* 我寫信向你通報最新的情況。

ap·proach¹ /ə`protʃ; əˈprəʊtʃ/ *v*

1 ►MOVE TOWARDS 向…移動◄ [I,T] to move towards or nearer to someone or something 走近; 靠近; 接近: *As they approached the wood a rabbit ran out of the trees.* 他們走近樹林的時候, 一隻兔子從樹叢裡跑了出來。| *The car swerved to avoid an approaching bus.* 小汽車突然轉向, 躲避一輛開過來的公共汽車。

2 ►ASK 請求◄ [T] to ask someone for something, or ask them to do something, especially when you are not sure they will be interested 接洽, 交涉: **approach sb for** *Will you be approaching the bank for a loan?* 你會向銀行要求貸款嗎? | **approach sb/sth about (doing) sth** *The charity approached several stores about giving food aid.* 慈善機構找了幾家商店, 請求他們給予食物援助。—see also 另見 APPROACHABLE

3 ►FUTURE EVENT 未來事件◄ [I,T] if an event or a particular time approaches, or you approach it, it is coming nearer and will happen soon 臨近: *Our vacation is approaching and we still can't decide where to go.* 我們的假期日益臨近, 可我們仍定不下來去哪兒。| *He was in his fifties and approaching retirement.* 他五十幾歲, 快到退休年齡了。

4 ►ALMOST REACH STH 幾乎到…◄ [I,T] to almost reach a particular high level or amount, or an extreme condition or state 接近: *temperatures approaching 35°C* 接近35攝氏度的溫度 | **nothing/not approaching** (=not at all close in amount) 差得遠 *Nothing approaching the $200 million was found by the auditors.* 審計員查到的數字離兩億美元尚差得很遠。

5 ►DEAL WITH 對付◄ [T] to begin to deal with a difficult situation in a particular way or with a particular attitude 對付, 處理: *I don't think refusing to negotiate is the right way to approach this problem.* 我認為拒絕談判不是處理這一問題的正確方法。

approach² *n* **1** [C] a method of doing something or dealing with a problem 方法; 步驟: **[+to]** *a new approach to teaching languages* 教授語言的新方法 **2** [U] movement towards or near to something 靠近; 接近; 臨近: *Our approach frightened the birds away.* 我們一靠近, 鳥全都受驚飛走了。**3** [C] a road, path etc that leads to a place, and is the main way of reaching it 通路, 入口: *The approach to the house was by a minor road.* 進入這幢房子要經過一條小路。**4** [C] a request from someone, asking you to do something for them 要求: **make an**

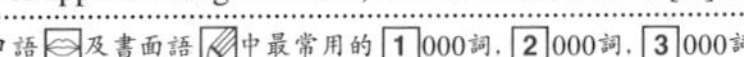

approach *They made approaches to the team to buy one of their players.* 他們與那支球隊洽談要買他們的一個球員。**5 the approach of** the approach of a particular time or event is the fact that it is getting closer ...的來臨[臨近]: *The leaves were turning brown with the approach of autumn.* 隨着秋天的臨近，樹葉變成了褐色。

ap·proa·cha·ble /ə`protʃəbḷ; ə'prəʊtʃəbəl/ *adj* friendly and easy to talk to 友善的; 易接近的: *The head teacher is very approachable.* 校長非常平易近人。—opposite 反義詞 UNAPPROACHABLE

ap·pro·ba·tion /ˌæprə`beʃən; ˌæprə'beɪʃən/ *n* [U] *formal* official praise or approval【正式】稱讚; 認可, 批准

1 1 **ap·pro·pri·ate¹** /ə`proprɪ·ɪt; ə'prəʊpri-ɨ̣t/ *adj* correct or suitable for a particular time, situation, or purpose 恰當的; 合適的: *At an appropriate moment I'll offer the visitors some coffee.* 在合適的時候，我會請來訪者喝咖啡。| **[+for]** *Your clothes are hardly appropriate for a job interview.* 你的服裝不太適合求職面試時穿。| **[+to]** *objectives and strategies which are appropriate to the markets* 適合市場要求的目標和策略 —opposite 反義詞 INAPPROPRIATE —**appropriately** *adv*: *Her new job started, appropriately enough, on the first of January.* 她的新工作正好從1月1日開始。—**appropriateness** *n* [U]

ap·pro·pri·ate² /ə`proprɪˌet; ə'prəʊprieɪt/ *v* [T] **1** to take something for yourself with no right to do this 挪用; 佔用; 盜用: *He is suspected of appropriating government funds.* 他被懷疑挪用政府資金。**2** to take something, especially money, to use for a particular purpose 撥出〔款項〕: **appropriate sth for** *Congress appropriated $5 million for the International Woman's Year.* 國會為國際婦女年撥款五百萬美元。—see also 另見 MISAPPROPRIATE

ap·pro·pri·a·tion /əˌproprɪ`eʃən; əˌprəʊpri'eɪʃən/ *n* [C, U] **1** the process of saving money for a special purpose, or the money that is saved, especially by a business or government 撥款: **[+of]** *the appropriation of $2 million for the new hospital* 給新醫院撥款二百萬美元 **2** the act of taking control of something without asking permission 擅用; 私佔: *the appropriation by the state of all large, profitable businesses* 國家把所有大型贏利企業據為己有

2 3 **ap·prov·al** /ə`pruvḷ; ə'pruːvəl/ *n* [U] **1** the fact of believing that someone or something is good or is doing the right things 讚許; 贊成, 同意: **win/earn sb's approval** *By doing well at school he hoped to win his parents' approval.* 他在學校表現不錯，希望以此得到父母的讚許。| **nod/smile/watch etc in approval** *The audience cheered, yelled and whistled in approval.* 觀眾發出歡呼聲、喊叫聲和口哨聲表示讚許。—opposite 反義詞 DISAPPROVAL **2** the act of officially accepting a plan, decision, or person 批准; 認可: *approval of the plans for the new science lab* 批准建立新科學實驗室的方案 | **for approval** *He submitted his credentials to the Medical Faculty for approval.* 他向醫學院遞交自己的資格證書希望得到認可。| **meet with sb's approval** (=be accepted by someone) 得到某人的批准 *The budget proposals met with the Senate's approval.* 預算提案得到了參議院的批准。| **seal of approval** (=statement that you accept something) 認可, 接受 *The IMF has given its seal of approval to the government's economic strategy.* 國際貨幣基金組織已經認同這個政府的經濟策略。**3** official permission to do something 准許, 允許, 許可: *We need parental approval before allowing students to go on field trips.* 我們需要得到家長的同意才會允許學生去野外考察。**4 on approval** if you buy something on approval, you have the right to return it to the shop if you decide you do not want it〔商品〕包退包換, 不滿意可退貨

2 2 **ap·prove** /ə`pruv; ə'pruːv/ *v* **1** [T] to officially accept a plan, proposal etc 批准; 認可: *The Senate approved a plan for federal funding of local housing programs.* 參議院批准了一項關於聯邦政府提供地方建房資金的計劃。**2** [I] to think that someone or something is good, right, or suitable 贊成, 同意: **[+of]** *Catherine's parents now approve of her marriage.* 凱瑟琳的父母現在同意她結婚。

approved school /·'· ·/ *n* [C,U] a special school in Britain, where children who have done something illegal are sent if they are under 18〔英國的〕少年感化院; 少年(罪)犯教養院

ap·prov·ing /ə`pruvɪŋ; ə'pruːvɪŋ/ *adj* showing support or agreement for something 讚許的; 贊成的: *The professor made no comment about the speech, but gave an approving nod.* 教授對這個演講未作評論，但點頭表示讚許。—**approvingly** *adv*: *She smiled approvingly at the child.* 她對孩子微笑着表示讚許。

approx. the written abbreviation of 縮寫= approximately

ap·prox·i·mant /ə`prɑksəmənt; ; ə'prɒksɨ̣mənt/ *n* [C] a consonant sound such as /w/ or /l/ made by air passing between the tongue or lip and another part of the mouth without any closing of the air passage 無擦通音, 無摩擦延續音

ap·prox·i·mate¹ /ə`prɑksəmɪt; ə'prɒksɨ̣mɨ̣t/ *adj* an approximate number, amount, or time is a little bit more or less than the exact number, amount etc 大致的, 大約的, 大概的: *What is the approximate cost of the materials?* 材料的大致費用是多少？—**approximately** *adv*: *The plane will be landing in approximately 20 minutes.* 飛機大約在20分鐘以後着陸。 3 3

Frequencies of the adverbs **approximately, about**, and **roughly** in spoken and written English 副詞 approximately, about 和 roughly 在英語口語和書面語中的使用頻率

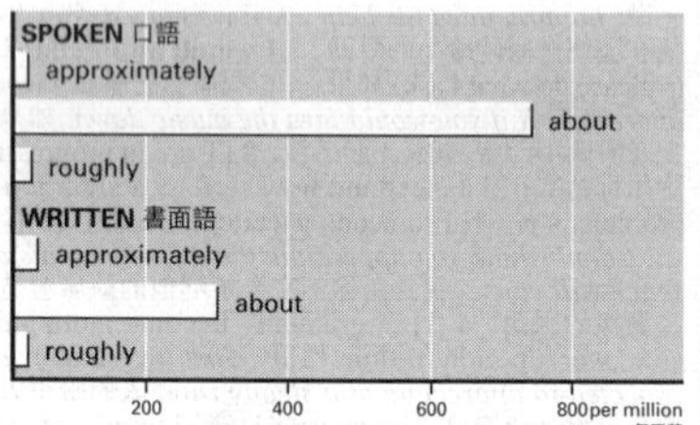

Based on the British National Corpus and the Longman Lancaster Corpus
據英國國家語料庫和朗文蘭卡斯特語料庫

All three adverbs are used to mean 'more or less' or 'not exactly'. The graph shows that in this meaning **about** is much more common than **approximately** in both spoken English and written English. **Roughly** is also more common than **approximately** in spoken English. 這三個副詞用來表示"大約"、"大概"的意思。本圖表顯示，表示此意時，about在口語和書面語中的使用頻率都遠遠高於 approximately。在口語中 roughly 也比 approximately 常用。

ap·prox·i·mate² /ə`prɑksəˌmet; ə'prɒksɨ̣meɪt/ *v* [I, linking verb 連繫動詞] *formal*【正式】**1** to be close to a particular number 接近: **[+to]** *Rainfall during the period we were there approximated to the yearly average.* 我們在那裡的那段時間降雨量接近年均水平。**2** to be similar to but not exactly the same as something 近似: **[+to]** *Your story only approximates to the real facts.* 你所説的僅僅是接近事實真相。

ap·prox·i·ma·tion /əˌprɑksə`meʃən; əˌprɒksɨ̣'meɪʃən/ *n* [C,U] **1** a number, amount etc that is not exact, but is almost correct 概算, 近似值: **rough approximation** (=not exact at all) 估算 *Could you give us a rough approximation of the likely cost?* 你能估算一下成本大概有多少嗎？**2** something that is similar to another thing, but not exactly the same 類似物: **[+of/to]** *It was the nearest approximation to a crisis she had ever experienced.* 這是她所經歷過的最近乎於危機的情況。

ap·pur·te·nance /ə`pɝtn̩əns; ə'pɜːtɪnəns/ *n* [C usually plural 一般用複數] **1** *formal* things that are an additional and less important part of something larger, for example possessions in a house【正式】附屬物, 附帶物 **2** *technical* an additional right or responsibility connected with owning property【術語】附帶權利[責任]

APR /ˌe pi `ɑr; ˌeɪ piː 'ɑː/ *n* [C usually singular 一般用單數] Annual Percentage Rate; the rate of INTEREST[1] (4) that you must pay when you borrow money 年率, 年利率

ap·rès-ski /ˌæpre `ski; ˌæpreɪ 'skiː◂/ *n* [singular] activities such as eating and drinking that you take part in after skiing (SKI[2]) 滑雪後的活動〔如吃喝東西等〕

a·pri·cot /`eprɪˌkɑt; 'eɪprɨkɒt/ *n* **1** [C] a small round fruit that is orange or yellow and has a single large seed 杏 —see picture on page A8 參見A8頁圖 **2** [U] the colour of this fruit 杏黃色 —see picture on page A5 參見A5頁圖 —**apricot** *adj*

A·pril /`eprəl; 'eɪprəl/ written abbreviation 縮寫為 **Apr** *n* [C,U] the fourth month of the year, between March and May 四月: **on April the sixth/the fifteenth etc** *BrE*【英】/**on April sixth/fifteenth** *AmE*【美】*I arrived on April seventh.* 我於4月7日到達。| **on the sixth/fifteenth etc of April** *My new job starts on the second of April.* 我的新工作從4月2日開始。| **in April** *This office opened in April 1994.* 這個辦事處在1994年4月開始運作。| **this/last/next April** *I'm going to Africa next April.* 我明年4月去非洲。

April fool /ˌ·· '·/ *n* [C] someone who is tricked on April Fools' Day, or the trick that is played on them〔在4月1日〕愚人節時受愚弄的人; 在愚人節開的玩笑

April Fools' Day /ˌ·· '· ·/ also 又作 **All Fools' Day** *old-fashioned*【過時】*n* [singular] April 1st, a day when people play tricks on each other 愚人節

a pri·o·ri /ˌe praɪ`oraɪ; ˌeɪ praɪ'ɔːraɪ/ *adj, adv Latin* using previous experiences or facts to decide what the probable result or effect of something will be【拉丁】由因及果的[地], 演繹的[地]: *an a priori statement such as 'It is raining so the streets must be wet.'* "天正在下雨, 因此街道肯定是濕的"等推理

a·pron /`eprən; 'eɪprən/ *n* [C] **1** a piece of clothing that covers the front part of your clothes and ties around your waist, worn to keep your clothes clean, especially while cooking 圍裙 —see picture on page A10 參見A10頁圖 **2 tied to your mother's/wife's apron strings** too easily controlled by your mother or wife 受母親/妻子的擺佈 **3** also 又作 **apron stage** the part of the stage in a theatre that comes forward towards the people watching 台口〔舞台幕前部分〕 **4** the hard surface in an airport on which planes are turned around, loaded, unloaded etc 停機坪

ap·ro·pos¹ /ˌæprə`po; ˌæprə'pəʊ/ *adv, prep* **apropos of** used to introduce a new subject that is connected with something just mentioned 說到…, 關於, 就…而言〔用於引入與剛才話題有關的新話題〕: *He had nothing to say apropos of the latest developments.* 至於最新的進展, 他沒有甚麼要說的。| **apropos of nothing** (=not connected with previous conversation) 突然地, 毫無理由地〔改變話題〕*Apropos of nothing, he suddenly asked me if I liked cats!* 他突然沒頭沒尾地問我是否喜歡貓!

apropos² *adj* [not before noun 不用於名詞前] suitable for a particular situation 適時的, 恰當的: *I thought her remarks were very apropos.* 我認為她的話說得很合時宜。

apse /æps; æps/ *n* [C] the curved inside end of a building, especially the east end of a church 半圓室, 半圓形殿〔尤指教堂東端的半圓形建築〕

apt /æpt; æpt/ *adj* **1 apt to do something** having a natural tendency to do something 有做某事傾向的, 易於做某事的: *Some of the staff are apt to arrive late on Mondays.* 一些職員星期一常遲到。**2** exactly right for a particular situation or purpose 適當的, 恰當的: *an apt and telling remark* 既恰當又能說明問題的話 **3** *formal* quick to learn and understand【正式】敏捷的; 聰明的 —**aptness** *n* [U]

ap·ti·tude /`æptəˌtud; 'æptɨtjuːd/ *n* [C,U] natural ability or skill, especially in learning〔尤指學習方面的〕天資, 資質: **[+for]** *She has a real aptitude for drawing and painting.* 她在繪畫方面的確有天賦。

apt·ly /`æptlɪ; 'æptli/ *adv* **aptly named/described/called etc** named, described etc in a way that seems very suitable 命名/描述/稱呼等很恰當: *Lightfoot was aptly named; we never heard him enter.* "輕腳"這個名字起得好, 我們從未聽到過他進來的聲音。

aq·ua·lung /`ækwəˌlʌŋ; 'ækwəlʌŋ/ *n* [C] a piece of equipment that a swimmer wears on their back under water, that provides air for them to breathe〔潛水者揹在背上的〕水肺, 水中呼吸器

aq·ua·ma·rine /ˌækwəmə`rin; ˌækwəmə'riːn◂/ *n* **1** [C, U] a greenish blue jewel or the type of stone it comes from 海藍寶石 **2** [U] a greenish blue colour 藍綠色, 海藍色 —**aquamarine** *adj* —see picture on page A5 參見A5頁圖

aq·ua·plane¹ /`ækwəˌplen; 'ækwəpleɪn/ *n* [C] a thin board that you stand on while you are pulled over the water by a fast boat 滑水板

aquaplane² *v* [I] **1** to be pulled over the water on an aquaplane 滑水, 站在滑水板上滑行 **2** *BrE* if a car aquaplanes, it slides over a wet road in an uncontrolled way【英】〔汽車〕在積水的路面上失去控制而滑行; HYDROPLANE[2] (1) *AmE*【美】

a·quar·i·um /ə`kwɛrɪəm; ə'kweəriəm/ *n plural* **aquariums** *or* **aquaria** /-rɪə; -riə/ [C] **1** a clear glass or plastic container for fish and other water animals〔玻璃或塑料的〕養魚缸, 水族箱 **2** a building where people go to look at fish and other water animals 水族館

A·quar·i·us /ə`kwɛrɪəs; ə'kweəriəs/ *n* **1** [singular] the eleventh sign of the ZODIAC, represented by a person pouring water and believed to affect the character and life of people born between January 21 and February 19 寶瓶宮〔黃道第十一宮〕, 水瓶座 **2** [C] someone who was born between January 21 and February 19 出生於寶瓶宮[水瓶座]時段〔1月21日至2月19日〕的人

a·quat·ic /ə`kwætɪk; ə'kwætɪk/ *adj* **1** living or growing in water 水棲的; 水生的: *an aquatic plant* 水生植物 **2** involving water 水中的, 水上的: *aquatic sports* 水上運動 —**aquatically** /-klɪ; -kli/ *adv*

aq·ua·tint /`ækwəˌtɪnt; 'ækwətɪnt/ *n* [C,U] a method of producing a picture using acid on a sheet of metal, or a picture printed using this method 凹板腐蝕製版法, 銅版蝕鏤法; 用凹板腐蝕法印製成的圖畫

aq·ue·duct /`ækwɪˌdʌkt; 'ækwɨdʌkt/ *n* [C] a structure like a bridge, used to carry a water supply across a valley〔跨過山谷的〕高架渠, 渡槽

a·que·ous /`ekwɪəs; 'eɪkwiəs/ *adj technical* containing water or similar to water【術語】水的; 似水的; 含水的

aq·ui·line /`ækwəˌlaɪn; 'ækwɨlaɪn/ *adj* **1 aquiline nose** an aquiline nose has a curved shape like the beak of an EAGLE 鷹鉤鼻 **2** like an EAGLE 似鷹的

-ar /ɚ; ə/ *suffix* **1** [in nouns 構成名詞] the form used for -ER in certain words …人〔在某些詞中用以代替 -er〕: *a beggar* (=person who begs) 乞丐 **2** [in adjectives 構成形容詞] of or concerning something 與…有關的: *muscular strength* (=strength of muscles) 肌肉的力量 —see also 另見 -ULAR

Ar·ab /`ærəb; 'ærəb/ *n* [C] **1** someone whose language is Arabic and whose family have their origin in Arabia or the Middle East 阿拉伯人 **2** also 又作 **Arabian** *AmE*【美】a type of fast graceful horse 阿拉伯馬

ar·a·besque /ˌærə`bɛsk; ˌærə'besk/ *n* [C] **1** a position in BALLET 阿拉貝斯克舞姿〔一種芭蕾舞姿〕 **2** a decorative pattern of flowing lines 阿拉伯式花飾

A·ra·bi·an /ə`rebɪən; ə'reɪbiən/ *adj* from or connected with Arabia 阿拉伯的

Ar·a·bic /`ærəbɪk; 'ærəbɪk/ *n* [U] the language or

A

writing of the Arabs, which is the main language of North Africa, the Middle East, and Arabia 阿拉伯語 —**Arabic** *adj*

Arabic nu·me·ral /,··· '···/ *n* [C] a sign, such as 1, 2, or 3, used for numbers in the English alphabet and many others 阿拉伯數字 —see also 另見 ROMAN NUMERAL

ar·a·ble /ˈærəbl̩; ˈærəbəl/ *adj* **1 arable land/soil** arable land is suitable for growing crops 適於耕作的土地/土壤 **2** concerned with growing crops 與種植有關的

ar·bi·ter /ˈɑrbɪtɚ; ˈɑːbɪ̣tə/ *n* [C] **1** someone whose opinions have a lot of influence on what other people do 權威人士: *an arbiter of taste* 品味鑑賞方面的權威人士 **2** someone or something that settles an argument between two opposing sides 仲裁人; 公斷人: **be the final arbiter** (=to make the final decision) 是最終的決策者

ar·bi·trage /ˈɑrbətrɑʒ; ˈɑːbɪ̣trɑːʒ/ *n* [U] *technical* the process of buying something such as a COMMODITY (1) or CURRENCY (1) in one place and selling it in another place at the same time【術語】套利; 套匯; 套購 —**arbitrageur** /ˌɑbɪtrɑˈʒɝ; ˌɑːbɪ̣trɑːˈʒɜː/ *n* [C]

ar·bi·tra·ry /ˈɑrbəˌtrɛrɪ; ˈɑːbɪ̣trəri/ *adj* **1** decided or arranged without any reason or plan, often unfairly 專橫的, 武斷的, 霸道的: *Management is weak, morale low and punishment is arbitrary.* 管理不力, 士氣低落, 懲罰武斷。 **2** happening or decided by chance rather than a plan 任意的, 隨機的: *The figure of 20% is quite arbitrary.* 20% 這個數字是相當隨機的。—**arbitrariness** *n* [U] —**arbitrarily** /ˈɑrbəˌtrɛrɪlɪ; ˈɑːbɪ̣trərɪ̣li/ *adv*: *arbitrarily deprived of his duties* 專斷地剝奪了他的職責

ar·bi·trate /ˈɑrbəˌtret; ˈɑːbɪ̣treɪt/ *v* [I,T] to officially judge how an argument between two opposing sides should be settled 仲裁; 公斷: *A committee will arbitrate between management and unions.* 由一個委員會來仲裁資方和工會的爭端。—**arbitrator** *n* [C]

ar·bi·tra·tion /ˌɑrbəˈtreʃən; ˌɑːbɪ̣ˈtreɪʃən/ *n* [U] the process of judging officially how an argument should be settled 仲裁; 公斷: **go to arbitration** (=ask someone to arbitrate) 通過仲裁

ar·bo·re·al /ɑrˈborɪəl; ɑːˈbɔːriəl/ *adj technical* connected with trees or living in trees【術語】有關樹木的; 生活在樹上的

ar·bo·re·tum /ˌɑrbəˈritəm; ; ˌɑːbəˈriːtəm/ *n* [C] a place where trees are grown for scientific study〔供科學研究用的〕樹木園, 植物園

ar·bour *BrE*【英】, **arbor** *AmE*【美】/ˈɑrbɚ; ˈɑːbə/ *n* [C] a shelter in a garden made by making plants grow together on a frame shaped like an ARCH[1] (4)〔花園中長滿蔓藤的〕棚架, 籐架; 涼亭

arc /ɑrk; ɑːk/ *n* [C] **1** a curved shape 弧 (狀): *the arc of a rainbow* 彩虹的弧狀 **2** part of a curved line or a circle 弧線, 弧形: *The sun moves across the sky in an arc.* 太陽在天空以弧形運行。—see picture at 參見 CIRCLE[1] 圖 **3** a flash of light formed by the flow of electricity between two points 弧光, 電弧 —**arc** *v* [T]

ar·cade /ɑrˈked; ɑːˈkeɪd/ *n* [C] **1** a covered passage at the side of a row of buildings with PILLARS and arches (ARCH[1] (1)) supporting it on one side 拱廊 **2** a covered passage between two streets with shops on each side of it 拱廊式街道〔上有蓋頂, 兩邊有商店〕 **3** an AMUSEMENT ARCADE 遊樂場; 遊戲機室 **4** *BrE* also 又作 **shopping arcade** a large building or part of a building where there are many shops【英】室內購物商場

Ar·ca·di·a /ɑrˈkedɪə; ɑːˈkeɪdiə/ *n* [singular] *literary* a place or scene of simple pleasant country life【文】世外桃源, 淳樸愉快的田園生活

ar·cane /ɑrˈken; ɑːˈkeɪn/ *adj literary* secret and mysterious【文】祕密的, 神祕的: *the arcane mysteries and language of the perfume business* 香水行業的神祕特點和語言

arch- /ɑrtʃ; ɑːtʃ/ *prefix* of the highest class or rank; chief; main 最高等級的; 主要的: *an archbishop* (=a chief BISHOP) 大主教 | *our archenemy* (=our main worst enemy) 我們的頭號敵人 | *the company's archrivals* (=main competitors) 公司的主要競爭對手

arch[1] /ɑrtʃ; ɑːtʃ/ *n* [C] **1** a structure with a curved top and straight sides that supports the weight of a bridge or building 拱頂; 拱洞 **2** a curved structure above a door, window, or gate 拱門; 拱窗 **3** a curved structure of bones in the middle of your foot 足底弓 —see picture at 參見 FOOT[1] 圖 **4** something with a curved top and straight sides 弓狀物; 拱形物 —see picture on page A12 參見 A12 頁圖

arch[2] *v* [I,T] to form or make something form a curved shape 拱起, (使) 成拱形: *Two rows of trees arched over the driveway.* 兩排樹呈拱形彎向車道。| *She stretched her arms out and arched her back.* 她伸出手臂, 拱起了背。

arch[3] *adj* amused because you think you understand something better than other people 淘氣的; 調皮的: *an arch tone* 調皮的口吻 —**archly** *adv*: *"I think someone here has a little secret," she said archly.* "我認為這兒某個人有個小祕密。" 她狡黠地說。

ar·chae·ol·o·gy *especially BrE*【尤英】, **archeology** *AmE*【美】/ˌɑrkɪˈɑlədʒɪ; ˌɑːkiˈɒlədʒi/ *n* [U] the study of ancient societies by examining what remains of their buildings, graves, tools etc 考古學 —**archaeologist** *n* —**archaeological** /ˌɑrkɪəˈlɑdʒɪkl̩; ˌɑːkiəˈlɒdʒɪ̣kəl◂/ *adj*: *an archaeological dig* 考古發掘 —**archaeologically** /-kl̩ɪ; -kli/ *adv*

ar·cha·ic /ɑrˈke·ɪk; ɑːˈkeɪ·ɪk/ *adj* **1** old and no longer used 不再使用的: *The English used in the letter is an archaic form.* 這封信中使用的英語已過時了。 **2** old-fashioned and needing to be replaced 過時的, 陳舊的: *The central heating in the building is positively archaic.* 這幢建築的中央供暖系統已經非常陳舊了。 **3** connected to ancient times 古代的

ar·cha·is·m /ˈɑrkɪˌɪzəm; ɑːˈkeɪ-ɪzəm/ *n* [C] an old word or phrase that is no longer used〔不再使用的〕古詞, 古語

arch·an·gel /ˈɑrkˌendʒəl; ˈɑːkeɪndʒəl/ *n* [C] the chief ANGEL (1) in the Jewish, Christian, and Muslim religions〔猶太教、基督教和伊斯蘭教中的〕天使長, 大天使

arch·bish·op /ˈɑrtʃˈbɪʃəp; ˌɑːtʃˈbɪʃəp◂/ *n* [C] a priest of the highest rank, who is in charge of all the churches in a particular area 大主教

arch·bish·op·ric /ˌɑrtʃˈbɪʃəprɪk; ˌɑːtʃˈbɪʃəprɪk/ *n* [C] **1** the area governed by an archbishop 大主教的轄區 **2** the rank of archbishop 大主教的職銜

arch·dea·con /ˈɑrtʃˈdikən; ˌɑːtʃˈdiːkən◂/ *n* [C] a priest of a high rank in the Anglican church who works under a bishop〔英國國教的〕副主教

arch·di·o·cese /ˈɑrtʃˈdaɪəˌsɪs; ˌɑːtʃˈdaɪəsɪ̣s/ *n* [C] the area that is governed by an archbishop 大主教轄區

arch·duke /ˈɑrtʃˈdjuk; ˌɑːtʃˈdjuːk◂/ *n* [C] a prince who belonged to the royal family of Austria 大公〔昔日奧地利的皇太子〕

arch·en·e·my /,·ˈ···/ *n* [C] **1** the main enemy 大敵, 天字第一號敵人: *Lex Luthor, Superman's archenemy* 萊克斯·盧瑟, 超人的大敵 **2 the archenemy** *literary* the devil【文】魔王, 撒旦

ar·che·ol·o·gy /ˌɑrkɪˈɑlədʒɪ; ˌɑːkiˈɒlədʒi/ *n* [U] the American spelling of ARCHAEOLOGY archaeology 的美式拼法

ar·cher /ˈɑrtʃɚ; ˈɑːtʃə/ *n* [C] someone who shoots ARROWS (1) from a BOW[3] (1) 射箭運動員; 弓箭手

ar·cher·y /ˈɑrtʃərɪ; ˈɑːtʃəri/ *n* [U] the sport of shooting ARROWS (1) from a BOW[3] (1) 射箭 (運動)

ar·che·type /ˈɑrkəˌtaɪp; ˈɑːkɪtaɪp/ *n* [C] the most

typical example of something, because it has all the most important qualities 原型; 典型: *Merlin is the archetype of the wise old man.* 默林是智慧老人的典範。—**archetypal** /ˌɑrkɪˋtaɪpḷ; ˌɑːkɪˈtaɪpəl◂/ *adj*: *Byron was the archetypal Romantic hero.* 拜倫是典型的浪漫主義英雄。

ar·chi·pel·a·go /ˌɑrkəˋpɛləˌgo; ˌɑːkɪ̵ˈpeləgəʊ/ *n* [C] a group of small islands and the large area of sea around them 羣島; 羣島周圍的海域

3 **ar·chi·tect** /ˋɑrkəˌtɛkt; ˈɑːkɪ̵tekt/ *n* [C] **1** someone whose job is to design buildings 建築師, 設計師 **2 the architect of sth** the person who originally thought of an important and successful idea …的設計師〔偉大思想的倡導者〕: *Gorbachev was the architect of glasnost.* 戈爾巴喬夫是開放思想的設計師。

3 3 **ar·chi·tec·ture** /ˋɑrkəˌtɛktʃɚ; ˈɑːkɪ̵tektʃə/ *n* **1** [U] the style and design of a building or buildings 建築風格, 建築式樣 **2** [U] the art and practice of planning and designing buildings 建築學: *He studied architecture at university.* 他在大學裡修讀建築學。**3** [U] the structure and design of something 結構: *the architecture of DNA* DNA (脫氧核糖核酸) 的結構 **4** [C] *technical* the design of the inside of a computer【術語】電腦的內部設計; 架構 —**architectural** /ˌɑrkəˋtɛktʃərəl; ˌɑːkɪ̵ˈtektʃərəl◂/ *adj*: *architectural features* 建築特點 —**architecturally** *adv*: *Architecturally Chengdu is quite different from most of China.* 從建築學的角度看, 成都與中國大多數城市不一樣。

ar·chive /ˋɑrkaɪv; ˈɑːkaɪv/ *n* [C] **1 archives** a large number of records that provide information about the history of a country, organization, family etc 檔案, 案卷 **2** a place where a large number of historical records is stored 檔案館: *the State Archives in Paris* 巴黎的國家檔案館 —**archive** *adj*: *interesting archive material* 有趣的檔案資料 —**archival** /ɑrˋkaɪvḷ; ɑːˈkaɪvəl/ *adj*

ar·chi·vist /ˋɑrkəvɪst; ˈɑːkɪ̵vɪ̵st/ *n* [C] someone who works in an archive 檔案保管員

arch·way /ˋɑrtʃˌwe; ˈɑːtʃweɪ/ *n* [C] **1** a passage under an ARCH[1] (1) or arches 拱廊, 拱道 **2** an entrance under an arch 拱門: *He was standing in the archway outside the club.* 他站在俱樂部外的拱門內。

-archy /ɚkɪ, ɑrkɪ; əki, ɑːki/ *suffix* [in nouns 構成名詞] government; rule 治理; 統治: *anarchy* (=no government) 無政府 (狀態) | *monarchy* (=with one ruler) 君主政體

Arc·tic /ˋɑrktɪk; ˈɑːktɪk/ *n* **the Arctic** the large area of land surrounding the North Pole 北極; 北極地區

arctic *adj* **1** connected with or from the most northern part of the world 北極的 **2** extremely cold 極冷的: *arctic conditions* 極冷的環境

Arctic Cir·cle /ˌ·· ˋ··/ *n* [singular] an imaginary line drawn around the world at a certain distance from the most northern point (the North Pole) 北極圈 —compare 比較 ANTARCTIC CIRCLE —see picture at 參見 EARTH[1] 圖

arc weld·ing /ˌ· ˋ··/ *n* [U] a method of joining two pieces of metal together by heating them with a special tool (電) 弧焊 (接)

-ard /ɚd; əd/ *suffix* [in nouns 構成名詞] someone who is usually or always in a particular state 沉湎於…的人: *a drunkard* 酒鬼

ar·dent /ˋɑrdṇt; ˈɑːdənt/ *adj* **1** showing strong positive feelings about an activity and determination to succeed at it 熱心的; 熱烈的: *an ardent supporter of free trade* 自由貿易的熱心支持者 **2** *literary* showing strong feelings of love【文】顯示出熾熱愛情的; 熱情的: *an ardent suitor* 熱烈的求婚男子 —**ardently** *adv*

ar·dour *BrE*【英】, **ardor** *AmE*【美】/ˋɑrdɚ; ˈɑːdə/ *n* [U] **1** very strong positive feelings 激情, 熱誠: *They sang with real ardour.* 他們唱得很有激情。**2** *literary* strong feelings of love【文】熾熱的愛情

ar·du·ous /ˋɑrdʒuəs; ˈɑːdjuəs/ *adj* involving a lot of strength and effort 費力的, 艱巨的: *an arduous journey through the mountains* 艱難的山區旅行 —**arduously** *adv* —**arduousness** *n* [U]

are[1] /ɚ; ə, *strong* 強讀 ɑr; ɑː/ the present tense and plural of 'be' be的現在式複數

are[2] /ɑr; ɑː/ *n* [C] a unit of area 公畝 —see table on page C3 參見 C3 頁附錄

ar·e·a /ˋɛrɪə; ˈeəriə/ *n* [C] **1** a particular part of a country, town etc 地區; 區域: *a working-class area of Birmingham* 伯明翰的工人居住區 | *Many areas of Africa have suffered severe drought this year.* 今年, 非洲的許多地區都遭遇了嚴重的旱災。| **the surrounding area** (=the area around a place) 周圍地區 *The police have searched the farm and the surrounding area.* 警察已搜遍了農場及其附近地區。**2** a part of a house, office, garden etc that is used for a particular purpose 場所, 地方: *a no-smoking area* 禁煙場所 | *Come through into the dining area.* 進飯廳來。**3** a particular subject, range of activities, or group of related subjects 領域, 範圍, 方面: **[+of]** *reforms in the key areas of health and education* 衛生及教育關鍵領域的改革 **4** the amount of space that a flat surface or shape covers 面積: *a formula to calculate the area of a circle* 計算圓面積的公式 | *an area of 2,000 square miles* 2,000平方英里的面積 —see 見 **grey area** (GREY[1] (6)) 1 1

USAGE NOTE 用法説明: AREA

WORD CHOICE 詞語辨析: **area, part of the world/the country/town, region, district**

Area is the most general word for a part of the Earth's surface. An **area** can be small or large, and is not usually thought of as a fixed land division. area是指地球表面某一部分最常用的詞, 它所指的範圍可大可小, 通常並非固定劃分的地方: *the shopping/downtown area of the city* 城市的購物區/商業中心區 | *a rural area of the country* 該國的農村地區 | *the Houston area* 休斯敦地區。Informally you might talk instead about a **part of the world/the country/town**. 非正式場合可以用 part of the world/the country/town 來代替 area: *There's no video shop in our part of town.* 鎮上我們這一帶沒有影音商店。| *New England is a delightful part of the country* (usually 一般 = country area). 新英格蘭是一個很有趣的地方。

A **region** is usually large, is usually part of a country, and may or may not be thought of as a fixed land division. region常指較大的地方, 一般指國家的一部分, 可以是也可以不是固定劃分的地區: *the arctic region of Canada* 加拿大的北極地區 | *The southeast is the richest region in England.* 東南部是英格蘭最富裕的地區。

A **district** is smaller than a **region**, and is usually an officially fixed area of a country or city. district比region小, 通常是一國或一城市中正式固定劃分的區域: *the financial district of town* 城市的金融區 | *the central district of Hong Kong* 香港的市中心 | *the Lake District* 湖區

area code /ˋ··· ˌ·/ *n* [C] three numbers you use when you want to telephone someone in a different area of the US〔美國電話的〕地區代號 [编碼]; DIALLING CODE *BrE*【英】

a·re·na /əˋrinə; əˈriːnə/ *n* [C] **1** a building with a large flat central area surrounded by seats, where sports or entertainments take place 表演場地: *The bull was led into the arena.* 公牛被帶進競技場。**2 the political/public/international etc arena** all the activities and people connected with politics, public life etc 政治/公眾/國際等舞台: *Women are entering the political arena in larger numbers.* 越來越多的婦女進入政界。

aren't /ɑrnt; ɑːnt/ *v* **a)** the short form of 縮略式= are not: *They aren't here.* 他們不在這兒。**b)** the short form of 縮略式= am not, used in questions〔用於疑問句〕: *I am your friend, aren't I?* 我是你的朋友, 不是嗎?

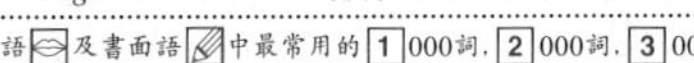

a·rête /æ`ret; ə'ret/ *n* [C] a part of a mountain that consists of a long line of raised rock with steep sides 峻嶺, 陡峭的山脊 —see picture on page A12 參見A12頁圖

ar·gent /`ardʒənt; 'ɑːdʒənt/ *n* [U] *poetic* a silver colour【詩】銀色 —**argent** *adj*

ar·gon /`argɑn; 'ɑːgɒn/ *n* [U] a chemically inactive gas that is found in the air and is sometimes used in electric lights 氬

ar·got /`argo; 'ɑːgəʊ/ *n* [C,U] informal expressions used by a particular group of people such as criminals 行話, 隱語, 黑話, 暗語

ar·gu·a·ble /`argjuəbḷ; 'ɑːgjuəbəl/ *adj* not certainly true or correct and therefore easy to doubt 有疑問的, 可爭辯的: *Whether or not Webb is the best person for the job is arguable.* 韋布是不是這個職務的最佳人選尚有商榷餘地。| **it is arguable that** (=you can show good reasons why it might be true) 有理由說 *It's arguable that legislation has little effect on young people's behaviour.* 有論據表明, 立法對年輕人的行為沒太大影響。—**arguably** *adv*: *Senna was arguably the greatest racing driver of all time.* 冼拿無疑是有史以來最了不起的賽車手。

1 1 **ar·gue** /`argju; 'ɑːgjuː/ *v*
1 ►DISAGREE 不同意◄ [I] to disagree with someone in words, often in an angry way 爭論, 爭吵: *Did you hear the couple next door arguing last night?* 昨晚你聽見隔壁的夫妻在爭吵嗎? | **[+with]** *I'm not going to argue with you, but I think you're wrong.* 我不想和你爭辯, 但是我認為你錯了。| **[+about]** *They were arguing about how to spend the money.* 他們就這錢怎麼花而爭論不休。| **[+over]** (=argue about something, especially about who should have something) 就…爭吵 *The family argued bitterly over who should inherit the house.* 這家人就誰應該繼承房產激烈地爭吵。
2 ►STATE 表明◄ [I,T] to state, giving clear reasons, that something is true, should be done etc 提出理由: *a well-argued case* 說理充分的案例 | **argue that** *Croft argued that a date should be set for the withdrawal of troops.* 克羅夫特認為應該確定撤軍的日期。| **argue for/against** (=argue that something should or should not be done) 據理力爭/反對 *You can argue against extending the airport on the grounds of cost.* 你可以以成本太高為理由提出反對擴建機場。| **argue the point** (=discuss something) 討論 *We could argue this point for hours without reaching any sensible conclusions.* 我們就這一點可以討論幾個小時而得不出合理的結論。
3 argue sb into/out of sth *especially BrE* to persuade someone to do or not do something【尤英】說服某人做某事/不做某事: *Joyce argued me into buying a new jacket.* 喬伊斯說服了我買一件新夾克衫。
4 ►SHOW CLEARLY 清楚表明◄ [T] *formal* to show that something clearly exists or is true【正式】顯示出, 表明: *The commissioner's statement argues a high level of police involvement.* 長官的陳述表明投入了很大警力。
5 argue the toss *BrE informal* to continue to argue about a decision that has been made and cannot be changed【英, 非正式】(對已決定的事)唱反調; 挑剔: *How stupid of me to argue the toss with the traffic policeman.* 我真蠢, 和交警去講理。

1 1 **ar·gu·ment** /`argjəmənt; 'ɑːgjᵾmənt/ *n* **1** [C] a situation in which two or more people disagree, often angrily 爭論, 爭辯, 爭吵: **[+with]** *an argument with my husband* 跟我丈夫的爭吵 | **[+about/over]** *The argument seemed to be about who was going to take the cat to the vet.* 爭論似乎是關於由誰帶貓去看獸醫。| **have an argument** *They were having an argument about the children.* 他們為孩子的事爭吵。| **get into an argument** *I got into an argument with the other driver.* 我和另一位司機吵了起來。| **win/lose an argument** *He lost his argument with the doctor.* 他說不過醫生。| **heated argument** (=very angry argument) 激烈的爭論 **2** [C] a set of reasons that show that something is true or untrue, right or wrong etc 論點, 論據: *Rose's argument is complex and ingenious.* 露絲的論點全面又富有見地。| **[+for/against]** *a powerful argument against smoking* 反對吸煙的有力論據 | **argument that** *the familiar argument that the costs outweigh the benefits* 得不償失這一常見的論點 **3** [U] the act of disagreeing or questioning something 異議; 爭議: **do sth without (further) argument** *Seamus accepted the suggestion without argument.* 謝默斯完全接受這個建議。| **for the sake of argument** (=in order to discuss all the possibilities) 打個比方, 假定 *Let's say for the sake of argument that you don't take the job, then what?* 假定說你不接受這個工作會怎麼樣?

ar·gu·men·ta·tive /ˌargjə`mɛntətɪv; ˌɑːgjᵾ'mentətɪv◂/ *adj* someone who is argumentative often argues or likes arguing 好爭辯的, 好爭吵的: *When he drinks he becomes argumentative.* 他一喝酒, 就愛理論。

ar·gy-bar·gy /ˌardʒɪ `bardʒɪ; ˌɑːdʒi 'bɑːdʒi/ *n* [U] *BrE spoken* arguments or quarrelling【英口】爭論; 爭吵

a·ri·a /`arɪə; 'ɑːriə/ *n* [C] a song that is sung by only one person in an OPERA or ORATORIO 獨唱曲; 詠嘆調

-arian /ɛrɪən; eəriən/ *suffix* **1** [in nouns 構成名詞] someone who is connected with or believes in a particular thing …派[主義]的人: *a vegetarian* (=someone who does not eat meat) 素食主義者 | *a librarian* (=someone who works in a library) 圖書館管理員 —see also 另見 -GENARIAN **2** [in adjectives 構成形容詞] for or connected with people of this type 涉及某種人的: *a vegetarian restaurant* 素食餐館 | *libertarian principles* 自由論者的原則

ar·id /`ærɪd; 'ærᵻd/ *adj* **1** arid land is extremely dry and cannot produce many crops 乾燥的, 乾旱的; 貧瘠的, 不毛的: *Much of Namibia is arid country.* 納米比亞的大部分地區乾旱貧瘠。**2** an arid discussion, period of time etc does not produce anything new 無創見的, 無新意的 —**aridity** /ə`rɪdətɪ; ə'rɪdᵻti/ *adj*

Ar·ies /`ɛriz; 'eəriːz/ *n* **1** [singular] the first sign of the ZODIAC, represented by a RAM (=male sheep), and believed to affect the character and life of people born between March 21 and April 20 白羊宮(黃道的第一宮), 白羊座 **2** [C] someone who was born between March 21 and April 20 出生於白羊宮時段(3月21日至4月20日)的人

a·right /ə`raɪt; ə'raɪt/ *adv old-fashioned*【過時】**1** correctly 正確地: *if I remember aright* 如果我沒有記錯的話 **2 set things aright** to settle problems or difficulties 解決問題[困難]

a·rise /ə`raɪz; ə'raɪz/ *v past tense* **arose** /ə`roz; ə'rəʊz/ *past participle* **arisen** /ə`rɪzn̩; ə'rɪzən/ [I] **1** if a problem or difficult situation arises, it begins to happen 發生: *A crisis has arisen in the Foreign Office.* 外交部發生了危機。**2** if something arises from or out of a situation, event etc, it is caused or started by that situation etc 由…引起: **[+from]** *Can we begin by discussing matters arising from the last meeting?* 我們是不是可以從討論由上次會議引起的問題開始? **3 when the need arises/should the need arise** when or if it is necessary 如果有必要: *Should the need arise for extra staff, we will contact you.* 如果有必要招聘更多的員工, 我們會和你聯繫。**4** *old-fashioned* to get out of bed, or stand up【過時】起牀; 起立; 起來: *Daniel arose at dawn.* 丹尼爾天亮就起牀了。**5** if something arises when you are moving towards it, you are gradually able to see it as you move closer 出現, 呈現: *As we sped down the highway, the lights of the city arose before us.* 我們在公路上疾馳, 城市的燈光映入眼簾。**6** *formal* if a group of people arise, they fight for or demand something they want【正式】起來(表示覺醒): *Arise and fight for your rights!* 起來, 為自己的權利而戰! —see 見 OCCUR (USAGE)

ar·is·toc·ra·cy /ˌærə`stɑkrəsɪ; ˌærᵻ'stɒkrəsi/ *n* **1** [C] the people in the highest social class, who traditionally have a lot of land, money, and power 貴族; 貴族階級: *dukes, earls, and other members of the aristocracy* 公爵、伯爵及其他貴族成員 | *the new LA rock 'aristocracy'* 洛杉

磯搖滾樂的"新貴們" —see also 另見 UPPER CLASS **2** [U] *technical* the system in which a country is governed by the people of the highest social class【術語】貴族政治 —compare 比較 DEMOCRACY

ar·is·to·crat /əˋrɪstəˌkræt; ˈærɪ̈stəkræt/ *n* [C] someone who belongs to the highest social class 貴族（成員）

ar·is·to·crat·ic /əˌrɪstəˋkrætɪk; ˌærɪ̈stəˈkrætɪk◂/ *adj* belonging to or typical of the aristocracy 貴族（似）的: *old, aristocratic families* 老式的貴族家庭 | *an aristocratic manner* 貴族氣派

a·rith·me·tic¹ /əˋrɪθməˌtɪk; əˈrɪθmətɪk/ *n* [U] the science of numbers involving adding, multiplying etc 算術 —compare 比較 MATHEMATICS

ar·ith·met·ic² /ˌærɪθˋmɛtɪk; ˌærɪθˈmetɪk◂/ also 又作 **ar·ith·met·i·cal** /-tɪkḷ; -tɪkəl/ *adj* involving or related to arithmetic 算術的 —**arithmetically** /-kḷɪ; -kli/ *adv*

arithmetic pro·gres·sion /ˌ····ˋ··/ *n* [C] a set of numbers in order of value in which a particular number is added to each to produce the next (as in 2, 4, 6, 8 …) 算術級數, 等差級數 —compare 比較 GEOMETRIC PROGRESSION

ark /ɑrk; ɑːk/ *n* [C] **1** a large ship 大船 **2 the Ark** in the Bible, the large boat built by Noah to save his family and the animals from a flood that covered the earth〔《聖經》中的〕挪亞方舟 **3 out of the Ark** *BrE informal* very old or old-fashioned【英, 非正式】極陳舊的; 過時的

Ark of the Cov·e·nant /ˌ···ˋ···/ *n* [singular] a box containing the laws of the Jewish religion that represented to the Jews the PRESENCE of God〔猶太教的〕約櫃

arm 臂; 上肢

1 1 **arm¹** /ɑrm; ɑːm/ *n* [C]
1 ▶BODY 身體◀ one of the two long parts of your body between your shoulders and your hands 手臂; 上肢: *Mom put her arms around me to comfort me.* 母親摟着我給我安慰。| *Pat appeared carrying a large box under his arm.* 帕特來了, 胳膊下面夾着個大盒子。| *a broken arm* 斷臂 | **with arms folded/crossed** (=with your arms bent so that they are resting against your body) 兩臂交叉 | **take sb by the arm** (=lead someone somewhere by holding their arm) 抓住某人的手臂 *Sid took me by the arm and hurried me out of the room.* 錫德拉着我的胳膊催促我趕快出了房間。| **take sb in your arms** (=gently hold someone with your arms) 擁抱某人 *Gerry took Fiona in his arms and kissed her.* 格里把菲奧娜抱在懷裡親吻。—see picture at 參見 BODY 圖
2 ▶WEAPONS 武器◀ arms [plural] weapons used for fighting wars 武器裝備: *The government is cutting arms expenditure.* 政府正在削減武器開支。| **take up arms (against sb)** (=get weapons and prepare to fight) 拿起武器（對付某人）*Boys as young as 13 are taking up arms to defend the city.* 連13歲的孩子都拿起武器保衛城市。| **lay down your arms** (=put your weapons down and stop fighting) 放下武器（停戰）| **under arms** *BrE* (=with weapons and ready to fight)【英】在備戰狀態中 *All available forces are under arms.* 所有兵種都處於備戰狀態中。—see also 另見 SMALL ARMS
3 ▶FURNITURE 家具◀ the arm of a chair, sofa etc is the part you rest your arms on〔椅子、沙發等的〕靠手臂, 扶手
4 ▶CLOTHING 衣服◀ the part of a piece of clothing that covers your arm; SLEEVE 袖子
5 arm in arm if you walk arm in arm with someone, you are walking next to them with your arm in theirs 臂挽着臂
6 be up in arms *informal* to be very angry and ready to argue or fight【非正式】〔氣得〕摩拳擦掌, 憤怒: *Residents are up in arms about plans for a new road along the beach.* 居民們對在海邊建新公路的計劃非常憤怒。
7 welcome sb/sth with open arms to show that you are happy to see someone or eager to accept an idea, plan etc 張開雙臂歡迎某人／舉雙手贊成某事: *We welcomed Henry's offer with open arms.* 我們舉雙手贊成亨利的提議。
8 give your right arm to be willing to do anything to get or do something 願付出一切: *I'd give my right arm to be 21 again.* 如果我能再回到21歲, 我願付出任何代價。
9 at arm's length if you hold something at arm's length, you hold it away from your body 一臂之距
10 keep sb at arm's length to avoid developing a relationship with someone 疏遠某人, 與某人保持一定距離: *Petra keeps all men at arm's length to avoid getting hurt.* 皮特拉跟所有的男人都保持一定距離, 以免自己受到傷害。
11 as long as your arm *informal* a list or written document that is as long as your arm is very long【非正式】〔名單或文字材料〕有胳臂那麼長, 冗長
12 ▶PART OF GROUP 團體的一部分◀ a part of a large group that is responsible for a particular type of activity 職能部門; 分支機構: *the political arm of a terrorist organization* 恐怖組織的政治部門
13 ▶OBJECT/MACHINE 物體/機器◀ the arm of an object or piece of machinery is the long thin part that looks or moves like an arm 臂（狀部件）: *the arm of a record player* 唱機的唱頭臂 —see picture at 參見 GLASS 圖
14 ▶DESIGN 設計◀ arms [plural] a set of pictures or patterns, usually painted on a SHIELD, that is used as the special sign of a family, town, university etc; COAT OF ARMS 盾徽, 盾形紋章
15 on your arm *old-fashioned* if a man has a woman on his arm, she is walking beside him holding his arm【過時】挽着你的胳膊走 —see also 另見 **arms akimbo** (AKIMBO), **babe in arms** (BABE (1)), **brothers in arms** (BROTHER¹ (5)), **fold sb/sth in your arms** (FOLD¹ (7)), **twist sb's arm** (TWIST¹ (9))

arm² *v* [T] **1** to provide weapons for yourself, an army, a country etc in order to prepare for a fight or a war 為…提供武器裝備, 武裝: **arm sb with sth** *We armed ourselves with whatever we could lay our hands on.* 我們用各種能找到的東西武裝自己。—see also 另見 ARMED (1), UNARMED **2** to provide all the information, power etc that are needed to deal with a difficult situation or argument 準備好, 裝備: *I've armed myself with all the facts I need to prove my point.* 我已準備好充分的事實來證明自己的觀點。

ar·ma·da /ɑrˋmɑdə; ɑːˈmɑːdə/ *n* [C] a large group of something, usually war ships 大批; 大羣〔尤指艦隊〕: *a vast armada of foreign visitors* 大批外國遊客

ar·ma·dil·lo /ˌɑrməˋdɪlo; ˌɑːməˈdɪləʊ/ *n* [C] a small animal that has a shell made of hard bone-like material, and lives in parts of North and South America 犰狳〔產於美洲的小動物, 身上有骨質硬殼〕

Ar·ma·ged·don /ˌɑrməˋgɛdṇ; ˌɑːməˈgedn/ *n*

[singular, U] a terrible battle that will destroy the world 〔會毀滅世界的〕大決戰: *a nuclear Armageddon* 核大戰

ar·ma·ment /ˈɑrməmənt; ˈɑːməmənt/ *n* **1** [C usually plural 一般用複數] the weapons and military equipment used in an army 軍備, 武器: *nuclear armaments* 核武器 **2** [U] the process of preparing an army or country for war by giving it weapons 武裝, 備戰(行動) —compare 比較 DISARMAMENT

ar·ma·ture /ˈɑrmətʃɚ; ˈɑːmətʃə/ *n* [C] **1** the part of a GENERATOR, motor etc that turns around to produce electricity, movement etc 〔發電機、電動機等的〕轉子, 電樞 **2** a frame that you cover with clay or other soft material to make a model 〔支撐塑像的〕骨架

arm·band /ˈɑrmˌbænd; ˈɑːmbænd/ *n* [C] **1** a band of material that you wear around your arm to show that you have an official position, or as a sign of MOURNING 臂章; 袖標; 〔服喪時戴的〕臂紗 **2** [usually plural 一般用複數] *BrE* one of two bands of plastic filled with air that you wear around your arms when you cannot swim【英】〔游泳用的充氣〕浮臂, 救生臂環

arm·chair[1] /ˈɑrmˌtʃɛr; ˈɑːmtʃeə/ *n* [C] a comfortable chair with sides that you can rest your arms on 扶手椅 —see picture at 參見 CHAIR[1] 圖

arm·chair[2] /ˈɑrmˌtʃɛr; ˈɑːmtʃeə/ *adj* **armchair traveller/critic etc** someone who talks or reads about being a traveller etc, but does not have any real experience of it 空談的旅行家/批評者等

3 3 **armed** /ɑrmd; ɑːmd/ *adj* **1** carrying weapons, especially a gun 帶武器的, 有裝備的: *The hostages were kept under armed guard.* 人質由武裝衛兵看守。| [+with] *The suspect is armed with a shotgun.* 疑犯身上帶着獵槍。| **heavily armed** (=with a lot of weapons) 有許多武器裝備的 *a heavily armed battleship* 重裝甲的戰艦 | **armed robbery** (=using guns) 持槍搶劫 | **armed combat** (=fighting with weapons) 槍戰 | **armed conflict** (=war) 武裝衝突 *This political dispute could lead to armed conflict.* 這一政治爭端可能會導致武力衝突。| **armed to the teeth** (=carrying a lot of weapons) 武裝到牙齒的; 全副武裝的 **2** having something such as knowledge or skills that make it possible for you to do something or deal with something difficult 帶備〔足夠的知識或技術〕的: [+with] *She came to the meeting armed with all the facts and figures to prove us wrong.* 她帶着能證明我們錯了的所有的事實和數字來參加會議。

armed forc·es /ˌ· ˈ··/ *n* **the armed forces** *plural* a country's military organizations, including the army, navy, and airforce 武裝力量; 武裝部隊

arm·ful /ˈɑrmˌful; ˈɑːmfʊl/ *n* [C] the amount of something that you can hold in one or both arms 〔單臂或雙臂的〕一抱(之量): [+of] *an armful of books* 一抱書

arm·hole /ˈɑrmˌhol; ˈɑːmhəʊl/ *n* [C] a hole in a shirt, dress, jacket etc that you put your arm through 〔衣服的〕袖孔

ar·mi·stice /ˈɑrməstɪs; ˈɑːmɨstɨs/ *n* [C] an agreement to stop fighting, usually for a short time 停戰, 休戰(協定) —compare 比較 CEASEFIRE, TRUCE

ar·mour *BrE*【英】, **armor** *AmE*【美】/ˈɑrmɚ; ˈɑːmə/ *n* [U] **1** metal or leather clothing that protects your body, worn by soldiers in battles in former times 〔舊時戰士在戰鬥中穿的〕盔甲: *a knight in shining armour* 穿着閃亮盔甲的騎士 | *suit of armor* 全套盔甲 **2** a strong metal layer that protects military vehicles 裝甲: *armour-clad warships* 裝甲戰艦 **3** a strong layer or shell that protects some plants and animals 〔動植物的〕硬殼, 硬皮 —see also 另見 **a chink in sb's armour** (CHINK[1] (3))

ar·moured *BrE*【英】, **armored** *AmE*【美】/ˈɑrmɚd; ˈɑːməd/ *adj* **1** armoured vehicles have an outside layer made of metal to protect them from attack 裝甲的: *armored personnel carriers* 裝甲運兵車 **2** an armoured army used armoured vehicles 配備裝甲車輛的: *an armoured division* 裝甲師

armoured car *BrE*【英】, **armored car** *AmE*【美】/ˌ·· ˈ·/ *n* [C] **1** a car that has special protection from bullets etc, used especially by important people 防彈車 **2** a military vehicle with a strong metal cover and usually a powerful gun 裝甲車

ar·mour·er *BrE*【英】, **armorer** *AmE*【美】/ˈɑrmərɚ; ˈɑːmərə/ *n* [C] someone who makes or repairs weapons and ARMOUR 〔製造或修理武器及裝甲的〕軍械士

armour-plat·ed *BrE*【英】, **armor-plated** *AmE*【美】/ˌ·· ˈ··◂/ *adj* something, especially a vehicle, that is armour-plated has an outer metal layer to protect it 〔尤指車輛〕裝甲的 —**armour plating** *n* [U] —**armour plate** *n* [U]

ar·mour·y *BrE*【英】, **armory** *AmE*【美】/ˈɑrmərɪ; ˈɑːməri/ *n* [C] a place where weapons are stored 軍械庫, 武器庫

arm·pit /ˈɑrmˌpɪt; ˈɑːmˌpɪt/ *n* [C] **1** the hollow place under your arm where it joins your body 腋(窩) —see picture at 參見 BODY 圖 **2** *AmE slang* a very unpleasant or ugly place【美俚】最差的地方, 骯髒的角落: *Butte is the armpit of Montana.* 巴特是蒙大拿州最差的地方。

arms con·trol /ˈ· ·ˌ·/ *n* [U] the attempts by powerful countries to limit the number and type of war weapons that exist 軍備控制

arms race /ˈ· ·/ *n* [C usually singular 一般用單數] the attempt by different countries to produce powerful weapons 軍備競賽: *the nuclear arms race* 核軍備競賽

ar·my /ˈɑrmɪ; ˈɑːmi/ *n* **1 the army** the part of a country's military force that is trained to fight on land in a war 陸軍: *He joined the army when he was 17.* 他17歲就參軍了。| [also+plural verb *BrE* 英] *The army are helping to clear up after the floods.* 洪水過後, 軍隊在幫助清理災後現場。| **be in the army** *Both my sons are in the army.* 我的兩個兒子都在當兵。**2** [C] a large organized group of people trained to fight on land in a war 武裝組織: *The rebel armies have taken control of the radio station.* 叛軍已經控制了廣播電台。| **raise an army** (=collect and organize an army to fight a battle) 組建軍隊 **3** [C] a large number of people or animals involved in the same activity 團體; 隊伍; 大羣: *The village hall is maintained by an army of volunteers.* 村禮堂由一支志願者隊伍維修。—compare 比較 AIRFORCE, NAVY

a·ro·ma /əˈromə; əˈrəʊmə/ *n* [C] a strong pleasant smell 芳香, 香氣, 香味: *the aroma of toast and fresh coffee* 烤麵包片和新鮮咖啡的香味

a·ro·ma·ther·a·py /əˌroməˈθɛrəpɪ; əˌrəʊməˈθerəpi/ *n* [U] a treatment that uses MASSAGE (=rubbing the body) with pleasant smelling natural oils to reduce pain and make you feel well 芳香劑療法, 香薰療法 —**aromatherapist** *n* [C]

ar·o·mat·ic /ˌærəˈmætɪk; ˌærəˈmætɪk◂/ *adj* having a strong, pleasant smell 芳香的: *aromatic oils* 芳香油 —**aromatically** /-klɪ; -kli/ *adv*

a·rose /əˈroz; əˈrəʊz/ the past tense of ARISE

a·round[1] /əˈraund; əˈraʊnd/ *adv* **1** used to say that something is placed or arranged so that it surrounds something else 四周, (在)周圍: *The winner held up his trophy, with many of the spectators crowded around.* 獲勝者高舉獎盃, 四周圍滿了觀眾。| *a bouquet of a dozen red roses, with a silver ribbon wrapped around* 用銀色絲帶紮着的一打紅玫瑰 | **all around** *The prison was set on an island, with high walls all around.* 監獄設在一個島上, 四周有高牆。**2** [only after verb 僅用於動詞後] used to say that someone or something is moving in a circular movement 旋轉; 圍繞: *She watched the cogs and wheels going around silently.* 她靜靜地看着齒輪和輪子在旋轉。**3 sit/stand/lie etc around** to sit, stand etc without doing anything in particular, especially so that people think you are wasting time 沒事閒坐着/站着/躺着等: *There were a few suspicious looking people hanging around outside.* 有幾個看起來可疑的人在外面遊蕩。**4 fool/mess etc around** used to mean that someone is wasting time by doing something stupid or dishonest 無所事事, 混日子; 胡鬧: *Stop messing around! I know you've hidden it.* 別胡鬧了！我知道你把它藏起來了。**5** [only after verb 僅用於動詞後] in many places or in many different parts of a particular area 到處, 四處: *Don't leave all your papers lying around – anyone could read them.* 不要到處亂放你的文件 —— 誰都能看到。| *When I finished college, I travelled around for a while before I got my first job.* 大學畢業以後, 我找到第一份工作之前到處旅遊了一段時間。| *Since it's your first day here, would you like me to show you around?* 這是你到這兒的第一天, 要我帶你到處走走嗎？ **6** if someone is around, they are in the same place as you 附近, 在近處: *He went down to the sports centre but there was no-one around that he knew.* 他去了體育中心, 但周圍沒有一個他認識的人。| *Why is there never a policeman around when you need one?* 需要警察的時候為甚麼附近就找不到呢？**7 the best ... around/the most exciting ... around etc** used to say that someone or something is the best, the most exciting thing of this kind 當前最佳的…/最令人激動的…等: *East 17 are one of the most popular groups around.* "East 17" 是當今最受歡迎的演唱組合之一。**8 get around to (doing) sth** to finally do something that you have been intending to do for a long time 找時間做某事; 終於去做某事〔指早就想做的事〕: *I'll get around to the decorating one of these days.* 這幾天我要找時間佈置一下。**9** facing in the opposite direction 轉過身: *Slowly he turned the boat around, hoping the patrol would not hear the engines.* 他慢慢將船調過頭去, 希望巡邏隊不會聽到發動機聲。**10 have been around** *informal* to have had experience of many different situations, so that you can deal with new situations confidently【非正式】生活經歷豐富; 見過世面 **11 2 feet/100 cms etc around** *AmE* having a CIRCUMFERENCE of 2 feet, 100 cms etc【美】周長 2 英尺/100 厘米等 —see also 另見 ROUND², ROUND³ (USAGE)

1 1 **around²** *prep* **1** used to say that something is placed or arranged so that it surrounds something else 環繞, 在…周圍: *The whole family were sitting around the dinner table chatting.* 全家人圍坐在飯桌旁聊天。| *She had a beautiful woollen shawl wrapped around her shoulders.* 她肩上圍着一條漂亮的羊毛披肩。**2** used to say that someone or something is moving in a circular movement 繞着…: *A few wolves were prowling around the deer's carcass.* 幾條狼在一隻鹿的屍體旁繞圈子。| *There are reports of a light aircraft flying around and around the Sears Tower.* 有報道說一架輕型飛機在希爾斯大廈上空來回盤旋。**3** in many places or parts of a particular area or place 到…四處, 在…各處: *We took a wander around the garden after breakfast.* 早餐後, 我們在花園裡到處走走。| *They have branches dotted around the country.* 他們的分支機構遍佈全國各地。| **all around** *There were flowers all around the apartment, making it look more homely.* 公寓裡到處是鮮花, 給人一種家的感覺。**4** if someone or something is around a particular place, they are in or near that place 在…附近, 在…近處: *I think he lives somewhere around the centre of town.* 我想他住在市中心附近的某個地方。| *Is there a bank around here?* 這附近有銀行嗎？ **5** if you move or go around something, you move around the side of it instead of going through or over it 繞過…: *If the gate is locked you'll have to go around the side of the house.* 如果大門鎖上了, 你們就得從房子側面繞過去。**6** if something is organized around a particular person or thing, it is organized according to their needs, ideas, beliefs etc 圍繞…, 以…為中心; 根據: *Why does everything have to be organised around what Callum wants to do?* 為甚麼一切都要按照卡勒姆的意願安排呢？| *Their whole society was built around their belief in their gods.* 他們的整個社會都建立在他們對諸神的信仰的基礎上。**7 get around** to avoid or solve a particular problem or difficult situation 逃避, 迴避; 用計防止: *How do we get around the problem of the new tax laws?* 我們怎樣才能避開新稅法的問題？**8 around 200/5000 etc** used when guessing a number, amount etc 200/5000 等左右: *There must have been around 40,000 people in the stadium.* 體育場裡肯定有四萬人左右。| **around about** *Most guests started to make their way home around about 10 o'clock.* 大多數客人在十點鐘左右開始回家。—see also 另見 ROUND³

a·rous·al /ə'rauzḷ; ə'raʊzəl/ *n* [U] excitement, especially sexual excitement 喚起;〔尤指性慾的〕激起

a·rouse /ə'rauz; ə'raʊz/ *v* [T] **1 arouse interest/expectations etc** to make you become interested, expect something etc 引起興趣/期望等: *Matt's behavior was arousing the interest of the neighbors.* 馬特的行為逐漸引起了鄰居的興趣。**2 arouse anger/fear/dislike etc** to make someone feel very angry, afraid etc 激起憤怒/恐懼/討厭等 **3** to make someone feel sexually excited 激起…的性慾 **4** *formal* to wake someone【正式】喚醒: **[+from]** *Anne had to be aroused from a deep sleep.* 不得不喚醒熟睡中的安妮。

ar·peg·gi·o /ɑr'pɛdʒɪˌo; ɑː'pedʒiəʊ/ *n* [C] the notes of a musical CHORD (1) played separately rather than all at once 琶音; 琶音和弦

arr 1 the written abbreviation of 縮寫= arranged by (由…) 改編, 改寫: *music by Mozart, arr Britten* 莫扎特原曲, 布里頓改編 **2** the written abbreviation of 縮寫= arrives or arrival

ar·raign /ə'ren; ə'reɪn/ *v* [T] *technical* to make someone come to court to hear what the court says their crime is【術語】提堂審訊, 傳訊: *arraigned on a charge of murder* 因被控謀殺而被提審 —**arraignment** *n* [C,U]

ar·range /ə'rendʒ; ə'reɪndʒ/ *v* **1** [I,T] to organize or make plans for something such as a meeting, party, or trip 安排, 籌劃: *James is arranging a big surprise party for Helen's birthday.* 詹姆斯正在為海倫張羅一個使她驚喜的生日聚會。| *I'd like to arrange a business loan.* 我想安排一項商業貸款。| **arrange to do sth** *Have you arranged to meet Mark this weekend?* 你安排了這個週末見馬克嗎？| **arrange for sb to do sth** *I've arranged for the window cleaner to come on Thursday.* 我已經安排好一個窗子清潔工星期四來。| **arrange sth with sb** *Beth arranged a meeting with the marketing director.* 貝思安排了和營銷經理見面。| **arrange for sth** *The company will arrange for a taxi to meet you at the airport.* 公司將安排一輛計程車去機場接你。| **arrange when/where/how etc** *We still have to arrange how to get home.* 我們還必須安排好怎樣回家。| **as arranged** *Matthew arrived at 2 o'clock as arranged.* 馬修於兩點鐘如約而至。**2** [T] to put a group of things or people in a particular order or position 整理, 排列, 佈置: *I've arranged my CDs in alphabetical order.* 我把我的雷射唱片按字母順序排好了。| **arrange sth in pairs/groups etc** *The children were arranged in lines according to height.* 孩子按身高排成幾隊。**3** [T] to write or change a piece of music so that it is suitable for particular instruments 改編〔樂曲〕: **[+for]** *a symphony arranged for the piano* 改編為鋼琴演奏曲的交響曲 2 2

arranged mar·riage /ˌ·ˌ· '··/ *n* [C,U] a marriage in which the parents choose a husband or wife for their child 包辦婚姻: *Arranged marriages are still common in the Indian community.* 包辦婚姻在印度社會仍然很普遍。

ar·range·ment /ə'rendʒmənt; ə'reɪndʒmənt/ *n* **1** [C usually plural 一般用複數] the things that you must organize so that an event, meeting etc can happen 安排, 籌劃, 準備: **[+for]** *What exactly are the arrangements for the wedding?* 婚禮到底是如何安排的？| **make arrangements** *The local newspaper made arrangements for an interview with Professor Stein.* 當地報紙安排對斯坦教授進行專訪。| **seating/travel/sleeping etc arrangements** *I'm not very happy about the sleeping arrangements.* 我對住宿安排不太滿意。**2** [C,U] some- 2 2

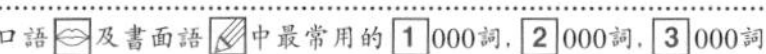

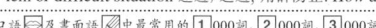

thing that has been organized or agreed on; agreement 議定之事, 協定: *Our loan is by special arrangement with the bank.* 我們的貸款是經與銀行特別協商確定的。| **come to some arrangement** (=make an agreement that is acceptable to everyone) 達成協議 *It would usually cost $500, but I'm sure we can come to some kind of arrangement.* 正常價格是500美元, 但我相信我們可以再協商。**3** [C,U] a group of things that have been arranged in an attractive or neat way, or the act of arranging a group of things in this way 整理[佈置、排列]好的東西: *a beautiful flower arrangement* 漂亮的插花樣式 **4** [C,U] a piece of music that has been written or changed for a particular instrument 改編曲: *an arrangement of an old folk song for chorus* 把一首傳唱已久的民歌改編成合唱曲

ar·rant /ˋærənt; 'ærənt/ *adj old-fashioned* used to emphasize how bad something is【過時】壞透的; 徹頭徹尾的, 極端的: *arrant nonsense* 一派胡言

ar·ray¹ /əˋre; ə'reɪ/ **1** [C usually singular 一般用單數] a group or collection of things, usually arranged so that you can see them all 排列, 陳列: *The museum has a vast array of uniforms and ceremonial robes.* 博物館展出一系列樣式繁多的制服和禮服。**2** [C usually singular 一般用單數] a group of people, especially people who are important or special 隊列, 一隊: *a dazzling array of acting talent* 一羣光彩奪目的演藝天才 **3** [C,U] *literary* fine clothes, especially those worn for a special occasion【文】盛裝: *The king came aboard with his guests and family in colourful array.* 國王穿着豔麗的盛裝與賓客和家人上了船。**4** [C] *technical* a set of numbers or signs, or of computer memory units, arranged in lines across or down【術語】(數字、符號的) 排列, 數列, 陣列; 數組

array² *v* [T usually passive 一般用被動態] **1** *literary* to arrange something in an attractive way【文】佈置, 排好 **2** *formal* to put soldiers in position ready for battle【正式】佈陣, 部署 **3** *literary* to dress in good quality chothes【文】身着盛裝, 打扮: *She came in arrayed in all her finery.* 她衣着華麗地來了。

ar·rears /əˋrɪrz; ə'rɪəz/ *n* [plural] **1 be in arrears** if someone is in arrears or if their payments are in arrears, they are late in paying something that they should pay regularly, such as rent 拖欠: *Teachers' pay is in arrears and the school says it can't afford to pay.* 教師的工資仍然拖欠着, 校方說沒錢支付。| **be four weeks/three months etc in arrears** *The rent money is two months in arrears.* 租金拖欠了兩個月。| **fall into arrears** (=become late with payments) 拖欠 **2** money that you owe someone because regular payments such as rent have not been paid at the right time 逾期欠款: *We've got 3 months arrears to pay on the video.* 我們買錄像機的錢有三個月的欠賬未付。**3 be paid in arrears** to be given your wages at the end of the period you have worked ... 之後付款: *a salary paid monthly in arrears* 每月後行支付的薪金

3 **ar·rest¹** /əˋrɛst; ə'rest/ *v* [T] **1** if the police arrest you, they take you away because they think you have done something illegal 逮捕, 拘捕: *Police arrested 26 demonstrators, over half of them women.* 警方逮捕了26名示威者, 其中一半以上是婦女。| **arrest sb for sth** *Wayne was arrested for dangerous driving.* 韋恩因危險駕駛被拘留。**2** *formal* to stop something happening or to make it happen more slowly【正式】抑制; 阻止: *drugs used to arrest the spread of the disease* 用於控制疾病蔓延的藥物 | *arrested development* 受到遏制的發展 **3 arrest your attention** *formal* to make you look or listen to something, because it is interesting or exciting【正式】引起你的注意; 吸引你: *Her warning tone arrested my attention.* 她警告的口氣引起我的注意。

arrest² *n* [C,U] the act of taking someone away and guarding them because they may have done something illegal 逮捕: **make an arrest** *The police made several arrests.* 警方逮捕了好幾個人。| **be under arrest** (=kept by the police) 被逮捕 *He's under arrest and awaiting trial.* 他被拘留候審。| **place/put sb under arrest** (=arrest someone) 逮捕某人

ar·riv·al /əˋraɪvl; ə'raɪvəl/ *n* **1** [U] the act of arriving somewhere 到達, 抵達: *the late arrival of the train* 火車誤點 | *Joe's sudden arrival spoiled all our plans.* 喬的突然到來破壞了我們所有的計劃。| **arrival at/in** *Shortly after our arrival in Turkey Lisa became very ill.* 我們到達土耳其不久, 莉莎就病倒了。| **on arrival** (=when you arrive) 到達時 *He was rushed to the hospital but was dead on arrival.* 他被急速送往醫院, 但到達時已死亡。**2 the arrival of** the time when an important new idea, method, or product is first used or discovered ...的到來[出現]: *The arrival of democracy has thrown the economy into chaos.* 民主的出現使經濟陷入混亂。**3 new arrival** someone who has just arrived in a particular place to live, work etc 新來的人: *New arrivals in the camp were greeted with suspicion.* 新來到營地的人都受到懷疑。**4** [C] a plane or train that arrives in an airport or station 進站列車; 進港飛機 —opposite 反義詞 DEPARTURE 3

ar·rive /əˋraɪv; ə'raɪv/ *v* [I] 2 1

1 ►GET SOMEWHERE 到某處◄ to get to the place you are going to 到達, 抵達: *Give me a call to let me know you've arrived safely.* 打個電話給我, 告訴我你已平安到達。| **arrive in/at/from** *Elaine should be arriving in the States about now.* 伊萊恩現在該到美國了。

2 ►BE DELIVERED 送到◄ if something arrives, it is brought or delivered to you 送達: *By the time the letter finally arrived, I'd heard the news.* 信最終送到時我早已知道消息了。

3 ►EVENT 事件◄ if an event or particular period of time arrives, it happens 發生; 降臨, 來到: *At last the day of the carnival arrived!* 狂歡節的日子終於來到了!

4 ►STH NEW 新事物◄ if a new idea, method, product etc arrives, it begins to exist or starts being used 出現; 起用: *Children don't play outside as much since computer games arrived.* 自從有了電腦遊戲, 孩子們就很少出外玩了。

5 ►BIRTH 出生◄ to be born 出生: *Sharon's baby arrived just after midnight.* 莎倫的孩子午夜剛過就出生了。

6 arrive at a conclusion/agreement/idea etc to reach an agreement etc after much effort 得出結論/達成協議/有了主意等: *After three weeks of confusion we arrived at the conclusion that there was a security leak.* 經過三個星期的混亂狀態, 我們得出結論: 安全措施有疏漏之處。

7 ►SUCCESS 成功◄ to achieve success 取得成功: *When he saw his name printed on the door he knew he'd arrived!* 當他看到自己的名字被印在門上, 他知道自己成功了。—see 見 REACH¹ (USAGE)

ar·ro·gance /ˋærəgəns; 'ærəgəns/ *n* [U] the quality of thinking that you are very important so that you behave rudely 傲慢: *The arrogance of that man – pretending he'd never seen us before!* 瞧那個人多傲慢! 裝作從來沒見過我們的樣子!

ar·ro·gant /ˋærəgənt; 'ærəgənt/ *adj* so proud of your own abilities or qualities that you behave as if you are much more important than anyone else 傲慢的, 趾高氣揚的, 目中無人的, 妄自尊大的: *I found him arrogant and overbearing.* 我發現他妄自尊大, 盛氣凌人。—**arrogantly** *adv*: *He strutted about the room arrogantly.* 他趾高氣揚地在屋子裡踱步。

ar·ro·gate /ˋærə͵get; 'ærəgeɪt/ *v* **arrogate sth to yourself** *formal* to claim that you have a particular right, position etc without having the legal right to it【正式】霸佔; 冒稱; 擅取: *Having seized power he arrogated to himself the right to change the law.* 他攫取大權以後, 便僭取了修改法律的權力。

ar·row /ˋæro; 'ærəʊ/ *n* [C] **1** a weapon like a thin straight stick with a point at one end that you shoot with a BOW³ (1) 箭, 矢 **2** a sign in the shape of an arrow, used to show people which direction to go in 箭號, 箭頭 (符號): *Follow the red arrows to the X-ray department.* 順着紅箭頭指的方向去X光科。—see also 另見 STRAIGHT ARROW

ar·row·head /ˈæroˌhɛd; ˈærəʊhed/ *n* [C] a sharp pointed piece of metal or stone fixed to one end of an arrow 箭鏃, 箭頭

ar·row·root /ˈæroˌrut; ˈærəʊruːt/ *n* [U] flour made from the root of a tropical American plant 葛粉

arse¹ /ɑrs; ɑːs/ *n BrE*【英】**1** [C] an impolite word for the part of your body that you sit on 屁股〔非禮貌用詞〕**2** [C] *spoken* an impolite word for a stupid and annoying person; arsehole【口】笨蛋, 飯桶〔非禮貌用詞〕: *Jake's such an arse, I don't know why she's going out with him!* 我不知道她為何跟傑克這種笨蛋交往! **3 my arse!** *spoken* an impolite way of saying that you do not believe something【口】胡扯!〔非禮貌說法〕: *He says he's got a new car? My arse! He hasn't got any money!* 他說他買了一輛新車? 胡扯! 他根本沒有錢! **4 shift/move your arse** *spoken* an impolite way of telling someone to hurry up【口】快點!〔非禮貌用語〕: *Come on! Shift your arse or we'll be late.* 快點! 不然我們就遲到了。**5 be right up sb's arse** *spoken* an impolite way of saying that someone is driving very close to the back of the car in front of them【口】就要撞到前車的尾部〔非禮貌用語〕—see also 另見 ASS, **pain in the arse/ass etc** (PAIN¹ (3)), SMART ARSE

arse² *v* [I] *BrE slang*【英俚】**can't/couldn't be arsed** to not do something because you are feeling too lazy 懶得做某事: *I just can't be arsed making my own lasagne this time – I'll buy one instead.* 這次, 我不想費事做意大利麵條了, 我去買一份。

arse about/around *phr v* [I] to waste time 浪費時間; 遊手好閒: *He's been arsing about in the garden all day.* 他整天在花園裡遊蕩。

arse·hole /ˈɑrsˌhol; ˈɑːshəʊl/ *n* [C] *BrE*【英】**1** *spoken* an impolite word for a stupid and annoying person【口】傻瓜蛋〔非禮貌用詞〕; ASSHOLE *AmE*【美】**2** an impolite word for the ANUS 屁眼, 肛門〔非禮貌用詞〕

ar·se·nal /ˈɑrsn̩əl; ˈɑːsənəl/ *n* [C] **1** a store of weapons 一大批儲備的武器: [+of] *The police found an arsenal of guns in the terrorist's hideout.* 警察在恐怖分子藏匿的地方發現了一大批槍枝。**2** a building where weapons are stored 武器庫, 軍火庫

ar·se·nic /ˈɑrsn̩ɪk; ˈɑːsənɪk/ *n* [U] a very poisonous substance sometimes used for killing rats 砷, 砒霜

ar·son /ˈɑrsn̩; ˈɑːsən/ *n* [U] the crime of deliberately making something burn, especially a building 縱火 (罪), 放火 (罪) —**arsonist** *n* [C]

1 1 **art¹** /ɑrt; ɑːt/ *n* **1** [U] the use of painting, drawing, SCULPTURE etc to represent things or express ideas 美術, 繪畫; 藝術: *an example of Indian art* 印度繪畫的典範 | **modern art** *the Museum of Modern Art* 現代美術館 **2** [U] objects that are produced by art, such as paintings, drawings etc 美術作品; 藝術品: *an art exhibition* 藝術作品展 **3** [U] the skill of drawing or painting 繪畫技巧: *He excelled at art at school.* 上學時他擅長繪畫。**4 the arts** [plural] art, music, theatre, film, literature etc all considered together 藝術〔指繪畫、音樂、戲劇、電影、文學等的統稱〕: *more government funding for the arts* 政府對文學藝術投入更多的資金 **5 arts** also 又作 **the arts** [plural] subjects of study that are not scientific, such as history, languages etc 人文學科, 文科 —see also 另見 HUMANITIES **6** [C,U] the ability or skill involved in doing or making something 技術; 技巧: **the art of doing something** *Television is ruining the art of conversation.* 電視簡直是在糟蹋談話藝術。| **be quite an art** (=be quite difficult) 需要些技巧, 不太容易 *Driving a car through central London is quite an art.* 開車穿過倫敦市中心還真需要點技術。| **have/get sth down to a fine art** (=do something very well) 把某事做得出色[精巧] *I've got the early morning routine down to a fine art.* 我把清晨的例行工作幹得很妥當。

art² *v* **thou art** *old use* used to mean 'you are' when talking to one person【舊】你是〔you are 的古說法〕

art dec·o /ˌɑr ˈdeko; ˌɑː ˈdekəʊ/ *n* [U] a style of art and decoration that uses simple shapes and was popular in Europe and America in the 1920s and 1930s〔20世紀20和30年代流行的一種〕裝飾派藝術 (風格)

art di·rec·tor /ˈ· ·ˌ··/ *n* [C] someone who organizes the clothes, lights, scenery etc for a film〔電影等的〕美術指導

ar·te·fact, artifact /ˈɑrtɪˌfækt; ˈɑːtɪ̈fækt/ *n* [C] an object such as a tool, weapon etc that was made in the past and is historically important 人工製品〔有史學價值的武器、工具等〕, 手工藝品: *an exhibition of ancient Egyptian artefacts* 古埃及器物展覽

ar·ter·i·al /ɑrˈtɪrɪəl; ɑːˈtɪəriəl/ *adj* [only before noun 僅用於名詞前] **1** involving the arteries 動脈的: *arterial blood* 動脈血 **2 arterial road/railway line etc** a main road, railway line etc 公路/鐵路幹線等

ar·ter·i·o·scle·ro·sis /ɑrˈtɪrɪˌosklɪˈrosɪs; ɑːˌtɪəriəʊsklɪ̈ˈrəʊsɪ̈s/ *n* [U] a disease in which your arteries become hard, which stops the blood from flowing through them smoothly 動脈硬化 (症)

ar·te·ry /ˈɑrtərɪ; ˈɑːtəri/ *n* [C] **1** one of the tubes that carries blood from your heart to the rest of your body 動脈 —compare 比較 VEIN (1) **2** a main road, railway line, river etc〔道路〕幹道; 鐵路幹線; 河的幹流

ar·te·si·an well /ɑrˈtiʒən ˈwɛl; ɑːˌtiːziən ˈwel/ *n* [C] a WELL⁴ (1) from which the water is forced up out of the ground by natural pressure 自流井, 噴水井

art·ful /ˈɑrtfəl; ˈɑːtfəl/ *adj* clever at deceiving people 狡猾的, 奸詐的: *He's an artful little devil and always gets what he wants.* 他是個狡詐的小傢伙, 總能得到想要的東西。—**artfully** *adj*: *artfully concealed pockets* 隱藏得很巧妙的衣袋 —**artfulness** *n* [U]

art gal·le·ry /ˈ· ˌ···/ *n* [C] a building where important paintings are kept and shown to the public 美術館, 藝術畫廊

art house /ˈ· ·/ *n* [C] a cinema that shows mainly foreign films or films made by small film companies 藝術影院

ar·thri·tis /ɑrˈθraɪtɪs; ɑːˈθraɪtɪ̈s/ *n* [U] a disease that causes a lot of pain in the joints of your body 關節炎 —**arthritic** /-ˈθrɪtɪk; -ˈθrɪtɪk/ *adj*: *arthritic fingers* 患關節炎的手指

ar·ti·choke /ˈɑrtɪˌtʃok; ˈɑːtɪ̈tʃəʊk/ *n* [C] **1** also 又作 **globe artichoke** a plant with thick pointed leaves that are eaten as a vegetable 朝鮮薊, 洋薊 —see picture on page A9 參見A9頁圖 **2** also 又作 **Jerusalem artichoke** a plant that has a root like a potato that you can eat 菊芋, 洋薑 —see picture on page A9 參見A9頁圖

ar·ti·cle /ˈɑrtɪkl̩; ˈɑːtɪkəl/ *n* [C] **1** a thing, especially one 2 1
of a group of things (一件) 物品: *Most of our wedding presents were household articles that we really needed.* 我們收到的結婚禮物大都是我們確實需要的家用器具。| **article of clothing/furniture/jewellery etc** *She didn't take much with her, just a few articles of clothing.* 她沒帶太多東西, 只帶了幾件衣服。**2** a piece of writing about a particular subject in a newspaper, magazine etc 文章, 論文, 專題: *Have you seen that article in the Star about stress management?* 你看到《星報》上那篇講述如何對付壓力的文章了嗎? **3** a part of a law or legal agreement, especially a numbered part 條款: *Article 1 of the constitution guarantees freedom of religion.* 憲法的第一條保障宗教信仰自由。**4** *technical* a word used before a noun to show whether the noun refers to a particular example of something or to a general example of something【術語】冠詞: **the definite article** (='the' in English) 定冠詞 | **the indefinite article** (='a' or 'an' in English) 不定冠詞 **5 articles** *BrE* an agreement by which someone finishes their education, especially as a lawyer, by working for a company【英】見習契約; 師徒合約 **6 an ar-**

ticle of faith something that you feel very strongly about so that it affects how you think or behave 信念, 信條

ar·ti·cled /ˋɑrtɪkḷd; ˈɑːtɪkəld/ *adj* someone who is articled to a company of lawyers, ACCOUNTANTs etc, is employed by that company while they are training to become a lawyer etc 訂有見習契約的: *an articled clerk* 訂有見習合約的文員

ar·tic·u·late¹ /ɑrˋtɪkjəlɪt; ɑːˈtɪkjʊlɪt/ *adj* **1** able to talk easily, clearly and effectively about things, especially difficult subjects 能清楚表達的; 口齒伶俐的: *bright, articulate 17-year-olds* 聰明的、表達能力強的17歲的青年人 —opposite 反義詞 INARTICULATE **2** writing or speech that is articulate is very clear and easy to understand even if the subject is difficult 表達清楚的; 發音清晰的 **3** *technical* having joints【術語】有關節的, 分節的: *Grasshoppers are articulate insects.* 蚱蜢是分節昆蟲。—**articulately** *adv* —**articulateness** *n* [U]

ar·tic·u·late² /ɑrˋtɪkjə,let; ɑːˈtɪkjʊleɪt/ *v* [I] **1** to express what you are thinking or feeling very clearly 清楚地表達: *muddled emotions that I found difficult to articulate* 難以表達清楚的糊塗情感 **2** to speak or pronounce your words clearly and carefully 口齒清楚地講話[發音]

ar·tic·u·la·ted /ɑrˋtɪkjə,letɪd; ɑːˈtɪkjʊleɪtɪd/ *adj* having two or more parts that are joined together by a moving joint 鉸接式的: **articulated bus/vehicle etc** *It's amazing how easily those articulated lorries turn corners.* 那些鉸接式貨車轉彎非常靈敏, 真令人稱奇。

ar·tic·u·la·tion /ɑr,tɪkjəˋleʃən; ɑː,tɪkjʊˈleɪʃən/ *n* **1** [U] the production of speech sounds 發音, 咬字: *clear articulation* 清晰的發音 **2** [U] the expression of thoughts or feelings in words〔思想、感情的〕表達: *the articulation of her suffering* 她對所受痛苦的傾訴 **3** [C] *technical* a joint, especially in a plant【術語】關節;〔植物的〕節

ar·ti·fact /ˋɑrtɪ,fækt; ˈɑːtɪfækt/ *n* [C] another spelling of ARTEFACT artefact 的另一種拼法

ar·ti·fice /ˋɑrtəfɪs; ˈɑːtɪfɪs/ *n formal*【正式】**1** [U] the use of clever tricks 訣竅, 竅門; 巧計: *Her charm was all artifice.* 她的魅力全在於她的計謀。**2** [C] a clever trick, especially one used to deceive someone 詭計

3 **ar·ti·fi·cial** /,ɑrtəˋfɪʃəl; ,ɑːtɪˈfɪʃəl◂/ *adj* [usually before noun 一般用於名詞前] **1** not made of natural materials or substances 人造的, 人工的: *artificial sweeteners* 人造甜味劑 **2** not real or natural but deliberately made to look real or natural 假的, 仿造的: *an artificial leg* 義肢 **3** artificial behaviour is not natural or sincere because someone is pretending to be something they are not 虛假的, 不真摯的, 矯揉造作的: *an artificial smile* 牽強的微笑 **4** happening because someone has made it happen and not as part of a natural process 人為的: *High import taxes give their goods an artificial advantage in the market.* 高進口稅使他們的產品在市場上獲得人為的優勢。—**artificially** *adv*: *Food prices are being kept artificially low.* 食品價格正被人為地控制在低水平。—**artificiality** /,ɑrtə,fɪʃɪˋælətɪ; ,ɑːtɪfɪʃiˈælɪti/ *n* [U]

artificial in·sem·i·na·tion /,···· ···ˋ··/ *n* [U] the process of making a woman or female animal PREGNANT (1) using a piece of equipment, rather than naturally 人工授精

artificial in·tel·li·gence /,···· ·ˋ···/ also 又作 **AI** *n* [U] the study of how to make computers do things that people can do, such as make decisions, see things etc 人工智能

artificial res·pi·ra·tion /,···· ··ˋ··/ *n* [U] a way of making someone breathe again when they have stopped by blowing air into their mouth; MOUTH-TO-MOUTH RESUSCITATION 人工呼吸

ar·til·le·ry /ɑrˋtɪlərɪ; ɑːˈtɪləri/ *n* **1** [U] large guns, especially ones on wheels or fixed in one place, such as on a ship 砲, 大砲 **2 the artillery** the part of the army that uses these weapons 砲兵

ar·ti·san /ˋɑrtəzṇ; ,ɑːtɪˈzæn/ *n* [C] someone who does skilled work with their hands; CRAFTSMAN 工匠, 手藝人

art·ist /ˋɑrtɪst; ˈɑːtɪst/ *n* [C] **1** someone who produces art, especially paintings or drawings 畫家, 美術家; 藝術家: *It's not always easy to earn a living as an artist.* 作為畫家, 謀生也不是易事。**2** a professional performer, especially in music, dance, or the theatre 藝術家; 藝人: *Many of the artists in the show donated their fee to charity.* 參加演出的許多藝人將演出收入捐給慈善事業。**3** *informal* someone who is extremely good at something【非正式】高手, 技術高超的人: *He's no ordinary baker, the man's an artist.* 他絕不是普通的麵包師, 簡直是個藝術大師。 3 2

ar·tiste /ɑrˋtist; ɑːˈtiːst/ *n* [C] a professional singer, dancer, actor etc who performs in a show 職業演藝人員, 藝人

ar·tis·tic /ɑrˋtɪstɪk; ɑːˈtɪstɪk/ *adj* **1** connected with art or culture 美術的, 藝術的; 美術家的, 藝術家的: *I'm not sure about the artistic merit of much of Dali's work.* 我不太肯定達里大部分作品的藝術價值。**2** showing skill or imagination in any of the arts 富於藝術想像力的, 有藝術才華的: *What a beautiful picture, I never realized you were so artistic.* 多美的畫! 我從來沒有意識到你這樣有藝術才華。**3** an artistic arrangement, design etc looks attractive and has been done with skill and imagination 有藝術技巧的; 有創意的: *food presented in an artistic way* 擺放得很精美的食品—**artistically** /-kḷɪ; -kli/ *adv*

art·ist·ry /ˋɑrtɪstrɪ; ˈɑːtɪstri/ *n* [U] skill in a particular artistic activity 創作天資; 藝術才華; 藝術性: *an example of the photographer's artistry* 攝影家藝術才華的範例

art·less /ˋɑrtlɪs; ˈɑːtləs/ *adj* natural, honest, and sincere 天真自然的, 純樸的; 不造作的: *She chatted away about her life with artless confidence.* 她充滿自信, 毫不造作地談起自己的生活。—**artlessly** *adj* —**artlessness** *n* [U]

art nou·veau /ˋɑr nuˋvo; ,ɑː nuːˈvəʊ/ *n* [U] a style of art that used pictures of plants and flowers, popular in Europe and America at the end of the 19th century 新藝術(派)〔19世紀末流行於歐美的一種裝飾藝術風格〕

arts and crafts /,· · ˋ·/ *n* [plural] the arts that involve making things with your hands, such as POTTERY etc 手工藝, 工藝(美術)

art·work /ˋɑrtwɝk; ˈɑːtwɜːk/ *n* [U] pictures that are made for a book or magazine, or for another product such as a computer PROGRAM 插圖

art·y /ˋɑrtɪ; ˈɑːti/ *BrE*【英】, **art·sy** /ˋɑrtsɪ; ˈɑːtsi/ *AmE*【美】*adj informal* someone who is arty knows a lot about art or does a lot of art【非正式】懂[搞]藝術的: *arty types gathered in a corner at the party* 懂藝術的人聚集在晚會的一角

arty-craft·y /,·· ˈ··◂/ *BrE*【英】, **art·sy craft·sy** /,ɑrtsɪ ˋkræftsɪ; ,ɑːtsi ˈkrɑːftsi◂/ *AmE*【美】*adj* someone who is arty-crafty makes things at home and does all kinds of art, especially in a way that is not very professional 自以為懂藝術的

art·y-fart·y /,ɑrtɪ ˋfɑrtɪ; ,ɑːti ˈfɑːti◂/ *BrE*【英】, **art·sy-fart·sy** /,ɑrtsɪ ˋfɑrtsɪ; ,ɑːtsi ˈfɑːtsi◂/ *AmE*【美】*adj informal* someone who is arty-farty tries too hard to show that they are interested in art【非正式】冒充對藝術感興趣的, 附庸風雅的

-ary /ɛrɪ; əri/ *suffix* **1** [in adjectives 構成形容詞] of or concerning something; that is something ...的; 與...有關的: *planetary bodies* (=that are PLANETs) 天體 | *customary* 習慣的 **2** [in nouns 構成名詞] someone connected with something 與...有關的人: *the beneficiaries of the will* (=people who get something good from it) 遺囑的受益人 | *a functionary* (=someone with duties) 小官員 **3** [in nouns 構成名詞] a thing or place connected with or containing things of a particular kind 與...有關的東西[場所]: *a library* (=containing books) 圖書館 | *an ovary* (=containing eggs) 卵巢

Ar·y·an /ˋɛrɪən; ˈeəriən/ *n* [C] someone from Northern Europe, especially someone with fair hair and blue eyes

雅利安人,〔尤指金髮碧眼的〕北歐人 —**Aryan** *adj*

1 1 **as¹** /əz; əz; *strong* 強讀 æz; æz/ *adv, prep* **1 as old/fat/clever etc as sb/sth** equally old, fat etc as someone or something else 像某人/某物一樣老/胖/聰明等: *My brother is not as old as me.* 我弟弟年紀沒我大。| *Her ring is twice as big as mine.* 她的戒指有我的兩個大。| **as soon as possible** (=as soon as you can) 盡快 | **just as clever/clean/happy etc** *Tina's clever, but her brother is just as clever.* 蒂娜聰明, 她的弟弟同樣聰明。—see also 另見 **as good as** (GOOD¹) **2 such as** for example 比如: *a heavy land horse such as a Suffolk* 像薩福克馬一樣能幹重活的馬 | *"There are plenty of opportunities for young people." "Oh yeah, such as?"* "年輕人有的是機會。""是嗎, 比方說?" | **such ... as** *The disease attacks such birds as parrots and canaries.* 這種病會侵襲像鸚鵡和金絲雀之類的鳥類。—see also 另見 **no such ... as** (SUCH¹ (6)) **3 as a teacher/mother/actor etc** used when you are describing someone's job or the main purpose of someone or something 作為老師/母親/演員等: *As parents we are concerned for our children's future.* 作為父母, 我們關注孩子的未來。| *Speaking as your doctor, I would not advise this.* 作為你的醫生, 我建議不要這樣。| *It's not bad as a first attempt.* 作為第一次嘗試, 這樣的結果已經不錯了。| *The children all dressed up as animals.* 孩子們都打扮成動物模樣。**4 as a result of sth** because of something 作為某事的結果: *Several businesses went under as a result of the recession.* 由於經濟衰退, 好幾家企業相繼倒閉。**5 be regarded as sth** to be considered to be something 被看作是某物: *'Novecento' is regarded by many as Bertolucci's best film.* 許多人認為《二十世紀》是〔意大利著名導演〕貝托魯奇最好的電影。—see also 另見 **as one** (ONE² (16))

1 1 **as²** *conjunction* **1** used in comparisons 像…一樣: *I can't run as fast as I used to.* 我跑得不如過去那樣快。| *Jim works in the same office as my sister does.* 吉姆和我妹妹在同一個辦公室工作。**2** in the particular way or manner mentioned 照…的方法, 正如…: *Do as I say!* 按我說的去做! | *We'd better leave things as they are until the police arrive.* 在警察到來以前, 我們最好保持現場原樣。| *As I mentioned in my last letter, I'll be back in Ohio in June.* 正如我上封信提到的, 我將在六月份回到俄亥俄州。| *David, as you know, has not been well lately.* 正如你所知, 戴維近來身體不大好。| **as usual** *Roberta was late as usual.* 羅伯塔和往常一樣又遲到了。**3** while or when (正當)…的時候: *I saw Peter as I was getting off the bus.* 我下公共汽車的時候看見了彼得。| *As time passed, things seemed to get worse.* 隨着時間的推移, 情況似乎變得更加糟糕了。**4** used to state why a particular situation exists or why someone does something 因為, 由於: *As we're both tired, let's just grab a takeaway.* 我們倆都累了, 來吃點外賣食品吧。| **seeing as** (=since) 因為, 既然 *A cup of tea? I hardly think so, seeing as I'm going out in about two minutes.* 來杯茶? 我想不必了, 你瞧, 我兩分鐘以後就走。**5** though 儘管, 雖然: *Unlikely as it might seem, I'm tired too.* 儘管看起來不像, 但我的確也累了。| *Try as she might, Sue couldn't get the door open.* 無論蘇怎樣努力, 她就是打不開門。| *As popular as he is, the President hasn't always managed to have his own way.* 儘管總統很受人歡迎, 但他也並非總能按自己的方式辦事。**6 so cold/heavy/quick etc as to... or such an idiot/a disaster etc as to...** used to show the reason that makes something happen or not happen 如此冷/重/快等以至於; 這麼個大傻瓜/這麼一場災難等以至於…: *The water was so cold as to make swimming quite impossible.* 水如此冷, 沒法游泳。| *How could he have been such an idiot as to trust them in the first place?* 首先, 他怎麼這樣傻, 竟信任他們呢? **7 so as to do sth** with the purpose of doing something 為了做某事: *The little boy ran off so as not to be caught.* 為了不被抓住, 小男孩跑開了。**8 as for sb/sth** *especially spoken* an expression meaning 'concerning'; used when you are starting to talk about someone or something new that is connected with what you were talking about before【尤口】至於, 就某人/某物而言: *Nick can stay, but as for you, you can get out of my sight.* 尼克可以留下來, 至於你, 最好不要讓我看見。**9 as yet** [used in negatives 用於否定句] until and including the present time 到現在為止(尚未): *We've had no word from Colin as yet.* 我們到現在為止也沒得到科林的任何消息。**10 as if.../as though... a)** in a way that suggests that something is true or not true 好像: *You look as if you've had a good time.* 你看起來好像玩得挺開心。| *It sounds as though she's been really ill.* 聽起來她好像真的病了。| *Mandy felt as if they were all ganging up on her.* 曼迪覺得他們好像在合夥對付她。| **as if to say** *Beckworth shook his head as if to say "don't trust her".* 貝克沃思搖搖頭, 好像是要說"別信她"。**b)** used to suggest a possible explanation for something although you do not think that this is the actual explanation 彷彿, 好像: *That news reporter always sounds as if he's drunk.* 那位新聞播音員聽上去老像喝醉酒了似的。| *You make it sound as if you have to go without food for days on end!* 你的話聽起來好像在說你不得不連續幾天不吃東西! **11 it's not as if...** used to say that something is definitely not true, about a situation or someone's behaviour 其實並不: *Why do they never go on holiday? I mean it's not as if they're poor, is it?* 他們為甚麼從來也不去度假呢? 我的意思是他們並不窮, 對嗎? | *I don't know why you're so frightened of her, it's not as if she's got any power over you.* 我不明白你為甚麼這樣怕她, 似乎她並沒有擺佈你的權力。**12 as if you would/as if you care/as if it matters** used to say that someone would definitely not do something, does not care etc or that something does not matter at all 就好像你會(做)/好像你很在乎/好像事關重大似的: *Margaret told me she'd never speak to me again! As if I cared.* (=I do not care at all) 瑪格麗特說她再也不會跟我說話了! 好像我會在乎似的。| *"I reckon Ken's deliberately ignoring us." "As if he would!"* (=he would not ignore us) "我猜肯是故意不理我們的。""他不會。" **13 as it is a)** according to the situation that actually exists, especially when that situation is different from what you expected or need 事實上, 實際情況是: *They hoped to finish the kitchen by Friday, but as it is they'll probably have to come back next week.* 他們希望星期五把廚房建完, 但事實上, 他們很可能下週還得回來。**b)** already 已經: *Just keep quiet, you're in enough trouble as it is.* 安靜點, 你的麻煩已經夠多了。**14 as from today/15th December/next June etc** also 又作 **as of today etc** starting from today, 15th December etc and continuing 從即日/12月15日/明年6月等起: *As from today, you are in charge of the office.* 從即日起, 你負責辦公室的工作。| *As of now, there will be no more paid overtime.* 從現在起不再有加班費。**15 as against** in comparison with 跟…相比: *Profits this year are $2.5 million as against $4 million last year.* 跟去年的(利潤)400萬美元相比, 今年的利潤是250萬美元。**16 as to whether/who/which etc** an expression meaning 'concerning' used when speaking about arguments and decisions 至於是否/誰/哪個等: *Frank was very uncertain as to whether it was the job for him.* 至於這工作是不是適合他, 弗蘭克實在拿不準。| *advice as to which suppliers to approach* 關於與哪些供應商接洽的建議 **17 as much as to say** *especially spoken* expressing something in actions rather than words【尤口】等於說: *He shrugged, as much as to say he wasn't interested.* 他聳了聳肩, 等於在說他不感興趣。**18 as it were** used when describing someone or something in a way that is not quite exact 可以說是: *Jim Radcliffe became our idol as it were, the man we all wanted to be.* 吉姆·拉德克利夫可以說是我們的偶像, 我們都想成為他那樣的人。**19 as to** according to a particular standard or principle 根據, 依照: *The fabrics were arranged as to size and colour.* 紡織品按規格和顏色排列。**20 as is/was/does etc** *formal* in the same way as someone or

something else is, does etc【正式】...也如此: *Eve's very tall, as was her mother.* 伊芙個子很高, 她媽媽個子也高。| *I voted Labour, as did my wife.* 我投了工黨的票, 我妻子也是。—see also 另見 **not as such** (SUCH[2] (4)), **as well** (WELL[1] (6)), **as well as** (WELL[1] (5)), **might just as well** (MIGHT[1] (8))

asap /ˌe ɛs e ˋpi; ˌeɪ es eɪ ˈpiː/ the abbreviation of 縮寫= 'as soon as possible'

as·bes·tos /æsˋbɛstəs; æsˈbestəs/ *n* [U] a grey mineral that does not burn easily, used as a building material or in protective clothing 石棉

as·cend /əˋsɛnd; əˈsend/ *v formal*【正式】**1** [I] to move up through the air 上升, 升高: *He could feel a current of warm air ascending from the street.* 他能感受到一股熱流從街上升騰起來。**2** [T] to climb 攀登, 爬: *We were walking on the forest path, ascending a steep slope.* 我們走在森林小路上, 順着一個陡峭的山坡往上爬。**3** [I,T] to lead up to a higher position 上升, 向上: *The stairs ascended in a graceful curve.* 樓梯呈優美的弧形向上盤旋。**4 ascend the throne** to become king or queen 登上王位, 登基 **5 in ascending order** if a group of things are arranged in ascending order, each thing is higher, or greater in amount, than the one before it 按升序排列 —opposite 反義詞 DESCEND

as·cen·dan·cy, ascendency /əˋsɛndənsɪ; əˈsendənsi/ *n* [U] a position of power, influence or control 優勢; 支配(地位): [+over/in] *He slowly gained ascendancy in the group.* 他漸漸地控制了這羣人。

as·cen·dant[1] /əˋsɛndənt; əˈsendənt/ also 又作 **ascendent** *n* **be in the ascendant** to be or become powerful or popular 有支配力; 佔有優勢: *During this period the trade union view was in the ascendant.* 這一時期, 工會的思想佔上風。

ascendant[2] also 又作 **ascendent** *adj* **1** becoming more powerful or popular 影響力漸大的; 佔優勢的 **2** rising 上升的

as·cen·sion /əˋsɛnʃən; əˈsenʃən/ *n* [U] the act of moving up 上升, 升高

as·cent /əˋsɛnt; əˈsent/ *n* **1** [C usually singular 一般用單數] a path or way up to the top of something, for example a mountain 向上的路; 上坡: *a rugged and abrupt ascent* 崎嶇陡峭的上坡路 **2** [C usually singular 一般用單數] the act of climbing something or moving upwards 上升, 攀登: *We rested in the valley before beginning the ascent.* 我們在開始攀登之前, 在山谷休息了一會兒。**3** [U] the process of becoming more important, powerful, or successful than before 演變, 前進: *the ascent of man to modern civilization* 人類朝着現代文明邁進 —opposite 反義詞 DESCENT (1, 2, 4)

as·cer·tain /ˌæsəˋten; ˌæsəˈteɪn/ *v* [I,T] *formal* to find out if a fact that you think is true is really true【正式】弄清, 確定, 查明: *The police were never able to ascertain the true facts.* 警察永遠也不能查出真相。| **[+how/when/why etc]** *He could not ascertain where the clouds ended and the snow-covered rocks began.* 他無法確定哪裡是雲層的邊緣, 哪裡是冰雪覆蓋的岩石的起點。—**ascertainable** *adj*

as·cet·ic /əˋsɛtɪk; əˈsetɪk/ *adj* living without any physical pleasures or comforts, especially for religious reasons〔尤指因宗教原因〕苦行的, 禁慾的: *the ascetic life of Buddhist monks* 佛教僧人的清苦生活 —**ascetic** *n* [C] —**ascetically** *adv* —**asceticism** *n* [U]

as·cot /ˋæskət; ˈæskɒt/ *n* [C] *AmE* a wide piece of material worn by men loosely folded around their neck inside their collar; CRAVAT【美】〔男人戴的〕領巾

as·cribe /əˋskraɪb; əˈskraɪb/ *v*

ascribe sth **to** sb/sth *phr v* [T] *formal*【正式】**1** to believe that something happens or exists because of someone or something else 把...歸(因)於: *The melody is ascribed to Bach.* 這首曲子被認為是巴赫所作。| *They ascribe the country's difficulties to the last government's policies.* 他們把國家的困境歸因於上屆政府的政策。**2** to believe something or someone has a particular quality 認為〔某人或某物〕具有...特點: *The Malays ascribe healing properties to this fruit.* 馬來人認為這種水果有治病的功效。—**ascribable** *adj* **[+to]**

a·sep·tic /əˋsɛptɪk; eɪˈseptɪk/ *adj* a wound that is aseptic is completely clean without any harmful BACTERIA〔傷口〕經消毒的, 無菌的

a·sex·u·al /eˋsɛkʃuəl; eɪˈsekʃuəl/ *adj* **1** not having sexual organs or having sex 無性器官的; 無性(別)的 **2 a)** not seeming to have any sexual qualities 無性別特徵的: *He strikes me as a completely asexual person.* 他給我的印象是個沒有性別特徵的人。**b)** not interested in sexual relations 無性慾的, 對性不感興趣的 —**asexually** *adv*: *a plant that reproduces asexually* 無性繁殖的植物

ash /æʃ; æʃ/ *n* [C,U] **1** the soft grey powder that remains after something has been burnt 灰, 灰燼: *cigarette ash* 香煙灰 | *The house burnt to ashes.* 那房子燒成了灰燼。**2** a very hard wood, or the tree, common in Britain and North America, that produces this 梣(樹), 白蠟樹 **3 ashes** [plural] the ash that remains when a dead person's body is burned 骨灰: *We scattered my father's ashes over the lake.* 我們把父親的骨灰撒入湖中。

a·shamed /əˋʃemd; əˈʃeɪmd/ *adj* [not before noun 不用於名詞前] **1** feeling shame because of something you have done 羞恥的; 內疚的; 慚愧的: **be ashamed of doing sth** *I was ashamed of having lied to my mother.* 我對向母親說謊的事感到很內疚。| **be ashamed that** *Barry was ashamed that he had lost his temper.* 巴里因自己發脾氣感到很慚愧。| **You ought to be ashamed (of yourself)** *spoken* (=used to tell someone they should feel guilty about something)【口】你應為自己的行為感到羞恥 *You ought to be ashamed of yourself – treating your sister like that!* 你應當為自己那樣對待妹妹感到羞愧! **2** feeling uncomfortable or upset, especially because someone does something that embarrasses you 感到不好意思的, 難為情的: **[+of]** *Sherry is at that age when kids are ashamed of their parents.* 謝麗正處於因父母而感到難為情的年紀。| **be ashamed to be/do sth** *That kind of behaviour makes me ashamed to be British.* 那種行為使我感到作為一個英國人很慚愧。—see 見 SHAME[1] (USAGE)

ash·can /ˋæʃˌkæn; ˈæʃkæn/ *n* [C] *AmE old-fashioned* a GARBAGE CAN【美, 過時】垃圾箱

ash·en /ˋæʃən; ˈæʃən/ *adj* being a pale grey colour like ash 灰色的: *her ashen face* 她面如土色

a·shore /əˋʃor; əˈʃɔː/ *adv* on or towards the shore of a lake, river, sea, or ocean 在岸上; 向岸上: *Brian pulled the boat ashore.* 布賴恩把船拉上岸。

ash·ram /ˋæʃrəm; ˈæʃrəm/ *n* [C] **1** a place where a Hindu holy man lives alone〔印度教高僧的〕靜修處 **2** a house where people live together practising the religion of Hinduism 印度教修行者住的修行屋

ash·tray /ˋæʃˌtre; ˈæʃtreɪ/ *n* [C] a small dish where you put used cigarettes 煙灰缸, 煙灰碟 —see picture at 參見 TRAY 圖

Ash Wednes·day /ˌ· ˈ··/ *n* [C,U] the first day of Lent 聖灰星期三〔四旬節的第一日〕

A·sian[1] /ˋeʃən; ˈeɪʃən/ *n* **1** *BrE* someone from Asia, especially India or Pakistan【英】亞洲人〔尤指印度或巴基斯坦人〕**2** *AmE* someone from Asia, especially Japan, China, Korea etc【美】亞洲人〔尤指日本人、中國人、朝鮮人等〕

A·sian[2] *adj* from Asia or related to Asia 亞洲的; 亞洲人的

Asian-A·mer·i·can /ˌ·· ·ˈ···/ *n* [C] an American citizen whose family was originally from Asia 亞裔美國人

a·side[1] /əˋsaɪd; əˈsaɪd/ *adv* **1 move/step aside** to move, step etc to the side 靠一邊/站到一邊: *I stepped aside just in time, and the car whizzed past.* 我及時地站到一邊, 汽車飛馳而過。**2 put/set/leave sth aside a)** to save part of an amount of money 留存一筆錢: *I've been setting aside a little money each week for our holiday.* 我

每週節省一點錢準備用來度假。**b)** to keep something separate or not use it because someone is going to buy or use it later 留出某物，撥出某物：*One of the rooms was set aside for a yoga class.* 留出一個房間上瑜伽課。**c)** to leave something to be considered at another time 把某事放置一邊〔以後再考慮〕：*Let's put this question aside for next week.* 我們先把這個問題擱一擱，下週再考慮。**3 brush/sweep sth aside** to treat someone's idea or statement in a way that shows you do not think it is important 不理會/不顧/漠視某事：*Mr. Coleman brushed my suggestion aside and asked for another question.* 科爾曼先生對我的建議不予理會，問了另一個問題。**4 aside from** *especially AmE*【尤美】**a)** except for 除…以外：*Aside from that one little problem, the day was perfect.* 除了那個小問題外，今天過得好極了。**b)** in addition to 此外：*Aside from physical problems, these patients also show a lot of hostility.* 這些病人除了身體方面的問題外，還表現出很多的敵意。**5** used to show that something you have just said is not as important as what you are going to say next 且不談，且不管：*These problems aside, we think the plan should go ahead.* 這些問題暫不說，我們認為這個計劃應馬上實施。

aside² *n* [C] **1** words spoken by an actor to the people watching a play, that the other characters in the play do not hear〔戲劇中的〕旁白 **2** a remark made in a low voice that you only intend certain people to hear 竊語，小聲說的話 **3** a remark or story that is not part of the main subject of a speech 離題的話

as·i·nine /ˈæsn̩ˌaɪn; ˈæsɪ̆naɪn/ *adj* extremely stupid or silly; RIDICULOUS 極愚蠢的，荒謬的：*What an asinine remark!* 多麼愚蠢的話！

[1] [1] **ask** /æsk; ɑːsk/ *v*

1 ►QUESTION 問題◄ [I,T] to say or write something in order to get an answer, a solution, or information 問，詢問，打聽，提問：*"What's your name?" she asked.* 她問："你叫甚麼名字？" | **ask a question** *That kid's always asking awkward questions.* 那孩子總是問一些不好回答的問題。| **ask who/what/where etc** *I was only asking how this could have happened.* 我只是問怎麼會發生這樣的事情。| **ask sb sth** *She asked an old man the way to the station.* 她向一位老人打聽去火車站該怎麼走。| **ask sb** *Don't ask him – he won't know anything about it.* 不要問他，他甚麼也不知道。| **ask if/whether** *Go and ask Pat whether he's coming tonight.* 去問問帕特他今天晚上是否來。| **ask (sb) about** *Visitors usually ask about the history of the place.* 參觀者常常問起這個地方的歷史。| **ask around** (=ask in a lot of places or ask a lot of people) 到處打聽 *I'm not sure where you can get a good mechanic – you'd better ask around.* 我不清楚你到哪兒能找到一個好的修理工，你最好多問問別人。

2 ►FOR HELP ETC 求助等◄ [I,T] to make a request for help, advice, information etc 要求，請求：*If you need anything, you only have to ask.* 你需要甚麼，只要提出來就行。| **ask sb to do sth** *Ask John to mail those letters tomorrow.* 請約翰明天把那些信寄出去。| **ask to do sth** *Karen asked to see whoever was in charge.* 卡倫請求見負責人。| **[+for]** *Some people find it difficult to ask for help.* 有些人發覺很難尋求別人幫助。| **ask if you can do sth** *Ask your dad if we can borrow his truck.* 問問你爸爸我們可否借他的卡車。—see 見 REQUEST² (USAGE)

3 ►PRICE 價格◄ [T] to want a particular amount of money for something you are selling 索要〔價格〕：**ask $50/£1,000 etc for** *I can't believe he's asking £2,000 for that old car.* 我真不敢相信那輛舊車他居然索價2,000英鎊。| **ask the earth/a fortune (for)** (=ask far too much money for something) 要價太高，開天價 *They're asking the earth for tickets – we just can't afford it.* 他們簡直是開天價，這樣的票價我們承受不起。

4 ►INVITE 邀請◄ [T] to invite someone to your home, to go out with you etc 邀請：**ask sb out** (=ask someone, especially someone of the opposite sex, to go to the theatre, a restaurant etc with you) 邀請某人〔特別是異性〕出去〔看電影、吃飯等〕*Jerry's too scared to ask her out.* 傑里沒有勇氣邀她出去。| **ask sb in** (=invite someone into your house, office etc) 邀請某人進去 *Don't leave them standing on the doorstep – ask them in!* 別讓他們在門口站着 —— 請他們進來！| **ask sb along** (=invite someone to go somewhere with you, especially when you are with a lot of other people) 請某人一起〔去〕*Get Bill to ask Sheila along.* 讓比爾叫希拉一起去。| **ask sb over** (=invite someone to come to your home) 邀請某人去你家

5 be asking for it *spoken* used to say that someone deserves something bad that happens to them【口】自找麻煩，自作自受：*I don't really care he got beat up on – he was asking for it.* 我才不在乎他挨打呢，他是自作自受的。

6 be asking for trouble to do something that is very likely to have a bad effect or result 自找麻煩：*He thinks anyone who completely trusts anyone else is asking for trouble.* 他認為一個人完全信賴別人是自找麻煩。

7 don't ask me *spoken* used to say you do not know the answer to something【口】別問我〔我不知道〕：*"Where's she gone then?" "Don't ask me!"* "她到底去哪兒了？""別問我！"

8 asking price the price that someone wants to sell something for 索價：*At an asking price of just £250, it's got to be a bargain.* 索價才250英鎊，那肯定便宜。

9 ask yourself to try to honestly discover the true reason for something 捫心自問，反思：*The government should ask itself where the responsibility for this mess really lies.* 政府應該深刻反思一下目前的困境責任究竟由誰來負。

10 for the asking if you can have something for the asking, you only have to ask for it and you can have it 只要你提出要求〔你就可以得到它〕

11 I ask you! *spoken* used to express surprise at and disapproval of something stupid that someone has done【口】你瞧瞧！〔表示不贊同、吃驚〕：*She sent her kids to camp dressed all in white. I ask you!* 她竟然讓孩子們全穿上白衣服去營地。你瞧瞧！—see 見 REQUEST² (USAGE)

USAGE NOTE 用法說明：ASK

WORD CHOICE 詞語辨析：**ask, want to know, inquire, question, interrogate**

Ask is the usual verb for questions. ask 是提問題常用的動詞：*"How are you doing?" she asked.* "你近來怎樣？"她問道。| *That's a stupid question to ask.* 那個問題問得很愚蠢。Often people use **want to know** when they are talking about what someone else has asked. 談到別人問甚麼時常用 want to know：*He wanted to know where I lived/the train times.* 他打聽我住在哪兒/火車時刻。

Inquire (or **enquire** *BrE*) has the same meaning but is more formal, and is not followed by a noun or pronoun object. inquire (或 enquire 英) 與 ask 意思相同，但較為正式，後面不能接名詞或代名詞受詞。At a meeting 在會上：*May I inquire what the committee proposes to do about this?/about the effectiveness of this policy?* (NOT 不用 *...inquire the effectiveness of this policy*). 我可否問一下委員會建議這件事怎麼做/這一政策的有效性？

To **question** a person is to ask them a lot of questions, especially officially, and to **interrogate** suggests that someone is being held by force and asked questions that they are unwilling to answer, for example by the police or an enemy. question a person (詢問某人) 是問很多問題，尤指正式的問話，而 interrogate (訊問) 含有強制要求回答他不願意回答的問題之意，如警察盤問或敵方審訊。

A

GRAMMAR 語法

Remember that you do not follow **ask** with a direct question, unless you are repeating the exact words. 切記, 除非是直接引語, 否則ask後不能直接跟一個問句: *Ask what sort of room he would like* (NOT 不用 *Ask what sort of room would he like*). 問他想要甚麼樣的房間。| *I asked "What sort of room would you like?"* 我問"你想要甚麼樣的房間?"

You **ask** people certain things without using *for* or *about*. 下列情況中, ask後不用for或about: *I asked him the way/his name/the price/the time/a favour/permission/his advice* (NOT 不用 *asked to him the way*). 我問他路/姓名/價格/時間/求他幫忙/請求他允許/向他諮詢。You usually **ask for** or **about** most other things. 以下情況ask後加for或about: *Ask one of our guides for directions to Lincoln Center.* 問我們的導遊去林肯中心的路線。| *He asked Sharon for a date* (NOT 不用 *He asked a date to Sharon*). 他請莎倫跟他約會。| *Can I ask you about the exam results?* (NOT 不用 *of the exam results*) 我能問你考試成績嗎?

a·skance /ə`skæns; əˈskæns/ *adv* **look askance (at)** to look at or consider something in a way that shows you do not believe it or approve of it〔不高興地〕側目,〔以懷疑的目光〕注視, 瞟視

a·skew /ə`skju; əˈskjuː/ *adv* not quite straight or in the right position 不正, 歪: *Matilda ran towards us with her hat askew.* 馬蒂爾達歪戴着帽子朝我們跑來。

a·slant /ə`slænt; əˈslɑːnt/ *adv* [not before noun 不用於名詞前] *formal* not straight up or down, but across at an angle【正式】斜着, 歪着 —**aslant** *adj*

 2 **a·sleep** /ə`slip; əˈsliːp/ *adj* [not before noun 不用於名詞前] **1** sleeping 睡着的: *Quiet! The baby is asleep.* 安靜點! 寶寶在睡覺。| **fast/sound asleep** (=very deeply asleep) 睡得很熟 *You'll be fast asleep by the time we get home.* 我們到家的時候, 你早就呼呼大睡了。**2 fall asleep a)** to begin to sleep 入睡: *I always fall asleep watching TV.* 我看電視時總是會睡着。**b)** *literary* used to mean that someone dies when you want to avoid saying this directly【文】長眠 **3** an arm or leg that is asleep has been in one position for too long, so you cannot feel it 發麻, 麻木 —see also 另見 **go to sleep** (SLEEP[2] (3)) **4 half asleep** not paying attention to something because you are tired 半睡眠狀態, 困倦

A/S level /ˌe `ɛs ˌlɛvl; ˌeɪ ˈes ˌlevəl/ *n* **1** [U] an examination in British schools, for pupils who have taken GCSEs and want to study a wider range of subjects than is possible at A LEVEL〔英國中學的〕高級補充程度會考〔為已通過普通中學教育證書考試的學生而設, 讓學生可學習多於高級程度所規定的科目〕**2** [C] an examination at this standard in a particular subject 高級補充程度會考的某學科考試

asp /æsp; æsp/ *n* [C] a small poisonous snake from North Africa 角蝰; 蝮蛇〔北非的一種小毒蛇〕

as·par·a·gus /ə`spærəgəs; əˈspærəgəs/ *n* [U] a long thin green vegetable with a point at one end 蘆筍, 石刁柏 —see picture on page A9 參見A9頁圖

 3 1 **as·pect** /`æspɛkt; ˈæspekt/ *n* **1** [C] one part of a situation, idea, plan etc that has many parts 方面: [+of] *Alcoholism affects all aspects of family life.* 酗酒影響家庭生活的各個方面。**2** [C] the direction in which a window, room, front of a building etc faces 朝向, 方位: *a south-facing aspect* (方向) 朝南 **3** [C,U] *formal* the appearance of someone or something【正式】面貌, 外觀, 神態: *Her face wore a melancholy aspect.* 她面帶憂傷。**4** [C,U] *technical* the form of a verb in grammar that shows whether an action is continuing, or happens always, repeatedly, or once【術語】〔動詞的〕體: *'He sings' differs from 'He is singing' in aspect.* He sings和He is singing的體不同。

as·pen /`æspən; ˈæspən/ *n* [C] a kind of tree of western North America with leaves that shake in the wind〔北美西部的〕顫楊, 大齒楊

as·per·i·ty /æs`pɛrətɪ; æˈsperɨti/ *n* [C,U] *formal* a way of speaking or behaving that is rough or severe【正式】〔說話、舉止等的〕粗魯, 刻薄: *the asperity of her manner* 她舉止的粗魯

as·per·sion /ə`spɝʒən; əˈspɜːʃən/ *n* **cast aspersions on** *formal* to make an unkind remark or an unfair judgment【正式】誹謗, 中傷, 誣蔑: *Are you casting aspersions on my wife's character?* 你是不是在誹謗我妻子的人格?

as·phalt /`æsfɔlt; ˈæsfælt/ *n* [U] a black sticky substance that becomes hard when it dries, used for making the surface of roads 瀝青, 柏油 —**asphalt** *v* [T]

as·phyx·i·a /æs`fɪksɪə; æsˈfɪksiə/ *n* [U] death caused by not being able to breathe 窒息(而死)

as·phyx·i·ate /æs`fɪksɪˌet; æsˈfɪksieɪt/ *v* [I,T] *technical* to be unable to breathe air or make someone unable to do so, especially to die or kill someone in this way; SUFFOCATE (1)【術語】(使)窒息(而死); (使)無法呼吸 —**asphyxiation** /æsˌfɪksɪ`eʃən; æsˌfɪksiˈeɪʃən/ *n* [U]

as·pic /`æspɪk; ˈæspɪk/ *n* [U] a clear brownish JELLY (3) eaten with meat 肉凍

as·pi·dis·tra /ˌæspɪ`dɪstrə; ˌæspɨˈdɪstrə/ *n* [C] a plant with broad green pointed leaves, often grown in houses 蜘蛛抱蛋〔一種長有寬而尖的綠葉、多擺設於室內的植物〕

as·pi·rant /ə`spaɪrənt; əˈspaɪərənt/ *n* [C+to/for] *formal* someone who hopes to get a position of importance or honour【正式】有志者, 有抱負者;〔名譽、地位的〕追求者

as·pi·rate[1] /`æspəˌret; ˈæspɨreɪt/ *v* [T] *technical* to make the sound of an 'H' when speaking, or to blow out air when pronouncing some consonants【術語】發字母H音, 發送氣音

as·pi·rate[2] /`æspərɪt; ˈæspɨrɨt/ *n* [C] *technical* the sound of the letter 'H', or the letter itself【術語】(字母)H音, 送氣音

as·pi·ra·tion /ˌæspə`reʃən; ˌæspɨˈreɪʃən/ *n* **1** [C usually plural 一般用複數, U] a strong desire to have or achieve something 強烈願望; 志向, 抱負: *Hannah has always had political aspirations.* 漢納在政治上一向有抱負。| [+of] *the aspirations of the working classes* 工人階級的強烈願望 **2** [U] the sound of air blowing out that happens when some CONSONANTs are pronounced, such as the /p/ in pin〔某些輔音字母發音的〕送氣音〈如pin一詞中p的發音〉

as·pire /ə`spaɪr; əˈspaɪə/ *v* [I] to desire and work towards achieving something important 追求, 渴望, 有志於: [+to/after] *It was clear that Mrs Thatcher aspired to the leadership of the party.* 顯然易見戴卓爾夫人立志成為該黨的領導人。| **aspire to do sth** *At that time, all serious artists aspired to go to Rome and paint.* 那時, 所有嚴肅的畫家都渴望去羅馬作畫。

as·pi·rin /`æspərɪn; ˈæsprɨn/ *n plural* **aspirins** *or* **aspirin** [C,U] a medicine that reduces pain, INFLAMMATION, and fever 阿士匹靈(藥片), 阿斯匹林

ass /æs; æs/ *n* [C]

1 ►PART OF BODY 身體的部分◄ *especially AmE* an impolite word for the part of your body that you sit on【尤美】屁股, 臀部〔非禮貌用語〕: *I tripped and fell flat on my ass.* 我絆倒了, 一屁股坐在地上。

2 get your ass in gear also 又作 **move your ass** *spoken* an impolite way of telling someone to hurry【口】趕快, 抓緊時間〔非禮貌用語〕: *Get your ass in gear, or you'll miss your plane!* 你他媽的快點, 不然你就趕不上飛機了!

3 get off your ass *AmE spoken* an impolite way of telling someone to stop being lazy【美口】別偷懶〔非禮貌用語〕: *If you want to pass this test, you'd better get off your ass and study!* 如果你想考試及格, 就要用功學習!

4 kick/whip sb's ass also 又作 **kick (some) ass** *AmE slang* to beat someone easily in a fight, game, or sport

【美俚】輕而易舉地戰勝某人: *Let's get out there and kick some ass.* 讓我們一鼓作氣, 打敗他們。

5 be on sb's ass *AmE spoken*【美口】**a)** an impolite way of saying that someone is annoying you by telling you to do things you do not want to do 老逼某人〔做不想做的事; 非禮貌說法〕: *My boss is on my ass all the time.* 我的老闆老逼着我幹。**b)** an impolite way of saying that someone is driving very close to the back of another car 快撞上前面汽車的屁股了〔非禮貌說法〕

6 get your ass over here *AmE spoken* an impolite way of telling someone to come quickly【美口】快點兒來〔非禮貌說法〕

7 my ass! *AmE spoken* an impolite way of saying that you do not believe something【美口】見鬼!〔表示不相信的非禮貌話法〕: *"He said he ran twenty miles." "Twenty miles my ass!"* "他說他跑了二十英里。" "二十英里, 見他的鬼!"

8 ►STUPID PERSON 笨人◄ *informal* a stupid, annoying person【非正式】傻瓜, 蠢人: **make an ass of yourself** (=do something stupid or embarrassing) 做傻事, 出洋相

9 sb doesn't know their ass from their elbow *AmE spoken* an impolite way of saying that someone is stupid【美口】大傻帽兒一個, 甚麼都不知道〔非禮貌說法〕

10 ►ANIMAL 動物◄ *old use* a DONKEY【舊】驢 —see also 另見 ARSE, **haul ass** (HAUL[1] (6)), **kiss sb's ass** (KISS), **pain in the arse/ass etc** (PAIN[1] (3)), **piece of ass** (PIECE[1] (22)), SMART ARSE

as·sail /əˋsel; əˈseɪl/ *v* [T] **1** [usually passive 一般用被動態] if a thought or feeling assails you, it worries or upsets you 困擾: *Carla was suddenly assailed by doubts.* 卡拉突然為各種疑慮所困擾。**2** to attack someone or something violently 猛烈攻擊, 打擊: **assail sb with sth** *The angry crowd assailed police with stones and bottles.* 憤怒的人羣用石頭和瓶子襲擊警察。

as·sai·lant /əˋselənt; əˈseɪlənt/ *n* [C] *formal* someone who attacks another person【正式】攻擊者: *Ms Hervey states that she could not see her assailant's face.* 赫維女士聲稱她看不清襲擊她的人的面孔。

as·sas·sin /əˋsæsɪn; əˈsæsɪ̣n/ *n* [C] someone who murders an important person 暗殺者, 刺客: *Kennedy's supposed assassin, Lee Harvey Oswald* 據說是暗殺甘迺迪的人李·哈維·奧斯瓦爾德

as·sas·sin·ate /əˋsæsn̩ˏet; əˈsæsɪ̣neɪt/ *v* [T] to murder an important person 暗殺, 行刺: *a plot to assassinate the President* 刺殺總統的陰謀 —see 見 KILL[1] (USAGE)

as·sas·sin·a·tion /əˏsæsn̩ˋeʃən; əˌsæsɪ̣ˈneɪʃən/ *n* [C,U] the act of assassinating someone 行刺, 暗殺: *a terrorist group plotting an assassination* 密謀暗殺的恐怖分子組織 | **assassination attempt** (=a situation in which someone tries but fails to assassinate someone) 行刺的企圖 —see also 另見 **character assassination** (CHARACTER (6))

3 **as·sault¹** /əˋsɔlt; əˈsɔːlt/ *n* [C,U] **1** the crime of attacking someone 攻擊, 襲擊(罪): *increases in violent assaults over the past decade* 近十年來暴力襲擊事件的增加 | **sexual assault** *three years in prison for sexual assault* 因犯強姦罪被監禁三年 **2** a military attack to take control of a place controlled by the enemy 襲擊, 攻佔: *the platoon's unsuccessful assault on the border positions* 那個士兵小隊未能攻佔邊境陣地 **3** an attempt to achieve something difficult, especially using physical force〔尤指靠體力〕攻破(難關): **[+on]** *an assault on Mt Everest* (=an attempt to climb it) 攀登珠穆朗瑪峯的嘗試 **4 assault on** a strong spoken or written criticism of someone else's ideas, plans etc 對...的抨擊[攻擊]: *the tobacco industry's recent assault on plans to ban cigarettes* 煙草行業最近對禁煙計劃的攻擊

assault² *v* [T] **1** to attack someone in a violent way 猛襲, 攻擊, 襲擊: *Policemen were assaulted by young demonstrators.* 警察遭到年輕示威者的襲擊。**2** to strongly criticize someone's ideas, plans etc 抨擊, 攻擊, 嚴厲批評: *The MP was assaulted with a barrage of abuse from angry strikers.* 這位議會議員遭到憤怒的罷工者連珠砲式的辱罵。**3** if a feeling assaults you, it affects you in a way that makes you uncomfortable or upset 使感到難受, 困擾: *The noise in the club assaulted our ears.* 俱樂部裡的噪音使我們的耳朵感到很不舒服。

assault and bat·ter·y /ˌ·ˌ· ·ˈ···/ *n* [U] *law* the official name for a violent attack and the threats that the attacker makes before it【法律】毆打罪, 威脅和暴力行為罪

assault course /·ˈ· ˌ·/ *n* [C] *BrE* an area of land with special equipment to climb, jump over, run through etc that is used for developing physical strength especially by soldiers【英】軍事訓練場地; OBSTACLE COURSE *AmE*【美】

as·say /əˋse; əˈseɪ/ *v* [T] **1** to test a metal 鑑定, 化驗, 分析〔金屬含量〕**2** *literary* to attempt to do something【文】嘗試〔做某事〕: *to assay the impossible* 嘗試做不可能成功的事 —**assay** /əˋse; əˈseɪ/ *n* [C]

as·se·gai /ˋæsəˏgaɪ; ˈæsɪ̣gaɪ/ *n* [C] a long thin wooden stick with an iron point, used as a weapon in southern Africa〔非洲南部人用的〕細木柄標槍, 長矛

as·sem·blage /əˋsɛmblɪdʒ; əˈsemblɪdʒ/ *n formal*【正式】**1** [C] a group of people or things that are together〔集合在一起的〕一羣人; 一批東西 **2** [U] the act of putting parts together in order to make something 組合, 裝配

as·sem·ble /əˋsɛmbḷ; əˈsembəl/ *v* **1** [I] if a group of people assemble in one place, they all go there together 集合, 聚集: *A large crowd had assembled opposite the American embassy.* 一大羣人聚集在美國大使館對面。**2** [T] to gather a large number of things or people together in one place 收集; 召集: *Over the years we've assembled a huge collection of old books.* 這麼多年來, 我們收集了大量的舊書。**3** [T] to put all the parts of something together 組裝, 裝配: *an easy-to-assemble kit* 很容易裝配的配套元件

as·sem·bly /əˋsɛmblɪ; əˈsembli/ *n* **1** [C] a group of people who are elected to make laws for a particular country or area 立法機構; 議會: *the New York State Assembly* 紐約州議會 **2** [C+of] a group of people who have gathered together for a particular purpose〔為特定目的〕聚集在一起的人 **3** [C,U] a regular meeting of all the teachers and pupils of a school 全校師生會議, 集會 **4** [U] the process of putting parts together in order to make something 組裝, 裝配: *instructions for assembly* 組裝說明(書) **5 the right of assembly/freedom of assembly** the right of any group to meet together in order to discuss things 集會的權利/自由 3 2

assembly line /·ˈ·· ·/ *n* [C] a system for making things in a factory in which the products move past a line of workers who each make or check one part 裝配線, 流水作業線

as·sem·bly·man /əˋsɛmblɪmən; əˈsemblimən/ *n* [C] *AmE* a male member of an ASSEMBLY (1)【美】男議員

as·sem·bly·wom·an /əˋsɛmblɪˏwʊmən; əˈsembliˌwʊmən/ *n* [C] *AmE* a female member of an ASSEMBLY (1)【美】女議員

as·sent¹ /əˋsɛnt; əˈsent/ *n* [U] *formal* approval or agreement from someone who has authority【正式】同意, 贊成: *a nod of assent* 點頭表示贊成 | **the Royal assent** (=act of officially signing a new law by the British King or Queen) 御准〔指英國國王或女王簽署新法令〕

assent² *v* [I+to] *formal* to agree to a suggestion, idea etc after considering it carefully【正式】〔經審慎考慮後〕同意, 贊成

as·sert /əˋsɝt; əˈsɜːt/ *v* [T] **1 assert your rights/independence etc** to state very strongly your right to do or have something 堅持自己的權利/獨立等 **2 assert yourself** to behave in a determined way so that people do not make you do things you do not want 堅持自己的想法: *You need to assert yourself more.* 你需要進一步堅持自己的想法。**3** to state firmly that something is true (堅決) 主張; 斷言: **assert that** *The professor asserted* *that there was nothing wrong with his theory.* 那位教授堅持認為自己的理論沒有錯誤。**4 assert itself** if an idea or belief asserts itself, it begins to influence something 產生影響: *Milton's influence asserts itself later in his poetry.* 米爾頓後期的詩歌產生了很大的影響。

as·ser·tion /ə`sɝʃən; ə'sɜːʃən/ *n* [C] something that you say or write that you strongly believe 斷言, 聲明, 主張: **assertion that** *Wilkinson kept repeating his assertion that he was innocent.* 威爾金森一再聲稱自己無罪。

as·ser·tive /ə`sɝtɪv; ə'sɜːtɪv/ *adj* behaving in a confident way so that people notice you 果斷的, 肯定的, 自信的 —**assertively** *adv* —**assertiveness** *n* [U]: *assertiveness training* 自信心的訓練[培養]

as·sess /ə`sɛs; ə'ses/ *v* [T] **1** to make a judgment about a person or situation after thinking carefully about it 評價, 評定: *It's difficult to assess the effects of the new legislation just yet.* 現在還難以評價新法令的效果。| **assess what/how etc** *We've tried to assess what went wrong.* 我們已試着判斷到底哪兒出了毛病。**2** to calculate the value or cost of something 估價, 估計: **assess sth at** *They assessed the value of the house at over $250,000.* 他們估計這所房子值二十五萬美元以上。

as·sess·ment /ə`sɛsmənt; ə'sesmənt/ *n* **1** [C,U] a process in which you make a judgment about a person or situation 評價, 估計: *What's your assessment of the situation in Northern Ireland?* 你是怎樣評價北愛爾蘭的形勢的? **2** [C,U] a calculation about the cost or value of something 核定額: *a tax assessment* 應納稅的核定額 —see also 另見 **continuous assessment** ((CONTINUOUS) (3))

as·ses·sor /ə`sɛsɚ; ə'sesə/ *n* [C] **1** someone who decides how well someone has done in an examination 評分人 **2** someone whose job is to calculate the value of something or the amount of tax someone should pay 估價員; 評稅員 **3** someone who knows a lot about a subject or activity and who advises a judge or an official committee〔在某種專業知識方面輔助法官或官方委員會工作的〕技術顧問, 助理

as·set /`æsɛt; 'æset/ *n* [C] **1** [usually plural 一般用複數] the things that a company owns, that can be sold to pay debts 資產, 財產 **2** [usually singular 一般用單數] something or someone that is useful because they help you succeed or deal with problems 有利條件; 長處; 有用的人: *A sense of humor is a real asset in this business.* 在這行業中, 幽默感是一大長處。| **be an asset to** *I think Rachel would be an asset to the department.* 我認為雷切爾對這個部門來講是個難得的人才。—compare 比較 LIABILITY —see also 另見 LIQUID ASSETS

asset strip·ping /`.. ,../ *n* [U] the practice of buying a company cheaply and then selling all the things it owns to make a quick profit 資產倒賣〔低價買進一家公司, 再將其全部資產賣出獲利〕

as·sev·e·rate /ə`sɛvə,ret; ə'sevəreɪt/ *v* [T+**that**] to state something very firmly and seriously 鄭重聲明, 斷言

ass·hole /`æshol; 'æshəʊl/ *n* [C] **1** an offensive word for someone you think stupid and annoying 蠢貨〔冒犯用詞〕**2** an offensive word for the ANUS 屁眼〔冒犯用詞〕—see also 另見 ARSEHOLE

as·sid·u·ous /ə`sɪdʒuəs; ə'sɪdjuəs/ *adj formal* very careful to make sure that something is done properly or completely【正式】專心致志的, 勤勉的: *an assiduous collector of folk songs* 堅持不懈的民歌收集者 —**assiduously** *adv* —**assiduity** /,æsə`duətɪ; ,æsɪ'djuːɪti/ *n* [U]

as·sign /ə`saɪn; ə'saɪn/ *v* [T] **1** to give someone a particular job or make them responsible for a particular person or thing 分配, 分派, 指派〔任務〕: **assign sb a job/duty/task** *I've been assigned the job of looking after the new students.* 指派給我的工作是照料新來的學生。| **assign sb to** *Jan's been assigned to the Asian Affairs Bureau.* 簡被派到亞洲事務部。**2** to decide that something should be done at or during a particular time 訂出, 確定〔時間或期限〕: *How much time have you assigned for the meeting?* 你給這個會定了多長時間? **3** *formal* to give money, equipment etc to someone or decide it should be used for a particular purpose【正式】把〔財產、設備等〕轉讓與: **assign sth to** *The US has already assigned a large part of its foreign aid budget to Rwanda.* 美國已經把對外援助預算中的很大一部分轉給了盧旺達。

as·sig·na·tion /,æsɪg`neʃən; ,æsɪg'neɪʃən/ *n* [C] a secret meeting, especially with someone you are having a romantic relationship with (祕密) 約會; 幽會: *a secret assignation at midnight* 午夜的祕密約會

as·sign·ment /ə`saɪnmənt; ə'saɪnmənt/ *n* **1** [C] a piece of work that is given to someone as part of their job, or that a student is asked to do〔分配的〕任務; 作業: *a history assignment* 歷史作業 | **on an assignment** *Joanna's going to Italy on a special assignment for her newspaper.* 喬安娜受委派到意大利去執行報社的一項特殊任務。**2** [U] the act of giving people particular jobs to do 分配, 指派〔任務〕: *the assignment of chores* 分配雜務

as·sim·i·late /ə`sɪml,et; ə'sɪmɪleɪt/ *v* **1** [T] to think about new ideas, information etc so that you feel ready to use them 吸收, 理解, 掌握: *It will take time to assimilate all these facts.* 充分理解這些事實需要時間。**2** [I,T] if people assimilate or are assimilated into a country or group, they become part of it and are accepted by other people in it 融入, 加入; (使) 同化: **[+into]** *women being assimilated into the workforce* 加入勞動者行列的婦女 **3** [T] *technical* if you assimilate food, you take it into your mouth and DIGEST[1] (1) it【術語】吸收, 消化〔食物〕

as·sim·i·la·tion /ə,sɪml`eʃən; ə,sɪmɪ'leɪʃən/ *n* [U] **1** the process of assimilating or being assimilated 吸收; 融合, 同化 **2** *technical* the process in which a sound in a word changes because of the effect of another sound next to it, for example the 'p' in 'cupboard'【術語】語音的同化〈如 cupboard 中的 p〉

as·sist[1] /ə`sɪst; ə'sɪst/ *v* **1** [I,T] to help someone to do something, especially by doing all the less important things so that they can spend time doing difficult things 幫助, 協助: **assist (sb) with/in** *I was employed to assist the manager with his duties.* 我受雇協助經理工作。**2** [T] to make it easier for someone to do something 使做…變得更容易: *They had no maps to assist them.* 他們沒地圖, 很不方便。—see 見 HELP[1] (USAGE)

assist[2] *n* [C] an action that helps another player on your team to make a point〔體育項目中的〕助攻

as·sist·ance /ə`sɪstəns; ə'sɪstəns/ *n* [U] help or support 幫助, 援助: *financial assistance* 財政援助 | *Can I be of any assistance?* (=can I help you?) 我能幫甚麼忙嗎? | **with the assistance of** *a report drawn up with the assistance of experts* 在專家的協助下起草的報告 | **come to sb's assistance** (=help someone) 幫助某人 *One of her fellow passengers came to her assistance.* 同車的一個乘客過來幫她。—see 見 HELP[1] (USAGE)

as·sis·tant[1] /ə`sɪstənt; ə'sɪstənt/ *adj* **assistant manager/director/cook etc** someone whose job is just below the level of manager, etc 助理經理/主任/廚師等

assistant[2] *n* [C] **1** someone who helps someone else in their work, especially by doing the less important jobs 助手, 助理, 副手: *a clerical assistant* 文書助理 **2** a SHOP ASSISTANT 商店店員 —see also 另見 PERSONAL ASSISTANT

assistant pro·fes·sor /.,.. .`../ *n* [C] the lowest rank of PROFESSOR (2) at an American university〔美國大學的〕助理教授

as·siz·es /ə`saɪzɪz; ə'saɪzɪz/ *n* [plural] *old use* a meeting of a court in which a judge who travelled to different towns in Britain dealt with cases【舊】〔英國的〕巡迴裁判庭 —**assize** *adj*

assn a written abbreviation of 縮寫= ASSOCIATION

assoc a written abbreviation of 縮寫= ASSOCIATION

as·so·ci·ate[1] /ə`soʃɪ,et; ə'səʊʃieɪt/ *v* **1** **associate sb/sth with** to make a connection in your mind between one thing or person and another 把某人/某事物與…聯繫起來: *I've never associated you with this place.* 我從未把你和這個地方聯繫在一起。| *People usually associate*

Japan with high tech consumer products. 人們一般把日本和高科技消費品聯想在一起。**2 be associated (with)** to be connected with a particular subject, activity, group etc 與...有關, 與...有瓜葛: *problems associated with cancer treatment* 與治療癌症有關的問題 | *I wouldn't want to be associated with McKey's project.* 我不想和麥基的項目有任何瓜葛。**3 associate with sb** to spend time with someone, especially a group who other people disapprove of 與〔他人不贊同的〕人交往[合夥, 結交]: *I don't like these layabouts you're associating with.* 我不喜歡你結交的這些遊手好閒的人。

as·so·ci·ate² /ə`soʃɪɪt; ə'səʊʃiɪ̯t/ *n* [C] **1** someone who you work or do business with 同事; (生意) 夥伴: *one of his business associates* 他生意上的一個夥伴 **2** someone who has an associate degree 準學位證書持有者

associate³ *adj* **associate member/director/head etc** someone who has some of the same rights or responsibilities as a member etc 非正式會員/副主任/副主管等

associated com·pa·ny /·,···· '···/ *n* [C] a company of which 20 to 50 per cent of the shares (SHARE² (5)) are owned by another company 聯營公司

associate de·gree /·,··· ·'·/ *n* [C] a degree given after two years of study at a JUNIOR COLLEGE in the US 副學士學位, 準學士學位〔美國兩年制初級大學的學位〕

associate pro·fes·sor /·,··· ·'··/ *n* [C] a PROFESSOR (2) at an American university whose job is above the level of ASSISTANT PROFESSOR and below the level of FULL PROFESSOR 副教授 —compare 比較 ASSISTANT PROFESSOR, FULL PROFESSOR

3 1 **as·so·ci·a·tion** /ə,sosɪ`eʃən; ə,səʊsi'eɪʃən/ *n* [C] **1** an organization that consists of a group of people who have the same aims, do the same kind of work etc 協會, 社團: *the Association of Master Builders* 建築師協會 | *an association to help families suffering from alcoholism* 旨在幫助那些遭受酗酒之害家庭的團體 —see also 另見 HOUSING ASSOCIATION **2** a connection with a particular person, organization, group etc 聯繫, 關係, 關聯: *his association with the Green Party* 他與綠黨的合作 **3** a feeling or memory that is connected with a particular place, event, word etc 聯想: *Scotland has all kinds of happy associations for me.* 蘇格蘭給我各種各樣愉快的聯想。**4 in association with** made or done together with another person, organization etc 與...合夥, 合作: *concerts sponsored by the Arts Council in association with several local businesses* 由藝術委員會和當地幾家企業合作承辦的音樂會 —see also 另見 FREE ASSOCIATION

Association foot·ball /·,···· '··/ *n* [U] *BrE formal* FOOTBALL (1)【英, 正式】足球 (運動)

as·so·nance /`æsənəns; 'æsənəns/ *n* [U] *technical* similarity in the vowel sounds of words that are close together in a poem, for example between 'born' and 'warm'【術語】〔聲音相似的〕諧音;〔尤指元音的〕母韻, 半韻, 半諧音〈如 born 和 warm 中的元音〉

as·sort·ed /ə`sɔrtɪd; ə'sɔːtɪ̯d/ *adj* of various different kinds 各種各樣的: *assorted sizes* 各種各樣的規格 | *assorted cookies* 什錦餅乾 —see also 另見 ILL-ASSORTED

as·sort·ment /ə`sɔrtmənt; ə'sɔːtmənt/ *n* [C] a mixture of different things or of various kinds of the same thing 各式各樣東西的混合; 什錦: **[+of]** *an odd assortment of knives and forks* 各式各樣的刀叉

asst the written abbreviation of 縮寫= ASSISTANT

as·suage /ə`swedʒ; ə'sweɪdʒ/ *v* [T] *literary* to make an unpleasant feeling less painful or severe; RELIEVE (1)【文】緩和, 減輕, 平息: *Nothing could assuage his guilt.* 沒有任何事能減輕他的罪疚感。

as·sume /ə`sum; ə'sjuːm/ *v* [T] **1** to think that something is true, although you have no proof of it 假定, 假設: **assume (that)** *I didn't see your car, so I assumed you'd gone out.* 我沒有看見你的汽車, 所以我以為你出去了。| *Assuming that the proposal is accepted, when are we going to get the money?* 假定這個建議被採納, 我們甚麼時候能拿到錢? | **we can safely assume** (=used to say that something is certain to happen) 我們可以肯定 *I think we can safely assume that interest rates will go up again soon.* 我認為我們可以肯定利率很快又會上調。| **assume guilt/innocence** (=assume that someone is guilty or not guilty of a crime) 認定〔某人〕有罪/無辜 **2 assume control/power/responsibilities etc** to start to do a job, especially an important one 開始控制/掌權/承擔責任等: *The President assumes his new responsibilities in January.* 總統一月份就任新職。**3 assume a manner/air/expression etc** *formal* to behave in a way that does not show how you really feel, especially in order to seem more confident, cheerful etc than you are【正式】裝出...的態度/樣子/表情等: *Andy assumed an air of indifference whenever her name was mentioned.* 每次提到她的名字, 安迪都表現出無所謂的樣子。**4** to start to have a particular quality or appearance 呈現出, 出現為: *The problem is beginning to assume massive proportions.* 問題開始顯出其嚴重性。**5** to be based on the idea that something else is correct; PRESUPPOSE 以...為先決條件, 預先假定: **assume (that)** *Your theory assumes that we are willing to pay for services by taxation.* 你的理論以我們願意通過稅收方式支付服務費為前提。

as·sumed /ə`sumd; ə'sjuːmd/ *adj* **under an assumed name** using a false name 用假名: *He registered at the hotel under an assumed name.* 他用假名登記入住酒店。

as·sump·tion /ə`sʌmpʃən; ə'sʌmpʃən/ *n* **1** [C] something that you think is true although you have no proof 假定, 假設: **make an assumption** *A lot of people make the assumption that poverty only exists in the Third World.* 許多人認為貧困僅僅存在於第三世界。| **on the assumption that** *I'm working on the assumption that the money will come through.* 我是在假定能拿到錢的情況下在工作。| **underlying assumption** (=a belief that is used to support a statement or idea, even though this belief may not be correct) 潛在的假設 *the underlying assumption that scientific progress is always a good thing* 認為科學進步總是件好事的潛在假設 **2** [U] *formal* the act of starting to have control or power【正式】霸佔, 承擔, 就任: **[+of]** *the assumption of responsibility* 承擔責任, 就職 2 2

as·sur·ance /ə`ʃurəns; ə'ʃʊərəns/ *n* **1** [U] a feeling of calm confidence in your own abilities, especially because you have a lot of experience; SELF-ASSURANCE 自信, 把握: *She spoke in a tone of quiet assurance.* 她以不慌不忙的自信口氣說話。**2** [C] a promise that you will definitely do something or that something will definitely happen, especially to make someone less worried 擔任, 保證: *Despite my repeated assurances Rob still looked very nervous.* 儘管我再三保證, 羅布看起來還是很緊張。| **assurance that** *I give you my personal assurance that the work will be done very soon.* 我個人向你保證, 這項工作將很快完成。**3** [U] *BrE technical* insurance against events that are certain to happen【英, 術語】保險; INSURANCE (1) *AmE*【美】—see also 另見 LIFE ASSURANCE

as·sure /ə`ʃur; ə'ʃʊə/ *v* [T] **1** to tell someone that something will definitely happen or is definitely true so that they are less worried 向...保證, 使確信, 讓...放心: **assure sb that** *Mom assured us that everything would be all right.* 媽媽向我們保證一切都不會有問題。| **I (can) assure you** *spoken*【口】*The document is genuine, I can assure you.* 我敢保證, 這文件是真的。| **assure sb of sth** *The dealer had assured me of its quality.* 經銷商向我保證質量。—see also 另見 **rest assured** (REST² (6)) **2 be assured of** to be able to feel certain that something will happen 有信心, 有把握: *The Liberal Democrats are assured of success in the local elections.* 自由民主黨人有把握在地方選舉中獲勝。**3** to make something certain to happen or to be achieved; ENSURE 確保, 提供保證: *Excellent reviews have assured the film's success.* 上佳的評論確保了該影片的成功。—see 見 INSURE (USAGE) 2 3

as·sured /ə`ʃurd; ə'ʃʊəd/ *adj* **1** confident about your own abilities; SELF-ASSURED 自信的: *an assured manner* 自信的態度 **2** certain to happen or to be achieved 確定的, 有把握的: *Her political future looks assured.* 她的政治前途看來是有把握的。**3 the assured** *BrE technical* someone whose life has been insured【英, 術語】已保壽險的人, 受保人

as·sur·ed·ly /ə`ʃʊrɪdlɪ; əˈʃʊərɪ̶dli/ *adv formal* definitely or certainly【正式】肯定地, 確定地: *as these three fine examples assuredly demonstrate* 的確, 正如這三個很好的例子所示範的

as·te·risk /`æstəˌrɪsk; ˈæstərɪsk/ *n* [C] a mark like a star (*), used especially to show something interesting or important 星號 (*) —**asterisk** *v* [T]

a·stern /ə`stɝn; əˈstɜːn/ *adv* in or at the back of a ship 在船尾; 向船尾

as·te·roid /`æstəˌrɔɪd; ˈæstərɔɪd/ *n* [C] one of the many small PLANETs between Mars and Jupiter〔火星與木星之間的〕小行星

asth·ma /`æzmə; ˈæsmə/ *n* [U] an illness that causes difficulties in breathing 氣喘; 哮喘 (病)

asth·mat·ic /æz`mætɪk; æsˈmætɪk/ *adj* suffering from asthma 患哮喘病的 —**asthmatic** *n* [C] —**asthmatically** /-klɪ; -kli/ *adv*

as·tig·ma·tis·m /ə`stɪgməˌtɪzəm; əˈstɪgmətɪzəm/ *n* [U] difficulty in seeing clearly that is caused by a change in the inner shape of the eye 散光, 散視 —**astigmatic** /ˌæstɪg`mætɪk; ˌæstɪgˈmætɪk◂/ *adj*

a·stir /ə`stɝ; əˈstɜː/ *adj* [not before noun 不用於名詞前] *literary*【文】**1** awake and out of bed 起牀的 **2** excited about something 激動的, 轟動的, 騷動的: *The whole village was astir as the visitors arrived.* 客人來到時, 全村為之哄動。

as·ton·ish /ə`stɑnɪʃ; əˈstɒnɪʃ/ *v* [T] to surprise someone very much 使〔某人〕吃驚, 使〔某人〕驚訝: *Diana astonished her family by winning three competitions in a row.* 黛安娜連續三次獲勝, 使家人感到驚訝。| **what astonishes someone is** *What astonishes me most is his complete lack of fear.* 最令我吃驚的是, 他一點兒也不恐懼。

as·ton·ished /ə`stɑnɪʃt; əˈstɒnɪʃt/ *adj* very surprised about something 對…感到吃驚的: *We climbed out of the hole, right in front of two astonished policemen.* 我們爬出洞, 恰好出現在兩個警察面前, 他們顯得很驚訝。| **astonished that** *The man seemed astonished that anyone would want to buy the house.* 這人顯得很驚訝, 居然有人想買這房子。| **astonished to see/hear/find etc** *We were astonished to find the temple still in its original condition.* 我們驚訝地發現該寺廟仍完好無損。

as·ton·ish·ing /ə`stɑnɪʃɪŋ; əˈstɒnɪʃɪŋ/ *adj* so surprising that it is difficult to believe 令人驚訝的: *an astonishing achievement* 驚人的成就 —**astonishingly** *adv*: *She looked astonishingly beautiful.* 她美得令人稱奇。

as·ton·ish·ment /ə`stɑnɪʃmənt; əˈstɒnɪʃmənt/ *n* [U] complete surprise 驚異, 驚訝: **in astonishment** *She stared at him in astonishment.* 她吃驚地看着他。| **to your astonishment** *To my astonishment, the keys were in the door.* 令我吃驚的是, 鑰匙就在門上。

as·tound /ə`staund; əˈstaʊnd/ *v* [T] to make someone very surprised or shocked 使震驚: *The judge's decision astounded everyone.* 法官的判決使大家深感震驚。—**astounded** *adj*: *an astounded look* 吃驚的眼光

as·tound·ing /ə`staundɪŋ; əˈstaʊndɪŋ/ *adj* so surprising that it is almost impossible to believe 令人震驚的: *house prices shooting up at an astounding rate* 房價以驚人的速度猛漲 —**astoundingly** *adv*: *astoundingly beautiful scenery* 異乎尋常的美景

as·tra·khan /ˌæstrə`kæn; ˌæstrəˈkæn◂/ *n* [U] black or grey fur used for making coats and hats〔製造衣帽的〕阿斯特拉罕羔羊皮

as·tral /`æstrəl; ˈæstrəl/ *adj formal* connected with stars【正式】星的, 關於星的: *astral bodies* 星體

a·stray /ə`stre; əˈstreɪ/ *adv* **1 go astray a)** to become lost 迷失, 迷路: *One of the documents has gone astray.* 有一份文件不見了。**b)** *humorous* to start behaving in an immoral way【幽默】走入歧途 **2 lead sb astray a)** *often humorous* to encourage someone to do bad or immoral things that they would not normally do【常幽默】把某人引入歧途: *His mother worries that the older boys will lead him astray.* 他母親擔心比他大的孩子會把他帶壞。**b)** to make someone believe something that is not true 誤導某人: *It's easy to be led astray by the reports in the papers.* 很容易受報紙上的內容誤導。

a·stride /ə`straɪd; əˈstraɪd/ *adv* with one leg on each side of something 跨坐地; 跨騎地; 跨在…上

as·trin·gent[1] /ə`strɪndʒənt; əˈstrɪndʒənt/ *adj* **1** *technical* able to make your skin less oily or stop a wound from bleeding【術語】收斂 (性) 的; 止血的: *an astringent lotion* 收斂性美容液 **2** criticizing someone very severely 嚴厲的, 尖刻的: *astringent remarks* 尖刻的言辭 —**astringency** *n* [U]

astringent[2] *n* [C,U] *technical* a substance used to make your skin less oily or to stop a wound from bleeding【術語】收斂劑; 止血藥

astro- /æstro; æstrəʊ/ *prefix* concerning the stars, the PLANETs, or space (關於) 星球 [天體, 宇宙, 太空] 的: *an astronaut* (=someone who travels in space) 宇航員, 太空人 | *astrophysics* (=science of the stars) 天體物理學

as·trol·o·ger /ə`strɑlədʒɚ; əˈstrɒlədʒə/ *n* [C] someone who uses astrology to tell people about their character, life, or future 占星 (術) 家

as·trol·o·gy /ə`strɑlədʒɪ; əˈstrɒlədʒi/ *n* [U] the study of the relationship between the movements of the stars and their influence on people and events 占星術 —see also 另見 ZODIAC —**astrological** /ˌæstrə`lɑdʒɪkl; ˌæstrəˈlɒdʒɪkəl◂/ *adj* —**astrologically** /-klɪ; -kli/ *adv*

as·tro·naut /`æstrəˌnɔt; ˈæstrənɔːt/ *n* [C] someone who travels and works in a SPACECRAFT 宇航員, 太空人

as·tro·nom·i·cal /ˌæstrə`nɑmɪkl; ˌæstrəˈnɒmɪkəl◂/ *adj* **1** astronomical prices, costs etc are extremely high 極巨大的; 天文數字的 **2** connected with the study of the stars 星的, 天體的, 天文 (學) 的 —**astronomically** /-klɪ; -kli/ *adv*: *astronomically high rents* 巨額租金

as·tron·o·my /ə`strɑnəmɪ; əˈstrɒnəmi/ *n* [U] the scientific study of the stars 天文學

as·tro·phys·ics /ˌæstro`fɪzɪks; ˌæstrəʊˈfɪzɪks/ *n* [U] the scientific study of the chemical structure of the stars and the forces that influence them 天體物理學 —**astrophysical** *adj* —**astrophysicist** /-`fɪzəsɪst; -ˈfɪzɪ̶sɪ̶st/ *n* [C]

as·tro·turf /`æstrotɝf; ˈæstrəʊtɜːf/ *n* [U] *trademark* an artificial surface, like grass, that is used in sports such as football【商標】阿斯特羅人造草皮〔用於體育運動, 如足球〕

as·tute /ə`stut; əˈstjuːt/ *adj* able to understand situations or behaviour very well and very quickly, especially so that you can get an advantage for yourself 精明的, 敏銳的; 狡黠的: *a particularly astute electoral move* 一個特別明智的選舉步驟 | *astute investments* 精明的投資 —**astutely** *adv* —**astuteness** *n* [U]

a·sun·der /ə`sʌndɚ; əˈsʌndə/ *adv* **be torn asunder** *literary* to be broken violently into many pieces【文】破成碎塊, 散成碎片: *The boat was torn asunder on the rocks.* 船被礁石撞成碎片。

a·sy·lum /ə`saɪləm; əˈsaɪləm/ *n* **1** [U] protection given to someone by a government because they have escaped from fighting or political trouble in their own country (政治) 避難, (政治) 庇護 —see also 另見 POLITICAL ASYLUM **2** [C] *old use* a MENTAL HOSPITAL【舊】瘋人院, 精神病院

a·sym·met·ri·cal /ˌesɪ`mɛtrɪkl; ˌeɪsɪ̶ˈmetrɪkəl/ also 又作 **a·sym·met·ric** /-`mɛtrɪk; -ˈmetrɪk◂/ *adj* **1** having two sides that are different in shape 不對稱的, 不勻稱的: *asymmetrical patterns* 不對稱圖案 **2** *formal* not equal【正式】不相等的 —opposite 反義詞 SYMMETRICAL —

asymmetrically /-klɪ; -kli/ *adv*

a·symp·to·mat·ic /eˌsɪmptəˋmætɪk; æˌsɪmptəˈmætɪk/ *adj* if someone or the illness that they have is asymptomatic, there are no signs of the illness 無症狀的

1 1 **at** /ət; ət; *strong* 強讀 æt; æt/ *prep* **1** used to show a point in space where someone or something is, or where an event is happening 在…〔表示地點〕: *We'll meet at my house.* 我們將在我家見面。| *a huge queue at the bus stop* 公共汽車站的長隊 | *They sat down at a corner table.* 他們在角落的桌旁坐下。| **at Jack's/Sue's etc** (=at Jack's house, Sue's house etc) 在傑克/蘇等的家裡 *Pete's round at Mel's.* 皮特在梅爾家附近。| **at the doctor's/the bank/the airport etc** (=at a place you go to for a particular purpose) 在診所/銀行/機場等 *Guess who I met at the dentist's?* 猜猜我在牙科診所遇到了誰? **2 at a party/club/funeral etc** at an event while it is taking place 在聚會/俱樂部/葬禮上等: *I met my wife at a disco.* 我在的士高[迪斯科]舞廳遇見了我的妻子。| *They're all out at the cinema.* 他們都出去看電影了。**3 at school/work etc** regularly going to school, work etc 上學/上班等: *Is Jessica still at school?* (=does she go to school regularly) 傑西卡還上學嗎? **4 at lunch/dinner etc** eating your lunch, dinner etc 在吃午飯/晚餐等: *I'm sorry, Pam's at lunch just now.* 對不起, 帕姆現在在吃午飯。**5** used to show an exact time 在…〔表示確切的時間〕: *The film starts at 8 o'clock.* 電影在八點鐘開始。| **at the moment** (=now) 現在, 此刻 *We're really busy at the moment.* 我們現在很忙。**6** used to show a particular period of time during which something happens 在…(期間): *My husband often works at night.* 我丈夫經常在晚上工作。| *We like to go to Midnight Mass at Christmas.* 聖誕節時我們喜歡去做子夜彌撒。**7** used to show the person or thing that an action is directed or aimed at 對着…; 朝…方向: *Protesters threw rotten eggs at the speakers .* 抗議者向演講者扔臭雞蛋。| *Jake shot at the deer but missed.* 傑克朝鹿開了一槍, 但沒打中。| *Look at that!* 看那個! | *Stop shouting at the kids all the time.* 別總是衝着孩子大喊大叫。**8** used to show the thing that caused an action or feeling 對…; 由於…: *The children all laughed at his jokes.* 孩子們聽了他說的笑話都大笑起來。| *I'm surprised at you!* 你讓我吃驚! | *Dad got really mad at me for scratching the car.* 爸爸對我劃壞了汽車感到很生氣。**9** used to show the subject or activity that you are considering when making a judgment about someone's ability 在…方面: *Barbara's getting on really well at her new job.* 芭芭拉在新的工作崗位上幹得真不錯。| *Rosa's a genius at chemistry.* 羅莎在化學方面是個天才。| **good/bad etc at (doing) sth** *Luis was always good at maths.* 路易斯總是很擅長數學。| *Matt's bad at handling people.* 馬特不擅長跟人打交道。**10** used to show a continuous state or activity 處於…〔表示情況、狀態〕: *two nations at war* 處於交戰狀態的兩國 | *Many children are still at risk from neglect or abuse.* 許多孩子仍處於沒人照顧或受虐待的危險中。| *Granny's at peace now.* (=dead) 奶奶已故世了。| **at large** (=if someone or something dangerous is at large they are in a particular area and may harm or kill someone) 〔危險人物或野獸〕自由的, 逍遙的, 未被捕的 *rumours of a black panther at large* 一隻黑豹在任意出沒的傳言 —see picture on page A1 參見A1頁圖 **11** used to show a price, rate, level, age, speed etc 以…; 在…〔表示價格、比率、水準、年齡、速度等〕: *old books selling at 10 cents each* 以每本一角錢(的價格)出售的舊書 | *The house was sold at a price of £250,000.* 房子以二十五萬英鎊的價格售出。| *You should have more sense at your age.* 你這個年齡不應該這樣不懂事。| *The car was going at about 50 mph.* 汽車以每小時50英里的速度行駛。| *Amanda rode off at a gallop.* 阿曼達匆匆忙忙地騎馬走了。**12 at least/worst/most etc** the least, worst etc thing possible 至少/最糟/至多等: *John has to practise for at least half an hour every day.* 約翰每天至少得練半小時。| *At worst, up to 50% of the population could be affected.* 最壞的情況就是50%的人可能受到影響。| **at the very least/most/worst etc** *That car's worth £250 at the very most.* 那輛汽車充其量也就值250英鎊。| **at its/her/their best etc** *The garden is at its best in June.* 花園在六月的景色最美。| *This was Sampras at his most powerful.* 這是處於巔峯期的森柏斯。**13** used to show that you are trying to do something but are not succeeding or completing it 〔勉強地〕在〔做某事〕: *George was just picking at his food.* 喬治在挑挑揀揀地吃東西。| *Sarah took another sip at her wine.* 莎拉又啜了一小口酒。| *I clutched at the rope but missed.* 我伸手去抓繩子, 但沒抓着。**14 at sb's invitation/command** because someone asks or orders you to do something 應某人之邀/據某人之命令: *Rachel attended the dinner at the chairman's command.* 雷切爾在主席的囑咐下參加了晚宴。**15 at that a)** also or besides 也, 還, 而且: *It's a new idea, and a good one, at that.* 這是個新主意, 還是個好主意哩。**b)** after something happens or as a result of it; then 隨即, 然後: *Tess called him a liar and at that he stormed out of the room.* 苔絲說他是個騙子, 他一聽便氣沖沖地走出了房間。—see also 另見 **leave it at that** (LEAVE[1] (12)) **16 at a time** at the same time 每次; 同時: *Ben was putting chocolates in his mouth two at a time.* 本每次往嘴裡放兩塊巧克力。**17 where it's at** *informal* used to describe a place or activity that is very popular, exciting, and fashionable【非正式】流行[精彩, 時尚]的場所或活動: *This Hacienda Club is where it's at.* 這種西班牙農場式的俱樂部很流行。—see also 另見 **(not) at all** (ALL[3]) —see picture on page A1 參見A1頁圖

at·a·vis·tic /ˌætəˋvɪstɪk; ˌætəˈvɪstɪk◂/ *adj formal* atavistic feelings are very basic human feelings, that people have felt since humans have existed【正式】返祖的; 原始的

ate /et; eɪt/ the past tense of EAT

-ate /ɪt, et; ɪ̗t, eɪt/ *suffix* **1** [in adjectives 構成形容詞] full of or showing a particular quality 充滿…的, 有…特點的: *very affectionate* (=showing love) 多情的 **2** [in verbs 構成動詞] to make something have a particular quality 使…: *to activate* (=make active) 使活躍, 使活動 | *to regulate* (=make regular; control) 使有規律, 使合乎規範 **3** [in nouns 構成名詞] a group of people with certain duties〔具有某種職責的〕人: *the electorate* (=voters) 選民 | *an inspectorate* 檢查員, 監察員 **4** [in nouns 構成名詞] the job, rank, or degree of a particular type of person 職務, 身分, 狀況: *She was awarded her doctorate.* (=the degree of doctor) 她獲頒授博士學位。**5** *technical* [in nouns 構成名詞] a chemical salt formed from a particular acid【術語】(…酸的)鹽: *phosphate* 磷酸鹽 —**-ately** /ɪtlɪ; ɪ̗tli/ [in adverbs 構成副詞]: *fortunately* 幸運地; 幸好

a·the·is·m /ˋeθɪˌɪzəm; ˈeɪθi-ɪzəm/ *n* [U] the belief that God does not exist 無神論 —**atheist** *n* [C] —**atheistic** /ˌeθɪˋɪstɪk; ˌeɪθiˈɪstɪk◂/ —**atheistical** *adj*

ath·lete /ˋæθlit; ˈæθliːt/ *n* [C] someone who is good at or who often does sports 運動員: *a natural athlete* 天生的運動員

athlete's foot /ˌ·· ˈ·/ *n* [U] a medical condition in which the skin cracks between your toes 腳癬, 香港腳

ath·let·ic /æθˋlɛtɪk; æθˈletɪk/ *adj* **1** physically strong and good at sport 強壯的, 擅長運動的: *Sven was tall, blonde, and athletic looking.* 斯文個子高, 一頭金髮, 看上去像個運動員。**2** connected with athletics 運動的

ath·let·ics /æθˋlɛtɪks; æθˈletɪks/ *n* [U] *BrE* sports such as running and jumping【英】體育, 田徑(項目); TRACK AND FIELD *AmE*【美】

-athon /əθɑn; əθən/ *suffix* [in nouns 構成名詞] *informal* an event in which a particular thing is done for a very long time, especially to collect money【非正式】〔尤指為籌錢〕持續時間很長的事件, 馬拉松式的活動: *a swimathon* 長距離游泳比賽 | *a talkathon* 馬拉松式的冗長演說

a·thwart /ə`θwɔrt; ə'θwɔːt/ *prep literary* across【文】橫跨過

-ation /eʃən; eɪʃən/ *suffix* [in nouns 構成名詞] the act, state, or result of doing something ...動作(造成的狀態或結果): *an examination of the contents* (=examining them) 對內容的檢查 | *the combination of several factors* 幾種因素的綜合

a·tish·oo /ə`tɪʃu; ə'tɪʃuː/ *spoken* a word used to represent the sound you make when you SNEEZE【口】阿嚏〔打噴嚏的聲音〕

-ative /ətɪv; ətɪv/ *suffix* [in adjectives 構成形容詞] liking something or tending to do something or show a particular quality 喜歡...的; 有...傾向或特點的: *talkative* (=liking to talk a lot) 喜歡說話的, 多嘴的 | *argumentative* (=enjoying arguments) 喜歡爭論的 | *imaginative* (=showing imagination) 富於想像力的

at·las /`ætləs; 'ætləs/ *n* [C] a book of maps 地圖集, 地圖冊: *a world atlas* 世界地圖冊

ATM /ˌe ti `ɛm; ˌeɪ tiː 'em/ *n* [C] *AmE* a machine outside a bank that you use to get money from your account【美】自動櫃員機, 自動提款機; CASHPOINT *BrE*【英】

2 **at·mo·sphere** /`ætməsˌfɪr; 'ætməsfɪə/ *n* [C,U] **1 the atmosphere** the mixture of gases that surrounds the Earth 大氣(層) **2** the air inside a room〔室內的〕空氣: *a smoky atmosphere* 煙霧彌漫的空氣 **3** the feeling that an event or place gives you 氣氛, 環境: *The atmosphere at home's been depressing since they had that fight.* 自從那次他們打架以來, 家裡的氣氛日漸沉鬱。| **atmosphere of crisis/optimism etc** *An atmosphere of optimism dominated the party conference.* 黨的會議在樂觀的氣氛中進行。

at·mo·spher·ic /ˌætməs`fɛrɪk; ˌætməs'ferɪk◂/ *adj* **1** [only before noun 僅用於名詞前] related with the Earth's atmosphere 大氣(層)的; 有關大氣的: *atmospheric pressure* 氣壓 **2** beautiful and mysterious 有神祕美感的; 製造氣氛的: *atmospheric music* 能製造氣氛的音樂

at·mo·spher·ics /ˌætməs`fɛrɪks; ˌætməs'ferɪks/ *n* [plural] continuous cracking noises that sometimes interrupt radio broadcasts〔無線電的〕大氣干擾; 天電

at·oll /`ætɑl; 'ætɒl/ *n* [C] a CORAL[1] island in the shape of a ring 環狀珊瑚島, 環礁: *an atomic bomb detonated on Bikini Atoll in the Pacific* 一顆原子彈在太平洋的比基尼島上爆炸

at·om /`ætəm; 'ætəm/ *n* [C] **1** the smallest part of an ELEMENT (1) that can exist alone or combine with other substances to form MOLECULES 原子 **2** a very small amount of something 一點兒: *There isn't an atom of truth in it.* 那裡面沒有絲毫的真實性。

atom bomb /'·· ·/ also 又作 **atomic bomb** /·,·· '·/ *n* [C] a NUCLEAR bomb that splits atoms to cause an extremely large explosion 原子彈

a·tom·ic /ə`tɑmɪk; ə'tɒmɪk/ *adj* **1** related to the energy produced by splitting atoms or the weapons that use this energy 原子的; 原子能的; 核能的: *atomic warfare* 核戰爭 | *an atomic submarine* 原子能潛艇 **2** connected with the atoms in a substance 原子的; 與原子有關的: *atomic weight* 原子量

atomic en·er·gy /·,·· '···/ *n* [U] NUCLEAR ENERGY 原子能, 核能

at·om·izer /`ætəmˌaɪzə; 'ætəmaɪzə/ *n* [C] a thing used to make a liquid such as PERFUME[1] (1) come out of a bottle in very small drops like mist 霧化器, 噴霧器: *a perfume atomizer* 噴霧香水瓶 | *a paint atomizer* 噴塗器

a·ton·al /e`tonl; eɪ'təʊnl/ *adj* a piece of music that is atonal is not based on a particular KEY[2] (4)〔音樂〕無調的 —**atonally** *adv* —**atonality** /ˌeto`nælətɪ; ˌeɪtəʊ'næləti/ *n* [U]

a·tone /ə`ton; ə'təʊn/ *v* [I] *formal* to do something to show that you are sorry for having done something wrong【正式】贖(罪); 彌補〔過失等〕: [+for] *Richard was anxious to atone for his thoughtlessness.* 理查德急切地想彌補自己考慮不周的過失。

a·tone·ment /ə`tonmənt; ə'təʊnmənt/ *n* [U] *formal* something you do to show that you are sorry for having done something wrong【正式】贖罪, 謝罪; 彌補過失

a·top /ə`tɑp; ə'tɒp/ *prep literary* on top of something【文】在...頂上, 在...上面

-ator /etə; eɪtə/ *suffix* [in nouns 構成名詞] someone or something that does something 做...動作的人; 起...作用的事物: *a narrator* (=someone who tells a story) 敘事人 | *a generator* (=machine that produces electricity) 發電機

A to Z /ˌe tə `zi; ˌeɪ tə 'zed/ *n* [C] *trademark* a book with maps that show every street in a British city【商標】〔英國的〕城市指南

at-risk /ˌ· '·◂/ *adj* **at-risk children/patients etc** people who need special care because they are likely to be in danger from violent parents, to become ill etc 需要特別保護的孩子/病人等: **at-risk register** (=an official list of people in this situation) 需特別保護人員名單

at·ri·um /`etrɪəm; 'eɪtriəm/ *n* [C] **1** one of the two spaces in the top of your heart that push blood into the VENTRICLES 心房 **2** a large high open space in a tall building〔高樓大廈的〕中庭, 天井

a·tro·cious /ə`troʃəs; ə'trəʊʃəs/ *adj* extremely bad or showing no ability to do something at all 兇殘的; 惡劣的, 糟糕的, 差勁的: *atrocious weather* 惡劣的天氣 | *Her singing was atrocious.* 她的演唱很差勁。| *atrocious housing conditions* 惡劣的居住條件 —**atrociously** *adv* —**atrociousness** *n* [U]

a·troc·i·ty /ə`trɑsətɪ; ə'trɒsəti/ *n* [C usually plural 一般用複數, U] an extremely cruel and violent action, especially during a war〔尤指戰爭中的〕暴行: *one of the worst atrocities of the Vietnam War* 越南戰爭中最駭人聽聞的暴行

at·ro·phy /`ætrəfɪ; 'ætrəfi/ *v* [I,T] to become weak or make something become weak because of lack of use or lack of blood (使)萎縮, (使)衰退: *therapy to prevent the leg muscles from atrophying* 防止腿部肌肉萎縮的療法 —**atrophy** *n* [U]

at·tach /ə`tætʃ; ə'tætʃ/ *v* [T] 

1 ►CONNECT 連接◄ to connect one thing to another 繫; 綁; 貼; 固定; 連接; 附上: **attach sth to** *Attach a recent photograph to your application form.* 申請表上請貼一張近照。| **be attached to** *a small battery attached to a little loudspeaker* 裝在小喇叭上的一節小電池 | *The web was only attached to the leaf by one thread.* 蜘蛛網只有一根細絲吊在葉子上。

2 ►LIKE 喜歡◄ be attached to to like someone or something very much, because you have known them or had them for a long time 喜歡, 依戀: *It's easy to become attached to the children you work with. Too attached, sometimes.* 很容易喜歡上和你相處的孩子們。有時候會喜歡過頭。

3 attach importance/significance etc to believe that something is important 重視, 認為...很重要: *People attach too much importance to economic forecasts.* 人們把經濟預測看得過於重要。

4 attach blame if you attach blame or if blame attaches to someone, they have done something wrong 與...有牽連

5 ►FEELING/QUALITY 感覺/質量◄ be attached to if a quality, feeling, idea etc is attached to a person, thing or event, it is connected with them 與...聯繫起來: *It's easy to let the emotions attached to one situation spill over into others.* 一件事中產生的情緒很容易會加諸於其他事情上。

6 ►ORGANIZATION/COMPANY 組織/公司◄ be attached to sth a) to work for part of a particular organization, especially for a short period of time〔尤指短期地〕為...工作: *He was attached to the foreign affairs department of a Japanese newspaper.* 他在一家日本報紙的外事部門工作。**b)** to be part of a bigger organization 附屬於..., 屬於...的一個分支: *The Food Ministry is attached*

to the Ministry of Agriculture. 糧食部隸屬於農業部。

at·taché /ˌætəˈʃe; əˈtæʃeɪ/ *n* [C] someone who works in an EMBASSY, and deals with a particular subject〔在大使館工作並處理某類問題的〕專員, 隨員: *a cultural attaché* 文化專員

attaché case /·ˈ·· ·/ *n* [C] a thin case used for carrying business documents 手提公文包

at·tach·ment /əˈtætʃmənt; əˈtætʃmənt/ *n* **1** [C,U] a feeling that you like or love someone or something and that you would be unhappy without them 喜愛, 愛慕, 依戀: **[+to/for]** *I did feel a certain sense of attachment for the strange old guy.* 我的確對這古怪的老人感到有些依戀。 **2** [U] belief in and loyalty towards a particular idea 信仰, 忠誠: **[+to/for]** *old people's attachment to traditional customs and ways* 老人們對傳統習慣和生活方式的篤信 **3** [C] a part that you can put onto a machine to make it do different things 附件, 附屬物, 附加裝置: *a versatile food mixer that comes with a range of attachments* 有許多附件的多用途食品攪拌器 **4 on attachment** working for a particular organization, especially for a short period of time 為…短期工作: *He was sent on attachment to their offices in Hong Kong.* 他被派到他們在香港的辦事處工作。

2 1 **at·tack¹** /əˈtæk; əˈtæk/ *n*

1 ▶VIOLENCE AGAINST SB 針對某人的暴力行為◀ [C] an act of deliberately using violence against someone 暴力事件, 打鬥: **[+on]** *There have been several attacks on foreigners recently.* 最近發生了幾次針對外國人的暴力事件。

2 ▶IN A WAR 在戰爭中◀ [C,U] the act of using weapons against an enemy in a war 進攻, 襲擊, 攻擊: *The attack began at dawn.* 進攻在拂曉開始。| **[+on]** *a carefully planned attack on Iraqi air bases* 對伊拉克空軍基地的一次計劃周密的襲擊 | **be/come under attack** *Once again we came under attack from enemy fighter planes.* 我們又一次遭到敵人戰鬥機的攻擊。| **launch an attack** (=start an attack) 發動襲擊

3 ▶CRITICISM 批評◀ [C,U] a statement that criticizes someone strongly 抨擊, 攻擊, 非難, 責罵: **[+on]** *recent attacks on the Prime Minister* 最近對首相的抨擊 | **be/come under attack** (=be strongly criticized) 遭到猛烈的抨擊 *The company came under attack for the firing of 50 employees.* 公司因解雇了 50 名員工而受到猛烈抨擊。| **go on the attack** (=start to criticize someone severely) 嚴厲批評

4 ▶ACTIONS TO STOP STH 阻止某事的行動◀ [C,U] actions intended to get rid of or stop something such as a system, a set of laws etc〔對體制、法律等的〕處理, 解決: **[+on]** *Mrs Thatcher's attack on the welfare state* 戴卓爾夫人對福利狀況的處理

5 ▶ILLNESS 疾病◀ [C] a sudden short period of suffering from an illness, especially an illness that you have often 突然發作: *an attack of asthma* 哮喘發作

6 ▶SPORT 體育◀ [C,U] **a)** an attempt by a group of players to make a GOAL (2) 進攻 **b)** the group of players on a team whose job is to make a GOAL (2) 進攻隊員: *the Arsenal attack* 阿仙奴隊的進攻球員

7 an attack of fear/panic/anxiety etc a short period of time when you feel frightened, worried etc 一陣恐懼/驚慌/焦慮等: *panic attacks* 陣陣驚慌 —see also 另見 HEART ATTACK

2 2 **attack²** *v*

1 ▶ATTACK SOMEONE 攻擊某人◀ [I,T] to deliberately use physical violence against someone 襲擊, 毆打: *Jim was attacked by a man in the park.* 吉姆在公園裡遭到一個男人的襲擊。| *dogs trained to attack on command* 經訓練一聽到命令就攻擊的狗 | **attack sb with sth** *She started attacking the burglar with a piece of wood.* 她開始用一塊木頭猛打進屋行竊的小偷。

2 ▶IN A WAR 在戰爭中◀ [I,T] to start using guns, bombs etc against an enemy in a war 進攻, 攻擊, 襲擊: *The village had been attacked by the French airforce.* 這個村子遭到法國空軍的襲擊。

3 ▶CRITICIZE 批評◀ [T] to criticize someone or something very strongly 抨擊, 攻擊, 責難: *The senator made a speech attacking Clinton's healthcare program.* 這位參議員發表演說抨擊克林頓的衛生保健計劃。| **attack sb for sth** *The article attacked the government for its policy on education.* 這篇文章抨擊了政府的教育政策。

4 ▶SPORT 體育◀ [I,T] to move forward and try to make a GOAL (2) 進攻: *Brazil began to attack more in the second half of the match.* 巴西隊下半場加強了進攻。

5 ▶BEGIN DOING 開始做◀ [T] to begin doing a job or dealing with a problem with determination and eagerness 着手處理, 投入: *She immediately set about attacking the problem.* 她立即着手處理該問題。

6 ▶DISEASE 疾病◀ [T] to damage part of someone's body 給…造成傷害; 侵襲, 侵蝕: *a cruel disease that attacks the central nervous system* 一種破壞中樞神經系統的兇殘疾病

at·tain /əˈten; əˈteɪn/ *v* [T] *formal*【正式】**1** to succeed in reaching a particular level or in getting something after trying for a long time 達到, 獲得, 贏得: *More women are attaining positions of power in public life.* 越來越多的婦女在公共生活中獲得權位。**2** to reach a high level 達到, 漲到: *Share prices attained a high of $3.27.* 每股價格漲到 3.27 美元之高。—**attainable** *adj*: *This target should be attainable.* 這個目標應該能實現。

at·tain·ment /əˈtenmənt; əˈteɪnmənt/ *n formal*【正式】**1** [U] success in getting something or reaching a particular level 獲得, 達到, 實現: *the attainment of happiness* 獲得幸福 **2** [C] something that you have succeeded in getting or learning, such as a skill 成就, 造詣, 學識, 技能

at·tempt¹ /əˈtɛmpt; əˈtempt/ *n* [C] **1** an act of trying to do something, especially something difficult 努力, 嘗試, 企圖〔尤指較難的事情〕: **attempt to do sth** *All attempts to control inflation have failed.* 所有為控制通貨膨脹而作出的嘗試都失敗了。| **[+at]** *He made one last attempt at the world record.* 他為打破世界記錄作了最後一次努力。| **make no attempt** *The protestors made no attempt to resist arrest.* 抗議者對逮捕未進行抵抗。| **in an attempt to do sth** *In an attempt to diffuse the tension I suggested that we break off for lunch.* 為了消除緊張感, 我建議我們停下來去吃午飯。**2 an attempt on sb's life** an act of trying to kill someone, especially someone famous or important 企圖謀殺某人〔尤指名人或重要人物〕 2 1

attempt² *v* [T] to try to do something that is difficult, dangerous, or has never been done before 試圖, 嘗試, 企圖: **attempt to do sth** *Every time I've attempted to convince her, I've failed completely.* 每一次我都試圖說服她, 但全然不起作用。| **attempt sth** *Weather conditions prevented them from attempting the jump.* 天氣狀況使他們無法試跳。 2 2

at·tend /əˈtɛnd; əˈtend/ *v* **1** [I,T] to go to an event such as a meeting or a class 參加, 出席, 到場: *Only 7 people attended the meeting.* 只有七個人參加會議。| *Please let us know if you are unable to attend.* 如你不能出席, 請通知我們。—see 見 JOIN¹ (USAGE) **2** [I,T] to go regularly to a school, church etc 上〔學〕, 去〔教堂〕: *All children between the ages of 5 and 16 must attend school.* 所有 5 至 16 歲的孩子必須上學。**3** [T] *formal* to happen or exist at the same time as something【正式】陪伴, 伴隨…而至: *the peculiar atmosphere which attends such an event* 籠罩着這事件的古怪氣氛 **4** [T] to look after someone, especially because they are ill 看護, 照料 2 2

attend to sb/sth *phr v* [T] **1** to deal with business or personal matters 處理, 料理〔生意或個人事務〕: *I may be late – I have got one or two things to attend to.* 我也許會遲到, 我有一兩件事要處理。**2** to help a customer in a shop or a restaurant to buy or order something〔在商店或飯店〕照顧, 接待〔顧客〕—see 見 JOIN¹ (USAGE)

A

Frequencies of **attend** and **go to** in spoken and written English 在英語口語和書面語中 attend 和 go to 的使用頻率

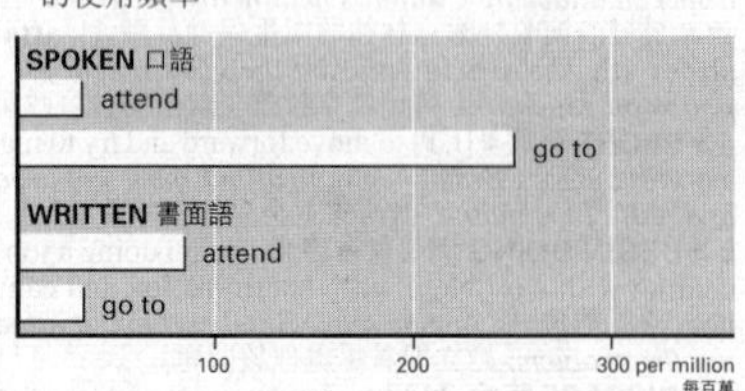

Based on the British National Corpus and the Longman Lancaster Corpus
據英國國家語料庫和朗文蘭卡斯特語料庫

Both verbs are used to mean 'be at an event'. The graph shows that in this meaning **go to** is much more common than in spoken English. In written or formal English **attend** is more common. 這兩個動詞都用於表示"參加"的意思。本圖表顯示, 口語中用於此意時, go to 的使用頻率遠遠高於 attend。在書面語和正式用語中 attend 則更為常用。

at·tend·ance /ə`tɛndəns; ə'tendəns/ *n* **1** [C] the number of people who attend a game, concert, meeting etc 出席人數, 出席者: **high/low attendance** *a low attendance at class of 84's reunion* 84 年畢業班校友聚會出席人數很少 **2** [C,U] the number of times that you go to a meeting, class etc that is held regularly 出席(率), 到場(次數): *Many students have a very poor attendance record.* 許多學生到課率很低。**3 be in attendance** *formal* to be at a special or important event【正式】出席, 參加: *Over 2000 people were in attendance at yesterday's demonstration.* 有二千多人參加了昨天的示威遊行。**4 be in attendance on sb** *formal* to look after someone or serve them【正式】照顧[待候]某人 —see also 另見 **dance attendance on** (DANCE[1] (5))

at·tend·ant¹ /ə`tɛndənt; ə'tendənt/ *n* [C] **1** someone whose job is to look after or help customers in a public place 服務員: *a car-park attendant* 停車場的服務員 **2** someone who looks after a very important person, such as a king or queen 侍從, 隨從; 衞士

attendant² *adj formal*【正式】**1** connected with or caused by something 伴隨的, 隨之而來的, 附帶的: *nuclear power, with all its attendant risks* 核能以及伴隨的危險 **2** going with or being with someone in order to help them 隨侍的, 負責照料的, 服務的, 服侍的

1 1 **at·ten·tion** /ə`tɛnʃən; ə'tenʃən/ *n*

1 ►WATCHING/LISTENING CAREFULLY 仔細看/聽◄ **a) pay attention** to carefully listen to or watch something that is happening, or to be careful about what you are doing 注意, 專心, 留心: *The teacher got angry with me when I didn't pay attention.* 當我不專心聽講時, 老師很生氣。| **[+to]** *The TV was on but Di wasn't paying much attention to it.* 電視開着, 可是黛沒怎麼注意看。| **pay no attention to** (=used to tell someone to ignore what someone says because it is not true or not important) 對〔某人的話〕不要在意 *Don't pay any attention to him – he's always saying stupid things.* 別對他太在意, 他總是說些蠢話。| **pay little attention to/not pay much attention to** (=behave in a way that shows that you do not think something or someone is very important) 對〔某人或某事〕不太在意 *We heard noises coming from upstairs, but we didn't pay much attention to them.* 我們聽到了樓上有動靜, 但我們沒太在意。**b) give sb/sth your attention** to listen to someone or study something carefully, especially so that you can deal with a problem 傾聽某人/專注於某事: **give sb your full/undivided attention** *Now he's gone, I can give you my undivided attention.* 現在他已經走了, 我可以把全部注意力都放在你身上。

2 ►INTEREST 興趣◄ **a)** [U] the interest that people show in someone or something 興趣; 關心, 關注: *She was flattered by all the attention he was giving her.* 他對她很關心, 她感到非常高興。| **give sth attention** *The press has given the story a lot of attention.* 新聞界對這個報道給予很大關注。| **the centre of attention** (=a person who everyone looks at and is interested in) 人們注視的中心(人物) *Some people enjoy being the centre of attention.* 有些人喜歡成為別人關注的對象。| **the focus of attention** (=the situation that people are most concerned about or consider to be most important) 關注的焦點 *The focus of attention has shifted away from domestic issues.* 人們關注的焦點已不再是國內問題。| **hold/keep sb's attention** (=make someone continue to be interested in something) 一直吸引某人的興趣 *Follett keeps the reader's attention throughout the book.* 福利特的書從頭到尾都吸引着讀者的興趣。| **attention span** (=the period of time during which you continue to be interested in something) 注意廣度〔能集中於某事的時間〕*Children generally have a short attention span.* 一般說來, 孩子們能集中注意力的時間較短。

3 ►MAKE SB NOTICE 使某人注意到◄ **a) attract/catch/get sb's attention** to make someone notice you, especially because you want to speak to them or you need their help 吸引/引起/得到某人的注意: *She tried to attract the waiter's attention.* 她設法吸引服務員的注意。**b) attract attention** if someone or something attracts attention, people notice them, especially because they look very interesting or unusual 引人注目: *The band members couldn't go out in the street because they attracted too much attention.* 樂隊成員不能到街上去, 因為他們太引人注目了。**c) get attention** to make someone notice you and be interested in what you are doing 吸引注意力: *Children are often bad in order to get attention.* 孩子們常常淘氣, 以吸引別人的注意力。**d) draw attention to** to make people notice and be concerned about something 使人們關注...: *The article was intended to draw attention to the situation in Cambodia.* 這篇文章旨在呼籲人們關注柬埔寨的局勢。**e) draw attention away from** to make people stop being concerned about something such as a social problem 轉移人們對...的注意力 **f) bring sth to sb's attention** to tell someone, especially someone in authority, about something such as a problem 使某事引起某人注意: *The matter was first brought to my attention earlier this year.* 今年較早時, 我第一次注意到這個問題。**g) come to sb's attention** if something such as a problem comes to the attention of someone in authority, they find out about it 吸引某人的注意力, 發現

4 ►REPAIR/TREATMENT 修理/處理◄ [U] **a)** something you do to repair or clean something, or make it work or be able to be used 維修, 保養: *Honda 50cc for sale. Needs some attention.* 本田 50cc 出售, 需要小修。**b)** treatment given to someone who is ill or injured 護理: *medical attention* 醫療護理

5 ►CARE 關心◄ [C,U] things that you do to help someone which show that you like them 照顧: *Pets need a lot of care and attention.* 寵物需要很多的關心和照顧。

6 ►SOLDIERS 士兵◄ **stand to attention/be at attention** to stand up straight in neat lines 站直, 立正: **attention!** (=used when ordering a group of soldiers to stand up straight) 立正!〔軍隊口令〕

7 ►SPEECH/ANNOUNCEMENT 演說/通知◄ **a) may/could I have your attention?** *spoken* used in a formal situation when you want people to listen to you【口】大家請安靜一下好嗎?〔用於正式場合〕**b) thank you for your attention** *spoken* used at the end of a speech or statement to thank people for listening【口】〔用於演講結束時〕謝謝大家

8 ►LETTER 信◄ **for the attention of** used on the front of an official letter when you want a particular person to read it or deal with it …親啟: *for the attention of the manager* 經理親啟

at·ten·tive /ə'tɛntɪv; ə'tentɪv/ *adj* **1** listening or watching someone carefully because you are interested in them 關注的; 注意的, 專心的; 注意聽的: *The professor was pleased to have such an attentive audience.* 聽眾如此專心聽講讓教授非常高興。**2** making sure someone has everything they need 照顧周到的: **[+to]** *The crew were attentive to the passengers' needs.* 乘務人員很留意乘客的需要。—opposite 反義詞 INATTENTIVE —**attentively** *adv*: *He listened attentively and with growing interest.* 他專心地聽着, 越來越感興趣。—**attentiveness** *n* [U]

at·ten·u·ate /ə'tɛnju,et; ə'tenjueɪt/ *v* [T] *formal* to make something weaker or have less effect【正式】使變細; 使變弱; 使效果差; 稀釋: *an attenuated measles vaccine* 麻疹減毒疫苗 —**attenuation** *n* [U]

at·test /ə'tɛst; ə'test/ *v* **1** [I,T] to show or prove that something is true 證明, 作為(…的)證據: **[+to]** *Luxurious furnishings attested to the wealth of the owner.* 豪華的家具說明主人很有錢。**2** [T] to officially state that you believe something is true, especially in a court of law 作證, 證實

at·tes·ta·tion /,ætɛs'teʃən; ,æte'steɪʃən/ *n* [C,U] *formal* a legal statement made by someone in which they say that something is definitely true【正式】證明, 證實, 證詞

at·tic /'ætɪk; 'ætɪk/ *n* [C] a space or room under the roof of a house often used for storing things 閣樓; 頂樓: *She went to college consigning her collection of cuddly toys to the attic.* 她去上大學, 把心愛的玩具都放到了閣樓裡。—see picture on page A4 參見A4頁圖

at·tire /ə'taɪr; ə'taɪə/ *n* [U] *formal* clothes【正式】服裝, 衣服: *formal evening attire* 晚禮服

at·tired /ə'taɪrd; ə'taɪəd/ *adj* [not before noun 不用於名詞前] *formal* dressed in a particular way【正式】…穿着的, …打扮的: *more suitably attired for a rave than for school* 打扮得更適合於狂歡聚會而不適合於上學

1 **at·ti·tude** /'ætə,tud; 'ætɪtjuːd/ *n* **1** [C,U] the opinions
1 and feelings that you usually have about something 態度, 心態; 感覺: **[+towards]** *Pete's attitude towards women really scares me.* 皮特對婦女的態度真讓我害怕。**2** [C,U] the way that you behave towards someone or in a particular situation, especially when this shows how you feel 姿態: *an aggressive attitude* 一副挑釁的架勢 | *As soon as they found out I was a doctor their whole attitude changed.* 他們一發現我是醫生, 整個態度都變了。| **attitude problem** (=behaviour that shows that you do not like to help people or do what you should do) 態度問題 | **have a good/bad attitude** *He has a bad attitude towards his schoolwork.* 他對功課的態度不端正。**3** [U] *informal* a style of dressing, decorating etc that shows you have the confidence to do unusual and exciting things without caring what other people think【非正式】我行我素的打扮: **with attitude** *a coat with attitude* 顯示自我風格的大衣

2 **at·tor·ney** /ə'tɝnɪ; ə'tɜːni/ *n* [C] *AmE* a lawyer【美】律
2 師 —see 見 LAWYER (USAGE)

attorney gen·e·ral /·,·· '···/ *n* [C] the chief lawyer in a state or of the government in the US〔美國聯邦或州的〕司法部長; 首席檢察官

2 **at·tract** /ə'trækt; ə'trækt/ *v* [T] **1** to make someone in-
2 terested in something, or make them want to take part in something 吸引, 引起〔興趣、關注等〕: **attract sb to sth** *What attracted me most to the job was the chance to travel.* 這份工作最吸引我的是有旅行的機會。| **attract interest/attention etc** *The story has attracted a lot of interest in the media.* 這則報道引起了傳媒的廣泛關注。**2 be attracted to** to feel that you like someone and want to have a sexual relationship with them 喜愛, 為…所吸引: *I'm not usually attracted to blond men.* 我通常不喜歡金髮男人。**3** to make someone like or admire something or feel romantically interested in someone 吸引; 引誘: *I guess it was his eyes that attracted me first.* 我想是他的眼睛先迷住了我。**4** to make someone or something move towards another thing 招引; 吸引: *Leftover food attracts flies.* 剩飯剩菜招引蒼蠅。| *low rents designed to attract new businesses to the area* 低租金旨在吸引更多新企業到這地區來

at·trac·tion /ə'trækʃən; ə'trækʃən/ *n* **1** [C,U] a feeling 3
of liking someone, especially in a sexual way 喜愛, 喜歡: *The attraction between them was almost immediate.* 他們幾乎是一見鍾情。**2** [C] something interesting or enjoyable to see or do 吸引人之物, 有魅力之物, 誘惑物: **tourist attraction** (=a place that many tourists visit) 旅遊景點 | **the main attraction** (=the most popular place, person, or activity) 最受歡迎的人; 最吸引人的地方; 最精彩的活動 *The beautiful beaches are the island's main attraction.* 美麗的海灘是這個島吸引人的主要之處。**3** [C,U] a feature or quality that makes something seem interesting or enjoyable 吸引力, 誘惑力: **[+of]** *Being your own boss is one of the attractions of owning your own business.* 自己當老闆是發展自己事業的其中一個吸引之處。**4** [C,U] *technical* a force which makes things move together or stay together【術語】吸引力: *gravitational attraction* 重力, 萬有引力

at·trac·tive /ə'træktɪv; ə'træktɪv/ *adj* **1** someone who 2
is attractive is good looking, especially in a way that 2
makes you sexually interested in them 有吸引力的, 誘人的: *an attractive young woman* 嫵媚動人的年輕女子 | **find sb attractive** *I must admit I've never found him particularly attractive.* 我必須承認我從未發覺他有甚麼特別迷人的地方。**2** pleasant to look at 好看的, 漂亮的, 美觀的: *Kitchen utensils should be attractive as well as functional.* 廚房用具應該既美觀又實用。—see 見 BEAUTIFUL (USAGE) **3** having qualities that make you want to accept something or be involved in it 有吸引力的, 引人入勝的: **[+to]** *a political movement that is very attractive to the younger generation* 對年輕一代很有吸引力的政治運動 | **attractive offer/proposition/package etc** *It's a very attractive offer, and I'll have to give it serious thought.* 這是個非常好的建議, 我會認真考慮一下。—**attractively** *adv* —**attractiveness** *n* [U]

at·trib·u·ta·ble /ə'trɪbjʊtəbl; ə'trɪbjʊtəbəl/ *adj* [not before noun 不用於名詞前] likely to be caused by something 可歸因於…的: **[+to]** *Death was attributable to gunshot wounds.* 死因可能是槍傷。

at·tri·bute¹ /ə'trɪbjut; ə'trɪbjuːt/ *v*

attribute sth **to** sb/sth *phr v* [T] **1** to say that a situation or event is caused by something 把…歸因於…: *The fall in the number of deaths from heart disease is generally attributed to improvements in diet.* 心臟病死亡人數的下降通常歸因於日常飲食的改善。**2** to say that someone was responsible for saying or writing something, painting a famous picture etc 認為…屬於: *a saying usually attributed to Confucius* 一般認為是孔子說的一句名言 **3** to say that someone or something has a particular quality 具有…特性 —**attribution** /,ætrə'bjuʃən; ,ætrɪ'bjuːʃən/ *n* [U]

at·tri·bute² /'ætrə,bjut; 'ætrɪbjuːt/ *n* [C] a quality or feature, especially one that is considered to be good or useful 特性, 特質, 屬性: *What attributes should a good manager possess?* 一名優秀的經理應該具有甚麼樣的特點?

at·trib·u·tive /ə'trɪbjətɪv; ə'trɪbjʊtɪv/ *adj* describing and coming before a noun〔置於名詞前〕起修飾作用的, 起定語作用的, 限定的: *In the phrase 'big city', 'big' is an attributive adjective, and in the phrase 'school bus', 'school' is a noun in an attributive position.* 在big city這個詞組中, big是起修飾作用的形容詞; 而在school bus這個詞組中, school是起修飾作用的名詞。—**attributively** *adv*

at·tri·tion /ə'trɪʃən; ə'trɪʃən/ *n* [U] the process of gradually destroying your enemy or making them weak by attacking them continuously 消耗, 消磨: *a war of attri-*

A

tion 消耗戰

at·tuned /ə`tund; ə'tjuːnd/ *adj* [not before noun 不用於名詞前] familiar with the way someone thinks or behaves so that you can react to them in a suitable way 合拍的, 協調的, 適應的: [+to] *British companies still aren't really attuned to the needs of the Japanese market.* 英國公司還沒有完全適應日本市場的需求。

a·typ·i·cal /e`tɪpɪkl; eɪ'tɪpɪkəl/ *adj* not typical or usual 非典型的, 不同尋常的

au·ber·gine /`obɚˌʒin; 'əʊbəʒiːn/ *n* [C,U] *BrE* a large dark purple vegetable【英】茄子; EGGPLANT *AmE*【美】—see picture on page A9 參見A9頁圖

au·burn /`ɔbɚn; 'ɔːbən/ *adj* auburn hair is a reddish brown colour 紅褐色的, 茶色的 —see picture on page A6 參見A6頁圖

auc·tion¹ /`ɔkʃən; 'ɔːkʃən/ *n* [C] a public meeting where land, buildings, paintings etc are sold to the person who offers the most money for them 拍賣: **put sth up for auction** (=try to sell something at an auction) 把某物交付拍賣 *The house was put up for auction.* 這所房子被交付拍賣了。| **auction house** (=a company that arranges auctions) 拍賣行

auction² *v* [T+off] to sell something at an auction 拍賣

auc·tio·neer /ˌɔkʃən`ɪr; ˌɔːkʃə'nɪə/ *n* [C] someone who is in charge of an auction and tells people the prices of the goods 拍賣人

au·da·cious /ɔ`deʃəs; ɔː'deɪʃəs/ *adj* brave and shocking 大膽的; 愚勇的; 膽大妄為的: *an audacious robbery* 鋌而走險的搶劫 —**audaciously** *adv*

au·dac·i·ty /ɔ`dæsətɪ; ɔː'dæsəti/ *n* [U] the quality of having enough courage to take risks or say impolite things 魯莽, 大膽無禮, 放肆: **have the audacity to do sth** *I can't believe he had the audacity to ask me for more money!* 我真不敢相信, 他竟厚顏無恥地還向我要錢!

au·di·ble /`ɔdəbl; 'ɔːdəbəl/ *adj* a sound that is audible is loud enough for you to hear it 聽得見的: *an audible sigh of relief* 聽得見的舒氣聲 | **barely audible** (=difficult to hear) 難以聽到的 *His voice was barely audible above the roar of the crowd.* 人聲嘈雜, 幾乎聽不見他的說話聲。—opposite 反義詞 INAUDIBLE —**audibly** *adv* —**audibility** /ˌɔdə`bɪlətɪ; ˌɔːdə'bɪləti/ *n* [U]

au·di·ence /`ɔdɪəns; 'ɔːdiəns/ *n* [C] **1** a group of people who watch and listen to someone speaking or performing in public 聽眾; 觀眾: *The audience began clapping and cheering.* 觀眾開始鼓掌歡呼。**2** the number or kind of people who regularly watch or listen to a particular programme〔某節目的〕固定觀眾[聽眾]（人數）: *The show attracts a regular audience of about 20 million.* 這個節目吸引了大約2,000萬固定觀眾收看。| **target audience** (=the kind of people that a programme, advertisement etc is supposed to attract)〔節目、廣告等〕針對的觀眾[聽眾] **3** a formal meeting with a very important person 謁見, 覲見, 正式拜會: *The princess was granted an audience with the Pope.* 公主獲准謁見教皇。

au·di·o /`ɔdɪˌo; 'ɔːdiəʊ/ *adj* [only before noun 僅用於名詞前] related to recording and broadcasting sound 音頻的, 聲頻的: *an audio signal* 聲頻信號

au·di·o·tape /`ɔdɪoˌtep; 'ɔːdiəʊteɪp/ *n* [C,U] *technical* a long thin band of MAGNETIC material used to record sound【術語】錄音磁帶

au·di·o·ty·pist /`ɔdɪoˌtaɪpɪst; 'ɔːdiəʊˌtaɪpɪst/ *n* [C] *BrE* someone whose job is to type letters that have been recorded【英】錄音打字員〔聽錄音打字的人員〕

au·di·o·vis·u·al /ˌɔdɪo`vɪʒuəl; ˌɔːdiəʊ'vɪʒuəl◂/ *adj* involving the use of recorded pictures and sound 視聽的; 視聽教學的: *audiovisual equipment* 視聽教學設備

au·dit /`ɔdɪt; 'ɔːdɪt/ *v* [T] **1** to officially examine a company's financial records in order to check that they are correct 查…的賬目, 審計, 稽查 **2** *AmE* to attend a university course without having to take any examinations【美】旁聽〔大學課程〕—**audit** *n* [C]: *the annual audit* 年度審計

au·di·tion¹ /ɔ`dɪʃən; ɔː'dɪʃən/ *n* [C] a short performance by an actor, singer etc that someone judges to decide if they are good enough to act in a play, sing in a concert etc〔面試時〕試聽, 試唱, 試演: *He failed the audition for the part of the prince.* 他試演王子的角色但失敗了。

audition² *v* [I,T] to perform in an audition or judge someone in an audition 進行試演[試唱]; 要求〔某人〕試演[試唱]: [+for] *She's auditioning for Ophelia in 'Hamlet'.* 她在試演《哈姆雷特》中的奧菲莉婭一角。| **audition sb (for)** *They auditioned over 2000 people for 'Grease'.* 他們安排了兩千多人為音樂劇《油脂》進行試演。

au·di·tor /`ɔdɪtɚ; 'ɔːdɪtə/ *n* [C] someone whose job is to officially examine a company's financial records 稽核員, 查賬員, 審計員

au·di·to·ri·um /ˌɔdə`torɪəm; ˌɔːdɪ'tɔːriəm/ *n* [C] **1** the part of a theatre where people sit when watching a play, concert etc 聽眾席; 觀眾席 **2** a large building used for concerts or public meetings 禮堂; 音樂廳

au·di·to·ry /`ɔdəˌtorɪ; 'ɔːdɪtəri/ *adj* [only before noun 僅用於名詞前] *technical* connected with the ability to hear【術語】聽覺的

au fait /ˌo `fe; əʊ 'feɪ/ *adj* **be au fait with** to be familiar with a system or way of doing something 精通; 熟悉: *I'm not really au fait with the computer system yet.* 我還沒有真正熟悉這套電腦系統。

Aug the written abbreviation of 縮寫= AUGUST

au·ger /`ɔgɚ; 'ɔːgə/ *n* [C] a tool used for making a hole in wood or in the ground 螺旋鑽, 鑽孔機

aught /ɔt; ɔːt/ *pron* **1** *old use* anything【舊】任何事物 **2 for aught I know/care** *old use* used when saying that something may be true but you are not sure or do not care about it【舊】據我所知/我才不管呢

aug·ment /ɔg`mɛnt; ɔːg'ment/ *v* [T] *formal* to increase the value, amount, effectiveness etc of something【正式】增大; 提高; 加強: *new taxes intended to augment government income* 旨在增加政府收入的新稅制

au·gur /`ɔgɚ; 'ɔːgə/ *v* [T] **1 augur well** *formal* to be a sign that something will be successful【正式】是好兆頭, 主吉: *His unfriendly manner did not augur well for our interview.* 他不友好的舉止預示着我們的會面不會有好結果。**2** *literary* to be a sign that a particular thing will happen in the future【文】預卜, 預示, 預言

au·gu·ry /`ɔgjərɪ; 'ɔːgjʊri/ *n* [C] *literary* a sign of what will happen in the future【文】前兆, 預兆, 徵兆

Au·gust /`ɔgəst; 'ɔːgəst/ *written abbreviation* 縮寫為 **Aug** *n* [C,U] the eighth month of the year, between July and September 八月: **in August** *The new offices open in August 2003.* 新辦事處於2003年8月開始辦公。| **last/next August** *I moved here last August.* 我去年八月搬到這裡。| **on August 6th** [also 又作 **on 6th August** *BrE* 英] *The new store opened on August 6th.* 新商店是8月6日開業的。

au·gust /ɔ`gʌst; ɔː'gʌst/ *adj literary* old, famous, and respected【文】威嚴的, 令人敬畏的, 莊嚴的

auk /ɔk; ɔːk/ *n* [C] a black and white seabird with short wings 海雀

au lait /o `le; əʊ 'leɪ/ *adj French* with milk【法】加牛奶的: *café au lait* 牛奶咖啡

Auld Lang Syne /ˌold læŋ `saɪn; ˌɔːld læŋ 'zaɪn/ a Scottish song that people sing when they celebrate the beginning of the new year at 12 o'clock (MIDNIGHT) on December 31st《過去的好時光》〔蘇格蘭民歌〕

aunt /ænt; ɑːnt/ *n* [C] **1** the sister of your father or mother, or the wife of your father's or mother's brother 姑母; 姨母; 嬸嬸; 伯母; 舅母: *Aunt Mary* 瑪麗姑媽 —see picture at 參見 FAMILY 圖 **2** a woman who is a friend of a small child's parents 阿姨, 大媽, 大娘 —see also 另見 AGONY AUNT

aunty, auntie /`æntɪ; 'ɑːnti/ *n* [C] *informal* aunt【非正式】阿姨, 大媽, 大娘

au pair /ˌo `pɛr; ˌəʊ 'peə/ *n* [C] a young woman who

stays with a family in a foreign country to learn the language and to look after their children 做換工的姑娘〔住在外國人家裡以學習外語並幫助做家務或照看孩子的女留學生〕

au·ra /ˋɔrə; ˈɔːrə/ [C] a quality or feeling that seems to surround or come from a person or a place 氣氛, 氣息, 韻味: **[+of]** *Hollywood still has an aura of glamour about it.* 荷里活的藝術氛圍仍然具有魅力。

au·ral /ˋɔrəl; ˈɔːrəl/ *adj* connected with the sense of hearing, or with someone's ability to understand a language 聽覺的, 聽力的 —**aurally** *adj*

au·re·ole /ˋɔrɪˌol; ˈɔːriəʊl/ *n* [C] *literary* a bright circle of light; HALO【文】光環, 光輪; 光暈

au re·voir /ˌo rəˋvwɑr; ˌəʊ rəˈvwɑː/ *interjection French* goodbye【法】再見, 再會

au·ri·cle /ˋɔrɪkl; ˈɔːrɪkəl/ *n* [C] one of the two spaces inside the top of your heart〔心臟的〕心房, 心耳

au·ro·ra bo·re·a·lis /əˌrɔrə bɔrɪˋælɪs; əˌrɔːrə bɔːriˈeɪlɪs/ *n* [singular] bands of moving light that you can see in the night sky in the far north; the NORTHERN LIGHTS 北極光

aus·pic·es /ˋɔspɪsɪz; ˈɔːspɪsɪz/ *n* [plural] **under the auspices of** *formal* with the help and support of a particular organization【正式】在…的資助下: *a relief project set up under the auspices of the United Nations* 由聯合國資助的救濟項目

aus·pi·cious /ɔˋspɪʃəs; ɔːˈspɪʃəs/ *adj formal* likely to be successful【正式】吉利的, 吉祥的: *It was an auspicious moment for a meeting between the heads of state.* 這正是兩國領導人會晤的大好時機。

Aus·sie /ˋɔsɪ; ˈɒzi/ *n* [C] *informal* someone from Australia【非正式】澳大利亞人, 澳洲人 —**Aussie** *adj*

aus·tere /ɔˋstɪr; ɔːˈstɪə/ *adj* **1** plain and simple and without any decoration 樸實的, 古樸的: *the austere grandeur of the old church* 簡樸莊嚴的古教堂 **2** someone who is austere is very strict and looks very serious 嚴肅的 **3** an austere way of life is very simple and has few things to make it comfortable or enjoyable 簡樸的, 艱苦的, 苦修的 —**austerely** *adv*

aus·ter·i·ty /ɔˋstɛrətɪ; ɔːˈsterɪti/ *n* [U] **1** the quality of being austere 樸實, 樸素, 艱苦 **2** bad economic conditions in which people do not have much money to spend〔經濟的〕緊縮, 節約: *a time of great austerity after the war* 戰後經濟緊縮時期

Aus·tra·la·sian /ˌɔstrəlˋeʒən; ˌɒstrəˈleɪʒən◂/ *adj* connected with Australasia 澳大拉[利]西亞〔包括澳大利亞、新西蘭及附近諸島〕的

Aus·tra·li·an /ɔˋstreljən; ; ɒˈstreɪliən/ *n* [C] someone from Australia 澳大利亞人, 澳洲人 —**Australian** *adj*: *Australian English* 澳大利亞英語

Aus·tri·an /ˋɔstrɪən; ˈɒstriən/ *n* [C] someone who is from Austria 奧地利人 —**Austrian** *adj*

Austro- /ɔstro; ɒstrəʊ/ *prefix* **1** Australian and 澳大利亞和…的: *Austro-Malayan* 澳大利亞－馬來的 **2** Austrian and 奧地利和…的: *Austro-Hungarian* 奧匈帝國的

au·tar·chy /ˋɔtɑrkɪ; ˈɔːtɑːki/ *n* [U] *formal* a system of government in which one person or group has unlimited power【正式】個人專制, 獨裁

au·tar·ky /ˋɔtɑrkɪ; ˈɔːtɑːki/ *n technical*【術語】**1** [U] an economic system in which a country produces all the things it needs as opposed to buying them from another country 自給自足(政策) **2** [C] a country that has this economic system 實行自給自足政策的國家

au·then·tic /ɔˋθɛntɪk; ɔːˈθentɪk/ *adj* **1** done or made in the traditional or original way 正宗的, 原汁原味的: *authentic Chinese food* 正宗的中國食品 **2** a painting, document, book etc that is authentic has been proved to be by a particular person 原作的, 真跡的, 原創的 **3** based on facts 可靠的, 真實的: *an authentic account* 真實可信的說法 —**authentically** /-klɪ; -kli/ *adv*

au·then·tic·ate /ɔˋθɛntɪˌket; ɔːˈθentɪkeɪt/ *v* [T] to prove that something is true or real 證明〔某物〕是真的, 鑑定…之真實性: *authenticated reports of human rights violations* 經證實的違反人權情況的報告 —**authentication** /ɔˌθɛntɪˋkeʃən; ɔːˌθentɪˈkeɪʃən/ *n* [U]

au·then·tic·i·ty /ˌɔθənˋtɪsətɪ; ˌɔːθenˈtɪsɪti/ *n* [U] the quality of being real or true 真實性, 確實性, 可靠性: *to establish the painting's authenticity* 鑑定這幅繪畫作品的真實性

au·thor¹ /ˋɔθɚ; ˈɔːθə/ *n* [C] **1** someone who writes books 作者, 作家, 著作人: *Jeffrey Archer, successful author and politician* 傑弗里·阿切爾, 成功的作家和政治家 | **the author** (=the person who wrote a particular book)〔某部書的〕作者 *It's clear that the author is a woman.* 顯然, 這部書的作者是位女性。**2** *formal* the person who starts a plan or idea【正式】〔計劃、主張的〕創始人, 發起者: *the author of the plan* 這個計劃的倡議者 2

author² *v* [T] to be the writer of a book, report etc 創作, 寫作

au·thor·ess /ˋɔθərɪs; ˈɔːθərɪs/ *n* [C] a woman who writes books 女作家, 女作者

au·thor·i·tar·i·an /əˌθɑrəˋtɛrɪən; ɔːˌθɒrɪˈteəriən◂/ *adj* strictly forcing people to obey a set of rules or laws that are often wrong or unfair 獨裁的, 專制的: *an authoritarian regime* 獨裁政權 | *a cruel and authoritarian father* 嚴酷專制的父親 —**authoritarian** *n* [C] —**authoritarianism** *n* [U]

au·thor·i·ta·tive /əˋθɑrəˌtetɪv; ɔːˈθɒrɪtətɪv/ *adj* **1** an authoritative book, account etc is respected because the person who wrote it knows a lot about the subject 權威性的, 可信的, 可靠的: *Lewis's authoritative account of the history of aviation* 路易斯對航空工業歷史的權威性敘述 **2** behaving or speaking in a confident determined way that makes people respect and obey you 權威的, 有威信的, 威嚴的 —**authoritatively** *adv*

au·thor·i·ty /əˋθɑrətɪ; ɔːˈθɒrɪti/ *n* 

1 ►POWER 權力◄ [U] the power you have because of your official position or because people respect your knowledge and experience 權力, 權威, 威信: *None of us questioned my father's authority.* 對於父親的權威, 我們誰都沒有質疑。| **the voice of authority** (=a way of speaking that makes people respect you) 權威的口氣 *Witten spoke with the voice of authority.* 威滕以權威的口氣說話。

2 the authorities the people or organizations that are in charge of a particular country or area 當局, 官方; 當權者: *British police are cooperating with the Malaysian authorities.* 英國警方正在和馬來西亞當局合作。

3 ►ORGANIZATION 組織◄ [C] an official organization or a local government department which controls public affairs, provides public services etc 公共事業機構: *the Brewer Transit Authority* 啤酒運輸部門 | **local authority** *BrE*【英】*You can claim housing benefit from the local authority.* 你可以向地方政府申請領取住房津貼。

4 I have it on good authority used to say that you are sure that something is true because you trust the person who told you about it 我完全相信

5 ►EXPERT 專家◄ [C] someone who knows a lot about a subject and whose knowledge and opinions are greatly respected 權威人士, 大師, 泰斗: **[+on]** *Professor Erikson is one of the world's leading authorities on tropical disease.* 埃里克森教授在熱帶疾病方面是世界權威之一。

6 ►PERMISSION 允許◄ [C,U] official permission to do something〔正式的〕許可, 授權: *Whose authority are you acting on?* 是誰授權你這樣做的?

au·thor·i·za·tion also 又作 **-isation** *BrE*【英】/ˌɔθərəˋzeʃən; ˌɔːθəraɪˈzeɪʃən/ *n* [C,U] official permission to do something, or the document giving this permission 授權(書), 許可(證): *You need special authorization to park here.* 在此停車要有特別的許可。

au·thor·ize also 又作 **-ise** *BrE*【英】/ˋɔθəˌraɪz; ˈɔːθəraɪz/ *v* [T] to give official or legal permission for something 授權, 批准, 許可, 委任: **authorize sb to do sth** *I'm not*

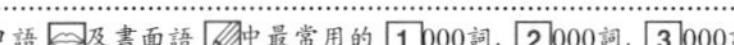

A

authorized to answer your questions. 我沒有得到授權回答你的問題。

authorized cap·i·tal /,··· '···/ *n* [U] the largest amount of money a company is allowed to get by selling shares (SHARE[2] (5)) 法定股本, 額定股本〔公司獲准發行的股份金額〕

Authorized Ver·sion /,··· '··/ *n* [singular] the English translation of the Bible made in England in 1611《聖經》欽定本

au·thor·ship /ˈɔθɚ,ʃɪp; ˈɔːθəʃɪp/ *n* [U] **1** the fact that you have written a particular book, document etc 原作者; 作者身分, 著作權: *There's no evidence to dispute his claim to authorship.* 沒有證據可以駁斥他提出的著作權。**2** *formal* the profession of writing books【正式】寫作職業

au·tis·m /ˈɔtɪzəm; ˈɔːtɪzəm/ *n* [U] a severe mental illness that affects children and prevents them from communicating with other people 孤獨症, 自閉症〔尤指兒童因大腦障礙而無法與人建立正常的人際關係〕—**autistic** /ɔˈtɪstɪk; ɔːˈtɪstɪk/ *adj*: *an autistic child* 患孤獨症的孩子

au·to /ˈɔto; ˈɔːtəʊ/ *adj AmE old-fashioned* connected with cars【美, 過時】汽車的: *the auto industry* 汽車工業

auto- /ɔtə; ɔːtəʊ/ *prefix* **1** of or by yourself 自己 (做) 的: *an autobiography* (=book about your own life, written by yourself) 自傳 **2** working by itself without human operation 自動的: *an autopump* 自汲唧筒

au·to·bi·og·ra·phy /,ɔtəbaɪˈɑgrəfɪ; ,ɔːtəbaɪˈɒgrəfi/ *n* **1** [C] the story of your life written by yourself 自傳 **2** [U] literature that is concerned with people writing about their own lives 自傳體文學 —**autobiographic** /,ɔtəbaɪəˈgræfɪk; ,ɔːtəbaɪəˈgræfɪk◂/ *adj* —**autobiographical** *adj* —**autobiographically** /-klɪ; -kli/ *adv* —compare 比較 BIOGRAPHY

au·toc·ra·cy /ɔˈtɑkrəsɪ; ɔːˈtɒkrəsi/ *n* **1** [U] a system of government in which one person or group has unlimited power 專制統治, 獨裁政體 **2** [C] a country governed in this way 專制[獨裁]國家

au·to·crat /ˈɔtə,kræt; ˈɔːtəkræt/ *n* [C] **1** someone who makes decisions and gives orders to people without asking them for their opinion 獨斷專行的人 **2** someone who has unlimited power to govern a country 獨裁者, 獨裁統治者 —**autocratic** /,ɔtəˈkrætɪk; ,ɔːtəˈkrætɪk◂/ *adj*: *his autocratic control of the White House staff* 他對白宮職員的專斷控制 —**autocratically** /-klɪ; -kli/ *adv*

au·to·cross /ˈɔtokrɔs; ˈɔːtəʊkrɒs/ *n* [U] *BrE* a sport in which cars race around a grass field【英】汽車越野賽

au·to·cue /ˈɔtokju; ˈɔːtəʊkjuː/ *n* [C] a machine that shows the words that someone must say while they are being filmed for a television programme〔電視的〕自動提示器, 電子提詞器

au·to·graph[1] /ˈɔtə,græf; ˈɔːtəgrɑːf/ *n* [C] a famous person's signature that they give to someone who admires them〔名人的〕親筆簽名: *Can I have your autograph?* 我可以要你的簽名嗎?

autograph[2] *v* [T] if a famous person autographs a book, photo etc, they sign it〔名人〕在…上親筆簽名

auto-im·mune dis·ease /,ɔtoɪmjun dɪˈziz; ,ɔːtəʊɪmjuːn dɪˈziːz/ *n* [U] a condition in which substances that normally prevent illness in the body, attack and harm parts of it instead 自身免疫病

au·to·mak·er /ˈɔto,mekɚ; ˈɔːtəʊ,meɪkə/ *n* [C] *AmE* a company that makes cars【美】汽車製造商: *US automakers* 美國汽車製造商

au·to·mat /ˈɔtə,mæt; ˈɔːtəmæt/ *n* [C] *trademark AmE* a restaurant where you put money in machines to get food【商標, 美】自助餐館〔用自動售貨機賣食物的快餐店〕

au·to·mate /ˈɔtə,met; ˈɔːtəmeɪt/ *v* [T] to change to a system where jobs are done or goods are produced by machines instead of people 使自動化

au·to·ma·ted /ˈɔtə,metɪd; ˈɔːtəmeɪtɪd/ *adj* using machines to do a job or industrial process 自動化的: *a highly automated factory* 高度自動化的工廠

au·to·mat·ic[1] /,ɔtəˈmætɪk; ,ɔːtəˈmætɪk◂/ *adj* **1** an automatic machine, car etc is designed to be operated in a simple way using only a few controls 自動的, 自動化的: *an automatic rifle* 自動步槍 | *an automatic time switch* 自動定時開關 **2** something that is automatic always happens as a result of something you have done, especially because of a rule or law 必然發生的: *Littering results in an automatic fine of $500.* 亂丟垃圾按規定要罰 500 美元。**3** done without thinking, especially because you have done the same thing many times before 不自覺的, 無意識的, 不假思索的: *It seems difficult to remember at first, but after a while it becomes automatic.* 起初記起來似乎很難, 但是過了一段時間就自然記住了。 3

automatic[2] *n* [C] **1** a weapon that can fire bullets continuously 自動武器 **2** a car with a system of gears (GEAR[1] (1)) that operate themselves without the driver needing to change them 自動汽車, 有自動變速器的汽車

au·to·mat·i·cally /,ɔtəˈmætɪklɪ; ,ɔːtəˈmætɪkli/ *adv* **1** without thinking about what you are doing 不假思索地, 無意識地: *"Of course," I replied automatically.* "當然了。"我不假思索地回答。**2** as the result of a situation 必然會發生地: *As a student you are automatically entitled to a grant.* 作為一名學生, 你自然有權得到助學金。**3** by the action of a machine, without a person making it work 自動地: *The doors opened automatically as we approached.* 我們走近時, 門自動開了。

automatic pi·lot /,···· '··/ *n* [C] a machine that flies a plane by itself without the need for a pilot〔飛機上的〕自動駕駛儀

automatic trans·mis·sion /,···· ·'··/ *n* [U] a system that operates the gears (GEAR[1] (1)) of a car without the driver needing to change them〔汽車的〕自動變速器

au·to·ma·tion /,ɔtəˈmeʃən; ,ɔːtəˈmeɪʃən/ *n* [U] the use of machines instead of people to do a job or industrial process 自動化 (操作)

au·tom·a·ton /ɔˈtɑmə,tɑn; ɔːˈtɒmətən/ *n* [C] **1** someone who seems to be unable to feel emotions 沒有感情的人 **2** a machine, especially one in the shape of a human, that moves without anyone controlling it 自動操作裝置, 機器人

au·to·mo·bile /ˈɔtəmə,bil; ˈɔːtəməbiːl/ *n* [C] *AmE* a car【美】汽車: *the automobile industry* 汽車工業

au·ton·o·mous /ɔˈtɑnəməs; ɔːˈtɒnəməs/ *adj* **1** having the power to govern a region, country etc without being controlled by anyone else〔地區、國家等〕自治的, 有自治權的: *an autonomous state* 自治州 **2** *formal* having the ability to work and make decisions by yourself without any help from anyone else【正式】有自立能力的, 自主的 —**autonomously** *adv*

au·ton·o·my /ɔˈtɑnəmɪ; ɔːˈtɒnəmi/ *n* [U] **1** freedom to govern a region, country etc without being controlled by anyone else 自治, 自治權: *a political system that allows a high degree of local autonomy* 允許地方有高度自治權的政治體制 **2** the ability to make your own decisions without being influenced by anyone else 自立能力, 自主能力: *the autonomy of the individual* 每個人的自主能力

au·to·pi·lot /ˈɔto,paɪlət; ˈɔːtəʊ,paɪlət/ *n* [C] AUTOMATIC PILOT〔飛機上的〕自動駕駛儀

au·top·sy /ˈɔtɑpsɪ; ˈɔːtɒpsi/ *n* [C] *especially AmE* an examination of a dead body to discover the cause of death【尤美】屍體剖檢, 驗屍; POSTMORTEM *BrE*【英】

au·to·sug·ges·tion /,ɔtosəgˈdʒɛstʃən; ,ɔːtəʊsəˈdʒestʃən/ *n* [U] *technical* the process of making someone believe or feel something, without them realizing that you are doing this【術語】自我暗示 (法)

au·tumn /ˈɔtəm; ˈɔːtəm/ also 又作 **fall** *AmE*【美】*n* [C, U] the season between summer and winter, when leaves change colour and the weather becomes slightly colder 秋天, 秋季: *autumn mists* 秋天的霧靄

au·tum·nal /ɔ`tʌmnḷ; ɔː'tʌmnəl/ *adj* connected with or typical of autumn 秋季的; (似) 秋天的: *autumnal colours* 秋天的色調

aux the written abbreviation of 縮寫= AUXILIARY, especially of 尤為 AUXILIARY VERB

aux·il·ia·ry¹ /ɔg`zɪljərɪ; ɔːg'ziljəri/ *adj* **1** auxiliary workers provide additional help for another group of workers, especially nurses or soldiers 輔助的: *an auxiliary nurse* 輔助的護理人員 | *auxiliary staff* 輔助員工 **2** an auxiliary motor, piece of equipment etc is kept ready to be used if the main one stops working properly 補充的; 備用的: *an auxiliary power supply* 備用的供電設備

auxiliary² *n* [C] **1** a worker who provides additional help for another group of workers, especially nurses or soldiers 輔助人員: *a nursing auxiliary* 護理輔助人員 **2** an auxiliary verb 助動詞: *a modal auxiliary* 情態助動詞

auxiliary verb /·,··· '·/ *n* [C] a verb that is used with another verb to show its tense, person (PERSON (6)), mood (MOOD (6)) etc. In English the auxiliary verbs are 'be', 'do', and 'have' (as in 'I am running', 'I didn't go', 'they have gone') and all the MODALs. 助動詞〔與另一個動詞連用表示動詞時態、人稱及語態的一種動詞, 在英語中為 be, do, have 以及所有情態動詞〕

AV an abbreviation of 縮寫= AUDIO VISUAL

a·vail¹ /ə`vel; ə'veɪl/ *n* **be to no avail/be of no avail** if something you do is to no avail or of no avail, you do not succeed in getting what you want 沒結果, 無效果: *We searched the whole area but all to no avail: Robbie had disappeared.* 我們搜遍了整個地方但毫無結果, 羅比失蹤了。

avail² *v* **avail yourself of** *formal* to accept an offer or use an opportunity to do something【正式】利用: *He availed himself of this privilege.* 他利用了這項特權。

[1] [1] **a·vail·a·ble** /ə`veləbḷ; ə'veɪləbəl/ *adj* **1** something that is available is able to be used or can easily be bought or found 可獲得的; 可用的: *Now available in paperback!* 現可以買到平裝本了! | *We've already used up all the available space.* 可用的空間我們都用上了。| [**+for**] *The university is trying to make more accommodation available for students.* 大學設法為學生提供更多的住處。| [**+to**] *an increase in the number of jobs available to women* 婦女就業機會的增加 | **readily/freely available** (=very easy to obtain by anyone) 容易得到的 *Drugs like crack are freely available.* 強效純可卡因一類的毒品隨處可以得到。| **every available** (=every one that you can get) 每個能找到的 *Every available ambulance was rushed to the scene of the accident.* 所有能找得到的救護車都迅速趕往出事地點。**2** [not before noun 不用於名詞前] someone who is available is not busy and has enough time to talk to you 有暇的, 可接待客人的: *The president was not available for comment.* 總統沒時間對此事發表評論。**3** someone who is available does not have a wife, BOYFRIEND etc, and therefore may want to start a new romantic relationship with someone else 未婚的; 未有伴侶的 —**availability** /ə,velə`bɪlətɪ; ə,veɪlə'bɪlɨti/ *n* [U]: *the availability of affordable housing* 人們買得起的住房供應

av·a·lanche /`ævḷ,æntʃ; 'ævəlɑːnʃ/ *n* [C] **1** a large mass of snow, ice, and rocks that falls down the side of a mountain 雪崩: *Two skiers were killed in the avalanche.* 有兩名滑雪者在雪崩中喪生。**2 an avalanche of** a very large number of things such as letters, messages etc that arrive suddenly at the same time 雪片般的, 大量的

av·ant-garde /,ævɑn `gɑrd; ,ævɔːŋ 'gɑːd◂/ *adj* **1** avant-garde music, literature etc is extremely modern and often seems strange or slightly shocking 前衛的, 先鋒派的: *an avant-garde play* 先鋒派話劇 **2 the avant-garde** the group of artists, writers, musicians etc who produce avant-garde books, paintings etc 前衛派〔畫家、作家、音樂家等〕: *a member of the avant-garde* 前衛派成員

av·a·rice /`ævərɪs; 'ævərɨs/ *n* [U] *formal* a desire to have a lot of money that is considered to be too strong; GREED【正式】貪得無厭, 貪婪 —**avaricious** /,ævə`rɪʃəs; ,ævə'rɪʃəs◂/ *adj* —**avariciously** *adv*

Ave the written abbreviation of 縮寫= AVENUE (1) 大街: *36, Rokesly Ave* 羅克士利大街36號

a·venge /ə`vɛndʒ; ə'vendʒ/ *v* [T] *literary* to do something to hurt or punish someone because they have harmed or offended you【文】報…之仇, 為…雪恥: *He wanted to avenge his brother's death.* 他要為弟弟的死復仇。—**avenger** *n* [C]

av·e·nue /`ævə,nu; 'ævɨnjuː/ *n* [C] **1 Fifth Avenue/Shaftesbury Avenue etc** used in the names of streets in a town or city 第五大街/莎夫茨伯里大街等 **2** a possible way of achieving something 方法, 途徑: *We explored every possible avenue, but couldn't find a solution.* 我們探討了所有可能的途徑, 但沒能找到解決辦法。**3** *BrE* a road or broad path between two rows of trees, especially one leading to a big house【英】〔通向房子的〕兩旁有樹的小路: *an avenue of chestnut trees* 兩側有栗子樹的小路 [3]

a·ver /ə`vɝ; ə'vɜː/ *v* [T] *formal* to say something firmly and strongly because you are sure that it is true【正式】斷言; 堅稱

av·e·rage¹ /`ævərɪdʒ; 'ævərɪdʒ/ *adj* **1** [only before noun 僅用於名詞前] the average amount is the amount you get when you add together several quantities and divide this by the total number of quantities 平均(數)的: *Average earnings in the state are about $1500 a month.* 這個國家的平均月收入約為1500美元。| *What's the average rainfall for July?* 七月份的平均降雨量為多少? | *an average speed of 200 kph* 平均時速200公里 **2** an average amount or quantity is not unusually big or small 中等的, 適中的: **(of) average height/build/intelligence etc** (=not tall or short, fat or thin etc) 中等個子/身材/智力等 *I'd say he was of average height.* 我會說他是中等身材。**3** having qualities that are typical of most people or things 平常的, 普通的: *The average student spends about two or three hours a night doing homework.* 一般學生每晚要花兩三個小時做作業。| *In an average week I drive about 250 miles.* 平常我每週開車250英里。**4** neither very good nor very bad 不好不壞的, 一般的: *There was nothing special about the film – it was just average.* 這部電影沒甚麼特別之處, 很一般。 [2] [2]

average² *n* **1** [C] the amount calculated by adding together several quantities, and then dividing this amount by the total number of quantities 平均數: *The average of 3, 8 and 10 is 7.* 3、8、10 的平均數為7。| *House prices have gone up by an average of 2%.* 房價平均上漲了2%。**2 on average** based on a calculation about how many times something usually happens, how much money someone usually gets, how often people usually do something etc 平均來看: *On average men smoke more cigarettes than women.* 平均來看男子比女子吸煙多。| *Japanese people on average live much longer than Europeans.* 日本人的平均壽命要比歐洲人長得多。**3** [C, U] the usual level or amount for most people or things in a group 平均水平: **above/below average** (=better or worse than average) 高於/低於平均水平 *Susie's school work is well above average.* 蘇茜的學業成績遠遠高於平均水平。| **the national average** *I suppose the national average is about £20,000 per year.* 我假定全國的平均水平是每年兩萬英鎊。—see also 另見 **law of averages** (LAW (11)) [2]

average³ *v* [linking verb 連繫動詞] **1** to usually do something or usually happen a particular number of times, or to usually be a particular size or amount 平均做; 平均是: *I suppose I average about five cups of coffee a day.* 我想我平均每天喝大約五杯咖啡。| *The fish averages about two inches in length.* 這些魚平均兩英寸長。**2** to calculate the average of figures 算出…的平均數

average out *phr v* **1** [T **average** sth ↔ **out**] to calculate the usual number of times that something happens, the usual size of something, or the average amount of a

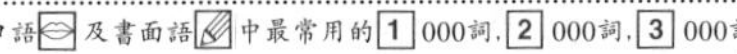

group of figures 算出…的平均數: *I averaged out the total increase at about 10%.* 我算出總增長為平均 10% 左右。**2** [linking verb 連繫動詞 **+to/at**] to usually result in a particular number or amount 達到平均量: *The weekly profits average out at about $1000.* 每週平均利潤達到 1,000 美元左右。

a·verse /ə`vɝs; ə'vɜːs/ *adj* **1 not be averse to** used to say that someone likes to do something sometimes, especially something that is slightly wrong or bad for them 並不反對; 不太討厭, 並非完全不喜歡: *I don't smoke cigarettes, but I'm not averse to the occasional cigar.* 我不吸煙, 但我不反對偶爾抽一支雪茄。**2 be averse to** *formal* to be unwilling to do something or to dislike something【正式】不願意做, 討厭做

a·ver·sion /ə`vɝʒən; ə'vɜːʃən/ *n* [singular,U] a strong dislike of something or someone 厭惡, 討厭, 反感: [**+to**] *Despite his aversion to publicity, Arnold was persuaded to talk to the press.* 儘管不喜歡張揚, 阿諾德還是被說服接受傳媒採訪。| **have an aversion to** *I have an aversion to housework.* 我討厭做家務。

a·vert /ə`vɝt; ə'vɜːt/ *v* [T] **1** to prevent something unpleasant from happening 防止, 避免: *The tragedy could have been averted if the crew had followed safety procedures.* 如果乘務人員按照安全規則操作, 這場悲劇本來是可以避免的。**2 avert your eyes/gaze etc** to look away from something that you do not want to see 轉移目光: *Lockwood averted his eyes as she undressed.* 洛克伍德在她脱衣時把目光轉移開。

a·vi·a·ry /`evɪˌɛrɪ; 'eɪviəri/ *n* [C] a large CAGE where birds are kept 大鳥籠, 鳥舍

a·vi·a·tion /ˌevɪ`eʃən; ˌeɪvi'eɪʃən/ *n* [U] **1** the science or practice of flying in aircraft 航空, 航空學, 飛行(術) **2** the industry that makes aircraft 航空工業

a·vi·a·tor /`evɪˌetɚ; 'eɪvieɪtə/ *n* [C] *old-fashioned* a pilot【過時】飛機駕駛員, 飛行員

av·id /`ævɪd; 'ævɪ̈d/ *adj* **avid reader/listener/fan etc** someone who does something, listens to something etc as much as they can 熱心的讀者/聽眾/發燒友等: *an avid collector of old jazz records* 爵士樂舊唱片的熱心收藏者

av·o·ca·do /ˌævə`kado; ˌævə'kɑːdəʊ◂/ also 又作 **avocado pear** /ˌ···· '·/ *n* [C] a fruit with a thick green or dark purple skin that is green inside and has a large seed in the middle 鱷梨, 牛油果

2 1 **a·void** /ə`vɔɪd; ə'vɔɪd/ *v* [T] **1** to do something to prevent something bad from happening 避免, 防止: *The other car swerved, trying to avoid a collision.* 另一輛車猛然轉彎, 以避免撞車。| **avoid doing sth** *This leaflet tells you how to avoid getting ill while travelling.* 這小冊子告訴你怎樣在旅行期間防止生病。**2** to deliberately stay away from someone or something 迴避, (故意)避開: *Jon was embarrassed and tried to avoid us the next day.* 喬恩很尷尬, 第二天設法躲着我們。| *I managed to avoid the worst of the traffic.* 我設法避開了最擁擠的車流。| **avoid sb/sth like the plague** (=stay away from someone or something completely, especially because they are very unpleasant) 像躲避瘟疫一樣地避開某人/某物 *I used to avoid that class like the plague.* 我曾經像躲瘟疫一樣避開那門課。**3** to deliberately not do something, especially because it is dangerous, unpleasant etc 逃避: *Loopholes are a way of legally avoiding taxes.* 鑽稅法的空子是合法逃稅的一種方法。| **avoid doing sth** *Organic gardeners try to avoid using pesticides.* 施有機肥的園丁設法不用殺蟲劑。

a·void·ance /ə`vɔɪdn̩s; ə'vɔɪdəns/ *n* [U] the act of avoiding someone or something 迴避, 避開, 避免: [**+of**] *the avoidance of issues such as domestic violence* 避免家庭暴力事件之類的問題 | **tax avoidance** (=legal ways of not paying tax) 避稅 *millions of dollars in lost revenue due to tax avoidance* 因避稅而損失了幾百萬美元的稅收

av·oir·du·pois /ˌævɚdə`pɔɪz; ˌævədə'pɔɪz/ *n* [U] the system of weighing things that uses the standard measures of the OUNCE (1), POUND[1] (1), and TON (1) 常衡〔以盎司、磅、噸為稱量標準的衡制〕—compare 比較 METRIC SYSTEM

a·vow /ə`vaʊ; ə'vaʊ/ *v* [T] *formal* to say or admit publicly something you believe or promise【正式】承認, 公開聲明: *He avowed his commitment to Marxist ideals.* 他承認信奉馬克思主義理想。—**avowal** *n* [C,U]: *an avowal of love* 公開表示愛慕

a·vowed /ə`vaʊd; ə'vaʊd/ *adj* [only before noun 僅用於名詞前] admitted or said publicly 承認的, 公開聲明的: *an avowed atheist* 公開的無神論者

a·vun·cu·lar /ə`vʌŋkjəlɚ; ə'vʌŋkjɪ̈lə/ *adj* being like an uncle; kind and concerned about someone who is younger 叔伯般的; 關心備至的: *an avuncular pat on the shoulder* 像叔伯般地輕拍肩膀 —**avuncularly** *adv*

a·wait /ə`wet; ə'weɪt/ *v* [T] *formal*【正式】**1** to wait for something 等待: *Several men are awaiting trial for robbery.* 幾個人因搶劫正在等待受審。**2** if a situation, event etc awaits you, it is going to happen in the future 將發生在…; 期待: *A terrible surprise awaited them at Mr Tumnus' house.* 在圖姆納斯先生家, 一件可怕的意外將降臨到他們頭上。—see 見 WAIT[1] (USAGE)

a·wake[1] /ə`wek; ə'weɪk/ *adj* [not before noun 不用於名 3
詞前] **1** not sleeping 醒着的: **be awake** *"Are you awake?" Julie whispered from the door.* "你醒了嗎?"朱莉在門口輕聲問。| *Les shook her awake.* 萊斯把她搖醒。| **wide awake** (=completely awake) 完全醒着, 沒有睡意 *The baby was wide awake at midnight.* 這個嬰兒在半夜還毫無睡意。| **keep sb awake** (=prevent someone from sleeping) 讓某人無法入睡 *The noise of the traffic kept me awake.* 交通噪音使我無法入睡。| **stay awake** *One of us ought to stay awake and keep watch.* 我們當中一個人應該醒着值夜。| **lie awake** *I lay awake worrying about my exams.* 我躺在牀上睡不着, 擔心考試的事。**2 be awake to** to understand a situation and its possible effects 注意到, 意識到: *The company is awake to the potential of these ideas.* 公司注意到了這些意見的潛在作用。

awake[2] *v past tense* **awoke** /ə`wok; ə'wəʊk/ *past participle* **awoken** /ə`wokən; ə'wəʊken/ [I,T] **1** to wake up, or to make someone wake up (使)醒來, 喚醒: *The child awoke and began to cry.* 孩子醒來後就開始哭。**2** if something awakes an emotion or if an emotion awakes, you suddenly begin to feel that emotion 喚起, 激發起: *A dull resentment awoke within him.* 他內心突然感到一種隱約的忿恨情緒。

awake sb ↔ **to** sth *phr v* [T] to make someone understand a situation and its possible effects 使領悟, 使醒悟; 意識到: *Artists finally awoke to the aesthetic possibilities of photography.* 畫家終於領悟了攝影的美學潛在價值。

a·wak·en /ə`wekən; ə'weɪkən/ *v formal*【正式】**1** [T] if something awakens an emotion, it makes you suddenly begin to feel that emotion 激發起, 喚起: *We need to awaken a new faith in the hearts of non-believers.* 我們需要喚起無信仰者內心的一種新的信念。**2** [I,T] to wake up or to make someone wake up (使)醒來, 吵醒: *The noise outside awakened him.* 外面的噪音吵醒了他。

awaken sb ↔ **to** sth *phr v* [T] to make someone understand a situation and its possible effects 使領悟, 使醒悟; 使意識到: *We must awaken people to the danger to the environment.* 我們必須讓人們意識到對環境造成的危害。

a·wak·en·ing /ə`wekənɪŋ; ə'weɪkənɪŋ/ *n* [C] **1** an occasion when you suddenly realize that you understand something or feel something 醒, 覺醒, 醒悟: *the adolescent's sexual awakening* 青春期的性萌動 | **rude awakening** (=an occasion when you suddenly realize that something is not true or is unpleasant) 猛然覺醒 *Anyone who thinks marriage will be bliss forever is in for a rude awakening.* 認為婚姻會是永遠幸福的人都會

猛然覺醒。**2** the act of waking from sleep 醒來

2 1 **a·ward[1]** /əˋwɔrd; əˈwɔːd/ *n* [C] **1** something such as a prize or money given to someone to reward them for something they have done 獎, 獎賞, 獎金, 獎品: *Meryl Streep won the best actress award.* 梅麗史翠普獲最佳女演員獎。**2** something, especially money, that is officially given to someone as a payment or judgment 報酬, 薪水, 工資: *The nurses' pay award was not nearly as much as they had expected.* 護士的工資遠沒有預想的那麼多。

3 **award[2]** *v* [T] **1** to officially give someone something such as a prize or money to reward them for something they have done 給予, 授予: **be awarded sth** *Einstein was awarded the Nobel Prize for his work in quantum physics.* 愛因斯坦因在量子物理學方面的成就獲諾貝爾獎。| **award sb sth** *The university awarded her a scholarship.* 大學給她頒發獎學金。**2** to officially decide that someone should receive a payment or judgment 判給, 裁定: **be awarded sth** *After seven years of litigation, he was awarded $750,000 compensation.* 經過七年的訴訟, 他終於獲得七十五萬美元的賠償。| **award sb sth** *Management have awarded all factory employees a 5% pay rise.* 資方給所有員工加薪5%。

1 1 **a·ware** /əˋwɛr; əˈweə/ *adj* [not before noun 不用於名詞前] **1** if you are aware that something such as a problem or a dangerous situation exists, you realize that it exists 意識到的, 明白的, 知道的: **aware that** *Were you aware that your son was having difficulties at school?* 你知道你兒子在學校學習有困難嗎? | **[+of]** *Most smokers are perfectly aware of the dangers of smoking.* 大多數吸煙者完全知道吸煙的危害。| **make sb aware of sth** *It's time someone made him aware of the effects of his actions.* 該有人讓他意識到他所作所為造成的後果了。| **not that I'm aware of** *spoken*【口】*"Does she have any problems with her marriage?" "Not that I'm aware of."* "她的婚姻出現了問題嗎?" "據我所知沒有。" | **well/acutely aware** (=very aware) 完全/敏鋭地知道 *Sara was well aware of Francesca's fear of heights.* 莎拉完全知道弗朗西斯卡有畏高症。**2** if you are aware of something, you notice it, especially because you can see, hear, or smell it 意識到的, 注意到的, 察覺到的: **aware that** *I gradually became aware that there was someone else in the room.* 我逐漸意識到房間裡還有別人在場。| **[+of]** *He was aware of a faint smell of gas.* 他察覺到隱約有一股煤氣味。**3** understanding a lot about what is happening around you and paying attention to it, especially because you realize possible dangers and problems 有…意識的: **politically/socially/environmentally etc aware** *Nowadays everyone's much more environmentally aware.* 如今, 大家的環境意識強多了。**4 so/as far as I am aware** *spoken* used when you want to emphasize that there may be things that you do not know about a situation【口】就我所知: *So far as I'm aware this is the first time a British rider has won the competition.* 就我所知, 這是英國騎師第一次贏得這項競賽。

3 **a·ware·ness** /əˋwɛrnɪs; əˈweənɪ̌s/ *n* [U] **1** knowledge or understanding of a particular subject or situation 意識: *political awareness* 政治意識 | **raise awareness** (=improve people's knowledge) 提高認識 *Health officials have tried to raise awareness about AIDS among teenagers.* 衛生部門官員一直在努力提高青少年對愛滋病的認識。**2** the ability to notice something using your senses 感悟能力: **[+of]** *an artist's awareness of light and color* 畫家對光和顏色的感悟能力

a·wash /əˋwɑʃ; əˈwɒʃ/ *adj* [not before noun 不用於名詞前] **1** covered with water or another liquid 被水或其他液體淹沒的 **2** containing too many things or people of a particular kind 充斥的, 泛濫的: **[+with]** *TV nowadays is awash with soap operas.* 如今的電視充斥着肥皂劇。

1 1 **a·way[1]** /əˋwe; əˈweɪ/ *adv* **1** to or at a distance from someone or something 離開; 距離…: *Go away!* 走開! | *Dinah was crying as she drove slowly away.* 黛娜一面慢慢地把車開走一面在哭。| **[+from]** *The police tried to keep people away from the accident.* 警察設法阻止人們走近事故現場。| **turn/look away (from sb/sth)** (=turn so that you are not looking at someone or something) 移開視線 **2** if someone is away from school, work or home they are not there 不在〔上班、上學等〕: **[+from]** *You must bring a note from your parents if you've been away from school.* 缺了課必須補交家長的便條。| **away with flu/measles/a cold etc** (=not at school, work etc because you are ill) 由於患了流感/麻疹/感冒等病缺勤 **3 3 miles/5 kilometres etc away** at a distance of 3 miles, 5 kilometres etc from someone or something 離…三英里/五公里等: *Geneva is about 20 miles away.* 日內瓦離這兒大約20英里遠。**4 2 days/3 weeks etc away** if an event is 2 days, 3 weeks etc away, it will happen after 2 days etc have passed 離…還有兩天/三週等: *Christmas is only a month away.* 再過一個月就是聖誕節了。| *We live minutes away from the sea.* (=it only takes minutes to get there) 我們住的地方離海邊只有幾分鐘的路。**5** into a safe or enclosed place 放到〔一個安全的地方〕, 放進: *Put your money away, I'm paying.* 把你的錢收起來, 我來付。**6** so as to be gone or used up 消失; 用完: *The music died away.* 音樂聲消失了。| *The farm was swept away in the flood.* 農場被洪水沖垮了。| *Ruben gave all his money away to charity.* 魯賓把所有的錢都送給了慈善機構。| *Support for the Democrats has dropped away.* 支持民主黨的人已經減少了。| *The young lovers danced the night away.* (=danced all night) 這對年輕情侶跳舞跳了一整夜。| *Cut away all the dead wood.* 把所有的枯木都砍掉。**7** used to emphasize a continuous action 一直, 繼續不斷地: *Sue was singing away to herself in the bath.* 蘇在浴室裡一直唱着歌。| *They've been hammering away all day.* 他們整天都在不停地用錘子敲打東西。**8** if a team is playing away, it is playing a game at its opponent's sports field, STADIUM etc 在客場〔比賽〕: *Liverpool are playing away at Everton on Saturday.* 利物浦隊星期六在埃弗頓客場進行比賽。**9 away with sb/sth!** *literary* used to tell someone to take someone or something away【文】把某人/某物帶走!: *Away with the prisoner!* 把囚犯帶走! **10 be away** *ScotE* to go or leave a place【蘇格蘭】走, 離開: *He's just away to the shops.* 他剛走, 去商店了。| *We're away tomorrow.* (=we're leaving tomorrow) 我們明天走。—see also 另見 **far and away** (FAR[1] (9)), **right away** (RIGHT[2] (2))

away[2] *adj* [only before noun 僅用於名詞前] an away game or match is played at your opponent's field or sports hall〔比賽〕客場的, 在對方場地進行的 —opposite 反義詞 HOME[3] (4)

awe[1] /ɔ; ɔː/ *n* [U] **1** a feeling of great respect and admiration for someone or something 敬畏, 畏怯: **with awe/in awe** *Kate gazed at the mountains with awe.* 凱特敬畏地注視着羣山。| **fill sb with awe** *The sight of so many jewels in one place filled them with awe.* 一個地方有這麼多珠寶, 使他們大為驚嘆。**2 be/stand in awe of sb** to have great respect and admiration for and sometimes a slight fear of someone 對某人非常敬畏: *Because of his reputation as a dancer we were all rather in awe of him.* 他作為一個舞蹈家非常有名望, 所以我們對他非常敬畏。

awe[2] *v* [T usually singular 一般用單數] *formal* if you are awed by someone or something, you feel great respect and admiration for them, and are often slightly afraid of them【正式】使敬畏; 使畏懼: *The girls were awed by the splendor of the cathedral.* 那些女孩對大教堂的壯觀景象大為驚嘆。—**awed** *adj*: *an awed silence* 出於敬畏的沉默

awe-in·spir·ing /ˈ· ·,··/ *adj* extremely impressive in a way that makes you feel great respect and admiration 令人敬畏的, 令人欽佩的: *a truly awe-inspiring achievement* 真正令人敬佩的成就

awe·some /ˋɔsəm; ˈɔːsəm/ *adj* **1** extremely impressive,

serious, or difficult so that you feel great admiration, worry, or fear 令人畏懼的, 可怕的: *an awesome responsibility* 一項令人驚懼的責任 | *the awesome sweep of the scenery* 令人嘆為觀止的景色 **2** *AmE informal* very good【美, 非正式】很好的, 了不起的: *Their last concert was really awesome.* 他們最後的那場音樂會真不錯。—**awesomely** *adv*

awe·strick·en /ˈ· ˌ··/ *adj* = AWESTRUCK

awe·struck /ˈɔˌstrʌk; ˈɔːstrʌk/ *adj* feeling extremely impressed by the importance, difficulty, or seriousness of someone or something 肅然起敬的, 充滿敬畏的; 感到驚懼的: *She gazed awestruck at the jewels.* 她充滿驚奇地注視着那些珠寶。

1 **aw·ful¹** /ˈɔfl; ˈɔːfəl/ *adj* **1** very bad or unpleasant 糟糕的, 惡劣的, 難受的: *The weather was awful.* 天氣很糟糕。| *a really awful book* 十分差劣的書 | *These canned apricots taste awful!* 這些罐頭杏真難吃! | *I felt awful about not being able to help.* 我幫不上忙, 心裡好難受。**2** [only before noun 僅用於名詞前] *spoken* used to emphasize how much or how good, bad etc something is【口】非常: **an awful lot** (=a very large amount) 非常多的 *I have an awful lot of work to do this week.* 這星期我有一大堆工作要做。| *It made him look an awful fool.* 這使他看起來像個大笨蛋。**3 look/feel awful** to look or feel ill 看上去/感覺像生病了: *You look awful – what's wrong with you?* 你看上去臉色不好, 出甚麼事了? **4** *literary* making you feel great admiration or fear【文】令人敬畏的 —**awfulness** *n* [U]

awful² *adv* [+adj/adv] *AmE spoken* very【美口】非常: *That kid's awful cute, with her red curls.* 那孩子一頭紅鬈髮, 十分可愛。

aw·ful·ly /ˈɔflɪ; ˈɔːfəli/ *adv spoken* very【口】非常: *It's awfully cold in here. Is the heater on?* 這兒非常冷, 取暖器開了嗎?

a·while /əˈhwaɪl; əˈwaɪl/ *adv especially literary* for a short time【尤文】暫時, 片刻

2 **awk·ward** /ˈɔkwəd; ˈɔːkwəd/ *adj* **1** making you feel so embarrassed that you are not sure what to do or say 尷尬的, 為難的: *The more she tried to get out of the situation, the more awkward it became.* 她越是想擺脱困境, 越變得不知所措。| *an awkward pause* 令人尷尬的短暫沉默 | **make things awkward** (=cause trouble and make a situation very difficult) 使事情變得難辦, 使情況變得棘手 *She could make things very awkward if she wanted to.* 如果她想那樣做, 她會把事情弄得很難辦。**2** not convenient 不方便的: *I'm sorry, have I called at an awkward time?* 對不起, 我的電話打得是否不是時候? **3** moving or behaving in a way that does not seem relaxed or comfortable, especially because you feel nervous or embarrassed 笨拙的, 不靈活的; 彆扭的: *I felt a bit awkward on my first day there, but I soon settled in.* 我第一天到那兒感到有點彆扭, 但很快就習慣了。| *an awkward wave* 笨拙的揮手動作 | *an awkward teenager* 不靈巧的少年 **4** difficult to use or handle 難用的, 不好操作的: *The camera has a lot of small buttons, which makes it rather awkward to use.* 那照相機有許多小按鈕, 用起來不大方便。**5** an awkward person is deliberately unhelpful 難相處的, 不好應付的: **[+about]** *I wish you'd stop being so bloody awkward about everything.* 我希望你不要再處處與人為難。| **an awkward customer** (=someone who is difficult to deal with) 難侍候的顧客 —**awkwardly** *adv*: *"Are you the head tutor ..." she began awkwardly.* "你是校長嗎..." 她有些不好意思地問。—**awkwardness** *n* [U]

awl /ɔl; ɔːl/ *n* [C] a pointed tool for making holes in leather〔在皮革上鑽孔用的〕鑽子, 錐子

aw·ning /ˈɔnɪŋ; ˈɔːnɪŋ/ *n* [C] a sheet of material outside a shop, tent etc to keep off the sun or the rain 篷, (帆)布篷

a·woke /əˈwok; əˈwəʊk/ the past tense of AWAKE

a·wok·en /əˈwokən; əˈwəʊkən/ the past participle of AWAKE

AWOL /ˌe ˌdʌblju o ˈɛl; ˌeɪ ˌdʌbəljuː əʊ ˈel/ *adj* absent without leave; absent from your army group without permission 擅離職守的: **go AWOL** *Two soldiers had gone AWOL the night before.* 前一晚, 有兩個士兵擅離職守。

a·wry /əˈraɪ; əˈraɪ/ *adj* **1 go awry** if something goes awry, it does not happen in the way that was planned 出岔子, 走樣的, 違背正道的: *My carefully laid plans had already gone awry.* 我精心設計的計劃已經出了岔子。**2** not in the correct position 歪的: *He rushed out, hat awry.* 他匆忙出去, 帽子都戴歪了。

aw shucks /ˌɔ ˈʃʌks; ˌɔː ˈʃʌks/ *interjection AmE* used in a joking way to show that you feel embarrassed or sad【美】羞怯的, 難為情的

axe¹ also 又作 **ax** *AmE*【美】/æks; æks/ *n* [C] **1** a tool with a heavy metal blade on the end of a long handle, used to cut down trees or split pieces of wood 斧頭, 長柄斧 **2 give sb the axe** *informal* to dismiss someone from their job【非正式】解雇[開除]某人 **3 give sth the axe** *informal* to get rid of something such as a plan, a system, or a service【非正式】砍掉[取消]某事物 **4 have an axe to grind** to do or say something again and again because you want to persuade people to accept your ideas or beliefs 別有企圖, 另有打算: *I have no political axe to grind.* 我沒有甚麼政治企圖。

axe² also 又作 **ax** *AmE*【美】*v* [T] *informal*【非正式】**1** to suddenly dismiss someone from their job 突然解雇, 突然開除: *plans to axe half the workforce* 裁員一半的計劃 **2** to get rid of a plan, system, or service, or reduce the amount of money that is spent on something 砍掉, 取消, 廢止: *Student grants have been axed.* 學生助學金被取消了。

ax·i·om /ˈæksɪəm; ˈæksiəm/ *n* [C] *formal* a rule or principle that is generally considered to be true【正式】公理, 規律, 原則, 原理

ax·i·o·mat·ic /ˌæksɪəˈmætɪk; ˌæksiəˈmætɪk◂/ *adj formal* not needing to be proved because you can easily see that it is true; SELF-EVIDENT【正式】公理的, 不需證明的, 不言自明的 —**axiomatically** /-klɪ; -kli/ *adv*

ax·is /ˈæksɪs; ˈæksɪ̥s/ *n plural* **axes** /-siz; -siːz/ [C] *technical*【術語】**1** the imaginary line around which a large round object, such as the Earth, turns 軸, 軸線: *The Earth rotates on an axis between the North and South Poles.* 地球繞着南北兩極之間的地軸自轉。—see picture at 參見 EARTH¹ 圖 **2** a line drawn across the middle of a regular shape that divides it into two equal parts〔將規則形狀平分成相等的兩部分的〕中心線 **3** either of the two lines of a GRAPH, by which the positions of points are measured 參考軸線, 基準線, 坐標軸

ax·le /ˈæksḷ; ˈæksəl/ *n* [C] the bar connecting two wheels on a car or other vehicle 輪軸, 車軸 —see picture at 參見 BICYCLE¹ 圖

ay·ah /ˈaɪə; ˈaɪə/ *n* [C] *IndE, PakE* a nurse who looks after children【印, 巴】保姆, 女傭

a·ya·tol·lah /ˌaɪəˈtolə; ˌaɪəˈtɒlə/ *n* [C] a religious leader of the Shiite Muslims, especially a very powerful one 阿亞圖拉〔伊斯蘭什葉派宗教領袖〕

aye¹ /aɪ; aɪ/ *adv* **1** used to say yes when voting 是! 贊成! 對!〔用於表決時〕: **the ayes have it** (=used to say that most people in a meeting have voted in favour of something) 贊成者佔多數 —opposite 反義詞 NAY **2** *dialect* a word meaning yes, used especially in Scotland【方言】是! 對! 同意!〔尤用於蘇格蘭〕

aye² /e; eɪ/ *adv ScotE old use or poetic* always【蘇格蘭, 舊或詩】永遠地, 永久地, 永恆地

az·ure /ˈæʒə; ˈæʒə/ *adj* having a bright blue colour like the sky 天藍色的, 蔚藍的 —**azure** *n* [U]

B, b

B

B, b /bi; biː/ *plural* **B's, b's** *n* [C] the second letter of the English alphabet 英語字母表的第二個字母

B *n* **1 a)** the seventh note in the musical SCALE[1] (8) of C major B 音〔C 大調音階中的第七個音〕 **b)** the musical KEY[2] (4) based on this note B 調 **2** a mark given to a student's work, to show that it is good but not excellent B 級, 乙級, 乙等〔表示學業成績良好〕: *I got a B in History.* 我歷史得了個 B。—see also 另見 B-MOVIE, B-SIDE

b the written abbreviation of 縮寫= born: *Andrew Lanham, b 1885* 安德魯·拉納姆, 生於1885年

B & B /ˌbi ənd ˋbi; ˌbiː ənd ˈbiː/ the written abbreviation of 縮寫= BED AND BREAKFAST

BA /ˌbi ˋe; ˌbiː ˈeɪ/ *n* [C] Bachelor of Arts; the title of a first university degree in a subject such as literature, history etc 文學士: *Susan Potter, BA* 蘇姍·波特, 文學士 —compare 比較 BSC

baa /bɑ; bɑː/ *v* [I] to make a sound like a sheep 咩〔發出羊叫聲〕—**baa** *n* [C]

bab·ble¹ /ˋbæbḷ; ˈbæbəl/ *v* **1** [I,T] to speak quickly in a way that is difficult to understand or sounds silly 含糊不清地說; 嘮嘮叨叨: *I have no idea what he was babbling on about.* 我根本不知道他在嘮叨些甚麼。**2** [I] to make a sound like water moving over stones 發出潺潺流水聲 —**babbler** *n* [C]

babble² *n* [singular] **1** the confused sound of many people talking at the same time 嘈雜的說話聲: *the babble of a crowded party* 聚會上人羣唧唧喳喳的說話聲 **2** a sound like water moving over stones 潺潺聲

babe /beb; beɪb/ *n* **1** *literary* a baby【文】嬰兒: **babe in arms** (=one that has to be carried) 懷裡的嬰兒 **2** a word for an attractive young woman 寶貝兒〔用於稱呼年輕貌美的女子〕 **3** a way of speaking to a young woman, often considered offensive 小妞〔對年輕女子的稱謂, 通常被認為具有冒犯性〕 **4** a way of speaking to someone you love, especially your wife or husband 親愛的〔對自己的愛人, 尤指對妻子或丈夫的稱呼〕 **5 babe in the woods** *AmE* someone who can be easily deceived【美】容易上當受騙的人: *He was like a babe in the woods when he first came to New York.* 剛到紐約時, 他經常上當受騙。

ba·bel /ˋbebḷ; ˈbeɪbəl/ *n* [singular,U] the confusing sound of many voices talking together 嘈雜聲: *a babel of French and Italian* 有人說法語、有人說意大利語的混雜聲

ba·boon /bæˋbun; bəˈbuːn/ *n* [C] a large monkey that lives in Africa and South Asia 狒狒〔產於非洲和南亞〕

ba·bu, baboo /ˋbɑbu; ˈbɑːbuː/ *n* [C] **1** *IndE old-fashioned* an Indian title of respect【印, 過時】巴布〔印度人的尊稱〕 **2** *BrE* an Indian CLERK or government official of low rank【英】〔印度人〕書記員

1 1 **ba·by** /ˋbebɪ; ˈbeɪbi/ *n plural* **babies** [C]

1►CHILD 兒童◄ a very young child who has not yet learned to speak or walk 嬰兒: *A baby was crying upstairs.* 樓上有嬰兒在哭。| *They have a five-year-old boy and a baby girl.* 他們有一個五歲的男孩和一個出生不久的女孩。| **have a baby** (=give birth to a baby) 生孩子 *I think she had the baby in June.* 我認為她是六月份生孩子的。| **be expecting a baby** (=have a baby developing inside your body) 有孕 —see 見 CHILD (USAGE)

2►ANIMAL/PLANT 動物/植物◄ a very young animal or plant 幼獸; 雛鳥; 幼苗: *baby birds* 雛鳥 | *baby carrots* 胡蘿蔔苗

3►BROTHER/SISTER 兄弟/姐妹◄ a younger child in a family, often the youngest〔兄弟姐妹中〕年紀最小的一個: *He's the baby of the family.* 他在家裡年紀最小。

4►WOMAN 女人◄ *AmE spoken*【美口】**a)** a way of speaking to someone that you love 親愛的〔用於稱呼愛人〕: *Mike baby, could you get me a glass of water?* 親愛的邁克, 你能給我拿杯水來嗎? **b)** a way of speaking to a young woman, often considered offensive 小妞〔對年輕女子的稱呼, 通常被認為具有冒犯性〕

5►SILLY 傻的◄ someone who is not behaving in a sensible way 幼稚的人: *Don't be such a baby – take your medicine!* 別這麼孩子氣 —— 吃藥吧!

6►RESPONSIBILITY 責任◄ *informal* something special that someone has developed or is responsible for【非正式】差事, 任務, 分內之事: *Don't ask me about the building contract – that's Robert's baby.* 不要問我關於建築合同的事 —— 那是羅伯特管的。

baby blues /ˈ·· ·/ *n* [plural] *informal* a feeling of DEPRESSION (1a) that some women suffer from after they have had a baby【非正式】產後憂鬱症: *an attack of the baby blues* 患上產後憂鬱症

baby boom·er /ˈ·· ˌ··/ *n* [C] someone born during a period when a lot of babies were born, especially between 1946 and 1964〔尤指 1946 年至 1964 年間〕生育高峯期出生的人

baby car·riage /ˈ·· ˌ··/ *n* [C] *AmE* a thing like a small bed with four wheels, used for taking a baby from one place to another【美】手推嬰兒車, 嬰兒推車; PRAM *BrE*【英】—compare 比較 PUSHCHAIR —see picture at 參見 PRAM 圖

baby-faced /ˈ·· ·/ *adj* a baby-faced adult has a face like a child 娃娃臉的

Ba·by·gro /ˋbebɪˌgro; ˈbeɪbigrəʊ/ *n* [C] *BrE trademark* a piece of clothing for a baby, that covers their whole body【英, 商標】〔嬰兒穿的〕連身服

ba·by·hood /ˋbebɪˌhud; ˈbeɪbihʊd/ *n* [U] the period of time when you are a baby 嬰兒期, 幼兒期

ba·by·ish /ˋbebɪ-ɪʃ; ˈbeɪbi-ɪʃ/ *adj* like a baby or suitable for a baby 嬰兒似的, 孩子氣的: *The games were a little babyish for nine-year-olds.* 這些遊戲對九歲的孩子來說太容易了一點。

baby milk /ˈ·· ·/ *n* [U] *BrE* dried milk mixed with water and fed to babies instead of breast milk【英】〔用以替代母乳的〕嬰兒奶粉; FORMULA (5) *AmE*【美】

ba·by·sit /ˋbebɪˌsɪt; ˈbeɪbisɪt/ *v past tense and past participle* **babysat** /-ˌsæt; -sæt/ *present participle* **babysitting** [I,T] to take care of children while their parents are away for a short time〔臨時受雇代外出的父母〕照料(小孩) —**babysitting** *n* [U]: *She earns some extra cash from babysitting.* 她幫人家照看孩子掙些額外收入。| *a babysitting service* 照看孩子的服務

ba·by·sitter /ˋbebɪˌsɪtɚ; ˈbeɪbiˌsɪtə/ *n* [C] **1** someone who takes care of children while their parents are away for a short time〔代外出的父母照料小孩的〕臨時保姆 **2** *AmE* someone who is paid to look after children while their parents are at work【美】保姆, 靠照看小孩為生的人; CHILDMINDER *BrE*【英】

baby talk /ˈ·· ·/ *n* [U] sounds or words that babies use when they are learning to talk 兒語, 嬰兒牙牙學語聲

baby tooth /ˈ·· ·/ *n plural* **baby teeth** [C] a tooth from the first set of teeth that young children have 乳牙; MILK TOOTH *BrE*【英】

baby walk·er /ˈ·· ˌ··/ *n* [C] a frame on wheels that is used to support a baby while it is learning to walk〔幼兒〕學步車

bac·ca·lau·re·ate /ˌbækəˋlɔrɪət; ˌbækəˈlɔːriət/ *n* [C] the last examination you take in French schools and some international schools〔法國和一些國際學校的〕中學畢業考試

bac·ca·rat /ˌbækəˋrɑ; ˈbækərɑː/ *n* [U] a card game usually played for money 巴卡拉紙牌遊戲〔一種賭博方式〕

bac·cha·na·li·an /ˌbækəˋnelɪən; ˌbækəˈneɪliən◂/ *adj literary* a bacchanalian party, celebration etc involves alcohol, sex, and uncontrolled behaviour【文】狂飲作樂的: *a bacchanalian orgy* 狂飲作樂的鬧宴

B

bac·cy /ˋbækɪ; ˈbæki/ *n* [U] *slang* tobacco【俚】煙草

bach /bætʃ; bætʃ/ *v* **bach it** *AmE old-fashioned* if a man baches it, he lives on his own and looks after himself【美, 過時】〔男子〕過單身生活

bach·e·lor /ˋbætʃələ; ˈbætʃələ/ *n* [C] a man who has never been married 未婚男子, 單身漢: **confirmed bachelor** (=a man who intends never to marry) 決定終身不結婚的男子, 決心當一輩子光棍的人 | **eligible bachelor** (=a rich young man who has not yet married) 條件不錯的未婚男子

bachelor flat /ˈ··· ˌ·/ *n* [C] a set of rooms where an unmarried man lives 單身男子公寓

bachelor par·ty /ˈ··· ˌ··/ *n* [C] *AmE* a party for men only, especially the night before a man's wedding【美】〔尤指在某男子結婚前一晚舉行的〕單身漢聚會; STAG NIGHT *BrE*【英】

bachelor's de·gree /ˈ··· ·ˌ·/ *n* [C] the first level of university degree; BA 學士學位

ba·cil·lus /bəˋsɪləs; bəˈsɪləs/ *n plural* **bacilli** /-laɪ; -laɪ/ [C] *technical* a rod-shaped BACTERIA, of which some types cause diseases【術語】桿菌, 病菌

S1 W1 **back**[1] /bæk; bæk/ *adv*

1 ►RETURN 回原處◄ in or into the place or position where someone or something was before 回到原處; 恢復原狀: *Freddie was supposed to be back at the hotel by six.* 弗雷迪應該在六點鐘前回到旅館。| *Put that book back where you found it!* 把那本書放回原處! | *"We'd better go back," she said regretfully.* "我們最好回去。"她懊悔地說。—see graph at 參見 RETURN[1] 圖表

2 ►AS BEFORE 如前◄ in or into the condition that someone or something was in before 恢復原來的狀態: *I just couldn't get back to sleep.* 我再也睡不着了。| *This brings me back to my point about the state of the economy.* 這使我又回到了我對經濟情況的看法。

3 ►HOME TOWN 故鄉◄ in a place where you or your family lived before 回到〔故鄉〕: **[+in/at etc]** *Back in Manitoba we used to skate on the lakes in winter.* 過去在故鄉曼尼托巴時, 我們常常在冬天去湖上滑冰。| *Back home we never did things this way.* 過去在家時, 我們從來不這樣做事。

4 ►NOT FORWARDS 不向前◄ in the direction that you have come from 向後面; 在後面: *George glanced back to see if he was still being followed.* 喬治往後瞧了一眼, 看看是不是仍有人在跟蹤自己。| *He took a few steps back, then took the photo.* 他向後退了幾步, 然後拍照。

5 ►REPLY 回覆◄ as a reply or reaction to what someone has done 回覆, 回答: *Can you ask Mr Clark to call me back?* 你可以請克拉克先生給我回個電話嗎? | *I'll pay you back on Friday.* 我星期五再還錢給你。| *I grinned back at him.* 我也朝他咧嘴笑笑。

6 ►AGAIN 再◄ once again 再次, 又一次: *Play the tape back for me, will you?* 把磁帶再給我放一遍, 好嗎? | *Let's go back over these figures just to make sure we're right.* 讓我們重新算一下這些數字以確保正確。

7 sit/lie/lean back to sit or lie in a comfortable, relaxed way 舒舒服服地坐/躺/倚着: *Sit back, relax, and enjoy the show!* 坐好, 放鬆一下, 好好欣賞節目吧!

8 ►THE PAST 過去◄ in or towards an earlier time 以前, 從前, 過去, 追溯至: **[+in/on]** *Back in the fifties, children respected their elders.* 追溯到五十年代, 孩子們尊敬長輩。| **three years/two months etc back** (=three years ago etc) 三年/兩個月等以前 *If I'd known three years back that stocks were going to crash, I'd have sold everything.* 如果我三年前知道股票會暴跌, 我早就全賣掉了。

9 ►AWAY FROM SB 離開某人◄ away from the person who is speaking 後退〔離開說話人〕: *Stay well back! Let the ambulance through.* 向後退!讓救護車過去。

10 ►AWAY FROM STH 離開某物◄ away from a surface or area 離開表面: *Pull back the bandage and see if the wound is healing.* 把繃帶拉下來, 看看傷口是不是在癒合。| *The clouds rolled back and suddenly there was sunlight.* 雲層逐漸散開, 陽光突然出現了。

11 back and forth if someone or something goes back and forth, they go in one direction then back to where they started from, and keep repeating this movement 來來回回: *The shuttle bus runs back and forth between the airport and the downtown area.* 班車往返於機場與市中心之間。| *pacing back and forth in the waiting room* 在等候室裡來回踱步

12 ►BOOK 書◄ towards the beginning of a book 往前, 往回: *There's a picture six pages further back.* 書再往回翻六頁有一幅圖。

13 pay/get sb back (for) to do something unpleasant to someone because they have done something unpleasant to you or someone you care about 回擊某人, 還擊某人: *I'll pay him back for hurting my sister – just you wait!* 他傷害我妹妹, 我會予以回擊的。你等着瞧!

14 go back on a promise/agreement etc to do the opposite of what you promised to do 食言/違約: *You can trust Kate – she'll never go back on her word.* 你可以信任凱特, 她從不食言。

back 背部, 背脊

John's shirt is on back to front *BrE*【英】/on backwards *AmE*【美】. 約翰的襯衫前後穿反了。

They stood back to back. 他們背靠背站着。

back[2] *n* [C] S1 W1

1 ►BODY 身體◄ a) the side of a person's or animal's body that is opposite the chest and goes from the neck to the top of the legs〔人或動物的〕背部, 背脊, 後背: *He lifted the bag of golf clubs onto his back.* 他拿起裝有高爾夫球棒的袋子揹到背上。| *The cat arched its back and hissed.* 那隻貓拱起背發出嘶嘶聲。| **on your back** (=with your back on the ground) 仰臥 *They lay on their backs and gazed at the sky.* 他們仰躺着凝望天空。| **with your back to** *Stand with your back to the wall and don't move.* 背靠牆站着, 別動。—see picture at 參見 HORSE[1] 圖 **b)** the bones that go from your neck to the top of your legs 脊骨: *He broke his back in a motorbike accident.* 在一場摩托車事故中, 他摔斷了脊梁。

2 ►PART 部分◄ the part of something that is furthest from the direction in which it moves or faces 後面, 後部: **[+of]** *He kissed her on the back of her head.* 他在她後腦勺上親了一下。| *I think there's enough room for your stuff in the back of the truck.* 我看卡車後部有足夠的地方裝你這些東西。| **at the back** *a small shop with* *an office at the back* 後面有一間辦公室的小商店 —see 見 FRONT[1] (USAGE) | **in back (of)** *AmE* (=in or at the back of something)【美】在…後面 *When we go on long journeys by car the kids always ride in back.* 我們開車長途旅行時, 孩子們總是坐在車的後座。| **round the back/out (the) back** *BrE informal* (=behind a house or other building)【英, 非正式】在房屋[建築物]的後面 *We keep the bikes in a shed out the back.* 我們把腳踏車放在屋後的車棚裡。—opposite 反義詞 FRONT[1] (3)

3 ▶SURFACE 表面◀ the less important side or surface of something such as a paper or card 較為不重要的一面; 背面, 反面: *Paul scribbled his address on the back of an envelope.* 保羅把他的地址草草地寫在信封的背面。| *On the back of the canvas we can see the date: 1645.* 在油畫的背面我們可以看到日期: 1645 年。

4 ▶CHAIR 椅子◀ the part of a seat that you lean against when you are sitting 椅背, 靠背: **[+of]** *He rested his arm on the back of the sofa.* 他把一隻胳膊放在沙發的靠背上。

5 ▶BOOK/NEWSPAPER 書/報紙◀ the last pages of a book or newspaper〔書的〕後面;〔報紙的〕最末版: **[+of]** *The index is at the back of the book.* 索引在書的末尾。

6 ▶FOOTBALL ETC 足球等◀ one of the defending players on a football or hockey team 後衛

7 at your back a) behind you 在…後面: *They had the wind at their backs as they set off.* 他們出發時順風。**b)** *literary* supporting you【文】支持: *Caesar marched into Rome with an army at his back.* 凱撒在軍隊的支持下長驅直入羅馬。

8 at/in the back of your mind a thought or feeling that is at the back of your mind is influencing you even though you are not thinking about it 頭腦中有…的印象: *At the back of Joe's mind was the feeling that he had seen this place before.* 喬隱約記得以前見過這個地方。

9 back to back a) with the backs towards each other 背靠背: *Stand back to back and we'll see who is taller.* 讓我們背靠背站着就能看出誰比較高了。—see also 另見 BACK-TO-BACK **b)** *especially AmE* happening one after the other【尤美】連續地, 一個接一個地: *a marathon basketball tournament with games played back to back* 比賽一場接一場的馬拉松式籃球聯賽

10 back to front *BrE* in an incorrect position so that what should be the back is at the front; backwards【英】前後倒置: *You've got your sweater on back to front.* 你把毛衣前後穿反了。

11 behind sb's back if you do something behind someone's back, you do it without them knowing 背着某人, 背地裡: *She's the kind of person who talks about you behind your back.* 她是那種在背後講閒話的人。

12 get/put sb's back up *informal* to annoy someone【非正式】使某人生氣, 使某人產生反感, 惹怒某人: *You'll just put people's backs up if you're aggressive all the time.* 如果你總是那樣好鬥, 你只會把別人惹怒。

13 get off my back *spoken* used to tell someone to stop annoying you or asking you to do things you do not want to do【口】別囉嗦了: *Do me a favour and get off my back!* 勞駕, 別煩我好不好!

14 know sth back to front *BrE*【英】, **know sth backwards** *especially AmE*【尤美】if you know or learn something back to front, you know it very thoroughly 對某事了解得很透徹: *You can't fool her! She knows the regulations back to front!* 你騙不了她! 她對這些規則簡直滾瓜爛熟!

15 know somewhere like the back of your hand to know a place extremely well 對某地方瞭如指掌: *I'll drive, if you want – I know New York like the back of my hand.* 如果你願意, 我來開車, 我對紐約瞭如指掌。

16 the back of beyond *informal especially BrE* a very distant place that is difficult to get to【非正式, 尤英】遙遠偏僻的地方: *They live on a farm somewhere in the back of beyond.* 他們住在一個非常偏僻的農場。

17 be (flat) on your back to be so ill that you cannot get out of bed 病得不能下牀: *He's been flat on his back with flu for three weeks.* 他得了流感, 已卧牀三週了。

18 be on sb's back *informal* to be trying to make someone do things they do not want to do【非正式】非讓某人做…不可, 硬要某人做…: *Dad's on my back about my homework, so I can't go out tonight.* 爸爸非要我做作業不可, 所以我今晚不能出去。

19 put your back into it *informal* to work extremely hard at something【非正式】全力以赴, 發奮做某事: *If we really put our backs into it, we could finish today.* 如果我們加把勁, 今天能幹完。

20 have your back to the wall *informal* to be in a very difficult position with no choice about what to do【非正式】陷入絕境; 被逼得走投無路

21 low-backed/straight-backed/narrow-backed etc with a low, straight, narrow etc back 低背的/直背的/窄背的等: *a high-backed chair* 高背椅

22 turn your back on to refuse to be involved with something 對…不予理睬; 拒絕幫助: *So many of them just turn their backs on their religion when they leave home.* 他們當中有許多人在離開家鄉後就不再在意原來所信仰的宗教了。

back³ *adj* [only before noun 僅用於名詞前] **1** at the back 後面的, 後部的: *a back room* 後屋 | *the back page* 封底 | *a back seat* 後座 —see also 另見 BACK DOOR **2** behind something 在…後面的: *in the backyard* 在後院 **3** from the back 從後面的: *a back view* 從後往前看 | *Go in the back way so you won't be seen.* 從後面的路走不會有人看見你。**4 back street/lane/road etc** a street etc that is away from the main streets 偏僻的街/巷/路等: *a little shop in a back street behind the station* 車站後面街上的小商店 **5 back rent/taxes/pay** money that someone owes from an earlier date 拖欠的租金/稅款/工資 **6 back issue/copy/number** an old copy of a magazine or newspaper 過期的報刊雜誌: *a pile of back copies of 'Punch' magazine* 一疊舊《潘趣》雜誌〔1841 年創刊於倫敦的漫畫雜誌〕**7** *technical* a back vowel sound is made by raising your tongue at the back of your mouth【術語】〔元音〕舌後的, 舌根的

back⁴ *v*

1 ▶MOVE SB 移動某人◀ [I always+adv/prep, T always+adv/prep] to move backwards, or make someone else move backwards (使) 後退, (使) 退出: **back towards/across etc** *Stanley backed slowly across the stage.* 斯坦利緩緩地退出舞台。

2 ▶MOVE VEHICLE 移動車輛◀ [I,T] to make a car move backwards; REVERSE[1] (2) 後退, 倒退, 倒車: **back (sth) into/out of etc** *If you back your car out of the driveway I can get mine in.* 你把車退出車道, 我的車才能開進去。—see picture on page A3 參見 A3 頁圖

3 ▶SUPPORT 支持◀ [T] to support someone or something, especially with money, power, or influence 支持, 鼓勵, 資助: *The bill is backed by environmental lobbyists.* 這個議案得到了環保說客的支持。| *government-backed loans* 政府資助的貸款

4 ▶BACK SURFACE 背面◀ [T usually passive 一般用被動態] to put something on the back surface of a flat piece of material 以…為背襯, 用…裝背襯: *Back the photo with strong cardboard.* 用結實的硬紙板作這張照片的背襯。| *a plastic-backed shower curtain* 以塑料作背襯的浴簾

5 ▶BE BEHIND 在後面◀ [T usually passive 一般用被動態] to be at the back of something or behind it 在…的後邊: *It was a sunny spot, backed by a wall.* 這是個陽光充足的地方, 後邊有一道牆。

6 ▶MUSIC 音樂◀ [T usually passive 一般用被動態] if musicians back a singer or another musician, they play music that makes the main performer sound better 伴奏

7 ▶HORSE/DOG RACE 賽馬/賽狗◀ [T] to risk money on whether a horse, dog, team etc wins something 下賭注於: *We backed Eliamana but it finished fourth.* 我們都下注於埃里亞馬娜, 但牠最後得了個第四。

8 back the wrong horse to support a person, group etc that loses 下錯了賭注, 支持了輸家
9 ►WIND 風◄ [I] *technical* if the wind backs, it changes direction, moving around the COMPASS (1) in the direction North-West-South-East【術語】逆時針轉, 逆轉

back away *phr v* [I] **1** to move backwards, away from something, especially because you are afraid, shocked etc〔尤指因恐懼或震驚而〕躲開; 向後退, 退縮: **[+from]** *The waiter backed away from the table, bowing slightly.* 男服務員從桌旁向後退, 欠身鞠了個躬。**2** to gradually stop taking part in something or supporting something 逐漸退出, 不再支持: *Imperceptibly, the Government has backed away from the plan.* 政府逐漸地不再支持這個計劃。

back down *phr v* [I] to accept defeat in an argument, opinion, or claim 放棄〔觀點、意見、要求〕; 承認〔錯誤〕; 認輸: *When presented with the evidence, the suspect backed down.* 拿出證據後, 疑犯終於認罪。

back off *phr v* [I] *especially AmE*【尤美】**1** to move backwards, away from something 退後: *Back off, you're crowding me.* 往後退, 別擠我。**2** to stop trying to force someone to do or think something 不再逼使〔某人〕做[考慮]〔某事〕: *I think you should back off for a while and leave Alan to make his own decision.* 我認為你應該暫時不要逼迫艾倫, 讓他自己去決定。**3** to gradually stop taking part in something or supporting something 逐漸退出, 不再支持: *Jerry backed off when he realized how much work was involved.* 傑里意識到有多少工作要做之後, 便退出了。

back onto sth *phr v* [T] if a building backs onto something such as a river or field, its back faces it〔建築物〕背後靠近, 背對着

back out *phr v* [I] to decide not to do something that you had promised to do 不履行〔諾言、合同等〕, 打退堂鼓, 食言, 違約: **[+of]** *They backed out of the contract at the last minute.* 他們在最後一分鐘退出了合同。

back up *phr v* **1** [T **back** sb/sth ↔ **up**] to say that what someone is saying is true 證實〔某人〕的說法; 支持〔某人〕的說法: *Peggy would back me up if she were here.* 佩吉要是在這兒, 一定會支持我的說法。| *The videotape evidence backed up the manager's story.* 錄像帶這一證據證實了經理的話。**2** [I,T **back** sth ↔ **up**] to make a copy of the information on a computer PROGRAM or DISK 複製(磁碟) **3** [I,T **back** sth ↔ **up**] to make a car go backwards 倒(車): *Get out of the way – the truck's backing up!* 讓開, 卡車在倒車! —see picture on page A3 參見A3頁圖 **4** [I] to move backwards 向後移動: *Back up a bit so that everyone can see.* 往後點兒讓大家都能看得見。—see also 另見 BACKUP

back·ache /ˋbæk͵ek; ˈbækeɪk/ *n* [C,U] a pain in your back 背痛

back·bench /͵bækˋbɛntʃ; ͵bækˈbentʃ◂/ *n* [C] *BrE* the seats in the British parliament where ordinary MPS (MP (1)) sit【英】後座議員席位: *the backbenches* 後座議員們 —compare 比較 FRONTBENCH

back·bench·er /͵bækˋbɛntʃɚ; ͵bækˈbentʃə◂/ *n* [C] *BrE* an ordinary British Member of Parliament rather than one of the party leaders【英】後座議員〔不擔任政黨領袖的普通議員〕: *Angry backbenchers are threatening to vote against the government.* 憤怒的後座議員們威脅要投票反對政府。

back·bit·ing /ˋbæk͵baɪtɪŋ; ˈbækbaɪtɪŋ/ *n* [U] unpleasant or cruel talk about someone who is not present 背後說人的壞話: *All this backbiting is destroying company morale.* 所有這些流言蜚語都在影響公司的士氣。—**backbiter** *n* [C]

back·board /ˋbæk͵bord; ˈbækbɔːd/ *n* [C] the board behind the basket in the game of BASKETBALL 籃板 —see picture on page A22 參見A22頁圖

back·bone /ˋbækˋbon; ˈbækbəʊn/ *n* **1** [C] the row of connected bones that go down the middle of your back; SPINE (1) 脊骨, 脊柱 **2 the backbone of** the most important part of an organization, set of ideas etc 骨幹; 支柱; 主力, 中堅: *The manufacturing sector forms the backbone of the country's economy.* 製造業是這個國家經濟的支柱。**3** [U] moral strength 骨氣, 毅力: *The army'll give 'em some backbone!* 部隊會鍛鍊他們的毅力!

back·break·ing /ˋbæk͵brekɪŋ; ˈbækbreɪkɪŋ/ *adj* backbreaking work is physically very difficult and makes you very tired〔工作〕累死人的, 非常繁重的

back·chat /ˋbæk͵tʃæt; ˈbæktʃæt/ *n* [U] *BrE* a reply to someone who is telling you what to do【英】頂嘴, 回嘴; BACKTALK *AmE*【美】: *None of your backchat, do your homework!* 不要頂嘴, 做你的作業吧!

back·cloth /ˋbæk͵klɔθ; ˈbæk-klɒθ/ *n* [C] **1** a painted cloth hung across the back of a stage〔舞台後部的〕背景幕布 **2** the conditions or situation in which something happens〔事件的〕背景: *Against this backcloth of industrial turmoil, violence was always likely.* 在工人騷亂的情況下, 很可能發生暴力事件。

back·comb /ˋbæk͵kom; ˈbæk-kəʊm/ *v* [T] *BrE* to comb your hair against the way it grows in order to style it and make it look thicker【英】倒梳(頭髮)〔使之蓬鬆〕; TEASE[1] (4) *AmE*【美】

back coun·try /ˈ· ͵··/ *n* [U] **1** *especially AustrE* a country area where few people live【尤澳】偏遠地區 —compare 比較 BUSH **2** *AmE* an area, especially in the mountains, away from roads and towns【美】偏遠山區

back·date /ˋbæk͵det; ͵bækˈdeɪt/ *v* [T] to make something have its effect from an earlier date 追溯到, 從〔過去某個日期〕開始生效: **backdate sth from/to** *The pay increase agreed in June will be backdated to January.* 六月同意增加的工資將從一月份算起。—compare 比較 ANTEDATE, POSTDATE

back door /͵· ˈ·/ *n* [C] **1** a door at the back or side of a building 後門, 旁門, 側門 **2 get in through the back door** to achieve something by having an unfair secret advantage 走後門: *His father works for them so he got in through the back door.* 他父親給他們做事, 所以他走了後門。

back·door /ˋbæk͵dɔr; ˈbækdɔː/ *adj* [only before noun 僅用於名詞前] secret, or not publicly stated as your intention 祕密的, 不公開的: *In what amounts to a backdoor income tax increase, the Chancellor chose to freeze personal tax allowance.* 財政大臣決定凍結個人免稅額, 這就等於暗暗地提高了個人所得稅。

back·drop /ˋbæk͵drɑp; ˈbækdrɒp/ *n* [C] **1** *literary* the scenery behind something that you are looking at【文】背景: *the stunning backdrop of the Alps* 極其優美的阿爾卑斯山遠景 **2** the conditions or situation in which something happens〔事件的〕背景: *The depression was the backdrop for Steinbeck's greatest works.* 斯坦貝克最著名的作品都是以大蕭條時期作為歷史背景的。**3** a painted cloth hung across the back of a stage〔舞台後部的〕背景幕布

back·er /ˋbækɚ; ˈbækə/ *n* [C] someone who supports a plan, especially by providing money 支持者, 贊助者, 資助者: *We're still trying to find backers for the housing development scheme.* 我們還在努力為住房開發計劃尋找贊助商。

back·fire /ˋbæk͵faɪr; ͵bækˈfaɪə/ *v* [I] **1** if a plan or action backfires, it has the opposite effect to the one you intended 發生意外; 產生事與願違的結果 **2** if a car backfires, it makes a sudden loud noise because the engine is not working correctly〔汽車引擎〕逆火, 回火

back for·ma·tion /ˈ· ·͵··/ *n* [C] *technical* a new word formed from an older word, for example 'televise' formed from 'television'【術語】逆構詞, 逆成詞

back·gam·mon /ˋbæk͵gæmən; ˈbækgæmən/ *n* [U] a game for two players, using flat round pieces and DICE[1] (1) on a special board 西洋十五子棋, 西洋雙陸棋〔一種供兩人玩、以擲骰子決定棋子行進的遊戲〕

back·ground /ˋbæk͵graʊnd; ˈbækgraʊnd/ *n* **1** [C] someone's family history, education, social class etc 出

身，個人背景: *He's always going on about his working class background.* 他老是埋怨自己出身於工人階級家庭。| *a background in computer engineering*（有）電腦工程背景 **2** [C,U] the events in the past that explain why something has happened in the way that it has〔事情發生時的〕背景情況: *Without knowing the background to the case, I couldn't possibly comment.* 因為不了解案件的背景情況，我不可能加以評論。| **background information/details/data etc** *With a bit more background information the report will be fine.* 再加點兒背景資料，這個報告會很不錯。**3** [C] the pattern or colour on top of which something has been drawn, printed etc 背景，後景；底色: *red lettering on a white background* 白底紅色字母圖案 **4 in the background a)** behind the main thing that you are looking at 在不顯眼的位置；在背景中: *In the background of this photo you can see a few of my old college friends.* 在這幅照片的背景中，你可以看到我的幾個大學時的老朋友。**b)** someone who keeps or stays in the background tries not to be noticed 在不被人注意[不顯眼]的位置: *A couple of waiters hovered in the background.* 幾個服務員在不被人注意的地方來回走動。**c)** a sound that is in the background is present but is not the main thing that you are listening to 隱約的[地]: *In the background I could hear the sound of traffic.* 我隱約能夠聽到來往的車輛聲。**5** [C,U] the sounds that you can hear apart from the main thing that you are listening to 背景聲；雜音: **background noise/music/a lot of background noise** *an irritating background noise of tinny music* 聲音不大、令人煩躁的音樂雜聲

back·hand /ˋbækˋhænd; ˈbækhænd/ *n* [C usually singular 一般用單數] a hit in tennis and some other games in which the back of your hand is turned in the direction of the hit〔網球等的〕反手擊球（技術）—**backhand** *adj* —see picture on page A23 參見 A23 頁圖

back·hand·ed /ˋbækˋhændɪd; ˌbækˈhændɪ̈d◂/ *adj* **1** a backhanded remark or COMPLIMENT[1] (1) seems to express praise or admiration but in fact means the opposite 間接的，轉彎抹角的，諷刺挖苦的: *'Brave' can be a backhanded way of saying 'crazy'.* "勇敢"可以是轉彎抹角地在説"發瘋"。**2** a backhanded shot etc is made with a backhand 反手擊球的，用反手的

back·hand·er /ˋbækˋhændɚ; ˈbækhændə/ *n* [C] **1** a hit or shot made with the back of your hand 反手一擊 **2** *BrE informal* money that you pay illegally and secretly to get something done【英，非正式】賄賂；回扣: *Investigators estimate that £35m had been spent on bribes and backhanders.* 調查者估計用於賄賂和回扣的金額達三千五百萬英鎊。

back·hoe /ˋbækˌho; ˈbækhəʊ/ *n* [C] a large digging machine used for making roads etc〔築路用的〕挖掘機

back·ing /ˋbækɪŋ; ˈbækɪŋ/ *n* **1** [U] support or help, especially with money 支持，幫助，資助 **2** [C] material that is used to make the back of an object 襯墊物，背襯 **3** [C] the music that is played with a singer's voice to make it sound better〔音樂〕伴奏 —**backing** *adj*

back·lash /ˋbækˌlæʃ; ˈbæklæʃ/ *n* [C] a strong but usually delayed reaction against recent events, especially against political or social developments〔對重大事件的〕強烈反應，反衝: **backlash against** *The 1970s saw the first backlash against the emerging women's movement.* 20 世紀 70 年代正在興起的婦女運動首次遭到強烈抵制。| *The rise in violent crime provoked a backlash against the liberal gun-control laws.* 暴力罪案的增加引起了對鬆散的槍支管制法的強烈不滿。

back·log /ˋbækˌlɔg; ˈbæklɒg/ *n* [usually singular 一般用單數] a large amount of work, especially that should already have been completed 積壓未辦之事，積壓的工作: *a backlog of letters* 很多未處理的信

back·pack¹ /ˋbækˌpæk; ˈbækpæk/ *n* [C] *especially AmE* a bag carried on your back, often supported by a light metal frame, used especially by climbers and walkers【尤美】〔尤指登山者或步行者所用的〕背包，行囊；RUCKSACK *BrE*【英】

backpack² *v* [I] *especially AmE* to go walking and camping carrying a BACKPACK[1]【尤美】揹着背包徒步旅行；野外露營: *backpacking along the Appalachian trail* 沿着阿巴拉契亞山路揹包徒步旅行 —**backpacker** *n* [C]

back pas·sage /ˌ· ˈ··/ *n* [C] a word meaning ANUS (=the hole where food waste comes out of your body) used to avoid offending people 肛門〔婉詞〕

back·ped·al /ˋbækˌpɛdl; ˌbækˈpedl/ *v* **backpedalled, backpedalling** *BrE*【英】, **backpedaled, backpedaling** *AmE*【美】[I] **1** to start to change your opinion about something that you had promised 變卦，改變主意，出爾反爾: *They are backpedalling on the commitment to cut taxes.* 他們曾經承諾減税，但現在變卦了。**2** to PEDAL[2] (2) backwards on a bicycle〔騎腳踏車時〕倒踩腳踏板

back·room boy /ˋbækrum ˌbɔɪ; ˈbækrʊm ˌbɔɪ/ *n* [usually plural 一般用複數] *informal especially BrE* someone such as an engineer or scientist, whose work is important but who does not get much attention or fame【非正式，尤英】幕後籌劃者；從事祕密研究工作的人員

back seat /ˌ· ˈ·◂/ *n* **1** [C] a seat at the back of a car, behind where the driver sits 汽車後座 **2 back seat driver a)** a passenger in the back of a car who gives unwanted advice to the driver about how to drive 對司機指手畫腳、亂指揮其駕駛的後座乘客 **b)** *especially AmE* someone in business or politics who tries to control things that they are not really responsible for【尤美】干涉與自己職責無關的事情的人，多管閒事的人

back·side /ˋbækˋsaɪd; ˈbæksaɪd/ *n informal* the part of your body that you sit on【非正式】屁股，臀部

back·slap·ping /ˋbækˌslæpɪŋ; ˈbækslæpɪŋ/ *n* [U] noisy cheerful behaviour when people praise each other's achievements more than they deserve（過分）喧鬧的歡慶〔指相互慶賀成功〕—**backslapper** *n* [C]

back·slash /ˋbækˌslæʃ; ˈbækslæʃ/ *n* [C] a line (\) used in writing to separate words, numbers, or letters 反向斜線符號

back·slide /ˋbækˌslaɪd; ˌbækˈslaɪd/ *v* [I] to start doing the bad things that you used to do, especially after having improved your behaviour 倒退，退步，故態復萌: *I haven't had a cigarette for two months, but recently I'm afraid I've begun to backslide.* 我已經兩個月沒有抽煙了，但最近又開始抽起來。—**backslider** *n* [C]

back·space /ˋbækˌspes; ˈbækspeɪs/ *n* [usually singular 一般用單數] the part of a TYPEWRITER that you press to move backwards towards the beginning of the line〔打字機的〕退格鍵

back·spin /ˋbækˌspɪn; ˈbækspɪn/ *n* [U] a turning movement in a ball that has been hit so that the top of the ball turns backwards as the ball travels forwards 倒[迴]旋球

back·stage /ˋbækˋstedʒ; ˌbækˈsteɪdʒ◂/ *adv* **1** behind the stage in a theatre, especially in the actors' dressing rooms 在後台〔尤指演員化妝室〕**2** in private, especially within the secret parts of an organization 祕密地，背地裡，在幕後: *That's the official line, but who knows what really goes on backstage?* 這是官方的路線方針，但誰知道幕後情況怎麼樣？—**backstage** *adj*

back·stairs /ˋbækˌstɛrz; ˈbæksteəz/ *adj* [only before noun 僅用於名詞前] secret and probably unfair 祕密的，暗地裡的；中傷的，不正當的: *backstairs influence* 暗中的影響力

back·street /ˈ· ·/ *adj* backstreet activities are often illegal and done badly 私下的，偷偷摸摸的: *a backstreet abortion* 非法墮胎

back·stroke /ˋbækˌstrok; ˈbækstrəʊk/ *n* [singular] a way of swimming on your back by moving first one arm then the other backwards while kicking your feet 仰泳，背泳

back·talk /ˋbækˌtɔk; ˈbæktɔːk/ *n* [U] *AmE* a rude reply to someone who is telling you what to do【美】頂嘴，回嘴；BACKCHAT *BrE*【英】

back-to-back /ˌ· · ˈ·◂/ *n* [C] *BrE* a house in a row or

TERRACE (1) built with its back touching the back of the next row of houses【英】背靠背的房子

back·track /ˈbæk,træk; ˈbæktræk/ *v* [I] **1** to change your beliefs, statements etc so that they are not as strong as they were earlier 退縮, 取消諾言, 出爾反爾: *Clinton seemed to be backtracking on his policy on Bosnia.* 克林頓在波斯尼亞的政策上似乎有所退縮。**2** to return by the same way that you came 原路返回

B

back·up /ˈbæk,ʌp; ˈbækʌp/ *n* [C,U] **1** something or someone used to provide support and help when it is needed 備用品; 後備人員, 支援人員: *Army units can only operate if they have sufficient backup.* 有足夠的後備力量時部隊才能作戰。**2 backup plan/system/generator** a plan or system that can be used if the main one does not work 備用計劃/系統/發電機

back·ward /ˈbækwəd; ˈbækwəd/ *adj* **1** [only before noun 僅用於名詞前] made in a direction towards what is behind you 向後的, 後退的: *She went without a backward glance.* 她頭也不回地走了。**2** developing slowly and less successfully than most others 落後的; 遲鈍的: *some of the more backward countries* 一些更落後的國家 | *a backward child* 遲鈍的孩子 —compare 比較 FORWARD[2] —**backwardly** *adv* —**backwardness** *n* [U]

2 **back·wards** /ˈbækwədz; ˈbækwədz/ also 又作 **backward** *AmE*【美】*adv* **1** towards the back, the beginning, or the past 向後地, 倒退地; 回顧地: *She pushed me and I fell backwards into the chair.* 她推了我一下, 我倒退回椅子裡。| *Can you say the alphabet backwards?* 你能倒背英文字母表嗎? **2** moving or facing the opposite direction to the usual one 背向前地; 倒轉地, 逆向地: *He walked backwards away from the King.* 他後退着從國王身邊走開。| *You've got your hat on backwards!* 你把帽子前後戴反了! **3** towards a worse state 每況愈下地, 退步地: *The new measures are seen by some as a major step backwards.* 有些人認為新措施是一個大倒退。**4 backwards and forwards** first in one direction and then in the opposite direction, usually many times 來回地, 忽前忽後地 **5 bend over/lean over backwards (to do sth)** to try as hard as possible to help or please someone 拚命, 竭盡全力〔幫助或取悅某人〕: *We bent over backwards to help them.* 我們盡了最大努力幫助他們。**6 know sth backwards** *BrE*【英】, **know sth backwards and forwards** *AmE*【美】to know something very well or perfectly 對某事瞭如指掌, 熟知某事: *All the actors know the play backwards and forwards.* 所有演員對這個劇本都可以倒背如流。—compare 比較 FORWARD[1]

back·wa·ter /ˈbæk,wɔtə; ˈbækwɔːtə/ *n* **1** a very quiet place not influenced by outside events or new ideas 與世隔絕的地方; 閉塞的地方: *a rural backwater* 一個與世隔絕的村莊 **2** a part of a river away from the main stream, where the water does not move〔河流的〕回水, 死水, 滯水

back·woods /ˈbækˈwudz; ˈbækwudz/ *n* [plural] a distant and undeveloped area away from any towns 邊遠落後地區

back·woods·man /ˈbækˈwudzmən; ˈbækwudzmən/ *n* [C] **1** someone who lives in the backwoods 邊遠地區的居民 **2** *BrE* a member of a political party or parliament, especially the House of Lords, who is not very active politically and only sometimes votes, attends meetings etc【英】政治上不很積極的政黨成員〔尤指上議院議員只在有時參加會議或投票活動〕

back·yard /ˈbækˈjɑrd; ,bækˈjɑːd◂/ *n* **1** *BrE* a square flat area behind a house, covered with a hard surface【英】〔鋪了硬地面的〕後院 **2** *AmE* an area of land behind a house, usually covered with grass【美】〔常指有草皮的〕後院, 後花園: *The old man grew vegetables in his backyard.* 老人在屋後園子裡種了蔬菜。

3 **ba·con** /ˈbekən; ˈbeɪkən/ *n* [U] **1** salted or smoked meat from the back or sides of a pig, often served in narrow thin pieces〔通常切成薄片的〕鹹豬肉, 熏豬肉: **bacon and eggs** (=bacon and eggs cooked in hot fat and served together) 熏豬肉煎蛋 —see also 另見 MEAT **2 bring home the bacon** *informal* to provide enough money to support your family【非正式】掙錢養家 —see also 另見 **save sb's bacon** (SAVE[1])

bac·te·ri·a /bækˈtɪrɪə; bækˈtɪəriə/ *n* [plural] *singular* **bacterium** very small living things related to plants, some of which cause disease; MICROBES 細菌 —compare 比較 VIRUS (1,2) —**bacterial** *adj*: *a bacterial infection* 細菌感染

bac·te·ri·ol·o·gy /ˈbæk,tɪrɪˈɑlədʒɪ; bæk,tɪəriˈɒlədʒi/ *n* [U] the scientific study of bacteria 細菌學 —**bacteriologist** *n* [C] —**bacteriological** /ˈbæk,tɪrɪəˈlɑdʒɪkl; bæk,tɪəriəˈlɒdʒɪkəl/ *adj*

Bac·tri·an cam·el /,bæktrɪən ˈkæml; ,bæktriən ˈkæməl/ *n* [C] a CAMEL from Asia with two HUMPS[1] (2)〔亞洲的〕雙峯駱駝

bad[1] /bæd; bæd/ *adj comparative* 比較級 **worse** /wɜs; wɜːs/ *superlative* 最高級 **worst** /wɜst; wɜːst/

1 ▶HARMFUL 有害的◀ unpleasant, harmful, or likely to cause problems 不好的, 令人不快的, 糟糕的: *I have some bad news for you.* 我給你帶來了壞消息。| *I thought things couldn't possibly get any worse.* 我想事情不會變得更糟了。| *It's bad enough being woken by the baby without you keeping me awake as well.* 就算你沒有讓我醒着, 給那嬰孩吵醒我已經夠受了。—opposite 反義詞 GOOD[1] (2)

2 ▶LOW QUALITY 低質量◀ low in quality or below an acceptable standard 差的, 不符合標準的: *The failure of the company was due to bad management.* 公司因經營不善而破產。| *Your handwriting is so bad I can hardly read it.* 你寫的字太差, 我幾乎認不出來。| *bad teachers and a lack of funds* 老師水平低且缺乏資金 —opposite 反義詞 GOOD[1] (1)

3 ▶WRONG 錯的◀ morally wrong or evil〔道德品質〕壞的: *He's a bad man – keep away from him.* 他是個壞人, 離他遠一點兒。—opposite 反義詞 GOOD[1] (16)

4 ▶SERIOUS 嚴重的◀ serious or severe 嚴重的, 厲害的: *He is recovering from a bad accident.* 他在經歷了一場嚴重的事故後正逐漸康復。| *The pain was really bad.* 痛得真厲害。

5 bad time/moment etc a time at which it is very unlucky for something to have happened 不適當的時候: *It's a bad time to have to borrow money, with interest rates so high.* 現在借款真不是時候, 利率這麼高。

6 bad for you harmful to you or to your health 對健康有害: *Too much salt can be bad for you.* 食用過多的鹽對你身體不好。| *It is bad for a young girl to be on her own so much.* 一個小姑娘要完全靠自己, 身體吃不消。

7 ▶FOOD 食物◀ food that is bad is not safe to eat because it has decayed 已變質的, 腐爛的: *This fish has gone bad.* 這魚變質了。| *bad apples* 爛蘋果

8 bad at maths/tennis/drawing etc having no skill or ability in a particular activity 不擅長數學/網球/繪畫等: *I'm really bad at chess.* 我棋下得不好。| *Strategic thinking is what so many companies are bad at.* 許多公司都不善於進行戰略思考。

9 bad heart/leg/back etc a heart, leg etc that is injured or does not work correctly 心臟/腿/背等有病[不舒服]: *I haven't been able to do much because of my bad back.* 我因為背傷不能夠做太多工作。| *Ouch, that was my bad foot!* 哎唷!那是我受了傷的腳!

10 ▶SWEARING 詛咒◀ bad language contains swearing or rude words 詛咒的, 污穢的: *all these TV programmes with their violence and bad language* 所有這些充滿暴力和污言穢語的電視節目

11 in a bad temper/mood feeling annoyed or angry 脾氣/心情不好: *I didn't mean to take my bad temper out on you.* 我不是故意對你發脾氣的。

12 ▶GUILTY 內疚◀ feel bad to feel ashamed or sorry about something 感到遺憾[內疚]: *I felt bad about not being able to come last night.* 我昨天晚上沒能來, 非常抱歉。

13 go from bad to worse to become even more unpleasant or difficult 越來越壞, 每況愈下: *The evening went from bad to worse as more and more people left the party.* 越來越多的人離開, 使晚會變得越來越沒意思。
14 be in a bad way *informal especially BrE* to be very ill, unhappy, injured, or in serious trouble【非正式, 尤英】病情嚴重; 不高興; 受傷; 處於困境: *She was in a bad way after the funeral.* 葬禮之後, 她非常難受。
15 get a bad name to lose people's respect or trust 名聲不好:[+for] *The bar had a bad name and was avoided by all the locals.* 這個酒吧名聲不好, 當地人都不願意去。
16 bad egg/lot/sort/type *BrE old-fashioned* someone who is morally bad or cannot be trusted【英, 過時】壞人, 壞蛋, 壞傢伙
17 bad penny someone or something that causes trouble and is difficult to avoid 令人討厭卻又難以避開的人[事]: **turn up like a bad penny** (=suddenly appear) 突然出現 *Sure enough, Steve turned up at the party, like a bad penny.* 史蒂夫果然在晚會上出現, 真討厭。
18 be taken bad *informal especially BrE* to become ill【非正式, 尤英】生病: *He was taken bad in the middle of the night.* 他在半夜裡發病了。
19 in bad faith if someone does something in bad faith they are behaving dishonestly and have no intention of keeping a promise 存心不良, 背信棄義: *In order to sue, you have to prove that the company was acting in bad faith.* 要打官司, 你必須證明該公司有欺詐行為。
20 bad news *informal* someone or something that always causes trouble【非正式】討厭的人[事物]: *Look, just avoid him, I warn you. He's bad news!* 喂, 離他遠點兒, 我警告你, 他不是個好東西!
21 bad form *BrE old-fashioned* socially unacceptable behaviour【英, 過時】不禮貌的行為: *It's bad form to argue with the umpire.* 跟裁判員爭辯是一種不禮貌的行為。
22 bad blood angry or bitter feeling between people; HOSTILITY 惡感, 敵意, 仇恨: *There's too much bad blood between them.* 他們之間的敵意太深。

Frequencies of the adjective **bad** in spoken and written English 形容詞bad在英語口語和書面語中的使用頻率

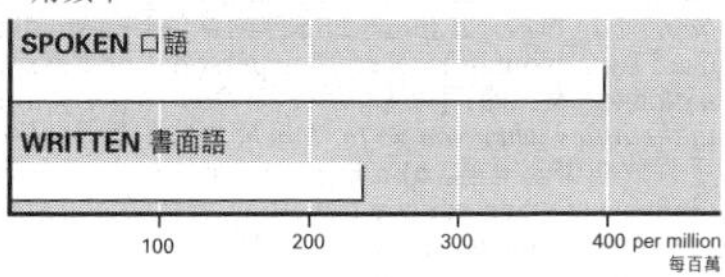

Based on the British National Corpus and the Longman Lancaster Corpus
據英國國家語料庫和朗文蘭卡斯特語料庫

This graph shows that the adjective **bad** is much more common in spoken English than in written English. This is because it is used in some common spoken phrases. 本圖表顯示, 形容詞bad在英語口語中的使用頻率遠遠高於書面語, 因為口語中一些常用片語是由 bad 構成的。

bad *(adj)* **SPOKEN PHRASES**
含 bad 的口語片語

23 not bad *especially BrE* used to say that something is good, or better than you expected【尤英】挺不錯: *"How are you?" "Oh, not bad."* "你身體怎麼樣?" "還行。" | *That's not a bad idea.* 那個主意不錯。| *"Did you enjoy the course?" "Oh it wasn't too bad."* "你喜歡這門課嗎?" "噢, 還可以。"
24 too bad a) used to say that you do not care that something bad happens to someone 咎由自取, 自找的: *"I'm going to be late now!" "Too bad, you should have gotten up earlier."* "我要遲到了!" "活該, 誰叫你那麼晚才起牀。" **b)** used to say that you are sorry that something bad has happened to someone 太可惜, 真遺憾: *It's too bad that you couldn't come to the party last night.* 你昨晚沒能來參加聚會, 真遺憾。 **c)** *BrE old-fashioned* used to say that something is very annoying or unreasonable【英, 過時】沒道理, 很煩人, 太不像話: *They can't increase the price like that, it's just too bad!* 他們不能這樣亂漲價, 太不像話了!
25 bad girl/boy used when a child behaves badly 淘氣的女孩/男孩: *Bad girl! Put that glass down!* 淘氣丫頭! 把玻璃杯放下!
26 it's not that bad/it's not as bad as all that used to say that something is not as bad as someone says it is 並不像別人說的那樣糟糕: *"Yuk! This cheese is revolting!" "Oh, come on, it's not as bad as all that."* "呸! 這乾酪都臭了!" "喲, 得了, 沒那麼嚴重!"
27 not too bad/not so bad used to say that something is not as bad as expected 並不像預期的那樣糟糕: *The exams weren't so bad after all.* 考試並不像想的那樣差。
28 it's bad enough... used to say that you already have one problem, so that you cannot worry about or deal with another one ...已經夠受的了: *It's bad enough having to bring up three kids on your own without having to worry about money as well!* 就算不需要同時擔心錢的問題, 要獨力撫養三個孩子已經夠糟糕!
29 sth can't be bad used to persuade someone that something is good or worth doing 那不錯: *You only pay £10 deposit and no interest: that can't be bad, can it?* 你只付十英鎊保證金, 又不用付利息, 那可是不錯, 對吧? —see also 另見 **make the best of a bad job** (JOB (18)), —**badness** *n* [U]

bad[2] *n* **1 take the bad with the good** accept not only the good things in life but also the bad things 好壞都忍受; 既能享樂, 又能吃苦 **2 to the bad** *informal* if you are a particular amount to the bad you are that much poorer or you owe that much【非正式】負債: *Thanks to your mistake, I'm £500 to the bad!* 由於你的錯誤, 我欠下了 500 英鎊的債! **3 go to the bad** *old-fashioned* to begin living in a wrong or immoral way【過時】開始學壞, 墮落

bad debt /ˌ· ˈ·/ *n* [C] a debt that is unlikely to be paid 呆賬, 壞賬

bad·die, baddy /ˈbædɪ; ˈbædi/ *n* [C] *BrE informal* someone who is bad, especially in a book or film【英, 非正式】(尤指小說、電影等中的)壞蛋

bade /bæd; bæd/ the past tense and past participle of BID[3]

badge /bædʒ; bædʒ/ *n* [C] **1** *BrE* a small piece of metal, cloth, or plastic with a picture or words on it, worn to show rank, membership of a group, support for a political idea or belief, etc【英】徽章, 證章; 標記, 象徵: *They were wearing badges that said 'Nuclear Power – No thanks!'.* 他們佩戴着印有"核能 — 別客氣了!"字樣的徽章。| *a school blazer with a badge sewn on it* 縫着徽章的學校運動服 —compare 比較 BROOCH —see picture at 參見 SIGN[1] 圖 **2** a small piece of metal that you wear or carry that shows you have an official position, for example that you are a police officer (佩戴在身上以顯示官職的)徽章〈如警徽〉 **3** a small piece of cloth with a picture on it, given to SCOUTS[1] (1), GUIDES[1] (4) etc to show what skills they have learned (給童子軍等的)布製徽章: *I got my music badge today.* 今天我得到了音樂徽章。**4 badge of office** an object which shows that you have an official position 職位標識物: *Mayors wear chains around their necks as badges of office.* 市長們戴着象徵職位的項鏈。

bad·ger[1] /ˈbædʒə; ˈbædʒə/ *n* [C] an animal which has

black and white fur, lives in holes in the ground, and is active at night 獾, 穴熊

badger² *v* [T] to try to persuade someone by asking them something several times; PESTER 糾纏着要, 煩擾: *The children badgered me into taking them to the cinema.* 孩子們纏着我要我帶他們去看電影。| **badger someone to do something** *They kept badgering him to get a home computer.* 他們一直纏着要他買一台家用電腦。

bad guy /ˈ· ·/ *n* [C] *AmE informal* someone who is bad, especially in a book or film【美, 非正式】〔尤指小說或電影中的〕壞蛋: *Screen hero Kevin Costner is playing the bad guy for once.* 銀幕英雄奇雲告士拿這次扮演一個壞蛋。

bad·i·nage /ˌbædṇˈɑʒ; ˈbædɪnɑːʒ/ *n* [U] *formal or humorous* playful joking talk【正式或幽默】開玩笑, 打趣

bad·lands /ˈbædˌlændz; ˈbædlændz/ *n* [plural] an area of unproductive land in North America with rocks and hills that have been worn into strange shapes by the weather〔尤指北美的〕荒原, 怪石嶙峋的不毛之地

bad·ly /ˈbædlɪ; ˈbædli/ *adv comparative* 比較級 **worse** *superlative* 最高級 **worst** **1** in an unsatisfactory or unsuccessful way 壞, 差, 拙劣地: *The company has been very badly managed.* 這家公司管理不善。| *Pearce played pretty badly in yesterday's semi-final.* 皮爾斯在昨天的半決賽中表現很差。| *badly made furniture* 做工粗糙的家具 | **do badly** (=not be successful) 不成功 *Rob did very badly in the History exam.* 羅伯的歷史考得很差。**2** to a great or serious degree 嚴重地, 厲害地, 大大地, 非常: *He's been limping badly ever since the skiing accident.* 自那次滑雪事故後, 他的腿一直跛得很厲害。| *She badly wanted to be chosen for the school hockey team.* 她非常渴望入選學校的曲棍球隊。| **badly in need of** (=needing something very much) 急需, 非常需要 *He's badly in need of a haircut.* 他急需理髮。| **go badly wrong** (=if a situation goes badly wrong it becomes very difficult or serious) 變得十分困難[嚴重] *Things started to go badly wrong for Eric after he lost his job.* 埃里克失去工作後, 生活開始變得很艱難。**3 think badly of** to have a bad opinion of someone or something 對…有看法[有意見]: *I'm sure they won't think badly of you if you tell them you need some time away from work.* 我肯定, 如果你告訴他們你需要離開工作崗位一段時間, 他們不會對你有甚麼意見。

badly-off /ˌ·· ˈ·/ *adj comparative* 比較級 **worse-off** *superlative* 最高級 **worst-off** [not before noun 不用於名詞前] **1** not having much money; poor 缺錢的, 貧窮的: *We're too badly-off to have a holiday.* 我們太窮, 沒有錢度假。**2 badly-off for** not having enough of something that is needed 不足的, 缺乏的: *The school is rather badly-off for equipment.* 學校相當缺乏設備。—opposite 反義詞 WELL-OFF

bad·min·ton /ˈbædmɪntən; ˈbædmɪntən/ *n* [U] a game like tennis but played with a SHUTTLECOCK (=small feathered object) instead of a ball 羽毛球 —see picture on page A23 參見A23 頁圖

bad-mouth /ˈ· ·/ *v* [T] *informal especially AmE* to criticize someone or something【非正式, 尤美】說…的壞話, 謾罵, 批評: *Her former colleagues accused her of bad-mouthing them in public.* 她以前的同事指責她在公開場合說他們的壞話。

bad-off /ˌ· ˈ·◂/ *adj AmE* not having much money; poor【美】缺錢的, 貧窮的

bad-tem·pered /ˌ· ˈ··◂/ *adj* easily annoyed or made angry 脾氣不好的, 急性子的: *He was known as a bad-tempered recluse.* 大家都知道他脾氣很壞, 不愛與人來往。

baf·fle¹ /ˈbæfl; ˈbæfəl/ *v* [T] if something baffles someone, they cannot understand or explain it at all 使困惑, 難倒: *The question baffled me completely.* 這個問題把我徹底難倒了。—**bafflement** *n* [U] —**baffling** *adj*: *a baffling mystery* 令人不解的謎

baffle² *n* [C] *technical* a board, sheet of metal etc that controls the flow of air, water, or sound into or out of something【術語】〔控制空氣、水流或聲音進出的〕隔板; 折流板; 隔音板

bags 袋, 包, 囊

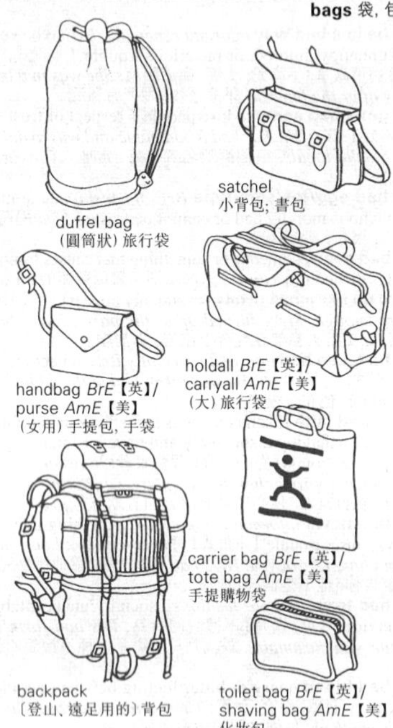

bag¹ /bæg; bæg/ *n* [C]

1 ▶CONTAINER 容器◀ **a)** a container made of paper, cloth etc, which usually opens at the top 袋, 包, 囊: *a paper bag* 紙袋 | *a sports bag* 運動背包 **b)** a small bag used by a woman to carry her personal possessions; HANDBAG〔女士的〕手提袋, 手提包: *Don't leave your bag in the office when you go for lunch.* 去吃午飯時, 不要把手袋放在辦公室裡。**c)** a large bag used to carry your clothes etc when you are travelling 旅行袋: *Just throw your bags in the back of the car.* 把你的行李放在車後好了。—see picture at 參見 CONTAINER 圖

2 ▶AMOUNT 數量◀ the amount that a bag will hold 一袋的量, 一(滿)袋: [+of] *two bags of rice per family per month* 每戶每月兩袋大米

3 ▶WOMAN 婦女◀ *spoken* an insulting word for an unpleasant or unattractive woman【口】醜婆娘; 邋遢女人: *You silly old bag!* 你這愚蠢的醜老太婆!

4 ▶HUNTING 打獵◀ [usually singular 一般用單數] the number of birds or animals that someone catches when they go hunting〔一次打獵所獲的〕捕獵物: *We had a good bag that day.* 那天我們獵獲甚豐。

5 ▶A LOT OF 許多◀ **bags of** *spoken especially BrE* a lot of something; plenty【口, 尤英】很多: *She's got bags of money.* 她有的是錢。| *We're not late, we've got bags of time.* 我們沒遲到, 還有很多時間。

6 pack your bags *informal* to leave a place where you have been living, usually after an argument【非正式】〔通常在爭吵之後〕收拾行李; 走人: *We told her to pack her bags at once.* 我們告訴她立刻收拾行李走人。

7 ▶EYES 眼睛◀ dark circles or loose skin around your eyes, usually because of old age or being tired 眼袋

8 bag of bones *informal* a very thin person or animal 【非正式】骨瘦如柴的人[動物]

9 in the bag *informal* certain to be won or achieved 【非正式】囊中之物; 十拿九穩, 穩操勝券: *We're sure to win, the match is in the bag.* 我們肯定能贏, 這場比賽已穩操勝券。

10 ►TROUSERS 褲子◄ **bags** [plural] *BrE old-fashioned* loose-fitting trousers【英, 過時】肥褲子, 寬鬆的褲子: *Oxford bags* 牛津式的肥褲子

11 ►INTERESTED 感興趣的◄ **sb's bag** *informal* something that someone is very interested in or very good at 【非正式】某人的愛好; 某人的強項, 某人最擅長之事: *Sorry, computers aren't really my bag.* 對不起, 電腦並不是我的強項。

12 bag and baggage with all your possessions 連同所有財物, 帶着全部家當: *They threw her out of the house bag and baggage.* 他們把她連人帶東西全都攆出了房子。—see also 另見 BAGS, SLEEPING BAG, **let the cat out of the bag** (CAT (2)), **be left holding the bag** (HOLD¹ (20)), **a mixed bag** (MIXED (6))

bag² *v* **bagged, bagging 1** [T] to put materials or objects into bags 把〔東西〕裝進袋[包]裡 **2** [T] *informal* to kill or catch animals or birds【非正式】獵捕〔獸或鳥〕: *We bagged a rabbit.* 我們抓到了一隻兔子。**3** [T] *informal* to manage to get something that a lot of people want 【非正式】佔有, 搶佔, 據為己有[用]: *Try to bag a couple of seats at the front.* 想辦法在前邊佔幾個座位。**4** [I] also 又作 **bag out** *informal* to hang loosely, like a bag【非正式】〔像袋子一樣〕鬆散下垂, 鼓脹

bag sth ↔ **up** *phr v* [T] to put small objects or loose substances into bags 把…裝入袋中: *We bagged up the money before we closed the shop.* 我們在關上店門之前把錢裝進袋子裡。

bag·a·telle /ˌbægəˋtɛl; ˌbægəˈtel/ *n* **1** [U] a game played on a board with small balls that must be rolled into holes 九穴桌球遊戲 **2** [singular] something that is small and unimportant compared to everything else 小事, 瑣事: *It cost about £25, a mere bagatelle for someone as rich as her.* 它價格在25英鎊左右, 對她這樣有錢的人來說只是區區之數, 不足掛齒。

ba·gel /ˋbegḷ; ˈbeɪgəl/ *n* [C] a small ring-shaped type of bread 麵包圈

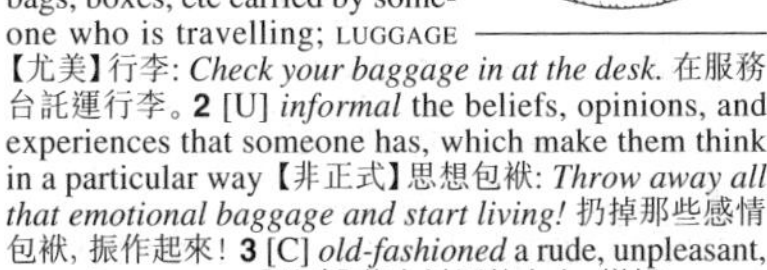
bagel 麵包圈

bag·ful /ˋbægfʊl; ˈbægfʊl/ *n plural* **bagfuls** *or* **bagsful** [C] the amount a bag can hold 一袋的量

bag·gage /ˋbægɪdʒ; ˈbægɪdʒ/ *n* **1** [U] *especially AmE* the cases, bags, boxes, etc carried by someone who is travelling; LUGGAGE 【尤美】行李: *Check your baggage in at the desk.* 在服務台託運行李。**2** [U] *informal* the beliefs, opinions, and experiences that someone has, which make them think in a particular way【非正式】思想包袱: *Throw away all that emotional baggage and start living!* 扔掉那些感情包袱, 振作起來! **3** [C] *old-fashioned* a rude, unpleasant, annoying woman【過時】惹人討厭的女人; 鸞婦

baggage car /ˈ·· ˌ·/ *n* [C] *AmE* the part of a train where boxes, bags etc are carried【美】〔火車的〕行李車

baggage room /ˈ·· ·/ *n* [C] *AmE* a place, usually in a station, where you can leave your bags and collect them later【美】行李寄存處

bag·gy /ˋbægɪ; ˈbægi/ *adj* baggy clothes hang in loose folds〔衣服等〕寬鬆下垂的, 肥大的: *She was wearing jeans and a baggy T-shirt.* 她穿着牛仔褲和又寬又大的T恤。

bag la·dy /ˈ· ˌ··/ *n* [C] a homeless woman who walks around carrying all her possessions with her 露宿街頭、無家可歸的女人, 女流浪者

bag·pipes /ˋbægˌpaɪps; ˈbægpaɪps/ *n* [plural] a musical instrument played especially in Scotland in which air stored in a bag is forced out through pipes to produce the sound〔蘇格蘭的〕風笛 —**bagpipe** *adj*

bags /bægz; bægz/ *spoken BrE*【口, 英】**Bags I!** used by children to claim something that they want 給我!〔孩子要東西時說的話〕: *Bags I the biggest cake!* 給我最大的蛋糕!

ba·guette /bæˋgɛt; bæˈget/ *n* [C] a long thin LOAF of bread, made especially in France〔尤指法式〕長棍麵包

bah /bɑ; bɑː/ *interjection* used to show disapproval of something 呸!〔表示不贊同或輕蔑〕: *Bah! That's stupid.* 呸! 真蠢!

bail¹ /bel; beɪl/ *n* [U] **1** money left with a court of law to prove that a prisoner will return when their TRIAL¹ (1) starts 保釋金: **release sb on bail/grant sb bail** (=let someone out of prison when bail is paid) 交保釋金後釋放某人/允許保釋某人 *She was released on bail of £5,000.* 她在交納5,000英鎊保釋金後獲釋。| **be on bail** (=be waiting for your trial after bail has been paid) 在保釋期間 *While on bail, Marshall committed another assault.* 馬歇爾在保釋期間又犯了襲擊罪。| **stand bail/put up bail** (=pay the bail for someone to be let out) 為某人提供保釋金, 保釋某人 *His father stood bail for him.* 他父親做他的保釋人。**2** one of the two small pieces of wood laid on top of the STUMPS¹ (4) in a game of CRICKET (2)〔板球〕三柱門上的橫木

bail² *v*

bail out *phr v* **1** [T **bail** sb ↔ **out**] to leave a large sum of money with a court so that someone can be let out of prison while waiting for their TRIAL¹ (1)〔交保釋金〕把〔某人〕保釋出來: *Clarke's family paid £500 to bail him out.* 克拉克的家人交了500英鎊保釋他出來。**2** [I, T **bail** sth ↔ **out**] also 又作 **bale out** *BrE*【英】to remove water from the bottom of a boat 從〔船底〕舀出水 **3** [T **bail** sb/sth ↔ **out**] to provide money to get someone or something out of financial trouble〔提供經費〕幫助…擺脫困境: *You can't expect the taxpayer to bail out the car industry indefinitely.* 你不能指望納稅人無限期地幫助汽車工業擺脫困境。**4** [I] *AmE*【美】**a)** to escape from a plane, using a PARACHUTE¹ 跳傘逃脫 **b)** *informal* to leave a place or situation as quickly as you can【非正式】快速逃離, 逃脫; **bale out** (BALE²) *BrE*【英】

bai·ley /ˋbelɪ; ˈbeɪli/ *n* [C] an open area inside the outer wall of a castle 城堡內之庭院, 城堡外庭

bai·liff /ˋbelɪf; ˈbeɪlɪf/ *n* [C] **1** *BrE* an official of the legal system who can take people's goods or property when they owe money【英】〔查封財產或貨物的〕查封官, 執達吏: *Last year, all his furniture was seized by bailiffs.* 去年, 他所有的家具都被查封官查封了。**2** *AmE* an official of the legal system who watches prisoners and keeps order in a court of law【美】法警, 庭吏 **3** *BrE* someone who looks after a farm or land that belongs to someone else【英】農場管理人; 農場主[地主]的管家

bail-out /ˈ· ·/ *n* [C] *informal* financial help given to a person or a company that is in difficulty【非正式】〔緊急財政〕援助: *The directors were hoping for a government bail-out to save the company.* 董事們都希望政府能出資幫助, 以解公司燃眉之急。

bain ma·rie /ˌbæn məˋri; ˌbæn məˈriː/ *n* [C] *French* a pan for cooking things gently usually by cooking them in another pan of water【法】雙層蒸鍋

bairn /bɛrn; beən/ *n* [C] *ScotE, N EngE*【蘇格蘭, 英格蘭北部】**1** a baby 嬰兒 **2** a child 孩子

bait¹ /bet; beɪt/ *n* [singular,U] **1** food used to attract fish, animals, or birds so that you can catch them 餌, 誘餌: *Worms make excellent fish bait.* 蚯蚓是極佳的魚餌。| **take the bait** (=eat it and be caught) 上鉤 **2** something used to make someone do something, buy something etc 引誘物, 誘餌: **take the bait** (=accept what someone is offering) 接受條件 *The customer takes the bait and that's it, you've got another sale.* 顧客接受了條件, 這一來你又做成了一筆生意。**3 rise to the bait** to become angry when someone is deliberately trying to make you angry 上當發火, 中圈套: *Senator O'Brien just* *smiled, refusing to rise to the bait.* 奥布賴恩參議員只是笑了笑, 沒有中計發火。

bait² *v* [T] **1** to put bait on a hook to catch fish or in a trap to catch animals 在〔魚鉤或捕獸器〕上裝餌 **2** to deliberately try to make someone angry by criticizing them, using rude names etc 故意激怒〔某人〕, 使〔某人〕受苦: *The other children took a vicious pleasure in baiting him.* 其他的孩子都在惡意地取笑他。**3 bear-baiting/badger-baiting etc** the activity of attacking a wild animal with dogs 用狗來襲擊熊/獾等〔野獸〕

baize /bez; beɪz/ *n* [U] thick cloth, usually green, used especially to cover tables on which games such as BILLIARDS are played 桌面呢〔多為綠色, 尤用來鋪於枱球等桌面上〕

3 **bake** /bek; beɪk/ *v* **1** [I,T] to cook something using dry heat, in an OVEN 烘, 烤, 焙: *I'm baking some bread.* 我在烤些麵包。| *baked potatoes* 烤馬鈴薯 —see picture on page A10 參見A10頁圖 **2** [I,T] to make something become hard by heating it 烘乾, 燒硬: *In former times, bricks were baked in the sun.* 過去, 磚塊是放在陽光下曬乾的。**3** [I] *informal* to be too hot【非正式】過熱: *Open a window it's baking in here!* 開開窗吧, 這兒熱得像火爐! —see also 另見 HALF-BAKED

baked beans /ˌ· ˈ·/ *n* [U] a dish consisting of beans cooked in a sauce made from tomatoes etc〔加番茄醬的〕烘豆

Ba·ke·lite /ˈbekəˌlaɪt; ˈbeɪkəlaɪt/ *n* [U] *trademark* a hard plastic used especially in the 1930s and 1940s【商標】〔尤指20世紀30和40年代使用的〕酚醛電木; 酚醛塑料

bak·er /ˈbekɚ; ˈbeɪkə/ *n* [C] **1** someone who bakes bread and cakes, especially in order to sell them in a shop 麵包師, 糕點師 **2 baker's** *especially BrE* a shop that sells bread, cakes etc; bakery【尤英】麵包店, 糕點屋

baker's doz·en /ˌ·· ˈ··/ *n* [singular] *old-fashioned* thirteen of something【過時】一打加一, 十三

bak·er·y /ˈbekərɪ; ˈbeɪkəri/ also 又作 **baker's** *BrE*【英】/ˈbekɚz; ˈbeɪkəz/ *n* [C] a place where bread and cakes are baked, or a shop where they are sold 麵包[糕餅]烘房; 麵包[糕餅]店

bak·ing pow·der /ˈ·· ˌ··/ *n* [U] a powder used in baking cakes to make them light 發(酵)粉

baking sheet /ˈ·· ·/ *n* [C] a baking tray 烘烤盤

baking so·da /ˈ·· ˌ··/ *n* [U] BICARBONATE OF SODA 小蘇打

baking tray /ˈ·· ·/ *n* [C] a flat piece of metal that you bake food on 烤盤 —see picture at 參見 TRAY 圖

bak·sheesh /ˌbækˋʃiʃ; ˌbækˈʃiːʃ/ *n* [U] money that people in the Middle East give to poor people, to someone who has helped them, or as a BRIBE〔中東地區的〕小費, 賞錢; 賄賂

bal·a·cla·va /ˌbæləˋklɑvə; ˌbæləˈklɑːvə◂/ *n* [C] *especially BrE* a warm WOOLLEN hat that covers most of your head and face【尤英】盔式大絨帽〔遮蓋住大部分頭和面部的羊毛帽〕

bal·a·lai·ka /ˌbæləˋlaɪkə; ˌbæləˈlaɪkə/ *n* [C] a musical instrument with strings on a three-sided box, played especially in Russia 巴拉萊卡琴〔尤指俄國的三角琴〕

2 2 **bal·ance¹** /ˈbæləns; ˈbæləns/ *n*

1 ►STEADY 穩定的◄ [U] a state in which all your weight is evenly spread so that you do not fall 平衡: *You need a good sense of balance to ride a bicycle.* 騎腳踏車要有良好的平衡感。| **lose your balance** (=be unable to stay steady and not fall) 失去平衡 *I lost my balance and fell on my face.* 我失去平衡, 臉着地摔倒了。| **keep your balance** (=manage to stay steady and not fall, especially when this is difficult) 保持平衡

2 ►EQUALITY 均等◄ [singular] a state in which opposite forces or influences have or are given equal importance 均衡, 均勢, 平衡: **[+between]** *the delicate balance between man and nature* 人與自然之間微妙的平衡 | **[+of]** *a realistic balance of work and relaxation* 勞逸結合, 工作與娛樂的實際平衡 | **strike a balance** (=manage to balance opposing forces) 兩全其美 *We need to strike a balance between the needs of the community and the rights of the individval.* 我們必須處理好社會需要與個人權利之間的平衡。—opposite 反義詞 IMBALANCE

balance 平衡

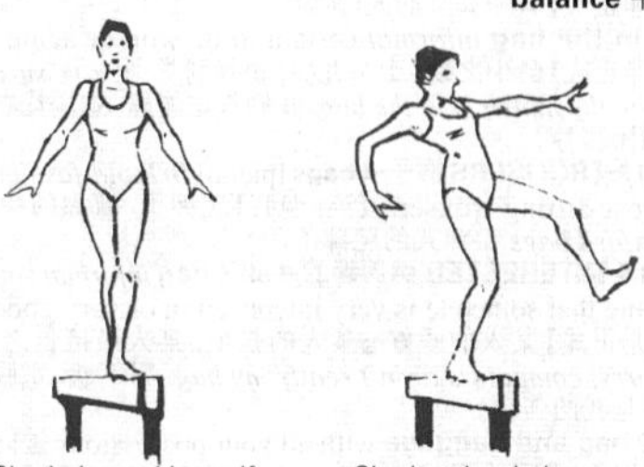

She balanced herself. 她使自己保持平衡。 She lost her balance. 她失去了平衡。

3 on balance if you think something on balance, you think it after considering all the facts 全面考慮之後, 權衡利弊, 總的說來: *I think on balance I prefer the old system.* 總的說來, 我覺得自己更喜歡舊體制。

4 off balance a) unable to stay steady or upright 沒站穩的, 失去平衡的: *I was still off balance when he hit me again.* 沒等我站穩, 他又朝我打過來。**b)** surprised or confused 吃驚的, 糊塗的: **throw sb off balance** *The abrupt question threw her off balance and she couldn't reply.* 那突如其來的問題把她搞糊塗了, 她不知道怎樣回答。

5 the balance of evidence/probability etc the most likely answer or result produced by opposing information, reasons etc 從各方面的證據/可能性等來看: *The balance of evidence suggests that at least some of the politicians received money.* 從各方面的證據來看, 至少有一些政客收了錢。

6 ►FOR WEIGHING 用於稱重量◄ [C] an instrument for weighing things by seeing whether the amounts in two hanging pans are equal 天平, 秤

7 ►BANK 銀行◄ [C] the amount of money that you have in your bank account 餘數, 餘額, 差額, 結餘: *Could you tell me what my balance is please?* 你能告知我的戶口還有多少餘額嗎?

8 ►THE REST 其餘的◄ [singular] the amount of something that remains after some has been used or spent 剩餘(部分): **[+of]** *I'd like to take the balance of my vacation in September.* 我想在九月份用完我剩餘的假期。

9 ►OPPOSITE FORCE 相反的力◄ [singular] a force or influence on one side which equals an opposite force or influence 平衡力; 制衡作用; 抵銷因素: *They work well together – her steadiness acts as a balance to his clever but impractical ideas.* 他們共事合作得很好, 她的穩健沉着對他那巧妙但卻不切實際的想法起了制衡作用。

10 be/hang in the balance if the future or success of something hangs in the balance, you cannot yet know whether the result will be bad or good 懸而未決: *Meanwhile the fate of the refugees continues to hang in the balance.* 同時, 難民的命運仍然懸而未決。

11 tip/swing the balance to influence the result of an event 影響事態的結果: *Your letter of recommendation swung the balance in his favour.* 你的推薦信使情況變得對他有利。

balance² *v*

1 ►KEEP STEADY 保持穩定◄ [I,T] to get into a steady position, without falling to one side or the other, or to put something into this position (使)平穩, (使)保持平衡: **balance sth on** *She balanced the cup on a huge pile of books.* 她把杯子穩穩地放在一大堆書上。| **[+on]** *He turned around, balancing awkwardly on one foot.* 他轉

過身去，笨拙地用一隻腳站穩。

2 ▶BE EQUAL TO 等於◀ [I,T] to be equal to something else in weight, amount, or importance（使）〔重量、數量、重要性等〕均衡，相抵，相等：*Exports must go down to balance decreased imports.* 必須減少出口以便和下降的進口保持平衡。

3 ▶GO WELL WITH 與…相配◀ [T] to have an opposite effect to something else, so that a good result is achieved 使〔兩種相反的效果〕適中：*just enough sugar to balance the acidity of the fruit* 加足夠的糖中和一下水果的酸味

4 ▶KEEP STH EQUAL 保持某物均衡◀ [T] to try to give equal importance to two things 平衡好，處理好：*a working mother, balancing home and career* 能處理好家庭和事業兩者關係的上班工作的母親 | **balance sth with** *She had learned to balance working efficiency with good human relationships.* 她已經學會協調，既要提高工作效率，又要保持良好的人際關係。

5 ▶THINK ABOUT 思考◀ [T] to consider the importance of something in relation to the importance of something else 權衡，斟酌，比較：**balance sth against** *The courts must balance the liberty of the few against the security of the many.* 法庭必須權衡少數人的自由和多數人的安全之間的關係。

6 balance the books/budget to show or make sure that the money that has been spent is equal to the money that is available 使收支平衡

balance beam /ˈ·· ˌ·/ *n* [C] a long narrow wooden board on which a GYMNAST performs〔體操〕平衡木

bal·anced /ˈbælənst; ˈbælənst/ *adj* **1** giving equal attention to all sides or opinions; fair 公平的，合理的；均衡的，調和的：*balanced and impartial reporting of the election campaign* 對競選活動公正而無偏袒的報道 **2** not giving too much importance to one thing; SENSIBLE 不偏不倚的；平和的：*a balanced outlook on life* 平和的生活態度 **3** arranged to include things or people of different kinds in the right amount 均衡的：*a balanced programme of events* 合理的節目安排 | **balanced diet** (=containing the right foods in the right amounts) 均衡飲食

balance of pay·ments /ˌ·· · ˈ··/ *n* [singular] the difference between what a country spends in order to buy goods and services abroad, and the money it earns selling goods and services abroad 國際收支差額；國際收支平衡

balance of pow·er /ˌ·· · ˈ··/ *n* **the balance of power** a situation in which political or military strength is shared evenly〔政治或軍事的〕力量均勢：**hold the balance of power** (=be able to make either side more powerful than the other by supporting them) 舉足輕重，掌握決定權 *In a hung parliament the centre parties hold the balance of power.* 在各黨派勢均力敵的議會裡，中間黨派的地位舉足輕重。

balance of trade /ˌ·· · ˈ·/ *n* the difference in value between the goods a country buys from abroad and the goods it sells abroad 貿易差額

balance sheet /ˈ·· ·/ *n* [C] a statement of how much money a business has earned and how much money it has paid for goods and services 資產負債表，決算表〔顯示收支總差額的報告表〕：*a healthy balance sheet despite the recession* 儘管經濟衰退，收支仍然平衡

bal·co·ny /ˈbælkənɪ; ˈbælkəni/ *n* [C] **1** a structure you can stand on that sticks out from the upstairs wall of a building 陽台 **2** the seats upstairs at a theatre〔戲院的〕樓座，樓廳 — see picture at 參見 THEATRE 圖

bald /bɔld; bɔːld/ *adj* **1** having little or no hair on your head 禿（頭）的：*His bald head was badly sunburnt.* 他的禿頭被陽光嚴重灼傷。| **go bald** (=gradually lose your hair) 逐漸禿頂 **2** not having enough of what usually covers something 光禿的，磨光的，掉光的：*The car's tires are completely bald.* 這輛汽車的車胎完全磨光了。**3 bald statement/language/truth etc** a statement etc that is correct but gives no additional information to help you understand or accept what is said 不加修飾[直話直說]的聲明/語言/道理等 —**baldness** *n* [U]

bald ea·gle /ˌ· ˈ··/ *n* [C] a large North American bird with a white head and neck that is the national bird of the US 白頭鷲，禿鷹〔產於北美，美國國鳥〕

bal·der·dash /ˈbɔldɚˌdæʃ; ˈbɔːldədæʃ/ *n* [U] *old-fashioned* talk or writing that is silly nonsense【過時】胡言亂語，廢話

bald-faced /ˌ· ˈ·◂/ *adj AmE* making no attempt to hide that you know what you are doing or saying is wrong; BAREFACED【美】厚顏無恥的；露骨的

bald·ing /ˈbɔldɪŋ; ˈbɔːldɪŋ/ *adj* a balding man is losing the hair on his head 漸漸變禿的：*a spare, already balding man in his mid-thirties* 一位瘦弱的、已開始禿頂的三十五六歲的男人

bald·ly /ˈbɔldlɪ; ˈbɔːldli/ *adv* in a way that is true but makes no attempt to be polite 直言不諱地，直截了當地，赤裸裸地：*To put it baldly, stop smoking or you'll be dead in a year.* 坦白說吧，你如果不戒煙，最多活一年。

bale¹ /bel; beɪl/ *n* [C] a large quantity of something such as paper or hay that is tightly tied together especially into a block 大捆，大包：*a bale of straw* 一大捆稻草

bale² *v* [T] to tie something such as paper or hay into a large block 把〔紙、乾草等〕綁成一大捆

bale out *phr v* [I] *BrE*【英】**1** to escape from an aircraft by PARACHUTE¹ 跳傘逃生 **2** to leave a place or situation as quickly as you can 迅速離開；**bail out** (BAIL² (4)) *AmE*【美】

bale·ful /ˈbelfəl; ˈbeɪlfəl/ *adj literary* expressing anger, hatred, or a wish to harm someone【文】邪惡的，惡毒的，帶威脅性的：*a baleful look* 充滿惡意的目光 —**balefully** *adv*

balk¹ also 又作 **baulk** *BrE*【英】/bɔk; bɔːk/ *v* **1** [I] to not want to or refuse to do something that is difficult, or frightening 畏縮不前，猶豫，打退堂鼓：**[I+at]** *Perry seemed interested, but balked when he heard the price.* 佩里似乎感興趣，但一聽價錢就猶豫了。**2** [I+at] if a horse balks at a fence etc, it stops suddenly and refuses to jump or cross it〔馬在障礙物前〕突然站住 **3** [T] to stop someone or something from getting what they want 阻止，妨礙：*eager young men balked by rules and regulations* 為規章制度所限的熱情高漲的年輕人 **4** *AmE* to stop, in BASEBALL, in the middle of the action of throwing the ball to the player who is trying to hit it【美】〔棒球投手在投球時〕做假動作，佯投

balk² also 又作 **baulk** *BrE*【英】*n* [C] a thick rough wooden beam 梁木，粗木枋

bal·ky /ˈbɔkɪ; ˈbɔːki/ *adj AmE* refusing to do what you are asked or expected to do【美】倔強的，聽不進別人的話的：*He's a balky man to have to work with.* 他是個不好共事的人。

ball¹ /bɔl; bɔːl/ *n* [C] (S1) (W2)

1 ▶TO PLAY WITH 用來玩的◀ a round object that is thrown, kicked, or hit in a game or sport 球：*Bounce that ball to me.* 把球彈給我。| *a tennis ball* 網球

2 ▶ROUND SHAPE 圓形◀ something formed or rolled into a round shape 球狀物：*a ball of string* 線團 | *Shape the dough into balls.* 把麵團做成球狀。

3 the ball of the foot/hand/thumb the rounded part of the foot at the base of the toe, rounded part of the hand at the base of the thumb or fingers 大腳趾底部的肉球/手心圓肉/拇指球 —see also 另見 EYEBALL¹ (1) —see picture at 參見 FOOT¹ 圖

4 a fast/good/curved etc ball a ball that is thrown, hit, or kicked fast etc in a game or sport 快球/好球/弧圈球等：*He hit a long ball to right field.* 他向右半場踢了一個長傳球。

5 no ball a ball that is thrown too high, low etc towards someone trying to hit it, in the games of CRICKET (2) or ROUNDERS〔板球或圓場棒球的〕投球犯規〔球投得太高或太低〕

6 ▶BASEBALL 棒球◀ *AmE* a ball thrown in BASEBALL that a player is not expected to hit because it is not within the correct area【美】〔棒球運動中投手投出的〕壞球

7 **►BULLET** 子彈◄ a round bullet fired from a type of gun that was used in the past 彈丸, 球形子彈
8 **on the ball** *informal* thinking or acting quickly【非正式】機警的; 有見識的; 效率高的: *We need an assistant who's really on the ball.* 我們需要一名真正內行的助手。
9 **set/start the ball rolling** to begin an activity or event or make sure it continues 使事情開始[繼續進行]: *Let's start the ball rolling with a few suggestions.* 讓我們提幾條建議作為開始。
10 **the ball is in your court** it is your turn to take action or to reply 現在輪到你〔作出反應或採取行動〕: *I've sent him a letter, now the ball's in his court.* 我已經給他發了信, 下面就看他的了。
11 **►DANCE** 跳舞◄ a large formal occasion at which people dance 舞會
12 **have a ball** *informal* to have a very good time【非正式】玩得很開心: *We had a ball at the party last night.* 昨晚聚會我們玩得很開心。
13 **balls** [plural] **a)** TESTICLES 睾丸 **b)** *taboo spoken* courage or determination【諱, 口】膽量: *It's not going to be easy. It'll take fight, guts and balls.* 這不容易。這需要鬥志、勇氣和膽量。**c)** *BrE taboo spoken* something that is stupid or wrong; nonsense【英, 諱, 口】胡說八道: *That's a load of balls!* 那簡直是放屁!
14 **a ball of fire** someone who has a lot of energy and is active and successful 精力充沛、積極向上的人
15 **the whole ball of wax** *AmE informal* the whole thing; everything【美, 非正式】一切, 全部, 所有
16 **ball-buster/ball-breaker** *AmE slang*【美俚】**a)** a problem that is very difficult to deal with 棘手的問題 **b)** an offensive word for a woman who uses her authority over men〔冒犯用語〕對男人發號施令的女人 —see also 另見 BALLS, **not play ball** (PLAY¹ (24))

ball² *v* [T] **1** also 又作 **ball up** to form something into a small round shape so that it takes up less space 把〔某物〕弄成球狀 **2** *AmE spoken taboo* to have sex with a woman【美口, 諱】和〔女人〕發生性關係
ball sth ↔ **up** *phr v AmE spoken* to make a situation confused or difficult to deal with【美口】弄糟: *No, we're not going now, Lindsay's managed to ball everything up.* 不, 我們現在不走。林賽把事情搞得一團糟。—see also 另見 BALLS-UP

bal·lad /ˋbæləd; ˈbæləd/ *n* [C] **1** a short story in the form of a poem 敍事詩歌 **2** a simple song, especially a popular love song 民歌, 歌謠; 流行的情歌

bal·last¹ /ˋbæləst; ˈbæləst/ *n* [U] **1** heavy material that is carried by a ship to make it more steady in the water〔使船隻保持平穩的〕壓艙物 **2** material such as sand that is carried in a BALLOON¹ (2) and can be thrown out to make it rise〔起穩定氣球或操縱高度作用的〕沙囊, 壓載物 **3** broken stones that are used as a surface under a road, railway lines etc〔道路、鐵路等鋪路基用的〕道砟, 石碴

ballast² *v* [T] to fill or supply something with ballast 給〔船〕放壓艙物; 給〔氣球等〕放沙囊; 為〔鐵路〕鋪道砟

ball bear·ing /ˌ· ˈ··/ *n* [C] **1** an arrangement of small metal balls moving in a ring around a bar so that the bar can turn more easily 滾珠軸承 **2** one of these metal balls 滾珠

ball boy /ˈ· ·/ *n* [C] a boy who picks up tennis balls for people playing in important tennis matches〔在網球比賽中為球員拾球的〕球僮 —see picture at 參見 TENNIS 圖

ball·cock /ˋbɔlˌkɑk; ˈbɔːlkɒk/ *n* [C] a hollow floating ball on a stick that opens and closes a hole, to allow water to flow into a container, for example in a TOILET (1) 浮球閥, 浮球栓, 浮球旋塞

bal·le·ri·na /ˌbæləˋrinə; ˌbæləˈriːnə/ *n* [C] a woman who dances in ballets 芭蕾舞女演員

bal·let /ˋbæle; ˈbæleɪ/ *n* **1** [C] a performance in which a special style of dancing and music tell a story without any speaking 芭蕾舞劇; 芭蕾舞曲: *Tchaikovsky wrote several famous ballets.* 柴可夫斯基創作了好幾部著名的芭蕾舞曲。**2** [U] this type of dancing 芭蕾舞(藝術) **3** [C] a group of ballet dancers who work together 芭蕾舞團: *the Bolshoi ballet* (俄國)大劇院芭蕾舞團

ballet danc·er /ˈ·· ˌ··/ *n* [C] someone who dances in ballets 芭蕾舞演員

ball game /ˈ· ·/ *n* **1** *AmE* a BASEBALL game【美】棒球比賽 **2** *BrE* any game played with a ball【英】球類比賽 **3 a whole new ball game** a situation that is very different from the one you are used to 完全不同的情況: *I used to be a teacher, so working in an office is a whole new ball game.* 我以前是教師, 因此辦公室工作對我是件全新的事。

ball girl /ˈ· ·/ *n* [C] a girl who picks up tennis balls for people playing in important tennis matches〔在網球比賽中為球員拾球的〕女球僮

bal·lis·tic mis·sile /bəˌlɪstɪk ˋmɪsl; bəˌlɪstɪk ˈmɪsaɪl/ *n* [C] a MISSILE (1) that is guided up into the air and then falls freely 彈道導彈, 彈道飛彈

bal·lis·tics /bəˋlɪstɪks; bəˈlɪstɪks/ *n* [U] the scientific study of the movement of objects that are thrown or fired through the air, such as bullets shot from a gun 彈道學, 發射學

bal·loon¹ /bəˋlun; bəˈluːn/ *n* [C] **1** a small brightly coloured rubber bag that can be filled with air and used as a toy or decoration for parties 玩具氣球, 裝飾性氣球 **2** a large bag of strong light cloth filled with gas or heated air so that it can float in the air 熱氣球: *hot air balloons drifting toward the horizon* 朝着遠處地平線飄去的熱氣球 **3** the circle drawn around the words spoken by the characters in a CARTOON〔卡通漫畫中表示人物對白的〕氣球狀對話框 **4 balloon payment** *AmE* money borrowed that must be paid back in one large sum after several smaller payments have been made【美】〔分期付款中〕最後一筆數目特大的償付額: *a $10,000 balloon payment due in two years* 最後一筆兩年後到期應付的一萬美元的分期付款額 **5 go down like a lead balloon** *informal* if a joke, remark etc goes down like a lead balloon, people do not laugh or react as you expected【非正式】〔笑話、講話等〕未達到預期效果

balloon² *v* [I] **1** to get bigger and rounder 膨脹, 鼓起來: [**+out/outwards/up**] *His cheeks ballooned out as he played his trumpet.* 他吹喇叭時, 兩頰都鼓了起來。**2** to become larger in amount 膨脹, 增加: *Mitch's business debts ballooned to $20,000 in just one year.* 只過了一年, 米奇的商業債務就迅速增加到二萬美元。

bal·loon·ing /bəˋlunɪŋ; bəˈluːnɪŋ/ *n* [U] the sport of flying in a balloon 乘熱氣球飛行(運動) —**balloonist** *n* [C]

bal·lot¹ /ˋbælət; ˈbælət/ *n* **1** [C,U] a system of secret voting or an occasion when you vote in this way 無記名投票〔選舉或表決〕: *The Club's officers are always chosen by ballot.* 俱樂部的官員一直都是無記名投票選出來的。**2** [C] a piece of paper on which you make a secret vote; BALLOT PAPER〔無記名〕投票用紙, 選票 **3** [C] the number of votes recorded; POLL¹ (3) 投票總數, 投票結果

ballot² *v* [I,T] to vote or to decide something by a vote 進行無記名投票; 通過投票選出[決定]: *The chairman is elected by balloting all the shareholders.* 董事長是經全體股東投票選出的。

ballot box /ˈ·· ·/ *n* **1** [C] a box that ballot papers are put in after voting 投票箱 **2 the ballot box** the system or process of voting in an election 投票(法): *The people have expressed their views through the ballot box.* 人們通過投票的方式表達自己的意見。

ballot pa·per /ˈ·· ˌ··/ *n* [C] a piece of paper on which you record your vote 選票

ball park /ˈ· ·/ *n* **1** *especially AmE* a field for playing BASEBALL, with seats for watching the game【尤美】〔有看台的〕棒球場 **2 in the right ball park** *informal* close to the amount, price etc that you want or are thinking about【非正式】大致正確; 差不多: *Their estimate is definitely in the right ball park.* 他們的估計肯定大致是正確的。**3 a ball park figure** a number or amount that is almost but not exactly correct 大致正確的數字: *He said $25,000 but it's just a ball park figure.* 他說是二萬五千美元, 不過這只是個大致的數目。

ball·play·er /ˋbɔlˏpleɚ; ˈbɔːlˌpleɪə/ *n* [C] *AmE* someone who plays BASEBALL【美】棒球運動員

ball·point /ˋbɔlˏpɔɪnt; ˈbɔːlpɔɪnt/ also 又作 **ballpoint pen** /ˏ·· ˈ·/ *n* [C] a pen with a ball at the end that rolls thick ink onto the paper 圓珠筆, 原子筆 —see picture at 參見 PEN¹ 圖

ball·room /ˋbɔlˏrum; ˈbɔːlrʊm/ *n* [C] a very large room used for dancing on formal occasions 舞廳, 舞場

ballroom danc·ing /ˏ·· ˈ··/ *n* [U] a type of dancing that is done with a partner and has different steps for particular types of music, such as the WALTZ¹ (1) 交際舞, 交誼舞〈如華爾茲等〉

balls¹ /bɔlz; bɔːlz/ *interjection taboo* used to show strong disapproval or disappointment【諱】〔表示強烈反對或失望〕胡說八道: *Balls to that! I'm not working Saturday morning!* 胡說!我星期六上午不工作!

balls² *v*

balls sth ↔ **up** *phr v BrE taboo slang* to do something very badly or unsuccessfully【英, 諱, 俚】把…弄得一團糟: *He totally ballsed up his exams.* 他考試全考砸了。

balls-up /ˈ· ·/ *n BrE taboo slang* something that has been done very badly or unsuccessfully【英, 諱, 俚】弄得一團糟的事, 爛攤子: *Nigel made a complete balls-up of the arrangements.* 奈傑爾把安排全搞亂了。

ball·sy /ˋbɔlzɪ; ˈbɔːlzi/ *adj AmE spoken* brave and determined【美口】膽識過人的: *He's a ballsy kind of guy.* 他是個膽識過人的傢伙。

bal·ly /ˋbælɪ; ˈbæli/ *adj, adv BrE old-fashioned* an expression meaning BLOODY¹ used to avoid offending other people【英, 過時】討厭的[地], 見鬼的[地]

bal·ly·hoo /ˋbælɪˏhu; ˌbæliˈhuː/ *n* [U] *informal* a situation in which people publicly express a lot of anger, excitement etc【非正式】大吹大擂, 譁眾取寵: *After all the promotional ballyhoo, the film flopped.* 儘管搞了大吹大擂的宣傳, 這部電影還是不賣座。

balm /bɑm; bɑːm/ *n* [C,U] **1** an oily liquid with a strong, pleasant smell that you rub into your skin, often to reduce pain〔塗抹用的藥用〕油, 膏, 止痛膏 **2** *literary* something that gives you comfort【文】安慰(物), 慰藉(物): *Her words were a balm to my shredded nerves.* 她的話對我紛亂的心緒多少是些安慰。

balm·y /ˋbɑmɪ; ˈbɑːmi/ *adj* balmy air, weather etc is warm and pleasant〔空氣、天氣等〕溫和的, 宜人的: *a balmy summer night* 宜人的夏夜

ba·lo·ney /bəˋlonɪ; bəˈləʊni/ *n* [U] *informal*【非正式】**1** something that is silly or not true; nonsense 胡說, 鬼話: *"Don't give me that baloney," he said, winking at Christopher.* 他朝克里斯托弗眨了眨眼說: "別胡說。" **2** *AmE* BOLOGNA【美】博洛尼亞香腸, 大香腸

bal·sa /ˋbɔlsə; ˈbɔːlsə/ *n* [C,U] a tropical American tree or the wood from this tree, which is very light〔美洲熱帶地區產的〕白塞木樹; 白塞木, 輕木

bal·sam /ˋbɔlsəm; ˈbɔːlsəm/ *n* [C,U] BALM, or the tree that produces it 香脂冷杉; 〔上述植物的〕香脂, 香膠

bal·us·trade /ˏbæləˋstred; ˌbæləˈstreɪd/ *n* [C] a row of upright pieces of stone or wood with a bar along the top, especially around a BALCONY〔尤指陽台周圍的〕扶手, 欄杆

bam·boo /bæmˋbu; ˌbæmˈbuː◂/ *n* [C,U] a tall tropical plant with hollow stems that are used for making furniture 竹, 竹子

bam·boo·zle /bæmˋbuzl̩; bæmˈbuːzəl/ *v* [T] *informal* to deceive, trick, or confuse someone【非正式】欺騙, 愚弄, 蒙蔽

3 **ban¹** /bæn; bæn/ *n* [C] an official order that forbids something from being used or done 禁止, 禁令: *The President supports a global ban on nuclear testing.* 總統支持全球性禁止核試驗。—see also 另見 TEST BAN

ban² *v* **banned, banning** [T] to say that something must not be done, seen, used etc 禁止, 取締: *Smoking is banned in the building.* 大樓內禁止吸煙。| **ban sb from doing sth** *Charlie's been banned from driving for a year.* 查理被禁止駕車一年。| **banned book/film/video etc** (=a book etc that is illegal) 禁書/禁止上映的電影/禁播錄像等

ba·nal /ˋbenl̩; bəˈnɑːl/ *adj* ordinary and not interesting, because of a lack of new or different ideas 平淡無奇的, 平庸的, 陳腐的: *a banal piece of writing* 平庸之作 —**banality** /bəˋnælətɪ; bəˈnælɪ̣ti/ *n* [C,U]

ba·na·na /bəˋnænə; bəˈnɑːnə/ *n* [C] a long curved tropical fruit with a yellow skin 香蕉 —see picture on page A8 參見 A8 頁圖

banana re·pub·lic /ˌ·ˈ·· ·ˈ··/ *n* [C] *informal* an insulting word for a small poor country with weak government that depends on financial help from abroad【非正式】香蕉共和國〔侮辱性詞語, 指政府軟弱, 經濟不發達, 需依賴他國財政援助的小國〕

ba·na·nas /bəˋnænəz; bəˈnɑːnəz/ *adj informal*【非正式】**1** crazy or silly 發瘋的; 愚蠢的: *People think Mr Allen is bananas because he talks to his plants.* 人們都認為艾倫先生發瘋了, 因為他對着他的植物說話。**2 go bananas** become very angry or excited 變得十分氣憤[激動]: *Dad will go bananas when he sees this.* 爸爸看到這個會氣瘋的。

banana skin /·ˈ·· ˌ·/ *n* [C] *BrE informal* an embarrassing mistake made by someone in a public position, especially a politician or someone in a government【英, 非正式】引起麻煩[使人出洋相]的事件: *This incident could turn into another banana skin for the government.* 這件事可能使政府再次出洋相。

banana split /ˌ·· ˈ·/ *n* [C] a sweet dish with bananas and ICE CREAM 香蕉新地, 香蕉船〔用香蕉和冰淇淋做成的甜點〕

band¹ /bænd; bænd/ *n* [C]

1 ▶MUSIC 音樂◀ a group of musicians, especially a group that plays popular music〔尤指演奏流行音樂的〕樂隊, 樂團: **jazz/rock/big etc band** (=a band that plays JAZZ etc) 爵士樂隊/搖滾樂隊/大樂團等 *He plays saxophone in a little-known jazz band.* 他在一個不知名的爵士樂隊裡吹薩克斯管。| **band leader/singer** (=someone who leads a band, or sings with a band) 樂隊領班/主唱 2 2

2 ▶GROUP OF PEOPLE 人羣◀ a group of people formed because of a common belief or purpose 一夥, 一羣, 一幫: *a small band of enthusiasts* 一小羣熱心者

3 ▶PIECE OF MATERIAL 材料◀ a flat, narrow piece of material with one end joined to the other to form a circle 繫物的帶子; 箍帶: *papers held together with a rubber band* 用橡皮筋綁在一起的文件 | *a wide silk band* 寬絲帶

4 ▶PATTERN 圖形◀ a thick coloured line 條紋: *There are orange bands around the snake's back.* 這條蛇的背部有橙色條紋。

5 tax/income/age etc band a particular range of tax, income etc in which a group of people belong 稅收/收入/年齡等範圍: *people within the $20,000 – $30,000 income band* 收入在二萬至三萬元這個範圍的人

6 ▶RADIO 無線電◀ *technical* a range of radio signals【術語】波段, 頻帶

band² *v* [T] to put a band of colour or material on or around something 給…加上條紋邊框, 給…鑲邊

band together *phr v* [I] to unite in order to achieve something 團結起來, 聯手: *The two parties banded together to form an alliance.* 兩黨團結起來結成聯盟。

ban·dage¹ /ˋbændɪdʒ; ˈbændɪdʒ/ *n* [C] a narrow piece of cloth that you tie around a wound or around a part of the body that has been injured 繃帶

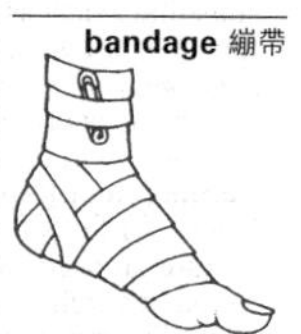
bandage 繃帶

bandage² also 又作 **bandage up** *v* [T] to tie or cover a part of the body with a bandage 用繃帶包紮: *The nurse bandaged up his sprained ankle.* 護士用繃帶包紮他

扭傷了的腳踝。

Band-Aid /'· ·/ *n* [C] *AmE trademark* a piece of thin material that is stuck to the skin to cover cuts and other small wounds【美, 商標】邦迪牌創可貼〔一種護創膠布〕; PLASTER[1] (3) *BrE*【英】; ELASTOPLAST *BrE*【英】

ban·dan·na, bandana /bænˋdænə; bænˈdænə/ *n* [C] a large brightly coloured piece of cloth you wear around your head or neck 印花大圍巾, 大頭巾: *hair tied up in a scarlet bandanna* 紮着鮮紅頭巾的頭髮

B and B /ˌbi ənd ˋbi; ˌbiː ənd ˈbiː/ the abbreviation of 縮寫= BED AND BREAKFAST: *a small B and B in the Cotswolds* 科茨沃爾德的一家提供住宿和早餐的小旅店

band·box /ˋbændˌbɑks; ˈbændbɒks/ *n* [C] a box for keeping hats in〔裝帽子的〕圓筒形盒

ban·deau /bænˋdo; ˈbændəʊ/ *n plural* **bandeaux** /-ˋdoz; -dəʊz/ [C] a band of material that you wear around your head to keep your hair in place 束髮帶

ban·dit /ˋbændɪt; ˈbændʒt/ *n* [C] someone who robs people, especially one of group of people who attack travellers 強盜, 土匪, 歹徒: *Beware of bandits in the mountains.* 當心山裡的土匪。—see also 另見 ONE-ARMED BANDIT —**banditry** *n* [U]

band·mas·ter /ˋbændˌmæstɚ; ˈbændˌmɑːstə/ *n* [C] someone who CONDUCTs a military band, BRASS (2) band etc〔軍樂隊、銅管樂隊等的〕樂隊指揮

ban·do·lier /ˌbændəˈlɪr; ˌbændəˈlɪə/ *n* [C] a belt that goes over someone's shoulder and is used to carry bullets〔斜掛於肩膀的〕子彈帶

bands·man /ˋbændzmən; ˈbændzmən/ *n* [C] a musician who plays in a military band, BRASS (2) band etc〔軍樂隊、銅管樂隊等的〕樂隊隊員

band·stand /ˋbændˌstænd; ˈbændstænd/ *n* [C] a structure that has a roof but no walls and is used by a band playing music in a park〔有頂蓋的〕室外音樂演奏台

band·wa·gon /ˋbændˌwægən; ˈbændˌwægən/ *n* [C] **climb/jump on the bandwagon** to begin to do something that a lot of other people are doing 趕浪頭, 順應潮流, 隨大流: *Everyone seems to be jumping on the environmental bandwagon.* 大家似乎都順應潮流, 開始關注環境問題。

ban·dy[1] /ˋbændɪ; ˈbændi/ *adj* bandy legs curve outwards at the knees 兩膝向外曲的, 羅圈腿的 —**bandy-legged** *adj*

bandy[2] *v* **bandy words (with)** *old-fashioned* to quarrel with someone【過時】(與某人) 爭吵, 鬥嘴

bandy sth **about** *phr v* [T] to mention an idea, name, remark etc several times, especially to impress someone 口頭傳播, 隨便散播: *Several different figures have been bandied about – which is correct?* 有好幾個不同的數字到處在傳, 究竟哪個是對的?

bane /ben; beɪn/ *n* [singular] something that causes trouble or makes people unhappy 禍根; 災星: **be the bane of** *Drugs are the bane of the inner cities.* 毒品是城市中心區的禍根。| **the bane of sb's life/existence** (=a cause of continual trouble or unhappiness) 某人一生麻煩[不幸]的緣由 *Ask any laser printer user what the bane of their life is and they'll tell you – replacing the toner.* 問任何一個使用激光打印機的人, 他最不願意做的事是甚麼, 他會告訴你 —— 那就是更換碳粉。

bane·ful /ˋbenfəl; ˈbeɪnfəl/ *adj literary* evil or bad【文】邪惡的; 有害的 —**banefully** *adv*

S3 **bang**[1] /bæŋ; bæŋ/ *n* **1** [C] a sudden loud noise caused by something such as a gun or an object hitting a hard surface 砰; 啪〔槍聲或重物相碰的聲音〕: *The front door slammed with a loud bang.* 前門砰的一聲關上了。**2** [C] a hard knock or hit against something 猛擊, 猛撞; 重打: *That was a nasty bang on the head.* 頭撞得可不輕。**3 bangs** [plural] *AmE* hair cut straight across your forehead【美】〔頭髮的〕前劉海; FRINGE[1] (1) *BrE*【英】—see picture on page A6 參見 A6 頁圖 **4** [singular] *AmE informal* a strong feeling of pleasure【美, 非正式】快感, 樂趣: *She got a real bang out of seeing the kids in the school play.* 看到孩子們在演學校裡排演的戲劇時, 她高興極了。**5 go off with a bang** to happen in a very successful way 極為成功, 大受歡迎: *The party really went off with a bang!* 聚會真的棒極了!

bang[2] *v*

1 ▶KNOCK/HIT STH 碰到某物◀ [I,T] to hit something hard against something else, making a loud noise 猛敲; 砰然重擊: *She banged the phone down.* 她把電話啪的一聲放下。| **[+on]** *They were banging on the door with their fists.* 他們用拳頭使勁地敲門。

2 ▶CLOSE STH 關上某物◀ [I always+adv/prep, T] to close something violently making a loud noise, or to make something close in this way 很響地使勁關 (門): *She banged the door and stomped up the stairs.* 她砰的一聲關上門, 噔噔地上了樓。| **bang shut** *The window banged shut.* 窗戶砰的一聲關上了。

3 ▶MAKE NOISE 發出響聲◀ [I] to make a loud noise or noises 砰砰作響: **[+about/around/away]** *I could hear the garage door banging in the wind.* 我能聽見車庫的門被風吹得砰砰作響。

4 ▶HIT STH 碰撞某物◀ [T] to hit a part of your body or something you are carrying against something, especially by accident; BUMP[1] (1)〔意外地〕撞擊: *Bobby fell and banged his knee.* 博比摔倒了, 膝蓋撞了一下。| *I slipped and banged the guitar against the door.* 我滑了一跤, 結他撞到了門上。

5 be banging your head against a brick wall *informal* to be wasting your efforts by doing something that does not produce any results【非正式】白費氣力, 枉費心機: *Trying to teach that class is like banging your head against a brick wall.* 想要教那個班的學生學點東西完全是白費氣力。

6 ▶HAVE SEX 性交◀ [T] *taboo* to have sex with someone【諱】與〔某人〕發生性關係

bang on *phr v* [I] *BrE informal* to talk continuously about something in a boring way【英, 非正式】囉嗦個沒完: **[+about]** *I'm tired of politicians banging on about family values.* 我厭倦了政治家沒完沒了地談論家庭的價值觀。

bang sth ↔ **out** *phr v* [T] *informal*【非正式】**1** to play a tune or song loudly and badly on a piano〔在鋼琴上〕使勁亂敲地彈奏〔樂曲、歌曲〕**2** to write something in a hurry, especially on a TYPEWRITER〔尤指在打字機上〕匆忙趕寫: *Danielle banged out a few letters, before going home for the day.* 丹尼爾在當天回家前匆忙地寫了幾封信。

bang sb/sth ↔ **up** *phr v* [T] **1** *BrE slang* to put someone in prison【英俚】監禁 **2** *AmE informal* to seriously damage something【美, 非正式】使…嚴重受損: *a banged-up old Buick* 嚴重毀壞的舊別克轎車

bang[3] *adv* **1** *informal* directly or exactly【非正式】直接地; 準確地; 正巧, 恰恰: *The train arrived bang on time.* 火車準點到達。**2 bang on** *spoken* exactly correct【口】完全正確: *Yes! Your answer's bang on!* 對! 你的答案完全正確! **3 bang goes** *spoken* used to show that you are unhappy because something you had hoped for will not happen【口】完蛋了, 告吹了: *£750 to repair the car? Bang goes my holiday.* 花 750 英鎊修汽車? 那我度假的事就泡湯了。**4** *spoken* in a sudden, violent way【口】突然, 猛然: *He slowed down, and bang! The car behind crashed straight into us!* 他減速後, 後面的車突然直撞向我們!

bang[4] *interjection* used to make a sound like a gun or bomb 砰〔用作模仿槍聲或炸彈的聲響〕: *"Bang, bang – you're dead," Tommy shouted.* "砰, 砰 —— 打死你了。" 湯米喊道。

bang·er /ˋbæŋɚ; ˈbæŋə/ *n* [C] *BrE informal*【英, 非正式】**1** a SAUSAGE 香腸 **2** an old car in bad condition 破舊的汽車, 老爺車: *Gary's finally scrapped that old banger of his.* 加里終於丟棄了他那輛老爺車。**3** a type of noisy FIREWORK〔聲音很響的一種〕爆竹

ban·gle /ˋbæŋgl; ˈbæŋgəl/ *n* [C] a solid band of gold,

silver etc that you wear loosely around your wrist as jewellery 手鐲

bang-up /ˈ· ·/ *adj AmE informal* very good【美, 非正式】非常好的, 很棒的: *He did a bang-up job fixing the plumbing.* 他把水管修得棒極了。

ban·ish /ˈbænɪʃ; ˈbænɪʃ/ *v* [T] **1** to not allow someone or something to stay in a particular place 驅逐, 趕走; 驅除, 排除: **banish sth from/to** *The children were banished to the backyard.* 孩子們被趕到後院裡去了。**2** to send someone away permanently from their country or the area where they live, especially as an official punishment 放逐; 驅逐出境〔尤指作為官方懲罰〕: **banish sb from/to** *Many Soviet dissidents were banished to Siberia.* 許多持不同政見的前蘇聯人士被流放到西伯利亞。**3 banish sb/sth (from your mind)** to try to stop thinking about something, especially something that worries you 不再想某人／某物 —**banishment** *n* [U]

ban·is·ter /ˈbænɪstɚ; ˈbænɨstə/ *n* [C] a row of upright sticks with a bar along the top, that stops you from falling over the edge of stairs〔樓梯的〕欄杆, 扶手 —see picture on page A4 參見 A4 頁圖

ban·jo /ˈbændʒo; ˈbændʒəʊ/ *n* [C] a musical instrument with four or more strings, a long neck and a round body used especially in COUNTRY AND WESTERN music 班卓琴

口1 書1 **bank[1]** /bæŋk; bæŋk/ *n* [C]

1 ▶MONEY 錢◀ a) a business that keeps and lends money and provides other financial services 銀行: *The major banks have announced an increase in interest rates.* 幾家大銀行已宣布提高利率。**b)** a local office of a bank 銀行(營業廳): *I have to go to the bank at lunch time.* 午飯時我得去銀行。

2 ▶RIVER/LAKE 河/湖◀ land along the side of a river or lake 岸, 堤: *Roger pushed the boat away from the bank.* 羅傑把船從岸邊推走。—see 見 SHORE[1] (USAGE)

3 ▶PILE 堆◀ a large pile of earth, sand, snow etc〔土、沙、雪等的〕大堆, 埂, 壟: *There were steep banks of snow at the sides of the road.* 路旁有許多尖形的雪堆。

4 blood/sperm/organ etc bank a place where human blood etc is stored until someone needs it 血庫／精子庫／器官庫等

5 cloud/fog bank etc a large mass of clouds, mist etc 雲團／霧團等

6 bank of televisions/elevators/computers etc a large number of machines, television screens etc arranged close together in a row 緊密排成一列的電視／電梯／電腦等

7 ▶GAME 遊戲◀ the money in a GAMBLING game that people can win 莊家的賭本 —see also 另見 **break the bank** (BREAK[1] (32))

8 ▶ROAD 路◀ a slope made at a bend in a road or RACETRACK to make it safer for cars to go around〔為使車輛安全拐彎而設於公路或跑道拐彎處的〕內側斜坡 —see also 另見 BOTTLE BANK, MEMORY BANK

bank[2] *v*

1 ▶MONEY 錢◀ [T] to put or keep money in a bank 把〔錢〕存入銀行: *Did you bank that check?* 你把支票存入銀行了嗎?

2 ▶PARTICULAR BANK 某銀行◀ [I] to keep your money in a particular bank 把(錢)存入某家銀行: [+with] *Who do you bank with?* 你把錢存入哪家銀行?

3 ▶TURN 轉◀ [I] to make a plane, MOTORCYCLE, or car slope to one side when turning〔飛機、摩托車、汽車等轉彎時〕傾斜飛行[行駛]: *The plane banked, and circled back toward us.* 飛機傾斜着飛行, 繞圈子朝着我們飛回來。

4 ▶PILE/ROWS 堆/排◀ also 又作 **bank up** *BrE* [T] to arrange something into a pile or into rows【英】把…堆起來[排成行]: *The walls of the space center are banked high with electronic equipment.* 航天中心的牆上排滿了電子儀器。

5 ▶CLOUD/MIST 雲/霧◀ also 又作 **bank up** [T] to form a mass of cloud, mist etc 聚集成〔雲團、霧團等〕: *Banked clouds promised rain.* 雲團密佈, 預示有雨。

6 ▶FIRE 火◀ also 又作 **bank up** [T] to cover a fire with wood, coal etc to keep it going for a long time 封〔火〕, 壓〔火〕: *Josie banked up the fire to last till morning.* 喬西把爐火封好, 這樣火可以保持到第二天早晨。

bank on sb/sth *phr v* [T] to depend on something happening or someone doing something 依靠, 指望: **bank on sb doing sth** *We were banking on John being there to show us the way.* 我們指望約翰在那裡告訴我們走哪條道。

bank·a·ble /ˈbæŋkəbl; ˈbæŋkəbəl/ *adj informal* a bankable person or quality is likely to help you get money, success etc【非正式】可靠的, 可獲利的: *They need a bankable star for the movie.* 他們需要一個富有號召力的明星來為這部電影賺錢。

bank ac·count /ˈ· ·,·/ *n* [C] an arrangement between a bank and a customer that allows the customer to pay in and take out money 銀行賬戶

bank bal·ance /ˈ· ,··/ *n* [singular] the amount of money someone has in their bank account 銀行存款; 賬戶餘額

bank book /ˈ· ·/ *n* [C] a book in which a record is kept of the money you put into and take out of your bank account (銀行)存摺; PASSBOOK *AmE*【美】

bank card /ˈ· ·/ *n* [C] **1** *AmE* a CREDIT CARD provided by your bank【美】信用卡, 銀行卡 **2** *BrE* a CHEQUE CARD【英】(銀行)支票保付卡, 銀行支票證

bank draft /ˈ· ·/ also 又作 **banker's draft** *n* [C] **1** a cheque for one bank to another, especially a foreign bank, to pay a certain amount of money to a person or organization〔銀行與銀行, 尤指外國銀行之間的〕銀行匯票

bank·er /ˈbæŋkɚ; ˈbæŋkə/ *n* [C] **1** someone who works in a bank in an important position 銀行家; 經營銀行業務者 **2** the player who is in charge of the money in some games〔牌戲或賭博的〕莊家

banker's card /ˈ·· ·/ *n* [C] *BrE* a CHEQUE CARD【英】(銀行)支票保付卡, 銀行支票證

banker's or·der /,·· ˈ··/ *n* [C] *BrE* a STANDING ORDER【英】長期自動轉賬委託

bank hol·i·day /,· ˈ···/ *n* [C] **1** *BrE* an official holiday when banks and most businesses are closed【英】銀行假日; 公眾假期: *Next Monday is a bank holiday.* 下星期一是銀行假日。| *stuck in the bank holiday traffic* 被困在公眾假期的交通堵塞之中 | **bank holiday weekend** (=a weekend on which there is a bank holiday on Friday or Monday)〔星期一或星期五〕銀行假日的週末, 週末銀行假日 *Are you going away for the bank holiday weekend?* 週末是銀行假日, 你要外出嗎? **2** *AmE* a day during the week when banks are closed by law【美】非週末法定銀行休息日; 銀行停業期

bank·ing /ˈbæŋkɪŋ; ˈbæŋkɪŋ/ *n* [U] the business of a bank 銀行業: *the international banking system* 國際銀行業體制

bank man·a·ger /ˈ· ,···/ *n* [C] someone who is in charge of a local bank 銀行(分行)經理

bank note /ˈ· ·/ *n* [C] *especially BrE* a piece of paper money of a particular value that you use to buy things【尤英】鈔票, 紙幣

bank rate /ˈ· ·/ *n* [C] *technical* the rate of INTEREST[1] (4) decided by a country's main bank【術語】〔中央銀行所定的〕貼現率

bank·roll[1] /ˈbæŋk,rol; ˈbæŋkrəʊl/ *n* [C] a supply of money 資金, 財源

bankroll[2] *v* [T] *informal* to provide the money that someone needs for a business, a plan etc【非正式】對…融資, 為…提供資金; 資助: *a software company bankrolled by the Samsung Group* 由三星集團提供資金的軟件公司

bank·rupt[1] /ˈbæŋkrʌpt; ˈbæŋkrʌpt/ *adj* **1** unable to pay your debts 資不抵債的; 破產的: *Seventeen years of war left the country bankrupt.* 十七年的戰爭使這個國家負債累累。**2 go bankrupt** to be unable to pay your debts and to have to sell your property and goods 破產; 倒閉: *The recession has made many small companies go bankrupt.* 經濟衰退使許多小企業破產。**3** completely lacking a particular good quality 缺乏〔某種美德〕的; 淪

喪的: *The opposition attacked the government as morally bankrupt.* 反對黨攻擊政府道德敗壞。

bankrupt² *v* [T] to make a person, business or country bankrupt or very poor 使破產; 使極其貧困: *Legal fees almost bankrupted us.* 訴訟費幾乎使我們破產。

bankrupt³ *n* [C] someone who has officially said that they cannot pay their debts 破產者

bank·rupt·cy /ˋbæŋkrʌptsɪ; ˈbæŋkrʌptsi/ *n* **1** [C,U] the state of being unable to pay your debts 破產; 倒閉: *There has been a sharp increase in bankruptcies in the last two years.* 近兩年破產個案急劇增加。**2** [U] a total lack of a particular good quality 缺乏道德: *the moral bankruptcy of this materialistic society* 道德淪喪的實利主義社會

bank state·ment /ˈ· ˌ··/ *n* [C] a document sent regularly by a bank to a customer that lists the amounts of money taken out of and paid into their BANK ACCOUNT 銀行結單

banned /bænd; bænd/ *adj* not officially allowed to meet or exist 被禁止的; 被取締的: *Leaders of the banned party were arrested last night.* 被取締黨派的領導人昨晚遭到逮捕。

ban·ner¹ /ˋbænɚ; ˈbænə/ *n* [C] **1** a long piece of cloth on which something is written, often carried between two poles〔通常用兩根竿子撐開的〕橫幅標語: *Crowds of people carrying banners joined the demonstration.* 成羣結隊的人打着橫幅標語加入了遊行示威的隊伍。—see picture at 參見 DEMONSTRATION 圖 **2** *literary* a flag【文】旗幟 **3** a belief or principle 信仰: *Many of the poor and unemployed rallied to the Communist banner.* 許多窮人和失業者都團結在共產主義的旗幟下。| **under the banner of** (=claiming to support a principle) 在…的旗幟下, 在…的名義下, 為了…的事業 *The party fought the election under the banner of social justice.* 該黨以維護社會正義的名義參加競選。

banner² *adj AmE* excellent【美】優秀的, 極好的: *a banner year for American soccer* 美國足球成績突出的一年

banner head·line /ˌ·· ˈ··/ *n* [C] words printed in very large letters across the top of the first page of a newspaper〔報紙的〕通欄大標題

ban·nock /ˋbænək; ˈbænək/ *n* [C] *especially ScotE* a flat cake made of OATMEAL or corn【尤蘇格蘭】燕麥[玉米]做的薄餅

banns /bænz; bænz/ *n* [plural] a public statement that two people intend to get married, made in a church in Britain〔在英國, 預先在教堂發布的〕結婚公告

ban·quet /ˋbæŋkwɪt; ˈbæŋkwɪ̤t/ *n* [C] a formal dinner for many people on an important occasion 宴會

banqueting hall /ˈ··· ˌ·/ also 又作 **banquet room** /ˈ·· ·/ *AmE*【美】*n* [C] a large room in which banquets take place 宴會廳

ban·shee /ˋbænʃi; bænˈʃiː/ *n* [C] a spirit whose loud cry is believed to be heard when someone is going to die〔傳說會大聲哭號以預報凶訊的〕報喪女妖

ban·tam /ˋbæntəm; ˈbæntəm/ *n* [C] a type of small chicken 矮腳雞

ban·tam·weight /ˋbæntəmˌwet; ˈbæntəmweɪt/ *n* [C] a BOXER (1) or WRESTLER who belongs to a group of a particular weight〔拳擊、摔跤〕最輕量級選手

ban·ter¹ /ˋbæntɚ; ˈbæntə/ *n* [U] conversation that has a lot of jokes and teasing (TEASE¹ (1)) remarks in it 玩笑, 戲謔, 妙語: *covering his shyness with a good deal of banter* 用許多逗樂的話掩蓋他的腼腆

banter² *v* [I] to joke with and TEASE someone 開玩笑, 逗樂 —**bantering** *adj* —**banteringly** *adv*

ban·yan /ˋbænjən; ˈbænjən/ *n* [C] an Indian tree with large branches that spread out and form new roots〔印度〕榕樹

bap /bæp; bæp/ *n* [C] *BrE* a round soft bread ROLL² (2)【英】麵包卷

bap·tis·m /ˋbæptɪzəm; ˈbæptɪzəm/ *n* [C,U] **1** a Christian religious ceremony in which someone is touched or covered with water to welcome them into the Christian faith, and sometimes to officially name them〔基督教的〕洗禮, 浸禮 **2 baptism of fire** a difficult or painful first experience of something〔戰〕火的洗禮; 初次的痛苦經歷[考驗]: *We went straight into battle the next day. It was a baptism of fire I'll never forget.* 第二天, 我們直接走上了戰場。這是我永生難忘的一次戰火的洗禮。—**baptismal** /bæpˋtɪzml̩; bæpˈtɪzməl/ *adj*

Bap·tist /ˋbæptɪst; ˈbæptɪ̤st/ *n* [C] a member of a Christian group that believes baptism should only be for people old enough to understand its meaning 浸禮會[浸信會]教友

bap·tize also 又作 **-ise** *BrE*【英】/bæpˋtaɪz; bæpˈtaɪz/ *v* [T] **1** to perform the ceremony of baptism on someone 給…施行洗禮 **2** to accept someone as a member of a particular Christian church by a ceremony of baptism 為…施行洗禮並吸納入教: *He was baptized a Roman Catholic.* 他受洗禮成為羅馬天主教徒。**3** to give a child a name in a baptism ceremony 洗禮時給〔某人〕命名: *She was baptized Sheila Jane.* 她受洗禮時被命名為希拉·簡。

bar¹ /bɑr; bɑː/ *n* [C]

1 ▶**PLACE TO DRINK IN** 飲酒場所◀ **a)** a place where alcoholic drinks are served 酒吧 —compare 比較 PUB **b)** *BrE* one of the rooms inside a pub【英】酒吧間: *The public bar was crowded.* 酒吧間裡人很多。

2 ▶**PLACE TO BUY DRINK** 買飲料處◀ a COUNTER¹ (1) where alcoholic drinks are served 出售酒的櫃台: *There were no free tables so they stood at the bar.* 沒有空桌子, 因此他們到酒吧櫃台邊站着。

3 coffee/snack/salad etc bar a place where a particular kind of food or drink is served 咖啡店/小吃店/沙拉自助櫃台等

4 ▶**BLOCK OF STH** 一塊東西◀ a small block of solid material that is longer than it is wide 條, 棒, 根: *a candy bar* 一塊糖 | *a bar of soap* 一塊肥皂 —see picture on page A7 參見 A7 頁圖

5 ▶**PIECE OF METAL/WOOD** 金屬/木頭◀ a length of metal or wood put across a door, window etc to keep it shut or to prevent people going in or out〔門, 窗等的〕閂; 橫木; 阻礙物: *A lot of houses had bars across the windows.* 許多房屋的窗戶上都有鐵條。

6 ▶**MUSIC** 音樂◀ a group of notes and rests (REST¹ (12)), separated from other groups by vertical lines, into which a line of written music is divided〔樂曲中的〕一小節: *She hummed a few bars of the song.* 她哼出了歌曲的幾小節。

7 a bar to (doing) sth something that prevents you from achieving something that you want 做某事的障礙: *Bad English is a bar to getting a good job.* 蹩腳的英語對找個好工作來說是個障礙。

8 ▶**GROUP OF LAWYERS** 律師◀ *law*【法律】**a) the bar** *BrE* the group of people who are BARRISTERS (=lawyers who have the right to speak in a court of law)【英】〔有資格出庭處理訴訟案件的〕大律師 **b)** *AmE* an organization consisting of people who are lawyers【美】律師界, 律師業

9 be called to the bar a) *BrE* to become a BARRISTER【英】成為大律師 **b)** *AmE* to become a lawyer【美】成為律師

10 ▶**PILE OF SAND/STONES** 沙/石堆◀ a long pile of sand or stones under the water at the entrance to a HARBOUR¹〔港口入口處的〕沙洲; 暗礁

11 ▶**COLOUR/LIGHT** 顏色/光◀ a narrow band of colour or light 線條, 條紋, 帶

12 ▶**UNIFORMS** 制服◀ a narrow band of metal or cloth worn on a military uniform to show rank〔軍服上的〕軍階槓; 綬帶

13 ▶**HEATER** 加熱器◀ the part of an electric heater that provides heat and has a red light〔電暖氣的〕電熱線[片]

14 behind bars *informal* in prison【非正式】在獄中

bar² *v* **barred, barring** [T] **1** also 又作 **bar up** to shut a door or window using a bar or piece of wood so that people cannot get in or out 閂上, 閂住〔門、窗〕**2** [T] to officially prevent someone from entering a place or from doing something 摒除, 排擠於…之外; 阻止: **bar sb from** *Members voted to bar women from the club.* 會員表決不允許婦女加入俱樂部。**3** to prevent people from going somewhere by placing something in their way 阻止通行; 阻擋, 阻攔: *The road ahead was barred by a solid line of policemen.* 前面的道路被警察的密集防線所阻攔。| **bar sb's way** (=prevent someone passing you by standing in front of them) 擋某人的道 *A security guard barred her way.* 警衛攔住了她。

bar³ *prep* **1** *formal* except【正式】除了…以外: *No work's been done in the office today, bar a little typing.* 除了打點兒字, 今天在辦公室沒做甚麼工作。**2 bar none** used to emphasize that someone is the best of a particular group 無人可比: *He's the most talented actor in the country, bar none.* 他是該國最有天份的演員, 無人可比。—see also 另見 BARRING

barb /bɑrb; bɑːb/ *n* [C] **1** the sharp curved point of a hook, ARROW (1) etc that prevents it from being easily pulled out〔魚鉤、箭頭等的〕倒鉤, 倒刺 **2** a remark that is clever and amusing, but also cruel 帶刺的話; 譏諷 —see also 另見 BARBED (2)

bar·bar·i·an /bɑrˋbɛrɪən; bɑːˈbeəriən/ *n* [C] **1** someone from a different tribe or land, who people believe to be wild and not CIVILIZED (1) 野蠻人, 未開化的人, 粗野的人: *The barbarians conquered Rome.* 野蠻人征服了羅馬。**2** someone who does not behave properly, does not show proper respect for education, art etc 大老粗; 無教養的人: *educational theories apparently written by barbarians* 顯然由未受過良好教育的人寫的教育理論

bar·bar·ic /bɑrˋbærɪk; bɑːˈbærɪk/ *adj* **1** very cruel and violent; BARBAROUS 野蠻的, 兇殘的: *a barbaric act of terrorism* 恐怖主義的暴行 **2** like or belonging to a wild or cruel group or society (似) 野蠻人的: *barbaric forest tribes* 野蠻的森林部落

bar·bar·is·m /ˋbɑrbəˌrɪzəm; ˈbɑːbərɪzəm/ *n* **1** [U] a state or condition in which people are not educated, behave violently etc 野蠻 (的生活方式), 未開化 (的狀態) **2** [U] cruel and violent behaviour 殘暴的行為, 粗野的舉止

bar·bar·i·ty /bɑrˋbærətɪ; bɑːˈbærɪ̣ti/ *n* [C,U] a very cruel act 殘暴; 暴行: *The barbarities of the last war must not be repeated.* 上次戰爭的暴行絕不能重演。

bar·bar·ous /ˋbɑrbərəs; ˈbɑːbərəs/ *adj* **1** shockingly cruel; BARBARIC 非常殘忍的, 兇殘的 **2** wild and not CIVILIZED (1) 野蠻的, 無禮的, 粗鄙的: *a savage, barbarous people* 兇猛野蠻的民族 —**barbarously** *adv*

barbecue 燒烤野餐

bar·be·cue¹ /ˋbɑrbɪˌkju; ˈbɑːbɪkjuː/ *n* [C] **1** a metal frame for cooking food on outdoors〔用於戶外的〕烤肉架 **2** an outdoor party during which food is cooked and eaten outdoors 燒烤野餐: *We had a barbecue on the beach.* 我們在海灘上舉行了燒烤野餐。

barbecue² *v* [T] to cook food on a metal frame over a fire outdoors〔用烤肉架〕燒烤〔肉〕: *barbecued chicken*〔用烤肉架燒的〕烤雞

barbed /bɑrbd; bɑːbd/ *adj* **1** a hook or arrow that has one or more sharp, curved points 有倒鉤[倒刺]的, 帶刺的 **2** a barbed remark is unkind 尖酸刻薄的: *a barbed comment on his appearance* 對他的外表所作的尖酸刻薄的評論

barbed wire also 又作 **barbwire** /ˌ· ˈ·◂/ *AmE*【美】*n* [U] wire with short, sharp points on it 帶刺鐵絲: *a high barbed wire fence* 高架帶刺鐵絲網

bar·bell /ˋbɑrˌbɛl; ˈbɑːbel/ *n* [C] *AmE* a metal bar with weights at each end, which you lift to make you stronger【美】啞鈴, 槓鈴

bar·ber /ˋbɑrbɚ; ˈbɑːbə/ *n* [C] **1** a man whose job is to cut men's hair and sometimes to SHAVE¹ (1) them〔以男性為服務對象的〕男理髮師 **2 barber's** *BrE* a shop where men's hair is cut【英】理髮店

bar·ber·shop /ˋbɑrbɚˌʃɑp; ˈbɑːbəʃɒp/ *n* [U] **1** a style of singing popular songs in four parts in close HARMONY 男聲四重唱〔用和聲法演唱流行歌曲〕: *a barbershop quartet* 男聲四重唱 **2** *AmE* a barber's【美】理髮店

barber's pole /ˌ·· ˈ·/ *n* [C] a pole with red and white bands used as a sign outside a barber's shop〔立於理髮店外作為招牌的〕旋轉標誌彩柱

bar·bi·can /ˋbɑrbɪkən; ˈbɑːbɪkən/ *n* [C] a tower for defence at the gate or bridge of a castle 碉堡, 橋頭堡, 更樓

bar·bie /ˋbɑrbɪ; ˈbɑːbi/ *n* [C] *BrE & AustrE informal* a BARBECUE【英和澳, 非正式】〔用於室外的〕烤肉架; 燒烤野餐

bar bil·liards /ˈ· ˌ··/ *n* [U] a game played in PUBs in Britain in which players use long sticks to push balls into holes on a table〔英國酒吧內的〕枱球, 桌球

bar·bi·tu·rate /ˌbɑrˋbɪtʃuret; bɑːˈbɪtʃʊrɪ̣t/ *n* [C,U] a powerful drug that makes people calm and puts them to sleep 巴比土酸鹽〔一種鎮靜劑、安眠藥〕

barb·wire /ˋbɑrbˌwaɪr; ˌbɑːbˈwaɪə◂/ *n* [U] *AmE* BARBED WIRE【美】帶刺鐵絲

bar chart /ˈ· ·/ *n* [C] *BrE* a picture of boxes of different heights, in which each box represents a different amount, for example an amount of profit made in a particular month【英】〔用長短不同的長條形表示數量的〕條形圖(表); BAR GRAPH *AmE*【美】—see picture at 參見 CHART¹ 圖

bar code /ˈ· ·/ *n* [C] a group of thin and thick lines from which a computer reads information about a product that is sold in a shop〔印刷在產品包裝上的〕條形碼, 條碼

bar code 條形碼, 條碼

0-582-84223-9

bard /bɑrd; bɑːd/ *n* [C] *literary* a poet【文】詩人

bare¹ /bɛr; beə/ *adj*

1 ►WITHOUT CLOTHES 未穿衣服◄ not covered by clothes 赤裸的: *Jonathan's bare feet made no sound in the soft sand.* 喬納森光着腳在鬆軟的沙灘上走, 一點聲音都沒有。

2 ►LAND/TREES 土地/樹木◄ not covered by trees or grass, or not having any leaves 葉子全落的; 光禿禿的: *a bare hillside* 光禿禿的山坡

3 ►ROOMS 房間◄ empty, not covered by anything, or not having any decorations 空的, 無裝飾的: *This room looks very bare – you need some pictures on the walls.* 房間顯得過於單調 — 你應該在牆上掛幾幅畫。

4 the bare facts/truth a statement that tells someone only what they need to know, with no additional details 暴露無遺的事實/赤裸裸的真相: *a journalist who is not content to simply record the bare facts* 不滿足於只記錄事實真相的記者

5 ►SMALLEST AMOUNT NECESSARY 最少必需量◄ [only before noun 僅用於名詞前] the very least amount of something that you need to do something 僅有的, 勉強的, 最低限度的: *He got 40% – a bare pass.* 他得了 40

分，剛好及格。| **the bare essentials/necessities** *The refugees fled, taking only the bare essentials.* 難民帶着僅夠維持生活的必需品逃難。| **the bare minimum** (=the smallest amount possible) 最少量 *carrying the bare minimum of equipment* 輕裝上陣 | **the barest** (=the smallest or simplest possible) 最少的；最簡單的 *We can provide only the barest outline of the plan.* 我們只能簡略地透露計劃的要點。

6 the bare bones the most important parts or facts of something without any detail 梗概: *the bare bones of the plan* 計劃的梗概

7 lay sth bare a) to uncover something that was previously hidden 顯示出某事物，使某事物暴露: *The excavation laid bare the streets of an ancient city.* 這次發掘挖出了一座古城的街道。**b)** to reveal something that was secret 揭露，揭發: *The investigation laid bare a million-dollar embezzlement racket.* 這次調查揭露了一宗挪用100萬元公款的犯罪勾當。

8 with your bare hands without using a weapon 赤手空拳: *He killed her with his bare hands.* 他赤手空拳殺死了她。—**bareness** *n*

bare² *v* [T] **1** to let something be seen, by removing something that is covering it 使暴露，使赤裸，露出: *The dog bared its teeth.* 狗露出了牙。**2 bare your soul** to reveal your most secret feelings 敞開心扉，剖白心事，訴説真情，披肝瀝膽

bare-assed /ˈbɛr ˌæst; ˌbeər ˈæst◂/ *adj AmE slang* having no clothes on【美俚】光屁股的，赤條條的

bare·back /ˈbɛrˌbæk; ˈbeəbæk/ *adj, adv* on the bare back of a horse, without a SADDLE¹ (1) 無馬鞍的[地]: *riding bareback* 騎無鞍馬

bare·faced /ˈbɛrˌfest; ˌbeəˈfeɪst◂/ *adj* a barefaced lie, remark etc is clear and makes no attempt not to offend someone 厚顏無恥的；露骨的；公然的: *What barefaced cheek – saying that to you!* 多麼厚顏無恥——竟然對你説那樣的話！

bare·foot /ˈbɛrˌfʊt; ˈbeəfʊt/ also 又作 **barefoot·ed** /ˈbɛrˌfʊtɪd; ˌbeəˈfʊtɨd◂/ *adj, adv* without shoes on your feet 赤腳的[地]: *kids going barefoot all summer* 整個夏天都光着腳的孩子們

bare·hand·ed /ˈbɛrˋhændɪd; ˌbeəˈhændɨd◂/ *adj, adv* having no GLOVES on, or having no tools or weapons 沒有戴手套的[地]；赤手空拳的[地]: *They fought barehanded.* 他們赤手空拳地搏鬥。

bare·head·ed /ˈbɛrˋhɛdɪd; ˌbeəˈhedɨd◂/ *adj, adv* without a hat on your head 光着頭的[地]，不戴帽的[地]: *You can't go out bareheaded in this weather!* 這樣的天氣你不能不戴帽子出去！

bare·leg·ged /ˈbɛrˋlɛgd; ˌbeəˈlegɨd/ *adj, adv* with no clothing on your legs 光着腿的[地]，沒穿襪子的[地]

bare·ly /ˈbɛrlɪ; ˈbeəli/ *adv* **1** in a way that almost does not happen, exist etc; just 幾乎沒有，僅僅，勉強地: *Her voice was so low, I could barely hear her.* 她說話的聲音很輕，我幾乎聽不見。| *We have barely enough money to live on.* 我們的錢只夠勉強度日。**2** in a way that is simple, with no decorations or details 貧乏地；簡陋地，幾乎無裝飾地: *The room was furnished barely.* 這房間陳設簡陋。**3** used to emphasize that something happens immediately after a previous action〔表示強調〕剛剛: *She'd barely sat down before he started firing questions at her.* 她剛坐下，他就開始向她提出一連串的問題。

barf /bɑrf; bɑːf/ *v* [I] *AmE informal* to VOMIT¹【美，非正式】嘔吐 —**barf** *n* [U] —**barfy** *adj*

bar·fly /ˈbɑrˌflaɪ; ˈbɑːflaɪ/ *n* [C] *AmE informal* someone who spends a lot of time in bars【美，非正式】泡酒吧的人，酒吧常客 —**barfly** *adj*

bar·gain¹ /ˈbɑrgɪn; ˈbɑːgɨn/ *n* [C] **1** something bought cheaply or for less than its usual price 便宜貨，廉價貨: *I might buy a TV, if I can find a bargain in the sales.* 如果我能在大減價中找到便宜貨，我也許會買台電視機。| **be a bargain** *These shoes are a bargain at $22.* 這些鞋每雙才22美元，很便宜。| **bargain holiday/clothes/prices etc** (=a holiday etc that is very cheap) 廉價假期/減價服裝/便宜的價錢等 | **bargain hunting** (=looking for things to buy at a cheap price) 到處找廉價貨買 *a bargain hunting housewife at the January sales* 在一月份減價促銷期間到處找廉價貨買的家庭主婦 **2** an agreement, made between two people or groups, to do something in return for something else 協議；交易: **make a bargain** *We've made a bargain that he'll do the shopping and I'll cook.* 我們已經講好了，他買東西我做飯。| **drive a hard bargain** (=succeed in making an agreement that is very much to your advantage) 達成非常有利於自己的協議 *Fischer was determined to drive a hard bargain.* 費希爾決心要達成有利自己的協議。| **keep your side of the bargain** (=do what you promised as part of an agreement) 履行協議 | **strike a bargain** (=reach an agreement) 達成協議 *Management and unions have struck a bargain over wage increases.* 資方和工會就增加工資的問題達成了協議。**3 into the bargain** *especially BrE* in addition to everything else【尤英】此外，外加，而且: *He was short, fat, and spotty into the bargain.* 他又矮又胖，而且一臉粉刺。**4 make the best of a bad bargain** to do the best you can under difficult conditions 困難時盡力而為；善處逆境，隨遇而安 —**bargainer** *n* [C]: *a wage bargainer* 工資談判者 —see 見 CHEAP¹ (USAGE)

bargain² *v* [I] to discuss the conditions of a sale, agreement etc 講價錢，討價還價；洽談（交易）條件: **[+for]** *bargaining for better pay* 要求提高薪水

bargain for sth *phr v* also 又作 **bargain on** sth [T usually in negatives 一般用於否定句] to expect that something will happen and make it part of your plans 考慮到，估計到，預料到: *We hadn't bargained for such heavy rain, and got really wet.* 我們沒料到會下這麼大的雨，結果渾身都濕透了。| **bargain on doing sth** *We can't bargain on finding the right house straight away.* 我們不能指望馬上就能找到合適的房子。| **more than you bargained for** (=more than you expected) 比預計的…得多 *His wife's angry reaction was more than he bargained for!* 他妻子生氣的程度比他所預料的要嚴重！

bargain base·ment /ˌ.. ˈ../ *n* [C] a part of a large shop, usually in the floor below ground level, where goods are sold at reduced prices〔通常設在大商場地下室的〕廉價商品部

bar·gain·ing /ˈbɑrgɪnɪŋ; ˈbɑːgənɪŋ/ *n* [U] **1** discussion in order to reach agreement about a sale, contract etc 討價還價；談（交易）條件: *The 4% pay raise was the result of some hard bargaining.* 經過一番艱苦的討價還價，才達成把工資提高4%的協議。**2 bargaining position** the power that a person or group has in a discussion or argument 談判中所處的地位

barge¹ /bɑrdʒ; bɑːdʒ/ *n* **1** [C] a large low boat with a flat bottom used mainly for carrying heavy goods on a CANAL (1) or river 駁船，平底載貨船 **2** a large rowing boat used for an important ceremony〔用槳划的〕大遊船，畫舫〔通常在舉行重要儀式時使用〕

barge² *v* [I always+adv/prep] to move somewhere in an awkward way, often hitting against things 笨拙地走動；亂碰亂撞: *She ran around the corner and barged into one of the teachers.* 她跑着繞過拐角，和一位老師撞了個滿懷。| **barge your way** *He barged his way through the room.* 他跌跌撞撞地穿過房間。

barge in *phr v* [I] to enter or rush in rudely 闖入: *I wish she wouldn't barge in like that.* 我希望她不會那樣闖進來。| **[+on]** *Her mother barged in on her and Mike when they were in bed together!* 她和邁克兩人正在牀上的時候，她母親闖入了房間！

barge in on *phr v* [T] to interrupt someone rudely 打斷〔別人的談話〕: *Dan's always barging in on other people's conversations.* 丹總是打斷別人的談話。

barg·ee /ˌbɑrˋdʒi; bɑːˈdʒiː/ *BrE*【英】, **barge·man** /ˈbɑrdʒmən; ˈbɑːdʒmən/ *AmE*【美】*n* [C] someone who drives or works on a barge 駁船船工

barge pole /ˈ· ·/ *n* [C] a long pole used to guide a barge〔駁船用的〕撐篙 —see also 另見 **wouldn't touch sth with a bargepole** (TOUCH[1] (12))

bar graph /ˈ· ·/ *n* [C] an American form of BAR CHART bar chart 的美語形式

bar·hop /ˈbɑrˌhɑp; ˈbɑːhɒp/ *v* [I] *AmE informal* to visit and drink at several bars, one after another【美, 非正式】串遊酒吧〔從一家酒吧喝到另一家酒吧〕; PUB-CRAWL *BrE*【英】

bar·i·tone /ˈbærəˌton; ˈbærə̍təʊn/ *n* [C] a male singing voice lower than a TENOR (1) and higher than a BASS[1] (1), or a male singer whose voice is in this range 男中音（歌手）

ba·ri·um /ˈbɛrɪəm; ˈbeəriəm/ *n* [U] a soft silvery-white metal 鋇

barium meal /ˌ··· ˈ·/ *n* [U] *technical* a chemical substance that you drink before you have an X-RAY[1] (2)【術語】鋇餐〔照 X 光前服用〕

bark¹ /bɑrk; bɑːk/ *v* **1** [I] to make the short, loud sound that dogs and some other animals make〔狗等動物〕吠, 叫: **[+at]** *The dog always barks at strangers.* 這條狗總是對着陌生人叫。**2** also 又作 **bark out** [T] to say something quickly in a loud voice 大聲嚷, 吼叫: *"Listen up!" the teacher barked.* "聽着!" 老師吼道。**3 bark up the wrong tree** *informal* to have a wrong idea, especially about how to get a particular result【非正式】打錯了主意; 認錯了目標: *You're barking up the wrong tree if you think Sam can help you.* 你要是認為薩姆能夠幫助你, 那你是找錯了對象。**4 bark at the moon** *AmE informal* to worry and complain about something that you cannot change, and that is not very important【美, 非正式】狂犬吠月, 徒勞無功; 杞人憂天 **5** [T] to rub the skin off your knee, elbow etc by falling or knocking against something 擦破〔皮〕: *I stumbled, barking my shins painfully against the step.* 我絆倒在台階上, 擦破了小腿的皮, 很痛。

bark² *n* [C,U] **1** the sharp, loud sound made by a dog 狗叫聲 **2** the outer covering of a tree 樹皮 **3** a loud sound or voice 響聲; 吼叫聲: *the bark of the guns* 槍砲聲 **4 sb's bark is worse than their bite** used to say that although someone talks in an angry way they would not behave violently 嘴巴兇, 心不狠 **5** *literary* BARQUE【文】三桅[四桅, 五桅]帆船

bar·keep·er /ˈbɑrˌkipɚ; ˈbɑːˌkiːpə/ also 又作 **bar·keep** /ˈbɑrˌkip; ˈbɑːkiːp/ *n* [C] *AmE* someone who serves drinks in a bar; BARTENDER【美】酒吧服務員

bark·er /ˈbɑrkɚ; ˈbɑːkə/ *n* [C] someone who stands outside a place at a CIRCUS (1), FAIR[3] etc shouting to people to come in〔在馬戲場、集市等外面〕大聲招攬顧客的人

bar·ley /ˈbɑrlɪ; ˈbɑːli/ *n* [U] a plant that produces a grain used for making food or alcohol 大麥

barley sug·ar /ˈ·· ˌ··/ *n* [C,U] *BrE* a hard sweet made of boiled sugar【英】麥芽糖

barley wine /ˌ·· ˈ·/ *n* [U] *BrE* a kind of very strong beer【英】大麥酒〔一種烈性啤酒〕

bar·maid /ˈbɑrˌmed; ˈbɑːmeɪd/ *n* [C] *BrE* a woman who serves drinks in a bar【英】酒吧女侍應

bar·man /ˈbɑrmən; ˈbɑːmən/ *n* [C] *BrE* a man who serves drinks in a bar【英】酒吧男侍應; BARTENDER *AmE*【美】

bar mitz·vah /ˌbɑr ˈmɪtsvə; ˌbɑː ˈmɪtsvə/ *n* [C] **1** the religious ceremony held when a Jewish boy reaches the age of 13 and is considered an adult in his religion〔為年滿 13 週歲的猶太男孩進行的〕受誡禮 **2** a boy for whom this ceremony is held 猶太受誡男孩

barm·y /ˈbɑrmɪ; ˈbɑːmi/ *adj BrE informal* slightly crazy【英, 非正式】精神有些錯亂的; 傻呵呵的

barn /bɑrn; bɑːn/ *n* [C] **1** a large farm building for storing crops, or for keeping animals in 穀倉, 糧秣房, 倉庫; 牲口棚 **2** *informal* a large, plain building【非正式】空蕩蕩的大房子: *a great barn of a house* 一所空蕩蕩的大房子

bar·na·cle /ˈbɑrnək̩l; ˈbɑːnəkəl/ *n* [C] a small sea animal with a hard shell that sticks firmly to rocks and the bottom of boats 藤壺〔附在岩石、船底的甲殼類動物〕

barn dance /ˈ· ·/ *n* [C] **1** a social event at which COUNTRY DANCING is performed 穀倉舞會〔社交集會, 會上有鄉村舞表演〕**2** *BrE* a dance performed at this type of event【英】穀倉舞 —compare 比較 SQUARE DANCE

bar·ney /ˈbɑrnɪ; ˈbɑːni/ *n* [C usually singular 一般用單數] *BrE informal* a noisy argument【英, 非正式】吵吵嚷嚷, 大吵大鬧

barn·storm /ˈbɑrnˌstɔrm; ˈbɑːnstɔːm/ *v* [I] *AmE* to travel from place to place making short stops to give political speeches, theatre performances, or aircraft flying shows【美】巡迴演講; 巡迴演出; 巡迴飛行表演 —**barnstormer** *n* [C] —**barnstorming** *adj*

barn·yard /ˈbɑrnˌjɑrd; ˈbɑːnjɑːd/ *n* [C] **1** a space surrounded by farm buildings; FARMYARD 穀倉場院, 農家糧倉旁的院子 **2 barnyard humor** *AmE* humour that is slightly rude【美】粗俗的幽默

ba·rom·e·ter /bəˈrɑmətɚ; bəˈrɒmə̍tə/ *n* [C] **1** an instrument for measuring changes in the air pressure and weather or calculating height above sea level 氣壓計, 晴雨表 **2** something that shows or gives an idea of changes that are happening 能顯示變化的事物;〔輿論的〕晴雨表; 變化的標記: *Infant mortality is a highly sensitive barometer of social conditions.* 嬰兒死亡率是反映社會狀況的一個非常敏感的晴雨表。—**barometric** /ˌbærəˈmɛtrɪk; ˌbærəˈmetrɪk◂/ *adj* —**barometrically** /-kl̩ɪ; -kli/ *adv*

bar·on /ˈbærən; ˈbærən/ *n* [C] **1** a man who is a member of the lowest rank of the British NOBILITY (1) or of a rank of European NOBILITY (1) 男爵〔英國貴族中爵位最低者或歐洲貴族的一個等級〕**2** a businessman with a lot of power or influence〔工商業〕巨頭, 大王: *conservative press barons like Beaverbrook* 像比弗布魯克這樣的保守派報業大王 | *Pakistani and Colombian drug barons* 巴基斯坦和哥倫比亞的大毒梟 —see also 另見 ROBBER BARON

bar·on·ess /ˈbærənɪs; ˈbærənə̍s/ *n* **1** [C] a woman who is a member of the lowest rank of the British NOBILITY (1)〔英國的〕女男爵 **2** the wife of a baron 男爵夫人

bar·on·et /ˈbærənɪt; ˈbærənə̍t/ *n* [C] a British KNIGHT[1] (2) lower in rank than a baron, whose title passes on to his son when he dies 準男爵〔英國最低的世襲爵位, 但不是貴族〕

bar·on·et·cy /ˈbærənɪtsɪ; ˈbærənə̍tsi/ *n* [C] the rank of a baronet 準男爵爵位

ba·ro·ni·al /bəˈronɪəl; bəˈrəʊniəl/ *adj* **1** a baronial room is very large and richly decorated 富麗堂皇的 **2** belonging to or involving BARONS (1) 男爵的; 與男爵有關的

bar·on·y /ˈbærənɪ; ˈbærəni/ *n* [C] the rank of BARON (1) 男爵爵位

ba·roque /bəˈrok; bəˈrɒk/ *adj* **1** belonging to the very decorated style of art, music, buildings etc, that was common in Europe in the 17th century 巴洛克風格的〔17 世紀時在歐洲流行的一種華麗的風格, 尤見於藝術、音樂及建築等方面〕: *elaborate baroque facades* 精心建造的具有巴洛克風格的大廈正面 **2** very detailed and complicated 精雕細琢的 —**baroque** *n* [singular]

barque /bɑrk; bɑːk/ *n* [C] a sailing ship with three, four, or five MASTS (=poles that the sails are fixed to) 三桅[四桅, 五桅]帆船

bar·rack /ˈbærək; ˈbærək/ *v* [I,T] **1** *BrE* to interrupt someone by shouting, sometimes pretending that you agree with them【英】(對...) 起哄; 喝倒采: *The minister was repeatedly barracked during his speech.* 部長在講話時多次被喝倒采。**2** *AustrE* to shout to show that you support somone or something【澳】吶喊助威

bar·racks /ˈbærəks; ˈbærəks/ *n* [plural] a group of buildings in which soldiers live 兵營, 營房

bar·ra·cu·da /ˌbærəˈkudə; ˌbærəˈkjuːdə/ *n* [C] a large tropical fish that eats flesh 梭子魚〔大型熱帶食肉海魚〕

bar·rage¹ /bəˈrɑʒ; ˈbærɑːʒ/ *n* **1** [C usually singular 一般用單數] the continuous firing of guns, especially large heavy guns, to protect soldiers as they move toward an enemy 掩護砲火: *a barrage of anti-aircraft fire* 高射砲火網 **2** [singular] a lot of questions, comments etc, that are said at the same time or very quickly after each other 連珠砲似的問題[評論等]: **[+of]** *Despite facing a barrage of criticism, Mr Rees pressed ahead with plans for Theatr Clwyd.* 儘管面對連珠砲似的批評, 里斯先生還是加緊推行建造克盧伊達劇院的計劃。

B

bar·rage² /ˋbɑrɪdʒ; ˈbærɑːʒ/ *n* [C] a wall of earth, stones etc built across a river to provide water for farming or to prevent flooding 攔河壩, 堰堤

barrage bal·loon /ˈ·· ·ˌ·/ *n* [C] a large bag that floats in the air to prevent enemy planes from flying near the ground〔阻止敵機低飛的〕阻攔氣球, 阻塞氣球

barred /bɑrd; bɑːd/ *adj* **1** a barred window, gate etc has bars across it〔門、窗等〕裝有鐵柵的, 上了閂的 **2** *formal* having bands of different colours【正式】有不同顏色條紋的: *red barred tail feathers* 有紅色條紋的尾羽 —see also 另見 BAR

3 **bar·rel¹** /ˋbærəl; ˈbærəl/ *n* [C] **1** a large curved container with a flat top and bottom, made of wood or metal〔中間鼓起的〕桶: *barrels of beer* 幾桶啤酒 —see picture at 參見 CONTAINER 圖 **2** also 又作 **barrelful** the amount of liquid that a barrel contains, used especially as a measure of oil 一桶之量: *Oil was $30 a barrel.* 石油每桶30美元。**3** the part of a gun that the bullets are fired through 槍[砲]管 —see picture at 參見 GUN¹ 圖 **4 have sb over a barrel** to put someone in a situation in which they are forced to accept or do what you want 使某人處於被動[不利]的地位: *The manager had us over a barrel – either we worked on a Saturday or we lost our jobs.* 經理迫使我們作出選擇, 要麼星期六工作, 要麼失去工作。**5 be a barrel of laughs** [often in negatives 常用於否定句] to be very enjoyable 很好玩: *The meeting wasn't exactly a barrel of laughs.* 那會議其實沒甚麼意思。—see also 另見 PORK BARREL, **scrape (the bottom of) the barrel** (SCRAPE¹ (6)), **lock, stock, and barrel** (LOCK² (3))

barrel² *v* **barreled, barreling** [I] *AmE informal* to move very fast, especially in an uncontrolled way【美, 非正式】飛奔; 高速行駛: *He barreled down the road at 90 miles an hour.* 他以每小時90英里的速度在公路上疾駛。

barrel-chest·ed /ˌ·· ˈ··◂/ *adj* a man who is barrel-chested has round chest that sticks out〔男性〕胸部厚實發達的

barrel or·gan /ˈ·· ˌ··/ *n* [C] a musical instrument that you play by turning a handle, used especially in former times 手搖風琴〔尤在舊時使用〕

bar·ren /ˋbærən; ˈbærən/ *adj* **1** land or soil that is barren has no plants growing on it 貧瘠的, 荒蕪的: *a barren mountainous area* 土地貧瘠的山區 **2** *old use* a woman or a female animal who is barren cannot produce children or baby animals; INFERTILE (2)【舊】〔婦女或雌性動物〕不孕的, 不生育的 **3** a tree or plant that is barren does not produce fruit or seeds 不結果實的, 不結籽的 **4** *literary* without any useful results【文】無用的; 無效果的: *a pointless and barren discussion* 毫無意義、沒有任何結果的討論

bar·rette /bəˋrɛt; bæˈret/ *n* [C] *AmE* a small metal or plastic object used to keep a woman's hair in place【美】〔女用〕髮夾; HAIR SLIDE *BrE*【英】

bar·ri·cade¹ /ˋbærəˌked; ˈbærɪkeɪd/ *n* [C] a temporary wall or fence across a road, door etc that prevents people from going through〔臨時的〕路障; 街壘: *Soldiers fired over the barricades at the rebels.* 士兵們在路障後邊朝叛亂分子開火。

barricade² *v* [T] to protect or close something by building a barricade 設路障於; 以障礙物阻塞: *Terrorists had barricaded themselves inside the embassy.* 恐怖分子在使館內築起工事固守。

3 **bar·ri·er** /ˋbærɪɚ; ˈbæriə/ *n* [C] **1** a type of fence or gate that prevents people from moving in a particular direction 障礙物; 柵欄; 關卡: *Crowds burst through the barriers and ran onto the pitch.* 人羣衝破柵欄跑進球場。**2** a rule, problem etc that prevents people from doing something, or limits what they can do〔阻止或妨礙人們做事的〕障礙: *an attempt to break down trade barriers* 打破貿易壁壘的嘗試 | **[+to]** *a psychological barrier to success* 阻礙成功的心理障礙 | **language barrier** (=inability to talk to someone because you speak a different language) 語言障礙 **3** a physical object that keeps two areas, people etc apart 屏障: **[+between]** *The mountains form a natural barrier between the two countries.* 羣山構成了兩國之間的天然屏障。**4 the 10 second/40% etc barrier** a level or amount of 10 seconds, 40% etc, that is seen as a limit which it is difficult to get beyond〔難以超越的〕10秒/40%等難關: *Sprint runners had by then broken the 10 second barrier.* 短跑運動員那時已經突破了10秒大關。—see also 另見 SOUND BARRIER

barrier reef /ˌ··· ˈ·/ *n* [C] a line of CORAL (=pink stone-like substance) separated from the shore by water 堡礁, 堤礁

bar·ring /ˋbɑrɪŋ; ˈbɑːrɪŋ/ *prep* unless there are 除非, 除了…以外: *Barring any last minute problems, we should finish the job tonight.* 除非最後一分鐘出問題, 否則我們今晚應該完成工作。

bar·ri·o /ˋbɑrɪo; ˈbæriəʊ/ *n* [C] *AmE* a part of an American town or city where many poor, Spanish-speaking people live【美】美國城鎮中說西班牙語的人集居的貧民區

bar·ris·ter /ˋbærɪstɚ; ˈbærɪstə/ *n* [C] a lawyer in Britain who can argue cases in the higher law courts〔英國有資格在高等法院出庭的〕訟務律師, 大律師 —compare 比較 SOLICITOR —see 見 LAWYER (USAGE)

bar·row /ˋbæro; ˈbærəʊ/ *n* [C] **1** a small vehicle like a box on wheels, from which fruits, vegetables etc used to be sold〔流動商販用的二輪或四輪〕手推車 **2** a large pile of earth like a small hill that was put over an important grave in ancient times 古塚, 古墓 **3** a WHEELBARROW 獨輪手推車

barrow boy /ˈ·· ·/ *n* [C] *BrE* a man or boy who sells fruit, vegetables etc from a barrow【英】推車售貨的男小販

Bart /bɑrt; bɑːt/ the written abbreviation of 縮寫= BARONET

bar·tend·er /ˋbɑrˌtɛndɚ; ˈbɑːˌtendə/ *n* [C] *AmE* someone who makes, pours, and serves drinks in a bar or restaurant【美】酒吧男侍; 酒保; BARMAN *BrE*【英】

bar·ter¹ /ˋbɑrtɚ; ˈbɑːtə/ *v* [I,T] to exchange goods, work, or services for other goods or services rather than for money 易貨貿易; 物物交換, 以物易物: **barter (with sb) for sth** *I had to barter with the locals for food.* 我只得和當地人換點食物。| **barter sth for sth** *They bartered farm products for machinery.* 他們拿農產品換機器。

barter² *n* [U] **1** a system of exchanging goods and services for other goods and services rather than using money 易貨貿易, 以貨易貨: *an economy based on barter* 以易貨貿易為基礎的經濟 **2** goods or services that are exchanged in this kind of system 易貨貿易中的商品[服務]: *Beads were used as barter in the early days of settlement.* 定居初期曾用念珠作為交換物。

bas·alt /bəˋsɔlt; ˈbæsɔːlt/ *n* [U] a type of dark green-black rock 玄武岩

base¹ /bes; beɪs/ *v* [T] to establish or use somewhere as the main place for your business or work 把基地設在…, 以…為基地: *a Denver-based law firm* 總部設在丹佛的法律事務所 

base sth **on/upon** sth *phr v* [T often passive 常用被動態] to use particular information or facts as a point from which to develop an idea, plan etc 以…為基礎, 以…為根據: *The film is based on a novel by Sinclair Lewis.* 該影片是根據辛克萊·劉易斯的小說改編的。

base² *n* 

1 ►LOWEST PART 最低的部分◄ [C usually singular 一般用單數] the lowest part of something, or the surface at the bottom of something 底部; 根基; 基礎: [+of] *There was a chip in the base of the glass.* 玻璃杯底部有個裂口。| *the base of a triangle* 三角形的底邊 | *Waves crashed and pounded at the base of the cliff.* 海浪衝擊拍打着懸崖的底部。

2 ▶KNOWLEDGE/IDEAS 知識/想法◀ [C] the most important part of something from which new ideas develop〔思想〕基礎: *India has a good scientific research base.* 印度有良好的科研基礎。| *This provides a good base for the development of new techniques.* 這為新技術的發展提供了良好的基礎。

3 ▶COMPANY/ORGANIZATION 公司/組織◀ [C, U] the main place from which a group, company, or organization controls its activities 基地, 根據地, 總部: *Cuba was seen as a base for Communist activity throughout Latin America.* 古巴被視為整個拉丁美洲共產主義活動的基地。| *Report back to base as soon as you see anything.* 看到任何情況立即向總部報告。

4 ▶MILITARY 軍事◀ [C] a place where people in a military organization live and work〔軍事〕基地: *a naval base* 海軍基地

5 ▶PEOPLE/GROUPS 人羣◀ [C usually singular 一般用單數] the people, money, groups etc from which a lot of support or power comes〔人、經濟等的〕基礎, 支柱: *an attempt to strengthen the city's economic base* 加強城市經濟基礎的努力 | **tax/customer base** (=all the people who pay tax or buy goods in a particular place) 稅收/顧客基礎 *A reputation for excellent service will expand our customer base.* 優質服務的信譽能擴大我們的顧客基礎。| **manufacturing base** (=all the factories, companies etc that produce goods in a country) 生產基礎 *The country's manufacturing base has shrunk by 20% during the recession.* 在經濟衰退的時候, 該國的製造業基地縮減了20%。—see also 另見 POWER BASE

6 ▶SUBSTANCE/MIXTURE 物質/混合物◀ [singular, U] the main part of a substance to which something else is later added 基礎成分, 主要成分: *paint with an oil base* 以油脂為主要成分的顏料

7 ▶BODY/PLANT 身體/植物◀ [C usually singular 一般用單數] the point where part of your body or part of a plant joins with the rest 基部; 連接處: *She had a dull ache at the base of her neck.* 她的脖子根下有點隱隱作痛。

8 ▶SPORT 體育◀ [C] one of the four places that a player must touch in order to get a point in games such as BASEBALL〔棒球等的〕壘

9 be off base *AmE informal* to be completely wrong【美, 非正式】完全錯誤, 大錯特錯: *His estimate for painting the kitchen seems way off base.* 他對粉刷廚房的估計似乎差得太遠了。

10 ▶CHEMISTRY 化學◀ [C] *technical* a chemical substance that combines with an acid to form a SALT[1] (4)【術語】鹼, 鹽基

11 ▶NUMBERS 數目◀ [C usually singular 一般用單數] *technical* the number in relation to which a number system or mathematical table is built up【術語】基數

12 touch base (with sb) to telephone someone who you live or work with, or make a short visit, while you are spending time somewhere else〔跟某人〕聯繫上 —see also 另見 **cover (all) the bases** (COVER[1] (13))

base³ *adj literary* not having good moral principles【文】卑鄙的, 下流的, 無恥的: *base passions* 庸俗的激情 —see also 另見 BASE METAL

3 2 **base·ball** /ˈbesˌbɔl; ˈbeɪsbɔːl/ *n* **1** [U] an outdoor game between two teams of nine players, in which players try to get points by hitting a ball and running around four bases (BASE[2] (8)) 棒球運動 —see picture on page A22 參見A22頁圖 **2** [C] the ball used in this game 棒球

baseball cap /ˈ·· ˌ·/ *n* [C] a hat that fits closely around your head with a round part that sticks out at the front 棒球帽 —see picture at 參見 CAP[1] 圖

base·board /ˈbesˌbɔrd; ˈbeɪsbɔːd/ *n* [C] *AmE* a narrow board fixed to the bottom of indoor walls where they meet the floor【美】〔地板與牆壁相接處的〕踢腳板, 壁腳板; SKIRTING BOARD *BrE*【英】

base·less /ˈbeslɪs; ˈbeɪsləs/ *adj formal* not based on facts or good reasons【正式】無根據的; 無緣無故的: *baseless accusations* 毫無根據的指控

base·line /ˈbesˌlaɪn; ˈbeɪslaɪn/ *n* **1** [C usually singular 一般用單數] *technical* a standard measurement or fact to which other measurements or facts are compared, especially in medicine or science【術語】〔尤指醫學或科學中的〕基線, 準線 **2** the line at the back of the court in games such as tennis or VOLLEYBALL〔網球場、排球場等的〕底線 —see picture at 參見 TENNIS 圖 **3** the area that a player must run in on a BASEBALL field〔棒球場的〕壘線

base·ment /ˈbesmənt; ˈbeɪsmənt/ *n* [C] a room or area that is under the level of the ground 地下室; 地庫 —see picture on page A4 參見A4頁圖

base met·al /ˌ· ˈ··/ *n* [C,U] a metal that is not very valuable, such as iron or lead 普通金屬〈如鐵、鉛等〉—compare 比較 NOBLE[1] (4)

base rate /ˈ· ·/ *n* [C] the standard rate of INTEREST[1] (4) on which a bank bases its charges 基本利率 —compare 比較 PRIME RATE

bas·es /ˈbesiz; ˈbeɪsiːz/ the plural of BASIS

bash¹ /bæʃ; bæʃ/ *v* [I,T] *informal*【非正式】**1** to hit someone or something hard, in a way that causes pain or damage 猛擊, 猛撞; 擊碎; 打傷: **bash sth on/against** *I bashed my toe against the door.* 我的腳趾頭撞到了門上。| **[+into/against]** *Jay bashed into a table in the dark.* 傑伊在黑暗中撞到了桌子。| **bash down/in/up etc** (=destroy something by hitting it often) 砸破, 打碎等 *Police bashed down the door to get in.* 警察破門而入。**2 union/government etc bashing** *BrE* strong criticism of unions, the government etc【英】猛烈抨擊工會/政府等 **3** to physically attack a type of person that you do not like 痛打〔某一類人〕: *gay bashing* 痛打同性戀者 —see also 另見 SQUARE-BASHING, **bible basher** (BIBLE (4))

bash away at sth *phr v* [T] *BrE informal* to continue working hard at something【英, 非正式】一直努力地〔做着某事〕: *I've been bashing away at this essay for hours.* 這篇文章我已經寫了好幾個小時了。

bash on sth *phr v* [I,T+**with**] *BrE informal* to continue working in order to finish something【英, 非正式】繼續努力工作: *Well, better bash on.* 嗯, 最好繼續努力。

bash² *n* [C] **1** *informal* a hard strong hit【非正式】猛擊, 痛打: *I gave him a bash on the nose.* 我朝他的鼻子猛擊了一拳。**2** *informal* a party or celebration【非正式】熱鬧的聚會; 痛快的玩樂, 狂歡: *a birthday bash* 生日聚會 **3 have a bash** *BrE spoken* to try to do something, especially when you are not sure that you will succeed【英口】試試看: **[+at]** *Why not have a bash at windsurfing?* 為甚麼不嘗試一下風帆滑浪?

bash·ful /ˈbæʃfəl; ˈbæʃfəl/ *adj* easily embarrassed in social situations; shy 靦腆的, 害羞的, 忸怩的: *a bashful smile* 靦腆的一笑 | *Many men are still bashful about discussing their feelings.* 很多男人在談論自己的感受時還是覺得難為情。—**bashfully** *adv* —**bashfulness** *n* [U]

Ba·sic /ˈbesɪk; ˈbeɪsɪk/ *n* [U] a commonly used computer language〔電腦的〕Basic 語言, 初學者通用符號指令

basic *adj* **1** forming the main or most necessary part of something 基礎的, 基本的, 根本的: *a meeting to discuss the basic structure of the department* 一個討論部門基本結構的會議 | *the basic principles of mathematics* 數學的基本原理 **2** at the simplest or least developed level 最簡單的, 最初級的: *My knowledge of German is pretty basic.* 我所掌握的德語知識是相當初級的。| *The farm lacks even basic equipment.* 這個農場連最基本的設備都沒有。**3 basic salary/pay etc** the amount of money that you are paid before any special payments are added 基本工資/底薪等 **4** [only before noun 僅用於名詞前] basic desires, rights etc, are ones that everyone has 最基

口語及書面語中最常用的 1 000詞, 2 000詞, 3 000詞

本的，起碼的：*Basic human rights are still denied in many countries.* 許多國家的人民連最基本的人權都沒有。—see also 另見 BASICS

1 **ba·sic·ally** /ˋbesɪkl̩ɪ; ˈbeɪsɪkli/ *adv* **1** [sentence adverb 句子副詞] *spoken* used when giving the most important reason or fact about something, or a simple explanation of something【口】基本上，本質上，從根本上講：*Basically, I just don't have enough money.* 基本上，我就是沒有足夠的錢。| *Well, basically, it's a matter of filling in a few forms.* 其實也就是填幾張表的事。**2** in the main or most important ways, without considering additional details or differences 基本地，基本上：*The two structures are basically the same.* 這兩種結構基本相同。| *He's basically a nice guy.* 他基本上是個好人。**3** in a very simple way, with only the things that are completely necessary 簡單地，初步地：*The office was very basically equipped.* 這辦公室的陳設很簡陋。

ba·sics /ˋbesɪks; ˈbeɪsɪks/ *n* [plural] the most important and necessary facts about something, from which other possibilities and ideas may develop 基礎；基本原則：*Once you know the basics, you can start experimenting with different methods.* 你一旦掌握了基本原則，就可以用各種不同的方法開始試驗。| **the basics of** *I learned the basics of first aid on a weekend course.* 我在一個週末班上學會了急救的基本知識。

basic train·ing /,‥ ˈ‥/ *n* [U] the period when a new soldier learns military rules and does a lot of exercise〔新兵入伍後的〕基本訓練

bas·il /ˋbæzl̩; ˈbæzəl/ *n* [U] a sweet-smelling HERB used in cooking 羅勒〔一種帶香味，可用於烹調的植物〕

ba·sil·i·ca /bəˋsɪlɪkə; bəˈsɪlɪkə/ *n* [C] a church in the shape of a long room with a round end 長方形廊柱大廳式教堂：*the basilica of St Peter's* 聖彼得大教堂

bas·i·lisk /ˋbæsə,lɪsk; ˈbæsɪ̣lɪsk/ *n* [C] an imaginary animal like a snake in ancient stories, supposed to be able to kill people by looking at them 蛇怪〔傳說中的蛇狀怪物，據說其目光能使人喪命〕

ba·sin /ˋbesn̩; ˈbeɪsən/ *n* [C] **1** *BrE* a round container fixed to the wall in a bathroom where you wash your hands and face; SINK[2] (2)【英】洗臉盆 **2** *BrE* a bowl for liquids or food【英】盆；大碗：*Pour the sauce into a basin.* 把調味汁倒入碗中。**3** also 又作 **ba·sin·ful** /ˋbesn̩fʊl; ˈbeɪsɪ̣nfʊl/ the amount of liquid that a basin can contain 一盆[一碗]之量：*a basin of hot water* 一盆熱水 **4** a bowl-shaped area containing water 水窪；貯水池：*Water splashed in the basin of the fountain.* 噴泉的水池水花四濺。**5** an area of land from which water runs down into a river 流域；盆地；低窪地：*the Amazon basin* 亞馬遜河流域 —see also 另見 PUDDING BASIN (1)

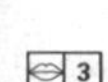
ba·sis /ˋbesɪs; ˈbeɪsɪ̣s/ *n plural* **bases** /-siz; -siːz/ [C] **1** the facts or ideas from which something can be developed 基礎；根據；基本原理：*Their claim had no basis in fact.* 他們的主張並沒有任何事實根據。| **[+for]** *The video will provide a basis for class discussion.* 錄像將為課堂討論提供基本內容。| **[+of]** *a lecture series that later formed the basis of a new book* 後來成了一本新書的基礎的一系列講座 **2 on the basis of** because of a particular fact or situation 在…的基礎上；根據…：*Employers are not allowed to discriminate on the basis of sex.* 雇主不允許有性別歧視。**3 on a daily/weekly etc basis** every day, week etc 按天/週等計算：*All rooms are cleaned on a daily basis.* 所有房間都是每天打掃一次。**4 on a voluntary/part-time etc basis** a system or agreement by which someone or something is VOLUNTARY[1] etc 自願性質/以兼職的形式等：*The machine has been installed on a trial basis.* 這台機器的安裝是試驗性的。

bask /bæsk; bɑːsk/ *v* [I] **1** to enjoy sitting or lying in the heat of the sun or a fire〔舒適地〕曬太陽[取暖]：**[+in]** *A lizard was basking in the heat of the afternoon sun.* 一條蜥蜴正在享受下午的陽光浴。**2** to enjoy the approval or attention that you are getting from other people 沉浸在〔別人的讚許中〕：**[+in]** *She basked in the admiration of her family and friends.* 她沉浸在家人和朋友的讚賞中。—see also 另見 **bask/bathe in sb's reflected glory** (GLORY[1] (4))

baskets 籃子；簍子；筐子

bas·ket /ˋbæskɪt; ˈbɑːskɪ̣t/ *n* [C] **1** a container made of thin pieces of plastic, wire, or wood woven together, used to carry things or put things in 籃子；簍子；筐子：*a shopping basket* 購物籃 | **clothes/laundry basket** (=for putting dirty clothes in) 洗衣籃 **2** a net with a hole at the bottom hung from a metal ring, through which the ball is thrown in BASKETBALL〔籃球運動的〕籃：**make/shoot a basket** (=get a point in the game) 投籃得分 —see also 另見 **put all your eggs in one basket** (EGG[1] (5)), WASTEPAPER BASKET —see picture on page A22 參見 A22 頁圖

bas·ket·ball /ˋbæskɪt,bɔl; ˈbɑːskɪ̣tbɔːl/ *n* [U] a game played indoors between two teams of five players, in which each team tries to win points by throwing a ball through a net, or the ball used in this game 籃球（運動）—see picture on page A22 參見 A22 頁圖

basket-case /ˈ‥ ‥/ *n* [C] *informal* someone who is so nervous or anxious that they cannot deal with simple situations【非正式】遇到點小事就緊張[焦慮]的人

bas·ket·ry /ˋbæskɪtrɪ; ˈbɑːskɪ̣tri/ also 又作 **bas·ket·work** /ˋbæskɪt,wɝk; ˈbɑːskɪ̣twɜːk/ *n* [U] **1** baskets or other objects made by weaving together thin dried branches 籃筐類〔總稱〕**2** the skill of making baskets 編製籃筐的技藝

basque /bæsk; bæsk/ *n* [C] a piece of underwear for a woman that covers her from under her arms to the top of her legs 巴斯克衫〔一種長過腰部的女士緊身內衣〕

bas-re·lief /,bɑ rɪˋlif; ,bɑː rɪˈliːf/ *n* [C,U] *technical* a style of art in which stone or wood is cut so that shapes are raised above the surrounding surface【術語】淺浮雕（作品）—compare 比較 HIGH RELIEF

bass[1] /bes; beɪs/ *n* **1** [C] a man whose singing or speaking voice is very low 男低音（歌手）**2** [singular] the part of a piece of music that this person sings 男低音部 **3** [U] the lower half of the whole range of musical notes〔樂譜的〕低音部 —compare 比較 TREBLE[3] (1) **4** [C] a BASS GUITAR 低音結他：**on bass** (=playing the bass guitar) 彈低音結他 *The band features Willie Dixon on bass.* 這

個樂隊由威利·狄克遜彈低音結他。**5** [C] a DOUBLE BASS 低音提琴 —**bass** *adj* —**bass** *adv*

bass² /bæs; bæs/ *n plural* **bass** *or* **basses** [C] a fish that can be eaten and lives both in rivers and the sea 鱸魚

bass clef /ˌbes ˋklɛf; ˌbeɪs ˈklef/ *n* [C] a sign (𝄢) at the beginning of a line of written music that shows that the top line of the STAVE¹ (1) is the A below MIDDLE C 低音譜號 —see picture at 參見 MUSIC 圖

bas·set /ˋbæsɪt; ˈbæsɪ̈t/ also 又作 **basset hound** /ˋ·· ·/ *n* [C] a dog with short legs and long ears used for hunting 巴斯特獵犬〔一種腿短、耳長的獵犬〕

bass gui·tar /ˌbes gɪˋtɑr; ˌbeɪs gɪˈtɑː/ also 又作 **bass** *n* [C] an electric musical instrument with six strings and a long neck, that plays low notes 低音(電)結他

bas·si·net /ˌbæsəˋnɛt; ˌbæsɪ̈ˈnet/ *n* [C] *AmE* a small bed that looks like a basket for a young baby【美】(嬰兒)搖籃;〔有篷蓋的〕嬰兒車

bas·sist /ˋbesɪst; ˈbeɪsɪ̈st/ *n* [C] someone who plays a BASS GUITAR or a DOUBLE BASS 低音結他手; 低音提琴手

bas·soon /bəˋsun; bəˈsuːn/ *n* [C] a very long wooden musical instrument with a low sound, that is held upright and played by blowing into a thin curved metal pipe 巴松管, 低音管

3 **bas·tard** /ˋbæstəd; ˈbɑːstəd/ *n* [C] **1** *slang* an offensive word for someone, especially a man, who you think is unpleasant【俚】〔冒犯用語〕討厭鬼, 臭小子, 壞蛋, 雜種: *The bastard went and told the police!* 那臭小子去報告了警察! **2** *spoken* an insulting or joking word for a man【口】傢伙〔對男子的蔑稱或戲稱〕: *The poor bastard's been sacked!* 那倒霉的傢伙被解雇了! | *You lucky bastard!* 你這傢伙真幸運! **3** *BrE spoken* something that causes difficulties or problems【英口】難事, 麻煩事: *This pan is a bastard to clean.* 這鍋刷起來真麻煩。**4** *old-fashioned* someone whose parents were not married when they were born【過時】私生子

bas·tard·ize also 又作 **-ise** *BrE*【英】/ˋbæstəˌdaɪz; ˈbɑːstədaɪz/ *v* [T] to spoil something by changing its good parts 使變低劣; 使不實: *a bastardized version of the play* 該戲劇粗劣的改編本

bas·tard·y /ˋbæstədɪ; ˈbɑːstədi/ *n* [U] *old use* the situation of having parents who were not married to each other when you were born【舊】私生子身分

baste /best; beɪst/ *v* [I,T] **1** to pour liquid or melted fat over meat that is cooking〔烹調時在肉上〕澆塗油脂 **2** to fasten cloth with long loose stitches, in order to hold it together so that you can SEW it properly later 用長針腳疏縫, 粗縫

bas·ti·on /ˋbæstʃən; ˈbæstiən/ *n* [C] **1** something that protects a way of life, principle etc that seems likely to change or disappear 堡壘〔指固守一種生活方式、準則等的事物〕: **[+of]** *These clubs are the last bastions of male privilege.* 這些俱樂部是男人特權的最後堡壘。**2** a place where a country or army has strong military defences 設防地區, 防衛據點: *Pearl Harbor was the principal American bastion in the Pacific.* 珍珠港曾是美國在太平洋的主要軍事據點。**3** *technical* a part of a castle wall that sticks out from the rest【術語】稜堡〔城堡和堡壘的突出部分〕

3 **bat¹** /bæt; bæt/ *n* [C]

1 ►ANIMAL 動物◄ a small animal like a mouse that flies around at night 蝙蝠 —see also 另見 FRUIT BAT

2 ►SPORT 體育◄ a) a long wooden stick with a special shape that is used in some sports and games 球棒: *a baseball bat* 棒球棒 **b)** *BrE* a round flat piece of wood with a handle, used to hit a ball in TABLE TENNIS【英】〔乒乓球〕球拍; PADDLE¹ (3) *AmE*【美】

3 be at bat to be the person who is trying to hit the ball in a game of BASEBALL〔棒球比賽中〕輪到擊球

4 do sth off your own bat *BrE informal* to do something without being told to do it【英, 非正式】主動地, 自覺地: *You did all this work off your own bat?* 你是自己主動完成這些工作的嗎?

5 do sth right off the bat *AmE informal* to do something immediately【美, 非正式】立刻去做: *I asked him to help, and he said yes right off the bat.* 我請他幫忙, 他馬上就答應了。

6 like a bat out of hell *informal* very fast【非正式】極快地, 飛快地: *I drove like a bat out of hell to the hospital.* 我飛快地開車趕往醫院。

7 old bat *spoken* an unpleasant old woman【口】老傢伙, 老太婆〔對老嫗的冒犯用語〕

8 have bats in the belfry *old-fashioned* to be slightly crazy【過時】有點兒古怪 —see also 另見 **as blind as a bat** (BLIND¹ (1c))

bat² *v* **batted, batting 1** [I,T] to hit the ball with a bat in CRICKET (2) or BASEBALL〔板球、棒球〕用球棒擊球 **2 not bat an eye/eyelid** *informal* to not seem to be shocked, surprised, or embarrassed【非正式】連眼都不眨; 泰然不動, 面不改色: *He didn't bat an eyelid when I said I was leaving.* 我說我要走的時候, 他一點也沒有表現出在乎的樣子。**3 bat your eyes/eyelashes** if a woman bats her eyes, she opens and closes them quickly, especially in order to look attractive to men〔女子〕使眼色〔以吸引男子〕 **4 go to bat for** *AmE informal* to help and support someone【美, 非正式】支持〔某人〕; 為〔某人〕出力: *Andy really went to bat for me when I was accused of stealing that money.* 我被指控偷錢的時候, 是安迪出面為我澄清的。**5 bat a thousand** also 又作 **bat a 1000** *AmE informal* to be very successful【美, 非正式】很有成就: *She's been batting a thousand ever since she got that new job.* 她得到那份新工作後, 表現非常出色。

bat sth ↔ **around** *phr v* [T] *informal* to discuss the good and bad parts of a plan, idea etc【非正式】討論, 商量

bat·boy /ˋbætbɔɪ; ˈbætbɔɪ/ *n* [C] a boy whose job is to look after the equipment of a BASEBALL team 棒球隊球僮

batch /bætʃ; bætʃ/ *n* [C] **1** a group of people or things that arrive or are dealt with together 一批; 一羣; 一組: *The second batch of student essays was due in.* 第二批學生作文該交上來了。**2** a quantity of food, medicine etc, that is produced or prepared at the same time〔食物、藥品等的〕一次生產量[投料量]

batch pro·ces·sing /ˌ· ˋ···/ *n* [U] a type of computer system in which the computer does several jobs one after the other, without needing instructions between each job〔電腦的〕成批處理

bat·ed /ˋbetɪd; ˈbeɪtɪ̈d/ *adj* **with bated breath** feeling very anxious or excited 屏着氣〔表示焦急或興奮〕: *We waited with bated breath for the results of the test to come through.* 我們屏住呼吸, 緊張地等待考試成績的發佈。

bath¹ /bæθ; bɑːθ/ *n plural* **baths** /bæðz, bɑːðz/ [C] **1** 2
BrE a large long container that you fill with water and 3
sit in to wash yourself【英】浴缸, 澡盆; BATHTUB *especially AmE*【尤美】: **run a bath** (=make water flow into a bath) 往浴缸裡放水 **2** an act of washing your body in a bath 洗澡, 沐浴: *After a week of camping, I really needed a bath.* 經過一週的露營之後, 我真得洗個澡。| **have a bath** *BrE*【英】/**take a bath** *AmE*【美】*Do I have time to take a bath before we go out?* 我洗個澡再出去, 來得及嗎? | **give sb a bath** (=wash someone in a bath) 給某人洗澡 **3** a container full of liquid in which something is placed for a particular purpose 缸; 盆; 池: *Plunge the fabric into a bath of black dye.* 把織物投入黑染料缸中。**4 baths a)** *BrE old-fashioned* a public building in which there is a swimming pool【英, 過時】〔室內〕公共游泳池 **b)** a public building where people could go in the past to wash themselves 澡堂, 公共浴室: *the Roman baths at Cirencester* 賽倫塞斯特的羅馬式公共浴室 **5 take a bath** *AmE informal* to lose money, especially in a business deal【美, 非正式】賠錢, 虧本: *We took a bath in the market over that stock.* 我們買那種股票賠了錢。—see also 另見 BIRDBATH, BUBBLE BATH, HIPBATH, **throw the baby out with the bath water** (THROW¹ (34)), TURKISH BATH

bath² *v BrE*【英】**1** [T] to wash someone in a bath 為〔某人〕洗澡; BATHE¹ (1) *AmE*【美】**2** [I] *old-fashioned* to wash yourself in a bath; BATHE¹ (1)【過時】洗澡

USAGE NOTE 用法說明: BATH

WORD CHOICE 詞語辨析: **bathe, bath, have/take a bath, bathtub, have a swim, take/have a dip, swimming bath(s), sunbathe, bathroom**

You **bathe** (*AmE*) or more formally in British English, **bath** to get clean. bathe〔美〕或較為正式的 bath〔英〕是把身體洗乾淨之意: *He baths/bathes every morning.* 他每天早上都洗澡。However, you are more likely to say that you **have a bath** (*BrE*) or **take a bath** (*AmE*). 但表示洗澡之意, 則多用 have a bath〔英〕或者 take a bath〔美〕: *I have/take a bath every day.* 我每天都洗澡。The thing that you **have/take a bath** in is a **bath** (*BrE*) or **bathtub** (*AmE*). 洗澡用的大盆或浴缸叫 bath〔英〕或 bathtub〔美〕。

You **bathe** something gently to make it clean especially for medical reasons. bathe 是指輕輕擦洗, 尤指用藥水把某種東西浸洗, 以進行治療: *to bathe a cut/your eyes* 洗傷口/眼睛。In British English you say that you **bath** a baby or a sick person, in American English you **bathe** them. 英國英語中說 bath a baby/a sick person (為小孩/病人洗澡), 而美國英語中則用 bathe。

You also **bathe** (*BrE*) when you go swimming, though this meaning is no longer common. bathe〔英〕也有游泳之意, 儘管這一意思現已不常用: *to bathe in the sea* (NOT 不用 *take a bath in the sea*) 在海裡游泳。You are more likely to use **have a swim** or **take/have a dip** in the sea or a swimming pool. 表示在海中或泳池裡游泳更常用的說法是 have a swim 或 take/have a dip。(A slightly old-fashioned word for **swimming pool** in British English is **swimming bath**. 英國英語中略為舊式的用法是把 swimming pool 說成 swimming bath)。You also **sunbathe** in the sun (NOT 不用 *have a sun bath*). sunbathe 是曬日光浴。

Often you say that you are going to the **bathroom** especially in American English, not because you are going to have a bath, but as a polite way of saying that you are going to the toilet. 在美國英語中 go to the bathroom 不是去洗澡之意, 而是去廁所的委婉說法。

SPELLING 拼法

Note the spelling of **bathing** and **bathed**. These words can be formed from **bath** with the pronunciation /ˈbɑθɪŋ/bæθt; ˈbɑːθɪŋ/bæθt/. But they can also be formed from **bathe**, with the pronunciation /ˈbeðɪŋ/beðd; ˈbeɪðɪŋ/beɪðd/. 注意 bathing 和 bathed 的拼法。這兩個單詞可以由 bath 而來, 讀作 /ˈbæθɪŋ/bæθt; ˈbɑːθɪŋ/bɑːθt/, 也可以由 bathe 而來, 讀作 /ˈbeðɪŋ/beðd; ˈbeɪðɪŋ/beðd/。

bath chair /ˈ· ·/ *n* [C] a special chair with wheels and a cover, used in the past for moving someone old or sick around〔舊時老人或病人用的〕帶篷輪椅 —compare 比較 WHEELCHAIR

bathe¹ /beð; beɪð/ *v* **1** [I,T] *especially AmE* to wash yourself or someone else in a bath【尤美】洗澡; 為〔某人〕洗澡; BATH² *BrE*【英】: *I bathed, washed my hair, and got dressed.* 我洗了澡, 洗了頭, 穿好衣服。**2** [I] *BrE old-fashioned* to swim in the sea, a river, or a lake【英, 過時】〔去海裡、河裡、湖裡〕游泳: *The children ran off to bathe.* 孩子們跑出去游泳了。**3** [T] to wash or cover part of your body with a liquid, especially as a medical treatment〔尤指用作醫療用途的〕洗, 浸, 泡: *Bathe the wound in antiseptic.* 用消毒劑洗一下傷口。**4 be bathed in light/moonlight etc** *literary* an area or building that is bathed in light has light shining onto it in a way that makes it look pleasant or attractive【文】沐浴於陽光/月光等之中: *The castle was bathed in golden autumn sunlight.* 城堡沐浴於金秋的陽光中。**5 be bathed in tears/sweat etc** *literary* to be covered in tears, sweat etc【文】眼淚汪汪/滿身大汗等 —see 見 BATH² (USAGE)

bathe² *n* [singular] *BrE old-fashioned* an occasion when you swim in the sea, a river, or a lake【英, 過時】〔在海裡、河裡或湖裡〕游泳: *They went for a bathe.* 他們去游泳了。

bath·er /ˈbeðɚ; ˈbeɪðə/ *n* **1** [C] *BrE old-fashioned* someone who is swimming in the sea, a river, or a lake【英, 過時】〔去海裡、河裡或湖裡的〕游泳者 **2 bathers** [plural] *AustrE* a piece of clothing that you wear for swimming; SWIMSUIT【澳】游泳衣

bath·ing /ˈbeðɪŋ; ˈbeɪðɪŋ/ *n* [U] *BrE old-fashioned* the activity of swimming in the sea, a river, or a lake【英, 過時】〔在海裡、河裡或湖裡〕游泳: *Is the beach safe for bathing?* 這海灘游泳安全嗎?

bathing cap /ˈbeðɪŋ ˌkæp; ˈbeɪðɪŋ kæp/ *n* [C] *old-fashioned* a special hat that you wear for swimming【過時】游泳帽

bathing cos·tume /ˈbeðɪŋ ˌkɑstum; ˈbeɪðɪŋ ˌkɒstjuːm/ *n* [C] *BrE old-fashioned* a bathing suit【英, 過時】泳裝, 游泳衣

bathing ma·chine /ˈbeðɪŋ məˌʃin; ˈbeɪðɪŋ məˌʃiːn/ *n* [C] a small wooden building on wheels in which people could change their clothes for swimming in the 18th and 19th centuries〔18、19 世紀時給游泳者使用的木製帶輪的〕更衣車

bathing suit /ˈbeðɪŋ ˌsut; ˈbeɪðɪŋ suːt/ *n* [C] a piece of clothing that you wear for swimming 游泳衣

bathing trunks /ˈbeðɪŋ ˌtrʌŋks; ˈbeɪðɪŋ trʌŋks/ *n* [C] *BrE old-fashioned* a piece of clothing worn by men for swimming【英, 過時】〔男子穿的〕游泳褲

bath mat /ˈ· ·/ *n* [C] a piece of thick cloth that you put on the floor next to the bath 浴室踏腳墊, 地巾

ba·thos /ˈbeθɑs; ˈbeɪθɒs/ *n* [U] a sudden change from a beautiful, moral, or serious subject to one that is ordinary, silly, or not important〔修辭〕突降法〔指由美好、莊重的突然轉為平庸可笑的手法〕: *a sentimental poem, trembling on the verge of bathos* 有點矯揉造作的傷感詩

bath·robe /ˈbæθˌrob; ˈbɑːθrəʊb/ *n* [C] a long loose piece of clothing shaped like a coat, that you wear especially before or after having a bath 浴袍, 浴衣 —compare 比較 DRESSING GOWN

bath·room /ˈbæθˌrum; ˈbɑːθrʊm/ *n* [C] **1** a room where there is a bath, BASIN (1) etc, and sometimes a toilet 浴室〔一般帶有廁所〕**2** *AmE* a room where there is a toilet【美】衛生間, 廁所: *Can you tell me where the bathroom is?* 你能告訴我衛生間在哪兒嗎? | **go to the bathroom** (=use a toilet) 去廁所 *Mommy, I have to go to the bathroom.* 媽媽, 我要上廁所。

bath salts /ˈ· ·/ *n* [plural] a substance that you put in bath water to make it smell nice 浴鹽〔使浴水帶香味〕

bath tow·el /ˈ· ··/ *n* [C] a large TOWEL (=piece of material for drying yourself) 浴巾

bath·tub /ˈbæθˌtʌb; ˈbɑːθtʌb/ *n* [C] *especially AmE* a long large container that you fill with water and sit or lie in to wash yourself【尤美】浴缸, 澡盆; BATH¹ (1) *BrE*【英】

bath·y·sphere /ˈbæθɪˌsfɪr; ˈbæθɪsfɪə/ *n* [C] *technical* a strong container used for going deep under the sea, especially to watch plants, animals etc【術語】〔可潛入深海中觀察海底生物生活情況的〕探海球, 潛水球

ba·tik /ˈbɑtik; bəˈtiːk/ *n* **1** [U] a way of printing coloured patterns on cloth that involves putting WAX¹ (1) over some parts of the cloth 蠟染法 **2** [C,U] cloth that has been coloured in this way 蠟染布 —see picture on page A16 參見 A16 頁圖

bat·man /ˈbætmən; ˈbætmən/ *n plural* **batmen** /-mən; -mən/ [C] *technical* an officer's personal servant in the British army【術語】〔英國軍官的〕勤務兵

bat·on /bæˈtɑn; ˈbætɒn/ *n* [C] **1** a short thin stick used by a CONDUCTOR (=the leader of a group of musicians) to direct the music〔樂隊指揮用的〕指揮棒 **2** a short light stick that is passed from one person to another during a race 接力棒 **3** *especially BrE* a short thick stick used as a weapon by a policeman; TRUNCHEON【尤英】警棍 **4** a short stick that is carried as a sign of a special office or rank 權杖, 官杖 **5** a light metal stick that is spun and thrown into the air by a MAJORETTE〔樂隊女指揮所用的〕金屬指揮杖

bats·man /ˈbætsmən; ˈbætsmən/ *n plural* **batsmen** /-mən; -mən/ [C] the person who is trying to hit the ball in CRICKET (2)〔板球〕擊球手

bat·tal·ion /bəˈtæljən; bəˈtæljən/ *n* [C] a large group of soldiers consisting of several companies (COMPANY (9))〔軍隊的〕營

bat·ten¹ /ˈbætn̩; ˈbætn/ *v* **1 batten down the hatches a)** to prepare yourself for a period of difficulty or trouble 準備面對困境 **b)** to firmly fasten the entrances to the lower part of a ship〔用壓條〕封艙 **2 batten on sb** *especially literary* to live well by using someone else's money, possessions etc【尤文】靠別人養肥自己

batten² *n* [C] a long narrow piece of wood that boards or TILEs are fastened to, or that is fixed to other pieces of wood to keep them in place 板條, 壓條

bat·ter¹ /ˈbætə; ˈbætə/ *v* [I always+adv/prep, T] to keep hitting something hard, especially in a way that causes damage 搗毀, 打爛; 拍打, 撞擊: **[+at/on/against etc]** *The waves battered against the shore.* 波浪拍打着海岸。—**battering** *n* [C,U]

batter² *n* **1** [C,U] a liquid mixture of flour, eggs, milk etc, used in cooking〔麵粉、雞蛋、牛奶等調成的〕麵糊: *Fry the fish in batter.* 將蘸上麵糊的魚油炸。**2** [C,U] *AmE* a thick mixture of flour, eggs, milk etc, used for making cakes【美】〔做薄餅用的〕麵糊 **3** [C] the person who is trying to hit the ball in BASEBALL〔棒球〕擊球手—see picture on page A22 參見 A22 頁圖

bat·tered /ˈbætəd; ˈbætəd/ *adj* **1** old and in bad condition 舊的, 破的: *a battered old suitcase* 破舊的衣箱 **2 battered women/children etc** women or children who have been violently treated by their husbands or fathers 遭受虐待的婦女/兒童等: *a shelter for battered wives* 受虐妻子的庇護所

bat·ter·ing ram /ˈ··· ˌ·/ *n* [C] a long heavy piece of wood used in wars in the past to break through walls or doors〔古代戰爭攻城時用於搗毀牆、門的〕破城錘

2 **bat·ter·y** /ˈbætərɪ; ˈbætəri/ *n*

1 ►ELECTRICITY 電◄ [C] an object that provides a supply of electricity for something such as a radio or a car 電池: *I need to change the batteries in the flashlight.* 我需要更換手電筒裡的電池。| **dead/flat battery** (=a battery that has stopped producing electricity) 廢電池—see picture at 參見 ENGINE 圖

2 ►HENS 母雞◄ [C] a row of small CAGEs in which chickens are kept to produce large numbers of eggs 層架式雞籠: *battery hens* 在層架式雞籠裡飼養的母雞 —compare 比較 FREE RANGE

3 ►GUNS 槍砲◄ [C] several large guns used together 砲組, 排砲: *Enemy anti-aircraft batteries immediately responded to the attack.* 敵人的高射砲火對襲擊迅速作出反應。

4 recharge your batteries *informal* to rest or relax in order to get back your energy【非正式】休息[放鬆]以恢復精神體力: *A week in the mountains should recharge my batteries.* 在山裡休息一個星期, 我的精神體力應該能恢復過來。

5 a battery of a group of many things of the same kind〔同類事物的〕一排, 一組, 一連串: *Mayer sat at his desk, surrounded by a battery of telephones.* 邁耶坐在桌旁, 被一排電話包圍着。

6 ►CRIME 罪行◄ [U] *law* the crime of hitting someone【法律】毆打罪 —see also 另見 ASSAULT AND BATTERY

2 **bat·tle¹** /ˈbætl; ˈbætl/ *n* [C]

1 ►BETWEEN ARMIES 軍隊之間◄ a fight between opposing armies, groups of ships etc, especially one that is part of a larger war〔尤指大型戰爭中的局部〕戰鬥, 戰役: *the Battle of Trafalgar*〔西班牙〕特拉法爾加戰役 | **in/into battle** *Her son was killed in battle.* 她兒子在戰鬥中陣亡。| *sending troops into battle* 派部隊參戰

2 ►BETWEEN OPPONENTS 對手之間◄ a situation in which opposing groups or people compete or argue with each other when trying to achieve success or control 較量, 競爭, 爭奪: *a long-running legal battle* 曠日持久的法律爭訟 | **[+for]** *The president's advisors were engaged in a battle for power.* 總統的顧問進行着一場權力之爭。| **[+between]** *a fierce ratings battle between rival TV stations* 相互競爭的電視台之間一場激烈的收視率之爭 | **[+with]** *an ongoing battle with my mother about eating properly* 我和母親有關均衡飲食的持續爭論

3 ►ATTEMPT 試圖◄ an attempt to solve a difficult problem or change an unpleasant situation 奮鬥, 抗爭: **[+against]** *The battle against AIDS will continue for years to come.* 和愛滋病的鬥爭還要持續很多年。| **fight a losing battle** (=try to achieve something that you cannot achieve) 做毫無希望的事情, 徒勞無功 *I try to get the kids to pick up their clothes, but I'm fighting a losing battle.* 我設法讓孩子自己收拾衣服, 可是他們不聽我的。

4 be half the battle to the most difficult or important part of what you have to do 成功了一半, 勝利大有希望: *If you can get an interview, that's half the battle.* 如果你能得到面試的機會, 成功就大有希望了。

5 a battle of wits a disagreement that opposing sides try to win by using their intelligence 智慧的較量: *It became a battle of wits between student and teacher.* 那成了師生間智慧的較量。

6 do battle (with) to argue with someone or fight against someone 與…爭論[鬥爭]: *We had to do battle with the authorities over planning permission for the house.* 關於批准建屋計劃的事, 我們必須和當局據理力爭。

7 the battle of the sexes the relationship between men and women when it is considered as a fight for power 男女之間權力的競爭

battle² *v* **1** [I,T] to be involved in a struggle or argument when you are trying to achieve something difficult or to deal with something unpleasant or dangerous 與…鬥爭, 與…搏鬥: **[+against/with]** *She had battled bravely against cancer for many years.* 她勇敢地與癌症抗爭了許多年。| *I found Maria battling with her maths homework.* 我發現瑪麗亞在努力地做數學作業。| **[+for]** *a pressure group battling for better schools* 為改善學校條件而鬥爭的壓力團體 | **battle to do sth** *Doctors battled to save his life.* 醫生們奮力挽救他的生命。| **battle sth** *AmE*【美】*I was already battling a cold.* 我的感冒快挺過去了。**2 battle it out** to keep fighting or opposing each other until one person or team wins 決出勝負: *I left Adrian and Jo battling it out for the trophy.* 我讓阿德里安和喬為獎盃一決高低。**3** [I] *literary* to take part in a fight or war【文】參戰; 與…作戰

bat·tle·axe *BrE*【英】, **battleax** *AmE*【美】/ˈbætl̩ˌæks; ˈbætl-æks/ *n* [C] **1** *informal* an unpleasant unfriendly woman who tries to control other people【非正式】悍婦 **2** a large AXE (=tool for cutting wood) used as a weapon in the past 戰斧

battle cruis·er /ˈ·· ˌ··/ *n* [C] a large fast ship used in war 戰列巡洋艦

battle cry /ˈ·· ·/ *n* [C usually singular 一般用單數] **1** a phrase used to encourage people, especially members of a political organization〔尤指政治組織的〕口號; 吶喊: *'Socialism Now!' was their battle cry.* "現在就實現社會主義!" 是他們的口號。**2** a loud shout used in war to encourage your side and frighten the enemy〔戰場上的〕吶喊

battle fa·tigue /ˈ·· ·ˌ·/ *n* [U] a type of mental illness caused by the frightening experiences of war, in which you feel very anxious and upset 戰爭疲勞症

bat·tle·field /ˈbætḷˌfild; ˈbætlfiːld/ also 又作 **bat·tle·ground** /ˈbætḷˌgraund; ˈbætlgraʊnd/ *n* [C] **1** a place where a battle is being fought or has been fought 戰場, 戰地 **2** a subject that people disagree or argue a lot about 鬥爭的主題; 爭論的問題: *The housing issue has become a political battleground.* 住屋問題已經變成了政治鬥爭的內容。

B

bat·tle·ments /ˈbætḷmənts; ˈbætlmənts/ *n* [plural] a low wall around the top of a castle, that has spaces to shoot guns or arrows (ARROW (1)) through〔城堡的〕雉堞; 城垛; 有槍眼的防禦牆

bat·tle·ship /ˈbætḷˌʃɪp; ˈbætlˌʃɪp/ *n* [C] the largest kind of ship used in war, with very big guns and heavy ARMOUR (2) 主力艦, 戰列艦

bat·ty /ˈbætɪ; ˈbæti/ *adj BrE informal* slightly crazy but not in an unpleasant or frightening way; ECCENTRIC[1] (1)【英, 非正式】有點瘋的; 古怪的

bau·ble /ˈbɔbḷ; ˈbɔːbəl/ *n* [C] **1** a cheap piece of jewellery 不值錢的飾物 **2** *BrE* a brightly coloured decoration that looks like a ball and is used to decorate a CHRISTMAS TREE【英】〔裝飾聖誕樹用的閃亮的〕球形小飾物

baud /bɔd; bɔːd/ *n* [C] *technical* a unit of measurement of the speed at which information is sent to or from a computer, for example through a telephone line【術語】波特〔發報、數據傳輸速率單位〕

baulk /bɔk; bɔːk/ a British spelling of BALK balk 的英式拼法

baux·ite /ˈbɔksaɪt; ˈbɔːksaɪt/ *n* [U] a soft substance that ALUMINIUM (=a type of metal) is obtained from 鋁礬土, 鋁土礦

bawd·y /ˈbɔdɪ; ˈbɔːdi/ *adj* bawdy songs, jokes, stories etc are about sex and are funny, enjoyable, and often noisy〔歌曲、笑話、故事等〕淫猥的; 娛人的: *the bawdy 18th century romp, 'Moll Flanders'* 18 世紀逗樂的小說《摩爾·福蘭德絲》—**bawdily** *adv* —**bawdiness** *n* [U]

bawdy house /ˈ·· ·/ *n* [C] *old use* a place where women have sex with men for money【舊】妓院

bawl /bɔl; bɔːl/ *v* **1** [I,T] also 又作 **bawl out** to shout in a loud unpleasant voice 叫嚷, 大喊: *The captain stood at the front, bawling orders.* 隊長站在前面, 喊着口令。**2** [I] to cry noisily 大哭, 號哭: *a baby bawling* 嬰兒的哭叫

bawl sb ↔ **out** *phr v* [T] *informal especially AmE* to speak angrily to someone because they have done something wrong【非正式, 尤美】痛罵, 大聲責備: *Mom bawled me out for the mess in my room.* 媽媽因我的房間太亂而責罵我。

bay[1] /be; beɪ/ *n* [C]
1 ►SEA 海◄ an area of the sea that curves inwards towards the land 灣, 海灣: *I had a view across the bay to white sand and pine trees.* 我能看到海灣那邊的白沙和松樹。| *Montego Bay*〔牙買加〕蒙特哥灣 —see picture on page A12 參見 A12 頁圖
2 keep/hold sth at bay to prevent something dangerous or unpleasant from happening or from coming too close 使…不能迫近, 遏制…: *The growling of dogs held the strangers at bay.* 狗的吠叫使陌生人無法靠近。| *Economic collapse was held at bay by aid from Russia.* 來自俄羅斯的援助使經濟不致崩潰。
3 ►AREA 地區◄ an area within a large room that is separated by shelves, walls etc〔建築物的〕開間, 隔間, 格距: *bays in a library* 圖書館書架間的空處
4 ►VEHICLES 車輛◄ a place where a vehicle can park for a short time〔可供車輛短暫停泊的〕停車間, 停車處: *The bus will depart from bay 3.* 公共汽車將從三號停車站開出。| *a loading bay* 裝卸場
5 ►TREE 樹◄ also 又作 **bay tree** a tree that has leaves which smell sweet and are often used in cooking 月桂樹
6 ►HORSE 馬◄ a horse that is a reddish brown colour 紅棕色的馬

bay[2] *v* [I] **1** if a dog bays, it makes a long high noise, especially when it is chasing something〔獵犬〕不停地吠叫: *the baying of the hounds* 獵犬不停的吠叫聲 **2** to make strong demands to get answers to questions or force someone to give you something 窮追: [**+for**] *a pack of tabloid reporters baying for blood* 一羣窮追不捨的小報記者 | *younger men baying at his heels* 緊跟着他的較年輕者

bay[3] *adj* a bay horse is a reddish-brown colour〔馬〕紅棕色的

bay leaf /ˈ· ·/ *n* [C] a sweet-smelling leaf from the bay tree, often used in cooking 月桂樹葉〔常用於煮食〕

bay·o·net[1] /ˈbeənɪt; ˈbeɪənə̍t/ *n* [C] a long blade that is fixed to the end of a RIFLE (=long gun)〔步槍上的〕刺刀, 槍刺

bayonet[2] *v* [T] to push the point of a bayonet into someone 用刺刀刺

bay·ou /ˈbaɪu; ˈbaɪuː/ *n* [C] a large area of water in the southeast US that moves very slowly and has many water plants〔美國東南部的〕水流緩慢、水草繁多的小河

bay win·dow /ˌ· ˈ··/ *n* [C] a window that sticks outwards from the wall of a house, usually with glass on three sides 凸窗〔凸出於牆壁之外三面有玻璃的窗戶〕

ba·zaar /bəˈzɑr; bəˈzɑː/ *n* [C] **1** a market or group of shops, especially in India or the Middle East〔尤指印度或中東的〕市場, 市集 **2** a sale held to collect money for a good purpose 義賣: *a charity bazaar* 慈善義賣會

ba·zoo·ka /bəˈzukə; bəˈzuːkə/ *n* [C] a long light gun that rests on your shoulder and is used especially for firing at tanks (TANK[1] (3))〔扛在肩上發射的反坦克〕火箭筒

BBC /ˌbi bi ˈsi; ˌbiː biː ˈsiː◂/ *n* **1** the British Broadcasting Corporation; the British radio and television company that is paid for by the state 英國廣播公司 **2 BBC English** a standard form of English pronunciation used in Britain; RP〔英國的〕標準發音

BB gun /ˈbi bi ˌgʌn; ˈbiː biː gʌn/ *n* [C] *AmE* a gun that uses air pressure to force out small round metal balls【美】氣槍; AIRGUN *BrE*【英】

BBQ *n* [C] an abbreviation for 縮寫= BARBECUE

BC /ˌbi ˈsi; ˌbiː ˈsiː/ before Christ; used after a date to show that it was before the birth of Christ 公元前: *The Great Pyramid dates from around 2600 BC.* 大金字塔建於公元前 2600 年左右。—compare 比較 AD

BCE /ˌbi si ˈi; ˌbiː siː ˈiː/ *especially AmE* before common era; used after a date to show that it is before the birth of Christ【尤美】公元前

be- /bɪ; bɪ/ *prefix* **1** in some verbs, means to treat as a particular thing 視作〔用於動詞〕: *Don't belittle him* (=say he is unimportant). 不要小看他。| *He befriended me* (=became my friend). 他成了我的朋友。**2** *literary* in some adjectives, means wearing a particular thing【文】佩戴, 穿戴〔用於部分形容詞〕: *a bespectacled boy* (=wearing glasses) 戴眼鏡的男孩 **3** *old use* completely; thoroughly【舊】完全, 徹底: *to besmear* (=make very dirty) 把…弄髒, 玷污

be[1] /bɪ; bi; *strong* 強讀 bi; biː/ *auxiliary verb* **1** used with a present participle to form the CONTINUOUS (4) tenses of verbs〔和現在分詞構成動詞的進行時態〕: **be doing sth** *Don't disturb me while I'm working.* 我工作的時候不要打擾我。| *Gemma was reading when her son called.* 吉瑪的兒子打電話來的時候, 她正在看書。| *They've been asking a lot of questions.* 他們已經問了許多問題了。| *He's always causing trouble.* 他總是惹麻煩。**2** used with past participles to form the PASSIVE[2]〔和過去分詞構成被動語態〕: *Smoking is not permitted.* 禁止吸煙。| *I was told about it yesterday.* 我昨天被告知了這件事。| *The house is being painted.* 房子正在上油漆。| *She has been invited to the party.* 她已被邀參加聚會。| *The flames could be seen several miles away.* 在幾英里外都能看到火焰。| *The police should have been informed about this.* 這件事本應向警察報告。**3** used to give an order or to tell someone about a rule〔表示命令或規則〕: *All* *guests are to vacate their rooms by 10 am on the day of their departure.* 所有退房的旅客必須在離開當日上午10點前騰出房間。| *The children are to be in bed when we get home.* 我們到家時, 孩子們就得睡覺。**4** used to show arrangements for the future〔表示將來的安排〕: *Audrey and Jimmy are to be married in June.* 奧德麗和吉米將在六月結婚。| *We were to have gone away last week but I was ill.* 我們本打算上週走, 可是我病了。| *I'll be leaving in about half an hour.* 我大約半個小時後離開。**5** used to show what someone should do or what should happen〔表示某人應該怎樣做或應該發生甚麼〕: *What am I to tell her* (=what should I tell her?) *when she finds out?* 一旦她發現了, 我該怎樣對她說呢? | *He is more to be* (=should be more) *pitied than blamed.* 他更應該得到憐憫而不是責備。**6** used to show what cannot or could not happen〔表示不能或不會發生甚麼〕: *We searched everywhere but the ring was nowhere to be found.* 我們找來找去, 但哪兒也找不着那隻戒指。**7** used to show what had to happen or what did happen〔表示不得不發生或已發生甚麼〕: *This discovery was to have a major effect on the treatment of heart disease.* 這個發現對心臟病的治療產生了重大影響。**8** used in CONDITIONAL[1] (2) sentences that describe a situation that does not or could not exist〔用於條件句, 表示虛擬語氣〕: *If I were to do that what would you say?* 如果我做了那件事, 你會說甚麼呢? | *Were we to offer you the job, would you take it?* 如果我們給你這份工作, 你會接受嗎? **9** *old use* used instead of 'have' to form the PERFECT[3] tenses of some verbs【舊】〔代替 have 構成某些動詞的完成時態〕: *Christ is risen* (=has risen) *from the dead.* 基督已從死裡復活。

1 1 **be²** *v* **1** [linking verb 連繫動詞] used to show that someone or something is the same as the subject〔表示某人或某事與主語相同〕: *It's me.* 是我。| *Lack of money is our biggest problem.* 缺錢是我們最大的問題。| *If I were you, I shouldn't do it.* 如果我是你, 我就不會這樣做。| **the problem/difficulty etc is doing sth** *The problem is explaining it to her in a tactful way.* 問題是怎樣用得體的方法向她解釋。| **the problem/difficulty etc is to do sth** *The difficulty is to know what to do for the best.* 困難的是要知道怎樣做最好。| **the fact/idea etc is (that)** *The fact is that you know too much.* 事實是你知道得太多了。**2** [I always +adv/prep] used to show position or time〔表示位置或時間〕: *Where is Simon?* 西蒙在哪兒? | *Jane's upstairs.* 簡在樓上。| *The principal's in his office.* 校長在辦公室。| *How long has she been here?* 她來這兒有多久了? | *The book is on the table.* 書在桌子上。| *The concert was last night.* 音樂會是在昨晚舉行的。| *The party is on Saturday.* 聚會將在星期六舉行。**3** [linking verb 連繫動詞] used to show that someone or something belongs to a group or has a particular quality〔表示某人或某物屬於一個羣體或具有某種特徵〕: *Snow is white.* 雪是白色的。| *Horses are animals.* 馬是動物。| *She wants to be a doctor when she leaves school.* 她畢業後想當醫生。| *These shoes are mine.* 這雙鞋是我的。| *We were hungry.* 我們餓了。| *I'm not ready.* 我沒準備好。| *Be careful!* 小心! | *It's hot today.* 今天很熱。| *A knife is for cutting with.* 刀子是用來切東西的。**4** used in short phrases and questions〔用於片語和疑問句中〕: *It's cold, isn't it?* 天氣真冷, 是吧? | *He isn't leaving, is he?* 他不是要走, 對吧? | *"That's not your coat!" "Yes it is!"* "那不是你的大衣!" "不, 是我的!" **5** [linking verb 連繫動詞] used after 'there' to show that something exists〔用在 there 之後表示某物的存在〕: *There's a hole in your trousers.* 你的褲子上有個洞。**6 be that as it may** *formal* used to say that even though you accept that something is true it does not change a situation【正式】即使那是真的; 儘管如此: *"James has been under a lot of pressure at work recently." "Be that as it may, he ought to spend time with his family."* "詹姆斯最近工作壓力很大。" "即使如此, 他也應該找時間陪伴家人。" **7** [I] to exist 存在: *That's just how it is.* 事情的經過就是這樣。**8** to remain in the same state or stay calm 維持原來的狀態; 保持鎮靜: *If the baby's sleeping, let her be.* 如果寶寶睡了, 就讓她睡吧。**9 let/leave sth be** to let a situation remain as it is without trying to change it 順其自然: *You just have to let some things be.* 有些事情你就必須順其自然。**10 the be-all and end all** the most important part of a situation or of someone's life 首要的事情; 最高的目標: *For Jim making money is the be-all and end all of his job.* 對吉姆來講, 掙錢是他追求的最高目標。

beach¹ /bitʃ; biːtʃ/ *n plural* **beaches** [C] an area of sand or small stones next to the sea or a lake 海灘, 沙灘: *It was a hot day, and the beach was already crowded with people.* 天氣很熱, 海灘上已經擠滿了人。—see picture on page A12 參見 A12 頁圖 —see 見 SHORE[1] (USAGE) 3 2

beach² *v* [T] **1** to pull a boat onto the shore away from the water 把〔船〕拖上岸 **2** if a WHALE (=large sea animal) beaches itself or is beached, it swims onto the shore and cannot get back in the water 使〔鯨〕擱淺

beach ball /ˈ· ·/ *n* [C] a large coloured plastic ball filled with air and used for playing games on the beach 沙灘球

beach bug·gy /ˈ· ˌ··/ *n* [C] a vehicle with very large tyres that can be driven on sand 海灘車〔在沙灘上用的裝有特大輪胎的機動車〕; DUNE BUGGY *AmE*【美】

beach chair /ˈ· ·/ *n* [C] *AmE* a folding chair with a seat and back made of cloth or plastic, which is used outdoors, especially at the beach; DECKCHAIR【美】〔尤指在海灘上使用的〕帆布躺椅 —see picture at 參見 CHAIR[1] 圖

beach·comb·er /ˈbitʃˌkomɚ; ˈbiːtʃˌkəʊmə/ *n* [C] someone who searches beaches for things that might be useful 沙灘拾荒者

beach·head /ˈbitʃˌhɛd; ˈbiːtʃhed/ *n* [C] an area of shore that has been taken from an enemy by force and can be used for landing soldiers on 灘頭陣地, 灘頭堡: *the Normandy beachheads* 諾曼第灘頭陣地

beach·wear /ˈbitʃˌwɛr; ˈbiːtʃweə/ *n* [U] clothes that you wear for swimming, lying on the beach etc 海灘裝, 沙灘裝

bea·con /ˈbikən; ˈbiːkən/ *n* [C] **1** a special tower with a bright light, or floating object that sends signals, used to warn boats that they are near the shore 燈塔 **2** a light that is put somewhere to warn or guide people, vehicles, or aircraft 燈標 **3** a radio or RADAR signal used by aircraft or boats to help them find their position and direction 無線電[雷達]信標 **4** *especially literary* a person, idea etc that guides or encourages you【尤文】指路明燈; 指引者; 楷模: *a beacon of hope in a dark world* 黑暗世界裡的希望之光 **5** a fire on top of a hill used in former times as a signal〔舊時的〕烽火(台) —see also 另見 BELISHA BEACON

bead /bid; biːd/ *n* [C] **1** one of a set of small, usually round pieces of glass, wood, plastic etc, that you can put on a string and wear as jewellery 珠子; 小珠: *a necklace of amber beads* 琥珀珠子串成的項鏈 **2** a small drop of liquid such as water or blood〔液體〕小珠, 小滴〈如水珠、血滴等〉: *Beads of sweat stood out on his brow.* 他的額頭上滲出了汗珠。**3 draw a bead on** to aim carefully before shooting a weapon〔射擊時〕瞄準 —see also 另見 WORRY BEADS

bead·ed /ˈbidɪd; ˈbiːdʒd/ *adj* **1** decorated with beads 帶珠子的, 有珠子作裝飾的 **2 beaded with sweat/perspiration** with drops of SWEAT (=liquid produced by your body when you are hot) on your skin 汗流浹背, 大汗淋漓

bead·ing /ˈbidɪŋ; ˈbiːdɪŋ/ *n* [U] **1** long thin pieces of wood or stone that are used as a decoration on the edges of walls, furniture etc〔牆壁、家具等的〕串珠狀懸飾 **2** a lot of beads sewn close together on clothes, leather etc as decoration〔衣服、皮革等上的〕串珠狀裝飾物

bea·dle /ˈbidl̩; ˈbiːdl/ *n* [C] **1** an officer in British churches in former times who helped the priest in various ways, especially by keeping order〔英國舊時教區的〕執事, 牧師助手 **2** an officer in some British universities who helps at special ceremonies〔英國一些大學舉行典禮時的〕儀仗官, 禮儀前導官

bead·y /ˈbidɪ; ˈbiːdi/ *adj* **1** beady eyes are small, round, and shiny〔眼睛〕珠子般的; 圓而亮的 **2 have/keep your beady eye(s) on** *humorous* to watch someone or something very carefully【幽默】睜大眼睛仔細地看

B

bea·gle /ˈbigl̩; ˈbiːgəl/ *n* [C] a dog with short legs and smooth fur, sometimes used to hunt rabbits 畢格爾犬〔短腿軟毛的獵兔犬〕

beak /bik; biːk/ *n* [C] **1** the hard pointed mouth of a bird 鳥嘴, 喙 **2** *humorous* a large pointed nose【幽默】鷹鈎鼻 **3** *BrE old-fashioned* a judge or a male teacher【英, 過時】法官; 男教師

bea·ker /ˈbikɚ; ˈbiːkə/ *n* [C] **1** *BrE* a drinking cup with straight sides and no handle, usually made of plastic【英】〔直身無柄的〕杯子 **2** a glass cup with straight sides that is used in chemistry for measuring and heating liquids〔實驗室用的〕燒杯, 量杯 —see picture at 參見 LABORATORY 圖

beam¹ /bim; biːm/ *n* [C]

1 ►LIGHT 光◄ a) a shining line of light from the sun, a lamp etc 光束, 光線: *We could see the beams of searchlights scanning the sky.* 我們可以看到搜索天空的探照燈光。**b)** a line of light, energy etc that you cannot see 束, 柱: *a laser beam* 激光束 | *The intruder passed through an infrared alarm beam.* 非法闖入者穿過了紅外線警報光束。

2 ►WOOD/METAL 木頭/金屬◄ a long heavy piece of wood or metal used in building houses, bridges etc 梁, 橫梁

3 ►SMILE 微笑◄ a wide happy smile 喜色, 笑容: *"Congratulations!" she said, with a beam of delight.* "恭喜你!" 她面帶喜色地說。

4 off (the) beam incorrect or mistaken 不正確的, 錯誤的, 不對頭的: *We tried to guess the price but we were way off beam.* 我們猜過價錢, 但我們猜的和實際價錢差得太遠了。

5 ►SPORT 體育◄ a long raised wooden bar used in GYMNASTICS, on which you balance and move〔體操〕平衡木

6 ►SHIP 船◄ *technical* the widest part of a ship from side to side【術語】船寬 —see also 另見 **broad in the beam** (BROAD¹ (12))

beam² *v* **1** [I] to smile very happily 笑, 眉開眼笑: *The captain beamed with satisfaction.* 上尉露出了滿意的微笑。| *"I got a place!" said Sara, beaming delightedly.* "我被錄取了!" 莎拉帶着喜悅的微笑說。**2** [T always+adv/prep] to send a radio or television signal through the air, especially to somewhere very distant 向…發送〔電波〕: *the first ever broadcast beamed across the Atlantic* 首次向大西洋彼岸發出的廣播信號 **3** [I,T] to send out a line of light, heat, energy etc 發光; 發熱; 發射: *The sun beamed through the clouds.* 陽光穿透了雲層。| *X-rays are beamed through the patient's body.* 用X光透視病人的身體。

beam-ends /ˌ· ˈ·/ *n* **be on your beam-ends** *BrE old-fashioned* to have almost no money【英, 過時】經濟拮据

3 **bean¹** /bin; biːn/ *n*

1 ►VEGETABLE 蔬菜◄ a) a seed from one of many types of climbing plants, that is often used as food 豆 **b)** a POD (=seed case) from a bean plant that is used as food when the seeds are young 豆莢: *green beans* 青豆莢 —see picture on page A9 參見 A9 頁圖

2 ►PLANT 植物◄ a plant that produces beans 豆科植物

3 ►COFFEE 咖啡◄ one of many types of seed that is used to make coffee, chocolate etc〔能製成咖啡或巧克力等的〕豆: *coffee beans* 咖啡豆 | *cocoa beans* 可可豆

4 be full of beans *informal* to be very eager and full of energy【非正式】生氣勃勃; 精力充沛: *It's the kids' party today and they're full of beans.* 今天是孩子們的聚會, 他們都充滿了朝氣。

5 not have a bean *informal* to have no money at all【非正式】身無分文: *I can't pay you – I haven't got a bean.* 我不能付錢給你 —— 我一分錢也沒有。

6 not know beans (about) *AmE informal* to know nothing at all about a subject【美, 非正式】〔對…〕一無所知

7 old bean *BrE old-fashioned* used by men when talking to a man they know well【英, 過時】老兄〔用於稱呼朋友〕—see also 另見 **spill the beans** (SPILL¹ (3))

bean² *v* [T] *informal* to hit someone on the head with an object【非正式】〔用東西〕打〔某人的〕頭部: *I was beaned on the head by a baseball.* 我的頭被棒球打了一下。

bean·bag /ˈbinˌbæg; ˈbiːnbæg/ *n* [C] **1** a very large cloth bag that is filled with pieces of soft plastic and used for sitting on 豆袋坐墊; 豆袋椅 **2** a small cloth bag filled with beans, used for throwing and catching in children's games〔兒童投擲遊戲用的〕豆袋

bean curd /ˈ· ·/ *n* [C] a soft white food made from SOYBEANS; TOFU 豆腐

bean feast /ˈ· ·/ *n* [C] *BrE informal* a party or celebration【英, 非正式】聚會; 慶祝會

bea·nie /ˈbinɪ; ˈbiːni/ *n* [C] *AmE* a small round hat that fits close to your head【美】無邊小便帽

bean·pole /ˈbinˌpol; ˈbiːnpəʊl/ *n* [C] *humorous* a very tall thin person【幽默】〔人〕瘦高個子

bean·sprout /ˈbinsˌpraut; ˈbiːnspraʊt/ *n* [C] the small white stem from a bean seed that is eaten as a vegetable 豆芽 —see picture on page A9 參見 A9 頁圖

bear¹ /bɛr; beə/ *v past tense* **bore** /bɔr; bɔː/ *past participle* **borne** /bɔrn; bɔːn/ [T]

1 can't bear a) to dislike something or someone so much that they make you very annoyed or impatient 忍受不了: *Oh, I can't bear that man – he really irritates me!* 我真受不了那個人 —— 他真的讓我很生氣! | *I just can't bear that kind of selfishness.* 我就是無法忍受那種自私。| **can't bear sb doing sth** *He can't bear people smoking while he's eating.* 他忍受不了人們在他吃飯的時候吸煙。**b)** to be so upset about something that you feel unable to accept it or let it happen 接受不了…的事實: *Please don't leave me all alone. I couldn't bear it.* 不要把我一個人留在這兒。我受不了。| **can't bear the thought of** *We just couldn't bear the thought of selling the farm.* 我們就是實在不敢想賣農場的事。| **can't bear to do sth** *Alison couldn't bear to leave and cried all the way to the airport.* 艾利森忍受不了離別之苦, 去機場的路上一直在哭。

2 bear in mind (that) to remember a fact or piece of information that is important or could be useful in the future 記住; 考慮到: *Bearing in mind that he's only ten, I think he did very well.* 考慮到他只有十歲, 我認為他做得非常好。| *I think that's excellent advice to bear in mind.* 我覺得那是個非常好的建議, 必須記住。

3 ►BE BRAVE 勇敢◄ to bravely accept or deal with a painful or unpleasant situation 忍受, 忍耐, 經受住: *She bore the pain with tremendous courage.* 她非常勇敢地忍受了痛苦。| *Listening to their screams was more than we could bear.* 聽他們尖叫我們可真受不了。| **grin and bear it** (=accept something unpleasant without complaining) 逆來順受; 苦笑着忍受; 默默承受 *It's no good moaning – you'll just have to grin and bear it.* 老是抱怨也沒有用 —— 你只能忍下來算了。

4 bear the costs/burden/expense etc *formal* to pay for something【正式】承擔費用/負擔/開支等: *As usual, the poorest members of society are bearing the burden of tax increases.* 一如既往, 社會上最貧窮的人承受着增稅的負擔。

5 bear responsibility/the blame etc *formal* to be responsible, accept the blame etc for something【正式】承擔責任/應受責備等: *In this case, the victim must bear some responsibility for the crime.* 在這起案件中, 受害

者本人必須承擔部分責任。

6 ►SUPPORT 支持◄ to support the weight of something 支撐〔重量〕: *I don't think the table is strong enough to bear your weight.* 我看這桌子承受不住你的重量。| *a load-bearing wall* 承重牆

7 doesn't bear thinking about so unpleasant or shocking that you prefer not to think about it 不堪設想: *The long-term consequences of a nuclear leak don't bear thinking about.* 核泄漏造成的長遠後果真是不堪設想。

8 bear a resemblance/relation etc to to be similar to or connected with someone or something else 與…相似/與…有關等: *George doesn't bear much resemblance to his father.* 喬治長得不太像他父親。| *The things she says bear little relation to what she actually does.* 她說的和她做的不大相符。

9 bear the strain/pressure etc to be strong enough or firm enough to continue despite problems 承受壓力等: *She suddenly became a big star, and their marriage was unable to bear the strain.* 她突然間成了大明星, 他們的婚姻承受不了這樣的壓力。

10 bear the brunt of to have to accept the most difficult or damaging part of something 首當其衝: *It's the junior staff who will bear the brunt of the redundancies.* 低級職員將首當其衝被裁員。

11 bear (sb) a grudge to continue to feel annoyed about something that someone did a long time ago 對〔某人〕懷恨在心: *Despite her treatment of him over the years, he bears her no grudges.* 儘管多年來她一直待他不好, 他並沒有懷恨在心。

12 bear fruit a) if a plan, decision etc bears fruit, it is successful, especially after a long period of time〔尤指計劃、決定等長時間之後〕有了成果; 成功了: *Our careful investments were finally bearing fruit.* 我們謹慎的投資終於得到了回報。**b)** if a tree bears fruit, it produces fruit〔果樹〕結果

13 ►SHOW SIGNS OF 顯出…的跡象◄ to show physical or emotional signs of a past experience 顯示; 具有, 帶有〔標記或特徵〕: *Jim proudly bears the scars of his rugby days.* 吉姆自豪地展示他當橄欖球員時留下的傷疤。

14 not bear examination/inspection etc to not be suitable or good enough to be tested or examined thoroughly 經受不住檢查/審查等: *This line of argument doesn't bear much examination.* 這樣的論據經不起推敲。

15 bring influence/pressure etc to bear (on) to use your influence or power to get what you want〔對…〕施加壓力; 敦促: *The tobacco companies are bringing pressure to bear on the government to stop the advertising ban.* 煙草公司向政府施壓, 促其取消香煙廣告的禁令。

16 bear witness to *formal* to show that something is true or exists【正式】證明, 作證: *Her latest film bears witness to her versatility as a director.* 她最近拍的電影證明她是一位多才多藝的導演。

17 bear right/left to turn towards the right or left 向右/左轉: *Bear left at the crossroads.* 在十字路口向左轉。| *The road bears round to the right.* 這條路過個環島向右轉。

18 ►BABY 嬰兒◄ *formal* to give birth to a baby【正式】生育: **bear sb a child/son/daughter** (=have their baby) 為某人生孩子/兒子/女兒 *She bore him three sons.* 她為他生了三個兒子。

19 bear yourself *formal* to walk, stand etc in a particular way, especially when this shows your character【正式】表現; 保持某種舉止: *Throughout the trial, she bore herself with great dignity.* 在整個審判過程中, 她都保持着端莊的舉止。

20 ►CARRY 攜帶◄ *literary* to carry someone or something, especially something important【文】運送; 攜帶; 傳運: *The emperor was borne along in a sedan chair.* 皇上是一路坐着轎子來的。| *A messenger arrived, bearing a message from the prince.* 來了一位使者, 帶來了王子的口信。

21 ►WIND/WATER 風/水◄ *literary* if the wind, sea, or air bears something, it moves it along【文】吹動; 傳送: *The sound of music was borne along on the wind.* 樂聲隨風飄送。

22 ►SIGN/MARK 記號/標記◄ *formal* to have or show a sign or mark【正式】帶有〔標記〕: *The letter bore no signature.* 這封信上沒有署名。

23 ►NAME/TITLE 姓名/頭銜◄ *formal* to have a particular name or title【正式】具有, 擁有〔名字或頭銜〕: *The chest bears the name of Chippendale.* 箱子上有〔英國著名家具公司〕奇本代爾公司的牌子。

24 bear sb no malice/ill will etc *formal* not to feel angry towards someone【正式】對某人沒有惡意/敵意等

Frequencies of the verbs **bear**, **stand**, and **endure** in spoken and written English 動詞 bear, stand 和 endure 在英語口語和書面語中的使用頻率

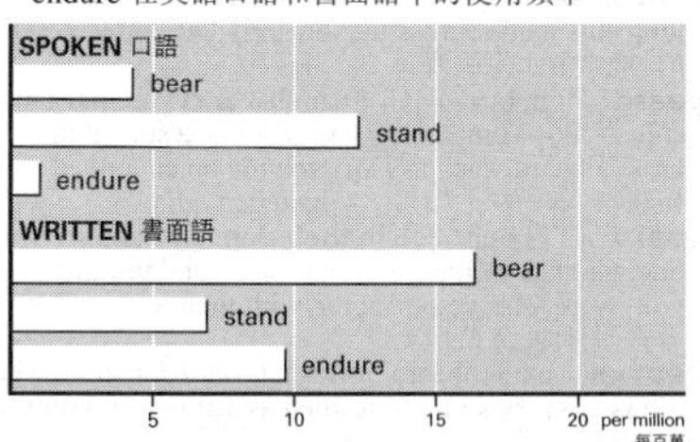

Based on the British National Corpus and the Longman Lancaster Corpus
據英國國家語料庫和朗文蘭卡斯特語料庫

All three verbs are used to mean 'accept or deal with an unpleasant situation'. The graph shows that in this meaning **stand** and **bear** are much more common than **endure** in spoken English. In written English, **bear** is the most common and **endure**, a formal word, is fairly common. 這三個動詞都用來表示"接受或應付令人不快的局面"。本圖表顯示, 作此意解釋時, stand 和 bear 在口語中的使用頻率遠遠高於 endure。在書面語中, bear 最常用; endure 語氣正式, 也相當常用。

bear down *phr v* **1 bear down on** to move quickly towards someone in a threatening way 向…逼近; 衝向: *His aunt bore down on him and insisted he joined them for dinner.* 他的姨媽跑到他身邊, 堅持要他和他們一起吃飯。| *A powerboat was bearing down on us.* 一艘汽艇向我們逼近。**2** [I] to use all your strength and effort to push or press down on something 使勁推; 使勁壓下 **3** [T **bear sb/sth ↔ down**] *formal* to defeat a person or deal successfully with a difficult situation【正式】壓倒; 征服; 打敗

bear on/upon sth *phr v* [T] *formal* to have a connection with something【正式】與…有聯繫, 與…有關

bear sb/sth **out** *phr v* [T] if facts or information bear out a claim, story, opinion etc, they help to prove that it is true 為…作證, 證實, 支持〔某種說法〕: *Recent evidence bears out the idea that students learn best in small groups.* 最新的證據顯示, 學生以小組方式學習效果最佳。| *Tell them what really happened. I'll bear you out.* 把真相告訴他們吧, 我會為你作證。

bear up *phr v* [I] to show courage or determination during a difficult or unpleasant time 支持住, 撐下去; 不氣餒: *How has he been bearing up since the accident?* 事故發生後, 他是怎樣挺過來的?

bear with sb/sth *phr v* [T] **1 bear with me** *spoken* used to ask someone politely to wait while you find out information, finish what you are doing etc【口】耐心等待; 別着急: *Bear with me a minute, and I'll check if Mr Garrard's in.* 請等一下, 讓我看看加勒德先生在不在。**2**

to be patient or continue to do something difficult or unpleasant 容忍, 忍耐: *I tried to bear with her tempers.* 我設法容忍她的壞脾氣。

bear² *n* [C] **1** a large strong animal with thick fur that eats flesh, fruit, and insects 熊 —see also 另見 TEDDY BEAR, POLAR BEAR **2** *technical* someone who sells shares (SHARE² (5)) or goods when they expect the price to fall【術語】〔股市或期貨〕看跌的人: **a bear market** (=when the value of business shares is falling) 熊市 **3** *informal* a big man who is rough or bad-tempered【非正式】粗暴魯莽的人, 脾氣暴躁的人 **4 be like a bear with a sore head** *informal* to be rude to people because you are feeling bad-tempered【非正式】脾氣暴躁

bear·a·ble /ˈbɛrəbl̩; ˈbeərəbəl/ *adj* something that is bearable is difficult or unpleasant, but you can deal with it 忍耐得住的, 可忍受的, 可容忍的: *His friendship was the only thing that made life bearable.* 唯有他的友情能使生活沒那麼艱難。—**bearably** *adv*

bear claw /ˈ· ·/ *n* [C] *AmE* fruit covered in PASTRY with long cuts made across the top【美】〔頂部帶有平行切條的〕熊掌形水果餡餅

3 **beard¹** /bɪrd; bɪəd/ *n* [C] **1** hair that grows around a man's chin 鬍鬚 —compare 比較 MOUSTACHE **2** something similar to a beard, such as hair growing on an animal's chin 鬚狀物〈如動物的鬍鬚〉—**bearded** *adj*

beard² *v* [T] **beard sb in their den** to go and see someone who has influence or authority, and tell them what you want, why you disagree with them etc 敢對有權勢者當面責問; 太歲頭上動土

bear·er /ˈbɛrə; ˈbeərə/ *n* [C] **1** *formal* someone whose job is to carry something such as a flag or a STRETCHER (=light bed for a sick person)【正式】持…的人; 抬[擔、揹]着…的人; 旗手 **2** someone who brings you information, a letter etc 帶信人: *I hate to be the bearer of bad news, but...* 我不願當一個帶來壞消息的人, 但是… **3** *law* the bearer of a legal document such as a PASSPORT is the person that it officially belongs to【法律】〔證件的〕持有者 **4** *IndE, PakE* a male servant【印, 巴】男僕

bear hug /ˈ· ·/ *n* [C] an action in which you put your arms around someone and hold them very tightly because you like them or are pleased to see them 緊緊的擁抱

bear·ing /ˈbɛrɪŋ; ˈbeərɪŋ/ *n* **1 have some/no etc bearing on** to have some influence, no influence etc on something 對…有/無影響等: *Recent market fluctuations have had a direct bearing on company policy.* 近期市場的波動對公司政策有直接影響。**2 lose your bearings** to become confused about where you are or what you should do next 迷失方向, 暈頭轉向: *I completely lost my bearings in the dark.* 漆黑中我一點兒也辨不清方向。**3 get your bearings** to find out exactly where you are, or feel confident that you know where you are 弄清自己的方位, 辨明方向: *Jim'll show you around and help you get your bearings.* 吉姆會帶你四處逛逛, 幫你熟悉一下這個地方。**4** [singular,U] the way in which you move, stand, or behave, especially when this shows your character 舉止, 風度 **5** [C] *technical* a direction or angle that is shown by a COMPASS (1)【術語】〔羅盤顯示的〕方向, 方位; 方位角 **6** [C] *technical* part of a machine that turns on another part, or in which a turning part is held【術語】〔機器的〕承座; 軸承

bear·ish /ˈbɛrɪʃ; ˈbeərɪʃ/ *adj* **1** rude or bad-tempered 沒禮貌的, 粗魯的; 暴躁的 **2 a)** a bearish market is one where the prices of shares (SHARE² (5)) are decreasing 行情看跌的 **b)** someone who is bearish expects the price of business shares to go down〔人〕預料股市行情下跌的 —**bearishly** *adv* —**bearishness** *n*

bear·skin /ˈbɛr,skɪn; ˈbeə,skɪn/ *n* **1** [C,U] the skin of a bear 熊皮 **2** [C] a tall hat made of black fur, worn by some British soldiers for special ceremonies〔一些英國士兵在特殊儀式上戴的〕黑色熊皮高帽

beast /bist; biːst/ *n* [C] **1** *literary* an animal, especially a large or dangerous one【文】〔尤指龐大或危險的〕野獸 **2** *old-fashioned especially spoken* someone who is cruel or unpleasant【過時, 尤口】令人討厭的人, 畜生, 禽獸: *You filthy beast!* 你這個下流的畜生! **3** *spoken* a job, problem etc that is difficult to deal with【口】難辦的事, 難題: *Can you undo this jar? It's a real beast to open.* 你能把這瓶子打開嗎? 它真難開。**4 the beast in sb** the part of someone's character that makes them experience hatred, strong sexual feelings, violence etc 人的獸性: *You bring out the beast in me. Come here!* 你激起了我的野性。過來!

beast·ly /ˈbistlɪ; ˈbiːstli/ *adj old-fashioned especially spoken* very unpleasant; nasty【過時, 尤口】令人不快的, 討厭的; 惡劣的: *What beastly weather!* 天氣真惡劣! —**beastly** *adv* —**beastliness** *n* [U]

beast of bur·den /,· · ˈ··/ *n* [C] *old use* an animal that does heavy work【舊】役畜, 力畜

beat¹ /bit; biːt/ *v past tense* **beat** *past participle* **beaten** /ˈbitn̩; ˈbiːtn/

1 ►DEFEAT 打敗◄ [T] **a)** to get the most points, votes etc in a game, race, or competition 擊敗, 打敗, 戰勝: *Brazil were beaten in the final 2-1.* 巴西隊在決賽中以 1 比 2 告負。| *I could always beat my brother at chess.* 每次下棋, 我都能贏我哥哥。| **beat sb hollow** (=defeat them easily)〔在比賽中〕輕取對方 **b)** to successfully deal with or defeat a problem that you have been struggling with 戰勝; 克服: *The Administration claims to have beaten inflation.* 政府宣稱已成功地遏制了通貨膨脹。—see 見 WIN¹ (USAGE)

2 ►HIT 打◄ [T] to hit someone or something many times with your hand or with a stick〔接連地〕打, 擊: *In those days children were often beaten at school.* 那些日子, 孩子們在學校經常挨打。| *I've been beating the rugs and I'm covered in dust.* 我一直在拍打地毯, 所以渾身全是灰塵。| **beat sb to death/beat sb unconscious etc** (=beat them until they die etc) 把某人打死/打昏等 | **beat sb black and blue** (=make marks on their body by beating them hard) 把某人打得青一塊紫一塊 | **beat the living daylights out of** *informal* (=beat someone very hard)【非正式】痛打, 狠揍

3 beat a record/score etc to do better than a record etc that already exists 打破記錄等: *The record set by Kierson in 1984 has yet to be beaten.* 基爾遜在 1984 年創下的記錄至今無人打破。

4 ►HIT AGAINST 碰撞◄ [I always+adv/prep] to knock or hit against something continuously〔連續〕撞擊, 拍打: **beat on/against etc** *Waves beat against the cliffs.* 海浪拍打着懸崖。| *We could hear the rain beating on the roof.* 我們可以聽到雨點拍打屋頂的聲音。

5 beat sb to it *informal* to get or do something before someone else, especially if you are both trying to do it first【非正式】趕在前面, 搶先一步: *I really wanted that car but someone else had beaten me to it.* 我很想要那輛車, 但有人搶先一步把它買了。

6 (it) beats me *spoken* used to say that you cannot understand or explain something【口】把我難住了: *"How can these kids afford clothes like that?" "Beats me."* "這些孩子怎麼買得起那樣的衣服?" "我也搞不清楚。"

7 ►MIX 混合◄ [T] to mix things together with a fork or machine when preparing food 攪拌, 攪打: *Beat the eggs until they are light and fluffy.* 把蛋液打到鬆軟不再黏稠。

8 ►DRUMS 鼓◄ [I,T] if you beat the drums or if drums beat, they make a regular continuous sound 擊(鼓), 打(鼓)

9 ►HEART 心◄ [I] when your heart beats, it moves in a regular RHYTHM (1) as it pumps your blood 跳(動): *He's still alive – I can feel his heart beating.* 他還活着——我能感覺到他的心跳。

10 ►WINGS 翅膀◄ [I,T] if a bird beats its wings or its wings beat, they move up and down quickly and regularly〔鳥〕拍打〔翅膀〕;〔翅膀〕有規律地動

11 you can't beat *spoken* used to say that someone or something is better than anything else【口】甚麼也比不上: *You can't beat motor racing for excitement and danger.* 甚麼也比不上賽車那樣刺激又驚險。
12 take some beating a) to be difficult to beat 難以戰勝: *Schumacher has 42 points, which will take some beating.* 舒馬赫得到 42 分, 要戰勝他不容易。**b)** to be better, more enjoyable etc than almost anything else of the same type 是最好的, 是最精彩的: *As a winter sports center, Edmonton takes some beating.* 作為冬季體育運動中心, 埃德蒙頓是最好的。
13 ►BE BETTER 更好◄ [T not in progressive 不用進行式] *spoken* to be much better and more enjoyable than something else【口】好多了, 強多了: *This job sure beats tending bar!* 這工作肯定比當酒吧侍應好多了!
14 beat the rush to do something earlier than normal in order to avoid problems when everyone does it 提前行動〔以避免人多麻煩〕: *Shop now and beat the Christmas rush!* 現在就去購物吧, 省得在聖誕節前商店擁擠時去湊熱鬧!
15 beat about/around the bush to avoid or delay talking about something embarrassing or unpleasant〔說話〕轉彎抹角, 旁敲側擊: *Stop beating about the bush and tell me why you're here.* 不要轉彎抹角了, 快告訴我你來幹甚麼。
16 beat the system to find ways of avoiding or breaking the rules of an organization, system etc, in order to achieve what you want 鑽制度[規章]的空子
17 beat it! *spoken* used to tell someone to leave at once because they are annoying you or should not be there【口】走開! 滾開!
18 beat your brains out *AmE informal* to think about something very hard and for a long time【美, 非正式】絞盡腦汁, 苦苦思索
19 beat the rap *AmE informal* to avoid being punished for something you have done【美, 非正式】逃脫懲罰
20 if you can't beat 'em, join 'em *spoken* used when you decide to take part in something although you disapprove of it, because everyone else is doing it and you cannot stop them【口】隨大流〔若阻止不了別人做某事, 那自己也加入一起幹〕
21 beat time to make regular movements or sounds to show the speed at which music should be played 打拍子: *a conductor beating time with his baton* 用指揮棒打拍子的樂隊指揮
22 can you beat that/it? *spoken* used to show that you are surprised or annoyed by something【口】〔表示驚訝或惱火〕竟有這等事? 豈有此理? 你聽到過[看見過]如此奇怪的人[事]嗎?: *He's taken the money and gone! Can you beat that?* 他把錢拿走了! 真是豈有此理!
23 beat a path (to sb's door) if people beat a path to your door, they are interested in something you are selling, a service you are providing etc 紛紛前來購買: *They'll be beating a path to your door after this ad.* 他們看過這則廣告後, 一定會紛紛前來搶購的。
24 to beat the band *AmE informal* in large amounts or with great force【美, 非正式】大量地; 大力地: *It's raining to beat the band.* 正下着傾盆大雨。
25 beat the heat *AmE informal* to make yourself cooler【美, 非正式】涼快一下: *Let's go swimming to beat the heat.* 我們去游泳吧, 涼快一下。
26 ►METAL 金屬◄ [T] to hit metal with a hammer in order to shape it or make it thinner 錘打, 〔用錘〕敲打
27 ►HUNTING 打獵◄ [I,T] to force wild birds and animals out of bushes, long grass etc so that they can be shot for sport 將獵物趕出〔草叢、樹叢等〕
28 beat your breast *literary* to show clearly that you are very upset or sorry about something【文】捶胸頓足〔表示憤怒或悲傷〕—see also 另見 BEATEN, BEATING

beat down *phr v* **1** [I] if the sun beats down, it shines very brightly and the weather is hot〔烈日〕曝曬 **2** [I] if the rain beats down, it is raining very hard〔雨〕下得很大 **3** [T **beat** sb ↔ **down**] to persuade someone to reduce a price 使〔某人〕壓低價錢, 殺價: **beat sb down to sth** *He wanted £4,500 for the car but I beat him down to £3,850.* 這輛車他要價4,500英鎊, 但最後給我壓到3,850英鎊。

beat off *phr v* **1** [T **beat** sb/sth ↔ **off**] to prevent someone who is trying to attack you, harm you, or compete against you 擊退, 打退, 趕跑: *efforts to beat off our business rivals* 為打敗我們的商業對手而作出的努力 | *We managed to beat off the dogs and run away.* 我們設法把狗打跑, 才得以脱身。**2** [I,T **beat** sb ↔ **off**] *AmE taboo slang* to MASTURBATE【美, 諱, 俚】手淫, 自瀆

beat out *phr v* **1** [T **beat** sth ↔ **out**] to put out a fire by beating it 撲滅〔火〕 **2** [T **beat** sth **out of** sb] to force someone to tell you something by beating them 拷打逼供: *I had the truth beaten out of me by my father.* 爸爸逼我說出了真相。**3** [T **beat** sth ↔ **out**] if drums beat out a RHYTHM (1) or you beat out a rhythm on the drums, they make a continuous regular sound 用鼓點奏出〔節拍〕 **4** [T **beat** sb ↔ **out**] *AmE* to defeat someone in a competition【美】戰勝, 打敗: *Roberts beat out Tony Gwynn for the Most Valuable Player Award.* 羅伯茨擊敗托尼·格溫獲得最有價值球員獎。

beat up *phr v* **1** [T **beat** sb ↔ **up**] to hurt someone badly by hitting them 痛打, 毆打; 打傷: *They claimed they had been beaten up by the police.* 他們聲稱曾被警察毒打。**2 beat up on** *AmE* to hit someone and harm them, especially someone younger or weaker than yourself【美】毆打; 欺負〔尤指弱小者〕 **3 beat up on yourself** *AmE informal* to blame yourself too much for something【美, 非正式】太過自責

beat² *n* **1** [C] one of a series of movements or hitting actions〔連續敲打的〕一擊, 敲擊: *a heartbeat* 心跳 | *the slow beat of the drum* 緩慢的鼓聲 **2** [C usually singular 一般用單數] a regular repeated noise 有規律而重複的聲音: **[+of]** *the beat of marching feet* 列隊行進的腳步聲 **3** [singular] the main RHYTHM (1) that a piece of music or a poem has〔音樂或詩歌的〕拍子, 節拍: *Try to follow the beat.* 儘量跟着拍子。**4** [C] one of the notes in a piece of music that sounds stronger than the other notes〔音樂〕強節奏 **5** [singular] the area of a town, city etc that a police officer regularly walks around〔警察的〕巡邏路線 3

beat³ *adj* [not before noun 不用於名詞前] *informal* very tired【非正式】疲憊不堪的: *I'm beat.* 我累極了。| **dead beat** *Come and sit down, you must be dead beat.* 過來坐下, 你一定累壞了。

beat·en /ˈbitn; ˈbiːtn/ *adj* [only before noun 僅用於名詞前] **1** beaten metal has been shaped with a hammer to make it thinner〔金屬〕鍛打的, 錘製而成的 **2** a beaten path, track etc has been made by many people walking the same way〔路等〕被踏成的, 走出來的: *a well beaten path through the forest* 人們在森林中踏出來的路 **3 off the beaten track** a place that is off the beaten track is not well known and is far away from the places that people usually visit〔地方〕不出名的; 人跡罕至的; 偏遠的

beat·er /ˈbitɚ; ˈbiːtə/ *n* [C] **1** an object that is designed to beat something 拍打器; 攪拌器: *an egg beater* 打蛋器 | *a carpet beater* (清理)地毯的撣子 **2** someone who forces wild birds or animals out of bushes, long grass etc so that they can be shot for sport〔把野生動物或鳥趕向獵人槍口的〕獵人助手 **3** *AmE informal* an old car in bad condition【美, 非正式】破舊的汽車, 老爺車

be·a·tif·ic /ˌbiəˈtɪfɪk; ˌbiːəˈtɪfɪk◄/ *adj literary* a beatific look, smile etc shows great peace and happiness【文】極樂的; 幸福的; 安息的 —**beatifically** /-klɪ; -kli/ *adv*

be·at·i·fy /bɪˈætəˌfaɪ; biˈætɪ̈faɪ/ *v* [T] if the Roman Catholic church beatifies someone who has died, it says officially that they are a holy or special person〔羅馬天主教〕為〔死者〕行宣福禮 —**beatification** /bɪˌætəfəˈkeʃən; biˌætɪ̈fɪ̈ˈkeɪʃən/ *n* [U]

beat·ing /ˈbitɪŋ; ˈbiːtɪŋ/ *n* [C] **1** an act of hitting someone many times as a punishment or in a fight 打, 擊; 痛打: **give sb a beating** (=beat them) 揍某人一頓 **2 take a beating** to lose very badly in a game or competition 慘敗, 敗北: *Our team took a real beating on Saturday.* 我隊在星期六遭到慘敗。—see also 另見 **take some beating** (BEAT[1] (12))

B

beat·nik /ˈbitnɪk; ˈbiːtnɪk/ *n* [C] one of a group of young people in the late 1950s and early 1960s, who did not accept the values of society and showed this by their clothes and the way they lived 反傳統一代成員,〔俗稱〕披頭族成員〔20世紀50年代末和60年代初出現於美國的反對世俗陳規和傳統生活方式的年輕人〕

beat-up /ˈ· ·/ *adj informal* a beat-up car, bicycle etc, is old and in bad condition【非正式】破舊的, 破爛的: *a beat-up old Ford Escort* 一輛破舊的福特護航艦牌汽車

beau /bo; bəʊ/ *n plural* **beaux** /boz; bəʊz/ or **beaus** [C] *old-fashioned*【過時】**1** a woman's close friend or lover〔女子的〕密友; 情人 **2** a fashionable, well-dressed man 花花公子, 紈袴子弟; 衣着入時的男子

Beau·jo·lais /ˌboʒəˈle; ˈbəʊʒəleɪ/ *n* [C,U] a type of French red wine 博若萊葡萄酒〔一種法國紅葡萄酒〕

beau-monde /bo ˈmɑnd; ˌbəʊ ˈmɒnd/ *n* [singular] *French* rich and fashionable people【法】富有時髦的人

beaut[1] /bjut; bjuːt/ *n* [singular] *AmE & AustrE informal* **a (real) beaut** used to say that something is either very good or very bad【美和澳, 非正式】好事; 醜事: *That last catch was a beaut.* 最後一個接球太棒了[真差勁]。

beaut[2] *adj AustrE informal* very good【澳, 非正式】棒的, 好的: *"Had a good day?" "It was beaut."* "今天好玩嗎?" "棒極了。"

beau·te·ous /ˈbjutɪəs; ˈbjuːtiəs/ *adj poetic* beautiful【詩】美麗的, 優美的: *the beauteous Helen of Troy* 特洛伊城美麗的海倫 —**beauteously** *adv*

beau·ti·cian /bjuˈtɪʃən; bjuːˈtɪʃən/ *n* [C] someone whose job is to give beauty treatments to your skin, hair etc 美容師; 美髮師

1 **beau·ti·ful** /ˈbjutəfəl; ˈbjuːtɪ̬fəl/ *adj* **1** someone or some-
2 thing that is beautiful is extremely good to look at and gives you a feeling of pleasure 美麗的, 美好的, 優美的: *She was even more beautiful than I had remembered.* 她比我記憶中的更美。| *a beautiful bunch of flowers* 美麗的花束 **2** very good 極好的, 妙極的: *a beautiful experience* 愉快的經歷 | *What a beautiful shot!* 多麼漂亮的槍法! | *The weather was beautiful.* 天氣好極了。—**beautifully** *adv*

USAGE NOTE 用法說明: BEAUTIFUL

WORD CHOICE 詞語辨析: **beautiful, pretty, handsome, good-looking, attractive, sexy**

Beautiful and **pretty** can be used of women, children, and things, but not usually of men, unless you want to suggest that they have female features. beautiful 和pretty 可以用來形容女子、孩子和事物, 但通常不用來形容男子, 除非這男子帶有女人氣: *a beautiful girl/house/view* 美麗的女孩/漂亮的房子/優美的景色 | *a pretty child/picture/voice* 漂亮的孩子/漂亮的圖畫/美妙的聲音。**Beautiful** is the strongest word to describe a very attractive appearance, it suggests that someone has almost perfect good looks. **Pretty** means good-looking in a more ordinary way, but not really beautiful. beautiful 語氣最強, 說明某人長得非常漂亮, 幾近完美。pretty 表示一般的漂亮, 但不是特別漂亮。

Handsome is not common in spoken English. It is usually used to describe men, especially if they have the strong regular features that men in romantic stories are supposed to have. A **handsome** woman is **good-looking** in a strong, healthy way. handsome 在英語口語中用得不多。它通常用於形容男子, 特別是在浪漫故事中的英俊男子。handsome 也可以用來形容女子, 表示強壯、健美的女性。

Good-looking can be used about men and women, but not usually about things. good-looking 既可形容男子, 也可形容女子, 但通常不用於形容事物: *Gina and Barry are a good-looking couple.* 吉納和巴里兩口子都很漂亮。**Attractive** can be used about men, women, and things. attractive 可以用來形容男子、女子和事物: *an attractive colour/idea/young man* 好看的顏色/好主意/有魅力的年輕男子。An **attractive** person may not be very **good-looking** but makes other people sexually interested in them, though not as much as if they are **sexy**. attractive 不一定是長得好看而是很有魅力、很性感, 但語氣上不像sexy 那樣強烈。

beau·ti·fy /ˈbjutəˌfaɪ; ˈbjuːtɪ̬faɪ/ *v* [T] to make someone or something beautiful 使美麗, 美化

beau·ty /ˈbjutɪ; ˈbjuːti/ *n* 3
1 ►APPEARANCE 外表◄ a) [U] a quality that a place 2
or person has that makes them very attractive to look at 美, 美麗, 漂亮: *Her beauty had faded over the years.* 這麼多年過去了, 她的美貌漸漸失色。| *an area of outstanding natural beauty* 景色優美的地方 | **beauty product/tip etc** (=a product etc that is supposed to make you more beautiful) 美容產品/美容小提示等 **b)** [C] *old-fashioned* a woman who is very beautiful【過時】美人: *She was considered a great beauty in her youth.* 她年輕時是個公認的大美人。

2 ►GOOD QUALITY 優質◄ [U] a quality that something such as a poem, song, emotion etc has, which gives you pleasure or joy 美感: *the beauty of Shakespeare's verse* 莎士比亞詩作之美

3 ►ADVANTAGE 長處◄ the beauty of a particularly good quality that makes something especially suitable or useful …的優點, …的好處, …的妙處: *The beauty of golf is that you can play it on your own.* 高爾夫球的好處在於可以一個人自己玩。

4 ►GOOD EXAMPLE 範例◄ [C] *spoken* a very good example of something or an object that is a particularly good, large, or pleasant one of its type【口】很好的樣品; 美好的事物: *We had a turkey at Easter – a real beauty it was.* 復活節時我們吃了火雞, 那真是美味。| *That black eye's a beauty, Justin!* 賈斯廷, 那被打青的眼睛真是夠漂亮的!

5 ►APPROVAL 贊同◄ (you) beauty! *AustrE spoken* used to show that you are very pleased by something【澳口】(你) 太好了! 棒極了!〔表示高興〕: *Look at this lunch. Beauty!* 看這頓中午飯, 太棒了! | *You beauty! You've made my day.* 你太好了! 你讓我太高興了!

6 beauty is in the eye of the beholder used to say that different people have different opinions about what is beautiful 情人眼裡出西施

beauty con·test /ˈ·· ˌ··/ *n* [C] a competition in which women are judged on how attractive they look 選美(比賽)

beauty mark /ˈ·· ·/ *n* [C] *AmE* a small dark mark on a woman's skin【美】美人痣, 美人斑; BEAUTY SPOT (2) *BrE*【英】

beauty par·lor /ˈ·· ˌ··/ *n* [C] *AmE* a beauty salon【美】美容院

beauty queen /ˈ·· ·/ *n* [C] the winner of a beauty contest 選美皇后〔選美比賽的優勝者〕

beauty sal·on /ˈ·· ˌ··/ *n* [C] a place in which you can receive beauty treatments for your skin, hair etc 美容院

beauty shop /ˈ·· ·/ *n* [C] *AmE* a beauty salon【美】美容院

beauty sleep /ˈ·· ·/ *n* [U] *humorous* enough sleep to keep you healthy and looking good【幽默】美容睡眠〔指

充分的睡眠有益於美容〕: *I need my beauty sleep.* 我需要睡個美容覺。

beauty spot /ˈ·· ·/ *n* [C] **1** a beautiful place in the countryside 名勝, 美景 **2** *BrE* a small dark mark on a woman's skin【英】美人痣, 美人斑; BEAUTY MARK *AmE*【美】—see picture on page A6 參見 A6 頁圖

bea·ver¹ /ˈbivɚ; ˈbiːvə/ *n* [C] a North American animal that has thick fur, a wide flat tail, and cuts down trees with its teeth 河狸, 海狸 —see also 另見 **eager beaver** (EAGER (3))

beaver² *v*

beaver away *phr v BrE informal* to work very hard, especially at writing or calculating something【英, 非正式】賣力地幹, 努力工作〔尤指寫作或計算〕: [+at] *He had been beavering away at his homework half the night.* 他整個晚上有一半的時間都在忙着做作業。

be·bop /ˈbi͵bɑp; ˈbiːbɒp/ *n* [U] a type of JAZZ music; BOP² (2) 博普爵士樂

be·calmed /bɪˈkɑmd; bɪˈkɑːmd/ *adj literary* a ship or boat that is becalmed cannot move because there is no wind【文】〔艦船〕因無風而靜止不動的

be·came /bɪˈkem; bɪˈkeɪm/ the past tense of BECOME

1 1 **be·cause** /bɪˈkɔz; bɪˈkɒz/ *conjunction* **1** for the reason that 因為: *I do it because I like it.* 我這樣做是因為我喜歡這樣做。| *She got the job because she was the best candidate.* 她得到了那份工作, 因為她是最佳人選。| *"Why can't I go?" "Because you're too young."* "我為甚麼不能去?" "因為你年紀太小了。" **2 because of** as a result of a particular thing or of someone's actions 因為, 由於: *He had to retire because of ill health.* 他因為健康狀況不佳, 所以不得不退休。| *Sandy's very upset and it's all because of you.* (=your fault) 桑迪很生氣, 這全都怪你。—see 見 OWING (USAGE) **3 just because...** *spoken* used to say that although one thing is true, it does not mean that something else is true【口】僅僅因為: *Just because I'm married doesn't mean that I don't want to see my old friends anymore.* 不能僅僅因為我結婚了就認為我不想再見老朋友。| *David seems to think that just because he's our boss he can talk to us anyway he wants.* 戴維似乎認為就因為他是我們的老闆, 他愛對我們說甚麼就說甚麼。

beck /bɛk; bek/ *n* **1** [C] *BrE* a small stream【英】小溪流, 山澗 **2 be at sb's beck and call** to always be ready to do what someone wants 聽命於某人: *I was tired of being at her beck and call all day long.* 我厭倦了整天受她指使。

beck·on /ˈbɛkən; ˈbekən/ *v* [I,T] **1** to make a signal to someone with your hand or arm, to show that you want them to come towards you〔招手〕示意, 召喚: [+to] *She beckoned to the child, who came running.* 她用手示意, 那孩子就跑過來了。| **beckon sb forward/to/towards etc** *I stood there till she beckoned me across the room.* 我一直站在那兒, 直到她示意我走到房間的那一邊。**2** if something such as money or happiness beckons, it is so attractive that you have to do something in order to get it 吸引, 引誘

1 1 **be·come** /bɪˈkʌm; bɪˈkʌm/ *v past tense* **became** /bɪˈkem; bɪˈkeɪm/ *past participle* **become 1** [linking verb 連繫動詞] to begin to be something, or to develop in a particular way 成為, 變成, 變得: *He became King at the age of 17.* 他 17 歲時成為國王。| *After the death of her father she became the richest woman in the world.* 她父親死後, 她成了世界上最富有的女人。| *The weather became warmer.* 天氣變得更暖和了。| *We soon became acclimatized to the warmer weather.* 我們很快就適應了較暖和的氣候。| *These constant delays are becoming a bit of a bore.* 這種經常性的耽擱成了令人討厭的事。| *She became increasingly anxious about her husband's strange behaviour.* 她對丈夫的異常行為越來越擔憂。| *He withdrew from the competition when it became clear that he stood no chance of winning.* 他知道自己在比賽中沒有獲勝的希望, 便退出了比賽。**2** [T not in progressive 不用進行式] *formal* to suit someone or be suitable for them【正式】適合, 適宜; 與...相稱: *This sort of behaviour hardly becomes a person in your position.* 這種行為與一個有你這樣地位的人簡直不相稱。**3 what has become of...?/whatever will become of...?** used to ask what has happened to someone, especially when you have not seen them for a long time, or what will happen to someone that you are worried about ... 怎麼樣了/...會怎麼樣: *Whatever will become of Sam when his wife dies?* 如果薩姆的妻子死了, 他會怎麼樣呢?

USAGE NOTE 用法說明: BECOME

WORD CHOICE 詞語辨析: **become, get, turn, go, come**

Become and **get** can be used with most types of adjective to describe changes in people and things. **Become** is more common in writing, and **get** in spoken English, especially where a quick change is involved. become 和 get 兩個動詞可以和大部分形容詞連用, 以描述人和事物的變化。become 在書面語中比較常用, 而 get 則多用於口語中, 特別是指變化非常快: *The sky became/got cloudy.* 天空變得多雲了。| *Crime is becoming more widespread.* 違法活動愈來愈普遍。| *It became clear that he was lying.* 他顯然在撒謊。| *It gets dark early now.* 現在天黑得早了。| *I'm getting wet standing here.* 站在這兒, 我都給淋濕了。| *Your dinner's getting cold.* 你的飯菜都涼了。

When things change colour, **turn** can be used, or less formally **go** (especially if the change does not last long). 說事物改變顏色時可用 turn, 非正式情況下也用 go〔尤其當變化不是長久性的〕。Compare 比較: *Jonathan turned/went pale when he heard the news.* 喬納森聽到這個消息時, 臉都變白了。| *It's that time of year when the leaves go/turn golden.* 那是一年中樹葉變成金黃色的時候。

Go can also be used when someone's mind or body changes for the worse. go 也可用於表示人的精神或身體朝壞的方面變化: *He went crazy/blind/deaf/bald* (but 但說 *He fell sick/ill*). 他瘋/瞎/聾/禿了。**Go** is used in a similar meaning with some things. go 也可用於表示某些事物向壞的方面變化: *The meat's gone bad.* 肉變壞了。| *Everything went wrong/haywire.* 所有的事情都一團糟。But in other situations **turn** is used. 但其他情況則用 turn: *The milk's turned/gone sour.* 牛奶變酸了。| *The situation turned nasty.* 局勢變得很嚴峻。

Come is used only in very few expressions where something gets better. come 只用於少數片語中, 表示事情向好的方面發展: *It came right in the end.* 結果挺好。| *All my dreams have come true* (NOT 這裡不用 *become/get* here). 我所有的夢想都成了現實。Otherwise people use **become** or **get** again. 除此以外, 人們還是用 become 或 get: *He eventually got better.* 他身體最終好了起來。

GRAMMAR 語法

Become is never followed by an infinitive though **come** can be. become 後面不接不定式, 但 come 可以: *After a while I came to like Chicago* (NOT 不用 *...became to like...*). 經過一段時間, 我逐漸喜歡上了芝加哥。

be·com·ing /bɪˈkʌmɪŋ; bɪˈkʌmɪŋ/ *adj old-fashioned*【過時】**1** clothes that are becoming make you look attractive〔衣服〕合適的, 相配的; 好看的 **2** words or actions that are becoming are suitable for you or for the situation you are in〔說話或行為〕適當的, 適宜的 —**becomingly** *adv*

bec·que·rel /bɛkˋrɛl; ͵bekəˈrel/ *n* [C] *technical* a unit for measuring RADIOACTIVITY (2)【術語】貝克雷爾〔放射性強度單位〕

B

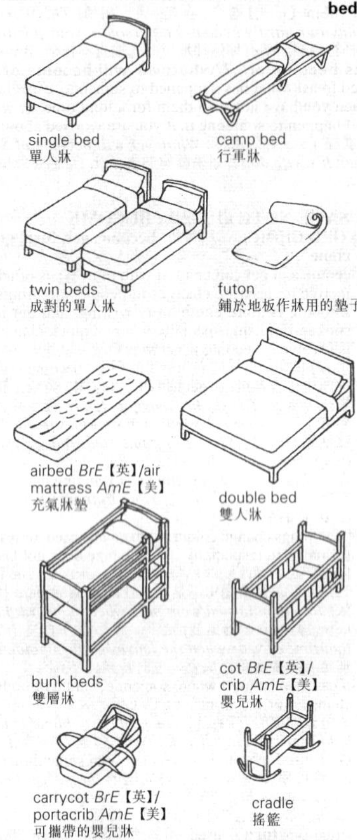

bed[1] /bɛd; bed/ *n*

1 ►SLEEP 睡眠◄ [C,U] a piece of furniture for sleeping on 牀: *a spare bed* 備用牀 | *a double bed* 雙人牀 | **in bed** *Simon lay in bed reading for hours.* 西蒙躺在牀上看了好幾個小時的書。| **go to bed** *In the end, she went to bed without any fuss.* 最後, 她毫無怨言地上牀睡覺了。| **make the bed** (=tidy the bed covers) 鋪牀 | **put sb to bed** *I'll just put the children to bed.* 我馬上就讓孩子們睡覺。| **get (sb) out of bed** *Sorry for calling so early – I hope I didn't get you out of bed.* 對不起, 這麼早給你打電話, 但願沒有打擾你休息。| **time for bed** (=time to go to sleep) 到了睡覺的時候 | **take to your bed** *old-fashioned* (=stay in bed because you are ill)【過時】〔因病〕卧牀

2 go to bed with *informal* to have sex with someone【非正式】和〔某人〕上牀〔發生性關係〕

3 get sb into bed *informal* to persuade someone to have sex with you【非正式】誘使某人發生性關係

4 ►RIVER/LAKE/SEA 河/湖/海◄ [C] the flat ground at the bottom of a river, lake, or sea〔河、湖或海的〕底部: *the sea bed* 海底

5 ►GARDEN 花園◄ [C] an area of a garden, park etc that has been prepared for plants to grow in 苗牀; 花圃; 花壇: *rose beds* 玫瑰花壇

6 ►ROCK 岩石◄ [C] a layer of rock 岩層 —see also 另見 BEDROCK (2)

7 ►BASE 基部◄ [singular] a layer of something that forms a base that other things are put on top of 底部; 地基, 基座: **[+of]** *The hut rests on a bed of concrete.* 小屋蓋在水泥地基上。| *prawns on a bed of lettuce* 鋪在生菜上面的大蝦

8 oyster/coral etc bed an area of the bottom of the sea where there are a lot of OYSTERs etc〔海底的〕牡蠣層/珊瑚層等

9 get out of bed (on) the wrong side *BrE*【英】, **get up on the wrong side of the bed** *AmE*【美】to feel slightly angry or annoyed for no particular reason 不對勁, 心情不好

10 not a bed of roses not a happy, comfortable, or easy situation 不一帆風順, 不稱心如意: *Life isn't always a bed of roses you know.* 要知道, 人生並非總是事事如意的。

11 you've made your bed and you must lie on it used to say that you must accept the bad results of your actions 自作自受, 自食其果

12 be brought to bed (of) *old use* to give birth to a baby【舊】生孩子

bed[2] *v* [T] **1** *old-fashioned* to have sex with someone【過時】與〔某人〕發生性關係 **2** also 又作 **bed out** to put plants into the ground so that they can grow 栽種於花壇[苗牀]裡 **3** to fix something firmly onto or into a base 固定在…上; 嵌入; 埋置: *The foundations were bedded in cement.* 地基嵌入水泥之中。

bed down *phr v* **1** [T **bed** sb/sth ↔ **down**] to make a person or animal comfortable for the night 使〔人或牲畜〕安睡 **2** [I] to make yourself comfortable for the night 使自己安睡: *Can I bed down on your sofa?* 我能睡在你的沙發上嗎?

bed and board /ˌ· · ˈ·/ *n* [U] food and a place to sleep 膳宿

bed and break·fast /ˌ· · ˈ··/ *n* [C, U] a private house or small hotel where you can sleep and have breakfast, or this type of place; B AND B 提供住宿和早餐的私人住家[小旅館]

be·daub /bɪˋdɔb; bɪˈdɔːb/ *v* [T usually passive 一般用被動態+**with**] *formal* to put paint, mud etc onto something in an untidy way【正式】亂塗, 抹; 弄髒

be·daz·zle /bɪˋdæzḷ; bɪˈdæzəl/ *v* [T] to make you think that someone or something is extremely impressive 使眼花繚亂; 使迷醉: *He is bedazzled by the status symbols of these crooks.* 這些代表着社會地位的權杖使他眼花繚亂。

bed bath /ˈ· ·/ *n* [C] a thorough body wash given to someone who cannot leave their bed 為卧病在牀的人洗的澡

bed·bug /ˋbɛdˌbʌg; ˈbedbʌg/ *n* [C] an insect that sucks blood and lives in houses, especially in beds 臭蟲; 牀虱

bed·cham·ber /ˋbɛdˌtʃembɚ; ˈbedˌtʃeɪmbə/ *n* [C] *old-use* a bedroom【舊】臥室

bed·clothes /ˋbɛdˌkloðz; ˈbedkləʊðz/ *n* [plural] the sheets, covers etc that you put on a bed 寢具, 鋪蓋〔包括被單、牀罩等牀上用品〕

bed·ding /ˋbɛdɪŋ; ˈbedɪŋ/ *n* [U] **1** sheets, covers etc that you put on a bed 牀上用品, 寢具, 鋪蓋 **2** something soft for animals to sleep on, such as dried grass or STRAW (=dried corn stems)〔供牲畜作窩的乾草等〕鋪墊物

be·deck /bɪˋdɛk; bɪˈdek/ *v* [T usually passive 一般用被動態] *literary* to decorate something such as a building or street by hanging things all over it【文】裝飾, 點綴: *a balcony bedecked with hanging baskets* 用吊籃裝飾的陽台

be·dev·il /bɪˋdɛvḷ; bɪˈdevəl/ *v* **bedevilled** *BrE*【英】**bedeviled** *AmE*【美】[T usually passive 一般用被動態] *formal* to cause a lot of problems and difficulties for someone or something【正式】搞糟, 攪擾; 使苦惱: *a society bedevilled by racial tensions* 被種族緊張關係搞得一團糟的社會 —**bedevilment** *n* [U]

bed·fel·low /ˋbɛdˏfɛlo; ˈbedˌfeləʊ/ *n* [C] **strange/odd/uneasy etc bedfellows** two or more people, ideas etc that are connected or working together in an unexpected way 奇怪的組合〔指兩個或兩個以上的人、觀點等出人意料地聯繫在一起〕: *Politics and ecology often make uneasy bedfellows.* 政治和生態經常會奇怪地聯繫在一起。

bed·head /ˋbɛdˏhɛd; ˈbedhed/ *n* [C] the part of a bed that is behind your head when you are sitting up 牀頭

bed·lam /ˋbɛdləm; ˈbedləm/ *n* [U] a wild noisy place or situation 喧鬧嘈雜的地方; 混亂: *The courtroom erupted into bedlam as the judge delivered his verdict.* 法官宣布判決結果時, 法庭裡頓時一片喧嘩。

bed lin·en /ˈ· ˌ··/ *n* [U] the sheets and PILLOWCASES for a bed 被單和枕套

Bed·ou·in /ˋbɛduɪn; ˈbeduɪn/ *n* [C] a member of an Arab tribe that traditionally lives in tents in the desert 貝都因人〔住在沙漠裡帳篷中的阿拉伯遊牧部落成員〕

bed·pan /ˋbɛdˏpæn; ˈbedpæn/ *n* [C] a low wide container used as a toilet by someone who has to stay in bed 〔病人在牀上用的〕便盆

bed·post /ˋbɛdˏpost; ˈbedpəʊst/ *n* [C] one of the four main supports at the corners of an old-fashioned bed 〔舊式牀的〕牀柱, 牀架杆

be·drag·gled /bɪˋdrægḷd; bɪˈdrægəld/ *adj* looking untidy and dirty, especially because you have been out in the rain 〔尤指淋雨後〕濕漉漉的; 又濕又髒的: *She came in wet and bedraggled.* 她又濕又髒地走了進來。

bed·rid·den /ˋbɛdˏrɪdṇ; ˈbedˌrɪdn/ *adj* unable to leave your bed, especially because you are old or ill 〔因年老或生病而〕臥牀不起的

bed·rock /ˋbɛdˋrɑk; ˈbedrɒk/ *n* [U] **1** the basic ideas and principles of a belief etc 基本事實, 基本原則; 根底, 基礎: *Their determination to remain independent was the bedrock on which the war effort rested.* 決心維護獨立是他們奮力作戰的思想基礎。**2** solid rock in the ground on top of which all the soil rests 基岩, 底岩, 牀岩

bed·roll /ˋbɛdˏrol; ˈbedrəʊl/ *n* [C] *AmE* a number of blankets (BLANKET[1] (1)) rolled together and used for sleeping outdoors【美】〔室外睡覺用的〕鋪蓋卷

1 2 **bed·room¹** /ˋbɛdˏrum; ˈbedrʊm/ *n* [C] **1** a room for sleeping in 臥室: *a hotel with 50 bedrooms* 有50間客房的旅館 **2 make/have bedroom eyes** to show that you are sexually attracted to someone 挑逗人, 勾引人

bed·room² *adj* a bedroom suburb is a place from which people travel to a city to work every day 郊外住宅區的; DORMITORY *BrE*【英】

bed·side /ˋbɛdˏsaɪd; ˈbedsaɪd/ *n* [C] the area around your bed 牀側, 牀邊: *Relatives have been at his bedside all week, hoping he will regain consciousness.* 親屬們整個星期都圍在他的牀邊, 希望他會恢復知覺。| **bedside lamp/table etc** (=next to your bed) 牀頭燈/桌等

bedside man·ner /ˌ·· ˈ··/ *n* [singular] a doctor's bedside manner is the way that they talk to the people that they are treating 醫生對病人的態度

bed·sit /ˌbɛdˋsɪt; ˌbedˈsɪt/ also 又作 **bed·sit·ter** /-ˋsɪtɚ; -ˈsɪtə/, **bed·sit·ting room** /ˌbɛdˋsɪtɪŋ rum; ˌbedˈsɪtɪŋ rʊm/ *n* [C] *BrE* a rented room used for both living and sleeping in【英】起居室兼臥室的兩用房間

bed·sore /ˋbɛdˏsɔr; ˈbedsɔː/ *n* [C] a sore place on your skin caused by lying in bed for a long time 〔長期臥牀引起的〕褥瘡

bed·spread /ˋbɛdˏsprɛd; ˈbedspred/ *n* [C] a decorative cover for a bed that goes on top of all the other covers 牀罩

bed·stead /ˋbɛdˏstɛd; ˈbedsted/ *n* [C] the wooden or metal frame of a bed 〔木製或金屬製的〕牀架

bed·time /ˋbɛdˏtaɪm; ˈbedtaɪm/ *n* [C,U] the time when you usually go to bed 就寢時間: *It's way past your bedtime!* 你該上牀睡覺的時間早過了! | *a bedtime story* 哄孩子睡覺時講的故事

bed wet·ting /ˈ· ˌ··/ *n* [U] the problem that some children have of passing URINE (=liquid from the body) while they are asleep 尿牀 —**bed-wetter** *n* [C]

bee /bi; biː/ *n* [C] **1** a black and yellow flying insect with a round body that makes HONEY (1) and can sting you 蜜蜂: *a swarm of bees* 蜂羣 —see also 另見 BUMBLEBEE **2 a busy bee** *spoken* someone who enjoys being busy or active【口】忙碌活躍的人 **3 have a bee in your bonnet** *informal* to think something is so important, so necessary etc that you keep mentioning it or thinking about it【非正式】腦海裡不斷地想着某一件事: *Dad's got a bee in his bonnet about saving electricity.* 爸爸一心想着要省電。**4 think you're the bee's knees** *BrE spoken* used to describe someone who thinks they are very clever, very good at something etc【英口】自以為非常出色: *She thinks she's the bee's knees around here.* 她認為自己是這裡最出色的人。**5 working/sewing etc bee** *AmE informal* an occasion when people, usually women, meet in order to do a particular type of work【美, 非正式】〔尤指婦女為某種工作而舉行的〕工作會/縫紉會等 —see also 另見 SPELLING BEE, **the birds and the bees** (BIRD (3))

Beeb /bib; biːb/ *n* **the Beeb** *spoken* the BBC【口】英國廣播公司

beech /bitʃ; biːtʃ/ *n* [C,U] a large tree with smooth grey BARK[2] (2) (=outer covering), or the wood from this tree 山毛櫸(木)

beef¹ /bif; biːf/ *n* **1** [U] the meat from a cow 牛肉: *roast beef* 烤牛肉 **2** [C] *informal* a complaint【非正式】牢騷, 怨言: *OK, so what's the beef this time?* 好了, 這一次又有甚麼苦要訴? **3 where's the beef?** *spoken especially AmE* used when you think someone's words and promises sound good, but you want to know what they actually plan to do【口, 尤美】葫蘆裡究竟賣甚麼藥? —see also 另見 BEEF TEA, CORNED BEEF 3

beef² *v* [I] *informal* to complain a lot【非正式】老發牢騷, 抱怨: [+**about**] *They're always beefing about something or other.* 他們總是就這樣那樣的事發牢騷。

beef sth ↔ **up** *phr v* [T] *informal* to improve something or make it more interesting, more important etc【非正式】加強; 改進; 充實: *a beefed up news story* 一個充實了內容的新聞報道 | *We need to beef the campaign up a bit.* 我們的宣傳活動要加把勁兒。

beef·bur·ger /ˋbifˏbɝgɚ; ˈbiːfbɜːgə/ *n* [C] *BrE* a HAMBURGER【英】漢堡包

beef·cake /ˋbifˏkek; ˈbiːfkeɪk/ *n* [C,U] *informal* a strong attractive man with large muscles, or men like this in general【非正式】〔肌肉發達的〕健美男子 —compare 比較 CHEESECAKE

Beef·eat·er /ˋbifˏitɚ; ˈbiːfˌiːtə/ *n* [C] a ceremonial guard at the Tower of London 倫敦塔的儀仗衛兵

beef·steak /ˋbifˏstek; ˈbiːfsteɪk/ *n* [C,U] STEAK (1) 牛排, 牛扒

beef tea /ˌ· ˈ·/ *n* [U] a hot drink made from BEEF[1] (1) that used to be given to people when they were ill 〔昔日給病人食用的〕牛肉湯, 牛肉汁

beef·y /ˋbifɪ; ˈbiːfi/ *adj informal* someone who is beefy is big, strong, and often quite fat【非正式】〔人〕大塊頭的, 強壯的, 肥實的

bee·hive /ˋbiˏhaɪv; ˈbiːhaɪv/ *n* [C] **1** a structure where bees (BEE (1)) are kept for producing HONEY (1) 蜂窩; 蜂箱 **2** a way of arranging a woman's hair in a high pile on the top of her head, which was popular in the 1960s 〔20世紀60年代流行的〕蜂窩式髮型

bee·line /ˋbiˏlaɪn; ˈbiːlaɪn/ *n* **make a beeline for** *informal* to go quickly and directly towards someone or something【非正式】迅速直奔, 逕直前往: *Rob always makes a beeline for beautiful women at parties.* 羅布在晚會上總是直奔向漂亮的女士。

been /bɪn; biːn/ **1** the past participle of BE **2 have/has been a)** used to say that someone has gone to a place and come back 曾到過〔某地〕: [+**to**] *I've never been to Japan.* 我從未去過日本。| **have been to do sth** *Have* *you been to see the Van Gogh exhibition yet?* 你去看過梵高畫展了嗎? **b)** *BrE* used to say that someone has come to a place and left again【英】來過〔某地〕: *The postman hasn't been yet.* 郵差還沒有來過。—see 見 GO[1] (3) **3 been there, done that** *spoken* used to say that you are no longer interested in doing something, because you already have a lot of experience of it【口】由於經歷太多而對某事失去興趣, 膩了

beep¹ /bip; biːp/ *v* **1** [I] if a machine beeps, it makes a short high sound〔機器〕嘟嘟響: *Why does the computer keep beeping?* 為甚麼電腦不斷嘟嘟響? **2** [I,T] if a car horn beeps or you make it beep, it makes a loud noise〔汽車喇叭〕鳴響; 按響

beep² *n* [C] **1** a short high sound made by an electronic machine 嘟嘟聲: *Leave your message after the beep.* 嘟聲過後請留言。**2** the sound of a car horn 汽車的喇叭聲音: *Look, there's Jan. Give her a beep.* 看, 那是簡, 按喇叭叫她一下。

beep·er /ˋbipɚ; ˈbiːpə/ *n* [C] a small machine that you carry with you, that makes short high electronic sounds to tell you that you must telephone someone; BLEEPER, PAGER 傳呼機

2 3 **beer** /bɪr; bɪə/ *n* **1** [U] an alcoholic drink made from MALT[1] (1) and hops (HOP[2] (4)) 啤酒: *a pint of beer* 一品脫啤酒 | *home-brewed beer* 家釀的啤酒 **2** [C] a glass, bottle, or can of beer 一杯[瓶, 罐]啤酒: *Do you fancy a beer?* 你想要杯啤酒嗎? **3 not all beer and skittles** *BrE old-fashioned* not just full of pleasure and enjoyment, but involving problems as well【英, 過時】並非只是吃喝玩樂 **—beery** *adj*

beer bel·ly /ˈ· ˌ··/ also 又作 **beer gut** /ˈ· ·/ *n* [C] an unattractive fat stomach caused by drinking too much beer 啤酒肚

beer mat /ˈ· ·/ *n* [C] a small circle of card that you put under a glass, especially in a bar〔尤指酒吧裡的〕啤酒杯墊

bees·wax /ˋbizˌwæks; ˈbiːzwæks/ *n* [U] **1** a substance produced by bees (BEE (1)), especially for making furniture polish and CANDLES 蜂蠟〔尤用於製造家具擦光油、蠟燭等〕**2 none of your beeswax** *AmE spoken* used to tell someone that what they have asked you is private or personal【美口】不關你的事

beet /bit; biːt/ *n* [C,U] **1** also 又作 **sugar beet** a vegetable that sugar is made from 甜菜 **2** *AmE* a plant with a round dark red root that you cook and eat as a vegetable【美】甜菜根; BEETROOT *BrE*【英】**3 red as a beet** *AmE informal* having a red face, especially because you are embarrassed【美, 非正式】〔尤指因尷尬而〕臉紅

bee·tle¹ /ˋbitḷ; ˈbiːtl/ *n* [C] one of many types of insect with a round hard, usually black, back 甲(殼)蟲

beetle² *v* [I always+adv/prep] *BrE informal* to go somewhere quickly, especially because you are trying not to be noticed【英, 非正式】趕緊離去; 悄悄溜掉: *He went beetling off down the corridor.* 他從走廊溜走了。

beet·root /ˋbitˌrut; ˈbiːtruːt/ *n* [C,U] **1** *BrE* a plant with a round dark red root that you cook and eat as a vegetable【英】甜菜根; BEET *AmE*【美】—see picture on page A9 參見 A9 頁圖 **2 go beetroot** *BrE informal* to become red in the face, especially because you are embarrassed【英, 非正式】〔尤指因尷尬而〕臉紅

be·fall /bɪˋfɔl; bɪˈfɔːl/ *v past tense* **befell** /-ˋfɛl; -ˈfel/ *past participle* **befallen** /-ˋfɔlən; -ˈfɔːlən/ [T] *formal* if something unpleasant or dangerous befalls you it happens to you【正式】〔不幸的事或災難〕降臨(到): *We prayed that no harm should befall them.* 我們祈求他們平安無事。

be·fit /bɪˋfɪt; bɪˈfɪt/ *v past tense and past participle* **befitted** [T] *formal* to be proper or suitable for someone【正式】適合, 適宜: *The chairman travelled club class, as befitted his status.* 主席乘坐商務艙旅行, 這樣符合他的身分。**—befitting** *adj* **—befittingly** *adv*

1 1 **be·fore¹** /bɪˋfɔr; bɪˈfɔː/ *conjunction* **1** earlier than the time when something happens 在…之前: *Say goodbye before you go.* 你臨走之前去道個別吧。| *It will be some time before we know the full results.* 再過些時間我們才能知道全部結果。**2** so that something bad does not happen 以防: *Put that money somewhere safe before it gets stolen.* 把錢放在安全的地方, 以防被人偷去。| *That dog ought to be destroyed before it attacks any more children.* 應該把那條狗殺死, 以防牠再傷害更多的孩子。**3** used to say that you are willing to suffer or do something unpleasant rather than do something that you do not want to do 寧願: *He will die before he tells them what they want to know.* 他寧願死也不願說出他們想知道的事。**4 before you know it** *spoken* used to say that something will happen very soon【口】說時遲, 那時快; 將快: *We'd better set off or it will be dark before we know it.* 天快要黑了, 我們得馬上出發。**5** used to warn someone not to laugh at, criticize etc someone or something because they have faults and weaknesses themselves 先不要〔嘲笑或批評別人〕: *Before the chairman starts attacking committee members he ought to remember his own mistakes.* 主席先不要抨擊委員會成員, 他應該知道自己也有錯。**6** used to warn someone that you will do something unpleasant or harmful to them if they do not do something 要不然; 否則: *Get out before I call the police.* 滾出去, 要不然我叫警察了。

before² *prep* **1** earlier than something〔時間上〕在…以前: *I usually take a shower before having my breakfast.* 我通常在吃早餐前洗個澡。| *The new road should be completed before the end of the year.* 這條新公路在年底前應該完工。| *He arrived home before me.* 他比我先到家。| *the day before yesterday* (=two days ago) 前天 —see 見 FRONT[1] (USAGE) **2** ahead of someone or something else in a list or order〔名單或次序上〕較…為先; 在…之前: *I think you were before me in the queue.* 我認為你排在我的前面。**3** in the same place, or in front of a person or crowd of people〔方位上〕在…面前: *Italy will face Brazil this afternoon before a crowd of 100,000 spectators.* 今天下午意大利隊將在十萬名觀眾面前迎戰巴西隊。**4** if something such as a report or evidence is put before a person or group of people they must consider it and make a decision about it〔報告或證據等〕擺在…面前; 供…考慮: *The proposal was put before the planning committee.* 該項建議已提交計劃委員會審議。**5** if one quality or person comes before another, it is more important than it〔重要性〕在…之前, 比…更重要: *I put my wife and kids before anyone else.* 我把妻子和孩子放在首要地位。| *Quality must come before quantity in my opinion.* 在我看來, 質量比數量更重要。**6** *formal* in front of【正式】在…前面: *The priest stood before the altar.* 那位教士站在聖壇前面。| *The great plain stretched out before them.* 展現在他們面前的是一望無際的平原。**7** if one place is before another place it is a particular distance in front of that place as you travel towards it 在〔某個地點〕前: *The pub is 100m before the church on the right.* 那家小酒館在教堂往前 100 米靠右側的地方。**8** *formal* if there is a job or situation before you, you have to do the job or face the situation soon【正式】〔工作、局面〕擺在…面前: *The task of emptying the house lay before us.* 我們面前的任務是把房間裡的東西都搬出去。**9** *formal* if a period of time is before you it is about to start and you can do what you want during it【正式】來臨; 等着: *We had a glorious summer afternoon before us to do as we pleased.* 我們有一個宜人的夏日下午做自己喜歡的事。**10** *formal* if you show a particular reaction before someone or something you react in that way【正式】面臨: *She trembled before the prospect of meeting him again.* 一想到又要跟他見面, 她直打顫。

before³ *adv* **1** at an earlier time 先前; 從前; 以前: *Haven't we met before?* 我們以前見過面吧? | *I thought she might take notice of what I said but she just carries on as before.* 我以為她注意到了我的話, 可是她表現得還是像以前一樣。| **the day/week/month before** *Last week she was* in Paris, and the week before she was in Rome. 上週她在巴黎, 前一週她在羅馬。| **before long** *I expect the bus will be here before long.* 我估計公共汽車很快就到。| *The kids were playing in the mud and before long they were covered in it.* 孩子們在爛泥地裡玩, 很快渾身上下都是泥。**2** *old use* ahead of someone or something else【舊】在…前面: *The king's herald walked before.* 國王的傳令官走在前面。

3 **be·fore·hand** /bɪˋfɔr͵hænd; bɪˈfɔːhænd/ *adv* before something else has happened or is done 事先, 預先, 事前: *The police need to be briefed beforehand on how to deal with this sort of situation.* 需要事先告訴警察怎樣處理這種情況。| *When you give a speech, it's natural to feel nervous beforehand.* 你在演講之前感到緊張是很自然的。

be·friend /bɪˋfrɛnd; bɪˈfrend/ *v* [T] *formal* to behave in a friendly way towards someone, especially someone who is younger or needs help【正式】以朋友態度對待〔尤指對較年輕者或需要幫助者〕: *They befriended me when I first arrived in London as a student.* 我初到倫敦求學時, 他們如同朋友一般地照顧我。

be·fud·dled /bɪˋfʌdl̩d; bɪˈfʌdəld/ *adj* completely confused 迷惑不解的; 極其糊塗的: *I felt befuddled by all these changes.* 所有這些變化都把我弄糊塗了。

beg /bɛg; beg/ *v*

1 I beg your pardon *spoken*【口】**a)** used to say sorry when you have made a mistake, or said something wrong or embarrassing 請原諒, 對不起: *Oh, I beg your pardon. I thought you meant next Tuesday.* 喲, 對不起, 我還以為你是指下星期二。**b)** used to show that you strongly disagree with something that someone has said, or think it is unacceptable 恕我不敢苟同〔表示不同意某人的觀點〕: *"Chicago's an awful place." "I beg your pardon, that's where I'm from!"* "芝加哥是個很糟糕的地方。" "請恕我不敢苟同, 我就是芝加哥人!" **c)** used to ask someone to repeat what they have just said 請再說一遍: *"The meeting's on Wednesday." "I beg your pardon." "I said the meeting's on Wednesday."* "會議星期三開。" "請您再說一遍好嗎?" "我說會議星期三開。"

2 ►ASK 要求◄ [I,T] to ask for something in an anxious or urgent way, because you want it very much 請求, 懇求: *She begged and pleaded with them until they finally gave in.* 她一再懇求, 最後他們終於讓步了。| **beg (sb) to do sth** *The children begged to come with us.* 孩子們一再懇求和我們一起來。| *I begged Helen to stay but she wouldn't listen.* 我懇求海倫留下來, 可她就是不聽。| **beg (sb) for sth** *I'm begging you for help, Greg.* 格雷格, 我懇請你幫忙。| **beg forgiveness/a favour/mercy etc** *Can I beg a favour?* 我可以請你幫個忙嗎? | **beg leave to do sth** *formal* (=ask permission to do something)【正式】請求獲准做某事

3 ►MONEY/FOOD 金錢/食物◄ [I,T] to ask people to give you food, money etc because you are very poor 乞求施捨, 乞討: *a begging letter* 乞求信 | **beg from sb** *a ragged child begging from passing shoppers* 向過路的購物者行乞的衣衫襤褸的孩子 | **beg (for) sth** *They were reduced to begging food in the streets.* 他們被迫淪落到在街上乞討食物。| **beg sth off sb** *spoken*【口】*Can I beg a cigarette off you?* 我能問你要枝香煙嗎?

4 I beg to differ *spoken formal* to say firmly that you do not agree with something that has been said【口, 正式】恕我不敢苟同: *I must beg to differ on this point.* 在這點上, 恕我不敢苟同。

5 beg the question to discuss something in a way that makes it seem that a fact is definitely true when in fact it may not be 以假定作為論據進行討論; 迴避問題的實質: *This planning proposal begs the question whether we need more sports facilities at all.* 這個建設計劃迴避了我們是否需要更多體育設施這一實質問題。

6 be going begging *spoken* if something is going begging, it is available for anyone who wants it【口】現成的, 可用的: *There's a bottle of wine going begging if anyone's interested.* 有一瓶葡萄酒在這裡, 如果有誰感興趣的話, 請隨便喝。

7 ►DOG 狗◄ [I] if a dog begs, it sits up with its front legs off the ground〔狗〕用後腿站立, 前腿舉於胸前

beg off *phr v* [I] to say that you cannot do something that you had agreed to do 懇求免除〔已經承諾的責任〕; 請求不做〔某事〕: *I'm sorry, but I'm going to have to beg off from the game tonight.* 對不起, 今晚的比賽我請求不去了。

be·get /bɪˋgɛt; bɪˈget/ *v past tense and past participle* **begot** /-ˋgɑt; -ˈgɒt/ *or past tense* **begat** /-ˋgæt; -ˈgæt/ *past participle* **begotten** /-ˋgɑtn̩; -ˈgɒtn/ [T] *formal*【正式】**1** *old use* to become the father of a child【舊】成為…之父 **2** to cause something or make it happen 招致: *Hunger begets crime.* 飢餓招致犯罪。

beg·gar¹ /ˋbɛgɚ; ˈbegə/ *n* [C] **1** someone who lives by asking people for food and money 乞丐: *There's been a huge increase in the number of beggars on London's streets.* 倫敦街頭的乞丐人數激增。**2 lucky/lazy/cheeky etc beggar** *BrE spoken* used to describe someone who you think is lucky, lazy etc, in a friendly way【英口】幸運/懶惰/無禮等的傢伙: *You lazy little beggar!* 你這懶惰的小傢伙! | *"How's Dave?" "The lucky beggar's in the south of France!"* "戴夫好嗎?" "這個幸運的傢伙正在法國南部!" **3 beggars can't be choosers** used to say that when you have no money, no power to choose etc, you have to accept whatever is available 既然落難, 就不要挑肥揀瘦; 飢不擇食

beggar² *v* [T] **1 beggar description/belief etc** *formal* to be impossible to describe, believe etc【正式】無法形容/相信等: *The scenery was so beautiful that it beggared description.* 景色之優美難以用言語來形容。**2** *formal* to make someone very poor【正式】使貧窮: *Drought combined with falling prices to beggar whole communities of farmers.* 乾旱加上糧食價格下跌使大批農民陷於貧困。

beg·gar·ly /ˋbɛgɚlɪ; ˈbegəli/ *adj literary* a beggarly amount of money is far too small【文】〔錢〕少得可憐的

beggar-my-neigh·bour /͵.. · ˈ../ *n* [U] a card game in which the aim is to get all your opponent's cards〔以吃光對手所有牌為勝的〕"吃光"紙牌遊戲

beg·gar·y /ˋbɛgərɪ; ˈbegəri/ *n* [U] *formal* the state of being very poor【正式】赤貧: *The failure of their farm reduced them to beggary.* 農場歉收使他們落到一貧如洗的境地。

be·gin /bɪˋgɪn; bɪˈgɪn/ *past tense* **began** /-ˋgæn; -ˈgæn/ *past participle* **begun** /-ˋgʌn; -ˈgʌn/ *v* [I,T] 1 1

1 ►START DOING/FEELING 開始做/感到◄ to start doing something or start feeling a particular way 開始; 着手: **begin to do sth** *We began to wonder if the train would ever arrive.* 我們開始懷疑火車到底會不會到。| **begin** *I'll begin when you're ready.* 你準備好了我就開始。| **begin sth** *She curled up in bed and began her book.* 她蜷卧在牀上, 開始讀書。| **begin doing sth** *I left teaching in 1990 and began working in my present job.* 我1990年離開了教學崗位, 開始做現在的工作。| **begin by doing sth** (=do or say something as the first part of an activity) 從做某事開始 *Can I begin by thanking you all for being here tonight?* 首先讓我感謝所有今晚到場的來賓。

2 ►START HAPPENING 開始發生◄ [I,T] if something begins, or you begin something, it starts to happen or exist 開始〔發生或存在〕: *Work on the new bridge will begin next year.* 修築新橋的工作將於下一年開始。| *It was the coldest winter since records began.* 這是有記錄以來最寒冷的冬天。| **[+at]** *The meeting begins at 10.30 am.* 會議在上午十點半開始。| **begin (sth) as** *Roger began his career as a model.* 羅傑是以當模特兒來開始他的事業的。

3 to begin with a) *especially spoken* used to introduce the first or most important point that you want to make【尤口】首先: *Well, to begin with, he shouldn't even have been driving my car.* 好吧, 首先他就不應該一直開我的

車。**b)** used to say that something was already in a particular condition before something else happened 原來: *I didn't break it! It was like that to begin with.* 不是我弄壞的！它原來就是那樣子。**c)** during the first part of a process or activity 剛開始的時候: *The kids helped me to begin with, but they soon got bored.* 起初孩子們都來幫忙，但他們很快就厭煩了。—see 見 FIRSTLY (USAGE)

4 ►SPEECH/BOOK 講話/書◄ [I] if a speech, book, word etc begins with something, it starts with a particular event, activity, letter etc 以…開頭: **[+with]** *'Psychosis' begins with a P.* psychosis（精神病）一詞以字母 p 開頭。

5 can't begin to understand/imagine etc *spoken* used to emphasize how difficult something is to understand etc【口】根本無法理解/想像等: *I can't begin to imagine how awful it must be to lose your child.* 我簡直無法想像你失去了孩子會有多難過。

This graph shows how common different grammar patterns of the verb **begin** are. 本圖表所示為動詞 begin 構成的不同語法模式的使用頻率。

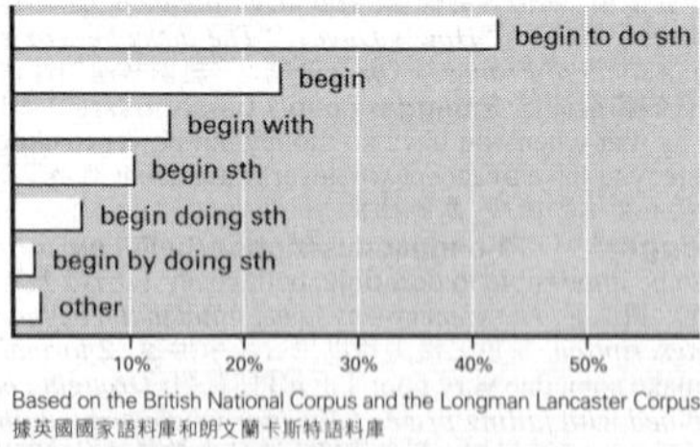

be·gin·ner /bɪˋgɪnɚ; bɪˈgɪnə/ *n* [C] **1** someone who has just started to do or learn something 生手; 初學者: *an absolute beginner* 一個不折不扣的初學者 **2 beginner's luck** unusual success that you have when you start something new 新手的好運

be·gin·ning /bɪˋgɪnɪŋ; bɪˈgɪnɪŋ/ *n* [C usually singular 一般用單數] **1** the start or first part of an event, story, period of time etc 開始, 開端, 起點: **[+of]** *It will be ready at the beginning of next week.* 將在下星期初準備就緒。| *The beginning of the film is very violent.* 這部電影的開頭充滿暴力鏡頭。| **in/at/from the beginning** (=at or from the time when a situation, process etc begins) 一開始; 初期 *We pay our rent at the beginning of every month.* 我們每個月的月初交房租。| *I said he would be trouble, right from the beginning.* 從一開始，我就說他是個麻煩。| **from beginning to end** *The whole trip was a disaster from beginning to end.* 整個旅程從頭到尾都是災難。—see 見 FIRSTLY (USAGE) **2 beginnings** [plural] the early part or early signs of something that later develops and becomes bigger, more important etc 起源; 開端: *the beginnings of the capitalist system* 資本主義制度的起源 | **from small/humble beginnings** *From humble beginnings in Atlanta, it had developed into a multinational corporation.* 該公司從亞特蘭大的一間小店起家，逐漸發展為跨國公司。**3 the beginning of the end** the time when something good starts to end or become less good〔好的事情〕結束[惡化]的先兆

USAGE NOTE 用法說明: BEGINNING

WORD CHOICE 詞語辨析: **at the beginning of, in the beginning**

Something that happens at the very start of an event or period of time happens **at the beginning of** it. at the beginning of 指的是一個事件或一段時間剛剛開始的時候: *At the beginning of the Civil War Fort Sumter was attacked* (NOT 不用 *in the beginning of it*). 南北戰爭剛開始時，薩姆特要塞遭到襲擊。| *There's a car chase at the beginning* (=at the start of the film).（電影）一開始有一個汽車追逐的場面。

If something happens **in the beginning** (not usually with *of*) it happens during a period of time near the start of an event or longer period of time. in the beginning〔一般不與 of 連用〕指一個事件的前一階段或初期: *In the beginning the South had some success* (=during the early part of the Civil War). 南北戰爭初期，南方取得了一些勝利。| *I was too shy to speak to her in the beginning* (=the first few times I saw her). 起初（幾次見面時）我太靦腆沒有和她說話。

SPELLING 拼法

Remember there are two 'n's in **beginning**. 記住 beginning 中的 n 要雙寫。

be·gone /bɪˋgɔn; bɪˈgɒn/ *interjection old use* used to tell someone to go away【舊】走開

be·go·ni·a /bɪˋgonɪə; bɪˈgəʊniə/ *n* [C] a plant with yellow, pink, red, or white flowers 秋海棠

be·got /bɪˋgɑt; bɪˈgɒt/ the past tense of BEGET

be·got·ten /bɪˋgɑtn̩; bɪˈgɒtn/ the past participle of BEGET

be·grudge /bɪˋgrʌdʒ; bɪˈgrʌdʒ/ *v* [T] **1** to feel JEALOUS of someone because they have something which you think they do not deserve 嫉妒: **begrudge sb sth** *We shouldn't begrudge her this success.* 我們不應該嫉妒她的成功。**2** to feel annoyed or unhappy that you have to pay something, give someone something etc 吝嗇; 捨不得給: **begrudge sb sth** *Surely you don't begrudge him the money for his education?* 想必你不會捨不得花錢讓他唸書吧？| **begrudge doing sth** *I begrudge spending so much money on train fares.* 我捨不得把這麼多錢花在火車票上。

be·guile /bɪˋgaɪl; bɪˈgaɪl/ *v* [T] **1** to persuade or trick someone into doing something, especially by saying nice things to them〔尤指用花言巧語〕欺騙, 哄騙: *Carr beguiled the voters with his good looks and grand talk.* 選民被卡爾那英俊的外表和他的偉論蒙騙了。**2** *literary* to do something that makes the time pass, especially in an enjoyable way【文】輕鬆地消磨〔時間〕; 消遣

be·guil·ing /bɪˋgaɪlɪŋ; bɪˈgaɪlɪŋ/ *adj* attractive and interesting, but often in a way that deceives you 迷人的; 誘人的: *The prospect of instant riches was too beguiling to ignore.* 瞬間暴富的前景太誘人了，不能放過。—**beguilingly** *adv*

be·gum /ˋbegəm; ˈbeɪgəm/ *n* [C] *IndE, PakE* a title of respect, used for married Muslim women, especially of high rank【印, 巴】穆斯林貴婦; 夫人〔對尤指地位高的已婚女子的尊稱〕

be·gun /bɪˋgʌn; bɪˈgʌn/ the past participle of BEGIN

be·half /bɪˋhæf; bɪˈhɑːf/ *n* **on behalf of** also 又作 **in behalf of** *AmE*【美】**a)** instead of someone, or as their representative 代表: *On behalf of everyone here, may I wish you a very happy retirement.* 我代表在座各位祝你退休愉快。| *The President can't be here today, so I'm going to speak in his behalf.* 總裁今天不能來，所以我將代表他發言。**b)** because of someone 由於〔某人〕: *Oh, don't go to any trouble on my behalf.* 不要因為我而麻煩你。

be·have /bɪˋhev; bɪˈheɪv/ *v* [I] **1** [always+adv/prep] to do things in a particular way 舉動; 表現: *I'm sorry about last night – I behaved like a child.* 對不起，昨天晚上我表現得太幼稚。**2** also 又作 **behave yourself** to behave in a way that people think is good or correct, by being polite and obeying people, not causing trouble etc 舉止規矩有禮; 檢點: *Will you children please behave!* 你們這些孩子能不能規矩一點！| *Did Peter behave himself while I was away?* 我不在時，彼得守規矩嗎？| **well-**

behaved/badly-behaved *a badly-behaved class* 不守規矩的班級 —opposite 反義詞 MISBEHAVE **3** [I] to do something according to natural laws 循自然規律運行: *Quantum mechanics is the study of the way atoms behave.* 量子力學是研究原子運動的學科。

2 1 **be·hav·iour** *BrE*【英】, **behavior** *AmE*【美】/bɪˋhevjɚ; bɪˈheɪvjə/ *n* [U] **1** the way that someone behaves 舉止, 行為: *Can TV violence cause aggressive behavior?* 電視中的暴力會導致攻擊性行為嗎? | **good/bad behaviour** *The headmaster will not tolerate bad behaviour in class.* 校長不會容忍班上不規矩的行為。| **[+towards]** *Her father's behaviour towards him was irrational.* 她父親對待他的態度是不理智的。**2 be on your best behaviour** to behave as well and politely as you can, especially in order to please someone 盡可能好地表現; 儘量行為檢點: *I want you both to be on your best behaviour at Grandad's.* 我希望你們倆在爺爺家要盡可能循規蹈矩。**3** the way that an object, animal, substance etc normally behaves 性能; 特點; 活動: *studying the behaviour of the AIDS virus* 研究愛滋病病毒的特性 —**behavioural** *adj*: *behavioural science* 行為科學 —**behaviourally** *adv*

be·hav·iour·is·m *BrE*【英】, **behaviorism** *AmE*【美】/bɪˋhevjərˏɪzəm; bɪˈheɪvjərɪzəm/ *n* [U] *technical* the belief that the scientific study of the mind should be based only on people's behaviour, not on what they say about their thoughts and feelings【術語】行為主義〔認為科學的心理研究應該以研究對象本身表現出的行為為依據, 而不應以人們對自己的思想感情所作的陳述為依據〕—**behaviourist** *n* [C]

be·head /bɪˋhɛd; bɪˈhed/ *v* [T] to cut off someone's head as a punishment 將…斬首, 殺…的頭〔尤指作為刑罰〕: *Charles I was beheaded in 1649.* 查理一世於 1649 年被斬首。

be·he·moth /bɪˋhimɑθ; bɨˈhiːmɒθ/ *n* [C] *literary* something that is very large【文】龐然大物: *five warships, including two 64,000-ton behemoths* 五艘戰艦, 包括兩艘六萬四千噸的巨艦

be·hest /bɪˋhɛst; bɪˈhest/ *n* [singular] **at the behest of** *formal* because someone has requested or ordered it【正式】在…的要求下, 在…的命令下

1 1 **be·hind¹** /bɪˋhaɪnd; bɪˈhaɪnd/ *prep* **1** at or towards the back of something 在[向]…後面: *The cat ran out from behind a tree.* 貓從樹後跑了出來。| *I got stuck behind a truck all the way to the airport.* 去機場時, 我的車一路上都被堵在一輛卡車的後面。| *Jane shut the door behind her.* 簡隨手關上身後的門。—see 見 FRONT¹ (USAGE) **2** not as successful or advanced as someone or something else 劣於; 落後於; 低於: *We're three points behind the other team.* 我們落後對方球隊三分。| *Mark's always behind the rest of his class in mathematics.* 馬克的數學成績總是不如班上的其他同學。| **behind schedule** (=not arriving or not ready at the right time) 延誤; 晚點 *The new building is already three months behind schedule.* 這幢新大廈的工期已經延誤了三個月。**3 what's behind sth** being the secret or hidden reason for something 某事幕後的原因: *I wonder what's behind this sudden change of plan.* 我想知道計劃突然改變的真正原因是甚麼。**4** supporting a person, idea etc 支持: *The workers are very much behind these proposals.* 工人們非常支持這些建議。| **behind sb/sth all the way** (=supporting someone or something totally) 全力支持某人/某事; 作某人/某事後盾 *We're behind you all the way on this one.* 這件事我們自始至終支持你。**5** responsible for a plan, idea etc or for organizing something 對…負責: *The police say that organized groups of children are behind the recent spate of thefts.* 警方說近期連串的偷竊案是由有組織的兒童集團所策劃的。| *The Rotary Club is behind the fund-raising for the new hospital.* 扶輪社負責新醫院的籌款工作。**6** if an unpleasant experience or situation is behind you it no longer upsets you or affects your life 置於…之後: *Now you can put all these worries behind you.* 現在你可以把這些煩惱全部撇在腦後了。**7** if you have experience behind you, you have learnt valuable skills or got important qualities that can be used 有…的〔經驗〕: *Marjorie's got ten years of experience as a social worker behind her.* 梅傑里已有十年作為社會工作者的經驗。**8** if a quality or attitude is behind an appearance you think that it exists in spite of being hidden〔隱藏〕在…後: *She suspected that a certain cynicism lay behind his cheerful exterior.* 她懷疑他開朗的外表後面隱藏着某種憤世嫉俗的心理。—see also 另見 **behind sb's back** (BACK² (11)), **behind bars** (BAR¹ (14))

behind² *adv* **1** at or towards the back of something 在後面; 向後: *an enormous desk with an old man sitting behind* 後面坐着一位老人的大桌子 | *The house has a huge garden behind.* 房子後面有個大花園。| **close behind/not far behind** *The motorcyclists came first, with the President's car following close behind.* 摩托車隊先行開路, 總統專車緊隨其後。**2 be/get behind** to be late or slow in doing something 遲; 慢; 落後: *This work should have been finished yesterday; I'm getting terribly behind.* 這項工作本應該昨天完成, 我已經大大地落後了。| **behind with** *We're already three months behind with the rent.* 我們的房租已經拖欠了三個月。**3 stay/remain behind** to stay in a place when other people have left it or gone somewhere else 留下來: *I decided to stay behind and look after the baby.* 我決定留下來照看嬰兒。**4 leave sth behind** to leave something in a place where you were before 留下某物; 忘了帶某物 **5 fall behind** to be less successful than other people 落後(於他人) 2 3

behind³ *n* [C] *informal* a word meaning BOTTOM¹ (7), sometimes used when you want to avoid saying this directly【非正式】臀部, 屁股

be·hind·hand /bɪˋhaɪndˏhænd; bɪˈhaɪndhænd/ *adv* **[+with, in]** *formal* late or slow in doing something or paying a debt【正式】遲; 慢; 過期; 拖欠

be·hold /bɪˋhold; bɪˈhəʊld/ *v past tense and past participle* **beheld** /bɪˋhɛld; bɪˈheld/ [T] *literary or old use* to see or to look at something【文或舊】見到, 看, 注視 —see also 另見 LO AND BEHOLD —**beholder** *n* [C]

be·hold·en /bɪˋholdən; bɪˈhəʊldn/ *adj* **feel/be beholden to** to feel that you have a duty to someone because they have done something for you 欠…人情; (對…)負有義務: *I hate feeling beholden to anyone.* 我不願欠任何人的人情。

be·hove /bɪˋhov; bɪˈhəʊv/ *BrE*【英】, **be·hoove** /bɪˋhuv; bɪˈhuːv/ *AmE*【美】*v* **it behoves you to do sth** *formal* you should do something because it is right or necessary or it will help you in some way【正式】某事是應當做的, 做某事是責無旁貸的

beige /beʒ; beɪʒ/ *n* [U] a pale dull yellowish brown colour 米黃色; 淺棕色 —**beige** *adj* —see picture on page A5 參見 A5 頁圖

be·ing¹ /ˋbiɪŋ; ˈbiːɪŋ/ *v* **1** the present participle of BE **2** used in explanations〔用於解釋〕由於: *Being a quiet sort of fellow, I didn't want to get involved.* 作為一個喜歡清靜的人, 我不想介入。| *You can't expect them just to ignore it, human nature being what it is.* 從人的本性來說, 你不能期望他們會就此不理此事。**3 being as** *spoken especially BrE* because; as【口, 尤英】因為: *He wasn't that keen to drive, being as he'd had a few drinks.* 他剛喝了點兒酒, 不太想開車。

being² *n* **1 come into being/be brought into being** to begin to exist 誕生; 出現; 存在: *a society that first came into being in 1912* 於 1912 年成立的協會 **2** [C] a living thing, especially a person 生物〔尤指人〕: *a human being* 一個人 | *strange beings from outer space* 來自外太空的奇怪生物 **3** [U] *literary* the most important quality or nature of something, especially of a person【文】〔尤指人的〕本質, 本性: **the core/roots/whole of sb's being** *The music seemed to touch the whole of her being.* 看來那支樂曲觸動了她整個身心。 2 3

be·jew·elled *BrE*【英】, **bejeweled** *AmE*【美】/bɪˋdʒuəld;

bɪˈdʒuːəld/ *adj* wearing jewels or decorated with jewels 戴珠寶的; 飾以珠寶的: *a bejewelled tiara* 鑲有寶石的冠狀頭飾

be·la·bour *BrE*【英】, **belabor** *AmE*【美】/bɪˈlebɚ; bɪˈleɪbə/ *v* [T] **1 belabour the point** to emphasize an idea or fact too strongly, especially by repeating it many times 反覆強調; 嘮叨 **2** to attack or criticize someone or something severely 嚴厲抨擊 **3** *old use* to beat someone or something hard【舊】痛打; 猛擊

B

be·lat·ed /bɪˈletɪd; bɪˈleɪtɪ̈d/ *adj* happening or arriving late 延誤的, 遲來的: *belated birthday greetings* 遲到的生日祝福 —**belatedly** *adv*

be·lay /bɪˈle; bɪˈleɪ/ *v* [I,T] *technical* to fix a rope on a ship by winding it under and over in the shape of a figure 8 on a special hook【術語】〔在船上〕將〔繩〕以8字形繫於特製的鉤上

belch /bɛltʃ; beltʃ/ *v* **1** [I] to let air from your stomach come out noisily through your mouth 打嗝: *He took a mouthful and belched loudly.* 他吃了一口, 接着大聲打起嗝來。—see also 另見 BURP (1) **2** [I] to give or send out large amounts of smoke, fire etc 噴出, 冒出〔煙、火等〕: *Blue smoke belched from the car's exhaust pipe.* 汽車的排氣管中冒出一股藍色的煙霧。—**belch** *n* [C]

be·lea·guered /bɪˈligɚd; bɪˈliːgəd/ *adj formal*【正式】**1** having many difficulties, especially because everyone is criticizing you or causing trouble for you 被煩擾的, 被纏住的: *beleaguered parents trying to discipline their children* 為管教孩子而煩惱的父母 **2** surrounded by an army and unable to escape 被圍困的

bel·fry /ˈbɛlfrɪ; ˈbelfri/ *n* a tower for a bell, especially on a church〔尤指教堂的〕鐘塔, 鐘樓 —see also 另見 **have bats in the belfry** (BAT[1] (8))

Bel·gian[1] /ˈbɛldʒən; ˈbeldʒən/ *n* [U] someone from Belgium 比利時人

Belgian[2] *adj* from or connected with Belgium 比利時的

be·lie /bɪˈlaɪ; bɪˈlaɪ/ *v* [T] *formal*【正式】**1** to give someone a false idea about something 使人對…產生錯覺; 使人對…誤解; 掩飾: *Her pleasant manner belied her true character.* 她討人喜歡的舉止掩蓋了她真實的為人。**2** to show that your words, hopes etc are false or mistaken 顯示〔言詞、希望等〕不真實; 證明…是虛假的: *Two large tears belied Rosalie's brave words.* 兩顆大大的淚珠暴露出羅莎莉並不像她自己所說的那樣勇敢。

S3 W2 **be·lief** /bɪˈlif; bɪ̈ˈliːf/ *n* **1** [singular,U] the feeling that something is definitely true or definitely exists 信心; 信念: *religious belief* 宗教信仰 | **[+in]** *a belief in God* 篤信上帝 | **[+that]** *a growing belief that war had become inevitable* 越來越相信戰爭不可避免 | **it is sb's belief that** *It is my belief that racism remains widespread in British society.* 我認為種族主義在英國社會中仍然普遍存在。| **in the belief that** (=because you think something is true) 因為相信 *She started taking money, in the mistaken belief that she would not be discovered.* 她誤以為自己不會被察覺, 開始偷起錢來。| **contrary to popular belief** (=although most people believe the opposite of this) 和人們一般的認識相反 *Contrary to popular belief, eating carrots does not improve your eyesight.* 和大家普遍的看法相反, 吃胡蘿蔔並不會改善視力。**2** [C] an idea that you believe to be true, especially one that forms part of a system of ideas 信仰; 信條: *political beliefs* 政治信仰 | **hold a belief** (=have a belief) 相信 *Some of them hold very right-wing beliefs.* 他們中的一些人持有很極端的右翼思想。**3** [singular] the feeling that something is good and can be trusted 信任, 信賴: **[+in]** *If you're selling, you have to have genuine belief in the product.* 如果你賣東西, 你必須對這產品真正有信心。| **shake sb's belief in** (=make them doubt what they believe) 動搖某人對…的信心 *The judge's decision shook my belief in the legal system.* 法官的判決動搖了我對法律制度的信心。**4 be beyond belief** to seem too strange or unreasonable to be true 難以置信: *These latest proposals are beyond belief!* 這些最新的提議令人難以置信! —see also 另見 **to the best of your belief** (BEST[3] (4)) —compare 比較 DISBELIEF, UNBELIEF

be·liev·a·ble /bɪˈlivəbḷ; bɪ̈ˈliːvəbəl/ *adj* something that is believable can be believed because it seems possible, likely, or real 可信的: *What I like about the book is that the characters are all very believable.* 我喜歡這本書的理由是: 書中的人物都很真實可信。—**believably** *adv*

be·lieve /bɪˈliv; bɪ̈ˈliːv/ *v* [not in progressive 不用進行式] S1 W1

1 ►BE SURE STH IS TRUE 確信某事是真的◄ [T] to be sure that something is true or that someone is telling the truth 相信: *You shouldn't believe everything you read.* 你不應該盡信你所讀到過的東西。| **believe (that)** *I can hardly believe he's only 25!* 我很難相信他只有25歲! | **believe sb** *I don't believe her – it can't be true.* 我不相信她的話, 那不可能是真的。| **believe sth of sb** *Stealing? I would never have believed it of him!* 偷竊? 我怎麼也不相信他會幹這種事! | **not believe a word of it** *spoken* (=not believe something at all)【口】壓根兒不相信

2 can't/don't believe *spoken* used to say that you are very surprised or shocked by something【口】不信: *It's still raining – I don't believe it!* 還在下雨 —— 我真不能相信! | *I can't believe he's expecting us to work on Sunday as well!* 我簡直不能相信他指望我們星期天也去上班! | *My mum couldn't believe it when I dyed my hair green.* 我媽媽簡直不敢相信我把頭髮染成了綠色。

3 believe it or not *spoken* used when you are going to say something that is true but surprising【口】信不信由你: *Well, believe it or not, they've given me a loan.* 不管你信不信, 他們已經給我貸了款。

4 would you believe it! *spoken* used when you are surprised or angry about something【口】你會相信嗎?〔表示驚訝或生氣〕: *And then he just walked out. Would you believe it!* 接着他便退席了。你能相信嗎?

5 believe (you) me *spoken* used to emphasize that something is definitely true【口】相信我: *There'll be trouble when they find out about this, believe you me!* 相信我, 這件事如果給他們發現了會很麻煩!

6 you'd better believe it! *spoken* used to emphasize that something is true【口】你該相信!

7 don't you believe it! *spoken* used to emphasize that something is definitely not true【口】千萬不要相信!

8 can't believe your eyes/ears *spoken* to be very surprised by something you see or hear【口】不敢相信自己的眼睛/耳朵: *I could hardly believe my eyes when he took a gun out of his pocket.* 他從衣袋裡掏出一把槍的時候, 我簡直不敢相信自己的眼睛。

9 if you believe that, you'll believe anything *spoken* used to say that something is definitely not true, and that anyone who believes it must be stupid【口】誰相信誰就是傻瓜

10 ►HAVE AN OPINION 持某觀點◄ [T] to think that something is true, although you are not completely sure 認為; 料想, 猜想: **believe (that)** *I believe you two have met already.* 我想你們倆已經見過面了。| **believe so/not** (=think that something is true or not) 認為/不認為是這樣 *"Have they arrived yet?" "Yes, I believe so."* "他們到了嗎?" "我想到了。" | **believe sb to be sth** *The jury believed Beyers to be innocent.* 陪審團認為拜爾斯是無罪的。| **be widely believed** (=a lot of people believe this) 人們普遍認為 *They are widely believed to be planning a takeover bid.* 人們普遍認為他們正計劃進行收購。| **have reason to believe (that)** (=have information that makes you believe something) 有理由相信 *We have reason to believe that she knew the victim quite well.* 我們有理由相信她對受害者很熟悉。

11 seeing is believing *usually spoken* used to say that you will only believe that something happens or exists when you actually see it【一般口】眼見為實

12 ►RELIGION 宗教◄ [I] to have a strong religious faith 篤信: *She says that those who believe will go to heaven.*

她說信教的人會進天堂。—see also 另見 **make believe** (MAKE[1] (18))

believe in *phr v* [T] **1** to be sure that someone exists 相信（…的存在）: *Do you believe in God?* 你相信有上帝嗎？| *It's amazing how many people believe in ghosts.* 有那麼多人相信有鬼魂，真令人吃驚。**2** to support or approve of something because you think it is good or right 相信（…的價值）: *I don't believe in all these silly diets.* 我不相信這些愚蠢的食譜。| **believe in doing sth** *They believe in letting children make their own mistakes.* 他們相信讓孩子自己犯點錯對他們有益處。**3** [T **believe in** sb] to be confident that someone can be trusted 信任，信賴: *The people want a President they can believe in.* 人民想要一個可信賴的總統。| *You've got to believe in yourself, or you'll never succeed.* 你必須相信自己，否則你永遠不會成功。

be·liev·er /bɪˋlivɚ; bɪ̇ˈliːvə/ *n* [C] **1** someone who believes in a particular god, religion, or system of beliefs 宗教信仰者；信徒 **2 be a (great) believer in** to believe strongly that something is good and brings good results 相信[深信]…的人: *I'm a great believer in co-ed schools.* 我深信男女同校大有益處。

Be·li·sha bea·con /bəˌliʃə ˋbikən; bəˌliːʃə ˈbiːkən/ *n* [C] one of two posts with a round flashing orange light on the top that stand by some road crossings in Britain〔英國的〕行人過道指示燈

be·lit·tle /bɪˋlɪtl; bɪˈlɪtl/ *v* [T] *formal* to make someone or something seem small or unimportant【正式】輕視；貶抑: *He tends to belittle his own efforts.* 他往往輕視自己的努力。

2 3 **bell** /bɛl; bel/ *n* [C] **1** a piece of electrical equipment that makes a ringing sound, used as a signal or to get someone's attention 鐘；鈴；電鈴: *The door bell rang but no-one answered it.* 門鈴響了，但沒有人應答。| *Ring the bell once to make the bus stop.* 按一下鈴讓公共汽車停下來。—see picture at 參見 BICYCLE[1] 圖 **2** [usually singular 一般用單數] the sound of a bell ringing as a signal or a warning 鐘聲；鈴聲: *I didn't hear the bell, did you?* 我沒有聽到鈴聲，你呢？| **the bell goes** (=makes a noise) 鈴響了 *The bell for the end of school went at 3.30.* 放學鈴在三點半響起。**3** a hollow metal object shaped rather like a cup, that makes a ringing sound when it is hit by a piece of metal that hangs down inside it 鐘；響鈴: *church bells* 教堂的鐘 **4 give sb a bell** *BrE spoken* to telephone someone【英口】給某人打電話: *I must give Vicky a bell later.* 我過一會兒必須給維基打個電話。**5** something in the shape of a bell, hollow and getting wider at the end 鐘狀物: *the bell of a flower* 鐘狀的花萼 —see also 另見 DIVING BELL, **ring a bell** (RING[2] (4)), **clear as a bell** (CLEAR[1] (10)), **sound as a bell** (SOUND[3] (5))

bel·la·don·na /ˌbɛləˋdɑnə; ˌbeləˈdɒnə/ *n* [U] **1** a poisonous plant; DEADLY NIGHTSHADE 顛茄〔一種有毒的植物〕**2** a substance from this plant, used as a drug〔用作藥物的〕顛茄劑

bell-bot·toms /ˈ· ˌ··/ *n* [plural] trousers with legs that become wider at the bottom 喇叭褲

bell·boy /ˋbɛlˌbɔɪ; ˈbelbɔɪ/ *n* [C] *BrE* a young man who carries bags, takes messages etc in a hotel【英】〔旅館中〕做雜役的青年男侍者；BELLHOP *AmE*【美】

belle /bɛl; bel/ *n* [C] *old-fashioned* a beautiful girl or woman【過時】美女，美人，佳麗: **the belle of the ball** (=the most beautiful girl at a dance or party) 舞會之花，舞會上最美的女子

belles-let·tres /ˌbɛl ˋlɛtrə; ˌbel ˈletrə/ *n* [U] *French* literature or writings about literary subjects【法】唯美文學；純文學

bell·hop /ˋbɛlˌhɑp; ˈbelhɒp/ *n* [C] *AmE* a young man who carries bags, takes messages etc in a hotel【美】〔旅館中〕做雜役的青年男侍者；BELLBOY *BrE*【英】

bel·li·cose /ˋbɛləˌkos; ˈbelɪkəʊs/ *adj literary* always wanting to fight or argue; AGGRESSIVE (1)【文】好戰的；好爭吵的；好鬥的 —**bellicosity** *n* [U]

bel·lig·er·ent /bəˋlɪdʒərənt; bɪ̇ˈlɪdʒərənt/ *adj* **1** very unfriendly and unpleasant 敵對的；好鬥的；好尋釁的: *a belligerent attitude* 敵對的態度 **2** [only before noun 僅用於名詞前] *formal* a belligerent country is at war with another country【正式】交戰中的 —**belligerence, belligerency** *n* [U]

bel·low[1] /ˋbɛlo; ˈbeləʊ/ *v* **1** [I, T] to shout loudly, especially in a low voice 咆哮；以低沉的聲音叫喊；大聲喝道: *Tony bellowed instructions from an upstairs window.* 托尼從樓上的窗戶那兒大喊該怎麼做。**2** [I] to make the deep hollow sound that a BULL[1] (1,2) makes〔公牛般〕吼叫

bellow[2] *n* **1** [C] the deep hollow sound that a BULL[1] (1,2) makes〔公牛的〕吼叫聲 **2 bellows** [plural] **a)** an object that you use to blow air into a fire〔送風催火的〕吹風器；風箱 **b)** part of a musical instrument, such as an ORGAN (2), that uses air to produce sound〔管風琴等的〕風箱

bell pep·per /ˈ· ˌ··/ *n* [C] *AmE* a hollow red, green, or yellow vegetable【美】燈籠椒；PEPPER[1] (3) *BrE*【英】，CAPSICUM

bell-ring·er /ˈ· ˌ··/ *n* [C] someone who rings church bells, usually as part of a team〔教堂的〕敲鐘人 —**bell-ringing** *n* [U]

bel·ly[1] /ˋbɛlɪ; ˈbeli/ *n* [C] 3

1 ►PERSON 人◄ a) your stomach 胃: *a full belly* 吃得飽飽的肚子 **b)** *BrE* the part of your body between your chest and your legs; ABDOMEN (1)【英】肚子，腹部: *She lay on her belly in the long grass.* 她趴在長長的草叢中。

2 ►ANIMAL 動物◄ the underneath of an animal's body 肚子 —see picture at 參見 HORSE[1] 圖

3 ►OBJECT 物體◄ a curved or rounded part of an object 腹狀部分: *the belly of a plane* 飛機的機腹 —see also 另見 POTBELLY

belly[2] *v*

belly out *phr v* [I, T **belly** sth ↔ **out**] to swell or become full, or to make something do this（使）鼓氣；（使）脹起: *The sails bellied out in the wind.* 船帆迎風鼓起。

bel·ly·ache[1] /ˋbɛlɪˌek; ˈbeli-eɪk/ *n* [C, U] a pain in your stomach 肚子痛，腹痛

bellyache[2] *v* [I] *informal* to complain a lot, especially about something unimportant【非正式】〔尤指對瑣事〕抱怨: [**+about**] *Stop bellyaching about it and get on with the job!* 別再發牢騷了，繼續工作吧！

belly but·ton /ˈ·· ˌ··/ *n* [C] *informal* the small round mark in the middle of your stomach; NAVEL【非正式】肚臍

belly dance /ˈ·· ·/ *n* [C] a dance from the Middle East performed by a woman using movements of her BELLY[1] (1b) and hips (HIP[1] (1)) 肚皮舞〔一種源於中東，由女性運用腹部和臀部動作表演的舞蹈〕—**belly dancer** *n* [C]

belly flop /ˈ·· ·/ *n* [C] a way of jumping into water, in which the front of your body falls flat against the surface of the water 俯跳入水時腹部平拍水面的跳水動作 —**bellyflop** *v* [I]

bel·ly·ful /ˋbɛlɪˌful; ˈbelifʊl/ *n* **have had a bellyful of** *informal* to be annoyed by something because you have heard or experienced too much of it【非正式】已經聽[受]夠了: *I've had a bellyful of your complaints.* 我已經聽夠了你的牢騷。

belly-land·ing /ˈ·· ˌ··/ *n* [C] the act of landing a plane without using special equipment〔飛機不用起落裝置〕以機腹着陸

belly laugh /ˈ·· ·/ *n* [C] *informal* a deep loud laugh【非正式】開懷大笑

be·long /bəˋlɔŋ; bɪˈlɒŋ/ *v* [I] **1** [always+adv/prep] to be in the right place or situation 處在（適當位置），該在: *Put that chair back where it belongs.* 把椅子放回原處。| *Wild animals like this don't belong in a zoo – they should be allowed to go free.* 這樣的野生動物不應該在動物園裡，應該放了牠們，給牠們自由。**2** to feel happy and comfortable in a place or situation, because you have the same interests and ideas as other people 能適應；感到自在 2 2

口語及書面語中最常用的 1 000詞，2 000詞，3 000詞

belong to *phr v* [T] **1** to be the property of 屬於: *The house belonged to my grandfather.* 這座房子原是屬於我祖父的。| *Who does this scarf belong to?* 這是誰的頭巾? **2** to be a member of a group or organization 是...的成員, 屬於〔某組織〕: *Do you belong to the tennis club?* 你是網球俱樂部的成員嗎? | *They were suspected of belonging to a terrorist organization.* 他們被懷疑是恐怖組織的成員。**3** to be connected with or form part of 與...有關; 是...的一部分: *The film belongs to a rich comic tradition.* 這部電影帶着濃厚的喜劇傳統。| *He belongs to a different generation.* 他是另一代的人。

be·long·ings /bəˋlɔŋɪŋz; bɪˈlɒŋɪŋz/ *n* [plural] the things that you own, especially those that you can carry with you 所有物; 財產, 財物: *Please ensure that you have all your belongings when you leave the train.* 下火車以前, 請檢查一下自己的物品是否齊全。

be·lov·ed /bɪˋlʌvɪd; bɪˈlʌvɨd/ *adj literary or humorous*【文或幽默】**1** a beloved place, thing etc is one that you love very much 心愛的, 鍾愛的, 喜愛的: *She returned at last to her beloved country.* 她終於回到了自己熱愛的祖國。| *He's always talking about his beloved computer!* 他總是在談論自己心愛的電腦! | [**+of/by**] *a slogan much beloved of politicians* 深受政治家喜愛的口號 **2 my/her etc beloved** the person that you love most 我/她等心愛的人: *It was a gift from my beloved.* 這是我心愛的人送給我的禮物。—see also 另見 **dearly beloved** (DEARLY (4))

2 2 **be·low¹** /bəˋlo; bɪˈləʊ/ *prep* **1** in a lower place or position than, or on a lower level than〔地方或位置〕在...的下面; 低於: *I'd like you to trim my hair just below the ears.* 請你把我的頭髮修剪到剛剛到耳朵下面。| *Fish were swimming below the surface of the water.* 魚在水面下游動。—see picture on page A1 參見 A1 頁圖 —see 見 UNDER¹ (USAGE) **2** less than a particular number, amount, level etc〔數量、水平等〕在...之下: *These families are living below the official poverty line.* 這些家庭生活在官方界定的貧窮線以下。| *Bank charges rose at a level slightly below that of inflation.* 銀行收費上漲的水平略低於通貨膨脹的水平。| **well/way below** (=very much lower than) 大大低於 *Sales figures for January were well below target.* 一月份的銷售數字遠遠低於原定指標。| **below average** (=not as good as the normal standard) 低於平均水平 *Tom's spelling is well below average.* 湯姆的拼寫遠遠低於平均水平。| **below freezing** (=if the temperature is below freezing it is less than zero degrees) 零度以下 **3** in a lower, less important job than someone else〔職位〕低於: *A captain is below a general.* 上尉的軍階比將軍低。

2 2 **below²** *adv* **1** in a lower place or position, or on a lower level 在較低處, 在較低的位置: *We looked down from the mountain at the valley below.* 我們從山上俯瞰下面的山谷。| *Jim lives on the fourth floor and Jean-Pierre is on the floor below.* 吉姆住在四樓, 讓－皮埃爾住在下面的一層。**2** on the lower level of a ship or boat 在船下層: *The Captain told the crew to go below.* 船長叫船員下到艙裡去。**3** less than a particular number, age, price etc〔數量、年齡、價格等〕以下, 低於: *Children of three and below pay half fare.* 三歲及三歲以下兒童半票。**4 10°/15°/20° below etc** if a temperature is 10°, 15°, 20° etc below, it is that number of degrees lower than zero 零下10/15/20度等 **5** mentioned or shown lower on the same page or on a later page 在(本頁)下文; 在後面一頁: *See p.85 below.* 見後面第85頁。| *The information below was compiled by our correspondent.* 以下資料是我們的記者收集整理的。**6** in a lower, less important rank or job 在較低級別: *officers of the rank of captain and below* 上尉及上尉以下的軍官 **7** *literary* on Earth rather than in Heaven【文】在世上, 在人間

2 3 **belt¹** /bɛlt; belt/ *n* [C]

1 ►CLOTHES 衣服◄ a band of leather, cloth etc that you wear around your waist 腰帶; 帶子 —see picture on page A17 參見A17頁圖

2 ►AREA 地區◄ a large area of land that has particular characteristics〔特定的〕區域, 地帶: *America's farming belt* 美國農業地區 | *the commuter belt* 乘[駕]車上下班者的居住區 —see also 另見 GREEN BELT

3 ►MACHINE PART 機器部件◄ a circular band of material such as rubber that connects or moves parts of a machine 傳動帶; 輸送帶 —see also 另見 CONVEYOR BELT, FAN BELT

4 below the belt *informal* a remark or criticism that is below the belt is unfair or cruel【非正式】不公道的; 不正當的: *That was a bit below the belt, Paul.* 保羅, 那樣做有點不光明正大。

5 have/get sth under your belt to have achieved something useful or important 獲得某物: *You need some work experience under your belt.* 你需要一些工作經驗。

6 (at) full belt *spoken* moving as quickly as possible【口】(以)全速地: *Willy was off down the road at full belt.* 威利飛快地開車上路。

7 give sb a belt *spoken* to hit someone hard【口】狠揍某人 —see also 另見 CHASTITY BELT, GARTER BELT, SUSPENDER BELT, **tighten your belt** (TIGHTEN (6))

belt² *v informal*【非正式】**1** [T] to hit someone or something hard 重打, 狠揍: *Dan belted the ball at goal.* 丹將球朝球門猛一腳踢去。**2** [I always+adv/prep] *BrE* to travel very fast【英】快速行進: [**+down/along etc**] *We were belting down the motorway at 90 miles per hour.* 我們以每小時90英里的速度在高速公路上疾駛。

belt sth ↔ **out** *phr v* [T] *informal* to sing a song or play an instrument loudly【非正式】引吭高歌; 高聲演奏〔樂器〕: *She was belting out old Broadway favourites.* 她在大聲地唱着受人喜愛的百老匯老歌。

belt up *phr v* [I] *BrE spoken* used to tell someone rudely to be quiet【英口】住口; 別做聲: *Belt up, for Christ's sake!* 看在耶穌的份上, 別說話!

belt·ed /ˋbɛltɪd; ˈbeltɨd/ *adj* fastened with a belt 繫皮帶的, 有皮帶的: *a tightly belted raincoat* 繫緊腰帶的雨衣

belt·way /ˋbɛlt͵we; ˈbeltweɪ/ *n* [C] *AmE* a road that goes around a city to keep traffic away from the centre【美】環城公路; RING ROAD *BrE*【英】

be·moan /bɪˋmon; bɪˈməʊn/ *v* [T] to complain or say that you are disappointed about something 抱怨; 嘆息; 惋惜: *As usual, they were all bemoaning the lack of decent training facilities.* 跟往常一樣, 他們都在抱怨沒有足夠的高質量培訓設施。

be·mused /bɪˋmjuzd; bɪˈmjuːzd/ *adj* looking as if you are confused 茫然的; 發呆的; 困惑的: *a bemused expression on his face* 他臉上茫然的神情

ben /bɛn; ben/ *n* [C] *ScotE* mountain; often used as part of a name【蘇格蘭】山〔常用作名稱的一部分〕: *Ben Nevis* 尼維斯山

bench¹ /bɛntʃ; bentʃ/ *n*

1 ►SEAT 座位◄ [C] a long seat for two or more people, used especially outdoors〔尤指戶外的〕長椅: *a park bench* 公園裡的長椅

2 ►COURT 法庭◄ the bench a) the seat where a judge or MAGISTRATE sits in a court of law 法官席: *Would the prisoner please approach the bench?* 請犯人走近法官席。**b)** the position of being a judge or MAGISTRATE in a court of law 法官: *He was appointed to the bench last year.* 他去年被任命為法官。| **serve/sit on the bench** (=work as a judge or MAGISTRATE) 擔任法官

3 ►POLITICS 政治◄ benches [plural] *BrE* the seats in the British parliament where members of a particular party sit【英】議員席: *There were shouts of 'resign!' from the Opposition benches.* 從反對黨的議員席傳來了"辭職!"的喊聲。

4 ►TABLE 桌子◄ [C] a long heavy table used for working on with tools or equipment 長形工作枱: *a carpenter's bench* 木工工作枱

5 ►SPORT 體育◄ [singular] a seat where members of

a sports team sit when they are not playing 候補隊員席 —see also 另見 FRONT BENCH, BACKBENCH

bench² *v* [T] *AmE* to remove a sports player from a game for a short time【美】罰〔場上運動員〕出場: *The number three has been benched for aggressive behaviour.* 三號運動員因為侵犯性行為被罰離場。

bench·mark /ˈbɛntʃˌmɑrk; ˈbentʃmɑːk/ *n* [C] **1** something that is used as a standard by which other things can be judged or measured 基準; 規範: *a benchmark for future pay negotiations* 給日後工資談判作參考的一個尺度 **2** a mark made on a building, post etc that shows its height above sea level, and is used to measure other heights and distances in a SURVEY¹ (3)〔測量用的〕水準(基)點

3 3 **bend¹** /bɛnd; bend/ *v past tense and past participle* **bent** /bɛnt; bent/

1 ►MOVE YOUR BODY 挪動身體◄ [I always+adv/prep] to move the top half of your body forwards or downwards 俯身; 彎腰: [**+towards/across etc**] *He bent towards me and whispered in my ear.* 他俯下身來對我耳語。| **bend over** (=bend your body at the waist) 彎腰 *She was bending over the basin, washing her hair.* 她彎着腰在臉盆裡洗頭。| **bend down** (=bend your body at the knees or waist) 彎身 *I bent down to lift the box off the floor.* 我彎下身從地上扛起箱子。

2 ►CURVE 曲線◄ a) [T] to push or press something into a curved shape or fold it at an angle 使彎曲: *Bend your arms and then stretch them upwards.* 兩臂彎曲然後向上伸展。| **bend sth back/away etc** *I'll bend the branches back so that you can get through.* 我把樹枝向後彎一下, 讓你過去。**b)** [I] to be in the shape of a curve or to change to this shape 呈彎形; 變彎曲: *The wire bent easily.* 這根金屬線容易彎曲。

3 bend the rules to do something that is not normally allowed, but will not cause serious problems, usually in order to help someone else 放寬規則; 通融: *You should really pay today, but we can bend the rules just this once.* 你真的應該今天付款, 這次我們就通融一下, 但下不為例。

4 bend over backwards (to do sth) to try very hard to be helpful 竭盡全力〔做某事〕: *I've been bending over backwards to get it done on time for them.* 我已盡了最大努力設法按時為他們完成任務。

5 bend sb's ear *spoken* to talk to someone, especially about something that is worrying you【口】和某人談心〔尤指談令人煩惱的事〕

6 on bended knee a) trying very hard to persuade someone to do something 努力勸說; 懇求: *If I go on bended knee to the boss, do you think she'd give me my job back?* 如果我懇求老闆, 你認為她會重新讓我上班嗎? **b)** in a kneeling position 跪着

7 bend your mind/efforts/thoughts etc to *formal* to give all your energy or attention to one activity, plan etc【正式】集中全力於..., 專心致志於...

bend² *n* [C] **1** a curved part of something, especially a road or river〔尤指道路或河流的〕彎曲處: *The taxi swung around the bend at a terrifying speed.* 計程車在以驚人的速度拐過彎道。| [**+in**] *a sharp bend in the river* 河流中一個急彎 **2** an action in which you bend a part of your body〔身體的〕彎曲(動作): *We started the session with a few knee bends to warm up.* 我們在上課前先做些活動膝蓋的動作來熱身。**3 the bends** [plural] a very painful and serious condition that divers get when they come up from under the sea too quickly 潛水夫病, 潛函病, 減壓病〔潛水員浮出水面過快引致的一種令人非常疼痛的病〕**4 drive sb round the bend** *spoken especially BrE* to annoy someone【口, 尤英】惹惱某人 **5 be/go round the bend** *spoken especially BrE* to be or become crazy【口, 尤英】發瘋: *You must be round the bend to let her treat you like that.* 你竟然讓她那樣對待你, 你一定是瘋了。

ben·der /ˈbɛndɚ; ˈbendə/ *n* [C] *BrE informal*【英, 非正式】**1 go on a bender** to drink a lot of alcohol at one time 酗酒, 縱酒 **2** an insulting word for a man who is attracted to other men; HOMOSEXUAL 男同性戀者〔侮辱性用語〕

bend·y /ˈbɛndɪ; ˈbendi/ *adj informal*【非正式】**1** easy to bend 易彎曲的: *a bendy rubber doll* 易彎曲的橡膠玩具娃娃 **2** with many curves or angles 彎彎曲曲的: *a bendy road* 一條彎彎曲曲的路

be·neath¹ /bɪˈniθ; bɪˈniːθ/ *prep formal*【正式】**1** in or to a lower position than something, or directly under something 在...之下; 在...正下方; 在...底下: *The dolphins disappeared beneath the waves.* 海豚在波濤下消失了。| *Jo enjoyed feeling the warm sand beneath her feet.* 喬很喜歡踏着腳下溫暖的沙子。| **give/buckle/tremble beneath the weight of** (=if something gives, buckles etc beneath the weight of something, it breaks or becomes weaker because it is supporting or carrying a heavy weight) 受...重壓而彎曲[變形] *The shelf was buckling beneath the weight of the books piled on it.* 書架在書的重壓下變了形。**2** in a lower, less important rank or job than someone else〔等級、職位等〕低於: *She would not speak to people she considered beneath her.* 她不願跟那些她認為比自己地位低的人講話。**3** not suitable for someone because of not being good enough 與...不相稱: **beneath you** *Vera considered it beneath her even to reply to the insult.* 薇拉認為回應這種侮辱性的言論有損自己的身分。**4** a feeling or attitude that is beneath another feeling or attitude is covered or hidden by it 被...所隱藏[掩蓋]: *Dave sensed that something more sinister lay beneath the woman's cheerful exterior.* 戴夫感覺到那個女人開朗的外表下隱藏着某種更陰險的東西。—see picture on page A1 參見 A1 頁圖 2

beneath² *adv formal* in or to a lower position【正式】在下面; 朝下: *Madge's skirt was too short and her petticoat was showing beneath.* 馬琪的裙子太短, 襯裙都露出來了。| *He was standing on the bridge gazing down at the river beneath.* 他站在橋上凝視着下面的河流。

Ben·e·dic·tine /ˌbɛnəˈdɪktɪn; ˌbenəˈdɪktɪn◂/ *n* [C] a member of a Christian religious order of MONKS 本篤會修士 —**Benedictine** *adj*

ben·e·dic·tine /ˌbɛnəˈdɪktin; ˌbenəˈdɪktiːn/ *n* [C, U] a strong alcoholic drink; type of LIQUEUR 本尼迪克特甜酒〔最初由本篤會修士釀造的一種烈酒〕

ben·e·dic·tion /ˌbɛnəˈdɪkʃən; ˌbenəˈdɪkʃən/ *n* [C, U] a Christian type of prayer said as a BLESSING (1) 祝福; 祝禱

ben·e·fac·tion /ˌbɛnəˈfækʃən; ˌbenəˈfækʃən/ *n formal*【正式】**1** [U] the act of doing something good, especially by giving money to someone who needs it 善行, 施惠; 捐款 **2** [C] money given in this way 慈善捐款

ben·e·fac·tor /ˈbɛnəˌfæktɚ; ˈbenəˌfæktə/ *n* [C] someone who gives money for a good purpose 行善者; 捐助人; 施主: *An anonymous benefactor donated $2 million.* 一位沒留姓名的捐助人捐款二百萬美元。

ben·e·fac·tress /ˈbɛnəˌfæktrɪs; ˈbenəfæktrəs/ *n* [C] *old-fashioned* a woman who gives money for a good purpose【過時】女施主; 女性捐助者

ben·e·fice /ˈbɛnəfɪs; ˈbenəfəs/ *n* [C] the pay and position of the priest of a Christian PARISH (1) 聖俸; 聖職

be·nef·i·cent /bəˈnɛfəsn̩t; bɪˈnefəsənt/ *adj formal* doing things to help people; generous【正式】行善的; 仁慈的; 寬厚的 —**beneficence** *n* [U] —**beneficently** *adv*

ben·e·fi·cial /ˌbɛnəˈfɪʃəl; ˌbenəˈfɪʃəl◂/ *adj* producing results that bring advantages 有益的, 有利的, 有用的: *beneficial effects* 裨益 | [**+to**] *an agreement that will be beneficial to both parties* 對雙方都有利的協議 —**beneficially** *adv*

ben·e·fi·cia·ry /ˌbɛnəˈfɪʃɪˌɛrɪ; ˌbenəˈfɪʃəri/ *n* [C] **1** someone who gets advantages from an action or change 受益者, 受惠者: *The rich were the main beneficiaries of the tax cuts.* 富人是減稅的主要受益者。**2** someone who receives money or property from someone else who has died〔遺囑中的〕受益人: [+of] *He was the chief beneficiary of his father's will.* 他是他父親遺囑中的主要受益人。

ben·e·fit[1] /ˋbɛnəfɪt; ˈbenɨfɪt/ *n* **1** [C,U] something that gives you advantages or improves your life in some way 好處, 益處, 裨益, 利益: *an aid program that has brought lasting benefits to the region* 給這一地區帶來長遠利益的援助計劃 | **have the benefit of** *She has had the benefit of a first-class education.* 她因受過一流教育而獲益。| **for sb's benefit** (=in order to help someone or to be useful to them) 為了幫助某人; 對某人有益 *All donations are used for the benefit of disabled children.* 所有的捐款都用於殘疾兒童的福利。| **reap the benefit** (=use and enjoy the advantages of something you have worked to achieve) 獲得益處 | **be of benefit** *formal* (=be useful or helpful in some way)【正式】有益的, 有好處的 *The new credit cards will be of great benefit to our customers.* 新信用卡將會為我們的客戶帶來很多好處。**2** [C,U] *BrE* money provided by the government to people who are sick or unemployed【英】〔政府提供給生病者及失業者的〕救濟金, 津貼; WELFARE (3) *AmE*【美】: *Are you sure you're getting all the benefits you're entitled to?* 你肯定得到了你有資格領取的所有補助嗎? | **housing/child/unemployment etc benefit** *How much unemployment benefit do you get?* 你得到多少失業救濟金? | **on benefit** (=receiving benefit) 領救濟金 *How long have you been on benefit?* 你領救濟金多久了? **3 benefit concert/performance/match** a concert, performance, etc arranged to make money for CHARITY (2) 慈善音樂會/義演/義賽: *a benefit concert for famine relief* 為饑荒災民籌款的慈善音樂會 **4 give sb the benefit of the doubt** to accept what someone tells you even though you think they may be lying 姑且相信某人 **5** [C usually plural 一般用複數] the money or other advantages that you get from insurance that you have 保險金, 保險賠償: *The benefits include full medical cover when travelling abroad.* 保險賠償包括你出國時的全額醫療費用。

benefit[2] *v* **1** [T] to bring advantages to someone or improve their lives in some way 有益於, 有利於, 對…有好處: *a trade agreement that will greatly benefit the developing world* 對發展中國家十分有利的一項貿易協定 **2** [I] to be helped by something 獲益, 受益, 得到好處: *I can see the advantages of this for you, but how will I benefit?* 我能看出這件事對你有益, 可是我能得到甚麼好處呢? | **[+from/by]** *Many thousands have benefited from the new treatment.* 千千萬萬的人受益於這種新的療法。

Ben·e·lux /ˋbɛnəlʌks; ˈbenɨlʌks/ *n* [singular] the countries of Belgium, the Netherlands, and Luxembourg considered as a group 比利時、荷蘭、盧森堡三國; 比荷盧聯盟

be·nev·o·lent /bəˋnɛvələnt; bɨˈnevələnt/ *adj* kind and generous 仁慈的, 仁愛的; 樂善好施的: *A benevolent uncle paid for her to have music lessons.* 一位仁慈的叔叔為她支付了音樂課的費用。| *a benevolent smile* 和藹的微笑 —**benevolence** *n* [U] —**benevolently** *adv*

Ben·ga·li[1] /bɛnˋgɔlɪ; benˈgɔːli/ *n* **1** [U] the language of Bangladesh or West Bengal 孟加拉語 **2** [C] someone from Bengal 孟加拉人

Bengali[2] *adj* from or connected with Bengal 孟加拉的

be·night·ed /bɪˋnaɪtɪd; bɪˈnaitɨd/ *adj* having no knowledge or understanding 愚昧的, 蒙昧無知的 —**benightedly** *adv*

be·nign /bɪˋnaɪn; bɪˈnaɪn/ *adj* **1** kind and gentle 慈祥的; 寬厚親切的: *He shook his head in benign amusement.* 他親切且滿心歡喜地搖了搖頭。**2** a benign TUMOUR (=unnatural growth in the body) is not likely to return after treatment〔腫瘤〕良性的 —compare 比較 MALIGNANT (1) —**benignly** *adv* —**benignity** /bɪˋnɪgnətɪ; bɪˈnɪgnɨti/ *n* [U]

bent[1] /bɛnt; bent/ the past tense and past participle of BEND[1]

bent[2] *adj* **1** something that is bent is no longer flat or straight 彎曲的: *The hinge was bent and the lid wouldn't shut properly.* 合葉彎了, 蓋子蓋不上。**2 bent on** completely determined to do something 下定決心(做)…; 專心於…, 埋頭於…: *He seems bent on success at all costs.* 他好像下定決心不惜任何代價一定要成功。| **bent on doing sth** *She's bent on becoming an actress.* 她一心要成為演員。—see also 另見 HELL-BENT **3** *informal especially BrE* financially dishonest and willing to use your official position unfairly【非正式, 尤英】〔經濟上〕不老實的, 收受賄賂的; 貪贓枉法的: *a bent policeman* 貪贓枉法的警察 **4** *BrE slang* an insulting word meaning HOMOSEXUAL【英俚】同性戀的〔侮辱性用語〕**5 bent out of shape** *slang especially AmE* very angry or upset【俚, 尤美】非常氣憤的; 相當不安的

bent[3] *n* [singular] *formal* special natural skill【正式】天賦; 特長: *He has an artistic bent.* 他有藝術天賦。

ben·zene /ˋbɛnzin; ˈbenziːn/ *n* [U] a liquid obtained from coal and used for making plastics 苯〔一種從煤提煉而成的液體, 用於製造塑膠〕

ben·zine /ˋbɛnzin; ˈbenziːn/ *n* [U] a liquid obtained from PETROLEUM and used to clean clothes 輕質汽油, 輕油精, 揮發油〔一種從石油提煉而成的液體, 用於清潔衣物〕

be·queath /bɪˋkwið; bɪˈkwiːð/ *v* [T] **1** to officially arrange for someone to have something that you own after your death 遺贈; 遺留: **bequeath sth to sb** *She bequeathed her collection of paintings to the National Gallery.* 她立下遺囑把自己的藏畫贈送給國家美術館。| **bequeath sb sth** *His father bequeathed him a fortune.* 他父親留給他一大筆財產。**2** to pass knowledge, customs etc to people who come after you or live after you〔把知識、風俗等〕傳給〔後人〕

be·quest /bɪˋkwɛst; bɪˈkwest/ *n* [C] *formal* money or property which you arrange to give to someone after your death【正式】遺產; 遺贈物: *a bequest of $5,000* 五千美元遺產

be·rate /bɪˋret; bɪˈreɪt/ *v* [T+for] *formal* to speak angrily to someone because they have done something wrong【正式】訓斥; 嚴責

be·reaved /bəˋrivd; bɨˈriːvd/ *adj formal*【正式】**1** having lost a close friend or relative because they have recently died〔剛剛〕喪失親友的: *a bereaved mother* 痛失孩子的母親 **2 the bereaved** the person or people whose close friend or relative has just died 死者的親友: *Our sympathies go to the bereaved.* 我們同情死者的親友。

be·reave·ment /bəˋrivmənt; bɨˈriːvmənt/ *n* [C,U] *formal* the fact or state of having lost a close friend or relative because they have died【正式】喪親(之痛); 喪友(之痛); 居喪: *depression caused by bereavement or divorce* 痛失親人或離婚導致的憂傷

be·reft /bɪˋrɛft; bɨˈreft/ *adj formal*【正式】**1 bereft of hope/meaning/life etc** completely without any hope etc 失去希望/意義/生命等: *The party's manifesto is bereft of new ideas.* 這個黨的宣言毫無新意。**2** feeling very sad and lonely 傷感的; 寂寞的: *He had left, and she felt completely bereft.* 他走了, 她深感孤寂。

be·ret /bəˋre; ˈbereɪ/ *n* [C] a round cap with a tight band around the head and a soft loose top part 貝雷帽〔扁圓無沿柔軟的小帽〕—see picture at 參見 CAP[1] 圖

ber·i·ber·i /ˌbɛrɪˋbɛrɪ; ˌberiˈberi/ *n* [U] a disease of the nerves caused by lack of VITAMIN B 腳氣(病)

berk, burk /bɝk; bɜːk/ *n* [C] *BrE spoken slang* a stupid person【英口, 俚】傻瓜: *I felt a berk in my jeans when everyone else was in suits.* 別人都穿套裝, 而我卻穿着牛仔褲, 感覺像個傻瓜一樣。

ber·ry /ˋbɛrɪ; ˈberi/ *n* [C] a small soft fruit with small seeds 漿果, 莓 —see picture on page A8 參見 A8 頁圖

ber·serk /bɝˋsɝk; bɜːˈsɜːk/ *adj* **go berserk** to become very angry and violent 狂怒, 暴跳如雷

berth[1] /bɝθ; bɜːθ/ *n* [C] **1** a place where a ship can stop and be tied up (船舶的) 泊位, 停泊處 **2** a place for someone to sleep in a ship or on a train; BUNK¹ (1) 〔船或火車上的〕臥鋪, 鋪位; 艙位 —see also 另見 **give sb/sth a wide berth** (WIDE¹ (7))

berth² *v* [I,T] to bring a ship into a berth or arrive at a berth (使)〔船〕停泊

ber·yl /ˋbɛrəl; ˈberl̩/ *n* [C] a valuable stone that is usually green or yellow 綠柱石, 綠玉

be·seech /bɪˋsitʃ; bɪˈsiːtʃ/ *v past tense and past participle* **besought** /bɪˋsɔt; bɪˈsɔːt/ *or* **beseeched** [T] *literary* to eagerly and anxiously ask someone for something 【文】懇求, 祈求, 哀求, 央求

be·seem /bɪˋsim; bɪˈsiːm/ *v* [T] *old use* to be suitable or proper for something 【舊】適合; 與…相稱

be·set /bɪˋsɛt; bɪˈset/ *v past tense and past participle* **beset** *present participle* **besetting** [T] *formal* 【正式】 **1** [usually passive 一般用被動態] to make someone experience serious problems or dangers 困擾, 使苦惱: *The business has been beset with financial problems.* 該企業為財務問題所困擾。 **2 besetting sin/weakness** *often humorous* a particular bad feature or habit 【常幽默】壞習慣, 惡習: *Mark's besetting sin is laziness.* 馬克最大的惡習是懶惰。

3 2 **be·side** /bɪˋsaɪd; bɪˈsaɪd/ *prep* **1** next to or very close to someone or something 在…旁邊, 在…近旁: *Wendy came up and sat beside me.* 温迪走過來, 坐在我身邊。| *We parked the car beside the sports hall.* 我們把車停在體育館旁邊。—see picture on page A1 參見A1 頁圖 **2** used to compare two people or things 與…相比: *This year's sales figures don't look very good beside last year's results.* 和去年相比, 今年的銷售額看來不佳。| *Pat looked big and clumsy beside her younger sister.* 帕特跟她妹妹比起來, 個子高, 但動作不靈巧。 **3 beside yourself** feeling so angry, excited etc that you find it difficult to control yourself〔由於氣憤、激動等而〕失去控制; 忘形: *He was beside himself with joy when his wife gave birth to their first child.* 妻子生下了第一個孩子時, 他欣喜若狂。 **4 beside the point** used to say that something that has been mentioned is not directly connected with the main subject or problem that you are talking about 離題, 與本題無關: *"How old is she?" "That's beside the point, the question is, can she do the job?"* "她多大了?" "那與本題無關, 問題是她能勝任這項工作嗎?"

be·sides¹ /bɪˋsaɪdz; bɪˈsaɪdz/ *prep* in addition to a point, statement etc that has just been mentioned 除了…之外: *Will there be anyone else we know at the party besides Will and Janet?* 除了威爾和珍妮特外, 聚會上還有我們認識的人嗎? | **besides doing sth** *Besides going to French evening classes twice a week she does yoga on Wednesdays.* 她除了每週兩晚學法語外, 星期三還練瑜伽。

besides² *adv* used when making another point or statement after one that you have already made 而且; 還有: *I don't want to go to the cinema; besides I'm feeling too tired.* 我不想去看電影, 再說我也太累了。| *My wife and I will be there and four of our friends besides.* 我和妻子會到場, 此外還有四位朋友。—see 見 MOREOVER (USAGE)

be·siege /bɪˋsidʒ; bɪˈsiːdʒ/ *v* [T] **1** to surround a city or castle with military force until the people inside let you take control 包圍; 圍攻; 圍困: *In April 655, Osman's palace in Medina was besieged by rebels.* 公元655年4月, 奧斯曼帝國在麥迪那的宮殿遭到叛軍圍攻。 **2** [usually passive 一般用被動態] if people, worries, thoughts etc, besiege you, you are surrounded by them〔人、煩惱、想法等〕包圍: *Miller was besieged by reporters and press photographers.* 米勒被記者和新聞攝影師團團圍住。 **3 be besieged with letters/demands/requests etc** to receive a very large number of letters, requests etc 被大量的信件/求助/請求等所困擾

be·smirch /bɪˋsmɝtʃ; bɪˈsmɜːtʃ/ *v* [T] *literary* 【文】 **besmirch sb's honour/reputation** to spoil the good opinion that people have of someone 敗壞[詆毀]某人的名譽

be·som /ˋbizəm; ˈbiːzəm/ *n* [C] a large brush made of sticks tied together around a long handle 長柄掃帚

be·sot·ted /bɪˋsɑtɪd; bɪˈsɒtɨd/ *adj* **be besotted (with)** to love or want someone or something so much that you cannot think or behave sensibly 痴迷(於); 沉醉(於); (為…)昏了頭: *He's completely besotted with her.* 他被她弄得神魂顛倒。

B

be·sought /bɪˋsɔt; bɪˈsɔːt/ the past tense and past participle of BESEECH

be·speak /bɪˋspik; bɪˈspiːk/ *v past tense* **bespoke** /bɪˋspok; bɪˈspəʊk/ *past participle* **bespoken** /bɪˋspokən; bɪˈspəʊkən/ [T] *literary* to be a sign of something 【文】顯示, 表示: *His easy manner bespoke a knowledge of the world.* 他從容不迫的舉止顯示出他很通達世故。

be·spec·ta·cled /bɪˋspɛktəkl̩d; bɪˈspektəkəld/ *adj* wearing glasses 戴眼鏡的

be·spoke /bɪˋspok; bɪˈspəʊk/ *adj BrE old-fashioned* a bespoke suit, coat etc has been specially made to fit one person 【英, 過時】〔服裝〕定做的

best¹ /bɛst; best/ *adj* [superlative of *good* good 的最高級] **1** better than anything else or anyone else in quality, skill, effectiveness etc 最好的: *He was the best teacher in the school.* 他是學校裡最好的老師。| *What's the best way to cook this fish?* 這種魚怎樣烹製最好? | *The best thing to do is to stop worrying.* 最好的辦法就是別再擔心。| **easily the best/by far the best** (=much better than anything else) 絕對是最好的 *I've read all her books but 'Middlemarch' is easily the best.* 她所有的書我都讀過, 但《米德爾馬奇》絕對是最好的。| **it's best to** *It's best to clean the wall before you paint it.* 油漆之前, 最好先把牆弄乾淨。 **2 best dress/shoes/clothes etc** clothing that you keep for special occasions 最好的穿着/鞋子/衣服等〔留待特殊場合才穿戴〕: *You ought to wear your best shirt.* 你應該穿上你最好的襯衫。 **3 best friend** the friend that you know and like better than anyone else 最好的朋友 **4 the next best thing** something that is not exactly what you want but is as similar to it as possible 僅次於最好的: *The next best thing to being with her was to phone and talk.* 能和她在一起最好了, 但打電話和她聊聊也不錯。 **5 best of all** used to introduce the one fact about a situation that is even better than the other good things 更好的是; 而且: *Yeah, my dad's getting a new car – and best of all, he's going to give me the old one!* 是啊, 我爸爸買了一輛新車。更好的是, 他會把舊車給我! —see also 另見 **be on your best behaviour** (BEHAVIOUR (2)), **your best bet** (BET² (3)), **the best/better part of** (PART¹ (6)) 1 1

best² *adv* [superlative of *well* well 的最高級] **1** in a way that is better than any other; most well 最好地: *It works best if you let it warm up first.* 如果先把它預熱一下, 用起來就最佳。| *The glacier can best be viewed from above.* 從上面看冰川最美。| *the best-dressed man in Paris* 巴黎穿得最講究的男人 **2** to the greatest degree; most 最, 極: *You know him best – you should ask him.* 你最熟悉他, 你應該去問他。| *Which did you like best, the music or the dancing?* 你最喜歡的是甚麼? 是音樂還是舞蹈? | *one of our best-loved old cathedrals* 我們最喜愛的舊教堂之一 **3 for reasons best known to herself/himself** used to say that you cannot understand why someone has done something 只有她/他自己才知道的原因: *For reasons best known to herself, she arrived dressed in a gorilla suit!* 出於只有她自己才知道的原因, 她打扮成一隻大猩猩到場! **4 as best you can** *spoken* as well as you can, even if this is not very good 【口】盡最大努力, 竭力: *I'll translate it as best I can, but my German is very rusty.* 我會盡力把它翻譯好, 可是我的德語已很生疏了。 **5 had best** *spoken* ought to 【口】應該; 最好: *You'd best stay at home till you get over that*

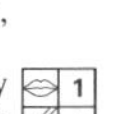

cold. 你最好留在家裡休息，直到感冒好了為止。

best³ *n* **1 a)** the best, most helpful, most successful etc situation or results that you can achieve 最佳；至上；至善：*We all want the best for our children.* 我們都希望給自己的孩子最好的東西。| *It's the best we can do in the circumstances.* 在這種情況下，我們所能做到最好的就是這樣了。**b)** the person or thing that is better than any other 最好之人；最佳之物：*She's the best of the new young writers.* 她是新一代年輕作家中最優秀的。**2 do your best** to try as hard as you can to do something 盡力而為；作出最大努力：*As long as you do your best we'll be happy.* 只要你盡力而為，我們就滿意了。| **do your best to do sth** *We'll do our best to finish it on time.* 我們會盡力按時把它完成。**3 at best** used to emphasize that something is not very good, pleasant, honest, etc even if you consider it in the best possible way 充其量；至多：*The city was at best an ordinary sort of place.* 這城市充其量只是個普通的地方。| *His answers were at best evasive, at worst very misleading.* 他的回答往好裡說是模棱兩可，往壞裡說是帶有誤導性。**4 to the best of your knowledge/belief/ability** used to say that something is as much as you know, believe, or are able to do 就某人所知/所信/能力所及：*I'm sure he'll do the work to the best of his ability.* 我相信他會竭盡全力做好這項工作。**5 the best of both worlds** a situation in which you have the advantages of two different things without any of the disadvantages 兩全其美；各取其長：*They live in a village but it's only an hour from London so they have the best of both worlds.* 他們住在一個村子裡，但離倫敦只有一小時的路程，所以他們能享受着兩者的優點。**6 at your best** performing as well or effectively as you are able to 在最佳狀態[巔峯]時：*At her best, she's a really stylish player.* 她處於最佳狀態時，是個很棒的運動員。| *He was never at his best early in the morning.* 在大清早他的狀態總不是最佳。**7 make the best of sth/make the best of a bad job** to accept an unsatisfactory situation, and do whatever you can to make it less bad 盡可能善用〔不能令人滿意的事物或處境〕；善處逆境：*We are stuck here so we might as well make the best of it.* 我們反正被困在這兒了，不如盡量利用這裡的條件做些甚麼。**8 the best of a bad lot** the least bad person or thing in a group of not very good people or things 差中選優 **9 all the best** used to express good wishes to someone for the future 一切順利！萬事如意！：*All the best for the New Year!* 新年萬事如意！**10 Sunday best** *old-fashioned* your best clothes, which you only wear on special occasions【過時】盛裝 **11 be for the best** *especially spoken* used to say that a particular event may not be as bad as it seems【尤口】也許不是件壞事：*I still don't want him to go but maybe it's for the best.* 我還是不希望他去，但這也許不是件壞事。**12 at the best of times** if something is not very good, pleasant etc at the best of times, it is usually even worse than this 即使在最好的情況下：*It's not a very exciting town at the best of times.* 即使在最好的時候，這個小鎮也不那麼熱鬧。

best⁴ *v* [T] *old use* to defeat someone【舊】擊敗，勝過

best-be·fore date /ˌ· ·ˈ· ˌ·/ *n* [C] a date on containers of food or drink that shows when they will be too old to eat or drink 最佳食用期，食品保質期

bes·ti·al /ˈbɛstʃəl; ˈbestiəl/ *adj* inhuman 野蠻的；獸性的：*Thousands of them had been murdered in the most bestial manner.* 他們當中有成千上萬的人被慘無人道地屠殺了。—**bestially** *adv*

bes·ti·al·i·ty /ˌbɛstʃɪˈæləti; ˌbestiˈæləti/ *n* [U] **1** sexual relations between a person and an animal 人獸交合，獸姦 **2** *formal* very cruel behaviour【正式】獸行，殘忍的行為

bes·ti·ar·y /ˈbɛstɪˌɛri; ˈbestiəri/ *n* [C] an old book about strange animals, written in the Middle Ages〔寫於中世紀的〕動物寓言集

be·stir /bɪˈstɝ; bɪˈstɜː/ *v* [T] **bestir yourself** *formal* to start to do things, after relaxing or being lazy【正式】發奮，振作精神

best man /ˌ· ˈ·/ *n* [singular] the man who helps the BRIDEGROOM (=the man getting married) at a wedding ceremony 男儐相，伴郎

be·stow /bɪˈsto; bɪˈstəʊ/ *v* [T] *formal* to give someone something of great value or importance【正式】給予；贈給；授予：**bestow sth on/upon** *honours bestowed on him by the Queen* 女王授予他的榮譽

be·stride /bɪˈstraɪd; bɪˈstraɪd/ *v past tense* **bestrode** /bɪˈstrod; bɪˈstrəʊd/ *past participle* **bestridden** /bɪˈstrɪdn̩; bɪˈstrɪdn/ [T] *literary* to sit or stand on or over something with one leg on each side of it【文】跨坐[立]於…上

best-sel·ler /ˌ· ˈ··/ *n* [C] a very popular book which many people buy 暢銷書 —**best-selling** *adj*: *a best-selling author* 暢銷書作者

bet¹ /bɛt; bet/ *v past tense and past participle* **bet** *or* **betted**, *present participle* **betting 1** [I, T] to risk money on the result of a race, game, competition, or other future event 下賭注；與…打賭：**bet (sb) that** *Sean bet that I wouldn't pass my exam.* 肖恩打賭說我考試不會及格。| **bet (sth) on** *She bet all her money on a horse that came last.* 她把賭注都壓在跑在最末的那匹馬上。| *No, I don't bet on my own team. It's bad luck.* 不，我不會在自己的球隊上下賭注，那樣會倒霉的。

Frequencies of the verb **bet** in spoken and written English 動詞bet在英語口語和書面語中的使用頻率

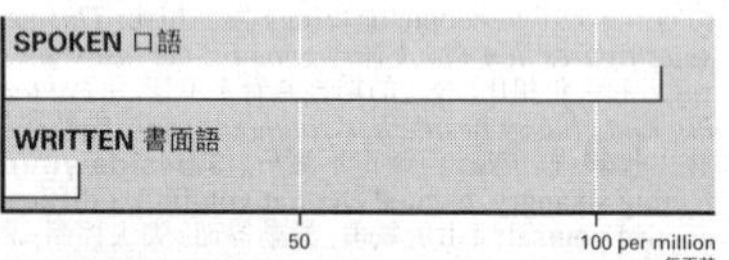

Based on the British National Corpus and the Longman Lancaster Corpus 據英國國家語料庫和朗文蘭卡斯特語料庫

This graph shows that the verb **bet** is much more common in spoken English than in written English. This is because it is used in some common spoken phrases. 本圖表顯示，動詞bet在口語中的使用頻率遠遠高於書面語，因為口語中很多常用片語是由bet構成的。

bet (*v*) **SPOKEN PHRASES**
含 bet 的口語片語

2 I bet a) used to say that you are fairly sure that something is true, something is happening etc, although you cannot prove this 我敢肯定；我敢預言：*I bet Nigel's sitting at home now laughing his head off.* 我敢肯定現在奈傑爾正坐在家裡笑個不停。| *I bet it's quite good actually.* 我肯定實際情況會不錯。| *I bet you she won't come.* 我有把握對你說她不會來。**b)** used to show that you understand or can imagine the situation that someone has just told you about 我相信；我想得出：*"The strawberries dipped in chocolate were gorgeous." "I bet!"* "草莓蘸巧克力味道好極了。" "我想一定不錯！" | *"God, I was so angry." "I bet you were."* "天哪，我當時生氣極了。" "我想你是的。" **c)** used when you are asking someone to guess something 我相信〔用於讓某人猜測〕：*I bet you'll never guess who I saw this morning.* 我想你永遠也猜不出我今早見到了誰。**d)** used to show that you do not believe what someone has just told you 我才不相信：*"I'm definitely going to give up smoking this time." "Yeah, I bet!"* "這次我肯定會戒煙。" "哼！我才不信！" **3 you bet!** used to emphasize that you agree with someone or are keen to do what they suggest 的確！當然！一定！一點不錯！：*"Going to the party on Saturday?" "You bet!"* "星期六去參加聚會嗎？" "當然啦！" **4 you can bet your life/your bottom dollar** used when you are sure that you know what someone will do or what will happen 確信，完全有把握: *You can bet your bottom dollar that relationship will end in tears.* 準沒錯，這種關係肯定以悲劇收場。

bet[2] *n* [C] **1** an agreement to risk money on the result of a race, game, competition etc 打賭: **have a bet on** *Mom had a bet on the Yankees and won $20.* 媽媽把賭注下在揚基隊上，結果贏了20美金。| **place a bet** (=choose a horse, team etc and bet on it)〔在…上〕下賭注 **2** money that you risk on a bet 賭金，賭注: *I've got a £10 bet on the National.* 我在國家隊上下了十英鎊的賭注。**3 your best bet** *spoken* used when advising someone of what to do【口】最好的辦法: *I think your best bet would be to go back to college and get more qualifications.* 我想你最好的辦法是回大學去，取得更多的資歷。**4 my bet is (that)** *spoken* used when saying what you expect to happen in the future【口】我認為…: *My bet is that she'll be famous in a few years' time.* 我估計她用不了幾年就會出名。**5 a good bet/a safe bet** an action or situation that is likely to be successful or does not involve much risk 極可能成功[穩妥]的做法[情況]: *If you're looking for long-term growth, the government's own saving certificates are a pretty good bet.* 如果你尋求長期增值，政府的儲蓄券是最保險的。**6 a safe bet/a sure bet (that)** *spoken* used to say that something seems almost certain【口】幾乎不成問題: *I think it's a pretty safe bet that he'll get the job.* 我想他得到這份工作應該不成問題。**7 do sth for a bet** to do something stupid, dangerous etc to win money from someone or to prove that you can do it 為打賭而做某事: *Sandra cut the manager's tie off for a bet!* 桑德拉為了打賭把經理的領帶剪掉了!

be·ta /ˋbetə; ˈbiːtə/ *n* **1** [singular] the second letter of the Greek alphabet, β or B 希臘字母表的第二個字母〔即β或B〕**2** [C] this letter given as a mark for good work by a student〔學生成績〕乙等，B等

beta-block·er /ˋ‥ ˌ‥/ *n* [C] a drug used to help prevent HEART ATTACKS 貝他阻斷劑〔一種用以預防心臟病的藥物〕

be·take /bɪˋtek; bɪˈteɪk/ *v past tense* **betook** /bɪˋtuk; bɪˈtuːk/ *past participle* **betaken** /bɪˋtekən; bɪˈteɪkən/ **betake yourself to** *literary* to go somewhere【文】前往，赴

be·tel /ˋbitl̩; ˈbiːtl/ *n* [U] a plant whose leaves have a fresh taste, and are chewed (CHEW[1] (2)) by people in Asia 蔞葉，蒟醬葉

betel nut /ˋ‥ ˌ/ *n* [C, U] small pieces of red nut with a bitter taste, that are wrapped in a betel leaf and chewed (CHEW[1] (2)) 檳榔果

bête-noire /ˌbet ˋnwɑr; ˌbet ˈnwɑː/ *n* [singular] *French* the person or thing that you dislike most【法】最令人憎恨[厭惡]的人[事物]

be·think /bɪˋθɪŋk; bɪˈθɪŋk/ *v past tense and past participle* **bethought** /bɪˋθɔt; bɪˈθɔːt/ **bethink yourself of** *old use* to remember something or think about something【舊】想到；考慮

be·tide /bɪˋtaɪd; bɪˈtaɪd/ *v* **woe betide you** used, especially humorously, to say that someone will be in trouble if they do something 天降禍於某人，某人會倒霉的〔尤為幽默用法〕: *Woe betide anyone who wakes the baby!* 誰要是把嬰兒吵醒，他一定會倒霉的!

be·times /bɪˋtaɪmz; bɪˈtaɪmz/ *adv old use* early or soon【舊】早；快

be·to·ken /bɪˋtokən; bɪˈtəʊkən/ *v* [T] *literary* to be a sign of something【文】預示；顯示…的徵兆

be·tray /bɪˋtre; bɪˈtreɪ/ *v* [T] **1** to be disloyal to someone who trusts you so that they are harmed or upset 背叛；對…不忠；出賣: **betray sb (to sb)** *What kind of man would betray his own sister to the police?* 甚麼樣的人會向警方出賣自己的妹妹? **2** to be disloyal to your country, for example by giving secret information to its enemies 叛國；泄露〔機密〕: *people who are prepared to betray their country for money* 那些準備為錢財而出賣國家利益的人 **3 betray your beliefs/principles/ideals etc** to stop supporting your old beliefs and principles, especially in order to get power or avoid trouble 背棄自己的信仰/原則/理想等 **4** [not in progressive or passive 不用進行式或被動態] to show feelings that you are trying to hide 暴露出〔真實情感或意圖〕: *The tremor in his voice betrayed his nervousness.* 他顫抖的聲音暴露出他很緊張。—**betrayer** *n* [C]

be·tray·al /bɪˋtreəl; bɪˈtreɪəl/ *n* [C,U] an act of betraying your country, friends, or someone who trusts you 背叛，出賣；泄露；暴露: *The tax increases are a ruthless betrayal of election pledges.* 增加稅收是對選舉諾言的無情背叛。

be·troth·al /bɪˋtroðəl; bɪˈtrəʊðəl/ *n* [C] *old use* an agreement that two people will be married; ENGAGEMENT (1)【舊】定親，訂婚

be·trothed /bɪˋtroðd; bɪˈtrəʊðd/ *adj old use*【舊】**1 be betrothed to** to have promised to marry someone 與…訂婚，和…定親 **2 sb's betrothed** the person that someone has agreed to marry 某人的未婚夫[妻] —**betroth** *v* [T]

bet·ter[1] /ˋbɛtɚ; ˈbetə/ *adj* [comparative of *good* good 的比較級] **1** more useful, interesting, satisfactory, effective, suitable etc 更好的，較好的: *Your stereo is better than mine.* 你的音響比我的好。| *a better job with a better salary* 一份更好且薪水更高的工作 | *It was one of the better Broadway shows I've seen.* 這是我所看過的百老匯演出中較好的一次。| *There must be a better way to do this.* 一定還有更好的辦法來做這件事。| *a better-quality car* 質量更好的汽車 | **much better/far better/a lot better** *It's a much better quality design than the previous model.* 這個設計質量比上一個型號要好得多。**2** [comparative of *well* well 的比較級] **a)** more healthy or less ill or painful than before〔健康狀況〕好轉的: *She is a little better today, the doctor says.* 醫生說她今天有些好轉。| *I'm feeling much better, thank you.* 我覺得好多了，謝謝你。| **feel better for** (=feel better as a result of) 因…感覺好些 *Go for a walk – you'll feel better for getting some fresh air.* 出去散散步吧，呼吸些新鮮空氣你會感覺好一點的。—see graph at 參見 IMPROVE 圖表 **b)** completely well again after an illness 痊癒的，康復的: *When you're better we can see about planning a trip.* 等你病好了，我們可以計劃去旅行。**3 get better a)** to improve 改善，變好，進步: *If the weather gets better we could go out for a walk.* 如果天氣好轉，我們可以外出散散步。| *Her English isn't really getting any better.* 其實她的英語沒甚麼進步。**b)** to recover from an illness or accident 康復，好轉: *Are you hungry Sally? I think you must be getting better.* 薩莉，你餓嗎?我想你一定是好些了。—see graph at 參見 RECOVER 圖表 **4 have seen better days** *informal* to be in a bad condition【非正式】狀態不佳: *The sofa has seen better days but the chairs are still okay.* 沙發已經不行了，但椅子還可以。**5 be no better than** to be almost as bad as 比…好不了多少: *He's no better than a thief.* 他比小偷好不了多少。**6 better still** used to say that something is even better than the first thing you mentioned〔比第一個提到的事物〕更好: *Go for a walk around the building, or better still around the block.* 圍着大樓走走吧，要是能圍着街區散步那就更好了。**7 against your better judgment** if you do something against your better judgment, you do it even though you think it may not be sensible 違心地: *Against our better judgment, we allowed her to stay.* 我們違心地允許她留下來。**8 sb's better nature** the part of someone's character that makes them want to be kind and generous, treat people well, etc 人性中善良的一面: *He's become a lot nicer recently. I think she's brought out his better nature.* 最近他變得友好了許多。我想她使他表現出了善良的本性。—see also 另見 **your better half/other half** (HALF[2] (9)), **best/better part of** (PART[1] (6)) —opposite 反義詞 WORSE[1]

B

S1 W1

Frequencies of the word **better** in spoken and written English 單詞better在英語口語和書面語中的使用頻率

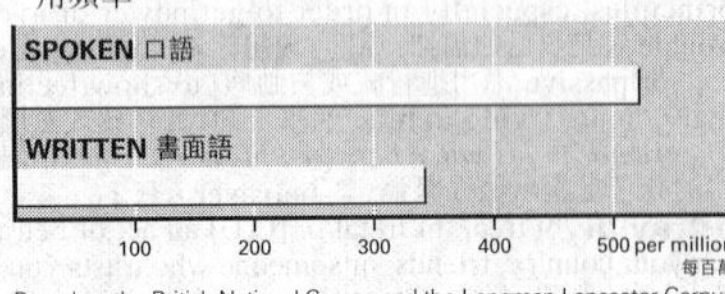

Based on the British National Corpus and the Longman Lancaster Corpus
據英國國家語料庫和朗文蘭卡斯特語料庫

This graph shows that the word **better** is more common in spoken English than in written English. This is because it is used in a lot of common spoken phrases. 本圖表顯示，單詞better在口語中的使用頻率高於書面語，因為口語中很多常用片語是由better構成的。

better (*adj*) **SPOKEN PHRASES**
含 better 的口語片語

9 sb had better a) used to give advice about what someone should do〔提出建議〕某人最好（還是）: *She'd better see a doctor if it gets any worse.* 她如果病情加重，最好去看醫生。**b)** used to threaten someone〔表示威脅〕某人最好…: *You'd better keep your mouth shut about this.* 關於這件事你最好閉上嘴。**10 that's better a)** used to praise or encourage someone 這樣好一些〔用以讚賞或鼓勵某人〕: *Try hitting the ball higher. That's better!* 試把球打高一點。有進步！**b)** used when trying to comfort someone or make them feel less upset 這就對了〔用以安慰某人〕: *Come on, give me a hug. There, that's better, isn't it?* 來吧，抱我一下。怎麼樣，這樣好一點了，對吧？**11 better** used to say that you or someone else should do something〔建議某人做某事〕最好還是: *Better go and phone her to check she's in.* 最好去給她打個電話，看看她在不在。**12 you'd be better/it would be better to do sth** used to suggest that someone should do one thing rather than another 你最好還是做某事: *It would be better to install a shower rather than a bath.* 安裝淋浴器比浴缸更好。**13 better luck next time** used to encourage someone who has done badly in an examination, competition etc 下次還有機會〔用來鼓勵在考試、比賽等中的失敗者〕**14 you'd be better off** used when suggesting that someone should do something differently or change their situation 你會更好的: *Believe me, you'd be better off without him, you really would!* 相信我，離開他你會過得更好，肯定會的！**15 what could be better...?/there's nothing better** used to say that something is perfect 還有甚麼〔比…〕更好的？/沒有〔比…〕更好的了: *Three weeks in the sun with nothing to do. What could be better?* 曬三個星期的太陽，甚麼事情也不用做。還有甚麼比這更好的？| *There's nothing better than a hot shower in the morning.* 沒有甚麼比早晨洗個熱水澡更好的了。**16 is that better?** used to ask someone if they are happier with something after you have changed it 是不是好一些？: *I'll put some more sugar in. There, is that better?* 我再多放些糖。這樣好些了吧？**17 it's better than doing sth** used to say that although your situation is not good, it is better than another situation 總比做某事要好: *Maybe I'm not well paid, but it's better than being out of a job.* 也許我的薪酬不高，但總比沒工作好。**18 better late than never** used to say that even if something happens late or someone arrives late, this is better than it not happening at all 遲做[到]總比不做[到]好 **19 better the devil you know** used to say that something bad that you know about is better than something bad you know nothing about 再壞的事情，了解總比不了解要好

better² *adv* [comparative of *well* well的比較級] **1** in a better way 更好地: *He can speak French a lot better than I can.* 他講法語比我好得多。| *Your bike will run better if you oil it.* 你給腳踏車上點油就會更好騎。| *The private schools tend to be better equipped.* 私立學校的設施往往較好。**2** to a higher degree; more 更，更加；更多地: *She knows this town better than you do.* 她比你更了解這個城鎮。| *I think I like the red one better.* 我想我比較喜歡那個紅的。| *Potter is better known for his TV work.* 波特更出名的是他的電視事業。**3 do better** to perform better or reach a higher standard 做得更好: *You'd do better if you practised more.* 你如果多練習，會做得更好。| *We did better than all the other schools.* 我們的成績比其他學校都好。**4 the sooner the better/the later the better etc** used to emphasize that you would prefer something to happen as soon as possible, as late as possible etc 越快越好/越晚越好等: *School finishes at the end of the week, and the sooner the better as far as I'm concerned.* 週末學校就放假了，在我看來，越早越好。**5 the bigger the better/the faster the better etc** used to emphasize that you want something to be as big as possible, as fast as possible etc 越大越好/越快越好等: *"Do you want me to bring a bottle of wine?" "Sure – the more the better!"* "你要我帶一瓶酒嗎？" "當然，越多越好！" **6 better off** richer than you were before〔比以前〕更富裕: *Today's pensioners are better off than they used to be.* 靠養老金生活的人過得比以前好。| *The average taxpayer will be $80 better off as a result of these changes.* 由於這些改變，納稅者平均將省下80美元。**7 go one better (than)** *informal* to do something more successfully than someone else【非正式】（比…）做得更好: *That was a good story but I can go one better.* 那個故事不錯，不過我可以講得更好。—compare 比較 WORSE³

better³ *n* **1 the better** used to mean the one that is better when you are comparing two similar people or things 更好的人[事物]: *It's hard to decide which one's the better.* 很難確定哪一個更好。**2 get the better of a)** if your feelings or wishes get the better of you, they make you behave in a way you would not normally behave 勝過，超越: *My curiosity finally got the better of me and I opened the letter.* 最終我還是按捺不住好奇，打開了信。| *I think her nerves got the better of her.* 我想她是太緊張了。**b)** to defeat someone or deal successfully with a problem 戰勝〔某人〕；成功地解決〔問題〕**3 for the better** in a way that improves the situation 有所好轉: *a definite change for the better* 明顯的好轉 | **take a turn for the better** (=improve) 有所改善，好轉 *The President's fortunes seem, at last, to have taken a turn for the better.* 總統的命運似乎終於朝好的方向轉變了。**4 be all the better for** *especially spoken* to be improved by a particular action, change etc【尤口】那就更好了: *I think it's all the better for that extra ten minutes' cooking.* 我想再煮上十分鐘會更好。**5 so much the better** used to say that something would be even better or bring even more advantages 這樣更好: *They usually cost about $50, but if you can get one for less, then so much the better.* 它們通常的價格是50美元左右，但如果你能便宜些買下來就更好了。**6 for better or (for) worse** used to say that something must be accepted, whether the results will be good or bad, because it cannot be changed 不管是好是歹: *This type of farming is, for better or worse, rapidly dying out.* 不管是好是壞，這種耕作方式很快就會絕跡。**7 your betters** *old-fashioned* people who are more important than you or deserve more respect【過時】上司；比自己地位高的人 —compare 比較 WORSE² —see also 另見 **elders and betters** (ELDER² (4))

better⁴ *v* [T] **1** to be better than something in quality, amount etc〔在質量、數額等方面〕勝過，超過，優於: *His total of five gold medals is unlikely to be bettered.* 他總共五塊金牌的記錄不大可能被超越。**2 better yourself** to improve your position in society by getting a better education or earning more money 提高自己的社會地位 **3** *formal* to improve something【正式】改善, 改進: *bettering the lot of the working classes* 改善工人階級的命運

bet·ter·ment /ˋbɛtɚmənt; ˈbetəmənt/ *n* [singular] *formal* improvement, especially in someone's social and economic position【正式】改善, 提高〔尤指個人的社會和經濟地位〕

be·tween¹ /bəˋtwin; bɪˈtwiːn/ *prep* **1** in or into the space or time that separates two things or people 在…之間: *I sat between Sue and Jane at the Christmas party.* 聖誕聚會時, 我坐在蘇和簡中間。| *There was a low brick wall between our garden and the field beyond.* 我們花園和外面田地之間有一道矮磚牆。**2** in the time that separates two events 在〔兩個事件〕之間: *Are there any public holidays between Christmas and Easter?* 聖誕節和復活節之間有公眾假日嗎? | *You shouldn't eat between meals.* 你不該在兩餐之間吃零食。**3** used to show a range of amounts, numbers, distances etc especially when guessing a particular amount, number etc 在…和…之間〔尤指在某特定數量、數目的範圍之內〕: *The project will cost between eight and ten million dollars.* 這項工程的花費在八百萬到一千萬美元之間。**4** used to show a connection between two places 連接…和…: *They're building a new road between Manchester and Sheffield.* 他們正在曼徹斯特和謝菲爾德之間建一條新公路。| *a regular air service between London and Paris* 倫敦和巴黎之間的定期航班 **5** used to show the relationship between two situations, things, people etc …與…之間 (的關係): *a long-standing friendship between Bob and Bryan* 鮑勃和布賴恩之間的長久友誼 | *cooperation between the two countries* 兩國之間的合作 | *a dispute between management and unions* 資方和工會之間的糾紛 **6** used to show the fact that something is divided or shared among several people, places, or things 在…和…之間〔分享〕: *Tom divided his money between his three children.* 湯姆把錢分給自己的三個孩子。| *Between the four of them they managed to lift her into the ambulance.* 他們四個人一齊動手把她抬上了救護車。| *We collected £17 between us.* 我們共收集到 17 英鎊。| **between doing sth** *Between cooking, writing, and running the farm Elsie was kept very busy.* 埃爾西既要做飯、寫作, 又要經營農場, 忙得不可開交。**7 in between** at a point in space or time between two places, events etc 介於…之間; 在其間: *In between school and university I did a three month crash course in Italian.* 在中學畢業後到上大學之前這段時間, 我上了三個月的意大利語速成班。| *It's somewhere in between New York and Chicago.* 它在紐約和芝加哥之間的某個地方。**8 between you and me** also 又作 **between ourselves** *spoken* used before telling someone something that you do not want them to tell anyone else【口】你我私下說說, 只限於我倆之間: *Between you and me, I think Schmidt's about to resign as chairman.* 這是我倆私下裡說的話, 我認為施米特即將辭去主席職務。**9 come between you** if something comes between two people, it causes an argument or problems between them 引起糾紛 **10** *especially spoken* used when it is difficult to give an exact description of, or name to something and you therefore have to compare it to two things that are similar to it【尤口】難以界定; 既有些像…, 又有些像…: *My job is between a bank-clerk and a messenger boy.* 我的工作既像個銀行職員, 又像個信差。

between² *adv* in or into the space that separates two things or people, or in the time that separates two events 〔空間或時間〕在其間, 當中, 中間: *So far I've had temporary jobs with long periods of unemployment between.* 到現在為止我一直在做臨時工, 其間還有很長一段時間沒有工作。| **in between** *She has breakfast and supper but doesn't eat anything in between.* 她只吃早餐和晚餐, 兩餐之間不吃任何東西。| *a house and stables with a yard in between* 中間隔着院子的房子和馬廄

USAGE NOTE 用法說明: BETWEEN

WORD CHOICE 詞語辨析: **between, among(st), with, shared by**

Between is usually used to talk about two or a few people or things, thought of separately or one after another. between 通常用於談及兩個或幾個獨立或相關的人或事物: *the differences between British and American English* 英國英語和美國英語之間的差異 | *the relationship between each member of the family and the other* (NOT 不用 *among*) 家庭成員之間的關係 | *the gaps between the fence posts* 籬笆木樁間的縫隙。In spoken English you will often hear things like 在口語中, 你經常會聽到這樣的用法: *Share this between the twelve of you.* (你們十二個人分享。), though some people think only **among** is correct where a group of more than two is involved. 但有些人認為超過兩個人應該用 among。

Among(st) is used to talk about a group of three or more people or things together, especially using nouns that name groups. among(st) 用於談論三個或三個以上的人或事物, 尤用於指作為一個整體而言的人或物: *The mountains were hidden among the clouds.* 羣山隱沒在雲中。| *Just talk amongst yourselves for a minute.* 你們互相傾談一會吧。| *Among the books he found one by Salinger* (*between the books* would suggest 暗示 'between two of them'). 在眾多的書中, 他發現了一本塞林格的作品。

Amongst is more formal than **among.** amongst 比 among 更正式。

Where there is little idea of anything different or separate being involved within a group, you can use **with** after adjectives and verbs or **shared by** with nouns. 如果一羣人或事物之間沒有甚麼差異或分不開, 可在形容詞或動詞後接 with, 或名詞後接 shared by: *This offer was very popular with our customers* (NOT 不用 *between*, though 但可用 *among* is possible). 這個優惠很受我們的顧客歡迎。| *I always eat with them* (NOT usually 一般不用 *among*). 我常和他們一起吃飯。| *the knowledge shared by the family* 全家人都有的知識 | *an opinion/a view shared by a lot of people* (or 或用 *among*) 許多人都持有的觀點

be·twixt /bəˋtwɪkst; bɪˈtwɪkst/ *prep* **1** *poetic or old use* between【詩或舊】在…之間; 在其間 **2 betwixt and between** *old-fashioned* not quite belonging to one group or to another【過時】既不屬於這種, 也不屬於那種; 兩者都沾點邊兒

bev·el /ˋbɛvl̩; ˈbevəl/ *n* [C] *technical*【術語】**1** a sloping edge or surface, usually along the edge of a piece of wood or glass〔常見於木材或玻璃邊緣上的〕斜邊, 斜面 **2** a tool for making this kind of edge or surface 斜角規 —**bevelled** *adj*: *bevelled glass* (邊緣) 切成斜面的玻璃

bev·elled /ˋbɛvl̩d; ˈbevəld/ *adj* with a sloping edge 成斜角的: *a mirror with bevelled edges* 邊緣切成斜面的鏡子

bev·er·age /ˋbɛvrɪdʒ; ˈbevərɪdʒ/ *n* [C] *formal* a hot or cold drink【正式】〔熱或冷的〕飲料: *alcoholic beverages* 含酒精的飲料

bev·y /ˋbɛvɪ; ˈbevi/ *n* [C] a large group of people of the same kind, especially girls or young women 一羣人〔尤指少女或年輕女子〕: [+of] *Tom swaggered in surrounded by a bevy of beauties.* 湯姆在一羣美女簇擁下大搖大擺地走了進來。

be·wail /bɪˋwel; bɪˈweɪl/ *v* [T] *literary* to express deep sadness or disappointment about something【文】為…而悲傷[痛惜]; 哀悼

be·ware /bɪˋwɛr; bɪˈweə/ *v* [I,T only in imperative and infinitive 僅用於祈使句及不定式] used to warn someone to be careful because something is dangerous 謹防, 當心, 注意: [+of] *Beware of the dog!* 當心有狗! | *Be-*

ware of doing anything to arouse suspicion. 謹防做出引起別人懷疑的事情。

be·wigged /bɪˋwɪgd; bɪˈwɪgd/ *adj formal* wearing a WIG【正式】戴着假髮的

be·wil·der /bɪˋwɪldə; bɪˈwɪldə/ *v* [T] to confuse someone 使迷惑; 使昏亂

be·wil·dered /bɪˋwɪldəd; bɪˈwɪldəd/ *adj* totally confused 困惑的; 不知所措的; 暈頭轉向的: *Benny looked around, a bewildered expression on his face.* 本尼環顧四周, 臉上帶着困惑的表情。

be·wil·der·ing /bɪˋwɪldərɪŋ; bɪˈwɪldərɪŋ/ *adj* confusing, especially because there are too many choices or things happening at the same time 令人困惑的; 令人感到茫無頭緒的: *There's a bewildering range of skin care products to choose from.* 可供選擇的護膚用品令人目不暇接。

be·wil·der·ment /bɪˋwɪldəmənt; bɪˈwɪldəmənt/ *n* [U] a feeling of being very confused 困惑; 昏亂

be·witch /bɪˋwɪtʃ; bɪˈwɪtʃ/ *v* [T] **1** to make someone feel so interested or attracted by something that they cannot think clearly 使着迷, 使心醉: *Tim's utterly bewitched by that woman.* 蒂姆完全被那個女人迷住了。| *a bewitching smile* 使人着迷的微笑 **2** to get control over someone by putting a magic SPELL² (1) on them 施魔力於…; 使着魔

2 1 **be·yond¹** /bɪˋjɑnd; bɪˈjɒnd/ *prep* **1** on or to the further side of something 在[向]…的那一邊; 越過: *Beyond the mountains was the border territory.* 山的那一邊是邊境地帶。—see picture on page A1 參見 A1 頁圖 **2** later than a particular time, date etc 遲於; 過了…以後: *The disco went on until beyond midnight.* 的士高一直跳到午夜以後。| *The new law extends the ban beyond 1998.* 新的法律將這條禁令延長至1998年後。**3** more or greater than a particular amount, level, or limit 超出〔某個數量、水平或限度〕: *Most people do not choose to work beyond the normal retirement age.* 大多數人過了通常的退休年齡後便不再工作。| *Inflation has now risen beyond the level of 5%.* 通貨膨脹已超出了5%的水平。**4** outside the range or limits of someone or something 超出…的範圍, 非…可及: *Such tasks are beyond the scope of your average schoolkid.* 這樣的任務非你這一般學生的能力可及。| *The light switch was beyond the child's reach.* 那電燈開關孩子是摸不到的。**5 beyond belief/doubt/recognition etc** used to say that you cannot believe something, doubt something etc 難以置信/毫無疑問/認不出來等: *The town centre had changed beyond all recognition.* 鎮中心已變得面目全非了。**6 be beyond sb** *especially spoken* to be too difficult for someone【尤口】對某人來說太難: *Algebra was always beyond me.* 代數對我來説一直很難。**7 it is beyond me why/what etc** *spoken* used to say that something seems completely stupid and you cannot understand the reason for it【口】我無法理解: *Why Joan ever married such an idiot in the first place is beyond me.* 首先我不明白瓊為甚麼會和這樣一個白痴結婚。**8** used like 'except' in negative sentences〔用於否定句〕除…以外: *Fred owns nothing beyond the clothes on his back.* 除了身上穿的衣服以外, 弗雷德一無所有。| *I can't tell you anything beyond what you know already.* 除了你已經知道的以外, 我無可奉告。

beyond² *adv* **1** on or to the further side of something 在更遠處; 往更遠處; 在那邊: *They crossed the mountains and headed for the valleys beyond.* 他們越過羣山, 到那邊的山谷去了。**2** later than a particular time, date etc 遲於某個時間[日期]: *What changes await us in the year 2000 and beyond?* 2000年及那以後會有甚麼樣的變化在等待着我們呢?

beyond³ *n* **the beyond** *literary* whatever comes after this life【文】來世, 再生

be·zique /bəˋzik; bɪ̆ˈziːk/ *n* [U] a card game for two or four players, using 64 cards 比齊克牌戲〔二人或四人玩的一種紙牌遊戲, 共用64張牌〕

bha·ji, bhajee /ˋbɑdʒi; ˈbɑːdʒiː/ *n* [C] a hot-tasting Indian vegetable cake cooked in BATTER (=a liquid mixture of flour, egg, and milk or water) 印式油餅〔蔬菜外裹以麵糊炸成的一種印度食品, 味辛辣〕: *onion bhajis* 印式洋葱油餅

bi- /baɪ; baɪ/ *prefix* two; twice; double 雙, 兩(倍): *bilingual* (=speaking two languages) 雙語的 | *to bisect* (=cut in two) 把…二等分 —compare 比較 SEMI- —see also 另見 DI-, TRI-

bi·an·nu·al /baɪˋænjuəl; baɪˈænjuəl/ *adj* happening twice each year 一年兩次的: *a biannual report* 半年度報告 —compare 比較 ANNUAL¹, BIENNIAL (1)

bi·as¹ /ˋbaɪəs; ˈbaɪəs/ *n* **1** [U singular] a tendency to consider one person, group, idea etc more favourably than others 偏見, 成見; 偏心: *a newspaper with a strong right-wing bias* 有強烈右翼偏見的報紙 | **[+against/towards/in favour of]** *There was a definite bias against commerce and science in the educational curriculum.* 該教育課程明顯歧視商科和理科。**2** [singular] a natural skill or interest in one particular area 專長; 偏愛: *Lydia has a strong artistic bias.* 莉迪亞有很強的藝術天分。**3 on the bias** in a DIAGONAL direction 偏斜地; 成對角地

bias² *v* **biased, biasing** *or* **biassed, biassing** [T] to unfairly influence attitudes, choices, or decisions 使有偏見; 使傾向一方

bias bind·ing /ˌ.. ˈ../ *n* [U] *BrE* cloth in the form of a narrow band, used when sewing edges【英】〔用於縫邊的〕斜裁布條

biased, biassed /ˋbaɪəst; ˈbaɪəst/ *adj* unfairly influenced in favour of or against one particular person, opinion etc 有偏見的; 偏袒一方的: *I admit I'm biased, but I think my son's performance was brilliant!* 我承認我有偏見, 但我認為我兒子的表演很出色! | **[+against/towards/in favour of]** *news reporting that was heavily biased towards the government* 極度偏袒政府的新聞報道

bias tape /ˌ.. ˈ./ *n* [U] *AmE* BIAS BINDING【美】〔用於縫邊的〕斜裁布條

bib /bɪb; bɪb/ *n* [C] **1** a piece of cloth or plastic tied under a baby's chin to protect its clothes when it is eating〔繫於幼兒下巴底下的〕圍嘴 **2** the upper part of an APRON (1), DUNGAREES, or overalls (OVERALL³ (2)), above the waist 圍裙[工裝褲]腰部以上的部分 **3 your best bib and tucker** *humorous* your best clothes【幽默】你最好的衣服

bi·ble, Bible /ˋbaɪbl; ˈbaɪbəl/ *n* **1 the Bible** the holy book of the Christian religion, consisting of the OLD TESTAMENT and the NEW TESTAMENT 基督教《聖經》〔包括《舊約全書》和《新約全書》〕**2** [C] a copy of the Bible 一本《聖經》**3** [singular] *informal* the most useful and important book on a particular subject【非正式】〔某一專業的〕權威書籍: *It's the anatomy student's bible!* 這是解剖學學生的寶典! **4 bible basher** *BrE*【英】, **bible thumper** *AmE*【美】an insulting expression for someone who tries to spread their own very strong Christian beliefs 基督教的狂熱傳道者〔侮辱性用法〕

bib·li·cal /ˋbɪblɪkl; ˈbɪblɪkəl/ *adj* connected with the Bible《聖經》的; 有關《聖經》的

biblio- /bɪblɪo; bɪbliəʊ/ *prefix* concerning books 與書籍有關: *a bibliophile* (=someone who likes books) 書籍愛好者

bib·li·og·ra·phy /ˌbɪblɪˋɑgrəfɪ; ˌbɪbliˈɒgrəfi/ *n* [C] **1** a list of all the books and articles used in preparing a piece of writing〔一篇文章的〕參考書目 **2** a list of everything that has been written about a particular subject〔有關某一專題的〕書目; 文獻目錄—**bibliographer** *n*

bib·li·o·phile /ˋbɪblɪəˌfaɪl; ˈbɪbliəfaɪl/ *n* [C] *formal* someone who likes books【正式】珍愛書籍者; 藏書家

bib·u·lous /ˋbɪbjələs; ˈbɪbjələs/ *adj humorous or formal* liking to drink too much alcohol【幽默或正式】嗜酒的

bi·cam·er·al leg·is·la·ture /baɪˌkæmərəl ˋlɛdʒɪsletʃə; baɪˌkæmərəl ˈledʒəsleɪtʃə/ *n* [C] *technical* a law-making body consisting of two parts, like the Senate and the House of Representatives in the US Congress【術語】兩院制的立法機關〈如美國國會的參、眾兩院〉

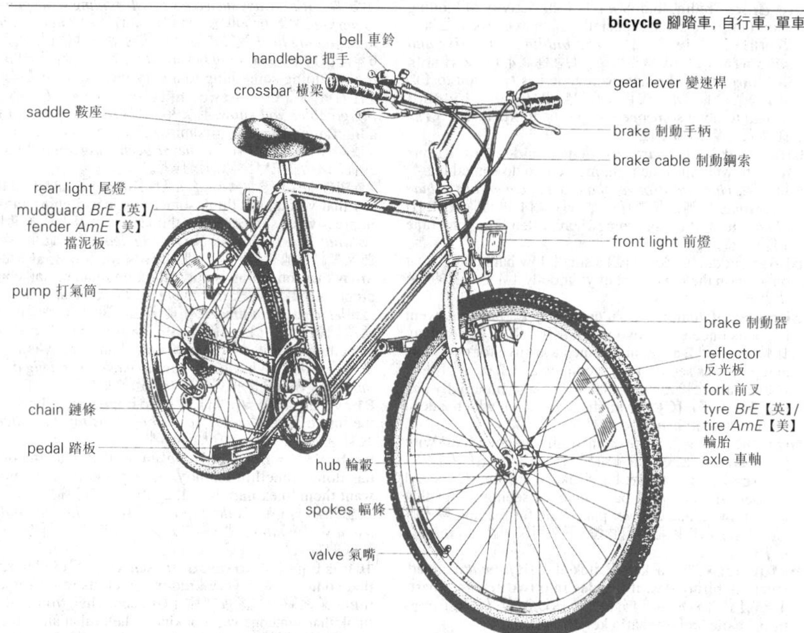

bi·car·bon·ate of so·da /baɪˌkɑrbənɪt əv ˋsodə; baɪˌkɑːbənət əv ˈsəʊdə/ also 又作 **bicarbonate**, also 又作 **bi·carb** /ˋbaɪˌkɑrb; ˈbaɪkɑːb/ *informal*【非正式】*n* [U] a chemical substance used especially in baking, and sometimes taken with water as a medicine 小蘇打, 碳酸氫鈉

bi·cen·te·na·ry /baɪˋsɛntəˌnɛrɪ; ˌbaɪsenˈtiːnəri/ *n* [C] *especially BrE* the day or year exactly 200 years after an important event【尤英】二百週年 (紀念) : *the bicentenary of Mozart's death* 莫扎特逝世二百週年紀念 —**bicentenary** *adj*

bi·cen·ten·ni·al /ˌbaɪsɛnˋtɛnɪəl; ˌbaɪsenˈteniəl/ *n* [C] *AmE* the day or year exactly 200 years after an important event【美】二百週年 (紀念) : *the bicentennial of the declaration of independence* 獨立宣言發表二百週年紀念 —**bicentennial** *adj*: *bicentennial celebrations* 二百週年慶祝活動

bi·ceps /ˋbaɪsɛps; ˈbaɪseps/ *n plural* **biceps** [C] the large muscle on the front of your upper arm〔上臂前側的〕二頭肌, 肱二頭肌 —see picture at 參見 BODY 圖

bick·er /ˋbɪkɚ; ˈbɪkə/ *v* [I+about/over/with] to argue, especially about something very unimportant〔尤指為瑣事〕爭吵, 口角: *I wish you two would stop bickering.* 我希望你們倆停止爭吵。

bi·cy·cle[1] /ˋbaɪsɪkḷ; ˈbaɪsɪkəl/ *n* [C] a two-wheeled vehicle that you ride by pushing its pedals (PEDAL[1] (1)) with your feet; BIKE 腳踏車, 自行車, 單車: *She goes to work on her bicycle.* 她騎腳踏車上班。| *Can James ride a bicycle yet?* 詹姆斯學會騎腳踏車了嗎?

bicycle[2] *v* [I always +adv/prep] *formal* to go somewhere by bicycle【正式】騎腳踏車[自行車, 單車]〔去某處〕—**bicyclist** *n* [C]

bid[1] /bɪd; bɪd/ *n* [C] **1** an offer to pay a particular price for something, especially at an AUCTION[1]〔尤指拍賣時的〕出價: [+for] *They put in the highest bid for the house.* 他們為這幢房子出了最高價。**2** an offer to do work or provide services for a specific price 投標: [+for] *rival bids for the cleaning contract* 對清潔合約的競爭性投標 **3** an attempt to achieve or obtain something〔為爭取某物而作出的〕努力: [+for] *a bid for power* 權力之爭 | **bid to do sth** *a desperate bid to free herself from a loveless marriage* 為擺脫她那段沒有愛情的婚姻而作出的不顧一切的努力 **4** a statement of how many points you hope to win in a card game〔玩紙牌者的〕叫牌

bid[2] *v past tense and past participle* **bid** *present participle* **bidding 1** [I,T] to offer to pay a particular price for goods, especially in an AUCTION[1]〔尤指拍賣時〕出價: **bid (sb) sth for** *She bid £100 for a Victorian chair.* 她為一把維多利亞時代的椅子出價 100 英鎊。| *What am I bid for lot 227? Shall we start at $500?* 我該為 227 號拍賣品出多少價呢? 我們從 500 美元開始好嗎? **2** [I] to offer to do work or provide services for a specific price, in competition with other offers 投標 (競爭) : [+for] *Three firms bid for the contract on the new buildings.* 有三家公司投標爭取承包新樓工程。**3** [I,T] to say how many points you think you will win in a game of cards〔玩紙牌時〕叫牌 —**bidder** *n* [C]

bid[3] *v past tense* **bade** /bæd; bæd/ *or* **bid** *past participle* **bidden** /ˋbɪdṇ; ˈbɪdn/ *or* **bid** *present participle* **bidding** *old use or literary*【舊或文】**1 bid sb good afternoon/good morning etc** to say good morning, good afternoon etc to someone 祝某人下午好/早安等 **2** [T] to order or tell someone what to do 命令, 吩咐: **bid sb (to) do sth** *The queen bade us to enter.* 女王吩咐我們進去。**3 bid fair to do sth** to seem likely to do something 有做某事的可能: *The good weather bids fair to hold.* 好天氣很可能持續下去。

bid·da·ble /ˋbɪdəbḷ; ˈbɪdəbəl/ *adj especially BrE* willing to do what you are told without arguing【尤英】聽話的; 順從的

bid·ding /ˈbɪdɪŋ; ˈbɪdɪŋ/ *n* [U] **1** the activity of bidding (BID[2] (1)) for goods, especially in an AUCTION[1]〔尤指拍賣時的〕競買, 喊價, 出價: *The bidding was brisk and sales went well.* 出價很踴躍, 生意進展不錯。**2 at sb's bidding** *formal* because someone has told you to【正式】按某人的要求; 按某人的吩咐 **3 do sb's bidding** *formal* to obey someone's requests or orders【正式】服從某人的要求[命令]

B

bide /baɪd; baɪd/ *v past tense* **bode** *or* **bided 1 bide your time** to wait until the right moment to do something 等待良機: *They are stronger than us and can afford to bide their time.* 他們比我們有實力, 可以耐心等待時機。**2** [I] *old use* to wait or stay somewhere, often for a long time【舊】等待, 久等

bi·det /bɪˋde; ˈbiːdeɪ/ *n* [C] a small, low bath that you sit on to wash the lower part of your body〔專洗下身的〕坐浴盆

bi·en·ni·al /baɪˋɛnɪəl; baɪˈeniəl/ *adj* **1** a biennial event happens once every two years 兩年一次的 —compare 比較 ANNUAL[1] **2** a biennial plant stays alive for two years and produces seeds in the second year〔植物〕兩年生的 —compare 比較 ANNUAL[2] (1), BIANNUAL —**biennially** *adv*

bier /bɪr; bɪə/ *n* [C] a frame like a table on which a dead body or COFFIN is placed 棺材架; 停屍架

biff /bɪf; bɪf/ *v* [T] *informal* to hit someone hard with your FIST【非正式】〔用拳頭〕狠打, 揍 —**biff** *n* [C]

bi·fo·cals /ˈbaɪˌfoklz; baɪˈfəʊkəlz/ *n* [plural] special glasses with an upper part made for seeing things that are far away, and a lower part made for reading 雙光眼鏡〔鏡片上部用以看遠處物體, 下部用以閱讀〕—**bifocal** *adj*

bi·fur·cate /ˈbaɪfəˌket; ˈbaɪfəkeɪt/ *v* [I] *formal* if a road, river etc bifurcates, it divides into two separate parts【正式】〔道路、河流等〕分為兩支[部分], 分叉 —**bifurcation** /ˌbaɪfəˋkeʃən; ˌbaɪfəˈkeɪʃən/ *n* [C,U]

S1 W1 **big** /bɪg; bɪg/ *adj comparative* 比較級 **bigger**, *superlative* 最高級 **biggest**

1 ►SIZE 尺寸◄ of more than average size, amount, weight etc 大的; 重的: *a big house* 大房子 | *Your baby's getting big!* 你的寶寶長大了! | *a big increase in prices* 價格的大幅度上漲 | *the biggest hotel in New York* 紐約最大的酒店 | *She had a big grin on her face.* 她咧嘴大笑。| **great big** *spoken* (=extremely big)【口】特大的 *There was this great big spider in the sink.* 洗滌槽裡有隻特大的蜘蛛。—see 見 WIDE[1] (USAGE)

2 ►IMPORTANT 重要的◄ important and serious 重大的, 重要的; 需認真對待的: *a big decision* 重大的決定 | *Buying your own house is a big commitment.* 給自己買房子可是件大事。

3 ►SUCCESSFUL/POWERFUL 成功的/強大的◄ *informal* successful or popular especially in business or entertainment【非正式】〔尤指在商業和娛樂業中〕極受歡迎的; 極成功的: *Rap music was really big in the 1980s.* 說唱音樂在20世紀80年代廣受歡迎。| *It's becoming quite a big area for tourism.* 這地方逐漸成為旅遊勝地。| [+in] *She's very big in the music business.* 她在音樂界很成功。| **make it big** (=become very successful) 取得成功 *After years as a small-time actor, he suddenly made it big in Hollywood.* 他做了多年的配角後, 在荷里活一舉成名。| **the big boys** (=the most powerful and influential people or companies) 極有影響力的人物[公司] *Small firms like ours can't really compete with the big boys.* 像我們這樣的小公司真的無法和大公司競爭。—see also 另見 BIG CHEESE, **big name** (NAME[1] (4)), BIG NOISE, **big shot** (SHOT[1] (17)), BIGTIME

4 ►OLDER 年長一些的◄ *spoken*【口】**a) big sister/brother** your older sister or brother 姐姐/哥哥 **b)** used especially when speaking to children to mean older or more grown-up 年紀大一些的; 長大了的: *Come on, don't cry. You're a big girl now.* 好了, 別哭。你現在是個大女孩了。

5 ►BAD 壞的◄ [only before noun 僅用於名詞前] *spoken* used to emphasize how bad something is【口】糟的〔表示強調〕: *It's always such a big hassle finding some place to park.* 找個地方停車總是件很麻煩的事。| *I never said that, you big liar!* 我從未説過那樣的話, 你這個大騙子!

6 ►A LOT 許多◄ [only before noun 僅用於名詞前] *informal* doing something to a very large degree【非正式】大量的: **a big eater/drinker/spender etc** *Des is a big gambler you know.* 你知道, 德斯是個大賭徒。| **be a big fan/admirer of** (=admire someone very much) 是〔某人〕的極度崇拜者 *I've never been a big fan of REM.* 我從來不是REM樂隊的崇拜者。

7 ►BIG DEAL 要事◄ *spoken*【口】**a) big deal!** used to say that you do not think something is as important or impressive as someone else thinks it is 有甚麼了不起!: *So what if he is upset about it? Big deal!* 他對此事不高興又怎樣? 他有甚麼了不起! **b) it's no big deal** used to say that something is not really important or not a big problem 沒甚麼問題: *It's no big deal if you can't come – just let us know in time.* 你不能來也沒問題, 只要及時告訴我們就行了。**c) make a big deal (out) of** to treat something as if it is more important than it really is 把…看得過於重要: *Why do you have to make such a big deal out of it?* 你為甚麼把這件事看得過於重要呢?

8 have big ideas/plans to have impressive plans for the future 有雄心大志: *I've got big plans for this place.* 我對這個地方已經有了大的計劃。

9 what's the big idea? *spoken* used when someone has done something annoying, especially when you want them to explain why they did it【口】你這是甚麼意思?: *Hey, what's the big idea? Who said you could use my computer?* 嘿! 你這是甚麼意思? 誰告訴你可以用我的電腦?

10 it is big of sb to do sth *spoken*【口】**a)** used to say that someone was very kind or generous to do something 某人做事很大度[慷慨] **b)** used when you really think that someone was not kind or helpful at all …真夠大方的〔說反話〕: *A whole £5! That was very big of her, I must say!* 總共五英鎊! 我説她也真夠大方的!

11 big money also 又作 **big bucks** *AmE informal* a lot of money, or the chance to earn a lot of money【美, 非正式】大筆的錢; 發財; 發財的機會: *You should go into merchant banking. That's where the big money is.* 你應該到商業銀行界去工作, 那裡才是掙大錢的地方。

12 big mouth *spoken* someone who has a big mouth cannot be trusted to keep things secret【口】多嘴多舌; 嘴巴不嚴: *Oh God, me and my big mouth!* 噢, 天哪, 我真是多嘴多舌! —see also 另見 BIGMOUTH

13 be/get too big for your boots *informal* to be too proud of yourself【非正式】自以為了不起, 自高自大; 擺架子

14 use/ward/wield the big stick *informal* to threaten to use your power to get what you want【非正式】揮舞大棒, 執行大棒政策〔用權力相威脅以達到自己的目的〕

15 big with child *old use* soon going to have a baby; PREGNANT【舊】快生孩子的; 有身孕的

16 big enchilada *humorous AmE* the most important person; the BOSS【幽默, 美】要人; 大亨; 老闆 —see also 另見 **think big** (THINK[1] (17)) —**bigness** *n* [U]

USAGE NOTE 用法説明: BIG

WORD CHOICE 詞語辨析: **big, large, great**

Big and **large** are both often used to talk about the measurements of things or groups, though **large** is slightly more formal and not so often used of people. 談事物或羣體的大小時, big和large都常用。但large較正式, 一般不用於指人: *That shirt doesn't fit me – it's too big/large.* 那件襯衫太大了, 不合我身。| *How big are you round the waist?* 你的腰圍有多大? | *a big crowd/company/gap* 一大羣人/大公司/大裂縫 | *a large family/city/university* 大家庭/大城市/規模很大的大學。—see also 另見 **fat** WORD CHOICE and 和 **wide** WORD CHOICE.

None of these words are used with uncountable nouns for things you can touch. 這兩個詞都不與不可數的具體名詞連用: *There was a lot of traffic/land/space* (NOT 不用 *big traffic, large land*). 有許多車輛/土地/空間。

Great means famous or important for something good, or, when it is used about ordinary people, just extremely nice. great意為著名的、重要的, 如指普通人意思是非常好的: *Rembrandt was a great painter.* 倫勃朗是一位偉大的畫家。| *Isn't Max a great guy?* 難道馬克斯不是個好人嗎? —see also 另見 **famous** WORD CHOICE.

Great used about the size of things or events is mainly found in literary writing or names and means 'very large and impressive'. great用於指事物或事件的大小時, 多見於文學作品或名稱中, 意為"巨大而令人印象深刻的": *the great city of Samarkand* 大撒馬爾罕市 | *A great crowd had gathered.* 聚集了一大羣人。| *a great banquet* 盛大的宴會 | *the Great Wall of China* 中國的萬里長城 Otherwise **great** is used very informally of things just to mean extremely good. 除此以外, great用於指物時是一個非正式的用法, 意為非常好的: *You look great!* 你看起來精神非常好! | *There's a great view from our hotel room.* 從我們旅館的房間裡能看到非常美麗的景色。| *We had a great time there* (=enjoyable, not necessarily long). 我們在那兒玩得很開心。

You would usually use **great** rather than **big** to describe the size or extent of things you cannot touch. 用於描述抽象事物的大小或程度時, 通常用great而不用big: *She showed great courage/talent/ability.* 她表現出很大的勇氣/聰明的才智/強的能力。| *We had great fun.* 我們過得很愉快。| *in great detail* 十分詳盡。Where both can be used, **great** is stronger and suggests more importance. 兩個詞都可以用時great比big語氣更強, 更強調重要性: *It's a big/great pleasure to see you.* 見到你很高興。| *great/big problem/opportunity/danger* 大問題/好機會/很大的危險。But note that you usually say 但要注意, 一般說: *a big difference/mistake/argument* 很大的差別/大錯/大的爭論 | *It isn't a big deal* (informal 非正式 = It's not serious or important). 沒甚麼了不起的。

Note that **large** (less often **great** or **big**) is used with these quantity words. 注意 large (較少用 great 或 big) 與下列表示數量的詞語連用: *a large amount/scale/number/quantity/extent/proportion/percentage/part/volume/area* 大量/大規模/很多/大量/很大程度/大比例/大百分比/大部分/大體積/大面積。But note only **great** is used in 但下列用法中只用 great: *a great deal* (=a lot) 許多 | *at great length* 很詳細地 | *a great height/age* 很高/高齡

big·a·my /ˋbɪgəmɪ; ˈbɪgəmi/ *n* [U] the crime of being married to two people at the same time 重婚(罪) —compare 比較 MONOGAMY, POLYGAMY —**bigamist** *n* [C] —**bigamous** *adj*

big bang the·o·ry /ˌ· ˈ· ˌ···/ *n* [singular] *technical* the idea that the universe began with a single large explosion (the 'big bang'), and that the pieces are still flying apart【術語】〔關於宇宙起源的〕大爆炸學說 —compare 比較 STEADY STATE THEORY

big brother, Big Brother /ˌ· ˈ··/ *n* [singular] any person, organization, or system that seems to want to control people's lives and restrict their freedom 專制的人[組織, 制度];"老大哥": *Increasingly, the state is taking a big brother role in this area.* 國家在這一領域日益起着老大哥的作用。

big busi·ness /ˌ· ˈ··/ *n* [U] **1** very large companies, considered as a powerful group with a lot of influence 大企業財團 **2** a product or type of activity that people spend a lot of money on 大買賣: *Dieting has become big business.* 節食減肥已經成了一個有利可圖的行當。

big cat /ˌ· ˈ·/ *n* [C] *not technical* a large animal of the cat family, such as a lion or tiger【非術語】大型貓科動物〈如獅、虎〉

big cheese /ˌ· ˈ·/ *n* [C] *informal, often humorous* an important and powerful person in an organization【非正式, 常幽默】要人, 大人物

big dipper /ˌ· ˈ··/ *n* [C] **1** a small railway in a FUNFAIR, with steep slopes and sharp curves to give an exciting ride〔遊樂場的〕雲霄飛車, 過山車 **2 the Big Dipper** *AmE* a group of seven bright stars seen only from northern parts of the world【美】北斗七星; the PLOUGH[1] (3) *BrE*【英】

big game /ˌ· ˈ·/ *n* [U] large wild animals hunted for sport, such as lions and ELEPHANTs 大獵物〈如獅、象〉: *a big game hunter* 獵捕大獵物的人

big·gie /ˋbɪgɪ; ˈbɪgi/ *n* [C] *informal* something very large, important, or successful【非正式】龐然大物; 重要事情; 大熱門: *I think their new CD is going to be a biggie.* 我想他們的新唱片會成為大熱門。

big gov·ern·ment /ˈ· ˌ···/ *n* [U] *AmE* too much government involvement in people's lives【美】大政府, 政府包辦〔指在太多方面干預人們生活的政府〕: *big government welfare policies* 政府全包的福利政策

big gun /ˌ· ˈ·/ *n* [C] *informal* a person or company that has a lot of power and influence【非正式】大人物, 要人; 有影響力的公司: *He's one of the party big guns.* 他是該黨的要人之一。

big·head /ˋbɪgˌhɛd; ˈbɪghed/ *n* [C] *informal* someone who thinks they are very important, clever etc【非正式】自高自大的人, 吹牛的人 —**bigheaded** /ˌbɪg ˋhɛdɪd; ˌbɪgˈhedɨd◂/ *adj*

big-heart·ed /ˌ· ˈ··◂/ *adj* very kind and generous 仁慈的; 大度的; 寬宏的 —**big-heartedly** *adv* —**big-heartedness** *n*

big·horn sheep /ˌbɪghɔrn ˋʃip; ˌbɪghɔːn ˈʃiːp/ *n* [C] a wild sheep with long, curved horns that lives in the mountains of western North America〔北美西部山區的〕大角羊

bight /baɪt; baɪt/ *n* [C] **1** a curve in a coast, like a BAY[1] (1) but not as curved 海岸線的彎曲部分, 大灣 **2** a LOOP[1] (1) made in the middle of a rope when tying a knot〔繩子中間的〕繩環, 繩套

Big Man on Cam·pus /ˌ· · · ˈ··/ *n* [C] *AmE informal* an important and popular male student at a college or university, especially someone who is good at sports【美, 非正式】大學校園裡有名氣的男學生, 校園名人〔特別是擅長體育者〕

big·mouth /ˋbɪgˌmaʊθ; ˈbɪgmaʊθ/ *n* [C] *informal* someone who cannot be trusted to keep secrets【非正式】多嘴的人, 守不住祕密的人

big name /ˌ· ˈ·/ *n* [C] a famous person or group, especially a musician, actor etc 知名人士[集團]〔尤指音樂家或演員等〕: *Poor attendance at the concert was put down to the lack of big names.* 由於缺少知名音樂家, 這場音樂會的入座率很低。

big noise /ˌ· ˈ·/ *n* [C] *informal* an important and powerful person in an organization【非正式】要人; 有影響力的人

big·ot /ˋbɪgət; ˈbɪgət/ *n* [C] someone who is bigoted 固執己見的人, 思想頑固的人, 執拗的人: *The new sergeant was a bigot, and viewed all black men with suspicion.* 新警官是個有着頑固種族思想的人, 對所有的黑人都持懷疑態度。

big·ot·ed /ˋbɪgətɪd; ˈbɪgətɨd/ *adj* having such strong opinions about race, religion, or politics that you are unwilling to listen to anyone else's opinions〔對種族、宗教或政治〕固執己見的, 頑固不化的: *The decision not to allow disabled athletes to take part was seen as petty* *and bigoted.* 不讓殘障運動員參加的決定被認為是狹隘而固執的。

big·ot·ry /ˋbɪgətrɪ; ˈbɪgətri/ *n* [U] bigoted behaviour or beliefs 偏執的行為[信念]: *sensational news stories that just encourage bigotry and intolerance* 只會導致偏執和不容異見的煽情新聞報道

big screen /ˌ· ˈ·/ *n* **the big screen** the cinema, rather than the television or theatre 電影院; 大銀幕: *His first big screen part was in a 1957 horror movie, 'The Count'.* 他的第一個銀幕角色出現在 1957 年的恐怖電影《伯爵》中。

big shot /ˈ· ·/ *n* [C] *informal* someone who has a lot of power or influence in a company or an area of business【非正式】要人, 大人物; 有權勢之人: *Pete Waterman, the record producer and music-biz big shot* 唱片監製、音樂界大亨皮特·沃特曼

big tick·et /ˈ· ˌ··/ *adj AmE informal* expensive【美, 非正式】昂貴的: *big ticket items such as cars or refrigerators* 汽車、冰箱等貴重商品

big time /ˈ· ·/ *n* **the big time** the position of being very famous or important, for example in the entertainment business or in politics〔演藝界或政治上的〕頭號地位; 最高成就; 第一流水平: *He really made it to the big time when his book was turned into a Hollywood movie.* 他的書被荷里活拍成電影後, 他真的成了名人。—**big-time** *adj*: *big-time cocaine dealers* 臭名遠揚的可卡因販賣者

big toe /ˌ· ˈ·/ *n* [C] the largest toe on your foot 大拇趾, 大腳趾頭 —see picture at 參見 FOOT[1] 圖

big top /ˌ· ˈ·/ *n* [C] the very large tent in which a CIRCUS (1) performance takes place〔馬戲團表演用的〕大帳篷

big wheel /ˌ· ˈ·/ *n* [C] *BrE* a machine used in AMUSEMENT PARKS, consisting of a very large upright wheel with seats hanging from it, which turns round slowly【英】〔遊樂場的〕大轉輪, 摩天輪; FERRIS WHEEL *AmE*【美】

big·wig /ˋbɪgˌwɪg; ˈbɪgwɪg/ *n* [C] *informal* an important person【非正式】大人物, 要人

bi·jou /ˋbiʒu; ˈbiːʒuː/ *adj* [only before noun 僅用於名詞前] a bijou house or apartment is small and fashionable 小巧雅致的: *a bijou residence in Mayfair* 梅菲爾區小巧雅致的住宅

2 **bike¹** /baɪk; baɪk/ *n* [C] **1** *informal* a bicycle or MOTORCYCLE【非正式】腳踏車, 自行車, 單車; 摩托車 **2 on your bike!** *BrE spoken* used to tell someone rudely to go away【英口】滾開!

bike² *v* [I always+adv/prep] *informal* to ride a bicycle【非正式】騎腳踏車[自行車, 單車]: *She bikes to work every day.* 她每天騎腳踏車上班。

bik·er /ˋbaɪkɚ; ˈbaɪkə/ *n* [C] someone who rides a MOTORCYCLE, especially as part of a group 摩托車手〔尤指某一組織的成員〕: *A biker's leather jacket says more about him than a thousand words.* 摩托車手穿的皮衣比言辭更能説明他的身分。

bi·ki·ni /bɪˋkinɪ; bȷ̍ˈkiːni/ *n* [C] a piece of clothing in two separate parts that women wear for swimming 比基尼式游泳衣, 三點式泳裝

bikini line /ˈ·ˌ·· ·/ *n* [C] the place on a woman's legs where the hair around her sexual organs stops growing 比基尼線〔女性生殖器官的毛髮停止生長的地方〕

bi·la·bi·al /baɪˋlebɪəl; baɪˈleɪbiəl/ *n* [C] *technical* a CONSONANT sound such as /p/ or /b/ that is made using both lips【術語】雙唇(輔)音〈如 /p/, /b/〉—see also 另見 LABIAL —**bilabial** *adj*

bi·lat·er·al /baɪˋlætərəl; baɪˈlætərəl/ *adj* **bilateral agreement/arrangement/treaty etc** an agreement etc between two groups or nations 雙邊協議/約定/條約等 —compare 比較 MULTILATERAL, UNILATERAL —**bilaterally** *adv*

bil·ber·ry /ˋbɪlˌbɛrɪ; ˈbɪlbəri/ *n* [C] a blue-black fruit that grows in Northern Europe or the bush it grows on 歐洲越橘

bile /baɪl; baɪl/ *n* [U] **1** a bitter green brown liquid formed in the LIVER (1), which helps you to DIGEST¹ (1) fats 膽汁 **2** *literary* anger and hatred【文】壞脾氣; 乖戾

bilge /bɪldʒ; bɪldʒ/ *n* **1** [C usually plural 一般用複數] the broad bottom part of a ship〔船的〕艙底 **2** [U] *old-fashioned informal* nonsense【過時, 非正式】廢話, 胡説

bi·lin·gual /baɪˋlɪŋgwəl; baɪˈlɪŋgwəl/ *adj* **1** written or spoken in two languages 雙語的; 包含兩種語言的: *a bilingual dictionary* 雙語詞典 **2** able to speak two languages equally well 會説兩種語言的: *Their kids are completely bilingual.* 他們的孩子能流利地説兩種語言。—**bilingual** *n* [C] —compare 比較 MONOLINGUAL, MULTILINGUAL

bil·i·ous /ˋbɪljəs; ˈbɪliəs/ *adj* **1** feeling sick〔因膽汁過多而〕感到不適的: *Fatty foods make some people bilious.* 多脂肪的食物會使一些人患上膽汁病。**2** bad-tempered 壞脾氣的; 暴躁的 —**biliousness** *n*

bilk /bɪlk; bɪlk/ *v* [T+out of] *informal* to cheat someone, especially by taking their money; SWINDLE¹【非正式】蒙騙〔尤指騙錢〕

bill¹ /bɪl; bɪl/ *n* [C]

1 ►PAYMENT 付款◄ **a)** a written list showing how much you have to pay for services you have received, work that has been done etc〔服務費用的〕賬單: **[+for]** *The bill for the repairs came to $650.* 修理費用總計 650 美元。| **pay/settle a bill** *Have you paid the phone bill?* 你付清電話費了嗎? **b)** *BrE* a list showing how much you have to pay for food you have eaten in a restaurant【英】〔餐費的〕賬單; CHECK² (7) *AmE*【美】: *Could we have the bill, please?* 請結賬。—see picture on page A15 參見 A15 頁圖

2 ►LAW 法律◄ a written proposal for a new law, which is brought to a parliament so that it can be discussed 議案, 法案: *a debate in Congress on the President's new transportation bill* 國會對總統的新運輸法案進行的辯論

3 ►MONEY 錢◄ *AmE* a piece of paper money【美】紙幣, 鈔票; NOTE¹ (5) *BrE*【英】: *a five-dollar bill* 一張五美元的鈔票

4 fill the bill/fit the bill to be exactly what you need 符合需要; 最為合適; 管用: *This car fits the bill perfectly. It's cheap and gets good mileage.* 這輛汽車很合適, 既便宜又省油。

5 ►CONCERT/SHOW ETC 音樂會/演出等◄ a programme of entertainment at a theatre, concert, cinema etc, with details of who is performing, what is being shown etc 節目單; 招貼, 海報: **top the bill** (=be the most important performer) 領銜主演 | **a double bill** (=a show in two parts) 雙劇目 *a great double bill with two classic horror movies* 兩部經典恐怖片同場放映

6 ►ADVERTISEMENT 廣告◄ a printed notice advertising an event 廣告; 招貼; 傳單

7 give sb/sth a clean bill of health to officially state that someone is in good health or that something is working correctly 給某人/某物開具健康良好證明[合格證明]: *Safety inspectors gave all the rides a clean bill of health.* 安全檢查員評定所有的騎馬道都符合安全標準。

8 ►BIRD 鳥◄ a bird's beak 鳥嘴, 喙

9 the old bill/the bill *BrE spoken* the police【英口】警察

bill² *v* [T] **1 be billed as** to be advertised or generally described in a particular way 被宣傳為: *The election was billed as the make-or-break point for the Liberals.* 這次選舉被宣傳為自由黨人的成敗關鍵。**2 be billed to play/appear etc** if someone is billed to perform somewhere, it has been advertised that they will perform there 海報上宣傳某人將演出/出場等: *He was billed to play three successive concerts.* 海報上宣傳他將連續演出三場音樂會。**3** to send someone a bill 給…開[送]賬單: *Clients will be billed monthly.* 按月給客戶開送賬單。**4 bill and coo** *literary or humorous* if two lovers are billing and cooing, they are kissing and talking softly【文或幽默】〔情侶間〕接吻和低聲地談情説愛, 卿卿我我

bill·board /ˋbɪlˌbɔrd; ˈbɪlbɔːd/ *n* [C] a large sign used for advertising 廣告牌[板]; HOARDING (2) *BrE*【英】

bil·let¹ /ˋbɪlɪt; ˈbɪlɪ̥t/ *n* [C] a private house where soldiers live temporarily 士兵臨時營舍〔通常為民房〕

billet² *v* [T+on/with] to put soldiers in private house to live there temporarily 給〔士兵〕提供住宿處

bil·let-doux /ˌbɪle ˋdu; ˌbɪleɪ ˈduː/ *n plural* **billets-doux** /ˌbɪle ˋduz; ˌbɪleɪ ˈduːz/ [C] *French humorous or literary* a love letter【法, 幽默或文】情書

bill·fold /ˋbɪlˌfold; ˈbɪlfəʊld/ *n* [C] *AmE* a small flat leather case, used for carrying paper money, credit cards etc in your pocket; WALLET (1)【美】〔裝鈔票和信用咭等的〕錢包, 皮夾子

bill·hook /ˋbɪlˌhʊk; ˈbɪlhʊk/ *n* [C] a tool consisting of a blade with a hooked point and a handle, used for cutting off tree branches etc〔剪枝等用的〕鉤鐮, 鈎刀

bil·liards /ˋbɪljədz; ˈbɪljədz/ *n* [plural] a game played on a cloth-covered table in which balls are hit with a CUE (=a long stick) against each other and into pockets at the edge of the table 枱球, 桌球, 撞球戲 —compare 比較 POOL¹ (3), SNOOKER¹ —**billiard** *adj* [only before noun 僅用於名詞前]: *a billiard table* 枱球桌 | *the billiard room* 枱球室

bill·ing /ˋbɪlɪŋ; ˈbɪlɪŋ/ *n* **give sb top/star billing** to name a particular performer, actor etc as being the most important person in a show, play etc 在海報上宣傳某人領銜主演

bil·lion /ˋbɪljən; ˈbɪljən/ *plural* **billion** or **billions** *number* **1** one thousand million 十億 —see 見 HUNDRED (USAGE) **2** *BrE old use* a million million【英舊】萬億 —**billionth** *determiner, n, pron, adv*

bill of ex·change /ˌ· · ˋ·/ *n* [C] *technical* a signed document ordering someone to pay someone else a particular amount of money【術語】匯票

bill of fare /ˌ· · ˋ·/ *n* [C] *old-fashioned* a list of the food that is served in a restaurant; MENU (1)【過時】〔餐館的〕菜單

bill of lad·ing /ˌ· · ˋ··/ *n* [C] *technical* a list of the goods being carried, especially on a ship【術語】〔尤指船運〕提(貨)單

bill of rights /ˌ· · ˋ·/ *n* [C] a written statement of the most important rights of the citizens of a country 人權法案; 權利法案: *One state has proposed the country adopt a bill of rights and replace the Queen as head of state with a president.* 有一個州提議該國採納一項人權法案, 用總統取代女王擔任國家元首。

bill of sale /ˌ· · ˋ·/ *n* [C] a written document showing that someone has bought something 賣據, 賣契

bil·low¹ /ˋbɪlo; ˈbɪləʊ/ *v* [I] **1** also 又作 **billow out** to swell out like a sail〔像帆一樣地〕鼓起, 揚起: *billowing skirts* 揚起的裙子 **2** *literary* to rise and roll in waves【文】在波濤中翻滾; 洶湧奔騰: *smoke billowing upwards* 滾滾上升的濃煙

billow² *n* [C usually plural 一般用複數] **1** *literary* a wave, especially a very large one【文】波濤; 巨浪 **2** a moving cloud or mass of something such as smoke or cloth 波濤般滾滾而來之物

bil·ly /ˋbɪlɪ; ˈbɪli/ also 又作 **bil·ly·can** /ˋbɪlɪˌkæn; ˈbɪlikæn/ *n* [C] *BrE, AustrE* a tin pot for cooking or boiling water when you are camping【英, 澳】〔露營時煮飯燒水用的〕鐵皮罐

billy club /ˋ·· ·/ *n* [C] *AmE old-fashioned* a short stick carried by a police officer【美, 過時】警棍; TRUNCHEON *BrE*【英】

billy-goat /ˋ·· ·/ *n* [C] *informal* a word for a male goat used especially by or to children【非正式】公山羊〔尤用於兒語〕—compare 比較 NANNY GOAT

billy-o /ˋ·· ·/ *n* **like billy-o** *BrE old-fashioned slang* very fast or with a lot of effort【英, 過時, 俚】很快地; 盡全力; 猛烈地: *We ran like billy-o!* 我們拚命跑。

bil·tong /ˋbɪlˌtɑŋ; ˈbɪltɒŋ/ *n* [U] *SAfrE* meat dried in the sun【南非】曬乾的肉

bim·bo /ˋbɪmbo; ˈbɪmbəʊ/ *n* [C] *informal* an insulting word for an attractive but unintelligent young woman【非正式】〔年輕貌美但頭腦簡單的〕女人〔侮辱性用語〕: *He picked up some bimbo at the club last night.* 他昨晚在俱樂部勾搭上了一個美豔女郎。

bi·month·ly /baɪˋmʌnθlɪ; baɪˈmʌnθli/ *adj* appearing or happening every two months or twice each month 兩月一次的; 一月兩次的: *bimonthly magazine* 雙月刊; 半月刊 —**bimonthly** *adv*

bin¹ /bɪn; bɪn/ *n* [C] **1** *BrE* a container for putting waste in【英】垃圾箱, 垃圾桶: *Throw it in the bin.* 把它扔到垃圾箱裡去。—see picture on page A10 參見 A10 頁圖 **2** a large container for storing things, such as goods in a shop or substances in a factory 大貯藏箱 2

bin² *v* **binned, binning** [T] *BrE informal* to throw something away【英, 非正式】扔掉: *"What should I do with this letter?" "Just bin it!"* "這封信我該怎麼處理?" "扔掉就是了!"

bi·na·ry /ˋbaɪnərɪ; ˈbaɪnəri/ *adj technical*【術語】**1 the binary system** a system of counting, used in computers, in which only the numbers 0 and 1 are used〔電腦運算系統〕二進制 **2** consisting of two parts; double 由兩部分組成的; 二元的; 雙重的: *a binary star system* 雙星系

bind¹ /baɪnd; baɪnd/ *v past tense and past participle* **bound** /baʊnd; baʊnd/

1 ►TIE/FASTEN 束/縛◄ [T] *formal or literary*【正式或文】**a)** to tie someone so that they cannot move or escape 捆, 綁: *They bound my arms and legs with rope.* 他們用繩子綁住我的雙臂和雙腿。| **bound and gagged** (=tied up, and with cloth tied around your mouth so you cannot speak) 身體被綁着, 嘴被堵住 **b)** also 又作 **bind up** to tie things firmly together with cloth or string〔用布或帶子〕束緊; 捆紮: *They bound his wounds.* 他們把他的傷口包紮好。

2 ►UNITE 聯合◄ [T] to form a strong emotional or economic connection between two people, countries etc 把…緊緊聯繫在一起; 使關係密切: **bind sth together** *Their shared experiences in war helped to bind the two communities together.* 共同的戰爭經歷使兩個團體的關係十分密切。

3 ►STICK TOGETHER 黏起來◄ [I,T] to stick together in a mass, or to make small pieces of something stick together (使)黏合; (使)凝結: *The flour mixture isn't wet enough to bind properly.* 這麵粉漿糊水不夠, 所以不黏。| **bind sth** *The rain will help to bind the soil.* 這場雨有助於使泥土黏合。

4 ►RESTRICT 限制◄ [T] to reduce someone's freedom of action, for example by giving them a duty or making them promise to do something 約束; 使負有義務: *regulations that could bind policy-makers in the future* 能於將來約束決策者的規定 | *The monks are bound by vows of silence.* 僧侶們必須遵守保持緘默的誓言。

5 ►STITCH 縫◄ [T] to strengthen or decorate something with a border of material 給…加上飾邊; 給…鑲邊: *The edges of the blanket were bound with ribbon.* 毯子有絲帶飾邊。

6 ►BOOK 書◄ [T] to fasten the pages of a book together and put them in a cover 裝訂 —see also 另見 BOUND

bind sb over *phr v* [T] *BrE law* to order someone to cause no more trouble by threatening them with legal punishment【英, 法律】命令〔某人〕具結[保證]不再鬧事: *bound over to keep the peace* 依法具結不得擾亂治安

bind² *n* **a bind** *informal* an annoying or difficult situation【非正式】窘境, 困境: *It's a real bind having to look after the children.* 要照顧這些孩子真令人為難。

bind·er /ˋbaɪndɚ; ˈbaɪndə/ *n* **1** [C] a removable cover for holding loose sheets of paper, magazines etc 活頁封面, 活頁夾 —see also 另見 RING BINDER **2** [C] a person or machine that fastens the parts of a book together〔書籍〕裝訂工; 裝訂機 **3** [C,U] a substance that makes things stick together 黏合物 **4** [C] *AmE* an agreement in which you pay something to show that you intend to buy some property【美】〔購買不動產時的〕臨時契約

bind·ing¹ /ˈbaɪndɪŋ; ˈbaɪndɪŋ/ *adj* **a binding contract/promise/agreement etc** a promise, agreement etc that must be obeyed 具有約束力[必須履行]的合同/承諾/協議等

binding² *n* **1** [C] a book cover 書籍的封面 **2** [U] material sewn or stuck along the edge of a piece of cloth for strength or decoration 鑲邊; 邊飾; 滾條

B

bind·weed /ˈbaɪndˌwid; ˈbaɪndwiːd/ *n* [U] a wild plant that winds itself around other plants 旋花屬植物; 旋花蔓

binge¹ /bɪndʒ; bɪndʒ/ *n* [C] *informal* a short period when you do too much of something, especially drinking alcohol【非正式】狂歡作樂; 大吃大喝〔尤指喝酒〕: *a week-long binge of shopping and theatre-going* 一週的瘋狂購物和看戲 | **on a binge** *Ken's gone on a binge with his mates.* 肯和他的夥伴一起飲酒作樂去了。

binge² *v* [I] *informal* to eat a lot of food in a short time, especially if you have an EATING DISORDER【非正式】〔尤因患飲食失調症而引起的〕暴食: [+on] *Whenever she's depressed she binges on chocolates.* 每當情緒低落時她就猛吃巧克力。

bin·go¹ /ˈbɪŋgo; ˈbɪŋgəʊ/ *n* [U] a game played for money or prizes in which numbers are chosen by chance and called out, and if you have the right numbers on your card you win 賓戈遊戲〔一種彩票式遊戲, 玩者持有一張有數字的牌, 如牌上的數字和開叫的號碼對上, 玩者便勝出〕: *Vera won £20 at bingo.* 薇拉玩賓戈贏了 20 英鎊。

bingo² *interjection old-fashioned* used when you have just done something successfully and are pleased【過時】瞧, 好, 妙〔對剛才成功做某事表示的興奮叫聲〕: *Bingo! That's the one I've been looking for.* 太好了! 這正是我一直在找的那一個。

bin lin·er /ˈ· ˌ··/ *n* [C] *BrE* a plastic bag used inside a bin (BIN¹ (1)) for holding waste【英】〔置於垃圾箱內的〕塑料垃圾袋

bin·man /ˈbɪnmæn; ˈbɪnmæn/ *n plural* **binmen** /-mɛn; -men/ [C] *BrE* someone who comes to people's houses to collect their waste【英】上門收垃圾的清潔工; GARBAGE COLLECTOR *AmE*【美】

bi·noc·u·lars /bɪˈnɑkjələ-z; bɪˈnɒkjʊləz/ *n* [plural] a pair of glasses like short telescopes (TELESCOPE¹), used for looking at distant objects 雙筒望遠鏡

binocular vi·sion /·ˌ··· ˈ··/ *n* [U] *technical* the ability to FOCUS (=see clearly with) both eyes on one object, which humans, monkeys, and some birds have【術語】〔人、猴及某些鳥類具有的〕雙眼視覺

bi·no·mi·al /baɪˈnomɪəl; baɪˈnəʊmiəl/ *n* [C] *technical* a mathematical expression that has two parts connected by the sign + or the sign –, for example 3x+4y or x–7【術語】〔數學〕二項式〈如 3x+4y 或 x–7〉 —**binomial** *adj*

bio- /baɪo; baɪəʊ/ *prefix* concerning living things 生物: *biochemistry* (=study of the chemistry of living things) 生物化學

bi·o·chem·is·try /ˌbaɪoˈkɛmɪstrɪ; ˌbaɪəʊˈkemɪstri/ *n* [U] the scientific study of the chemistry of living things 生物化學 —**biochemist** *n* [C] —**biochemical** *adj*

bi·o·de·gra·da·ble /ˌbaɪodɪˈgredəbl; ˌbaɪəʊdɪˈgreɪdəbəl◂/ *adj technical* materials, chemicals etc that are biodegradable are changed naturally by the action of BACTERIA into substances that are not harmful to the environment【術語】微生物可分解的, 可由微生物降解的

bi·og·ra·pher /baɪˈɑgrəfə-; baɪˈɒgrəfə/ *n* [C] someone who writes about someone else's life 傳記作者

bi·og·ra·phy /baɪˈɑgrəfɪ; baɪˈɒgrəfi/ *n* **1** [C] an account of a person's life written by someone else〔由他人撰寫的〕傳記: *Boswell's biography of Dr. Johnson* 鮑斯韋爾為約翰遜博士寫的傳記 **2** [U] the part of literature that consists of biographies 傳記文學 —compare 比較 AUTOBIOGRAPHY —**biographical** /ˌbaɪəˈgræfɪkḷ; ˌbaɪəˈgræfɪkəl◂/ *adj* —**biographically** /-kḷɪ; -kli/ *adv*

bi·o·lo·gi·cal /ˌbaɪəˈlɑdʒɪkḷ; ˌbaɪəˈlɒdʒɪkəl/ *adj* **1** connected with biology 生物學的; 與生物學有關的: *woman's biological function as a bearer of children* 婦女的生育能力 | *the biological sciences* 生物科學 **2 biological father/mother/parent** a child's natural parent, rather than someone who has become its parent through ADOPTION (1) 生父/生母/親生父[母]

biological clock /ˌ····· ˈ·/ *n* [singular] **1** *technical* the time system in plants and animals that controls behaviour such as sleeping and eating; BODY CLOCK【術語】生物鐘〔指植物和動物控制某些行為如吃、睡等的一個體系〕**2** *not technical* the idea that when a woman reaches a certain age, she will soon be too old to have a baby【非術語】受孕生理鐘〔指婦女到了一定年齡後不會生育的一種說法〕

biological con·trol /ˌ····· ·ˈ·/ *n* [U] a method of controlling PESTS (=small insects that harm or destroy crops) by using other insects, birds, or animals to kill them 生物控制〔指利用其他昆蟲、鳥雀或獸類對害蟲進行控制〕

biological war·fare /ˌ····· ˈ··/ *n* [U] methods of fighting a war in which BACTERIA are used to poison people, damage crops etc 生物戰, 細菌戰 —compare 比較 CHEMICAL WARFARE

bi·ol·o·gy /baɪˈɑlədʒɪ; baɪˈɒlədʒi/ *n* [U] **1** the scientific study of living things 生物學: *She has a degree in biology.* 她擁有生物學的學位。**2** the scientific laws that control the life of a particular type of animal, plant etc〔某種動物或植物的〕生活規律; 生態學: *the biology of bacteria* 細菌的生態學 —**biologist** *n* [C] —**biological** /ˌbaɪəˈlɑdʒɪkḷ; ˌbaɪəˈlɒdʒɪkəl◂/ *adj*: *biological washing powder* (=using special chemicals to wash clothes) 生物洗衣粉 —**biologically** /-kḷɪ; -kli/ *adv*

bi·o·mass /ˈbaɪoˌmæs; ˈbaɪəʊmæs/ *n* [U] *technical* plant and animal matter used to provide fuel or energy【術語】〔尤指用作燃料或提供能量的〕生物量

bi·on·ic /baɪˈɑnɪk; baɪˈɒnɪk/ *adj informal* much stronger or faster than a normal person usually because of having electronic arms or legs【非正式】〔由於身體某部分受電子操縱而〕具有超人力量[速度]的

bi·o·phy·sics /ˌbaɪoˈfɪzɪks; ˌbaɪəʊˈfɪzɪks/ *n* [U] the scientific study of matter and natural forces in living things 生物物理學

bi·o·pic /ˈbaɪoˌpɪk; ˈbaɪəʊˌpɪk/ *n* [C] *informal* a film that tells the story of someone's life【非正式】傳記影片: *'Great Balls of Fire', the biopic of Jerry Lee Lewis* 一部有關〔搖滾樂明星〕傑里·李·劉易斯生平的電影《大火球》

bi·op·sy /ˈbaɪɑpsɪ; ˈbaɪɒpsi/ *n* [C] the removal of cells, liquid etc from the body of someone who is ill, in order to find out more about their disease and its effects 活組織檢查, 活體檢視

bi·o·rhyth·ms /ˈbaɪoˌrɪðəmz; ˈbaɪəʊˌrɪðəmz/ *n* [plural] regular changes in the speed at which physical processes happen in your body, which some people believe can affect the way you feel and behave 生物節律〔一種據認為存在於生物體內的週期性的變化現象, 被認為會對情感和行為產生影響〕

bi·o·sphere /ˈbaɪəˌsfɪr; ˈbaɪəsfɪə/ *n* [singular] *technical* the part of the world in which animals, plants etc can live【術語】生物圈〔地球上生命可存在的區域〕

bi·o·tech·nol·o·gy /ˌbaɪotɛkˈnɑlədʒɪ; ˌbaɪəʊtekˈnɒlədʒi/ *n* [U] *technical* the use in science and industry of living things such as cells and BACTERIA, to make drugs or chemicals, destroy waste matter etc【術語】生物技術; 生物工藝學

bi·par·ti·san /baɪˈpɑrtəzṇ; ˌbaɪpɑːtɪˈzæn/ *adj* consisting of or representing two political parties 由兩黨組成的; 代表兩黨的: *Gore proposed a bipartisan committee drawn especially from both houses.* 戈爾提議成立一個由參、眾兩院議員組成的兩黨委員會。

bi·par·tite /baɪˈpɑrtaɪt; baɪˈpɑːtaɪt/ *adj* **1** *formal* shared by or agreed on by two different groups【正式】雙方同意的; 雙方共有的: *a bipartite treaty* 雙邊條約 **2** *technical* having two parts【術語】有兩部分的; 由兩部分構成的: *a bipartite leaf* 呈二深裂的葉子 —compare 比較 TRIPARTITE

bi·ped /ˋbaɪpɛd; ˈbaɪped/ *n* [C] *technical* an animal with two legs, including humans【術語】兩足動物〔包括人類〕—compare 比較 QUADRUPED —**bipedal** /ˋbaɪpɛdḷ; ˌbaɪˈpedl◂/ *adj*

bi·plane /ˋbaɪˌplen; ˈbaɪpleɪn/ *n* [C] an aircraft with two sets of wings, especially of a type built in the early 20th century 雙翼飛機〔尤指20世紀初期有兩層機翼的飛機〕—compare 比較 MONOPLANE

birch¹ /bɝtʃ; bɜːtʃ/ *n* **1** [C,U] a tree with smooth BARK (=outer covering) and thin branches, or the wood from this tree 樺樹; 樺木 **2 the birch** the practice of hitting people with a stick as a punishment 用樺條笞打的懲罰 —see also 另見 SILVER BIRCH

birch² *v* [T] to hit someone with a stick as a punishment〔用樺條〕抽打

S2 W2 **bird** /bɝd; bɜːd/ *n* [C]

1 ▶**BIRD** 鳥◀ a creature with wings and feathers that lays eggs and can usually fly 鳥: *The tree was full of tiny, brightly-coloured birds.* 樹上到處都是色彩鮮豔的小鳥。

2 a little bird told me *spoken* used to say that you know something, but you will not say how you found out【口】一個消息靈通的人告訴我: *A little bird told me that you've got engaged.* 有個消息靈通的人告訴我你訂婚了。

3 the birds and the bees *humorous* the facts about sex, especially as told to children【幽默】〔尤指對兒童講述的〕有關兩性的基本常識, 性知識

4 birds of a feather *informal* people of the same kind【非正式】同類的人; 志趣相投者

5 give sb the bird a) *AmE informal* to make a very rude sign by putting your middle finger up【美, 非正式】〔豎起中指〕對某人做下流手勢 **b)** *BrE* to make rude noises in order to show disapproval of a performer, public speaker etc【英】向〔演員、演講者等〕發噓聲, 喝倒采

6 a bird in the hand (is worth two in the bush) used to say that something you already have is worth more than something which is better, but which you cannot be sure of getting 已到手的東西(總比不一定能到手的東西強)

7 the bird has flown *informal* used to say that the person you are looking for has already left or escaped【非正式】要抓[找]的人跑[走]了

8 be (strictly) for the birds *AmE informal* to be silly, useless, or not practical【美, 非正式】愚蠢的; 毫無用處的; 不實用的

9 ▶**WOMAN** 女人◀ *BrE old-fashioned* a word meaning a young woman which some women think is offensive【英, 過時】年輕女子, 少女, 小妞〔一些女性視此詞為冒犯用語〕—see also 另見 DOLLY BIRD

10 ▶**PERSON** 人◀ *old-fashioned* a person of a particular type, especially one who seems strange or unusual【過時】怪人, 古怪[奇特]的傢伙: *He's a strange old bird.* 他是個古怪的老頭。

11 do bird *BrE slang* to spend a period of time in prison【英俚】蹲監獄 —see also 另見 **eat like a bird** (EAT (1a)), **early bird** (EARLY¹ (10)), **home bird** (HOME³ (5)), **kill two birds with one stone** (KILL¹ (10))

bird·bath /ˋbɝdˌbæθ; ˈbɜːdbɑːθ/ *n* a stone bowl filled with water for birds to wash in, usually in a garden〔通常在花園裡的〕鳥浴池

bird-brained /ˈ· ·/ *adj informal* stupid or thoughtless【非正式】愚蠢的; 欠考慮的

bird dog /ˈ· ·/ *n* [C] *AmE* a dog that is trained to find and bring back birds that have been shot for sport; GUN DOG【美】〔獵鳥時用的〕獵犬

bird·ie¹ /ˋbɝdɪ; ˈbɜːdi/ *n* [C] **1** *spoken* a word meaning a little bird, used especially by or to children【口】小鳥兒〔兒語〕**2** one STROKE¹ (10) less than PAR (=the usual number of strokes) in a game of GOLF〔高爾夫球中〕比標準桿數少一擊入洞, 小鳥球 **3** *AmE* the small object that you hit across the net in a game of BADMINTON【美】羽毛球; SHUTTLECOCK *BrE*【英】**4 watch the birdie** *old-fashioned* used to tell people that you are going to take a photograph of them【過時】看鏡頭〔準備按快門時說的一句話〕

birdie² *v* [T] to hit the ball into the hole in GOLF with one STROKE¹ (10) less than PAR (=the usual number of strokes)〔高爾夫球中〕以比標準桿數少一擊的成績打入(洞)

bird·lime /ˋbɝdˌlaɪm; ˈbɜːdlaɪm/ *n* [U] a sticky substance spread on branches to catch small birds〔塗在樹枝上捕小鳥用的〕黏鳥膠

bird of par·a·dise /ˌ· · ˈ···/ *n* [C] a brightly coloured bird from New Guinea 天堂鳥, 極樂鳥〔產自新幾內亞的一種色彩鮮豔的鳥〕

bird of pas·sage /ˌ· · ˈ··/ *n* [C] **1** a bird that flies from one area or country to another, according to the seasons 候鳥 **2** *literary* someone who never stays in the same place for long【文】漂泊不定的人

bird of prey /ˌ· · ˈ·/ *n* [C] a bird that kills other birds or small animals for food 猛禽: *The peregrine falcon, a rare bird of prey, is a protected species.* 稀有猛禽游隼是受保護物種。

bird·seed /ˋbɝdˌsid; ˈbɜːdsiːd/ *n* [U] a mixture of seeds for feeding birds〔餵鳥的〕鳥食

bird's-eye view /ˌ· · ˈ·/ *n* [singular] **1** a view of something from high above it 鳥瞰(圖),〔自高處俯視的〕全景: *From the plane we had an amazing bird's-eye view of the town.* 從飛機上, 我們看到一幅美妙的全城鳥瞰圖。**2** a general report or account of something, without many details 概述, 概要

bird·song /ˋbɝdˌsɔŋ; ˈbɜːdsɒŋ/ *n* [U] the musical noises made by birds 悅耳的鳥鳴: *Birdsong and the hum of insects filled the air.* 空中充滿了鳥囀和蟲鳴。

bird ta·ble /ˈ· ˌ··/ *n* [C] *BrE* a high wooden structure in a garden that you put seeds, bread etc on for birds to eat【英】鳥食台〔用來放置鳥食〕

bird-watch·er /ˈ· ˌ··/ *n* [C] someone who watches wild birds and tries to recognize different types 野鳥觀察者; 野鳥生態研究者 —**birdwatching** *n* [U]

bi·ret·ta /bəˋrɛtə; bȷ̍ˈretə/ *n* [C] a square cap worn by Roman Catholic priests〔天主教神職人員戴的〕法冠, 四角帽

bir·i·a·ni, biryani /ˌbɪrɪˋɑnɪ; ˌbɪriˈɑːni/ *n* [C,U] an Indian rice dish with meat, fish, or vegetables and spices (SPICE¹ (1))〔與肉、魚、蔬菜及香料一起烹製的〕印度燴飯

bi·ro /ˋbaɪro; ˈbaɪərəʊ/ *n* [C] *BrE trademark* a pen with a small ball at the end that rolls ink onto paper; BALLPOINT【英, 商標】"拜樂"牌圓珠筆, 原子筆: *Have you got a red biro?* 你有紅色的圓珠筆嗎? —see picture at 參見 PEN¹ 圖

birth /bɝθ; bɜːθ/ *n* **1 give birth (to)** if a woman gives birth, she produces a baby from her body 生育, 生孩子: *She gave birth to a fine healthy girl.* 她生了一個健康漂亮的女孩。**2** [C,U] the time when a baby comes out of its mother's body 出生; 分娩: *Congratulations on the birth of your daughter!* 恭喜你生了個女兒! | *Were you present at the birth?* 分娩時你在場嗎? | **at birth** *He only weighed three pounds at birth.* 他生下來時只有三磅重。**3** [U] the character, language, social position etc that you have because of the family or country you come from 出身; 血統; 家世, 家系: *of noble birth* 出身高貴 | *She is French by birth.* 她的父母是法國人。**4** [singular] the time when something new starts to exist〔新事物〕誕生, 出現: *the birth of an idea* 一個想法的萌生 | *the birth of a nation* 一個國家的誕生 **5 the town/country etc of your birth** the town, country etc where you were born 出生地/國等 S2 W2

birth cer·tif·i·cate /ˈ· ·ˌ···/ *n* [C] an official document that shows when and where you were born 出生證明書

birth con·trol /ˈ· ·ˌ·/ *n* [C] the practice of controlling, by various methods, the number of children you have; CONTRACEPTION 節育; 避孕: *a safe method of birth control* 安全的避孕方法

birth·day /ˋbɝθˌde; ˈbɜːθdeɪ/ *n* [C] **1** a day that is an exact number of years after the day when you were born 生日, 誕辰: *a birthday present* 生日禮物 | *It's my 21st birthday next week.* 下星期該到我的21歲生日了。| S2 W3

happy birthday! *spoken* (=what you say on someone's birthday)【口】生日快樂! **2 in your birthday suit** *humorous* not wearing any clothes【幽默】光着身子; 赤條條的; 一絲不掛的

birth·mark /ˋbɝθˏmɑrk; ˈbɜːθmɑːk/ *n* [C] a permanent red or brown mark on your skin that you have had since you were born 胎記, 胎痣: *Paul had a birthmark on his left cheek.* 保羅左臉頰上有塊胎痣。

birth·place /ˋbɝθˏples; ˈbɜːθpleɪs/ *n* [C usually singular 一般用單數] **1** the place where someone was born, especially someone famous〔尤指名人的〕出生地: *Stratford-upon-Avon was Shakespeare's birthplace.* 埃文河畔的斯特拉特福德是莎士比亞的出生地。**2** the place where something first started to happen or exist 發源地, 發祥地: *New Orleans is the birthplace of jazz.* 新奧爾良是爵士樂的發源地。

birth·rate /ˋbɝθˏret; ˈbɜːθreɪt/ *n* [C] the number of births for every 100 or every 1000 people in a particular year in a particular place 出生率: *a rapidly rising birthrate* 迅速上升的出生率 —compare 比較 DEATH RATE

birth·right /ˋbɝθˏraɪt; ˈbɜːθraɪt/ *n* [C usually singular 一般用單數] **1** a basic right that you believe you should have because of the family or country you come from 與生俱來的權利: *Freedom of speech is every American's birthright.* 言論自由是每個美國人與生俱來的權利。**2** property, money etc that you believe you should have because it comes from your family 本該繼承的(來自家族的)財產: *Charles felt cheated out of his birthright.* 查爾斯覺得本該由他來繼承的財產被人騙走了。

bir·y·a·ni /ˏbɪrɪˋɑnɪ; ˌbɪriˈɑːni/ *n* [C,U] another spelling of BIRIANI biriani 的另一種拼法

3 **bis·cuit** /ˋbɪskɪt; ˈbɪskɪ̣t/ *n* **1** [C] *BrE* a thin, flat, dry, usually sweet cake that is usually sold in packages or tins【英】餅乾: *chocolate biscuits* 巧克力餅乾 | *cheese and biscuits* 餅乾上塗乾酪 —compare 比較 COOKIE (1) **2** [C] *AmE* a type of bread baked in small round pieces【美】烤餅 **3** [U] a light yellowish-brown colour 淡褐色 **4 take the biscuit** *BrE informal* to be the most surprising, annoying etc thing you have ever heard【英, 非正式】所聽到過的最令人驚訝[討厭等]的事: *His latest excuse really takes the biscuit!* 他最近這個藉口真是令人驚訝!

bi·sect /baɪˋsɛkt; baɪˈsekt/ *v* [T] *technical* to divide something, especially a line or angle, into two equal parts【術語】把…一分為二; 把…二等分 —**bisection** /baɪˋsɛkʃən; baɪˈsekʃən/ *n* [U]

bi·sex·u·al¹ /baɪˋsɛkʃuəl; baɪˈsekʃuəl/ *adj* **1** sexually attracted to both men and women 對男女兩性都有性慾的 —compare 比較 HETEROSEXUAL, HOMOSEXUAL **2** having qualities or features of both sexes 具有雌雄兩性特徵的, 雌雄同體的, 兩性的: *a bisexual plant* 雌雄同株的植物 —**bisexually** *adv* —**bisexuality** /baɪˏsɛkʃuˋælətɪ; ˌbaɪsekʃuˈælɪ̣ti/ *n* [U]

bisexual² *n* [C] someone who is sexually attracted to both men and women 對男女兩性都有性慾的人, 雙性戀者: *a club for bisexuals* 雙性戀者俱樂部

3 **bish·op** /ˋbɪʃəp; ˈbɪʃəp/ *n* [C] **1** a priest with a high rank in the Christian religion, who is the head of all the churches and priests in a large area〔基督教某些教派管轄大教區的〕主教: *the Bishop of Durham* 達勒姆郡的主教 **2** a piece in the game of CHESS that can be moved any number of squares from one corner towards the opposite corner〔國際象棋的〕象

bish·op·ric /ˋbɪʃəprɪk; ˈbɪʃəprɪk/ *n* [C] **1** the area that a bishop is in charge of; DIOCESE 主教管轄的教區 **2** the position of being a bishop 主教之職位

bis·muth /ˋbɪzməθ; ˈbɪzməθ/ *n* [U] a grey-white metal that is often used in medicine〔金屬元素〕鉍

bi·son /ˋbaɪsn̩; ˈbaɪsən/ *n plural* **bison** *or* **bisons** [C] an animal like a large cow with long hair, which used to be common in North America; BUFFALO (2) 犎牛〔昔日常見於北美的一種野牛, 肩部長滿鬃毛〕: *ancient cave paintings of bison at Lascaux* 拉斯考克斯的古代犎牛洞穴壁畫

bisque /bɪsk; bɪsk/ *n* [U] a thick, creamy soup, especially one made from SHELLFISH〔尤指貝類煮成的〕奶油濃湯: *lobster bisque* 龍蝦奶油濃湯

bis·tro /ˋbistro; ˈbiːstrəʊ/ *n* [C] a small restaurant or bar 小酒吧; 小餐館

bit¹ /bɪt; bɪt/ *n* [C] 1 1

1 ▶SLIGHTLY/FAIRLY 略微/相當◀ **a bit** *informal, especially BrE*【非正式, 尤英】**a)** slightly, but not very; a little 有點兒; 稍微: *Could you turn the radio down a bit, please?* 請把收音機的音量稍微調低一點兒好嗎? | *Stay a bit longer – it's still early.* 再待一會兒吧, 還早着呢。| *I think you're a bit young to be watching this.* 我想你年紀還小, 不適合看這個。| **a bit more/less** *Would you like a bit more cake?* 要再來點兒蛋糕嗎? | **a bit like** (=a little similar) 有點兒像 *She's a bit like my sister.* 她有點兒像我妹妹。**b)** used when you mean 'very' or 'quite a lot', but you do not want to emphasize it too much 相當〔用於不想過分強調時〕: *It's all a bit depressing, really.* 這真的很令人沮喪。—see graph at 參見 LITTLE 圖表

2 ▶AMOUNT 量◀ *informal, especially BrE* a small amount, especially of something that is not a physical object【非正式, 尤英】一點兒; 一些: **[+of]** *Let me give you a bit of advice.* 讓我給你一些建議。| *We may need a bit of help.* 我們也許需要一些幫助。| *He still likes to do a bit of gardening.* 他仍然喜歡幹些園藝活。

3 ▶PIECE 件, 片◀ a small piece of something 一小塊; 一小片: **[+of]** *The floor was covered with bits of broken glass.* 地板上全是碎玻璃。| **break/smash/blow sth to bits** *The bridge was blown to bits by the blast.* 那座橋被炸得粉碎。| **fall to bits** *That old table's falling to bits.* 那張舊桌子已經散架了。

4 ▶PART 部分◀ *informal especially BrE* a part or piece of something larger【非正式, 尤英】部分; 片段; 小塊: *You can play on the grass, but keep off the muddy bits.* 你可以在草地上玩, 但要遠離泥窪。| **[+of]** *I liked the last bit of the film best.* 我最喜歡這部電影的結尾部分。

5 a good bit/quite a bit *especially BrE* a fairly large amount, or to a fairly large degree【尤英】不少; 頗多: *She knows quite a bit about European history.* 她懂得不少歐洲歷史方面的知識。| *She's quite a bit older than me.* 她比我大很多。

6 not a bit *especially BrE* not at all【尤英】一點兒都不: *You're not a bit like your brother, are you?* 你一點兒也不像你弟弟, 對吧? | *I wasn't a bit worried.* 我一點也不擔心。

7 every bit as just as much as 完全一樣; 同樣是: *I think she's every bit as pretty as her sister.* 我認為她和她妹妹長得一樣漂亮。

8 bit by bit *especially BrE* gradually【尤英】逐漸地, 一點一點地: *It's a slow process, but we're getting there bit by bit.* 這是個緩慢的過程, 但我們正逐步向目標邁進。

9 a bit at a time *especially BrE* in several small parts, not all at the same time【尤英】一次一點兒: *Just do a bit at a time.* 一次就幹一點兒。

10 ▶TOOL 工具◀ the sharp part of a tool for cutting or making holes〔工具的〕刀頭; 鑽頭: *a drill bit* 鑽頭

11 ▶FOR A HORSE 給馬用的◀ a metal bar that is put in the mouth of a horse and used for controlling its movements 馬嚼子, 馬銜 —see picture at 參見 HORSE¹ 圖

12 ▶COMPUTER 電腦◀ the smallest unit of information that can be used by a computer 位, 比特, 位元〔電腦使用的最小信息單位〕: *a 16-bit processor* 16 位處理器 —compare 比較 BYTE

13 a bit part a very small and unimportant acting job in a play or film 小角色, 配角: *He got a bit part in 'Coronation Street'.* 他在《加冕街》中扮演一個小角色。

14 bits and pieces/bits and bobs *BrE informal* any small things of various kinds【英, 非正式】各種零碎的小東西: *Let me get my bits and pieces together.* 讓我把自己的零星雜物收拾好。| *I still had a few bits and bobs of work left to do.* 我還有一些零碎的工作要做。

15 do your bit *BrE informal* to do your share of the work that needs to be done【英, 非正式】盡自己的本分: *I don't mind doing my bit, but I'm not organizing the whole thing on my own.* 我並不介意盡自己的本分, 但整件事情都由我一個人來組織我不幹。
16 get the bit between your teeth *BrE* to start doing something in a very determined way, so that you are not likely to stop until it is done【英】執意; 下定決心: *Once she'd got the bit between her teeth, there was no stopping her.* 她一旦下定決心要做某事, 甚麼也阻擋不了她。
17 take the bit between your teeth *AmE* to make a determined effort to deal with something difficult or unpleasant【美】下定決心處理棘手的事情; 全力以赴: *I just have to take the bit between my teeth and start writing that essay.* 我得狠下決心, 開始寫那篇文章。
18 ►US MONEY 美元◄ a) *AmE old use* 12½ cents【美舊】12.5 美分: *I wouldn't give you two bits for that old book.* 我不會花二十五美分買你的那本舊書。—see also 另見 **two bits** (TWO (7)) **b)** *BrE old use* a small coin【英舊】小硬幣: *a three-penny bit* 一枚三便士的硬幣
19 ►YOUNG WOMAN 年輕女子◄ also 又作 **a bit of stuff/fluff/skirt** *spoken* offensive expressions meaning a young woman, especially one who is sexually attractive【口】〔尤指性感的〕年輕女子, 小妞〔冒犯說法〕
20 a bit of all right *BrE informal* used to describe someone you think is sexually attractive【英, 非正式】風騷: *She's a bit of all right.* 她很風騷。
21 a bit on the side *BrE informal often humorous* the girlfriend or boyfriend of someone who is already married or involved in a sexual relationship with someone else【英, 非正式, 常幽默】情婦; 情夫 —see also 另見 **be champing at the bit** (CHAMP[1] (2)), **a bit of rough** (ROUGH[1] (17))

Frequencies of the noun **bit** in spoken and written English 名詞bit在英語口語和書面語中的使用頻率

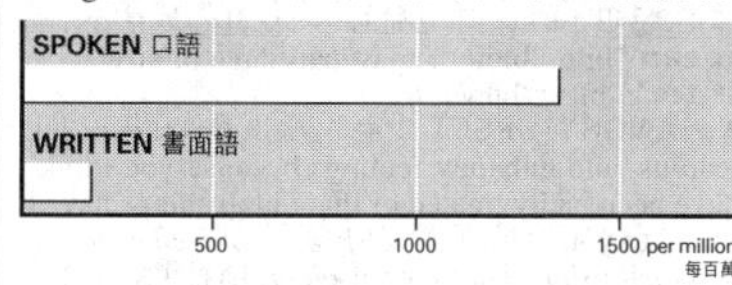

Based on the British National Corpus and the Longman Lancaster Corpus
據英國國家語料庫和朗文蘭卡斯特語料庫

This graph shows that the noun **bit** is much more common in spoken English than in written English. This is because **a bit** is more common than **a little** in spoken English, and **bit** is used in a lot of common spoken phrases. 本圖表顯示, 名詞bit在英語口語中的使用頻率遠遠高於書面語, 因為a bit在口語中比a little常用, 而且口語中很多常用片語是由 bit 構成的。

bit (*n*) SPOKEN PHRASES
含 bit 的口語片語

22 a bit of a problem/surprise/fool etc *BrE* a problem, surprise etc, but not a very big or serious one【英】有點問題/吃驚/愚蠢等: *The party was a bit of a disappointment in the end.* 聚會最後變得有點兒令人失望。| *I had a bit of a shock when I got home.* 我回到家時感到有點兒震驚。| *I'm afraid I'm in a bit of a hurry just now – I'll give you a ring later.* 恐怕我現在有點急事 —— 我過一會兒再給你打電話。
23 with a bit of luck *especially BrE* if things go well and there are no problems【尤英】進展順利的話: *With a bit of luck we should get it finished tomorrow.* 進展順利的話, 我們明天就能做完。
24 take a bit of doing/fixing etc *BrE* to be difficult to do, fix etc【英】難做/難修理等: *This new system takes a bit of getting used to, doesn't it?* 新體制還一時難以適應, 對吧?
25 play the piano a bit/speak French a bit etc *BrE* to be able to play the piano, speak French etc, but not particularly well or often【英】會彈一點兒鋼琴/會說一點兒法語等: *I used to act a bit when I was younger.* 我年輕的時候演過一點戲。
26 for a bit/in a bit *BrE* for or after a short period of time【英】一會兒/過一會兒: *Could you mind the baby for a bit?* 你能照顧嬰兒一會兒嗎? | *I'll see you in a bit then.* 那我們過一會兒見。
27 a bit much *BrE* used to say that something is not fair or reasonable【英】有點兒過分; 不公平; 不合理: *I thought it was a bit much, asking me to drive him all the way home.* 我認為他要我開車把他一路送到家是有點兒過分。
28 not a bit of it *especially BrE* used to say that something did not happen, even though you expected that it would【尤英】根本就沒有〔做某事〕: *He should at least have apologized, but not a bit of it.* 他最起碼也應該道個歉, 但他卻毫無表示。
29 the student bit/travelling bit etc the behaviour or experience that is typical of a student, of travelling etc 典型的學生所為/典型的旅遊經歷等: *Then she gave us the concerned mother bit.* 那時候她給了我們母愛般的關懷。| *He's really gone in for the whole hippy bit.* 其實, 他整個就是嬉皮士。

bit[2] the past tense of BITE[1]
bitch[1] /bɪtʃ; bɪtʃ/ *n* [C] **1** a female dog 母狗 **2** *informal* an insulting word for a woman that you dislike or think is unpleasant【非正式】潑婦, 狗婆娘, 婊子: *She's such a bitch.* 她這個潑婦。| *The silly bitch went and told the police.* 那個蠢婆娘去報告了警察。**3** *AmE spoken* something that causes problems or difficulties【美口】討厭的事: *I love that silk dress, but it's a bitch to wash.* 我很喜歡那條綢裙子, 就是洗起來太麻煩了。—see also 另見 SON OF A BITCH
bitch[2] *v* [I] *informal*【非正式】**1** to make unpleasant remarks about someone or something 說壞話: [+about] *We were all bitching about the boss when she walked in.* 老闆走進來的時候, 我們正在說她的壞話。**2** to complain continuously 沒完沒了地發牢騷, 埋怨: *Stop bitching!* 別再沒完沒了地發牢騷! | [+at] *AmE*【美】*He kept bitching at me for waking him up.* 他不停地埋怨我把他吵醒了。
bitch·in /ˈbɪtʃən; ˈbɪtʃən/ *adj AmE slang* very good; excellent【美俚】極好的, 極棒的: *That's a bitchin car!* 那輛車真棒! | *"We're going to the beach, wanna come?" "Bitchin! Let's go!"* "我們要去海灘, 你去嗎?" "好極了! 我們走吧!"
bitch·y /ˈbɪtʃɪ; ˈbɪtʃi/ *adj informal* unkind and unpleasant about other people【非正式】惡意的, 壞心眼兒的: *a bitchy remark* 刻薄的話 | *She can be really bitchy sometimes.* 她有時候很惡毒。—**bitchily** *adv* —**bitchiness** *n* [U]
bite[1] /baɪt; baɪt/ *v past tense* **bit** /bɪt; bɪt/ *past participle* **bitten** /ˈbɪtn; ˈbɪtn/ 2

bite 咬

1 ►WITH YOUR TEETH 用牙◄ [I,T] to cut or crush something with your teeth 咬: *Be careful! My dog bites.* 當心! 我的狗咬人。| *Do you bite your fingernails?* 你咬指甲嗎? | **[+into/through]** *biting into a juicy apple* 咬一口多汁的蘋果 | *They had to bite through the rope to escape.* 他們得把繩子咬斷才能逃脫。| **bite sth off** *a man whose arm had been bitten off by an alligator* 被鱷魚咬

掉一隻胳膊的男子
2 ►INSECT/SNAKE 蟲/蛇◄[I,T] if an insect or snake bites you, it injures you by making a hole in your skin 〔昆蟲〕叮, 螫; 〔蛇〕咬傷: *I was bitten all over by mosquitoes.* 我渾身都被蚊子叮了。
3 ►FISH 魚◄[I] if a fish bites, it takes food from a hook and so gets caught 吞餌, 上鈎
4 ►NOT SLIP 不滑◄[I] to hold firmly to a surface, or rest firmly against it; GRIP² (1) 抓緊; 卡緊; 咬住: [+into] *The ski's edge should bite into the snow.* 滑雪板的邊兒應該卡進雪裡。
5 ►HAVE AN EFFECT 有效◄[I] to have the effect that was intended, especially an unpleasant one 達到預期的(壞) 效果: *The new tobacco taxes have begun to bite.* 新的煙草稅已開始叫人吃不消。
6 bite your tongue to try hard to stop yourself from saying what you really think 強忍住不說: *She was really making me angry, but I bit my tongue.* 她真的讓我生氣, 但我忍着不作聲。
7 bite the dust a) to die, fail, or be defeated 死亡; 失敗; 被擊敗: *a welfare programme that bit the dust following budget cuts* 削減預算後告吹的福利計劃 **b)** to stop working completely 完全不好用; 報廢: *My old car's finally bitten the dust.* 我的老轎車終於報廢了。
8 bite the bullet *informal* to bravely accept something unpleasant【非正式】咬緊牙關忍受痛苦, 勇敢地面對: *Decisions have to be taken, and as director you have to bite the bullet.* 必須作出決定, 而你作為主任, 必須勇敢地面對現實。
9 bite sb's head off *informal* to answer someone or speak to them very angrily, when there is no good reason for doing this【非正式】發火; 蠻橫粗暴地說話[回答]: *I asked if she needed any help, and she bit my head off!* 我問她是否需要幫忙, 她卻對我很兇!
10 bite off more than you can chew to try to do more than you are able to do 試圖承擔力所不及的事
11 he/she won't bite *spoken* used to say that there is no need to be afraid of someone, especially someone in authority【口】不必怕他/她〔尤指權威人士〕: *Well go and ask him – he won't bite!* 去問問他 —— 不用怕他!
12 what's biting you/her etc? *spoken* used to ask why someone is annoyed or upset【口】甚麼事煩擾着你/她等? 愁甚麼呢?
13 once bitten twice shy used to say that if you have failed or been hurt once, you will be very careful next time 一次吃虧, 二次小心; 一朝被蛇咬, 十年怕井繩
14 bite the hand that feeds you to harm someone who has treated you well or supported you 恩將仇報; 以怨報德
15 be bitten by the bug/craze etc to develop a very strong interest in or desire for something 熱衷於, 迷上: *By then she had been bitten by the travel bug, and could not wait to go again.* 那時候她迷上了旅遊, 巴不得馬上再去一趟。

bite back *phr v* **1** [T **bite** sth ↔ **back**] to stop yourself from saying something or telling someone what you really feel 強忍着不說出來: *She bit back the insult that rose to her lips.* 她強忍着把到嘴邊的難聽話又嚥了回去。 **2** [I] to react strongly and angrily when someone criticizes you 回嘴; 反唇相譏: *Determined to bite back at car thieves, he wired his Sierra Cosworth to an electric fence.* 他決心要對竊車賊進行反擊, 於是把他那輛謝拉科斯沃思汽車用金屬線接到電圍欄上。

bite into sth *phr v* [T] to cut or press hard against a surface 咬進; 陷進; 砍入: *The knotted cord bit into my skin.* 那條打結的繩索勒進了我的皮膚。

3 **bite²** *n*
1 ►WITH YOUR TEETH 用牙◄[C] the act of cutting or crushing something with your teeth 咬(的動作): **give sb a bite** *The cat gave Mike a playful bite.* 貓頑皮地咬了邁克一口。| **have/take a bite of** (=bite a small piece from a larger piece of food) 咬一口 *Can I have a bite of your apple?* 我咬一口你的蘋果行嗎?
2 ►WOUND 傷◄[C] a wound made when an animal or insect bites you 被咬[叮, 螫]的傷口: *My face was covered in mosquito bites!* 蚊子叮得我滿臉是傷!
3 a bite (to eat) *spoken* a small meal【口】量少的一餐: *I haven't had a bite to eat all day.* 我從早到晚連一口東西都沒有吃。| *Let's grab a bite at the airport.* 我們在機場吃點東西吧。
4 ►COLD 冷◄[singular] a feeling of coldness 冷意, 寒意: *There's a real bite in the air tonight.* 今晚空氣中真的帶着一絲寒意。
5 ►TASTE 味道◄[U] a pleasantly sharp or bitter taste 辛辣; 苦澀: *I like cheese with a bit of bite.* 我喜歡吃帶點辣味的乾酪。
6 ►EFFECTIVENESS 效果◄[U] a special quality in a piece of speech or writing that makes its arguments or criticisms effective and likely to persuade people 〔演說或文章的〕犀利; 有說服力: *a political satire that lacked bite* 語言並不尖刻的政治諷刺作品
7 ►FISH 魚◄[C] an occasion when a fish takes the food from a hook 吞餌; 上鈎: *Sometimes I sit for hours and never get a bite.* 有時我坐上幾個鐘頭也沒有一條魚上鈎。
8 bite-size/bite-sized the right size to fit into your mouth easily 很小的, 一口大小的: *Cut them into bite-size pieces before serving.* 先切成小塊再端上桌。
9 another bite/a second bite at the cherry *BrE* a second chance to do something【英】第二次機會

bit·ing /ˈbaɪtɪŋ; ˈbaɪtɪŋ/ *adj* **1** a biting wind is unpleasantly cold 刺骨的: *A biting wind blew down from the hills.* 從山上吹來刺骨的寒風。**2** a biting criticism, remark is cruel or unkind 尖刻的: *biting sarcasm* 尖刻的諷刺 —**bitingly** *adv*

bit·map /ˈbɪtˌmæp; ˈbɪtmæp/ *n* [C] *technical* a computer image consisting of an arrangement of bits (BIT¹ (12))【術語】〔電腦〕位映像, 位圖: *bitmap fonts* 位圖字體

bit·sy /ˈbɪtsɪ; ˈbɪtsi/ *adj AmE informal* very small【美, 非正式】很小的, 一丁點兒的 —see also 另見 ITSY-BITSY

bit·ten /ˈbɪtn; ˈbɪtn/ the past participle of BITE¹

bit·ter¹ /ˈbɪtə; ˈbɪtə/ *adj*
1 ►ANGRY/UPSET 生氣的/心煩的◄ full of angry, jealous, and unhappy feelings because you think you have been badly treated or that unfair things have happened to you 氣憤的; 妒忌的; 鬱悶的: *He became bitter and disillusioned as he grew older.* 隨着年齡的增長, 他變得越來越憤憤不平, 不再抱任何幻想。| [+about] *They all lost their jobs when the company was taken over, and obviously they're very bitter about it.* 公司被接管後, 他們都失業了, 顯然他們對此憤憤不平。
2 ►CAUSING UNHAPPINESS 造成不快◄[only before noun 僅用於名詞前] making you feel very unhappy and upset 痛苦的, 心酸的, 慘痛的; 難以接受的: *Losing the election was a bitter humiliation.* 選舉失利是個奇恥大辱。| **a bitter disappointment/blow** *If he failed, it would be a bitter disappointment to his parents.* 如果他失敗了, 他的父母將會大失所望。| **from bitter experience** (=because of your own very unpleasant experiences) 有過慘痛的教訓 *We had learned from bitter experience not to trust their promises.* 我們有過慘痛的教訓, 不再相信他們的承諾。
3 ►FULL OF HATRED 充滿仇恨◄ a bitter argument, attack, struggle etc is one in which people oppose or criticize each other with strong feelings of hate and anger 激烈的; 諷刺的; 充滿敵意的; 怨憤的: *bitter opposition to the President's policies* 對總統的政策的激烈反對 | *bitter enemies* 死敵, 不共戴天之敵
4 ►TASTE 味道◄ having a strong taste like black coffee without sugar, or very dark chocolate 苦的, 有苦味的: *The medicine tasted bitter and the child spat it out.* 這藥太苦, 孩子把它吐了出來。—compare 比較 SWEET¹ (1), SOUR¹ (1)
5 ►COLD 冷◄ unpleasantly cold 刺骨的, 寒冷的: *a bitter*

east wind 寒冷的東風 | **bitter cold** *a bitter cold day in February* 二月裡寒冷徹骨的一天 —see 見 COLD[1] (USAGE)

6 to the bitter end continuing until the end, in spite of problems or difficulties 堅持到底; 拼到底: *She stayed with him to the bitter end, although it must have been horrible.* 她和他始終待在一起, 儘管這樣做肯定很不好受。

7 a bitter pill (to swallow) something very unpleasant that you have to accept 不得不接受的現實; 不得不忍受的恥辱: *His failure was a bitter pill to swallow.* 他的失敗是個難以吞嚥的苦果。—see also 另見 BITTERLY —**bitterness** *n* [U]

bitter[2] *n* **1** [C,U] *BrE* bitter beer of the type drunk in Britain, or a glass of this【英】〔一杯〕苦啤酒: *A pint of bitter, please.* 請來一品脫苦啤酒。—compare 比較 MILD **2 bitters** [U] a bitter liquid made from a mixture of plant products and used to add taste to alcoholic drinks 〔攙入酒精飲料中的〕苦味配劑

bit·ter·ly /ˋbɪtɚlɪ; ˈbɪtəli/ *adv* **1** in a way that makes you very unhappy, or shows that you are very unhappy 痛苦地; 憤恨地: *The boys complained bitterly about their chores.* 男孩們憤憤不平地抱怨要做家務。| *I was bitterly disappointed.* 我非常失望。| *a decision that she bitterly regretted* 一個令她痛悔不已的決定 **2 bitterly cold** very cold 極其寒冷的

bit·tern /ˋbɪtɚn; ˈbɪtən/ *n* [C] a brown European bird with long legs that lives near water and makes a deep sound 麻鳽〔產於歐洲的褐色長腿水鳥〕

bit·ter·sweet /ˌbɪtɚˋswit; ˌbɪtəˈswiːt◂/ *adj* **1** feelings, memories, or experiences that are bittersweet are happy and sad at the same time 苦樂參半的: *bittersweet memories of childhood* 對童年時代甜蜜而又辛酸的回憶 **2** a taste or smell that is bittersweet is both sweet and bitter at the same time 甜中帶苦的

bit·ty /ˋbɪtɪ; ˈbɪti/ *adj BrE informal* having too many small parts that do not seem to be connected to each other【英, 非正式】零碎的, 東拼西湊的, 不連貫的: *I thought the film was rather bitty.* 我認為那部影片有點兒七拼八湊。—**bittiness** *n* [U]

bi·tu·men /bəˋtumən; ˈbɪtʃʊmɪ̮n/ *n* [U] a sticky substance made from petrol products that is used for making the surface of roads 瀝青, 柏油 —**bituminous** /bɪˋtjumənəs; bɪ̮ˈtjuːmɪ̮nəs/ *adj*

bi·valve /ˋbaɪˌvælv; ˈbaɪvælv/ *n* [C] *technical* any sea animal that has two shells joined together, such as an OYSTER【術語】雙殼貝類〈如牡蠣〉

biv·ou·ac[1] /ˋbɪvʊˌæk; ˈbɪvu-æk/ *n* a temporary camp built outside without any tents〔無帳篷的〕露營(地), 野營(地)

bivouac[2] *v* **bivouacked, bivouacking** [I] to spend the night outside without tents in a temporary camp 露宿: *The climbers bivouacked halfway up the mountain.* 登山者在半山腰上露營過夜。

bi·week·ly /baɪˋwiklɪ; baɪˈwiːkli/ *adj, adv* **1** appearing or happening every two weeks; FORTNIGHTLY 兩週一次的[地]: *a biweekly magazine* 雙週刊 **2** appearing or happening twice a week; SEMIWEEKLY 一週兩次的[地]: *a biweekly television drama* 一週兩次的電視劇

biz /bɪz; bɪz/ *n* [singular] *informal* a particular type of business, especially one connected with entertainment【非正式】〔尤指與娛樂業有關的〕商業; 生意

bi·zarre /bɪˋzɑr; bɪ̮ˈzɑː/ *adj* very unusual or strange 古怪的; 奇異的: *a bizarre coincidence* 奇異的巧合 | *bizarre religious sects* 奇特的宗教派別 —**bizarrely** *adv*

blab /blæb; blæb/ *v* [I] *informal* to tell secret information to someone who is not supposed to know it【非正式】泄露祕密: [+to] *What if they blab to the newspapers?* 如果他們把消息透露給報社該怎麼辦?

blab·ber /ˋblæbɚ; ˈblæbə/ *v* [I] *informal* to talk in a silly or annoying way, especially for a long time【非正式】瞎說, 胡扯; 喋喋不休: [+on] *I wish she'd stop blabbering on about her boyfriends.* 我真希望她別再沒完沒了地講她那些男朋友的事。

blab·ber·mouth /ˋblæbɚˌmaʊθ; ˈblæbəmaʊθ/ *n* [C] *informal* someone who tells secrets because they always talk too much【非正式】饒舌者; 嘴巴不嚴的人; 泄漏祕密者

black[1] /blæk; blæk/ *adj* S1 W1

1 ►COLOUR 顏色◄ having the colour of night or coal 黑色的, 黑的: *a black evening dress* 黑色的晚禮服 | *The mountains looked black against the moon.* 在月光的襯托下, 羣山看上去黑乎乎的。| *She has short black hair.* 她留着黑色的短髮。—see picture on page A5 參見 A5 頁圖

2 ►PEOPLE 人◄ a) someone who is black is a member of a dark-skinned race, especially the Negro race 黑人血統的, 黑種的: *Over half the students here are black.* 這裡的學生中超過一半是黑人。**b)** [only before noun 僅用於名詞前] connected with or concerning black people 黑人的, 與黑人有關的: *politics from a black perspective* 黑人的政治見解 | *contemporary black music* 當代黑人音樂 —see 見 NEGRO (USAGE)

3 ►TEA/COFFEE 茶/咖啡◄ black coffee or tea does not have milk in it 不加奶的: *Two black coffees, please.* 來兩杯不加奶的咖啡。—opposite 反義詞 WHITE[1] (4)

4 ►DIRTY 髒的◄ very dirty 黑乎乎的, 髒的: *My hands were black from working on the car.* 我在修車, 手弄得很髒。

5 ►WITHOUT HOPE 沒有希望◄ sad and without much hope for the future; GLOOMY 無希望的; 情況不妙的; 前景暗淡的: *Things were beginning to look pretty black for us.* 看來情況開始對我們有些不妙。| *a feeling of black despair* 感到大失所望 | **a black day** (=when something very sad or upsetting happens) 極糟糕的一天, 極倒霉的一天 *It's been another black day for the motor industry, with announcements of major job losses.* 這天對汽車工業來說又是一個極為糟糕的日子, 許多工廠宣布大規模裁員。

6 ►ANGRY 生氣的◄ full of feelings of anger or hate 怒氣沖沖的; 充滿仇恨的: *I knew not to irritate him when he was in such a black mood.* 他正在氣頭上, 我知道不該去惹他。| *Denise gave me a black look.* 丹尼斯惡狠狠地瞪了我一眼。

7 not be as black as you are painted not be as bad as people say you are 並不像人們所說的那樣壞

8 ►EVIL 罪惡◄ *literary* very bad【文】非常壞的: *black deeds* 惡行 | *a blackhearted villain* 心腸狠毒的惡棍 —see also 另見 BLACKLY —**blackness** *n* [C]

black[2] *n* **1** [U] the dark colour of night or coal 黑色 **2** [U] black clothes 黑色的衣服: *You look good in black.* 你穿黑色衣服挺好看。**3** [C] someone who belongs to a dark-skinned race, especially the Negro race 黑人: *laws that discriminated against blacks* 歧視黑人的法律 —see 見 NEGRO (USAGE) **4 be in the black** to have money in your bank account〔銀行存款〕有盈餘, 有餘額 —opposite 反義詞 **be in the red** (RED[2] (5)) **5** [U] black paint, colour etc 黑色的染料[顏料等]: *Put some more black around your eyes.* 在你的眼圈上再塗些黑色眼影。

black[3] *v* [T] **1** *BrE* if a TRADE UNION blacks goods or blacks a company, it refuses to work with them【英】〔指工會〕抵制, 杯葛〔貨物、公司等〕**2** *old-fashioned* to make something black【過時】使變黑, 弄黑

black out *v* **1** [I] to lose consciousness; faint 失去知覺; 昏厥: *I completely blacked out after the accident.* 事故發生後, 我完全失去了知覺。**2** [T **black** sth ↔ **out**] to put a dark mark over something so that it cannot be seen 蓋住; 塗黑: *The censors had blacked out several words.* 審查員塗掉了幾個詞。**3** [T **black** sth ↔ **out**] to hide or turn off all the lights in a town or city, especially during war〔尤指戰時〕對〔城鎮或城市〕實行燈火管制 —see also 另見 BLACKOUT

black·a·moor /ˋblækəˌmʊr; ˈblækəmʊə/ *n* [C] *old use* an offensive word for a black person, especially a man

【舊】黑人〔冒犯用語, 尤指男子〕

black and blue /ˌ· · ˈ·◂/ *adj* skin that is black and blue has BRUISES (=dark marks) in it as a result of being hit〔皮膚被打得〕青一塊紫一塊的; 有瘀痕的: *Ron's been skiing. He's black and blue all over!* 羅恩滑雪去了, 渾身上下摔得青一塊紫一塊。

B

black and white /ˌ· · ˈ·◂/ *adj* **1** showing pictures or images only in black, white, and grey〔圖像或影片〕黑白的: *a black and white photo* 黑白照片 | *an old black and white TV* 一台舊的黑白電視機 **2** considering things in a very simple way, as if there are clear differences between good and bad, right and wrong etc 非黑即白的, 絕對化的: *a rather black and white presentation of the situtation* 對形勢用簡單的非好即壞的觀點進行的介紹 | **a black and white decision/issue/question** (=where the difference between two choices is completely clear) 絕對化[黑白分明]的決定/問題 **3 in black and white** in written form, and therefore definite 白紙黑字〔寫得清清楚楚〕; 以書面形式: *You'd better get a commitment in black and white first.* 你最好先得到一份書面形式的承諾。| *There it was in black and white – I'd passed the exam!* 白紙黑字寫着呢——我考試及格了!

black art /ˌ· ˈ·/ *n* [U] also 又作 **the black arts** [plural] BLACK MAGIC 巫術; 魔法

black·ball /ˋblækˏbɔl; ˈblækbɔːl/ *v* [T] to vote against someone, especially so that they cannot join a club or social group 投票反對〔某人〕參加某俱樂部[社會組織]; 排擠

black belt /ˌ· ˈ·/ *n* [C] **1** a high rank in some types of Eastern self-defence, especially JUDO and KARATE 黑腰帶級〔柔道、空手道等的最高等級〕 **2** someone who has this rank 黑腰帶級選手: *Sandy's a blackbelt in judo.* 桑迪是柔道黑腰帶級選手。

black·ber·ry /ˋblækˏbɛrɪ; ˈblækbəri/ *n* [C] the black or purple fruit of a type of BRAMBLE 黑莓 —see picture on page A8 參見A8頁圖

black·ber·ry·ing /ˋblækˏbɛrɪ·ɪŋ; ˈblækbəri-ɪŋ/ *n* [U] **go blackberrying** to go out picking blackberries 去採黑莓

black·bird /ˋblækˏbɝd; ˈblækbɜːd/ *n* [C] a common European and American bird, the male of which is completely black 黑唱鶇, 黑鸝〔產於歐洲及美洲, 其雄鳥遍體黑色〕

black·board /ˋblækˏbɔrd; ˈblækbɔːd/ *n* [C] a board with a dark smooth surface, used in schools for writing on with CHALK[1] (2) 黑板 —compare 比較 WHITEBOARD

black box /ˌ· ˈ·/ *n* [C] an electronic unit that controls or records information about a machine, especially on an aircraft; FLIGHT RECORDER〔尤指飛機的〕黑匣子, 飛行記錄器

black com·e·dy /ˌ· ˈ···/ *n* [C,U] a play, story etc that is funny, but also shows the unpleasant side of human life 黑色喜劇

black·cur·rant /ˌblækˋkɝənt; ˌblækˈkʌrənt◂/ *n* [C] **1** a European plant that grows in gardens and has small blueblack berries (BERRY) 黑醋栗, 黑加侖子 **2** a berry from this plant 黑醋栗豆, 黑加侖子果實: *blackcurrant juice* 黑加侖子汁 —compare 比較 REDCURRANT

Black Death /ˌ· ˈ·/ *n* [singular] the illness that killed large numbers of people in Europe and Asia in the 14th century 黑死病〔14世紀在歐亞蔓延的瘟疫〕—see also 另見 BUBONIC PLAGUE, PLAGUE[1] (2)

black e·con·o·my /ˌ· ˈ····/ *n* [singular] business activity that takes place unofficially, especially in order to avoid tax 地下經濟活動, 黑市經營〔指為逃避稅收而暗中進行的經濟活動〕—compare 比較 BLACK MARKET

black·en /ˋblækən; ˈblækən/ *v* **1** [I,T] to become black, or make something black (使)變黑; 把…弄黑: *Smoke had blackened the ceiling of the room.* 煙把房間的天花板熏黑了。**2 blacken sb's name/character/reputation etc** to say unpleasant things about someone in order to make other people have a bad opinion of them 玷污某人的名聲/品德/聲譽等

black En·glish /ˌ· ˈ··/ *n* [U] the variety of English spoken by some black people in the US 黑人英語〔某些美國黑人講的英語〕

black eye /ˌ· ˈ·/ *n* [C] darkness of the skin around your eye, because you have been hit〔被打成〕青黑色的眼眶: *Joe came home with a black eye.* 喬帶着青黑色的眼眶回家來。

black-eyed bean /ˌ· · ˈ·/ *BrE*【英】, **black-eyed pea** *AmE*【美】*n* [C] a small pale bean with a black spot on it 豇豆, 黑眼豆

black-eyed Su·san /ˌblæk aɪd ˋsuzn̩; ˌblæk aɪd ˈsuːzən/ *n* [C] a type of yellow or orange flower that grows in North America〔花朵中心呈黑色的〕金光菊

black gold /ˌ· ˈ·/ *n* [U] *informal* oil【非正式】石油

black goods /ˈ· ·/ *n* [plural] *BrE* pieces of equipment used in the house that are usually black, such as televisions or HI-FIS【英】黑色家用設備〈如電視、音響等〉—compare 比較 WHITE GOODS

black·guard /ˋblægɚd; ˈblægɑːd/ *n* [C] *old use* a man who treats other people very badly; SCOUNDREL【舊】惡棍, 流氓, 無賴

black·head /ˋblækˏhɛd; ˈblækhed/ *n* [C] a small spot on the skin, with a black centre 黑頭粉刺

black hole /ˌ· ˈ·/ *n* [C] **1** *technical* an area in outer space into which everything near it, including light, is pulled【術語】黑洞 **2** *informal* something that seems to keep using up all your money【非正式】無底洞〔指極耗費金錢的事物〕

black hu·mour /ˌ· ˈ··/ *n* [U] jokes, funny stories etc that deal with the unpleasant parts of human life 黑色幽默

black ice /ˌ· ˈ·/ *n* [U] an area of ice that is very difficult to see 黑冰: *dangerous driving conditions, with black ice in many areas* 遍地是黑冰的危險路面情況

black·ing /ˋblækɪŋ; ˈblækɪŋ/ *n* [U] *old-fashioned* a very thick liquid or polish that is put on objects to make them black【過時】黑色塗料

black·jack /ˋblækˏdʒæk; ˈblækdʒæk/ *n* [U] a card game 二十一點(牌戲)

black lead /ˌblæk ˋlɛd; ˌblæk ˈled/ *n* [U] a soft black substance; GRAPHITE 石墨, 炭精, 黑鉛

black·leg /ˋblækˏlɛg; ˈblækleg/ *n* [C] *BrE* someone who continues to work when other workers are on strike (STRIKE[2] (1))【英】罷工期間繼續上班的人; 拒不參加罷工者; 工賊

black·list[1] /ˋblækˏlɪst; ˈblækˌlɪst/ *n* [C] a list of people, countries, products etc that are disapproved of, and should therefore be avoided or punished 黑名單: *Friends of the Earth have produced a blacklist of environmentally damaging products.* 地球之友已經開列了一份破壞環境的產品的黑名單。

blacklist[2] *v* [T] to put a person, country, product etc on a blacklist 將…列入黑名單: *I've been blacklisted by the insurance companies just because of one silly accident!* 僅僅由於一次糊塗的事故, 保險公司已將我列入黑名單!

black lung /ˌ· ˈ·/ *n* [U] *AmE informal* a lung disease caused by breathing in coal dust over a long period of time【美, 非正式】黑肺病, 煤肺病〔因長期吸入煤塵而導致的肺病〕

black·ly /ˋblæklɪ; ˈblækli/ *adv literary* in an angry, threatening, or unpleasant way【文】陰險地; 氣沖沖地; 惡狠狠地: *clouds blackly looming* 陰雲密佈

black mag·ic /ˌ· ˈ··/ *n* [U] magic that is believed to use the power of the Devil for evil purposes 巫術; 魔法 —see also 另見 WHITE MAGIC

black·mail[1] /ˋblækˏmel; ˈblækmeɪl/ *v* [T] to demand money or favours from someone by threatening to tell secrets about them 敲詐; 勒索; 訛詐: **blackmail sb into doing sth** *Don't think you can blackmail me into helping you!* 不要以為你能要挾我來幫你! —**blackmailer** *n* [C]

blackmail² *n* [U] **1** the practice of getting money from someone or making them do what you want by threatening to tell secrets about them 敲詐; 勒索; 訛詐 **2** an attempt to make someone do what you want by making threats or by making them feel guilty if they do not 威逼; 恐嚇; 挾人就範: *Staff who refused to work on Sundays faced losing their jobs – it was sheer blackmail.* 拒絕星期天上班的員工都要面臨失業的危險 —— 這純粹是要挾。| **emotional blackmail** (=by making someone feel guilty) 用感情手段逼某人 *She had already tried emotional blackmail to stop him leaving.* 她已經嘗試了用感情手段阻止他離開。

black Ma·ri·a /ˌblæk məˈraɪə; ˌblæk məˈraɪə/ *n* [C] *BrE old-fashioned* a vehicle used by the police to move prisoners【英, 過時】囚車

black mar·ket /ˌ· ˈ··◂/ *n* [C] the system by which people illegally buy and sell foreign money, goods that are difficult to obtain etc 黑市(交易): [+in] *There's a thriving black market in vehicle parts.* 汽車零件的黑市交易很興隆。| **on the black market** *The exchange rate for dollars was much higher on the black market.* 黑市上美元的兑換率高得多。| *black market cigarettes* 黑市香煙 —compare 比較 BLACK ECONOMY

black mar·ket·eer /ˌ· ··ˈ·/ *n* [C] someone who sells things on the black market 黑市商人

Black Mus·lim /ˌ· ˈ··/ *n* [C] a member of a group of black people who believe in the religion of Islam and want a separate black society 黑人穆斯林〔指信奉伊斯蘭教, 並要建立獨立黑人社會的黑人組織成員〕

black·out /ˈblækˌaut; ˈblækaʊt/ *n* [C] **1** a period of darkness caused by a failure of the electricity supply 停電: *The storm caused a sudden blackout and brought down telephone lines.* 風暴導致突然間停電, 電話線也颳斷了。**2** a period during a war when all the lights in a town etc must be turned off〔戰時的〕燈火管制 **3** an occasion when you suddenly lose consciousness 突然間的知覺喪失: *You'll have to go to the doctor if you keep getting these blackouts.* 如果你經常突然間失去知覺, 就必須去看醫生。**4** a situation in which particular pieces of news or information are not allowed to be reported〔新聞〕封鎖, 刪除〔對報道等的〕: *A news blackout was imposed during the peace negotiations.* 在和談期間實施新聞封鎖。

black pep·per /ˌ· ˈ··/ *n* [U] pepper made from crushed seeds from which the dark outer covering has not been removed 黑胡椒(粉)

black pud·ding /ˌ· ˈ··/ *n* [C,U] *BrE* a kind of thick dark SAUSAGE made from animal blood and fat【英】血腸〔用動物的血和脂肪製成的粗黑香腸〕

black sheep /ˌ· ˈ·/ *n* [C usually singular 一般用單數] someone who is regarded by other members of their family or group as a failure or embarrassment 害羣之馬;〔集體中的〕敗類: *She's the black sheep of the family.* 她是個敗家子。

Black·shirt /ˈblækˌʃɝt; ˈblækʃɜːt/ *n* [C] a member of a FASCIST organization with a black shirt as part of its uniform〔法西斯組織〕黑衫黨黨員

black·smith /ˈblækˌsmɪθ; ˈblækˌsmɪθ/ *n* [C] someone who makes and repairs things made of iron, especially HORSESHOES 鐵匠, 鍛工〔尤指馬蹄鐵匠〕

black spot /ˈ· ·/ *n* [C] *especially BrE*【尤英】**1** part of a road where accidents often happen 交通事故多發路段, 交通黑點: *an accident black spot* 交通黑點 **2** a place or area where there are more problems than usual 經常出亂子的地區: *the worst unemployment black spots* 失業問題最嚴重的地區

black·strap mo·las·ses /ˌblækstræp məˈlæsɪz; ˌblækstræp məˈlæsɪ̈z/ *n* [U] *AmE* the darkest, thickest MOLASSES (=thick sweet liquid) produced when sugar is taken from sugar plants【美】赤糖糊

black·thorn /ˈblækˌθɔrn; ˈblækθɔːn/ *n* [C] a European bush that has small white flowers 黑刺李〔一種開白色小花的歐洲灌木〕

black-tie /ˌ· ˈ·◂/ *adj* a black-tie party or social occasion is one at which people wear EVENING DRESS (=special formal clothes)〔社交場合〕穿晚禮服的: *Jan and George are having a party – it's black-tie.* 簡和喬治要參加一個必須穿晚禮服的聚會。—compare 比較 WHITE-TIE

black·top /ˈblækˌtɑp; ˈblæktɒp/ *n AmE*【美】**1** [U] a thick black sticky substance that becomes hard as it dries, used to cover roads; BITUMEN 瀝青, 柏油 **2** [singular] the surface of a road covered by this substance 鋪瀝青的路面: *We left the blacktop and drove along a forest road.* 我們離開了柏油路, 沿着一條森林小路行駛。

black wa·ter fe·ver /ˌ· ·· ˈ··/ *n* [U] a very severe form of the disease MALARIA 黑尿熱〔一種嚴重瘧疾〕

black wid·ow /ˌ· ˈ··/ *n* [C] a very poisonous type of SPIDER that is black with red marks 黑寡婦蜘蛛〔一種毒性極大的蜘蛛〕

blad·der /ˈblædɚ; ˈblædə/ *n* [C] **1** an organ of the body, that is shaped like a bag and contains URINE (=waste liquid from the body) until it is passed out of the body 膀胱 **2** a bag of skin, leather, or rubber, for example inside a football, that can be filled with air or liquid〔可充氣或充水的〕囊; 袋 —see also 另見 GALL BLADDER

blade /bled; bleɪd/ *n* [C] **1** the flat cutting part of a tool or weapon 刀刃; 刀鋒; 刀片: *Keep the blade of your penknife sharp.* 讓你的小摺刀刀刃保持鋒利。| *a packet of razor blades* 一小盒剃刀刀片 —see picture at 參見 TOOL¹ and 及 SWORD 圖 **2** the flat wide part of an object that pushes against air or water 槳葉; 螺旋槳葉; 葉片狀物: *the blade of an oar* 槳葉 | *a ceiling fan with polished blades* 帶有精緻葉片的吊扇 **3** a long flat leaf of grass or a similar plant〔狹長而扁平的〕草葉; 葉片: *a blade of grass* 草葉 **4** the metal part on the bottom of an ICE SKATE〔溜冰鞋的〕冰刀 —see also 另見 SHOULDER BLADE S3

blag /blæg; blæg/ *v* [I,T] *BrE slang* to obtain something you want by talking in a clever way【英俚】通過花言巧語得到好處; 巧妙地得到: *He blagged his way in by saying he was a friend of the owner.* 他自稱是老闆的一位朋友, 從而巧妙地混了進去。

blah¹ /blɑ; blɑː/ *n* [U] **1 blah, blah, blah** *spoken* used when you do not need to complete what you are saying because it is boring or because the person you are talking to already knows it【口】諸如此類的等等: *The answer to question 3, 'which South American country has blah, blah, blah?' is Argentina.* 第三題"哪個南美洲國家有甚麼甚麼?"的答案是阿根廷。**2** *BrE spoken* remarks or statements that are boring and do not mean much【英口】廢話; 乏味的話語: *the usual blah about everyone working harder* 要大家都努力幹的陳詞濫調 S2

blah² *adj AmE spoken*【美口】**1** not having an interesting taste, appearance, character etc 枯燥的; 單調的; 乏味的: *The decor of the house was kind of blah.* 這幢房子佈置得有點單調。**2** slightly unwell or unhappy 不舒服的; 不愉快的: *I feel really blah today.* 今天我真的有點不舒服。

blame¹ /blem; bleɪm/ *v* [T] **1** to say or think that someone or something is responsible for something bad 責怪, 指摘; 把…歸咎於: *It's not fair to blame me – it's not my fault we lost.* 責怪我是不公平的 —— 我們輸了又不是我的錯。| **blame sb/sth for** *Mom blamed herself for Danny's problems.* 丹尼出了問題, 媽媽把責任歸咎於自己。| *The report blames poor safety standards for the accident.* 報告把事故的起因歸咎於沒能達到安全標準。| **blame sth on** *Don't go trying to blame it on me!* 別想賴我! | **be to blame** (=be responsible for something bad) 應(為…)承擔責任; 該(因…)受到責備 *You're not to blame for what happened.* 發生這種事情不能怪你。**2 don't blame me** *spoken* used when you are advising someone not to do something【口】不要怪我〔用於勸告某人不要做某事〕: *Buy it then, but don't blame me when it breaks down.* 那就買下吧, 可是壞了別怪我。**3 I don't blame you/them etc** *spoken* used to say that you think S2 W3 it was right or reasonable for someone to do what they did【口】我理解某人的做法: *"She's left her husband." "I don't blame her, after the way he treated her."* "她離開她的丈夫了。" "他那樣對待她, 也難怪她這樣做。" **4 only have yourself to blame** *spoken* used to say that someone's problems are their own fault【口】只能怪你自己: *If he fails his exams, he'll only have himself to blame.* 如果他考試不及格, 那只能怪他自己。**5** to criticize someone or something 批評; 責難: **blame sb/sth for** *The documentary was blamed for its one-sided presentation of the strike.* 人們紛紛批評那部紀錄片只片面地反映了這場罷工。

blame² *n* [U] responsibility for a mistake or for something bad〔對錯誤或壞事應負的〕責任: **[+for]** *The government cannot escape blame for the state of the economy.* 對於當前的經濟現狀, 政府難逃其責。| **get the blame** (=be blamed) 受到責難 *I always get the blame for his mistakes!* 我總是因他的錯誤而背黑鍋! | **take the blame** (=say that something is your fault) 承擔責任 *You can't expect Terry to take all the blame.* 你不能指望特里承擔全部責任。| **put/lay the blame on** (=say that something is someone else's fault) 把責任推到...身上 *The other driver kept trying to put the blame on me.* 另一個司機竭力把責任往我身上推。

blame·less /ˈblemlɪs; ˈbleɪmləs/ *adj formal* not guilty of anything bad; INNOCENT¹ (1)【正式】無罪的; 無可指責的; 清白的: *I don't think he's entirely blameless.* 我看他並非完全沒有過錯。| *a blameless life* 清白的一生 —**blamelessly** *adv*

blame·wor·thy /ˈblemˌwɝðɪ; ˈbleɪmˌwɜːði/ *adj formal* deserving blame or disapproval【正式】該受責備的: *blameworthy conduct* 應受譴責的行為

blanch /blæntʃ; blɑːntʃ/ *v* **1** [I] to become pale because you are frightened or shocked〔因害怕或震驚而〕變得(臉色)蒼白: *Robin swallowed and blanched. "Oh, God! Pregnant!"* 羅賓嚥了一下口水, 臉色蒼白地說: "哦, 天哪, 懷孕了!" **2** [T] to put vegetables, fruit, or nuts into boiling water for a short time 用沸水燙〔蔬菜、水果、堅果等〕: *Blanch the peaches and remove the skins.* 把桃子用沸水燙一燙, 然後去皮。**3** [T] to make a plant become pale by keeping it away from light 使〔植物不見陽光而〕變白

blanc·mange /bləˈmɑnʒ; bləˈmɒnʒ/ *n* [C,U] *BrE* a cold sweet food made from CORNFLOUR, milk, and sugar【英】牛奶凍〔用玉米粉、牛奶和糖製成的甜食〕

bland /blænd; blænd/ *adj* **1** without any excitement, strong opinions, or special character 平和的, 溫和的; 無動於衷的: *The principal made a few bland comments about the value of education.* 校長對教育的重要性作了一些不痛不癢的論述。| *Their music is pleasant enough, but a little bland.* 他們的音樂很動聽, 但缺少激情。**2** food that is bland has very little taste〔食物〕淡而無味的: *a rather bland potato soup* 口味相當淡的馬鈴薯湯 —**blandly** *adv* —**blandness** *n* [U]

blan·dish·ments /ˈblændɪʃmənts; ˈblændɪʃmənts/ *n* [plural] *formal* praise and nice remarks about someone that are intended to persuade them or influence someone【正式】奉承, 討好, 甜言蜜語: *She was immune to both their threats and their blandishments.* 她既不怕他們的威逼, 也不為他們的甜言蜜語所動。

3 **blank¹** /blæŋk; blæŋk/ *adj* **1** showing no expression, understanding, or interest 無表情的; 漠然的; 不感興趣的: *Her eyes were blank and stared right through me.* 她目光呆滯, 直勾勾地望着我。| *a blank look* 毫無表情的眼神 **2** without any writing, print, or recorded sound 無字跡的; 空白的: *Leave the last page blank.* 讓最後一頁空着。| *a blank cassette* 一盒空白磁帶 **3 go blank a)** to be suddenly unable to remember something 腦子突然一片空白, 怎麼也想不起來: *When I got into the exam room I just panicked and my mind went completely blank.* 一進考場, 我就慌亂起來, 腦子裡一片空白。**b)** to stop showing any images, writing etc〔屏幕等〕一片空白: *Suddenly the screen went blank.* 屏幕上突然一片空白。—see also 另見 BLANK VERSE —**blankly** *adv* —**blankness** *n* [U]

blank² *n* [C] **1** an empty space on a piece of paper, where you are supposed to write a word or letter 空白處: *Use this information to fill in the blanks on your form.* 請在表格的空欄處填寫這些資料。**2 my mind's a blank** *spoken* used to say that you cannot remember something【口】腦子裡一片空白, 怎麼也想不起來: *I'm trying to think of his name, but my mind's a complete blank.* 我努力在想他的名字, 但怎麼也想不起來。**3** a CARTRIDGE (=container for a bullet in a gun) that contains an explosive but no bullet〔有火藥而無彈頭的〕空彈: *Soldiers fired blanks into the crowd.* 士兵向人羣發射空彈。—see also 另見 **draw a blank** (DRAW¹ (36)) —**blankness** *n* [U]

blank³ *v* **1** [I] *AmE* to be suddenly unable to remember something【美】突然記不起, 腦子突然一片空白: *I blanked in the oral exam.* 考口試時, 我腦子一片空白。**2** [T] *BrE spoken* to ignore someone who you would usually greet or speak to【英口】不理睬: *Why did she blank Phil when he came in?* 菲爾進來的時候, 她為甚麼沒理人家?

blank sth ↔ **out** *phr v* [T] *informal*【非正式】**1** to cover something so that it cannot be seen 塗掉, 刪去: *The actual names had been blanked out.* 真實姓名被塗掉了。**2** to completely forget something, especially deliberately〔尤指故意地〕全部忘記: *I tried to blank out everything he had said from my mind.* 我盡量把他的話從腦海中全部抹去。

blank car·tridge /ˌ· ˈ··/ *n* [C] a CARTRIDGE (1) that contains an explosive but no bullet〔有火藥而無彈頭的〕空彈

blank cheque *BrE*【英】, **blank check** *AmE*【美】/ˌ· ˈ·/ *n* [C] **1** a cheque that has been signed, but has not had the amount written on it〔簽過名而未填寫金額的〕空白支票 **2 give sb a blank cheque/check** to give someone permission to do whatever they think is necessary in a particular situation 給某人以全權[自由處理權]

blan·ket¹ /ˈblæŋkɪt; ˈblæŋkɪt/ *n* [C] **1** a cover for a bed, usually made of wool 毯子, 毛氈 **2** a thick covering or area of something 厚覆蓋層: **[+of]** *The valley was covered with a blanket of mist.* 山谷為霧靄所籠罩。—see also 另見 WET BLANKET

blanket² *v* [T usually passive 一般用被動態] to cover something with a thick layer 覆蓋; 籠罩: **[+in/with]** *All the rooftops were blanketed in snow.* 家家戶戶的屋頂上都覆蓋着積雪。

blanket³ *adj* [only before noun 僅用於名詞前] **blanket statement/rule/ban etc** a statement, rule etc that affects everyone or includes all possible cases 全面[適用於所有人]的陳述/規定/禁止等: *a blanket ban on the use of aerosols* 全面禁止使用噴霧器 | *We sent out a blanket mailing to every member of Congress.* 我們給所有的國會議員都寄發了郵件。

blank·e·ty-blank /ˌblæŋkɪtɪ ˈblæŋk; ˌblæŋkəti ˈblæŋk/ *adj* [only before noun 僅用於名詞前] *AmE spoken* used to show annoyance when you want to avoid swearing【美口】該死的: *The blankety-blank key is stuck!* 該死的鑰匙卡住了!

blank verse /ˌ· ˈ·/ *n* [U] poetry that has a fixed RHYTHM (1) but does not RHYME² (1) 無韻詩: *Shakespeare's blank verse* 莎士比亞的無韻體詩 —compare 比較 FREE VERSE

blare /blɛr; bleə/ *v* [I,T] to make a very loud unpleasant noise 刺耳地大聲鳴響: *Horns blared in the street outside my hotel window.* 我住的旅館的窗外傳來街上的汽車喇叭聲。| *blaring sirens* 發出刺耳聲音的警報器 | **blare out** *a stereo blaring out rock music* 正在高聲播放搖滾樂的立體聲音響設備 —**blare** *n* [singular]

blar·ney /ˈblɑrnɪ; ˈblɑːni/ *n* [U] *informal especially BrE* pleasant but untrue things that you say to someone in order to trick or persuade them【非正式, 尤英】甜言蜜語; 奉承話

bla·sé /blɑˈze; ˈblɑːzeɪ/ *adj* not worried or excited about things that most people think are important, impressive etc 漠不關心的; 無動於衷的; 不感興趣的; 厭倦的: *He's very blasé about money now that he's got that job.* 他得到了那份工作, 對錢也就無所謂了。

blas·pheme /blæs`fim; blæs'fiːm/ *v* [I+**against**] to speak in a way that insults God or people's religious beliefs, or to use the names of God and holy things when swearing 褻瀆〔上帝等〕; 辱罵, 中傷, 口出惡言 —**blasphemer** *n* [C]

blas·phe·my /`blæsfɪmɪ; 'blæsfɪ̵mi/ *n* [C,U] something you say or do that is insulting to God or people's religious beliefs 對上帝的褻瀆; 褻瀆的言辭 —**blasphemous** *adj*: *The book has been widely condemned as blasphemous.* 人們普遍譴責這本書帶有褻瀆意味。—**blasphemously** *adv*

blast¹ /blæst; blɑːst/ *n*

1 ▶**AIR/WIND** 空氣/風◀ [C] a sudden strong movement of wind or air 一陣疾風; 一股氣流: [+**of**] *A blast of cold air swept through the hut.* 一股寒氣衝進了小屋。

2 ▶**EXPLOSION** 爆炸◀ [C] an explosion, or the very strong movement of air that it causes 爆炸; 爆炸引起的氣浪, 衝擊波: *Thirty-six people died in the blast.* 有三十六人在爆炸中喪生。

3 ▶**NOISE** 噪聲◀ [C] a sudden very loud noise 突然的巨大聲響: *a blast of rock music* 一陣震耳欲聾的搖滾樂 | *The guard gave a blast on his whistle and we were off.* 警衛猛吹了一下哨子, 我們就離開了。

4 (at) full blast as strongly, loudly, or fast as possible 全力地; 全速地; 開足馬力: *The radiators were on full blast, but it was still freezing.* 暖氣已開到最大, 但還是冷得要命。| *a radio going at full blast* 音量開到最大的收音機

5 ▶**FUN** 樂趣◀ [singular] *AmE informal* an enjoyable and exciting experience【美, 非正式】歡樂而刺激的經歷: *The concert was a blast.* 音樂會很好聽。| *We had a blast at the fair.* 我們在遊樂場上玩得很開心。

blast² *v*

1 ▶**EXPLODE** 爆炸◀ [I,T] to break a mass of rock into pieces using explosives 爆破〔尤指岩石〕: [+**through**] *We had to blast our way through 50 metres of solid rock.* 我們不得不炸通50米堅固的岩石。| **blast sth through/in** *Slowly they blasted a path through the mountains.* 他們緩慢地在山間炸開一條路。

2 blast! also 又作 **blast her/it etc** *spoken* used when you are very annoyed about something【口】真討厭! 真該死! 〔表示厭煩〕: *Oh blast! I've forgotten my key.* 真討厭! 我忘了帶鑰匙。

3 ▶**MUSIC** 音樂◀ also 又作 **blast out** [I,T] to produce a lot of loud noise, especially music 發出許多響亮的聲音〔尤指音樂〕: *a radio blasting out pop music* 大聲播放流行音樂的收音機 | *Dance music blasted from the stereo.* 立體聲音響在播放很響的跳舞音樂。

4 ▶**AIR/WATER** 空氣/水◀ [T] to direct air or water at something with great force 向…噴射〔氣或水〕: *Coral can be cleaned by blasting it with a strong jet of water.* 可以用強水流將珊瑚噴洗乾淨。

5 ▶**ATTACK** 攻擊◀ [T] to attack a place or person using bombs or heavy guns 用炸彈[重砲]襲擊: *The town was blasted out of existence.* 整個城鎮被炸為平地。

6 ▶**CRITICIZE** 批評◀ [T] to criticize something very strongly 抨擊, 猛烈批評: *The Senator blasted their plans for educational aid.* 這位參議員猛烈抨擊他們的教育援助計劃。

7 blast sb's hopes to destroy someone's hope of doing something 使某人的希望破滅: *Injury on the team has blasted our hopes of reaching the final.* 隊中有球員受傷使我們進軍決賽的希望破滅了。

8 ▶**DESTROY** 毀壞◀ [T] *literary* to make something dry up and die, especially because of heat or cold【文】〔以高熱或嚴寒〕使枯萎; 摧毀: *Every green thing was blasted by the icy breath of winter.* 冬天的寒氣使所有綠色植物都凋謝了。

blast off *phr v* [I] if a SPACECRAFT blasts off, it leaves the ground〔航天器〕離地升空; 發射 — see also 另見 BLAST-OFF

blas·ted /`blæstɪd; 'blɑːstɪ̵d/ *adj* [only before noun 僅用於名詞前] *spoken* used to express annoyance【口】該死的, 討厭的〔表示厭煩〕: *I wish that blasted baby would stop crying!* 我希望那討厭的嬰孩別再哭了!

blast fur·nace /'· ˌ··/ *n* [C] a large industrial structure in which iron is separated from the rock that surrounds it〔煉鐵的〕高爐, 鼓風爐

blast-off /'· ·/ *n* [U] the moment when a SPACECRAFT leaves the ground〔航天器的〕離地升空時刻: *10 seconds to blast-off* 離航天器離地升空還差十秒 —see also 另見 **blast off** (BLAST²)

bla·tant /`bletn̩t; 'bleɪtənt/ *adj* something bad that is blatant is very clear and easy to see, but the person responsible for it does not seem embarrassed or ashamed 公然的; 露骨的: *a blatant abuse of power* 公然濫用職權 | *blatant discrimination* 毫不掩飾的歧視 —**blatantly** *adv* —**blatancy** *n* [C]

blath·er /`blæðɚ; 'blæðə/ *v* [I+**about**] to talk for a long time about things that are not important 廢話連篇; 胡扯 —**blather** *n* [C,U]

blaze¹ /blez; bleɪz/ *v* **1** [I] to burn very brightly and strongly 熊熊燃燒: *The room was warm and cosy, with a fire blazing in the hearth.* 房間溫暖而舒適, 壁爐裡的火在熊熊地燃燒着。**2** [I] to shine with a very bright light 發光, 照亮: *The house still blazed with lights although it was midnight.* 儘管已是午夜, 屋子裡仍然燈火通明。**3** also 又作 **blaze away** [I] to fire bullets rapidly and continuously 快速而連續地射擊: *An enemy plane roared overhead, its guns blazing.* 一架敵機在上空轟鳴, 不斷地開槍掃射。**4 blaze a trail** to develop important new methods or make important new discoveries 做開路先鋒, 起先導作用: *The company has blazed a trail in robotic technology.* 這家公司在機械人技術方面開拓了新路。**5 be blazed across/all over** if something is blazed across a newspaper etc, it is written in a way that everyone will notice 使廣為人知地刊登: *News of their divorce was blazed across all the tabloids.* 小報都在顯著位置刊登了他們離婚的消息。—see also 另見 BLAZING

blaze² *n*

1 ▶**FIRE** 火◀ **a)** [singular] the strong bright flames of a fire 火焰; 烈火: *We soon had a cheerful blaze.* 我們很快燃起了明亮的火焰。**b)** [C] a big dangerous fire 危險的大火: *Wind fanned the blaze, making it impossible for the firefighters to continue.* 風使火勢越來越猛, 消防隊員無法繼續滅火。

2 ▶**LIGHT/COLOUR** 光/顏色◀ [singular] very bright light or colour〔光線、色彩等的〕光輝, 閃耀; 五彩繽紛: [+**of**] *a blaze of sunshine* 太陽的光輝 | *The garden is a blaze of colour at this time of year.* 這個時節, 花園裡花團錦簇, 萬紫千紅。

3 ▶**GUNS** 槍砲◀ [singular] the rapid continuous firing of a gun 急促而連續的射擊: [+**of**] *a blaze of machine gun fire* 一陣機槍的掃射

4 a blaze of anger/hatred/passion etc a sudden show of very strong emotion 突發的怒氣/仇恨/激情等: *He was surprised by the sudden blaze of anger in her eyes.* 他對她眼裡突然冒出的怒火感到吃驚。

5 in a blaze of glory/publicity etc receiving a lot of praise or public attention 在盛讚/公眾矚目之下等: *Our team finished the season in a blaze of glory, winning the championship with ease.* 我們的球隊在一片讚揚聲中結束了本季的比賽, 輕而易舉地取得了冠軍。

6 what the blazes/who the blazes etc *spoken old-fashioned* used to emphasize a question when you are annoyed【口, 過時】到底在搞甚麼/是誰等〔用於加強問題的語氣, 表示厭煩〕: *What the blazes is going on here?* 這裡究竟在搞甚麼鬼?

7 like blazes *old-fashioned* as fast, as much, or as strongly as possible【過時】盡可能地: *We're going to have to work like blazes to get it done on time!* 我們得拚

命幹，才能按時完成！

8 go to blazes *spoken old-fashioned* used to angrily tell someone to go away【口，過時】滾開

9 ►MARK 記號◄ [C usually singular 一般用單數] a white mark, especially one down the front of a horse's face〔尤指馬鼻上的一條〕白斑 —see also 另見 ABLAZE

blaz·er /ˋblezə; ˈbleɪzə/ *n* [C] a JACKET (=piece of clothing like a short coat), sometimes with the special sign of a school, club etc on it〔有時帶有學校、俱樂部等標記的〕上衣: *a school blazer* 印有校名的外衣

blaz·ing /ˋblezɪŋ; ˈbleɪzɪŋ/ *adj* [only before noun 僅用於名詞前] **1** extremely hot 熾熱的: *a blazing August afternoon* 一個炎熱的八月天的下午 **2** full of strong emotions, especially anger 強烈的〔尤指怒氣〕: *He jumped to his feet in a blazing fury.* 他暴跳如雷。| **blazing row** (=very angry argument) 憤怒的爭吵

bla·zon¹ /ˋblezn̩; ˈbleɪzən/ *n* [C] a COAT OF ARMS 盾形紋章，盾徽

blazon² *v* [T] **be blazoned on/across etc** to be written or shown on something in a very noticeable way 炫示，(大肆) 宣揚

bleach¹ /blitʃ; bliːtʃ/ *n* [U] a chemical used to make things white or to kill GERMs 漂白劑: *I spilled bleach on my blue trousers and ruined them.* 漂白劑濺到我的藍褲子上，褲子給毀了。

bleach² *v* [T] to make something white, especially by using chemicals or sunlight 使〔顏色〕變淡，使變白; 漂白; 曬白: *bleached blonde hair* 褪色的金髮 | *Driftwood lined the shore, bleached by the sun.* 浮木排列在岸邊，已曬得褪了色。

bleach·ers /ˋblitʃəz; ˈbliːtʃəz/ *n* [plural] *AmE* seats arranged in rows with no roof covering them, where you sit to watch sport【美】〔體育場的〕露天看台 (座位): *We had a good view from the bleachers.* 我們在露天看台上看得很清楚。

bleak /blik; bliːk/ *adj* **1** without anything to make you feel cheerful or hopeful 沒有希望的; 令人沮喪的: *bleak news* 令人沮喪的消息 | **a bleak outlook/prospect/future** *With no money and no job, my prospects seemed bleak.* 又沒工作又沒錢，我的前景似乎很暗淡。**2** cold and without any pleasant or comfortable features 陰冷的; 陰鬱的: *a bleak January afternoon* 一月裡一個陰冷的下午 | *The landscape was bleak and bare.* 景色一片淒涼。—**bleakly** *adv* —**bleakness** *n* [U]

blear·y /ˋblɪrɪ; ˈblɪəri/ also 又作 **bleary-eyed** /ˌ.. ˈ.◂/ *adj* unable to see very clearly, because you are tired or have been crying〔因疲勞或流淚〕視力模糊的; 睡眼惺忪的: *Bleary-eyed, she pulled on her robe and went to the kitchen to make coffee.* 她睡眼惺忪地穿上睡袍去廚房煮咖啡。—**blearily** *adv* —**bleariness** *n* [U]

bleat /blit; bliːt/ *v* [I] **1** to make the sound that a sheep or goat makes〔羊〕咩咩地叫 **2** *informal* to complain in a silly or annoying way【非正式】低聲訴苦; 埋怨: *Oh stop bleating!* 別再訴苦了！—**bleat** *n* [C]

bleed /blid; bliːd/ *v past tense and past participle* **bled** /blɛd; bled/

1 ►BLOOD 血◄ a) [I] to lose blood, especially because of an injury〔尤指因受傷〕流血，出血: *Your nose is bleeding.* 你的鼻子流血了。| **bleed profusely** (=bleed a lot) 血流如注 *Marc lay on the ground, bleeding profusely.* 馬克躺在地上，鮮血直流。**b)** [T] to take some blood from someone's body in order to treat a disease 給...放血〔以治療疾病〕

2 ►MONEY 錢◄ [T] to make someone pay an unreasonable amount of money 榨取〔某人〕錢財; 勒索: *She bled him for every last cent.* 她榨盡了他的每一分錢。| **bleed sb dry/white** (=take all their money) 榨乾某人的錢財 *developing countries that had been bled dry by massive loan repayments* 需要償還大量貸款而被榨乾錢財的發展中國家

3 my heart bleeds *spoken* used to say that you feel a lot of sympathy for someone, but often in a joking way when you do not think someone deserves any sympathy【口】我的心在流血〔感到悲傷或同情，常用於玩笑〕: *You can't afford a third car? My heart bleeds!* 你買不起第三輛汽車？我真同情你！| [**+for**] *My heart bleeds for those poor children.* 我為那些可憐的孩子感到悲傷。

4 ►AIR/LIQUID 空氣/液體◄ [T] to remove air or liquid from a system in order to make it work properly, for example from a heating system 抽掉〔氣體或液體〕: *We need to bleed the radiators.* 我們要把暖氣裝置中的水放掉。

5 ►COLOUR 顏色◄ [I] to spread from one area of cloth or paper to another 滲開: *Wash it in cold water so the colours don't bleed.* 用冷水洗以防滲色。

bleed·er /ˋblidə; ˈbliːdə/ *n* [C] *BrE spoken* a rude word for someone, especially a man, that you dislike【英口】討厭的傢伙〔尤指男子〕

bleed·ing¹ /ˋblidɪŋ; ˈbliːdɪŋ/ *adj* [only before noun 僅用於名詞前] *BrE spoken* used to emphasize something when you are angry【英口】該死的，討厭的〔用於加強語氣，表示生氣〕: *Get your bleeding hands off my car!* 拿開你那討厭的手，別碰我的車！

bleeding² *n* [U] the condition of losing blood from your body 流血: *We tied his arm up tightly to stop the bleeding.* 我們把他的胳膊緊緊纏住以止血。

bleeding heart /ˌ.. ˈ./ also 又作 **bleeding heart lib·e·ral** /ˌ.. . ˈ.../ *n* [C] *informal* someone who feels sympathy for poor people or criminals, in a way that you think is not practical or helpful【非正式】心腸過軟的人; 假同情者〔指不實際或無助益地同情窮人和罪犯的人〕

bleep¹ /blip; bliːp/ *n* [C] a high electronic sound〔電子儀器發出的〕嗶嗶聲: *The shrill bleep of the telephone woke him up.* 電話刺耳的嗶嗶聲吵醒了他。

bleep² *v* **1** [I] to make a high electronic sound 發出嗶嗶聲: *The computer will bleep when it has completed the search.* 電腦完成搜索時會發出嗶嗶聲。**2** [T] *BrE informal* to let someone know, through their bleeper, that you want them to telephone you【英，非正式】〔用傳呼機〕召喚〔某人〕**3** [T] also 又作 **bleep out** to prevent an offensive word being heard on television or the radio by making a high electronic sound〔電視或收音機中〕用嗶嗶聲蓋過〔說話〕: *All the swear words had been bleeped out.* 所有的粗話都被嗶嗶聲蓋過了。

bleep·er /ˋblipə; ˈbliːpə/ *n* [C] *BrE* a small machine that you carry with you, that makes short high electronic sounds to tell you that you must telephone someone; BEEPER, PAGER【英】傳呼機

blem·ish¹ /ˋblɛmɪʃ; ˈblemɪʃ/ *n* [C] a small mark, especially a mark on someone's skin or on the surface of an object, that spoils its appearance 瑕疵，污點，疤痕

blemish² *v* [T often passive 常用被動態] to spoil the appearance, beauty, or perfection of something 有損...的完美; 玷污 —see also 另見 UNBLEMISHED —**blemished** *adj*

blench /blɛntʃ; blentʃ/ *v* [I] to make a sudden movement backwards because you are frightened〔因害怕而〕退縮，退避，畏縮

blend¹ /blɛnd; blend/ *v* **1** [T] to thoroughly mix together soft or liquid substances to form a single smooth substance 混和，摻合，調和: *Blend the sugar, eggs, and flour.* 把糖、雞蛋和麵粉和在一起。**2** [I,T] to combine different features or characteristics in a way that produces an effective or pleasant result, or to become combined in this way 交融; 揉合: *an exciting narrative that blends fact and legend* 融合了事實和傳說的精彩敘述 | [**+with/together**] *The aroma of woodsmoke blended with the smell of cooking.* 木頭燃燒的香味和烹調的氣味混合在一起。**3** [T usually passive 一般用被動態] *technical* to produce tea, tobacco, WHISKY etc by mixing several different types together【術語】〔用不同品種的茶、煙草、威士忌等〕混合調製

blend in *phr v* [I] if something blends in with the things around it, it matches the background very well or suitably 協調; 和諧: [**+with**] *The old house blends in per-*

fectly with the gentle Hampshire countryside. 這所老房子和寧靜的漢普郡鄉村十分協調。

blend² *n* [C] **1** a product such as tea, tobacco, or WHISKY that is a mixture of several different types 混合物, 混成品 **2** a mixture of different qualities, characteristics, people etc, that combine together well 不同品質[特性, 人]的巧妙組合: *an excellent team, with a nice blend of experience and youthful enthusiasm* 既有經驗又有年輕人的熱忱的一支優秀隊伍

blend·er /ˋblɛndɚ; ˈblendə/ *n* [C] an electric machine that you use to mix liquids and soft foods together〔食品〕攪拌器

3 **bless** /blɛs; bles/ *v past tense and past participle* **blessed** *or* **blest** /blɛst; blest/ [T] **1 be blessed with** to have a special ability, good quality etc 有幸得到, 被賦予: *Fortunately we're both blessed with good health.* 幸運的是我們倆都有健康的身體。| *Nicole had not been blessed with a sense of humour.* 尼科爾天生一點幽默感也沒有。 **2** to ask God to protect someone or something 祈求上帝祝福[保祐], 求神賜福於: *May God bless you and keep you safe from harm.* 願上帝保祐你平安無事。**3** to make something holy 使神聖; 視…為聖物; 讚頌: *Then the priest blesses the bread and wine.* 然後牧師將餅和酒聖潔化。**4 bless you!** *spoken*【口】**a)** what you say when someone SNEEZES 長命百歲!〔別人打噴嚏時說〕**b)** *old-fashioned* used to thank someone for doing something for you【過時】謝謝〔某人〕**5 bless him/her etc** *spoken* used to show that you are fond of someone, amused by them, or pleased by something they have done【口】真不錯; 幹得好〔表示喜歡或滿意〕: *"Tim can tie his shoelaces now, Mum." "Can he, bless him!"* "蒂姆會繫鞋帶了, 媽媽。" "是嗎, 好孩子。" | *Bless her little heart.* 這個小寶貝她真行。**6 bless my soul/I'll be blessed!** *spoken old-fashioned* used to express surprise【口, 過時】我的天哪!〔表示吃驚〕

bless·ed /ˋblɛsɪd; ˈblesɪ̸d/ *adj* **1** [only before noun 僅用於名詞前] *spoken* used to express annoyance【口】該死的, 倒霉的〔表示煩惱〕: *Now where have I put that blessed book?* 這該死的書我到底放哪兒了? **2** [only before noun 僅用於名詞前] very enjoyable or desirable 令人愉快的, 可喜的, 快樂的: *a few moments of blessed silence* 令人愜意的片刻寧靜 **3** holy 神聖的; 受上帝祝福的, 有福的: *Blessed are the peacemakers.* 使人和睦的人有福。| *the Blessed Virgin* 聖母馬利亞 —**blessedly** *adv* —**blessedness** *n* [U]

bless·ing /ˋblɛsɪŋ; ˈblesɪŋ/ *n*

1 ►STH GOOD/HELPFUL 好的/有幫助的事物◄ [C] something that you have or something that happens which is good because it improves your life, helps you in some way, or makes you happy 幸事, 幸運, 福氣: *This rain will be a blessing for the farmers.* 對農民來說, 這場雨真是一場甘霖。| **be a (great/real) blessing** *The dishwasher has been a real blessing!* 有洗碗碟機可真是享福! | **it is a blessing (that)** *It's a blessing no-one was badly hurt.* 沒有人受重傷, 真是幸運。

2 a mixed blessing a situation that has both good and bad parts 有利亦有弊的事物: *Getting that job was rather a mixed blessing, as it left me very little time to spend with my family.* 得到那份工作有利也有弊, 因為我很少有時間和家人在一起了。

3 blessing in disguise something that seems to be bad or unlucky at first, but which you later realize is good or lucky 表面上帶來麻煩或不愉快而實際上使人得福的事; 禍中得福; 壞事變好事

4 count your blessings used to tell someone to remember how lucky they are, especially when they are complaining about something 想想你有多幸運; 不要身在福中不知福

5 ►APPROVAL 贊同◄ [U] someone's approval or encouragement for a plan, activity, idea etc 准許, 同意; 鼓勵: **with sb's blessing** *They were determined to marry, with or without their parents' blessing.* 不管父母同意與否, 他們都決心要結婚。| **give your blessing to** *The Defense Department has given its blessing to the disarmament proposals.* 國防部已經批准了裁軍的提議。

6 ►FROM GOD 上帝賜予的◄ [C,U] protection and help from God, or words spoken to ask for this〔上帝的〕祝福, 賜福; 保祐; 恩典: *The priest gave the blessing.* 牧師做了祈禱。

bleth·er /ˋblɛðɚ; ˈbleðə/ *v* [I+**on**] *especially ScotE* to talk about things that are not important【尤蘇格蘭】瞎說一通, 胡扯; 喋喋不休 —**blether** *n* [C,U]

blew /blu; bluː/ *v* the past tense of BLOW¹

blight¹ /blaɪt; blaɪt/ *n* [singular] **1** an unhealthy condition of plants in which parts of them dry up and die〔植物〕枯萎病 **2** something that makes people unhappy or that spoils their lives or the environment they live in〔導致煩惱或不幸的〕壞因素; 陰影: *Her guilty secret was a blight on her happiness.* 那使她感到內疚的祕密給她的幸福蒙上了一層陰影。| *the blight of poverty* 貧窮的陰影

blight² *v* [T] to spoil or damage something, especially by preventing people from doing what they want to do 使枯萎; 摧殘; 使某人遭遇挫折: *a disease which, though not fatal, can blight the lives of its victims* 雖說不會致命, 卻足以使患者飽受折磨的一場疾病 | *a country blighted by poverty* 一個為貧窮所困擾的國家 —**blighted** *adj*: *blighted hopes* 破滅的希望

blight·er /ˋblaɪtɚ; ˈblaɪtə/ *n* [C] *BrE old-fashioned*【英, 過時】**1** used to talk about someone that you feel sorry for or JEALOUS of 令人同情[妒忌]的傢伙: *Poor old blighter.* 可憐的老人。| *You lucky blighter!* 你這走運的傢伙! **2** a bad or unpleasant person 令人討厭的人

bli·mey /ˋblaɪmɪ; ˈblaɪmi/ *interj BrE spoken* used to express surprise【英口】哎呀! 天啊!〔表示驚愕〕: *Blimey, look at that!* 天啊, 你看!

Blimp /blɪmp; blɪmp/ *n* [C] someone, especially an old man, with very old-fashioned political ideas 老頑固, 老保守 —**Blimpish** *adj*

blimp *n* [C] **1** a small AIRSHIP (=type of aircraft without wings) 小型飛艇 **2 Blimp** a COLONEL BLIMP 老頑固, 老保守〔源自漫畫中一個老派保守人物布林普上校〕

blind¹ /blaɪnd; blaɪnd/ *adj* 2 3

1 ►CAN'T SEE 看不見◄ **a)** unable to see 瞎的, 盲的, 失明的: *He was nearly blind in one eye.* 他的一隻眼睛幾近失明。| **go blind** (=become blind) 失明 *In later stages of the disease, sufferers often go blind.* 在此病晚期, 患者常會失明。**b) the blind** [plural] people who are unable to see 盲人: *talking books for the blind* 盲人有聲讀物 **c) as blind as a bat** *humorous* not able to see well【幽默】甚麼也看不見: *I'm as blind as a bat without my glasses.* 我不戴眼鏡, 就甚麼也看不見。

2 ►IGNORE 忽視◄ **a) be blind to** to completely fail to notice or realize something 對…缺乏識別能力的: *They seemed to be blind to the consequences of their decision.* 他們似乎看不到這項決策可能帶來的後果。**b) turn a blind eye (to)** to deliberately ignore something that you know should not be happening (對…) 視而不見, (對…) 假裝看不見: *The boss sometimes turns a blind eye to smoking in the office.* 老闆有時對在辦公室吸煙假裝看不見。**c) not take a blind bit of notice** *especially spoken* to completely ignore what someone else is doing, especially in a way that is annoying【尤口】對…熟視無睹; 不把…當一回事

3 not make a blind bit of difference *BrE informal* used to emphasize that whatever someone says or does will not change the situation at all【英, 非正式】沒有一點兒區別; 於事無補; 無任何作用

4 ►FEELINGS 感覺◄ **a) blind faith/loyalty/hate etc** strong feelings that you have without thinking about why you have them 盲目的信仰/忠誠/仇恨等: *an unreasoning, blind hatred* 不理智的盲目仇恨 **b) blind panic/rage** strong feelings that are out of your control 盲目的恐慌/無端的憤怒: *In a moment of blind panic she had pulled the trigger and shot the man dead.* 她在無名的恐懼中扣

B

動了扳機，將那男子擊斃。

5 blind corner/bend/curve a corner on a road that you cannot see beyond when you are driving 看不到的角落/拐彎處

6 the blind leading the blind *often humorous* used to say that people who do not know much about what they are doing are guiding or advising others who know nothing at all【常幽默】盲人給瞎子引路; 瞎指揮

7 ►AIRCRAFT 飛機◄ blind flying/landing using only instruments to fly an aircraft because you cannot see through cloud, mist etc 只靠儀表操作進行飛行/着陸

8 blind drunk *BrE informal* extremely drunk【英，非正式】爛醉如泥

9 swear blind to say very firmly that something is definitely true 固執地說; 一口咬定: *Phil swears blind it wasn't him.* 菲爾發誓說那不是他幹的。—see also 另見 BLINDLY —**blindness** *n* [U]

blind² *v* [T] **1** to permanently destroy someone's ability to see 使永久失去視力: *He had been blinded in the war.* 他在戰爭中雙目失明。**2** to make it difficult for someone to see for a short time 使目眩: *Opening the door, I was immediately blinded by the glare.* 一開門，一股強光照得我一時甚麼也看不見。**3** to make someone lose their good sense or judgement and be unable to see the truth about something 使不理解; 使失去判斷力: *blinded by emotion* 被情感蒙住了眼睛 | **blind sb to** *He had tremendous charm, which blinded us to his dishonesty.* 他外表很有魅力，使我們沒有看清他的虛偽。**4 blind sb with science** to confuse or trick someone by using complicated language 用專業術語蒙騙某人 —see also 另見 **effing and blinding** (EFF (1))

blinds 窗簾; 百葉窗

roller blind *BrE*【英】/ window shade *AmE*【美】捲簾

Venetian blind 百葉窗簾

blind³ *n* [C] **1** a covering that can be pulled down over a window; WINDOW SHADE〔能上下捲疊的〕窗簾; 百葉窗 —see also 另見 ROLLER BLIND, WINDOW SHADE *AmE*【美】, VENETIAN BLIND, SHADE¹ (2b) **2** a trick or excuse to stop someone from discovering the truth 障眼物; 掩飾; 藉口: *Her accent was a blind – she isn't really an American.* 她的口音是一種掩飾，其實她不是美國人。**3** *AmE* a small shelter where you can watch birds or animals without being seen by them【美】〔尤指狩獵時〕窺視獵物的隱蔽處，埋伏處; HIDE² (1) *BrE*【英】

blind al·ley /,· '··/ *n* [C] **1** a small narrow street with no way out at one end 死胡同，死巷 **2** an attempt to achieve something, which does not produce useful results 行不通的方法

blind date /,· '·/ *n* [C] an arranged meeting between a man and woman who have not met each other before 從未晤面的男女間的約會

blind·er /ˈblaɪndə; ˈblaɪndə/ *n* **1** [singular] *BrE informal* an excellent performance, especially in sport【英，非正式】〔尤指體育比賽中〕上佳的表現: *He played an absolute blinder!* 他在比賽中的表現真是太棒了! **2 blinders** [plural] *AmE* things fixed beside a horse's eyes to prevent it seeing objects on either side【美】〔繫於馬眼旁使之不能側視的〕馬眼罩; BLINKERS *BrE*【英】

blind·fold¹ /ˈblaɪnd,fold; ˈblaɪndfəʊld/ *n* [C] a piece of cloth that covers someone's eyes to prevent them from seeing anything 蒙眼布; 障眼物

blindfold² *v* [T] to cover someone's eyes 蒙住〔某人的〕眼睛: *Blindfold the prisoner!* 把囚犯的眼睛蒙上!

blind·fold³ *adv* also 又作 **blindfolded** /ˈblaɪnd,foldɪd; ˈblaɪndfəʊldɪd/ **1** with your eyes covered 蒙着眼地 **2 can do sth blindfold** *informal* used to say that it is very easy for you to do something because you have done it so often【非正式】閉上眼都能做某事

blind·ing /ˈblaɪndɪŋ; ˈblaɪndɪŋ/ *adj* **1 blinding light/flash etc** a very bright light that makes you unable to see properly 刺眼的光/閃光等 **2 blinding headache/pain etc** a headache, pain etc that is so strong that it makes you unable to think or behave normally 極其嚴重的頭痛/疼痛等 **3** *BrE spoken* excellent【英口】最佳的，很棒的: *It's a blinding tape, really funny.* 這錄音帶棒極了，真有趣。—**blindingly** *adv*: *blindingly obvious* 極其明顯

blind·ly /ˈblaɪndlɪ; ˈblaɪndli/ *adv* **1** not thinking about something or trying to understand it 盲目地: *Don't just blindly accept what you're told.* 不要盲目地相信別人的話。**2** not seeing or noticing what is around you 漫無目標地，胡亂地: *He felt around blindly for the matches.* 他瞎摸着找火柴。

blind man's buff /,· · '·/ *n* [U] a children's game in which one player whose eyes are covered tries to catch the others 捉迷藏〔遊戲〕

blind·side /ˈblaɪndsaɪd; ˈblaɪndsaɪd/ *v* [T] *AmE informal*【美，非正式】**1** to hit someone unexpectedly from the side 從側面偷襲〔某人〕: *blindsided by a bus at the intersection* 在十字路口冷不防被公共汽車撞着 **2** to give someone an unpleasant surprise 給〔某人〕一個不愉快的意外: *I was blindsided by his suggestion.* 我對他的建議感到很驚訝。

blind spot /'· ·/ *n* [C] **1** something that you are unable or unwilling to understand 不理解的事物; 偏見，無知: *I have a blind spot where computers are concerned.* 我對電腦一竅不通。**2** the part of the road that you cannot see when you are driving a car〔駕駛者視角〕看不見的地方，死角: *The other car was in my blind spot – I just hadn't seen it!* 另一輛車在我視線的死角處——我正巧沒看見! **3** the point in your eye where the nerve enters, which is not sensitive to light 盲點〔眼神經無光感處〕

blink¹ /blɪŋk; blɪŋk/ *v* **1** [I,T] to shut and open your eyes quickly 眨眼: *I blinked as I came out into the sunlight.* 我走出來到太陽底下時直眨眼睛。**2** [I] if lights blink, they shine unsteadily or go on and off rapidly〔燈光〕時閃時滅，閃爍: *The light on your answering machine is blinking.* 你的電話答錄機上的指示燈在閃爍。**3 not (even) blink** to not seem at all surprised 絲毫不驚奇: *She didn't even blink when I told her how much it would cost.* 當我告訴她那件東西的價錢時，她甚至連眼睛都沒眨一下。**4 before you could blink** *spoken* extremely quickly【口】沒等你眨眼，很快地

blink² *n* **1 on the blink** *spoken* not working properly【口】失靈，出毛病: *The radio's on the blink again.* 收音機又出毛病了。**2 the blink of an eye** a very short period of time 一眨眼工夫，瞬間 **3** [C] the action of quickly shutting and opening your eyes 眨眼

blink·ered /ˈblɪŋkəd; ˈblɪŋkəd/ *adj* **1** having a limited view of a subject or refusing to accept or consider ideas that are new or different 狹隘的，有偏見的; 保守的: *blinkered and outdated attitudes* 狹隘而又守舊的態度 **2** a horse that is blinkered is wearing blinkers〔馬〕戴眼罩的

blink·ers /ˈblɪŋkəz; ˈblɪŋkəz/ *n* [plural] **1** *BrE* pieces of leather fixed beside a horse's eyes to prevent it seeing objects on either side【英】〔繫於馬眼旁使之不能側視的〕馬眼罩; BLINDERS *AmE*【美】**2** *AmE informal* the small lights on a car that you flash on and off to show which direction you are turning【美，非正式】〔汽車上的〕轉向指示燈; WINKERS *BrE*【英】

blink·ing /ˋblɪŋkɪŋ; ˈblɪŋkɪŋ/ *adj* [only before noun 僅用於名詞前] *BrE spoken* used to show that you are annoyed【英口】該死的, 討厭的〔表示厭煩〕: *Whose blinking idea was it to come to this awful place?* 誰的鬼主意, 要來這麼個破地方?

blip /blɪp; blɪp/ *n* [C] **1** a short high electronic sound or a flashing light on the screen of a piece of electronic equipment〔電子儀器發出的〕嗶嗶聲; 屏幕上的信號, 光點: *blips on a radar screen* 雷達屏幕上的光點 **2** a short pause or change in a process, or activity, especially when the situation gets worse for a while before it improves again 暫時中斷[變化]: *The drop in sales is only a temporary blip.* 銷售的下降只是暫時的。

bliss /blɪs; blɪs/ *n* [U] perfect happiness or enjoyment 極樂, 無上幸福, 福祐, 至福: *wedded bliss* 美滿婚姻 | *I didn't have to get up till 11 – it was sheer bliss.* 我可以睡到十一點, 真幸福啊!

bliss·ful /ˋblɪsfəl; ˈblɪsfəl/ *adj* **1** extremely happy or enjoyable 極其幸福的; 樂而忘憂的: *blissful sunny days* 陽光明媚的日子 **2 blissful ignorance** a situation in which you do not yet know about something unpleasant 對〔不幸之事〕毫不察覺 —**blissfully** *adv*: *Jean's now married and blissfully happy.* 瓊已經結婚了, 生活得美滿幸福。

blis·ter¹ /ˋblɪstɚ; ˈblɪstə/ *n* [C] **1** a swelling on your skin containing clear liquid, caused for example by a burn or continuous rubbing〔皮膚上因燙傷、摩擦而起的〕疱, 水泡: *New shoes always give me blisters.* 新鞋總使我的腳起泡。 **2** a swelling on the surface of metal, rubber, painted wood etc〔金屬、橡膠或油漆過的木料等表面的〕氣泡, 浮泡

blister² *v* [I,T] to develop blisters or make blisters form 起泡; 使起水泡: *The paint will blister in the heat.* 油漆遇高温會起泡。—**blistered** *adj*: *Before long, my hands were blistered from all the digging.* 由於一直在挖, 我的手很快就起了泡。

blis·ter·ing /ˋblɪstərɪŋ; ˈblɪstərɪŋ/ *adj* **1** extremely hot 炎熱的, 酷熱的: *the blistering heat of the desert* 沙漠中的酷熱 **2 blistering attack/criticism etc** very critical remarks expressing anger and disapproval 猛烈的攻擊/批評等: *She launched into a blistering attack on her boss.* 她開始猛烈地攻擊老闆。—**blisteringly** *adv*: *Cover up as the sun can be blisteringly hot.* 遮蓋一下吧, 陽光會很酷熱。

blithe /blaɪð; blaɪð/ *adj* **1** seeming not to care or worry about the effects of what you do 漫不經心的, 毫不在乎的: *a blithe disregard for the facts* 完全漠視事實 **2** *literary or old use* cheerful and having no worries【文或舊】無憂無慮的, 快樂的 —**blithely** *adv*: *Mollie strolled blithely into the yard.* 莫利悠閒地蹓躂着進了院子。

blith·er·ing /ˋblɪðərɪŋ; ˈblɪðərɪŋ/ *adj* **blithering idiot** *spoken* someone who has done something very stupid【口】愚蠢的傢伙, 傻瓜

blitz /blɪts; blɪts/ *n* [usually singular 一般用單數] **1** a sudden military attack, especially from the air 閃電般的猛烈襲擊〔尤指空襲〕; 閃電戰 **2 have a blitz on** *informal* to work very hard to completely finish something that needs to be done【非正式】努力地把…辦妥: *We'll have to have a blitz on the house before your parents arrive.* 在你父母到來以前, 我們必須把屋子打掃乾淨。—**blitz** *v* [T]

blitzed /blɪtst; blɪtst/ *adj especially AmE informal* very tired or very drunk【尤美, 非正式】非常疲勞的; 爛醉如泥的

bliz·zard /ˋblɪzɚd; ˈblɪzəd/ *n* [C] **1** a severe snow storm 暴風雪: *We got stuck in a blizzard that night.* 那天晚上, 我們被暴風雪所圍困。—see picture on page A13 參見A13頁圖 **2** *AmE informal* a sudden large amount of something that you must deal with【美, 非正式】大量〔要處理的事〕: *a blizzard of memos* 一大堆備忘錄要處理

bloat·ed /ˋblotɪd; ˈbləʊtɨ̣d/ *adj* full of liquid, gas, food etc, so that you look or feel much larger than normal 發脹的, 膨脹的; 臃腫的: *They've fished a bloated carcass out of the river.* 他們從河裡撈上來一具發脹了的動物屍體。| *I feel really bloated after that meal.* 吃完飯後, 我覺得肚子很脹。

bloa·ter /ˋblotɚ; ˈbləʊtə/ *n* [C] a large fat fish eaten smoked 醃熏魚

blob /blɑb; blɒb/ *n* **1** a very small round mass of liquid or sticky substance 一滴, 一小團: **[+of]** *a blob of honey* 一滴蜂蜜 —see picture on page A7 參見A7頁圖 **2** something far away that cannot be clearly seen〔遠處〕模糊的事物, 一小點: *The church spire was just a distant blob.* 遠處的教堂尖塔只能隱約看見。

bloc /blɑk; blɒk/ *n* [usually singular 一般用單數] a large group of people or countries with the same political aims, working together 集團, 陣營: *the former Soviet bloc* 前蘇聯陣營 —see also 另見 EN BLOC

block¹ /blɑk; blɒk/ *n* [C] S2 W2

1 ►SOLID MASS 固體◄ a solid mass of hard material such as wood or stone with straight sides 一大塊〈如木、石等通常有直切邊的堅硬物體〉: **[+of]** *a block of ice* 一大塊冰 —see picture on page A7 參見A7頁圖

2 ►STREET/STREETS 街◄ a) *AmE* the distance along a city street from where one street crosses it to the next【美】街段: *It's three blocks to the store from here.* 這兒到那家商店隔三條馬路。| *She lives down the block.* 她住在街尾。**b)** the four city streets that form a square around an area of buildings 街區: *Let's walk around the block before we go in.* 我們先圍着這街區走一圈再進去。

3 ►LARGE BUILDING 大樓◄ a large building divided into separate parts 棟, 座, 幢: *a block of flats* 一棟住宅樓宇 | *a tower block* 一座高層建築 | *office blocks* 辦公大樓 —see picture on page A4 參見A4頁圖

4 ►QUANTITY OF THINGS 數量◄ a quantity of things considered as a single unit 一組, 一批, 一套, 一疊: **[+of]** *a block of shares in a business* 企業的大宗股票 | *Highlight this block of text.* 突出課文的這一部分。

5 block booking/voting an arrangement that is made for a whole group, to buy something or to vote together 成批購買/集體投票

6 ►UNABLE TO THINK 不能思考◄ [usually singular 一般用單數] the temporary loss of your normal ability to think, learn, write etc 阻滯: **mental/writer's block** *She has a mental block about speaking French.* 她腦子堵塞了, 一句法語也説不出來。

7 ►STOPPING MOVEMENT 阻止行動◄ [usually singular 一般用單數] something in a pipe, road etc that stops things moving through or along it 障礙物, 堵塞物

8 the block a solid block of wood on which someone's head was cut off as a punishment, in former times〔昔時的〕斷頭台: *He was prepared to go to the block for his beliefs.* 他準備好了為自己的信仰掉腦袋。

9 lay/put your head on the block to risk destroying other people's opinion of you by doing or saying something 冒着敗壞自己名聲的危險

10 ►SPORT 體育◄ a movement in sport that stops an opponent going forward 攔擋(動作)

11 ►INFORMATION 信息◄ a physical unit of stored information on a MAGNETIC TAPE or DISK 信息組〔指磁帶或磁盤上儲存信息的物理單位〕

12 ►PRINTING 印刷◄ a piece of wood or metal with words or line drawings cut into it, for printing 印版, 版墊, 襯版, 木印板

13 ►LAND 土地◄ *AustrE, NZE* a large piece of land【澳, 新西蘭】一大片土地: *a ten acre block near the city* 城市附近一塊十英畝的土地 —see also 另見 BLOCK CAPITALS, BUILDING BLOCK, **be a chip off the old block** (CHIP¹ (6)), **I'll knock your block off** (KNOCK¹ (4)), **stumbling block** (STUMBLE (4))

block² *v* [T] **1** also 又作 **block up** to prevent anything moving through a narrow space by placing something across it or in it 阻擋, 堵塞: *Your truck is blocking the road.* 你的卡車堵住了道路。| *My nose is blocked up* S3 *with this cold.* 由於傷風，我的鼻子不通氣。**2** to stop something happening, developing, or succeeding 阻止，妨礙，阻撓: *The Senate blocked publication of the report.* 參議院阻撓這個報告的發表。**3** also 又作 **block off** to be in front of someone so that they cannot see a view, light, the sun etc 擋住〔視線〕: *Can you move? You're blocking my light.* 你挪一下行嗎？你擋住了光。**4 block sb's way** to stand in front of someone, so that they cannot go past 擋住某人的去路: *The teacher stood at the entrance, blocking the children's way.* 老師站在入口處，擋住了孩子們的路。**5** *technical* to limit the use of a particular country's money【術語】限制使用〔某國貨幣〕: *a blocked currency* 凍結的貨幣

block sth ↔ **in/out** *phr v* [T] to make a drawing of something that gives a general idea but is not exact 草擬；畫…的簡略圖: *I'll just block in the main buildings.* 我僅把主要建築的草圖勾畫出來。

block sth ↔ **off** *phr v* [T] to completely close a road or path 封閉，封鎖〔道路〕

block sth ↔ **out 1** to stop light passing 擋〔光〕: *a heavy curtain blocking out the light* 擋光的厚窗簾 **2** [I, T **block** sth ↔ **out**] to stop yourself thinking about something, or remembering it 不去想: *a memory so terrible that she tried to block it out* 她努力不去想的可怕的回憶

block·ade[1] /blɑˋked; blɒˈkeɪd/ *n* [usually singular 一般用單數] the surrounding of an area by soldiers or ships to stop people or supplies leaving or entering〔對某地的〕封鎖: *a naval blockade* 海上封鎖 | **lift/raise the blockade** (=to end a blockade) 解除封鎖 | **impose a blockade** *They've imposed an economic blockade on the country.* 他們對該國實行了經濟封鎖。

blockade[2] *v* [T] to put a place under a blockade 封鎖: *The ships blockaded the port.* 船隻封鎖了港口。

block·age /ˈblɑkɪdʒ; ˈblɒkɪdʒ/ *n* **1** [C] something that is stopping movement in a narrow place 堵塞物；障礙，阻礙: *a blockage in the pipe* 管子內的堵塞物 **2** [U] the state of being blocked or prevented 被阻，堵塞〔狀態〕

block and tack·le /,· · ˈ··/ *n* [usually singular 一般用單數] a piece of equipment made with wheels and ropes, used for lifting heavy things〔搬提重物的〕滑車裝置，滑輪組，絞轆

block·bust·er /ˈblɑkˌbʌstɚ; ˈblɒkˌbʌstə/ *n* [C] **1** *informal* a book or film that is very good or successful【非正式】轟動一時的電影〔書籍〕: *the latest blockbuster from Hollywood* 荷里活最新大片 **2** a very powerful bomb 爆炸力巨大的炸彈

block cap·i·tals /,· ˈ···/ *n* [plural] letters in their large form, eg A, B, C, rather than a, b, c 大寫字母: *Complete the form in block capitals.* 用大寫字母填寫表格。

block·head /ˈblɑkˌhɛd; ˈblɒkhed/ *n* [C] *informal* a very stupid person【非正式】大笨蛋，大傻瓜: *You silly blockhead!* 你這傻瓜！

block·house /ˈblɑkˌhaus; ˈblɒkhaʊs/ *n* [C] a small strong building used as a shelter from enemy guns 碉堡；掩體

block let·ters /,· ˈ··/ *n* [plural] block capitals 大寫字母

block par·ty /ˈ· ,··/ *n* [C] *AmE* a party held in the street for all the people living in the area【美】〔為居住在同一街區裡所有人舉辦的〕街頭聚會

3 **bloke** /blok; bləʊk/ *n* [C] *BrE informal* a man【英，非正式】人，傢伙: *The new bloke next door seems a bit weird.* 隔壁新來的那個傢伙看起來有點古怪。

blok·ish /ˈblokɪʃ; ˈbləʊkɪʃ/ *adj BrE humorous* if you do blokish things, you behave in a traditionally male way【英，幽默】〔男性〕傳統的；傳統上由男人完成的: *playing football, fixing the car and other blokish activities* 踢足球、修汽車及其他男人做的事 —**blokishness** *n* [U]: *amiable blokishness* 和藹的男性舉止

blond /blɑnd; blɒnd/ *adj* **1** another spelling of BLONDE blonde 的另一種拼法 **2** a man who is blond has pale or yellow hair〔男子〕金髮的

blonde[1] /blɑnd; blɒnd/ *adj* **1** blonde hair is pale or yellow in colour〔頭髮〕金色的，淺色的 **2** a woman who is blonde has pale or yellow hair〔女子〕金髮的，淺色頭髮的 3

blonde[2] *n* [C] *informal* a woman with pale or yellow-coloured hair【非正式】金髮女人，淺色頭髮的女人: *a beautiful blonde* 金髮美女 3

blood[1] /blʌd; blʌd/ *n* 1

1 ►IN YOUR BODY 身體內◄ [U] the red liquid that your heart pumps round your body 血，血液: *She lost a lot of blood in the accident.* 她在事故中流了很多血。| **give/donate blood** (=have blood taken from you and stored, to be used to treat someone else) 獻血，捐血 | **draw blood** (=make someone bleed) 使〔某人〕出血 *The dog bit her but failed to draw blood.* 狗咬了她，但沒出血。 1

2 have sb's blood on your hands to have caused someone's death 雙手沾滿某人的鮮血，導致某人死亡

3 in cold blood in a cruel and deliberate way 冷血地，殘忍地；蓄意地: *He murdered the old man in cold blood.* 他殘忍地殺害了那位老人。

4 make your blood boil to make you extremely angry 使某人怒火中燒: *The way they treat those people really makes my blood boil.* 他們這樣對待那些人真使我非常氣憤。

5 make your blood run cold to make you feel extremely frightened 令某人毛骨悚然: *The sudden scream made my blood run cold.* 突然的尖叫聲嚇得我毛骨悚然。

6 it's like getting blood out of a stone used when you find it difficult to persuade someone to give you or tell you something 猶如想從石頭裡榨出血來〔指要從某人身上獲得某物或探聽某事很困難〕

7 blood is thicker than water used to say that family relationships are more important than any other kind 血濃於水；疏不間親

8 be after sb's blood to be angry enough to want to hurt or injure someone 恨透了某人；恨不得咬某人一口

9 sb's blood is up someone is extremely angry and determined to do something about it 動怒，激動，衝動: *They tried to stop me, but my blood was up.* 他們設法阻止我，但我怒不可遏。

10 ►YOUR FAMILY/GROUP 家庭/團體◄ [U] the family or group to which you belong from the time that you are born 血統，血緣；家世，門第: *There's French blood on his mother's side.* 他母親有法國血統。

11 be/run in sb's blood if an ability or tendency is in, or runs in, someone's blood, it is natural to them and others in their family 家傳的；天賦的

12 sweat blood to work extremely hard to achieve something 拚命工作: *Beth sweated blood over that article.* 貝思嘔心瀝血地寫那篇文章。

13 new/fresh blood new members in a group or organization who bring new ideas and energy 新血，新增的成員: *It's good to have some new blood in the department.* 系裡增添了新成員是件好事。

14 young blood *old-fashioned* a word for a fashionable young man【過時】時尚的年輕人 —see also 另見 **bad blood** (BAD[1] (22)), BLUE-BLOODED, RED BLOOD CELL, WHITE BLOOD CELL, **your own flesh and blood** (FLESH[1] (5))

blood[2] *v* [T] **1** *BrE* to give someone their first experience of an activity, especially a difficult or unpleasant one【英】使〔某人〕取得初次經驗〔尤指在困難或不愉快的活動中〕**2** to give a hunting dog its first taste of blood 使〔獵犬〕初嘗血腥味

blood-and-guts /,· · ˈ·◂/ *adj AmE informal* full of action or violence【美，非正式】激烈的，猛烈的；充滿暴力的: *a blood-and-guts struggle between the two teams* 兩隊之間的激烈爭奪

blood-and-thun·der /,· · ˈ··◂/ *adj* [only before noun 僅用於名詞前] *BrE* a blood-and-thunder film or story is full of exciting and violent action【英】〔電影、小説等〕充滿血腥和暴力場面的

blood bank /ˈ· ·/ *n* [C] a store of human blood to be used in hospital treatment 血庫

blood·bath /ˈblʌdˌbæθ; ˈblʌdbɑːθ/ *n* [singular] the violent killing of many people at one time 血洗; 大屠殺

blood broth·er /ˌ· ˈ··/ *n* [C] a man who promises loyalty to another, often in a ceremony in which the men's blood is mixed together 歃血盟誓的兄弟, 結盟的拜把兄弟

blood count /ˈ· ·/ *n* [C] a medical examination of someone's blood to see if it contains the right substances in the right amounts 血球計數, 血細胞計數: *Her blood count is very low.* 她的血細胞計數很低。

blood·cur·dling /ˈblʌdˌkɝdlɪŋ; ˈblʌdˌkɜːdlɪŋ/ *adj* extremely frightening 令人心驚膽戰的, 令人毛骨悚然的: *a bloodcurdling shriek* 令人毛骨悚然的尖叫聲

blood do·nor /ˈ· ˌ··/ *n* [C] someone who gives their blood to be used in the treatment of other people 獻血者, 捐血者

blood feud /ˈ· ·/ *n* [C] a quarrel that lasts for many years between people or families and in which each side murders or injures members of the other side〔家族之間多年的〕宿仇, 血仇

blood group /ˈ· ·/ *n* [C] *BrE* one of the classes into which human blood can be separated, including A, B, AB and O【英】血型〔分為 A 型、B 型、AB 型和 O 型〕; BLOOD TYPE *AmE*【美】

blood heat /ˈ· ·/ *n* [U] the normal temperature of the human body, about 37°C 人體血溫〔約 37°C〕

blood·hound /ˈblʌdˌhaund; ˈblʌdhaʊnd/ *n* [C] a large dog with a very good sense of smell, often used for hunting〔嗅覺靈敏, 常用於追蹤的〕大警犬, 大獵犬

blood·less /ˈblʌdlɪs; ˈblʌdləs/ *adj* **1** without killing or violence 不流血的; 沒有暴力的: *a bloodless coup* 不流血的政變 **2** a bloodless part of your body is very pale 無血色的, 蒼白的: *His lips were thin and bloodless.* 他的嘴唇又薄又蒼白。**3** lacking in human feeling 無情的, 冷酷的 —compare 比較 BLOODY² —**bloodlessly** *adv* —**bloodlessness** *n* [U]

blood·let·ting /ˈblʌdˌlɛtɪŋ; ˈblʌdˌletɪŋ/ *n* [U] **1** killing people; BLOODSHED 流血, 殺戮: *The violence was a foretaste of the bloodletting to come.* 這次暴力事件預示着一場殺戮將要發生。**2** the medical practice in former times of treating people who were ill by removing some of their blood〔古代醫療的〕放血(術) **3** the reduction of the number of people working for an organization 裁員

blood lust /ˈ· ·/ *n* [U] a strong desire to be violent 殺戮慾

blood mon·ey /ˈ· ˌ··/ *n* [U] **1** money paid for murdering someone 付給(受雇)殺手的酬金 **2** money paid to the family of someone who has been murdered 償付給被害人親屬的撫恤金

blood or·ange /ˈ· ˌ··/ *n* [C] an orange with red juice〔具深紅汁液的〕血橙

blood poi·son·ing /ˈ· ˌ···/ *n* [U] *technical* a serious medical condition in which an infection spreads from a small area of your body through your blood【術語】血中毒, 敗血症

blood pres·sure /ˈ· ˌ··/ *n* [U] the force with which blood travels through your body, that can be measured by a doctor 血壓: *high blood pressure* 高血壓

blood-red /ˌ· ˈ·◂/ *adj* dark red, like blood 血紅(色)的: *blood-red lipstick* 血紅色的唇膏

blood re·la·tion /ˈ· ·ˌ··/ *n* [C] someone related to you by birth rather than by marriage 血緣關係, 血親, 骨肉

blood·shed /ˈblʌdˌʃɛd; ˈblʌdʃed/ *n* [U] the killing of people, usually in fighting or war〔常指在搏鬥或戰爭中的〕流血, 殺戮, 殘殺: *taking action to stop the bloodshed* 採取行動阻止流血事件

blood·shot /ˈblʌdˌʃɑt; ˈblʌdʃɒt/ *adj* bloodshot eyes are slightly reddish in colour〔眼睛〕充血的, 有血絲的

blood sport /ˈ· ·/ *n* [C] a sport that involves the killing of animals or birds 以獵殺〔鳥獸〕為樂的運動[活動]: *a demonstration against blood sports* 一場抗議捕殺鳥獸的遊行

blood·stain /ˈblʌdˌsten; ˈblʌdsteɪn/ *n* [C] a mark or spot of blood 血污, 血跡 —**bloodstained** *adj*: *a bloodstained handkerchief* 血跡斑斑的手帕

blood·stock /ˈblʌdˌstɑk; ˈblʌdstɒk/ *n* [U] horses that have been bred for racing〔用於賽馬的〕純種馬: *a bloodstock auction* 純種馬拍賣

blood·stream /ˈblʌdˌstrim; ˈblʌdstriːm/ *n* [singular] the blood as it flows around your body 循環於體內的血液, 血流: *The drug is injected directly into the bloodstream.* 藥物直接注射入血液中。

blood·suck·er /ˈblʌdˌsʌkɚ; ˈblʌdˌsʌkə/ *n* [C] **1** a creature that sucks blood from the body of other animals 吸血的動物; 吸血蟲 **2** *informal* someone who always uses other people's money or help【非正式】吸血鬼, 剝削者

blood·thirst·y /ˈblʌdˌθɝstɪ; ˈblʌdˌθɜːsti/ *adj* **1** eager to kill and wound, or enjoying seeing killing and violence 嗜殺成性的; 耽於暴力的: *ruthless and bloodthirsty warriors* 殘暴的鬥士 **2** describing or showing violence 涉及暴力的: *The film was too bloodthirsty for me.* 這部電影暴力鏡頭太多, 我不喜歡。—**bloodthirstily** *adv* —**bloodthirstiness** *n* [U]

blood trans·fu·sion /ˈ· ·ˌ··/ *n* [C] the process of putting blood into someone's body as a medical treatment 輸血

blood type /ˈ· ·/ *n* [C] *AmE* one of the classes into which human blood can be separated, including A, B, AB, and O【美】血型〔分為 A 型、B 型、AB 型和 O 型〕; BLOOD GROUP *BrE*【英】

blood ves·sel /ˈ· ˌ··/ *n* [C] **1** any of the tubes through which blood flows in your body 血管 —see picture at 參見 TEETH 圖 **2 burst a blood vessel** to become very angry or upset about something 大動肝火: *My dad nearly burst a blood vessel when I told him I quit college.* 我告訴爸爸我從大學退學時, 他氣得血管都要炸了。

blood·y¹ /ˈblʌdɪ; ˈblʌdi/ *adj, adv spoken especially BrE* (S3 W3) used to emphasize what you are saying in a slightly rude way【口, 尤英】很, 太, 十分, 非常〔用於以不太禮貌的方式加強語氣〕: *It's bloody cold out there!* 外邊的天氣可真冷! | *It serves you bloody well right.* 你這是活該。| *What a bloody cheek!* 真不要臉! | *Bloody hell!* 該死的! | **not bloody likely** (=definitely not) 絕對不行; 休想 *"Are you going to go with him?" "Not bloody likely."* "你要和他一塊兒去嗎?" "絕對不行。"

bloody² *adj* **1** covered in blood or bleeding 流血的; 血淋淋的, 染滿血的 **2** with a lot of killing and injuries 血腥的; 傷亡慘重的; 殘忍的: *a bloody battle* 傷亡慘重的戰役 **3 scream/yell bloody murder** *AmE informal* to protest in a loud, very angry way【美, 非正式】大聲憤怒地抗議: *She was furious – screaming bloody murder at the manager!* 她勃然大怒, 對經理大聲吼叫! **4 bloody but unbowed** harmed by events but not defeated by them 受到…的傷害但沒有被擊垮: *He emerged from the discussions bloody but unbowed.* 討論終於完結了, 他雖受到猛烈抨擊, 但沒有被擊垮。**5** *BrE old-fashioned* unpleasant and nasty or unkind【英, 過時】討厭的; 惡劣的; 不友好的

bloody³ *v* [T] *formal* to injure someone so that blood comes, or to cover something with blood【正式】使〔某人〕受傷(流血): *The boy punched Jack and bloodied his nose.* 那個男孩用拳猛擊傑克, 致使他鼻子流血。

bloody-mind·ed /ˌ·· ˈ··◂/ *adj BrE informal* deliberately making things difficult for other people【英, 非正式】故意作對的; 有意刁難的; 頑固的: *Stop being so bloody-minded!* 不要再故意刁難人了! —**bloody-mindedly** *adv* —**bloody-mindedness** *n* [U]

bloom¹ /blum; bluːm/ *n* **1** [C,U] a flower or flowers 花: *beautiful red blooms* 美麗的紅花 | *a mass of bloom on* *the apple trees* 蘋果樹上的花團 **2 in (full) bloom** with the flowers fully open〔花朵〕盛開, 怒放 **3** [U singular] a covering of fine powder that forms on fruit such as GRAPES or PLUMS〔葡萄或李子等水果表面的一層〕粉霜, 粉衣 **4 the bloom of youth/love etc** *literary* the best or happiest time when you are young【文】豆蔻年華; 全盛時期

B

bloom² *v* [I] **1** to produce flowers or to open as flowers 開花;〔花〕盛開 **2** to become happy and healthy or successful 精神煥發; 興旺: *Anne has bloomed since she got her new job.* 安妮有了新工作後容光煥發。

bloom·er /ˈblumɚ; ˈbluːmə/ *n* **1 bloomers** [plural] **a)** *old-fashioned* women's underwear like loose trousers that end at your knees【過時】〔長及膝部的女用〕燈籠內褲 **b)** short loose trousers that end in a tight band at your knees worn by women in Europe and America in the late 19th century〔19世紀末歐美婦女所穿的長及膝部的〕燈籠褲 **2** [C] *BrE humorous, old-fashioned* an embarrassing mistake in front of other people【英, 幽默, 過時】〔在大庭廣眾前犯的〕錯誤, 差錯, 洋相; BLOOPER (1) *AmE*【美】

bloom·ing /ˈblumɪŋ; ˈbluːmɪŋ/ *adj, adv BrE spoken* used for emphasizing a remark or statement【英口】太, 很, 非常〔用於加強語氣〕: *It's blooming ridiculous!* 這真是太荒唐了! | *Blooming heck! – look at this!* 活見鬼! 看看這個!

bloop·er /ˈblupɚ; ˈbluːpə/ *n* [C] *AmE informal*【美, 非正式】**1** an embarrassing mistake made in front of other people〔在大庭廣眾前犯的〕錯誤, 差錯, 洋相; BLOOMER (2) *BrE*【英】: *I made a real blooper yesterday.* 昨天我大出洋相。**2** a ball in BASEBALL that is high and slow and easy to catch or hit〔棒球中的〕高吊下旋球

blos·som¹ /ˈblɑsəm; ˈblɒsəm/ *n* [C,U] **1** a flower or all the flowers on a tree or bush〔指樹或灌木的〕花, 花簇: *orange blossom* 香橙花 **2 in (full) blossom** with the flowers open 鮮花盛開

blossom² *v* [I] **1** if trees blossom, they produce flowers 開花: *a blossoming apple tree* 正在開花的蘋果樹 **2** also 又作 **blossom out** to become happier, more beautiful, more successful etc 變快樂了; 變漂亮了; 興旺: *Pete has really blossomed out in his new school.* 皮特到了新學校真的進步了。

blot¹ /blɑt; blɒt/ *v* **blotted, blotting** [T] **1** to dry a wet surface by pressing soft paper or cloth on it〔用軟紙或布等〕吸乾 **2 blot your copybook** *informal* to do something that spoils the idea that people have of you【非正式】玷污自己的名聲

blot sth ↔ **out** *phr v* [T] to cover or hide something completely 把…遮住, 遮蓋; 塗去; 隱藏: *Thick, white smoke completely blotted out the sun.* 濃重的白煙完全遮住了陽光。| *She had blotted out all her memories of the accident.* 她已經抹去了對那場事故的所有記憶。

blot sth ↔ **up** *phr v* [T] to remove liquid from a surface by pressing a soft cloth, paper etc onto it〔用軟布或紙張等〕擦乾, 吸乾

blot² *n* [C] **1** a mark or spot that spoils something or makes it dirty 污點, 污漬: *ink blots* 墨水漬 **2** a building, structure etc that is ugly and spoils the appearance of a place 破壞了某地方景致的東西〈如樓房等〉: **a blot on the landscape** *That new power station is a real blot on the landscape.* 那座新建的電站真是煞風景。**3** something that spoils the good opinion other people have of you〔尤指名譽的〕污點, 瑕疵: *The Colonel's confession is a blot on the army's honor.* 上校的供詞玷污了軍隊的名譽。

blotch /blɑtʃ; blɒtʃ/ *n* [C] a pink or red mark on the skin, or a coloured mark on something〔皮膚上的〕斑; 疤;〔衣服等上的〕污漬 —**blotchy** *adj* —**blotched** *adj*

blot·ter /ˈblɑtɚ; ˈblɒtə/ *n* [C] **1** a large piece of blotting paper kept on the top of a desk 吸墨紙 **2** *AmE* a book in which an official daily record is kept【美】記事本, 臨時記錄簿: *the police blotter* 警察臨時記事本

blotting pa·per /ˈ·· ˌ··/ *n* [U] soft thick paper used for drying wet ink on a page after writing 吸墨紙

blot·to /ˈblɑto; ˈblɒtəʊ/ *adj BrE old-fashioned* drunk【英, 過時】爛醉的

blouse /blaus; blaʊz/ *n* [C] a shirt for women 女式寬鬆短衫, 女襯衫: *a silk blouse* 絲質女襯衫

blow up 爆炸; 吹氣

The car blew up. 汽車爆炸了。

Roald's blowing up a balloon. 羅阿爾德在吹氣球。

blow¹ /blo; bləʊ/ *v past tense* **blew** /blu; bluː/ *past participle* **blown** /blon; bləʊn/

1 ►WIND MOVING 風移動◄ [I] if the wind or a current of air blows, it moves〔風〕吹, 颳: *A cold breeze was blowing.* 寒風在吹。

2 ►WIND MOVING STH 風吹動某物◄ [I usually+adv/prep, T] to move something, or to be moved, by the force of the wind or a current of air 吹動; 颳走: *Her hair was blowing in the breeze.* 她的頭髮在微風中飄揚。| *A sudden draught blew the door shut.* 一陣突如其來的穿堂風把門颳上了。

3 ►AIR FROM YOUR MOUTH 嘴裡呼出的空氣◄ [I, T] to send out a current of air from your mouth 吹氣; 噴氣: *She blew on her coffee to cool it down.* 她把咖啡吹涼。

4 ►MAKE A NOISE 弄出聲響◄ [I,T] to make a sound by passing air through a musical instrument or a horn 吹奏; (使) 鳴響: *The whistle blew for halftime.* 哨子聲響起, 上半場結束。

5 ►VIOLENCE 暴力◄ [T] to damage or destroy something violently with an explosion or by shooting 炸毀, 摧毀: **blow sth away/out/off** *The explosion blew the ship right out of the water.* 爆炸將船掀出水面。

6 ►LOSE MONEY 損失金錢◄ [T] *informal* to spend all your money at one time in a careless way【非正式】亂花, 揮霍: *He's blown all his wages on a new stereo.* 他花掉所有的工資買了一台新的立體聲音響。

7 ►LOSE AN OPPORTUNITY 失去機會◄ [T] *informal* to lose a good opportunity by making a mistake or by being careless【非正式】失掉, 斷送: *We've blown our chances of getting that new contract.* 我們失去了得到那份新合同的機會。

8 ►SURPRISE/ANNOYANCE 驚訝/煩惱◄ **blow/blow me/blow that etc** *BrE spoken* used to show surprise, annoyance, or determination【英口】真沒料到; 糟糕〔表示驚訝、煩惱或決心〕: *Blow me if she didn't just run off!* 她沒有逃走才怪呢! | *Blow it! I forgot to phone Jane.* 糟糕! 我忘了給簡打電話。

9 ▶MAKE A SHAPE 造成某形狀◀ [T] to make or shape something by sending out a current of air from your mouth 吹製: **blow a bubble** (=make a ball shape) 吹泡泡 | **blow glass** (=shape glass by blowing into it when it is very hot) 吹製玻璃(器皿)
10 blow sth (up) out of all proportion to make something seem much more serious or important than it is 小題大作; 誇大
11 ▶LEAVE 離開◀ **blow town** *AmE slang* to leave a place quickly【美俚】匆忙離開
12 ▶ELECTRICITY STOPS 電力中斷◀ [I,T] if an electrical FUSE[1] (1) blows, or a piece of electrical equipment blows a FUSE[1] (1), the electricity suddenly stops working because a thin wire has melted〔保險絲〕燒斷
13 ▶TYRE 輪胎◀ [I,T] if a tyre blows or if a car blows a tyre, it bursts 爆裂, (使)破裂
14 ▶MAKE A SECRET KNOWN 泄密◀ to make known a secret about someone or something 泄露〔祕密〕: *Your coming here has blown the whole operation.* 你來這兒使整個行動泄了密。| **blow sb's cover** (=make known what someone's real job or name is) 公開某人的真實身分 *It is believed Ames blew the cover of up to twenty agents.* 據信艾姆斯公開了二十個間諜的身分。| **blow the gaff** *BrE slang* (=tell something secret, especially without intending to)【英俚】泄露祕密, 告密
15 blow hot and cold *informal* to keep changing your attitude towards someone or something【非正式】(對…)反覆無常, 忽冷忽熱, 搖擺不定: *I can't tell what he wants – he keeps blowing hot and cold.* 我也不知道他要甚麼, 他一直拿不定主意。
16 blow sb a kiss to kiss your hand and then pretend to blow the kiss towards someone 給某人一個飛吻: *She blew him a kiss from across the street.* 她從街對面向他飛吻。
17 blow your mind *informal* to make you feel very surprised and excited by something【非正式】使驚喜, 使吃驚: *Meeting her after so many years really blew my mind.* 多年以後再見到她真令我喜出望外。—see also 另見 MIND-BLOWING
18 blow your nose to clean your nose by forcing air through it into a cloth or a piece of soft paper 擤鼻涕
19 blow sth sky-high a) to destroy an idea, plan etc by showing that it cannot be true or effective 粉碎; 使破滅: *This new information blows his theory sky-high.* 這個新信息徹底粉碎了他的理論。**b)** to completely destory a building or structure with an explosion 把…炸得粉碎, 徹底摧毀
20 blow your top/stack *informal* to become extremely angry quickly or suddenly【非正式】勃然大怒, 大發雷霆
21 blow your own trumpet/horn *informal* to praise yourself for your own achievements【非正式】自吹自擂, 自誇: *You have to blow your own trumpet sometimes – no one else'll do it for you.* 有時你必須自我吹噓一下, 沒有人會代你那樣做的。
22 blow the whistle on *informal* to bring something that is wrong to the attention of an authority or the public【非正式】〔向有關當局或公眾〕揭發〔錯事〕, 揭露
23 blow a gasket/fuse *informal* to become very angry and upset【非正式】大怒, 暴跳如雷: *Don't tell her that, she'll blow a fuse!* 別告訴她, 她會大發雷霆的!

blow away *phr v informal, especially AmE*【非正式, 尤美】**1** [T **blow** sb ↔ **away**] to kill someone by shooting them with a gun 槍殺: *One move and I'll blow you away!* 動一動我就開槍打死你! **2** [T **blow** sb ↔ **away**] to defeat someone completely, especially in a game〔尤指在比賽中〕徹底戰勝〔某人〕: *Nancy blew away the rest of the skaters.* 南希戰勝了其他的滑冰運動員。**3** [T **blow** sb ↔ **away**] to completely surprise someone, especially with something they admire〔尤指用某人羨慕的東西〕使大為驚訝

blow down *phr v* [I,T] if the wind blows something down, or if something blows down, the wind makes it fall 吹倒, 颳倒: **blow sth ↔ down** *trees blown down in the gale* 被大風颳倒的樹木

blow in *phr v* [I] *informal, especially AmE* to arrive unexpectedly【非正式, 尤美】突然到來: *Jim blew in about an hour ago – did you see him?* 吉姆大約一小時前突然來了, 你見到他了嗎?

blow sb/sth **off** *phr v* [T] *AmE slang* to treat someone or something as unimportant【美俚】視〔某人或某事〕不重要, 不重視, 輕視: *It seems crazy that they blew off Jurassic Park when they were choosing best movies.* 他們真傻, 在選擇最佳影片時竟然沒有瞧上《侏羅紀公園》。

blow out *phr v* **1** [I,T] if you blow a flame or a fire out, or if it blows out, it stops burning 吹滅; 熄滅: **blow sth ↔ out** *Blow out all the candles.* 吹滅所有的蠟燭。| *The match blew out before I could light the candles.* 沒等我點燃蠟燭, 火柴就滅了。**2** [I] if a tyre blows out, it bursts〔車胎〕爆裂 **3** [T] **blow itself out** if a storm blows itself out, it ends〔風暴〕停止: *We sheltered in a barn waiting for the storm to blow itself out.* 我們躲在穀倉裡, 等風暴停止。**4** [T **blow** sb ↔ **out**] **a)** *AmE spoken* to easily defeat someone【美口】輕而易舉地戰勝: *We blew them out 28 – zero.* 我們以 28 比 0 大勝他們。**b)** *BrE spoken* to disappoint someone by not meeting them or not doing what you have agreed to【英口】失約; 失信於〔某人〕: *He blew me out again last night – I've had enough.* 昨晚他又一次失約, 我可受夠了。**5** [I] if an oil or gas well blows out, oil or gas suddenly escapes〔油井或氣井〕井噴

blow over *phr v* **1** [I,T] if the wind blows something over, or it blows over, the wind makes it fall 颳倒: *Our fence blew over in the storm.* 我們的籬笆被風暴颳倒了。| **blow sth ↔ over** *You could get blown over in a hurricane.* 颶風會把你颳倒。**2** [I] if a storm blows over, it comes to an end〔暴風雨等〕停止, 平息; 過去 **3** [I] if an argument or unpleasant situation blows over, it no longer seems important or is forgotten〔重要性〕消失; 被遺忘: *They weren't speaking to each other, but I think it's blown over now.* 他們互相之間不說話, 但我想現在一切都過去了。

blow up *phr v* **1** [I,T] to destroy something, or to be destroyed, by an explosion 炸毀, (使)炸得粉碎: *The plane blew up in midair.* 飛機在半空中爆炸。| **blow sth ↔ up** *Rebels attempted to blow up the bridge.* 叛亂分子企圖炸毀橋梁。**2** [T **blow** sth ↔ **up**] to fill something with air or gas 給…充氣, 打氣: *Stop at the gas station and we'll blow up the tyres.* 在加油站停一下, 我們要給輪胎打氣。**3** [T **blow** sth ↔ **up**] if you blow up a photograph, you make it larger 放大〔照片〕: *How much would it cost to have this photo blown up?* 把這張照片放大要多少錢? **4** [I] if bad weather blows up, it suddenly arrives〔惡劣天氣〕來臨: *It looks as though there's a storm blowing up.* 暴風雨好像就要來了。**5** [I] if a situation, argument etc blows up, it suddenly becomes important or dangerous〔形勢、爭論等〕變得嚴峻: *A crisis had blown up over the peace talks.* 和談出現了危機。**6** [I] to become very angry with someone 大發雷霆: *Jenny's father blew up when she didn't come home last night.* 珍妮昨晚沒回家, 她的父親大為光火。

blow² *n* [C] W3
1 ▶HARD HIT 重擊◀ a hard hit with the hand, a tool, or a weapon 重擊: *a blow on the head* 在頭上的一記重擊 | *three heavy blows from the hammer* 用錘重擊三下
2 ▶BAD EFFECT 壞效果◀ something that has a bad effect on your confidence or on the possibility of success〔對信心、成功的可能性等的〕打擊: **[+to]** *Her rejection was a serious blow to his pride.* 她的拒絕使他的自尊心受到沉重打擊。| **deal a blow** *Withdrawal of government funding dealt a serious blow to the project.* 政府資金的撤出嚴重打擊了這項工程。
3 ▶UNHAPPY EVENT 不幸事件◀ an event that makes you very unhappy or shocks you 突然的打擊; 不幸: *Her*

mother's death was a terrible blow. 她母親的去世對她是一個可怕的打擊。
4 ►BLOWING 吹◄ [C] an action of blowing〔指動作〕吹: *It took three blows to put out the candles.* 吹了三下才把蠟燭吹滅。
5 come to blows to quarrel seriously and start hitting each other 打起來: *They almost came to blows over the money.* 他們為錢的事差一點兒打起來。
6 soften/cushion the blow to help someone accept something unpleasant or bad 緩和…的打擊
7 ►WIND 風◄ [singular] a strong wind or storm 勁風; 風暴 —see also 另見 BODY BLOW, **strike a blow for** (STRIKE[1] (12))

blow-by-blow /ˌ· · ˈ·◂/ *adj* [only before noun 僅用於名詞前] a blow-by-blow story, account etc gives all the details of an event as they happened〔敘述〕極其詳盡的: *Jenny bored us all with a blow-by-blow account of her night out.* 珍妮極其詳盡地敘述她晚上外出的事, 我們都聽煩了。

blow-dry /ˈ· ·/ *v* [T] to dry hair and give it shape by using an electric dryer〔用吹風機〕吹乾〔頭髮〕; 把〔頭髮〕吹出髮型 —**blow-dry** *n* [C]: *a cut and blow-dry* 剪髮並吹風

blow·er /ˈbloɚ; ˈbləʊə/ *n* [C] **1** a machine that blows out air 吹風機, 鼓風機: *a snow blower for clearing the path* 清掃小徑的吹雪機 **2 on the blower** *BrE old-fashioned* on the telephone in order to talk to someone【英, 過時】打電話: *Get on the blower to him at once.* 馬上打電話給他。—see also 另見 GLASSBLOWER

blow-fly /ˈ· ·/ *n* [C] a fly that lays its eggs on meat or wounds〔產卵於腐肉、創口的〕麗蠅, 綠頭蒼蠅

blow-hard /ˈ· ·/ *n* [C] *AmE informal* someone who talks about themselves too much【美, 非正式】自吹自擂者

blow-hole /ˈ· ·/ *n* [C] **1** a hole in the surface of ice to which water animals such as seals (SEAL[1] (1)) come to breathe〔海豹等動物游去呼吸的結冰水面上的〕冰孔 **2** a hole in the top of the head of a WHALE, DOLPHIN etc through which they breathe〔鯨魚、海豚等的〕噴水孔, 鼻孔

blow job /ˈ· ·/ *n* [C] *taboo slang* the practice of touching a man's sexual organs with your lips and tongue to give him sexual pleasure【諱, 俚】口交

blow-lamp /ˈ· ·/ *n* [C] *BrE* a piece of equipment that produces a small very hot flame, used especially for removing paint【英】噴燈; BLOWTORCH *AmE*【美】

blown /blon; bləʊn/ the past participle of BLOW[1]

blow·out /ˈbloˌaut; ˈbləʊaʊt/ *n* [C] **1** a sudden bursting of a TYRE 輪胎爆裂: *A blow-out at this speed could be really dangerous.* 輪胎在這樣的車速下爆裂是很危險的。**2** [usually singular 一般用單數] *informal* a big expensive meal or large social occasion【非正式】美餐, 盛宴; 大型社交活動 **3** a sudden uncontrolled escape of oil or gas from a well〔油井或氣井的〕井噴 **4** *AmE informal* an easy victory over someone in a game【美, 非正式】〔比賽中〕輕而易舉的勝利

blow·pipe /ˈbloˌpaɪp; ˈbləʊpaɪp/ *n* [C] a tube through which you can blow small stones, poisoned arrows (ARROW (1)) etc, used as a weapon〔作為武器用的〕吹箭筒, 吹矢槍

blow·torch /ˈbloˌtɔrtʃ; ˈbləʊtɔːtʃ/ *n* [C] *AmE* a piece of equipment that produces a small very hot flame, used especially for removing paint【美】噴燈; BLOW-LAMP *BrE*【英】

blow-up /ˈ· ·/ *n* [C] **1** a photograph, or part of a photograph, that has been made larger 放大的照片 **2** [usually singular 一般用單數] a sudden moment of anger 發脾氣: *I think they've had a blow-up again.* 我想他們又吵架了。—see also 另見 **blow up** (BLOW[1])

blow·y /ˈbloɪ; ˈbləʊi/ *adj BrE informal* windy【英, 非正式】颳風的, 風大的

blow·zy, blowsy /ˈblauzɪ; ˈblaʊzi/ *adj* a blowzy woman is fat and looks untidy〔婦女〕體胖而又穿着邋遢的

blub·ber[1] /ˈblʌbɚ; ˈblʌbə/ *v* **1** also 又作 **blub** [I] to cry noisily, especially in a way that annoys people 號哭: *Stop blubbering, for heaven's sake!* 天哪, 別再哇哇地哭個不停了! **2** also 又作 **blubber out** [T] to say something while crying noisily 邊哭邊說; 哭訴: *"It's not my fault," she blubbered.* "這不是我的錯。"她哭訴道。

blubber[2] *n* [U] the fat of sea animals, especially WHALES 海獸脂肪〔尤指鯨脂〕

bludge /blʌdʒ; blʌdʒ/ *v* [I,T] *AustrE, NZE slang* to get something without working or paying for it【澳, 新西蘭, 俚】(向人) 索取; 不勞而獲 —**bludger** *n* [C]

blud·geon[1] /ˈblʌdʒən; ˈblʌdʒən/ *v* [T] **1** [+into/out of] to force someone to do something by making threats or arguing with them 強迫, 威脅〔某人做某事〕 **2** to hit someone several times with something heavy 用重物接連重擊〔某人〕: *bludgeoned to death* 被重擊致死

bludgeon[2] *n* [C] a heavy stick with a thick end, used as a weapon〔作武器用的〕大頭棒

blue[1] /blu; bluː/ *adj*
1 ►COLOUR 顏色◄ the colour of the clear sky or of the sea on a fine day 藍色的, 蔚藍色的, 青色的: *the blue water of the lake* 蔚藍色的湖水 | *a dark blue raincoat* 深藍色的雨衣 —see picture on page A5 參見A5頁圖
2 ►SAD 悲傷的◄ [not before noun 不用於名詞前] *informal* sad and without hope; DEPRESSED (1a)【非正式】憂鬱的, 沮喪的, 悲觀的: *That song always makes me feel blue.* 那首歌曲總使我傷感。
3 ►CONCERNED WITH SEX 與性有關的◄ *informal* concerned with sex in a way that might offend some people【非正式】色情的, 淫猥的: *Some of his jokes were a bit blue.* 他的某些笑話有點下流。—see also 另見 BLUE FILM
4 once in a blue moon *informal* hardly ever【非正式】難得有一次, 極為罕見: *I only ever see him once in a blue moon.* 我難得見到他。
5 scream/yell blue murder *informal* to shout very loudly in protest against something or because you are in pain【非正式】大聲抗議; 大聲呼救
6 do sth till you're blue in the face *informal* to do something a lot but without achieving what you want【非正式】盡力去做仍無法成功: *You can argue till you're blue in the face, she won't change her mind.* 不管你怎麼說, 她也不會改變主意的。
7 blue with cold extremely cold 凍得發紫
8 talk a blue streak *AmE informal* to talk a lot without stopping【美, 非正式】喋喋不休, 說個沒完
9 go blue if your skin goes blue, you become blue because you are cold or cannot breathe properly〔因寒冷或不能呼吸而〕臉色發青
10 like blue blazes *AmE informal* extremely【美, 非正式】非常, 極其: *It hurts like blue blazes!* 疼極了!

blue[2] *n* **1** [C,U] the colour that is blue 藍色: *the rich greens and blues of the tapestry* 掛毯濃豔的藍綠色調 | *She nearly always dresses in blue.* 她幾乎總穿藍色衣服。**2 blues** [plural] a slow sad style of music that came from the southern US 勃魯斯音樂〔起源於美國南方的一種緩慢、憂鬱的樂曲〕: *a blues singer* 勃魯斯歌手 —see also 另見 RHYTHM AND BLUES **3 the blues** [plural] *informal* feelings of sadness【非正式】憂鬱, 沮喪: *Don't be surprised if you get the blues for a while after your baby is born.* 如果你在生完孩子後出現暫時的憂鬱, 你不必感到驚訝。**4 out of the blue** *informal* unexpectedly【非正式】出乎意料地, 突如其來地: *a phone call from Jane right out of the blue* 出乎意料地接到了簡打來的電話 —see also 另見 **a bolt from/out of the blue** (BOLT[1] (3)) **5 boys in blue** *informal* the police【非正式】警察 **6** [C] **Blue** *BrE* someone who has represented Oxford or Cambridge University at a sport, or the title given to such a person【英】校隊選手, "藍色選手"〔給予曾代表牛津或劍橋大學運動隊參賽隊員的一種榮譽〕: *a rugger Blue* 橄欖球隊的"藍色選手" **7 the blue** *lite-*

rary the sea or the sky【文】海洋; 天空

blue[3] *v* [T] *BrE informal* to spend money in a way that is careless or not very responsible【英, 非正式】濫用〔錢〕, 揮霍: *John blued all his money on drink.* 約翰把他所有的錢都花在酗酒上。

blue ba·by /ˈ· ˌ··/ *n* [C] a baby whose skin is slightly blue when it is born because it has a heart problem〔出生時因心臟有先天性缺陷而〕皮膚發青的嬰兒

blue·beard /ˈbluˌbɪrd; ˈbluːbɪəd/ *n* [C] a man who marries and kills one wife after another 藍鬍子〔一個連續娶妻殺妻的男人〕

blue·bell /ˈbluˌbɛl; ˈbluːbel/ *n* [C] a small plant with blue flowers that grows in woods 藍色風鈴草

blue·ber·ry /ˈbluˌbɛrɪ; ˈbluːbəri/ *n* [C,U] the small blue fruit of a bushy plant, or the plant itself 藍莓漿果, 紫漿果; 烏飯樹, 藍莓: *blueberry pie* 藍莓餡餅 —see picture on page A8 參見 A8 頁圖

blue·bird /ˈbluˌbɝd; ˈbluːbɜːd/ *n* [C] a small blue bird that lives in North America〔北美的〕藍色知更鳥, 藍鶇

blue-blood·ed /ˌ· ˈ··◂/ *adj* belonging to a royal or NOBLE[1] (3) family 貴族血統的, 名門出身的: *a blue-blooded French duchess* 有貴族血統的法國女公爵 —**blue-blood** *n* [U]

blue book /ˈ· ·/ *n* [C] **1** *BrE* an official report, usually by a committee, printed by the British Government【英】藍皮書〔由英國政府印行、通常為某個委員會的官方報告〕 **2** *AmE* a book with a blue cover that is used in American colleges for writing answers to examination questions【美】〔美國大學生筆試用的〕藍色封面的答題冊, 藍皮簿

blue·bot·tle /ˈbluˌbɑtl̩; ˈbluːˌbɒtl/ *n* [C] a large blue fly 青蠅

blue cheese /ˌ· ˈ·/ *n* [C, U] a kind of cheese with blue lines and a strong taste〔帶有藍色黴菌條紋的〕藍乳酪

blue chip /ˌ· ˈ·◂/ *adj* a blue-chip company or INVESTMENT (1) is profitable and safe〔公司或投資〕穩賺錢的, 可靠的, 藍籌(股)的: *blue chip stocks and shares* 熱門債券和股票 —**blue chip** *n* [C]

blue-col·lar /ˌ· ˈ··◂/ *adj* [only before noun 僅用於名詞前] blue-collar workers do hard or dirty work with their hands 藍領階級的, 體力勞動者的 —compare 比較 PINK-COLLAR, WHITE-COLLAR

blue-eyed boy /ˌ· · ˈ·/ *n* [C usually singular 一般用單數] *informal* a man or boy who is liked and approved of by someone in authority【非正式】(男) 寵兒: *John was always the blue-eyed boy at school.* 約翰在學校裡總是寵兒。

blue film /ˌ· ˈ·/ *n* [C] *BrE informal* a film showing sexual activity; BLUE MOVIE【英, 非正式】色情電影

blue·fish /ˈbluˌfɪʃ; ˈbluːˌfɪʃ/ *n plural* **bluefish** [C] a sea fish that is a bluish colour and is caught for sport and to eat off the North American coast〔北美產的〕青魚

blue·grass /ˈbluˌgræs; ˈbluːgrɑːs/ *n* [U] **1** a type of music from the southern and western US, played on instruments such as the GUITAR and VIOLIN 藍草鄉村音樂〔美國鄉村音樂, 起源於南部和西部, 通常用結他或小提琴演奏〕 **2** a type of grass found in North America, especially in Kentucky 六月禾〔一種禾本科植物, 生長在北美, 尤在肯塔基州〕

blue gum /ˈ· ·/ *n* [C] a tall Australian tree that is a type of EUCALYPTUS〔產於澳洲的〕藍桉樹

blue·jay /ˈbluˌdʒe; ˈbluːˌdʒeɪ/ *n* [C] a common large North American bird with blue feathers〔北美產的〕藍背樫鳥

blue jeans /ˌ· ˈ·/ *n* [plural] *AmE* dark blue trousers made in a heavy material; JEANS【美】牛仔褲

blue law /ˈ· ·/ *n* [C] *AmE* a law to control sexual morals, the drinking of alcohol, working on Sundays etc【美】〔管理性道德、喝酒、星期日工作等的〕清教徒法規, 藍色法規; LICENSING LAWS *BrE*【英】

blue mo·vie /ˌ· ˈ··/ *n* [C] a film showing sexual activity 色情電影

blue·print /ˈbluˌprɪnt; ˈbluːˌprɪnt/ *n* [C] **1** a plan for achieving something 計劃, 設想: *a blueprint for the reform of the tax system* 税制改革計劃 **2** a photographic print of a plan for a building, machine etc 藍圖

blue rib·bon /ˌ· ˈ··/ also 又作 **blue riband** *n* [C] *AmE* a small piece of blue material that you give to the first-prize winner of a competition【美】藍綬帶〔頒發給競賽優勝者作為一等獎標誌〕—**blue ribbon** *adj*: *a blue-ribbon recipe* 一流的食譜

blue-rinse /ˌ· ˈ·◂/ *adj BrE*【英】**blue-rinse brigade** *humorous* used to describe older women with traditional RIGHT WING values【幽默】具傳統右翼思想的老年婦女, 黑髮幫 —see also 另見 RINSE[2] (2)

blue-sky /ˈ· ·/ *adj* [only before noun 僅用於名詞前] *AmE* blue-sky tests etc are done to test ideas and not for any practical purpose【美】〔測試等〕純理論的; 不切實際的

blue·stock·ing /ˈbluˌstɑkɪŋ; ˈbluːˌstɒkɪŋ/ *n* [C] *BrE old-fashioned* a very well-educated woman【英, 過時】有學者氣派的女性, 才女

bluff[1] /blʌf; blʌf/ *v* [I,T] to pretend that you will do something bad or that you are someone else, especially to get something you want when you are in a difficult or dangerous situation 虛張聲勢, 嚇唬; 欺騙: *"I'm an accredited British envoy," he bluffed.* "我是官方派來的英國使節。"他嚇唬說。| **bluff your way out of/through/past** (=get out of a difficult situation by deceiving someone) 以欺騙手段擺脱困境 *They bluffed their way past the prison guard.* 他們蒙騙了獄警逃走了。| **bluff it out** (=escape trouble by continuing to deceive someone) 繼續蒙騙以脱離困境 | **bluff sb into doing sth** *Rob bluffed the interviewers into believing he'd had lots of experience.* 羅布蒙騙面試考官讓他們認為自己很有經驗。

bluff[2] *n* **1** [C,U] an attempt to deceive someone by making them think you will do something when you have no intention of doing it 虛張聲勢, 嚇唬: *Her threat to fire me was little more than a bluff.* 她威脅説要開除我, 但那不過是嚇唬人而已。**2 call sb's bluff** to tell someone to do what they threaten because you believe they have no intention of doing it and you want to prove it 促使某人實行其所威脅要做的事; 接受某人挑戰 **3** [C] a very steep cliff or slope 峭壁, 懸崖, 陡岸

bluff[3] *adj* behaving in a loud, cheerful way, without always considering the way other people feel 率直的, 爽快的, 粗率的: *He tried in his bluff, good-natured way to comfort her.* 他試着用率直而溫厚的方式安慰她。—**bluffly** *adv* —**bluffness** *n* [U]

blu·ish /ˈbluɪʃ; ˈbluːɪʃ/ *adj* slightly blue 淺藍色的; 帶青色的: *Her skin had a bluish tinge.* 她的皮膚有點發藍。

blun·der[1] /ˈblʌndɚ; ˈblʌndə/ *n* [C] a careless or stupid mistake 愚蠢的錯誤, 疏忽: *A last-minute blunder by the goalkeeper cost them the match.* 守門員最後一分鐘的疏忽使他們輸掉了這場比賽。

blunder[2] *v* **1** [I always+adv/prep] to move in an unsteady way, as if you cannot see properly 踉踉蹌蹌地走, 跌跌撞撞: **blunder around/about/into** *I could hear someone blundering around downstairs.* 我能聽到樓下有人在跌跌撞撞地走動。**2** [I] to make a big mistake, especially because you have been careless or stupid 犯愚蠢的錯誤; 出漏子: *They blundered badly when they appointed him as Chairman.* 他們犯了一個很愚蠢的錯誤, 就是任命他為主席。—**blunderer** *n* [C]

blun·der·buss /ˈblʌndɚˌbʌs; ˈblʌndəbʌs/ *n* [C] a type of gun used in the past〔老式的〕短程散彈槍

blun·der·ing /ˈblʌndərɪŋ; ˈblʌndərɪŋ/ *adj* [only before noun 僅用於名詞前] careless or stupid 粗心的; 愚蠢的: *You blundering idiot! What did you do that for?* 你這個愚蠢的傻瓜!你為甚麼要那樣做?

blunt[1] /blʌnt; blʌnt/ *adj* **1** not sharp or pointed 鈍的, 不鋒利的, 不尖的: *All I could find was a blunt pencil.* 我只能找到一枝鈍鉛筆。—opposite 反義詞 SHARP[1] (11) —see picture at 參見 SHARP[1] 圖 **2** speaking in an honest way even if this upsets people〔說話〕不客氣的, 直言不諱的, 耿直的: *Jan was straightforward and blunt as always.* 簡總是那樣坦率, 直言不諱。—see also 另見 BLUNTLY —**bluntness** *n* [U]

blunt² *v* [T] **1** to make a feeling less strong 減弱: *The bad weather blunted their enthusiasm for camping.* 糟糕的天氣減弱了他們去露營的熱情。**2** to make the point of a pencil or the edge of a knife less sharp 把〔鉛筆尖或刀〕弄鈍

blunt·ly /ˋblʌntlɪ; ˈblʌntli/ *adv* speaking in a direct, honest way that sometimes upsets people〔說話〕不客氣地, 直言不諱地: *"You've drunk too much," she said bluntly.* "你喝得太多了。"她不客氣地説。| **to put it bluntly** *spoken*【口】*To put it bluntly, she's not up to the job.* 恕我直言, 她不適合這份工作。

blur¹ /blɝ; blɜː/ *n* [singular] **1** [C] a shape that you cannot see clearly 模糊不清的事物: *Everything's a blur without my glasses.* 不戴眼鏡我眼前一片模糊。| *the blur of headlights in the distance* 遠處隱隱約約的汽車前燈 **2** an unclear memory of something 模糊的記憶: *The events of that day gradually became a blur in her mind.* 那天發生的事在她的腦海中逐漸變得模糊。

blur² *v* **1** [I,T] to become difficult to see or make something difficult to see, because the edges are not clear (使) 模糊, (使) 看不清楚: *The ships on the horizon seemed to blur before my eyes.* 遠處地平線上的船隻看上去似乎模模糊糊的。**2** [I,T] to make the difference between two ideas, subjects etc less clear (使) 不明朗, (使) 不清楚: *The differences between the two political parties have slowly blurred.* 兩黨之間的分歧慢慢地已不再明顯。—see also 另見 BLURRED —**blurry** *adj*: *a few blurry photos of their holiday together* 幾張他們在一起度假時拍的模糊照片

blurb /blɝb; blɜːb/ *n* [C] a short description giving information about a book, new product etc 書的內容提要; 新產品的簡介

blurred 模糊的

The words were blurred without his glasses.
他不戴眼鏡字就變得模糊了。

blurred /blɝd; blɜːd/ *adj* **1** unclear in shape, or making it difficult to see shapes〔形狀〕模糊的: *a blurred photo* 一張模糊的照片 **2** difficult to remember or understand clearly〔記憶〕模糊的; 不太好理解的: *blurred memories* 模糊的記憶

blurt /blɝt; blɜːt/ *v*

blurt sth ↔ **out** *phr v* [T] to say something suddenly and without thinking, usually because you are nervous or excited〔尤指因緊張或激動而〕不假思索地說出, 脱口說出, 說漏嘴: *Peter blurted the news out before we could stop him.* 我們還沒來得及阻止, 彼得就脱口說出了那個消息。

blush¹ /blʌʃ; blʌʃ/ *v* [I] **1** to become red in the face, usually because you are embarrassed〔因難為情而〕臉紅: *He blushes every time he speaks to her.* 他每次和她說話都臉紅。**2** to feel ashamed or embarrassed about something 感到不好意思; 慚愧: **blush to do sth** *I blush to think of the things I did when I was younger.* 想起我年輕時做過的事, 我就感到羞愧難當。**3 the blushing bride** *humorous* a young woman on her wedding day【幽默】含羞的新娘 —**blushingly** *adv*

blush² *n* **1** [C] the red colour on your face that appears when you are embarrassed 臉紅, 赧顏: *She felt a blush come to her cheeks when her name was mentioned.* 她的名字被提到時, 她感到一陣臉紅。**2 spare my blushes** *old-fashioned* used to say that someone is praising you too much【過時】讓我臉紅, 使我難為情 **3 at first blush** *literary* when first thought of or considered【文】猛一看, 乍看時: *At first blush this discovery would seem to confirm his theory.* 乍一看, 這項發現似乎證實了他的理論。**4** [U] *AmE* blusher【美】胭脂霜 [粉]

blush·er /ˋblʌʃɚ; ˈblʌʃə/ *n* [U] cream or powder used for making your cheeks look red or pink 胭脂霜 [粉]; blush *AmE*【美】

blus·ter /ˋblʌstɚ; ˈblʌstə/ *v* [I] **1** to speak in a loud, angry way 咆哮, 叫嚷, 叱喝: *He was inclined to bluster when his authority was challenged.* 當他的權威受到挑戰時, 他就會聲嘶力竭地喊叫。**2** if the wind blusters, it blows violently〔風〕狂吹 —**bluster** *n* [U] —**blustering** *adj*: *blustering wintry weather* 狂風怒吼的寒冷天氣

blus·ter·y /ˋblʌstərɪ; ˈblʌstəri/ *adj* blustery weather is very windy〔天氣〕惡劣的; 狂風大作的: *a cold and blustery day* 寒風凜冽的一天 —see picture on page A13 參見A13頁圖

blvd the written abbreviation of 縮寫= BOULEVARD

B-mov·ie /ˋbi ˌmuvɪ; ˈbiː ˌmuːvi/ *n* [C] a cheaply-made film of low quality〔廉價製作、質量不高的〕二流影片

BO /ˌbi ˋo; ˌbiː ˈəʊ/ *n* [U] body odour; an unpleasant smell from someone's body caused by sweat 體臭, 狐臭

bo·a /ˋboə; ˈbəʊə/ *n* [C] **1** also 又作 **boa con·strict·or** /ˈ‥ ·ˌ‥/ a large snake that is not poisonous, but kills animals by crushing them 大蟒蛇 **2** a FEATHER BOA〔一種長蛇形〕女用羽毛圍巾

boar /bɔr; bɔː/ *n* [C] **1** a wild pig (公) 野豬 **2** a male pig 公豬

boards 板; 牌子

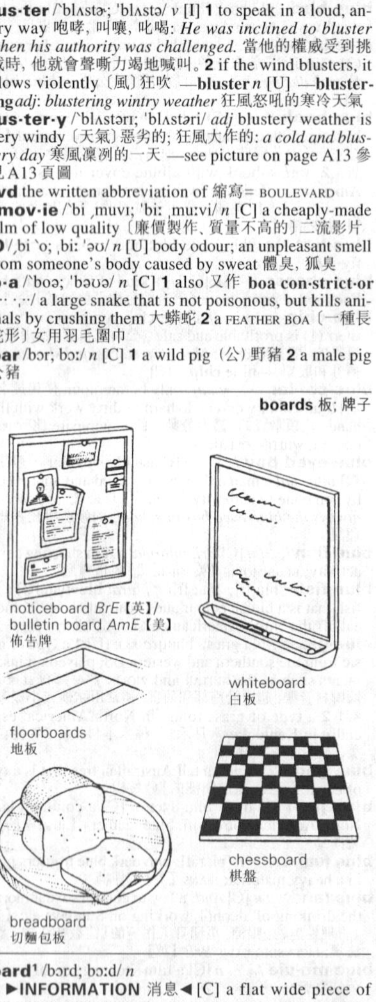

noticeboard *BrE*【英】/
bulletin board *AmE*【美】
佈告牌

whiteboard
白板

floorboards
地板

chessboard
棋盤

breadboard
切麵包板

board¹ /bɔrd; bɔːd/ *n*

1 ►INFORMATION 消息◄ [C] a flat wide piece of

wood, plastic etc that shows a particular type of information〔顯示資料用的〕硬質板; 佈告牌, 公告牌: *I wrote the examples up on the board.* 我把例子寫在黑板上。| *Can I put this notice on the board?* 我可以把這個啟事貼在佈告牌上嗎? | *I'll check the departure board for train times.* 我會到佈告板處查一下火車的開車時間。—see also 另見 NOTICEBOARD, SCOREBOARD

2 ►FOR PUTTING THINGS ON 供放東西用◄ [C] a flat piece of wood, plastic, card etc that you use for a particular purpose such as cutting things on, or for playing indoor games〔特殊用途的〕平板: *Cut the bread on the board, not the table!* 把麵包放在切板上切, 不要放在桌上切! | *Where's the chessboard?* 棋盤在哪兒? —see also 另見 BREADBOARD, CHOPPING BOARD

3 ►GROUP OF PEOPLE 人羣◄ [C also+plural verb *BrE* 英] a group of people in an organization who make the rules and important decisions 理事會, 委員會, 董事會;〔官方的〕局, 部: *a board meeting* 委員會會議 | **sit on a board** *He sits on the hospital management board.* 他是醫院管理委員會委員。| **board of directors** *There is still only one woman on the board of directors.* 董事會中仍然只有一位女性。

4 ►FOR BUILDING 用於建築◄ [C] a long thin flat piece of wood used for making floors, walls, fences etc〔長薄〕木板: *We'll have to take the boards up to check the wiring.* 我們必須把地板撬起來檢查一下電線。—see also 另見 FLOORBOARD (1)

5 on board on a ship or plane 在船上; 在飛機上: *The ship went down with all its crew on board.* 船和船上的全體船員一起下沉。—compare 比較 ABOARD

6 take sth on board to listen to and accept a suggestion, idea etc 接受〔建議、想法等〕: *The school refused to take any of the parents' criticisms on board.* 學校拒絕接受家長們提出的任何批評。

7 go by the board if a plan goes by the board, it is no longer possible〔計劃、安排等〕落空, 失敗: *We just don't have the time – so our idea about meeting to discuss it has had to go by the board.* 我們根本沒時間, 所以我們本來打算開會討論一下這件事的想法只好告吹了。

8 across the board if a plan or situation happens across the board, it affects everyone in a particular group, place etc 全面地, 涉及全體地: *We're aiming to increase productivity across the board.* 我們的目標是全面提高生產效率。

9 ►MEALS 膳食◄ [U] the meals that are provided for you when you pay to stay somewhere 膳食: *I pay $100 a week for room and board.* 我每週付100美元膳宿費。| **full/half board** (=all or some meals)〔旅館等〕供一日三餐的/供部分膳食的

10 ►THEATRE 劇場◄ **the boards** [plural] the stage in a theatre 舞台 —see also 另見 **tread the boards** (TREAD[1] (6))

11 ►SPORT 體育◄ **boards** [plural] *AmE* the low wooden wall around the area in which you play ICE HOCKEY【美】〔冰球場四周的〕護板

12 college/medical boards *AmE* examinations that you take in the US when you apply to a college or medical school【美】大學/醫學院的入學考試 —see also 另見 ABOVE BOARD, DIVING BOARD, DRAWING BOARD, IRONING BOARD, SURFBOARD, **sweep the board** (SWEEP[1] (9))

board² *v* **1** [I,T] *formal* to get on a bus, plane, train etc in order to travel somewhere【正式】登上〔巴士、飛機、火車等交通工具〕: *Passengers are asked to board half an hour before departure time.* 乘客須在起飛[開車]前半小時登機[上車]。**2** [I] if a plane or ship is boarding, passengers are getting onto it 登機; 上船: *Flight N654 for Kathmandu is now boarding at Gate 16.* 飛往加德滿都的N654號航班現在由16號門登機。**3** [I always+adv/prep] to stay in a room in someone's house that you pay for〔在某人家裡〕寄宿; 寄膳: *I board with the Nicholsons during the week.* 週一到週五我寄宿在尼科爾森家。**4** [I] to stay at a school at night as well as during the day 在校寄宿: *The students board during the week and go home at weekends.* 學生們平日住在學校裡, 週末才回家。

board sth ↔ **out** *phr v* [T] *BrE* to pay money and arrange for an animal to stay somewhere【英】把〔動物〕寄養〔在某處〕: *We'll have to board the cat out while we're away.* 我們外出期間, 得給貓找個地方寄養。

board sth ↔ **up** *phr v* [T] to cover a window or door with wooden boards 用〔木板〕遮住 [堵上]: *All the windows were boarded up and the place looked totally deserted.* 所有的窗子都被堵上了, 整個地方看起來很荒涼。

board·er /ˈbɔrdɚ; ˈbɔːdə/ *n* [C] **1** a student who stays at a school during the night, as well as during the day 寄宿生, 住校生 **2** someone who pays to live in another person's house with some or all of their meals provided; LODGER〔住在他人家裡的〕寄宿者, 寄膳宿者

board game /ˈ· ·/ *n* [C] an indoor game played on a specially designed board made of thick card or wood 棋類遊戲

board·ing /ˈbɔrdɪŋ; ˈbɔːdɪŋ/ *n* [U] **1** the act of getting on a ship, plane etc in order to travel somewhere 登機; 上船: *Boarding is now taking place at Gate 38.* 38號門現在開始登機。**2** narrow pieces of wood that are fixed side by side, usually to cover a broken door or window 並排的木板

boarding card /ˈ·· ·/ *n* an official card that you have to show before you get onto a plane 登機證

boarding house /ˈ·· ·/ *n* [C] a private house where you pay to sleep and eat; GUESTHOUSE 供膳宿的私人住房 —compare 比較 PENSION[3]

boarding pass /ˈ·· ·/ *n* [C] a boarding card 登機證

boarding school /ˈ·· ·/ *n* [C] a school where students live as well as study 寄宿學校 —compare 比較 DAY SCHOOL

board·room /ˈbɔrdˌrum; ˈbɔːdruːm/ *n* [C] a room where the directors (DIRECTOR (1)) of a company have meetings 董事會會議室

board·walk /ˈbɔrdˌwɔk; ˈbɔːdwɔːk/ *n* [C] *AmE* a raised path made of wood, usually built next to the sea【美】〔常在海濱〕用木板鋪成的小道 —compare 比較 PIER (2)

boast¹ /bost; bəʊst/ *v* **1** [I,T] to talk too proudly about your abilities, achievements, or possessions because you want to make other people admire you 誇口, 誇耀, 吹噓: *"I can do better than any of them," she boasted.* "我能比他們任何人都做得好。" 她誇口說。| **[+about]** *I'm fed up hearing Jan boast about her new job.* 我已聽膩了簡誇耀她的新工作。| **[+of]** *He enjoyed boasting of his wealth.* 他喜歡誇耀自己的財富。| **boast that** *She was boasting that she could speak six languages fluently.* 她吹噓說她能流利地講六種語言。**2** [T] if a place, object, or organization boasts a good feature, it has that good feature〔地方、物體或機構〕擁有〔好的事物或特徵〕: *Few teams can boast such a good record in European football.* 在歐洲足球壇中沒有幾支隊伍擁有這樣好的記錄。| *The hotel boasts the finest view in Wales.* 這家旅館擁有威爾斯最好的風景。—**boaster** *n* [C]

boast² *n* [C] **1** something that you like telling people because you are proud of it 引以為豪的事物: *One of her proudest boasts is that her daughter is a doctor.* 她最值得驕傲的事之一是她的女兒是醫生。**2 no idle boast** used to say that something is not a boast but that it is true 決非吹牛

boast·ful /ˈbostfəl; ˈbəʊstfəl/ *adj* talking too proudly about yourself 好自誇的, 自吹自擂的: *We all got drunk and became very loud and boastful.* 我們都喝醉了, 扯着嗓門自吹自擂起來。—**boastfully** *adv* —**boastfulness** *n* [U]

boat /bot; bəʊt/ *n* [C] **1** a vehicle that travels across water 小船, 小舟, 小艇: *a fishing boat* 漁船 | *a rowing boat* 划艇 | **by boat/in a boat** *We went up the river by boat.* 我們乘小船在河中逆流而上。**2** *informal* a ship, especially one that carries passengers【非正式】輪船〔尤指客輪〕: *We're getting the night boat to Zeebrugge.* 我們乘晚上的船去澤布呂赫。**3 be in the same boat (as)** to be in the same unpleasant situation as someone else

S1 W2

處於相同的倒霉境地; 面臨同樣的危險: *We're all more or less in the same boat, so there's no use complaining.* 我們的處境差不多, 所以抱怨也沒用。**4 push the boat out** *BrE informal* to spend a lot of money on something, especially on celebrating an event【英, 非正式】不惜多花錢慶祝一番: *They really pushed the boat out for their daughter's wedding.* 他們為女兒的婚禮確實花了不少錢。**5 rock the boat** to express a different attitude, opinion, idea etc from what other people are used to, in a way that upsets them 破壞良好[舒適]的現狀; 擾亂正常秩序: *They rocked the boat by refusing to come to the firm's Christmas lunch.* 他們興風作浪, 拒絕參加公司的聖誕午餐會。—see also 另見 GRAVY BOAT, SAUCE BOAT, **burn your bridges/boats** (BURN[1] (22)), **miss the boat/bus** (MISS[1] (5))

boat·er /ˈbotɚ; ˈbəʊtə/ *n* [C] a hard STRAW (1a) hat with a flat top 平頂硬草帽 —see picture at 參見 HAT 圖

boat hook /ˈ· ·/ *n* [C] a long pole with an iron hook at the end, used to pull or push a small boat〔一端有鉤, 用來鉤住或推開小船的〕鉤篙

boat·house /ˈbotˌhaʊs; ˈbəʊthaʊs/ *n* [C] a building by the side of water that boats are kept in〔水邊停放船隻的〕船庫, 棚屋

boat·ing /ˈbotɪŋ; ˈbəʊtɪŋ/ *n* [U] the activity of travelling in a small boat for pleasure 划船, 乘遊艇: **go boating** *Let's go boating on the lake.* 我們到湖上划船去吧。

boat·man /ˈbotmən; ˈbəʊtmən/ *n* [C] a man who you pay to take you out in a boat or for the use of a boat 出租小船的船主; 船夫; 槳手

boat peo·ple /ˈ· ˌ··/ *n* [plural] people who escape from bad conditions in their country in small boats 乘小船出逃的難民, 船民

boat·swain /ˈbosn̩; ˈbəʊsən/ *n* [C] an officer on a ship whose job is to organize the work and look after the equipment; BOSUN〔船上的〕水手長; 掌帆長

boat train /ˈ· ·/ *n* [C] a train that takes people to or from ships in a port〔與港口船隻配合的〕聯運火車

Bob /bɑb; bɒb/ *n* **Bob's your uncle!** *BrE spoken* used to say that something will be easy to do【英口】沒問題! 放心吧!: *Just copy the disk, and Bob's your uncle!* 複製磁盤吧, 沒問題的!

bob[1] *v*

1 ►MOVE IN WATER 水中移動◄ [I] to move up and down when floating on the surface of water〔在水面上〕上下快速移動: **bob up and down** *The boat was bobbing up and down on the waves.* 小船在波濤中上下顛簸。

2 ►MOVE SOMEWHERE 移往某處◄ [I always+adv/prep] to move quickly in a particular direction 沿某個方向快速移動: **[+up/down/out etc]** *She bobbed down behind the wall to avoid being seen.* 她快速俯身躲到牆後以免讓人看見。

3 bob your head to move your head down quickly as a way of showing respect, greeting someone or agreeing with them 點頭〔表示尊敬、問候或贊同〕: *Seymour bobbed his head respectfully and said, "Good evening, Sir."* 西摩禮貌地點點頭說: "先生, 晚上好。"

4 bob (sb) a curtsy to make a quick, small CURTSY to someone 迅速地行半屈膝禮

5 ►HAIR 頭髮◄ [T] to cut someone's hair so that it is the same length all the way round their head 剪短〔頭髮〕: *I'm going to get my hair bobbed.* 我要把頭髮剪短。—see picture at 參見 HAIRSTYLE 圖

6 bob for apples to play a game in which you try to pick up apples floating in water, using only your mouth 咬蘋果〔指試圖用口咬住漂浮在水上的蘋果的遊戲〕

bob[2] *n* [C] **1** a way of cutting hair so that it is the same length all the way round your head 短齊髮(髮式) —see picture at 參見 HAIRSTYLE 圖 **2** a quick up and down movement of your head, or body, to show respect, agreement, greeting etc 點頭; 屈膝〔表示尊敬、贊同、問候等〕: *The maid gave a little bob and left the room.* 女僕略微點了點頭, 然後離開了房間。**3** [plural] *informal* a SHILLING (=coin used in the past in Britain)【非正式】〔舊時的英國硬幣〕一先令: *In those days the train fare was three bob.* 那時候火車票要花三先令。—see also 另見 **bits and bobs** (BIT[1] (14))

bob·bin /ˈbɑbɪn; ˈbɒbɪn/ *n* [C] a small round object that you wind thread onto, especially for a SEWING MACHINE 線軸, 繞線筒, 管筒 —compare 比較 REEL[1] (1a)

bob·ble[1] /ˈbɑbl̩; ˈbɒbəl/ *n* [C] *BrE* a small soft ball, usually made of wool, that is used especially for decorating clothes【英】〔用於裝飾的〕小羊毛球, 小絨球: *Her pullover had bobbles on the front.* 她的套頭毛衣前面有幾個小絨球。—**bobbly** *adj*: *My sweater's gone all bobbly.* 我的針織套衫都起球了。

bobble[2] *v* [T] *AmE* to drop or hold a ball in an uncontrolled way; FUMBLE (3)【美】漏接〔球〕, 失掉〔球〕: *The shortstop bobbled the ball and the runner ran home.* 游擊手接球失誤, 跑壘者跑回本壘。

bobble hat /ˈ·· ·/ *n* [C] *BrE* a WOOLLEN hat with a bobble on the top【英】〔頂上飾有小絨球的〕毛絨帽

bob·by /ˈbɑbɪ; ˈbɒbi/ *n* [C] *BrE informal old-fashioned* a policeman【英, 非正式, 過時】警察

bobby pin /ˈ·· ·/ *n* [C] *AmE* a thin piece of metal bent into a narrow U shape that you use to hold your hair in place【美】小髮夾; HAIRGRIP *BrE*【英】—see picture at 參見 PIN[1] 圖

bobby socks, bobby sox /ˈ·· ·/ *n* [plural] *AmE* girls' short socks that have the tops turned over【美】〔女孩穿的〕短襪

bob·cat /ˈbɑbˌkæt; ˈbɒbkæt/ *n* [C] a large North American wild cat that has no tail; LYNX 短尾貓〔一種北美野貓〕

bobs /bɑbz; bɒbz/ *n* [plural] —see 見 **bits and bobs** (BIT[1] (14))

bob·sleigh /ˈbɑbˌsle; ˈbɒbsleɪ/ also 又作 **bobsled** /ˈbɑbˌslɛd; ˈbɒbsled/ *n* **1** [C] a small vehicle with two long thin metal blades instead of wheels, that is used for racing down a special ice track 雪橇〔一種供比賽用的雪上小型車輛, 可在結冰的賽道上高速下滑〕 **2** [U] a sports event in which people race against each other in bobsleighs 雪橇比賽: *Sixteen teams took part in the 400m bobsleigh.* 有十六支隊伍參加了400米雪橇比賽。—**bobsleigh** *v* [I]

bob·tail /ˈbɑbˌtel; ˈbɒbteɪl/ *n* [C] **a)** a horse or dog whose tail has been cut short 截短尾巴的馬[狗] **b)** a tail that has been cut short 截短了的尾巴 —see also 另見 **ragtag and bobtail** (RAGTAG (2))

bob·white /ˈbɑbˋhwaɪt; ˈbɒbwaɪt/ *n* [C] a bird from North America, often shot for sport; QUAIL[1] (1) 山齒鶉〔產於北美〕

boche /bɑʃ; bɒʃ/ *n* **the Boche** an offensive word meaning the Germans or German soldiers, used in Britain during the First and Second World Wars 德國佬, 德國鬼子〔第一次世界大戰和第二次世界大戰時對德國士兵的冒犯用語〕

bod /bɑd; bɒd/ *n* [C] **1** *BrE spoken* a person【英口】人, 傢伙: *We had to write to some bod at head office to ask for a refund.* 我們只好給總公司的人寫封信要求退款。**2** *informal* someone's body【非正式】身體: *Move your bod, will you!* 挪動一下身子, 好不好! **3 odd bod** *informal* a strange person【非正式】古怪的人: *He's a bit of an odd bod but very pleasant.* 他有點古怪, 但挺友善的。

bode /bod; bəʊd/ *v* **1** the past tense of BIDE **2 bode well/ill (for)** *especially literary* to be a good or bad sign for the future【尤文】預示…的吉/凶: *The results of the opinion poll do not bode well for the Democrats.* 民意調查的結果預示着民主黨人的前景並不樂觀。

bodge /bɑdʒ; bɒdʒ/ also 又作 **bodge up** *n* [singular] *spoken* a mistake or something that is not as good as it should be【口】差錯, 失誤; 比預想的要糟得多的東西: *The builders have made a complete bodge of the kitchen.* 建築工人把廚房蓋得一團糟。—see also 另見 BOTCH — **bodge** *v* [T]

body 身體

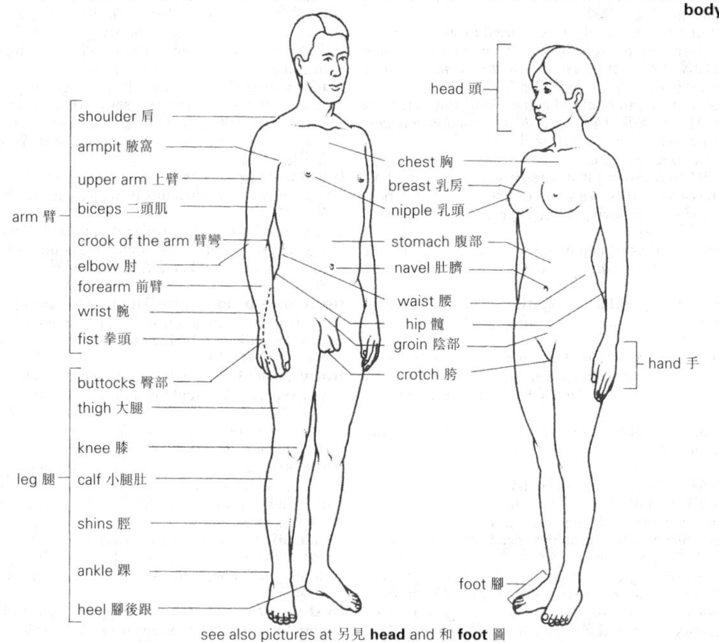

see also pictures at 另見 **head** and 和 **foot** 圖

bod·ice /ˈbɑdɪs; ˈbɒdɪ̣s/ *n* [C] **1** the part of a woman's dress above her waist 女服腰以上的部分 **2** a tight-fitting woman's WAISTCOAT worn over a BLOUSE in former times〔舊時的〕女式緊身馬甲 **3** *old use* a piece of woman's underwear that covered the upper part of her body; CORSET (1)【舊】緊身女胸衣

bod·i·ly[1] /ˈbɑdlɪ; ˈbɒdɪ̣li/ *adj* [only before noun 僅用於名詞前] related to the human body 身體的, 肉體的: *Many bodily changes occur during adolescence.* 身體的許多變化都是在青春期發生的。| *bodily sensations* 身體的知覺

bodily[2] *adv* **1** by moving the whole of your or someone else's body 全身地: *He lifted the child bodily aboard.* 他把孩子一把抱到車上。**2** by moving a large object in one piece 整體地, 全部地: *The column was transferred bodily to a new site by the bank of the river.* 那條圓柱被整根轉送到河邊的一個新地點。

bod·kin /ˈbɑdkɪn; ˈbɒdkɪ̣n/ *n* [C] a long thick needle without a point〔鈍頭〕粗長針

1 1 **bod·y** /ˈbɑdɪ; ˈbɒdi/ *n plural* **bodies**

1 ►SB'S BODY 身體◄ [C] the physical structure of a person or animal〔人或動物的〕身體, 軀體: *Many teenagers are self-conscious about their bodies.* 許多青少年對自己的身體感到害羞。| **body heat/temperature/weight etc** *Babies undergo a rapid increase in body weight during the first weeks.* 嬰兒的體重在剛剛出生的頭幾週迅速增加。| **body image** (=the mental picture that you have of your own body) 頭腦中自己身體的形象 *negative feelings associated with a changed body image* 由頭腦中自己身體形象的改變而引發的負面情緒 | **the body beautiful** (=an idea of the perfect body) 最佳體型 *products designed to help you achieve the body beautiful* 專門設計使人達到最佳體型的產品

2 ►DEAD BODY 遺體◄ [C] the dead body of a person 屍體: *Neighbours were called in to identify the body.* 鄰居們被叫來辨認屍體。

3 ►GROUP OF PEOPLE 人羣◄ [C] a group of people who work together to do a particular job or who are together for a particular purpose 團體, 機構, 羣體: [+of] *Two hundred years ago a body of settlers established themselves on the island.* 二百年前, 一羣移民來到這個島上定居。| **governing body** (=a body that controls the work or activities of an organization or group) 管理機構[部門] | **student body** (=all the students in a particular school or college) 全體學生 *We have a student body from a wide range of background.* 我們有各種各樣背景的學生。| **public body** (=group of people involved in government) 政府公務人員

4 a body of a) a large amount or collection of something 大量的: **body of knowledge/information/literature etc** *Researchers used vast bodies of information to arrive at their findings.* 研究人員利用大量資料取得了研究成果。**b)** the main, central, or most important part of something〔事物的〕主要[最大]部分, 主體: *The bedrooms were connected to the body of the house by a long corridor.* 臥室通過一條長走廊與房屋的主體相連。| *the main body of the report* 報告的主要部分

5 in a body if people do something in a body, they do it together in large numbers 全體, 一起: *The demonstrators marched in a body to the main square.* 遊行示威者一起朝着主廣場走去。

6 ►CENTRAL PART 中央部位◄ [C] the central part of a person or animal's body, not including the head, arms, legs or wings〔除頭和四肢或翅膀以外的〕軀幹部: *Nick has short legs but a long body.* 尼克腿短體長。

7 ►SEPARATE OBJECT 分開的物體◄ [C] *technical* an object that is separate from other objects【術語】物體

8 ►VEHICLE 車輛◄ [C] the main structure of a vehicle not including the engine, wheels etc 車身: *The body's beginning to rust.* 車身開始生鏽。

9 ►HAIR 毛髮◄ [U] if your hair has body, it is thick and healthy 茂盛, 濃密

10 **over my dead body** *spoken* used to show that you are determined to prevent something from happening【口】除非我死了, 休想: *He'll come to the meeting over my dead body.* 有我在, 他休想來開會。

11 **long/thick etc bodied** having a long, thick etc body 身材細長/粗壯等: *They were thick-bodied men accustomed to hard labour.* 他們身材粗壯, 習慣幹重活。—see also 另見 ABLE-BODIED

12 **full/medium/light bodied** used to describe how much FLAVOUR (=taste) a wine or beer has, with full bodied wine or beer having the strongest taste〔酒〕味道醇厚/較濃郁/清淡

13 **body and soul** completely 全身心地, 完全地: *She threw herself body and soul into her work.* 她全心全意地投入工作。

14 **keep body and soul together** to continue to exist with only just enough food, money etc 勉強維持生活, 掙錢糊口

15 ►CLOTHES 衣服◄ [C] *BrE* a type of tight fitting shirt worn by women that fastens between their legs【英】女式緊身衣; BODY SUIT *AmE*【美】—see picture at 參見 UNDERWEAR 圖

16 **body of water** a large area of water such as a lake 水域〈如湖泊〉

USAGE NOTE 用法說明: BODY

WORD CHOICE 詞語辨析: **body, figure, build**

A **body** consists of someone's arms, legs, head etc and may be healthy, skinny, dead etc. body包括人的雙臂、雙腿、頭等, 可能是健康、瘦弱或死亡的: *I like to look after my body.* 我要照顧好自己的身體。If you say someone has a *lovely/good/beautiful body* this may suggest you find them sexually attractive. 如果說某人有 a lovely/good/beautiful body (可愛的/好的/健美的身體), 則指這個人很性感。

Your **figure** is the shape of your **body**. **Figure** is usually used about women. figure 指的是人的身材或體型, 多用於女性: *She has a really good figure.* 她的身材真好。| *I won't have a cake, thanks. I'm watching my figure* (=trying not to get fat). 謝謝, 我不吃蛋糕, 我怕發胖。

Build can be used for the size and shape of both men and women. build 既可指男性也可以指女性的胖瘦和體態: *a man/woman of small/heavy/slim build* 體型瘦小/強壯/修長的男子 [女子]

body ar·mour /'·· ,··/ *n* [U] clothing worn by the police that protects them against bullets 防彈衣

body bag /'·· ·/ *n* [C] a large bag in which a dead body is removed 運屍袋: *Men will not volunteer to fight once they see the body bags returning.* 人們一旦看到運送回來的運屍袋就不會自告奮勇去打仗了。

body blow /'·· ·/ *n* [C] **1** a serious loss, disappointment, or defeat 嚴重損失; 大挫折; 大敗北: *Hopes of economic recovery were dealt a body blow by this latest announcement.* 最新公佈的消息對經濟復蘇的希望是個沉重打擊。**2** a hard hit between your neck and waist during a fight 上半身〔頸與腰之間〕受到的重擊

body build·ing /'·· ,··/ *n* [U] an activity in which you do hard physical exercise in order to develop big muscles 健美運動 —**body builder** *n* [C]

body clock /'·· ·/ *n* [C] the system in your body that controls types of behaviour which happen at regular times, such as sleeping or eating; BIOLOGICAL CLOCK 生理時鐘, 人體生物鐘

body count /'·· ,·/ *n* [C] the number of enemy dead after a period of fighting, or the process of counting their bodies〔敵方〕死亡人數統計; 清點死亡人數

bod·y·guard /'bɑdɪˌgɑrd; 'bɒdigɑːd/ *n* [C] **1** someone whose job is to protect an important person〔重要人物的〕貼身衛士, 保鏢, 警衛員: *The Senator arrived, surrounded by personal bodyguards.* 這位參議員在保鏢的簇擁下抵達。**2** a group of people who work together to protect an important person 警衛隊

body lan·guage /'·· ,··/ *n* [U] changes in your body position and movements that show what you are feeling or thinking 身體語言, 肢體語言: *It was obvious from Luke's body language that he was nervous.* 盧克的動作表明他很緊張。

body o·dour /'·· ,··/ *n* [C] the natural smell of someone's body, especially when this is unpleasant; BO 人體氣味; 狐臭, 體臭

body pol·i·tic /,·· '···/ *n* [singular] *formal* all the people in a nation forming a state under the control of a single government【正式】政治實體; 國家;〔被視為一個整體的〕民族

body pop·ping /'·· ,··/ *n* [U] a type of dancing in which the dancer makes short, sudden movements that make them look like a machine or ROBOT (1)〔模仿機器人動作的〕扭身舞, 噗啪舞

body search /'·· ·/ *n* [C] a thorough search for drugs, weapons etc, that might be hidden on someone's body 搜身; 搜身檢查: *They did a body search on all the passengers before they boarded the plane.* 他們在乘客登機前逐一進行了安全檢查。—**body-search** *v* [T]

body snatch·er /'·· ,··/ *n* [C] someone in the past who dug up dead bodies and sold them to doctors for scientific study〔舊時賣死屍給醫生作研究的〕掘墓盜屍者

body spray /'·· ·/ *n* [U] a chemical substance that you put onto your body to make it smell nice 爽身露

body stock·ing /'·· ,··/ *n* [C] a close-fitting piece of clothing that covers the whole of your body 連身[一件式]緊身衣

body suit /'·· ·/ *n* [C] *AmE* a type of tight fitting shirt worn by women that fastens between their legs【美】女緊身衣; BODY (15) *BrE*【英】

bod·y·work /'bɑdɪˌwɝk; 'bɒdiwɜːk/ *n* [U] the metal frame of a vehicle, not including the engine, wheels etc〔汽車的〕車身: *The bodywork's beginning to rust.* 汽車車身開始生鏽。

Bo·er[1] /bɔr; bɔː/ *n* [C] someone from South Africa whose family came from Holland 布爾人〔荷蘭血統的南非白人〕

Boer[2] *adj* connected with the Boers 布爾人的, 與布爾人有關的: *the Boer War* 布爾戰爭〔1899-1902 年英國人與布爾人的戰爭〕

bof·fin /'bɑfɪn; 'bɒfən/ *n* [C] *BrE*【英】**1** *old-fashioned* a scientist【過時】科學家, 科技人員 **2** *informal* someone who is very clever but not fashionable【非正式】聰明但不合時尚的人: *He was always a bit of a boffin, even at school.* 他很聰明, 但總是有點不合時尚, 即使在學校時也是如此。

bog[1] /bɑg; bɒg/ *n* **1** [C,U] an area of wet muddy ground that you can sink into 沼澤, 泥塘 —compare 比較 MARSH, SWAMP[1] **2** [C] *BrE slang* a toilet【英俚】廁所

bog[2] *v*

bog sb ↔ **down** *phr v* [T] **1** to become too involved in thinking about or dealing with one particular thing 沉湎於; 被...拖住; 使不可自拔: [+in] *Don't let yourself get bogged down in minor details.* 不要陷入這些枝節問題而不能自拔。**2** to become stuck in muddy ground and be unable to move 使陷入泥沼中

bog off *phr v* [I] **bog off!** *BrE spoken slang* used to tell someone rudely to go away【英口, 俚】滾開!: *Just bog off and leave me alone!* 滾開, 別煩我!

bo·gey /'bogɪ; 'bəʊgi/ *n* [C] **1** a problem or difficult situation that makes you feel anxious 使人焦慮的問題[局面]: **lay/put the bogey to rest** (=deal with the problem) 應對困難, 解決問題 *After six successive defeats, Athletico finally laid their bogey to rest with a 3-0 win.* 連輸六場後, 競技隊最終擺脫困境, 以3比0的比分獲勝。

2 also 又作 **bogy** a piece of MUCUS from inside your nose 鼻涕 **3** also 又作 **bogie, bogy** *technical* an example of taking one shot more than PAR (=the usual number of strokes) to get the ball into the hole in GOLF【術語】〔高爾夫球〕比標準桿數多一擊的進球 **4** a bogeyman 鬼怪, 怪物

bo·gey·man /ˈbogɪˌmæn; ˈbəʊgimæn/ *n* [C] an evil spirit, especially in children's imagination or stories; BOGEY (4)〔孩子想像中的或故事中的〕鬼怪, 怪物: *Beware of the bogeyman.* 當心妖怪。

bog·gle /ˈbɑgḷ; ˈbɒgəl/ *v* **1 the mind/imagination boggles** *informal* if your mind etc boggles when you think of something, it is difficult for you to imagine or accept it【非正式】不敢想; 簡直不敢相信; 聽得瞠目結舌: *"Did you know Keith's a father now?" "Good God, no, the mind boggles."* "你知道基思當了父親嗎?" "天啊, 不會吧, 我簡直不敢相信。" | **[+at]** *My mind boggles at the amount of work still to do.* 一想到還有那麼多工作要做, 我就不敢再想了。**2** [I] to be surprised or shocked by something 吃驚, 受驚: **[+at]** *It's a hell of a lot of money, even I boggle at it.* 那是很多很多錢, 連我都很吃驚。

bog·gy /ˈbɑgɪ; ˈbɒgi/ *adj* boggy ground is wet and muddy 泥濘的: *There was a boggy patch at the edge of the field.* 在田野的邊緣有一塊泥濘地。

bo·gie¹ /ˈbogɪ; ˈbəʊgi/ *n* [C] a BOGEY (3)〔高爾夫球〕比標準桿數多一擊的進球

bogie² *v* [T] to use one more than PAR (=the usual number of strokes) to get the ball into the hole in GOLF〔高爾夫球〕比標準桿數多一擊進球

bog roll /ˈ· ·/ *n* [C,U] *BrE slang* TOILET PAPER【英俚】衞生紙, 廁紙

bog stan·dard /ˌ· ˈ··◂/ *adj BrE informal* not special or interesting in any way; average【英, 非正式】一般的, 平常的, 普通的

bo·gus /ˈbogəs; ˈbəʊgəs/ *adj* not true or real, although someone is trying to make you think it is 假冒的, 偽造的: *bogus insurance claims* 偽造的保險索賠

bo·gy /ˈbogɪ; ˈbəʊgi/ *n* [C] a BOGEY (4) 鬼怪, 怪物

bo·he·mi·an /boˈhimɪən; bəʊˈhiːmiən/ *adj* living in a very informal or relaxed way and not accepting society's rules of behaviour 不拘於傳統的; 放蕩不羈的: *bohemian cafes frequented by artists, musicians, and actors* 畫家、音樂家和演員們經常光顧的新潮咖啡館 —**bohemian** *n* [C]

3 **boil¹** /bɔɪl; bɔɪl/ *v* **1** [I,T] when a liquid boils it is hot enough to turn into gas 使達到沸點, 煮沸, 燒開: *Put the spaghetti into plenty of boiling, salted water.* 把意大利粉放入大量煮沸的鹽水中。| **[+at]** *Water boils at 100 degrees centigrade.* 水在攝氏 100 度沸騰。| *We were advised to boil the water before drinking it.* 有人建議我們把水燒開後再喝。**2** [I,T] if something containing liquid boils, the liquid inside it is boiling (使)〔容器裡的液體〕沸騰: *The kettle's boiling! Shall I turn it off?* 水壺裡的水開了! 我把它關了好嗎? | **put sth on to boil** (=begin to heat something) 開始把…加熱 *I've put the potatoes on to boil.* 我已經把馬鈴薯加熱了。| **boiled dry** (=heated for too long so there is no liquid left) 煮乾 **3** [I, T] to cook something in boiling water〔用開水〕煮〔食物〕: *a boiled egg* 煮好的雞蛋 **4** [T] to wash clothes at a very high temperature〔用高溫水〕洗〔衣服〕: *I always boil the cotton sheets.* 我總是用熱水洗棉牀單。—see also 另見 BOILING POINT, **make your blood boil** (BLOOD¹ (4))

boil away *phr v* if a liquid boils away it disappears because it has been heated too much 煮乾, 汽化: *Oh no! The soup's almost boiled away.* 啊, 不好了! 湯幾乎要燒乾了。

boil down *phr v* **1** [I,T **boil sth ↔ down**] if a food or liquid boils down, it becomes less after cooking 煮稠, 濃縮: *Spinach tends to boil down a lot.* 菠菜一煮會縮掉許多。**2** [T] **boil sth down** to make information shorter by not including anything that is not necessary 壓縮〔資料等〕: *You can boil this down so that there are just two main categories.* 你可以將其簡化為兩大類。

boil down to sth *phr v* [T not in progressive 不用進行式] *informal* if a long statement, argument etc boils down to something, that is the main point or cause【非正式】相當於, 歸結為: *What it boils down to, is that no-one is willing to take on that kind of responsibility.* 歸結起來就是沒有人願意承擔那樣的責任。

boil over *phr v* [I] **1** if a liquid boils over, it rises and flows over the side of the container 沸騰而溢出: *Keep an eye on the milk; don't let it boil over.* 看着牛奶, 別讓它溢出來。**2** if a situation or an emotion boils over, the people involved stop being calm〔局面或感情〕控制不住: **[+into]** *The argument boiled over into a fight.* 爭論演變成了一場打鬥。

boil up *phr v* **1** [I] if a situation or emotion boils up, it reaches a dangerous level 發展到危險程度: *She could sense that trouble was boiling up at work.* 她能感受到工作中的麻煩到了危險程度。**2** [T **boil sth ↔ up**] to heat food or a liquid until it begins to boil 把…加熱, 煮沸: *Boil the fruit up with sugar.* 把水果加糖煮沸。

boil² *n* **1 the boil** the act or state of boiling 煮沸; 沸騰: **bring sth to the boil** *Bring the sauce to the boil and simmer for 10 minutes.* 把調味汁煮開, 然後用文火煨十分鐘。| **be coming to the boil** (=almost boiling) 快要開了 | **take sth off the boil** (=stop boiling something by taking it off the heat) 不再煮下去 **2** [C] a painful infected swelling under someone's skin 癤子, 疔: *The boy's body is covered in boils.* 這個男孩滿身是瘡。**3 go off the boil** *BrE* to become less good at something that you are usually very good at【英】生疏了: *Gower has gone off the boil in terms of batting lately.* 高爾最近的擊球水平有所下降。

boiled sweet /ˈ· ·/ *n* [C] *BrE* a hard SWEET² (1) that often tastes of fruit【英】〔常帶有水果味的〕硬糖; HARD CANDY *AmE*【美】

boil·er /ˈbɔɪlɚ; ˈbɔɪlə/ *n* [C] a container for boiling water that is part of a steam engine, or is used to provide heating in a house 鍋爐 3

boiler suit /ˈ·· ·/ *n* [C] *BrE* a piece of loose clothing like trousers and a shirt joined together, that you wear over your clothes to protect them【英】〔衣褲相連的〕工作服

boil·ing /ˈbɔɪlɪŋ; ˈbɔɪlɪŋ/ *adj* **1** very hot 滾熱的, 酷熱的: *Can I open a window? It's boiling in here.* 我可以開一扇窗嗎? 這兒太熱了。| **boiling hot** *It's been boiling hot all Summer.* 炎熱的天氣持續了整個夏天。—see 見 COLD¹ (USAGE) **2** very angry 非常氣憤的: *I was boiling with pent-up rage.* 我怒火中燒。 3

boiling point /ˈ·· ·/ *n* [C] **1** the temperature at which a liquid boils 沸點 **2** the point at which emotions get out of control and a situation stops being calm〔情緒或局面的〕爆發點: **reach boiling point** *Relations between the two countries have almost reached boiling point.* 兩國間的緊張關係已經達到白熱化的程度。

bois·ter·ous /ˈbɔɪstərəs; ˈbɔɪstərəs/ *adj* someone, especially a child, who is boisterous makes a lot of noise and has a lot of energy〔尤指兒童〕喧鬧的, 活躍的: *a class of boisterous five year olds* 一班愛吵鬧的五歲的孩子

bok choy /ˌbɑk ˈtʃɔɪ; ˌbɒk ˈtʃɔɪ/ *n* [U] another spelling of PAK CHOI pak choi 的另一種拼法 —see picture on page A9 參見 A9 頁圖

bold /bold; bəʊld/ *adj*

1 ►PERSON/ACTION 人/行動◄ not afraid of taking risks and making difficult decisions 果敢的, 冒險的, 無畏的: *a bold leader* 果敢的領導者 | *It's a bold venture starting a business these days.* 如今開設一家商號是個冒險之舉。

2 ►MANNER/APPEARANCE 舉止/外貌◄ so confident or determined that you sometimes offend people 唐突

B

的, 冒失的, 魯莽的, 放肆的: **as bold as brass** (=very confident and not showing enough respect) 厚顏無恥 *He came in here, as bold as brass, and asked if he could have his money back.* 他厚顏無恥地來到這兒, 問是否可以要回自己的錢。
3 ►COLOURS/SHAPES 顏色/形狀◄ very strong or bright so that you notice them 醒目的, 顯眼的, 輪廓清晰的: *bold geometric shapes* 清晰的幾何圖形
4 ►LINES/WRITING 線條/書寫◄ written or drawn in a very clear way 粗線條的; 粗大醒目的: **a bold hand** (=bold writing) 醒目的粗體字 *Her letter was written in a bold sloping hand.* 她的信是用粗大的斜體字寫的。
5 in bold (type) printed in letters that are darker and thicker than ordinary printed letters〔印刷〕用黑體字排印的: *The numbers in this dictionary are in bold type.* 這部詞典的數字是用黑體字排印的。
6 make so bold as to do sth *formal* to do something that other people feel is rude or not acceptable【正式】冒昧, 膽敢: *One of the staff made so bold as to ask what the director's salary was.* 一個職員冒昧地問主任的工資是多少。
7 if I may be so bold *spoken formal* used when asking someone a question, to show that you hope it will not offend them【口, 正式】恕我冒昧地問: *And what, if I may be so bold, is the meaning of this note?* 恕我冒昧地問一句, 這個註解是甚麼意思? —**boldly** *adv* —**boldness** *n* [U]

bold·face /ˈbold,fes; ˈbəʊldfeɪs/ *n* [U] *technical* a way of printing letters that makes them thicker and darker than normal【術語】黑體字, 粗體字 —**boldfaced** *adj*

bole /bol; bəʊl/ *n* [C] *literary* the main part of a tree; TRUNK (1)【文】樹幹

bo·le·ro¹ /bəˈlɛro; bəˈleərəʊ/ *n* [C] a type of Spanish dance, or the music for this dance〔西班牙〕波萊羅舞; 波萊羅舞曲

bol·e·ro² /boˈlɛro; ˈbɒlərəʊ/ *n* [C] a short jacket for a woman 女式短上衣

boll /bol; bəʊl/ *n* [C] the part of a cotton plant that contains the seeds〔棉桃的〕圓莢, 莢殼

bol·lard /ˈbɑləd; ˈbɒləd/ *n* [C] **1** *BrE* a short thick post in the street that is used to stop traffic entering an area or to show a JUNCTION more clearly【英】〔街道盡頭阻止汽車進入的〕安全柱, 矮柱;〔行人安全島的〕護柱 **2** a thick stone or metal post used for tying ships to when they are in port〔船上或碼頭上的〕繫纜柱

bol·lock /ˈbɑlək; ˈbɒlək/ *v* [T] *BrE slang* to tell someone angrily that you do not like what they have done【英俚】臭罵: *I'll bollock him for sticking his rubbish in my cupboard.* 他把亂七八糟的東西塞進了我的櫃子裡, 我要好好罵他一頓。

bol·lock·ing /ˈbɑləkɪŋ; ˈbɒləkɪŋ/ *n* [C] **give sb a bollocking** *BrE* to tell someone that you are very angry about something they have done【英】斥責[責罵]某人: *I expect I'll get a bollocking from my boss when she finds out.* 我估計老闆發現真相後我要挨她一頓臭罵。

bol·locks /ˈbɑləks; ˈbɒləks/ *n* [plural] *BrE slang*【英俚】**1** *spoken* used to say rudely that you think something is wrong or stupid【口】胡鬧; 廢話: *These statistics are total bollocks.* 這些統計數字完全是糊弄人的。| **a load of old bollocks** (=complete nonsense) 一派胡言, 胡說八道 *She's just talking a load of old bollocks.* 她簡直是一派胡言。**2** *spoken* a word used to emphasize that you are annoyed or angry【口】太糟糕了〔表示厭煩或生氣〕: *Oh bollocks! We've missed it.* 真糟糕! 我們沒有趕上。
3 bollocks to you/that/it etc *spoken* used when you refuse to accept or obey something【口】不要想〔表示不接受或不服從〕: *Oh yeah? Well, bollocks to you, mate!* 哦, 是嗎? 哼, 老兄, 你休想! **4** the two round male organs that produce SPERM; TESTICLES 睾丸

boll wee·vil /ˌ· ˈ··/ *n* [C] an insect that eats and destroys cotton plants 棉鈴象鼻蟲

bo·lo·gna /bəˈlonɪ; bəˈləʊni/ *n* a type of cooked meat often eaten in sandwiches 博洛尼亞香腸, 大香腸〔通常夾在三明治裡〕

bo·lo·ney /bəˈlonɪ; bəˈləʊni/ *n* [U] another spelling of BALONEY baloney 的另一種拼法

bo·lo tie /ˈbolo ˌtaɪ; ˈbəʊləʊ taɪ/ *n* [C] *AmE* a string worn around your neck that you fasten with a decoration【美】波洛領帶〔用飾扣繫住的一種細帶〕

Bol·she·vik /ˈbolʃə,vɪk; ˈbɒlʃəvɪk/ *n* [C] **1** someone who supported the COMMUNIST¹ party at the time of the Russian Revolution in 1917 布爾什維克〔在 1917 年俄國革命中支持共產黨的人〕**2** *old-fashioned* an insulting way of talking about a COMMUNIST² or someone who has strong left-wing views【過時】共產黨人; 極左翼分子〔侮辱性詞語〕—**bolshevik** *adj*

bol·shie, bolshy /ˈbolʃɪ; ˈbəʊlʃi/ *adj BrE informal* tending to be angry or annoyed and not to obey people【英, 非正式】易怒的; 不服從的; 愛爭吵的: *Jack was in one of his bolshie moods again!* 傑克又發牛脾氣了! —**bolshiness** *n* [U]

bol·ster¹ /ˈbolstə; ˈbəʊlstə/ *n* [C] a long firm PILLOW¹ (1) that you put under other pillows 長枕墊

bolster² also 又作 **bolster up** *v* [T] **1** to help someone to feel better and more positive 增強; 激勵: *I did my best to bolster up his confidence.* 我盡力增強他的自信心。**2** to improve something by supporting it〔通過支持〕改進: *a speech designed to bolster her chances at the election* 旨在增加她選舉獲勝機會的演講

bolt¹ /bolt; bəʊlt/ *n* [C]
1 ►LOCK 鎖◄ a metal bar that you slide across a door or window to fasten it〔門窗的〕金屬插銷
2 ►SCREW 螺釘◄ a screw with a flat head and no point, for fastening two pieces of metal together 螺栓
3 a bolt from out of the blue news that is sudden and unexpected 晴天霹靂; 飛來橫禍: *It was a bolt out of the blue when Alan resigned – completely unexpected.* 艾倫辭職的消息真是晴天霹靂, 令人意想不到。

bolt 螺栓; 金屬插銷; 弩箭
nut 螺帽
washer 墊圈
bolt 金屬插銷
bolt 弩箭

4 bolt of lightning lightning that appears as a white line in the sky 閃電, 霹靂 —see also 另見 THUNDERBOLT
5 make a bolt for (it) to suddenly try to escape from somewhere 急忙逃跑, 拔腿便跑
6 ►WEAPON 武器◄ a short heavy ARROW (1) that is fired from a CROSSBOW〔短而粗的〕弩箭, 矢
7 ►CLOTH 布◄ a large long roll of cloth 一卷, 一匹 —see also 另見 **shoot your bolt** (SHOOT¹ (20)), **the nuts and bolts of** (NUT¹ (6))

bolt² *v* **1** [I] **a)** to suddenly start to run very fast because you are frightened 奔, 竄: *The horse reared up and bolted.* 馬用後腿直立起來, 跑開了。**b)** to escape from somewhere 逃跑: *Kevin had bolted through the open window.* 凱文從開着的窗子逃走了。**2** also 又作 **bolt down** [T] to eat very quickly 狼吞虎嚥: *Don't bolt your food.* 不要狼吞虎嚥。**3** to fasten two things together using a BOLT¹ (2) 用螺栓扣住: *We had the safe bolted to the wall.* 我們用螺栓把保險櫃固定到牆上。**4** [I,T] to lock a door or window by sliding a bolt across 閂上〔門或窗〕

bolt³ *adv* **sit/stand bolt upright** to sit or stand with your back very straight 挺直地坐着/站着

bolt·hole /ˈbolt,hol; ˈbəʊlthəʊl/ *n* [C] a place where you can escape to and hide 避難所, 藏身處: *a bolthole in the country* 鄉下的藏身處

bomb¹ /bɑm; bɒm/ *n* [C]
1 ►WEAPON 武器◄ a weapon made of material that will explode 炸彈; 爆炸裝置: *A bomb was planted at the railway station.* 一枚炸彈被放置在火車站內。—see also

另見 ATOM BOMB, HYDROGEN BOMB, LETTER BOMB, NEUTRON BOMB, STINK BOMB, TIME BOMB
2 the bomb used to describe NUCLEAR WEAPONS, and especially the HYDROGEN BOMB 核彈, 核武器〔尤指氫彈〕: *a 'ban the bomb' campaign* "禁止核武器"運動
3 cost a bomb *BrE informal* to cost a lot of money 【英, 非正式】花費很多錢; 值很多錢
4 go like a bomb *BrE informal* 【英, 非正式】**a)** if a car goes like a bomb, it can travel very quickly〔車〕開得飛快 **b)** if a party goes like a bomb, it is very successful〔聚會〕非常成功
5 make a bomb *BrE informal* to get a lot of money by doing something 【英, 非正式】掙大錢: [**+out of**] *If you could get some of that cheap pottery back to England, you could make a bomb out of it.* 如果你能把那些廉價的陶器帶回英國, 就能賺大錢。

bomb² *v* **1** [T] to attack a place by leaving a bomb there, or by dropping bombs on it from a plane 轟炸, 向…投炸彈, 炸毀: *The town was heavily bombed in World War II.* 這座城鎮在第二次世界大戰中遭到猛烈轟炸。**2** [I] *BrE informal* to move or drive very quickly 【英, 非正式】疾行, 飛駛, 快速前進: [**+down/along/towards**] *Suddenly a police car came bombing down the high street.* 有一輛警車突然在大街上疾駛而過。**3** [I,T] *AmE informal* to fail a test very badly 【美, 非正式】〔考試〕不及格, 失敗: *I bombed my mid-term.* 我的期中考試不及格。**4** [I] *especially AmE* if a play bombs, it is not successful 【尤美】〔戲劇〕演砸了, 不成功: *His latest play bombed on Broadway.* 他最新的話劇在百老匯演砸了。
bomb sth ↔ **out** *phr v* [T] if a building or the people in it are bombed out, the building is completely destroyed 炸毀, 炸平: *a bombed out town* 被炸彈夷為平地的城鎮

bom·bard /bɑmˋbɑrd; bɒmˈbɑːd/ *v* [T] **1** to attack a place by firing a lot of guns or throwing bombs continuously at it〔用砲火連續地〕猛炸, 轟擊: *British ships began bombarding the port of Alexandria.* 英國戰艦開始猛轟亞歷山大港。**2** to continue asking someone a lot of questions criticizing them, or giving them a lot of information at once 連珠砲似地質問; 一下子提供很多信息: *Both leaders were bombarded with questions from the press.* 兩位領導人都遭到新聞記者連珠砲似的提問。

bom·bar·dier /ˌbɑmbɚˋdɪr; ˌbɒmbəˈdɪə◂/ *n* [C] **1** the person on a military aircraft responsible for dropping bombs〔飛機上的〕轟炸員, 投彈手 **2** a low rank in the Royal Artillery (=part of the British Army)〔英國皇家砲兵〕下士

bom·bard·ment /bɑmˋbɑrdmənt; bɒmˈbɑːdmənt/ *n* [U] a continuous attack on a place by big guns and bombs 砲轟, 轟炸: *Sarajevo is coming under heavy bombardment from Serb forces.* 薩拉熱窩正遭到塞族軍隊的猛烈轟擊。| **aerial bombardment** (=attack by planes dropping bombs) 飛機轟炸

bom·bas·tic /bɑmˋbæstɪk; bɒmˈbæstɪk/ *adj* bombastic language contains long important sounding words that have no real meaning 唱高調的; 誇大其辭的: *Pennant's pushy and bombastic manner* 彭南特咄咄逼人又善唱高調的作風 —**bombast** /ˋbɑmbæst; ˈbɒmbæst/ *n* [U]

bomb dis·po·sal /ˈ· ·ˌ··/ *n* [U] the job of dealing with bombs that have not exploded, and making them safe 未爆炸彈處理: **a bomb disposal expert/squad/unit etc** *Bomb disposal experts were called in to make the device safe.* 炸彈處理專家奉召到場以確保這個裝置的安全。

bombed /bɑmd; bɒmd/ *adj* [not before noun 不用於名詞前] *slang* very drunk or affected by illegal drugs 【俚】爛醉的; 吸了毒的: *I feel like going out and getting completely bombed.* 我想出去喝個不醉不歸。

bomb·er /ˋbɑmɚ; ˈbɒmə/ *n* [C] **1** a plane that carries and drops bombs 轟炸機 **2** someone who puts a bomb somewhere 投彈手; 放置炸彈的人

bomber jack·et /ˈ·· ˌ··/ *n* [C] a short jacket which fits tightly around your waist 緊身短上衣, 夾克衫, 短茄克

bomb·ing /ˋbɑmɪŋ; ˈbɒmɪŋ/ *n* [C,U] the use of bombs to attack a place 砲轟, 轟炸: **wave of bombings** (=series of attacks using bombs) 一連串爆炸 *Hundreds have been killed in the current wave of bombings.* 有好幾百人在近日發生的一連串爆炸事件中喪生。

bomb·proof /ˋbɑmˋpruf; ˈbɒmpruːf/ *adj* strong enough not to be damaged by a bomb attack 防彈的, 避彈的: *a bombproof shelter* 防空洞

bomb scare /ˈ· ·/ *n* [C] a situation where someone telephones and says that there is a bomb in a particular place 炸彈恐嚇: *a bomb scare in Central London* 恐嚇說在倫敦中心區放置了炸彈

bomb·shell /ˋbɑmˏʃɛl; ˈbɒmʃel/ *n* [C] *informal* 【非正式】**1** an unexpected and very shocking piece of news 令人震驚的消息; 突發意外事件: *His death came as a complete bombshell.* 他的死訊傳來, 令人深感震驚。**2 drop a bombshell** to suddenly tell someone a shocking piece of news 突然告訴某人一個令人震驚的消息 **3 blonde bombshell** *humorous* an extremely attractive woman with FAIR (=light coloured) hair 【幽默】金髮美人

bomb shel·ter /ˈ· ˌ··/ *n* [C] a room or building that is built to protect people from bomb attacks 防空建築, 防空洞

bomb site /ˈ· ·/ *n* [C] a place where a bomb has destroyed several buildings in a town 被炸後的廢墟: *They've pulled down so many buildings around here it looks like a bomb site.* 他們把這兒的許多建築物都推倒了, 看起來就像一片被轟炸後的廢墟。

bo·na fi·de, bonafide /ˋbonə ˋfaɪdɪ; ˌbəʊnə ˈfaɪdi/ *adj* **1** real, true and not intended to deceive someone 真正的; 真實的; 真誠的: *Only bona fide members are allowed to use the club pool.* 只有真正的會員才允許使用俱樂部的泳池。**2 bona fides** [plural] *BrE* if you check someone's bona fides, you check that they are who they say they are 【英】誠意, 真誠, 善意

bo·nan·za /bəˋnænzə; bəˈnænzə/ *n* [C] a lucky or successful situation where people can make a lot of money 走鴻運, 獲利之道, 致富之源: *Spielberg's movie ET was a box office bonanza.* 史匹堡的電影《E·T· 外星人》票房收入可觀。

bon·bon /ˋbɑnˏbɑn; ˈbɒnbɒn/ *n* [C] a type of round SWEET² (1) 巧克力夾心軟糖, 糖果

bonce /bɑns; bɒns/ *n* [C] *slang* your head 【俚】頭

bond¹ /bɑnd; bɒnd/ *n* [C] 3
1 ▶MONEY 錢◀ an official document promising that a government or company will pay back money that it has borrowed, often with INTEREST¹ (4) 債券, 證券, 公債: *My father put all his money into Canadian Northern Railway bonds.* 我父親把他所有的錢都投到了加拿大北方鐵路的債券上。| *furious trading on the bond market* 債券市場風起雲湧的交易
2 ▶UNITE 團結◀ something that unites two or more people or groups, such as love, or a shared interest or idea〔因共同利益或感情而使人連繫起來的〕紐帶, 維繫, 連結物, 關係: [**+between**] *the natural bond between mother and child* 母親和孩子之間一種自然的緊密關係 | [**+of**] *The two countries are linked by bonds of friendship going back many years.* 兩國之間的友好關係可追溯到許多年以前。| [**+with**] *He felt a strong bond with his audience.* 他感到自己和觀眾有着一種很緊密的聯繫。
3 bonds [plural] *literary* 【文】**a)** something that limits your freedom and prevents you from doing what you want 枷鎖, 桎梏, 限制人自由的東西: [**+of**] *the bonds of slavery* 奴隸制度的枷鎖 **b)** chains, ropes etc used for tying up a prisoner 鐐銬, 繩索: *The prisoners will be freed from their bonds.* 囚犯們將不再帶鐐銬。
4 ▶GLUE 膠(水)◀ the way in which two surfaces become fixed to each other using glue 結合, 黏合
5 ▶CHEMISTRY 化學◀ *technical* the chemical force that holds atoms together 【術語】化學鍵: *In each methane molecule there are four CH bonds.* 每一個甲烷分

子中有四個碳氫鍵。

6 a written agreement to do something, that makes you legally responsible for doing it 契約, 盟約

7 my word is my bond *formal* used to say that you will definitely do what you have promised【正式】我說的話(像契約一樣)可靠, 我一定會履行諾言

8 in/out of bond *technical* in or out of a BONDED WAREHOUSE【術語】〔進口貨物〕存入關棧中以待完稅/已完稅出關

bond² *v* **1** [I] if two things bond with each other, they become firmly fixed together, especially after they have been joined with glue〔尤指用膠水〕黏合: *It takes less than 10 minutes for the two surfaces to bond.* 兩個表面不到十分鐘就會黏到一起。**2** [I] to develop a special relationship with someone〔與某人〕培養一種特殊的關係: *the tendency to bond with others of the same sex* 與其他同性的人建立關係的趨勢 **3** [T] *technical* to keep goods in a bonded warehouse【術語】〔把貨物〕存入關棧 [保稅倉庫] 中

bond·age /ˈbɑndɪdʒ; ˈbɒndɪdʒ/ *n* [U] **1** the practice of being tied up for sexual pleasure〔為獲得性快感而進行的〕縛住手腳做愛, 捆綁起來做愛 **2** *literary* the state of being a slave【文】奴役: *Since the age of 13 he had been in bondage.* 他從13歲起就成了奴隸。**3** the state of having your freedom limited, or being prevented from doing what you want 束縛, 限制: *He wanted to be free from the bondage of social conventions.* 他想擺脫社會習俗的束縛。

bonded ware·house /ˌ·· ˈ··/ *n* [C] *technical* an official store for goods that have been brought into a country before tax has been paid on them【術語】〔海關的〕關棧, 保稅倉庫

bond·hold·er /ˈbɑndˌholdɚ; ˈbɒndˌhəʊldə/ *n* [C] *technical* someone who owns government or industrial bonds (BOND¹ (1))【術語】債券持有人

bond·ing /ˈbɑndɪŋ; ˈbɒndɪŋ/ *n* [U] **1** a process in which a special relationship develops between two or more people 親密關係的形成: *They're in the bar again doing some male bonding!* 他們一班男士又在酒吧裡談天說地, 聯絡感情了! **2** *technical* the connection of atoms【術語】〔原子的〕結合

S2 W2 **bone¹** /bon; bəʊn/ *n*

1 ►BODY 身體◄ [C] one of the hard parts that together form the frame of a human or animal body 骨頭, 骨: *The X-ray showed that the bone was broken in two places.* X光檢查顯示骨頭有兩處折斷。| **thigh/cheek/jaw etc bone** (=the bone in your thigh etc) 股骨/顴骨/頷骨等 *very prominent cheek bones* 非常突出的顴骨 | **big-boned/fine-boned/small-boned etc** (=with big etc bones) 骨頭粗大的/骨架勻稱的/骨架小的等 *Grace was a tall, big-boned woman.* 格雷斯是一個高大、粗壯的婦女。| **good/fine bone structure** (=someone with good bone structure has a well-shaped face) 臉形好, 臉部線條優美

2 have a bone to pick with sb *spoken* used to tell someone that you are annoyed with them and want to talk about it【口】對某人不滿, 對某人有抱怨

3 the bare bones the simplest and most important details of something 最基本的內容, 梗概: *This is just the bare bones of the plan – it's still in the early stages.* 這只是計劃的梗概, 一切還處於初步階段。

4 make no bones about (doing) sth to not feel nervous or ashamed about doing or saying something 對某事毫無顧忌, 對某事毫不躊躇: *We made no bones about our commitment to Marxism.* 我們毫不猶豫地獻身馬克思主義。

5 be chilled/frozen to the bone extremely cold 寒冷刺骨

6 a bone of contention something that causes arguments between people 爭執的原因: *The question of unpaid overtime became the main bone of contention.* 沒有付加班費的問題成了爭執的焦點。

7 a bag of bones someone who is much too thin 骨瘦如柴的人

8 bones [plural] *AmE* DICE¹ (1)【美】骰子

9 close to the bone a remark, statement etc that is close to the bone is close to the truth in a way that may offend someone 苛刻地揭露真相的; 露骨的: *Some of his jokes were a bit close to the bone.* 他的一些笑話有點露骨。

10 cut sth to the bone to reduce costs, services etc as much as possible〔把成本或服務等〕削減到最低程度

11 feel/know it in your bones to be certain that something is true, even though you have no proof and cannot explain why you are certain 從內心裡感到, 確信: *That boy's trouble, I can feel it in my bones.* 我從心底裡覺得那個男孩會帶來麻煩。

12 off the bone meat that is served off the bone has been cut away from the bone〔肉〕脫骨的

13 on the bone meat that is served on the bone is still joined to the bone〔肉〕帶骨的 —see also 另見 **as dry as a bone** (DRY¹ (1)), **work your fingers to the bone** (WORK¹ (27))

bone² *v* [T] to remove the bones from fish, or meat 剔掉…的骨頭, 去掉…的骨

bone up [I] *informal* to study hard for an examination【非正式】〔為考試等〕鑽研, 用功: *I'm having to bone up on criminal law for a test next week.* 我在用功溫習, 準備下週的刑法測驗。

bone chi·na /ˌ· ˈ··◂/ *n* [U] delicate and expensive cups, plates etc that are made partly with crushed bone 骨灰瓷

bone dry /ˌ· ˈ·◂/ *adj* completely dry 極乾的, 乾透的: *There had been no rain for months and the land was bone dry.* 幾個月沒下雨, 地都乾透了。

bone·head /ˈbonˌhɛd; ˈbəʊnhed/ *n* [C] *informal* a stupid person【非正式】笨蛋, 傻瓜

bone i·dle /ˌ· ˈ··◂/ *adj* extremely lazy 懶到極點的: *He's not stupid, just bone idle.* 他並不笨, 只是太懶。

bone mar·row /ˈ· ˌ··/ *n* the soft substance in the hollow centre of bones; MARROW (1) 骨髓: *a bone marrow transplant* 骨髓移植

bone meal /ˈ· ·/ *n* [U] a substance used to feed plants that is made of crushed bones〔用作肥料的〕骨粉

bon·er /ˈbonɚ; ˈbəʊnə/ *n* [singular] **1** *AmE taboo* an ERECTION (1)【美諱】(陰莖) 勃起狀態 **2** *AmE informal* a stupid or embarrassing mistake【美, 非正式】愚蠢可笑的錯誤; 令人尷尬的差錯

bone·shak·er /ˈbonˌʃekɚ; ˈbəʊnˌʃeɪkə/ *n* [C] *BrE humorous* an old vehicle that is in very bad condition【英, 幽默】破舊顛簸的車輛

bone-tired /ˌ· ˈ·◂/ *adj* [not before noun 不用於名詞前] *AmE informal* extremely tired【美, 非正式】累壞了的: *Dan sat in the rocker by the fire, bone-tired after his journey.* 丹坐在火邊的搖椅上, 旅途後累得精疲力竭。

bon·fire /ˈbɑnˌfaɪr; ˈbɒnfaɪə/ *n* [C] a large outdoor fire, either for burning waste, or for a party 篝火, 營火, 火堆: *There was a huge bonfire on Guy Fawkes' night.* 蓋依·福克斯之夜點起了盛大的篝火。

bonfire night /ˈ·· ˌ·/ *n* [singular] November 5th, when in Britain people light FIREWORKS and burn a GUY¹ (2) on a large outdoor fire; GUY FAWKES' NIGHT 篝火之夜, 營火之夜, 蓋依·福克斯之夜〔為紀念1605年蓋依·福克斯企圖炸毀倫敦議會, 英國於每年11月5日遊行, 放煙花並焚燒蓋依·福克斯的模擬像〕

bong /bɑŋ; bɒŋ/ *n* **1** [singular] a deep sound made by a large bell 洪亮的鐘聲 **2** [C] *slang* an object used for smoking CANNABIS in which the smoke goes through water to make it cool【俚】大麻葉煙槍

bon·gos, bongoes /ˈbɑŋgoz; ˈbɒŋgəʊz/ also 又作 **bongo drums** /ˈ·· ·/ *n* [plural] a pair of small drums that you play with your hands 小手鼓, 拉丁小鼓

bon·ho·mie /ˌbɑnəˈmi; ˈbɒnəmi/ *n* [U] *French especially literary* a friendly feeling among a group of people【法, 尤文】友好, 和藹, 性情隨和: *The atmosphere of* *bonhomie was suddenly gone.* 親切友好的氣氛突然消失了。

bonk¹ /bɑŋk; bɒŋk/ *v* [I,T] **1** *BrE slang humorous* to have sex with someone【英俚, 幽默】與…性交 **2** *informal* to hit someone lightly on the head or to hit your head on something by mistake【非正式】敲腦袋, 撞頭, 磕, 碰: *He fell, bonking his head against a tree.* 他摔倒了, 頭撞到一棵樹上。

bonk² *n* **1** [singular] *BrE slang humorous* the action of having sex【英俚, 幽默】性交, 性行為: *a quick bonk* 快速交合 **2** [C] *informal* the action of hitting someone lightly on the head, or hitting your head against something【非正式】打腦袋; 撞頭 **3** [C] *informal* a sudden short deep sound, for example, when something hits the ground【非正式】〔短促而低沉的〕碰撞聲

bon·kers /ˈbɑŋkɚz; ˈbɒŋkəz/ *adj BrE humorous*【英, 幽默】**1** slightly crazy 發瘋的: *Fly to Tokyo for one day? You must be bonkers!* 乘飛機去東京一天? 你準是發瘋了! **2 drive sb bonkers** to annoy someone 煩擾某人, 使人發瘋: *I wish they'd turn that bloody music down – it's driving me bonkers!* 我希望他們把這破音樂關輕些, 那聲音簡直要使我發瘋了!

bon mot /ˌbɑn ˋmo; ˌbɒn ˈməʊ/ *n* [C] *French* a clever remark【法】雋語, 機智的妙語

bon·net /ˈbɑnɪt; ˈbɒn¹̩t/ *n* [C] **1** *BrE* the metal lid over the front of a car【英】汽車引擎蓋: *I'll need to check under the bonnet.* 我需要查看一下引擎蓋的下面。—see picture on page A2 參見A2頁圖 **2) a)** a warm hat that a baby wears which ties under its chin〔在頦下繫帶的〕嬰兒帽 **b)** a type of hat that women wore in the past which tied under their chin and often had a wide BRIM¹ (1)〔舊時婦女用的, 在頦下有帶子、帽前有寬邊的〕包頭軟帽 —see also 另見 **have a bee in your bonnet** (BEE (3)) —see picture at 參見 HAT 圖

bon·ny /ˈbɑnɪ; ˈbɒni/ *adj especially ScotE*【尤蘇格蘭】**1** pretty and healthy 漂亮健康的, 健美的: *a bonny baby* 漂亮健康的嬰兒 **2** clever or skilful 聰明的; 熟練的: *a bonny fighter* 技術高超的拳擊手

bon·sai /ˈbɑnsaɪ; ˈbɒnsaɪ/ *n* [C,U] a tree that is grown so that it always stays very small, or the art of growing trees in this way 盆景, 盆栽(藝術) —**bonsai** *adj*

2 **bo·nus** /ˈbonəs; ˈbəʊnəs/ *n* [C] **1** money added to someone's wages, especially as a reward for good work 獎金; 紅利; 特別津貼: *People who stay more than two years in the job receive a special bonus.* 從事這個工作超過兩年者會得到一項特別津貼。**2** something good that you did not expect in a situation 沒有預料到的好事: **added bonus** *It's an added bonus being able to work at home.* 另一個好處是能在家工作。**3 no-claims bonus** a reduction in the cost of your car insurance when you do not make a claim in a particular year 未索賠鼓勵金〔一種汽車保險優惠〕

bon vi·vant /ˌbɑn viˋvɑnt; ˌbɒn viːˈvɒnt/ also 又作 **bon viveur** /-viˋvɝ; -viːˈvɜː/ *n* [C] *literary French* someone who enjoys good food and wine, and being with people【文, 法】講究飲食和生活的人, 享樂主義者

bon voy·age /ˌbɑn vwaɪˋɑʒ; ˌbɒn vwaɪˈɑːʒ/ *interjection French* used to wish someone a good journey【法】祝你一路順風

bon·y /ˈbonɪ; ˈbəʊni/ *adj* **1** someone or part of their body that is bony is very thin 骨瘦如柴的, 瘦得皮包骨的: *Her hand felt cold and bony.* 她的手摸起來又冷又瘦。**2** bony meat or fish contains a lot of small bones〔肉或魚〕多骨[刺]的 **3** a part of an animal that is bony consists mostly of bone〔動物身體部分〕多骨的

boo¹ /bu; buː/ *v* [I,T] **1** to shout 'boo' to show that you do not like a person, performance, idea etc 發噓聲〔表示反對或反感〕: *Some of the audience started booing.* 一些觀眾開始發出噓聲。**2 boo sb off (stage)** to shout 'boo' until a performer leaves the stage 喝倒采, 把某人哄下台: *His jokes were so bad he got booed off stage.* 他的笑話很粗俗, 被觀眾喝倒采哄下了台。

boo² *interjection* **1** *plural* **boos** a noise made by people who do not like a person, performance, idea etc〔表示反對或反感的〕噓聲 **2** a word you shout suddenly to someone as a joke in order to frighten them 喲!〔驚嚇別人時發出的聲音〕**3 wouldn't say boo to a goose** an expression used to describe a shy, quiet person 非常羞怯: *Christine wouldn't say boo to a goose.* 克莉斯蒂非常害羞。

B

boob¹ /bub; buːb/ *n* [C usually plural 一般用複數] **1** *slang* a woman's breast【俚】〔婦女的〕乳房, 奶子 **2** *BrE informal* a silly mistake【英, 非正式】愚蠢的錯誤 **3** *AmE old-fashioned* a stupid or silly person【美, 過時】傻瓜, 笨蛋

boob² *v* [I] to make a stupid mistake 出錯: *I think Jean's boobed again.* 我看吉恩又犯錯了。

boo-boo /ˈ· ·/ *n* [C] *informal* a word meaning a mistake【非正式】錯誤: *I made a bit of a boo-boo asking her about David!* 我向她打聽戴維真的是一個錯誤!

boob tube /ˈ· ·/ *n* [C] **1** *BrE* a piece of women's clothing made of stretchy material, that covers only her chest【英】(女子)彈力短上衣; TUBE TOP *AmE*【美】**2 the boob tube** *AmE informal* the TELEVISION (1)【美, 非正式】電視機: *sitting around watching the boob tube* 圍坐在一起看電視

boo·by /ˈbubɪ; ˈbuːbi/ *n* [C] *informal* a silly or stupid person【非正式】傻瓜, 蠢材

boo·by hatch /ˈ·· ·/ *n* [singular] *AmE old-fashioned* a mental hospital【美, 過時】精神病院

booby prize /ˈ·· ·/ *n* [C] a prize given as a joke to the person who is last in a competition〔指出於善意的玩笑而發給的〕末名獎

booby trap, booby-trap /ˈ·· ·/ *n* [C] **1** a hidden bomb that explodes when you touch something else that is connected to it 偽裝地雷[炸彈], 餌雷 **2** a HARMLESS trap that you arrange for someone as a joke〔開玩笑的〕陷阱, 機關, 惡作劇的把戲: *The booby trap was a bucket of water resting on top of the door.* 惡作劇的把戲是把一桶水放在門頂上。—**booby-trapped** *adj*

boog·er /ˈbugɚ; ˈbʊgə/ *n* [C] *AmE slang*【美俚】**1** used when describing a person or thing 傢伙; 東西: *You wouldn't want to meet him in a dark alley – he's a mean-looking booger.* 你不會想在黑暗的小巷裡見他, 他是一個看起來非常卑鄙的傢伙。—compare 比較 BUGGER **2** a thick piece of MUCUS from your nose 鼻涕

boo·gey·man /ˈbugɪˌmæn; ˈbuːgimæn/ *n* a BOGEYMAN 鬼怪, 怪物

boo·gie¹ /ˈbugɪ; ˈbuːgi/ *v* [I] *informal* to dance, especially to fast popular music【非正式】〔隨着快節奏的流行音樂〕跳舞: *Boogie on down!* 使勁跳吧!

boogie² *n* **1** also 又作 **boogie woo·gie** /ˈbugɪ ˋwugɪ; ˌbuːgi ˈwuːgi/ [U] *AmE* a type of music played on the piano with a strong fast RHYTHM (1)【美】布基伍基音樂〔用鋼琴演奏的一種節奏強勁的音樂〕**2** [C] *informal* a dance, especially to fast popular music【非正式】〔隨着快節奏的流行音樂而跳的〕舞蹈: *Do you fancy going for a boogie on Saturday?* 你喜歡星期六去跳舞嗎?

boo·hoo /ˌbu ˋhu; ˌbuː ˈhuː/ *interjection* a word used especially in children's stories to show that someone is crying 嗚嗚〔尤用於兒童故事中表示哭泣〕

book¹ /bʊk; bʊk/ *n* S1 W1

1 ►PRINTED BOOK 印刷的書◄ [C] a set of printed pages that are fastened together in a cover so that you can read them 書, 書籍: *I'm reading a book by Graham Greene.* 我正在讀〔英國小說家〕格雷厄姆·格林寫的一本書。| *Nothing beats curling up with a good book.* 甚麼也比不上蜷着身子看一本好書的感覺。

2 ►BOOK TO WRITE IN 寫字的本◄ [C] a set of sheets of paper fastened together in a cover so that you can write on them 本, 冊, 簿: *a note book* 筆記本 | **address/exercise etc book** (=a book for a particular purpose) 地址簿/練習本等

3 ►SET OF THINGS 成套的東西◄ [C] a set of things

such as stamps, matches or tickets, fastened together inside a paper cover 裝訂成冊之物
4 books [plural] **a)** ▶**ACCOUNTS** 賬目◀ written records of the accounts of a business 賬目, 賬簿, 會計簿: *Their books show a profit.* 他們的賬目本顯示有盈利。—see also 另見 **cook the books** (COOK¹ (5)) **b)** ▶**JOBS** 職業◀ the names of people who use a company's services, or who are sent by a company to work for other people〔顧客或雇員〕名冊: **on sb's books** *informal* (=employed by a company or organization)【非正式】受雇於某公司[機構]: *We have over 100 VDU operators on our books at the moment.* 目前, 我們在冊的視頻顯示器操作員超過一百人。
5 a closed book a subject that you do not understand or know anything about 不理解[一無所知]的學科[主題]; 謎: *Chemistry is a closed book to me.* 我對化學一竅不通。
6 one for the books *informal* used to say that something that has happened is unusual or surprising【非正式】新奇[不尋常]的事: *Look! Gaynor's buying the drinks. There's one for the books!* 看! 蓋納在買酒。這真是新鮮事!
7 be in sb's good/bad books *informal* used to say that someone is pleased or annoyed with you【非正式】令某人滿意/惱火
8 go by the book/do sth by the book to do something exactly according to rules or instructions 照章辦事, 循規蹈矩: *Tony's the sort of bloke who does everything by the book.* 托尼是那種甚麼都照章辦事的人。
9 in my book *usually spoken* used when giving your opinion【一般口】依我看: *She's all right in my book.* 依我看, 她沒甚麼事。
10 ▶**PART OF A BOOK** 書的部分◀ [C] one of the parts that a very large book such as the Bible is divided into 卷, 篇: **[+of]** *the Book of Isaiah*《以賽亞書》〔《聖經》中的一卷〕
11 bring sb to book *especially BrE* to punish someone for breaking laws or rules, especially when you have been trying to punish them for a long time【尤英】處罰某人, 責罰某人: *Terry was finally brought to book for fiddling the accounts.* 特里因在賬目上做手腳, 最終受到了懲罰。—see also 另見 STATUTE BOOK, **take a leaf out of sb's book** (LEAF¹ (2)), **read sb like a book** (READ¹ (13)), **suit sb's book** (SUIT² (5)), **a turn-up for the book** (TURN-UP (2)), **throw the book at** (THROW¹ (27))

2 **book²** *v* **1** [I,T] *BrE* to arrange with a hotel, restaurant, theatre etc to go there at a particular time in the future【英】預訂, 預購, 預約: *I've booked a table for two at Mario's tonight.* 今晚我在瑪里奧飯店預訂了兩個人的桌子。| *We need to book well in advance for Christmas.* 我們得在聖誕節以前早早預訂。| **booked up/fully booked** (=no rooms, tables etc available) 已被訂完, 訂滿 *I'm sorry, we're fully booked for the 14th.* 對不起, 14日的已全部被預訂了。| **booked solid** (=all the tickets etc have been sold)〔票等〕全部售完 *The show's booked solid for months to come.* 未來幾個月的演出門票都已售完。**2** [T] to arrange for someone such as a singer to perform on a particular date 預約〔某人〕演出: **booked up/fully booked** (=no time left to do any more performances) 演出時間已排滿 *We're booked up right through the summer season.* 我們整個夏季的演出時間都已排滿。**3** [T] when a police officer books someone, they write down their name, address etc because they have done something wrong〔尤指警察〕把…記錄在案: *Rebecca's been booked for speeding.* 麗貝卡因超速駕駛被記錄在案。**4** [T] *BrE* when a football REFEREE¹ (1) books a player who has broken the rules, they officially write down the player's name in a book【英】〔足球裁判〕記下〔犯規球員〕名字, 記名警告
book in/into *phr v BrE*【英】**1** [I] to arrive at a hotel and say who you are etc〔到達旅館後〕辦理入住登記手續: *I'll call you as soon as I've booked in at my hotel.* 我辦完入住登記手續就給你打電話。**2** [T **book** sb **in/into**] to arrange for someone to stay at a hotel 為…預訂旅館房間: *Could you book me in at the Hilton for tonight?* 你能為我在希爾頓酒店預訂今晚的房間嗎?
book sb **on** sth *phr v* [T] to arrange for someone to travel on a particular plane, train etc 為〔某人〕預訂〔飛機票或火車票〕: *She asked her secretary to book her on the next flight to London.* 她請祕書給她預訂下一班飛往倫敦的航班。

book·a·ble /ˈbukəbl̩; ˈbʊkəbəl/ *adj* **1** *BrE* tickets for a concert, performance etc that are bookable can be ordered before it happens【英】可預訂的 **2 bookable offence** an offence for which a football player can be punished by having their name written in the referee's (REFEREE¹ (1)) book〔會使足球裁判記名警告的〕犯規
book·bind·ing /ˈbukˌbaɪndɪŋ; ˈbʊkˌbaɪndɪŋ/ *n* [U] the art of fastening the pages of books inside a cover〔書籍的〕裝訂, 裝幀 —**bookbinder** *n* [C]
book·case /ˈbukˌkes; ˈbʊk-keɪs/ *n* [C] a set of shelves for keeping books on 書架, 書櫃: *a walnut bookcase* 胡桃木書櫃
book club /ˈ· ·/ *n* [C] a club that offers books cheaply to its members〔廉價賣書給會員的〕讀書會; 讀書俱樂部
book·end /ˈbukˌɛnd; ˈbʊkend/ *n* [C usually plural 一般用複數] one of a pair of objects that you put at the end of a row of books to prevent them from falling over 書擋, 書靠
book·ie /ˈbukɪ; ˈbʊki/ *n* [C] *BrE informal* a BOOKMAKER【英, 非正式】馬票商
book·ing /ˈbukɪŋ; ˈbʊkɪŋ/ *n* [C] **1** *BrE* an arrangement to travel by train, use a hotel room etc at a particular time in the future【英】預約, 預訂: **make a booking** *Can I make a booking for tonight?* 我可以預訂今晚的(票)嗎? | *cancel a booking* 取消預訂 **2** an arrangement made by a performer to perform at a particular time in the future 演出合同 **3** the act of writing a football player's name in a book as a punishment for breaking the rules〔足球員〕犯規被記名, 違章事件的記錄
booking of·fice /ˈ·· ˌ··/ *n* [C] *BrE* a place where you can buy train or bus tickets【英】售票處, 訂票處
book·ish /ˈbukɪʃ; ˈbʊkɪʃ/ *adj* **1** someone who is bookish is more interested in reading and studying than in sports or other activities 嗜書的; 好讀書的; 喜歡學習的: *Bill was the studious, bookish type.* 比爾是那種勤奮好學的人。**2** based on books rather than on practical experience 按書本行事的, 學究氣的
book·keep·ing /ˈbukˌkipɪŋ; ˈbʊkˌkiːpɪŋ/ *n* [U] the job or activity of recording the accounts of an organization 記賬, 簿記, 管賬
book·let /ˈbuklɪt; ˈbʊkl̩ɪt/ *n* [C] a very short book that usually contains information 小冊子: *free booklet on drug abuse* 關於濫用藥物的免費小冊子
book·mak·er /ˈbukˌmekɚ; ˈbʊkˌmeɪkə/ *n* [C] someone whose job is to collect money that people want to risk on the result of a race, competition etc, and who pays them if they guess correctly 馬票商, 經營(賽馬)賭注登記者
book·mark /ˈbukˌmɑrk; ˈbʊkmɑːk/ *n* [C] a piece of paper, leather etc that shows you the last page you have read in a book 書籤
book·mo·bile /ˈbukməˌbil; ˈbʊkməbiːl/ *n* [C] *AmE* a vehicle that contains a library and travels to different places so that people can use it【美】流動圖書館
book·plate /ˈbukˌplet; ˈbʊkpleɪt/ *n* [C] a decorated piece of paper with your name on it, that you stick in the front of your books〔貼在書中的〕藏書者標籤
book·rest /ˈbukˌrɛst; ˈbʊk-rest/ *n* [C] a metal or wood frame that holds a book upright so that you can read it without holding it in your hands 看書架〔供放置攤開的書用〕
book·sell·er /ˈbukˌsɛlɚ; ˈbʊkˌselə/ *n* [C] a person or company that sells books 書商
book·shelf /ˈbukˌʃɛlf; ˈbʊkʃelf/ *n plural* **bookshelves** /-ˌʃɛlvz; -ʃelvz/ [C] a shelf that you keep books on 書架

book·shop /ˈbuk͵ʃap; ˈbʊkʃɒp/ *n* [C] *especially BrE* a shop that sells books【尤英】書店; bookstore *AmE*【美】

book·stall /ˈbuk͵stɔl; ˈbʊkstɔːl/ *n* [C] *BrE* a small shop that has an open front and sells books and magazines, often at a station【英】書亭, 書報攤; NEWSSTAND *AmE*【美】

book·store /ˈbuk͵stɔr; ˈbʊkstɔː/ *n* [C] *AmE* a shop that sells books【美】書店; bookshop *BrE*【英】

book to·ken /ˈ· ͵··/ *n* [C] *BrE* a card that you can exchange for books【英】〔可兑換書刊的〕購書券, 書券: *My aunt always gives me a book token for Christmas.* 我的姨母在聖誕節時總給我購書券。

book va·lue /ˈ· ͵··/ *n* [C] the standard value that something such as a car of a particular age, style etc is supposed to have 賬面價值, 淨值, 實值

book·worm /ˈbuk͵wɝm; ˈbʊkwɜːm/ *n* [C] **1** someone who likes reading very much 極愛讀書的人, 書蟲, 書呆子 **2** an insect that eats books 蠹魚, 蛀書蟲

3 **boom¹** /bum; buːm/ *n*

1 ►INCREASE IN BUSINESS 業務增加◄ [singular] a rapid increase of business activity〔生意〕繁榮, 興旺, 景氣: [+in] *a sudden boom in the housing market* 房產市場的突然繁榮 | **consumer/investment/property etc boom** *the post-war property boom* 戰後的財富增長 | **boom years/times** *These are boom times for voluntary organizations.* 這是志願機構興起的時期。—see also 另見 BOOM TOWN

2 ►WHEN STH IS POPULAR 某事物流行之時◄ [singular] a period when something suddenly becomes very popular or starts happening a lot 流行時期: **jazz/aerobics etc boom** *the jazz boom of the 1950s* 20世紀50年代爵士樂的鼎盛時期

3 ►SOUND 聲音◄ [C] a deep loud sound that you can hear for several seconds after it begins, especially the sound of an explosion or a large gun 隆隆聲: *the dull boom of the cannons* 隱約傳來的大砲轟鳴聲 —see also 另見 SONIC BOOM

4 ►LONG POLE 長桿子◄ [C] **a)** a long pole on a boat that is attached to a sail at the bottom 帆的下桁, 帆桿 —see picture at 參見 YACHT 圖 **b)** a long pole used as part of a piece of equipment that loads and unloads things〔裝卸貨物時用的〕吊桿, 起重臂 **c)** a long pole that has a camera or microphone on the end〔一端掛照相機或麥克風的〕活動支架, 吊桿

5 ►ON A RIVER 在河上◄ [C] something that is stretched across a river or a BAY¹ (1) to prevent things floating down or across it〔橫攔於河面以阻止物件漂走的〕擋柵, 水柵

boom² *v* **1** also 又作 **boom out a)** [I] to make a loud deep sound 發低沉的聲音, 隆隆作響: *Guns boomed in the distance.* 遠處大砲隆隆作響。**b)** [T] to say something in a loud deep voice 用洪亮而低沉的聲音說: *"Come here, boy," boomed the headteacher.* "過來, 孩子。"校長用洪亮而低沉的聲音說。**2** [I usually in progressive 一般用進行式] if business, trade, or a particular area is booming, it is very successful〔商業、貿易等〕繁榮;〔城鎮等〕興起; 迅速發展: *The steel industry is booming.* 鋼鐵工業迅速發展。—**booming** *adj*

boom box /ˈ· ·/ *n* [C] *AmE informal* a GHETTO BLASTER【美, 非正式】手提錄音機

boo·me·rang¹ /ˈbuməˌræŋ; ˈbuːməræŋ/ *n* [C] a curved stick from Australia that flies in a circle and comes back to you when you throw it〔出自澳大利亞的拋出後可飛回的〕飛去來鏢, 回飛棒, 回力棒

boomerang² *v* [I] if a plan boomerangs on someone, it affects them instead of the person who it was intended to affect〔計劃〕起反作用, 自作自受, 自食其果

boom town /ˈ· ·/ *n* [C] a town or city that suddenly becomes very successful because there is a lot of new industry〔突然興旺起來的〕新興城市

boon /bun; buːn/ *n* [C usually singular 一般用單數] **1** something that is very useful and makes your life a lot easier 裨益, 恩物, 有用之物: *The new bus service will be a real boon to people in the village.* 新設的巴士服務對村民十分有用。**2** *old use* a FAVOUR¹ (1)【舊】恩惠

boon com·pan·ion /͵· ·ˈ··/ *n* [C] *literary* a very close friend【文】好友, 摯友

boon·docks /ˈbun͵daks; ˈbuːndɒks/ *n* [plural] *AmE informal* a place that is a long way from the nearest town【美, 非正式】偏僻鄉村, 荒僻的地方

boon·dog·gle /ˈbun͵dagl̩; ˈbuːn͵dɒgl/ *n* [singular] *AmE informal* an officially organized plan or activity that is very complicated and wastes a lot of time, money, and effort【美, 非正式】龐大而浪費的計劃 [活動]

boo·nies /ˈbuniz; ˈbuːniz/ *n* [plural] *AmE informal* boondocks【美, 非正式】偏僻鄉村, 荒僻的地方

boor /bur; bʊə/ *n* [C] *old-fashioned* a man who behaves in a very rude way【過時】粗魯[沒禮貌]的人〔指男子〕—**boorish** *adj*: *boorish behaviour* 粗魯的舉止 —**boorishly** *adv*

boost¹ /bust; buːst/ *v* [T] **1** to increase something such as production, sales etc because they are not as high as you want them to be 增加, 提高, 促進: *The advertising campaign is intended to boost sales.* 廣告宣傳活動旨在增加銷售。**2 boost sb's confidence/morale/ego** to make someone feel more confident and less worried 增強某人的自信心/士氣/自尊: *He regularly phones to boost her morale.* 他定期打電話鼓勵她。**3** to advertise something by discussing or praising it 吹捧, 大肆宣傳: *a special promotion to boost their new product* 為推銷他們的新產品而特別展開的宣傳活動 **4** also 又作 **boost up** to help someone reach a higher place by lifting them 向上推起, 托一把: *Can you boost me up onto the horse?* 你能幫忙把我托上馬嗎?

boost² *n* **1** [singular] something that helps someone be more successful and confident, or that helps something increase or improve 激勵, 鼓舞; 增加, 改進: [+to] *Last night's victory was a tremendous boost to the team.* 昨晚的勝利對球隊是一個巨大的鼓舞。| **give (sb/sth) a boost** *Being chosen to attend the conference gave Matthew a real boost.* 被選去出席會議給馬修以很大的激勵。| **ego/morale boost** (=an increase in confidence) 自我激勵 *He wanted a dizzy blonde as a boost to his ego.* 他想找一個傻乎乎的金髮姑娘以增強自己的自信心。**2** [U] an increase in the amount of power available to a ROCKET¹ (1), piece of electrical equipment etc〔火箭、電器等的〕動力增強, 助推 **3 give sb a boost (up)** to lift someone so that they can reach a higher place 推起, 托某人一把: *If I give you a boost up, could you reach the window?* 如果我托你一把, 你能夠到窗戶嗎?

boost·er /ˈbustɚ; ˈbuːstə/ *n* [C] **1** a small quantity of a drug that increases the effect of one that was given before, so that someone continues to be protected against a disease〔增強藥效的〕附加劑量, 加強劑 **2** something that helps someone be more successful or to feel more confident 令人鼓舞的事情: **morale booster** *The departmental party was a real morale booster.* 全系聚會對士氣是個很大的鼓舞。**3** a ROCKET¹ (1) that is used to provide additional power for a SPACECRAFT to leave the Earth 推進器; 升壓機; 放大器: *a giant booster rocket* 巨大的助推火箭 **4** *AmE* someone who gives a lot of support to a person, organization, or an idea【美】擁護者, 熱心支持者

booster cush·ion /ˈ·· ͵··/ *BrE*【英】also 又作 **booster seat, booster chair** /ˈ·· ·/ *AmE*【美】*n* [C] a special seat for a small child that lets them sit in a higher position in a car or at a table〔小孩子坐的〕墊高座

boot¹ /but; buːt/ *n* [C] 2 3

1 ►SHOE 鞋◄ a type of shoe that covers your whole foot and the lower part of your leg 靴子, 高腰鞋: *a pair of old army boots* 一雙舊軍靴

2 ►JOB 職業◄ *informal*【非正式】**a) get the boot** to be forced to leave your job 被開除, 被解雇 **b) give sb the boot** to dismiss someone from their job; SACK² (1) 解雇, 開除: *He was certain they would find out he'd been given the boot.* 他肯定他們會發現他已經被解雇了。

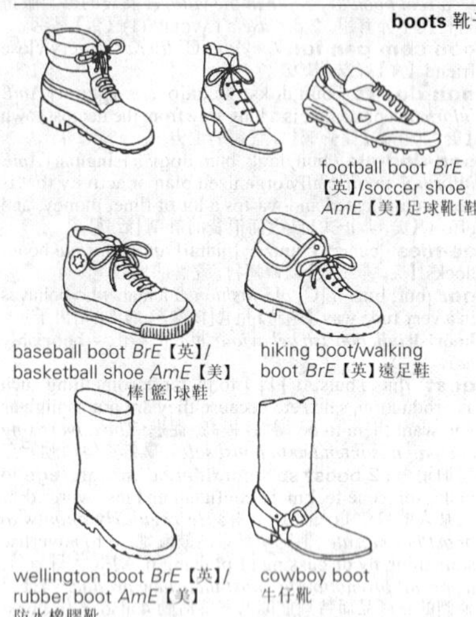

3 ►CAR 汽車◄ *BrE* an enclosed space at the back of a car, used for carrying bags etc【英】〔汽車後部的〕行李箱; TRUNK (2) *AmE*【美】: *At least the boot is of reasonable proportions.* 至少行李箱大小正合適。—see picture on page A2 參見A2頁圖

4 put the boot in *BrE informal*【英, 非正式】**a)** to say very unkind things to someone who is already upset 火上澆油: *I know you were angry with him but there was no need to put the boot in like that.* 我知道你對他生氣, 但也沒有必要火上澆油。**b)** to attack someone by kicking them repeatedly, especially when they are on the ground 猛踢〔已倒地的人〕

5 give sth a boot *informal* to give something a quick hard kick【非正式】用腳踢一下某物: *The door wouldn't open so I gave it a boot.* 門打不開, 所以我使勁踢了一腳。

6 the boot is on the other foot *BrE* used to say that you now have power over someone who used to have power over you【英】局勢逆轉; 此一時, 彼一時

7 to boot used at the end of a list of remarks to emphasize them 並且, 加之: *He is dishonest, and a coward to boot.* 他不誠實, 而且是個膽小鬼。—see also 另見 **be/get too big for your boots** (BIG (13)), **lick sb's boots** (LICK[1] (7)), **as tough as old boots** (TOUGH[1] (2))

boot² *v* **1** [T] *informal* to kick someone or something hard【非正式】踢: **boot sth/sb in/round/etc** *The goalkeeper booted the ball upfield.* 守門員一腳把球踢到對方半場。**2** [I,T] to make a computer ready to be used by putting in its instructions 進行〔電腦的〕引導啟動程序, 啟動 **3** [T] *AmE* to stop someone from moving their illegally parked vehicle by fixing a piece of equipment to the wheels【美】給〔違規停放的車輛〕加上鎖扣; CLAMP[1] (3) *BrE*【英】

boot sb ↔ **out** *phr v* [T] *informal* to force someone to leave a place, job, or organization, especially because they have done something wrong【非正式】趕走; 開除: *They were booted out of the pub for fighting.* 他們因為打架被逐出了酒館。

boot up *phr v* [I,T **boot sth up**] to make a computer ready to be used by putting in its instructions; BOOT² (2) 啟動〔電腦〕, 使〔電腦〕作好使用準備

boot camp /ˈ· ·/ *n* [C] a training camp for people who have just joined the US army, Navy, or Marine Corps〔美國海、陸軍或海軍陸戰隊的〕新兵訓練營

boot·ee, bootie /buˋti; ˈbuːtiː/ *n* [C] a short sock that a baby wears instead of a shoe〔嬰兒當鞋穿的〕毛絨襪, 毛絨鞋

booth /buθ; buːð/ *n* [C] **1** a small partly enclosed place where one person can do something privately, such as use the telephone or vote〔供一人使用的隔開的〕小間 **2** a tent where you can buy things, play games, or find out information, usually at a market or a FAIR³ (1)〔市場或遊樂場上的〕售貨棚, 攤位, 攤檔 **3** *especially AmE* a partly enclosed place in a restaurant with a table between two long seats【尤美】〔餐館內的〕雅座

boot·lace /ˋbutˏles; ˈbuːtleɪs/ *n* [C usually plural 一般用複數] a long piece of string that you use to fasten a boot 鞋帶, 靴帶

boot·leg¹ /ˋbutˏlɛg; ˈbuːtleg/ *adj* [only before noun 僅用於名詞前] bootleg alcohol or recordings are made and sold illegally 走私的; 非法製造及銷售的

bootleg² *n* [C] an illegal recording of a music performance 盜版唱片[錄音帶]: *You could tell from the bad printing that the CD was a bootleg.* 從粗劣的印刷可以看出這張唱片是盜版的。

boot·leg·ging /ˋbutˏlɛgɪŋ; ˈbuːtlegɪŋ/ *n* [U] illegally making or selling alcohol 非法私釀[銷售]酒 **—bootlegger** *n* [C] **—bootleg** *v* [I,T]

boot·lick·ing /ˋbutˏlɪkɪŋ; ˈbuːtˌlɪkɪŋ/ *n* [U] *informal* behaviour that is too friendly to someone in a position of authority, in order to get advantages for yourself【非正式】巴結, 獻媚, 拍馬屁 **—bootlicker** *n* [C] **—bootlicking** *adj*

boot sale /ˈ· ·/ *n* [C] *BrE* a CAR BOOT SALE【英】舊貨出售, 舊物集市

boot·straps /ˋbutˏstræps; ˈbuːtstræps/ *n* [plural] **pull/haul yourself up by your bootstraps** to improve your position and get out of a difficult situation by your own effort, without help from other people 靠自己的努力改善境遇

boot·y /ˋbutɪ; ˈbuːti/ *n* [U] *especially literary* valuable things that a group of people, especially an army that has just won a victory, take away or steal from somewhere【尤文】贓物; 戰利品

booze¹ /buz; buːz/ *n* [U] *informal* alcoholic drink【非正式】酒

booze² *v* [I] *informal* to drink alcohol, especially a lot of it【非正式】飲酒; 狂飲: *I expect Jon's out boozing with his mates.* 我估計喬恩出去和朋友一塊兒喝酒去了。

booz·er /ˋbuzɚ; ˈbuːzə/ *n* [C] *BrE informal*【英, 非正式】**1** a PUB 小酒館 **2** someone who often drinks a lot of alcohol 酒徒, 酒鬼, 豪飲者

booze-up /ˈ· ·/ *n* [C] *BrE informal* a party where people drink a lot of alcohol【英, 非正式】狂飲作樂的聚會

booz·y /ˋbuzɪ; ˈbuːzi/ *adj* showing signs of having drunk too much alcohol 酒醉的, 暴飲的: *boozy laughter* 醉酒的笑聲 **—boozily** *adv* **—booziness** *n* [U]

bop¹ /bɑp; bɒp/ *v* **bopped, bopping** *informal*【非正式】**1** [T] to hit someone, especially gently 輕打, 輕拍: *I bopped him on the head with my book.* 我用書拍了一下他的頭。**2** [I] *BrE* to dance to popular music【英】〔隨流行音樂〕起舞

bop² *n* [singular] **1** *BrE informal* a dance【英, 非正式】舞蹈: *It's ages since I had a really good bop.* 我已經好久沒有痛快地跳舞了。**2** another word for BEBOP bebop 的另一種說法

bo·rax /ˋbɔræks; ˈbɔːræks/ *n* [U] a mineral used for cleaning 硼砂

Bor·deaux /bɔrˋdo; bɔːˈdəʊ/ *n* [C] a wine that comes from the Bordeaux area in France〔法國〕波爾多葡萄酒

bor·del·lo /bɔrˋdɛlo; bɔːˈdeləʊ/ *n* [C] *especially literary* a house where men can pay to have sex; BROTHEL【尤文】妓院, 青樓

bor·der¹ /ˋbɔrdɚ; ˈbɔːdə/ *n* [C] **1** the official line that separates two countries, or the area close to this line 國界, 邊境, 邊界; 邊境地區: **[+between]** *The town lies on* *the border between the US and Mexico.* 該鎮位於美國和墨西哥交界。| [+with] *There has been renewed fighting along the border with Pakistan.* 沿巴基斯坦邊境一帶又有戰事。| **on the border** *Jeumont is a small town on the border between France and Belgium.* 丘蒙特是法國和比利時交界處的一個小鎮。| **cross the border** *The terrorists were stopped trying to cross the Spanish border.* 恐怖分子企圖跨越西班牙邊界時被攔住了。**2** a band along the edge of something, such as a picture or piece of material 邊, 邊飾: *writing paper with a black border* 帶有黑邊的書寫紙 **3** a band of soil containing plants at the edge of an area of grass 草地的邊緣部分,〔花園等邊緣狹長的〕綠化帶: *border plants such as dianthus* 石竹等種在草坪四周的植物

border² *v* [T] **1** to form a border around the edge of something 形成…的邊界, 毗鄰: *Large trees border the river and the streams.* 毗鄰河流和小溪的是大樹。| [+on] *The valley is bordered on both sides by high limestone cliffs.* 山谷的兩邊都是高聳的石灰岩懸崖。**2** if one country borders another country, it is next to it and shares a border with it 與…接壤

border on sth *phr v* [T] to be very close to reaching an extreme feeling or quality 近似, 接近: *excitement bordering on hysteria* 近乎歇斯底里的興奮

bor·der·land /ˈbɔrdə˞ˌlænd; ˈbɔːdəlænd/ *n* [C] **1** the land near the border between two countries 邊境地帶 **2** the borderland between two qualities is an unclear area that contains features of both of them 介乎於兩種狀況之間的狀態; 邊緣狀態

bor·der·line¹ /ˈbɔrdə˞ˌlaɪn; ˈbɔːdəlaɪn/ *adj* **borderline case/candidate/decision etc** a situation in which you are not sure whether someone or something is acceptable 難以確定的情況/候選人/決定等: *Borderline candidates will take an oral exam to decide their final result.* 對那些邊緣的候選人將進行一次口試決定最終的結果。

borderline² *n* **1** [singular] the point at which one quality, condition, emotion etc ends and another begins 介於兩種不同情況之間的不明確界線; 曖昧狀況, 含混的情景: *slipping gently over the borderline into sleep* 慢慢地進入睡眠的狀態 **2** [C] a border between two countries 分界線, 邊界, 國境線

bore¹ /bɔr; bɔː/ the past tense of BEAR¹

bore² *v* **1** [T] to make someone feel bored, especially by talking too much about something they are not interested in〔尤指以無聊的長話〕使〔人〕厭煩: *I'm sorry I spoke for so long – I hope I didn't bore you.* 對不起, 我說得太久了。我希望沒有使你感到厭煩。| **bore sb with** *My father's always boring us with his stories about the war.* 父親老是講他在戰爭中的經歷, 我們都厭煩了。| **bore sb to death/tears** (=make them very bored) 使某人煩得要命 **2** [I,T] to make a deep round hole in a hard surface 鑽(孔), 開鑿, 挖(洞): [+through/into] *To build the tunnel they had to bore through solid rock.* 為了建隧道, 他們必須鑽透堅硬的岩石。**3** [I+into] if someone's eyes bore into you, they look at you in a way that makes you feel uncomfortable〔令人不安地〕盯住看

bore³ *n* **1** [C] someone who is boring, especially because they talk too much about themselves〔尤指因過多談論自己而〕令人厭煩的人: *He was something of a bore – going on about his charity work all evening.* 他真煩人, 整個晚上都在講他的慈善工作。| **soccer/photography etc bore** (=someone who talks too much about photography etc) 一談起足球/攝影等就沒完沒了的人 **2** [singular] something that you have to do but do not want to do 令人厭煩的事: *Doing housework is a real bore.* 做家務真是件令人厭煩的事。**3 12-bore/small bore etc** the measurement of the size of the inside of a gun BARREL¹ (3)〔槍砲〕12毫米口徑/小口徑等 **4** a borehole 鑽孔, 井眼

3 **bored** /bɔrd; bɔːd/ *adj* tired and impatient because you do not think something is interesting, or because you have nothing to do 厭煩的, 不感興趣的: *Children easily get bored.* 孩子們很容易感到厭煩。| [+with] *I'm bored with the same old routine day after day.* 我厭倦了日復一日的例行事務。| **bored stiff/to tears/to death/out of your mind** (=extremely bored) 感到極度厭煩, 煩得要命 *You'd be bored stiff in a job like that.* 做這樣的工作你會煩死的。

USAGE NOTE 用法說明: BORED

WORD CHOICE 詞語辨析: **bored, boring, interested in, interesting, frightened of, frightening**

With pairs of adjectives like this, the one ending in **-ed** describes the person who has the feeling, the one ending in **-ing** describes whatever gives them that feeling. 在這些成對的形容詞當中, 以 -ed 結尾的形容詞描寫的是人有了這種感受, 而以 -ing 結尾的形容詞描寫的是使人產生這種感受的人或事物: *I got bored watching TV/talking to Susan.* 我厭倦了看電視/和蘇姍談話。| *TV/Susan was boring.* 電視/蘇姍真叫人煩。| *I'm interested in their summer courses* (NOT 不用 *I interested in...* or 或 *I was interesting in/on...* or 或 *I was interested of/on/with/about...*). 我對他們的夏季課程感興趣。| *Don't be frightened of it – it isn't really frightening.* 不要害怕, 其實並不可怕。

GRAMMAR 語法

You will hear people say they are *bored of* something but many people think only **bored with** is correct. 你會聽到有人說 be bored of, 但許多人認為 be bored with 才是正確的: *She's getting really bored with her job.* 她對自己的工作真的厭倦了。

bore·dom /ˈbɔrdəm; ˈbɔːdəm/ *n* [U] the feeling you have when you are bored 厭倦, 厭煩: *the sheer boredom of working in a factory* 在工廠裡工作真乏味

bore·hole /ˈbɔrˌhol; ˈbɔːhəʊl/ *n* [C] a deep hole made using special equipment, especially in order to get water or oil out of the ground 鑽孔, 井眼

boring 無趣的, 無聊的, 乏味的, 令人生厭的

The teacher/lecture is boring./The students are bored.
那個老師/那堂課枯燥無味。/學生們不感興趣。

bor·ing /ˈbɔrɪŋ; ˈbɔːrɪŋ/ *adj* not interesting in any way 2
無趣的, 無聊的, 乏味的, 令人生厭的: *Her husband is about the most boring person I've ever met.* 在我所見過的人當中, 她的丈夫差不多是最惹人厭煩的。| **deadly boring** (=very boring) 極度沉悶 *I always thought maths was deadly boring.* 我一直認為數學枯燥得要命。

born¹ /bɔrn; bɔːn/ a past participle of BEAR¹

born² *adj* 1
1 be born when a person or animal is born it comes out 2
of its mother's body, or out of an egg 出生, 誕生: *Forty lambs were born this spring.* 這個春季有四十頭羔羊出生。| [+in] *Swift was born in 1667.* 斯威夫特生於 1667

年。| *I was born in a small southern town in the USA.* 我在美國南部的一個小鎮出生。| [+at] *In those days most babies were born at home.* 那時候, 大多數嬰兒都是在家裡出生的。| [+on] *I was born on December 15th 1973.* 我於1973年12月15日出生。| **newly-born** (=recently born) 最近出生的, 出生不久的 *a newly-born baby* 新生兒, 初生嬰兒 | **be born into/to/of** (=be born in a particular situation, type of family etc) 出身為, 出生在…的家庭背景 *Frank was born into a wealthy family.* 弗蘭克出生於富有家庭。| **be born with** (=have a particular disease, type of character etc since birth) 天生有〔某種疾病、性格等〕 *Jenny was born with a cleft palate.* 珍妮天生腭裂。| **be born blind/deaf/etc** (=be blind, deaf etc when born) 生來便盲/聾等 | **be born lucky/unlucky etc** (=always be lucky, unlucky etc) 生來命好/命苦等 | **Australian/French etc born** (=born in or as a citizen of Australia etc) 在澳大利亞/法國等出生的 *Australian born rock icon Nick Cave* 在澳大利亞出生的搖滾偶像尼克·凱夫

2 be born to do/be sth to be very suitable for a particular job, activity etc 天生適合做〔某項工作、活動等〕

3 born leader/teacher/musician etc someone who has a strong natural ability to lead, teach etc 天生的領袖/教師/音樂家等

4 ▶START EXISTING 開始存在◀ [not before noun 不用於名詞前] something that is born starts to exist 產生, 誕生: *And so the concept of the jet engine was born.* 於是噴氣發動機的概念便誕生了。

5 born of/out of existing as a result of something 因為…而形成, 是…的產物: *Bill spoke with a cynicism born of bitter experience.* 比爾説話憤世嫉俗是因為他有過痛苦的經歷。

6 born and bred born and having grown up in a particular place and having the typical qualities of someone from that place 土生土長: *born and bred in Liverpool* 在利物浦土生土長

7 I wasn't born yesterday *spoken* used to tell someone you think is deceiving you that you are not stupid enough to believe them【口】不要拿我當三歲小孩

8 in all my born days *spoken old-fashioned* used to express surprise at something that you have never heard about or experienced before【口, 過時】在我的一生中, 有生以來: *Well, I've never heard of such a thing in all my born days!* 我有生以來從未聽説過這樣的事!

9 there's one born every minute *spoken* used to say that someone has been very stupid or easily deceived【口】隨時有人犯傻[上當]

10 be born under a lucky/unlucky star to always have good or bad luck in your life 生來就幸運/不幸 — see also 另見 NATURAL-BORN

11 be born with a silver spoon in your mouth to be born into a rich family 生在富貴人家

12 be born on the wrong side of the blanket *humorous* to have parents who were not married when you were born【幽默】父母婚前出生

born-a-gain /ˈ· ··/ *adj* **1 born-again Christian** someone who has become an EVANGELICAL Christian after having a religious experience 基督教再生教徒〔指經過悟性體驗後接受了基督教福音主義教派的人〕 **2 born-again nonsmoker/vegetarian etc** someone who has recently stopped smoking, eating meat etc, and who wants other people to do the same 重新振作起精神的戒煙者/戒葷食者等

borne[1] /bɔrn; bɔːn/ the past participle of BEAR[1]

borne[2] *adj* **1 water borne/sea borne/air borne etc** carried by water, the sea, air etc 由水/海洋/空氣等傳播[攜帶]的: *waterborne diseases* 由水傳播的疾病 **2 be borne in on/upon sb** if a fact is borne in on someone, they realize that it is true 意識到, 完全認識到: *Slowly it was borne in on the citizens that the enemy had surrounded the entire town.* 市民漸漸意識到敵人已經把整個城鎮包圍住了。

bo·rough /ˈbʌro; ˈbʌrə/ *n* [C] a town, or part of a large city, that is responsible for managing its own schools, hospitals, roads etc 享有某些自治權的市鎮[區]: *The New York borough of Queens* 紐約昆士(自治)區 | *Lambeth Borough Council* 蘭貝思自治區議會 2

borough coun·cil /,·· ˈ··/ *n* [C] *especially BrE* the organization that controls a borough【尤英】自治區[市]議會

bor·row /ˈbɑro; ˈbɒrəʊ/ *v* [I,T] **1** to use something that belongs to someone else and that you must give back to them later 向別人借, 借來, 借入: *Can I borrow your pen for a minute?* 我可以借你的筆用一下嗎? | **borrow sth from sb** *BrE*【英】*You are allowed to borrow 6 books from the library at a time.* 你每次可從圖書館借六本書。| **borrow heavily** (=borrow a lot of money) 借巨款 *They borrowed heavily from the bank to start their new business.* 他們向銀行貸了巨款來創辦新企業。—compare 比較 LEND (1), LOAN[2] (1) —see picture at 參見 LEND 圖 **2** to take or copy someone's ideas, words etc and use them in your own work, language etc (擅自)借用, 採用; 抄襲〔思想、文字等〕: *It is obvious that many ideas in the book have been borrowed.* 顯然, 這本書裡的許多思想都是拾人牙慧的。| [+from] *English borrows words from many languages.* 英語從很多不同的語言中借用了詞語。**3 borrow trouble** *AmE informal* to worry about something unnecessarily【美, 非正式】自尋煩惱 —see also 另見 **be living on borrowed time** (LIVE[1] (14)) 2 3

USAGE NOTE 用法説明: BORROW

WORD CHOICE 詞語辨析: **borrow, lend, loan, hire, rent, get/have the use of, let somebody use**

You **borrow** something **from** another person who is willing to **lend** it **to** you. 從別人那裡借是borrow, 別人借給你是lend: *I borrowed some money from my sister* (=my sister lent me some money/I was lent some money by my sister). 我向妹妹借了一些錢。〔妹妹借給我一些錢〕 You will hear some native speakers of English saying things like *My sister borrowed me the money,* but this is not considered to be correct. 某些英語國家的人會説 My sister borrowed me the money, 但這種説法不對。

In American English **loan** is often like **lend**. 在美國英語中loan常同於lend的意思: *The current administration has loaned this country a billion dollars.* 現政府給這個國家貸款十億美元。In British English **loan** (*v*) is usually used for when someone lends a possession for a long time to a museum etc so that everybody can see it. 在英國英語中loan通常指某人把藏品長期借給博物館以便大家能觀賞。

If you **borrow** money you have to pay it back later, and you may have to pay for the use of it as well, if you have borrowed it from a bank rather than a friend. If you **borrow** a car/video etc you give it back afterwards but you do not usually pay for the use of it, otherwise you would say **hire** or **rent**. 如果你borrow(借)錢, 你以後必須歸還, 如果你從銀行借錢, 而不是從朋友處借錢, 你還需支付利息。如果你borrow(借)車/錄像帶等, 歸還時不必付錢, 否則用hire或rent(租)。—see 見 **hire** WORD CHOICE

People do not usually use **borrow** or **lend/loan** for something that cannot be moved such as a room, house, or piece of land. If you pay for using this sort of thing you **hire** or **rent** it, otherwise you **get the use of** it from someone who is willing to **let you use** it. 對於房間、房子、土地等不移動的東西, 人們通常不説 borrow 或 lend/loan。如果你需付錢, 就用hire或rent, 否則你可以get the use of(使用), 因為別人let(讓)你免費用: *Could you let us use this hall?/Could we have the use of this hall?* 我們可以借用這個禮堂嗎?

bor·row·er /ˈbɑroɚ; ˈbɒrəʊə/ *n* [C] someone who is borrowing money 借款者, 借方: *Most borrowers pay 7% interest.* 大多數借款人支付 7% 的利息。

bor·row·ing /ˈbɑroɪŋ; ˈbɒrəʊɪŋ/ *n* **1** [C] something such as a word, phrase, or idea that has been copied from another language, book etc 借用的詞語, 外來語; 借來的概念: *Names such as Lloyd are Celtic borrowings.* Lloyd 之類的人名都是從凱爾特語中借用的詞語。| **[+from]** *His music is full of borrowings from other composers.* 他的音樂中有許多從其他作曲家那裡借用的元素。**2** [U] the practice of borrowing money 借錢, 貸款: *The banks announced that borrowing had increased.* 銀行宣布貸款有所增加。**3 borrowings** the total amount of money that a company or organization owes 欠款總額

borrowing pow·ers /ˈ··· ˌ··/ *n* [plural] the amount of money that a company is allowed to borrow, according to its own rules〔公司章程所規定的〕舉債能力; 借款權

bor·stal /ˈbɔrstəl; ˈbɔːstl/ *n* [C,U] *BrE old-fashioned* a special prison for criminals who are not old enough to be in an ordinary prison【英, 過時】〔少年罪犯的〕教養院, 少年感化院: *Shanie was sent to borstal when she was 14.* 薩妮 14 歲時被送進少年感化院。

bosh /bɑʃ; bɒʃ/ *interjection BrE old-fashioned* a word used when you think that what someone has said is silly or untrue【英, 過時】廢話, 胡說: *"I think Sally has lost weight." "Bosh! She looks fatter than ever."* "我認為薩莉瘦了。" "胡說! 她看起來比以前更胖了。" **—bosh** *n* [U]

bos·om /ˈbʊzəm; ˈbʊzəm/ *n* **1** [singular] the front part of a woman's chest, or the part of her clothes that covers it〔女人的〕胸部;〔衣服的〕胸襟 **2** [C usually plural 一般用複數] a woman's breast〔女人的〕乳房 **3 the bosom of the family/the Church etc** the situation where you feel safe because you are with people who love and protect you 家庭/教會等的溫暖 [安全感] **4** [singular] *literary* a word meaning someone's feelings and emotions, used especially when these are bad or unpleasant【文】內心情感: *Drury harboured bitterness and anger in his bosom.* 德魯里內心深處暗藏着痛苦和仇恨。**5 bosom friend/buddy** a very close friend 密友, 知己, 心腹之交: *We first met in high school and we've been bosom buddies ever since.* 我們在上中學時認識, 從那時起就成為了知心朋友。

bos·om·y /ˈbʊzəmɪ; ˈbʊzəmi/ *adj informal* having large breasts【非正式】胸部隆起的, 乳房豐滿的

2 3 **boss¹** /bɔs; bɒs/ *n* [C] **1** the person who employs you or who is in charge of you at work 老闆, 上司; 領班: *I'll have to ask my boss for a day off.* 我要向老闆請一天假。| **be your own boss** (=work for yourself rather than being employed by someone else) 自己當老闆 **2** *informal* a manager with an important position in a company or other organization【非正式】經理; 頭頭: *Prison bosses launched an investigation into major security lapses.* 監獄的頭兒對嚴重的保安失誤展開了調查。| *Bosses got pay increases of 75%, when the workers' pay was cut to £13,000.* 經理們的工資增加了75%, 而工人的工資則下降到 13,000 英鎊。**3** the person who is the strongest in a relationship, who controls a situation etc 控制局勢的人: *When you first start training a dog it's important to let him see that you're the boss.* 剛開始訓練狗時, 要讓狗知道一切由你作主。| **show sb who's boss** (=make someone realize that you are in control, not them) 讓某人知道誰是主子 **4** a round decoration on the surface of something such as the ceiling of an old building 圓形裝飾物, 飾球〈如舊式建築物的天花板上的浮凸飾物〉

boss² *v* [T] to tell people to do things, give them orders etc, especially when you have no authority to do it 對…發號施令, 指揮〔尤指無權這樣做時〕: **boss sb about** *BrE*【英】**/around** *I'm sick of him bossing us around like that. Who does he think he is?* 我已厭倦了他那樣對我們發號施令。他以為自己是誰呀?

boss³ *adj slang* very attractive or fashionable【俚】誘人的; 時髦的: *That's boss, that new computer game.* 那個新的電腦遊戲棒極了。

bos·sa no·va /ˌbɑsəˈnovə; ˌbɒsəˈnəʊvə/ *n* [C] a dance that comes from Brazil, or the music for this dance〔巴西〕波薩諾伐舞; 波薩諾伐舞曲

boss-eyed /ˌ· ˈ·◂/ *adj BrE* having both eyes looking in towards your nose; CROSS-EYED【英】內斜視的, 鬥雞眼的, 內斜眼的

boss·y /ˈbɔsɪ; ˈbɒsi/ *adj* **1** always telling other people what to do in a way that is annoying 愛發號施令的, 專橫的: *I like his approach to things – he can show people what to do without being bossy.* 我喜歡他做事的方式, 他能告訴別人做甚麼, 卻一點也不專橫。**2 bossy-boots** *BrE informal* someone who you think tells other people what to do too often【英, 非正式】愛發號施令的人: *Don't be such a bossy-boots. Let her decide for herself.* 別老愛指揮別人, 讓她自己做主吧。**—bossily** *adv* **—bossiness** *n* [U]

bo·sun /ˈbosn̩; ˈbəʊsən/ *n* [C] another spelling of BOATSWAIN boatswain 的另一種拼法

bo·tan·i·cal /bəˈtænɪkl̩; bəˈtænɪkəl/ *adj* [only before noun 僅用於名詞前] connected with plants or the scientific study of plants 植物 (學) 的 **—botanically** /-kl̩ɪ; -kli/ *adv*

botanical gar·den /ˌ·ˌ··· ˈ··/ *n* [C] a large public garden where many different types of flowers and plants are grown for scientific study 植物 (公) 園

bot·a·nist /ˈbɑtn̩ɪst; ˈbɒtən̩ɪst/ *n* [C] someone whose job is to make scientific studies of wild plants 植物學家

bot·a·ny /ˈbɑtn̩ɪ; ˈbɒtəni/ *n* [U] the scientific study of plants 植物學

botch¹ /bɑtʃ; bɒtʃ/ also 又作 **botch up** *v* [T] *informal* to do something badly, because you have been careless or because you do not have the skill to do it properly【非正式】〔因不經心或缺乏技術而〕把…做得拙劣: *The builders really botched up our patio.* 建築工人把我們的平台做得真拙劣。**—botcher** *n* [C]

botch² also 又作 **botch-up** /ˈ· ·/ *n* [C] *informal especially BrE* a piece of work, job etc that has been badly or carelessly done【非正式, 尤英】拙劣的活兒: **make a botch of** *I've just made an awful botch of my translation.* 我譯得一塌糊塗。| **botch job** *That repair was a botch job.* 修理工作幹得很差。

both /boθ; bəʊθ/ *predeterminer, determiner, pron* **1** used to talk about two people, things, situations etc together 兩者, 雙方, 倆: *Both Helen's parents are doctors.* 海倫的父母都是醫生。| *Both sides are keen to reach an agreement.* 雙方都很想達成協議。| *"I don't know which book to buy." "Why not buy both of them?"* "我不知道該買哪本書。" "為甚麼不兩本都買?" | *They both started speaking together.* 他們倆開始一起說起來。— compare 比較 EITHER² **2 both…and…** used to emphasize that something is true not just of one person, thing, or situation but also of another 不僅…而且…; 既…又…: *He's lived in both Britain and America.* 他在英國和美國都生活過。| *She can both speak and write Japanese.* 她不僅會說日語, 而且還會寫。| *We were treated with both tolerance and compassion.* 他們對待我們既有耐性又有同情心。 1 1

both·er¹ /ˈbɑðɚ; ˈbɒðə/ *v* 1 3

1 ►MAKE AN EFFORT 作出努力◄ [I,T] to make the effort to do something 費心, 盡力〔做某事〕, 因…操心: [**+about/with**] *BrE*【英】*I'm too busy to bother about fixing it now.* 我太忙, 現在沒空修理。| **(not) bother to do sth** *Unfortunately he didn't bother to check the exact wording of the contract before he signed it.* 遺憾的是, 他在簽字前沒有費心檢查一下合同上的確切措辭。| *Nobody listens to me. I don't know why I bother.* 沒人聽我的。我不知道自己為甚麼還要費那份勁。| **(not) bother doing something** *I don't know if Sally's coming to the party. I didn't bother asking.* 我不知道薩莉是否會參加聚會, 我沒有問她。| **don't/didn't/won't etc**

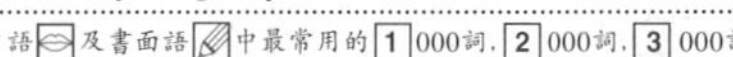

bother *"Do you want me to wait for you?" "No, don't bother."* "你想讓我等你嗎?" "不, 你不必了。"
2 ►WORRY 擔心◄ [I,T] to make someone feel slightly worried or upset (使) 擔心, (使) 苦惱: *Being in a crowd really bothers me.* 擁在人羣裡真使我苦惱。| **it bothers sb that** *It really bothered me that he'd forgotten my birthday.* 他把我的生日都忘記了, 真讓我感到沒勁兒。| **not bother sb** *Mandy hates walking home alone at night but it doesn't bother me.* 曼迪不願晚上一個人走回家, 可我無所謂。
3 ►ANNOY 使惱怒◄ [I,T] to annoy someone by interrupting them when they are trying to do something 打擾, 煩擾: *Danny, stop bothering me while I'm trying to work!* 丹尼, 我要工作的時候別再打擾我! | **bother sb about/with sth** *He didn't want to bother her with his financial problems on their honeymoon.* 他不想在蜜月期間因他的經濟問題使她掃興。
4 can't/couldn't be bothered *BrE* used to say that you do not want to do something because you do not have enough energy or interest【英】不想費神[沒有心思]去做某事: *I knew I ought to clean the car but I just couldn't be bothered.* 我知道我應該去洗車, 但我就是沒心思幹。| **can't/couldn't be bothered to do sth** *My parents could never be bothered to come and see me in the school play.* 我父母從來不肯來學校看我演話劇。
5 not bothered *especially BrE* if you are not bothered about something, it is not important to you【尤英】無所謂, 不在意: *"Which chair do you want?" "I'm not bothered."* "你要哪把椅子?" "我無所謂。" | **[+about]** *He's not really bothered about getting the facts right.* 事實對否他並不太在意。
6 sorry to bother you *spoken* used as a very polite way of telling someone you want their attention【口】對不起打擾你一下
7 ►FRIGHTEN 嚇唬◄ [T] to upset or frighten someone by repeatedly trying to hurt them, touch them sexually etc 騷擾; 恐嚇: *Is that man bothering you? Shall I call the police?* 那男人騷擾你了嗎? 要不要我報警?
8 hot and bothered angry and worried about something, especially unnecessarily〔尤指不必要地〕心急火燎的: *What are you getting all hot and bothered about? It's not that important.* 你為甚麼整天心急火燎的? 事情並沒有那麼重要。
9 not bother yourself/not bother your head to not take time or energy to do something or to think about something, either because it is not important or because it is too difficult 不為…操心[傷腦筋]: **[+with/about]** *Cliff didn't want to bother himself with masses of detail.* 克利夫不想為那些瑣事傷腦筋。
10 bother it/them etc *BrE old-fashioned* used to express a sudden feeling of annoyance about something【英, 過時】真討厭〔表示厭煩〕: *Oh bother it! The thread's broken again!* 真討厭! 線又斷了!

bother² *n* **1** [U] *especially BrE* trouble or difficulty that has been caused by small problems and that usually only continues for a short time【尤英】麻煩, 不便; 憂慮; 煩惱的事: *It's an old car but it's never caused me any bother.* 那是輛舊車, 但從來沒有為我帶來任何麻煩。| **[+with]** *Joe's been having a bit of bother with his back again recently.* 最近喬的後背又有點不適。| **it's no bother** *spoken* (=used to emphasize that you are happy to help someone and it is not much effort)【口】沒關係, 不費事 *"Thanks for your help." "It was no bother at all."* "謝謝你幫忙。" "這不算甚麼。" | **go to the bother (of doing sth)** (=make the effort to do something) 費神去做 *I'm not going to go to the bother of writing again. She never writes back.* 我再也不費神寫信了。她從不回信。| **give sb any bother/a lot of bother etc** *Are you sure the station is on your way? I don't want to give you any extra bother.* 你真的順道路過火車站嗎? 我不想給你添麻煩。| **save sb/yourself the bother (of doing sth)** *I should have phoned the shop first and saved myself the bother of going there.* 我本應該先給商店打個電話, 可以省得我費勁親自去一趟。**2** [singular] *BrE* a person or job that is annoying to deal with【英】難對付的事[人]: *Sorry to be such a bother but could you show me how the photocopier works?* 對不起, 麻煩你一下, 你能示範一下複印機怎樣用嗎?

bother³ *interjection BrE* used when you are slightly annoyed about something【英】真煩人! 真討厭!〔表示有些惱火〕: *Oh bother! I forgot to phone Jean.* 真糟! 我忘了給瓊打電話。

both·er·a·tion /ˌbɑðəˈreʃən; ˌbɒðəˈreɪʃən/ *interjection BrE old-fashioned* used when you are slightly annoyed【英, 過時】可惡〔表示有些惱火〕: *Botheration. I forgot my glasses.* 可惡, 我忘了戴眼鏡。

both·er·some /ˈbɑðəsəm; ˈbɒðəsəm/ *adj old-fashioned* slightly annoying【過時】引起麻煩的, 討厭的; 令人為難的: *She brushed his hand away like a bothersome fly.* 她像躲令人生厭的蒼蠅一樣撥開他的手。

bottles 瓶

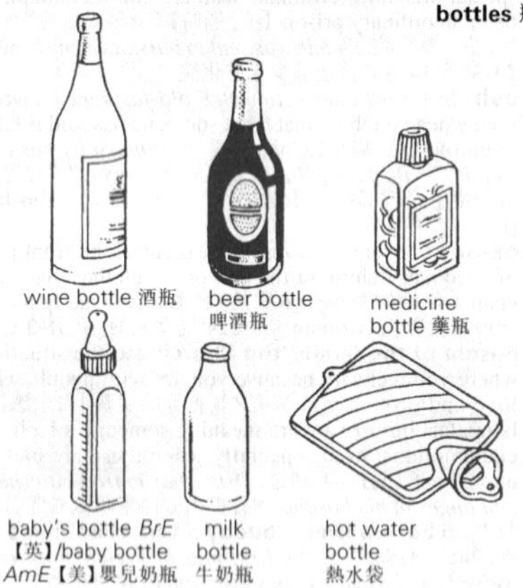

wine bottle 酒瓶
beer bottle 啤酒瓶
medicine bottle 藥瓶
baby's bottle *BrE*【英】/baby bottle *AmE*【美】嬰兒奶瓶
milk bottle 牛奶瓶
hot water bottle 熱水袋

bot·tle¹ /ˈbɑtl̩; ˈbɒtl/ *n*
1 ►CONTAINER 容器◄ [C] a container with a narrow top for keeping liquids in, usually made of plastic or glass 瓶: *Give the bottle a shake before you open it.* 開瓶前先搖一搖。| **[+of]** *a bottle of champagne* 一瓶香檳酒
2 ►AMOUNT OF LIQUID 一定量的液體◄ also 又作 **bottleful** [C] the amount of liquid that a bottle contains 一瓶之量: *Between us, we drank three bottles of wine.* 我們倆喝了三瓶酒。
3 ►MILK 牛奶◄ [singular] milk given to babies or young animals in a bottle rather than from their mother's breast〔餵嬰兒用的〕裝在奶瓶中的牛奶: *My first baby just wouldn't take a bottle at all.* 我的第一個孩子就是不肯喝牛奶。
4 ►COURAGE 勇氣◄ [U] *BrE informal* courage to do something that is dangerous or unpleasant【英, 非正式】勇氣, 膽量: *I never thought she'd have the bottle to do it!* 我從未想過她會有勇氣做這樣的事!
5 hit the bottle/take to the bottle to start drinking a lot of alcohol regularly, in order to forget your problems〔為了忘掉煩惱〕開始酗酒
6 be on the bottle to always be drinking a lot of alcohol 愛喝酒, 貪酒
7 bring a bottle *BrE*【英】, **bring your own bottle** *AmE*【美】used to describe a party to which you must bring your own alcoholic drink 自帶酒參加聚會

bottle² *v* [T] **1** to put a liquid, especially wine or beer, into a bottle after you have made it 把…裝進瓶中: *The wine is bottled at the vineyard.* 葡萄酒是在葡萄園裡裝

瓶的。**2** to put vegetables or fruit into special glass containers in order to preserve them 把〔蔬菜或水果〕裝瓶保存

bottle out *phr v* [I] *BrE informal* to suddenly decide not to do something because you are frightened【英, 非正式】因膽怯而決定不做某事, 打退堂鼓: *"Did you tell him?" "No, I bottled out at the last minute."* "你告訴他了嗎?" "沒有, 我在最後一分鐘退縮了。"

bottle sth ↔ **up** *phr v* [T] to deliberately not allow yourself to show a strong feeling or emotion 抑制〔感情〕, 勉強忍住: *It is far better to cry than to bottle up your feelings.* 哭出來比憋在心裡要好。

bottle bank /ˈ·· ·/ *n* [C] a container in the street that you put empty bottles into, so that the glass can be used again〔大街上〕回收玻璃器皿的空瓶箱

bot·tled /ˈbɑtḷd; ˈbɒtld/ *adj* **bottled water/beer etc** water, beer etc that is sold in a bottle 瓶裝水/啤酒等

bottle-feed /ˈ·· ·/ *v past tense and past participle* **bottle-fed** /-ˌfɛd; -fed/ [T] to feed a baby or young animal with milk from a bottle rather than from their mother's breast 用奶瓶餵 —**bottle-feeding** *n* [U]

bottle green /ˌ·· ˈ·◂/ *n* [U] a very dark green colour 深綠色 —**bottle green** *adj* —see picture on page A5 參見A5頁圖

bot·tle·neck /ˈbɑtḷˌnɛk; ˈbɒtlnek/ *n* [C] **1** a place in a road where the traffic cannot pass easily, so that there are a lot of delays 瓶頸路段, 交通阻塞點, 狹窄路段 **2** a delay in one stage of a process that makes the whole process take longer 障礙, 妨礙整個進度的工序: *Having only one person to do the clerical work has caused a real bottleneck.* 只有一個人做文書工作妨礙了整個進度。

bottle o·pen·er /ˈ·· ˌ···/ *n* [C] a small tool used for removing the metal lids from bottles 開瓶器

[1] [3] **bot·tom¹** /ˈbɑtəm; ˈbɒtəm/ *n*

1 ►LOWEST PART 最底部◄ the lowest part of something 底部, 基部; 下端, 末尾: **the bottom** *From the bottom the skyscraper looked as if it touched the clouds.* 從底下看, 那幢摩天大樓好像直插雲端。| **[+of]** *Hold the bottom of the pole and keep it upright.* 托住柱子的末端, 使其保持垂直。| **at the bottom** *Go downstairs and wait for me at the bottom.* 下樓去, 在底層等我。| **at the bottom of** *Sign your name at the bottom of the page.* 在這頁的末尾簽上名字。—opposite 反義詞 TOP¹ (1)

2 ►SEA/RIVER 海/河◄ the ground under a sea, river etc, or the flat land in a valley 水底; 海底; 河底: **the bottom** *the sea bottom* 海底 | **[+of]** *The bottom of the pool is very slippery.* 這個池塘的底部很滑。| **at/on the bottom of sth** *A body was found at the bottom of the canal.* 水渠的底部發現一具屍體。

3 ►LOWEST SIDE 最低面◄ the flat surface on the lowest side of an object〔物體的〕平底: **the bottom** *Take the price tag off the bottom.* 把底下的價格標籤拿掉。| **[+of]** *You have chewing gum stuck to the bottom of your shoe.* 你的鞋底黏上了口香糖。

4 ►CUP/BOX ETC 杯/盒等◄ the lowest inner surface of something such as a cup or container 容器的內底: **the bottom** *Yuk, this cup's got mould in the bottom.* 哗, 這個杯子底上都發黴了。| **[+of]** *The flour is at the bottom of the cupboard.* 麵粉在櫥櫃最下層。

5 ►LOWEST POSITION 最低的位置◄ the lowest position in an organization or company, or on a list etc 最低職位; 最後名次: **the bottom** *The team is at the bottom of the league.* 這支球隊排在聯賽最後一名。| **start at the bottom** *Higgins started at the bottom and worked his way up to managing director.* 希金斯從最基層幹起, 一級一級地升到了總經理的職位。| **the bottom of the ladder/pile** (=the lowest position in society, an organization etc) 基層; 最低職位[職務] —opposite 反義詞 TOP¹ (3)

6 the bottom of a road/garden etc *especially BrE* the part of a road, area of land etc that is furthest from where you are【尤英】路/花園等的盡頭: *There's a shop at the bottom of the street.* 街的盡頭有家商店。

7 ►BODY 身體◄ [C] the part of your body that you sit on; BUTTOCKS 臀部, 屁股: *I just sat on my bottom and slid down.* 我就坐着滑了下去。

8 ►CLOTHES 衣服◄ [C] also 又作 **bottoms** the part of a set of clothes that you wear on the lower part of your body〔兩件一套衣服中的〕褲子: *bikini bottom* 比基尼式內褲 | *pyjama bottoms* 睡褲

9 get to the bottom of to find out the cause of a problem or situation 找出〔某事〕的真相: *I'm going to get to the bottom of this!* 這件事情我要查個水落石出!

10 be at the bottom of to be the basic cause of a problem or situation 是…的根本原因: *I'm sure Carrie's disturbed childhood is at the bottom of her current problems.* 我敢肯定嘉麗不幸的童年是她目前問題的根本原因。

11 hit rock bottom/be at rock bottom to reach a very low level, or be in a very bad situation 到最低程度; 最糟糕情況: *Morale has hit rock bottom.* 士氣到了最低落的程度。| *We bought the house when prices were at rock bottom.* 我們在房價最低時買下了房子。

12 from the bottom of your heart in a very sincere way 從心底裡, 由衷地: *Thank you from the bottom of my heart.* 衷心感謝你。

13 big-bottomed/round-bottomed etc having a bottom or base that is big, round etc 底大的/圓底的

14 the bottom dropped out of sb's world used to say that something very bad suddenly happened to someone 厄運突然降臨到某人身上, 某人倒大霉

15 the bottom drops out of the market used to say that people stop buying a particular product 出現暴跌的情況

16 bottoms up! *spoken* used to tell someone to enjoy or finish their alcoholic drink【口】乾杯!

17 bottom gear the lowest GEAR¹ (1) of a vehicle〔機動車的〕低速擋

18 ►SHIP 船◄ [C] the part of a ship that is below water 船體在水下的部分

19 at bottom the way a person or situation really is, although they may seem different 實際上; 內心裡: *She's a good, kind person at bottom.* 她實際上是個熱心腸的好人。—compare 比較 TOP¹ —see also 另見 **you can bet your bottom dollar** (BET¹ (4)), **knock the bottom out of** (KNOCK¹ (17)), **from top to bottom** (TOP¹ (19))

bottom² *adj* [only before noun 僅用於名詞前] **1** in the lowest place or position 底下的: *The records are kept on the bottom shelf.* 錄音帶放在底下的架上。| *the bottom right hand corner of the page* 這頁的右下角 **2** the least important, successful etc 最無關緊要的; 最差的: *Tim is in the bottom 10% of his class.* 蒂姆排在班上最差的10%中。**3** *especially BrE* in the place furthest away from where you are【尤英】離得最遠的: *Most of the sheep were grazing in the bottom field.* 大多數羊在遠處的地裡吃草。 [1] [3]

bottom³ *v*

bottom out *phr v* [I] if a situation, price etc bottoms out, it stops getting worse or lower, usually before improving again〔局面在好轉前〕停止惡化;〔價格在回升前〕停止下跌: *The market price of oil got as low as $10 a barrel before it finally bottomed out.* 石油的市場價格降到每桶十美元的最低點後回升。

bottom drawer /ˌ·· ˈ·/ *n* [C] *BrE* all the things, especially things that you use in a house, that a woman collects to use when she is married【英】女子結婚前準備的衣物, 嫁妝; HOPE CHEST *AmE*【美】

bot·tom·less /ˈbɑtəmlɪs; ˈbɒtəmləs/ *adj* **1** a sea, hole etc that is bottomless is extremely deep 無底的, 深不可測的, 極深的 **2** seeming to have no end 無盡頭的: **a bottomless pit** *a bottomless pit of misery* 痛苦的深淵

bottom line /ˌ·· ˈ·/ *n* **the bottom line a)** the profit or the amount of money that a business makes or loses 賬本底線,〔賬目上〕盈虧一覽結算線: *Business today is* *only interested in the bottom line.* 現今的商家只對賬本底線感興趣。**b)** a situation or fact that exists and that you must accept, even though you may not like it 不得不接受的局面[事實]: *The bottom line is that drinking and driving can kill.* 事實是酒後駕車會出人命。**c)** the lowest amount of money that you are willing to pay or take for something 底價, 最低價: *"What's your bottom line for selling the car?" "I can go down to £450."* "你這輛車的最低售價是多少?""我能降到450英鎊。"

B

bot·tom·most /ˈbɑtəmˌmost; ˈbɒtəmˌməʊst/ *adj* [only before noun 僅用於名詞前] in the lowest, furthest, or deepest position or place 最低的; 最遠的; 最深的: *the bottommost reaches of the Amazon* 亞馬遜河最深的河段

bottom-up /ˌ·· ˈ·◂/ *adj BrE* a bottom-up plan is one in which you decide on practical details before thinking about general principles【英】〔計劃〕從細節到整體的, 從實際出發的, 基於具體事實的 —opposite 反義詞 TOP-DOWN

bot·u·lis·m /ˈbɑtʃəˌlɪzəm; ˈbɒtʃʊlɪzəm/ *n* [U] serious food poisoning caused by BACTERIA in preserved meat and vegetables 肉毒(桿)菌中毒, 臘腸毒菌病

bou·doir /buˈdwɑr; ˈbuːdwɑː/ *n* [C] **1** *old use* a woman's bedroom or private sitting room【舊】〔女子的〕閨房 **2** the bedroom seen as the place where sex happens 〔發生性關係的〕寢房: *secrets of the boudoir* 寢房的祕密

bouf·fant /buˈfɑnt; ˈbuːfɒŋ/ *adj* a bouffant hair style is one in which your hair is raised away from your head at the top 〔髮型〕蓬鬆的

bou·gain·vil·le·a /ˌbugənˈvɪlɪə; ˌbuːgənˈvɪliə/ *n* [C,U] a plant that has red or purple flowers and grows up walls 九重葛屬植物〔一種開紅、紫色花的攀緣植物〕

bough /baʊ; baʊ/ *n* [C] a main branch on a tree 粗大的樹枝, 主枝

bought /bɔt; bɔːt/ the past tense and past participle of BUY[1]

bouil·la·baisse /ˌbujəˈbes; ˌbuːjəˈbes/ *n* [C,U] a strong-tasting soup or STEW[1] (1) made of fish 濃味燉魚(湯)

bouil·lon /ˈbujɑn; ˈbuːjɒn/ *n* [C,U] a clear soup made by boiling meat and vegetables in water 肉菜清湯

bouillon cube /ˈ·· ·/ *n* [C] *AmE* a solid piece of dried meat or vegetables used in soups【美】〔經脫水的〕塊狀湯料; STOCK CUBE *BrE*【英】

boul·der /ˈboldɚ; ˈbəʊldə/ *n* [C] a large stone or piece of rock 巨石, 巨礫: *huge boulders choking the stream bed* 堵塞河牀的大石塊

boule·vard /ˈbuləˌvɑrd; ˈbuːlvɑːd/ *n* [C] **1 a)** *BrE* a wide road in a town, usually with trees along the sides【英】林蔭大道 **b)** *AmE* a wide road in a town or city【美】寬闊的街道 **2** written abbreviation 縮寫為 **Blvd** used as part of the name of a particular road ...大道〔街道名稱的一部分〕: *Sunset Boulevard* 夕陽大道

3 **bounce[1]** /bauns; baʊns/ *v*

1 ▶MOVE FROM A SURFACE 從某表面移動◀ [I,T] if a ball or other object bounces, it immediately moves away from a surface it has just hit, or you make it move in this way (使)〔球等〕彈回, (使)反彈, (使)跳起: **[+off]** *The ball bounced off the crossbar and into the net.* 球從球門的橫木彈進了球門網。| **bounce sth on/against etc** *The kids were bouncing stones against the walls.* 孩子們把石頭往牆上打。

bounce 反彈

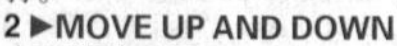

2 ▶MOVE UP AND DOWN 上下移動◀ [I] to move up and down, especially because you are hitting a surface that is made of rubber, has springs etc 跳上跳下, 蹦蹦跳跳: **[+on]** *Lyn was bouncing on the trampoline.* 林恩在彈牀上蹦跳。| **bounce up and down** *Stop bouncing up and down on the sofa.* 別再在沙發上跳上跳下了。

3 ▶CHEQUE 支票◀ [I,T] if a cheque bounces or a bank bounces a cheque, the bank will not pay any money because there is not enough money in the account of the person who wrote it (遭)退票, (被)拒付; 〔銀行〕拒付: *One bounced cheque could spell ruin for a new business.* 一張遭拒付的支票可以導致一個新商家的破產。

4 ▶WALK 走◀ [I always+adv/prep] to walk quickly and with a lot of energy 蹦蹦跳跳地走: **[+across/along/in etc]** *Olivia came bouncing into the room.* 奧利維亞蹦蹦跳跳地走進了房間。

5 ▶WHEN YOU MOVE 移動時◀ [I] if something bounces, it moves quickly up and down as you move 上下晃動: *Her hair bounced when she walked.* 她走路時, 頭髮上上下下地擺動。

6 bounce ideas off sb to ask someone for their opinion about an idea, a plan etc before you make a decision 徵求某人的意見

7 ▶LIGHT/SOUND 光/聲◀ [I,T] to REFLECT (1) from a surface 反射: **[+off]** *radio signals bouncing off the moon* 從月球反射回來的無線電信號

8 bounce sb on your knee to lift a child up and down on your knee 把孩子放在膝上上下顛着

9 be bounced into (doing) sth to be forced to decide something quickly or agree with a particular decision, because you have no time to think about it or you will seem to be wrong if you do not agree 急急忙忙地決定做某事: *Party members claimed that they had been bounced into choosing him as leader.* 黨員聲稱他們來不及考慮, 被迫選舉他為領導人。

bounce back *phr v* [I] to feel better quickly or become successful again after having a lot of problems 恢復元氣, 復蘇, 重新活躍: *In spite of the difficulties we always managed to bounce back.* 儘管困難重重, 我們總是設法重新振作起來。| *Becker bounced back in the second set.* 貝克爾在第二盤恢復了狀態。

bounce[2] *n* **1** [C] the action of moving up and down on a surface 跳起, 彈回, 反彈: *Try to catch the ball on the second bounce.* 球第二次彈起時就把它接住。**2** [U] the ability to move up and down on a surface, or that surface's ability to make something move up and down 彈性, 彈力: *The ball had completely lost its bounce.* 這球已經完全失去了彈力。**3** [U] a lot of energy 活力, 精力, 朝氣: *The dog has a shiny coat and is full of bounce.* 那隻狗有着亮閃閃的皮毛, 充滿活力。**4** [U] hair that has bounce is in very good condition and goes back to its shape if you press it 〔頭髮的〕彈性

bounc·er /ˈbaunsɚ; ˈbaʊnsə/ *n* [C] **1** someone whose job is to stand at the door of a club, bar etc and stop unwanted people coming in, or make people leave if they are behaving badly 〔夜總會、酒吧等的〕保安人員, 門衞, 保鏢 **2** a fast ball in CRICKET (2) that passes or hits the BATSMAN above the chest after it bounces 〔板球的〕反彈球〔指反彈後以高過擊球手胸部的高度經過或擊中擊球手的球〕

bounc·ing /ˈbaunsɪŋ; ˈbaʊnsɪŋ/ *adj* **bouncing baby/child** a very healthy baby or young child 健康的嬰兒/孩子

bounc·y /ˈbaunsɪ; ˈbaʊnsi/ *adj* **1** a bouncy ball etc quickly moves away from a surface after it has hit it 〔球等〕有彈性的; 彈起的 **2** a bouncy surface is made of a substance that makes people move up and down when they are on it 〔表面〕有彈性的, 彈力好的: *The bed is nice and bouncy.* 這牀彈性很強, 十分舒適。**3** someone who is bouncy is always very happy, confident, and full of energy 〔人〕快樂自信的, 精神飽滿的, 充滿朝氣的 **4** hair or material that is bouncy goes back to its shape when you press it 〔頭髮等〕有彈性的 —**bouncily** *adv* —**bounciness** *n* [U]

bound[1] /baund; baʊnd/ the past tense and past participle of BIND[1]

bound[2] *adj* [no comparative 無比較級]

1 be bound to to be very likely to do or feel a particular thing 很有可能, 肯定會: *Don't lie to her. She's bound to find out about it.* 別騙她, 她肯定會發現的。| **it is bound to be** (=used to say that something should have been expected) 當然, 早應料到 *"It's hot!" "Well, it was bound to be, I just took it out of the oven."* "真燙!" "當然了, 我剛從烤箱裡拿出來。" | **bound to happen** *"Why did Max die, Mom?" "He was an old dog, dear. It was bound to happen one day."* "馬科斯為甚麼死了, 媽媽?" "親愛的, 牠是一條老狗。這種事情遲早會發生。"

2 ▶DUTY/PROMISE 責任/許諾◀ **a) be bound (by)** if someone is bound by a law, promise, agreement etc, they have to do what it says 負有義務, 有責任受…約束, 理應…: *We are bound by agreements made at the time of the treaty.* 我們受到締結條約時達成的協議所約束。| **bound (by sth) to do sth** *If he's acting as auditor he's bound by law to report.* 如果他是個審計員, 按法律他有義務報告。| **legally bound** *The two parties are not legally bound until the contract has been signed.* 雙方在簽訂合同以後才有法律義務。**b) be/feel bound to do sth** to feel that you ought to do something 理應做某事, 應該做某事: *John felt bound to tell Katherine about the job, even though he didn't want to work with her.* 約翰感到應該告訴凱瑟琳關於那份工作的事, 儘管他不想和她共事。| **I'm bound to say (that)** *I'm bound to say I think you're taking a huge risk.* 我得說你在冒很大的風險。| **feel duty bound/honour bound to do sth** (=feel very strongly that you have to do or say something, especially because you think it is morally correct) 感到自己有義務做某事

3 ▶CONNECTED/INVOLVED 有聯繫的/涉及到的◀ **a) be bound up with sth** to be closely connected with a particular problem, situation etc 與某事有密切關係: *Henry's problems are all bound up with his mother's death when he was ten.* 亨利的問題都與他十歲時母親就去世了有關。**b) be bound up in sth** to be so involved in a difficult situation etc that you cannot think about anything else 忙於[熱衷於, 專心於]某事: *Jim's too bound up in his own worries to be able to help us.* 吉姆太專注於自己的煩惱事, 無法幫助我們。**c) be bound (together) by sth** to share a particular feature or quality 具有同樣的特點[性質]: *All the stories are bound by a common theme: jealousy.* 所有這些故事都有一個共同的主題: 妒忌。

4 ▶PLACE/DIRECTION 地方/方向◀ **a) bound for London/college etc** also 又作 **London/college etc bound** travelling towards or going to a particular place 前往倫敦/大學等: *The planes bound for Somalia carry food and medical supplies.* 飛往索馬里的飛機裝載着食品和醫療用品。| **homeward bound** (=going home) 返家途中 **b) northbound/southbound/eastbound/westbound** travelling in a particular direction 朝北/南/東/西行駛[航行]: *All eastbound trains have been cancelled due to faulty signals.* 由於信號錯誤, 所有東行的列車都已取消。

5 snow-bound/strike-bound/tradition-bound etc controlled or limited by something, so that you cannot do what you want or what other people want you to 由於大雪/罷工/傳統等的限制: *a fog-bound airport* 因大霧而無法正常運作的機場

6 ▶BOOK 書◀ a bound book is covered on the outside with paper, leather etc 用…裝訂好的, 有封面的: [+in] *a beautiful Bible bound in Moroccan leather* 一部摩洛哥皮面的精美的《聖經》| **leather/velvet etc bound** (=covered in leather, velvet etc) 皮面/天鵝絨面等

7 I'll be bound *old-fashioned* used when you are very sure that what you have just said is true【過時】我確信, 我敢肯定: *He had good reasons for doing that, I'll be bound.* 我確信, 他那樣做一定有道理。

8 bound form *technical* a part of a word that is always found in combination with another form, such as 'un' and 'er' in the words 'unknown' and 'speaker'【術語】〔不能獨立存在的〕黏附形式〈如在"unknown"和"speaker"中的"un"和"er"〉

bound[3] *v* **1** [I always+adv/prep] to run with a lot of energy, because you are happy, excited, or frightened 跳躍, 跳躍着前進, 蹦蹦跳跳地跑: **[+up/towards/across etc]** *Suddenly a huge dog came bounding towards me.* 一條大狗突然朝我跳過來。**2 be bounded by** if a country or area of land is bounded by something such as a wall, river etc it has the wall etc at its edge 以…為界, 形成…的界限: *a yard bounded by a rusty fence* 被生鏽的鐵柵欄隔開的院子 | *The US is bounded in the north by Canada and in the south by Mexico.* 美國北面與加拿大接壤, 南面與墨西哥毗鄰。

bound[4] *n*

1 by leaps and bounds/in leaps and bounds *BrE* if someone or something increases, develops etc by leaps and bounds, they increase etc very quickly【英】突飛猛進, 飛速發展: *Julie's reading is improving in leaps and bounds.* 朱莉的閱讀能力進步得很快。

2 out of bounds if a place is out of bounds, you are not allowed to go there 不得進入: [+to/for] *Parts of the complex are out of bounds to some personnel.* 這個綜合大樓的某些部分禁止一些人員進入。

3 ▶LIMITS 限制◀ **bounds** [plural] **a)** limits or rules that are given by law or exist because of social custom 界限, 極限, 限度, 止境: **stay/keep/remain within bounds** *Richards tried to stay within the bounds set by the financial controller.* 理查德盡力遵守財務總監作出的規定。| **keep sth within bounds** *Talking is permitted in the classroom as long as it is kept within bounds.* 只要是有限度的, 在教室裡談話是允許的。**b)** *old-fashioned* the edges of a town, city etc【過時】市[鎮]的邊緣

4 go beyond the bounds of decency/reason/good taste etc to not follow the rules that people normally follow when doing something 超出了得體/理性/雅趣等的限度

5 be within/beyond the bounds of possibility to be possible or impossible 可能/不可能: *Mike's version of events is unlikely, but not beyond the bounds of possibility.* 事情未必像邁克所描述的那樣, 但也不是不可能的。

6 know no bounds *formal* if someone's honesty, kindness etc knows no bounds, they are extremely honest etc【正式】無止境地, 極其地

7 in bounds/out of bounds inside or outside the legal playing area in a sport such as American football or BASKETBALL 界內/出界

8 ▶JUMP 跳◀ [C] a long or high jump made with a lot of energy 跳, 跳躍

bound·a·ry /ˈbaʊndərɪ; ˈbaʊndəri/ *n*

1 ▶EDGE 邊◀ [C] the official line that marks the edge of a town, country etc 分界線, 邊界: **[+between]** *the boundary between the US and Canada* 美國和加拿大的分界線 | **draw a boundary** (=decide where one town etc ends and another one starts) 確定分界線 | **boundary line** *the country's boundary line* 國界

2 ▶WALL/FENCE 牆/籬笆◀ [C] something such as a wall or fence that is intended to keep people or things separate 界限, 範圍: *staying within the boundary of the old city walls* 留在老城牆的範圍以內

3 ▶LIMIT 限制◀ [C usually plural 一般用複數] the highest or most extreme limit that something can reach 限度, 界限: [+of] *the boundaries of human knowledge* 人類知識的極限

4 ▶BETWEEN FEELINGS/QUALITIES ETC 感情/特質等之間◀ [C] the point at which one feeling, quality etc stops and another starts 分野: **[+of/between]** *People disagree about the boundaries of political parties.* 人們對政黨之間的分野觀點不一致。

5 push back the boundaries (of) to change the way

people think about an idea, belief etc, or greatly increase their knowledge of something 擴展…的領域: *Her new essay really pushes back the boundaries of literary theory.* 她的新論文確實拓展了文學理論的範圍。
6 ►CRICKET 板球◄ [C] the outer limit of the playing area in CRICKET (2), or a shot that sends the balls across this limit for points 球場邊界線; 擊球超過邊界線得分

B

bound·en /ˋbaundən; ˈbaʊndən/ *adj* **your bounden duty** *old-fashioned* something that you should do because it is morally correct【過時】分內的事, 應盡的義務

bound·er /ˋbaundɚ; ˈbaʊndə/ *n* [C] *BrE old-fashioned* a disapproving word for a man who has behaved in a way that you think is morally wrong【英, 過時】不道德的人: *The man's a bounder.* 那人是個無賴。

bound·less /ˋbaundlɪs; ˈbaʊndləs/ *adj* having no limit or end 無限的, 無量的, 無窮的: *enthusiasts with boundless energy for their hobby* 對自己的愛好有無窮精力的狂熱者 —**boundlessly** *adv* —**boundlessness** *n* [U]

boun·te·ous /ˋbauntɪəs; ˈbaʊntiəs/ *adj literary* very generous【文】慷慨的, 大方的

boun·ti·ful /ˋbauntəfəl; ˈbaʊntɪfəl/ *adj literary*【文】**1** if something is bountiful, there is more than enough of it 大量的, 充足的: *bountiful harvests* 大豐收 **2** generous 慷慨的: *bountiful God* 寬宏大量的上帝

boun·ty /ˋbauntɪ; ˈbaʊnti/ *n* **1** [C] an amount of money that is given to someone by the government as a reward for doing something, such as catching a criminal〔政府給予的〕獎勵金, 賞金: *The million-dollar bounty on Noriega's head shows how important it is he is brought to trial.* 懸賞百萬美元捉拿(巴拿馬獨裁者)諾列加, 說明把他繩之以法是多麼重要。**2** [U] *literary* the quality of being generous【文】慷慨, 好施, 仁愛

bounty hunt·er /ˋ·· ˌ··/ *n* [C] someone who catches criminals and brings them to the police in return for a reward 為獲得賞金而搜捕罪犯的人

bou·quet /buˋke; bəʊˈkeɪ/ *n* **1** [C] an arrangement of flowers, especially one that you give to someone 花束 **2** [C,U] the smell of a wine 酒的芳香: *a fruity bouquet* 有水果味的酒香

bour·bon /ˋbɝbən; ˈbʊəbən/ *n* [U] a type of American WHISKEY〔美國產的〕波旁威士忌酒

bour·geois[1] /burˋʒwa; ˈbʊəʒwɑː/ *adj* **1** too interested in having a lot of possessions and a high position in society 過分注重名利的, 追求物質享受的; 市儈的, 庸俗的: *the Sixties backlash against bourgeois materialism* 六十年代對過分注重名利的實利主義的強烈反對 **2** belonging to the MIDDLE CLASS 中產階級的 **3** belonging to or typical of the part of society that is rich, educated, owns land etc, according to MARXISM 資產階級的 —see also 另見 PETTY BOURGEOIS —compare 比較 PROLETARIAN

bourgeois[2] *n plural* **bourgeois** [C] **1** someone who is too interested in having a lot of possessions and a high position in society 過分追求物質享受的人, 過分看重名利的人 **2** a member of the MIDDLE CLASS 中產階級的一員 **3** someone who belongs to the part of society which is rich, educated, owns land etc, according to MARXISM 資產階級的一員 —compare 比較 PROLETARIAT

bour·geoi·sie /ˌburʒwaˋzi; ˌbʊəʒwɑːˈziː/ *n* **the bourgeoisie** the people in a society who are rich, educated, own land etc, according to MARXISM 資產階級

'bout /baut; baʊt/ *adv, prep spoken* about【口】關於: *"What are you talking 'bout?"* "你在談甚麼?"

bout /baut; baʊt/ *n* [C] **1 a bout of flu/nausea/depression etc** a short period of time during which you suffer from an illness 流感/噁心/抑鬱等的發作(時期) **2** a short period of time during which you do something a lot, especially something that is bad for you 一陣, 一回, 一場, 一番〔尤指做對自己有害的事情〕: *After a near fatal drinking bout, Joe decided to give up alcohol.* 在一次幾乎致命的狂飲之後, 喬決定戒酒。**3** a BOXING or WRESTLING match 拳擊[摔跤]比賽

bou·tique /buˋtik; buːˈtiːk/ *n* [C] a small shop that sells very fashionable clothes or other objects 出售流行服飾的小商店, 精品店

bou·ton·ni·ere /butṇˋɪr; buːˌtɒniˈeə/ *n* [C] *AmE* a flower that a man wears in the LAPEL of his suit, especially at a wedding【美】別在〔男士西服〕翻領上的花; BUTTONHOLE (2) *BrE*【英】

bo·vine /ˋbovaɪn; ˈbəʊvaɪn/ *adj* **1** *technical* connected with cows【術語】牛的 **2** slow and slightly stupid, like a cow 似牛的; 笨拙的; 遲鈍的, 緩慢的: *a bovine expression of contentment* 傻乎乎的滿意表情

bov·ver /ˋbɑvɚ; ˈbɒvə/ *n* [U] *BrE old-fashioned slang* violent behaviour, especially by a group of young men【英, 過時, 俚】〔尤指青少年〕打羣架, 鬥毆; 恐嚇行為: **bovver boy** (=someone who behaves in a violent way) 小流氓

bow[1] /bau; baʊ/ *v* **1** [I] to bend the top part of your body forward in order to show respect for someone important 鞠躬, 躬身行禮: **[+before/to etc]** *He bowed before the king.* 他向國王躬身行禮。**2** [I,T] to bend your body over something, especially in order to see it more closely 躬身向前看〔尤指為靠近些看〕: **[+over]** *Professor Teague sat at his desk, bowed over a book.* 蒂格教授坐在桌旁伏身看一本書。| **bow your head** (=bend your neck so that you are looking at the ground) 低頭, 俯首 | **bow your head in shame** *Phil stood there, his head bowed in shame.* 菲爾站在那兒, 羞愧地低下了頭。**3 be bowed (under sth)** to be bent because you are carrying something heavy on your back〔被背上重物〕壓得躬着身子 **4 bow and scrape** to show too much respect to someone in authority〔對人〕卑躬屈膝, 點頭哈腰

bow down *phr v* [I] **1** to bend forward from your waist, especially when you are already kneeling, in order to show respect 深度躬身致敬: **[+before/to etc]** *Maria bowed down before the statue.* 瑪麗亞在塑像前躬身致敬。**2 bow down to sb** *literary* to let someone give you orders or tell you what to do【文】向某人屈服; 屈從於某人

bow out *phr v* [I] **1** to stop taking part in an activity, job etc, especially one that you have been doing for a long time (從…)退出, 退場; 辭職: **bow out of sth** *Reeves thinks it is time for him to bow out of politics.* 里夫斯認為到了自己從政界退出的時候了。**2** to not do something that you have promised or agreed to do 不守信用, 背信棄義

bow to sb/sth *phr v* [T] to finally agree to do something that people want you to, even though you do not want to do it 向…讓步, 屈服於: *Congress may bow to public pressure and lift the arms embargo.* 國會也許會屈服於公眾的壓力, 解除武器禁運。

bow 蝴蝶結

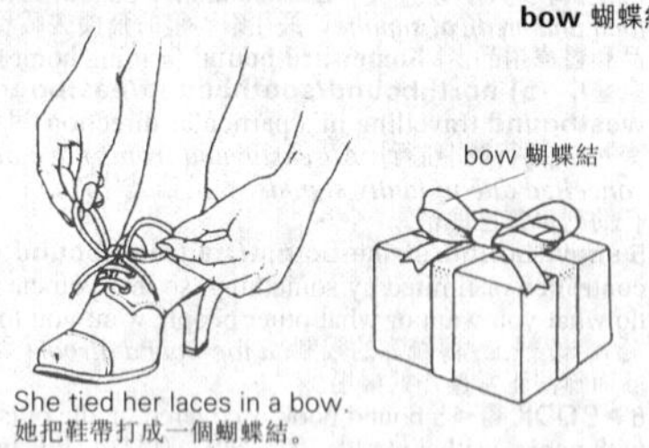

She tied her laces in a bow.
她把鞋帶打成一個蝴蝶結。

bow[2] /bau; baʊ/ *n* **1** [C] the act of bending the top part of your body forward to show respect for someone 鞠躬 **2** also 又作 **bows** the front part of a ship 船頭 —compare 比較 STERN[2] —see picture at 參見 YACHT 圖 **3 take a bow** if someone takes a bow, they come on the stage at the end of a performance so that people can APPLAUD them〔表演結束時〕謝幕

bow³ /bo; baʊ/ *n* **1** [C] a weapon used for shooting arrows (ARROW (1)), made of a long thin curved piece of wood 弓 **2** [C] a knot of cloth or string with a curved part on either side, used especially for decoration 蝴蝶結: *Ella wore a big bow in her hair.* 埃拉頭上戴着一隻大蝴蝶結。**3** [C] a long thin piece of wood with a tight string fastened along it, used to play musical instruments that have strings〔弦樂器的〕弓 **4 bow legs** legs that curve outwards at the knees 弓形腿, 羅圈腿 —see also 另見 **have more than one string to your bow** (STRING¹ (8))

bow⁴ /bo; baʊ/ *v* **1** [I] to bend or curve 彎曲, 彎成弓形 **2** [I,T] to play a piece of music on a musical instrument with a BOW³ (3) 用弓拉奏〔樂曲〕

bowd·ler·ize also 又作 **-ise** *BrE*【英】/ˈbaudləˌraɪz; ˈbaʊdləraɪz/ *v* [T] to remove the parts of a book, play etc that you think are offensive, and actually ruin it by doing this 刪除〔書本、劇本等中〕猥褻鄙俗的字句 —**bowdlerized** *adj*: *a bowdlerized version of 'Antony and Cleopatra'*〔莎劇〕《安東尼和克婁巴特拉》的刪節本

bow·el /ˈbauəl; ˈbaʊəl/ *n* **1 bowels** [plural] the system of tubes inside your body where food is made into solid waste material and through which it passes out of your body; INTESTINE 腸: **move/empty your bowels** (=get rid of solid waste from your body) 排大便 **2** [singular] one part of this system of tubes 腸道: *cancer of the bowel* 腸癌 **3 a bowel movement** *formal* an act of getting rid of solid waste from your body【正式】大解, 排便 **4 the bowels of sth** *literary* the lowest or deepest part of something【文】內部, 最深處: **the bowels of the earth** (=deep under the ground) 地球內部

bow·er /ˈbauɚ; ˈbaʊə/ *n* [C] *literary*【文】**1** a pleasant place in the shade under a tree, especially in a garden 樹蔭處: *a rose-scented bower* 有玫瑰香味的樹蔭 **2** *old use* a woman's bedroom【舊】閨房

bow·ing /ˈboɪŋ; ˈbəʊɪŋ/ *n* [U] the skill of using a BOW³ (3) to play a musical instrument 弓法〔用弓拉奏樂器的技巧〕

2 **bowl¹** /bol; bəʊl/ *n*

3 **1 ▶CONTAINER** 容器◀ [C] a wide round container that is open at the top, used to hold liquids, flowers etc 碗; 缽; 盤: *Mix all the ingredients thoroughly in a bowl.* 把所有的配料都放在一個碗裡徹底拌和。| [+of] *a bowl of fruit* 一盤水果 | **soup/salad/cereal etc bowl** (=a bowl to eat or serve soup, salad etc from) 湯碗/沙拉碗/麥米碗等

2 ▶AMOUNT 數量◀ also 又作 **bowlful** [C] the amount that a bowl will hold 一碗之量: [+of] *a bowl of rice* 一碗米飯

3 ▶GAME 遊戲◀ **a) bowls** [plural] *BrE* an outdoor game played on grass in which you try to roll big balls as near as possible to a small ball【英】(草地) 滾木球戲; LAWN BOWLING *AmE*【美】**b)** [C usually singular 一般用單數] a special game in American football played by the best teams after the normal playing season 美式足球季後賽: *the Rose Bowl* 玫瑰盃賽

4 ▶BALL 球◀ [C] *BrE* a ball that you use in the game of bowls【英】〔滾木球戲所用的〕木球

5 ▶SHAPE 形狀◀ [C] the part of an object such as a spoon, pipe, toilet etc that is shaped like a bowl 碗狀物, 物體的凹處〈如煙斗的斗、匙子舀物的部分、抽水馬桶的桶身等〉

6 ▶SPORT 體育◀ [C usually singular 一般用單數] *AmE* a large structure shaped like a bowl, where people go to watch special events; STADIUM【美】環形劇場; 橢圓形體育場: *the Hollywood Bowl* 荷里活環形劇場

bowl² *v* **1** [I,T] to roll a ball along a surface when you are playing the game of bowls〔玩滾木球戲時〕使 (球) 滾動 **2** [I,T] to throw a ball at the BATSMAN in CRICKET (2)〔玩板球時向擊球員〕投 (球) **3** also 又作 **bowl out** [T] to make a BATSMAN in CRICKET (2) have to leave the field, by hitting the WICKET (=set of sticks) behind him with a ball〔玩板球時以球擊中三柱門〕迫使〔擊球員〕出局

bowl along *phr v* [I] to travel or move very quickly and smoothly 平穩而快速地行駛[移動]: *We were really bowling along when suddenly the back wheel fell off.* 我們的汽車正平穩而快速地行駛, 突然間後輪掉了。

bowl sb ↔ **out** *phr v* [T] to make a BATSMAN in CRICKET (2) have to leave the field by hitting the WICKET (=set of sticks) behind him with a ball〔玩板球時以球擊中三柱門〕迫使〔擊球員〕出局

bowl sb/sth ↔ **over** *phr v* [T] **1** to accidentally hit someone so that they fall down, because you are running too quickly 撞倒: *Some kids running past bowled an old lady over.* 一些跑過的孩子把一位老婆婆撞倒了。**2** to surprise, please, or excite someone very much 使大為驚喜: *We were absolutely bowled over by the Parthenon.*〔希臘雅典的〕巴特農神殿使我們傾倒。

bow-legged /ˈboˌlɛgd; ˈbəʊˌlegd/ *adj* having legs that curve outwards at the knees 弓形腿的, 羅圈腿的, 外彎腿的

bowl·er /ˈbolɚ; ˈbəʊlə/ *n* [C] **1** a player in CRICKET (2) who throws the ball at a BATSMAN〔板球的〕投球手 **2** also 又作 **bowler hat** *especially BrE* a hard round black hat that business men sometimes wear【尤英】〔男用硬圓頂黑色〕常禮帽; DERBY (1) *AmE*【美】—see picture at 參見 HAT 圖

bowl·ing /ˈbolɪŋ; ˈbəʊlɪŋ/ *n* [U] **1** an indoor game in which you roll a large heavy ball along a wooden track in order to knock down a group of PINs (=wooden objects shaped like bottles) 保齡球: **go bowling** (=play this game) 玩保齡球 **2** the act of throwing a ball at the BATSMAN in CRICKET (2)〔玩板球時向擊球員〕投球

bowling al·ley /ˈ·· ˌ··/ *n* [C] a building where you go bowling 保齡球場

bowling ball /ˈ·· ·/ *n* [C] the heavy ball you use in the game of bowling 保齡球

bowling green /ˈ·· ·/ *n* [C] a piece of grass where you play the game of bowls (BOWL¹ (3a)) (草地) 滾木球場

bow·man /ˈbomən; ˈbəʊmən/ *n* [C] *old use* a soldier who shoots arrows (ARROW (1)) with a BOW³ (1)【舊】弓箭手

bow·sprit /ˈbauˌsprɪt; ˈbəʊˌsprɪt/ *n* [C] a long pole on the front of a boat that the ropes from the sails are fastened to 船首的斜桅〔繫船帆繩索的地方〕

bow tie /ˌbo ˈtaɪ; ˌbəʊ ˈtaɪ/ *n* [C] a short piece of cloth tied in the shape of a bow that men sometimes wear around their neck 蝶形領結 —see picture on page A17 參見 A17 頁圖

bow win·dow /ˌbo ˈwɪndo; ˌbəʊ ˈwɪndəʊ/ *n* [C] a window that curves outwards 弓形窗, 圓 [凸] 肚窗

bow-wow¹ /ˈbau ˈwau; ˈbaʊ waʊ/ *n* [C] a word meaning a dog, used by and to small children〔兒語〕狗狗

bow·wow² /ˈbauˈwau; ˌbaʊˈwaʊ/ *interjection* a word used to make the sound a dog makes, used by and to small children〔兒語〕汪汪〔即狗叫聲〕

box¹ /bɑks; bɒks/ *n* 1

1 ▶CONTAINER 容器◀ [C] a container for putting things in, especially one with four stiff straight sides 盒, 匣, 箱: [+of] *a box of tissues* 一盒紙巾 | *a matchbox* 火柴盒 | **cardboard/wooden box** *You need a filing cabinet, not all these cardboard boxes.* 你需要一個文件櫃, 不是這些硬紙板箱。| **toolbox/shoebox etc** (=used for keeping tools etc in) 工具箱/鞋盒等 —see picture at 參見 CONTAINER 圖 1

2 ▶AMOUNT IN A BOX 箱的容量◀ also 又作 **boxful** [C] the amount that a box can hold 一盒 [一箱] (之量): [+of] *a box of chocolates* 一盒巧克力

3 ▶SQUARE SHAPE 方形◀ [C] a small square on a page for people to write information in 方框, 方格: *Put an 'X' in the box if you would like to join our mailing list.* 如果你想加入我們的郵寄名單, 請在方框內寫上 X。

4 ►IN A THEATRE/COURT 在劇院/法庭中◄ [C] a small area of a theatre or court that is separate from where other people are sitting〔戲院的〕包廂;〔法庭的〕隔間: *the jury box* 陪審團席 —see picture at 參見 THEATRE 圖
5 box 25/450 etc an address at a POST OFFICE that people can use instead of their own address; PO BOX 25號/450號等郵政信箱
6 ►SPORTS FIELD 體育場地◄ [C] a special area of a sports field that is marked by lines and used for a particular purpose〔運動場地用線劃定的〕區: *a penalty box* 罰球區
7 ►WORN DURING SPORTS 運動時穿著的◄ [C] *BrE* a piece of plastic that a man wears over his sex organs to protect them when he is playing a sport, especially CRICKET (2)【英】〔尤指板球運動員的〕下體護身, 護罩
8 ►DEATH 死亡◄ [C] *informal* a COFFIN【非正式】棺材
9 ►TREE 樹◄ [C,U] a small tree that keeps its leaves in winter and is often planted around the edge of a garden or field, or the wood from this tree 黃楊〔一種冬天不落葉的小樹, 常種植在花園四周〕; 黃楊木: *a box hedge* 黃楊籬笆牆
10 give sb a box on the ears *old-fashioned* to hit someone on the side of their head【過時】打某人耳光
11 the box *informal* the television【非正式】電視: *What's on the box tonight?* 今晚有甚麼電視節目?
12 be out of your box *BrE slang* to be very drunk【英俚】爛醉 —see also 另見 BLACK BOX

box² *v* **1** [I,T] to fight someone as a sport by hitting them with your closed hands inside big leather GLOVES (2)(與...)進行拳擊比賽 **2** also 又作 **box up** [T] to put things in boxes 把...裝入箱[盒]內 —see also 另見 BOXED **3** [T] to draw a box around something on a page〔在紙上給某物〕畫框 **4 box sb's ears** *old-fashioned* to hit someone on the side of their head【過時】打耳光
box sb/sth ↔ **in** *phr v* [T] **1** to park so near to another car that it cannot move 緊挨着另一輛車停車 **2** to surround someone so that they are unable to move freely 封堵: *Steve Cram got boxed in on the final curve.* 史蒂夫·克拉姆在最後一個彎道被人擋住了。**3 feel boxed in a)** to feel that you cannot do what you want to do because a person or situation is limiting you 感覺施展不開, 感到被限制: *Married for only a year, Connie already felt boxed in.* 才結婚一年, 康尼已經感到受到了束縛。**b)** to feel that you cannot move freely, because you are in a small space〔被困在狹小的空間內而〕動彈不得
box sth ↔ **off** *phr v* [T] to separate a particular area from a larger one by putting walls around it 把...圈上, 隔開: *We're going to box off that corner to get extra storage space.* 我們要把那個角落隔開以擴大儲存空間。

box can·yon /ˈ· ,··/ *n* [C] *AmE* a deep narrow valley with very straight sides and no way out【美】〔無出口的〕峽谷

box·car /ˈbɑks,kɑr; ˈbɒkskɑː/ *n* [C] *AmE* a railway carriage with high sides and a roof, used for carrying goods【美】〔鐵路上的〕有蓋貨車, 棚車

boxed /bɑkst; bɒkst/ *adj* sold in a box or boxes 盒裝的: *a boxed set of CDs* 一套盒裝的雷射唱片

box end wrench /,· ·ˈ·/ *n* [C] *AmE* a type of WRENCH² (3) with a hollow end that fits over a NUT¹ (2) that is being screwed or unscrewed【美】套筒扳手; RING SPANNER *BrE*【英】—see picture at 參見 TOOL¹ 圖

box·er /ˈbɑksɚ; ˈbɒksə/ *n* [C] **1** someone who boxes (BOX² (1)), especially as a job〔尤指職業〕拳擊手 **2** a large dog with light brown short hair and a flat nose 拳師狗

boxer shorts /ˈ·· ,·/ *n* [plural] loose cotton underwear for men〔男用〕寬鬆純棉短褲, 平腳短褲 —see picture at 參見 UNDERWEAR 圖

box·ing /ˈbɑksɪŋ; ˈbɒksɪŋ/ *n* [U] the sport of fighting while wearing big leather GLOVES (2) 拳擊 (運動)

Boxing Day /ˈ·· ·/ *n* [C,U] *BrE* a national holiday in England and Wales, on the first day after Christmas Day that is not a Sunday【英】節禮日〔英格蘭及威爾斯的法定假日, 在聖誕節次日, 遇星期日順延, 按俗這天向郵遞員、雇員等送禮〕

box junc·tion /ˈ· ,··/ *n* [C] *BrE* a place marked with yellow painted lines where two roads cross each other【英】路口方形黃線區域

box lunch /ˈ· ·/ *n* [C] *AmE* a lunch that you take to school or work with you in a LUNCHBOX【美】〔尤指帶去學校或上班的〕盒裝午餐

box num·ber /ˈ· ,··/ *n* [C] *BrE* an address at the POST OFFICE that people can use instead of their own address【英】(郵政)信箱號碼

box of·fice /ˈ· ,··/ *n* **1** [C] the place in a theatre, cinema etc where tickets are sold〔戲院、電影院等的〕售票處 **2** [singular] used to describe how successful a film, play, or actor is, by the number of people who pay to see them 票房(價值): **do well/badly at the box office** (=be very successful or unsuccessful)〔電影〕賣座/不賣座 | **a (big) box office draw** (=a successful actor who many people will pay to see) 有票房號召力的演員

box room /ˈ· ·/ *n* [C] *BrE* a small room in a house where you can store things【英】〔家中的〕儲存室, 雜物室

boy¹ /bɔɪ; bɔɪ/ *n* [C]
1 ►CHILD 兒童◄ a male child or young man 男孩, 少年: *The boys all wanted to play football.* 這些男孩都想踢球。| **little boy** (=a young male child) 小男孩
2 ►SON 兒子◄ a son 兒子: *I love my boys, but I'd like to have a girl too.* 我喜歡我的兒子, 但希望再有個女兒。| **little boy** (=a young son) 小兒子 *How old is your little boy?* 你的小兒子多大了?
3 office/paper/delivery etc boy a young man who does a particular job 辦公室雜務員/送報員/送貨員等
4 the boys *informal* a group of men who are friends and often go out together【非正式】男性朋友們; 一羣男夥伴: *Friday's his night out with the boys.* 星期五晚上是他和一班男性朋友外出的時間。| **one of the boys** (=popular with a group of men) 男夥伴當中的一個
5 ►ANIMALS 動物◄ a way of addressing a male horse or dog〔對公馬或公狗說的〕傢伙: *Good boy!* 好傢伙!
6 ►JOB 工作◄ **boys** *informal*【非正式】**a)** a group of men who do the same job 一羣從事同一職業的男人: *Oh no! Wait until the press boys get hold of this story.* 不行! 要等新聞界的朋友採訪到這個新聞。**b)** men in the army, navy etc, especially those who are fighting in a war〔尤指在戰場上作戰的〕士兵, 戰友: *our boys on the front lines* 我們在前線的戰友們
7 boys will be boys used to say that you should not be surprised when boys behave badly, are noisy etc 男孩子總歸是男孩子〔指男孩子生性淘氣, 愛吵鬧〕
8 city/local/working-class boy *informal* a man of any age considered as being affected by the place and social group that he was born in【非正式】城市/本地/工人家庭出身的男人: *the classic story of a local boy who's made good* 一個本地小伙子最終成功的經典故事 | *I'm just a country boy.* 我不過是個鄉下孩子。
9 old boy/my dear boy *BrE old-fashioned* a friendly way for one man to speak to another man【英, 過時】老兄〔對男性講話時的招呼用語〕
10 *AmE taboo* an offensive way of addressing a black man【美諱】〔對黑人男性的蔑稱〕—see also 另見 BLUE-EYED BOY, **jobs for the boys** (JOB (5)), MAMA'S BOY, MUMMY'S BOY, OLD BOY, WIDE BOY

boy² *interjection spoken especially AmE*【口, 尤美】**1** also 又作 **oh boy** used when you are excited or pleased about something 好傢伙〔表示興奮、欣喜等〕: *Boy, that was a great meal!* 嘿, 那頓飯真不錯! **2 oh boy** used when you are slightly annoyed or disappointed about something 哎〔表示煩惱或失望〕: *Oh boy! Bethany's sick again.* 哎! 貝瑟尼又病了。

boy·cott¹ /ˈbɔɪ,kɑt; ˈbɔɪkɒt/ *v* [T] to refuse to buy something, use something, or take part in something as a way of protesting 抵制, 排斥, 杯葛; 拒絕參加: *We boy-*

cott all products tested on animals. 我們抵制所有拿動物做試驗的產品。

boycott² *n* [C] an act of boycotting something, or the period of time when it is boycotted 抵制行動, 杯葛行動: [**+of/on/against**] *a boycott on South African fruit in the 70s* 20世紀70年代抵制南非水果的活動

boy·friend /ˈbɔɪˌfrɛnd; ˈbɔɪfrend/ *n* [C] a man that you are having a romantic relationship with〔女子的〕男朋友: *Have you met Jilly's new boyfriend yet?* 你見過吉莉的新男朋友了嗎? —see also 另見 GIRLFRIEND

boy·hood /ˈbɔɪhʊd; ˈbɔɪhʊd/ *n* [U] the time of a man's life when he is a boy 男孩的童年, 少年時代: *boyhood memories* 童年的記憶 —see also 另見 GIRLHOOD

boy·ish /ˈbɔɪ-ɪʃ; ˈbɔɪ-ɪʃ/ *adj* **1** a man who is boyish looks or behaves like a boy in a way that is attractive〔指男人〕男孩似的, 男孩子氣的, 天真爛漫的: *boyish good looks* 男孩般的漂亮外貌 **2** a woman or girl who is boyish looks or behaves a little like a boy〔女人、女孩〕男孩似的, 男孩子氣的: *At 45 May still had a trim, boyish figure.* 都45歲了, 梅仍然保持着勻稱的、男孩般的身材。 —**boyishly** *adv* —**boyishness** *n* [U]

boy scout /ˌ· ˈ·/ *n* [C] a boy who is a member of an association for boys that teaches them practical skills and develops their characters; SCOUT¹ (1b) 童子軍 —see also 另見 GIRL SCOUT, GUIDE

boy won·der /ˌ· ˈ··/ *n* [C] a young man who is very successful 年輕有為的男子: *Robson, the boy wonder of the department* 系裡的年輕奇才羅伯遜

bo·zo /ˈbozo; ˈbəʊzəʊ/ *n plural* **bozos** [C] *informal* someone who you think is silly or stupid【非正式】笨蛋, 傻瓜: *Who's the bozo in the pyjamas?* 那個穿着睡衣褲的傻瓜是誰?

BPhil /ˌbi ˈfɪl; ˌbiː ˈfɪl/ *n* [C usually singular 一般用單數] Bachelor of Philosophy; a first or second degree that you may get after studying at a British university, but that is not as common as a BACHELOR'S DEGREE〔英國〕哲學學士

BR /ˌbi ˈɑr; ˌbiː ˈɑː/ *n* [singular] British Rail; the organization that controls the British railway system 英國鐵路公司

Br 1 the written abbreviation of 縮寫= BROTHER **2** the written abbreviation of 縮寫= BRITISH

bra /brɑ; brɑː/ *n* [C] a piece of underwear that a woman wears to support her breasts 乳罩, 胸罩 —see picture at 參見 UNDERWEAR 圖

brace¹ /bres; breɪs/ *v* **1** [T] to prepare for something unpleasant that is going to happen 準備迎接〔困難〕, 使振作精神: **brace yourself for** *Nancy braced herself for the inevitable arguments.* 南希為這場無可避免的爭論作好了準備。| **brace yourself to do** *Jean, you'd better brace yourself to hear bad news.* 瓊, 你得作好準備, 有壞消息相告。| **be braced for** *The entire castle was braced for an attack.* 整個城堡都準備好了抵抗襲擊。**2** [T] to push part of your body against something solid in order to make yourself more steady 把〔身體〕抵着〔某物, 以保持平衡〕, 使穩住: **brace sth against** *Gina braced her foot against the wall and pulled herself up.* 吉納用腳抵着牆站了起來。| **brace yourself** *Before he could brace himself she'd shoved him out of the door.* 他還沒站穩, 她就把他推出了門。**3** [T] to make something stronger by supporting it 支撐; 加固: *Wait until we've braced the ladder.* 等我們把梯子支撐住再說。**4** [I,T] to make your body or part of your body stiff in order to prepare to do something difficult〔使身體或身體某部分〕繃緊, 鼓足氣力: *Stuart braced his muscles and heaved the fridge aside.* 斯圖爾特繃緊肌肉, 把冰箱推到了一邊。

brace² *n*

1 ▶TEETH 牙齒◀ **a) brace** *BrE*【英】, **braces** *especially AmE*【尤美】a connected set of wires that children sometimes wear on their teeth to make them straight (兒童) 牙齒矯正器 **b)** [C] *BrE* a wire frame that children sometimes have to put over their teeth to make them straight【英】(兒童) 畸齒矯正鋼絲架

2 ▶SUPPORT 支持◀ **a)** [C] something that is used to strengthen, stiffen, or support something 支撐物, 支架: *Cath had to wear a neck brace after the accident.* 事故後, 凱絲只得戴上頸托。**b)** [C usually plural 一般用複數] *AmE* a metal support that someone with weak legs wears to help them walk【美】〔裝在腿上幫助腿力弱者行走的〕金屬支架; CALLIPERS *BrE*【英】

3 a brace of sth two birds or animals that have been killed for food or sport〔指鳥獸等獵獲物的〕一對, 一雙

4 ▶PRINTED SIGN 印刷符號◀ one of a pair of signs { } used to show that information written between them should be considered together 一對大括弧 { } 中的一個 —compare 比較 BRACKET¹ (1)

5 braces *BrE* two long pieces of material that stretch over someone's shoulders and fasten to their trousers at the front and the back to stop them falling down【英】〔褲子的〕吊帶, 背帶; SUSPENDERS *AmE*【美】

brace·let /ˈbreslɪt; ˈbreɪslɪ̈t/ *n* [C] a band or chain that you wear around your wrist or arm as a decoration 手鐲; 臂鐲 —compare 比較 BANGLE —see picture at 參見 JEWELLERY 圖

brac·ing /ˈbresɪŋ; ˈbreɪsɪŋ/ *adj* bracing air or weather is cold and makes you feel very awake and healthy〔空氣、天氣〕令人心神清爽的, 提神的: *a bracing sea breeze* 令人精神爽快的海風

brack·en /ˈbrækən; ˈbrækən/ *n* [U] a plant that often grows in forests and becomes reddish brown in the autumn 蕨; 羊齒植物

brack·et¹ /ˈbrækɪt; ˈbrækɪ̈t/ *n* [C] **1** [usually plural 一般用複數] **a)** *BrE* also 又作 **round bracket** one of the pair of signs ( ) put around words to show that the rest of the writing can be read and understood without these words【英】一對圓括弧 ( ) 中的一個; PARENTHESIS *AmE*【美】: **in brackets** *Last year's sales figures are given in brackets.* 去年的銷售數字寫在括弧中。—see picture at 參見 PUNCTUATION MARK 圖 **b)** *AmE*【美】**square bracket** *BrE*【英】a sign like this that is square [ ] 一對方括弧 [ ] 中的一個 **c) angle bracket** a sign like this that is shaped 〈 〉一對尖括弧〈 〉中的一個 —compare 比較 BRACE² (4)

2 income/tax/age etc bracket an income etc that is inside a particular range 收入等級 / 納稅等級 / 年齡組別等: *Peter's new job puts him in the highest tax bracket.* 彼得的新工作使他進入了最高的納稅階層。**3** a piece of metal, wood, or plastic, often in the shape of the letter L, fixed to a wall to support something such as a shelf〔釘在牆上的〕托架, 托座, 角撐架

bracket² *v* [T] **1** to put brackets around a written word, piece of information etc 把…放在括弧內: *Debit amounts are usually bracketed.* 賬簿上的借項數字通常標在括弧內。**2** to consider two or more people or things as being the same type 把…視為同類; 將…相提並論: [**+together/with**] *Women and minors were bracketed together for the legislation.* 立法時婦女和未成年人被歸為一類。

brack·ish /ˈbrækɪʃ; ˈbrækɪʃ/ *adj* brackish water is not pure because it is slightly salty〔水〕微鹹的, 略含鹽分的

brad /bræd; bræd/ *n* [C] *AmE* a small metal object like a button with two metal sticks that are put through several pieces of paper and folded down to hold the papers together【美】圓形紙夾; PAPER FASTENER *BrE*【英】

brad·awl /ˈbrædˌɔl; ˈbrædɔːl/ *n* [C] *especially BrE* a small tool with a sharp point for making holes; AWL【尤英】〔打孔用的〕小錐子, 打眼錐

brae /bre; breɪ/ *n* [C] *ScotE* a hill or slope【蘇格蘭】山坡; 斜坡

brag /bræg; bræg/ *v* **bragged, bragging** [I,T] to talk too proudly about what you have done, what you own etc; BOAST¹(1) 自誇, 吹噓: *"I came out top in the test," he bragged.* "我考試名列前茅。" 他吹噓道。| [**+about**] *Ben's always bragging about his success with women.*

本總是吹噓他對女人很有辦法。| **brag (that)** *Julia used to brag that her family had a villa in Spain.* 朱莉亞以前老吹噓她家在西班牙有一所別墅。

brag·ga·do·ci·o /ˌbrægəˋdoʃɪˌo; ˌbrægəˈdəʊʃiəʊ/ *n* [U] *especially literary* proud talk about something that you claim to own, to have done etc【尤文】大吹特吹, 自吹自擂

B

brag·gart /ˋbrægɚt; ˈbrægət/ *n* [C] someone who is always talking too proudly about what they own or have done 自誇者, 吹牛者

Brah·man /ˋbrɑmən; ˈbrɑːmən/ also 又作 **Brah·min** /ˋbrɑmɪn; ˈbrɑːmɪn/ *n* [C] someone belonging to the highest rank in the HINDU faith 婆羅門〔印度種姓四大等級中的最高等級, 即僧侶〕

braid¹ /bred; breɪd/ *n* **1** [U] a narrow band of material formed by twisting threads together, used to decorate the edges of clothes〔絲等編成的裝飾性〕帶子, 穗帶: *a jacket trimmed with red braid* 邊上鑲有紅色穗帶的夾克 **2** [C] *AmE* a length of hair that has been separated into three parts and then woven together【美】髮辮, 辮子; PLAIT² *BrE*【英】: **in braids** *Pippa always wears her hair in braids.* 皮帕總是梳着辮子。—**braided** *adj* —see picture at 參見 HAIRSTYLE 圖

braid² *v* [T] *especially AmE* to weave or twist together three pieces of hair or cloth to form one length【尤美】把...打成繩子; 把...編成辮子; PLAIT¹ *BrE*【英】

braille /brel; breɪl/ *n* [U] a form of printing with raised parts that blind people can read by touching the paper〔盲人用的〕盲文, 點字

brain¹ /bren; breɪn/ *n*

1 ►ORGAN 器官◄ [C] the organ inside your head that controls how you think, feel, and move 腦(子); 腦髓: *Messages from the brain are carried by the central nervous system.* 大腦的信息是通過中樞神經系統傳遞的。

2 ►INTELLIGENCE 智力◄ [U] also 又作 **brains** *plural* the ability to think clearly and learn quickly 智力, 智慧, 頭腦, 腦筋: *If you had any brains you'd know what I meant.* 如果你有點腦子, 你就會知道我的意思。

3 ►PERSON 人◄ [C] *informal* someone who is intelligent, with good ideas and useful skills【非正式】極聰明的人, 智者: *Some of our best brains are leaving the country to work in the US.* 我們當中的一些優秀人才離開本國到美國工作。—see also 另見 BRAIN DRAIN

4 have sth on the brain *informal* to be always thinking about something【非正式】一直想着某事, 牽掛着: *I've got that song on the brain today.* 今天我腦子裡一直想着那首歌。

5 be the brains behind sth to be the person who thought of and developed a particular plan, system, or organization, especially a successful one 出謀獻策的智囊, 主腦

6 brain dead a) in a state where your brain has stopped working properly even though your heart may still be beating 腦死亡 **b)** *informal* stupid and uninteresting, especially because you live a boring life【非正式】不會動腦子的, 愚蠢的: *If all she does is watch TV all day, no wonder she's brain dead.* 如果她整天就是看電視, 難怪她變得呆頭呆腦的。

7 pick sb's brains to ask someone a lot of questions about something that they know about 詳盡地向某人提問: *I need to pick your brains about this cashflow forecast.* 我需要向你詳細問問有關現金流轉預測的問題。

8 brain box *BrE informal* a very intelligent person【英, 非正式】智商高的人, 極聰明的人 —see also 另見 BIRD-BRAINED, HAREBRAINED, **beat your brains out** (BEAT¹ (18)), **rack your brain(s)** (RACK² (2))

brain² *v* [T] *spoken* to hit someone very hard on the head【口】重擊〔某人的〕頭部: *I'll brain you if you do that again!* 你再那樣做, 我就打破你的頭!

brain·child /ˋbrenˌtʃaɪld; ˈbreɪntʃaɪld/ *n* [singular] an idea, plan, organization etc that someone has thought of without any help from anyone else 智力產兒, 腦力勞動的成果: [+of] *The festival was the brainchild of Mayor Reeves.* 舉辦這個節日是里夫斯市長想出來的好主意。

brain dam·age /ˈ· ˌ··/ *n* [U] damage to someone's brain caused by an accident or illness 腦損傷: *Potts suffered severe brain damage in the crash.* 波茨的大腦在車禍中受到嚴重損傷。—**brain-damaged** *adj*

brain drain /ˈ· ·/ *n* **the brain drain** a movement of highly skilled or professional people from their own country to a country where they can earn more money 人才流失, 人才外流

brain·less /ˋbrenlɪs; ˈbreɪnləs/ *adj* completely stupid 沒有頭腦的, 傻的, 愚笨的: *What a brainless thing to do!* 這樣做很愚蠢! —**brainlessly** *adv*

brain scan /ˈ· ·/ *n* [C] a process in which detailed photographs of the inside of your brain are taken and examined by a doctor 腦部掃描(檢查)

brain·storm /ˋbrenˌstɔrm; ˈbreɪnstɔːm/ *n* **1 have a brainstorm** *BrE informal* to suddenly be unable to think clearly or sensibly【英, 非正式】一時糊塗: *I'm sorry, I must have had a brainstorm that afternoon.* 對不起, 那天下午我一定是一時糊塗了。**2** [singular] *AmE* a sudden clever idea【美】靈感, 突然想到的妙計; BRAINWAVE *BrE*【英】: **have a brainstorm** *Unless you have a brainstorm, I don't see how we're going to get out of this.* 除非你能想出一個妙法, 不然我看不出我們如何能擺脱困境。

brain·storm·ing /ˋbrenˌstɔrmɪŋ; ˈbreɪnstɔːmɪŋ/ *n* [U] the act of meeting with a group of people in order to try to develop ideas and think of ways of solving problems 集體解決難題, 大家出主意, 合力攻關: *a brainstorming session to come up with a slogan for the new shampoo* 為新洗髮劑想一條廣告標語的獻策會 —**brainstorm** *v* [I]

brain sur·geon /ˈ· ˌ··/ *n* [C] a doctor who performs operations on people's brains 腦外科醫生

brain teas·er /ˈ· ˌ··/ *n* [C] a difficult problem that you enjoy trying to solve〔測試頭腦機敏性的〕難題, 智力測驗遊戲

brain·wash /ˋbrenˌwɔʃ; ˈbreɪnwɒʃ/ *v* [T] to make someone believe something that is not true, by using force, confusing them, or continuously repeating it over a long period of time 對...進行洗腦, 把某種思想強加於, 強行灌輸: *Young people are being brainwashed by this religious group.* 這一宗教組織正在對年輕人進行洗腦。| **brainwash sb into doing sth** *Commercials can brainwash consumers into buying things they don't need.* 廣告宣傳能給消費者洗腦, 使他們購買一些他們並不需要的東西。—**brainwashing** *n* [U]

brain·wave /ˋbrenˌwev; ˈbreɪnweɪv/ *n* [C] **1** *BrE* a sudden clever idea【英】靈感, 突然想到的妙計; BRAINSTORM *AmE*【美】: *I've had a brainwave! Let's go this weekend instead.* 我突然想到了一個妙計, 我們改為這個週末去! **2** an electrical force that is produced by the brain and that can be measured 腦電波

brain·y /ˋbrenɪ; ˈbreɪni/ *adj informal* able to learn easily and think quickly; clever【非正式】聰明的, 多智的, 敏鋭的: *He always was the brainy one, except at maths.* 他總是很聰明, 只是數學差一些。

braise /brez; breɪz/ *v* [T] to cook meat or vegetables slowly in a small amount of liquid in a closed container 燉, 焖, 用文火煮 —**braised** *adj*

braising steak /ˈ·· ˌ·/ *n* [U] BEEF¹ (1) that needs long slow cooking 供燉〔煮〕的牛肉

brake¹ /brek; breɪk/ *n* [C] **1** a piece of equipment that makes a vehicle go more slowly or stop, usually operated by pressing on a bar with your foot or hand 煞車, 制動器, 車閘: *Remember to test your brakes regularly.* 記住定期檢查煞車裝置。| **put/slam on the brakes** also 又作 **apply the brakes** *formal*【正式】*Moira slammed on the brakes and skidded to a halt.* 莫伊拉猛踩煞車, 汽車滑動一下便停住了。—see also 另見 EMERGENCY BRAKE, HANDBRAKE —see picture at 參見 BICYCLE¹ 圖 **2 act/serve as a brake on sth** to make something slow or difficult 對某事物起抑制作用, 遏制某事物: *Rises in* *interest rates usually act as a brake on expenditure.* 利率的提高往往會起到抑制消費的作用。**3 put the brakes on sth** to stop something that is happening 阻止某事物: *Well, that pretty much puts the brakes on our plans.* 嗯, 這差不多使我們的計劃無法實現。

brake² *v* [I] to make a vehicle or bicycle go more slowly or stop by using its brake 煞車〔使減速或停住〕: **brake sharply/hard** (=brake quickly) 急煞車 *He braked sharply to avoid the dog.* 為了避開那條狗, 他突然急煞車。

brake flu·id /ˈ· ˌ··/ *n* [U] liquid used in certain kinds of brakes so that the different parts move smoothly 煞車油, 制動液

brake light /ˈ· ·/ *n* [C] a light on the back of a vehicle that comes on when you uses the brake〔位於汽車尾部, 煞車時即亮起的〕(紅色) 制動信號燈 —see picture on page A2 參見A2頁圖

brake shoe /ˈ· ˌ·/ *n* [C] one of the two curved parts that press against the wheel of a vehicle in order to make it go more slowly or stop 閘瓦, 制動瓦

bram·ble /ˈbræmbḷ; ˈbræmbəl/ *n* [C] a wild BLACKBERRY 懸鉤子屬植物〔尤指野生黑莓〕

bran /bræn; bræn/ *n* [U] the crushed outer skin of wheat or a similar grain that is separated from the rest of the grain when making white flour 麥麩; 糠; 穀皮

1 2 **branch¹** /bræntʃ; brɑːntʃ/ *n* [C]

1 ▶ON A TREE 樹上◀ a part of a tree that grows outwards from the TRUNK (=stem) and that has leaves, fruit, or smaller branches growing from it 樹枝: *a fallen tree branch* 掉下的樹枝

2 ▶IN A LOCAL AREA 在當地◀ a shop, office etc in a particular area that is part of a large company 分行; 分支機構: *The bank has branches all over the country.* 這家銀行在全國各地都有分行。| *a branch office in Boston* 設在波士頓的地方辦事處

3 ▶OF AN ORGANIZATION 某機構的◀ a part of a government or other organization that deals with one particular part of its work〔政府或機構的〕部門: *All branches of government are having to cut costs.* 政府所有部門都要削減開支。

4 ▶OF A SUBJECT 某學科的◀ one part of a large subject of study or knowledge 分科: **[+of]** *Newton developed a branch of mathematics called calculus.* 牛頓開創了一個數學分支, 稱為微積分。

5 ▶OF A FAMILY 某家族的◀ a group of members of a family who all have the same grandparents or ANCESTORS〔家族中的〕一支, 分支: *the wealthy South American branch of the family* 這個家族中一個南美洲的富裕分支

6 ▶SMALLER PART 較小的部分◀ a smaller less important part of something that leads away from the larger more important part of it 分支; 支線; 支流: *a branch of the river Arno* 阿諾河的支流

branch² *v* [I] to divide into two or more smaller, narrower, or less important parts 分支; 分岔: **branch into two** *When you reach Germain Street, the road branches into two.* 到了澤梅因大街, 路分岔為兩條。

branch off *phr v* [I] **1** if a road, passage, railway etc branches off from another road etc, it separates from it and goes in a different direction 分岔; 分支; 分道: **[+from]** *a passage branching off from the main tunnel* 從主隧道岔開的通道 **2** to leave a main road 離開主路[幹線], 走入岔道: **[+from/into]** *We branched off from the main road and turned down a country lane.* 我們離開幹道, 轉入一條鄉村小路。**3** to start talking about something different from what you were talking about before 岔開〔話題〕: **[+into]** *Then the conversation branched off into a discussion about movies.* 接着談話轉入對電影的討論。

branch out *phr v* [I] to do something different from what you usually do 擴大〔興趣、活動〕範圍, 開闢新的領域: *Don't be afraid to branch out and try new ideas.* 不要怕另闢蹊徑, 不妨嘗試新的想法。| **branch out into (doing) sth** *Profits were falling until the bookstore branched out into selling CDs and cassettes.* 書店在擴大營業範圍兼賣唱片和磁帶之前, 利潤一直在下降。

brand¹ /brænd; brænd/ *n* [C] **1** a type of product made by a particular company 商標, 牌子: **[+of]** *What brand of detergent do you use?* 你用甚麼牌子的洗滌劑? | **brand leader** (=the brand that sells the most) 主打品牌 | **brand loyalty** (=the tendency to always buy a particular brand) 品牌忠誠度 | **own brand** *BrE*【英】**store brand** *AmE*【美】(=made and sold by a particular store) 自有品牌 **2 brand of humour/politics/religion etc** a particular type of humour, politics etc 某種幽默/政治/宗教等: *a strange, macabre brand of humour* 一種怪異而可怕的幽默 **3** a mark made or burned on an animal's skin that shows who it belongs to〔標明牲畜所屬的〕烙印 **4** *literary* a piece of burning wood【文】一塊燃燒着的木頭 **5** *poetic* a sword【詩】劍

brand² *v* [T] **1** to describe someone or something as a very bad type of person or thing, often unfairly 給〔某人〕加上不公的污名: **brand sb as** *You can't brand all football supporters as hooligans.* 你不能給所有的足球迷都加上流氓的惡名。| **brand sb a liar/cheat/whore etc** *In those days, any unmarried mother was branded a whore.* 那時候, 任何未婚媽媽都會被加上淫婦的臭名。| **brand sb for life** *Stealing that money has branded Jim for life – no-one will trust him again.* 吉姆終身背上了偷錢的罪名, 再沒有人信任他。**2** [usually passive 一般用被動態] to make a mark on something, especially by burning, in order to show who it belongs to 給〔某物〕打上烙印〔以標明其主人〕: **brand sth with sth** *Each cow was branded with the ranch's logo.* 每頭母牛都烙上了該牧場的標誌。

brand·ed /ˈbrændɪd; ˈbrændɨd/ *adj* [only before noun 僅用於名詞前] a branded product is made by a well known company and has the company's name on it 有品牌(標誌)的

branding i·ron /ˈ·· ˌ··/ *n* [C] a piece of metal that is heated and used for burning marks on cattle or sheep, to show who they belong to〔在牲畜身上烙印用的〕烙鐵

bran·dish /ˈbrændɪʃ; ˈbrændɪʃ/ *v* [T+at] to wave something around in a dangerous or threatening way, especially a weapon (威脅性地) 揮舞〔尤指武器〕: *A man leapt out brandishing a kitchen knife.* 有一個男人跳了出來, 揮舞着一把菜刀。

brand name /ˈ· ˌ·/ *n* [C] the name given to a product by the company that makes it; TRADE NAME〔某商品的〕商標名稱, 商品名

brand-new /ˌ· ˈ·◂/ *adj* new and completely unused 全新的, 嶄新的, 未用過的

bran·dy /ˈbrændɪ; ˈbrændi/ *n* [C,U] a strong alcoholic drink made from wine, or a glass of this drink (一杯) 白蘭地(酒)

brandy but·ter /ˈ·· ˌ··/ *n* [U] a mixture of butter, sugar, and BRANDY, usually eaten with CHRISTMAS PUDDING〔通常和聖誕布丁一起吃的〕白蘭地黃油

brash /bræʃ; bræʃ/ *adj* **1** behaving too confidently and speaking too loudly 無禮的, 自以為是的; 急躁的, 莽撞的: *Brash, noisy journalists were crowding around the ambassador.* 粗魯吵鬧的記者擁擠着圍在大使身邊。**2** a brash building, place, or object attracts attention by being very colourful, large, exciting etc 醒目的; 刺眼的: *The painting was bold, brash and modern.* 這幅畫大膽、醒目, 而且現代。—**brashly** *adv* —**brashness** *n* [U]

brass /bræs; brɑːs/ *n*

1 ▶METAL 金屬◀ [U] a very hard bright yellow metal that is a mixture of COPPER (1) and ZINC 黃銅〔銅鋅合金〕: **brass bed/knob/button etc** *an old brass bedstead* 老式銅牀架

2 the brass (section) the people in an ORCHESTRA or band who play musical instruments made of brass, such as the TRUMPET¹ (1), horn etc〔管弦樂隊等的〕銅管樂器部

3 have the brass *informal* to have the self-confidence and lack of respect to do something that is rude【非正式】厚着臉皮, 厚顏無恥: **have the brass to do sth** *I didn't think she'd have the brass to tell him to his face.* 我認為她不會厚着臉皮當面告訴他。

4 ▶DECORATIONS 裝飾◀ [C,U] an object made of brass, usually with a design cut into it, or several brass objects 黃銅飾品, 黃銅器

B

5 ▶IN CHURCH 教堂裡◀ [C] a picture and writing on brass, placed on the wall or floor of a church in memory of someone who died〔為紀念已故者而嵌在教堂地板上或掛在牆壁上刻有肖像等的〕黃銅紀念牌

6 get down to brass tacks *informal* to start talking about the real business of a meeting【非正式】言歸正傳, 談實質性問題, 談正事

7 ▶PEOPLE IN TOP JOBS 身居高位者◀ **the brass** *AmE informal* people who hold the most important positions【美, 非正式】要員; TOP BRASS *BrE*【英】

8 it's brass monkeys/brass monkey weather *BrE spoken* used to say that it is very cold【英口】極其寒冷的: *It's brass monkeys out there today.* 今天外邊特別冷。

9 ▶MONEY 錢◀ [U] *BrE informal* money【英, 非正式】錢

10 brass hat *especially BrE slang* a military officer with a high rank【尤英, 俚】高級軍官 —see also 另見 **as bold as brass** (BOLD (2))

brass band /ˌ· ˈ·/ *n* [C] a band consisting mostly of brass musical instruments such as TRUMPETs, horns etc 銅管樂隊

brassed off /ˌbræst ˋɔf; ˌbrɑːst ˈɒf/ *adj BrE informal* tired and annoyed【英, 非正式】厭倦的, 厭煩的: [+with] *I'm really brassed off with the way he treats me.* 我真厭倦了他這樣對待我。

bras·se·rie /ˌbræsəˋri; ˈbræsəri/ *n* [C] a cheap, informal restaurant usually serving French food〔出售法國食品的〕啤酒店, 小餐館

bras·si·ere /brəˋzɪr; ˈbræziə/ *n* [C] *formal* a BRA【正式】乳罩, 胸罩

brass knuck·les /ˌ· ˈ··/ *n* [plural] *AmE* a set of metal rings worn over your KNUCKLEs, used as a weapon【美】指節銅套〔一種武器〕; KNUCKLE-DUSTER *BrE*【英】

brass rub·bing /ˈ· ˌ··/ *n* [C,U] the act of making a copy of a BRASS (5) in a church by putting a piece of paper over it and rubbing it with a soft pencil, or a picture made in this way〔對黃銅紀念牌上的文字等進行的〕拓印, 摹拓

brass·y /ˋbræsɪ; ˈbrɑːsi/ *adj* **1** yellowish in colour like BRASS (1) 黃銅色的 **2** sounding hard and loud like the sound made by a BRASS (2) musical instrument 聲音像銅管樂器的 **3** a woman who is brassy is too loud, confident, or brightly dressed〔婦女〕吵吵嚷嚷的, 說話無禮的; 打扮豔麗的: *Who's that brassy woman with Les?* 和賴思在一起的潑婦是誰?

brat /bræt; bræt/ *n* [C] *informal* a child, especially a badly behaved one【非正式】小壞蛋, 淘氣鬼: **spoilt/spoiled brat** *That kid of theirs is a real spoilt brat.* 他們的那個孩子真是個寵壞了的淘氣鬼。

bra·va·do /brəˋvɑdo; brəˈvɑːdəʊ/ *n* [U] behaviour that is deliberately intended to show how brave and confident you are 故作勇敢, 逞強的行動, 虛張聲勢: *youthful bravado* 年輕人的逞強行為

3 **brave¹** /brev; breɪv/ *adj* **1** facing danger, pain, or difficult situations with courage and confidence 勇敢的, 無畏的: *a brave cancer victim* 勇敢的癌症患者 | *It was very brave of you to tell her the truth.* 你真勇敢, 把事實真相告訴了她。**2** very good 美好的, 極好的: *his original brave intentions* 他本來的善意 | **a brave attempt** *Fran didn't win, but it was a brave attempt.* 弗蘭沒有贏, 但這是一次很好的嘗試。**3 put on a brave face/front** to pretend that you are happy when you are really very upset 強裝歡笑 —**bravely** *adv*

brave² *v* [T] to deal with a difficult, dangerous, or unpleasant situation 勇敢地面對: *Braving their parents' displeasure, they announced their engagement.* 他們不顧父母的不滿, 宣布訂婚。| **brave the elements** (=go out in bad weather) 在惡劣的天氣下外出, 頂風冒雨

brave sth ↔ **out** *phr v* [T] to deal bravely with something that is frightening or difficult 勇敢地應對

brave³ *n* **1** [plural] brave people 勇士: *Today we remember the brave who died in the last war.* 我們今天來紀念那些在上一次戰爭中英勇犧牲的人。**2** [C] a young fighting man from a Native American tribe 印第安部落的青年武士

brav·e·ry /ˋbrevərɪ; ˈbreɪvəri/ *n* [U] actions, behaviour, or an attitude that shows courage and confidence 勇敢的行為[態度]; 勇氣: *an act of great bravery* 大無畏的行為

bra·vo /ˋbrɑvo; ˈbrɑːvəʊ/ *interjection* used to show your approval when someone, especially a performer, has done something very well 好〔表演精彩時的喝采聲〕: *Bravo! Encore!* 好極了! 再來一個!

bra·vu·ra /brəˋvjʊrə; brəˈvjʊərə/ *n* [U] **1** the act of showing a lot of skill in the way you perform, write, paint etc, especially when you do something very difficult 出色的演出[寫作, 繪畫等] **2** the act of showing great courage 氣勢磅礡, 雄壯

braw /brɔ; brɔː/ *adj ScotE*【蘇格蘭】**1** a braw woman is beautiful, especially because she is big and strong 漂亮的〔尤指高大、健壯的女人〕**2** braw weather is good〔天氣〕晴朗的

brawl¹ /brɔl; brɔːl/ *n* [C] a noisy quarrel or fight among a group of people, especially in a public place〔尤指在公共場所的〕爭吵; 打(羣)架: *a drunken brawl in the street* 街上的酒後毆鬥 —**brawler** *n* [C]

brawl² *v* [I] to quarrel or fight in a noisy way, especially in a public place〔尤指在公共場所〕打(羣)架; 爭吵

brawn /brɔn; brɔːn/ *n* [U] **1** physical strength, especially when compared with intelligence 體力: *Mina has the brains, I have the brawn.* 米納有頭腦, 我有體力。**2** *BrE* meat from a pig's head that has been boiled and pressed in a container and is often served in thin flat pieces【英】〔用豬頭肉煮成的〕碎肉凍; HEADCHEESE *AmE*【美】

brawn·y /ˋbrɔnɪ; ˈbrɔːni/ *adj* very large and strong 強壯的; 肌肉發達的: *His brawny arms glistened with sweat.* 他強壯的胳膊上的汗水閃閃發光。

bray /bre; breɪ/ *v* [I] **1** if a DONKEY brays, it makes a loud sound〔驢〕發出叫聲 **2** if someone brays, they laugh or talk in a loud, slightly unpleasant way 發出近似驢叫的聲音 —**bray** *n* [C] —**braying** *adj*

bra·zen¹ /ˋbreznֽ; ˈbreɪzən/ *adj* **1** behaving in an immoral way without being embarrassed or ashamed 厚顏無恥的, 恬不知恥的: **a brazen hussy** (=a woman who behaves this way, especially sexually) 不知羞恥的蕩婦 **2 brazen lie/attitude** a lie or bad attitude that is shocking because the person responsible is not ashamed of it 無恥的謊言/態度 **3** *literary* having a shiny yellow colour【文】黃銅色的, 金黃色的

brazen² *v*

brazen sth ↔ **out** *phr v* [T] to deal with a situation that is difficult or embarrassing for you by appearing to be confident rather than ashamed〔面對困難或尷尬的處境時〕厚着臉皮幹

bra·zen·ly /ˋbreznֽlɪ; ˈbreɪzənli/ *adv* without showing or feeling any shame 厚顏無恥地: *She brazenly admitted she had spent the night with Greg.* 她厚顏無恥地承認那天晚上她和格雷格在一起。

bra·zi·er /ˋbreʒɚ; ˈbreɪziə/ *n* [C] a metal container that holds a fire and is used to keep people warm in the outside〔供人們取暖的〕火盆

breach¹ /britʃ; briːtʃ/ *n* **1 breach of the law/rules/agreement etc** an action that breaks a law, rule, or agreement between people, groups, or countries 違反[破壞, 不履行]法律/規章/協議等: *a clear breach of the*

1994 Trade Agreement 明顯違背1994年的貿易協議 | **be in breach of sth** *We will expel any member found to be in breach of the rules.* 我們將開除任何被發現違反規定的成員。| **breach of contract** *If they fail to deliver the goods, we will sue them for breach of contract.* 如果他們不發貨, 我們就控告他們違約。**2 breach of confidence/trust/etiquette etc** an action that breaks the rules of what people consider good or moral behaviour 泄密/失信/違反禮節等: *Bond shook the Queen's hand in a deliberate breach of etiquette.* 邦德故意違反禮節和女王握手。| *The company regards revealing confidential information as a serious breach of trust.* 公司把泄露機密資料視為嚴重的背信棄義的行為。**3** [C] a serious disagreement between people, groups, or countries with the result that they do not have a good relationship any more〔友好關係的〕破裂, 裂痕: *Britain could not risk a breach with the US over sanctions.* 在制裁問題上, 英國不會冒與美國決裂之險。| **heal the breach** (=make people etc stop disagreeing and be friends again) 修補裂痕, 重歸於好 **4 breach of the peace** *BrE law* an action such as fighting that annoys people in a public place【英, 法律】擾亂治安 **5 step into the breach** to help by doing someone else's job or work when they are suddenly unable to do it 代理別人的工作 **6** [C] a hole or broken place in a wall or similar structure, especially one made during a military attack〔尤指被砲火轟開的〕缺口, 破洞: *a breach in the castle wall* 城堡牆上被攻破的缺口 **7 a breach of security/duty etc** the result of someone breaking a system, not doing their duty etc 違反安全原則/失職等: *There had been a major breach of security at the air base.* 在空軍基地發生了一宗嚴重違反安全規則的事故。

breach² *v* [T] **1** to break a hole in a wall or similar structure so that something can pass through 攻破, 在...造成缺口: *The storm had breached the sea wall in two places.* 風暴在海堤上造成兩處缺口。**2** to break a law, rule, agreement etc 違背, 違反〔法律、規定、協議等〕: *The committee ruled that Payne was guilty of breaching the rules on sponsorship.* 委員會裁定佩恩違反了贊助規則。

2 3 **bread** /brɛd; bred/ *n* [U] **1** a common important food made from flour, water, and YEAST 麵包: *Would you like some bread with your soup?* 你喝湯時要吃點麵包嗎? | **a loaf of bread** (=a large piece of bread that you buy and cut into pieces) 一條麵包 | **a slice of bread** (=a thin piece of bread that you cut from a loaf) 一片麵包 | **white/brown bread** (=bread baked with white or brown flour) 白/黑麵包 **2** *old-fashioned* money【過時】錢 **3 your/sb's bread and butter** *informal* the work that provides you with most of the money that you need in order to live【非正式】生計; 謀生之道: *I don't write just for fun – it's my bread and butter.* 我寫作並非只為了樂趣, 它是我的謀生之道。**4 earn your (daily) bread** to earn the money that you need in order to live 謀生, 掙錢糊口 **5 know which side your bread is buttered on** to know who to be nice to in order to get advantages for yourself 知道該奉迎誰以謀求自己的利益 —see also 另見 FRENCH BREAD, SLICED BREAD

bread-and-but·ter /ˌ· · '··◂/ *adj* [only before noun 僅用於名詞前] **bread-and-butter question/issue** *BrE* a question that is concerned with the most important and basic things【英】生計的問題; 最基本的問題: *bread-and-butter political issues such as jobs and housing* 就業和住房等有關民生的政治問題

bread·bas·ket /ˈbrɛdˌbæskɪt; ˈbredˌbɑːskɪ̈t/ *n* **1** [C] a basket for holding or serving bread 麵包籃 **2** [singular] the part of a country or other large area that provides most of its food 重要的產糧區, 糧倉: *Zambia could be the breadbasket of Africa.* 贊比亞可能成為非洲重要的產糧區。

bread bin /'· ·/ *n* [C] *BrE* a container for keeping bread in so that it stays fresh【英】〔用來保持麵包新鮮的〕麵包箱[盒] —see picture on page A10 參見A10頁圖

bread·board /ˈbrɛdˌbɔrd; ˈbredbɔːd/ *n* [C] a wooden board on which you cut bread 切麵包板 —see picture at 參見 BOARD¹ 圖

bread·box /'· ·/ *n* [C] *AmE* a BREAD BIN【美】麵包箱[盒]

bread·crumbs /ˈbrɛdˌkrʌmz; ˈbredkrʌmz/ *n* [plural] very small pieces of bread left after cutting bread, or deliberately prepared for cooking 麵包屑: *Coat the fish with breadcrumbs and fry in a little oil.* 把魚裹上麵包屑, 然後放入少量油裡煎。

bread·ed /ˈbrɛdɪd; ˈbredɪ̈d/ *adj* covered in breadcrumbs 沾滿麵包屑的: *breaded plaice* 沾滿麵包屑的鰈魚

bread·fruit /ˈbrɛdˌfrut; ˈbredfruːt/ *n* [C,U] a large tropical fruit that looks like bread 麵包果

bread·line /ˈbrɛdˌlaɪn; ˈbredlaɪn/ *n* **1 be/live on the breadline** to be extremely poor 非常窮, 勉強維持生活 **2 be near/below the breadline** to be quite poor or extremely poor, according to official standards 接近/低於最低生活標準線

breadth /brɛdθ; bredθ/ *n* **1** [C,U] the distance from one side of something to the other; width 寬度; 闊度: *What is the breadth of this room?* 這個房間有多寬? | **5 metres/3 feet etc in breadth** *The boat measured eight feet in breadth.* 船的寬度為八英尺。—compare 比較 LENGTH (1), WIDTH (1) **2 breadth of vision/mind/outlook etc** an ability to consider and understand a range of ideas, attitudes, and customs that are very different from your own 眼光廣闊/心胸開闊/看法全面等: *a statesman with the breadth of vision of Abraham Lincoln* 像亞伯拉罕·林肯那樣虛懷若谷的政治家 **3** [U] the fact or quality of including a great variety of people, subjects etc 廣博, 淵博; 廣度: *a novel of the breadth and magnitude of Tolstoy's 'War and Peace'* 像托爾斯泰的《戰爭與和平》那樣氣勢恢宏的長篇小說 **4** [C,U] the quality of being very large from one side to the other 幅員遼闊, 廣闊: *the breadth of the ocean* 廣闊的海洋 —see also 另見 BROAD, HAIR'S BREADTH, **the length and breadth of** (LENGTH (6))

breadth·ways /ˈbrɛdθˌwez; ˈbredθweɪz/ also 又作 **breadth·wise** /-ˌwaɪz; -waɪz/ *adj, adv* with the broad side nearest to the person who is looking at it 橫向的[地]; 橫着的[地]: *The box should fit in the case breadthways.* 這盒子應該橫着放進大箱子。

bread·win·ner /ˈbrɛdˌwɪnɚ; ˈbredˌwɪnə/ *n* [C] the member of a family who earns the money to support the others 掙錢養家的人

break¹ /brek; breɪk/ *v past tense* **broke** /brok; brəʊk/ 1 1
past participle **broken** /ˈbrokən; ˈbrəʊkən/

1 ►IN PIECES 成片◄ **a)** [T] to make something separate into two or more pieces, for example by hitting it, dropping it, or bending it 使破裂, 打碎; 折斷: *The thieves got in by breaking a window.* 竊賊破窗而入。| **break sth in two/in half/into pieces etc** *He broke the roll in two and handed a piece to me.* 他把麵包卷掰成兩半, 遞了一塊給我。**b)** [I] to separate into two or more pieces 破裂〔成兩部分或更多塊〕, 破碎; 斷裂: *The frames are made of plastic and they tend to break easily.* 這些框架是塑料製的, 很容易碎裂。

2 ►PART OF YOUR BODY 身體的部分◄ [T] to damage part of your body, especially a bone, and make it split into two or more pieces 骨折, 摔斷: *She fell downstairs and broke her hip.* 她摔下了樓, 髖部骨折。

3 ►NOT WORKING 不能再用◄ **a)** [T] to damage something such as a machine so that it cannot work or be used 損壞, 弄壞, 摔壞: *Someone's broken my camera – I can't get it to focus properly.* 不知道是誰摔壞了我的照相機, 我無法調準焦距。| *There's no point in buying him expensive toys, he'll only break them.* 不用給他買貴重的玩具, 他只會把它們弄壞。**b)** [I] if something such as a part of a machine breaks, it stops working〔機器部件等〕失靈, 壞了: *I think the spring's broken.* 我覺得是彈簧斷了。

B

4 ►SURFACE/SKIN 表面/皮膚◄ [I,T] if the surface of something breaks or if you break it, it splits or gets a hole in it 弄破…的表面, 裂開, 破損: *The seal on the jar did not seem to have been broken.* 罐子的密封條似乎沒有打開過。

5 ►RULE/LAW ETC 規定/法律等◄ [T] to disobey a rule, law etc 不遵守, 觸犯: *Anyone who rides a motorbike without a helmet is breaking the law.* 騎摩托車不戴頭盔是違法的。

6 ►PROMISE/AGREEMENT 諾言/協議◄ **break a promise/break an agreement/break your word** to not do what you have promised to do or signed an agreement to do 違背諾言/違反協議/食言: *I felt I had to take her to the film – I didn't want to break my promise.* 我認為必須帶她去看電影, 我不想食言。

7 break free/break loose to escape from someone or somewhere by using force 用力掙脫; 逃跑: *I managed to break free by elbowing him in the stomach.* 我用胳膊肘頂他的肚子設法逃脫了。

8 break loose if violent feelings or a violent situation breaks loose, they suddenly start to happen 迸發, 爆發: **all hell broke loose** (=people started behaving in a wild, uncontrolled way) 亂作一團 *The moment the shot rang out all hell broke loose.* 槍響時人們亂作一團。

9 break even to neither make a profit nor lose money 不賠不賺, 不盈不虧, 收支相抵: *Things have been so bad we'll be lucky if we break even.* 情況很糟糕, 如果我們能不賠不賺, 就算幸運了。

10 break a habit to stop wanting to keep doing something, especially something that you should not do 改掉某習慣〔尤指壞習慣〕: *Smoking is a difficult habit to break.* 吸煙是一個難以改掉的習慣。

11 why break the habit of a lifetime? *humorous spoken* used when telling someone that you expect that they will behave in the same way that they have always done, and make the same mistakes【幽默, 口】你不總是這樣嗎?(為甚麼要改掉你畢生的習慣呢?): *"I'd better hurry up or I'll be late." "Why break the habit of a lifetime?"* "我得抓緊時間, 不然就遲到了。""你不總是這樣嗎?"

12 break sb's heart to make someone very unhappy by ending a relationship with them or by doing something that they do not want you to do 使某人傷心[心碎]: *He's really good looking – I expect he broke all the girls' hearts when he was at school.* 他的確很帥, 我猜想他在求學時期傷盡了女孩子的心。| *It'll break your father's heart if you tell him you're giving up college.* 如果你告訴你爸爸不上大學了, 會使他很傷心。

13 you're breaking my heart/it's breaking my heart *humorous spoken* used when saying jokingly that you are very sad about something, even though you are not【幽默, 口】你真讓我心痛

14 break your neck *spoken* to hurt yourself very badly, especially by falling onto the ground【口】摔壞, 跌傷〔尤指摔倒在地〕: *The path was really icy and I was lucky I didn't break my neck.* 小路結滿了冰, 我很幸運沒摔着。

15 I'll break his/her neck *spoken* used when threatening to hurt someone because you are very angry about what they have done【口】我要打扁他/她: *If I get hold of the guy who hit my car I'll break his neck.* 如果我抓到撞我的車的那個傢伙, 我會打扁他。

16 break the back of to finish the main or worst part of something 完成…的主要的[最艱難的]部分: *The engineers are confident they have broken the back of the problem.* 那些工程師相信他們已經克服了難關。

17 break your back *spoken* to work very hard to try and do something【口】拚死拚活地幹; 盡最大的努力: *We've been breaking our backs trying to get the work done on time.* 我們一直在拚命幹, 爭取如期完成任務。

18 break sb's fall to stop someone from falling straight onto the ground, so that they are not badly hurt 阻止某人摔倒, 使某人免於受傷: *Luckily some trees at the bottom of the cliff broke his fall.* 幸運的是, 懸崖底下的一些樹擋住了他使他免於受傷。

19 break a record to do something even faster or even better than the previous best time, amount etc 破記錄: *Christie has broken his own European record in the 100 meters.* 克里斯蒂打破了他自己保持的100米歐洲記錄。| **break all records** (=to be much better or much more successful than anything before) 突破以前的記錄 *This year's sales performance is expected to break all records.* 今年的銷售成績有望突破以前的記錄。

20 break for lunch/coffee/dinner etc to stop for a short time in order to have lunch, a drink etc 休息(一段時間)吃午飯/喝咖啡/吃晚飯等: *At 12.30 we'll break for lunch, and start again at 2 o'clock.* 十二點半, 我們休息吃午飯, 兩點鐘再開始幹。

21 break sb's concentration/flow/train of thought to interrupt someone and stop them from being able to continue thinking or talking about something 分散某人的注意力; 打斷某人的談話/思路: *I never listen to music when I'm working – it breaks my concentration.* 我工作時從不聽音樂, 那樣會分散我的注意力。

22 ►END A SITUATION 終止某情況◄ [T] to stop an unpleasant situation from continuing 結束, 終止, 打破: **break the monotony** *We took turns driving, in order to try and break the monotony.* 我們輪流開車, 以打破旅途的單調。| **break the deadlock/stalemate** (=end a situation in which an agreement or a solution cannot be found) 打破僵局 *a way of ending the deadlock in Bosnia* 打破波斯尼亞僵局的方法

23 break a strike to force workers to end a STRIKE² (1) 迫使〔工人〕結束罷工: *threats to use the army to break the 10-month-old strike* 威脅動用武力結束長達十個月的罷工

24 break the silence/calm to end a period of silence or calm by talking or making a noise 打破寂靜/平靜: *The silence was broken by a burst of machine-gun fire.* 一陣機槍聲打破了沉寂。

25 break your silence to start talking about something in public after refusing to do so for a long time 打破沉默: *She has finally broken her silence about the divorce.* 她終於打破沉默, 談論自己離婚的事。

26 break your links/ties/connection etc to end your connection or relationship with a person, group, organization etc 斷絕關係: *The US broke all diplomatic links with North Korea for a 3 month period.* 美國中止了和北韓的所有外交聯繫長達三個月。

27 break sb to completely destroy someone's chances of success or make them feel that they cannot continue 斷送了某人的前程, 毀了某人: *the scandal that finally broke him* 最終毀了他的醜聞

28 break sb's spirit/resolve to make someone stop trying to achieve something, or start doing what you want 瓦解某人的士氣/決心: *They could not break her spirit.* 他們無法瓦解她的士氣。

29 break ranks to behave differently from the other members of a group, who are expecting you to support them 不支持所屬的團體: *No one in the party was prepared to break ranks and vote against their leader.* 黨內所有的成員都準備團結一致, 全投領導人的票。

30 break the ice a) to make people who have just met each other less nervous and more willing to talk, for example at a party or meeting 打破沉默 [冷場]: *Sharon tried to break the ice by suggesting that we all play a game.* 沙倫想打破沉默, 建議我們玩個遊戲。**b)** to do something that shows you want to end an argument, quarrel etc 為結束爭端而努力: *Yeltsin offered a ceasefire to the rebels in an attempt to break the ice.* 葉利欽向反叛者提出停火建議, 試圖結束爭端。

31 it won't break the bank used to say that you can afford to buy something 花得起錢: *It's time we had a holiday, and it won't break the bank.* 我們該去度假了, 我們出得起這錢。

32 break the bank to win more money in a game of

cards than a CASINO or a DEALER (3) is able to pay you 赢了(莊家)全部的錢

33 break fresh/new ground to do something completely new that no one has ever done before, or find out new information about a subject 開闢新的領域; 作出新發現: *Researchers claim they are breaking new ground and are getting closer to discovering the causes of the disease.* 研究者聲稱他們正在作出新的發現, 即將找出這種疾病的誘因。

34 break cover to move out of a place where you have been hiding so that you can be seen 從隱藏處出來: *One of the rhinos broke cover and charged straight at them.* 一頭犀牛突然竄出, 直向他們衝來。

35 break camp to pack tents and other equipment and leave the place where you have been camping 開拔, 拔營

36 ►DAY/DAWN 白天/黎明◄ [I] if the day or the dawn breaks, light starts to shine in the sky (天)剛亮, 破曉: *We arrived at Narita just as the dawn was breaking.* 天剛蒙蒙亮, 我們就到達成田機場。

37 ►STORM 暴風雨◄ [I] if a storm or the MONSOON breaks, it suddenly begins 來臨, 突然出現: *Bonington's team were nearing the summit when the monsoon broke.* 伯寧頓的小組即將到達頂峯時, 季風突然來臨。

38 ►WEATHER 天氣◄ [I] if the weather breaks, it suddenly changes 突變

39 ►WAVE 波浪◄ [I] if a wave breaks, the top part starts to fall down, usually because it is hitting or getting near the shore 落下; 沖擊: *waves breaking against the foot of the cliffs* 海浪拍打着峭壁的底部

40 ►VOICE 嗓門◄ [I] if a boy's voice breaks, it becomes lower and starts to sound like a man's voice〔男孩發育時的嗓音〕變低變粗, 變聲: *I was in the school choir until my voice broke.* 變聲前我一直是學校合唱隊隊員。

41 ►NEWS 新聞◄ [I] if news about an important event breaks, it finally becomes known 傳開: *The Watergate scandal was about to break.* 水門事件醜聞很快就要被傳開。

42 ►CODE 代碼◄ [T] to succeed in understanding what the letters or numbers in a secret CODE¹ (4) mean 破解, 破譯: *Polish scientists broke the Enigma code shortly before World War II.* 就在第二次世界大戰爆發前不久, 波蘭科學家破譯了"謎語"密碼。

43 break wind to allow gas to escape from your BOWEL*s*, making a noise and an unpleasant smell; FART¹ (1) 放屁

44 break (sb's) serve to win a game in tennis when your opponent is serving (SERVE¹ (10))〔網球〕破對方發球(局)得分: *Courier broke Sampras' serve in the first game of the third set.* 古利拉在第三盤第一局破了森柏斯的發球局。

45 break! used when telling BOXER*s* or WRESTLER*s* to stop fighting〔告訴拳擊手或摔跤手〕分開!

46 break a leg! *humorous spoken* used to wish someone good luck【幽默, 口】祝你走運!

break away *phr v* [I] **1** to leave a group or political party to form another group, usually because of a disagreement〔從團體或政黨中〕脫離出去: **[+from]** *The Nottingham miners broke away from the NUM to form their own union.* 諾丁漢礦工脫離了全國礦工總會, 組成了自己的工會。**2** to move away from someone or something〔從…〕逃脫, 掙脫, 逃離: **[+from]** *They kissed, then she broke away from him and ran to the window.* 他們親吻, 然後她從他懷裡掙脫出去, 向窗子跑去。

break down *phr v*

1 ►MACHINE 機器◄ [I] if a large machine, especially a car, breaks down, it stops working 停止運轉, 出故障: *The elevators in this building are always breaking down.* 這幢樓裡的電梯總出故障。

2 ►FAIL 失敗◄ [I] if a discussion, system etc breaks down, it fails because there are problems 失敗, 遭受挫折: *Peace talks have broken down over the question of reparations.* 和談因戰後賠款問題而破裂。

3 ►DOOR 門◄ [T **break** sth ↔ **down**] if you break down a door, you hit it so hard that it breaks and falls to the ground 弄壞, 打破

4 ►CHANGE FIXED IDEAS 改變固有想法◄ [T **break** sth ↔ **down**] to change the fixed ideas or feelings that someone or a group of people have so that they agree with yours 改變〔某人固有的觀點〕: *It'll be difficult to break down their prejudices about lesbians.* 很難改變他們對女同性戀者的固有偏見。

5 ►CHANGE CHEMICALLY 化學變化◄ [I,T] if a substance breaks down or something breaks it down, it changes as a result of a chemical process (把…)分解: **break** sth ↔ **down** *Bacteria break down the animal waste to form methane gas.* 細菌把動物糞便分解形成沼氣。

6 ►CRY 哭喊◄ [I] to be unable to stop yourself crying, especially in public 感情失去控制, 失聲痛哭〔尤指在公共場合〕: *If I go to the funeral, I'll break down.* 要是去參加葬禮, 我會忍不住痛哭。

7 ►BECOME ILL 生病◄ [I] to become mentally or physically ill 精神崩潰; 身體垮掉: *If Tim carries on working like this, he'll break down sooner or later.* 如果蒂姆還繼續這樣工作, 遲早會崩潰。

8 ►MAKE STH SIMPLE 使某事物變得簡單◄ [T **break** sth ↔ **down**] to separate something such as a job or report into parts, especially so that it is easier to do or understand 把…分類, 把…分成: *a recipe that breaks down the making of creme brulee into simple steps* 把做蛋奶凍分成幾個簡單步驟的烹飪法 —see also 另見 BREAKDOWN (4)

break for sth *phr v* [T] *AmE* to suddenly run or drive somewhere, especially in order to escape from someone【美】突然跑向, 將車開到〔某地, 尤指想逃跑〕: *Sharkey broke for the exit, but got nabbed.* 夏基跑向出口, 但被抓住了。

break in *phr v* **1** [I] to enter a building by using force, in order to steal something 闖入〔行竊〕: *Someone broke in and took several computers.* 有人闖入屋內, 偷走了幾台電腦。—see also 另見 BREAK-IN **2** [T **break** sb/sth ↔ **in**] to make a person or animal get used to a certain way of behaving or working 使習慣於; 馴〔動物〕: *Don't worry about doing the accounts, we'll break you in gently.* 不要擔心做會計工作, 我們會讓你慢慢熟悉的。**3** [I] to join a conversation by interrupting someone or saying something suddenly 打斷, 插嘴: **[+with]** *Dad would occasionally break in with a suggestion.* 爸爸總會不時插話, 提出建議。| **[+on]** *Sorry to break in on you, but your wife is on the line.* 對不起, 打斷你, 你的妻子打電話找你。**4** [T **break** sth ↔ **in**] to make new shoes or boots less stiff and more comfortable, by wearing them 使〔新鞋〕逐漸舒適合腳

break into sth *phr v* [T]

1 ►STEAL 偷竊◄ to enter a building by using force, in order to steal something 闖入〔行竊〕: *Thieves broke into the bank vault by digging a tunnel.* 竊賊挖了一個通道闖入銀行金庫。

2 break into a run/gallop/trot etc to suddenly start running etc 突然奔跑: *Suzie heard footsteps behind her and broke into a run.* 蘇絲聽到身後的腳步聲拔腿就跑。

3 break into a sweat to start sweating (SWEAT² (1)) 開始出汗: *The game was over before I'd even broken into a sweat!* 我還沒有出汗, 比賽就結束了!

4 ►NEW BUSINESS ACTIVITY 新的商業活動◄ to become involved in a new activity, especially a business activity 參與〔尤指商業活動〕: *British Airways is trying to break into the American market.* 英國航空公司正設法打入美國市場。

5 ►MONEY 金錢◄ to start to spend money that you did not want to spend (勉強)動用一部分: *We'll have to break into the £500 your dad gave us.* 我們不得不動用

你爸爸給的500英鎊。

6 ▶INTERRUPT 打斷◀ to interrupt an activity by saying or doing something 打擾, 打斷: *Sorry to break into your lunch hour, but I must speak to you urgently.* 對不起, 打擾你們吃午飯了, 但我有要緊事要說。

7 break into tears/laughter/cheers etc to suddenly start crying, laughing etc 突然大哭／大笑／歡呼起來等

break sb **of** sth *phr v* [T] to make someone stop having a bad habit 使某人改掉〔壞習慣〕: *What can we do to break him of sucking his thumb?* 我們怎樣才能使他改掉吮吸拇指的習慣?

break off *phr v* **1** [I,T] to suddenly stop doing something, especially talking to someone（使）突然結束, 中斷〔尤指談話〕: *Fay told her story, breaking off now and then to wipe the tears from her eyes.* 費伊講述自己的故事, 不時停下來擦去眼裡的淚水。| **break sth ↔ off** *I broke off the conversation and answered the phone.* 我中斷了談話去接電話。**2** [T **break** sth ↔ **off**] to stop a relationship 中止〔關係〕, 斷絕: **break off relations/an engagement** *Britain was about to break off diplomatic relations with Libya.* 英國正要和利比亞斷絕外交關係。**3** [T] to break a piece from the main part of something（使）折斷: **break sth ↔ off** *I broke off a piece of bread.* 我掰下一塊麵包。| **break sth off sth** *Why don't you break a branch off the tree and make a walking stick?* 你為甚麼不折下一根樹枝當手杖?

break out *phr v* [I]

1 ▶WAR/FIRE ETC 戰爭／火災等◀ if something unpleasant such as a fire, war, or disease breaks out, it starts to happen〔不愉快之事〕爆發, 突然發生: *Several scuffles broke out in the crowd.* 人羣中發生了幾場混戰。

2 ▶ESCAPE 逃跑◀ to escape from a prison or similar place 逃出: **[+of]** *a plan to break out of jail* 越獄計劃 —see also 另見 BREAKOUT

3 ▶CHANGE YOUR LIFE 改變生活◀ to change the way you live or behave, especially because you feel bored 改變生活方式: **break out of a routine/rut etc** *I've got to break out of the same old dull routine or I'll go crazy.* 我必須擺脱老一套的常規, 不然我會瘋的。

4 break out in spots/a rash etc if you break out in spots etc, a lot of red spots appear on your skin 出疹子: *Talcum powder makes me break out in a rash.* 爽身粉使得我長滿了疹子。

5 break out in a sweat to start sweating (SWEAT² (1)) 出汗

break through *phr v* **1** [I,T] to force a way through something 突破; 突圍: **break through sth** *At dawn 300 tanks prepared to break through the enemy lines.* 拂曉時, 300輛坦克準備突破敵人的防線。**2** [I,T] if the sun or light breaks through, you can see it through something such as clouds or mist〔太陽或光從雲霧中〕透出來 **3** [T **break through** sth] to deal successfully with something, especially unreasonable behaviour or bad feelings 克服〔尤指不合理行為或不好的感覺〕: *How could I break through his reserve?* 我該怎樣做才能讓他開口呢? —see also 另見 BREAKTHROUGH

break up *phr v*

1 ▶BREAK INTO PIECES 碎成片◀ [I,T] to break or make something break into many small pieces 打碎; 碎開; 斷開: *The stricken tanker began to break up on the rocks.* 油船觸礁後開始斷裂。| **break sth ↔ up** *Jim started to break the ice up on the frozen lake.* 吉姆開始砸碎湖面上結的冰。

2 ▶SEPARATE 分開◀ [T **break** sth ↔ **up**] to separate something into several smaller parts 把…分成幾部分: *I want to plant more bushes to break up the garden a bit.* 我想多種一點矮樹叢把花園隔成幾部分。

3 ▶FIGHT 打架◀ [I,T] if a fight etc breaks up or someone breaks it up, the people stop fighting each other 停止; 制止〔鬥毆〕: **break** sth ↔ **up** *Three policemen were needed to break up the fight.* 需要三名警察制止這場鬥毆。| **break up a demonstration/meeting etc** *The army is on hand to break up any demonstrations against the regime.* 部隊隨時可以制止反對政權的示威活動。

4 ▶MARRIAGE/ORGANIZATION 婚姻/組織◀ [I,T] if a marriage, group of people, or organization breaks up, the people in it separate and do not live or work together any more 破裂; 解散, 瓦解: *If a parent dies, the family may break up.* 如果父母中有一人去世, 這個家就可能散了。—see also 另見 BREAKUP (1)

5 ▶CROWD 人羣◀ [I] if a crowd or meeting breaks up, people start to leave 散開, 散場

6 ▶SCHOOL 學校◀ [I] *BrE* if a school or the students of a school break up, they begin a holiday【英】開始放假: **[+for]** *When do you break up for Easter?* 你們甚麼時候開始放復活節假?

7 ▶MAKE SB LAUGH 引某人笑◀ [T] *AmE* to say or do something that is so funny that people cannot stop laughing【美】使〔人〕捧腹大笑: **break sb up** *Hal really broke me up with that story about the alligator.* 哈爾講的短吻鱷的故事讓我笑破肚皮。

break with sb/sth *phr v* [T] **1** to leave a group of people or an organization, especially because you have had a disagreement with them 與…斷絕關係; 與…決裂: **break with sb/sth over sth** *Powell broke with the Conservative Party over Europe.* 由於在歐洲問題上觀點不一致, 鮑威爾與保守黨斷絕了來往。**2 break with tradition/the past** to stop following old customs and do something in a completely different way 與傳統／過去決裂

break² *n*

1 ▶A REST 休息◀ **a)** [C] a period of time when you stop what you are doing in order to rest, eat etc 小憩, 間歇, 中間休息: **without a break** *Larry had worked all day without a break.* 拉里一整天都在工作, 沒有休息。| **tea/coffee/lunch break** *It's time for a coffee break.* 該喝杯咖啡休息一下了。| **have/take a break** *Let's take a ten minute break.* 讓我們休息十分鐘。**b)** [C] a short holiday 短暫的假期: **weekend break** *a travel agent specializing in weekend breaks* 專門辦理週末度假的旅行社 | **the Easter/Christmas etc break** (=the public or school holiday at Easter etc) 復活節／聖誕節等假期 **c)** [U] also 又作 **break time** *BrE* the time during the school day when classes stop and teachers and students can rest, eat, play etc【英】課間休息; RECESS¹ (2) *AmE*【美】: *I'll speak to you at break.* 課間休息時我有話對你說。

2 ▶A PAUSE IN STH 暫停◀ **a)** [C] a period of several weeks or years during which something stops, before continuing again 休假: **[+in]** *a welcome break in my normal routine* 我正常公事中難得的休假 | **career break** *Demi Moore planned to take a career break to have children.* 狄美·摩亞計劃暫停工作生孩子去。**b)** [C] a pause in a conversation or in what someone is saying〔談話的〕暫停: **[+in]** *She waited for a break in the conversation.* 她等待談話暫停。**c)** also 又作 **commercial break** a pause for advertisements during a television or radio programme 廣告時間: *Join us again after the break.* 廣告之後繼續收看我們的節目。

3 ▶END/CHANGE 結束/變化◀ [singular] an occasion when you end a relationship with a person, organization etc, or change the way that things have always been done in the past 中止關係; 改變生活習慣: **[+from]** *Medieval thought represents a sharp break from that of the Greeks.* 中世紀思想意味着與古希臘思想的斷然決裂。| **[+with]** *In a break with tradition, they held their wedding at home.* 他們打破傳統, 在家舉行婚禮。| **a clean break** (=a very clear and definite end to a relationship) 徹底斷絕關係 *I don't want a messy divorce, just a quick, clean break.* 我不希望拖泥帶水地離婚, 離就快點離, 徹底離。| **make the break** *She's wanted to leave Dave for years, and last week she finally made the break.* 她多年來都想離開戴夫, 上週她終於離開了。

4 ▶A SPACE 空隙◀ [C] a space between two things or between two parts of something 裂口, 裂縫; 破裂: *The sun shone through a break in the clouds.* 陽光從雲層的

縫隙中透出來。| **a break in the weather** (=a short period of good weather) 短時間的好天氣

5 ►A CHANCE 機會◄ [C] *informal* a sudden or unexpected chance to do something, especially be successful in your job【非正式】機會; (好) 運氣: **big/lucky break** *My big break came when I was spotted singing in a club by a talent scout.* 我的好運來了, 一位星探發現我在俱樂部唱歌唱得不錯。

6 make a break for sth to suddenly start running towards something in order to escape from a place 向…方向逃去: *As soon as the guard's back was turned they made a break for the door.* 守衛剛一轉過身, 他們就趕快向門口跑去。| **make a break for it** (=try to escape) 企圖逃跑

7 ►BROKEN PLACE 破處◄ [C] the place where a bone in your body has broken 骨折的地方: *It's a nasty break, the bone has splintered.* 骨折很嚴重, 骨頭已裂成碎片。

8 give sb/sth a break! *spoken* used when you want someone to stop talking about something or doing something because it is annoying you【口】住口!; 住手!: *I'm sick of hearing about your problems. Just give it a break.* 你的問題我聽厭了, 別說了。

9 give me a break! *AmE spoken* used when you do not believe something someone has said【美口】我才不信呢!

10 ►TENNIS 網球◄ also 又作 **break of serve** [C] a situation in a game of tennis in which you win a game when your opponent is serving (SERVE¹ (10))〔網球〕破對方發球 (局) 得勝: **break point** (=the moment when if you win the point, you win a game) 賽點〔比賽中決定勝負的一刻〕

11 ►POINTS 分◄ [C] the number of points won by a player when it is their turn to hit the ball in a game such as BILLIARDS or SNOOKER¹〔枱球或彩色桌球〕在一次擊球機會中連續得分

12 the break of day *literary* the time early in the morning when it starts getting light【文】黎明, 拂曉

break·a·ble /ˋbrekəbl̩; ˈbreɪkəbəl/ *adj* made of a material such as glass or clay that breaks easily 易破碎的

break·age /ˋbrekɪdʒ; ˈbreɪkɪdʒ/ *n* **1 breakages** [plural] things that have been broken, especially things that belong to someone else that you must pay for 破損物: *a £5 deposit on hiring glasses, in case of breakages* 租眼鏡時交五英鎊押金以防毀壞 **2** [U] *formal* the act of breaking【正式】破損; 毀壞

break·a·way /ˋbrekə͵we; ˈbreɪkəweɪ/ *adj* **breakaway group/party/movement** a breakaway group etc has been formed by people who left another group because of a disagreement 另立門戶的集團/黨/運動: *the breakaway state of Slovenia* 分離出來的斯洛文尼亞 —**breakaway** *n* [C]

break·dance /ˋbrek͵dæns; ˈbreɪkdɑːns/ *v* [I] to do a type of dance involving ACROBATIC movements 跳霹靂舞 —**breakdancing** *n* [U] —**breakdancer** *n* [C]

break·down /ˋbrek͵daʊn; ˈbreɪkdaʊn/ *n* **1** [C,U] the failure of a system or relationship〔系統〕故障; 損壞;〔關係〕破裂: *Family breakdown can lead to behavioral problems in children.* 家庭破裂會導致孩子的行為出問題。| **[+in]** *a serious breakdown in relations between the two countries* 兩國關係的嚴重破裂 | **[+of]** *the gradual breakdown of authority* 權威的逐漸喪失 **2** also 又作 **nervous breakdown** [C] a serious medical condition in which someone becomes mentally ill and is unable to deal with even the simplest situations 精神崩潰: **have/suffer a breakdown** *After the trial Paul had a breakdown.* 審訊後, 保羅崩潰了。**3** [C] an occasion when a car or a piece of machinery breaks and stops working〔汽車或機器〕故障 **4** [C] a written statement explaining the details of something such as a bill or the cost of a plan 分類, 分析: **[+of]** *Can you prepare a full breakdown of labour costs?* 你能準備一份詳細的勞工成本分類清單嗎?

breakdown truck /ˈ·· ͵·/ also 又作 **breakdown lor·ry** /ˈ·· ͵··/ *n* [C] *BrE* a vehicle with special equipment used to pull a car that does not work to a place where it can be repaired【英】〔拖走拋錨汽車的〕牽引車, 拖車; TOWTRUCK *AmE*【美】

break·er /ˋbrekɚ; ˈbreɪkə/ *n* [C] a large wave with a white top that rolls onto the shore〔沖擊岸邊帶有白色浪頭的〕碎浪, 浪花

break·e·ven /brekˋivən; ͵breɪkˈiːvən◂/ *n* [U] the level of business activity at which a company is making neither a profit nor a loss 不賠不賺; 收支平衡: **breakeven point** *The firm should reach breakeven point after one year.* 一年後這家公司應該達到收支平衡點。—see also 另見 **break even** (BREAK¹ (9))

break·fast /ˋbrɛkfəst; ˈbrekfəst/ *n* [C,U] the meal you have in the morning 早餐: **have sth for breakfast** *We had coffee and toast for breakfast.* 我們早餐喝咖啡, 吃烤麵包片。| **working breakfast** (=a breakfast at which you talk about business) 工作早餐 —see also 另見 BED AND BREAKFAST, CONTINENTAL BREAKFAST, **make a dog's breakfast/dinner of sth** (DOG¹ (8)) —**breakfast** *v* [I+on]

breakfast tel·e·vi·sion /͵·· ˈ····/ *n* [U] *BrE* television programmes that are broadcast in the early part of the morning【英】晨播電視節目

break-in /ˈ· ·/ *n* [C] an act of entering a building illegally and by force, especially in order to steal things〔尤指為盜竊〕非法強行進入, 闖入: *Since the break-in we've had all our locks changed.* 自從上次有人非法闖入後, 我們換了所有的鎖。—see also 另見 **break in** (BREAK¹)

breaking and en·ter·ing /͵·· · ˈ···/ *n* [U] *law* the crime of entering a building illegally and by force【法律】破門侵入 (罪)

break·neck /ˋbrek͵nɛk; ˈbreɪknek/ *adj* **at breakneck speed** extremely and often dangerously fast 以危險的高速〔開車〕

break·out /ˋbrek͵aʊt; ˈbreɪkaʊt/ *n* [C] an escape from a prison, especially one involving a lot of prisoners 逃脫, (結夥) 越獄; 突圍

break·through /ˋbrek͵θru; ˈbreɪkθruː/ *n* [C] an important new discovery in something you are studying, especially one made after trying for a long time 突破; 重大進展: **make a breakthrough** *Scientists have made a major breakthrough in the treatment of cancer.* 科學家在癌症治療上取得了重大突破。

break·up /ˋbrek͵ʌp; ˈbreɪkʌp/ *n* [C,U] **1** the act of ending a marriage or relationship〔婚姻或關係的〕破裂: *the consequences of marital breakup on children* 婚姻破裂對孩子的影響 **2** the separation of a group, organization, or country into smaller parts, especially because it has become weaker or there are serious disagreements 分裂; 解散; 分離; 瓦解; 崩潰: **[+of]** *the breakup of the Soviet Union* 蘇聯的解體

break·wa·ter /ˋbrek͵wɔtɚ; ˈbreɪk͵wɔːtə/ *n* [C] a large strong wall built out into the sea to protect the shore from the force of the waves 防波堤: *forming a natural breakwater against the sea* 形成一道抵禦海浪的天然防波堤

breast¹ /brɛst; brest/ *n*

1 ►PART OF A WOMAN'S BODY 婦女身體的部位◄ [C] one of the two round raised parts of a woman's body that produce milk when she has a baby 乳房: *a woman with a baby at the breast* 正在給嬰兒哺乳的婦女 | *breast cancer* 乳腺癌 —see picture at 參見 BODY 圖

2 ►CHEST 胸部◄ [C] the part of your body between your neck and your stomach, especially the upper part of this area 胸部, 胸口: *Dick cradled her photograph against his breast.* 迪克把她的照片輕輕貼在胸前。

3 ►PART OF A BIRD 鳥的部位◄ [C] the front part of a bird's body 胸脯: *a robin with a red breast* 紅色胸脯的知更鳥

4 ►MEAT 肉◄ [U] meat that comes from the front part

of the body of a bird such as a chicken 胸脯肉: *turkey breast* 火雞胸脯肉

5 make a clean breast of it/things to admit that you have done something wrong 和盤托出, 完全供認, 坦白: *Why not make a clean breast of it and tell them you took the money?* 為甚麼不和盤托出, 告訴他們是你拿的錢?

B

6 single-breasted/double-breasted a coat, dress etc that is single-breasted etc has one or two rows of buttons down the front〔衣服〕單排扣/雙排扣的

7 bare-breasted/small-breasted/red-breasted etc having bare etc breasts 袒胸的/小胸脯的/紅色胸脯的等

8 ►EMOTIONS 感情◄ [C] *literary* where your feelings of sadness, love, anger, fear etc come from【文】胸懷; 心情, 內心: *a troubled breast* 心煩意亂 —see also 另見 **beat your breast** (BEAT[1] (28))

breast² *v* [T] **1** to reach the top of a hill or slope 登上〔山頂〕**2** to push against something with your chest 以胸部觸; 挺胸面對

breast·bone /ˈbrɛstˋbon; ˈbrestbəʊn/ *n* [C] a long flat bone in the front of your chest to which the top seven pairs of RIBS[1] (1) are connected 胸骨 —see picture at 參見 SKELETON 圖

breast-feed /ˈbrɛst,fid; ˈbrestfiːd/ *v past tense and past participle* **breast-fed** /-,fɛd; -fed/ [I,T] to feed a baby with milk from your breast rather than from a bottle 用母乳餵養, 哺乳 —compare 比較 SUCKLE, NURSE[2] (6)

breast·plate /ˈbrɛst,plet; ˈbrestpleɪt/ *n* [C] a leather or metal protective covering worn over the chest by soldiers during battles in former times〔古時士兵打仗時穿的〕護胸甲, 胸鎧

breast-pock·et /,· ˈ··/ *n* [C] a pocket on the outside of a shirt or JACKET (1), above the breast 胸前口袋

breast·stroke /ˈbrɛst,strok; ˈbrest-strəʊk/ *n* [U] a way of swimming in which you push your arms out and then bring them back in a circle towards you while bending your knees towards your body and then kicking out 蛙泳

S3 W2 **breath** /brɛθ; breθ/ *n*

1 ►AIR YOU BREATHE 呼吸的氣◄ a) [U] the air that you take in and out of your lungs when you breathe 氣息, 呼吸: *Paul smelt the cigarette smoke on her breath.* 保羅聞到她的呼吸中帶煙草味。| **bad breath** (=breath that smells unpleasant) 口臭 **b)** the process of breathing in and out 呼吸〔過程〕: *Her breath was coming more easily now.* 她的呼吸現在順暢多了。**c)** [U, singular] the air in your lungs or the act of breathing it in 一口氣,(一次)呼吸: *Let your breath out slowly.* 慢慢地呼氣。| **take a (big/deep) breath** (=breathe in once)(深深地)吸一口氣 *Shaun took a deep breath and dived in.* 肖恩深深地吸了口氣, 然後跳入水中。| **be out of breath** (=have difficulty breathing because you have just been running, climbing stairs etc) 上氣不接下氣 | **get your breath back** (=breathe normally again after running or making a lot of effort) 喘過氣來 *At the top of the stairs she stopped to get her breath back.* 她到了樓梯頂時停下來喘口氣。| **short of breath** (=unable to breath easily, especially because you are unhealthy) 呼吸急促, 喘不過氣〔尤指不適時〕

2 a breath of fresh air a) something that is new and different in a way you find exciting and enjoyable 一股新風, 新的活力: *Osborne's play brought a breath of fresh air to the British theatre.* 奧斯本的戲劇給英國戲劇界帶來了生氣。**b) take a breath of fresh air** to go outside because it is unpleasantly hot where you are〔去戶外〕呼吸新鮮空氣

3 hold your breath a) to breathe in and close your mouth to keep the air in your lungs 屏住呼吸: *I just held my breath and prayed I wouldn't sneeze.* 我屏住呼吸, 祈求自己不要打噴嚏。**b)** to wait anxiously to see what is going to happen 屏息以待: *We held our breath while Mr Evans read the exam results.* 埃文斯先生宣讀考試成績時, 我們都屏息而聽。

4 take your breath away to be so beautiful or exciting that you feel as if you nearly stop breathing〔因美麗或激動〕使人目瞪口呆, 使大吃一驚: *a view that takes your breath away* 美得讓人驚訝的景色

5 under your breath in a quiet voice so that no one can hear you 低聲地: *"Son of a bitch," he muttered under his breath.* "畜生。"他低聲說。

6 in the same breath a) used to say that someone has said two things at once that are so different from each other they cannot both be true 連着說〔自相矛盾的話〕: *They said that women should have equal pay, and added in the same breath that men need more money.* 他們說婦女應得到同樣的報酬, 接着又說男人需要更多的錢。**b)** if you mention two people or things in the same breath, you show that you think they are alike 歸於同一類, 非常相像: *a player who has been mentioned in the same breath as Pete Sampras* 和皮特·森柏斯相提並論的運動員

7 with your last/dying breath at the moment when you are dying 臨終時: *With his last breath he cursed his captors.* 他臨終時詛咒捉拿他的人。

8 a breath of air/wind *literary* a slight movement of air【文】一絲微風: *Scarcely a breath of air disturbed the stillness of the day.* 整天幾乎沒有一絲風。

9 be the breath of life to sb to be the most important thing in someone's life〔某人生命中〕最重要的東西, 不可缺少的東西 —see also 另見 **with bated breath** (BATED), **catch your breath** (CATCH[1] (23)), **draw breath** (DRAW[1] (23)), **gasp for breath** (GASP[1] (2)), **save your breath** (SAVE[1] (15)), **waste your breath** (WASTE[2] (2))

breath·a·lyse *BrE*【英】, **breathalize** *AmE*【美】/ˈbrɛθə,laɪz; ˈbreθəl-aɪz/ *v* [T] to make someone breathe into a special piece of equipment in order to see if they have drunk too much alcohol【美】對…作呼氣測醉檢查

breath·a·lys·er *BrE*【英】, **breathalyzer** *AmE*【美】/ˈbrɛθə,laɪzɚ; ˈbreθəl-aɪzə/ *n* [C] *trademark* a piece of equipment used by the police to see if drivers have drunk too much alcohol【商標】呼氣測醉器

breathe /brið; briːð/ *v*

1 ►AIR 空氣◄ [I,T] to take air into your lungs and send it out again 呼吸: *When you get an asthma attack you can't breathe.* 哮喘病發作時你會喘不過氣來。| *People are concerned about the quality of the air they breathe.* 人們關注他們呼吸的空氣的質量。| **breathe deeply** (=take in a lot of air) 深深地吸口氣

2 ►BLOW 吹◄ [I,T] to blow air or smoke out of your mouth 呼氣; 噴出…氣味: **[+on]** *Roy breathed on his hands and rubbed them together vigorously.* 羅伊在雙手上哈了一口氣, 然後用力互相摩擦。| **breathe sth over sb** *The fat man opposite was breathing garlic all over me.* 對面的那個胖男人衝我呼出的氣滿是大蒜味。

3 breathe again/more easily to relax because something dangerous or frightening has finished 鬆一口氣: *The all-clear was given and we could breathe again.* 解除空襲警報的信號發出了, 我們可以鬆口氣了。

4 breathe a sigh of relief to no longer be worried about something that had been worrying or frightening you 輕鬆地舒了口氣

5 be breathing down sb's neck to pay very close attention to what someone is doing in a way that makes them feel nervous or annoyed 緊盯某人; 嚴密監視某人: *How can I concentrate with you breathing down my neck all the time?* 你總是這樣盯着我, 我怎麼能集中精力?

6 not breathe a word to not tell anyone anything at all about something, because it is a secret 不透露風聲: *Don't breathe a word, it's supposed to be a surprise.* 不要把這事說出去, 讓別人有個驚喜。

7 ►WINE 酒◄ [I] if you let wine breathe, you open the

bottle to let the air get to it before you drink it 透氣; 散發香味
8 ►SAY STH QUIETLY 輕聲説◄ [T] to say something very quietly, almost in a whisper 輕聲説話; 低語: *"Wait," he breathed.* "等一下。" 他輕聲說。
9 breathe your last *literary* to die【文】斷氣, 死
10 breathe life/excitement/enthusiasm into sth to change a situation so that people feel more excited or interested 給…注入生命/刺激/熱情: *Let's hope Doug can breathe a bit of life into these rather dull people.* 讓我們希望多戈能給這些沉悶的人們注入新的生命。
11 breathe fire to behave and talk very angrily 發火

breathe in *phr v* **1** [I] to take air into your lungs 吸氣: *The doctor made me breathe in while he listened to my chest.* 醫生聽我胸部時要我吸氣。**2** [T **breathe** sth ↔ **in**] to breathe air, smoke, a particular kind of smell etc into your lungs 把〔空氣、煙霧等〕吸入肺中: *They may be in danger of breathing in asbestos dust.* 他們有吸入石棉塵埃的危險。

breathe out *phr v* **1** [I] to send air out from your lungs 呼氣: *Jim breathed out deeply.* 吉姆深深地呼了一口氣。**2** [T **breathe** sth ↔ **out**] to send out air, oxygen, a particular kind of smell etc 排出〔某種氣體〕: *Green plants breathe out oxygen in sunlight.* 在陽光下, 綠色植物排出氧氣。

breath·er /ˋbriðɚ; ˈbriːðə/ *n* **have/take a breather** *informal* to stop what you are doing for a short time in order to rest【非正式】休息一下, 喘一口氣 —see also 另見 HEAVY BREATHER

breath·ing /ˋbriðɪŋ; ˈbriːðɪŋ/ *n* [U] the process of breathing air in and out 呼吸: **heavy breathing** (=loud breathing) 沉重的呼吸 *When I picked up the phone all I heard was heavy breathing.* 我拿起聽筒, 只聽到沉重的呼吸聲。

breathing space /ˈ·· ·/ *n* [C,U] a short time when you stop doing something difficult, tiring etc, so that you have time to think more clearly about a situation 喘息的時間; 歇息的機會

breath·less /ˋbrɛθlɪs; ˈbreθləs/ *adj* **1** having difficulty breathing, especially because you are very tired, excited, or frightened 氣喘吁吁的, 喘不過氣來的: *The long climb left Jan feeling breathless.* 長時間的攀登使簡感到喘不過氣來。**2** unpleasantly hot with no fresh air or wind 使人窒息的, 令人透不過氣的: *the breathless heat of a midsummer night in Rome* 羅馬仲夏夜令人透不過氣的炎熱 —**breathlessly** *adv* —**breathlessness** *n* [U]

breath·tak·ing /ˋbrɛθˌtekɪŋ; ˈbreθˌteɪkɪŋ/ *adj* very impressive, exciting, or surprising 使人興奮的, 激動人心的, 驚險的; 令人驚嘆的: *the breathtaking natural beauty of the rain forests* 熱帶雨林令人驚嘆的自然美景 | *a man of quite breathtaking stupidity* 令人驚愕的愚蠢之人 —**breathtakingly** *adv*

breath test /ˈ· ˌ·/ *n* [C] a test in which the police make a car driver breathe into a special bag to see if he has drunk too much alcohol 呼氣測醉試驗

breath·y /ˋbrɛθɪ; ˈbreθi/ *adj* if someone's voice is breathy, you can hear their breath when they speak 〔尤指嗓音〕帶有氣音的, 帶喘息聲的

breech birth /ˋbritʃ ˌbɝθ; ˈbriːtʃ bɜːθ/ also 又作 **breech de·liv·e·ry** /ˈ· ·ˌ···/ *n* [C] a birth in which the lower part of a baby's body comes out of its mother first 臀位分娩

breech·es /ˋbrɪtʃɪz; ˈbrɪtʃɨz/ *n* [plural] short trousers that fasten just below the knees 〔長及膝蓋的〕束腳短褲; 馬褲: *riding breeches* 馬褲

3 **breed¹** /brid; briːd/ *v past tense and past participle* **bred** /brɛd; bred/ **1** [I] if animals breed they have babies 〔動物〕繁殖, 下崽, 下蛋: *Eagles breed during the cooler months of the year.* 鷹在一年中較涼爽的季節繁殖。**2** [T] to keep animals or plants in order to produce babies or new plants, or in order to develop new or better animals or plants 育種, 飼養繁殖; 培植; 改良(品種): *commercially bred animals* 商業化繁殖的動物 **3** [T] to cause a particular feeling or condition 引起; 釀成, 招致〔一般指不良之事〕: *living conditions that breed violence and despair* 產生暴力與絕望的生活條件 **4 breed like rabbits** to produce a lot of babies quickly, especially more than you think is desirable 生太多的孩子 —see also 另見 WELL-BRED

breed² *n* [C] **1** a type of animal or plant, especially one that people have kept to breed, such as cats, dogs, and farm animals 〔尤指人工培育的動植物〕品種: *Spaniels are my favourite breed of dog.* 西班牙獵犬是我最喜歡一種狗。**2** a particular kind of person or type of thing 〔人或物的〕某種類型: **a rare/dying breed** *Honest salesmen are a rare breed nowadays.* 如今誠實的推銷員已是非常難得。| **a new breed of** *the first of a new breed of satellites* 第一顆新型人造衛星

breed·er /ˋbridɚ; ˈbriːdə/ *n* [C] someone who breeds animals or plants as a job 育種者; 飼養者; 繁殖者; 栽培者: *a dog breeder* 育狗人

breed·ing /ˋbridɪŋ; ˈbriːdɪŋ/ *n* [U] **1** the act or process of animals producing babies 生殖, 繁殖: **breeding season** (=the time of the year when an animal has babies) 繁殖季節 **2** the activity of keeping animals or plants in order to produce new or better types 培育, 育種: *the breeding of pedigree dogs* 純種狗的繁育 | **breeding stock** (=animals you keep to breed from) 種畜 **3** polite social behaviour that someone learns from their family 教養: *The young lieutenant had an air of wealth and good breeding.* 這位年輕中尉具有富有人家受過良好教育的氣度。

breeding ground /ˈ·· ·/ *n* [C] **1** a place or situation where something bad or harmful grows and develops 〔尤指壞事物的〕滋生地, 温床: [+**for**] *overcrowded slums that are breeding grounds for crime* 過分擁擠的貧民窟是滋生罪惡的温牀 **2** a place where animals go in order to breed 繁殖場: *In spring, the birds migrate north to their breeding grounds.* 春天, 鳥兒遷徙到北方的繁殖地。

breeze¹ /briz; briːz/ *n* [C] **1** a gentle wind 微風, 和風: *flowers waving in the breeze* 在微風中搖曳的花朵 —see picture on page A13 參見 A13 頁圖 **2 be a breeze** *informal* to be something that is very easy to do【非正式】不費吹灰之力的事 —see also 另見 **shoot the breeze** (SHOOT¹ (8))

breeze² *v* [I always+adv/prep] to walk somewhere in a calm confident way 飄然出現; 信步走進: [+**in/into/out etc**] *She just breezed into my office and said she wanted a job.* 她信步走進我的辦公室, 說想找份工作。

breeze through sth *phr v* [T] to finish a piece of work or pass an exam very easily 輕鬆完成; 輕鬆通過: *She breezed through the exam.* 她毫不費力地通過了考試。

breeze-block /ˈ· ·/ *n* [C] *BrE* a light brick used in building, made of CEMENT and CINDERS【英】煤渣混凝土空心磚, 煤渣磚; CINDER BLOCK *AmE*【美】

breez·y /ˋbrizɪ; ˈbriːzi/ *adj* **1** a breezy person is cheerful, confident, and relaxed 愉快的; 輕鬆自信的: *a breezy and relaxed air of confidence* 充滿自信的輕鬆神情 **2** breezy weather is when the wind blows quite strongly 〔天氣〕有微風的 —**breezily** *adv* —**breeziness** *n* [U]

breth·ren /ˋbrɛðrən; ˈbreðrən/ *n* [plural] *old-fashioned* a way of addressing or talking about the members of an organization or association, especially a religious group【過時】教友(們); 會友(們); 弟兄(們)

breve /briv; briːv/ *n* [C] *BrE* a musical note which continues for twice as long as a SEMIBREVE【英】〔樂曲的〕倍全音符, 二全音符; DOUBLE WHOLE NOTE *AmE*【美】

bre·vi·a·ry /ˋbrivɪˌɛrɪ; ˈbriːviəri/ *n* [C] a prayer book used in the Roman Catholic church 〔羅馬天主教神職人員的〕每日祈禱書, 簡本大日課經

brev·i·ty /ˋbrɛvətɪ; ˈbrevɨti/ *n* [U] **1** the quality of expressing something in very few words 簡潔, 簡練 **2** shortness of time 短暫, 短促: *In the interests of brevity I will summarize my views.* 為簡潔起見, 我會概述一下我的觀點。

brew¹ /bru; bru:/ *v* **1** [T] to make beer 釀造〔啤酒〕**2** [I, T] if tea or coffee brews or you brew it, you pour boiling water over it to make it ready to drink 沖, 泡, 沏 **3** [I] if something unpleasant is brewing, it will happen soon〔不快之事〕醞釀: *There's trouble brewing at work.* 工作中要有麻煩了。

brew up *phr v* [I] *BrE informal* to make a drink of tea【英, 非正式】泡 [沏] 茶

B

brew² *n* [C] a drink such as tea or beer 釀造[沖泡]的飲料〈如茶或啤酒〉—see also 另見 HOME BREW

brew·er /ˈbruə; ˈbru:ə/ *n* [C] a person or company that makes beer 釀啤酒者; 啤酒公司

brew·er·y /ˈbruərɪ; ˈbru:əri/ *n* [C] a place where beer is made, or a company that makes beer 啤酒廠

bri·ar, brier /ˈbraɪə; ˈbraɪə/ *n* **1** [C,U] a wild bush with prickly branches 歐石南, 荊棘 **2** [C] a tobacco pipe made from a briar 歐石南根煙斗

bribe¹ /braɪb; braɪb/ *v* [T] to pay money to someone to persuade them to help you, especially by doing something dishonest 賄賂, 收買: **bribe sb to do sth** *We bribed the doorman to let us in.* 我們賄賂守門人讓我們進去。| **bribe sb for sth** *prisoners bribing guards for cigarettes* 犯人賄賂獄警想要香煙

bribe² *n* [C] an amount of money or something valuable that you give someone to persuade them to help you or to do something dishonest 賄賂〔尤指錢〕: *a New York judge charged with accepting bribes* 一名被指控收受賄賂的紐約法官 —compare 比較 PAYOLA

brib·er·y /ˈbraɪbərɪ; ˈbraɪbəri/ *n* [U] dishonestly giving money to someone in order to persuade them to do something that will help you 行賄; 受賄: *We tried persuasion, bribery and threats, but the guard still wouldn't let us pass.* 我們試着說服警衛, 賄賂他, 威脅他, 他就是不讓我們過去。| *He was arrested on suspicion of accepting bribery.* 他因涉嫌受賄而被捕。| **bribery and corruption** (=bribery and dishonest behaviour) 貪污腐化

bric-a-brac /ˈbrɪk ə ˌbræk; ˈbrɪk ə ˌbræk/ *n* [U] small objects that are not worth very much money but are interesting or attractive 小飾品, 小擺設

2 3 **brick¹** /brɪk; brɪk/ *n* **1** [C,U] a hard block of baked clay used for building walls, houses etc 磚: *a brick wall* 磚牆 **2** [C] *BrE* a small square block of wood, plastic etc used as a toy【英】積木玩具 **3** [C] *old-fashioned* a good person who you can depend on when you are in trouble【過時】可靠的人, 好心人: *Janet's a real brick.* 珍妮特是個很可信賴的人。**4 you can't make bricks without straw** used to say you cannot do a job if you do not have the necessary materials 巧婦難為無米之炊 —see also 另見 **bang your head against a brick wall** (BANG² (5)), **drop a brick** (DROP¹ (34)), **come down on sb like a ton of bricks** (TON (5))

brick² *v*

brick sth ↔ **off** *phr v* [T] to separate an area from a larger area by building a wall of bricks 用磚牆隔開: *Some of the rooms had been bricked off.* 有幾間房已用牆隔開。

brick sth ↔ **up/in** *phr v* [T] to fill or close a space by building a wall of bricks in it 用磚堵住 [圍住]: *bricked up windows* 用磚堵住的窗戶

brick·lay·er /ˈbrɪkˌleə; ˈbrɪkˌleɪə/ *n* [C] someone whose job is to build walls, buildings etc with bricks 泥瓦匠, 砌磚工人 —**bricklaying** *n* [U]

brick·work /ˈbrɪkˌwɜk; ˈbrɪkwɜ:k/ *n* [U] bricks, or the way they have been used to build a wall, house etc 砌磚工程; 磚建築物; 〔建築物的〕磚結構: *The brickwork was cracked and in need of repair.* 磚牆出現裂縫, 需要修補。

brick·yard /ˈbrɪkˌjɑrd; ˈbrɪkjɑ:d/ *n* [C] a place where bricks are made 磚廠; 磚窑

brid·al /ˈbraɪdl; ˈbraɪdl/ *adj* **1** concerning a bride or a wedding 新娘的; 婚禮的: *a bridal car* 結婚花車 **2 the bridal party** the group of people who arrive at the church with the bride 隨新娘一起去教堂的人 **3 bridal suite** a special set of rooms in a hotel for a newly married couple〔酒店中的〕新婚套房 **4 bridal shower** *AmE* a party for a woman who is going to be married, given by her friends and family【美】〔朋友和家人〕為即將出嫁的新娘舉辦的送禮會

bride /braɪd; braɪd/ *n* [C] a woman at the time she gets married or just after she is married 新娘: *You may kiss the bride.* 你可以吻新娘了。

bride·groom /ˈbraɪdˌgrum; ˈbraɪdgru:m/ also 又作 **groom** *n* [C] a man at the time he gets married, or just after he is married 新郎

brides·maid /ˈbraɪdzˌmed; ˈbraɪdzmeɪd/ *n* [C] a girl or woman, usually unmarried, who helps the bride on her wedding day and is with her at the wedding 女儐相; 伴娘

bride-to-be /ˌ· · ˈ·/ *n* [C] a woman who is going to be married soon 快要當新娘的女子, 準新娘: *That's Jonathan's bride-to-be.* 那是喬納森的準新娘。

bridge¹ /brɪdʒ; brɪdʒ/ *n* [C]

1 ►OVER A RIVER/ROAD ETC 在河/路等的上方◄ a structure built over a river, road etc, that allows people or vehicles to cross from one side to the other 橋, 橋梁

2 ►CONNECTION 連接◄ something that provides a connection between two things; LINK² (1)〔事物之間的〕橋梁, 紐帶, 聯繫: *The training programme is seen as a bridge between school and work.* 該培訓計劃被視為學校與工作之間的橋梁。

3 ►SHIP 船◄ the raised part of a ship from which the officers control it 船橋, 艦橋, 駕駛台

4 ►CARD GAME 紙牌戲◄ [U] a card game for four players who play in pairs 橋牌

5 the bridge of your nose the bony upper part of your nose between your eyes 鼻梁

6 ►PAIR OF GLASSES 眼鏡◄ the part of a pair of glasses that rests on the bridge of your nose〔眼鏡的〕鼻梁架 —see picture at 參見 GLASS¹ 圖

7 ►MUSICAL INSTRUMENT 樂器◄ a small piece of wood under the strings of a VIOLIN or GUITAR, used to keep them in position〔弦樂器的〕弦柱, 弦馬, 琴馬

8 ►FOR TEETH 用於牙齒的◄ a small piece of metal for keeping false teeth in place〔假牙上的〕齒橋 —see also 另見 **build bridges** (BUILD¹ (7)), **burn your bridges** (BURN¹ (22)), **cross that bridge when you come to it** (CROSS¹ (8)), **be (all) water under the bridge** (WATER¹ (7))

bridge² *v* [T] **1** to build or form a bridge over something 在…上架橋: *a fallen tree bridging the stream* 倒下的樹橫跨在小溪上 **2 bridge the gap (between)** to reduce or get rid of the difference between two things 彌合差距: *an attempt at bridging the economic gap between North and South* 旨在彌合南北經濟差距的努力

bridge·head /ˈbrɪdʒˌhɛd; ˈbrɪdʒhed/ *n* [C] a strong position far forward in enemy land from which an army can go forward or attack 橋頭堡, 橋頭陣地

bridging loan /ˈ·· ˌ·/ *n* [C] *BrE* an amount of money lent by a bank to cover the period between buying a new house and selling the old one【英】〔銀行提供的短期〕過度性貸款

bri·dle¹ /ˈbraɪdl; ˈbraɪdl/ *v* **1** [T] to put a bridle on a horse 給〔馬〕套上籠頭 **2** [I,T] to show you are angry about something, especially by making a sudden upward movement of your chin (對…) 表示憤怒〔尤指猛然昂首〕: *She bridled at his autocratic tone.* 她揚起頭對他的專斷口氣嗤之以鼻。

bridle² *n* [C] a set of leather bands put around a horse's head and used to control its movements 馬籠頭; 馬勒 —see picture at 參見 HORSE¹ 圖

bridle path /ˈ·· ·/ also 又作 **bri·dle·way** /ˈbraɪdlˌwe; ˈbraɪdlweɪ/ *n* [C] a path intended for horse-riding, and not suitable for cars〔不能通車的〕騎馬專用道

Brie /bri; briː/ *n* [U] a soft French cheese 布里乾酪〔法國產的一種軟乾酪〕

2 2 **brief**[1] /brif; briːf/ *adj*

1 ►TIME 時間◄ continuing for a short time 短時間的; 短暫的: *a brief visit* 短暫的訪問

2 have a brief word to have a short conversation 說幾句話: *Could I have a brief word with you, Mr Thomas?* 托馬斯先生, 我能和你說幾句話嗎?

3 be brief to say or write something using only a few words, especially because there is little time 長話短說

4 ►SPEECH/LETTER 演講/信◄ using very few words or including few details 簡潔的, 簡明的: *a brief note of thanks* 簡短的感謝信

5 in brief a) in as few words as possible 簡而言之; 簡單地說: *We should, in brief, invest heavily in digital systems.* 簡而言之, 我們應該大量投資於數碼化系統。**b)** without any details 粗略地, 梗概地: *a report in brief* 簡報

6 someone who is brief does not say very much to someone, often in a rude way 唐突無禮的;〔說話〕草草的: *She was very brief with me when I asked about the contracts.* 當我問她合同的事, 她只草草說了兩句。

7 ►CLOTHES 衣服◄ clothes which are brief are short and cover only a small area of your body 短的, 暴露的: *a very brief bikini* 非常暴露的比基尼泳裝

brief[2] *n* [C] **1** official instructions that explain what someone's job is, what their duties are, how they should behave etc 簡短命令, 工作指示: *The architects's brief is to design an extension that is modern but blends with the rest of the building.* 建築師指示擴建部分建築物的設計既要現代, 又要與其餘的建築物保持和諧。**2** a short spoken or written statement giving facts about a law case 案情摘要, 案情簡介 **3 briefs** [plural] men's or women's underwear worn on the lower part of the body 貼身短內褲, 三角褲

brief[3] *v* [T] to give someone all the necessary information about a situation, so that they are prepared for it 作簡單的指示; 為…提供資訊: **brief sb on sth** *The president has been fully briefed on the current situation in Haiti.* 總統已掌握了有關海地當前局勢的情況。—compare 比較 DEBRIEF

brief·case /ˈbrifˌkes; ˈbriːfkeɪs/ *n* [C] a case used for carrying papers or documents 公文包, 公事包 —see picture at 參見 SUITCASE 圖

brief·ing /ˈbrifɪŋ; ˈbriːfɪŋ/ *n* [C,U] information or instructions that you get before you have to do something 簡要指示; 情況簡介; 簡報會

2 3 **brief·ly** /ˈbriflɪ; ˈbriːfli/ *adv* **1** for a short time 短暫地, 短時間地: *We stopped off briefly in London on our way to Geneva.* 我們去日內瓦途中, 在倫敦作了短暫停留。**2** in as few words as possible 概括地, 簡潔地, 簡要地: *Sonia explained briefly what we were to do.* 索尼亞簡要地說明了我們要做的事。| [sentence adverb 句子副詞] *Briefly, I think we should accept their offer.* 簡而言之, 我認為我們應該接受他們的建議。

bri·er /ˈbraɪɚ; ˈbraɪə/ *n* [C] a BRIAR 歐石南, 荊棘

brig /brɪg; brɪg/ *n* [C] a ship with two MASTs (=poles) and large square sails 方帆[橫帆]雙桅船

3 **bri·gade** /brɪˈged; brɪˈgeɪd/ *n* [C] **1** a large group of soldiers forming part of an army〔軍隊的〕旅 **2** an insulting word for a group of people who have the same beliefs 幫, 夥〔侮辱性詞語〕: *the antinuclear brigade* 反對使用核能的那一夥人 —see also 另見 FIRE BRIGADE

brig·a·dier /ˌbrɪgəˈdɪr; ˌbrɪgəˈdɪə◂/ *n* [C] a high military rank in the British Army or the person who has this rank 准將 —see table on page C6 參見 C6 頁附錄

brigadier-gen·e·ral /ˌ··· ˈ···/ *n* [C] a high army rank or someone holding this rank 准將 —see table on page C6 參見 C6 頁附錄

brig·and /ˈbrɪgənd; ˈbrɪgənd/ *n* [C] *literary* a thief, especially one of a group that attacks people in mountains or forests【文】歹徒; 土匪; 強盜; 山賊

brig·an·tine /ˈbrɪgənˌtin; ˈbrɪgəntiːn/ *n* [C] a ship like a BRIG but with fewer sails 縱橫帆雙桅帆船

bright /braɪt; braɪt/ *adj* 2 2

1 ►LIGHT 光線◄ shining strongly or with plenty of light 光亮的; 閃光的; 發光的: *bright sunlight* 燦爛的陽光 | *bright lights* 燈火通明 | *a new, bright, fully air-conditioned office* 明亮的、全空調的新辦事處

2 ►INTELLIGENT 聰明的◄ intelligent and likely to be successful 聰穎的: *Rosa's a bright child – she should do well at school.* 羅莎是一個聰明的孩子, 在學校裡成績應該不錯。| **(have) a bright idea** *We've no money and the last bus has gone. Any bright ideas?* 我們身上沒錢了, 最後一班公共汽車也開走了。有甚麼好主意嗎?

3 ►COLOURS 顏色◄ bright colours are strong and easy to see 鮮豔的, 鮮亮的: *bright red* 鮮紅色 | *Wash bright colours separately.* 顏色鮮豔的衣服要分開洗。

4 ►CHEERFUL 高興的◄ cheerful or full of life 生氣勃勃的; 歡快的; 興高采烈的: *a bright smile* 燦爛的笑容 | [+with] *Her eyes were bright with excitement.* 她十分興奮, 雙眼流露出喜悅的神色。

5 as bright as a button clever and full of life 聰明活潑的

6 not too/very bright a) if your future is not too bright, there is no reason to hope that good things will happen〔前景〕暗淡的: *The future doesn't look too bright for these youngsters on the dole.* 這些靠救濟金生活的年輕人前途暗淡。**b)** *informal* not sensible【非正式】不明智的: *That wasn't very bright, was it?* 那樣很不明智, 對吧?

7 look on the bright side to see the good points in something that is bad in other ways 看光明的一面, 抱樂觀態度: *Look on the bright side – not having a holiday will mean you save money!* 往好處想, 不去度假還省錢呢!

8 bright and early very early in the morning 大清早: *Max was up bright and early, keen to get started.* 麥克斯一大早就起來了, 急着開始工作。

9 bright spark *informal* an intelligent person, often used jokingly about someone who has done something stupid【非正式】聰明人〔常用作反話〕: *What bright spark forgot to turn the oven off?* 甚麼人這麼聰明, 忘了關烤爐?

10 bright and breezy cheerful and confident 快樂而自信的

11 have a bright future/have bright prospects to be likely to be successful in whatever you do as a job 前途光明, 前途遠大

12 bright-eyed and bushy-tailed *humorous* keen to start doing something, especially because it is new or interesting【幽默】躍躍欲試的

13 the bright lights the interesting exciting life that people are supposed to have in big cities 大城市五光十色的生活: *June went off in search of the bright lights in London.* 瓊去倫敦追求大城市五光十色的生活了。

14 bright spot an event or a period of time that is more pleasant when everything else is unpleasant 亮點〔指在其他事情都很糟糕時的一件令人高興的事或一段快樂的時光〕: *The only bright spot of the weekend was our trip to the theatre.* 這個週末我們唯一高興的事就是去看戲。—**brightly** *adv*: *The sun shone brightly.* 太陽光芒四射。—**brightness** *n* [U]

bright·en /ˈbraɪtn̩; ˈbraɪtn/ *v* **1** [T] to make something brighter in colour 使…更鮮豔 **2** [I] to become brighter in colour, or to shine with more light 發光; 明亮: *The sky had already begun to brighten.* 天空已開始亮起來。**3** [I,T] to become happier or more excited, or make someone else feel like this (使) 高興, (使) 興奮: *His expression brightened when I mentioned the money.* 我一提到錢, 他便高興起來。

brighten sth ↔ **up** *phr v* **1** [T] to make something more attractive or interesting 使更漂亮; 使更有趣: *New curtains would brighten up this room.* 新窗簾會使這個

房間變得漂亮些。**2** [I] to start to become happy again 重新高興起來: *She brightened up as soon as she saw us.* 她一看見我們便高興起來。**3** [I] to become brighter 變得晴朗: *The weather soon brightened up.* 天氣很快就放晴了。

brights /braɪts; braɪts/ *n* [plural] *AmE* car HEADLIGHTS when they are on as brightly as possible【美】〔汽車開着的〕車頭燈 —see also 另見 HIGH BEAM

brill¹ /brɪl; brɪl/ *adj BrE spoken* very good; BRILLIANT¹ (3)【英口】非常好的; 優秀的

brill² *n* [C] a European fish with a thin flat body〔歐洲產的〕菱鮃

bril·liance /ˈbrɪljəns; ˈbrɪljəns/ *n* [U] **1** a very high level of intelligence or skill 才華: *Hendrix's brilliance as a rock guitarist has never been matched.* 作為一個搖滾結他手, 亨德里克斯的才華無人能比。**2** brightness of colour〔顏色〕鮮豔

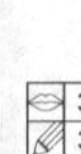

bril·liant¹ /ˈbrɪljənt; ˈbrɪljənt/ *adj* **1** brilliant light or colour is very bright and strong 光亮的, 光輝奪目的, 燦爛的: *The stage was flooded with brilliant light.* 舞台被燈光照得通亮。| *brilliant reds and blues* 色彩繽紛的紅藍色調 **2** extremely good, clever, or skilful 輝煌的; 聰穎的, 才華橫溢的: *Cox's performance was brilliant.* 考克斯演技精湛。| **a brilliant idea** *Hugh came up with a brilliant idea for a book.* 修想出了寫一本書的絕妙主意。**3** *BrE* excellent【英】優秀的, 好極的: *"How was your holiday?" "It was brilliant!"* "你假期過得怎麼樣?" "太棒了!" **4** very successful 極成功的: *a long and brilliant career* 長久而出色的事業 —**brilliantly** *adv*

brilliant² *n* [C] *technical* a precious stone cut with a lot of surfaces that shine【術語】多面形鑽石〔寶石〕

bril·lian·tine /ˈbrɪljənˌtin; ˈbrɪljəntiːn/ *n* [U] an oily substance used on men's hair〔男用〕潤髮油

Bril·lo pad /ˈbrɪlo ˌpæd; ˈbrɪləʊ pæd/ *n* [C] *trademark* a ball of wire filled with soap, used for cleaning pans【商標】潔鍋球

brim¹ /brɪm; brɪm/ *n* [C] **1** the bottom part of a hat that sticks out to protect you from sun and rain 帽簷, 帽邊 —see picture at 參見 HAT 圖 **2 be full to the brim (with)** if a container such as a glass is full to the brim, it is as full as possible 滿得要溢出來: *Dave poured whisky till the glass was full to the brim.* 戴夫往杯子裡倒了滿滿的威士忌酒。

brim² *v* **brimmed, brimming** [I] to be very full of something 注滿, 充盈: [+with] *Andy's eyes brimmed with tears.* 安迪熱淚盈眶。| *Eve was brimming with confidence.* 伊夫充滿了自信。

brim over *phr v* [I] **1** if a container is brimming over, it is so full of something that this is coming out over its top edge 滿到溢出來:[+with] *The barrel was brimming over with water.* 桶裡的水滿到溢出來了。**2 brim over with confidence/excitement etc** to be very confident, excited etc 充滿自信/喜悅之情等

brim·ful, brimfull /ˈbrɪmˋfʊl; ˈbrɪmˌfʊl/ *adj* [not before noun 不用於名詞前] very full 滿到邊的; 溢出的; 充滿的: [+of/with] *John is brimful of ambition, and ready to fight his way to the top.* 約翰野心勃勃, 決心奮鬥到最高層。

brim·stone /ˈbrɪmˌston; ˈbrɪmstəʊn/ *n* [U] *old use* SULPHUR【舊】硫磺 —see also 另見 **fire and brimstone** (FIRE¹ (13))

brin·dled /ˈbrɪndl̩d; ˈbrɪndld/ *adj* a brindled cow, cat etc is brown with marks or bands of another colour〔牛、貓等〕褐色底帶斑紋的

brine /braɪn; braɪn/ *n* [U] **1** water which contains a lot of salt, used for preserving food 濃鹽水: *sardines in brine* 用鹽水醃製的沙丁魚 **2** sea water 海水

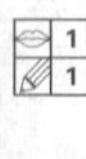

bring /brɪŋ; brɪŋ/ *v past tense and past participle* **brought** /brɔt; brɔːt/ [T] **1** to take someone or something to the place you are now, to the place you are going to, or to the place that you have been talking about 帶來; 拿來; 領來: *Did you bring anything to drink?* 你帶了甚麼喝的來嗎? | *Sheila was at the party and she brought that awful Ronnie with her!* 希拉參加了聚會, 還帶來了那個討厭的龍尼! | **bring sb sth** *Could you bring me that chair?* 你可以把那把椅子拿給我嗎? **2** to cause something such as a problem or reaction 造成, 引起, 導致: *The minister's speech brought an angry reaction from the Teachers' Association.* 部長的講話激起了教師聯合會的憤怒。| *This whole venture has brought nothing but trouble!* 這整個的冒險行動帶來的只有麻煩! **3 bring with it** if a change, action etc brings with it something such as a problem or advantage, the two things are connected and come together 伴隨而來: *Every scientific advance brings with it its own risks.* 每一項科學進展都帶有風險。**4** if something such as an event or fact brings people to a place, it makes them go there 促使某人去...: *The discovery of gold brought thousands of prospectors flocking to the Transvaal.* 由於發現了金子, 成千上萬的淘金者湧向〔南非〕德蘭士瓦。**5 bring charges** if the police bring charges against someone, they decide to charge them with a crime 起訴: *There was a six-month investigation, but eventually no charges were brought.* 調查進行了六個月, 但最終沒有提出起訴。**6 not bring yourself to do sth** if you cannot bring yourself to do something, you cannot make yourself do it 實在不忍心做某事: *She couldn't bring herself to touch it.* 她實在不忍摸一下。**7 bring sth into being** *formal* to make something start to exist【正式】成立, 建立; 產生: *The bureau was brought into being during the Second World War.* 該局是第二次世界大戰時成立的。**8 bring sth to the boil** to heat liquid until it starts to boil 把某物燒開[煮開] **9 bring tears to your eyes/bring a lump to your throat** to make you start to feel strong emotions such as pity, sadness, or happiness 使人熱淚奪眶而出/使人哽咽: *To see them meet after all this time, it really brings a lump to your throat!* 看到他們分開這麼久後重逢, 真使人感到唏噓不已! **10 bring sth to an end/a close/a conclusion etc** to make something finish or stop 結束[停止]某事: *It's time we brought this whole sordid affair to a close.* 我們該結束這整件卑鄙的事情了。**11 bring sth to bear** *formal* to use pressure, influence etc to change a situation【正式】對...施加壓力, 敦促: *Unfair pressure has been brought to bear upon the strikers to make them return.* 用不正當的手段對罷工的工人施加了壓力迫使他們復工。**12 bring sth to sb's attention/notice** *formal* to tell someone about something【正式】使某人注意某事, 提醒某人注意某事: *Thank you for bringing this mistake to our attention.* 謝謝你提醒我們注意這個錯誤。**13 what brings you here?** *spoken* used to show that you are surprised to see someone【口】是甚麼風把你吹來了? **14 bring home the bacon** *informal* to earn the money that your family needs to live【非正式】掙得養家餬口的錢 —see also 另見 **bring sth to a head** (HEAD¹ (45)), **bring sb to heel** (HEEL¹ (9)), **bring sb to their senses** (SENSE¹ (6)), **bring sth home to sb** (HOME² (4)), **bring sb/sth to their knees** (KNEE¹ (6))

bring sth ↔ **about** *phr v* [T] to make something happen 引起, 導致, 造成: *Computers have brought about many changes in the workplace.* 電腦給工作場所帶來了很多變化。

bring sb/sth **around/round** *phr v* [T] **1 bring the conversation around/round to** to deliberately and gradually introduce a new subject into a conversation 轉移話題: *I'll try to bring the conversation around to the subject of money.* 我會試圖把話題轉到金錢方面。**2** to make someone become conscious again 使...恢復知覺: *We managed to bring her round with some smelling salts.* 我們設法用嗅鹽使她恢復了知覺。**3** to manage to persuade someone to do something or to agree with you 説服〔某人〕做〔某事〕; 使同意某種觀點: *Give me a day or two and I'll see if I can bring her around.* 給我一兩天時間, 看我能否使她回心轉意。**4** to bring someone or something to someone's house 把某人[某物]帶到...: *If I* *bring it round tomorrow you can check it out.* 如果我明天帶來, 你可以核對一下。

bring back *phr v* [T] **1** [**bring** sth ↔ **back**] to start to use something such as a law, method, or process that was used in the past 使恢復: *They should bring back the death penalty, that's what I think!* 他們應該恢復死刑, 那就是我的想法! | *bringing back the old electric trams* 恢復舊時的有軌電車 **2** [**bring back** sth] to make you remember something 使想起, 使憶起: *The smell of new paper always brings back memories of school.* 新紙張的氣味總是使我回想起上學時的日子。**3** [**bring** sth ↔ **back**] to take something or someone with you when you come back from somewhere 把…帶回來: **bring sb back sth** *Hey, Freddie! Bring me back a few beers would ya!* 嗨, 弗雷迪! 給我帶回幾瓶啤酒好嗎? | **bring sth back (for sb)** *I brought these back from Kenya for the children.* 這些是我從肯尼亞帶回來給孩子們的。**4 it brings us/me back to** used when you want to talk about a particular problem again 這使我們/我再回到〔某問題〕: *This brings us back to the important question of money.* 這使我們又回到錢這一重要問題上。

bring sb/sth ↔ **down** *phr v* [T] **1** to fly an aircraft down to the ground and stop 使〔飛機〕降落: *He brought the Cessna down in a hay-meadow by the river.* 他把賽斯那小型飛機降落在河邊的牧草場上。**2** to move your arm or a weapon, tool etc quickly downwards 放下, 使向下: *He brought down the axe with a thud.* 他砰的一聲用斧子砍了下去。**3** to shoot at a plane, bird or animal so that it falls to the ground 射下, 打落: *A bomber had been brought down by anti-aircraft fire.* 一架轟炸機被防空砲火擊落。**4 bring down the government/president etc** to force the government etc to stop ruling 推翻政府/總統等 **5** to knock someone over in a game of football, RUGBY etc〔運動中〕撞倒: *Klinsmann was brought down on the edge of the area.* 克林斯曼在球場邊緣被撞倒了。

bring sth ↔ **down on/upon** *phr v* [T] *formal* to make something bad happen to someone, especially yourself【正式】使〔壞事〕發生在…, 使…落在〔某人自己〕身上: *His recklessness brought down disaster on the whole family.* 他的魯莽給全家帶來了災難。

bring sth ↔ **forth** *phr v* [T] *formal* to produce something or make it appear【正式】產生; 使出現; 生產, 生育: *a tragic love affair that brought forth only pain* 只能帶來痛苦的愛情悲劇

bring sth ↔ **forward** *phr v* [T] **1** to change an arrangement in the future so that something happens sooner 將…提前: *The meeting's been brought forward to Thursday.* 會議已經提前到星期四舉行。**2 bring forward legislation/plans/policies etc** to officially introduce plans etc for people to discuss 提出法案/計劃/政策等: *The government has brought forward a plan to tackle urban crime.* 政府提出了一項解決城市犯罪的計劃。**3** *technical* to move the total from one set of calculations onto the next page, so that more calculations can be done【術語】把〔賬目〕結轉〔到次頁〕: *The balance brought forward is £21,765.* 結轉到次頁的餘額是21,765英鎊。

bring in *phr v* [T] **1** [**bring in** sth] to earn a particular amount or produce a particular amount of profit 盈利; 賺錢: *The sale of the house only brought in about £45,000.* 房子只賣了約四萬五千英鎊。**2** [**bring** sb ↔ **in**] to allow or invite someone to become involved in a discussion, INVESTIGATION etc 使〔某人〕參加: *It all became very serious and the police were brought in.* 事態變得很嚴重, 警察奉召到場。| *Could I just bring in some members of the audience to get their views?* 我可以邀請一些觀眾來, 聽取他們的意見嗎? **3 bring in a verdict** when a court or JURY brings in a verdict, it says whether someone is guilty or not 宣判, 裁決

bring sb/sth ↔ **off** *phr v* [T] **1** to succeed in doing something very difficult 使成功; 圓滿完成〔困難的事〕: *Together they brought off a daring diamond robbery.* 他們一起終於做成了一樁大膽的鑽石搶劫案。**2** *technical* to help people to leave a ship that is sinking【術語】幫助〔他人〕逃離沉船, 救出〔沉船受害者〕

bring sth ↔ **on** *phr v* [T] **1** to make something bad or unpleasant happen 引起, 導致; 惹來: *a bad cold brought on by going out in the rain* 因冒雨外出導致的重感冒 | *Whatever has brought this on? Have I upset you somehow?* 這到底是怎麼搞的? 我惹你不高興了嗎? **2** to make plants or crops grow faster 加速〔農作物〕生長: *The hot weather has really brought on the roses.* 炎熱的天氣真的使玫瑰生長得更好。

bring sth **on/upon** sb *phr v* [T] to make something bad happen to someone 引起〔尤指不愉快的事〕; 招來, 惹來: *You have brought disaster on the whole village!* 你給整個村子帶來了災難!

bring out *phr v* [T] **1** [**bring** sth/sb ↔ **out**] to make something easier to see, taste, notice etc 使…明顯; 顯示出; 使…得以發揮: *The oregano really brings out the flavour of the meat.* 牛至果然使肉的味道更鮮美。| *Fatherhood seems to have brought out his sense of responsibility.* 當父親後, 他似乎有了責任感。**2 bring out the best/worst in sb** to make someone behave in the best or worst way that they can 把某人最好的方面/最醜陋的一面誘發出來: *Alcohol just brings out the worst in her.* 喝酒把她最醜陋的一面都誘發出來了。**3** [**bring** sth ↔ **out**] to produce a book, record etc to be sold to the public 推出〔書籍、唱片等〕: *The Food Association has brought out a handy guide.* 食品協會推出了一本簡易手冊。**4** [**bring** sb **out**] to make someone feel more confident, happy, and friendly 使更自信, 使不再害羞: *When he went to college it really brought him out.* 上了大學後, 他的自信心增強了。**5** [**bring** sb ↔ **out**] *BrE* to make workers stop working and go on strike (STRIKE[2] (1))【英】使罷工: *They are threatening to bring out the power workers next.* 他們威脅說下一步將煽動電力工人罷工。

bring sb **out in** *phr v* [T] *BrE* if something brings you out in spots, a RASH[2] (1) etc, it makes spots etc appear on your skin【英】使長出〔斑點、疹等〕: *Chocolate always brings me out in spots.* 一吃巧克力, 我總會長丘疹。

bring sb **round** —see 見 **bring sb around/round**

bring sb **through** (sth) *phr v* [T] to help someone to successfully deal with a very difficult event or period of time 使脫離 (險境); 使渡過 (難關): *It was Churchill, above all, who brought us through the war.* 最重要的是, 是丘吉爾使我們安全渡過了戰爭的難關。

bring sb **together** *phr v* [T] to introduce two people to each other or to be the thing that does this 使聯合, 使攜手: *What brought them together was their mutual love of opera.* 是對歌劇的共同愛好使他們兩人走到了一起。

bring sb/sth ↔ **up** *phr v* [T] **1** to mention a subject or start to talk about it 提出〔議題〕: *Why did you have to bring up the subject of money?* 你為甚麼非要提錢這個話題? | *I shall bring up this question at the next meeting.* 我將在下次會議上提出這個問題。—see 見 RAISE[1] (USAGE) **2** [usually passive 一般用被動態] to educate and care for a child until it is grown up 養育, 教養〔孩子〕: *He left her to bring up three young children on her own.* 他留下她獨自撫養三個年幼的孩子。| **be brought up (as) a Catholic/Muslim etc** *I was brought up a Lutheran.* 我是在路德教的教育下長大的。| **be brought up to do sth** *In my day, children were brought up to respect the law.* 在我小時候, 孩子們都接受教育要遵守法律。**3** *BrE* to VOMIT[1] something up from your stomach【英】嘔吐: *He can't eat anything without bringing it up.* 他吃甚麼都會吐。**4 bring sb up short/with a start** to make someone suddenly stop talking or doing something 使某人突然停住: *Her question brought me up short.* 她的問題使我突然停住了。**5 bring sb up on a charge of theft/treason etc** to charge someone with a particular crime 指控某人盜竊/叛國等

USAGE NOTE 用法説明: BRING

WORD CHOICE 詞語辨析: **bring, take, fetch, carry**

Bring means to take someone or something with you to the place where you are now, to your home, or to the place you have been talking about. bring 表示"帶來", 即把某人或某物帶到你所在的地方、你的家裡, 或你所說的地方: *They came to my party and brought me a present.* 他們來參加我的聚會, 並給我帶來一份禮物。| *When I'm next in San Francisco, bring your new boyfriend to see me.* 我下次到三藩市時, 把你新認識的男朋友帶來看我。| *Have you brought your camera?* 你把照相機帶來了嗎? **Bring** is also used in the same way for taking something towards the person being spoken to or talked about. bring 也用於指把某物帶給交談的對象或所談及的人: *Hold on, I'll bring you a towel.* 稍等一下, 我給你拿條毛巾來。| *They brought her everything she needed.* 他們把她需要的東西都帶來了。

Take involves moving in the opposite direction to **bring**. take 是"帶去", 和 bring 的方向相反: *We went to her party and took her a present.* 我們去參加她的聚會, 並帶給她一份禮物。| *When I'm in San Francisco I'll take you to Alcatraz.* 我到了三藩市, 就帶你去阿爾卡特拉斯島。| *Take your camera when you go out* (NOT usually 這裡一般不用 *carry* here). 外出時把照相機帶上。| *Can you take me home now?* 你現在能帶我回家嗎?

Fetch in British English means to go and get something or someone and bring them back. fetch 在英國英語中指去取某物或接某人並將其帶回: *Can you fetch Janice from the station?* 你能去車站把賈尼斯接回來嗎? **Carry** does not give any idea as to the direction of movement, but suggests that you are holding something in your arms or with your hands. carry 意為"帶", 不含任何方向的意思, 而是指用雙臂或用雙手攜帶: *Will you carry the baby/the groceries for me?* 你能幫我抱一下孩子/拿一下食品雜貨嗎?

bringing-up /ˌ·· ˈ·/ *n* [singular] *AmE* the care and training that parents give their children when they are growing up; UPBRINGING【美】養育, 撫養; 教養

brink /brɪŋk; brɪŋk/ *n* **1 be on the brink of** to be almost in a new and very different situation 在…的邊緣, 處在…關頭: *Karl is on the brink of a brilliant acting career.* 卡爾即將開始輝煌的演藝生涯。**2 the brink of** *literary* the edge of a very high place such as a cliff【文】〔峭壁等的〕邊緣

brink·man·ship /ˈbrɪŋkmənˌʃɪp; ˈbrɪŋkmənʃɪp/ *BrE*【英】, **brinks·man·ship** /ˈbrɪŋksmən-; ˈbrɪŋksmən-/ *AmE*【美】*n* [U] a method of gaining political advantage by pretending that you are willing to do something very dangerous 邊緣政策, 冒險政策

brin·y /ˈbraɪnɪ; ˈbraɪni/ *adj* water that is briny contains a lot of salt 鹽水的; 很鹹的

bri·oche /ˈbrioʃ; ˈbriːɒʃ/ *n* [C] a type of sweet bread made with flour, eggs, and butter 黃油蛋糕卷

bri·quette /brɪˈkɛt; brɪˈket/ *n* [C] a block of pressed coal dust, to burn in a fire or BARBEQUE 煤磚, 煤餅

brisk /brɪsk; brɪsk/ *adj* **1** quick and full of energy 輕快的; 活潑的; 精力充沛的: *a brisk walk* 輕快的步行 **2** quick, practical and showing that you want to get things done quickly 敏捷的, 反應快的: *She spoke in a brisk tone.* 她用爽快的語氣說話。**3** trade or business that is brisk is very busy, with a lot of products being sold〔生意〕興隆的 **4** weather that is brisk is cold and clear〔天氣〕清新涼爽的 —**briskly** *adv* —**briskness** *n* [U]

bris·ket /ˈbrɪskɪt; ˈbrɪskɪ̵t/ *n* [U] meat from an animal's chest, especially a cow〔動物, 尤指牛的〕胸肉

bris·tle[1] /ˈbrɪsl; ˈbrɪsəl/ *n* [C,U] **1** short stiff hair that feels rough 短而硬的毛髮; 鬍茬: *His chin was covered with bristles.* 他滿下巴都是鬍茬。**2** a short stiff hair, wire etc that forms part of a brush〔製刷子用的〕鬃毛 —see picture at 參見 BRUSH[1] 圖

bristle[2] *v* [I] **1** to behave in a way that shows you are very angry or annoyed 顯得憤怒: **[+with]** *bristling with rage* 怒髮衝冠 | **[+at]** *He bristled at the mere suggestion.* 只要稍微提一下, 他就怒不可遏。**2** if an animal's hair bristles, it stands up stiffly because the animal is afraid or angry〔動物因驚慌或憤怒而毛髮〕豎立; 硬挺

bristle with sth *phr v* [T] to have a lot of something or be full of something 到處都是…; …重重, …叢生: *a battleship bristling with guns* 佈滿了大砲的戰艦

bris·tly /ˈbrɪslɪ; ˈbrɪsli/ *adj* **1** bristly hair is short and stiff〔毛髮〕短而硬的 **2** a bristly part of your body has short stiff hairs on it〔身體部位〕長滿硬毛的: *a bristly chin* 鬍子拉茬的下巴

Brit /brɪt; brɪt/ *n* [C] *informal* someone from Britain【非正式】英國人

britch·es /ˈbrɪtʃɪz; ˈbrɪtʃɪ̵z/ *n* [plural] *AmE* trousers【美】褲子

Brit·ish /ˈbrɪtɪʃ; ˈbrɪtɪʃ/ *adj* **1** from or connected with Great Britain 不列顛的, 英國的: *the British government* 英國政府 **2 the British** people from Britain 英國人

British Broad·cast·ing Cor·po·ra·tion /ˌ·· ˈ··· ··ˌ··/ *n* the BBC 英國廣播公司

Brit·ish·er /ˈbrɪtɪʃɚ; ˈbrɪtɪʃə/ *n* [C] *AmE* someone from Britain【美】英國人

British Isles /ˌ·· ˈ·/ *n* the group of islands that includes Great Britain, Ireland, and the smaller islands around them 不列顛羣島

British Sum·mer Time /ˌ·· ˈ·· ·/ *n* [U] the time one hour ahead of Greenwich Mean Time, that is used in Britain from late March to late October 英國夏令時間〔每年從三月底至十月底比格林尼治標準時間提前一小時〕—compare 比較 DAYLIGHT SAVING TIME

Brit·on /ˈbrɪtn̩; ˈbrɪtn/ *n* [C] *formal* someone from Britain【正式】英國人: *the ancient Britons* 古代英國人

brit·tle /ˈbrɪtl̩; ˈbrɪtl/ *adj* **1** hard but easily broken 脆的, 易碎的: *The branches were dry and brittle.* 那些樹枝乾而易斷。**2** a system, relationship etc that is brittle is easily damaged or destroyed 不牢固的: *a very brittle friendship* 很不牢固的友誼 **3** showing no warm feelings 冷淡的: *a brittle laugh* 冷笑

bro /bro; brəʊ/ *n* [C] *spoken*【口】**1** your brother 兄弟; 弟弟; 哥哥 **2** *AmE* a way of greeting a friend【美】兄弟, 哥兒們〔招呼用語〕

broach /brotʃ; brəʊtʃ/ *v* [T] **1 broach the subject/question/matter etc** to mention a subject that may be embarrassing, unpleasant or cause an argument 提及話題/問題/事情等〔尤指尷尬或會引起爭論的話題〕: *It's often difficult to broach the subject of sex.* 性的話題通常不太好開口。**2** to open a bottle or BARREL[1] (1) containing wine, beer etc 開啟〔酒瓶、桶等〕

broad[1] /brɔd; brɔːd/ *adj*

1 ▶WIDE 寬的◀ a road, river, or part of someone's body etc that is broad is wide 寬的, 闊的: *We went along a broad carpeted passage.* 我們沿着一條鋪着地毯的寬闊走廊走了過去。| *He was six feet tall, with broad shoulders and slender hips.* 他身高六英尺, 寬肩瘦臀。| **6 feet/3 metres etc broad** *The track was three metres broad.* 車道有三米寬。—compare 比較 NARROW

2 ▶INCLUDING A LOT 包括很多◀ including many different kinds of things 廣博的; 豐富的; 廣泛的: **broad range/spectrum of** *She has a very broad range of interests.* 她興趣非常廣泛。| **broad category/field/area etc** *In general, the paintings fall into two broad categories.* 一般而言, 繪畫分為兩大類。

3 ▶GENERAL 總的◀ concerning the main ideas or parts of something rather than all the details 粗略的, 概括的, 一般的; 廣義的: **broad sense/term/definition etc** *This is education in the broadest sense of the word.* 這是從最廣義上說的教育。| **broad consensus/agreement etc** *All the members were in broad agreement.* 所有成員大

體上達成了共識。
4 ►LARGE AREA 大面積◄ covering a large area of land or water 遼闊的, 廣大的, 廣袤的: *They came to a broad expanse of water.* 他們來到一片廣闊的水域。
5 broad grin/smile a big smile which clearly shows that you are happy 開懷大笑: *"A great win," he said with a broad grin.* "一次巨大的勝利。"他大笑着說。
6 in broad daylight if something such as a crime happens in broad daylight, it happens in the daytime when you would expect someone to prevent it 大白天; 光天化日: *The attack happened in broad daylight, in one of the busiest parts of town.* 襲擊事件發生在大白天, 是在城鎮最繁華的地段。
7 ►WAY OF SPEAKING 說話方式◄ a broad ACCENT[1] (1) clearly shows where you come from 口音重的: *a broad Scottish accent* 濃重的蘇格蘭口音
8 broad hint/sarcasm a HINT (=suggestion) etc that is very clear and easy to understand 明白的暗示/諷刺: *dropping broad hints about what she wanted for Christmas* 明白地暗示出她聖誕節想要甚麼
9 broad humour/wit etc humour etc that is slightly rude 略有些粗俗的幽默/機智等
10 it's as broad as it's long *spoken* used to say that it does not matter which of two things you choose, because neither is clearly better【口】反正都一樣; 半斤八兩; 不分高低
11 have a broad back to be easily able to deal with hardwork, problems etc 輕鬆應對困難
12 broad in the beam *informal* having large or fat HIPS【非正式】屁股肥大的
13 a broad church an organisation that contains a wide range of opinions 容納多種觀點的組織: *The Labour Party has to be a broad church.* 工黨必須是一個允許多種見解的政黨。—see also 另見 BREADTH

broad² *n* **1 the Broads** used in the names of some wide parts of rivers in Eastern England〔尤指英格蘭東部由河川變寬而成的〕湖沼地區: *the Norfolk Broads* 諾福克郡湖沼地區 **2** [C] *AmE spoken* an offensive way of referring to a woman【美口】女人, 娘兒們〔冒犯性用語〕

broad·band /ˈ· ˌ·/ *n* [U] *technical* a system of sending radio signals which allows several messages to be sent at the same time【術語】〔無線電〕寬頻帶, 寬波段

broad bean /ˌ· ˈ·/ *n* [C] *BrE* a round pale green bean【英】蠶豆; FAVA BEAN *AmE*【美】—see picture on page A9 參見 A9 頁圖

broad·brush, broad-brush /ˈbrɔdˌbrʌʃ; ˈbrɔːdbrʌʃ/ *adj* dealing only with the main parts of something, and not with the details 粗略的, 概括的: *a broadbrush strategy for increasing sales* 提高銷量的綱要性策略

broad·cast¹ /ˈbrɔdˌkæst; ˈbrɔːdkɑːst/ *n* [C] a programme on the radio or on television〔電台或電視的〕廣播節目; 播送節目: *a radio news broadcast* 電台新聞廣播 | **live broadcast** (=a programme that you see or hear at the same time as the events are happening) 實況轉播

broadcast² *v past tense and past participle* **broadcast 1** [I,T] to send out radio or television programmes 廣播; 播送: *The interview was broadcast live across Europe.* 這次訪問向歐洲各地現場直播。**2** [T] to tell something to a lot of people 使廣為傳播, 散佈: *There was no need to broadcast the fact that he lost his job.* 沒有必要大肆宣揚他丟了工作這件事。

broad·cast·er /ˈbrɔdˌkæstɚ; ˈbrɔːdkɑːstə/ *n* [C] someone who speaks on radio or television programmes 播音員: *a well-known journalist and broadcaster* 著名的新聞記者和播音員

broad·cast·ing /ˈbrɔdˌkæstɪŋ; ˈbrɔːdkɑːstɪŋ/ *n* [U] the business of making television and radio programmes〔電視或電台的〕廣播工作; 廣播事業: *a career in broadcasting* 從事廣播事業

broad·en /ˈbrɔdn̩; ˈbrɔːdn/ *v* **1** [T] to increase something such as knowledge, experience, or your range of activities 使擴大, 使增加: *Broaden your knowledge of English with this book.* 看這本書來增進你的英語知識。| **broaden your horizons** (=increase your activities and opportunities) 開闊視野 **2** [I,T] to make something broader or to become broader 加寬; (使) 變寬: *The road broadened into an imposing avenue.* 這條路被拓寬成一條壯觀的大街。**3 broaden your mind** if an experience broadens your mind, it makes it easier for you to accept other people's beliefs, ways of doing things etc 開闊你的胸襟, 增長你的見識: *Travel broadens the mind.* 旅遊使人開闊胸襟。
broaden out *phr v* [I] to gradually become wider 逐漸變寬: *The river broadens out at this point.* 河流在這裡開始變寬。

broad gauge /ˈ· ·/ *n* [C] a size of railway track that is wider than the normal size〔鐵路的〕寬軌

broad jump /ˈ· ·/ *n* [U] *AmE* a sport in which you try to jump as far as possible; LONG JUMP【美】跳遠

broad·loom /ˈbrɔdˌlum; ˈbrɔːdluːm/ *n* [U] *technical* CARPET[1] (1) that is woven in a single wide piece【術語】寬幅地毯

broad·ly /ˈbrɔdlɪ; ˈbrɔːdli/ *adv* **1** in a general way, covering the main facts rather than details 大體上說來, 總體上來講: *She knows broadly what to expect.* 她大致知道等待她的將會是甚麼結果。| **broadly speaking** *There are, broadly speaking, four types of champagne.* 香檳酒大致上分為四種。| **broadly similar** *We reached broadly similar conclusions.* 我們得出大致相同的結論。**2 smile/grin broadly** to have a big smile on your face which clearly shows that you are happy or amused 開懷地笑 **3 broadly based** including a range of different things or subjects 多方面的, 全面的: *a broadly based approach to education* 全方位的教育方法

broad·mind·ed, broad-minded /ˈbrɔdˈmaɪndɪd; ˌbrɔːdˈmaɪndɪd◂/ *adj* willing to respect opinions or behaviour that are very different from your own 氣量大的, 心胸開闊的, 能容納不同意見的: *Her parents were broadminded, tolerant and liberal.* 她的父母心胸開闊, 寬容而開明。—opposite 反義詞 NARROW-MINDED —compare 比較 SMALL-MINDED —**broad-mindedly** *adv* —**broad-mindedness** *n* [U]

broad·sheet /ˈbrɔdˌʃit; ˈbrɔːdʃiːt/ *n* [C] a newspaper printed on large sheets of paper, especially a serious newspaper that people respect〔尤指嚴肅的〕寬幅報紙—compare 比較 TABLOID

broad·side¹ /ˈbrɔdˌsaɪd; ˈbrɔːdsaɪd/ *n* [C] **1** a strong criticism of someone or something especially a written one〔尤指書面的〕猛烈抨擊: *Can the government survive this latest broadside from its own supporters?* 政府能否頂住其支持者最近的猛烈抨擊? **2** an attack in which all the guns on one side of a ship are fired at the same time 舷砲齊射

broadside² *AmE*【美】, **broadside on** *BrE*【英】*adv* with the longest side facing something 側向地: [+to] *I brought the boat in broadside to the beach.* 我把船划進來, 側面對着海灘。

broadside³ *v* [T] *especially AmE* to crash into the side of another vehicle【尤美】撞上〔另一輛車的〕側面

broad·sword /ˈbrɔdˌsɔrd; ˈbrɔːdsɔːd/ *n* [C] a heavy sword with a broad flat blade 大砍刀; 闊劍

bro·cade /broˈked; brəˈkeɪd/ *n* [U] thick heavy decorative cloth which has a pattern of gold and silver threads 織錦, 錦緞: *brocade curtains* 錦緞窗簾 —**brocaded** *adj*

broc·co·li /ˈbrɑkəlɪ; ˈbrɒkəli/ *n* [U] a green vegetable that has short branch-like stems 花莖甘藍; 花椰菜, 西蘭花菜 —see picture on page A9 參見 A9 頁圖

bro·chure /broˈʃur; ˈbrəʊʃə/ *n* [C] a thin book giving information or advertising something 小冊子: *a glossy holiday brochure* 印刷精美的度假宣傳小冊子

brogue /brog; brəʊg/ *n* [C] **1** a thick strong leather shoe with a pattern in the leather 粗革厚底皮鞋; 拷花皮鞋 —see picture at 參見 SHOE[1] 圖 **2** [usually singular 一般用單數] an ACCENT (=way of pronouncing words), especially the one used by the Irish or Scottish people〔尤指愛爾

蘭人或蘇格蘭人說英語時的〕土腔

broil /brɔɪl; brɔɪl/ *v* [T] *AmE* to cook something under direct heat, or over a flame on a BARBECUE[1] (1)【美】烤; 焙; 炙; GRILL[1] (1) *BrE*【英】: *broiled chicken* 烤雞

broil·er /ˋbrɔɪlɚ; ˈbrɔɪlə/ *n* [C] **1** *AmE* a special area of a STOVE[1] (1) used for cooking food under direct heat【美】烤架, 烘烤爐; GRILL[2] (1) *BrE*【英】**2** *AmE* a very hot day【美】大熱天 **3** a broiler chicken〔適於燒烤的〕嫩雞

broiler chick·en /ˈ·· ˌ··/ *n* [C] a chicken that is suitable to be cooked by broiling〔適於燒烤的〕嫩雞

broil·ing /ˋbrɔɪlɪŋ; ˈbrɔɪlɪŋ/ *adj AmE* broiling weather, sun etc makes you feel extremely hot【美】酷熱的, 灼熱的: *a day in the broiling sun* 酷熱難耐的一天

broke[1] /brok; brəʊk/ the past tense of BREAK[1]

broke[2] *adj* [not before noun 不用於名詞前] **1** having no money 破產的, 身無分文的: *I'm fed up with being broke all the time.* 我已受夠了一文不名的日子。| **flat broke** *AmE*【美】, **stony broke** *BrE*【英】(=completely broke) 完全破產的, 一文不名的 **2 go broke** if a company or business goes broke, it can no longer operate because it has no money 破產: *A lot of small businesses went broke in the recession.* 在經濟衰退中, 許多小型企業都破產了。**3 go for broke** *informal* to take big risks trying to achieve something【非正式】孤注一擲: *Why not go for broke and set up your own business?* 你為何不冒個險自己開一家店呢?

bro·ken[1] /ˋbrokən; ˈbrəʊkən/ the past participle of BREAK[1]

S3 W3 **broken[2]** *adj*

1 ▶PIECE OF EQUIPMENT 設備◀ not working properly 壞的, 不能使用的: *The vacuum cleaner's broken again.* 吸塵器又壞了。| **get broken** (=become broken) 出毛病, 出故障 *Somehow the heaters got broken.* 不知甚麼原因, 取暖器壞了。

2 ▶OBJECT 物體◀ in small pieces because it has been hit, dropped etc 破的; 破碎的; 損壞的; 斷裂的: *Mind the broken glass.* 當心碎玻璃。| **get broken** (=become broken) 損壞 *It got broken in the mail.* 這東西在郵寄過程中損壞了。—see picture on page A18 參見A18頁圖

3 ▶BONE 骨頭◀ cracked because you have had an accident 折斷的: *a broken leg* 摔斷了的腿

4 ▶INTERRUPTED 斷續的◀ interrupted and not continuous 被打斷的; 斷斷續續的: *a broken white line* 白色的虛線 | **broken sleep** (=with interruptions) 時斷時續的睡眠 *sixteen nights of broken sleep because of the baby* 由於嬰兒吵, 十六個夜晚只能斷斷續續地睡點覺

5 ▶PERSON 人◀ extremely mentally or physically weak because you have suffered a lot 衰弱的; 沮喪的: *He returned a broken man.* 他回來時很沮喪。

6 broken agreement/promise etc a promise etc in which someone did not do what they promised 未被遵守的協議/承諾等

7 broken English/French etc English, French etc that is spoken very slowly by someone who only knows a little of the language 蹩腳[不流利]的英語/法語等

8 broken home a family that no longer lives together because the parents have divorced (DIVORCE[2] (1))〔夫妻離異造成的〕破裂家庭

9 broken marriage a marriage that has ended because the husband and wife do not live together any more 破裂的婚姻

10 a broken heart a feeling of extreme sadness, especially because someone you love has died or left you 破碎的心

broken-heart·ed /ˌ·· ˈ··◂/ *adj* extremely sad, especially because someone you love has died or left you 傷心的, 心碎的: *He dumped her for no apparent reason, and left her broken-hearted.* 他莫名其妙地拋棄了她, 使她傷心欲絕。—**broken-heartedly** *adv*

bro·ker[1] /ˋbrokɚ; ˈbrəʊkə/ *n* [C] someone who buys and sells shares (SHARE[2] (5)) in a company, INSURANCE (1), foreign money etc for other people 經紀人, 掮客; 中間人, 代理商: *an insurance broker* 保險經紀人

broker[2] *v* [T] **broker a deal/settlement/treaty etc** to arrange the details of a deal etc so that everyone can agree to it 就交易/協議/條約等進行調停

bro·ker·age /ˋbrokərɪdʒ; ˈbrəʊkərɪdʒ/ *n* [U] **1** the business of being a broker 經紀業; 掮客業務 **2** the amount of money a broker charges 佣金, 手續費, 經紀費 **3 brokerage house/firm** a company of brokers, or the place where they work 經紀行

brol·ly /ˋbrɑlɪ; ˈbrɒli/ *n* [C] *BrE informal* an UMBRELLA (1)【英, 非正式】雨傘

bro·mide /ˋbromaɪd; ˈbrəʊmaɪd/ *n* **1** [C,U] a chemical compound, sometimes used in medicine to make people feel calm 溴化物; 溴化劑 **2** [C] *formal* a statement which is intended to make someone less angry but which is not effective【正式】老生常談, 陳詞濫調

bronc /brɑŋk; brɒŋk/ *n* [C] *informal* a BRONCO【非正式】野馬

bron·chi·al /ˋbrɑŋkɪəl; ˈbrɒŋkiəl/ *adj* affecting the bronchial tubes 支氣管的: *a bronchial infection* 支氣管感染

bronchial tube /ˈ··· ˌ·/ *n* [C usually singular 一般用單數] one of the small tubes that take air into your lungs 支氣管 —see picture at 參見 RESPIRATORY 圖

bron·chi·tis /brɑŋˋkaɪtɪs; brɒŋˈkaɪtɪ̢s/ *n* [C] an illness which affects your bronchial tubes and makes you cough 支氣管炎 —**bronchitic** /-ˋkɪtɪk; -ˈkɪtɪk/ *adj*

bron·co /ˋbrɑŋko; ˈbrɒŋkəʊ/ *n* [C] a wild horse from the western US〔美國西部的〕野馬: *a bucking bronco* 跳起的野馬

bron·to·sau·rus /ˌbrɑntəˋsɔrəs; ˌbrɒntəˈsɔːrəs/ *n* [C] a large DINOSAUR with a small head and a long neck 雷龍〔以植物為食的一種恐龍〕

Bronx cheer /ˌbrɑŋks ˋtʃɪr; ˌbrɒŋks ˈtʃɪə/ *n* [C] *AmE* a rude sound you make by putting your tongue between your lips and blowing【美】譏笑聲, 噓聲; 喝倒采; RASPBERRY (2) *BrE*【英】

bronze[1] /brɑnz; brɒnz/ *n* **1** [U] a hard metal that is made of a mixture of COPPER (1) and TIN[1] (1) 青銅, 古銅 **2** [U] the dark red-brown colour of bronze 青銅色, 古銅色 **3** [C] a work of art such as a STATUE (=model of a person), made of bronze 青銅器; 青銅藝術品 **4** [C] a BRONZE MEDAL 銅(獎)牌

bronze[2] *adj* **1** made of bronze 青銅製的: *a bronze statuette by Degas*〔法國畫家〕德加塑造的小青銅雕像 **2** having the red-brown colour of bronze 青銅色的, 古銅色的

Bronze Age /ˈ· ·/ *n* [singular] the time, between about 6,000 and 4,000 years ago, when bronze was used for making tools, weapons etc 青銅器時代〔距今約4,000至6,000年〕—compare 比較 IRON AGE, STONE AGE

bronzed /brɑnzd; brɒnzd/ *adj* having skin that is attractively brown because you have been in the sun〔皮膚因日曬而呈〕古銅色的

bronze med·al /ˌ· ˈ··/ *n* [C] a MEDAL made of bronze given to the person who comes third in a race or competition 銅牌, 銅(獎)章 —**bronze medallist** *n* [C] —see also 另見 GOLD MEDAL, SILVER MEDAL

brooch /brotʃ; brəʊtʃ/ *n* [C] a piece of jewellery that you fasten to your clothes 胸針, 飾針; PIN[1] (2) *AmE*【美】—see picture at 參見 PIN[1] 圖

brood[1] /brud; bruːd/ *v* [I] **1** to keep thinking for a long time about something that you are worried, angry, or upset about 沉思; 憂思; 深思: *After the argument Simon sat in his room, brooding.* 爭吵之後, 西蒙坐在房間裡沉思。| **[+over/about/on]** *There's no point brooding over it – she's gone.* 老是想這件事也沒用, 反正她已經走了。**2** if a bird broods, it sits on its eggs to make the young birds break out 孵卵, 抱窩

brood[2] *n* [C] **1** a family of young birds all born at the same time〔尤指雛鳥的〕一窩 **2** *humorous* a family with a lot of children【幽默】一家的孩子們: *Mary has a whole brood of grandchildren.* 瑪麗有一大幫孫兒女。

brood·er /ˋbrudɚ; ˈbruːdə/ *n* [C] **1** a heated structure for young birds to live in 孵化器 **2** someone who broods

a lot 沉思的人

brood·ing /ˋbrudɪŋ; ˈbruːdɪŋ/ *adj* mysterious and threatening 神祕莫測的: *a brooding menacing atmosphere* 神祕而不祥的氣氛 —**broodingly** *adv*

brood·y /ˋbrudɪ; ˈbruːdi/ *adj* **1** silent because you are thinking or worrying about something 悶悶不樂的, 抑鬱的; 沉思的: *Damian's been really broody lately.* 達米安近來一直悶悶不樂。**2** *informal* wishing that you had a baby【非正式】想要孩子的: *I get broody when I see baby clothes in shop windows.* 我一看到櫥窗裡的嬰兒服裝, 就想自己也有個孩子。**3** if a female bird is broody, it wants to lay eggs or to sit on them to make the young birds break out〔雌鳥〕想孵卵的, 要抱窩的 —**broodily** *adv* —**broodiness** *n* [U]

brook¹ /bruk; brʊk/ *n* [C] a small stream 小河, 溪流: *a babbling brook* 潺潺的小溪

brook² *v* **not brook sth/brook no sth** *formal* to not allow or accept something【正式】不容忍…: *He would brook no interruptions from subordinates.* 他不容忍自己的下屬打岔。

broom /brum; bruːm/ *n* **1** [C] a large brush with a long handle, used for sweeping floors 掃帚 —see picture at 參見 BRUSH¹ 圖 **2** [U] a large bush with small yellow flowers that grows on unused land 金雀花

broom·stick /ˋbrumˌstɪk; ˈbruːmˌstɪk/ *n* [C] a broom with a long handle and small sticks tied at one end that a WITCH (1) is supposed to fly on in children's stories〔童話中女巫騎坐的〕長掃帚柄

Bros the written abbreviation of 縮寫= Brothers, used in the names of companies 兄弟公司〔用於公司名稱〕: *Jones Bros., tailors* 瓊斯兄弟服裝公司

broth /brɔθ; brɒθ/ *n* [U] thick soup with meat, rice, or vegetables 肉湯; 米湯; 菜湯: *chicken broth* 雞湯 —see also 另見 SCOTCH BROTH

broth·el /ˋbrɑθəl; ˈbrɒθəl/ *n* [C] a house where men pay to have sex with PROSTITUTES 妓院

1 1 **broth·er¹** /ˋbrʌðɚ; ˈbrʌðə/ *n* [C] **1** a male who has the same parents as you (同胞) 兄弟; 哥; 弟: *This is a picture of my brother Andrew.* 這是我弟弟安德魯的照片。| **elder/older/younger/little etc brother** *My younger brother is a doctor.* 我弟弟是一名醫生。—see picture at 參見 FAMILY 圖 **2** a male member of a group with the same interests, religion, profession etc as you 弟兄; (男性) 同胞; 同仁; 同行; 會友: *Brothers, we must stand together to fight the inequalities of the system!* 弟兄們, 我們必須為反對不平等的制度而並肩戰鬥! **3** *plural* **brothers** or **brethren** a male member of a religious group, especially a MONK〔同教會的男性〕教友, 主內兄弟; 僧侶; 修士: *Brother Justin* 賈斯廷修士 **4** *AmE* a member of a FRATERNITY (=a club of male university students)【美】〔男學生的〕大學生聯誼會, 兄弟會 **5 brothers in arms** soldiers who have fought together in a war 戰友 —see also 另見 BIG BROTHER, BLOOD BROTHER

brother² *interjection AmE* used to express annoyance or surprise【美】哇! 呀! 哎!〔表示不耐煩、驚訝〕: *Oh brother! Did he really say that?* 啊! 他真那樣說的嗎?

broth·er·hood /ˋbrʌðɚˌhud; ˈbrʌðəhʊd/ *n* **1** [U] a feeling of friendship between people 手足情, 同胞之愛: *peace and brotherhood among men* 男人間的親睦關係 **2** [C] an organization or society formed for a particular purpose, especially a religious one〔宗教的〕兄弟會: *the Franciscan brotherhood* 聖方濟各兄弟會 **3** [C] *old-fashioned* a union of workers in a particular trade【過時】同業工會 **4** [U] the relationship between brothers 兄弟關係, 手足之情

brother-in-law /ˈ·· · ˌ·/ *n plural* **brothers-in-law** *or* **brother-in-laws** [C] **1** the brother of your husband or wife 內兄; 內弟; 大伯; 小叔 **2** the husband of your sister 姐夫; 妹夫 **3** the husband of your husband or wife's sister 連襟〔配偶之姐妹的丈夫〕—see picture at 參見 FAMILY 圖

broth·er·ly /ˋbrʌðɚlɪ; ˈbrʌðəli/ *adj* showing the helpfulness, love, loyalty etc that you would expect a brother to show 情同手足的, 兄弟的, 兄弟般的: *brotherly love* 兄弟之愛 | *He offered me some brotherly advice.* 他給我提了一些兄弟般的勸告。—**brotherliness** *n* [U]

brough·am /ˋbruəm; ˈbruːəm/ *n* [C] a light carriage used in the past which had four wheels and a roof and was pulled by a horse〔古時由一匹馬拉的〕四輪箱型馬車

brought /brɔt; brɔːt/ the past tense and past participle of BRING

brou·ha·ha /bruˋhɑhɑ; ˈbruːhɑːhɑː/ *n* [U] *old-fashioned* unnecessary noise and activity; COMMOTION【過時】喧鬧, 嘈雜; 騷亂

brow /brau; braʊ/ *n* **1** [C] the part of your face above your eyes and below your hair; FOREHEAD 額: **mop/wipe your brow** (=dry your brow with your hand or a piece of cloth when you are hot or nervous) 擦額頭 (上的汗) | **crease/wrinkle/knit etc your brow** (=tighten the skin on your brow, making lines appear when you are angry or thinking very hard) 緊鎖眉頭 *"I don't understand," he said, wrinkling his brow.* "我不懂。"他緊鎖眉頭說。**2** an EYEBROW 眉, 眉毛 **3 the brow of the hill** *especially BrE* the top part of a slope or hill【尤英】斜坡的上部

brow·beat /ˋbrauˌbit; ˈbraʊbiːt/ *v past tense* **browbeat** *past participle* **browbeaten** /-ˌbitn̩; -biːtn/ [T+**into**] to make someone do something by continuously asking them to, especially in an unpleasant threatening way〔聲色俱厲地〕威逼, 恫嚇: *The witness was being browbeaten under cross-examination.* 證人被盤問時受到威逼。

brown¹ /braun; braʊn/ *adj* **1** having the colour of earth, wood, or coffee 褐色的; 棕色的: *I'd like a pair of dark brown shoes please.* 我想買一雙深棕色的皮鞋。| *brown bread* 黑麵包 **2** having skin that has been turned brown by the sun〔皮膚被太陽曬得〕黝黑的: *You're very brown – have you been on vacation?* 你皮膚曬得很黑, 是不是去度假了? | **brown as a berry** (=very brown)〔皮膚〕黝黑的 *She came back as brown as a berry.* 她回來時皮膚曬得黝黑。 2 2

brown² *n* [C,U] the colour of earth, wood, or coffee 褐色; 棕色: *the different browns and greens of the landscape* 深淺不同的褐色及綠色的景觀 —see picture on page A5 參見 A5 頁圖

brown³ *v* [I,T] **1** to heat food so that it turns brown or to become brown in this way by being heated (使)〔食品〕燒成褐色: *First brown the meat in a frying pan.* 首先將肉在油鍋裡炸成褐色。**2** to become brown because of the sun's heat or to make something brown in this way〔太陽〕(使) 變成褐[棕]色: *The children's faces were browned by the sun.* 孩子們的臉被太陽曬得黑黝黝的。**3 browned off** *BrE informal* annoyed and bored【英, 非正式】厭煩的, 厭倦的

brown-bag /ˈ· ·/ *v* [I] *AmE*【美】**1** to bring your LUNCH to work, usually in a small brown paper bag 自帶〔牛皮紙袋裝的〕午餐上班: *I'm brown-bagging it this week.* 這週我要自己帶午餐上班。**2** to bring your own alcohol to a restaurant which does not serve alcohol 自帶酒上餐館〔把酒帶到不供應酒的餐館〕—**brown-bagging** *n* [U]

brown goods /ˈ· ·/ *n* [plural] *BrE* electrical goods bought to provide entertainment at home, such as televisions and computers【英】棕色商品〔指電視機、電腦等〕—compare 比較 WHITE GOODS

Brown·ie /ˋbraunɪ; ˈbraʊni/ also 又作 **Brownie Guide** /ˈ·· ·/ *n* **1 the Brownies** the part of the Girl Guides Association that is for younger girls 幼年女童子軍 **2** [C] a member of this organization 幼年女童子軍成員

brownie *n* [C] **1** a thick flat American chocolate cake 果仁巧克力蛋糕: *fudge brownies* 乳脂果仁巧克力蛋糕 **2 get/earn brownie points** *informal* if you do something to get brownie points you want people to praise you【非正式】想得到別人的表揚

brown-nose /ˈ· ·/ *v* [I,T] *informal* to try to make your manager, teacher etc like you by being very nice to them【非正式】拍馬屁, 巴結: *You're not going to get that promotion just by brown-nosing!* 你單靠拍馬屁是不會升職

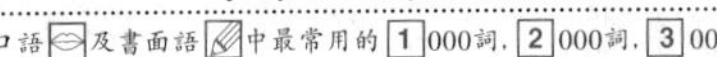

的！—**brown-nose** *n* [C]

brown out /ˈ· ·/ *n* [C] *AmE* a power failure affecting some but not all the electrical lights in an area【美】部分停電

brown rice /,· ˈ·/ *n* [U] rice which still has its outer layer 糙米

brown·stone /ˈbraun,ston; ˈbraʊnstəʊn/ *n* **1** [U] a type of reddish-brown stone, often used for building〔建築用的〕褐（砂）石 **2** [C] a house in the US with a front made of this stone, common in New York City 褐（砂）石房屋〔多見於紐約市〕: *office buildings side by side with the more elegant brownstones* 與精緻的褐（砂）石房子緊挨着的辦公大樓

browse /brauz; braʊz/ *v* [I] **1** to look through the pages of a book, magazine etc without a particular purpose, just reading the most interesting parts 隨意翻閱，瀏覽〔書刊等〕: **[+through]** *I was browsing through a newspaper when I spotted your name.* 我在翻閱一張報紙時突然發現了你的名字。**2** to look at the goods in a shop without wanting to buy any particular thing 瀏覽商品: *Can I help you, madam, or are you just browsing?* 夫人，您想買甚麼，還是隨便看看？**3** **[+on]** if a goat, DEER etc browses, it eats plants〔牲畜〕吃草 **4** to search computer material 搜索電腦資料，瀏覽: *a fast effective browsing tool* 快速高效的瀏覽工具

bruise¹ /bruz; bruːz/ *n* [C] **1** a purple or brown mark on your skin that you get because you have fallen, been hit etc 青瘀，傷痕，擦傷 **2** a mark on a piece of fruit that spoils its appearance〔水果的〕擦痕，碰傷

bruise² *v* [I,T] **1** if part of your body bruises or if you bruise it, it gets hit or hurt and a bruise appears 使碰傷，擦傷，使成淤傷: *She fell off her bike and bruised her knee.* 她從腳踏車上摔下來，擦傷了膝蓋。**2** if a piece of fruit bruises or is bruised, it gets a bruise by being hit, dropped etc（使）〔水果〕碰傷，擦傷 —**bruising** *n* [U]: *severe bruising to the face and head* 面部和頭部嚴重擦傷

bruised /bruzd; bruːzd/ *adj* **1** **bruised ribs/knee/elbow etc** a part of your body with a bruise on it 挫傷的肋骨/膝蓋/胳膊肘等 **2** upset or emotionally harmed by an experience 受傷害的；受挫的

bruis·er /ˈbruzə; ˈbruːzə/ *n* [C] *informal* a big strong rough man【非正式】彪形大漢: *Two ugly bruisers barred the door.* 兩個醜陋的彪形大漢擋住了門。

bruit /brut; bruːt/ *v*

bruit sth ↔ **abroad** *phr v* [T] *formal* to tell a lot of people about something【正式】傳播，散佈

brunch /brʌntʃ; brʌntʃ/ *n* [C,U] a meal eaten in the late morning, as a combination of breakfast and LUNCH 早午餐〔早餐和午餐併為一頓吃〕

bru·nette /bruˈnɛt; bruːˈnet/ *n* [C] a woman with dark brown hair 深褐色頭髮的女子: *a slim brunette* 長着深褐色頭髮的苗條女子

brunt /brʌnt; brʌnt/ *n* **bear/take the brunt of sth** to receive the worst part of an attack, criticism etc 受到最嚴厲的批評[攻擊]; 首當其衝: *The southern part of the town bore the brunt of the attack.* 城市的南部受到最嚴重的襲擊。

3 **brush¹** /brʌʃ; brʌʃ/ *n*

1 ►FOR CLEANING 用於清掃◄ [C] an object that you use for cleaning, painting etc, made with a lot of hairs, bristles (BRISTLE¹ (2)), or thin pieces of plastic fixed to a handle 刷子；毛刷；畫筆；毛筆: *a hairbrush* 髮刷 | *Get a brush and sweep up all that rubbish.* 拿把刷子來，把這些垃圾都清除掉。

2 [singular] a movement which brushes something, to remove dirt, make something smooth, tidy etc〔動作〕刷[梳，擦]，拂拭: *I'll just give my hair a quick brush.* 我就很快梳一下頭髮。

3 ►TOUCH 接觸◄ [singular] a quick light touch, made by chance when two things or people pass each other 輕觸，輕擦: *the brush of her silk dress as she walked past* 她走過時，她的綢衣輕輕地擦過

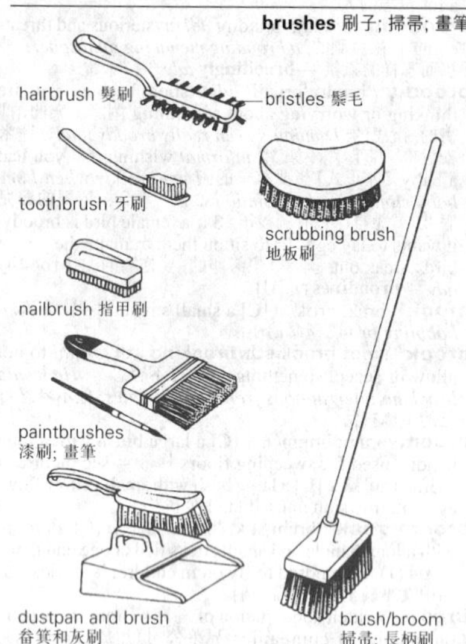

4 ►BUSHES/TREES 灌木/樹◄ [U] **a)** *AmE* small bushes and trees covering an open area of land【美】灌木林，雜樹叢 **b)** branches which have broken off bushes and trees 折斷的樹枝；柴枝

5 a brush with death/a brush with the law etc an occasion when something bad almost happens to you, but you just manage to avoid it 差一點送命/犯法等

6 ►TAIL 尾巴◄ [C] the tail of a FOX¹ (1) 狐狸尾巴 —see also 另見 **daft as a brush** (DAFT (1))

brush² *v* **1** [T] to clean something or make something smooth and tidy using a brush〔用刷子〕刷，掃，拂拭: *Don't forget to brush your teeth.* 不要忘記刷牙。**2** [T always+adv/prep] to remove something with a brush or with your hand 刷掉；拂去: **brush sth off/away etc** *Brush the crumbs off your jacket, you messy thing.* 把上衣上的麵包屑刷掉，你這髒傢伙。| *He brushed his hair out of his eyes.* 他把擋住眼睛的頭髮梳了上去。**3** [I always+adv/prep, T] to touch someone or something lightly by chance when passing them 輕擦而過: **[+against]** *I felt her hair brush against my arm.* 我感到她的頭髮輕拂着我的胳膊。| **brush sth** *The car brushed the hedges of the narrow lane.* 汽車輕輕擦過小路旁的樹籬。**4** **brush yourself down** *BrE*【英】, **brush yourself off** *AmE*【美】to tidy yourself, especially after a fall, by using your hands to brush your clothes etc〔用手〕撣掉自己身上的塵土: *I got up, brushed myself down, and carried on walking.* 我爬起來，撣了撣身上的塵土，繼續往前走。

brush sb/sth ↔ **aside** *phr v* [T] to refuse to listen to or consider something 不理會，不顧，漠視: *He simply brushed all my objections aside.* 他根本不顧我的種種反對意見。

brush sth ↔ **down** *phr v* [T] to clean your clothes or an animal thoroughly using a brush〔用刷子〕徹底刷洗

brush sth ↔ **off** *phr v* [T] refuse to listen to someone or their ideas, especially by ignoring them or saying something rude 漠視，充耳不聞: *The President brushed off their pleas for an investigation.* 總統拒絕了他們調查的請求。

brush up (on) sth *phr v* [I] to quickly practise and improve your skills or knowledge 溫習，複習: *I must brush up on my French before I go to Paris.* 去巴黎之前，我要好好溫習一下法語。

brushed /brʌʃt; brʌʃt/ *adj* [only before noun 僅用於名詞前] a brushed cloth has been specially treated to make it feel much softer 拉毛的, 起絨的: *brushed cotton* 起絨棉布

brush-off /ˈ· ·/ *n* [singular] a clear sign that you do not want someone's friendship, invitations etc 拒絕, 碰釘子: **give sb the brush-off** *I thought Andy liked me, but he gave me the brush-off.* 我以為安迪喜歡我, 可是他讓我碰了一鼻子灰。

brush·wood /ˈbrʌʃˌwud; ˈbrʌʃwʊd/ *n* [U] small dead branches broken from trees or bushes 折斷的小樹枝

brush·work /ˈbrʌʃˌwɝk; ˈbrʌʃwɜːk/ *n* [U] the particular way in which someone puts paint on a picture using a brush 畫法; 繪畫風格

brusque /brʌsk; bruːsk/ *adj* using very few words in a way that seems rude but is not intended to be 莽撞的; 粗魯的; 唐突的: *He was rather brusque on the phone.* 他在電話上説話有些粗魯。—**brusquely** *adv*: *"You'd better leave," she said brusquely.* "你最好離開。"她無禮地說。—**brusqueness** *n* [U]

brus·sels sprout /ˌbrʌsl̩z ˈspraut; ˌbrʌsəlz ˈspraʊt/ *n* [C] a small round green vegetable with many tightly folded leaves 球芽甘藍(菜), 抱子甘藍; SPROUT² (1) — see picture on page A9 參見A9頁圖

bru·tal /ˈbrutl̩; ˈbruːtl/ *adj* **1** very cruel and violent 無情的, 殘酷的, 野蠻的, 兇殘的: *a brutal and savage crime* 野蠻殘暴的罪行 **2** unkind and not sensitive to people's feelings 不講情面的, 不顧他人感情的: **brutal honesty/frankness etc** *They told us all the details with brutal honesty.* 他們絲毫不講情面, 把所有的細節都告訴了我們。—**brutally** *adv*: *brutally honest* 極其直率的 —**brutality** /bruˈtælətɪ; bruːˈtæləti/ *n* [C,U]: *the brutalities of war* 戰爭的殘酷[野蠻]

bru·tal·ize also 又作 **-ise** *BrE*【英】/ˈbrutl̩ˌaɪz; ˈbruːtəl-aɪz/ *v* [T usually passive 一般用被動態] **1** to affect someone so badly that they lose their normal human feelings 使殘忍; 使變無情: *brutalized by their experiences in jail* 因坐過牢而變得無情 **2** to treat someone in a cruel or violent way 虐待: *systematically abused and brutalized* 遭到蓄意辱罵和虐待 —**brutalization** /ˌbrutl̩əˈzeʃən; ˌbruːtəl-aɪˈzeɪʃən/ *n* [U]

brute¹ /brut; bruːt/ *n* [C] **1** *often humorous* a man who is rough, cruel and not sensitive【常幽默】無人性的傢伙〔尤指男人〕: *Don't hit him, you brute!* 別打他, 你這個沒人性的傢伙! **2** *literary* an animal, especially a large or strong one【文】〔尤指大或強壯的〕畜生, 動物, 獸

brute² *adj* **brute force/strength etc** physical strength rather than thought or intelligence 暴力/蠻勁等: *He won, not so much by skill as by brute force.* 他贏了, 但不是靠技巧, 而是靠蠻勁。

brut·ish /ˈbrutɪʃ; ˈbruːtɪʃ/ *adj* showing no human intelligence or feeling 畜生似的, 獸性的, 沒有人性的 —**brutishly** *adv* —**brutishness** *n* [U]

Bryl·creem /ˈbrɪlkrim; ˈbrɪlkriːm/ *n* [U] *trademark* a type of oil used on men's hair to make it shiny and smooth【商標】"百利"牌男用髮膏

BS /ˌbi ˈɛs; ˌbiː ˈes/ *n* [U] *AmE informal*【美, 非正式】an abbreviation of 縮寫= BULLSHIT

BSc /ˌbi ɛs ˈsi; ˌbiː es ˈsiː/ Bachelor of Science; a first university degree in a science subject 理學士: *Barbara Stone, BSc* 芭芭拉·斯通理學士 —compare 比較 BA

BSE /ˌbi ɛs ˈi; ˌbiː es ˈiː/ *n* [U] bovine spongiform encephalitis; a deadly brain disease in cows 牛海綿狀腦病, 瘋牛病

B-side /ˈbi saɪd; ˈbiː saɪd/ *n* [C] the less important side of a record〔唱片的〕B面

BST /ˌbi ɛs ˈti; ˌbiː es ˈtiː/ *n* [U] the abbreviation of 縮寫 = British Summer Time

bub /bʌb; bʌb/ *n* [C] *AmE slang* used to speak to a man, especially when you are angry【美俚】老弟, 老兄〔生氣時用語〕: *Hey, what do you think you're doing, bub?* 老兄, 你這是在幹甚麼?

bub·ble¹ /ˈbʌbl̩; ˈbʌbəl/ *n* [C] **1** a ball of air in liquid〔液體中的〕氣泡; 泡沫: *When water boils, bubbles rise to the surface.* 水開時, 水面會起泡泡。| *soap bubbles* 肥皂泡 | **blow bubbles** *She was blowing bubbles in her milk with a straw.* 她把吸管放進牛奶裡吹泡泡。**2** a small amount of air trapped in a solid substance〔固體中的〕氣泡: *Examine the glass carefully for bubbles.* 仔細檢查一下玻璃, 看有沒有氣泡。**3** also 又作 **speech bubble** *BrE* a circle around the words said by someone in a CARTOON (1)【英】〔卡通畫人物對白的〕話框 **4 prick/burst the bubble** to make someone suddenly realize the unpleasant truth about something that seemed wonderful or perfect 使〔希望或信心〕破滅: *The relationship was great at first but that bubble soon burst.* 起初關係很好, 但很快就吹了。**5 burst sb's bubble** to destroy someone's beliefs or hopes about something 使某人的信心[希望]成為泡影: *Coming second in the contest really burst his bubble.* 在比賽中位居第二使他的希望成為泡影。**6** a large clear plastic tent used to protect a seriously ill person from infection〔防止病人感染的隔離〕透明圓罩

bubble² *v* **1** [I] to produce bubbles 起泡, 冒泡; 沸騰: *Heat the cheese until it bubbles.* 把乳酪加熱到冒泡。| [+up] *The cola bubbled up when I unscrewed the lid.* 當我打開瓶蓋, 可樂飲料的泡冒了出來。**2** [I] to make the sound that water makes when it boils〔水沸騰時〕發出噗噗聲: [+away] *The water was bubbling away on the stove.* 爐子上的水正發出噗噗的沸騰聲。**3** [I] also 又作 **bubble over** to be excited 洋溢, 興奮: [+with] *bubbling over with enthusiasm* 充滿熱情

bubble and squeak /ˌ·· · ˈ·/ *n* [U] a British dish of potatoes and CABBAGE (1) mixed together and cooked in fat 捲心菜煎馬鈴薯

bubble bath /ˈ·· ·/ *n* **1** [U] a liquid soap that smells pleasant and makes bubbles in your bath water 泡沫液 **2** [C] a bath with this in the water 泡泡浴

bubble gum¹ /ˈ·· ·/ *n* [U] a type of CHEWING GUM that you can blow into a BUBBLE¹ (2) 泡泡糖

bubble gum² *adj AmE* connected with children between about seven and thirteen years old【美】七到十三歲兒童的: *a magazine aimed at the bubble gum set* 以七到十三歲兒童為對象的雜誌

bubble jet print·er /ˈ·· · ˌ··/ *n* [C] a type of machine for printing from a computer that sprays ink onto the paper 噴墨打印機

bub·bly¹ /ˈbʌblɪ; ˈbʌbli/ *adj* **1** full of BUBBLES 充滿泡沫的 **2** someone who is bubbly always seems cheerful, friendly, and eager to do things 活潑的; 生龍活虎的, 生氣勃勃的: *Angie's irresistibly bubbly personality* 安吉十分討人歡喜的活潑個性

bubbly² *n* [U] *informal* CHAMPAGNE【非正式】香檳酒

bu·bon·ic plague /buˌbɑnɪk ˈpleg; bjuːˌbɒnɪk ˈpleɪg/ *n* [U] a very serious disease spread by rats, that killed large numbers of people in the Middle Ages 腺鼠疫 —see also 另見 BLACK DEATH, PLAGUE¹ (2)

buc·ca·neer /ˌbʌkəˈnɪr; ˌbʌkəˈnɪə/ *n* [C] **1** someone who attacks ships at sea and steals from them; PIRATE¹ (3) 海盜 **2** someone who succeeds, especially in business, by using any method, including cheating〔尤指生意場上〕不擇手段的人

buck¹ /bʌk; bʌk/ *n* [C] S1

1 ►MONEY 錢◄ *AmE, AustrE informal* a dollar【美, 澳, 非正式】元: *He owes me ten bucks.* 他欠我十美元。| **big bucks** (=a lot of money) 許多錢 | **make a fast buck** (=make some money quickly, often dishonestly) 一下子賺得一筆錢〔常指不義之財〕

2 pass the buck to try to blame someone else or make them responsible for something that you should deal with 推諉責任: *You were the one who took on this job. Don't try to pass the buck.* 是你接手這項工作的, 別想推諉責任。

3 the buck stops here used to say that you are the person who is responsible when no-one else will accept the responsibility 責任到此不能再推

4 ►MALE ANIMAL 雄性動物◄ *plural* **buck** or **bucks** a male DEER, rabbit etc 雄鹿; 雄兔 —compare 比較 DOE

5 feel/look like a million bucks *AmE informal* to feel or look very healthy, happy, and beautiful【美, 非正式】感覺精神非常好/看上去很精神

6 buck naked *AmE informal* wearing no clothes at all【美, 非正式】赤身裸體的

7 ►WELL-DRESSED MAN 穿戴整齊的男子◄ a well-dressed young man in early 19th-century England〔英國19世紀初的〕紈袴子弟; 花花公子: *a Regency buck* 攝政時期的紈袴子弟

buck² *v*

1 ►HORSE 馬◄ [I] if a horse bucks, it kicks its back feet into the air, or jumps with all four feet off the ground 弓背躍起

2 ►THROW SB 摔某人◄ [T] to throw a rider off by jumping in this way〔馬〕跳起來把〔騎手〕摔下

3 ►CAR 汽車◄ [I] *AmE* if a car bucks, it moves forward in a way which is not smooth, but stops and starts suddenly【美】〔汽車〕顛簸行駛

4 ►OPPOSE 反對◄ *informal* to oppose something in a direct way; RESIST【非正式】反抗; 抵抗: **[+against/at]** *Initially he bucked against her restraints, but later came to accept them.* 起初, 他反抗她的管束, 但後來逐漸順從了。| **buck the system** (=avoid the usual rules) 反抗現行制度 *natural rebels, with the guts it takes to buck the system* 天生的反叛者, 有勇氣反抗這種制度 | **buck a trend** *The growth of the company has bucked the current recessionary trend in the industry.* 公司的發展頂住了該行業目前衰退的趨勢。

buck for sth *phr v* [T] to try very hard to get something, especially a good position at work 努力爭取〔尤指好的職位〕: *He's bucking for promotion.* 他在努力爭取升職。

buck up *phr v* **1** [I,T **buck** sb **up**] to become more cheerful or make someone more cheerful (使)振作精神, (使)快活起來: *Come on, buck up, things aren't that bad!* 來吧, 不要灰心, 事情還沒那麼糟糕! **2 buck up!** *BrE spoken* used to tell someone to hurry up【英口】加油! 快點!: *Buck up, John! We'll be late.* 約翰, 快點! 我們要遲到了。**3 buck your ideas up** *BrE informal* used to tell someone to try harder to improve their behaviour or attitude【英, 非正式】力圖改進; 加緊工作[學習]

buck·a·roo /ˌbʌkəˋru; ˌbʌkəˈruː/ *n* [C] *AmE informal* a word meaning COWBOY (1), used especially when speaking to children【美, 非正式】牛仔〔尤對兒童用語〕

buck·board /ˋbʌkˌbɔrd; ˈbʌkbɔːd/ *n* [C] a light vehicle which has four wheels and is pulled by a horse, used in the US in the 19th century〔尤指美國19世紀單匹馬拉的〕四輪平板馬車

bucked /bʌkt; bʌkt/ *adj* [not before noun 不用於名詞前] *BrE old-fashioned* very pleased【英, 過時】振奮的, 高興的, 歡欣鼓舞的: **[+at/by]** *We were bucked at the news.* 這消息使我們歡欣鼓舞。

2 **buck·et¹** /ˋbʌkɪt; ˈbʌkɪ̈t/ *n* [C]

1 ►CONTAINER 容器◄ an open container with a handle, used for carrying and holding things, especially earth or water 桶: *a bucket of water* 水桶

2 also 又作 **bucketful** the quantity of liquid that a bucket can hold 一桶之量: **[+of]** *It took four buckets of water to wash the car.* 洗汽車用了四桶水。

3 ►PART OF MACHINE 機器部件◄ a part of a machine shaped like a large bucket and used for moving earth, water etc 鏟斗; 勺斗; 戽斗

4 by the bucket/bucketful *informal* in large quantities【非正式】一桶一桶地, 大量地: *drinking beer by the bucket* 狂飲啤酒

5 sweat/weep buckets *informal* to SWEAT¹ (1) or cry a lot【非正式】大量出汗/嚎啕大哭

6 in buckets *informal* if rain comes down in buckets, it is raining very heavily【非正式】〔雨〕傾盆而下 —see also 另見 **kick the bucket** (KICK¹ (12)), **a drop in the bucket** (DROP² (8))

bucket² *v*

bucket down *phr v* [I] *BrE informal* to rain very hard【英, 非正式】〔雨〕傾盆而下: *It's been bucketing down all day.* 傾盆大雨已下了一整天。

bucket shop /ˈ‥ ˌ/ *n* [C] *BrE informal* a business that sells cheap tickets for air travel【英, 非正式】廉價機票分銷店

buck·le¹ /ˋbʌkl; ˈbʌkəl/ *v* **1** [I,T] to fasten a buckle or be joined together with a buckle 用扣環扣住[扣緊]: *The strap buckles at the side.* 帶子是在側面扣的。| **buckle sth** *buckle a satchel* 扣上書包 | **buckle sth on/up/together** *Lou was buckling on his revolver.* 盧把左輪手槍扣掛在身上。**2** [I,T] to become bent or curved because of heat or pressure, or to make something bend or curve in this way〔因高温、壓力等〕(使)彎曲; 扭曲; (使)變形: *The rails buckled under the intense heat of the fire.* 鐵軌在火焰的高温作用下變了形。**3** [I] if your knees or legs buckle, they become weak and bend 腿軟, 站不直: *I felt a blow and my knees started to buckle.* 我感到挨了一擊, 腿一軟站不住了。

buckle down *phr v* [I] to start working seriously 開始認真從事; 埋頭於: **[+to]** *You'd better buckle down to some revision now.* 你該認真複習了。

buckle up *phr v* [I] *especially AmE* to fasten your SEAT BELT in a car, aircraft etc【尤美】繫上安全帶

buckle² *n* [C] a metal fastener used for joining the two ends of a belt or STRAP¹, for fastening a shoe, bag etc, or for decoration〔皮帶等的〕金屬扣環, 扣子; 帶扣 —see picture at 參見 FASTENER 圖

buck·ler /ˋbʌklɚ; ˈbʌklə/ *n* [C] *especially literary* a small circular SHIELD¹ (1a) with a raised centre【尤文】小圓盾

buck·ram /ˋbʌkrəm; ˈbʌkrəm/ *n* [U] stiff cloth, used in the past for covering books, making the stiff parts of clothes etc 硬粗布〔尤指舊時用來做書的封面或使衣服挺直的粗布〕

Buck's Fizz /ˌbʌks ˋfɪz; ˌbʌks ˈfɪz/ *n* [C,U] a mixture of CHAMPAGNE and orange juice, or a glass of this 香檳橙汁飲料

buck·shee /ˌbʌkˋʃi; ˌbʌkˈʃiː◂/ *adv BrE old-fashioned* without payment; free【英, 過時】免費地 —**buckshee** *adj*

buck·shot /ˋbʌkˌʃɑt; ˈbʌkʃɒt/ *n* [U] a lot of small metal balls that you fire together from a gun〔打獵用的〕散彈槍子彈

buck·skin /ˋbʌkˌskɪn; ˈbʌkˌskɪn/ *n* [U] strong soft leather made from the skin of a DEER or goat 鹿皮; 硝好的羊皮

buck teeth /ˌ· ˈ·/ *n* [plural] teeth that stick forward out of your mouth 齙牙, 獠牙 —**buck-toothed** /ˌ· ˈ·◂/ *adj*

buck·wheat /ˋbʌkˌhwit; ˈbʌkwiːt/ *n* [U] a type of small grain used as food for chickens, and for making FLOUR 蕎麥

bu·col·ic /bjuˋkɑlɪk; bjuːˈkɒlɪk/ *adj literary* connected with the countryside【文】鄉村的; 田園生活的: *a church, lovely in its bucolic setting* 座落在美麗田園中的教堂 —**bucolically** /-klɪ; -kli/ *adv*

bud 芽; 苞; 蓓蕾

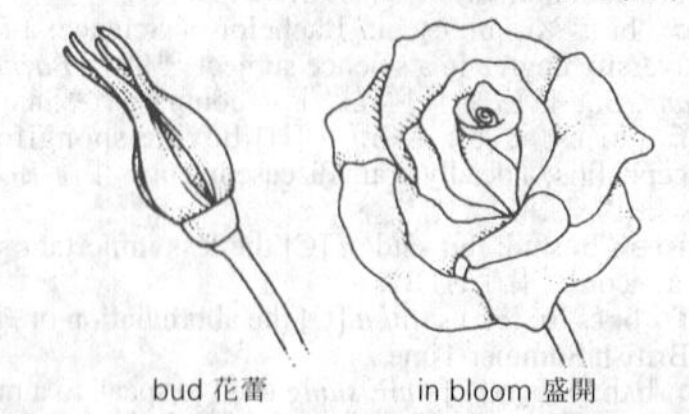

bud¹ /bʌd; bʌd/ *n* [C] **1** a young tightly rolled up flower or leaf before it opens 芽; 苞; 蓓蕾: *rose buds* 玫瑰花苞 |

in bud (=having buds but no flowers yet) 含苞待放 | **come into bud** (=start to produce buds) 長出花蕾 **2** *AmE informal*【美, 非正式】BUDDY 老兄; 喂 —see also 另見 COTTON BUD, TASTE BUD, **nip sth in the bud** (NIP[1] (3))

bud[2] *v* **budded, budding** [I] to produce buds 發芽, 長出花蕾, 含苞

Bud·dhis·m /ˈbudɪzəm; ˈbʊdɪzəm/ *n* [U] a religion of east and central Asia, based on the teaching of Gautama Buddha 佛教 —**Buddhist** *n* [C] —**Buddhist** *adj*

bud·ding /ˈbʌdɪŋ; ˈbʌdɪŋ/ *adj* **1 budding singer/actor/writer etc** someone who is just starting to sing, act etc and will probably be successful at it 初露頭角的歌手/演員/作家等 **2** [only before noun 僅用於名詞前] beginning to develop 開始發展的; 成長中的: *a budding relationship* 開始發展的關係

bud·dy /ˈbʌdɪ; ˈbʌdi/ *n* [C] **1** *informal* a friend【非正式】朋友, 夥伴: *We're good buddies.* 我們是好朋友。**2** *AmE spoken* used to speak to a man you do not know; BUD[1] (2)【美口】老兄; 喂〔用於稱呼不認識的男子〕: *Hey, buddy! This your car?* 喂, 老兄! 這是你的車嗎? **3** someone who offers to look after and become a friend to a person who has AIDS 愛滋病患者之友〔指自願照顧並善待愛滋病患者的人〕

buddy-bud·dy /ˈ·· ˌ··/ *adj AmE informal* very friendly with someone【美, 非正式】十分友好的

buddy sys·tem /ˈ·· ˌ··/ *n* [C] *AmE* a system in which two people help each other or keep each other safe【美】〔兩人互相照顧的〕結伴制

budge /bʌdʒ; bʌdʒ/ *v* [I,T usually in negatives 一般用於否定句] *informal*【非正式】**1** to move, or move someone or something from one place to another (使) 稍微移動: *Come on – budge. I can't get past.* 嘿, 挪一下, 我過不去。| **budge sth** *The car was stuck in the snow and we couldn't budge it.* 汽車陷在雪地裡, 我們怎麼動都動不了。| **[+from]** *Will hasn't budged from his room all day.* 威爾整天都在自己的房間裡。**2** to make someone change their opinion (使某人) 改變主意: *It's no good, Dad won't budge.* 沒有用, 爸爸不會改變主意的。| **not budge an inch** (=not change at all) 寸步不讓, 一點也不改變

bud·ge·ri·gar /ˈbʌdʒərɪˌgɑr; ˈbʌdʒərɪgɑː/ *n* [C] a small brightly-coloured bird that people keep at home as a pet; BUDGIE 虎皮鸚鵡

1 2 **bud·get**[1] /ˈbʌdʒɪt; ˈbʌdʒɪ̍t/ *n* [C] **1** a plan of how a person or organization will spend the money that is available in a particular period of time, or the money itself 預算: *planning the annual budget* 制定年度預算 | **[+of]** *a welfare program with a budget of $2 billion* 預算為二十億美元的福利計劃 | **defence/advertising etc budget** (=money available for defence etc) 國防經費/廣告費等預算 | **over/under budget** (=having spent more or less than the amount allowed in a budget) 〔支出〕高於/低於預算 | **budget deficit** (=a situation in which more money has been spent than is available) 預算赤字 | **balance the budget** (=make sure that only money available is spent) 保持收支平衡 | **be on a tight budget** (=not have much money to spend) 財政緊張, 經濟拮据 **2** an official statement that a government makes about how much it intends to spend and what taxes will be necessary 政府預算案

budget[2] *v* **1** [I] to carefully plan and control how much you spend 〔精心地〕制定預算; 按預算來安排 (開支): *We'll just have to budget more sensibly in the future.* 今後我們必須更合理地安排開支。| **budget for** (=plan how much you need for something) 為…計劃開支 *We've budgeted for a new car next year.* 我們已計劃好了明年買汽車的開支。**2** [I,T] to plan carefully how much of something will be needed (為…) 作出安排: *She's learned how to budget her time carefully.* 她已經學會了怎樣精心安排自己的時間。

budget[3] *adj* [only before noun 僅用於名詞前] very low in price; cheap 經濟的, 特價的, 便宜的: *a budget flight* 低價航班

bud·get·a·ry /ˈbʌdʒɪˌtɛrɪ; ˈbʌdʒɪ̍təri/ *adj* connected with the way money is spent in a budget 預算的: *budgetary restrictions* 預算限制

bud·gie /ˈbʌdʒɪ; ˈbʌdʒi/ *n* [C] *BrE* a small brightly-coloured bird that people keep at home as a pet; BUDGERIGAR【英】虎皮鸚鵡

buff[1] /bʌf; bʌf/ *n* **1** [C] **film/computer/jazz etc buff** someone who is interested in films, computers etc and knows a lot about them 影迷/電腦迷/爵士樂迷等 **2** [U] a pale yellow-brown colour 淺[暗]黃色, 米色 —see picture on page A5 參見 A5 頁圖 **3 in the buff** *old-fashioned* having no clothes on; NAKED【過時】赤身裸體的, 一絲不掛的

buff[2] *v* [T] to make a surface shine by polishing it with a dry cloth 〔用軟布〕擦亮: *Buff to a shine after waxing.* 打蠟之後用軟布擦亮。

buf·fa·lo /ˈbʌflˌo; ˈbʌfələʊ/ *n plural* **buffalos, buffaloes,** or **buffalo** [C] **1** an African animal similar to a large cow with long curved horns 水牛 —see also 另見 WATER BUFFALO **2** a BISON 北美野牛, 犎牛

buff·er[1] /ˈbʌfɚ; ˈbʌfə/ *n* [C]

1 ►PROTECTION 保護◄ something that protects something else 緩衝物: *The trees act as a buffer against strong winds.* 這些樹木起到了緩衝強風的作用。

2 ►RAILWAY 鐵路◄ one of the two special metal springs on the front or back of a train or at the end of a railway track to take the shock if the train hits something 〔鐵路車輛或鐵軌末端的〕緩衝器

3 buffer zone an area between two armies, which is intended to separate them so that they do not fight 〔軍事〕緩衝地帶

4 buffer state a smaller peaceful country between two larger countries, which makes war between them less likely 緩衝國: *Part of the settlement was to create a Serbian buffer state.* 協議的部分內容是建立塞爾維亞緩衝國。

5 ►COMPUTER 電腦◄ a place in a computer's memory for storing information temporarily 緩衝存儲器

6 ►PERSON 人◄ *BrE old-fashioned* an old man who seems silly【英, 過時】老傢伙, 老糊塗: *You stupid old buffer!* 你這老糊塗!

7 ►FOR POLISHING 用於擦拭◄ something used to polish a surface 〔用於擦亮表面的〕拋光工具: *Where's my nail buffer?* 我的指甲銼在哪裡?

8 hit the buffers *informal* an official discussion that hits the buffers does not have a successful result【非正式】受挫

buffer[2] *v* [T] to reduce the bad effects of something 緩衝, 緩和, 緩解: *buffering the effects of the recession* 緩解經濟衰退造成的影響

buf·fet[1] /bəˋfe; ˈbʊfeɪ/ *n* [C] **1** a place in a railway station, bus station etc where you can buy and eat food or drink 快餐部, 飲食櫃台 **2** a meal of cold food at a party or other occasion, in which people serve themselves at a table and then move away to eat 自助餐: **buffet lunch/supper** *We had a buffet lunch for Hayley's christening.* 我們安排了一頓自助午餐慶祝海利受洗。| **finger buffet** (=with food that you eat with your hands) 可用手拿食物吃的自助餐 **3** *BrE* the part of the train where you can buy food and drink; DINING CAR【英】〔火車上的〕餐車 **4** a piece of furniture in which you keep the things you use to serve and eat a meal 餐具架[櫃]

buffet[2] /ˈbʌfɪt; ˈbʌfɪ̍t/ *v* [T usually passive 一般用被動態] **1** if wind, rain, or the sea buffets something, it hits it with a lot of force 〔風、雨等〕猛裂襲擊: *London was buffeted by storms last night.* 倫敦昨晚遭到暴風雨的襲擊。**2** *literary* to treat someone unkindly【文】打擊, 傷害: *weary of being buffeted by life* 厭倦了生活的打擊 —**buffeting** *n* [C]

buffet sb/sth **about** *phr v* [I] to knock or hit something and make it move 撞[擊]得〔某人或某物〕移動

buf·foon /bəˋfun; bəˈfuːn/ *n* [C] *old-fashioned* someone who does silly things that make you laugh【過時】丑角; 粗俗而愚蠢的人 —**buffoonery** *n* [U]

bug¹ /bʌg; bʌg/ *n* [C] **1** *especially AmE* a small insect, especially one that people think is unpleasant【尤美】小蟲子 **2** *informal* an illness that people catch very easily from each other but is not very serious【非正式】小毛病: **pick up a bug** (=get a bug) 得(小)病 | **tummy/stomach bug** (=illness affecting your stomach) 肚子/胃不舒服 **3 the travel/ski/parachuting etc bug** *informal* a sudden strong interest in doing something that usually lasts only a short time【非正式】對旅行/滑雪/跳傘等突然着迷: *bitten by the fitness bug* 對健身着了迷 **4** a small fault in the system of instructions that operates a computer〔電腦程序等的〕故障, 毛病 —see also 另見 DEBUG **5** a small piece of electronic equipment for listening secretly to other people's conversations 竊聽器

bug² *v* **bugged, bugging** [T] **1** *informal* to annoy【非正式】打擾; 激怒; 使厭煩: *It really bugs me when the car behind me drives too close.* 後面的汽車離我太近, 真令我惱怒。**2** to put a BUG¹ (5) somewhere secretly in order to listen to conversations 給…裝竊聽器; 竊聽: *Do you think the room is bugged?* 你認為這房間裝了竊聽器嗎?

bug·a·boo /ˋbʌgəˏbu; ˈbʌgəbuː/ *n* [C] *old-fashioned* an imaginary thing or person that children are scared of【過時】嚇人的東西; 妖怪

bug·bear /ˋbʌgˏbɛr; ˈbʌgbeə/ *n* [C] something that makes people feel worried or scared 使人煩惱[擔心]的東西; 無謂的恐慌: *the old bugbear – racism* 讓人不安的老問題 — 種族主義

bug-eyed /ˏbʌgˋaɪd; ˌbʌgˈaɪd◂/ *adj* having eyes that stick out 眼睛瞪大的, 眼球突出的

2 **bug·ger¹** /ˋbʌgə; ˈbʌgə/ *n* [C] *spoken especially BrE*【口, 尤英】**1** *taboo* someone who is very annoying or unpleasant【諱】壞蛋, 可鄙的傢伙: *Bill's an obnoxious little bugger.* 比爾是個令人討厭的小搗蛋鬼。**2** a rude word meaning someone that you pretend to be annoyed with, although you actually like them 傢伙, 小子〔粗魯但實際上表示親昵〕: *What are you doing, you daft bugger?* 你這笨傢伙在幹甚麼? **3** a rude word meaning a job or activity that is very difficult 麻煩的事物; 令人頭痛的事: *Having to commute so far is a real bugger.* 必須跑這麼遠的路上下班真是件麻煩事。**4 bugger all** a rude expression meaning nothing, used especially when you are angry 甚麼也沒有〔粗話〕: *There's bugger all we can do about the car now.* 現在我們對這輛車屁辦法都沒有。| **bugger all help/thanks/work etc** (=none at all) 一點兒也不幫忙/感謝/行不通等 *I got bugger all thanks for driving my boss to the airport.* 我開車送老闆到機場, 他連句感謝話都沒說。**5 play silly buggers** a rude expression meaning to behave in a stupid way that annoys other people 胡鬧: *Stop playing silly buggers and get on with your homework!* 別瞎胡鬧了, 趕快做作業吧! **6** *taboo* a man who regularly has ANAL SEX, especially with other men or boys【諱】雞姦者

bugger² *v* [T] *BrE*【英】**1 bugger (it)!** *spoken* a rude expression used when you are angry because something bad has happened【口】該死!; 見鬼!: *Bugger it! The car battery is dead.* 活見鬼! 汽車電池沒電了。**2 I'll be buggered/bugger me!** *spoken* a rude expression used when you are surprised about something【口】該死的!〔表示非常驚奇〕**3 bugger the ...** *slang* used to say that you do not care about the person or thing you are talking about【俚】管他是誰; 管它怎麼樣: *Bugger the expense, I'm going to buy it!* 別管多貴, 我都要把它買下來! **4 I'll be buggered if...** *slang* used to say angrily that you will not do something【俚】如果…我就該死…: *I'll be buggered if I help them any more.* 如果我再幫他們, 我就是個該死的傢伙。**5** *taboo or law* to have ANAL sex with someone【諱或法律】與…雞姦, 犯雞姦罪

bugger about also 又作 **bugger around** *phr v BrE*【英】**1** [I] to behave in a stupid way or waste time 胡鬧, 瞎折騰: *Stop buggering about and get on with your work.* 別瞎胡鬧了, 幹你的活。**2** [T **bugger sb about**] to cause unnecessary problems for someone 給〔某人〕添麻煩, 煩擾: *Don't let Peter bugger you about, tell him to leave.* 別讓彼得再煩擾你了, 叫他離開。

bugger off *phr v* [I often imperative 常用於祈使句] *BrE* an impolite expression meaning to go away, or leave a place, which is very rude when used directly【英】走開, 滾開: *Bugger off and leave me alone!* 走開, 離我遠點! | *Simon's always buggering off home early.* 西蒙總是很早就滾回家去。

bugger sth ↔ up *phr v* [T] *BrE* to do something stupid that ruins something or causes trouble【英】損害; 搞糟: *You really buggered up our plans by arriving late.* 你這一遲到, 真把我們的計劃搞砸了。

bug·gered /ˋbʌgəd; ˈbʌgəd/ *adj* [not before noun 不用於名詞前] **1** *BrE slang* a rude word meaning extremely tired【英俚】精疲力盡的: *That's the last time I work so late. I'm buggered!* 這是我最後一次工作得這麼晚。我累壞了! **2** *BrE slang* a rude word meaning completely ruined or broken【英俚】損壞的: *The washing machine's buggered.* 洗衣機壞了。**3 I'm buggered** *BrE spoken* used to say that you are very surprised by something or cannot understand it【英口】我很吃驚: *I'm buggered if I know why they didn't come!* 我真奇怪他們為甚麼沒有來!

bug·ger·y /ˋbʌgərɪ; ˈbʌgəri/ *n* [U] *BrE law* ANAL sex【英, 法律】雞姦

bug·gy /ˋbʌgɪ; ˈbʌgi/ *n* [C] **1** *BrE* a light folding chair on wheels that you push small children in【英】摺疊式輕便嬰兒車; STROLLER *AmE*【美】**2** a light carriage pulled by a horse〔一匹馬拉的〕輕型馬車 **3** *AmE* a thing like a small bed on wheels, that a baby lies in【美】〔嬰兒可躺在裡面的〕嬰兒車; PRAM *BrE*【英】

bu·gle /ˋbjugḷ; ˈbjuːgəl/ *n* [C] a musical instrument like a TRUMPET¹ (1) which is used in the army to call soldiers 號角; 軍號, 喇叭 —**bugler** *n* [C]

build¹ /bɪld; bɪld/ *v past tense and past participle* **built** /bɪlt; bɪlt/

1 ►MAKE STH 製作某物◄ [I,T] to make something, especially a building or something large 建房; 建築, 建造, 蓋; 造: *Are they going to build on this land?* 他們要在這塊地上建房子嗎? | **build sb sth** *Nick said he'd build us a fitted wardrobe.* 尼克説他要為我們造一個尺寸合適的大衣櫃。

2 ►MAKE STH DEVELOP 使某物發展◄ [T] to make something develop or form 使發展; 使構成; 創建, 建立; 樹立; 培養: *Kate's working hard to build a career.* 凱特工作很努力, 想開創一番事業。| **build (up) a picture of sb/sth** (=form a clear idea about someone or something) 對某人/某物有清楚的認識 *The police are trying to build up a picture of Haig's daily routine.* 警方在設法弄清黑格的日常活動規律。

3 ►FEELING 感情◄ [I,T] if a feeling builds or you build it, it increases gradually over a period of time 發展, 增進, 加劇: *Tension is building between the two countries.* 兩國的緊張關係在加劇。

4 well-built/brick-built etc used for describing how large someone is, what something is made of, or how it was built 體格強壯的/磚結構的等: *a heavily-built man* 體格非常強壯的男人 | *a brick-built house* 磚砌的房子

5 be built of to be made using particular materials 由〔某些材料〕建成: *a cottage built of Cumbrian slate* 用坎伯蘭石板造的小屋

6 be built on/around to happen as a result of something 建立在…之上: *The company's success is built on its very popular home computers.* 公司的成功全靠其很暢銷的家用電腦。

7 build bridges to try to establish a better relationship between people who do not like each other 溝通〔尤指在對立的人之間〕

build sth ↔ in *phr v* [T usually passive 一般用被動

態] to make something so that it is a permanent part of a wall, room etc 把…嵌[插, 建, 裝]入

build sth ↔ **into** *phr v* [T] **1** to make something so that it is a permanent part of a wall, room etc 把…嵌[插, 建, 裝]入 **2** to make something a permanent part of a system, agreement etc 使成為某物不可分的部分: *A completion date was built into the contract.* 完成日期已訂入了合同。—see also 另見 BUILT-IN

build on sth *phr v* **1** [T **build** sth ↔ **on**] to add another room etc to a building in order to have more space 擴建, 增建 **2** [**build on** sth] to use your achievements as a base for further development 以…作為發展的基礎: *Now we must build on our success in Italy.* 我們必須以在意大利的成功作為基礎。—see also 另見 **be built on** (BUILD[1] (6))

build up *phr v*

1 ►PRAISE 讚揚◄ [T **build** sb/sth ↔ **up**] to praise someone or something so that other people think they are really good 吹捧, 讚揚, 宣傳: *You have to build kids up – make them feel important.* 你必須多表揚孩子, 讓他們覺得自己重要。

2 ►MAKE STRONGER 使強壯◄ [T **build** sb ↔ **up**] to make someone well and strong again, especially after an illness 幫助〔某人〕逐步恢復體力〔尤指病後〕: *Build your mother up with nourishing food.* 讓你母親多吃點營養食品, 使她逐步恢復體力。

3 ►FEELING 感情◄ [I,T **build** sth ↔ **up**] if a feeling builds up or you build it up, it increases gradually over a period of time 增強; 增加: *Try and build up his confidence a bit.* 設法讓他增加對自己的信心。

4 ►INCREASE GRADUALLY 逐漸增加◄ [I,T **build** sth ↔ **up**] if a substance, force, or activity builds up somewhere or you build it up, it gradually becomes bigger and stronger 逐漸增加; 擴大: *Both sides have built up huge stockpiles of arms.* 雙方都已大量增加武器貯備。—see also 另見 BUILD-UP (1)

5 build up sb's hopes to unfairly encourage someone to think that they will get what they hope for〔以不正當的方式〕讓某人懷有希望

build up to sth *phr v* [T] to prepare for a particular moment or event 為某個時刻的到來做準備: *I could tell she was building up to some kind of announcement.* 我能看得出她準備向大家宣布些甚麼事。—see also 另見 BUILD-UP (3)

build² *n* [singular,U] the shape and size of someone's body 體格; 體形: *a powerful build* 強壯的體格 —see 見 BODY (USAGE)

3 **build·er** /ˋbɪldɚ; ˈbɪldə/ *n* [C] *especially BrE* a person or a company that builds or repairs buildings【尤英】建築工人; 建築商; 建造者

builders' mer·chant /ˈ·· ˌ··/ *n* [C] *BrE* a company that stores and sells building materials such as bricks, cement, and sand【英】建材公司; 建材商

1 1 **build·ing** /ˋbɪldɪŋ; ˈbɪldɪŋ/ *n* [C] **1** a structure such as a house, church, or factory, that has a roof and walls 建築(物): *one of the tallest buildings in the world.* 世界上最高的建築之一 **2** [U] the process or business of building things 建築, 建造; 建築業: *The next major step is the building of a gym.* 下一個重要舉措是建一個體育館。| **building costs/programmes/regulations etc** *Building costs will have to be reduced.* 建築成本必須降低。

building block /ˈ·· ·/ *n* [C] **1** a block of wood or plastic for young children to build things with 積木 **2 building blocks** [plural] the pieces or parts which together make it possible for something big or important to exist 成分, 構成要素: *Amino acids are the fundamental building blocks of protein.* 氨基酸是構成蛋白質的基本成分。

building con·trac·tor /ˈ·· ·ˌ··/ *n* [C] someone whose job is to organize the building of a house, office, factory etc 建築承包商

building site /ˈ·· ·/ *n* [C] a place where a house, factory etc is being built 建築工地

building so·ci·e·ty /ˈ·· ·ˌ···/ *n* [C] *BrE* a type of bank that you pay money into in order to save it and earn interest and that will lend you money to buy a house or apartment【英】購房[房屋]互助協會〔接受會員存款並付給利息, 會員購房可貸款的商業機構〕; SAVINGS AND LOAN ASSOCIATION *AmE*【美】

build-up /ˈ· ·/ *n* **1** [U singular] an increase over a period of time 增長; 加強; 集結; 儲備: *a heavy build-up of traffic on the motorway* 高速公路上交通流量的急劇增長 **2** [C] a description of someone or something in which you say they are very special or important〔尤指預先的〕輿論宣傳, 吹捧: **give sb a big build-up** *The presenter gave her a big build-up.* 節目主持人事前對她大肆吹捧。**3** [C] the length of time spent preparing an event 準備時間: [+**to**] *the long build-up to the opening of the Channel Tunnel* 海峽隧道開通的漫長準備期 —see also 另見 **build up** (BUILD[1])

built /bɪlt; bɪlt/ the past tense and past participle of BUILD[1]

built-in /ˌ· ˈ·◄/ *adj* forming a part of something that cannot be separated from it 作為固定裝置而建造的, 裝在結構裡的; 固定的; 內在的: *a built-in microphone* 內置的麥克風 —see also 另見 **build in** (BUILD[1])

built-up /ˌ· ˈ·◄/ *adj* a built-up area has a lot of buildings and not many open spaces 佈滿建築物的: *speeding in a built-up area* 在一個建築物密集的地區疾駛

bulb /bʌlb; bʌlb/ *n* [C] **1** the glass part of an electric light, that the light shines from; LIGHT BULB 燈泡: *a 100 watt bulb* 100瓦的燈泡 —see picture at 參見 LIGHT[1] 圖 **2** a root shaped like a ball that grows into a flower or plant〔植物的〕球莖, 鱗莖, 球根: *tulip bulbs* 鬱金香球莖

bul·bous /ˋbʌlbəs; ˈbʌlbəs/ *adj* fat and round and unattractive 又圓又胖的: *a bulbous nose* 蒜頭鼻子, 圓圓的鼻子

bulge¹ /bʌldʒ; bʌldʒ/ *n* [C] **1** a curved mass on the surface of something, usually caused by something under or inside it 膨脹, 鼓起部: *The wallet made a fat bulge in his pocket.* 錢包把他的口袋撐得鼓鼓的。**2** a sudden temporary increase in the amount or level of something 驟增, 膨脹, 暴漲: *a bulge in the birthrate* 出生率驟增 —**bulgy** *adj*: *bulgy-eyed* 眼睛凸出的

bulge² *v* [I] **1** also 又作 **bulge out** to stick out in a rounded shape, especially because something is very full or too tight 鼓起: [+**with**] *His pockets were bulging with candy.* 他的口袋裡鼓鼓囊囊塞滿了糖塊。**2** [+**with**] *informal* to be very full of people or things【非正式】塞滿, 充滿

bul·gur /ˋbʌlgɚ; ˈbʌlgə/ *n* [U] a type of wheat which has been dried and broken into pieces 碾碎的乾小麥

bu·lim·i·a /bjuˋlɪmɪə; bjuːˈlɪmiə/ *n* [U] an illness in which a person cannot stop themselves from eating too much, and then vomits (VOMIT[1]) in order to control their weight 易飢症, 食慾過盛症 —**bulimic** *adj*

bulk¹ /bʌlk; bʌlk/ *n* **1 the bulk (of sth)** the main or largest part of something〔某物的〕主要部分; 大半: *the bulk of the workforce* 大部分的勞動力 **2** [C usually singular 一般用單數] a big mass of something 團, 大塊 **3** [U] the size of something or someone 體積; 尺寸; 塊頭: *The dough will rise until it is double in bulk.* 麵團發酵後體積能膨脹到原來的兩倍。**4 in bulk** if you buy goods in bulk, you buy large amounts each time you buy them 整批的, 大批的

bulk² *adj* **1 bulk buying/orders etc** the buying etc of goods in large quantities at one time 大批[大量]購買/訂購等 **2** [only before noun 僅用於名詞前] bulk goods are sold or moved in large quantities 大批的, 大量的: *bulk flour for commercial bakeries* 為商用麵包烘房提供的大量麵粉 **3 bulk mail** the posting of large amounts of mail for a smaller cost than usual 大宗[大量]郵件寄送

bulk³ *v* **bulk large** *literary* to be the main or most important part of something【文】顯得重要, 起重大作用

bulk sth ↔ **out** *phr v* [T] to make something look bigger or thicker, by adding something else 使膨脹; 使

看起來更厚實[豐滿]; 充實: *We can bulk out the report with lots of diagrams.* 我們可以加許多圖表使報告更充實。

bulk·head /ˈbʌlkˌhɛd; ˈbʌlkhed/ *n* [C] a wall which divides the structure of a ship or aircraft into separate parts〔船等的〕艙壁, 隔離壁

B

bulk·y /ˈbʌlki; ˈbʌlki/ *adj* **1** something that is bulky is bigger than other things of its type and is difficult to carry or store 龐大的, 笨重的, 體積大的; 寬大的: *a bulky parcel* 笨重的包裹 | *a new elastic that is less bulky* 不那麼粗的新鬆緊帶 **2** someone who is bulky is big and heavy 又高又胖的 —**bulkiness** *n* [U]

bull¹ /bʊl; bʊl/ *n* [C]

1 ►MALE COW 公牛◄ an adult male animal of the cattle family 公牛: *A mean-looking bull was standing in the path.* 小路上站着一頭兇惡的公牛。

2 ►MALE ANIMAL 雄性動物◄ the male of some other large animals such as the ELEPHANT or WHALE 雄性動物〈如象或鯨等身軀龐大的動物〉

3 take the bull by the horns to bravely or confidently deal with a difficult, dangerous, or unpleasant problem 挺身面對困難: *She decided to take the bull by the horns and ask him outright.* 她決定挺身而出, 直截了當去問他。

4 ►NONSENSE 廢話◄ [U] *AmE informal* nonsense or something that is completely untrue【美, 非正式】大話; 廢話, 空話: *You never went to Hawaii – that's pure bull.* 純屬吹牛, 你從未去過夏威夷。

5 be like a bull in a china shop to keep knocking things over, dropping things, breaking things etc 笨手笨腳到處闖禍

6 like a bull at a gate if you move somewhere like a bull at a gate, you move there very fast, ignoring everything in your way 猛烈地; 兇猛地

7 ►RELIGION 宗教◄ an official statement from the POPE 教皇訓諭[詔書]

8 ►CENTRE 中心◄ the centre of a TARGET¹ (3) that you are shooting at 靶心

9 ►BUSINESS 商業◄ someone who buys shares (SHARE² (5)) because they expect prices to rise〔股票投機中的〕多頭; 股市看漲的人 —compare 比較 BEAR² (2) —see also 另見 **like a red rag to a bull** (RED¹ (6)), **shoot the bull** (SHOOT¹ (8))

bull² *interjection slang* used to say that you do not believe or agree with what someone has said【俚】廢話! 胡說!: *Bull! Where did you get that idea?* 廢話! 你怎麼會有那種想法?

bull·dog /ˈbʊlˌdɔg; ˈbʊldɒg/ *n* [C] a powerful dog with a large head, a short neck, and short thick legs 鬥牛犬

bulldog clip /ˈ·· ˌ·/ *n BrE* [C] a small metal object that shuts tightly to hold papers together【英】〔夾紙用的〕金屬夾

bull·doze /ˈbʊlˌdoz; ˈbʊldəʊz/ *v* [T] **1** to destroy buildings etc with a bulldozer〔用推土機〕推倒 **2** to push objects such as earth and rocks out of the way with a bulldozer〔用推土機〕推平, 平整 **3 bulldoze sb into (doing) sth** to force someone to do something that they do not really want to do 強迫某人做某事

bull·doz·er /ˈbʊlˌdozɚ; ˈbʊldəʊzə/ *n* [C] a powerful vehicle with a broad metal blade, used for moving earth and rocks, destroying buildings etc 推土機

bul·let /ˈbʊlɪt; ˈbʊlɪt/ *n* [C] a small piece of metal that you fire from a gun 槍彈, 子彈, 彈頭: *a bullet through the heart* 穿透心臟的子彈 | **bullet holes/wounds etc** *The door was riddled with bullet holes.* 門上到處是彈孔。—compare 比較 SHELL¹ (2), SHOT¹ (4) —see also 另見 PLASTIC BULLET, **bite the bullet** (BITE¹ (8)) —see picture at 參見 GUN¹ 圖

bul·le·tin /ˈbʊlətɪn; ˈbʊlətɪn/ *n* [C] **1** a news report on radio or television〔廣播或電視中的〕新聞簡報 **2** an official statement that is made to inform people about something important 公告; 公報; 告示 **3** a letter or printed statement that a group or organization produces to tell people its news〔尤指團體出版的〕小報; 會刊

bulletin board /ˈ··· ˌ·/ *n* [C] **1** *AmE* a board on the wall that you put information or pictures on【美】佈告牌[欄]; NOTICEBOARD *BrE*【英】: *a windows bulletin board due out next year* 明年到期的窗式佈告欄 —see picture on page A14 參見A14頁圖 **2 electronic bulletin board** a place in a computer information system where you can read or leave messages〔電腦的〕電子佈告牌

bullet proof /ˈ··· ·/ *adj* something that is bullet proof is designed to stop bullets from going through it 防彈的

bull·fight /ˈbʊlˌfaɪt; ˈbʊlfaɪt/ *n* [C] a type of entertainment popular in Spain, in which a man fights and kills a BULL¹ (1) 鬥牛 —**bullfighter** *n* [C] —**bullfighting** *n* [U]

bull·finch /ˈbʊlˌfɪntʃ; ˈbʊlˌfɪntʃ/ *n* [C] a small grey and red European bird 紅腹灰雀

bull·frog /ˈbʊlˌfrɑg; ˈbʊlfrɒg/ *n* [C] a kind of large FROG that makes a loud noise 牛蛙

bull-head·ed /ˌ· ˈ··◄/ *adj* determined to get what you want without really thinking enough about it 愚笨固執的; 任性的 —**bull-headedly** *adv* —**bull-headedness** *n* [U]

bull·horn /ˈbʊlˌhɔrn; ˈbʊlhɔːn/ *n* [C] *AmE old-fashioned* a piece of equipment that you hold up to your mouth to make your voice louder【美, 過時】手提式擴音器, 喇叭筒; MEGAPHONE *BrE*【英】

bul·lion /ˈbʊljən; ˈbʊljən/ *n* [U] bars of gold or silver 金[銀]條, 金[銀]塊: *gold bullion* 金條

bul·lish /ˈbʊlɪʃ; ˈbʊlɪʃ/ *adj* **1** [not before noun 不用於名詞前] feeling confident about the future〔對未來〕有信心的; 樂觀的: *very bullish about the company's prospects* 對公司的前景充滿信心 **2** *technical* in a business market that is bullish the prices of shares (SHARE² (5)) tend or seem likely to rise【術語】股票行情看漲的, 做多頭的 —**bullishly** *adv* —**bullishness** *n* [U]

bull·necked /ˌbʊlˈnɛkt; ˌbʊlˈnekt◄/ *adj* having a short and very thick neck〔指人〕頸部短粗的

bul·lock /ˈbʊlək; ˈbʊlək/ *n* [C] a young male cow that cannot breed 小閹牛

bull pen /ˈ· ·/ *n* [C] *AmE*【美】**1** the area in a BASEBALL field in which PITCHERs practise throwing〔棒球場中的〕投球練習區 **2** the PITCHERs of a BASEBALL team〔棒球運動中的〕投球手

bull·ring /ˈbʊlˌrɪŋ; ˈbʊlˌrɪŋ/ *n* [C] the place where a BULLFIGHT is held 鬥牛場

bull ses·sion /ˈ· ˌ··/ *n* [C] *AmE informal* an occasion when a group of people meet to talk in a relaxed and friendly way【美, 非正式】閒聊, 輕鬆而友好的交談: *an all-night bull session* 通宵漫談

bull's-eye 靶心

The arrow hit the bull's-eye. 箭正中靶心。

bull's-eye /ˈ· ·/ *n* [C] **1** the centre of a TARGET¹ (3) that you try to hit when shooting or in games like darts (DART² (2)) 靶心 **2** *BrE* a large hard round sweet【英】大塊圓形硬糖

bull·shit¹ /ˈbʊlˌʃɪt; ˈbʊlˌʃɪt/ *n* [U] *informal* a rude word meaning something that is stupid and completely untrue【非正式】瞎扯, 胡說八道, 廢話: *Forget all that bullshit and listen to me!* 別管那些廢話, 聽我說! | **a**

load of bullshit *Your so-called plan is a load of bullshit.* 你的所謂計劃不過是一堆廢話。

bullshit² *v* [I,T] *informal* a rude word meaning that something said is stupid or completely untrue, especially in order to deceive or impress someone【非正式】胡說, 瞎吹, 亂說: *Don't believe him, he's probably bullshitting.* 別信他的, 他可能在亂說。—**bullshitter** *n* [C]

bull ter·ri·er /ˌ· ˈ···/ *n* [C] a strong short-haired dog 短毛㹴〔原產於英國, 為鬥牛犬和㹴交配生的雜種犬〕—see also 另見 PIT BULL TERRIER

bul·ly¹ /ˈbulɪ; ˈbʊli/ *n* [C] someone who uses their strength or power to frighten or hurt someone who is weaker 恃強淩弱者, 以大欺小者; 流氓, 暴徒: *Bullies are often cowards.* 欺負人者常常是懦夫。

bully 欺侮

bully² *v* [T] to threaten to hurt someone or frighten them, especially someone smaller or weaker 欺侮, 以大欺小, 威逼 —**bullying** *n* [U]: *an attempt to tackle the problem of bullying in schools* 為解決學校裡有人以大欺小的問題所作出的嘗試

bully off *phr v* [I] to start a game of HOCKEY (1)〔曲棍球〕比賽開始 —**bully-off** *n* [C]

bully³ *adj* **bully for you/him etc** *spoken* used when you do not think that someone has done anything special but they want you to praise them【口】好極了〔用於表示贊同某人的做法, 但不一定出於真心〕: *Yes. I know you've done all the dishes. Bully for you!* 是的, 我知道你把碗碟都洗了。太好了!

bully beef /ˈ·· ·/ *n* [U] *BrE* CORNED BEEF【英】罐裝鹹牛肉

bully boy /ˈ·· ·/ *n* [C] *BrE informal* someone who behaves in a violent and threatening way【英, 非正式】惡棍, 流氓, 暴徒

bul·rush /ˈbulˌrʌʃ; ˈbʊlrʌʃ/ *n* [C] a tall plant that looks like grass and grows by water 寬葉香蒲; 燈心草

bul·wark /ˈbulwɚk; ˈbʊlwək/ *n* [C] **1** something that protects you from an unpleasant situation 保障; 堡壘; 保護物: [+against] *The Soviet Union was our only bulwark against fascism.* 蘇聯是保護我們不受法西斯統治的唯一保障。**2 bulwarks** [plural] the sides of a boat or ship above the DECK¹ (1)〔船的〕舷牆 **3** a strong structure like a wall, built for defence 掩體, 壁壘, 堡壘

3 **bum¹** /bʌm; bʌm/ *n* [C] *informal*【非正式】**1** *AmE* someone, especially a man, who has no home or job, and who asks people for money【美】流浪乞丐; 無業遊民 **2** *BrE* the part of your body that you sit on; BOTTOM¹ (3)【英】屁股 **3 beach/ski etc bum** someone who spends all their time on the beach, skiing (SKI²) etc without having a job 沉湎於海灘/滑雪等的人 **4** someone who is very lazy 懶鬼

bum² *v* **bummed, bumming** [T] *slang* to ask someone for something such as money, food, or cigarettes【俚】乞討

bum around *phr v slang*【俚】**1** also 又作 **bum about** [I] to spend time lazily doing nothing 遊手好閒, 遊蕩 **2** [T **bum around** sth] to travel around in an unplanned way living very cheaply 漫遊: *a year bumming around Australia* 在澳大利亞漫遊一年

bum³ *adj* [only before noun 僅用於名詞前] *slang* bad and useless【俚】蹩腳的, 毫無價值的: *It must be a bum copy. It sounds terrible!* 這肯定是粗劣的複製品, 音質太差勁!

bum bag /ˈ· ·/ *n* [C] a small bag that you wear around your waist to hold money, keys etc 腰包

bum·ble /ˈbʌmbl̩; ˈbʌmbəl/ *v* [I] **1** also 又作 **bumble on** to speak in a confused way so that no-one can understand you 含糊不清地說: *I really don't know what Karl was bumbling on about.* 我真不知道卡爾在嘟囔些甚麼。**2** also 又作 **bumble around** to move in an unsteady way 笨拙地行動

bum·ble·bee /ˈbʌmbl̩ˌbi; ˈbʌmbəlbiː/ *n* [C] a large hairy BEE 大黃蜂, 熊蜂

bum·bling /ˈbʌmblɪŋ; ˈbʌmblɪŋ/ *adj* [only before noun 僅用於名詞前] behaving in a careless way and making a lot of mistakes 粗心大意的, 常出錯的: *bumbling incompetence* 笨手笨腳, 不能勝任

bumf, bumph /bʌmf; bʌmf/ *n* [U] *BrE informal* boring written information that you have to read【英, 非正式】令人乏味的文件; 無大用處的印刷品: *I got a load of bumf from the gas board.* 我從煤氣公司得到了一大堆無用的印刷品。

bum·mer /ˈbʌmɚ; ˈbʌməʳ/ *n* **a bummer** *slang* a situation that is disappointing or annoying【俚】令人失望[煩惱]的情形: *It was a real bummer being ill on holiday.* 在假期生病真掃興。

bump¹ /bʌmp; bʌmp/ *v* **1** [I always+adv/prep, T] to hit 3
or knock against something 猛碰, 撞: [+against/into etc] *It was so dark I bumped into a tree.* 天太黑, 我撞到了樹上。| **bump sth on/against etc** *I bumped my head on the ledge.* 我的頭撞到了壁架上。**2** [I always+adv/prep] to move up and down as you move forward, especially in a vehicle〔車輛〕顛簸而行: [+along/across etc] *The bus bumped along the rutted road.* 公共汽車沿着有車轍的路顛簸而行。

bump into sb *phr v* [T] to meet someone that you know when you were not expecting to 巧遇, 邂逅, 碰見: *I bumped into Jean in town this morning.* 今天上午我在城裡遇見了瓊。

bump sb ↔ **off** *phr v* [T] *informal* to kill someone【非正式】殺死〔某人〕

bump sth ↔ **up** *phr v* [T] *informal* to suddenly increase something by a large amount【非正式】突然大幅度提高, 增加: *In the summer they bump up the prices by ten percent.* 在夏天, 他們把價格突然提高了10%。

bump² *n* [C] **1** an area of skin that is raised up because you have hit it on something〔撞擊造成的〕腫塊: *How did you get that bump over your eye?* 你眼睛上的腫塊是怎麼回事? **2** a small raised area on a surface 隆起之處: *bumps on the road* 路面隆起之處 **3** *informal* a slight accident in which your car hits something but you are not hurt【非正式】〔汽車〕碰撞: *Jim had a bump in the car.* 吉姆的汽車顛了一下。**4** the sound of something hitting a hard surface 砰然一聲; 撞擊聲: *We heard a bump in the next room.* 我們聽到隔壁房間傳來砰的一聲。| **fall/sit down etc with a bump** *Don sat down with a bump.* 唐撲通一屁股坐了下去。

bump·er¹ /ˈbʌmpɚ; ˈbʌmpə/ *n* [C] **1** *BrE* a bar fixed on the front and back of a car to protect it if it hits anything【英】〔汽車車身前後的〕保險槓; FENDER (1) *AmE*【美】—see picture on page A2 參見A2頁圖 **2 bumper-to-bumper** bumper-to-bumper traffic is very close together and moving slowly 一輛緊跟一輛

bumper² *adj* [only before noun 僅用於名詞前] unusually large 特大的; 豐盛的: *a bumper crop* (莊稼)大豐收 | *a bumper edition of a magazine* 特大版的雜誌

bumper car /ˈ·· ·/ *n* [C] a small electric car that you drive in a special area at a FUNFAIR and deliberately try to hit other cars 碰碰車

bumper stick·er /ˈ·· ˌ··/ *n* [C] a sign on the BUMPER¹ (1) of a car, with a humorous, political, or religious message 貼在汽車保險槓上的小標語〔內容為幽默的、政治性的或宗教的語句〕

bumph /bʌmf; bʌmf/ *n* [U] another spelling of BUMF bumf的另一種拼法

bump·kin /ˈbʌmpkɪn; ˈbʌmpkɪn/ *n* [C] *informal* someone from the countryside who is considered to be stupid【非正式】鄉巴佬, 土包子

bump·tious /ˈbʌmpʃəs; ˈbʌmpʃəs/ *adj* too proud of your abilities in a way that annoys other people 自吹自擂的, 自高自大的, 自負的 —**bumptiously** *adv* —**bumptiousness** *n* [U]

bump·y /ˈbʌmpɪ; ˈbʌmpi/ *adj* **1** a bumpy surface is flat but has a lot of raised parts so it is difficult to walk or drive on it 高低不平的: *a bumpy lane* 凸凹不平的車道 **2** a bumpy journey by car or plane is uncomfortable because of bad road or weather conditions〔旅程〕顛簸的 **3 have a bumpy ride/time** to have a lot of problems for a long time 走過相當漫長坎坷的道路/度過相當長的困難時期: *Professional soccer has had a bumpy ride in the US.* 職業足球在美國走過了漫長坎坷的道路。—opposite 反義詞 SMOOTH[1]

bun /bʌn; bʌn/ *n* [C] **1** *BrE* a small round sweet cake【英】小圓糕點: *a sticky bun* 一個黏乎乎的小圓點心 **2** *especially AmE* a small round type of bread【尤美】小圓麵包: *a hamburger bun* 漢堡包 **3** a hairstyle in which a woman with long hair fastens it in a small round shape at the back of her head〔盤在腦後的〕圓髮髻—see picture at 參見 HAIRSTYLE 圖 **4 have a bun in the oven** *BrE humorous* to be PREGNANT (=going to have a baby)【英, 幽默】懷孕, 有喜

S2 **bunch**[1] /bʌntʃ; bʌntʃ/ *n* **1 bunch of flowers/keys/grapes etc** a group of flowers, keys etc that are fastened or held together 一束花/一串鑰匙/一串葡萄等 **2** [singular] *informal* a group of people【非正式】〔人〕一羣, 一夥: *Our new neighbours are a weired bunch.* 我們的新鄰居是一夥很古怪的人。**3 the pick of the bunch** the best among a group of people or things 佼佼者 **4** [singular] *especially AmE* a large number of people or things, or a large amount of something【尤美】大量: [+of] *The doctor asked me a bunch of questions.* 醫生問了我一連串問題。**5 in bunches** *BrE* if a girl wears her hair in bunches, she ties it together at each side of her head【英】〔把頭髮分在兩邊〕紮成兩簇 **6 thanks a bunch** an expression meaning thank you very much, used jokingly when you are not grateful at all 多謝了〔玩笑説法, 表示毫無感激之意〕

bunch[2] *v* also 又作 **bunch together, bunch up 1** [I] to stay close together in a group 聚成堆[羣]: *The children bunched together in groups in the playground.* 孩子們你一羣我一夥地聚在操場上。**2** [T] to tighten part of your body 繃緊〔身體的一部分〕: *Sean bunched his fists and strode towards them.* 肖恩握緊拳頭, 大步朝他們走去。**3** [T] to hold or tie things together in a bunch 將〔東西〕綁成一束 **4** [I,T] to pull material together tightly in folds 使起褶

bun·dle[1] /ˈbʌndl; ˈbʌndl/ *n* [C] **1** a group of things such as papers, clothes, or sticks that are fastened or tied together 捆, 把, 紮, 束 **2** [singular] *informal* a lot of money【非正式】一大筆錢: **cost a bundle** *The trip will cost a bundle and we can't pay for it ourselves.* 旅行要花一大筆錢, 我們自己支付不起。| **make a bundle** (=earn or win a lot of money) 賺了大筆錢 **3 be a bundle of nerves** *informal* to be very nervous【非正式】極度緊張 **4 be a bundle of fun/laughs** *informal* an expression meaning a person or situation that is fun or makes you laugh, often used jokingly when they are not fun at all【非正式】出洋相: *You were a bundle of fun last night. What's wrong?* 昨晚你大出洋相, 到底是怎麼回事? **5 not go a bundle on sth** *BrE informal* to not like something very much【英, 非正式】不太喜歡某事物: *Jim never drank, and certainly didn't go a bundle on gambling.* 吉姆從不喝酒, 而且肯定也不太喜歡賭博。

bundle[2] *v* **1** [T always+adv/prep] to quickly push someone or something somewhere because you are in a hurry or you want to hide them 匆匆打發〔某人〕; 把〔某物〕亂塞: **bundle sb into/through etc** *They bundled Perez into the car, and drove off.* 他們把佩雷斯推上汽車, 然後開走了。**2** [I always + adv/prep] to move somewhere quickly in a group 塞進, 擠進: [+into/through etc] *Six of us bundled into a taxi.* 我們六個人擠進了計程車。

bundle sb **off** *phr v* [T] to send someone somewhere in a hurry 匆匆把〔某人〕送往某地

bundle up *phr v* **1** [T **bundle** sth ↔ **up**] to make a bundle by tying things together 把…紮緊, 把…捆上: *Bundle up the newspapers and take them to the skip.* 把這些報紙捆在一起扔進廢物桶裡。**2** [I,T **bundle sb up**] to dress warmly because it is cold (給)〔某人〕穿上暖和的衣服

bung[1] /bʌŋ; bʌŋ/ *n* [C] **1** a round piece of rubber, wood etc used to close the top of a container (大) 塞子 —see picture at 參見 LABORATORY 圖 **2** *BrE slang* money given to someone secretly, and usually illegally, to make them do something【英俚】賄賂

bung[2] *v* [T always+adv/prep] *BrE informal* to put something somewhere quickly and without thinking carefully【英, 非正式】投, 扔, 擲; 亂放: **bung sth in/on etc** *Can you bung these clothes in the washing machine?* 你能把這些衣服扔進洗衣機嗎?

bung sth ↔ **up** *phr v* [T] **1** to block a hole by putting something in it 阻塞, 塞住 **2 be bunged up** *informal* to find it difficult to breathe because you have a COLD【非正式】〔因傷風而鼻子〕不通氣

bun·ga·low /ˈbʌŋgəˌlo; ˈbʌŋgələʊ/ *n* [C] **1** *BrE* a house which is all on ground level【英】平房 **2** *AmE* a small house which is often on one level【美】單層小屋 —see picture on page A4 參見 A4 頁圖

bun·gee cord /ˈbʌndʒɪ ˌkɔrd; ˈbʌndʒi ˌkɔːd/ *n* [C] *AmE* a thick rope that stretches and has hooks on each end【美】〔用於綁緊跳的〕有彈性的繩

bungee jump·ing /ˈbʌndʒɪ ˌdʒʌmpɪŋ; ˈbʌndʒi ˌdʒʌmpɪŋ/ *n* [U] the activity of attaching yourself to something such as a bridge with a bungee cord, then jumping off so you BOUNCE in the air 綁緊跳, 笨豬跳, 蹦極跳〔把自己用一根有彈性的繩繫在橋等物體上, 然後跳下, 再彈回空中的一種運動〕

bung·hole /ˈbʌŋˌhol; ˈbʌŋhəʊl/ *n* [C] a hole for emptying or filling a BARREL[1] (1) 桶孔, 桶口

bun·gle /ˈbʌŋgl; ˈbʌŋgəl/ *v* [T] to do something unsuccessfully, because you have made stupid or careless mistakes 做壞, 搞糟: *The whole police operation was bungled.* 整個警察行動給弄得一團糟了。—**bungle** *n* [C] —**bungler** *n* [C] —**bungling** *n* [U] —**bungled** *adj*: *a bungled rescue attempt* 一次失敗的救援行動

bun·ion /ˈbʌnjən; ˈbʌnjən/ *n* [C] a painful red sore area on the first joint of your big toe 拇趾囊腫, 拇囊炎腫

bunk[1] /bʌŋk; bʌŋk/ *n* **1** [C] a narrow bed that is fixed to the wall, for example on a train or ship〔火車、船上的〕卧鋪, 靠壁牀鋪, 鋪位 **2 bunk beds** [plural] two beds that are fixed together, one on top of the other 雙層牀 —see picture at 參見 BED[1] 圖 **3 do a bunk** *BrE informal* to suddenly leave a place without telling anyone【英, 非正式】逃走; 擅自離開 **4** [U] *informal* nonsense; BUNKUM【非正式】瞎説, 廢話: *What a load of bunk!* 一大堆廢話!

bunk[2] *v* [I] *informal* also 又作 **bunk down** to lie down to sleep in a particular place【非正式】〔在某處〕睡下: *You can bunk down on the sofa for tonight.* 今晚你可以在沙發上過夜。

bunk off *phr v BrE informal* [I,T **bunk off** sth] to stay away from somewhere such as school or to leave somewhere early without permission【英, 非正式】擅自離開; 逃走: *I think I'll bunk off classes this afternoon.* 我想今天下午我要逃課。

bun·ker /ˈbʌŋkə; ˈbʌŋkə/ *n* [C] **1** a place where you store coal, especially on a ship or outside a house〔尤指船上或屋外的〕煤倉 **2** a strongly built shelter for soldiers, usually underground 掩體, 地堡, 掩蔽壕 **3** *BrE* a large hole on a GOLF course, filled with sand【英】〔高爾夫球場的〕沙坑; SANDTRAP *AmE*【美】—see picture on page A23 參見 A23 頁圖

bunk·house /ˋbʌŋkˌhaʊs; ˈbʌŋkhaʊs/ *n* [C] a building where workers sleep 工棚; 簡易工人宿舍

bun·kum /ˋbʌŋkəm; ˈbʌŋkəm/ *n* [U] *informal* nonsense【非正式】廢話, 胡說八道

bunk-up /ˌ· ˋ·/ *n BrE* [singular] *informal* an act of pushing someone up from below to help them get higher【英, 非正式】〔幫助別人攀登時向上的〕一推, 一托

3 **bun·ny** /ˋbʌnɪ; ˈbʌni/ also 又作 **bunny rab·bit** /ˋ·· ˌ··/ *n* [C] a word for a rabbit, used especially by or to children 兔子〔尤為兒語〕

bun·sen bur·ner /ˌbʌnsn̩ ˋbɝnɚ; ˌbʌnsən ˈbɜːnə/ *n* [C] a piece of equipment that produces a hot gas flame, for scientific EXPERIMENTs 本生燈〔實驗室用的一種煤氣燈〕—see picture at 參見 LABORATORY 圖

bunt /bʌnt; bʌnt/ *v* [I] *AmE* to deliberately hit the ball a short distance in a game of BASEBALL【美】〔棒球比賽中的〕觸擊 —**bunt** *n* [C]

bun·ting /ˋbʌntɪŋ; ˈbʌntɪŋ/ *n* [U] small paper or cloth flags on strings, used to decorate buildings and streets on special occasions〔用繩子穿成一長串的〕小彩旗

buoy[1] /ˋbuɪ; bɔɪ/ *n* [C] an object that floats on the sea to mark a safe or dangerous area 浮標, 航標

buoy[2] also 又作 **buoy up** *v* [T] **1** to make someone feel happier or more confident 振奮…的精神; 鼓舞: *buoyed by a two goal lead* 為領先兩分而振奮 **2** to keep profits, prices etc at a high level 維持〔利潤、價格等的高水平〕: *The company's profits were buoyed by a successful publishing venture.* 由於出版風險項目的成功運作, 這家公司維持了較高水平的利潤。**3** to keep something floating 使浮起

buoy·an·cy /ˋbɔɪənsɪ; ˈbɔɪənsi/ *n* [U] **1** the ability of an object to float〔物體在液體裡的〕浮性: *the buoyancy of light wood* 輕質木材的浮性 **2** the power of a liquid to make an object float 浮力: *Salt water has more buoyancy than fresh water.* 鹽水的浮力比淡水大。**3** a feeling of cheerfulness and belief that you can deal with problems easily 自信; 樂觀 **4** the ability of prices, a business etc to quickly get back to a high level after a difficult period〔價格、營業狀況等的〕維持力; 恢復力; 上漲行情; 增長趨勢

buoy·ant /ˋbɔɪənt; ˈbɔɪənt/ *adj* **1** cheerful and confident 輕鬆愉快的; 自信的: *Phil was in buoyant mood.* 菲爾心情很愉快。**2** buoyant prices etc tend to rise 趨於上升的; 上漲的: *a buoyant economy* 欣欣向榮的經濟 **3** able to float or keep things floating 有浮力的, 易浮起的: *Cork is a very buoyant material.* 軟木塞是一種極易浮起的材料。—**buoyantly** *adv*

bur /bɝ; bɜː/ *n* [C] another spelling of BURR burr 的另一種拼法

Bur·ber·ry /ˋbɝbərɪ; ˈbɜːbəri/ *n* [C] *trademark* a kind of RAINCOAT【商標】柏帛麗牌雨衣

bur·ble /ˋbɝbl̩; ˈbɜːbəl/ *v* **1** [I,T] to talk about something in a confused way that is difficult to understand 嘟嘟囔囔地說; 嘮叨: *Maggie kept burbling away about how difficult things were.* 瑪吉滔滔不絕地說情況太糟。**2** [I] to make a sound like a stream flowing over stones 發出潺潺聲; 潺潺而流 —**burble** *n* [C]

burbs /ˌbɝbz; bɜːbz/ *n* **the burbs** *AmE informal* the SUBURBs (=areas around a city)【美, 非正式】郊區

3 **bur·den**[1] /ˋbɝdn̩; ˈbɜːdn/ *n* **1** [C] something difficult or
3 worrying that you are responsible for 重擔, 負擔: **heavy burden** *We're in no position to take on another heavy financial burden.* 我們無法承受又一個沉重的經濟負擔。**2** [singular] *formal* the main meaning of what someone is saying【正式】要點, 要旨, 主旨 **3 the burden of proof** *law* the duty to prove that something is true【法律】舉證責任 **4** something that is carried; load 擔子; 負荷 —see also 另見 BEAST OF BURDEN

burden[2] *v* **1 be burdened by** to have a lot of problems because of a particular thing 被…所困擾; 承受…的負擔: *a big company burdened by debt* 債務纏身的大公司 —see also 另見 UNBURDEN **2 be burdened with** to be carrying something heavy 負載着, 揹負着: *burdened with grocery bags* 揹着沉重的食品袋

bur·den·some /ˋbɝdn̩səm; ˈbɜːdnsəm/ *adj* causing problems or additional work 成為負擔的, 累贅的; 令人煩惱的: *burdensome responsibilities* 繁重的責任

bu·reau /ˋbjuro; ˈbjʊərəʊ/ *n plural* **bureaux** /-roz; -rəʊz/ *BrE*【英】, **bureaus** *AmE*【美】[C] **1** an office or organization that collects or provides information 提供[收集]消息的辦事處[機構]: *an employment bureau* 職業介紹所 **2** *especially AmE* a government department or a part of a government department【尤美】〔政府部門的〕司; 局; 處; 署: *the Federal Bureau of Investigation* 聯邦調查局 **3** *BrE* a large desk or writing table【英】大書桌, 大寫字枱 **4** *AmE* a piece of furniture with several drawers, used to keep clothes in; CHEST OF DRAWERS【美】五斗櫥, 衣櫃

bu·reauc·ra·cy /bjuˋrɑkrəsɪ; bjʊəˈrɒkrəsi/ *n* **1** [U] a complicated official system which is annoying or confusing because it has a lot of rules, processes etc 官僚制度; 官僚政治; 官僚機構; 官僚主義: *plans to eliminate unnecessary bureaucracy* 消除不必要的官僚體制的計劃 **2** [C,U] the officials who are employed rather than elected to do the work of a government, business etc 官僚〔指雇用而非選舉之政府官員的總稱〕;〔工商業的〕高級管理人員

bu·reau·crat /ˋbjurəˌkræt; ˈbjʊərəkræt/ *n* [C] someone who works in a bureaucracy and uses official rules very strictly 官僚; 官僚主義者; 官僚作風的人

bu·reau·crat·ic /ˌbjurəˋkrætɪk; ˌbjʊərəˈkrætɪk◂/ *adj* involving a lot of complicated official rules and processes 官僚的; 官僚主義的 —**bureaucratically** /-kl̩ɪ; -kli/ *adv*

bureau de change /ˌbjuro de ˋʃɑndʒ; ˌbjʊərəʊ də ˈʃɒndʒ/ *n* [C] *French* an office or shop where you can change foreign money【法】外幣兌換所[店]

bur·geon /ˋbɝdʒən; ˈbɜːdʒən/ *v* [I] *formal* to grow or develop quickly【正式】急速增長[發展]

bur·geon·ing /ˋbɝdʒənɪŋ; ˈbɜːdʒənɪŋ/ *adj* increasing or developing very quickly 迅速發展的: *a project to improve water supplies to Denver's burgeoning population* 為適應丹佛迅速增加的人口而改善供水的項目

burg·er /ˋbɝgɚ; ˈbɜːgə/ *n* [C] **1** a flat round piece of finely cut BEEF[1] (1), which is cooked and usually eaten in a bread ROLL[2] (2); a HAMBURGER 漢堡包: **cheeseburger** (=a burger with cheese on top of the meat) 乳酪漢堡包 **2 vegeburger/nutburger** something like a HAMBURGER but made of vegetables, nuts etc 素餡/果仁漢堡包

burgh /bɝg; ˈbʌrə/ *n* [C] *ScotE* a BOROUGH【蘇格蘭】享有某些自治權的城鎮

bur·gher /ˋbɝgɚ; ˈbɜːgə/ *n* [C] *old use* someone who lives in a particular town【舊】〔自治市的〕市民

bur·glar /ˋbɝglɚ; ˈbɜːglə/ *n* [C] someone who gets into houses, shops etc to steal things 小偷, 竊賊 —compare 比較 ROBBER, THIEF —see also 另見 CAT BURGLAR

burglar a·larm /ˋ·· ·ˌ·/ *n* [C] a piece of equipment that makes a loud noise when a burglar gets into a building 防盜警報器[鈴] —see picture at 參見 ALARM[1] 圖

bur·gla·rize /ˋbɝgləˌraɪz; ˈbɜːgləraɪz/ *v* [T] *AmE* to get into a building and steal things from it or from the people inside【美】入室行竊, 闖入…行竊; burgle *BrE*【英】

bur·glar·y /ˋbɝglərɪ; ˈbɜːgləri/ *n* [C,U] the crime of getting into a building to steal things 入室盜竊(罪): *Burglaries in the area have risen by 5%.* 這一地區的入室盜竊罪上升了 5%。

bur·gle /ˋbɝgl̩; ˈbɜːgəl/ *v* [T] *BrE* to get into a building and steal things from it or from the people inside【英】闖入…行竊; burglarize *AmE*【美】: *We've been burgled three times!* 我們(家)已經三次被盜! —see 見 STEAL[1] (USAGE)

bur·gun·dy /ˈbɝɡəndɪ; ˈbɜːɡəndi/ *n* **1** [C,U] red or white wine from the Burgundy area of France〔法國勃艮第地區產的〕葡萄酒 **2** [U] a dark red colour 深(紫)紅色 —see picture on page A5 參見A5頁圖

bur·i·al /ˈbɛrɪəl; ˈberiəl/ *n* [C,U] the act or ceremony of putting a dead body into a grave 埋葬; 葬禮

burk /bɝk; bɜːk/ *n* [C] another spelling of BERK berk的另一種拼法

B

bur·lap /ˈbɝlæp; ˈbɜːlæp/ *n* [U] *AmE* a type of thick rough cloth【美】〔打包用的〕粗麻布, 麻袋布; HESSIAN *BrE*【英】

bur·lesque¹ /bɝˈlɛsk; bɜːˈlesk/ *n* **1** [C,U] speech, acting, or writing in which a serious subject is made to seem silly or an unimportant subject is treated in a serious way 滑稽諷刺講話[演出, 文字] **2** *AmE* a performance involving a mixture of comedy and STRIPTEASE, popular in America in the past【美】〔美國舊時的〕滑稽歌舞雜劇〔常包括脫衣舞〕: *a burlesque house* 雜耍表演場

burlesque² *v* [T] to make a serious subject seem silly to amuse people 諷刺, 嘲弄, 使滑稽化

bur·ly /ˈbɝlɪ; ˈbɜːli/ *adj* a burly man is big and strong 壯實的, 魁梧的: *burly rugby players* 壯實的橄欖球員 —**burliness** *n* [U]

burn¹ /bɝn; bɜːn/ *v past and past participle* **burnt** /bɝnt; bɜːnt/ *or* **burned**

① FIRE 火
② CHEMICALS 化學品
③ KILL 殺死
④ PRODUCE POWER/LIGHT 產生力/光
⑤ FEELING/EMOTION 感覺/感情
⑥ MONEY 錢
⑦ CARS 汽車
⑧ OTHER MEANINGS 其他意思

① FIRE 火

1 ►PRODUCE HEAT 產生熱◄ [I] to produce heat and flames 燃燒: *Is the fire still burning?* 火還在燃燒嗎?

2 ►DESTROY WITH FIRE 燒毀◄ [I,T] to be destroyed by fire or destroy something with fire 焚燒, 燒毀: **burn sth** *I burnt all his old letters.* 我把他的舊信全燒了。

3 burn to the ground/burn to ashes if a building burns to the ground, it is completely destroyed by fire 燒成灰燼

4 burn sth to a crisp/cinder to burn something until it is black, especially by cooking it for too long 將某物燒黑〔尤指烹調時間過長〕—see picture on page A10 參見A10頁圖

5 ►DAMAGE BY FIRE 燒壞◄ [I,T] to damage something or hurt someone with fire or heat, or be hurt or damaged in this way (使)燒傷[壞], (使)燙傷[壞], (使)燒焦: *I've burnt my hand.* 我燙傷了手。| *Quick, the toast's burning!* 快! 麵包烤焦了! | **burn a hole in** *Be careful you don't burn a hole in the chair with your cigarette.* 小心點, 別讓煙頭把椅子燒個洞。

② CHEMICALS 化學品

6 [T] to damage or destroy something by a chemical action; CORRODE 腐蝕, 燒毀

③ KILL 殺死

7 be burned to death/burned alive to be killed in a fire 被活活燒死

8 burn sb at the stake to kill someone by tying them to a post on top of a fire 把某人活活燒死在火刑柱上

④ PRODUCE POWER/LIGHT 產生力/光

9 [I,T] if you burn a FUEL, or if it burns, it is used to produce power, heat, light etc 點, 燒: *The central heating boiler burns oil.* 中央供暖鍋爐燒油。

10 ►SHINE 發光◄ [I] if a light or lamp burns, it shines or produces light 發光, 照亮: *A light was burning in her window.* 她窗子裡亮着燈。

⑤ FEELING/EMOTION 感覺/感情

11 [I,T] to feel unpleasantly hot or make part of your body feel like this 使發燒; 刺痛; 感覺火辣[灼熱, 刺痛]: *I'm afraid the ointment might burn a bit.* 恐怕這種油膏會使皮膚有灼熱感。

12 ►BE EMBARRASSED 感到尷尬◄ [I] if your face or cheeks are burning, they feel hot because you are embarrassed or upset 臉發燒[熱]

13 be burning with rage/desire etc to feel an emotion very strongly 怒火中燒/產生強烈的慾望等

14 be burning to do sth to want to do something very much 心急如焚地要做某事: *Hannah's burning to tell you her news.* 漢娜心急如焚地要告訴你她的消息。

15 it burns me/her/John etc that *AmE* used to say that something makes someone feel angry or jealous【美】〔某事〕使我/她/約翰等感到氣憤[妒忌]: *It really burns me the way they treat us.* 他們那樣對待我們, 使我很氣憤。

16 be/get burned to be emotionally hurt by someone or something 感情受到傷害

⑥ MONEY 錢

17 burn a hole in your pocket if money is burning a hole in your pocket, you want to spend it as soon as you can 急於把錢花掉

18 burn your fingers/get your fingers burned *informal* to suffer the unpleasant results of something that you have done【非正式】自作自受; 自食其果: *George got his fingers badly burned when the travel company collapsed.* 旅行公司倒閉了, 喬治這是自作自受。

19 be/get burned to lose a lot of money, especially in a business deal〔尤指生意上〕賠了很多錢: *A lot of people got burned buying junk bonds.* 很多人因買垃圾債券而損失慘重。

⑦ CARS 汽車

20 ►GO FAST 快速行進◄ [I always+adv/prep] to travel very fast 高速行進: **[+along/through/up etc]** *a sports car burning up the motorway* 一輛在高速公路上疾駛的跑車

21 burn rubber *AmE informal* to start a car moving so quickly that the tyres become very hot and make a loud high noise【美, 非正式】〔因起動太快〕車胎發燙發出響聲

⑧ OTHER MEANINGS 其他意思

22 burn your bridges/boats *informal* to do something that you cannot change, that often makes a situation difficult for you【非正式】破釜沉舟, 自絕後路

23 burn the candle at both ends *informal* to work too hard for too long【非正式】過分消耗體力, 起早貪黑地幹, 廢寢忘食

24 burn the midnight oil *informal* to work or study until late at night【非正式】熬夜工作[讀書], 開夜車

burn away *phr v* [I,T] if something burns away or is burned away, it is destroyed or reduced to something much smaller by fire 燒掉, 燒毀, 燒光

burn down *phr v* **1** [I,T **burn** sth ↔ **down**] if a building burns down or is burned down, it is destroyed by fire〔建築物〕被燒毀 **2** [I] if a fire burns down, the flames become weaker and it produces less heat 火力減弱, 火頭變小 —compare 比較 **burn out** (BURN[1]), **burn up** (BURN[1])

burn sth ↔ **off** *phr v* [T] **1** to remove something by burning it 燒掉: *farmers burning off the stubble from the fields* 農民把田裡的茬子燒掉 **2 burn off energy/fat/calories etc** to use energy etc by doing physical exercise 消耗能量/脂肪/熱量等: *I think I'll go for a walk and burn off a few calories!* 我想散散步, 消耗點兒熱量!

burn out *phr v*

1 ▶FIRE 火◀ [I,T **burn** sth **out**] if a fire burns out or burns itself out, it stops burning because there is no coal, wood etc left 燒盡, 燃盡

2 be burnt out if something is burnt out, the inside of it is destroyed by fire 被燒空: *The hotel was completely burnt out; only the walls remained.* 旅館完全燒空, 僅剩四壁。

3 burn yourself out to ruin your health and feel very tired through working too hard, drinking too much alcohol etc〔因工作過累、酗酒等而〕元氣大傷, 精力耗盡;〔身體〕搞垮

4 ▶ENGINE 發動機◀ [I,T **burn** sth ↔ **out**] if an engine or electric wire burns out or is burned out, it stops working because it has been damaged by getting too hot 燒壞

5 ▶AIRCRAFT 飛機◀ [I] if a ROCKET[1] (1) or JET[1] (1) burns out, it stops operating because all its FUEL has been used 燃油用盡 —see also 另見 BURNOUT (1)

burn up *phr v*

1 ▶DESTROY 摧毀◀ [I,T **burn** sth ↔ **up**] if something burns up or is burnt up, it is completely destroyed by fire or great heat 燒毀, 燒盡

2 ▶BURN BRIGHTER 燒得更亮◀ [I] if a fire burns up, it gets stronger and brighter〔火〕旺起來, 燒起來

3 ▶BE HOT 變熱◀ [I] *spoken* if someone is burning up, they are very hot【口】〔人〕感到很熱

4 ▶MAKE SB ANGRY 使某人生氣◀ [T **burn** sb **up**] *informal especially AmE* to make someone angry【非正式, 尤美】使〔某人〕氣憤: *The way he treats her really burns me up.* 他那樣對待她, 令我十分氣憤。

5 be burned up with anger/jealousy etc to have your mind full of a strong emotion 怒火中燒/妒火中燒等

6 burn up energy/fat/calories etc to use energy etc by doing physical exercise 消耗能量/脂肪/熱量等

USAGE NOTE 用法說明: BURN

SPELLING 拼法

In American English the past tense and past participle of the verb is **burned**. 在美國英語中, 該詞的過去式和過去分詞都是 burned: *She burned a hole in my new shirt.* 她把我的新襯衫燒了個洞。In British English **burnt** is used, though **burned** is also used, especially when the action goes on for some time. 在英國英語中, 過去式和過去分詞是 burnt; 但也用 burned, 特別指動作已進行一段時間: *The fire burned brightly.* 火燒得很旺。| *I've burnt my hand.* 我把手燒傷了。| *The house burnt down.* 房子被燒毀了。

In both American and British English, **burnt** is used when the word is used as an adjective. 用作形容詞時, 美國英語和英國英語都作 burnt: *burnt toast* 烤焦的麵包 | *a burnt tree* (=made black by burning) 燒焦的樹

This is also true of 以上規則也適用於下列對應詞 **spoiled/spoilt, learned/learnt, spilled/spilt, spelled/spelt, smelled/smelt,** and, with a pronunciation difference as well 但有些詞的發音不同, **leaned/leant, leaped/leapt, dreamed/dreamt, kneeled/knelt**. e.g. 如 *I learned English for ten years.* 我學過十年英語。| *a spoilt child* 寵壞的孩子

3 **burn²** *n* [C] **1** an injury or mark caused by fire, heat, or acid〔因火、高溫或酸引起的〕灼傷; 燙傷; 傷痕: **severe/minor burns** (=burns that are serious or not serious) 嚴重/輕度燒傷 **2 the burn** *informal* a painful hot feeling in your muscles when you exercise a lot【非正式】〔大量鍛鍊使肌肉產生的〕熱痛感: *Go for the burn.* 去鍛鍊一下肌肉, 使其產生熱痛感。**3** *especially ScotE* a small stream【尤蘇格蘭】溪流

burn·er /ˈbɝnɚ; ˈbɜːnə/ *n* [C] **1** *AmE* the part of an OVEN or heater that produces heat or a flame【美】燃燒器 [爐]; 爐頭, 火眼; GAS RING *BrE*【英】: *a gas burner* 煤氣爐頭 —see picture at 參見 FONDUE 圖 **2 put sth on the back burner** *informal* to delay dealing with something until a later time【非正式】推遲〔做某事〕: *We've had to put the vacation plans on the back burner because of Bob's ill health.* 由於鮑勃身體欠佳, 我們只好推遲度假計劃。

burn·ing¹ /ˈbɝnɪŋ; ˈbɜːnɪŋ/ *adj* [only before noun 僅用於名詞前] **1** on fire 燃燒着的: *You could see the burning house for miles around.* 你可以在幾英里之外看到正在燃燒的房子。**2** feeling very hot 感到發燙的: *burning cheeks* 發燙的雙頰 **3 burning ambition/need etc** a very strong need etc 雄心勃勃/急切需要等: **burning ambition** *My burning ambition is to travel around the world.* 我極其渴望環遊世界。**4 burning question/issue** a very important and urgent question 急待解決的問題: *The burning question is, will Rob agree to come?* 當務之急是, 鮑勃會同意來嗎?

burning² *adv* **burning hot** very hot 滾燙的, 酷熱的

bur·nish /ˈbɝnɪʃ; ˈbɜːnɪʃ/ *v* [T] to polish metal until it shines 打磨, 拋光擦亮; 使光滑 —**burnished** *adj*: *burnished copper* 磨光的黃銅

bur·nous also 又作 **burnoose** *AmE*【美】/bɚˈnus; bɜːˈnuːs/ *n* [C] a long loose dress or coat worn by Arab men and women〔阿拉伯人穿的〕帶包頭巾的長袍

burn·out /ˈbɝnˌaʊt; ˈbɜːnaʊt/ *n* [C,U] **1** the time when a ROCKET[1] (1) or JET[1] (1) has finished all of its FUEL and stops operating〔火箭等燃料用盡時的〕熄滅 **2** a state in which you have ruined your health by working too hard〔因拼命工作導致的〕精疲力竭: *teachers suffering from burnout* 精疲力竭的教師們

burnt¹ /bɝnt; bɜːnt/ the past tense and past participle of BURN[1]

burnt² *adj* **1** damaged or hurt by burning 燒壞的, 燒傷的: *The cake's a little bit burnt, I'm afraid.* 恐怕蛋糕有點烤糊了。**2 burnt offering a)** something that is offered as a gift to a god by being burnt on an ALTAR (1) 燔祭, 供品〔炙熟以祭神之牲畜或果菜〕**b)** *humorous* food that you accidentally burnt while you were cooking it【幽默】燒焦的食物 3

burp /bɝp; bɜːp/ *v informal*【非正式】**1** [I] to pass gas noisily from your stomach out through your mouth; BELCH (1) 打嗝 **2** [T] to help a baby to do this, especially by rubbing or gently hitting its back〔按摩或輕拍其背部〕幫助〔嬰兒〕打嗝 —**burp** *n* [C]

burr /bɝ; bɜː/ *n* [C] **1** a fairly quiet regular sound like something turning quickly; WHIRR 顫音; 嗡嗡聲; 嘎嘎聲: *the burr of a sewing machine* 縫紉機的嘎嘎聲 **2** a way of pronouncing English with a strong 'r' sound〔發英語 r 音時顫動小舌的〕粗喉音 **3** also 又作 **bur** the seed container of some plants, covered with PRICKLES[1] (1) that make it stick to things〔某些植物〕帶芒刺的種子殼, 刺果, 針毬

bur·ri·to /bəˈrito; bəˈriːtəʊ/ *n plural* **burritos** [C] Mexican dish made with a TORTILLA (=flat thin bread) folded around meat or beans with cheese〔包有肉或乾酪的〕玉米麵餅

bur·ro /ˈbɝo; ˈbʊrəʊ/ *n plural* **burros** [C] *especially AmE* a DONKEY (1), usually a small one【尤美】(小) 毛驢

bur·row¹ /ˈbɝo; ˈbʌrəʊ/ *v* **1** [I always+adv/prep, T] to make a hole or passage in the ground 掘洞; 鑽洞: *burrowing a hole* 挖個洞 | [**+into/under etc**] *The dog managed to burrow under the fence.* 那隻狗設法從籬笆底下鑽了過去。**2** [T always+adv/prep] to press your body close to someone or under something because you want to get warm, feel safe etc 偎依, 緊靠: **burrow sth into/under etc** *The baby burrowed her head into my shoulder.* 寶寶把頭緊靠在我的肩膀上。**3** [I always+adv/prep] to search for something that is hidden in a container or under other things 尋找, 翻找: [**+into/through etc**] *Helen burrowed into her pocket for a handkerchief.* 海倫把手伸進口袋裡掏手帕。

burrow² *n* [C] a passage in the ground made by a rabbit or FOX¹ (1) as a place to live〔動物, 尤指兔子或狐狸所掘的〕洞穴

bur·sar /ˈbɝsɚ; ˈbɜːsə/ *n* [C] *especially BrE* someone at a school or college who deals with the accounts and office work【尤英】〔大中學校的〕財務[行政]主管

bur·sa·ry /ˈbɝsərɪ; ˈbɜːsəri/ *n* [C] *BrE* an amount of money given to someone so that they can study at a university or college; SCHOLARSHIP【英】〔大學的〕獎學金

burst 脹破

The balloon burst.
汽球吹破了。

burst¹ /bɝst; bɜːst/ *v past tense and past participle* **burst**

1 ►BREAK OPEN 裂開◄ [I,T] if something bursts or if you burst it, it breaks open or apart suddenly and violently so that its contents come out (使) 破裂; (使) 爆裂; (使) 脹破; (使) 爆炸: *You're going to burst the balloon, if you're not careful.* 一不小心, 你會把氣球弄爆的。

2 bursting with so full of something that there is no room for any more 充滿: *The barracks were bursting with refugees.* 兵營裡擠滿了難民。

3 ►MOVE SUDDENLY 突然移動◄ [I always+adv/prep] to move somewhere suddenly or quickly, especially into or out of a place 衝, 闖, 突然出現: [**+through/into/in etc**] *Don't burst into my bedroom without knocking!* 別不敲門就闖入我的臥室!

4 burst open to suddenly be open 突然開了: *The door burst open to reveal Francis holding a tray.* 門突然開了, 可以看到弗朗西絲拿着一個托盤。

5 be bursting to do sth *informal* to want to do something very much【非正式】迫不急待要做某事: *Mona's bursting to tell you the news.* 莫娜急不及待地要告訴你這個消息。

6 be bursting with pride/confidence/energy etc to be very proud, confident etc 充滿自豪/自信/精力等

7 be bursting *informal* to need to go to the toilet very soon【非正式】〔大小便〕憋不住了

8 full to bursting so full that there is no room for any more〔吃得〕太飽: *I can't eat any more, I'm full to bursting!* 我不能再吃了, 我已經撐飽了!

9 bursting at the seams so full that nothing else can fit inside 脹滿 —see also 另見 **burst sb's bubble** (BUBBLE¹ (5)), **burst the bubble** (BUBBLE¹ (4))

burst in on/upon sb/sth *phr v* [T] to interrupt something at an embarrassing moment 突然闖入, 打擾; 突然插嘴: *I burst in on the meeting thinking that the room was empty.* 我以為房間是空的, 沒想到打擾了人家的會議。

burst into sth *phr v* [T] **1** to suddenly begin to make a sound, especially to start singing, crying, or laughing 突然…起來〔尤指哭、笑、唱等〕: *The audience burst into applause.* 觀眾爆發出一陣掌聲。| **burst into song** *Everyone on the bus burst into song as we got closer to home.* 當我們快到家時, 公共汽車上所有的人都大聲唱起來。| **burst into tears** *Benny suddenly burst into tears.* 本尼突然放聲大哭。**2 burst into flames** to suddenly start to burn very strongly 突然起火〔尤指火勢失去控制〕: *The plane crashed into the hillside and burst into flames.* 飛機撞到山坡上, 一下子燃燒起來。

burst out *phr v* **1 burst out laughing/crying etc** to suddenly start to laugh, cry etc 突然大笑/大哭等: *They all burst out laughing at the expression on her face.* 看到她臉上的表情, 他們都大笑起來。**2** [T] to suddenly say something forcefully 突然說出: *"I don't believe it!" she burst out angrily.* 她憤憤然脱口而出: "我才不信呢!" —see also 另見 OUTBURST (1)

burst² *n* [C] **1** the act of something bursting or the place where it has burst 破裂, 爆炸; 噴出; 裂口: *a burst in the water pipe* 水管上的裂口 **2 a burst of sth a)** a short sudden effort or increase in activity 突然用力, 加速: *a burst of speed on the last lap* 最後一圈突然加速 **b)** a short sudden and usually loud sound 突發的響聲: *sharp bursts of machine gun fire* 一陣陣刺耳的機關槍聲 **c)** a sudden strong feeling or emotion 情感的突然爆發: *bursts of violent temper* 突然大發脾氣, 勃然大怒

bur·then /ˈbɝðən; ˈbɜːðən/ *n* [C] *literary* a BURDEN【文】重擔, 負擔

bur·ton /ˈbɝtn̩; ˈbɜːtn/ *n* **gone for a burton** *BrE spoken* lost, broken, or dead【英口】遺失了; 損壞了; 死了: *This radio's gone for a burton.* 這台收音機不響了。

bur·y /ˈbɛrɪ; ˈberi/ *v* [T]

1 ►PUT SB IN GRAVE 將某人埋入墳墓◄ to put someone who has died in a grave 埋葬: **bury sb in/at etc** *Gretta wanted to be buried at St Peter's.* 格里塔希望自己安葬在聖彼得公墓。

2 have buried sb to have had someone you love die 經歷親人的死亡: *Jessie has already buried two husbands.* 傑西先後已有兩位丈夫過世。

3 ►PUT STH UNDER EARTH 將某物埋入土中◄ to put something under the earth, often in order to hide it 埋藏

4 ►COVER WITH STH 用某物覆蓋◄ [usually passive 一般用被動態] to cover something with other things so that it cannot be found 被…埋住: **bury sth under/beneath etc** *The climbers were buried under a pile of rocks.* 登山者被埋在一堆岩石中。

5 ►FEELING/MEMORY 感覺/記憶◄ to ignore a feeling or memory and pretend that it does not exist 把〔感情〕埋在心裡: *a deeply buried memory* 深藏心裡的回憶

6 bury your face/head etc (in sth) to press your face etc into something soft, usually to get comfort, to avoid someone, or to be able to smell something 把臉/頭等伸到…裡去: *Noel turned away, burying his face in the pillow.* 諾埃爾轉過身, 把頭埋在枕頭底下。| **bury your face/head in your hands** (=cover your face etc with your hands because you are very upset) 用手捂住臉/頭

7 dead and buried completely finished and no longer important 不再重要的: *All the prewar ideas about defence are now dead and buried.* 戰前關於防禦的所有設想現在都已毫無意義。

8 bury the hatchet/bury your differences to agree to stop arguing about something and become friends again 拋棄前嫌, 重歸於好

9 ►PUSH STH INTO A SURFACE 將某物嵌入表面◄ to push something, especially something sharp, into something else with a lot of force〔尤指用尖利之物〕用力插入: *The dog buried its teeth in my leg.* 狗使勁咬住我的腿。| **bury itself** (=be pushed, thrown, or shot somewhere and stick there) 把…推[投, 扎]進去 *The knife buried itself in the wall a few inches from my head.* 刀扎在牆上離我的頭只有幾英寸。

10 bury yourself in your work/studies etc to give all your attention to something 埋頭工作/學習等: *After the divorce, she buried herself in her work.* 離婚後, 她埋頭於工作。

11 bury your head in the sand to ignore an unpleasant situation and hope it will stop if you do not think about it 採取鴕鳥政策, 閉眼不看現實

1 2 **bus¹** /bʌs; bʌs/ *n plural* **buses** also 又作 **busses** *AmE* 【美】[C] a large vehicle that people pay to travel on 公共汽車, 巴士; 大客車: *Hurry up or we'll miss the bus!* 快點, 不然我們就趕不上公共汽車了! | **by bus** *I go to work by bus.* 我乘公共汽車上班。| **bus driver/fare etc** *The bus fare is 60p.* 公共汽車車費是60便士。

bus² *v* **bussed, bussing** also 又作 **bused, busing** *AmE* 【美】[T] **1** to take a group of people somewhere in a bus that you HIRE (=pay to use) for the journey 用租用的大客車運送: **bus sb to/into etc** *Children had to be bussed to neighbouring schools.* 得用大客車把孩子們送往附近的學校。**2** *AmE* to take away dirty dishes from the tables in a restaurant 【美】收拾〔餐館飯桌上的髒碗碟〕: **bus tables** *Shelley had a job bussing tables.* 謝利得到一份收拾飯桌的工作。

bus·boy /ˈbʌsˌbɔɪ; ˈbʌsbɔɪ/ *n* [C] *AmE* a young man whose job is to help in a restaurant by taking away dirty dishes 【美】餐館侍應生的手下雜工〔負責收拾髒碗碟的年青男子〕

bus·by /ˈbʌzbɪ; ˈbʌzbi/ *n* [C] a tall fur hat worn by some British soldiers〔某些英國士兵戴的〕毛皮高頂帽

bush /bʊʃ; bʊʃ/ *n* [C] **1** a low thick plant smaller than a tree and with a lot of thin branches 灌木, 矮樹叢: *a rose bush* 玫瑰叢 **2 the bush** wild country that has not been cleared, especially in Australia or Africa〔尤指澳大利亞或非洲的〕未開墾的叢林地 —see also 另見 **beat about the bush** (BEAT¹ (15))

bush ba·by /ˈ· ˌ··/ *n* [C] a small African animal that lives in trees and has large eyes and ears, and a long tail〔非洲的〕嬰猴, 眼鏡猿

bushed /bʊʃt; bʊʃt/ *adj* [not before noun 不用於名詞前] *informal* very tired【非正式】筋疲力盡的

bush·el /ˈbʊʃəl; ˈbʊʃəl/ *n* [C] a unit for measuring grain or vegetables equal to 8 gallons or 36.4 litres 蒲式耳〔穀物、蔬菜、水果等的容量單位, 等於36.4升〕—see also 另見 **hide your light under a bushel** (HIDE¹ (7)) —see table on page C5 參見C5頁附錄

bush league /ˈ· ·/ *adj AmE informal* badly done or of such bad quality that it is not acceptable【美, 非正式】做得差的, 幹得不好的: *His work is still strictly bush league.* 嚴格地講, 他的工作還是做得很差。

bush·man /ˈbʊʃmən; ˈbʊʃmən/ *n* [C] **1 Bushman** a member of a southern African tribe who live in the bush〔非洲〕布須曼人 **2** someone who lives in the Australian BUSH (2)〔生活在澳大利亞的〕叢林人

bush tel·e·graph /ˌ· ˈ···/ *n* [U] *BrE humorous* the way in which people pass important news to each other very quickly【英, 幽默】小道消息: *I'd better warn you, the bush telegraph here works faster than the speed of light.* 我想提醒你, 在這裡小道消息傳播得比光速還快。

bush·whack /ˈbʊʃˌhwæk; ˈbʊʃwæk/ *v AmE*【美】**1** [T] to attack someone suddenly from a hidden place; AMBUSH² 伏擊, 偷襲 **2** [I,T] to push or cut your way through thick trees or bushes 在叢林中開道, 披荊斬棘 —**bushwhacker** *n* [C]

bush·y /ˈbʊʃɪ; ˈbʊʃi/ *adj* bushy hair or fur grows thickly〔毛髮〕濃密的, 多毛的: *a bushy tail* 毛茸茸的尾巴 —**bushiness** *n* [U] —see picture on page A6 參見A6頁圖

1 1 **busi·ness** /ˈbɪznɪs; ˈbɪznəs/ *n*

① WORK DONE BY COMPANIES 公司業務
② COMPANY 公司
③ SUBJECT 事務
④ STH THAT CONCERNS YOU 與你有關的事
⑤ WORK TO BE DONE 要做的工作
⑥ OTHER MEANINGS 其他意思

① WORK DONE BY COMPANIES 公司業務

1 [U] the activity of buying or selling goods or services that is done by companies 商業, 買賣, 生意, 業務: *Students on the course learn about all aspects of business.* 學這門課程的學生要了解商業各方面的知識。| **in business** *Most of my family are in business.* 我家裡大多數人都經商。| **do business with** *We do a lot of business with Italian companies.* 我們與意大利公司有許多業務來往。| **the business community** (=important people who work in business) 商會; 商界 *The policy is backed by the international business community.* 這項政策得到了國際商界的支持。

2 be in business/go into business to be operating as a company or to begin operating as a company 做生意, 經商, 辦公司: *Pam's going into business with her sister.* 帕姆要和姐姐一起做生意。

3 go out of business to stop operating as a company 停業, 關門: *Higher interest rates will drive smaller firms out of business.* 高利率會迫使一些小商號倒閉。

4 ►AMOUNT OF COMPANY WORK 公司業務量◄ [U] the amount of work a company is doing or its value 營業額, 交易量: *We're now doing twice as much business as we did last year.* 我們現在的營業額是去年的兩倍。| **business is good/bad/slow etc** *Business is slow during the summer.* 今年夏天的生意清淡。| **drum up business** (=increase it) 招攬生意 *Sidney's doing the rounds of the customers, trying to drum up business.* 錫德尼在走訪顧客, 以招攬生意。

5 ►NOT PLEASURE 並非樂趣◄ [U] work that you do as part of your job 差事: **on business** *Chris is in London this week, on business.* 克里斯本星期在倫敦出差。| **business trip/lunch/meeting etc** *I try to avoid too many business lunches.* 我盡量避開過多的業務應酬午餐。

6 business is business used to say that profit is the most important thing to consider 公事公辦: *Harry may be a friend but business is business, and he's not the best man for the job.* 哈里也許是朋友, 但公事公辦, 他不是這項工作的最佳人選。

② COMPANY 公司

7 [C] an organization such as a shop or factory which produces or sells goods or services 商店; 企業; 公司; 事務所; 工廠: *Paul's decided to start his own business.* 保羅決定創辦自己的公司。| **run a business** *Mrs Taylor runs an office equipment business.* 泰勒夫人經營着一家辦公設備公司。

8 the advertising/printing/shipping etc business work or a job involved with advertising, printing etc 廣告業/印刷業/航運業等: *Steve works in the movie business.* 史蒂夫從事電影業。

③ SUBJECT 事務

9 ►SUBJECT/EVENT 事務/事件◄ [singular] a subject, event, or activity that you have a particular opinion of

事情; 議題; 事務; 業務: *Politics is a serious business.* 政治是一件嚴肅的事情。| *Tanya found the whole business ridiculous.* 坦亞發現整件事情都很荒謬。

10 ►STH UNCLEAR 不清楚的事物◄ [U] used when you talk about something in general and do not give any details 工作, 事務: *He handles the mail and all that business.* 他負責處理郵件之類的工作。

B

④ **STH THAT CONCERNS YOU** 與你有關的事

11 none of your business *spoken* not something that you have a right to know about【口】與你無關: *I know it's none of my business, but what did you decide?* 我知道這不關我的事, 但你是怎樣決定的? | *It's none of your business how much I weigh.* 我體重多少不關你的事。

12 mind your own business a) *spoken* used to tell someone that something is private and you do not want them to ask about it or know about it【口】不要多管閒事: *"Where did you go last night?" "Mind your own business!"* "你昨晚去哪兒了?" "別多管閒事!" **b)** to do your normal activities, without showing any interest in what other people are doing 做自己的事〔不關心他人在做甚麼〕: *I was driving along, minding my own business, when the police pulled me over.* 我在專心開車, 突然警察示意我靠邊停下。

13 not your business not something that you are responsible for or that affects you 不關你的事

14 your/sb's business something that affects you but not other people, so other people have no right to know about it 你的/某人的私事: *"Are you going out with Kate tonight?" "That's my business".* "你今晚和凱特一起出去嗎?" "那是我的私事。"

15 make it your business to do sth to make a special effort to do something 特意努力做某事, 認為是自己應做的事: *Ruth made it her business to get to know the customers.* 露絲認為了解顧客是自己應做的事。

⑤ **WORK TO BE DONE** 要做的工作

16 [U] work that must be done in a particular job or period of time 職責, 本分, 任務: *We discussed this week's business.* 我們討論了本週的任務。| **[+of]** *the routine business of government* 政府的日常事務

17 get down to business to start dealing with an important subject 着手處理重要問題, 認真幹起來: *We'd better stop chatting and get down to business.* 我們最好閒話少說, 着手辦正事吧。

18 business as usual used to tell you that a shop or business is working normally when you might think it was closed 照常營業

19 any other business subjects to be discussed in a meeting after the main subjects have been dealt with〔會上主要議題討論之後待議的〕其他問題

⑥ **OTHER MEANINGS** 其他意思

20 be in business *informal* to have all that you need to start doing something【非正式】準備就緒: *Gillian brought the food, Jack the wine and I had some rugs to sit on, so we were in business.* 吉莉安帶來了食品, 傑克帶來了酒, 我找了一些坐的毯子, 我們一切已準備就緒。

21 mean business *informal* to be determined to do something even if it involves harming someone or making them upset【非正式】當真, 說話算數: *I could tell from the look on his face that he meant business.* 我能從他的面部表情上看出他是認真的。

22 go about your business to do the things that you normally do 做自己的事, 從事自己的工作: *ordinary people going about their business* 為自己的事奔波的普通人

23 have no business doing sth/have no business to do sth to behave wrongly in doing something 無權做某事, 不應該做某事: *He was very drunk and had no business driving.* 他喝酒太多, 不能開車。

24 like nobody's business *spoken* very well, very much, or very fast【口】很好地; 很多地; 很快地: *Wanda can play the piano like nobody's business.* 萬達鋼琴彈得很好。

25 not in the business of doing sth not planning to do something, because it is thought to be wrong〔因認為錯誤而〕沒有做某事的計劃 [意圖]: *This government is not in the business of increasing public spending.* 這屆政府沒有增加公共支出的打算。

26 (it's) the business *BrE slang* used to say that something is very good or works well【英俚】很好, 工作性能好: *Have you seen David's new car? It's the business.* 你見過戴維的新汽車嗎? 真不錯。—see also 另見 BIG BUSINESS, **funny business** (FUNNY (3)), **monkey business** (MONKEY[1] (3)), SHOW BUSINESS

business card /'·· ,·/ *n* [C] a card that shows the business person's name, position, company, and address〔印有姓名、職務、公司和地址的〕商務名片 —see picture on page A14 參見A14頁圖

business class /'·· ·/ *n* [U] travelling conditions on an aircraft that are more expensive than TOURIST CLASS but not as expensive as FIRST CLASS (1)〔飛機上的〕二等艙, 商務客位 —compare 比較 ECONOMY CLASS

business end /'·· ·/ *n* **the business end (of sth)** *informal* the end of a tool or weapon that does the work or causes the damage【非正式】〔工具或武器〕起作用的一端, 實用部分: *the business end of a gun* 槍管

business hours /'·· ·/ *n* [plural] the normal hours that shops and offices are open 營業時間; 辦公時間

busi·ness·like /ˈbɪznɪsˌlaɪk; ˈbɪznəs-laɪk/ *adj* effective and practical in the way that you do things 處事務實的, 有效率的, 講究實際的: *a businesslike manner* 務實的態度

busi·ness·man /ˈbɪznɪsˌmæn; ˈbɪznəsmən/ *n plural* **businessmen** /-ˌmən; -mən/ [C] **1** a man who works at a fairly high level in a company 商人; 實業家, 從事工商業的人士 **2 be a good businessman** to know how to deal with money and be successful in business 生財有道

business park /'·· ,·/ *n* [C] an area where many companies and businesses have buildings and offices 商業區

business plan /'·· ,·/ *n* [C] a document which explains what a company wants to do in the future〔公司〕未來的發展計劃

business stud·ies /'·· ,··/ *n* [plural] a course of study on economic and financial subjects 商業學

business suit /'·· ,·/ *n* [C] *AmE* a suit that a man wears during the day, especially in the office【美】〔尤指日常在辦公室穿的〕西服, 西裝; LOUNGE SUIT *BrE*【英】

busi·ness·wom·an /ˈbɪznɪsˌwʊmən; ˈbɪznəsˌwʊmən/ *n plural* **businesswomen** /-ˌwɪmɪn; -ˌwɪmɪn/ [C] **1** a woman who works at a fairly high level in a company 女商人; 女實業家, 從事工商業的女性 **2 be a good businesswoman** to know how to deal with money and be successful in business 生財有道

busk /bʌsk; bʌsk/ *v* [I] *BrE* to play music in a public place in order to earn money【英】街頭賣藝 —**busker** *n* [C]

bus lane /'· ·/ *n* [C] a part of a wide road that only buses are allowed to use 公共汽車專用車道

busman's hol·i·day /ˌbʌsmənz ˈhɒlədeɪ; ˌbʌsmənz ˈhɒlədi/ *n* [singular] a holiday spent doing the same work as you do in your job 照常工作的節假日, 有名無實的假日

bus pass /'· ·/ *n* [C] a special ticket giving cheap or free bus travel〔用於乘搭公共汽車的〕優惠[免費]乘車證

buss /bʌs; bʌs/ *v* [T] *AmE* to kiss someone in a friendly rather than sexual way【美】親吻〔表示友好〕: *politicians* *bussing babies* 政治家親吻幼兒

bus·ser /ˈbʌsɚ; ˈbʌsə/ *n* [C] *AmE* someone who works in a restaurant taking away dirty dishes【美】〔餐館裡收拾髒碗碟的〕勤雜工

bus shel·ter /ˈ· ˌ··/ *n* [C] *especially BrE* a small structure with a roof that keeps people dry while they are waiting for a bus【尤英】公共汽車候車亭

bus sta·tion /ˈ· ˌ··/ *n* [C] a place where buses start and finish their journeys 公共汽車總站

bus stop /ˈ· ·/ *n* [C] a place at the side of a road, marked with a sign, where buses stop for passengers 公共汽車站

bust¹ /bʌst; bʌst/ *v past tense and past participle* **bust** *BrE*【英】, **busted** *especially AmE*【尤美】[T] *informal*【非正式】

1 ►BREAK 弄破◄ to break something 打爛, 打碎, 弄壞: *I bust my watch this morning.* 今早我把手錶摔壞了。| *Tony busted the door down.* 托尼把門砸爛了。

2 ►POLICE 警察◄ *informal*【非正式】**a) bust sb (for sth)** if the police bust someone, they charge them with a crime 指控某人（犯有某種罪行）**b)** if the police bust a place, they go into it to look for something illegal 查抄〔住宅〕, 突擊搜查〔非法物品〕: *The party was busted by the vice squad.* 警察緝捕隊突擊搜查該聚會。

3 bust a gut *informal* to try extremely hard to do something【非正式】竭盡全力: *I bust a gut trying to finish that work on time.* 我竭盡全力, 希望如期完成那項工作。

4 ...or bust! *informal* used to say that you will try very hard to go somewhere or do something【非正式】一定要去[做]: *San Francisco or bust!* 我一定要去三藩市!

5 ►MILITARY 軍事的◄ *especially AmE* to give someone a lower military rank as a punishment; DEMOTE【尤美】貶降...的軍階; 使降職

6 ►BURST◄ *AmE* to burst【美】使爆裂

bust out *phr v* [I] *informal* to escape from a place, especially prison【非正式】逃跑; 越獄

bust up *phr v informal*【非正式】**1** [I] to argue angrily and stop being lovers, partners, or friends〔關係〕破裂: *They bust up after six years of marriage.* 他們結婚六年後離異了。**2** [T **bust** sth ↔ **up**] to prevent something from continuing 打斷, 搞糟: *Angry protesters bust up the meeting.* 憤怒的抗議者打斷了會議。**3** [T **bust** sth ↔ **up**] *AmE* to damage or break something【美】損壞, 弄壞: *Hey! Don't bust up my bar!* 喂! 不要砸我的酒吧! —see also 另見 BUST-UP

bust² *n* [C] **1** a model of someone's head, shoulders and upper chest, made of stone or metal〔用石頭或金屬製造的〕半身塑像: [+**of**] *a bust of Beethoven* 貝多芬的半身塑像 **2** a woman's breasts, or the part of her clothes that covers her breasts〔婦女或其衣服的〕胸部 **3** a measurement around a woman's breast and back 胸圍: *Do you have this bra in a bigger bust size?* 你有胸圍比這大一號的乳罩嗎? **4** *informal* a situation in which the police go into a place looking for something illegal【非正式】拘捕, 搜查, 突襲: *major drugs bust* 毒品大搜查

bust³ *adj* [not before noun 不用於名詞前] *informal*【非正式】**1 go bust** a business that goes bust cannot continue operating 生意失敗, 破產, 倒閉: *Dad lost his job when the firm went bust.* 公司破產後, 爸爸失去了工作。**2** broken 破的, 壞的: *The television's bust again.* 電視又壞了。

bus·ter /ˈbʌstɚ; ˈbʌstə/ *n AmE spoken* used to speak to a man who is annoying you or who you do not respect【美口】小子〔對男子的蔑稱〕: *You're under arrest, buster!* 小子, 你被捕了!

bus·tle¹ /ˈbʌsl̩; ˈbʌsəl/ *v* [I always+adv/prep] to move around quickly, looking very busy 忙亂, 忙忙碌碌: [+**about/round etc**] *Madge bustled round the room putting things away.* 馬奇忙着在房間裡收拾東西。

bustle² *n* **1** [singular] busy and usually noisy activity 忙碌; 熙攘; 喧鬧: [+**of**] *a continual bustle of people coming and going* 川流不息的來往人羣 —see also 另見 **hustle and bustle** (HUSTLE² (1)) **2** [C] a frame worn by women in the past to hold out the back of their skirts〔舊時婦女用來撐裙子的〕裙撐, 腰墊

bus·tling /ˈbʌslɪŋ; ˈbʌsəlɪŋ/ *adj* a bustling place is very busy 繁忙的, 熱鬧的

bust-up /ˈ· ·/ *n* [C] *informal*【非正式】**1** a very bad quarrel or fight 爭吵, 吵架: *Cathy and I had a real bust-up yesterday.* 我和凱茜昨天實實在在地吵了一架。**2** [C] the end of a relationship〔關係的〕破裂: *the bust-up of their marriage* 他們婚姻的破裂 —see also 另見 **bust up** (BUST¹)

B

bust·y /ˈbʌstɪ; ˈbʌsti/ *adj informal* a woman who is busty has large breasts【非正式】〔婦女〕乳房大的

bus·y¹ /ˈbɪzɪ; ˈbɪzi/ *adj*

1 ►WORKING NOW 在工作◄ someone who is busy at a particular time is working and is not available 忙碌的; 正在工作的: *She's busy now, can you phone later?* 她現在正忙, 你晚些時候打電話來好嗎? | [+**with**] *Mr Haynes is busy with a customer at the moment.* 海恩斯先生此時正忙着接待一位顧客。

2 busy doing sth giving something a lot of your time and attention 忙於做某事: *Rachel's busy studying for her exams.* 雷切爾正忙於温習準備考試。

3 ►TIME 時間◄ a busy period is full of work or other activities 繁忙的: *December is the busiest time of year for shops.* 十二月份是一年中商店最繁忙的時期。

4 ►PLACE 地方◄ a busy place is very full of people or vehicles and movement 熱鬧的, 忙碌的: *We live on a very busy road.* 我們住的那條大街很熱鬧。| *a busy office* 忙碌的辦公室

5 ►WORKS HARD 辛苦操勞◄ having very little free time because you always have so much to do 操勞的: *a busy mother of four with a full time job* 既有全職工作, 又要照看四個孩子的勞碌母親

6 keep sb/yourself busy to find plenty of things to do 使某人/自己忙碌: *I kept myself busy to take my mind off smoking.* 我讓自己忙於工作, 不去想吸煙。

7 ►TELEPHONE 電話◄ *especially AmE* a telephone that is busy, is being used【尤美】〔電話〕佔線的; ENGAGED (2) *BrE*【英】: *I'm sorry, the line's busy at the moment, can you try later?* 對不起, 電話佔線。你過一會兒再打好嗎?

8 ►PATTERN 圖案◄ a pattern or design that is busy is too full of small details〔圖案或設計〕過於繁雜的, 瑣碎的

9 as busy as a bee very active 忙得不亦樂乎: *The children have been as busy as bees making a collage this afternoon.* 今天下午, 孩子們一直在做拼貼畫, 忙得不亦樂乎。—**busily** *adv*

busy² *v* [T] **busy yourself with** to use your time dealing with something 使自己忙於: *He busied himself with answering letters.* 他忙着回覆信件。

bus·y·bod·y /ˈbɪzɪˌbɑdɪ; ˈbɪziˌbɒdi/ *n* [C] someone who is too interested in other people's private activities 好管閒事的人: *You interfering old busybody!* 你這愛管閒事的老傢伙!

busy Liz·zie /ˌbɪzɪ ˈlɪzɪ; ˌbɪzi ˈlɪzi/ *n* [C] a small plant with bright flowers 鳳仙花

bus·y·work /ˈbɪzɪˌwɝk; ˈbɪziwɜːk/ *n* [U] *AmE* work that seems to be producing a result but is really only keeping someone busy【美】勞而無功的事

but¹ /bət; bət; *strong* 強讀 bʌt; bʌt/ *conjunction*

1 in spite of something, or not as you would expect 但是, 然而, 儘管如此: *The situation looked desperate but they didn't give up hope.* 形勢看來十分危急, 但他們並沒有放棄希望。| *The car was very cheap but it's been extremely reliable.* 這汽車雖然便宜, 但性能很可靠。**2** used to add another statement to one that you have already made, to say that both things are true 但與此同時; 另一方面; 不過; 誠然...但: *These changes will cost quite a lot, but they will save us money in the long run.* 這些改動相當費錢, 但從長遠的角度看能為我們省錢。| *an expensive but*

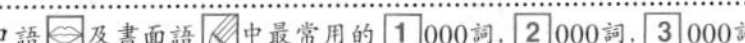

immensely useful book 一本很貴卻大有用處的書 **3** used like however, to explain why something did not happen, why you did not do something etc 只因為, 只可惜: *He would have won easily, but he fell and broke his leg.* 他本來勝利在望, 可惜跌倒把腿摔斷了。| *I'd like to go but I'm too busy.* 我很願意去, 可是實在太忙。**4** used after a negative to emphasize that it is the second part of the sentence that it is true 毋寧說, 而是: *They own not one but three houses.* 他們擁有不是一幢, 而是三幢房子。| *The purpose of the scheme is not to help the employers but to provide work for young people.* 這個計劃的目的不是為了幫助雇主, 而是為青年人提供工作機會。| **no choice/alternative etc but to...** *We had no alternative but to fire him.* 我們別無選擇, 只得解雇他。| **no question/doubt but that...** (=used to say that you are sure that something is true) 毫無疑問 *There's no doubt but that Evans is guilty.* 毫無疑問, 埃文斯是有罪的。**5 but for** without 要不是: *But for these interruptions the meeting would have finished half an hour ago.* 要不是幾次中斷, 會議半小時前就開完了。**6 but then (again)** *spoken* 【口】**a)** used before a statement that makes what you have just said seem less true, useful, or valuable 然而, 不過: *We could ask John to help again, but then I don't want to bother him.* 我們是可以再求約翰幫忙, 不過我不想麻煩他。**b)** used before a statement that may seem surprising, to say that it is not really surprising 但另一方面, 不過: *Apparently Dinah hasn't been to work all week, but then she always was unreliable, wasn't she?* 黛娜好像一個星期都沒來上班, 不過, 她不總是這樣不可靠嗎? **7** used to express strong feelings such as anger, surprise etc 嘿, 天哪〔用於表示強烈的情感, 如憤怒、驚訝等〕: *But that's marvellous news!* 喔, 這真是個好消息! **8 you cannot but.../you could not but...** *formal* used to say that you have to do something or cannot stop yourself from doing it 【正式】禁不住, 情不自禁: *I could not but admire her.* 我不由得對她產生了敬慕之情。**9** used to emphasize a word or statement〔用來加強重複部分的語氣〕: *It'll be a great party – everyone, but everyone, is coming.* 這將是一次重大的聚會 —— 每個人, 對, 是每個人都會來。**10** used to change the subject of a conversation 無論如何, 反正, 好〔用於改變話題〕: *But now to the main question.* 好, 現在談談主要問題。**11** [usually in negatives 一般用於否定句] *literary* used to emphasize that a statement includes every single person or thing 【文】無一例外地: *Not a day goes by but that I think of Geoff.* (=I think of Geoff every day) 我每天都想起傑夫。

USAGE NOTE 用法說明: BUT

WORD CHOICE 詞語辨析: **but, however**

But is very frequent in spoken English, where it is often used at the beginning of a sentence. but 經常用於口語, 作為句子的開頭: *"I read it in a newspaper." "But newspapers aren't always right!"* "我從報上讀到這消息。" "但報紙並不總是正確的!"

But is also used in writing, though not usually at the beginning of a sentence. **However** is used especially in more formal writing, often with commas before and after it in the middle of a sentence. but 也用於書面語, 但通常不放在句首。however 尤其用在正式文體中, 位於句子中間, 前後用逗號隔開: *This had been reported in a newspaper. One must remember, however, that newspapers are not always accurate.* 這 (消息) 在報上已有報道。然而, 必須記住, 報上的內容也不總是準確的。

GRAMMAR 語法

But or **however** is never used in a main clause beside another clause with **although**. 當子句用 although 時, 主句不用 but 或 however: *Although they're very busy, I think they enjoy it* (NOT 不用 *...but/however I think they enjoy it*). 雖然他們很忙, 但我認為他們喜歡這樣。You can begin a clause with *but although,* or *however although.* but although 或 however although 可用於引導子句: *I tried doing the accounts, but although I know some maths I found it very difficult* (=and I know some maths but I still found it difficult). 我試着算賬, 雖然我懂些數學, 但仍覺得很難。

but² *prep* **1** apart from; except 除...以外: *What can we do but sit and wait?* 我們除了坐等, 還能做些甚麼呢? | *I could come any day but Thursday.* 除了星期四, 我哪天都能來。| **nothing but** (=used when talking about a bad quality or situation to emphasize how bad it is) 完完全全〔強調質量或情況很糟〕*This car's been nothing but trouble.* 這輛車, 除了添麻煩, 甚麼用處也沒有。| **anything but** (=used to say that a person or situation does not have a good quality) 根本不, 一點也不 *Those receptionists are anything but helpful.* 那些接待人員一點也不幫忙。**2 the last but one/the next but two etc** *especially BrE* the last or next thing or person except for one, two etc 【尤英】倒數第二/相隔兩個等: *Pauline and Derek live in the next house but one.* (=they live two houses away from us) 波林和德里克住的房子和我們隔着一座。

but³ *adv* **1** *especially literary* only 【尤文】只能, 僅僅, 不過, 至少, 剛剛, 好歹: *You can but try.* 你只能試試看。**2** *AmE spoken* used to emphasize what you are saying 【美口】非常, 極其〔用於加強語氣〕: *Go there but fast!* 去吧, 可要快呀! | *They're rich, but I mean rich!* 他們有錢, 我是說很有錢!

but⁴ /bʌt; bʌt/ *n* **no buts (about it)** *spoken* used to say that there is no doubt about something 【口】不容置疑, 毫無疑問: *No buts, you are going to school today!* 沒甚麼可以辯解的, 你今天必須上學!

bu·tane /ˈbjuten; ˈbjuːteɪn/ *n* [U] a gas stored in liquid form, used for cooking and heating 丁烷〔用於煮食、取暖的氣體〕

butch /bʊtʃ; bʊtʃ/ *adj informal* 【非正式】**1** a woman who is butch looks, behaves, or dresses like a man〔女子外表、舉止、穿着〕男性化的 **2** a man who is butch seems big and strong, and typically male〔男子〕有男子氣的

butch·er¹ /ˈbʊtʃɚ; ˈbʊtʃə/ *n* [C] **1** someone who owns or works in a shop that sells meat 屠宰商; 肉販 **2 the butcher's** a shop where you can buy meat 肉店, 肉鋪 **3** someone who has killed a lot of people cruelly and unnecessarily 劊子手; 屠夫 **4 have/take a butcher's** *BrE slang* to have a look at something 【英俚】看一眼

butcher² *v* [T] **1** to kill animals and prepare them to be used as meat 屠宰〔牲口〕**2** to kill people cruelly or unnecessarily, especially in large numbers 血腥屠殺 **3** *informal* to spoil something by working carelessly 【非正式】弄壞, 搞糟: *That hairdresser really butchered my hair!* 理髮師把我的頭髮理壞了!

butch·er·y /ˈbʊtʃərɪ; ˈbʊtʃəri/ *n* [U] **1** cruel and unnecessary killing 殘殺, 屠殺: *the butchery of battle* 戰場上的血腥屠殺 **2** the preparation of meat for sale 屠宰業

but·ler /ˈbʌtlɚ; ˈbʌtlə/ *n* [C] the main male servant of a house 男管家, 僕役長

butt¹ /bʌt; bʌt/ *n* [C]

1 be the butt of to be the person or thing that other people often make jokes about 成為...的笑柄: *Paul quickly became the butt of everyone's jokes.* 保羅很快成了大家取笑的對象。

2 ►CIGARETTE 香煙◄ the end of a cigarette after most of it has been smoked 煙蒂, 煙頭

3 ►GUN 槍◄ the thick end of the handle of a gun〔工具等〕粗大的一端, 柄: *a rifle butt* 槍托

4 ►CONTAINER 容器◄ a large round container for collecting or storing liquids 大桶: *a rainwater butt* 裝雨水的大桶

5 ▶ACT OF STRIKING STH 打擊某物◀ the act of striking someone with your head 用頭頂
6 ▶PART OF YOUR BODY 身體部分◀ *AmE informal* the part of your body that you sit on; BUTTOCK【美, 非正式】屁股 —see also 另見 **a pain in the ass/butt** (PAIN¹ (3))
7 get your butt in/out/over *AmE spoken* used to rudely tell someone to go somewhere or do something【美口】別老坐着; 快起來〔粗魯地告訴某人去某處或做某事〕: *Get your butt out of that bathroom now.* 馬上從衞生間裡出來。

butt² *v* [I,T] **1** to hit or push against something or someone with your head〔用頭〕頂, 撞 **2** if an animal butts someone, it hits them with its horns〔用角〕牴

butt in *phr v* [I] **1** to interrupt a conversation rudely 插嘴: *Stop butting in!* 別再插嘴! **2** *AmE* to become involved in a private situation that does not concern you【美】管閒事: *Things were going real well until you had to butt in!* 在你沒參與以前, 情況本來挺好的!

butt out *phr v* [I] *AmE spoken* used to tell someone to stop being involved in something【美口】不要管: *This has got nothing to do with you, so just butt out!* 這件事與你無關, 別瞎管了!

butte /bjut; bjuːt/ *n* [C] *AmE* a hill with steep sides and a flat top【美】〔有平頂和陡坡的〕孤山, 孤峯

2 **but·ter¹** /ˈbʌtɚ; ˈbʌtə/ *n* [U] **1** a solid yellow food made from milk or cream that you spread on bread or use in cooking 黃油, 牛油: *Beat the butter and sugar together.* 把黃油和糖放在一起攪打。**2 butter wouldn't melt in sb's mouth** used to say that someone seems to be very kind and sincere but is not really 某人裝出一副忠厚善良的樣子 —**buttery** *adj*

butter² *v* [T] to spread butter on something 塗黃油於…: *buttered toast* 抹了黃油的烤麵包片

butter sb ↔ **up** *phr v* [T] *informal* to say nice things to someone so that they will do what you want【非正式】奉承, 討好〔某人〕: *Don't think you can butter me up that easily.* 不要以為你那麼容易討好我。

but·ter·ball /ˈbʌtɚˌbɔl; ˈbʌtəbɔːl/ *n* [C] *AmE informal* someone who is fat, especially a child【美, 非正式】肥胖兒

butter bean /ˈ‥ ˌ/ *n* a large pale yellow bean 利馬豆 —see picture on page A9 參見 A9 頁圖

but·ter·cream /ˈbʌtɚˌkrim; ˈbʌtəkriːm/ *n* [U] a soft mixture of butter and sugar used inside or on top of cakes〔蛋糕表面或裡面的〕奶油

but·ter·cup /ˈbʌtɚˌkʌp; ˈbʌtəkʌp/ *n* [C] a small shiny yellow wild flower 毛茛

but·ter·fat /ˈbʌtɚˌfæt; ˈbʌtəfæt/ *n* [U] the natural fat in milk 乳脂

but·ter·fin·gers /ˈbʌtɚˌfɪŋgɚz; ˈbʌtəˌfɪŋgəz/ *n* [singular] *informal* someone who often drops things they are carrying or trying to catch【非正式】拿不穩東西的人

but·ter·fly /ˈbʌtɚˌflaɪ; ˈbʌtəflaɪ/ *n* [C] **1** a type of insect that has large wings, often with beautiful colours 蝴蝶 **2 have butterflies (in your stomach)** *informal* to feel very nervous before doing something【非正式】〔做某事前〕情緒緊張, 心裡發慌: *I always get butterflies before an exam.* 考試前我總是很緊張。**3 butterfly stroke** a way of swimming by lying on your front and moving your arms together over your head 蝶泳 **4** someone who usually moves on quickly from one activity or person to the next 輕浮易變的人

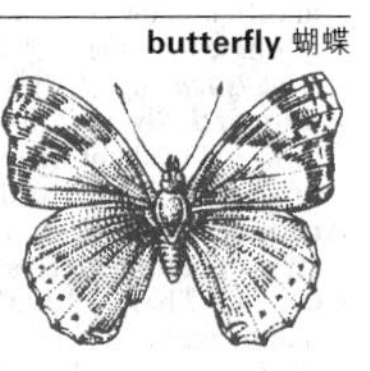
butterfly 蝴蝶

butterfly nut /ˈ‥ ˌ ˌ/ *n* [C] a WING NUT 蝶形螺母

but·ter·milk /ˈbʌtɚˌmɪlk; ˈbʌtəˌmɪlk/ *n* [U] the liquid that remains after butter has been made 脫脂乳, 酪乳

but·ter·scotch /ˈbʌtɚˌskɑtʃ; ˈbʌtəskɒtʃ/ *n* [U] a type of sweet made from butter and sugar boiled together 黃油硬糖, 奶油糖果

butt·hole /ˈbʌtˌhol; ˈbʌthəʊl/ *n* [C] *AmE taboo slang*【美, 諱, 俚】**1** someone's ANUS 屁眼 **2** used to insult someone 笨蛋〔侮辱性用詞〕: *You butthole!* 你這傻瓜!

but·tock /ˈbʌtək; ˈbʌtək/ *n* [C usually plural 一般用複數] one of the fleshy parts of your body that you sit on 屁股, 臀部 —see picture at 參見 BODY 圖

but·ton¹ /ˈbʌtn̩; ˈbʌtn/ *n* **1** [C] a small round flat object on your shirt, coat etc which you pass through a hole to fasten it 鈕扣, 扣子: **do up/undo a button** (=fasten or unfasten a button) 繫上/解開扣子 —see picture at 參見 FASTENER 圖 **2** [C] a small round object on a machine that you press to make it work 按鈕: *Press the pause button.* 按暫停鍵。—see also 另見 PUSH-BUTTON **3** *AmE* a small metal or plastic BADGE (1,2), often with a message on it【美】〔印有文字的〕金屬〔塑料〕小徽章 **4 button nose/eyes** a nose or eyes that are small and round 小而圓的鼻子/眼睛 **5 on the button** *informal especially AmE* exactly right, or at exactly the right time【非正式, 尤美】非常準確, 準時 —see also 另見 **as bright as a button** (BRIGHT (5)) 2

button² *v* [I,T] also 又作 **button up 1** to fasten clothes with buttons or to be fastened with buttons 用鈕扣扣住, 扣上…的扣子: *I don't like pants that button at the side.* 我不喜歡在側面繫扣的褲子。| *Sam, make sure Nina buttons up her jacket.* 薩姆, 要確保尼娜把上衣扣好。**2 button it!** *spoken* used to tell someone impolitely to stop talking【口】住嘴!

button-down /ˈ‥ ˌ/ *adj* a button-down shirt or collar has the ends of the collar fastened to the shirt with buttons〔襯衫〕領尖有扣子的 —see picture on page A17 參見 A17 頁圖

but·ton·hole /ˈbʌtn̩ˌhol; ˈbʌtnhəʊl/ *n* [C] **1** a hole for a button to be put through to fasten a shirt, coat etc 鈕孔, 鈕扣眼 —see picture on page A17 參見 A17 頁圖 **2** *BrE* a flower you fasten to your clothes【英】扣在鈕孔內或別在衣服上的花; BOUTONNIERE *AmE*【美】

button-through /ˈ‥ ˌ/ *adj BrE* a button-through dress or skirt fastens from the top to the bottom with buttons【英】〔衣服〕從上到下都帶鈕扣的

but·tress¹ /ˈbʌtrɪs; ˈbʌtrəs/ *n* [C] a brick or stone structure built to support a wall 扶壁, 撐牆, 扶垛

buttress² *v* [T] to support a system, idea, argument etc, especially by providing money〔尤指用錢〕支持〔某一體制、主張、論點等〕: *The evidence seemed to buttress their argument.* 證據似乎支持他們的論點。

but·ty /ˈbʌtɪ; ˈbʌti/ *n* [C] *BrE informal* a SANDWICH【英, 非正式】三明治

bux·om /ˈbʌksəm; ˈbʌksəm/ *adj* a woman who is buxom is attractively large and healthy and has big breasts〔女性〕豐滿健美的

buy¹ /baɪ; baɪ/ *v past tense and past participle* **bought** / 1
bɔt; bɔːt/ **1 a)** [I,T] to get something by paying money 1
for it 買, 購: *Where did you buy that dress?* 那條裙子你在哪兒買的? | **buy sb sth** *Let me buy you a drink.* 我來請你喝杯酒。| **buy sth for** *Sally's buying new curtains for the bedroom.* 薩莉在為臥室買新窗簾。| **buy sth from sb** *I bought this from an old guy in the market.* 這是我在市場上從一個老人那裡買到的。| **buy sth for $10/£200 etc** *I bought it for two bucks at a garage sale.* 我在一處在宅前出售舊物的攤檔上以兩美元買來的。| **buy sth for a song** (=buy something very cheaply) 某物買得便宜極了 —opposite 反義詞 SELL¹ (1) **b)** [T] if a sum of money buys something, that is what you can get with it 夠買, 能買: *A dollar doesn't buy much these days.* 如今一元買不了甚麼東西。**2 buy time** to get more time to do something, especially by making excuses 爭取時間; 〔尤指找藉口〕設法拖延: *Tell them we've got problems with the software, it might buy us more time.* 就說我們的軟件出了問題, 這樣可以爭取些時間。**3** [T] *infor-*

mal to believe an explanation or reason, especially one that is not very likely to be true【非正式】接受, 相信: *We could say it was an accident, but he'd never buy that.* 我們可以說這是一次意外, 可他怎麼也不會相信。**4** [T] *AmE informal* to pay money to someone, especially someone in an official position, in order to persuade them to do something dishonest; BRIBE【美, 非正式】賄賂, 買通: *They say the judge was bought.* 他們說那位法官被買通了。**5 (have) bought it** *informal* to be killed, especially in an accident or war【非正式】〔尤指在意外事故或戰爭中〕遇難: *Vic bought it somewhere in the desert.* 維克在沙漠中遇難。

buy in sth *phr v* [T] *BrE* to buy something in large quantities【英】大量買進: *We'd better buy in more beer for the party.* 我們最好多買些啤酒聚會時喝。

buy into sth *phr v* [T] **1** to buy part of a business or organization, especially because you want to control it 買進〔企業的股份〕: *Clegg used the money to buy into a printing business.* 克萊格買進了一家印刷廠的股份。**2** *informal* to believe an idea【非正式】相信〔觀點〕

buy sb ↔ **off** *phr v* [T] to pay someone money to stop them causing trouble or threatening you; BRIBE[1] 買通〔某人〕, 向〔某人〕行賄; 用錢疏通

buy out *phr v* **1** [T **buy** sb/sth ↔ **out**] to buy someone's shares (SHARE[2] (5)) of a business that you previously owned together, so that you have complete control 全部收購〔股權、產權〕—see also 另見 BUYOUT **2** [T **buy** sb **out of** sth] to pay money so that someone can leave an organization such as the army before their contract has finished 出錢買回自由〔尤指出錢提前退伍〕

buy up sth ↔ *phr v* [T] to quickly buy as much as you can of something such as land, tickets, food etc〔迅速地〕囤積, 大量買下〔土地、票券、食品等〕: *Much of the land has been bought up by property developers.* 大部分地皮都給房地產開發商買下來了。

Frequencies of the verbs **buy, get** and **purchase** in spoken and written English 動詞 buy, get 和 purchase 在英語口語和書面語中的使用頻率

Based on the British National Corpus and the Longman Lancaster Corpus
據英國國家語料庫和朗文蘭卡斯特語料庫

All three verbs are used to mean 'get something by paying for it'. The graph shows that in this meaning **get** is extremely common in spoken English. However, **get** is informal and is not at all common in written English. **Purchase** is used in formal or business contexts. It is not very common and is used more in written English than in spoken English. 這三個動詞都用來表示"付款購得"。本圖表顯示, 作此意解釋時, get 在口語中極其常用。但 get 語氣不正式, 書面語中很少見。purchase 用於正式文體或商業性文體中。這個詞不太常用, 在書面語中出現的頻率比在口語中高。

buy² *n* **be a good/bad buy** to be worth or to be not worth the price you paid 買得合算/不合算: *The wine is a good buy at £3.49.* 這葡萄酒每瓶3.49英鎊, 很合算。—see 見 CHEAP[1] (USAGE)

buy·er /ˈbaɪə; ˈbaɪə/ *n* [C] **1** someone who buys something expensive such as a house or car 購買者, 買主: *We hope lower house prices will attract more buyers.* 我們希望低廉的房價會吸引更多的買主。—opposite 反義詞 SELLER (1) **2** someone whose job is to choose and buy the goods for a shop or company 採購員, 進貨員, 買手

buyer's mar·ket /ˌ·· ˈ··/ *n* [singular] a situation in which there is plenty of something available so that buyers have a lot of choice and prices tend to be low 買方市場 —opposite 反義詞 SELLER'S MARKET

buy·out /ˈbaɪaʊt; ˈbaɪaʊt/ *n* [C] a situation in which someone gains control of a company by buying all or most of its shares (SHARE[2] (5)) 全部買下, 收購全部[大部分]股份[權]: *a management buyout* 管理層收購

buzz¹ /bʌz; bʌz/ *v*

1 ►MAKE A SOUND 發聲◄ [I] to make a continuous sound, like the sound of a BEE 發出嗡嗡聲: *The machine made a loud buzzing noise.* 機器發出很大的嗡嗡聲。

2 ►MOVE AROUND 四處移動◄ **a)** [I always+adv/prep] to move around in the air making a continuous sound like a BEE〔蜜蜂等〕嗡嗡地飛: **buzz round/around/about** *A fly buzzed round the room.* 有一隻蒼蠅在房間裡嗡嗡地亂飛。**b)** to move quickly and busily around a place 在〔某個地方〕忙轉: **buzz around/round/about** *I spent the day buzzing around town in Dad's car.* 那天我就開着爸爸的車在鎮上兜了一天。

3 ►EXCITEMENT 激動◄ [I] if a group of people or a place is buzzing, people are making a lot of noise because they are excited 發出一陣興奮的說話聲: [+with] *Lineker had the crowd buzzing with excitement.* 萊恩科使人羣發出一陣興奮的說話聲。

4 sb's head/mind is buzzing (with sth) if your head or mind is buzzing with thoughts, ideas etc, you cannot stop thinking about them 某人的頭腦中不住地想 (某事)

5 ►EARS 耳朵◄ [I] if your ears or head are buzzing you can hear a continuous low unpleasant sound 耳鳴

6 ►CALL 呼叫◄ [I+for, T] to call someone by pressing a BUZZER 用蜂音器召喚〔某人〕: *I'll just buzz my secretary and ask for the file.* 我用蜂音器叫祕書送來文件。

7 ►AIRCRAFT 飛機◄ [T] *informal* to fly an aircraft low and fast over buildings, people etc【非正式】低空掠過

buzz off *phr v* [I] *spoken*【口】**1 buzz off!** used to tell someone impolitely to go away 走開! 滾開! **2** to go away 離開, 走開: *I've finished everything, so I'll buzz off now.* 事情我都辦完了, 現在我要走了。

buzz² *n* **1** [C] a continuous noise like the sound of a BEE 嗡嗡聲, 嗞嗞聲 —see picture on page A19 參見A19頁圖 **2** [singular] the sound of people talking a lot in an excited way〔人們〕興奮的談笑聲: [+of] *a buzz of anticipation* 期待的議論聲 **3** [singular] *informal* a strong feeling of excitement, pleasure, or success【非正式】興奮之感; 喜悅心情: **give sb a buzz** *You know Steve, driving fast gives him a real buzz.* 你了解史蒂夫, 開快車使他感到刺激。**4 give sb a buzz** *informal* to telephone someone【非正式】給某人打電話 **5 the buzz** *informal* unofficial news or information that is spread by people telling each other【非正式】小道消息: *The buzz is that Jack is leaving.* 人們都傳傑克要離開。

buz·zard /ˈbʌzəd; ˈbʌzəd/ *n* [C] **1** *BrE* a type of large HAWK[1] (1) (=hunting bird)【英】鵟, 鵖鵰 **2** *AmE* a type of large bird that eats dead animals【美】美洲兀鷹

buzz·cut /ˈbʌzˌkʌt; ˈbʌzkʌt/ *n* [C] *AmE* a very short style of cutting hair【美】平頭 (髮型)

buzz·er /ˈbʌzə; ˈbʌzə/ *n* [C] a small electric machine that buzzes (BUZZ[1] (1)) when you press it 蜂音器: *Press the buzzer if you know the answer.* 如果你知道答案, 就按搶答器。

buzz saw /ˈ· ·/ *n* [C] *AmE* a SAW[2] (1) with a round blade that is spun around by a motor; CIRCULAR SAW【美】〔電動〕圓鋸

buzz·word /ˈbʌzwɜd; ˈbʌzwɜːd/ *n* [C] a word or phrase from one special area of knowledge that people suddenly think is very important〔重要的〕專門術語, 時髦語: *The* *'information superhighway' became a buzzword in the 90s.* "信息高速公路"在20世紀90年代成了時髦語。

by-, bye- /baɪ; baɪ/ *prefix* less important 次要的: *a by-product* (=something made in addition to the main product) 副產品 | *a by-election* (=one held between regular elections) 補(缺)選(舉)

by¹ /baɪ; baɪ/ *prep* **1** used especially with a PASSIVE¹ (2) verb to show the person or thing that does something or makes something happen 被, 由〔尤用於被動語態動詞之後〕: *I was attacked by a dog.* 一條狗向我撲了過來。| *The building was designed by a famous architect.* 該建築物是由一位著名建築師設計的。| *We are all alarmed by the rise in violent crime.* 我們都對暴力犯罪的增加感到震驚。**2** using or doing a particular thing 通過; 用…; 靠…; 乘…: *You can reserve the tickets by phone.* 你可以用電話訂票。| *Send it by airmail.* 用航空郵件寄吧。| *I know her by sight.* (=recognize her face) 我能認出她來。| **by doing sth** *She earns her living by selling insurance.* 她以推銷保險為生。| **by train/plane/car** *We're travelling to London by train.* 我們乘火車去倫敦。**3** passing through or along a particular place 經過, 沿, 順, 經由: *They came in by the back door.* 他們從後門進來的。| *It's quicker to go by the country route.* 走鄉村那條路會更快。**4** beside or near something 靠近, 在…旁: *She stood by the window looking out over the fields.* 她站在窗邊眺望遠處的田野。| *Jane went and sat by Patrick.* 簡走過去坐在帕特里克身旁。**5** if you move or travel by someone or something, you go past them without stopping 經過…〔的旁邊〕: *He walked by without noticing me.* 他走過我身旁而沒有注意到我。| *I go by the Vicarage every day on my way to work.* 我每天去上班都要經過牧師的住宅。**6** used to show the name of someone who wrote a book, produced a film, wrote a piece of music etc 由…所創作[編著, 導演]: *the 'New World Symphony' by Dvorak* 由德沃夏克創作的《新世界交響曲》**7** not later than a particular time, date etc 不遲於, 在…之前: *The documents need to be ready by next Friday.* 文件最遲需在下星期五準備好。| *I reckon the film should be over by 9.30.* 我估計九點半電影該演完了。**8** according to a particular rule, method, or way of doing things 按照, 依據: *You've got to play by the rules.* 你必須按規則比賽。| *Profits were £6 million, but by their standards this is low.* 利潤達到六百萬英鎊, 但按照他們的標準, 這還不算多。**9** used to show the amount or degree of something 數量[程度]達到…: *The price of oil fell by a further $2 a barrel.* 每桶油價又下跌了兩美元。| *I was overcharged by £3.* 他們多收了我三英鎊。| **by far** (=by a large amount or degree) …得多〔指量和程度〕 *Godard's first film was better by far.* 戈達德的第一部電影要好得多。**10** used to show the part of a piece of equipment or of someone's body that someone takes or holds〔表示承受動作的身體或物體的部分〕: *He took her by the arm and led her across the road.* 他牽着她的手, 領她過了馬路。| *She grabbed the hammer by the handle.* 她抓住錘子的柄。**11** used when expressing strong feelings or making serious promises 對…發誓〔表示強烈的情感或莊嚴的承諾〕: *By God, I'll kill that boy when I see him!* 我對上帝發誓, 我要是看見這小子, 非殺了他不可! **12** used between two numbers that you are multiplying or dividing 用…乘以[除以]…得: *What's 48 divided by 4?* 48除以4等於多少? **13** used when giving the measurements of a room, container etc 乘以, 見方: *a room 15 metres by 23 metres* 一間15米寬23米長的房間 **14** used to show a rate or quantity 以…為單位計: *We're paid by the hour.* 按小時給我們計酬。**15 day by day/bit by bit etc** used to show the way in which something happens 一天一天地/一點一點地等: *Day by day he grew weaker.* 他一天比一天衰弱。**16** used to show the situation or period of time during which you do something or something happens 在…情況下; 在…期間: *You could ruin your eyes reading by torchlight.* 在手電筒光下看書會損害你的眼睛。| **by day/night** *a tour of Paris by night* 夜遊巴黎 **17** used to show the connection between one fact or thing and another 就…來説〔表示一個事實與另一個事實間的關係〕: *Colette's French by birth.* 科利特的出生地為法國。| *It's fine by me if you want to go.* 你要去我覺得沒有問題。**18** as a result of an action or situation 由於: **by accident** *I saw Maureen quite by accident in the supermarket the other day.* 那天, 我碰巧在超級市場遇見了莫琳。| **by mistake** *I managed to delete an afternoon's work on the computer by mistake.* 由於疏忽, 我竟然把一下午在電腦中做的內容全刪去了。**19** if a woman has children by a particular man, that man is the children's father 與〔某男子〕所生: *Ann's got two children by her previous husband.* 安與前夫生了兩個孩子。**20 (all) by yourself** completely alone 單獨, 獨自: *Dave spent Christmas all by himself.* 戴夫獨自一人過聖誕節。

by² *adv* **1** if someone or something moves or goes by, they go past〔由旁邊〕經過: *As I was standing on the platform the Liverpool train went whizzing by.* 我站在月台上, 開往利物浦的火車飛馳而過。| *Ten years had gone by since I had last seen Marilyn.* 自從我上次見過瑪莉琳, 已經過了十年了。| *James walked by without even looking in my direction.* 詹姆斯沒有朝我這兒看就走了過去。**2** beside or near someone or something 在附近: *A crowd of people were standing by waiting for an announcement.* 一大羣人站在旁邊等待消息的發佈。**3 put/keep/lay sth by etc** to put something somewhere in order to use it in the future〔將某物〕存放起來, 收着: *Her mother gave her a dinner service to put by for when she got married.* 她母親給了她一套餐具以備結婚時用。**4 call/stop/go by** to go to someone's house in order to visit them for a short time 短暫訪問: *Why don't you stop by for a drink after work?* 下班後為何不過來喝點甚麼? **5 by and large** *especially spoken* used when talking generally about someone or something【尤口】大體上, 一般地說, 總的説來: *Charities are, by and large, exempt from income tax.* 一般來說, 慈善團體免交所得税。**6 by the by** *spoken* used when mentioning something that may be interesting but is not particularly important【口】順便説一下: *By the by, Ian said he might call round tonight.* 順便告訴你, 伊恩說他也許今天晚上會過來。**7 by and by** *especially literary* soon【尤文】不久, 很快

bye- /baɪ; baɪ/ *prefix* another spelling of BY- by-的另一種拼法

bye¹ /baɪ; baɪ/ also 又作 **bye-bye** /ˌ· ˈ·/ *interjection informal* goodbye【非正式】再見, 拜拜: **bye for now** (=used to say that you will see or speak to someone again soon) 一會兒見

bye² *n* [C] a situation in a sports competition in which a player or a team does not have an opponent to play against and continues to the next part of the competition 輪空〔指體育比賽中因沒有對手而直接進入下一輪比賽〕

bye-byes /ˈ· ·/ *n* **go (to) bye-byes** *BrE* an expression meaning go to sleep, used by or to children【英】去睡覺〔兒語〕

by·e·lec·tion, bye-election /ˈ· ·ˌ··/ *n* [C] *especially BrE* a special election to replace a politician who has left parliament or died【尤英】〔英國議會的〕補缺選舉

by·gone /ˈbaɪˌgɔn; ˈbaɪgɒn/ *adj* **bygone age/era/days etc** an expression meaning a period of time in the past 過去的時期/年代/歲月等: *The buildings reflect the elegance of a bygone era.* 這些建築物反映了過去年代的典雅。

by·gones /ˈbaɪˌgɔnz; ˈbaɪgɒnz/ *n* **let bygones be bygones** to forget something bad that someone has done to you and forgive them 過去的事就讓它過去吧

by·law /ˈbaɪˌlɔ; ˈbaɪlɔː/ *n* **1** [C] a law made by a local government that people in that area must obey (地方)法規 **2** *AmE* a rule made by an organization to control the people who belong to it【美】〔組織、社團的〕章程, 會章

by-line /ˈ· ·/ *n* [C] a line at the beginning of some writing in a newspaper or magazine giving the writer's name〔報刊文章開頭的〕作者署名行

by·pass¹ /ˈbaɪˌpæs; ˈbaɪpɑːs/ *n* [C] **1** a road that goes around a town or other busy area rather than through it 旁道, 間道, 小路 **2** *technical* a tube that allows gas or liquid to flow around something rather than through it【術語】旁通管, 分流器, 輔助管 **3 heart bypass/bypass surgery** an operation to direct blood through new VEINS (=blood tubes) outside the heart 心臟搭橋手術, 旁道管手術

B

bypass² *v* [T] **1** to avoid the centre of a city by driving around it 避開; 繞…而行 **2** to avoid obeying a rule, system, or someone in an official position 繞過正常手續或規章: *Francis bypassed the complaints procedure and wrote straight to the director.* 弗朗西絲繞過正常的投訴程序, 直接寫信給董事。

by·play /ˈbaɪˌple; ˈbaɪpleɪ/ *n* [U] something that is less important than the main action, especially in a play〔尤指戲劇中的〕穿插動作; 枝節

by-prod·uct /ˈ·ˌ··/ *n* [C] **1** something additional that is produced during a natural or industrial process 副產品: *milk by-products such as whey* 如乳清等牛奶的副產品 **2** an unplanned additional result of something that you do 意外收穫, 額外收穫; 附帶的結果 —compare 比較 END PRODUCT

byre /baɪr; baɪə/ *n* [C] *BrE old-fashioned* a farm building in which cattle are kept; COWSHED【英, 過時】牛棚

by·stand·er /ˈbaɪˌstændɚ; ˈbaɪˌstændə/ *n* [C] someone who watches what is happening without taking part; ONLOOKER 旁觀者, 局外人, 看熱鬧的人: **innocent bystander** *Several innocent bystanders were killed by the blast.* 有幾個無辜的旁觀者在爆炸中喪生。

byte /baɪt; baɪt/ *n* [C] *technical* a unit of computer information equal to eight bits (BIT¹ (12))【術語】字節;〔由八位元構成的〕位元組

by·way /ˈbaɪˌwe; ˈbaɪweɪ/ *n* [C] a small road or path which is not used very much 偏僻小路, 旁道

by·word /ˈbaɪˌwɝd; ˈbaɪwɜːd/ *n* [C] **1 be a byword for** to be so well-known for a particular quality that your name is used to represent that quality 成為…的代名詞: *The political system had become a byword for fraud.* 該政治體制成了詐騙的代名詞。**2** [singular] a phrase or saying that is very well-known 口頭禪; 俗語

by·zan·tine /ˈbɪzənˌtin; baɪˈzæntaɪn/ *adj formal* complicated and difficult to understand【正式】錯綜複雜的; 弄不明白的: *the byzantine complexity of our tax laws* 我們繁雜難懂的稅務法

C,c

C, c /si; siː/ *plural* **C's, c's** *n* [C] **1** the third letter of the English alphabet 英語字母表的第三個字母 **2** the number 100 in the system of ROMAN NUMERALS 羅馬數字 100

c 1 the written abbreviation of 縮寫= CENTIMETRE(s) 厘米 **2** a written abbreviation of 縮寫= CIRCA (=about) 大約, 左右: *born c 1830* 生於 1830 年前後 **3** the written abbreviation of 縮寫= CUBIC 立方 **4** the written abbreviation of 縮寫= COPYRIGHT when printed inside a small circle 版權, 著作權〔印在小圓圈內〕

C[1] /si; siː/ *n* **1 a)** the first note in the musical SCALE[2] (8) of C MAJOR[1] (4) C 音〔C 大調音階中的第一個音〕**b)** the musical KEY[1] (4) on this note C 音調 **2** a mark given to a student's work to show that it is of average quality C 級, 丙級, 丙等〔表示學業成績中等〕

C[2] the written abbreviation of 縮寫= CELSIUS 攝氏: *Water boils at 100°C.* 水在攝氏 100 度時沸騰。

C&W /ˌsi ən ˋdʌbəlju; ˌsiː ən ˈdʌbəljuː/ *n* [U] COUNTRY AND WESTERN (=type of music) 鄉村和西部音樂

ca a written abbreviation of 縮寫= CIRCA (=about) 大約, 左右: *dating from ca 1900* 可追溯到 1900 年左右

cab /kæb; kæb/ *n* [C] **1** a taxi 出租車, 的士, 計程車: **call (sb) a cab** (=telephone for a taxi) (為某人) 叫一輛計程車 **2** the part of a bus, train or TRUCK[1] (1) in which the driver sits〔公共汽車、火車或貨車的〕司機室, 駕駛室 **3** a carriage pulled by horses that was used like a taxi in former times〔舊時的〕出租馬車

ca·bal /kəˋbæl; kəˈbæl/ *n* [C] a small group of people who make secret plans, especially in order to have political power〔尤指為獲取政權的〕陰謀小集團

cab·a·ret /ˌkæbəˋre; ˈkæbəreɪ/ *n* **1** [C,U] entertainment, usually with music, songs, and dancing, performed in a restaurant or club while the customers eat and drink〔餐廳或夜總會的〕卡巴萊歌舞表演 **2** [C] a restaurant or club where this is performed 卡巴萊〔指有歌舞表演的餐廳或夜總會〕: *the most famous Parisian cabaret, the Moulin Rouge* 最著名的巴黎卡巴萊夜總會 —— 紅磨坊

cab·bage /ˋkæbɪdʒ; ˈkæbɪdʒ/ *n* **1** [C,U] a large round vegetable with thick green or purple leaves 捲心菜, 洋白菜, 甘藍 —see picture on page A9 參見 A9 頁圖 **2** [C] *BrE informal*【英, 非正式】**a)** someone who is lazy and shows no interest in anything 對一切都不感興趣者, 胸無大志者 **b)** someone who cannot think, move, speak etc as a result of brain injury; VEGETABLE (2) 植物人

cab·bie, cabby /ˋkæbɪ; ˈkæbi/ *n* [C] *informal* a taxi driver【非正式】出租車[計程車]司機

ca·ber /ˋkebɚ; ˈkeɪbə/ *n* [C] a long heavy wooden pole that is thrown into the air as a test of strength in sports competitions in Scotland〔蘇格蘭體育競賽中用於投擲比試的〕長樹幹, 長木柱: *tossing the caber* 扔木樁, 擲樹幹

cab·in /ˋkæbɪn; ˈkæbɪ̥n/ *n* [C] **1** a small house, especially one built of wood in an area of forest or mountains〔尤指建於山上或林中的〕小木屋 **2** a small room on a ship in which you live or sleep〔船上的〕艙 **3** an area inside a plane where the passengers sit or where the pilot works〔飛機上的〕客艙; 駕駛艙: *the First Class cabin* 飛機頭等艙

cabin boy /ˋ·· ·/ *n* [C] a young man who works as a servant on a ship 船艙的男服務員[侍應生]

cabin class /ˋ·· ·/ *n* [U] travelling conditions on a ship that are better than TOURIST CLASS but not as good as FIRST CLASS (1)〔船上的〕二等艙

cabin cruis·er /ˋ·· ˌ··/ *n* [C] a large motor boat with one or more cabins for people to sleep in〔有臥艙的〕大遊艇

cab·i·net /ˋkæbənɪt; ˈkæbɪ̥nɪ̥t/ *n* [C] **1** [also+plural verb *BrE* 英] the politicians with important positions in a government who meet to make decisions or advise the leader of the government 內閣: *a cabinet meeting* 內閣會議 **2** a piece of furniture with doors and shelves or drawers, used for storing or showing things〔有擱板、拉門或抽屜的〕貯藏櫃, 陳列櫃: *a drinks cabinet* 酒櫃 —see also 另見 FILING CABINET 2 2

cabinet-mak·er /ˋ··· ˌ··/ *n* [C] someone whose job is to make good quality wooden furniture 細木工, 家具木工

cabin fe·ver /ˋ·· ˌ··/ *n* [U] *AmE* a state in which you feel bad-tempered, because you have not been outside for a long time【美】〔長期足不出戶而引起的〕幽閉煩躁症

ca·ble[1] /ˋkebl̩; ˈkeɪbəl/ *n* **1** [C] a plastic or rubber tube containing wires that carry telephone messages, electronic signals etc 電纜 **2** [C,U] a thick strong metal rope used on ships, to support bridges etc 纜繩 **3** [U] CABLE TELEVISION 有線電視: *a cable channel* 有線頻道 **4** [C] a TELEGRAM 電報 3

cable[2] *v* [I,T] to send someone a CABLE[1] (4) 發電報: **cable sb sth** *I cabled Mary the good news.* 我用電報把這個好消息告訴了瑪麗。

cable car /ˋ·· ·/ *n* [C] **1** a vehicle pulled by a moving CABLE[1] (2), used to take people to the top of mountains 登山纜車, 吊車 **2** a vehicle used in cities, that is pulled along by a moving CABLE[1] (2)〔城市內的〕索道車

cable car 登山纜車, 吊車

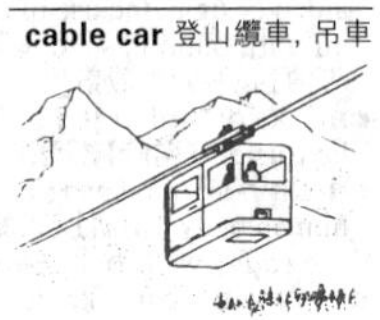

ca·ble·gram /ˋkebl̩ˌgræm; ˈkeɪbəlgræm/ *n* [C] a TELEGRAM 電報

cable rail·way /ˋ·· ˌ··/ *n* [C] a railway on which vehicles are pulled up steep slopes by a moving CABLE[1] (2)〔登山〕纜車鐵路

cable stitch /ˋ·· ·/ *n* [C,U] a knotted pattern of stitches used in KNITTING 纜繩狀針織法

cable tel·e·vi·sion /ˌ·· ˋ··· ˌ·· ··ˋ··/ also 又作 **cable TV** /ˌ·· ·ˋ·/ *n* [U] a system of broadcasting television programmes by CABLE[1] (1) 有線電視 —compare 比較 SATELLITE TELEVISION

ca·boo·dle /kəˋbudl; kəˈbuːdl/ *n* **the whole (kit and) caboodle** *informal* everything【非正式】全部: *slash costs by abolishing the whole caboodle: ballot papers, polling booths, even town halls* 大幅降低費用的辦法是取消所有的選票、投票站, 甚至市政廳

ca·boose /kəˋbus; kəˈbuːs/ *n* [C] *AmE* the part of a train where the official in charge of it travels, usually at the back【美】列車車長車廂〔通常在列車末尾〕; GUARD'S VAN *BrE*【英】

cab rank /ˋ· ·/ *n* [C] *BrE* a place where taxis wait【英】計程車[出租車]候客站, 的士站; CABSTAND *AmE*【美】

cab·ri·o·let /ˌkæbrɪəˋle; ˈkæbriəleɪ/ *n* [C] a car with a roof that can be folded back; CONVERTIBLE[2] 摺篷式汽車

cab·stand /ˋkæbˌstænd; ˈkæbstænd/ *n* [C] *AmE* a place where taxis wait for customers【美】計程車[出租車]候客站, 的士站; TAXI RANK *BrE*【英】

ca·cao /kəˋkɑo; kəˈkaʊ/ *n* [C] the seed from which chocolate and COCOA are made 可可豆

cache[1] /kæʃ; kæʃ/ *n* [C] a number of things that have been hidden, or the place where they have been hidden

隱藏物; 隱藏處: *Police found a cache of explosives in a garage in South London.* 警方在倫敦南部發現一個藏有許多炸藥的車庫。

cache² *v* [T] to hide something in a secret place 隱藏; 貯藏

cach·et /ˈkæʃe; ˈkæʃeɪ/ *n* [U] *formal* if something has cachet, people think it is especially good and desirable 【正式】聲望; 〔高貴的〕身分: *a good college but without the cachet of Harvard or Yale* 一所不錯的、但聲望不及哈佛或耶魯的大學

cack-hand·ed /ˌkæk ˋhændɪd; ˌkæk ˈhændɪ̣d◂/ *adj BrE informal* careless or tending to drop things; CLUMSY (1) 【英, 非正式】笨手笨腳的

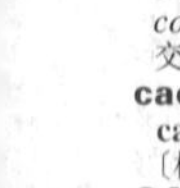

cack·le¹ /ˋkækl; ˈkækəl/ *v* [I] **1** to laugh in a loud unpleasant way, making short high sounds 刺耳地咯咯笑: *Rumplestiltskin rubbed his hands and cackled with delight.* 朗波斯狄特斯金一邊搓着手一邊開心地發出咯咯的笑聲。**2** when a chicken cackles, it makes a loud unpleasant sound 〔雞〕咯咯地叫

cackle² *n* **1** [C,U] a short high unpleasant laugh 咯咯刺耳的笑聲: *loud cackles of amusement* 因覺得好玩而發出的咯咯大笑 **2 cut the cackle** *BrE old-fashioned* used to tell someone to stop talking about unimportant things 【英, 過時】〔用於要求某人〕停止閒扯, 別再饒舌了

ca·coph·o·ny /kəˋkɑfənɪ; kəˈkɒfəni/ *n* [singular] a loud unpleasant mixture of sounds 刺耳嘈雜的聲音: *a cacophony of car horns and shouting* 汽車喇叭聲與喊叫交織在一起的嘈雜聲 —**cacophonous** *adj*

cac·tus /ˋkæktəs; ˈkæktəs/ *n plural* **cacti** /-taɪ; -taɪ/ or **cactuses** [C] a prickly plant that grows in hot dry places 〔植物〕仙人掌

CAD /ˌsi e ˋdi, kæd; ˌsiː eɪ ˈdiː, kæd/ *n* [U] computer-aided design; the use of COMPUTER GRAPHICS to plan cars, aircraft, buildings etc 電腦輔助設計; 〔汽車、飛機、建築等的〕電腦圖形設計

cad /kæd; kæd/ *n* [C] *old-fashioned* a man who cannot be trusted 【過時】不可信賴的男人, 無賴 —**caddish** *adj*

ca·dav·er /kəˋdævɚ; kəˈdævə/ *n* [C] *technical* a dead human body 【術語】〔人的〕屍體: *He looked like a walking cadaver.* 他看上去枯槁憔悴。

ca·dav·er·ous /kəˈdævərəs; kəˈdævərəs/ *adj formal* looking extremely pale, thin, and unhealthy 【正式】面色灰白的, 形容枯槁的: *cadaverous cheeks* 蒼白的臉頰

CAD/CAM /ˋkædkæm; ˈkædkæm/ *n* [U] computer-aided design and manufacture; the use of computers to plan and make industrial products 電腦輔助設計和製造; 電腦輔助生產系統

cad·dy¹ /ˋkædɪ; ˈkædi/ *n* [C] **1** also 又作 **caddie** someone who carries the GOLF CLUBS for someone who is playing GOLF 〔受雇為打高爾夫球的人背球棒的〕球僮 **2** a small box for storing tea 茶葉盒, 茶葉罐

caddy², caddie *v* [I+for] to carry GOLF CLUBS for someone who is playing GOLF 當〔某人的〕高爾夫球僮 —see picture on page A23 參見 A23 頁圖

ca·dence /ˋkedn̩s; ˈkeɪdəns/ *n* [C] **1** the way someone's voice rises and falls, especially when reading out loud 〔尤指大聲朗讀時音調的〕抑揚頓挫 **2** *technical* a set of CHORDS at the end of a line or piece of music 【術語】〔樂曲、樂章的一組〕結尾和弦, 終止式

ca·den·za /kəˋdɛnzə; kəˈdenzə/ *n* [C] *technical* a difficult part of a CONCERTO in which the performer plays without the ORCHESTRA to show their skill 【術語】〔協奏曲中獨奏的〕華彩樂段

ca·det /kəˋdɛt; kəˈdet/ *n* [C] **1** someone who is training to be an officer in the army, navy, air force, or police force 〔軍官學校或警官學校的〕學員 **2** someone who is in a CADET CORPS 軍訓隊員

cadet corps /·ˈ· ·/ *n* [C] an organization that gives simple military training to pupils in some British schools 〔英國某些學校中給學生進行軍訓的〕軍訓隊(組織)

cadge /kædʒ; kædʒ/ *v* [I,T] *BrE informal* to ask someone for food or cigarettes because you do not have any or do not want to pay 【英, 非正式】乞討; 索取; MOOCH *AmE* 【美】: **cadge sth from/off** *I managed to cadge a lift from Joanna.* 我設法硬是搭上了喬安娜的便車。—**cadger** *n* [C]

Cad·il·lac /ˋkædɪlæk; ˈkædɪlæk/ *n* [C] *trademark* 【商標】**1** a very expensive and comfortable car made by an American company 卡迪拉克轎車 **2** *AmE informal* something that is regarded as the highest quality example of a particular type of product 【美, 非正式】精品, 一流名牌產品; ROLLS ROYCE *BrE* 【英】: *the Cadillac of stereo systems* 立體音響系統中的精品

cad·mi·um /ˋkædmɪəm; ˈkædmiəm/ *n* [U] a type of metal used in batteries (BATTERY (1)) 鎘

ca·dre /ˋkɑdɚ; ˈkɑːdə/ *n formal* [C also+plural verb *BrE* 英] a small group of specially trained people in a profession, political party, or military force 【正式】骨幹隊伍: *a cadre of highly trained scientists* 一批受過嚴格培訓的骨幹科學家

cae·sar·e·an /sɪˋzɛrɪən; sɪ̣ˈzeriən/ also 又作 **caesarean section** /·,···ˈ··/ *n* [C] an operation in which a woman's body is cut open to take a baby out 剖腹產(手術); C-SECTION *AmE* 【美】

cae·su·ra /sɪˋʒʊrə; sɪˈzjʊərə/ *n* [C] *technical* a pause in the middle of a line of poetry 【術語】〔一行詩中間的〕停頓

café /kæˋfe; ˈkæfeɪ/ *n* [C] **1** a small restaurant where you can buy drinks and simple meals 咖啡館, 小餐館 **2** a place on a computer NETWORK¹ (4), where people with similar interests discuss things electronically 網絡聊天室: *You can set up a special interest café on e-mail or Internet.* 你不妨設立一個關於電子郵件和互聯網的專題聊天室。

caf·e·te·ri·a /ˌkæfəˋtɪrɪə; ˌkæfɪ̣ˈtɪəriə/ *n* [C] a restaurant where you choose your own food and carry it to the table, often in a factory, college etc 〔工廠、學校等的〕自助餐廳, 食堂: *the school cafeteria* 學校食堂

caf·e·tiere /ˌkæfəˋtjɛr; ˌkæfəˈtjeə/ *n* [C] a special pot for making coffee, with a metal FILTER¹ (1) that you push down 〔帶有金屬濾器的〕咖啡壺

caff /kæf; kæf/ *n* [C] *informal BrE* a café 【非正式, 英】咖啡館, 小餐館

caf·feine /ˋkæfin; ˈkæfiːn/ *n* [U] a substance in tea and coffee that makes you feel more active 咖啡因[鹼]

caf·tan /ˋkæftæn; ˈkæftæn/ *n* [C] a long loose piece of clothing like a coat, usually made of silk or cotton and worn in the Middle East 〔中東地區人穿的絲質或棉質的〕寬鬆長袍

cage¹ /kedʒ; keɪdʒ/ *n* [C] a structure made of wires or bars in which birds or animals can be kept 籠子

cage 籠子

cage² *v* **1** [T] to put or keep something in a cage 把…放[關]進籠中: *caged birds* 籠中鳥 **2 feel caged in** to feel uncomfortable and annoyed because you cannot go outside 感覺被束縛, 行動無自由

cag·ey /ˋkedʒɪ; ˈkeɪdʒi/ *adj informal* unwilling to tell people definitely what your plans, intentions, or opinions are 【非正式】〔言談〕小心謹慎的, 謹言慎行的: [+about] *Senator King is being very cagey about whether he'll run for president.* 金參議員對是否參選總統含糊其詞。—**cagily** *adv* —**caginess** *n*

ca·goule /kəˋgul; kəˈguːl/ *n* [C] *BrE* a thin coat with a HOOD (=cover for your head) that stops you from getting wet 【英】帶風帽的薄雨衣

ca·hoots /kəˋhuts; kəˈhuːts/ *n* **be in cahoots (with)** to be working secretly with another person or group, especially in order to do something dishonest 與…合夥; 與…共謀[勾結]: *Perhaps O'Brien was in cahoots with the thieves.* 奧布賴恩可能與小偷有勾結。

cairn /kɛrn; keən/ *n* [C] a pile of stones, especially at the top of a mountain, to mark a place〔尤指在山頂作為標記的〕石堆, 石標

cais·son /ˈkesn̩; ˈkeɪsən/ *n* [C] **1** a large box filled with air, that allows people to work under water〔水下作業用的〕沉箱 **2** a large box for carrying AMMUNITION (1) 彈藥箱

ca·jole /kəˋdʒol; kəˈdʒəʊl/ *v* [I,T] to gradually persuade someone to do something by being nice, etc〔用甜言蜜語〕哄騙, 勸誘: **cajole sb into doing sth** *Can't you cajole her into coming?* 難道你不能哄她來嗎?

2 3 **cake¹** /kek; keɪk/ *n* **1** [C,U] a soft sweet food made by baking a mixture of flour, fat, sugar and eggs 蛋糕, 糕餅: *a birthday cake* 生日蛋糕 | *Would you like a slice of chocolate cake?* 來塊巧克力蛋糕怎麼樣? —compare 比較 BISCUIT **2 fish cake/rice cake etc** fish, rice etc that has been formed into a flat round shape and then cooked 魚肉餅/米餅等 **3** [C] a small block of something 塊: [+of] *a cake of soap* 一塊肥皂 **4 be a piece of cake** *spoken* to be very easy【口】很容易做到的事, 輕鬆愉快的事: *"How do you do that?" "It's a piece of cake! Watch!"* "你怎麼做?" "很簡單! 看着!" **5 take the cake** *AmE informal* to be worse than anything else you can imagine【美, 非正式】糟糕透頂; **take the biscuit** (BISCUIT (4)) *BrE*【英】: *I've heard some pretty dumb ideas, but that takes the cake!* 我聽到過許多餿主意, 但那一個是最蠢的! **6 you can't have your cake and eat it** *spoken* used to tell someone that they cannot have the advantage of something without its disadvantages【口】兩者不可兼得 **7 a slice of the cake** a part of the money, help etc that is available for everyone to share〔人人都可分享到的財物、幫助等的〕份額 —see also 另見 **sell like hot cakes** (HOT CAKE)

cake² *v* **1 be caked with/in** to be covered with a layer of something thick and hard 厚厚地塗上[沾上]...: *Look at your boots! They're caked with mud.* 看看你的靴子! 沾滿了泥巴! **2** [I] if a substance cakes, it forms a thick hard layer when it dries〔乾後〕結成硬塊

cake·hole /ˈkekˌhol; ˈkeɪk-həʊl/ *n* [C] *BrE spoken* someone's mouth【英口】嘴巴: *Shut your cakehole!* 閉嘴!

cake pan /ˈ· ·/ *n* [C] *AmE* a CAKE TIN (1)【美】蛋糕烤盤

cake tin /ˈ· ·/ *n* [C] *BrE*【英】**1** a metal container in which you bake a cake 蛋糕烤盤 —see picture at 參見 PAN¹ 圖 **2** a metal container with a lid, that you keep a cake in 裝蛋糕的有蓋金屬盒

cake·walk /ˈkekˌwɔk; ˈkeɪkwɔːk/ *n* [singular] *AmE informal* a very easy victory【美, 非正式】輕易取得的勝利

cal·a·bash /ˈkæləˌbæʃ; ˈkæləbæʃ/ *n* [C] a large tropical fruit with a shell that can be dried and used as a bowl〔產於熱帶的〕加拉巴果〔其殼乾燥後可作碗用〕, 葫蘆

cal·a·brese /ˈkæləbris; ˈkæləbriːs/ *n* [U] a type of BROCCOLI 花莖甘藍, 西蘭花菜, 花椰菜

cal·a·mine lo·tion /ˈkæləˌmaɪn ˋloʃən; ˈkæləmaɪn ˌləʊʃən/ *n* [U] a pink liquid for sore, itchy or sunburnt (SUNBURN) skin 爐甘石藥水〔粉紅色護膚藥水, 可防止皮膚疼痛、瘙癢或日曬後的疼痛〕

ca·lam·i·ty /kəˋlæmətɪ; kəˈlæməti/ *n* [C] a terrible and unexpected event that causes a lot of damage or suffering 災難, 禍患: *It would be a calamity for the farmers if the crops failed again.* 如果收成再不好, 將會給農民造成很大的災難。—**calamitous** *adj* —**calamitously** *adv*

cal·ci·fy /ˈkælsəˌfaɪ; ˈkælsəfaɪ/ *v* [I,T] *technical* to become hard, or make something hard, by adding LIME¹ (3)【術語】(使) 石灰質化, (使) 鈣化; (使) 硬化

3 **cal·ci·um** /ˈkælsɪəm; ˈkælsiəm/ *n* [U] a simple chemical substance in bones, teeth, and CHALK¹ (1) 鈣

cal·cu·la·ble /ˈkælkjələbl̩; ˈkælkjələbəl/ *adj* something that is calculable can be measured by using numbers 能計算的: *clear and calculable beneficial effects* 清楚而且可以算出來的效益

cal·cu·late /ˈkælkjəˌlet; ˈkælkjəleɪt/ *v* [T] **1** to find out how much something will cost, how long something will take etc, by using numbers 計算, 核算: *Oil prices are calculated in dollars.* 油價以美元計算。| **calculate how much/how many etc** *I'm trying to calculate how much paint we need.* 我試着算算看我們需要多少塗料。| **calculate (that)** *Sally calculated that she'd have about £100 left.* 莎莉算了一下, 自己還會剩下大約 100 英鎊。**2** to guess something using as many facts as you can find 估算, 估計: *It's difficult to calculate what effect all these changes will have on the company.* 很難估計這些變化將會給公司帶來甚麼樣的影響。**3 be calculated to do sth** to be intended to have a particular effect 旨在, 用意在於; 打算; 適於 (做) ...: *a comment calculated to annoy traditionalists in the party* 旨在惹怒黨內傳統人士的評論 2 3

calculate on sth *phr v* [T] if you calculate on something you are depending on it for your plans to succeed 指望, 期望: *We're calculating on an early start.* 我們指望可以一早出發。| **calculate on sb/sth doing sth** *Ken hadn't calculated on Polson refusing his offer.* 肯恩並未料到波爾森會拒絕自己的提議。

cal·cu·lat·ed /ˈkælkjəˌletɪd; ˈkælkjəleɪtəd/ *adj* **1** a calculated crime or dishonest action is deliberately and carefully planned 故意的, 蓄意的; 有計劃的; 存心欺騙的: *a calculated attempt to deceive the American public* 蓄意欺騙美國公眾的企圖 **2 take a calculated risk** to do something that involves a risk after thinking carefully about what might happen 冒預料到的風險 —see also 另見 CALCULATE —**calculatedly** *adv*

cal·cu·lat·ing /ˈkælkjəˌletɪŋ; ˈkælkjəleɪtɪŋ/ *adj* making careful and clever plans to get what you want, without caring about anyone else 有算計的, 工於心計的, 用盡心機 (作損人利己之事) 的: *a criminal with a cold, calculating mind* 一個冷酷而工於心計的罪犯

cal·cu·la·tion /ˌkælkjəˋleʃən; ˌkælkjəˈleɪʃən/ *n* **1** [C,U] 2 a way of using numbers in order to find out an amount, price, or value 計算; 推斷; 預測, 估計: *Dee looked at the bill and made some rapid calculations.* 迪睞着賬單, 同時進行着速算。**2** [U] careful planning in order to get what you want 盤算, 深思熟慮, 慎重的計劃

cal·cu·la·tor /ˈkælkjəˌletɚ; ˈkælkjəleɪtə/ *n* [C] a small 3 electronic machine that can do calculations such as adding and multiplying 計算器[機]: *a solar calculator* (=working using the power of the sun) 太陽能電池計算器[機]

cal·cu·lus /ˈkælkjələs; ˈkælkjələs/ *n* [U] the part of mathematics that deals with changing quantities, such as the speed of a falling stone or the slope of a curved line 微積分

cal·dron /ˈkɔldrən; ˈkɔːldrən/ *n* [C] the American spelling of CAULDRON cauldron 的美式拼法

cal·en·dar /ˈkæləndɚ; ˈkæləndə/ *n* [C] **1** pages printed to show the days, weeks, and months of a particular year, that you hang on the wall 日曆, 月曆 **2** *AmE*【美】**a)** a book with separate spaces or pages for each day of the year, on which you write down the things you have to do〔日曆〕記事簿; DIARY (2) *BrE*【英】**b)** all the things you plan to do in the next days, months etc 日程表; 一覽表: *The President's calendar is already very full.* 總統的日程表早已排得滿滿的。**3** a system for dividing time, that fixes the event from which all years are measured and arranges days into months and years 曆法: *the Gregorian calendar* 公曆, 陽曆 **4** all the events in a year that are important for a particular organization or activity〔某個團體或某項活動預定一年內要辦的〕大事日程表: *The Derby is a major event in the racing calendar.* 打比馬賽在賽馬日程表上是一項重要的賽事。

calendar month /ˌ··· ˈ··/ *n* [C] **1** one of the twelve months of the year 曆月: *Salaries will be paid at the end of the calendar month.* 工資在每個月月底發放。**2** a period of time from a specific date in one month to the same date in the next month〔指某月中的某日至下月中同一日的〕滿一個月的時間

calendar year /ˌ··· ˈ·/ *n* [C] a period of time from January 1st to December 31st 曆年

calf /kæf; kɑːf/ *n plural* **calves** /kævz; kɑːvz/ [C] **1** the part of the back of your leg between your knee and your ANKLE〔人腿的〕腓, 小腿肚 —see picture at 參見 BODY 圖 **2** the baby of a cow, or of some other large animals such as the ELEPHANT 小牛, 牛犢;〔象等某些大動物的〕仔, 幼獸 **3 be in calf** if a cow is in calf, it is going to have a baby〔母牛〕懷孕的 —see also 另見 **kill the fatted calf** (KILL[1] (14))

C

calf love /ˈ· ·/ *n* [U] PUPPY LOVE 青少年時期的初戀

cal·i·ber /ˋkæləbɚ; ˈkælɨbə/ *n* the American spelling of CALIBRE calibre 的美式拼法

cal·i·brate /ˋkæləˌbret; ˈkælɨbreɪt/ *v* [T] *technical* to mark an instrument or tool so that you can use it for measuring【術語】標定, 劃分, 校準〔測量器的〕刻度

cal·i·bra·tion /ˌkælɪˋbreʃən; ˌkælɨˈbreɪʃən/ *n* [U] *technical* a set of marks on an instrument or tool used for measuring【術語】〔測量儀器上的〕刻度

cal·i·bre *BrE*【英】, **caliber** *AmE*【美】/ˋkæləbɚ; ˈkælɨbə/ *n* **1** [U] the level of quality or ability that someone or something has achieved〔人的〕能力, 才幹;〔事物的〕質量, 水準: *We've been lucky in the high calibre of directors we've been able to recruit.* 我們很幸運, 能夠招聘到高水平的領導人才。**2** [C] *technical*【術語】**a)** the width of the inside of a gun or tube〔槍砲或管子的〕內徑, 口徑 **b)** the width of a bullet〔子彈的〕彈徑, 直徑

cal·i·co /ˋkæləˌko; ˈkælɪkəʊ/ *n* [U] **1** *BrE* heavy cotton cloth that is usually white【英】厚白棉布 **2** *AmE* light cotton cloth with a small printed pattern【美】薄印花棉布 **3 calico cat** *AmE* a cat that has black, white and brown fur【美】〔毛皮黑白棕色相間的〕花斑貓

cal·i·pers /ˋkælɪpɚz; ˈkælɨpəz/ *n* [plural] the American spelling of CALLIPERS callipers 的美式拼法

ca·liph /ˋkelɪf; ˈkeɪlɨf/ *n* [C] a MUSLIM ruler 哈里發〔伊斯蘭教國家的教主和統治者〕

ca·li·phate /ˋkælɪˌfet; ˈkeɪlɨfeɪt/ *n* [C] the country a caliph rules, or the period of time when they rule it 哈里發統治的國家[時期]

cal·is·then·ics /ˌkæləsˋθɛnɪks; ˌkælɨsˈθenɪks/ *n* [plural] the American spelling of CALLISTHENICS callisthenics 的美式拼法

calk /kɔk; kɔːk/ *v* [T] an American spelling of CAULK caulk 的美式拼法

call[1] /kɔl; kɔːl/ *v*

① HAVE/USE A NAME 叫做/稱呼
② DESCRIBE SB/STH 描述某人/某事物
③ TELEPHONE 打電話
④ SAY STH LOUDLY 高聲說出某事
⑤ TELL/ORDER 告知/命令
⑥ VISIT 拜訪
⑦ AGREE 同意
⑧ ARRANGE STH 安排某事
⑨ OTHER MEANINGS 其他意思

① HAVE/USE A NAME 叫做/稱呼

1 [T] **be called sth** to have a particular name or title 名稱, 名叫: *They have a three-year-old son called Matthew.* 他們有個三歲的兒子, 名叫馬修。| *What was that book called?* 那本書的書名是甚麼?

2 [T] to use a particular name or title when you speak to someone 稱呼, 叫: *My name's Alan, but you can call me Al.* 我的名字是阿倫, 但你們可以叫我阿爾。| *Do you want to be called Miss or Ms?* 你願意被稱為小姐還是女士? | **call sb by** *I prefer to be called by my middle name.* 我喜歡別人叫我的中間名。

3 [T] to give someone or something the name they will be known by in the future 為〔某人或某事物〕取名: **call sb/sth sth** *They've decided to call the baby Louise.* 他們決定給寶寶取名為路易絲。

② DESCRIBE SB/STH 描述某人/某事物

4 [T] to use a particular word or phrase to describe someone or something that clearly shows what you think of them 認為…是…, 視為: **call sb/sth sth** *Are you calling me a liar?* 你認為我是個說謊者嗎? | *You may call it harmless fun, but I call it pornography.* 你可能認為這是毫無惡意的玩笑, 但是我卻認為這是黃色的。

5 call yourself sth to claim that you are a particular type of person, although you do nothing to show this is true 自稱為…, 自我描繪成是…: *He calls himself a Christian, but I've never seen him go to church.* 他稱自己是基督徒, 但我從未見他去過教堂。

6 call sb names to insult someone by using unpleasant words to describe them 辱罵某人: *The other kids used to call me names.* 別的孩子過去常常辱罵我。—see also 另見 **call a spade a spade** (SPADE (3))

③ TELEPHONE 打電話

7 [I,T] to telephone someone (給某人) 打電話: *I tried calling last night but you weren't home.* 昨晚我試着給你打電話, 但你不在家。| *He said he'd call me later to make arrangements.* 他說稍後會給我打電話作出安排。—see 見 TELEPHONE[1] (USAGE)

8 [T] to ask someone to come to you by telephoning them 打電話請某人: *I think we should call the doctor.* 我想我們應該打電話請醫生來。| *I swear, I'm gonna call the cops!* 我發誓, 我會打電話報警! —see graph at 參見 TELEPHONE[2] 圖表 —see also 另見 **call in**

9 call collect *AmE* to make a telephone call that is paid for by the person who receives it【美】打對方付費電話; **reverse the charges** (REVERSE[1] (5)) *BrE*【英】

④ SAY STH LOUDLY 高聲說出某事

10 [I,T] to say or shout something loudly so that someone can hear you 喊, 叫: *I thought I heard Dad calling me.* 我想我聽到爸爸叫我了。| **[+through/down/up]** *"I'm coming!" she called down the stairs.* "我就來!" 她朝樓下喊道。

11 [T] also 又作 **call out** to read names or numbers in a loud voice in order to get someone's attention 點名: *OK, when I call your name, go and stand in line.* 好! 我點到你的名字時, 你就過去站到隊列中。

⑤ TELL/ORDER 告知/命令

12 [T] to ask or order someone to come to you, either by speaking loudly or sending them a message〔高聲或傳信〕召喚[命令]〔某人〕來: **call sb into/over** *Later, the boss called Dan into her office.* 後來, 老板把丹恩叫進她的辦公室。| **call sb up/down** *AmE*【美】*Marcie got called up to the Principal's office for smoking.* 瑪西因為抽煙被叫到了校長辦公室。

13 [T usually passive 一般用被動態] to tell someone that they must come to a law court or official committee 傳召〔到法庭等〕: **call sb to do sth** *They were called to give evidence at the trial.* 他們被傳召到庭

訊中作證。

14 be/feel called to do sth if you are called to do something, you feel that God is telling you to do it 感到〔受上帝〕召喚: *Simon felt called to do missionary work.* 西蒙感覺到是上帝在召喚自己從事傳教的工作。

15 call sb/sth to order *formal* to tell people to obey the rules of a formal meeting【正式】命令…遵守議事規程: *I now call this meeting to order.* 現在, 我請大家遵守議事規程。

⑥ **VISIT** 拜訪

16 [I] *BrE*【英】also 又作 **call round** to stop at a house or other place for a short time to see someone or do something〔短時間〕拜訪〔某人〕,〔短時間〕逗留〔以便做某事〕: *The milkman called while you were out.* 你不在時, 送牛奶的人來過。| **call on sb** *We thought we'd call on James on the way home.* 我們想, 回家的路上我們應該拜訪一下詹姆斯。| **call at sth** *I called at the drycleaner's to collect your suit.* 我去了乾洗店取你的衣服。

⑦ **AGREE** 同意

17 call it £10/2 hours etc *spoken* used to ask someone to agree with a particular suggestion you are making, especially in order to make things simpler【口】就算作10英鎊/兩小時等: *"I owe you £10.20." "Oh, call it £10!"* "我欠你十英鎊二十便士。" "喔, 就算十英鎊吧。"

18 call it a draw if two opponents in a game call it a draw, they agree that neither of them has won 打成平局, 不分勝負 —see also 另見 **call it quits** (QUITS (2))

⑧ **ARRANGE STH** 安排某事

19 call a meeting/election/rehearsal etc to arrange for something to happen at a definite time 召集會議/選舉/排練等: *We've called an emergency meeting of the governors.* 我們已召集了州長舉行緊急會議。

20 call a huddle *AmE informal* to arrange for people to come together to have a meeting【美, 非正式】召集會議

⑨ **OTHER MEANINGS** 其他意思

21 call into question to make people uncertain about whether something is right or true〔使人對某事〕產生疑問: *I feel that my competence is being called into question here.* 我覺得自己的能力在這裡受到了懷疑。

22 call it a day *informal* to decide to stop working, especially because you have done enough or you are tired【非正式】今天(的工作)就到此為止: *Come on, let's call it a day and go home.* 好了, 今天我們就到此為止, 回家吧。

23 call attention to to ask people to pay attention to a particular subject or problem 提請注意: *May I call your attention to item seven on the agenda.* 請大家注意議程上的第七項。

24 ►TRAINS 火車◄ [I+at] if a train calls at a place, it stops there for a short time 短暫停留: *This train will call at all stations to Broxbourne.* 這輛開往布羅克思本的火車沿途所有車站都停。

25 call the tune/shots *informal* to be in a position of authority so that you can give orders and make decisions【非正式】發號施令; 操縱

26 call sth to mind a) to remind you of something 使回憶起: *Don't those two call to mind the days when we were courting?* 難道他們倆沒讓我們回憶起戀愛的日子? **b)** to remember something 想起: *Can you call to mind when you last saw her?* 你記得最後一次見到她是甚麼時候嗎?

27 ►GAMES/SPORTS 遊戲/體育◄ [I,T] to guess which side of a coin will land upwards when it is thrown in the air, in order to decide who will play first in a game 拋硬幣決定先後次序: *It's your turn to call.* 輪到你來拋硬幣了。—see also 另見 SO-CALLED, **call sb's bluff** (BLUFF² (2))

call back *phr v* **1** [I,T] to telephone someone again, especially because one of you was not in or was busy〔對方打來電話時因不在或繁忙而事後〕回電話: *No problem, I'll call back later.* 沒問題, 我過會兒再回電話。| **call sb back** *Can you ask John to call me back when he gets in?* 約翰來後讓他給我回電話好嗎? **2** [I] *BrE* to return to a place you have been to earlier, especially a house or a shop【英】再來〔尤指某所房子或商店〕: *I'll call back with my car and pick up the painting.* 我會開車再來取這幅畫。

call by *phr v* [I] *BrE informal* to stop and visit someone when you are near the place where they live or work【英, 非正式】順路拜訪: *I thought I'd call by and see how you were.* 我想我會順路去看看你怎麼樣了。

call sb/sth ↔ **down** *phr v* [T] *literary* to pray loudly that something unpleasant will happen to someone or something【文】〔大聲〕祈求降禍於…: *calling down the wrath of God* 祈求上帝降怒

call for sb/sth *phr v* [T] **1** to need a particular action, behaviour, quality etc 需要〔某種行動、舉止、品質等〕: *Really, Susan, that kind of attitude just isn't called for.* 真的, 蘇珊, 那種態度根本沒必要。—see also 另見 UNCALLED-FOR **2** to ask strongly and publicly for money, justice etc in order to change a situation 要求, 呼籲: *farmers calling for larger government subsidies* 呼籲政府給予更多補貼的農民 **3** *BrE* to meet someone at their home in order to take them somewhere【英】(去)接〔某人〕: *I'll call for you at 8 o'clock.* 我8點鐘來接你。**4** *AmE* to say that something is likely to happen, especially when talking about the weather【美】預測〔尤指天氣〕: *The forecast calls for more rain.* 天氣預報說還會下雨。

call sth ↔ **forth** *phr v* [T] *formal* to make something such as a quality appear so that you can use it; SUMMON【正式】喚起, 引起, 激起

call in *phr v* [I] **1** to telephone somewhere, especially the place where you work, to tell them where you are, what you are doing etc〔尤指向工作單位〕打電話匯報: **call in sick** (=telephone to say you are too ill to come to work) 打電話請病假 **2** [T **call** sb ↔ **in**] to ask someone to come and see you to help you with a difficult situation 請…來〔幫助〕: *Police have been called in to help find missing Sandra Day, aged 7.* 已經請了警察幫忙尋找失蹤的七歲小孩桑德拉·戴。**3 call in a loan/favour** to ask someone to pay back money or to help you with something because you helped them earlier 討還債款; 要求回報 **4** [I+at/on] *BrE* to visit a person or place while you are on your way somewhere else【英】順路拜訪, 順路探望: *Could you call in on Mum on your way home?* 你回家時能順便探望一下媽媽嗎?

call sb/sth ↔ **off** *phr v* [T] **1** to order a dog or person to stop attacking someone 叫〔狗或人〕…走開〔以免攻擊人〕: *Call off the alsatian – it's frightening my son.* 把狼狗叫走, 牠在嚇唬我兒子。**2** to decide that a planned event will not take place; CANCEL 取消, 撤銷〔原計劃的活動〕: *There's no rush now – the game's been called off.* 現在不用匆匆忙忙的了, 比賽已經取消了。**3 call off a strike/search etc** to decide officially that something should be stopped after it has already started 下令停止罷工/搜尋等: *Rescuers had to call off the search due to worsening weather.* 由於天氣惡化, 救援人員決定停止搜尋。

call on/upon sb/sth *phr v* [T] **1** to visit someone for a short time 短暫訪問: *Why don't you call on my sister when you're in Brighton?* 你到了布里季頓時何不順便探望一下我姐姐? **2** to formally ask someone to do something〔正式〕要求〔某人做某事〕: **call on sb to do sth**

The UN has called on both sides to observe the ceasefire. 聯合國已要求雙方遵守停火協議。

call out *phr v* **1** [I,T **call** sth ↔ **out**] to say something loudly 大聲說出: *Call out the numbers so that we can hear them at the back.* 大聲報出那些數字，讓我們在後面坐的人也能聽見。**2** [T **call** sb/sth ↔ **out**] **a)** to order an organization to help, especially in a dangerous situation〔尤指在出現某種險情時〕召喚[命令]〔某個組織〕出動: *The National Guard has been called out to help fight fires.* 國民警衛隊已奉令幫助滅火。**b)** *BrE* to order workers to go on strike (STRIKE² (1))【英】命令〔工人〕罷工

call up *phr v* **1** [I,T] **call** sb ↔ **up** *informal especially AmE* to telephone someone【非正式，尤美】給〔某人〕打電話 **2** [T **call** sb ↔ **up** *BrE* 英] to officially order someone to join the army, navy, or air force 徵召…入伍; DRAFT² (2) *AmE*【美】: *I was called up three months after war broke out.* 戰爭爆發三個月後，我被徵召入伍。**3** [T **call** sb ↔ **up**] to choose someone for a national sports team, especially football 挑選〔某人〕入國家隊〔尤指足球隊〕: *Hurst was called up for the game against Mexico.* 赫斯特入選國家隊，參加和墨西哥隊的比賽。**4** [T **call** sth ↔ **up**] if you call up information on a computer, you make the computer show it to you〔在電腦上〕顯示[調出]資訊 **5** [T **call** sb/sth **up**] to make something appear again after it has gone or been forgotten 使回憶起來; 召回: *calling up the spirits of the dead* 召回死者的靈魂

call² *n*

1 ►TELEPHONE 電話◄ [C] **a)** an attempt to speak to someone by telephone（一次）通話; 電話: *Were there any phone calls for me while I was out?* 我不在時有人給我來過電話嗎? | **get/receive a call** *I got a call from Jane in Australia last week.* 上週我接到珍從澳大利亞打來的電話。| **give sb a call** *I'll give you a call at the weekend.* 週末我會給你打電話。| **make a call** *It's cheaper to make calls after 6pm.* 下午 6 點後打電話便宜些。| **take a call** (=answer a call) 接電話 *I'll take the call in my office.* 我會在辦公室裡接電話。| **return a call** (=telephone someone who tried to telephone you earlier) 回電話 **b)** a telephone call asking a doctor, the police etc to go somewhere where they are needed 給〔醫生、警察等打的〕求助電話: *We're getting calls about a disturbance at a pub in Camden.* 我們接到電話，說卡姆登一家小酒吧裡發生了騷亂。

2 be on call if someone such as a doctor or engineer is on call, they are ready to go and help whenever they are needed as part of their job〔醫生、工程師等〕待命的，隨叫隨到的: *Don't worry, there's a doctor on call 24 hours a day.* 別擔心，全天 24 小時都有一位醫生值班。

3 ►SHOUT/CRY 叫/喊◄ [C] **a)** the sound or cry that a bird or animal makes〔鳥或動物的〕叫聲 **b)** a shout or cry that you make to get someone's attention〔引起他人注意的〕呼喊聲

4 ►VISIT 拜訪◄ [C] a visit, especially for a particular reason〔尤指特殊原因的〕短暫拜訪: *Sorry, Doctor Pugh is out on a call at the moment.* 對不起，皮尤醫生現在出診去了。| **pay/make a call (on)** (=visit someone) 拜訪某人 *Why not pay a call on your aunt while you're in Leeds?* 你到了利兹時何不探訪一下你姨媽?

5 there isn't much call for used to say that something is not popular or is not needed 沒有需求，不需要: *There isn't much call for black and white televisions these days.* 如今黑白電視機的需求量並不大。

6 there is no call for *spoken* used to tell someone that their behaviour is wrong and unnecessary【口】沒有理由，沒必要: *There's no call for swearing – I'm doing my best!* 沒必要罵人，我正竭盡全力!

7 ►REQUEST/ORDER 要求/命令◄ [C] a request or order for someone to do something or go somewhere 號召，呼籲: *a strike call* 罷工號召 | **call for sb to do sth** *There have been calls for the secretary to resign.* 有人要求部長辭職。

8 ►PLANE 飛機◄ [C] an official message at an airport that a plane for a particular place will soon leave 航班起飛前對旅客的通知: *This is the last call for flight BA872 to Moscow.* 這是飛往莫斯科的 BA872 航班起飛前的最後一次通知。

9 ►DECISION 決定◄ [singular] **a)** the decision made by a REFEREE (=judge) in a sports game〔體育運動比賽中裁判員的〕判決 **b)** *AmE informal* a decision【美，非正式】決定: **make a call** (=decide) 作決定 | **easy/hard call** (=a difficult or easy decision) 簡單/困難的決定 | **it's your call** *spoken* (=it's your decision)【口】這是你自己的決定

10 have first call on a) to have the right to be the first person to use something 具有〔使用某物的〕優先權 **b)** to be the first person that someone will help because you are important to them 處於優先〔受助的〕地位

11 the call of *literary* the power that a place or way of life has to attract someone【文】吸引力，魅力: *the call of the sea* 大海的魅力

12 the call of nature a need to URINATE (=pass liquid from your body) 要小便 —see also 另見 **be at sb's beck and call** (BECK (2)), PORT OF CALL, ROLL-CALL

call box /ˈ· ·/ *n* [C] **1** *AmE* a public telephone beside a road used to telephone for help【美】路邊求救電話 **2** *BrE* a small structure that is partly or completely enclosed, containing a public telephone【英】公用電話亭; PHONE BOOTH *AmE*【美】

call·er /ˈkɔlɚ; ˈkɔːlə/ *n* [C] **1** someone making a telephone call 打電話者: *An anonymous caller warned the police about the bomb.* 有人打匿名電話警告警方說有炸彈。**2** someone who visits your house 到訪者: *If you're not sure who the caller is, ask to see some identification.* 如果你無法確定來訪者的身分，可以要求看看他的證件。

call girl /ˈ· ·/ *n* [C] a PROSTITUTE who makes arrangements to meet men by telephone 電話應召女郎

cal·lig·ra·phy /kəˈlɪgrəfɪ; kəˈlɪgrəfi/ *n* [U] the art of producing beautiful writing using special pens or brushes, or the writing produced this way 書法（藝術）; 筆跡 —**calligrapher** *n* [C]

call-in /ˈ· ·/ *n* [C] *AmE* a radio or television programme in which people telephone to give their opinions【美】〔電台或電視台的〕電話熱線節目; PHONE-IN *BrE*【英】

call·ing /ˈkɔlɪŋ; ˈkɔːlɪŋ/ *n* [C] **1** a strong desire or feeling of duty to do a particular kind of work, especially religious work; VOCATION (3)〔神的〕感召;〔從事某種工作的〕強烈衝動; 使命感 **2** *formal* someone's profession or trade【正式】職業，行業

calling card /ˈ·· ·/ *n* [C] *AmE* a small card with a name and often address printed on it, that people used to give to people they visited; VISITING CARD【美】名片

cal·li·pers *BrE*【英】, **calipers** *AmE*【美】/ˈkælɪpɚz; ˈkæləpəz/ *n plural* **1** a tool used for measuring thickness, the distance between two surfaces, or the DIAMETER (=inside width) of something 測徑規; 卡鉗; 兩腳規 **2** *BrE* metal bars that someone wears on their legs to help them walk【英】〔裝在雙腿上幫助行走的〕金屬條; BRACE² (2b) *AmE*【美】

cal·lis·then·ics *BrE*【英】, **calisthenics** *AmE*【美】/ˌkæləsˈθɛnɪks; ˌkæləsˈθenɪks/ *n* [U] a set of physical exercises that are intended to make you thin and healthy 健美（體）操，健身操

call let·ters /ˈ· ˌ··/ *n* [plural] *AmE* a name made up of letters and numbers used by people operating communication radios to prove who they are【美】〔無線電〕呼號; CALL SIGN *BrE*【英】

call op·tion /ˈ· ˌ··/ *n* [C] *technical* the right to buy a particular number of shares (SHARE² (5)) at a different price within a fixed period of time【術語】〔股票的〕看漲期權, 認購期權, 購買選擇權〔指按規定的價格和日期購買一定數量的股票的權利〕

cal·lous /ˋkæləs; ˈkæləs/ *adj* not caring that other people are suffering 無情的, 冷漠的: *We were shocked at the callous disregard for human life.* 對人的生命的無情漠視令我們震驚。| *the callous slaughter of thousands of seals* 數千隻海豹被殘殺 —**callously** *adv* —**callousness** *n* [U]

cal·loused /ˋkæləst; ˈkæləst/ *adj* calloused skin is rough and covered in CALLUS*es*〔皮膚〕硬結的, 起老繭的

cal·low /ˋkælo; ˈkæləʊ/ *adj literary* young and without experience; IMMATURE【文】年輕幼稚的, 不成熟的: *a callow youth* 幼稚的年輕人

call sign /ˈ· ·/ *n* [C] *BrE* a name made up of letters and numbers used by people operating communication radios to prove who they are【英】〔電台的〕呼號, 呼叫信號; CALL LETTERS *AmE*【美】

call-up /ˈ· ·/ *n* [C] *BrE* an order to join the army, navy etc【英】〔服兵役的〕徵召令; DRAFT[1] (2) *AmE*【美】: *He got his call-up papers in July.* 他在七月收到徵召入伍的命令。—see also 另見 **call up** (CALL[1])

cal·lus /ˋkæləs; ˈkæləs/ also 又作 **callosity** /kəˋlɑsətɪ; kəˈlɒsɪ̈ti/ *n* [C] an area of thick hard skin 硬皮, 老繭: *The rowers had calluses on their hands.* 槳手們的手上都長滿了老繭。

3 **calm**[1] /kɑm; kɑːm/ *adj* **1** quiet and without excitement, nervous activity, or strong feeling 鎮靜的, 沉着的; 心平氣和的: *Richard spoke with calm authority.* 李察講話時沉着而威嚴。| *Keep calm, and try not to panic!* 沉住氣, 別驚慌! **2** weather that is calm is not windy〔天氣〕無風的 **3** a sea, lake etc that is calm is smooth or has only gentle waves〔海洋、湖泊等〕平靜的, 風平浪靜的 —**calmly** *adv* —**calmness** *n* [U]

calm[2] *n* [U] **1** a situation that is quiet and peaceful 平靜; 安靜; 寧靜: *They remained on the terrace after dinner, enjoying the calm of the evening.* 晚餐後他們仍然坐在平台上, 享受着夜晚的寧靜。**2 the calm before the storm** a calm peaceful situation before a big argument, problem etc 暴風雨前的平靜

calm[3] *v* [T] to make someone or something quiet after strong emotion or nervous activity 使平靜, 使安靜, 使鎮定: *Charlie tried to calm the frightened children.* 查理努力安撫受驚的孩子。

calm (sb/sth ↔) **down** *phr v* [I,T] to become quiet after strong emotion or nervous activity, or make someone or something become quiet (使) 平靜 (下來), (使) 鎮定: *Calm down and tell me what happened.* 冷靜點, 告訴我發生了甚麼事。

Cal·or gas /ˋkælɚ gæs; ˈkælə gæs/ *n* [U] *BrE trademark* a type of gas that is sold in metal containers and used where there is no gas supply【英, 商標】卡樂氣, 罐裝液化氣

cal·o·rie /ˋkælərɪ; ˈkæləri/ *n* [C] **1** a unit for measuring the amount of ENERGY that food will produce 卡 (路里)〔食物的熱量單位〕: *An average potato has about 90 calories.* 一個普通的馬鈴薯含有大約 90 卡路里。| *a calorie-controlled diet* 控制熱量的飲食 | *Burn off the calories with this new exercise bike.* 使用這新買的健身腳踏車把熱量消耗掉。**2** *technical* the amount of heat that is needed to raise the temperature of one gram of water by one degree centigrade【術語】卡路里〔熱量單位, 即將一克水的溫度提升一攝氏度所需要的熱量〕**3 count your calories** to control your weight, especially by calculating the number of calories you eat〔通過計算自己的卡路里攝取量來〕控制體重

cal·o·rif·ic /ˌkæləˋrɪfɪk; ˌkæləˈrɪfɪk◂/ *adj* **1** food that is calorific tends to make you fat〔食物〕含熱量的, 使人發胖的 **2** *technical* producing heat【術語】產生熱量的

ca·lum·ni·ate /kəˋlʌmnɪˌet; kəˈlʌmni-eɪt/ *v* [T] *formal* to say untrue and unfair things about someone; SLANDER[2]【正式】誣蔑, 誹謗, 中傷

cal·um·ny /ˋkæləmnɪ; ˈkæləmni/ *n* **1** [C] an untrue and unfair statement about someone intended to give people a bad opinion of them 誣蔑, 誹謗, 誣陷之詞 **2** [U] the act of saying things like this 中傷 —see also 另見 SLANDER[1]

cal·va·ry /ˋkælvərɪ; ˈkælvəri/ *n* [C] a model that represents the death of Jesus Christ 耶穌受難像

calve /kæv; kɑːv/ *v* [I] to give birth to a CALF (=young cow) 生小牛

calves /kævz; kɑːvz/ *n* the plural of CALF

Cal·vin·is·m /ˋkælvɪnɪzəm; ˈkælvɪ̈nɪzəm/ *n* [U] the Christian religious teachings of John Calvin, based on the idea that events on Earth are controlled by God and cannot be changed by humans〔基督教〕加爾文教[主]義〔是其創始人約翰·加爾文的教條, 根據此種思想, 地球上發生的一切都由上帝控制, 人類無法左右〕

Cal·vin·ist /ˋkælvɪnɪst; ˈkælvɪ̈nɪ̈st/ *adj* **1** following the teachings of CALVINISM 加爾文教派的, 追隨加爾文主義的 **2** also 又作 **Calvinistic** /ˌkælvəˋnɪstɪk; ˌkælvɪ̈ˈnɪstɪk◂/ having severe moral standards and tending to disapprove of pleasure; PURITANICAL 清教主義的, 道德觀念十分嚴格的 —**Calvinist** *n* [C]

ca·lyp·so /kəˋlɪpso; kəˈlɪpsəʊ/ *n* [C] a West Indian song based on subjects of interest in the news "加力騷" 即興歌曲〔起源於西印度羣島, 以時事為主題〕

ca·lyx /ˋkelɪks; ˈkælɪks/ *n plural* **calyxes** or **calyces** [C] the green outer part of a flower that protects it before it opens 花萼

cam /kæm; kæm/ *n* [C] a wheel or part of a wheel that is shaped to change circular movement into backwards and forwards movement 凸輪

ca·ma·ra·de·rie /ˌkɑməˋrɑdərɪ; ˌkæməˈrɑːdəri/ *n* [U] friendliness between people who like each other or work together as part of a group 同志[同事]情誼, 友情: *camaraderie of soldiers in the trenches* 士兵們在戰壕裡建立的情誼

cam·ber /ˋkæmbɚ; ˈkæmbə/ *n* [C,U] *technical* a slight curve from the centre to the side of a road or other surface that makes water run off to the side【術語】〔道路或其他表面的〕中凸形, 拱勢〔中間高兩邊低的彎度, 以使水向兩邊流〕

cam·bric /ˋkembrɪk; ˈkeɪmbrɪk/ *n* [U] thin white cloth made of LINEN (2) or cotton 細白棉布, 麻紗

cam·cor·der /ˋkæmˌkɔrdɚ; ˈkæmˌkɔːdə/ *n* [C] a VIDEO camera and recorder in one machine, that you can carry around 手提攝錄機

camcorder 手提攝錄機

came /kem; keɪm/ the past tense of COME

cam·el /ˋkæml̩; ˈkæməl/ *n* [C] a large desert animal with a long neck and either one or two HUMP*s* (=large raised parts) on its back 駱駝

cam·el·hair /ˋkæml̩hɛr; ˈkæməlheə/ *n* [U] a thick yellowish brown cloth usually used for making coats 駝絨, 駱駝呢

ca·mel·li·a /kəˋmilɪə; kəˈmiːliə/ *n* [C] a red, pink, or white flower like a rose 山茶 (花)

cam·em·bert /ˋkæməmˌbɛr; ˈkæməmbeə/ *n* [C,U] a small round French cheese, that is white outside and yellow inside〔產於法國的外白內黃的小圓形〕卡門貝乾酪

cam·e·o /ˋkæmɪˌo; ˈkæmi-əʊ/ *n plural* **cameos** [C] **1** a short appearance in a film or play by a well-known actor〔由名演員演的〕電影[戲劇]片段: *Denholm Eliot in a cameo role as a butler* 德諾姆·艾略特在一個片段中飾演管家的角色 **2** a small piece of jewellery with a raised figure or shape fixed to a flat surface of a different colour 多彩浮雕寶石 **3** a short piece of writing that gives a clear idea of a person, place, or event〔對人物、地方、事件的〕特寫; 小品

C

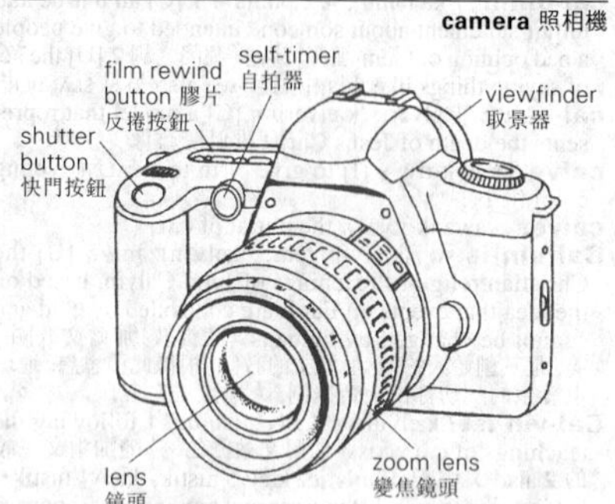

2 3 **cam·e·ra** /ˋkæmərə; ˈkæmərə/ *n* [C] **1** a piece of equipment used to take photographs or moving pictures 照相機; 攝影機 **2** the part of the equipment used for making television pictures that changes images into electrical signals (電視) 攝像機 **3 in camera** a law case that is held in camera takes place secretly or privately〔訴訟案〕不公開審理地, 祕密地, 私下地

cam·e·ra·man /ˋkæmərə͵mæn; ˈkæmərəmən/ *n* [C] someone who operates a camera for films or television〔電影或電視的〕攝影師

camera-shy /ˈ··· ·/ *adj* not liking to have your photograph taken 不喜歡照相的

cam·i·knick·ers /ˋkæmɪ͵nɪkəz; ˈkæmiˌnɪkəz/ *n* [plural] *BrE* a piece of women's underwear that combines CAMISOLE and KNICKERS【英】〔女裝〕連褲緊身內衣

cam·i·sole /ˋkæmə͵sol; ˈkæmɪsəʊl/ *n* [C] a short piece of women's underwear worn on the top half of the body〔女裝〕短內衣, 貼身胸衣 —see picture at 參見 UNDERWEAR 圖

cam·o·mile, chamomile /ˋkæmə͵maɪl; ˈkæməmaɪl/ *n* [C,U] a plant with small white and yellow flowers that are sometimes used to make tea 洋甘菊, 黃春菊: *camomile tea* 甘菊茶

cam·ou·flage[1] /ˋkæmə͵flɑʒ; ˈkæməflɑːʒ/ *n* **1** the way in which the colour or shape of something makes it difficult to see in the place where it lives 偽裝: *The insect's colour provides camouflage from its enemies.* 該昆蟲的顏色為其提供了躲避天敵的偽裝。**2** a way of hiding something, especially a military object, using branches, paint etc〔尤指軍事目標的〕偽裝: *anti-aircraft camouflage netting* 防空偽裝網 **3** behaviour that is designed to hide something 偽裝, 掩飾: *Aggression is often a camouflage for insecurity.* 侵略常常是缺乏安全感的掩飾。

camouflage[2] *v* [T] to hide something by making it look the same as the things around it, or by making it seem like something else〔用偽裝〕遮掩, 掩飾: *The trucks were well camouflaged with branches.* 卡車都用樹枝妥善地遮掩起來。| *symptoms of illness camouflaged by other factors* 被其他因素掩蓋的疾病症狀

3 3 **camp**[1] /kæmp; kæmp/ *n* **1** [C,U] a place where people stay in temporary shelters, such as tents, usually for a short time 營地: *Let's go back to the camp – it's getting dark.* 我們回營地吧, 天快黑了。| **break camp** (=take down a tent or shelter you have been using) 撤營, 拔營 **2 prison/labour etc camp** a place where people are kept for a particular reason, when they do not want to be there 戰俘營/勞改營等: *a refugee camp* 難民營 —see also 另見 CONCENTRATION CAMP **3** [C,U] a place where young people go to relax and take part in activities, often as members of an organization〔青少年的〕活動營地, 度假營地: *scout camp* 童子軍營地 | *summer camp* 夏令營 —see also 另見 DAY CAMP, HOLIDAY CAMP **4** [C] a group of people or organizations who have the same ideas or principles, especially in politics〔尤指政治上的〕陣營, 派別, 集團: *the extreme right-wing camp of the party* 該黨的極右翼派別

camp[2] *v* [I] **1** to set up a tent or shelter and stay there for a short time 紮營, 宿營, 露營: *We'll camp by the river for the night, and move on tomorrow.* 我們今晚在河邊宿營, 明天繼續前進。| *camping equipment* 露營裝備 **2 go camping** to visit an area and stay in a tent 去露營: *We went camping in the mountains last weekend.* 上週末我們到山裡露營。

camp out *phr v* [I] **1** to sleep outdoors, usually in a tent〔通常指在帳篷裡〕露宿 **2** to stay somewhere where you do not have all the usual things that a house has〔在不具備基本住宿條件的地方〕勉強暫住: *We'll just have to camp out until our furniture arrives.* 在家具運到之前, 我們只好對付着住一下了。

camp sth ↔ **up** *phr v* [T] *informal* to deliberately behave in a funny, unnatural way, with too much movement or expression【非正式】做出誇張的舉動

camp[3] *adj informal*【非正式】**1** a man who is camp moves or speaks in the way that people used to think was typical of HOMOSEXUALs〔男子〕舉止言行像同性戀的; 娘娘腔的 **2** clothes, decorations etc that are camp are very strange, bright, or unusual〔衣服、裝飾等〕稀奇古怪的: *Only you could get away with wearing that outfit – it's so camp!* 只有你才會穿上那套行頭 —— 它看上去十分古怪!

cam·paign[1] /kæmˋpen; kæmˈpeɪn/ *n* [C] **1** a series of actions intended to achieve a particular result, especially in politics or business〔政治或商業性的為取得某個結果的〕運動; (宣傳) 活動: [+ **for**] *a campaign for equal rights* 爭取平等權利的運動 | [+**against**] *educational campaigns against smoking* 反吸煙的教育運動 | *an advertising campaign* 廣告宣傳活動 **2** a series of battles, attacks etc intended to achieve a particular result in a war〔軍事〕戰役

campaign[2] *v* [I] to lead or take part in a series of actions intended to achieve a particular result 發起[參加]〔旨在獲得某種效果的〕運動: [**+for/against**] *a group campaigning against the destruction of the rainforests* 發起反對毀壞雨林運動的團體 —**campaigner** *n* [C]

cam·pa·ni·le /͵kæmpəˋnili; ˌkæmpəˈniːli/ *n* [C] a high bell tower that is usually separate from any other building〔通常與其他建築分立的〕鐘樓

cam·pa·nol·o·gy /͵kæmpəˋnɑlədʒɪ; ˌkæmpəˈnɒlədʒi/ *n* [U] the skill of ringing bells 鳴鐘術 —**campanologist** *n* [C]

camp bed /͵· ˈ·/ *n* [C] *especially BrE* a light, narrow bed that folds flat and is easy to carry【尤英】行軍牀; 摺疊牀; 露營牀; COT (2) *AmE*【美】—see picture at 參見 BED[1] 圖

camp·er /ˋkæmpɚ; ˈkæmpə/ *n* [C] **1** someone who is staying in a tent or shelter 露營者 **2** *AmE* a sort of room fitted onto or pulled behind a large vehicle that has cooking equipment and beds in it【美】〔食宿用具俱全的〕野營車 **3 happy camper** *spoken* someone who seems to be happy with their situation【口】滿足於現狀者

camp·fire /ˋkæmp͵faɪr; ˈkæmpfaɪə/ *n* [C] a fire made outdoors by people who are camping 營火, 篝火

camp fol·low·er /ˈ· ͵···/ *n* [C] **1** someone who supports an organization or a political party, but who is not actually a member of the main group〔黨派組織的〕追隨者, 附和者 **2** someone who was not a soldier but who followed an army from place to place to provide services, especially in the past〔尤指舊時〕隨軍提供服務的平民

camp·ground /ˋkæmp͵graʊnd; ˈkæmpgraʊnd/ *n* [C] *AmE* an area where people can camp, that often has a water supply and toilets【美】〔有供水和廁所的〕(野) 營地; CAMPSITE *BrE*【英】

cam·phor /ˋkæmfɚ; ˈkæmfə/ *n* [U] a white substance with a strong smell, that is used especially to keep insects away 樟腦

camp rob·ber /ˈ· ͵··/ *n* [C] a grey North American bird that does not seem afraid of people and often flies away with food〔常叼走食物的不怕人的北美〕灰噪鴉

camp·site /ˈkæmpˌsaɪt; ˈkæmpsaɪt/ *n* [C] **1** *BrE* an area where people can camp, that often has a water supply and toilets【英】〔有供水和廁所的〕(野) 營地; CAMPGROUND *AmE*【美】**2** *AmE* a place, usually within a CAMPGROUND, where one person or group can camp【美】〔野營地內可供一人或一羣人使用的〕紮營地

camp·stool /ˈkæmpˌstul; ˈkæmpstuːl/ *n* [C] a small folding seat with no back 輕便摺櫈

cam·pus /ˈkæmpəs; ˈkæmpəs/ **1** the land and buildings of a university or college〔大學或學院的〕校園 **2 big man on campus** *AmE* someone who is well-known for being involved in a lot of student activities, and thinks they are important because of this【美】校園大人物〔指因參與許多學生活動而聞名者〕

cam·shaft /ˈkæmˌʃæft; ˈkæmʃɑːft/ *n* [C] a metal bar that a CAM is fastened to in an engine 凸輪軸

1 1 **can[1]** /kən; kən; *strong* 強讀 kæn; kæn/ *v* [modal verb] **1** to be able to 能, 有能力: *He's so tall he can touch the ceiling.* 他那麼高, 手能碰到天花板。| *This machine can perform two million calculations per second.* 這台機器每秒能夠運算二百萬次。| *I can't remember where I put it.* 我不記得把它放在哪裡了。| *They have everything that money can buy.* 他們擁有金錢所能買到的一切。| *The police still haven't found her, but they're doing all they can.* 警方還沒有找到她, 但是正在盡一切努力去做。**2** *spoken* used when asking someone to do something or give you something【口】〔用於拜託、請求〕可以…嗎? 能…嗎?: *Can I have a cigarette please?* 能給我一支香煙嗎? | *Can you help me lift this box?* 你能幫我抬起這個箱子嗎? **3** *especially spoken* to have permission to do something or to be allowed to do something【尤口】允許, 可以: *You can't play football here.* 你們不可以在這裡踢足球。| *"Can we go home now please?" "No you can't."* "我們現在可以回家了嗎?" "不, 不可以。" | *The goalkeeper can't handle the ball outside the penalty area.* (=it is against the rules) 守門員不可以在罰球區外用手觸球。**4** to have a particular skill or know how to do a particular activity 懂得, 會: *Gabriella can speak French, Russian, and Italian.* 加布里拉會說法語、俄語和意大利語。| *Can you drive?* 你會開車嗎? **5** used to show what is possible or likely 有可能, 會: *I am confident that a solution can be found.* 我有信心會找到解決的辦法。| *There can be no doubt that he is guilty.* 他有罪, 這是毋庸置疑的。| *The word "bank" can have several different meanings.* "bank"這個詞可有幾種不同的意思。| *Can he still be alive after all this time?* 過了這麼長的時間, 他還可能活着嗎? **6** used with verbs connected with the five senses and with verbs connected with thinking〔與表示感官和思維的動詞連用〕: *I can hear you easily from here.* 從這裡我可以很容易聽到你說話。| *You can really taste the garlic in that soup.* 你確實可以嚐出湯裡的大蒜味。| *I can't understand why you're so upset.* 我不明白你為甚麼如此不安。| *You can imagine how annoyed she was!* 你可以想像出她有多惱怒! **7** [usually in questions and negatives 一般用於疑問句和否定句] used especially when you think there is only one possible answer to a question or one possible thing to do in a particular situation 只能: *Jill's left her husband but can you blame her after the way he treated her?* 吉爾離開了丈夫, 但在她丈夫那樣對待她之後, 你能責怪她嗎? | *It's a very kind offer, but I really can't accept it.* 這個提議很好, 但我真的不能接受。**8** to have to do something; must 必須, 不得不: *If you won't keep quiet you can get out!* 如果你不保持安靜, 那就只好請你出去了! **9** used especially in expressions of surprise〔尤用於表示驚訝〕究竟…; 可能…嗎?: *What can it possibly be?* 這究竟是甚麼呢? | *You can't be serious!* 你不會是認真的吧! | *They can't have arrived already surely!* 他們絕對不可能已經到了! **10** used to show what sometimes happens or how someone sometimes behaves〔用於表示偶爾的可能性〕有時可能會: *It can be quite cold here at night.* 這裡夜間有時可能很冷。| *Gerard can be annoying, I know.* 我知道, 傑拉爾德有時會令人相當討厭的。

Frequencies of the verb **can** in spoken and written English 動詞can在英語口語和書面語中的使用頻率

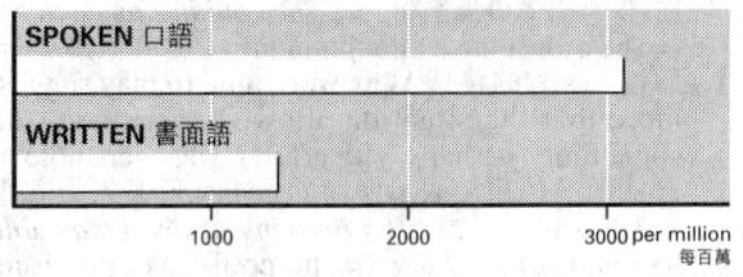

Based on the British National Corpus and the Longman Lancaster Corpus
據英國國家語料庫和朗文蘭卡斯特語料庫

This graph shows that the verb **can** is much more common in spoken English than in written English. This is because it is used a lot in questions and has some special uses in spoken English. 本圖表顯示動詞can在英語口語中比書面語中常見得多。這是因為它大量使用於疑問句中, 而且在英語口語中有某些特別用法。

USAGE NOTE 用法說明: CAN

WORD CHOICE 詞語辨析: **can, may, could, might, be allowed to, let, do/would you mind if..., be able to**

In everyday conversation, **can** is used much more commonly than **may** to talk about permission. 在日常會話中, can要比may更常用於表示許可: *You can go now* (=you are allowed to go). 你現在可以走了〔=你被允許離開〕。Some people say that **may** is more correct, however, its use tends to be limited to formal contexts. When talking about permission in the past, people often use **was/were allowed to** or change the sentence and use **let**. 有人說may較正確, 不過它的用法多局限於正式的語體。當談論過去的許可時, 人們經常使用was/were allowed to或者改變句子而使用let: *He was allowed to leave at ten.* 他獲准十點鐘離開。| *I let him leave at ten* (=I allowed him to go and he did). 我讓他十點鐘離開〔=我允許他離開, 然後他也這麼做了〕。When you are asking permission, **could** (also **might**, especially in American English) is often used instead of **can**, because it seems less direct and more polite. 當你要求得到許可時, 經常用could〔might亦可, 尤其在美國英語中〕而不用can, 這是因為它似乎不那麼直截了當, 而且較為禮貌: *Could I borrow your car?* 我可以借用你的汽車嗎? **May** is more formal, and is used especially by officials. For example at an airport. may較為正式, 而且尤其常被官員使用。例如在機場時: *May I see your passport, madam?* 夫人, 我可以看一下你的護照嗎? In everyday English people often say **Do/would you mind if...** or **Is it alright if...** when asking permission. 在日常英語中要求得到許可時, 人們常說Do/would you mind if... 或 Is it alright if...: *Do you mind if I smoke?* 我抽煙你介意嗎?

Can is also used to say that you have the ability to do something. can還用於表示你具有做某事的能力: *I can swim now* (=I am able to swim). 我現在會游泳了。To talk about something you will have the ability to do in the future, you use **will be able to** 談論將來有能力做某事時, 要用 will be able to: *I'll be able to speak better if I practise more.* 我如果多練習, 就會講得更好。For past ability either **could** or **was/were able to** is used, but sometimes with slightly different meaning. 對於過去的能力, 要使用could或者was/were able to, 不過有時意義略有差別。**Could** often suggests more someone's ability that they had for some time (but perhaps did not use). could 較多地用於表示某人在某時期內擁有的能力〔不過也許不一定使用〕: *I could swim when I was eight* (=I knew how to). 我八歲時就會游泳〔=我懂得怎麼游〕。| *She couldn't buy a ticket* (=She didn't have enough money). 她無法購票〔=她沒有足夠的錢〕。**Was/were able to** may suggest more that the situation allowed someone to do something (perhaps with effort). was/were able to 可能較多地用於表示當時的情況允許某人做某事〔也許要付出努力〕: *By arriving at two I was able to swim for an hour* (=The pool was open long enough to allow this). 由於我兩點鐘到達, 得以游了一個小時〔=游泳池開放時間足夠長, 允許這麼做〕。| *I wasn't able to buy a ticket* (=There were none left/I didn't manage to get one). 我沒有買到票〔=沒有票了/我沒能買到〕。**Used to be able to** is used to talk about something that you could do before, but can no longer do now. used to be able to 用於談論過去能夠做到但是現在已無法再做到的事: *He used to be able to run a 100 metres in under 10 seconds, but he's getting a bit old these days.* 他過去能在十秒內跑完一百米, 但是如今他有點兒老了。

When you are talking about something that is not certain, you often use **may**, or, with more doubt, **might** or **could**. 談論不確定的某事時, 常用 may, 或者有更多疑問時, 常用 might 或 could: *The road may/might/could be blocked* (=Perhaps/It is possible the road is blocked). 道路可能被封鎖了。| *The road could be blocked* (=It is possible to block the road). 可以把道路封鎖起來。For past time **may have/might have/could have** are used 對於過去的時間, 則使用 may have/might have/could have: *There may have been an accident* (=Perhaps there was an accident). 可能發生了一些事故。*Might* or *could have* would be more often used here when we now know that there was no accident. 在知道沒有發生過事故時, might 或 could have 更為常用。

Can is usually used to ask whether something is possible. can 通常用來詢問某事是否可能: *Can this really be true?* (=Is it possible this is true?) 這事會是真的嗎? and to say that something is not possible 而且也用來表示某事是不可能的: *That can't be true.* 那不可能是真的。Again **could** shows more doubt (and is commoner in American English) 同樣地, could 表示較大的疑問〔而且在美國英語中較常見〕: *Could that really be true?* 那事會是真的嗎?

Can is often used with verbs related to the senses and the mind, such as *see, hear, feel, believe.* can 經常和諸如 see, hear, feel, believe 等與感官以及思想有關的動詞連用: *Look at this photo – can you see somebody famous in it?* 看看這張照片, 你能看到一些名人嗎?

GRAMMAR 語法

Remember **can, could, may** and **might** are NEVER used with the *to* infinitive of a verb. 記住, can, could, may 和 might 從不與帶 to 的動詞不定式連用: *I can help you* (NOT 不用 *I can to help you*). 我可以幫你。

2 **can²** /kæn; kæn/ *n* [C] **1** a metal container in which food or drink is preserved without air 罐頭: *a Coke can* 可樂罐 | **[+of]** *All we've got is a couple of cans of soup.* 我們所擁有的不過是幾個罐頭湯。—see picture at 參見 CONTAINER 圖 **2** a special metal container that keeps the liquid inside it under pressure, releasing it as a SPRAY² (1) when you press the button on the lid〔特製的壓力〕噴罐: *a can of hairspray* 一罐噴髮膠 **3** *especially AmE* a metal container with a lid that can be removed, used for holding liquid【尤美】有蓋金屬圓罐[桶]: *Two large cans of paint ought to be enough.* 兩大桶油漆應該夠了。**4 can of worms** a very complicated situation that causes a lot of problems when you start to deal with it 極為棘手[困難、麻煩]的局面: *I just don't know what to do – every solution I can think of would just open up a whole new can of worms.* 我不知道該怎麼辦 —— 每個我能想到的解決方案只會開啟一個全新的棘手的局面而已。**5 in the can** *informal* a film that is in the can is complete and ready to be shown【非正式】〔影片〕已拍攝好隨時可放映的 **6 the can** *slang*【俚】**a)** a prison 監獄 **b)** *AmE* a toilet【美】廁所 —see also 另見 **carry the can** (CARRY¹ (31))

can³ *v* **canned, canning** [T] *especially AmE*【尤美】**1** to preserve food by putting it into a metal container from which all the air is removed 製成罐頭 —see also 另見 CANNED (1) **2** *AmE informal* to dismiss someone from a job; SACK² (1)【美, 非正式】解雇, 開除 **3 can it!** *AmE spoken* used to tell someone to stop talking or making noise【美口】閉嘴!

Ca·na·di·an ba·con /kə͵nediən ˋbekən; kə͵neɪdiən ˈbeɪkən/ *n* [U] *AmE* meat from the back or sides of a pig, served in thin, narrow pieces【美】加拿大式熏豬肉; BACON *BrE*【英】

ca·nal /kəˋnæl; kəˈnæl/ *n* [C] **1** a passage dug out of the ground, either to connect two areas of water so boats can travel between them, or to bring or remove water from somewhere 運河: *the Panama Canal* 巴拿馬運河 **2** a passage in the body of a person or animal〔人或動物體內的〕管, 道 —see also 另見 ALIMENTARY CANAL

canal boat /ˈ·ˌ· ·/ *n* [C] a long narrow boat that is used on a canal 運河船〔行駛於運河上的狹長船隻〕

can·a·lize also 又作 **-ise** *BrE*【英】/ˋkænḷ͵aɪz; ˈkænəl-aɪz/ *v* [T] **1** *formal* to direct the actions, energy, etc of a person or group to one particular purpose; CHANNEL² (1)【正式】把…納入〔某種軌道〕; 把…引向某一目標 **2** to make a river deeper, straighter etc, especially in order to prevent flooding 挖深[修直、加寬]河道 —**canalization** /kə͵næləˋzeʃən; ͵kænəlaɪˈzeɪʃən/ *n* [U]

can·a·pé /ˋkænəpɪ; ˈkænəpeɪ/ *n* [C] a small piece of bread with cheese, meat, fish, etc on it, served with drinks at a party〔加有乳酪、肉、魚等的〕小片麵包〔通常在聚會上配飲料食用〕

ca·nard /kəˋnɑrd; kæˈnɑːd/ *n* [C] *French* a deliberately false report or piece of news【法】謠傳, 謊報; 假新聞

ca·nar·y /kəˋnɛrɪ; kəˈneəri/ *n* [C] a small yellow bird that sings and is often kept as a pet 金絲雀

ca·nas·ta /kəˋnæstə; kəˈnæstə/ *n* [U] a card game in which two sets of cards are used 凱納斯特紙牌戲〔用兩副紙牌一起玩的遊戲〕

can·can /ˋkænkæn; ˈkænkæn/ *n* [C] a fast dance from France danced by women in a show in which they kick their legs high into the air 肯肯舞, 康康舞〔由女子表演的、把腿高高踢起的一種法國快節奏舞蹈〕

can·cel /ˋkænsḷ; ˈkænsəl/ *v* **cancelled, cancelling** *BrE*【英】**canceled, canceling** *AmE*【美】[T] **1** to arrange that a planned activity or event will not now happen 取消: *The football game had been cancelled due to rain.* 足球比賽因天雨取消。**2** to end an agreement or arrangement that exists in law 中止〔協議、安排等〕; 廢除: *I've cancelled my subscription to the magazine.* 我已停止訂閱那本雜誌。

cancel sth ↔ **out** *phr v* [T] to have an equal but opposite effect on something, so that a situation does not change 抵銷; 中和: *The losses in our overseas division have cancelled out this year's profits.* 我們海外分部的虧損抵銷了今年的盈利。

can·cel·la·tion /͵kænsəˋleʃən; ͵kænsəˈleɪʃən/ *n* [C,U] a decision or statement that a planned or regular activity will not happen 取消, 作廢: *The restaurant is fully booked for tonight, but sometimes there are cancellations.* 這家餐廳今天晚上全訂滿了, 但有時會有取消訂桌的。

Can·cer /ˈkænsɚ; ˈkænsə/ *n* **1** [singular] the fourth sign of the ZODIAC represented by a CRAB[1] (1), and believed to affect the character and life of people born between June 22 and July 22 巨蟹座 **2** [C] someone who was born between June 22 and July 22 出生於巨蟹座時段的人〔即在6月22日至7月22日之間出生的人〕

2 2 **cancer** *n* **1** [C,U] a very serious disease in which cells in one part of the body start to grow in a way that is not normal, often causing death 癌(症): *Smoking causes lung cancer.* 吸煙引起肺癌。| *cancer of the jaw* 顎[頜]癌 **2** [C] an activity that is increasing, and causes a lot of harm 弊病, 社會惡習: *Corruption is the cancer of society.* 貪污腐敗是社會的毒瘤。—**cancerous** *adj*: *a cancerous growth* 癌性瘤狀物

can·de·la·brum /ˌkændḷˈebrəm; ˌkændʒˈlɑːbrəm/ *n* [C] a decorative holder for several candles or lamps 〔可插數支蠟燭或燈泡的〕裝飾性燭[燈]台

can·did /ˈkændɪd; ˈkændʒd/ *adj* directly truthful, even when the truth may be unpleasant or embarassing 坦誠的, 率直的; 直言不諱的: *The Governor's brutally candid assessment struck a new blow to Mr Major's reputation.* 州長無情的直率評價對梅傑先生的聲譽是一個新的打擊。—see also 另見 CANDOUR —**candidly** *adv*

can·di·da /ˈkændɪdə; ˈkændʒdə/ *n* [U] *technical* a FUNGUS that causes an infection in the mouth and throat of children or in a woman's VAGINA; THRUSH[1] (2)【術語】念珠菌

can·di·da·cy /ˈkændɪdəsɪ; ˈkændʒdʒsi/ also 又作 **candidature** /ˈkændɪdətʃɚ; ˈkændʒdətʃə/ *especially BrE*【尤英】*n* [C,U] the position of being one of the people who are competing to be elected 候選人資格[身分]

2 **can·di·date** /ˈkændəˌdet; ˈkændʒdʒt/ *n* [C] **1** someone who is being considered for a job or is competing to be elected 候選人; 候補人: **[+for]** *They're interviewing three candidates for the post of sales manager.* 他們正在面試三個應徵做銷售經理的人選。**2** *especially BrE* someone who is taking an examination【尤英】應考人, 投考者 **3** a person, group, or idea that is suitable for something or likely to get something 極有可能有某結局的人[羣體、觀點等]: **[+for]** *You smoke, drink, and never get any exercise: you're a prime candidate for a heart attack!* 你又抽煙又喝酒, 可是從不做運動, 最有可能得心臟病!

can·died /ˈkændɪd; ˈkændid/ *adj* [only before noun 僅用於名詞前] boiled or baked in sugar as a means of preservation 糖漬的, 蜜餞的: *candied cherries* 蜜餞櫻桃

3 **can·dle** /ˈkændḷ; ˈkændl/ *n* [C] **1** a round stick of WAX[1] (1) around a WICK (=piece of string) that is burnt to provide light 蠟燭 **2 can't hold a candle to** *informal* to be not as good as someone or something else【非正式】遠遜於, 簡直不能與…相比: *When it came to giving a good party, no one could hold a candle to the Andersons.* 說到舉辦一個好的聚會, 誰也比不上安德森夫婦。—see also 另見 **burn the candle at both ends** (BURN[1] (23))

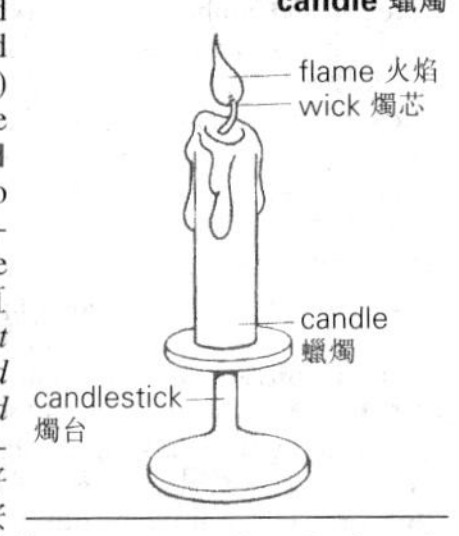

candle 蠟燭

can·dle·light /ˈkændḷˌlaɪt; ˈkændl-laɪt/ *n* [U] the light produced when a candle burns 燭光

candle-lit /ˈ·· ·/ *adj* lit by candles 用燭光照明的: *a candle-lit dinner for two* 雙人燭光晚餐

can·dle·stick /ˈkændḷˌstɪk; ˈkændlˌstɪk/ *n* [C] a specially shaped metal or wooden stick that you put a candle into 燭台 —see picture at 參見 CANDLE 圖

can·dle·wick /ˈkændḷˌwɪk; ˈkændlˌwɪk/ *n* [U] **1** also 又作 **candlewicking** thick, soft cotton thread 燭芯 **2** cloth decorated with patterns of raised rows of this thread 燭芯紗〔有凸起花紋的織物〕

can-do /ˌ· ˈ·/ *adj* [only before noun 僅用於名詞前] *informal* willing to try anything and expect that it will work【非正式】敢於嘗試的: *a can-do attitude towards work* 敢於嘗試的工作態度

can·dour *BrE*【英】, **candor** *AmE*【美】/ˈkændɚ; ˈkændə/ *n* [U] sincere HONESTY and truthfulness 誠心誠意, 坦率; 正直: *I appreciate your candour in this matter.* 我很欣賞你在此事中表現出的坦誠。—see also 另見 CANDID

can·dy /ˈkændɪ; ˈkændi/ *n* [C,U] *AmE* sweet food made of sugar or chocolate, or a piece of this【美】糖果, 巧克力糖果; SWEET[2] (1) *BrE*【英】—see graph at 參見 SWEET[2] 圖表 3

candy ap·ple /ˈ·· ˌ··/ *n* [C] *AmE* TOFFEE APPLE【美】太妃糖蘋果

candy cane /ˈ·· ·/ *n* [C] *AmE* a stick of hard red and white sugar with a curved end【美】棒糖〔紅白相間弧形端的條形硬糖〕

can·dy·floss /ˈkændɪˌflɑs; ˈkændiflɒs/ *n* [U] *BrE* sticky threads of pink sugar wound around a stick and eaten as a sweet【英】棉花糖; COTTON CANDY *AmE*【美】

can·dy-striped /ˈ·· ˌ·/ *adj* candy-striped cloth has narrow coloured lines on a white background 白底有彩色條子花紋的〔布〕

candy strip·er /ˈkændɪ ˌstraɪpɚ; ˈkændi ˌstraɪpə/ *n* [C] *AmE* a young person, usually a girl, who does unpaid work as a nurse's helper in a hospital in order to learn about hospital work【美】醫院的實習女助護

cane[1] /ken; keɪn/ *n* **1** [C] a long thin stick with a curved handle used to help someone walk 手杖, 拐杖 —see also 另見 STICK **2** [U] thin pieces of the stems of plants used for making furniture, baskets etc〔用來製家具、籃子等的〕藤料: *a cane chair* 藤椅 **3** [C] a long, hard, yellow stem of a BAMBOO, used for supporting other plants in the garden〔用來支撐花木的〕竹莖, 竹料 **4** [singular] a long thin stick used especially in former times by teachers to hit children with as a punishment〔舊時老師用來懲治學生的〕藤條, 藤杖

cane[2] *v* [T] to punish someone, especially a child, by hitting them with a long thin stick 用藤條鞭打〔以示懲罰〕

ca·nine /ˈkenaɪn; ˈkeɪnaɪn/ *adj* being or related to dogs 狗的, 犬科動物的: *a canine welfare organization* 愛狗組織 | *his canine companion, Rex* 他的狗夥伴雷克思

canine tooth /ˈ·· ·/ *n* [C] one of four sharp pointed teeth in the front of the human mouth; EYE TOOTH〔人的〕犬齒 —see picture at 參見 TEETH 圖

can·is·ter /ˈkænɪstɚ; ˈkænʒstə/ *n* [C] **1** a round metal case that bursts when thrown or fired from a gun, scattering what is inside 霰彈筒: *Police fired canisters of tear gas into the crowd.* 警察向人羣施放催淚彈。**2** a small round container, usually made of metal, for keeping food, liquid etc in〔裝食品、液體等的〕金屬小圓桶[罐]: *discovered an early copy of 'Napoleon' in an old film canister* 在一個陳舊的電影膠片桶裡發現了《拿破崙》的早期拷貝 **3** a round metal container of gas〔圓形的金屬〕氣體儲存罐

can·ker /ˈkæŋkɚ; ˈkæŋkə/ *n* [C,U] **1** an evil influence that spreads quickly and is difficult to destroy 腐敗因素; 禍害: *the canker of violence in modern society* 現代社會的暴力惡習 **2** a disease that affects trees or plants〔花木的〕枝枯病, 根瘤病 —**cankerous** *adj* —**cankered** *adj*

can·na·bis /ˈkænəbɪs; ˈkænəbʒs/ *n* [U] an illegal drug obtained from HEMP plants and smoked in cigarettes 大麻

canned /kænd; kænd/ *adj* **1** canned food is preserved in a round metal container〔食物〕罐裝的; TINNED *BrE*【英】: *canned tomatoes* 罐頭番茄[西紅柿] **2 canned music/laughter etc** music, laughter etc that has been recorded and is used on television or in radio programmes〔在電視或電台節目中使用的〕預錄音樂/預錄笑聲 **3** [never before noun 永不用於名詞前] *slang* drunk【俚】喝醉酒的

can·nel·lo·ni /ˌkænəˋlonɪ; ˌkænḷˈləʊni/ *n* [U] small tubes of PASTA filled with meat and sometimes cheese, and covered in SAUCE[1]〔塞有肉或乾酪並且澆汁的〕粗通心粉

can·ne·ry /ˋkænərɪ; ˈkænəri/ *n* [C] a factory where food is put into cans 罐頭食品廠

can·ni·bal /ˋkænəbḷ; ˈkænɪ̈bəl/ *n* [C] **1** someone who eats human flesh 食人肉者: *the cannibal killer, Jeffrey Dahmer* 食人肉殺人狂傑弗里·達瑪 **2** an animal that eats the flesh of other animals of the same kind 同類相食的動物 —**cannibalism** *n* [U] —**cannibalistic** /ˌkænəbḷˋɪstɪk; ˌkænɪ̈bəˈlɪstɪk◂/ *adj*

C

can·ni·bal·ize also 又作 **-ise** *BrE*【英】/ˋkænəbḷˌaɪz; ˈkænɪ̈bəlaɪz/ *v* [T] to take something apart, especially a machine, so that you can use its parts to build something else 拆卸利用, 拆取〔機器零部件〕作為他用

can·non[1] /ˋkænən; ˈkænən/ *n* [C] a large, heavy, powerful gun, usually fixed to two wheels, used in the past〔舊時的雙輪〕大砲; 加農砲

cannon[2] *v* [I always+adv/prep] to hit or knock into someone or something, especially while running〔尤指奔跑中〕撞到, 碰到: *She came hurtling round the corner and cannoned straight into me.* 她從拐角處猛衝過來, 和我撞了個滿懷。

can·non·ade /ˌkænənˋed; ˌkænəˈneɪd/ *n* [C] a continuous heavy attack by large guns 連續猛烈砲擊

can·non·ball /ˋkænənˌbɔl; ˈkænənbɔːl/ *n* [C] a heavy iron ball fired from an old type of large gun〔舊時的球狀〕砲彈

cannon fod·der /ˈ·· ˌ··/ *n* [U] *informal* ordinary members of the army, navy etc whose lives are not considered to be very important【非正式】砲灰〔指普通士兵〕

can·not /ˋkænɑt; ˈkænɒt/ *modal verb* **1** a negative form of 'can'. can 的否定形式: *Mrs Armstrong regrets that she cannot accept your kind invitation.* 阿姆斯特朗夫人對無法接受你的邀請感到很遺憾。**2 cannot but** *formal* used to say that you feel you have to do something【正式】不得不, 不能不, 必須: *One cannot but admire her determination.* 人們不能不佩服她的決心。

can·ny /ˋkænɪ; ˈkæni/ *adj* **1** clever, careful, and not easily deceived, especially in business or politics〔尤指在生意或政治方面〕精明的, 機警的, 不易上當的: *a canny political advisor* 精明的政治顧問 **2** *ScotE* nice, good【蘇格蘭】溫和善良的: *a canny lass* 溫和善良的少女 —**cannily** *adv*

canoe 獨木舟

ca·noe[1] /kəˋnu; kəˈnuː/ *n* [C] a long light boat that is pointed at both ends and which you move along using a PADDLE[1] (1) 獨木舟 —see also 另見 **paddle your own canoe** (PADDLE[2] (5))

canoe[2] *v* [I] to travel by canoe 划獨木舟, 乘獨木舟 —**canoeist** *n* [C]

can·on /ˋkænən; ˈkænən/ *n* [C] **1** a Christian priest who has special duties in a CATHEDRAL〔基督教〕大教堂教士會成員 **2** a piece of music in which a tune is started by one singer or instrument and is copied by each of the others 卡農〔一種複調樂曲〕 **3** *formal* a generally accepted rule or standard on which an idea, subject, or way of behaving is based【正式】準則, 標準, 規範: *Her behaviour offends all the canons of good taste.* 她的行為不符合高雅的標準。**4** *formal* a list of books or pieces of music that are officially recognized as being the work of a certain writer【正式】全集, 書目; 真本(書目): *the Shakespearian canon* 莎士比亞著作集 **5** an established law of the Christian church 基督教教規, 基督教教會法

ca·non·i·cal /kəˋnɑnɪkḷ; kəˈnɒnɪkəl/ *adj* **1** according to CANON LAW 按照教規的 **2** *technical* in the simplest mathematical form【術語】〔數學方程式等〕典型的; 標準的

can·on·ize also 又作 **-ise** *BrE*【英】/ˋkænənˌaɪz; ˈkænənaɪz/ *v* [T] to officially state that a dead person is a SAINT (1) 把〔死者〕封為聖人 —**canonization** /ˌkænənaɪˋzeʃən; ˌkænənaɪˈzeɪʃən/ *n* [C,U]

canon law /ˌ·· ˈ·/ *n* [U] the laws of Christian Church 基督教教會法

ca·noo·dle /kəˋnudḷ; kəˈnuːdl/ *v* [I] *BrE old-fashioned* if two people canoodle, they kiss and hold each other in a sexual way【英, 過時】愛撫, 摟抱

can o·pen·er /ˈ· ˌ···/ *n* [C] *especially AmE* a tool for opening a can of food【尤美】開罐器, 罐頭刀; TIN OPENER *BrE*【英】—see picture on page A10 參見 A10 頁圖

can·o·py /ˋkænəpɪ; ˈkænəpi/ *n* [C] **1** a cover fixed above a bed, seat etc as a decoration or as a shelter〔牀或座位上的〕頂罩, 罩篷, 華蓋 **2** *literary* something that spreads above you like a roof【文】像天篷的東西: *a canopy of branches* 樹枝交織成的天篷 —**canopied** *adj*

canst /kənst; kənst; *strong* 強讀 kænst; kænst/ *v* **thou canst** *old use* used to mean 'you can' when talking to one person【舊】〔談話時用於表示〕你可以, 你能

can't /kænt; kɑːnt/ **1** the short form of 縮略式= cannot: *I can't understand what this means.* 我不懂這是甚麼意思。| *You can swim, can't you?* 你會游泳, 不是嗎? **2** used as the opposite of 'must', to say that something is impossible or unlikely. 不可能, 不太可能〔must 的反義詞〕: *They can't have gone out because the light's on.* 他們不可能出去了, 因為燈還亮着。

cant[1] /kænt; kænt/ *n* **1** [U] insincere talk about moral or religious principles by someone who is pretending to be better than they really are〔有關道德或宗教的〕假話, 偽善的話: *a politician's cant about family values* 政客關於家庭價值的虛假言辭 **2** [U] special words used by a particular group of people, especially in order to keep things secret 行話, 隱語, 黑話: *thieves' cant* 小偷的黑話 **3** [C] a sloping surface or angle 斜面; 斜坡; 斜角

cant[2] *v* [I,T] to lean, or make something lean (使)傾斜

cantab /ˋkæntæb; ˈkæntæb/ used after the title of a degree from Cambridge University 劍橋大學的〔用於學位名稱後〕: *Jane Smith MA (Cantab)* 簡·史密斯, 劍橋大學文學碩士

can·ta·loup, cantaloupe /ˋkæntḷˌop; ˈkæntəluːp/ *n* [C, U] a type of MELON with a hard green skin and sweet orange flesh 羅馬甜瓜; 皺皮香瓜 —see picture on page A8 參見 A8 頁圖

can·tan·ker·ous /kænˋtæŋkərəs; kænˈtæŋkərəs/ *adj* bad-tempered and complaining a lot 脾氣壞而且愛嘮叨的: *a cantankerous old man* 脾氣壞而且愛嘮叨的老頭 —**cantankerously** *adv* —**cantankerousness** *n* [U]

can·ta·ta /kænˋtɑtə; kænˈtɑːtə/ *n* [C] a piece of religious music sung by a CHOIR and single performers 康塔塔, 大合唱〔一種由獨唱、重唱和合唱組成的宗教樂曲〕

can·teen /kænˋtin; kænˈtiːn/ *n* [C] **1** a place in a factory, school etc where meals are provided, usually quite cheaply〔工廠或學校等的〕食堂, 餐廳: *lunch in the works' canteen* 在工廠食堂裡吃午餐 **2** a small container in which water or other drink is carried by soldiers, travellers etc〔士兵、旅行者攜帶的〕水壺 **3** *BrE* a set of knives, forks and spoons in a box【英】一盒(全套)刀、叉、湯匙餐具

canter[1] /ˋkæntɚ; ˈkæntə/ *v* [I,T] to ride or make a horse run quite fast, but not as fast as possible (使)〔馬〕以普通速度跑

can·ter[2] *n* **1** [singular] the movement of a horse when it is running fairly fast, but not as fast as possible〔馬的〕普通跑步, 中速跑 **2** [C] a ride on a horse at this speed 騎馬中速跑 **3** a short or quick journey 短暫旅程: *Paris is now only a canter away due to the Channel Tunnel.* 由於有了海峽隧道, 現在去巴黎只需很短的時間。

can·ti·cle /ˈkæntɪkḷ; ˈkæntɪkəl/ *n* [C] a short religious song usually using words from the Bible〔歌詞一般取自《聖經》的〕讚美詩, 聖歌

can·ti·le·ver /ˈkæntḷˌivɚ; ˈkæntəliːvə/ *n* [C] a beam that sticks out from an upright post or wall and supports a shelf, the end of a bridge etc 托臂, 懸臂, 懸臂梁, 支架

can·to /ˈkænto; ˈkæntəʊ/ *n plural* **cantos** [C] one of the parts into which a very long poem is divided〔長詩中的〕篇章

can·ton /kænˈtɑn; ˈkæntɒn/ *n* [C] one of the areas with limited political powers that make up a country such as Switzerland 小行政區〈如瑞士的州〉

Can·to·nese /ˌkæntəˈniz; ˌkæntəˈniːz◂/ *n* [U] a Chinese language spoken in Southern China and Hong Kong 粵語, 廣東話

can·ton·ment /kænˈtonmənt; kænˈtuːnmənt/ *n* [C] *technical* a camp for soldiers【術語】軍營, 駐地

can·tor /ˈkæntɚ; ˈkæntə/ *n* [C] **1** a man who leads the prayers and songs in a Jewish religious service〔猶太教儀式中的〕帶領祈禱和唱詩者 **2** the leader of a CHOIR in a church〔教堂唱詩班的〕領唱者

can·vas /ˈkænvəs; ˈkænvəs/ *n* **1** [U] strong cloth used to make bags, tents, shoes etc 帆布 **2** [C] a painting done with oil paints, or the piece of cloth it is painted on 油畫(布) **3 under canvas** *BrE* in a tent【英】在帳篷內: *We spent the night under canvas.* 我們在帳篷裡過夜。

can·vass /ˈkænvəs; ˈkænvəs/ *v* **1** [I,T] to try to get information, support for a political party etc, by going from place to place within an area and talking to people 遊說; 拉選票; 徵求意見: *The company canvassed 600 people who use their product.* 公司徵求了600名產品使用者的意見。| *We'll have to canvass the entire area before the referendum.* 在公民投票前我們得在全區拉選票。**2** [T] to talk about a problem, suggestion etc in detail〔詳細〕討論: *The suggestion is being widely canvassed as a possible solution to the dispute.* 這項建議作為解決爭端的可行辦法, 正受到廣泛的討論。—**canvass** *n* [C] —**canvasser** *n* [C]

can·yon /ˈkænjən; ˈkænjən/ *n* [C] a deep valley with very steep sides of rock that usually has a river running through it〔兩邊為峭壁, 谷底常有溪流的〕峽谷

cap. also 又作 **caps.** the written abbreviation of 縮寫= capital letter (CAPITAL[1] (3)) 大寫字母

caps 帽子

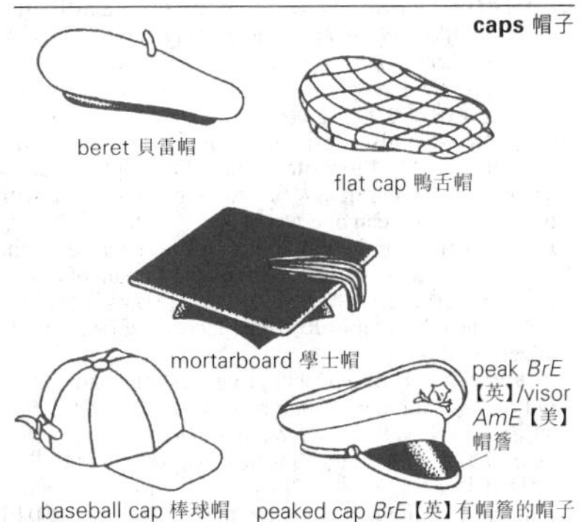

see also picture at 另見 **hat** 圖

3 **cap¹** /kæp; kæp/ *n* [C]

1 ▶HAT 帽子◀ **a)** a type of soft flat hat that has a curved part sticking out at the front〔有帽簷的〕帽子 **b)** a covering that fits very closely to your head and is worn for a particular purpose〔緊蓋住頭部的〕帽子, 便帽: *a swimming cap* 泳帽 | *a shower cap* 浴帽 **c)** a special type of hat that is worn by a particular profession or group of people〔表示職業或所屬團體的〕制服帽: *a nurse's cap* 護士帽

2 ▶TOP/COVERING 罩, 蓋◀ a protective covering that you put on the end or top of an object〔對物件起保護作用的〕罩, 蓋, 套: *Make sure that you put the cap back on that pen.* 務必把筆帽套上。—see also 另見 ICE CAP, TOECAP

3 go cap in hand (to) to ask someone for something, especially money, in a very polite way that makes you seem unimportant 恭敬地請求, 謙卑地要求: *going cap in hand to the bank for a loan* 謙卑地懇求銀行貸款

4 if the cap fits *spoken* used to say that someone should regard a remark as criticism of them if they think that the criticism is suitable【口】批評中肯, 恰如其分: *I never said you were a liar, but if the cap fits...* 我從未說過你撒謊, 但如果情況屬實…

5 ▶EXPLOSIVE 爆炸物◀ a small paper container with explosive inside it, used especially in toy guns 啪啪紙, 火藥紙〔玩具槍中用的紙包火藥〕

6 ▶LIMIT 限度◀ an upper limit that is put on the amount of money that can be spent or borrowed in a particular situation〔金額的〕最高限額: *a cap on local council spending* 地方委員會支出的最高限額

7 ▶SEX 性行為◀ a CONTRACEPTIVE made of a round piece of rubber that a woman puts inside her VAGINA〔婦女避孕用的〕子宮帽

8 set your cap at *old-fashioned* if a woman sets her cap at a man, she tries to attract him, especially in order to marry him【過時】〔女子〕向〔男子〕示愛, 追求〔尤指為嫁給某人〕—see also 另見 **a feather in your cap** (FEATHER[1] (2)), **put on your thinking cap** (THINKING[1])

cap² *v* **capped, capping** [T] **1** to say or do something that is better, worse, funnier etc than what someone else has just said or done 勝過, 超越: *She capped my story with an hilarious account of the party.* 她對晚會繪聲繪色的描述, 使得我所講的故事黯然失色。**2 to cap it all** *spoken* used before describing the worst, funniest etc part at the end of a story or description【口】〔用於故事或描述的結尾〕最有趣[糟糕]的是: *And to cap it all, I found I'd left my purse at home!* 最糟糕的是, 我發現把錢包忘在家裡了。**3 be capped with** to have a particular substance on top 為…所覆蓋, 為…所籠罩: *snow-capped mountains* 白雪覆蓋的羣山 | *a graceful tower capped with a gilded dome* 美麗的鍍金圓頂塔 **4** *BrE* to choose someone for a national sports team【英】把…選入〔國家隊〕: *He's been capped three times for England.* 他三次入選英格蘭隊 **5** to cover a tooth with a special white substance 給〔牙齒〕上釉 **6** *BrE* to put a limit on the amount of money that can be charged or spent, especially by local government【英】〔尤指地方政府〕對〔收費或開支〕規定上限

ca·pa·bil·i·ty /ˌkepəˈbɪlətɪ; ˌkeɪpəˈbɪləti/ *n* [C] **1** the natural ability, skill, or power that makes you able to do something 能力, 才能: *a child's language capability* 兒童的語言能力 | **capability to do sth** *A willingness and a capability to change are necessary to meet the market's needs.* 願意並能夠作出調整, 這對於滿足市場需求是很必要的。| **beyond sb's capabilities** (=too difficult for someone) 超過某人的能力 *I have a good knowledge of French, but simultaneous translation is beyond my capabilities.* 我法語不錯, 但是做同聲傳譯卻不是我力所能及的。**2** the ability that a country has to take a particular kind of military action〔一國的〕軍事能力: *a nuclear weapons capability* 核武力 S3

ca·pa·ble /ˈkepəbḷ; ˈkeɪpəbəl/ *adj* **1 capable of (doing) sth** having the skills, power, intelligence etc needed to do something 有能力(做某事): *I don't think Banks is capable of murder.* 我認為班克斯沒有能力謀殺。| *The company isn't capable of handling an order that large.* S2 W2

那家公司沒有能力應付那麼大的訂單。**2** skilled or very good at doing something 熟練的: *a very capable doctor* 一位非常能幹的醫生 —**capably** *adv*

ca·pa·cious /kə`peʃəs; kə'peɪʃəs/ *adj formal* able to contain a lot【正式】容量大的: *a capacious suitcase* 大手提箱 —**capaciousness** *n* [U]

ca·pa·ci·tor /kə`pæsətə; kə'pæsɪ̇tə/ *n* [C] a piece of equipment that collects and stores electricity 電容器

ca·pac·i·ty /kə`pæsətɪ; kə'pæsɪ̇ti/ *n* **1** [singular] the amount of space a container, room etc has to hold things or people 容量, 容積; 容納力: **[+of]** *The fuel tank has a capacity of 12 gallons.* 這個燃料箱的容量為12加侖。| *seating capacity of 500* 500個座位 | **capacity crowd** (=one that fills all the seats in a room, hall etc) 座無虛席 *The orchestra played to a capacity crowd in the Queen Elizabeth Hall.* 管弦樂團在伊莉莎白女王大廳的演奏座無虛席。| **filled to capacity** (=completely full) 擠滿; 滿座 **2** [C,U] someone's ability to do something 能力, 才能: **[+for]** *a child's capacity for learning* 孩子的學習能力 | *an infinite capacity for love* 無限的愛 | **capacity to do sth** *a capacity to think in an original way* 創造性的思維能力 **3** [singular] *formal* someone's job, position, or duty; ROLE (1)【正式】職位; 地位; 身分; 職責: *Rollins will be working in an advisory capacity on this project.* 羅林斯將以顧問的身分參與此項目。| **do sth in your capacity as** *I attended in my capacity as chairman of the safety committee.* 我是以安全委員會主席的身分參加的。**4** [singular,U] the amount of something that a factory, company, machine etc can produce or deal with〔工廠、公司、機器等的〕產量, 生產力: *Our factories have been working at full capacity all year.* 我們的工廠全年都滿負荷生產。

ca·par·i·soned /kə`pærəsn̩d; kə'pærɪ̇sənd/ *adj* in medieval times a caparisoned horse was one covered in a decorated cloth〔中世紀的馬〕配有華麗馬衣的

cape /kep; keɪp/ *n* [C] **1** a long loose piece of clothing without SLEEVEs that fastens around you neck and hangs from your shoulders 斗篷, 披風, 披肩 **2** a large piece of land surrounded on three sides by water 海角, 岬: *the Cape of Good Hope* 好望角

ca·per¹ /`kepə; 'keɪpə/ *v* [I always+adv/prep] to jump about and play in a happy, excited way〔快樂地〕跳躍, 雀躍: *lambs capering in the fields* 在田野裡跳躍嬉戲的羔羊

caper² *n* [C] **1** a small dark green part of a flower used in cooking to give a sour taste to food〔用作調味料的〕續隨子花芽 **2** *informal* a planned activity, especially an illegal or dangerous one【非正式】欺詐, 違法行為: *If he thinks I'm going along with him on this caper, he's wrong.* 如果他認為我會跟他一塊兒去幹這種違法的事, 那麼他就錯了。**3** a short jumping or dancing movement 快速跳躍動作, 快速舞步: **cut a caper** (=dance with little steps or jumps) 雀躍地跳舞[蹦跳]

ca·pil·la·ry /`kæpl̩ˌɛrɪ; kə'pɪləri/ *n* [C] **1** a very small tube as thin as a hair 毛細管 **2** the smallest type of BLOOD VESSEL (=tube carrying blood) in the body 毛細血管

capillary at·trac·tion /·ˌ··· ·'··/ also 又作 **capillary ac·tion** /·ˌ··· '··/ *n* [U] *technical* the force that makes a liquid rise up a narrow tube【術語】毛細管作用, 毛細管引力

cap·i·tal¹ /`kæpətl̩; 'kæpɪ̇tl/ *n*

1 ►CITY 城市◄ [C] an important town or city where the central government of a country, state etc is 首都; 首府; 省會: *Albany is the capital of New York State.* 奧爾巴尼是紐約州的首府。

2 ►FINANCIAL 金融的◄ [singular,U] money or property, especially when it is used to start a business or to produce more wealth 資本, 資金: *You'll need more capital if you want to open your own business.* 自己創辦企業的話需要更多的資金。—see also 另見 WORKING CAPITAL, VENTURE CAPITAL

3 ►LETTER 字母◄ [C] a letter of the alphabet written in its large form as it is, for example at the beginning of someone's name 大寫字母 —compare 比較 LOWER CASE

4 ►CENTRE OF ACTIVITY 活動中心◄ [C] a place that is a centre for an industry, business, or other activity〔工商業及其他活動的〕中心: *Hollywood is the capital of the movie industry.* 荷里活是電影業的中心。

5 make capital out of to use a situation or event to help you get an advantage 利用..., 從...中撈一把[獲益]: *The Republicans are sure to make capital out of the closure of the plant.* 共和黨人一定會從該廠的倒閉中撈取好處的。

6 ►BUILDING 建築物◄ the top part of a COLUMN (=a long stone post used in some buildings) 柱頭, 柱頂

capital² *adj* **1 capital letter** a letter that is written or printed in its large form 大寫字母 —compare 比較 LOWER CASE **2 capital offence/crime** an offence etc that is punished by death 可處死刑的罪 **3** *old-fashioned* excellent【過時】極好的: *That's a capital suggestion!* 那建議好極了!

capital as·sets /ˌ··· '··/ *n* [plural] *technical* machines, buildings, and other property belonging to a company【術語】固定資產, 資本資產

capital gains /ˌ··· '·/ *n* [plural] profits you make by selling your possessions 資本收益〔出售固定資產所得的收益〕

capital gains tax /ˌ··· '· ·/ *n* [C] a tax that you pay on profits that you make when you sell your possessions 資本收益稅

capital goods /'··· ˌ·/ *n* [plural] goods such as machines or buildings that are made for the purpose of producing other goods 資本貨物〔指機器等用來製造其他商品的貨物〕—compare 比較 CONSUMER GOODS

capital in·ten·sive /ˌ··· ·'···◂/ *adj* a capital intensive business, industry etc needs a lot of money for it to operate properly〔工業〕資本密集的 —compare 比較 LABOUR-INTENSIVE

cap·i·tal·is·m /`kæpətl̩ˌɪzəm; 'kæpɪ̇tl-ɪzəm/ *n* [U] a system of production and trade based on property and wealth being owned privately, with only a small amount of industrial activity by the government 資本主義 —compare 比較 COMMUNISM

cap·i·tal·ist¹ /`kæpətl̩ɪst; 'kæpɪ̇tl-ɪ̇st/ *n* [C] **1** someone who supports capitalism 資本主義者: *the class struggle between workers and capitalists* 工人與資本主義者之間的階級鬥爭 **2** someone who owns or controls a lot of money and lends it to businesses, banks etc to produce more wealth 資本家

capitalist² also 又作 **cap·i·ta·lis·tic** /ˌkæpɪtl`ɪstɪk; ˌkæpɪ̇tl'ɪstɪk◂/ *adj* using or supporting capitalism 資本主義的: *Marx argued against the capitalist system.* 馬克思反駁資本主義制度。| *capitalist societies of the rich West* 富足的西方資本主義社會

cap·i·tal·ize also 又作 **-ise** *BrE*【英】/`kæpətl̩ˌaɪz; 'kæpɪ̇tl-aɪz/ *v* [T] **1** to write a letter of the alphabet using a CAPITAL¹ (3) letter 把...大寫 **2** to supply a business with money so that it can operate 給〔公司〕提供資金 **3** *technical* to calculate the value of a business based on the value of its shares (SHARE² (5)) or on the amount of money it makes【術語】〔根據公司的股票價值或其收益〕核定〔公司〕的資本 —**capitalization** /ˌkæpətl̩ə`zeʃən; ˌkæpɪ̇tl-aɪ'zeɪʃən/ *n* [U]

capitalize on sth *phr v* [T] to get as much advantage out of a situation, event etc as you can 盡量榨取, 充分利用: *We are well-placed to capitalize on the growth of cable TV.* 我們有條件從有線電視的發展中得到好處。

capital lev·y /ˌ··· '··/ *n* [C] *technical* a tax on private or industrial wealth that is paid to the government【術語】資本稅

capital pun·ish·ment /ˌ··· '···/ *n* [U] punishment by legal killing 死刑, 極刑

capital trans·fer tax /ˌ··· '·· ˌ·/ *n* [C,U] *BrE* a tax paid when you receive money, either as a gift or when someone dies【英】資本轉移稅 —see also 另見 INHERITANCE TAX

cap·i·ta·tion /ˌkæpəˋteʃən; ˌkæpɪ̵ˈteɪʃən/ *n* [C] a tax or payment of the same amount from each person 人頭稅; 按人收費

Cap·i·tol /ˋkæpətḷ; ˈkæpɪ̵tl/ *n* **1 the Capitol** the building in Washington D.C. where the US Congress meets〔位於華盛頓市的〕美國國會大廈 **2** [C] the building or group of buildings of the central government of one of the 50 states of the US〔美國各州的〕州議會大廈

Capitol Hill /ˌ··· ˈ·/ *n* [singular] **1** the US Congress 美國國會 **2** the hill where the Capitol building stands〔美國〕國會山

ca·pit·u·late /kəˋpɪtʃəˌlet; kəˈpɪtʃʊleɪt/ *v* [I] **1** to accept or agree to something that you have been opposing until now 屈服, 不再反對, 停止抵抗: *Helen finally capitulated and let her son have a car.* 海倫最後作出讓步, 同意讓兒子買一輛車。**2** *formal* to accept defeat by your enemies in a war; SURRENDER¹ (1)【正式】投降 —**capitulation** /kəˌpɪtʃəˋleʃən; kəˌpɪtʃʊˈleɪʃən/ *n* [C,U]

ca·pon /ˋkepɑn; ˈkeɪpən/ *n* [C] a male chicken that has had its sex organs removed to make it grow big and fat〔供食用的〕閹雞

cap·puc·ci·no /ˌkæpəˋtʃino; ˌkæpʊˈtʃiːnəʊ/ *n* [C,U] Italian coffee made with hot milk and with chocolate powder on top 意大利白咖啡〔一種加熱牛奶, 上面撒有巧克力粉的意大利式咖啡〕

ca·price /kəˋpris; kəˈpriːs/ *n* **1** [C,U] a sudden and unreasonable change of mind or behaviour 任性; 反覆無常, 多變: *the caprices of a spoilt child* 嬌生慣養兒童的任性 **2** [U] the tendency to change your mind suddenly or behave in an unexpected way 反覆無常的傾向

ca·pri·cious /kəˋprɪʃəs; kəˈprɪʃəs/ *adj* **1** likely to change your mind suddenly or behave in an unexpected way 反覆無常的; 任性的: *as capricious and manipulative as her mother had been* 像她母親一樣任性並有操縱慾 **2** changing quickly and suddenly 善變的: *a capricious wind* 變幻莫測的風 —**capriciously** *adv*

Cap·ri·corn /ˋkæprɪˌkɔrn; ˈkæprɪkɔːn/ *n* **1** [singular] the tenth sign of the ZODIAC represented by a goat and believed to affect the character and life of people born between December 22 and January 19 摩羯宮, 摩羯[山羊]座 **2** [C] someone who was born between December 22 and January 19 生於摩羯[山羊]座時段〔即 12 月 22 日至 1 月 19 日〕的人

cap·si·cum /ˋkæpsɪkəm; ˈkæpsɪkəm/ *n* [C,U] *technical* a kind of PEPPER (=a green, red, or yellow vegetable)【術語】〔青色、紅色、黃色〕辣椒

cap·size /ˋkæpˌsaɪz; kæpˈsaɪz/ *v* [I,T] if a boat capsizes or if you capsize it, it turns over in the water (使)〔船〕傾覆

cap·stan /ˋkæpstən; ˈkæpstən/ *n* [C] **1** a round machine shaped like a drum, used to wind up a rope that pulls or lifts heavy objects 絞盤, 捲揚機; 起錨機 **2** the round bar that goes round to move the TAPE¹ (12) in a TAPE RECORDER〔錄音機的〕主動輪, 旋轉軸

cap·sule /ˋkæpsḷ; ˈkæpsjuːl/ *n* [C] **1** a plastic container shaped like a very small tube with medicine inside that you swallow whole〔藥物〕膠囊 **2** the part of a SPACECRAFT in which people live and work〔太空船的〕密封艙〔太空人生活和居住的地方〕

3 **cap·tain¹** /ˋkæptɪn; ˈkæptɪ̵n/ *n* [C] **1** someone who commands a ship or aircraft 艦長; 船長; 機長: *The Captain and crew welcome you aboard.* 船長和船員們歡迎你登船。**2** a rank in the navy, army or US Air Force or Marines〔陸軍〕上尉;〔空軍〕(英) 上校, (美) 上尉;〔海軍〕上校 —see also 另見 GROUP CAPTAIN —see table on page C6 參見 C6 頁附錄 **3** someone who leads a team or other group of people 隊長, 組長: *Julie's the school tennis captain.* 朱莉是學校網球隊隊長。**4 captain of industry** someone who owns an important company 工業界巨子[大亨], 實業巨頭

captain² *v* [T] to lead a group or team of people and be their captain 擔任…指揮, 率領

cap·tain·cy /ˋkæptənsɪ; ˈkæptɪ̵nsi/ *n* [C,U] the position of being captain of a team, or the period during which someone is captain 隊長職位; 隊長任期

cap·tion /ˋkæpʃən; ˈkæpʃən/ *n* [C] words printed above or below a picture in a book or newspaper or on a television screen to explain what the picture is showing〔圖片、報刊文章、電視等的〕題目, 標題; 說明文字

cap·tious /ˋkæpʃəs; ˈkæpʃəs/ *adj literary* always criticizing unimportant things【文】吹毛求疵的

cap·ti·vate /ˋkæptəˌvet; ˈkæptɪ̵veɪt/ *v* [T often passive 常用被動態] to attract someone very much 使着迷; 迷住, 吸引: *I was captivated by his charm and good looks.* 我被他的魅力與帥氣迷倒了。

cap·ti·va·ting /ˋkæptəˌvetɪŋ; ˈkæptɪ̵veɪtɪŋ/ *adj* very attractive 極為迷人的: *a captivating smile and beautiful eyes* 迷人的微笑和美麗的雙眼

cap·tive¹ /ˋkæptɪv; ˈkæptɪv/ *adj* **1** [only before noun 僅用於名詞前] unable to move about freely because of being kept in prison or in a small space 被監禁的, 被關押的: *Captive soldiers passed by in chains.* 被關押的士兵戴着鎖鏈走過。| *captive animals* 關在籠子裡的動物 **2 take/hold sb captive** to keep someone as a prisoner 俘虜/關押某人: *The American officers were held captive for three months.* 那些美國軍官被關押達三個月之久。**3 captive audience** people who listen or watch someone or something because they have to, not because they are interested 被迫看[聽]…的聽眾[觀眾]

captive² *n* [C] someone who is kept as a prisoner, especially in a war 戰俘, 俘虜, 囚徒

cap·tiv·i·ty /kæpˋtɪvətɪ; kæpˈtɪvɪ̵ti/ *n* [U] the state of being kept in a prison, CAGE etc and not allowed to go where you want 被俘 (的狀態), 拘禁, 囚禁; 束縛: *The hostages were released from captivity.* 人質從囚禁中被釋放出來了。| **in captivity** *Many animals do not breed well when kept in captivity.* 許多動物被關入籠中就繁殖得不好。

cap·tor /ˋkæptɚ; ˈkæptə/ *n* [C] someone who is keeping another person prisoner 捉拿者, 捕捉者: *He managed to escape from his captors.* 他設法從捉他的人那裡逃了出來。

cap·ture¹ /ˋkæptʃɚ; ˈkæptʃə/ *v* [T] 3

1 ▶PERSON 人◀ to catch someone in order to make them a prisoner 俘虜, 逮捕: *Government troops have succeeded in capturing the rebel leader.* 政府軍成功捕獲了叛亂分子的頭目。

2 ▶PLACE 地方◀ to get control of a place that previously belonged to an enemy by fighting for it〔用武力從敵人手中〕奪取〔某地〕: *The town of Moulineuf was captured after a siege lasting ten days.* 經過長達十天的圍攻, 莫林那輔鎮終於被攻陷了。

3 ▶ANIMAL 動物◀ to catch an animal after chasing or following it 捕獲

4 ▶BOOK/PAINTING/FILM 書/畫/電影◀ to succeed in showing or describing a situation or feeling using words or pictures〔用文字、圖片〕記錄下: *These photographs capture the essence of working-class life at the turn of the century.* 這些相片記錄了世紀之交時工人階級的生活實況。

5 capture sb's imagination/attention etc to make someone feel very interested and attracted 引起某人想像/吸引某人注意等: *His stories of foreign adventure captured my imagination.* 他所講的外國歷險故事使我心馳神往。

6 capture sb's heart to seem attractive to someone so that they become very fond of you or love you 贏得某人的好感[愛意]

7 ▶BUSINESS/POLITICS 商業/政治◀ to get something that previously belonged to one of your competitors 奪得, 搶佔: *Japanese firms have captured over 60% of the electronics market.* 日本公司已經搶佔了超過 60% 的電子市場。

8 ▶COMPUTERS 電腦◀ *technical* to put something in

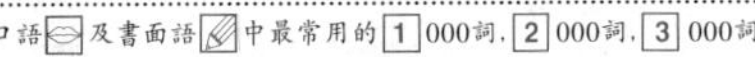

a form that a computer can use【術語】〔電腦〕把…變換成可用於電腦的形式; 記錄: *The data is captured by an optical scanner.* 該數據是通過光學掃描器記錄下來的。**9 ►CHESS** 國際象棋◄ to remove one of your opponent's PIECE*s* from the board in CHESS〔在國際象棋比賽中〕吃掉〔對方一子〕

capture² *n* **1** [U] the act of catching someone in order to make them a prisoner 捕獲, 俘虜: *The two soldiers somehow managed to avoid capture.* 這兩名士兵設法逃過了被俘的命運。**2 the capture of Rome/Jerusalem etc** the act of getting control of a place that previously belonged to an enemy 佔領羅馬/耶路撒冷等

1 1 **car** /kɑr; kɑː/ *n* [C] **1** a small vehicle with four wheels and an engine, that you use to travel from one place to another 汽車: *I go to work by car.* 我開車去上班。| *Cars were parked on both sides of the road.* 路兩邊都停着汽車。—see picture on page A2 參見A2頁圖 **2 sleeping/dining/buffet car** a train carriage used for sleeping etc〔火車〕臥鋪車廂/餐車 **3** *AmE* a train carriage【美】〔火車〕車廂 **4** the part of a lift, BALLOON¹ (2), or AIRSHIP in which people or goods are carried〔電梯的〕升降室, 機廂; 〔氣球、飛艇等的〕吊艙; 座艙; 貨艙

ca·rafe /kə`ræf; kə'ræf/ *n* [C] a glass container with a wide neck, used for serving wine or water at meals 寬頸玻璃瓶, 飲料瓶

car a·larm /'· ·,·/ *n* [C] a special system for protecting cars against thieves that makes a loud noise if anyone touches the car 汽車防盜警報器

car·a·mel /`kærəml; 'kærəməl/ *n* **1** [C] a brown sweet made of sticky boiled sugar〔含有焦糖的〕糖果 **2** [U] burnt sugar used for giving food a special taste and colour〔食品調味或調色用的〕焦糖 —see also 另見 CRÈME CARAMEL —**caramelize** *v* [I,T]

car·a·pace /`kærə,pes; 'kærəpeɪs/ *n* [C] *technical* a hard shell on the outside of some animals such as CRAB*s* or TORTOISE*s*, that protects them【術語】〔蟹或龜等的〕甲殼

car·at /`kærət; 'kærət/ *n* [C] **1** also 又作 **karat** *AmE*【美】a measurement that shows how pure gold is 開〔黃金的純度單位〕: *a 22-carat gold chain* 22開的金鏈 **2** a measurement equal to 200 MILLIGRAM*s* on the scale of measurement for the weight of jewels 克拉〔寶石重量單位, 相等於200毫克〕

car·a·van /`kærə,væn; 'kærəvæn/ *n* [C] **1** *BrE* a vehicle that a car can pull and in which people can live and sleep when they are on holiday【英】〔帶有食宿設備的〕旅行拖車; TRAILER (1) *AmE*【美】**2** *BrE* a covered vehicle pulled by a horse in which people such as gipsies (GIPSY) live【英】〔吉卜賽人居住的〕大篷車, 有篷馬車; WAGON (1) *AmE*【美】**3** a group of people with animals or vehicles who travel together for protection through dangerous areas such as deserts〔帶着牲口、車輛等穿越沙漠等危險地帶的〕旅行隊

car·a·van·ning /`kærəvænɪŋ; 'kærəvænɪŋ/ *n* [U] *BrE* the practice of having holdays in a caravan【英】乘旅行拖車外出度假: *a caravanning holiday in Cornwall* 乘旅行拖車在康沃爾度假

car·a·van·se·rai /,kærə`vænsə,raɪ; ,kærə'vænsəraɪ/ *n* [C] a hotel with a large open central area, used in the past in Eastern countries by groups of people and animals travelling together〔舊時東方國家裡供旅行隊過夜且有停車大院子的〕旅店, 客棧

car·a·way /`kærə,we; 'kærəweɪ/ *n* [C,U] a plant whose strongtasting seeds are used to give a special taste to food〔其籽有特殊香味, 可做調味料的〕葛蒿, 葛縷子, 香旱芹

car·bine /`kɑrbaɪn; 'kɑːbaɪn/ *n* [C] a short light RIFLE (=type of gun) 卡賓槍

car·bo·hy·drate /,kɑrbo`haɪdret; ,kɑːbəʊ'haɪdreɪt/ *n* **1** [C,U] *technical* one of several food substances such as sugar which consist of oxygen, HYDROGEN and CARBON (1), and which provide your body with heat and energy【術語】碳水化合物, 醣類 **2** [C usually plural 一般用複數] foods such as rice, bread, and potatoes that contain carbohydrates 含碳水化合物的食品〈如米飯、麵包、馬鈴薯等〉

car·bol·ic a·cid /kɑr`bɑlɪk `æsɪd; kɑː,bɒlɪk 'æsɪ̠d/ *n* [U] a liquid that kills BACTERIA, used for preventing the spread of disease or infection 石碳酸

carbolic soap /·,·· '·/ *n* [U] a strong soap made from coal TAR¹ (1) 石碳酸皂

car bomb /'· ·/ *n* [C] a bomb hidden inside a car 汽車炸彈

car·bon /`kɑrbən; 'kɑːbən/ *n* **1** [U] a simple substance that exists in a pure form as diamonds, GRAPHITE etc or in an impure form as coal, petrol etc 碳 **2** [C,U] CARBON PAPER 複寫紙 **3** [C] a CARBON COPY (1) 複寫本, 副本

car·bon·at·ed /`kɑrbənetɪd; 'kɑːbəneɪtɪ̠d/ *adj* carbonated drinks contain small BUBBLE*s*〔飲料〕含二氧化碳的: *carbonated spring water* 有汽礦泉水

carbon black /'·· ·/ *n* [U] a black powder made by partly burning oil, wood etc, used for making rubber〔用於生產橡膠的〕碳黑

carbon cop·y /,·· '··/ *n* [C] **1** a copy, especially of something that has been typed (TYPE² (1)), made using CARBON PAPER 複寫本, 副本 **2** someone or something that is very similar to another person or thing 極為相似的人[物]: [+of] *The robbery is a carbon copy of one that took place last year.* 這宗搶劫案與去年發生的那宗極為相似。

carbon dat·ing /,·· '··/ *n* [U] a method used to find out the age of very old objects 碳年代測定法

carbon di·ox·ide /,·· ·'··/ *n* [U] the gas produced when animals breathe out, when carbon is burned in air, or when animal or vegetable substances decay 二氧化碳

car·bon·if·er·ous /,kɑrbə`nɪfərəs; ,kɑːbə'nɪfərəs◄/ *adj* producing or containing carbon or coal 碳質的, 產碳的; 含煤的; 碳紀的: *carboniferous rocks* 石碳紀形成的岩石

car·bon·ize also 又作 **-ise** *BrE*【英】/`kɑrbən,aɪz; 'kɑːbənaɪz/ *v* [I,T] to change or make something change into CARBON (1) by burning without air (使) 碳化, (使) 焦化 —**carbonized** *adj*

carbon mo·nox·ide /,·· ·'··/ *n* [U] a poisonous gas produced when CARBON (1), especially petrol, burns in a small amount of air 一氧化碳

carbon pa·per /'·· ,··/ *n* [C,U] thin paper with a blue or black substance on one side, that you put between sheets of paper when typing (TYPE² (2)) in order to make copies 複寫紙

carbon tet·ra·chlo·ride /,kɑrbən tɛtrə`klɔraɪd; ,kɑːbən tetrə'klɔːraɪd/ *n* [U] a colourless liquid used for cleaning dirty marks off clothes 四氯化碳〔用於去除衣服上污跡的一種無色液體〕

car boot sale /,·'· ,·/ *n* [C] *BrE* a sale in a CAR PARK or other open space, where people sell things from the back of their cars【英】舊貨出售, 舊物集市〔在停車場等地方將舊物放在汽車的行李箱中出售〕

car·bo·run·dum /,kɑrbə`rʌndəm; ,kɑːbə'rʌndəm/ *n* [U] an extremely hard substance made from CARBON (1) and SILICON used for polishing things 金剛砂, 碳化硅

car·boy /`kɑrbɔɪ; 'kɑːbɔɪ/ *n* [C] a large round bottle used for holding dangerous chemical liquids〔用來裝載危險化學溶液的〕圓形大瓶

car·bun·cle /`kɑrbʌŋkl; 'kɑːbʌŋkəl/ *n* [C] **1** a large painful lump under someone's skin 癰〔生於皮下組織的化膿性炎症〕**2** a red jewel, especially a GARNET (1) 紅寶石, 〔尤指〕石榴石

car·bu·ret·tor *BrE*【英】, **carburetor** *AmE*【美】/`kɑrbə,retə; ,kɑːbjʊ̠'retə/ *n* [C] a part of a car engine that mixes the air and petrol which burns in the engine to provide power〔汽車引擎的〕汽化器, 化油器 —see picture at 參見 ENGINE 圖

car·cass /`kɑrkəs; 'kɑːkəs/ *n* [C] **1** the body of a dead animal, especially one that is ready to be cut up as meat 動物屍體〔屠宰後用作肉食的牲畜軀體〕**2 shift/move**

your carcass! *spoken* used to tell someone to move from the place where they are sitting or standing【口】挪挪窩！躲開！**3** the decaying outer structure of a building, vehicle, or other object〔建築物、汽車等的〕殘骸，骨架

car·cin·o·gen /kɑr`sɪnədʒən; kɑːˈsɪnədʒən/ *n* [C] a substance that can cause CANCER 致癌物(質)

car·cin·o·gen·ic /ˌkɑrsənəˋdʒɛnɪk; ˌkɑːsɪnəˈdʒenɪk◂/ *adj* likely to cause CANCER 致癌的: *the carcinogenic effects of high-fat diets* 高脂飲食的致癌性

car·ci·no·ma /ˌkɑrsəˋnomə; ˌkɑːsə̩ˈnəʊmə/ *n* [C] *technical* a CANCER【術語】癌

[1] [2] **card¹** /kɑrd; kɑːd/ *n*

1 library/membership/identity etc card a small piece of plastic or paper that shows that someone belongs to a particular organization, club etc 圖書館／會員／身分等證件: *Employees must show their ID cards at the gate.* 雇員必須在門口出示身分證件。

2 ▶BIRTHDAY/CHRISTMAS ETC 生日/聖誕等◀ [C] a piece of thick stiff paper with a picture on the front, that you send to people on special occasions 賀卡: *Did you remember to send Val a birthday card?* 你記得給瓦爾寄生日賀卡了嗎？

3 ▶HOLIDAY 假期◀ [C] a card with a photograph or picture on one side, that you send to someone when you are on holiday; POSTCARD 明信片: *Don't forget to send us a card from Greece!* 別忘了從希臘給我們寄張明信片！

4 ▶INFORMATION 資料◀ [C] a small piece of stiff paper or plastic that shows information about someone or something, especially one that is part of a set used for storing information 檔案卡片: *a card index system* 卡片索引系統 | *an expansion card for 386 machines* 386 電腦的擴充卡

5 ▶STIFF PAPER 卡片紙◀ [U] *BrE* thick stiff paper【英】厚紙片，(硬) 紙板

6 ▶BANK 銀行◀ [C] a small piece of plastic that you use to pay for goods or to get money from a special machine at a bank 信用卡; 借記卡: *Lost or stolen cards must be reported immediately.* 信用卡丢失或被盜必須馬上掛失。—see also 另見 CHARGE CARD, CHEQUE CARD, CREDIT CARD

7 ▶GAMES 遊戲◀ [C] a small piece of thick stiff paper with numbers and signs or pictures on, that is one of a set of fifty two used to play games such as POKER (1) or BRIDGE¹ (4) 紙牌，撲克牌: **play cards** (=play a game with cards) 玩牌 | **a pack of cards** (=a complete set of cards) 一副牌

8 cigarette/football/baseball etc card a small piece of thick stiff paper with a picture on one side that is part of a set which people collect 香煙牌／足球卡／棒球卡等〔可收集成套〕

9 ▶BUSINESS 商務◀ [C] a small piece of thick stiff paper that shows your name, job, and the company you work for; BUSINESS CARD; VISITING CARD 名片: *I'll leave my card and you can contact me when it suits you.* 我留下一張名片，你可以在方便的時候跟我聯繫。

10 be on the cards *BrE*【英】, **be in the cards** *AmE*【美】to seem likely to happen 很可能發生: *Another resignation could be on the cards.* 可能又有人要遞交辭呈。

11 play your cards right to deal with a situation in the right way so that you are successful in getting what you want 處理得當，做事精明: *If he plays his cards right Tony might get a promotion.* 如果東尼處事得當的話，他可能會得到提升。

12 put/lay your cards on the table to tell people what your plans and intentions are in a clear, honest way 攤牌，公開自己的打算[立場]: *I think it's time I put my cards on the table. You see, I'm not really a student.* 我想該說出真相了。其實我根本不是學生。

13 play/keep your cards close to your chest to keep your plans, thoughts, or feelings secret〔對自己的計劃、想法、感覺等〕祕而不宣，守口如瓶

14 hold all the cards *informal* to have all the advantages in a particular situation so that you can control what happens【非正式】佔盡優勢，掌握局勢

15 get/be given your cards *BrE informal* to have your job taken away from you【英，非正式】被解雇[免職]，失業

16 have another card up your sleeve to have another advantage that you can use to be successful in a particular situation 另有一張王牌，另有致勝法寶

17 best/strongest/winning/trump card something that gives you a big advantage in a particular situation 最厲害的一張王牌，撒手鐧: *The promise of tax cuts proved, as always, to be the Republican Party's trump card.* 一如以往，許諾減稅是共和黨的王牌。

18 sb's card is marked if someone's card is marked, they have done something that makes people in authority disapprove of them 某人留下了污點，某人上了黑名單

19 ▶AMUSING/UNUSUAL PERSON 滑稽/與眾不同的人◀ [singular] *old-fashioned* an amusing or unusual person【過時】逗人發笑的人，活寶: *Old Fred's a real card, isn't he!* 老弗雷德真是個活寶，對吧！

20 [C] the thing inside a computer that the chips (CHIP¹ (4a)) are fixed to, that allows the computer to do specific things〔電腦的〕卡，插件

21 ▶TOOL 工具◀ [C] *technical* a tool that is similar to a comb and is used for combing, cleaning and preparing wool or cotton for spinning (SPIN¹ (2))【術語】〔梳理送紡前的羊毛、棉花等的〕梳毛[棉]機

22 ▶FOOTBALL 足球◀ [C] a small piece of stiff red or yellow paper, shown to a player who has done something wrong in a game of football 紅牌，黃牌

card² *v* [T] **1** to comb, clean, and prepare wool or cotton, before making cloth〔用梳毛機等〕梳理 **2** *AmE* to ask someone to show a card proving that they are old enough to be in a particular place, especially a bar【美】要…出示證件〔尤指在酒吧等場所以檢查對方是否夠年齡入內〕

car·da·mom /ˋkɑrdəməm; ˈkɑːdəməm/ *n* [C,U] the seeds of an Asian fruit, used to give a special taste to Indian and Middle Eastern food 小豆蔻〔一種亞洲產果實的種子，用於調味〕

card·board¹ /ˋkɑrdˌbɔrd; ˈkɑːdbɔːd/ *n* [U] a stiff brown material like very thick paper, used especially for making boxes〔尤指可用於製紙箱的〕(硬) 紙板，卡紙: *We covered the hole with a sheet of cardboard.* 我們用一塊紙板擋住了洞。

cardboard² *adj* **1** made from cardboard 硬紙板製的: *a cardboard box* 硬紙板盒 **2** [only before noun 僅用於名詞前] seeming silly and not real 顯得愚蠢的; 不真實的: *a romantic novel full of cardboard characters* 充滿虛構人物的浪漫小說

cardboard cit·y /ˌ.. ˋ../ *n* [C] an area usually in a large town or city where people who have no home sleep outside using cardboard boxes to try to keep warm〔大城市內露宿者住的〕紙板區，板房區

cardboard cut-out /ˌ.. ˋ. ./ *n* [C] **1** a picture drawn on cardboard so that it can stand up on a surface〔畫在硬紙板上可豎立的〕圖樣[形] **2** a person or character in a book, film etc who seems silly or unreal〔作品或電影等中的〕虛構人物，胡亂編造的角色

card-car·ry·ing /ˋ. ˌ.../ *adj* **card-carrying member** someone who has paid money to an organization and is a keen member of it 正式成員: *a card-carrying member of the Labour Party* 工黨的一名正式黨員

card cat·a·log /ˋ. ˌ.../ *n* [C] *AmE* a box of cards that contain information about something and are arranged in order, for example in a library【美】〔圖書館等內的〕卡片目錄，卡片索引; CARD INDEX *BrE*【英】

card·hold·er /ˋkɑrdˌholdɚ; ˈkɑːdˌhəʊldə/ *n* [C] someone who has a CREDIT CARD〔信用卡的〕持卡人

car·di- /kɑrdɪ; kɑːdi/ *prefix* another form of the prefix CARDIO- 前綴 cardio- 的另一種形式

car·di·ac /ˋkɑrdɪˌæk; ˈkɑːdi-æk/ *adj* [only before noun

僅用於名詞前] *technical* connected with the heart【術語】心臟的; 心臟病的: **cardiac arrest/failure** (=when the heart stops working) 心搏停止/心力衰竭

car·di·gan /ˈkardɪgən; ˈkɑːdɪgən/ also 又作 **car·die** /ˈkardɪ; ˈkɑːdi/ *BrE informal*【英, 非正式】*n* [C] a knitted JACKET[1] (1) or SWEATER, fastened at the front with buttons〔胸前開扣的〕毛線衣,〔開襟〕羊毛衫

car·di·nal[1] /ˈkardṇəl; ˈkɑːdənəl/ *n* [C] **1** a priest of high rank in the Roman Catholic Church〔羅馬天主教會的〕紅衣主教, 樞機主教 **2** a North American bird of which the male is a bright red colour 紅衣鳳頭鳥, 北美紅雀〔雄鳥毛色亮紅〕**3** a CARDINAL NUMBER 基數

cardinal[2] *adj* [only before noun 僅用於名詞前] very important or basic 最重要的, 主要的; 基本的: *Having clean hands is one of the cardinal rules when preparing food.* 做飯前首先要把手洗乾淨。| **cardinal error** (=very serious and basic mistake) 重大的失誤

cardinal num·ber /,··· ˈ··/ *n* [C] a number such as 1, 2 or 3, that shows how many of something there are 基數〈如 1, 2, 3〉—compare 比較 ORDINAL NUMBER

cardinal point /,··· ˈ·/ *n* [C] *technical* one of the four main points (north, south, east, or west) on a COMPASS (1)【術語】〔羅盤上的〕基本方位〔指北、南、東、西〕

cardinal sin /,··· ˈ·/ *n* [C] **1** *informal* something bad or stupid that you must avoid doing【非正式】愚蠢的失誤: *the cardinal sin of ignoring public opinion* 無視公眾輿論的愚蠢失誤 **2** a serious SIN[1] (1) in the Christian religion〔基督教中的〕主罪

cardinal vir·tue /,··· ˈ··/ *n* [C] *formal* a moral quality that someone has which people greatly respect or value【正式】大德, 基本德性, 基本道德

card in·dex /ˈ·,··/ *n* [C] *BrE* a box of cards that contain information about something and are arranged in order, for example in a library【英】〔圖書館等的〕卡片目錄, 卡片索引; CARD CATALOG *AmE*【美】

cardio- /kardɪo; kɑːdiəʊ/ *prefix* also 又作 **cardi-** /kardɪ; kɑːdi/ *technical* concerning the heart【術語】(有關)心臟的: *a cardiograph* (=instrument that measures movements of the heart) 心電圖儀, 心動描記器

car·di·ol·o·gy /ˌkardɪˈalədʒɪ; ˌkɑːdiˈɒlədʒi/ *n* [U] the study or science of the heart 心臟病學

card phone /ˈ· ·/ *n* [C] a public telephone in which you must use a special plastic card rather than coins 卡式公用電話

card·sharp /ˈkardˌʃarp; ˈkɑːdʃɑːp/ also 又作 **card·sharp·er** /-ˌʃarpɚ; -ˌʃɑːpə/ *n* [C] someone who cheats when playing cards in order to make money 靠詐術玩紙牌贏錢的人, 以賭博騙錢的人

card ta·ble /ˈ· ,··/ *n* [C] a small light table that you can fold, used for playing cards 牌桌〔供玩牌用, 桌子可摺疊〕

card vote /ˈ· ·/ *n* [C] *BrE* a way of voting at a TRADE UNION meeting in which your vote represents the votes of all the members of your organization【英】憑卡投票法〔指工會大會上的一種投票方法, 每位代表所投的票的作用相當於他代表的所有人投的票〕

S1 W3 **care**[1] /kɛr; keə/ *v* [I,T]

1 ▶OBJECTS/EVENTS 物體/事件◀ to feel that something is important, so that you are interested in it, worried about it etc 關心; 在意; 擔心: **[+about]** *The only thing he seems to care about is money.* 他好像只在乎錢。| **care who/what/how etc** *Don't you care what happens to them?* 你難道不擔心他們出甚麼事嗎? | *I don't care whether we win or lose.* 我不在乎我們是贏還是輸。

2 ▶PEOPLE 人們◀ to mind about what happens to someone, because you like or love them 關心, 在乎: *I care about him, and hate to see him hurt like this.* 我關心他, 很不願意看見他傷成這個樣子。| *She felt that nobody cared.* 她覺得無人在乎。

3 who cares? *spoken* used to say that something does not worry or upset you because it is not important【口】有誰在乎呢?: *It's rather old and scruffy, but who cares?* 這東西又舊又破, 但又有誰在意呢?

4 couldn't care less *spoken* used to say rudely that you do not care at all about something【口】不在乎〔粗魯的說法〕: *I really couldn't care less what you think!* 你怎麼想的, 關我甚麼事!

5 what do I/you/they care? *spoken* used to say that someone does not care at all about something【口】我/你(們)/他們在乎甚麼呢?〔表示對某事毫不在乎〕: *What do I care? It's your responsibility now!* 這關我甚麼事呢? 現在是你的責任了!

6 as if I cared! *spoken* used to say that something is not important to you at all【口】我才不在乎呢!: *As if I cared whether he comes with us or not!* 他是否會跟我們一起來我才不在乎呢!

7 for all sb cares *spoken* used to say that something does not matter at all to someone【口】毫不在乎: *We could be starving for all they care!* 我們即使在挨餓, 他們也不在乎。

8 not care to *old-fashioned* not to like to do something【過時】不喜歡做某事: *She doesn't care to spend much time with her relatives.* 她不喜歡花太多時間跟親戚待在一起。

9 I wouldn't care to *spoken* used to say that you think that something would be an unpleasant experience【口】我不想, 我不願意: *I wouldn't care to meet him in a dark alley!* 我不想在黑暗的巷子裡和他見面!

10 would you care to? *spoken formal* used to ask someone politely whether they want to do something【口, 正式】要不要…? …怎麼樣?〔禮貌說法〕: *Would you care to join us for a drink?* 要不要跟我們一起喝一杯? —see also 另見 CARING

care for sb/sth *phr v* [T] **1** to look after someone who is not able to look after themselves 照顧, 照料: *She cared for her father all through his long illness.* 她在父親長期臥病期間一直照料着他。| *The children are being well cared for.* 孩子們得到了悉心的照料。**2** [usually in negatives and questions 一般用於否定句和疑問句] *formal* to like or want something or someone【正式】喜歡, 想要: *Would you care for a drink?* 要喝點甚麼嗎? | *I don't much care for his parents.* 我不太喜歡他的父母。

care[2] *n* S W

1 ▶LOOKING AFTER SB/STH 照料某人/某物◀ [U] the process of looking after someone or something, especially because they are weak, ill, old etc 照顧, 照料, 護理: *high standards of medical care* 高水準的醫療服務 | *They shared the care of the children.* 他們共同照顧孩子。| *advice on skin care* 皮膚護理的建議 —see also 另見 DAY CARE, INTENSIVE CARE

2 ▶CAREFULNESS 小心◀ [U] carefulness to avoid damage, mistakes etc 小心, 謹慎, 注意: *Fragile – handle with care.* 易碎, 小心輕放! —see also 另見 **tender loving care** (TENDER[1] (4))

3 take care to be careful 當心, 注意: *It's very icy, so take care on the roads.* 路上結冰了, 小心。| **take care (that)** *Take care that you don't drop it!* 當心別掉地上! | **take care to do sth** *Take care to keep the power cable away from the blade.* 注意把電線與刀片分開。| **take care with/over sth** *Paul always takes great care over his appearance.* 保羅一向很注意自己的外表。

4 take care of a) to look after someone or something 照看, 照料: *Who's taking care of the dog while you're away?* 你不在時誰來照看你的狗? **b)** to deal with all the work, arrangements etc that are necessary for something to happen 處理, 對付, 注意: *Her secretary always took care of the details.* 細節問題總是由她的祕書來處理。| *Don't worry about your accommodation – it's all taken care of.* 別擔心你的住宿問題, 一切都解決了。**c)** an expression meaning to pay for something; used when you want to avoid saying this directly〔婉轉說法〕承擔〔費用〕: *We'll take care of the fees.* 我們將會承擔費用。

5 take care! *spoken* used when saying goodbye to family or friends【口】保重! 珍重!: *Bye! Take care! See you on Sunday.* 再見, 請多保重! 週日再見。

6 in care *BrE* a child who is in care is being looked after in a local council home, not by their parents【英】〔地方當局對兒童進行〕收養, 監護: **take sb into care** *When he was sent to prison, the children were taken into care.* 他入獄時, 孩子們就由收養所照料。

7 ▶PROBLEM/WORRY 麻煩/憂慮◀ [C,U] *literary* something that causes problems and makes you anxious or sad【文】惱人之事, 煩惱; 憂慮: *At last I felt free from my cares.* 我終於擺脫了煩惱。| **not have a care in the world** (=not have any problems or worries) 無憂無慮 | **take the cares of the world on your shoulders** (=worry about other people's problems as well as your own) 憂國憂民

8 care of used when sending letters to someone at someone else's address; c/o 由…轉交〔寫在信封上, 略作 c/o〕

9 driving without due care and attention *BrE law* the crime of driving a car without being careful enough【英, 法律】不小心駕駛罪

10 have a care! *spoken old-fashioned* used to tell someone to be more careful【口, 過時】小心點! 仔細點!〔用於提醒〕

ca·reen /kəˋrin; kəˈriːn/ *v* [I always+adv/prep] *AmE* to move quickly forwards making sudden sideways movements; LURCH【美】〔車輛等〕歪歪斜斜地疾駛: **[+down/over/along]** *The car careened around the corner and skidded to a halt.* 那輛車左搖右晃地疾駛過街角, 打滑着停了下來。

2 2 **ca·reer¹** /kəˋrɪr; kəˈrɪə/ *n* [C] **1** a job or profession that you have been trained for and intend to do for several years 職業, 事業: *a career in banking* 從事銀行業 | *He realized that his acting career was over.* 他意識到自己的演藝事業已結束。| **career change** (=when you start a completely different job or profession) 改行 | **career structure** (=the opportunities that you have to move upwards in your job or profession) 職業結構〔發展或提升的種種機會〕—see 見 JOB (USAGE) **2 career soldier/teacher etc** someone who intends to be a soldier, teacher etc for most of their life, not just for a particular period of time 職業士兵/教師等 **3** the period of time in your life that you spend doing a particular activity 生涯; (一段)工作經歷, 履歷: *She had not had a very impressive school career up till then.* 在那以前, 她在學校裡的表現並不怎麼樣。| *My career as an English teacher didn't last long.* 我的英語教師生涯沒持續多久。

career² *v* [I always+adv/prep] to move forwards very fast and often without control〔常指失控地〕猛衝: **[+down/along/towards]** *The truck careered down the hill and into a tree.* 那輛卡車直衝下山, 一頭撞到一棵樹上。

career break /·ˈ· ˌ·/ *n* [C] a short period of time when you do not work in your usual job or profession, for example because you want to look after your children 職業中斷〔指在一段時間裡暫時不去工作, 例如為了照顧孩子〕

career coun·sel·or /·ˈ· ˌ···/ *n* [C] *AmE* a CAREERS OFFICER【美】就業顧問, 就業指導人員

ca·reer·ist /kəˋrɪrɪst; kəˈrɪərɪst/ *n* [C] *especially AmE* someone whose career is more important to them than anything else so that they will do whatever is necessary to be successful【尤美】名利心重的人, 一心想飛黃騰達的人; 野心家 —**careerist** *adj* —**careerism** *n* [U]

careers of·fic·er /·ˈ· ˌ···/ also 又作 **careers ad·vis·er** /·ˈ· ·ˌ··/ *n* [C] *BrE* someone whose job is to give people advice about what jobs and professional training might be suitable for them【英】就業顧問, 就業指導人員; CAREER COUNSELOR *AmE*【美】

career wom·an /·ˈ· ˌ··/ *n* [C] a woman whose career is very important to her, so that she may not want to get married or have children 事業型女性: *a fiercely independent career woman* 非常獨立的女強人

care·free /ˋkɛrˌfri; ˈkeəfriː/ *adj* having no worries or problems 無憂無慮的, 無牽掛的: *With the exams over, we felt happy and carefree at last.* 考試結束了, 我們感到非常高興, 一身輕鬆。| *Travel in carefree comfort to your hotel near Paris.* 輕鬆舒適地旅行到巴黎附近的旅館入住。

care·ful /ˋkɛrfəl; ˈkeəfəl/ *adj* **1 (be) careful!** *spoken* used to tell someone to think about what they are doing so that they do not have an accident【口】小心點! **2** trying to avoid damaging, harming, or losing something 謹慎的, 小心翼翼的: *a careful driver* 謹慎的司機 | **careful to do sth** *I was careful not to say anything about it to the boss.* 我很謹慎, 甚麼也沒告訴老板。| **[+with]** *Be careful with that vase – it's very fragile.* 小心那隻花瓶, 它很易碎。| **careful who/what/how etc** *Be careful how you handle those glasses.* 你搬動那些玻璃杯時要當心。| *I had taught them to be careful crossing the road.* 我教他們過馬路時要當心。| **[+about]** *Mara was extremely careful about what she ate.* 瑪拉在飲食方面極為謹慎。| **careful (that)** *We were very careful that he didn't find out.* 我們非常小心, 因此他並未發覺。**3** paying a lot of attention to detail, so that something is done correctly and thoroughly 細心的; 周密的: *After careful consideration, we've decided to accept their offer.* 我們經過周密的考慮之後, 決定接受他們的提議。| *a careful study of all aspects of the problem* 對問題全面周密的研究 **4 careful with money** not spending more money than you need to 花錢謹慎 **5 you can't be too careful** *spoken* used to say that you should do everything possible to avoid problems or danger【口】越小心越好 —**carefulness** *n* [U] 1 2

This graph shows how common different grammar patterns of the adjective **careful** are. 本圖表所示為形容詞careful構成的不同語法模式的使用頻率。

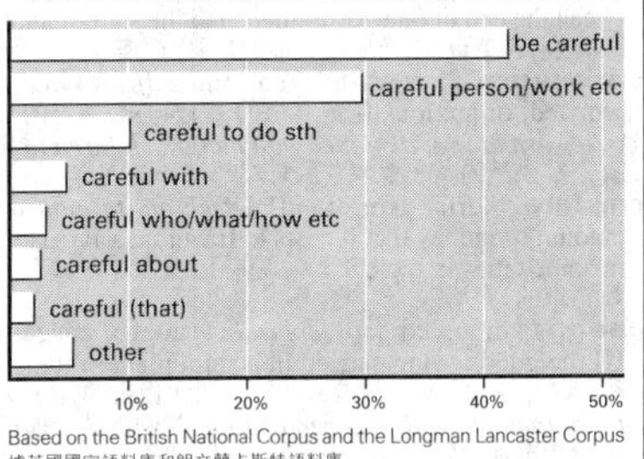

Based on the British National Corpus and the Longman Lancaster Corpus
據英國國家語料庫和朗文蘭卡斯特語料庫

care·ful·ly /ˋkɛrfəlɪ; ˈkeəfəli/ *adv* in a careful way 小心地; 仔細地: *I carried the bowl carefully in both hands.* 我雙手小心翼翼地捧着碗。| **carefully planned/chosen etc** *a carefully planned operation* 精心策劃的行動 2 2

care·giv·er /ˋkɛrˌgɪvɚ; ˈkeəˌgɪvə/ *n* [C] *AmE* someone who takes care of a child or sick person【美】〔小孩或病人的〕看護者, 護理員

care la·bel /ˈ· ˌ··/ *n* [C] a small piece of cloth in a piece of clothing that tells you how to wash it〔衣服上說明洗滌方法的〕洗滌標籤

care·less /ˋkɛrlɪs; ˈkeələs/ *adj* **1** not paying enough attention to what you are doing, so that you make mistakes, damage things etc 不小心的, 粗心的; 疏忽的: *I had been careless and left the window unlocked.* 我太粗心了, 忘記了關窗戶。| *a careless student* 粗心大意的學生 **2** done without much effort or attention to detail 草率的, 敷衍的: *This is a very careless piece of work – do it again!* 這工作幹得太馬虎了, 重做吧! | *a careless mistake* 疏忽造成的錯誤 **3** natural and not done with any deliberate effort or attention 漫不經心的, 自然的: *He ran a hand through his hair with a careless gesture.* 他漫不經心地用手理了理頭髮。| *careless charm* 天生[自然流露]的迷人風采 **4 careless of** *formal* deliberately ignoring something【正式】〔故意〕不在乎, 不理會: *She turned* *and, careless of the pain, headed blindly for the door.* 她轉過身, 忍住痛楚, 盲目地朝門口走去。**5** *rare* without problems or worries; CAREFREE【罕】無憂無慮的 —**carelessly** *adv* —**carelessness** *n* [U]

care pack·age /ˈ· ˌ··/ *n* [C] *AmE* a package of food, sweets etc that is sent to someone living away from home, especially a student at college【美】〔尤指從家裡寄給遠方在校生的〕愛心包裹

car·er /ˋkɛrɚ; ˈkeərə/ *n* [C] *BrE* someone who stays at home to look after a relative who is old, ill etc【英】〔在家照料年老、生病等的親人的〕照料者

ca·ress[1] /kəˋrɛs; kəˈres/ *v* [T] **1** to gently touch someone in a way that shows you love them 愛撫, 撫摸: *She lovingly caressed the baby's cheek.* 她親切地撫摸寶寶的臉頰。**2** *poetic* to touch something gently, in a way that seems pleasant or romantic【詩】輕撫, 輕拍: *Waves caressed the shore.* 波浪輕輕地拍打着海岸。

caress[2] *n* [C] a gentle loving touch or kiss 愛撫, 撫摸; 親吻

car·et /ˋkærət; ˈkærɨt/ *n* [C] *technical* the mark (ʎ) or (ʌ) used in writing and printing to show where something is to be added【術語】脱字號, 補字符號

care·tak·er /ˋkɛrˌtekɚ; ˈkeəˌteɪkə/ *n* [C] **1** *BrE* someone whose job is to look after a building, especially a school【英】〔尤指學校等建築物的〕管理員; JANITOR *AmE*【美】**2** someone who looks after a house or land while the person who owns it is not there〔主人不在時照料其房地產的〕看管人 **3** *AmE* someone who looks after other people, especially a teacher, parent, nurse etc【美】照看人, 保護人; 監護人〔尤指老師、父母、護士等〕

caretaker gov·ern·ment /ˈ··· ˌ···/ *n* [C] a government that has power only for a short period of time between the end of one government and the start of another〔舊政府已下台、新政府產生前的〕看守政府

care·worn /ˋkɛrˌwɔrn; ˈkeəwɔːn/ *adj* looking sad, worried, or anxious 飽經憂患的, 因操心而憔悴的: *the careworn face of a mother with hungry children to feed* 有一羣飢餓的孩子要餵養的母親那憔悴的面容

car·fare /ˋkɑrfɛr; ˈkɑːfeə/ *n* [U] *AmE old-fashioned* the amount of money that it costs to travel on a TROLLEY (3) in some cities in the US【美, 過時】〔美國一些城市內有軌電車的〕車費

car·go /ˋkɑrgo; ˈkɑːgəʊ/ *n plural* **cargoes** *or* **cargos** [C, U] the goods being carried in a ship, plane, TRUCK[1] (1) etc〔船、飛機、卡車等裝載的〕(一批) 貨物: *We sailed from Jamaica with a cargo of rum.* 我們滿載一船朗姆酒從牙買加啟航。| *a cargo vessel* 貨船

car·hop /ˋkɑrˌhɑp; ˈkɑːhɒp/ *n* [C] *AmE old-fashioned*【美, 過時】**1** someone who takes care of your car if you are staying a large hotel〔大酒店中為顧客服務的〕看車人 **2** someone who carries food to people's cars at a DRIVE-IN restaurant 路邊汽車餐廳的侍者

Car·ib·be·an /ˌkærəˋbiən; ˌkærɨˈbiːən◂/ *adj* from or connected with the islands in the Caribbean Sea 加勒比海 (諸島) 的 —**Caribbean** *adj*: *Caribbean literature* 加勒比海文學

car·i·bou /ˋkærəˌbu; ˈkærɨbuː/ *n* [C] a North American REINDEER 北美馴鹿

car·i·ca·ture[1] /ˋkærɪkətʃɚ; ˈkærɪkətʃʊə/ *n* **1** [C] a funny drawing of someone that makes some of their features look bigger or more amusing than they really are〔人物〕漫畫: *Newspapers often have caricatures of politicians.* 報紙上經常登載政客的漫畫。**2** [C] a description of someone that shows only some parts of their character, especially parts that are silly or amusing 諷刺畫[文]: *a caricature of a semi-educated village teacher* 對一個半文盲鄉村教師的諷刺描寫 **3** [U] the skill of making pictures, or writing about people in this way 漫畫手法

caricature[2] *v* [T] to draw or describe someone in a way that makes them seem silly or stupid 把…畫成漫畫, 用漫畫表現[諷刺]; 使滑稽化: *They are always being caricatured as hardworking bores.* 他們總是被漫畫畫成勤勞但卻令人厭煩的人。

car·i·ca·tur·ist /ˋkærɪkətʃərɪst; ˈkærɪkətʃʊərɨst/ *n* [C] someone who draws or writes caricatures 漫畫家

car·ies /ˋkɛriz; ˈkeəriz/ *n* [U] *technical* decay in someone's teeth【術語】齲齒: *dental caries* 蛀牙

car·ill·on /ˋkærəˌlɑn; ˈkærɨljən/ *n* [C] a set of bells in a tower that are controlled from a piano KEYBOARD[1] (1), or a tune played on these bells〔鐘樓上可用鍵盤彈奏的〕組鐘 (樂曲), 排鐘 (樂曲)

car·ing /ˋkɛrɪŋ; ˈkeərɪŋ/ *adj* **1** someone who is caring thinks about what other people need or would like, and tries to help them 關心照顧人的; 提供幫助的: *a warm and caring man* 熱心助人者 | *a very caring attitude* 非常樂於助人的態度 **2 be past caring** *informal* to not worry about something because you are very tired, upset, or worried about something else【非正式】無暇顧及,〔因沮喪、勞累等而〕無心考慮 **3 caring profession** a job that involves looking after other people 關心照顧人的職業: *Like most of the caring professions, nursing is very badly paid.* 和大多數照顧人的職業一樣, 護理的報酬很低。

car·jack·ing /ˋkɑrˌdʒækɪŋ; ˈkɑːˌdʒækɪŋ/ *n* [C,U] the crime of forcing the driver of a car to drive you somewhere or give you their car, by using threats and violence 劫車 —compare 比較 HIJACKING —**carjacker** *n* [C] —**carjack** *v* [T]

car·mine /ˋkɑrmɪn; ˈkɑːmɨn/ *n* [U] a deep purplish red colour 紫紅色, 洋紅色, 胭脂紅 —**carmine** *adj*

car·nage /ˋkɑrnɪdʒ; ˈkɑːnɪdʒ/ *n* [U] the killing and wounding of lots of people, especially in a war〔尤指戰爭中的〕大屠殺, 殘殺: *The battlefield was a scene of terrible carnage.* 戰場上是一片可怕的大屠殺景象。

car·nal /ˋkɑrnḷ; ˈkɑːnl/ *adj* a word meaning connected with the body or sex, used especially in religious language 肉體的, 性慾的, 肉慾的〔尤用於宗教語言〕: *carnal desires* 肉慾 —**carnally** *adv*

car·na·tion /kɑrˋneʃən; kɑːˈneɪʃən/ *n* [C] a white, pink, or red flower that smells sweet and is often worn as a decoration at formal ceremonies 康乃馨 (花)

car·ne /ˋkɑrnɪ; ˈkɑːni/ *n* [U] —see 見 CHILLI (1)

car·ne·li·an /kɑrˋniljən; kɑːˈniːliən/ *n* [C] another spelling of CORNELIAN cornelian 的另一種拼法

car·ney /ˋkɑrnɪ; ˈkɑːni/ *n* [C] *AmE*【美】another spelling of CARNY carny 的另一種拼法

car·ni·val /ˋkɑrnəvḷ; ˈkɑːnɨvəl/ *n* **1** [C,U] a celebration with dancing, drinking, and a PROCESSION (1) through the streets 狂歡 (節); 嘉年華會: *Carnival in Rio* 里約熱內盧的嘉年華會 | *the Notting Hill carnival* 諾丁山狂歡節 | *the carnival atmosphere after they won the game* 他們贏得比賽後的狂歡氣氛 **2** [C] *AmE* a noisy outdoor event at which you can ride on special machines and play games for prizes【美】遊樂場, 流動遊藝場〔喧鬧的戶外活動, 有機動遊戲、攤位遊戲等〕; FUNFAIR *BrE*【英】**3** [C] *AmE* an event held at a school in which students play games for prizes【美】〔學校的〕遊園會, 嘉年華會

car·ni·vore /ˋkɑrnəˌvor; ˈkɑːnɨvɔː/ *n* [C] **1** an animal that eats flesh 肉食動物 —compare 比較 HERBIVORE, OMNIVORE **2** *humorous* someone who eats meat【幽默】食葷的人 —compare 比較 VEGETARIAN —**carnivorous** *adj*

car·ny, carney /ˋkɑrnɪ; ˈkɑːni/ *n* [C] *AmE informal* someone who works in a CARNIVAL (2)【美, 非正式】流動遊藝場的工作[表演]人員

car·ob /ˋkærəb; ˈkærəb/ *n* [U] the fruit of a Mediterranean tree, that tastes similar to chocolate and is sometimes eaten instead of chocolate〔產於地中海地區的〕角豆樹果實〔其味道與巧克力相似〕

car·ol[1] /ˋkærəl; ˈkærəl/ also 又作 **Christmas carol** *n* [C] a traditional Christmas song (聖誕) 頌歌

carol[2] *v* **carolled, carolling** *BrE*【英】**caroled, caroling** *AmE*【美】[I] to sing carols or other songs in a lively way〔歡樂地〕唱聖誕頌歌〔或其他歌曲〕

ca·rot·id ar·te·ry /kəˋrɑtɪd ˏɑrtərɪ; kəˈrɒtɪ̣d ˌɑːtəri/ *n* [C] *technical* one of the two arteries (ARTERY (1)) in your neck, that supply blood to your head【術語】頸動脈

ca·rouse /kəˋraʊz; kəˈraʊz/ *v* [I] *literary* to drink a lot, be noisy, and laugh loudly【文】痛飲, 狂飲歡鬧—**carousal** *n* [C,U]

car·ou·sel, carrousel /ˏkæruˋzɛl; ˌkærəˈsel/ *n* [C] **1** *AmE* a machine with wooden horses on it that turns round and round, which people can ride on for fun; MERRY-GO-ROUND (1)【美】旋轉木馬 **2** the circular moving belt that you collect your bags and cases from at an airport〔機場的〕旋轉式行李傳送帶 **3** a circular piece of equipment that you put slides (SLIDE[2] (4)) into for showing on SLIDE PROJECTOR〔幻燈放映機上的〕幻燈片卡盤

carp[1] /kɑrp; kɑːp/ *v* [I usually in progressive 一般用於進行式] to complain about something or criticize someone continually 挑剔, 找岔, 吹毛求疵: *Stop carping!* 別挑剔了!

carp[2] *n plural* **carp** [C] a large fish that lives in lakes, pools, and rivers, which you can eat 鯉魚

car·pal tun·nel syn·drome /ˏkɑrpḷ ˋtʌnḷ ˏsɪndrom; ˌkɑːpəl ˈtʌnl ˌsɪndrəʊm/ *n* [U] *technical* a medical condition in which someone gets a lot of pain and weakness in their wrist【術語】腕管綜合症

car park /ˋ· ·/ *n* [C] *BrE*【英】**1** an open area where cars can park 露天停車場; PARKING LOT *AmE*【美】**2** an enclosed building for cars to park in 公共停車房, 多層停車場; PARKING GARAGE *AmE*【美】

car·pen·ter /ˋkɑrpəntɚ; ˈkɑːpɪ̣ntə/ *n* [C] someone whose job is making and repairing wooden objects 木匠, 木工

car·pen·try /ˋkɑrpəntrɪ; ˈkɑːpɪ̣ntri/ *n* [U] the skill or work of a carpenter 木工手藝; 木匠業

3 3 **car·pet[1]** /ˋkɑrpɪt; ˈkɑːpɪ̣t/ *n* **1** [C,U] heavy woven material for covering floors or stairs, or a piece of this material 地毯: *a beautiful Persian carpet* 一張美麗的波斯地毯 | **fitted carpet** (=one that is cut to fit the shape of a room) 固定的地毯 —compare 比較 RUG (1) **2 carpet of leaves/flowers etc** *literary* a thick layer of leaves etc【文】滿地的樹葉/花等 —see also 另見 MAGIC CARPET, **sweep sth under the carpet** (SWEEP[1] (13))

carpet[2] *v* [T] **1** [usually in passive 一般用被動態] to cover a floor with carpet 在…上鋪地毯: *a carpeted corridor* 鋪有地毯的走廊 **2** *informal especially BrE* to blame someone for something they have done; REPRIMAND【非正式, 尤英】斥責, 責備, 責罵 **3 carpeted with grass/flowers etc** *literary* covered with a thick layer of grass etc【文】覆蓋着一層厚厚的草/花等

car·pet·bag /ˋkɑrpɪtˏbæg; ˈkɑːpɪtbæg/ *n* [C] a bag used for travelling, usually made of carpet 毛毯製的旅行袋

car·pet·bag·ger /ˋkɑrpɪtˏbægɚ; ˈkɑːpɪ̣tˌbægə/ *n* [C] someone who tries to become active in the political life of another area for their own advantage, especially someone from the North of the US active in the South in the 1860s and 1870s 提包客, 外來政客〔尤指 19 世紀 60 至 70 年代間, 在美國南方政壇上活躍的北方人〕

carpet bomb /ˋ·· ˏ·/ *v* [T] to drop a lot of bombs over a small area to destroy everything in it 對…進行地毯式轟炸

car·pet·ing /ˋkɑrpɪtɪŋ; ˈkɑːpɪ̣tɪŋ/ *n* [U] heavy woven material for making CARPETs 做地毯的料子

carpet slip·per /ˋ·· ˏ··/ *n* [C] a type of soft shoe that you wear indoors〔室內穿的〕地毯拖鞋

carpet sweep·er /ˋ·· ˏ··/ *n* [C] a simple machine for sweeping CARPETs 地毯清掃器

car pool[1] /ˋ· ·/ *n* [C] **1** a group of car owners who agree to drive everyone in the group to work, school etc on different days so that only one car is used at a time 合夥用車者〔指一羣有汽車的人達成協議, 輪流用自己的車送大家上班、上學等〕**2** a group of cars owned by a company or other organization that its members can use; MOTOR POOL〔公司等擁有的供其工作人員使用的〕公車隊

car pool[2] *v* [I] *AmE* if a group of people car pool, they agree to drive everyone in the group to work, school etc on different days so that only one car is used at a time【美】合夥用車

car·port /ˋkɑrˏpɔrt; ˈkɑːpɔːt/ *n* [C] a shelter for a car that has a roof and one or two walls, often built against the side of a house〔靠牆搭建的〕敞棚式汽車間, 停車棚 —compare 比較 GARAGE[1] (1)

car·rel /ˋkærəl; ˈkærəl/ *n* [C] a small enclosed space with a desk and a light for one person to use in a library〔圖書館內供一個讀者使用的帶枱燈和書桌的〕小單間

car·riage /ˋkærɪdʒ; ˈkærɪdʒ/ *n* **1** [C] a vehicle with wheels that is pulled by a horse, used in former times〔舊時的〕馬車 **2** [C] *BrE* one of the connected parts of a train that passengers sit in【英】〔鐵路〕客車車廂; CAR (3) *AmE*【美】**3** [U] *formal* the way someone walks and moves their head and body【正式】儀態, 姿態, 舉止 **4** something with wheels that is used to move a heavy object, especially a gun 車架; (有輪) 砲架 **5** [U] *formal especially BrE* the act of moving goods from one place to another or the cost of moving them【正式, 尤英】運輸, 搬運; (貨) 運費 **6** [C] the movable part of a machine that supports another part〔機器的〕滑架; 溜板; 拖板: *the carriage of a typewriter* 打字機的滑架 —see also 另見 BABY CARRIAGE 3

C

carriage clock /ˋ·· ·/ *n* [C] a small clock inside a glass case with a handle on top 旅行鐘, 便攜式時鐘

car·riage·way /ˋkærɪdʒˏwe; ˈkærɪdʒweɪ/ *n* [C] *BrE* the part of a road that a single line of traffic moves along【英】馬路; 行車道 —see also 另見 DUAL CARRIAGEWAY

car·ri·er /ˋkærɪɚ; ˈkæriə/ *n* [C] **1** a company that moves goods or passengers from one place to another 運輸公司 **2** a military vehicle or ship used to move soldiers, weapons etc〔運送武器、士兵等的〕軍車; 運輸艦 —see also 另見 AIRCRAFT CARRIER **3** *technical* someone who passes a disease to other people without having it themselves【術語】帶菌者, 病媒〔指傳播疾病而自身卻不受其害者〕**4** a metal frame that is fixed to a bicycle or other vehicle and holds bags etc〔固定在腳踏車等上的金屬〕攜物架 **5** a carrier bag 手提購物袋

carrier bag /ˋ··· ˏ·/ *n* [C] *BrE* a bag that you are given in a shop, to carry the things you have bought【英】手提購物袋 —see picture at 參見 BAG[1] 圖

carrier pi·geon /ˋ··· ˏ··/ *n* [C] a PIGEON (=type of bird) that has been trained to carry messages 信鴿

car·ri·on /ˋkærɪən; ˈkæriən/ *n* [U] dead flesh that is decaying 腐屍; 腐肉: *Some birds feed on carrion.* 有些鳥類以動物的腐屍為食物。

car·rot /ˋkærət; ˈkærət/ *n* **1** [C,U] a plant with a long thick orange pointed root that you eat as a vegetable 胡蘿蔔, 紅蘿蔔 —see picture on page A9 參見 A9 頁圖 **2** [C] *informal* something that is promised to someone in order to try and persuade them to work harder【非正式】〔為使某人做某事而給予的〕報酬, 好處, 獎品; 許諾: **carrot and stick approach/method etc** (=a way of persuading someone to do something using a mixture of promises and threats) 胡蘿蔔加大棒[威逼利誘]的方法

car·rot·y /ˋkærətɪ; ˈkærəti/ *adj* hair that is carroty is orange〔頭髮〕胡蘿蔔色的, 橘紅色的

car·rou·sel /ˏkæruˋzɛl; ˌkærəˈsel/ *n* [C] another spelling of CAROUSEL carousel 的另一種拼法

car·ry[1] /ˋkærɪ; ˈkæri/ *v* **carried, carrying** 

1 ►LIFT AND TAKE 提拿◄ [T] to take something somewhere in your hands or arms, on your back etc 提; 拿; 抱; 帶; 扛; 揹; 搬: *A porter helped me carry my luggage.* 一位搬運工人幫我搬行李。| *Let me carry that for you.* 讓我幫你拿吧。| **carry sth around/out/to etc** *I'm not carrying it around all day!* 我才不會整天到處帶着它呢! —see 見 BRING (USAGE)

2 ►VEHICLE/SHIP/PLANE 車/船/飛機◄ [T] to take people or things from one place to another 運送: **carry sth to/down/away etc** *The ship was carrying oil from Kuwait to Japan.* 這艘船把石油從科威特運到日本。| **carry sb/sth** *a coach carrying 44 American tourists* 載

有44個美國遊客的長途客車

3 ▶HOW STH IS MOVED 輸送方式◀ [T] if a pipe, river, wire etc carries something such as liquid or electricity, the liquid etc flows along it 輸送, 傳送: **carry sth along/through/across etc** *Pipes carry the water across the desert.* 輸水管穿過沙漠把水輸送出去。| *Soil from the river banks is carried down towards the sea.* 河水把河兩岸的泥土沖向海裡。| **carry sth** *Two lines are dedicated to carrying teletext data.* 有兩條線路專門用來傳送電視文字數據。| **be carried out to sea/downstream etc** (=be taken somewhere by a current of water) 被沖到大海/下游等

4 ▶DISEASE 疾病◀ [T] if a person, animal, or insect carries a disease the disease is spread by them 傳播〔疾病〕: *Brown rats carried the plague.* 褐色的老鼠傳播這種瘟疫。| *Many serious diseases are carried by insects.* 許多嚴重的疾病都是由昆蟲傳播的。

5 carry sth in your head/mind to remember information that you need, without writing it down 將某事記在腦海中: *He was required to carry a detailed map of the airport in his head.* 他被要求把那個機場的詳細地圖記在腦子裡。

6 ▶HAVE WITH YOU 隨身帶着◀ [T] to take money, a weapon, or something that you need, with you in your pocket, on your belt, in your bag etc 攜帶; 佩戴: *I don't usually carry that much cash on me.* 我身上通常不帶那麼多現金。| **carry a gun/knife etc** *The police here don't carry guns.* 這裡的警察不帶槍。| **carry arms** (=carry weapons) 攜帶武器 *a society where men carried arms as a matter of course* 一個把攜帶武器視為理所當然的社會

7 ▶SHOP 商店◀ [T] if a shop carries goods, it has a supply of them for sale 備有〔貨物〕供銷售: **carry a range/selection** *Selfridges carries a good range of sports equipment.* 塞爾弗里奇商店備有多種運動器材供選購。| *I'm afraid we don't carry that line any more.* 恐怕我們不會再進那種貨了。

8 be carrying too much weight/extra pounds etc to weigh too much 超重; 超載, 多載: *He's carrying at least ten kilos too many around.* 他帶的東西至少超重了十公斤。

9 ▶BUILDING 建築物◀ [T] if a pillar, wall etc carries something, it supports the weight of that thing 支撐, 支持: *These two columns carry the whole roof.* 這兩根柱子支撐着整個屋頂。

10 be/get carried away to be so excited, angry, interested etc that you are no longer really in control of what you do or say, or you forget everything else 忘乎所以, 忘形: *Sorry I shouted – I get a little carried away at times!* 對不起, 我不應該吼叫, 我有時有點控制不住。| *We got carried away by the beauty of the music.* 美妙的音樂讓我們忘乎所以。

11 carry yourself well/stiffly etc to stand and move in a particular way 舉止優雅/僵硬等: *He carried himself upright, like the old soldier he was.* 他站得筆直, 彷彿是一個老兵。

12 ▶CHILD 孩子◀ [T] *old-fashioned* if a woman is carrying a child, she is PREGNANT (=going to have a baby) 【過時】懷孕

13 ▶NEWSPAPER/BROADCAST 報紙/廣播◀ [T] if a newspaper or a television or radio broadcast carries a piece of news, an advertisement etc, it prints it or broadcasts it 登載; 廣播; 報道: *The trade press carried details of the new laws.* 貿易新聞報道了新法例的詳細內容。

14 ▶LABEL/WRITING 標籤/書寫◀ [T] if an object, container etc carries a warning, information etc it is written on it 印有, 寫有: *These new perfumes carry an 'exclusive' tag.* 這些新的香水印有"專營"標籤。| *a card carrying details of your blood group* 一張寫有你血型詳情的卡片

15 carry insurance/a guarantee etc to have insurance etc 具有保險/保用期等: *All our products carry a 12 month guarantee.* 我們所有的產品均有一年的保用期。

16 ▶HAVE A QUALITY 具有某種特質◀ [T] to have a particular quality such as authority or confidence that makes you believe or not believe someone 具有〔某種特質如權威性、信心等〕: *Her manner carried an unmistakable air of authority.* 她的舉止具有毋庸置疑的權威性。| **carry conviction** (=to seem very sure about something) 〔對某事〕非常確信 *Matthew's voice did not carry much conviction.* 馬修的聲音聽起來並不太堅定。| **carry weight** (=to have some influence over someone) 有影響力 *Her views carry a lot of weight with the committee.* 她的觀點對委員會有很大的影響力。

17 ▶CRIME 犯罪◀ [T] if a crime carries a particular punishment, that is the usual punishment for the crime 被判處〔某種懲罰〕: *Rape carries the death penalty here.* 強姦在這裡要判處死刑。| *a serious crime which carries a long jail sentence* 會被判處長期徒刑的嚴重罪行

18 carry a (heavy) load/burden to have a lot of work to do or a lot of responsibility for something 承擔〔大量〕工作/重任: *Each team member is expected to carry a fair share of the workload.* 每個組員都應平分工作量。

19 ▶USELESS PERSON 無用者◀ [T] if you carry someone who is not doing as much as they should, you manage without the work they should be doing, or the money they should be earning 扶助, 資助, 援助; 供養: *The team simply can't afford to carry anyone.* 隊裡根本供養不起任何閒人。

20 carry sth too far/to extremes/to excess to do or say too much about something 把某事做[說]得太過分: *Don't you think you're carrying discipline a bit too far? They're only children!* 你不覺得你的懲罰有點太過分了嗎? 他們不過是孩子!

21 carry sb to victory/to the top etc to be the reason that a person or group is successful 使某人獲勝/成功: *It's that extra enthusiasm that will carry you to the top.* 那份額外的熱情會使你成功的。

22 ▶PERSUADE 說服◀ [T] if someone carries a group of people, they persuade those people to support them 贏得…的支持: *Her tearful pleas carried the meeting.* 她聲淚俱下的請求贏得了與會者的同情。

23 carry the day to persuade a group of people to support you 獲得…的支持[贊同]: *His appeal to common sense was what finally carried the day.* 他藉着情理最終贏得了大家的支持。

24 as fast as his/her legs could carry him/her as fast as possible 飛快, 盡快: *She ran to her mother as fast as her legs could carry her.* 她飛快地跑向母親。

25 carry all/everything before you *literary* to be completely successful in a struggle against other people【文】獲得極大成功, 大獲全勝

26 ▶VOTE 投票◀ **be carried** if a suggestion, proposal etc is carried, most of the people at an official meeting vote for it and it is accepted〔建議、提議等〕獲得通過: *The amendment to the bill was carried unanimously.* (=everyone agreed to it) 修正法案獲得一致通過。| **be carried by 20 votes/50 votes etc** (=20, 50 etc more people voted for something than voted against it) 以20票/50票等的優勢獲得通過 *The motion to ban the sale of guns was carried by 76 votes.* 禁止出售槍支的動議以76票的優勢獲得通過。| **declare sth carried** (=to state officially that something has been accepted) 宣布某事獲通過 *I declare the resolution carried.* 我宣布該項決議獲得通過。

27 ▶SOUND/SMELL 聲音/氣味◀ [I] if a sound or smell carries to a particular place, it goes as far as that place 傳到: *The sounds of laughter carried as far as the lake.* 笑聲一直傳到湖邊。

28 carry one/two/three etc to put a number into the next row to the left when you are adding numbers together〔做加法時將數字〕進一位/二位/三位等: *Nine and three make twelve, put down two and carry one.* 9加3等於12, 先寫下2, 然後進1。

29 ▶BALL 球類◀ [I] if the ball carries a particular distance in GOLF, CRICKET (2) etc, that is how far it travels when it is hit〔高爾夫球、板球等〕能打出（...的距離）
30 carry a torch for sb to be in love with someone who does not love you 對某人鍾情[單相思]
31 carry the can (for sb/sth) *BrE informal* to be blamed or punished for something that is someone else's fault as well as your own【英, 非正式】(為某人/某事) 獨自承擔責任[揹黑鍋]: *Why am I always left to carry the can?* 為甚麼總讓我揹黑鍋?
32 carry a tune to sing correctly 唱準音調 —see also 另見 CARDCARRYING, CARRIER, CASH AND CARRY, **fetch and carry** (FETCH (4))

carry sth ↔ **forward** *phr v* [T] **1** to move a total to the next page for adding to other numbers 將〔賬目〕轉入次頁 **2** to make an amount of something such as money or holiday time available for use at a later time 把〔金錢或假期〕結轉, 結存〔留待日後使用〕

carry sb/sth ↔ **off** *phr v* [T] **1** to do something difficult successfully 成功地完成〔困難的任務、職責等〕: *It's a demanding role, but I'm sure she'll be able to carry it off.* 這是一個富有挑戰性的角色, 但我深信她能勝任。**2** to win a prize 贏得, 獲得〔獎品、榮譽等〕: *Jackie carried off most of the awards that evening.* 傑基那天晚上贏得了大部分的獎項。

carry on *phr v* **1** [I,T **carry on** sth] *especially BrE* to continue doing something【尤英】繼續做; 堅持: *Don't stop – carry on, everyone!* 大家別停下來, 繼續幹! | **carry on doing sth** *We all carried on singing as if nothing odd was happening.* 我們繼續歌唱, 就像甚麼怪事也沒發生過一樣。| **carry on with sth** *Please carry on with your work.* 請繼續幹你們的工作吧。| **carry on as normal/as usual/as you are/regardless** *I think we should just carry on as we are for now.* 我想現在我們應該照常進行下去。**2** [I] to continue moving 繼續走; 繼續行進: *We carried on down the freeway for a while.* 我們沿着高速公路繼續行進了一會兒。| *Carry straight on until you get to the traffic lights.* 一直走到紅綠燈那裡為止。**3** [T **carry on** sth] to continue something that has been started by someone else 繼續〔某人未完成的事業、工作等〕; 繼承: *He is relying on his son to carry on the family business.* 他指望兒子繼承家業。| *When she left I carried on her research.* 她離開後, 我便繼續進行她那項研究。**4** [T **carry on** sth] to do something for a period of time 繼續開展[進行]下去: *Negotiations were being carried on, in spite of the fighting.* 儘管還有戰鬥, 但談判仍然繼續進行。| **carry on a conversation** *They carried on a curious conversation, never looking at each other.* 他們進行了一次奇特的談話, 雙方從不看對方一眼。**5** [I] *spoken* to behave in a silly, excited, or anxious way【口】大吵大鬧: *Stop carrying on, you two!* 你們倆別吵了! | *Anyone would think they owned the business, the way they carry on!* 看他們大吵大鬧的樣子, 誰都會認為他們是老闆! **6** [I] *old-fashioned* to have a sexual relationship with someone, when you should not【過時】與...有不正當性關係: *She's been carrying on with the milkman, I'm certain of it.* 我肯定她跟那個送牛奶的有曖昧關係。

carry sth ↔ **out** *phr v* [T] **1** to do something that needs to be organized and planned 實行, 進行; 執行: *They are carrying out urgent repairs.* 他們正在進行搶修。| *A survey is now being carried out nationwide.* 正在進行一次全國性的調查。| *It won't be an easy plan to carry out.* 那並不是一項容易實行的計劃。**2 carry out a promise/a threat/an intention/an order etc** to do something that you have said you will do or that someone has asked you to do 履行承諾/實行威脅/實現目的/執行命令等: *We carried out her instructions to the letter.* 我們不折不扣地執行了她的指示。

carry sth ↔ **over** *phr v* [T] **1** if something is carried over into a new set of conditions, it continues to exist when conditions change〔情況變化時〕繼續下去: *aspects of the dream which are carried over into wakefulness* 清醒時仍然殘存的夢境 **2** to carry something forward 往後延; 積存: *Holiday time can be carried over into next year.* 假期可以積存至明年。

carry through *phr v* [T] **1** [**carry** sth **through**] to complete or finish something successfully, in spite of difficulties 實現, 完成: *I'm determined to carry this through.* 我決意完成此事。**2 carry sb through (sth)** to help someone to manage during an illness or a difficult period 幫助〔某人〕度過〔患病、困難等時期〕; 使度過難關: *Her confidence carried her through.* 信心使她度過了難關。

carry[2] *n* [C,U] *technical* the distance a ball or bullet travels after it has been thrown, hit or fired【術語】〔球〕被拋擲的距離;〔槍的〕射程

car·ry·all /ˈkærɪˌɔl; ˈkæri-ɔːl/ *n* [C] *AmE* a large soft bag or case【美】大手提包, 裝雜物的大袋子; HOLDALL *BrE*【英】—see picture at 參見 BAG[1] 圖

car·ry·cot /ˈkærɪˌkɑt; ˈkærikɒt/ *n* [C] *BrE* a small bed used for carrying a baby【英】手提式嬰兒牀; PORTACRIB *AmE*【美】—see picture at 參見 BED[1] 圖

carrying charge /ˈ··· ˌ·/ *n* [C] *AmE* a charge added to the price of something you have bought by INSTALLMENT PLAN (=paying over several months)【美】〔分期付款購物的〕附加費用

carry-on[1] /ˈ·· ·/ *n* [singular] *BrE spoken* behaviour or a situation that is silly or annoying【英口】愚蠢[令人惱火]的行為[局面]: *What a carry-on!* 真不像話! —see also 另見 **carry on** (CARRY[1])

carry-on[2] *adj* [only before noun 僅用於名詞前] carry-on cases or bags are ones that passengers take onto a plane with them〔行李箱、手提包等〕可隨身帶着登機的

carry-out /ˈ·· ·/ *n* [C] *AmE, ScotE* food that you can take away from a restaurant to eat somewhere else, or a restaurant that sells food like this【美, 蘇格蘭】外賣食品; 外賣餐館; TAKEAWAY *BrE*【英】

carry-o·ver /ˈ·· ˌ··/ *n* [singular] **1** something that affects an existing situation but is the result of a past one 遺留物; 殘存物; 剩貨: **[+from]** *Grandma is still frugal, a carry-over from the war years.* 外婆仍然保持着戰爭年代留下來的儉樸作風。**2** an amount of money that has not been used and is available to use later 結轉金額: **[+of]** *a carry-over of funds to next year's budget* 結轉到下年預算中的資金 —see also 另見 **carry over** (CARRY[1])

car·sick /ˈkɑrˌsɪk; ˈkɑːˌsɪk/ *adj* feeling sick because you are travelling in a car 暈車的 —**carsickness** *n* [U]

cart[1] /kɑrt; kɑːt/ *n* [C] **1** a vehicle with two or four wheels that is pulled by a horse and used for carrying heavy things〔兩輪或四輪的〕馬車 —see also 另見 HANDCART **2** *AmE* a large wire basket on wheels that you use in a SUPERMARKET【美】〔超級市場中的〕手推車; TROLLEY (1) *BrE*【英】**3** *AmE* a small table with wheels, used to move and serve food and drinks【美】〔送食物和飲品的〕手推餐車; TROLLEY (2) *BrE*【英】**4 put the cart before the horse** to do things in the wrong order 本末倒置; 前後顛倒 —see also 另見 **upset the apple cart** (UPSET[1] (5))

cart[2] *v* [T always+adv/prep] **1** *informal* to carry something that is awkward or heavy【非正式】搬運〔笨重物品等〕: *I was really tired after carting all that furniture upstairs.* 我把那些家具搬到樓上後, 真的筋疲力盡了。**2** to carry something in a cart 用車裝運: **[+away]** *The corn sacks were carted away.* 裝有穀物的袋子被車子運走了。

cart sb **off** *phr v* [T] *informal* to take someone away, especially to prison【非正式】帶走, 抓走〔尤指進監獄〕: *The police carted him off this morning.* 今天早上警察把他抓走了。

car tax /ˈ· ·/ *n* [C,U] ROAD TAX 公路稅, 通行稅

carte blanche /ˈkɑrt ˋblɑnʃ; ˌkɑːt ˈblɑːnʃ/ *n* [U] complete freedom to do whatever you like in a particular situation, especially to spend money〔尤指開支方面的〕全權, 自由處理權: **give sb carte blanche** *We were given carte blanche to redecorate the hotel.* 我們獲授予全權重新裝修酒店。

C

car·tel /ˋkartl; kɑːˈtel/ *n* [C] a group of companies who agree to fix prices to limit competition so that they can increase their profits 卡特爾, 同業聯盟〔多家公司為限制競爭和增加利潤而結成的固定價格聯盟〕: *an illegal international oil cartel* 非法的國際石油同業聯盟

cart·er /ˋkartɚ; ˈkɑːtə/ *n* [C] *old use* someone whose job is to drive a CART[1] (1)【舊】馬車夫, 趕車人

cart·horse /ˋkarthɔrs; ˈkɑːthɔːs/ *n* [C] a large strong horse, often used for pulling heavy loads〔常用於拉重物的〕大馬, 役馬

car·ti·lage /ˋkartḷɪdʒ; ˈkɑːtəlɪdʒ/ *n* [C,U] a strong stretchy substance, or piece of this, that is around the joints in a person or animal's body 軟骨 (組織)

cart·load /ˋkart͵lod; ˈkɑːtləʊd/ *n* [C] the amount that a CART can hold 一貨車的裝載量: **[+of]** *cartloads of hay* 數車乾草

car·tog·ra·phy /karˋtagrəfɪ; kɑːˈtɒgrəfi/ *n* [U] the skill or practice of making maps 地圖製作法; 製圖學 —**cartographer** *n* [C]

car·ton /ˋkartn; ˈkɑːtn/ *n* [C] **1** a box made of CARDBOARD (=stiff paper) or plastic that contains food or drink 硬紙盒, 厚紙箱; 塑料盒: *a carton of fruit juice* 一盒果汁 | *a milk carton* 牛奶盒 —see picture at 參見 CONTAINER 圖 **2** *AmE* a large container with smaller containers of goods inside it【美】〔可內置小容器的〕盒箱,〔裝了一定量商品的〕容器: *a carton of cigarettes* 一條香煙

3 **car·toon** /karˋtun; kɑːˈtuːn/ *n* [C] **1** a funny drawing in a newspaper, often including humorous remarks about news events (諷刺) 漫畫, 幽默畫 —compare 比較 COMIC STRIP **2** a short film that is made by photographing a series of drawings 卡通 (片), 動畫片 **3** a drawing that is used as a model for a painting or other work of art 草圖, 底圖

car trans·port·er /ˈ·· ͵··/ *n* [C] a large vehicle on the road or railway, that carries several new cars to a place where they will be sold〔將新車運往銷售地的〕車輛運輸車[火車]

car·tridge /ˋkartrɪdʒ; ˈkɑːtrɪdʒ/ *n* [C] **1** a metal, CARDBOARD, or plastic tube containing explosive and a bullet that you use in a gun 彈藥筒, 彈殼; 子彈 **2** the small part of a RECORD PLAYER containing the STYLUS (=needle) that takes sound signals from the record〔電唱機上裝唱針的〕唱頭, 針匣 **3** a container with ink, film, or MAGNETIC TAPE in it, that you put into a pen, camera, or TAPE RECORDER〔鋼筆的〕墨水囊, 筆芯;〔裝膠卷的〕暗盒;〔裝卡式錄音磁帶的〕盒子

cartridge pa·per /ˈ·· ͵··/ *n* [U] *BrE* thick strong paper used for drawing on【英】〔繪畫用的〕厚白紙, 圖畫紙

cart·track /ˈ· ·/ *n* [C] a narrow road with a rough surface, usually on a farm〔常指農場上路面不平的〕小路, 小徑

cart·wheel /ˋkart͵hwil; ˈkɑːt-wiːl/ *n* [C] a movement in which you turn right over by throwing your body sideways onto your hands while bringing your legs over your head 側手翻, 側身筋斗 —**cartwheel** *v* [I]

carve /karv; kɑːv/ *v* **1** [I,T] to cut a large piece of cooked meat into smaller pieces using a big knife 把〔熟肉〕切成小塊;〔從熟肉上〕割下薄片: *Carve the lamb into slices and arrange in a hot serving dish.* 把羊肉切成片後擺放在一個熱的盤子裡。—see picture on page A11 參見 A11 頁圖 **2** [T] to cut shapes out of solid wood or stone 雕, 刻; 把〔木、石等〕雕成〔某物〕: *Michelangelo carved this figure from a single block of marble.* 米開朗基羅用一塊大理石雕刻出這個人像。**3** [T] to cut a pattern or letter on the surface of something 刻〔圖形或字母〕: **carve sth on/in etc** *Someone had carved their initials on the tree.* 有人將自己姓名的起首字母刻在樹上。

carve sth ↔ **out** *phr v* [T] **carve out a career/niche/reputation etc** to become successful and be respected 開創出事業/謀得合適的職位/贏得名聲: *She's carved out a very successful career as a photographer.* 她成為了一個非常成功的攝影師。

carve sb/sth ↔ **up** *phr v* [T] **1** if two or more people, governments etc carve something up, they divide it into separate parts and share it between them even though this is wrong 瓜分, 分割: *They ruthlessly carved up Poland.* 他們無情地瓜分了波蘭。—see also 另見 CARVE-UP **2** *BrE informal* to drive past another car going in the same direction and then turn in front of it too quickly【英, 非正式】快速超車, 快速切入別人的行車線

carv·er /ˋkarvɚ; ˈkɑːvə/ *n* [C] **1** someone who carves 雕刻師, 雕工; 切肉人 **2** a big knife used for cutting meat; CARVING KNIFE 切肉刀

car·ver·y /ˋkarvərɪ; ˈkɑːvəri/ *n* [C] *BrE* a restaurant that serves ROAST[3] meat【英】烤肉餐廳

carve-up /ˈ· ·/ *n* [singular] an arrangement between two or more people, governments etc by which they divide something among themselves even though this is wrong 瓜分, 分割

carv·ing /ˋkarvɪŋ; ˈkɑːvɪŋ/ *n* **1** [C] an object or pattern made by cutting a shape in wood or stone for decoration 雕刻物[品]; 雕刻圖案 **2** [U] the activity or skill of carving 雕刻工作; 雕刻藝術; 雕刻技巧

carving fork /ˈ·· ·/ *n* [C] a large fork used to hold cooked meat firmly while you are cutting it〔切肉時用來按住肉塊的〕大餐叉, 切肉叉

carving knife /ˈ·· ·/ *n* [C] a large knife used for cutting cooked meat (大的) 切肉刀 —see picture at 參見 KNIFE[1] 圖

car wash /ˈ· ·/ *n* [C] a place where there is special equipment for washing cars 洗車處, 洗車場

car·y·at·id /͵kærɪˋætɪd; ͵kæriˈætəd/ *n* [C] *technical* a PILLAR (1) in the shape of a female figure【術語】女像柱〔雕成女性形狀的建築物支柱〕

Cas·a·no·va /͵kæsəˋnovə; kæsəˈnəʊvə/ *n* [C] a man who has had, or says he has had, a lot of lovers (聲稱) 擁有許多情婦的男子, 大情人: *a man with a reputation as a womaniser, a Casanova* 有風流浪子名聲的玩弄女性者

cas·bah /ˋkæzba; ˈkæzbɑː/ *n* [C] an ancient Arab city or the market in it 阿拉伯古城, 卡斯巴; 阿拉伯古城中的市場

cas·cade[1] /kæsˋked; kæˈskeɪd/ *n* [C] **1** a small steep WATERFALL that is one of several together 小瀑布〔大瀑布的分支〕**2** something that hangs down in large quantities 瀑布狀物: **[+of]** *Her hair fell over her shoulders in a cascade of curls.* 她的鬈髮瀑布般垂落在肩頭。

cascade[2] *v* [I always+adv/prep] to flow, fall or hang down in large quantities 瀑布似地落下; 大量傾瀉: *Geraniums cascaded over the balcony.* 天竺葵從陽台上垂了下來。| *a cascading stream* 傾瀉而下的河流

case[1] /kes; keɪs/ *n*

1 ►EXAMPLE 例證◄ [C] an example of a particular situation, problem etc 事例, 實例: *In some cases, it is necessary to operate.* 在某些情況下, 動手術是必要的。| **[+of]** *an extreme case of anorexia* 一個厭食的極端例子 | **case in point** (=a clear example of a situation, problem etc that you are discussing or explaining) 明顯的例子 *This latest policy is a case in point.* 這項最新的政策就是一個明證。| **classic case of** (=a typical example of a situation, problem etc) 典型例證 *a classic case of food poisoning* 食物中毒的典型例子

2 ►SITUATION 情況◄ [C usually singular 一般用單數] a situation that exists, especially as it affects a particular person or group〔尤指影響某人或羣體的〕狀況, 情形; 場合: **be the case** *This was found to be the case in many third-world countries.* 在許多第三世界國家裡都出現這種情況。| **it is the case (that)** *It is simply not the case that standards have fallen.* 說水準已下降, 這根本不符合事實。| **in sb's case** *In Sandra's case, the reasons are less easy to pinpoint.* 就桑德拉的情況來說, 較難找出原因。| *I'm not supposed to let anyone in without a card, but I'll make an exception in your case.* 我本來不可以讓任何沒有證件的人進去的, 但就你的情況來說, 我就破一回例。| **understate/overstate the case** (=make a situation seem less or more serious than it really is) 把情況淡化/誇大

3 in that case *spoken* used to describe what you will do, or what will happen, as a result of a particular situation or event【口】如果是那樣的話: *"I'm afraid I can't come after all." "Well, in that case I'm not going either."* "我恐怕終究來不了。""好吧, 如果是那樣的話, 我也不去了。"
4 in any case *spoken* used to say that a fact or part of a situation stays the same even if other things change【口】不管怎樣, 無論如何: *We have to go past your house in any case, so we'll take you home.* 不管怎樣, 我們都要經過你家, 所以我們會送你回去。
5 (just) in case *especially spoken*【尤口】**a)** as a way of being safe from something that might happen or might be true 以防萬一: *Take an umbrella, in case it rains.* 帶把傘吧, 以防下雨。| *I'm sure Harry will remember, but why not give him a ring just in case?* 我肯定哈里會記得, 但為防萬一, 為甚麼不給他打個電話呢? **b)** *AmE* if【美】如果, 假使: *In case I'm late, start without me.* 假如我來晚了, 你們就先開始吧。
6 it's a case of *spoken* used before describing a situation, especially the one you are now in【口】情況是…: *We don't want to sell the car, but it's a case of having to.* 我們並不想賣掉汽車, 但這是沒有辦法的事。| *It's a case of too many people and not enough jobs.* 情況是人多職位少。
7 in case of used to describe what you should do in a particular situation, especially on official notices 要是…, 在…的時候〔尤用於官方告示〕: *In case of fire, break the glass.* 如發生火警, 請打碎玻璃。
8 ►BOX/CONTAINER 箱子/容器◄ [C] **a)** a large box or container in which things can be stored or moved 大箱子, 大容器: *a packing case* 包裝箱 | *a case of wine* 一箱葡萄酒 **b)** a special box used as a container for holding or protecting something 盒(子), 匣(子); 櫥, 櫃; 套, 罩; 殼: *a jewellery case* 首飾盒 | *The exhibits were all in glass cases.* 展品都放在玻璃罩裡。**c)** *BrE* a SUITCASE【英】手提箱: *Shall I take your cases down to the car?* 要我把你的箱子拿到車上嗎? —see also 另見 BOOKCASE, BRIEFCASE, PILLOWCASE
9 ►LAW/CRIME 法律/罪行◄ [C] **a)** a question or problem that will be dealt with by a law court 訴訟案件; 官司; 個案: *a libel case* 誹謗案 | **win/lose a case** *They lost their case in the High Court, and had to pay damages.* 高等法院判他們輸了官司, 他們得賠償損失。**b)** all the reasons that one side in a legal argument can give against the other side〔訴訟中一方的〕理由, 論據, 證據, 申述: *the case for the prosecution* 控方的論據 | **have a case** (=have enough good arguments to go to a law court) 有足夠的證據起訴 *The police have a clear case against him.* 警方掌握了不利於他的確鑿證據。**c)** an event or set of events that need to be dealt with by the police (犯罪)案件, 事件: *investigating a murder case* 調查一宗謀殺案 | **be on the case** (=be in charge of dealing with a particular crime) 負責〔某個〕案件 *Inspector Hacker is on the case.* 哈克督察負責此案。
10 ►REASON/ARGUMENT 理由/論據◄ [C,U] the facts, arguments, or reasons for doing something, supporting something etc 事實, 論據, 理由: **[+for/against]** *the case against hanging* 反對絞刑的理由 | *There may be a case for abandoning the scheme altogether.* 或許有理由全盤否決該計劃。| **make out a case for** (=provide good reasons for something) 為…提供充分的理由 *I'm sure we can make out a good case for a pay rise.* 我確信我們能夠提出增加工資的充分理由。
11 get off my case *spoken* used to tell someone to stop criticizing you or complaining about you【口】別再批評[埋怨]我了: *OK, OK, just get off my case already!* 好了, 好了, 不要再埋怨我了!
12 be on sb's case *informal* to be criticizing someone continuously【非正式】不停地抱怨[指責]某人: *Dad's always on my case about something or another.* 爸爸老是不停地抱怨我這抱怨我那。
13 ►PERSON 人◄ [C] someone who is being dealt with by a doctor, a SOCIAL WORKER, the police etc 病人, 患者; 社會工作者的工作對象; 由警方監管的人 —see also 另見 **sad case** (SAD (4)), NUTCASE, BASKET-CASE
14 ►GRAMMAR 語法◄ [C,U] *technical* the way in which the form of a word changes, showing its relationship to other words in a sentence【術語】格: *case endings* 格詞尾 —see also 另見 LOWER CASE, UPPER CASE

case² *v* [T] **1 be cased in** to be completely surrounded by a material or substance 被包圍: *The reactor will be cased in metal.* 反應器將用金屬包起來。**2 case the joint** *slang* to look around a place that you intend to steal from in order to find out information【俚】〔為行竊而〕預先偵察, 窺探 —see also 另見 CASING

case·book /ˈkes͵bʊk; ˈkeɪsbʊk/ *n* [C] a detailed written record kept by a doctor, SOCIAL WORKER, or police officer of the cases (CASE¹ (13)) they have dealt with 病歷; 〔社會工作者的〕記錄簿; 〔警察的〕案件檔案

case his·tory /ˈ· ˌ···/ *n* [C] a detailed record of someone's past illnesses, problems etc that a doctor or SOCIAL WORKER studies 病歷; 〔社會工作者的工作對象的〕個案史

case law /ˈ· ·/ *n* [U] *law* a type of law that is based on decisions judges have made in the past【法律】判例法〔以從前判決的案例為依據的法律〕

case·load /ˈkes͵lod; ˈkeɪsləʊd/ *n* [C] the number of people a doctor, SOCIAL WORKER etc has to deal with〔醫生、社會工作者等的〕工作量

case·ment /ˈkesmənt; ˈkeɪsmənt/ *n* [C] a window that opens like a door with HINGES¹ at one side〔像門那樣開關的〕門式窗

case stud·y /ˈ· ˌ··/ *n* [C] a detailed account of the development of a particular person, group, or situation that has been studied over a period of time 個案研究

case work /ˈ· ·/ *n* [U] work that a SOCIAL WORKER does which is concerned with the problems of a particular person or family that needs help 社會(福利)工作, 社會輔導工作 —**caseworker** *n* [C]

cash¹ /kæʃ; kæʃ/ *n* [U] **1** money in the form of coins or notes rather than cheques, CREDIT CARDS etc 現款, 現金: **in cash** *I'm bringing $400 in traveller's cheques and $100 in cash.* 我將帶400美元的旅行支票和100美元的現金。—see 見 MONEY (USAGE) | **pay in cash** (=not by cheque etc) 用現金付賬 | *Is there any discount if I pay in cash?* 如果我付現金, 有折扣嗎? | **hard cash** (=notes and coins only) 現金, 現款 *In terms of hard cash, we've raised over £200 and in pledges about £8,500.* 我們已籌得超過200英鎊現金和大約8500英鎊的承諾捐款。**2** *informal* money【非正式】錢: *The company's a bit short of cash right now.* 公司現在現款有點緊。| **be strapped for cash** (=not have enough money) 缺錢 **3 pay cash** to pay immediately using a cheque or cash, but not by adding a debt to your account〔用現金或支票〕付現, 當場付款: *Are you paying cash or do you have a trade account?* 你付現款還是有結算賬戶? | **cash bonus/sale/deposit** (=one in which a direct payment is made) 現金獎勵/現金銷售/現金存款 **4 cash down** if you pay for something cash down, you pay for it before you receive it 預付 **5 cash on delivery** COD; used to mean that the customer pays the person delivering the goods to them 貨到付款 —see also 另見 PETTY CASH S2 W2

cash² *v* [T] **cash a cheque/postal order/draft etc** to exchange a cheque etc for the amount of money it is worth 把支票/郵政匯票/匯票等兑成現金: *Can you cash my traveller's cheques here?* 你們這兒可以把我的旅行支票兑成現金嗎? | *Where can I get this cashed?* 我到哪兒能把這(張支票)兑現? —**cashable** *adj*: *cashable at any bank* 可以在任何一家銀行兑現的 S3

cash in *phr v* **1** [I] to make a profit from a situation in a way that other people think is wrong or unfair〔靠不正當手段〕賺錢; 利用: **[+on]** *He's just cashing in on the fact that his father is a big movie director.* 他不過是利用他父親是個大導演來賺錢。**2** [T **cash** sth ↔ **in**] to exchange something such as an insurance POLICY (2) for its value in money 把〔保險單等〕兑成現金 **3 cash in your chips** *humorous* to die【幽默】死; 完蛋; 報銷

cash up also 又作 **cash out** *AmE*【美】*phr v* [T] to add up the amount of money received in a shop in a day so that it can be checked〔收銀員在打烊後〕結賬

cash and car·ry /ˌ· · ˈ··/ *n* [C] a very large shop where customers representing a business or organization can buy large amounts of goods at cheap prices 現款自運商店

cash·book /ˈkæʃˌbuk; ˈkæʃbʊk/ *n* [C] a book in which you keep a record of money received and paid out 現金賬簿

C

cash box /ˈ· ·/ *n* [C] a small metal box with a lock that you keep money in 錢箱, 銀箱

cash card /ˈ· ·/ *n* [C] a special plastic card used for getting money from a machine outside a bank〔用於自動提款機的〕自動提款卡 —compare 比較 CHEQUE CARD, CREDIT CARD, DEBIT CARD

cash cow /ˈ· ·/ *n* [C] the part of a business you can always depend on to make enough profits 穩賺項目; 搖錢樹; 財源: *seeing the product as a high-yielding cash cow, requiring little investment in the mature stage of its life-cycle* 把那種產品視為一棵巨大的搖錢樹, 在其成熟期不需要甚麼投資

cash crop /ˈ· ·/ *n* [C] a crop grown in order to be sold rather than to be used by the people growing it 商品農作物 —compare 比較 SUBSISTENCE CROP

cash desk /ˈ· ·/ *n* [C] the desk in a shop where you pay〔商店的〕收款台, 櫃台, 付款處

cash dis·count /ˌ· ˈ··/ *n* [C] an amount by which a seller reduces a price if the buyer pays immediately or before a particular date 現金折扣〔指因現款購貨或在某段時間前付款而給予的優惠折扣〕

cash dis·pens·er /ˈ· ·ˌ··/ *n* [C] *especially BrE* a CASH MACHINE【尤英】自動提款機

ca·shew /ˈkæʃu; ˈkæʃuː/ *n* [C] **1** a small curved nut 腰果 **2** the tropical American tree that produces this〔熱帶美洲的〕腰果樹

cash flow /ˈ· ·/ *n* [singular,U] **1** the movement of money coming into a business as income and going out as wages, materials etc 現金流轉: *maintaining a healthy cash flow* 維持良好的現金流轉 **2 have cash flow problems** to not have enough money 發生現金周轉問題

cash·ier¹ /kæˈʃɪr; kæˈʃɪə/ *n* [C] someone whose job is to receive or pay out money in a shop, bank, hotel etc〔商店、銀行、旅館等的〕櫃台出納[收賬]員

cashier² *v* [T] to force an officer to leave the army, navy etc because they have done something wrong 罷免; 革除〔軍官的〕職務

cash-in-hand /ˌ· · ˈ·◂/ *adj* a cash-in-hand payment is made in the form of notes and coins so that there is no record of the payment 用現金支付[結算]的

cash·less /ˈkæʃləs; ˈkæʃlǝs/ *adj* done or working without using actual money 不用現金的, 轉賬的: *a cashless transaction between two banks* 兩家銀行間的非現金交易 | *the cashless society* 不用現金的社會

cash ma·chine /ˈ· ·ˌ·/ *n* [C] a machine in or outside a bank from which you can obtain money with a special plastic card 自動櫃員機, 自動提款機; CASH DISPENSER *especially BrE*【尤英】, ATM *AmE*【美】

cash·mere /ˈkæʃmɪr; ˈkæʃmɪə/ *n* [U] a type of fine soft wool 開士米羊毛織品; 克什米爾產細羊毛: *I wish I could afford a cashmere sweater.* 我希望我能買得起一件開士米羊毛衫。

cash·point /ˈkæʃpɔɪnt; ˈkæʃpɔɪnt/ *n* [C] *BrE* a cash machine【英】自動提款機

cash reg·is·ter /ˈ· ˌ···/ *n* [C] a machine used in shops to keep the money in and record the amount of money received from each sale; TILL² 現金收入記錄機, 現金出納機, 收銀機

cash-strapped /ˈ· ·/ *adj* not having enough money 缺錢的, 財政困難的: *higher school meal prices imposed by a cash-strapped county council* 郡議會因財政困難而導致較高的學校伙食費

cas·ing /ˈkesɪŋ; ˈkeɪsɪŋ/ *n* [C] an outer layer of metal, rubber etc that covers and protects something such as a wire or tyre〔包在電線或輪胎等物體外面起保護作用的〕罩, 殼, 套; 管; 外胎

ca·si·no /kəˈsino; kəˈsiːnəʊ/ *n plural* **casinos** [C] a place where people try to win money by playing card games or ROULETTE 賭場: *Doesn't that club have a casino upstairs?* 那家俱樂部樓上不是有賭場嗎?

cask /kæsk; kɑːsk/ *n* [C] a round wooden container used for storing wine or other liquids, or the amount of liquid contained in this〔裝酒或其他液體的〕小木桶; 一桶之量: *a cask of rum* 一桶朗姆酒

cas·ket /ˈkæskɪt; ˈkɑːskǝt/ *n* [C] **1** a small decorated box in which you keep jewellery and other valuable objects〔裝珠寶等貴重物品的〕小盒, 小箱 **2** *especially AmE* a COFFIN【尤美】棺材

cas·sa·va /kəˈsɑvə; kəˈsɑːvə/ *n* [C,U] a tropical plant with thick roots that you can eat, or the flour made from these roots 木薯; 木薯澱粉

cas·se·role¹ /ˈkæsəˌrol; ˈkæsərəʊl/ *n* [C] **1** food that is cooked slowly in liquid in a covered dish in the OVEN 燉鍋[砂鍋]菜餚: *chicken casserole* 砂鍋雞 **2** a deep covered dish used for cooking food in the oven 燉鍋, 砂鍋

casserole² *v* [T] to cook food in a casserole 用燉鍋[砂鍋]烹飪

cas·sette /kəˈsɛt; kəˈset/ *n* [C] **1** a small flat plastic case containing MAGNETIC TAPE, that can be used for playing or recording sound〔錄音帶的〕卡式盒: *Now available on cassette or CD!* 現有盒式磁帶和雷射唱片兩種產品出售! **2** a closed container with photographic film in it, that can be fitted into a camera〔攝影膠卷的〕暗盒, 膠卷盒

cassette play·er /·ˈ· ˌ··/ *n* [C] a piece of electrical equipment used for playing cassettes 盒式磁帶錄音機

cassette re·cord·er /·ˈ· ·ˌ··/ *n* [C] a piece of electrical equipment used for recording sound or for playing cassettes on; TAPE RECORDER 盒式磁帶錄音機

cas·sock /ˈkæsək; ˈkæsək/ *n* [C] a long, usually black, piece of clothing worn by priests〔牧師穿的, 多為黑色的〕法衣, 長袍

cast¹ /kæst; kɑːst/ *v past tense and past participle* **cast**

1 cast (a) light on/onto a) to provide new information which makes something easier to understand 使〔某事〕更為清楚; 闡明; 論述: *research findings that cast new light on the origin of our universe* 為宇宙起源提出新的論點的研究發現 **b)** *literary* to send light onto a surface【文】把光線投在...表面: *The candle cast a flickering light on the wall.* 燭光映在牆上搖曳不定。

2 cast a shadow *literary*【文】**a)** if something casts a shadow over an event, period of time etc, it makes people feel less happy or hopeful because they are worried about it〔在心理上〕投下陰影, 使不快: **[+over]** *My father's illness cast a shadow over the wedding celebrations.* 我父親的病使婚禮籠罩着一層陰影。**b)** to make a shadow appear on a surface or area〔在某一表面或區域上〕投下影子: **[+on/over/across etc]** *The oak tree casts a long shadow across the lawn in the afternoon.* 到了下午, 橡樹在草坪上投下長長的樹影。

3 ►LOOK 看◄ a) cast a look/glance *literary* to look at someone or something【文】看[瞅]一眼: **[+at/towards/around etc]** *Sandra waited, casting nervous glances over her shoulder.* 桑德拉等待着, 不時緊張地看看身後。**b) cast an eye over** to check or look at something quickly 迅速地檢查[看]: *Could you just cast an eye over these figures before I show them to the bank?* 在我把這些數字交給銀行之前, 你能先檢查一下嗎?

4 cast doubt on to make people feel less certain about something 使懷疑, 使不確信: *Preliminary results from an Anglo-French trial cast doubts on the usefulness of* *the drug.* 英法兩國試用的初步結果使人們對這種藥物的療效有所懷疑。

5 cast a vote also 又作 **cast a ballot** *AmE*【美】to vote in an election 投票: *Barely one in three voters will bother to cast a ballot on February 26th.* 僅有三分之一的選民願意在2月26日那天去投票。

6 cast a spell on/over a) to use magic words or ceremonies to change someone or something 給…下咒語, 用咒語迷惑: *She's a witch! She'll cast a spell on you if she sees you in the wood!* 她是巫婆！如果她看見你在林子裡, 就會對你唸魔咒！**b)** to make someone feel very strongly attracted and keep their attention completely 把…迷住, 深深吸引: *Within minutes Sinatra's voice had cast its spell on the audience.* 短短幾分鐘之內, (美國著名流行歌手) 仙納杜拉的歌聲就迷倒了所有聽眾。

7 cast your mind back to try to remember something that happened a long time ago 回想, 回顧, 追憶: [+to] *Cast your mind back to your first day at school.* 回想你第一天上學的情況。

8 cast sth from your mind if you cast worries, fears, doubts etc from your mind, you stop feeling worried, afraid etc 忘卻某事〔指煩惱、恐懼、疑惑等〕, 把某事丟到腦後

9 cast aspersions on *formal* to make unfavourable remarks about someone or something【正式】批評; 詆毀, 中傷: *Under the censorship rules, they could not cast aspersions on a foreign power.* 在這種審查制度下, 他們無法對外國強權進行批評。

10 ►METAL 金屬◄ [T] to pour liquid metal, plastic etc into a MOULD (=specially shaped container), or to make an object in this way 澆鑄; 按模鑄造: *a statue of a horse cast in bronze* 青銅澆鑄的馬塑像

11 ►ACTOR 演員◄ [T] to choose which people will act particular parts in a play, film etc〔為戲劇、電影等〕挑選〔演員〕

12 cast sb as/cast sb in the role of to regard or describe someone as a particular type of person 評價; 描述: *Clarke's trying to cast me in the role of the villain in all of this.* 克拉克在這整件事上都想把我說成是個壞人。

13 ►FISHING 捕魚◄ [I,T] to throw a fishing line or net into the water 拋(釣絲); 撒(網): *There's a trick to casting properly.* 正確地撒網[垂釣]是有訣竅的。

14 ►THROW 拋◄ [T always+adv/prep] *literary* to throw something somewhere【文】投, 拋, 扔, 丟: *Sparks leapt as more wood was cast onto the bonfire.* 往火堆中丟入更多的木頭時, 火花不停地四濺。

15 cast sb into prison/into a dungeon/into Hell etc *literary* to force someone to go somewhere unpleasant【文】把…關進監獄/地牢/地獄等: *Memet should, in her opinion, be cast into prison.* 她認為應該把梅梅特關入大牢。

16 be cast away to be left alone on a lonely shore or island, as a result of your ship sinking〔因沉船而〕流落荒島: *If you were cast away on a desert island, what would you miss most?* 如果你因沉船而流落在荒島上, 你會最想念甚麼?

17 be cast down *literary* to feel sad and discouraged【文】沮喪, 灰心: *Malcolm too seemed quite cast down.* 馬爾科姆似乎也相當沮喪。

18 cast your net wide to consider or try as many things as possible in order to find what you want 想盡方法尋找, 千方百計搜羅: *We'll be casting our net wide to get the right person for the job.* 我們將盡力從各方物色能勝任此項工作的人選。

19 ►CAST ITS SKIN 蛻皮◄ if a snake casts its skin, it gets rid of the top layer〔蛇〕蛻皮

20 cast a shoe if a horse casts a shoe, it loses one of them〔馬〕掉一個蹄鐵

21 cast a horoscope to calculate the details of someone's HOROSCOPE 用占星術算命

22 cast pearls before swine to offer something that is very valuable or beautiful to someone who does not understand how valuable it is 把好東西送給不識貨的人; 明珠暗投; 對牛彈琴 —see also 另見 **the die is cast** (DIE[2] (3)), **throw in/cast your lot with** (LOT (16))

cast about/around for sth *phr v* [T] to try to think of something to do or say 考慮, 計劃: *Having retired early, I am casting about for a way to supplement my income.* 因為退休早, 我正想辦法增加收入。

cast sb/sth ↔ **aside** *phr v* [T] to get rid of someone or something because you no longer like them or they are no longer useful〔因不喜歡或無用而〕把…丟在一旁, 對…置之不理: *When Henry became King, he cast aside all his former friends.* 亨利當上國王後就不理他以前的朋友了。| **cast aside your inhibitions/doubts etc** (=get rid of your feelings of shyness, doubt etc) 消除顧忌/疑惑等

cast off *phr v* **1** [T **cast** sb/sth ↔ **off**] *literary* to get rid of something or someone【文】擺脫, 放棄, 丟掉: *a haven of tranquility where you can cast off the strains and stresses of life* 能讓你擺脫生活的緊張和壓力的安靜地方 **2** [I,T **cast** sth ↔ **off**] to untie the rope that fastens your boat to the shore so that you can sail away〔船隻〕解纜起航 **3** [I,T **cast** sth ↔ **off**] to finish a piece of KNITTING by taking the last stitches off the needle in a way that stops them from coming undone〔編織〕收針

cast on *phr v* [I,T **cast** sth ↔ **on**] to start a piece of KNITTING by making the first stitches on the needle〔編織〕起針

cast sb/sth ↔ **out** *phr v* [T] *literary* to force someone or something to go away【文】把…趕走, 驅逐: *an exorcist who casts out demons* 驅魔法師

cast sth ↔ **up** *phr v* [T] if the sea casts up something, it brings it onto the shore〔海水〕把…沖上岸: *A body had been cast up on the rocks.* 一具屍體被海水沖上了岩石。

cast[2] *n* [C]

1 ►ACTORS 演員◄ all the people who act in a play or film 演員陣容, 全體演員: *Films like 'Ben Hur' have a cast of thousands.* 像《賓虛》一類的電影, 演員多達數千人。

2 ►ON YOUR BODY 人體上◄ a hard protective case used around a part of your body to support a broken bone〔固定骨折用的〕石膏: *a plaster cast* 石膏 | *Murray has his leg in a cast.* 默里的腿用石膏固定着。

3 ►FOR SHAPING METAL 澆鑄◄ **a)** a MOULD (=specially shaped container) into which you pour liquid metal, plastic etc in order to make an object of a particular shape 鑄模, 模子 **b)** an object made in this way 鑄件, 鑄造品

4 cast of (sb's) mind/features *formal* the way someone thinks, behaves, or looks【正式】(某人的) 思維方式/特徵: *a philosophical cast of mind* 具有哲理的思維方式

5 ►IN FISHING 釣魚◄ the act of throwing a fishing line 拋釣絲

6 have a cast in your eye *old-fashioned* to have a problem with your eye which forces it to look to the side【過時】〔眼睛〕斜視

7 ►COLOUR 顏色◄ a small amount of a particular colour 色調: *Sage leaves have a silvery cast.* 鼠尾草的葉子是帶點銀色的。

8 ►EARTH 泥土◄ a small pile of earth thrown out of the ground by WORMs when they make a hole〔蚯蚓鑽洞時翻到地面的〕小土堆

cas·ta·nets /ˌkæstəˋnɛts; ˌkæstəˈnets/ *n* [plural] a musical instrument made of two small round pieces of wood or plastic that you knock together in your hand 響板〔一種樂器〕

cast·a·way /ˋkæstəˏwe; ˈkɑːstəweɪ/ *n* [C] someone who is left on a lonely shore or island after their ship has sunk 沉船後漂流到孤島的人

caste /kæst; kɑːst/ *n* [C,U] **1** one of the fixed and unchangeable social classes into which people are born in

India, or the system of having these classes〔印度社會的〕種姓; 種姓制度 **2** a group of people who have the same position in society 社會階層[等級]: **lose caste** *BrE* (=lose your social position)【英】失去社會地位

cas·tel·lat·ed /ˋkæstəˌletɪd; ˈkæstəleɪtəd/ *adj technical* built to look like a castle【術語】構造似城堡的: *a castellated bell tower* 如城堡似的鐘樓

cast·er, castor /ˋkæstɚ; ˈkɑːstə/ *n* [C] **1** a small wheel fixed to the bottom of a piece of furniture so that it can move in any direction〔家具的〕小腳輪, 滾輪 **2** *BrE* a small container with holes in the top, used to spread sugar, salt etc on food【英】〔頂端有小孔, 用來撒糖、鹽等的〕調味瓶; SHAKER (1) *AmE*【美】

C

caster sug·ar, castor sugar /ˈ·· ˌ··/ *n* [U] *BrE* sugar with very small grains used for cooking【英】細白砂糖

cast·i·gate /ˋkæstəˌget; ˈkæstəgeɪt/ *v* [T] *formal* to criticize or punish someone severely【正式】嚴厲責罵, 斥責; 嚴懲 —**castigation** /ˌkæstəˋgeʃən; ˌkæstəˈgeɪʃən/ *n* [U]

cast·ing /ˋkæstɪŋ; ˈkɑːstɪŋ/ *n* **1** [U] the process of choosing the actors for a film or play 挑選演員, 分派角色: *a casting director* 負責挑選演員的導演 **2** [C] an object made by pouring liquid metal, plastic etc into a MOULD (=specially shaped container) 鑄造品, 鑄件 **3 the casting couch** *humorous* a situation in which an actress is persuaded to have sex in return for a part in a film, play etc【幽默】以肉體換角色〔女演員為了獲演某個角色而以肉體作為交換條件〕

casting vote /ˈ·· ˌ·/ *n* [C usually singular 一般用單數] the vote of the person in charge of a meeting, which can be used to make a decision when there is an equal number of votes supporting and opposing a proposal〔當贊成和反對票數相等時, 由會議主持人所投的〕決定性一票

cast i·ron /ˌ· ˈ··/ *n* [U] a type of iron that is hard, breaks easily, and is shaped in a MOULD[1] (2) 鑄鐵; 生鐵

cast-i·ron /ˌ· ˈ··◂/ *adj* **1 a cast-iron excuse/alibi/guarantee etc** an excuse etc that is very certain and cannot fail 理由充分的藉口/無懈可擊的辯解/強而有力的保證等 **2** made of cast iron 鑄鐵製的, 生鐵做的: *a cast-iron frying pan* 生鐵煎鍋 **3** extremely strong or determined 極為強壯的; 堅定不移的: *You need a cast-iron stomach to eat Imran's curry!* 你要吃伊姆蘭的咖喱, 就要有個強健的胃!

3 **cas·tle** /ˋkæsl; ˈkɑːsəl/ *n* [C] **1** a very large strong building, built in the past as a safe place that could be easily defended against attack 城堡, 堡壘: *Warwick Castle* 沃里克城堡 **2** one of the pieces used in a game of CHESS; ROOK[1] (2)〔國際象棋中的〕車 **3 castles in the air** plans or hopes that you have that are unlikely ever to become real; DAYDREAMS 空想, 空中樓閣, 異想天開

cast-off /ˈ· ·/ *adj* [only before noun 僅用於名詞前] cast off clothes or other goods are not wanted or have been thrown away〔衣物、東西〕被丟棄的, 廢棄的

cast-offs /ˈ· ·/ *n* [C] clothes that you do not wear any more and give to someone else〔自己不穿而贈人的〕舊衣服: *As the youngest of five kids I was always dressed in other people's cast-offs.* 我是五個孩子中年紀最小的一個, 所以總穿別人穿過的舊衣服。

cast·or /ˋkæstɚ; ˈkɑːstə/ *n* [C] another spelling of CASTER caster 的另一種拼法

castor oil /ˌ·· ˈ·◂/ *n* [U] a thick oil made from the seeds of a plant and used in the past as a medicine to make the BOWELs empty〔舊時用作輕瀉劑的〕蓖麻油

castor sug·ar /ˈ·· ˌ··/ *n* [U] another spelling of CASTER SUGAR caster sugar 的另一種拼法

cas·trate /ˋkæstret; kæˈstreɪt/ *v* [T] to remove the sexual organs of a male animal or a man 閹割〔雄性動物或男性〕—**castration** /ˌkæsˋtreʃən; kæˈstreɪʃən/ *n* [U]

cas·u·al /ˋkæʒuəl; ˈkæʒuəl/ *adj*

1 ►NOT CARING 不在意◄ not caring or seeming not to care about something 漫不經心的, 隨隨便便的, 不放在心上的: *His casual manner annoyed me.* 他無所謂的態度使我惱怒。| *Karla tried to sound casual, but her excitement was obvious.* 卡拉盡量說得好像漫不經心, 但她的興奮卻是顯而易見的。

2 ►CLOTHES 衣服◄ casual clothes are comfortable clothes that you wear in informal situations 便裝的, 非正式場合穿的: *casual shoes* 便鞋

3 casual worker/employment/labour etc a worker, employment etc that a company uses or offers only for a short period of time 臨時工/短期工作[職位]等: *They're making do with casual staff.* 他們將就着使用臨時工。

4 ►WITHOUT ATTENTION 不注意◄ without any clear aim or serious interest 漫無目的的, 不認真的, 隨便的: *a casual glance at the Times* 隨便翻了翻《泰晤士報》| **casual observer** (=someone not looking very carefully) 大意的觀察者 *Even to the most casual observer it was obvious she was sick.* 即使是最大意的人也能看出她顯然是生病了。

5 ►NOT PLANNED 非計劃的◄ happening by chance without being planned 偶然的, 碰巧的: *a casual meeting* 巧遇 | **casual remark** (=something you say for no particular reason) 隨意的言辭

6 casual sex sex that you have without intending to have a serious relationship with the other person 隨意的[不負責任的]性關係

7 casual visitor/user etc someone who does not often visit a place, use something etc 偶然來訪的客人/不固定的使用者等: *a casual user of the library service* 偶爾去去圖書館的人 —**casually** *adv*: *a casually dressed young man* 穿着隨便的年輕人 —**casualness** *n* [U]

cas·u·al·ty /ˋkæʒuəltɪ; ˈkæʒuəlti/ *n* **1** [C] someone who is hurt or killed in an accident or battle〔事故或戰鬥中的〕傷者; 死者: *First reports of the air crash tell of more than 50 casualties.* 據最初的空難報道, 傷亡人數已超過50人。| **heavy casualties** (=a lot of people hurt or killed) 傷亡慘重 **2 be a casualty of** someone or something that suffers as a result of a particular event or situation 是〔某事件或情況造成的〕受害者[犧牲品]: *The Safer City Project became a major casualty of financial cutbacks.* 城市安全工程成了財政削減下的最大犧牲品。**3 Casualty** [U] *BrE* the part of a hospital that people are taken to when they are hurt in an accident or suddenly become ill【英】急救室, 急症室, 急診室; EMERGENCY ROOM *AmE*【美】: *Steph works nights in Casualty.* 史蒂夫在急救室上夜班。

cas·u·ist /ˋkæʒuɪst; ˈkæʒuəst/ *n* [C] *formal* someone who is skilled in casuistry【正式】詭辯家

cas·u·is·try /ˋkæʒuɪstrɪ; ˈkæʒuəstri/ *n* [U] *formal* the use of clever but often false arguments to answer moral or legal questions【正式】詭辯(術)

ca·sus bel·li /ˋkesəs ˋbɛlaɪ; ˌkɑːsəs ˈbeli/ *n* [C] *Latin* an event or political action which directly causes a war【拉丁】引起戰爭的事件, 開戰的理由

cat /kæt; kæt/ *n* [C]

1 ►ANIMAL 動物◄ **a)** a small animal with four legs that is often kept as a pet or used for catching mice (MOUSE (1)) 貓 **b)** a large animal that is related to this, such as a lion or tiger 貓科動物〈如獅、虎〉

2 let the cat out of the bag to tell a secret, especially without intending to〔尤指無意中〕洩露祕密, 露出馬腳

3 put/set the cat among the pigeons to cause trouble by doing or saying something that upsets people, causes arguments etc〔以引人反感的言行〕惹出亂子, 引起軒然大波

4 play cat and mouse with to let someone think they are getting or doing what they want, then prevent them from getting or doing it 把…當作玩物, 愚弄[某人]

5 like a cat on hot bricks *BrE*【英】, **like a cat on a hot tin roof** *AmE*【美】so nervous or anxious that you cannot keep still or keep your attention on one thing 像熱鍋上的螞蟻, 坐立不安, 心神不定

6 ►WOMAN 女人◄ *old-fashioned* an insulting word for a woman who you think is unkind or unpleasant【過

時】惡毒的女人〔此詞具侮辱性〕—see also 另見 CATTY, **raining cats and dogs** (RAIN² (4)), **there's not enough room to swing a cat** (ROOM¹ (2))

cat·a·clys·m /ˈkætəˌklɪzəm; ˈkætəklɪzəm/ *n* [C] *literary* a violent and sudden event or change, such as a serious flood or EARTHQUAKE【文】〔突發的〕劇變; 災難〈如洪水、地震〉—**cataclysmic** /ˌkætəˋklɪzmɪk; ˌkætəˈklɪzmɪk/ *adj*

cat·a·comb /ˋkætəˌkom; ˈkætəkuːm/ *n* [C usually plural 一般用複數] an area of passages and rooms below the ground where dead people are buried 地下墓穴

cat·a·falque /ˋkætəˌfælk; ˈkætəfælk/ *n* [C] a decorated raised structure on which the dead body of an important person is placed before their funeral 靈柩台

Cat·a·lan /ˋkætḷən; ˈkætəlæn/ *n* [U] a language spoken in part of Spain around Barcelona〔西班牙巴塞羅那周邊地區使用的〕加泰隆語

cat·a·lep·sy /ˋkætəˌlɛpsɪ; ˈkætəlepsi/ *n* [U] a medical condition in which you cannot control your movements so that your body becomes stiff like a dead body or remains in whatever position it is placed 僵直症, 強直性昏厥 —**cataleptic** /ˌkætəˋlɛptɪk; ˌkætəˈleptɪk◂/ *adj*

3 **cat·a·logue¹** also 又作 **catalog** *AmE*【美】/ˋkætḷˌɔg; ˈkætəlɒg/ *n* [C] **1** a book containing pictures and information about goods that you can buy 商品目錄, 購物指南: *the Sears catalog* 西爾斯公司商品目錄 **2 catalogue of failures/disasters/errors etc** a series of failures, disasters etc that happen one after the other and never seem to stop 一連串的失敗/災難/錯誤等: *the latest addition to the catalogue of terrorist crimes* 恐怖主義罪行錄上的最新補充 **3** a list of all the objects, paintings etc at an EXHIBITION (1) or sale, of all the books in a library etc〔展覽會或拍賣會上所有物品、繪畫的〕目錄, 一覽表;〔圖書館的〕目錄(冊)

catalogue² also 又作 **catalog** *AmE*【美】*v* [T] **1** to put a list of things into a particular order and write it in a catalogue 為…編目錄, 把…列入目錄中 **2** to give a list of all the events or qualities connected with someone or something 把〔與某人或某物有關的事件或特點〕列出

ca·tal·y·sis /kəˋtæləsɪs; kəˈtælɪsɪs/ *n* [U] the process of making a chemical reaction quicker by adding a catalyst 催化作用, 觸媒作用

cat·a·lyst /ˋkætḷɪst; ˈkætl-ɪst/ *n* [C] **1** a substance that makes a chemical reaction happen more quickly without being changed itself 催化劑; 觸媒 **2** something or someone that causes an important change or event to happen 導致重大變化的人[事物]; 促進因素: **[+for]** *The police beatings served as a catalyst for the escalation of violence.* 警察打人事件是這場暴力升級的導火線。—**catalytic** /ˌkætḷˋɪtɪk; ˌkætəˈlɪtɪk◂/ *adj*

catalytic con·vert·er /ˌ····ˈ··/ *n* [C] a piece of equipment fitted to the EXHAUST¹ (1) of a car that reduces the amount of poisonous gases sent out into the air when the engine is operating〔安裝在汽車排氣裝置上的〕催化式排氣淨化器

cat·a·ma·ran /ˌkætəməˋræn; ˌkætəməˈræn/ *n* [C] a sailing boat with two separate HULLs (=the part that goes in the water) 雙體船

cat-and-dog /ˌ··ˈ·/ *adj* [only before noun 僅用於名詞前] *BrE informal* a cat-and-dog life is full of quarrels and arguments【英, 非正式】〔生活〕爭吵不休的, 充滿爭吵的, 不和睦的

cat·a·pult¹ /ˋkætəˌpʌlt; ˈkætəpʌlt/ *n* [C] **1** a large weapon used in former times to throw heavy stones, iron balls etc〔古時用的, 能彈射巨石、鐵球的〕石弩, 弩砲 **2** *BrE* a small stick in the shape of a Y with a thin band of rubber fastened over its ends, used by children to throw stones【英】〔小孩玩的〕彈弓; SLINGSHOT *AmE*【美】**3** a piece of equipment used to send an aircraft into the air from a ship〔艦上的〕飛機起飛器, 起動器

catapult² *v* **1** [T always+adv/prep] to push or throw something very hard so that it moves through the air very quickly 把…彈出去, 把…射出去: **catapult sb into/over/out etc** *Sam was catapulted into the air by the force of the blast.* 山姆被爆炸所產生的衝力拋到空中。**2 catapult sb to fame/stardom etc** to suddenly make someone very famous 使…一舉成名: *The movie 'Rebel Without a Cause' catapulted James Dean to stardom.* 電影《阿飛正傳》使占士甸一砲走紅。

cat·a·ract /ˋkætəˌrækt; ˈkætərækt/ *n* [C] **1** a medical condition of the eye in which the LENS (3) of your eye becomes white instead of clear, so that you cannot see 白內障 **2** *literary* a large WATERFALL【文】大瀑布

ca·tarrh /kəˋtɑr; kəˈtɑː/ *n* [U] an uncomfortable condition in which your nose and throat are almost blocked with thick liquid, for example when you have a cold 卡他,〔鼻、喉等的〕黏膜炎

ca·tas·tro·phe /kəˋtæstrəfɪ; kəˈtæstrəfi/ *n* [C,U] **1** a terrible event in which there is a lot of destruction or many people are injured or die 大災難; 嚴重的不幸: *the catastrophe of a worldwide conflict* 一場世界性衝突所造成的大災難 | *The oil spill threatens an unparalleled ecological catastrophe.* 漏油可能會造成一場前所未有的生態大災難。**2** an event or situation which is extremely bad for the people involved 麻煩, 困境, 不利的局面: *If the contract is cancelled, it'll be a catastrophe for everyone concerned.* 如果合同取消, 對有關各方都是個大災難。| *It's a minor catastrophe, isn't it? Plymouth losing?* 只是個小失利, 對吧? 普利茅斯隊要輸球了吧? —**catastrophic** /ˌkætəsˋtrɑfɪk; ˌkætəˈstrɒfɪk◂/ *adj*: *a catastrophic fall in the price of rice* 大米價格的災難性下跌 —**catastrophically** /-kḷɪ; -kli/ *adv*

cat·a·ton·ic /ˌkætəˋtɑnɪk; ˌkætəˈtɒnɪk◂/ *adj technical* caused or affected by a condition in which you cannot think, speak, or move any part of your body【術語】(患)倔強症的, (患)強直性昏厥的: *a catatonic trance* 強直性昏厥狀態

cat·bird seat /ˋkætbɝd ˌsit; ˈkætbɜːd ˌsiːt/ *n AmE informal*【美, 非正式】**be (sitting) in the catbird seat** to be in a position where you have an advantage 處於有利地位

cat bur·glar /ˈ· ˌ··/ *n* [C] a thief who gets into a building by climbing up walls, pipes etc〔爬牆、攀水管等入屋行竊的〕飛賊

cat·call /ˋkætˌkɔl; ˈkætkɔːl/ *n* [C] a loud whistle or shout expressing dislike or disapproval of a speech or performance〔表示反對或喝倒采的〕口哨聲; 尖叫聲: *jeers and catcalls from the audience* 來自觀眾的嘲笑和噓聲 —**catcall** *v* [I]

catch¹ /kætʃ; kætʃ/ *v past tense and past participle* **caught** 1 1

1 ►STOP/TRAP SB 抓住某人◄ [T] **a)** to stop someone after you have been chasing them and prevent them from escaping 抓住, 捉住: *"You can't catch me!" she yelled, running away across the field.* "你抓不到我的!" 她大聲喊道, 一邊穿過田野逃跑了。| *If the guerillas catch you, they will kill you.* 要是游擊隊抓到你, 他們會殺了你。**b)** if the police catch a criminal, they find the criminal and stop him or her from escaping 捕獲, 逮住〔罪犯〕: *State police have launched a massive operation to catch the murderer.* 州警方展開了大規模行動搜捕兇手。| *The jewel thieves were never caught.* 偷盜珠寶的竊賊仍然逍遙法外。

2 ►FIND SB DOING STH 發現某人做某事◄ [T] to find or see someone while they are actually doing something wrong or illegal 撞見, 發現; 當場抓住〔某人正在幹壞事〕: **catch sb doing sth** *I caught Howard reading my private letters.* 霍華德在看我的私人信件時讓我撞見了。| **catch sb in the act (of)/catch sb red-handed** (=catch someone in the middle of doing something bad) 當場抓住 *a shoplifter caught in the act* 被當場抓住的商店扒手 | *They say Buster was caught red-handed.* 他們說巴斯特被當場捉住。| **catch sb at it** *BrE spoken*【英口】*We know he's been cheating, but we've never caught* *him at it.* 我們知道他一直在行騙，不過我們從來沒有當場抓到過他。

3 ►FIND SB UNPREPARED 出其不意◄ **catch sb unawares/catch sb off guard/catch sb on the hop** *BrE* to do something or happen when someone is not expecting it and not ready to deal with events【英】使某人吃驚／措手不及／猝不及防: *a night attack that caught the enemy unawares* 令敵人措手不及的夜襲 | *Her question caught him off guard.* 她的問題讓他猝不及防。| *The dramatic fall in share prices caught even the experts on the hop.* 股票價格暴跌甚至連專家也始料不及。| **be caught napping** *informal* (=not be ready to deal with something unexpected that happens)【非正式】〔對突發事件〕措手不及 | **catch sb with their pants/trousers down** *informal* (=make someone feel embarrassed by arriving or doing something when they are not ready)【非正式】〔出其不意地出現或做某事〕令某人措手不及

C

4 ►ANIMAL/FISH 動物/魚類◄ [T] to trap an animal or fish by using a trap, net, or hook, or by hunting it〔用陷阱、網、鉤等〕捕，捉〔動物或魚類〕: *It's a useless cat, no good at catching mice.* 這是一隻沒用的貓，一點也不會抓老鼠。| *Last time we went fishing I caught a huge trout.* 我們上次去釣魚時我釣到一條大鱒魚。| *catching butterflies* 捕捉蝴蝶

5 ►HOLD 持着◄ **a)** [I,T] to get hold of and stop an object such as a ball that is moving through the air 接住〔在空中移動的物體〕: *Watch – if you throw the ball, Bouncer can catch it in his mouth.* 注意看，如果你把球拋出，邦瑟能用嘴接住。| *"Chuck me over those cigarettes, would you?" "Here you are. Catch!"* "把那些香煙扔給我，好嗎?" "給你。接住!" —see picture on page A22 參見A22頁圖 **b)** [T] to suddenly take hold of someone 突然抓住〔某人〕: *She stumbled forward but Calum caught her in his arms.* 她朝前絆了一下，但是卡勒姆用雙臂抱住了她。| **catch hold of** *Miss Perry caught hold of my sleeve and pulled me back.* 佩莉小姐抓住我的袖子，把我拉了回來。

6 ►ILLNESS 病◄ [T] to get a disease or illness 患〔病〕，感染上…: *My sister has mumps. I hope I haven't caught it.* 我妹妹得了流行性腮腺炎。我希望自己沒有被傳染。| **catch sth from/off** *I think I'm getting the flu – I must have caught it off Gerry.* 我想我得了流感，一定是從傑里那兒傳染的。| **catch your death (of cold)** (=get a very bad cold) 得重感冒 *Don't stand out there in the rain. You'll catch your death.* 別站在外面淋雨。你會得重感冒的。

7 catch a train/plane/bus to get on a train etc in order to travel, or to be in time to get it 趕火車／飛機／公共汽車: *Every morning I catch the 7:15 train to London.* 每天早晨我乘7點15分的列車去倫敦。| *There's a train in now. If you run, you'll just catch it.* 現在有一班火車，你跑步就能趕上。| **have a train etc to catch** *I have to hurry – I have a bus to catch.* 我得趕快，我得趕上搭那輛巴士。—see 見 REACH[1] (USAGE)

8 ►BE IN TIME 及時◄ [T] to not be too late to see something, talk to someone etc 及時趕上: *I managed to catch her just as she was leaving.* 我趕在她要離開時見到了她。| **catch the post** *BrE* (=post letters in time for them to be collected that day)【英】趕上收信的時間寄信 —opposite 反義詞 MISS[1] (5)

9 ►GET STUCK 被卡住◄ [I,T] if your hand, finger, clothing etc catches or is caught in something, it becomes stuck or fastened there (被) 夾住; (被) 卡住; (被) 鉤住: *"What happened to your finger?" "It got caught in the car door."* "你的手指頭怎麼啦?" "被車門夾了一下。" | *Bobby caught his shirt on a wire fence.* 博比的襯衫被柵欄鐵絲鉤住了。

10 catch sb's attention/interest/imagination etc if something catches your attention etc, you notice it or feel interested in it 引起某人的注意／興趣／想像等: *The unusual panelling on the wall caught our attention.* 牆上那不尋常的鑲板引起了我們的注意。| *a story that will catch the imagination of every child* 能夠激發每個孩子想像力的故事 | **catch sb's eye** (=get sb's attention) 吸引某人的注意 *We need big, bold headlines – something to catch the reader's eye.* 我們需要大字黑體的標題，以便能夠引起讀者的注意。

11 ►HEAR/UNDERSTAND 聽見/理解◄ **not catch sth** to not hear or not understand what someone says 沒聽到，沒聽清; 沒聽懂: *Could you say that again? I didn't catch the last bit.* 你可以再說一遍嗎? 我沒聽清最後一部分。| *I'm afraid I didn't catch your name.* 我恐怕沒聽清你的名字。| *Did you catch the announcement?* 你聽到那個通知了嗎?

12 ►NOTICE 注意◄ [T not in progressive 不用進行式] to see or notice something for a moment〔短暫地〕見到，注意到: **catch sight of/catch a glimpse of** *I suddenly caught sight of her in the crowd.* 我突然在人羣中看見了她。| *Fans waited at the airport hoping to catch a glimpse of Gloria Estefan.* 歌迷守候在機場，希望能一睹格洛麗亞·艾斯特芬的風采。| **catch a whiff of** (=notice a smell for a moment)〔短暫地〕聞到〔某種氣味〕*Brad caught a whiff of smoke in the air.* 布萊德猛然聞到空氣中有一股煙味。

13 ►DESCRIBE WELL 成功描述◄ [T] to show or describe very successfully the character or quality of something, in a picture, a piece of writing etc〔圖畫、文章等〕成功地描述〔某物的性質或特點〕: *a novel that catches the mood of pre-war Britain* 生動地刻劃出戰前英國的社會氣氛的小說

14 ►BURN 燃燒◄ **a) catch fire** if something catches fire, it starts to burn accidentally 着火: *Two farm workers died when a barn caught fire.* 穀倉失火，兩名農場工人死亡。—see 見 FIRE[1] (USAGE) **b)** [I] if a fire catches it starts to burn 開始燃燒: *For some reason the charcoal isn't catching.* 不知怎的木炭點不着。

15 you won't catch me doing sth *spoken* used to say that you would never do something【口】別指望我會做某事: *You won't catch me ironing all his cotton shirts!* 別指望我會熨燙他所有的棉布襯衫!

16 be caught up in to be involved in something unwillingly 被迫捲入〔某事〕: *Children who were caught up in the crime are getting a lot of media attention.* 被脅迫參與犯罪的孩子得到媒體的大量關注。

17 catch yourself doing sth to suddenly realize that you are doing something 突然意識到自己在做某事: *Monica sometimes caught herself envying her students.* 莫妮卡有時會突然意識到自己在嫉妒學生。

18 ►PROBLEM 麻煩◄ [T] to discover a problem and stop it from developing any more 發現〔麻煩並阻止其進一步發展〕: *This kind of cancer can be cured, provided it is caught early enough.* 這種癌症發現得早的話是可以治癒的。

19 ►HIT 擊打◄ [T] to hit someone 打〔某人〕: **catch sb on the chin/face etc** *I caught him on the chin with a heavy punch.* 我一記重拳打在他的下巴上。

20 ►SPORT 體育運動◄ **a)** also 又作 **catch out** [T] to end a player's INNINGS in CRICKET (2) by taking and holding a ball hit off their BAT[1] (2a) before it touches the ground〔板球未着地前〕接住球使〔擊球手〕出局 **b)** [I] to be the CATCHER in a game of BASEBALL〔棒球比賽中〕充當接球手

21 ►BE PUNISHED 受懲罰◄ **you'll catch it** *BrE spoken* used to tell someone that they are going to be in trouble because they have done something wrong【英口】〔因做錯事〕你要吃苦頭了: *You'll catch it if your mother finds out where you've been.* 如果你媽發現你去過那種地方，你準要捱罵。

22 ►IN A BAD SITUATION 處於困境◄ **be caught in/without etc** to be in a situation that is difficult, because you cannot easily get out of it or because you do not have what you need〔因為無法克服困難或缺少所需的東西而〕處於困境: *We got caught in a rainstorm on the way here.* 來這裡的路上我們遇上了暴風雨。| *an actor caught without a script* 因缺劇本而感到為難的演員

23 catch your breath a) to stop breathing for a moment because something has surprised, frightened or shocked you〔因驚訝、恐懼、震驚而〕屏息 **b)** to pause for a moment after a lot of physical effort in order to breathe normally again 喘口氣, 緩口氣: *Hang on a minute, let me catch my breath!* 稍等一下, 讓我喘口氣!
24 ►SHINE ON 照射◄ [T] if the light catches something or if something catches the light, the light shines on it making it look bright (被) 光〔照射〕: *The sunlight caught her hair and turned it to gold.* 陽光照在她的頭髮上, 使之變成了金色。
25 ►CONTAINER 容器◄ [T] if a container catches liquid, it is in a position where the liquid falls into it 接住, 盛住〔水等液體〕: *Steve! Bring me something to catch the drips under this pipe.* 史蒂夫! 幫我拿個東西過來接住水管的滴水。
26 catch the sun *informal* to become sunburned (SUNBURN) so that your skin is red【非正式】皮膚被曬紅: *You've caught the sun on the back of your neck.* 你的脖子背後被曬紅了。

catch at sth *phr v* [T] to try to take hold of something 試圖抓住: *"You mean there's a real fire?" Heather caught at his arm.* "你是說真的失火了?" 希瑟用力抓住他的手臂。

catch on *phr v* [I] **1** to become popular and fashionable 流行: *It was a popular style in Britain but it never really caught on in America.* 這在英國是個受歡迎的款式, 但是在美國卻從來沒有真正流行起來。**2** to begin to understand or realize something (開始) 明白, 意識到: **[+to]** *It was a long time before the police caught on to what he was really doing.* 過了好長時間警方才搞清楚他其實在幹甚麼。

catch sb ↔ **out** *phr v* [T] *BrE*【英】**1** to make someone make a mistake, especially in order to prove that they are lying 識破〔錯誤〕, 故意使某人犯錯〔尤指為了證明某人撒謊〕: *It's a useful technique for handling people who are trying to catch you out.* 對付那些想讓你犯錯的人, 這可是個很有用的技巧。**2** if an unexpected event catches you out, it puts you in a difficult situation, because you were not ready to deal with it (使) 遭遇不測情況: *Didn't they ever tell you they in fact got caught out by the weather?* 難道他們沒告訴你他們實際上遇到了壞天氣嗎?

catch up *phr v* **1** [I,T] to improve so much that you reach the same standard as other people in your class, group etc〔水平〕追上, 趕上〔別人〕: *If you miss a lot of lessons, it's very difficult to catch up.* 如果你錯過了許多課, 就很難趕上了。| **[+with]** *At the moment our technology is more advanced, but other countries are catching up with us.* 目前我們的科技比較先進, 不過其他國家正在趕上來。**2** [I, T] to come from behind and reach someone in front by going faster 追上; 超過: **[+with]** *Drive faster, they're catching up with us.* 開快點, 他們要趕上我們了。| **catch sb up** *You go on ahead. I'll catch you up later.* 你先走, 我稍後就追上你。**3** [I] to do what needs to be done because you have not been able to do it until now 趕做, 補做: **[+on]** *I have some work to catch up on.* 我還有一些工作趕着要做。| *a chance to catch up on some sleep* (=after a period without enough sleep) 可以補睡一會兒的機會 | *You have a lot of catching up to do.* 你還有很多事情要補做。

catch up with sb *phr v* [T] **1** to finally find someone who has been doing something illegal and punish them〔終於〕抓住並懲罰〔罪犯〕: *It took six years for the law to catch up with them.* 警察花了六年時間才終於逮住他們。**2** if troubles, duties etc catch up with you, you cannot avoid them any longer〔麻煩、職責等〕纏身

catch² *n* **1** [C] *informal* a hidden problem or difficulty; SNAG¹(1)【非正式】陷阱, 隱患, 圈套, 詭計: *The rent is only £40 a week – there must be a catch somewhere.* 房租每週只需40鎊, 這裡面一定有些古怪。| **the catch is (that)** *The catch is that you can't enter the competition unless you've spent $100 in the store.* 圈套就在於, 你得在該店消費100美元, 否則你就進不了比賽。**2** [C] a hook or something similar for fastening a door or lid and keeping it shut 鎖鉤; 掛鉤, 吊扣 **3** [C] an act of catching a ball that has been thrown or hit 接球 (動作): *Hey! Nice catch!* 嘿! 多漂亮的接球! **4** [C] an amount of fish that has been caught〔魚的〕捕獲量: *Local fishermen are reporting record catches.* 當地漁民稱捕魚量創了紀錄。**5** [U] a simple game in which two or more people throw a ball to each other 接球遊戲: *Let's go outside and play catch.* 我們到外面去玩拋球接球吧。**6 be a good catch** *old-fashioned* if a man is a good catch, he is regarded as a very desirable husband, because he is rich and good-looking【過時】是理想的丈夫〔長得帥氣而且富有〕

catch-22 /ˌkætʃ twɛntɪˈtu; ˌkætʃ twentiˈtuː/ *n* [U] a situation in which you cannot do one thing until you do another thing, but you cannot do that until you have done the first thing, with the result that you can do neither 左右為難, 無法擺脫的困境, 進退維谷: **catch-22 situation** *It's a catch-22 situation – without experience you can't get a job and without a job you can't get experience.* 這是個無法擺脫的困局: 沒有經驗就找不到工作, 找不到工作你就沒有經驗。

catch·all¹ /ˈ· ·/ *adj* intended to include all situations or possibilities 無所不包的: **catch-all clause/list etc** *a vague catchall clause in an employment contract* 雇用合同裡一條模糊的無所不包的條款

catch·all² *n* [C] *AmE* a drawer, cupboard etc where you put any small objects【美】放置各種小雜物的抽屜[櫥櫃等]

catch crop /ˈ· ·/ *n* [C] a vegetable crop that grows quickly, planted between two rows of another crop 間種作物, 填閒作物〔在兩行主要作物之間快速生長的蔬菜類農作物〕

catch·er /ˈkætʃɚ; ˈkætʃə/ *n* [C] the player who sits on his heels behind the BATTER² (3) in a game of baseball〔棒球運動中的〕接球手 —see picture on page A22 參見A22頁圖

catch·ing /ˈkætʃɪŋ; ˈkætʃɪŋ/ *adj* [not before noun 不用於名詞前] *informal*【非正式】**1** a disease or illness that is catching is infectious〔疾病〕傳染 (性) 的: *Well, I hope it's not catching.* 嗯, 我希望這種病沒有傳染性。**2** an emotion or feeling that is catching spreads quickly among people〔情感〕具有感染力的

catch·ment ar·e·a /ˈkætʃmənt ˌɛrɪə; ˈkætʃmənt ˌeəriə/ *n* [C] **1** the area that a school takes its students from, that a hospital takes its patients from etc〔學校〕學生來源的區域;〔醫院〕病人集中的地區 **2** the area that a river or lake gets water from〔為河流或湖泊供水的〕集水區, 匯水盆地

catch·pen·ny /ˈ· ··/ *adj old-fashioned* cheap and of bad quality but made to look attractive【過時】價廉質劣但外表吸引的, 花哨而不值錢的

catch·phrase /ˈkætʃˌfrez; ˈkætʃfreɪz/ *n* [C] a short well-known phrase used regularly by an entertainer or politician, so that people think of that person when they hear it〔演員或政客常用的〕時髦話, 流行的詞句

catch·word /ˈkætʃˌwɝd; ˈkætʃwɜːd/ *n* [C] a word or phrase that is easy to remember and is repeated regularly by a political party, newspaper etc; SLOGAN〔政黨、報刊等的〕代表性口號, 標語

catch·y /ˈkætʃɪ; ˈkætʃi/ *adj* **catchy song/tune** a song or tune that is pleasant and easy to remember〔歌曲、曲調〕悅耳易記的: *a catchy advertising slogan like 'Go to Work on an Egg'* 朗朗上口的廣告標語如"吃個雞蛋去上班" —**catchily** *adv*

cat·e·chis·m /ˈkætəˌkɪzəm; ˈkætəˌkɪzəm/ *n* [singular] a set of questions and answers about the Christian religion that people learn in order to become full members of a church〔基督教的〕教理問答

cat·e·chize also 又作 **-ise** *BrE*【英】/ˈkætəˌkaɪz; ˈkætəkaɪz/ *v* [T] to teach someone about a religion by using a series of questions and answers 用問答法向〔某

人〕傳授教義

cat·e·gor·i·cal /ˌkætəˋgɔrɪkl; ˌkætɪ̣ˈgɒrɪkəl◂/ *adj* a categorical statement is a clear statement that something is definitely true 確實的, 明確的: **categorical denial/statement/assurance etc** *Can you give us a categorical assurance that no jobs will be lost?* 你能否明確向我們保證不會出現失業?

cat·e·gor·i·cally /ˌkætəˋgɔrɪklɪ; ˌkætɪ̣ˈgɒrɪkli/ *adv* in such a sure and certain way that there is no doubt 確定無疑地, 斷然地, 明確地: **categorically deny/refuse etc** *Forbes has categorically denied his guilt all along.* 福布斯自始至終都斷然否認他有任何過錯。

cat·e·go·rize also 又作 **-ise** *BrE*【英】/ˋkætəgəˌraɪz; ˈkætɪ̣gəraɪz/ *v* [T] to put people or things into groups according to what type they are, or to say which group they are in; CLASSIFY 對…進行分類; 把…列作: *The population is categorized according to age, sex, and socio-economic group.* 按年齡、性別和社會經濟羣體對人口進行分類。| **categorize sth/sb as** *Keene doesn't like to be categorized as a socialist.* 基尼不喜歡人們把他列為社會主義者。—**categorization** /ˌkætəgəraɪˋzeʃən; ˌkætɪ̣gəraɪˈzeɪʃən/ *n* [C,U]

S2 W2 **cat·e·go·ry** /ˋkætəˌgɔrɪ; ˈkætɪ̣gəri/ *n* [C] a group of people or things that all have the same particular qualities 類別, 種類, 範疇: **fall into a category** (=belong to a category) 屬於某類 *Voters fall into three main categories.* 選民分為三大類。

ca·ter /ˋketɚ; ˈkeɪtə/ *v* [I,T] to provide and serve food and drinks at a party, meeting etc, usually as a business〔在聚會、會議等上〕(為…)承包伙食; 承辦酒席: **[+for/at]** *Who's catering at your daughter's wedding?* 誰承辦你女兒的婚宴? | **cater sth** *AmE*【美】*Shouldn't we get bids for catering the 20th class reunion?* 我們難道不該爭取為第二十屆班級聚會提供酒水等服務嗎?

cater for sb/sth *phr v* [T] to provide a particular group of people with everything that they need or want 為…提供服務; 滿足…的要求: *a holiday company that caters more for the elderly* 一家較多為老年人提供假日活動的公司

cater to sb/sth *phr v* [T] to provide something that a particular type of person wants but that you think is bad, stupid etc 迎合, 投合: *It's the kind of movie that caters to the worst side of human nature.* 這是那種迎合人性陰暗面的電影。

ca·ter·er /ˋketərɚ; ˈkeɪtərə/ *n* [C] a person or company that is paid to provide and serve food and drinks at a party, meeting etc〔聚會、會議等的〕酒席承辦者: *What time will the caterers get here?* 飲食承辦人甚麼時候到?

ca·ter·ing /ˋketərɪŋ; ˈkeɪtərɪŋ/ *n* [U] the activity of providing and serving food and drinks at parties for money 承辦飲食服務: *Who did the catering?* 誰承辦酒席? —see also 另見 SELF-CATERING

cat·er·pil·lar /ˋkætɚˌpɪlɚ; ˈkætəˌpɪlə/ *n* [C] **1** a small creature like a WORM with a lot of legs that feeds on leaves and is the LARVA of a BUTTERFLY or other insect 毛蟲〔蝴蝶等昆蟲的幼蟲〕**2** also 又作 **caterpillar track** a belt made of metal plates that is fastened over the wheels of a heavy vehicle to help it to move over soft ground〔重型車輛的〕履帶 **3** also 又作 **caterpillar tractor** a heavy vehicle that is fitted with these belts 履帶式拖拉機

cat·er·waul /ˋkætɚˌwɔl; ˈkætəwɔːl/ *v* [I] to make a loud high unpleasant noise like the sound a cat makes 發出〔貓叫似的〕刺耳聲 —**caterwaul** *n* [singular]

cat flap /ˈ· ·/ *n* [C] an entrance to the house for your pet cat, consisting of a piece of wood or plastic which hangs down over a hole at the bottom of the door, and which can swing open 供家貓進出房屋的吊門

cat·gut /ˋkætgʌt; ˈkætgʌt/ *n* [U] strong thread made from the INTESTINES of animals and used for the strings of musical instruments〔用來製作琴弦的〕腸線, 腸弦

ca·thar·sis /kəˋθɑrsɪs; kəˈθɑːsɪ̣s/ *n* [C,U] *formal* a way of dealing with bad or strong feelings and emotions, by expressing or experiencing them through writing, talking, DRAMA etc【正式】〔通過寫作、戲劇等〕宣泄情感 —**cathartic** /-tɪk; -tɪk/ *adj*: *It was actually a cathartic experience to write my autobiography.* 寫自傳確實是我一次宣泄情感的經歷。

ca·the·dral /kəˋθidrəl; kəˈθiːdrəl/ *n* [C] a very large church, which is the main church of a particular area under the control of a BISHOP (1) 大教堂,〔主教控制的〕教區總教堂: *Durham cathedral* 達勒姆大教堂 | **cathedral city** (=one with a cathedral) 教區總教堂所在城市

cath·er·ine wheel /ˋkæθərɪn hwil; ˈkæθərɪ̣n wiːl/ *n* [C] a round FIREWORK that spins around 輪轉煙火

cath·e·ter /ˋkæθɪtɚ; ˈkæθɪ̣tə/ *n* [C] a thin tube that is put into your body to take away liquids〔置入體內以導出液體的〕導(液)管 —**catheterize** also 又作 **-ise** *BrE*【英】*v* [T]

cath·ode /ˋkæθod; ˈkæθəʊd/ *n* [C] *technical* the negative ELECTRODE from which electric current leaves a piece of equipment like a BATTERY (1)【術語】陰極, 負極—compare 比較 ANODE

cathode ray tube /ˌ·· ˈ· ·/ *n* [C] a piece of equipment used in televisions and computers, in which negative ELECTRONS from the cathode produce an image on a screen 陰極射線管, 電子射線管

Cath·o·lic /ˋkæθəlɪk; ˈkæθəlɪk/ *adj* connected with the Roman Catholic Church 與(羅馬)天主教有關的: *a Catholic school* 天主教學校 —**Catholic** *n* [C] —**Catholicism** /kəˋθɑləˌsɪzəm; kəˈθɒlɪ̣sɪzəm/ *n* [U]

catholic *adj formal*【正式】**have catholic tastes** to like a wide variety of things 興趣廣泛的 —**catholicity** /ˌkæθəˋlɪsətɪ; ˌkæθəˈlɪsɪ̣ti/ *n* [U]

cat·kin /ˋkætkɪn; ˈkætkɪn/ *n* [C] *especially BrE* a soft flower that grows in long thin groups and hangs from the branches of trees such as the WILLOW or BIRCH[1]【尤英】〔柳樹、樺樹等的〕葇荑花序; 楊花; 柳絮

cat lit·ter /ˈ· ˌ··/ *n* [U] a substance that people put down in boxes for cats that live indoors, so that they can pass waste from their BOWELS into it 貓沙

cat·nap /ˋkætnæp; ˈkætnæp/ *n* [C] *informal* a very short sleep【非正式】瞌睡, 小睡: *"Where's Grandma?" "She's having a catnap."* "奶奶在哪?" "她正在小睡。" —**cat nap** *v* [I]

cat-o'-nine-tails /ˌkæt ə ˋnaɪn ˌtelz; ˌkæt ə ˈnaɪn teɪlz/ *n* [C] a whip made of nine strings with knots on the end, used in the past for punishing people〔舊時用於懲罰人的由九根末尾帶結的繩子組成的〕九尾鞭

CAT scan /ˋkæt skæn; ˈkæt skæn/ *n* [C] the image produced by a CAT scanner 電腦化X射線軸向分層造影掃描圖

CAT scan·ner /ˋkæt ˌskænɚ; ˈkæt ˌskænə/ *n* [C] an electronic machine used in a hospital to look inside someone's body 電腦化X射線軸向分層造影掃描器

cat's cra·dle /ˌ· ˈ··/ *n* [U] a game children play with string which they wind around the fingers of both hands to make different patterns〔小孩玩的〕翻繩遊戲〔用線繩繞於手指上翻出各種花樣的遊戲〕

cat's eye /ˈ· ·/ *n* [C] one of the line of small flat objects fixed in the middle of the road, that shine when lit by car lights, to guide traffic in the dark〔置於道路中間, 黑暗中可藉車燈發光的〕道路反光裝置

cat's paw /ˈ· ·/ *n* [C] *old-fashioned* someone who does unpleasant or dangerous jobs because someone else has ordered them to【過時】奉命做危險或不愉快事情的人, 爪牙, 傀儡

cat suit /ˈ· ·/ *n* [C] a tight piece of women's clothing that covers all of the body and legs in one piece 女式緊身連衣褲

cat·sup /ˋkætsəp; ˈkætsəp/ *n* [U] *AmE*【美】an American spelling of KETCHUP ketchup 的美式拼法

cat·te·ry /ˋkætərɪ; ˈkætəri/ *n* [C] *BrE* a place where you can leave cats to be looked after while you are away from home【英】〔臨時寄養貓的〕貓屋, 貓窩

cat·tle /ˋkætl; ˈkætl/ *n* [plural] cows and BULLS kept on a farm for their meat or milk 牛〔指菜牛或奶牛〕: *herds of cattle* 一羣羣牛 | **20/100 etc head of cattle** (=20, 100 etc cattle) 20/100 頭牛

cattle grid /ˈ·· ·/ *BrE*【英】, **cattle guard** *AmE*【美】*n* [C] a set of bars placed over a hole in the road, so that animals cannot go across but cars can 攔畜溝柵〔鋪在路中坑洞的若干木棒, 汽車可通過而牲畜則走不過去〕

cat·tle·man /ˈkætlmən; ˈkætlmən/ *n* [C] someone who looks after or owns cattle 養牛人, 牧牛工人

cattle mar·ket /ˈ·· ˌ··/ *n* [C] *BrE*【英】**1** a place where cattle are bought and sold 牛市場 **2** *informal* a disapproving word for a beauty competition or a social event where women are judged only by their sexual attractiveness【非正式】〔只以色相取人的〕選美比賽

cattle truck /ˈ·· ·/ *n* [C] *BrE* a vehicle or part of a train that is made to carry cattle【英】運牛的卡車[火車(車廂)]

cat·ty /ˈkætɪ; ˈkæti/ *adj* someone who is catty is unpleasant and often says nasty things about people 愛說惡毒的話的, 壞心眼的, 令人討厭的: *She's a liar. Does that sound catty, too?* 她是個騙子。這聽起來是否也有點刻薄? —**cattily** *adv* —**cattiness** *n* [U]

catty-cor·ner /ˈ·· ˌ··/ *adv AmE*【美】KITTY CORNER 成對角線地, 斜線地

cat·walk /ˈkætˌwɔk; ˈkætwɔːk/ *n* [C] **1** a long raised path that MODELs walk on in a fashion show〔時裝模特兒走的〕伸展台 **2** a temporary structure for walking on, built around the outside of buildings or between them when they are being built or repaired〔臨時的〕步行小道

Cau·ca·sian /kɔˈkeʒən; kɔːˈkeɪziən/ *adj* someone who is Caucasian belongs to the race that has white or pale skin 高加索(人)的, 白種人的 —**Caucasian** *n* [C]

cau·cus /ˈkɔkəs; ˈkɔːkəs/ *n* [C] a group of people in a political party, who meet to discuss and decide on political plans〔政黨的〕決策者, 決策層

cau·dal /ˈkɔdl; ˈkɔːdl/ *adj technical* at or related to an animal's tail【術語】〔動物〕尾部的 —**caudally** *adv*

caught /kɔt; kɔːt/ the past tense and past participle of CATCH[1]

caul·dron, caldron /ˈkɔldrən; ˈkɔːldrən/ *n* [C] a large round metal pot for boiling liquids over a fire〔煮液體用的〕大鍋: *a witch's cauldron* 女巫的大鍋 —see picture at 參見 WITCH 圖

cau·li·flow·er /ˈkɔləˌflauə; ˈkɒlɪˌflaʊə/ *n* [C,U] a garden vegetable with green leaves around a large firm white centre 菜花, 花椰菜 —see picture on page A9 參見 A9 頁圖

cauliflower cheese /ˌ···· ˈ·/ *n* [U] *BrE* the white part of a cauliflower cooked and eaten with cheese SAUCE【英】乳酪菜花

cauliflower ear /ˌ···· ˈ·/ *n* [C] an ear permanently swollen into a strange shape, especially as a result of an injury〔尤指因受傷而造成的〕開花耳朵

caulk, calk /kɔk; kɔːk/ *v* [T] to fill the holes or cracks in something, especially a ship, with an oily or sticky substance that keeps water out〔用防水物料〕填塞〔船等的漏洞或裂縫〕

caus·al /ˈkɔzl; ˈkɔːzəl/ *adj* **1 causal relationship/link/connection etc** a relationship etc that exists between two or more events or situations, where one causes the other to happen 因果關係/聯繫等: *a causal relationship between unemployment and crime* 失業和犯罪之間的因果關係 **2** *technical* a causal CONJUNCTION (3), for example 'because', introduces a statement about the cause of something【術語】表示原因的〔連接詞〕—**causally** *adv*

cau·sal·i·ty /kɔˈzælətɪ; kɔːˈzæləti/ *n* [U] *formal* the relationship between a cause and the effect that it has【正式】因果關係, 因果性

cau·sa·tion /kɔˈzeʃən; kɔːˈzeɪʃən/ *n* [U] *formal*【正式】**1** the action of causing something to happen or exist 導致; 起因, 惹起 **2** causality 因果關係, 因果性

caus·a·tive /ˈkɔzətɪv; ˈkɔːzətɪv/ *adj formal*【正式】**1** acting as the cause of something 起因的, 成為…的原因的: *causative factors* 起因 **2** *technical* a causative verb expresses an action that causes something to happen or be【術語】〔動詞〕使役的 —**causatively** *adv*

cause¹ /kɔz; kɔːz/ *n* [S2] [W1]

1 ▶WHAT CAUSES STH 起因◀ [C] a person, event, or thing that makes something happen 原因, 起因: **[+of]** *What was the cause of the accident?* 那場事故的起因是甚麼? | *The doctor had recorded the cause of death as heart failure.* 醫生記錄了死亡的原因為心臟衰竭。| **root/underlying etc cause** (=the basic cause) 根本/基本原因 *The root cause of the crime problem is poverty.* 貧困是產生犯罪問題的根本原因。| **cause and effect** (=the idea or fact of one thing directly causing another) 因果 —see 見 REASON¹ (USAGE)

2 ▶GOOD REASON 恰當理由◀ [U] something that makes it right or fair for you to feel or behave in a particular way 理由, 根據, 緣故: **[+for]** *There is no cause for alarm.* 沒有理由驚慌。| **cause for complaint** (=a reason to complain) 抱怨的理由 *I've got no cause for complaint – I'm doing all right.* 我沒有理由抱怨 —— 我一切都好。| **cause for concern** (=a reason to be worried) 擔心的理由 *The patient's condition is giving cause for concern.* 病人的狀況令人擔憂。| **have good cause to** *God knows he's got good cause to be relieved.* 上帝知道他有充分的理由得到解脫。| **with/without good cause** *Many people are worried about the economy, and with good cause.* 許多人正為經濟狀況擔心, 這是有充分的理由的。

3 ▶STH YOU SUPPORT 支持的事物◀ a) [C] an organization, principle, or aim that a group of people support or fight for 極力維護[支持]的組織[原則、目標]: *How many of them are sympathetic to our cause?* 他們當中有多少人支持我們的事業? | **[+of]** *her lifelong devotion to the cause of women's rights* 她對女權運動終生不渝的獻身 **b) be in/for a good cause** if something you do is for a good cause, it is worth doing because it is intended to help other people, especially through a CHARITY (2) 為了正義的事業, 〔尤指〕為慈善: *Well, I don't mind giving if it's for a good cause.* 嗯, 如果是為慈善的話, 我不介意捐贈。

4 make common cause (with) *formal* to join with other people or groups for a particular purpose【正式】〔為某目的〕與…共同合作[齊心合力]: *Faced by an enemy on their territory, the French parties tried to make common cause.* 面對侵犯領土的敵人, 法國各黨派都團結起來。

5 ▶LAW 法律◀ [C] a case that is brought to a court of law 訴訟案件 —see also 另見 **lost cause** (LOST¹ (13))

cause² *v* [T] [S1] [W1] to make something happen 導致, 引起, 使發生: *Heavy traffic is causing long delays on the freeway.* 擁擠的交通造成高速公路上的長時間耽誤。| **cause sb/sth to do sth** *A dog ran into the road, causing the cyclist to swerve.* 一隻狗跑到了道路上, 使得那位騎腳踏車的人突然轉向。| **cause concern/uncertainty/embarrassment etc** (=make people feel worried, unsure, embarrassed etc) 使人感到擔憂/不知所措/尷尬等 *The constant changes of policy have caused a great deal of uncertainty in the workforce.* 政策的不斷改變使得勞動大軍感到疑惑。| **cause sb trouble/problems/inconvenience etc** *Jimmy's behaviour is causing me a lot of problems.* 吉米的所作所為給我帶來許多麻煩。| **cause offence** (=offend someone) 冒犯〔某人〕*I'm sorry; I didn't mean to cause offence.* 對不起, 我不是有意冒犯的。

USAGE NOTE 用法說明: CAUSE

GRAMMAR 語法

Something can **cause** death/crime/trouble etc, or **cause** somebody inconvenience/a problem etc. cause 可以表示某事物導致死亡/犯罪/麻煩等, 或為某人帶來不便/問題等: *His behaviour caused everyone a lot of worry* (NOT 不用 *caused to everyone...*). 他的行為使大家非常擔心。

Something can **cause** someone or something **to** do something. cause可以用於表示某事物使某人或某物做某事: *The disease caused his face to swell* (NOT *caused that his face swelled,* or *caused his face swell,* though you could say less formally ...*made his face swell*). 這種病使他的臉腫起來了〔不用caused that his face swelled, 或 caused his face swell. 雖然較隨便的說法可以是 ...made his face swell〕。

SPELLING 拼法

Remember the difference between **cause**, and *because* and *of course.* 記住 cause, because 和 of course之間的區別。

C

cause cé·lè·bre /ˌkoz sɛˋlɛbrə; ˌkəʊz seˈlebrə/ *n* [C] *French* an event or legal case that a lot of people become interested in, because it is an exciting subject to discuss or argue about【法】轟動一時的事件; 引起公眾關注的訴訟案

cause·way /ˈkɔzˌwe; ˈkɔːzweɪ/ *n* [C] a raised road or path across wet ground or through water〔穿越濕地或水面的〕墊高的堤道, 砌道

caus·tic /ˈkɔstɪk; ˈkɔːstɪk/ *adj* **1** a caustic substance can burn through things by chemical action〔物質〕苛性的; 腐蝕性的 **2** a caustic remark criticizes someone in a way that is unkind but often cleverly humorous〔語言〕尖刻的; 諷刺的 —**caustically** /-klɪ; -kli/ *adv*

caustic so·da /ˌ.. ˈ../ *n* [U] a very strong chemical substance that you can use for some difficult cleaning jobs〔清潔用的〕燒鹼; 苛性鈉

cau·ter·ize also 又作 **-ise** *BrE*【英】/ˈkɔtəˌraɪz; ˈkɔːtəraɪz/ *v* [T] *technical* to burn a wound with hot metal or a chemical to stop the blood or stop it becoming infected【術語】〔用燒灼劑或烙鐵〕烙, 燒灼〔傷口以消毒或止血〕

cau·tion¹ /ˈkɔʃən; ˈkɔːʃən/ *n* **1** [U] the quality of being very careful, not taking any risks, and trying to avoid danger 小心, 謹慎, 慎重: **with caution** *We must proceed with caution.* 我們必須謹慎行事。| **great/extreme caution** *the need for extreme caution when handling these animals* 安置這些動物需要極為小心 | **treat sth with caution** (=think carefully about something because it might not be true) 仔細斟酌某事 *Evidence given by convicted criminals should always be treated with caution.* 對已被判刑的罪犯所提供的證據應經常予以仔細審察。**2** **word/note of caution** a warning to be careful 警示, 警告〔某人小心〕: *One note of caution, don't let your children try this trick.* 提醒你, 不要讓你的孩子嘗試這種把戲。**3** **throw/fling/cast caution to the winds** to start to take more risks in what you do or say 不顧一切/魯莽行事: *Throwing all caution to the winds, she swung around to face him.* 她不顧一切地轉身面對他。**4** [C] *BrE* a spoken official warning given by someone in authority when you have done something wrong that is not a serious crime【英】〔給犯了輕罪的人的〕正式(口頭)警告, 訓誡: *The judge let him off with a caution.* 法官給他一個訓誡就釋放了他。**5** [singular] *old-fashioned* an amusing person【過時】滑稽有趣的人

caution² *v* [T] **1** to warn someone that something might be dangerous, difficult etc 警告, 告誡, 提醒: **caution sb about/ against** *Geraldine cautioned the boys about talking to strange men.* 傑拉爾丁告誡孩子不要隨便和陌生人說話。| **caution (sb) that** *Foreign Office officials were quick to caution that these remarks did not mean there would be a new peace initiative.* 外交部官員迅速告誡說這些評論並不意味着會有新的和平舉措。**2** *BrE* to warn someone officially that the next time they do something illegal they will be punished【英】給某人正式警告: **caution sb for/about** *She got cautioned for speeding.* 她因開快車而被警告。

cau·tion·ar·y /ˈkɔʃənˌɛrɪ; ˈkɔːʃənəri/ *adj* giving a warning or advice 警告的, 告誡的: *a cautionary note on the abuse of power* 對濫用職權的警告 | **cautionary tale** (=the story of an event that can be used to warn people) 警世故事 *It's a cautionary tale about how not to buy a computer.* 那是一個關於如何不買電腦的告誡性故事。

cau·tious /ˈkɔʃəs; ˈkɔːʃəs/ *adj* careful to avoid danger or risks 小心的, 謹慎的, 慎重的: *a cautious driver* 一位謹慎的司機 | **cautious about doing sth** *I've always been very cautious about giving my address to strangers.* 我總是很小心, 不輕易把我的地址給陌生人。| **cautious optimism** (=hopes for a good result while being careful not to expect too much) 審慎的樂觀 —**cautiously** *adv*: *Sara opened the door cautiously and peeped in.* 莎拉小心翼翼地打開門往裡面瞧。—**cautiousness** *n* [U]

cav·al·cade /ˌkævḷˋked; ˌkævəlˈkeɪd/ *n* [C] a line of people on horses or in cars or carriages moving along as part of a ceremony〔作為禮儀一部分的〕騎馬隊; 車隊

Cav·a·lier /ˌkævəˋlɪr; ˌkævəˈlɪə◂/ *n* [C] a supporter of the King against parliament in the English Civil War of the 17th century〔英國17世紀內戰中的〕保王黨成員 —compare 比較 ROUNDHEAD

cavalier *adj* not caring or thinking about other people's feelings 滿不在乎的, 隨便的, 輕漫的: *The complaints show these companies have been treating the issue in a cavalier way.* 這些投訴說明這些公司在處理這一事件時態度輕率。

cav·al·ry /ˈkævḷrɪ; ˈkævəlri/ *n* [U] **1** the part of an army that fights on horses, especially in the past〔尤指舊時的〕騎兵(部隊) **2** the part of a modern army that uses tanks (TANK¹ (3)) 坦克部隊, 裝甲兵部隊

cav·al·ry·man /ˈkævḷrɪmən; ˈkævəlrimən/ *n* [C] a soldier who fights on a horse 騎兵

cave¹ /kev; keɪv/ *n* [C] a large natural hole in the side of a cliff or hill, or under the ground 洞穴; 山洞; 岩洞; 窖洞 —see picture on page A12 參見A12頁圖

cave² *v*

cave in *phr v* [I] **1** if the top or sides of something cave in, they fall down or inwards 塌落, 坍塌, 陷下: [+on] *The roof of the tunnel just caved in on us.* 隧道頂坍塌壓住了我們。**2** to finally stop opposing something, especially because someone has persuaded or threatened you〔尤指因某人勸說或威脅而〕停止反對; 屈服, 投降: *You don't know, they might cave in straight away and give us what we want.* 你不知道, 他們可能馬上就會屈服, 給我們所要求的東西。—**cave-in** *n* [C]

ca·ve·at /ˈkevɪˌæt; ˈkeɪviæt/ *n* [C] *formal* a warning that you must pay attention to something before you make a decision or take a particular action【正式】〔做決定或行動前必須注意的〕警告, 提醒

caveat emp·tor /ˈkevɪˌæt ˋɛmptɔr; ˌkeɪviæt ˈemptɔː/ *n* [U] *Latin* the principle that when goods are sold, the buyer is responsible for checking the quality of the goods【拉丁】〔買主〕購物前驗貨(原則)

cave·man /ˈkevˌmæn; ˈkeɪvmæn/ *n* [C] **1** someone who lived in a CAVE¹ many thousands of years ago〔史前時代的〕穴居人 **2** *informal* a man who behaves rudely or violently【非正式】野蠻人, 舉止粗野的人: *He used caveman tactics of rough behaviour towards women.* 他對待婦女極其野蠻無禮。

cav·ern /ˈkævən; ˈkævən/ *n* [C] a large CAVE¹ 大洞穴

cav·ern·ous /ˈkævənəs; ˈkævənəs/ *adj* a cavernous room, space, or hole is very large and deep〔房間、空間〕像大洞穴的, 大而深的: *a cavernous dining hall* 一個很大的食堂 —**cavernously** *adv*

cav·i·ar, caviare /ˌkævɪˋɑr; ˈkæviɑː/ *n* [U] **1** the preserved eggs of various large fish, eaten as a special very expensive food 魚子醬 **2** **caviar to the general** *BrE literary* something that only a sensitive and educated person can enjoy or understand【英, 文】曲高和寡的事物, 陽春白雪

cav·il /ˈkævḷ; ˈkævəl/ *v* **cavilled, cavilling** *BrE*【英】**caviled, caviling** *AmE*【美】[I+at] *formal* to make unnecessary complaints about someone or something【正

式】無端指責, 挑剔, (對...) 吹毛求疵

cav·ing /ˈkevɪŋ; ˈkeɪvɪŋ/ *n* [U] the sport of going deep under the ground in CAVE*s* 洞穴探察; SPELUNKING *AmE*【美】

cav·i·ty /ˈkævətɪ; ˈkævəti/ *n* [C] **1** *formal* a hole or space inside something【正式】腔, 洞, 窟窿 **2** *technical* a hole in a tooth made by decay【術語】蛀牙洞

cavity wall /ˈ··· ˌ·/ *n* [C] a wall consisting of two walls with a space between them to keep out cold and noise〔防寒或隔音的〕夾層牆, 空心牆

cavity wall in·su·la·tion /ˌ··· · ··ˈ··/ *n* [U] a substance put inside a cavity wall to keep heat inside a building 空心牆保暖材料

ca·vort /kəˈvɔrt; kəˈvɔːt/ *v* [I] to jump or dance around noisily in a playful or sexual way 狂舞; 跳躍; 亂跳亂蹦: *Pictures appeared in newspapers of the two of them cavorting on a beach.* 報紙上登出了他們兩人在海灘上歡呼雀躍的照片。

caw /kɔ; kɔː/ *n* [C] the loud unpleasant sound made by some types of bird, especially the CROW[1] (1)〔尤指烏鴉等鳥類難聽的〕哇哇的叫聲 —**caw** *v* [I]

cay /ki; kiː/ *n* [C] *AmE* a very small low island formed of CORAL[1] or sand【美】珊瑚島, 沙洲

cay·enne pep·per /ˌkeɪɛnˈpɛpɚ; ˌkeɪen ˈpepə/ *n* [U] the red powder made from a PEPPER[1] (3) that has a very hot taste (紅) 辣椒粉

cay·man /ˈkemən; ˈkeɪmən/ *n* [C] a South American animal like an ALLIGATOR〔南美的〕短吻鱷

CB /ˌsi ˈbi; ˌsiː ˈbiː◂/ *n* [U] Citizen's Band; a radio on which people can speak to each other over short distances, especially when they are driving 民用波段〔尤其用於人們駕車時近距離通話的無線電通訊方式〕—**CB-er** *n* [C]

CBE /ˌsi bi ˈi; ˌsiː biː ˈiː/ *n* [C] Commander of the British Empire; an honour given to some British people for things they have done for their country 大英帝國勳章

cc 1 carbon copy to; used at the end of a business letter to show that you are sending a copy to someone else 副本交, 抄送呈交: *To Neil Fry, cc. Anthea Baker, Matt Fox* 交: 尼爾·弗賴伊, 副本交: 安西婭·貝克, 馬特·福克斯 **2** the abbreviation of 縮寫= CUBIC CENTIMETRE 立方厘米: *a 200 cc engine* 200 立方厘米的發動機[引擎]

CCTV[1] the written abbreviation of 縮寫= CLOSED CIRCUIT TELEVISION 閉路電視, 有線電視

CCTV[2] the written abbreviation of 縮寫= China Central Television 中國中央電視台

CD /ˌsi ˈdi; ˌsiː ˈdiː◂/ *n* [C] compact disc; a small circular piece of hard plastic on which high quality recorded sound or large quantities of information can be stored〔電腦的〕光盤, 光碟; 激光[雷射]唱片

CD player 激光[雷射]唱片機

CD player /ˈ·ˈ· ˌ··/ *n* [C] a piece of equipment used to play COMPACT DISC*s* 激光[雷射]唱片機

CD-ROM /ˌsi di ˈrɑm; ˌsiː diː ˈrɒm/ *n* [C,U] compact disc read-only memory; a CD on which large quantities of information can be stored to be used by a computer 唯讀光碟, 只讀光盤, 光盤只讀存儲器 —see picture on page A14 參見 A14 頁圖

CDT /ˌsi di ˈti; ˌsiː diː ˈtiː/ *n* [U] Craft, Design, and Technology; a practical subject studied in British schools 工藝、設計和技術課〔英國學校開設的一門實用學科〕

cease[1] /sis; siːs/ *v* [I,T] *formal* to stop doing something or stop happening【正式】停止, 終止, 結束: **cease (doing) sth** *The company ceased trading at 6 pm today.* 這家公司今天下午 6 點就停止交易了。| *It rained all day without ceasing.* 雨不停地下了一整天。| **cease sth** *The committee decided to cease financial support.* 委員會決定終止財政支持。| **cease to do sth** *Most people had already ceased to obey the curfew.* 大多數人早已不再遵守宵禁的命令了。| **cease to exist** *The town which Joyce wrote about has long since ceased to exist.* 喬伊斯所描寫的那個小鎮早已不復存在了。| **cease fire!** (=used to order soldiers to stop shooting)〔命令士兵〕停止射擊! 停火! —see also 另見 CEASEFIRE, **wonders will never cease** (WONDER[2] (6)) W3

cease[2] *n* **without cease** *formal* without stopping【正式】不停地, 持續地

cease·fire /ˈsisˌfaɪr; ˈsiːsfaɪə/ *n* [C] an agreement to stop fighting for a period of time, especially so that a more permanent agreement can be made 停火[停戰]協議: *negotiating a ceasefire* 為達成停火協定而談判 —compare 比較 ARMISTICE, TRUCE

cease·less /ˈsislɪs; ˈsiːsləs/ *adj formal* happening or existing for a long time without changing or stopping【正式】不停的, 持續的, 不斷的: *the ceaseless fight against crime* 對犯罪的不停打擊 —**ceaselessly** *adv*

ce·dar /ˈsidɚ; ˈsiːdə/ *n* **1** [C] a large EVERGREEN[2] tree with leaves shaped like needles 雪松, 西洋杉 **2** also 又作 **cedarwood** [U] the hard reddish wood of this tree that smells pleasant 雪松木, 杉木

cede /sid; siːd/ *v* [T] *formal* to give something such as an area of land or a right to a country or person, especially when you are forced to【正式】〔尤指被迫〕割讓〔領土或主權〕, 把...讓給 —see also 另見 CESSION

ce·dil·la /sɪˈdɪlə; sɪˈdɪlə/ *n* [C] a mark put under the letter 'c' in French and some other languages, to show that it is an 's' sound instead of a 'k' sound. It is written 'ç'.〔加在法語或其他一些語言的 c 字母下的〕下加符, 尾形符〔表示應讀成 /s/ 而不是 /k/〕

Cee·fax /ˈsifæks; ˈsiːfæks/ *n* [U] *trademark* an information service that has no sound and is provided on television by the BBC in Britain【商標】〔英國廣播公司提供的〕圖文電視

cei·lidh /ˈkelɪ; ˈkeɪli/ *n* [C] an evening entertainment with Scottish or Irish singing and dancing 同樂會〔有蘇格蘭或愛爾蘭歌舞的晚間娛樂活動〕

ceil·ing /ˈsilɪŋ; ˈsiːlɪŋ/ *n* [C] **1** the inner surface of the top part of a room 天花板, 頂篷 —compare 比較 ROOF[1] (2) **2** the largest number or amount of something that is officially allowed 上限, 最高限度: *a budget ceiling of $5000* 上限為 5000 美元的預算 | *The government imposed a ceiling on imports of foreign cars.* 政府對進口外國汽車的數量實行了上限規定。**3** *technical* the greatest height an aircraft can fly at or the level of the clouds【術語】最大飛行高度, 升限; 雲幕高度 —see also 另見 **glass ceiling** (GLASS[1] (7)) S3 W3

ce·leb /səˈlɛb; səˈleb/ *n* [C] *informal* a CELEBRITY【非正式】名人, 明星

cel·e·brant /ˈsɛləbrənt; ˈseləbrənt/ *n* [C] someone who performs or takes part in a religious ceremony 主持[參加]宗教儀式的人

cel·e·brate /ˈsɛləˌbret; ˈseləbreɪt/ *v* **1** [I,T] to show that an event or occasion is important by doing something special or enjoyable 慶祝: *It's Dad's birthday and we're going out for a meal to celebrate.* 今天是爸爸的生日, 我們打算出去吃飯, 慶祝一下。| *We've bought champagne to celebrate Jan's promotion.* 我們買了香檳來慶賀傑恩的提升。| **celebrate sth** *My folks are celebrating their 50th anniversary.* 我父母正在慶祝他們的 50 週年紀念。| **celebrate Christmas/Thanksgiving etc** W3

C

The Chinese celebrate their New Year in January or February. 中國人在一月或二月慶祝他們的新年。**2** [T] *formal* to praise someone or something in speech or writing【正式】〔口頭或書面〕讚揚, 讚美, 歌頌: *poems that celebrate the joys of love* 讚美愛情之歡樂的詩歌 **3** to perform a religious ceremony, especially the Christian Mass 主持〔宗教儀式, 尤指彌撒〕

cel·e·brat·ed /ˋsɛləbretɪd; ˈseləbreɪtəd/ *adj* famous; talked about a lot 著名的, 聞名的: *a celebrated professor* 一位著名的教授 | *a celebrated legal case* 一宗備受關注的法律案件

3 **cel·e·bra·tion** /ˌsɛləˋbreʃən; ˌseləˈbreɪʃən/ *n* **1** [C] an occasion or party when you celebrate something 慶祝會, 慶祝活動: *I don't feel like getting involved in any New Year's celebrations.* 我不想參加任何新年慶祝活動。**2** [U] the act of celebrating 慶祝: **in celebration of** (=in order to celebrate something) 為...舉行慶祝活動 *There'll be a reception in celebration of the Fund's 70th Anniversary.* 為了慶祝基金會成立70週年, 將會舉行一個招待會。

cel·e·bra·to·ry /ˋsɛləbrətɔrɪ; ˌseləˈbreɪtəri◂/ *adj* [only before noun 僅用於名詞前] done in order to celebrate a particular event or occasion 表示慶祝的, 為了慶祝的: *Join us for a celebratory drink in the bar.* 和我們一起去酒吧喝一杯慶祝一下。

ce·leb·ri·ty /səˋlɛbrətɪ; səˈlebrəti/ *n* **1** [C] a famous person, especially someone in the entertainment business 〔尤指娛樂界的〕名人, 明星 **2** [U] *formal* the state of being famous; fame【正式】著名; 名譽, 名聲

ce·ler·i·ty /səˋlɛrətɪ; səˈlerəti/ *n* [U] *formal* great speed【正式】迅速, 快速

cel·e·ry /ˋsɛlərɪ; ˈseləri/ *n* [U] a vegetable with long pale green stems that you can eat cooked or uncooked 芹菜: *a stick of celery* 一根芹菜 —see picture on page A9 參見A9頁圖

ce·les·ti·al /səˋlɛstʃəl; səˈlestiəl/ *adj formal*【正式】**1** related to the sky or heaven 天空的, 天上的; 天堂的: **celestial bodies** (=the sun, moon, stars etc) 天體〔太陽、月亮、星星等〕**2** *literary* very beautiful【文】極美的, 異常美麗的

cel·i·bate /ˋsɛləbɪt; ˈseləbət/ *adj* not married and not having sex, especially because of your religious beliefs 〔尤指因宗教原因而〕獨身的; 禁慾的: *Catholic priests are required to be celibate.* 天主教神父按要求不能結婚。—**celibate** *n* [C] —**celibacy** /-bəsɪ; -bəsi/ *n* [U]: *a vow of celibacy* 奉行獨身的誓言

1 **cell** /sɛl; sel/ *n* [C] **1** the smallest part of a living thing that can exist independently 細胞: *cancer cells* 癌細胞 | *red blood cells* 紅血球 **2** a small room in a prison, MONASTERY, or CONVENT where someone sleeps 小囚室, 牢房; 〔修道院的〕斗室, 單人房間 **3** a piece of equipment for producing electricity from chemicals, heat, or light 電池: *alkaline battery cells* 鹼性電池 **4** a small group of people who are working secretly as part of a larger political organization 〔政治組織的〕分部, 祕密活動小組: *a terrorist cell* 恐怖分子小組 **5** a small space that an insect or other small creature has made to live in or use 〔蜂巢中單個的〕小蜂窩, 蜂房: *the cells of a honeycomb* 蜂巢的蜂房

cel·lar /ˋsɛlɚ; ˈselə/ *n* [C] **1** a room under a house or other building, often used for storing things 地窖, 地下貯藏室 **2** a store of wine belonging to a person, restaurant etc 〔私人或餐館的〕酒窖

cel·lar·age /ˋsɛlərɪdʒ; ˈselərɪdʒ/ *n* [U] **1** the charge for storing something in a cellar 地窖貯藏費 **2** the size of a cellar 地窖的面積

cell di·vi·sion /ˈ· ·ˌ··/ *n* [C,U] the process by which plant and animal cells increase their numbers 細胞分裂

cel·list /ˋtʃɛlɪst; ˈtʃeləst/ *n* [C] someone who plays the cello 大提琴演奏者

cel·lo /ˋtʃɛlo; ˈtʃeləʊ/ *n* [C] a large musical instrument shaped like a VIOLIN that you hold between your knees and play by pulling a special stick across wire strings 大提琴

Cel·lo·phane /ˋsɛləˌfen; ˈseləfeɪn/ *n* [U] *trademark* thin transparent material used for wrapping things【商標】〔包裝用的〕玻璃紙

cell·phone /ˋsɛlˌfon; ˈselfəʊn/ *n* [C] a cellular phone 手提電話, 移動電話, 手機

cel·lu·lar /ˋsɛljəlɚ; ˈseljələ/ *adj* **1** consisted of or related to the cells of plants or animals 細胞的, 由細胞組成的 **2** **cellular blanket/clothes etc** loosely woven covers, clothes etc that keep you warm 有網眼的毯子/外衣等 **3** having a lot of holes; POROUS 多孔的: *cellular rock* 多孔的岩石

cellular phone /ˌ··· ˈ·/ *n* [C] a telephone that you can carry around with you, that works from a system that uses a network of radio stations to pass on signals 〔利用電台網通訊的〕手提電話, 移動電話, 手機

cel·lu·lite /ˋsɛljulaɪt; ˈseljəlaɪt/ *n* [U] fat that is just below someone's skin and makes it look uneven and unattractive 皮下脂肪團

cel·lu·loid /ˋsɛljəˌlɔɪd; ˈseljəlɔɪd/ *n trademark*【商標】**1** **on celluloid** on cinema film 攝在電影膠片上, 在電影裡: *Chaplin's comic genius is preserved on celluloid.* 卓別林的喜劇天才在電影裡被保存下來。**2** [U] a plastic substance made mainly from CELLULOSE (2) that used to be made into photographic film 賽璐珞〔舊時用以製作攝影膠片的材料〕

cel·lu·lose /ˋsɛljəˌlos; ˈseljələʊs/ *n* [U] **1** the material that the cell walls of plants are made of and that is used to make plastics, paper etc 細胞膜質; 纖維素 **2** also 又作 **cellulose acetate** *technical* a plastic that is used for many industrial purposes, especially making photographic film and explosives【術語】醋酸纖維素〔工業上用於製造攝影膠卷和炸藥〕

Cel·si·us /ˋsɛlsɪəs; ˈselsiəs/ abbreviation 縮寫為 **C** *n* [U] a temperature scale in which water freezes at 0° and boils at 100°; CENTIGRADE 攝氏溫度: *12° Celsius* 攝氏12度 —**Celsius** *adj*: *a Celsius thermometer* 攝氏溫度計

Cel·tic /ˋsɛltɪk; ˈkeltɪk/ *adj* related to the Celts, an ancient European people, or to their languages 凱爾特人的; 凱爾特語的

ce·ment¹ /səˋmɛnt; sɪˈment/ *n* [U] **1** a grey powder made from LIME¹ (3) and clay, that becomes hard when it is mixed with water and allowed to dry, and that is used in building 水泥: *I think he's outside mixing cement and laying bricks.* 我想他正在外面和水泥砌磚。**2** a thick sticky substance that becomes very hard when it dries and is used for filling holes or sticking things together 膠接劑, 接合劑

cement² *v* [T] **1** also 又作 **cement over** to cover something with cement 在...上抹水泥 **2** to make a relationship between people or countries firm and strong 加強, 鞏固〔關係、友誼〕: *His marriage to Lucy Brett cemented important business ties with her family.* 他和露茜·布雷特的婚姻鞏固了與她家族的重要商業聯繫。

cement mix·er /ˈ·ˌ ˌ··/ *n* [C] a machine with a round drum that turns around, into which you put cement, sand, and water to make CONCRETE; CONCRETE MIXER 水泥[混凝土]攪拌機

cem·e·tery /ˋsɛməˌtɛrɪ; ˈsemətri/ *n* [C] a piece of land, usually not belonging to a church, in which dead people are buried 〔通常不屬於教會的〕公墓, 墓地 —compare 比較 CHURCHYARD, GRAVEYARD

cen·o·taph /ˋsɛnəˌtæf; ˈsenətɑːf/ *n* [C] a MONUMENT built to remind you of soldiers, sailors etc who were killed in a war and are buried somewhere else 〔為葬於別處的陣亡將士立的〕紀念碑

cen·sor¹ /ˋsɛnsɚ; ˈsensə/ *n* [C] someone whose job is to examine books, films, letters etc and remove anything considered to be offensive, morally harmful, or politically dangerous 〔書刊、電影、書信等的〕檢查員, 監察員, 審查官

censor² *v* [T] to examine books, films, letters etc to remove anything that is considered offensive, morally harmful, or politically dangerous etc 審查〔書刊、電影、信件等〕

cen·so·ri·ous /sɛn`sɔrɪəs; sen'sɔːriəs/ *adj formal* always looking for mistakes and faults in other people and wanting to criticize them【正式】愛挑剔的, 苛評的, 吹毛求疵的: *She didn't used to be so censorious of others' behaviour.* 她過去並不是那麼挑剔別人的行為的。—**censoriously** *adv* —**censoriousness** *n* [U]

cen·sor·ship /`sɛnsɚ͵ʃɪp; 'sensəʃɪp/ *n* [U] the practice or system of censoring something 審查 (制度), 檢查 (體制): *the censorship of television programmes* 電視節目審查制度

cen·sure¹ /`sɛnʃɚ; 'senʃə/ *n* [U] *formal* the act of expressing strong disapproval and criticism【正式】嚴厲譴責, 批評: *a vote of censure* 不信任票

censure² *v* [T] *formal* to officially criticize someone for something they have done wrong【正式】嚴厲批評, 正式譴責: *The inspector was officially censured for his handling of the demonstration.* 這名督察因處理這次示威不當而受到官方譴責。

cen·sus /`sɛnsəs; 'sensəs/ *n plural* **censuses** [C] **1** an official process of counting a country's population and finding out about the people 人口普查 **2** an official process of counting something for government planning〔官方進行的〕統計, 調查: *a traffic census* 交通情況調查

1 1 **cent** /sɛnt; sent/ *n* [C] **1** 0.01 of the main unit of currency in some countries, or a coin worth this amount. For example, there are 100 cents in one US dollar. 分; 分幣〔一美元或某些十進制貨幣單位的百分之一〕 **2 put in your two cents' worth** *AmE* to give your opinion about something, when other people do not want to hear it【美】〔未獲邀請而〕發表意見 —see also 另見 **red cent** (RED¹ (8))

cen·taur /`sɛntɔr; 'sentɔː/ *n* [C] a creature in ancient Greek stories with the head, chest, and arms of a man and the body and legs of a horse〔希臘神話中的〕人頭馬怪物, 半人半馬怪物

cen·te·nar·i·an /͵sɛntə`nɛrɪən; ͵sentɪ̵'neəriən/ *n* [C] someone who is 100 years old or older 百歲〔或百歲以上〕老人

cen·te·na·ry /`sɛntə͵nɛrɪ; sen'tiːnəri/ also 又作 **cen·ten·ni·al** /sɛn`tɛnɪəl; sen'teniəl/ *AmE*【美】*n* [C] the day or year exactly 100 years after a particular event 一百週年 (紀念): *a concert to mark the centenary of the composer's birth* 為該作曲家百年誕辰而舉辦的音樂會

cen·ter /`sɛntɚ; 'sentə/ *n v* the American spelling of CENTRE centre 的美式拼法

centi- /sɛntə; sentɪ̵/ *prefix* also 又作 **cent-** /sɛnt; sent/ **1** 100 一百: *a centipede* (=creature with 100 legs) 蜈蚣 [百足蟲] **2** 100th part of a unit 百分之一: *a centimetre* (=0.01 metre) 厘米 (=0.01米) —see table on page C4 參見C4 頁附錄

Cen·ti·grade /`sɛntə͵gred; 'sentɪ̵greɪd/ *n* [U] CELSIUS 攝氏度 —**Centigrade** *adj*

cen·ti·gram, centigramme /`sɛntə͵græm; 'sentɪ̵græm/ *n* [C] a unit for measuring weight. There are 100 centigrams in one gram. 厘克〔百分之一克〕—see table on page C3 參見 C3 頁附錄

cen·time /`sɑntim; 'sɒntiːm/ *n* [C] 0.01 of a FRANC or some other units of money, or a coin worth this amount 生丁〔百分之一法郎〕, 分; 分幣

cen·ti·me·tre *BrE*【英】, **centimeter** *AmE*【美】/`sɛntə͵mitɚ; 'sentɪ̵͵miːtə/ written abbreviations 縮寫為 **c** and **cm** *n* [C] a unit for measuring length. There are 100 centimetres in one metre. 厘米〔百分之一米〕—see table on page C3 參見 C3 頁附錄

cen·ti·pede /`sɛntə͵pid; 'sentɪ̵piːd/ *n* [C] a small creature like a WORM with a lot of very small legs 百足蟲, 蜈蚣

cen·tral /`sɛntrəl; 'sentrəl/ *adj* **1** [only before noun, no comparative 僅用於名詞前, 無比較級] a central organization, system etc makes decisions or controls the operation of a whole country or large organization 中心的, 中央的: *central planning* 中心計劃 | *the central committee of the Chinese Communist Party* 中國共產黨中央委員會 | *I'm not advocating central government.* 我不主張建立中央政府。| *All the money is allocated from a central fund.* 所有的資金都是從一個中央基金下撥的。**2** [only before noun, no comparative 僅用於名詞前, 無比較級] in the middle of an object or an area 中心的, 中部的, 在中間的: *Central Asia* 中亞 | *The houses face onto a central courtyard.* 這些房子都面向一個中心院子。**3** more important and having more influence than anything else 重要的, 主要的: *Owen played a central role in the negotiations.* 歐文在這次談判中扮演了重要角色。| **[+to]** *The inevitability of mass poverty is central to Malthus's argument.* 馬爾薩斯的中心論點是人民大眾的貧窮是無可避免的。| **of central importance** *Environmental issues are rapidly taking a position of central importance in the political debate.* 環境問題在這次政治辯論中很快成為中心議題。| **central idea/theme/concern etc** *A responsible press was a central theme running through the speech.* 這次演講的中心主題是出版社的責任感問題。**4** a place that is central is easy to reach because it is near the middle of a town or area 靠近中心區的; 易於到達的: *The house is near Leicester Square, it's very central.* 這房子在萊斯特廣場附近, 很好找。—**centrally** *adv*: *Our office is very centrally situated.* 我們的辦事處位於市中心。—**centrality** /͵sɛn`trælətɪ; sen'trælɪ̵ti/ *n* [C]

central bank /͵·· '·/ *n* [C] a national bank that does business with the government, and controls the amount of money available and the general system of banks 中央銀行

central gov·ern·ment /͵·· '···/ *n* [C,U] the government of a whole country, as opposed to LOCAL GOVERNMENT 中央政府

central heat·ing /͵·· '··/ *n* [U] a system of heating buildings in which water or air is heated in one place and then sent around the rest of the building through pipes and RADIATORS or VENTS 中央暖氣系統, 集中供熱設備

cen·tral·is·m /`sɛntrəl͵ɪzəm; 'sentrəlɪzəm/ *n* [U] a way of governing a country or controlling an organization in which one central group has power and tells people in other places what to do 中央集權制[主義], 集中制

cen·tral·ize also 又作 **-ise** *BrE*【英】/`sɛntrəl͵aɪz; 'sentrəlaɪz/ *v* [T] to organize the control of a country or organization so that one central group has power and tells people in other places what to do 使…處於中央的控制之下, 實行中央集權制: *an attempt to centralize the economy* 實行中央管理經濟的嘗試 —compare 比較 DECENTRALIZE —**centralized** *adj*: *centralized planning* 中央統一計劃 —**centralization** /͵sɛntrələ`zeʃən; ͵sentrəlaɪ'zeɪʃən/ *n* [U]

central lock·ing /͵·· '··/ *n* [U] a system for locking the doors on a car in which all the locks are operated when you turn the key in one lock〔汽車的〕中央鎖閉系統

central nerv·ous sys·tem /͵·· '·· ͵··/ *n* [C] the main part of your NERVOUS SYSTEM consisting of your brain and your SPINAL CORD 中樞神經系統

central pro·ces·sing u·nit /͵·· '··· ͵··/ *n* [C] a CPU〔電腦的〕中央處理機[器]

central res·er·va·tion /͵·· ··'··/ *n* [C] *BrE* a narrow piece of ground that separates the two parts of a MOTORWAY【英】〔公路的〕中央分道區; MEDIAN¹ (1) *AmE*【美】—see picture on page A3 參見A3 頁圖

cen·tre¹ *BrE*【英】, **center** *AmE*【美】/`sɛntɚ; 'sentə/ *n* 1 1
1 ►MIDDLE 中間◄ [C] the middle of a space, area, or object, especially the exact middle〔空間、地域或物體的〕(正) 中間, 中心 (點): *Draw a line through the centre of the circle.* 劃一條線通過那個圓形的中心。| *Tony only likes chocolates with soft centres.* 東尼只愛吃軟夾心巧克力。| **[+of]** *There was an enormous oak table in the centre of the room.* 房間中央有一張巨大的橡木桌子。
2 ►PLACE/BUILDING 地方/建築物◄ [C] a place or

building which is used for a particular purpose or activity〔供進行某種活動用的〕中心（場所、建築物等）: *the Fred Hutchinson Cancer Research Centre* 弗雷德·哈欽森癌症研究中心 | *a huge new suburban shopping centre* 位於郊區的新建大型購物中心 | *I'll just get a cab to the conference centre.* 我會坐計程車去會議中心。— see also 另見 GARDEN CENTRE, JOB CENTRE

3 ►CENTRE OF ACTIVITY 活動中心◄ [C] a place where most of the important things happen that are connected with a particular business or activity〔商業或其他活動的〕中心（地區）: *a major banking centre* 一個主要的銀行業中心 | *It's not exactly a cultural centre like Paris.* 這並不完全是像巴黎那樣的文化中心。| [+of] *The main Control Room is the centre of the communications system.* 主控制室是通訊系統的中心。| *a centre of academic excellence* 學術中心

4 ►OF A TOWN 城鎮的◄ [C] *BrE* the part of a town or city where most of the shops, restaurants, cinemas, theatres etc are【英】〔集中了大部分商店、餐廳、電影院、劇院等的〕城鎮的中心; DOWNTOWN *AmE*【美】: **city/town centre** *parking facilities in the town centre* 市中心的停車設施

5 centre of population/urban centre an area where a large number of people live 人口密集地區: *Nuclear installations are built well away from the main centres of population.* 核設施建在遠離人口密集的地區。

6 ►OF ATTENTION/INTEREST 與注意力/興趣相關的◄ someone or something to which people give a lot of attention〔注意、關注的〕中心: **be the centre of attention** *Betty just loves being the centre of attention.* 貝蒂總是喜歡成為人們關注的焦點。| **be at the centre of a row/dispute/controversy etc** (=be the person or thing most involved in a quarrel etc and therefore getting the most attention) 成為爭吵/爭論/議論的焦點

7 ►IN POLITICS 政治上◄ **the centre** a MODERATE (=middle) position in politics which does not support extreme ideas 中間派[立場], 温和派: *The party's new policies show a swing towards the centre.* 該黨的新政策顯示出一種傾向中間立場的轉變。| **left/right of centre** *As far as I can tell, her political views are slightly left of centre.* 據我所知, 她的政治觀點屬中間稍稍偏左。

8 ►IN SPORT 運動◄ [C] a player in games such as football or BASKETBALL who plays in or near the middle of the field or playing area〔足球、籃球等的〕中鋒: *the Sonics' six-foot-four-inch centre* 超音速隊六尺四寸高的中鋒

centre² *BrE*【英】, **center** *AmE*【美】*v* [T] to move something to a position at the centre of something else 集中; 使…處於中心位置: *The title isn't quite centred on the page, is it?* 標題並不在這頁的正中間, 是嗎?

centre on/upon *phr v* [T] if your attention centres on something or someone, or is centred on them, you pay more attention to them than anything else〔注意力〕集中於…: *The debate centred on the morality of fox hunting.* 這次辯論集中於獵狐行為是否道德的問題上。| **be centred on** *Anyone could see that his interest was centred on Bess.* 誰都能看出, 他的興趣集中在貝絲身上。

centre around also 又作 **centre round** *BrE*【英】*phr v* [I,T] if your thoughts, activities etc centre around something or are centred around it, it is the main thing that you are concerned with or interested in 以…為中心, 集中於: *In the 16th century, village life centred around religion.* 16世紀時, 鄉村生活是以宗教為中心的。

cen·tre·fold *BrE*【英】, **centerfold** *AmE*【美】/ˈsɛntɚˌfold; ˈsentəfəʊld/ *n* [C] **1** the two pages that face each other in the middle of a magazine or newspaper〔報紙或雜誌的〕中心頁跨頁版面 **2** a picture covering these two pages, especially one of a young woman with no clothes on 中心跨頁的圖片〔尤指年輕裸女的圖片〕

centre for·ward /ˌ·· ˈ··/ *n* [C] an attacking player who plays in the centre of the field in football〔足球的〕中鋒

centre of grav·i·ty /ˌ··· ˈ···/ *n* [singular] the point in any object on which it can balance〔物體的〕重心

cen·tre·piece *BrE*【英】, **centerpiece** *AmE*【美】/ˈsɛntɚˌpis; ˈsentəpiːs/ *n* [C] **1** a decoration, especially an arrangement of flowers in the middle of a table 置於桌子中央的裝飾品〔尤指鮮花〕**2** [singular] the most important, noticeable or attractive part of something 最重要[最具吸引力]的部分: [+of] *The centrepiece of Bevan's policy was the National Health Service.*〔前英國工黨領袖〕貝文的政策最核心的一項是國民保健制度。

cen·tri·fu·gal force /sɛnˈtrɪfjugl̩ ˈfɔrs; ˌsentrɪˈfjuːgəl◂ ˈfɔːs/ *n* [U] *technical* a force which makes things move away from the centre of something when they are moving around the centre【術語】離心力

cen·tri·fuge /ˈsɛntrəˌfjudʒ; ˈsentrɪ̵fjuːdʒ/ *n* [C] a machine that spins a container around very quickly so that the heavier liquids and any solids are forced to the outer edge or bottom 離心機, 離心分離機

cen·trip·e·tal force /sɛnˌtrɪpətl̩ ˈfɔrs; senˌtrɪpɪ̵tl ˈfɔːs/ *n* [U] *technical* a force which makes things move towards the centre of something【術語】向心力

cen·trist /ˈsɛntrɪst; ˈsentrɪ̵st/ *adj* having political beliefs that are not extreme; MODERATE¹ (2)〔政治上的〕中間派的, 温和派的 —**centrist** *n* [C]

cen·tu·ri·on /sɛnˈturɪən; ˌsenˈtʃʊəriən/ *adj* an army officer of ancient Rome, who was in charge of about 100 soldiers〔古羅馬軍團的〕百人隊隊長, 百夫長

cen·tu·ry /ˈsɛntʃərɪ; ˈsentʃəri/ *n* [C] **1** one of the 100-year periods counted forwards or backwards from the year of Christ's birth 一世紀: *twentieth-century art forms such as Cubism* 二十世紀的藝術形式如立體主義 | *the worst air disaster this century* 本世紀最大的空難 | **at the turn of the century** (=in or around the year 2000) 世紀之交 **2** a period of 100 years 一百年 **3** 100 runs (RUN² (17)) made by one player in the game of CRICKET (2) in one INNINGS〔一名板球運動員在一局所得的〕一百分

CEO /ˌsi i ˈo; ˌsiː iː ˈəʊ/ *n* [C] Chief Executive Officer; the person with the most authority in a large company 行政總裁

ce·phal·ic /səˈfælɪk; sɪ̵ˈfælɪk/ *adj technical* connected with or affecting your head【術語】頭（部）的; 影響頭部的

ce·ram·ics /səˈræmɪks; sɪ̵ˈræmɪks/ *n* **1** [U] the art of making pots, bowls, TILES etc, by shaping pieces of clay and baking them until they are hard 陶[瓷]器製法; 陶瓷工藝 **2** [plural] things that are made this way 陶[瓷]器: *an exhibition of ceramics at the crafts museum* 工藝博物館的陶[瓷]器展覽 —**ceramic** *adj*: *ceramic tiles* 瓷磚

ce·re·al /ˈsɪrɪəl; ˈsɪəriəl/ *n* **1** [C,U] a breakfast food made from grain and usually eaten with milk〔通常與牛奶一起吃、作為早餐的〕穀類食品 **2** [C] a plant grown to produce grain for foods, such as wheat, rice etc 穀類植物, 穀物〈如小麥、稻穀等〉: *cereal crops* 穀類作物

cer·e·bel·lum /ˌsɛrəˈbɛləm; ˌserɪ̵ˈbeləm/ *n* [C] *technical* the bottom part of your brain that controls your muscles【術語】小腦

cer·e·bral /səˈribrəl; ˈserɪ̵brəl/ *adj* **1** *technical* connected with or affecting your brain【術語】腦的, 大腦的; 影響大腦的: *cerebral hemorrhage* 腦出[溢]血 **2** thinking or explaining things in a very complicated way that takes a lot of effort to understand 要運用智力的; 訴諸理性的: *If I'd wanted something cerebral on a Friday night, I'd have stayed at home and read Proust!* 星期五的晚上如果我想要理性點, 我會待在家裡讀讀〔法國小說家〕普魯斯特的書! | *a cerebral film* 一部引人深思的電影

cerebral pal·sy /ˌ··· ˈ··/ *n* [U] a disease caused by damage to the brain before or during birth which results in difficulties of movement and speech 大腦性麻痹, 腦癱

cer·e·bra·tion /ˌsɛrəˈbreʃən; ˌserɪ̵ˈbreɪʃən/ *n* [U] *formal* the process of thinking【正式】大腦活動, 思維, 思考

cer·e·mo·ni·al¹ /ˌsɛrəˈmonɪəl; ˌserɪ̵ˈməʊniəl◂/ *adj* used in a ceremony or done as part of a ceremony 禮儀的, 儀

式的: *the Mayor's ceremonial duties* 市長的禮儀性職責 | *Native American ceremonial robes* 美洲印第安人的禮袍

ceremonial² *n* [C,U] a special ceremony or the practice of having ceremonies 典禮, 儀式: *an occasion for public ceremonial* 公眾儀式場合

cer·e·mo·ni·ous /ˌsɛrəˋmonɪəs; ˌserɪˈməʊniəs◂/ *adj* paying great attention to formal, correct behaviour, as if you were in a ceremony 隆重的; 講究禮儀的 —**ceremoniously** *adv*: *He ceremoniously burnt the offending documents in the bin.* 他鄭重其事地把那些令人討厭的文件放在垃圾桶裡燒了。—**ceremoniousness** *n* [U]

cer·e·mo·ny /ˋsɛrəˌmonɪ; ˈserɪməni/ *n* **1** [C] a formal or traditional set of actions used at an important social or religious event 典禮, 儀式: *the wedding ceremony* 婚禮 | *a graduation ceremony* 畢業典禮 **2** [U] the special actions and formal words traditionally used on particular occasions 禮儀, 禮節: *The queen was crowned with due ceremony.* 女王按照規定的禮儀加冕。**3 without ceremony** in a very informal way, without politeness 隨意地; 無禮地: *Without further ceremony, Ed pushed back his chair and went out.* 艾德不再講甚麼禮貌, 把椅子往後一推, 走了出去。—see also 另見 **not stand on ceremony** (STAND¹ (45))

ce·rise /səˋriz; səˈriːz/ *n* [U] bright pinkish red 鮮紅色, 櫻桃紅 —**cerise** *adj*

cert /sɝt; sɜːt/ *n* **be a (dead) cert** *BrE informal* to be certain to happen or to succeed【英, 非正式】必然發生的, 確定的: *So you reckon that this horse is a dead cert to win?* 那麼你認為這匹馬一定會贏嗎?

cert. the written abbreviation of 縮寫= CERTIFICATE

cer·tain¹ /ˋsɝtn̩; ˈsɜːtn/ *determiner, pronoun* **1** a certain thing, person, place etc is a particular thing, person etc that you are not naming or describing exactly 某, 某些, 某個: *You can get cheaper fares on certain days of the year.* 在每年的某些日子, 你可以買到較為便宜的車票。| *There are certain things I just can't discuss with my mother.* 有些事情我是不能和母親商量的。| **certain of** *formal* (=several particular people or things in a group)【正式】〔羣體中的〕某些〔人或物〕*Certain of the older members objected strongly to the proposal.* 某些年長的成員強烈反對此項建議。**2** some, but not a lot 一些, 若干: **a certain amount of** *a certain amount of flexibility* 一定的靈活性 | **to a certain extent/degree** (=in a limited way, but not completely) 在某程度上 *I agree with you to a certain extent but there are other factors to consider.* 在某程度上我同意你的看法, 但還有其他一些因素需要考慮。**3 a certain a)** enough of a particular quality to be noticed 稍微的, 一些的, 一定量的: *There's a certain prestige about going to a private school.* 上私立學校還是有可炫耀之處的。**b)** *formal* used to talk about someone you do not know but whose name you have been told【正式】〔用於談論不認識但知其名的〕某某, 某位: *There's a certain Mrs Myles on the phone for you.* 有位叫邁爾斯太太的人正打電話找你。

This graph shows how common different grammar patterns of the adjective **certain** are. 本圖表所示為形容詞certain構成的不同語法模式的使用頻率。

certain (that)
be certain
for certain
certain of
certain who/what/how etc
certain to do sth
other

0% 10% 20% 30% 40%

Based on the British National Corpus and the Longman Lancaster Corpus
據英國國家語料庫和朗文蘭卡斯特語料庫

certain² *adj* **1** [not before noun 不用於名詞前] confident and sure, without any doubts 肯定的, 確定的, 毫無疑問的: *Just so we're absolutely certain, can I check these figures?* 為使我們能絕對確定, 我能核查一下這些數字嗎? | **certain (that)** *We're certain that by tomorrow, Mr Knowles, you'll have an answer.* 諾爾斯先生, 我們肯定你明天就能得到答覆。| **certain who/what/how etc** *I'm not certain whether there's a bus service on Sundays.* 我不確定星期天是否也有巴士服務。| **[+about/of]** *Now are you certain about that?* 現在你能確定了嗎? | *I'm not quite certain of how much is left in that account.* 我不能確定那賬戶還剩多少錢。**2 know/say for certain** to know something without any doubt 確切知道/肯定地說: *"How much will the repairs cost?" "I couldn't say for certain."* "修理要多少錢?" "我說不準。" **3 make certain a)** to do something in order to be sure that something will happen 使確實; 確保: **make certain (that)** *Can you draw Harry a map just to make certain he'll find the hotel?* 你能給哈里畫張地圖以確保他能找到那家旅館嗎? **b)** to check that something is correct or true 核實〔某事〕, 把…弄清楚: **[+of]** *I suggest you make certain of your facts before you accuse anybody.* 我建議你在指責別人之前先核實一下你所掌握的事實。**4** if something is certain, it will definitely happen or is definitely true 肯定會發生的, 必然的: *a business facing certain bankruptcy* 一家肯定會面臨破產的公司 | **it is certain (that)** *It now seems certain that Pam will lose her license.* 現在看來帕姆一定會丟掉執照的。| **certain to do sth** *There's one boy who's certain to succeed!* 有個男孩一定會成功的! | **it is not certain who/what/how etc** *It's not certain where he lived.* (=no one knows definitely) 沒有人確切地知道他住哪兒。

cer·tain·ly /ˋsɝtn̩lɪ; ˈsɜːtnli/ *adv* [sentence adverb 句子副詞] **1** without any doubt; of course 的確, 一定, 毫無疑問, 當然: *Certainly we'll consider your suggestion, Alan.* 阿倫, 我們當然會考慮你的提議。| *That certainly does change the situation.* 那的確使情況有所變化。| *"Not smoking has made a real difference." "It certainly has."* "不抽煙確實大不相同。" "這當然了。" —see 見 OF COURSE (USAGE), SURELY (USAGE)

Frequencies of the adverb **certainly** in spoken and written English 副詞certainly在英語口頭和書面語中的使用頻率

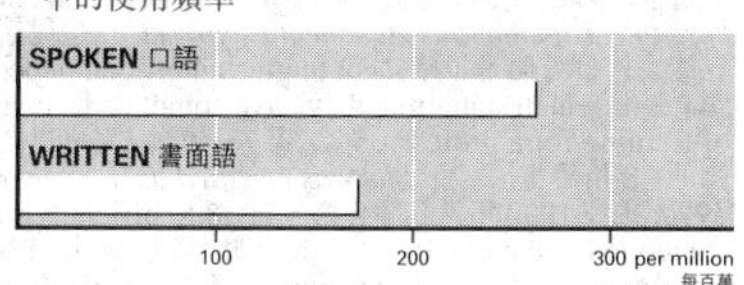

Based on the British National Corpus and the Longman Lancaster Corpus
據英國國家語料庫和朗文蘭卡斯特語料庫

This graph shows that the adverb **certainly** is more common in spoken English than in written English. This is because it has some special uses in spoken English. 本圖表顯示, 副詞certainly在英語口語中的使用頻率遠遠高於書面語。這是因為它在英語口語中有一些特殊的用法。

certainly (*adv*) **SPOKEN PHRASES**
含 certainly 的口語片語

2 used to agree or give your permission 當然〔用於表示同意或允許〕: *"I'd like a beer, please." "Certainly, sir."* "請給我來杯啤酒。" "好的, 先生。" | *"Can I come along?" "Certainly."* "我可以一塊兒來嗎?" "當然可以。" **3 certainly not!** used to disagree completely, or to refuse to give permission 當然不!: *"Did you break my camera?" "Certainly not!"* "是你弄壞了我的相機嗎?" "當然不是!"

cer·tain·ty /ˈsɝtn̩tɪ; ˈsɜːtnti/ *n* **1** [C] something that is definitely true or that will definitely happen 確定[確實]的事; 必然會發生的事: *It's a certainty that prices will go up soon.* 價格不久就會上漲, 這是肯定的事。| *Dying's the only certainty in this life.* 死亡是一生中唯一確定的事。**2** [U] the state of being completely certain 確實(性), 確信, 確知: *Nowadays there's less certainty about church teachings.* 如今, 人們對宗教教義並不是那麼深信無疑了。| **with certainty** *You can't say with any certainty where you might be in the future.* 誰也無法肯定自己將來會是甚麼樣的。

cer·ti·fi·ab·le /ˈsɝtəˌfaɪəbl; ˈsɜːtɪ̣faɪəbəl/ *adj* **1** *informal* crazy, especially in a way that is dangerous【非正式】〔尤指近乎危險地〕瘋狂的: *If you ask me, that man is certifiable.* 要我說, 那個人就是瘋子。**2** *especially AmE* good enough or correct enough to be officially approved【尤美】〔好或正確得〕可獲正式通過的: *a certifiable statement* 可證明的陳述 | *grade A certifiable beef* A級合格牛肉

3 3
cer·tif·i·cate /sɚˈtɪfəkɪt; səˈtɪfɪkət/ *n* [C] **1** an official document that states that a fact or facts are true 證明書, 證書: **birth/death/marriage certificate** (=giving details of someone's birth, death, or marriage) 出生/死亡/結婚證明書 **2** an official paper stating that you have completed a course of study (畢業)文憑, 成績合格證書

cer·tif·i·cat·ed /sɚˈtɪfəˌketɪd; səˈtɪfɪkeɪtɪ̣d/ *adj especially BrE* having successfully completed a training for a profession【尤英】完成專業培訓的, 授予證明書的, 合格的, 取得執照的: *a certificated nurse* 持有證書的合格護士 —**certification** /sɚˌtɪfəˈkeʃən; sɜˌtɪfɪ̣ˈkeɪʃən/ *n* [U]

certified mail /ˌ··· ˈ·/ *n* [U] *AmE* a method of sending mail in which the fact that you have sent it is recorded and the person it is sent to must sign their name to prove they have received it【美】掛號郵件; RECORDED DELIVERY *BrE*【英】

certified pub·lic ac·coun·tant /ˌ··· ˌ·· ·ˈ··/ *n* [C] a CPA 執業會計師

cer·ti·fy /ˈsɝtəˌfaɪ; ˈsɜːtɪ̣faɪ/ *v* [T] **1** to state that something is correct or true, especially after some kind of test〔尤指經過某種檢驗〕證明, 證實, 核證: *You have to get these accounts certified by an auditor.* 這些賬目必須由審計師核實。| **certify sb/sth** *Remember that gas boiler we had that was certified dangerous?* 記得我們那台被證實是很危險的燃氣鍋爐嗎? | **certify (that)** *Sign here to certify that this statement is correct.* 在這兒簽名以證實這個聲明是正確的。**2** to give an official paper to someone which states that they have completed a course of training for a profession 給〔某人〕頒發(完成專業培訓的)合格證書[文憑]: *She was certified as a teacher in 1990.* 她在1990年獲教師合格證書。**3** to officially state someone to be mentally ill 正式證明〔某人〕有精神病

cer·ti·tude /ˈsɝtəˌtud; ˈsɜːtɪ̣tjuːd/ *n* [U] *formal* the state of being or feeling certain about something【正式】確信, 確定, 自信

ce·ru·le·an /səˈrulɪən; sɪ̣ˈruːliən/ *adj technical or literary* deep blue like a clear sky【術語或文】蔚藍, 天藍色

cer·vi·cal /ˈsɝvɪkl̩; ˈsɜːvɪkəl/ *adj technical*【術語】**1** related to the neck 頸(部)的: *cervical vertebrae* (=the bones in the back of your neck) 頸椎骨 **2** related to the cervix 子宮頸的: *cervical cancer* 子宮頸癌

cervical smear /ˌ··· ˈ·/ *n* [C] *technical* a test for CANCER of a woman's CERVIX【術語】子宮頸塗片檢查; PAP SMEAR *AmE*【美】

cer·vix /ˈsɝvɪks; ˈsɜːvɪks/ *n* [C] the narrow passage into a woman's UTERUS 子宮頸

ce·sar·e·an /sɪˈzɛrɪən; sɪ̣ˈzeəriən/ *n* [C] another spelling of CAESAREAN caesarean 的另一種拼法

ces·sa·tion /sɛˈseʃən; seˈseɪʃən/ *n* [C,U+of] *formal* a pause or stop【正式】〔暫時〕休止, 停止, 中斷: *a cessation of hostilities* (=when the fighting stops in a war) 休戰

ces·sion /ˈsɛʃən; ˈseʃən/ *n* [C,U] *formal* the act of giving up land, property, or rights, especially to another country after a war, or something that is given up in this way【正式】〔尤指戰後一國土地、財產、權利等的〕割讓, 讓與: *John's cession of his kingdom in 1213* 1213年約翰讓出了他的王國。—see also 另見 CEDE

cess·pit /ˈsɛsˌpɪt; ˈsesˌpɪt/ *n* [C] **1** also 又作 **cesspool** /ˈsɛsˌpul; ˈsesˌpuːl/ a large hole or container under the ground in which waste from a building, especially from the toilets, is collected 污水坑; 化糞池 **2** a place or situation in which people behave immorally 污穢的場所: *For weeks the affair threatened to be a cesspit of scandal.* 幾個星期來, 這一事件眼看就要成為醜聞的滋生源。

ce·tac·ean /sɪˈteʃən; sɪˈteɪʃən/ *n* [C] *technical* a MAMMAL (=an animal which feeds its babies on milk) that lives in the sea, such as a WHALE【術語】鯨目動物〈如鯨〉—**cetacean** *adj*

cf used in writing to introduce something else that should be compared or considered〔用於文章〕參照; 比較

CFC /ˌsi ɛf ˈsi; ˌsiː ef ˈsiː/ *n* also 又作 **chlorofluorocarbon** a gas used in FRIDGES and AEROSOL cans, now believed to be responsible for damaging the OZONE LAYER 含氯氟烴

cha-cha /ˈtʃɑ tʃɑ; ˈtʃɑː tʃɑː/ also 又作 **cha-cha-cha** /ˌ· · ˈ·/ *n* [C] a dance from South America with small, fast steps 恰恰舞〔源自南美的一種快節奏舞蹈〕

chafe /tʃef; tʃeɪf/ *v* **1** [I,T] if a part of your body chafes or if something chafes it, it becomes sore because of something rubbing against it (使)擦傷; (使)擦痛: *Put a soft pad under the saddle to avoid chafing the horse's back.* 在馬鞍下放一個軟墊子以免擦傷馬背。**2** [T] to rub part of your body to make it warm 把〔身上某一部位〕擦熱 **3** [I] to be or become impatient or annoyed〔因…而〕惱怒, 焦躁, 不耐煩: **[+at/under]** *Some hunters are chafing under the new restrictions.* 某些獵人對這些新的限制感到十分惱怒。

chaff[1] /tʃæf; tʃɑːf/ *n* [U] **1** the HUSKs (=outer seed covers) separated from grain before it is used as food 糠; 穀物的外殼 **2** dried grasses and plant stems used for food for farm animals〔作飼料用的〕乾草, 草料, 秣 —see also 另見 **separate the wheat from the chaff** (WHEAT (3))

chaff[2] *v* [T] *old-fashioned* to make jokes about the person you are talking to, in a friendly way【過時】〔善意地〕戲弄, 對〔某人〕開玩笑

chaf·finch /ˈtʃæfɪntʃ; ˈtʃæfɪntʃ/ *n* [C] a common small European bird 蒼頭燕雀〔歐洲常見的一種小鳥〕

chafing dish /ˈ·· ·/ *n* [C] a container with a HEATER under it, used for cooking food in or for keeping food warm at the table〔在餐桌上烹飪或使食物保溫的〕火鍋

chag·rin[1] /ʃəˈgrɪn; ˈʃægrɪn/ *n* [U] *formal* annoyance and disappointment because something has not happened the way you hoped【正式】懊惱, 失望: **to sb's chagrin** *To the chagrin of the Pentagon, the USSR exploded a nuclear bomb in 1949.* 讓五角大樓大為懊惱的是, 蘇聯於1949年引爆了一枚核彈。

chagrin[2] *v* **be chagrined** *formal* to feel annoyed and disappointed【正式】感到失望, 感到懊惱: *Dale was chagrined that she wasn't impressed.* 令戴爾感到失望的是她沒有被感動。

chain[1] /tʃen; tʃeɪn/ *n*

1 ►JOINED RINGS 連接在一起的環◄ [C,U] a series of rings, usually made of metal, which are joined together in a line and used for fastening things, supporting weights, decoration etc 鏈子, 鏈條: *Look at the gold chain Tim bought me!* 看, 蒂姆買給我的金項鏈! | *a length of chain* 一段鏈子 | *a bridge supported on heavy chains* 由粗鐵索承受着重量的橋 | *We had to stop and put chains on the tires.* 我們只好停車, 在輪胎上加上鏈條。| **a bicycle chain** (=that makes the wheels turn) 腳踏車鏈條 | **chain of office** *BrE* (=a decoration worn by some officials at ceremonies)【英】〔官員在儀式場合佩戴的〕鏈徽 —see picture at 參見 BICYCLE[1] 圖

2 chain of events/circumstances etc [C] a connected series of events etc 一系列[一連串]的事件/情況等: *the*

chain of events that led to World War I 引發第一次世界大戰的一系列事件 —see also 另見 CHAIN OF COMMAND, FOOD CHAIN

3 ►SHOPS/HOTELS 商店/旅館◄ [C] a number of shops, hotels, cinemas etc owned or managed by the same company or person 連鎖店, 連鎖集團: **[+of]** *a chain of restaurants* 連鎖餐廳 | **hotel/restaurant/retail etc chain** *a major American hotel chain* 美國一家主要的酒店連鎖集團

4 ►CONNECTED LINE 連接線◄ [C] people, mountains, islands etc forming a line 連成一行的人[山; 島嶼]: *the largest mountain chain in North America* 北美最大的山脈 | *Everybody link arms to make a chain.* 大家挽臂形成人鏈。

5 ►PRISONER 囚犯◄ **chains** [plural] chains fastened to a prisoner's legs and arms, to prevent them from escaping〔鎖住囚犯四肢的〕鐐銬, 鎖鏈: **in chains** *There were a number of men in chains, all sentenced to death.* 有幾個人被鎖鏈鎖着, 他們都被判處了死刑。

6 ►BUYING A HOUSE 購屋◄ [C usually singular 一般用單數] *BrE* a number of people buying houses in a situation where each person must complete the sale of their own house before they can buy the next person's house【英】〔一些人先賣舊屋再買新屋的〕鏈式購屋法, 連環購房鏈

7 ►MEASURE 度量◄ [C] a measurement of length, used in the past 鏈〔舊時的長度單位〕—see table on page C4 參見C4頁附錄

chain² *v* **1** to fasten someone or something to something else, especially in order to prevent them from escaping or being stolen〔尤指為防逃跑或被盜而〕鎖在一起, 拴住, 束縛: **chain sb/sth up** *She wouldn't chain her dog up, and it got killed on the main road.* 她總不把狗拴起來, 結果狗在大路上被壓死了。| **chain sb/sth together** *convicts working all chained together* 鎖在一起從事勞動的罪犯 | **chain sb/sth to sth** *There's a bicycle chained to the railings out front.* 有一輛腳踏車拴在前面的欄杆上。**2 be chained to something** to have your freedom restricted because of a responsibility you cannot escape 受到〔責任〕的束縛: *With a sick husband she's chained to the house all day.* 由於丈夫生病, 她終日被困在家裡。

chain gang /ˈ· ·/ *n* [C] a group of prisoners chained together to work outside their prison 用鏈子拴在一起服勞役的囚犯

chain let·ter /ˈ· ˌ··/ *n* [C] a letter sent to several people asking them to send a copy of the letter to several more people 連鎖信〔寄給數人的信, 要求每個收信人複製數份再寄給他人, 如此延續下去〕

chain mail /ˈ· ·/ *n* [U] a piece of protective clothing made by joining small metal rings together, worn by soldiers in the past〔舊時軍人穿的〕鎖子甲, 連環甲

chain of com·mand /ˌ· · ·ˈ·/ *n* [C] a system in an organization by which decisions are made and passed from people at the top of the organization to people lower down 指揮系統; 指揮鏈; 行政管理系統: *Symonds is third in the chain of command.* 西蒙茲是第三把交椅。

chain re·ac·tion /ˌ· ·ˈ··/ *n* [C] a series of related events or chemical reactions, each of which causes the next 連鎖反應; 鏈式反應: *A student playing with chemicals set off a chain reaction in a public toilet and blew it to bits.* 一個學生在公廁裡玩化學品, 導致一系列連鎖反應, 把廁所炸成了一片廢墟。

chain saw /ˈ· ·/ *n* [C] a tool used for cutting wood, consisting of a circular chain fitted with teeth and driven by a motor 鏈鋸 —compare 比較 CIRCULAR SAW —see picture at 參見 TOOL¹ 圖

chain-smoke /ˈ· ·/ *v* [I,T] to smoke cigarettes continuously 一支接一支地抽〔煙〕—**chain-smoker** *n* [C]

chain stitch /ˈ· ·/ *n* [C,U] a way of sewing in which each new stitch is pulled through the last one〔鈎針或製繡品的〕鏈狀針法

chain store /ˈ· ·/ *n* [C] one of a group of shops, all of which are owned by one organization; MULTIPLE STORE 連鎖店 —see also 另見 CHAIN¹ (3)

chairs 椅子

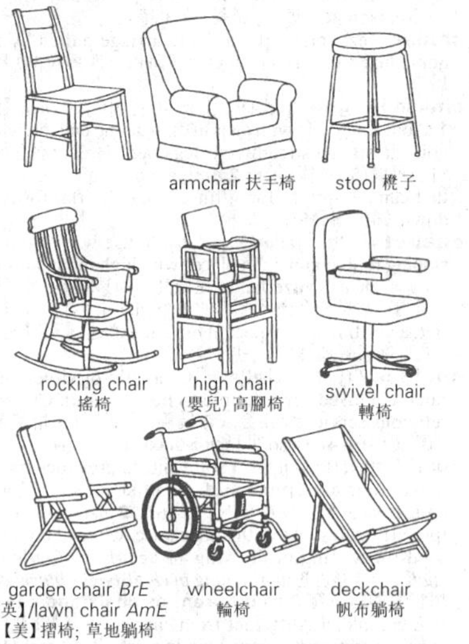

armchair 扶手椅
stool 櫈子
rocking chair 搖椅
high chair (嬰兒)高腳椅
swivel chair 轉椅
garden chair *BrE*【英】/lawn chair *AmE*【美】摺椅; 草地躺椅
wheelchair 輪椅
deckchair 帆布躺椅

chair¹ /tʃɛr; tʃeə/ *n* **1** [C] a piece of furniture for one person to sit on, which has a back, a seat, and four legs 椅子: *Grandpa's in his favorite chair by the fireplace.* 祖父坐在火爐邊他最喜歡的椅子上。**2** [singular] the position of being in charge of a meeting, or the person who is in charge of it〔會議的〕主持人, 主席; 主席的席位[職位]: *Address your questions to the chair, please.* 請向主席提出你的問題。| **be in the chair** *Who will be in the chair at tomorrow's meeting?* 誰主持明天的會議? **3** [C] the position of being a professor 大學教授的職位: **[+of]** *a new Chair of Medicine* 一位新任醫學教授 **4 the chair** *informal especially AmE* the punishment of death by electric shock given in an ELECTRIC CHAIR【非正式, 尤美】電椅死刑 S1 W2

chair² *v* [T] to be the CHAIRPERSON of a meeting 擔任〔會議〕主席[主持人]: *The commission of inquiry was chaired by a well-known judge.* 調查委員會由一位知名的法官擔任主席。

chair·lift /ˈtʃɛrˌlɪft; ˈtʃeəlɪft/ *n* [C] a line of chairs hanging from a moving wire, used for carrying people up and down mountains, especially when they are skiing (SKI²)〔載運乘客上下山的〕纜車吊椅

chair·man /ˈtʃɛrmən; ˈtʃeəmən/ *n plural* **chairmen** /-mən; -mən/ [C] **1** someone, especially a man, who is in charge of a meeting or directs the work of a committee or organization〔尤指男性的〕主席;〔委員會或組織的〕負責人: *Potts was elected chairman of the education committee.* 波茨當選為教育委員會主席。**2** *BrE* someone who is in charge of a large company or organization【英】〔大組織、大公司的〕董事長; 委員長; 理事長; 總裁: *I think he was the chairman of a big building society before he came here.* 我認為他來這兒之前是一個大型房屋協會的會長。 S3 W1

chair·man·ship /ˈtʃɛrmənˌʃɪp; ˈtʃeəmənʃɪp/ *n* **the chairmanship** the position of being a chairman, or the time when someone has this position 主席職位; 主席任期: *A committee was set up under the chairmanship of Edmund Compton.* 成立了一個以艾德蒙·康普頓為主席的委員會。

chair·per·son /ˈtʃɛrˌpɝsn̩; ˈtʃeəˌpɜːsən/ *n plural* **chair-**

persons [C] someone who is in charge of a meeting or directs the work of a committee or organization〔主持會議或指導某組織或委員會工作的〕主席; 議長; 主持人
chair·wom·an /ˈtʃɛr,wʊmən; ˈtʃeə,wʊmən/ *n plural* **chairwomen** /-,wɪmɪn; -,wɪmɪn/ [C] a woman who is a chairperson 女主席; 女議長; 女主持人
chaise /ʃez; ʃeɪz/ *n* [C] a light carriage pulled by one horse, used in former times〔舊時由一匹馬拉的〕輕便馬車
chaise longue /ˈʃez ˈlɔŋ; ,ʃeɪz ˈlɒŋ/ *n* [C] *French*【法】**1** a long chair[1] (1) with an arm only at one end, on which you can sit and stretch your legs out〔僅在一端有扶手可坐可躺的〕長椅, 躺椅 **2** *AmE* a long chair with a back that can be upright for sitting, or can lie flat for lying down【美】摺疊椅, 長靠椅
chal·et /ʃæˈle; ˈʃæleɪ/ *n* [C] **1** a house with a steeply sloping roof, common in places with high mountains and snow such as Switzerland〔屋頂陡斜的〕木造農舍, 坡頂小木屋〔常見於多山及多雪的地方如瑞士〕**2** *especially BrE* a small house, especially in a HOLIDAY CAMP【尤英】〔尤指度假營地裡的〕小屋
chal·ice /ˈtʃælɪs; ˈtʃælɪ̈s/ *n* [C] a gold or silver decorated cup used for example to hold wine in Christian religious services〔用金或銀裝飾的〕酒杯〔尤指基督教的聖餐杯〕—see also 另見 **poisoned chalice** (POISON[2] (7))
chalk[1] /tʃɔk; tʃɔːk/ *n* [U] **1** soft white or grey rock formed a long time ago from the shells of small sea animals; LIMESTONE 白堊: *chalk hills* 白堊山地 **2** also 又作 **chalks** [plural] small sticks of this substance, white or coloured, used for writing or drawing 粉筆: *a box of coloured chalks* 一盒彩色粉筆 | *writing in chalk on the blackboard* 黑板上的粉筆字 **3 as different as chalk and cheese** *BrE* completely different from each other【英】截然不同的 —see also 另見 **not by a long chalk** (LONG[1] (16))
chalk[2] *v* [T+up/on] to write, mark, or draw something with chalk 用粉筆寫[標記, 繪畫]
chalk sth ↔ **up** *phr v* [T] *informal*【非正式】**1** to succeed in getting something, especially points in a game 贏得〔尤指比分〕; 取得: *Seattle chalked up another win last night over Denver.* 西雅圖隊昨晚又戰勝了丹佛隊。**2** to record what someone has done, what someone should pay etc 記下〔所做的事、賬目等〕: *You can chalk the drinks up to my account.* 你可以把酒錢記到我的賬上。**3 chalk it up to experience** to accept a failure or disappointment calmly and regard it as an experience that you can learn something from 平靜地接受失敗並從中汲取教訓
chalk·board /ˈtʃɔk,bɔrd; ˈtʃɔːkbɔːd/ *n* [C] *AmE* a BLACKBOARD【美】黑板: *Thanks, but the janitor cleans the chalkboard.* 謝謝, 但是應該由管理員把黑板擦乾淨。
chalk·y /ˈtʃɔkɪ; ˈtʃɔːki/ *adj* similar to chalk or containing chalk (像) 粉筆的; (像) 白堊的: *white chalky soil* 白色的白堊質土壤 | *I can't stand those chalky tasting antacid tablets.* 我受不了那些味如粉筆的抗酸藥片。—**chalkiness** *n* [U]
chal·lenge[1] /ˈtʃælɪndʒ; ˈtʃælɪ̈ndʒ/ *n*
1 ►STH DIFFICULT 棘手的事◄ [C,U] something that tests strength, skill, or ability especially in a way that is interesting 挑戰, 具有挑戰性的事物, 考驗〔某人〕能力的事物: *I liked the speed and challenge of racing.* 我喜歡賽車的速度和挑戰。| **face a challenge** (=be ready to deal with one) 迎接挑戰 *The White House has to face yet another foreign policy challenge.* 白宮不得不面臨外交政策的又一挑戰。| **meet a challenge/rise to a challenge** (=successfully deal with one) 迎接/接受挑戰 *a new and vibrant initiative to meet the challenge of the 21st century* 一項迎接21世紀挑戰的充滿生氣的新舉措
2 ►QUESTIONING OF RIGHTNESS 對公正性的質疑◄ [C] a refusal to accept that something is right and legal〔對某事的正確性、合法性等的〕質疑: [+to] *a direct challenge to the Governor's authority* 對總督的權威性提出直接的質疑 | *feminist challenges to the traditional social order* 女權主義對傳統社會秩序的質疑
3 ►INVITATION TO COMPETE 挑戰◄ a suggestion to someone that they should try to defeat you in a fight, game etc 挑戰,〔比賽等的〕提議: *The champions are ready to accept a challenge from any team that is a serious contender.* 冠軍隊早已準備好接受任何一隊有實力的隊伍的挑戰。
4 ►A DEMAND TO STOP 停止的命令◄ [C] a demand from someone such as a guard to stop and give proof of who you are, and an explanation of what you are doing 喝停盤問
5 ►IN LAW 法律方面◄ [C] *law* a statement made before the beginning of a court case that a JUROR is not acceptable【法律】〔開庭前律師〕反對某人任陪審團成員的聲明: *Each lawyer may issue up to six challenges.* 每名律師最多可以提出六次反對某人任陪審員的聲明。
challenge[2] *v* [T] **1** to refuse to accept that something is right or legal 質疑〔某事的正確性、合法性等〕, 對...表示懷疑: *What happens if the Finance Committee challenges us on these figures?* 如果財政委員會不相信這些數字, 那我們怎麼辦? | *political offenders who challenge the authority of our law courts* 懷疑我們法庭的權威性的政治犯 | **challenge sb to do sth** *I challenge Dr Carver to deny his involvement!* 我質問卡弗博士敢不敢否認他與此事有關聯! **2** to invite someone to compete or fight against you 向...挑戰; 邀請〔某人〕比賽: **challenge sb to sth** *After lunch Carey challenged me to a game of tennis.* 午飯後, 凱里邀我進行了一場網球比賽。—compare 比較 DARE[1] (5) **3** to test the skills or abilities of someone or something; STIMULATE 考驗...的技術[能力]; 激發; 激勵: *I'm really at my best when I'm challenged.* 接受考驗時正是我處於最佳狀態的時候。| **challenge sb to do sth** *Every teacher ought to be challenging kids to think about current issues.* 所有老師都應激勵學生思考當前發生的問題。**4** to stop someone and demand proof of who they are, and an explanation of what they are doing 喝停盤問〔某人的身分、意圖等〕: *We were challenged by the sentry guarding the gate.* 我們被守門的哨兵攔住查問。**5** *law* to state that a JUROR is not acceptable before a TRIAL[1] (1) begins【法律】〔開審前在選定陪審員時〕對 (某候選陪審員) 表示反對 —**challenger** *n* [C]
chal·lenged /ˈtʃælɪndʒd; ˈtʃælɪ̈ndʒd/ *adj* **visually/physically/mentally challenged** *AmE* an expression for describing someone who has difficulty doing things because of blindness etc, used when you want to avoid saying this directly【美】盲人/殘疾人士/智障者〔委婉的說法〕
chal·leng·ing /ˈtʃælɪndʒɪŋ; ˈtʃælɪ̈ndʒɪŋ/ *adj* difficult in an interesting or enjoyable way 具有挑戰性的; 需充分發揮能力的: *Teaching young children is a challenging and rewarding job.* 教育兒童是一項具有挑戰性和有價值的工作。| *a challenging problem* 一個富有挑戰性的難題 —**challengingly** *adv*
cham·ber /ˈtʃembɚ; ˈtʃeɪmbə/ *n* **1** [C] an enclosed space, especially in your body or inside a machine〔人體內或某些機器中的〕室; 腔: *a combustion chamber* 燃燒室 | *The heart has four chambers.* 心臟有四個心室。**2** [C] a room used for a special purpose, especially an unpleasant one 作特殊用途的房間〔尤指令人不快者〕: **gas/torture chamber** (=used for killing people by gas or for hurting them) 毒氣/用刑室 **3** [C] a large room in a public building used for important meetings 大會議室, 會議廳: *the council chambers* 議事室; 會議室 **4** [C] one of the two parts of a parliament or of the US Congress. For example, in Britain the upper chamber is the House of Lords and the Lower Chamber is the House of Commons〔美國〕參[眾]議院;〔英國〕上[下]議院 **5** [C] *old use* a bedroom or private room【舊】私人房間, 寢室: *the Queen's private chambers* 女王的私人起居室 **6 chambers** [plural] *especially BrE* an office or offices used by BARRISTERS or judges【尤英】〔大律師或法官的〕辦公室; 事務所 **7** [C] the place inside a gun where you put the bullet 槍膛, 砲膛 —see picture at 參見 GUN[1] 圖

cham·ber·lain /ˋtʃembɚlɪn; ˈtʃeɪmbəlɪ̣n/ *n* [C] an important official who manages things like cooking, cleaning, buying food etc in a king's or NOBLEMAN's court〔國王或貴族的〕管家, 侍從; 宮廷內臣

cham·ber·maid /ˋtʃembɚˌmed; ˈtʃeɪmbəmeɪd/ *n* [C] a female servant or worker whose job is to clean and tidy bedrooms, especially in a hotel〔尤指旅館裡的〕女服務員; 打掃房間的女僕

chamber mu·sic /ˋ·· ˌ··/ *n* [C] CLASSICAL music written for a small group of instruments〔古典〕室內樂

chamber of com·merce /ˌ·· · ˋ··/ *n* [C] a group of business people in a particular town or area, working together to improve trade〔某地的〕商會

chamber or·ches·tra /ˋ·· ˌ···/ *n* [C] a small group of musicians who play CLASSICAL music together〔演奏古典音樂的〕室內樂隊

chamber pot /ˋ·· ·/ *n* [C] a round container for URINE used in a bedroom and kept under the bed in the past 夜壺, 尿壺

cha·me·le·on /kəˋmilɪən; kəˈmiːliən/ *n* [C] **1** a LIZARD that can change its colour to match the colours around it 變色龍[蜥蜴] **2** someone who changes their ideas, behaviour etc to fit different situations 善變的人, 見風使舵的人, 改變想法以適應情況的人: *He was a chameleon, able to blend with the customs and people he was living among.* 他是一個適應能力很強的人, 能夠融入周圍的人和風俗習慣。

cham·ois /ˋʃæmɪ; ˈʃæmwɑː/ *n* **1** [C] a wild animal like a small goat that lives in the mountains of Europe and SW Asia〔生活在歐洲及亞洲西南部山區的〕岩羚羊 **2** also 又作 **chamois leather** /ˋ·· ˋ··/ [C,U] soft leather prepared from the skin of chamois, sheep, or goats and used for cleaning or polishing, or a piece of this leather〔由羚羊、綿羊、山羊等的皮製成的〕軟皮革

cham·o·mile /ˋkæməˌmaɪl; ˈkæməmaɪl/ *n* [C,U] another spelling of CAMOMILE camomile 的另一種拼法

champ[1] /tʃæmp; tʃæmp/ *v* [I,T] **1** to bite food noisily; CHOMP 大聲咀嚼〔食物〕 **2 be champing at the bit** to be unable to wait for something patiently 急不及待

champ[2] *n* [C] a CHAMPION[1] (1) 冠軍: *The Cowboys are the next World Champs!* 牛仔隊是下一個世界冠軍!

cham·pagne /ʃæmˋpen; ʃæmˈpeɪn/ *n* [U] a French white wine with a lot of BUBBLEs, drunk on special occasions〔法國〕香檳酒

cham·pers /ˋʃæmpɚz; ˈʃæmpəz/ *n* [U] *BrE informal* champagne【英, 非正式】香檳酒

2 **cham·pi·on[1]** /ˋtʃæmpɪən; ˈtʃæmpiən/ *n* [C] **1** someone or something that has won a competition, especially in sport〔尤指體育比賽中的〕冠軍, 第一名: *the world heavyweight boxing champion* 世界重量級拳擊冠軍 | **reigning champion** (=the champion at the present time) 現任冠軍 **2 champion of** someone who publicly fights for and defends an aim or principle, such as the rights of a group of people〔為某目標或原則如某羣人的權利而奮鬥的〕鬥士: *a champion of women's rights* 女權捍衛者

champion[2] *v* [T] to publicly fight for and defend an aim or principle, such as the rights of a group of people 公開為〔某目標或原則〕而鬥爭; 維護: *championing the cause of religious freedom* 維護宗教自由的事業

2 **cham·pi·on·ship** /ˋtʃæmpɪənˌʃɪp; ˈtʃæmpiənʃɪp/ *n* **1** [C] also 又作 **championships** [plural] a competition to find which player, team, etc is the best in a particular sport 錦標賽, 冠軍賽: *the women's figure skating championships* 女子花樣滑冰錦標賽 **2** [C] the position or period of being a champion; TITLE[1] (5) 冠軍地位, 冠軍稱號: *fighting for the world championship* 爭奪世界冠軍 **3** [U+of] the act of championing something or someone〔對某事或某人的〕支持, 維護

chance[1] /tʃæns; tʃɑːns/ *n*

1 ▶POSSIBILITY 可能性◀ [C,U] how possible or likely it is that something will happen, especially something that you want 機會, 可能性: **chance/chances of** *What are her chances of survival?* 她生還的可能性有多大? | **there's a chance (that)** *There's always the chance that something will go wrong.* 總有可能會出現問題。| **a good/fair/slight chance (of)** *The day will be cloudy with a slight chance of some rain later tonight.* 天氣將轉陰, 今晚稍後可能會下雨。| **some/no/little chance** *There seems to be little chance of a ceasefire.* 看來停火的可能性不大。| **chances are** *spoken* (=used to say that something is likely)【口】很可能… *Chances are they'll be out when we call.* 很可能我們去拜訪時他們不在。| **a fifty-fifty chance** (=when the chances of something happening or not happening are equal) 50% 的可能性 | **a chance in a million** (=a chance that you are very unlikely to have again) 難得的機會; 少有的機會 *I couldn't pass up going to Japan; it was a chance in a million.* 我不能放棄日本之行, 這可是個千載難逢的機會。| **a million to one chance** (=when something is extremely unlikely to happen) 幾乎不可能

2 ▶HOW LIKELY TO SUCCEED 成功的機率◀ **a) sb's chances** how likely it is that someone will succeed 某人成功的可能性: *Ryan will be a candidate in next month's elections, but his chances are not good.* 瑞安是下月選舉的候選人之一, 但他當選的機會不大。| **not fancy/not rate sb's chances** *BrE* (=think someone is unlikely to succeed)【英】認為某人不可能成功 **b) stand/have a chance (of)** if someone or something stands a chance of doing something, it is possible that they will succeed 有希望…: **stand a good chance** (=be likely to succeed) 很可能會成功 *If we did move to London, I'd stand a much better chance of getting a job.* 如果我們真的搬到倫敦, 那我找到工作的可能性就會大得多。| **have an outside chance** (=have a slight chance of success) 成功的機會很小 | **have a sporting chance** (=have a fairly good chance of success) 成功的可能性相當大 | **have a fighting chance** (=have a small but real chance of success if a great effort can be made) 需付出極大的努力才有成功的可能 **c) be in with a chance** if a competitor is in with a chance, it is possible that they will win 有成功[獲勝]的可能; 可能達到目標: *There're three of us going for promotion, but I figure I'm in with a chance.* 我們有三個人在爭取得到提升, 但我認為我還是有機會勝出的。

3 by any chance *spoken* used to ask politely whether something is true【口】也許, 可能〔用於禮貌地問某事是否屬實〕: *Are you Mrs Grant, by any chance?* 你可能就是格蘭特太太吧?

4 any chance of... *spoken* used to ask whether you can have something or whether something is possible【口】能…嗎〔用於詢問是否能擁有某物或某事是否可能〕: *Any chance of a cup of coffee?* 我能要杯咖啡嗎? | *Any chance of you coming to the party on Saturday?* 星期六你是否會來參加聚會?

5 no chance!/fat chance! *spoken* used to emphasize that you are sure something could never happen【口】絕對不可能!: *"Maybe your brother would lend you the money?" "Huh, fat chance!"* "也許你哥哥會借錢給你呢?" "哼! 絕不可能!"

6 on the off chance if you do something on the off chance, you do it hoping for a particular result, although you know it is not likely 希望〔某事〕發生, 對…抱有一線希望: *I didn't really expect her to be at home. I just called on the off chance.* 我並不指望她會在家, 我只是打個電話看看。

7 ▶OPPORTUNITY 機會◀ [C] a time or situation which you can use to do something that you want to do 機會, 機遇, 有利時機: **chance to do sth** *Ralph was waiting for a chance to introduce himself.* 拉爾夫正在等待機會介紹自己。| [+of] *our only chance of escape* 我們逃走的唯一機會 | **have/get a chance** *I never get a chance to relax these days.* 我近來一直沒機會好好放鬆一下。| **give sb a chance** *I can explain everything if you'll just* *give me a chance.* 如果你能給我機會, 我會解釋這一切。| **take the chance** (=use the opportunity) 把握機會 *You should take the chance to travel while you're still young.* 你應該趁年輕抓緊機會旅遊。| **grab the chance/jump at the chance** (=eagerly and quickly use an opportunity)〔趕緊〕抓住機會 *You're so lucky. If someone invited me over to Florida, I'd jump at the chance.* 你真幸運。如果有人邀請我去佛羅里達的話, 我會迫不及待地抓住這個機會。| **miss a chance** (=fail to use the opportunity) 錯過機會 *Denise never misses the chance of a free meal.* 丹尼斯從不錯過任何吃免費餐的機會。| **a second chance/another chance** (=another chance after you have failed the first time) 第二次機會 *Students will be given further training and a second chance to pass the exam.* 學生們將受到進一步的訓練, 並獲得一次補考的機會。| **last chance** *Friday is your last chance to see the show before it closes.* 星期五是閉幕前你觀看那個表演的最後機會。| *You really ought to be punished, but I'll give you one last chance.* (=opportunity to behave well) 你真該受到懲罰, 不過我會給你最後一次機會。| **the chance of a lifetime** (=an opportunity you are not likely to get more than once) 千載難逢[一生難得]的機會 | **now's your chance** *spoken* (=used to tell someone to do something immediately because there is a good opportunity)【口】你的機會到了 *Quick! Now's your chance to ask her, before she leaves.* 快點!在她走前可是問她的好機會。| **given half a chance** *spoken* (=if someone were given even a small opportunity)【口】稍有機會 *Rick could do really well, given half a chance.* 如果你給里克一丁點機會, 他一定能幹得很出色的。

8 ►RISK 冒險◄ take a chance to do something that involves risks 冒險: *The rope might break but that's a chance we'll have to take.* 繩子可能會斷, 但我們只能冒這個險了。| **take chances** *After losing $20,000 on my last business venture, I'm not taking any chances this time.* 上次買賣我損失了20,000美元, 這次我不會冒任何風險了。| **take a chance on** (=take a chance hoping things will happen in the way you want) 希望事情如願 *I haven't reserved a table. I'm taking a chance on the restaurant not being full.* 我沒預定座位, 但願餐廳不會客滿。

9 ►LUCK 運氣◄ [U] the way some things happen without being planned or caused by people 巧合, 偶然: *Success is rarely a matter of chance. You have to work at it.* 成功很少靠運氣。你得為此而努力。| **by chance** (=without being planned or intended) 偶然地; 碰巧地 *I bumped into her quite by chance in Oxford Street.* 我在牛津大街碰巧遇到她。| **pure/sheer/blind chance** (=nothing except chance) 純屬巧合 *It was pure chance that they ended up working in the same office in the same town.* 真巧, 結果他們在同一個小鎮的同一個辦公室裡工作。| **as chance would have it** (=happening in a way that was not expected or intended) 湊巧, 碰巧 *As chance would have it, the one time I wanted to see her, she wasn't in.* 真巧, 我就這麼一次想見她, 她卻不在。

10 chance would be a fine thing! *spoken* used to mean that the thing you want to happen is very unlikely【口】要有這樣的機會就好了!〔用於表示希望發生的事是不可能的〕: *"If he asked me to marry him, I might say yes." "Chance would be a fine thing!"* (=he's unlikely to ask) "如果他向我求婚, 我會答應的。" "要能這樣就好了!"〔=他不可能會求婚〕—see also 另見 **a game of chance** (GAME¹ (11))

USAGE NOTE 用法說明: CHANCE

WORD CHOICE 詞語辨析: **chance, opportunity, occasion**

Both **chance** and **opportunity** can be used for a situation that is suitable for doing something that you want to do. chance 和 opportunity 都可以用來指適於做某事的良機: *I'll have a chance/an opportunity to visit Niagara Falls when I'm in the States.* 我在美國的時候將有機會去看看尼亞加拉大瀑布。You can *get/take/grab/jump at/miss the opportunity/chance* to do something and *give someone the opportunity/chance* to do something. 你可以有/利用/抓住/錯失一個機會做某事以及給某人一個機會做某事。

Chance is also used to say it is possible that something might happen. chance也指某事有可能發生: *There is a chance that I'll see him* (=perhaps I'll see him). 我有可能見到他。

An **occasion** is a moment when something happens, especially when the same thing happens several times. occasion 指某事發生的時刻, 尤指同樣的事反覆發生: *I met her on several occasions* (=several times). 我遇到她好幾次了。| *On this occasion I was late* (NOT *In this occasion...* or just *This occasion...*). 這次我遲到了〔不能用 In this occasion..., 也不能只用 This occasion...〕。An **occasion** can also be an event. occasion也可以指事件: *Christmas is a special occasion.* 聖誕節是一個特殊的節日。

In formal English **occasion** (usually [U]) can also mean 'reason'. 在正式英語中, occasion〔通常為不可數名詞〕也可指"原因、理由": *The poor service gave them occasion to complain* (=caused them to complain). 糟糕的服務給了他們投訴的理由。

SPELLING 拼法

Remember the two 'p's in **opportunity**. 要記住opportunity 一詞中有兩個 p。

chance² *v* **1** *informal* to do something that you know involves a risk【非正式】冒險〔做某事〕: **chance it** *If we creep in quietly, maybe no one will notice. Anyway, let's chance it.* 如果我們悄悄地爬進去, 也許沒人會注意到。不管怎樣, 我們就來冒這個險吧。| **chance your luck** *You may lose all your money, but you'll just have to chance your luck like everyone else.* 你可能會輸光所有的錢, 但你必須像其他人那樣試試運氣。**2** *literary* to happen in an unexpected and unplanned way【文】偶然[碰巧]發生: **chance to do sth** *She chanced to be passing when I came out of the house.* 我從屋裡出來時她恰巧經過。| **it chanced that** *It chanced that we were both working in Paris that year.* 湊巧的是, 那一年我們都在巴黎工作。

chance on/upon sb/sth *phr v* [T] to find something or meet someone when you are not expecting to 與...不期而遇, 碰上: *Henry chanced upon some valuable coins in the attic.* 亨利無意中在閣樓裡發現了一些很珍貴的硬幣。

chance³ *adj* [only before noun 僅用於名詞前] not planned; ACCIDENTAL 偶然的, 意外的: *Their chance meeting brought them back together after seven years apart.* 分別七年後的偶然相遇使他們再走在一起。

chan·cel /ˈtʃænsḷ; ˈtʃɑːnsəl/ *n* [C] the part of a church where the priests and the CHOIR (=singers) sit〔供牧師和唱詩班坐的〕聖壇

chan·cel·ler·y /ˈtʃænsələrɪ; ˈtʃɑːnsələri/ *n* [C] **1** the building in which a CHANCELLOR has his office 大臣官邸; 總理官署; 大法官的辦公處 **2** the officials who work in a CHANCELLOR's office 大臣[大法官等]辦公處中的全體官員 **3** the offices of an official representative of a foreign country; CHANCERY 大使館[領事館]的辦公室

chan·cel·lor /ˈtʃænsələ; ˈtʃɑːnsələ/ *n* [C] **1** the Chancellor of the Exchequer〔英國〕財政大臣 **2 a)** the person who officially represents a British university on special occasions〔英國大學的〕名譽校長 **b)** the person in charge of an American university〔美國大學的〕負責人, 校長 **3** the chief minister of some countries〔某些國家的〕總理, 首相: *Willy Brandt, the former West German Chancellor* 前西德總理威利·勃蘭特

Chan·cel·lor of the Ex·cheq·uer /,... ·····'··/ *n* [C] the British government minister in charge of taxes and government spending〔英國〕財政大臣

chan·ce·ry /ˈtʃænsərɪ; ˈtʃɑːnsəri/ *n* [singular] **1** *especially BrE* a government office that collects and stores official papers【尤英】檔案館[室], 公文保管處 **2** the part of the British system of law courts which deals with EQUITY (4) 衡平法院〔以正義公平即衡平為總原則, 審理不屬普通法範圍的案件的法院〕**3** the offices of an official representative of a foreign country; CHANCELLERY 外國大使[領事]館的辦公處

chanc·y /ˈtʃænsɪ; ˈtʃɑːnsi/ *adj informal* uncertain or involving a lot of risk【非正式】不確定的; 冒險的: *Acting professionally is a chancy business.* 專業表演是個有風險的行業。—**chanciness** *n* [U]

chan·de·lier /ˌʃændḷˈɪr; ˌʃændəˈlɪə/ *n* [C] a large round structure for holding CANDLEs or lights that hang from the ceiling and is decorated with many small pieces of glass 枝形吊燈

chand·ler /ˈtʃændlə; ˈtʃɑːndlə/ *n* [C] *old use* someone who makes or sells candles【舊】製造[出售]蠟燭者 —see also 另見 SHIP'S CHANDLER

1 1 **change¹** /tʃendʒ; tʃeɪndʒ/ *v*

1 ►BECOME DIFFERENT 變得不同◄ [I,T] to become different 變化, 改變: *Susan has changed a lot since I last saw her.* 自從我上次看見蘇珊以來, 她變了許多。| **changing circumstances/attitudes etc** *Animals must be able to adapt to changing conditions in order to survive.* 為了生存, 動物必須能夠適應不斷變化的環境。| **change out of all recognition** (=change completely) 變得完全認不出 *The town I grew up in has changed out of all recognition.* 我成長生活的小鎮已經徹底地變樣了。| **change colour** *The leaves are slowly changing colour.* 葉子正在慢慢變色。| **not change your spots** (=never change your character or habits) 本性[習慣]不改

2 ►MAKE STH/SB DIFFERENT 使某物/某人不同◄ [T] to make something or someone different 使變化, 改變: *plans to change the voting system* 改變選舉制度的計劃 | *Having a baby changes your life completely.* 有了孩子會使你的生活徹底改變。

3 ►FROM ONE THING TO ANOTHER 從某物變成另一物◄ [I,T] to stop having or doing one thing and start having or doing something else instead 轉變; 轉換: **change (from sth) to sth** *We've changed from traditional methods of production to an automated system.* 我們已從傳統的生產方式改變為自動化系統。| **change your name/address/job etc** *Emma refused to change her name when she married.* 艾瑪結婚後不願意改姓。| **change jobs/cars etc** (=change from one to another) 換工作/車等 | **change course/direction** (=start to move in a different direction) 改變方向 *Our ship changed course and headed south.* 我們的船改變了航向駛向南方。| **change the subject** (=talk about something else) 換個話題 *I'm sick of politics. Let's change the subject.* 我討厭政治, 我們換個話題吧。| **change tack** (=try a different method of dealing with a situation) 改變策略 *Perhaps my cold reaction persuaded him to change tack in his dealings with the committee.* 或許是我冷淡的反應令他在和委員會打交道時改變了策略。| **change sides** (=leave one side and join the other one) 改變立場 *Paul decided to change sides halfway through the debate.* 辯論進行到一半的時候保羅決定改變立場。| **change ends** (=to move to opposite ends of a TENNIS COURT or football field during a game)〔網球賽或足球賽中的〕交換場地 *The two teams change ends at half-time.* 下半場開賽時, 兩隊交換了場地。

4 change your mind to change your decision, plan, or opinion about something 改變主意: **[+about]** *If you change your mind about the job, just give me a call.* 如果你對這份工作改變了主意, 打電話給我。

5 ►CLOTHES 衣服◄ **a)** [I,T] to take off your clothes and put on different ones 換(衣服): *I'm just going upstairs to change.* 我正要上樓去換衣服。| **[+into/out of]** *Why don't you change into something more comfortable?* 你為甚麼不換上更舒適的衣服呢? | *It's time you changed your socks.* 你該換雙襪子了。| **get changed** (=put on different clothes) 換衣服 **b)** [T] to put fresh clothes on a baby or fresh covers on a bed 給〔嬰兒〕換(衣服); 〔給牀〕換(牀單): *I'm just going to change the baby.* 我正要給寶寶換尿布。

6 ►REPLACE STH 取代某事物◄ [T] to put something new in place of something old, damaged, or broken 替換; 更換: *Can you change the light bulb for me?* 你能替我換個燈泡嗎? | *changing a tyre* 換輪胎

7 ►EXCHANGE GOODS 換貨◄ [T] to exchange something that you have bought, or that a customer has bought from you, especially because there is something wrong with it〔尤指因商品有問題而〕換〔貨物〕: *I bought these gloves for my daughter, but they're too large. Can I change them for a smaller size?* 我給女兒買的這副手套太大了, 我能換副小一點的嗎?

8 ►EXCHANGE MONEY 換錢◄ [T] **a)** to exchange a larger unit of money for smaller units that add up to the same value 換成〔零錢〕: *Can you change a £20 note?* 你能幫我把這20英鎊換成零錢嗎? **b)** to exchange money from one country for money from another 兌換〔貨幣〕: **change sth into/for** *I want to change my sterling into dollars.* 我想把英鎊換成美元。

9 ►TRAINS/BUSES 火車/公共汽車◄ [I,T] to get out of one train or bus and into another in order to continue your journey 換車, 轉車: **[+at]** *Passengers for Liverpool should change at Crewe.* 前往利物浦的乘客要在克魯轉車。| **change trains/buses** *You can travel all the way to Paris without having to change trains.* 你可以坐火車直達巴黎, 無須轉車。| **all change!** *BrE* (=used to tell passengers to get off a train because it does not go any further)【英】全部下車!〔到終點站後司機叫列車乘客下車時的用語〕

10 change hands if property changes hands, it passes from one owner to another 易手; 易主: *The house has changed hands three times in the last two years.* 在過去的兩年中, 這房子已轉手三次了。

11 change places (with) a) to give someone your place and take their place (和...)換位置: *Would you mind changing places with me so I can sit next to my friend?* 你能和我換一下座位, 讓我坐在朋友旁邊嗎? **b)** to take someone else's social position or situation in life instead of yours 交換地位[環境]: *She may be very rich, but I wouldn't want to change places with her.* 她也許很有錢, 但我不願意和她交換位置。

12 change gear to put the engine of a vehicle into a higher or lower GEAR¹ (1) in order to go faster or slower〔汽車的〕換排擋: **change into/out of** *Change into second gear as you approach the corner.* 靠近轉彎處時你要換成二擋。| **change up/down** *BrE*【英】*Change down before you get to the hill.* 上坡時你要換成低速擋。

13 change your tune to start expressing a different attitude and reacting in a different way, after something has happened〔某事發生後〕改變論調[態度]: *When I offered him a share of the profits, he soon changed his tune.* 當我提出分給他一些利潤時, 他立刻改變了態度。

14 ►WIND 風◄ [I] if the wind changes, it starts to blow in a different direction 改變風向 —see also 另見 **chop and change** (CHOP¹ (5))

change sth ↔ **around** *phr v* [T] to move things into different positions 改變〔物件的〕位置: *When we'd changed the furniture around, the room looked quite different.* 我們把家具改變位置後, 房間看上去大不一樣了。

change into *phr v* [T] **1** [**change into** sth] to become something different 變成: *When the princess kissed the frog, it changed into a handsome prince.* 公主吻了青蛙之後, 牠立刻變成了一位英俊的王子。**2** [**change** sth/sb **into** sth] to make something or someone become something different 把...變成...: *You can't change iron into gold.* 你無法使鐵變成金。

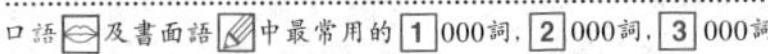

change² *n*

1 ►THINGS BECOMING DIFFERENT 事情變得不同◄ [C,U] the process or result of something or someone becoming different 變化, 改變, 變更: **[+in]** *a change in the weather* 天氣的變化 | *I've noticed a big change in Louise since she got married.* 我發覺路易絲結婚後有了很大的變化。| *changes in the immigration laws* 移民法的修改 | *Many old people find it hard to cope with change.* 許多老年人難以適應變化。| **[+of]** *a change of temperature* 溫度的變化 | **change for the better/worse** (=a change that makes a situation better or worse) 好轉/轉壞 *When Bill Clinton was elected, we all believed the new administration would be a change for the better.* 比爾·克林頓當選後, 我們都相信新政府會有所改善的。| **change of heart** (=change in someone's attitude) 改變態度 *He didn't want kids at first but recently he's had a real change of heart.* 他起初不想要孩子, 但最近卻改變了主意。

2 ►FROM ONE THING TO ANOTHER 從一物到另一物◄ [C] the fact of one thing or person being replaced by another 替換: **[+of]** *a change of government* 政府的更替 | *a change of address* 更改地址 | **change from sth to** *the change from city life to living right out in the countryside* 從城市生活轉變成鄉村生活 | *The car needs an oil change.* 這輛車需要換油。

3 ►PLEASANT NEW SITUATION 令人高興的新狀況◄ [singular] a situation or experience that is different from what happened before, and is usually interesting or enjoyable〔有趣或令人愉快的〕轉變: **[+from]** *Roast lamb is a welcome change from the usual junk food.* 老吃垃圾食品, 改吃一次烤羊便深受歡迎。| **for a change** *Let's go out to a restaurant for a change.* 我們換換口味上飯館去吃飯吧! | **it makes a change** *spoken* (=used to say that something is different from usual and better)【口】不同尋常, 變好了 *"The train was on time today." "Well, that makes a change."* "火車今天很準時。" "哦, 真是難得。" | **change of scene/air etc** (=a stay in a different place that is pleasant) 換個〔好〕環境 *How about a week by the sea? The change of air would do you good.* 到海邊度假一個禮拜怎麼樣? 換換環境對你有好處。

4 ►MONEY 錢財◄ [U] **a)** the money that you get back when you have paid for something with more money than it costs 找回的零錢: *I waited for the shopkeeper to hand me my change.* 我等店主找錢。**b)** money in the form of coins 硬幣, 零錢: **in change** *I have about a dollar in change.* 我有大約一美元的零錢。| **change for £1/$10** (=coins that you give someone in exchange for the same money in a larger unit) 一英鎊/十美元的硬幣 *Excuse me, have you got change for a pound?* 對不起, 你能幫我把一英鎊換成零錢嗎? | **loose change** *Matt emptied the loose change from his pockets.* 瑪特把口袋裡的零錢都掏了出來。| **small change** (=coins of low value) 零錢, 小錢 *When travelling by bus in a strange place, have small change ready.* 在陌生的城市乘搭公共汽車, 要準備好零錢。—see 見 MONEY (USAGE)

5 change of clothes/underwear etc an additional set of clothes that you have with you, for example when you are travelling 備換的衣服/內衣等

6 ►TRAIN/BUS 火車/公共巴士◄ [C] a situation in which you get off one train or bus and get on another in order to continue your journey 換車, 轉車

7 get no change out of *spoken* to get no useful information or help from someone【口】從〔某人那兒〕得不到有用的資料[幫助]: *I wouldn't bother asking Richard, you'll get no change out of him.* 我不會去問李察, 你從他那兒不會得到任何有用的幫助的。—see also 另見 **ring the changes** (RING² (6))

change·a·ble /ˈtʃendʒəbl̩; ˈtʃeɪndʒəbəl/ *adj* likely to change or changing often 可變的; 易變的; 常變化的: *The weather was very changeable.* 這天氣變化無常。—**changeably** *adv*—**changeableness** *n* [U]—**changeability** /ˌtʃendʒəˈbɪlətɪ; ˌtʃeɪndʒəˈbɪləti/ *n* [U]

changed /tʃendʒd; tʃeɪndʒd/ *adj* **1 a changed man/woman** someone who has become very different from what they were before as a result of a powerful experience〔由於某種經歷後〕有很大改變的: *Since she stopped drinking, she's a changed woman.* 自從戒酒後她整個人都變了。**2 changed circumstances** a change in someone's financial situation 經濟狀況的改變: *When planning ahead, be aware of the possibility of changed circumstances.* 在為將來作計劃時, 要注意經濟狀況變化的可能性。

change·less /ˈtʃendʒlɪs; ˈtʃeɪndʒləs/ *adj literary* never seeming to change【文】不變的, 永恒的: *a changeless desert landscape* 毫無變化的沙漠景觀 —**changelessly** *adv*

change·ling /ˈtʃendʒlɪŋ; ˈtʃeɪndʒlɪŋ/ *n* [C] *literary* a baby that is said to have been secretly exchanged for another baby by fairies (FAIRY (1))【文】〔傳說中〕被〔仙女〕調換的嬰兒

change of life /ˌ· · ˈ·/ *n* [singular] the MENOPAUSE 更年期, 絕經期

change·o·ver /ˈtʃendʒˌovɚ; ˈtʃeɪndʒˌəʊvə/ *n* [C] a change from one activity, system, or way of working to another〔活動、體制或工作方法的〕改變, 轉變, 變更: *working to ensure that the changeover to the new method is as smooth as possible* 努力確保改用新方法能夠順利進行

change purse /ˈ· ·/ *n* [C] *AmE* a small bag in which coins are kept【美】放零錢的小錢包; PURSE¹ (1) *BrE*【英】—see picture at 參見 PURSE¹ 圖

change ring·ing /ˈ· ˌ··/ *n* [U] the art of ringing a set of bells in an order that keeps changing 敲奏組鐘的技藝

changing room /ˈ·· ·/ *n* [C] a room where people change their clothes when they play sports〔運動場等內的〕更衣室; LOCKER ROOM *AmE*【美】

chan·nel¹ /ˈtʃænl; ˈtʃænl/ *n* [C]

1 ►TELEVISION 電視◄ a television station and all the programmes broadcast by it 頻道: *We watched the news on Channel 4.* 我們看了第四頻道的新聞節目。| *This is boring – I'm going to switch to another channel.* 這節目太無聊了 —— 我要換台。

2 ►RADIO 廣播◄ a particular range of SOUND WAVES which can be used to send and receive radio messages〔發送和接收無線電信號的〕波道

3 ►SYSTEM OF INFORMATION 信息系統◄ also 又作 **channels** [plural] a system or method that you use to send or obtain information about a particular subject〔傳遞或獲得資料的〕途徑; 手段; 渠道: *If you go through official channels, your application will take months.* 如果通過正式途徑, 你的申請要幾個月才能批准。

4 ►FOR WATER 水◄ a passage that water or other liquids flow along 管道; 水渠, 水溝: *an irrigation channel* 灌溉渠

5 ►SEA/RIVER 海洋/河流◄ **a)** a passage of water connecting two seas 海峽: **the Channel** (=the English Channel) 英吉利海峽 **b)** the deepest part of a river, HARBOUR¹, or sea passage, especially one that is deep enough to allow ships to sail in 航道

6 ►IN A SURFACE 在表面◄ a long deep line cut into a surface or a long deep space between two edges; GROOVE¹ (1)〔在表面形成的〕槽, 溝: *Slide the plastic door strip into the channel provided.* 把細塑料門條插進槽中。

7 ►WAY TO EXPRESS YOURSELF 表達方式◄ a way of expressing your thoughts, feelings, or physical energy〔表達思想、感情或發泄精力的〕方式, 渠道, 途徑: *The kids need a channel for all that energy.* 孩子們需要一種途徑去發揮他們的精力。

channel² *v* **channelled, channelling** *BrE*【英】**channeled, channeling** *AmE*【美】[T] **1** to control and direct something such as money or energy towards a particular purpose 把〔錢或精力等〕導向〔某一特定目的〕; 引導: **channel sth into** *Nancy channels her creativity into her home life.* 南茜把她的創造才能用於她的家庭生活中。| **channel sth through** *The famine relief money was* *channelled through the UN.* 饑荒救濟款項是通過聯合國分發的。**2** to cut a long deep line in something 在〔某物上〕形成槽: *Water had channelled grooves in the rock.* 水在岩石上形成了一道道深槽。**3** to send water through a passage〔透過管道〕輸送〔水等〕: *An efficient irrigation system channels water to the crops.* 有效的灌溉系統把水輸送給莊稼。

channel hop /ˈ‥ ˌ/ *BrE*【英】, **channel surf** *AmE*【美】*v* [I] to repeatedly change from one television channel to another, only watching a few minutes of any programme 跳頻道〔指看電視時不斷換頻道〕

chan·nel·ling *BrE*【英】, **channeling** *AmE*【美】/ˈtʃænl̩-ɪŋ; ˈtʃænl-ɪŋ/ *n* [U] a practice based on the belief that messages can be received from other PLANETS or from dead people 接收外太空信息; 通靈術 —**channeller** *n* [C]

chant¹ /tʃænt; tʃɑːnt/ *v* [I,T] **1** to repeat a word or phrase again and again〔有節奏地反覆地〕唱, 喊叫: *an angry crowd chanting slogans and waving banners* 反覆地喊着口號並揮動着旗幟的憤怒的人羣 **2** to sing or say a religious song or prayer in a way that involves singing phrases on one note 吟唱, 背誦〔讚美詩等〕: *a priest chanting the liturgy* 背誦禱文的牧師

chant² *n* [C] **1** words or phrases that are repeated again and again by a group of people 有節奏的一再重複的話語: **take up a chant** *Dave took up the crowd's chant of "More Jobs! More Money!"* 大衛也加入人羣中, 不停地喊着"增加職位! 增加工資!" **2** a regularly repeated tune, often with many words sung on one note, especially used for religious prayers 反覆唱的調子〔尤指聖歌〕—see also 另見 GREGORIAN CHANT —**chanter** *n* [C]

chan·try /ˈtʃæntrɪ; ˈtʃɑːntri/ also 又作 **chantry cha·pel** /ˌ‥ ˈ‥/ *n* [C] a small church or part of a church paid for by someone so that priests can pray for them there after they die〔施主為祈求冥福而捐建的〕小教堂

chan·ty also 又作 **chantey** *AmE*【美】/ˈʃæntɪ; ˈʃænti/ *n* [C] a song sung by sailors as they did their work in former times; SHANTY〔舊時水手唱的〕船歌; 船夫號子

Cha·nu·kah /ˈhɑnəkə; ˈhɑːnəkə/ *n* HANUKKAH〔紀念古代以色列戰功顯赫年代的〕獻殿節, 光明節

cha·os /ˈkeɑs; ˈkeɪ-ɒs/ *n* [U] **1** a situation in which everything is happening in a confused way and nothing is organized or arranged in order 大混亂; 紊亂; 無秩序狀態: **complete/utter/absolute chaos** *There was absolute chaos when the air controllers came out on strike.* 航空調度員罷工時出現了極度混亂的場面。| **in chaos** (=in a state of chaos) 淩亂不堪 *I arrived home to find the house in chaos.* 我回到家中, 發現家裡一片淩亂。**2** the state of the universe before there was any order〔天地未形成前〕宇宙的混沌狀態

cha·ot·ic /keˈɑtɪk; keɪˈɒtɪk/ *adj* a chaotic situation is one in which everything is happening in a confused way 混亂的, 毫無秩序的: *Traffic conditions tonight are chaotic.* 今晚的交通狀況一片混亂。

3 **chap** /tʃæp; tʃæp/ *n BrE informal*【英, 非正式】**1** [C] a man, especially a man you know and like〔尤指你認識和喜歡的〕小伙子, 傢伙: *a decent sort of chap* 一個正派的小伙子 **2 chaps** [plural] protective leather covers worn over your trousers when riding a horse〔騎馬時穿的〕皮套褲

chap·ar·ral /ˌʃæpəˈræl; ˌʃæpəˈræl/ *n* [U] *AmE* land on which small OAK trees grow close together【美】叢林, 茂密的 (橡) 樹林

chap·book /ˈtʃæpˌbʊk; ˈtʃæpbʊk/ *n* [C] *AmE* a small printed book, usually consisting of writings about literature or poetry【美】〔文學或詩歌〕小冊子

chap·el¹ /ˈtʃæpl̩; ˈtʃæpəl/ *n* **1** [C] a small church or a room in a hospital, prison etc in which Christians pray and have religious services〔醫院、監獄等中的〕小教堂, 小禮拜堂 **2** [C] a small church or a room or area in a church with its own ALTAR used especially for private prayer and religious services〔教堂內的〕私人祈禱處; 附屬小禮拜堂: *a wedding chapel in Las Vegas* 拉斯維加斯的一個婚禮禮拜堂 **3** [C] **a)** a building in England or Wales where Christians who are Nonconformists have religious services〔英格蘭或威爾斯不屬於英國國教的〕教堂 **b)** a Roman Catholic church in Scotland〔蘇格蘭的〕天主教教堂 **4** [U] the religious services held in a chapel〔小教堂裡的〕禮拜儀式: **go to chapel** *Betham goes to chapel every Sunday.* 貝瑟姆每個星期天都去教堂做禮拜。**5** [C] *BrE* the members of a UNION (=workers' organization) in the newspaper or printing industry【英】〔報業或印刷業的〕工會會員

chapel² *adj BrE informal* Nonconformist【英, 非正式】非英國國教的: *He's chapel but his wife is Roman Catholic.* 他不信奉英國國教, 但是他的妻子是天主教徒。

chap·e·rone¹, chaperon /ˈʃæpəˌron; ˈʃæpərəʊn/ *n* [C] **1** an older woman in former times who went out with a young unmarried woman on social occasions and was responsible for her behaviour〔舊時在社交場合陪伴未婚女子並負責監督其行為的〕年長女伴;〔女〕監護人: *I will only allow it if you have Maria as a chaperone.* 除非瑪麗亞陪你去, 我才會允許。**2** *AmE* someone, usually a parent or teacher, who attends school dances or visits to help watch the children【美】〔為幫助監護孩子而參加學校晚會或參觀的〕家長; 老師

chaperone², chaperon *v* [T] to go out somewhere with a woman as her chaperone 當〔某人〕的年長女伴; 監護; 陪伴

chap·lain /ˈtʃæplɪn; ˈtʃæplɪ̈n/ *n* [C] a priest or other religious minister responsible for the religious needs of a club, the army, a hospital, etc〔社團、軍隊或醫院等的〕牧師: *the prison/school chaplain* 監獄/學校牧師 —see 見 PRIEST (USAGE)

chap·lain·cy /ˈtʃæplɪnsɪ; ˈtʃæplɪ̈nsi/ *n* [C] the position of a chaplain or the place where a chaplain works 牧師的職位; 牧師的辦公處

chap·let /ˈtʃæplɪt; ˈtʃæplɪ̈t/ *n* [C] *literary* a band of flowers worn on the head【文】〔戴在頭上的〕花冠

chapped /tʃæpt; tʃæpt/ *adj* chapped lips or hands are sore, dry, and cracked, especially as a result of cold weather or wind〔尤指因寒冷或風導致唇、手〕乾燥的, 皸裂的 —**chap** *v* [T]

chap·ter /ˈtʃæptɚ; ˈtʃæptə/ *n* [C] S3 W1

1 ►IN A BOOK 書中◄ one of the parts into which a book is divided 章節: *I've only read as far as Chapter 5.* 我只讀到了第五章。

2 ►PERIOD 時期◄ a particular period or event in someone's life or in history〔人生或歷史的〕一段時期: **[+of]** *That summer an important chapter of my life came to an end.* 那個夏天, 我一生中一個重要的時期結束了。

3 ►PRIESTS 教士◄ all the priests connected with a CATHEDRAL, or a meeting of these priests 大教堂的所有教士; 大教堂全體教士的會議

4 ►CLUB 俱樂部◄ *especially AmE* the local members of a large organization such as a club【尤美】〔俱樂部的〕地方分會: *the San Fernando Valley chapter of the Sierra Club* 山林俱樂部在聖費爾南多山谷的分部

5 give/quote sb chapter and verse to give someone exact details about where to find some information 提供〔資料的〕確實出處

6 a chapter of accidents *BrE* a series of unfortunate events coming one after another【英】一連串的災禍[意外事件]

chap·ter·house /ˈtʃæptɚˌhaus; ˈtʃæptəhaʊs/ *n* [C] a building where the priests connected with a CATHEDRAL meet〔供大教堂教士集會用的〕教士禮堂

char¹ /tʃɑr; tʃɑː/ *v past tense and past participle* **charred, charring** **1** [I,T] to burn something so that its outside becomes black (把…) 燒焦: *Roast the peppers until the skin begins to char and blister.* 把這些辣椒烤到表皮發黑起泡為止。—see also 另見 CHARRED **2** [I] *BrE old-fashioned* to work as a cleaner in a house, office, public building etc【英, 過時】〔在家庭、辦公室、公共建築等〕當清潔工

char² *n* **1** [C] *BrE old fashioned* a CHARWOMAN【英, 過

時】清潔女工 **2** [U] *BrE old-fashioned* tea【英, 過時】茶: *a cup of char* 一杯茶

char·a·banc /ˈʃærə͵bæŋ; ˈʃærəbæŋ/ *n* [C] *BrE old-fashioned* a large comfortable bus used for pleasure trips【英, 過時】〔大而舒適的〕旅行客車, 大型遊覽車

1 1 **char·ac·ter** /ˈkærɪktɚ; ˈkærᵻktə/ *n*

1 ►ALL SB'S QUALITIES 某人所有的品質◄ [C usually singular 一般用單數] the particular combination of qualities that makes someone a particular kind of person〔某人的〕個性, 性格, 氣質: *There is a serious side to her character.* 她性格當中也有嚴肅的一面。| **be in/out of character** (=be typical or untypical of someone's character) 符合/不符合…的個性 *I can't believe she lied to me – it seems so out of character.* 想不到她會對我撒謊, 這不符合她的個性。| **the English/French etc character** *Openness is at the heart of the American character.* 坦誠是美國人性格的核心。—see 見 CHARACTERISTIC[1]

2 ►QUALITIES OF STH 某物的特徵◄ [singular,U] the particular combination of features and qualities that makes a thing or place different from all others〔某物或某地的〕特色, 特點: *the unspoilt character of the coast* 海岸未被破壞的特徵 | **[+of]** *In only ten years the whole character of the school has changed.* 僅僅十年間這所學校的所有特點都改變了。| **in character** *Liquids are different in character from both solids and gases.* 液體的特性與固體和氣體有所不同。

3 ►INTERESTING QUALITY 有趣的特點◄ [U] a quality that makes someone or something special and interesting〔使某人或某物特別或有趣的〕特徵: *These new houses have very little character.* 這些新房子並沒有甚麼特別之處。

4 ►MORAL STRENGTH 道德力量◄ [U] a combination of qualities such as courage and loyalty that are admired and regarded as valuable 人格, 好的品質, 品性: *a woman of great character* 一個品格高尚的婦人 | **character building** (=activity aimed at developing these qualities) 品德培養 *outdoor programs that are meant to be character building* 旨在培養優良品格的戶外活動計劃

5 ►PERSON 人物◄ [C] **a)** a person in a book, play, film etc〔書、劇本、電影等中的〕人物, 角色: *Hardy's main character is a young milkmaid whose life ends in tragedy.* 哈迪筆下的主要人物是一個最終以悲劇收場的年輕擠奶姑娘。**b)** a person of a particular kind, especially a strange or dishonest one 人;〔尤指〕怪人: *a couple of suspicious-looking characters standing outside the house* 站在門外的幾個神情可疑的人 **c) be a character** to be an interesting, and unusual person 有趣的人; 不同尋常的人: *Kurt's quite a character – he has so many tales to tell.* 庫爾特是個很特別的人 —— 他有許多不同的經歷。

6 ►REPUTATION 聲譽◄ [U] *formal* reputation【正式】名譽, 名聲, 聲譽: *a man of previous good character* 從前擁有良好聲譽的人 | **a slur on your character** (=something that harms your character in other people's opinion) 毀壞名譽之事 | **character assassination** (=a cruel and unfair attack on someone's character) 人身攻擊, 誹謗

7 ►LETTER/SIGN 字母/符號◄ [C] a letter, mark, or sign used in writing, printing, or computing〔書寫、印刷或電腦的〕字; 字體; 符號: *Chinese characters* 漢字

char·ac·ter·ise /ˈkærɪktə͵raɪz; ˈkærᵻktəraɪz/ *v* a British spelling of CHARACTERIZE characterize 的英式拼法

3 2 **char·ac·ter·is·tic**[1] /͵kærɪktəˈrɪstɪk; ͵kærᵻktəˈrɪstɪk◄/ *n* [C usually plural 一般用複數] a quality or feature of something or someone that is typical of them and easy to recognize〔人或物的〕特徵, 特性, 特色: *A characteristic of this species is the blue stripe on its back.* 這物種有個特徵, 那就是其背部有藍色的條紋。| *Obstinacy remains one of Gail's less endearing characteristics.* 固執一直是蓋爾不太討人喜歡的一個特點。

characteristic[2] *adj* very typical of a particular thing or of someone's character 典型的; 獨特的; 表現〔人或物的〕特性的: *Larry, with characteristic generosity, invited us all back to his house.* 本性慷慨大方的拉里邀請我們所有人回到他家去。| **[+of]** *The flint walls are characteristic of the local architecture.* 燧石牆是當地建築的一大特色。—**characteristically** /-klɪ; -kli/ *adv*

char·ac·ter·i·za·tion /͵kærɪktərəˈzeʃən; ͵kærᵻktəraɪˈzeɪʃən/ *n* **1** [C,U] the way in which a writer makes a person in a book, film, or play seem like a real person〔書、電影等中的〕人物塑造, 角色刻劃: *He writes exciting stories but his characterization is weak.* 他寫的故事很有趣, 但人物的塑造卻缺乏力度。**2** [U] the way in which the character of a real person or thing is described〔人物性格或事物特徵的〕描述, 刻劃, 表現: **characterization of sb/sth as** *the characterization of the enemy as 'cruel fanatics'* 敵人被描繪成"殘酷的狂熱分子"

char·ac·ter·ize also 又作 **-ise** *BrE*【英】/ˈkærɪktə͵raɪz; ˈkærᵻktəraɪz/ *v* [T] **1** to be typical of a person, place, or thing〔人、地方或事物〕以…為特徵, 以…為典型: *Bright, vibrant colours characterize his paintings.* 他的畫以明亮輕快的色彩為特徵。**2** to describe the character of someone or something in a particular way; PORTRAY 描述…的特性; 描繪: **characterize sb as sth** *I would characterize Captain Hill as a born leader of men.* 我認為希爾上校是一個天生的領導者。

char·ac·ter·less /ˈkærəktɚlɪs; ˈkærᵻktələs/ *adj* not having any special or interesting qualities 無特色的; 平凡的: *snack-bars selling mass-produced, characterless food* 出售沒有特色的大眾食品的小吃店

character ref·e·rence /ˈ··· ͵···/ *n* [C] REFERENCE (4) 介紹信, 推薦信

cha·rade /ʃəˈred; ʃəˈrɑːd/ *n* **1 charades** [U] a game in which one person acts the meaning of a word or phrase and the others have to guess what it is 手勢字謎遊戲 **2** [C] a situation in which people pretend that something is true and behave as if it were true, when everyone knows it is not really true 顯而易見[容易識破]的偽裝: *Their marriage is an empty charade, continued only for the sake of the children.* 他們的婚姻已經形同虛設, 只是為了孩子的緣故才繼續維持着。

char·broil /ˈtʃɑr͵brɔɪl; ˈtʃɑːbrɔɪl/ *v* [T] *AmE* to cook food over a very hot charcoal fire【美】炭烤, 炭炙 —**charbroiled** *adj*

char·coal /ˈtʃɑr͵kol; ˈtʃɑːkəʊl/ *n* [U] a black substance obtained by burning wood, that can be used as FUEL, or sticks of this substance used for drawing 木炭;(畫用)炭筆: *a sketch drawn in charcoal* 用炭筆畫的素描 | *a charcoal grill* 木炭燒烤架

chard /tʃɑrd; tʃɑːd/ *n* [U] a vegetable with large leaves 莙薘菜, 牛皮菜; 瑞士甜菜

charge[1] /tʃɑrdʒ; tʃɑːdʒ/ *n*

1 ►PRICE 價格◄ [C,U] the amount of money you have to pay for goods or services 費用, 價錢: *Gas charges will rise in July.* 七月份煤氣價格將上漲。| **[+for]** *When you buy a suit, there is no charge for any alterations.* 買了西服後可以免費修改。| **free of charge** (=at no cost) 免費 *Your order will be delivered free of charge within a ten-mile limit.* 在十英里範圍之內, 你將享有免費送貨的服務。| **at no extra charge** (=without having to pay more money) 不需額外付費 —see 見 COST[1] (USAGE)

2 ►CONTROL 控制◄ **a) be in charge (of)** to be the person who controls or is responsible for a group of people or an activity 負責…, 掌管…: *Who's in charge around here?* 這兒誰負責? | *the officer in charge of the investigation* 負責調查的長官 —see 見 CONTROL[1] (USAGE) **b) put sb in charge (of)** to give someone complete responsibility over an activity, group of people, organization etc 讓…全權負責: *I've been put in charge of the team.* 我被指派負責這個隊。**c) take charge (of)** to take control of a situation, organization, or group of people 控制, 掌管〔局面、組織或人〕: *Harry will take charge of the department while I'm away.* 我不在時由哈里負責部門的事務。

3 ►RESPONSIBILITY/CARE FOR 責任/照料◄ **a) be**

in/under sb's charge if someone or something is in your charge, you are responsible for looking after them 由…照料[照顧]: *The child was in my charge when he ran away.* 他離家出走後，孩子便由我照顧。| *The files were left in your charge.* 這些文件由你負責處理。**b)** [C] *formal* someone that you are responsible for looking after【正式】被照顧的人: *Sarah bought some chocolate for her three young charges.* 莎拉給自己照顧的三個小孩買了些巧克力。

4 ▶THAT SB IS GUILTY 某人有罪◀ [C] an official statement made by the police saying that someone is guilty of a crime 指控，控告，罪名: **[+against]** *The charge against her was arson.* 她被控縱火。| **on a charge** *Young appeared in court on a murder charge.* 楊格因被控謀殺罪而出庭。| **charge of burglary/theft/fraud etc** *Owen is facing a charge of armed robbery.* 歐文面臨一項持械行劫的控罪。| **bring/press/prefer charges** (=state officially that someone is guilty of a crime) 正式起訴 *As it was his first offence, the store agreed not to press charges.* 由於是初犯，那家商店同意不起訴他。| **drop the charges** (=decide to stop making charges) 撤銷控訴

5 ▶BLAME 責備◀ [C] a written or spoken statement blaming someone for doing something bad or illegal; ALLEGATION〔書面或口頭的〕指責，批評，責備: *the charge of being an uncaring mother* 被指責為一個漠不關心的母親 | *a group which earlier rejected the charge that it had put undue pressure on the Prime Minister* 一個早前否認指控說它對首相過分施壓的團體 | **counter a charge** (=say that a charge is untrue) 駁斥指控 | **lay/leave yourself open to a charge of** (=be likely to be blamed for something) 可能遭到非議[指責] *The procedures the doctor followed laid him open to charges of negligence.* 那位醫生所採用的程序使他有可能被指責為疏忽。

6 ▶ATTACK 進攻◀ [C] an attack in which soldiers, wild animals etc rush with great force against someone〔士兵或野生動物等〕猛烈的攻擊

7 ▶ELECTRICAL FORCE 電力◀ [U] an electrical force that is put into a piece of electrical equipment such as a BATTERY (1) 電荷；電量: **on charge** (=taking in a charge of electricity) 在充電 *Leave the battery on charge all night.* 讓電池充一晚上的電。

8 ▶EXPLOSIVE 爆炸物◀ [C] an amount of explosive, especially the amount needed to work successfully〔一定量的〕炸藥

9 ▶STRENGTH OF FEELINGS 感情的力量◀ [U] the power of strong feelings〔感情的〕力量；感染力: *a novel with a strong emotional charge* 一部具有強烈感染力的小說

10 get a charge out of sth *AmE* to be excited by something and enjoy it very much【美】從〔某事〕得到快樂[刺激、興奮]: *I got a real charge out of seeing my niece take her first steps.* 看到姪女踏出第一步，我高興極了。

11 ▶AN ORDER TO DO STH 命令◀ [C] *formal* an order to do something【正式】命令，指示，吩咐: **a charge to do sth** *The old servant fulfilled his master's charge to care for the children.* 老僕人按照主人的吩咐照料小孩。—see also 另見 **reverse the charges** (REVERSE[1] (5))

1 **charge**[2] *v*

2 **1 ▶MONEY** 錢◀ **a)** [I,T] to ask someone a certain amount of money for something you are selling（向…）收費；開價: **charge sb £10/$50 etc (for sth)** *The restaurant charged us £40 for the wine.* 餐廳收我們40英鎊的酒水錢。| **[+for]** *We won't charge for delivery if you pay now.* 如果現在付款，我們將免費送貨上門。**b) charge sth to sb's account** to record the cost of something on someone's account, so that they can pay for it later 把某物記在某人的賬上: *Charge the room to the company's account.* 把房間費用記在公司的賬下。**c)** [T] *AmE* to pay for something with a CREDIT CARD【美】用信用卡付賬: *I charged the shoes on Visa.* 我用維澤信用卡付了這鞋子的錢。| **charge it** *"Do you have enough cash for that?" "No, but I can charge it."* "你有足夠的現金支付嗎?" "不夠，但我可以刷卡。"

2 ▶RUSH/ATTACK 衝擊/攻擊◀ **a)** [I,T] to deliberately rush quickly towards someone or something in order to attack them 進攻，衝鋒；衝向: **[+at/towards/into]** *a three-ton rhino charging towards us* 一頭重三噸向我們衝來的犀牛 | **charge sb** *We drew our swords and charged the enemy.* 我們拔劍向敵人衝去。**b)** [I always+ adv/prep] to deliberately run or walk somewhere quickly 快步走向[跑向]: **[+around/through/out etc]** *At playtime, the children charged wildly out of the building.* 一到活動時間，孩子們便瘋狂地跑出了屋子。

3 ▶WITH A CRIME 有罪◀ [T] to state officially that someone is guilty of a crime 控告；指控: **be charged with** *The man they arrested last night has been charged with murder.* 昨晚他們逮捕的那人被控犯有謀殺罪。

4 ▶BLAME SB 指責某人◀ [T] *formal* to say publicly that you think someone has done something wrong【正式】〔公開〕指責，責備: **charge that** *Labour's Bryan Gould charged that Mr Mellor acted 'improperly'.* 工黨的布賴恩·古爾德公開指責梅勒先生的所作所為是"不恰當的"。

5 ▶ELECTRICITY 電◀ [I,T] if a battery charges or if you charge it, it takes in and stores electricity（使）充電: *If the light comes on, the battery isn't charging.* 如果指示燈亮了，就表示電池沒在充電。

6 ▶ORDER SB 命令某人◀ [T] *formal* to order someone to do something or make them responsible for it【正式】吩咐，命令: **be charged with doing sth** *The commission is charged with investigating all the alleged breaches of the rules.* 委員會受命調查所有違規行為的指控。

7 ▶GUN 槍◀ [T] *old use* to load a gun【舊】給〔槍〕裝子彈

8 ▶GLASS 杯子◀ [T] *formal* to fill a glass【正式】斟滿〔杯〕: *Charge your glasses and drink a toast to the happy couple.* 把酒杯斟滿，為這幸福的一對乾杯。

charge·a·ble /ˈtʃɑrdʒəbl̩; ˈtʃɑːdʒəbəl/ *adj* **1** chargeable costs must be paid 應付費的；可記在某人賬上的: *Living expenses are chargeable to my account.* 生活開支可記在我的賬上。**2** chargeable assets or gains have to have tax paid on them 應交稅的 **3** a chargeable offence is serious enough for the police to officially state that you are guilty of it 可被指控[控告]的

charge ac·count /ˈ· ·,·/ *n* [C] *AmE* an account you have at a shop that allows you to take goods away with you now and pay later; CREDIT ACCOUNT【美】〔客戶購貨用的〕信用[賒欠]賬戶

charge card /ˈ· ·/ *n* [C] a plastic card that you can use to buy goods in a particular shop and pay for them later〔可賒購貨物的〕記賬卡，簽賬卡

charged /tʃɑrdʒd; tʃɑːdʒd/ *adj* a charged situation or subject makes people feel very angry, anxious, or excited, and is likely to cause arguments or violence 引起強烈感情的；〔氣氛〕緊張的: **highly charged** *a highly charged press conference* 一個氣氛緊張的記者招待會

char·gé d'af·faires /ʃɑrˋʒe dæˋfɛr; ˌʃɑːʒeɪ dæˈfeə/ *n* [C] *French* an official who represents their government during the absence of an AMBASSADOR or in a country where there is no ambassador【法】代辦〔代理大使職務的外交代表〕

charge hand /ˈ· ·/ *n* [C] *BrE* a worker in charge of other workers whose position is below that of a FOREMAN (1)【英】副領班，副監工

charge nurse /ˈ· ·/ *n* [C] a nurse in charge of one part of a hospital 護士長；責任護士

charg·er /ˈtʃɑrdʒɚ; ˈtʃɑːdʒə/ *n* [C] **1** a piece of equipment used to put electricity into a BATTERY (1) 充電器 **2** *literary* a horse that a soldier or KNIGHT rides in battle【文】戰馬，軍馬

charge sheet /ˈ· ·/ *n* [C] a record kept in a police station of the names of people the police have stated are guilty of a particular crime〔警察局中的〕案件記錄; 被起訴者名簿

char·i·ot /ˈtʃærɪət; ˈtʃæriət/ *n* [C] a vehicle with two wheels pulled by a horse, used in ancient times in battles and races〔古時用於戰爭或比賽的雙輪〕馬車; 戰車

char·i·o·teer /ˌtʃærɪəˈtɪr; ˌtʃæriəˈtɪə/ *n* [C] the driver of a chariot 馬車夫; 雙輪戰車駕御者

cha·ris·ma /kəˈrɪzmə; kəˈrɪzmə/ *n* [U] a powerful attractive personal quality that has a strong influence over other people and makes them admire you 個人魅力; 超凡氣質: *Few Presidents have had the charisma of Kennedy.* 沒有幾個總統擁有像甘迺迪那樣非凡的個人魅力。

char·is·mat·ic /ˌkærɪzˈmætɪk; ˌkærɪ̈zˈmætɪk◂/ *adj* **1** able to attract and influence other people because of a powerful personal quality you have 有吸引力的; 有感召力的; 有魅力的: *Martin Luther King was a very charismatic speaker.* 馬丁·路德·金是個很有感召力的演説家。**2 charismatic church/movement** groups of Christians who believe that God can give them special powers, for example the power to cure illness〔自認為得到神授的特殊能力的〕神授能力基督教派/運動

char·i·ta·ble /ˈtʃærətəbl̩; ˈtʃærɪ̈təbəl/ *adj* **1** kind and sympathetic in the way you judge people 仁慈的; 寬容的; 具有同情心的: *Let's be charitable and say he didn't know the car was stolen.* 我們寬容點吧, 就當他不知道車已被偷了。—opposite 反義詞 UNCHARITABLE **2** concerned with giving help to the poor 慈善的: *a charitable institution* 慈善機構 —**charitably** *adv*

2 3 **char·i·ty** /ˈtʃærətɪ; ˈtʃærɪ̈ti/ *n* **1** [U] money or gifts given to help people who are poor, sick etc 救濟(金), 施捨(物): *All the money raised by the concert will go to charity.* 演奏會所得的收入將全部用作善款。| *refugees living on charity* 靠救濟過活的難民 **2** [C] an organization that collects money or goods in order to help people who are poor, sick etc 慈善機構, 慈善團體: *Several charities sent aid to the flood victims.* 好幾個慈善機構已向水災災民給予了援助。| **charity event/walk/concert etc** (=an event organized to collect money for a charity) 為慈善事業籌款的活動/步行/演唱會等 **3** [U] a kind sympathetic attitude you have when judging or criticizing someone 寬容, 寬厚, 寬大: **show charity** *The newspaper stories reporting his suicide showed little charity.* 報紙對他自殺的報道顯得很不寬容。**4 charity begins at home** you should help your own family, country etc before you help other people 慈善始於家庭, 施捨先及親友

charity shop /ˈ‥ ˌ·/ *n* [C] *BrE* a shop that sells things given by people in order to collect money for a charity【英】〔以銷售義捐商品來募集善款的〕慈善商店

char·la·dy /ˈtʃɑrˌledɪ; ˈtʃɑːˌleɪdi/ *n* [C] *BrE old-fashioned* a CHARWOMAN【英, 過時】〔打掃房子、辦公室、大廈的〕清潔女工

char·la·tan /ˈʃɑrlətn̩; ˈʃɑːlətən/ *n* [C] someone who pretends to have special skills or knowledge 假充內行的騙子: *The man's a complete charlatan, only in it for the money.* 那個人是個徹頭徹尾的大騙子, 這麼做純粹為了錢。

Charles·ton /ˈtʃɑrlztən; ˈtʃɑːlstən/ *n* **the Charleston** a quick dance popular in the 1920s 查爾斯頓舞〔20世紀20年代流行的一種快節奏舞蹈〕

char·ley horse /ˌtʃɑrlɪ ˈhɔrs; ˌtʃɑːli ˈhɔːs/ *n* [C singular] *AmE informal* a pain in a large muscle, for example in your leg, caused by the muscle becoming tight; CRAMP[1] (1)【美, 非正式】肌肉痙攣, 抽筋

char·lie /ˈtʃɑrlɪ; ˈtʃɑːli/ *n* [C] *BrE spoken* a stupid person【英口】笨蛋, 蠢人: **feel a right/proper charlie** (=feel very stupid) 覺得自己很蠢

charm[1] /tʃɑrm; tʃɑːm/ *n* **1** [C,U] a pleasant quality someone or something has that makes people like them, feel attracted to them, or be easily influenced by them 魅力, 魔力, 吸引力; 可愛之處: *Dick still has a certain boyish charm.* 迪克仍保有一種稚趣。| *the charms of rural life* 鄉村生活的魅力 | **turn on the charm** (=use your charm) 施展魅力 *Wait till Grace turns on the charm, you won't be able to resist.* 等到葛蕾絲向你展現她的魅力時, 你將會無法抗拒。**2** a piece of magic which involves saying special words; SPELL[2] (1) 魔法; 咒語 **3** a very small object worn on a chain or BRACELET that people think will bring them good luck〔裝在手鏈、手鐲上表示吉祥的〕小裝飾品; 護身符: *a small gold horseshoe worn as a lucky charm* 作為吉祥物的金鑄馬蹄形掛墜 **4 work like a charm** to work perfectly or immediately 完全[迅速]地奏效: *I don't know what you sprayed on the roses, but it worked like a charm.* 我不知道你給這些玫瑰噴了甚麼, 但它非常管用!

charm[2] *v* [T] **1** to attract someone and make them like you, especially so that you can easily influence them 迷住, 吸引: *Collette was charmed by the stranger's elegant manners and rugged good looks.* 科萊特被這位陌生人優雅的舉止和粗獷而英俊的外表深深吸引住。**2** to gain power over someone or something by using magic 向…施魔法, 用魔法控制 **3 have/lead a charmed life** to be lucky all the time, so that although you are often in dangerous situations nothing ever harms you 總是幸運的, 總能逢凶化吉的 —**charmed** *adj*

charm·er /ˈtʃɑrmɚ; ˈtʃɑːmə/ *n* [C] someone who uses their charm to please or influence people 使人着迷的人: *Even at ten years old, he was a real charmer.* 早在十歲時他就是個討人喜歡的人。—see also 另見 SNAKE CHARMER

charm·ing /ˈtʃɑrmɪŋ; ˈtʃɑːmɪŋ/ *adj* very pleasing or attractive; nice 迷人的, 有魅力的, 有吸引力的: *What a charming house!* 多漂亮的房子啊! | *Harry can be charming when he wants.* 哈里樂意時非常迷人。—**charmingly** *adv*

charm school /ˈ· ·/ *n* [C] *especially AmE* a school where young women were sometimes sent in the past to learn how to behave politely and gracefully【尤美】〔舊時年輕女子就讀的〕禮儀學校

char·nel house /ˈtʃɑrnl̩ ˌhaus; ˈtʃɑːnl haʊs/ *n* [C] *literary* a place where the bodies and bones of dead people are stored【文】存骸所; 骨灰堂; 停屍間

charred /tʃɑrd; tʃɑːd/ *adj* burnt black 烏黑的, 黑色的, 焦黑的: *the charred remains of a corpse* 焦黑的屍骸

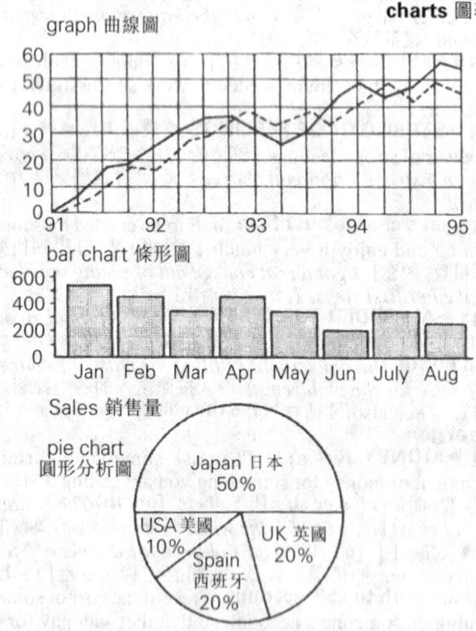

chart[1] /tʃɑrt; tʃɑːt/ *n* [C] **1** information that is clearly arranged in the form of a simple picture, sets of figures, GRAPH etc, or a piece of paper with this information on it 圖表, 圖: *a flow chart* 流程圖 | *a weather chart* 天氣圖

2 a detailed map, especially of an area of the sea 地圖;〔尤指〕海圖, 航海圖 **3 the charts** a list, which comes out weekly, of the most popular records〔流行歌曲每週〕排行榜: **top the charts** *Madonna's song topped the charts for over ten weeks.* 麥當娜的歌曲連續十多週穩居榜首。—see also 另見 BAR CHART, PIE CHART, FLOW CHART

chart² *v* [T] **1** to record information about a situation or set of events over a period of time in order to see how it changes or develops 給…製圖; 記述: *a study charting the steady progress of women in the 19th century* 記述19世紀婦女穩步發展的一個研究 **2** to make a map of an area of land or sea, or draw lines on a map to show where you have travelled 繪製…的地圖[海圖]; 把〔途經路線〕繪入地圖[海圖] —see also 另見 UNCHARTED

3 **char·ter¹** /ˋtʃɑrtɚ; ˈtʃɑːtə/ *n* **1** [C] a statement of the principles, duties, and purposes of an organization〔組織的〕原則, 章程, 憲章, 宣言: *freedoms embodied in the UN Charter* 聯合國憲章所體現的自由 **2** [singular] *BrE informal* a law or official decision that seems to give someone the right to do something most people consider morally wrong【英, 非正式】授予特種權利的法令; 特許狀; 特權: *Proposals to cut customs staff amount to little more than a drug-smuggler's charter.* 削減海關人員數量的提議差不多等於給予毒品走私者特權。**3** [C] a signed statement from a government or ruler which allows a town, organization, or university to officially exist and have special rights〔政府或統治者特許城鎮、組織或大學存在並享有特權的〕許可證 **4** [U] the practice of paying money to a company to use their boats, aircraft, etc〔船、飛機等的〕包租: *boats available for charter* 可供包租的船

charter² *v* [T] **1** to pay for the use of a plane, boat, train etc 包租〔飛機、船、火車等〕: *a chartered plane* 包機 **2** to say officially that a town, organization, or university officially exists and has special rights 特許成立〔城鎮、組織或大學〕—see 見 HIRE¹ (1)

chartered ac·coun·tant /ˌ‥ ‥ˈ‥/ *n* [C] *BrE* an ACCOUNTANT who has successfully completed special examinations【英】特許會計師; CPA *AmE*【美】

charter flight /ˈ‥ ˌ/ *n* [C] a low cost journey in a plane on which all the places have been paid for in advance by travel companies for their customers 包機旅行[航班] —compare 比較 **scheduled flight** (SCHEDULE²)

charter mem·ber /ˌ‥ ˈ‥/ *n* [C] *AmE* an original member of a club or organization【美】〔俱樂部或某組織的〕元老, 創始成員; FOUNDER MEMBER *BrE*【英】

char·treuse /ʃɑrˋtruz; ʃɑːˈtrɜːz/ *n* [U] **1** a strong green or yellow alcoholic drink 沙特勒茲酒, 蕁麻酒〔一種呈綠色或黃色的烈性酒〕**2** a bright green colour 黃綠色

chart-top·ping /ˈ‥ ˌ‥/ *adj* **chart-topping record/group/hit etc** a record, group etc that has sold the most records in a particular week〔某週內〕高居榜首的唱片/樂隊/歌曲等

char·wom·an /ˋtʃɑrˌwʊmən; ˈtʃɑːˌwʊmən/ *n* [C] *BrE old-fashioned* a woman who works as a cleaner, especially in someone's house【英, 過時】〔尤指打掃住宅的〕清潔女工

char·y /ˋtʃɛrɪ; ˈtʃeəri/ *adj* **be chary of doing sth** to be unwilling to risk doing something 小心的, 謹慎的: *Many census authorities have been chary of asking for information on sensitive subjects such as ethnic background.* 許多人口普查機構在問及諸如種族背景等敏感問題時, 都十分謹慎。

3 **chase¹** /tʃes; tʃeɪs/ *v*

1 ►FOLLOW 跟隨◄ [I,T] to quickly follow someone or something in order to catch them 追逐, 追趕; 追捕: *Outside in the yard, kids were yelling and chasing each other.* 外面院子裡, 孩子們叫喊着在互相追逐。| **chase sb along/down/up etc** *The dog spotted a cat and chased it up a nearby tree.* 狗發現了一隻貓並把牠趕到了附近的一棵樹上。| **chase sb away/off** (=chase someone in order to make them leave) 趕走, 驅逐 *Harry chased the boys off with a stick.* 哈里用一根棍子把男孩子們趕了出去。| [+after] *A favorite game was to chase after a passing farm cart and try to grab its tailboard.* 追逐路過的農用車, 並設法抓住其尾板是人們喜歡的一項遊戲。

2 ►HURRY 趕快◄ [I always+adv/prep] *especially BrE* to rush or hurry somewhere【尤英】急忙趕往: **around/up/down etc** *Mum's been chasing round the shops all day.* 媽媽整天忙於在商場購物。

3 ►TRY TO GET STH 試圖得到某物◄ [I+after, T] to use a lot of time and effort trying to get something such as work or money 努力贏得, 設法獲得: *The solicitor's doing everything she can to chase the contract.* 那個律師正盡全力要爭取到這份合同。

4 ►MAN/WOMAN 男人/女人◄ [T] to try hard to make someone notice you and pay attention to you, because you want to have a sexual relationship with them 追求, 求愛: *It was embarrassing – Louise spent the entire party chasing me.* 整個宴會期間路易絲都在追求我, 真是令人尷尬。

5 ►METAL 金屬◄ [T] *technical* to decorate metal with a special tool【術語】鏤刻, 雕鏤〔金屬製品〕: *chased silver* 雕鏤銀器

6 chase the dragon *slang* to smoke the drug HEROIN【俚】吸食海洛因

chase sb/sth ↔ **up** *phr v* [T] **1** to remind someone to do something they promised to do for you 提醒某人〔實踐諾言〕: *I had to chase Dick up to get those reports I asked for last week.* 我得去提醒迪克, 要他去拿我上個星期問他要的那些報告。**2** to try to make something happen or arrive more quickly, because it has been taking too long 加速…的發生進程, 催促: *Can you chase up those photos for me by tomorrow?* 你明天能把這些照片趕洗出來嗎?

chase² *n* **1** [C] the act of following someone or something quickly in order to catch them 追逐, 追趕; 追捕: *The movie began with a dramatic car chase.* 影片是以一場激烈的汽車追逐開始的。**2 give chase** *literary* to chase someone or something【文】追逐〔某人或某物〕: *The hounds gave chase across the fields.* 獵狗追逐着穿過田野。—see also 另見 PAPER CHASE, WILD-GOOSE CHASE

chas·er /ˋtʃesɚ; ˈtʃeɪsə/ *n* [C] a weaker alcoholic drink which is drunk after a strong one, or a stronger alcoholic drink which is drunk after a weak one 飲烈酒後喝的淡酒; 飲淡酒後喝的烈酒: *a pint of bitter and a whisky chaser* 一品脫啤酒後再來點威士忌

chas·m /ˋkæzəm; ˈkæzəm/ *n* **1** [C] a very deep space between two high areas of rock, especially one that is dangerous〔尤指危險的〕裂隙, 深坑, 深淵, 峽谷: *a rope bridge across the chasm* 峽谷上的繩索吊橋 **2** [singular] a big difference between the opinions, experience, ways of life, etc of different groups of people, especially when this means they cannot understand each other〔不同的人在觀點、經歷、生活方式等方面無法相互理解的〕巨大差距, 分歧: *the chasm between rich and poor* 窮人和富人之間的鴻溝

chas·sis /ˋʃæsɪ; ˈʃæsi/ *n plural* **chassis** /ˋʃæsis; ˈʃæsiːz/ [C] **1** the frame on which the body, engine, wheels etc of a vehicle are built〔汽車的〕底盤; 車架 **2** the landing equipment of a plane〔飛機的〕機架; 起落架

chaste /tʃest; tʃeɪst/ *adj* **1** *old-fashioned* having very high personal moral standards in your sexual behaviour【過時】純潔的, 貞潔的; 正派的: *Wives are expected to remain chaste, whatever their husbands' behaviour.* 不管丈夫做出了甚麼行為, 妻子都被要求保持貞節。—compare 比較 CELIBATE —see also 另見 CHASTITY **2** simple and plain in style〔風格〕簡單明了的 —**chastely** *adv*

chas·ten /ˋtʃesn̩; ˈtʃeɪsən/ *v* [T usually passive 一般用被動態] to make someone realize that their behaviour is wrong or mistaken 懲戒, 責罰; 磨鍊〔某人〕: *Party workers have returned to their home towns, chastened by their overwhelming defeat.* 受到重創後, 這些黨的工作者返回了自己的家鄉。

chas·tise /tʃæsˋtaɪz; tʃæˈstaɪz/ *v* [T] **1** *formal* to criti-

C

cize someone severely【正式】嚴厲譴責, 指責, 責備: *He should be chastised for his insolence.* 他傲慢無禮, 應該受到指責。**2** *old-fashioned* to physically punish someone【過時】體罰 —**chastisement** *n* [C,U]

chas·ti·ty /ˈtʃæstətɪ; ˈtʃæstᵻti/ *n* [U] the principle or way of behaving in which you do not behave in a way that is sexually immoral, especially for religious reasons 貞潔, 貞節, 貞操

chastity belt /ˈ··· ,·/ *n* [C] a special belt with a lock, used in former times to prevent women from having sex〔舊時防止婦女私通用的〕貞操帶

2 **chat¹** /tʃæt; tʃæt/ *n* [C,U] *especially BrE* an informal friendly conversation【尤英】閒談, 聊天: *Drop in for a chat if you have an hour to spare this evening.* 如果今晚能抽出一小時的話, 到我家裡來聊聊天吧! | **have a chat** *We had a chat about the old days.* 我們聊了聊過去的時光。—see also 另見 BACKCHAT

chat² **chatted, chatting** *v* [I] *especially BrE* also 又作 **chat away** to talk in a friendly informal way, especially about things that are not important【尤英】閒談, 聊天: *Danny and Paul chatted away like old friends.* 丹尼和保羅像老朋友似的在聊天。| **[+about]** *We sat in the café for hours chatting about our experiences.* 我們在咖啡室裡坐了幾個小時, 大談各自的經歷。| **[+with/to]** *Helen chatted with most of the guests at the party.* 海倫在晚會上跟大多數客人都攀談了。

chat sb ↔ **up** *phr v* [T] *BrE* to talk to someone in a way that shows you are sexually attracted to them【英】與…搭訕, 與…調情: *We found Doug in the bar trying to chat up a waitress.* 我們看見道格在酒吧裡想要和女侍應搭訕。

chat·eau /ʃæˈto; ˈʃætəʊ/ *n plural* **chateaux** /-toz; -təʊz/ or **chateaus** [C] a castle or large country house in France〔法國的〕城堡; 鄉間大別墅; 莊園

chat·e·laine /ˈʃætl̩,en; ˈʃætl-eɪn/ *n* [C] **1** *formal* the female owner, or wife of the owner, of a large country house or castle in France【正式】〔法國的〕鄉間別墅[城堡]女主人 **2** a short thin chain fastened to a woman's belt, used in the past for carrying keys〔舊時女子繫在腰帶上用以懸掛鑰匙的〕鑰匙鏈

chat line /ˈ· ·/ *n* [C] *BrE* a telephone service that people call to talk to other people who have called the same service【英】聊天熱線〔一種電信服務, 打電話到該熱線的人互相之間可以進行通話〕

chat show /ˈ· ·/ *n* [C] *BrE* a television or radio show on which people are asked questions and talk about themselves【英】〔電視或電台的〕清談節目; TALK SHOW *AmE*【美】

chat show host /ˈ· · ,·/ *n BrE* the person who introduces people and asks questions on a chat show【英】訪談節目主持人, 清談節目主持人

chat·tel /ˈtʃætl̩; ˈtʃætl/ *n* [C] *law old-fashioned* something that belongs to you【法律, 過時】動產; 私人財產: *In those days women and children were considered chattels.* 在那個時代, 婦女和兒童被視為個人財產。—see also 另見 GOODS AND CHATTELS

chat·ter¹ /ˈtʃætɚ; ˈtʃætə/ *v* [I] **1** to talk quickly in a friendly way without stopping, especially about things that are not serious or important 嘮叨, 喋喋不休: **[+to]** *You've been chattering to Tom on the phone for ages.* 你在電話上和湯姆嘮叨很久了。**2** if birds or monkeys chatter, they make short high sounds〔鳥類或猴子的〕鳴叫; 啁啾; 吱吱叫 **3** if your teeth are chattering, you are so cold or frightened your teeth are knocking together and you cannot stop them〔因寒冷或恐懼而使牙齒〕打顫; 咯咯作響 **4 the chattering classes** *BrE* those people in society who are keen to discuss and have opinions about important or fashionable ideas, subjects, and events【英】整天發表議論的人; 愛好評論的人

chatter² *n* [U] **1** a friendly informal conversation about something unimportant 聊天, 閒談; 嘮叨 **2** a series of short high sounds made by some birds or monkeys〔鳥類或猴子的〕鳴叫聲; 啾啾叫聲; 吱吱的叫聲 **3** a hard quick repeated sound made by your teeth knocking together or by machines〔牙齒打顫的〕咯咯聲;〔機器的〕震顫聲: *the chatter of the printer* 打印機發出的吱吱聲

chat·ter·box /ˈtʃætɚ,bɑks; ˈtʃætəbɒks/ *n* [C] *informal* someone, especially a child, who talks too much【非正式】喋喋不休的人, 話匣子〔尤指小孩〕

chat·ty /ˈtʃætɪ; ˈtʃæti/ *adj especially BrE*【尤英】**1** liking to talk a lot in a friendly way 愛閒聊的, 愛談天的, 健談的: *Lorna's normally very quiet, but she was quite chatty yesterday.* 洛娜平時話不多, 但昨天卻非常健談。**2** a piece of writing that is chatty has a friendly informal style〔文章〕很隨意的, 閒談式的: *a chatty letter* 一封聊天式的信

chat-up line /ˈ· · ,·/ *n* [C] *BrE* something that someone says in order to start a conversation with someone they find sexually attractive【英】挑逗的話, 輕佻的話, 搭訕的話; LINE¹ (23) *AmE*【美】

chauf·feur¹ /ˈʃofɚ; ˈʃəʊfə/ *n* [C] someone whose job is to drive a car for someone else〔受雇為他人開車的〕司機

chauffeur² *v* [T] **1** to drive a car for someone as your job 專職為…開汽車 **2** also 又作 **chauffeur around** to drive someone in your car, especially when you do not want to〔尤指非情願地〕開車載〔某人〕到處去: *I seem to spend most of Saturday chauffeuring the kids around.* 我似乎星期六大都要開車載孩子到處去。

chauf·feuse /ʃoˈfɝz; ʃəʊˈfɜːz/ *n* [C] a woman whose job is to drive a car for someone else〔受雇為他人開車的〕女司機

chau·vin·is·m /ˈʃovɪn,ɪzəm; ˈʃəʊvᵻnɪzəm/ *n* [U] **1** a strong belief that your country is better or more important than any other 盲目的愛國主義, 沙文主義, 本國至上主義: *cultural chauvinism* 文化沙文主義 **2** the attitude that your own sex is better, more intelligent, or more important than the other sex, especially the male sex 大男[女]子主義, 男性[女性]至上主義: **male chauvinism** *The club is a bastion of male chauvinism.* 該俱樂部是捍衛大男子主義的堡壘。

chau·vin·ist /ˈʃovɪnɪst; ˈʃəʊvᵻnᵻst/ *n* [C] **1** someone, especially a man, who believes that their own sex is better and more important than the other sex 本性別至上主義者〔尤指大男子主義者〕: **male chauvinist (pig)** *My boss is a male chauvinist who thinks no woman could do his job.* 我的老闆是個大男子主義者, 他認為沒有女人能勝任他的工作。**2** someone who believes that their own country is better or more important than any other country 盲目愛國者; 沙文主義者 —**chauvinist** *adj*

chau·vi·nis·tic /,ʃovɪˈnɪstɪk; ,ʃəʊvᵻˈnɪstɪk◂/ *adj* **1** having the belief that your own country is better or more important than any other country 盲目愛國的, 沙文主義的: *a chauvinistic dislike of all things foreign* 盲目愛國而排斥一切舶來品 **2** having the attitude that your own sex is better or more important than the other sex, especially that men are more important than women 本性別至上主義的〔尤指大男子主義的〕—**chauvinistically** /-klɪ; -kli/ *adv*

cheap¹ /tʃip; tʃiːp/ *adj*

1 ►**PRICE** 價格◄ not at all expensive, or lower in price than you expected 便宜的, 不貴的, 廉價的: *You're just not going to find a cheap leather coat.* 你是買不到便宜的皮衣的。| *the cheapest TV on the market* 市場上最便宜的電視 | **dirt cheap** (=extremely low in price) 極廉價的, 極便宜的 *These CDs are dirt cheap.* 這些雷射唱片便宜極了。—see 見 ECONOMIC (USAGE)

2 ►**CHARGING LESS** 要價較少的◄ charging a low price 要價低的: *Which store do you suppose is cheaper?* 你認為哪家店的東西較便宜? | *As taxi companies go, they're quite cheap.* 就計程車公司而言, 他們算是便宜。| **cheap and cheerful** *BrE* (=simple and charging a low price, but pleasant)【英】價廉物美的 *a cheap and cheerful bistro, popular with students* 一家很受學生歡迎的既便宜又舒適的小餐館

3 ►**BAD QUALITY** 劣質的◄ low in price and quality,

or not worth much 價廉質劣的; 無價值的, 不值錢的: *Cheap wine gives me a headache.* 喝了低價劣質的酒, 我頭會痛。| *You don't think these earrings look too cheap?* 你難道不覺得這副耳環很低俗嗎? | **cheap and nasty** *BrE* (=very low in price and quality)【英】低價劣質的 *cheap and nasty T-shirts* 價廉質差的T恤
4 ►CHEAP TO USE 花費低的◄ not costing much to use or to employ 便宜的, 價格低的: *I'll have to have a cheaper car, this one uses too much gas.* 我只能買一輛較便宜的車, 這輛車太耗油了。| **cheap labour** *multinational clothing companies exploiting cheap child labour in Bangladesh* 在孟加拉剝削廉價童工的跨國製衣公司
5 ►NOT DESERVING RESPECT 不值得尊敬◄ showing a lack of honesty, moral principles, or sincere feelings, and therefore difficult to respect 不值得尊敬的, 卑鄙的, 可恥的: *It makes me feel cheap, but I can't face seeing Mother.* 這讓我覺得可恥, 但我無法面對教母。| **(just) some cheap sth** *He acts like I'm just some cheap little bimbo.* 他表現得就像我只是個下賤的壞女人。| *This is not some cheap pastime! This is art!* 這不是粗鄙的娛樂消遣! 這是藝術! | **cheap thrill** (=excitement that you do not have to work hard for or pay for) 容易得來的[粗鄙的]刺激 *Glue-sniffing is a cheap thrill, and a trend among some schoolchildren.* 吸膠毒簡單刺激, 在學童中間甚為流行。| **cheap remark/joke etc** (=one that attacks people who cannot defend themselves) 低級的評論/玩笑
6 ►NOT GENEROUS 不大方的◄ *AmE* not liking to spend money【美】小氣的, 吝嗇的; MEAN² (2) *BrE*【英】: *Frank's so cheap that he re-uses Christmas wrapping paper.* 弗蘭克真吝嗇, 他竟使用用過的聖誕禮物包裝紙。
7 on the cheap spending less money than is needed to do something properly 沒有付足錢的, 便宜的, 廉價的: *I'm not surprised the roof is leaking – the landlord does everything on the cheap.* 屋頂漏水我一點也不奇怪 —— 房東做甚麼都貪圖便宜。
8 cheap at the price/at any price of such high value, or so good or useful, that the cost is not important 無論價格多麼高都值得
9 life is cheap used to say that it is not important if people die 某人的死無足輕重: *Everyone carried a gun or knife during the war, and life was cheap.* 打仗時所有人都持槍帶刀的, 生命簡直不值錢。—**cheaply** *adv*: *a cheaply furnished room* 一個配置廉價家具的房間 — **cheapness** *n* [U]

USAGE NOTE 用法說明: CHEAP
WORD CHOICE 詞語辨析: **cheap, low-priced, inexpensive, not cost a lot, reasonable, good value, a good buy, a bargain, a steal, a snip, low**
Saying that something is **cheap** often suggests it is also bad in quality. 如說某物 cheap, 往往也暗示其質量不高: *Buying cheap shoes is not a good idea in the long run.* 從長遠看, 買便宜質劣的鞋是不划算的。| *That necklace looks really cheap and nasty.* 那條項鏈看起來真是既便宜又難看。**Low-priced** and **inexpensive** do not suggest this, but are not so common in informal spoken English. low-priced 和inexpensive則無此含義, 但在非正式口語中不那麼常用: *The university needs more low-priced accommodation.* 這所大學需要更多便宜些的住宿設施。In everyday English people often just say that something **doesn't cost a lot/much**. 在日常英語中, 人們說某東西不值錢, 用doesn't cost a lot/much。
If you want to say that something is good and does not cost as much as it might, you say it is **reasonable, good value**, or **a good buy** 如果你想說一件東西質量好而價格又不高, 你可以說它是 reasonable, good value 或 a good buy: *$200 for a leather jacket seems pretty reasonable to me.* 對我來說, 200美元買件皮夾克, 不算貴。
If something is **a bargain** it cost very much less than you expected to pay. In informal conversation people often say instead that something is **a steal** (American English) or **a snip** (British English). 如果一件東西是 a bargain, 那就是說它的價格比你預期的要低得多。在非正式談話中, 人們往往以 a steal〔美國英語〕或 a snip〔英國英語〕代替 a bargain。
The cost of something, a bill, someone's salary etc can be **low** or **reasonable** but not **cheap**. 某物的成本、賬單或工資薪水等只能用 low 或 reasonable, 但不能說 cheap。

cheap² *adv* at a low price 便宜地, 廉價地: *Sharon has some really nice furniture she picked up cheap in a sale.* 莎倫在一次大減價時低價買了些很好的家具。| *They're selling linen off cheap in Lewis's.* 劉易斯的店在削價賣掉日用織品。| **sth does not come cheap** (=something is expensive) 某物不便宜 *Houses like that don't come cheap.* 那樣的房子是很貴的。| **(be) going cheap** (=selling for a lower price than usual) 降低價格, 廉價出售 *Ask if they've got any flights going cheap.* 去問問他們有沒有降價的航班。
cheap·en /ˈtʃipən; ˈtʃiːpən/ *v* **1** [T] to make something or someone seem to have lower moral standards than they had before 降低身分, 貶低: **cheapen yourself by doing sth** *Don't cheapen yourself by accepting their bribe.* 不要因為接受他們的賄賂而降低了自己的身分。**2** [I,T] to become or make something become lower in price or value (使)減價, (使)降價: *The dollar's increase in value has cheapened imports.* 美元增值使進口商品便宜了。
cheap·skate /ˈtʃipˌsket; ˈtʃiːpskeɪt/ *n* [C] *informal* someone who does not like spending money and does not care if they behave in an unreasonable way to avoid spending it【非正式】小氣鬼, 守財奴, 吝嗇鬼: *The cheapskate didn't even offer to pay for the cab.* 這個小氣鬼竟然連計程車費都不肯付。
cheat¹ /tʃit; tʃiːt/ *v* **1** [I] to behave in a dishonest way in order to win or to get an advantage, especially in a competition, game, or examination〔尤指在競賽、遊戲或考試中〕欺騙; 作弊: *You're doing it again, you're trying to cheat!* 你又來這一套了, 又想騙人! | **[+at]** *Jack always cheats at cards.* 傑克玩紙牌時總是作弊。| **that's cheating** *Hey, don't look at the next page – that's cheating!* 嘿, 別看下一頁 —— 那是作弊! **2** [T] to trick or deceive someone who trusts you 騙取: *Don't just jump to conclusions that you've been deliberately cheated.* 不要這麼快就下結論, 說你一直被人故意欺騙。| **cheat sb (out) of sth** *Guy figures he was cheated out of that job by office politics.* 蓋伊估計自己是因為辦公室的爾虞我詐而丟了那份工作的。**3 feel cheated** to feel that you have been treated wrongly or unfairly and have not got what you deserve 感覺不公平, 被騙: *I feel cheated really. I was meant to go to France and now it's only Leeds.* 我真的感到被騙了, 本來我該去法國的, 結果只去了利茲。**4 cheat death/fate etc** to manage to avoid death etc even though it seemed that you would not be able to 逃避[逃脫]死亡/命運等
cheat on sb *phr v* [T] to be unfaithful to your husband, wife, or sexual partner by secretly having sex with someone else 對〔配偶或性伴侶〕不忠: *I think Winnie's been cheating on me, but I can't prove it.* 我認為溫妮一直對我不忠, 但我卻無法證實。
cheat² *n* [C] **1** someone who is dishonest and cheats 騙子; 作弊者: *I saw you look at that card, you cheat!* 我看見你偷看了那張牌, 你這個騙子! **2 a cheat** something that is dishonest or unfair 作弊, 欺騙行為; 不公平的事: *That's a cheat! The box is half empty!* 這是個騙局! 這個盒子是半空的!
check¹ /tʃɛk; tʃek/ *v* [S1] [W2]
1 ►FIND OUT 發現◄ [I,T] to do something in order to

find out whether something that you think is correct, true, or safe really is correct, true, or safe 檢查, 核對, 查驗: *"Are all the windows shut?" "I'll just go and check."* "所有的窗戶都關上了嗎?""我去檢查一下。" | **check sth** *I'll check my calendar and get back to you.* 我要查查我的日程安排, 然後再答覆你。| **[+that]** *They're entitled to check that the will is valid, of course.* 當然, 他們有權去驗證那份遺囑是否有效。| **[+whether/how/who etc]** *Let me just check whether the potatoes are cooked.* 我去看看馬鈴薯煮好了沒有。| **[+for]** *Have these cables been checked for faults?* 有沒有對這些電纜進行過故障檢查? | **check sth against/with sth** (=compare something with something else to see whether they are the same) 與…相比較 *Upon delivery, the items are checked against the original order.* 送貨時, 所有的貨物都要對照原訂單檢查一遍。| **double check** (=look at something twice to be sure about something) 再次檢查以確定 *Double check all the spellings, especially of people's names.* 再檢查一遍拼寫, 尤其是人名的拼寫。

2 ▶ASK SB 詢問某人◀ [I] to ask someone for permission to do something or ask whether something is correct 詢問; 徵求同意; 核實: *I'm not authorized to give you a refund – I'll have to check first.* 我無權給你退款 —— 我必須先徵得同意才行。| **[+that]** *We'd better check that these are the right pills.* 我們最好詢問一下, 看看這些藥丸是不是對的。| **[+whether/how/who etc]** *Let's stop and check whether this is the right road.* 停一下, 看看是否走對了路線。| **check with sb** *It's wise to check with your doctor before going on a diet.* 在節食之前先諮詢一下醫生是明智之舉。

3 ▶NOT DO STH 不做某事◀ [T] to suddenly stop yourself from saying or doing something because you realize it would be better not to 克制〔自己〕; 停止[阻止]〔自己〕做〔某事〕: *Susan quickly turned aside, checking an urge to laugh out loud.* 蘇珊很快轉過臉去, 努力憋着不笑出聲來。| **check yourself** *"You shouldn't have..." he checked himself, trying to stay calm.* "你不應該..."他停下來, 努力保持平靜。

4 ▶STOP STH 停止某事◀ [T] to stop something bad from getting worse or continuing to happen etc 阻礙, 制止; 抑制: *Speed bumps will be installed to check the neighborhood traffic.* 將在路上安裝汽車減速墩以控制附近的交通狀況。

5 ▶MAKE A MARK 作標記◀ [T] *AmE* to make a mark (√) next to an answer, something on a list etc to show that it is correct or that you have dealt with it【美】給〔答案、清單的項目等〕打勾號; TICK² (2) *BrE*【英】

6 ▶BAGS/CASES ETC 袋子/箱子等◀ [T] *AmE* to leave your bags etc at an official place so they can be put on a plane or a train, or to take someone's bags in order to do this【美】托運〔行李〕; 接受托運〔行李〕: *Any luggage over 5 kilos must be checked.* 行李超過五公斤就必須托運。

check in *phr v* **1** [I,T **check** sb **in**] to go to the desk at a hotel or airport and report that you have arrived〔在旅館〕登記辦理入住手續;〔在機場〕辦理登機手續: *You need to check in one hour before the flight.* 你必須在飛機起飛前一小時辦理登機手續。| **check in at** *Let's check in at the hotel before we get something to eat.* 我們吃東西前先去旅館辦理入住手續吧。—see also 另見 CHECK-IN **2** [T **check** sth ↔ **in**] *AmE* to take a book you have borrowed back to a library【美】〔到圖書館〕歸還〔圖書〕

check sth ↔ **off** *phr v* [T] to write a mark next to something on a list when you have dealt with it or made sure that it is correct 在〔處理過或核對過的項目後〕打勾: *Check off the names as people arrive.* 人們到達後就在他們的名字旁邊打勾。

check out *phr v*

1 ▶MAKE SURE 確定◀ **a)** [T **check** sth ↔ **out**] to make sure that something is actually true, correct, or acceptable; INVESTIGATE 調查, 檢查, 核實, 查證: *Why don't I check out the bar and see if it's OK?* 我為甚麼不查看一下門閂, 看看它是否行呢? | **check it out (with)** *Check it out if you don't believe me.* 如果不相信我的話, 你可以去核實一下! **b)** [I] if information checks out, it is proven to be true, correct, or acceptable 證實是對的, 得到證實, 查證無誤的: *If your credit record checks out, they give you a $1000 limit right away.* 如果你的信用記錄被證實是可靠的, 他們會立即給你1000美元的透支額。

2 ▶LOOK AT SB/STH 看某人/物◀ [T **check** sb/sth ↔ **out**] to look at someone or something because they are interesting or attractive〔因某人或物有趣或吸引人而〕盯着看: *Hey, check this out!* 嘿, 看這個!

3 ▶GET INFORMATION 獲得資料◀ [T **check** sb ↔ **out**] *informal* to get information about someone, especially to find out if they are suitable for something【非正式】了解…的情況: *It's routine, they check members out before letting them join.* 這是例行公事, 他們對每個入會者都要事先了解一下。

4 ▶TEST STH 檢測某物◀ [T **check** sth ↔ **out**] to test something to find out if it works, how it works, whether it is suitable for what you want etc 檢測〔某物〕: *In here, they stripped down the aircraft and checked them out for airworthiness.* 在這兒, 他們把飛機拆開以檢測它是否達到適於飛行的標準。

5 ▶HOTEL 旅館◀ [I] to leave a hotel after paying the bill 辦理退房手續, 結賬退房: *We checked out at noon.* 我們中午就退房了。

6 ▶BOOKS 書籍◀ [T **check** sth ↔ **out**] *AmE* to borrow books from a library【美】〔從圖書館〕借出〔書〕: *The library allows you to check out six books at a time.* 圖書館允許每次借六本書。—see also 另見 CHECKOUT

check sth ↔ **over** *phr v* [T] **1** to look closely at something to make sure it is correct or acceptable 檢查; 查看: *Will you check over my essay before I hand it in?* 你能在我交論文之前幫我仔細檢查一下嗎? **2** to examine someone to make sure they are healthy 體檢, 健康檢查: *They've checked her over and given her all these tests and she's fine.* 他們對她做了身體檢查和所有這些測試, 結果是她很健康。

check up on sb *phr v* [T] to try and make sure that someone is doing what they said they would do or what you want them to do, especially secretly〔尤指祕密地〕調查, 查核〔某人〕: *Are you trying to check up on me, or what?* 你是在調查我嗎, 還是怎麼地?

check on sb *phr v* [T] to make sure that someone is safe, has everything they need, etc 檢查; 查看〔某人是否安全等〕: *Honey, can you go upstairs and check on the kids?* 親愛的, 你能上樓看看孩子的情況嗎?

check² *n*

1 ▶ON SAFETY/CORRECTNESS/TRUTH ETC 安全/正確/真實等◀ [C] an act of finding out if something is safe, correct, true, or in the condition it should be〔以確保某物安全、正確、真實等的〕檢查; 查核: *the airport's routine security checks* 機場的例行安全檢查| **[+on]** *the need for tighter checks on arms sales* 需要對武器買賣進行更為嚴格的檢查 | **have a check** *Have a check in your bag first and see if it's there.* 先檢查一下你的袋子, 看是否在那兒。| **eye/blood pressure/dental etc check** (=done to make sure you are healthy) 眼科/血壓/牙齒等的檢查 | **carry out a check (on)** *We will carry out a check on options available to you.* 我們將對可供你選擇的方案進行檢查。| **spot check** (=a quick check of one thing among a group of things, that you do without warning) 抽查, 事先不告知的檢查 *Customs officers will do spot checks for drugs and other illegal goods.* 海關人員將進行抽查以檢查是否有毒品和其他違禁物品。

2 keep a check (on sb/sth) to watch or listen to something or someone regularly or continuously, in order to control something or gather information 監視; 監聽: *Keep a check on your speed.* 要隨時檢查你的速度。| *Their phones had even been tapped to keep a check on their activities.* 他們的電話甚至被安裝了竊聽器, 以監視他們的活動。

3 run/do a check to organize an examination of something or someone in order to find out information 進行檢查[調查]: **run a check on sb** *Troy's staying late to run some background checks on suspects.* 特洛伊在熬夜調查疑犯的背景。| **do a check for sth** *I'd better do a check for gas leaks.* 我最好檢查一下看是否有煤氣泄漏。**4 ►A CONTROL ON STH** 控制某事◄ something that controls something else and stops it from getting worse, continuing to happen etc 制止(手段), 抑制(手段), 控制: *Higher interest rates will act as a check on public spending.* 高利率會抑制公眾消費。| **keep/hold sb/sth in check** (=keep someone or something under control) 控制某人[物] *It was obvious she was barely holding her temper in check.* 很明顯, 她幾乎不能控制自己的脾氣了。**5 ►PATTERN** 圖案◄ [C,U] a pattern of squares, especially on cloth〔尤指布料上的〕方格圖案: *I don't like checks or stripes, just plain colors.* 我不喜歡方格或條紋, 我喜歡素色的。| **a check shirt/jacket etc** (=made with this cloth) 格子襯衫/夾克等 —see also 另見 CHECKED —see picture on page A16 參見A16頁圖 **6 ►FROM YOUR BANK** 從銀行◄ [C] *AmE* one of a set of printed pieces of paper that you can sign and use instead of money to pay for things【美】支票; CHEQUE *BrE*【英】: **[+for]** *a check for $30* 一張30美元的支票 | **by check** *Is it okay to pay by check?* 可用支票支付嗎? **7 ►IN A RESTAURANT** 在餐館◄ [C] *AmE, ScotE* a list that you are given in a restaurant showing what you have eaten and how much you must pay; BILL¹ (1b)【美, 蘇格蘭】賬單 —see picture on page A15 參見A15頁圖 **8 ►FOR YOUR COAT/BAG** 衣物/袋子◄ *AmE*【美】**a) coat check/hat check** a place in a restaurant, theatre etc where you can leave your coat, bag etc to be guarded until you go home〔餐館、劇院等的〕衣帽寄存處 **b)** [C] a ticket that you are given so you can claim your things from this place 存放單, 寄存物品的憑證 **9 ►MARK** 記號◄ [C] *AmE* a mark (√) that you put next to an answer to show that it is correct or next to something on a list to show that you have dealt with it【美】〔表示答案正確或某事項已處理的〕勾號; TICK¹ (1) *BrE*【英】 **10 ►CHESS** 國際象棋◄ [U] the position of the KING (=most important piece) in CHESS when it can be directly attacked by the opponent's pieces〔國際象棋中〕被"將軍"的局面〔王棋處於被攻擊的位置上〕

check·book /ˈtʃɛkˌbʊk; ˈtʃekbʊk/ *n* [C] *AmE* a small book of checks that your bank gives you【美】支票簿; CHEQUEBOOK *BrE*【英】

checked /tʃɛkt; tʃekt/ *adj* checked cloth has a regular pattern of differently coloured squares 有不同顏色方格圖案的: *a checked blouse* 格子女襯衫

check·er /ˈtʃɛkɚ; ˈtʃekə/ *n* **1** [C] *AmE* someone who works at the CHECKOUT in a SUPERMARKET【美】〔超級市場的〕收銀員 **2 checkers** [U] a game that two people play with 12 round pieces each, in which the purpose is to take the other player's pieces by jumping over them with your pieces 西洋跳棋; draughts (DRAUGHT¹ (2)) *BrE*【英】—see also 另見 CHINESE CHEQUERS

check·er·board /ˈtʃɛkɚˌbɔrd; ˈtʃekəbɔːd/ *n* [C] *AmE* a board used to play checkers, with 32 white squares and 32 black squares【美】西洋跳棋棋盤〔由32個白格和32個黑格所構成〕; DRAUGHTBOARD *BrE*【英】

check·ered also 又作 **chequered** *BrE*【英】/ˈtʃɛkɚd; ˈtʃekəd/ *adj* **1** having a pattern made up of squares of two different colours 有方格[格子]圖案的: *a checkered tablecloth* 方格桌布 | *checkered tiles in the bathroom* 浴室裡的方格瓷磚 **2 have a checkered history/past/career etc** to have had periods of failure as well as successful times in your past 成敗參半的歷史/過去/事業等: *The company has a pretty checkered history. I'd think carefully before investing.* 這家公司的業績時好時壞, 投資前我會謹慎考慮。

checkered flag also 又作 **chequered flag** *BrE*【英】/ˌ·· ˈ·/ *n* [C] a flag covered with black and white squares that is waved at the beginning and end of a motor race〔汽車賽開始和結束時用的〕黑白格子旗

check-in /ˈ· ·/ *n* **1** [singular] a place where you report your arrival, especially at an airport〔尤指在機場的〕辦理登機手續處[櫃台]: *Make sure you're at the check-in by 5:30.* 務必要在5點30分之前到機場辦好登機手續。| **check-in desk** *BrE*【英】, **check-in counter** *AmE*【美】 *Go to the check-in desk in zone C.* 去C區的辦理登機手續櫃台。**2** [U] the process of reporting your arrival, especially at an airport〔尤指到機場〕辦理登機手續: *The whole check-in process seems to take forever.* 辦理登機手續所花的時間太長了。—see also 另見 **check in** (CHECK¹)

checking ac·count /ˈ·· ·ˌ·/ *n* [C] *AmE* a bank account that you can take money out of at any time【美】活期存款賬戶; 支票存款賬戶; CURRENT ACCOUNT *BrE*【英】—compare 比較 DEPOSIT ACCOUNT

check·list /ˈtʃɛkˌlɪst; ˈtʃekˌlɪst/ *n* [C] a list that helps you by reminding you of the things you need to do for a particular job or activity〔核對用的〕清單, 檢查單: *The guide contains a handy checklist of points to look for when buying a car.* 這本指南載有買車時便於查閱的要點一覽表。

check·mate /ˈtʃɛkˌmet; ˈtʃekmeɪt/ *n* [C,U] the position of the KING (=most important piece) in CHESS at the end of the game, when it is being directly attacked and cannot escape〔國際象棋中的〕將軍, 將死〔王棋被將死的位置〕

check·out /ˈtʃɛkˌaʊt; ˈtʃek-aʊt/ *n* **1** [C] the place in a SUPERMARKET where you pay for the goods you have collected〔超級市場的〕付款處, 收銀台: *Why can't they have more checkouts open?* 為甚麼他們不多開幾處收銀台呢? **2** [C,U] the time by which you must leave a hotel room〔旅店的〕退房時間: *Checkout is at noon.* 退房時間是中午12點之前。—see also 另見 **check out** (CHECK¹)

check·point /ˈtʃɛkˌpɔɪnt; ˈtʃekpɔɪnt/ *n* [C] a place, especially on a border, where an official person examines vehicles or people〔尤指邊境的〕關卡; 檢查站: *Vehicles were stopped at the checkpoint.* 汽車在檢查站被攔住(檢查)。

check·room /ˈtʃɛkˌrum; ˈtʃek-rʊm/ *n* [C] *AmE* a place in a restaurant, theatre etc where you can leave your coat, bags etc to be guarded【美】〔餐館、劇院等供存放袋子或衣服等的〕寄存處; 衣帽間; CLOAKROOM (1) *BrE*【英】

check stub /ˈ· ·/ *n* [C] the American spelling of CHEQUE STUB cheque stub 的美式拼法

check·up, check-up /ˈtʃɛkˌʌp; ˈtʃek-ʌp/ *n* [C] a general medical examination that a doctor or DENTIST gives you to make sure you are healthy 體格[健康]檢查

ched·dar /ˈtʃɛdɚ; ˈtʃedə/ *n* [U] a hard, smooth, usually yellow or orange cheese 切達乾酪, 車打芝士〔一種光滑的硬乳酪, 通常呈黃色或橙色〕

cheek¹ /tʃik; tʃiːk/ *n* **1** [C] the soft round area of flesh on each side of your face below your eye 面頰; 臉蛋兒: *Would you let him kiss you on the cheek?* 你會讓他吻你的臉頰嗎? | *the smooth pink cheeks of a baby* 嬰兒粉嫩光滑的臉蛋兒 —see picture at 參見 HEAD¹ 圖 **2** [singular, U] *BrE* disrespectful or rude behaviour, especially towards someone in a position of authority【英】〔尤指對權威〕無禮[放肆]的行為; 厚顏無恥: *I've had enough of that boy's cheek.* 我受夠了那男孩的粗魯無禮。| **have the cheek to do sth** *Billy had the cheek to say it was boring round here, right in front of Nan.* 比利竟當着南恩的面無禮地說這兒單調乏味。| **have a cheek** *They've got a cheek, charging her for a call when it's her own phone!* 他們真是厚顏無恥, 她用自己的電話竟向她收錢! **3 what a cheek!** *BrE spoken* used to show surprise that someone has behaved rudely or without enough respect【英口】真不要臉! **4 cheek by jowl** if people live or work cheek by jowl they live or work very close together 緊緊靠着, 親密地在一起: *Families were living cheek by jowl in impossible conditions.* 一個個的家庭擠在惡劣的環境裡一起生活。**5 cheek to cheek** if two people dance

W 3

C

cheek to cheek, they dance very close to each other in a romantic way 面貼面地〔跳舞〕**6 turn the other cheek** to deliberately avoid reacting in an angry or violent way when someone has hurt or upset you〔對傷害自己的人〕不還手, 不加報復; 抑制住怒氣 **7** [C] *informal* one of the two soft fleshy parts of your bottom; BUTTOCK【非正式】屁股 **8 red-cheeked/hollow-cheeked/rosy-cheeked etc** having red, hollow etc cheeks 面色紅潤/雙頰凹陷的等: *He was a merry-faced, ruddy-cheeked little man.* 他個子很小, 一張臉總是紅撲撲、笑嘻嘻的。—see also 另見 **tongue in cheek** (TONGUE (3))

C

cheek² *v* [T] *BrE* to speak rudely or disrespectfully to someone, especially to someone older such as your teacher or parents【英】〔尤指對師長〕無禮地說話; SASS *AmE*【美】: *Don't you cheek your mother like that! Go and apologise!* 不要對你母親如此無禮地說話! 去道歉!

cheek·bone /ˈtʃikˌbon; ˈtʃiːkbəʊn/ *n* [C usually plural 一般用複數] one of the two bones above your cheeks, just below your eyes 顴骨, 頰骨

cheek·y /ˈtʃikɪ; ˈtʃiːki/ *adj BrE*【英】**1** rude or disrespectful, especially towards someone older such as a teacher or parent〔尤指對師長〕厚臉皮的, 不敬的, 放肆的: *Don't be so cheeky!* 別這麼無禮! | *The cheeky devil!* 這個無禮的傢伙! | **cheeky monkey** *Cheeky monkey! Get your hand out of the biscuit tin.* 你這個厚臉皮的人! 把手從餅乾罐中拿開! **2** *approving* disrespectful or not proper, but in a way that is amusing rather than rude【褒】調皮的, 搞笑的: *a scruffy little boy with a cheeky grin* 面露調皮微笑的邋遢小男孩 | *a rather cheeky mini skirt* 太露的迷你裙 —**cheekily** *adv* —**cheekiness** *n* [U] —see also 另見 SASSY

cheep /tʃip; tʃiːp/ *v* [I] if a young bird cheeps, it makes a weak, high noise〔雛鳥〕吱吱叫: *baby birds cheeping for food* 嗷嗷待哺的小鳥 —**cheep** *n*

cheer¹ /tʃɪr; tʃɪə/ *n* [C] **1** a shout of happiness, praise, approval, or encouragement 歡呼, 喝采, 讚美聲: **a cheer rises/goes up** *A deafening cheer rose from the crowd as the band walked onto the stage.* 當樂隊走上舞台時, 人羣中發出了震耳欲聾的歡呼聲。| **give a cheer** *Everyone gave a cheer when Gilmore crawled out of the wreck, unhurt.* 當吉爾摩從廢墟中毫髮無傷地爬出來時, 大家都歡呼起來。**2 three cheers for sb!** used to tell a group of people to shout three times as a way of showing support, happiness, thanks etc 給〔某人〕三聲歡呼!: *Three cheers for the birthday girl!* 給生日的女孩三聲歡呼! **3** [U] *formal or literary* a feeling of happiness and confidence【正式或文】歡愉, 快活; 樂觀: *Christmas cheer* 聖誕節的歡欣 —see also 另見 CHEERS **4** [C] a special CHANT (=kind of poem) that the crowds at a US sports game shout in order to encourage their team to win〔美國體育運動中的〕加油聲, 鼓舞聲

cheer² *v* **1** [I,T] to shout as a way of showing happiness, praise, approval, or support of someone or something 歡呼, 喝采: *Everybody cheered when the firemen arrived.* 消防員到達時, 大家都歡呼起來。| **cheer sb** *It says here that thousands packed the city centre to cheer her.* 這兒報道說成千上萬的人湧到市中心向她歡呼喝采。**2** [T usually passive 一般用被動態] to make someone feel more hopeful when they are worried 鼓勵; 安慰: *cheering news* 鼓舞人心的消息 | *Kerrie was visibly cheered when we finally saw a light in the distance.* 當我們最終看見遠處的燈光時, 克里顯然受到鼓舞而振作了起來。

cheer sb/sth ↔ **on** *phr v* [T] to shout encouragement at a person or team to help them do well in a race or competition〔在比賽中〕為…加油; 打氣: *They were behind by two touchdowns and she was still cheering them on!* 雖然他們比對方少了兩次觸地得分, 但她仍在為他們加油!

cheer up *phr v* **1** [I,T] to become less sad, or to make someone feel less sad (使) 高興起來, (使) 振作起來: *He'll cheer up if you get him a beer.* 給他杯啤酒, 他的情緒就會好起來。| **cheer** sb ↔ **up** *I'm taking Angie out to cheer her up.* 我要帶安吉到外面轉轉, 讓她振作起來。**2 cheer up!** *spoken* used to tell someone not to be so sad【口】振作些! 別發愁啦!: *"Cheer up, Mandy!" "Oh, I'm all right, really."* "別發愁, 曼迪!" "噢, 我很好, 真的沒事!" **3 cheering up** the act of trying to make someone feel less sad 鼓舞, 鼓勵: **need/want cheering up** *Craig needs cheering up. What should we do?* 要給克雷格打打氣, 我們該做些甚麼呢? | *All I want is a little cheering up.* 我現在需要的只是一些鼓勵。

cheer·er /ˈtʃɪrə; ˈtʃɪərə/ *n* [C] *AmE* someone who shouts encouragement at a person or team to help them do well in a race or competition【美】啦啦隊員: *the loudest cheerer in the grandstand* 在看台上叫得最響的啦啦隊員

cheer·ful /ˈtʃɪrfəl; ˈtʃɪəfəl/ *adj* **1** behaving in a way that shows you are happy, for example by smiling or being very friendly 快樂的, 興高采烈的; 開朗的: *Despite feeling ill, she managed to keep cheerful.* 她儘管身體不舒服, 但仍極力保持精神愉快。| **a cheerful grin/smile/face** (=showing that you are happy) 快活的笑容/微笑/面容 *Nancy gave me a cheerful grin and waved me over.* 南希向我快樂地一笑, 招手示意我過去。**2** something that is cheerful makes you feel happy because it is so bright or pleasant 令人愉快的; 令人振奮的: *I must say I like a cheerful kitchen.* 我得說我喜歡看起來令人愉快的廚房。| *a cheerful letter full of good news* 一封寫滿好消息的令人振奮的信 **3** tending to be happy most of the time 樂觀的: *Basically I'm a cheerful person.* 我基本上是個性格開朗的人。**4** [only before noun 僅用於名詞前] a cheerful attitude shows that you are willing to do whatever is necessary in a happy way 願意的, 樂意的, 欣然的: *cheerful enthusiasm for the job* 對工作積極進取的熱情 —see also 另見 **cheap and cheerful** (CHEAP¹ (2)) —**cheerfully** *adv*: *"Morning!" she called cheerfully.* "早安!" 她高興地說。—**cheerfulness** *n* [U]

cheer·i·o /ˈtʃɪrɪˌo; ˌtʃɪəriˈəʊ/ *interjection BrE informal* goodbye【英, 非正式】再見

cheerleader 啦啦隊隊員

pompom 絨球

cheer·lead·er /ˈtʃɪrˌlidə; ˈtʃɪəˌliːdə/ *n* [C] a member of a team of young women who encourage a crowd to cheer at a US sports game by shouting special words and dancing 啦啦隊隊員: *cheerleaders practicing their routines* 正在進行例行訓練的啦啦隊

cheer·lead·ing /ˈtʃɪrˌlidɪŋ; ˈtʃɪəˌliːdɪŋ/ *n* [U] **1** the activity of being a cheerleader 當啦啦隊隊員: *a cheerleading uniform* 啦啦隊的制服 **2** *AmE* the act of loudly supporting an organization, idea etc and not being willing to listen to criticism of it【美】大力支持

cheer·less /ˈtʃɪrlɪs; ˈtʃɪələs/ *adj* cheerless weather, places, or times make you feel sad, bored, or uncomfortable〔天氣、地方或時期〕不快樂的; 陰鬱的; 沉悶的; 慘淡的: *the dark, cheerless rooms upstairs* 樓上黑暗陰森的房間 | *a grey and cheerless day* 灰暗慘淡的一天 —**cheerlessly** *adv* —**cheerlessness** *n* [U]

cheers /tʃɪrz; tʃɪəz/ *interjection* **1** used when you lift a glass of alcohol before you drink it, in order to say that you hope the people you are drinking with will be happy and have good health 乾杯〔用於祝酒〕**2** *BrE informal* thank you【英, 非正式】謝謝 **3** *BrE informal* goodbye【英, 非正式】再見

cheer·y /ˋtʃɪrɪ; ˈtʃɪəri/ *adj* cheerful, or making you feel happy 歡快的, 高興的; 令人愉快的: *a cheery greeting* 愉快的問候 | *Oh she's fine, as cheery as ever.* 哦, 她很好, 和往常一樣精神飽滿。—**cheerily** *adv*

2 3 **cheese** /tʃiz; tʃiːz/ *n* [C,U] **1** a solid food made from milk, which is usually yellow or white in colour, and can be soft or hard 乾酪, 乳酪, 芝士: *half a pound of cheese* 半磅乳酪 | *a cheese sandwich* 乳酪三明治 | *a selection of English cheeses* 精選英國乳酪 | **cow's/goat's/sheep's cheese** (=from the milk of a cow etc) 牛奶/山羊奶/綿羊奶製成的乾酪 **2 say cheese** used to tell people to smile when you are going to take their photograph 笑一笑〔照相時叫人微笑說的話〕: *Come on everybody, say cheese!* 來, 大家笑一笑! —see also 另見 BIG CHEESE, **as different as chalk and cheese** (CHALK[1] (3))

cheese·board /ˋtʃizˌbɔrd; ˈtʃiːzbɔːd/ *n* [C] **1** a board used to cut cheese on〔切乾酪用的〕乾酪板 **2** a board used for serving a variety of cheeses 盛乾酪的板 —see picture on page A15 參見 A15 頁圖

cheese·bur·ger /ˋtʃizˌbɝgɚ; ˈtʃiːzbɜːgə/ *n* [C] a HAMBURGER cooked with a piece of cheese on top of the meat 乾酪[芝士]漢堡包

cheese·cake /ˋtʃizˌkek; ˈtʃiːzkeɪk/ *n* **1** [C,U] a cake made from a mixture containing soft cheese 乳酪蛋糕 **2** [U] *old-fashioned* photographs of pretty women with few clothes on【過時】顯示性感女郎肉體美的照片 —compare 比較 BEEFCAKE

cheese·cloth /ˋtʃizˌklɔθ; ˈtʃiːzklɒθ/ *n* [U] thin cotton cloth used for putting around some kinds of cheeses, and sometimes for making clothes 乾酪包布〔一種薄棉布, 可包乳酪, 也可製衣〕

cheesed off /ˌtʃizd ˋɔf; ˌtʃiːzd ˈɒf/ *adj BrE informal* bored and annoyed with something【英, 非正式】感到厭煩的; 厭倦的: *You sound cheesed off. What's the matter?* 聽上去你很不耐煩, 怎麼啦?

cheese·par·ing /ˈ· ˌ··/ *n* [U] *BrE* behaviour that shows you are unwilling to give or spend money【英】花錢斤斤計較; 吝嗇, 小氣 —**cheeseparing** *adj*

chee·tah /ˋtʃitə; ˈtʃiːtə/ *n* [C] a member of the cat family that has long legs and black spots on its fur, and can run extremely fast 獵豹

chef /ʃɛf; ʃef/ *n* [C] a skilled cook, especially the chief cook in a hotel or restaurant 廚師;〔尤指旅館或餐館的〕主廚, 廚師長: *a pastry chef* 糕餅師傅 —see picture on page A15 參見 A15 頁圖

chef d'oeu·vre /ʃe ˋdœvrə; ˌʃeɪ ˈdɜːvrə/ *n* [C] *French formal* the best piece of work by a painter, writer, etc; MASTERPIECE【法, 正式】〔畫家、作家等的〕傑作

Chel·sea bun /ˌtʃɛlsɪ ˋbʌn; ˌtʃelsi ˈbʌn/ *n* [C] *BrE* a small, round, sweet cake with dried fruit in it【英】切爾西葡萄乾麵包

chem·i·cal[1] /ˋkɛmɪkl; ˈkemɪkəl/ *n* [C] a substance used in chemistry or produced by chemistry 化學品: *mixing chemicals in a test tube* 把化學物質在試管中混合

chemical[2] *adj* connected with or used in chemistry, or made by a chemical process 化學的; 化學上的; 用化學方法製造的: *the chemical composition of bleach* 漂白劑的化學成分 | *the chemical industry* 化學工業 | *chemical engineering* 化學工程 —**chemically** /-klɪ; -kli/ *adv*: *Chemically, the two substances are very similar.* 在化學性質方面, 這兩種物質是很相近的。

chemical re·ac·tion /ˌ··· ·ˈ··/ *n* [C,U] a natural process in which the atoms of chemicals mix and arrange themselves differently to form new substances 化學反應

chemical war·fare /ˌ··· ˈ··/ *n* [U] methods of fighting a war using chemical weapons 化學戰 —compare 比較 BIOLOGICAL WARFARE

chemical weap·on /ˌ··· ˈ··/ *n* [C] a poisonous substance, especially a gas, used as a weapon in war 化學武器〔尤指毒氣〕

che·mise /ʃəˋmiz; ʃəˈmiːz/ *n* [C] **1** a piece of women's underwear worn on the top half of her body〔女式〕寬鬆內衣 **2** a simple dress that hangs straight from a woman's shoulders 寬鬆連衣裙

chem·ist /ˋkɛmɪst; ˈkemɪst/ *n* [C] **1** a scientist who has a special knowledge in chemistry 化學家 **2** *BrE* someone who is trained to prepare drugs and medicines, who works in a shop【英】藥劑師; DRUGGIST *AmE*【美】—compare 比較 PHARMACIST 3

chem·is·try /ˋkɛmɪstrɪ; ˈkemɪstri/ *n* [U] the science that is concerned with studying the structure of substances and the way that they change 化學 —compare 比較 PHYSICS 2

chemistry set /ˈ··· ˌ·/ *n* [C] a box containing equipment for children to do simple chemistry at home〔供兒童做簡單化學實驗用的〕化學箱, 盒裝化學實驗套件

chem·ist's /ˋkɛmɪsts; ˈkemɪsts/ *n* [C] *BrE* a shop where medicines and TOILETRIES are sold【英】藥店, 藥房; DRUGSTORE *AmE*【美】—see also 另見 PHARMACY

chem·o·ther·a·py /ˌkimoˋθɛrəpɪ; ˌkiːməʊˈθerəpi/ *n* [U] the use of drugs to control and try to cure CANCER〔治療癌症的〕化學療法, 化學治療

che·nille /ʃəˋnil; ʃəˈniːl/ *n* [U] twisted thread with a surface like a soft brush, or cloth made from this and used for decorations, curtains etc 雪尼爾花線; 繩絨線; 繩絨線織物

cheque /tʃɛk; tʃek/ *n* [C] *BrE* one of a set of printed pieces of paper that you can sign and use instead of money to pay for things【英】支票: [+**for**] *a cheque for £200* 一張200英鎊的支票 | **write a cheque** *How much should I write the cheque for?* 我該開多少錢的支票? | **by cheque** (=with a cheque) 用支票付 *Can I pay by cheque?* 我能用支票付款嗎? | **cash a cheque** (=get cash by writing a cheque) 兌現支票; CHECK *AmE*【美】—see also 另見 DRAFT[1] (3), BLANK CHEQUE, TRAVELLERS CHEQUE 2

chequebook 支票簿

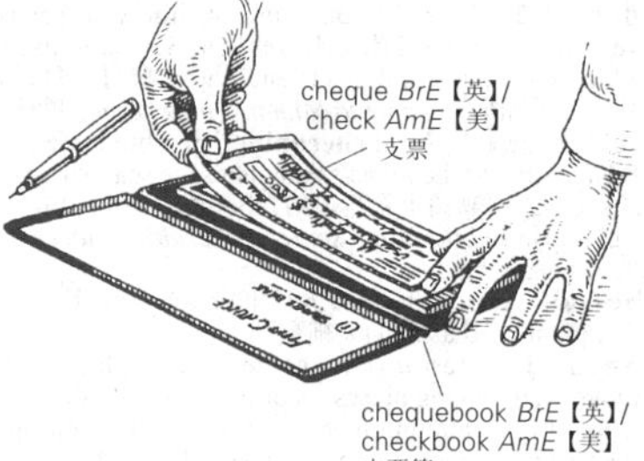

cheque·book /ˋtʃɛkˌbʊk; ˈtʃekbʊk/ *n* [C] *BrE* a small book of cheques that your bank gives you【英】支票簿; CHECKBOOK *AmE*【美】

chequebook jour·nal·is·m /ˌ·· ˈ····/ *n* [U] *BrE* low quality writing in newspapers that pay large amounts of money for details of famous people's private lives【英】支票新聞; 低級的新聞稿〔指斥巨資獲取有關名人私生活詳情的拙劣新聞報道〕

cheque card /ˈ· ·/ also 又作 **cheque guarantee card** /ˌ· ··ˈ· ·/ *n* [C] *BrE* a card given to you by your bank that you must show when you write a cheque, which promises that the bank will pay out the money written on the cheque【英】支票保付卡, 銀行支票證 —compare 比較 CASH CARD, CREDIT CARD, DEBIT CARD

chequ·ered /ˋtʃɛkɚd; ˈtʃekəd/ *adj* a British spelling of CHECKERED checkered 的英式拼法

chequered flag /ˌ·· ˈ·/ *n* [C] a British spelling of CHECK-

ERED FLAG checkered flag 的英式拼法

cheq·uers /ˈtʃɛkɚz; ˈtʃekəz/ *n* —see 見 CHINESE CHEQUERS

cheque stub *BrE*【英】, **check stub** *AmE*【美】/ˈ· ·/ *n* [C] the part of a cheque that is left when you tear it out of a cheque book, used for recording the amount you have spent 支票存根

cher·ish /ˈtʃɛrɪʃ; ˈtʃerɪʃ/ *v* [T usually passive 一般用被動態] **1** to love someone or something very much and take care of them well 珍愛, 珍惜, 鍾愛: *his most cherished possession* 他最珍愛的物品 **2** to be very important to someone 視為珍貴[重要]: **cherished hopes/dreams/ideas etc** *one of our cherished hopes, a community centre for the village* 我們心中懷有的一個希望是為村子建一個社區活動中心 | *cherished memories* 珍藏在心底的回憶

che·root /ʃəˈrut; ʃəˈruːt/ *n* [C] a CIGAR with both ends cut straight〔兩端切平的〕方頭雪茄煙

3 **cher·ry** /ˈtʃɛrɪ; ˈtʃeri/ *n* **1** [C] a small red or black round fruit with a long thin stem 櫻桃: *a bunch of cherries* 一串櫻桃 | *cherry tart* 櫻桃餡餅 —see picture on page A8 參見 A8 頁圖 **2 a)** [C] also 又作 **cherry tree** the tree on which this fruit grows 櫻桃樹 **b)** [U] the wood of this tree, used for making furniture 櫻桃木 **3** a bright red colour 櫻桃紅, 鮮紅 **4 the cherry on the cake/on the top** something additional that you did not expect, that is pleasant to have 意外收穫 —see also 另見 **another bite/a second bite at the cherry** (BITE[2] (9))

cherry bomb /ˈ·· ·/ *n* [C] *AmE* a large round red FIRECRACKER (=small loud explosive)【美】櫻桃爆竹

cherry bran·dy /,·· ˈ··/ *n* [U] a sweet alcoholic drink that tastes of cherries 櫻桃白蘭地

cherry-pick /ˈtʃɛrɪ,pɪk; ˈtʃeripɪk/ *v* [I,T] to choose exactly the things or people you want, from a group 挑選

cherry to·ma·to /ˈ·· ·,··/ *n plural* **cherry tomatoes** [C] a very small TOMATO 櫻桃番茄, 聖女果〔一種很小的番茄〕

cher·ub /ˈtʃɛrəb; ˈtʃerəb/ *n* [C] **1** a picture or figure of a fat, pretty, usually male child with small wings, used as a decoration 小天使, 普智天使〔繪畫或雕塑中有翅膀的小男孩〕 **2** *informal* a young pretty child who behaves very well【非正式】漂亮乖巧的兒童 **3** *spoken* used to address a young child in a friendly way【口】寶貝〔對小孩的一種昵稱〕: *Come to Mummy, my cherub!* 寶貝, 到媽媽這兒來! **4** *plural* **cherubim** /ˈtʃɛrəbɪm; ˈtʃerʊbɪm/ *biblical* one of the ANGELs that guard the seat where God sits【聖經】〔護衛上帝寶座的〕小天使 —**cherubic** /tʃəˈrubɪk; tʃəˈruːbɪk/ *adj*: *a smile of cherubic innocence* 天使般的純真笑容

cher·vil /ˈtʃɝvɪl; ˈtʃɜːvɪl/ *n* [U] a strong-smelling garden plant used as a HERB 細葉芹

chess /tʃɛs; tʃes/ *n* [U] a game for two players, who move their playing pieces according to fixed rules across a board in an attempt to CHECKMATE (=trap) their opponent's KING (=most important piece) 國際象棋

chess·board /ˈtʃɛs,bɔrd; ˈtʃesbɔːd/ *n* [C] a square board with 64 black and white squares, each square being next to a square of a different colour, on which chess is played 國際象棋棋盤 —see picture at 參見 BOARD[1] 圖

chess·man /ˈtʃɛsmæn; ˈtʃesmæn/ also 又作 **chesspiece** /ˈtʃɛspis; ˈtʃespiːs/ *n plural* **chessmen** /-mɛn; -men/ [C] any of the 16 black or 16 white playing pieces used in the game of chess〔國際象棋〕棋子

2
3 **chest** /tʃɛst; tʃest/ *n* [C] **1** the front part of your body between your neck and your stomach 胸部, 胸腔: *a hairy chest* 毛茸茸的胸脯 | *The doctor is going to listen your chest, Cindy.* 仙迪, 醫生要聽診你的胸部。—see also 另見 FLAT-CHESTED —see picture at 參見 BODY 圖 **2** a large, strong box that you use to store things in or to move your personal possessions from one place to another 箱, 大箱子: *We keep the summer clothes in a chest in the attic.* 我們把夏天穿的衣服放在閣樓上的大箱子裡。| *a blanket chest* 毛氈箱 —see also 另見 CHEST OF DRAWERS, HOPE CHEST, MEDICINE CHEST, TEA CHEST, WAR CHEST **3 get something off your chest** to tell someone about something that has been worrying or annoying you for a long time, so that you feel better afterwards 傾吐心中的煩惱

ches·ter·field /ˈtʃɛstɚ,fild; ˈtʃestəfiːld/ *n* [C] a soft comfortable SOFA, usually covered with leather 長沙發

chest·nut[1] /ˈtʃɛsnʌt; ˈtʃesnʌt/ *n* **1** [C] a smooth red-brown nut that you can eat 栗子: *roast chestnuts* 炒栗子 | *chestnut stuffing* 栗子餡 **2** also 又作 **chestnut tree** [C] the tree on which this nut grows 栗子樹 **3** [U] a reddish brown colour 栗色, 紅棕色 **4** [C] a horse that is this colour 紅棕色的馬, 栗色馬 **5 an old chestnut** a joke or story that has been repeated many times 老掉牙的故事[笑話] **6** [C] a HORSE CHESTNUT 七葉樹; 七葉樹的果實 —see also 另見 WATER CHESTNUT

chestnut[2] *adj* red-brown in colour 栗色的, 紅棕色的: *her chestnut hair* 她的紅棕色頭髮

chest of drawers /,· · ˈ·/ *n* a piece of furniture with drawers, used for storing clothes〔有抽屜的〕五斗櫥, 衣櫃; BUREAU (4) *AmE*【美】

chest·y /ˈtʃɛstɪ; ˈtʃesti/ *adj* **1** *informal especially BrE* having a lot of CATARRH (=thick liquid) in your lungs【非正式, 尤英】患胸部疾病的; 有胸病徵狀的: *a chesty cough* 發自胸腔的咳嗽 | *He was a bit chesty, so I didn't send him to school.* 他胸部有點不舒服, 所以我沒有讓他上學。**2** *informal* an impolite word used to describe a woman with large breasts【非正式】〔非禮貌用語, 指女人〕乳房突出的, 有大乳房的

chev·a·lier /,ʃɛvəˈlɪr; ,ʃevəˈlɪə/ *n* [C] *French*【法】**1** a title for someone who has a high rank in a special association in France 騎士: *a Chevalier of the Legion of Honour* 法國勳級會榮譽軍團騎士 **2** a member of the lowest rank of the French NOBILITY in the past〔舊時法國〕爵位最低的貴族

che·val mir·ror /ʃəˈvæl ,mɪrɚ; ʃəˈvæl mɪrə/ *n* [C] a long mirror in a frame which stands upright without being fixed to a wall〔裝於直立架上的〕鑲框的長鏡, 穿衣鏡

chev·ron /ˈʃɛvrən; ˈʃevrən/ *n* [C] **1** a pattern in a V shape V形圖案 **2** a piece of cloth in the shape of a V which a soldier has on their SLEEVE (1) to show their rank〔表示軍人等級的〕V形臂章

chew[1] /tʃu; tʃuː/ *v* **1** [I,T] to bite food several times before swallowing it 咀嚼; 嚼碎: *This meat's so tough I can hardly chew it!* 這塊肉太硬, 我幾乎咬不動! | [+at/on] *a dog chewing on a bone* 在啃着一根骨頭的狗 **2** [I,T] to bite something repeatedly in order to taste it or because you are nervous〔因緊張等〕不停地嚼, 咬: *We gave the dog an old shoe to chew on.* 我們扔了一隻舊鞋給狗咬。| *Stop chewing your nails – it's disgusting.* 別再咬指甲了, 叫人受不了。**3 chew the cud a)** if a cow or sheep chews the cud, it repeatedly bites food it has brought up from its stomach〔牛、羊等〕反芻 **b)** *informal* to think very carefully before making a decision【非正式】〔在作出決定前〕仔細考慮, 斟酌 **4 chew the fat** *informal* to have a long, friendly conversation【非正式】促膝長談, 閒聊 —see also 另見 **bite off more than you can chew** (BITE[1] (10))

chew on sth *phr v* [T] **chew on it** *informal* to think about something carefully for a period of time【非正式】仔細考慮, 深思

chew sb **out** *phr v* [T] *AmE, informal* to talk angrily to someone in order to show them that you disapprove of what they have done【美, 非正式】嚴厲責備〔某人〕: *I know I'm late, you don't have to chew me out!* 我知道我遲到了, 但你沒有必要大聲責備我呀!

chew sth ↔ **over** *phr v* [T] to think carefully about a question, problem, idea etc. over a period of time 仔細考慮〔問題、意見等〕: *Let me chew it over for a few days, and then I'll let you have my answer.* 讓我仔細考慮幾天後再給你答覆。

chew sth ↔ **up** *phr v* [T] to bite something repeatedly with your teeth so that you can make it smaller or softer and swallow it 嚼碎, 咀嚼: *That dog's chewed the carpet up again!* 那頭狗又在咬地毯了。

chew[2] *n* [C] **1** the act of biting something repeatedly with the teeth 嚼, 咀嚼 **2** something such as a sweet you chew or special tobacco which you chew but do not swallow 咀嚼物〈如口香糖、煙草〉: *a chew of tobacco* 一塊嚼煙草

chewing gum /ˈ·· ·/ *n* [U] a type of sweet, that you chew for a long time but do not swallow 口香糖

chew·y /ˋtʃuɪ; ˈtʃuːi/ *adj* food that is chewy has to be chewed a lot before it is soft enough to swallow〔食物〕需多嚼的, 難嚼碎的: *chewy toffees* 難嚼的太妃糖 | *wonderfully chewy chocolate brownies* 耐嚼的美味巧克力蛋糕

Chey·enne /ʃaɪˋæn; ʃaɪˈæn/ *n* **1 the Cheyenne** a Native American people that live in the West of the US 夏延族〔美國西部的美洲土著〕**2** [C] a member of the Cheyenne people 夏延人

chic /ʃik; ʃiːk/ *adj* very fashionable and expensive and showing good judgment of what is attractive and good style 時髦的; 漂亮的; 雅致的: *a chic black dress* 一條時髦的黑色連衣裙 | *Provençal cuisine has become very chic.* 普羅旺斯式的烹調大受歡迎。| *a chic restaurant* 一家時髦的餐廳 —**chic** *n* [U]

chi·cane /ʃɪˋken; ʃɪˈkeɪn/ *n* [C] an S shaped bend in a straight road, especially on a track for racing cars〔尤指賽車跑道上的〕S形彎道

chi·ca·ne·ry /ʃɪˋkenərɪ; ʃɪˈkeɪnəri/ *n* [U] *formal* the use of clever plans or actions to deceive people【正式】詭計, 欺騙, 詐騙: *The legal system got to the truth and settled cases fairly and without chicanery.* 法律部門查清事實真相, 公正嚴明地處理所有案件。

Chi·ca·no /tʃɪˋkɑno; tʃɪˈkɑːnəʊ/ *n* [C] *plural* **Chicanos** *AmE* a US citizen who was born in Mexico or whose family came from Mexico【美】墨西哥裔美國人 —**Chicano** *adj*

chi-chi /ˋʃi ʃi; ˈʃiː ʃiː/ *adj informal* stylish or attractive, especially in a way that you think uses too much decoration【非正式】時髦的; 吸引人的; 過分豔麗的: *a chi-chi nightclub* 富麗堂皇的夜總會

chick /tʃɪk; tʃɪk/ *n* [C] **1** a baby bird 小鳥: *a robin chick* 幼知更鳥 **2** a word meaning a young woman, that some people think is offensive 少女; 少婦〔有些人認為此詞具冒犯性〕

chick-a-dee /ˋtʃɪk ə ˏdi; ˈtʃɪk ə diː/ *n* [C] a North American bird with a black head 山雀〔一種北美小鳥, 頭部呈黑色〕

2 **chick·en[1]** /ˋtʃɪkɪn; ˈtʃɪkɪ̣n/ *n*

1 ▶BIRD 鳥◀ [C] a common farm bird that is kept for its meat and eggs 雞: *He keeps chickens on his farm.* 他在農場裡養雞。—see also 另見 HEN, COCK[1] (1), ROOSTER

2 ▶MEAT 肉◀ [U] the meat from this bird eaten as food 雞肉: *roast chicken* 烤雞 | *fried chicken* 炸雞 | *chicken soup* 雞湯

3 ▶SB WHO IS NOT BRAVE 懦夫◀ [C] *informal* someone who is not at all brave; COWARD【非正式】膽小鬼, 懦夫: *Don't be such a chicken!* 別那麼膽小!

4 ▶GAME 遊戲◀ [U] a game in which children must do something dangerous to show that they are brave〔兒童玩的〕比試膽量的遊戲

5 which came first, the chicken or the egg? used to say that it is difficult or impossible to decide which of two things came first or which action is the cause and which is the effect 先有雞, 還是先有蛋?〔表示因果難以區分〕

6 a chicken and egg situation/problem/thing etc a situation in which it is impossible to decide which part caused another and which is the effect of another 因果難以區分的狀況/問題/事情等

7 your chickens have come home to roost your bad or dishonest actions in the past have caused the problems that you have now 惡有惡報, 自作自受 —see also 另見 **don't count your chickens before they're hatched** (COUNT[1] (8)), SPRING CHICKEN

chicken[2] *v*

chicken out *phr v* [I] *informal* to decide at the last moment not to do something you said you would do because you are afraid【非正式】〔因害怕而〕臨陣退縮: **chicken out of doing sth** *I knew you'd chicken out of telling Dad you want to leave school.* 我知道你最終會不敢告訴爸爸你想退學的事。

chicken[3] *adj* [not before noun 不用於名詞前] *informal* not brave enough to do something【非正式】沒勇氣的, 膽小的: *Your brother is chicken.* 你哥哥是膽小鬼。

chick·en·feed /ˋtʃɪkɪnˏfid; ˈtʃɪkɪ̣nfiːd/ *n* [U] *informal* an amount of money that is so small that it is almost not worth having【非正式】一筆小數額的錢: *The bank offered to lend us £1,000, but that's chickenfeed compared to what we need.* 銀行答應借給我們1,000英鎊, 但這與我們需要的數目相比, 簡直微不足道。

chicken-fried steak /ˌ·· · ˈ·/ *n* [C,U] *AmE* a thin piece of BEEF[1] (1) covered in BREADCRUMBS and cooked in hot fat【美】〔外裹麵包屑的〕炸牛排

chicken-heart·ed /ˌ·· ˈ··◂/ also 又作 **chicken-livered** *adj* not brave; COWARDLY 膽小的, 怯懦的

chick·en·pox /ˋtʃɪkɪnˏpɑks; ˈtʃɪkɪ̣npɒks/ *n* [U] an infectious illness which causes a slight fever and spots on your skin 水痘

chicken run /ˈ·· ·/ *n* [U] an area surrounded by a fence where you keep chickens〔四周設欄以養雞的〕雞欄

chick·en·shit /ˋtʃɪkɪnˏʃɪt; ˈtʃɪkɪ̣nʃɪt/ *n* [C] *AmE informal* a rude word meaning someone who is not at all brave; COWARD【美, 非正式】膽小鬼, 懦夫〔不禮貌說法〕

chicken wire /ˈ·· ·/ *n* [U] a type of thin wire net used to make fences for chickens〔做雞欄的〕細鐵絲網

chick-pea /ˈ· ·/ *n* [C] a large brown PEA which is cooked and eaten; GARBANZO 鷹嘴豆

chick·weed /ˋtʃɪkˏwid; ˈtʃɪkwiːd/ *n* [U] a garden WEED[1] (1) with small white flowers 捲耳; 繁縷〔園子裡開白色小花的一種雜草〕

chic·le /ˋtʃɪkḷ; ˈtʃɪkəl/ *n* [U] the GUM (=thick juice) of a tropical American tree used in making CHEWING GUM 糖膠樹膠〔可製口香糖〕

chic·o·ry /ˋtʃɪkərɪ; ˈtʃɪkəri/ *n* [U] a European plant with blue flowers whose leaves are eaten and whose roots are sometimes used as coffee 菊苣; ENDIVE (2) *AmE*【美】

chide /tʃaɪd; tʃaɪd/ *v past tense* **chided** *or* **chid** /tʃɪd; tʃɪd/ *past participle* **chided, chid** *or* **chidden** /ˋtʃɪdṇ; ˈtʃɪdn/ [I,T] *literary* to speak angrily to someone because you do not approve of something they have done; REBUKE【文】呵斥, 指責: *"You naughty children!" she chided.* 她呵斥道:"你們這些淘氣鬼!" | **chide sb for sth** *Louise often chided her son for his idleness.* 路易絲常常責罵兒子懶惰。| **chide sb for doing sth** *Mr Jones chided the children for not wearing their coats.* 瓊斯先生責怪孩子沒有穿大衣。

chief[1] /tʃif; tʃiːf/ *adj* **1** most important; main 最重要的, 主要的: *One of the chief causes of crime today is drugs.* 毒品是如今引發犯罪的主要原因之一。| *the prosecution's chief witness* 控方的主要證人 —see also 另見 CHIEFLY **2** highest in rank 最高級的, 首席的: *the chief accountant* 首席會計師 | *the chief political correspondent of the Washington Post*《華盛頓郵報》的首席政治記者 **3 chief cook and bottle washer** *humorous* someone in charge of an event, especially someone who must do a lot of small unimportant jobs to make sure it is a success【幽默】事必躬親的負責人; 百管部長; 當家: *"Is there any more wine?" "Ask my husband, he's chief cook and bottle washer today!"* "還有酒嗎?" "去問我丈夫, 他今天當了百管部長!" S2 W2

chief[2] *n* [C] W3

1 ▶RULER OF TRIBE 部落統治者◀ a ruler of a tribe 部落首領, 酋長: *an American Indian tribal chief* 美洲印第安人部落的酋長

2 ►SB IN CHARGE OF AN ORGANIZATION 組織的領導人◄ the most important person in a company or organization 總裁; 主管人; 領袖; 最高領導人: *the chief of Austria's army intelligence* 奧地利軍事情報司令 | *Industry chiefs yesterday demanded tough measures against inflation.* 工業巨頭們昨天要求採取強硬措施對付通貨膨脹的問題。
3 the chief *informal* the person in charge of the company or organization you work for【非正式】老闆, 頭兒: *The chief wants to see you right away.* 老闆要你立刻去見他。
4 big/great white chief *humorous* the person in charge of a group of people, company, organization etc【幽默】首領; 頭目; 上司
5 too many chiefs and not enough Indians used to say there are too many people saying how something should be done and not enough people doing it 官多兵少; 動嘴的多, 動手的少
6 ►MAN 人◄ *BrE old-fashioned* used to speak in a friendly way to a man you think is more important than you【英, 過時】〔用作表示客氣的稱呼〕

chief con·stab·le /ˌ· ˈ···/ *n* [C] a police officer in charge of the police in a large area of Britain【英】〔英國一大地區的〕警察局局長

Chief Ex·ec·u·tive /ˌ· ·ˈ···/ *n AmE* **the Chief Executive** the President of the US【美】美國總統

chief executive of·fic·er /ˌ· ·ˈ··· ˌ···/ *n* [C] the person with the most authority in a large company〔公司的〕行政總裁

chief in·spect·or /ˌ· ·ˈ··◂/ *n* [C] a British police officer of middle rank〔英國的〕警察總督察, 總巡官

chief jus·tice /ˌ· ˈ··◂/ *n* [C] the most important judge in a court of law, especially of the US Supreme Court〔尤指美國的〕高等法院院長; 首席法官

chief·ly /ˈtʃifli; ˈtʃiːfli/ *adv* mostly but not completely; mainly 大部分地; 主要地: *The work consists chiefly of interviewing members of the public.* 這份工作主要是採訪公眾。| *I lived abroad for years, chiefly in Italy.* 我長年住在國外, 大多住在意大利。

chief of staff /ˌ· · ˈ·/ *n plural* **chiefs of staff** [C] **1** an officer of high rank in the army, navy etc who advises the officer in charge of a particular military group or operation 參謀長 **2** an official of high rank who advises the man in charge of an organization or government〔政府或組織中的〕高級顧問; 參事; 參謀: *the White House chief of staff* 白宮參謀長

Chief Rab·bi /ˌ· ˈ··/ *n* **the Chief Rabbi** the main leader of the JEWISH religion in a country 首席拉比, 猶太教會領袖〔一國內的猶太教主要領導人〕

chief su·per·in·ten·dent /ˌ· ···ˈ··◂/ *n* [C] a British police officer of high rank〔英國警察的〕總警司, 警務長

chief·tain /ˈtʃiftın; ˈtʃiːftən/ *n* [C] the leader of a tribe or a Scottish CLAN 族長; 酋長;〔蘇格蘭高地氏族的〕宗族長; 首領 —**chieftainship** *n* [C,U]

Chief Whip /ˌ· ˈ·/ *n* **the Chief Whip** an important member of a British political party whose job is to make sure that members of his party elected to parliament obey party orders 黨鞭〔英國政黨中的要員, 負責確保該黨議員遵從黨令〕

chif·fon /ʃɪˈfɑn; ˈʃɪfɒn/ *n* [U] a soft thin silk or NYLON material that you can see through 雪紡綢, 薄綢: *a pink chiffon ballgown* 粉紅色的薄綢禮服

chi·gnon /ˈʃinjɑn; ˈʃiːnjɒn/ *n* [C] *French* a smooth knot of hair that a woman wears at the back of her head【法】〔女人的〕髮髻

chi·hua·hua /tʃɪˈwɑwɑ; tʃɪˈwɑːwə/ *n* [C] a very small dog from Mexico with smooth hair 奇瓦瓦[吉娃娃]狗〔毛光滑的小狗, 產自墨西哥〕

chil·blain /ˈtʃɪlˌblen; ˈtʃɪlbleɪn/ *n* [C] a painful red place on your fingers or toes that is caused by cold and a weak supply of blood〔手指或腳趾上的〕凍瘡

child 小孩, 兒童

child /tʃaɪld; tʃaɪld/ *n* [C] *plural* **children** /ˈtʃɪldrən; ˈtʃɪldrən/
1 ►YOUNG PERSON 小孩◄ a young person from the time they are born until they are aged 14 or 15〔14到15歲之前的〕小孩, 兒童: *We've always competed, ever since we were children.* 我們總是相互競爭, 從小如此。| *Can you sell me a bike suitable for a seven-year-old child?* 你能賣給我一輛適合七歲兒童騎的腳踏車嗎? | **as a child** (=when you were a child) 孩提時, 兒時 *As a child I remember Grandma singing me to sleep.* 我記得當我還是個孩子時, 外婆總是唱着歌讓我入睡。| **a child killer/victim/prostitute etc** (=a child who is a killer etc) 兒童兇手/兒童受害者/雛妓等
2 ►SON/DAUGHTER 兒女◄ a son or daughter of any age 兒子; 女兒; 孩子: *How many children did Victoria have?* 維多利亞有幾個孩子? | *We'll come if we can find a babysitter for the children.* 如果我們能找到人臨時看孩子, 我們就會來。| *Is this her first child?* (=is this her first PREGNANCY?) 這是她的第一個孩子嗎? | **have a child** (=give birth) 生孩子, 分娩 | **an only child** (=someone with no brothers or sisters) 獨生子[女]
3 ►SB INFLUENCED BY AN IDEA 受某想法影響者◄ someone who is very strongly influenced by the ideas and attitudes of a particular person or period of history 深受某人[某時期]影響的人: *Thatcher's children are finding that the world has moved on.* 深受戴卓爾的思想影響的人正發覺世界已經向前發展。| **[+of]** *a real child of the sixties* 真正屬於六十年代的人
4 ►SB WHO IS LIKE A CHILD 孩子氣的人◄ someone who is not very experienced in doing something, or who behaves like a child 幼稚的人, 行為像孩子的人: *Richard's such a child – he can't even do his own washing and cooking.* 李察簡直像個孩子 — 他甚至不會洗衣和做飯。
5 children should be seen and not heard an expression meaning that children should be quiet and not talk, used when you disapprove of the way the children are behaving 小孩子應該少說話〔用來叫小孩子安靜的一句話〕
6 be with child *old use* to be PREGNANT【舊】懷孕
7 be heavy/great with child *old use* to be nearly ready to give birth【舊】大腹便便即將臨盆的 —see also 另見 CHILD'S PLAY

USAGE NOTE 用法說明: CHILD
WORD CHOICE 詞語辨析: **child, baby, infant, toddler, teenager, adolescent, youth, young people, kid**
A very young **child** is a **baby** or more formally an **infant** 年紀很小的小孩叫做 baby, 或較正式的說法是 infant: *Many infants have died in the refugee*

camps. 許多嬰兒在難民營裡夭折。A child who has just learned to walk is a **toddler**. 剛學步的小孩叫做 toddler。

Young people aged 13 to 19 are **teenagers** and a younger teenager may also be called an **adolescent**, but this word is rather formal, and may show a negative attitude. 13-19 歲的青少年叫 teenagers, 年齡小些的少年還可叫做 adolescent, 但這個詞相當正式, 而且略帶貶義: *a group of giggly adolescent girls* 一羣嘰嘰喳喳的少女

The word **youth** is often used for an older male teenager (15+) in official reports about crimes or bad behaviour. youth 一詞常用於正式報告中指犯罪或行為不端的年齡較大〔15 歲以上〕的男性青年: *The police are seeking two youths who raped a teenage girl.* 警方正在搜捕兩名強姦了一個少女的男青年。In official names **youth** includes both sexes. 在正式名稱中 youth 可指男或女: *a youth club/group/scheme/worker/centre/hostel* 青年俱樂部/青年團體/青年人計劃/青年工作者/青少年中心/青年旅館 Often the phrase **young people** is used for this age group in everyday English. 在日常英語中, 多用 young people 來指這個年齡組別的青年: *a disco full of young people dancing* 擠滿了在跳舞的年輕人的的士高舞廳

Kid is informal and used both for **child** (up to around 14) kid〔非正式〕可以用來指 child〔大約 14 歲以下〕: *The kids are playing in the yard* 孩子們在院子裡玩耍, and for **young people**. 也可以用來指 young people: *We met a group of college kids.* 我們遇見了一羣年輕的大學生。

GRAMMAR 語法

Remember the plural of **child** is **children**, never *childs* or *childrens*. 記住 child 的複數形式為 children, 不是 childs 或 childrens。But in the possessive form you say 但所有格中應為: *this child's education* 這個孩子的教育 | *these children's education* 這些孩子的教育

child·bear·ing /ˈtʃaɪld͵bɛrɪŋ; ˈtʃaɪld͵beərɪŋ/ *n* [U] **1** the process of giving birth to a baby 懷孩子, 分娩, 生孩子 **2 childbearing age** the time in a woman's life when she can have babies 育齡

child ben·e·fit /͵· ˈ···/ *n* [U] an amount of money that the British government gives to families with children 兒童津貼〔英國政府發給兒童的父母, 直到兒童到某一年齡為止〕

child·birth /ˈtʃaɪld͵bɝθ; ˈtʃaɪldbɜːθ/ *n* [U] the act of having a baby 分娩, 生孩子: *His mother died in childbirth.* 他的母親死於難產。

child·care /ˈtʃaɪld͵kɛr; ˈtʃaɪldkeə/ *n* [U] an arrangement in which someone who is trained to look after children cares for them while the parents are at work 兒童看護, 兒童照管: *The company pays £20 a week towards childcare.* 公司每週發 20 英鎊兒童看護費。

child·hood /ˈtʃaɪld͵hʊd; ˈtʃaɪldhʊd/ *n* [C,U] the period of time when you are a child 童年; 兒童時代: *I had a happy childhood.* 我有一個快樂的童年。—see also 另見 SECOND CHILDHOOD

child·ish /ˈtʃaɪldɪʃ; ˈtʃaɪldɪʃ/ *adj* **1** related to or typical of a child 孩子的; 孩子般的: *a high childish laugh* 孩子般的大笑 **2** behaving in a silly way that makes you seem much younger than you really are 傻氣的, 孩子氣的, 幼稚的: *Stop messing around, it's so childish.* 別搗亂, 太孩子氣了。—compare 比較 CHILDLIKE —**childishly** *adv* —**childishness** *n* [U]

child·less /ˈtʃaɪldlɪs; ˈtʃaɪldləs/ *adj* having no children 無子女的: *a childless couple* 一對沒有兒女的夫妻 —**childlessness** *n* [U]

child·like /ˈtʃaɪld͵laɪk; ˈtʃaɪldlaɪk/ *adj* having qualities that are typical of a child, especially qualities such as INNOCENCE and trust 孩子般的, 像孩子似的; 天真無邪的: *an expression of childlike innocence* 天真爛漫的表情 —compare 比較 CHILDISH

child·min·der /ˈtʃaɪld͵maɪndɚ; ˈtʃaɪld͵maɪndə/ *n* [C] *BrE* someone who is paid to look after young children while their parents are at work【英】〔孩子父母外出工作時受雇〕照看孩子的人; BABYSITTER *AmE*【美】—**childminding** *n* [U]

child prod·i·gy /͵· ˈ···/ *n* [C] a child who is unusually skilful at doing something such as playing a musical instrument 神童, 天才兒童; 有特殊才能的兒童

child·proof /ˈtʃaɪld͵pruf; ˈtʃaɪldpruːf/ *adj* something that is childproof is designed to prevent a child from opening, damaging, or breaking it 對孩童安全的; 不會被孩童弄壞的; 能防止孩童瞎摸弄的: *a childproof lock* 對兒童安全的鎖

chil·dren /ˈtʃɪldrən; ˈtʃɪldrən/ *n* the plural of CHILD

children's home /ˈ·· ·/ *n* [C] a place in Britain where children live if their own parents cannot look after them〔英國的〕兒童之家, 兒童收容所

child's play /ˈ· ·/ *n* [U] something that it is very easy to do 容易的事, 小兒科的事: *Cracking such a simple code was child's play to him.* 破譯這麼簡單的代碼對他來說是輕而易舉的事。

child sup·port /ˈ· ͵·ˈ/ *n* [U] *AmE* money that someone pays regularly to their former wife or husband in order to support their children【美】〔付給前配偶的〕子女贍養費, 子女撫養費; MAINTENANCE (2) *BrE*【英】

chil·i /ˈtʃɪlɪ; ˈtʃɪli/ *n* [C,U] the American spelling of CHILLI chilli 的美式拼法

chill[1] /tʃɪl; tʃɪl/ *v* **1** [I,T] if you chill something such as food or drink or if it chills, it becomes very cold but does not freeze (使) 冷卻, (使) 變冷: *Chill the champagne in a bucket of ice.* 把香檳放在冰桶裡冷卻。| *Serve the melon chilled.* 端上冰的甜瓜。**2** [T usually passive 一般用被動態] to make someone very cold 使〔某人〕感到很冷: **chilled to the bone/marrow** *Come and sit by the fire, you look chilled to the bone.* 過來坐在火爐邊, 你看上去冷壞了。**3** [T] *literary* to frighten someone, especially by seeming very cruel or violent【文】〔尤指以殘忍和暴力的手段〕使…不寒而慄, 使…寒心: *The look in her eye chilled me.* 她眼中的神情讓我不寒而慄。**4** [T] *literary* if you chill someone's hopes or keenness for doing something, you discourage them【文】使失望; 使〔熱情〕冷卻

chill out *phr v* [I] *especially AmE* to relax completely instead of feeling angry, tired, or nervous【尤美】完全放鬆, 不緊張: *Chill out, man, I didn't mean to insult you.* 老兄, 放輕鬆些, 我無意冒犯你。

chill[2] *n* **1** [singular] a feeling of coldness 寒冷, 寒氣: *There's a real chill in the air.* 空氣中透着寒意。| **take the chill off** (=heat something slightly) 稍稍加熱 *Heat the baby's milk just enough to take the chill off.* 把寶寶的牛奶温一下。**2** [C] a feeling of fear caused by something that is very unpleasant or cruel 害怕; 心寒: *Her description of the massacre sent a chill through the audience.* 她對大屠殺的描述讓觀眾膽戰心驚。| **send a chill down sb's spine** (=make them feel very frightened) 使某人非常恐懼 **3** [C] a mild illness with a fever 小感冒, 輕微發燒: **catch a chill** *It began to snow on the way home and I caught a nasty chill.* 在回家的路上天開始下雪, 我就因此着涼了。**4** [singular] a way of behaving or speaking that is very unfriendly 不友好, 冷漠, 冷淡: *There was a marked chill in his voice when he answered.* 他回答時語氣中有明顯不友好的意味。

chill[3] *adj* unpleasantly cold 寒冷的, 寒氣襲人的: *a chill wind* 寒風

chil·ler /ˈtʃɪlɚ; ˈtʃɪlə/ *n* [C] *informal* a film or book that is intended to frighten you【非正式】恐怖書; 恐怖電影: *the black magic chiller, 'Rosemary's Baby'* 巫術恐怖電影《魔鬼怪嬰》

chil·li *BrE*【英】, **chili** *AmE*【美】/ˈtʃɪlɪ; ˈtʃɪli/ *n plural* chillies, chilies **1** [U] a dish made with beans and usually meat cooked with chillies 辣味牛肉豆子〔一種用牛肉、豆和辣椒做成的菜餚〕: **chilli con carne** (=this dish made with meat) 辣味牛肉豆子 **2** [C] a small, thin type of PEPPER[1] (3) with a very strong, hot taste 辣椒 **3** [U] a hot-tasting red powder made from this PEPPER[1] (3) and used in cooking 辣椒粉

chil·ling /ˋtʃɪlɪŋ; ˈtʃɪlɪŋ/ *adj* something that is chilling makes you feel frightened, especially because it is cruel, violent, or dangerous 令人毛骨悚然的, 令人害怕的: *the chilling sound of wolves howling* 令人毛骨悚然的狼嚎

chilli pow·der /ˈ·· ,··/ *n* [U] CHILLI (3) 辣椒粉

chil·lum /ˋtʃɪləm; ˈtʃɪləm/ *n* [C] *slang* a type of pipe used for smoking CANNABIS【俚】吸食大麻用的煙斗

chill·y /ˋtʃɪlɪ; ˈtʃɪli/ *adj* **1** cold enough to make you feel uncomfortable 寒冷的, 嚴寒的: *The wind's a bit chilly.* 這風有點兒寒冷。**2** unfriendly 冷漠的, 不友好的: *The speech met with a chilly reception.* 這次演講的反應很冷淡。—see 見 COLD[1] (USAGE) —**chilliness** *n* [singular, U]

chilly bin /ˈ·· ·/ *n* [C] *NZE* a large container used for keeping food or drink cold【新西蘭】〔儲藏食物或飲料的〕冷藏箱, 冷藏櫃

chi·mae·ra /kaɪˋmɪrə; kaɪˈmɪərə/ *n* [C] another spelling of CHIMERA chimera 的另一種拼法

chime[1] /tʃaɪm; tʃaɪm/ *v* **1** [I,T] if a bell or clock chimes, it makes a ringing sound, especially to tell you what time it is (使) 鐘響; 報時: *The grandfather clock chimed six.* 大擺鐘敲六點鐘了。**2** [I+with] to be the same as something else or to have the same effect 與…協調; 與…一致: *Her views on art chime completely with mine.* 她對藝術的見解和我的完全一樣。

chime in *phr v* [I] to say something in a conversation, especially to agree with what someone has just said 插話〔表示贊同〕: *"We'll miss you too," the children chimed in.* 那些孩子插嘴道:"我們也會想念你的。"

chime[2] *n* [C] **1** a ringing sound made by a bell or clock 鐘聲; 鈴聲: *the chime of the doorbell* 門鈴聲 **2 chimes** [plural] a set of bells or other objects that produce musical sounds〔可敲出音樂的〕一組鐘

chi·me·ra, chimaera /kaɪˋmɪrə; kaɪˈmɪərə/ *n* [C] **1** an imaginary creature that breathes fire and has a lion's head, a goat's body, and a snake's tail 客米拉〔神話中獅頭、羊身、蛇尾的吐火女怪〕**2** something, especially an idea or hope, that is not really possible and can never exist 幻想; 妄想: *trying to present that impossible chimera, 'a balanced view'* 努力提出那種不可能的妄想, 一種"平衡觀點"

chi·me·ri·cal /kaɪˋmɛrɪkl̩; kaɪˈmerɪkəl/ *adj literary* imaginary or not really possible【文】幻想的; 不切實際的; 虛幻的

chim·ney /ˋtʃɪmnɪ; ˈtʃɪmni/ *n* [C] **1** a pipe inside a building that goes from a fire to the roof in order to let smoke out 煙囪, 煙筒: *a factory chimney belching smoke* 冒出濃煙的工廠煙囪 —see picture on page A4 參見 A4 頁圖 **2** a narrow opening in tall rocks or cliffs that you can climb up〔可容人攀登的〕岩石裂縫 **3** the glass cover that is put over the flame in an oil lamp〔煤油燈的〕玻璃燈罩

chimney breast /ˈ·· ·/ *n* [C] *BrE* the part of a wall in a room that encloses a chimney【英】壁爐腔

chimney-piece /ˈ·· ·/ *n* [C] *BrE* a decoration, usually made of brick or stone, built above a FIREPLACE【英】壁爐架; 壁爐台

chimney pot /ˈ·· ·/ *n* [C] a short wide pipe made of baked clay or metal, that is fixed to the top of a CHIMNEY 煙囪管帽 —see picture on page A4 參見 A4 頁圖

chimney stack /ˈ·· ·/ *n* [C] *BrE*【英】**1** the tall CHIMNEY of a building such as a factory〔工廠等的〕高煙囪; SMOKESTACK *AmE*【美】**2** a group of small chimneys on a roof〔屋頂上多煙道的〕煙囪體, 組合煙囪

chimney sweep /ˈ·· ·/ *n* [C] someone whose job is to clean CHIMNEYs using special long brushes 煙囪清掃工

chim·pan·zee /,tʃɪmpænˋzi; ˌtʃɪmpænˈziː/ also 又作 **chimp** /tʃɪmp; tʃɪmp/ *informal*【非正式】*n* [C] an intelligent African animal that is like a monkey without a tail〔非洲產的〕黑猩猩

chin /tʃɪn; tʃɪn/ *n* [C] **1** the front part of your face below your mouth 頦, 下巴: *She sat with her chin in her hands.* 她雙手托着下巴坐着。—see picture at 參見 HEAD[1] 圖 **2 (keep your) chin up!** *spoken* used to tell someone to make an effort to stay cheerful when they are in a difficult situation【口】不要氣餒! 不要灰心!: *Chin up! It'll be over soon.* 振作點! 很快就會過去的了。

chi·na /ˋtʃaɪnə; ˈtʃaɪnə/ *n* [U] **1** a hard white substance produced by baking a type of clay at a high temperature 瓷, 瓷料: *china teacups* 瓷茶杯 **2** also 又作 **chinaware** plates, cups etc made of china 瓷製品, 瓷器: *We were given a lot of china as wedding presents.* 許多人送瓷器給我們作結婚禮物。

Chi·na·town /ˋtʃaɪnə,taun; ˈtʃaɪnətaʊn/ *n* [C,U] an area in a city where there are Chinese restaurants, shops, and clubs, and where a lot of Chinese people live 中國城, 華人區, 唐人街

chin·chil·la /tʃɪnˋtʃɪlə; ˌtʃɪnˈtʃɪlə/ *n* **1** [C] a small South American animal bred for its fur〔皮毛具有高價值的〕絨鼠[栗鼠] **2** [U] the pale grey fur of the chinchilla 絨鼠[栗鼠]的毛皮

Chi·nese[1] /tʃaɪˋniz; ˌtʃaɪˈniːz◂/ *n* **1** [U] the language of China 漢語, 中文 **2 the Chinese** people from China 中國人, 漢人 **3** [C] *BrE informal* a meal of Chinese food, or a restaurant that sells Chinese food【英, 非正式】中國菜, 中餐; 中餐館

Chinese[2] *adj* from or connected with China 中國的

Chinese che·quers *BrE*【英】, **Chinese checkers** *AmE*【美】/,·· ˈ··/ *n* [U] a game in which you move small balls from hole to hole on a board in the shape of a star 中國跳棋, 波子棋

Chinese fire drill /,·· ˈ· ·/ *n* [singular] *AmE informal* a very confusing situation【美, 非正式】混亂的局面

Chinese lan·tern /,·· ˈ··/ *n* [C] a small box made of thin paper that you put a light inside as a decoration 紙燈籠

Chinese leaves /,·· ˈ·/ *n* [U] a type of CABBAGE eaten especially in East Asia 白菜, 青菜〔尤在東亞地區食用〕—see picture on page A9 參見 A9 頁圖

Chinese medi·cine /,·· ˈ··/ *n* [U] a kind of medicine that uses HERBs (=dried plants) and ACUPUNCTURE 中國醫學, 中醫

Chinese whis·pers /,·· ˈ··/ *n* [U] *BrE* the passing of information from one person to another, and then others, when the information gets slightly changed each time【英】〔以訛傳訛或道聽途說的〕閒言碎語, 傳話: *Chinese whispers started about child abuse in Cleveland and developed into a national scandal.* 在克里夫蘭發生的虐兒事件竟由開始時的閒言碎語演變成了一樁全國性的醜聞。

Chink /tʃɪŋk; tʃɪŋk/ *n* [C] a very offensive word for a Chinese person 中國佬〔對中國人的蔑稱〕

chink[1] *n* **1** [C] a small hole in a wall, or between two things that join together, that lets light or air through 裂縫; 裂口; 縫隙: *The sun came through a chink in the curtains.* 陽光從窗簾的縫隙中照了進來。**2** [C] a high ringing sound made by metal or glass objects hitting each other〔金屬、玻璃等互相碰擊發出的〕叮噹聲: *the chink of coins* 硬幣叮噹作響的聲音 **3 a chink in sb's armour** a weakness in someone's character, argument etc that you can use to attack them〔性格、論點等的〕漏洞; 弱點

chink[2] *v* [I,T] if glass or metal objects chink or you chink them, they make a high ringing sound when they knock together (使) 叮噹響: *They chinked their glasses and drank a toast to the couple.* 他們相互碰杯, 向那對夫婦敬酒。

chin·less /ˋtʃɪnlɪs; ˈtʃɪnləs/ *adj* **1** having a chin that is small or slopes inwards 沒有下巴的, 下巴內縮的 **2** *BrE* lacking courage or determination【英】沒有勇氣的; 猶豫不決的 **3 chinless wonder** a young man from an upper class family who is weak and stupid 無用愚蠢的紈絝子弟

chi·no /ˋtʃino; ˈtʃiːnəʊ/ *n* **1** [U] a strong material made of woven cotton 絲光斜紋布 **2 chinos** [plural] trousers made from this material 絲光斜紋布褲子

chin·strap /ˈtʃɪnˌstræp; ˈtʃɪnstræp/ *n* [C] a band of cloth under your chin to keep a hat or HELMET in place〔繫於頦下固定帽子或頭盔用的〕頦帶

chintz /tʃɪnts; tʃɪnts/ *n* [U] smooth cotton cloth that is printed with flowery patterns and used for making curtains, furniture covers etc〔作窗簾或家具套等用的〕印花棉布: *pink chintz curtains* 粉紅色花窗簾

chintz·y /ˈtʃɪntsɪ; ˈtʃɪntsi/ *adj* **1** covered with chintz 印花棉布面子的: *a chintzy sofa* 印花棉布面沙發 **2** *AmE informal* cheap and badly made【美, 非正式】廉價劣質的, 做工粗糙的: *a chintzy chest of drawers* 做工粗糙的五斗櫥 **3** *AmE informal* unwilling to give people things or spend money; STINGY【美, 非正式】小家子氣的, 吝嗇的: *We don't need to be chintzy over the Christmas presents this year.* 我們今年買聖誕禮物不需要太小氣。

chin up /ˈ· ·/ *n* [C] *AmE* an exercise in which you hang on a bar and pull yourself up until your chin is above the bar; PULL-UP【美】引體向上〔在單槓上做的體能鍛鍊〕

chin·wag /ˈtʃɪnˌwæg; ˈtʃɪnwæg/ *n* [singular] *informal especially BrE* an informal conversation; CHAT[1]【非正式, 尤英】談天, 閒聊 —**chinwag** *v* [I]

2 **chip[1]** /tʃɪp; tʃɪp/ *n* [C]

3 **1 ▶MARK 記號◀** a small hole or mark on a plate, cup etc where a piece has broken off〔物品碰損後留下的〕瑕疵, 缺口: **[+in]** *There's a chip in this plate.* 這個盤子有個缺口。

2 ▶PIECE 片, 塊◀ a small piece of wood, stone, metal etc that has broken off something〔木、石、金屬等的〕碎片, 碎屑: *Wood chips covered the floor of the workshop.* 車間地板上滿是木屑。—see picture on page A7 參見A7頁圖

3 a) ▶FOOD 食物◀ *BrE* a long thin piece of potato cooked in oil【英】炸馬鈴薯[土豆]條; FRENCH FRY *AmE*【美】: *fish and chips* 炸魚和炸薯條 **b)** *AmE* a thin, flat round piece of potato cooked in very hot oil and eaten cold【美】炸薯片; CRISP[1] *BrE*【英】

4 ▶COMPUTER 電腦◀ a) a small piece of SILICON that has a set of complicated electrical connections on it and is used to store and PROCESS[2] (4) information in computers 微型集成電路片, 芯片, 矽片 **b)** the main MICROPROCESSOR of a computer 微處理器

5 have a chip on your shoulder to easily become offended or angry because you think you have been treated unfairly in the past〔因感到委屈而〕好爭吵, 好生氣; 記恨: *He's always had a chip on his shoulder about not going to university.* 他因沒能上大學而心懷憤懣。

6 be a chip off the old block *informal* to be very similar to your mother or father in appearance or character【非正式】〔外貌或性格〕酷似父親[母親]

7 ▶GAME 遊戲◀ a small flat coloured piece of plastic used in GAMBLING to represent a particular amount of money〔用於賭錢的〕籌碼

8 ▶SPORT 體育運動◀ a kick in football, RUGBY etc that makes the ball go high into the air for a short distance〔足球、橄欖球等運動中將球踢到空中的短距離的〕撮球

9 when the chips are down *spoken* a serious or difficult situation, especially one in which you realize what is really true or important【口】在重要關頭, 在緊急時刻: *When the chips are down, you've only got yourself to depend on.* 在緊要關頭, 你只有靠自己了。

10 have had your chips *BrE informal* to be in a situation in which you no longer have any hope of improvement【英, 非正式】失勢; 完蛋 —see also 另見 BLUE CHIP, **cash in your chips** (CASH[2]), COW CHIP

chip[2] *v* **chipped, chipping 1** [I,T] if something such as a plate chips or if you chip it, a small piece of it breaks off accidentally (使) 掉碎片; (使)〔邊緣等〕稍有破損; 弄缺: *Gary fell and chipped one of his front teeth.* 加里摔了一跤, 碰掉一顆門牙。| *These cheap plates chip really easily.* 這些廉價的盤子很容易碰破。**2** [T] to cut potatoes into thin pieces ready to be cooked in hot oil 將〔馬鈴薯〕切成小片[條] **3** [T] to hit or kick a ball in football, RUGBY etc so that it goes high into the air for a short distance〔足球、橄欖球等〕撮踢〔球〕

chip sth ↔ **away** *phr v* [T] to remove something, especially something hard that is covering a surface, by hitting it with a tool so that small pieces break off〔用工具將硬覆蓋物一點一點地〕清除, 劇掉: *Sandy chipped away the plaster covering the tiles.* 辛迪劇掉了瓷磚上的灰泥。| **[+at]** *Archaeologists were carefully chipping away at the rock.* 考古學家正仔細地敲那塊岩石。

chip away at sth *phr v* [T] to gradually make something less effective or destroy it〔逐步〕削弱; 損害: *The emphasis on testing has chipped away at teachers' autonomy.* 強調測試已逐步削弱了老師的自主權。

chip in *phr v* **1** [I] to interrupt a conversation by saying something that adds more detail 插嘴, 插話: *They kept chipping in with facts and figures.* 他們不時地插話, 提供一些事實和數據。**2** [I,T] if each person in a group chips in, they each give a small amount of money so that they can buy something together 共同出錢, 湊錢: *I'd like to chip in if you're getting Mike a birthday present.* 如果你要給邁克買生日禮物的話, 我也想湊一份。

chip sth ↔ **off** *phr v* [T] to remove something by breaking it off in small pieces〔一點一點〕去掉: *Bert chipped the paint off the front door and varnished it.* 伯特將前門上的油漆刮去, 塗上清漆。

chip·board /ˈtʃɪpˌbɔrd; ˈtʃɪpbɔːd/ *n* [U] a type of board made from small pieces of wood pressed together with glue 刨花板; 碎木膠合板

chip·munk /ˈtʃɪpmʌŋk; ˈtʃɪpmʌŋk/ *n* [C] a small American animal similar to a SQUIRREL[1] with black lines on its fur 花鼠, 金花鼠, 花栗鼠〔產於美洲, 背部有黑白花紋〕

chip·o·la·ta /ˌtʃɪpəˈlɑtə; ˌtʃɪpəˈlɑːtə◂/ *n* [C] *BrE* a small thin SAUSAGE【英】奇珀拉特小香腸

chip pan /ˈ· ·/ *n* [C] *BrE* a deep pan with a wire basket inside used for cooking food in hot oil, especially chips (CHIP[1] (3))【英】〔尤指炸薯條用的, 內有濾油網架的〕深平底鍋

chipped /tʃɪpt; tʃɪpt/ *adj* a cup, plate etc that is chipped has a small piece broken off the edge of it〔杯子、盤子等〕邊緣有缺口的 —see picture on page A18 參見A18頁圖

chip·per /ˈtʃɪpɚ; ˈtʃɪpə/ *adj AmE* cheerful and active【美】興高采烈的; 活潑的; 輕快的; 精力充沛的: *Grandma's over her illness and feeling pretty chipper again.* 奶奶病好了, 又恢復了以前的輕快幹練。

chip·pings /ˈtʃɪpɪŋz; ˈtʃɪpɪŋz/ *n* [plural] *BrE* small pieces of stone used when putting new surfaces on roads or railway tracks【英】〔鋪路或鐵軌用的〕碎石

chip shop /ˈ· ·/ also 又作 **chip·py** /ˈtʃɪpɪ; ˈtʃɪpi/ *informal*【非正式】*n* [C] *BrE* a shop that cooks and sells FISH AND CHIPS and other food【英】〔烹製及出售炸魚薯條及其他食物的〕薯條店

chi·rop·o·dist /kaɪˈrɑpədɪst; kɪ̵ˈrɒpədɪst/ *n* [C] *BrE* someone who is trained to examine and treat foot injuries and diseases【英】足病醫生; PODIATRIST *AmE*【美】—**chiropody** *n* [U]

chi·ro·prac·tic /ˌkaɪrəˈpræktɪk; ˈkaɪrəpræktɪk/ *n* [U] a way of treating illness by pressing on and moving the bones in someone's SPINE (1)〔對脊柱的〕指壓療法; 按摩療法 —**chiropractor** *n* [C]

chirp /tʃɝp; tʃɜːp/ also 又作 **chirrup** *v* [I] **1** if a bird or insect chirps, it makes short high sounds〔鳥或昆蟲〕發啁啾聲; 吱喳叫, 唧唧叫 **2** to speak in a cheerful, high voice 嘁嘁喳喳地說: *"Yes, all finished," he chirped.* "不錯, 全部完了。" 他喜氣洋洋地說。—**chirp** *n* [C]

chirp·y /ˈtʃɝpɪ; ˈtʃɜːpi/ *adj BrE informal* cheerful and active【英, 非正式】快活的; 活潑的: *You're very chirpy this morning – have you had some good news?* 你今天上午興高采烈的——有甚麼好消息嗎? —**chirpily** *adv* —**chirpiness** *n* [U]

chir·rup /ˈtʃɪrəp; ˈtʃɪrəp/ *v* [I] CHIRP〔鳥或昆蟲〕吱喳叫; 嘁嘁喳喳地說

chis·el[1] /ˈtʃɪzl; ˈtʃɪzəl/ *n* [C] a metal tool with a sharp edge, used to cut wood or stone 鑿子, 鑿刀 —see picture at 參見 TOOL[1] 圖

chisel[2] *v* **chiselled, chiselling** *BrE*【英】**chiseled, chiseling** *AmE*【美】[T] **1** to use a chisel to cut wood or stone into a particular shape〔用鑿子〕鑿; 雕; 刻: **chisel sth into/from/in etc** *Martin chiselled a hole in the door for the new lock.* 馬丁在門上鑿了一個洞以便安裝新鎖。 **2** *old-fashioned* to cheat or deceive someone, by getting more than you deserve【過時】哄騙, 欺騙 —**chiseller** *BrE*【英】**chiseler** *AmE*【美】*n* [C]

chit /tʃɪt; tʃɪt/ *n* [C] **1** an official note that shows that you are allowed to have something 便條; 字據; 賬單; 收條: *Take the chit to the counter and collect your books.* 把這張便條拿到櫃台取書。**2** *old-fashioned* a young woman who behaves badly and does not respect older people【過時】冒失的女孩[少婦]; 黃毛丫頭

chit-chat /ˈ· ·/ *n* [U] *informal* conversation about things that are not very important【非正式】聊天, 閒談: *boring social chit-chat* 乏味的社交客套話

chit·ter·lings /ˈtʃɪtə·lɪŋz; ˈtʃɪtəlɪŋz/ also 又作 **chit·lings** /ˈtʃɪtlɪŋz; ˈtʃɪtlɪŋz/ **chitlins** /-lɪnz; -lənz/ *n* [plural] the INTESTINE of a pig eaten as food, especially in the southern US〔尤在美國南部供食用的〕豬小腸

chit·ty /ˈtʃɪtɪ; ˈtʃɪti/ *n* [C] *BrE informal* a CHIT (1)【英, 非正式】便條; 字據; 收條; 賬單

chiv·al·rous /ˈʃɪvl̩rəs; ˈʃɪvəlrəs/ *adj* a man who is chivalrous behaves in a polite, kind, generous, and honourable way, especially towards women〔男子〕有騎士風範的; 對〔女士〕彬彬有禮的; 體貼殷勤的: *a chivalrous attitude towards the loser* 對輸家的騎士風度 —**chivalrously** *adv*

chiv·al·ry /ˈʃɪvl̩rɪ; ˈʃɪvəlri/ *n* [U] **1** behaviour that is honourable, kind, generous, and brave, especially men's behaviour towards women 騎士品質〈如仁慈、慷慨、勇猛、對女士彬彬有禮等〉**2** a system of religious beliefs and honourable behaviour that KNIGHTS in the Middle Ages were expected to follow〔中世紀的〕騎士制度[精神]

chive /tʃaɪv; tʃaɪv/ *n* [C usually plural 一般用複數] a long thin green plant that looks and tastes like an onion, and is used in cooking〔烹調用的〕香葱, 蝦夷葱

chiv·vy, chivy /ˈtʃɪvɪ; ˈtʃɪvi/ *v* **chivvied, chivvying** [T] *BrE* to try to make someone do something more quickly, especially in an annoying way【英】催促, 嘮叨: **chivvy sb along/up** *Go and see if you can chivvy the kids up a bit.* 去看看你能不能催孩子們快點。

chlo·ride /ˈklɔraɪd; ˈklɔːraɪd/ *n* [C,U] *technical* a chemical compound that is a mixture of chlorine and another substance【術語】氯化物: *sodium chloride* 氯化鈉, 食鹽

chlo·ri·nate /ˈklɔrɪˌnet; ˈklɔːrəneɪt/ *v* [T] to add chlorine to water to kill BACTERIA〔在水中〕加氯〔消毒〕

chlo·rine /ˈklɔrin; ˈklɔːriːn/ *n* [U] a greenish-yellow gas that is a chemical ELEMENT (=simple substance) and is often used to keep the water in swimming pools clean 氯, 氯氣

chlo·ro·fluo·ro·car·bon /ˌklɔroflʊəroˈkɑrbən; ˌklɔːrəʊflʊərəʊˈkɑːbən/ *n* [C] *technical* a CFC【術語】含氯氟烴

chlor·o·form /ˈklɔrəˌfɔrm; ˈklɒrəfɔːm/ *n* [U] a liquid that makes you become unconscious if you breathe it 氯仿, 哥羅仿, 三氯甲烷 —**chloroform** *v* [T]

chlo·ro·phyll /ˈklɔrəˌfɪl; ˈklɒrəfɪl/ *n* [U] the green-coloured substance in plants 葉綠素

choc /tʃɑk; tʃɒk/ *n* [C] *BrE informal* a CHOCOLATE (2)【英, 非正式】巧克力糖, 朱古力糖

choc·a·hol·ic /ˌtʃɑkəˈhɔlɪk; ˌtʃɒkəˈhɒlɪk/ *n* [C] another spelling of CHOCOHOLIC chocoholic 的另一種拼法

choc·cy /ˈtʃɑkɪ; ˈtʃɒki/ *n* [C] *BrE spoken* a CHOCOLATE (2)【英口】巧克力糖, 朱古力糖

choc-ice /ˈ· ·/ *n* [C] *BrE* a small block of ICE CREAM covered with chocolate【英】巧克力冰淇淋, 紫雪糕〔表面裹有一層巧克力的冰磚〕

chock /tʃɑk; tʃɒk/ *n* [C] a block of wood or metal put in front of a wheel, door etc to prevent it from moving〔固定車輪、門等的〕墊木; 塞塊; 楔子 —**chock** *v* [T]

chock-a-block /ˌtʃɑk ə ˈblɑk; ˌtʃɒk ə ˈblɒk◂/ *adj* [not before noun 不用於名詞前] full of people or things that are very close to each other 擠得滿滿的: **[+with]** *Disneyland was chock-a-block with people that day.* 迪士尼樂園那天擠滿了人。

chock-full /ˌ· ˈ·◂/ *adj* [not before noun 不用於名詞前] *informal* completely full【非正式】裝滿的, 塞滿的: **[+of]** *The bus was chock-full of people.* 公共汽車上擠滿了人。

choc·o·hol·ic also 又作 **chocaholic** /ˌtʃɑkəˈhɔlɪk; ˌtʃɒkəˈhɒlɪk/ *n* [C] someone who likes chocolate very much and eats it all the time 嗜吃巧克力的人

choco·late /ˈtʃɑkəlɪt; ˈtʃɒkl̩t/ *n* **1** [U] a sweet brown food eaten for pleasure or used to give foods such as cakes a special sweet taste 巧克力, 朱古力: *a chocolate bar* 一條巧克力 | **chocolate cake/cookie/ice cream etc** (=cake etc that tastes of chocolate) 巧克力味蛋糕/曲奇餅/冰淇淋等 | **milk chocolate** (=chocolate made with a lot of milk in it) 牛奶巧克力 | **dark** *AmE*【美】**/plain** *BrE*【英】**chocolate** (=chocolate that does not have much milk in it) 純巧克力 | **plain** *AmE*【美】**/cooking** *BrE*【英】**chocolate** (=chocolate with no milk in it, used for cooking) 烹調用純巧克力 | **white chocolate** (=chocolate that is white) 白巧克力 **2** [C] a small sweet that consists of something such as a nut or CARAMEL covered with chocolate 巧克力糖, 朱古力糖: *a box of chocolates* 一盒巧克力糖 **3** [C,U] a hot sweet drink made with milk and chocolate, or a cup of this drink 巧克力飲料; 一杯巧克力飲料

chocolate box /ˈ·· ·/ *adj* [only before noun 僅用於名詞前] *BrE informal* very pretty, but in a way that seems false or artificial【英, 非正式】漂亮得有點太假[人工化]的: *a chocolate box village* 圖畫般的村莊

chocolate chip cook·ie /ˌ··· ˈ··/ *n* [C] a kind of flat COOKIE containing small pieces of chocolate 巧克力碎曲奇

choco·lat·ey /ˈtʃɑkələtɪ; ˈtʃɒkl̩ti/ *adj* tasting or smelling of chocolate 巧克力味的

choice[1] /tʃɔɪs; tʃɔɪs/ *n*

1 ►ABILITY TO CHOOSE 選擇能力◄ [singular,U] the right to choose or the chance to choose between several things 選擇權: *Nowadays both men and women are able to exercise choice as to whom they marry.* 如今, 男女都能由自己選擇與誰人結婚。| **[+between]** *a genuinely free choice between candidates* 對候選人真正自由的選擇 | **[+of]** *a choice of accommodation* 食宿的選擇 | **have a choice** (=be able to choose) 能選擇, 有選擇的餘地 | **give sb a choice** *I'll give you a choice – we can go to the movies or out for a meal.* 我讓你來選擇 — 我們可以去看電影, 也可以出去吃飯。| **have no choice** (=be forced to do something because it is the only thing you can do) 沒有選擇餘地 *I had to go back. I was short of money and had no choice.* 我必須回去。我缺錢, 沒有別的選擇。| **leave sb with no choice** (=be forced to do something because it is the only thing you can do) 使某人別無選擇 *He was left with no choice but to resign.* 他別無選擇, 只能辭職。

2 ►ACT OF CHOOSING 選擇行為◄ [C] the act of choosing something 選擇, 挑選: *The board denied that financial considerations had influenced their choice.* 董事會否認說財政考慮影響了他們的選擇。| **[+of]** *Alf left the choice of where they would go to Jenny.* 阿爾夫讓珍妮決定到哪兒去。| **make a choice** (=choose) 作出選擇 *You should find out more before making your final choice.* 你在作最後選擇之前, 應該找出更多的資料。

3 ►RANGE TO CHOOSE FROM 選擇範圍◄ [singular] the range of people or things that you can choose from 選擇範圍: *There's a small general store in town, but I don't think there will be much choice.* 鎮上有一家小雜貨店, 但我想那裡的貨物品種不會很多。| **[+of]** *There is a choice of dozens of magazines aimed at women* readers. 可供女性讀者選擇的雜誌有幾十種。| **have a choice** *In your exam you will have a choice of five questions.* 考試中, 共有五個問題供你選擇。

4 ▶THING CHOSEN 選定的東西◀ [C usually singular 一般用單數] the person or thing that someone has chosen 被選中的東西[人], 抉擇: *The choices you make now will affect you for many years.* 你現在所作出的抉擇將會影響你許多年。| **[+of]** *The choice of Cannes as the venue for the conference was inspired.* 人們想到了於康城舉行會議的主意。| **first/second etc choice** *Italy was our second choice – all the flights to Greece were booked up.* 去意大利是我們的第二選擇, 因為飛往希臘的全部航班都已訂購一空了。

5 ▶THING YOU MAY CHOOSE 可以選擇的東西◀ [C] one of several things that you can choose 可供選擇之物: *The computer will show you several search choices.* 電腦將給你展示好幾種搜索辦法。

6 of your choice chosen by you without anything limiting what you can choose from 自選的, 隨便選擇: *Chill and serve with the garnishes of your choice.* 冷卻後加一些自己喜歡的裝飾菜再端上去。

7 by choice if you do something by choice, you do it because you want to do it and not because you are forced to do it 自己選擇的, 自願的: *The government has claimed that many people are homeless by choice.* 政府聲稱許多人流離失所是出於自願的。

8 the drug/treatment/newspaper etc of choice the thing that a certain group of people prefer to use 首選的藥/治療方法/報紙等: *It is the drug of choice for this type of illness.* 這是治療這種病的首選藥。—see also 另見 CHOOSE, HOBSON'S CHOICE

choice[2] *adj* **1** *formal* of a very high quality or standard, used especially of food【正式】〔尤指食物〕上等的, 精選的; 品質優良的: *choice apples* 優質蘋果 | *a choice collection of antique books* 一套精選的古書 **2** choice meat, especially BEEF[1] (1), is of a standard that is good but not the best〔尤指牛肉〕中上級的: *choice steak* 中上級牛排 **3 a few choice words/phrases** if you use a few choice words, you say exactly what you mean in an angry way 尖刻的話, 刻薄的話: *He dismissed the objection in a few choice words.* 他用幾句尖刻的話駁斥了反對的意見。

choir /kwaɪr; kwaɪə/ *n* [C] **1** a group of people who sing together, especially in a church or school〔學校或教堂等的〕唱詩班; 合唱團 **2** [usually singular 一般用單數] the part of a church in which the choir sits〔教堂中〕唱詩班的席位

choir·boy /ˈkwaɪrˌbɔɪ; ˈkwaɪəbɔɪ/ *n* [C] a young boy who sings in a church choir 唱詩班的男童歌手

choir loft /ˈ· ·/ *n* [C] *AmE* the part of a church, usually at the front, in which the choir sits【美】〔教堂中的〕唱詩班樓座

choir·mas·ter /ˈkwaɪrˌmæstɚ; ˈkwaɪəˌmɑːstə/ *n* [C] *BrE* someone who trains a choir【英】唱詩班的指揮; DIRECTOR (3) *AmE*【美】

choke[1] /tʃok; tʃəʊk/ *v*

1 ▶STOP BREATHING 停止呼吸◀ [I,T] to prevent someone from breathing, or to be prevented from breathing, because your throat is blocked or because there is not enough air (使) 窒息, (使) 呼吸困難: *The fumes were choking me.* 煙嗆得我呼吸困難。| **[+on]** *He choked to death on a fish bone.* 他被一根魚骨噎死。

2 ▶INJURE 傷害◀ [T] to prevent someone from breathing and hurt them by putting your hands around their throat and pressing on it 掐住…的脖子: *Stop it – you're choking me!* 住手——你讓我透不過氣來了!

3 ▶BLOCK 堵塞◀ [I,T] to fill an area or passage so that it is difficult to move through it 阻塞, 塞住, 堵塞: *Weeds choked the canal.* 雜草把水道塞住了。| *The roads were choked with traffic.* 路被川流不息的車輛堵塞了。

4 ▶VOICE 聲音◀ [I,T] if your voice is choked or you choke with laughter or anger, your emotions make your voice sound strange and not very loud 哽咽;〔笑得或氣得〕說不出話來: **[+with]** *"She's been raped," he said in a voice choked with emotion.* "她被姦污了。"他悲不自抑地哽咽着說。

5 ▶SAY STH 說出某事◀ [T] also 又作 **choke** sth ↔ **out** to say something one word or phrase at a time in a strange voice, because you are very upset or angry or because you have been laughing 哽住; 一字一頓地說: *"George," he choked out, "is that you, George?"* "喬治,"他一字一頓地說道:"是你嗎, 喬治?"

6 ▶SPORTS 體育◀ [I] *AmE informal* to fail at doing something, especially a sport, because there is a lot of pressure on you【美, 非正式】〔因有壓力而〕失敗, 輸: *They choked in the playoffs and lost the series 4 games to 2.* 他們在季後賽中未能發揮水準, 以 4:2 輸了比賽。

7 ▶PLANTS 植物◀ [T] to kill a plant by surrounding it with other plants that take away its light and room to grow 扼殺, 使枯萎: *The thistles choked the corn.* 那些薊把玉米全壓死了。

8 choke a horse *AmE spoken* if something is big enough to choke a horse, it is very big or larger than usual【美口】異常大: *a wad of bills big enough to choke a horse* 一大疊賬單

choke sth ↔ **back** *phr v* [T] to control your anger, sadness etc so that you do not show it 抑制, 強忍住: *I stood there trembling and trying to choke back the tears.* 我站在那裡, 渾身顫抖, 強忍住淚水。

choke sth ↔ **down** *phr v* [T] **1** to eat something with difficulty, especially because you are ill or upset 嚥, 硬吞〔食物〕: *He managed to choke down a sandwich.* 他勉強吞下一份三明治。**2** to choke something back 抑制, 強忍住

choke off *phr v* [T] to prevent someone from doing something or stop something happening 制止, 阻止; 壓制: *A higher interest rate will choke off the demand for money.* 高利率會減少貨幣需求。

choke up *phr v* [I] **be choked up** to be very upset about something 對…緊張; 不知所措: *She and Mark broke up last week, and she's pretty choked up about it.* 她和馬克上週鬧翻了, 對此她心煩意亂。

choke[2] *n* **1** [C] a piece of equipment in a vehicle that controls the amount of air going into the engine, and that is used to help the engine start〔汽車引擎的〕阻氣門 **2** [U] the controlling of the amount of air going into an engine by using this piece of equipment 用阻氣門阻氣: *Give it a bit more choke.* 把阻氣門開大一點兒。**3** [C] the act or sound of choking 窒息; 噎; 嗆[塞]住的聲音

choke chain /ˈ· ·/ *n* [C] a chain that is fastened around the neck of a dog to control it〔控制狗隻用的〕狗頸圈

choke·cher·ry /ˈtʃokˌtʃɛrɪ; ˈtʃəʊktʃeri/ *n* [C] a North American tree that produces small sour fruit 北美稠李樹

choked /tʃokt; tʃəʊkt/ *adj* [not before noun 不用於名詞前] *BrE* upset or angry【英】不安的; 生氣的; 心煩意亂的: *I was really choked to hear he'd died.* 聽到他的死訊, 我難過得說不出話來。

chok·er /ˈtʃokɚ; ˈtʃəʊkə/ *n* [C] a piece of jewellery or narrow cloth that fits closely around your neck 短項鏈; 剛好圍住脖子的項圈

chok·y, chokey /ˈtʃokɪ; ˈtʃəʊki/ *n* [U] **in choky** *BrE old-fashioned* in prison【英, 過時】被拘留; 蹲監獄

chol·er /ˈkɑlɚ; ˈkɒlə/ *n* [U] *literary* bad temper【文】怒氣, 暴躁脾氣

chol·e·ra /ˈkɑlərə; ˈkɒlərə/ *n* [U] a serious disease of the stomach and BOWELS that is caused by bad water or infected food 霍亂

chol·e·ric /ˈkɑlərɪk; ˈkɒlərɪk/ *adj literary* bad-tempered or angry【文】脾氣壞的; 生氣的: *an unbalanced choleric individual* 精神錯亂、脾氣暴躁的人

cho·les·te·rol /kəˈlɛstəˌrol; kəˈlestərɒl/ *n* [U] a chemical substance found in fat, blood, and other cells in your body, which doctors think may cause heart disease 膽固醇

chomp /tʃɑmp; tʃɒmp/ *v* [I+away/on] to bite food noisily 大聲地嚼: *chomping away on an apple* 大聲嚼着蘋果

choo-choo /ˈtʃu tʃu; ˈtʃuː tʃuː/ *n* [C] *spoken* a word meaning a train, used by or to children【口】〔兒語〕火車

1 1 **choose** /tʃuz; tʃuːz/ *v past tense* **chose** /tʃoz; tʃəʊz/ *past participle* **chosen** /ˈtʃozn̩; ˈtʃəʊzən/ [I,T] **1** to decide which one of a number of things, possibilities, people etc that you want because it is the best or most suitable 挑選, 選擇; 選取; 選中: **choose sth** *The party has finally chosen a woman as leader.* 這個政黨最終選了一位女士當領導。| **choose to do sth** *He chose to learn German rather than French in school.* 他在學校選修德語而非法語。| *Eleanor was chosen to play the role of Juliet.* 伊琳諾被選中扮演朱麗葉的角色。| **choose** *I don't know which one to get. You choose.* 我不知道該要哪個, 你選吧。| **[+between]** *Maria was forced to choose between happiness and duty.* 瑪麗亞被迫在幸福與責任之間作出選擇。| **choose whether/which/when etc** *You should choose where we eat – I don't mind.* 你來選擇到哪兒吃飯吧 —— 我無所謂。| **choose from** *a story chosen from a collection of fairy tales* 從一部童話故事集選出的一個故事 **2** to decide or prefer to do something or behave in a particular way 情願; 選定; 決定: *We can, if we choose, take the case to appeal.* 要是我們願意, 我們可以把案件上訴。| **choose to do sth** *We chose to ignore her rudeness.* 我們決定不理會她的無禮。**3 there is little/nothing to choose between** used when you think that two or more things are equally good and you cannot decide which is better 兩者不相上下[同樣的好], 難以取捨: *There was little to choose between the two candidates.* 兩名候選人不相上下。—see also 另見 CHOICE[1]

This graph shows how common different grammar patterns of the verb **choose** are. 本圖表所示為動詞 choose 構成的不同語法模式的使用頻率。

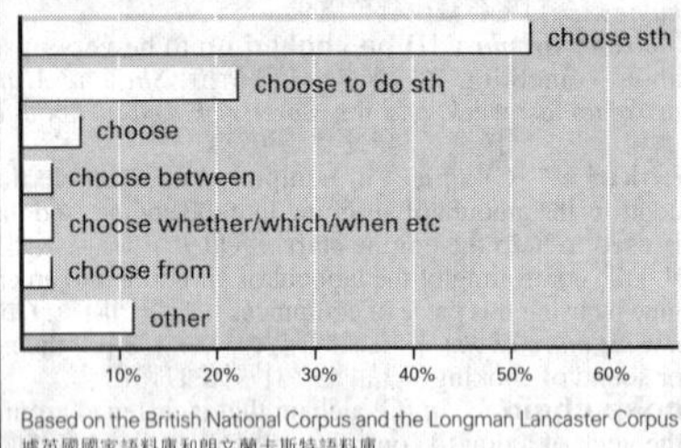

Based on the British National Corpus and the Longman Lancaster Corpus
據英國國家語料庫和朗文蘭卡斯特語料庫

choos·y, choosey /ˈtʃuzɪ; ˈtʃuːzi/ *adj especially BrE* someone who is choosy will only accept food, clothes, jobs etc that they consider to be very good; PICKY【尤英】愛挑剔的, 過分講究的: *She didn't much like the job, but she knew she couldn't afford to be choosy.* 她不太喜歡那份工作, 但她知道自己不能太挑剔。

chop[1] /tʃɑp; tʃɒp/ *v* **chopped, chopping**

1 ▶CUT STH 切某物◀ [T] also 又作 **chop up** to cut something such as food or wood into smaller pieces 將〔食物、木材等〕切碎; 劈開: *Can you chop some firewood?* 你能劈些木柴嗎? | **chop sth into pieces/chunks/segments** *Chop an onion into pieces.* 把洋葱切碎 —see picture on page A11 參見 A11 頁圖

2 ▶REDUCE STH 減少某物◀ [T] to reduce by a large amount the money that can be spent〔大幅度〕削減: *Next year's budget has been chopped by fifty percent.* 明年的財政預算被大幅度削減了百分之五十。

3 ▶SWING A TOOL 揮舞工具◀ [I] to swing a heavy tool such as an AXE[1] (1) in order to cut something〔用斧頭等〕砍, 劈: **[+away/at]** *Ben's been chopping away at that tree for two hours now.* 班恩砍那棵樹已有兩個小時了。

4 ▶MAKE A PATH 開路◀ [T] to make a path by cutting down plants 開路, 闢路: *The leader chopped a rough trail through the jungle.* 隊長在叢林中開闢出一條崎嶇的小路。| **chop your way through** *We chopped our way through the underbrush.* 我們披荊斬棘, 穿過了灌木叢。

5 chop and change *BrE informal* to keep changing your mind【英, 非正式】不停改變主意; 變化無常

6 ▶HIT STH 打中某物◀ [T] to hit something by moving your hand downward quickly and suddenly〔用手向下〕砸: *I chopped his wrist and he dropped the knife.* 我猛砸一下他的手腕, 使他手上的刀掉了下來。

chop sth ↔ **down** *phr v* [T] to make a tree or strong plant fall down by cutting it with a sharp tool such as an AXE[1] (1)〔用斧頭等利器〕砍倒, 伐倒

chop sth ↔ **off** *phr v* [T] to remove something by cutting it with a sharp tool such as an AXE[1] (1) so that it is no longer connected to something else〔用斧等〕砍掉, 砍斷: *Charles I had his head chopped off.* 查理一世被斬首了。

chop[2] *n* [C]

1 ▶MEAT 肉◀ a small flat piece of meat on a bone, usually cut from a sheep or pig〔羊、豬等〕帶骨的肉塊: *a grilled pork chop* 烤豬排

2 get the chop *BrE informal*【英, 非正式】**a)** to lose your job 被辭退, 被解雇: *Six more salesmen got the chop yesterday.* 昨天又有六名推銷員被炒了魷魚。**b)** to officially stop something or reduce the amount you are paying for it 被中止; 被削減: *The project got the chop in the last board meeting.* 這個項目在上一次董事會上被取消了。

3 be for the chop *BrE informal* to be very likely to be closed or stopped【英, 非正式】很可能停止[關閉]: *One of the three factories is for the chop.* 三家廠中有一家可能要關掉。

4 ▶WITH YOUR HAND 用手◀ a sudden downward movement with your hand 掌劈〔尤用掌側〕: *a karate chop* 空手道的切擊

5 ▶WITH A TOOL 用工具◀ the act of hitting something once with a sharp tool such as an AXE[1] (1)〔用斧頭等利器等〕砍, 劈

6 the chops *informal* the part of your face that includes your mouth and jaw【非正式】顎, 下巴: *I hit him in the chops.* 我打了他的下巴。

chop-chop /ˌ· ˈ·/ *interjection especially BrE* an expression used when you want someone to hurry【尤英】〔用於催促〕快點: *Come on! Chop-chop!* 來吧! 趕快!

chop·per /ˈtʃɑpɚ; ˈtʃɒpə/ *n* [C] **1** *BrE* a large square knife used for cutting large pieces of meat【英】大砍刀; 屠刀 **2** *informal* a HELICOPTER【非正式】直升飛機 **3** a type of MOTORCYCLE on which the front wheel is in front of the bars you use to control the vehicle instead of underneath them〔前輪位於車把之前的〕摩托車 **4 choppers** [plural] *slang* teeth【俚】牙齒

chopping board /ˈ·· ·/ also 又作 **chopping block** *n* [C] *especially BrE* a large piece of wood or plastic that you cut meat or vegetables on【尤英】砧板; CUTTING BOARD *AmE*【美】

chop·py /ˈtʃɑpɪ; ˈtʃɒpi/ *adj* choppy water has many small waves and is very rough to sail on〔水面〕浪花起伏的, 波浪滔滔的 —**choppiness** *n* [U]

chop·stick /ˈtʃɑpˌstɪk; ˈtʃɒp-stɪk/ *n* [C usually plural 一般用複數] one of the two thin sticks that you use to eat food in many countries in Asia 筷子 —see picture at 參見 STICK[2] 圖

chop su·ey /ˌtʃɑp ˈsuɪ; ˌtʃɒp ˈsuːi/ *n* [U] a Chinese dish made of pieces of vegetables and meat served with rice 炒雜碎〔用肉、蔬菜炒成的中國菜〕

cho·ral /ˈkɔrəl; ˈkɔːrəl/ *adj* [only before noun 僅用於名詞前] involving singing by a CHOIR (=group of people), or intended to be sung by a choir 唱詩班的; 合唱的; 合唱團的: *choral music* 唱詩班音樂 | *a choral concert* 合唱團音樂會

cho·rale /koˈræl; kɒˈrɑːl/ *n* [C] a piece of music praising God usually sung in a church by a CHOIR (=group of people)

讚美詩, 聖歌: *a Bach chorale* 巴赫譜曲的讚美詩

choral so·ci·e·ty /ˈ·· ,···/ *n* [C] *BrE* a group of people who sing together【英】合唱團

chord /kɔrd; kɔːd/ *n* [C] **1** a combination of two or more musical notes played at the same time〔音樂的〕和弦, 和音 **2 strike/touch a chord** to do or say something that people feel is familiar or true 引起〔某人〕內心共鳴; 打動: *His writings struck a chord in the hearts of the rebellious students.* 他的作品在那些反叛學生的心中引起了共鳴。**3** *technical* a straight line joining two points on a curve【術語】〔連接曲線上兩點的〕弦 —see picture at 參見 CIRCLE[1] 圖

chore /tʃɔr; tʃɔː/ *n* [C] **1** a job that you have to do regularly, especially work that you do to keep a house clean 家庭雜務; 日常零星工作: *household chores* 家庭雜務 **2** something you have to do that is very boring and unpleasant 令人厭煩的工作: *I find motorway driving a chore.* 我覺得在高速公路上駕車是件煩人的事。

chor·e·og·raph /ˈkɔriə,græf; ˈkɒriəgrɑːf/ *v* [T] to arrange how dancers should move during a performance 設計舞蹈動作, 編舞

chor·e·og·ra·phy /,kɔriˋɑgrəfi; ˌkɒriˈɒgrəfi/ *n* [U] the art of arranging how dancers should move during a performance 編舞(藝術); 舞蹈設計 —**choreographer** *n* [C]

chor·is·ter /ˈkɔrɪstə; ˈkɒrɪstə/ *n* [C] a singer in a CHOIR, especially a boy in a school choir that sings in a church 合唱團團員; 〔尤指〕唱詩班的男童歌手

chor·tle /ˈtʃɔrtḷ; ˈtʃɔːtl/ *v* [I] to laugh because you are amused or pleased about something 哈哈笑, 咯咯笑: *Harry chortled with delight.* 哈里高興地哈哈大笑。—**chortle** *n* [C]

cho·rus[1] /ˈkɔrəs; ˈkɔːrəs/ *n* [C]

1 ▶SONG 歌曲◀ the part of a song that is repeated after each VERSE (=main part in a song) 副歌, 疊句: *Everyone joined in the chorus.* 唱到歌曲的副歌時, 大家也跟着齊唱起來。

2 ▶SINGERS 歌手◀ a large group of people who sing together 合唱團, 歌詠隊: *the university chorus* 大學合唱團 —compare 比較 CHOIR (1)

3 ▶MUSIC 音樂◀ a piece of music written to be sung by a large group of people 合唱曲: *the Hallelujah Chorus* 哈利路亞合唱曲

4 ▶GROUP IN MUSICAL PLAY 音樂劇中的歌舞隊◀ a group of singers, dancers, or actors who act together in a show but do not have the main parts 歌舞隊: *a member of the chorus in the musical '42nd Street'* 音樂劇《第四十二街》歌舞隊的成員

5 a chorus of thanks/disapproval/protest etc something expressed by many people at the same time 異口同聲的感謝/反對/抗議: [+of] *Peggy's announcement brought a chorus of congratulation.* 佩姬的宣布引來一片祝賀聲。

6 in chorus if people say something in chorus, they say the same thing at the same time 一起; 同時; 一致: *"Mom!" the kids cried in chorus.* "媽!"孩子們同時叫了一聲。

7 a) ▶PLAY 戲劇◀ in ancient Greek plays, the chorus is the group of actors who gives explanations or opinions about the play〔古希臘戲劇中〕解釋劇情的演員 **b)** in English drama of the early 1600s, the chorus is usually one person who gives explanations or opinions about the play, especially at the beginning or the end〔17世紀早期英國戲劇中在開場或終場時〕進行解説者

chorus[2] *v* [T] if two or more people chorus something, they say it at the same time 同時説, 異口同聲地説: *"Good morning," we chorused.* "早安。"我們齊聲説道。

chorus girl /ˈ·· ·/ *n* [C] a woman who sings and dances in a group in a play or film〔戲劇或電影中的〕歌舞隊女演員

chorus line /ˈ·· ·/ *n* [C] a group of people who sing and dance together, especially while standing in a straight line, in a play or film〔戲劇或電影中的〕歌舞隊, 〔尤指〕排成一列的歌舞隊

chose /tʃoz; tʃəʊz/ the past tense of CHOOSE

cho·sen /ˈtʃozn; ˈtʃəʊzən/ the past participle of CHOOSE —see also 另見 WELL-CHOSEN

chow[1] /tʃaʊ; tʃaʊ/ *n* **1** [U] *slang* food【俚】食物, 食品: *It's chow time!* 該吃飯啦! **2** also 又作 **chow chow** /ˈ· ·/ [C] a dog with long thick fur and a dark-coloured tongue that first came from China 雄獅狗〔原產於中國的一種狗, 毛厚, 舌呈藍黑色〕

chow[2] *v*

chow down *phr v* [I] *AmE informal* to eat【美, 非正式】吃: *We were chowing down on powdered donuts.* 我們在吃糖粉油炸麵圈餅。

chow·der /ˈtʃaʊdə; ˈtʃaʊdə/ *n* [U] a thick soup usually made with CLAMS or fish, vegetables, and milk 雜燴海鮮湯, 周打湯

chow·der·head /ˈtʃaʊdə,hɛd; ˈtʃaʊdəhed/ *n* [singular] *AmE slang* a stupid person【美俚】傻瓜, 笨蛋

chow mein /ˈtʃaʊ ˋmen; ˌtʃaʊ ˈmeɪn/ *n* [U] a Chinese dish made with meat, vegetables and NOODLES 炒麵

Christ[1] /kraɪst; kraɪst/ *n* **1** also 又作 **Jesus Christ, Jesus** the man on whose life, death and teaching Christianity is based, believed to be the son of God 基督, 耶穌基督 —see 見 JESUS[1] (USAGE) **2 the Christ** the religious leader who Christians believe saves the world 救世主

Christ[2] *interjection* used to express annoyance, surprise etc 天哪!〔表示厭煩、吃驚等〕: *Christ! I've left my keys at home.* 天哪! 我把鑰匙留在家裡了。

chris·ten /ˈkrɪsn; ˈkrɪsən/ *v* [T] **1** to be officially given your name at a Christian religious ceremony soon after you are born 為…施洗禮, 〔在洗禮儀式上〕為…命名: **be christened** *She was christened Sarah.* 她在洗禮時給取名為莎拉。**2** to invent a name for someone because it describes them well 給…起綽號[雅號]: *Tony's colleagues christened him Romeo.* 東尼的同事給他起了綽號叫羅密歐。**3** *BrE informal* to use something for the first time【英, 非正式】首次使用: *We haven't christened the new dinner service yet.* 我們還未用過這套新餐具。

Chris·ten·dom /ˈkrɪsndəm; ˈkrɪsəndəm/ *n* [U] *old-fashioned* all the Christian people or countries in the world【過時】〔全世界所有的〕基督教徒; 基督教國家

chris·ten·ing /ˈkrɪsnɪŋ; ˈkrɪsənɪŋ/ *n* [C,U] a Christian religious ceremony at which someone is officially given their name and becomes a member of a Christian church 洗禮〔給某人施洗禮命名的儀式〕

Chris·tian[1] /ˈkrɪstʃən; ˈkrɪstʃən/ *n* [C] **1** a person who believes in the ideas taught by Jesus Christ or belongs to a Christian church 基督徒 **2** *informal* a good person【非正式】正派的人, 高尚的人, 好人

Christian[2] *adj* **1** believing the ideas taught by Jesus Christ, or belonging to a Christian church 基督教的; 信奉基督教的; 屬基督教教會的: *Christian ministers* 基督教牧師 **2** based on the ideas taught by Jesus Christ 基督教義的: *Christian doctrine* 基督教教義 **3** also 又作 **christian** behaving in a good, kind way 仁慈的, 慈悲的: *Laughing at his misfortune wasn't a very christian act.* 嘲笑他的不幸不是仁慈的行為。

Christian e·ra /,·· ˈ··/ *n* [singular] the period from the birth of Christ to the present 基督紀元; 公元; 西曆紀元

Chris·ti·an·i·ty /,krɪstʃɪˋænətɪ; ˌkrɪstiˈænǝti/ *n* [U] the religion based on the life and teachings of Jesus Christ 基督教

Christian name /ˈ·· ·/ *n* [C] the name someone is given when they are christened (CHRISTEN (1)), or someone's first name 教名〔洗禮時所取名字〕, 名字; GIVEN NAME *especially AmE*【尤美】: *His Christian name is Michael.* 他名叫米高。

Christian Sci·ence /,·· ˈ··/ *n* [U] a religion started in America in 1866, which includes the belief that illnesses can be cured by faith 基督教科學派〔1866年於美國創立, 主張靠信仰即可治癒疾病的教派〕—**Christian Scientist** *n* [C]

Christ·mas /ˈkrɪsməs; ˈkrɪsməs/ *n* [C,U] **1** also 又作

Christmas Day December 25th, the day when Christians celebrate the birth of Christ 聖誕節〔12月25日〕: *Are you going home for Christmas?* 你回家過聖誕節嗎? **2** the period before and after this day 聖誕節節期: *It snowed all over Christmas.* 整個聖誕節期間都在下雪。

Christmas cake /ˈ·· ·/ *n* [C,U] a special cake eaten in Britain at Christmas〔英國人聖誕節時吃的〕聖誕蛋糕

Christmas card /ˈ·· ·/ *n* [C] a card that you send to friends and relatives at Christmas with your good wishes 聖誕(賀)卡

Christmas car·ol /ˌ·· ˈ··/ *n* [C] a Christian song sung at Christmas; CAROL[1] 聖誕頌歌

Christmas cook·ie /ˌ·· ˈ··/ *n* [C] a COOKIE eaten in the US at Christmas〔美國人聖誕節時吃的〕聖誕小甜餅

Christmas crack·er /ˌ·· ˈ··/ *n* [C] a brightly coloured tube of paper containing a small toy that two people pull at Christmas parties 聖誕彩包爆竹〔一種拉開時噼啪作響的彩紙筒, 裡面裝有小玩具〕

Christmas Day /ˌ·· ˈ·/ *n* [C,U] December 25th, the day when Christians celebrate the birth of Christ 聖誕節〔12月25日, 基督徒慶祝耶穌誕生的日子〕

Christmas din·ner /ˌ·· ˈ··/ *n* [C] a special meal eaten on Christmas Day, consisting mainly of TURKEY (2) and vegetables, followed by Christmas pudding 聖誕大餐

Christmas Eve /ˌ·· ˈ·/ *n* [C,U] the day before Christmas Day 聖誕前夕, 平安夜, 聖誕夜

Christmas pud·ding /ˌ·· ˈ··/ *n* [C] a PUDDING containing a lot of dried fruit eaten at Christmas 聖誕布丁

Christmas stock·ing /ˌ·· ˈ··/ *n* [C] a long sock which children leave out on Christmas Eve to be filled with presents 聖誕襪〔小孩子在聖誕夜掛起來盛放禮物的長襪子〕

Christ·mas·sy /ˋkrɪsməsɪ; ˈkrɪsməsi/ *adj informal* typical of or connected with Christmas【非正式】聖誕節的; 與聖誕節有關的: *a nice Christmassy feeling* 一種美妙的過聖誕節的感覺

Christ·mas·time /ˋkrɪsməsˌtaɪm; ˈkrɪsməstaɪm/ *n* [U] the period during Christmas when people celebrate 聖誕節節期

Christmas tree /ˈ·· ·/ *n* [C] a FIR tree either real or artificial that you decorate specially for Christmas 聖誕樹

chro·mat·ic /kroˋmætɪk; krəʊˈmætɪk/ *adj* **1** connected with or containing bright colours 彩色的, 顏色鮮豔的 **2** related to the musical scale which consists of SEMITONES 半音(階)的: *the chromatic scale* 半音階

chrome /krom; krəʊm/ *n* [U] a hard ALLOY (=a combination of metals) of chromium and other metals used for covering objects with a shiny protective surface 鉻合金

chrome yel·low /ˌ· ˈ··◂/ *n* [U] a very bright yellow colour 鉻黃色, 鮮黃色

chro·mi·um /ˋkromɪəm; ˈkrəʊmiəm/ *n* [U] a blue or white metal that is an ELEMENT (=simple substance) and is used for covering objects with a shiny protective surface 鉻: *chromium plated* 鍍鉻的

chro·mo·some /ˋkroməˌsom; ˈkrəʊməsəʊm/ *n* [C] *technical* a part of every living cell that is shaped like a thread which controls the character, shape etc that a plant or animal has【術語】染色體: *x and y chromosomes* x 和 y 染色體

chron- /krɑn; krɒn/ *prefix* another form of the prefix CHRONO- 前綴 chrono- 的另一種形式

chron·ic /ˋkrɑnɪk; ˈkrɒnɪk/ *adj* [usually before noun 一般用於名詞前] **1** a chronic disease or illness is one that cannot be cured〔疾病〕慢性的, 長期的: *He's been suffering from chronic arthritis for years now.* 他患慢性關節炎好幾年了。**2** a problem or difficulty that you cannot get rid of or that keeps coming back〔問題、困難〕長期的, 反覆出現的: *a chronic shortage of language teachers* 語文教師長期不足 | *chronic unemployment* 長期的失業問題 **3 chronic alcoholic/gambler etc** someone who suffers from a particular problem or type of behaviour for a long time and cannot stop 酒鬼/沉迷賭博的人: *Jake was a chronic alcoholic who could not hold down a job.* 傑克酗酒成性, 甚麼工作也幹不長。**4** *BrE informal* extremely bad【英, 非正式】惡劣的; 糟透的: *Don't go to that new restaurant, I've heard the food's chronic.* 不要去那家新餐館, 聽說那兒的食物糟透了。—**chronically** /-klɪ; -kli/ *adv*: *chronically ill* 長期患病的

chron·i·cle¹ /ˋkrɑnɪkl; ˈkrɒnɪkəl/ *n* [C] a written record of a series of events, especially historical events, written in the order in which they happened 編年史, 年代記: [+of] *The book provides a detailed chronicle of the events leading up to his death.* 這本書詳細記載了導致他死亡的一系列事件。

chronicle² *v* [T] to give an account of a series of events in the order in which they happened 將〔一系列事件〕載入編年史中; 記錄〔大事〕: *The effect of her parents' separation on her childhood is carefully chronicled in the book.* 父母分居對她童年造成的影響都詳細地記載在這本書中。—**chronicler** *n* [C]

chrono- /krɑno; krɒnəʊ/ also 又作 **chron-** *prefix* concerning time 有關時間的: *a chronometer* (=instrument for measuring time very exactly) 精密記時儀器

chron·o·graph /ˋkrɑnəˌgræf; ˈkrɒnəgrɑːf/ *n* [C] a scientific instrument for measuring and recording periods of time 計時儀[器]; 秒錶

chron·o·log·i·cal /ˌkrɑnəˋlɑdʒɪkl; ˌkrɒnəˈlɒdʒɪkəl◂/ *adj* arranged according to when something happened 按時間先後順序排列的: **chronological order** *Put the following battles in chronological order.* 將下列戰爭按時間順序排列出來。—**chronologically** /-klɪ; -kli/ *adv*

chro·nol·o·gy /krəˋnɑlədʒɪ; krəˈnɒlədʒi/ *n* [U] the science of giving times and dates to events 年代學

chro·nom·e·ter /krəˋnɑmətɚ; krəˈnɒmɪtə/ *n* [C] a very exact clock for measuring time, used for scientific purposes 精密記時鐘錶

chrys·a·lis /ˋkrɪslɪs; ˈkrɪsəlɪs/ *n* [C] a MOTH or BUTTERFLY at the stage of development when it has a hard outer shell, before being a LARVA and an adult 蝶蛹; 蛾蛹

chry·san·the·mum /krɪsˋænθəməm; krɪˈsænθɪməm/ *n* [C] a garden plant with large brightly coloured flowers 菊(花)

chub·by /ˋtʃʌbɪ; ˈtʃʌbi/ *adj* fat in a pleasant healthy-looking way 圓圓胖胖的; 豐滿的: *I was chubby even as a baby.* 我還是嬰孩時就胖嘟嘟的。| *chubby cheeks* 圓胖的臉頰 —**chubbiness** *n* [U] —see 見 FAT¹ (USAGE)

chuck¹ /tʃʌk; tʃʌk/ *v* [T] *informal*【非正式】**1** to throw something in a careless or relaxed way〔胡亂或隨便地〕扔, 拋: **chuck sth on/out of/into etc** *Tania chucked her bag down on the sofa.* 塔尼亞把袋子胡亂扔在沙發上。| **chuck sb sth** *Chuck me that magazine, would you?* 把那本雜誌扔給我好嗎? **2 chuck sb** *BrE* to end a romantic relationship with someone【英】甩掉〔某人〕: *Why did Judy chuck him?* 為甚麼茱迪會甩了他呢? **3 chuck sb under the chin** to gently touch someone under their chin, especially a child 輕撫…的下巴〔尤對小孩〕

chuck sth ↔ **away/out** *phr v* [T] to throw something away 扔掉: *We had to chuck a lot of stuff out when we moved.* 我們搬家時, 不得不扔掉很多雜物。

chuck sb ↔ **out** *phr v* [T] to make someone leave a place, especially because they are behaving badly 迫使〔某人〕離開; 趕走, 攆走: *We got chucked out of the pub last night.* 昨晚我們被攆出酒館。

chuck sth ↔ **in** *phr v* [T] *BrE* to stop doing something, especially something that is boring or annoying【英】停止; 放棄: *What on earth made him chuck his job in so suddenly?* 究竟是甚麼原因使他這麼突然地辭掉工作呢?

chuck up *phr v* [I,T] *especially BrE slang* to VOMIT¹【尤英, 俚】嘔吐: *I was chucking up all night.* 我吐了一晚上。

chuck² *n* **1** [C] part of a machine that holds something so that it does not move〔機器的〕卡盤, 夾盤 **2** *spoken* a word used to address someone in some parts of Northern England【口】嗨〔英格蘭北部一些地區稱呼的用語〕

chuck·le /ˋtʃʌkḷ; ˈtʃʌkəl/ *v* [I] to laugh quietly 低聲輕笑; 暗自笑: *What are you chuckling about?* 你在偷笑甚麼? —**chuckle** *n* [C]

chuck·le·head /ˋtʃʌkḷˌhɛd; ˈtʃʌkəlhed/ *n* [C] *AmE informal* a stupid person【美, 非正式】傻瓜, 笨蛋

chuck steak /ˌ·ˈ·/ *n* [U] meat that comes from just above the shoulder of an animal〔動物的〕頸肉; 牛肩肉排

chuck wag·on /ˈ· ˌ··/ *n* [C] *AmE old-fashioned* a vehicle that carries food for a group of people【美, 過時】流動炊事車

chuffed /tʃʌft; tʃʌft/ *adj BrE informal* very pleased or happy【英, 非正式】愉快的, 高興的: *He's really chuffed about passing the exam.* 他因通過考試而滿心歡喜。

chug /tʃʌg; tʃʌg/ *v* **chugged, chugging** [I always+adv/prep] if a car, train etc chugs, it moves slowly making a repeated low sound〔汽車、火車等〕發出嘎嚓聲地緩慢前進: [**+along/up/around etc**] *The boat chugged out of the harbour.* 小船突突地響着駛出港口。—**chug** *n* [C usually singular 一般用單數]

chug-a-lug /ˈ· ·ˌ·/ *v* [T] *AmE informal* to drink all of something in a glass or bottle without stopping【美, 非正式】一口氣喝完: *He chug-a-lugged the entire thing.* 他咕嚕咕嚕一口氣全喝完了。

chum¹ /tʃʌm; tʃʌm/ *n* [C] *old-fashioned* a good friend【過時】好朋友: *Freddie's an old school chum of mine.* 弗雷迪是我的一位老校友。

chum²

chum up *phr v* [I] *old-fashioned* to become someone's friend【過時】(與…)成為朋友: [**+with**] *She soon chummed up with the girl in the next room.* 她不久就與隔壁房間的女孩成了好朋友。

chum·my /ˋtʃʌmɪ; ˈtʃʌmi/ *adj old-fashioned* friendly【過時】友好的 —**chummily** *adv* —**chumminess** *n* [U]

chump /tʃʌmp; tʃʌmp/ *n* [C] *BrE*【英】**1** *old-fashioned* someone who is silly or not very clever【過時】傻瓜, 笨蛋 **2 chump chop/steak** a thick piece of meat with a bone in it 厚肉塊/大塊牛排 **3 be off your chump** *old-fashioned* to be doing or intend to do something extremely silly【過時】發瘋, 發狂

chun·der /ˋtʃʌndɚ; ˈtʃʌndə/ *v* [I] *informal* to VOMIT¹【非正式】嘔吐

chunk /tʃʌŋk; tʃʌŋk/ *n* [C] **1** a large piece of something that does not have an even shape 厚塊, 大塊: [**+of**] *a chunk of cheese* 一大塊乳酪 —see picture on page A7 參見A7頁圖 **2** a large part or amount of something 大量; 大部分: *The rent takes a large chunk out of my monthly salary.* 房租佔去我薪水中的一大部分。| *It's sad to see another chunk of the old Liverpool gone.* 看到利物浦老城很大一部分又消失了, 真傷心。

chunk·y /ˋtʃʌŋkɪ; ˈtʃʌŋki/ *adj* **1** thick, solid and heavy 厚重的: *She wore a lot of chunky silver jewellery.* 她戴着很多沉甸甸的銀首飾。**2** someone who is chunky has a broad, heavy body〔人〕壯實的

1 **church** /tʃɝtʃ; tʃɜːtʃ/ *n* **1** [C] a building where Chris-
1 tians go to worship 教堂, 禮拜堂 **2** [U] the religious ceremonies in a church〔教堂的〕禮拜儀式: *Mrs Dobson invited us to dinner after church.* 多布森太太邀請我們做完禮拜後到她家吃飯。**3 the church** the profession of the CLERGY (=priests and other people employed by the church) 牧師(的職位); 神職人員 **4** [singular,U] the institution of the Christian religion〔基督教〕教會: *separation of church and state* 政教分離

church·go·er /ˋtʃɝtʃˌgoɚ; ˈtʃɜːtʃˌgəʊə/ *n* [C] someone who goes to church regularly 常去教堂做禮拜的人

church·key /ˋtʃɝtʃˌki; ˈtʃɜːtʃkiː/ *n* [C] *AmE informal*【美, 非正式】a BOTTLE OPENER 開瓶器

church·man /ˋtʃɝtʃˌmən; ˈtʃɜːtʃmən/ *n* [C] *plural* **churchmen** /-mən; -mən/ a priest; CLERGYMAN 牧師; 神職人員

Church of Eng·land /ˌ· · ˈ··◂/ *n* **the Church of England** the state church in England, the official leader of which is the Queen or King 英國國教會, 英國聖公會 —**Church of England** also 又作 **C of E** *adj*

Church of Scot·land /ˌ· · ˈ··◂/ *n* [singular] the state church in Scotland 蘇格蘭長老會

church school /ˈ· ˌ·/ *n* [C] a school in Britain that is partly controlled by the church〔英國的〕教會學校

church·war·den /ˋtʃɝtʃˋwɔrdṇ; ˌtʃɜːtʃˈwɔːdn/ *n* [C] someone who looks after church property and money〔負責教會財產和財務的〕教會執事

church·yard /ˋtʃɝtʃˌjɑrd; ˈtʃɜːtʃjɑːd/ *n* [C] a piece of land around a church where people are buried〔在教堂周圍的〕教堂墓地

churl·ish /ˋtʃɝlɪʃ; ˈtʃɜːlɪʃ/ *adj* bad-tempered or impolite 脾氣不好的; 無禮的: *It seemed churlish to refuse his invitation.* 不接受他的邀請似乎不太禮貌。—**churl** *n* [C] —**churlishly** *adv* —**churlishness** *n* [U]

churn¹ /tʃɝn; tʃɜːn/ *n* [C] **1** a container used for shaking milk in order to make it into butter〔製造黃油的〕攪乳器 **2** *BrE* a large metal container used to carry milk in【英】〔金屬〕奶桶 —see picture at 參見 CONTAINER 圖

churn² *v* **1** [I] if your stomach churns you feel sick because you are nervous or frightened〔胃因緊張或驚慌而〕劇烈攪動: *My stomach was churning on the day of the exam.* 考試那天我的胃裡直翻騰。**2** [T] to make milk by using a churn〔用攪乳器〕攪〔乳〕**3** also 又作 **churn up** [I,T] if water churns or if it is churned, it moves about violently (使)〔水〕劇烈翻騰

churn sth ↔ **out** *phr v* [T] to produce large quantities of something, especially without caring about quality〔不顧質量〕大量生產, 粗製濫造: *The factory churns out thousands of these awful plastic toys every week.* 這家工廠每週生產出成千上萬個這類劣質的塑料玩具。

churn up *phr v* **1** [T **churn** sth ↔ **up**] to damage the surface of something, especially by walking on it or driving a vehicle over it〔尤指由於行走或車輛輾壓而〕損壞〔某物的表面〕: *The lawn had been churned up by the tractor.* 拖拉機將草坪破壞了。**2** [T **churn** sb **up**] to make someone upset or angry 使〔人〕緊張[生氣]: *The argument had left her feeling all churned up.* 這場爭論使她感到非常生氣。**3** [I,T] to CHURN² (3) (使)〔水〕劇烈翻騰

chute /ʃut; ʃuːt/ *n* [C] **1** a long narrow structure that slopes down, used for sliding things from one place to another or for people to slide down 滑道; 斜槽; 溜槽; 滑梯: *The pool had the added attraction of a water chute.* 那個泳池的又一吸引人之處是一條水上滑梯。**2** *informal* a PARACHUTE¹【非正式】降落傘

chut·ney /ˋtʃʌtnɪ; ˈtʃʌtni/ *n* [U] a mixture of fruits, hot-tasting seeds and sugar, that is eaten with meat or cheese 酸辣醬〔水果、辣籽、糖等混合物, 與肉或乳酪一起食用〕: *mango chutney* 芒果酸辣醬

chutz·pah /ˋhʊtspə; ˈhʊtspə/ *n* [U] *slang* too much confidence, which is often considered to be rude; NERVE¹ (3)【俚】厚臉皮; 放肆, 肆無忌憚: *He wouldn't have the chutzpah to deliver that message.* 他不至於臉皮那麼厚去傳遞那個消息。

CIA /ˌsi aɪ ˋe; ˌsiː aɪ ˈeɪ/ *n* **the CIA** the Central Intelligence Agency; the department of the US government that collects information about other countries, especially secretly〔美國〕中央情報局 —compare 比較 FBI

ciao /tʃaʊ; tʃaʊ/ *interjection informal* used to say goodbye【非正式】再見!

ci·ca·da /sɪˋkedə; sɪ̇ˈkɑːdə/ *n* [C] an insect that lives in hot countries, has large transparent wings, and makes a high singing noise 蟬

cic·a·trice /ˋsɪkətrɪs; ˈsɪkətrɪs/ also 又作 **cic·a·trix** /-trɪks; -trɪks/ *n* [C] *technical* a mark remaining from a wound; SCAR¹ (1)【術語】疤痕; 痂; 傷痕

ci·ce·ro·ne /ˌsɪsəˋronɪ; ˌsɪsəˈrəʊni/ *n* [C] *literary* someone who shows tourists interesting places; GUIDE¹ (1a)【文】觀光導遊

CID /ˌsi aɪ ˋdi; ˌsiː aɪ ˈdiː/ *n* **the CID** the Criminal Investigation Department; the department of the British police

that deals with very serious crimes〔英國〕刑事偵緝部
-cide /saɪd; saɪd/ *suffix* [in nouns 構成名詞] another form of the suffix -ICIDE 後綴 -icide 的另一種形式: *genocide* (=killing a whole race of people) 種族屠殺 —**-cidal** [in adjectives 構成形容詞] —**-cidally** [in adverbs 構成副詞]
ci·der /ˋsaɪdɚ; ˈsaɪdə/ *n* [C,U] **1** *BrE* an alcoholic drink made from apples or a glass of this drink【英】(一杯) 蘋果酒 **2** *AmE* also 又作 **sweet cider** a non-alcoholic drink made from apples or a glass of this drink【美】(一杯) 蘋果汁 —see also 另見 HARD CIDER *AmE*【美】
ci·gar /sɪˋgɑr; sɪˈgɑː/ *n* [C] a thing that people smoke made from tobacco leaves that have been rolled into a thick tube shape 雪茄煙
2 3 **cig·a·rette** /ˌsɪgəˋrɛt; ˌsɪgəˈret/ *n* [C] a thin tube of paper filled with finely cut tobacco that people smoke 香煙: *a packet of cigarettes* 一包香煙
cigarette butt /ˈ·ˈ· ˌ·/ also 又作 **cigarette end** *especially BrE*【尤英】*n* [C] the part of a cigarette that remains when someone has finished smoking it 煙蒂, 煙頭
cigarette hol·der /ˈ·ˈ· ˌ··/ *n* [C] a narrow tube for holding a cigarette 香煙煙嘴
cigarette light·er /ˈ·ˈ· ˌ··/ also 又作 **lighter** *n* [C] a small object that produces a flame for lighting cigarettes, CIGARS etc 打火機
cigarette pa·per /ˈ·ˈ· ˌ··/ *n* [C,U] thin paper used to make your own cigarettes 捲煙紙
cig·gy /ˋsɪgɪ; ˈsɪgi/ *n* [C] *BrE spoken* a cigarette【英口】香煙
ci·lan·tro /sɪˋlɑntro; sɪ̇ˈlɑːntrəʊ/ *n* [U] *AmE* the strong-tasting leaves of a small plant, used for giving a special taste to food, especially in Asian and Mexican cooking【美】〔尤用於亞洲和墨西哥菜中調味的〕芫荽葉; CORIANDER *especially BrE*【尤英】
C-in-C /ˌsi ɪn ˋsi; ˌsiː ɪn ˈsiː/ *n* an abbreviation of 縮寫= COMMANDER IN CHIEF
cinch[1] /sɪntʃ; sɪntʃ/ *n* [singular] *informal*【非正式】**1** something that is very easy 極容易的事情: *"How was the exam?" "Oh, it was a cinch!"* "考試怎麼樣?" "噢, 容易得很!" **2** something that will definitely happen 必然發生的事: *It's an absolute cinch that this horse is going to win!* 這匹馬肯定會贏!
cinch[2] *v* [T] *AmE*【美】**1** to pull a belt, STRAP[1] etc tightly around something 給…繫上帶子 **2** to do something so that you can be sure something will happen 確保, 穩保: *They cinched a place in the play-off.* 他們在季後賽中穩奪一個席位。
cinch[3] *adj AmE* **cinch belt/strap etc** a thin belt etc, made of ELASTIC[1], that you pull so that it is very tight【美】有彈性的帶子
cinc·ture /ˋsɪŋktʃɚ; ˈsɪŋktʃə/ *n* [C] *literary* a belt【文】束帶, 腰帶
cin·der /ˋsɪndɚ; ˈsɪndə/ *n* [C usually plural 一般用複數] a very small piece of burnt wood, coal etc 煤渣; 炭渣; 爐渣: *a cold hearth full of cinders* 滿是爐渣的冷卻了的爐床 | **burnt to a cinder** (=completely burnt) 烤焦 *The cake was burnt to a cinder.* 蛋糕給烤焦了。
cinder block /ˈ·· ·/ *n* [C] *AmE* a large brick for building made from CEMENT and cinders【美】煤渣磚; BREEZE-BLOCK *BrE*【英】
cinder track /ˈ·· ·/ *n* [C] a race track covered with cinders 煤渣跑道
cine- /sɪnɪ; sɪni/ *prefix BrE* concerning films or the film industry【英】電影 (業) 的: *a cine-camera* 電影攝影機
cine-cam·e·ra /ˋsɪnɪˌkæmərə; ˈsɪni ˌkæmərə/ *n* [C] *BrE* a camera for making moving films, rather than photographs【英】電影攝影機
cine-film /ˋsɪnɪ fɪlm; ˈsɪni fɪlm/ *n* [U] *BrE* film used in a cine-camera【英】電影膠片
3 **cin·e·ma** /ˋsɪnəmə; ˈsɪnɪ̇mə/ *n especially BrE*【尤英】**1** [C] a building in which films are shown 電影院; MOVIE THEATER *AmE*【美】: *What's on at the cinema?* 電影院在上映甚麼電影? **2** [singular,U] the skill or industry of making films 電影製作; 電影業: *a leading figure in Italian cinema* 意大利電影界數一數二的人物
cin·e·mat·ic /ˌsɪnəˋmætɪk; ˌsɪnɪ̇ˈmætɪk◂/ *adj* connected with films for the cinema 電影的: *a lack of cinematic output* 電影作品的缺乏
cin·e·ma·to·gra·phy /ˌsɪnəməˋtɑgrəfɪ; ˌsɪnɪ̇məˈtɒgrəfi/ *n* [U] *technical* the skill or study of making films【術語】電影攝影術[學]; 電影製片術[學]: *with impressive cinematography by Robert Surtees* 羅伯特·瑟蒂斯高超的攝影術 —**cinematographer** *n* [C]
cin·na·mon[1] /ˋsɪnəmən; ˈsɪnəmən/ *n* [U] a sweet-smelling substance used for giving a special taste to cakes etc 桂皮香料; 肉桂
cinnamon[2] *adj* having a light yellowish-brown colour 淺黃褐色的, 肉桂色的
ci·pher[1], **cypher** /ˋsaɪfɚ; ˈsaɪfə/ *n* [C] **1** a system of secret writing; CODE[1] (4) 密碼; 暗號 **2** someone who is not important and has no power or influence 不重要[無影響力]的人: *a mere cypher* 無足輕重的人物 **3** *literary* the number 0; zero【文】〔數字〕零
cipher[2] *v* [T] to put a message into CODE (=a system of secret writing) 把…譯成密碼 —compare 比較 DECIPHER
cir·ca /ˋsɝkə; ˈsɜːkə/ *prep formal* used before a date to show that something happened on nearly, but not exactly that date【正式】〔用於日期前〕大約: *manuscripts dating from circa 1100* 可追溯到大約 1100 年的手稿
cir·ca·di·an /sɝˋkedɪən; sɜːˈkeɪdiən/ *adj* [only before noun 僅用於名詞前] *technical* connected with a period of 24 hours, used especially when talking about changes in people's bodies【術語】〔尤指體內變化〕晝夜節律的, 生理節奏的, 以 24 小時為週期的
cir·cle[1] /ˋsɝkl̩; ˈsɜːkəl/ *n* [C]

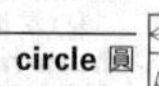

circle 圓

1 ►SHAPE 形狀◄ a completely round shape, like the letter O 圓 (形): *Draw a circle 10cm in diameter.* 畫一個直徑10厘米的圓。| *Cut the pastry into circles.* 將油酥麵團切成圓狀。| **perfect circle** (=exactly round) 完美的圓 —see picture at 參見 SHAPE[1] 圖
2 ►GROUP OF PEOPLE/THINGS 一組人/物◄ a group of people or things forming a round shape 排成一圈的人[物]: *The children stood round in a circle.* 小孩們站成一圈。| *a circle of chairs* 一圈椅子
3 ►SOCIAL GROUP 社會團體◄ also 又作 **circles** a group of people who know each other 圈子, …界: *a large circle of friends* 交友甚廣 | *well-known in fashionable circles* 在時裝界很出名 | **move in different circles** (=have different friends, jobs, interests etc) 有不同的活動圈子〔有不同朋友、職業、愛好等〕
4 political/literary/scientific etc circles the people who are involved in politics, literature, science etc 政界/文學界/科學界等: *These ideas have caused an uproar in literary and academic circles.* 這些看法在文學界和學術界引起了軒然大波。
5 ►THEATRE 劇院◄ *BrE* the upper floor of a theatre, that has seats arranged in curved rows【英】〔有半圓形樓座的〕樓廳包廂; BALCONY (2) *especially AmE*【尤美】—see picture at 參見 THEATRE 圖
6 go round in circles to think or argue about something without deciding anything or making progress 繞圈子; 白忙, 瞎忙: *Let's have a break – we're just going round in circles.* 休息一下吧 — 我們忙了半天也沒個頭緒。
7 come/turn full circle if a process, argument etc comes full circle, it ends in the same situation in which it began 循環, 兜了一圈回到原位; 週而復始: *By August her*

feelings had turned full circle. 到八月份, 她的心情好似兜了一個圈又和原來一樣了。—see also 另見 **square the circle** (SQUARE[3] (6)), VICIOUS CIRCLE

circle² *v* **1** [T] to draw a circle around something 圍繞; 在…上畫圈; 圈出: *Circle the correct answer.* 將正確答案圈出來。**2** [I,T] to move around in a circle in the air〔在空中〕盤旋: *The plane circled the airport before landing.* 飛機着陸前在機場上空盤旋了一會兒。

cir·clet /ˋsɝklɪt; ˈsɜːklɨ̥t/ *n* [C] a narrow band of gold, silver, or jewels worn around someone's head or arms〔戴在頭上或手臂上的〕環狀飾物

3 **cir·cuit** /ˋsɝkɪt; ˈsɜːkɨ̥t/ *n* [C] **1** a path that forms a circle around an area, or a journey along this path 環形道路; 環行: *We did a circuit of the old city walls.* 我們繞着舊城牆走了一圈。**2** a track that cars, MOTORBIKES etc race around 賽車道 **3 the tennis/lecture/cabaret etc circuit** all the places that are usually visited by someone who plays tennis etc 網球運動員/演講者/歌舞團等巡迴表演[比賽等]的地方: *a well-known entertainer on the club circuit* 到各夜總會巡迴表演的一位著名演員 **4** the complete circle that an electric current travels 電路, 線路 **5 do circuits** *BrE informal* to do CIRCUIT TRAINING【英, 非正式】循環訓練 —see also 另見 PRINTED CIRCUIT, SHORT CIRCUIT

circuit board /ˈ·· ·/ *n* [C] a set of connections between points on a piece of electrical equipment which uses a thin line of metal to CONDUCT (=carry) the electricity; PRINTED CIRCUIT 電路板, 印刷電路

circuit break·er /ˈ·· ˌ··/ *n* [C] a piece of equipment that stops an electric current if it becomes dangerous (電流) 斷路器

circuit court /ˈ·· ˌ·/ *n* [C] a court of law that happens in a small town when a judge visits from a larger town 巡迴法院

cir·cu·i·tous /sɝˋkjuɪtəs; sɜːˈkjuːɨ̥təs/ *adj* **circuitous route/course etc** a way of getting from one place to another that is longer than the most direct way 迂迴的路線 —**circuitously** *adv*

cir·cuit·ry /ˋsɝkɪtrɪ; ˈsɜːkɨ̥tri/ *n* [U] a system of electric circuits 電路系統

circuit train·ing /ˈ·· ˌ··/ *n* [U] *BrE* several different exercises done quickly after each other, in order to make you able to do sport better【英】循環訓練法

cir·cu·lar¹ /ˋsɝkjələ; ˈsɜːkjᵿlə/ *adj* **1** shaped like a circle 圓形的, 環形的: *a circular table* 圓桌 **2** moving around in a circle 循環的; 環行的: *a circular bus route* 環行公共汽車路線 **3 circular argument/discussion etc** an argument in which you always return to the same statements or ideas that were expressed at the beginning 循環論證/討論 —**circularity** /ˌsɝkjəˋlærətɪ; ˌsɜːkjᵿˈlærɨ̥ti/ *n* [U]

circular² *n* [C] a printed advertisement, notice etc that is sent to lots of people at the same time〔同時送達很多人的〕印刷品; 通知, 通告

cir·cu·lar·ize also 又作 **-ise** *BrE*【英】/ˋsɝkjələˌraɪz; ˈsɜːkjᵿləraɪz/ *v* [T] to send printed notices or advertisements to a lot of people 給…發通知[傳單等]; 傳閱〔文件等〕

circular saw /ˌ··· ˈ·/ *n* [C] a round metal blade with small sharp parts around the edge, used for cutting wood 圓鋸 —compare 比較 CHAIN SAW

cir·cu·late /ˋsɝkjəˌlet; ˈsɜːkjᵿleɪt/ *v* **1** [I,T] to move around within a system, or to make something do this (使) 循環: *Blood circulates around the body.* 血液在全身循環。**2** [I] if information, facts, ideas etc circulate, they become known by many people 流傳; 傳播; 散佈 **3** [T] to send goods, information etc to people 發送; 傳播: *His agent circulated several copies of the book.* 他的代理人發送了幾冊書。**4** [I] to move around a group, especially at a party, taking to many different people; MINGLE (2)〔在聚會上〕到處走動, 來回周旋 —**circulatory** /ˋsɝkjələˌtorɪ; ˌsɜːkjᵿˈleɪtəri/ *adj*

cir·cu·la·tion /ˌsɝkjəˋleʃən; ˌsɜːkjᵿˈleɪʃən/ *n* **1** [C,U] the movement of blood around your body 血液循環: *Exercise improves the circulation.* 運動有助於促進血液循環。**2** [U] the exchange of information, money etc from one person to another in a group or society〔資料、貨幣等的〕流通: **in circulation** *Several thousand of the fake notes are in circulation.* 市面上流通着幾千張偽鈔。**3** [singular] the average number of copies of a newspaper or magazine that are usually sold each day, week, month etc〔報紙、雜誌的〕發行量, 銷售量: *Circulation fell when the price was increased to 45p.* 價格漲到45便士後, 發行量便下降了。**4 out of circulation** *informal* not taking part in social activities for a period of time【非正式】不參加社交活動: *Sandy's out of circulation until after her exams.* 桑迪直至考完試後才參加社交活動。**5** [C,U] the movement of liquid, air etc in a system〔液體、空氣等的〕流通, 環流

circum /sɝkəm; sɜːkəm/ *prefix* all the way round something 環繞…: *to circumnavigate the world* (=sail round it) 環遊世界 | *to circumvent* (=avoid something by finding a way round) 迴避

cir·cum·cise /ˋsɝkəmˌsaɪz; ˈsɜːkəmsaɪz/ *v* [T] **1** to cut off the skin at the end of the PENIS (=male sex organ) 割去〔男性的〕包皮 **2** to cut off the CLITORIS of a female 切除〔女性的〕陰蒂

cir·cum·ci·sion /ˌsɝkəmˋsɪʒən; ˌsɜːkəmˈsɪʒən/ *n* [C,U] the act of circumcising someone, or an occasion when a baby is circumcised as part of a religious ceremony 包皮切除術; 陰蒂切除術; 割禮

cir·cum·fer·ence /sɚˋkʌmfərəns; səˈkʌmfərəns/ *n* **1** [C,U] the distance measured around the outside of a circle 圓周; 周長: *the circumference of the Earth* 地球的周長 | *3 metres in circumference* 周長三米 —see picture at 參見 CIRCLE[1] 圖 **2** [singular] the measurement around the outside of any shape; PERIPHERY 周線, 周界;〔任何形狀物體的〕周邊的長度 —**circumferential** /sɚˌkʌmfəˋrɛnʃəl; səˌkʌmfəˈrenʃəl/ *adj* —see table on page C5 參見C5頁附錄

cir·cum·flex /ˋsɝkəmˌflɛks; ˈsɜːkəmfleks/ *n* [C] a mark placed above a letter in a French word to show its pronunciation, for example, ô〔標在法文元音字母上〕表示音調的符號 —compare 比較 GRAVE[3], ACUTE (7)

cir·cum·lo·cu·tion /ˌsɝkəmloˋkjuʃən; ˌsɜːkəmləˈkjuːʃən/ *n* [C,U] *formal* the practice of using too many words to express an idea, instead of saying it directly【正式】婉轉曲折的說法, 迂迴的說法 —**circumlocutory** /ˌsɝkəmˋlɑkjəˌtorɪ; ˌsɜːkəmˈlɒkjᵿtəri/ *adj*

cir·cum·nav·i·gate /ˌsɝkəmˋnævəˌget; ˌsɜːkəmˈnævɨ̥geɪt/ *v* [T] to sail completely around the Earth, an island etc 環繞〔地球或島嶼等〕航行 —**circumnavigation** /ˌsɝkəmnævəˋgeʃən; ˌsɜːkəmnævɨ̥ˈgeɪʃən/ *n* [C,U]

cir·cum·scribe /ˌsɝkəmˋskraɪb; ˈsɜːkəmskraɪb/ *v* [T] **1** [often passive 常用被動態] *formal* to limit power, rights, or abilities; RESTRICT【正式】約束, 限制: *All our minds are heavily circumscribed by habit.* 我們的思維深受習慣的制約。**2** *technical* to draw a line around something【術語】在…周圍畫線: *a circle circumscribed by a square* 正方形中的圓形 —**circumscription** /ˌsɝkəmˋskrɪpʃən; ˌsɜːkəmˈskrɪpʃən/ *n* [U]

cir·cum·spect /ˋsɝkəmˌspɛkt; ˈsɜːkəmspekt/ *adj* **1** thinking carefully about things before doing them; CAUTIOUS 小心的, 謹慎的: *The journalist was circumspect, only tentatively linking the escape with the murder.* 這名記者很謹慎, 只是試探性地將出逃與謀殺聯繫起來。**2** a circumspect action or answer is done or given only after careful thought〔行動、答案〕深思熟慮的, 考慮周到的 —**circumspectly** *adv* —**circumspection** /ˌsɝkəmˋspɛkʃən; ˌsɜːkəmˈspekʃən/ *n* [U]

cir·cum·stance /ˋsɝkəmˌstæns; ˈsɜːkəmstæns/ *n* **1 circumstances** [plural] the conditions that affect a situation, action, event etc 情況, 情形: *The rules can only be waived in exceptional circumstances.* 這些規定只有在特殊情況下才可予以豁免。| **in suspicious circumstances** (=in a way that makes you think something illegal or dishonest has happened) 情形可疑 *He was found* 1 1

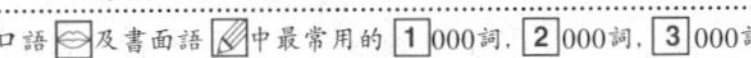

dead in suspicious circumstances. 他被發現死亡，死因很可疑。| **extenuating circumstances** (=things that have happened which excuse or explain someone's bad behaviour or actions) 情有可原的情況 **2 under/in no circumstances** used to emphasize that something must definitely not happen 決不，無論如何都不: *Under no circumstances are you to leave the house.* 你無論如何也不能離開這屋子。**3 under/in the circumstances** used to say that a particular situation makes an action, decision etc necessary or acceptable when it would not normally be 在這種情況下，情形既然如此: *The result was the best that could be expected under the circumstances.* 在這種情況下，這是我們能期待的最好的結果。**4** [U] the combination of facts, events etc that influence your life, and that you cannot control 無法控制的因素；環境；境遇: **force of circumstance** *Force of circumstance compelled us to leave.* 形勢所迫，我們不得不走。| **victim of circumstance** (=someone who is harmed because of the situation they are in, not because they have done anything wrong) 局勢的犧牲品，環境的受害者 **5 live in reduced circumstances** *old-fashioned* to have much less money than you used to have【過時】財政狀況不佳，經濟拮据 **6 pomp and circumstance** *literary* grand ceremonial activity, especially on a formal or important occasion【文】盛大隆重的場面

cir·cum·stan·tial /ˌsɝkəm`stænʃəl; ˌsɜːkəm'stænʃəl◂/ *adj* **1 circumstantial evidence** *law* facts that make you believe something probably happened, but do not definitely prove that it did【法律】有充分的細節但無法證實的證據，間接推測的證據 **2 circumstantial account/description etc** *formal* a description etc that includes all the details【正式】詳細的敍述/描述 —**circumstantially** *adv*

cir·cum·vent /ˌsɝkəm`vɛnt; ˌsɜːkəm'vent/ *v* [T] **1** to avoid a problem or rule that restricts you , especially in a clever or dishonest way〔尤指巧妙地〕迴避；規避: *The company opened an account abroad, in order to circumvent the tax laws.* 該公司在國外開設了一個賬戶，以逃避（本國的）稅法。**2** *formal* to change the direction in which you are travelling in order to avoid something【正式】〔為避免…而〕改道，繞過: *We went north in order to circumvent the mountains.* 我們為避開羣山，改向北行進。—**circumvention** /-`vɛnʃən; -'venʃən/ *n* [U]

cir·cus /`sɝkəs; 'sɜːkəs/ *n* **1** [C] a group of people and animals who travel around performing skilful tricks as entertainment 馬戲團: **circus act** (=a trick performed in a circus) 馬戲表演 | **circus ring** (=the round area where tricks are performed) 馬戲表演場 **2** [singular] *informal* a meeting, group of people etc that is very noisy and uncontrolled【非正式】亂哄哄的聚會，熱鬧的場面: *The first day of school is always such a circus.* 開學第一天總是那麼鬧哄哄的。**3** [C] in ancient Rome, a place where fights, races etc took place, with seats built in a circle〔古羅馬的〕圓形競技場 **4** [singular] *BrE* used sometimes as the name of a round open area where several streets join together【英】〔數條街道相匯聚的〕圓形廣場: *Piccadilly Circus* 皮卡迪利廣場

cirque /sɝk; sɜːk/ *n* [C] *technical* a CORRIE【術語】冰圍地，冰斗 —see picture on page A12 參見A12頁圖

cir·rho·sis /sɪ`rosɪs; sə̇'rəʊsə̇s/ *n* [U] a serious disease of the LIVER (1), often caused by drinking too much alcohol 肝硬化〔常由過度飲酒引起〕

cir·rus /`sɪrəs; 'sɪrəs/ *n* [U] a form of cloud that is light and shaped like feathers, high in the sky 卷雲 —compare 比較 CUMULUS, NIMBUS (1)

CIS /ˌsi aɪ `ɛs; ˌsiː aɪ 'es/ *n* the Commonwealth of Independent States; the name given to a group of states of which the largest is Russia 獨立國家聯合體，獨聯體

cis·sy /`sɪsɪ; 'sɪsi/ *n* [C] *BrE informal* SISSY【英，非正式】娘娘腔的男子 —**cissy** *adj*

cis·tern /`sɪstən; 'sɪstən/ *n* [C] a container in which water is stored inside a building〔建築物內的〕水箱；貯水槽

cit·a·del /`sɪtədḷ; 'sɪtədəl/ *n* [C] **1** a strong FORT (=small castle), intended to be somewhere people can go for safety if their city is attacked 城堡；要塞；堡壘 **2 the citadel of sth** *literary* a place or situation in which an idea, principle, system etc that you think is important is kept safe; STRONGHOLD【文】保衞…的地方；有保障的地方: *the last citadel of freedom* 自由的最後堡壘

ci·ta·tion /saɪ`teʃən; saɪ'teɪʃən/ *n* **1** [C] an official statement about someone's character or actions, especially one saying that they have been brave in battle〔尤指對作戰英勇者的〕表彰；嘉獎狀: *a citation for bravery* 英勇嘉獎狀 **2** [C] a line taken from a book, speech etc; QUOTATION (1) 引文，引句，引語 **3** [U] an occasion when someone cites or is cited 引用，引證

cite /saɪt; saɪt/ *v* [T] **1** to mention something as an example, especially one that supports, proves, or explains an idea or situation 引證，援引: **cite sth as sth** *Several factors have been cited as the cause of the student unrest.* 好幾個因素被引證來說明學生動亂的起因。**2** to give the exact words of something that has been written in order to support an opinion or prove an idea; QUOTE[1] (1) 引用，引述: *the passage cited above* 上面引用的段落 **3** to call someone to appear before a court of law 傳召；傳訊〔到法院〕: *Two managers had been cited for similar infractions.* 兩名經理因為類似的違法行為而被傳訊。**4** to mention someone by name in a court case 傳喚: *Penny was cited in the divorce proceedings.* 彭尼被傳喚去辦離婚案。**5** *formal* to mention someone because they deserve praise【正式】嘉獎；表揚，表彰: **cite sb for sth** *Joe was cited for bravery.* 喬因表現勇敢而受到表彰。

cit·i·fied /`sɪtɪˌfaɪd; 'sɪtɪfaɪd/ *adj* connected with the city or the way people in cities live, especially when this is considered bad 城市的；城市生活的: *a rural area that has become industrialized and citified* 已被工業化和城市化的農村地區

cit·i·zen /`sɪtəzṇ; 'sɪtə̇zən/ *n* [C] **1** someone who lives in a particular town, country, or state and has rights and responsibilities there 市民，城鎮居民: *teaching our children to be good citizens* 教育我們的孩子成為好公民 **2** someone who belongs to a particular country, whether they are living there or not 公民，國民: *tax advantages for British citizens living and working abroad* 給在國外工作和生活的英國公民的稅務優惠 —compare 比較 NATIONAL[2] **3 second-class citizen** someone who feels unimportant because of the way other people treat them 二等公民: *I was made to feel like a second-class citizen as soon as I walked through the door.* 我一進門時就感覺像二等公民。—see also 另見 SENIOR CITIZEN

cit·i·zen·ry /`sɪtəzṇrɪ; 'sɪtə̇zənri/ *n* [U] all the citizens in a particular place 全體公民[市民]

citizen's ar·rest /ˌ··· ·'·/ *n* [C] the act of taking someone to a police station because you think they have done something wrong 公民（對罪犯）採取的逮捕行動: **make a citizen's arrest** *The stallholder made a citizen's arrest.* 那個攤販逮捕了罪犯。

Cit·i·zens' Band /ˌ··· '·◂/ *n* [U] —see 見 CB

cit·i·zen·ship /`sɪtəzṇˌʃɪp; 'sɪtə̇zənʃɪp/ *n* [U] the legal right of belonging to a particular country 公民權利；公民身分: **French/US/Brazilian citizenship** *an application for French citizenship* 申請法國國籍[公民資格] | **dual citizenship** (=belonging to two different countries) 雙重國籍 *dual citizenship of Canada and the US* 加拿大和美國雙重國籍

cit·ric ac·id /ˌsɪtrɪk `æsɪd; ˌsɪtrɪk 'æsə̇d/ *n* [U] a weak acid found in some fruits, such as lemons 檸檬酸

cit·ron /`sɪtrən; 'sɪtrən/ *n* [C] a fruit like a LEMON (1) but bigger 香櫞，枸櫞

cit·ron·el·la /ˌsɪtrə`nɛlə; ˌsɪtrə'nelə/ *n* [U] an oil used for keeping insects away〔驅蟲用的〕香茅油

cit·rus /`sɪtrəs; 'sɪtrəs/ also 又作 **citrus tree** /'·· ·/ *n* [C] a type of tree that produces citrus fruits 柑橘屬果樹 —**citrus, citrous** /`sɪtrəs; 'sɪtrəs/ *adj*

citrus fruit /'·· ·/ *n* [C,U] a fruit with a thick skin such as an orange or LEMON (1) 柑橘屬水果〈如橙子、檸檬〉—see picture on page A8 參見A8頁圖

1 1 **cit·y** /ˈsɪtɪ; ˈsɪti/ *n* **1** [C] a large important town, especially one with a CATHEDRAL〔尤指擁有大教堂的〕城市, 都市: *New York City* 紐約市 | *a capital city* 首府, 首都 | **city dweller** (=someone who lives in a city) 城市居民, 城市人 **2** the people who live in a city 全市居民: *The city has been living in fear since last week's earthquake.* 上週地震後, 全市居民都生活在恐懼中。**3 the City** *BrE* the area of London which is Britain's financial centre, and the important institutions there【英】倫敦城: **city banker/stockbroker etc** (=a banker etc who works in the city) 倫敦商業區的銀行家/證券經紀人等 —see also 另見 INNER CITY

city cen·tre /ˌ·· ˈ··/ *n* [C] *BrE* the main shopping or business area in a city【英】市中心; DOWNTOWN *AmE*【美】

city desk /ˈ·· ·/ *n* [C] *AmE* a department of a newspaper that deals with local news【美】〔報社的〕本地新聞部

city ed·it·or /ˈ·· ˌ···/ *n* [C] **1** also 又作 **financial editor** *BrE* a JOURNALIST responsible for the financial part of a newspaper【英】負責財經新聞的編輯 **2** *AmE* a JOURNALIST responsible for local news【美】負責本地新聞的編輯

city fa·ther /ˌ·· ˈ··/ *n* [C usually plural 一般用複數] *old use* a member of the group of people who govern a city【舊】市政府官員; 市議員

city hall /ˌ·· ˈ·/ *n* [C,U] *AmE* the local government of a city and the building it uses as its offices【美】市政府(大樓), 市政廳

city plan·ning /ˌ·· ˈ··/ *n* [U] *AmE* the study of the way cities work, so that roads, houses, services etc can be provided effectively【美】城市規劃; TOWN PLANNING *BrE*【英】

city slick·er /ˌ·· ˈ··/ *n* [C] someone who lives and works in a city and has no experience of anything outside it〔對城市以外的情況毫無體驗的〕城裡人, 城市居民

city-state /ˌ·· ˈ·/ *n* [C] a city, especially in former times, that forms an independent state with the surrounding country area〔尤指舊時的〕城邦: *the city-state of Athens* 雅典城邦

cit·y·wide /ˈsɪtɪˌwaɪd; ˈsɪtiwaɪd/ *adj especially AmE* involving all the areas of a city【尤美】全市範圍的: *a citywide campaign to fight racism* 全市範圍的反種族主義運動

civ·et /ˈsɪvɪt; ˈsɪvɨt/ *n* **1** [C] also 又作 **civet cat** a small animal like a cat, that lives in Asia and Africa〔產於亞洲和非洲的〕靈貓, 麝香貓 **2** [U] a strong-smelling liquid from a civet cat, used to make PERFUME 靈貓香〔用作香料〕

civ·ic /ˈsɪvɪk; ˈsɪvɪk/ *adj* [only before noun 僅用於名詞前] **1** connected with a town or city 城鎮的; 城市的: *the civic authorities* 市當局 | **civic centre** (=an area in a city where all the public buildings are) 市中心 **2** connected with the people who live in a town or city 市民的, 公民的: *It is your civic duty to vote in the local elections.* 在地區選舉中投票是你的公民義務。| **civic pride** (=people's pride in their own city) 市民對自己城市的自豪感

civ·ics /ˈsɪvɪks; ˈsɪvɪks/ *n* [U] *especially AmE* a school subject dealing with the rights and duties of citizens and the way government works【尤美】公民(學)科; 市政學

civ·ies /ˈsɪvɪz; ˈsɪviz/ *n* [plural] CIVVIES 便服〔非軍服〕

2 2 **civ·il** /ˈsɪvḷ; ˈsɪvəl/ *adj* **1** [only before noun 僅用於名詞前] connected with the people who live in a country 公民的; 民間的: *civil order* 公民秩序 | **civil conflict/disturbance/unrest etc** (=fighting etc between different groups of people living in the same country) 民間衝突/騷動/騷亂等 *the continuing civil conflict in Rwanda* 盧旺達持續不斷的民間衝突 | **civil liberty/liberties** (=the freedom that the people in a country have to behave and think as they wish within the law) 公民自由 **2** [only before noun 僅用於名詞前] connected with the ordinary people or things in a country rather than the military ones 普通公民的; 平民的; 民用的; 非軍事的: *The military and civil authorities are working together to quell the unrest.* 軍隊和地方當局正聯手鎮壓騷亂。**3** [only before noun 僅用於名詞前] involving or dealing with private legal matters, not with criminal ones 民事的: *Many civil cases can be settled out of court.* 許多民事案件都可以在法庭外解決。—see also 另見 CIVIL LAW —compare 比較 CRIMINAL[1] (2) **4** polite in a formal and not a friendly way 客氣的; 文明的; 有禮貌的: *Try at least to be civil.* 至少要盡量禮貌一點。

civil de·fence /ˌ·· ·ˈ·/ *n* [U] **1** the organization of ordinary rather than military people to help defend their country from military attack 民防 **2 civil defences** *plural* the things a country does to prepare for a military attack by an enemy 民防工事: *We need to strengthen our civil defences.* 我們需要加強民防工事。

civil dis·o·be·di·ence /ˌ·· ··ˈ···/ *n* [U] action that breaks the law usually taken by a large number of people to protest against something done by the government〔人民針對政府的〕非暴力反抗, 不合作主義

civil en·gi·neer·ing /ˌ·· ··ˈ··/ *n* [U] the planning, building, and repair of roads, bridges, large buildings, etc 土木工程 —**civil engineer** *n* [C]

ci·vil·ian /səˈvɪljən; sɨˈvɪljən/ *n* [C] anyone who is not a member of the army, navy, airforce, or police〔與軍人、警察相對的〕平民, 百姓; 文職人員: *the killing of innocent civilians during the bombing campaign* 轟炸中對無辜平民的屠殺 —**civilian** *adj*: *a return to civilian government after years of military rule* 軍事統治許多年後恢復文官政府

ci·vil·i·ty /səˈvɪlətɪ; sɨˈvɪlɨti/ *n* **1** [U] polite behaviour which most people consider normal 禮貌, 客氣, 謙恭: *Please have the civility to knock before you enter next time.* 下次你進來時要有點禮貌 —— 先敲門。**2 civilities** [plural] *formal* something that you say or do in order to be polite【正式】禮儀; 客套話: *We exchanged civilities when we were neighbours but nothing more.* 我們還是鄰居時, 也只是互相客氣地打個招呼而已。

civ·i·li·za·tion also 又作 **-isation** *BrE*【英】/ˌsɪvḷəˈzeʃən; ˌsɪvəl-aɪˈzeɪʃən/ *n* **1** [C,U] a society that is well organized and developed 文明(社會): *contemporary American civilization* 當代美國文明 | **[+of]** *the ancient civilizations of Greece and Rome* 希臘和羅馬的古代文明 **2** [U] all the societies in the world considered as a whole 文明世界: *The book explores the relationship between religion and civilization.* 本書探索了宗教和文明世界之間的關係。**3** [U] the process in which societies become developed and organized 開化; 教化 **4** [U] *humorous* a place where you feel comfortable or where there is plenty to do【幽默】現代文明生活: *After a week in the mountains all I wanted to do was get back to civilization!* 在山裡過了一週後, 我一心只想回到文明生活!

civ·i·lize also 又作 **-ise** *BrE*【英】/ˈsɪvḷˌaɪz; ˈsɪvəl-aɪz/ *v* [T] *BrE often humorous* to make someone behave in a more sensible or gentle way【英, 常幽默】教化; 使開化, 使文明: *men who need to be domesticated and civilized* 需要馴化和教化的人

civ·i·lized also 又作 **-ised** *BrE*【英】/ˈsɪvḷˌaɪzd; ˈsɪvəl-aɪzd/ *adj* **1** being well organized and developed socially 開化的, 文明的: *Such things should not be allowed to happen in a civilized society.* 文明社會不容許發生此類事情。**2** pleasant and comfortable 令人愉快的, 舒適宜人的: *"This is very civilized," she said, lying back in the sun with a gin and tonic.* "太舒服了。"她說, 一邊躺在陽光下喝着摻奎寧水的杜松子酒。**3** behaving in a polite sensible way instead of getting angry 心平氣和的; 有禮貌的: *Let's try and be civilized about this, shall we?* 我們盡量心平氣和地對待這件事, 好嗎?

civil law /ˌ·· ˈ·/ *n* [U] the area of law deals with the affairs of private citizens rather than with crime 民法, 民事法

civil lib·er·ty /ˌ·· ˈ···/ *n* [U] also 又作 **civil liberties** [plural] the right of all citizens to be free to do whatever they want while respecting the rights of other people 公

民自由

civil list /ˈ·· ·/ *n* [singular] the sum of money given every year by Parliament to the King or Queen of Britain and to some other people〔英國議會每年批給王室的〕王室費

civil rights /ˌ·· ˈ·/ *n* [plural] the rights that every person should have, such as the right to vote or to be treated fairly by the law, whatever their sex, race, or religion 公民權: **civil rights campaigner/movement etc** *50,000 people attended the civil rights demonstration.* 有 50,000 人參加了民權示威遊行。—see also 另見 BILL OF RIGHTS

civil ser·vant /ˌ·· ˈ··/ *n* [C] someone employed in the civil service 公務員; 文職人員

civil ser·vice /ˌ·· ˈ··/ *n* [singular] the government departments that manage the affairs of the country 政府文職機構, 公職, 行政部門

civil war /ˌ·· ˈ·/ *n* [C,U] a war in which opposing groups of people from the same country fight each other in order to gain political control 內戰

civ·vies, civies /ˈsɪvɪz; ˈsɪviz/ *n* [plural] *slang* ordinary clothes, as opposed to military uniform, used mainly by people in the army, navy, or airforce【俚】便服〔非軍服〕: *sailors on leave wearing their civvies* 穿着便服的休假水兵

civ·vy /ˈsɪvɪ; ˈsɪvi/ *n* [C] *BrE*【英】**1** *slang* a word meaning someone who is not in the army, navy, or airforce, used mainly by people who are or have been in the armed forces【俚】平民〔該詞主要為現役或退役軍人使用〕**2 civvy street** *old-fashioned* ordinary life as it is lived outside the army, navy, or airforce【過時】平民生活; 非軍人生活

cl the written abbreviation of 縮寫= CENTILITRE

clack /klæk; klæk/ *v* **1** [I,T] if you clack something or if it clacks, it makes a continuous short hard sound 發出咔嗒聲; 使咔嗒咔嗒地響 **2** [I] *informal* if tongues are clacking, people are talking a lot about something shocking or surprising【非正式】嘰嘰喳喳談論, 嘮叨: *News of her pregnancy had already set tongues clacking in the neighbourhood.* 她懷孕的消息引起了鄰居間嘰嘰喳喳的議論。—**clack** *n* [singular]

clad /klæd; klæd/ *adj* **1** *literary* wearing a particular kind of clothing【文】穿〔某種特別的〕衣服的: *a model clad in silk and lace* 穿着鑲有花邊的絲綢服裝的模特兒 | **warmly/poorly/scantily clad** (=dressed in a particular way) 穿得暖暖的/衣衫襤褸的/衣着單薄的 **2 snow-clad/ivy-clad etc** covered in a particular thing 積雪覆蓋的/爬滿常春藤的等: *an armor-clad ship* 裝甲艦[船]

clad·ding /ˈklædɪŋ; ˈklædɪŋ/ *n* [U] a cover of hard material that protects the outside of a building, tank, or engine 覆面〔建築物外壁、容器或引擎表面的保護層〕

1 1 **claim¹** /klem; kleɪm/ *v* **1** [T] to state that something is true, even though it has not been proved 聲稱; 斷言; 主張: **claim (that)** *Gascoigne claimed he'd been dining with friends at the time of the murder.* 加斯科因聲稱兇案發生時自己正與朋友進餐。| **claim to be** *She claims to be a descendant of Charles Dickens.* 她宣稱自己是查理斯·狄更斯的後裔。| **claim to have done** *Doctors claimed to have discovered a cure for the disease.* 醫生聲稱已經找到了治療該病的方法。| **claim responsibility/innocence/credit** (=say officially that you are responsible, innocent etc) 聲稱有責任/無辜/有功勞 **2** [I,T] to officially demand or receive money from an organization 索賠; 索取: **[+on]** *You can claim on the insurance if you have an accident while on vacation.* 如果你度假期間出了事可向保險公司索賠。| *The government intends to make legal aid harder to claim.* 政府打算加大法律援助的難度。| **claim benefit/an allowance/damages** (=officially receive money because you do not have a job, are injured etc) 申領救濟金/申領補助/要求賠償金 **3** [T] to state that you have a right to something or to take something that belongs to you 認領; 要求; 索取〔應得的權利或財物〕: *Viscount Lander will claim the title on his father's death.* 蘭德子爵在父親去世後會繼承爵位。| *Lost property can be claimed between 10 a.m. and 4 p.m.* 可於上午十點至下午四點認領失物。**4** [T] if a war, accident etc claims lives, people die because of it 奪去, 奪走〔生命〕: *The Kobe earthquake has so far claimed over 3000 lives.* 神戶的地震已經奪去了三千多人的生命。**5** [T] if something claims someone's attention or time, they have to consider it carefully 值得; 需要〔花時間或精力〕: *The issue of a united Ireland continues to claim our undivided attention.* 愛爾蘭統一這一問題值得我們繼續密切注意。

claim² *n* [C] 2

1 ►MONEY 金錢◄ **a)** a request for money, especially money that you have a right to〔根據權利而提出的〕要求, 索款: **[+for]** *claims for compensation* 要求賠償 | **make a claim/put in a claim** *They put in a claim on the insurance for the stolen luggage.* 他們在行李被偷後向保險公司提出索賠要求。| **pay claim** (=a request made by workers for more money) 工資要求 | **claim form** (=an official form that you must fill in in order to get money from an organization) 索賠申請表 **b)** the sum of money you request when making such a claim 索賠金額: *The insurance company cannot meet such enormous claims.* 保險公司不能滿足如此巨額的索賠。 1

2 ►STATEMENT 聲明◄ a statement that something is true, even though it has not been proved 聲稱; 斷言; 主張: **claim that** *Dino denies claims that he is involved in a drugs ring.* 迪諾否認自己和販毒集團有關係的說法。| **claim to do/be sth** *the Democratic claim to be the party of women's rights* 民主黨聲稱是婦女權利之黨 | **make a claim** *Photographs make a claim to portray reality in a way that paintings never can.* 照片有着繪畫永遠達不到的真實性。| **make no claim to do something** (=used to say that you do not pretend to be able to do something) 不自稱會做某事 *I make no claim to understand the complexities of the situation.* 我不敢斷言自己對這局勢各種複雜的細節都了解。| **dispute a claim** (=say publicly that a statement is not true) 就某種說法提出質疑

3 ►FOR PRAISE/RESPECT ETC 用於表揚/尊敬等◄ something that you say or do, that shows that you deserve to be successful 應得的權利[資格]: **[+to]** *Judging by last night's performance Ryan must have a claim to a place on the Olympic team.* 從瑞安昨晚的表現來看, 他應該入選奧運隊。

4 ►TO OWN OR TAKE SOMETHING 擁有或拿某物◄ a right to have or get something such as land, a title etc that belongs to you 所有權: **[+to]** *No one can dispute Oliver's claim to the inheritance.* 沒有人能對奧利弗的繼承權提出質疑。| **have a claim on/to sth** *Surely they have a rightful claim to their father's land.* 的確, 他們對父親的土地擁有合法的所有權。

5 lay claim to sth to say that you have a right to own something 聲稱對某物擁有所有權: *Ellen resented the stranger who laid claim to her brother's fortune.* 艾倫對那個自稱對她哥哥的財產有繼承權的陌生人感到憤恨。

6 stake your claim to say that you have a right to own something, especially when other people also say they have a right to own it 聲稱對…擁有所有權〔尤指當別人也同時作出相同的聲明〕: *If you want some of the furniture now's the time to stake your claim.* 如果你想要一些家具的話, 現在就該去表明你擁有所有權。

7 claim to fame an expression meaning a reason why someone or something is famous, often used jokingly when mentioning something that is not very important 出名的原因〔常為戲謔說法, 一般指實際上並不怎麼重要的東西〕: *My main claim to fame is that I once shook Elvis' hand.* 我之所以出名, 主要是因為我和〔貓王〕艾爾維斯握過手。

8 have a claim on sb to have a right to demand someone's time, attention etc 有權得到〔某人的〕注意; 有權佔用〔某人的〕時間: *She seems to think she's got an exclusive claim on my time.* 她似乎覺得她有特權佔用我的時間。

9 ►LAND 土地◄ something such as a piece of land that contains valuable minerals 要求得到的東西〔如含有礦

產的土地〉—see also 另見 **jump a claim** (JUMP[1] (19))

clai·mant /ˈklemənt; ˈkleɪmənt/ *n* [C] **1** someone who claims something, especially money, from the government, a court etc because they think they have a right to it 申請人; 要求者; 索賠人: *The company was ordered to recompense the claimant for damages.* 該公司接到命令要向索賠人的損失作出賠償。**2** someone who makes a claim, for example under a WILL[2] (2) 繼承人; 認領人

clair·voy·ant /klɛrˈvɔɪənt; kleəˈvɔɪənt/ *n* [C] someone who says they can see what will happen in the future 聲稱能夠預見未來的人; 有洞察力的人 —**clairvoyance** *n* [U] —**clairvoyant** *adj*

clam[1] /klæm; klæm/ *n* [C] **1** a SHELLFISH that you can eat, which has a shell in two parts that open and close 蛤; 蛤蜊; 蜆 **2** *AmE informal* someone who does not say what they are thinking or feeling【美, 非正式】嘴緊的人, 沉默寡言的人 **3 as happy as a clam** *AmE informal* very happy【美, 非正式】非常高興; 相當滿足

clam[2] *v*

clam up *phr v* [I] *informal* to suddenly stop talking, especially when you are nervous or shy【非正式】〔尤指因緊張、害羞而〕拒不開口, 沉默不語: *I just clammed up when her father came in.* 她父親進來後, 我乾脆不說話了。

clam·bake /ˈklæmˌbek; ˈklæmbeɪk/ *n* [C] *AmE* an informal party by the sea where clams are cooked and eaten【美】海濱烤蛤野餐聚會

clam·ber /ˈklæmbɚ; ˈklæmbə/ *v* [I always+adv/prep] to climb slowly, using your hands and feet〔手腳並用, 費力地〕攀登, 爬: **[+up/over/to etc]** *They clambered over the slippery rocks.* 他們爬上了滑溜的岩石。

clam·my /ˈklæmɪ; ˈklæmi/ *adj* feeling wet, cold, and sticky in a way that is unpleasant 冷濕的, 感覺滑膩的, 黏糊糊的: *clammy with sweat* 因為出汗而黏黏的 —**clammily** *adv* —**clamminess** *n* [U]

clam·our[1] *BrE*【英】, **clamor** *AmE*【美】/ˈklæmɚ; ˈklæmə/ *n* [singular,U] **1** a very loud noise, often made by a large group of people or animals 吵鬧聲, 嘈雜聲: *the clamour of factory machinery* 工廠機器的轟鳴聲 **2** strong feeling expressed loudly by a large group of people〔一大批人的〕強烈要求[呼聲]: **[+for]** *the clamour for an all-out strike* 強烈要求全體罷工 —**clamorous** *adj*

clamour[2] *BrE*【英】, **clamor** *AmE*【美】*v* [I] **1** [always+adv/prep] to demand something loudly 大聲疾呼; 強烈要求: **[+for]** *The audience were on their feet clamouring for more.* 觀眾站了起來, 高聲要求再來一曲。**2** to talk or shout loudly 大聲講話; 大聲呼喊: *Children clamoured in the playground.* 孩子們在操場上大聲喊叫。

clamp[1] /klæmp; klæmp/ *v* [T] **1** [always+adv/prep] to fasten or hold two things together using a clamp〔用夾鉗〕夾住, 夾緊: **clamp sth together/onto etc** *Clamp the two parts together until the glue dries.* 用夾鉗把這兩部分夾緊, 直到膠水乾了再鬆開。**2** [always+adv/prep] to put or hold something in a position where it does not move 固定: **clamp sth over/between/around etc** *He clamped a hand over my mouth.* 他用手捂住我的嘴。**3** *BrE* to put a clamp on a car that is illegally parked【英】〔給非法停放的車輛〕上夾鉗; BOOT[2] (3) *AmE*【美】

clamp down *phr v* [I] to take firm action to stop a crime or other illegal activity happening 取締; 壓制; 箝制; 鎮壓: **[+on]** *The police are really clamping down on drunk drivers.* 警方正在嚴厲制裁酒後駕車者。

clamp[2] *n* [C] **1** a piece of equipment for fastening or holding things together 夾子, 夾具, 夾鉗 **2** a piece of equipment fastened to the wheel of a car that is parked illegally〔固定非法停放車輛的〕夾鉗, 車輪固定夾; DENVER BOOT *AmE*【美】

clamp·down /ˈklæmpˌdaʊn; ˈklæmpdaʊn/ *n* [C usually singular 一般用單數] sudden firm action that is taken to try and reduce crime 嚴禁; 取締; 鎮壓, 壓制

clan /klæn; klæn/ *n* [C] **1** a large group of families that often share the same name 宗族, 氏族: *the Campbell clan* 坎貝爾宗族 **2** *humorous* a word meaning a large family, used especially when they are all together on a special occasion【幽默】〔尤指在特殊場合聚在一起的〕大家族; 一大家人: *The whole clan will be here over Christmas.* 我們那一大幫親戚聖誕節期間將會來這裡住。

clan·des·tine /klænˈdɛstɪn; klænˈdestɪn/ *adj* clandestine activities or organizations are secret 祕密的, 暗中從事的: *a clandestine affair* 祕密事務

clang /klæŋ; klæŋ/ *v* [I,T] if a metal object clangs or if you clang it, it makes a loud ringing sound (使) 發出叮噹聲 —**clang** *n* [singular]

clang·er /ˈklæŋɚ; ˈklæŋə/ *n* **drop a clanger** *BrE informal* to make a careless remark that upsets or embarrasses someone very much【英, 非正式】失言失禮; 犯了明顯的錯誤

clang·our *BrE*【英】, **clangor** *AmE*【美】/ˈklæŋɚ; ˈklæŋə/ *n* [U] the hard ringing sound that is made when metal is hit〔由金屬發出的〕鏗鏘聲; 叮噹聲

clank /klæŋk; klæŋk/ *v* [I,T] if a metal object clanks or if you clank it, it makes a loud heavy sound (使)〔金屬〕發出噹啷聲 —**clank** *n* [C]: *the clank of machinery* 機器的噹啷聲

clans·man /ˈklænzmən; ˈklænzmən/ *n* [C] a male member of a CLAN 宗族[氏族]的男成員

clans·wom·an /ˈklænzˌwʊmən; ˈklænzˌwʊmən/ *n* [C] a female member of a CLAN 宗族或[氏族]的女成員

clap[1] /klæp; klæp/ *v* **clapped, clapping 1** [I] to hit your hands together loudly and continuously to show that you enjoyed a performance or that you approve of something 拍手, 鼓掌: *The crowd roared with approval and clapped.* 人羣發出一片喝采鼓掌聲。—see picture on page A20 參見 A20 頁圖 **2 clap your hands a)** to hit your hands together loudly and continuously to show that you approve, agree, or have enjoyed something 鼓掌 **b)** to hit your hands together to attract someone's attention or to stop them doing something 拍手〔引起某人的注意或示意某人停止〕: *She clapped her hands and shouted, "Rosie, stop that now!"* 她拍了拍手, 喊道: "羅茜, 停!" **3 clap sb on the back/shoulder etc** to hit someone lightly with your open hand in a friendly way or to show that you are amused 輕拍某人的背部/肩膀等 **4 clap eyes on** *BrE informal* to suddenly see someone or something【英, 非正式】突然看見: *Until this morning I'd never clapped eyes on him.* 今早以前我從來沒有見過他。**5 clap your hand on/over etc** to put your hand somewhere quickly and suddenly 突然把手放到: *Babs clapped her hand over her mouth saying, "My God, I think I left the oven on."* 巴布斯突然用手掩住嘴說: "天哪, 我想我沒把烤箱關掉。" **6 clap hold of** to take hold of someone or something suddenly 突然抓住: *I clapped hold of him by the shoulder and pushed him out of the front door.* 我猛地一把抓住他的肩膀, 把他推出前門。**7 clap sb in prison/jail/irons** to suddenly put someone in prison or chains 把某人投進監獄 —**clapping** *n* [U]

clap[2] *n* **1** [singular] a sudden loud sound that you make when you hit your hands together, especially to show that you enjoyed something or that you agree 拍手 (聲), 鼓掌 (聲): **give sb a clap** *BrE*【英】*Come on everyone, let's give Tommy a clap.* 來吧各位, 我們都來為湯米鼓掌吧。**2 a clap on the back/shoulder** an act of hitting someone on the back or shoulder to show that you are friendly or amused〔表示友好的〕輕拍背部/肩膀 **3 a clap of thunder** a loud sound made by thunder 雷鳴聲 **4 the clap** *slang* GONORRHOEA【俚】淋病

clap·board /ˈklæbɚd; ˈklæpbɔːd/ *n* [C,U] *AmE* a set of boards that cover the outside walls of a building, or one of these boards【美】〔建築物的〕外牆護牆板, 隔板; WEATHERBOARD (1) *BrE*【英】: *a clapboard house* 裝有護牆板的房子

clapped-out /ˌ· ˈ·◂/ *adj BrE informal* a clapped-out car, machine etc is in very bad condition because it is old and has been used a lot【英, 非正式】〔汽車、機器等〕破

舊的, 破爛的

clap·per /ˈklæpɚ; ˈklæpə/ *n* [C] **1** the metal thing inside a bell that hits it to make it ring 鐘錘; 鈴錘 **2** *BrE* a piece of equipment used by farmers that makes a noise to frighten birds away【英】〔農夫用以轟鳥的〕響板 **3 run like the clappers** *BrE informal* to run extremely fast【英, 非正式】飛快地奔跑: *You'll have to run like the clappers if you want to catch that bus.* 你得快跑才能趕上那輛公共汽車。

clap·trap /ˈklæpˌtræp; ˈklæptræp/ *n* [U] *informal* stupid talk【非正式】胡說; 譁眾取寵的話

C

clar·et /ˈklærət; ˈklærət/ *n* [C,U] **1** red wine from the Bordeaux area of France〔法國波爾多地區產的〕紅葡萄酒 **2** [U] a dark red colour 暗紫紅色 —**claret** *adj*

clar·i·fied but·ter /ˌ... ˈ../ *n* [U] butter that has been made clean and pure by heating it〔通過加熱而〕提純的黃油[牛油]

clar·i·fy /ˈklærəˌfaɪ; ˈklærɪ̈faɪ/ *v* [T] to make something clearer and easier to understand 澄清, 講清楚, 闡明: *Can you clarify that statement?* 你能把那句話的意思講清楚一點嗎? | **clarify how/what etc** *The report aims to clarify how these conclusions were reached.* 那份報告旨在闡明這些結論是如何得出的。| **clarify your position** (=tell people what you think about a particular subject and what you intend to do about it)〔對某問題〕闡明立場 *Reporters asked the Congressman to clarify his position on welfare reform.* 記者們要求該國會議員闡明他在福利改革問題上的立場。—**clarification** /ˌklærəfəˈkeʃən; ˌklærɪ̈fɪ̈ˈkeɪʃən/ *n* [U]

clar·i·net /ˌklærəˈnɛt; ˌklærɪ̈ˈnet/ *n* [C] a musical instrument shaped like a long black tube, which you play by blowing into it and pressing keys (KEY² (3)) to change the notes 單簧管, 黑管 —**clarinettist** *n* [C]

clar·i·on call /ˈklærɪən ˌkɔl; ˈklæriən ˌkɔːl/ *n* [C] a strong and direct request for people to do something 強烈的呼喚

clar·i·ty /ˈklærəti; ˈklærɪ̈ti/ *n* [U] the quality of expressing ideas or thoughts in a clear way 清晰, 清楚; 易懂: *the clarity and precision of his prose* 他的散文思路清晰嚴謹 | **clarity of vision/purpose** *Churchill's clarity of vision impressed all who knew him.* 邱吉爾的遠見卓識給所有認識他的人留下了深刻的印象。

clash¹ /klæʃ; klæʃ/ *v* **1** [I] if two armies, or groups of people clash, they suddenly start fighting each other (發生)衝突: *Troops clashed near the border.* 軍隊在邊境附近發生衝突。| [+with] *Police have clashed with demonstrators again today.* 今天警方和遊行示威羣眾再次發生衝突。**2** [I] if two people or groups of people clash, they argue because their opinions and beliefs are very different〔因意見分歧而〕爭論, 爭執: [+with] *Democrats clashed with Republicans in a heated debate.* 民主黨人和共和黨人進行了激烈的爭論。**3** [I] if two colours or patterns clash, they look very bad together〔顏色、花樣〕不相配, 不協調: [+with] *That purple tie clashes with your red shirt.* 那條紫色領帶和你的紅襯衫不相配。**4** [I] if two events clash, they happen at the same time in a way that is inconvenient〔兩件事情〕撞期: [+with] *Unfortunately the concert clashed with Ann and Jim's dinner party.* 真可惜, 音樂會與安和吉姆的晚宴撞期了。**5** [I,T] if two pieces of metal clash or if you clash them, they make a loud ringing sound (使)發出〔金屬相碰的〕撞擊聲: *The cymbals clashed.* 鐃鈸碰擊作響。

clash² *n* [C] **1** a short fight between two armies or groups of people 衝突; 打鬥: *border clashes* 邊境衝突 **2** an argument between two people or groups of people 爭論, 交鋒: *a clash of temperament* 脾氣不合 | [+between] *angry clashes between Tory and Labour ministers* 保守黨和工黨部長們的激烈交鋒 | **personality clash** (=a situation in which two people do not like each other) 性格上難以相容 **3** a loud sound made by two metal objects being hit together〔金屬〕碰撞聲: *the clash of swords* 劍的撞擊聲 **4** a combination of two colours, designs etc that look bad together〔顏色、花樣等的〕不相配, 不協調 **5** a situation in which two events happen at the same time in a way that is inconvenient〔時間上的〕衝突, 撞期: *a scheduling clash on TV* 電視節目時間的衝突

clasp¹ /klæsp; klɑːsp/ *n* **1** [C] a small metal object for fastening a bag, belt, piece of jewellery etc 鉤; 扣子; 扣環 **2** [singular] a tight hold; GRIP¹ (1) 緊握; 緊抱: *the firm, reassuring clasp of her hand* 她那堅定而使人放心的握手

clasp² *v* [T] **1** to hold someone or something tightly, closing your fingers or arms around them 握緊; 抱緊; 抓住: *A baby monkey clasps its mother's fur tightly.* 小猴子緊緊地抓住母猴的毛。| **clasp sb/sth in your hands/arms** *She clasped the photograph in her hands.* 她將照片緊握在手中。| **clasp sb to your chest/bosom** (=hold someone tightly because you love them or are upset, frightened etc) 抱住; 摟住 **2** to fasten something with a clasp〔用扣環〕扣住; 鉤住

clasp knife /ˈ. ./ *n* [C] a large knife with blades that fold into the handle; JACK-KNIFE¹ (1) 大摺刀

class¹ /klæs; klɑːs/ *n*

1 ►IN A SOCIETY 社會上◄ a) [C] one of the groups in a society that people can be divided into according to their jobs, income, the kind of family they have etc 階級, 社會等級: *the professional classes* 專業階層 | **class differences/distinctions/privileges etc** *Class divisions are as evident in Britain today as ever.* 不論現在或以前階級劃分在英國都同樣明顯。—see also 另見 LOWER CLASS, MIDDLE CLASS, UPPER CLASS, WORKING CLASS **b)** [U] the system in which people are divided into such groups 社會等級制度: **class system** *The old class system is slowly disappearing.* 舊的社會等級制度正在慢慢消失。

2 ►GROUP OF STUDENTS 學生羣◄ [C] a group of pupils or students who are taught together 班, 班級, 年級: *We're in the same class in math.* 我們上數學課是在同一個班的。| [also+plural verb *BrE* 英] *My class are going on an outing to the Lake District.* 我們班要去湖區郊遊。

3 ►TEACHING PERIOD 教學時段◄ [C,U] a period of time during which someone teaches a group of people, especially in a school (一節)課, 上課, 上課時間; LESSON (2) *BrE*【英】: **in class** (=during the class) 上課時 *No talking in class!* 課堂上不許講話! | **take a class** *BrE* (=teach a class)【英】講課 | **geography/French/cooking class** (=a period of time during which a particular subject is taught) 地理/法語/烹飪課

4 ►LESSONS 課◄ [C] *AmE* a set of classes you attend in order to study a particular subject【美】(一門)課程; COURSE¹ (3) *BrE*【英】: *a class in photography at night school* 夜校的攝影課程

5 ►COLLEGE 學院◄ [C] *especially AmE* a group of students who finished studying together in the same year【尤美】同屆學生: *I missed a semester and couldn't graduate with my class.* 我漏了一學期課, 所以沒能和同學一起畢業。| **the class of 1965/1973 etc** *The class of '69 spent almost as much time protesting as learning.* 69年畢業的同學花在抗議和學習上的時間幾乎一樣多。

6 ►OF ANIMALS/PLANTS ETC 動/植物等的◄ [C] a group of people, animals, or other things that can be considered or studied together because they are similar in some way〔動、植物分類學上的〕綱

7 ►QUALITY 質量◄ [C] a group into which people or things are divided according to their quality〔人或事物的〕等級: *You get a nicer class of people living in this area.* 這個地區居住着較高修養的人。| **in a class of its own** (=used to say someone or something is excellent) 極好的, 一流的 *Your mother's cooking is in a class of its own.* 你母親的烹飪技術一流。| **not in the same class** (=not as good as someone or something) 不及, 不如, 不能與…相比擬 *He's not in the same class as her at tennis.* 他在網球方面和她是沒法相比的。—see also 另見 BUSINESS CLASS, CABIN CLASS, CLUB CLASS, ECONOMY CLASS, FIRST CLASS, HIGH-CLASS, LOW-CLASS, SECOND CLASS, THIRD CLASS, TOURIST CLASS

8 ▶STYLE 風格◀ [U] *informal* style or skill that you show in the way you do something, that makes people notice and admire you【非正式】〔風格、技巧等的〕優雅, 出眾, 令人讚賞: **have/show class** *The team showed real class in this afternoon's match.* 這支隊伍在下午的比賽中確實表現出眾。| **class player/actress etc** (=very good player, actress, etc) 一流的運動員/女演員等 | **class act** (=used to describe someone who is very skilful, attractive etc) 出類拔萃的人 *The company's very well managed, the class act of the industry.* 這家公司經營得非常好, 在該行業中是數一數二的。
9 ▶DEGREE 學位◀ [C] *BrE* one of the three levels into which a university degree is divided according to the quality of the work【英】〔大學學位的〕等級: *a second class degree* 二等[級]學位

class² *v* [T often passive 常用被動態] to consider people, things etc as belonging to a particular group, especially according to an official system 把…歸類; 把…看作: **class sb/sth as** *Heroin and cocaine are classed as hard drugs.* 海洛因和可卡因被看作是毒性極強的毒品。

class ac·tion /ˌ· ˈ··◂/ *n* [C,U] *AmE* a LAWSUIT arranged by a group of people for themselves and also for others with the same problem【美】集體控告[訴訟]

class-con·scious /ˈ· ˌ··/ *adj* always judging other people according to the social class they belong to 有階級意識的 —**class-consciousness** *n* [U]

3 **clas·sic¹** /ˈklæsɪk; ˈklæsɪk/ *adj* **1** a classic book, play, film etc is important or special and remains popular for a long time 經典的: *The Coca-Cola bottle is one of the classic designs of the last century.* 可口可樂瓶是上個世紀的經典設計之一。**2** of excellent quality 極優秀的, 第一流的: *Roy scored a classic goal in the 90th minute.* 羅伊在90分鐘時踢進了漂亮的一球。**3** a classic style of art or clothing is attractive in a simple traditional way 式樣簡樸的, 傳統式樣的: *a classic raincoat* 傳統式樣的雨衣 **4 a classic example/case etc** a very typical example of something, sometimes in an impressive or humorous way 典型例子/情況等: *Tom made the classic mistake of trying to drive away without releasing the handbrake.* 湯姆犯了一個典型的錯誤, 那就是沒有鬆開手煞車就想開車。

classic² *n* [C] **1** a book, play, or film that is important and has been popular for a long time 名著; 經典作品; 傑作: *'La Grande Illusion' is one of the classics of French cinema.* 《大幻影》是法國電影中的經典作品之一。**2** something that is very good and one of the best examples of its kind 典範: *The 1976 semi-final between Borg and Gerulaitis was a classic.* 1976年〔瑞典網球名將〕博格和格魯來提斯間的半決賽堪稱一絕。**3 classics** [plural] the language, literature, and history of Ancient Rome and Greece 古羅馬、古希臘的語言、文學及歷史: *Judith studied classics at Oxford.* 朱迪斯在牛津讀古典文化課程。**4 that's (a) classic!** *spoken* used when you think something is extremely funny【口】太滑稽了!

3 **clas·si·cal** /ˈklæsɪkl; ˈklæsɪkəl/ *adj* **1** based on or belonging to a traditional style or set of ideas, especially in art or science〔尤指藝術、科學〕經典的; 傳統的, 正統的: *classical physics, as opposed to quantum physics* 與量子物理學相對的經典物理學 **2** connected with the language, literature etc of Ancient Greece and Rome 古典的; 古典派的; 與古希臘、羅馬有關的: **classical education** (=an education that includes studying Latin and Greek)〔包括希臘文與拉丁文的〕古典教育

classical mu·sic /ˌ··· ˈ··/ *n* [U] music that people consider to be serious and that has been popular for a long time 古典音樂

clas·si·cis·m /ˈklæsəˌsɪzəm; ˈklæsɪsɪzəm/ *n* [U] a style of art that is simple, regular, and does not show too much emotion, based on the models of Ancient Greece or Rome 古典主義; 古典風格 —compare 比較 REALISM, ROMANTICISM

clas·si·cist /ˈklæsəsɪst; ˈklæsɪsɪst/ *n* [C] someone who studies classics (CLASSIC² (3)) 古典主義者; 古典學者

clas·si·fi·ca·tion /ˌklæsəfəˈkeʃən; ˌklæsɪfɪˈkeɪʃən/ *n* **1** [U] a process in which you put something into the group or class it belongs to 歸類, 分類, 分級: *the classification of wines according to quality* 把葡萄酒按質分類 **2** [C] a group or class into which something is put 類別, 等級: *job classifications* 工作類別

clas·si·fied /ˈklæsəˌfaɪd; ˈklæsɪfaɪd/ *adj* classified information or documents are ones which the government has ordered to be kept secret〔資料或文件〕保密的, 機密的

classified ad /ˌ··· ˈ·/ also 又作 **classified** *BrE*【英】*n* [C] a small advertisement you put in a newspaper if you want to buy or sell something〔報紙上的〕分類廣告; SMALL AD, WANT AD *AmE*【美】

classified di·rec·to·ry /ˌ··· ·ˈ···/ *n* [C] *BrE* a book that gives a list of the addresses and telephone numbers of companies under the title of their job or business【英】分類電話號碼簿

clas·si·fy /ˈklæsəˌfaɪ; ˈklæsɪfaɪ/ *v* [T] **1** to decide what group a plant, animal, book etc belong to according to a system〔依據某系統〕將…分類: **classify sth as** *Is this plant classified as a moss or a lichen?* 這種植物歸為苔蘚還是歸為地衣? **2** to regard people or things as belonging to a particular type because they have the same physical features, qualities etc 把…歸入一類[一個等級] —**classifiable** *adj*

class·is·m /ˈklæsɪzəm; ˈklɑːsɪzəm/ *n* [U] the belief that one social class, especially the one you belong to, is better than another 階級偏見 —**classist** *adj*

class·less /ˈklæslɪs; ˈklɑːsləs/ *adj* **1** a classless society is one in which people are not divided into different social classes〔社會〕不分階級[階層]的 **2** a classless person does not clearly belong to one particular social class〔人〕不屬於某一特定階級[階層]的 —**classlessness** *n* [U]

class·mate /ˈklæsˌmet; ˈklɑːsmeɪt/ *n* [C] a member of the same class in a school, college or, in the US, a university 同班同學

class·room /ˈklæsˌrum; ˈklɑːs-rʊm/ *n* [C] a room that you have lessons in at a school or college 教室, 課室 3 3

class strug·gle /ˌ· ˈ··/ *n* [singular,U] the Marxist theory that social reality is a continuing struggle for political and economic power between CAPITALISTS (=the owners of property, factories etc) and the PROLETARIAT (=the workers)〔馬克思主義學說中資產階級與無產階級的〕階級鬥爭

class·work /ˈklæsˌwɝk; ˈklɑːswɜːk/ *n* [U] school work done by students in a class rather than at home 課堂作業 —compare 比較 HOMEWORK (1)

class·y /ˈklæsɪ; ˈklɑːsi/ *adj informal* fashionable and expensive【非正式】昂貴時髦的; 高級的, 上等的: *classy restaurants* 高級餐廳

clat·ter /ˈklætɚ; ˈklætə/ *v* **1** [I,T] if heavy hard objects clatter, or if you clatter them, they make a loud unpleasant noise (使) 發出撞擊聲: *The tray fell clattering to the ground.* 盤子啪啦一聲掉在地上。**2** [I alway+adv/prep] to move quickly and noisily 急速而發出響聲地走: **clatter over/down/along etc** *The horse went clattering over the cobbles.* 馬咔噠咔噠地走過卵石鋪成的街道。—**clatter** *n* [singular,U]: *the clatter of dishes* 盤碟相碰的噹啷聲

clause /klɔz; klɔːz/ *n* [C] **1** a part of a written law or legal document covering a particular subject of the whole law or document〔法律等文件中的〕條款, 項目: *A confidentiality clause was added to the contract.* 合同中加上了一條保密條款。**2** *technical* a group of words that contains a subject and a verb, but which is usually only part of a sentence【術語】從句, 分句, 子句 —compare 比較 PHRASE¹ (2) 

claus·tro·pho·bi·a /ˌklɔstrəˈfobɪə; ˌklɔːstrəˈfəʊbiə/ *n* [U] a strong fear of being in a small enclosed space or among a crowd of people 幽閉恐懼症 —compare 比較 AGORAPHOBIA

claus·tro·pho·bic /ˌklɔstrəˈfobɪk; ˌklɔːstrəˈfəʊbɪk◂/ *adj* **1** feeling extremely anxious when you are in a small

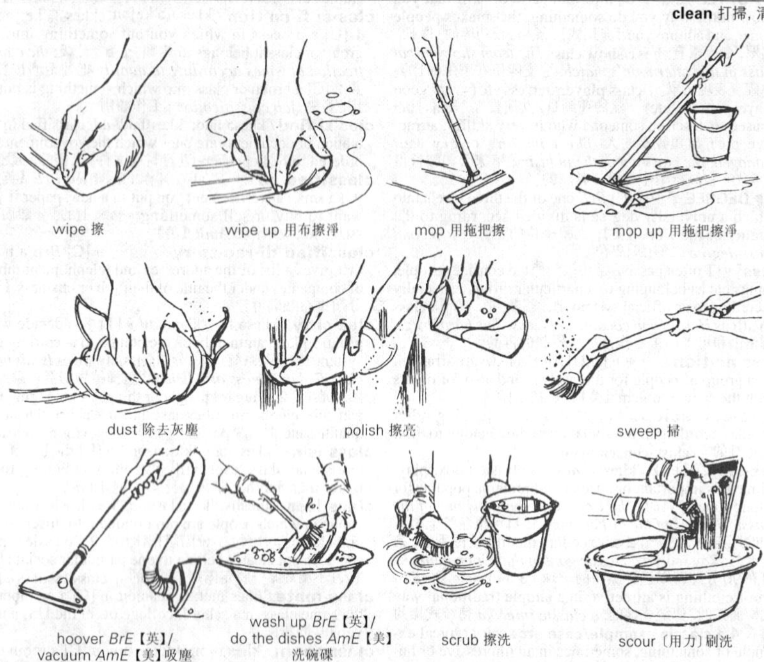

enclosed space 有幽閉恐懼症的: *I get claustrophobic in elevators.* 在電梯裡, 我有種幽閉恐懼症。**2** making you feel anxious and uncomfortable as if you are enclosed in a small space〔場所〕導致幽閉恐懼症的: *a claustrophobic atmosphere* 一種能導致幽閉恐懼症的氣氛

clav·i·chord /ˈklævəˌkɔrd; ˈklævɪ̩kɔːd/ *n* [C] a musical instrument like a piano that was played especially in the past〔尤舊時用的〕擊弦古鋼琴; 翼琴

clav·i·cle /ˈklævəkl̩; ˈklævɪkəl/ *n* [C] *technical* a COLLARBONE【術語】鎖骨 —see picture at 參見 SKELETON 圖

claw¹ /klɔ; klɔː/ *n* [C] **1** a sharp curved nail on the toe of an animal or bird〔鳥、獸的〕爪: *The cat dug his claws into my leg.* 那隻貓用爪子抓我的腿。**2 get your claws into sb a)** if a woman gets her claws into a man, she shows that she is determined to marry him 決心嫁給某人 **b)** to say unpleasant things about someone in order to upset them 攻擊某人, 中傷某人: *Wait till the papers get their claws into him.* 一直等到報紙攻擊他為止。**3** [usually plural 一般用複數] the part of the body of some insects and sea animals that is used for attacking and holding things〔昆蟲、蝦、蟹等的〕螯, 鉗 —see picture at 參見 CRAB¹ 圖 **4** the curved end of a tool or machine used for pulling nails out of wood and lifting things 拔釘爪, 起釘器: *a claw hammer* 拔釘鎚

claw² *v* [I,T] **1** to tear or pull at something using claws〔用爪〕抓; 撕: [+at] *The cat keeps clawing at the rug.* 貓不停地用爪子抓地毯。**2** to try very hard to get hold of something 奮力抓住: *Mary clawed at her husband's sleeve, trying to stop him.* 瑪麗使勁拽住丈夫的衣袖, 想要阻止他。| **claw your way up/along/across etc** (=move somewhere slowly by holding tightly onto things as you move) 慢慢地攀[爬]

claw sth ↔ **back** *phr v* [T] **1** to get back something that you had lost, by working very hard 奪回, 撈回; 設法彌補: *Through aggressive advertising, the company managed to claw back its share of the market.* 該公司通過大做廣告, 成功地奪回了它的那部分市場。**2** *BrE* if a government claws back money that ordinary people have been allowed to keep or get, it gets it back by increasing taxes【英】〔政府用增加稅款的手段〕收回〔減免的稅款〕

clay /kle; kleɪ/ *n* [U] heavy sticky soil that can be used for making pots, bricks etc 黏土 —see also 另見 **feet of clay** (FOOT¹ (24)) —**clayey** *adj*

clay pi·geon shoot·ing /ˌ·ˈ·· ˌ··/ *n* [U] *BrE* a sport in which you shoot at pieces of hard clay that are thrown up into the air【英】泥鴿射擊運動〔射擊用黏土製成的盤形飛靶〕; SKEET SHOOTING *AmE*【美】

clean¹ /klin; kliːn/ *adj*

1 ▶WITHOUT DIRT 無塵的◀ without any dirt or marks 清潔的, 乾淨的: *Are your hands clean?* 你的手乾淨嗎? | *a clean towel* 乾淨的毛巾 | **sweep/scrub etc sth clean** *Wipe that sink clean when you're done.* 洗完後將水槽擦乾淨。| **clean and tidy/neat** *Try to keep your room clean and tidy.* 保持房間整潔。| **spotlessly clean** (=very clean) 一塵不染的 *a spotlessly clean kitchen* 一塵不染的廚房

2 ▶HABITS/APPEARANCE 習慣/外表◀ behaving in a way that keeps things clean or having a clean appearance 愛清潔的: *Cats are wonderfully clean creatures.* 貓是極愛乾淨的動物。

3 ▶AIR/WATER 空氣/水◀ containing nothing that is dirty or harmful, such as poisons 純淨的; 無病菌的: *Smell that clean air!* 呼吸一下那潔淨的空氣!

4 ▶FAIR/LEGAL 公平/合法的◀ **a)** done in a fair or legal way 公平的; 不作弊的; 合法的: *a clean fight* 公平的打鬥 **b)** showing that you have followed the rules or the law 無過失[違法]記錄的: *a clean driving licence* 無違規記錄的駕駛執照 | *Well, she has a clean record.* (=she

is not a criminal) 嗯, 她無違法記錄。
5 ►JOKES/HUMOUR 玩笑/幽默◄ not offensive or not dealing with sex 不猥褻的, 不下流的; 正派的; 無挑釁性的: **good, clean fun** *Oh, don't get mad – it was just good, clean fun!* 噢, 不要生氣——只不過開了個正派的玩笑! | **keep it clean** (=used to tell someone not to do or say anything morally offensive) 保持清白 | **clean living** (=a way of life in which you do not drink, take drugs, or behave in an immoral way) 清白的生活
6 make a clean breast of it to admit that you have done something wrong so that you no longer feel guilty 全盤托出, 坦白供認
7 a clean break a) a quick sudden separation from a person, organization, place etc 〔與某人或機構等〕一刀兩斷, 脱離關係; 決裂: *Den left the next day, needing to make a clean break.* 因為要徹底脱離關係, 丹恩第二天就走了。**b)** a break in a bone or other object that is complete and has not left any small pieces 徹底斷裂, 折斷
8 ►SMOOTH 平滑的◄ having a smooth or regular edge or surface 表面光滑的; 邊緣整齊的: *a clean cut* 整齊的切口
9 come clean *informal* to finally tell the truth or admit that you have done something wrong【非正式】最終認錯; 坦白交代, 承認: **[+about]** *It's time you came clean about your affair.* 該承認你做的事了吧。
10 a clean sheet/slate a situation that shows that someone has behaved well or not made any mistakes 過去無過錯記錄的: *Jed looked forward to starting life again with a clean sheet.* 傑德期望清清白白地重新做人。
11 a clean bill of health a report that says you are healthy or that a machine or building is safe 健康狀況良好證明書; 機器[建築物]狀況良好證明: *Inspectors gave the factory a clean bill of health.* 檢查員證實該工廠狀況良好。
12 a clean sweep a) a complete change in a company or organization, made by getting rid of people 〔公司或機構的〕大換班; 大改變 **b)** a victory in all parts of a game or competition, especially by winning the first three places 〔在比賽中〕大獲全勝〔尤指獲前三名〕: *The 200m race was a clean sweep for France.* 法國運動員包攬了200米賽跑的全部獎牌。
13 ►PAPER 紙◄ a piece of paper that is clean has not yet been used 未用過的, 新的
14 a clean copy a piece of writing that contains no mistakes 〔文稿〕無錯誤的
15 ►WITHOUT WEAPONS/DRUGS 無武器/無毒品◄ [not before noun 不用於名詞前] *slang* not having any hidden weapons or illegal drugs【俚】沒有私帶武器[毒品]的: *They searched him at the airport, but he was clean.* 他們在機場對他進行了搜查, 但他身上沒有違禁品。
16 ►NOT HAVING DRUGS 不吸毒的◄ [not before noun 不用於名詞前] no longer taking illegal drugs 不再吸毒的: *Dave's been clean for two years now.* 戴夫已經戒毒兩年了。
17 ►POWER/ENERGY 動力/能源◄ producing energy or power without causing POLLUTION 無污染的: **clean energy** (=energy that is produced safely) 無污染的能源
18 ►MOVEMENT 運動◄ a clean movement in sport is skilful and exact 〔體育運動〕動作乾淨利落的
19 as clean as a new pin *BrE*【英】**as clean as a whistle** very clean 非常清潔的 —see also 另見 CLEANLY, CLEAN-CUT, **keep your nose clean** (NOSE[1] (13)) —**cleanness** *n* [U]

1 3 **clean²** *v* **1** [I,T] to remove dirt from something by rubbing or washing 把…弄乾淨, 使清潔, 清理: *Your shoes need cleaning.* 你的鞋該刷一刷了。—see also 另見 DRY-CLEAN, SPRING-CLEAN **2** [I] to clean a building or other people's houses as your job 〔作為工作〕打掃衞生: *Anne comes in to clean twice a week.* 安妮每週來清掃兩次。**3** [T] to cut out the inside parts of an animal or bird that you are going to cook 給〔準備食用的動物、家禽等〕開膛取出內臟 **4 clean your plate** to eat all your food 〔把食物〕吃完, 吃光

clean sb/sth **out** *phr v* [T] **1** [**clean** sth ↔ **out**] to make the inside of a room, house etc clean or tidy 把〔房間、屋子的內部〕打掃乾淨: *We'd better clean out the attic this week.* 我們本週最好清掃一下閣樓。**2** [**clean** sb/sth ↔ **out**] *informal* to steal everything from a place or all someone's possessions【非正式】把〔某處〕盜竊一空, 偷光: *Burglars completely cleaned the place out.* 竊賊將所有東西都偷光了。**3** [**clean** sb **out**] *informal* if something expensive cleans someone out, they spend all their money on it so that they have none left【非正式】用[耗]盡…的錢財: *The Paris trip cleaned us out.* 巴黎之旅把我們的錢全用光了。

clean up *phr v* **1** [I,T] to make something completely clean and tidy 打掃乾淨; 清理: *We spent all Saturday morning cleaning up.* 我們整個星期六上午都在打掃清理。| *a plan to clean up the bay* 清理海灣的計劃 **2** [I,T] to wash yourself after you have got very dirty 把〔身體〕洗乾淨: **clean sb/yourself up** *Let me just go clean myself up.* 讓我去洗一洗。| **get cleaned up** *Dad's upstairs getting cleaned up.* 爸爸在樓上洗澡。**3 clean up your act** *informal* to start behaving in a responsible way【非正式】改掉不良行為: *If you don't clean up your act I'll kick you out.* 如果你不改掉壞習慣, 我就讓你滾蛋。**4** [I] *informal* to win a lot of money or make a lot of money in a business deal【非正式】賺得[贏得]一大筆錢: *We really cleaned up at the races today!* 今天的賽馬確實讓我們發了財! **5** [T **clean** sth ↔ **up**] to improve moral standards in a place or organization 肅清, 整頓〔秩序、治安〕: *It's high time British soccer cleaned up its image.* 英式足球該改善一下它的形象了。—see also 另見 CLEAN-UP

clean³ *adv informal* used to emphasize the fact that an action or movement takes place completely and thoroughly【非正式】〔行為、動作〕完全地; 徹底地: **clean away/through/past** *The robbers got clean away.* 竊賊逃得無影無蹤。| *The knife went clean through his finger.* 小刀穿透他的手指。| **clean forget** (=forget completely) 忘得一乾二淨 *Sorry, I clean forgot your birthday.* 對不起, 我完全忘了你的生日。

clean⁴ *n* [singular] a process in which you clean something 清理, 打掃: *The car needs a good clean.* 車子需要好好地洗一洗。

clean-cut /ˌ· ˈ·◂/ *adj* someone who is clean-cut looks neat and clean 外貌整潔體面的: *clean-cut college boys* 外表整潔體面的男大學生

clean·er /ˈklinɚ; ˈkliːnə/ *n* [C] **1** someone whose job is to clean other people's houses, offices etc 清潔工人 **2** a machine or substance used for cleaning 清潔器; 清潔劑: *a vacuum cleaner* 真空吸塵器 **3 the cleaner's** a DRY CLEANER's 洗衣店, 乾洗店 **4 take sb to the cleaner's** *informal*【非正式】**a)** to cheat someone out of all their money or possessions 騙光某人的錢, 使…破產 **b)** to defeat someone completely 徹底打敗[擊敗]: *The Lakers took the Bulls to the cleaner's, winning 96–72.* 湖人隊以96-72大勝公牛隊。 3

clean·ing /ˈklinɪŋ; ˈkliːnɪŋ/ *n* [U] a process in which you clean other people's houses, offices etc 〔為他人的住宅、辦公室等作的〕清理, 打掃: **the cleaning** *Liz comes on Thursday to do the cleaning.* 莉茲星期四來打掃〔房間〕。

cleaning lady /ˈ·· ˌ··/ also 又作 **cleaning woman** *n* [C] a woman who cleans offices, houses etc as her job 清潔女工

clean-limbed /ˌ· ˈ·◂/ *adj* tall and active-looking 高大靈活的: *a clean-limbed athlete* 一個高大靈活的運動員

clean·li·ness /ˈklɛnlɪnəs; ˈklenlinǝs/ *n* [U] the practice of keeping yourself or the things around you clean 〔保持〕清潔; 〔保持〕衞生

clean·ly /ˈklinlɪ; ˈkliːnli/ *adv* quickly and smoothly with just one movement 利落地: *The branch snapped cleanly in two.* 樹枝整整齊齊地斷成兩截。

cleanse /klɛnz; klenz/ *v* [T] **1** to get rid of any dirt from a wound or from your skin 使清潔, 清洗〔傷口或皮膚〕: *Use a piece of gauze to cleanse the cut.* 用一塊棉紗清洗

C

傷口。**2** [+of/from] *biblical* to make someone no longer guilty for things they have done wrong【聖經】使…免除罪惡, 使…清白, 淨化

cleans·er /ˈklɛnzə; ˈklenzə/ *n* [C,U] **1** a liquid used for removing dirt or MAKE-UP (1) from your face 潔面乳 **2** a chemical liquid or powder used for cleaning surfaces inside a house, office etc 清潔劑; 去污粉: *cream cleanser for the bathroom* 浴室清潔乳劑

clean-shav·en /,· ˈ··◂/ *adj* a man who is clean-shaven does not have hair on his face 鬍子刮得很乾淨的 —see picture on page A6 參見A6頁圖

clean-up /ˈ· ·/ *n* [C usually singular 一般用單數] a process by which you get rid of dirt or waste from a place 清掃; 掃除: *a clean-up program designed to tackle car pollution* 清除汽車污染的計劃 | **clean-up campaign/programme/measures** *The mayor launched the clean-up campaign.* 市長發起了清潔運動。

clear¹ /klɪr; klɪə/ *adj*

1 ▶EASY TO UNDERSTAND 易懂的◀ expressed in a simple and direct way so that people understand 清楚的, 明白的: *clear instructions* 清楚的指示 | *You must never do that again. Is that clear?* 不許你再那樣做, 明白嗎? | **be clear on** *The rules are quite clear on the point.* 在這一點上各項規定都明白易懂。| **clear to sb** *Is all this clear to you?* 你全都明白了嗎? | **make sth clear** (=express something strongly) 清楚地闡述 *Taylor's book makes the subject exquisitely clear.* 泰勒的書很清楚地闡釋了這一主題。| **make it clear (that)** *Mr Tate made it clear there was to be no compromise.* 泰特先生清楚地說明沒有商量的餘地。| **make yourself clear** (=express something well) 表達清楚 *To make yourself clear without using facial expressions can be very difficult.* 很難不藉助面部表情而清楚地表達自己。| **get sth clear** *Let's get one thing clear; you have my wholehearted support.* 你要明白一件事, 我全力支持你。| **Do I make myself clear?** (=used when you are angry and are telling someone to do or not to do something) 你聽明白我的意思了嗎? *If I catch you smoking again you're grounded. Do I make myself clear?* 如果再讓我發現你抽煙, 我就要你好看, 我的話你聽清楚了嗎? | **a clear picture/idea** (=a good understanding) 清晰的理解 | **crystal clear** (=very easy to understand) 很容易理解

2 ▶IMPOSSIBLE TO DOUBT 無疑◀ impossible to doubt, question, or be mistaken about 無可置疑的; 明白無誤的, 明確的; 明顯的: *clear evidence of guilt* 有罪的確鑿證據 | *They won by a clear majority.* 他們以明顯的多數獲勝。| **clear whether/why/how etc** *It is not yet clear whether we will benefit or not.* 我們是否會獲益目前還不清楚。| **it is clear that** *It is clear that this situation cannot last much longer.* 很明顯這種局勢維持不了多久。| **become clear** *It has become increasingly clear that privileges have been abused.* 特權被濫用了, 這一點是越來越清楚了。| **a clear case/example of sth** *a clear case of theft* 一宗無可置疑的偷竊案

3 ▶CERTAIN 確定◀ **be clear** to feel certain that you know or understand something 確信的; 充分了解的: [+about/on] *Are you all clear now about what you have to do?* 大家全都清楚自己要幹甚麼了嗎? | **clear whether/what/how etc** *I'm still not really clear how this machine works.* 這台機器該怎樣操作, 我還不大清楚。

4 ▶SUBSTANCE/LIQUID 物質/液體◀ transparent 透明的: *a clear gel* 透明的凝膠

5 ▶WATER/AIR 水/空氣◀ clean and fresh 清澈的; 清新的: *a crystal clear mountain lake* 水晶般清澈的山湖

6 clear sky/day etc without clouds, mist, smoke etc 晴朗的天空 / 日子等

7 ▶EYES 眼睛◀ very pure in colour and without any redness 亮晶晶的, 明亮的

8 ▶SKIN 皮膚◀ smooth and without any red spots 光潔的

9 ▶EASY TO SEE 易見的◀ easy to see 看得清楚的: *The photo was fuzzy, not clear at all.* 照片很模糊, 一點都看不清楚。

10 ▶EASY TO HEAR 易聽見的◀ easy to hear, and therefore easy to understand 聽得清的; 易懂的: *a clear speaking voice* 口齒清楚 | *The radio reception isn't very clear.* 收音機的接收不太清晰。| **clear as a bell** (=very easy to hear and understand) 像鐘聲一般清晰洪亮

11 ▶AFTER TAX 稅後◀ a clear amount of profit, wages etc is what is left after taxes have been paid on it; NET³ (1)〔工資、收入等完稅後〕淨得的: *I get £200 a week clear.* 我每週的純收入為200英鎊。| **a clear $10,000/£400 etc** *It pays a clear $30,000 per year.* 每年淨得30,000美元。

12 a clear month/two clear weeks/five clear days etc used to say that you have a whole month, two weeks etc to do something without having to do anything else 整整一個月 / 兩個星期 / 五天〔指該段時間全被用於做某事〕

13 see your way clear (to doing sth) *informal* to have the necessary time or willingness to be able to do something【非正式】認為 (做某事) 適當;願意, (做某事): *I was hoping you could see your way clear to lending me $150.* 我希望你會願意借給我150美元。

14 a clear conscience the knowledge that you have done the right thing 問心無愧: *Now I've explained what happened, I can go with a clear conscience.* 我已經將所發生的事情向你解釋清楚了, 我現在問心無愧。

15 ▶NOT BLOCKED 無阻塞的◀ not covered or blocked by anything that stops you from doing or seeing what you want 暢通的; 無阻礙的; 無遮蓋的: *Finally! A clear desk.* 桌子終於整理乾淨了! | **clear view/look** *From the top floor you get a clear view of the bay.* 從頂層可將海灣一覽無遺。

16 ▶NOT BUSY 不忙的◀ without any planned activities or events 沒事的; 不忙的; 空閒的: *Next Monday is clear; shall we meet then?* 下週一有空, 我們那時見面, 怎麼樣?

17 a clear head the ability to think clearly and quickly 思維敏銳的; 頭腦清晰的: *I won't drink now – I'll need a clear head to face Susan.* 我不喝 (酒) 了 — 我要以清醒的頭腦面對蘇姍。

18 be clear of to not touch something or to be ahead of someone or something 不擋路的; 不妨礙的: *He parked the car clear of the entrance.* 他將車停在不擋進口處的地方。| *United are clear of their nearest rivals.* 聯隊毫無敵手。

19 as clear as mud *spoken humorous* used to say that something is very difficult to understand【口, 幽默】一點都不清楚, 極難理解 —see also 另見 ALL CLEAR, CLARITY, CLEARLY, **the coast is clear** (COAST¹ (2)) —**clearness** *n* [U]

clear² *v*

1 ▶SURFACE/PLACE 表面/地方◀ [T] to make a surface or place emptier or tidier by removing things that cover it 清除; 清理: **clear sth of** *The room had been cleared of all his possessions.* 他房間裡的東西都被清理掉了。| **clear a space for** (=move things so that there is room for something else) 為…騰出地方 *Sally cleared a space on her desk for the computer.* 莎莉騰出書桌的一角放電腦。| **clear the table** (=take plates, forks, knives etc off the table after you have eaten) 收拾餐桌

2 ▶UNBLOCK 清除障礙◀ [T] to remove something that is blocking something else or causing a problem 清理〔障礙〕; 清除〔麻煩〕: *Snowploughs have been out clearing the roads.* 掃雪車一直在清掃路面。| **clear sb/sth from sth** *Police cleared crowds from the area.* 警察把人羣從該地區驅走了。

3 ▶OF A CRIME/BLAME ETC 關於犯罪/責任的◀ [T usually passive 一般用被動態] to prove that someone is not guilty of something 證明…無罪; 洗脫…的嫌疑: *Rawlings was cleared after new evidence was produced.* 提出新的證據後, 羅林斯終被證明是無罪的。| **clear sb of (doing) sth** *Maya was cleared of manslaughter.* 美雅已被證明沒有犯誤殺罪。| **clear sb's name** *He fought for years to clear his name.* 他多年來奮力地為自己洗清罪名。

4 ▶GIVE/GET PERMISSION 給予/得到許可◀ [T] **a)** to give or get official permission for something to be done 批准; 使得到…的許可: *The plans have not yet been cleared by the council.* 這幾項計劃尚未得到議會的批准。| **clear sth with sb** *I'll have to clear that with my boss first.* 此事我要先取得老闆的批准。**b)** to give official permission for a person, ship, or aircraft to enter or leave a country 允許〔入境或出境〕: *The plane took off as soon as it was cleared.* 飛機一得到許可就起飛了。

5 clear sth through customs/clear customs to be allowed to take things through customs (CUSTOM (4)) 允許通過海關, 清關

6 ▶WEATHER 天氣◀ [I] if the weather, sky, mist etc clears, conditions become brighter or easier to see through 變晴朗: *We'll wait till the fog clears.* 我們要等到大霧散去。

7 ▶LIQUID 液體◀ [I] if a liquid clears, it becomes more transparent 變清澈

8 ▶CHEQUE 支票◀ [I,T] if a cheque clears or if a bank clears it, the money is moved from one bank to another 〔經由銀行〕結算; 兑現

9 clear a debt/loan to get rid of a debt by paying what you owe 還清債務/貸款

10 ▶EARN 賺◀ [T] *informal* to earn a particular amount of money after taxes have been paid on it【非正式】淨賺: *Diane clears £20,000 a year.* 戴安娜每年淨賺 20,000 英鎊。

11 clear a fence/hurdle/wall etc to jump over a fence etc without touching it〔不接觸地〕越過籬笆/欄架/牆等

12 clear your head/mind to stop worrying or thinking about something or get rid of the effects of drinking too much alcohol 不再想着〔某事〕; 保持清醒; 放鬆: *A good walk might clear my head a bit.* 好好散散步也許可讓我的頭腦清醒一點。

13 clear the air to talk calmly and seriously with someone in order to try to end an argument and feel better 盡釋前嫌; 消除隔閡[誤解]

14 clear the decks to do a lot of work that needs to be done before you can do other things 準備行動: *I'm trying to clear the decks before Christmas.* 我在作過聖誕節的準備。

15 clear your throat to cough in order to be able to speak properly 清嗓子

16 ▶FACE/EXPRESSION 面部/表情◀ [I] if your face or expression clears, you stop looking worried or angry 放鬆; 不擔心: *Her brow cleared and she smiled.* 她舒展眉頭, 笑了。

17 ▶JOB/DUTY 工作/職責◀ [T] to deal with work that needs to be done 做, 幹: *Look! I've got all this to clear before the week-end.* 看! 週末前我要把這些全幹完。

18 ▶SKIN 皮膚◀ [I] to no longer have spots 去除斑點, 變得光潔

19 clear the way for to make preparations so that a process can happen 掃清道路, 給…做好準備: *This agreement will clear the way for further talks.* 這個協議將為進一步會談掃清道路。

20 ▶MESSAGE 信息◀ [T] *technical* to discover the meaning of a message in a secret language; DECODE (1)【術語】破譯, 破解〔密碼〕

clear away *phr v* [I,T] to make a place look tidier by putting things back where they belong 收拾, 整理: *Come on children, time to start clearing away.* 孩子們, 來吧, 該整理整理了。| **clear sth ↔ away** *Let's clear these files away.* 我們來把這些文件收拾好吧。

clear off *phr v* [I] *BrE informal* to leave a place quickly【英, 非正式】迅速離開: *They cleared off when they saw the police coming.* 他們看到警察過來便馬上離開了。| **clear off!** *spoken* (=used to tell someone angrily to go away)【口】滾開!

clear out *phr v* **1** [I,T] to make a place tidy by removing unwanted things 清除〔雜物〕; 騰出空間: **clear sth ↔ out** *It's time I cleared those drawers out.* 我該把那些抽屜裡的東西清理一下了。**2** [I] to leave a place or building quickly 迅速離開: *I'll give you ten minutes to clear out of here.* 我給你十分鐘時間離開這兒。| **clear out!** *spoken* (=used to tell someone angrily to go away)【口】滾開! —see also 另見 CLEAR-OUT

clear up *phr v* **1** [I,T] to make a place look tidier by putting things back where they belong 收拾, 整理; 拾掇: *We'd better start clearing up.* 我們最好開始收拾吧。| **clear sth up** *Come on, Jamie, clear those toys up.* 快點, 傑米, 把那些玩具收拾起來。**2** [T **clear** sth ↔ **up**] to find the whole explanation for something that is strange and hard to understand, such as a crime 説明; 解釋, 解答: *The Dreyfus case was never completely cleared up.* 德萊弗斯一案一直沒能完全弄清楚。**3** [T **clear** sth ↔ **up**] to make sure that everyone involved in something understands all the facts and agrees, so that there will be no problems 澄清, 闡明: *There are a couple of points we need to clear up before the meeting begins.* 開會前, 我們還需澄清幾點。**4** [I] if the weather clears up, it gets better〔天氣〕好轉, 轉晴 **5** [I] if an illness or infection clears up, it disappears〔疾病或感染〕痊癒, 消失

clear up after sb *phr v* [T] to make somewhere clean and tidy after someone else has made it dirty and untidy 替〔某人〕收拾: *I'm sick of clearing up after you!* 我討厭替你收拾爛攤子!

clear[3] *adv* **1** away from or out of the way 不接觸; 不靠近; 遠離: *They managed to pull her clear of the wreckage.* 他們設法將她從殘骸中拖了出來。**2 keep/stay/steer clear (of)** to avoid someone or something because of possible danger or trouble 避開, 躲開〔以免於危險或麻煩〕: *Steer clear of Marilyn, she's a troublemaker.* 離瑪麗琳遠點, 她經常招惹麻煩。**3 see clear** *especially AmE* to see something that is a long way away clearly【尤美】清晰地看到〔遠景〕: *You can see clear to the mountains today.* 今天你們可以清晰地看到遠處的羣山。—see also 另見 **loud and clear**

clear[4] *n* **in the clear a)** not guilty of something 清白, 無罪: *If Middlemass had spoken to Potter at 8:45, Potter was in the clear.* 如果説米德爾馬斯跟波特在 8 點 45 分談過話, 那麼波特就是清白的。**b)** no longer having a particular illness or infection 健康, 無疾病

clear·ance /ˈklɪrəns; ˈklɪərəns/ *n* **1** [C,U] the amount of space around one object that is needed to avoid it touching another object 空隙, 餘隙; 空間: *The clearance between the bridge and the top of the bus was only ten centimetres.* 橋和公共汽車頂部的距離只有十厘米。**2** [U] a process in which official permission is given for a person, ship , or aircraft to leave or enter a country 許可, 批准〔如准予船隻或飛機出入境〕: *The pilot requested clearance for an emergency landing.* 飛機師要求准予緊急降落。**3** [C,U] a process by which a cheque goes from one bank to another〔支票的〕交換結算, 兑現 **4** [C,U] the removal of unwanted things from a place 清除, 清理: **slum/land/snow clearance** *a slum clearance project* 貧民窟清拆計劃 **5** [U] SECURITY CLEARANCE 安全[保安]審查

clearance sale /ˈ·· ·/ *n* [C] an occasion when goods in a shop are sold cheaply in order to get rid of them 大甩賣, 清倉大賤賣

clear-cut[1] /ˌ· ˈ·◂/ *adj* **1** definite or easy to understand 明確的; 易懂的: *There's no clear-cut distinction between severe depression and mental illness.* 嚴重的抑鬱症與精神病之間並沒有明顯的區別。**2** having a definite outer shape 清晰的, 輪廓分明的: *the clear-cut outline of the mountains* 羣山清晰的輪廓

clear-cut[2] *n* [C] *AmE* an area of forest that has been completely cut down【美】砍伐精光的林區

clear-head·ed /ˌ· ˈ··◂/ *adj* thinking clearly 頭腦清醒的 —**clearheadedly** *adv* —**clear-headedness** *n* [U]

clear·ing /ˈklɪrɪŋ; ˈklɪərɪŋ/ *n* [C] a small area where there are no trees in the middle of a wood〔樹林中的〕小塊空地

clearing bank /ˈ·· ˌ·/ *n* [C] one of the banks in Britain

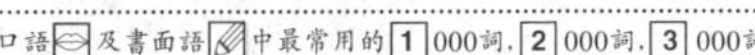

that uses a clearing house when dealing with other banks〔英國的〕票據交換銀行, 清算銀行

clearing house /ˈ‥ ˌ/ *n* [C] a central office that deals with financial affairs of clearing banks 票據交換所

clear·ly /ˈklɪrlɪ; ˈklɪəli/ *adv* **1** [sentence adverb 句子副詞] used to show that what you are saying is true and cannot be doubted; OBVIOUSLY 毫無疑問地, 顯然地, 明顯地: *Clearly, the situation is more complicated than we first thought.* 很明顯, 局勢要比我們當初預料的複雜。**2** in a way that is easy to see, hear, or understand 清楚地, 明白地: *Please speak clearly.* 請說得清楚點。**3** in a way that is sensible 明智地, 清醒地: *What's wrong with you today? You're not thinking clearly.* 你今天怎麼了? 頭腦不清醒。

clear-out /ˈ· ·/ *n* [C usually singular 一般用單數] *BrE* a process in which you get rid of unwanted objects or possessions【英】清除, 清理: **have a clear-out** *I must have a clear-out one of these days.* 我這兩天得進行一次大清理。

clear-sight·ed /ˌ· ˈ··◂/ *adj* able to understand a problem or situation well 有眼光的, 有見識的: *a clear-sighted analysis* 有見識的分析 —**clear-sightedly** *adv* —**clear-sightedness** *n* [U]

clear·way /ˈklɪrˌwe; ˈklɪəweɪ/ *n* [C] a road in Britain on which vehicles must not stop〔英國的〕禁停路

cleat /klit; kliːt/ *n* [C] **1** a small bar with two short arms around which ropes can be tied, especially on a ship〔尤指船上繫繩用的〕羊角; 繫索耳 **2** [usually plural 一般用複數] one of a set of pieces of rubber, iron etc fastened to the bottom of a shoe to stop it slipping〔釘在鞋底上的〕防滑條 —see picture at 參見 STUD[1] 圖 **3 cleats** [plural] *AmE* a pair of shoes with these pieces【美】防滑鞋 —compare 比較 **spikes** (SPIKE[1] (2))

cleav·age /ˈklivɪdʒ; ˈkliːvɪdʒ/ *n* [C,U] **1** the space between a woman's breasts〔婦女的〕乳溝 **2** *formal* a difference between two people or things that often causes problems or arguments【正式】分裂; 裂痕; 分歧

cleave /kliv; kliːv/ *v* [T] *past tense* **cleaved, clove** /klov; kləʊv/ **cleft** /klɛft; kleft/ *past participle* **cleaved, cloven** /ˈklovən; ˈkləʊvən/ **cleft** *formal*【正式】**1** [I always+adv/prep][T always+adv/prep] to cut something into separate parts using a heavy tool or to be able to be cut in this way 劈開; 割開; 裂開: *The wooden door had been cleft in two.* 木門被劈成了兩半。**2** [T] to divide something into two completely separate parts 徹底分開: *Class divisions have cleft the society.* 階級劃分將社會割裂開來。**3 cleave the air/darkness etc** to move quickly through the air etc 迅速地穿過空氣/黑暗: *His fist cleft the air.* 他迅速出拳。

cleave to sb/sth *phr v* [T] **1** *formal* to continue to think that a method, belief etc is true or valuable, even when this seems unlikely【正式】忠於; 堅持, 堅守: *John still cleaves to his romantic ideals.* 約翰仍堅持他的浪漫理想。**2** to stick to someone or something or seem to surround them 依戀〔某人〕; 貼住, 黏住〔某物〕

cleav·er /ˈklivɚ; ˈkliːvə/ *n* [C] a heavy knife for cutting up large pieces of meat 剁肉刀, 切肉的大菜刀

clef /klɛf; klef/ *n* [C] a sign at the beginning of a line of written music to show the PITCH[1] (6) of the notes〔置於五線譜一行之首表示高低音的〕譜號: *the treble clef etc* 高音譜號等

cleft[1] /klɛft; kleft/ *n* [C] a natural crack in the surface of rocks or the Earth etc〔地球、岩石等表面的〕裂縫, 裂口: *a deep cleft in his chin* 他下巴上的一條深疤

cleft[2] *adj* **be in a cleft stick** *BrE* to be in a very awkward situation【英】進退兩難, 陷於窘境

cleft[3] a past tense and past participle of CLEAVE

cleft pal·ate /ˌ· ˈ··/ *n* [C] a split in the top of someone's mouth that makes it difficult for them to speak clearly 腭裂; 兔唇

clem·a·tis /ˈklɛmətɪs; ˈklemətɪ̱s/ *n* [C,U] a plant with spreading branches and white, yellow, or purple flowers 鐵線蓮, 女萎〔一種開白、黃或紫色花的攀緣植物〕

clem·ent /ˈklɛmənt; ˈklemənt/ *adj formal*【正式】**1** willing not to punish someone too severely 寬大的, 仁慈的 **2** clement weather is neither too hot nor too cold; MILD[1] (1)〔氣候〕溫和的 —opposite 反義詞 INCLEMENT —**clemency** *n* [U] —**clemently** *adv*

clem·en·tine /ˈklɛmənˌtin; ˈkleməntiːn/ *n* [C] a kind of small, sweet orange 小甜橘 —see picture on page A8 參見 A8 頁圖

clench /klɛntʃ; klentʃ/ *v* [T] **clench your fists/teeth/jaw etc** to hold your hands, teeth etc together tightly, usually because you feel angry or determined〔因憤怒或下決心而〕握緊拳頭/咬緊牙關: *She muttered "Go away" through clenched teeth.* 她咬緊牙說了一句"滾開"。

clere·sto·ry /ˈklɪrˌstɔrɪ; ˈklɪəstəri/ *n* [C] *technical* the upper part of the wall of a large church, that has windows in it and rises above the lower roofs【術語】〔大教堂內的〕天窗, 氣窗

cler·gy /ˈklɝdʒɪ; ˈklɜːdʒi/ *n* **the clergy** [plural] the priests in the Christian church〔基督教的〕神職人員: *the power of the clergy in the Middle Ages* 中世紀教會的權力

cler·gy·man /ˈklɝdʒɪmən; ˈklɜːdʒimən/ *n* [C] *plural* **clergymen** /-mən; -mən/ a male priest in the Christian church 神職人員中的一員; 牧師; 教士 —see 見 PRIEST (USAGE)

cler·gy·wom·an /ˈklɝdʒɪˌwʊmən; ˈklɜːdʒiˌwʊmən/ *n* [C] *plural* **clergywomen** /-ˌwɪmɪn; -ˌwɪmɪn/ a female priest in the Christian church 女神職人員; 女牧師; 女教士

cler·ic /ˈklɛrɪk; ˈklerɪk/ *n* [C] *old-fashioned* a member of the clergy【過時】牧師; 教士; 神職人員

cler·i·cal /ˈklɛrɪkl; ˈklerɪkəl/ *adj* **1** connected with office work 文書的, 辦事員的: *a clerical error* 筆誤 **2** connected with priests 神職人員的; 牧師的; 教士的: *a clerical collar* 牧師領

clerk[1] /klɝk; klɑːk/ *n* [C] **1** someone who keeps records or accounts in an office 辦事員; 文員; 簿記員; 職員: *a clerk in a commercial firm* 一家商業公司的文員 **2** an official in charge of the records of a court, town council etc〔法庭、市政廳等負責管理文書的〕文書, 書記員 **3** *AmE* someone who deals with people arriving in a hotel【美】〔旅店的〕接待員: *Leave the keys with the desk clerk.* 把鑰匙交給櫃台服務員。**4** *AmE old-fashioned* someone who serves people in a shop【美, 過時】〔商店的〕售貨員, 店員 **5** *old use* a priest in the Church of England【舊】〔英國教會的〕牧師

clerk[2] *v* [I] *informal especially AmE* to work as a clerk【非正式, 尤美】當文書[售貨員、接待員]

clerk of works /ˌ· · ˈ·/ *n* [C] *BrE* someone who is in charge of repairs to the buildings in a particular place【英】〔負責某一建築物維修工程的〕工程管理員; 現場監工

clev·er /ˈklɛvɚ; ˈklevə/ *adj* **1** *especially BrE* able to learn and understand things quickly; INTELLIGENT【尤英】聰明的, 才思敏捷的: *a clever student* 聰明的學生 | *You tied your shoes up yourself? What a clever girl!* 是自己把鞋繫好的嗎? 多聰明的小姑娘! **2** able to use your intelligence to get what you want, especially in a slightly dishonest way 耍小聰明的, 滑頭的: *a clever lawyer's tricks* 滑頭律師所耍的花招 **3** *especially BrE* skilful at doing a particular thing【尤英】靈巧的, 伶俐的: *Bill's very clever with his hands.* 比爾雙手很靈巧。| **clever at doing sth** *Deborah's clever at getting people to cooperate.* 狄波拉善於讓人們合作。**4** designed in an unusual way that is very effective 機敏的; 巧妙的: *What a clever little gadget!* 多麼巧妙的小玩意! | *Now that's a clever idea.* 真是好主意! **5** *BrE spoken* used jokingly when someone has done something silly or stupid【英口】真聰明! 〔用於開玩笑地表示某人幹了一件蠢事〕: *"When I got to the library I found I'd left the books at home." "That was clever!"* "到了圖書館我才發現把書忘在家裡了。" "是嗎, 真行!" **6 clever clogs/dick** *BrE spoken* used to describe someone who is annoying because they are always right or always think they are right【英口】自以為聰明的人: *All right, clever clogs, we'll do it your way!* 好了, 聰明的傢伙, 我們就按你的方式辦! **7 be too clever**

by half *BrE spoken* to be annoying because you are confident about your own intelligence or abilities【英口】精明過頭的 —**cleverly** *adv* —**cleverness** *n* [U]

cli·ché /kli`ʃe; 'kliːʃeɪ/ *n* [C] an expression that is used too often and has lost most of its meaning 陳詞濫調, 老生常談, 老套: *the old cliché that a chain is only as strong as its weakest link* 常言道, 鏈條的強度取決於其最薄弱的一環。—**clichéd** *adj*

3 **click** /klɪk; klɪk/ *v* **1** [I,T] to make a short hard sound or make something produce this sound (使) 發出咔嗟聲: *The man opposite kept clicking his ballpoint pen.* 對面的男士一直把圓珠筆弄得咔嗟作響。| **click your fingers/tongue** (=make a short hard sound with your fingers or tongue, especially in order to get someone's attention or to express annoyance) 打響指/彈舌頭發出嘖嘖聲 | **click your heels** (=knock the heels of your shoes or boots together in a way that soldiers do) 腳後跟咔嗟相碰 (立正) | **click shut/click into place** *The bolt clicked into place.* 門閂咔嗟一聲栓上了。**2** [I] *informal* to suddenly understand or realize something【非正式】突然明白, 恍然大悟: **it clicked (with sb)** *It suddenly clicked. The man at the station must have been her brother.* (我) 突然明白了, 車站上的那個人一定是她哥哥。| *For ages I couldn't do algebra, then one day it clicked.* 很久以來我一直弄不懂代數, 有一天, 我卻突然頓悟了。**3** [I] *informal* to like someone and share their ideas, opinions etc【非正式】喜歡〔某人〕; 與…有相同興趣[愛好]: *Petra and I clicked straight away.* 彼得拉和我一拍即合。

click on sth *phr v* [T] to press a button on a computer MOUSE (2) in order to do a computer operation〔使用電腦鼠標〕點擊 —**click** *n* [singular]

3 1 **cli·ent** /`klaɪənt; 'klaɪənt/ *n* [C] someone who pays for services or advice from a person or organization 客戶, 客人, 顧客: *meeting with an important client* 與一位重要的客戶會晤

cli·en·tele /ˌklaɪən`tɛl; ˌkliːən'tel/ *n* [singular] all the people who regularly use a shop, restaurant etc〔定期光顧某商店、餐館等的所有〕顧客, 主顧: *a very select clientele* 一批高級的顧客

client state /ˌ·· '·◂/ *n* [C] a country that is dependent on the support and protection of a more powerful country〔依賴大國的〕附庸國

cliff /klɪf; klɪf/ *n* [C] a high rock with a very steep side, near the sea〔海邊的〕懸崖, 峭壁 —see picture on page A12 參見 A12 頁圖

cliff·hang·er /`klɪfˌhæŋɚ; 'klɪfˌhæŋə/ *n* [C] a situation or competition that makes you feel very excited or nervous because you have to wait a long time to see how it will end〔直到最後方見分曉的〕競爭, 搏鬥; 扣人心弦的比賽: *The election in Russia was a real cliffhanger.* 這次俄羅斯大選是一場真正扣人心弦的競爭。—**cliffhanging** *adj*

cli·mac·tic /klaɪ`mæktɪk; klaɪ'mæktɪk/ *adj* a climactic period of time or situation is one in which very important or exciting events happen 高潮的, 形成高潮的: *the hero, dodging bullets in the movie's climactic scene* 在電影的高潮場面中躲閃子彈的主角

3 **cli·mate** /`klaɪmɪt; 'klaɪmə̩t/ *n* [C] **1** a situation that exists at a particular time, especially one which involves people's opinions and attitudes〔某一時期社會上的〕風氣; 思潮; 趨勢: **social/political/economic climate** *Small businesses are finding it hard to survive in the present economic climate.* 小企業發現在當前的經濟形勢下很難生存。| **climate of suspicion/hostility/distrust** *a climate of growing racial intolerance* 漸濃的種族不相容風氣 **2** the typical weather conditions in a particular area 氣候: *Los Angeles' warm, dry climate* 洛杉磯溫暖乾燥的氣候 **3** an area with particular weather conditions 氣候帶, 地帶: *I could not bear living in a tropical climate.* 我不能忍受在熱帶地區生活。

cli·mat·ic /klaɪ`mætɪk; klaɪ'mætɪk/ *adj* [only before noun 僅用於名詞前] connected with the weather in a particular area 氣候的: *climatic conditions* 氣候情況

cli·max¹ /`klaɪmæks; 'klaɪmæks/ *n* [C usually singular 一般用單數] **1** the most exciting or important part of a story or experience that normally comes near the end 高潮, 頂點: [**+of**] *the climax of an exciting expedition* 一次刺激驚險的遠征的高潮 | **reach a climax** *The opera reaches its climax in the third act.* 歌劇在第三幕達到高潮。**2** an ORGASM 性高潮

climax² *v* **1** [I,T] if a situation, process, or story climaxes it reaches its most important or exciting part 達到頂點[高潮]: [**+in**] *Her determination and hard work climaxed in her appointment as chairwoman.* 她的決心和勤奮以被任命為主席而達到了頂點。**2** [I] to have an ORGASM 達到性高潮

climb¹ /klaɪm; klaɪm/ *v* 2

1 ►MOVE UP/DOWN 向上/下移動◄ [I always+adv/prep, T] to move up, down, or across something, especially something tall or steep, using your feet and hands〔手腳並用地〕攀登, 〔向上或下〕爬: [**+up/down/along etc**] *Some spectators climbed onto the roof to get a better view.* 一些觀看者爬到了屋頂上, 以便看得更清楚。| **climb a wall/tree/mountain etc** *The kids are always climbing trees.* 孩子們經常在爬樹。

2 ►WITH DIFFICULTY 艱難地◄ [I always+adv/prep] to move into, out of, or through something slowly and awkwardly 吃力地爬〔進、出〕: [**+through/over/into etc**] *Ian managed to climb through a hole in the hedge.* 伊恩設法爬過了樹籬上的一個洞。| **climb into/out of clothes** (=put on or remove clothing slowly) 費力地穿上/脱下衣服

3 ►SPORT 體育運動◄ [I,T] to climb mountains as a sport 爬山, 登山: *Sir Edmund Hillary was the first man to climb Mount Everest.* 艾德蒙·希拉里爵士是第一個登上珠穆朗瑪峯的人。—see also 另見 CLIMBING

4 ►PATH/SUN/PLANE 小路/太陽/飛機◄ [I] to move gradually to a higher position 徐徐上升; 爬高; 冒起: [**+into/up etc**] *The path climbs high into the hills.* 小路緩緩通向山頂。| *The plane slowly began to climb.* 飛機開始慢慢地往上升。

5 ►PLANT 植物◄ [I] to grow up a wall or other structure 沿…攀緣而上: *Ivy climbed up the front of the building.* 常春藤沿着建築物前部攀緣而上。

6 ►TEMPERATURE/PRICES ETC 溫度/價格等◄ [I] to increase in number, amount, or level 上升; 上漲: *The temperature was climbing steadily.* 氣温在穩步上升。| [**+to**] *The original estimate of $500 million has now climbed to a staggering $1300 million.* 原先估算的 5 億美元現在竟已驚人地漲到 13 億美元。

7 ►IN A LIST 在名單上◄ [I,T] to move higher in a list of teams, records etc as you become more popular or successful 排名升高: [**+to**] *Madonna's new record has climbed to number 2 in the US charts.* 麥當娜的新唱片已躍居美國排行榜第二位。

8 ►IN YOUR LIFE/PROFESSION 生活中/事業中◄ [I,T] to move to a better position in your social or professional life 提高〔社會地位〕; 晉升: *Steve climbed rapidly in the firm.* 史提夫在公司裡晉升得很快。| **climb the ladder** (=become more successful) 取得更大成功

9 be climbing the walls *spoken* to become extremely anxious, annoyed, or impatient【口】極度憂慮[煩惱、不耐煩]: *When Colin hadn't arrived home by midnight I was climbing the walls.* 科林半夜裡還沒回家, 使我非常擔心。

climb down *phr v* [I] *informal* to admit that you were wrong, especially after being certain that you were right【非正式】認錯; 退讓, 讓步 —**climb-down** *n* [singular]: *a humiliating climb-down* 丢人的屈服

climb² *n* [C usually singular 一般用單數] **1** a process in which you go up towards a place and that usually involves a lot of effort 攀登: *It's quite a climb to the fifth floor!* 爬到五樓, 可不簡單! | *a tough climb to the top of the hill* 艱難地爬上山頂 **2** an increase in value or amount 增值; 上升: *After a fairly steady climb, prices stabilized at around $1.65 a litre.* 價格穩步上升後穩定在每升 1.65 美元左右。**3** an improvement in your professional or social position〔職位或社會地位的〕提高; 晉升 **4** a process in which someone or something gets a higher position in a list because of being popular or successful〔名次的〕攀升: **a climb up the charts/table/league etc** *a sensational climb up the charts for Elton's new album* 艾爾頓那張新專輯的排名大幅度攀升 **5** a steep rock or cliff you climb up 攀登的陡峭懸崖: *You'll need a rope for that climb.* 你需要一根繩索爬上那座峭壁。

climb·er /ˈklaɪmə; ˈklaɪmə/ *n* [C] **1** someone who climbs as a sport 登山運動員 **2** a person or animal that can climb easily 善於攀爬的人[動物]: *Monkeys are good climbers.* 猴子善於攀爬。**3** a plant that grows up a wall or other structure 攀緣植物 —see also 另見 **social climber**

C

climb·ing /ˈklaɪmɪŋ; ˈklaɪmɪŋ/ *n* [U] the sport of climbing mountains or rocks〔體育運動〕登山: **climbing boots/equipment etc** *Remember to bring climbing boots.* 記得帶備登山鞋。| **rock/mountain climbing** *Rock climbing can be very dangerous.* 攀岩運動可能會很危險。| **go climbing** (=climb mountains or rocks as a sport) 去登山[攀岩]

climb·ing frame /ˈ·· ,·/ *n* [C] *BrE* a structure for children to climb on, made from metal bars, wood, or rope【英】〔兒童玩的〕攀爬架; JUNGLE GYM *AmE*【美】

climb·ing i·ron /ˈ·· ,··/ *n* [C usually plural 一般用複數] a small piece of metal with sharp points that is fastened under boots to make climbing less difficult or dangerous; CRAMPON〔登山靴上的〕鐵爪器, 鐵釘助爬器

clime /klaɪm; klaɪm/ *n* [C] *poetic* CLIMATE【詩】氣候: *They retired to sunnier climes.* 他們退休後到陽光明媚的地方居住。

clinch[1] /klɪntʃ; klɪntʃ/ *v* **1** [T] to succeed in getting or winning something after trying very hard 最終獲[贏]得: **clinch the deal/contract** *It was the BM40's superior design that clinched the deal.* 最終達成交易是因為BM40的優良設計。| **clinch the contest/championship/title etc** *Germany scored twice in the last ten minutes to clinch the championship.* 德國隊在最後十分鐘連進兩球, 從而獲得冠軍。**2 clinch it** *informal* if an event, situation, process etc clinches it, it makes someone finally decide to do something that they were already thinking of doing【非正式】使〔某人〕最終下決心: *The offer of a company car clinched it and I accepted the job.* 公司提出為我提供專車, 使我決定接受那份工作。**3** [I] if two people clinch, they hold each other's arms tightly, especially when they are fighting 扭打成一團 **4** [T] to fix a nail firmly by bending the point over 敲彎釘頭使釘牢[固定]

clinch[2] *n* [C] **1** a situation in which two people hold each other's arms tightly, especially when they are fighting〔尤指兩人打架時的〕扭抱 **2** a situation in which two people who love each other hold each other tightly; EMBRACE[2]〔相愛的人之間的〕擁抱

clinch·er /ˈklɪntʃə; ˈklɪntʃə/ *n* [C] *informal* a fact or remark that ends an argument or discussion【非正式】〔結束爭論或討論的〕事實[意見、論點]; 結尾: *The clincher came when police found his fingerprints on the stolen car.* 警方在被偷的汽車上發現了他的指紋, 這就可以下定論了。

cline /klaɪn; klaɪn/ *n* [C] *technical* a series of very small differences in a group of things of the same kind; CONTINUUM【術語】漸變性; 連續體

cling /klɪŋ; klɪŋ/ *v past tense and past participle* **clung** /klʌŋ; klʌŋ/ [I] **1** [always+adv/prep] to hold someone or something tightly, especially because you do not feel safe〔尤指感覺不安全而〕緊緊抓住[抱住]: **[+to/on/at etc]** *I clung onto Duncan for comfort.* 我緊緊抱住鄧肯尋求安慰。**2** [always+adv/prep] to stick to someone or something or seem to surround them 纏着; 黏着: **[+to/around etc]** *His wet shirt clung to his body.* 他的濕襯衫緊緊地黏在身上。**3** to stay close to someone all the time because you are too dependent on them or do not feel safe 挨近, 貼近; 依附: *Some children tend to cling on their first day at school.* 有些小孩在上學第一天會有眷戀的傾向。

cling to sth *phr v* [T] if you cling to a belief, idea, or feeling, you continue to think that it is true even when this seems extremely unlikely 堅持, 忠於: **cling to the hope that** *We clung to the hope that we might see her again one day.* 我們一直抱着希望終有一天能再見到她。

cling·film /ˈklɪŋfɪlm; ˈklɪŋfɪlm/ *n* [U] *BrE trademark* very thin transparent plastic used to cover food and keep it fresh【英, 商標】保鮮塑料薄膜; PLASTIC WRAP *AmE*【美】

cling·y /ˈklɪŋɪ; ˈklɪŋi/ also 又作 **clinging** /ˈklɪŋɪŋ; ˈklɪŋɪŋ/ *adj* **1** someone who is clingy is too dependent on another person 過於依賴別人的: *a timid, clingy child* 一個膽小且依賴性強的孩子 **2** clingy clothing or material sticks tightly to your body and shows its shape〔衣服或布料〕緊身的

clin·ic /ˈklɪnɪk; ˈklɪnɪk/ *n* [C] **1** a building, often part of a hospital, where people come for special medical treatment or advice 診所; 〔醫院的〕門診部: **dental/family planning/ante-natal clinic** *I'll meet you at the family planning clinic.* 在家庭計劃中心見。**2** *especially BrE* a period of time during which doctors give treatment or advice to people with particular health problems【尤英】門診時間: **hold a clinic** *The baby clinic is held on Monday afternoons.* 嬰兒門診在週一下午。**3** a meeting during which a professional person gives advice or help to people〔有專家回答問題的〕座談會, 諮詢會: *an M.P.'s clinic* 下議院議員的座談會 —compare 比較 SURGERY (3) **4** *AmE* a place where medical treatment is given at a low cost【美】〔醫療費用低廉的〕醫務室 **5** *especially AmE* a small hospital in an area far away from large cities which provides medical treatment【尤美】衛生所, 診所〔遠離大城市提供醫療服務的小醫院〕: *a rural health clinic with ten to fifteen beds* 有十至十五張病牀的鄉村診所 **6** *AmE* a group of doctors who work together and share the same offices【美】〔醫院的〕科, 室; PRACTICE[1] (5) *BrE*【英】**7** an occasion when medical students are taught how to decide what illness a patient has and how to treat it〔醫科學生的〕臨牀實習 (課)

clin·i·cal /ˈklɪnɪkḷ; ˈklɪnɪkəl/ *adj* **1** [only before noun 僅用於名詞前] clinical work, training etc is practical medical work that is done in a hospital or clinic 臨牀的: *The drug has undergone a number of clinical trials.* 該藥已經經過了多次的臨牀試驗。| *clinical medicine* 臨牀醫學 **2** connected with a hospital or clinic 診所的; 醫院的 **3** considering only the facts and not seeming influenced by personal feelings 冷靜的; 客觀的; 不偏不倚的: *He regarded her suffering with clinical detachment.* 他以一種超然的態度對待她的苦難。**4** a clinical building or room is very plain and clean but not attractive or comfortable 簡樸的: *The walls were painted a clinical white.* 牆給漆成樸素的白色。—**clinically** /-kḷɪ; -kli/ *adv*: *clinically tested* 臨牀試驗過的

clinical ther·mom·e·ter /,··· ·ˈ···/ *n* [C] a THERMOMETER for measuring the temperature of your body 體溫表[計]

clink[1] /klɪŋk; klɪŋk/ *v* [I,T] if two glass or metal objects clink or if you clink them, they make a short ringing sound (使) 發出叮噹響: **clink glasses** *I clinked glasses with the other guests.* 我和其他客人碰了杯。

clink[2] *n* **1** [singular] the short ringing sound made by metal or glass objects hitting each other〔金屬或玻璃物品碰撞發出的〕叮噹聲: *the clink of glasses* 碰杯聲 —see picture on page A19 參見 A19 頁圖 **2** *slang* prison【俚】牢房: *They threw him in the clink for two years.* 他們把他投進牢房, 關了兩年。

clink·er /ˈklɪŋkə; ˈklɪŋkə/ *n* **1** [C,U] the hard material like rocks which is left after coal has been burnt 爐渣, 煤渣, 燒結塊 **2** [singular] *AmE* a bad note in a musical performance【美】奏[唱]錯的音: *The singer hit a real clinker.* 那個歌手唱錯了音。**3** [singular] *AmE old-fashioned* something or someone that is a total failure【美, 過時】徹底失敗的東西[人]: *That movie was a total clinker.* 那部電影是一個徹徹底底的失敗。

clip¹ /klɪp; klɪp/ *n*
1 ▶**FOR FASTENING** 使緊固◀ [C] a small metal or plastic object for holding or fastening things together 迴形針; 夾子: *Fasten the microphone clip to your shirt front.* 把麥克風夾在襯衫前面。| **hair clip** (=a piece of metal or plastic for keeping hair in the right place) 髮夾 —see also 另見 BULLDOG CLIP, PAPERCLIP
2 ▶**CUT** 剪割◀ [singular] a process in which you make something shorter or tidier by cutting it 修剪: *I'll have to give that hedge a clip.* 我得把樹籬修剪一下了。
3 ▶**FILM** 電影◀ [C] a short part of a film that is shown by itself 剪下的一段電影: *clips from Mel Gibson's new movie* 米路吉遜的新片剪輯
4 **a clip round the ear/earhole** *BrE informal* a short blow on the side of someone's head【英, 非正式】一記耳光
5 ▶**GUN** 槍◀ [C] a container for bullets which passes them rapidly into the gun so that they can be fired 子彈夾
6 ▶**NEWSPAPER** 報紙◀ [C] an article that is cut from a newspaper or magazine for a particular reason 剪報
7 **$100/50 cents etc a clip** *AmE informal* if things cost $100, 50 cents etc a clip, they cost that amount of money each【美, 非正式】一次[每個]〔收費〕100美元/50美分
8 **at a good/fair etc clip** quickly 迅速地: *Traffic was going by at a fair clip.* 往來車輛的速度很快。
9 ▶**WOOL** 羊毛◀ [C] *AustrE, NZE* the total amount of wool that is taken from a group of sheep at one time【澳, 新西蘭】一次剪下的羊毛量

clip² *v* **clipped, clipping**
1 ▶**FASTEN** 緊固◀ [I always+adv/prep, T] to fasten something together or to be fastened together using a CLIP¹ (1) 夾住, 扣住: **clip sth into/onto/together etc** *The invoices had been carefully clipped together.* 發票已經仔細地夾在一起了。| **[+on/to etc]** *The keys will clip onto your belt.* 鑰匙會別在你的皮帶上。
2 ▶**CUT** 剪割◀ [T] to cut small amounts of something in order to make it tidier 修剪; 剪除: *clipping the hedge* 修剪樹籬
3 ▶**CUT FROM NEWSPAPER** 從報上剪下◀ [T always+adv/prep] to cut an article or picture from newspaper, magazine etc〔從報紙、雜誌上〕剪下: **clip sth out of/from** *Elsa clipped the article out of the evening paper.* 愛爾莎從晚報上剪下了這篇文章。
4 ▶**HIT** 打中◀ [T] to hit the surface of something quickly but hard 迅速用力的擊打, 猛擊: *The bullet clipped the car's side mirror.* 子彈猛地擊中汽車的側鏡。
5 ▶**REDUCE** 減少◀ [T] to slightly reduce an amount, quantity etc 減少, 減低: *Gunnell clipped a second off the world record.* 岡納爾將世界紀錄縮短了一秒。
6 **clip sb's wings** to restrict someone's freedom, activities, or power 限制…的自由[行動]; 削弱…的權力: *Getting married has really clipped his wings.* 結婚確實限制了他的自由。
7 **clip sb round the ear/earhole** *BrE informal* to hit someone quickly on the side of the head【英, 非正式】打某人耳光
8 ▶**TICKET** 票◀ [T] to make a hole in a bus or train ticket to show that it has been used〔於車票上〕打洞
9 **clip your words** to say words in a quick, short, and not very friendly way 不友好地快速說話

clip·board /ˈklɪpˌbɔrd; ˈklɪpbɔːd/ *n* [C] a small flat board with a clip¹ (1) on top used for holding pieces of paper so that you can write on them 有夾子的書寫板

clip-clop /ˌ· ˈ·/ *n* [singular] the sound made by a horse as it walks on a hard surface〔馬在硬路面上走發出的〕得得聲 —**clip-clop** *v* [I]

clip joint /ˈ· ·/ *n* [C] *slang* a restaurant or NIGHTCLUB that charges too much for food, drinks etc【俚】索價昂貴的飯店[夜總會]

clip-on /ˈ· ·/ *adj* [only before noun 僅用於名詞前] fastened to something with a CLIP¹ (1) 用夾子夾住的: *clip-on earrings* 夾式耳環 —**clip-on** *n* [C] —see picture at 參見 JEWELLERY 圖

clipped /klɪpt; klɪpt/ *adj* **1** cut so that it is short and neat 剪短的; 整齊的: *a neatly clipped hedge* 修剪整齊的樹籬 **2** a clipped voice is quick and clear but not very friendly 說話急促的

clip·per /ˈklɪpɚ; ˈklɪpə/ *n* [C] **1 clippers** [plural] a special tool with two blades for cutting small pieces from something 剪(子): *nail clippers* 指甲剪 **2** a fast sailing ship used in the past〔舊時的〕快速帆船

clip·ping /ˈklɪpɪŋ; ˈklɪpɪŋ/ *n* [C] **1** an article or picture that has been cut out of a newspaper or magazine; CUTTING¹ (2) 剪報 **2** [usually plural 一般用複數] a small piece cut from something bigger 剪下物: *He swept the hedge clippings into a heap.* 他把修剪下來的樹籬枝杈掃成一堆。

clique /klik; kliːk/ *n* [C] a small group of people who think they are special and do not let other people join them 派系; 小圈子; 小集團: *A small clique of right-wingers controls local affairs.* 一小撮右翼分子控制了地方事務。

cliqu·ey /ˈklikɪ; ˈkliːki/ also 又作 **cliquish** /ˈklikɪʃ; ˈkliːkɪʃ/ *adj* a cliquey organization, club etc has a lot of cliques or is controlled by them 小集團的, 派系的: *That tennis club is too cliquey for my liking.* 那個網球俱樂部太排他, 我不喜歡。

clit·o·ris /ˈklɪtərɪs; ˈklɪtərɪs/ *n* [C] a part of a woman's outer sexual organs where she can feel sexual pleasure 陰蒂, 陰核

Cllr *BrE*【英】the written abbreviation of 縮寫= COUNCILLOR

cloak¹ /klok; kləʊk/ *n* **1** [C] a warm piece of clothing like a coat without SLEEVES that hangs loosely from your shoulders 斗篷, 披風 **2** [singular] an organization, activity, or way of behaving that deliberately protects someone or keeps something secret 偽裝; 掩蓋物: **[+for]** *The political party is used as a cloak for terrorist activities.* 那個政黨只不過是搞恐怖活動的偽裝。| **under the cloak of** *prejudice and hypocrisy hiding under the cloak of religion* 在宗教掩飾下的偏見和虛偽

cloak² *v* [T usually passive 一般用被動態] **1** to deliberately hide facts, feelings etc so that people do not see or understand them 掩蓋, 掩飾〔事實、情感等〕: **cloaked in secrecy** *The early stages of the talks have been cloaked in secrecy.* 初期的會談一直在祕密中進行。**2 cloaked in darkness/rust/snow etc** *literary* covered in darkness, rust etc【文】在黑暗中/鐵鏽下/雪下等

cloak-and-dag·ger /ˌ· · ˈ·· ◂/ *adj* [usually before noun 一般用於名詞前] a cloak-and-dagger situation, activity etc, is very secret and mysterious, often in a way that seems unnecessary 祕密的; 神祕離奇的: *Cloak-and-dagger tactics were used to get the bill through Parliament.* 使用了一些祕密的手段使法案在國會中通過。| **cloak-and-dagger stuff** (=mysterious activities or ways of behaving) 祕密活動, 詭祕的行為 *I'm sick of all this cloak-and-dagger stuff.* 我討厭所有這些祕密的行動。

cloak·room /ˈklokˌrum; ˈkləʊkrʊm/ *n* [C] **1** a small room where you can leave your coat 衣帽間; 衣帽寄存處; COATROOM *AmE*【美】**2** *BrE* a word meaning a room in a public building where there are toilets, used because you want to avoid saying this directly【英】廁所, 洗手間, 化妝室; REST ROOM *AmE*【美】: *Excuse me, where's the ladies' cloakroom?* 對不起, 女洗手間在甚麼地方?

clob·ber¹ /ˈklɑbɚ; ˈklɒbə/ *v* [T] *informal*【非正式】**1** to hit someone very hard 狠打, 揍: *I'll clobber you if you say that again.* 如果你再那麼說, 我就揍你。**2** to defeat someone very easily in a way that is embarrassing for the team that loses 徹底擊敗: *The Dallas Cowboys clobbered the Buffalo Bills last night.* 昨晚達拉斯牛仔隊大破水牛比爾隊。**3** to affect someone or something badly, especially by making them lose money 使…遭受沉重損失: *companies clobbered by foreign competitors* 受到國外競爭者沉重打擊的公司 **4** to punish someone severely when they break a law 嚴懲: *Motorists caught driving without insurance will be clobbered.* 沒有保險的摩托車手駕車將受到嚴厲懲罰。

clobber² *n* [U] *informal especially BrE* someone's

possessions, especially their clothes【非正式, 尤英】隨身帶的東西; 衣物: *Don't forget all your clobber if you're staying the night.* 如果在外面過夜, 別忘了帶衣服。| **fishing/swimming/football clobber etc** (=clothes and equipment needed for a particular activity) 漁具/泳衣/足球衣物

cloche /klɒʃ; klɒʃ/ *n* [C] **1** a hat shaped like a bell, worn by women in the 1920s〔20世紀20年代的〕鐘形女帽 **2** a glass or transparent plastic cover put over young plants to protect them during cold weather〔保護幼嫩植物不受嚴寒侵襲的〕鐘形玻璃罩, 透明塑料罩

2 3 **clock¹** /klɑk; klɒk/ *n* [C] **1** an instrument in a room or on a public building that shows what time it is (時) 鐘: *The clock was ticking on the mantelpiece.* 時鐘在壁爐台上嘀嗒作響。| **the clock strikes three/half past four etc** *The church clock struck midnight.* 教堂鐘敲響了午夜的鐘聲。| **the clock says...** (=the clock shows a particular time) 時鐘顯示〔...點〕| **by the hall/kitchen/church etc clock** (=according to a particular clock) 根據大堂/廚房/教堂的鐘 *It's 4:30 by the kitchen clock.* 廚房的鐘指明現在是4點30分。| **wind (up) the clock** (=turn a key in a clock so that it keeps working) 上發條 | **set the clock by sth** (=change the time on a clock according to the time on the television, radio etc)〔根據電台、電視等的報時〕調整[校正]時間 | **set the clock for sth** (=turn a screw at the back of a clock so that it will ring at a certain time) 撥好鬧鐘 *Mary set her clock for 6:30 a.m..* 瑪麗把鬧鐘撥定在早上6點30分。| **the clock is slow/fast** (=used to show that the clock is showing an earlier or later time than the actual time) 鐘慢/快了 *Your clock's ten minutes slow.* 你的鐘慢了十分鐘。| **clock face** (=the front part of a clock with the numbers on) 鐘面 —see also 另見 ALARM CLOCK, CARRIAGE CLOCK, CUCKOO CLOCK, GRANDFATHER CLOCK —compare 比較 WATCH² (1) **2 put the clock(s) back** *especially BrE*【尤英】**set the clock(s) back** *AmE*【美】to change the time shown on the clock to an earlier time, when the time changes officially〔根據官方時間〕將時鐘撥慢 **3 put the clock(s) forward** *BrE*【英】**set the clock(s) ahead** *AmE*【美】to change the time shown on the clock to a later time, when the time changes officially〔根據官方時間〕將時鐘撥快 **4 put/turn the clock back** to go back to the ideas or methods tried before instead of doing things in a new or modern way 倒退, 開倒車, 倒行逆施: *The new employment bill will put the clock back fifty years.* 新的雇用法案簡直是倒退了五十年。**5 put the clock back/forward** to remember a particular time in the past or imagine a time in the future 讓時光倒流/前進: *It put the clock back forty years seeing that old Bette Davis movie.* 看貝特·戴維斯的那部老片使時光倒流了四十年。**6 around the clock/round the clock** *BrE* all day and all night without stopping【英】晝夜, 日以繼夜地, 日夜不停地: *Charles has been working round the clock preparing the case.* 查爾斯日以繼夜地忙於準備那個案子。**7 against the clock a)** if you work against the clock, you work as quickly as you can because you do not have much time 加快工作, 搶時間: *We're working against the clock to get this proposal finished.* 我們正加緊完成這份建議書。**b)** if you run, swim etc against the clock, you run or swim a particular distance as fast as possible 盡可能快地, 拚命地 **8 watch the clock** to keep looking at the clock to see what time it is because you are bored〔因感到厭煩而〕盯着時鐘 **9 live by the clock** to organize your life so that you always do the same things at the same time and are never late〔生活〕有規律, 有條不紊 **10 the twenty-four hour clock** a system for measuring time in which the hours of the day and night have numbers from 0 to 23 二十四小時制時鐘 **11 start/stop the clock** to start or stop measuring how much time is left in a game or sport that has a time limit〔在比賽中〕開始/停止計時: *They stopped the clock when Baggio was injured.* 巴治奧受傷後暫停計時。**12 the clock a)** an instrument in a vehicle that measures how many miles or kilometres it has travelled〔汽車上的〕行車里程計: *The car had 43,000 miles on the clock.* 里程表上顯示這輛車已行駛了43,000英里。**b)** an instrument in a vehicle that measures the speed at which it is travelling 車速表[計] **13 run out the clock/kill the clock** *AmE* if a team runs out the clock at the end of a game, it does not allow the opponents to get the ball so that they cannot earn points【美】〔在比賽末段〕消磨時間不讓對方得分 —see also 另見 BIOLOGICAL CLOCK, BODY CLOCK, DANDELION CLOCK, TIME CLOCK

clock² *v* [T] **1** to travel at a particular speed, or to measure the speed at which someone or something is travelling 以...速度行駛; 測出, 記下〔速度〕: *The police clocked him at 95 miles an hour on the freeway.* 警察測出他在公路上行駛的時速為95英里。**2** to record the time taken to travel a certain distance 記錄〔所花的〕時間, 為...計時: **clock sb at** *She was clocked at 59 seconds for the first lap.* 她跑第一圈花了59秒。**3 clock this/that!** *BrE spoken* used to tell someone to notice or pay attention to something【英口】注意〔看〕! **4 clock sb one** *BrE informal* to hit someone【英, 非正式】毆打某人, 揍某人: *I clocked him one in the eye.* 我打中他的眼睛。**5 clock a car** *BrE slang* to change the number of miles shown on the CLOCK¹ (12) of a car, in order to sell it for more money【英俚】〔為了使汽車賣更高價而〕更改里程表 (數字)

clock in/on *phr v* [I] to record on a special card the time you arrive at or begin work; punch in (PUNCH¹)〔用特製的卡片〕記錄上班的時間; 打上班卡: *I clock on at 8:30.* 我8點30分打上班卡。

clock off/out *phr v* [I] to record on a special card the time you stop or leave work; punch out (PUNCH¹)〔用特製的卡片〕記錄下班的時間; 打下班卡: *I'm clocking off early today.* 我今天要早點下班。

clock up sth *phr v* [T] to reach a particular number or amount 達到〔某一數量〕: *The Dodgers have clocked up six wins in a row so far this season.* 本賽季到目前為止閃避者隊已連勝六場。| *I clocked up 90,000 miles in my Ford.* 我的福特車已跑了90,000英里。

clock-ra·di·o /ˌ· ˈ···/ *n* [C] a clock that can be set to turn on a radio in order to wake someone up 收音機鬧鐘

clock·watch·ing /ˈklɑkˌwɑtʃɪŋ; ˈklɒkˌwɒtʃɪŋ/ *n* [U] the practice of looking often at a clock to see what time it is because you are bored or want to stop working 老是看鐘等下班的行為 —**clockwatcher** *n* [C]

clock·wise /ˈklɑkˌwaɪz; ˈklɒk-waɪz/ *adv* in the same direction in which the hands (HAND¹ (40)) of a clock move 順時針方向地: *Screw the lid on clockwise.* 順時針方向擰緊蓋子。—**clockwise** *adj* —opposite ANTICLOCKWISE *BrE*【英】, COUNTERCLOCKWISE *AmE*【美】

clock·work /ˈklɑkˌwɝk; ˈklɒk-wɜːk/ *n* [U] **1** clockwork toys, trains, soldiers etc have machinery inside them to make them move when you turn a key〔玩具上的〕發條裝置 **2 go like clockwork** if something you have arranged goes like clockwork, it happens in exactly the way you planned 準確地; 順利地: *The concert went like clockwork.* 音樂會進行得很順利。**3 (as) regular as clockwork** very regular 非常準時的; 極有規律的: *Walter came round every Friday, regular as clockwork.* 沃特每逢週五便過來, 非常有規律。**4 with clockwork precision/accuracy** in an extremely exact way 極精確地

clod /klɑd; klɒd/ *n* [C] **1** a lump of mud or earth 土塊, 泥塊 —see picture on page A7 參見A7頁圖 **2** *informal* a stupid person who behaves insensitively【非正式】傻瓜, 笨蛋 —**cloddish** *adj*

clod·hop·per /ˈklɑdˌhɑpɚ; ˈklɒdˌhɒpə/ *n* [C] **1** *informal* someone who is awkward and rough【非正式】笨拙的人, 粗人 **2 clodhoppers** [plural] *humorous* a pair of heavy strong shoes【幽默】結實笨重的鞋子

clog¹ /klɑg; klɒg/ *v* also 又作 **clog up** [I,T] if something clogs a road, pipe etc, or a road or a pipe clogs, it gradually becomes blocked and no longer works properly 阻塞, 塞住; 阻礙: *Don't put potato peelings down the drain,* *they'll clog up the pipe.* 不要把馬鈴薯皮削在水槽裡，會堵塞水管的。| **clog sth with** *The roads were clogged with traffic.* 路上交通阻塞。—**clogged** *adj*: *clogged pores* 堵塞的毛孔

clog² *n* [C usually plural 一般用複數] a shoe made of wood with a leather top that covers the front of your foot but not your heel 木底鞋, 木屐 —see also 另見 **clever clogs** (CLEVER (6)) **pop your clogs** (POP¹ (9)) —see picture at 參見 SHOE¹ 圖

clois·ter¹ /ˈklɔɪstɚ; ˈklɔɪstə/ *n* [C] **1** [usually plural 一般用複數] a covered passage that surrounds one side of a square garden in a church, MONASTERY etc〔修道院等的〕迴廊 **2** a building where MONKs or NUNs live 修道院

cloister² *v* **cloister yourself (away)** to spend a lot of time alone in a room or building, especially because you need to study or work〔尤指因學習或工作而〕使自己與世隔絕

clois·tered /ˈklɔɪstɚd; ˈklɔɪstəd/ *adj* **1** protected from the difficulties and demands of ordinary life 隱居的, 隱匿的: *a cloistered existence* 隱居生活 **2** a cloistered building contains cloisters 修道院的

clone¹ /klon; kləʊn/ *n* [C] **1** *technical* an animal or plant produced in an ASEXUAL way from a particular cell and looking exactly like this cell【術語】克隆, 無性繁殖 **2** *technical* a computer that can use SOFTWARE that was written for a different computer【術語】仿製電腦: *an IBM clone* 仿製 IBM 型號的電腦 **3** *informal* someone or something that seems to be an exact copy of someone or something else【非正式】極為相似的人[物]: *She's a bit of a Madonna clone.* 她和麥當娜就像一個模子裡出來的。

clone² *v* [T] to make an exact copy of a plant or animal by taking a cell from it and developing it artificially 使…無性繁殖

clonk /klɑŋk; klɒŋk/ *n* [singular] the sound made when a heavy object falls to the ground or hits another heavy object 咚的響聲 —**clonk** *v* [I,T]

clop /klɑp; klɒp/ *v* **clopped, clopping** [I] if a horse clops, its hooves (HOOF¹ (1)) make a loud sound as they touch the ground〔馬蹄〕發出嘚嘚聲 —**clop** *n* [singular] —**clopping** *n* [singular]

1 1 **close¹** /kloz; kləʊz/ *v*

1 ►SHUT 關◄ [I,T] to shut something so that there is no longer a space or hole, or to become shut in this way 關, 閉合: *Ann closed her book and stood up.* 安合上書站了起來。| **close a door/window/gate** *Would you mind if I closed the window?* 我可以把窗戶關了嗎? | **close the curtains/blinds/shutters** *Close the curtains – it's getting dark.* 把窗簾拉上吧 — 天快黑了。| **close your eyes** *Beth closed her eyes and tried to sleep.* 貝斯合上眼睛想睡。—see 見 OPEN² (USAGE)

2 ►NO LONGER EXIST 不再存在◄ also 又作 **close down** [I,T] if a company, shop etc closes or you close it, it stops operating permanently〔永久性〕關閉, 停業: *We have reluctantly decided to close the factory.* 我們極不情願地決定關閉該廠。

3 ►FOR A PERIOD OF TIME 一個時期◄ also 又作 **close up** [I,T] if a shop or building closes or you close it, it stops being open to the public for a period of time; SHUT¹ (5)〔暫時性〕關閉, 歇業: *The shops close at six.* 商店六點打烊。

4 ►BOOK/SPEECH ETC 書/言語等◄ [I always+adv/prep, T always+adv/prep] if a book, play, speech etc closes or someone closes it, it ends in a particular way 使結束, 使停止: **close sth/with/by etc** *The Prime Minister closed his speech by making an appeal for peace.* 首相以呼籲和平結束了演講。| **[+with/by/when]** *The novel closes when the family are re-united in Prague.* 小說以一家人在布拉格團聚為結尾。| **closing remarks** (=something that you say at the end of an official talk or speech) 閉幕辭

5 close an account to stop having an account with a bank 撤銷賬戶

6 ►FINANCIAL/ECONOMIC 金融的/經濟的◄ [I always+adv/prep] if business shares (SHARE² (5)) or CURRENCY (1) closes at a particular price, they are worth that amount at the end of a day's trade on the STOCK MARKET〔股市〕以…價格收盤: **[+at/down etc]** *Portland shares closed only 4p down at 112p.* 波特蘭股票以 112 點收盤, 僅跌了 4 點。

7 close a deal/sale/contract etc to successfully arrange a business deal, sale etc 做成生意/買賣/達成協議等

8 ►OFFER 開價◄ [I] to finish on a particular date 在〔某一日〕結束: *Special offer closes June 3.* 特殊優惠到 6 月 3 日結束。

9 ►DISTANCE/DIFFERENCE 距離/差異◄ [I,T] to make the distance or difference between two things smaller 拉近, 減少〔分歧〕: *Society needs to close the gap between rich and poor.* 社會需要縮小貧富間的差距。| *The other car was closing on us fast.* 另一輛汽車迅速地趕上來。

10 ►REDUCE ACTIVITIES ETC 減少活動等◄ [T] to make an activity or opportunity no longer available 使…不再存在: *The legislation closes a lot of loopholes in the tax law.* 該項立法填補了稅法中的很多漏洞。

11 be closed if a particular subject is closed, you are no longer willing to discuss it 不再談論某話題: *It was a regrettable incident but I now consider the matter closed.* 這個事件非常令人遺憾, 但是我認為現在不要再談論它了。

12 ►HOLD STH 抓握某物◄ [I always+adv/prep, T always+adv/prep] if someone's hands, arms etc close around something or they close them around something, they hold it firmly〔手〕抓握; 抱緊: **[+around/round/over etc]**: *The baby's tiny hand closed over Ken's finger.* 嬰兒的小手緊緊抓住肯恩的手指。

13 ►WOUND 傷口◄ also 又作 **close up** [I,T] if a wound closes or you close it, it grows back together and becomes healthy, or you sew it together for it to become healthy 合攏, 合上: *The surgeon closed the incision neatly.* 外科醫生乾淨利落地縫合了切口。

14 close ranks a) if people close ranks, they join together to protect each other, especially because their group, organization etc is being criticized 團結〔戰鬥〕**b)** if soldiers close ranks, they stand closer together〔士兵〕列隊靠攏;〔排成〕密集隊形

15 close the book(s) on sth to stop working on something, especially a police inquiry, because it is impossible to continue 終止,〔警察〕停止〔盤問〕—see also 另見 CLOSED, CLOSING DATE, CLOSING TIME, **close/shut the door on** (DOOR (16)), **close your eyes to sth** (EYE¹ (39))

close down *phr v* **1** [I,T **close** sth ↔ **down**] if a company, shop etc closes down or is closed down, it stops operating permanently 關閉, 停業 **2** [I] *BrE* to stop broadcasting radio or television programmes at the end of the day【英】〔電台、電視台在一天的播送後〕結束播送節目: *BBC 2 closes down at 12:45 tonight.* 今晚英國廣播公司第二台於 12 點 45 分停止廣播。

close in *phr v* [I] **1** to move closer to someone or something, especially in order to attack them 包圍, 合攏; 靠近: *The snake closed in for the kill.* 蛇湊近來準備捕食。| **[+on/around/upon etc]** *The gang closed in on Larry brandishing sticks.* 那幫人揮舞着棍子向拉里圍攏過來。**2** if the night, bad weather etc closes in, it becomes darker or gets worse〔天〕變黑;〔天氣〕變壞 **3** if the days close in, they become shorter because it is autumn〔白天〕變短

close sth ↔ **off** *phr v* [T] to separate a road, room etc from the area around it so that people cannot go there or use it 隔絕, 封鎖: *One of the lanes is closed off for repairs.* 一條車道由於要維修而被封閉了起來。

close out *phr v* [T] *AmE* if a store closes out a type of goods, they sell all of them cheaply【美】〔商店以低價〕清倉出售, 拋售存貨: **close sth ↔ out** *We're closing out this line of swimwear.* 我們正在削價銷售這種游泳衣。

close up *phr v* **1** [I,T **close** sth ↔ **up**] if a shop or building closes up or is closed up, it stops being open to the public for a period of time〔商店暫時〕停業; 歇業;〔建築物〕關閉; 封閉 **2** [I,T] if a group of people close up, they move nearer together 靠近, 靠攏: **close up the**

ranks! (=used to order soldiers to stand closer together)〔口令〕隊伍靠攏! **3** [I,T] if a wound closes up or if something closes it up, it grows together or is sewn together and becomes healthy again〔傷口〕癒合; 縫合 **4** [I] to deliberately not show your true emotions or thoughts 掩飾, 掩蓋〔感情或思想〕: *Every time I ask Jenny about it she just closes up.* 每次我詢問珍妮這件事, 她只是遮掩搪塞。

close with sb/sth *phr v* [T] *BrE*【英】**1** to agree to do a business deal with someone 同意; 與…達成協議: *It was such a good offer that I closed with him on the spot.* 報價非常好, 我當場就跟他拍板了。**2** *literary* to begin a fight or battle【文】開始戰鬥: *The two armies closed with each other around about midday.* 接近中午的時候雙方軍隊開始短兵相接。

close² /klos; kləʊs/ *adj*

① **NEAR** 靠近的
② **LIKELY** 可能的
③ **CAREFUL** 小心的
④ **SIMILAR** 類似的
⑤ **ALMOST LOST/DANGEROUS ETC** 幾近丟失/危險的等
⑥ **FRIENDLY** 友好的
⑦ **ALMOST CORRECT** 幾乎正確的
⑧ **SPOKEN PHRASES** 口語片[短]語
⑨ **OTHER MEANINGS** 其他意思

① NEAR 靠近的

1 ▶**NEAR IN SPACE** 空間上靠近的◀ not far 近的: *The shops on Roland Way are the closest.* 羅蘭德路上的商店是最近的。| [+to] *They chose a spot close to the river for their picnic.* 他們選擇了一個離河不遠的地方進行野餐。| **in close proximity** *The new housing estate is in close proximity to a nuclear power station.* 新的住宅區靠近核電站。

2 **at close range/quarters** very near 近距離地: *The victim had been shot at close range.* 被害者是近距離被槍殺的。

3 ▶**NEAR IN TIME** 時間上靠近的◀ near to something in time〔時間上〕接近的: [+to] *Your birthday's close to mine.* 你的生日和我的生日相隔不長。

② LIKELY 可能的

4 ▶**LIKELY TO HAPPEN** 可能發生的◀ seeming likely to happen or to do something soon 可能的, 接近的: [+to] *close to death* 離死亡不遠 | **close to doing sth** *The two countries are close to signing a peace agreement.* 兩國即將簽署和平協議。

③ CAREFUL 小心的

5 a close examination, inspection, observation is one in which you look at something very carefully and thoroughly 徹底而仔細的, 嚴密的: **take a close look at sth** *Take a closer look at the photo; doesn't it remind you of someone?* 你再仔細地看看那照片, 沒有讓你想起一個人嗎? | **keep a close watch/eye on** (=watch someone or something very carefully) 細心地看 *I'll keep a close eye on the kids; don't worry.* 我會當心看管小孩們的, 不要擔心。

6 **close confinement/arrest** if a prisoner is kept in close confinement or under close arrest, someone guards them carefully to make sure they do not escape 嚴密囚禁/拘押

④ SIMILAR 類似的

7 if two things are close, they are very similar 酷似的: [+to] *There was a look of resentment in her eyes which was close to hatred.* 她眼中有一種近乎敵意的怨恨目光。

8 **close to sth** if a number or amount is close to another number or amount, it is similar to it〔數量上〕接近某物: *During the recession, the country's growth rate was close to zero.* 蕭條時期, 該國的經濟增長率幾乎是零。

⑤ ALMOST LOST/DANGEROUS ETC 幾近丟失/危險的等

9 ▶**COMPETITION/ELECTIONS ETC** 比賽/選舉等◀ won or lost by a very small amount 幾乎平手的, 勢均力敵的, 難分高下的: **close game/contest etc** *a close match that could have gone either way* 輸贏都有可能的勢均力敵的比賽 | **a close second/third etc** (=almost finish a competition in the position ahead of the one you actually get) 與第一/二名相差很近的第二/三名

10 **be too close to call** if a competition, election, or result is too close to call the two sides have almost exactly the same number of votes, points etc〔比賽、競選、結果〕勢均力敵

11 ▶**ALMOST DANGEROUS/EMBARRASSING** 幾乎危險的/令人尷尬的◀ *spoken* used when you have only just managed to avoid a dangerous or embarrassing situation【口】險些〔造成危險或尷尬局面〕: **that was close** *"Phew, that was close," Frank said as he swerved to avoid the cyclist.* "咳, 真險,"弗蘭克在側身躲過腳踏車手後說道。| **a close call/shave/thing** (=a situation in which something dangerous, embarrassing etc almost happens) 勉強脫險/死裡逃生/九死一生

⑥ FRIENDLY 友好的

12 if two people are close, they like or love each other very much 親近的, 親密的: *Mom and I are much closer now than we were when I was a teenager.* 我和媽媽現在的關係比起在我十幾歲時更親密了。| [+to] *I felt closer to Rob that evening than ever before.* 那晚我覺得和羅伯比以前更親近了。| **close friends** *Fiona and I have always been close friends.* 我和菲奧娜一直都是密友。

13 **close relation/relative** a member of your family such as your brothers, sisters, parents etc 近親〈如家庭成員〉

14 **keep in close contact/touch** if two people keep in close contact, they see, talk to, or write to each other regularly 保持密切聯繫

15 **close association/connection/link etc** if a relationship, association etc is close, the people in it work or talk together a lot 密切的關係/聯繫/接觸等: *The school encourages close links between teachers and parents.* 學校鼓勵老師和家長多接觸。| **close cooperation** *What we need now is closer cooperation between the club and supporters.* 我們現在需要的是俱樂部與資助人之間更密切的合作。| **close partners/colleagues** *Dr Henke and I were close colleagues on the research project.* 亨克博士和我曾是該研究項目的親密同事。

⑦ ALMOST CORRECT 幾乎正確的

16 **you're close/that's close** *spoken* used to tell someone that they have almost guessed or answered some-

thing correctly【口】差不多, 你快猜對了: *"Where did you go on holiday this year – Turkey?" "You're close, we went on a 10 day tour to Syria."* "你今年去哪兒度假了? 土耳其嗎?" "差不多是那一帶。我們去敍利亞旅行了10天。"
17 close, but no cigar *AmE spoken* used when something someone does or says is almost correct or successful【美口】差不多, 但並非完全如此: *It was close, but no cigar for the Dodgers as they lost to the Reds 4-3.* 差不多讓你猜中了, 閃避者隊以4:3敗給紅色隊。

⑧ SPOKEN PHRASES 口語片[短]語
18 the closest thing to/the closest you'll get to something that is very similar to, but not exactly the same as the thing mentioned 最接近…的事物/你所能達到的最接近的事物: *The island was the closest thing to an earthly paradise I can imagine.* 那個島是我所想到的最接近人間仙境的地方。
19 too close for comfort if something that happens is too close for comfort, it frightens you or makes you nervous 使人驚恐[緊張]的: *That car came around the corner just a little too close for comfort.* 那輛車從拐角開出來, 嚇了我一跳。
20 close to home a) if something unpleasant happens close to home, you are directly affected by it because you see it in your daily life 發生在身邊: *It's one thing seeing violence on the television but when it happens so close to home it's a different matter.* 在電視上看到暴力是一回事, 但是暴力在你身邊發生又是另一回事。**b)** if a remark or criticism is close to home, it makes someone feel embarrassed or uncomfortable 令人尷尬[不舒服]的: *Allegations of elitism were too close to home as far as the committee was concerned.* 就該委員會而言, 提出精英主義的說法太令人不悅了。

⑨ OTHER MEANINGS 其他意思
21 ►WEATHER 天氣◄ very warm in a way that is uncomfortable because there seems to be no air 悶熱的: *It's very close today.* 今天很悶熱。
22 ►SECRET 祕密◄ [not before noun 不用於名詞前] unwilling to tell people your thoughts or feelings; SECRETIVE 遮掩的, 守口如瓶的: **[+about]** *Wanda's always been very close about her past.* 温達對她的過去一直守口如瓶。
23 ►NOT GENEROUS 不大方◄ [not before noun 不用於名詞前] not generous; MEAN[2] (2) 吝嗇的: **[+with]** *You won't get a penny out of him, he's very close with his money.* 你別想從他那兒得到一分錢, 他吝嗇得很。
24 close shave/haircut a process in which someone's hair is cut very close to the skin on the face or head 剪得很短的鬍子/頭髮
25 close print/stitches etc print etc with little space between the letters, lines etc 密密麻麻的印出的字/針腳等: *I find it difficult to read such close print.* 這樣密密麻麻的字, 我很難讀下去。
26 close work a process or activity which involves looking at or handling things in a very skilful and careful way 精細的工作: *Embroidery is very close work.* 刺繡是個很精細的工作。
27 close vowel *technical* a close vowel is pronounced with only a small space between the tongue and the top of the mouth【術語】閉元音 **—closeness** *n* [U] —see also 另見 **close to the bone** (BONE[1] (9)), **play your cards close to your chest** (CARD[1] (13))

3 2 **close[3]** /klos; kləʊs/ *adv* **1** not far away; near 不遠, 接近地: **[+to]** *Ships can anchor close to the shore there.* 船可以在離海岸不遠處下錨。| **close by** *The Abbots live quite close by.* 阿博特一家住得很近。| **close at hand/close together** (=very near) 近在咫尺/緊挨着 *Three men were standing very close together on the corner.* 三個人緊挨着站在角落裡。| **close behind** *James heard footsteps close behind him.* 詹姆士聽到緊跟身後的腳步聲。| **get close** *I couldn't get close enough to see what was happening.* 我不能走到近前看究竟發生了甚麼事。| **stay/keep close** *We must all stay close together.* 我們大家必須留在一塊兒。| **hold/draw sb close** (=hold someone against your body because you love them or want to protect them) 摟緊/拉近某人 *He drew her close to him.* 他把她拉到自己身邊。**2 close up/close to/up close** from only a short distance away 靠近: *When I saw her close up I realised she wasn't Jane.* 我看到她走近後才意識到她不是簡。**3 close on/close to** used when you are guessing a number, age, amount etc or cannot give the exact number etc 幾乎, 差不多: *The walk took three whole days and covered close on forty miles.* 我們整整走了三天, 大約有四十英里。**4 close to sth** to be very similar to something 與某事物極為相似: *When I saw Henry with another woman I felt something close to jealousy.* 當我看到亨利和另一個女人在一起時, 我感到頗有些嫉妒。**5 come close to (doing) sth** to almost do something 差點兒〔做〕: *I tell you I was so angry I came close to hitting her.* 我告訴你我很生氣, 差點兒打了她。| *She came close to tears when she heard the news.* 聽到這樣的消息, 她差點兒掉下眼淚。**6** near to the surface of something 接近表面地, 短到齊根地: *An electric razor doesn't really shave as close as a blade.* 電動剃鬚刀其實沒有刀片刮得乾淨。**7 run sb close** to be almost as successful, skilful etc as someone else 和某人差不多一樣成功[熟練等]: *Maxwell runs him close as one of this country's most exciting musicians.* 麥克斯威爾差不多是該國最優秀的音樂家之一。—see also 另見 **sail close to the wind** (SAIL[1] (6))

close[4] /kloz; kləʊz/ *n* **1** [singular] *formal* the end of an activity or of a period of time【正式】〔活動或一段時間的〕結束, 末尾: **the close of** *They returned home tired but happy at the close of the day.* 天黑時他們回到家裡, 雖然很累, 但很高興。**2 bring sth to a close** end a meeting, lesson etc 結束, 停止: *The chairman brought the meeting to a close by thanking everyone for their hard work.* 主席在感謝了每個人的辛勞後, 宣布會議結束。**3 come/draw to a close** if a period of time or an activity draws to a close, it ends 結束, 終止: *And so, as 2003 draws to a close let's look at some of the major events of the year.* 因此, 在2003年即將結束之際, 讓我們回顧一下本年度發生的一些重大事件。

close[5] /klos; kləʊs/ *n* **1** [C] *BrE* a word used in street names for a road that has only one way in or out【英】〔用於街道名稱〕死巷, 死胡同: *They live at 26 Hillside Close.* 他們住在希爾賽得巷26號。**2** the area and buildings surrounding a CATHEDRAL〔大教堂的〕周圍地區

close-cropped /ˌklos ˈkrɑpt; ˌkləʊs ˈkrɒpt◄/ *adj* close-cropped grass or hair is cut very short〔草或頭髮〕剪得很短的

closed /klozd; kləʊzd/ *adj* **1** shut, especially overnight or for a certain period of time 關閉的: *The shops are closed on Sundays.* 商店星期天關門。| **closed to the public/visitors etc** *The gardens are closed to visitors in winter.* 花園在冬天不對遊客開放。**2** restricted to a particular group of people 只限特定人羣的: **closed membership** *The golf club has closed membership.* 該高爾夫球俱樂部只有限定的會員參加。**3** not willing to accept ideas or influences from outside 閉關自守的, 不受外來影響: **closed society/world/way of life** *Army officers and their families live in a very closed world.* 軍官及其家屬生活在一個非常封閉的世界裡。| **closed mind** (=someone who has a closed mind does not accept new ways of thinking or doing things) 閉塞僵化的思想[頭腦] **4 behind closed doors** if official meetings or decisions take place behind closed doors, they take place secretly 不公開地, 祕密地 **5 a closed book** a subject or problem that someone knows or understands nothing about 一無所知[毫不理解]的學科[問題]: *Most of mathematics is just a closed book to me.* 3

我對大多數數學科目都幾乎一竅不通。

closed cir·cuit tel·e·vi·sion /,· ··'····/ *n* [C,U] a system in which cameras send pictures to television sets that is used in many public buildings to protect them from crime 閉路電視

closed-door /,· '·/ *adj* [only before noun 僅用於名詞前] closed-door meetings or talks take place secretly 祕密的

close·down /ˋkloz`daʊn; 'kləʊzdaʊn/ *n* **1** [C] a situation in which work in a company, factory etc is stopped, especially permanently〔公司、工廠等〕停工, 關閉 **2** [C, U] *BrE* the end of radio or television broadcasts each day【英】〔每天廣播或電視節目的〕停止播送

C

closed sea·son /,· '··/ *n* [C] the American form of CLOSE SEASON close season 的美語形式

closed shop /,·'·◂/ *n* [C] a company, factory etc where all the workers must belong to a particular TRADE UNION 只雇用某一工會會員的企業

close-fist·ed /ˌklos `fɪstɪd; ˌkləʊs 'fɪstɪ̵d◂/ *adj* unwilling to spend money; TIGHT-FISTED 吝嗇的, 小氣的

close-fit·ting /ˌklos `fɪtɪŋ; ˌkləʊs 'fɪtɪŋ◂/ *adj* close-fitting clothes are tight and show the shape of your body 〔衣服〕緊身的

close-grained /ˌklos `grend; ˌkləʊs 'greɪnd◂/ *adj* close-grained wood has a fine natural pattern〔木頭〕紋理細密的

close-knit /ˌklos `nɪt; ˌkləʊs 'nɪt◂/ also 又作 **closely-knit** /,·· '·◂/ *adj* a close-knit group of people have strong friendly relationships with each other 緊密連結在一起的: *a close-knit community* 關係密切的社區

S2 W2 **closely** /ˋkloslɪ; 'kləʊsli/ *adv* **1** if you look at or study something closely, you look at it etc hard, trying to notice everything about it 仔細地, 嚴密地: **watch sb closely** *The detective was watching him closely, waiting for a reply.* 偵探緊緊地盯着他, 等待答覆。**2** if two things are closely connected or related, there is a strong connection between them or they are very much like each other 密切地, 緊密地: *These two subjects were closely linked, and it makes sense to consider them together.* 這兩個問題密切相關, 放在一起考慮是明智的。| **closely resembles** *Their dialect closely resembles that of the northern provinces.* 他們的方言非常接近於北部各省的口音。**3** in a way that makes things close together 緊跟地, 擁擠地: *a flash of lightning, closely followed by thunder* 一道閃電, 緊接着便是雷聲 | *We were so closely packed in the elevator, I could hardly move.* 電梯裡如此擁擠不堪, 我幾乎動彈不了。

close-mouthed /ˌklos `maʊðd; ˌkləʊs 'maʊðd◂/ *adj* not willing to say much because you are trying to keep a secret 口緊的

close·out /ˋkloz,aut; 'kləʊzaʊt/ *adj* **closeout sale/price** *AmE* a sale or price that is to get rid of goods cheaply【美】清倉大拍賣/清倉拍賣價: *There's a close-out sale on swimwear at Penney's this week.* 本週彭尼店在清倉拍賣泳衣。—**closeout** *n* [C]

close sea·son /ˋklos ˌsizn̩; 'kləʊs ˌsiːzən/ *n* [C] *BrE* 【英】**1** the period each year when particular animals, birds, or fish cannot legally be killed for sport 禁漁期, 禁獵期; CLOSED SEASON *AmE*【美】—opposite 反義詞 OPEN SEASON **2** the period during the summer when football teams do not play important games〔夏季足球隊不舉行重大比賽時的〕足球休賽季節

close-set /ˌklos `sɛt; ˌkləʊs 'set◂/ *adj* close-set eyes are near to each other〔眼睛〕緊靠在一起的: *Lessing's angry, close-set eyes followed him.* 萊辛憤怒得皺起雙眼緊緊地盯着他。

S3 **clos·et¹** /ˋklazɪt; 'klɒzɪ̵t/ *n* [C] **1 come out of the closet a)** to tell people that you are HOMOSEXUAL after hiding the fact 公開自己的同性戀身分 **b)** to admit you believe something or to discuss something that was previously kept secret 公開承認相信〔某事〕; 公開以前保密的事 **2** *especially AmE* a cupboard built into the wall of a room from the floor to the ceiling【尤美】壁櫥: *Jean had a closet full of clothes that most teenages would kill for.* 吉恩有滿滿一櫃子大部分青少年夢寐以求的衣服。—compare 比較 WARDROBE **3** *old use* a small room where people went to study, pray etc alone【舊】密室; 祈禱室 —see also 另見 WATER CLOSET, **a skeleton in the closet** (SKELETON (4))

closet² *adj* **closet homosexual/alcoholic etc** someone who is a HOMOSEXUAL, ALCOHOLIC etc but who does not want to admit it 不願公開承認的同性戀/酗酒者等: *Not all teachers are closet radicals.* 不是所有老師都不願意承認自己是激進分子的。

closet³ *v* [T, usually passive 一般用被動態] to shut someone in a room away from other people in order to be alone or to discuss something private 把…關在小房間裡; 把…引進密室會談: **closet yourself away** *Bill closeted himself away in his study for hours on end.* 比爾把自己關在書房裡一連好幾個小時了。

close-up /ˋklos ˌʌp; 'kləʊs ʌp/ *n* [C] a photograph taken from very near 特寫照片, 近景照: *a close-up of the kitten's face* 小貓的臉部特寫 | **in close up** (=from very near) 近鏡頭特寫 *Much of the movie is shot in close-up.* 這部電影不少鏡頭都是特寫。

clos·ing¹ /ˋklozɪŋ; 'kləʊzɪŋ/ *adj* [only before noun 僅用於名詞前] happening or done at the end of a period of time or event 結尾的, 結束的: **closing remarks/words/speech/ceremony** *Yeltsin's closing speech was a call for a referendum on land ownership.* 葉利欽在閉幕辭中號召就土地所有權問題舉行全民投票。| **closing stages/seconds/minutes etc** *The UN was set up during the closing stages of the Second World War.* 聯合國是在第二次世界大戰將要結束時成立的。

closing² *n* [U] another word for CLOSURE closure 的另一種說法

closing date /'·· ,·/ *n* [C] the last date on which it is possible to make a request to do something 限期, 截止日期: *Closing date for applications is 6th August.* 申請的截止日期為 8 月 6 日。

closing time /'·· ·/ *n* [C,U] the time when a PUB in Britain must stop serving drinks and close〔英國酒吧的〕打烊時間, 停止營業時間: *Finish your drinks please – it's well past closing time!* 請快點喝完 — 已經過了打烊時間很久了!

clo·sure /ˋkloʒɚ; 'kləʊʒə/ *n* [C,U] **1** a process in which a factory, school, hospital etc permanently stops operating or providing services 關閉, 倒閉, 停業: *Today the government announced the closure of Bart's Hospital in London.* 今天政府宣布關閉倫敦的巴特醫院。**2 closure of a road/bridge etc** a process in which a road, bridge etc is blocked for a short time so that people cannot use it 道路/橋等的封閉

clot¹ /klat; klɒt/ **clotted, clotting** *v* [I,T] if blood or milk clots or if something clots it, it becomes thicker and more solid as it dries (使)〔血液或牛奶等〕凝結成塊 —see also 另見 CLOTTED CREAM

clot² *n* [C] **1** a thick almost solid mass formed when blood or milk dries〔血液或牛奶等的〕凝塊 **2** *BrE informal* a stupid person【英, 非正式】笨蛋, 呆子: *What did you put the matches in the fridge for, you clot?* 笨蛋, 你把火柴放入冰箱裡面幹嗎?

cloth /klɔθ; klɒθ/ *n* **1** [U] material used especially for making clothes 布料: *cotton cloth* 棉布 **2** [C] a piece of cloth used to cover a table; TABLECLOTH 桌布 **3** [C] a piece of cloth used for a particular purpose〔用作某一用途的〕一塊布: *She rubbed at the stain with a damp cloth.* 她用濕布擦去了污跡。| **dishcloth/floorcloth etc** *Tim grabbed a dishcloth and mopped up.* 蒂姆抓起抹布, 擦了起來。—see picture on page A10 參見 A10 頁圖 **4 the cloth** *literary* used to mean priests in the Christian church considered as a group【文】牧師, 教士 **5 make sth up out of whole cloth** *AmE informal* if a story, explanation, etc is made up out of whole cloth, it is not true【美, 非正式】虛構[编造]某事: *I could tell his excuse was made up out of whole cloth.* 我知道他的藉口是編出來的。

cloth cap /ˌ· ˈ·/ *n* [C] *BrE* a soft flat cap with a stiff pointed piece at the front【英】布帽, 工作帽

clothe /kloð; kləʊð/ *v* [T usually passive 一般用被動態] *literary*【文】**1** to put clothes on your body 給…穿衣: *Helen was clothed in a simple dress of brown wool.* 海倫穿了一件樸素的棕色毛衫。| **fully/partly/brightly clothed etc** (=dressed in a particular way) 穿得整齊/不整齊/鮮豔的等 *The children lay on the bed, fully clothed and fast asleep.* 孩子們躺在牀上, 衣服也沒有脫就熟睡了。**2** to provide clothes for yourself or other people 為…提供衣服: *Volunteers ensure that the children are adequately clothed.* 志願者保證孩子們有足夠的衣服穿。**3 be clothed in** *literary* to be completely covered by something【文】覆蓋; 籠罩: *an angel clothed in flames* 火焰圍繞的天使

clothes 衣服

clothes 衣服

cloth/material 布料

waterproof clothing 防水服裝

garments/articles of clothing (幾件) 衣服

2 2 **clothes** /kloz; kləʊðz/ *n* [plural] the things that people wear to cover their body or keep warm 衣服, 衣物: *I need some new clothes.* 我需要幾件新衣服。| **work/school clothes** (=clothes suitable for work or school) 工作服/校服

USAGE NOTE 用法說明: CLOTHES

WORD CHOICE 詞語辨析: **clothes, clothing, piece/item of clothing, garment, something to wear, cloth, material, fabric, dress**

Clothes is the usual word for things we wear. clothes 是我們所穿衣服的常用詞: *She's got some beautiful clothes* (NOT 不用 *cloths*). 她有幾件漂亮衣服。

Clothing [U] is a more formal word for **clothes** in general. 一般來說, clothing〔不可數〕比 clothes 更正式: *The workers here all have to wear protective clothing* (NOT 不用 *clothings*). 這兒的工人都必須穿防護服。| *a clothes/clothing shop* 服裝店. When you are talking about clothes for a particular event, you often say **something to wear**. 如果是特定場合穿的服裝, 則是 something to wear: *It's Gloria's wedding tomorrow and I haven't got anything to wear* (=I have no suitable clothes). 明天是歌莉亞的婚禮, 我還沒有合適的衣服穿。

Clothes is not used with numbers, and in conversation if you want to talk about one **piece/item of clothing** you would usually call it by its name. clothes 不能用數字來形容, 如果說 piece/item of clothing 通常要具體說出是甚麼服裝: *I want to buy a new coat* (NOT 不用 *a new cloth/clothing*). 我想買一件新外衣。**Garment** [C] is a rather formal word for a single **piece of clothing**. garment〔可數〕是正式用語, 指 a piece of clothing。On a shop notice 商店裡有如此告示: *Only three garments may be taken into the fitting room* (NOT 不用 *three clothes*). 只能帶三件衣服去試衣間。

Clothes are made from various kinds of **material, fabric** or **cloth** [U], such as woven wool, silk, cotton or acrylic. clothes 是由各種不同的材料 (material)、織物 (fabric) 或布料 (cloth) 製成: *I brought back a lovely piece of cloth from Thailand to make a dress out of.* 我從泰國帶了一塊很好看的布料回來, 準備做一條連衣裙。A **cloth** ([C] with plural **cloths**) is a piece of cloth, used for cleaning surfaces, dishes etc. a cloth (複數 cloths) 指用來擦物體表面、碟子等的布: *Oh dear, I've spilt my beer – have you got a cloth?* 天哪, 啤酒濺出來了, 你有抹布嗎?

A **dress** [C] is a kind of clothing worn by women. dress〔可數〕是指女性所穿的連衣裙: *What a pretty dress she's wearing!* 她穿的連衣裙多漂亮啊! In certain expressions **dress** [U] is used to mean a particular type of **clothes**. 在某些用語中 dress〔不可數〕是指特種類型的 clothes。*The men were expected to wear casual dress/formal evening dress/national dress/fancy dress for the dinner.* 參加宴會的男士應該穿便裝/正式的晚禮服/民族服裝/奇裝異服。

clothes bas·ket /ˈ· ˌ··/ *n* [C] *especially BrE* a large basket for clothes that need to be washed, dried, or ironed (IRON²)【尤英】放〔待洗、待乾或待燙〕衣物的籃子

clothes brush /ˈ· ·/ *n* [C] a brush used to remove dirt, dust etc from clothes 衣刷

clothes hang·er /ˈ· ˌ··/ *n* [C] a HANGER 衣架

clothes·horse /ˈklozˌhɔrs; ˈkləʊðzhɔːs/ *n* [C] **1** *BrE* a frame on which you hang clothes to dry indoors【英】〔室內的〕晾衣架 **2** *AmE informal* someone who thinks too much about clothes and who likes to have many different clothes【美, 非正式】講究穿着的人

clothes·line /ˈklozˌlaɪn; ˈkləʊðzlaɪn/ *n* [C] a rope on which you hang clothes to dry outdoors〔戶外的〕晾衣繩; WASHING LINE *BrE*【英】

clothes peg /ˈ· ˌ·/ *BrE*【英】**clothespin** /ˈklozˌpɪn; ˈkləʊzˌpɪn/ *AmE*【美】*n* [C] a wooden or plastic object that you use to fasten wet clothes to a clothesline 衣夾 —see picture at 參見 PIN¹ 圖

cloth·i·er /ˈkloðɪɚ; ˈkləʊðiə/ *n* [C] *old-fashioned* someone who makes or sells men's clothes or material for clothes【過時】男裝裁縫, 男士服裝商, 布販子

cloth·ing /ˈkloðɪŋ; ˈkləʊðɪŋ/ *n* [U] clothes considered as a group, especially the clothes someone is wearing, or a particular type of clothes 衣服, 衣着: *Remember to bring a change of clothing.* 記着帶一身換洗衣服。| **clothing manufacturer/industry** *Clothing manufacturers have reported a drop in profits.* 製衣商說利潤下降了。| **item/article of clothing** *Bring several warm items of clothing.* 帶幾件暖和的衣服來。| **waterproof/protective clothing** *Lab workers should wear protective clothing.* 實驗室工作人員應穿防護服。

clotted cream /ˌ·· ˈ·/ *n* [U] thick cream made by slowly heating milk and taking the cream from the top 濃縮奶油

clo·ture /ˈklotʃɚ; ˈkləʊtʃə/ *n* [C] *AmE technical* a way of ending an argument over a BILL¹ (2) in the US government and forcing a vote on it【美, 術語】終止辯論提付表決

cloud¹ /klaud; klaʊd/ *n* **1** [C,U] a white or grey mass in the sky that consists of very small drops of water 雲: 3 3

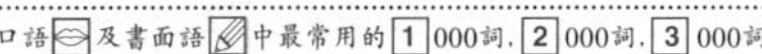

Dark clouds gathered overhead. 頭頂烏雲密佈。**2 a cloud of dust/smoke/gas etc** a mass of dust etc in the air 一團塵土/煙霧/氣體等 **3** [C] something that makes you feel afraid or worried 陰影, 烏雲: **[+of]** *The clouds of war began to threaten our peaceful life.* 戰爭的陰雲開始威脅到我們平靜的生活。| **a cloud on the horizon** (=something that threatens to spoil a happy situation) 麻煩的跡象, 不快 *The only cloud on the horizon was her mother's illness.* 唯一令人擔憂的是她母親病了。| **cast a cloud** (=spoil a happy situation) 破壞高興的氛圍 *The news that several competitors had been taking drugs cast a cloud over the event.* 有幾名選手服用藥物的消息令比賽蒙上了陰影。**4 on cloud nine** *informal* very happy about something【非正式】興奮, 高興: *Adam was on cloud nine after the birth of his son.* 亞當在兒子出生後欣喜若狂。**5 under a cloud** *informal* if someone is under a cloud, people have a bad opinion of them because they have done something wrong【非正式】遭嫌棄, 受懷疑: *He left the company under a cloud.* 他因不被信任而離開了公司。**6 be/live in cloud-cuckoo-land** to think that a situation is much better than it actually is in a way that makes you seem stupid 生活在理想境界: *If Ben thinks he's getting a pay rise, he's living in cloud-cuckoo-land.* 假如班恩認為自己會獲加薪的話, 那他是想入非非。**7 every cloud has a silver lining** used to say that there is something good even in a situation that seems very sad or difficult 黑暗中總有一線光明 —see also 另見 **have your head in the clouds** (HEAD¹ (11))

cloud² *v*
1 ►GLASS 玻璃◄ also 又作 **cloud over/up** [I,T] if a transparent material such as glass clouds or something clouds it, you cannot see through it properly any more (使) 變模糊, 使不清晰: *Steam had clouded the windows up.* 水蒸氣使窗玻璃變得模糊不清。
2 ►LIQUID 液體◄ also 又作 **cloud up** [I,T] if a liquid clouds or if something clouds it, it becomes less clear (使) 變渾濁: *Don't shake the barrel, you'll cloud the beer.* 不要搖晃酒桶, 你會把啤酒搖渾的。
3 ►THOUGHTS/MEMORIES 想法/記憶◄ [T] to make someone less able to think clearly or remember things 搞糊塗: **cloud sb's judgement/memory** *Don't let your personal feelings towards this woman cloud your judgement.* 不要讓你對這位婦人的個人感情影響了你的判斷力。
4 cloud the issue to make a subject or problem difficult to understand by introducing ideas or information that are not connected with it〔用無關信息〕使問題複雜化: *Bringing in unnecessary details at this stage will only cloud the issue.* 在這個時候加插一些不必要的細節只會使問題複雜化。
5 ►FACE 面部◄ also 又作 **cloud over** [I,T] if someone's expression clouds or if something clouds it, they start to look angry or sad〔臉色〕陰沉, (使) 憂鬱: *His face clouded when he saw her.* 他看到她時, 臉就沉了下來。
6 ►SPOIL STH 破壞某事物◄ [T] to make something less pleasant than it should have been 沖淡, 毀壞: *Half a billion people vote in a general election clouded by violence and charges of pollrigging.* 在這次因暴力事件和被指控有人操縱選票而蒙上了陰影的大選中, 有五億人投了票。
7 ►COVER WITH CLOUD 被雲籠罩◄ [T] to cover something with clouds〔雲〕籠罩: *Thick mist clouded the mountaintops.* 濃霧籠罩着山頂。
cloud over *phr v* [I] **1** if the sky clouds over, it becomes dark because it is full of black clouds〔天空〕陰雲密佈, 烏雲翻滾: *The sky's really clouding over; I think we're in for a storm.* 天空佈滿了烏雲, 我看我們將遇到一場暴風雨。**2** [I] if someone's expression clouds over, they start to look angry or sad〔臉色〕陰沉: *Anne's face clouded over as she remembered.* 安妮一想起來臉色就沉了下來。

cloud·bank /ˈklaudˌbæŋk; ˈklaʊdbæŋk/ *n* [C] a thick mass of low cloud 低垂濃密的雲團

cloud·burst /ˈklaudˌbɝst; ˈklaʊdbɜːst/ *n* [C] a sudden storm 驟雨, 大暴雨

cloud·ed /ˈklaudɪd; ˈklaʊdɪd/ *adj* **1** not clear or transparent 模糊不清的; 不透明的: *clouded glass* 不透明的玻璃 **2** a clouded face or expression shows that someone is unhappy or angry 愁容滿面的; 面露慍色的

cloud·less /ˈklaudlɪs; ˈklaʊdləs/ *adj* a cloudless sky is clear and bright 晴朗的, 無雲的: *sip exotic cocktails under a cloudless sky* 在晴朗的天空下啜飲外國雞尾酒

cloud·y /ˈklaudɪ; ˈklaʊdi/ *adj* **1** cloudy weather is dark because the sky is full of clouds 多雲的, 陰天的: *cloudy with outbreaks of rain* 陰天有陣雨。**2** cloudy liquids are not clear or transparent〔液體〕渾濁的, 不透明的 **3** cloudy thoughts, memories etc are not very clear or exact〔思想、想法、記憶等〕模糊的, 不清晰的

clout¹ /klaut; klaʊt/ *n* **1** [U] *informal* the power or authority to influence other people's decisions【非正式】〔影響他人決定的〕力量; 權勢: *His job carries a lot of clout.* 他的工作舉足輕重。**2** [C] *informal* a hard blow given with the hand【非正式】〔用手〕猛擊: *I'll give you a clout round the ear!* 我要讓你清醒清醒!

clout² *v* [T] *informal* to hit someone hard【非正式】猛擊〔某人〕: *Dad clouted me before I had a chance to explain.* 我還沒來得及解釋, 爸爸就狠狠揍了我一下。

clove¹ /klov; kləʊv/ *n* [C] **1** a SPICE (=something used to give a special taste to food) that has a strong smell, is black, and looks like a pin 丁香; 丁香花苞; 丁香香料 **2 a clove of garlic** one of the parts of a GARLIC root (=a plant similar to an onion) 一瓣大蒜

clove² a past tense of CLEAVE

clo·ven /ˈklovən; ˈkləʊvən/ a past participle of CLEAVE

cloven hoof /,.. ˈ./ *n* [C] a HOOF that is divided into two parts 偶蹄: *Sheep and goats have cloven hooves.* 綿羊和山羊都是偶蹄類動物。

clo·ver /ˈklovɚ; ˈkləʊvə/ *n* [U] **1** a small plant with three leaves on each stem 三葉草, 苜蓿 **2 in clover** *informal* living comfortably because you have plenty of money【非正式】生活舒適而富裕, 養尊處優

clo·ver·leaf /ˈklovɚˌlif; ˈkləʊvəliːf/ *n* [C] **1** the leaf of a clover plant 苜蓿葉, 三葉草的葉子 **2** a network of curved roads which connect two main roads where they cross 苜蓿葉形立體交叉路口

clown¹ /klaun; klaʊn/ *n* [C] **1** someone who entertains people in a CIRCUS (1) by dressing in funny clothes, and doing things to make people laugh〔馬戲團的〕小丑 **2** someone who often makes jokes or behaves in a funny way 愛開玩笑的人, 詼諧的人: *Frankie was a bit of a clown – always up to mischief and practical jokes.* 法蘭基有點滑稽 —— 總愛弄些惡作劇, 開開玩笑。| **class clown** (=someone in a school class who behaves in a funny or silly way)〔在班上常鬧笑話的〕課堂小丑 **3** a stupid or annoying person 蠢人; 討厭的人: *I can't understand what she sees in that clown.* 我不理解她在那個蠢貨身上看到了甚麼優點。**4 make a clown of yourself** *informal* to do something stupid or embarrassing【非正式】出洋相

clown 小丑

clown² *v* also 又作 **clown around/about** [I] to behave in a silly or funny way 做蠢事; 胡鬧: *Stop clowning around, you lot, and get back to your seats!* 別胡鬧了, 你們這羣傢伙, 都回到座位上去!

clown·ish /ˈklaunɪʃ; ˈklaʊnɪʃ/ *adj* silly or stupid 愚蠢的; 滑稽的 —**clownishly** *adv* —**clownishness** *n* [U]

cloy /klɔɪ; klɔɪ/ *v* [I] if something sweet or pleasant cloys, it begins to annoy you because there is too much of it

〔因過量而〕厭倦，發膩: *Her sweet submissive smile began to cloy after a while.* 不一會兒，她那過分甜蜜柔順的笑容開始讓人厭煩。

cloy·ing /ˈklɔɪ-ɪŋ; ˈklɔɪ-ɪŋ/ *adj* **1** a cloying attitude or quality annoys you because it is too pleasant 令人膩煩的: *cloying sentimentality* 令人生厭的多愁善感 **2** cloying food or smells are sweet and make you feel sick 甜得發膩的: *the cloying stench of cheap perfume* 廉價香水發出的刺鼻香味

cloze test /ˈkloz ˌtɛst; ˈkləʊz test/ *n* [C] a test in which students have to write the correct words into the spaces that have been left empty in a short piece of writing 填空測驗

1 1 **club¹** /klʌb; klʌb/ *n* [C]

1 ►FOR AN ACTIVITY/SPORT 活動/體育的◄ [also+plural verb *BrE* 英] an organization for people who share a particular interest or enjoy similar activities, such as sports or politics 俱樂部: *the Ramblers Club* 漫步者俱樂部 | **rugby/golf/squash club etc** (=a club for people who play a particular sport) 橄欖球/高爾夫球/壁球俱樂部等 | **join a club** *It costs £15 to join the club.* 參加這個俱樂部要交15英鎊。| **belong to a club** *She belongs to the local tennis club.* 她是當地網球俱樂部會員。

2 ►PROFESSIONAL SPORT 職業體育運動◄ a professional organization including the players, managers, and owners of a sports team 〔職業體育的〕俱樂部: *Tottenham Hotspur Football Club* 托特納姆熱刺足球俱樂部 | [also+plural verb *BrE* 英] *The club have added a new fast bowler to their line-up.* 該俱樂部新吸收了一名板球快投手。| **ball club** *AmE* (=a BASEBALL team)【美】棒球隊

3 ►FOR MEN 男人的◄ an organization, usually for men only, where they can relax and enjoy social activities 社交俱樂部

4 ►BUILDING 建築◄ the building or place where people who belong to an organization meet in order to do activities or play sports 俱樂部會所: *There's a party at the golf club.* 在那家高爾夫球俱樂部有個聚會。

5 book/record club etc an organization which people join in order to buy books, records etc cheaply 讀書/唱片等俱樂部〔其會員可以低價購買書籍、唱片等〕

6 ►FOR DANCING/MUSIC 舞蹈/音樂的◄ a place where usually young people go to dance, listen to music, and meet socially 俱樂部; 夜總會: *a jazz club* 爵士樂俱樂部 | *Shall we go to a club?* 我們去夜總會怎樣?

7 ►FOR HITTING BALL 擊球的◄ a special stick used in GOLF to hit the ball; GOLF CLUB (2)〔高爾夫球等的〕球棒

8 ►WEAPON 武器◄ a thick heavy stick used to hit people or things 大頭棒，棍棒

9 ►IN CARD GAMES 紙牌遊戲◄ **a)** a black shape with three leaves printed on cards for games 梅花 **b)** the SUIT (=group of cards) that has this shape printed on them 一手梅花牌: *the ace of clubs* 梅花A

10 in the club *BrE humorous* if a woman is in the club, she is going to have a baby; PREGNANT【英，幽默】懷孕的

11 join the club *BrE*【英】, **welcome to the club** *AmE*【美】used after someone has described a bad situation that they are in, to tell them that you are in the same situation 我們都一樣(糟) —see also 另見 COUNTRY CLUB, **fan club** (FAN[1] (1)), YOUTH CLUB

club² *v* **clubbed, clubbing** [T] to hit someone hard with a thick heavy object〔用棍棒〕打: **club sb to death** (=kill someone by hitting them several times with a heavy object) 用棍棒打死某人

club together *phr v* [I] *BrE* to share the cost of something with other people【英】分擔費用: *We clubbed together to buy her a present.* 我們湊錢給她買了一份禮物。

club·ba·ble /ˈklʌbəbl̩; ˈklʌbəbəl/ *adj BrE old-fashioned* interesting and good at talking in a friendly and relaxed way with other people【英，過時】合羣的; 好交際的

club·bing /ˈklʌbɪŋ; ˈklʌbɪŋ/ *n* **go clubbing** *BrE informal* to go regularly to NIGHTCLUBs【英，非正式】定期去夜總會

club class /ˈ· ·/ *n* [U] the area in a plane where the seats are more expensive than in the normal area, but are not as expensive as FIRST CLASS〔價格介於普通艙和頭等艙之間的〕飛機二等艙，商務艙

club foot /ˌ· ˈ·/ *n* **1** [C] a foot that has been badly twisted since birth and that prevents someone from walking properly〔先天性〕畸形足 **2** [U] the medical condition of having a club foot 足畸形 —**club-footed** *adj*

club·house /ˈklʌbˌhaus; ˈklʌbhaʊs/ *n* [C] a building used by a club, especially a sports club〔尤指體育〕俱樂部會所(大樓)

club sand·wich /ˌ· ˈ··/ *n* [C] a large SANDWICH[1] (1) consisting of three pieces of bread with two different kinds of cold food between them 公司三明治，總匯三明治〔通常為三片烤麵包，中間夾兩層不同的冷食〕

club so·da /ˌ· ˈ··/ *n* [C,U] *AmE* a drink consisting of water filled with gas BUBBLEs (1)【美】蘇打水; SODA WATER *BrE*【英】

cluck¹ /klʌk; klʌk/ *v* **1** [I] if a chicken clucks, it makes a short, low sound〔雞〕咯咯叫 **2** [I,T] to express sympathy or disapproval by saying something, or by making a short low noise with your tongue〔人用舌〕發咯咯聲〔以示同情或反對〕: **[+over/around/about]** *The women stood together clucking over her scandalously short skirt.* 那些女人站成一堆，嘰嘰呱呱議論着她那有傷風化的短裙。—**clucking** *adj*

cluck² *n* [C usually singular 一般用單數] **1** a low short noise made by hens〔母雞的〕咯咯聲 **2** a sound made with your tongue, used to show disapproval or sympathy〔人用舌發出的〕咯咯聲〔常表反對或同情〕: *a disapproving cluck* 表示反對的咯咯聲 **3** *especially AmE* a stupid person【尤美】蠢蛋，傻瓜: *You dumb cluck, why'd you tell him?* 你這個笨蛋，你為甚麼要告訴他?

clue¹ /klu; kluː/ *n* [C] **1** an object or piece of information that helps someone solve a crime or mystery 線索，提示: *He didn't know who had sent the letter, and the envelope provided no clue.* 他不知道誰寄了這封信，信封上也沒有任何線索。| **[+to/about]** *We now have a clue to the time at which the murder took place.* 我們現在對謀殺發生的時間有了一點線索。| **search for clues** *Our search for clues proved fruitless.* 我們沒有找到任何線索。**2** a question that you must solve in order to find the answer to a CROSSWORD or PUZZLE[2] (2)〔縱橫填字謎的〕提示語 | **give sb a clue** *I'll give you a clue, Kevin, it's a kind of bird.* 我給你個提示吧，凱文，那是一種鳥。**3 not have a clue** *informal*【非正式】**a)** to know nothing at all about the answer to a question or about how to do something 一無所知: *"Do you know how to switch this thing off?" "I'm afraid I haven't got a clue."* "你知道怎麼關上這個嗎?""恐怕我對此一無所知。" | **not have a clue where /why etc** *We haven't got a clue where they could have disappeared to.* 對他們躲到哪裡去了，我們毫無頭緒。**b)** to be very stupid, or very bad at a particular activity 很愚蠢; 很笨拙: *Myra just hits her kids when they start crying; she hasn't got a clue.* 孩子們一開始哭，邁拉就打他們。她真蠢。| **[+about]** *No point asking Jill, she hasn't got a clue about maths.* 問吉爾沒有用，她對數學一竅不通。| **not have a clue how/why etc** *Evans hasn't got a clue how to get on with people.* 艾文斯根本不懂如何與人相處。**4** a reason why something happens that you find by studying events, someone's behaviour etc 緣由，根源: *Childhood experiences may provide a clue as to why some adults develop phobias.* 童年經歷可能是一些成年人患恐懼症的緣由。 2

clue² *v*

clue sb ↔ **in** *phr v* [T] *informal* to give someone information about something【非正式】給〔某人〕提供線索; 告知: *Mark clued me in on how the computer system works.* 馬克告訴我電腦系統是如何運作的。

clued-up /ˌ· ˈ·/ *BrE*【英】**clued-in** *AmE*【美】*adj informal* knowing a lot about something【非正式】所知甚多的: *Ask Margaret, she's pretty clued-up about that sort of thing.* 去問瑪嘉烈, 她對那種事情知道得很清楚。

clue·less /ˈkluləs; ˈkluːləs/ *adj informal* having no understanding or knowledge of something【非正式】無線索的, 一無所知的: *He was completely clueless about the rules of the game.* 他對這項遊戲的規則一無所知。

C

clump¹ /klʌmp; klʌmp/ *n* **1** [C] a group of trees, bushes, or other plants growing very close together〔樹、灌木或其他植物的〕叢; 簇, 羣: **[+of]** *a clump of grass* 草叢 **2** [C] a piece of earth or mud 土塊 **3** [singular] the sound of someone walking with heavy steps 沉重的腳步聲: *I heard the clump of Ralph's boots going up the stairs.* 我聽見拉爾夫上樓時皮靴發出的沉重腳步聲。

clump² *v* **1** [I always+adv/prep] to walk with slow noisy steps 以沉重的步子行走: **[+up/down/along etc]** *Grandpa clumped along in his workboots.* 爺爺穿着工作靴, 邁着沉重的步子。 **2** [I always+adv/prep, T always+adv/prep] to put something heavy down with a loud noise 把某物重重放下: *She clumped the books down on the desk.* 她把那些書重重地放在書桌上。

clump together *phr v* [I,T] if separate objects clump together, or are clumped together they form a group or solid mass (使) 密集成叢; (使) 凝集成塊: *Rinse the rice to prevent the grains clumping together.* 把米淘一下, 以免米粒黏在一起。

clum·sy /ˈklʌmzɪ; ˈklʌmzi/ *adj* **1** moving in an awkward way and tending to break things 笨拙的, 不靈活的: *At 17, she was clumsy, shy and awkward.* 17歲時, 她做事笨手笨腳, 又害羞又不靈活。| *a clumsy attempt to catch the ball* 試圖接球的笨拙動作 | *"Look, you've just knocked that cup over." "Sorry, how clumsy of me."* "看, 你把茶杯碰倒了。" "對不起, 我真是笨手笨腳的。" **2** a clumsy object is not easy to use and is often large and heavy 龐大粗重的 **3** said or done carelessly or in a way that is not delicate and sensitive 粗糙的; 不得體的; 不細心的: *David made a clumsy but well-meaning attempt to comfort us.* 大衛好意地想安慰我們, 儘管有些笨拙。| **clumsy excuse/apology** *Becky stammered a clumsy apology.* 貝琪結結巴巴地道了個歉。—**clumsily** *adv* —**clumsiness** *n* [U]

clung /klʌŋ; klʌŋ/ the past tense and past participle of CLING

clunk /klʌŋk; klʌŋk/ *n* [singular] a loud sound made when two solid objects hit each other〔物體相撞發出的〕哐啷的一聲 —**clunk** *v* [I,T]

clunk·er /ˈklʌŋkɚ; ˈklʌŋkə/ *n* [C] *AmE informal* an old car or other machine that does not work well【美, 非正式】破舊的汽車[機器]

clunk·y /ˈklʌŋkɪ; ˈklʌŋki/ *adj* clunky shoes are heavy with thick SOLES (=bottoms)〔鞋〕厚底的

clus·ter¹ /ˈklʌstɚ; ˈklʌstə/ *n* [C] **1** a group of things of the same kind that are very close together 串, 束, 簇; 羣, 組: **[+of]** *a cluster of low farm buildings* 一羣低矮的農舍 **2** a group of people all in the same place〔聚集在同一地方的〕一羣人 **3** *AmE* a small piece of metal pinned to a soldier's uniform to show a high class of honour【美】〔別在軍服上代表較高榮譽的〕小金屬獎章

cluster² *v* [I always+adv/prep, T always+adv/prep] if a group of people or things cluster somewhere or are clustered somewhere, they form a small group in that place (使) 叢生; 羣集: **[+around/together etc]** *A group of children had clustered around the toy shop window.* 一羣孩子團團圍在玩具店的櫥窗前。

cluster bomb /ˈ·· ˌ·/ *n* [C] a bomb that sends out smaller bombs when it explodes 榴霰彈, 子母彈, 集束炸彈 —**cluster-bomb** *v* [T]

clutch¹ /klʌtʃ; klʌtʃ/ *v* [I] to hold something or someone tightly, especially because you are frightened, in pain, or do not want to lose something 緊握, 緊抓: *Tom fell to the ground clutching his stomach.* 湯姆跌倒在地, 緊緊捂着肚子。| *A woman clutching a baby stole an elderly woman's purse.* 一個懷抱嬰兒的婦女偷了一個老年婦人的錢包。

clutch at *phr v* **1** [T] to try hard to hold something, especially when you are in a dangerous situation〔尤指危險時〕努力抓住〔某物〕: *Suzie clutched desperately at the muddy river bank.* 蘇濟拚命地想抓牢泥濘的河堤。 **2 clutch at straws** to try hard to find a sign of hope or a solution, even when these are not likely to exist, in a difficult or dangerous situation〔在困境或險境中〕極力抓住渺茫的生存希望; 急不暇擇: *The doctors are really clutching at straws with this new treatment, but they've tried everything else.* 醫生們嘗試這種新療法其實是把死馬當活馬醫, 但他們也已試過其他所有治療方法了。

clutch² *n* **1** [C] the PEDAL¹ (2) that you press with your foot when driving a vehicle in order to change GEAR¹ (1) | **let in the clutch/let out the clutch** (=put your foot on or take your foot off the clutch) 接合/分離離合器 **2 clutches** *plural* the power, influence, or control that someone has 掌握, 控制, 統治: **in sb's clutches** (=controlled or influenced by someone) 在某人控制之下 *Many state organizations fell into the clutches of the Mafia.* 許多國家機構都落入黑手黨的控制之中。 **3** [singular] a tight hold that someone has on something 緊握, 緊抓: *I shook myself free of her clutch.* 我從她的緊抱中掙脫出來。 **4 a clutch of** a small group of similar things 一小羣; 一小簇: **a clutch of eggs/chickens** (=a group of eggs which a hen produces at one time, or the chickens born from these eggs) 一窩蛋/雞 **5 when it comes to the clutch** *AmE informal* when a difficult situation happens【美, 非正式】有困難的時候: *When it comes to the clutch, you can always count on Tom.* 有困難時, 你都可以依靠湯姆。

clutch bag /ˈ· ·/ *n* [C] a small bag that women carry in their hand, used especially on formal social occasions 女用無帶皮包〔尤用於正式社交場合〕

clut·ter¹ /ˈklʌtɚ; ˈklʌtə/ also 又作 **clutter up** *v* [T] **1** to cover or fill a space or room with too many things, so that it looks very untidy 亂堆, 塞滿: *Piles of books and papers cluttered his desk.* 他的書桌堆滿了書本和文件。| **be cluttered (up) with** *The front room was cluttered up with ornaments and antique furniture.* 前面的房間堆滿了裝飾品和古董家具。 **2** to fill your mind with unnecessary information 使〔心裡〕充滿〔不必要的信息〕: *Don't clutter up your mind with useless detail.* 別盡想些無關緊要的細節。—**cluttered** *adj*

clutter² *n* [singular,U] a large number of things that are scattered somewhere in an untidy way 雜亂的東西: *Could you get rid of some of that clutter in your bedroom?* 你能把你臥室那些雜物清理掉一些嗎?

cm the written abbreviation of 縮寫= CENTIMETRE

CNN /ˌsi ɛn ˋɛn; ˌsiː en ˈen/ *n* [U] Cable News Network; an American organization that broadcasts television news programmes to countries all over the world〔美國〕有線新聞網

C-note /ˈsi ˌnot; ˈsiː nəʊt/ *n* [C] *AmE slang* a 100 dollar note【美俚】一百元面值的鈔票

C.O. /ˌsi ˋo; ˌsiː ˈəʊ◂/ *n* [C] Commanding Officer; an officer who commands a military unit 指揮官

Co. /ko; kəʊ/ **1** the abbreviation of 縮寫= COMPANY: *James Smith & Co.* 詹姆士·史密斯公司 **2 and co** *spoken* used after mentioning a person or thing to mean the other people or things that you consider to belong to their group【口】及其一夥; 以及類似的種種: *I can't say I'm looking forward to seeing Angela and co again.* 我可不想再看見安琪拉和她那一夥人了。 **3** the written abbreviation of 縮寫= COUNTY 郡; 縣: *Co. Durham* 達勒姆郡

c/o the written abbreviation of 縮寫= care of; used especially in addresses when you are sending a letter or parcel to someone who is living in someone else's house etc〔書信用語〕由…轉交: *John Hammond, c/o Dowling Music College, Bethesda, Maryland* 煩由馬里蘭州貝塞斯達道林音樂學院轉交約翰·哈蒙德

co /ko; kəʊ/ *prefix* **1** together with 和…一起, 共同: *to coexist* (=exist together or at the same time) 共存 | *co-education* (=of boys and girls together) 男女合校教育 **2** doing something with someone else as an equal or with less responsibility 和…一起做; 輔助…做, 副: *my co-author* (=someone who wrote the book with me) 我的共同著者 | *the co-pilot* (=someone who helps a pilot) 飛機副駕駛員

coach¹ /kotʃ; kəʊtʃ/ *n* [C]
1 ▶IN A SPORT 體育運動中◀ [C] someone who trains a person or team in a sport〔體育〕教練: *a tennis coach* 網球教練 —see 見 TEACH (USAGE)
2 ▶IN A SCHOOL SUBJECT 課程中◀ [C] *especially BrE* someone who gives special instruction to a student in a particular subject, especially so that they can pass an examination【尤英】私人教師, 家庭教師
3 ▶BUS 巴士◀ [C] *BrE* a bus with comfortable seats used for long journeys【英】〔內有舒適座椅的〕長途公共汽車; BUS¹ *AmE*【美】: *We went to Paris by coach.* 我們坐長途公共汽車去巴黎。
4 ▶IN A TRAIN 乘火車◀ [C] *BrE* one of the parts of the train in which the passengers sit【英】旅客車廂; CAR (3) *AmE*【美】
5 ▶PULLED BY HORSES 由馬拖拉的◀ [C] a large carriage pulled by horses 公共馬車, 四輪大馬車
6 ▶A CLASS OF TRAVEL 旅行座位等級◀ [U] *AmE* the cheapest type of seats on a plane or train【美】普通旅客車廂;〔飛機的〕二等艙: *We flew coach out to Atlanta.* 我們坐二等艙飛往亞特蘭大。

coach² *v* [I,T] **1** to teach a person or team the skills they need for a sport 當教練, 訓練, 培訓, 指導: *Nigel coaches a cricket team in his spare time.* 奈傑爾業餘時間擔任一個板球隊的教練。**2** *especially BrE* to give someone special instruction in a particular subject, especially so that they can pass an examination【尤英】為…補習, 輔導: **coach sb in/for** *Chorley had to be coached in most subjects for the first two terms.* 頭兩個學期, 喬利的大多數科目都得請人補習。**3** to give someone instruction in what they should say or do in a particular situation〔演講、表演等方面〕予以指導: **coach sb in sth** *The Callaghan girl must be carefully coached in the story she will tell in court.* 必須好好指導一下那個來自卡拉漢的女孩如何在法庭陳述該事件。

coach·buil·der /ˈkotʃˌbɪldɚ; ˈkəʊtʃˌbɪldə/ *n* [C] *BrE* a worker who builds the main outer structure of a car【英】汽車車身製造工

coach·ing /ˈkotʃɪŋ; ˈkəʊtʃɪŋ/ *n* [U] **1** a process in which you teach a person or team the skills they need for a sport 教授, 訓練: **tennis/football/rugby coaching etc** *tennis coaching sessions* 網球訓練課 **2** a process in which you give a student special instruction in a particular subject〔對學生的〕輔導(工作)

coach·load /ˈkotʃˌlod; ˈkəʊtʃləʊd/ *n* [C] all the people travelling in a COACH¹ (3), especially when it is full〔尤指滿座的〕長途公共汽車的全體乘客: *coachloads of football supporters* 一滿車一滿車的足球迷

coach·man /ˈkotʃmən; ˈkəʊtʃmən/ *n* [C] someone who drove a COACH¹ (5) pulled by horses in the past〔舊時的〕馬車御者, 馬車伕

coach sta·tion /ˈ· ˌ··/ *n* [C] *BrE* the place where people begin or end their journeys on buses that travel a long distance【英】長途公共汽車(總)站

coach·work /ˈkotʃˌwɝk; ˈkəʊtʃwɜːk/ *n* [U] *BrE* the main outer structure of a car【英】〔汽車的〕車身

co·ag·u·late /koˈæɡjəˌlet; kəʊˈæɡjʊleɪt/ *v* [I,T] if a liquid coagulates or something coagulates it, it becomes thick and almost solid (使)凝結, (使)凝固: *The heat will coagulate the egg mixture.* 熱量會使蛋花凝固。—**coagulation** /koˌæɡjəˈleʃən; kəʊˌæɡjʊˈleɪʃən/ *n* [U]

coal /kol; kəʊl/ *n* **1** [U] a black mineral which is dug from the earth and burnt to produce heat 煤: *Bring in some coal for the fire.* 往火裡加點煤。| *the coal industry* 煤炭工業 **2** [C usually plural 一般用複數] a piece of coal, especially one that is burning〔尤指燃燒着的〕煤塊 **3 carry/take coals to Newcastle** *BrE informal* to take something to a place where there is already plenty of it available【英, 非正式】多此一舉, 徒勞無功 **4 haul/rake/drag sb over the coals** to speak angrily to someone because they have done something wrong 責備某人, 申斥某人

coal bunk·er /ˈ· ˌ··/ *n* [C] a small building or large container where coal is stored 儲煤倉[庫, 室]

co·a·lesce /ˌkoəˈlɛs; ˌkəʊəˈles/ *v* [I] *formal* if objects or ideas coalesce, they combine to form one single group【正式】聯合, 合併: *These three themes coalesce at the end of the book.* 在本書結尾時, 這三個主題融而為一。—**coalescence** *n* [U]

coal·face /ˈkolˌfes; ˈkəʊlfeɪs/ *n* **1** [C] the part of a coal mine where the coal is cut from the earth〔採煤礦井中的〕採煤工作面, 採煤區 **2 at the coalface** *BrE* actually doing a particular kind of work rather than planning or managing it【英】在實際工作崗位〔而不是計劃或管理工作〕: *These new methods will help teachers working at the coalface.* 這些新的方法將對老師的實際教學有所助益。

coal·field /ˈkolˌfild; ˈkəʊlfiːld/ *n* [C] an area where there is coal under the ground 煤田

coal gas /ˈ· ·/ *n* [U] gas produced by burning coal, used especially for electricity and heating 煤氣 —compare 比較 NATURAL GAS

coal·hole /ˈkolˌhol; ˈkəʊlhəʊl/ *n* [C] *BrE* a small underground room where coal is stored【英】〔地下〕儲煤室

coal·house /ˈkolˌhaus; ˈkəʊlhaʊs/ *n* [C] a small building where coal is stored 煤庫

Coal·ite /ˈkolaɪt; ˈkəʊlaɪt/ *n* [U] *trademark* a substance similar to coal that does not produce smoke when it is burned【商標】科萊特無煙燃料

co·a·li·tion /ˌkoəˈlɪʃən; ˌkəʊəˈlɪʃən/ *n* **1** [C] a union of two or more political parties that allows them to form a government or fight an election together〔政黨之間的〕同盟, 聯合: *a three-party coalition* 三黨聯盟 | **coalition government** (=a government consisting of different political parties) 聯合政府 **2** [C] a group of people who join together to achieve a particular purpose, usually a political one〔常為達某種政治目的而組成的〕同盟: *policies designed by a coalition of public officials and local businessmen* 由政府官員及地方商人共同制定的政策 **3** [U] a process in which two or more political parties or groups join together 結合, 聯合

coal·man /ˈkolmən; ˈkəʊlmən/ *n* [C] a man who delivers coal to people's houses 運煤工人; 送煤工人

coal mine /ˈ· ·/ also 又作 **coal pit** *n* [C] a mine from which coal is dug 煤礦

coal scut·tle /ˈ· ˌ··/ *n* [C] a specially shaped container with a handle for carrying coal 煤斗, 煤桶

coal tar /ˈ· ·/ *n* [U] a thick black sticky liquid made by heating coal without air, from which many drugs and chemical products are made 煤焦油: *coal tar soap* 煤焦油皂

coarse /kɔrs; kɔːs/ *adj* **1** having a rough surface that feels slightly hard 粗的, 粗糙的: *Hannah's skin was coarse from years of working outdoors.* 由於常年在戶外工作, 漢納的皮膚很粗糙。**2** consisting of threads or parts that are thicker or larger than usual 粗線條構成的; 粗的: *The coarse sand was hot and rough under her feet.* 她腳下的粗沙又燙又扎腳。**3** talking in a rude and offensive way, especially about sex 粗俗的; 猥褻

的; 粗鲁的: *coarse jokes* 猥亵的笑話 —**coarsely** *adv* —**coarseness** *n* [U]

coarse fish·ing /ˌ·ˈ··/ *n* [U] *BrE* the sport of catching fish other than TROUT or SALMON in rivers and lakes【英】捕捉淡水魚比賽〔鱒魚及鮭魚除外〕

coars·en /ˈkɔrsn̩; ˈkɔːsən/ *v* [I,T] **1** to become thicker or rougher, or to make something thicker or rougher (使) 變粗, (使) 粗糙: *Hard work had coarsened his hands.* 艱苦的工作使他的手變得粗糙。| *His face swollen and puffy, the features coarsened by over-indulgence.* 因過度放縱, 他的臉變得臃腫肥胖、粗俗難看。**2** to become or to make someone become less polite in the way they talk or behave, especially about sex (使) 變粗魯, (使) 變粗俗, (使) 變猥褻: *Drinking had coarsened his sexual appetites.* 酗酒使他變得猥褻下流。

3 3 **coast¹** /kost; kəʊst/ *n* [C] **1** the area where the land meets the sea 海岸, 海濱; 沿海地區: *We drove along the Pacific coast to Seattle.* 我們駕車沿着太平洋海岸去西雅圖。| **on the coast** (=on the land near the sea) 在沿海地區 *I used to live in a small village on the coast of Brittany.* 我過去住在布列塔尼海邊的一個小村莊。| **off the coast** (=in the sea near the land) 在近海的 *a small island off the coast of Scotland* 蘇格蘭近海的一座小島 | **coast to coast** (=from one coast of a country to the other coast of the same country) 從〔一國〕此岸到彼岸 *They walked coast to coast across England.* 他們徒步穿越了英格蘭全境。—see 見 SHORE (USAGE) **2** **the coast is clear** *informal* if the coast is clear, it is safe for you to do something without risking being seen or caught【非正式】危險已過: *We raced towards them as soon as the coast was clear.* 危險一過去, 我們立刻奔向他們。

coast² *v* [I] **1** [always+adv/prep] to move in or on a vehicle, especially down a hill, without using any effort or any power from the engine〔尤指乘坐運載工具向下坡〕靠慣性滑行: **[+down/around/along etc]** *Bev coasted downhill on her bicycle.* 貝夫騎着腳踏車靠着慣性滑下山坡。**2** to achieve something without having to try very hard 輕易得到: *Janey's teacher says she's just coasting and could do even better if pushed.* 珍妮的老師說, 她學起來毫不費力, 如果加把勁會學得更好。| **[+to/through]** *Polls predict that the party will coast to victory in the next election.* 民意測驗預測說, 該政黨會在下次選舉中輕鬆勝出。**3** *AmE* to slide down a hill covered in snow on a SLEDGE¹【美】〔乘雪橇〕向下滑: *The kids went coasting all afternoon.* 孩子們整個下午都在乘雪橇滑下山坡。**4** to sail along the coast while staying close to land 沿海航行, 近海航行

coast·al /ˈkostl; ˈkəʊstl/ *adj* [only before noun 僅用於名詞前] in the sea or on the land near the coast 近海的, 沿海的, 海岸的: *the coastal waters of Britain* 英國的近海水域

coast·er /ˈkostɚ; ˈkəʊstə/ *n* [C] **1** a small thin object on which you put a glass, or cup, to protect a table from heat or liquids〔杯子等的〕墊子, 托子 **2** a ship that sails from port to port along a coast, but does not go further out to sea 沿海航行的輪船 —see also 另見 ROLLER COASTER

coaster brake /ˈ·· ·/ *n* [C] *AmE* a BRAKE¹ on some types of bicycle that works by moving the pedals (PEDAL¹ (1)) backwards【美】〔腳踏車的〕腳剎車, 倒輪式剎車

coast·guard /ˈkostˌgɑrd; ˈkəʊstgɑːd/ *n* **1 the Coastguard** [also+plural verb *BrE* 英] the organization that helps swimmers and ships that are in danger and helps prevent illegal activities such as SMUGGLING 海岸警衛隊: *The operation required the cooperation of the Coastguard.* 該行動需要海岸警衛隊的合作。**2** [C] a member of this organization 海岸警衛隊隊員

coast·line /ˈkostˌlaɪn; ˈkəʊstlaɪn/ *n* [C] the land on the edge of the coast, especially the shape of this land as seen from the air〔尤指從空中鳥瞰的〕海岸線, 海岸地形: *rocky coastline* 多岩石的海岸地貌

coats 大衣, 外套, 短上衣

anorak *BrE*【英】/ wind breaker *AmE*【美】帶風帽的夾克〔短風雨衣〕 | donkey jacket *BrE*【英】厚外衣 | denim jacket 牛仔衣

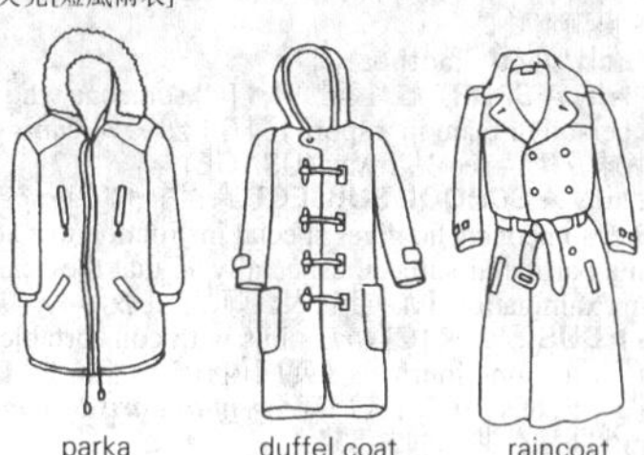

parka 風雪大衣 | duffel coat 連帽粗呢外套 | raincoat 雨衣

coat¹ /kot; kəʊt/ *n* [C] **1** a piece of clothing that is worn over your clothes to protect them or to keep you warm 大衣, 外套: *The lab assistants wear long white coats.* 那個實驗室助手穿着白色的長外套。| **put on/take off your coat** *Billy! Put your coat on, it's cold outside!* 比利! 穿上外套, 外面很冷! **2** *BrE old-fashioned or AmE* a piece of clothing that covers the top part of your body and is worn as part of a suit; JACKET (1)【英, 過時或美】〔常指套裝一部分的〕短上衣: *A business suit usually consists of matching pants, coat, and vest.* 一套西服套裝通常由配套的褲子、上衣及背心構成。**3** the fur, wool, or hair that covers an animal's body〔動物的〕皮毛: *a dog with a glossy coat* 皮毛光滑的狗 **4** a thin layer of a liquid or other substance that you spread thinly over a surface〔表面的〕覆蓋物; 塗層: **[+of]** *He applied a light coat of varnish.* 他上了一層清漆。**5 white-coated/fur-coated/winter-coated etc** wearing a white, fur etc coat 穿着白色/毛皮/冬天穿等的外套 —see also 另見 **cut your coat according to your cloth** (CUT¹ (34)), MORNING COAT

coat² *v* [T] **1** to cover something, especially food, with a thin layer of liquid or another substance 覆蓋; 蓋; 塗上: *Dust coated the furniture and everything smelled damp.* 家具上沾滿了灰塵, 所有的東西聞起來都有股濕濕的味道。| **coat sth with/in** *Herring is good coated in oatmeal and fried.* 油煎塗燕麥片的鯡魚很好吃。**2 metal-coated/plastic-coated etc** covered with a thin layer of metal etc 金屬塗層/塑料塗層等的 **3 sugar-coated a)** covered with sugar 塗了糖的 **b)** making something seem more attractive, desirable etc than it really is 甜言蜜語的, 過於美化的, 言過其實的: *The program depicts a sugar-coated version of family life.* 該節目過於美化了家庭生活。

coat check /ˈ· ·/ *n* [C] *AmE* a room in a public building where you can leave your coat while you are in the building; CLOAKROOM【美】衣帽間

coat hang·er /ˈ· ˌ··/ *n* [C] an object that you use to hang up clothes on; HANGER 衣架

coat·ing /ˈkotɪŋ; ˈkəʊtɪŋ/ *n* [C] a thin layer of something that covers a surface 塗層, 外層, 覆蓋層: *The tank's metal coating is made from a mixture of copper and zinc.* 油箱的金屬塗層是銅和鋅的合金。

coat of arms /ˌ· · ˈ·/ *n* [C] *plural* **coats of arms** a set of pictures or patterns painted on a SHIELD¹ (3) and used as the special sign of a family, town, university etc〔用作家族、城鎮、大學等標誌的〕(盾形) 紋章, 盾徽

coat of mail /ˌ· · ˈ·/ *n* [C] a coat made of metal rings that was worn to protect the top part of a soldier's body in the Middle Ages〔中世紀士兵的〕鎖子鎧甲

coat rack /ˈ· ·/ *n* [C] a board or pole with hooks on it that you hang coats on〔有掛鉤的〕掛衣架 —see picture on page A15 參見 A15 頁圖

coat·room /ˈkotˌrum; ˈkəʊtrʊm/ *n* [C] *AmE* a room in a public building where you may leave your coat, hat etc while you are there; CLOAKROOM (1)【美】衣帽間

coat·stand /ˈkotˌstænd; ˈkəʊtstænd/ *n* [C] a tall pole with hooks at the top that you hang coats on 衣帽架

coat·tails /ˈkotˌtelz; ˈkəʊt-teɪlz/ *n* [plural] **1 (ride/hang) on sb's coattails** if you achieve something on someone's coattails, you achieve it with the help or influence of someone powerful 在…的提攜下, 緊跟…之後: *A number of Republican congressmen were elected on Reagan's coattails.* 在列根的提攜下, 一些共和黨國會議員當選。**2** the cloth at the back of a TAILCOAT that is divided into two pieces〔燕尾服的〕燕尾

coax /koks; kəʊks/ *v* **1** [I,T] to persuade someone to do something that they do not want to do by talking to them in a kind, gentle, and patient way 勸誘; 哄; 誘導: *"Please, Vic, come with us," Nancy coaxed.* "求你了, 維克, 跟我們一塊兒來吧。" 南茜哄勸道。| **coax sb into/out of doing (sth)** *We had to coax Alan into going to school.* 我們得哄着阿倫去上學。| **coax sb to do sth** *The bear coaxed its cubs to enter the water.* 那頭熊哄着幼熊下水。| **coax sb down/out/back etc** *I managed to coax her round to my point of view.* 我成功地說服她同意我的觀點。**2** [T] to make something such as a machine do something by dealing with it in a slow, patient, and careful way 耐心地擺弄〔機器等〕: **coax sth out of/from sth** *He coaxed a fire out of some dry grass and twigs.* 他用一些乾草和小樹枝小心翼翼地生了個火。| **coax sth down/round/back etc** *We coaxed the pennies out of the piggybank with the blade of a knife.* 我們用刀片耐心地將硬幣從小豬撲滿中取出。—**coaxing** *n* [U] —**coaxingly** *adv*

cob /kɑb; kɒb/ *n* [C] **1** a CORNCOB 玉米棒子芯 **2** *BrE* a round LOAF of bread【英】圓頭麵包 **3** a type of large nut from the HAZEL[1] tree; COBNUT 歐洲榛子 **4** a type of horse that is strong and has short legs 一種壯實的矮腳馬 **5** a male SWAN[1] 雄天鵝

co·balt /ˈkobɔlt; ˈkəʊbɔːlt/ *n* [U] **1** a shiny silver-white metal that is a chemical ELEMENT (=simple substance), and that is used to make some metals and to give a blue colour to some substances 鈷; 鈷類顏料 **2** a bright blue-green colour 鈷藍色: *the parrot's cobalt feathers* 鸚鵡的鈷藍色羽毛 —**cobalt** *adj*

cob·ber /ˈkɑbɚ; ˈkɒbə/ *n* [C] *AustrE, NZE informal* a word meaning a friend, used especially by men talking to other men【澳, 新西蘭, 非正式】哥們, 夥伴, 朋友〔常用於男性間〕

cob·ble¹ /ˈkɑbl̩; ˈkɒbəl/ *v* [T] **1** *old-fashioned* to repair or make shoes【過時】修〔鞋〕; 製〔鞋〕 **2** to put COBBLESTONES on a street 用鵝卵石鋪路

cobble sth ↔ **together** *phr v* [T] *informal* to quickly make something that is useful but not perfect【非正式】〔匆忙而草率地〕拼湊: *The diplomats cobbled together an agreement.* 外交官們匆忙達成了一項協議。| *She cobbled together a tent from a few pieces of string and a sheet.* 她用幾根細繩和一張牀單胡亂地搭了一個帳篷。

cobble² *n* [C] a cobblestone 鵝卵石, 圓石

cob·bled /ˈkɑbl̩d; ˈkɒbəld/ *adj* a cobbled street is covered with cobblestones〔街道〕鋪鵝卵石的

cob·bler /ˈkɑblɚ; ˈkɒblə/ *n* [C] **1** *AmE* cooked fruit covered with a sweet, bread-like mixture【美】酥皮水果餡餅: *peach cobbler* 酥皮桃餡餅 **2** someone who makes and repairs shoes 鞋匠 **3 cobblers** *BrE spoken informal* something that someone says which you think is stupid or untrue【英口, 非正式】蠢話; 假話: **a load of (old) cobblers** *I've never heard such a load of old cobblers in my life!* 我這輩子還沒聽說過那樣的蠢話!

cob·ble·stone /ˈkɑbl̩ˌston; ˈkɒbəlstəʊn/ *n* [C] a small round stone set in the ground, especially in the past, to make a hard surface for a road 鵝卵石, 圓石〔用以鋪路等〕

cob·nut /ˈkɑbˌnʌt; ˈkɒbnʌt/ *n* [C] a nut from the HAZEL[1] tree; COB (3) 歐洲榛子

co·bra /ˈkobrə; ˈkəʊbrə/ *n* [C] a poisonous African or Asian snake that can spread the skin of its neck to make itself look bigger 眼鏡蛇

cob·web /ˈkɑbˌwɛb; ˈkɒbweb/ *n* [C] **1** a net of sticky threads made by a SPIDER to catch insects 蜘蛛網; SPIDERWEB *AmE*【美】**2 blow/brush/clear the cobwebs away** to do something, especially go outside, in order to help yourself to think more clearly and have more energy〔通過外出散步等〕恢復精神, 使頭腦清醒 —**cobwebbed** *adj* —**cobwebby** *adj*

co·ca /ˈkokə; ˈkəʊkə/ *n* [U] a South American bush whose leaves are used to make the drug COCAINE 古柯〔一種南美灌木, 其葉可提煉可卡因〕

Coca-Co·la /ˌ·· ˈ··/ *n* [C,U] *trademark* a sweet brown non-alcoholic drink【商標】可口可樂

co·caine /koˈken; kəʊˈkeɪn/ *n* [U] a drug, usually in the form of a white powder, that is taken illegally for pleasure or used in some medical situations to prevent pain 可卡因, 古柯鹼: *Jimmy was high on cocaine.* 吉米吸了可卡因, 精神恍惚。—see also 另見 CRACK² (10)

coc·cyx /ˈkɑksɪks; ˈkɒksɪks/ *n plural* **coccyxes** *or* **coccyges** /kɑkˈsaɪdʒiz; kɒkˈsaɪdʒiːz/ [C] *technical* the small bone at the bottom of your SPINE (1); TAILBONE【術語】尾骨 —see picture at 參見 SKELETON 圖

coch·i·neal /ˌkɑtʃəˈnil; ˌkɒtʃəˈniːl◂/ *n* [U] a red substance used to give food a red colour 胭脂蟲紅〔用於給食物染上紅色的一種物質〕

coch·le·a /ˈkɑklɪə; ˈkɒkliə/ *n plural* **cochleas** *or* **cochleae** /-lɪi; -li-aɪ/ [C] *technical* a part of the inner ear【術語】耳蝸

cock¹ /kɑk; kɒk/ *n*

1 ▶CHICKEN 雞◀ [C] *especially BrE* an adult male chicken【尤英】公雞; ROOSTER *AmE*【美】—see also 另見 COCK-A-DOODLE-DOO

2 ▶SEX ORGAN 性器官◀ [C] *taboo* a PENIS【諱】陰莖, 雞巴

3 cock and bull story a story or excuse that is silly and unlikely but is told as if it were true 荒誕無稽的故事; 編造的藉口: *She gave me some cock and bull story about the dog eating her homework.* 她對我編了一個荒唐的故事, 說狗吃掉了她的家庭作業。

4 ▶CONTROL FLOW 控制流動◀ [C] something that controls the flow of liquid out of a pipe or container; TAP[1] (1) 龍頭; 旋塞; 閥門 —see also 另見 BALLCOCK, STOPCOCK

5 ▶MALE BIRD 雄鳥◀ [C] an adult male bird of any kind 雄鳥, 雄禽: *a cock robin* 一隻雄性知更鳥

6 ▶MAN 男人◀ [C] *BrE old-fashioned* a word used by a man when talking to another man he knows well【英, 過時】老兄, 夥計〔用於男性之間的稱呼〕

7 cock of the walk *old-fashioned* if you describe someone as behaving like the cock of the walk, they are behaving as if they were better or more important than other people【過時】逞威風的頭領; 稱王稱霸的人 —see also 另見 **half cocked** (HALF[1] (11))

cock² *v* [T] **1** to lift a part of your body so that it is upright, or hold a part of your body at an angle 豎起, 翹起〔身體的一部分〕; 將〔身體的一部分〕轉向一邊: *Paul cocked his head to one side as he considered my idea.* 保羅側着頭, 考慮着我的主意。| *The little dog cocked a leg against the lamppost and urinated.* 那隻小狗將一條腿翹在街燈柱上撒尿。**2** to pull back the HAMMER[1] (5) of a gun so that it is ready to be fired 扳起〔槍的〕扳機 **3** to put your hat on at an angle; TILT[1] (1) 歪戴〔帽子〕 **4 keep an ear cocked** *informal* to pay close attention because

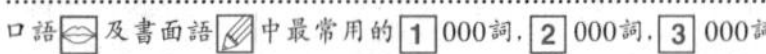

you want to be sure you hear something you expect or think may happen【非正式】豎起耳朵聽: *She kept an ear cocked for the sound of Joe's key in the front door.* 她豎起耳朵聽着喬轉動鑰匙開前門的聲音。**5 cock a snook** *BrE informal* to show clearly that you do not respect someone or something【英, 非正式】嗤之以鼻, 不屑一顧: **[+at]** *The artist cocked a snook at the critics by exhibiting an empty frame.* 為表示對評論界的不屑, 該藝術家展出了一副空畫框。

cock sth ↔ **up** *phr v* [T] *BrE informal* to spoil something such as an arrangement or plans, especially by making a stupid mistake【英, 非正式】把〔安排或計劃〕搞砸, 弄糟: *His secretary really cocked up his travelling schedule and he's furious about it.* 他的祕書確實把他的出差日程弄得一團糟, 他對此憤怒不已。—see also 另見 COCK-UP

C

cock·ade /kɑk`ed; kɒ'keɪd/ *n* [C] a small piece of cloth used as a decoration on a hat to show rank, membership of a club etc〔顯示級別、身分等的〕帽徽, 帽上的花結

cock-a-doo·dle-doo /ˌkɑk ə ˌdudl̩ `du; ˌkɒk ə ˌdu:dl 'du:/ *n* [C] the loud sound made by an adult male chicken〔公雞啼叫的〕喔喔聲

cock-a-hoop /ˌkɑk ə `hup; ˌkɒk ə 'hu:p/ *adj* [not before noun 不用於名詞前] pleased and excited about something, especially something you have done 得意洋洋的, 興高采烈的: **[+at/about]** *Robert's cock-a-hoop about his new job.* 羅伯特對他的新工作頗為得意。

cock-a-leek·ie /ˌkɑk ə `likɪ; ˌkɒk ə 'li:ki/ *n* [U] a type of Scottish soup made with chicken, vegetables, and LEEKS〔蘇格蘭〕雞肉韭菜湯

cock·a·ma·mie /ˌkɑkə`memɪ; ˌkɒkə'meɪmi◂/ *adj AmE informal* a cockamamie story or excuse is not believable or does not make sense【美, 非正式】荒謬的, 蹩腳的: *What cockamamie idea will he think up next?* 他還會冒出甚麼荒謬的想法?

cock·a·too /ˌkɑkə`tu; ˌkɒkə'tu:/ *n* [C] an Australian PARROT[1] (1) with a lot of feathers on the top of its head〔澳洲〕鳳頭鸚鵡, 葵花鸚鵡

cock·chaf·er /`kɑkˌtʃefɚ; 'kɒktʃeɪfə/ *n* [C] a European BEETLE (=a kind of insect) that damages trees and plants 金龜〔產於歐洲的一種害蟲〕

cock·crow /`kɑkˌkro; 'kɒk-krəʊ/ *n* [U] *literary* the time in the early morning when the sun rises; DAWN[1] (1)【文】黎明, 雞鳴時分

cocked hat /ˌ· '·/ *n* [C] **1 knock/beat sb/sth into a cocked hat** to be a lot better than someone or something else 遠遠勝過某人/某物: *My mother is such a good cook she knocks everybody else into a cocked hat.* 媽媽的廚藝高超, 無人能及。**2** a hat with the edges turned up on three sides, worn in the past〔舊時〕帽沿上捲的三角帽

cock·e·rel /`kɑkərəl; 'kɒkərəl/ *n* [C] a young male chicken 小公雞

cocker span·iel /ˌkɑkɚ `spænjəl; ˌkɒkə 'spænjəl/ *n* [C] a dog with long ears and long silky fur 獵用小獵犬

cock-eyed /ˌ· '·◂/ *adj informal*【非正式】**1** an idea, situation, plan etc that is cock-eyed is strange and not practical 荒謬的, 不切實際的: *The whole idea is completely cock-eyed.* 這個主意整個兒荒唐透頂。**2** not straight but set at an angle 傾斜的, 歪的: *I think you put that shelf up cock-eyed.* 我覺得你把那個書架放歪了。

cock fight /'· ·/ *n* [C] a sport, illegal in many countries, in which two male chickens are made to fight 鬥雞〔在許多國家為非法的一項活動〕—**cockfighting** *n* [U]

cock·horse /`kɑkhɔrs; ˌkɒk'hɔ:s/ *n* [C] *old use* a HOBBYHORSE【舊】木馬, 竹馬

cock·le /`kɑkl̩; 'kɒkəl/ *n* [C] **1** a common European SHELLFISH that is often used for food 鳥蛤 **2 warm the cockles of sb's heart** to make someone feel happy and full of good feelings towards other people 使人由衷地感到高興: *Seeing her delight in her new baby just warms the cockles of your heart.* 看到她有了小寶寶而幸福的樣子, 你會由衷地為她高興。

cock·le·shell /`kɑkl̩ˌʃɛl; 'kɒkəlʃel/ *n* [C] **1** the heart-shaped shell of the cockle 鳥蛤殼 **2** *literary* a small light boat【文】輕舟, 小船

cock·ney /`kɑknɪ; 'kɒkni/ *n* **1** [C] someone, especially a WORKING CLASS person, who comes from the eastern area of London 倫敦東區佬〔尤指工人階層〕**2** [U] a way of speaking English that is typical of someone from this area 倫敦東區土話 —**cockney** *adj*

cock·pit /`kɑkˌpɪt; 'kɒkˌpɪt/ *n* [C] **1** the area in a plane, small boat, or racing car where the pilot or driver sits〔飛機的〕駕駛艙;〔小船的〕舵手座;〔賽車的〕駕駛座 —see pictures at 參見 AIRCRAFT and 和 YACHT 圖 **2** a small, usually enclosed area where COCK FIGHTs took place in former times 鬥雞場

cock·roach /`kɑkˌrotʃ; 'kɒk-rəʊtʃ/ *n* [C] a large black insect often found in old or dirty houses 蟑螂; ROACH (1) *AmE*【美】

cocks·comb /`kɑksˌkom; 'kɒks-kəʊm/ *n* [C] **1** the red flesh that grows from the top of a male chicken's head〔公雞的〕雞冠 **2** also 又作 **coxcomb** the cap worn by a JESTER (=someone employed to amuse a king in the past) 小丑[弄臣]戴的帽子

cock·suck·er /`kɑkˌsʌkɚ; 'kɒkˌsʌkə/ *n* [C] *AmE taboo* an insulting way of talking to a man【美, 諱】狗雜種, 混蛋〔尤指男性〕

cock·sure /`kɑk`ʃur; ˌkɒk'ʃʊə/ *adj informal* too confident of your abilities or knowledge, in a way that is annoying to other people【非正式】過於自信的, 自以為是的: *He seemed to be rather cocksure, this young man.* 這個年輕人看來太過自負了。

cock·tail /`kɑkˌtel; 'kɒkteɪl/ *n* [C] **1** an alcoholic drink made from a mixture of different drinks 雞尾酒 **2 seafood/prawn/lobster cocktail** a mixture of small pieces of fish, PRAWNs, or LOBSTER, served cold and eaten at the beginning of a meal〔西餐作為第一道進食的〕涼拌海鮮/對蝦/龍蝦 **3 fruit cocktail** a mixture of small pieces of fruit 什錦水果粒 **4** a mixture of dangerous substances, especially one that you eat or drink〔尤指服用的〕危險品混合物: *a lethal cocktail of pain-killers and amphetamines* 由鎮痛劑和苯丙胺混合而成的致命物質 —see also 另見 MOLOTOV COCKTAIL

cocktail dress /'·· ˌ·/ *n* [C] a formal dress for wearing to parties or other evening social events〔正式場合穿的〕(晚)禮服

cocktail lounge /'·· ˌ·/ *n* [C] a public room in a hotel, restaurant etc, where alcoholic drinks may be bought〔旅館、餐廳等供應酒類飲料的〕休息室, 酒吧間

cocktail par·ty /'·· ˌ··/ *n* [C] a party at which alcoholic drinks are served and for which people usually dress formally 雞尾酒會

cocktail shak·er /'·· ˌ··/ *n* [C] a container in which cocktails are mixed 雞尾酒調酒器

cocktail stick /'·· ·/ *n* [C] a short pointed stick on which small pieces of food are served 取食籤〔用來挑起小塊食物〕—see picture at 參見 STICK[2] 圖

cocktail wait·ress /'·· ˌ··/ *n* [C] *AmE* a woman who serves drinks to people sitting at tables in a BAR[1] (1)【美】酒吧女侍應

cock-up /'· ·/ *n* [C] *BrE spoken* something that has been done very badly, so that it spoils someone's plans or arrangements【英口】混亂, 一團糟: *God, what a cock-up!* 天哪! 這真糟透了!

cock·y /`kɑkɪ; 'kɒki/ *adj informal* too confident about yourself and your abilities, especially in a way that annoys other people【非正式】驕傲自大的, 趾高氣揚的: *He's very clever, but far too cocky.* 他非常聰明, 但是太狂妄自大了。—**cockily** *adv* —**cockiness** *n* [U]

co·coa /`koko; 'kəʊkəʊ/ *n* [U] **1** also 又作 **cocoa powder** a brown powder made from the crushed cooked seeds of a tropical tree, used to make chocolate and to give a chocolate taste to foods 可可粉 **2** a sweet hot drink made with this powder, sugar, and milk or water 可可飲料〔由可可粉、糖及奶或水製成〕: *a cup of cocoa* 一杯可可

cocoa bean /ˈ·· ·/ *n* [C] the small seed of a tropical tree, that is used to make cocoa 可可豆

cocoa but·ter /ˈ·· ˌ··/ *n* [U] a fat obtained from the seeds of a tropical tree, used in making some COSMETICS 可可油〔可製化妝品等〕

co·co·mat /ˋkokəˌmæt; ˈkəʊkəmæt/ *n* [U] *AmE* COCONUT MATTING【美】椰衣墊

co·co·nut /ˋkokənʌt; ˈkəʊkənʌt/ *n* **1** [C] the large brown seed of a tropical tree, which has a hard shell containing white flesh that you can eat and a milky liquid 椰子 —see picture on page A8 參見 A8 頁圖 **2** [U] the white flesh of this seed, often used in cooking 椰肉: *shredded coconut* 椰絲

coconut mat·ting /ˌ··· ˈ··/ *n* [U] *BrE* a rough material used to cover floors that is made from the outer part of a coconut shell【英】〔用椰殼纖維製成的〕椰衣墊; cocomat *AmE*【美】

coconut milk /ˈ··· ˌ·/ *n* [U] the liquid inside a coconut 椰子汁

coconut shy /ˈ··· ˌ·/ *n plural* **coconut shies** [C] *BrE* a game in which you try to knock coconuts off posts by throwing balls at them【英】一種以球投落椰子的遊戲

co·coon[1] /kəˋkun; kəˈkuːn/ *n* [C] **1** a silk cover that young MOTHS and other insects make to protect themselves while they are growing 繭; 卵袋 **2** something that wraps around you completely, especially to protect you〔用以包裹全身的〕保護性衣物; 防護膜: [+of] *The baby peered out of its cocoon of blankets.* 寶寶從裹在身上的毛毯中向外張望。

cocoon[2] *v* [T] to protect or surround someone or something completely, especially so that they feel safe 緊裹; 密封〔以感覺安全〕: [+in] *cocooned in a reassuring network of friends and relatives* 處在朋友和親戚們的層層保護中 —**cocooned** *adj: a rich, cocooned existence on the East Side*〔曼哈頓〕東區的富人

COD /ˌsi o ˋdi; ˌsiː əʊ ˈdiː/ the abbreviation of 縮寫= cash on delivery; a situation in which you pay for goods when they are delivered to you 貨到付款

cod /kɑd; kɒd/ *n* **1** [C] a large sea fish that lives in the North Atlantic 鱈魚 **2** [U] the white flesh of this fish, eaten as food 鱈魚肉: *Cod and chips twice, please.* 請來雙份的鱈魚和薯條。

co·da /ˋkodə; ˈkəʊdə/ *n* [C] **1** an additional part at the end of a piece of music that is separate from the main part〔樂曲、樂章的〕尾聲, 結束樂段 **2** a separate piece of writing at the end of a work of literature or a speech〔文學作品或演說詞的〕結尾, 結局

cod·dle /ˋkɑdl; ˈkɒdl/ *v* [T] to treat someone in a way that is too kind and gentle and that protects them from pain or difficulty 悉心照料; 溺愛, 嬌縱: *Don't coddle the child – he's fine!* 別太慣着那孩子 —— 他沒事兒!

2 **code**[1] /kod; kəʊd/ *n* [C]

2 **1** ▶**BEHAVIOUR** 行為◀ a set of rules that tell people how to behave in their life or in certain situations 行為準則; 道德規範: **code of conduct/behaviour** *Fry rejected the accepted code of behaviour and married one of his servants.* 弗賴伊衝破傳統規範的約束, 與他的一個傭人結了婚。

2 ▶**RULES/LAWS** 規章/法律◀ a set of written rules or laws 法典, 法規: *Each state in the US has a different criminal and civil code.* 美國各州都制定了不同的刑法及民法法規。| **dress code** (=rule about what clothes you must wear in a school, business etc) 衣着規則

3 code of practice a set of rules that people in a particular business or profession agree to obey 行業規則: *The film industry wants to produce a code of practice for employers.* 電影界希望為雇主們制定一套行規。

4 ▶**SECRET MESSAGE** 祕密信息◀ a system of words, letters, or signs that you use instead of ordinary words when you are writing something that you want to keep secret 密碼; 代碼; 代號: **in code** *Send your reports in code.* 用密碼將你的報告發送過來。| **break/crack a code** (=manage to understand a secret code) 破譯密碼

5 ▶**SIGNS GIVING INFORMATION** 信息符號◀ a set of numbers, letters, or signs that show what something is or give information about it 編碼, 編號, 標記: *Most countries have some form of postal code that speeds mail delivery.* 大多數國家都有一套郵政編碼以加快郵遞速度。—see also 另見 BAR CODE, POSTCODE, ZIP CODE

6 ▶**TELEPHONES** 電話◀ also 又作 **dialling code, STD code** *BrE* the group of numbers that come before a telephone number when you are calling from a different area【英】長途電話區號; AREA CODE *AmE*【美】: *What's the code for Aberdeen?* 阿伯丁的區號是多少?

7 ▶**COMPUTERS** 電腦◀ a set of instructions that tell a computer what to do〔電腦的〕編碼 —see also 另見 MACHINE CODE, SOURCE CODE

8 ▶**SOUNDS/SIGNALS** 聲音/信號◀ a system of sounds or signals that represent words or letters when they are sent by machine〔電報等發出的〕電碼: *a telegraphic code* 一份電碼 —see also 另見 MORSE CODE

code[2] *v* [T] **1** to put a set of numbers, letters, or signs on something to show what it is or give information about it 把…編碼[編號]: *Product orders should be coded according to where they will be shipped.* 產品訂單必須按照運送地點編號。**2** to put a message in code so that it is secret 把…編成密碼 **3 colour code** to mark a group of things with different colours so that you can tell the difference between them 顏色編碼 —**coded** *adj*: *a coded message* 用密碼編成的信息

co·deine /ˋkodɪˌin; ˈkəʊdiːn/ *n* [U] a drug used to stop pain 可待因〔用以鎮痛的藥物〕

code name /ˈ· ·/ *n* [C] a name that keeps secret someone's real name or a real plan〔情報人員、計劃等的〕代號 —**code name** *v* [T]

co·dex /ˋkodɛks; ˈkəʊdeks/ *n* [C] *plural* **codices** /-dɪsiz; -dʒsiːz/ *technical* an ancient book written by hand【術語】〔古籍的〕手抄本: *a sixth-century codex* 一本公元六世紀時的手抄本

cod·fish /ˋkɑdˌfɪʃ; ˈkɒdˌfɪʃ/ *n* [C] a COD 鱈魚; 鱈魚肉

cod·ger /ˋkɑdʒɚ; ˈkɒdʒə/ *n* [C] *informal* **old codger** an old man【非正式】老傢伙: *He's a charming old codger.* 他是個很有魅力的老頭兒。

co·di·fy /ˋkɑdəˌfaɪ; ˈkəʊdʒfaɪ/ *v* [T] to arrange laws, principles, facts etc in a system 將〔法律、條例、事實等〕編集成典; 編纂 —**codification** /ˌkɑdəfəˋkeʃən; ˌkəʊdʒfʒˈkeɪʃən/ *n* [C,U]

cod-liver oil /ˌ· ·· ˈ·◂/ *n* [U] a yellow oil from a fish that contains a lot of substances that are important for good health 魚肝油

cod·piece /ˋkɑdˌpis; ˈkɒdpiːs/ *n* [C] a piece of coloured cloth worn by men in the 15th and 16th centuries to cover the opening in the front of their trousers〔15、16 世紀時男褲前面開口處的〕下體蓋片, 遮陰布

cods·wal·lop /ˋkɑdzˌwɑləp; ˈkɒdzˌwɒləp/ *n* [U] *BrE spoken*【英口】**a load of codswallop** something that someone says which you think is stupid or untrue 胡說八道, 一派胡言

co·ed[1] /ˋkoˋɛd; ˌkəʊˈed◂/ *adj* using a system in which students of both sexes are educated together 男女同校的: *The university became coed in 1967.* 這所大學在 1967 年開始實行男女同校。

coed[2] *n* [C] *AmE old-fashioned* a woman student at a university【美, 過時】〔大學的〕女生

co·ed·u·ca·tion /ˌkoɛdʒəˋkeʃən; ˌkəʊedjʊˈkeɪʃən/ *n* [U] a system in which students of both sexes are educated together 男女同校（制） —**coeducational** *adj formal*【正式】

co·ef·fi·cient /ˌkoəˋfɪʃənt; ˌkəʊʒˈfɪʃənt/ *n* [C] *technical* the number by which something that varies is multiplied【術語】係數: *In 8pq the coefficient of pq is 8.* 8pq 的 pq 係數為 8。

co·e·qual /ˌko`ikwəl; ˌkəʊ'iːkwəl◂/ *adj formal* if people are coequal, they have the same rank, ability, importance etc【正式】〔級別、能力、重要性等方面〕相等的: *three managers of coequal status* 三個同等級別的經理 —**coequally** *adv*

co·erce /ko`ɝs; kəʊ'ɜːs/ *v* [T] to force someone to do something they do not want to do by threatening them 強制; 脅迫; 迫使: **coerce sb into doing sth** *The rebels coerced the villagers into hiding them from the army.* 反叛者強迫村民們將他們隱藏起來, 以逃脱軍隊的搜捕。

co·er·cion /ko`ɝʒən; kəʊ'ɜːʃən/ *n* [U] the use of threats or orders to make someone do something they do not want to do 強迫; 脅迫, 逼迫: *Soames said he had been under coercion when he confessed.* 索姆斯説自己是迫於壓力才不得已招供的。

C

co·er·cive /ko`ɝsɪv; kəʊ'ɜːsɪv/ *adj* using threats or orders to make someone do something they do not want to do 強制的; 脅迫的: *coercive measures to reduce absenteeism* 減少曠工現象的高壓措施 —**coercively** *adv*

co·e·val /ko`ivḷ; kəʊ'iːvəl/ *adj formal* happening or existing during the same period of time【正式】同時代的; 同年代的: [+with] *The development of stone tools was coeval with the appearance of farming settlements.* 石器的發展與農業部落的出現處於同一時期。

co·ex·ist /ˌko·ɪg`zɪst; ˌkəʊɪg'zɪst/ *v* [I] *formal* to exist at the same time or in the same place, especially peacefully【正式】〔尤指和平地〕共存, 共處: [+with] *great wealth coexisting with extreme poverty* 龐大的財富與極度貧困同時存在

co·ex·ist·ence /ˌko·ɪg`zɪstəns; ˌkəʊɪg'zɪstəns/ *n* [U] *formal*【正式】**1** the state of existing together at the same time or in the same place 共存, 同時存在: *the coexistence of the traditional novel with experimental writing* 傳統小説與實驗寫作的共存 **2 peaceful coexistence** if two or more countries or people have a peaceful coexistence, they are not fighting one another 和平共處 —**coexistent** *adj*

C of E /ˌsi əv `i; ˌsiː əv 'iː/ *n BrE* an abbreviation for 縮寫= Church of England【英】英國國教, 英國聖公會

1 2 **cof·fee** /`kɔfɪ; 'kɒfi/ *n* [U] **1** a hot, dark brown drink that has a slightly bitter taste 咖啡: *Do you want a cup of coffee?* 你要來杯咖啡嗎? | **black coffee** (=coffee with no milk added) 不加牛奶的咖啡, 黑咖啡 | **white coffee** *BrE* (=coffee with milk added)【英】加牛奶的咖啡 **2** [C] *especially BrE* a cup of this drink【尤英】一杯咖啡: *Who wants a coffee?* 誰想要一杯咖啡? **3** a brown powder that you use to make coffee 咖啡〔粉〕: *a pound of coffee* 一磅咖啡〔粉〕| **instant coffee** (=a powder that you use to make coffee quickly) 即溶咖啡 **4** [U] a light brown colour 咖啡色, 淺褐色 —see picture on page A5 參見 A5 頁圖 —see also 另見 **wake up and smell the coffee** (WAKE[1])

coffee bar /'‥ ·/ *n* [C] *BrE* a small restaurant that serves coffee and other non-alcoholic drinks, sandwiches (SANDWICH[1] (1)) and cakes etc【英】小型咖啡館 —compare 比較 COFFEE SHOP

coffee bean /'‥ ·/ *n* [C] the seed of a tropical tree that is used to make coffee 咖啡豆

coffee break /'‥ ·/ *n* [C] a short time when you stop working to have a cup of coffee; TEA BREAK〔工作間隙喝咖啡的〕休息時間

cof·fee·cake /`kɔfɪˌkek; 'kɒfikeɪk/ *n* [C,U] **1** *AmE* a sweet heavy cake usually eaten with a cup of coffee【美】咖啡蛋糕〔喝咖啡時吃的一種甜糕點〕**2** *BrE* a cake tasting of coffee【英】咖啡味的糕點

coffee grind·er /'‥ ˌ‥/ *n* [C] a small machine that crushes coffee beans 咖啡豆研磨機

coffee house /'‥ ·/ *n* [C] a restaurant that serves coffee, cakes etc 咖啡館

coffee ma·chine /'‥ ·ˌ·/ *n* [C] a machine that gives you a cup of coffee, tea etc, when you put money in it〔飲料〕自動售賣機

cof·fee·mak·er /`kɔfɪˌmekɚ; 'kɒfiˌmeɪkə/ *n* [C] an electric machine that makes a pot of coffee 煮咖啡器, 咖啡壺

coffee mill /'‥ ·/ *n* [C] a COFFEE GRINDER 咖啡豆研磨機

coffee morn·ing /'‥ ˌ‥/ *n* [C] *BrE* a social occasion when a group of people meet to talk and drink coffee, and usually give money to help a church or another organization【英】〔通常為募捐而舉行的〕咖啡早茶會

coffee pot /'‥ ·/ *n* [C] a container from which coffee is served 咖啡壺

coffee shop /'‥ ·/ *n* [C] **1** *AmE* a restaurant that serves cheap meals【美】小吃部 **2** *BrE* a place in a large shop or a hotel that serves meals and non-alcoholic drinks【英】〔大型商店或旅館供應餐點、飲料的〕咖啡廳

coffee ta·ble /'‥ ˌ‥/ *n* [C] **1** a low table on which you put cups, newspapers etc 茶几, 矮茶几, 咖啡桌 **2 coffee table book** a large expensive book that usually has a lot of pictures in it and is meant to be looked at rather than read〔裝潢精美而內容空洞的〕大開本精裝圖書[畫冊]

cof·fer /`kɔfɚ; 'kɒfə/ *n* [C] **1 coffers** the money that an organization, government, etc, has available to spend 資金: *What happened to the money put into the union coffers three years ago?* 三年前注入工會的那筆資金哪裡去了? **2** a large strong box often decorated with jewels, silver, gold etc, and used to hold valuable or religious objects 珠寶盒, 珠寶箱; 保險箱 **3** a cofferdam 圍堰; 潛水箱; 沉箱

cof·fer·dam /`kɔfɚˌdæm; 'kɒfədæm/ *n* [C] a large box filled with air that allows people to work under water 圍堰,〔用於水下工作的〕潛水箱; 沉箱

cof·fin /`kɔfɪn; 'kɒfɪ̥n/ *n* [C] a long box in which a dead person is buried or burnt 棺材, 靈柩; CASKET *AmE*【美】—see also 另見 **a nail in sb's/sth's coffin** (NAIL[1] (3))

cog /kɑg; kɒg/ *n* [C] **1** a wheel with small bits sticking out around the edge, that fit together with the bits of another wheel as they turn around in a machine 齒輪 **2** one of the small bits that stick out on a cog 嵌齒; 輪齒 **3 a cog in the machine/wheel** someone who is not important or powerful, who only has a small job or part in a large business or organization 無足輕重的人物, 小人物

cog 齒輪

cog 輪齒

co·gent /`kodʒənt; 'kəʊdʒənt/ *adj formal* something such as an argument that is cogent is reasonable, so that people are persuaded that it is correct【正式】令人信服的, 有説服力的: **cogent argument/ reasons/answers etc** *Professor Calder presented a cogent examination of the facts.* 考爾德教授做了一個令人信服的測試, 證明了這些事實。—**cogently** *adv* —**cogency** *n*

cog·i·tate /`kɑdʒəˌtet; 'kɒdʒɪ̥teɪt/ *v* [I+about/on] *formal* to think carefully and seriously about something【正式】仔細考慮 —**cogitation** /ˌkɑdʒə`teʃən; ˌkɒdʒɪ̥'teɪʃən/ *n* [U]

co·gnac /`konjæk; 'kɒnjæk/ *n* [C,U] a kind of BRANDY (=strong alcoholic drink) made in France, or a glass of this drink〔法國〕干邑白蘭地(酒); 一杯干邑白蘭地(酒)

cog·nate[1] /`kɑgnet; 'kɒgneɪt/ *adj* cognate words or languages have the same origin〔詞語、語言〕同源的

cognate[2] *n* [C] a word in one language that has the same origin as a word in another language 同源詞: *The German 'hund' is a cognate of the English 'hound'.* 德語 "hund" 是英語 "hound" 的一個同源詞。

cog·ni·tion /kɑg`nɪʃən; kɒg'nɪʃən/ *n* [U] **1** *formal* understanding【正式】理解, 領悟 **2** *technical* the process by which you see or hear something, recognize it, and understand it【術語】認識, 認知: *the regions of the brain* *that are responsible for memory and cognition* 大腦主管記憶與認知的區域

cog·ni·tive /ˋkɑgnətɪv; ˈkɒgn⅟tɪv/ *adj formal or technical* related to the process of knowing, understanding, and learning something【正式或術語】認知的, 認知過程的: *cognitive psychology* 認知心理學 —**cognitively** *adv*

cog·ni·zance also 又作 **cognisance** *BrE*【英】/ˋkɑgnəzəns; ˈkɒgn⅟zəns/ *n* [U] *formal*【正式】**1** knowledge or understanding of something 知道, 認識 **2 take cognizance of** to understand something and consider it when you take action or make a decision 注意到; 承認

cog·ni·zant also 又作 **cognisant** *BrE*【英】/ˋkɑgnɪzənt; ˈkɒgn⅟zənt/ *adj* [not before noun 不用於名詞前] having knowledge or information about something; AWARE 知道的, 認識到的, 了解的: *Colby was cognizant of these goals, but was unmoved by them.* 科爾比注意到了這些目標, 但卻不為所動。

cog·no·men /kɑgˋnomən; kɒgˈnəʊmən/ *n* [C] **1** *formal* a name used instead of someone's real name, or a description added to someone's name, for example 'the Great' in 'Alexander the Great'【正式】綽號, 外號 **2** *technical* a SURNAME (=last name or family name), especially in ancient Rome【術語】〔尤指古羅馬人的〕姓氏

co·gno·scen·ti /ˌkɑnjoˋʃɛnti; ˌkɒnjəʊˈʃentiː/ *n* **the cognoscenti** people who have special knowledge about a particular subject, especially art, literature, or food〔尤指藝術、文學、食品等方面的〕行家, 鑑賞家

cog·wheel /ˋkɑgˌhwil; ˈkɒg-wiːl/ *n* [C] a COG (1) 齒輪

co·hab·it /koˋhæbɪt; ˌkəʊˈhæb⅟t/ *v* [I] *formal* to live with another person as though you were married【正式】〔男女〕同居 —**cohabitation** /ˌkohæbɪˋteʃən; kəʊˌhæb⅟ˈteɪʃən/ *n* [U]

co·here /koˋhɪr; kəʊˈhɪə/ *v* [I] *formal*【正式】**1** if the ideas or arguments in a piece of writing cohere, they are connected in a clear and reasonable way〔思想、論據等〕連貫, 有條理, 一致 **2** if two objects cohere, they stick together 黏着, 黏合, 附着

co·her·ence /koˋhɪrəns; kəʊˈhɪərəns/ also 又作 **co·her·en·cy** /-rənsɪ; -rənsi/ *n* [U] **1** a reasonable connection or relation between ideas, arguments, statements etc 連貫(性), 條理(性), 一致(性): *An overall theme will help to give your essay coherence.* 圍繞一個主旨將使你的文章連貫緊湊。**2** if a group has coherence, its members are connected or united because they share common aims, qualities, or beliefs 凝聚(力): *A common religion ensures the coherence of the tribe.* 共同的宗教信仰確保了該部落的凝聚力。

co·her·ent /koˋhɪrənt; kəʊˈhɪərənt/ *adj* **1** if a piece of writing, set of ideas etc is coherent, it is easy to understand because the information is presented in an orderly and reasonable way 連貫的, 有條理的, 一致的: *Finally! A textbook that provides a coherent approach to the subject.* 終於有了一本連貫地闡述該主題的課本。**2** if someone is coherent, they are talking in a way that is clear and easy to understand〔話語等〕條理清楚的, 易於理解的: *My head hurt so much I couldn't give a coherent answer.* 我的頭傷得很重, 我無法回答得很清楚。—**coherently** *adv*

co·he·sion /koˋhiʒən; kəʊˈhiːʒən/ *n* [U] **1** if there is cohesion among a group of people, a set of ideas etc, all the parts or members of it are connected or related in a reasonable way to form a whole 團結, 凝聚(力): *Religious beliefs can provide cohesion in diverse societies.* 宗教信仰能夠為多元的社會提供凝聚力。**2** a close relationship, based on grammar or meaning, between two parts of a sentence or a larger piece of writing〔句子、文章等的〕緊湊 —**cohesive** /-hisɪv; -hiːsɪv/ *adj* —**cohesively** *adv* —**cohesiveness** *n* [U]

co·hort /ˋkohɔrt; ˈkəʊhɔːt/ *n* [C] a word meaning a person or group of people who support a particular leader, used especially when you disapprove of them 追隨者, 黨羽: *Get the Mayor and his crooked cohorts out of City Hall!* 把市長和他那羣狡詐的黨徒趕出市政廳!

coif·fure /kwɑˋfjʊr; kwɒˈfjʊə/ *n* [C] *formal* the way someone's hair is arranged; HAIRDO【正式】髮型, 髮式 —**coiffured** *adj*

coil¹ /kɔɪl; kɔɪl/ *v* [I,T] to wind or twist into a series of rings, or to make something do this; SPIRAL³ (1)(使)捲纏; (使)盤繞: *snakes coiled in the grass* 盤在草叢中的蛇 | **coil sth** *Please coil the cords neatly before you put them away.* 請你把那些細繩捲好後放在一邊。—**coiled** *adj*

coil² *n* [C] **1** a continuous series of circular rings into which something such as wire or rope has been wound or twisted (一)卷, (一)圈, (一)匝: [+of] *Coils of barbed wire were stretched around the compound.* 院子四周圍着一圈圈帶倒刺的鐵絲網。**2** a wire or a metal tube in a continuous circular shape that produces light or heat when electricity is passed through it〔電路的〕線圈; 繞組: *the coil in a light bulb* 燈絲 **3** the part of a car engine that sends electricity to the SPARK PLUGS〔汽車發動機的〕盤管 —see picture at 參見 ENGINE 圖 **4** a CONTRACEPTIVE that is a flat curved piece of metal or plastic that is fitted inside a woman's UTERUS; IUD〔子宮〕避孕環

coin¹ /kɔɪn; kɔɪn/ *n* **1** [C] a piece of metal, usually flat and round, that is used as money 硬幣 —compare 比較 BILL¹ (3), NOTE¹ (5) **2 toss/flip a coin** to choose or decide something by throwing a coin into the air and guessing which side of it will show when it falls 拋硬幣決定〔某事〕: *Let's toss a coin to see who goes first.* 讓我們拋硬幣決定誰先去。**3 the other side of the coin** a different or opposite way of thinking about something 事情的另一面: *Children should learn to respect the police, but the other side of the coin is that the police should earn that respect.* 孩子們應該學會尊重警察, 但反過來, 警察也必須以行動贏得這種尊敬。**4 two sides of the same coin** two problems or situations that are so closely connected that they are really just two parts of the same thing 同一事情密切相關的兩個方面: *You can't cure poverty without also doing something about improving education; they're two sides of the same coin.* 不提高教育水平就無法根治貧困; 它們是密切相關的兩個方面。**5** [U] money in the form of metal coins 錢幣, 硬幣 **6 pay sb back in their own coin** *BrE old-fashioned* to treat someone in the same unpleasant way as they have treated you【英, 過時】以其人之道還治其人之身, 以牙還牙

coin² *v* [T] **1** to invent a new word or expression, especially one that many people start to use 創造, 杜撰〔新字等〕: *The term 'Information Highway' was coined a few years ago.* "信息高速公路"這個術語是幾年前造出來的。**2 to coin a phrase** *spoken* used as a joke when you have just said something so familiar and ordinary that it is funny【口】套句老話說, 常言說得好: *"Alone at last," he said, "to coin a phrase!"* 他說"套句老話, 最後還是獨身一人。" **3 coin money/coin it** *BrE spoken* to earn a lot of money very quickly【英口】大發其財, 暴富: *That new restaurant on the corner must be coining it.* 街角那家新開的餐館一定財源滾滾。**4** to make pieces of money from metal 鑄〔幣〕

coin·age /ˋkɔɪnɪdʒ; ˈkɔɪnɪdʒ/ *n* **1** [U] the system of money used in a country〔一國的〕貨幣制度: *Britain did not use decimal coinage until 1971.* 英國直到1971年才使用十進位幣制。**2** [C] a word or phrase that has been recently invented 新造的詞彙[片語]: *The phrase 'glass ceiling' is a fairly recent coinage.* "玻璃頂篷"是最近新造的一個詞語。**3** [U] the use of new words or phrases 新詞[片語]的使用 **4** [U] the making of coins 鑄幣, 造幣

co·in·cide /ˌkoɪnˋsaɪd; ˌkəʊ⅟nˈsaɪd/ *v* [I] **1** to happen at the same time as something else, especially by chance; CONCUR (2) 巧合; 同時發生: *Suspects are interviewed in separate rooms to see if their stories coincide.* 嫌疑犯

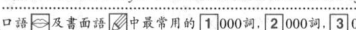

被放在不同房間詢問口供, 看看他們的說法是否吻合。| [+with] *The Suez crisis happened to coincide with the uprising in Hungary.* 蘇伊士運河危機碰巧發生在匈牙利的內亂時期。| **be planned/ timed/arranged to coincide** *The Queen's visit has been planned to coincide with the school's 200th anniversary.* 女王的訪問被安排在該校200週年校慶期間。**2** [not in progressive 不用進行式+with] if two people's ideas, opinions etc coincide, they are the same〔想法、觀點等〕相符, 一致

co·in·ci·dence /ko`ɪnsədəns; kəʊ'ɪnsɨdəns/ *n* **1** [C,U] a surprising and unexpected situation in which two things that are connected happen at the same time, in the same place, or to the same people 巧合, 巧事; 同時發生: *What a coincidence! I didn't know you were going to be in Geneva too!* 真是碰巧! 我原本不知道你也要去日內瓦! | **by coincidence** *My mother is called Anna, and by a funny coincidence my wife's mother is also called Anna.* 我媽媽叫安娜, 有趣的是碰巧我丈母娘也叫安娜。| **be sheer/pure coincidence** (=happen completely by chance) 純屬巧合 | **not a coincidence/ more than coincidence** (=used when you think something did not happen by chance) 蓄意, 非巧合 *It can't be a coincidence that four jewelry stores were robbed in one night.* 一夜之間, 四家珠寶店被劫, 這不可能是巧合。**2** [singular] *formal* if there is a coincidence between two ideas, opinions etc, the ideas etc are the same【正式】〔思想、觀點等的〕一致, 相符: [+of] *a coincidence of opinion among the board members* 董事會成員的共識

co·in·ci·dent /ko`ɪnsədənt; kəʊ'ɪnsɨdənt/ *adj formal* existing or happening at the same place or time【正式】同時[同地]發生的; 同時[同地]存在的; 巧合的

co·in·ci·den·tal /ko,ɪnsə`dɛntl; kəʊ,ɪnsɨ'dentl/ *adj* happening completely by chance without being planned 巧合的, 碰巧的: **purely/completely coincidental** *Any similarity between this film and real events is purely coincidental.* 本片與真實事件如有雷同, 純屬巧合。— **coincidentally** *adv* [sentence adverb 句子副詞]: *Coincidentally, two of the men came up with similar improvements concerning pumps.* 非常湊巧, 其中兩人對水泵提出了相似的改進意見。

co·in·sur·ance /,ko·ɪn`ʃʊrəns; ,kəʊɪn'ʃʊərəns/ *n* [U] *AmE*【美】**1** a type of insurance in which the payment is split between two people, especially between an employer and a worker 共同保險〔尤指雇主與雇員共同承擔的保險〕: *health coinsurance* 健康共同保險 **2** insurance that will only pay for part of the value of something 部分保險

co·in·sure /,ko·ɪn`ʃʊr; ,kəʊɪn'ʃʊə/ *v* [T] *AmE* to buy or provide insurance in which the payment is split between two people, or insurance that will only pay for part of the value of something【美】購買[提供]共同[部分]保險

coir /kɔɪr; kɔɪə/ *n* [U] the rough material that covers the shell of a COCONUT, used for making MATS, ropes etc〔用於製做墊子、繩子等的〕椰子殼的粗纖維

co·i·tus /`koɪtəs; 'kəʊɨtəs/ *n* [U] *technical* the act of having sex; SEXUAL INTERCOURSE【術語】性交 —**coital** *adj*

coke /kok; kəʊk/ *n* **1 Coke** [C,U] *trademark* the drink COCA-COLA【商標】可口可樂: *Regular fries and a large Coke, please.* 請來一客普通裝炸薯條和一大杯可樂。**2** [U] *informal* COCAINE【非正式】可卡因, 古柯鹼 **3** [U] a solid black substance produced from coal and burned to provide heat 焦炭, 焦煤

Col. *n* the written abbreviation for 縮寫= COLONEL

col[1] /kɑl; kɒl/ *n* [C] a low point between two high places in a mountain range; PASS[2] (5) 山口, 山坳

col[2] the written abbreviation for 縮寫= COLUMN

col- /kəl; kəl/ *prefix* the form used for CON- before l 前綴 con- 的一種形式〔用在l前面〕: *to collaborate* (=work together) 合作

co·la /`kolə; 'kəʊlə/ *n* [C,U] a brown, sweet, CARBONATED drink 可樂〔一種甜味棕褐色碳酸飲料〕: *a can of cola* 一罐可樂

col·an·der /`kʌləndɚ; 'kʌləndə/ *n* [C] a metal or plastic bowl with a lot of small holes in the bottom and sides, used to separate liquid from food〔過濾或淘洗食物用的〕濾鍋, 濾器

cold[1] /kold; kəʊld/ *adj*

1 ►OBJECTS/SURFACES/LIQUIDS/ROOMS ETC 物體/表面/液體/房間等◄ having a low temperature 溫度低的, 冷的: *a blast of cold air* 一股冷空氣 | *We slept on the cold ground.* 我們睡在冰冷的地上。| **feel cold** *The office always feels so cold first thing on Monday morning.* 星期一早晨, 這辦公室總讓人覺得很冷。| **ice/ stone/freezing cold** (=very cold) 非常冷, 冰冷 *The radiator is stone cold; isn't the heating working?* 暖氣管冰涼的, 是不是暖氣停了? | **as cold as ice** (=very cold) 冰冷的 | **go cold** *BrE*【英】/**get cold** (=become cold) 變冷 *My tea's gone cold.* 我的茶已經涼了。| *Come and eat or your dinner will get cold!* 過來吃飯吧, 再不吃就涼了! —see picture at 參見 HOT[1] 圖

2 ►WEATHER 天氣◄ when there is cold weather, the temperature of the air is very low〔天氣〕冷的, 寒冷的: *It was so cold this morning I had to scrape the ice off my windshield.* 今天早晨太冷了, 我不得不把擋風玻璃上的冰刮掉。| **cold winter/evening/January etc** *the coldest winter on record* 有史以來最冷的一個冬天 | **be cold out/outside** *Put on a coat; it's cold out.* 穿上外套, 外面很冷。| **get cold** (=become cold) 變冷 *The weather gets colder around the middle of October.* 十月中旬左右, 天氣開始轉涼。| **turn cold** (=become cold or colder, especially suddenly)〔尤指突然〕變冷

3 ►PEOPLE 人們◄ **be/feel/look/get cold** if you are cold, your body is at a low temperature 感到冷: *Could you turn up the heater, I'm cold.* 你能把取暖器打開嗎? 我很冷。| **be blue with cold** (=be so cold that your skin looks slightly blue) 凍得發紫 | **as cold as ice** (=very cold) 冰涼的 *My feet are as cold as ice.* 我的腳冰涼。

4 ►LACKING FEELING 缺乏情感◄ lacking normal human feelings such as sympathy, pity, humour etc 冷漠的, 冷酷的: *a cold, calculated murder* 一宗冷酷、預謀的謀殺(案) | *He's a very cold man, very aloof and arrogant.* 他是個冷漠的人, 難於接近, 而且十分傲慢。

5 ►UNFRIENDLY 不友好的◄ unfriendly and behaving as though you do not care much about other people 冷淡的, 不友好的, 不熱情的: *Martin was really cold towards me at the party.* 那次聚會上, 馬丁對我十分冷淡。

6 ►FOOD EATEN COLD 冷餐食品◄ cold food is cooked but not eaten hot〔食物〕冷的, 涼的: *We brought cold chicken and a bottle of wine to the picnic.* 我們買來冷雞肉和一瓶紅酒準備野餐。| *a cold buffet which the guests helped themselves to* 客人自助的冷餐會

7 get/have cold feet *informal* to suddenly feel that you are not brave enough to do something you planned to do【非正式】臨陣退縮, 膽怯: *You're not getting cold feet about marrying him, are you?* 你不會在要嫁給他時打退堂鼓吧?

8 give sb the cold shoulder *informal* to deliberately ignore someone or be unfriendly to them, especially because they have upset or offended you【非正式】故意冷落某人, 冷待某人

9 cold (hard) cash *AmE informal* money in the form of paper money and coins rather than cheques or CREDIT CARDS【美, 非正式】現款

10 leave sb cold to not feel interested in or affected by something in any way 未打動某人, 未引起...的興趣: *Opera just leaves me cold – I can't understand why people like it.* 我對歌劇沒甚麼興趣——我不明白為甚麼人們喜歡它。

11 cold shower a SHOWER[1] (2) without any hot water 冷水淋浴: **take a cold shower** (=used to tell someone to stop feeling sexually excited) 不要性衝動

12 ►TRAIL/SCENT 痕跡/氣味◄ if someone's trail or scent is cold, you cannot find out which way they have gone because it has been a long time since they passed a

particular place〔痕跡、氣味等〕已變淡的: *We had the dogs after him, but the trail had gone cold.* 我們已經派出獵犬追蹤他, 但他留下的氣味已經很淡了。
13 ►GAME 遊戲◄ [never before noun 永不用於名詞前] used in a children's game, to say that someone is far away from the hidden object they are trying to find〔兒童遊戲中〕遠離隱藏物的; 遠未猜中的: *You're getting colder!* 你猜得越來越離譜了!
14 ►LIGHT/COLOUR 光線/顏色◄ a cold colour or light reminds you of things that are cold〔色、光等〕給人冷淡感的, 冷的: *The moon shone with a cold, clear light.* 月亮發出清冷的光。| **in the cold light of day** (=in the morning, when you see things clearly) 在清晨 *In the cold light of day, we wondered whether we'd made the right decision.* 天大亮後, 我們懷疑自己是否作出了正確的決定。
15 cold steel *literary* a weapon such as a knife or sword【文】〔刀、劍等〕利器 —see also 另見 **in cold blood** (BLOOD[1] (3)), **cold fish** (FISH[1] (8)), **blow hot and cold** (BLOW[1] (15)), **cold comfort** (COMFORT[1] (7)), **pour cold water over/on** (POUR (7)), **a cold sweat** (SWEAT[2] (3)) —**coldly** *adv* —**coldness** *n* [U]

USAGE NOTE 用法說明: COLD
WORD CHOICE 詞語辨析: **cold, cool, hot, warm, chilly, freezing, boiling, baking, heated**
Cold means at a lower temperature than **cool**, often one that is not comfortable. **Cool** often suggests a pleasantly low temperature. cold 的寒冷程度高於 cool, 常指令人不適的寒冷。cool 則指使人舒服的涼爽感: *I hate cold weather.* 我討厭冷天氣。| *It's lovely and cool in here.* 這兒天氣涼爽, 感覺舒服極了。
In the same way, **hot** suggests a higher temperature than **warm**, or a temperature which would not be comfortable for a long period. **Warm** often suggests a pleasantly high temperature. 同樣, hot 所指的溫度高於 warm, 常指令人不舒服的持續高溫。warm 則指令人愉悦的暖和感: *The handle is too hot to touch.* 那個手柄熱得沒法碰。| *I could lie in a warm bath for hours.* 我可以在溫水中泡上幾個小時。
When talking of **cold** air or weather people often say it is **chilly** or, if it is very cold, **freezing** or **bitterly cold**. Very **hot** weather is **boiling** or **baking**. Cold weather may be called **the cold**. 人們談論寒冷的 (cold) 空氣或天氣通常會説 chilly, 如果十分寒冷, 則用 freezing 或 bitterly cold。非常炎熱的天氣用 boiling 或 baking。冷天氣可稱為 the cold: *My feet were purple with the cold* (=because of the cold, NOT 不用 *purple because of cold*). 天很冷, 我的腳凍得發紫。| *I don't like the cold* (NOT 不用 *I don't like cold*). 我不喜歡冷天。
A cold is an illness. a cold 指感冒: *My nose runs when I have a cold* (NOT 不用 *have cold*). 我感冒時流鼻涕。| *I've caught a cold from my husband* (NOT 不用 *caught cold*). 我從丈夫處染了感冒。Compare 比較: *I got cold waiting for the bus without a coat* (=felt cold, not the same as *...got a cold* = caught the illness). 等公共汽車時, 我沒有穿外套, 覺得很冷。
When talking about people's character or behaviour, **cold** usually means lacking any emotion or friendly feelings. 描述人的性格或行為時, cold 通常指冷漠或不友好: *a cold start* 一個冷淡的開端 | *His manner towards her was very cold.* 他對她的態度極為冷漠。**Cool** can mean less friendly, enthusiastic etc than usual. cool 則指沒有平常那麼友好或熱情: *When Bill arrived, more than an hour later, he got a rather cool reception.* 比爾一個多小時後趕到的時候, 受到了冷淡的接待。**Cool** can also mean calm and not getting excited or showing your emotions. cool 亦指冷靜的、平靜的: *a cool head in a crisis* 危機時刻冷靜的頭腦。**Warm** often means friendly and welcoming. warm 則指友好的、好客的: *a warm smile* 友好的微笑
Heated arguments, discussions etc are ones in which people disagree and get angry. 用 heated 形容爭論、討論等指氣氛熱烈。

cold[2] *n* **1** [U] **the cold** a very low temperature outside 冷, 寒冷: *Don't go out in the cold without your coat!* 外面天氣很冷, 穿上外套再出去吧! **2** [C] a slight illness that makes it difficult to breathe through your nose and makes your throat hurt 感冒, 傷風: *I've got a bad cold.* 我得了重感冒。| **catch a cold** (=become ill) 得感冒 *Keep your feet dry so you don't catch a cold.* 雙腳保持乾燥, 就不會感冒。| **catch your death of cold** (=used to warn someone that they may become very ill if they do not keep themselves warm in cold weather) 得重感冒 —see also 另見 COMMON COLD **3 come in from the cold** to become accepted or recognized, especially by a powerful group of people 被〔團體〕承認[接納] **4 leave sb out in the cold** *informal* to not include someone in an activity【非正式】把某人排擠在〔集體活動〕之外, 不理睬某人: *If you don't start working harder, you'll be left out in the cold when it comes time for promotion.* 如果你不開始努力工作, 晉升時就沒你的份。

cold[3] *adv* **1** *AmE* suddenly and completely【美】完全地, 徹底地; 突然地, 貿然地: *Then Paul stopped cold. "What was that noise?"* 保羅突然停下來問道: "那是甚麼聲音?" **2 out cold** unconscious, especially because you have been hit on the head〔尤指頭被擊打後〕不清醒地: **knock sb (out) cold** (=hit someone so that they become unconscious) 將某人打暈 **3** without preparation 無準備地: *I can't just get up there and make a speech cold!* 我無法毫無準備就上去演講!
cold-blood·ed /,· '··◄/ *adj* **1** a cold-blooded animal, such as a snake, has a body temperature that changes with the temperature of the air or ground around it〔動物〕冷血的〈如蛇〉—compare 比較 WARM-BLOODED **2 cold-blooded killer/murder/violence etc** a person or their actions that show they feel no pity and do not care if other people suffer 無情的[殘酷的]殺手/謀殺犯/暴行等 —**cold-bloodedly** *adv* —**cold-bloodedness** *n* [U]
cold call /,· '·/ *n* [C] if someone who is selling something makes a cold call, they telephone someone they have never met and try to sell something〔無事先接觸而打給潛在主顧的〕冷不防電話
cold cream /'· ·/ *n* [U] a thick, white, sweet-smelling, oily cream used for cleaning your face and making it softer 冷霜, 潤膚膏
cold cuts /'· ·/ *n* [plural] *especially AmE* thinly cut pieces of various types of cold cooked meat【尤美】什錦肉片冷盤
cold-heart·ed /,· '··◄/ *adj* behaving in a way that shows no pity or sympathy 鐵石心腸的, 冷酷無情的 —**cold-heartedly** *adj* —**cold heartedness** *n* [U]
cold snap /'· ·/ *n* [C] a sudden short period of extremely cold weather 寒汛(期), 冷汛(期); 乍冷, 驟冷
cold sore /'· ·/ *n* [C] a painful spot on your lips or inside your mouth that you may get when you are ill with a cold〔傷風、感冒時出現的〕唇瘡疹, 嘴邊瘡疹
cold spell /'· ·/ *n* [C] a period of several days or weeks when the weather is much colder than usual 寒潮期
cold stor·age /,· '··/ *n* [U] **1** if you keep something such as food in cold storage, you keep it in a cold place so that it will stay fresh and in good condition 冷藏 **2 put/go/be in cold storage** to not take action on a plan or idea until later in the future 把〔計劃或主意〕擱置起來: *We'll have to put the project into cold storage until we can get the funding.* 我們將不得不擱置這項工程, 直到我們得到所需的資金。

cold store /ˈ· ·/ *n* [C] a very cold room that is kept cold by a machine and used to store food, fur coats etc to keep them fresh or in good condition〔存放食品、動物毛皮等的〕冷藏庫

cold sweat /ˌ· ˈ·/ *n* [singular] a reaction by your body when you are nervous or afraid, in which you SWEAT[1] (1) but still feel cold 冷汗: *The thought of the trial made him break out in a cold sweat.* 一想到審判, 他就渾身冒冷汗。

cold tur·key /ˌ· ˈ··/ *n* [U] **go cold turkey** to suddenly stop taking a drug you are addicted to and to experience a sort of illness because of it 突然停止服用毒品而感到不舒適: *Marcia went cold turkey off heroin.* 瑪西婭突然戒了海洛因。

cold war /ˌ· ˈ·◂/ *n* [singular;U] an unfriendly political relationship between two countries who do not actually fight each other, usually used of the unfriendly relationship between the US and the USSR after the Second World War 冷戰

cole·slaw /ˋkolˌslɔ; ˈkəʊlslɔː/ *n* [U] a SALAD made with thinly cut raw CABBAGE (1) 涼拌捲心菜絲

co·ley /ˋkolɪ; ˈkəʊli/ *n* [C,U] a large North Atlantic sea fish or the flesh of this fish eaten as food 綠青鱈魚（肉）

col·ic /ˋkɑlɪk; ˈkɒlɪk/ *n* [U] if a baby suffers from colic, it has severe pain in its stomach and BOWELS (1) 胃絞痛, 急性腹痛 —**colicky** *adj*

co·li·tis /kəˋlaɪtɪs; kəˈlaɪtɪ̞s/ *n* [U] *technical* an illness in which part of your COLON (2) swells, causing pain【術語】結腸炎

col·lab·o·rate /kəˋlæbəˌret; kəˈlæbəreɪt/ *v* [I] **1** to work together with someone in order to achieve something, especially in science or art〔尤指在科學、藝術等方面〕合作, 協作: **[+on/with]** *He was one of the scientists who collaborated with Oppenheimer on the atomic bomb.* 他是與奧本海默一起從事原子彈研究的科學家之一。| **collaborate to do sth** *The gallery and the university collaborated to mount an exhibition of rare drawings.* 該畫廊與那所大學合作舉辦了一次畫作珍品展。| **collaborate in doing sth** *Watson and Crick collaborated in discovering the structure of DNA.* 沃森和克里克合作致力於揭示 DNA 的結構。**2 [+with]** to be disloyal to your country by helping an enemy army or government that has taken control of your country 通敵, 與〔佔領者〕合作

col·lab·o·ra·tion /kəˌlæbəˋreʃən; kəˌlæbəˈreɪʃən/ *n* [U] **1 [+between/with]** the act of working together with another person or group to achieve something, especially in science or art〔尤指在科學、藝術等方面的〕合作, 協作: **in collaboration with** *The company is building the centre in collaboration with the Institute of Offshore Engineering.* 該公司正與海洋工程學院合建這座中心。**2 [+with]** help given to an enemy army or government that has taken control of your country〔與敵人或佔領者〕勾結, 通敵

col·lab·o·ra·tive /kəˋlæbəretɪv; kəˈlæbərətɪv/ *adj* [only before noun 僅用於名詞前] **collaborative effort/work/project etc** involving two or more people working together to achieve something 合力/合作/協作項目等

col·lab·o·rat·or /kəˋlæbəretə; kəˈlæbəreɪtə/ *n* [C] **1** someone who helps their country's enemies, for example by giving them information, when the enemy has taken control of their country 通敵者,〔與佔領者〕勾結者: *Their job was to identify enemy collaborators.* 他們的工作是找出通敵者。**2** someone who works with other people in order to achieve something, especially in science or art〔尤指在科學、藝術等方面的〕合作者, 協作者: *collaborators on a biography of Dickens* 協作出版狄更斯傳記的工作人員

col·lage /kəˋlɑʒ; ˈkɒlɑːʒ/ *n* **1** [C] a picture made by sticking other pictures, photographs, cloth etc onto a surface〔把畫片、照片、布塊等黏貼而成的〕拼貼畫 **2** [U] the art of making such pictures 拼貼藝術

col·la·gen /ˋkɑlədʒən; ˈkɒlədʒən/ *n* [U] a PROTEIN substance, sometimes put into women's face creams 膠原（蛋白）

col·lapse[1] /kəˋlæps; kəˈlæps/ *v* 3

1 ►STRUCTURE 結構◄ [I] if a building, wall, piece of furniture etc collapses, it suddenly falls down because its structure is weak or because it has been hit with a sudden violent force 倒坍; 塌下: *The roof is in danger of collapsing.* 屋頂有倒塌的危險。| *Uncle Ted's chair collapsed under his weight.* 泰德叔叔的椅子承受不了他的重量而垮掉了。

2 ►FAIL 失敗◄ [I] if a system, idea, or organization collapses, it suddenly fails or becomes too weak to continue〔系統、觀點、組織等〕突然失敗, 垮掉, 崩潰, 瓦解: *The business finally collapsed because of rising debts.* 由於債務增加, 該商號最後垮了。

3 ►ILLNESS 疾病◄ [I] to suddenly fall down or become unconscious because you are ill〔因病〕突然倒下［昏倒］: *He collapsed with a heart attack while he was dancing.* 他跳舞時心臟病突發而倒下了。

4 ►SIT 坐◄ to suddenly sit down, especially because you are very tired〔尤指因精疲力竭而〕突然坐倒: *I was so exhausted when I got home, I just collapsed on the sofa.* 我到家時已經精疲力盡, 一屁股癱坐在沙發上。

5 ►MAKE STH SMALLER 使某物變小◄ [I,T] if a piece of furniture or equipment collapses or you collapse it, you can fold it so that it becomes smaller〔家具、儀器等〕摺疊起來; 套縮起來: *The legs on our card table collapse so we can store it in the closet.* 我們的牌桌桌腿可以摺疊, 我們可以把牌桌放進壁櫥中。

6 ►MEDICAL 醫療的◄ [I] if a lung or a BLOOD VESSEL collapses, it suddenly becomes flat, so that it no longer has any air or blood in it〔肺或血管〕突然萎陷

collapse[2] *n*

1 ►BUSINESS/SYSTEM/IDEA ETC 業務/系統/想法等◄ [singular,U] a sudden failure in the way something works, so that it cannot continue 突然失敗; 突然瓦解: *The country's economic collapse led to political chaos.* 該國的經濟崩潰導致了政治動亂。

2 ►BUILDING/STRUCTURE/FURNITURE ETC 建築/結構/家具等◄ [U] the act of suddenly falling down because of a weakness in something's structure or because something has hit it violently 突然倒坍: *the collapse of an apartment building during the earthquake* 地震時一幢公寓倒塌

3 ►ILLNESS 疾病◄ [singular] a sudden illness that makes you fall down or become unconscious〔因突發的疾病導致的〕昏倒, 昏迷;〔健康的〕垮掉

4 ►MONEY/PRICES ETC 錢/價格等◄ [singular] a sudden decrease in the value of something〔貨幣、價格等的〕突然貶值, 暴跌: *the collapse of the stock market in 1987* 1987 年股市的暴跌

col·lap·si·ble /kəˋlæpsəbl̩; kəˈlæpsɪ̞bəl/ *adj* something collapsible can be folded so that it takes less space 可摺疊的; 可套縮的: *a collapsible bicycle* 可摺疊式自行車

col·lar[1] /ˋkɑlə; ˈkɒlə/ *n* [C]

1 ►CLOTHING 衣服◄ a stiff band of material on a shirt, dress, or coat that fits around someone's neck 衣領, 領子 —see picture on page A17 參見 A17 頁圖

2 ►CAT/DOG 貓/狗◄ a narrow band of leather or plastic that is fastened around an animal's neck〔動物脖子上的〕頸圈, 項圈

3 hot under the collar *spoken* angry or excited 生氣的, 憤怒的, 激動的: *Calm down! There's no need to get all hot under the collar.* 冷靜一下！沒必要這麼激動。

4 ►COLOURED FUR/FEATHERS 彩色毛皮/羽毛◄ a band of fur, feathers, or skin around an animal's neck that is a different colour from the rest of the fur etc〔動物頸部的〕毛色別於身體其他部分的條紋

5 ►WORK ANIMAL 役畜◄ a thick leather ring put over the shoulders of a work animal to help it pull machinery or a vehicle 軛,〔馬具等〕頸圈

6 ►MACHINE 機器◄ a part of a machine that is shaped

like a ring 箍; 墊圈; 束套; 套管
7 ▶POLICE 警察◀ *slang* if the police make a collar, they catch a criminal【俚】捕獲, 逮捕 —see also 另見 BLUE-COLLAR, WHITE-COLLAR, DOG COLLAR

collar² *v* [T] *informal*【非正式】**1** to catch someone and hold them so that they cannot escape 抓住; 逮捕: *The police collared him before he could get out of the country.* 警察在他逃出國之前逮捕了他。**2** to find someone so that you can talk to them 找到〔某人〕談話: *See if you can collar Tim. I need to know when he'll be ready.* 看你能不能把蒂姆找來談談話。我要知道他甚麼時候會準備好。

col·lar·bone /ˋkɑlə˞ˏbon; ˈkɒləbəʊn/ *n* [C] one of the pair of bones that go from the bottom part of your neck to your shoulders 鎖骨 —see picture at 參見 SKELETON 圖

col·lard greens /ˋkɑlə˞d ˋgrinz; ˌkɒləd ˈgriːnz/ *n* a green leafy vegetable cooked and eaten as food 羽衣甘藍〔可食用〕

collar stud /ˈ·· ·/ *n* [C] an object like a button, used to fasten old-fashioned collars to shirts 領扣〔把老式的領子扣在襯衣上用〕

col·late /kəˋlet; kəˈleɪt/ *v* [T] **1** to arrange sheets of paper in the correct order before they are in a book etc〔裝釘前〕檢點〔印張〕, 配〔頁〕; 整理〔印張等〕: *a photocopier that collates and staples* 能整理和裝訂書頁的複印機 **2** *formal* to gather information together, examine it carefully, and compare it with other information to find any differences【正式】校對, 核對, 校勘

col·lat·e·ral¹ /kəˋlætərəl; kəˈlætərəl/ *n* [U] *technical* property or other goods that you promise to give someone if you cannot pay back the money they lent you; SECURITY (4)【術語】擔保品, 抵押品: **put sth up as collateral** (=promise it in this way) 將某物作為抵押品

collateral² *adj formal*【正式】**1** connected with something or happening as a result of it, but not as important 附屬的, 附帶的, 次要的: *A collateral aim of better education is reducing unemployment.* 提高教育水平有一個附帶的目標, 即減少失業。**2** collateral relatives are members of your family who are not closely related to you〔親戚〕旁系的, 非直系的

col·la·tion /kəˋleʃən; kəˈleɪʃən/ *n formal*【正式】**1** [U] the examination and comparing of information 校對, 校勘 **2** [U] the arranging of sheets of paper in the correct order〔裝釘前的〕配頁; 整理 **3** [C] *formal* a small, usually cold meal【正式】小吃〔一般指冷食〕

3 2 **col·league** /ˋkɑlig; ˈkɒliːg/ *n* [C] someone you work with, used especially by professional people or managers 同事, 同僚: *a colleague of mine at the bank* 我在銀行的一位同事

1 2 **col·lect¹** /kəˋlɛkt; kəˈlekt/ *v*
1 ▶BRING TOGETHER 集合一起◀ [T] to get things of the same type from different places and bring them together 收集, 採集; 使集中: *Researchers spent 6 months collecting facts and figures.* 調查人員們花了六個月的時間收集事實和數據。| *Could you collect some branches for a fire?* 你可以去收集一些樹枝生個火嗎?
2 ▶KEEP OBJECTS 保存物品◀ [T] to get and keep objects because you think they are attractive or interesting 收藏: *The family's been collecting modern art for thirty years.* 這個家庭收藏現代藝術品已經有三十年了。
3 ▶MONEY 錢◀ **a)** [T] to ask for or obtain money you are owed or something you have won 收〔賬、債或稅等〕; 獲得; 領取: *He's collected his second gold medal of these Olympics.* 他已經獲得了他的第二枚奧林匹克運動會金牌。**b) collect (money) for sth** to ask people to give you money for a particular purpose 為…籌款[集資]: *We're collecting for Save the Children.* 我們在為"拯救兒童基金"籌款。
4 ▶INCREASE IN AMOUNT 增加數量◀ [I,T] if something collects in a place or you collect it there, it gradually increases in amount 聚集, 增加: *Rain collected in pools on the uneven road.* 起伏不平的路上積了一攤攤的雨水。| *solar panels for collecting the sun's heat* 採集太陽熱能的太陽能電池板
5 ▶CROWD 羣◀ [I] to come together gradually to form a group of people 聚集: *A crowd was beginning to collect around the scene of the accident.* 人羣開始聚集在事故現場。
6 ▶DUST/DIRT 塵/土◀ [T] to become covered in dust etc 積〔灰等〕: *All the furniture had collected a fine layer of dust.* 所有家具都積了薄薄的一層灰塵。
7 ▶TAKE SB/STH FROM A PLACE 從某處帶走某人/物◀ [T] *especially BrE* to come to a particular place in order to take someone or something away【尤英】領取; 接走: *Martin's gone to collect the children from school.* 馬丁已經去學校接孩子們了。
8 collect yourself/collect your thoughts etc to make an effort to remain calm and think clearly and carefully about something 使〔自己〕鎮靜; 集中〔思想〕: *He paused for a moment to collect himself, then pushed open the door.* 他停了停, 努力鎮定自己, 然後推開那扇門。

collect² /kəˋlɛkt; kəˈlekt/ *adv AmE*【美】**1 call/phone sb collect** when you telephone someone collect, the person who receives the call pays for it 打受話人付費電話 **2 collect call** a telephone call paid for by the person who receives it 由受話人付費的電話

col·lect³ /ˋkɑlɛkt; ˈkɒlɪkt/ *n* [C] a short prayer in some Christian services〔某些基督教儀式中的〕短禱文

col·lect·a·ble /kəˋlɛktəbl̩; kəˈlektəbəl/ also 又作 **col·lect·i·ble** /-əbl̩; -ɪ̵bəl/ *adj* something that is collectable is likely to be bought and kept as part of a group of similar things, especially because it might increase in value 可收集的; 適於收藏的: *Art Deco glassware is very collectable right now.* 裝飾派藝術玻璃製品現在非常有收藏價值。

col·lect·ed /kəˋlɛktɪd; kəˈlektɪ̵d/ *adj* **1** in control of yourself and your thoughts, feelings, etc. 鎮定的, 泰然自若的 **2 collected works** all of someone's books, poems etc printed in one book or set of books〔某人的作品等〕全集

col·lect·i·ble /kəˋlɛktəbl̩; kəˈlektbəl/ also 又作 **collectable** *n* [C] an object that you keep as part of a group of similar things 收藏品: *Miss Kelly's house was full of collectibles, displayed on every possible surface.* 凱莉小姐的房子裡, 在每個能擺東西的地方都擺滿了收藏品。

col·lec·tion /kəˋlɛkʃən; kəˈlekʃən/ *n* 2 1
1 ▶SET/GROUP 套/組◀ **a)** [C] a set of similar things that are kept or brought together because they are attractive or interesting〔一批〕收藏品: *a stamp collection* 一批郵票收藏品 | **[+of]** *a magnificent collection of prehistoric tools* 一批珍貴的史前工具收藏品 **b)** [C] a group of things that are put together〔一批〕收集的東西: *A collection of empty wine bottles stood on the back porch.* (房子)後面的門廊陳列着一批空酒瓶。
2 ▶MONEY 錢◀ **a)** [C] the act of asking for money from people for a particular purpose 募捐: **have a collection** *Every Christmas we have a collection and give the money to a charity.* 每個聖誕節我們都會募捐, 將所得的款項捐給慈善機構。| **take (up) a collection** *We'll be taking up a collection at the end of tonight's service.* 我們在今晚的儀式之後將舉行捐款活動。**b)** [U] the act of obtaining money that is owed to you 收賬, 收債: *Resistance to the new tax is making collection difficult.* 人們拒絕繳納新稅使徵稅變得困難。
3 ▶TAKING STH AWAY 拿走某物◀ [C,U] the act of taking something from a place, especially when this is done regularly〔尤指定期的〕收取: *Garbage collections are made every Tuesday morning.* 每星期二早上收一次垃圾。
4 ▶BRINGING TOGETHER 集合一起◀ [U] the act of bringing together things of the same type from different places to form a group 收集, 採集: *the collection of reliable data* 可靠數據的收集
5 ▶CLOTHES 衣服◀ [C] a number of different pieces

of clothing designed by someone for a particular time of year 特定季節的時裝: *the Paris spring collections* 巴黎春季時裝展

6 ►PEOPLE 人們◄ [C usually singular 一般用單數] a group of people, especially people you think are strange or unusual in some way〔尤指奇特的〕一羣人: *There was an interesting collection of people at the wedding.* 那次婚禮聚集了一羣有趣的人。

7 ►BOOKS/MUSIC 書/音樂◄ [C] several stories, poems, pieces of music etc that are in one book or on one record〔書本、音樂的〕全集; 專輯: *a new collection of Frost's poetry* 新的弗洛斯特詩集

collection box /·ˈ·· ˌ·/ *n* [C] a container with a small opening in the top into which people put money for CHARITY (2) 募捐箱

collection plate /·ˈ·· ˌ·/ *n* [C] a large, almost flat dish in which you put money during some religious services 募捐盤

col·lec·tive¹ /kəˋlɛktɪv; kəˈlektɪv/ *adj* [only before noun 僅用於名詞前] involving a group, or shared or made by every member of a group 集體的; 共同的; 共有的: **collective decision/responsibility etc** *a collective decision on the part of the management* 管理層的共同決定

collective² *n* [C] **1** a group of people who work together to run something such as a business or farm 集體企業[農莊]人員 **2** the business or farm that is run by this group 集體經營的企業[農莊]

collective bar·gain·ing /·ˌ·· ˈ···/ *n* [U] the discussions held between employers and a union in order to reach agreement on wages, working conditions etc〔勞資雙方就工資、工作條件等進行的〕集體談判

collective farm /·ˌ·· ˈ·/ *n* [C] a large farm that is owned by the government and controlled by the farm workers〔由農業工人管理的〕(國營) 集體農莊

col·lec·tive·ly /kəˋlɛktɪvlɪ; kəˈlektɪvli/ *adv* as a group 集體地, 共同地: *The islands, which are northwest of Australia, are collectively known as Indonesia.* 澳大利亞西北方諸島嶼統稱為印度尼西亞。

collective noun /·ˌ·· ˈ·/ *n* [C] *technical* a noun, such as 'committee' or 'family', that is the name of people or things considered as a unit【術語】集合名詞

col·lec·tiv·is·m /kəˋlɛktɪvˌɪzəm; kəˈlektɪvɪzəm/ *n* [U] a political system in which all businesses, farms etc are owned by the government 集體主義 (制度) —**collectivize** *v* [T] —**collectivist** *adj*

col·lec·tor /kəˋlɛktɚ; kəˈlektə/ *n* [C] **1** someone whose job is to collect taxes, tickets, debts etc 收稅人; 收票員; 收款人 **2** someone who collects things that are interesting or attractive 收集者; 收藏家: *a coin collector* 錢幣收藏家 **3 collector's item** something that a collector would like to have 值得收藏的東西; 可收藏的東西: *Original teddy bears have become real collectors' items.* 第一批玩具熊已經成為值得收藏的東西。

col·lege /ˋkɑlɪdʒ; ˈkɒlɪdʒ/ *n*

1 ►ADVANCED EDUCATION 高級教育◄ [C,U] **a)** *especially BrE* a school for advanced education, especially in a particular subject or skill【尤英】學院; 技術專科學校: *a teacher training college* 師範學院 —see also 另見 SIXTH FORM COLLEGE **b)** *AmE* a school for advanced education where you can get a BACHELOR'S DEGREE【美】大學,〔大學的〕本科部: *Which colleges have you applied to?* 你申請了哪些大學? | **college campus/class/graduate etc** *Many firms will only hire college graduates.* 許多公司將只雇用本科畢業生。| **go to college** (=attend a college or university) 上大學 —see also 另見 JUNIOR COLLEGE —compare 比較 UNIVERSITY

2 ►PART OF UNIVERSITY 大學的部分◄ [C] one of the groups of teachers and students that form a separate part of some universities, especially in Britain〔尤指在英國附屬於大學的〕學院: *Trinity College, Cambridge* 劍橋三一學院

3 ►BUILDINGS 建築物◄ [C] the buildings used by any of these organizations 學院[學校] (的建築物)

4 ►STUDENTS AND TEACHERS 師生◄ [C also+plural verb *BrE* 英] the students and teachers of one of these organizations 學院的全體師生: *The whole college turned up to the memorial service.* 該學院全體師生都出席了紀念儀式。

5 ►ORGANIZATION 組織◄ [C] a group of people who have special rights and duties within a profession or organization 學會, 協會, 社團: *the Royal College of Nursing* 皇家護理學會 —see also 另見 ELECTORAL COLLEGE

6 ►SCHOOL 學校◄ [C] *BrE* a word used in the name of some large schools, especially PUBLIC SCHOOLs【英】公學, 書院;〔規模大的〕中學

college boards /ˌ·· ˈ·/ *n* [plural] a set of examinations that students in the US must take in order to enter a college or university〔美〕大學入學考試

col·le·gi·ate /kəˋlidʒɪɪt; kəˈliːdʒiət/ *adj* **1** involving or related to a college 大學的; 學院的: *inter-collegiate competition* 大學之間的競爭 **2** organized into colleges 由學院組成的: *a collegiate university* 由學院組成的大學

col·lide /kəˋlaɪd; kəˈlaɪd/ *v* [I] **1** to hit something or someone that is moving in a different direction from you 碰撞; 相撞: *Two supertankers collided in the rough seas.* 兩艘超級油輪在波濤洶湧的海面上相撞。| **[+with]** *Donna swerved to avoid colliding with a taxi.* 唐娜猛然轉變方向, 以免和一輛計程車相撞。**2** to have an argument with a person or group, especially on a particular subject 衝突, 抵觸: **[+with]** *The President has again collided with Congress over his budget plans.* 總統在預算計劃上又一次與國會發生衝突。

col·lie /ˋkɑlɪ; ˈkɒli/ *n* [C] a middle sized dog with long hair, kept as a pet or trained to look after sheep 柯利牧羊犬 —see picture at 參見 DOG¹ 圖

col·li·er /ˋkɑljɚ; ˈkɒliə/ *n* [C] *BrE*【英】**1** *formal* someone whose job is to cut coal in a mine; MINER【正式】煤礦工人 **2** a ship that carries coal 運煤船

col·lie·ry /ˋkɑljərɪ; ˈkɒljəri/ *n* [C] *BrE* a COAL MINE and the buildings and machinery connected with it【英】〔包括地面建築和設備等在內的〕煤礦

col·li·sion /kəˋlɪʒən; kəˈlɪʒən/ *n* [C,U] **1** an accident in which two or more people or vehicles hit each other while moving in different directions 碰撞 (事件): **[+with]** *The school bus was involved in a collision with a truck.* 這輛校車與一輛貨車相撞。| **head-on collision** (=between two vehicles moving directly towards each other)〔車輛〕迎頭相撞 **2 [+between]** a strong disagreement between two people or groups 衝突, 抵觸 **3 be on a collision course a)** to behave in a way that will cause a serious disagreement or even a war 勢將發生衝突: *Environmentalists and loggers are on a collision course, with no compromise in sight.* 環保主義者與伐木工人勢將發生衝突, 看來沒有任何妥協的餘地。**b)** to be moving in a direction in which you will hit another person or vehicle 將會發生碰撞

col·lo·cate /ˋkɑloˌket; ˈkɒləkeɪt/ *v* [I+with] *technical* when words collocate, they are often used together and sound natural together【術語】〔詞語的〕組合, 連用, 搭配 —**collocate** /ˋkɑlәkәt; ˈkɒləkɪt/ *n* [C]

col·lo·ca·tion /ˌkɑloˋkeʃən; ˌkɒləˈkeɪʃən/ *n* [U] *technical* [C,U] the way in which some words are often used together, or a particular combination of words used in this way【術語】〔詞語等習慣上的〕組合, 搭配; 連用: *"Commit a crime" is a typical collocation in English.* "commit a crime" 是英語中一個典型的搭配。

col·loid /ˋkɑlɔɪd; ˈkɒlɔɪd/ *n* [C] *technical* a mixture of substances in which one substance is completely mixed with another but not DISSOLVEd【術語】膠體; 膠質; 膠態 —compare 比較 SUSPENSION (4)

col·lo·qui·al /kəˋlokwɪəl; kəˈləʊkwiəl/ *adj* language or words that are colloquial are used mainly in conversation rather than in writing or formal speech 口語的, 會

話的 —**colloquially** *adv*

col·lo·qui·al·is·m /kəˋlokwɪəl͵ɪzəm; kəˈləʊkwiəlɪzəm/ *n* [C] an expression or word used mainly in conversation 口語體, 會話體, 口語用詞

col·lo·quy /ˋkɑləkwɪ; ˈkɒləkwi/ *n* [C] *formal* a conversation【正式】會話, 談話 —compare 比較 SOLILOQUY

col·lude /kəˋlud; kəˈluːd/ *v* [I] *formal* to work with someone secretly, especially in order to cheat or deceive other people【正式】共謀, 勾結, 串通: [+with] *He was accused of colluding with the occupying forces.* 他被控與佔領軍勾結。

col·lu·sion /kəˋluʒən; kəˈluːʒən/ *n* [U] *formal or law* a secret agreement that two or more people make in order to do something dishonest【正式或法律】共謀, 勾結, 串通

col·ly·wob·bles /ˋkɑlɪ͵wɑbḷz; ˈkɒli͵wɒbəlz/ *n* **the collywobbles** *BrE informal* an uncomfortable feeling that you get when you are very nervous【英, 非正式】緊張感, 焦慮感

co·logne /kəˋlon; kəˈləʊn/ *n* [U] a liquid that smells slightly of flowers or plants that you put on your neck or wrists 科隆香水, 古龍水 —compare 比較 PERFUME[1] (1)

co·lon /ˋkolən; ˈkəʊlən/ *n* [C] **1** the sign (:) that is used in writing and printing to introduce an explanation, example, QUOTATION (1) etc 冒號 —compare 比較 SEMICOLON —see picture at 參見 PUNCTUATION MARK 圖 **2** *technical* the lower part of the BOWELS, in which food is changed into waste matter【術語】結腸 —see picture at 參見 DIGESTIVE SYSTEM 圖

colo·nel /ˋkɝnḷ; ˈkɜːnl/ *n* [C] a high rank in the Army, Marines, or the US Air Force, or someone who has this rank〔陸軍、海軍陸戰隊或美國空軍的〕上校軍銜; 上校 —see table on page C6 參見C6頁附錄

Colonel Blimp /͵·· ˈ·/ *n* [C] *BrE* an old man with very old-fashioned ideas, who thinks he is important【英】老頑固, 守舊分子

co·lo·ni·al[1] /kəˋlonɪəl; kəˈləʊniəl/ *adj* **1** connected with or related to a country that controls and rules other countries 殖民地的: *a major colonial power* 主要的殖民地強國 **2** made in a style that was common in the US in the 18th century〔18世紀美國〕殖民地時期製造的; 仿殖民地時期式樣的: *a large colonial house* 一棟殖民時期製造的大宅子 **3** connected with the US when it was under British rule〔指美國獨立前〕受英國殖民統治時期的: *an old colonial port on the coast*〔美國〕海岸邊英國殖民地統治時期的舊港口 **4** *BrE* behaving in a way that shows you believe you are better than the people in the foreign country where you live【英】殖民主義者的: *He still has a colonial mentality.* 他仍然懷有殖民主義的倨傲心理。—see also 另見 COLONY

colonial[2] *n* [C] someone who lives in a COLONY but who is a citizen of the country that rules the colony 殖民地居民

co·lo·ni·al·is·m /kəˋlonɪəl͵ɪzəm; kəˈləʊniəlɪzəm/ *n* [U] the principle or practice in which a powerful country rules a weaker one and establishes its own trade and culture there 殖民主義; 殖民政策 —compare 比較 IMPERIALISM

co·lo·ni·al·ist /kəˋlonɪəlɪst; kəˈləʊniəlǐst/ *n* [C] a supporter of colonialism 殖民主義者 —**colonialist** *adj*: *a savage colonialist war* 野蠻的殖民主義戰爭

col·o·nist /ˋkɑlənɪst; ˈkɒlənǐst/ *n* [C] someone who settles in a new colony 開拓殖民地者; 殖民者: *Dutch colonists in South America* 南美的荷蘭殖民者

col·o·nize /ˋkɑlə͵naɪz; ˈkɒlənaɪz/ *v* [T] to establish political control over an area or over another country, and send your citizens there to settle 開拓〔某地〕成殖民地 —**colonization** /͵kɑlənaɪˋzeʃən; ͵kɒlənaɪˈzeɪʃən/ *n* [U] —**colonizer** *n* [C]

col·on·nade /͵kɑləˋned; ͵kɒləˈneɪd/ *n* [C] a row of upright stone posts that usually support a roof or row of arches 柱廊 —**colonnaded** *adj*

col·o·ny /ˋkɑlənɪ; ˈkɒləni/ *n* [C] **1** a country or area that is under the political control of a more powerful country, usually one that is far away 殖民地: *Algeria was formerly a French colony.* 阿爾及利亞以前是法屬殖民地。—see also 另見 CROWN COLONY, DOMINION (3), PROTECTORATE **2** a group of people who live in a colony 移民隊, 殖民團 **3** one of the 13 areas of land on the east coast of North America that later became the United States〔美國獨立前的〕13個州之一: *Connecticut was one of the original colonies.* 康涅狄格是美國獨立前的最初十三個州之一。**4** a particular group of people or the place where they live 聚集人羣; 聚居地[區]: *an artists' colony* 一個藝術家聚居區 | *a leper colony* 一個麻風患者聚居地 **5** a group of animals or plants of the same type that are living or growing together 羣; 羣體; 集羣; 菌落: *Breeding colonies of rare birds were threatened by the oil spill.* 溢出的石油威脅到珍稀鳥類羣體的繁衍。

C

col·or /ˋkʌlɚ; ˈkʌlə/ the American spelling of COLOUR colour 的美式拼法

col·o·ra·tion /͵kʌləˋreʃən; ͵kʌləˈreɪʃən/ *n* [U] the way something is coloured or the pattern these colours make; COLOURING 着[配]色 (法), 染色 (法)

col·o·ra·tu·ra /͵kʌlərəˋturə; ͵kɒlərəˈtʊərə/ *n* **1** [U] a difficult piece of music that is meant to be sung fast〔聲樂的〕花腔; 花腔音樂 **2** [C] a woman, especially a SOPRANO, who sings this type of music 花腔女高音

col·or·ize *AmE*【美】, **col·our·ize** also 又作 **-ise** *BrE*【英】/ˋkʌlɚ͵aɪz; ˈkʌləraɪz/ *v* [T] to add colour to an old film that was made in black and white 着彩色於〔黑白影片〕—**colourization** *n* [U]

color line /ˈ·· ·/ *n* [singular] *AmE* the set of laws or social customs in some places that prevents people of different races from going to the same places or taking part in the same activities【美】〔種族歧視制度下的〕種族分界線, 膚色障礙; COLOUR BAR *BrE*【英】: *Friendship across the color line was rare then.* 那時超越種族界線的友誼是極為稀少的。

co·los·sal /kəˋlɑsḷ; kəˈlɒsəl/ *adj* extremely large 巨大的, 龐大的: *a colossal statue* 巨大的雕像 | *Their secret to success was manufacturing cheap goods on a colossal scale.* 他們成功的祕訣是大量製造廉價商品。—**colossally** *adv*

co·los·sus /kəˋlɑsəs; kəˈlɒsəs/ *n* [C] someone or something that is very big or very important 巨大的人[物]; 偉人; 極重要的人[物]: *An intellectual colossus like Leonardo comes along only once in a generation.* 像列奧納多〔達·芬奇〕那樣的天才, 一代人中也才出一個。

colour[1] *BrE*【英】, **color** *AmE*【美】/ˋkʌlɚ; ˈkʌlə/ *n* [S1] [W1]

1 ▶A COLOUR 一種顏色◀ [C] red, blue, yellow, green, brown, purple etc 色彩, 彩色: *"What colour are your eyes?" "They're brown."* "你的眼睛是甚麼色的?" "褐色的。" | *My favourite colour is purple.* 我最喜歡紫色。| **light/bright/pastel etc colour** *Children like bright colours.* 孩子們喜歡鮮豔的色彩。| **be an orange/greenish etc colour** *It was kind of an orange-red colour.* 它帶點橘紅色。—see picture on page A5 參見A5頁圖

2 ▶COLOUR IN GENERAL 顏色的通稱◀ [C,U] the appearance of something, especially something with a lot of different colours 色, 顏色: *Chameleons can change colour to match their surroundings.* 變色龍能夠隨着環境改變身體的顏色。| *I had always wanted to go to New England to see the fall colours.* (=the colours of the trees) 我一直都想着去新英格蘭觀看秋日的各種色調。

3 in (full) colour a television programme or film that is in colour contains colours such as red, green, and blue rather than just black and white〔電視節目、電影等〕彩色的

4 ▶SB'S RACE 某人的種族◀ [C,U] how dark or light someone's skin is, which shows which race they belong to〔不同人種的〕膚色: *people of all colours* 各色人種 | *discrimination on the basis of color* 對有色人種的歧視 —see also 另見 COLOURED

5 ▶SB'S FACE 某人的臉◀ [C,U] the general appearance and colour of a person's skin, especially when this shows the state of their health or emotions 臉色; 氣色;

血色: *Well, you look better than you did. You've got some colour in your face now.* 不錯, 你看起來比以前好多了。現在你臉上已經有些血色了。| **a high colour** (=a red colour in someone's face that shows they are ill)〔臉部因生病而呈現的〕紅暈, 潮紅

6 ►SUBSTANCE 物質◄ [U] a substance that makes something red, blue, yellow etc 顏料; 染料: *After a few washes, dark clothes begin to lose their colour.* 洗了幾次以後, 深色衣服就開始褪色。

7 ►STH INTERESTING 趣事◄ [U] interesting and exciting details or qualities that a place or person has 生動, 趣味: *The old market is lively, full of colour and activity.* 那個舊市場熱鬧非凡, 充滿趣味與活力。| **add/give colour to** (=make something more interesting) 使…更生動有趣 *A few illustrations or anecdotes will add colour to your report.* 添加一些例子或趣聞軼事將使你的報告增色。

8 lend/give colour to sth to make something, especially something unusual, appear likely or true 使〔尤指不尋常的事〕顯得可信[真實]: *We now have independent evidence that lends colour to the accusation of fraud.* 我們如今有獨立的證據, 證明其犯有欺詐罪。

9 off colour a) not in good health 不健康的: *You look a little off colour today.* 你今天看起來氣色有點不太好。**b)** jokes, stories etc that are off-colour are rude and often about sex 粗俗的; 下流的, 齷齪的, 色情的

10 colours [plural] **a)** the colours that are used as a sign to represent a team, school, club etc〔代表球隊、學校、俱樂部等標誌的〕標誌色: *The national colours of Italy are green, white, and red.* 意大利的國旗顏色是綠、白、紅三色。**b)** *especially BrE* a flag, RIBBON, BADGE etc that you wear or carry to show that you belong to or support a team, school etc【尤英】〔表示屬於或支持某團隊、學校等而佩戴或手持的〕旗幟; 緞帶; 徽章

11 show yourself in your true colours to behave in a way that shows what your real character is, especially if you are unpleasant or dishonest 露出真面目

12 see the colour of sb's money *spoken* to have definite proof that someone has enough money to pay for something【口】確信某人有支付能力: *"A whiskey, please." "Let's see the colour of your money first."* "請來杯威士忌。" "讓我們先看看你是不是有足夠的錢。"

13 nail your colours to the mast to say clearly what your opinion is on a particular subject 闡明你的觀點

colour in *BrE*【英】**/color in** *AmE*【美】着色

colour² *BrE*【英】, **color** *AmE*【美】*v* **1** [T] to make something coloured rather than just black, white, or plain 給…着色[染色]: *Do you colour your hair or is it naturally red?* 你是染了髮, 還是本來就是紅色的? | **colour sth red/blue etc** *Sunset came and coloured the sky a brilliant red.* 日落時分, 天空被染上了一片豔麗的紅色。**2** also 又作 **colour in** [I,T] use coloured pencils to put colours inside the lines of a picture〔用彩筆〕着色, 填色: *As a kid, I used to love colouring in shapes.* 童年時候, 我常常喜歡給各種圖形填色。**3** [I] when someone colours, their face becomes redder because they are embarrassed〔因尷尬而〕臉紅 **4** [T] **colour sb's judgment/opinions/attitudes etc** to influence the way someone thinks about something, especially so that they become less fair or reasonable 使某人的判斷/觀點/態度等帶有偏見: *Don't you think your opinions are coloured by prejudice?* 你不認為你的觀點帶有偏見嗎? —see also 另見 **colour code** (CODE² (3))

colour³ *BrE*【英】, **color** *AmE*【美】*adj* **colour television/photograph/monitor etc** a television etc that produces or shows pictures in colour rather than in black, white and grey 彩色電視/照片/監視器等 —opposite 反義詞 MONOCHROME

colour bar *BrE*【英】, **color bar** *AmE*【美】/ˈ‥ ·/ *n* [C usually singular 一般用單數] a set of laws or social customs that prevent people of different races from going to the same places or taking part in the same activities〔法律上或社會上對有色人種設置的〕種族分界限, 膚色障礙; COLOR LINE *AmE*【美】

colour-blind *BrE*【英】, **color-blind** *AmE*【美】/ˈ‥ ·/ *adj* **1** unable to see the difference between all or some colours 色盲的 **2** treating people from different races equally and fairly 沒有種族成見的: *The law should be colour-blind.* 法律不應存在種族歧視。—**colour-blindness** *n* [U]

colour-co·or·di·nat·ed *BrE*【英】, **color-coordinated** *AmE*【美】/ˈ‥ ·,‥‥/ *adj* clothes, decorations etc that are colour-coordinated have colours which look good together〔衣服、裝飾等〕顏色協調的 —**colour-coordination** /,‥ ‥ˈ‥/ *n* [U]

col·oured¹ *BrE*【英】, **colored** *AmE*【美】/ˈkʌlɚd; ˈkʌləd/ *adj* **1** having a colour such as red, blue, yellow etc, rather than being black, white, or plain 有顏色的, 彩色的: *colored glass* 彩色玻璃 | *brightly coloured tropical birds* 色彩斑斕的熱帶鳥類 **2** an offensive word for someone who belongs to a race of people with dark or black skin 有色人種的〔冒犯用詞〕—see 見 NEGRO (USAGE) **3** *SAfrE* someone whose parents or grandparents were both white and black【南非】〔白人與有色人種所生的〕混血兒

coloured² *BrE*【英】, **colored** *AmE*【美】*n* [C] an offensive word for someone belonging to a race of people with dark skin 有色人種的人〔尤指黑人, 帶歧視性稱呼〕—see 見 NEGRO (USAGE)

col·our·fast *BrE*【英】, **colorfast** *AmE*【美】/ˈkʌlɚ-ˌfæst; ˈkʌləfɑːst/ *adj* cloth that is colourfast will not lose its colour when it is washed〔衣料〕不褪色的, 不掉色的 —**colourfastness** *n* [U]

col·our·ful *BrE*【英】, **colorful** *AmE*【美】/ˈkʌlɚfəl; ˈkʌləfəl/ *adj* **1** having bright colours or a lot of different colours 富於色彩的, 顏色鮮豔的: *a colourful display of flowers* 一場色彩繽紛的花展 **2** interesting, exciting, and full of variety 有聲有色的, 富於刺激性的, 生動有趣的: **colourful career/life/period etc** *Charlie Chaplin had a long and colourful career.* 查理·卓別林的演藝生涯漫長而豐富多彩。| **colourful character/figure** (=someone who is interesting and unusual) 有趣且不尋常的人物 *The old galley cook was the most colourful character on the ship.* 那個老廚師是整條船上最有趣的人。**3** colourful language, speech etc uses a lot of swearing〔語言、演説等〕大量使用咒罵語的 —**colourfully** *adv*

col·our·ing *BrE*【英】, **coloring** *AmE*【美】/ˈkʌlərɪŋ; ˈkʌlərɪŋ/ *n* **1 food colouring** a substance used to give a particular colour to food 食物色素 **2** [U] the colour of someone's skin, hair, and eyes〔皮膚、頭髮及眼睛等的〕顏色: *Mandy has her mother's fair colouring.* 曼迪的膚色和她母親的一樣白。**3** [U] the colours of an animal, bird, or plant〔動物、鳥類或植物的〕顏色, 色彩, 色調: *The black and yellow colouring of some insects acts as a warning to predators.* 某些昆蟲身上呈現黑黃色是對天敵的一種警告。

col·our·less *BrE*【英】, **colorless** *AmE*【美】/ˈkʌlɚlɪs; ˈkʌləlǝs/ *adj* **1** having no colour 無色的: *Water is a col-*

orless liquid. 水是一種無色的液體。**2** not interesting or exciting; DULL[1] (1) 無趣味的; 不刺激的; 不生動的: *Everything about this town seems drab and colourless to me.* 在我看來, 這個鎮的所有一切既單調又無趣。—**colourlessly** *adv* —**colourlessness** *n* [U]

colour scheme *BrE*【英】, **color scheme** *AmE*【美】/ˈ·· ·/ *n* [C] the combination of colours that someone chooses for a room, painting etc〔房間、畫作等的〕色彩設計, 色調搭配: *a sophisticated colour scheme* 老練的色彩設計

colour sup·ple·ment /ˈ·· ,···/ *n* [C] *BrE*【英】a magazine printed in colour and given free with a newspaper, especially a Sunday newspaper〔尤指星期日隨報附送的〕彩色增刊

Colt /kolt; kəʊlt/ *n* [C] *trademark* a kind of PISTOL【商標】科爾特牌手槍: *a Colt 45* 科爾特45型手槍

colt *n* [C] a young male horse 雄性小馬駒 —compare 比較 FILLY

colt·ish /ˈkoltɪʃ; ˈkəʊltɪʃ/ *adj* a young person or animal that is coltish has a lot of energy but moves in an awkward way 活蹦亂跳的; 活潑的: *her long coltish limbs* 她那修長富有活力的四肢

col·um·bine /ˈkɑləm,baɪn; ˈkɒləmbaɪn/ *n* [C] a garden plant with delicate leaves and bright flowers that hang down 耬斗菜〔園藝植物〕

2 **col·umn** /ˈkɑləm; ˈkɒləm/ *n* [C] **1** a tall, solid, upright,
2 stone post used to support a building or as a decoration 支柱; 柱, 圓柱: *a graceful Ionic column* 一根典雅的愛奧尼亞式圓柱 **2** a long moving line of people or things〔人或物排成的移動的〕(一)隊, (一)列; 縱行[列]: *A long, winding column of soldiers marched through the streets.* 一長隊士兵沿着街道蜿蜒前進。**3** one of two or more lines of print that go down the page of a newspaper or book and that are separated from each other by a narrow space〔報刊上的〕欄: *Turn to Page 5, column 2.* 翻到第5頁第2欄。**4** a line of numbers or words written under each other that goes down a page〔數字、單詞的〕列: *Add up the numbers in each column separately.* 分別將各列數字相加。**5** an article on a particular subject or by a particular writer that appears regularly in a newspaper or magazine〔報紙、雜誌的〕專欄(文章): *a weekly column* 每週專欄 | *She writes the gardening column in the Express.* 她為《快報》撰寫園藝專欄。**6** something that has a long, thin shape, like a column 柱狀物: **[+of]** *a column of smoke* 一柱輕煙 —see also 另見 FIFTH COLUMN, PERSONAL COLUMN, SPINAL COLUMN

col·umn·ist /ˈkɑləmɪst; ˈkɒləmɪ̵st/ *n* [C] someone who writes articles, especially about a particular subject, that appear regularly in a newspaper or magazine〔報刊、雜誌的〕專欄作家

com- /kəm; kəm/ *prefix* the form used for CON- before b, m, or p〔前綴con-的一個形式, 用於b, m或p前〕: *compassion* (=sympathy) 同情

co·ma /ˈkomə; ˈkəʊmə/ *n* [C] a state in which someone remains unconscious for a long time, usually caused by a serious illness or injury〔因重病或重傷而引起的〕昏迷: **be/lie in a coma** *Marina Stefani, 25, has been in a coma for the past four months.* 25歲的瑪麗娜·史蒂芬尼在過去的四個月裡一直處於昏迷狀態。

co·ma·tose /ˈkomə,tos; ˈkəʊmətəʊs/ *adj* **1** *technical* in a coma【術語】昏迷的 **2** *informal* so tired that you cannot think properly【非正式】〔因疲倦而〕呆滯的, 麻木的: *Working till you're comatose doesn't help anybody.* 工作到倦極麻木對誰都沒好處。

comb[1] /kom; kəʊm/ *n* **1** [C] a flat piece of plastic, metal etc with a row of thin teeth on one side, used for making your hair tidy 梳子 **2** [C] a small flat piece of plastic, metal etc with a row of thin teeth on one side, used for keeping your hair back or for decoration〔將頭髮固定於腦後或作裝飾用的〕梳狀飾物, 髮插 **3** [singular] a process in which you make your hair tidy or straight using a comb 梳理: *Your hair needs a good comb.* 你的頭髮需要好好梳理一下。**4** [C] the red piece of flesh that grows on top of a male chicken's head〔公雞的〕雞冠, 肉冠 **5** [C] a HONEYCOMB 蜂巢 —see also 另見 FINE-TOOTH COMB

comb[2] *v* [T] **1** to make hair or fur tidy or straight using a comb 梳, 梳理: *Your hair's a mess! Go comb it.* 你的頭髮亂七八糟的! 去梳一梳。**2** to search a place thoroughly 徹底搜尋, 四處搜查: **comb sth for** *The police combed the woods for the missing boy.* 警察在林子裡徹底搜查, 尋找那個失蹤的男孩。

comb sb/sth ↔ **out** *phr v* [T] **1** to make hair or fur straight and smooth using a comb 梳理〔頭髮、毛髮等〕: *It took over an hour to comb out all the tangles in Buster's fur.* 將巴斯特的毛髮梳理乾淨花了一個多小時。**2** *informal* to get rid of unnecessary people from within a group【非正式】裁減〔冗員〕**3** **[+from]** to find and collect specific pieces of information from a larger amount of information〔在大量信息中〕搜尋並收集專門信息 —**comb out** *n* [singular]

comb through *phr v* [T] to search through a lot of objects or information in order to find a specific thing or piece of information〔在大量物件、信息中〕仔細搜尋: *Marta combed through a box of old photographs, looking for the baby portrait.* 瑪爾塔在一盒舊照片中找尋那張嬰兒照。

com·bat[1] /ˈkɑmbæt; ˈkɒmbæt/ *n* **1** [U] organized fighting, especially in a war〔尤指戰爭中的〕戰鬥: **active/armed combat** *These troops have very little experience of active combat.* 這些軍隊沒有多少實戰經驗。| **in combat (with)** *Corporal Gierson was killed in combat.* 吉爾森下士陣亡了。| **combat mission/activity/unit etc** *The women were excluded from the combat units.* 婦女不得參加戰鬥小組。| **combat plane/jacket/boots** *A combat plane flew overhead.* 一架戰鬥機飛越上空。| **locked in mortal combat** (=fighting until one of the opponents dies) 決一死戰, 殊死的戰鬥 **2** [C] a fight or battle 鬥爭; 格鬥: **[+between/against]** *a combat between good and evil* 善惡之爭 | **single combat** (=a formal fight between only two people) 一對一的格鬥

com·bat[2] /ˈkɑmbæt; ˈkɒmbæt/ *v* **combatted, combatting** *BrE*【英】[T] *formal*【正式】**1** to take action in an organized way in order to oppose something bad or harmful 與…鬥爭: *a neighborhood watch system to help combat crime* 幫助打擊犯罪的鄰里警報系統 | *new strategies to combat inflation* 與通貨膨脹作鬥爭的新戰略 **2** to fight against an enemy or opponent in order to try and defeat them 與…戰鬥

com·ba·tant /ˈkɑmbətənt; ˈkɒmbətənt/ *n* [C] someone who fights in a war 戰鬥人員, 戰士

combat fa·tigue /ˈ·· ·,·/ *n* [U] *technical* BATTLE FATIGUE【術語】戰鬥疲勞症

com·ba·tive /kəmˈbætɪv; ˈkɒmbətɪv/ *adj* ready and willing to fight or argue 好鬥的; 好爭論的: *a combative committee member* 一位好鬥的委員 —**combatively** *adv* —**combativeness** *n* [U]

com·bi·na·tion /,kɑmbəˈneʃən; ,kɒmbɪ̵ˈneɪʃən/ *n* **1** [C, 3
U] two or more different things, qualities, substances 2
etc that are used or put together 結合, 聯合; 混合: *a perfect wine and food combination* 美酒佳餚的完美組合 | **[+of]** *A combination of factors may be responsible for the increase in cancer.* 各種因素的綜合作用可能導致癌症發病率的上升。| *a screen heroine who is a combination of the modern and the traditional* 一位融合了傳統與現代氣質的銀幕女星 | *A combination of tact and authority was needed to deal with the situation.* 處理這類情況需要機智, 也需要加以威懾。| **in combination (with)** *Certain drugs which are safe when taken separately are lethal in combination.* 某些藥品在分開服用時是安全的, 但在混合服用時則會致命。**2** [C] a number of things chosen from a group and put in a particular order 組合, 搭配: *Certain combinations of sounds are*

C

not possible in English. 在英語中, 某些音是不可能組合的。| *an unusual combination of colours* 不尋常的色彩搭配 **3** [C] the series of numbers or letters you need to open a combination lock〔密碼鎖的〕號碼組合: *I've forgotten the combination for my bicycle lock!* 我忘記了腳踏車鎖的號碼組合了! **4 a winning combination** a mixture of different people or things that work successfully together 成功的搭擋; 默契的組合 **5** [U] *especially AmE* used before a noun in some phrases to mean that something does more than one job or uses more than one method【尤美】組合物; 合併體: *a combination of washer and dryer* 洗衣和脱水兩用洗衣機 | *combination chemotherapy* 混和式化學療法 **6 combinations** [plural] *BrE old-fashioned* a piece of underwear covering the upper part of your body and legs, worn especially in the past; UNION SUIT【英, 過時】〔尤指舊時穿的〕連衣褲

combination lock /··'·· ·/ *n* [C] a lock which can only be opened by using a series of numbers or letters in a particular order 號碼[密碼]鎖, 轉字鎖

com·bine¹ /kəm`baɪn; kəm'baɪn/ *v* **1** [I,T] if you combine two or more different things, ideas, or qualities or if they combine, they begin to exist or work together (使) 結合; (使) 組合: *I'm looking for a job in which I can combine the different aspects of my experience so far.* 我正在尋找一份能結合應用我的不同經驗的工作。| **combine to do sth** *Several factors had combined to harm our friendship.* 幾個因素湊在一起, 傷害了我們的友誼。| **combine sth with** *The new software package combines power with maximum flexibility.* 這種新的套裝軟件既有大功率, 又極為靈巧。| **combined with** *Heat treatment is most effective if combined with regular physiotherapy.* 熱療若與定期的物理療法結合使用最為有效。| **combined effect/effects** (=the result of two or more different things used or mixed together) 共同作用/效果 *The combined effects of the heat and too much alcohol made Sheila feel nauseous.* 由於氣温太高與過量酒精的共同作用, 希拉覺得一陣噁心。**2** [I,T] if two or more different substances, liquids etc combine or if you combine them, they mix or join together to produce a new single substance, liquid etc (使) 化合, (使) 組合, 調和: **combine to do sth** *Different amino acids combine to form proteins.* 不同種類的氨基酸組合形成蛋白質。| **combine sth** *Combine all the ingredients in a salad bowl.* 將所有材料放在沙律碗中調拌。| **combine sth with** *Steel is produced by combining iron with carbon.* 鋼是由鐵加碳製造而成。**3** [T] to do two very different activities at the same time 同時做〔兩件完全不同的事〕: **combine sth with** *You can't combine studying for your exams with a wild social life!* 你不能在備考的同時到處瘋着去玩! | **combine sth and sth** *It's no easy task combining family responsibilities and a full-time job!* 在盡到家庭責任的同時又要從事全職工作, 這可不是件容易的事! | **combine business with pleasure** (=work and enjoy yourself at the same time) 既工作又娛樂 **4** [I,T] if two or more groups, organizations etc combine or if you combine them, they join or work together in order to do something (使) 聯合〔以達成某項目〕; 合併: **combine to do sth** *Two of the smaller groups had combined to form one large team.* 這些小羣體中有兩個已經聯合成立了一個較大的派系。| **combine sth** *a report on the advantages of combining small village schools* 一份關於合併小型鄉村學校的好處的報告

com·bine² /`kɑmbaɪn; 'kɒmbaɪn/ *n* [C] **1** also 又作 **combine harvester** a machine used by farmers to cut grain, separate the seeds from it, and clean it 聯合收割機 **2** a group of people or organizations who work together for a particular purpose〔為某一目的而組成的〕聯盟, 聯合 (體): *The factory was sold to a British combine after the war.* 戰後該公司被賣給了一家英國聯合企業。

com·bined /kəm`baɪnd; kəm'baɪnd/ *adj* **1** [only before noun 僅用於名詞前] done, made, or achieved by several people or groups working together 結合的, 聯合的, 共同的: **combined effort/action/operation** *"Who cooked the dinner?" "Well, it was a combined effort really."* "誰做的這頓飯?" "哦, 其實是大家一起做的。" | **combined salaries** (=the total amount of money that two or more people earn)〔兩人或多人〕共同賺得的錢 **2** having two very different feelings at the same time〔情感〕複雜的, 矛盾的: *Ann felt a combined relief and sadness.* 安既舒了口氣, 又覺得難過。

combining form /·'·· ·/ *n* [C] *technical* a form of a word that has a meaning but cannot be used alone, and is used with other words to make new ones such as 'Anglo', meaning 'English', in the word 'Anglo-American'【術語】複合用詞; 構詞成分〔如 "Anglo-American" 中的 "Anglo"〕

com·bo /`kɑmbo; 'kɒmbəʊ/ *n* [C] *informal*【非正式】**1** a small band that plays JAZZ¹ (1) or dance music〔演奏爵士樂或舞曲的〕小型樂隊 **2** *AmE* any combination of different things, especially a meal at a FAST FOOD restaurant【美】〔尤指快餐店的〕雜燴飯; 混合物: *I'll have the fish combo to go.* 我要帶一份魚燴飯走。

com·bus·ti·ble /kəm`bʌstəbl; kəm'bʌstəbəl/ *adj* able to burn easily 可燃的, 易燃的: *Alcohol is highly combustible.* 酒精非常易燃。

com·bus·tion /kəm`bʌstʃən; kəm'bʌstʃən/ *n* [U] **1** the process of burning 燃燒 **2** *technical* chemical activity which uses oxygen to produce light and heat【術語】〔產生高温和光的〕燃燒 **3 combustion chamber** the enclosed space in which combustion happens 燃燒室 — see also 另見 INTERNAL COMBUSTION ENGINE

come¹ /kʌm; kʌm/ *v past tense* **came** /kem; keɪm/ *past participle* **come**

① **MOVE** 移動
② **TRAVEL** 旅行
③ **ARRIVE** 到達
④ **REACH A CONDITION/STATE** 達到某種條件/狀態
⑤ **HAPPEN/EXIST** 發生/存在
⑥ **REACH AS FAR AS** 直到達
⑦ **SPOKEN PHRASES** 口語片語
⑧ **IN AN ORDER/POSITION** 處於某個次序/位置
⑨ **OTHER MEANINGS** 其他意思
⑩ **PHRASAL VERBS** 片語動詞

① **MOVE** 移動

1 [I] a word meaning to move towards someone, or to visit or arrive at a place, used when the person speaking or the person listening is in that place 來; 來到; 來臨: *Come a little closer.* 走近點兒。| *Sarah's coming later on.* 莎拉一會兒就來。| *I've come about the job you advertised.* 我來應徵你招聘的職位。| **[+to/towards/here etc]** *Come here and look at this.* 到這兒來看看這個。| *When are you coming back?* 你甚麼時候回來? | **come and do sth** *Can I come and see you tomorrow?*

我明天能來看看你嗎？| **come to do sth** *A man comes to clean the windows on Fridays.* 每星期五都有人來擦窗戶。| **come for sb** (=in order to take them somewhere) 來接某人 *When is Anton coming for you?* 安東甚麼時候來接你？| **come running/flying/speeding etc** *Jess came flying round the corner and banged straight into me.* 傑斯從拐角處飛跑出來，和我撞個滿懷。| **come to dinner/lunch** *What day are your folks coming to dinner?* 你們大家甚麼時候過來吃頓飯呀？

2 ▶MOVE WITH SB 與某人同行◀ [I] to move to a particular place with the person who is speaking 同行，同來: *Can Billy come too?* 比利也能來嗎？| **[+with]** *Would you like to come to the concert with me?* 你願意和我一起去聽音樂會嗎？| **[+along]** *There's room for one more, if you want to come along.* 如果你想一道來的話，還有夠一個人的位置。

② TRAVEL 旅行

3 [I] to travel a particular distance or in a particular way to reach the place you are in or talking about〔尤指沿特定的路線〕到達；至: *We rode back the way we had come.* 我們沿着來時的路線騎了回去。| **come by/on/with etc** *Did you come on a coach or by train?* 你是乘長途公共汽車還是火車來的？| **come far/miles/a long way etc** *Some of the birds have come thousands of miles to winter here.* 一些鳥飛了數千英里到這兒來過冬。| *It would be a shame to have come all this way and not see them.* 老遠趕來卻沒有見着他們，太可惜了。

③ ARRIVE 到達

4 [I] to arrive or be sent somewhere 來到；被送至〔某處〕: *The phone bill has come at a bad time.* 這張電話費賬單來得真不是時候。

5 ▶TIME/EVENT 時間/事件◀ [I] if a time or event comes, it arrives or happens〔時間、事件〕到來；發生: *The moment had come for me to break the news to her.* 是時候讓我將這個消息告訴她了。| *Christmas seems to come earlier every year.* 聖誕似乎一年比一年來得早。| **coming soon** (=used especially in advertisements) 即將〔上演、來貨等〕〔尤用於廣告〕 *Coming soon, to a theater near you!* 即將上演，就在你附近的一家劇院！| **the time is coming/will come** *The time will come when you'll thank me for this.* 你就要為此而感謝我了。

④ REACH A CONDITION/STATE 達到某種條件/狀態

6 come to sth an expression used in some phrases, meaning to reach a particular state or position 得出某物；達到某種狀態[境地]: **come to a decision/the conclusion** *I've come to the conclusion that we've made a mistake.* 我已經得出了結論，那就是我們犯了個錯誤。| **come to power/trial etc** *When does Alan's case come to court?* 艾倫的案子何時提到法庭受審？| **come to an end/halt/stop etc** *Yes, I saw the van come to a screeching halt right there.* 是的，我看見那輛貨車就在那兒嘎的一聲停了下來。

7 come open/undone etc to become open etc 鬆開，解開: *Your shoelace is coming untied.* 你的鞋帶鬆了。| *The bottle came open in my bag!* 我袋子裡的那個瓶子開了！—see also 另見 **a dream come true** (DREAM¹ (5))

8 come to do sth to begin to do something, especially to have a particular feeling or opinion about someone or something as a result of time or experience 開始做某事〔尤指隨着時間或經歷的增長，開始對某人或某物產生特殊感情或特定看法〕: *In time you may come to like it here.* 你最終可能會喜歡這兒的。| *That's the kind of behavior we've come to expect from him.* 那正是我們期待他會表現出來的品行。| *You've come to mean a lot to me.* 你開始對我變得很重要。

9 come into sth to begin to be in a particular state or position 變成，成為；進入〔狀態〕: *As we turned the corner, the town came into view.* 我們拐過街角，小鎮就出現在眼前。| *The new law comes into effect next month.* 這項新法律下個月開始生效。

⑤ HAPPEN/EXIST 發生/存在

10 [I] to happen or appear 發生；出現: *Your chance will come one day.* 你的機會總有一天會出現的。| *No good will come from all this.* 這麼做不會有好結果。| **sth comes and goes** *"How's the pain?" "Well, it comes and goes."* "疼得怎麼樣了？""哦，一陣兒一陣兒地疼。" | **come in twos/threes etc** (=happen two, three etc times, closely together) 接二連三地 *Trouble always comes in threes.* 禍不單行。

11 [I] to exist 存在: **come in different shapes and sizes** *Cats come in many shapes and sizes.* 貓的體形各異，大小也不一樣。

12 as nice/as stupid etc as they come extremely nice, stupid etc 極好的/極蠢的等: *Don't get Bill angry – he's as mean as they come.* 別惹比爾生氣 — 他小氣得不得了。

13 take it as it comes to accept something exactly as it happens or is given to you, without trying to change it or plan ahead 原樣接受；既來之，則安之: *For the moment I'm just taking each day as it comes.* 我現在只是得過且過。

14 the best/worst is yet to come used to say that better or worse things can be expected to happen in the future 最好的/最壞的還在後頭

15 come what may whatever happens 無論發生甚麼: *Come what may, I'll never leave you.* 無論發生甚麼，我永遠也不會離開你。

16 come to pass *literary* to happen after a period of time【文】〔一段時間以後〕發生: *It came to pass that they had a son.* 斗轉星移，他們喜得一子。

⑥ REACH AS FAR AS 直到達

17 [I always+adv/prep] to reach a particular place 到達〔某處〕: **come up to/down to etc** *The water is pretty deep – it comes right up to my neck.* 水相當深 — 直淹到了我的脖子。| *Carrie's hair comes down to her waist.* 卡麗的頭髮長及腰部。

Frequencies of the verb **come** in spoken and written English 動詞 come 在英語口語和書面語中的使用頻率

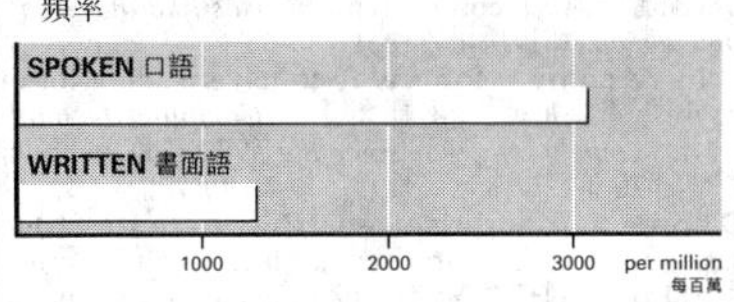

Based on the British National Corpus and the Longman Lancaster Corpus 據英國國家語料庫和朗文蘭卡斯特語料庫

This graph shows that the verb **come** is much more common in spoken English than in written English. This is because it is used in a lot of common spoken phrases. 本圖表顯示動詞 come 在英語口語中比在書面英語中較為常用。這是因為很多常用口語片語是由 come 構成的。

⑦ SPOKEN PHRASES 口語片語

18 here comes John/Shelia etc used when someone is coming towards you and you want the person you are with to notice them 約翰/希拉等來了: *Look out, here comes the boss!* 小心，老闆過來了！

19 how come? used to ask someone why something has happened 怎麼會…?: *How come Tyler's still here?* 泰勒怎麼還在這兒?

20 come to think of it/come to that used when you

want to add something you have just realized or been reminded of 還有…;〔剛好想起〕說起來…: *It was really fun – come to think of it, I should write Jim a thank-you note.* 這可真是有趣 —— 哦, 說起來, 我應該給吉姆寫張感謝便條。| *I haven't seen her for weeks – or her parents, come to that.* 我好幾個星期沒見到她了 —— 哦, 也沒見到她的父母。

21 come again? used to ask someone to repeat what they have just said 再說一遍好嗎?

22 come July/next year/the wedding etc at a particular time in the future 將要到來的七月/明年/婚禮等: *Come Monday, we'll be in our new house.* 下星期一我們將住進新房子。

23 come (now) *old-fashioned* used to comfort or gently encourage someone【過時】〔用於安慰或鼓勵〕好了; 行了: *Come, Sarah, don't cry.* 好了, 莎拉, 別哭了。

24 come, come!/come now *old-fashioned* used to tell someone that you do not accept what they are saying or doing【過時】〔表示不贊同〕哦, 不; 別這樣: *Come now, try to be more polite.* 別這樣, 盡量禮貌點。

25 don't come the innocent/victim etc with me *BrE* used to tell someone not to pretend to you that they are innocent, a victim etc【英】別在我面前裝無辜/可憐等: *Don't come the poor struggling artist with me. You're just lazy!* 別在我面前裝成個可憐巴巴勉強過活的藝術家。你就是懶!

⑧ IN AN ORDER/POSITION 處於某個次序/位置

26 [I always+adv/prep] to be in a particular position or rank in order, importance, or quality〔在級別、順序、重要性、質量上〕處於: **come before/after** *The singing comes before the Mayor's speech.* 歌曲之後是市長發言。| **come first/second etc** *"How was the tournament?" "We came last."* (=we did not win any games) "比賽結果如何?" "我們排在最後。" | *My family always comes first.* (=is the most important thing in my life) 我的家庭在我心中總是最重要的。

⑨ OTHER MEANINGS 其他意思

27 ►BE SOLD/AVAILABLE 出售/有供應◄ [I] to be sold, produced, or available 在出售; 生產中; 有供應: *Yogurt comes in many flavors.* 出售的酸乳酪有多種口味。| *The camera comes complete with batteries.* 這種相機配有電池。| **come cheap** *Houses like that don't come cheap.* 那種房子不便宜。

28 have come a long way to have made a lot of progress 有長足進步, 有極大發展: *Computer technology has come a long way since the 1970's.* 電腦技術自20世紀70年代以來已經取得了極大的進步。

29 come as a surprise/relief/blow etc (to sb) to make someone feel surprised, RELIEVED etc 使…驚奇/鬆一口氣/受到打擊等: *The news came as a complete shock to him.* 這個消息對他震撼極大。| **it comes as no surprise that** (=used to say that you were expecting something) 意料之中, 未出乎意料 *It comes as no surprise that their marriage is over.* 他們婚姻的結束並不出人意料。

30 come of age a) to reach an age, usually 18 or 21, when you are considered by law to be an adult 成年; 達到法定年齡〔通常為18或21歲〕**b)** if an artist, style, or organization comes of age, they reach their best, most successful period of time〔藝術、風格、組織等〕處於巔峯, 達到黃金時期: *Mozart's music came of age when the baroque style was at its height.* 在巴羅克藝術風格最盛行的時候, 莫扎特的音樂也達到了巔峯。

31 come easily/naturally (to sb) to be easy for someone to do, say etc 對…而言很容易/自然: *Acting has always come naturally to her.* 表演對她來說總是很容易的。

32 years/weeks/days etc to come used to emphasize that something is still in the future or will continue into the future 未來幾年/幾週/幾天等: *Nuclear waste will remain hazardous for generations to come.* 核廢料仍將對未來幾代人產生危險。—see also 另見 COMING¹

33 ►SEX 性◄ [I] *slang* to have an ORGASM【俚】達到性高潮

34 come to hand things that come to hand are easy to reach or use, or are easily available 唾手可得: *Just use whatever comes to hand.* 只要抓到甚麼就用甚麼。

35 come to mind if someone or something comes to mind, you think of them when you are trying to find a solution to something 進入腦海, 想到, 記起: *We need a new secretary. Does anyone good come to mind?* 我們需要一名新秘書。想到甚麼好的人選嗎?

36 come to life a) to become exciting or seem almost real 恢復生氣; 逼真: *When he reads out loud, Papa makes stories come to life.* 爸爸大聲朗讀故事, 讀得活靈活現。**b)** to wake up or begin to grow again 甦醒: *spring buds coming to life* 又開始重新綻放的春芽兒

37 come clean *informal* to admit that you have done something wrong【非正式】認錯, 全盤招供: **[+about]** *I think you should come clean about where you were last night.* 你必須老實交待昨晚去了哪兒。

38 come right out and say sth to speak in a direct, often surprising way 坦言, 直截了當地說〔常指出人意料地〕: *Susie came right out and asked Bert what he thought of her.* 蘇茜直截了當地問伯特他對她的看法。

39 not know whether you are coming or going *informal* to feel confused because you are doing too many things, so that nothing is organized【非正式】〔因事情過多而〕不知所措, 毫無頭緒

40 come good/right *BrE informal* to end or finish well or correctly【英, 非正式】圓滿結束: *Don't worry, it'll all come right in the end.* 別擔心, 最後一切都會好起來的。

⑩ PHRASAL VERBS 片語動詞

come about *phr v* [I] **1** to happen, especially in a way that seems impossible to control 發生; 產生〔尤指不受控制地〕: **how did it come about that** *How did it come about that humans speak so many different languages?* 人類是怎麼會說這麼多種語言的? **2** when a ship comes about, it changes direction〔船〕轉向, 改變方向

come across *phr v* **1** [T not in passive 不用被動態] to meet, find, or discover someone or something by accident or by chance 偶遇; 偶然發現: *He had never come across a person quite like Sheila.* 他從沒遇到過像希拉這樣的人。| *I came across some old photos in the attic.* 我在閣樓上偶然翻到一些舊照片。**2** [I] **a)** if an idea comes across to someone, they understand it clearly 被理解: *Your point really came across at the meeting.* 你在會議上的觀點確實被大家了解了。**b)** if someone comes across in a particular way, they give other people that feeling or opinion about them 給人的印象是: *He came across as being rather arrogant.* 他給人的印象是相當傲慢。| **come across well/badly** *I don't think I came across very well in the interview.* 我想我在那次面試中表現不太好。| **come across as (being) sth** *Sometimes you come across as being nervous.* 有時你顯得很緊張。

come across with sth *phr v* [T] *BrE spoken*【英口】**come across with the goods** to provide money or information when it is needed 給予所需錢財; 提供所需資料

come after sb *phr v* [T not in passive 不用被動態] to look for someone until you find them so you can hurt them, punish them, or get something from them 查找〔某人〕: *I heard the tax people are coming after him for unpaid VAT.* 我聽說稅務人員正為他未繳增值稅而找他。

come along *phr v* [I] **1 be coming along** *informal*

to be developing, or improving, especially in education or health【非正式】〔尤指教育或健康〕進步, 進展: [+with] *How's Martin coming along with his English?* 馬丁的英語學得怎麼樣了? | *Mother's coming along nicely, thank you.* 媽媽恢復得很好, 謝謝你。**2** to appear or arrive at a time you do not expect or cannot know about 出現; 來到; 發生: *Take any job opportunity that comes along.* 抓住任何工作機會。| *A bus should come along any minute now.* 公共汽車隨時都可能會來。**3 a)** to follow someone somewhere 跟隨: *Do you mind if I come along with you?* 如果我跟你來你會不會介意? **b)** to go somewhere with someone 跟〔某人〕去: *You go on ahead – I'll come along later.* 你先走 —— 我隨後就來。**4 come along!** *especially BrE spoken*【尤英口】**a)** used to tell someone to hurry up 快點, 趕快: *Come along now, children.* 現在得快點兒, 孩子們。**b)** used to encourage someone to try harder 加油, 加把勁: *Come along, surely someone knows the answer.* 盡量想一下, 肯定有人知道答案。

come apart *phr v* [I] **1** to split or fall into pieces without anyone using force 破裂; 崩潰, 垮掉: *The book just came apart in my hands.* 書在我手上就那麼散開來了。**2 come apart at the seams** to become unable to deal with a situation, or impossible to be dealt with 無力處置; 無法處理: *It felt as if his whole life was coming apart at the seams.* 看來他的整個人生似乎徹底完了。

come around *phr v* [I] **1** *AmE* to visit someone at home or at the place where they are【美】拜訪, 探訪: *Mind if I come around after work?* 介不介意我下班後順便拜訪一下? **2** *AmE* to change your opinion so that you now agree with someone【美】回心轉意, 改變觀點: *It took some persuading, but he finally came around.* 勸服他花了些功夫, 但他最後還是回心轉意了。**3** if a regular event comes round, it arrives or happens as usual〔如往常一樣〕發生; 降臨: *Thanksgiving comes around so quickly, doesn't it?* 這麼快又要到感恩節了, 不是嗎? **4** *AmE* to become conscious again【美】再度甦醒, 恢復知覺: *It was three weeks before she came around.* 三個星期以後她才甦醒過來。

come at sb/sth *phr v* [T not in passive 不用被動態] **1** to move towards someone in a threatening way 撲向, 向...逼近: *Meg came at me with a knife.* 梅格拿着刀向我衝過來。**2** if pieces of information, images etc come at you, you feel confused because there are a lot of them all at the same time〔大量資訊、圖像等〕湧向, 湧至 **3** *informal* to consider or deal with a problem【非正式】考慮; 處理〔問題〕: *We need to come at the problem from a different angle.* 我們需要換個角度來考慮這個問題。

come away *phr v* [I] **1** if part of something comes away from something else, it becomes separated when you are using it normally 脫落, 脫離: *I didn't break it! The handle came away in my hand.* 不是我折斷的! 這個手柄是我一碰就掉下來的。**2** to leave a place 離開〔某地〕: *Come away, Ben. There's going to be trouble.* 離開吧, 班恩, 會有麻煩的。

come back *phr v* [I] **1 it's all coming back to me** *spoken* to say that you are finally beginning to remember something【口】終於記起來 **2** to become fashionable or popular again 再度時髦, 重新流行: [+in] *Mini-skirts have come back in this season.* 迷你裙在本季又開始流行了。**3** to reply in a forceful, quick, and often unkind way; RETORT[1] 回嘴, 反駁, 駁斥: [+at] *I don't want anyone coming back at me over this.* 我不希望任何人在這一點上駁斥我。| [+with] *coming back with a nasty retort* 迅速有力地駁斥 —see also 另見 COMEBACK

come before sb *phr v* [T] *formal* to be sent to a person or group in authority in order to be considered or judged【正式】被提交...討論[處置]: *When you come before the judge, tell the whole truth.* 到法官面前, 你要講出所有的真相。

come between sb *phr v* [T not in passive 不用被動態] **1** to cause trouble between two or more people 離間, 挑撥: *Why should a little argument come between friends?* 為甚麼一點小爭吵要惹得朋友反目呢? **2** to prevent someone from giving enough attention to something 妨礙〔某人〕做〔某事〕: *I don't let anything come between me and my work.* 我不會讓任何事情妨礙我的工作。

come by sth *phr v* [T not in passive 不用被動態] **1** to obtain something that is rare or difficult to find 弄到, 獲得: *How on earth did you come by these tickets?* 你到底是怎麼弄到這些票的? | **be hard to come by** (=to be difficult to obtain or find) 難於得到; 難以發現 *Jobs are hard to come by these days.* 如今工作很難找。**2** *AmE* to make a short visit to a place on your way to somewhere else【美】順路拜訪, 順道看望: *I'll come by the house and get my stuff later, OK?* 我順便去一下那幢房子, 然後再去拿東西, 好嗎?

come down *phr v* [I]

1 ►BECOME LOWER 變低◄ **a)** if a price, level etc comes down, it becomes lower〔價格、水平等〕下降, 降低: *Wait to buy a house until interest rates come down.* 等利率調低時再去買房子吧。**b)** [+to] to offer or accept a lower price 提出[接受]低價: *Do you think the dealer would come down at all?* 你認為那個商人會降價嗎?

2 ►TRAVEL SOUTH 南行◄ to travel south or away from an important place such as a big city, to the place where the speaker is 南下,〔從大城市〕來到: *Come down for the weekend sometime.* 甚麼時候來這兒度週末。| [+to] *Are you coming down to Knoxville for Christmas?* 你來諾克斯維爾過聖誕嗎?

3 ►BUILDING 建築物◄ if a building comes down, it is destroyed by being pulled down〔建築〕被拆毀

4 come down on the side of also 又作 **come down in favour of** to decide to support someone or something after thinking about a problem for a long time〔深思熟慮之後〕決定支持某人[某事]

5 come down in sb's opinion/estimation to do something that makes someone respect you less 在某人心中地位下降: *John really came down in my opinion after that.* 從那以後約翰在我心目中的地位一落千丈。

6 come down in the world to become poorer or less successful than you used to be. 落泊, 潦倒; 失勢

7 come (back) down to earth to suddenly have to start dealing with ordinary practical problems after ignoring them for a time 跌回現實, 回到現實中: *"Charles!" He stopped day-dreaming and came back down to earth, startled.* "查理士!"他從白日夢中驚醒過來回到現實, 滿臉驚訝。

8 ►DRUGS 毒品◄ [+off/from] *informal* to stop being affected by a powerful drug such as HEROIN or LSD that you have taken【非正式】〔毒品藥性過後〕清醒過來

9 ►LEAVE UNIVERSITY 離開大學◄ [+from] *BrE* to leave a university, especially Oxford or Cambridge, after completing a period of study【英】〔尤指在牛津或劍橋大學結業後〕離校

come down on sb/sth *phr v* [T not in passive 不用被動態] to punish someone or criticize them severely 嚴懲; 痛斥: **come down on sb for doing sth** *My parents really came down on me for being out so late.* 我父母因為我在外留得太晚, 實實在在地教訓了我一頓。| **come down hard on** (=punish someone very severely) 非常嚴厲地懲罰 *We're going to come down hard on car theft.* 我們將嚴厲打擊盜車行為。| **come down like a ton of bricks** (=punish someone extremely severely) 極為嚴厲地懲罰〔某人〕

come down to sb/sth *phr v* [T not in passive 不用被動態] **1** if a complicated situation or problem comes down to something, it is the single most important point or choice 歸結為: **it comes down to** *It all came down to a choice between cutting wages or cutting staff.* 歸根到底, 就是在減薪或裁員之中作出選擇。**2** if a document, object, idea etc comes down to someone, it has survived from a long time ago until the present 落到…手中; 傳到…手裡: *The text which has come down to us is only a fragment of the original.* 那本課本到我們手裡的時候已經破爛不全了。

come down with sth *phr v* [T not in passive 不用被動態] *informal* to become ill with something infectious, especially something that is not very serious【非正式】染上〔病〕, 患〔小病〕: *I think I'm coming down with a cold.* 我想我得了感冒了。

come for sth/sb *phr v* [T] **1** to arrive to collect someone or something 來接; 來拿: *I've come for the carpet I ordered.* 我來取我訂購的毛毯。| *Shall I come for you at about six then?* 那麼我大概六點來接你好嗎? **2** to try to harm someone or take them away where they do not want to go 試圖傷害; 強行帶走: *When the secret police come for you, you'll talk, believe me!* 祕密警察來抓你的時候, 你肯定會説的, 相信我好了!

come forward *phr v* [I] **1** to offer yourself for a job, election etc 毛遂自薦, 自告奮勇, 主動爭取: **[+as]** *More women are coming forward as candidates than ever before.* 比起以前, 較多的女性主動自薦為候選人。| **come forward to do sth** *We need more volunteers to come forward to help.* 我們需要更多志願者來幫忙。**2** to offer help to someone in authority who needs it or has asked for it〔向有需要的官方人士〕提供幫助: **[+with]** *A young girl has come forward with a description of the attacker.* 一位年輕女孩對該襲擊者作了一番描述。

come from sb/sth *phr v* [T not in progressive 不用進行式] **1** to have started, been produced or first existed in a particular place, thing or time 始於; 產自; 來自: *Where do you come from originally?* 你老家是哪兒? | *Milk comes from cows.* 牛奶是從奶牛身上擠出來的。| *The passage she quoted came from Dickens.* 她引用的那段話出自狄更斯的作品。**2 coming from him/her/you etc** *spoken* used to criticize what someone has said because they say one thing and behave in the opposite way【口】可不是這麼回事〔用於指責某人表裡不一〕: *Pretentious? Me? That's rich, coming from you!* 自命不凡? 我? 真好笑, 你竟説這話! **3 come from doing sth** also 又作 **come of doing sth** to be the result of doing something 是某事的結果: *"I feel sick." "That's what comes from drinking too much."* "我覺得噁心。" "那是因為你喝太多的緣故。"

come in *phr v* [I]

1 ►ARRIVE 到達◄ to arrive or be received 到達; 接到: *As long as money's coming in, I'm happy.* 只要錢到了, 我就開心了。| *Reports are coming in of a bad earthquake in Mexico.* 傳來了墨西哥發生強烈地震的消息。| *Jenny's train comes in at eight.* 珍妮坐的火車八點到。

2 ►ENTER 進入◄ to enter a room or house 進入〔房間或屋子〕: *Come in! Take a seat.* 進來! 坐下吧。

3 ►BE INVOLVED 被捲入◄ **a)** to be involved in a plan, deal etc 捲入, 參與: *We need financial advice – that's where Kate comes in.* 我們需要財政諮詢 —— 那正是用得着凱特的地方。| **[+on]** *It'll cost you $1000 to come in on the scheme.* 參與該計劃將花掉你 1000 美元。**b)** to interrupt or enter a conversation or discussion 打斷[加入]談話[討論]: *Excuse me, can I come in here?* 對不起, 我能在這兒打斷一下嗎?

4 ►BECOME FASHIONABLE 變得時髦◄ to become fashionable or popular to use 流行起來; 開始被採用: *When platform shoes came in I thought they looked ridiculous.* 當厚底鞋剛流行時, 我覺得那種鞋看起來很可笑。—opposite 反義詞 **go out** (GO¹)

5 come in first/second etc to finish first, second etc in a race or competition〔在競賽中〕得第一名/第二名等: *I came in a long way behind everyone else.* 我遠遠地落在其他人身後。

6 come in useful/handy to be useful 有用, 用得上: *Bring some rope along; it might come in handy.* 帶上一些繩子, 可能派得上用場。

7 ►SEA 海◄ when the TIDE (=level of the sea) comes in, it rises〔潮〕漲 —opposite 反義詞 **go out** (GO¹) —see also 另見 **come in from the cold** (COLD² (3))

come in for sth *phr v* [T] **come in for criticism/blame/scrutiny** to be criticized, blamed etc for something 挨批評, 受責備: *The police came in for a lot of criticism for excess brutality.* 警方因為過度使用暴力而遭到大量批評。

come into sth *phr v* [T, not in passive 不用被動態] **1 come into money/a fortune** to receive money, land etc after someone has died; INHERIT (1) 繼承遺產 **2** to be involved in something 捲入〔某事〕: *Mary, a minor character, doesn't come into the story much.* 瑪麗是個配角, 在故事中沒有多少敍述。**3 luck/love/pride etc doesn't come into it!** *spoken* used to say that what someone has just mentioned is completely unimportant【口】沒有絲毫運氣/愛情/得意等: *"Your brother was very lucky to win." "It was skill – luck didn't come into it."* "你兄弟贏得真有運氣。" "那是技巧 —— 一點兒也不是運氣。" **4 come into fashion** to become a popular thing to wear or do 變得流行, 風行: *A-line skirts are coming into fashion again.* A 字裙重新流行起來了。**5 come into your own** to become very good, useful, or important in a particular situation〔在某一特殊情況下〕顯示出用處[重要性]: *On icy roads like these, a four-wheel drive really comes into its own.* 在這種冰封的路面上, 四輪驅動車是再合適不過的了。

come of sth *phr v* [T] to result from something 由於…而產生, 是…的結果: *Nothing came of my attempts to find her.* 我試圖找到她, 但沒有任何結果。| *"I'm fat." "That's what comes of not exercising."* "我很胖。" "那是由於不運動的結果。"

come off *phr v* **1** [I,T not in passive 不用被動態] to stop being connected to something or stop sticking to something 脱落, 掉落, 分開: *How did your button come off?* 你的鈕扣怎麼掉的? | **[+onto]** *Some wet paint came off onto her hands.* 一些濕漆沾到她的手上。| **come off sth** *The hook came off the wall when I hung my coat on it.* 我把外套掛到牆上的時候, 掛鉤掉下來了。**2 come off well/badly etc a)** to happen well, badly etc 發生, 進行良好/糟糕等: *Despite the problems, the wedding came off very well.* 儘管有這些問題, 婚禮還是進行得非常順利。**b)** to do something successfully, badly etc 做得成功/失敗: *The vice-president came off badly in the TV debate.* 那位副總統在電視辯論中表現糟糕。**3 come off it!** *spoken*【口】**a)** used to tell someone that you think they are lying, or saying something stupid 別撒謊了, 別説蠢話: *"I can't stand Claire." "Come off it, Joe, you asked her out last week!"* "我真受不了克萊爾。" "別裝蒜了, 喬, 你上星期還約她出去呢!" **b)** used to tell someone to stop doing or saying something annoying 別吵了, 別鬧了: *Come off it, Dave, that's enough now!* "別鬧了, 戴夫, 該鬧夠了!" **4** [I] to have the intended effect; succeed 達到預期效果; 成功: *Irene tried, but her joke didn't quite come off.* 艾琳試了一下, 但她的玩笑沒怎麼起到作用。**5 come off heroin/tranquillizers etc** to stop taking a drug that is ADDICTIVE (=makes you want to keep taking it) 戒除海洛因/鎮靜劑等

come on *phr v*

1 ►START 開始◄ [I] **a)** if a light or machine comes on, it starts working〔燈、機器等〕打開; 開動: *A dog started barking and lights came on in the house.* 一隻狗開始吠叫, 屋裡的燈亮了起來。**b)** if a slight illness comes on, you start to have it 患〔小病〕: *I can feel a headache coming on.* 我覺得頭有點疼。**c)** if a televi-

sion or radio programme comes on, it starts〔電視或電台節目〕開始, 啟播: *What time does the movie come on?* 電影甚麼時候開始? **d) it comes on to do sth** *BrE spoken* it starts to do something【英口】開始做〔某事〕, 開始發生: *It came on to rain.* 開始下雨了。
2 come on! *spoken*【口】**a)** used to tell someone to hurry up 快點: *Come on, we'll be late!* 快點兒, 我們要遲到了! **b)** also 又作 **come along!** *BrE*【英】used to encourage someone to try harder 加油, 加把勁: *Come on, guys, you can do it!* 加油, 小夥子們, 你們一定會成功! **c)** used to encourage someone to be more cheerful 高興一點, 樂觀一點: *Come on, let's see a smile.* 高興點, 笑一笑。**d)** used to show someone that you know that what they have just said was not true or right 別逗了; 算了吧, 得了吧: *Oh come on, don't lie to me!* 哦, 得啦, 別對我撒謊! **e)** used to make someone angry enough to want to fight you, or to do something they would not normally do〔用於挑釁對方〕來呀, 來吧: *Come on, then, hit me! I dare you!* 那就來吧, 打我呀! 諒你也不敢!
3 be coming on to be improving or making progress, especially in education or health〔尤指在教育或健康方面〕改善, 提高: [+**with**] *How are you coming on with your training?* 你的訓練進展得怎麼樣?
4 ▶DISCOVER 發現◀ [T **come on** sb/sth] to find or discover someone or something by chance 偶然找到, 偶然發現: *Turning the corner, I came on a group of picnickers.* 拐過街角, 我碰上一羣野餐的人。
5 come on strong *informal* to make it very clear to someone that you think they are sexually attractive【非正式】獻殷勤, 向〔某人〕表示強烈好感

come on to sb/sth *phr v* [T] **1** *spoken* to move forward in a speech or discussion to a new subject【口】〔演講或討論中〕轉到〔新話題〕: *I'll come on to this question in a few moments.* 待會兒我會談到這個問題。**2** *informal* if someone comes on to another person, they make it very clear that they are sexually interested in them【非正式】對〔某人〕表示好感, 獻殷勤

come out *phr v* [I]
1 ▶BECOME KNOWN 被知道◀ to become publicly known, especially after being hidden 顯露; 泄露: *It was several weeks before the truth of the matter came out.* 事實真相幾個星期以後才得到披露。
2 ▶BECOME CLEAR 變清楚◀ if a fact comes out when you consider something, it becomes much easier to see than it was before〔事實〕變得清楚: *The family resemblances come out strongly in the wedding photos.* 在結婚合照上, 這個家庭的成員明顯長得很像。
3 ▶BECOME AVAILABLE 成為有售的◀ if a book, record etc comes out, it becomes publicly available〔書、唱片等〕出版; 發行: *A second edition will come out next year.* 第二版將在明年出版。
4 ▶BE SAID 被說到◀ if something you say comes out in a particular way, that is how it sounds or how it is understood〔詞語、言語〕說出, 道出: *The words came out in little more than a whisper.* 這些話是悄悄說出的。| **come out all wrong** (=not sound the way you had intended) 與想表達的意思完全不同
5 ▶FINISH IN A PARTICULAR WAY 以特別的方式結束◀ **come out well/badly/ahead etc** to finish an action, process etc in a particular way or with a particular result 結果不錯/很糟/很成功等: *If you spend a little more time on your work now, you'll come out ahead in the end.* 如果你現在能在工作上多花一點兒時間, 你最終會成為佼佼者的。| *I can never get cakes to come out right.* 我從來都做不好蛋糕。
6 ▶SAY PUBLICLY 公開說◀ [always+adv/prep] to say publicly that you strongly support or oppose a particular plan, belief etc 公開表示〔贊同或反對的〕觀點: [+**for/against etc**] *The board of directors has come out strongly in favour of a merger.* 董事會強烈地公開表示支持一項合併。| **come out and say/state etc sth** *No one will come out and say it, but basically they can't stand her.* 沒人會出來說甚麼, 不過基本上他們都受不了她。
7 ▶DISAPPEAR 消失◀ if colour or a mark comes out, it disappears, especially because it has been washed〔尤指經過水洗後顏色、污漬〕褪去, 消失: *Ink stains will usually come out if you use a little methanol.* 如果你用一點兒甲醇, 墨水跡通常能洗掉。
8 ▶SUN 太陽◀ if the sun, moon, or stars come out, they appear in the sky〔太陽、月亮、星辰〕出現, 顯現
9 ▶FLOWER 花◀ if a flower comes out, it opens〔花朵〕開放: *I love it when the snowdrops start to come out.* 我喜歡開始綻放的雪花蓮。
10 ▶PHOTOGRAPH 照片◀ if a photograph or a subject of a photograph comes out, it looks the way the photographer wanted it to〔照片等〕顯像, 洗出: *Some of the wedding photos didn't come out.* 有些結婚照沖洗不出來。| *That sunset really came out well, didn't it?* 那張日落的照片的確照得很好, 不是嗎?
11 ▶HOMOSEXUAL 同性戀的◀ [+**to**] if someone comes out, they say openly that they are HOMOSEXUAL 公開宣布〔自己為同性戀〕
12 ▶WORKER 工作者◀ *BrE* to refuse to work; STRIKE² (1)【英】罷工, 舉行罷工: *The teachers are coming out in support of their pay claim.* 教師們正在舉行罷工, 以支持他們提出增加工資的要求。
13 ▶GIRL 女孩◀ *old-fashioned* if a young woman comes out, she is formally introduced into UPPER-CLASS society, usually at a dance【過時】〔尤指女孩通過舞會〕正式進入上流社交界

come out in sth *phr v* [T not in passive 不用被動態] *BrE*【英】**come out in spots/a rash etc** to become partly covered by marks because you are ill or sensitive to particular foods or drugs〔因生病或過敏而〕出疹子: *If I eat eggs, I come out in a rash.* 我一吃雞蛋身上就出疹子。

come out with sth *phr v* [T not in passive 不用被動態] *informal* to say something, especially suddenly or in a way that is not expected【非正式】〔尤指突然地或出乎意料地〕說出, 提出: *Tanya came out with a really stupid remark.* 坦亞突然冒出一句蠢話。

come over *phr v* **1** [I] **a)** to visit someone's house or the place where they are 來訪, 拜訪: *Can I come over and see you on Friday night?* 我可以星期五晚上來拜訪你嗎? **b)** to make a journey, from another country and travelling east or west, to a place where you are now〔從別國、遠方等〕過來: [+**to/from**] *When did your family first come over to America?* 你的家人第一次來美國是甚麼時候? **2** [T **come over sb** not in passive 不用被動態] if a strong feeling comes over someone, they suddenly experience it 突然感到: *A wave of sleepiness came over me.* 我突然覺得很睏。| **not know what has come over sb** (=be unable to explain someone's strange behaviour) 無法解釋某人的古怪行為 *I'm sorry I was so rude – I don't know what came over me!* 對不起, 我不該那麼失禮 —— 我不知道自己是怎麼了! **3** [I] **a)** if an idea comes over to someone, they understand it clearly〔觀點〕被理解 **b)** if someone comes over in a particular way, they give other people that feeling or opinion about them 表現為; 顯得: [+**as**] *I don't think I came over as a confident manager at the interview.* 我覺得我在面試中表現得不像個自信的經理人。**4 come over (all) shy/nervous etc** *informal especially BrE* to become shy, nervous etc【非正式, 尤英】變得害羞/緊張等

come round *BrE*【英】*phr v* [I] **1** to visit someone at home or at the place where they are 順路來訪, 拜訪: *Why don't you come round for lunch?* 你為甚麼不順道來吃午飯呢? **2** to change your opinion so that you now agree with someone 回心轉意; 改變立場[觀點]: [+**to**] *I'm sure Bradley will come round to our way of thinking.* 我肯定布萊德里會改變立場, 同意我們的想法的。**3** if a regular event comes round, it arrives or happens as usual

〔如往常〕降臨, 發生: *Your birthday's coming round again, isn't it?* 你的生日又快到了, 是不是? **4** to become conscious again 恢復知覺, 甦醒: *Kim was muttering, and seemed to be coming round.* 金正在咕噥着發出聲音, 看來要甦醒了。

come through *phr v* **1 a)** [I] if a piece of news, a result etc comes through, it becomes known or heard 〔消息、結果等〕公開; 被知曉: *Listen! There's something coming through on the radio now.* 聽! 現在收音機裡有甚麼消息要播送。| *We're still waiting for our exam results to come through.* 我們仍然在等待考試成績公佈。**b)** if an official document comes through, it arrives 〔官方文件的〕到達: *Has your giro come through yet?* 你的銀行轉賬到了嗎? **2** [T **come through** sth] to continue to live, exist, be strong, or succeed after a difficult or dangerous time 經歷…而活着; 安然度過: *We're so relieved that Bill came through the operation all right.* 比爾的手術成功了, 這讓我們大大鬆了口氣。| *Amazingly, our house came through the storm without much damage.* 我們的房子在那場暴風雨中沒受多大損壞, 這真是奇蹟。

come through with sth *phr v* [T] to give people something important, especially when they have been worried that you would not produce it in time 交出; 交付; 提供: *Our representative in Hong Kong finally came through with the figures.* 我們在香港的代表最終提供了數據。

come to *phr v*

1 ►REACH A STATE 達到某種狀態◄ [T **come to** sth] **a) it has come to this** *spoken* used to express shock that a situation has become so bad【口】竟糟到這種地步, 竟如此糟糕: *"I want back all the jewellery I gave you." "So, it's come to this, has it, our wonderful marriage?"* "我想要回所有我給你的首飾。" "那麼, 我們美滿的婚姻已經這麼糟了嗎?" **b)** to reach a particular state or position, especially a bad one 落到…田地; 至於…地步: *All those years, and in the end it came to nothing.* 那麼多年, 最後卻落得一事無成。| *If it comes to a fight, you can depend on me!* 如果要打架的話, 你可以放心, 有我呢! **c) what's it all coming to?/what's the world coming to?** *spoken* used to show how shocked or disappointed something has made you feel【口】這是怎麼回事? 這有甚麼意思? 〔用於表示震驚或失望〕

2 come to £20/$30 etc to be a total amount of £20, $30 etc 總額為 20 英鎊/30 美元等: *That comes to £23.50, madam.* 總共 23.50 英鎊, 夫人。

3 [T not in passive 不用被動態] if a thought or idea comes to you, you realize or remember it, especially suddenly 〔想法、主張等〕突然被…憶起, 被想起: *The solution came to him in a flash.* 他靈機一動, 想到了解決方法。| *I've forgotten her name, but maybe it'll come to me later.* 我忘了她的名字, 不過以後也許會想起來的。

4 [I] to become conscious again 恢復知覺, 甦醒: *When Jack came to, he was lying in an alley and his wallet was gone.* 傑克醒過來的時候, 他正躺在一個巷子裡, 錢包已經不見了。

5 when it comes to *informal*【非正式】**a)** on the subject of 涉及, 談到: *I can use a computer, but when it comes to repairing them, I know nothing.* 我會使用電腦, 但若談到修理, 我就一竅不通了。**b)** when you are dealing with something 處理, 處置: *When it comes to relationships, everyone makes mistakes.* 在處理人際關係的時候, 每個人都會犯錯誤的。

6 have sth coming (to you) *informal* to deserve to be punished or to have something bad happen to you【非正式】(你) 活該遭報應: *"Ron's been expelled from school." "Well, he had it coming."* "羅恩被學校開除了。" "哦, 他活該。" | *I hope you get what's coming to you, you sod!* 你這個卑鄙的傢伙, 我希望你會遭報應!

7 come to yourself *old-fashioned informal* to gain control of your emotions again【過時, 非正式】重新控制自己, 恢復自制力

come under sth *phr v* [T not in passive 不用被動態] **1** to be governed, controlled, or influenced by something 受…管轄[支配, 影響]: *Your case comes under the jurisdiction of the county courts.* 你的案子由郡法庭進行審理。| *All doctors come under the same rules of professional conduct.* 所有醫生都要遵守同樣的職業行為規範。**2 come under attack/fire/scrutiny** to be attacked, shot at etc 被襲擊/槍擊/監視: *Some members in the party have come under attack from radicals in recent weeks.* 最近幾週, 該黨的一些成員遭到激進分子攻擊。**3** if a piece of information comes under a particular title, subject etc, it can be found there in a book, library etc 可在…之下查到; 列在…下: *'Phobias' – that will come under Psychology in section twelve.* "恐懼症" —— 這個詞可以在第十二節 "心理學" 下查到。—see also 另見 **come under the hammer** (HAMMER¹ (2))

come up *phr v* [I]

1 ►APPEAR OR HAPPEN 出現或發生◄ a) to be mentioned or suggested as something to be considered or given attention 被提到, 被討論, 被考慮: *A lot of new questions came up at the meeting.* 在此次會議上, 許多新問題被提了出來。| *Your name came up in our conversation once or twice.* 你的名字在我們談話時被提到一兩次。**b) be coming up** if an important event is coming up, it is being arranged and will happen soon 即將開始, 即將到來: *Don't you have a birthday coming up soon?* 你的生日不是快到了嗎? **c)** if a legal case comes up, it is dealt with in a court of law 開庭審理: *Your case comes up next week.* 你的案件下週開庭審理。**d)** if a job or position comes up, it becomes available 〔工作或職位〕出現空缺: *A vacancy has come up in the accounts department.* 會計部空出了一個職位。

2 ►TRAVEL NORTH 北行◄ to travel north or towards an important place such as a big city 北上, 去大城市: [+to] *Why don't you come up to New York for the weekend?* 你為甚麼不去紐約度週末呢?

3 ►MOVE NEAR 靠近◄ to move near someone or something, especially by walking 〔尤指步行〕走近: [+to/behind etc] *Come up to the front of the room so everyone can see you.* 走到房間前面來, 讓大家都能看見你。| *Aagh! Don't come up behind me like that!* 哎喲! 別那樣從後面走近我。

4 ►SUN/MOON 太陽/月亮◄ a) when the sun or moon comes up, it rises 〔太陽或月亮〕升起: *The sun was coming up by the time I finished the essay.* 我完成那篇文章的時候, 太陽已冉冉升起。**b)** when a plant comes up, it begins to be seen above the ground 〔植物從地上〕長出, 發芽: *Look, the daffodils are coming up.* 看, 水仙花發芽了。**c)** when food comes up, it rises back from your stomach after being swallowed 〔食物〕嘔出, 吐出: *I suddenly felt nauseous and then the whole lot came up.* 我突然覺得噁心, 剛吃的東西一股腦兒全吐了出來。

5 ►PROBLEM 問題◄ if a problem or difficulty comes up, it suddenly appears or starts to affect you 突然出現〔問題、困難〕: **sth comes up** *Sorry I can't go with you – something has suddenly come up.* 對不起, 我不能跟你一起去了 —— 我突然有急事。

6 coming (right) up! *spoken* used to say that something, especially food or drink, will be ready very soon【口】〔尤指食品、飲料〕馬上就來, 立刻就好: *"Two martinis, please." "Coming up!"* "請來兩杯馬丁尼。" "馬上就來!"

7 come up in the world to become richer or more successful in society 更富有, 更成功: *She had come up in the world since her days on the flower stall.* 自從她擺了個花攤以來, 她的日子過得越來越優裕了。

8 ►BEGIN AT UNIVERSITY 開始上大學◄ *BrE* to begin studying at a university, especially Oxford or Cambridge【英】〔尤指在牛津或劍橋〕入學, 就讀

come up against sth/sb *phr v* [T not in passive 不用被動態] to have to deal with opposition, problems, unfairness etc; ENCOUNTER[1] (1) 得處理[面對]〔反對意見、問題或不公正〕: *You've got no idea of what you're going to come up against.* 你想不到將會面對甚麼。

come up for sth *phr v* **1** [T] **come up for review/re-examination etc** to have a fixed time in the future when something will be examined, changed etc 定期回顧/檢查等: *The new regulations come up for review in April.* 這些新規則在四月份將予以檢討。
2 come up for re-election/selection to reach the time when people have to vote about whether you should continue in your political position 到重新選舉期

come upon sth/sb *phr v* [T not in passive 不用被動態] *literary* to find or discover something or someone by chance【文】〔偶然〕遇見; 發現: *Suddenly I came upon a clearing in the wood.* 我在林中突然發現一片空地。

come up to sth *phr v* [T] to be as good as something else or as an expected standard 比得上; 達到〔標準〕: *This doesn't come up to the standard of your usual work.* 這次你的工作不及你一貫的水準。—see also 另見 **not come/be up to scratch** (SCRATCH[2] (3))

come up with sth *phr v* [T] **1** to think of an idea, plan, reply etc 想出, 提出〔主意、計劃、回答等〕: *Is that the best excuse you can come up with?* 那就是你能想出的最好藉口嗎? | *Someone had better come up with a solution fast.* 最好有人能盡快想出解決辦法。**2** to produce a sum of money that is needed 提供〔所需錢款〕: *How am I supposed to come up with $10,000?* 我怎麼能拿得出一萬美元來?

C

come[2] *n* [U] *slang* a man's SEMEN (=the liquid he produces during sex)【俚】精液

come·back /ˈkʌmˌbæk; ˈkʌmbæk/ *n* [C usually singular 一般用單數] **1 make/stage a comeback** if a person, activity, style etc makes a comeback, they become popular again after being unpopular for a long time 東山再起; 復原: *The miniskirt made a comeback in the late 1980s.* 迷你裙在20世紀80年代末期又再度流行。**2** a quick reply that is often clever, funny, and insulting; RETORT[2] (1)〔機智、幽默或尖刻的〕回答; 反駁: *I couldn't think of a good comeback.* 我想不出甚麼巧妙的回答。—see also 另見 **come back** (COME[1]) **3** a way of getting payment or a reward for something wrong or unfair that has been done to you 得到補償[補救]的方法: *Check your contract carefully, or you may have no comeback if something goes wrong.* 仔細檢查一下你的合同, 否則如果出了甚麼差錯, 你可能得不到任何補償。

co·me·di·an /kəˈmidiən; kəˈmiːdiən/ *n* [C] **1** someone whose job is to tell jokes and make people laugh〔講笑話或演滑稽戲的〕演員 **2** *old use* someone who plays funny characters in plays or films【舊】喜劇演員; 滑稽演員

co·me·di·enne /kəˌmidiˈɛn; kəˌmiːdiˈen/ *n* [C] *old-fashioned* a female comedian【過時】女喜劇演員; 女滑稽演員

come·down /ˈkʌmˌdaun; ˈkʌmdaʊn/ *n* [C usually singular 一般用單數] *informal* a situation that is not as good, important, interesting etc as the situation you had previously【非正式】落泊, 潦倒; 失勢: *The 'King of Wall Street' is bankrupt! What a comedown!* "華爾街之王"破產了! 真是落魄! —see also 另見 **come down** (COME[1])

com·e·dy /ˈkɑmədɪ; ˈkɒmədi/ *n* **1** [C,U] a play, film etc that is intended to entertain people and make them laugh 喜劇: *a comedy starring Eddie Murphy* 由〔美國黑人喜劇演員〕艾迪·墨菲主演的一部喜劇 | *Come to Comedy Night at the Albion!* 到阿爾比恩的喜劇之夜去! **2** [U] the quality in something such as a book or play that makes people laugh; HUMOUR[1] (1) 喜劇性, 喜劇成分; 幽默: *Can't you see the comedy of the situation?* 你不覺得這種情況滑稽嗎? —see also 另見 BLACK COMEDY, SITUATION COMEDY

comedy of man·ners /,... · '../ *n* [C] a comedy that makes the behaviour of a particular group, especially the UPPER CLASS, seem silly〔諷刺某一羣體, 尤其是上流社會的〕風俗喜劇

come-hith·er /,· '../ *adj old-fashioned* **come-hither look/eyes** a way of looking at someone that shows you think they are sexually attractive【過時】挑逗的眼神/誘惑的目光

come·ly /ˈkʌmlɪ; ˈkʌmli/ *adj literary* a comely woman has an attractive appearance【文】〔女性〕標致的, 秀麗的 —**comeliness** *n* [U]

come-on /'· ·/ *n* [C] **1** *informal* something that a business offers cheaply or free in order to persuade you to buy something【非正式】〔商業的〕促銷品; 贈品: *The competition for a free trip is just a come-on.* 爭取免費旅行的比賽不過是一種商業促銷行為。**2 give sb the come-on** *BrE spoken* to behave in a way that shows someone very clearly that you are sexually interested in them【英口】勾引, 挑逗 —see also 另見 **come on** (COME[1])

com·er /ˈkʌmə; ˈkʌmə/ *n* **all comers** *informal* anyone who is interested, especially anyone who wants to take part in a competition【非正式】參加者; 來者: *The contest is open to all comers.* 該項競賽對所有人開放。—see also 另見 LATECOMER, NEWCOMER

co·mes·ti·bles /kəˈmɛstəblz; kəˈmestəbəlz/ *n* [plural] *formal* food【正式】食物, 食品

com·et /ˈkɑmɪt; ˈkɒmət/ *n* [C] an object in space like a bright ball with a long tail that moves around the sun 彗星: *Halley's comet* 哈雷彗星

come·up·pance /kʌmˈʌpəns; kʌmˈʌpəns/ *n* [singular] *informal* a punishment or something bad that happens to you which you really deserve【非正式】應得的懲罰; 報應: **get your comeuppance** *You'll get your comeuppance one day, you'll see!* 瞧着吧, 總有一天你會得到報應的!

com·fort[1] /ˈkʌmfət; ˈkʌmfət/ *n* 3

1 ►EMOTIONAL 情感的◄ [U] a feeling of being more calm, cheerful, or hopeful after you have been worried or unhappy 安慰, 慰藉: *I looked to my family for comfort when things got difficult at work.* 工作中遇到困難時, 我向家人尋求安慰。| **bring/give comfort** *The service is there to give the advice and comfort people need.* 那裡的服務在於為人們提供所需的建議及撫慰。| **take/draw/derive comfort from** *Mrs. Oliphant drew great comfort from the familiar hymns.* 奧里芬特夫人從熟悉的聖歌中得到極大的安慰。| **it's no/some/any comfort** *If it's any comfort, we didn't win anything either.* 就算有點安慰, 我們也沒有贏得甚麼。

2 ►PHYSICAL 身體的◄ [U] a feeling of being physically relaxed and satisfied, so that nothing is hurting you, making you feel too hot or cold etc 舒適感, 滿足感: **for comfort** *I usually dress for comfort rather than style.* 我的衣着通常講究舒適而非追求時尚。| **too cold/hot/high etc for comfort** (=physically unpleasant for a particular reason) 因太冷/熱/高等而身體不適 | **in comfort/in the comfort of** *Now you can watch your favorite movies in the comfort of your own home.* 現在你可以舒舒服服地在自己家裡看你最喜歡的電影了。| **built/made/designed for comfort** *a new climbing boot designed for comfort and safety* 一種新型舒適安全的登山鞋

3 ►MONEY/POSSESSIONS 錢/財產◄ [U] a way of living in which you have all the possessions, money etc that you need or want 舒適, 安逸: *I intend to retire in comfort!* 我想在退休後過上安逸的生活!

4 comforts [plural] the things that make your life more pleasant and comfortable, especially things that are not necessary 使生活舒適之物; 奢侈品: **all the comforts of home** *The beach cabin has all the comforts of home.* 那座海濱小屋有一切家用舒適品。| **material comforts** (=money and possessions) 金錢, 財產 | **creature comforts** (=things such as comfortable chairs and warm rooms) 物質享受〈如舒適的椅子、温暖的房間〉*Alicia was too fond of her creature comforts to go camping.* 艾麗西亞十分喜愛家裡的舒適享受, 不想去露營。

5 ▶SB/STH THAT HELPS 有用的人/物◀ [C] someone or something that helps you feel happier or calmer when you have been worried or unhappy 安慰者; 慰藉物: **be a comfort to** *Jerry's been a real comfort to me since Max died.* 馬克斯去世後, 傑里成了我真正的安慰。| **comfort eating/shopping etc** (=eating etc that makes you feel better) 讓人好受[給人撫慰]的飲食/購物等 | **it's a comfort** *It's a comfort to know there's someone to keep an eye on the kids.* 知道有人照料着那些孩子, 真令人安慰。

6 too close/near etc for comfort something that is too close for comfort makes you feel worried, unhappy, or uncomfortable, because it is dangerous in some way〔因危險而〕使人憂慮[不快, 不適]的事情: *The cars were whizzing past us much too close for comfort.* 汽車緊貼着我們身邊呼嘯而過, 令我們提心吊膽。

7 cold/small comfort a small piece of good news that does not make you feel better about a bad situation 不起作用的安慰: *The promise that I might one day be rehoused was cold comfort.* 對於將來可給我提供新居所的承諾, 並不令人覺得欣慰。—**comfortless** *adj*

comfort² *v* [T] to make someone feel calmer and more hopeful by being kind and sympathetic to them when they are worried or unhappy 安慰, 慰問: *Nothing I could do or say could comfort Diane when her son died.* 戴安娜的兒子死後, 我不論做甚麼或說甚麼都無法安慰她。—**comforting** *adj* —**comfortingly** *adv*

2 3 **com·for·ta·ble** /ˈkʌmfətəbḷ; ˈkʌmftəbəl/ *adj*

1 ▶FEELING PHYSICALLY COMFORTABLE 身體感覺舒適的◀ feeling physically relaxed and satisfied, without feeling any pain or being too hot, cold etc〔人〕舒適的, 舒坦的; 滿意的: *I was so comfortable and warm in bed I didn't want to get up.* 牀上又舒服又暖和, 我一點都不想起來。| **make yourself comfortable** *Sit down and make yourself comfortable while I put the kettle on.* 請坐, 別客氣, 我燒點開水。

2 ▶CLOTHES/FURNITURE/PLACES ETC 衣服/家具/地方等◀ making you feel physically relaxed and satisfied 舒適的; 令人滿意的: *Joyce has a comfortable apartment in Portland.* 喬伊絲在波特蘭有一所舒適的公寓。| *comfortable shoes* 舒服的鞋 | **comfortable to sit/lie/stand on etc** *Is your chair comfortable to sit on?* 你的椅子坐上去舒服嗎?

3 ▶NOT WORRIED 不擔憂的◀ if you are comfortable with an idea, person, or activity, you do not feel worried about it 放心的; 欣慰的: *I'm not comfortable with the idea of you having a motorcycle.* 你騎摩托車這主意讓我不放心。| **feel comfortable** *an office environment you can feel comfortable in* 令人舒心的辦公環境

4 ▶MONEY 錢◀ having enough money to live on without worrying about paying for things 寬裕的, 小康的: *The Austins aren't rich, but they're comfortable.* 奧斯汀一家並不富有, 但他們手頭還算寬裕。

5 ▶ILL/INJURED 生病的/受傷的◀ if someone who is ill or injured is comfortable, they are not in too much pain〔患者或傷者〕感覺不太疼痛的

6 ▶RACE/COMPETITION 賽跑/競賽◀ a number of points or a distance that will allow you to win easily 輕鬆獲勝的, 輕鬆贏得的: *Cantona scored to give United a comfortable 3-0 lead at half-time.* 坎通納的進球使得聯隊在上半場結束時以三比零輕鬆領先。

7 ▶BELIEF/IDEA/OPINION 信仰/念頭/意見◀ a belief etc that you do not think very seriously about and that ignores problems or difficulties〔信仰等〕忽略困難的; 不嚴謹的: *the comfortable middle class belief that everyone who works hard will succeed* 認為每個人只要努力工作就會成功的過於樂觀的中產階級信念 —**comfortably** *adv* —see also 另見 UNCOMFORTABLE

com·fort·er /ˈkʌmfətə; ˈkʌmfətə/ *n* [C] **1** someone who comforts you 安慰者, 慰問者 **2** *AmE* a cover for a bed that is filled with a soft warm material such as feathers【美】〔鋪牀的〕被子; DUVET *BrE*【英】**3** *old use* a warm SCARF【舊】暖和的圍巾

com·fy /ˈkʌmfɪ; ˈkʌmfi/ *adj spoken* comfortable【口】舒適的, 舒服的: *a comfy chair* 舒適的椅子

com·ic¹ /ˈkɑmɪk; ˈkɒmɪk/ *adj* amusing you and making you want to laugh 滑稽的, 好笑的: *a comic performance* 滑稽表演 | **comic writer/actress/performer etc** (=someone who writes or performs things that make you laugh) 喜劇作家/女演員/演出者等 | **comic relief** (=a situation in a serious story that makes you relax a little because it is funny)〔情節嚴肅的故事中的〕喜劇情節 | **comic verse/song etc** (=a song etc that entertains you and makes you laugh) 滑稽詩/歌曲等 —opposite 反義詞 TRAGIC (2)

comic² also 又作 **comic book** /ˈ·· ·/ *AmE*【美】*n* [C] **1** a magazine for children that tells a story using comic strips 連環漫畫, 連環漫畫冊 **2** someone whose job is to tell jokes and make people laugh; COMEDIAN 喜劇演員: *a stand-up comic* 一位說笑話的喜劇演員

com·i·cal /ˈkɑmɪkḷ; ˈkɒmɪkəl/ *adj* behaviour or situations that are comical are funny in a strange or unexpected way 滑稽的, 荒誕可笑的: *The cat looked so comical with the bow on its head!* 那隻貓頭上打着個蝴蝶結, 看上去太滑稽了! —**comically** /-klɪ; -kli/ *adv*

comic op·e·ra /ˌ·· ˈ···/ *n* [C,U] an OPERA with an amusing story in which the singers speak as well as sing 喜歌劇

comic strip /ˈ·· ·/ *n* [C] a series of drawn pictures inside boxes that tell a story 連環漫畫 —compare 比較 CARTOON (1)

com·ing¹ /ˈkʌmɪŋ; ˈkʌmɪŋ/ *n* **1 the coming of sth/sb** the time when something new begins, especially something that will cause a lot of changes 某事物/某人的到來[降臨]: *With the coming of railways, new markets opened up.* 隨着鐵路的建成, 新市場開放了。**2 comings and goings** *informal* the movements of people as they arrive at and leave places【非正式】來來往往, 進進出出: *Mrs Williams next door knows all the comings and goings of everyone in the neighbourhood.* 隔壁的威廉斯夫人清楚地知道每個鄰居的進進出出。

coming² *adj* [only before noun 僅用於名詞前] *formal* happening soon【正式】即將發生的: *the clouds of the coming storm* 暴風雨前的烏雲 —see also 另見 UP-AND-COMING

coming of age /ˌ·· · ˈ·/ *n* [singular] the point in a young person's life, usually the age of 18 or 21, at which their society considers them to be an adult 成年〔通常為 18 歲或 21 歲〕

com·ma /ˈkɑmə; ˈkɒmə/ *n* [C] the mark (,) used in writing and printing to show a short pause 逗號 —see also 另見 INVERTED COMMA —see picture at 參見 PUNCTUATION MARK 圖

com·mand¹ /kəˈmænd; kəˈmɑːnd/ *n*

1 ▶ORDER 命令◀ [C] an order that should be obeyed 命令; 指示: *Fire when I give the command.* 我一下命令就開火。

2 ▶CONTROL 控制◀ [U] the control of a group of people or a situation 指揮; 管轄; 控制: **be in command** *Judge Hathaway was in complete command of the courtroom.* 哈撒韋法官完全控制了法庭的局面。| **have sth under your command** *We suspect that Don Sacco* *has several gangs under his command.* 我們懷疑唐·薩科手下有幾幫匪徒。| **take command** (=begin controlling and making decisions) 掌握，開始控制 *Janet took command of the situation and got everyone out of the building safely.* 珍尼特控制了局勢並讓所有人安全撤離那棟建築。| **at sb's command** (=available to be used by someone whenever they want) 服從某人，聽從某人吩咐 *Each congressman has a large staff at his command.* 每位國會議員都有一大羣下屬聽從吩咐。| **have command** *Flynn had command of a squadron on the Western Front.* 弗林在西線指揮一支中隊。

3 ▶MILITARY 軍事的◀ [C also+plural verb *BrE* 英] **a)** a part of an army, navy etc that is controlled separately and has a particular job 部隊；兵團：*pilots of the Southern Air Command* 南方空軍團的飛行員 **b)** a group of officers or officials who give orders 司令部；指揮部：*Are you criticizing the High Command?* 你是在指責最高司令部嗎？**c)** the group of soldiers that an officer is in control of〔同一軍官統率的〕部隊，軍隊

4 have (a) command of to have a good knowledge of something, especially a subject such as a language 掌握，精通〔尤指語言〕：*Jill has an impressive command of French.* 吉爾精通法語，令人印象深刻。

5 ▶COMPUTER 電腦◀ [C] an instruction to a computer to do something〔電腦的〕指令

6 at your command if you have a particular skill at your command, you are able to use that skill well and easily〔技能等〕嫻熟，運用自如：*a carpenter with years of experience at his command* 一位經驗老到的木匠

7 be in command of yourself/your faculties to be able to control your emotions and thoughts 控制自己〔指情緒、思想等〕：*Kathleen walked in, tall, slim, confident and in total command of herself.* 凱瑟琳走了進來，她身材修長，滿懷自信，神態自如。

command[2] *v*

1 ▶ORDER 命令◀ [I,T] to tell someone officially to do something, especially if you are a military leader, a king etc〔尤指軍官、國王等〕命令，下令：**command sb to do sth** *Captain Picard commanded the crew to report to the main deck.* 皮卡特船長命令全體船員到主甲板上集合。| **command that** *The General commanded that the regiment attack at once.* 將軍下令該團立刻發起進攻。

2 ▶LEAD THE MILITARY 率領軍隊◀ [I,T] to be responsible for giving orders to a group of people in the army, navy etc 統率；指揮〔軍隊〕：*He commands the 4th Battalion of the Scots Guard.* 他統率蘇格蘭衛隊第四營。

3 ▶DESERVE AND GET 應得並獲得◀ [T] to get something such as attention or respect because you are important or popular 贏得；博得〔尊敬、注意等〕：*Dr. Young commands a great deal of respect as a surgeon.* 揚醫生是德高望重的外科醫生。| *"Supermodels" can command extremely high fees.* "超級模特兒"能夠獲取巨額報酬。

4 ▶CONTROL 控制◀ [T] to control something 對…有支配權；掌握：*The party which commands a majority of seats in Parliament forms the government.* 由在議會擁有多數席位的黨派組成政府。

5 ▶VIEW 景色◀ if a place commands a view, you can see something clearly from it 俯瞰；眺望；清楚地看到：*The Ramses Hilton commands a magnificent view of Cairo.* 在拉姆西斯－希爾頓酒店滿眼都是開羅的美景。

com·man·dant /ˌkɑmənˋdænt; ˌkɒmənˈdænt/ *n* [C] the chief officer in charge of a military organization 司令官，指揮官：*the commandant of a prison camp* 監獄長

com·man·deer /ˌkɑmənˋdɪr; ˌkɒmənˈdɪə/ *v* [T] to take someone else's property for your own use, especially during the war〔尤指戰爭時期〕徵用，強徵〔私人財產〕：*The local hotel was commandeered for the wounded.* 當地的賓館被徵用，以安置傷員。

com·mand·er /kəˋmændɚ; kəˈmɑːndə/ *n* [C] **1** an officer of any rank who is in charge of a group of soldiers or a particular military activity 指揮官，長官：*the American Commander, General Otis* 美軍指揮官奧帝斯將軍 | *our platoon commander* 我們的排長 **2** a high rank in the navy, or someone who holds this rank 海軍中校 —see table on page C6 參見C6頁附錄 **3** a British police officer of high rank 英國高級警官 —see also 另見 WING COMMANDER

commander in chief /·,·· · ˈ·/ *n* [C usually singular 一般用單數] someone of high rank who is in control of all the military organizations in a country or of a specific military activity 總司令；最高統帥：*The Queen is Commander in Chief of the British armed forces.* 女王是英國軍隊的最高統帥。

com·mand·ing /kəˋmændɪŋ; kəˈmɑːndɪŋ/ *adj* **1** having the authority or position that allows you to give orders 指揮的，統率的：*a commanding officer* 指揮官 | *Japan's commanding economic position* 日本在經濟領域的領導地位 **2** making people respect and obey you 令人肅然起敬的；威嚴的：*Papa's commanding presence* 爸爸那威嚴的氣度 **3** a commanding view or position is one from which you can clearly see a long way 居高臨下的，視野開闊的 **4** being in a position from which you are likely to win a race or competition easily 遙遙領先的，勝券在握的：*a commanding lead* 遙遙領先

com·mand·ment /kəˋmændmənt; kəˈmɑːndmənt/ *n* [C] **1** one of the ten rules given by God in the Bible that tell people how they must behave 戒律〔《聖經》所指的十誡之一〕**2** *literary* a command【文】命令

command mod·ule /·ˈ· ,··/ *n* [C] *technical* the part of a space vehicle from which its activities are controlled【術語】〔太空船的〕指令艙，指揮艙

com·man·do /kəˋmændo; kəˈmɑːndəʊ/ *n plural* **commandos** or **commandoes** [C] **1** a soldier or a small group of soldiers who are specially trained to make quick attacks into enemy areas 突擊隊(員)：*a commando raid* 突擊隊的一次偷襲 **2 the commandoes** a UNIT (1) of the British Royal Marines〔英國皇家海軍陸戰隊的〕小隊

command per·form·ance /·,· ·ˈ··/ *n* [C usually singular 一般用單數] a special performance at a theatre that is given at the request of a king, president etc 奉命專場演出；御前演出

command post /·ˈ· ·/ *n* [C] the place from which military leaders and their officers control activities 指揮部，司令部

com·mem·o·rate /kəˋmɛməˌret; kəˈmeməreɪt/ *v* [T] to do something to show that you remember and respect someone important or an important event in the past 慶祝，為…舉行紀念活動：*a parade to commemorate the town's bicentenary* 慶祝該鎮建鎮200週年的遊行 —**commemorative** /kəˋmɛmərətɪv; kəˈmemərətɪv/ *adj*: *a commemorative plaque* 紀念牌匾

com·mem·o·ra·tion /kəˌmɛməˋreʃən; kəˌmeməˈreɪʃən/ *n* [U] something that makes you remember and respect someone important or an important event in the past 紀念；紀念活動：**in commemoration of** *a service in commemoration of those who died in the war* 紀念戰爭死難者的儀式

com·mence /kəˋmɛns; kəˈmens/ *v* [I,T] *formal* to begin or to start something【正式】開始；着手：[+with] *A trial commences with opening statements.* 審判以宣讀開庭詞開始。| **commence sth** *Your first evaluation will be six months after you commence employment.* 你工作六個月後，將接受第一次業務評估。| **commence doing sth** *You may commence reading, Jeremy.* 傑里米，你可以開始看書了。

Frequencies of **commence**, **start** and **begin** in spoken and written English 英語口語和書面語中 commence, start 和 begin 的使用頻率

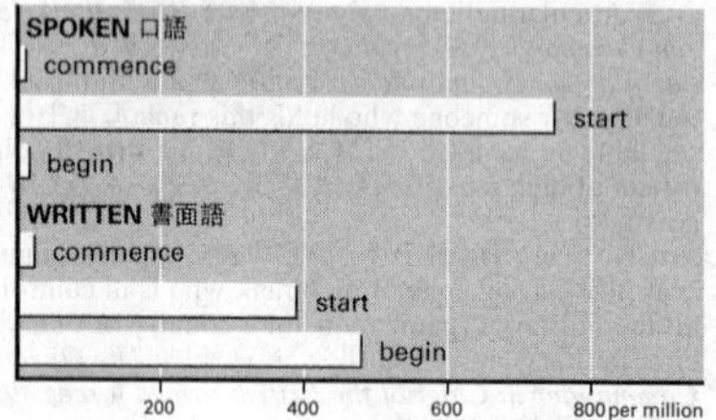

Based on the British National Corpus and the Longman Lancaster Corpus 據英國國家語料庫和朗文蘭卡斯特語料庫

This graph shows that in spoken English **start** is the most common of the three verbs. In written English **begin** is the most common. **Commence**, a formal word, is the least common of the three verbs in spoken and written English. 本圖表顯示, 在英語口語中 start 是三個動詞中最常用的。在書面語中 begin 最常用。commence 是一個正式的詞, 在英語口語和書面語中是三個動詞中最不常用的。

com·mence·ment /kə`mɛnsmənt; kə'mensmənt/ *n formal*【正式】**1** [C,U] beginning 開始, 開端: **[+of]** *the commencement of the proceedings* 訴訟程序的開始 **2** [C] *AmE* a ceremony at which university, college, or high school students receive their DIPLOMAS; GRADUATION【美】〔大學及高中的〕畢業典禮

com·mend /kə`mɛnd; kə'mend/ *v* [T] *formal*【正式】**1** to praise or approve of someone or something, especially publicly〔尤指公開地〕讚揚: **commend sb for sth** *A Chester man was commended for his public-spirited action.* 一位切斯特的男性居民由於熱心公益而受到表揚。| **highly commended** *Bartholomew's work has been highly commended.* 巴棱羅繆的作品大受好評。**2** to tell someone that something is good or deserves attention; RECOMMEND 推薦, 推崇: *I commend this bill to the House.* 我向議院提交了這項議案。| **not have much to commend it** (=not be satisfactory) 不令人滿意的 *The hotel doesn't have much to commend it.* 這家旅館實在不能令人滿意。**3** *old use* to give someone to someone else to take care of【舊】託…照顧, 把…交託給

com·men·da·ble /kə`mɛndəbḷ; kə'mendəbəl/ *adj formal* deserving praise【正式】值得稱讚的, 值得表揚的: *a highly commendable effort* 值得高度稱讚的努力 | *Baldwin answered with commendable frankness.* 伯德溫回答時所表現的坦誠令人讚許。—**commendably** *adv*

com·men·da·tion /ˌkɑmən`deʃən; ˌkɒmən'deɪʃən/ *n* [C,U] *formal* an official statement praising someone, especially someone who has been brave or very successful【正式】〔尤指對勇敢或很成功的人所作的正式的〕稱讚, 表揚

com·men·su·rate /kə`mɛnʃərɪt; kə'menʃərḷt/ *adj formal* matching something in size, quality, or length of time【正式】〔在尺寸、質量或時間長度上〕與…相當的; 相稱的: **[+with]** *a salary commensurate with your experience* 與你的經驗相稱的工資

1 2 **com·ment¹** /`kɑmɛnt; 'kɒment/ *n* **1** [C,U] an opinion that you express about someone or something 意見, 評論: *Does anyone have any questions or comments?* 有誰有問題或意見嗎? | **make a comment (on/about)** *The police chief made no comment about the bomb attack.* 警察總長對炸彈襲擊事件保持緘默。| **be fair comment** *BrE spoken* (=be criticism that is reasonable or deserved)【英口】作出合理的批評; 應得的評論 **2** [U] criticism or discussion of something someone has said or done〔對某人所說或所做事情的〕批評; 議論: *The Prime Minister's speech received much comment in the press.* 新聞界對首相的演說議論紛紛。| **no comment** *spoken* (=used by people in public life when they do not want to answer questions about a subject)【口】無可奉告〔政治家等人不想回答問題時使用〕**3 be a comment on** to be a sign of the bad quality of something 是〔反映事物不足之處的〕標誌, 特徵: *The number of adults who cannot read is a comment on the quality of our schools.* 成人文盲的數量是我們學校教育質量差的反映。

comment² *v* [I,T] to express an opinion about someone or something 評論; 發表意見: **[+on]** *People were always commenting on my sister's looks.* 人們總是對我妹妹評頭論足。| **comment that** *Some critics have commented that the film is unnecessarily violent.* 一些評論家批評這部電影充斥着不必要的暴力。 2

com·men·ta·ry /`kɑmənˌtɛrɪ; 'kɒməntəri/ *n* **1** [C] a spoken description of an event, given while the event is happening, especially on the television or radio〔尤指在電視或電台上對實況進行的〕解說, 報道: *Stop shouting! I can't hear the baseball commentary.* 別吵啦! 我聽不見棒球解說了。| **[+on]** *Do they have a commentary on the parade?* 他們會對這次遊行進行實況報道嗎? | **running commentary** (=a continuous description of something)〔對某一事件進行的〕連續報道 **2** [C,U] something such as a book or article that explains or discusses a book, poem, idea etc〔對書、詩歌、思想等的〕評說; 註釋: *political commentary* 政論 **3 be a sad commentary on** to be a sign of how bad a particular situation is〔情況或局勢〕令人沮喪[不容樂觀]的表現: *The whole incident was a sad commentary on the state of British football.* 整個事件是英國足球現狀不容樂觀的表現。

com·men·tate /`kɑmənˌtet; 'kɒmənteɪt/ *v* [I+on] to describe an event, such as a sports game on television or radio 為〔體育比賽等〕作解說

com·men·ta·tor /`kɑmənˌtetɚ; 'kɒmənteɪtə/ *n* [C] **1** someone who knows a lot about a particular subject, and who writes about it or discusses it on the television or radio 評論員: *political commentators* 政治評論員 **2** someone who describes an event as it is happening on television or radio 實況播音員; 實況解說員: *David Vine, the BBC's commentator on winter sports* 戴維·瓦因——英國廣播公司冬季運動的解說員 | *a sports commentator* 體育賽事的解說員

com·merce /`kɑmɝs; 'kɒmɜːs/ *n* [U] **1** the buying and selling of goods and services; TRADE¹ (1) 買賣, 貿易; 商務; 商業: *measures promoting local commerce and industry* 促進當地商業和工業發展的措施 **2** *old-fashioned* relationships and communication between people【過時】聯繫; 交流 —see also 另見 CHAMBER OF COMMERCE

com·mer·cial¹ /kə`mɝʃəl; kə'mɜːʃəl/ *adj* **1** related to business and the buying and selling of goods and services 商業的; 商務的: *Our top priorities must be profit and commercial growth.* 我們要以利潤和貿易增長作為重點。**2** related to the ability of a product or business to make a profit〔產品、經營〕能賺錢的, 營利的: *Gibbons failed to see the commercial value of his discovery.* 吉本斯沒有意識到自己的發現所具有的商業價值。| **a commercial success/failure** *The film was a huge commercial success.* 這部電影的票房收入非常可觀。**3** [only before noun 僅用於名詞前] a commercial product is one that is produced in large quantities and sold to the public rather than only to other businesses〔產品〕商品化的: *All commercial milk is pasteurized.* 牛奶產品都是經過殺菌的。**4** commercial business or activity produces goods and services in large quantities 大量生產的〈如產品和勞務〉: *a large commercial fish farm* 大型商業養魚場 **5** more concerned with money than with quality 商業化的〔更注視金錢而忽視質量的〕: *I used to like their music but they've become very commercial.* 過去我很喜歡他們的音樂, 但他們已經變得純粹是以賺錢為目的

了。**6 commercial radio/TV/channel etc** radio or television broadcasts that are produced by companies that earn money through advertising〔靠商業廣告維持的〕電台/電視/頻道等

3 **commercial**² *n* **1** [C] an advertisement on television or radio〔電視或電台的〕商業廣告: *a soap powder commercial* 肥皂粉廣告 **2 commercial break** the time when advertisements are shown during a television or radio programme 廣告時間〔電視或電台節目中插播廣告的時間〕

commercial bank /ˌ.. ˈ./ *n* [C] *technical* the kind of bank that provides services for customers and businesses and that is used by most ordinary people【術語】商業銀行

com·mer·cial·is·m /kəˈmɝʃəlˌɪzəm; kəˈmɜːʃəlɪzəm/ *n* [U] the principle or practice of being more concerned with making money from buying and selling goods than you are about their quality 營利主義, 利潤第一: *the commercialism of modern culture* 現代文化的實利主義

com·mer·cial·ize /kəˈmɝʃəlˌaɪz; kəˈmɜːʃəlaɪz/ also 又作 -ise *BrE*【英】*v* [T] **1** [usually passive 一般用被動態] to be more concerned with making money from something than about its quality 使商業化, 使成為營利手段: *Christmas has become so commercialized nowadays.* 聖誕節現已變得如此商業化了。**2** to sell something to the public in order to make a profit, especially something that would not usually be sold 使商品化〔尤指通常不銷售的東西〕: *commercializing space launches to help pay for more space research* 把太空發射商品化以支付更多的太空研究費用 —**commercialization** /kəˌmɝʃələˈzeʃən; kəˌmɜːʃəlaɪˈzeɪʃən/ *n* [U]

com·mer·cial·ly /kəˈmɝʃəlɪ; kəˈmɜːʃəli/ *adv* **1** [sentence adverb 句子副詞] considering whether a business or product is making a profit 從商業角度來看: *Commercially, the movie was a flop.* 從商業角度來看, 這部電影一敗塗地。| **commercially viable** *The project is no longer commercially viable.* 這個項目從商業角度看不再可行。**2** produced or used in large quantities as a business 大量生產[使用]: *commercially farmed land* 商業農場的土地 **3** if a new product is commercially available, you can buy it in shops 經營上, 營業上

commercial trav·el·ler /ˌ.. ˈ.../ *n* [C] *BrE old-fashioned* someone who travels from place to place selling goods for a company【英, 過時】巡迴推銷員

com·mie /ˈkɑmɪ; ˈkɒmi/ *n* [C] *especially AmE* an insulting word for a COMMUNIST【尤美】共黨分子〔蔑稱〕

com·mis·e·rate /kəˈmɪzəˌret; kəˈmɪzəreɪt/ *v* [I+with] *formal* to express your sympathy for someone who is unhappy about something【正式】憐憫, 同情〔某人的不幸〕

com·mis·e·ra·tion /kəˌmɪzəˈreʃən; kəˌmɪzəˈreɪʃən/ *n formal*【正式】**1** [U] a feeling of sympathy for someone when something unpleasant has happened to them 憐憫, 同情 **2 commiserations** [plural] used to express sympathy to someone, especially someone who has lost a competition〔尤指對某人在比賽中落敗的〕同情: *our commiserations to the losing team* 我們對落敗球隊的同情

com·mis·sar·i·at /ˌkɑməˈsɛrɪət; ˌkɒmɪˈseəriət/ *n* [C] a military department that is responsible for supplying food 軍需部〔負責提供食品〕

com·mis·sa·ry /ˈkɑməˌsɛrɪ; ˈkɒmɪsəri/ *n* [C] **1** *BrE* an officer in the army who is in charge of food supplies【英】軍需官 **2** *AmE* a shop that supplies food and other goods in a military camp【美】軍營商店 **3** *AmE* a place where you can eat in a large organization such as a film STUDIO (2), factory etc【美】〔電影製片廠、工廠等的〕餐廳食堂

1 **com·mis·sion**¹ /kəˈmɪʃən; kəˈmɪʃən/ *n*
1 **1 ▶PEOPLE** 人們◀ [C] a group of people who have been given the official job of finding out about something or controlling something 調查團; 考察團; 委員會: *The Government has set up a commission to suggest improvements to the education system.* 政府已經成立一個委員會, 負責提出建議, 改善教育體制。

2 ▶MONEY 錢◀ [C,U] an amount of money that is paid to someone according to the value of the goods they have sold 佣金; 酬金; 回扣: *The dealer takes a 20% commission on the sales he makes.* 這個商人收取銷售額的20%作為佣金。| **be on commission** (=be paid according to what you sell) 薪水根據銷售額來計算

3 ▶JOB 工作◀ [C] **a)** a request for an artist or musician to make a piece of art or music, for which they are paid 聘請, 委託〔藝術家或音樂家, 要求他創作一件作品〕: *a commission from the Academy for a new sculpture* 來自學院的委託, 要求製作一尊新雕塑 **b)** *formal* a duty or job that you ask someone to do【正式】委派, 任命

4 out of commission a) not working or not able to be used at the present time 不能工作; 暫時失靈: *One of the ship's anchors was out of commission.* 船的一個錨壞了。**b)** *informal* ill or injured【非正式】生病的; 受傷的

5 ▶ARMY/NAVY ETC 陸軍/海軍等◀ [C] an officer's position in the army, navy etc and the authority that is given to them〔軍隊中的〕軍官地位; 軍官職權

6 ▶CRIME 罪行◀ [U] *formal* the commission of a crime is the act of doing it【正式】犯罪

7 in commission if a military ship is in commission, it is still being used by the navy〔船艦〕仍在服役的

commission² *v* [T] **1** to formally ask someone to write an official report, produce a work of art for you etc 委託〔寫正式報告等〕: *We'll be commissioning a report on teenage alcoholism.* 我們將委託人寫青少年酗酒現象的報告。| **commission sb to do sth** *I've been commissioned to write a new play!* 有人託我寫一部新劇本! **2 be commissioned** be given an officer's rank in the army, navy etc〔在軍隊中〕被授予軍官軍銜

com·mis·sion·aire /kəˌmɪʃənˈɛr; kəˌmɪʃəˈneə/ *n* [C] *BrE* someone whose job is to stand at the entrance to a hotel, theatre, or cinema and help people【英】〔旅館、劇院、電影院的〕看門人; DOORMAN *AmE*【美】

commissioned of·fi·cer /ˌ.. ˈ.../ *n* [C] a military officer who has a commission 執勤軍官

com·mis·sion·er /kəˈmɪʃənɚ; kəˈmɪʃənə/ *n* [C] **1** someone who is officially in charge of a government department in some countries 部長: *Commissioner Addo is responsible for Education.* 阿杜部長負責教育部的工作。**2** the head of the police department in some parts of the US〔美國部分地區的〕警察部長 **3** a member of a COMMISSION¹ (1) 委員 **4 commissioner for oaths** *BrE* a lawyer who may legally be a WITNESS to particular legal documents【英】宣誓公證人〔在法律上能負責見證簽署文件的律師〕

com·mit /kəˈmɪt; kəˈmɪt/ *v* **committed, committing** [T] 2
1 ▶CRIME 罪行◀ to do something wrong or illegal 犯〔錯誤、罪行〕: **commit a crime** *Women commit fewer crimes than men.* 女性比男性的的犯罪率低。| **commit murder/rape/adultery etc** *Brady committed a series of brutal murders.* 布拉迪犯下了一系列殘忍的謀殺案。| **commit suicide** (=kill yourself deliberately) 自殺 2

2 ▶SAY THAT SB WILL DO STH 保證某人會做某事◀ to say that someone will definitely do something or must do something 使承擔義務, 作出保證: **commit sb to sth** *My agent has already committed me to an appearance.* 我的代理人已保證我會出場。| **commit sb to doing sth** *The contract commits him to playing for the team for the next three years.* 合約規定以後三年他要為球隊效力。

3 commit yourself to say that you will definitely do something 答應, 承諾: *You don't have to commit yourself at this stage.* 在這個階段你不必承諾甚麼。| *We can't commit ourselves to any concrete proposals.* 我們不能允諾支持甚麼具體的建議。| **commit yourself to doing sth** *Sorry, I've already committed myself to working for Clive.* 對不起, 我已經答應為克萊夫工作了。| **not**

C

commit yourself (=refuse to say whether you will do something) 拒絕允諾 *Roxburgh decided that it would be wiser not to commit himself.* 羅克斯伯格認為不許諾比較明智。

4 ►MONEY/TIME 金錢/時間◄ to decide to use money, time, people etc for a particular purpose 撥出…供使用, 調撥: **commit sth to sth** *A large amount of money has been committed to this project.* 已經撥了一大筆錢給這項工程。

5 ►PRISON/HOSPITAL 監獄/醫院◄ to order someone to be put in a hospital or prison 把…關進監獄[醫院], 監禁: *You're crazy! You ought to be committed!* 你瘋了！你該進精神病院！

6 commit sth to memory to learn something so that you remember it 牢記某事

7 commit sth to paper to write something down 寫下某事

com·mit·ment /kəˈmɪtmənt; kəˈmɪtmənt/ *n* **1** [C] a promise to do something or to behave in a particular way 承諾: *Jim's afraid of emotional commitments.* 吉姆害怕感情上的承諾。| [+to] *a commitment to equal pay and opportunities* 承諾提供平等的工資和機會 **2** [U] the hard work and loyalty that someone gives to an organization, activity etc〔對某一組織、某項活動等所付出的〕辛勞, 忠誠, 奉獻: *I was impressed by the energy and commitment shown by the players.* 我對選手們表現出的活力和奉獻的精神印象深刻。| [+to] *Her commitment to work is beyond question.* 她的敬業精神是不容置疑的。**3** [C] something that you have previously arranged to do at a certain time and that prevents you from doing anything else at that time 承諾的事: *She's got several teaching commitments over the summer.* 整個夏天她答應要進行幾項教學活動。**4** [C] an amount of money that you have to pay regularly and that prevents you from spending your money on other things 承付款項, 債務: *a heavy mortgage commitment* 一筆數額巨大的抵押貸款債務 **5** [U] *especially AmE* the use of money, time, people etc for a particular purpose【尤美】〔為某種目的, 錢、時間和人力等的〕使用, 花費: *The plan involves commitment of money and staff time.* 這個計劃涉及資金的使用和職員工作時間的安排。

com·mit·tal /kəˈmɪtl; kəˈmɪtl/ *n* [C,U] **1** the process in which a court sends someone to a mental hospital or prison 送入精神病院; 收監 **2** *formal* the burying or cremating (CREMATE) of a dead person【正式】下葬; 火化

com·mit·ted /kəˈmɪtɪd; kəˈmɪtɪ̣d/ *adj* willing to work very hard at something 樂於獻身的, 盡責的: *a committed group of environmentalists* 一羣兢兢業業的環境保護論者

com·mit·tee /kəˈmɪtɪ; kəˈmɪti/ *n* **1** [C] a group of people chosen to represent a larger group in order to do a particular job, make decisions etc 委員會: *He's on the finance committee.* 他是財政委員會的成員。| [also+plural verb *BrE*【英】] *The committee have decided to raise membership fees for next year.* 委員會已決定提高明年的會費。**2 welcoming committee** a group of people often sent by a large organization to welcome an important visitor〔由大型組織派出的〕歡迎團

com·mode /kəˈmod; kəˈməʊd/ *n* [C] **1** *BrE* a piece of furniture shaped like a chair that can be used as a TOILET【英】〔座椅式〕便桶 **2** *AmE dialect* a TOILET【美, 方言】馬桶 **3** *old use* a piece of furniture with drawers or shelves【舊】衣櫃, 五斗櫥

com·mo·di·ous /kəˈmodɪəs; kəˈməʊdiəs/ *adj formal* a house or room that is commodious is very big【正式】〔房子或房間〕寬敞的, 大的 —**commodiously** *adv*

com·mod·i·ty /kəˈmɑdətɪ; kəˈmɒdɪ̣ti/ *n* [C] **1** a product that can be sold to make a profit 商品: *agricultural commodities* 農業商品 **2** *formal* a useful quality【正式】有用的性質; 有用的東西: *Time is a precious commodity.* 時間是寶貴的財富。

com·mo·dore /ˈkɑməˌdɔr; ˈkɒmədɔː/ *n* [C] **1** a high rank in the navy, or someone who has this rank 海軍准將 —see table on page C6 參見C6頁附錄 **2** the CAPTAIN in charge of a group of ships that are carrying goods 商船隊隊長

com·mon¹ /ˈkɑmən; ˈkɒmən/ *adj*

1 ►A LOT/LARGE AMOUNT 大量◄ existing in large numbers or happening often and in many places 大量的; 常見的, 多發的: *Heart disease is one of the commonest causes of death.* 心臟病是致命的最常見原因之一。| [+among] *Bad dreams are fairly common among children.* 小孩做惡夢是司空見慣的。| **it is common for sth to happen** *It's very common for new fathers to feel jealous of the baby.* 新爸爸常常會妒嫉自己的寶寶。| **common belief/assumption/practice etc** *It's a common but false assumption that all mentally ill people are violent.* 有一種普遍但是錯誤的觀點, 認為所有精神病人都很兇暴。

2 ►SAME/SIMILAR 相同的/類似的◄ [usually before noun 一般用於名詞前, no comparative 無比較級] common aims, beliefs, ideas etc are shared by several people or groups〔目的、信仰、思想等〕共同的: *They had a satisfying sense of working towards a common goal.* 他們朝同一目標努力的這種意識令人滿意。| [+to] *a theme that is common to all her novels* 她全部小說中的共同主題 | **common ground** (=shared opinions, beliefs etc among people who are usually separate)〔一般有分歧的人的觀點、信仰等〕共同基礎 *The two parties met to establish some common ground.* 兩個黨派為達成共識而會面。

3 ►SHARED BY EVERYONE 共有◄ [usually before noun 一般用於名詞前, no comparative 無比較級] belonging to or shared by everyone in a society〔社會〕共有的, 公共的: [+to] *These problems are common to all societies.* 這些問題是所有社會的通病。| **the common good** (=the advantage of everyone) 公益 *Do they seriously think they're acting for the common good?* 他們自問真是從公眾利益出發來考慮的嗎? | **common knowledge** (=something everyone knows) 眾所周知的事 *In a small town everyone's actions are common knowledge.* 在一個小鎮上每個人的一舉一動都難以逃過大家的眼睛。| **common land** (=owned by the public) 公有土地 | **by common consent** (=agreed by everyone) 一致同意 *Joe was chosen as captain by common consent.* 大家一致通過選舉喬為隊長。

4 common courtesy/decency a polite way of behaving that you expect from people 通常的禮貌, 禮節: *It's only common courtesy to write and thank them for the present.* 寫信感謝他們送禮只是出於通常的禮貌。

5 ►ORDINARY 普通的◄ [only before noun 僅用於名詞前, no comparative 無比較級] ordinary and not special in any way 普通的, 平凡的: *The common people will not benefit from these reforms.* 老百姓將不會從這些改革中受益。| *common salt* 食鹽 | **the common man** (=ordinary people) 普通人 | **common-or-garden** *BrE slang* (=very common and ordinary)【英俚】很普通, 很一般

6 ►PERSON 人◄ *especially BrE old-fashioned* an offensive word for someone from a low social class【尤英, 過時】粗鄙的, 劣等的〔對下層社會成員的冒犯用語〕: *Stop that! People will think we're common.* 別那樣！別人會以為我們是粗人。| **as common as muck** *BrE* (=extremely common)【英】極其普通的

7 common practice a usual or accepted way of doing things 慣例: *Sending kids away to school was common practice among the upper classes.* 上層階級家庭將孩子送往寄宿學校是慣例。

8 the common touch the ability of someone in a position of power or authority to talk to and understand ordinary people 平易近人的品質: *He's made it to the top without losing the common touch.* 他雖已晉升高位, 卻仍然平易近人。

common² *n* **1 have sth in common (with sb)** to have the same interests, attitudes etc as someone else (與某

人）有相同的興趣、態度等: *To my surprise, I found I had a lot in common with this stranger.* 令我吃驚的是，我發現自己和這個陌生人有許多共同點。**2 have sth in common (with sth)** if objects or ideas have something in common, they share the same features（與某事物）有相同的特點: *Their methods have a lot in common.* 他們的方法有很多相同之處。**3 in common with sb/sth** in the same way as someone or something else 與某人/某物一樣: *In common with a lot of other countries, we're in an economic recession.* 同許多別的國家一樣，我國也處在經濟蕭條時期。**4** [C] a large area of grass in a village that people walk or play sport on〔村莊裡〕公用草地 **5** *technical* having the same relationship to two or more quantities【術語】與兩個以上的量關係相同的: *5 is a common factor of 10 and 20.* 5是10和20的公約數。

common cold /ˌ·· ˈ·/ *n* [C] a slight illness in which your throat hurts and it is difficult to breathe normally 感冒，傷風

common de·nom·i·na·tor /ˌ·· ·ˈ····/ *n* [C] **1** an attitude or quality that all the different members of a group have 共同點〔一組織中不同成員共有的態度或品質〕: *The common denominator in these very different schemes is that they aim to reduce pollution.* 這些計劃很不相同，它們的共同點是以減少污染為目標。**2** *technical* a number that can be divided exactly by all the DENOMINATORs (=bottom number) in a set of fractions (FRACTION (2))【術語】公分母 **3 the lowest common denominator** the least attractive, least intelligent people or features in a situation 最無知的人[特點]，最無趣的人[特點]: *trashy TV programs that appeal to the lowest common denominator* 滿足低級趣味的低劣電視節目

com·mon·er /ˈkɑmənɚ; ˈkɒmənə/ *n* [C] someone who is not a member of a NOBLE[1] (3) family 平民: *Sarah Ferguson was a commoner before she married the Duke Of York.* 在嫁給約克公爵之前，莎拉·費格遜是個平民。

common frac·tion /ˌ·· ˈ··/ *n* [C] *AmE* a FRACTION[1] (2) that is shown by a number above and a number below a line, such as ½, rather than as a DECIMAL[2]【美】普通分數，簡分數; VULGAR FRACTION *BrE*【英】

common law[1] /ˈ·· ·/ *adj* [only before noun 僅用於名詞前] **1 common-law marriage/husband/wife** a relationship that is considered to be a marriage because the man and woman have lived together for a long time 同居[事實]婚姻/夫/妻〔由於男女長期同居而被認為具有婚姻關係〕**2** according to or related to COMMON LAW[2] 根據習慣法的; 有關普通法的: *common law rules* 習慣法條例

common law[2] /ˌ·· ˈ·/ *n* [U] the law of England that has developed from common customs and the decisions of judges rather than from laws made by Parliament 普通法，習慣法〔即普遍的習俗和法官的判決發展而來而不是議會制定的英國法律〕

3 **com·mon·ly** /ˈkɑmənlɪ; ˈkɒmənli/ *adv* usually or by most people 通常，一般地，由大多數人〔同意等〕: *commonly agreed principles* 一般人同意的原則 | *Sodium chloride is more commonly known as salt.* 氯化鈉一般稱為鹽。

Common Mar·ket /ˌ·· ˈ··◂/ *n* **the Common Market** *old-fashioned* the EUROPEAN UNION【過時】共同市場〔歐盟的前身〕

common noun /ˌ·· ˈ·/ *n* [C] *technical* in grammar, a common noun is any noun that is not the name of a particular person, place, or thing【術語】普通名詞〔在語法中，任何不是某人、某地或某物的名詞都是普通名詞〕: *'Book' and 'sugar' are common nouns.* book和sugar是普通名詞。—compare 比較 PROPER NOUN —see also 另見 NOUN

com·mon·place[1] /ˈkɑmənˌples; ˈkɒmənpleɪs/ *adj* happening or existing in many places, and therefore not special or unusual 平常的; 平凡的; 不足為奇的: *Car thefts are commonplace in this part of town.* 在城市的這個地段偷車是家常便飯。

commonplace[2] *n* **1** [C usually singular 一般用單數] something that happens or exists in many places, so that it is not unusual 平常的事，司空見慣的事: *One-parent families are now a commonplace in our society.* 在我們的社會中單親家庭現在是很平常的。**2 the commonplace** ordinary or boring 一般，沒有特色，單調乏味: *In my view, his paintings verge on the commonplace.* 我認為他的畫幾近平庸。

common room /ˈ·· ·/ *n* [C] *BrE* a room in a school or college that a group of teachers or students use when they are not teaching or studying【英】〔中小學或大學的〕教師、學生休息室

Com·mons /ˈkɑmənz; ˈkɒmənz/ *n* **the Commons** the larger and more powerful of the two parts of the British parliament, whose members are elected by citizens〔英國議會的〕下議院〔議員由公民選舉產生〕: *enough votes to force a bill through the Commons* 能使某議案在下議院強行通過的足夠選票 | **in the Commons** (=among the Members of Parliament) 在下議院議員之間 —compare 比較 **the Lords** (LORD (2))

common sense /ˌ·· ˈ·◂/ *n* [U] the ability to behave in a sensible way and make practical decisions 常識: *Use your common sense for once!* 請你也用一次常識來判斷吧！—**common-sense** *adj*: *a common-sense approach to the economy* 按常理來處理經濟的政策

com·mon·wealth /ˈkɑmənˌwɛlθ; ˈkɒmənwelθ/ *n* **1 the Commonwealth** an organization of about 50 countries that were once part of the British EMPIRE (1) and which are now connected politically and economically 英聯邦〔由曾屬於大英帝國的約50個國家組成〕: *the Commonwealth Games* 英聯邦運動會 **2** [C] *formal* an association of countries with political or economic links【正式】〔由在政治或經濟上有聯繫的國家組成的〕聯合體: *In 1991 the USSR became the Commonwealth of Independent States.* 1991年蘇聯變成了"獨立國家聯合體"。

com·mo·tion /kəˈmoʃən; kəˈməʊʃən/ *n* [singular, U] sudden noisy activity 突然的混亂，喧鬧: *They heard a commotion downstairs.* 他們聽見樓下一陣騷動。| **cause a commotion** *The bar was packed, and the winning touchdown caused an immense commotion.* 酒吧裡擠滿了人，決勝負的觸地得分引起了極大的騷動。

com·mu·nal /ˈkɑmjunḷ; ˈkɒmjʊnəl/ *adj* **1** shared by a group, especially a group of people who live together〔為同一羣體所〕共有的，公共的，社區的: *a communal bathroom* 一個公用浴室 **2** involving people from many different races, religions, or language groups 種族間的; 教派間的: *rising communal tension in India* 印度日趨嚴重的種族對抗

com·mune[1] /ˈkɑmjun; ˈkɒmjuːn/ *n* [C] **1** a group of people who live together and who share the work and their possessions〔生活在一起、分享財產、分擔職責的〕羣居團體，社區 **2** a group of people who work as a team, especially on a farm, and give what they produce to the state 公社〔尤指在農場上合作生產的一羣人，他們的產品交與國家〕**3** the smallest division of local government in countries such as France and Belgium〔法國和比利時等國〕最小的地方行政區

com·mune[2] /kəˈmjun; kəˈmjuːn/ *v* [I] *formal* to share your thoughts and feelings with someone or with nature without using words【正式】與〔某人或大自然〕無言地進行思想感情交流，溝通: *communing with nature* 與自然界契合

com·mu·ni·ca·ble /kəˈmjunɪkəbḷ; kəˈmjuːnɪkəbəl/ *adj* **1** a communicable illness is infectious〔疾病〕傳染性的 **2** able to be communicated 可傳達的: *Her ideas were not easily communicable to others.* 她的想法不容易傳達給他人。—**communicably** *adv*

com·mu·ni·cant /kəˈmjunɪkənt; kəˈmjuːnɪkənt/ *n* [C] someone who receives COMMUNION (2) regularly in the Christian church〔基督教會中〕按時領受聖餐者

com·mu·ni·cate /kəˈmjunəˌket; kəˈmjuːnɪkeɪt/ *v* S3 W3
1 ►EXPRESS 表達◄ [T] to express your thoughts and

feelings clearly, so that other people understand them 表達, 傳達〔思想、感情〕: *A baby communicates its needs by crying.* 嬰兒用哭聲來表達需要。| **communicate sth to sb** *Without meaning to, she communicated her anxiety to her child.* 她無意中向孩子透露了她的焦慮。| **communicate itself** *Dissatisfaction with working conditions communicated itself throughout the workforce.* 工人間流露出對工作條件的不滿。

2 ►EXCHANGE INFORMATION 交流信息◄ [I,T] to exchange information or conversation with other people, using words, signs etc〔用符號等〕與〔他人〕交流信息; 交談: *He learnt how to use sign language to communicate with deaf customers.* 他學會了用手語與失聰的顧客交談。

C

3 ►CONTACT 聯繫◄ [I] *formal* to contact someone, especially by telephone or by writing a letter【正式】〔尤指用電話、書信等〕與他人聯繫

4 ►UNDERSTAND 理解◄ [I] if two people communicate, they can easily understand each other's thoughts and feelings 溝通〔思想、情感〕: [+with] *Parents sometimes find it difficult to communicate with their teenage children.* 孩子長到十幾歲, 父母有時會發覺難以與他們交流。

5 ►ROOMS 房間◄ [I] if rooms or parts of a building communicate, you can get directly to one from the other〔不同房間或樓房的不同部分〕互通, 相連

6 ►DISEASE 疾病◄ [T usually passive 一般用被動態] to pass a disease from one person or animal to another〔疾病〕傳染: *research into how the AIDS virus is communicated* 對愛滋病病毒傳染途徑的研究

2 1 **com·mu·ni·ca·tion** /kəˌmjunəˋkeʃən; kəˌmjuːnɪ̆ˈkeɪʃən/ *n* **1** [U] the process by which people exchange information or express their thoughts and feelings 信息交流; 思想感情表達: *Good communication is vital in a large organization.* 在一個龐大組織中良好的溝通是極為重要的。| **means of communication** *Radio was the pilot's only means of communication.* 無線電曾經是飛行員唯一的通訊手段。**2 communications** [plural] **a)** ways of sending information, especially using radio, telephone or computers 各種通訊手段〔尤指無線電、電話或電腦〕: *Modern communications enable more and more people to work from home.* 各種現代通訊手段使越來越多的人能在家裡工作。**b)** ways of travelling and sending goods, such as roads, railways etc 交通: [+with] *Paris has good communications with many European cities.* 巴黎與許多歐洲城市之間的交通便捷。**3** [C] *formal* a letter, message or telephone call【正式】函件; 信息; 電話通訊: *a communication from the Ministry of Defence* 來自國防部的函件 **4 communication skills** ways of expressing yourself well so that other people will understand 溝通技巧: *a week's course in improving communication skills* 提高交流技巧的一週課程 **5 be in communication with** *formal* to talk or write to someone regularly or occasionally【正式】〔定期或偶爾〕與〔某人〕交談[通信]

communication cord /·,··'·· ·/ *n* [C] *BrE* a chain that a passenger pulls to stop a train in an EMERGENCY (=a sudden dangerous situation)【英】〔在發生緊急情況時, 火車乘客拉動要求停車的〕緊急制動索

communications sat·el·lite /·,··'·· ,···/ *n* [C] a piece of equipment in space that travels around the Earth and is used for radio, television, and telephone signals around the world 通訊衛星

com·mu·ni·ca·tive /kəˋmjunəˌketɪv; kəˈmjuːnɪ̆kətɪv/ *adj* **1** able to talk easily to other people 健談的, 善於言談的: *It's hard to know what she's thinking; she's not very communicative.* 很難知道她的想法, 她不太愛說話。**2** relating to the ability to communicate, especially in a foreign language 表達能力〔尤指外語〕: *students' communicative skills* 學生們的交流技能

com·mu·nion /kəˋmjunjən; kəˈmjuːnjən/ *n* **1** [U] *formal* a special relationship with someone or something in which you feel that you understand them very well【正式】〔與某人或某物之間的〕情感交融: [+between/with] *He sought meaningful communion with another human being.* 他尋求與另一個人進行有意義的溝通。**2** [U] also 又作 **Holy Communion** the Christian ceremony in which people eat bread and drink wine as signs of Christ's body and blood 聖餐〔一種基督教儀式〕**3** [C] *formal* a group of people or organizations that share the same religious beliefs【正式】教會; 教派, 宗教團體: *He belongs to the Anglican communion.* 他是聖公會的教徒。

com·mu·ni·qué /kəˌmjunəˋke; kəˈmjuːnɪ̆keɪ/ *n* [C] an official report or announcement 公報: *The palace has issued a communiqué denying the paper's allegations.* 宮廷發表公報否認報紙上的指控。

Com·mu·nis·m /ˋkɑmjʊˌnɪzəm; ˈkɒmjʊ̆nɪzəm/ *n* [U] **1** a political system in some countries in which the government controls the production of all food and goods, and which has no different social classes 共產主義制度 **2** the belief in this political system 共產主義的信念

Com·mu·nist[1] /ˋkɑmjʊnɪst; ˈkɒmjʊ̆nɪ̆st/ *adj* connected with Communism 共產主義的: *Communist countries* 共產主義國家 | *a communist regime* 共產主義政權

Communist[2] *n* [C] **1** someone who is a member of a political party that supports Communism 共產黨員, 共產黨人 **2** someone who believes in Communism 共產主義者

communist bloc /,··· '·/ *n* [singular] the group of countries, mostly in Eastern Europe, that had Communist governments and supported the former Soviet Union 共產主義集團〔指曾經有共產黨政府並支持前蘇聯的國家, 這些國家大都在東歐〕

com·mu·ni·ty /kəˋmjunətɪ; kəˈmjuːnɪ̆ti/ *n*

1 ►PEOPLE 人們◄ [C, also+plural verb *BrE* 英] *BrE* all the people who live in the same area, town etc【英】〔同住一地的人所構成的〕社區: *an arts centre built to serve the whole community* 為整個社區服務的藝術中心 | **community affairs/needs/relations etc** *We meet once a month to discuss community problems.* 我們每月開會一次討論社區問題。| **community spirit** (=the desire to be friendly with and help other people who live in the same community) 社區精神〔指同一社區內友好互助的精神〕

2 ►PARTICULAR GROUP 特定團體◄ **sense of community** the feeling that you belong to a group of people because you live in the same area 社區歸屬感〔居住在同一地的人們所有的一種歸屬感〕

3 [C] a group of people who share the same nationality or religion or who are similar in another way〔由同國籍、同宗教等構成的〕羣體; 社區: *There are many different ethnic communities living in New York.* 紐約有許多不同民族聚居羣體。| *the gay community* 同性戀羣體

4 the community society and the people in it 社會; 公眾: *The trend is towards reintegrating mentally ill people into the community.* 目前的趨勢是將精神病人重新融入社會中。| **the international community** (=all the countries of the world) 國際社會 —see also 另見 EC

5 ►PLANTS/ANIMALS 植物/動物◄ [C] a group of plants or animals that live in the same environment 羣落〔生長或生活在同一環境中的植物或動物羣〕: *Communities of otters are slowly returning to several British rivers.* 水獺羣落又慢慢地回到幾條英國河流裡。

community cen·tre *BrE*【英】**community center** *AmE*【美】/·'··· ,·/ *n* [C] a place where people from the same area can go for social events, classes etc 社區活動中心

community chest /·'··· ,·/ *n* [C] *AmE* money that is collected by the people and businesses in an area to help poor people【美】〔救濟窮困者的〕社區福利金, 公益金

community col·lege /·'··· ,··/ *n* [C,U] a college in the US that students can go to for two years in order to learn a skill or to prepare for university; JUNIOR COLLEGE 社區學院〔美國兩年制學院, 學生學一項技藝或大學預科課程〕

com·mu·ni·ty prop·er·ty /ˌ·ˈ··· ˌ···/ *n* [U] *law* property such as houses or land, that is considered to be owned by both a husband and wife in US law【法律】夫妻共有財產〔美國法律視為夫妻共有的房屋、土地等財產〕

community ser·vice /ˌ·ˌ··· ˈ··/ *n* [U] **1** work that someone does without being paid to help other people 社區服務〔指為他人提供的無償服務〕**2** a punishment given for some crimes, in which the criminal has to do useful work to help people 社區服務〔一種懲罰, 由犯人為他人做一些有益的工作〕

com·mu·ta·ble /kəˋmjutəbl̩; kəˈmjuːtəbəl/ *adj* **1** *law* a punishment that is commutable can be made less severe【法律】可減刑的 **2** payments that are commutable can be exchanged for another type of payment〔支付方式〕可以改換的

com·mu·ta·tion /ˏkɑmjʊˋteʃən; ˌkɒmjʊˈteɪʃən/ *n* **1** [C, U] a reduction in how severe a punishment is 減刑: *commutation of a death sentence to life* 將死刑減為無期徒刑 **2** [U] *formal* the act of replacing one method of payment with a different method【正式】〔支付方式的〕替換 **3** [C] *technical* a payment of one type made instead of an equal payment of another type【術語】抵償(金)

com·mu·ta·tive /kəˋmjutətɪv; kəˈmjuːtətɪv/ *adj technical* a mathematical operation that is commutative can be done in any order【術語】〔數學運算順序〕交換, 可換的〔指順序不影響結果〕

com·mute¹ /kəˋmjut; kəˈmjuːt/ *v* **1** [I] to regularly travel a long distance to get to work 經常去遙遠的地方上班, 通勤: **[+to/from/between]** *Jim commutes from Weehawken to Manhattan every day.* 吉姆每天上下班往來於威霍肯與曼哈頓之間。**2** [T] to change the punishment given to a criminal to one that is less severe 減刑: **commute a sentence (to)** *The sentence was later commuted to life imprisonment.* 這個判決後來減刑為終身監禁。**3 commute sth for/into sth** to exchange one thing, especially one kind of payment, for another 把某物改換為另一物〔尤指支付方式〕: *He commuted his pension for a lump sum.* 他把按時分期領取的退休金改為一次領清。

commute² *n* [C usually singular 一般用單數] *especially AmE* the journey to work every day【尤美】每天去上班的路程: *My morning commute takes 45 minutes.* 我早上上班路上要花45分鐘。

commuters 每日去遙遠的地方上班的人

com·mut·er /kəˋmjutɚ; kəˈmjuːtə/ *n* [C] someone who travels a long distance to work every day 每日去遙遠的地方上班的人, 通勤者: *a carriage full of home-going commuters* 車廂裡擠滿了下班回家的人

commuter belt /ˌ·ˈ·· ˌ·/ *n* [C] an area around a large city from which many people travel to work every day 大城市四周的居住地帶〔許多人每天從那裡出發去工作地點〕

comp /kɑmp; kɒmp/ *n* [C] **1** *AmE informal* a ticket for a play, sports game etc that is given away free【美, 非正式】〔戲劇、體育比賽等〕招待券, 免費券 **2** *BrE spoken* a COMPREHENSIVE SCHOOL【英口】綜合中學

com·pact¹ /kəmˋpækt; kəmˈpækt/ *adj* **1** small and easy to carry 小巧便攜的: *a compact camera* 小巧的照相機 **2** small but arranged so that everything fits neatly into the space available 小而緊湊的: *The dormitory rooms were compact, with a desk, bed and closet built in.* 宿舍房間雖小卻安排緊湊, 配有現成的書桌、牀和壁櫥。**3** firmly and closely packed together; DENSE (1) 緊密的; 密集的: *The bushes grew in a compact mass.* 灌木長成茂密的一片。**4** small but solid and strong 矮小結實的, 壯實的: *a small compact-looking man* 個子矮小、看上去卻很結實的男人 **5** expressing things clearly in only a few words 簡潔的 **—compactly** *adv* **—compactness** *n* [U]

com·pact² /ˋkɑmpækt; ˈkɒmpækt/ *n* [C] **1** a small flat container with a mirror, containing powder for a woman's face〔內有鏡子的〕女式化妝粉盒 **2** *AmE* a small car【美】小型汽車 **3** *formal* an agreement between two or more people, countries etc【正式】〔人與人、國與國之間的〕協定

com·pact³ /kəmˋpækt; kəmˈpækt/ [T] *v* to press something soft or something made of small pieces together, so that it becomes smaller or more solid〔將某柔軟或由小塊組成的物質〕壓緊, 壓實 **—compacted** *adj*

compact disc /ˌ·· ˈ·/ *n* [C] a small circular piece of hard plastic on which music, or large quantities of information can be stored; CD 雷射[激光]唱片;〔電腦〕光碟, 光盤: *The new album is available on vinyl, cassette, or compact disc.* 這張新專輯的塑膠唱片、錄音帶、激光唱片都可以買到。

compact disc play·er /ˌ·· ˈ· ˌ··/ *n* [C] CD PLAYER 雷射[激光]唱機

com·pan·ion /kəmˋpænjən; kəmˈpænjən/ *n* [C] **1** someone you spend a lot of time with especially someone you are travelling with or a friend 同伴; 同行者: *His dog became his closest companion during the last years of his life.* 他的狗成了他晚年最親密的伴侶。| **constant companion** (=someone you are always with) 形影不離的夥伴 **2** one of a pair of things that go together or can be used together 構成一對的兩件物品中的一件: **[+to]** *This book is a companion to the author's first work.* 這本書是作者第一部作品的姊妹篇。| **companion volume/album/statement etc** *Paul Simon has just released a companion album to his Greatest Hits.* 保羅·西蒙剛剛發行了他《最流行的歌曲集》的姊妹集。**3** someone, especially a woman, who is paid to live or travel with an older person 伴侶〔尤指受雇陪一位老人一起生活或旅行的人, 尤為女子〕**4** used as part of the title of a book on a particular subject, especially a book that explains something 手冊, 指南〔用於書名〕 W3

com·pan·io·na·ble /kəmˋpænjənəbl̩; kəmˈpænjənəbəl/ *adj* pleasantly friendly 和善的; 友善的: *They sat together in companionable silence.* 他們友好地默默坐在一起。**—companionably** *adv*

com·pan·ion·ship /kəmˋpænjənʃɪp; kəmˈpænjənʃɪp/ *n* [U] a friendly and comfortable relationship with someone 友誼; 友好交往: *When Stan died, it was the companionship I missed.* 史坦死後, 我懷念我們的友情。

com·pan·ion·way /kəmˋpænjənˏwe; kəmˈpænjənweɪ/ *n* [U] the steps going from one DECK (=level) of a ship to another deck 升降口扶梯〔兩層船艙之間的梯子〕

com·pa·ny /ˋkʌmpənɪ; ˈkʌmpəni/ *n* S1 W1

1 ►BUSINESS 公司◄ [C] an organization that makes or sells goods or services in order to get money 公司: *Craig got a job working for an insurance company.* 克雷格在保險公司找到了一份工作。| [also+plural verb *BrE* 英] *The company are hoping to expand their operations abroad.* 公司想把業務擴展到國外。| **manage/run a company** *In ten years Geoff went from working in the mail room to running the company.* 在十年之間, 戈夫從收發員晉升到管理整家公司。| **set up/start a company** *The company was set up just after the war.* 這家公司是戰後不久創建的。| **a company goes bankrupt/bust/out of business** (=stops doing business because it owes so much money) 公司〔由於負債過多而〕破產/倒閉 *Quite a few companies went bankrupt in the late 1980s.* 在20世紀80年代後期有相當數量的公司破產。| **company directors/employees/policy etc** *It's not company policy to exchange goods without a receipt.* 調換貨品而不具備發票, 這不是公司的政策。—see also 另見 PUBLIC COMPANY

2 ►OTHER PEOPLE 別人◄ [U] another person, or other people, that you can talk to or who stop you feeling lonely 同伴, 朋友: *They obviously enjoy each other's company.* 顯然他們兩個在一起非常高興。| **keep sb company** *Rita's husband is away for the week, so I thought I'd go over and keep her company.* 麗塔的丈夫這個星期外出不在家, 所以我想我應該去她那兒給她作伴。| **be good company** (=if someone is good company, you enjoy being with them) 好夥伴 | **as company** *Bessie was glad to have the dog as company.* 貝茜很高興有這隻狗為伴。| **in sb's company/in the company of sb** (=with someone) 與某人在一起 *I couldn't help feeling uneasy in the company of such an important man.* 和如此重要的人物在一起, 我不由自主地感到不自在。| **in company with sb** (=together with another person or with a group) 和…一起 *He left for New York, in company with the orchestra.* 他與樂隊一同出發去紐約。

3 ►GUESTS 客人◄ [U] a guest or guests who are visiting you in your home, or someone who is coming to see you 客人: **have company** *It looks like the Hammills have company – there are three cars in the driveway.* 哈米爾斯家好像有客人, 他家的汽車道上停了三輛汽車。| **expect company** (=be waiting for guests to arrive) 等待客人到來 *We're expecting company this evening.* 今晚我們有客人要來。

4 ►FRIENDS 朋友◄ [singular, U] the group of people that you are friends with or that you spend time with 同伴, 夥伴: **in pleasant/elevated etc company** *She was too shy to mix in such elevated company.* 她太害羞, 與高貴的客人格格不入。| **the company sb keeps** (=the people you spend time with) 某人交往的人 *People do tend to judge you by the company you keep.* 人們往往根據你交往的人來判斷你的為人。| **bad company** (=people who do things you disapprove of) 不良的夥伴, 損友 *Parents worry that their children are being led into bad company.* 父母擔心自己的孩子被引誘去與壞人交往。| **not like the company sb is keeping** (=disapprove of the people someone is friends with) 不喜歡某人的朋友 | **keep company with sb** *old-fashioned* (=spend time with someone) 【過時】與某人作伴

5 ►PERFORMERS 表演者◄ [C] a group of actors, dancers, or singers who work together 劇團, 歌舞團體: *Our local theatre gets a lot of touring companies.* 我們本地劇院常有巡迴演出團表演。

6 be in good company used to tell someone that important or respected people have done something similar to what they have done, so they should not be ashamed 〔用於告訴某人〕有地位的人也做過類似的事〔因此他用不着感到慚愧〕

7 ►GROUP 人羣◄ [U] a group of people who are together in the same place, often for a particular purpose or for social reasons 〔為某種目的或社交原因而聚集在一起的〕一羣人: *These remarks made the assembled company burst into sudden applause.* 這番話使與會者爆發出熱烈掌聲。| **in company** (=surrounded by other people, especially at a formal or social occasion) 在大庭廣眾之中〔尤指在正式或社交場合〕 *Parents need to teach their children how to behave in company.* 父母應當教導孩子怎樣在別人面前舉止得體。

8 and company *especially spoken* used after a person's name to mean that person and their friends 【尤口】〔用於某人的名字之後表示此人〕及其朋友: *"Who's going to the party?" "Jim and company, I guess."* "誰會去參加晚會?" "我想吉姆和他的朋友們會去。"

9 ►ARMY 軍隊◄ [C] a group of about 120 soldiers who are usually part of a larger group 連〔約120個士兵組成, 常為較大支部隊的一部分〕

10 two's company, three's a crowd used to suggest that two people would rather be alone together than have other people with them 兩人為伴, 三人不歡〔用來表示寧可只有兩個人而不要更多的人加入他們〕

11 in company with sth if something happens in company with something else, both things happen at the same time 與另一件事同時發生: *Democracy progressed in company with the emancipation of women.* 民主制度是與婦女解放同時發展的。—see also 另見 **part company** (PART[2] (3)), **present company excepted** (PRESENT[1] (5))

company car /,··· '·/ *n* [C] a car that your employer gives you while you work for them 公司給雇員使用的汽車

company law /,··· '·/ *n* [U] the area of law that concerns how businesses operate and what their duties are to each other, to customers, and to governments 公司法

company sec·re·ta·ry /,··· '····/ *n* [C] *BrE* a member of a company who deals with money, legal matters etc 【英】公司祕書〔公司裡負責財務、法律事務等的職員〕

com·pa·ra·ble /ˋkɑmpərəbl̩; 'kɒmpərəbəl/ *adj* **1** similar to something else in size, number, quality etc, so that you can make a comparison 〔在大小、數量、質量等方面〕類似的, 同類的, 相當的: *A comparable car would cost far more abroad.* 一輛同等的汽車在國外的價格高很多。| **[+with/to]** *Is the pay rate comparable to that of other companies?* 這個工資比率可以和別的公司相比吧? | **comparable in size/importance etc** *The planet Pluto is comparable in size to the moon.* 冥王星的大小與月球相當。**2** being equally important, good, bad etc 〔重要性、好壞等〕同等的, 可相提並論的: *In my view these two artists just aren't comparable.* 我認為這兩位藝術家不能相提並論。| **[+with/to]** *His poetry is hardly comparable with Shakespeare's.* 他的詩不能與莎士比亞的詩相提並論。—**comparability** /ˌkɑmpərəˋbɪlətɪ; ˌkɒmpərə'bɪlɪ̣ti/ *n* [U]

com·pa·ra·bly /ˋkɑmpərəblɪ; 'kɒmpərəbli/ *adv* in a similar way or to a similar degree 類似地; 在相似程度上: *Earnings have risen comparably in the industrial sector.* 在工業部門利潤也以相當的幅度增長。

com·par·a·tive[1] /kəmˋpærətɪv; kəm'pærətɪv/ *adj* **1** **comparative comfort/freedom/wealth etc** comfort, freedom etc that is fairly satisfactory when compared to another state of comfort etc 相對的舒適/自由/財富等: *After a lifetime of poverty, his last few years were spent in comparative comfort.* 他窮了一輩子, 晚年相對而言還過得比較舒適。**2** **comparative beginner/newcomer/genius etc** someone who is not really a beginner etc, but who seems to be one when compared to other people 相對的初學者/新來者/天才等: *After living here five years, we're still considered comparative newcomers.* 我們在這裡生活了五年, 可是與別人相比我們仍被視為新來的。**3** **comparative study/analysis/literature etc** a study etc that involves comparing something to something else 比較研究/分析/文學等: *a comparative study of different sociological groups* 對不同社會集團的比較研究 **4** the comparative form of an adjective or adverb shows an increase in size, degree etc when it is considered in relation to something else. For example, 'bigger' is the comparative form of 'big', and 'more comfortable' is the comparative form of 'comfortable'. 比較級的〔指形容詞、副詞的比較級形式〕

comparative[2] *n* **the comparative** the form of an adjective or adverb that shows an increase in size, degree etc when something is considered in relation to something else. For example, 'bigger' is the comparative of 'big', and 'more comfortable' is the comparative of 'comfortable.' 〔形容詞、副詞的〕比較級形式〈如 bigger 是 big 的比較級, more comfortable 是 comfortable 的比較級〉

com·par·a·tive·ly /kəmˋpærətɪvlɪ; kəm'pærətɪ̣vli/ *adv*

as compared to something else or to a previous state 相對地; 比較地: *The children were comparatively well-behaved today.* 今天孩子們比較乖。| **comparatively speaking** *This part of the coast is still unspoiled, comparatively speaking.* 相比而言, 這部分海岸尚未受到破壞。

1 1 **compare[1]** /kəm`pɛr; kəm'peə/ *v*

1 ▶SIMILAR/DIFFERENT 類似的/不同的◀ [T] to consider two or more things, people, ideas etc, in order to show how they are similar to or different from each other 比較: *The report compares the different types of home computer currently available.* 這份報告比較了目前可以買到的不同型號的家用電腦。| **compare sth to/with** *There is nothing to compare with a nice cold drink when you get home after work.* 下班回家後, 沒有甚麼能比得上喝上一杯可口的冷飲。| **compare and contrast** (=an expression used when telling students to write about the similarities and differences in works of literature, or art) 比較對照〔用來要學生論述文學或藝術作品之間的異同〕
2 compared to/with used when considering the size, quality, or amount of something in relation to something similar〔尺寸、質量、數量〕與…相比: *Compared to our small apartment, our uncle's house seemed like a palace.* 跟我們的小公寓房比起來, 叔叔的房子就像是宮殿一般。| *Statistics show a 20% reduction in burglary compared with last year.* 統計數字表明, 與去年相比, 盜竊案下降了20%。
3 ▶LIKE/EQUALLY GOOD 像/同樣好◀ [T] to say that something or someone is like someone or something else, or that it is equally good, large etc〔表示某物、某人與另一物、另一人〕相像或一樣好, 一樣大等: **compare sth/sb to** *You can't compare the war in Somalia to the Vietnam War.* 你不能將索馬里那場戰爭比作越南戰爭。
4 does not compare if something or someone does not compare with something else, it is not as good, large etc 不能相比: *My old car was a real beauty. This one just doesn't compare.* 我從前那輛車真是漂亮, 這一輛就差得遠了。
5 ▶BETTER/WORSE 較好/較糟◀ to be better or worse in some way than someone or something else〔在某方面〕比〔某人/某物〕好[差]: **[+with]** *How does life in Britain compare with life in the States?* 與美國的生活相比, 英國的生活如何? | **compare favourably/unfavourably** *The imported fabrics are 30% cheaper and compare very favorably in quality.* 進口布料價格要便宜30%, 而且質地不錯。
6 compare notes if two people compare notes, they talk about something they have both done, in order to see if they have the same opinions, ideas etc about it〔兩人對所做過的事〕交換意見: *The pair got together in Paris to compare notes on current research.* 那兩個人在巴黎見面以交換意見, 討論研究的最新情況。

compare[2] *n* **beyond/without compare** *literary* a quality that is beyond compare is the best of its kind【文】無可比擬; 無可匹配: *a beauty and an elegance beyond compare* 無以倫比的美麗與優雅

3 2 **com·pa·ri·son** /kəm`pærəsn̩; kəm'pærɪ̆sən/ *n*

1 ▶COMPARING 比較◀ [U] the process of comparing two people or things〔兩人或兩物的〕比較: **[+with]** *Comparison with the director's earlier movies seems inevitable.* 對比導演早期的電影看來是不可避免的。| **by comparison** (=compared to someone or something else) 相比之下 *After months of being in a tropical climate, Spain seemed cool by comparison.* 在熱帶氣候裡呆了幾個月後, 西班牙相比之下似乎很涼爽。| **for comparison** (=for the purpose of comparing) 為了比較 *He showed us the original text for comparison.* 他讓我們看了原文以作比較。| **in comparison with/to** (=compared to someone or something else) 與…相比 *In comparison with the States, the UK is tiny.* 和美國相比較, 英國很小。| **invite comparison** (=if an object, idea etc invites comparison with something else, it reminds you of it so that you compare them) 某物、某想法等使人想到另一物, 因而對它們進行比較 *Her paintings invite comparison with those of the early Impressionists.* 她的畫不由得讓人將它們與早期印象派作品相比較。| **on comparison** (=after you have compared two things to see if they are similar or different) 在比較之後 *On comparison, the Escort was the more reliable car.* 經過比較, 證明"護航艦"牌車子更為可靠。| **stand/bear comparison** (=compare favourably with someone or something) 比得上, 不亞於 *Irving's work bears comparison with the best of the modern novelists.* 歐文的作品可與最出色的現代小說作品相媲美。
2 ▶JUDGEMENT 判斷◀ [C] a statement or examination that considers how similar or different two people, places, things etc are 比較; 比較報告: **[+of]** *a comparison of smog levels in Chicago and Detroit* 對芝加哥和底特律煙霧水平所作的比較 | **[+between]** *a comparison between the two novels* 對這兩部小說的比較
3 ▶BE LIKE STH 像某物◀ [C] a statement that someone or something is like someone or something else 比擬, 比喻: **[+to]** *The comparison of the mall to a zoo seemed entirely appropriate.* 將購物中心比作動物園好像非常合適。| **make a comparison** (=consider the similarities between two things) 作比較〔顯示兩者之間的共同點〕 *You can't make a comparison between American and Japanese schools – they're too different.* 你不能將美國和日本的學校相提並論, 它們太不相同了。| **draw a comparison** (=show a similarity between two ideas or things) 作出比較〔顯示兩者間的一個共同點〕 *It's tempting to draw a comparison between this and the Watergate scandal.* 將這件事和水門醜聞相比: 這個想法實在很有誘惑力。
4 there's no comparison *spoken* used when you think that someone or something is much better than someone or something else【口】不能相比〔用來表示某人或某物比另一人或物好得多〕: *There's just no comparison between the junk he sings now and his earlier songs.* 他現在唱的這些垃圾歌曲不能與他以前的歌相比。
5 ▶GRAMMAR 語法◀ [U] a word used in grammar meaning the way an adverb or adjective changes its form to show whether it is COMPARATIVE[1] (4) or SUPERLATIVE[1] (2)〔形容詞或副詞的〕比較(變化)

com·part·ment /kəm`pɑrtmənt; kəm'pɑːtmənt/ *n* [C] **1** one of the separate areas into which a plane, ship, or train is divided〔火車、飛機、輪船上的〕車廂, 艙: *a non-smoking compartment* 無煙車廂 **2** one of the separate parts of something such as a desk or box, where you can keep things〔書桌或盒子的〕分隔間: *Put the ice cream back in the freezer compartment.* 將冰淇淋放回冷凍室。—see also 另見 GLOVE COMPARTMENT

com·part·men·tal·ize also 又作 **-ise** *BrE*【英】/ˌkɑmpɑrt`mɛntlaɪz; ˌkɒmpɑːt'mentlaɪz/ *v* [T] to divide things into separate groups, especially according to what type of things they are〔尤指根據事物的種類〕劃分, 分類 —**compartmentalized** *adj* —**compartmentalization** /ˌkɑmpɑrtˌmɛntl̩ə`zeʃən; ˌkɒmpɑːtˌmentl-aɪ'zeɪʃən/ *n* [U]

com·pass /`kʌmpəs; 'kʌmpəs/ *n* **1** [C] an instrument that shows directions 指南針, 羅盤: *a map and compass* 一張地圖和一個指南針 | **compass point** (=one of the 32 marks on a compass that shows you the exact direction) 羅盤上的方位刻度 **2** [C] an instrument that you use to draw circles or measure distances on maps 圓規; 兩腳規 **3** [U] *formal* the area or range of subjects that someone is responsible for or that is discussed in a book【正式】〔某人負責或書中論述的〕範圍: **[+of]** *Within the brief compass of a single page the author covers most of the major points.* 在短短一頁的篇幅中, 作者涵蓋了大部分主要觀點。

com·pas·sion /kəm`pæʃən; kəm'pæʃən/ *n* [U] a strong feeling of sympathy for someone who is suffering, and a desire to help them 憐憫; 同情: **[+for]** *compassion for the poor and sick* 對窮人和病人的同情 | **feel/show compassion** *"Come have a drink," offered Cook, feeling* *compassion.* 庫克心生同情，說道:“來喝一杯。” | **be filled with compassion** (=feel a lot of compassion) 充滿了憐憫

com·pas·sion·ate /kəm`pæʃənɪt; kəm'pæʃənət/ *adj* feeling sympathy for people who are suffering 充滿憐憫同情的: *a caring, compassionate man* 滿懷關愛憐憫的人 | *a compassionate smile* 充滿同情的微笑 —**compassionately** *adv*

compassionate leave /·,··· ˈ·/ *n* [U] special permission to have time away from work because one of your relatives has died or is very ill〔由於親屬去世或病重而特許的〕事假

com·pat·i·bil·ity /kəm,pætə`bɪlətɪ; kəm,pætəˈbɪləti/ *n* [U] **1** the ability to exist or be used together without causing problems 相容〔能夠並存或同時使用而不致產生問題〕 **2** *technical* the ability of one piece of computer equipment to be used with another one, especially when they are made by different companies【術語】〔電腦設備的〕兼容性

com·pat·i·ble[1] /kəm`pætəbl; kəm'pætəbəl/ *adj* **1** *technical* compatible machines, methods, ideas etc can exist together or be used together without causing problems【術語】相容的，兼容的〔機器、方法、想法等能共存或配套使用而不致產生問題〕: *The new software is IBM compatible* (=can be used with IBM computers). 這個新軟件與IBM機兼容。| **[+with]** *The project is not compatible with the company's long-term aims.* 這項計劃與公司長遠目標相違背。**2** two people that are compatible are able to have a good relationship 能和諧相處的

compatible[2] *n* [C] a piece of computer equipment that can be used with another piece, especially one made by a different company〔尤指另一公司製造的〕電腦兼容設備: *IBM compatibles* IBM兼容機

com·pat·ri·ot /kəm`petrɪət; kəm'pætriət/ *n* [C] someone who was born in or is a citizen of the same country as someone else; COUNTRYMAN 同國人，同胞: *Stich defeated his compatriot Becker in the quarter final.* 史廸治在四分之一決賽中擊敗了他的同胞碧加。

com·pel /kəm`pɛl; kəm'pel/ *v* **compelled, compelling** [T] **1** to force someone to do something 強迫; 逼迫: **compel sb to do sth** *reports that children were compelled to participate in bizarre rituals* 關於孩子們被迫參加古怪儀式的報道 | **feel compelled to do sth** (=feel very strongly that you must do something) 強烈感到必須做某事 *Harrison felt compelled to resign because of the allegations in the press.* 由於新聞界的指控，哈里森強烈地感到他必須辭職。**2** *formal* to make people have a particular feeling or attitude【正式】使發生; 引起〔某種感情或態度〕: *His appearance on stage compelled the audience's attention.* 他一出現在舞台上就吸引了觀眾的注意力。—compare 比較 IMPEL

com·pel·ling /kəm`pɛlɪŋ; kəm'pelɪŋ/ *adj* **1** extremely interesting or exciting 令人激動的，極為有趣的: *a compelling personality* 極有吸引力的性格 **2 compelling argument/reason/cases etc** an argument etc that makes you feel it is true or that you must do something about it 令人信服的論點/理由/案例等: *He felt a compelling need to tell someone about his idea.* 他急需把自己的想法告訴別人。—**compellingly** *adv*

com·pen·di·ous /kəm`pɛndɪəs; kəm'pendiəs/ *adj formal* a book that is compendious gives information in a short but complete form【正式】扼要的，簡明的 —**compendiously** *adv*

com·pen·di·um /kəm`pɛndɪəm; kəm'pendiəm/ *n plural* **compendiums** *or* **compendia** /-dɪə; -diə/ [C] *formal*【正式】**1** a book that contains a complete collection of facts, drawings etc on a particular subject 手冊，大全〔關於某題目的詳盡資料、圖解等〕: *a cricketing compendium* 板球運動手冊 **2** *BrE* a set of different BOARD GAMES in one box【英】〔裝在一個盒子裡的〕一套幾種棋盤遊戲

com·pen·sate /`kɑmpən,set; 'kɒmpənseɪt/ *v* **1** [I] to replace or balance something good that has been lost or is lacking, by providing or doing something equally good 彌補，補償: *Because my left eye is so weak, my right eye has to work harder to compensate.* 因為我左眼視力差，右眼就要辛苦點來彌補一下。| **[+for]** *Her intelligence more than compensates for her lack of experience.* 她才智過人，因此雖然經驗不足，也遊刃有餘。**2** [I,T] to pay someone money because they have suffered injury, loss or damage 賠償，補償: **compensate sb for sth** *The firm agreed to compensate its workers for their loss of earnings.* 公司同意補償工人的收入損失。

com·pen·sa·tion /,kɑmpən`seʃən; ,kɒmpən'seɪʃən/ *n* **1** [U] money that someone pays you because they have harmed or hurt you in some way 補償費，賠償金: **[+for]** *compensation for injuries at work* 工傷補償金 | **in compensation** *The plane was cancelled, and all we got in compensation was a free meal.* 航班取消，我們的補償僅僅是一頓免費餐。| **as compensation** *The workers were given 30 days' pay as compensation.* 工人獲得30天的薪金作為補償。| **pay sb compensation** *The idea is that criminals should pay compensation to their victims.* 這個想法就是罪犯應對受害者作出賠償。| **seek/claim compensation** (=ask officially for compensation) 正式要求賠償 | **award/grant compensation** (=pay compensation) 給予補償 *The court awarded Jamieson £15,000 compensation.* 法院裁定給予傑米森1萬5千英鎊賠償。**2** [C,U] something that makes a sad or an unpleasant situation better or happier〔舒緩不佳的境遇的〕補償物，賠償物: *One of the few compensations of being unemployed was seeing more of the family.* 失業帶來的少數好處之一就是能更多地與家人在一起。| **by way of compensation** (=in order to make a situation better) 為了使情況改善 *By way of compensation he offered to take her out for a meal.* 他主動提出請她吃飯，以此作為一種補償。**3** [C,U] actions, behaviour etc that replace or balance something that is lacking〔行為舉止等作為〕彌補，補償: **[+for]** *Linda's aggressiveness is really just a compensation for her feelings of insecurity.* 琳達的咄咄逼人實際上只是對她缺乏安全感的一種補償。| **as compensation** *Lip reading can act as compensation for loss of hearing.* 唇讀可以作為對聽力喪失的補償。

com·pen·sa·to·ry /kəm`pɛnsə,torɪ; ,kɒmpən'seɪtəri◂/ *adj* [usually before noun 一般用於名詞前] **1** intended to reduce the harmful effects of something or to make them easier to bear 彌補性質的，補償性質的 **2** compensatory payments are paid to someone who has been harmed or hurt in some way 賠償的: *She was awarded a large sum in compensatory damages.* 她得到了一大筆錢來賠償她的損失。

com·pere /`kɑmpɛr; 'kɒmpeə/ *n* [C] *BrE* someone who introduces the people who are performing in a television programme, theatre show etc【英】〔電視節目、舞台表演等〕節目主持人; EMCEE *AmE*【美】: *He plays a sleazy, no-talent TV compere.* 他扮演一名格調低下而又缺少才華的電視節目主持人。—**compere** *v* [I,T] *BrE*【英】| *UTV's Pamela Ballentine will compere the show.* UTV台的帕美拉·巴倫坦將主持這次的演出。

com·pete /kəm`pit; kəm'piːt/ *v* [I]

1 ▶PERSON/BUSINESS 人/企業◀ to try to be more successful than another person or organization, especially in business 競爭〔尤指商業方面〕: **[+with]** *They found themselves competing with foreign companies for a share of the market.* 他們發現自己在與外國公司爭奪市場份額。| **[+for]** *She and her sister are always competing for attention.* 她和她姐姐[妹妹]老是爭寵。| **[+against]** *businesses competing against each other* 相互競爭的企業 | **compete to do sth** *Several advertising agencies are competing to get the contract.* 幾家廣告代理商在競爭，力求得到這份合同。| **can't compete** (=be unable to compete, especially with something bigger or better) 無法競爭〔尤指與比自己強大的對手〕*Small, independent bookstores simply can't compete with the big* national chains. 規模小的個體書店怎麼樣也競爭不過大型的全國連鎖店。

2 ►IN A COMPETITION 競賽中◄ to take part in a competition or sporting event 參加比賽: *How many runners will be competing in the marathon?* 有多少賽跑運動員將參加本次馬拉松?

3 can't compete with sb/sth to not be as interesting, attractive etc as someone or something else 敵不過某人/某物: *Melinda was plain and knew she couldn't compete with her sister where boys were concerned.* 梅琳達相貌平平, 她知道在吸引男孩子這方面自己比不上姐姐[妹妹]。

4 ►SOUND/SMELL 聲音/氣味◄ [I+with] if a sound or smell competes with another sound or smell, you can hear both equally well 同時聽見[聞到]: *The songs of the birds competed with the sound of the church bells.* 鳥與教堂鐘聲齊鳴。

5 ►IDEAS/ARGUMENTS 想法/論點◄ if two ideas, arguments, claims etc compete with each other, they cannot both be right 競爭, 對抗

com·pe·tence /ˋkɑmpətəns; ˈkɒmpɪ̣təns/ *n* **1** [U] the ability and skill to do what is needed 稱職; 勝任: *No one questioned his competence as a doctor.* 沒有人懷疑過他當醫生的能力。| *a high level of managerial competence* 高水平的管理才幹 **2** [U] *law* the legal power of a court of law to hear and judge something in court【法律】(法院審判案件的)權限; 管轄權 **3** [U] a special area of knowledge 知識範圍: *It is not within my competence to make such judgements.* 做這種判斷不在我知識範圍之內。**4** [C] a skill needed to do a particular job (做某種工作所必須的)技能: *Typing is considered by most employers to be a basic competence.* 大多數雇主認為打字是一種基本技能。

com·pe·tent /ˋkɑmpətənt; ˈkɒmpɪ̣tənt/ *adj* **1** having enough skill or knowledge to do something to a satisfactory standard 能幹的, 勝任的: *She's a highly competent linguist.* 她是一位非常有才幹的語言學家。| **competent to do sth** *I don't feel competent to give an opinion at the moment.* 我目前還沒有足夠的把握來發表看法。**2** a piece of work, performance etc that is competent is satisfactory but not especially good 合格的, 令人滿意的(但不見得特別好): *The workmen did a competent job.* 這些工人活幹得不錯。**3** [not before noun 不用於名詞前] having the legal power to deal with something in a court of law 有權在法庭上處理某事: **be competent to do sth** *This court is not competent to hear your case.* 這個法庭無權審理你的案子。—**competently** *adv*

com·pet·ing /kəmˋpitɪŋ; kəmˈpiːtɪŋ/ *adj* **competing claims/interests/theories etc** competing claims etc are two claims that cannot both be accepted 互相爭奪、要求承認的聲稱/利益/理論等: *We've got several competing priorities to decide between.* 我們有好幾項緊急事情需要決定處理順序。

1 1 **com·pe·ti·tion** /ˌkɑmpəˋtɪʃən; ˌkɒmpɪ̣ˈtɪʃən/ *n* **1** [U] a situation in which people or organizations compete with each other 競爭: **[+between]** *Sometimes there's a lot of competition between children for their mother's attention.* 為了得到母親的寵愛, 有時孩子們會相互競爭。| **[+for]** *Competition for the job was intense.* 該職位競爭很激烈。| **[+among]** *This price reduction is due to competition among suppliers.* 這次的降價源於供貨商之間的競爭。| **be in competition with** (=be competing with) 與…競爭 | **fierce/stiff/intense etc competition** *There is fierce competition between the three leading soap manufacturers.* 三大肥皂製造商之間競爭很激烈。| **in the face of competition** (=in a situation where you are competing) 面對競爭 *In the face of such strong competition, small grocery stores are going out of business.* 面對如此強大的競爭, 小雜貨店紛紛倒閉。**2** [singular,U] the people or groups that are competing against you, especially in business or in a sport 競爭對手: **the competition** *Going to trade fairs is an ideal opportunity to size up the competition.* 參加貿易商品展覽會是估量對手的理想機會。| **no/not much/little etc competition** (=no one who is likely to be better than you) 沒有/不太多/極少更強的對手 *Lewis is bound to win the race; there's just no competition.* 里維斯注定要獲勝, 因為根本沒有比他更強的對手。| **a lot of/considerable/fierce etc competition** (=people who are very strong or skilful) 許多強的/相當多強的/強勁的對手 *The team overcame fierce competition for their place in the finals.* 這支球隊戰勝了強勁的對手, 打進決賽。| **foreign competition** (=companies from other countries that you are competing with) 來自外國企業的競爭 **3** [C] an organized event in which people or teams compete against each other, especially using their skill (尤指運用技能的)比賽: *United were knocked out of the competition in the first round.* 曼聯隊在第一輪比賽中就敗下陣來。| *a crossword competition* 填字遊戲比賽 | **competition to do sth** *a competition to find a designer for the new airport building* 為新機場大樓招聘設計師而舉行的競賽 | **win/lose a competition** *Who won the volleyball competition?* 誰贏了這次排球比賽? | **enter a competition** *Teams from high schools all over the state have entered the competition.* 全州各地中學的運動隊都參加了這次比賽。

com·pet·i·tive /kəmˋpɛtətɪv; kəmˈpetɪ̣tɪv/ *adj* **1** a competitive situation is one in which people or organizations try very hard to be more successful than others 充滿競爭的: *an extremely competitive market* 競爭非常激烈的市場 | **highly/fiercely/intensely competitive** *Advertising is an intensely competitive business.* 廣告業是一個競爭激烈的行業。**2** products or prices that are competitive are cheaper than others but still of good quality 具有競爭力的(指比較便宜而質量不減的商品或價格): *The hotel offers a high standard of service at competitive rates.* 酒店以優惠的價格提供高標準的服務。**3** someone who is competitive is determined to be more successful than other people 好勝的: *I hate playing tennis with Steve. He's too competitive.* 我討厭和史蒂夫打網球, 他只能贏不能輸。**4 competitive edge** a strong desire to win or do well that gives someone an advantage 好勝的鋒芒(因強烈的求勝慾望而佔有的優勢): *The team seems to have lost their competitive edge in recent months.* 在最近幾個月裡這支運動隊的鋒芒似乎削弱了。—**competitively** *adv* 2 3

com·pet·i·tive·ness /kəmˋpɛtətɪvnəs; kəmˈpetɪ̣tɪvnɪ̣s/ *n* [U] **1** the ability of a company or a product to compete with others 競爭力: *New machinery has enhanced the company's productivity and competitiveness.* 新機器提高了公司的生產力, 增強了競爭力。**2** the desire to be more successful than other people 好勝, 要強: *Her enthusiasm and competitiveness rubbed off on everyone.* 她的熱情和好強感染了每一個人。

com·pet·i·tor /kəmˋpɛtətɚ; kəmˈpetɪ̣tə/ *n* [C] **1** a person, team, company etc that is competing with another 競爭者: *The firm's major competitors are all in France.* 公司主要的競爭對手都在法國。**2** someone who takes part in a competition 選手, 參賽者: *Two of the competitors failed to turn up for the race.* 兩名參賽者比賽時沒有出場。

com·pi·la·tion /ˌkɑmpɪˋleʃən; ˌkɒmpɪ̣ˈleɪʃən/ *n* **1** [C] a book or list, record etc which is made up of different pieces of information, songs etc 輯, 集, 集子: **compilation album/cassette** *a compilation album of Christmas music* 聖誕音樂匯編唱片集 **2** [U] the process of making a book, list, record etc from different pieces of information, songs etc 編纂, 編輯; 匯編: *the compilation of a dictionary* 詞典的編纂

com·pile /kəmˋpaɪl; kəmˈpaɪl/ *v* [T] **1** to make a list, record etc using different pieces of information, songs etc 編輯, 編纂; 編製; 匯編: *The document was compiled by the Department of Health.* 這份文件是由衛生部編輯的。| **compile sth from/for sth** *These notes were com-*

piled from lectures and seminars. 這些筆記是由講座和研討會記錄整理而成的。**2** to put a set of instructions into a computer in a form that you can understand and use 編譯〔電腦用語〕

com·pil·er /kəmˋpaɪlɚ; kəmˈpaɪlə/ *n* [C] **1** someone who collects different pieces of information or facts to be used in a book, report, or list 編輯者, 編纂者 **2** a set of instructions in a computer that changes a computer language known to the computer user into the form needed by the computer〔電腦的〕編譯程序

com·pla·cen·cy /kəmˋplesn̩sɪ; kəmˈpleɪsənsi/ *n* [U] a feeling of satisfaction with what you have achieved which makes you stop trying to improve or change things 自滿, 故步自封: *There are no grounds for complacency in today's competitive environment.* 在今天這種充滿競爭的環境下, 沒有理由自滿。

com·pla·cent /kəmˋplesn̩t; kəmˈpleɪsənt/ *adj* pleased with what you have achieved so that you stop trying to improve or change things 自滿的; 得意的: *There's a danger of becoming complacent if you win a few games.* 如果你贏了幾場比賽就會有自滿的危險。| **[+about]** *We simply cannot afford to be complacent about the future of our car industry.* 我們沒有資格對汽車業的前景沾沾自喜。—**complacently** *adv*

2 3 **com·plain** /kəmˋplen; kəmˈpleɪn/ *v* **1** [I,T not in passive 不用被動態] to say that you are annoyed, dissatisfied, or unhappy about something or someone 抱怨; 不滿, 發牢騷: *They've already been given a 10% raise so why are they complaining?* 已經給他們加薪 10%, 他們怎麼還在抱怨? | *"You never ask my opinion about anything," Rod complained.* 羅德抱怨道:"你從來都不問問我的意見。" | **[+about]** *She often complains about not feeling appreciated at work.* 她因為感到自己在工作上不受賞識而常常抱怨。| **complain (that)** *People complain that they don't get enough information.* 人們抱怨得不到足夠的信息。| **complain to sb** *Neighbours complained to the police about the dogs barking.* 鄰居因為狗吠擾民向警察投訴。| **complain bitterly** *Employees complained bitterly about working conditions.* 雇員對工作條件極為不滿。**2 can't complain** *spoken* used to say that a situation is satisfactory generally in spite of the fact there may be a few problems【口】〔雖然有些問題, 但〕(總體上) 還算滿意: *Old age is creeping up, but I can't complain.* 老年悄然而至, 但一切還算滿意。

complain of sth *phr v* [T] to say that you feel ill or have a pain in a part of your body 訴說有…病痛, 訴苦: *Dan's been complaining of severe headaches recently.* 丹最近總是說頭疼得厲害。

com·plain·ant /kəmˋplenənt; kəmˈpleɪnənt/ *n* [C] *law* someone who makes a formal complaint in a court of law; PLAINTIFF【法律】原告

2 3 **com·plaint** /kəmˋplent; kəmˈpleɪnt/ *n* **1** [C,U] a written or spoken statement in which someone complains about something〔口頭或書面的〕投訴: *The sales assistants were trained to deal with customer complaints in a friendly manner.* 售貨員都受過培訓以禮貌的態度處理顧客的投訴。| **[+about]** *We have received a number of complaints about your conduct.* 針對你的行為我們收到幾宗投訴。| **[+against]** *All complaints against police officers are carefully investigated.* 針對警察的所有投訴都予以仔細調查。| **complaint that** *We are concerned by complaints that children are being bullied.* 我們十分關心有關孩子們受到欺侮的投訴。| **make a complaint** (=complain formally to someone) 正式投訴 *If you wish to make a complaint you should see the manager.* 如果你要投訴, 應該去找經理。| **have/receive a complaint** *The BBC received a stream of complaints about the programme.* 關於這個節目英國廣播公司收到許多投訴。| **file/lodge/submit a complaint** *formal* (=complain officially to someone)【正式】正式〔向某人〕投訴 *"I wish to lodge an official complaint." the woman said.* 那女人說道, "我要提出正式投訴。" | **letter of complaint** *The Council received over 10,000 letters of complaint.* 市議會收到一萬多封投訴信件。| **reason/cause/grounds for complaint** *Anyone dismissed because of their race has legitimate grounds for complaint.* 由於種族的原因而被解雇的人都有正當的投訴理由。| **complaints procedure** (=a system for dealing with official complaints) 投訴程序 **2** [C] something that you complain about 投訴的事物: *Our main complaint is the poor standard of service.* 我們投訴的主要是服務質量差。**3** [C] an illness that affects a particular part of your body 疾病: *Mr Riley is suffering from a chest complaint.* 萊雷先生患了胸部疾病。| *minor skin complaints* 皮膚上的小毛病

com·plai·sance /kəmˋplezn̩s; kəmˈpleɪzəns/ *n* [U] *formal* willingness to do what pleases other people【正式】遷就, 殷勤 —**complaisant** *adj* —**complaisantly** *adv*

com·plect·ed /kəmˋplɛktɪd; kəmˈplektɪ̣d/ *adj* **fair/dark complected** *AmE* having fair or dark skin【美】皮膚白皙/黝黑的

com·ple·ment¹ /ˋkɑmpləmənt; ˈkɒmplɪ̣mənt/ *n* [C] **1** someone or something that emphasizes the good qualities of another person or thing 補足物; 補充; 使完備之物: **[+to]** *A fine wine is a complement to a good meal.* 美酒佳餚, 相得益彰。**2** the number or quantity needed to make a group complete 足數, 足額, 全數〔指使某物齊全的數目或數量〕: **a full complement (of)** (=all the people or things that form a complete group)〔構成一個完整羣體的〕所有的人[物] *Each new cell will carry its full complement of chromosomes.* 每個新的細胞都包含全部數量的染色體。**3** *technical* a word or phrase in grammar that follows a verb and describes the subject of the verb【術語】補語: *In 'John is cold' and 'John became chairman', 'cold' and 'chairman' are complements.* 在 John is cold 和 John became chairman 中, cold、chairman 是補語。**4** *technical* an angle that together with another angle already mentioned makes 90 degrees【術語】餘角 —compare 比較 COMPLIMENT¹

com·ple·ment² /ˋkɑmpləˏmɛnt; ˈkɒmplɪ̣ment/ *v* [T] to show up the good qualities in someone or something, or make them seem more attractive (使)〔優點〕顯現; 使更具吸引力: *The white silk of her blouse complements her olive skin perfectly.* 白色的綢襯衫完美地襯托出她橄欖色的皮膚。| *Sally's tact and reserve complemented John's go-getting attitude.* 莎莉的機智與沉穩使約翰勇敢進取的態度更為突出。—compare 比較 COMPLIMENT²

com·ple·men·ta·ry /ˌkɑmpləˋmɛntərɪ; ˌkɒmplɪ̣ˈmentəri◂/ *adj* **1** making someone or something better or more attractive by emphasizing its good qualities or having qualities that the other person or thing lacks 補充的; 補足的: *The computer and the human mind have different but complementary abilities.* 電腦與人腦各自不同卻又互為補充。**2** *technical* two angles that are complementary add up to 90 degrees【術語】餘角的; 互為餘角的

com·plete¹ /kəmˋplit; kəmˈpliːt/ *adj* **1** a word used to emphasize that a quality you are describing is as great or extreme as possible 十足的, 完全的: *Their engagement came as a complete surprise to me.* 他們訂婚使我大吃一驚。| *The police were in complete control of the situation.* 警方已完全控制了局勢。| **a complete idiot/failure/wimp etc** *I felt a complete fool.* 我覺得自己是個十足的傻子。**2** having all parts, details, facts etc included and with nothing missing 完整的, 全部的, 整個的: *The captain ordered a complete baggage check.* 船長命令對行李進行徹底檢查。| *Buy one of those plates every month until your collection is complete.* 你每月買一隻這套碟子, 直到買齊。| *The party didn't seem complete without Clare.* 沒有克萊爾這個晚會顯得不完整。| **the complete works of** (=a book or books containing every play, story or poem by a particular person) …的作品全集 *the complete works of Shakespeare* 莎士比亞全集 **3** [not before noun 不用於名詞前] finished 已完成的; 已

結束的: *The work on the new building is nearly complete.* 新樓房工程已接近完工。**4 complete with** having equipment or features 裝備有〔某設備〕, 具有〔某特點〕: *The house comes complete with swimming pool and sauna.* 這棟房子配備有游泳池和桑拿浴設備。**5 the complete footballer/host etc** someone who is good at all parts of an activity 全能的足球員/周到的晚會主持人等: *Best's vision and ball control made him the complete footballer.* 貝斯開闊的視野和極佳的控球能力使他成為全能的足球員。—**completeness** *n* [U]

2 1 **complete²** *v* [T] **1** to finish doing something especially when it has taken a long time 結束, 完成〔尤指經歷長時間之後〕: *The students have just completed their course.* 學生剛剛完成了他們的課程。| *The building took two years to complete.* 這幢大樓花了兩年才建成。**2** to make something whole or perfect by adding what is missing 使完整, 使圓滿: *This exercise involves completing sentences.* 這個練習訓練填充句子。| *He only needs one more stamp to complete his collection.* 他只差一個郵票, 就收集全了。| **complete a form/questionnaire** (=give information that is needed) 填表格/填寫問卷

com·plet·ed /kəm`plitɪd; kəmˈpliːtɪ̈d/ *adj* containing all the necessary parts or answers needed to finish something 完整的; 已完成的: *Send your completed form to the following address.* 請將已填好的表格寄往下列地址。

1 2 **com·plete·ly** /kəm`plitlɪ; kəmˈpliːtli/ *adv* in every way; totally 完全地, 全部地, 徹底地: *I completely forgot that it was his birthday yesterday.* 我完全忘了昨天是他的生日。| [+adj/adv] *She was bored with work and wanted to do something completely different.* 她對工作感到厭煩, 想幹點截然不同的事。| *I felt completely relaxed.* 我覺得完全放鬆下來了。

com·ple·tion /kəm`pliʃən; kəmˈpliːʃən/ *n* [U] **1** the state of being finished 完成, 結束: **near completion** (=almost finished) 接近完成 *The new houses are nearing completion.* 那些新房子即將建成。| **completion date** (=the time by which something must or will be finished) 完成的日期; 完成的限期 *The builders have given us December 22nd as a completion date.* 建築商將竣工日期定在12月22日。**2** the act of completing or finishing something 完成, 完結: [+of] *The job is subject to your satisfactory completion of the training course.* 你能否得到這份工作取決於你能否圓滿完成培訓課程。| **on completion** *We paid them on completion of the work.* 他們把工作完成後, 我們付了款。**3** the final point in the sale of a property, such as a house, when the documents have all been signed and all the money paid 銷售完成〔指在房屋等財產銷售中, 契約等已簽訂, 錢款都已付清〕

3 2 **com·plex¹** /kəm`plɛks; ˈkɒmpleks/ *adj* **1** consisting of many different parts or processes that are closely connected 複雜的〔指由許多密切聯繫的部分或過程構成的〕: *There is a complex network of roads round the city.* 這座城市周圍有一個複雜的道路網絡。| *Photosynthesis is a highly complex process.* 光合作用是一個非常複雜的過程。**2** difficult to understand or deal with 難以理解的, 難處理的; 複雜的: *Mental illness is by its nature very complex.* 精神病就其本質來說是十分複雜的。| *a complex problem* 一個複雜的問題 **3** *technical* a complex word or sentence contains a main part and one or more other parts【術語】〔詞、句〕複合

com·plex² /ˈkɑmplɛks; ˈkɒmpleks/ *n* [C] **1** a group of buildings that are close together, or a large building containing smaller buildings that are used for the same purpose 綜合樓羣〔由眾多大樓或一座主樓和諸多輔樓組成〕: *They are building a vast new shopping complex in the town.* 他們正在市區興建一處巨大的綜合性商場。| **leisure/sports/cinema complex** *a 12-screen cinema complex* 擁有12個放映廳的電影院 **2** an emotional problem in which someone is unnecessarily anxious about something or thinks too much about something 情結, 誇大的情緒反應: **have a complex about sth** *She's has some kind of a complex about her nose.* 她對自己的鼻子感到莫名其妙的擔心。| **give sb a complex** *You'll give Graham a complex if you keep going on about how fat he is.* 如果你老是對格雷厄姆說他有多胖, 就會惹得他心緒不寧。**3 a complex of roads/regulations etc** a large number of things which are closely connected and difficult to understand 縱橫交織的道路網/紛繁蕪雜的條例等 —see also 另見 INFERIORITY COMPLEX, OEDIPUS COMPLEX, PERSECUTION COMPLEX

com·plex·ion /kəm`plɛkʃən; kəmˈplekʃən/ *n* **1** [C] the natural colour or appearance of the skin on your face 面色; 面容: *Drinking lots of water is good for the complexion.* 多喝水對面色有好處。| **a pale/ruddy complexion etc** (=a pale, red face etc) 面色蒼白/臉色紅潤等 **2** [singular] the general character or nature of something 一般性質; 一般特徵: **put a (whole) new complexion on** (=change a situation) 使〔某事〕大為改觀 *These latest findings have put a whole new complexion on the affair.* 最近的這些發現使這件事大為改觀。

com·plex·i·ty /kəm`plɛksɪtɪ; kəmˈpleksɪ̈ti/ *n* [U] **1** the state of being complicated 複雜性, 錯綜複雜: *Many claimants are put off by the sheer complexity of insurance company rules.* 許多索賠人往往由於保險公司十分複雜的規章制度而作罷。**2 the complexities of** the problems and difficulties involved in a situation or process〔某局勢或過程中〕所牽涉的問題和困難: *the complexities of the tax laws* 稅法的錯綜複雜

com·pli·ance /kəm`plaɪəns; kəmˈplaɪəns/ *n* [U] *formal*【正式】**1** OBEDIENCE to a rule, agreement, or demand 服從, 聽從, 遵守〔規則、協議、要求〕: *Compliance with the law is expected of all citizens.* 所有公民都要遵守法律。| **in compliance with** *In compliance with her wishes, she was buried next to her husband.* 依照她的願望, 她被葬在丈夫旁邊。**2** the tendency to agree too willingly to someone else's wishes or demands 過於順從, 屈從: *Her compliance with everything we suggested made it difficult to know what she really felt.* 她對我們所有的提議言聽計從, 使人難以了解她真正的想法。

com·pli·ant /kəm`plaɪənt; kəmˈplaɪənt/ *adj* willing to obey, or agree to other people's wishes and demands〔對他人的意願和要求〕順從的; 聽從的, 服從的: *He soon settled down and became a compliant patient.* 他很快就安靜下來, 成了安分的病人。—**compliantly** *adv* —see also 另見 COMPLY

com·pli·cate /ˈkɑmplə͵ket; ˈkɒmplɪ̈keɪt/ *v* [T] **1** to make a problem or situation more difficult 使〔問題或情況〕更複雜, 更麻煩: *The situation is complicated by the fact that I've got to work late on Friday.* 我週五得加班, 這使情況更複雜了。| **to complicate matters/things** *Just to complicate things, the car has broken down!* 汽車拋錨了, 使事情更加麻煩! **2** [usually passive 一般用被動態] to make an illness worse 使〔疾病〕惡化: *a heart condition complicated by pneumonia* 因肺炎而惡化的心臟病

com·pli·cat·ed /ˈkɑmplə͵ketɪd; ˈkɒmplɪ̈keɪtɪ̈d/ *adj* **1** difficult to understand or deal with 難懂的; 難處理的: *They had to begin the complicated task of sorting out his legal affairs.* 他們不得不着手整理他的法律事務, 這是件繁雜的工作。| *a complicated set of instructions* 一組複雜難懂的說明 | **extremely/highly complicated** *a highly complicated situation* 極其複雜的情況 **2** consisting of many closely related or connected parts 結構複雜的: *The human brain is an incredibly complicated organ.* 人腦是一個結構極其複雜的器官。 2

com·pli·ca·tion /͵kɑmplə`keʃən; ͵kɒmplɪ̈ˈkeɪʃən/ *n* **1** [C,U] a problem or situation that makes something more difficult to understand or deal with 使複雜化的問題[情況]: *The fact that the plane was late added a further complication to our journey.* 飛機誤點給我們的旅行帶來更大麻煩。**2** [C, usually plural 一般用複數] a medical problem or illness that happens while someone is already ill and makes medical treatment more difficult 併發症: *Pneumonia is one of the common complications faced by bed-ridden patients.* 肺炎是臥牀病人所面臨的

常見併發症之一。

complicit /kəmˋplɪsət; kəmˈplɪsɪ̣t/ *adj* involved in or knowing about a situation, especially one that is morally wrong or dishonest 同謀的, 串通一氣的: *They exchanged complicit smiles.* 他們相視而會心微笑。| **complicit in sth** *The careers of the officers complicit in the cover-up were ruined.* 由於參與掩飾真相, 這些軍官的前途都毀掉了。

com·plic·i·ty /kəmˋplɪsətɪ; kəmˈplɪsɪ̣ti/ *n* [U] *formal* a process in which someone is involved in a crime or illegal activity together with other people【正式】共犯, 同謀; 串通: [+in] *Jennings denied complicity in the murder.* 詹寧斯否認自己參與了謀殺案。

com·pli·ment[1] /ˋkɑmpləmənt; ˈkɒmplɪ̣mənt/ *n* [C] **1** a remark that expresses admiration of someone or something 讚美; 恭維〔話〕: *"You have lovely hair", Bob told Emma, who blushed at the compliment.* 鮑勃對愛瑪說"你的頭髮真美", 這句恭維話讓愛瑪臉都紅了。| *Maria's used to receiving compliments on her appearance.* 瑪利亞已經習慣於接受別人對她容貌的讚美。| **pay sb a compliment** (tell someone that they look nice, have done something well, etc) 恭維某人; 讚美某人 | **take sth as a compliment** (=be pleased about what someone has said about you) 這麼說我很高興 *"James described you as a bold, brave feminist." "Oh well, I'll take that as a compliment."* "詹姆士說你是位大膽無畏的女權主義者。" "是嗎? 他這麼講我很高興。" | **shower sb with compliments** (=praise someone very much) 對某人百般恭維 | **return a compliment** (=say something nice to someone after they have said something nice to you) 回敬〔別人的〕稱讚 | **fish for compliments** (=try to make someone say something nice about you, usually by asking them a question) 引誘別人來誇獎自己〔一般通過提問〕**2 pay sb the compliment of doing sth** to do something that shows you trust someone else and have a good opinion of them 對某人做某事表示信任和好感: *They paid me the ultimate compliment of electing me as their representative.* 他們選我為他們的代表, 顯示了對我的高度信任。**3 compliments** *plural* used to express praise, admiration or good wishes 致意; 讚美; 祝賀: **my compliments to the chef** (=used to tell someone that they cook very well) 向廚師致意〔用於稱讚人善於烹飪〕*This Stilton and celery soup is delicious; my compliments to the chef!* 這種斯提爾頓乾酪和芹菜湯太好吃了, 請向廚師致謝! | **compliments of the season** (=used as a spoken or written greeting at Christmas and New Year) 謹致節日祝賀〔口頭或書面祝賀, 用於聖誕節和新年時〕**4 a) with the compliments of.../with our compliments** an expression printed on a small piece of paper used by a company or organization when they send goods or information ...向您致意 / 我們謹向您致意〔公司或其他機構運貨或傳信時印於小紙條上的用語〕: *With the compliments of J. Nocuold & Son* 那古爾德父子公司向您致意 **b)** used when a person or company gives you something such as a free ticket, meal etc 問候, 致意〔某人或某公司向你贈送諸如戲票、餐飲時使用〕: *Please accept these tickets with our compliments.* 幾張戲票請收下, 順致問候。**5 a) return the compliment** to do something to help someone after they have helped you 回禮, 答謝: *Thanks for helping me move the furniture; I'll try to return the compliment one day.* 謝謝你幫我搬家具, 我哪一天也會設法答謝。**b)** to say or do something unpleasant to someone after they have behaved badly towards you〔在受到別人無禮對待之後〕回敬〔某人〕: *"Gemma called you a fat liar." "Gee thanks. Remind me to return the compliment."* "姬瑪說你滿嘴謊話。" "嘿, 謝謝。請提醒我回敬她。" **6 back-handed compliment** *BrE*【英】, **left-handed compliment** *AmE*【美】something that someone says to you which is unpleasant and pleasant at the same time〔同時包含貶低及讚美的〕恭維話: *"A lot of people seem to resent you, but I like you", she said. Talk about a back-handed compliment.* "似乎許多人討厭你, 但我喜歡你。" 她說。此所謂既貶低又讚美的話。—compare 比較 COMPLEMENT[1]

com·pli·ment[2] /ˋkɑmplə͵mɛnt; ˈkɒmplɪ̣ment/ *v* [T] to say something nice to someone in order to praise them 讚美, 恭維: **compliment sb on sth** *Bob complimented me on my new hairstyle.* 鮑勃稱讚我的新髮型。—compare 比較 COMPLEMENT[2]

com·pli·men·ta·ry /͵kɑmpləˋmɛntərɪ; ͵kɒmplɪ̣ˈmentəri◂/ *adj* **1** expressing admiration, praise or respect 讚美的, 讚揚的; 尊敬的: *Your teacher made some very complimentary remarks about your work.* 你的老師對你的作業大加稱讚。| [+about] *Donleavy was highly complimentary about Coleman's work.* 鄧利維高度讚揚了科爾曼的工作。**2** given free to people 免費的: *There was a complimentary bottle of champagne in the hotel room.* 賓館房間內有一瓶免費供應的香檳。| **complimentary ticket/seat etc** *We've got two complimentary tickets for the Barcelona game.* 我們有兩張觀看巴塞羅那隊來比賽的贈票。

compliment slip /ˈ··· ͵·/ *n* [C] a small piece of paper with a company's name and address on it, that it sends with goods instead of a proper letter 致意便條〔印有公司名稱及地址, 附在向顧客寄送的商品上〕

com·pline /ˋkɑmplɪn; ˈkɒmplɪ̣n/ *n* [U] a Christian church service held late in the evening, especially in the Roman Catholic church〔尤指羅馬天主教的〕晚禱 —compare 比較 EVENSONG, VESPERS

com·ply /kəmˋplaɪ; kəmˈplaɪ/ *v* [I] *formal* to do what you have to do or are asked to do【正式】服從, 遵守: [+with] *Failure to comply with the regulations will result in prosecution.* 不遵守規則將招致起訴。—see also 另見 COMPLIANCE

com·po·nent /kəmˋponənt; kəmˈpəʊnənt/ *n* [C] one of several parts that together make up a whole machine or system〔機器或系統的〕零件; 成分; 組成部分: *The repair shop sells electrical components.* 修理店出售電器零件。| *Counselling is an important component of our rehabilitation programme.* 諮詢服務是我們康復計劃中的重要一環。—compare 比較 CONSTITUENT[1] (2)

com·port /kəmˋport; kəmˈpɔːt/ *v* **comport yourself** *formal* to behave yourself in a particular way【正式】行動, 表現: *He always comported himself in an exemplary manner.* 他的行為舉止始終可為人表率。—**comportment** *n* [U]

com·pose /kəmˋpoz; kəmˈpəʊz/ *v* **1 be composed of** to be formed from a group of substances or parts 由...組成: *Water is composed of hydrogen and oxygen.* 水由氫和氧組成。**2** [T not in progressive 不用進行式] if different things or people compose something else, they combine together to form it 組成, 構成: *the individual letters that compose a word* 組合成詞的單個字母 **3** [I, T] to write a piece of music 作曲: *Could you compose a piece for the concert?* 你能為音樂會創作一支曲子嗎? **4 compose a letter/poem/speech etc** to write a letter, poem etc, thinking very carefully about it as you write it 寫信 / 詩 / 講稿等: *compose a letter of complaint* 寫一封投訴信 **5 compose your thoughts/features** to make yourself feel or look calm 鎮靜心情 / 使外表平靜: *He felt he needed a quiet place where he could compose his thoughts.* 他覺得自己需要一個安靜的地方以平靜思緒。| **compose yourself** (=try hard to become calm after feeling very angry, upset, or excited)〔生氣、煩躁、激動後〕極力使自己平靜下來 **6** [T] to arrange the parts of a painting, photograph or scene etc in a way that achieves a particular result〔為達到特殊效果而〕為〔繪畫、照片場景〕構圖: *The photographer will need plenty of time to compose the shot.* 攝影師需要足夠的時間來為他這幅照片構圖。

com·posed /kəmˋpozd; kəmˈpəʊzd/ *adj* seeming calm and not upset or angry 看起來平靜的, 鎮定的: *He appeared very composed despite the stress he was under.* 儘管壓力很大, 他看起來仍十分鎮定。

com·pos·er /kəm`pozɚ; kəm'pəʊzə/ *n* [C] someone who writes music 作曲家

com·po·site¹ /kəm`pɑzɪt; 'kɒmpəzɨt/ *adj* [only before noun 僅用於名詞前] made up of different parts or materials 由不同成分或原料組成的: *a composite problem* 一道複合題 | *composite molecules* 合成分子

composite² *n* [C] **1** something made up of different parts or materials〔由不同成分或材料組成的〕複合物, 混合物: *Behaviour is a composite of individual and group influences.* 行為是個體與集體影響的混合物。| *If she wants to be a model, she'll need a composite of good photographs.* 她如果想做模特兒, 就需要一批多種多樣的高質量照片。**2** a method used by the police for producing a picture of a possible criminal from descriptions given by a WITNESS or WITNESSes 合成照片〔警方根據證人描述製作用以識別罪犯的方法〕; IDENTIKIT *BrE*【英】

3 **com·po·si·tion** /ˌkɑmpə`zɪʃən; ˌkɒmpə'zɪʃən/ *n*

1 ►MAKING A WHOLE 構成整體◄ [U] the way in which something is made up of different parts, things, members etc 組成, 構成: *There were dramatic changes in the composition of the committee after the election.* 選舉之後, 委員會的構成發生了大變動。| [+of] *He's doing research into the chemical composition of plants.* 他正在研究植物的化學構成。| **in composition** *The suburbs are mainly working class in composition.* 各個郊區的人口主要是勞工階級。

2 ►MUSIC/ART ETC 音樂/藝術等◄ **a)** [C] a piece of music or art, or a poem〔音樂、美術、詩歌〕作品: *She's very fond of Bach's later compositions.* 她十分喜愛巴赫的後期作品。**b)** [U] the art or process of writing pieces of music, poems etc〔音樂、詩歌等的〕創作; 作曲; 寫作

3 ►PHOTOGRAPH/PICTURE 照片/圖畫◄ [U] the way in which the different parts that make up a photograph or painting are arranged 照片、繪畫等的佈局: *The composition of these photographs is superb.* 這些照片的佈局極為精巧。

4 ►SCHOOL SUBJECT 學校科目◄ [C,U] *old-fashioned* a short piece of writing about a particular subject that is done especially at school【過時】作文〔尤指學生作業〕: *a 400-word composition about Autumn* 一篇以秋天為題的 400 字作文

5 ►PRINTING 印刷◄ [U] *technical* the process of arranging words, pictures etc on a page before they are printed【術語】排字; 排版

com·pos·i·tor /kəm`pɑzɪtɚ; kəm'pɒzɨtə/ *n* [C] someone who arranges letters, pictures etc on a page before they are printed 排字[版]工人

com·pos men·tis /`kɑmpəs `mɛntɪs; ˌkɒmpəs 'mentɨs/ *adj* [not before noun 不用於名詞前] *often humorous* able to think clearly and be responsible for your actions【常幽默】心智健全的: *It's too early in the morning – I'm not compos mentis!* 大清早的 —— 我還不太清醒呢!

com·post¹ /`kɑmpost; 'kɒmpɒst/ *n* [U] a mixture of decayed plants, leaves etc used to improve the quality of soil 堆肥, 混合肥料: **compost heap** (=a place in a garden where you pile decayed leaves, plants etc in order to make compost) 堆肥處

compost² *v* [T] **1** to make plants, leaves etc into compost 將〔植物、樹葉等〕製成堆肥 **2** to put compost onto soil 給〔土壤〕施堆肥

com·po·sure /kəm`poʒɚ; kəm'pəʊʒə/ *n* [singular, U] a calm feeling which you have when you feel confident about dealing with a situation 冷靜, 鎮定: **keep/maintain your composure** (=stay calm) 保持冷靜 *They maintained an admirable composure throughout the ordeal.* 他們在那場考驗中始終保持着令人佩服的鎮靜。| **lose your composure** (=get angry or upset) 生氣, 慌張煩躁 | **recover/regain your composure** (=become calm after feeling angry or upset)〔心情〕恢復平靜

com·pote /`kɑmpot; 'kɒmpɒt/ *n* [C,U] fruit cooked in sugar and water and eaten cold 糖水水果〔用糖和水烹調的水果, 通常冷食〕

com·pound¹ /`kɑmpaʊnd; 'kɒmpaʊnd/ *n* [C] **1** *technical* a substance containing atoms from two or more elements (ELEMENT (1))【術語】化合物: *Sulphur dioxide is a compound of sulphur and oxygen.* 二氧化硫是硫與氧的化合物。**2** a combination of two or more things or qualities that make up a situation 由兩件或更多事情, 兩種或更多情況結合造成的局勢: *social unrest caused by a compound of unemployment and poverty* 失業與貧困並存所導致的社會動蕩 **3** an area that contains a group of buildings and is surrounded by a fence or wall 四周有籬笆或圍牆的建築羣: *a prison compound* 監獄大院 **4** *technical* a noun or adjective made up of two or more words【術語】複合名詞; 複合形容詞: *The noun 'flower shop' and the adjective 'self-made' are compounds.* 名詞 flower shop 及形容詞 self-made 均為複合詞。

compound² *adj* **1 compound eye/leaf etc** *technical* a single eye, leaf etc that is made up of two or more parts or substances【術語】複眼/複葉等 **2 compound noun/adjective** *technical* a noun or adjective that is made up of two or more words【術語】複合名詞/複合形容詞

com·pound³ /kəm`paʊnd; kəm'paʊnd/ *v* [T] **1** to make a difficult situation even worse by adding more problems 使惡化, 加重: **be compounded by** *Our difficulties were compounded by the language barrier.* 我們因語言障礙而加重了困難。**2** to make something by mixing different parts or substances together 使混合; 使合成; 使化合: *Scientists are able to compound an increasing number of substances to produce new drugs.* 科學家們能夠通過混合越來越多的不同物質來製造新藥品。**3** *AmE* to pay INTEREST¹ (4) that is calculated on both the sum of money and the INTEREST¹ (4)【美】以複利計算支付〔利息〕: *My bank compounds interest quarterly.* 我的銀行按季度以複利計算支付利息。

compound frac·ture /ˌ·· '··/ *n* [C] *technical* a broken bone that cuts through someone's skin【術語】哆開骨折, 有創骨折

compound in·terest /ˌ·· '··/ *n* [U] INTEREST¹ (4) that is calculated on both the sum of money lent or borrowed and on the unpaid INTEREST already earned or charged 複利 —compare 比較 SIMPLE INTEREST

com·pre·hend /ˌkɑmprɪ`hɛnd; ˌkɒmprɪ'hend/ *v* [I,T not in progressive 不用進行式] *formal* to understand something that is complicated or difficult【正式】理解, 領悟〔複雜或困難事物〕: *Even scientists do not comprehend these phenomena.* 即使是科學家也不理解這些現象。| **comprehend how/why/what etc** *I fail to comprehend how this was allowed to happen.* 我不理解怎麼會允許這種事發生。| **fully comprehend** (=understand completely) 徹底理解

com·pre·hen·si·ble /ˌkɑmprɪ`hɛnsəbl; ˌkɒmprɪ'hensɨbəl/ *adj* easy to understand 易於理解的: *The book offers an easily comprehensible explanation of the subject.* 這本書對這個主題提供了淺顯易懂的解釋。| [+to] *Such detailed analyses are not comprehensible to the average person.* 如此詳細的分析對於一般人來說並不容易懂。—opposite 反義詞 INCOMPREHENSIBLE —**comprehensibly** *adv* —**comprehensibility** /ˌkɑmprɪˌhɛnsə`bɪlətɪ; ˌkɒmprɪhensɨ'bɪlɨti/ *n* [U]

com·pre·hen·sion /ˌkɑmprɪ`hɛnʃən; ˌkɒmprɪ'henʃən/ *n* **1** [U] the ability to understand something 理解(力): *a reasonable comprehension of the subject* 對這個主題的較深入理解 | **beyond (sb's) comprehension** (=impossible to understand) 不能理解, 無法理解 *How she managed to pass her exam after doing so little work is beyond my comprehension.* 她沒有怎麼用功就通過了考試, 這讓我無法理解。**2** [U] knowledge of what a situation is really like 了解: *Most politicians have no real comprehension of what it is like to be poor.* 大多數政治家對於甚麼是貧困並無真正的了解。**3** [C,U] an exercise given to students to test how well they understand written or spoken language 閱讀[聽力]理解測試: **reading/listening comprehension** (=a piece of written or spoken language which tests how well students understand) 閱讀/聽力理解測試

3 **com·pre·hen·sive** /ˌkɑmprɪˋhɛnsɪv; ˌkɒmprɪˈhensɪv◂/ *adj* **1** including all the necessary facts, details, or problems that need to be dealt with; thorough 詳盡的; 全面的; 徹底的: *There was a comprehensive inspection of the nuclear plant.* 對核工廠進行了一次全面的視察。| **comprehensive study/list/coverage etc** *a comprehensive account of the events leading up to the Second World War* 對導致第二次世界大戰的各種事件的詳盡敘述 | **comprehensive insurance/cover/policy** (=a type of insurance that pays for damage whether it is caused by you or someone else) 綜合保險〔指損失不論是否投保人造成, 都得到補償〕**2 comprehensive education/system** a system of education in which pupils of different abilities go to the same school or are taught in the same class 綜合教育/體系 —**comprehensively** *adv* —**comprehensiveness** *n* [U]

comprehensive school /··ˈ·· ˌ·/ also 又作 **comprehensive** *n* [C] a state school in Britain for pupils of different abilities over the age of 11〔英國招收年滿 11 歲不同資質學生的〕綜合中學: *Kylie goes to the local comprehensive.* 凱麗上的是本地的綜合中學。

com·press[1] /kəmˋprɛs; kəmˈpres/ *v* **1** [I,T] if you compress something it is pressed so that it takes up less space 壓緊; 壓縮: **compress sth into** *The machine compresses old cars into blocks of scrap metal.* 機器把舊汽車壓成一塊塊的廢鋼鐵。| **compressed air/gas etc** *Compressed gas was escaping through a hole in the cylinder.* 壓縮的氣體當時正在從汽缸的一個孔中逸出。**2** [T] to write or express something using fewer words 壓縮〔文字或話語〕: *Try to compress and simplify your notes so that they are easier to learn.* 盡量壓縮並簡化你的筆記, 這樣學起來比較容易。**3** [T usually passive 一般用被動態] to reduce the amount of time that it takes for something to happen or be done 壓縮〔做某事的時間〕: **compress sth into** *What would normally have been a three-year training course had to be compressed into eighteen months.* 在正常情況下需要三年的培訓課程不得不被壓縮到十八個月。—**compressible** *adj* —**compression** /-ˋprɛʃən; -ˈpreʃən/ *n* [U]

com·press[2] /ˋkɑmprɛs; ˈkɒmpres/ *n* [C] a small thick piece of material that you put on part of someone's body to stop blood flowing out or to make it less painful〔用以止血、止痛等的〕敷布, 壓布: **cold/hot compress** *Apply a cold compress to the injured part of the limb.* 將冷敷布敷在肢體的受傷處。

com·pres·sor /kəmˋprɛsɚ; kəmˈpresə/ *n* [C] a machine or part of a machine that compresses air or gas 壓氣機[機器中的氣體壓縮器]

3 **com·prise** /kəmˋpraɪz; kəmˈpraɪz/ *v* [not in progressive 不用進行式] *formal*【正式】**1** [linking verb 連繫動詞] to consist of particular parts, groups etc 包括, 由…構成: *The house comprises 2 bedrooms, a kitchen, and a living room.* 這座房子有兩間臥室、一間廚房以及一間起居室。| **be comprised of** *The city's population is largely comprised of Asians and Europeans.* 這座城市的人口主要由亞洲人與歐洲人構成。**2** [T] if different people or things comprise something they combine together to form it 構成; 組成: *Women comprise a high proportion of part-time workers.* 兼職人員中婦女構成很大一部分。—see also 另見 CONSTITUTE

USAGE NOTE 用法说明: COMPRISE

WORD CHOICE 詞語辨析: **make up, consist of, compose, comprise, include, constitute**

Things **consist of** or **are made up of** a series of parts, or more formally **are composed of/comprise** all their parts 事物如果由一系列部分組成, 通常用 consist of 或 are made of; 更正式則用 are composed of/comprise: *New York City comprises Manhattan, Queens, Brooklyn, The Bronx and Staten Island.* 紐約市由曼哈頓、皇后區、布魯克林、布朗克斯以及斯坦登島組成。| *a street composed mainly of detached houses* (NOT 不用 *composed by/from*) 主要由獨立的房屋構成的街道 | *a family made up of six people* 一個由六個人組成的家庭 | *Dinner consisted of a starter, a main course and a dessert* (NOT 不用 *consisted in/on* or 或 *was consisted of*). 這頓晚飯由一個開胃菜、一道主菜和甜點組成。

You will sometimes hear native speakers using **comprise** with *of*, but some people think this is incorrect 有時你會聽見英美人在 comprise 後面用 of, 但有人認為這種用法不正確: *The company comprised of/is comprised of five divisions.* 這家公司由五個部門組成。

If you only mention some of the parts, you use **include**. 如果僅僅提及一個整體中的某些部分, 則使用 include: *New York City includes Brooklyn and Queens.* 紐約市包括布魯克林區及皇后區。

All the parts of something together **make up** or more formally **constitute** or (less frequently) **comprise** the whole. 組成某物的所有部分合在一起構成一個整體用 made up, 比較正式時用 constitute 或 comprise〔不十分常用〕: *Manhattan, Queens, Brooklyn, The Bronx and Staten Island constitute/comprise New York City.* 曼哈頓、皇后區、布魯克林、布朗克斯和斯坦登島構成紐約市。| *How many people make up a basketball team?* 一支籃球隊由多少人組成?

GRAMMAR 語法

These words are not used in progressive tenses in these meanings. 這些詞用於上述意思時不能使用進行時態。

com·pro·mise[1] /ˋkɑmprəˌmaɪz; ˈkɒmprəmaɪz/ *n* **1** [C, U] an agreement between two people that is achieved by both people accepting less than they wanted at first〔由於雙方讓步而達成的〕折衷; 妥協: *Compromise is an inevitable part of marriage.* 妥協是婚姻不可避免的一個部分。| **reach a compromise** *Talks continue in the hope that the two factions will reach a compromise.* 談判繼續下去, 希望雙方能達成妥協。| **make a compromise** *Everybody has to be prepared to make compromises.* 每個人都必須準備作出讓步。**2** [C] an idea or thing that is the result of an agreement between two people or groups who want different things 折衷辦法[協議]: **[+between]** *The treaty represents a political compromise between the two nations.* 這一條約體現了兩國間的一次政治妥協。

compromise[2] *v* **1** [I] to reach an agreement with someone by both of you accepting less than you wanted at first 妥協, 讓步: *She was forced to compromise in order to avoid a major argument.* 為了避免一場激烈爭論, 她被迫讓步。| **[+on]** *We managed to compromise on a price for the car.* 我們終於就汽車的價格達成妥協。| **[+with]** *Can't you boys compromise with each other? Play football this morning and tennis this afternoon.* 你們男孩子難道就不能各讓一步嗎? 今天早上踢足球, 下午打網球。**2 compromise your principles/beliefs/ideas etc** to do something that is against your principles etc and which therefore seems dishonest or shameful 違背原則/放棄信仰/背棄理想等: *He tried to make money without compromising his moral values.* 他努力在不違背自己道德標準的前提下賺錢。| **compromise yourself** (=do something dishonest or embarrassing that puts you in a difficult position)〔做不光彩的事情而〕使自己處於困境 **3 compromise your chances** to spoil the chances of something good happening 使自己喪失機會: *That kind* *of behaviour will compromise your chances of promotion.* 那種行為將使你失去晉升的機會。

com·pro·mis·ing /ˋkɑmprəˏmaɪzɪŋ; ˈkɒmprəmaɪzɪŋ/ *adj* making it seem or proving that you have done something morally wrong or embarrassing 使處於理虧[難堪]境地的: **compromising situation/position etc** *The magazine had shown him in a compromising position with his political researcher.* 該雜誌暴露了他和他的政治研究員一段不光彩的經歷。| **compromising letter/photograph/picture etc** *A large number of compromising letters fell into the hands of Tsarist investigators.* 大批可能惹麻煩的信件落在了沙皇調查官員的手中。

comp·trol·ler /kənˋtrolɚ; kənˈtrəʊlə/ *n* [C] *formal* an official title for a CONTROLLER (2)【正式】審計員, 審計官

com·pul·sion /kəmˋpʌlʃən; kəmˈpʌlʃən/ *n* **1** [C] a strong and unreasonable desire that is difficult to control〔難以克制的〕強烈慾望, 衝動: *Constantly washing her hands became a compulsion that needed treatment.* 她不停地洗手, 這已成為一種需要治療的衝動。| **compulsion to do sth** *I had a sudden compulsion to hit her.* 我突然有種想要揍她的衝動。**2** [singular, U] a force or influence that makes someone do something〔使某人做某事的〕力量; 影響: **compulsion to do sth** *Please note that you are under no compulsion to sign the agreement.* 請注意, 您是否簽此協議, 完全自願。—see also 另見 COMPEL

com·pul·sive /kəmˋpʌlsɪv; kəmˈpʌlsɪv/ *adj* **1** compulsive behaviour is very difficult to stop or control, and is often a result of or a sign of a mental problem 難以抑制的〔難以抑制的行為往往是精神病的一種症候〕: *Compulsive spending is often a symptom of deep unhappiness.* 肆意地揮霍常常是內心鬱悶的一種徵兆。**2 a compulsive liar/gambler/drinker etc** someone who has such a strong desire to lie etc that they are unable to control it 有強烈說謊/賭博/酗酒等的慾望而無法自制的人 **3** a book, programme etc that is compulsive is so interesting that you cannot stop reading or watching it 吸引人的; 有趣的: **compulsive reading/viewing** (=very interesting to read or watch) 引人入勝的書刊/有趣的電視節目 *'Gardening World' – compulsive viewing for gardeners.* "園藝世界"── 園藝愛好者百看不厭的節目。—**compulsively** *adv* —**compulsiveness** *n* [U]

com·pul·so·ry /kəmˋpʌlsərɪ; kəmˈpʌlsəri/ *adj* something that is compulsory must be done because it is the law or because someone in authority orders you to; OBLIGATORY 規定的; 強迫的; 義務的: *In Britain, education is compulsory between the ages of 5 and 16.* 在英國5歲至16歲是義務教育時期。| *compulsory lay-offs* 強迫解雇 —**compulsorily** *adv* —compare 比較 VOLUNTARY¹ (4)

com·punc·tion /kəmˋpʌŋkʃən; kəmˈpʌŋkʃən/ *n* [U] *formal* a deep feeling of shame or guilt【正式】羞愧; 內疚; 懊悔

com·pu·ta·tion /ˏkɑmpjəˋteʃən; ˌkɒmpjʊˈteɪʃən/ *n* [C, U] *formal* the process of calculating or the result of calculating【正式】計算; 計算的結果

com·pute /kəmˋpjut; kəmˈpjuːt/ *v* [I,T] *formal* to calculate a result, answer, sum etc【正式】計算〔結果、答案、總數等〕

1 1 **com·put·er** /kəmˋpjutɚ; kəmˈpjuːtə/ *n* [C] an electronic machine that can store information and do things with it according to a set of instructions called a PROGRAM 電腦, 計算機: *the latest computer software* 最新的電腦軟件 | *a new computer-controlled heating system* 一套全新的由電腦控制的供暖系統 | *The doctor has all the patient's details on computer.* 醫生在電腦中儲存了這名病人的全部情況。| **computer system/analysis/applications/networks etc** *We've just had a new computer system installed at work.* 我們剛剛在工作單位安裝了新的電腦系統。| **computer literacy** (=basic knowledge of and ability to use computers) 基礎電腦知識和運用電腦的能力 | **computer literate** (=able to use a computer) 會使用電腦的 —see also 另見 MICROCOMPUTER, MINICOMPUTER, PERSONAL COMPUTER, LAPTOP

Computer-aid·ed de·sign /·ˏ·· ·· ·ˋ·/ *n* [U] CAD 電腦輔助設計

computer dat·ing a·gency /·ˏ·· ˈ·· ˏ···/ *n* [C] a company that uses computers to try to find suitable partners for people by matching their interests etc 電腦婚姻介紹所

computer game /·ˈ·· ˏ·/ *n* [C] a game that you play on a computer 電腦遊戲

computer graph·ics /·ˏ·· ˈ··/ *n* [plural] the pictures and images that you see on a computer screen 電腦圖像

com·put·er·ize also 又作 -ise *BrE*【英】/kəmˋpjutəˏraɪz; kəmˈpjuːtəraɪz/ *v* [T] to use a computer to control an operation, system etc 用電腦操作: *They have decided to computerize the accounts department.* 他們已經決定讓會計部門用電腦操作。| *Our local supermarket now has a fully computerized checkout system.* 我們本地的超級市場現在已經有了一套全電腦化的收費系統。—**computerization** /kəmˏpjutərəˋzeʃən; kəmˌpjuːtəraɪˈzeɪʃən/ *n* [U]

computer mod·el·ling /·ˏ·· ˈ···/ *n* [U] the representation of a problem, situation, or real object in a form in which you can see it from all angles on a computer 電腦模型製作, 電腦模擬〔指在電腦上以可以從各種角度觀察的形式呈現一個問題、局面或實物〕: *computer modelling of the city's traffic flow* 城市交通情況的電腦模擬

computer pro·gram /·ˏ·· ˈ··/ *n* [C] a list of instructions that you need to give to a computer in order to make it do a particular thing 電腦程序 —**computer programmer** *n* [C]

computer sci·ence /·ˏ·· ˈ··/ *n* [U] the study of computers and what they can do 電腦科學, 計算機科學: *a BSc in Computer Science* 電腦科學的理學士

computer vi·rus /·ˏ·· ˈ··/ *n* [C] a VIRUS (3) 電腦病毒

com·put·ing /kəmˋpjutɪŋ; kəmˈpjuːtɪŋ/ *n* [U] the use of computers as a job or in business etc 電腦應用: *Have you ever done any computing?* 你以前幹過電腦應用的工作嗎?

com·rade /ˋkɑmræd; ˈkɒmrɪ̈d/ *n* [C] **1** *formal* a friend, especially someone who shares difficult work or danger【正式】〔尤指共患難的〕朋友: *He misses his comrades from his days in the Army.* 他想念服役時結識的戰友。**2** someone who is a fellow member of a union, political party etc at the same time as you are, used especially of people in Communist groups 同志〔指與你同屬一個工會或政黨的成員, 多為共產黨團體中的人使用〕: *Comrades, please support this motion.* 同志們, 請支持這項動議。—**comradely** *adj*

comrade in arms /ˏ··· ˈ·/ *n* [C] someone who has worked, fought with you or worked with you to achieve particular aims 戰友

com·rade·ship /ˋkɑmrædˏʃɪp; ˈkɒmrɪ̈dʃɪp/ *n* [U] *formal* friendship and loyalty among people who work together, fight together etc【正式】〔一同工作、戰鬥的人們之間的〕友誼, 忠誠, 同志情誼: *It was the spirit of comradeship that made victory possible.* 正是同志情誼的精神使勝利成為可能。

Con the written abbreviation of 縮寫= CONSERVATIVE or 或 conservative party

con- /kən; kən/ *prefix* together; with 與…一起, 與…一道: *a confederation* 聯邦 | *to conspire* (=plan together) 合謀

con¹ /kɑn; kɒn/ *v* **conned, conning** [T] *informal*【非正式】**1** to get money from someone by deceiving them 騙錢; 詐騙: **con sb out of** *He conned me out of £5!* 他從我這裡騙走了五英鎊! **2** to persuade someone to do something by deceiving them 誘騙: **con sb into doing sth** *We were conned into signing the contract.* 我們上當了, 簽了這個合同。

con² *n* [C] **1** a method or process of getting money from someone, especially by pretending to be someone else〔尤指假冒身分的〕詐騙: *There are hardly any chocolates in this box at all – what a con!* 這個盒子裡沒有甚麼巧克力 —— 真是騙人! —see also 另見 MOD CONS, **the pros and cons** (PRO[1] (3)) **2** *slang* a prisoner【俚】犯人, 囚犯

con-artist /'· ,··/ *n* [C] *informal* someone who tricks or deceives people in order to get money from them【非正式】騙子, 行騙者

con·cat·e·nation /kən,kætṇ`eʃən; kɒn,kætʒ'neɪʃən/ *n* [C,U] *formal* a series of events or things joined together one after another【正式】一連串事件[物品]: *a strange concatenation of events* 一連串怪事

con·cave /,kɑn`kev; ,kɒn'keɪv◂/ *adj* a concave surface is curved inwards in the middle 凹的, 凹面的 —opposite 反義詞 CONVEX

con·cav·i·ty /kɑn`kævətɪ; kən'kævʒti/ *n formal* **1** [U] the state of being concave 凹陷 **2** [C] a place or shape that is curved inwards 凹陷處; 凹面; 凹處

con·ceal /kən`sil; kən'siːl/ *v* [T] *formal*【正式】**1** to hide something carefully 隱匿, 隱藏: *Customs officers found the cannabis concealed inside the case.* 海關官員發現了藏在箱子裡的大麻。| *The path was concealed by long grass.* 小路被掩蓋在深深的草叢中。**2** to hide your real feelings or the truth 隱藏真實感情; 隱瞞真相: **conceal sth from sb** *Don't try to conceal anything from me.* 甚麼事都別想瞞我。—**concealment** *n* [U]

con·cede /kən`sid; kən'siːd/ *v*

1 ►ADMIT STH IS TRUE 承認某事是真的◄ [T] to admit that something is true or correct although you wish it was not true (不得不) 承認: *"You could be right I suppose", Sheila conceded.* 希拉承認道:"我想你可能是對的。" | **concede (that)** *I concede that he's a good runner, but I still think I can beat him.* 我承認他是出色的賽跑運動員, 可是我仍然相信自己能戰勝他。

2 ►ADMIT DEFEAT 認輸◄ [I,T] to admit that you are not going to win a battle, argument, or game because you are not strong enough or good enough to win 承認 (失敗), 認 (輸): *The army conceded and the enemy claimed victory.* 軍隊承認戰敗, 敵人宣稱勝利。| **concede defeat** *Matthew kept on arguing, unwilling to concede defeat.* 馬休不斷地爭辯, 不願意認輸。

3 concede a goal/point etc to not be able to stop your opponent from getting a goal, point etc during a game 不能阻止對方進球/得分等: *Manchester United were unlucky to concede a goal before half-time.* 在上半場比賽, 曼徹斯特聯隊不幸被對方攻進一球。

4 ►GIVE STH AS A RIGHT 給予權利◄ [T] to give something to someone as a right or PRIVILEGE (1) 給予〔某人權利〕: **concede sth to** *The richer nations will never concede equal status to the poorer countries.* 富裕的國家決不會給窮國同等的地位。

5 ►GIVE STH UNWILLINGLY 不情願地給予◄ [T] to give something to someone unwillingly after trying to keep it〔在試圖保留之後不情願地〕讓予: **concede sth to** *After the First World War Germany conceded a lot of land to her neighbours.* 第一次世界大戰之後, 德國把許多土地割讓給鄰國。—see also 另見 CONCESSION

con·ceit /kən`sit; kən'siːt/ *n* **1** [U] an attitude that shows you have too high an opinion of your own abilities or importance; CONCEITEDNESS 自負, 自高自大: *The conceit of the woman – it's unbelievable!* 這個女人的自高自大程度 —— 真是不可思議! **2** [C] *technical* an unusual, cleverly expressed comparison of two very different things, especially in poetry【術語】〔尤指詩歌中〕別出心裁的比喻

con·ceit·ed /kən`sitɪd; kən'siːtʒd/ *adj* behaving in a way that shows you think you are very clever, skilful, beautiful etc 自負的, 驕傲自滿的, 自高自大的: *He's a conceited little so-and-so.* 他是一個自命不凡的小混蛋。—**conceitedly** *adv*: *"I knew that", he said conceitedly.* "那件事情我知道。" 他大模大樣地說。

con·cei·te·dness /kən`sitɪdnɪs; kən'siːtʒdnʒs/ *n* [U] CONCEIT 自負, 自傲

con·cei·va·ble /kən`sivəbḷ; kən'siːvəbəl/ *adj* able to be believed or imagined 可以相信的, 可想像的: *He could talk intelligently on almost any conceivable subject.* 幾乎甚麼能想到的話題他都能說得頭頭是道。| *What conceivable reason could they have for doing such crazy things?* 真想不出來他們有甚麼理由做這麼瘋狂的事? | **conceivable (that)** *It is conceivable that the peace mission will succeed.* 有理由相信和談代表團是會成功的。—opposite 反義詞 INCONCEIVABLE —**conceivably** *adv*

con·ceive /kən`siv; kən'siːv/ *v* **1** [T] to think of a new idea, plan etc and develop it in your mind 構思; 設想; 想出: *Scientists first conceived the idea of the atomic bomb in the 1930's.* 在 20 世紀 30 年代科學家第一次有了原子彈的設想。**2** [T] *formal* to imagine a particular situation【正式】想像〔某一具體情況〕: **conceive what/why/how etc** *I find it difficult to conceive why the government introduced the policy in the first place.* 先不說別的, 首先就很難想像政府為甚麼要推行這項政策。| **conceive of sth** *I can't conceive of any reason why we can't come.* 我想像不出我們有甚麼理由不能來。| **conceive of doing sth** *I would never conceive of treating someone the way Helen treats John.* 我不能想像有人會像海倫對待約翰那樣對待別人。**3** [I,T] to become PREGNANT 懷孕; 受孕: *fertility treatment for women who have difficulty conceiving* 對受孕困難的女性進行治療

con·cen·trate[1] /`kɑnsṇ,tret; 'kɒnsəntreɪt/ *v* **1** [I] to think very carefully about something that you are doing 專注, 專心; 集中注意力: *Keep the noise down will you – I'm trying to concentrate.* 把聲音弄小點, 行嗎? 我正在集中精力。| **[+on]** *She was too distracted to concentrate properly on her book.* 她心煩意亂, 根本無法專心讀書。**2 be concentrated on/in/around etc** to be present in particularly large numbers or amounts in a particular place 集中於; 匯集於: *Italian industry is concentrated mainly in the north of the country.* 意大利的工業主要集中在該國北部。| *The mass of the sphere is concentrated at its center.* 這個球體的質量聚在它的中心。**3** [T] if something concentrates the mind it makes you think very clearly 使…頭腦清醒: *Relaxing in a jacuzzi concentrates the mind wonderfully.* 在熱水渦流式浴缸中放鬆使人精神百倍。**4** [T] to make a liquid stronger by removing some of the water from it 濃縮〔液體〕

concentrate sth ↔ **on** *phr v* [T] to pay particular attention to something, work particularly hard at it etc, and make that the most important thing you are doing 把注意力集中於, 全神貫注於: *The discussion concentrated on improving the company's image.* 討論集中於如何改善公司的形象。| **concentrate your attention/efforts/thoughts etc on** *Virgos should concentrate their efforts on work this month.* 處女座出生的人這個月應把注意力集中在工作上面。

concentrate[2] *n* [C,U] a substance or liquid which has been made stronger by removing the water from it 濃縮物; 濃縮液: *orange concentrate* 濃縮橙汁

con·cen·trat·ed /`kɑnsṇ,tretɪd; 'kɒnsəntreɪtʒd/ *adj* **1** a concentrated liquid or substance is made stronger by removing water from it 濃縮的: *concentrated hydrochloric acid* 濃鹽酸 | *concentrated orange juice* 濃縮橙汁 **2** [only before noun 僅用於名詞前] showing determination to do something 全神貫注的; 全力以赴的: *He made a concentrated effort to improve his work.* 他集中力量改進自己的工作。

con·cen·tra·tion /,kɑnsṇ`treʃən; ,kɒnsən'treɪʃən/ *n* **1** [U] the ability to think about something carefully or for a long time 專心, 集中注意力: *Her work as a simultaneous translator requires strong powers of concentration.* 她作為即時傳譯員需要很強的聚精會神的能力。**2** [U] a process in which you put a lot of attention, energy etc into a particular activity 集中注意力, 集中精力: **[+on]**

Concentration on strengthening the team's defence is essential. 集中力量加強球隊的防守是必要的。**3** [C,U] a large amount of something in one place or area 在一處大量集中某事物: [+of] *There is an increasing concentration of power in central government.* 越來越多的權力集中於中央政府。**4** [C] *technical* the amount of a substance contained in a liquid【術語】〔液體中某物質的〕濃度: *a high concentration of sulphuric acid* 濃度高的硫酸

concentration camp /ˌ‥ˈ‥ ˌ/ *n* [C] a prison where large numbers of ordinary people are kept, especially during a war, and are treated extremely cruelly 集中營

con·cen·tric /kənˋsɛntrɪk; kənˈsentrɪk/ *adj technical* having the same centre【術語】同中心的: *concentric circles* 同心圓 —compare 比較 ECCENTRIC[1] (2)

concentric 同中心的

concentric circles 同心圓

eccentric circles 不同心圓

3 2 **con·cept** /ˋkɑnsɛpt; ˈkɒnsept/ *n* [C] someone's idea of how something is, or should be done 概念, 觀念; 想法: *a revolutionary concept in industry* 工業上的革命性概念 | [+of] *It's difficult to grasp the concept of infinite space.* 要領會無限空間的概念很困難。

con·cep·tion /kənˋsɛpʃən; kənˈsepʃən/ *n* **1** [C,U] a general idea about what something is like, or a general understanding of something 概念; 觀念, 思想; 想法: [+of] *He's got a really strange conception of friendship.* 他對友誼有一種非常獨特的見解。| **have no conception of** *You've no conception of what conditions are like.* 你對情況一無所知。**2** [U] a process in which someone forms a plan or idea 構思, 構想, 設想: *The conception of the book took five minutes, but writing it took a year.* 這本書的構思花了五分鐘, 而寫出來卻花了一整年。**3** [C,U] the process by which male and female sex cells join together in a woman's body and the woman becomes PREGNANT 受孕, 懷孕

con·cep·tu·al /kənˋsɛptʃuəl; kənˈseptʃuəl/ *adj formal* based on ideas【正式】概念的: *the conceptual framework of the play* 這部劇的概念框架 —**conceptually** *adv*

conceptual art /ˌ‥ˈ‥ ˈ/ *n* [U] *technical* art in which the main aim of the artist is to show an idea【術語】概念藝術〔以顯示概念為目的的藝術〕

con·cep·tu·al·ize also 又作 **-ise** *BrE*【英】/kənˋsɛptʃuəlˌaɪz; kənˈseptʃuəlaɪz/ *v* [I,T] to form an idea 形成概念, 使概念化: *two schools of thought that conceptualize things differently* 對事物進行不同詮釋的兩個思想派別

1 1 **con·cern[1]** /kənˋsɝn; kənˈsɜːn/ *n*

1 ▶WORRY 擔憂◀ a) [C] something that worries you 擔心的事, 關切的事: *The main concern is that the health of the employees will be at risk.* 最令人擔憂的事是雇員的健康將面臨威脅。**b)** [U] a feeling of worry, especially about something such as a social problem, someone's health etc 憂慮; 擔心: *The recent rise in crime is a matter of considerable public concern.* 近來犯罪增多是民眾極為關切的事。| [+about/over] *There is growing concern about the effects of pollution on health.* 對於污染影響健康的關注越來越強烈。| **concern for sb** *A government spokesman expressed concern for the lives of the hostages.* 一位政府的發言人對人質的生命安全表示擔憂。| **cause concern/be a cause for concern** *The depletion of the ozone layer is causing widespread concern among scientists.* 臭氧層的銳減在科學家之間引起廣泛關注。

2 be of concern (to sb) if something is of concern to you, it is important to you and you feel worried about it 令〔某人〕感到擔心的; 是〔某人〕所關心的: *The rise in unemployment is of great concern to the government.* 失業率的上升是政府關心的一件大事。

3 [C,U] something that is important to you or that involves you 與某人有關的事, 對某人重要的事: *His main concern is to be able to provide for his family.* 他主要關心的是能夠養活他一家人。

4 ▶FEELING FOR SB 對某人的情感◀ [singular, U] a feeling of wanting someone to be happy and healthy 關心; 關懷: [+for] *parents' loving concern for their children* 父母對子女的關愛

5 sb's concern if something is your concern, you are responsible for it 由某人負責的事: *The money side of the business is your concern.* 企業的財務管理是你的職責。

6 not sb's concern/none of sb's concern if something is not your concern, you are not interested in it and you do not need to worry about it or become involved in it 某人不感興趣的事; 與某人無關的事: *How much money I earn is none of your concern.* 我賺多少錢與你不相干。

7 ▶BUSINESS 企業◀ [C] a business or company 企業; 公司: *The restaurant is a family concern.* 這家餐館是一個家庭開辦的。| **a going concern** (=a business that is financially successful) 一家生意興隆的企業

concern[2] *v* [T] **1** if an activity, situation, rule etc concerns you, it affects you or involves you〔活動、情況、規則等〕對…有影響; 與…相關: *The tax changes will concern large corporations rather than small businesses.* 税收上的變化影響到的是大公司而不是小企業。**2** [not in passive 不用被動態] to make someone feel worried or upset 使憂慮, 使擔心: *The fact that she spends so much time on her own really concerns me.* 她很多時間都是一人獨處, 這真讓我擔心。**3** [not in passive 不用被動態] if a story, book, report etc concerns someone or something, it is about them〔故事、書、報告等〕與…有關, 關於: *This article concerns a man who was wrongly imprisoned.* 這篇文章寫的是一個被冤枉而入獄的人。**4 concern yourself with/about sth** to become involved in something because you are interested in it or because it worries you 關心, 擔心: *More and more people are concerning themselves with environmental problems.* 越來越多的人關心起環境問題。**5 to whom it may concern** an expression written at the beginning of a formal letter when you do not know the name of the person you want to communicate with〔寫在正式信函開頭的一句套話, 用於寫信人不知道收信人的姓名時〕—see also 另見 CONCERNED 3

con·cerned /kənˋsɝnd; kənˈsɜːnd/ *adj* 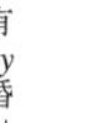

1 [not before noun 不用於名詞前] involved in something or affected by it〔與某事〕有關的, 有牽連的: *The affair is greatly regretted by everyone concerned.* 所有相關人士都對此事感到極為遺憾。| *Divorce is very painful, especially when children are concerned.* 離婚是非常痛苦的, 如果離婚的夫婦有孩子的話, 尤其痛苦。| [+in] *Everyone concerned in the incident was questioned by the police.* 所有與這個事件有關的人都受到警方盤問。| [+with] *all the people concerned with children's education* 所有關心兒童教育問題的人

2 ▶WORRIED 憂慮◀ worried about something 焦急的, 擔憂的: *Concerned parents approached the school about the problem.* 焦慮的家長就此問題與校方聯繫。| [+about] *Ross has never been particularly concerned about what other people think of him.* 羅斯對別人如何看待自己從來不太在意。| [+for] *Rescuers are concerned for the safety of two men trapped in the mine.* 拯救隊隊員對困在礦下的兩個人的安全感到擔憂。| **concerned that** *He's concerned that he won't get his money back.* 他擔心無法拿回自己的錢。—see 見 NERVOUS (USAGE)

3 as far as I'm concerned *spoken* used when giving your opinion about something or saying how it affects you, especially when you do not care what other people think【口】在我看來; 就我而言〔用於陳述自己對某事的看法或對自己有何影響, 尤指不在乎別人怎麼說〕: *As far as I'm concerned the whole idea is crazy.* 在我看來, 這

一想法十分荒唐。

4 ▶BE IMPORTANT TO 對…是重要的◀ [never before noun 不用於名詞前] believing that something is important 關切的, 關心的: **[+with]** *Congressmen seem to be far more concerned with getting elected than with passing legislation.* 看來眾議員們關心自己當選遠比關心立法更多。| **be concerned to do sth** *We are concerned to sort this out as quickly as possible.* 我們關切的是儘快把這件事處理掉。

5 where/as far as sth is concerned *spoken* used when saying what particular thing you are talking about【口】就…而言〔用來表明你在談論一件甚麼樣的事情〕: *Where money is concerned, I always try to be very careful.* 凡是涉及錢的地方, 我總是盡量小心謹慎。

C

6 ▶LOVE/CARE 愛/關心◀ caring about someone and whether they are happy and healthy 掛念的: **[+for/about]** *How can you expect me not to be concerned about my own son?* 你怎麼會以為我不掛念我的兒子呢?

7 be concerned with if a book, story etc is concerned with a person, subject etc it is about that subject〔書、故事等〕關於, 與…有關: *This story is concerned with a Russian family in the 19th century.* 這個故事寫的是19世紀的一個俄國家庭。—**concernedly** /kənˈsɜ˞nədlɪ; kənˈsɜːnɪ̣dli/ *adv*

3 **con·cern·ing** /kənˈsɜ˞nɪŋ; kənˈsɜːnɪŋ/ *prep formal* a word meaning 'about', used to show you are talking or writing about a particular thing or person【正式】關於: *Police are anxious to hear any information concerning his whereabouts.* 警方急於得悉有關他的下落的任何消息。

3 3 **con·cert** /ˈkɑnsɜ˞t; ˈkɒnsət/ *n* [C] **1** a performance given by musicians 音樂會: *We went to a concert of Vivaldi's 'Four Seasons'.* 我們去聽了維瓦爾第的《四季》音樂會。| *a pop concert* 流行歌曲音樂會 **2 in concert (with)** *formal*【正式】**a)** people who do something in concert do it together after having agreed on it 與…一起〔行動〕: *The various governments decided to act in concert over this matter.* 各個政府決定採取一致行動處理這個問題。**b)** playing or singing at a concert〔在音樂會上〕演出: *Michael Jackson in concert at the Palladium* 在帕拉迪姆劇場舉行演唱會的米高積遜

con·cert·ed /kənˈsɜ˞tɪd; kənˈsɜːtɪ̣d/ *adj* **concerted effort/attempt/action etc** a concerted effort etc is done by people working together in a carefully planned and very determined way 一致的努力/嘗試/行動等: *a concerted campaign to raise public awareness of environmental issues* 提高公眾對環境問題重視程度的聯合行動 —**concertedly** *adv*

con·cert·go·er /ˈkɑnsɜ˞tˌgoɚ; ˈkɒnsətˌgəʊə/ *n* [C] someone who often goes to concerts 音樂會的常客

concert hall /ˈ··· ·/ *n* [C] a large public building where concerts are performed 音樂會堂, 音樂廳

con·cer·ti·na¹ /ˌkɑnsɚˈtinə; ˌkɒnsəˈtiːnə/ *n* [C] a small musical instrument like an ACCORDION that you hold in your hands and play by pressing in from each side 六角形手風琴〔用雙手從兩端向內推擠來演奏的樂器〕

concertina² *v past and past participle* **concertinaed** [I] *BrE* if something concertinas, it folds together upon itself【英】摺襉狀壓縮[摺疊]: *The bonnet of the car had concertinaed as a result of the crash.* 汽車車蓋由於撞擊而皺縮。

con·cert·mas·ter /ˈkɑnsɚtˌmæstɚ; ˈkɒnsətˌmɑːstə/ *n* [C] *AmE* the most important VIOLIN player in an ORCHESTRA【美】〔交響樂團中的〕首席小提琴手

con·cer·to /kənˈtʃɛrto; kənˈtʃɜːtəʊ/ *n plural* **concertos** [C] a piece of music for one or more SOLO¹ (2) instruments and an ORCHESTRA 協奏曲

con·ces·sion /kənˈsɛʃən; kənˈseʃən/ *n*

1 ▶STH YOU ALLOW SB 讓與某人之物◀ [C] something that you allow someone to have in order to end an argument or a disagreement〔為了結束爭端而〕讓步: **make a concession** *We will never make any concessions to terrorists.* 我們決不向恐怖分子作出任何讓步。—see also 另見 CONCEDE

2 ▶A RIGHT 權利◀ [C] a special right that a particular person or group of people is allowed to have, for example by the government or an employer〔政府或雇主等許可的〕特權; 特許權: *tax concessions* 稅收優惠 | *Greyhound Inc won the concession of running hotels in Glacier Park.* "灰狗"公司獲得了在冰川公園開設旅館的特權。

3 ▶PRICE REDUCTION 降價◀ [C] *BrE* a reduction in the price of tickets, FARE*s* etc for certain groups of people, for example old people or children【英】〔對特殊羣體, 如老人、兒童, 在票價等費用上的〕價格優惠

4 concessions [plural] *AmE* the things sold at a concession stand【美】營業攤點上出售的商品

5 ▶ACT OF ALLOWING 許可行為◀ [U] *formal* the act of giving or allowing something as a right【正式】容許; 許可

6 ▶RIGHT TO SELL STH 銷售權◀ [C] *AmE* the right to sell something within the building of a larger business, or the area you are allowed to sell something in【美】在較大商店內部銷售商品的權利或銷售點: *a hamburger concession in the mall* 大商場裡的漢堡包店

con·ces·sion·aire /kənˌsɛʃənˈɛr; kənˌseʃəˈneə/ *n* [C] *informal* someone who has been given a CONCESSION (2), especially to run a business【非正式】某一特許權的獲得者〔尤指做生意的權利〕

con·ces·sion·ar·y /kənˈsɛʃənˌɛrɪ; kənˈseʃənəri/ *adj* **1** given as a concession 特許的; 讓步的; 讓與的 **2** *BrE* specially reduced in price, for example for old people or children【英】特別〔為老年人或兒童等〕降價的: *Local authorities have the power to set up concessionary fare schemes.* 本地當局有權制定降價乘車方案。

concession stand /·ˈ·· ˌ·/ *n* [C] *AmE* a small business that sells food, drinks or SOUVENIR*s* at sporting events, places that tourists visit and some theatres【美】〔體育比賽場地、旅遊景點和某些劇院開設的出售食品、飲料或紀念品的〕營業攤點, 小商店

con·ces·sive clause /kənˌsɛsɪv ˈklɔz; kənˌsesɪv ˈklɔːz/ *n* [C] *technical* a CLAUSE (2), often introduced by 'although,' that introduces a fact or idea that seems to be the opposite of the main fact or idea. For example, the sentence 'Although it's old, it works well.' begins with a concessive clause.【術語】讓步從句〔指常以 although 引導的從句。例如在"Although it's old, it works well.(這東西雖然舊了, 但仍然很好用。)"中, 就以一個讓步從句開頭〕

conch /kɑntʃ; kɒntʃ/ *n* [C] the large twisted shell of a tropical sea animal that looks like a SNAIL 海螺殼

con·chie /ˈkɑntʃɪ; ˈkɒntʃi/ *n* [C] *BrE old-fashioned informal* an insulting word for a CONSCIENTIOUS OBJECTOR【英, 過時, 非正式】〔因宗教或道德的原因而〕拒絕服兵役者〔侮辱性詞語〕

con·ci·erge /ˌkɑnsɪˈɛrʒ; ˌkɒnsiˈeəʒ/ *n* [C] *French*【法】**1** someone who looks after a building, usually by watching the entrance to see who comes in and goes out, especially in France〔尤指法國的〕看門人, 樓房管理員 **2** *especially AmE* someone whose job in a hotel is helping guests, for example by giving them advice about local restaurants etc【尤美】旅館內協助客人的服務人員〈如介紹當地餐館等〉

con·cil·i·ate /kənˈsɪlɪˌet; kənˈsɪlieɪt/ *v* [T] *formal* to do something to make people more likely to stop arguing, especially by giving them something they want【正式】安撫; 調停: *Negotiators were called in to conciliate between the warring factions.* 談判人員被請來在交戰的兩派之間進行調解。—**conciliator** *n* [C]

con·cil·i·a·tion /kənˌsɪlɪˈeʃən; kənˌsɪliˈeɪʃən/ *n* [U] the process of trying to get people to agree 說服; 調解: *peaceful negotiation attempts at conciliation through compromise* 通過妥協達成和解的和平談判努力

con·cil·i·a·tory /kənˈsɪlɪəˌtorɪ; kənˈsɪliətəri/ *adj* doing something that is intended to make someone stop arguing with you 和解的, 調停的: **conciliatory gesture/mes-**

sage/tone etc *We'd like to offer you free theater tickets as a conciliatory gesture.* 我們想送你幾張戲票以示和解。

con·cise /kən`saɪs; kən'saɪs/ *adj* short and clear, with no unnecessary words 簡潔的; 簡明的: *a concise explanation* 簡明的解釋 —**concisely** *adv* —**conciseness** also 又作 **concision** /kən`sɪʒən; kən'sɪʒən/ *formal n* [U]【正式】

con·clave /`kɑŋklev; 'kɒŋkleɪv/ *n* [C] a private and secret meeting 祕密會議: *A conclave of cardinals was held to elect a new pope.* 紅衣主教舉行了祕密會議選舉一位新教皇。

3 2 **con·clude** /kən`klud; kən'klu:d/ *v* [T] **1** to decide that something is true after considering all the information you have 作出結論, 斷定: **conclude that** *The enquiry concluded that the accident had been caused by human error.* 調查結論認為這次事故是人為失誤造成的。| **conclude from sth that** *Davis concludes from an analysis of traffic accidents that the speed limit should be lowered.* 戴維斯通過對交通事故的分析認定應該降低時速限制。**2** [T] to complete something you have been doing, especially for a long time 完成, 結束: **conclude your work/investigation/research etc** *I will be publishing my results only when I have concluded my research.* 我完成了研究才會發表結論。**3** [I always+adv/prep,T] to end something such as a meeting or speech by doing or saying one final thing〔以做某事或講某話來〕結束〔會議或演說〕: **[+with/on/as/by etc]** *The session usually concludes with an informal discussion.* 會議通常以一場非正式的討論作為結束。| **conclude sth** *We were finally able to conclude the meeting and go home.* 最後我們總算結束了會議回家去。| **conclude sth with/by etc** *The service was concluded with a hymn.* 禮拜以唱聖歌結束。**4 conclude an agreement/treaty/contract etc** to finish arranging an agreement etc successfully 達成協議/締結條約/簽訂合同等: *After months of negotiations they concluded the sale.* 經過幾個月的談判之後, 他們訂立了銷售合同。

con·clu·ding /kən`kludɪŋ; kən'klu:dɪŋ/ *adj* **concluding sentence/remark/stages etc** the last sentence, stage etc in an event or piece of writing 結束句/語/階段等: *He makes his position perfectly clear in the concluding paragraph.* 在最後一段他清楚地表明了自己的觀點。

2 2 **con·clu·sion** /kən`kluʒən; kən'klu:ʒən/ *n* **1** [C] something you decide after considering all the information you have 結論: *These are the report's main conclusions.* 這些就是這篇報告的主要結論。| **[+that]** *Becky came to the conclusion that he must have forgotten.* 貝基得出結論, 認為他肯定已經忘記了。| **lead to/point to/support the conclusion (that)** *All the evidence pointed to the conclusion that he was guilty.* 所有證據都表明他是有罪的。| **draw a conclusion** *From these facts we can draw some conclusions about how the pyramids were built.* 從這些事實我們可以得出一些關於金字塔是如何建造的結論。| **jump to conclusions** (=decide that something is true too quickly, without knowing all the facts) 匆忙地下結論, 草率下結論 *Don't jump to conclusions – just because they're late doesn't mean they've had an accident!* 別輕易下結論, 他們遲到並不意味着他們出事了! **2** [C] the end or final part of something 結尾, 末尾: *I found the conclusion of his book very interesting.* 我認為他的書的結尾非常有意思。**3 in conclusion** used in a piece of writing or a speech to show that you are about to finish what you are saying 總而言之〔用於文章或講話的末尾, 表明即將結束〕: *In conclusion, I would like to say how much I have enjoyed myself today.* 最後, 我想說我今天很開心。**4** [U] the final arrangement of something such as a business deal 締結, 簽訂: **[+of]** *the conclusion of a peace treaty* 和平條約的簽訂 **5 be a foregone conclusion** to be certain to happen even though it has not yet officially happened 是預料之中的結果: *The outcome of the battle was a foregone conclusion.* 戰鬥的結果早在預料之中。

con·clu·sive /kən`klusɪv; kən'klu:sɪv/ *adj* something that is conclusive is certainly true, so there is no doubt or uncertainty 令人確信的; 毫無疑問的: **conclusive proof/evidence/findings etc** *The investigation failed to provide any conclusive evidence.* 調查未能提供任何令人信服的證據。—opposite 反義詞 INCONCLUSIVE —**conclusively** *adv*

con·coct /kən`kɑkt; kən'kɒkt/ *v* [T] **1** to invent a clever story, excuse, or plan, especially in order to deceive someone 編造; 捏造; 虛構: *John concocted an elaborate excuse for being late.* 約翰為遲到編了一個巧妙的藉口。**2** to make something especially food or drink, by mixing different things, especially things that are not usually combined〔食物、飲料的〕配製, 調配, 拼湊: *Jean concocted a great meal from the leftovers.* 簡把剩菜剩飯調配成一頓美餐。

con·coc·tion /kən`kɑkʃən; kən'kɒkʃən/ *n* [C] something, especially a drink, made by mixing different things, especially things that are not usually combined〔尤指不常混合的酒的〕配製物, 調配物: *She offered him a green concoction with fruit floating in it.* 她給他一杯綠色的調製飲料, 上面有水果漂浮。

con·com·i·tant[1] /kən`kɑmətənt; kən'kɒmɪtənt/ *adj formal* existing or happening together, especially as a result of something【正式】伴隨的, 並存的: *war with all its concomitant sufferings* 戰爭及由戰爭引起的一切苦難 —**concomitantly** *adv*

concomitant[2] *n* [C] *formal* something that often or naturally happens with something else **[+of]**【正式】伴隨物: *Deafness is a frequent concomitant of old age.* 耳聾常隨老年而出現。

con·cord /`kɑŋkɔrd; 'kɒŋkɔ:d/ *n* [U] **1** *formal* the state of having a friendly relationship, so that you agree on things and live in peace【正式】一致, 和諧, 協調 **2** *technical* in grammar, concord between words happens when they match correctly, for example when a plural noun has a plural verb following it【術語】詞與詞在語法上的搭配一致〈如複數動詞跟隨複數名詞〉

con·cor·dance /kən`kɔrdṇs; kən'kɔ:dəns/ *n* **1** [U] the state of being similar to something else or in agreement with it 一致; 協調: *the concordance between the proposals* 兩項建議間的一致性 **2** [C] *technical* an alphabetical list of all the words used in a book or set of books by one writer, with information about where they can be found and usually about how they are used【術語】〔某作家在某(套)書中所用的全部詞語的〕索引: *a Shakespeare concordance* 莎士比亞詞語索引 | *computerized concordances* 電腦化詞語索引

con·cor·dant /kən`kɔrdṇt; kən'kɔ:dənt/ *adj formal* being in agreement or having the same regular pattern【正式】一致的; 屬於同一規格[模式]的

con·course /`kɑŋkors; 'kɒŋkɔ:s/ *n* [C] **1** a large hall in a building such as an airport or train station where crowds of people can gather〔火車站、飛機場等的〕大廳 **2** a large crowd that has gathered together 聚集的人羣: *a large concourse of people* 一大羣人

con·crete[1] /`kɑnkrit; 'kɒŋkri:t/ *adj* **1** made of concrete 3
混凝土的: *a concrete floor* 混凝土地板 **2** clearly based on fact, rather than on beliefs or guesses 有真憑實據的: *concrete information about the identity of the murderer* 關於兇手身分的確實資料 —compare 比較 ABSTRACT[1] (2) **3** definite and specific rather than general 具體的: *Have you got any concrete proposals as to what we should do?* 我們應該做些甚麼, 你有沒有具體的建議? —**concretely** *adv*

con·crete[2] *n* [U] a substance used for building that is made by mixing sand, very small stones, cement, and water 混凝土

con·crete[3] *v* [T] to cover something such as a path, wall etc with concrete 用混凝土澆築[覆蓋]〔小路、牆等〕

C

concrete jun·gle /ˌ.. ˈ../ *n* [C usually singular 一般用單數] an unpleasant area in a city that is full of big ugly buildings and has no open spaces 水泥叢林〔指到處是醜陋的高樓林立, 沒有開曠空地的城區〕

concrete mix·er /ˈ.. ˌ../ *n* [C] a CEMENT MIXER 混凝土攪拌機

con·cu·bi·nage /kɑnˋkjubənɪdʒ; kɒnˈkjuːbɪnɪdʒ/ *n* [U] *formal* the system or practice of living together as man and wife without being married【正式】姘居, 同居

con·cu·bine /ˋkɑŋkjuˌbaɪn; ˈkɒŋkjʊbaɪn/ *n* [C] a woman who lives with and has sex with a man who already has a wife or wives, but who is socially less important 妾; 姨太太

con·cur /kənˋkɝ; kənˈkɜː/ *v* **concurred, concurring** [I] *formal*【正式】**1** to agree with someone or have the same opinion as them〔與某人〕意見一致, 同意: **[+with]** *The judge stated that he concurred with the ruling.* 法官表示同意此項裁決。**2** to happen at the same time; COINCIDE (1) 同時發生的事: **concur to do sth** *Everything concurred to produce the desired effect.* 所有的事情都在同一時間發生, 產生了預期的效果。

con·cur·rence /kənˋkɝəns; kənˈkʌrəns/ *n formal*【正式】**1** [U] agreement 同意: **[+with]** *Jules expressed his concurrence with the suggestion.* 朱爾斯表示同意這個建議。**2** [C] an example of events, actions etc happening at the same time 同時發生的事: **[+of]** *a strange concurrence of events* 機緣巧合下發生的一系列事件

con·cur·rent /kənˋkɝənt; kənˈkʌrənt/ *adj* **1** existing or happening at the same time 同時存在或發生的: *He is serving two concurrent prison sentences.* 他在監獄裡同時為兩項判決服刑。**2** *formal* in agreement【正式】同意的, 一致的: **[+with]** *My opinions are concurrent with yours.* 我的觀點與你一致。—**concurrently** *adv*: *two prison sentences to run concurrently* 同時生效的兩項徒刑判決

con·cuss /kənˋkʌs; kənˈkʌs/ *v* [T often passive 常用被動態] if something hits your head and concusses you, it makes you lose consciousness or feel sick for a short time because your brain is temporarily damaged 使腦震蕩: *The driver of the car was badly concussed.* 汽車司機給撞成了嚴重的腦震蕩。

con·cus·sion /kənˋkʌʃən; kənˈkʌʃən/ *n* [U] a small amount of damage to the brain that makes you lose consciousness or feel sick for a short time, usually caused by something hitting your head 腦震蕩

con·demn /kənˋdɛm; kənˈdem/ *v* [T]

1 ►DISAPPROVE 責備◄ to say very strongly that you do not approve of something or someone, especially because you think it is morally wrong 指責, 譴責: *Politicians were quick to condemn the bombing.* 政治家很快就對炸彈爆炸事件予以譴責。| **condemn sth/sb as** *The law has been condemned as an attack on personal liberty.* 這項法律被指責為對人身自由的侵犯。| **condemn sb/sth for doing sth** *She knew that society would condemn her for leaving her children.* 她知道會因為遺棄孩子而受到社會的譴責。

2 ►PUNISH 懲罰◄ to give someone a severe punishment after deciding they are guilty of a crime 給…判罪, 給…判刑: **condemn sb to death** *The prisoner was condemned to death.* 這名犯人被判處死刑。

3 ►FORCE TO DO STH 強迫做某事◄ if a particular situation condemns someone to something, it forces them to live in an unpleasant way or to do something unpleasant 迫使〔某人〕處於不幸的境地; 迫使〔某人〕做不願做的事: **condemn sb to sth** *people condemned to a life of poverty* 被迫一輩子受窮的人 | **condemn sb to do sth** *A significant proportion of such children are condemned to fail.* 那些孩子中的很大一部分是注定通不過的。

4 ►BUILDING 建築物◄ to state officially that a building is not safe enough to be used 宣告某樓房不適於居住: *an old house that had been condemned* 一幢已被宣布為危房的老房子

5 ►SHOW GUILT 表明有罪◄ if the way you look or behave condemns you, it shows that you are guilty of something〔某人的神情或舉止〕表明…有罪: *His nervousness condemned him.* 他緊張的神情表明他是有罪的。

con·dem·na·tion /ˌkɑndɛmˋneʃən; ˌkɒndəmˈneɪʃən/ *n* [C,U] an expression of very strong disapproval of someone or something 責難, 譴責, 責備: **[+of]** *Condemnation of the latest violence came from all political parties.* 所有的政黨都對最近發生的暴力事件進行了譴責。

con·dem·na·to·ry /kənˋdɛmnəˌtɔrɪ; kənˈdemnətəri/ *adj* expressing strong disapproval 表示強烈譴責的

con·demned /kənˋdɛmd; kənˈdemd/ *adj* someone who is condemned is going to be punished by being killed 被判死刑的

condemned cell /.ˌ. ˈ./ *n* [C] *BrE* a room for a prisoner who was going to be punished by death【英】死刑犯的牢房

con·den·sa·tion /ˌkɑndɛnˋseʃən; ˌkɒndenˈseɪʃən/ *n* **1** [U] small drops of water that are formed when gas changes to liquid〔氣體冷凝形成的〕水滴: *There was a lot of condensation on the windows.* 窗戶上有許多露水。**2** [U] *technical* the process of change from gas to liquid【術語】凝結, 冷凝: *the condensation of steam into water* 蒸汽冷凝成水 **3** [C,U] *formal* the act of making something shorter【正式】縮短, 壓縮: *the condensation of his report* 對他所寫報告的壓縮

con·dense /kənˋdɛns; kənˈdens/ *v* **1** [I,T] if gas condenses or is condensed, it becomes a liquid as it becomes cooler (使)凝結, (使)冷凝: *Steam condensed on the bathroom mirror.* 蒸汽在浴室的鏡子上冷凝成水。| **[+into]** *The gaseous metal is cooled and condenses into liquid zinc.* 氣態的金屬被冷卻並冷凝成為液態鋅。**2** [T] to make a liquid thicker by removing some of the water 濃縮: *condensed soup* 濃湯 **3** [T] to make something that is spoken or written shorter, by not giving as much detail or using fewer words to give the same information 將〔講話或文章〕壓縮: **condense sth into sth** *This whole chapter could be condensed into a few paragraphs.* 這一整章可以縮寫為幾個段落。

condensed milk /.ˌ. ˈ./ *n* [U] a type of thick sweet milk sold in cans 濃縮牛奶, 煉乳 —compare 比較 EVAPORATED MILK

con·dens·er /kənˋdɛnsɚ; kənˈdensə/ *n* [C] **1** a piece of equipment that makes a gas change into liquid 冷凝器 **2** a machine for storing electricity, especially in a car engine 電容器

con·de·scend /ˌkɑndɪˋsɛnd; ˌkɒndɪˈsend/ *v* [I] **1** to behave as if you think you are better or more important than other people〔行為舉止〕顯示出自以為高人一等: *She'd be a better teacher if she didn't condescend to her students.* 她如果不是傲慢地對待學生的話, 她會是一個較好的老師。**2** to do something in a way that shows you think it is below your social or professional position 屈尊, 俯就, 降低身分: **condescend to do sth** *The managing director condescended to have lunch with us in the canteen.* 總經理屈尊來到食堂與我們一起吃午飯。—**condescension** /-ˋsɛnʃən; -ˈsenʃən/ *n* [U]

con·de·scend·ing /ˌkɑndɪˋsɛndɪŋ; ˌkɒndɪˈsendɪŋ◄/ *adj* behaving as though you think you are better or more important than other people 帶着優越感的: *Professor Hutter's manner is extremely condescending.* 哈特教授的態度極為傲慢。—**condescendingly** *adv*

con·di·ment /ˋkɑndəmənt; ˈkɒndɪmənt/ *n* [C] *formal* a powder or liquid, such as salt or KETCHUP that you use to give special taste to food【正式】〔鹽、番茄醬等〕調味品, 佐料

con·di·tion[1] /kənˋdɪʃən; kənˈdɪʃən/ *n*

1 ►STATE 狀態◄ [singular] the state that something is in 狀況, 狀態: **[+in]** *What sort of condition is your new house in?* 你的新房子目前是甚麼狀況? | **[+of]** *The garden was in a condition of total neglect.* 這個花園完全是荒蕪一片。| **be in good/bad/perfect/awful etc condi-**

tion *The car has been well maintained and is in excellent condition.* 汽車一直保養得很好，處於極佳狀態。| **in that condition** *spoken* (=in a bad state)【口】狀態不好 *You can't wear a jacket in that condition!* 這樣破的夾克衫你不能穿！

2 a) conditions [plural] the situation in which people live or work, especially the physical things such as pay or food that affect the quality of their lives〔生活或工作的〕條件: **working/driving/living etc conditions** *Poor working conditions lead to demoralized and unproductive employees.* 工作條件差導致雇員工作積極性不高，生產率低下。| **under excellent/terrible etc conditions** *The people are living in makeshift tents under the most appalling conditions.* 人們在極其惡劣的條件下住在臨時帳篷裡。**b)** the weather at a particular time, especially when you are considering how this will affect you〔某特定時期的〕天氣情況〔尤指會對人產生影響時〕: *Police are advising people to stay at home until weather conditions improve.* 警方建議人們待在家裡直到天氣情況好轉。| **freezing/stormy/icy conditions** *Blizzard conditions are making the roads extremely hazardous.* 大風雪天使道路極為危險。**c)** all the things that affect the way something happens〔影響某事發生的〕情況，條件: *The experiment must be done under laboratory conditions.* 這項試驗必須在實驗室條件下進行。

3 ►AGREEMENT/CONTRACT 協議/合同◄ [C] something that is stated in a contract or agreement that must be done 條款，條件: *Have you read the conditions of employment carefully?* 你有沒有仔細閱讀關於雇傭的條款？| [+for] *There were strict conditions for letting us use their information.* 讓我們使用他們的資料有嚴格的條件。| **lay down/impose conditions** (=state what must be done) 規定/強加條件 *The allies laid down several conditions for their continued support.* 各盟國對繼續給予支持規定了幾項條件。| **meet/satisfy a condition** (=obey what is demanded by a condition) 滿足要求，滿足條件 *The bank agreed to extend the loan if certain conditions were met.* 如果某些條件得到了滿足銀行同意延長這項貸款的期限。| **under the conditions of sth** *Under the conditions of the agreement the work must be completed by the end of the month.* 按照協定的條款工作必須在月底前完成。| **on condition that/on one condition** (=only if a particular thing happens) 只有在某條件下 *Ron lent me the money on condition that I pay it back next month.* 羅恩把錢借我，條件是下月歸還。

4 ►STH THAT MUST BE DONE 必做的事◄ [C] something that must happen first before something else can happen 先決條件，前提: [+for/of] *Finance ministers claimed that all the conditions for an economic revival were in place.* 財政部長們聲稱經濟復蘇的一切條件都已齊備。

5 ►AN ILLNESS 疾病◄ [C] an illness or health problem that affects you permanently or for a very long time 長期疾病: *People suffering from this condition should not smoke.* 得這種病的人不應該吸煙。| **a heart/lung etc condition** *She has a serious heart condition.* 她有嚴重心臟病。

6 ►STATE OF HEALTH 健康狀態◄ [U, singular] a person or animal's state of health〔人或動物的〕健康狀況: *The hospital described his condition as 'satisfactory'.* 醫院將他的身體情況描述為"令人滿意"。| **out of condition** (=unhealthy or unfit) 身體不佳 *The horse is still out of condition after a serious illness.* 生了一場大病後，這匹馬的健康情況依然不佳。| **in no condition to do sth** (=too ill, drunk, or upset to be able to do something)〔因病重、酒醉或生氣而〕不能做某事 *After a whole bottle of wine he was in no condition to drive.* 喝下一整瓶酒後，他不能開車了。

7 on no condition never, in no possible situation 絕對不可: *This equipment should on no condition be used by untrained staff.* 沒有受過訓練的人員絕對不可以操作這個設備。

8 ►SITUATION OF GROUP 羣體狀況◄ [singular] the situation or state of a particular group of people 某一羣人的狀況: *Few people can really appreciate the condition of the poor in our cities.* 很少人能真正體會到我們城市中窮人的狀況。

condition[2] *v* [T] **1** to make a person or an animal think or behave in a certain way by influencing or training them over a period of time〔通過影響或訓練〕使習慣於; 使適應: *People are conditioned by the society and age they live in.* 人們受到他們所生活的社會和時代的制約。| **condition sb to do sth** *The animals were conditioned to expect food at the sound of the bell.* 這些動物受過訓練，一聽見鈴聲就知道有食物可吃了。—see also 另見 CONDITIONING **2** *formal* to control or decide the way in which something can happen or exist【正式】控制; 制約: *What I buy is conditioned by the amount I earn.* 我買些甚麼是由我掙多少錢決定的。**3** to keep hair or skin healthy by putting a special liquid on it〔對頭髮、皮膚〕保養，養護: *This shampoo conditions your hair as well as washing it.* 這種洗髮劑既可洗髮又可護髮。—see also 另見 CONDITIONER

con·di·tion·al[1] /kən`dɪʃənl; kənˈdɪʃənəl/ *adj* **1** if an offer, agreement etc is conditional, it will only be done if something else happens〔幫忙、協議等〕有條件的: **be conditional on/upon** *a conditional acceptance* 有條件的接受 | *His agreement to buy our house was conditional on our leaving all the furniture in it.* 他同意買我們的房子，條件是要把所有家具留下。—opposite 反義詞 UNCONDITIONAL **2** in grammar, a conditional sentence is one that begins with 'if' or 'unless' and expresses something that must be true or happens before something else can be true or happen〔語法上〕條件的〔條件句以 if (如果) 或 unless (除非) 開頭〕—**conditionally** *adv*

conditional[2] *n* [C] a sentence or CLAUSE (2) that is expressed in a conditional form 條件句; 條件子[從]句

conditional dis·charge /·,··· '··/ *n* [C usually singular 一般用單數] a judgment made by a court that allows someone who has done something illegal not to be punished as long as they obey rules set by the court 有條件的釋放〔指一種法庭裁決，允許有違法行為的人在遵守法庭規定的情況下不受懲罰〕

con·di·tion·er /kən`dɪʃənə; kənˈdɪʃənə/ *n* [C,U] **1** a liquid that you put onto your hair after washing it to make it softer 護髮素 **2** a liquid that you wash clothes in to make them softer 織物柔軟劑，衣物柔順劑

con·di·tion·ing /kən`dɪʃənɪŋ; kənˈdɪʃənɪŋ/ *n* [U] the process by which people or animals are trained to behave in a particular way when particular things happen 條件作用，形成條件反射的過程: *Most adults are unaware of the social conditioning they have been subject to since childhood.* 大部分成年人都沒有意識到自己自童年以來受社會環境潛移默化的過程。—see also 另見 AIR CONDITIONING

con·do /ˈkɑndo; ˈkɒndəʊ/ *n* [C] *AmE informal* a CONDOMINIUM【美，非正式】公寓; 公寓樓

con·dole /kən`dol; kənˈdəʊl/ *v*

condole with sb *phr v* [T] *formal* to express sympathy for someone's problems【正式】對別人的困難表示同情

con·do·lence /kən`doləns; kənˈdəʊləns/ *n* [C usually plural 一般用複數, U] sympathy for someone who has had something bad happen to them, especially when someone has died〔尤指有人去世時〕同情，悼唁: *a letter of condolence* 悼唁信 | **send/offer your condolences** (=formally express your sympathy when someone has died) 表示哀悼，致哀 *I'd like to offer my condolences to the victim's parents.* 我謹對受害人的父母表示哀悼。—compare 比較 COMMISERATION

con·dom /ˈkɑndəm; ˈkɒndəm/ *n* [C] a thin rubber bag that a man wears over his PENIS (=sex organ) during sex, to prevent a woman having a baby, or to protect against disease 保險套，避孕套

con·do·min·i·um /ˌkɑndə`mɪnɪəm; ˌkɒndəˈmɪniəm/ *n*

[C] **1** *especially AmE* one apartment in a building with several apartments, each of which is owned by the people living in it【尤美】公寓（樓裡的一套住宅）**2** a building containing several of these apartments 公寓樓

con·done /kən`don; kən'dəʊn/ *v* [T] to accept or forgive behaviour that most people think is morally wrong 寬恕，原諒〔一般人認為不道德的行為〕: *I cannot condone the use of violence under any circumstances.* 我不能原諒在任何情況下使用暴力。

con·dor /`kɑndɚ; 'kɒndɔː/ *n* [C] a very large South American VULTURE (=a bird that eats dead animals) 南美洲禿鷹，兀鷲

con·duce /kən`djus; kən'djuːs/ *v*
conduce to/towards sth *phr v* [T] *formal* to help to produce a particular quality or state【正式】有助於

con·du·cive /kən`djusɪv; kən'djuːsɪv/ *adj* **be conducive to** *formal* if a situation is conducive to something such as work, rest etc, it provides conditions that make it easy for you to work【正式】有助於，有益於: *With so much noise outside, the room is hardly conducive to work.* 外面這麼吵，在這個房間裡簡直無法工作。

3 2 **con·duct¹** /kən`dʌkt; kən'dʌkt/ *v*
1 conduct a survey/experiment/inquiry etc to carry out a particular process, especially in order to get information or prove facts〔尤指為獲取信息或證實某事時〕進行調查/實驗/調查研究等: *The company conducted a survey to find out local reaction to the leisure centre.* 公司進行了一次調查，研究當地人對休閒中心的反應。
2 ►MUSIC 音樂◄ [I,T] to stand in front of a group of musicians and direct their playing 指揮: *The orchestra is conducted by John Williams.* 這個交響樂團由約翰·威廉斯指揮。
3 ►ELECTRICITY/HEAT 電/熱◄ [T] if something conducts electricity or heat, it allows the electricity or heat to travel along or through it 傳導: *Plastic and rubber won't conduct electricity, but copper will.* 塑料和橡膠不導電，但銅是導電的。
4 ►SHOW SB STH 帶某人參觀◄ [T always+adv/prep] to show someone a building or place by leading them around it 帶領某人參觀某地: *The guide conducted us round the castle.* 導遊陪伴我們遊覽了古堡。
5 conduct yourself *formal* to behave in a particular way, especially in a situation where people judge you by the way you behave【正式】行為，表現〔尤指人們藉此作出評判〕: *Public figures have a duty to conduct themselves responsibly.* 公眾人物必須行為端正負責。

3 **con·duct²** /`kɑndʌkt; 'kɒndʌkt/ *n* [U] *formal*【正式】**1** the way someone behaves, especially in public, in their job etc〔社會、職業等〕行為舉止: *The reporter was accused of unprofessional conduct.* 這個記者被指責違反職業操守。**2** the way a business, activity etc is organized〔某項生意、活動的〕組織安排；管理；經營: *There was great dissatisfaction with the conduct of the negotiations.* 對談判的進行情況存在極大的不滿。

con·duc·tion /kən`dʌkʃən; kən'dʌkʃən/ *n* [U] the passage of electricity through wires, heat through metal, water through pipes etc〔電、熱的〕傳導；〔水的〕輸送

con·duc·tive /kən`dʌktɪv; kən'dʌktɪv/ *adj technical* able to conduct electricity, heat etc【術語】〔對電、熱等〕具有傳導性的: *Copper is a very conductive metal.* 銅是一種傳導性極強的金屬。—**conductivity** /ˌkɑndʌk`tɪvətɪ; ˌkɒndʌk'tɪvəti/ *n* [U]

con·duc·tor /kən`dʌktɚ; kən'dʌktə/ *n* [C] **1** someone who stands in front of a group of musicians or singers and directs their playing or singing〔樂隊、合唱隊的〕指揮 **2** someone whose job is to collect payments from passengers on a bus or train〔火車、公共汽車〕售票員 **3** something that allows electricity or heat to travel along it or through it〔電或熱的〕導體: *Wood is a poor conductor of heat.* 木頭的導熱性能極差。**4** *AmE* someone who is in charge of a train or the workers on a train【美】〔火車的〕列車長

con·duc·tress /kən`dʌktrɪs; kən'dʌktrɪs/ *n* [C] *old-fashioned* a female conductor【過時】〔火車、公共汽車〕女售票員

con·duit /`kɑndʊɪt; 'kɒndɪt/ *n* [C] **1** a pipe or passage through which water, gas, a set of electric wires etc pass〔水、氣、電線等的〕管道，導管 **2** a connection between two things that allows people to pass ideas, news, money, weapons, drugs etc from one place to another〔傳遞信息、新聞、金錢、武器、毒品等的〕渠道，通道: *The countries have been a conduit for the arms supplied to the terrorists.* 這些國家一直是向恐怖分子供應武器的通道。

cone¹ /kon; kəʊn/ *n* [C] **1** a solid or hollow shape with a round base, sloping sides, and a point at the top, or something with this shape 圓錐體 **2** an object shaped like a large cone that is put on a road to prevent cars from going somewhere or to warn drivers about something〔公路上阻止車輛通行或向司機發出警示的〕圓錐形路標 **3** the fruit of a PINE¹ (1) or FIR tree 球果 —see also 另見 CONIFER **4** a piece of thin, cooked cake, shaped like a cone, that you put ICE CREAM (2) in〔裝冰淇淋的〕圓錐形蛋卷; CORNET (2) *BrE*【英】

cone² *v*
cone sth **↔ off** *phr v* [T] to close a road or part of a road by putting a row of cones across it or along it 用圓錐形路標封閉〔道路或部分道路〕

co·ney /`konɪ; 'kəʊni/ *n* [C] another spelling of CONY cony 的另一種拼法

con·fab /`kɑnfæb; 'kɒnfæb/ *n* [C] *informal* a conversation that is private and friendly【非正式】友好的私下交談: *We'll have a quick confab to talk about what he wants.* 我們將簡單地談談他的需要。

con·fab·u·late /kən`fæbjəˌlet; kən'fæbjʊleɪt/ *v* [I] *formal* to talk together【正式】交談

con·fab·u·la·tion /kənˌfæbjə`leʃən; kənˌfæbjʊ'leɪʃən/ *n* [C] *formal* a private conversation【正式】私下交談

con·fec·tion /kən`fɛkʃən; kən'fekʃən/ *n* [C] *formal* a beautifully prepared sweet food【正式】製作精美的糖果〔甜點心〕

con·fec·tion·er /kən`fɛkʃənɚ; kən'fekʃənə/ *n* [C] someone who makes or sells sweets, cakes etc〔製作或出售糖果、冰淇淋、糕點等的〕甜食商

confectioner's sug·ar /·'··· ˌ··/ *n* [U] *AmE* a kind of sugar that is very powdery【美】〔生產糖果用的〕糖粉; ICING SUGAR *BrE*【英】

con·fec·tion·e·ry /kən`fɛkʃənˌɛrɪ; kən'fekʃənəri/ *n* **1** [U] sweets, cakes etc 糖果，糕餅 **2** [C] a shop that sells sweets, cakes etc 糖果糕餅店

con·fed·e·ra·cy /kən`fɛdərəsɪ; kən'fedərəsi/ *n* [C] a union of people, parties, or states, especially for political purposes or trade〔尤指為政治或貿易目的〕聯盟，同盟

con·fed·e·rate¹ /kən`fɛdərɪt; kən'fedərɪt/ *n* [C] **1** someone who helps someone else do something, especially something secret or illegal 共犯，同謀，黨羽: *It was important that they didn't think he was John's confederate in the robbery.* 重要的是他們不認為他和約翰同謀搶劫。**2** a member of a confederacy 聯盟者，同盟者，盟友；盟國

confederate², Confederate *adj* belonging to a confederacy or the Confederacy 聯盟的；〔美國南北戰爭時期〕南部邦聯的: *The Confederate Army* 南部邦聯軍隊

con·fed·e·rate³ /kən`fɛdəˌret; kən'fedəreɪt/ *v* [I,T] to combine or to combine something in a confederacy（使）聯合[結盟]: [+with] *In 1949 Newfoundland was confederated with Canada through a referendum.* 1949年紐芬蘭通過全民公決與加拿大結盟。

con·fed·e·ra·tion /kənˌfɛdə`reʃən; kənˌfedə'reɪʃən/ *n* [C] a confederacy 聯盟；同盟

con·fer /kən`fɝ; kən'fɜː/ *v* **conferred, conferring** *formal*【正式】**1** [I] to discuss something with other people, so that everyone can express their opinions and decide on something 商談，商議，討論: [+with] *The congresswoman is conferring with her advisors on the matter.* 這位女國會議員正就此事與顧問商議。**2 confer a title/de-**

gree/honour etc [T] to officially give someone a title etc, especially as a reward for something they have achieved 授予稱號/學位/榮譽等: **[+on/upon]** *An honorary degree was conferred on him by the University.* 大學授予他一個榮譽學位。—**conferment** *n* [C,U]

con·fe·rence /ˋkɑnfərəns; ˈkɒnfərəns/ *n* [C] **1** a large formal meeting where a lot of people discuss important matters such as business or politics, especially for several days 會議〔指很多人參加討論重要事宜的大型會議, 尤指歷時數天的會議〕: **[+on]** *a scientific conference on the ozone layer* 討論臭氧層問題的科學會議 | **hold a conference** (=have a conference) 舉行會議 | **attend a conference** (=go to a conference) 出席會議 *Representatives from over 100 countries attended the International Peace Conference in Geneva.* 來自一百多個國家的代表出席了在日內瓦舉行的國際和平大會。| **conference centre/table/room** (=a building, table etc used for conferences) 會議中心/會議桌/會議室 *The university has a conference centre in the mountains.* 這所大學在山中建有一處會議中心。—see also 另見 PRESS CONFERENCE **2** a private meeting for a few people to have formal discussions 少數人參加的私下會議: **[+with]** *After a brief conference with his aides, he left for the airport.* 和他的助手進行簡短的討論後, 他動身去機場。| **have/hold a conference** *Everyone go and rest, and we'll have a conference about our next move later.* 大家都出去休息一下, 過一會兒我們再開會討論下一步怎麼辦。| **in conference** *The manager cannot see you now; she's in conference.* 經理現在不能見你, 她正在開會。**3** *AmE* a group of teams that play against each other; LEAGUE[1] (1) 【美】〔運動〕聯合會: *College football has two main conferences, the Pac Ten and the Big Ten.* 大學美式足球有兩大聯合會: 太平洋十強和十強。

conference call /ˈ··· ˌ·/ *n* [C] a telephone call in which several people in different places can all talk to each other 電話會議

con·fess /kənˋfɛs; kənˈfes/ *v* [I,T] **1** to admit that you have done something wrong or illegal, especially to the police〔尤指向警察〕坦白, 招認, 招供: *After three hours of questioning the suspect broke down and confessed.* 經過三個小時的審問, 嫌疑犯崩潰了, 招認了一切。| **confess to doing sth** *Edwards confessed to being a spy for the KGB.* 愛德華茲承認為克格勃當間諜。| **confess that** *She confessed that she killed her husband.* 她承認是她殺死了自己的丈夫。| **confess to murder/a crime/robbery etc** *Occasionally people confess to crimes they haven't committed just to get attention.* 有時人們會承認自己並未犯的罪行, 只是為了受到注意。**2** to admit something that you feel embarrassed about 承認〔使自己尷尬的事情〕: **confess that** *Marsha confessed that she didn't really know how to work the computer.* 瑪莎承認她其實並不會使用電腦。| **confess to doing sth** *He confessed to having a secret admiration for his opponent.* 他承認私底下很欽佩他的對手。| **confess yourself puzzled/baffled etc** *The police have confessed themselves baffled by this strange and savage crime.* 警方已經承認對這一怪異而野蠻的罪行感到無從下手。| **I (must) confess** *spoken* (=used when admitting something you feel slightly embarrassed about) 【口】我(必須)承認〔用於承認自己略感尷尬的事〕*I must confess I don't visit my parents as often as I should.* 我必須承認我並沒有像我應該做到的那樣經常去看我的父母。**3** to tell a priest or God about the wrong things you have done so that you can be forgiven〔向神父或上帝〕懺悔

con·fessed /kənˋfɛst; kənˈfest/ *adj* [only before noun 僅用於名詞前] having admitted publicly that you have done something 已公開承認的, 已招供的: *a confessed criminal* 已經招供的罪犯 —see also 另見 SELF-CONFESSED —**confessedly** /-ˋfɛsɪdlɪ; -ˈfesɨdli/ *adv*

con·fes·sion /kənˋfɛʃən; kənˈfeʃən/ *n* **1** [C] a formal statement that you have done something wrong or illegal 供認, 招供: *The police officer wrote down every word of Smith's confession.* 警察記錄下史密斯招供時所說的每一個字。| **[+of]** *a confession of failure* 承認失敗 | **make a confession** *At 3 a.m. Higgins broke down and made a full confession.* 在凌晨三點, 辛吉斯崩潰了並交代了一切。**2** [C,U] a private statement to a priest about the bad things that you have done〔對神父作的〕懺悔, 告解 **3** [C] *formal* a statement of what your religious beliefs are 【正式】關於自己宗教信仰的聲明: *a confession of faith* 信仰聲明

con·fes·sion·al[1] /kənˋfɛʃənḷ; kənˈfeʃənəl/ *n* [C] a place in a church, usually an enclosed room, where a priest hears people make their confessions〔教堂裡的〕告解室

confessional[2] *adj* confessional speech or writing contains private thoughts or facts that you normally want to keep secret, especially private information about things you have done that were wrong 自白的; 懺悔的

con·fes·sor /kənˋfɛsɚ; kənˈfesə/ *n* [C] the priest who someone regularly makes their confession to 常聽取某人告解的神父

con·fet·ti /kənˋfɛtɪ; kənˈfeti/ *n* [U] small pieces of coloured paper that you throw over a man and woman who have just been married, especially when they come out of church〔婚禮時向新郎新娘拋撒的〕五彩紙屑〔尤在他們步出教堂時〕

con·fi·dant /ˌkɑnfəˋdænt; ˈkɒnfɨdænt/ *n* [C] someone you tell your secrets to or who you talk to about personal things 知己, 密友, 心腹朋友

con·fi·dante /ˌkɑnfəˋdænt; ˈkɒnfɨdænt/ *n* [C] a female confidant 女性知己[密友]

con·fide /kənˋfaɪd; kənˈfaɪd/ *v* [T] **1** to tell someone you trust about personal things that you do not want other people to know 吐露〔自己的隱私〕: **confide to sb that** *He confided to his friends that he didn't have much hope for his marriage.* 他私下告訴他的朋友說他對自己的婚姻不抱太大的希望。**2** *formal* to give something you value to someone you trust so they look after it for you 【正式】將貴重物品託付給某人照管: **confide sth to sb** *He confided his money to his brother's safe-keeping.* 他把錢託付給他弟弟保管。

confide in sb *phr v* [T] to tell someone about something very private or secret, especially a personal problem, because you feel you can trust them 向某人吐露個人隱私: *It's important to have someone that you can confide in.* 有個能向他說心腹話的人是很重要的。

con·fi·dence /ˋkɑnfədəns; ˈkɒnfɨdəns/ *n*

1 ►FEELING SB/STH IS GOOD 認為某人/物好◄ [U] the feeling that you can trust someone or something to be good, work well, or produce good results 信任, 信賴: **[+in]** *Our first priority is to maintain the customer's confidence in our product.* 我們優先考慮的是如何保持顧客對我們產品的信任。| **have confidence in** *We have every confidence in your abilities.* 我們對你的能力非常有信心。| **win/gain/lose sb's confidence (in)** *Opinion polls show that voters have lost confidence in the administration.* 民意調查顯示選民對當局已失去信任。| **inspire/restore/undermine confidence (in)** (=make people feel more or less confident about something or someone) 激起/恢復/破壞信任 *These miscarriages of justice have undermined confidence in our legal system.* 這些冤案錯案破壞了人們對我們司法制度的信任。| **show confidence (in)** *Middle-aged people generally do not show as much confidence in what the future holds as do the young.* 總的來說中年人不像青年人那樣對未來充滿希望。

2 ►BELIEF IN YOURSELF 自信◄ [U] the belief that you have the ability to do things well or deal with situations successfully 自信, 信心: *Joyce always had an abundance of confidence. She seemed to fear no one.* 喬伊絲總是滿懷信心, 她好像不畏懼任何人。| **lack confidence/be lacking in confidence** *She's a good student but she lacks confidence in herself.* 她是好學生, 但缺乏自信。|

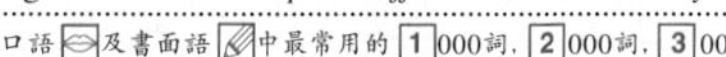

lack of confidence *A lack of confidence seems to be her main problem.* 缺乏自信心看來是她的主要問題。| **give sb confidence** *Living on her own in a foreign country for a year gave her a lot of confidence.* 獨自在國外生活了一年大大地增強了她的自信。| **give sb the confidence to do sth** *Good training will give a beginner the confidence to enjoy skiing.* 良好的訓練會使初學者有信心來享受滑雪的樂趣。| **restore/lose confidence** *Going back to work restored my confidence and made me feel more capable.* 回到工作崗位使我重獲自信, 並使我覺得自己更加能幹了。| **boost/shake sb's confidence** (=make someone feel more or less confident) 增強/動搖某人的信心 *Julie's confidence was badly shaken by her car accident.* 車禍極大地動搖了朱莉的自信心。

3 ►FEELING STH IS TRUE 確信某事確實◄ [U] the feeling that something is definite or true 確信, 堅信, 篤信: *How can anyone say with confidence that the recession is over?* 怎麼會有人能確切地説蕭條已經結束? | **have confidence that** *At that time he had little confidence that God existed.* 在那時他不怎麼相信上帝存在。

4 ►FEELING OF TRUST 信任感◄ [U] a feeling of trust in someone, so that you can tell them something and be sure they will not tell other people 信賴, 信任: **have/gain/get sb's confidence** (=make someone feel they can trust you) 擁有/獲得/得到某人的信任 *It took me a long time to gain his confidence, but he trusts me now.* 我花了很長時間來贏得他的信任, 不過現在他很信任我。| **in (strict) confidence** (=if you tell someone something in confidence, you tell them in secret and they must not tell anyone else) 必須(絕對)保密 *I'm giving you this information in the strictest confidence.* 我告訴你這個消息, 你要絕對保密。| **take sb into your confidence** (=tell someone something secret) 將祕密告訴某人 *Tanya took Liane into her confidence about her marital problems.* 塔尼婭向利安娜透露了她婚姻問題的祕密。

5 ►A SECRET 祕密◄ [C] a secret or a piece of information that is private or personal 知心話; 祕密: *They spent their evenings drinking wine by the fire and sharing confidences.* 他們每天晚上都坐在火爐旁一邊喝酒, 一邊閒談心腹事。—see also 另見 VOTE OF CONFIDENCE, VOTE OF NO CONFIDENCE

confidence-build·ing /'··· ,··/ *adj* an event, action etc that is confidence-building increases your confidence 增強自信心的: *The outdoor training is meant to be a confidence-building exercise for youngsters.* 戶外訓練是用來增強青少年自信心的一種訓練方式。

confidence trick /'··· ,·/ *n* [C] *formal* a dishonest trick played on someone in order to get their money; CON² (1)【正式】詐騙 —**confidence trickster** *n* [C]

S2 W3 **con·fi·dent** /ˈkɑnfədənt; ˈkɒnfɪdənt/ *adj* **1** sure that you can do something or deal with a situation successfully 有信心的: *He gave her a confident smile.* 他自信地對她微笑。| **be confident about** *Joyce is very confident about using computers.* 喬伊絲對使用電腦非常自信。**2** [not before noun 不用於名詞前] very sure that something is going to happen or that you will be able to do something 確信的; 有把握的: **be confident (that)** *We are confident that next year's profits will be higher.* 我們確信明年的利潤會增加。—see also 另見 SELF-CONFIDENT —**confidently** *adv*

con·fi·den·tial /ˌkɑnfəˈdɛnʃəl; ˌkɒnfɪˈdenʃəl◄/ *adj* **1** spoken or written in secret and intended to be kept secret 機密的; 機要的: *a confidential naval report on the failure of equipment* 有關設備失靈的海軍機要報告 | **keep sth confidential** *Doctors are required to keep patients' records completely confidential.* 醫生必須對病人的病歷絕對保密。| **strictly confidential** (=completely confidential) 絕密的 *What I'm telling you is strictly confidential.* 我告訴你的是絕密的事。**2** a confidential way of speaking or behaving shows that you do not want other people to know what you are saying〔言談舉止〕神祕的: *His voice sank into a confidential whisper as he mentioned who was involved.* 當説到有誰涉及時, 他把聲音壓低, 悄聲低語起來。**3** a confidential secretary or CLERK¹ (1) is one who is trusted with secret information〔祕書、人員〕機要的, 心腹的, 極受信任的 —**confidentially** *adv*

con·fi·den·ti·al·i·ty /ˌkɑnfəˌdɛnʃɪˈælətɪ; ˌkɒnfɪdenʃiˈæləti/ *n* [U] a situation in which you trust someone not to tell secret or private information to anyone else 機密, 祕密; 保密: *The relationship between attorneys and their clients is based on confidentiality.* 律師和委託人之間的關係是建立在保密的基礎之上的。| **breach of confidentiality** (=an occasion when someone tells a secret) 違反保密責任 *It is a breach of confidentiality for a priest to reveal what someone has said in the confessional.* 神父把某人告解所説的事情泄露出來是違反了保密的原則。

con·fid·ing /kənˈfaɪdɪŋ; kənˈfaɪdɪŋ/ *adj* behaving in a way that shows you want to tell someone about something that is private or secret 信任他人的: *She allowed a confiding note to enter her voice.* 她讓語調流露出一種對人的信任。—**confidingly** *adv*: *She spoke gaily, innocently, and confidingly.* 她愉快地與人交談, 那麼天真, 那麼信賴別人。

con·fig·u·ra·tion /kənˌfɪgjəˈreʃən; kənˌfɪgjʊˈreɪʃən/ *n* [C,U] **1** *formal or technical* the shape or arrangement of the parts of something; LAYOUT【正式或術語】構造, 結構; 佈局: [+of] *the configuration of pistons in an engine* 發動機內活塞的佈局 **2** *technical* the combination of equipment needed to run a computer system【術語】〔電腦設備的〕配置

con·fig·ure /kənˈfɪgjɚ; kənˈfɪgə/ *v* [T] *technical* to arrange something, especially computer equipment, so that it works with other equipment【術語】配置〔尤指電腦設備〕

W **con·fine** /kənˈfaɪn; kənˈfaɪn/ *v* [T]

1 ►LIMIT 限制◄ to keep someone or something within the limits of a particular activity or subject; RESTRICT 把…局限於; 把…限制於: **be confined to** *The police cadet's duties were confined to taking statements from the crowd.* 警官學校學員的責任只限於記錄人羣所作的口供。| *a former editor now confined to organizing the letter page* 現在只限於編排讀者來信版面的前任編輯 | **confine yourself to sth** *We must confine ourselves to the subject at hand.* 我們的討論應當限制在眼前的這個話題。

2 be confined to a) to affect or happen to only one group of people, or in only one place or time 局限於〔某一羣體、地點或時間〕: *This disease is not just confined to children.* 這種病不只發生在兒童身上。**b)** to have to stay in a place, especially because you are ill〔尤指因病〕只能待在〔某地〕: *an elderly woman confined to a small apartment* 只能在一套小居室內活動的老婦人 | **confined to a wheelchair** (=unable to walk) 行動只能靠輪椅 *Although confined to a wheelchair, she is very active in church life.* 雖然她只能依靠輪椅行動, 她對教堂的活動仍非常積極。

3 ►KEEP SB IN A PLACE 監禁某人◄ to keep someone in a place that they cannot leave, such as a prison 監禁, 禁閉: **confine sb to** *Any soldier who leaves his post will be confined to the barracks.* 任何擅離職守的士兵都將被關在營房裡, 不准外出。| **be confined in** *He was allegedly confined in a narrow, dark room for two months.* 據説他被監禁在一個既狹窄又黑暗的房間裡, 關了兩個月。

4 ►STOP SPREADING 阻止擴散◄ to stop something bad from spreading to another place 限制, 阻止: **confine sth to sth** *Fire fighters quickly confined the blaze to the factory floor.* 消防隊員很快就把火勢控制在工廠的車間範圍內。

5 ►STAY IN BED 臥牀◄ [usually passive 一般用被動態] to make someone stay in bed because they are ill 使…臥牀休息: *I had flu and was confined to bed.* 我感冒了, 只得臥牀休息。

con·fined /kənˈfaɪnd; kənˈfaɪnd/ *adj* a confined space or area is one that is very small〔指空間或面積〕有限

的, 狹窄的: *It wasn't easy to sleep in such a confined space.* 在如此狹小的空間裡睡覺實在不容易。

con·fine·ment /kən`faınmənt; kən'faınmənt/ *n* **1** [U] the act of putting someone in a room, prison etc, or the state of being there 監禁, 關押; 禁閉: *her years of confinement* 她坐牢的那些年 | *They were held in confinement for three weeks.* 他們被關押了三個禮拜。—see also 另見 SOLITARY CONFINEMENT **2** [C,U] an act of giving birth to a child; LYING-IN 分娩; 產期

con·fines /`kɑnfaınz; 'kɒnfaınz/ *n* [plural] limits or borders 界限, 範圍: **within/beyond the confines of** *within the confines of the prison* 在監獄範圍內

con·firm /kən`fɝm; kən'fɜːm/ *v* [T] **1** to show that something is definitely true, especially by providing more proof 證實, 證明: *The new evidence has confirmed the first witness's story.* 新證據證實了第一個證人的說法。| **confirm that** *Research has confirmed that the risk is higher for women.* 研究證實這種危險對婦女的威脅更大。| **confirm what** *The new results confirm what most of us knew already.* 新成果證實我們大多數人已經知道的東西。**2** to make an idea or feeling stronger or more definite 使〔想法、感覺〕鞏固, 更堅定, 加強: *This just confirms my fears.* 這只加深了我的恐懼。| **confirm you in your belief/opinion/view etc (that)** (=make you believe something more strongly) 使信念/意見/觀點等更加確實 *The expression on his face confirmed me in my suspicions.* 他臉上的表情證實了我的懷疑。**3** to say that something is definitely true 證實: *The President refused to confirm the rumor.* 總統拒絕證實這個謠言。| **confirm that** *Walsh confirmed that the money had been paid.* 沃爾什證實那筆錢已經支付。| **confirm what** *My brother will confirm what I have told you.* 我弟弟將證實我跟你說過的話。**4** to tell someone that a possible arrangement, date, or time is now definite 肯定, 確認〔安排、日期等〕: *Could you confirm the dates we discussed?* 你能確認我們討論的日期嗎? | **be confirmed in office** (=be formally accepted in a new position of responsibility, especially as leader of a country) 正式就職〔尤指擔任國家領導人〕**5 be confirmed** to be made a full member of the Christian church in a special ceremony 行堅信典禮〔從而正式成為基督教會成員〕

con·fir·ma·tion /ˌkɑnfɚ`meʃən; ˌkɒnfə'meıʃən/ *n* [C, U] **1** a statement etc that says that something is definitely true, or the act of stating this 證實, 證明: [+of] *There's still no official confirmation of the report.* 這則報告仍未得到官方證實。| **confirmation that** *verbal confirmation that payment has been made* 對已經付款的口頭證明 **2** a letter etc that tells you that a possible arrangement, date, time etc is now definite 〔安排、日期、時間等的〕確認函: *I'm still waiting for confirmation from them about my visit.* 我仍在等他們對我拜訪行程的確認函。**3** a religious ceremony in which someone is made a full member of the Christian church 堅信禮

con·firmed /kən`fɝmd; kən'fɜːmd/ *adj* **a confirmed bachelor/alcoholic/vegetarian etc** someone who seems completely happy with the way of life they have chosen 誓不結婚的單身漢/無可救藥的酒鬼/堅定的素食主義者等

con·fis·cate /`kɑnfısˌket; 'kɒnfɪ̈skeıt/ *v* [T] to officially take private property away from someone, usually as a punishment 把…充公, 沒收: *Miss Williams confiscated all our sweets.* 威廉斯小姐沒收了我們所有的糖果。—**confiscation** /ˌkɑnfıs`keʃən; ˌkɒnfɪ̈'skeıʃən/ *n* [C,U] *the confiscation of pornographic material* 對淫穢物品的沒收 —**confiscatory** /kən`fıskəˌtorı; 'kɒnfɪ̈skeıtəri/ *adj*

con·fla·gra·tion /ˌkɑnflə`greʃən; ˌkɒnflə'greıʃən/ *n* [C] *formal*【正式】**1** a very large fire that destroys a lot of buildings, forests etc 大火 **2** a violent situation or war 衝突; 戰爭: *a nuclear conflagration* 核衝突

con·flate /kən`flet; kən'fleıt/ *v* [T] *formal* to combine two or more things to form a single new thing【正式】合併, 混合: *This idea conflates two issues.* 這個想法來源於兩點。—**conflation** /-`fleʃən; -'fleıʃən/ *n* [C,U]

con·flict¹ /`kɑnflıkt; 'kɒnflıkt/ *n* [C,U] **1** a state of disagreement or argument between people, groups, countries etc〔意見等〕衝突, 相左: *serious political conflict* 嚴重的政治衝突 | **[+over]** *conflicts over wage settlements* 對工資協議的爭執 | **[+between]** *the conflict between tradition and innovation* 傳統與革新的衝突 | **in conflict** *permanently in conflict with her superiors* 與她的上級處於無休止的矛盾之中 | **come into conflict** (=start arguing with) 發生爭執 *She had often come into conflict with her mother-in-law.* 她經常與婆婆發生爭執。**2** a situation in which you have to choose between two or more opposite needs or influences〔在對立的需要或影響之間選擇的〕矛盾, 衝突: **[+between]** *a conflict between the demands of one's work and one's family* 工作和家庭之間的矛盾 | **in conflict with** *The principles of democracy are sometimes in conflict with political reality.* 民主原則有時與政治現實發生衝突。**3** fighting or a war 戰鬥; 戰爭: *a violent conflict* 劇烈的武裝衝突 | **armed conflict** *the frightening prospect of armed conflict* 發生武裝衝突的恐怖前景 **4** a situation in which you have two opposite feelings about something 矛盾心理: *an agonizing state of inner conflict* 折磨人的內心矛盾 **5 conflict of interest/interests a)** a situation in which you cannot do your job fairly because you will be affected by the decision you make 利益衝突: *There is a growing conflict of interest between her position as a politician and her business activities.* 她作為政客的地位和她的商務活動之間的利益衝突日益嚴重。**b)** a situation in which different people want different things〔不同人之間的〕利益衝突

con·flict² /kən`flıkt; kən'flıkt/ *v* [I] if two ideas, beliefs, opinions etc conflict, they cannot exist together or both be true 矛盾, 衝突, 抵觸: **[+with]** *This conflicts with the police evidence.* 這與警方的證據相矛盾。| **conflicting opinions/demands/interests etc** *I had rung a few friends, and been given a great deal of conflicting advice.* 我打電話給幾個朋友, 他們給我許多相互衝突的建議。

con·flu·ence /`kɑnfluəns; 'kɒnfluəns/ *n* [singular+of] **1** *technical* the place where two or more rivers flow together【術語】〔河的〕匯合點, 合流處 **2** the point at which two or more ideas, principles etc are very similar〔不同意見、原則的〕相似之處 —**confluent** *adj*

con·form /kən`fɔrm; kən'fɔːm/ *v* [I] **1** to behave in the way that most other people in your group or society behave 像大多數人一樣行事: *the pressure on schoolchildren to conform* 促使小學生循規蹈矩的力量 **2 conform to a law/rule etc** to obey a law, rule etc 遵守法律/規定等: *You must conform to the rules or leave the school.* 你要麼遵守規定, 要麼離開學校。| *conform to the official safety standards* 遵守官方的安全準則 **3 conform to the pattern/model/ideal etc** *formal* to happen or develop in the way that is normal or that you expect【正式】遵照模式/範例/理想等 —see also 另見 CONFORMIST —**conformer** *n* [C] —**conformance** *n* [U]

con·for·ma·tion /ˌkɑnfɔr`meʃən; ˌkɒnfɔː'meıʃən/ *n* [C, U] *technical* the shape of something or the way in which it is formed【術語】形狀; 構造: *the conformation of the earth* 地球的構造

con·form·ist /kən`fɔrmıst; kən'fɔːmɪ̈st/ *adj* thinking and behaving like everyone else, because you do not want to be different 墨守成規的, 老一套的: *conformist thinking* 守舊的想法 —**conformist** *n* [C] *his refusal to be a conformist* 他拒絕墨守成規

con·for·mi·ty /kən`fɔrmətı; kən'fɔːmɪ̈ti/ *n* [U] *formal*【正式】**1** behaviour that obeys the accepted rules of society or a group, and is the same as that of most other people 遵守, 依照〔公認準則的行為〕: *an emphasis on conformity and control* 對循規蹈矩和操縱的強調 | **[+to]** *conformity to an agreed standard of taste* 符合公認的口味標準 **2 in conformity with** *formal* in a way that obeys rules, customs etc【正式】與〔規定、習俗等〕一致,

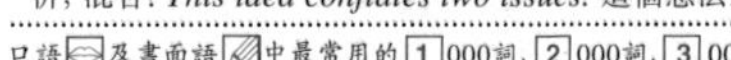

符合: *We must act in conformity with the local regulations.* 我們必須遵守當地的法規。

con·found /kɑnˋfaʊnd; kənˈfaʊnd/ *v* [T] **1** to confuse and surprise people by being unexpected 以出乎意料的行為使人困惑或驚訝: *His amazing recovery confounded the medical specialists.* 他神奇的康復使醫學專家感到困惑。**2** *formal* to defeat an enemy, plan etc【正式】挫敗〔敵人、計劃等〕**3** *formal* if a problem etc confounds you, you cannot understand it or solve it【正式】〔問題等〕把…難住, 使不知所措: *Her question completely confounded me.* 她提的問題把我完全搞糊塗了。**4 confound it/him/them** *old-fashioned* used to show that you are annoyed【過時】討厭, 該死

con·found·ed /kənˋfaʊndɪd; kənˈfaʊndɨd/ *adj* [only before noun 僅用於名詞前] *old-fashioned* used to show that you are annoyed【過時】討厭的; 該死的: *That confounded dog has run away again!* 那條該死的狗又跑掉了!

con·fra·ter·ni·ty /ˌkɑnfrəˋtɝnətɪ; ˌkɒnfrəˈtɜːnɨti/ *n* [C] a group of people, especially religious people who are not priests, who work together for some good purpose〔宗教、慈善事業等的〕團體; 社團

con·frère /ˋkɑnfrɛr; ˈkɒnfrə/ *n* [C] *French, formal* a friend or someone you work with【法, 正式】朋友; 同事

con·front /kənˋfrʌnt; kənˈfrʌnt/ *v* [T] **1** to behave in a threatening way towards someone, as though you are going to attack them 以暴力相威脅: *Opening the door, he found himself confronted by a dozen policemen with guns.* 他開門時發現自己面對着十二名帶槍的警察。**2** to deal with something very difficult or unpleasant in a brave and determined way 勇敢地面對; 正視: *We try to help people confront their problems.* 我們試圖幫助人們正視問題。**3** [usually passive 一般用被動態] to suddenly appear and need to be dealt with 突然面臨: *On my first day at work I was confronted with the task of chairing a meeting.* 我第一天上班就面臨主持一個會議的任務。**4** to accuse someone of doing something by showing them the proof 對質, 當面對證: **confront sb with the evidence/proof** *When the police confronted her with the evidence, she admitted everything.* 當警察當面向她出示證據時, 她承認了一切。

con·fron·ta·tion /ˌkɑnfrʌnˋteʃən; ˌkɒnfrənˈteɪʃən/ *n* [C,U+with/between] **1** a situation in which there is a lot of angry disagreement between two people or groups with very different opinions〔兩人或兩羣人之間〕怒氣沖沖的意見衝突: *She had stayed in her room to avoid another confrontation.* 她待在自己的房間裡以避免另一次的衝突。**2** a fight or battle 戰鬥, 戰役

con·fron·ta·tion·al /ˌkɑnfrʌnˋteʃənḷ; ˌkɒnfrənˈteɪʃənəl◂/ *adj* intended to cause arguments or make people angry 故意尋釁或叫人生氣的: *a confrontational style of government* 對抗式的統治方式

con·fuse /kənˋfjuz; kənˈfjuːz/ *v* [T] **1** to make someone feel that they cannot think clearly or do not understand 使困惑; 把〔某人〕弄糊塗: *Don't give me so much information – you're confusing me!* 別告訴我這麼多——你會把我弄糊塗的! **2** to think wrongly that one person, thing, or idea etc is someone or something else〔把人、物或想法〕混淆, 弄錯: **confuse sb/sth with** *I always confuse you with your sister – you look so alike.* 我總是把你和你妹妹搞混, 你們太像了。| *Donald Reagan, not to be confused with former President Ronald Reagan* 唐納德·里根, 不要把他與前總統朗奴·列根混淆 **3 confuse the issue/matter/argument etc** to make it even more difficult to think clearly about a situation or problem or to deal with it 使問題/事情/爭論等更加難以弄清或處理: *He kept asking unnecessary questions which only confused the issue.* 他不停地問些無關緊要的問題, 只有使這個問題更複雜。

3 **con·fused** /kənˋfjuzd; kənˈfjuːzd/ *adj* **1** unable to understand clearly what someone is saying or what is happening 困惑的, 糊塗的: *I am totally confused. Could you explain that again?* 我完全糊塗了, 你能再解釋一遍嗎? | **[+about]** *If you're confused about anything, phone my office.* 如果你對甚麼事有疑問, 給我辦公室打電話。**2** not clear or not easy to understand 不清楚的; 混亂的; 分不清的: *There was an argument and a confused fight followed.* 爭吵過後是一場混亂的打鬥。| *a lot of confused ideas* 許多混淆的觀念 —**confusedly** /-ˋfjuzdlɪ; -ˈfjuːzɨdli/ *adv*

con·fus·ing /kənˋfjuzɪŋ; kənˈfjuːzɪŋ/ *adj* difficult to understand because there is no clear order or pattern 令人困惑的, 模糊不清的, 難懂的: *The instructions were so confusing I've done it all wrong.* 那些説明模糊不清, 我全做錯了。| *It was a very confusing situation.* 這是非常混亂的局面。—**confusingly** *adv* 3

con·fu·sion /kənˋfjuʒən; kənˈfjuːʒən/ *n* [U] **1** a state of not understanding what is happening or what something means because it is not clear 困惑; 混亂: **[+about/over/as to]** *There was some confusion as to whether we had won or lost.* 不清楚我們究竟是輸了還是贏了。| **create/lead to confusion** *This complicated situation has led to considerable confusion.* 這種複雜的局勢造成了相當的混亂。**2** a situation in which someone wrongly thinks that one person, thing, or idea is someone or something else 辨別不清; 混淆, 錯認: *To avoid confusion, the teams wore different colours.* 為了避免混淆, 各球隊穿上不同顏色的服裝。| **[+between]** *confusion between 'tax avoidance' and 'tax evasion'* "避稅"和"逃稅"之間的混淆 **3** a feeling of not being able to think clearly what you should say or do, especially in an embarrassing situation 慌亂; 窘迫: *His confusion at meeting her there was quite apparent.* 他在那裡和她不期而遇, 明顯地表現得不知所措。| **in confusion** *She stopped in confusion as everyone turned to look at her.* 當每個人轉頭看她時, 她窘迫地停了下來。**4** a very confusing situation, usually with a lot of noise and action, so that it is difficult to understand or control 混亂, 騷亂: *a scene of indescribable confusion* 難以形容的混亂景象 3 3

con·fute /kənˋfjut; kənˈfjuːt/ *v* [T] *formal* to prove that a person or belief is completely wrong【正式】駁倒, 完全否定 —**confutation** /ˌkɑnfjuˋteʃən; ˌkɒnfjuːˈteɪʃən/ *n* [C,U]

con·ga /ˋkɑŋgə; ˈkɒŋgə/ *n* [C,U] a Latin American dance in which people hold onto each other and dance in a line, or the music for this 康茄舞〔一種拉丁美洲舞蹈〕; 康茄舞曲

con·geal /kənˋdʒil; kənˈdʒiːl/ *v* [I] if a liquid such as blood congeals, it becomes thick or solid〔血液等液體〕凝結

con·ge·ni·al /kənˋdʒinjəl; kənˈdʒiːniəl/ *adj* pleasant in a way that makes you feel comfortable and relaxed 宜人的; 令人舒適愉快的: **[+to]** *The club provides a social atmosphere which is congenial to the average business man.* 俱樂部提供一種社交氛圍, 使一般的商人都覺得非常舒適。—**congenially** *adv*

con·gen·i·tal /kənˋdʒɛnətḷ; kənˈdʒenɨtl/ *adj* **1** a congenital medical condition or disease has affected someone since they were born〔病症等〕先天的: *congenital abnormalities* 先天畸形 | *congenital defect* 先天性缺陷 **2** existing as a part of your character and unlikely to change 天生的; 根深蒂固的: *his congenital inability to make decisions* 他優柔寡斷的天性 | *a congenital liar* 生性好説謊的人 —**congenitally** *adv*

con·ger eel /ˌkɑŋgɚ ˋil; ˌkɒŋgər ˈiːl/ *n* [C] a large fish that looks like a snake 康吉鰻

con·ges·ted /kənˋdʒɛstɪd; kənˈdʒestɨd/ *adj* **1** a congested street, city etc is very full of traffic 交通擁擠的, 車輛阻塞的: *congested air space* 擁擠的空中交通 **2** a part of your body that is congested is very full of liquid, usually blood or MUCUS〔身體某部位〕充血[黏液]的 —**congestion** /-ˋdʒɛstʃən; -ˈdʒestʃən/ *n* [U]: *traffic congestion* 交通擁擠

con·glom·e·rate /kənˋglɑmərɪt; kənˈglɒmərɨt/ *n* **1** [C] a large business organization consisting of several different companies that have joined together 大型聯合企業: *a large multinational conglomerate* 大型跨國聯合企業 **2** [C,U] *technical* a rock consisting of different sizes of stones held together by clay【術語】礫岩 **3** [C] a group of things gathered together 聚集物

con·glom·e·ra·tion /kənˌglɑməˋreʃən; kənˌglɒməˈreɪʃən/ *n* [C+of] a group of many different things gathered together 聚集物

con·grats /kənˋgræts; kənˈgræts/ *n* [plural] *informal* CONGRATULATIONS【非正式】祝賀, 恭喜

con·grat·u·late /kənˋgrætʃəˌlet; kənˈgrætʃʊleɪt/ *v* [T] **1** to tell someone that you are happy because they have achieved something or because something nice has happened to them 祝賀, 向...道喜: *He never even stopped to congratulate me.* 他甚至都不停下來向我祝賀。| **congratulate sb on** *She congratulated me warmly on my exam results.* 她熱情地祝賀我考試取得好成績。**2 congratulate yourself (on)** to feel pleased and proud of yourself because you have achieved something or something good has happened to you 為自己高興, 感到自豪: *I congratulated myself on my good fortune.* 我為自己的好運氣感到高興。—**congratulation** /kənˌgrætʃəˋleʃən; kənˌgrætʃʊˈleɪʃən/ *n* [U] —**congratulatory** /kənˋgrætʃələˌtorɪ; kənˌgrætʃʊˈleɪtəri/ *adj*

3 **con·grat·u·la·tions** /kənˌgrætʃəˋleʃənz; kənˌgrætʃʊˈleɪʃənz/ *n* [plural] **1** words saying you are happy that someone has achieved something 祝賀的話語: *Give Marie my congratulations and tell her I'll come soon.* 替我恭喜瑪麗並告訴她我很快就來。**2** an expression used when you want to congratulate someone 恭喜, 祝賀: *"I've just passed my driving test!" "Congratulations!"* "我剛剛通過駕駛執照考試!" "恭喜你!" | **[+on]** *Congratulations on a superb performance!* 對這場精彩的演出表示祝賀!

con·gre·gate /ˋkɑŋgrɪˌget; ˈkɒŋgrɪgeɪt/ *v* [I] to come together in a group 聚合, 聚集: *Crowds began to congregate to hear the President's speech.* 人羣開始聚集起來, 聆聽總統的演講。

con·gre·ga·tion /ˌkɑŋgrɪˋgeʃən; ˌkɒŋgrɪˈgeɪʃən/ *n* [C also+plural verb *BrE* 英] **1** a group of people gathered together in a church 會眾〔在教堂裡聚集的人羣〕: *The congregation knelt to pray.* 會眾下跪祈禱。**2** the people who usually go to a particular church 會眾〔通常去某教堂做禮拜的人羣〕: *Several members of the congregation were sick.* 常來這裡做禮拜的幾個人病了。—**congregational** *adj*

Con·gre·ga·tion·al·is·m /ˌkɑŋgrɪˋgeʃənlˌɪzəm; ˌkɒŋgrɪˈgeɪʃənəlɪzəm/ *n* [U] one type of Christianity, in which each congregation is responsible for making its own decisions〔基督教〕公理主義; 公理制度〔一種基督教教派, 主張各教堂的會眾自行管理自己的事務〕—**Congregational** *adj* —**Congregationalist** *n* [C]

con·gress /ˋkɑŋgrəs; ˈkɒŋgres/ *n* **1** [C,U] a formal meeting of representatives of different groups, countries etc, to discuss ideas, give information etc 代表大會: *the annual congress of the miners' union* 礦工工會的年度代表大會 **2** [C] the group of people chosen or elected to make the laws in countries 國會; 議會 **3 Congress** the group of people elected to make laws in the US, consisting of the Senate and the House of Representatives〔由參議院和眾議院組成的〕美國國會: *The President has lost the support of Congress.* 總統失去了國會支持。—**congressional** /kənˋgrɛʃənḷ; kənˈgreʃənəl/ *adj* [only before noun 僅用於名詞前]: *a congressional committee* 國會委員會

con·gress·man /ˋkɑŋgrəsmən; ˈkɒŋgrɪsmən/ *n* [C] a man who is a member of a congress, especially the US House of Representatives 國會議員〔尤指美國眾議員〕: *Congressman Stephen Richards Rojack* 史蒂芬·理查茲·羅傑眾議員

con·gress·wom·an /ˋkɑŋgrəsˌwʊmən; ˈkɒŋgrɪsˌwʊmən/ *n* [C] a woman who is a member of a congress, especially the US House of Representatives 女國會議員〔尤指美國眾議員〕: *an interview with Congresswoman Anne Harding* 對安妮·哈丁眾議員的採訪

con·gru·ent /ˋkɑŋgruənt; ˈkɒŋgruənt/ *adj* **1 [+with]** *formal* fitting together well; suitable【正式】相配的; 符合的; 合適的 **2** *technical* congruent triangles (TRIANGLE (1)) are the same size and shape【術語】〔三角形〕全等的 —**congruence** *n* [U] —**congruently** *adv* —opposite 反義詞 INCONGRUENT

con·gru·ous /ˋkɑŋgruəs; ˈkɒŋgruəs/ *adj* **[+with]** fitting together well; suitable 相配的; 符合的; 合適的 —**congruity** /kənˋgruətɪ; kənˈgruːɪti/ *n* [C,U] —opposite 反義詞 INCONGRUOUS

con·ic /ˋkɑnɪk; ˈkɒnɪk/ *adj* connected with or shaped like a CONE[1] (1) 圓錐的; 圓錐形的

con·i·cal /ˋkɑnɪkḷ; ˈkɒnɪkəl/ *adj* shaped like a CONE[1] (1) 圓錐形的: *There were several huts with conical roofs.* 有幾間帶圓錐形屋頂的小屋。

conic sec·tion /ˌ·· ˋ··/ *n* [C] *technical* a shape made in GEOMETRY when an imaginary flat surface is passed through a CONE[1] (1)【術語】圓錐曲線, 二次曲線

co·ni·fer /ˋkonəfɚ; ˈkəʊnɪfə/ *n* [C] a tree that has leaves like needles that stay on it during the winter and brown cones (CONE[1] (3)) that contain its seeds 針葉樹 —**coniferous** /koˋnɪfərəs; kəˈnɪfərəs/ *adj*

conj the written abbreviation of 縮寫= CONJUNCTION

con·jec·ture[1] /kənˋdʒɛktʃɚ; kənˈdʒektʃə/ *n formal*【正式】**1** [U] the act of thinking of reasons, explanations etc without having very much information to base them on 推測, 猜測: *She didn't know the facts, so what she said was pure conjecture.* 她並不了解實際情況, 所以她說的只是猜測。| *conjecture about their role in the affair* 對他們在該事件中起的作用的猜測 **2** [C] an idea or opinion formed by guessing 根據推測所形成的想法或意見, 猜想: *My results show that this conjecture was, in fact, correct.* 我得到的結果證明這個測想實際上是正確的。—**conjectural** *adj*

conjecture[2] *v* [I,T] *formal* to form an idea or opinion without having much information to base it on; guess【正式】推測, 猜測: **[+that]** *It seems reasonable to conjecture that these conditions breed violence.* 有理由推斷這些情況會引發暴力。

con·join /kənˋdʒɔɪn; kənˈdʒɔɪn/ *v* [I,T] *formal* to join together or make things or people do this【正式】(使) 結合; (使) 聯合; (使) 連接

con·joint /kənˋdʒɔɪnt; kənˈdʒɔɪnt/ *adj* joined together, united 結合的; 聯合的 —**conjointly** *adv*: *conjointly working for peace* 共同謀求和平

con·ju·gal /ˋkɑndʒʊgḷ; ˈkɒndʒʊgəl/ *adj* [only before noun 僅用於名詞前] *formal* connected with marriage【正式】婚姻的; 夫妻之間的: *They lived together in conjugal bliss.* 他們婚姻生活非常幸福。

con·ju·gate /ˋkɑndʒəˌget; ˈkɒndʒʊgeɪt/ *v technical*【術語】**1** [I] if a verb conjugates, it has different grammatical forms to show different tenses etc〔動詞〕詞形變化: *The verb 'to go' conjugates irregularly.* 動詞 to go 詞形變化不規則。**2** [T] if you conjugate a verb, you state the different grammatical forms that it can have 列舉〔動詞〕的詞形變化

con·ju·ga·tion /ˌkɑndʒəˋgeʃən; ˌkɒndʒʊˈgeɪʃən/ *n* [C] *technical*【術語】**1** a set of verbs in languages such as Latin that conjugate in the same way〔拉丁語等語言中〕詞形變化相同的一組動詞 **2** the way that a particular verb conjugates 某一動詞的所有詞形變化

con·junc·tion /kənˋdʒʌŋkʃən; kənˈdʒʌŋkʃən/ *n* **1 in conjunction with** working, happening, or being used with someone or something else 與...共同, 連同: *The worksheets are designed to be used in conjunction with the new course books.* 這些練習活頁是專供與新課本一起使用的。**2** [C] a combination of different things that have come together by chance 不同事物的巧合: *a happy*

C

conjunction of events 諸多事件令人高興的巧合 **3** [C] *technical* a word such as 'but', 'and', or 'while' that connects parts of sentences, phrases, or clauses (CLAUSE (2))【術語】連詞

con·junc·tive /kən`dʒʌŋktɪv; kən'dʒʌŋktɪv/ also 又作 **con·junct** /`kɑndʒʌŋkt; 'kɒndʒʌŋkt/ *n* [C] *technical* a word that joins phrases together【術語】連詞 —**conjunctive** also 又作 **conjunct** /`kɑndʒʌŋkt; 'kɒndʒʌŋkt/ *adj*: *a conjunctive adverb* 連接副詞

con·junc·ti·vi·tis /kən͵dʒʌŋktə`vaɪtɪs; kən͵dʒʌŋktɪ'vaɪtɨs/ *n* [U] a painful and infectious disease of the eye that makes it red 結膜炎

C

con·junc·ture /kən`dʒʌŋktʃɚ; kən'dʒʌŋktʃə/ *n* [C] *formal* a combination of events or situations, especially one that causes problems【正式】〔事件或情況的〕同時發生: *the historic conjuncture from which Marxism arose* 馬克思主義產生的歷史性因緣

con·jure /`kʌndʒɚ; 'kʌndʒə/ *v* **1** [I,T] to perform clever tricks in which you seem to make things appear, disappear, or change as if by magic 變魔術; 用魔術變出: *The magician conjured a rabbit out of his hat.* 魔術師從帽子裡變出一隻兔子。**2** [T] to make something appear or happen unexpectedly 使〔某物〕突然出現[發生] **3 a name to conjure with a)** the name of a very important person 重要人物的名字 **b)** a very long name that is difficult to say 拗口的名字

conjure sth ↔ **up** *phr v* [T] **1** to bring a thought, picture, idea, or memory to someone's mind 使浮現於腦海; 使想起: *The word 'China' conjured up a whole new set of images in his mind.* "中國"這個詞使他在腦海中浮現出一幅幅全新的景象。**2** to make something appear when it is not expected, as if by magic 魔術般變出〔某物〕: *Somehow we have to conjure up another $10,000.* 無論如何我們要再弄到 10,000 美元。**3** to make the spirit of a dead person appear by saying special magic words 唸咒使〔鬼魂〕出現

con·jur·er, conjuror /`kʌndʒərɚ; 'kʌndʒərə/ *especially BrE n* [C] someone who entertains people by performing clever tricks in which things appear, disappear, or change as if by magic【尤英】變戲法的人; 魔術師

con·jur·ing /`kʌndʒərɪŋ; 'kʌndʒərɪŋ/ *n* [U] the skill of performing clever tricks in which you seem to make things appear, disappear, or change as if by magic 變戲法, 變魔術

conk[1] /kɑŋk; kɒŋk/ *n* [C] *BrE slang* a nose【英俚】鼻子

conk[2] *v* [T] *slang* to hit someone hard, especially on the head【俚】重擊〔某人, 尤指頭部〕

conk out *phr v* [I] *informal*【非正式】**1** if a machine or car conks out, it suddenly stops working〔機器、汽車〕突然失靈, 突然出故障: *Our car conked out on the way home.* 我們的車在回家的路上突然拋錨了。**2** *especially AmE* if someone conks out, they fall asleep because they are very tired【尤美】〔因疲勞而〕睡着: *I got home from work and I just conked out on the sofa.* 下班回到家, 我躺在沙發上就睡着了。

con·ker /`kɑŋkɚ; 'kɒŋkə/ *n* [C] *BrE*【英】**1** the large shiny brown seed of the HORSE CHESTNUT tree 七葉樹果 **2 conkers** *BrE* a children's game in which you try to break your opponent's conker by hitting it with your own【英】康克戲〔一種兒童遊戲, 各方用自己的七葉樹果努力擊破對方的七葉樹果〕

con·man /`kɑnmæn; 'kɒnmæn/ *n* [C] someone who tries to get money from people by tricking them〔詐取錢財的〕騙子

2 2 **con·nect** /kə`nɛkt; kə'nekt/ *v*

1 ▶JOIN 連接◀ [T] to join two or more things together 連結, 連接: *This railway line connects London and Edinburgh.* 這條鐵路線連接着倫敦和愛丁堡。| **connect sth to/with** *Connect the speakers to the record player and plug it in.* 將揚聲器連在唱機上, 再插上插頭。| **connecting passage/door etc** (=one that joins two rooms, buildings etc) 通道/相通的門等 *We'd like two rooms with connecting doors.* 我們想要有門相通的兩間房。

2 ▶REALIZE 意識到◀ [T] to realize that two facts, events, or people are related to each other 意識到兩個事實/事件/人是互相關聯的 *She did not connect the two events in her mind.* 在她心裡她沒有把這兩件事聯繫在一起。| **connect sb/sth with** *They did not at first connect her with the crime.* 起初他們並未將她與這宗罪案聯繫在一起。

3 ▶ELECTRICITY/GAS ETC 電/煤氣等◀ [T] to join something to the main supply of electricity, gas, or water, or to the telephone network 將某物與電源、煤氣、水的主要管道或電話網絡連接起來: *Has the phone been connected yet?* 電話接上了嗎? —opposite 反義詞 DISCONNECT

4 ▶TELEPHONES 電話◀ [T] to join two telephone lines so that two people can speak 給…接通電話: *Please hold the line. I'm trying to connect you.* 請別掛, 我正在為您接通。

5 ▶TRAINS/BUSES 火車/巴士◀ [I] if one train, bus etc connects with another, it arrives just before the other one leaves so that you can continue your journey〔火車、公共汽車等〕銜接: *I missed the connecting flight.* 我錯過了銜接的飛機。| **[+with]** *This train connects with the one to Glasgow.* 這班火車與去格拉斯哥的那班銜接。

6 ▶HIT STH 擊打某物◀ [I] *AmE* to succeed in hitting someone or something【美】擊中: *He swung at the ball, but didn't connect.* 他向球揮去, 卻沒擊中。

7 ▶UNDERSTAND PEOPLE 理解他人◀ [I+with] *especially AmE* if people connect, they feel that they like each other and understand each other【尤美】與人關係融洽: *They valued her ability to empathize and connect with others.* 他們重視她能對別人表示同情和融洽相處。

connect sth ↔ **up** *phr v* [I,T] to join something to the main supply of electricity, gas, or water, or to the telephone network 將某物與電源、煤氣、水的主要管道或電話網絡連接: *Is the washing machine connected up yet?* 洗衣機插了電源嗎?

con·nect·ed /kə`nɛktɪd; kə'nektɨd/ *adj* **1** if two things are connected, they are joined together 連接的, 相連的: *The two continents were once connected.* 這兩塊大陸曾經是相連的。| **[+to]** *The wire is connected to an electrode.* 電線與一個電極相連。**2** if two facts, events, etc are connected, they affect each other or are related to each other 相關的, 關聯的: **[+with]** *problems connected with drug abuse* 與濫用毒品相關的問題 | **closely connected** *The two ideas are closely connected, and should be dealt with together.* 這兩種觀念密切相連, 應該共同處理。**3 connected with sb** having a social or professional relationship with someone 與某人有社交[職業]關係: *Aren't they connected with his father's business in some way?* 他們與他父親的企業難道沒有甚麼聯繫嗎? **4 well connected** having important or powerful friends or relatives 與權貴有關係的

con·nec·tion also 又作 **connexion** *BrE*【英】/kə`nɛkʃən; kə'nekʃən/ *n* 

1 ▶STH THAT CONNECTS THINGS 關聯◀ [C] the way in which two facts, ideas, events etc are related to each other, and one is affected or caused by the other 聯繫, 關聯: **[+between]** *the connection between smoking and cancer* 吸煙與癌症間的關係 | **[+with]** *His statement had no connection with anything that had gone before.* 他的聲明與此前發生的任何事情都無關。| **find/establish a connection** (=prove or discover that something is connected with something else) 發現/證明某事與另一件事有聯繫 *Police have so far failed to establish a connection between the two murders.* 到目前為止警方還未能將兩宗兇殺案聯繫起來。| **make a connection** (=realize that there is a connection) 意識到有聯繫 *The evidence was there in the file but no one made the connection.* 證據就在檔案裡, 但沒有人意識到這裡存在

着聯繫。—see 見 RELATIONSHIP (USAGE)

2 ▶JOINING THINGS TOGETHER 將事物連接起來◀ [U] the joining together of two or more things 連接: *Connection to the water mains takes only a few minutes.* 接上總水管只要幾分鐘。

3 in connection with concerning something 關於; 有關: *The police are interviewing two men in connection with the robbery.* 警方正在查問與搶劫案有關的兩個人。

4 ▶ELECTRICAL WIRE 電線◀ [C] a wire or piece of metal joining two parts of a machine or electrical system 電線; 起連接作用的金屬: **loose connection** (=one that is not joined properly) 接觸不良 *My radio isn't working properly – I think it's got a loose connection.* 我的收音機出毛病了——我想是線路接觸不良。

5 ▶TRAIN/BUS ETC 火車/公共汽車等◀ [C] a train, bus, or plane which is arranged to leave at a time which allows passengers from an earlier train, bus, or plane to use it to continue their journey 銜接火車[公共汽車、飛機等]: *If this train gets delayed we'll miss our connection to Paris.* 如果這輛火車晚點, 我們就會誤了去巴黎的銜接火車。

6 ▶ROAD/RAILWAY ETC 公路/鐵路等◀ [C] a road, railway etc that joins two places and allows people to travel between them〔公路、鐵路等連接兩地的〕交通線: *Cheshunt has good rail connections to London, with trains every half hour.* 切森特與倫敦有良好的鐵路交通線, 每半個小時就有火車往返。

7 ▶PEOPLE 人們◀ **connections** [plural] **a)** people who you know who can help you by giving you money, finding you a job etc〔能夠幫你的〕人事關係: *He used his Mafia connections to find Pablo another job.* 他運用黑手黨的關係為帕伯羅找到另一份工作。**b)** people who are related to you, but not very closely〔較遠的〕親戚: *He is English, but has Irish connections.* 他是英格蘭人, 卻有愛爾蘭的親戚。—see 見 RELATIONSHIP (USAGE)

8 ▶TELEPHONE 電話◀ if you have a bad connection on the telephone, you are unable to hear properly because there is a lot of noise in the telephone 電話連接: *We had such a bad connection we gave up.* 我們通話效果極差, 只好掛斷。

con·nec·tive[1] /kə'nɛktɪv; kə'nektɪv/ *adj* joining two or more things together 連接的: *a lack of connective knowledge* 缺乏融會貫通的知識

connective[2] *n* [C] *technical* a word that joins phrases, parts of sentences etc【術語】連詞

connective tis·sue /·,·· '··/ *n* [U] parts of the body such as muscle or fat, that support or join organs and other body parts together 結締組織〈如肌肉等〉

con·ne·xion /kə'nɛkʃən; kə'nekʃən/ *n* a British spelling of CONNECTION connection 的英式拼法

conning tow·er /'·· ,··/ *n* [C] *technical* the structure on top of a SUBMARINE (=underwater ship)【術語】〔潛水艇頂部的〕瞭望塔

con·nip·tion fit /kə'nɪpʃən ,fɪt; kə'nɪpʃən ˌfɪt/ *n* [C] *AmE, humorous* a way of behaving which shows that you are very angry【美, 幽默】激怒; 歇斯底里發作: **have/throw a conniption fit** *My mother threw a conniption fit when I didn't come home till two in the morning.* 我凌晨兩點才回家, 我母親因此大發雷霆。

con·nive /kə'naɪv; kə'naɪv/ *v* [I] **1** to not try to stop something wrong from happening 放任; 默許〔錯誤事情〕: [+at] *He would not be the first politician to connive at a shady business deal.* 他不會是第一個默許不正當商業交易的政客。**2 connive to do sth** to work together secretly to achieve something, especially something wrong; CONSPIRE 祕密合謀; 串通: *They connived with their mother to deceive me.* 他們與他們的母親串通來騙我。—**connivance** *n* [C]: *We could not have escaped without the connivance of the guards.* 如果不是警衛默許, 我們是逃不出來的。

con·niv·ing /kə'naɪvɪŋ; kə'naɪvɪŋ/ *adj* behaving in a way that does not prevent something wrong from happening, or actively helps it to happen 縱容的; 默許的; 串通的: *He knew all along, the conniving bastard!* 他一直都是知道的, 這個同流合污的混蛋!

con·nois·seur /ˌkɑnə'sɝ; ˌkɒnə'sɜː/ *n* [C] someone who knows a lot about something such as art, food, music etc〔藝術、食品、音樂等〕鑑賞家, 鑑定家: *a wine connoisseur* 葡萄酒鑑定家

con·no·ta·tion /ˌkɑnə'teʃən; ˌkɒnə'teɪʃən/ *n* [C] a feeling or an idea that a word makes you think of that is not its actual meaning 隱含意義; 聯想的含義: *'Bermuda', with its connotations of sun, sea and sand* "百慕大"以及它給人對於陽光、海洋和沙灘的聯想 | *a negative connotation* 負面的涵義—compare 比較 DENOTATION—**connotative** /'kɑnəˌtetɪv; 'kɒnəteɪtɪv/ *adj*

con·note /kə'not; kə'nəʊt/ *v* [T] *formal* if a word connotes something, it makes you think of feelings and ideas that are not its actual meaning【正式】〔字、詞〕使人聯想到〔某些感覺和想法〕; 暗含: *The word 'plump' connotes cheerfulness.* "豐滿"這個詞使人聯想到高興、開朗。—compare 比較 DENOTE

con·nu·bi·al /kə'nubɪəl; kə'njuːbiəl/ *adj* **connubial bliss** *formal* the state of being happily married【正式】婚姻美滿: *living in connubial bliss* 生活在幸福的婚姻中

con·quer /'kɑŋkɚ; 'kɒŋkə/ *v* **1** [I,T] to take land by attacking people or win it by fighting a war 征服: *The Normans conquered England in 1066.* 諾曼人於1066年征服英格蘭。**2** [I,T] to defeat an enemy 擊敗, 戰勝: *The Zulus conquered all the neighbouring tribes.* 祖魯人打敗了所有相鄰的部落。**3** [T] to gain control over something that is difficult, using a lot of effort 克服; 制伏: *Gemma felt ashamed that she hadn't been able to conquer her fear.* 吉瑪因未能克服她的恐懼而感到羞愧。| *efforts to conquer inflation* 克服通貨膨脹的努力 **4** [T] to succeed in climbing to the top of a mountain when no one has ever climbed it before 成功登上〔從未有人攀登過的山頂〕 **5** [T] to become very successful in a place〔在某地〕大獲成功: *English comedians find it difficult to conquer America.* 英國喜劇演員認為要征服美國觀眾絕非易事。| **conquer sb's hearts** (=make someone love you) 博得某人的歡心 *She had conquered the hearts of the local people.* 她贏得了當地人民的喜愛。—**conqueror** *n* [C] —**conquering** *adj*: *conquering heroes* 戰勝的英雄們

con·quest /'kɑŋkwɛst; 'kɒŋkwest/ *n* **1** [singular,U] the act of defeating an army or taking land by fighting 擊敗, 征服: *the Norman Conquest* 諾曼人的征服 **2** [C] land that is won in a war 佔領地, 征服的土地: *French conquests in Asia* 法國在亞洲的佔領地 **3** [C] *often humorous* someone that you have persuaded to love you or to have sex with you【常幽默】愛情的俘虜: *He boasts about his many conquests.* 他吹噓自己征服了許多女孩的芳心。**4** [singular] the act of gaining control of or dealing successfully with something that is difficult or dangerous 攻克, 征服〔艱難、危險事物〕: [+of] *the conquest of space* 征服太空

con·quis·ta·dor /kɑn'kwɪstəˌdɔr; kɒn'kwɪstədɔː/ *n* [C] [plural] conquerors of Mexico, Central and South America in the 16th century 16世紀墨西哥、中美洲、南美洲的征服者

con·san·guin·i·ty /ˌkɑnsæŋ'gwɪnətɪ; ˌkɒnsæŋ'gwɪnəti/ *n* [U] *formal* the state of being members of the same family【正式】血緣; 血親關係

con·science /'kɑnʃəns; 'kɒnʃəns/ *n* [C,U]

1 ▶MIND 思想◀ the part of your mind that tells you whether what you are doing is morally right or wrong 良知, 良心: *Be guided by your conscience.* 讓你的良心來指引你。| **a social conscience** (=a moral sense of how society should be) 社會良知 | **a guilty/bad conscience** (=feel guilty because you have done something wrong) 負疚的心情 *It was his guilty conscience that made him offer to help.* 他是因為心中有愧才提出要幫忙的。| a

clear conscience (=a feeling that you have done nothing wrong) 無愧良心 *Well at least I can face them all with a clear conscience.* 至少我可以問心無愧地面對他們。| **a twinge/pang of conscience** (=guilty feeling) 一陣內疚的感覺 *Ian felt a pang of conscience at having misjudged her.* 伊恩因為冤枉了她而感到負疚。| **have no conscience (about sth)** (=not feel guilty about something) (對某事) 沒有負疚感 *They've no conscience at all about cheating.* 他們一點也不因為行騙而受到良心譴責。| **a prisoner of conscience** (=someone who is in prison because of their political or religious beliefs) 政治犯, 思想犯 | **a matter of conscience** (=something that you must make a moral judgment about) 良心問題 *I can't tell you what to do – it's a matter of conscience.* 我無法告訴你該如何辦 —— 這是一個事關良心的問題。**2 on your conscience** if you have something on your conscience it makes you feel guilty 內疚, 受到良心的譴責: *If anything happens to her I'll always have it on my conscience.* 如果她出甚麼問題, 我將永遠受到良心譴責。**3 prick your conscience** if an action or event pricks your conscience, it makes you feel guilty 使良心不安: *The dog's sad look pricked her conscience and she took him home.* 那隻狗可憐的神情使她良心不安, 她便帶牠回家了。

4 clear your conscience to make yourself stop feeling guilty by telling someone about what you did wrong〔承認錯誤〕解除內疚感: *Terry decided to clear his conscience and confess.* 特里決心解除自己心中的內疚感, 便坦白了。

5 in all conscience *formal* if you cannot in all conscience do something, you cannot do it because you think it is wrong【正式】憑良心不能做某些事情〔因為它是錯的〕: *I couldn't in all conscience tell him that his job was safe.* 憑良心我不能對他說那份工作很保險。

6 in good conscience if you do something in good conscience, you do it because you think it is the right thing to do 憑良心應該做某事情〔因為它是正確的〕: *statements made in good conscience* 憑良心做出的陳述

conscience clause /'·· ,·/ *n* [C] a part of a law that says that the law does not have to be obeyed by people who feel that it would be morally wrong to obey it〔法律的〕道德條款〔說明如果有人認為遵守這條法律違反道德, 可以不必遵守〕

conscience-strick·en /'·· ,··/ also 又作 **conscience-smitten** *adj* very sorry that you have done something wrong 良心不安的, 受良心譴責的: *Kate hurried home, conscience-stricken at leaving her mother alone.* 凱特匆忙趕回家, 因為讓母親獨自一人感到十分內疚。

con·sci·en·tious /ˌkɑnʃɪ`ɛnʃəs; ˌkɒnʃi'enʃəs◂/ *adj* showing a lot of care and attention 認真的; 細心負責的: *a conscientious and methodical worker* 一個工作認真, 有條不紊的人 —**conscientiously** *adv* —**conscientiousness** *n* [U]: *praised for her conscientiousness* 她因認真負責受到稱讚

conscientious ob·jec·tor /,···· ·'··/ *n* [C] someone who refuses to become a soldier because of their moral or religious beliefs〔由於道德或宗教的原因〕拒服兵役者 —see also 另見 DRAFT DODGER

con·scious /`kɑnʃəs; 'kɒnʃəs/ *adj* **1** [not before noun 不用於名詞前] noticing or realizing something; AWARE 注意到的; 意識到的: **conscious of (doing) sth** *I was very conscious of the fact that I had to make a good impression.* 我非常明白必須給人留下一個好印象。| **conscious that** *I was conscious that she was ill at ease.* 我注意到她有點局促不安。**2** awake and able to understand what is happening around you 清醒的: *The driver was still conscious when the ambulance reached the scene of the accident.* 當救護車趕到事故現場時, 司機仍然神志清醒。**3 a conscious effort/decision/attempt etc** an effort etc that is deliberate and intended 特意做出的努力/決定/嘗試等: *Vivien had made a conscious effort to be friendly.* 維維恩有意地努力表示友善。**4 safety-conscious/fashion-conscious etc** thinking a lot about safety, fashion etc 特別注意安全的/十分關注時尚的等: *recipes for calorie-conscious slimmers* 為特別注意熱量攝取的減肥者準備的食譜 —see also 另見 SELF-CONSCIOUS —opposite 反義詞 UNCONSCIOUS[1] —**consciously** *adv*

con·scious·ness /`kɑnʃəsnɪs; 'kɒnʃəsn̩s/ *n* **1** [U] the condition of being awake and able to understand what is happening around you 神志清醒: **lose consciousness** (=go into a deep sleep) 失去知覺 *David lost consciousness at eight o'clock and died a few hours later.* 戴維在八點鐘失去知覺, 幾小時後便去世了。| **regain consciousness** (=wake up) 恢復知覺 *She could faintly hear voices as she began to regain consciousness.* 當她開始恢復知覺時, 她能隱約聽見聲音。**2** [U] your mind and your thoughts 思想, 意識: *Even the most important issues eventually fade from your consciousness.* 就連最重要的事情最終都會從你的思想意識中淡出。**3** [U] someone's ideas, feelings, or opinions about politics, life etc 觀念, 感覺, 意見: *The experience helped to change her political consciousness.* 這次經歷有助於改變她的政治觀點。**4** [singular] the state of knowing that something exists or is true; AWARENESS 感知; 察覺: *a consciousness of danger* 對危險的意識 —see also 另見 STREAM OF CONSCIOUSNESS

consciousness rais·ing /'···· ,··/ *n* [U] the process of making people understand and care more about a moral, social, or political problem〔對道德、社會或政治問題的〕意識提高

con·script[1] /kən`skrɪpt; kən'skrɪpt/ *v* [T+into] **1** to make someone join the army, navy etc 徵召〔入伍〕: *young Frenchmen who were conscripted into the army and forced to fight in Algeria* 徵召入伍被迫在阿爾及利亞作戰的年輕法國人 **2** to make someone become a member of a group or take part in a particular activity 吸納…為成員, 使加入 —compare 比較 RECRUIT[1]

con·script[2] /`kɑnskrɪpt; 'kɒnskrɪpt/ *n* [C] someone who has been made to join the army, navy etc 徵召入伍者 —compare 比較 RECRUIT[2]

con·scrip·tion /kən`skrɪpʃən; kən'skrɪpʃən/ *n* [U] the practice of making people join the army, navy etc; DRAFT[1] (2a) 徵兵 —see also 另見 NATIONAL SERVICE

con·se·crate /`kɑnsɪˌkret; 'kɒns̩kreɪt/ *v* [T] **1** to officially state in a special religious ceremony that a place or building is holy and can be used for religious purposes〔舉行特別宗教儀式〕宣布〔某地〕為神聖 **2** to officially state in a special religious ceremony that someone is now a priest, BISHOP (1) etc〔舉行特別宗教儀式〕宣布〔某人〕為牧師[主教]等 —**consecrated** *adj*: *consecrated ground* 聖地 —**consecration** /ˌkɑnsɪ`kreʃən; ˌkɒns̩'kreɪʃən/ *n* [U]

con·sec·u·tive /kən`sɛkjətɪv; kən'sekjʊtɪv/ *adj* consecutive numbers or periods of time follow one after the other without any interruptions 連續的, 不間斷的: *It had rained for four consecutive days.* 雨接連下了四天。—**consecutively** *adv*: *Number the pages consecutively.* 請用連續的數字編頁碼。

con·sen·sus /kən`sɛnsəs; kən'sensəs/ *n* [singular,U] an opinion that everyone in a group will agree with or accept 共同意見, 一致看法, 共識: **reach a consensus on** *The EC Council of Finance Ministers failed to reach a consensus on the pace of integration.* 歐共體財政部長會議未能就一體化的速度達成共識。| **consensus politics** (=political ideas and actions that everyone accepts in a general way) 代表民意的政治觀點[行動]

con·sent[1] /kən`sɛnt; kən'sent/ *n* [U] **1** permission to do something especially by someone in authority or by someone who is responsible for something 許可, 允許: **without sb's consent** *He took the car without the owner's consent.* 他沒有得到車主的許可, 就把車開走了。| **give your consent** (=allow something to happen) 許可 —see also 另見 AGE OF CONSENT **2** agreement about something 同意, 贊同: **by common consent** (=with most people agreeing) 得到大多數人的同意 *The chairman was elected by common consent.* 主席是經大多數人同意選舉的。| **by mutual consent** (=by agreement between both the people or groups of people involved) 經雙方同意 *divorce by mutual consent* 雙方同意離婚 **3 with one consent** *old use* if people do something with one consent, they all agree to do it【舊】全體一致同意 —see also 另見 ASSENT, DISSENT

consent² *v* [I] to give your permission for something or agree to do something 同意, 允許: [+to] *Her father reluctantly consented to the marriage.* 她父親勉強答應了這門婚事。

consenting ad·ult /ˌ·ˌ·· ˈ··/ *n* [C] *law* someone who is considered to be old enough to decide whether they want to have sex【法律】成年人〔指已到達某年齡, 可以自行決定是否與人發生性關係的人〕—see also 另見 AGE OF CONSENT

3 **con·se·quence** /ˈkɑnsəˌkwɛns; ˈkɒnsᵻkwəns/ *n* **1** [C]
2 something that happens as a result of a particular action or set of conditions 後果: *the harmful social consequences of high levels of unemployment* 高失業率給社會帶來的不良後果 | *The safety procedures had been ignored, with potentially tragic consequences.* 安全程序被忽視, 可能帶來悲慘的後果。| **take/suffer/face the consequences (of sth)** (=to accept the bad results of something you have done) 承擔/遭受/面對(某事的)後果 *He broke the law, and now he must face the consequences of his actions.* 他觸犯了法律, 現在必須承擔自己的行為帶來的後果。**2 as a consequence (of sth)/in consequence (of sth)** *formal* as a result of something【正式】因為; 由於: *the rise in sea levels predicted as a consequence of global warming* 由於全球氣候變暖而預測的海平面升高 **3 of little/no/any consequence** *formal* of little importance or value【正式】不重要的/無足輕重的: *Your opinion is of little consequence to me.* 你的意見對我而言不重要。

con·se·quent /ˈkɑnsəˌkwɛnt; ˈkɒnsᵻkwənt/ *adj formal* happening as a result of a particular event or situation【正式】隨之發生的; 由某事引起的: *the rise in inflation and consequent fall in demand* 通貨膨脹的上升和隨之而來的需求下降 —compare 比較 SUBSEQUENT

con·se·quen·tial /ˌkɑnsəˈkwɛnʃəl; ˌkɒnsᵻˈkwenʃəl◂/ *adj formal*【正式】**1** happening as a direct result of a particular event or situation 隨之發生的: *redundancy and the consequential loss of earnings* 裁員以及隨之而來的收入損失 **2** important; SIGNIFICANT 重要的, 意義重大的: *a consequential decision* 重要的決定 —opposite 反義詞 INCONSEQUENTIAL —**consequentially** *adv*

3 **con·se·quent·ly** /ˈkɑnsəˌkwɛntlɪ; ˈkɒnsᵻkwəntli/ *adv* [sentence adverb 句子副詞] as a result 結果, 所以: *We talked until the early hours, and consequently I overslept.* 我們聊到凌晨, 結果我睡過頭了。| *The bank refused to give the company more time. Consequently, it went bankrupt.* 銀行拒絕給這家公司更多的寬限, 結果它倒閉了。—see 見 THUS (USAGE)

con·ser·van·cy /kənˈsɝvənsɪ; kənˈsɜːvənsi/ *n* [U] *BrE*【英】**1** a group of officials who control and protect an area of land, a river etc〔河道、土地等的〕管理局, 管理機構: *the Thames Conservancy* 泰晤士河管理局 **2** the protection of natural things such as animals, plants, forests etc; CONSERVATION (1)〔動植物、森林等的〕保護

3 **con·ser·va·tion** /ˌkɑnsəˈveʃən; ˌkɒnsəˈveɪʃən/ *n* [U]
3 **1** the protection of natural things such as animals, plants, forests etc, to prevent them being spoiled, or destroyed〔動植物、森林等的〕保護: *wildlife conservation* 野生生物保護 **2** the act of preventing something from being lost or wasted 保存, 保護: [+of] *conservation of energy* 能源保護

conservation a·re·a /ˌ··ˈ·· ˌ···/ *n* [C] **1** an area where animals and plants are protected〔動植物的〕保護區 **2** an area where interesting old buildings are protected and new buildings are carefully controlled〔保護特色古舊建築物並且控制新建築物的〕保護區

con·ser·va·tion·ist /ˌkɑnsəˈveʃənɪst; ˌkɒnsəˈveɪʃənᵻst/ *n* [C] someone who works to protect animals, plants etc or to protect old buildings〔動植物等或古舊建築〕保護工作者 —**conservationism** *n* [U]

con·ser·va·tis·m /kənˈsɝvətɪzəm; kənˈsɜːvətɪzəm/ *n* [U] **1** dislike of change and new ideas 守舊, 保守主義: *people's innate conservatism in matters of language* 人們在語言方面的天生守舊 **2** also 又作 **Conservatism** the political belief that society should change as little as possible 政治保守, 因循守舊 **3 Conservatism** the political beliefs of the Conservative Party 保守黨的政治主張

con·ser·va·tive¹ /kənˈsɝvətɪv; kənˈsɜːvətɪv/ *adj* **1 Conservative** belonging to or concerned with the Conservative Party in Britain〔英國〕保守黨的: *Conservative policies* 保守黨的政策 | *a Conservative MP* 保守黨下議院議員 **2** not liking changes or new ideas 因循守舊的, 不喜變化的: *a very conservative attitude to education* 對於教育非常守舊的態度 **3** not very modern in style, taste etc; traditional〔式樣、口味等〕不時興的, 傳統的: *a very conservative suit* 一套非常老式的衣服 **4 a conservative estimate/guess** a guess which is deliberately lower than the real amount 保守的估計/猜測: *At a conservative estimate, the holiday will cost about £1,500.* 根據保守的估計, 假期要花費約 1,500 英鎊。—**conservatively** *adv*

conservative² *n* [C] **1 Conservative** someone who supports or is a member of the Conservative Party in Britain 英國保守黨的支持者; 保守黨黨員 **2** someone who does not like changes in ideas or fashion 因循守舊者, 保守者: *Aunt May is a real conservative. She's totally opposed to mothers going out to work.* 梅姨是個真正的保守派, 她完全不贊成做了母親的婦女外出工作。

Conservative Par·ty /·ˈ··· ˌ··/ *n* **the Conservative Party** a British political party on the RIGHT 保守黨〔英國右翼政黨〕

con·ser·va·toire /kənˌsɝvəˈtwɑr; kənˈsɜːvətwɑː/ *n* [C] *BrE* a school where people are trained in music or acting【英】音樂學院; 戲劇學院; CONSERVATORY *AmE*【美】

con·ser·va·to·ry /kənˈsɝvəˌtorɪ; kənˈsɜːvətəri/ *n* [C] **1** a room with glass walls and a glass roof, where plants are grown, that is usually added on to the side of a house 溫室, 玻璃暖房 **2** *AmE* a school where people are trained in music or acting【美】音樂學院; 戲劇學院; CONSERVATOIRE *BrE*【英】

con·serve¹ /kənˈsɝv; kənˈsɜːv/ *v* [T] **1** to protect something and try to prevent it from changing or being damaged 保護; 保存: *We must conserve our woodlands for future generations.* 我們必須為後代保護林地。**2** to use as little water, energy etc as possible so that it is not wasted 節約〔水、能源等〕: *conserving electricity* 節約電

con·serve² /ˈkɑnsɝv; ˈkɒnsɜːv/ *n* [C,U] *formal* fruit that is preserved by being cooked with sugar; JAM¹ (1)【正式】蜜餞; 果醬

con·sid·er /kənˈsɪdɚ; kənˈsɪdə/ *v* 1
1 ▶THINK ABOUT 考慮◀ [I,T] to think about something, especially about whether to accept something or do something 考慮, 細想〔尤指是否接受或做某事〕: *He paused to consider his options.* 他停下來考慮應該作何選擇。| *Any reasonable offer will be considered.* 任何合理報價都將予以考慮。| **consider doing sth** *I'm considering applying for that job.* 我在考慮是否申請那份工作。| **consider where/how/why etc** *We're still considering where to move to.* 我們仍在考慮搬到哪裡去。**2 ▶HAVE AN OPINION 有某種看法◀** [T] to think of someone or something in a particular way 對某人/某事 1

有某種看法: **consider sb/sth (to be) wise/important etc** *A further increase in interest rates is now considered unlikely.* 進一步上調利率現在被認為不大可能。| **consider sth an honour/a duty etc** *I consider it a great honour to be invited.* 承蒙邀請深感榮幸。| **consider sb (to be) a fool/hero etc** *Liz Quinn was considered an excellent teacher.* 莉茲·奎因被認為是一位優秀的教師。
3 consider yourself lucky to think you are fortunate 自認幸運: *Consider yourself lucky you weren't in the car at the time.* 你當時不在車裡, 你應該感到慶幸。
4 ►REMEMBER TO THINK OF 記得考慮◄ [T] to remember to think carefully about something before making a judgment or a decision〔在作出判斷或決定前〕仔細考慮: *Before you resign you should consider the effect it will have on your family.* 你辭職前要考慮一下這會給你家庭帶來怎樣的影響。| **consider that** *If you consider that she's only been studying English for six months, she speaks it very well.* 如果考慮到她學英語才六個月, 她的英語可以説講得非常好了。| **consider what/how/who etc** *Have you considered how difficult it is for these refugees?* 你有沒有考慮過這些難民會有多麼艱難?
5 ►PEOPLE'S FEELINGS 人們的感情◄ [T] to think about someone or their feelings etc and try to avoid upsetting or hurting them 體諒, 體貼: *God, you're so selfish! You've got to learn to consider other people!* 天啊, 你太自私了! 你必須學會替別人着想!
6 ►DISCUSS FORMALLY 正式討論◄ [T] to discuss something such as a report or problem, so that you can make a decision about it 討論: *The committee has been considering the report.* 委員會一直在討論這份報告。
7 ►LOOK AT 注視◄ [T] *formal* to look at someone or something carefully【正式】仔細端詳: *Henry considered the sculpture with an expert eye.* 亨利以專家的眼光審視這尊雕塑。
8 be considering your position *formal* to be deciding whether or not to leave your job【正式】正在考慮是否辭去職務

2 1 **con·sid·e·ra·ble** /kən`sɪdərəbl; kən'sɪdərəbəl/ *adj* fairly large, especially large enough to have an effect or be important 相當大的〔尤指大到足以產生某種影響的程度〕: *She has considerable influence with the President.* 她對總統有相當大的影響。| *A statue was erected at considerable public expense.* 豎起了一座雕像, 花了公眾不少錢。—compare 比較 INCONSIDERABLE

3 3 **con·sid·e·ra·bly** /kən`sɪdərəblɪ; kən'sɪdərəbli/ *adv* **considerably more/colder/higher etc** much more, much colder etc 多得多/冷得多/高得多等: *It's considerably colder today.* 今天冷多了。

con·sid·er·ate /kən`sɪdərɪt; kən'sɪdərɪ̥t/ *adj* always thinking of what other people need or want and taking care not to upset them 關切的, 體貼的; 替他人着想的: *Diana is a considerate boss who is always willing to listen.* 黛安娜是一位體貼的老闆, 她總是樂於聽取意見。| **considerate of sb (to do sth)** *It was very considerate of you to let us know you were going to be late.* 你讓我們知道你會遲到, 真是考慮周到。—opposite 反義詞 INCONSIDERATE —**considerately** *adv* —**considerateness** *n* [U]

1 2 **con·sid·e·ra·tion** /kən͵sɪdə`reʃən; kən͵sɪdə'reɪʃən/ *n*
1 ►THOUGHT 思想◄ [U] *formal* careful thought and attention【正式】考慮, 斟酌: **under consideration** (=being discussed and thought about so that an official decision can be made) 在討論中, 在研究中, 在考慮中 *There are several amendments under consideration.* 好幾項修正案正在討論中。| **due/long consideration** *After due consideration, I have decided to tender my resignation.* 在作適當的考慮後, 我決定遞交辭呈。| **give sth your fullest consideration** (=think about it very carefully before making an official decision) 在作正式決定前充分考慮某事
2 take sth into consideration to remember to think about something important when you are making a decision or judgement〔在作出決定或判斷之前〕考慮到某事: *Your teachers will take your recent illness into consideration when marking your exams.* 你的老師在批改你的試卷時, 會考慮到你最近生病這一情況的。
3 ►STH THAT AFFECTS A DECISION 影響決定的因素◄ [C] something that you must think about when you are planning to do something, which affects what you decide to do 須考慮的因素: *Political rather than economic considerations influenced the location of the new factory.* 影響新工廠位置的是政治因素而不是經濟原因。
4 ►KINDNESS 善意◄ [U] the quality of thinking about other people's feelings and taking care not to upset them 體貼, 體諒: **out of consideration for** *The murdered woman's name has not been released, out of consideration for her parents.* 為了保護她父母, 沒有公布被謀殺婦女的姓名。| **show consideration for** *Jeff never shows any consideration for his mother's feelings.* 傑弗從來不體諒她母親的心情。
5 of no consideration/of little consideration *formal* if something is of no consideration it is not at all important【正式】毫不重要的
6 in consideration of *formal* as payment for something【正式】〔為某事所付的〕報酬: *a small payment in consideration of your services* 作為答謝你幫忙的一點報酬
7 ►MONEY 金錢◄ [singular] *formal* a payment for a service【正式】服務費, 酬金: **for a small consideration** *I might be able to help you, for a small consideration.* 我也許能夠效勞, 但要收少許費用。

con·sid·ered /kən`sɪdəd; kən'sɪdəd/ *adj* **1 considered opinion/judgement etc** an opinion based on careful thought 仔細考慮過的意見/判斷等 **2 well/poorly/highly considered** thought to be good, bad etc 評價很好/不好/很高: *Her paintings are very well considered abroad.* 她的畫在國外評價很高。**3 all things considered** *usually spoken* used to say what you believe after thinking about all the facts【一般口】從各個方面考慮之後, 全面考慮之後: *All things considered, I'm sure we made the right decision.* 總而言之, 我認為我們的決定是正確的。

con·sid·er·ing[1] /kən`sɪdərɪŋ; kən'sɪdərɪŋ/ *prep conjunction* used when describing a situation, before stating a fact that you know has had an effect on that situation 考慮到, 鑑於〔用來描繪某一情況, 常用於陳述對該情況有所影響的某事實之前〕: *Considering the strength of the opposition, we did very well to score two goals.* 考慮到對方實力強大, 我們能攻進兩球就很不錯了。| **considering that/who/how etc** *John did quite well in his exams considering how little he studied.* 考慮到約翰才學了那麼一點點, 他考得已算不錯了。

considering[2] *adv spoken* used at the end of a phrase when you are expressing an opinion about something in spite of another fact【口】細細想來, 通盤考慮〔用於短詞末尾, 表示"儘管…"〕: *Mum didn't look too bad, considering.* 從各方面看, 媽媽的氣色並不是太差。

con·sign /kən`saɪn; kən'saɪn/ *v* [T] *formal*【正式】**1** to put someone or something somewhere, especially in order to get rid of them〔尤指為丟棄而〕移走; 處置: **consign sb/sth to** *I consigned his letter to the dustbin.* 我把他的信扔進了垃圾桶。| *She preferred to take care of her mother at home, rather than consigning her to institutional care.* 她情願在家裡照顧她母親, 而不願交給養老院照顧。| **consign sb/sth to the flames** *literary* (=burn someone or something)【文】燒毀, 焚燒, 火化 *The body was consigned to the flames.* 屍體被火化了。**2** to send or deliver something to someone who has bought it 運送〔商品給購買者〕**3** to make someone or something be in a particular situation, especially an unpleasant one 使…陷於〔某種令人不快的境地〕: **consign sb/sth to** *consigning Cambodia to a decade of civil war* 使柬埔寨陷入十年內戰

con·sign·ee /͵kɑnsaɪ`ni; ͵kɒnsaɪ'niː/ *n* [C] *technical* the person that something is delivered to【術語】收件人, 收貨人

con·sign·ment /kən`saɪnmənt; kən'saɪnmənt/ *n* **1** [C] a quantity of goods delivered at the same time 同時運送的一批貨物: [+of] *a new consignment of computer games* 一批新託運的電腦遊戲 **2** [U] the act of delivering things 運送, 託運

con·sign·or, consigner /kən`saɪnɚ; kən'saɪnə/ *n* [C] *technical* the person who sends goods to someone else【術語】寄件人, 發貨人, 託運人

3 **con·sist** /kən`sɪst; kən'sɪst/ *v*

consist in sth *phr v* [T not in progressive 不用進行式] *formal* to be based on or depend upon something【正式】在於, 決定於: *The beauty of Venice consists largely in the style of its ancient buildings.* 威尼斯的美麗主要在於城中古建築物的風格。

consist of sth *phr v* [T not in progressive 不用進行式] used to say what something is made of when it contains a number of parts or things 由…組成, 由…構成: *Bolognaise sauce consists of minced beef, onion, tomatoes, garlic and seasoning.* 博洛尼亞肉醬由碎牛肉、洋蔥、番茄、大蒜和佐料調製而成。

con·sis·ten·cy /kən`sɪstənsɪ; kən'sɪstənsi/ *n* **1** [U] the quality of always being the same or always being good 連貫性, 前後一致: *Replies to these questions showed no real consistency.* 對這些問題的答案前後並不一致。—opposite 反義詞 INCONSISTENCY **2** [C,U] how firm or thick a mixture is 堅實度; 濃度: *Beat the butter and sugar until the mixture has the consistency of thick cream.* 將黃油和糖攪拌, 直到它具有稠奶油的濃度。

3
3 **con·sis·tent** /kən`sɪstənt; kən'sɪstənt/ *adj* **1** always having the same beliefs, behaviour, attitudes, quality etc〔信仰、行為、態度、品質等〕一貫的, 一致的: *one of the most consistent players on the tennis circuit* 網球巡迴賽場上常勝不衰的運動員之一 | *a consistent supporter of constitutional rights* 憲法權利一貫的支持者 **2** continuing to develop in the same way 穩定發展的, 持續不變的: *a consistent improvement in the country's economy* 該國經濟的持續好轉 **3** a consistent argument or idea is organized so that each part agrees with the others〔論點或看法〕前後一致的 **4 be consistent with** if something that is said, written, or done is consistent with a particular idea or piece of information, it says the same thing or follows the same principles〔所說、所寫或所做的事與某一觀點或信息〕相一致的, 相吻合的: *This evidence is not consistent with what you said earlier.* 這項證據與你先前所說矛盾。—opposite 反義詞 INCONSISTENT —**consistently** *adv*: *I'm fed up with your consistently negative attitude.* 你一貫的消極態度令我感到厭煩。

con·so·la·tion /ˌkɑnsə`leʃən; ˌkɒnsə'leɪʃən/ *n* [C,U] someone or something that makes you feel better when you are sad or disappointed 安慰; 起安慰作用的人[物]: *It was some consolation for me to know that I had only failed by 2%.* 知道自己只差 2% 就及格多少是一種安慰。

consolation prize /.‥'‥ ·/ *n* [C] a prize that is given to someone who has not won a competition 鼓勵獎, 安慰獎: *Ten runners-up each received a T-shirt as a consolation prize.* 十名冠軍以下的優勝者每人得到一件T恤衫作為安慰獎。

con·sol·a·to·ry /kən`sɑləˌtorɪ; kən'sɒlətəri/ *adj formal* intended to make someone feel better【正式】安慰的, 撫慰的

con·sole¹ /kən`sol; kən'səʊl/ *v* [T] to make someone feel better when they are feeling sad or disappointed 安慰, 慰藉, 安撫: *No one could console her when Peter died.* 彼得死後沒人能安慰她。| **console sb with** *Console yourself with the thought that no one was injured!* 沒有人受傷, 這是值得慶幸的!

con·sole² /`kɑnsol; 'kɒnsəʊl/ *n* [C] **1** a flat board that contains the controls for a machine, piece of electrical equipment, computer etc〔機器、電子設備、電腦的〕操縱台盤, 控制台盤: *a games console* 遊戲機操縱盤 **2** a special cupboard in which a television, computer etc is fitted〔放置電視機、電腦等的〕櫥櫃

con·sol·i·date /kən`sɑləˌdet; kən'sɒlɪ̈deɪt/ *v* [I,T] **1** to make your position of power stronger and more likely to continue, or maintain the same level of achievement, profit, success etc so that it seems likely to continue 加強〔實力地位〕, 鞏固〔成就、利潤、成功等〕: *His successful negotiations with the Americans helped him to consolidate his position.* 他與美國人的成功談判鞏固了他的地位。| *Canon has consolidated its hold on the European market.* 佳能加強了它在歐洲市場的地位。**2** to join together a group of companies, organizations etc, or to become jointed together 將〔公司、組織等〕合併, 聯合 **3** to combine several jobs, duties etc together 將〔幾個職位、職責等〕合併 —**consolidated** *adj* —**consolidation** /kənˌsɑlə`deʃən; kənˌsɒlɪ̈'deɪʃən/ *n* [C,U]

con·som·mé /ˌkɑnsə`me; kən'sɒmeɪ/ *n* [U] clear soup made from meat or vegetables 用肉或蔬菜製作的清湯

con·so·nance /`kɑnsənəns; 'kɒnsənəns/ *n* **1 in consonance with** *formal* agreeing with something or existing together without any problems【正式】與某物一致或協調相處 **2** [C,U] *technical* a combination of musical notes that sound pleasant; HARMONY (1)【術語】〔音樂〕協和音, 和音

con·so·nant¹ /`kɑnsənənt; 'kɒnsənənt/ *n* [C] **1** a speech sound made by partly or completely stopping the flow of air through the mouth 輔音 **2** a letter that represents one of these sounds. The letters 'a', 'e', 'i', 'o', and 'u' represent vowels, and all the other letters are consonants 輔音字母〔a, e, i, o, u 五個字母代表元音, 所有其他字母均是輔音〕

consonant² *adj* **1 consonant with** *formal* not seeming to show that a statement or belief is wrong【正式】一致的, 符合的: *This policy is scarcely consonant with the government's declared aims.* 這項政策與政府公布的目標簡直自相矛盾。**2** *technical* being a combination of musical notes that sounds pleasant【術語】協和音的

con·sort¹ /`kɑnsɔrt; 'kɒnsɔːt/ *n* [C] **1 in consort (with sb)** *formal* doing something together with someone【正式】(與某人) 一起〔做某事〕: *The prince ruled in consort with his father.* 王子與他的父親共同執政。**2** the wife or husband of a ruler 統治者的配偶 —see also 另見 PRINCE CONSORT **3** a group of people who play music from former times or the group of old-fashioned instruments they use〔演奏往日音樂的〕一羣樂師; 一批老式樂器

con·sort² /kən`sɔrt; kən'sɔːt/ *v formal* [I+with/together] to spend time with someone who other people disapprove of【正式】與名聲不好的人結交; 勾結: **consorting with the enemy** (=spending time with and helping the enemies of your country) 與敵人朋比為奸

con·sor·ti·um /kən`sɔrtɪəm; kən'sɔːtiəm/ *n plural* **consortiums** *or* **consortia** [C] a combination of several companies, banks etc working together to buy something, build something etc〔公司、銀行等為了進行購買或建築而組成的〕財團, 聯合企業

con·spec·tus /kən`spɛktəs; kən'spektəs/ *n* [C] *formal* a short report giving the most important ideas of a subject【正式】大綱, 簡要報告

con·spic·u·ous /kən`spɪkjuəs; kən'spɪkjuəs/ *adj* **1** someone or something that is conspicuous is very easy to notice, especially because they are different from everything or everyone else around them 顯著的, 顯眼的; 與眾不同的: *I felt very conspicuous in my suit – everyone else was in jeans.* 我覺得自己穿套裝很顯眼, 因為別人都是穿牛仔褲。**2** unusually good, bad, skilful etc; REMARKABLE 引人注目的: *The campaign had been a conspicuous success.* 這次活動取得了令人矚目的成功。**3**

conspicuous by your absence used to say that people noticed that you were not in the place you should have been 缺席引人注意 —opposite 反義詞 INCONSPICUOUS —**conspicuously** *adv* —**conspicuousness** *n* [U]

con·spi·ra·cy /kən`spɪrəsɪ; kən'spɪrəsi/ *n* [C,U] a secret plan made by two or more people to do something that is harmful or illegal 密謀, 陰謀: **conspiracy to (do) sth** *a conspiracy to smuggle drugs into the country* 走私毒品到這個國家的陰謀 | **conspiracy against** *a conspiracy against the elected government* 反對民選政府的陰謀 | **conspiracy of silence** (=an agreement to keep quiet about something that should not be a secret) 對不該保密的事緘口不談的密約 | **conspiracy theory** (=the idea that an event was caused by a conspiracy) 陰謀論〔某事件是由陰謀所導致的觀點〕*conspiracy theories about President Kennedy's assassination* 認為甘迺迪總統被暗殺是一項陰謀的各種觀點

con·spi·ra·tor /kən`spɪrətə; kən'spɪrətə/ *n* [C] someone who is involved in a secret plan to do something harmful or illegal 陰謀家

con·spi·ra·to·ri·al /kən͵spɪrə`tɔrɪəl; kən͵spɪrə'tɔːriəl/ *adj* **1** connected with a secret plan to do something harmful or illegal 陰謀的: *conspiratorial discussions* 策劃陰謀的討論 **2 conspiratorial grin/giggle/wink etc** one between two people who know a secret 詭祕的微笑/傻笑/眨眼等〔指掌握了某一祕密的兩人之間交換的神色等〕—**conspiratorially** *adv*

con·spire /kən`spaɪr; kən'spaɪə/ *v* [I] **1** to plan something harmful or illegal together secretly 密謀; 共謀; 搞陰謀: **conspire (with sb) to do sth** *He had conspired with an accomplice to rob the bank.* 他與一個同謀祕密策劃搶劫這家銀行。| **conspire against sb** *Mentally ill people sometimes believe that relatives are conspiring against them.* 精神病人有時會認為親戚密謀暗算他。**2** if events conspire to make something happen, they happen at the same time and make something bad happen〔事件〕湊在一起, 共同導致: **conspire to do sth** *Technological failure and atmospheric conditions conspired to make take-off impossible.* 技術故障和大氣情況湊在一起使飛機不能起飛。

con·sta·ble /`kɑnstəbḷ; 'kʌnstəbəl/ *n* [C] a British police officer of the lowest rank〔英國最低級別的〕警察 —see also 另見 PATROLMAN (1)

con·stab·u·la·ry /kən`stæbjə͵lɛrɪ; kən'stæbjələri/ *n* [C] *BrE* the police force of a particular area or country【英】〔某國家或地區的〕警察部隊 —see also 另見 PATROL[2] (2)

con·stan·cy /`kɑnstənsɪ; 'kɒnstənsi/ *n* [U] *formal*【正式】**1** the quality of staying the same even though other things change 堅定不移; 經久不變; 持久性: *constancy of purpose* 目標堅定 **2** loyalty and faithfulness to a particular person 忠實, 忠貞: *constancy between husband and wife* 夫妻間的忠誠

2 2 **con·stant**[1] /`kɑnstənt; 'kɒnstənt/ *adj* **1** staying the same for a period of time 始終如一的, 恆久不變的: *A thermostat kept the temperature constant.* 恆溫器保持溫度恆久不變。**2** happening all the time or regularly 持續不斷的, 經常發生的: *Sam was in constant pain.* 薩姆感到疼痛不止。**3** *literary* loyal and faithful【文】忠實的, 忠誠的: *a constant friend* 忠實的朋友

constant[2] *n* [C] *technical*【術語】**1** a number or quantity that never varies 常數, 恆量 **2** *formal* something that stays the same even though other things change【正式】不變的事; 恆定的事物 —compare 比較 VARIABLE[1]

3 3 **con·stant·ly** /`kɑnstəntlɪ; 'kɒnstəntli/ *adv* all the time, or very often 持續不斷地; 經常地: *As I walked through the town, I was constantly reminded of my childhood.* 當我步行穿過市鎮時, 見到的景象使我不斷地回憶起我的童年。| **constantly changing** *the constantly changing membership of our group* 我們這個羣體不斷變化的成員

con·stel·la·tion /͵kɑnstə`leʃən; ͵kɒnstə'leɪʃən/ *n* [C] **1** a group of stars that forms a particular pattern and has a name 星座 **2 a constellation of** *literary* a group of people or things that are similar【文】一羣〔相似的人或物〕: *a constellation of famous television performers* 一羣著名電視演員

con·ster·na·tion /͵kɑnstə`neʃən; ͵kɒnstə'neɪʃən/ *n* [U] a feeling of shock or worry, especially one that makes it difficult to think about what to do; DISMAY[1] 驚愕; 驚恐; 驚惶失措: *The thought of living alone filled her with consternation.* 想到要獨自生活使她充滿驚恐。

con·sti·pa·tion /͵kɑnstə`peʃən; ͵kɒnstə'peɪʃən/ *n* [U] the condition of finding it difficult to empty your bowels (BOWEL (1)) 便祕 —**constipated** *adj*

con·sti·tu·en·cy /kən`stɪtʃuənsɪ; kən'stɪtʃuənsi/ *n* [C] 3 **1** an area of the country that elects a representative to a parliament〔選舉議會議員的〕選區: *John Major, speaking from his Huntingdon constituency* 馬卓安在他的亨廷登郡選區發表講話 **2** [also+plural verb *BrE* 英] the people who live and vote in a particular area 選區的全體選民 —compare 比較 WARD[1] (2) **3** any group that supports or is likely to support a politician or a political party〔政治家或政黨的〕支持者, 擁護者: *The Unions were no longer the constituency of the Labour Party alone.* 工會不再單獨支持工黨。

con·sti·tu·ent[1] /kən`stɪtʃuənt; kən'stɪtʃuənt/ *n* [C] **1** someone who votes and lives in a particular area represented by one politician 選區的選民 **2** one of the parts that combine to form something 成分; 構成部分: *the constituents of gunpowder* 火藥的成分 —compare 比較 COMPONENT

constituent[2] *adj* [only before noun 僅用於名詞前] being one of the parts that makes a whole 構成的, 組成的: *the EC and its constituent members* 歐洲共同體及其成員國

con·sti·tute /`kɑnstə͵tut; 'kɒnstətjuːt/ *v* **1** [linking verb 連繫動詞, not in progressive 不用進行式] if several parts constitute something, they form it together; make up (MAKE[1]) 組成, 構成: *the 50 states that constitute the USA* 組成美國的50個州 —see also 另見 COMPRISE **2** [linking verb 連繫動詞, not in progressive 不用進行式] to be considered to be something 被視為: *Boarding a train without a ticket constitutes a breach of the regulations.* 無票乘火車被視為違反規章。**3** [T] *formal* to make something from a number of different parts【正式】將不同部分組成〔某物〕

con·sti·tu·tion /͵kɑnstə`tjuʃən; ͵kɒnstə'tjuːʃən/ *n* **1** [C] the system of basic laws and principles that a DEMOCRATIC country is governed by, which cannot easily be changed by the political party in power 憲法: *The First Amendment of the Constitution guarantees freedom of speech.* 憲法第一條修正案保證言論自由。**2** [singular] the ability of your body to fight disease and illness 體質: **have a strong/good/weak etc constitution** *She's got a strong constitution – she'll recover in no time.* 她體質很好, 很快就會痊癒。**3** [C] *formal* the way something is formed and how it is organized【正式】組成; 結構: [+of] *objections to the constitution of the committee* 對委員會組成方式的反對 **4** the system of rules and principles that an organization is governed by〔某組織的〕法規; 章程

con·sti·tu·tion·al[1] /͵kɑnstə`tjuʃənḷ; ͵kɒnstə'tjuːʃənəl◂/ *adj* **1** officially allowed or limited by the system of rules of a country or organization 憲法[章程]規定的; 合乎憲法[章程]的: *The government can't refuse to hold an election; it's not constitutional.* 政府不能拒絕舉行選舉, 那是違反憲法的。| **a constitutional monarchy** (=a country ruled by a king or queen whose power is restricted by a constitution) 君主立憲制 —opposite 反義詞 UNCONSTITUTIONAL **2** connected with the constitution of a country or organization 憲法[章程]的: *a constitutional crisis* 憲法危機 | **a constitutional amendment**

(=a change to the original constitution) 憲法修正 **3** connected with someone's health and their ability to fight illness 體質上的 —see also 另見 CONSTITUTIONALLY

constitutional² *n* [C] *old-fashioned* a walk you take because it is good for your health【過時】保健散步

con·sti·tu·tion·al·is·m /ˌkɑnstəˋtjuʃənḷɪzəm; ˌkɒnstɪ̣ˈtjuːʃənəlɪzəm/ *n* [U] the belief that a government should be based on a constitution 立憲主義〔主張政府組織等由憲法規定的信仰〕—**constitutionalist** *n* [C]

con·sti·tu·tion·al·i·ty /ˌkɑnstəˌtjuʃənˋælətɪ; ˌkɒnstɪ̣tjuːʃəˈnælɪ̣ti/ *n* [U] the quality of being acceptable according to the constitution 符合憲法, 合憲性: *The senator questioned the constitutionality of the proposed law.* 這位參議員質疑這項法案是否合乎憲法。

con·sti·tu·tion·al·ly /ˌkɑnstəˋtjuʃənḷɪ; ˌkɒnstɪ̣ˈtjuːʃənəli/ *adv* **1** in a way that obeys the rules of a country 依照憲法: *The government must always act constitutionally.* 政府必須時刻依照憲法行事。**2** in a way that is related to someone's character or health and physical ability 就體質而言; 就性格而言

con·strain /kənˋstren; kənˈstreɪn/ *v* [T] **1** to stop someone from doing what they want to do 限制; 阻止某人做他想做的事: **constrain by** *Many women feel constrained by their family's demand.* 許多婦女感覺她們受到家庭生活的束縛。**2** to prevent something from developing and improving 阻止, 抑制, 使某事不能發展、改進: *Our research has been constrained by lack of funding.* 我們的研究由於缺乏資金而受到限制。

con·strained /kənˋstrend; kənˈstreɪnd/ *adj* **1 constrained to do sth** feeling that you are forced to do something 被迫做某事: *In the recession companies felt constrained to make job cuts where possible.* 在經濟蕭條時期, 各公司都被迫盡可能地削減職位。**2** a constrained smile, manner etc seems too controlled and is not natural〔微笑、態度等〕強裝出來的; 拘謹的; 不自然的 —**constrainedly** /kənˋstrenɪdlɪ; kənˈstreɪnɪ̣dli/ *adv*

3 **con·straint** /kənˋstrent; kənˈstreɪnt/ *n* **1** [C] something that limits your freedom to do what you want; RESTRICTION 限制; 束縛; 約束力: [+on] *These new policies place additional constraints on housing projects.* 這些新政策對住房建造工程設置了額外的限制。| **financial/legal/cultural etc constraints** *Financial constraints limited her choice of accommodation.* 財力上的限制使她不能隨意選擇住處。**2** [U] control over the way people are allowed to behave, so that they cannot do what they want 行為約束: *freedom from constraint* 不受限制 **3 under constraint** if you do something under constraint, you do it because you have been forced to 被強迫

con·strict /kənˋstrɪkt; kənˈstrɪkt/ *v* [T] **1** to make something smaller, narrower, or tighter 壓縮; 壓緊; 使收縮, 使收緊 **2** to limit someone's freedom to do what they want 限制人們的行動自由: *Poverty constricts people's choices.* 貧困限制了人們的選擇餘地。—**constricted** *adj* —**constriction** *n* [C,U] —**constrictive** *adj*

3 **con·struct¹** /kənˋstrʌkt; kənˈstrʌkt/ *v* [T] **1** to build a large building, bridge, road etc 建造, 構築: *The Golden Gate Bridge was constructed in 1933-1937.* 金門橋建於 1933-1937 年。| **be constructed of/from etc** *huge skyscrapers constructed entirely of concrete and glass* 完全用混凝土和玻璃建成的摩天大樓 **2** to form something such as a sentence, argument, or system by joining words, ideas etc together 組成, 構成〔句子、論點、體系等〕: *attempts to construct a programme that will meet the educational needs of every child* 為滿足每一個兒童的教育需要制定一項計劃的嘗試 **3** *technical* to draw a mathematical shape【術語】繪製幾何圖形, 作圖: *Construct a square on this line.* 以這條線段為一邊作一個正方形。

con·struct² /ˋkɑnstrʌkt; ˈkɒnstrʌkt/ *n* [C] **1** an idea formed by combining pieces of knowledge 構想; 概念: *the central constructs of role theory* 角色理論的中心概念 **2** *formal* something that is built or made【正式】建造物; 構成物

con·struc·tion /kənˋstrʌkʃən; kənˈstrʌkʃən/ *n* 

1 ▶BUILDINGS/ROADS ETC 建築/道路等◀ [U] the process or method of building large buildings, bridges, roads etc 建造, 建築: *Local labor is used in the construction of the dam.* 建築大壩用的是本地的勞動力。| *the construction industry* 建築業 | **construction site** (=the place where something is being constructed) 建築工地 | **under construction** (=being built) 在建造之中 *When we got to the hotel, it was still under construction.* 我們到達酒店時, 它還在建築之中。

2 ▶MAKING STH USING MANY PARTS 使用許多部件製作某物◀ [U] the process or method of building or making something using many parts 建造, 構造: *Titanium is used in the construction of aircraft fuselages.* 鈦用來建造飛機的機身。

3 ▶PHRASE 片[短]語◀ [C] the order in which certain words are put together in a sentence, phrase etc〔詞在片[短]語或句子中的〕結構; 句法關係: *difficult grammatical constructions* 艱深的語法結構

4 ▶STH BUILT 建造物◀ [C] *formal* something that has been built【正式】建築物; 建造物: *a strange construction made of wood and glass* 用木頭和玻璃建造的奇特建築物

5 ▶IDEAS/KNOWLEDGE 思想/知識◀ [U] the method or process of forming something from knowledge or ideas 根據知識或思想建立理論: *the construction of sociological theory* 社會學理論的創立

6 of simple/strong etc construction *formal* built in a simple way, built to be strong etc【正式】構造簡單/堅固等: *Your home is not secure if the doors are not of strong construction.* 如果門建得不堅固的話, 你的房子就不安全。

7 put a construction on *formal* to think that a statement has a particular meaning or that something was done for a particular reason【正式】理解〔話語的含意、行動的原因等〕: *The judge put an entirely different construction on his remarks.* 法官對他的陳述作了完全不同的解釋。—**constructional** *adj*

con·struc·tive /kənˋstrʌktɪv; kənˈstrʌktɪv/ *adj* **1** intended to be helpful and to suggest improvements, rather than to upset or offend people 建設性的: **constructive advice/criticism** *I don't mind constructive criticism but if you're just going to insult me I'm not staying.* 我不介意建設性的批評, 但如果你只是想侮辱我, 我就不會留在這裡了。**2** having a good effect or likely to produce good results 積極的, 有益的: *Young people in inner cities need constructive outlets for their energy.* 市中心貧民區的年輕人需要有積極的途徑來發泄自己的精力。—**constructively** *adv* —**constructiveness** *n* [U]

con·struc·tor /kənˋstrʌktɚ; kənˈstrʌktə/ *n* [C] a company or person that builds things 建築公司; 建築商

con·strue /kənˋstru; kənˈstruː/ *v* **1 construe sth as** to understand a remark or action in a particular way 將某事解釋[理解]為: *Party leaders felt that such an action would be construed as political persecution.* 政黨領導人認為那樣的行為可以解釋為政治迫害。**2** [I,T] to translate each word in a piece of writing, especially one in Greek or Latin〔尤指對希臘文或拉丁文文章〕逐字直譯

con·sub·stan·ti·a·tion /ˌkɑnsəbˌstænʃɪˋeʃən; ˌkɒnsəbstænʃiˈeɪʃən/ *n* [U] *technical* the belief that the real body and blood of Christ are present in the bread and wine offered by the priest at a Christian religious service【術語】聖體共在論〔認為基督的聖體、聖血與聖餐共在之說〕

con·sul /ˋkɑnsḷ; ˈkɒnsəl/ *n* [C] **1** a representative of the government who lives in a foreign country in order to help and protect citizens of their own country who live there 領事: *the French Consul in Addis Ababa* 法國駐亞

的斯亞貝巴的領事 **2** one of the two chief public officials of the ancient Roman republic, each elected for one year〔古羅馬共和國時期任期一年的〕二執政官之一 —**consular** *adj*: *a consular official* 領事館官員 —**consulship** *n* [C,U]

con·su·late, Consulate /ˋkɑnslɪt; ˈkɒnsjʊlət/ *n* [C] the official building in which a consul lives and works 領事館

3 3 **con·sult** /kənˋsʌlt; kənˈsʌlt/ *v* [I,T] **1** to ask for information or advice from someone because it is their job to know about it 諮詢; 請教: *If symptoms persist, consult a doctor without delay.* 如果症狀繼續存在的話, 馬上去請教醫生。| **consult sb about sth** *An increasing number of clients are consulting them about Social Security changes.* 越來越多的客戶向他們諮詢有關社會保障制度的變化。**2** to ask for someone's permission or to discuss something with someone so that you can make a decision together 取得〔某人〕的允許; 與〔某人〕商量共同決定: *I can't believe you sold the car without consulting me!* 我無法相信你不經我允許就把車給賣了!| **[+with]** *The President consulted with European leaders before taking action.* 總統在採取行動以前曾與歐洲領導人商議。**3** to look for information in a book, map, list etc 查閱: *Have you consulted a dictionary?* 你查過字典了嗎?

C

con·sul·tan·cy /kənˋsʌltənsɪ; kənˈsʌltənsi/ *n* [C] a company that gives advice and training in a particular area to people in other companies 諮詢公司, 顧問公司

3 3 **con·sul·tant** /kənˋsʌltənt; kənˈsʌltənt/ *n* [C] **1** someone who has a lot of experience and whose job it is to give advice and training in a particular area 顧問: *a management consultant* 經營管理顧問 **2** *BrE* a senior hospital doctor who has a lot of knowledge about a particular kind of medical treatment【英】高級顧問醫生; 會診醫生; SPECIALIST (2) *AmE*【美】

3 3 **con·sul·ta·tion** /ˌkɑnsʌlˋteʃən; ˌkɒnsəlˈteɪʃən/ *n* **1** [U] a discussion in which people who are affected by a decision can say what they think should be done 商量, 磋商: *Parents are demanding a greater consultation over their children's future.* 家長們要求對子女的未來進行更廣泛的磋商。| **in consultation with** (=with the agreement and help of someone) 經與…協商 *The decision was made in consultation with union members.* 這項決定是通過與工會會員協商後作出的。**2** [U] advice given by a professional person 建議; 意見: *The school counselor was always available for consultation.* 學校的輔導員隨時都準備接受諮詢。**3** [C] a meeting with a professional person, especially a doctor, for advice or treatment〔與專業人士, 尤指醫師, 進行的〕會面〔以作諮詢、治療等〕: *A follow-up consultation was arranged for two weeks' time.* 安排了兩個星期的後續會面。**4** [U] the act of looking for information or help in a book 查閱: *Leaflets were regularly displayed for consultation by students.* 活頁材料定期展出供學生查閱參考。

con·sul·ta·tive /kənˋsʌltətɪv; kənˈsʌltətɪv/ *adj* providing advice and suggesting solutions to problems 諮詢的; 顧問的: *a consultative document* 一份諮詢性的文件

con·sult·ing¹ /kənˋsʌltɪŋ; kənˈsʌltɪŋ/ *n* [U] the service of providing financial advice to companies 財務諮詢[顧問]服務

consulting² *adj* providing financial or other types of advice to companies 財務諮詢[顧問]的; 諮詢[顧問]的: *a major international consulting firm* 一家主要的國際諮詢機構

consulting room *n* [C] *BrE* a room where a doctor sees patients【英】診查室, 診症室

con·sume /kənˋsum; kənˈsjuːm/ *v* [T] **1** to use time, energy, goods etc 消耗; 消費: *As a country, we consume a lot more than we produce.* 作為一個國家, 我們的消費遠遠多於生產。**2 time-consuming** something that is time-consuming takes a long time 耗費時間的: *a very time-consuming process* 非常耗費時間的過程 **3** *formal* to eat or drink something【正式】吃; 喝: *He's able to consume vast quantities of food.* 他能吃掉大量的食物。**4 consumed with** if you are consumed with a feeling, you feel it very strongly and cannot forget it 被〔某種情感〕所折磨: *He was consumed with guilt after the accident.* 那次事故以後他深感內疚。**5** *formal* if fire consumes something, it destroys it completely【正式】〔大火〕(徹底) 燒毀 —see also 另見 CONSUMING

con·sum·er /kənˋsumə; kənˈsjuːmə/ *n* [C] someone who buys and uses products and services 消費者: *a wider choice of goods for the consumer* 可供消費者選擇的品種更多的商品 —compare 比較 PRODUCER (1) 2 2

consumer con·fi·dence /ˌ·ˌ·· ˈ···/ *n* [U] a measure of how satisfied people are with the present economic situation, as shown by how much money they spend 消費者信任度[信心]: *Consumer confidence was reported to hit an all-time low in September.* 據報道, 九月份的消費者信心跌到了歷史的最低點。

consumer du·ra·bles /ˌ·ˌ·· ˈ···/ *BrE n* [plural] large things such as cars, televisions, or furniture that you do not buy often or regularly【英】耐用消費品; DURABLE GOODS *AmE*【美】

consumer goods /·ˈ·· ˌ·/ *n* [plural] goods such as food, clothes, and equipment that people buy, especially to use in the home 消費品, 日常生活資料 —compare 比較 CAPITAL GOODS

con·sum·er·ism /kənˋsumərɪzəm; kənˈsjuːmərɪzəm/ *n* [U] **1** the idea or belief that the buying and selling of products is the most important or useful activity for an individual and a society 消費主義〔認為買賣商品是個人和社會最重要或最有益的活動的想法或信念〕**2** actions to protect people from unfair prices, advertising that is not true etc 保護消費者利益的行為

consumer price in·dex /·ˌ·· ˈ· ˌ··/ *n* [C] *AmE* a list of the prices of products that is prepared to show how much prices have increased during a particular period of time【美】消費品價格指數; RETAIL PRICE INDEX *BrE*【英】

consumer so·ci·e·ty /·ˈ·· ·ˌ···/ *n* [C] a society in which the buying of products and services is considered extremely important 消費社會

con·sum·ing /kənˋsumɪŋ; kənˈsjuːmɪŋ/ *adj* [only before noun 僅用於名詞前] a consuming feeling is so strong that it controls you and often has a bad effect on your life〔感情〕強烈的, 支配人的〔往往是有害的〕: *It was her consuming ambition to become party leader.* 成為政黨領袖是她的強烈願望。| **consuming passion** (=something you are extremely interested in) 極強烈的愛好 *Sandy's consuming passion is still the martial arts.* 桑迪最強烈的愛好仍然是武術。

con·sum·mate¹ /kənˋsʌmɪt; kənˈsʌmɪt/ *adj formal*【正式】**1** very skilful 技藝高超的: *a great performance from a consummate actress* 技藝高超的女演員的精彩表演 **2** complete and perfect in every way 圓滿的, 完美的: *a consummate example of Picasso's artistry* 畢加索藝術天才的一個完美的例證 **3** used to emphasize how bad someone or something is 極其(差)的: *a man with a consummate lack of tact* 完全不懂策略的人 —**consummately** *adv*

con·sum·mate² /ˋkɑnsəˌmet; ˈkɒnsəmeɪt/ *v* [T] *formal*【正式】**1** to make a marriage or a relationship complete by having sex〔經同房〕使〔婚姻〕完成 **2** to make something complete or perfect 使完成, 使圓滿

con·sum·ma·tion /ˌkɑnsəˋmeʃən; ˌkɒnsəˈmeɪʃən/ *n* [U] *formal*【正式】**1** the act of making a marriage or relationship complete by having sex 圓房,〔經同房而〕完婚 **2** *formal* the point at which something is complete or perfect【正式】圓滿; 完美, 極至: *the consummation of his ambitions* 他雄心壯志的實現

con·sump·tion /kənˋsʌmpʃən; kənˈsʌmpʃən/ *n* [U] **1 ►AMOUNT OF STH USED** 消耗量◄ the amount of oil, electricity etc that is used〔油、電等的〕消耗量: *Fuel consumption has risen dramatically in the last few years.* 在過去幾年中, 燃料的消耗量急劇增加。

2 ▶EATING/DRINKING 吃/喝◀ *formal* the act of eating or drinking【正式】吃; 喝: *The consumption of alcohol was forbidden according to their religion.* 按照他們的宗教, 喝酒是禁止的。| **fit/unfit for human consumption** (=safe or not safe for people to eat) 適合/不適合人類食用 *The meat was declared unfit for human consumption.* 這種肉已被宣布不適合人類食用。
3 ▶BUYING 購買◀ the act of buying and using products 購買, 消費: *The consumption of luxury goods is governed by psychological values like social prestige.* 奢侈品的消費是由諸如社會聲望這樣的心理價值決定的。| **conspicuous consumption** (=buying expensive goods in order to show other people how rich you are) 炫耀性消費
4 ▶AMOUNT OF FOOD/DRINK 吃/喝的量◀ the amount of food or drink that is eaten or drunk〔食物的〕食用量, 消耗量: *Patients are advised to cut down on their consumption of alcohol.* 病人被建議減少喝酒。
5 ▶ILLNESS 疾病◀ a word used in the past for the lung disease TUBERCULOSIS〔舊時指〕肺結核
6 for sb's consumption if a piece of information or remark is for a particular person or group's consumption, it is intended to be heard or read by them 僅供某人[某些人]聆聽或閱讀: *secret policy documents that are not for public consumption* 不供公眾閱讀的機密政策文件
con·sump·tive /kən`sʌmptɪv; kən'sʌmptɪv/ *adj* a word used in the past to describe someone who had the lung disease TUBERCULOSIS〔舊時指〕患肺結核的 —**consumptive** *n* [C]
cont. the written abbreviation for 縮寫= CONTAINING, CONTENTS, CONTINUED, CONTINENT
3 2 **con·tact¹** /`kɑntækt; 'kɒntækt/ *n*
1 ▶COMMUNICATION 交流◀ [U] communication with a person, organization, country etc 聯繫, 聯絡; 交往: **[+with]** *He's not had any contact with his son for months.* 他已經有好幾個月沒有和他的兒子聯繫了。| **[+between]** *There is very little contact between the two tribes.* 這兩個部落間幾乎沒有甚麼交往。| **be/get/stay in contact (with)** *We stay in contact with each other by telephone.* 我們通過電話保持聯繫。| **make/lose contact with** (=succeed in communicating or stop communicating with someone) 與〔某人〕取得/失去聯繫 *I've lost contact with most of my school friends.* 我已經與大部分同學失去了聯繫。| **put sb in contact (with)** (=make it possible for someone to communicate with another person by giving them that person's address or telephone number) 使某人得以(與…)取得聯繫 *Sarah put me in contact with an expert in the field.* 莎拉幫我與該領域的一個專家取得了聯繫。
2 ▶TOUCH 觸摸◀ [U] a state in which two people or things touch each other 接觸: **[+with]** *Children need close physical contact and interaction with a caring adult.* 孩子們需要與有愛心的大人有親密的身體接觸和交流。| **[+between]** *This disease is spread by contact between the animals.* 這種疾病在動物間通過接觸傳播。| **in contact (with)** *For a second, his hand was in contact with mine.* 他的手很快地碰了一下我的手。| **come into contact (with)** *She screamed as her body came into contact with the water.* 當她的身體碰到水的一剎那她尖叫了起來。| **on contact (with)** (=at the moment of touching something) 與…接觸的剎那 *The bomb exploded on contact with the ground.* 炸彈與地面一接觸就爆炸了。| **contact points/ area/surfaces etc** *The contact points of the two surfaces must be clean and dry.* 這兩個表面的接觸點必須既乾淨又乾燥。
3 come into contact with sb to meet someone 會見某人: *Diana dazzled everyone who came into contact with her.* 黛安娜使每個見到她的人都為之傾倒。
4 ▶PERSON WHO CAN HELP 能提供幫助的人◀ [C] a person you know who may be able to help you or give you advice about something〔能提供幫助或建議的〕熟人: *He has a lot of contacts in the media.* 在傳媒界他有很多熟人。
5 ▶SITUATION/PROBLEM 局勢/問題◀ [U] experience of dealing with a particular kind of situation or problem〔處理某種局面或問題的〕經驗: **bring sb into contact with sth** *Pat's job brought her into contact with the problems people face when they retire.* 帕特的工作使她接觸到人們退休時面臨的問題。
6 point of contact a) a place that you go to or a person that you meet when dealing with an organization 聯繫點; 聯繫人: *Primary health care teams are the first point of contact for users of the health service.* 初級保健護理隊是這項保健服務用戶最初的聯繫人。**b)** a way in which two very different things are connected 聯繫點; 接合點: *It's difficult to find a point of contact between theory and practice.* 很難在理論和實踐之間找到聯繫。
7 ▶ELECTRICAL PART 電路元件◀ [C] an electrical part that completes a CIRCUIT (4) when it touches another part〔電路的〕觸點; 接頭
8 ▶EYES 眼睛◀ [C] a contact lens 隱形眼鏡 —see also 另見 **eye contact** (EYE¹ (9))
contact² *v* [T] to write to or telephone someone〔寫信、打電話〕聯繫〔某人〕: *Give the names of two people who can be contacted in case of emergency.* 給出兩個人的名字, 在緊急情況下可以給他們打電話。 3 2
contact³ *adj* [only before noun 僅用於名詞前] **1** a contact number or address is a telephone number or address where someone can be found if necessary 可供聯繫的〔電話號碼或地址〕: *The school requires a contact number for each child.* 學校要求每個孩子都有一個聯絡電話號碼。**2** contact explosives or chemicals become active when they touch something〔炸藥或化學物質〕憑接觸起作用的: *Contact poisons are widely used in pest control.* 接觸性毒藥廣泛用於防治蟲害。
contact lens /'‥ ˌ/ *n* [C] a small round piece of plastic you put on your eye to help you see clearly 隱形眼鏡
con·ta·gion /kən`tedʒən; kən'teɪdʒən/ *n* [C,U] **1** *technical* a situation in which a disease is spread by people touching each other【術語】〔疾病〕接觸傳染: *The danger of contagion was now very small.* 接觸傳染的危險現在非常小。**2** *technical* a disease that can be passed from person to person by touch【術語】接觸傳染病 **3** *formal* a feeling or attitude that spreads quickly from person to person【正式】〔感情、態度的〕感染; 蔓延
con·ta·gious /kən`tedʒəs; kən'teɪdʒəs/ *adj* **1** a disease that is contagious can be passed from person to person by touch〔疾病〕接觸傳染的 **2** a person who is contagious has a disease that can be passed to another person by touch 患接觸傳染病的: *The patient is still highly contagious.* 這個病人仍然有很強的傳染性。**3** if a feeling, attitude, or action is contagious, other people quickly begin to feel it, believe it, do it etc〔感情、態度、行動〕感染性的; 蔓延的: *Her enthusiasm was contagious.* 她的熱情很有感染力。—**contagiousness** *n* [U] —**contagiously** *adv*
con·tain /kən`ten; kən'teɪn/ *v* [T] **1** to have something inside, or have something as a part 包含; 容納; 裝盛: *He opened the bag, which contained a razor, soap and a towel.* 他打開袋子, 裡面有一把剃鬍刀、香皂和一條毛巾。| *The letter contained important information about Boulestin's legal affairs.* 這封信含有關於布里斯汀法律事務的重要資料。**2** to keep a strong feeling or emotion under control 克制〔強烈的感情〕: *Jane couldn't contain her amusement a moment longer.* 簡樂得再也忍不住了。| **contain yourself** (=keep your emotions under control) 克制自己 *He was so excited he could hardly contain himself.* 他太激動了, 再也無法控制自己。**3** to stop something from spreading or escaping 抑制, 控制: *Doctors are struggling to contain the epidemic.* 醫生正在努力控制流行病。—see also 另見 SELF-CONTAINED **4** *formal* to surround an area or an angle【正式】包圍〔區域或角〕: *How big is the angle contained by these two sides?* 這兩條邊之間的角有多大? 2 1

C

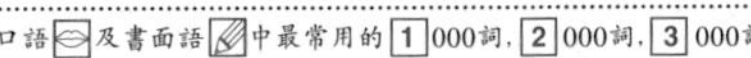

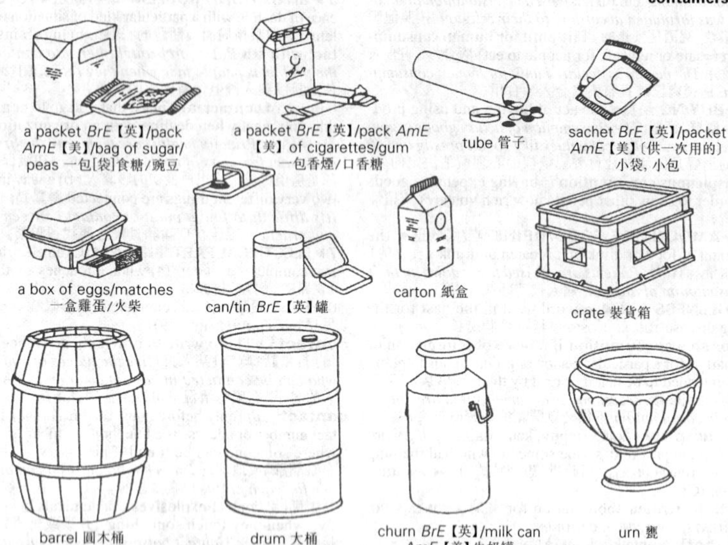

con·tain·er /kən`tenɚ; kən'teɪnə/ *n* [C] **1** something such as a box or bowl that can be used for keeping things in 容器: *Ice cream comes in plastic containers.* 冰淇淋是用塑料容器包裝出售的。**2** a very large metal box in which goods are packed to make it easy to lift or move them onto a ship or vehicle 集裝箱, 貨櫃: *The deck was full of big cargo containers.* 甲板上堆滿了大型貨物集裝箱。

con·tain·ment /kən`tenmənt; kən'teɪnmənt/ *n* [U] **1** the act of keeping something under control 控制; 抑制: *containment of public expenditure* 控制公共支出 **2** the use of political actions to prevent an unfriendly country from becoming more powerful 遏制〔對敵國的政策〕: *a policy of containment* 遏制政策

con·tam·i·nant /kən`tæmənənt; kən'tæmɪ̥nənt/ *n* [C] *technical* a poisonous substance that makes something impure【術語】污染物, 致污物

con·tam·i·nate /kən`tæmə,net; kən'tæmɪ̥neɪt/ *v* [T] **1** to make a place or substance dirty and dangerous by adding something to it, for example chemicals or poison 把…弄髒, 污染: *fears that dumped waste might contaminate water supplies* 對傾倒的垃圾可能會污染水源的憂慮 **2** to influence something in a way that has a bad effect 毒害; 使變壞 —**contamination** /kən,tæmə`neʃən; kən,tæmɪ̥'neɪʃən/ *n* [U]

con·tam·i·nat·ed /kən`tæmə,netɪd; kən'tæmɪ̥neɪtɪ̥d/ *adj* **1** water, food etc that is contaminated has dangerous or harmful things in it, such as chemicals or poison 〔水、食物等〕被污染的: *Several outbreaks of infection have been traced to contaminated food.* 幾次傳染病爆發的源頭都已經查明是被污染的食物。**2** influenced in a way that produces a bad effect 變壞的, 變劣的

contd. the written abbreviation for 縮寫 = CONTINUED

con·tem·plate /`kɑntəm,plet; 'kɒntəmpleɪt/ *v* **1** [T] to think about something that you intend to do in the future 打算, 想, 考慮: *Aren't you a little young to be contemplating marriage?* 你想結婚是不是有點早了? | **contemplate doing sth** *I've never even contemplated leaving my job.* 我從來連想都沒想過辭職。**2** [T] to accept the possibility that something is true 預期; 視…為可能: **too dreadful/horrifying etc to contemplate** *The thought of the letter never having reached him was too terrible to contemplate.* 只要一想到那封信沒有送達他那裡, 這便令人恐懼得不敢想下去。**3** [I,T] to think seriously about something for a long time, especially in order to understand it better 深思; 細想: *contemplating the meaning of life* 仔細思考生命的意義

con·tem·pla·tion /,kɑntəm`pleʃən; ,kɒntəm'pleɪʃən/ *n* [U] quiet, serious thinking about something, especially in order to understand it better 沉思, 冥想, 默想: *The monks spend an hour in contemplation each morning.* 那些修道士每天早上默禱一個小時。

con·tem·pla·tive[1] /kən`tɛmplətɪv; kən'templətɪv/ *adj* spending a lot of time thinking seriously and quietly 沉思的, 冥想的, 默想的: *a contemplative mood* 沉思的心境 —**contemplatively** *adv*

contemplative[2] *n* [C] *formal* someone who spends their life thinking deeply about religious matters【正式】沉思冥想思考宗教問題的人

con·tem·po·ra·ne·ous /kən,tɛmpə`renɪəs; kən,tempə'reɪniəs/ *adj formal* happening in the same period of time; CONTEMPORARY (2)【正式】發生於同一時期的: [+with] *Built in the 13th and 14th centuries, they are contemporaneous with many of the great Gothic cathedrals.* 它們建於13和14世紀, 和許多偉大的哥特式大教堂屬於同一個時期。—**contemporaneously** *adv* —**contemporaneity** /kən,tɛmpərə`niətɪ; kən,tempərə'ni:ɪ̥ti/ *n* [U]

con·tem·po·ra·ry[1] /kən`tɛmpə,rɛrɪ; kən'tempərəri/ *adj* **1** belonging to the present time; MODERN 當代的: **contemporary music/art/dance etc** *an exhibition of contemporary Japanese prints* 當代日本版畫的展覽 **2** happening or existing in the same period of time 發生[存在]於同一時代的

contemporary[2] *n* [C] someone who was in a particular place or who lived at the same time as someone else 同時代的人; 同輩: *Oswald was much admired by his contemporaries at the Royal Academy.* 奧斯瓦爾德在皇家藝術學會中很受同時代人的敬仰。

con·tempt /kən`tɛmpt; kən'tempt/ *n* [U] **1** a feeling that someone or something is not important and deserves no respect 輕蔑, 輕視, 鄙視: **[+for]** *His contempt for his fellow students was quite obvious.* 他對同學的鄙視之情非常明顯。| **with contempt** *He had been treated with nothing but contempt ever since he arrived.* 他從到達時起就一直受到輕視。| **hold sb in contempt** (=feel contempt for someone) 鄙視某人 *They'd always held that family in contempt.* 他們一直鄙視那家人。| **beneath contempt** (=so unacceptable that you have no respect for the person involved) 為人不齒 *That sort of behavior is simply beneath contempt.* 那種行為簡直為人所不齒。**2** disobedience or disrespect towards a court of law〔對法庭的〕輕蔑罪: **in contempt of** *He was found in contempt of the order.* 他被裁定為蔑視法庭命令。| **contempt of court** (=not doing what a judge or court of law has told you to do) 蔑視法庭（罪） **3** complete lack of fear towards something difficult or dangerous 不顧〔困難、危險〕: *contempt for danger* 不顧危險

con·temp·ti·ble /kən`tɛmptəbl̩; kən'temptəbəl/ *adj* so unacceptable that you have no respect for the person involved 可鄙的; 卑劣的: *They were portrayed as contemptible cowards.* 他們被刻畫為可鄙的膽小鬼。—**contemptibly** *adv*

con·temp·tu·ous /kən`tɛmptʃuəs; kən'temptʃuəs/ *adj* **1** showing that you feel that someone or something is not important and deserves no respect 輕蔑的, 表示輕蔑的; 傲慢不恭的: *Cordelia threw him a contemptuous look.* 科迪莉婭輕蔑地朝他看了看。| **be contemptuous of** *He was openly contemptuous of his elder brother.* 他公開蔑視他大哥。**2** not feeling any fear in a dangerous situation 不顧危險的: *Contemptuous of the risks, she ran into the burning building.* 她不顧危險衝進燃燒着的大樓。—**contemptuously** *adv*

con·tend /kən`tɛnd; kən'tend/ *v* **1** [I] to compete against someone in order to gain something 競爭; 奮爭: *contending for the World Heavyweight Title* 競爭世界重量級冠軍 **2** [T+that] to argue or state that something is true 聲稱, 斷言, 主張: *Some astronomers contend that the universe may be younger than previously believed.* 有些天文學家聲稱宇宙可能比原先認為的要年輕。

contend with sth *phr v* [T] **have to contend with sth/have sth to contend with** to have to deal with something difficult or unpleasant 必須處理[應付]某事: *He had to contend with a lot of shouting and jeering from the audience.* 他不得不應付觀眾發出的大喊大叫和嘲笑聲。

con·tend·er /kən`tɛndɚ; kən'tendə/ *n* [C] someone who takes part in a competition or a situation in which they have to compete with other people 競爭者: *a serious contender for the Democratic nomination* 大有希望獲得民主黨提名的人

2 2 **con·tent¹** /`kɑntɛnt; 'kɒntent/ *n* **1 contents** [plural] **a)** the things that are inside a box, bag, room etc 容納的東西: *The box had fallen over, and some of the contents had spilled out.* 箱子翻了, 裡面的一些東西散落出來。| *The customs official rummaged through the contents of the briefcase.* 海關官員徹底搜查了公事包裡的物品。**b)** the things that are written in a letter, book etc〔信、書等的〕內容: *If the contents of this letter become known to the Foreign Secretary, there would be grave consequences.* 如果信的內容被外交大臣知道的話, 會帶來嚴重的後果。| **table of contents** (=a list at the beginning of a book, which shows the different parts into which the book is divided) 目錄, 目次 | **contents page** (=the page in a book on which the table of contents appears) 目錄頁 **2** [singular] the amount of a substance that is contained in something 含量: *the fat content of cheese* 乾酪的脂肪含量 **3** [singular] the ideas, facts, or opinions that are contained in a speech or a piece of writing〔演講或文章的〕內容: *They said they liked the content of your article, but the style wasn't quite right for the magazine.* 他們說喜歡你文章的內容, 但是文章的風格不太適合那本雜誌。

con·tent² /kən`tɛnt; kən'tent/ *adj* [not before noun 不 3
用於名詞前] **1** happy and satisfied 滿意的, 滿足的: *Tarka lay drowsy and content in the sun.* 塔卡昏昏欲睡, 心滿意足地躺在陽光下。| **content to do sth** *John is quite content to watch television for hours at a stretch.* 約翰非常滿足於一連幾小時不停地看電視。| **[+with]** *She is content with her job at the moment.* 她現在對自己的工作非常滿意。**2 not content with** if someone is not content with doing something, they do not think that it is good enough, and so want to do more 對…不滿足: *Not content with sentencing him to ten years in prison, the judge ordered that he leave the country on his release.* 法官對判他入獄十年仍不滿足, 還命令他服刑期滿後馬上離開這個國家。

content³ *n* [U] **1** *literary* a feeling of quiet happiness and satisfaction【文】滿意, 滿足 **2 do sth to your heart's content** to do something as much as you want 盡情[心滿意足]地做某事: *We sang away to our hearts' content.* 我們盡情地唱個不停。

content⁴ *v* [T] **1 content yourself with sth** to do or have something that is not what you really wanted, but is still satisfactory 使自己滿足[甘心]於某事: *This is all I have, so you'll have to content yourself with £5 for the moment.* 我只有這點錢, 所以現在只能給你五英鎊, 你就將就將就吧。**2** to make someone feel happy and satisfied 使滿意; 使滿足: *I was no longer satisfied with the life that had hitherto contented me.* 我已經不滿足於過去我一直感到滿意的生活了。

con·tent·ed /kən`tɛntɪd; kən'tentɪ̣d/ *adj* happy and satisfied because your life is good 滿意的; 滿足的: *a fat and contented black cat* 一隻肥胖而顯得心滿意足的黑貓 —**contentedly** *adv*: *The baby gurgled contentedly in its crib.* 嬰兒在嬰兒牀上滿足地咯咯笑。

con·ten·tion /kən`tɛnʃən; kən'tenʃən/ *n* **1** [C] *formal* an opinion that someone expresses【正式】論點, 主張: *Her main contention is that doctors should do more to encourage people to lead healthy lives.* 她的主要觀點是醫生應該更多地鼓勵大家過健康的生活。**2** [U] *formal* argument and disagreement between people【正式】爭論, 爭端; 口角: *The issue of subsidies is a great source of contention in Europe.* 補貼問題在歐洲是極易引發爭論的問題。**3 a bone of contention** a subject that causes disagreement or argument 引起爭論的話題: *Their aunt's will has always been a bone of contention between them.* 姑母的遺囑一直是引起他們爭吵的話題。**4 in contention** *formal* being the subject of argument and disagreement【正式】是爭論、不和的主題: *The issue is no longer in contention.* 這問題不再讓人爭論了。

con·ten·tious /kən`tɛnʃəs; kən'tenʃəs/ *adj* **1** causing a lot of argument and disagreement between people 引起爭論的; 有爭議的: *Animal welfare did not become a contentious issue until the late 1970s.* 直到 20 世紀 70 年代晚期, 動物的福利才成為一個有爭議的話題。**2** someone who is contentious often argues with people 愛爭論的 —**contentiously** *adv* —**contentiousness** *n* [U]

con·tent·ment /kən`tɛntmənt; kən'tentmənt/ *n* [U] the state of being happy and satisfied 滿意; 滿足: *He gave a sigh of contentment, turned over and went to sleep.* 他滿意地哈了口氣, 轉身睡着了。—opposite 反義詞 DISCONTENT

con·test¹ /`kɑntɛst; 'kɒntest/ *n* [C] **1** a competition 比賽, 競賽: *a beauty contest* 選美比賽 **2** a struggle to win control or power 競爭, 爭奪, 角逐: *the contest for leadership of the party* 爭奪該黨的領導權 **3 no contest** used to mean that you will easily be the best or win the contest 輕易獲勝, 輕取

con·test² /kən`tɛst; kən'test/ *v* [T] **1** to say formally that you do not accept something or do not agree with it 對…提出質疑; 抗辯: *His brothers are contesting the will.* 他的兄弟對遺囑提出質疑。**2** to compete for something or try to win it 競爭, 爭奪, 角逐: *contesting a seat on the council* 爭奪議會的席位

con·tes·tant /kənˋtɛstənt; kən'testənt/ *n* [C] someone who competes in a contest 競爭者; 選手; 參加競賽者: *The next contestant is Vera Walker of Lincoln.* 下一個參賽者是來自林肯的薇拉·沃克。

3 1 **con·text** /ˋkɑntɛkst; 'kɒntekst/ *n* [C] **1** the situation, events, or information that are related to something, and that help you to understand it better 場合; 環境; 周圍情況; 背景: *These changes must be seen in their historical and social context.* 這些變化必須放在它的社會和歷史環境中來看待。| **in context** (=considered together with the related situation, events etc rather than considered alone) 結合環境來考慮 *I think we need to look at these events in context.* 我認為我們需要從全局來看待這些事件。**2** the words and sentences that come before and after a particular word, and that help you to understand the meaning of the word 上下文, 語境: *'Mad' can mean 'foolish', 'insane', or 'angry', depending on the context.* 在不同的上下文中, mad 的意思可以是"愚蠢的"、"發瘋的"或"生氣的"。**3 take/quote sth out of context** to repeat a sentence or statement, without describing the situation in which it was said, with the result that it seems to mean something different 斷章取義: *Jones was furious that the papers had quoted his remarks completely out of context.* 報紙引他的話完全是斷章取義, 瓊斯因此十分氣憤。

con·tex·tu·al /kənˋtɛkstʃuəl; kən'tekstʃuəl/ *adj* relating to a particular context 與上下文[環境]有關的: *contextual information* 根據上下文而確定的信息 **—contextually** *adv*

con·tex·tu·al·ize also 又作 **-ise** *BrE*【英】/kənˋtɛkstʃuəlaɪz; kən'tekstʃuəlaɪz/ *v* [T] to consider something together with the situation, events, or information that relate to it, rather than alone 把…與有關背景一併考慮 **—contextualization** /kənˌtɛkstʃuəlaɪˋzeʃən; kənˌtekstʃuəlaɪ'zeɪʃən/ *n* [U]

con·tig·u·ous /kənˋtɪgjuəs; kən'tɪgjuəs/ *adj* [+with] *formal* next to something, or near something in time or order【正式】〔時間、順序上〕相鄰的, 相近的: [+with] *Canada is contiguous with the US along much of its border.* 加拿大的邊界大部分與美國接壤。**—contiguously** *adv* **—contiguity** /ˌkɑntəˋgjuətɪ; ˌkɒntɪ'gjuːɪti/ *n* [U]

con·ti·nence /ˋkɑntənəns; 'kɒntɪnəns/ *n* [U] *formal* the practice of controlling your desire for sex【正式】節慾

con·ti·nent¹ /ˋkɑntənənt; 'kɒntɪnənt/ *n* [C] **1** a large mass of land surrounded by sea 洲; 大洲; 大陸: *the continents of Asia and Africa* 亞非大陸 **2 the Continent** *especially BrE* Western Europe not including Britain【尤英】〔不包括英國的〕西歐大陸: *a holiday on the Continent* 在西歐大陸上度假

continent² *adj* **1** able to control your BLADDER (1) and bowels (BOWEL (1)) 有排便節制力的 **2** *old use* controlling your desire to have sex【舊】禁慾的, 自我節制性慾的 —opposite 反義詞 INCONTINENT

con·ti·nen·tal¹ /ˌkɑntəˋnɛntl; ˌkɒntɪ'nentl◂/ *adj* **1** [only before noun 僅用於名詞前] belonging to the North American continent 北美大陸的: *The continental United States does not include Hawaii.* 美國大陸不包括夏威夷。**2** relating to a large mass of land 大陸的, 大陸性的: *birds and reptiles from continental South America* 從南美大陸來的鳥類和爬行動物 **3** *especially BrE* belonging to or in the European continent【尤英】歐洲大陸的: *We visited all the major continental cities.* 我們去了所有重要的歐洲大陸城市。**4** characteristic of the warmer countries in Western Europe 具有西歐溫暖國家風格的: *That café looks very continental with its tables set out on the pavement like that.* 那家咖啡館把咖啡桌擺放在人行道上, 看起來很有西歐大陸溫暖國家的風情。

continental² *n* [C] *BrE old-fashioned* someone who comes from Europe but not from Britain【英, 過時】歐洲大陸人〔不包括英國人〕

continental break·fast /ˌ.... '../ *n* [C] a breakfast consisting of coffee and bread with butter and JAM¹ (1)〔包括咖啡、麵包、黃油和果醬的〕歐洲大陸式早餐, 清淡早餐 —compare 比較 ENGLISH BREAKFAST

continental drift /ˌ.... '../ *n* [U] *technical* the very slow movement of the continents (CONTINENT¹ (1)) across the surface of the Earth【術語】大陸漂移

continental shelf /ˌ.... './ *n plural* **continental shelves** [C] *technical* the part of a CONTINENT¹ (1) that slopes down under the ocean and ends in a steep slope down to the bottom of the ocean【術語】大陸架

con·tin·gen·cy /kənˋtɪndʒənsɪ; kən'tɪndʒənsi/ *n* **1** an event or situation that might happen in the future, especially one that might cause problems〔可能發生的〕意外事件, 不測事件: **contingency plan** (=a plan that you make in order to deal with a problem that might happen) 應變計劃 *contingency plans to cope with a major computer failure* 應付重大電腦故障的應變計劃 **2 contingency fee** *AmE* an amount of money that a lawyer in the US will be paid only if the person they are advising wins in court【美】勝訴酬金〔勝訴才付給律師的酬勞〕

con·tin·gent¹ /kənˋtɪndʒənt; kən'tɪndʒənt/ *adj formal* dependent on something that is uncertain or that will happen in the future【正式】因情況而變的, 視條件而定的: [+on/upon] *Further investment would be contingent upon the company's profit performance.* 進一步的投資取決於公司的利潤收益。**—contingently** *adv*

contingent² *n* [C also+plural verb *BrE* 英] **1** a group of people who all have the same aim or are from the same area, and who are part of a larger group 代表團: *Has the Scottish contingent arrived yet?* 蘇格蘭代表團到了沒有? **2** a group of soldiers sent to help a larger group〔軍隊的〕分遣隊: *A large contingent of field artillery was dispatched.* 已派出了一大隊野戰砲兵。

con·tin·u·al /kənˋtɪnjuəl; kən'tɪnjuəl/ *adj* **1** continuing for a long time without stopping 持續的, 不間斷的: *five weeks of continual rain* 一連下了五個星期的雨 | *The hostages lived in continual fear of violent death.* 人質長期生活在暴力死亡的恐懼之中。**2** repeated often and over a long period of time; frequent 多次重複的, 頻繁的: *The continual trips to my mother's house took up a lot of my time.* 經常去看母親花費了我很多的時間。**3** used to describe actions that are repeated many times over a period of time and are annoying 頻繁而討厭的: *I wish you'd stop that continual chattering!* 我希望你不要再嘮叨個沒完! **—continually** *adv*: *continually reassessing the situation* 再三估計形勢

USAGE NOTE 用法說明: CONTINUAL

WORD CHOICE 詞語辨析: **continual(ly), continuous(ly)**

Continual describes separate actions (often annoying actions you do not like) which are repeated over a period of time. continual 形容在一段時間內多次重複的獨立動作〔常指令人不快的動作〕: *These continual interruptions are driving me mad.* 這些沒完沒了的插話快使我發瘋了。| *She's continually flying off to different places.* 她不停地飛往不同的地方。

Continuous especially describes things and events that go on without a break. continuous 尤指沒有間斷的事物或事件: *The police formed a continuous line round the building.* 警察在建築物周圍圍成一圈。| *This product is the result of years of continuous development.* 這個產品是幾年來不停開發的結果。| *We landed after flying continuously for 16 hours.* 我們在連續飛行了 16 小時後着陸。

The uses just described are regarded by many as the correct ones, but native speakers often use **continuous(ly)** also, like **continual(ly)**, to describe repeated separate actions. 以上描述的用法很多人認為是正確的, 但是母語是英語的人往往也用 continuous(ly) 來形容多次重複的獨立動作: *There* were continuous interruptions. 一直有人插話。As a result, **continuous(ly)** is much more frequent in spoken English. Where both might be used, **continuous(ly)** may carry less of the idea that the repeated action is annoying. 因此 continuous(ly) 在英語口語中更常用。在兩個詞都能用的場合，continuous(ly) 表示反覆動作令人不快的信息較少: *It rained continuously all summer, which was good for the rice crop.* 整個夏天都在下雨，這對稻米有好處。Compare 比較: *It rained continually all summer, which completely spoiled our vacation.* 整個夏天不停地下雨，徹底破壞了我們的假期。

con·tin·u·ance /kən`tɪnjuəns; kənˈtɪnjuəns/ *n* **1** [singular, U] the state of continuing for a long period of time 持續; 連續, 繼續: *the continuance in power of the Nationalist party* 民族主義政黨繼續掌權 **2** [C usually singular 一般用單數] *law* the act of allowing the events in a court of law to stop for a period of time, usually so a lawyer can find more facts about the case【法律】延期審理

con·tin·u·a·tion /kən͵tɪnju`eʃən; kənˌtɪnjuˈeɪʃən/ *n* **1** [U] the act or state of continuing for a long period without stopping 繼續; 持續: *A royal child will ensure the continuation of the family line.* 皇室的孩子可以為家族延續香火。**2** [C] something that follows after something else without stopping or changing 繼續部分: **[+of]** *The present economic policy is a continuation of the earlier one.* 現在的經濟政策是以前政策的延續。**3** [C] something that is joined to something else as if it were part of it 延續物, 接續物: **[+of]** *The Baltic Sea is a continuation of the North Sea.* 波羅的海是北海的延伸。

1 1 **con·tin·ue** /kən`tɪnju; kənˈtɪnjuː/ *v* **1** [I,T] to keep happening, existing, or doing something for a longer period of time without stopping (使) 繼續; (使) 延續: *He will be continuing his education in the US.* 他會在美國繼續上學。| *The fighting continued for a week.* 戰鬥持續了一個星期。**[+with]** *Continuing with this argument is very pointless.* 繼續這場爭論毫無意義。| **continue to do sth** *Silvina continued to work after she had had her baby.* 西爾維娜生小孩後繼續工作。| **continue doing sth** *They continued talking after the meal.* 他們飯後繼續談話。**2** [I,T] to start again after an interruption〔中斷後〕再繼續: *After a brief ceasefire the fighting continued.* 經過短暫的停火後戰鬥又繼續了。| **continue doing sth** *Are you going to continue seeing her when she comes back?* 她回來後你打算再跟她見面嗎? **3** [I] to walk, travel, or go further on or along 繼續走[旅行, 前行]: **[+down/in/after etc]** *We continued along the road for some time.* 我們繼續沿着這條路走了一段時間。**4** [I,T] to say something else after you have been interrupted 繼續說, 接着說: *"And so," he continued, "we will try harder next time."* "因此，"他接着說，"我們下一次會更加努力。" —see also 另見 CONTINUAL, DISCONTINUE

This graph shows how common different grammar patterns of the verb **continue** are. 本圖表所示動詞 continue 的常見不同語法模式的使用頻率。

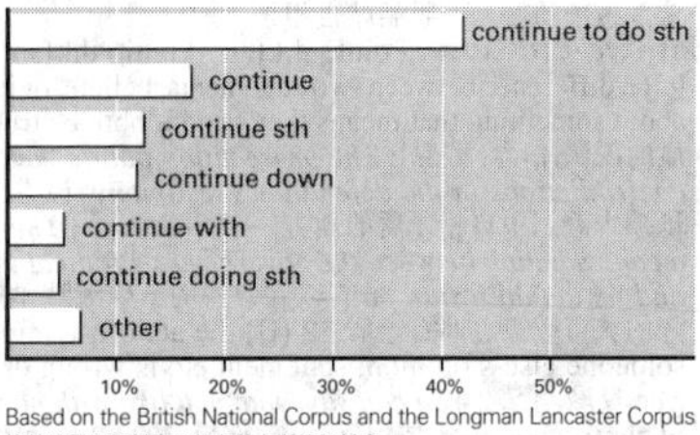

continue to do sth
continue
continue sth
continue down
continue with
continue doing sth
other

10% 20% 30% 40% 50%

Based on the British National Corpus and the Longman Lancaster Corpus
據英國國家語料庫和朗文蘭卡斯特語料庫

con·tin·ued /kən`tɪnjud; kənˈtɪnjuːd/ *adj* [only before noun 僅用於名詞前] continuing to happen for a long time, or happening many times 繼續的, 連續的; 反覆的, 頻繁的: *The continued failure of the police caused a public outcry.* 警方接連失職導致公眾的強烈抗議。| *continued press speculation* 持續的媒體揣測

continuing ed·u·ca·tion /·,··· ··'··/ *n* [U] education provided for adults outside the formal educational system, usually by means of classes that are held in the evening 持續教育, 成人教育

con·ti·nu·i·ty /͵kɑntə`nuətɪ; ˌkɒntəˈnjuːəti/ *n* [U] **1** the continuing of an event, system etc over a long period of time, without problems happening when there is a change 連續(性), 持續(性), 連貫(性): *We should ensure continuity of care between hospital and home.* 我們應當保證醫院和家庭之間保健的連續性。**2** *technical* the organization of a film or television programme to give the appearance that the action happens without pauses or interruptions【術語】〔電影的〕場景串聯, 〔電視的〕節目串聯

C

con·tin·u·o /kən`tɪnjuo; kənˈtɪnju-əʊ/ *n* [C] *technical* a musical part consisting of a line of low notes with figures showing the higher notes that are to be played with them【術語】〔音樂的〕數字低音, 通奏低音

con·tin·u·ous /kən`tɪnjuəs; kənˈtɪnjuəs/ *adj* **1** continuing to happen or exist without stopping or without any interruptions 持續的, 不間斷的, 連續的: *The brain needs a continuous supply of blood.* 大腦需要不斷地供血。| *The Blood Transfusion Service has a long and continuous tradition of public service.* 輸血站擁有長久而持續的為公眾服務的傳統。**2** something such as a line that is continuous does not have any spaces or holes in it〔線等〕連續的, 不間斷的 **3 continuous assessment** *BrE* a way of judging how well a student is doing by looking at the work they do during the year rather than by testing them in an examination【英】〔對學生成績的〕連續性評估〔有別於只用考試評定〕**4** *technical* the continuous form of a verb is used to show that an action or activity is continuing to happen, and is shown in English by the verb 'be', followed by a PRESENT PARTICIPLE, as in 'I was waiting for the bus'【術語】〔語法〕進行式[時]的 —**continuously** *adv* 2 3

con·tin·u·um /kən`tɪnjuəm; kənˈtɪnjuəm/ *n* [C] *plural* **continuums** *or* **continua** /-juə; -juə/ something that changes or develops very gradually, so that each part is very similar to previous and following parts; CLINE 統一體; 連續體: *a learning continuum along which all learners fit* 適合所有學習者的連續學習過程

con·tort /kən`tɔrt; kənˈtɔːt/ *v* [I,T] to twist something so that it does not have its normal shape, and looks strange or unattractive, or to twist in this way (使) 扭曲: **[+with]** *His face was contorted with rage.* 他的臉由於氣憤而扭曲了。

con·tor·tion /kən`tɔrʃən; kənˈtɔːʃən/ *n* [U] **1** the act of twisting something so that it does not have its normal shape, and looks strange or unattractive, or the fact of being twisted in this way 扭曲: *the involuntary contortion of muscles brought on by the illness* 由疾病引起的肌肉不由自主的扭曲 **2** [C] a twisted position or movement that looks strange 扭曲狀[姿勢]: *They turned as they danced with the most amazing contortions.* 他們一邊跳舞一邊轉圈, 舞姿扭曲的幅度令人驚訝。**3** [C] complicated activity in order to do something 複雜的活動: *He went through a series of amazing contortions to get Karen a work permit.* 他過五關斬六將才為凱倫取了一個工作許可證。

con·tor·tion·ist /kən`tɔrʃənɪst; kənˈtɔːʃənɪst/ *n* [C] someone who entertains people by twisting their body into strange and unnatural shapes and positions 柔體雜技演員

con·tour /`kɑntʊr; ˈkɒntʊə/ *n* [C] **1** the shape of the outer edges of something such as an area of land or someone's body 外形; 輪廓: *the contours of the hills and ridges* 小山和山脊的輪廓 | *the contour of her face* 她臉的輪廓 **2** also 又作 **contour line** a line on a map that connects points of equal height above sea level, which together with others show hills, valleys etc〔地圖上的〕等高線

con·toured /ˋkɑnturd; ˈkɒntʊəd/ *adj* **1** shaped to fit closely next to something else, or in a shape like this 成…的輪廓的: *The cushion was still warm, contoured to the shape of his body.* 墊子還是溫的, 還留下了他的坐印。**2** having an attractive, curved shape 線條迷人的; 輪廓優美的: *the smoothly contoured lines and attractive styling of this sofa* 這張沙發流暢的輪廓和迷人的風格

C

contra- /kɑntrə; kɒntrə/ *prefix* **1** acting to prevent something 反, 防 (止): *contraceptive devices* (=against CONCEPTION) 避孕用具 **2** opposite (與…) 相對: *plants in contradistinction to animals* 有別於動物的植物

con·tra·band /ˋkɑntrə͵bænd; ˈkɒntrəbænd/ *n* [U] goods that are brought into a country illegally, especially without tax being paid on them 走私貨; 禁運品: *contraband steel imported illegally into Turkey* 走私運進土耳其的鋼材 —**contraband** *adj*

con·tra·bass /͵kɑntrəˋbes; ͵kɒntrəˈbeɪs/ *n* [C] a DOUBLE BASS 低音提琴

con·tra·cep·tion /͵kɑntrəˋsɛpʃən; ͵kɒntrəˈsepʃən/ *n* [U] the practice of making it possible for a woman to have sex without having a baby, or the methods for doing this; BIRTH CONTROL 避孕; 節 (制生) 育: *The pill is a popular method of contraception.* 服用避孕藥是一種通用的避孕方法。

con·tra·cep·tive /͵kɑntrəˋsɛptɪv; ͵kɒntrəˈseptɪv◂/ *n* [C] a drug, object, or method used to make it possible for a woman to have sex without having a baby 避孕藥物[用具, 方法]: *You can get free contraceptives from the family planning clinic.* 你可以從計劃生育門診部免費獲得避孕藥。—**contraceptive** *adj* [only before noun 僅用於名詞前]: *a contraceptive device* 避孕用具

S2 W1 **con·tract¹** /ˋkɑntrækt; ˈkɒntrækt/ *n* [C] **1** a formal written agreement between two or more people, which says what each person must do for the other 契約; 合同: *His contract of employment specifies that he must get at least one month's training.* 他的雇傭合同明確寫明他要接受至少一個月的培訓。| **[+with]** *Tyler has just agreed a seven year contract with a Hollywood studio.* 泰勒剛剛與荷里活的一家製片廠簽訂了七年的合同。| **sign a contract** *Read the contract carefully before you sign it.* 簽署合同以前要仔細閱讀。| **enter into a contract** *They have just entered into a lucrative contract with a clothing store.* 他們剛剛與一家服裝店訂立了一份有利可圖的契約。| **be on a contract/be under contract** (=be working for someone with whom you have a contract) 跟與你訂立合同的人工作 | **be in breach of contract** (=have done something that is not allowed by the contract) 違約 *If they don't get the test version of the software to us by tomorrow they'll be in breach of contract.* 如果他們到明天還沒有把軟件的測試版交給我們, 他們就違約了。**2 subject to contract** if an agreement is subject to contract, it has not yet been agreed formally by a contract〔達成協議但還〕須簽訂合約: *We've agreed to their offer on our house, subject to contract.* 我們接受了他們對房子的出價, 簽訂合約就成交了。**3** *informal* an agreement to kill a person for money【非正式】刺殺協議: *There is a contract out on him and he's in hiding.* 有人雇殺手殺他, 他就躲了起來。

con·tract² /kənˋtrækt; kənˈtrækt/ *v* **1** [I] to become smaller or narrower 縮小; 收縮; 縮短: *Metal contracts as it becomes cool.* 金屬冷卻時收縮。| *The economy continues to contract, raising fears of further political problems.* 經濟繼續緊縮, 進一步加劇了人們對未來政治問題的恐懼。—opposite 反義詞 EXPAND (1) **2** [T] *formal* to begin to have an illness【正式】感染〔疾病〕, 患〔病〕: *He contracted pneumonia.* 他得了肺炎。**3 contract to do sth** to sign a contract in which you agree formally that you will do something 簽合同做…: *They contracted to work fixed hours each week.* 他們訂立合同確定每個星期固定的工作時數。**4 contract a marriage/alliance etc** to agree formally that you will marry someone or have a particular kind of relationship with them 訂立婚約/盟約等: *Most of the marriages were contracted when the brides were very young.* 大部分的婚約是在新娘很年輕的時候訂立的。

contract in *phr v* [I] *formal especially BrE* to agree or promise, especially officially, to take part in something【正式, 尤英】同意參與; 訂約加入: *They contracted in to the share deal.* 他們同意參與股份交易。

contract out *phr v* **1** [T **contract** sth ↔ **out**] to arrange to have a job done by a person or company outside your own organization 把〔工作等〕承包出去: *The company has contracted the catering out to an outside firm.* 這家公司已經把承辦酒席包給了外面的一家公司。**2** [I] [+of] *formal especially BrE* to agree or promise, especially officially, not to take part in something such as a PENSION SCHEME【正式, 尤英】同意不加入〔退休金計劃等〕

contract bridge /,·· ˈ·/ *n* [U] a form of the card game BRIDGE¹ (4), in which one of the two pairs say how many tricks (TRICK (11)) they will try to win 定約橋牌

con·trac·tion /kənˋtrækʃən; kənˈtrækʃən/ *n* **1** [C] *technical* a very strong and painful movement of a muscle, especially of the muscles around the WOMB during the process of birth【術語】肌肉攣縮〔尤指分娩時子宮收縮〕**2** [U] the process of becoming smaller or narrower 收縮; 縮小; 縮短: *the contraction of metal as it cools* 金屬冷卻時的收縮 **3** [C] a shortened form of a word or words〔詞的〕縮約形式: *'Haven't' is a contraction of 'have not'.* haven't 是 have not 的縮約形式。

con·trac·tor /ˋkɑntræktɚ; kənˈtræktə/ *n* [C] a person or company that makes an agreement to do work or provide goods in large amounts for another company 承包者; 承包商: *a roofing contractor* 蓋屋頂的承包商

con·trac·tu·al /kənˋtræktʃuəl; kənˈtræktʃuəl/ *adj* agreed in a contract 合同規定的, 依據合同的: *College teachers have a contractual obligation to research and publish.* 大學教師依據合同有從事研究和發表作品的義務。—**contractually** *adv*

con·tra·dict /͵kɑntrəˋdɪkt; ͵kɒntrəˈdɪkt/ *v* **1** [T] to disagree with something by saying that it is wrong or not true, especially by saying that the opposite is true 反駁; 抗辯; 否認: **contradict sb** *Don't contradict your father!* 不要頂撞你的父親! | **flatly contradict** *The article flatly contradicts what the lobbyists have claimed.* 這篇文章與說客所宣稱的完全兩樣。**2** [T] if one statement, story etc contradicts another statement etc, the facts in it are different so that both statements cannot be true〔說法、真相等〕與…抵觸, 與…發生矛盾: *The witnesses' statements contradicted each other and the facts remained unclear.* 目擊者的說法各不相同, 事實還是不清楚。**3 contradict yourself** to say something that is the opposite of what you said before 自相矛盾: *The stupid fool can't speak two sentences without contradicting himself.* 這個愚蠢的傻瓜一說話就自相矛盾。

con·tra·dic·tion /͵kɑntrəˋdɪkʃən; ͵kɒntrəˈdɪkʃən/ *n* **1** [C] a difference between two statements, beliefs, or ideas about something that means they cannot both be true 矛盾的說法[信念、觀點]: *The prosecution pointed out the contradictions in the defendant's testimony.* 控方指出了被告證詞中自相矛盾的地方。| **[+between]** *There is a contradiction between the government's radical ideas and its actual urban policy.* 在政府的激進觀點和其實際的城市政策之間有矛盾。**2** [U] the act of saying that someone else's opinion, statement etc is wrong or not true 反駁, 否認: *You can say what you like without fear of contradiction.* 不要怕反駁, 說你想說的。**3 a contradiction in terms** a combination of words that seem to mean opposite things, so that the phrase has no clear meaning 用詞上的自相矛盾: *'Permanent revolution' is a contradiction in terms.* "不斷革命"是用詞上的自相矛盾。**4 in (direct) contradiction to** in a way that is opposite to a belief or statement 與…矛盾: *Your behavior is in direct contradiction to the principles you claim to have.* 你的行為與你所宣稱的原則互相矛盾。

con·tra·dic·to·ry /ˌkɑntrəˋdɪktərɪ; ˌkɒntrəˈdɪktəri◂/ *adj* two statements, beliefs etc that are contradictory, are different and therefore cannot both be true 矛盾的; 抵觸的: *The witnesses gave two completely contradictory accounts.* 目擊者給了兩份完全互相矛盾的證詞。—see also 另見 SELF-CONTRADICTORY

con·tra·dis·tinc·tion /ˌkɑntrədɪˋstɪŋkʃən; ˌkɒntrədɪˈstɪŋkʃən/ *n* [C] **in contradistinction to** *formal* as opposed to【正式】與…相區別; 與…相對比: *plants in contradistinction to animals* 有別於動物的植物

con·tra·flow /ˋkɑntrəflo; ˈkɒntrəfləʊ/ *n* [C,U] *BrE* a temporary arrangement on a large road by which traffic in both directions uses only one side of the road because the other side is being repaired【英】〔由於公路另一側修路而暫時實行的〕一側雙向行駛

con·trail /ˋkɑntrel; ˈkɒntreɪl/ *n* [C] *AmE* a line of white steam made in the sky by a plane【美】〔飛機在空中飛行留下的〕凝結尾流, 拉煙

con·tral·to /kənˋtrælto; kənˈtræltəʊ/ *n* [C] the lowest female singing voice, or a woman who has this voice 女低音(歌手)

con·trap·tion /kənˋtræpʃən; kənˈtræpʃən/ *n* [C] *informal* a strange looking piece of equipment or machinery, especially one that you think is unlikely to work well【非正式】奇妙的機械裝置; 怪模怪樣的玩意兒〔尤指不大可能正常工作的〕: *a funny old contraption for pumping up water* 抽水用的可笑的破舊玩意兒

con·tra·ri·wise /ˋkɑntrɛrɪˌwaɪz; ˈkɒntrəriwaɪz/ *adv old-fashioned* in the opposite way or direction; CONVERSE[3]【過時】反之, 相反地

con·tra·ry[1] /ˋkɑntrɛrɪ; ˈkɒntrəri/ *n formal*【正式】**1 on the contrary** used for showing that you disagree completely with what has just been said 正相反, 恰恰相反〔用於表示強烈不贊同別人剛說的話〕: *It wasn't a good thing; on the contrary it was a huge mistake.* 那不是件好事, 恰恰相反, 是個巨大的錯誤。**2 to the contrary** showing that the opposite is true 意思相反; 完全不同: *Unless there is evidence to the contrary, we ought to believe them.* 除非證據相反, 否則我們應該相信他們。**3 the contrary** the opposite of what has been said or suggested 相反; 反面; 對立面: *They say he is guilty, but I believe the contrary.* 他們說他有罪, 可我認為他無罪。

contrary[2] *adj* **1** contrary ideas or opinions are completely different from each other and opposed to each other 相反的, 相對的: *Two contrary views emerged in the discussion.* 討論中出現了兩個相反的意見。**2** someone who is contrary deliberately does things differently from the way that other people do them, or from the way that people expect 故意作對的, 對抗的: *Evans was his usual contrary self.* 埃文斯依然故我, 還是故意與人作對。**3 contrary to** if something is contrary to someone's belief or opinion, it is true even though that person believes or thinks the opposite 與…相反〔用於表示與別人觀點相反的事實〕: *Contrary to popular belief the desert can be a beautiful place.* 正好與人們想像的相反, 沙漠也可以是美麗的地方。**4** *formal* contrary weather conditions are ones that cause difficulties【正式】〔天氣〕不作美的, 不合人意的: *Contrary winds delayed the boats' return.* 逆風耽誤了船的歸航。—**contrariness** *n* [U]

2 **con·trast**[1] /ˋkɑntræst; ˈkɒntrɑːst/ *n* **1** [C,U] a difference between people, ideas, or things etc that are compared 差異, 差別: **[+between]** *The contrast between the two sisters surprised him.* 兩姐妹的差別讓他大吃一驚。**2 in contrast/by contrast** used when you are comparing objects or situations and saying that they are completely different from each other 與…相反/相比之下: *Their old house had been large and spacious; by contrast the new London flat seemed cramped and dark.* 他們的老房子又大又寬敞, 相比之下, 倫敦的那套新公寓又窄又暗。| **in contrast to** *Mary was short and plump, in contrast to her mother who was tall and willowy.* 瑪麗又矮又胖, 與她媽媽的修長苗條形成對比。| **in sharp/marked/stark etc contrast to** *The foreign visitors were wealthy and glamorous, in complete contrast to the poverty-stricken locals.* 外國遊客的富有和魅力與當地人的貧困形成鮮明的對比。**3** [C] something that is very different from something else 對照物, 明顯的對比物: **[+to]** *The blue skies of the holiday brochure were such a contrast to this dreary rain-sodden March day.* 宣傳度假的小冊上的藍天與這陰雨連綿的三月天構成明顯的對比。**4** [U] the differences in colour, or between light and dark, used in paintings or photographs for artistic effect〔繪畫、照片中顏色、明暗的〕反差: *The artist has used contrast marvelously in his paintings.* 這個藝術家在他的繪畫中巧妙地運用了顏色的反差。**5** [U] the degree of difference between the light and dark parts of a television picture〔電視畫面的〕對比度, 襯度: *Can you adjust the contrast please?* 請你調整一下對比度好嗎?

con·trast[2] /kənˋtræst; kənˈtrɑːst/ *v* **1** [T] to compare two things, ideas, people etc to show how different they are from each other 使成對比, 使成對照: **contrast sth with sth** *In the film, the peaceful life of a farmer is contrasted with the violent existence of a gangster.* 電影中, 農夫平靜的生活與歹徒的打打殺殺形成對比。**2** [I] if two things contrast, the difference between them is very easy to see and is sometimes surprising 形成對照; 對比之下現出區別: **[+with]** *The snow was icy and white, contrasting with the brilliant blue sky.* 雪既冰且白, 與明亮的藍天形成對照。| **contrast sharply/strikingly with** (=be extremely different from) 與…截然不同 *These results contrast sharply with other medical tests carried out in Australia.* 這些結果與在澳大利亞進行的其他醫療檢測的結果截然不同。

con·tras·ting /kənˋtræstɪŋ; kənˈtrɑːstɪŋ/ *adj* two or more things that are contrasting are different from each other, especially in a way that is interesting or attractive 對比的, 對照的(尤指耐人尋味的、漂亮的): *a blue shirt with a contrasting collar* 有截然不同顏色領子的藍襯衫

con·tra·vene /ˌkɑntrəˋvin; ˌkɒntrəˈviːn/ *v* [T] *formal* to do something that is not allowed according to a law or rule【正式】與…相抵觸, 違背〔法律、法規〕: *Milk from an unhealthy cow may contravene public health regulations.* 不健康奶牛產的奶會違反公共衛生規定。

con·tra·ven·tion /ˌkɑntrəˋvɛnʃən; ˌkɒntrəˈvenʃən/ *n* **1** [C,U] the act of doing something that is not allowed by a law or rule 抵觸, 違反: *Sending the troops was a contravention of the treaty.* 派遣軍隊違反條約。**2 in contravention of** in a way that is not allowed by a law or rule 與〔法律、規定等〕抵觸, 與…相違: *They employed minors in contravention of the law.* 他們違法雇傭未成年人。

con·tre·temps /ˋkɑntrətɑn; ˈkɒntrətɒŋ/ *n plural* contretemps [C] *French often humorous*【法, 常幽默】**1** an argument 爭論: *I had a little contretemps with Mr Willard on the phone.* 我與威拉德先生在電話裡發生了一點爭論。**2** an unlucky and unexpected event, especially an embarrassing one 不幸的意外事; 令人窘困的意外事

con·trib·ute /kənˋtrɪbjut; kənˈtrɪbjuːt/ *v* **1** [I,T] to give money, help, ideas etc to something that a lot of other people are also involved in 捐獻; 捐助; 出一分錢; 出一分力: **contribute to/towards sth** *Most people contributed something towards the new church buildings.* 大部分人都為教堂的新建築捐獻了點錢。| **contribute sth to/towards sth** *The volunteers contribute huge amounts of their own time to the project.* 自願者把自己大量的時間花在這個計劃上。**2 contribute to sth** to help to cause something 對某事起促成作用: *Various factors contributed to his downfall.* 各種因素促成了他的倒台。**3** [I,T] to write articles, stories, poems etc for a newspaper or magazine〔給報紙、雜誌等〕撰稿; 投稿: *one of several authors contributing to the book* 為這本書撰稿的作者之一

con·tri·bu·tion /ˌkɑntrəˋbjuʃən; ˌkɒntrɪˈbjuːʃən/ *n* **1** [C] something that you give or do in order to help something be successful 捐獻物; 貢獻物: **[+to/towards]** *Einstein was awarded the Nobel Prize for his contribution to Quantum Theory.* 愛因斯坦因對量子論的貢獻而被授予諾貝爾獎。| **make a contribution** *Day centres for the elderly make a valuable contribution to the overall service.* 照顧老人的日託所為整個服務事業作出可貴的貢獻。**2** [C] an amount of money that you give in order to help pay for something 捐款: **[+to/towards]** *We are asking for contributions to disaster relief.* 我們在為賑災募捐。| **make a contribution** *Would you like to make a contribution to the hospital rebuilding fund?* 你願為醫院重建基金捐錢嗎? **3** [C] a regular payment that you make to your employer or to the government to pay for benefits that you will receive when you are no longer working, for example a PENSION[1]〔保險金、養老金等的〕分攤額 **4** [C] a story, poem, or piece of writing that you write and that is printed in a magazine or newspaper 投送的稿件: *This week's issue has contributions from several well-respected journalists.* 本期週刊有幾篇德高望重的新聞記者的文章。**5** [U] the act of giving money, time, help etc 捐獻: *All the money has been raised by voluntary contribution.* 所有這些錢都是靠自願捐獻籌措的。

con·trib·u·tor /kənˋtrɪbjətɚ; kənˈtrɪbjʊtə/ *n* [C] **1** someone who writes a story, article etc that is printed in a magazine or newspaper 撰稿人, 投稿人: **[+to]** *I became a regular contributor to the paper, writing film reviews.* 我成了這份報紙的定期撰稿人, 寫電影評論。**2** someone who gives money, help, ideas etc to something that a lot of other people are also involved in 捐款人; 捐助人; 做出貢獻的人: **[+to]** *Dr Win was a major contributor to the research.* 溫博士是這項研究的主要捐款人。**3** *formal* someone or something that helps to cause something to happen【正式】導致某事的人[事]; 起作用的人[因素]: **[+to]** *Order and quiet are important contributors to a good learning environment.* 安靜有序是良好的學習環境的重要因素。

con·trib·u·to·ry /kənˋtrɪbjəˌtɔri; kənˈtrɪbjʊtəri/ *adj* **1** [only before noun 僅用於名詞前] being one of the causes of a particular result 導致…: *Smoking is a contributory cause of lung cancer.* 抽煙是導致肺癌的一個因素。**2** a contributory PENSION[1] or insurance plan is one that is paid for by the workers as well as by the company〔退休金計劃、保險金計劃〕由雇主與雇員共同出錢的 —opposite 反義詞 NONCONTRIBUTORY

contributory neg·li·gence /·ˌ···ˈ···/ *n* [U] *law* failure to take enough care to avoid or prevent an accident, so that you are partly responsible for any loss or damage caused【法律】共同過失〔由於過失造成事故, 因此應承擔部分責任〕

con trick /ˈ··/ *n* [C] a CONFIDENCE TRICK 詐騙

con·trite /ˋkɑntraɪt; ˈkɒntraɪt/ *adj* feeling guilty and sorry for something bad that you have done 悔罪的, 悔悟的, 痛悔的: *her contrite expression* 她懊悔的表情 —**contritely** *adv* —**contrition** /kənˋtrɪʃən; kənˈtrɪʃən/ *n* [U]

con·triv·ance /kənˋtraɪvəns; kənˈtraɪvəns/ *n* **1** [C,U] a clever plan to get something for yourself by deceiving someone, or the practice of doing this 計謀; 詭計: *Their story was a clumsy contrivance to persuade me to help them.* 他們的故事是一個蹩腳的詭計, 想說服我幫助他們。**2** [C] a machine or piece of equipment that has been made or invented for a special purpose 發明物, 新裝置: *a steam-driven contrivance used in 19th century clothing factories* 19 世紀製衣廠使用的蒸汽動力裝置

con·trive /kənˋtraɪv; kənˈtraɪv/ *v* [T] **1** to arrange an event or situation in a clever way, especially secretly or by deceiving people 謀劃, 策劃: *He managed to contrive a meeting between Janet and her ex-boyfriend.* 他設法策劃珍妮特與她以前的男朋友相會。**2** *formal* to succeed in doing something in spite of difficulties【正式】設法做到: **contrive to do sth** *She didn't speak any English, but we contrived to communicate using sign language.* 她一點英語也不會說, 但是我們設法用手勢來交流。**3** to make or invent something in a clever way, especially because you need it suddenly〔尤指由於突然的需要而〕造出; 想出; 發明; 設計: *Peter had contrived a tolerable substitute for our sled.* 彼得拼湊了一種過得去的裝置來代替我們的雪橇。

con·trived /kənˋtraɪvd; kənˈtraɪvd/ *adj* a story, situation etc that is contrived has been written or arranged in a way that seems false and not natural〔故事、情節等〕不自然的; 勉強的: *The film had a ridiculously contrived story line.* 這部電影的故事情節荒謬且牽強。

con·trol[1] /kənˋtrol; kənˈtrəʊl/ *n*

1 ►MAKE SB/STH DO WHAT YOU WANT 控制某人/物◄ [U] the ability or power to make someone or something do what you want 掌握; 控制; 支配; 管理; 抑制: *Generally your driving's OK, but your clutch control isn't very good.* 總的來說你的駕駛還是可以的, 但是你對離合器的控制不是很好。| **[+of/over]** *Babies are born with very little control over their movements.* 嬰兒先天的控制運動能力很差。| **have control of/over** *I prefer living alone because I feel I have more control over my life.* 我寧願一個人生活, 因為我覺得這樣更能支配自己的生活。| **under control** (=being controlled or dealt with successfully) 在控制之中 *Don't worry, everything's under control.* 不要擔心, 一切都在控制之中。| **out of control** (=no longer possible to be controlled) 不受控制, 不受支配 *The car spun out of control and hit a tree.* 汽車失去控制, 撞在了一棵樹上。| **get out of control** (=become impossible to control) 失去控制 *The street party went on, getting louder and louder and more out of control.* 街頭聚會還在繼續, 聲音越來越大而且更加失控。| **lose control (of)** (=not be able to control something any longer) 失去 (對…的) 控制 *He took a corner too fast, and lost control of the car.* 他轉彎太急了, 汽車失去了控制。| **beyond/outside sb's control** (=impossible for you to control) 無法/不受控制 *Ten people had been killed, and it was obvious that the situation had gotten beyond the control of the authorities.* 已經有十個人被殺了, 很明顯, 當局已經控制不住局勢了。| **take/gain control (of)** (=gain the ability to control something) 得到/取得〔對…的〕控制 *Students are encouraged to take control of their own learning, rather than just depending on the teacher.* 學生被鼓勵要自己掌握學習, 而不只是依靠老師。| **circumstances beyond sb's control** (=a situation that you cannot control) 不受控制的情況 *Tonight's performance has been cancelled due to circumstances beyond our control.* 今晚的演出取消了, 事非得已。

2 ►POLITICAL/MILITARY POWER 政治/軍事權力◄ [U] the power to rule or govern a place, or the fact that you have more power than other political parties 統治; 管理; 管制: **have control of/over** *By the end of the year, the rebels had control of the northern territories.* 到年底, 叛亂分子已經控制了北部的領土。| **gain/take control (of)** (=get control of a place that someone else was controlling) 取得控制… *When the communists gained control they abolished the monarchy.* 共產黨取得政權後取消了君主制。| **lose control** (=not be able to control a place any longer) 失去控制 *The Democrats have just lost control of Congress.* 民主黨人失去了在國會的主導地位。| **be/come under sb's control** *The whole of this area came under Soviet control.* 整個地區都在蘇聯的統治之下。| **under the control of** (=being controlled by a political party etc) 受…的控制[支配] *The* *government has been overthrown and the country is now under the control of the military.* 政府被推翻了，現在整個國家都在軍隊的控制之下。| **under British/Communist/enemy control** *The city is now under Serbian control.* 這個城市現在在塞爾維亞人的控制之下。| **regain control** (=gain control after you had lost it) 重獲支配權 *The Conservatives are hoping to regain control of the seats taken from them in the last election.* 保守黨人希望重新獲得在上次選舉中失去的席位。| **have overall control** *BrE* (=have more members of your political party in a council than other parties have, so that you control the council)【英】〔在議會中〕佔多數席位，佔支配地位 | **assume control** (=get control of a country by defeating the government using military power)〔用軍隊〕取得政權 *Lij Iyasu seized the palace and assumed control of the country.* 利傑·伊亞速攻佔了皇宮並且控制了該國。

3 ►WAY OF LIMITING STH 限制措施◄ [C,U] a method or law for limiting the amount or growth of something 管制（措施）: **[+of]** *the control of inflation* 通貨膨脹的抑制 | *control of pests and diseases* 害蟲和疾病控制 | **[+on]** *The authorities imposed strict controls on the movement of cattle.* 當局對牛的運送進行了嚴格的控制措施。| **arms control** (=control of the amount of weapons a country has) 軍備控制 *An arms control agreement between the superpowers has just been announced.* 兩個超級大國之間剛剛簽訂了軍備控制協議。| **crowd control** *Crowd control is a problem for the police at these demonstrations.* 對警察來講，在這些示威遊行中控制人羣是個難題。| **tight/rigid controls** (=strict controls) 嚴格的管制 *The government favours the introduction of tighter controls on immigration.* 政府贊同對移民進行更加嚴格的管制。| **rent/price/wage etc controls** *Rent controls ensured that no one paid too much for housing.* 租金管制保證沒有人會付太高的房租。

4 ►DISEASE/FIRE ETC 疾病/火等◄ [U] the ability to stop something dangerous from getting worse or affecting more people〔對危險物的〕抑制，控制: **have sth under control** *Firefighters now have the blaze under control.* 消防隊員已經使火勢得到了控制。| **bring sth under control** *The plant was given six months to bring the pollution under control.* 給工廠六個月時間控制污染。| **keep sth under control** *Johnson's been struggling for years to keep his drinking under control.* 約翰遜多年來一直在努力控制自己的飲酒量。

5 ►ABILITY TO CONTROL EMOTIONS 情感克制力◄ [U] the ability to remain calm even when you feel very angry, upset, or excited 克制: *It took a lot of control, but she managed not to cry.* 那需要很大的克制力，但是她終於沒哭出來。| **lose control** (=become extremely angry or upset and not be able to control your behaviour)〔感情〕失去控制 *Jim made me so mad, I just lost control and hit him.* 詹姆讓我非常生氣，我失去控制打了他。| **self-control** (=the ability to behave calmly even when you feel very upset, angry etc) 自我克制 | **regain control** (=succeed in behaving calmly again after you have been upset or angry) 重新平靜下來 *She felt tears welling up inside her again, but she managed to regain control.* 她又感到要流淚但是她盡量重新平靜下來。

6 be in control a) to be able to control a situation, organization, or area because you have more power than anyone else 控制着〔局勢、組織或地區〕: **[+of]** *The anti-government forces are still in control of the area.* 反政府勢力現在仍控制着該地區。**b)** to be able to control your emotions, deal with problems, and organize your life well 克制住〔感情〕: *Weber's one of those guys who always seems to be in control.* 韋伯是一個彷彿總能控制住自己的人。**c)** to manage to control a difficult situation 控制了〔困難局面〕: **[+of]** *The police chief assured reporters that he was in control of events.* 警察總長向記者保證局面在他的控制之中。

7 ►COMPANY/ORGANIZATION 公司/組織◄ [U] the power to make all the important decisions in an organization or part of an organization 控制力；支配力: **take control (of)** *Anne Williams will take control of the research division on August 5th.* 安妮·威廉斯會在 8 月 5 日起管研究部。| **have control of** (=own a larger part of a company than other people so that you control that company)〔因擁有較多股本而〕控制〔公司〕 *The Johnson family has effective control of the company, owning almost 60% of the shares.* 約翰遜家族有效地控制那家公司，掌握近 60% 的股份。| **lose control (of)** (=not be able to control a company etc any longer) 失去（對…的）控制 *McAllister lost control of the company in 1988.* 麥克阿里斯特在 1988 年失去了對那家公司的控制權。| **under the control of** (=being controlled by someone) 在…的控制下 *The college was under the control of a group of trustees.* 這所大學在一羣理事的管理之下。

8 ►MACHINE/VEHICLE 機器/車輛◄ [C] the thing that you press or turn to make a machine, vehicle, television etc work〔機器、車輛、電視等的〕控制[操縱]裝置: *Who's got the control for the video?* 誰拿了錄像機的控制器? | *the volume control of a television set* 電視機的音量控制器 | **be at the controls** (=be controlling a vehicle or aircraft) 操縱；駕駛… *The co-pilot is at the controls.* 副駕駛員在操縱飛機。—see also 另見 REMOTE CONTROL

9 ►SKILL 技術◄ [U] the ability to make very skilful movements with a ball, pencil, tool etc 控球[運筆、使用工具等]的技巧: *Johnson passes with good control, over to Abdul-Jabber.* 莊遜非常熟練地傳給渣巴。

10 ►AIRCRAFT ETC 飛機等◄ [U] the people who direct an activity, especially by giving instructions to an aircraft or SPACECRAFT 指揮人員；操縱人員: *air-traffic control* 空中交通調度員

11 ►SCIENTIFIC TEST 科學測試◄ *technical*【術語】[C] **a)** a person, group etc against which you compare another person or group that is very similar, in order to see if a particular quality is caused by something or happens by chance 對照人[組]: **control group/population** *A control group of nonsmoking women were compared to four groups of women smokers.* 一個不抽煙婦女的對照組和四個抽煙婦女組進行了比較。**b)** a thing that you already know the result for that is used in a scientific test, in order to show that your method is working correctly 對照物 —see also 另見 CONTROLLED EXPERIMENT

12 ►COMPUTER 電腦◄ also 又作 **control key** [singular] a particular button on a computer that allows you to do certain operations 控制鍵: *Press control and F2 to exit.* 按控制鍵和 F2 退出來。

13 ►YOUR BODY 身體◄ the ability to control the movements of your body by using your muscles when dancing or doing physical exercise〔跳舞或體育鍛鍊時對身體的〕控制力

14 ►CHECKING SOMETHING 檢查某物◄ [U] the process of checking that something is correct, or the place where this is done 檢查；檢查站: *passport control* 護照檢查（站） | *stock control* 庫存管理 —see 見 BIOLOGICAL CONTROL, BIRTH CONTROL, QUALITY CONTROL, REMOTE CONTROL

control² *v* **controlled, controlling** [T] 

1 ►MAKE SB/STH DO WHAT YOU WANT 支配某人/某物◄ to make someone or something do what you want or behave in the way you want them to behave 支配；指揮；管理: *The teacher can't control the class.* 這老師管不住這個班。| *a huge company controlling half the world's coffee trade* 控制全球一半咖啡貿易的大公司

2 ►MACHINE/PROCESS/SYSTEM 機器/過程/系統◄ to make a machine, process, or system work in a particular way 控制；管理: *This button controls the temperature in the building.* 這個按鈕控制這座建築物內的溫度。| **control how/what/which etc** *The valves in the heart control how quickly the blood is pumped around the body.* 心臟的瓣膜掌管着血液輸送到身體各處的速度。

3 ►LIMIT 限制◄ if a government etc controls something, it uses laws or other methods to limit the amount or growth of something 管制; 管束: *Development in areas of outstanding natural beauty is strictly controlled.* 在風景區搞開發受到嚴格的限制。
4 ►POLITICAL/MILITARY POWER 政治/軍事權力◄ to rule or govern a place, or to have more power than other political parties 統治; 支配: *The Democrats continued to control the House until 1994.* 民主黨人對眾議院的控制一直持續到1994年。| **Labour/Republican/Democrat controlled** *a Conservative-controlled council* 由保守黨人控制的地方議會
5 ►DISEASE/FIRE ETC 疾病/火等◄ to stop something dangerous from getting worse or affecting more people 抑制, 控制〔危險物〕: *The Ministry of Health has set up a programme to control the spread of AIDS.* 衛生部已經制定了一套抑制愛滋病傳播的計劃。
6 ►EMOTION 情緒◄ if you control your emotions, you succeed in behaving calmly and sensibly, even though you feel angry, upset, or excited 克制, 自制: *Sarah just can't control her temper.* 莎拉根本控制不了自己的脾氣。| **control yourself** (=succeed in behaving calmly and sensibly, even though you feel angry etc) 自我克制 *She annoyed me intensely, but I managed to control myself and remain polite.* 她使我非常煩, 但是我盡量克制自己並保持禮貌。
7 ►VOICE/EXPRESSION 聲音/表情◄ if you control your voice or the expression on your face, you make it seem normal, so that people cannot see that you are upset, angry, or excited 控制〔嗓音或表情, 以免表露情緒〕: *He controlled his voice, betraying nothing but a casual interest.* 他控制着嗓音, 只表現出泛泛的興趣。
8 ►ANIMALS 動物◄ to kill animals when there are so many of them that they cause problems 節制, 調節〔動物數量〕: *measures to control rats in the city's sewers* 節制城市下水道中老鼠數量的措施
9 ►BUSINESSES/ORGANIZATIONS 企業/組織◄ to make sure that something is done correctly 確保, 保證: *The company strictly controls the quality of its products.* 這家公司嚴格控制其產品的質量。

USAGE NOTE 用法説明: CONTROL
WORD CHOICE 詞語辨析: **control, manage, run, be in charge of, check on, inspect, monitor**
Most meanings of **control** *(n,v)* involve the idea of a person or other force having the power to change or stop something, without the people or things affected being able to do anything about it. People, organizations, machines etc **control** other people, organizations, their own or other's actions, events, etc, sometimes from far away. control 的大部分意思包含一個人或別的力量有能力改變或制止某事, 而被影響的人或物對此則無能為力。control 的主體是人、組織、機器等, 對象有時遠在別處, 包括其他人、組織、主體自己或別人的行動、事件等。
Where you want to give the idea of people directing businesses etc, where the other people involved are nearby and perhaps allowed some say in the activity, you may use **manage**, **run**, or **be in charge of**. 指人管理商業等, 被管理的人就在附近而且或許有發言權, 可以用 manage, run 或 be in charge of: *He's managing/running an electrical shop/project group/rock band.* 他經營一家電器商店/管理一個項目組/領導一個搖滾樂隊。| *Margaret is in charge of the school while Mrs Williams is away.* 威廉斯太太不在的時候瑪格麗特掌管學校。
When you want to talk about people, things, or activities, in order to see if they are correct, but without directly affecting them, you may use **check on** or **inspect**. 談論人、事物或活動, 想要知道他們是不是正確, 但是不直接影響他們, 可以用 check on 或 inspect: *We need to check on our sales.* 我們需要檢查我們的銷售額。| *The department is going to be inspected next week.* 這個部門下個星期要接受檢查。| *a security check* 安全檢查。**Control** means the same as **check on** only in a few contexts, and usually only as the noun. control 與 check on 只在少數上下文中的意思一樣, 而且通常只用作名詞: *quality control* 質量檢查 | *stock control* 庫存管理
Monitor is a word meaning to watch and check on someone or something over a period of time. This can be done by a person or by a machine, often in a technical or official context. monitor 的意思是在一段時期中觀察並檢查某人或某物。這可以由人或機器來完成, 通常用在技術性或正式的環境中。

control key /-ˈ· ·/ *n* [C] a particular button on a computer that allows you to do certain operations〔電腦的〕控制鍵
con·trol·la·ble /kənˋtroləbl̩; kənˈtrəʊləbəl/ *adj* possible to be controlled 可管理的, 可操縱的, 可控制的: *Central heating makes the temperature of your home easily controllable.* 中央供暖系統使家中的溫度可輕易控制。
con·trolled /kənˋtrold; kənˈtrəʊld/ *adj* **1** calm and not showing emotion, even if you feel angry, afraid etc 自制的, 克制的: *Her voice was resonant and controlled as she delivered her resignation speech.* 當她在作辭職演講時聲音洪亮而且是克制的。**2** a movement, action, situation etc that is controlled is one that is carefully and deliberately done in a particular way, or made to have particular qualities 受控制的; 受限制的: *The chicks are hatched in a controlled environment.* 小雞是在一個受控制的環境中孵化的。**3** limited by a law or rule 受法律[規則]管制的: *controlled parking zones* 受管制的停車區
controlled drug /·,· ˈ·/ *n* [C] *law* a drug that is illegal to possess or use【法律】管制藥物
controlled ex·per·i·ment /·,· ·ˈ···/ *n* [C] *technical* a scientific test done in a place where you can control all the things that might affect the test【術語】受控試驗, 控制性試驗: *a controlled experiment to determine the effects of light and nutrients on plant growth* 確定光線及各種營養素對植物生長產生的影響的控制性試驗
controlled sub·stance /·,· ˈ··/ *n* [C] *law* a drug that is illegal to possess or use【法律】管制藥物: *Heroin is a controlled substance.* 海洛因是一種管制藥物。
con·trol·ler /kənˋtrolɚ; kənˈtrəʊlə/ *n* [C] **1** someone who is in charge of a particular organization or part of an organization 控制者; 管理者; 指揮者: *the Controller of Channel 4* 第4頻道的管理者 **2** also 又作 **comptroller** *formal* someone who is in charge of the money received or paid out by a company or government department【正式】審計員; 審計官
controlling in·terest /·,·· ˈ··/ *n* [C usually singular 一般用單數] *technical* if you have a controlling interest in a company, you own enough shares (SHARE[2] (5)) to be able to make decisions about what happens to the company【術語】〔對一家公司的〕控股權益
control room /-ˈ· ·/ *n* [C] the room that a process, service, large machine, factory etc is controlled from 控制室
control tow·er /-ˈ· ,··/ *n* [C] a tall building in an airport from which people direct the movement of aircraft on the ground and in the air〔機場的〕控制塔
con·tro·ver·sial /ˌkɑntrəˋvɝʃəl; ˌkɒntrəˈvɜːʃəl◄/ *adj* causing a lot of disagreement, because many people have strong opinions about the subject being discussed 引起爭論的, 有爭議的: *Contraception is still a controversial issue in this part of the world.* 在該地區節育仍是個有爭議的問題。| **a controversial plan/decision etc** *a highly controversial plan to flood the valley in order to*

build a hydro-electric dam 一個為了建水電站而要淹沒山谷的有很大爭議的計劃 | **a controversial figure** (=someone who does things that are controversial) 有爭議的人物 *Maxwell soon became a controversial figure in the world of big business.* 馬克斯韋爾很快就在大企業界成為一個有爭議的人物。—**controversially** *adv*

con·tro·ver·sy /ˋkɑntrəˌvɝsɪ; ˈkɒntrəvɜːsi/ *n* [C,U] a serious argument or disagreement, especially about something such as a plan or decision, that continues for a long time 爭論; 辯論; 爭議: *The proposals to reduce the strength of the army have been the subject of much controversy.* 削減軍隊力量的提議已經招來很多爭議。| *a political controversy* 政治爭論 | **[+over/about/surrounding]** *the controversy surrounding the nuclear energy program* 圍繞核能項目的爭論

con·tu·ma·cious /ˌkɑntjuˋmeʃəs; ˌkɒntjʊˈmeɪʃəs◂/ *adj formal* unreasonably disobedient【正式】拒不服從的 —**contumaciously** *adv*

con·tume·ly /kənˋtuməlɪ; ˈkɒntjuːmli/ *n* [C,U] disrespectful and offensive behaviour or language 謾罵; 傲慢的行為; 侮辱行為

con·tuse /kənˋtuz; kənˈtjuːz/ *v* [T] *technical* to BRUISE[2] 【術語】挫傷

con·tu·sion /kənˋtjuʒən; kənˈtjuːʒən/ *n* [C,U] *technical* a BRUISE[1] or BRUISING【術語】挫傷

co·nun·drum /kəˋnʌndrəm; kəˈnʌndrəm/ *n* [C] **1** a confusing and difficult problem 難題; 複雜問題: *I don't know the answer – it's a conundrum.* 我不知道答案, 這是個難題。**2** a trick question asked for fun; RIDDLE[1] (1) 謎語

con·ur·ba·tion /ˌkɑnɚˋbeʃən; ˌkɒnɜːˈbeɪʃən/ *n* [C] a group of towns that have spread and joined together to form an area with a high population, often with a large city as its centre〔由中心大城市及衛星城鎮構成的〕集合城市, 大都市圈: *urban conurbations on the west coast* 西海岸的集合城市

con·va·lesce /ˌkɑnvəˋlɛs; ˌkɒnvəˈles/ *v* [I] to spend time getting well after an illness 病後療養; 康復: *After her operation my wife was sent abroad to convalesce.* 我妻子手術後被送到國外去療養。

con·va·les·cence /ˌkɑnvəˋlɛsn̩s; ˌkɒnvəˈlesəns/ *n* [singular] the length of time a person spends getting well after an illness〔病後的〕康復期, 恢復期: *a long and painful convalescence* 漫長而且痛苦的恢復期

con·va·les·cent /ˌkɑnvəˋlɛsn̩t; ˌkɒnvəˈlesənt◂/ *n* [C] a person spending time getting well after an illness 康復期病人 —**convalescent** *adj*: *a convalescent nursing home* 康復期病人護理療養院

con·vect /kənˋvɛkt; kənˈvekt/ *v* [I] *technical* to move heat by convection【術語】對流傳熱

con·vec·tion /kənˋvɛkʃən; kənˈvekʃən/ *n* [U] the movement in a gas or liquid caused by warm gas or liquid rising, and cold gas or liquid sinking〔氣體、液體的〕對流: *Warm air rises by convection.* 熱空氣依靠對流作用上升。

convection ov·en /·ˈ·· ˌ··/ *n* [C] a special OVEN that makes hot air move around inside it so that all the parts of the food get the same amount of heat 對流烤箱

con·vec·tor /kənˋvɛktɚ; kənˈvektə/ also 又作 **convector hea·ter** /·ˈ·· ˌ··/ *n* [C] an electrical heater that uses hot air 對流加熱器

con·vene /kənˋvin; kənˈviːn/ *v* [I,T] *formal* if a group of people convene, or someone convenes them, they come together, especially for a formal meeting【正式】聚集, 集合; 開會: *The President's foreign policy advisers convened for an emergency session.* 總統的外交政策顧問們召開緊急會議。| *Shouldn't we convene a meeting about this?* 我們不應當為此事召集一個會議嗎?

con·ve·ni·ence /kənˋvinjəns; kənˈviːniəns/ *n* **1** [U] the quality of being suitable for a particular purpose, especially because it is easy to use or saves you time 方便, 便利; 合宜: *Many women prefer the convenience of working at home while their children are small.* 很多婦女在她們的孩子還小的時候寧可在家裡工作, 因為這樣比較方便。| **for convenience** *We bought this house for convenience; it's near the shops and the railway station.* 為了方便起見我們買了這座房子, 它靠近商店和火車站。**2** [U] what is easiest and best for a particular person〔個人的〕便利; 自在, 舒適: **for sb's convenience** *I'm not going to organize my day entirely for your convenience!* 我不打算完全為了你的方便而安排我的時間! | **suit sb's convenience** *We can call at your home at any time to suit your convenience.* 我們可以在你方便的任何時候去你家。| **at sb's convenience** (=at a time that is best and easiest for someone) 在某人方便的時候 *Meetings are always arranged at the management's convenience and staff are expected to fit in.* 會議總是安排在管理人員最方便的時候, 希望員工去配合。**3 at your earliest convenience** *formal* as soon as possible; usually in letters【正式】儘快〔常用於書信〕: *We should be grateful if you would reply at your earliest convenience.* 盼早日回覆, 非常感謝! **4** [C] something that is useful because it saves you time or means that you have less work to do 便利措施; 帶來方便的裝置: *The supermarket offers a bag-packing service, as a convenience to customers.* 為方便顧客, 這家超市提供袋裝服務。**5** also 又作 **public convenience** [C usually plural 一般用複數] *formal* a public toilet【正式】公共廁所 **6 a marriage of convenience** a marriage that has been agreed for a particular purpose, not because the two people love each other 基於利害關係的婚姻: *In the past most royal marriages were marriages of convenience, arranged for political reasons.* 過去大部分的皇室婚姻是基於政治原因的婚姻。

convenience food /·ˈ··· ˌ·/ also 又作 **convenience foods** *n* [C,U] food that is frozen, or in tins, packages etc, and can be prepared quickly and easily 方便食品〈如速凍食品、罐裝食品等〉: *People with busy lifestyles tend to rely more and more on convenience foods.* 生活節奏快的人越來越傾向於吃方便食品。

convenience store /·ˈ··· ˌ·/ *n* [C] *AmE* a shop where you can buy food, alcohol, magazines etc, that is often open 24 hours each day【美】便民店, 便利店 —see also 另見 CORNER SHOP

con·ve·ni·ent /kənˋvinjənt; kənˈviːniənt/ *adj* **1** helpful for you because it saves you time or does not spoil your plans or cause you problems 方便的; 便利的; 合宜的: *I find going to the supermarket once a month the most convenient way to shop.* 我發現一個月去一次超級市場購物最合適。| **convenient for sb** *Is three o'clock convenient for you?* 三點鐘你方便嗎? | **convenient time/moment** *I'm afraid this isn't a very convenient time – could you call back later?* 我想現在不是很合適, 你能稍後再打電話來嗎? **2** near and easy to reach 附近的; 方便的: *The bus stop around the corner is probably the most convenient.* 拐角處的公共汽車站可能是最方便的了。| **convenient for sth** *Our house is very convenient for schools and stores.* 我們的房子離學校和商店很近。—opposite 反義詞 INCONVENIENT 3

con·ve·ni·ent·ly /kənˋvinjəntlɪ; kənˈviːniəntli/ *adv* **1** in a way that is helpful for you because it saves you time or does not spoil your plans or cause you problems 方便地; 便利地; 合宜地: *The results can be summarized conveniently in the following table.* 在接下來的圖表中, 結果可以很容易地被總結出來。**2** in a place that is near or easily reached 近便; 便利: *The hotel is conveniently situated near the airport.* 這家酒店坐落在機場附近。**3** if someone has conveniently forgotten, ignored, lost etc something, they are pretending to have forgotten etc because this helps them to avoid doing something 故意〔忘記、不理會、丟失等〕: *Mary conveniently forgot that she had promised to help clean the kitchen.* 瑪麗故意忘記曾答應過要幫忙打掃廚房。

con·vent /ˋkɑnvɛnt; ˈkɒnvənt/ *n* [C] a building or set of buildings where NUNs live 女修道院 —see also 另見 CONVENT SCHOOL

con·ven·tion /kən`vɛnʃən; kən'venʃən/ *n* **1** [C,U] behaviour and attitudes that most people in a society consider to be normal and right 慣例; 常規; 習俗: *The handshake is a social convention.* 握手是一種社會習俗。| *She went against all convention and married outside her religion.* 她離經叛道, 與信其他宗教的人結了婚。| **by convention** *By convention, the bride's father gives her away at her wedding.* 按照習俗, 新娘的父親在婚禮上把她交給新郎。—see 見 HABIT (USAGE) **2** [C] a formal agreement, especially between countries, about particular rules or behaviour〔國際性的〕公約; 協定: *the European convention on human rights* 歐洲人權公約 —compare 比較 PACT, TREATY **3** [C] a large formal meeting for people who belong to the same profession or organization 大會, 會議: *a teacher's convention* 教師大會 **4** [C] a method or style often used in literature, art, the theatre etc to achieve a particular effect〔文學、藝術上的〕傳統手法: *The omniscient narrator is a convention of the nineteenth century novel.* 無所不知的敍述者是十九世紀小說採用的一種傳統手法。

con·ven·tion·al /kən`vɛnʃənḷ; kən'venʃənəl/ *adj* **1** [only before noun 僅用於名詞前] a conventional object or way of doing something is of a type that has been used or available for a long time and is considered the usual type 按慣例的; 因襲的; 傳統的: *The water purifying system fits neatly under a conventional sink unit.* 水淨化系統裝在傳統的水槽下面, 十分簡便。**2** always following the opinions and behaviour that most people in a society consider to be normal, right, and socially acceptable but sometimes slightly boring〔觀點、行為〕守舊的, 傳統的: *Her opinions are rather narrow and conventional.* 她的觀點相當狹窄而且守舊。| **[+in]** *John is fairly conventional in his tastes.* 約翰的趣味相當傳統。—opposite 反義詞 UNCONVENTIONAL **3 the conventional wisdom** the opinion that most people consider to be normal and right 公眾意見, 普遍看法: *This idea has become part of the conventional wisdom of a whole generation of educationalists.* 這個觀點已經成為一整代教育工作者的普遍看法的一部分。**4** [only before noun 僅用於名詞前] conventional weapons and wars are not NUCLEAR ones〔武器、戰爭〕常規的, 非核子的 **5 conventional medicine** the usual form of medicine practised in most European and North American countries; WESTERN MEDICINE 傳統的西方醫學 —**conventionally** *adv* —**conventionality** /kənˌvɛnʃən`æləti; kənˌvenʃə'nælǝti/ *n* [U]

conventional ov·en /·'··· ˌ··/ *n* [C] an ordinary OVEN, not a MICROWAVE¹(1) 普通烤箱〔非微波爐〕: *This will take 3 minutes in a microwave, or 25 minutes in a conventional oven.* 這在微波爐中要煮3分鐘, 在普通烤箱中要25分鐘。

convent school /'·· ˌ·/ *n* [C] a school for girls that is run by Roman Catholic NUNS〔由天主教會修女管理的〕女修道院學校

con·verge /kən`vɝdʒ; kən'vɜːdʒ/ *v* [I] **1** to come from different directions and meet at the same point 會合, 集中: *The two streams converge here to form a river.* 兩條溪流在這裡匯合成一條河。**2** if groups of people converge in a particular place, they come there from many different places and meet together to form a large crowd〔人羣〕聚集, 聚會, 匯集: **[+on]** *The two armies converged on the enemy capital.* 兩支軍隊在敵人的首都會師。**3** if different ideas or aims converge, they become the same〔觀點、目標〕趨同: *Here the two distinct theories converge.* 在這裡兩個完全不同的理論趨於一致。—opposite 反義詞 DIVERGE

con·ver·sant /kən`vɝsṇt; kən'vɜːsənt/ *adj* [not before noun 不用於名詞前] **1** *formal* having knowledge or experience of something【正式】熟悉的; 有經驗的: **[+with]** *Are you fully conversant with the facts of the case?* 你完全熟悉這個案件的情況嗎? **2** *AmE* able to hold a conversation in a foreign language, but not to be able to speak it perfectly【美】有某種外語的會話能力但不精通: **[+in]** *He's conversant in French but not really fluent.* 他會說法語但不是很流利。

con·ver·sa·tion /ˌkɑnvɚ`seʃən; ˌkɒnvə'seɪʃən/ *n* **1** [C] an informal talk in which people exchange news, feelings, and thoughts〔非正式的〕談話, 交談, 會話: *a telephone conversation* 電話交談 | *He stood silent in the doorway, unwilling to interrupt their conversation.* 他靜靜地站在門口, 不想打斷他們的談話。| **have/hold a conversation** *I had a long conversation with my brother on his birthday.* 我在弟弟的生日那天和他談了很久。| **carry on a conversation** (=have a conversation) 談話 *It's impossible to carry on a conversation with all this noise in the background.* 在這麼喧鬧的環境中談話是不可能的。| **turn a conversation to sth** (=begin talking about something) 開始談論某事 *The conversation turned to the subject of Sarah's new boyfriend.* 談話的主題轉到莎拉的新男友身上。**2** [U] informal talk in which people exchange news, feelings, and thoughts 會話, 談話: *the buzz of conversation* 談話的嗡嗡聲 | **make conversation** (=talk to someone in an informal way that actually needs some effort to think of what to say) 搭訕, 說應酬話 *I'm not very good at making polite conversation.* 我不太擅長說應酬話。| **be in conversation with** (=be talking to someone) 與…交談 *In today's programme, three well-known artists are in conversation with Jenny Murray.* 在今天的節目中, 有三位知名的藝術家要和珍妮·默里談話。**3 get into conversation** *especially BrE*【尤英】also 又作 **get into a conversation** *especially AmE*【尤美】to begin to talk to someone, especially someone you do not know 開始〔與陌生人〕交談: *I got into conversation with the bus driver today, and he told me that fares are going up again soon.* 我今天跟公共汽車司機攀談, 他告訴我車費不久又會漲價。

con·ver·sa·tion·al /ˌkɑnvɚ`seʃənḷ; ˌkɒnvə'seɪʃənəl◂/ *adj* **1** a conversational style, phrase etc is informal and commonly used in conversation〔風格、用語等〕會話(體)的, 談話式的: *Business letters are not usually written in conversational style.* 寫商業信件通常不用口語體。**2** concerning or relating to conversation 談話的, 會談的: *I go to evening classes to do conversational German.* 我去夜校學習德語口語。—**conversationally** *adv*

con·ver·sa·tion·al·ist /ˌkɑnvɚ`seʃənḷɪst; ˌkɒnvə'seɪʃənəlǝst/ *n* [C] someone whose conversation is intelligent, amusing, and interesting 健談者: *a good conversationalist* 善於談話的人

conversation piece /··'·· ˌ·/ *n* [C] something that provides a subject for conversation, often said in a joking way about objects that seem very strange or ugly 可作話題的東西, 談話題材

con·verse¹ /kən`vɝs; kən'vɜːs/ *v* [I] *formal* to talk informally, or to have a conversation【正式】談話, 交談: **[+with]** *It's difficult to converse rationally with people who hold extremist views.* 同持有過激觀點的人是難以理性地交談的。

con·verse² /`kɑnvɝs; 'kɒnvɜːs/ *n formal* **the converse** the converse of a fact, word, statement etc is the opposite of it【正式】反面的事實[詞、陳述]: *I think the converse of what you just said is true.* 我認為你剛才所說的對立面是正確的。

con·verse³ /kən`vɝs; 'kɒnvɜːs/ *adj formal* a converse opinion, belief, statement etc is the opposite opinion etc【正式】〔觀點、信仰、陳述等〕相反的: *I hold the converse opinion.* 我持相反的意見。

con·verse·ly /kən`vɝslɪ; kən'vɜːsli/ *adv formal* used when one situation is the opposite of another【正式】相反地; 另一方面: *$1 will buy 100 yen. Conversely, 100 yen will buy $1.* 1美元可以買100日元; 反過來說, 100日元能買1美元。

con·ver·sion /kən`vɝʒən; kən'vɜːʃən/ *n* [C,U] **1** the act or process of changing something from one form, purpose, or system to a different one 轉變; 轉化; 轉換; 換算: **[+into]** *The company buys raw material such as* *wool for conversion into cloth.* 這家公司買進羊毛等原材料生產成布料。| **[+of]** *The conversion of the old classrooms into a new library has greatly improved the school.* 舊教室改建成新圖書館大大改善了這所學校。| **[+to]** *The British conversion to the metric system took place in the 1970s.* 英國改用公制是在 20 世紀 70 年代。| **house conversion** (=the act or process of changing a large house into several apartments) 房屋改建 *a company that does house conversions* 從事房屋改建的公司 **2** an act of changing from one religion or belief to a different one 宗教的改變; 皈依; 歸附: **[+to]** *His sudden conversion to the anti-nuclear movement may make voters suspicious.* 他突然轉到反核運動一方, 可能會使選民生疑。| **[+from]** *Her conversion from the Protestant to the Catholic faith surprised many people.* 他從新教轉信羅馬天主教使很多人很吃驚。**3** a score that you can make in RUGBY football by kicking the ball over the top part of the GOAL (3) 〔橄欖球中將球踢過球門的橫木而獲得的〕附加得分

3 **con·vert¹** /kən`vɝt; kən'vɜːt/ *v* **1** [I,T] to change or make something change from one form, system, or purpose to a different one (使) 轉變; (使) 轉化; (使) 轉換: **convert sth to/into sth** *This is part of the process of converting iron into steel.* 這是把鐵煉成鋼的步驟的一部分。| **[+to]** *The whole office converted to a new computer system last year.* 去年, 整個辦公室換了一個新的電腦系統。| *Our house is a converted barn.* 我們的房子是由倉庫改造的。**2** [I] to be able to be changed from one object into another 可變為另一物體: **[+to/into]** *This sofa converts to a bed.* 這張沙發可以變成牀。| *I can't see how this plastic sheet converts into a tent.* 我不能相信這張塑料布是怎麼變成一頂帳篷的。**3** [I,T] to change or make someone change their opinion or habit (使) 改變意見〔習慣〕: **[+to]** *I've converted to decaffeinated coffee.* 我改飲不含咖啡因的咖啡。| **convert sb to sth** *My daughter has finally converted me to Guns n' Roses.* 我的女兒終於使我轉而喜歡〔重金屬搖滾樂隊〕"槍砲與玫瑰"。**4** [I,T] to change or make someone change from one religion or belief to another (使) 皈依: **[+to]** *Anne has converted to Islam recently.* 安妮最近皈依了伊斯蘭教。

con·vert² /`kɑnvɝt; 'kɒnvɜːt/ *n* [C] someone who has been persuaded to change their opinion and accept a particular religion or belief 皈依宗教者; 改變信仰者: *a convert to Christianity* 改信基督教的人

con·vert·er, convertor /kən`vɝtɚ; kən'vɜːtə/ *n* [C] a machine that changes the form of things, especially one that makes steel from melted iron 轉換器; 〔尤指煉鋼的〕轉爐

con·ver·ti·ble¹ /kən`vɝtəbḷ; kən'vɜːtɨbəl/ *adj* **1** an object that is convertible can be folded or arranged in a different way so that it can be used as something else 可轉換的, 可改變的: *They bought a convertible sofa-bed.* 他們買了一張摺疊式沙發牀。**2** money that is convertible can be exchanged for the money of another country 〔貨幣〕可兑換的 **3** a car that is convertible has a roof that you can fold back or remove 〔汽車〕開篷的: *a convertible sports car* 開篷跑車 **4** *technical* a financial document such as an insurance arrangement or BOND¹ (1) that is convertible can be changed, or exchanged for something else【術語】〔證券等〕可兑換的: *convertible life insurance policy* 可兑換的人壽保險單 —**convertibility** /kən,vɝtə`bɪlətɪ; kən,vɜːtɨ'bɪlɨti/ *n* [U]

convertible² *n* [C] a car with a soft roof that you can fold back or remove 開篷〔敞篷〕汽車 —compare 比較 HARDTOP —see also 另見 CABRIOLET

con·vex /,kɑn`vɛks; ,kɒn'veks◂/ *adj* curved outwards like the surface of the eye 凸出的; 凸面的: *a convex lens* 凸透鏡 | *a convex mirror* 凸鏡 —**convexly** *adv* —**convexity** /kən`vɛksətɪ; kən'veksɨti/ *n* [C,U] —opposite 反義詞 CONCAVE

con·vey /kən`ve; kən'veɪ/ *v* [T] **1** to express what you are thinking or feeling without stating it directly 傳達; 表達〔想法、感情〕: *His tone conveyed an unmistakable warning.* 他的語氣確定無疑地傳達出警告的意味。| *Jan's office conveyed an impression of efficiency and seriousness.* 簡的辦公室給人留下高效和莊重的印象。**2** to communicate information or a message 傳遞〔信息〕; 傳送; 傳播: *All this information can be conveyed in a simple diagram.* 所有這些信息可以通過簡單的圖表來傳達。| *Please convey my best wishes to her.* 請代我向她表示最好的祝願。**3** *formal* to take or carry something from one place to another【正式】傳送〔物件〕; 輸送; 運送: *Your luggage will be conveyed to the hotel by taxi.* 你的行李將由出租車送到酒店。**4** *law* to legally change the possession of property from one person to another【法律】把〔財產〕讓與; 轉讓

C

con·vey·ance /kən`veəns; kən'veɪəns/ *n* **1** [C] *formal* a vehicle【正式】運輸工具; 交通工具: *There was no conveyance available, so we were obliged to walk.* 找不到交通工具了, 我們不得不行走。**2** [U] *formal* the act of taking something from one place to another【正式】傳送; 運送 **3** [C] *law* a legal document that gives land, property etc from one person to another【法律】產權轉讓證書

con·vey·anc·ing /kən`veənsɪŋ; kən'veɪənsɪŋ/ *n* [U] *law* the work done, usually by a lawyer, to change the possession of property, especially a house, from one person to another【法律】財產〔尤指房子〕轉讓的法律手續

con·vey·or, conveyer /kən`veɚ; kən'veɪə/ *n* [C] **1** a person or thing that carries or communicates something 運送者; 傳達者; 運輸裝置: *the conveyer of good news* 好消息的傳送者 **2** a conveyor belt 傳送帶

conveyor belt /·'·· ·/ *n* [C] a long continuous moving band of rubber, cloth, or metal, used for moving goods or partly finished products from one place to another in a factory, or bags from one place to another in an airport 傳送帶, 輸送帶

con·vict¹ /kən`vɪkt; kən'vɪkt/ *v* [T] to prove or officially announce that someone is guilty of a crime after a TRIAL¹ (1) in a law court 證明〔宣判〕…有罪: **be convicted of sth** *Buxton was convicted of rape.* 巴克斯頓被判犯強姦罪。| *a convicted murderer* 被判有罪的謀殺犯 —opposite 反義詞 ACQUIT

con·vict² /`kɑnvɪkt; 'kɒnvɪkt/ *n* [C] someone who has been proved to be guilty of a crime and sent to prison 已決犯; 囚犯: *There was a report on the news about an escaped convict.* 有一則關於越獄犯的新聞報道。

con·vic·tion /kən`vɪkʃən; kən'vɪkʃən/ *n* **1** [C] a very strong belief or opinion 堅定的信仰〔主張〕: *a woman of strong political convictions* 一位有堅定政治信仰的婦女 **2** [U] the feeling of being sure about something and having no doubts 深信, 堅信: *The speech lacked style and conviction.* 這篇演講缺乏風格和説服力。| *"Maybe it was all a mistake," said Tom, without conviction.* "或許那完全是個錯誤。"湯姆猶猶豫豫地説。| **carry conviction** (=show that someone feels sure about something and has no doubts) 有説服力 *Their shouts and threats carried little conviction.* 他們的喊叫和威脅幾乎沒有説服力。**3** [C] a decision in a court of law that someone is guilty of a crime 裁定有罪: *They had no previous convictions.* 他們沒有前科。| **[+for]** *This was her third conviction for theft.* 這是她第三次被判犯盜竊罪。**4** [U] the process of proving that someone is guilty in a court of law 定罪: *The trial and conviction of Jimmy Malone took over three months.* 審判吉米·馬隆和給他定罪用了三個多月的時間。—opposite 反義詞 ACQUITTAL —see also 另見 **have the courage of your convictions** (COURAGE (2)) 3

con·vince /kən`vɪns; kən'vɪns/ *v* [T] **1** to make someone feel certain that something is true 使確信; 使信服: *Her arguments didn't convince me.* 她的論點不能説服我。| **convince sb (that)** *I managed to convince them that the story was true.* 我終於使他們相信那故事是真的。| **convince sb of sth** *We finally convinced them of* 3 3 *our innocence.* 我們終於使他們相信我們是無辜的。**2** to persuade someone to do something 說服, 勸服: **convince sb to do sth** *I've been trying to convince Jean to come with me.* 我一直在設法說服吉恩跟我們一起來。

con·vinced /kən`vɪnst; kən'vɪnst/ *adj* **1 be convinced** to feel certain that something is true 確信的; 信服的: *Molly agreed, but she did not sound very convinced.* 莫莉同意了, 但是她聽起來不像很信服。| *I was convinced that we were doing the right thing.* 我確信我們做的事情是正確的。| **convinced of sth** *We are all convinced of his innocence.* 我們都相信他是無辜的。| **convinced (that)** *I felt convinced that they were right.* 我相信他們是正確的。**2 convinced Muslim/Christian etc** someone who believes very strongly in a particular religion 信仰堅定的穆斯林/基督徒等

con·vinc·ing /kən`vɪnsɪŋ; kən'vɪnsɪŋ/ *adj* **1** making you believe that something is true or right 有說服力的, 使人信服的: *You're not a very convincing liar!* 你是一個難以讓人信服的說謊者! | *There is now convincing evidence that smoking causes lung cancer.* 現在有令人信服的證據說明吸煙能導致肺癌。**2 a convincing victory/win** an occasion when a person or team wins a game by a lot of points 大勝 —**convincingly** *adv*

con·viv·i·al /kən`vɪvɪəl; kən'vɪviəl/ *adj* friendly and pleasantly cheerful 歡樂的; 友好的: *a convivial atmosphere* 友好的氣氛 | *She seemed to be in a convivial mood.* 她看起來心情愉悅。—**convivially** *adv* —**conviviality** /kən͵vɪvɪ`ælətɪ; kən͵vɪvi'æləti/ *n* [U]

con·vo·ca·tion /͵kɑnvə`keʃən; ͵kɒnvə'keɪʃən/ *n formal* 【正式】**1 a)** [U] an organization of church officials or members of some universities that holds formal meetings〔由教會領袖或一些大學中的人員組成的〕會議召集團體 **b)** [C] formal meetings held in this way〔教會的正式〕會議;〔大學的〕校務會議: *He first gave the speech at a German university convocation in March.* 他第一次作這個演講是三月份在德國大學的一次會議上。**2** [U] the process of arranging for a large meeting to be held〔大型會議的〕召集, 召開 **3** [C] *AmE* the ceremony held when students have passed their examinations and are leaving university 【美】〔大學〕畢業典禮

con·voke /kən`vok; kən'vəʊk/ *v* [T] *formal* to tell people that they must come together for a formal meeting 【正式】召開〔會議〕

con·vo·lut·ed /`kɑnvə͵lutɪd; 'kɒnvəlu:tɪd/ *adj* **1** complicated and difficult to understand 不易理解的, 費解的: *The whole thing was written in the most convoluted and obscure language possible.* 通篇語言隱晦難解得無以復加。| *a convoluted argument* 錯綜複雜的論據 **2** *formal* having many twists and bends 【正式】旋繞的, 彎曲的: *They used some convoluted glass apparatus for measuring the expansion of the gas.* 他們使用某種彎曲的玻璃器皿來測量該氣體的膨脹度。—**convolutedly** *adv*

con·vo·lu·tion /͵kɑnvə`luʃən; ͵kɒnvə'lu:ʃən/ *n* [C usually plural 一般用複數] **1** the complicated details of a story, explanation etc, which make it difficult to understand 錯綜複雜的細節: *It was an effort to follow the endless convolutions of the plot.* 要弄懂無休止的錯綜複雜的情節不太容易。**2** a fold or twist in something which has many of them 卷曲, 盤繞: *the many convolutions of the small intestine* 小腸的許多卷曲

con·voy[1] /`kɑnvɔɪ; 'kɒnvɔɪ/ *n* [C] **1** a group of vehicles or ships travelling together 車隊; 船隊: *A convoy of lorries arrived bringing supplies of food and medicine.* 卡車隊滿載着食物和藥品到達了。| **in convoy** *We decided to travel in convoy so that no-one could lose their way.* 我們決定結隊而行以防有人迷路。**2** a group of armed vehicles or ships whose purpose is to travel with others in order to protect them 護送車隊; 護送艦隊: *They were escorted through the danger area by a naval convoy.* 在海軍護航隊的保護之下他們通過危險地區。| **under convoy** (=protected by a convoy) 由護送隊保護 *The weapons were sent under convoy.* 武器在護送之下運走。

convoy[2] *v* [T] to travel with something in order to protect it 護送; 護航: *Battleships helped to convoy much-needed supplies to Britain in 1917.* 1917 年, 軍艦幫助護送急需物資到英國。

con·vulse /kən`vʌls; kən'vʌls/ *v* **1** [I] if a part of your body convulses, it moves violently and you are not able to control it〔身體某部分〕劇烈震動; 劇烈抖動: *He sat down, his shoulders convulsing with sobs.* 他坐下來, 他的肩膀由於抽泣而劇烈抖動。**2** [I] if you convulse, your body shakes violently and you are not able to control it, especially because of illness or injury 痙攣; 抽搐 **3 be convulsed with laughter/anger** to be laughing so much or feel so angry that you shake and are not able to stop yourself 笑得前仰後合/氣得發抖

con·vul·sion /kən`vʌlʃən; kən'vʌlʃən/ *n* **1** [C usually plural 一般用複數] an act of shaking violently and uncontrollably because you are ill 驚厥; 痙攣; 抽搐: *His temperature was very high and he started having convulsions.* 他的體温很高並開始抽搐。**2 be in convulsions** *informal* to be laughing a lot 【非正式】笑得前仰後合: *The story was so funny, we were in convulsions.* 這個故事太有趣了, 我們笑得前仰後合。

con·vul·sive /kən`vʌlsɪv; kən'vʌlsɪv/ *adj* sudden, violent and impossible to control 突然的; 劇烈的; 不能控制的: *The drunken man made convulsive efforts to stand up.* 這個醉漢突然跌跌撞撞地想站起來。—**convulsively** *adv*

co·ny, coney /`konɪ; 'kəʊni/ *n* **1** [C] *old use* a rabbit 【舊】家兔 **2** [U] rabbit fur used for making coats 兔毛皮

coo[1] /ku; ku:/ *v* [I] **1** to make the low soft cry of a DOVE[1] (1) or PIGEON〔鴿子等〕咕咕地叫 **2** to make soft quiet sounds 低聲細語: *He was cooing in her ear.* 他低聲向她耳語。—see also 另見 **bill and coo** (BILL[2] (4)) —**coo** *n* [C]

coo[2] *interjection* used to express surprise 啊, 呀〔表示驚訝〕: *Coo! That must have cost a lot!* 啊, 那一定花了很多錢!

cook[1] /kʊk; kʊk/ *v* **1** [I,T] to prepare food for eating by using heat 烹調; 煮, 燒: *Mmm! That's delicious! Where did you learn to cook like that?* 嗯! 太香了! 你從哪裡學燒菜的? | **cook dinner/supper/a meal etc** *I'm tired. Will you cook dinner today?* 我累了, 今天你能做晚飯嗎? | **cook sth for sb** *Sarah cooked lasagne for her parents when they visited.* 莎拉在她父母來看她的時候給他們燒寬麵條吃。| **cook sb sth** *He decided to cook his parents a special meal for their wedding anniversary.* 他決定為父母的結婚紀念日做一頓特殊的飯菜。**2** [I] to be prepared for eating by using heat 被燒煮: *The potatoes are cooking and will be ready in ten minutes.* 馬鈴薯正在煮, 十分鐘就會好。**3** [T] *informal* to change facts, numbers etc dishonestly, for your own advantage; FALSIFY 【非正式】竄改; 捏造: *I'm sure the police have been cooking the evidence to get more convictions.* 我敢肯定, 警察為了使更多人被判有罪而捏造證據。**4 be cooking** *informal* being planned in a secret way 【非正式】祕密計劃; 密謀: *Everyone in the office has been whispering this morning – I'm sure there's something cooking.* 今天早上辦公室裡的每個人都低聲耳語, 肯定有事要發生了。**5 cook the books** to dishonestly change official records and figures in order to steal money 做假賬: *The company accountant was charged with cooking the books.* 這家公司的會計被指控做假賬。**6 cook sb's goose** to get someone into serious trouble 使某人陷入極大麻煩: *It would really cook his goose if I told his wife where he was last night.* 如果我告訴他妻子昨天晚上他在哪兒, 他麻煩就大了。**7 be cooking with gas** *AmE spoken* used to say that someone is doing something very well 【美口】幹得很好, 幹得優秀

cook sth ↔ **up** *phr v* [T] **1** to make a meal quickly, often using food that has been left from a previous meal〔匆忙地〕煮燒, 做〔飯〕: *I volunteered to cook up a risotto using the rice from last night.* 我自願用昨晚的米

飯做雞肉煨飯。**2** *informal* to invent a story or excuse in order to prevent someone blaming you for something【非正式】捏造; 编造: *Rachel cooked up some story about her car breaking down, to explain why she was so late.* 雷切爾編造說她的車拋錨了, 以此來解釋為甚麼她遲到了。

cook[2] *n* [C] **1** someone who prepares and cooks food as their job 廚師, 炊事員: *Jane works as a cook in a local restaurant.* 簡在本地的一家餐館裡做廚師。—compare 比較 CHEF **2 be a good/excellent etc cook** to be good at preparing and cooking food 好的/出色的廚師: *My dad's a really good cook.* 我爸爸是一個真正出色的廚師。**3 too many cooks (spoil the broth)** used when you think there are too many people trying to do the same job at the same time, so that the job is not done well 廚師太多燒壞湯〔用來形容人多誤事〕—see also 另見 **chief cook and bottle washer** (CHIEF[1] (3))

cook·book /ˈkʊkˌbʊk; ˈkʊkbʊk/ *n* [C] *AmE* a book that tells you how to prepare and cook food【美】烹飪書; 食譜; COOKERY BOOK *BrE*【英】

cook-chill /ˌ· ˈ·◂/ *adj BrE* cook-chill foods have already been cooked when you buy them, and are stored at a low temperature, but not frozen【英】冷藏熟食

cooked /kʊkt; kʊkt/ *adj* cooked food is not raw and is ready for eating〔食物〕熟的; 煮熟的; 燒好的: *cooked meats* 熟肉

cook·er /ˈkʊkɚ; ˈkʊkə/ *n* [C] *BrE*【英】**1** a large piece of equipment for cooking food on or in 廚灶; 爐具; STOVE[1] (2) *AmE*【美】—see picture on page A10 參見A10頁圖 **2** a fruit, especially an apple, that is suitable for cooking but not for eating raw 適宜煮食而不宜生吃的水果〔尤指蘋果〕

cook·e·ry /ˈkʊkərɪ; ˈkʊkəri/ *n* [U] *BrE* the art or skill of cooking【英】烹飪法; 烹飪術; COOKING[1] (1) *AmE*【美】: *Jane's favourite subject at school is cookery.* 珍妮在學校最喜歡的科目是烹飪課。| *French provincial cookery* 法國的地方烹飪法

cookery book /ˈ··· ˌ·/ *n* [C] *BrE* a book that tells you how to prepare and cook food【英】烹飪書; 食譜; COOKBOOK *AmE*【美】

cook·house /ˈkʊkˌhaʊs; ˈkʊkhaʊs/ *n* [C] *old-fashioned* an outdoor kitchen where you cook food, especially in a military camp【過時】〔尤指軍營的〕露天廚房; 野營廚房; 戶外廚房

cook·ie /ˈkʊkɪ; ˈkʊki/ *n* [C] **1** *especially AmE* a flat, dry, sweet cake usually sold in packets【尤美】小甜餅, 甜餅乾; BISCUIT (1) *BrE*【英】: *Karen had a glass of milk and a cookie.* 凱倫喝了一杯牛奶, 吃了一個小甜餅。**2 tough/smart cookie** *informal* someone who is clever, successful, and strongly defends what they believe in【非正式】聰明、成功、意志堅定的人 **3 that's the way the cookie crumbles** *informal* used when something unpleasant has happened to say that you must accept things the way they are, even though you do not like it【非正式】生米已煮成熟飯〔指不合意的事已發生, 不得不接受〕**4** *AmE old-fashioned* an attractive young woman【美, 過時】漂亮的年輕女子 **5** *ScotE*【蘇格蘭】= a BUN (1)

cookie cut·ter /ˈ·· ˌ··/ *n* [C] *AmE*【美】**1** an instrument that cuts cookies into special shapes before you bake them 餅乾成型切割刀 **2** something that is almost exactly the same as other things of the same type, and is not interesting in any way 千篇一律的東西; 俗套的東西: *The new business park was totally different from the cookie cutter approach of the other buildings in the area.* 這個新的商業園完全不同於該地區其他建築千篇一律的處理方法。

cookie sheet /ˈ·· ·/ *n* [C] *AmE* a flat piece of metal that you bake food on【美】餅乾烘製板; BAKING TRAY

3 **cook·ing**[1] /ˈkʊkɪŋ; ˈkʊkɪŋ/ *n* [U] **1** the act of making food and cooking it 燒飯, 做飯: *I hate cooking.* 我討厭燒飯。**2** food made in a particular way or by a particular person〔用特殊方法或由特定的人烹調的〕飯菜: *Gail's cooking is always good.* 蓋爾做的菜總是很可口。| *Indian cooking* 印度菜 | **home cooking** (=good food like you get in your own house) 家庭飯菜

cooking[2] *adj* [only before noun 僅用於名詞前] **1** suitable for or used in cooking 烹飪用的; 適合烹飪用的: *Fry the vegetables in cooking oil.* 用烹調油炒蔬菜。**2** *AmE* doing something very well【美】做得非常好的: *The band is really cooking tonight.* 這個樂隊今天晚上演奏得棒極了。

cooking ap·ple /ˈ·· ˌ··/ *n* [C] a kind of apple used in cooking 煮熟吃的蘋果 —compare 比較 EATING APPLE

cooking oil /ˈ·· ·/ *n* [U] oil from plants, such as sunflowers or olives (SUNFLOWER or OLIVE (2)) 烹飪油

cook·out /ˈkʊkˌaʊt; ˈkʊk-aʊt/ *n* [C] *AmE informal* a party or occasion when a meal is cooked and eaten outdoors【美, 非正式】在露天煮吃的野餐

cook·ware /ˈkʊkwɛr; ˈkʊkweə/ *n* [U] containers and equipment used for cooking 烹飪用具, 炊具

cool[1] /kul; kuːl/ *adj* 3

1 ►TEMPERATURE 溫度◄ low in temperature, but not cold, often in a way that feels pleasant 涼的, 涼爽的: *There was a cool breeze blowing off the sea.* 涼爽的微風從海上吹來。| *sipping a cool drink* 吸一口涼飲料 —see 見 COLD (USAGE)

2 ►CALM 冷靜的◄ calm and not nervous, upset, embarrassed etc 冷靜的; 沉着的: *Now just stay cool. Everything's OK.* 好了, 保持冷靜, 一切都沒事。| **(as) cool as a cucumber** (=very calm) 泰然自若, 極為冷靜 *Robert walked into the exam looking cool as a cucumber.* 羅伯特走進考場時看上去泰然自若。| **cool customer** (=someone who behaves calmly in a difficult situation)〔困境中〕保持冷靜的人 | **cool head** (=ability to remain calm in a difficult situation) 頭腦冷靜 *The job is quite demanding, so we need someone with a cool head.* 這項工作的要求很高, 所以我們需要一個頭腦冷靜的人。| **cool, calm, and collected** (=calm) 冷靜 *Although she was nervous before the interview she managed to appear cool, calm and collected.* 她在面試前儘管緊張, 面試時卻泰然自若。

3 ►NOT FRIENDLY 不友好的◄ behaving in a way that is not as friendly as you expect 冷漠的; 冷淡的: *Her gaze was decidedly cool.* 她的凝視顯然是冷漠的。| **[+towards]** *The boss didn't actually say anything critical, but he was very cool towards me.* 老闆實際上並沒有指責我甚麼, 但是對我卻很冷淡。

4 ►FASHIONABLE 時髦的◄ *informal* very attractive, fashionable, relaxed etc, in a way that people admire【非正式】極有魅力的, 時髦的; 放鬆的; 酷的: *You look really cool in those sunglasses.* 你戴着太陽眼鏡確實很酷。

5 it's cool *spoken* used to say that something is not a problem【口】沒問題, 好辦: *Don't worry about the work – it's cool!* 不要擔心工作, 沒問題的!

6 ►COLOUR 顏色◄ a cool colour is one, such as blue or green, that makes you think of cool things 冷色的,〔顏色〕給人涼爽感覺的

7 a cool million/hundred thousand etc *informal* a surprisingly large amount of money that someone seems to earn very easily【非正式】輕易賺來的大筆錢: *He earns a cool half million every year.* 他每年輕易就賺到五十萬。—**coolness** *n* [U] —**coolly** *adv* —**coolish** *adj*

cool[2] *v* **1** [I,T] also 又作 **cool down** to become cool or cooler, or make something do this (使) 變涼: *You'll need to let your tea cool before you drink it.* 在飲用前, 你需要把茶涼一涼。| *They opened the windows to cool the room down.* 他們打開窗子使房間涼快下來。**2** [I] if a feeling, emotion, or relationship cools, it becomes less strong〔感情、情緒、關係等〕冷下來; 冷卻; 變淡: *Our initial enthusiasm cooled when we saw how much work was involved.* 當我們看到要做多少工作時, 我們最初的熱情冷卻了。**3 cool it** *spoken*【口】**a)** used to tell someone to stop being angry, violent etc 用於要別人冷靜下 3

來: *That's enough arguing, you two – cool it!* 你們兩個不要再爭論了，冷靜點。**b)** to stop putting as much effort into something, or pressure on someone as you have been 沉住氣；慢慢來: *The more you chase after him, the less likely he is to go out with you. You'd better cool it a bit.* 你越追求他他就越不會跟你來往，你最好沉住氣。**4 cool your heels** to be forced to wait 被迫等候: *The receptionist kept me cooling my heels for at least an hour.* 接待員至少讓我空等了一個小時。

cool down *phr v* **1** [I,T] to become cool or cooler, or make something do this（使）冷卻下來，（使）變涼: *Let the engine cool down, and then try starting it.* 讓引擎冷卻下來，然後再發動試試。| **cool sth ↔ down** *Blow on your cocoa to cool it down.* 吹吹你的可可使它涼下來。**2** [I] to become calm after being angry 冷靜下來: *His father took a long time to cool down after their last argument.* 自從他們上一次的爭論之後，他父親過很長時間才冷靜下來。

cool off *phr v* [I] **1** to return to a normal temperature after being hot〔溫度〕涼下來；涼快下來: *We'd been in the sun all day, so went for a swim to cool off.* 我們已經在太陽底下待了一天了，因此我們去游泳涼快涼快。**2** to become calm after being angry 冷靜下來: *Maybe you should go away and cool off before we talk anymore.* 或許你應該出去冷靜一下，然後我們再來談。

cool³ *n* **1 the cool** a temperature that is pleasantly cold 涼爽〔的氣溫〕: [+of] *They went for a stroll in the cool of the evening.* 他們在涼爽的夜晚出去散步。**2 keep your cool** to remian clam in a frightening or difficult situation 保持冷靜 **3 lose your cool** to stop being calm in an annoying or frightening situation 失去冷靜: *I couldn't help it, I just lost my cool and started shouting at him.* 我無法自制，失去了冷靜，開始對他大喊大叫。

cool⁴ *adv* **play it cool** to behave in a calm way because you do not want someone to know that you are really nervous, angry etc 冷靜對待；鎮定應付: *Don't worry, just listen to what they say and play it cool.* 不要擔心，好好聽他們說甚麼，然後冷靜處理。

coo·lant /ˈkulənt; ˈkuːlənt/ *n* [C,U] *technical* a liquid or gas used to cool something, especially an engine【術語】冷卻劑 —see picture at 參見 ENGINE 圖

cool·box /ˈkulˌbɑks; ˈkuːlbɒks/ also 又作 **cool·bag** /ˈkulˌbæg; ˈkuːlbæg/ *n* [C] *BrE* a container that keeps food and drink cool and fresh, which you use on a PICNIC¹ (1)【英】〔儲藏野餐食物的〕冰盒；冰袋；COOLER (2) *AmE*【美】

cool·er /ˈkulɚ; ˈkuːlə/ *n* [C] **1** a container in which something, especially drinks, is cooled or kept cold 冷卻器；冰桶: *Mike went to fetch a bottle of wine from the cooler.* 邁克從冰桶拿來一瓶酒。**2** *AmE* a coolbox【美】冰盒；冰袋 **3** *AmE* a machine that provides AIRCONDITIONING【美】空氣調節器，空調設備 **4 the cooler** *slang* prison【俚】牢房

cool-head·ed /ˌ· ˈ··◂/ *adj* not easily excited or upset 頭腦冷靜的，沉着的: *We need a quick-thinking, cool-headed person for the job.* 我們需要一個思路敏捷、頭腦冷靜的人來做這份工作。

coo·lie /ˈkulɪ; ˈkuːli/ *n* [C] *old-fashioned* an unskilled worker who is paid very low wages, especially in parts of Asia【過時】〔尤指在亞洲某些地區的〕苦力

cooling-off pe·ri·od /ˌ·· ˈ· ˌ···/ *n* [C] **1** a period of time when two people or groups who are arguing about something can go away and think about how to improve the situation 冷卻期〔爭論的兩個人或組織停止爭吵考慮如何改善狀況的時期〕**2** a period of time after you have signed some types of sales agreement, when you can change your mind about buying something 冷卻期〔在簽訂銷售合同後，可以改變想法的一段時間〕: *a 14-day cooling-off period on a pension plan* 一個退休金計劃的 14 天冷卻期

cooling sys·tem /ˈ·· ˌ··/ *n* [C] a system for keeping the temperature in a machine, engine etc low 冷卻系統: *a fault in the power station's cooling system* 發電站冷卻系統的故障

cooling tow·er /ˈ·· ˌ··/ *n* [C] a large, round, tall building, used in industry for making water cool 冷卻塔

coon /kun; kuːn/ *n* [C] **1** *AmE informal* a RACCOON【美，非正式】浣熊 **2** *taboo* a very offensive word for a black person【諱】黑鬼 **3 in a coon's age** *AmE informal* in a long time【美，非正式】長時間: *This is the best meal I've had in a coon's age!* 好久沒吃到這樣好的一頓飯了！

coon·skin /ˈkunskɪn; ˈkuːnskɪn/ *adj* made from the skin of a RACCOON 浣熊毛皮製的: *pictures of traders in coonskin caps* 戴着浣熊皮帽子的商人的圖畫

co-op /ˈkoɑp; ˈkəʊɒp/ *n* [C] a COOPERATIVE² 合作社

coop¹ /kup; kuːp/ *n* [C] a building for small animals, especially chickens 禽舍；雞籠

coop² *v*

coop sb/sth ↔ up *phr v* [T usually passive 一般用被動態] to restrict the freedom of someone or something by keeping them in a place that is too small 把…關在狹小的地方: [+in] *The fresh air felt good after being cooped up in the house for so long.* 在房子裡關了這麼久，呼吸新鮮空氣的感覺非常好。

coo·per /ˈkupɚ; ˈkuːpə/ *n* [C] someone who makes barrels (BARREL¹ (1)) 製桶[修桶]工人

co·op·e·rate also 又作 **co-operate** *BrE*【英】/koˈɑpəˌret; kəʊˈɒpəreɪt/ *v* [I] **1** if two people or groups cooperate, they work together in order to achieve a result that is good for both of them 合作，協作: *a classroom ethos which enables children to cooperate* 使得孩子們互相合作的課堂風氣。| [+with] *Leopards cooperate with each other when hunting game.* 豹在追捕獵物時互相合作。| [+in] *Russia and the US are cooperating in joint space ventures.* 俄羅斯和美國合作進行太空探索。| **cooperate to do sth** *Aid agencies and the UN are cooperating to deliver supplies to the area.* 援助機構和聯合國合作向該地區派送物資。| **cooperate closely** (=work a lot together to achieve something) 親密合作 **2** to help someone willingly when they ask for your help 配合；協助: [+with] *I will advise my client to cooperate fully with the police.* 我會勸說我的當事人與警方全力配合的。

co·op·e·ra·tion also 又作 **co-operation** *BrE*【英】/koˌɑpəˈreʃən; kəʊˌɒpəˈreɪʃən/ *n* [U] **1** things that you do with someone else to achieve a common purpose 合作，協作: [+between] *a lack of cooperation between police and fire services* 警察和消防隊之間缺少合作 | **in cooperation with** *The film was produced in cooperation with KBC of Australia.* 這部電影是與澳大利亞 KBC 公司聯合製作的。**2** help that is willingly given 配合: *Have your passports ready, and thank you for your cooperation.* 請把你們的護照準備好，謝謝你們的配合。| **full/complete cooperation** *If we're going to succeed, I'll need your full cooperation.* 如果我們想成功，我需要你們的全力合作。

co·op·e·ra·tive¹ also 又作 **co-operative** *BrE*【英】/koˈɑpərətɪv; kəʊˈɒpərətɪv/ *adj* **1** willing to cooperate; helpful 合作的: *a cooperative witness* 合作的目擊者 | *The woman in the bank wasn't very cooperative.* 銀行裡的那位婦女不太合作。**2** done or operated by people working together 合作進行的: *The Food Stamp Program is a cooperative activity of local, state and Federal governments.* 食物券計劃是由地方、州和聯邦政府合作進行的。**3 cooperative factory/firm/association etc** a cooperative firm etc is operated by people working together as a cooperative 合作工廠/公司/機構等

cooperative² also 又作 **co-operative** *BrE*【英】*n* [C] an organization such as a company or factory in which all the people working there own an equal share of it; CO-OP 合作社: **housing/farm cooperative** *The produce is supplied by a farm cooperative.* 這些農產品是由農業合作社提供的。

co-opt also 又作 **co-opt** /koˈɑpt; kəʊˈɒpt/ *v* [T] *formal*【正式】**1** to add someone to an organization such as a committee, sometimes against their will, by the agreement of all the other members〔某組織的成員〕推舉[增選]...為新成員〔有時被推舉人並不願意〕: *The Student's Union can have a maximum of 5 coopted members.* 學生會最多可以增選五人。| **coopt sb onto/into sth** *Mr King has been coopted onto the board.* 金先生被推選進董事會。**2** to include someone in something, especially against their will 強加於, 強行拉攏: *a vision of the world which coopts and misrepresents us* 一個既強加於我們又醜化我們的世界觀

co·or·di·nate¹ also 又作 **co-ordinate** *BrE*【英】/ko`ɔrdn̩,et; kəʊ'ɔːdɪ̣neɪt/ *v* [T] **1** to organize an activity so that the people involved in it work well together and achieve a good result 協調〔多人參加的活動〕: *Harris is coordinating a campaign to make people aware of the importance of exercise.* 哈里斯正在協調一個使人們意識到鍛鍊身體的重要的運動。**2** to make the movements of the parts of your body work well together when performing a particular action 協調〔身體的動作〕: *a young child unable to coordinate her movements* 無法協調動作的幼兒

co·or·din·ate² also 又作 **co-ordinate** *BrE*【英】/ko`ɔrdn̩ɪt; kəʊ'ɔːdɪ̣nɪ̣t/ *n* [C] **1** *technical* one of a set of numbers which give the exact position of a point on a map, computer screen etc【術語】坐標 **2 coordinates** *plural* women's clothes that can be worn together because their colours match〔在顏色上搭配能夠一起穿的〕配套女裝

coordinate³ also 又作 **co-ordinate** *BrE*【英】*adj technical*【術語】**1** equal in importance or rank 同等的; 並列的: *coordinate clauses in a sentence joined by 'and'* 一個句子中用and連接的並列子句 —compare 比較 SUBORDINATE¹ **2** involving the use of coordinates 坐標的

coordinating con·junc·tion /·'···· ·,··/ *n* [C] a word such as 'and' or 'but', which joins two clauses of the same type 並列連接詞

co·or·di·na·tion /ko,ɔrdn̩`eʃən; kəʊ,ɔːdɪ̣'neɪʃən/ *n* [U] **1** the way in which your muscles move together when you perform a movement〔肌肉的〕協調: *Too much alcohol affects your coordination.* 喝酒太多會影響你的動作協調。**2** the act of coordinating 協調, 調和: *the careful coordination of research* 研究工作的精心協調

co·or·di·na·tor /ko`ɔrdn̩etɚ; kəʊ'ɔːdɪ̣neɪtə/ *n* [C] someone who organizes the way people work in an activity 協調人

coot /kut; kuːt/ *n* [C] **1** a small black and white water bird with a short beak 白骨頂〔水鳥〕**2 old coot** *AmE informal* an old man who you think is strange or unpleasant【美, 非正式】老怪人: *crazy old coot* 瘋狂的老怪人

coo·ties /`kutɪz; 'kuːtiz/ *n* [plural] *AmE informal*【美, 非正式】**1** *old use* lice (LOUSE¹ (1)) that you have in your hair【舊】體蝨 **2 have cooties** *spoken* used by children to insult another child【口】有體蝨〔兒童用來羞辱人的話〕: *Jenny has cooties!* 珍妮長蝨子了!

3 **cop¹** /kɑp; kɒp/ *n* [C] **1** *informal* a police officer【非正式】警察: *a motorcycle cop* 騎摩托車的警察 **2 not be much cop** *BrE slang* to not be very good【英俚】不大好: *The film wasn't much cop, was it?* 這部電影不怎麼樣, 是嗎? **3 it's a fair cop** *BrE spoken humorous* used when someone has discovered that you have done something wrong and you want to admit it【英口, 幽默】抓得好, 抓得有理〔犯錯被人發現時用於承認〕

cop² *v* **copped, copping** [T] *slang*【俚】**1 cop it** *BrE spoken* to be punished【英口】挨罰: *You'll cop it from your Mum when she finds out!* 如果你媽媽發現的話, 你倒霉了! **2 cop (a load of) this** *BrE spoken* used to say look at or listen to this【英口】聽; 看〔用於引人注意〕**3 cop hold of** [only in imperative 僅用於祈使句] *BrE spoken* used to tell someone to take or hold something【英口】請拿着...: *Cop hold of my bag while I go and get the tickets.* 我去取票的時候, 請拿着我的提包。**4 cop a plea** *AmE* to agree to say you are guilty of a crime in order to receive a less severe punishment【美】承認有罪以求輕判 **5 cop a feel** *AmE* to touch someone in a sexual way when they do not want you to【美】〔調情時〕撫摸〔而對方並不同意〕

cop off *phr v* [I,T] *BrE slang* to meet someone and start a sexual relationship with them【英俚】與...見面並開始性關係: *So, what's the gossip? Did you cop off?* 那麼, 流言是甚麼呢? 你們發生性關係了嗎? | **[+with]** *Who was it he copped off with at the Christmas Party?* 在聖誕晚會上他與誰勾搭上了?

cop out *phr v* [I,T] *slang* to not do something that you are supposed to do【俚】逃避〔責任〕: *It's your turn to sing – you can't cop out now.* 該你唱了, 你不能賴喲。—see also 另見 COP OUT

cope¹ /kop; kəʊp/ *v* [I] **1** to succeed in dealing with a difficult problem or situation〔成功地〕應付, 對付: *I've never driven a big van before, but I'm sure I can cope.* 我從來沒有駕駛過大貨車, 但是我一定能應付得了。| **[+with]** *A family and a full time job is a lot to cope with.* 照顧家庭加上一份全職工作需要花很大精力。**2** if a machine or system can cope with a particular amount of work, it can do it〔機器或系統〕能處理; 能應付: *The system can cope with up to 40 terminals.* 這個系統可以處理多達40台終端機。 2 2

cope² *n* [C] a long loose piece of clothing worn by priests on special occasions〔教士在特別日子穿的〕長袍, 法衣

cop·i·er /`kɑpɪɚ; 'kɒpiə/ *n* [C] a machine that quickly makes photographic copies of documents; PHOTOCOPIER 複印機; 影印機

co·pi·lot /`ko,paɪlət; 'kəʊ,paɪlət/ *n* [C] a pilot who shares the control of an aircraft with the main pilot 飛機副駕駛員

cop·ing /`kopɪŋ; 'kəʊpɪŋ/ *n* [C,U] a layer of rounded stones or bricks at the top of a wall or roof〔牆頂或屋頂的〕護頂; 蓋頂

co·pi·ous /`kopɪəs; 'kəʊpiəs/ *adj* existing or being produced in large quantities 豐富的, 大量的: *Jill sat through the meeting and made copious notes.* 吉爾參加了整個會議, 並做了大量的筆記。—**copiously** *adv*: *Then she wept copiously.* 接着她淚如泉湧。

cop out /'· ·/ *n* [C] *slang* an occasion when you do or say something in order to avoid doing what you should do, or the actual words you use to make this excuse【俚】逃避責任; 逃避責任的藉口

cop·per /`kɑpɚ; 'kɒpə/ *n* **1** [U] a reddish-brown metal used for making wire 銅 **2 coppers** [plural] *BrE* money of low value made of this metal or of BRONZE¹ (1)【英】銅幣: *He pulled a pawn ticket and a few coppers out of his pocket.* 他從口袋裡掏出一張當票和幾枚銅幣。**3** [U] a reddish-brown colour 紅棕色: *flowing copper hair* 瀑布般的紅棕色頭髮 **4** [C] *BrE informal* a police officer【英, 非正式】警察

copper beech /,·· '·/ *n* [C] a large tree with purple-brown leaves 紫葉歐洲山毛櫸

cop·per·head /`kɑpɚ,hɛd; 'kɒpəhed/ *n* [C] a poisonous yellow and brown North American snake 銅頭蝮蛇

cop·per·plate /`kɑpɚ,plet; 'kɒpəpleɪt/ *n* [U] neat, regular, curving handwriting with the letters all joined together in a very specific style, used especially in the past 圓形草體〔西方字母的手寫體, 字體工整, 筆畫彎曲, 字母互相連接, 過去尤其常用〕

copse /kɑps; kɒps/ also 又作 **cop·pice** /`kɑpɪs; 'kɒpɪ̣s/ *n* [C] a group of trees or bushes growing close together; a small wood 矮樹叢; 灌木叢; 小樹林

cop shop /'· ·/ *n* [C] *informal* the office from which the police work; POLICE STATION【非正式】警察局

cop·u·la /`kɑpjələ; 'kɒpjɪ̣lə/ *n* [C] *technical* a type of verb that connects the subject of a sentence to its COMPLEMENT¹ (3)【術語】連繫動詞; 繫詞: *In the sentence 'The house seems big', 'seems' is the copula.* 在句子 The house seems big 中, seems 是連繫動詞。

cop·u·late /`kɑpjə,let; 'kɒpjɪ̣leɪt/ *v* [I] *technical* to have sex【術語】交媾; 交配 —**copulation** /ˌkɑpjəˋleʃən; ˌkɒpjʊˈleɪʃən/ *n* [U]

cop·u·la·tive /ˋkɑpjəˌletɪv; ˈkɒpjʊlətɪv/ *n* [C] *technical* a word or word group that connects other word groups【術語】連繫的, 繫詞的 —**copulative** *adj*

1
2
cop·y¹ /ˋkɑpɪ; ˈkɒpi/ *n* **1** [C] something that is made to be exactly like another thing 複製件; 副本: *I haven't got the original letter, but I have got a copy.* 我沒有信的原件, 但有複印件。| **[+of]** *Please send a copy of your marriage certificate.* 請交一份你的結婚證書複印件給我。| **make a copy** *I made a copy of the ad and sent it to my brother.* 我把這個廣告複製了一份送給弟弟。**2** [C] one of many books, magazines etc that are all exactly the same〔書、雜誌等的〕一冊; 一份: **[+of]** *He was reading a copy of the daily newspaper.* 他在讀一份日報。**3** [U] *technical* written material that is to be printed in a newspaper, magazine etc【術語】準備排印的書面材料: *All copy must be on my desk by Monday morning.* 星期一早上以前所有稿子必須送到我的桌子上。**4 make good copy** *informal* to be interesting news【非正式】成為〔新聞報道的〕好材料 —see also 另見 FAIR COPY, HARD COPY, SOFT COPY

copy out 抄寫

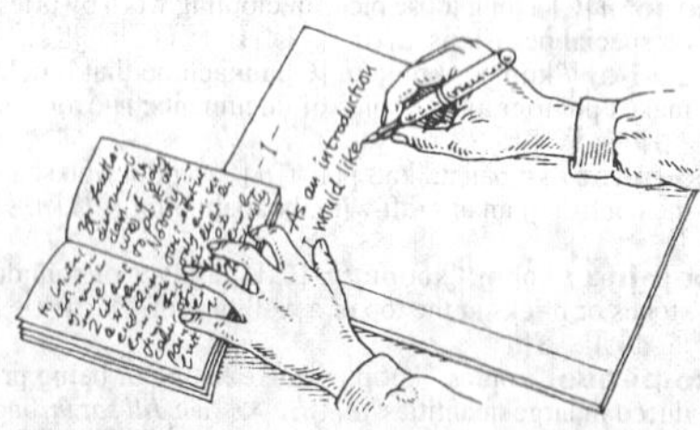

2
copy² *v* **1** [T] to make something exactly like another thing 複製, 抄寫: *Could you copy this letter and send it out, please?* 你能把這封信複製一份並把它投遞出去嗎? **2** [T] to deliberately do things that someone else has done, or do things in the same way that someone else does them 模仿; 仿效: *Street fashion tends to copy the ideas of the top fashion designers.* 街頭時裝往往模仿頂級時裝設計師的理念。**3** [I,T] to cheat in an examination, school work etc by looking at someone else's work and writing the same thing that they have 抄襲: **[+off]** *If I catch anyone copying off their neighbor, they'll be sent to the principal's office!* 如果我抓住有誰抄襲鄰座, 我會把他送到校長室! | **[+from]** *Jeremy had copied from the girl next to him.* 傑里米曾抄襲他鄰座的女孩。

copy sth ↔ **out** *phr v* [T] *BrE* to write something again exactly as it is written somewhere else【英】抄寫: *The monks copied their manuscripts out by hand.* 修道士用手抄出文稿。| *Just copy out of the book.* 照抄這本書吧。

cop·y·book¹ /ˋkɑpɪˌbʊk; ˈkɒpibʊk/ *n* [C] a book used in the past containing examples of good handwriting to copy 字帖, 習字簿 —see also 另見 **blot your copybook** (BLOT¹ (2))

copybook² *adj* [only before noun 僅用於名詞前] *BrE* completely suitable or correct【英】完全合適[正確]的: *a copybook answer* 完全正確的答案

cop·y·cat /ˋkɑpɪˌkæt; ˈkɒpikæt/ *n* [C] **1** *informal* a word used by children to criticize someone who copies other people's clothes, behaviour, work etc【非正式】模仿他人行為[衣着等]的人〔兒童用語〕**2 copycat crime/killing etc** a crime, murder etc which is similar to a famous crime that another person has done 模仿性的犯罪/模仿他人的兇殺等

copy ed·i·tor /ˈ·· ˌ···/ *n* [C] someone whose job is to be sure that the words in a book, newspaper etc are ready to be printed 文字編輯

cop·y·ist /ˋkɑpɪɪst; ˈkɒpi-ɪst/ *n* [C] someone who made written copies of documents, books etc in the past 抄寫員, 謄寫員

cop·y·right /ˋkɑpɪˌraɪt; ˈkɒpiraɪt/ *n* [C,U] the legal right to be the only producer or seller of a book, play, film, or record for a specific length of time 版權; 著作權: *Who owns the copyright of this book?* 誰擁有這本書的版權? | *an infringement of copyright* 侵犯版權 —**copyright** *adj* —**copyright** *v* [T]

cop·y·writ·er /ˋkɑpɪˌraɪtɚ; ˈkɒpiˌraɪtə/ *n* [C] someone who writes the words for advertisements 廣告文字撰稿人

coq au vin /ˌkɑk o ˋvæn; ˌkɒk əʊ ˈvæn/ *n* [U] *French* a dish of chicken cooked in red wine【法】酒燜雞

coq·ue·try /ˋkokɪtrɪ; ˈkɒkɪtri/ *n* [C,U] *literary* behaviour that is typical of a coquette【文】〔女人的〕賣弄風情

co·quette /koˋkɛt; kəʊˈket/ *n* [C] *literary* a woman who frequently tries to attract the attention of men without having sincere feelings for them; FLIRT²【文】賣弄風情的女人 —**coquettish** *adj* —**coquettishly** *adv*

cor /kɔr; kɔː/ *interjection BrE spoken* used when you are very surprised or impressed by something【英口】老天爺〔表示吃驚、震驚〕

cor- /kə, kɔr; kə, kɒ/ *prefix* the form used for CON- before r 在 r 前代替 con-: *to correlate* (=connect together) 使相互關聯

cor·a·cle /ˋkɑrəkl̩; ˈkɒrəkəl/ *n* [C] a small round boat that you move with a PADDLE¹ (1) 科拉科爾小舟

cor·al¹ /ˋkɔrəl; ˈkɒrəl/ *n* [U] a hard red, white, or pink substance formed from the bones of very small sea creatures, that is often used to make jewellery 珊瑚: *a coral necklace* 珊瑚項鏈

coral² *adj* pink or reddish orange in colour 珊瑚色的, 粉紅色的, 橘紅色的

coral reef /ˌ·· ˈ·/ *n* [C] a line of hard rocks formed by coral, found in warm sea water that is not very deep 珊瑚礁

cor an·glais /ˌkɔr ɔŋˋgle; ˌkɔːr ˈɒŋgleɪ/ *n* [C] *especially BrE* a long wooden musical instrument which is like an OBOE but with a lower sound【尤英】英國管〔一種木管樂器, 似雙簧管〕; ENGLISH HORN *especially AmE*【尤美】

cor bli·mey /ˌkɔr ˋblaɪmɪ; ˌkɔː ˈblaɪmi/ also 又作 **blimey** *interjection BrE old-fashioned* used to express surprise【英, 過時】哎呀〔表示驚訝〕

cord¹ /kɔrd; kɔːd/ *n* **1** [C,U] a piece of thick string or thin rope 粗線; 細繩; 索, 帶: *We need some cord to hang the picture.* 我們需要一些細繩來掛畫。| *He pulled explosives and some tangled cord from his bag.* 他從他的包裡掏出一些炸藥和亂糟糟的細繩。**2 cords** [plural] trousers made from a thick strong cotton cloth with thin raised lines on it 燈芯絨褲子 **3** [C,U] *especially AmE* an electrical wire or wires with a protective covering, usually for connecting electrical equipment to the supply of electricity【尤美】電線: *the phone cord* 電話線 | *How much cord do you need to connect the washing machine?* 連接洗衣機你需要多少電線? **4** [C] *AmE* a specific quantity of wood cut for burning in a fire【美】考得〔木柴單位〕: **[+of]** *We use three cords of wood in a winter.* 一個冬天我們要用三考得的木柴。—see also 另見 **cut the cord** (CUT¹ (29)), COMMUNICATION CORD, CORDLESS, SPINAL CORD, UMBILICAL CORD, VOCAL CORDS

cord² *v* [T] to tie or connect something with rope, string, etc 用繩索[線]捆紮[連接]: *Bundles of hay were corded and tossed onto the wagon.* 一捆捆乾草被紮好扔到馬車上。

cord·age /ˋkɔrdɪdʒ; ˈkɔːdɪdʒ/ *n* [U] rope or cord in general, especially on a ship 繩索〔總稱〕; 船用索具

cor·di·al¹ /ˋkɔrdʒəl; ˈkɔːdiəl/ *n* [C,U] **1** *BrE* sweet fruit juice that you add water to before you drink it【英】〔加

水後飲用的〕果汁: *a lime cordial* 酸橙果汁 **2** *AmE old-fashioned* a strong sweet alcoholic drink; LIQUEUR【美, 過時】烈性甜酒; 甜露酒: *We were offered an after-dinner cordial.* 給我們上了一杯飯後甜露酒。

cordial² *adj* friendly but quite formal and polite 熱誠的; 友好的〔但比較正式、有禮〕: *a cordial note from Mrs Thomas* 湯姆斯太太寫來的熱誠的便條 —**cordiality** /kɔrˈdʒælətɪ; ˌkɔːdiˈælɪ̥ti/ *n* [U]

cor·di·al·ly /ˈkɔrdʒəlɪ; ˈkɔːdiəli/ *adv* **1** in a friendly but polite and formal way 熱誠地; 誠摯地: *You are cordially invited to our wedding on May 9.* 熱誠邀請你5月9日參加我們的婚禮。**2 cordially disliked/hated** to dislike someone very strongly 強烈厭惡/憎恨: *He was cordially disliked by the whole street.* 整條街的人都非常討厭他。

cor·dite /ˈkɔrdaɪt; ˈkɔːdaɪt/ *n* [U] a smokeless explosive used in bullets and bombs 無煙火藥

cord·less /ˈkɔrdləs; ˈkɔːdləs/ *adj* a piece of equipment that is cordless is not connected to its power supply by wires〔設備〕無線的: *a cordless phone* 無線電話

cor·don¹ /ˈkɔrdn̩; ˈkɔːdn/ *n* [C] a line of police officers, soldiers, or vehicles put around an area to stop people going there 警戒線: *The police immediately put up a cordon around the scene of the accident.* 警察立即在事故現場周圍設置了警戒線。

cordon² *v*

cordon sth ↔ **off** *phr v* [T] to surround and protect an area with police officers, soldiers, or vehicles 設置警戒線圍起: *Police have cordoned off the street where the murder took place.* 警察在發生謀殺案的街道周圍設置了警戒線。

cor·don bleu /kɔrˈdɔ̃ ˈblœ; ˌkɔːdɒn ˈblɜː/ *adj* [only before noun 僅用於名詞前] concerning food cooked to the highest standard 烹飪手藝一流的: **cordon bleu chef** (=someone who is trained to prepare food to this standard) 手藝高超的廚師

cor·du·roy /ˈkɔrdəˌrɔɪ; ˈkɔːdʒərɔɪ/ *n* [U] a thick strong cotton cloth with thin raised lines on it, used for making clothes 燈芯絨, 條絨布: *a corduroy jacket* 燈芯絨夾克 —see picture on page A16 參見A16頁圖

3 **core¹** /kɔr; kɔː/ *n* [C]

1 ►FRUIT 水果◄ the hard central part of fruit such as an apple〔蘋果等的〕果心: *Remove the cores, fill with raisins and cinnamon, and bake the apples for 40 minutes.* 去除果心, 填入葡萄乾和肉桂, 然後把蘋果烤40分鐘。

2 ►CENTRAL PART 中心部分◄ the most important or central part of something〔事物的〕核心, 最重要部分: **[+of]** *Houston is the central core of a metropolitan area of about 2.6 million residents.* 休斯頓是一個有大約260萬居民的大都市的核心部分。

3 core values/beliefs/concerns the values etc that are most important to someone 最重要的標準/最重要的信仰/最關心的問題

4 ►PEOPLE 人們◄ a number of people who form a strong group which is very important to an organization〔組織的〕核心成員: *The club was beginning to develop a core of young people who were very active in the community.* 這個俱樂部開始培養一批在社區裡非常活躍的年輕核心成員。

5 to the core in a way that affects all of your feelings or your character 十分地; 徹底地: *That woman is rotten to the core!* 那個女人壞透了! | *When I saw the accident, I was shaken to the core.* 我看到事故, 十分震驚。

6 ►PLANETS 行星◄ the central part of the Earth or any other PLANET 地心;〔天體的〕核心

7 ►NUCLEAR REACTOR 核反應堆◄ the central part of a NUCLEAR REACTOR〔核反應堆的〕活性區

core² *v* [T] to take the centre from a piece of fruit 去掉〔水果的〕果心

core cur·ric·u·lum /ˌ· ·ˈ···/ *n* [U] the basic subjects that someone must study in school 基礎課程

co·re·li·gion·ist /ˌkorɪˈlɪdʒənɪst; ˌkəʊrɪ̥ˈlɪdʒənɪ̥st/ *n* [C] *formal* someone who is a member of the same religion as you【正式】信奉同一宗教的人, 教友

cor·er /ˈkɔrə; ˈkɔːrə/ *n* [C] a specially shaped knife for taking the hard centres out of fruit 去果心的刀

co·res·pon·dent /ˌkorɪˈspɑndənt; ˌkəʊrɪ̥ˈspɒndənt/ *n* [C] *law* someone whose name is given in a DIVORCE¹ (1) because they have had sex with the wife or husband of the person who wants the divorce【法律】共同被告〔在離婚訴訟中被指與原告的配偶通姦的人〕—compare 比較 RESPONDENT

core time /ˈ· ·/ *n* [U] the period during the middle part of the day when an office or other place of work that has FLEXITIME expects all its people to be working〔彈性工作時間制中所有人員都在上班的〕核心上班時間〔多為每天中間的一段時間〕

cor·gi /ˈkɔrgɪ; ˈkɔːgi/ *n plural* **corgis** [C] a small dog with short legs and a pointed nose 柯基犬〔一種腿短鼻尖的小狗〕: *the Queen's famous corgis* 女王的著名柯基犬

co·ri·an·der /ˌkɔrɪˈændə; ˌkɒriˈændə/ *n* [U] *BrE* a plant used to give a special taste to food, especially in Indian cooking【英】芫荽, 香菜; CILANTRO *AmE*【美】

Co·rin·thi·an /kəˈrɪnθɪən; kəˈrɪnθiən/ *adj* of a style of Greek architecture that uses decorations of leaves cut into stone 科林斯式建築風格的〔一種希臘建築的風格, 其裝飾特點是在石上雕刻葉子〕: *a Corinthian column* 科林斯式柱

cork¹ /kɔrk; kɔːk/ *n* **1** [U] the BARK (=outer part) of a tree from southern Europe and North Africa, used to make things 軟木橡樹的樹皮: *cork mats* 軟木橡樹皮墊子 **2** [C] a long round piece of cork which is put into the top of a bottle, especially a wine bottle, to keep liquid inside 木瓶塞, 軟木塞

cork² *v* [T] to close a bottle by blocking the hole at the top tightly with a long, round piece of cork 用軟木塞塞緊 —opposite 反義詞 UNCORK

cork·age /ˈkɔrkɪdʒ; ˈkɔːkɪdʒ/ *n* [U] the charge made by a hotel or restaurant for allowing people to drink alcoholic drinks which they bought somewhere else〔對自帶酒顧客收取的〕開瓶費

corked /kɔrkt; kɔːkt/ *adj* corked wine tastes bad because a decaying cork has allowed air into the bottle〔酒由於瓶塞腐朽而〕味道不佳的, 帶瓶塞味的

cork·er /ˈkɔrkə; ˈkɔːkə/ *n* [C] *BrE old-fashioned* someone or something you think is very good【英, 過時】出類拔萃的人[物] —**corking** *adj*

cork·screw¹ /ˈkɔrkskru; ˈkɔːkskruː/ *n* [C] a tool made of twisted metal which you use to pull a CORK¹ (2) out of a bottle〔拔木瓶塞的〕瓶塞鑽 —see picture on page A10 參見A10頁圖

corkscrew² *adj* [only before noun 僅用於名詞前] twisted or curly; SPIRAL¹ 螺旋型的: *corkscrew curls* 螺旋式的鬈髮

cor·mo·rant /ˈkɔrmərənt; ˈkɔːmərənt/ *n* [C] a large black sea bird which has a long neck and eats fish 鸕鶿

corn /kɔrn; kɔːn/ *n* **1** [U] *BrE* grains of plants such as 3
wheat, BARLEY, and OATS or their seeds【英】穀物; 穀粒 **2** [U] *AmE, AustrE*【美, 澳】**a)** a tall plant with large yellow grains at the top, which is cooked whole and eaten as a food; MAIZE 玉米 **b)** the grains of this plant 玉米粒 —see also 另見 SWEETCORN **3** [C] a painful area of thick hard skin on your foot 雞眼, 肉刺

corn·ball /ˈkɔrnˌbɔl; ˈkɔːnbɔːl/ *adj* [only before noun 僅用於名詞前] *AmE informal* cornball humour is too simple, old-fashioned, unoriginal, and silly【美, 非正式】〔幽默感〕陳腐的, 過時的; 愚蠢的: *At lunchtime he bored us with these awful cornball jokes.* 吃午飯的時候, 他說了這些糟糕的老掉牙的笑話, 讓我們覺得很無趣。

corn bread /ˈ· ·/ *n* [U] bread made from CORNMEAL 玉米粉麵包

corn chip /ˈ· ·/ *n* [C] crushed MAIZE formed into a small flat piece and cooked in oil, eaten especially in the US 炸玉米片

C

corn cir·cle /ˈ· ,··/ also 又作 **crop circle** *n* [C] patterns that appeared in British farm fields which some people believe were made by creatures from another world〔有些人認為是由外星人製作的〕農田圈

corn·cob /ˈkɔrn,kɑb; ˈkɔːnkɒb/ also 又作 **cob** *n* [C] the top part of a MAIZE plant after its yellow grains have been removed 玉米穗軸, 玉米芯

corn·crake /ˈkɔrn,krek; ˈkɔːnkreɪk/ *n* [C] a European bird with a loud sharp cry 秧雞

corn dol·ly /ˈ· ,··/ *n* [C] a figure made from the heads and stems of wheat plants, made especially in former times to celebrate the HARVEST[1] (1) 稻草人

cor·ne·a /ˈkɔrnɪə; ˈkɔːniə/ *n* [C] the transparent protective covering on the outer surface of your eye〔眼球的〕角膜 —**corneal** *adj*: *an operation for a corneal graft* 角膜移植手術 —see picture at 參見 EYE[1] 圖

corned beef /,kɔrnd ˈbif; ,kɔːnd ˈbiːf◂/ *n* [U] *BrE*【英】**1** a kind of pressed cooked BEEF[1] (1) sold in a tin 罐裝牛肉 **2** *AmE* beef that has been covered in salt water and SPICES to preserve it【美】鹹牛肉

cor·ne·li·an /kɔrˈniljən; kɔːˈniːliən/ *n* [U] a red or white stone used in jewellery 紅玉髓, 光玉髓〔石〕

cor·ner[1] /ˈkɔrnə; ˈkɔːnə/ *n*

1 ▶WHERE TWO LINES/EDGES MEET 角◀ [C] the point at which two lines or edges meet 角; 角落: *He pulled a dirty handkerchief out by its corner and waved it at me.* 他捏住髒手帕的一角拉出來向我揮動。| **in/on the corner** *Write your name in the top left-hand corner of the page.* 把你的名字寫在紙的左上角。| **three-cornered/four-cornered etc** *a three-cornered hat* 三角帽

2 ▶ROADS 道路◀ [C often singular 常用單數] **a)** the point where two roads meet 拐角處: **on/at the corner** *He stopped at the corner of 5th and Main to buy a newspaper.* 他在第5街和主街拐角處停下來買報紙。**b)** a point in a road where it turns sharply〔路上的〕急轉彎: *I think the gas station should be just around the next corner.* 我想加油站應該就在下一個轉彎處。

3 ▶CORNER OF A ROOM/BOX 房間/箱子的角落◀ [C often singular 常用單數] the place inside a room or box where two walls or sides meet〔房間、箱子內部的〕角: **in/at the corner** *Jim and his cousin sat in the corner talking about people back home.* 吉姆和他的堂兄坐在角落裡談論家裡人。

4 ▶MOUTH 嘴◀ [C] the corners of your mouth are the sides of your mouth 嘴角: *A small smile appeared at the corners of his mouth.* 他的嘴角露出淺淺的微笑。

5 ▶DIFFICULT SITUATION 困境◀ [singular] a difficult situation that is difficult to escape from 困境; 絕路: **force sb into a corner** *The president is likely to be forced into a corner over his latest plans for welfare spending.* 總統有可能因為最近的福利開支計劃被逼入困境。| **tight corner** (=very difficult situation) 絕路, 絕境

6 ▶SPORT 體育◀ [C] **a)** a kick in SOCCER that one team is allowed to take from one of the corners of their opponent's end of the field〔足球的〕角球 —see picture on page A23 參見 A23 頁圖 **b)** any of the four corners of the area in which the competitors fight in BOXING or WRESTLING 拳擊[摔跤]場的角

7 ▶DISTANT PLACE 遠方◀ [C] a distant place in another part of the world 遠方; 天涯海角: **[+of]** *She's gone off to do voluntary work in some remote corner of the world.* 她已離開, 去了世界的某個偏僻角落做志願工作。| **the four corners of the Earth/world** (=all the distant places in the world) 四面八方, 世界各地 *People came from the four corners of the world to see this spectacle.* 人們從世界各地來觀看這奇境。

8 see sth out of the corner of your eye to notice something accidentally, without turning your head towards it or looking for it 偶然看到, 不經意看到: *Out of the corner of her eye she saw the dog running towards her.* 她從眼角瞟去, 看到狗向她跑來。

9 just around the corner likely to happen soon 即將來臨: *Economic recovery is just around the corner.* 經濟很快就會恢復。

10 turn a corner to start to improve 渡過難關, 轉危為安: *She's been ill for a long time, but the doctors think she's turned a corner now.* 她已經病了很長時間, 但是醫生相信她已經渡過難關, 開始康復。

11 cut corners to do things too quickly, and not as carefully as you should, especially to save money or time〔為了節省金錢或時間而〕馬虎從事: *Don't try to cut corners when you're decorating.* 在裝飾的時候不要圖省事。

12 cut a corner to go across the corner of something, especially a road, instead of keeping to the edges 抄近路, 走捷徑

13 have a corner on the market to have a position in which you control all of the supply of a particular type of goods 壟斷: *The company had a corner on the silver market.* 這家公司壟斷白銀市場。—see also 另見 KITTY-CORNER

corner[2] *v* **1** [T] to force a person or animal into a position from which they cannot easily escape 把〔人或動物〕困住, 把…逼入絕境: *As the dog was cornered, it began to growl threateningly.* 狗被逼到無路可走的時候, 開始狂吠。| *Janet cornered Marty in the hall.* 珍妮特把瑪蒂困在大廳裡。**2 corner sb** also 又作 **back sb into a corner** to put someone into a position in which they cannot choose to do what they want to do 使某人陷入困境: *They have backed us into a corner – if we don't accept their terms, we'll lose our jobs.* 他們使我們進退維谷, 如果我們不接受他們的條件就會失業。**3 corner the market** to gain control of the whole supply of a particular kind of goods 壟斷: *They're trying to corner the market by buying up all the wheat in sight.* 他們企圖通過買進現有的全部小麥來壟斷市場。**4** [I] if a car corners, it goes around a corner or curve in the road〔車輛〕轉彎

corner shop /ˈ·· ·/ *n* [C] *BrE* a usually small shop, usually but not always on a corner, that sells food, cigarettes, and other things needed every day【英】街頭小店 —see also 另見 CONVENIENCE STORE

cor·ner·stone /ˈkɔrnə,ston; ˈkɔːnəstəʊn/ *n* [C] **1** a stone set at one of the bottom corners of a building, often put in place at a special ceremony 基石; 奠基石: *The mayor laid the cornerstone for the new city hall yesterday.* 市長昨天給新的市政大廳奠基。**2** something that is extremely important because everything else depends on it 基礎; 基本: **[+of/for]** *Trust and commitment are the cornerstones of any marriage.* 信任和忠誠是任何婚姻的基礎。—compare 比較 FOUNDATION STONE

cor·net /ˈkɔrnɪt; ˈkɔːnɪt/ *n* [C] **1** a musical instrument like a TRUMPET[1](1) often used in military bands 短號 **2** *BrE* a thin container shaped like a cone that you eat ICE-CREAM from【英】〔裝冰淇淋的〕圓錐形蛋卷 —see also 另見 CONE

corn ex·change /ˈ· ·,·/ *n* [C] a place where corn used to be bought and sold 穀物交易市場

corn·flakes /ˈkɔrn,fleks; ˈkɔːnfleɪks/ *n* [plural] small flat pieces of crushed corn, usually eaten at breakfast with milk and sugar 玉米片〔通常加牛奶和糖在早餐時吃〕

corn·flour /ˈkɔrnflaʊə; ˈkɔːnflaʊə/ *n* [U] *BrE* fine white flour made from corn, used in cooking to make liquids thick【英】〔精磨〕玉米粉; 玉米麵; CORNSTARCH *AmE*【美】

corn·flow·er /ˈkɔrn,flaʊə; ˈkɔːnflaʊə[r]/ *n* [C] a wild plant with blue flowers 矢車菊

cor·nice /ˈkɔrnɪs; ˈkɔːnɪs/ *n* [C] a decorative area at the top edge of a wall or PILLAR (1) 上楣, 飛檐

cor·niche /kɔrˈniʃ; kɔːˈniːʃ/ *n* [C] a road built along a coast 濱海路

Cor·nish /ˈkɔrnɪʃ; ˈkɔːnɪʃ/ *adj* from or related to Cornwall 康沃爾郡的

Cornish pas·ty /,·· ˈ··/ *n* [C] *BrE* a folded piece of

PASTRY (1), baked with meat and potatoes in it, usually for one person to eat【英】康沃爾餡餅

corn liq·uor /ˈ· ˌ··/ also 又作 **corn whiskey** *n* [U] a strong American alcoholic drink made from corn 玉米威士忌酒

corn·meal /ˈkɔrnˌmil; ˈkɔːnmiːl/ *n* [U] flour made from MAIZE 玉米粉; 玉米麵

corn on the cob /ˌ· · · ˈ·/ *n* [U] the top part of a MAIZE plant, cooked and eaten whole 玉米棒子

corn pone /ˈkɔrn pon; ˈkɔːnpəʊn/ *n* [U] a kind of American bread made from cornmeal〔一種美國〕玉米餅

corn·row /ˈkɔrnro; ˈkɔːnrəʊ/ *n* [C] a way of arranging hair, especially by women of West Indian and West African origin, in which hair is put into small tight plaits (PLAIT²) in lines along your head "玉米壠"式髮型〔西印度羣島和西非地區黑人婦女編成一排排辮子的髮型〕

corn·starch /ˈkɔrnˌstartʃ; ˈkɔːnstɑːtʃ/ *n* [U] *AmE* cornflour【美】玉米粉; 玉米麵

corn syr·up /ˌ· ˈ··/ *n* [U] a very sweet thick liquid made from MAIZE, used in cooking 玉米糖漿

cor·nu·co·pi·a /ˌkɔrnəˈkopɪə; ˌkɔːnjʊˈkəʊpiə/ *n* [singular] **1** a decorative container in the shape of an animal's horn, full of fruit and flowers, used to represent plenty〔象徵豐饒的〕角飾, 角狀盛器 **2** a lot of good things 許多好東西, 大量好東西: *the cornucopia of delights on display* 很多令人賞心悅目的展品

corn whis·key /ˈ· ˌ··/ *n* [U] CORN LIQUOR 玉米威士忌酒

corn·y /ˈkɔrnɪ; ˈkɔːni/ *adj informal* not new, different, interesting, or surprising【非正式】陳舊的; 平凡的; 乏味的: *My dad loves telling corny jokes.* 我爸爸喜歡講過時的笑話。| *I know it sounds corny, but I dream about her every night.* 我知道那聽起來有點老一套, 但是我確實每天晚上都夢到她。—**cornily** *adv* —**corniness** *n* [U]

co·rol·la·ry /ˈkɔrəˌlɛrɪ; kəˈrɒləri/ *n* [C] *formal* something that is the direct result of something else【正式】直接的結果; 必然的推論: *This is the inevitable corollary of his determination to succeed.* 這是他一心想要成功不可避免的結果。

co·ro·na /kəˈronə; kəˈrəʊnə/ *n* [C] the shining circle of light seen around the sun when the moon passes in front of it in an ECLIPSE¹ (1) 日冕

cor·o·na·ry /ˈkɔrəˌnɛrɪ; ˈkɒrənəri/ *adj* concerning or about the heart 心臟的, 與心臟有關的: *coronary disease* 心臟病

cor·o·na·tion /ˌkɔrəˈneʃən; ˌkɒrəˈneɪʃən◂/ *n* [C] the ceremony at which someone is officially made king or queen 加冕典禮

cor·o·ner /ˈkɔrənɚ; ˈkɒrənə/ *n* [C] someone whose job is to discover the cause of someone's death, especially if they died in a sudden or unusual way〔調查死因的〕驗屍官: *The coroner recorded a verdict of death by natural causes.* 驗屍官判定是自然死亡。

cor·o·net /ˈkɔrənɪt; ˈkɒrənɪt/ *n* [C] **1** a small CROWN¹ (1a) worn by princes or other members of a royal family, especially on formal occasions〔王子或王族戴的〕小冠冕 **2** anything that you wear on your head that looks like a CROWN¹ (1b) 冠狀頭飾: *a coronet of flowers* 花環頭飾

corp /kɔrp; kɔːp/ **1** the abbreviation of 縮寫= CORPORAL¹ **2** the abbreviation of 縮寫= CORPORATION

cor·po·ra /ˈkɔrpərə; ˈkɔːpərə/ *n* [plural] plural of CORPUS

cor·po·ral¹ /ˈkɔrpərəl; ˈkɔːpərəl/ *n* [C] a low rank in the army, air force etc〔陸軍、空軍等的〕下士 —see table on page C6 參見C6頁附錄

corporal² *adj formal literary* of or about the body【正式, 文】肉體的; 身體的

corporal pun·ish·ment /ˌ··· ˈ···/ *n* [U] a way of officially punishing someone by hitting them, especially in schools and prisons〔尤指學校和監獄中的〕體罰: *Corporal punishment was abolished in Britain in 1986.* 英國於1986年取消了體罰。

2 **cor·po·rate** /ˈkɔrpərɪt; ˈkɔːpərɪt/ *adj* [only before noun 僅用於名詞前] **1** belonging to or connected with a business 公司的: *This policy is a key feature of our long-term corporate planning.* 這項政策是本公司長期計劃的一個重要特色。**2** shared by or involving all the members of a group 團體的; 全體的: *corporate responsibility* 集體責任 | *corporate identity* 企業標誌 **3** forming a single group 合為一體的: *The university is a corporate body made up of several different colleges.* 這所大學由幾個不同的學院組成。**4 corporate hospitality** ways in which companies entertain their customers in order to gain business〔為了獲得商業機會而進行的〕公司招待 —**corporately** *adv*

cor·po·ra·tion /ˌkɔrpəˈreʃən; ˌkɔːpəˈreɪʃən/ *n* [C] **1** a big company, or a group of companies acting together as a single organization 大型公司; 大企業; 企業集團: *He works for a large American corporation.* 他為一家美國大公司工作。| *a multinational corporation* 跨國公司 **2** *BrE old use* a group of people elected to govern a town or city【英, 舊】市鎮當局; 市議會 **3 corporation tax** a tax paid by companies on their profits 公司(利潤)稅 3 2

cor·po·re·al /kɔrˈporɪəl; kɔːˈpɔːriəl/ *adj formal*【正式】**1** related to the body as opposed to the mind, feelings, or spirit 身體的, 肉體的: *He paid little attention to corporeal needs like food.* 他很少注意各種肉體的需要, 如食物。**2** able to be touched; MATERIAL² (2) 物質的; 有形的

corps /kɔr; kɔː/ *n* **1** a group in an army with special duties and responsibilities 特殊部隊; 特殊兵種: *the medical corps* 醫療部隊 **2** *technical* a trained army unit made of two or more DIVISIONS (=group of soldiers)【術語】軍〔軍隊編制單位, 至少由兩個師組成〕**3** a group of people who work together to do a particular job 共同工作的一羣人: *the president's press corps* 總統記者團

corpse /kɔrps; kɔːps/ *n* [C] the dead body of a person 屍體: *Her corpse was found floating in the river.* 她的屍體被發現漂浮在河上。

cor·pu·lent /ˈkɔrpjələnt; ˈkɔːpjələnt/ *adj formal* very fat【正式】肥胖的; 臃腫的: *He was a corpulent, pompous, and short-tempered little man.* 他是一個肥胖、自負、脾氣暴躁的小男人。—**corpulence** *n* [U]

cor·pus /ˈkɔrpəs; ˈkɔːpəs/ *n plural* **corpora** /-pərə; -pərə/ *or* **corpuses** [C] **1** *formal* a collection of all the writing of a particular kind or by a particular person【正式】〔某種作品的〕總集; 〔某人的〕全集: *They aim to study the entire corpus of Shakespeare's works.* 他們的目標是研究莎士比亞的全部著作。**2** *technical* a collection of information or material to be studied【術語】研究材料的匯總; 資料庫: *a corpus of spoken English* 英語口語資料庫 —see also 另見 HABEUS CORPUS

cor·pus·cle /ˈkɔrpəsl; ˈkɔːpəsəl/ *n* [C] one of the red or white cells in the blood 血球, 血細胞

cor·ral¹ /kəˈræl; kəˈrɑːl/ *n* [C] an enclosed area where cattle, horses etc can be temporarily kept, especially in North America〔尤指北美臨時關牛馬等的〕畜欄

corral² *v* **-ll-** [T] **1** to make animals move into a corral 把〔牲畜〕趕入畜欄: *They corralled the cattle before loading them onto the truck.* 在把牛裝上車以前, 他們把牛趕入畜欄。**2** to keep people in a particular area in order to control them 把〔人〕限制在某地方: *They corralled the protesters, keeping them away from the president's car.* 他們把抗議者趕到一邊, 使他們遠離總統的車。

cor·rect¹ /kəˈrɛkt; kəˈrekt/ *adj* **1** without any mistakes 正確的, 無誤的: *I'm not sure of the correct spelling.* 我不確定正確的拼法。| *Make sure you replace the parts in the correct order.* 要確定你按正確的順序更換部件。**2** suitable and right for a particular situation 恰當的, 正確的: *What's the correct procedure in cases like this?* 像這種案件的正確程序是甚麼? | *When lifting heavy weights it is very important that your back is in the cor-*

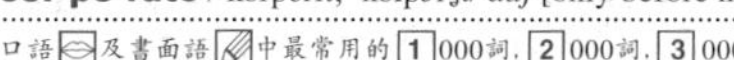
口語及書面語中最常用的 1 000詞, 2 000詞, 3 000詞

rect position. 在舉重物時, 背部保持恰當的姿勢是很重要的。**3** correct behaviour is formal and polite〔行為〕合乎禮節的; 得體的: *Simpson always knew what was correct and proper.* 辛普森總是知道甚麼是得體和合適的。—**correctly** *adv* —**correctness** *n* [U] —opposite 反義詞 INCORRECT

3 **correct²** *v* [T]

1 ►SHOW STH IS WRONG 表示某事錯誤◄ to show someone that something is wrong, and make it right 改正; 糾正: *Correct my pronunciation if it's wrong.* 如果我的發音錯了, 請予以糾正。| *I'd like to correct the impression that library work is boring.* 我希望糾正圖書館工作枯燥的印象。| **correct sb** (=tell someone that what they have said is wrong) 指出...說的話中的錯誤

2 ►IMPROVE BY CHANGING 改正◄ to make something work the way it should 校正; 矯正: *Some eyesight problems are relatively easy to correct.* 有些視力問題相對來講是容易矯正的。

3 ►EXAMS/ESSAYS ETC 考試/文章等◄ to make marks on a piece of written work to show the mistakes in it 批改: *She spent the whole evening correcting exam papers.* 她花了整個晚上批改試卷。

4 correct me if I'm wrong *spoken* used when you are not sure that what you are going to say is true or not【口】如果我錯了, 請予以糾正: *Correct me if I'm wrong, but didn't you say you were going to London today?* 如果我錯了就請予以糾正, 但是你不是說過今天要去倫敦嗎?

5 I stand corrected *formal spoken* used to admit that something you have said is wrong after someone has told you it is wrong【正式, 口】我承認有錯, 我接受批評指正

cor·rec·tion /kəˋrɛkʃən; kəˈrekʃən/ *n* **1** [C] a change made in something in order to correct it 修改, 糾正: *The page was covered in crossings-out and corrections.* 這一頁上全是叉號和所做的改正。| **make a correction** *She makes all her corrections with a green pen.* 她所有的改正都是用綠筆做的。**2** [U] the act of changing something in order to make it right or better 改正; 糾正 **3** *spoken* used to say that what you have just said is wrong and you want to change it【口】改正一下: *That figure was 30,000 ... correction, make that 31,000.* 那數字是30,000──改正一下, 是31,000。

correctional fa·cil·i·ty /·ˈ···, ·ˈ···/ *n* [C] *AmE technical or humorous* a prison【美, 術語或幽默】監獄

correction flu·id /·ˈ·· ˌ··/ *n* [U] *formal* a special white liquid used for covering written mistakes【正式】修正液, 塗改液

cor·rec·ti·tude /kəˋrɛktəˌtud; kəˈrektɪtjuːd/ *n* [U] *formal* correctness of behaviour【正式】〔行為的〕正當, 端正

cor·rec·tive¹ /kəˋrɛktɪv; kəˈrektɪv/ *adj formal* intended to make a fault or mistake right again【正式】改正的; 糾正的: *corrective treatment* 矯正治療 | *This condition may require corrective surgery.* 這種情況或許需要矯正手術。—**correctively** *adv*

corrective² *n* [C] *formal* something that is intended to correct a fault or mistake【正式】糾正物: **[+to]** *The idea is that this will function as a corrective to complacency.* 該觀點認為這會對自滿情緒起糾正的作用。

cor·rel·ate¹ /ˋkɔrəˌlet; ˈkɒrɪleɪt/ *v* [I,T] if two or more facts, ideas etc correlate, or you correlate them, they are closely connected or one causes another (使)相互關聯: *They found that the two sets of results seemed to be correlated.* 他們發現這兩組結果看起來是互相關聯的。| **[+with]** *Scientists have been unable to correlate their findings with recent increases in radioactivity levels.* 科學家不能把他們的發現和最近增長的輻射水平聯繫起來。

cor·re·late² /ˋkɔrəˌlɪt; ˈkɒrɪlɪt/ *n* [C] either of two things that correlate with each other 相關的事物

cor·re·la·tion /ˌkɔrəˋleʃən; ˌkɒrɪˈleɪʃən/ *n* **1** [C,U] a connection between two ideas, facts etc, especially when one may be the cause of the other 相互關係; 關聯; 因果關係: **[+between]** *They found a strong correlation between urban deprivation and poor health.* 他們發現城市中的貧困和健康狀況差有很密切的聯繫。| **[+with]** *There was also some correlation with social class.* 與社會階級也有些關係。**2** [U] the process of correlating two or more things 聯繫(的過程)

cor·rel·a·tive¹ /kəˋrɛlətɪv; kəˈrelətɪv/ *adj* **1** two or more facts, ideas etc that are correlative are closely related or dependent on each other 密切相關的; 互相依賴的: *correlative theories and beliefs* 相關的理論和信仰 | *Profits were directly correlative to the popularity of the product.* 利潤和產品的受歡迎程度有直接的關係。**2** *technical* two words that are correlative are frequently together but not usually used next to each other【術語】〔詞語〕關聯的〔指經常一起使用但一般並不連續的詞〕: *'Either' and 'or' are correlative conjunctions.* either和or是關聯連詞。

correlative² *n* [C] *formal* one of two or more facts, ideas etc that are closely related or that depend on each other【正式】相關物

cor·re·spond /ˌkɔrəˋspand; ˌkɒrɪˈspɒnd/ *v* [I] **1** if two things or ideas correspond, the parts or information in one relate to the parts or information in the other 符合; 相一致: *The two halves of the document did not correspond.* 這份文件的前後兩半不相符。| **[+with/to]** *The numbers correspond to distinct points on the map.* 這些數字與地圖上不同的點相對應。**2** to be very similar or the same as something else 相類似, 相當: **[+to]** *The French 'baccalauréat' roughly corresponds to British 'A-levels'.* 法國的baccalauréat與英國的高級程度考試大體上相類似。**3** to write letters to someone and receive letters from them 通信: *For the next three years they corresponded regularly.* 在接下來的三年裡他們經常通信。| **[+with]** *She stopped corresponding with him after the death of her mother.* 她母親死後她不再與他通信。

cor·re·spon·dence /ˌkɔrəˋspandəns; ˌkɒrɪˈspɒndəns/ *n* [U] **1** letters exchanged between people, especially official or business letters 信件〔尤指公函或商業信函〕: *A secretary came in twice a week to deal with his correspondence.* 一個秘書每個星期來兩次處理他的信件。**2** the process of sending and receiving letters 通信: *All correspondence between us must cease.* 我們必須停止一切通信。**3** a relationship or connection between two or more ideas or facts 關係; 聯繫: **[+between]** *There was no correspondence between the historical facts and Johnson's account of them.* 這些歷史事實和約翰遜對其表述之間沒有關聯。

correspondence course /··ˈ·· ˌ·/ *n* [C] a course of lessons in which the student works at home and sends completed work to their teacher by mail 函授課程: *I'm taking a correspondence course in business studies.* 我正在上商務函授課程。

cor·re·spon·dent¹ /ˌkɔrəˋspandənt; ˌkɒrɪˈspɒndənt/ *n* [C] **1** someone who is employed by a newspaper or a television station etc to report news from a particular area or on a particular subject 新聞記者: *Our correspondent in South Africa sent this report.* 我們的駐南非記者送來了這份報道。| *the political correspondent for The Times*《泰晤士報》的政治新聞記者 **2** someone who writes letters 通信者: **good/bad correspondent** (=someone who is good or bad at writing letters regularly) 勤於/疏於寫信的人 *I'm not a very good correspondent, I'm afraid.* 我想我不太勤於寫信。

correspondent² *adj formal* being right for a particular situation【正式】適合的; 一致的: **[+with]** *The result was correspondent with the government's wishes in this matter.* 這個結果與政府的希望在這件事上是一致的。

cor·re·spon·ding /ˌkɔrəˋspandɪŋ; ˌkɒrɪˈspɒndɪŋ◂/ *adj* [only before noun 僅用於名詞前] **1** caused by or dependent on something you have already mentioned 相應的, 由此引起的: *The war, and the corresponding fall in trade, have had a devastating effect on the country.* 戰爭以及由此所導致的貿易量的下降對這個國家有致命的影響。**2** having similar qualities or a similar position to something you have already mentioned; matching; EQUIVALENT[1] 相似的;〔位置〕對應的; 相符合的; 相等的: *The corresponding chromosome in the other parent was found to be defective.* 父母中一人身上對應的染色體被發現有缺陷。—**correspondingly** *adv*

2 3 **cor·ri·dor** /ˈkɔrədɚ; ˈkɒrɨdɔː/ *n* [C] **1** a long, narrow passage between two rows of rooms in a building or a train, with doors leading off it 通道; 走廊: *Room 101 is at the end of the corridor.* 101房間在走廊的盡頭。| *She hurried down the corridor.* 她沿着走廊匆匆而去。**2** a narrow area of land, within a bigger area, that has different qualities or features from the land that surrounds it〔陸地上與周邊地區有不同性質或特徵的〕走廊; 地帶: *the industrial corridor that connects Queretaro with Mexico City* 連接克雷塔羅和墨西哥城的工業地帶 | *the Polish corridor* 波蘭走廊 **3 corridors of power** the places where important government decisions are made 權力走廊, 權力核心〔政府的決策場所〕: *Who can tell what really goes on in the corridors of power?* 權力走廊裡到底發生了甚麼, 誰能說得清?

corrie /ˈkɔrɪ; ˈkɒri/ *n* [C] a deep bowl-shaped area on a mountain 山側圓形凹地 —see picture on page A12 參見A12頁圖

cor·rob·o·rate /kəˈrɑbəˌret; kəˈrɒbəreɪt/ *v* [T] *formal* to provide information that supports or helps to prove someone else's statement, idea etc【正式】〔提供資料〕證實: *We now have new evidence to corroborate the defendant's story.* 我們現在有新證據來證實被告人的證詞。—**corroboration** /kəˌrɑbəˈreʃən; kəˌrɒbəˈreɪʃən/ *n* [U] —**corroborative** /kəˈrɑbəˌretɪv; kəˈrɒbərətɪv/ *adj*

cor·rode /kəˈrod; kəˈrəʊd/ *v* [I,T] if metal corrodes or something corrodes it, it is slowly destroyed by the effect of water, chemicals etc 腐蝕; 侵蝕: *All the electrical components have corroded.* 所有電器部件都被腐蝕了。

cor·ro·sion /kəˈroʒən; kəˈrəʊʒən/ *n* [U] **1** the gradual destruction of substances such as metal by the effect of water, chemicals etc 腐蝕; 侵蝕 **2** a substance such as RUST (=red weakened metal) that is produced by the process of corrosion 腐蝕而成之物〈如鏽〉

cor·ro·sive /kəˈrosɪv; kəˈrəʊsɪv/ *adj* **1** a corrosive liquid such as an acid can destroy metal, plastic etc 腐蝕性的; 侵蝕性的: *Danger! Corrosive material.* 危險!腐蝕性物質。**2** gradually making something weaker, and possibly destroying it 有害的, 逐步起損害作用的: *Fear of unemployment is having a corrosive effect on the country's economy.* 失業的恐懼正對這個國家的經濟逐步帶來損害。

cor·ru·gated /ˈkɔrəˌgetɪd; ˈkɒrəgeɪtɨd/ *adj* in the shape of waves or folds, or made like this in order to give something strength 起皺的, 波紋的; 有瓦楞的: *corrugated cardboard* 瓦楞紙 | *corrugated iron* 瓦楞鐵 —**corrugation** /ˌkɔrəˈgeʃən; ˌkɒrəˈgeɪʃən/ *n* [C]

corrugated 有瓦楞的

corrugated iron 瓦楞鐵

cor·rupt[1] /kəˈrʌpt; kəˈrʌpt/ *adj* **1** using your power in a dishonest or illegal way in order to get an advantage for yourself 貪污受賄的, 腐敗的: *Corrupt judges have taken millions of dollars in bribes.* 貪污的法官接受了幾百萬美元的賄賂。**2** very bad morally 有傷風化的, 道德敗壞的; 邪惡的: *a corrupt society* 墮落的社會 **3** something that is corrupt is not pure or is not the way it was made or intended 訛誤的; 不純粹的 —see also 另見 INCORRUPTIBLE —**corruptly** *adv* —**corruptness** *n* [U]

corrupt[2] *v* [T] **1** to encourage someone to start behaving in an immoral or dishonest way; PERVERT[1] (2) 使道德敗壞; 使腐敗: *Young prisoners are being corrupted by the older, long term offenders.* 年輕的囚犯被年紀較大、刑期長的囚犯帶壞了。| *They say power corrupts.* 他們說權力能使人腐化。**2** to change the traditional form of something, such as a language, so that it becomes worse than it was 破壞〔語言等〕的純潔 **3** to change the information in a computer, so that the computer does not work properly any more 破壞〔電腦中的信息〕—**corruptible** *adj* —**corruptibility** /kəˌrʌptəˈbɪlətɪ; kəˌrʌptɨˈbɪlɨti/ *n* [U]

cor·rup·tion /kəˈrʌpʃən; kəˈrʌpʃən/ *n* **1** [U] dishonest, illegal, or immoral behaviour, especially from someone with power 貪污; 賄賂; 受賄; 腐敗: *The Chief Executive is being investigated for alleged corruption.* 總裁由於涉嫌受賄正在接受調查。**2** [C usually singular 一般用單數] a changed form of something, for example a word〔詞等〕變化了的形式: *The word Thursday is a corruption of Thor's Day.* Thursday是由Thor's Day演變而來的。

cor·sage /kɔrˈsɑʒ; kɔːˈsɑːʒ/ *n* [C] a group of small flowers that a woman fastens to her clothes on a special occasion such as a wedding〔女服上用於婚禮等特殊場合的〕裝飾花束

cor·sair /ˈkɔrsɛr; ˈkɔːseə/ *n* [C] *old use* the name of a North African PIRATE[1] (3), or their ship【舊】〔古代北非的〕海盜; 海盜船

corse /kɔrs; kɔːs/ *n* [C] *old use or poetical* a CORPSE【舊或詩】屍體

cor·set /ˈkɔrsɪt; ˈkɔːsɨt/ *n* [C] **1** a tightly fitting piece of underwear that women wore in the past to make them look thinner〔古代婦女穿來保持苗條的〕緊身褡 **2** a strong, tightly fitting piece of clothing that supports your back when it is injured〔穿來支承受傷背部的〕圍腰, 胸衣

cor·tege /kɔrˈtɛʒ; kɔːˈteɪʒ/ *n* [C] a line of people, cars etc that move along slowly in a funeral 送葬行列

cor·tex /ˈkɔrtɛks; ˈkɔːteks/ *n plural* **cortices** /-təsiz; -tɨsiːz/ [C] *technical* the outer layer of an organ such as your brain【術語】皮層; 皮質; 腦皮層 —**cortical** /ˈkɔrtɪkl̩; ˈkɔːtɪkəl/ *adj*

cor·ti·sone /ˈkɔrtɪˌson; ˈkɔːtɨzəʊn/ *n* [U] a HORMONE that is used especially in the treatment of diseases such as ARTHRITIS 可的松〔用於治風濕症的激素〕

cor·us·ca·ting /ˈkɔrəsˌketɪŋ; ˈkɒrəskeɪtɪŋ/ *adj formal* flashing with light【正式】閃光的; 閃爍的: *coruscating jewels* 閃亮的珠寶

cos[1] /kəz; kəz/ *conjunction nonstandard*【不規範】an 1
abbreviation of 縮寫= because

cos[2] /kɑs; kɒs/ *n* the abbreviation of 縮寫= COSINE

cosh[1] /kɑʃ; kɒʃ/ *n* [C] *BrE informal* a heavy weapon in the shape of a short thick pipe【英, 非正式】〔作武器用的〕短棒

cosh[2] *v* [T] *informal especially BrE* to hit someone with a cosh【非正式, 尤英】用短棒打

co·sig·na·to·ry /ˌkoˈsɪgnəˌtorɪ; ˌkəʊˈsɪgnətəri/ *n* [C] *formal* one of a group of people who sign a legal document for their department, organization, country etc【正式】連署人: *We will need both cosignatories to sign the cheque.* 我們需要兩位連署人都簽署支票。

co·sine /ˈkosaɪn; ˈkəʊsaɪn/ *n* [C] *technical* the measurement of an ACUTE (6) angle in a TRIANGLE (1) with a RIGHT ANGLE that is calculated by dividing the length of the side next to it by the length of the HYPOTENUSE【術語】〔數學的〕餘弦 —compare 比較 SINE

cos·met·ic /kɑzˈmɛtɪk; kɒzˈmetɪk/ *adj* [only before noun 僅用於名詞前] **1** dealing with the outside appearance rather than the important part of something; SUPERFICIAL (1) 裝門面的; 表面的: *We're making a few cosmetic changes to the house before we sell it.* 我們在賣這所房子以前, 會對它的門面稍作裝修。| **cosmetic ex-**

ercise (=something you do that looks good but does not achieve anything) 裝門面的事 **2** intended to make your hair or skin look more attractive 化妝的; 美容的: *the cosmetic industry* 美容化妝品業 | *Are you on the diet for health or cosmetic reasons?* 你節食是為了健康還是為了美容?

cos·me·ti·cian /ˌkazməˋtɪʃən; ˌkɒzməˈtɪʃən/ *n* [C] someone who is professionally trained to put cosmetics on other people 美容師

cos·met·ics /kazˋmɛtɪks; kɒzˈmetɪks/ *n* [plural] creams, powders etc that you use on your face and body in order to look more attractive 化妝品

C

cosmetic sur·ge·ry /·ˌ·· ˈ···/ *n* [U] medical operations that improve your appearance after you have been injured, or because you want to feel more attractive 整容外科手術

cos·mic /ˋkazmɪk; ˈkɒzmɪk/ *adj* **1** connected with space or the universe 宇宙的 **2** extremely large 廣大無邊的; 極大的: *a scandal of cosmic proportions* 特大醜聞 — **cosmically** /-klɪ; -kli/ *adv*

cosmic ray /ˌ·· ˈ·/ *n* [C usually plural 一般用複數] a stream of RADIATION (2) reaching the Earth from space 宇宙射線

cos·mog·o·ny /kazˋmagənɪ; kɒzˈmɒgəni/ *n* [C,U] the origin of the universe, or a set of ideas about this 宇宙起源; 宇宙起源論

cos·mol·o·gy /kazˋmalədʒɪ; kɒzˈmɒlədʒi/ *n* [U] the science of the origin and structure of the universe, especially as studied in ASTRONOMY 宇宙論

cos·mo·naut /ˋkazməˌnɔt; ˈkɒzmənɔːt/ *n* [C] an ASTRONAUT from the former Soviet Union〔前蘇聯的〕宇航員, 太空人

cos·mo·pol·i·tan¹ /ˌkazməˋpalətn̩; ˌkɒzməˈpɒlɪtən◂/ *adj* **1** a cosmopolitan place consists of people from many different parts of the world〔某地的人〕來自世界各地的: *the cosmopolitan bustle of San Francisco* 三藩市來自世界各地的人們熙熙攘攘 **2** a cosmopolitan person, belief, opinion etc shows a wide experience of different people and places〔人〕見識廣的;〔信仰、意見等〕兼容並包的: *Brigitta has such a cosmopolitan outlook on life.* 布麗吉特對生活有一種恢宏大度的觀點。

cosmopolitan² *n* [C] someone who has travelled a lot and feels at home in any part of the world 遊歷四方的人; 四海為家的人

cos·mos /ˋkazməs; ˈkɒzmɒs/ *n* **the cosmos** the whole universe, especially when you think of it as a system 宇宙

cos·set /ˋkasɪt; ˈkɒsɪt/ *v* [T] to give someone as much care and attention as you can, especially when it is too much 寵愛; 嬌養; 縱容: *No-one in the family gets as much cossetting as that cat!* 家中沒有誰比那隻貓更受寵愛!

S1 W1 **cost¹** /kɔst; kɒst/ *n*

1 ►MONEY PAID 付出的錢◄ [C] the amount of money that you have to pay in order to buy, do, or produce something 費用; 成本: *I'll give you $15 to cover the cost of the gas.* 我會給你 15 美元來支付汽油費用。| **at a cost of** *The new building's going up at a cost of $82 million.* 這座新建築物要花費 8200 萬美元。| **high/low cost** *a low cost source of electric power* 發電的低成本能源 | **full cost** *If no scholarships or other aid are available, students will have to pay the full cost of their education.* 如果得不到獎學金或別的資助, 學生要支付他們的全部學習費用。| **cost of living** (=the cost of buying all the food, clothes etc that you need to live) 生活費 *The cost of living rose two percent in the last year.* 在過去的一年中生活費增加了百分之二。| **at no extra cost** *A cassette/radio is included at no extra cost.* 一盒磁帶/一台收音機包含在內, 不需另外付費。

2 ►LOSS/DAMAGE 損失/損壞◄ [C,U] something that you lose, give away, damage etc in order to achieve something 代價; 犧牲: **at (a) cost to** *Duncan always puts Hannah's needs before his own, at considerable cost to himself.* 鄧肯總是把漢娜的需要放在自己的需要之上, 因此付出相當大的代價。| **whatever the cost** (=no matter how much work, money, risk etc is needed) 無論如何 *He's determined to win, whatever the cost.* 他無論如何決心要獲勝。| **at all costs** (=whatever happens) 不惜任何代價 *We must avoid a scandal at all costs.* 我們必須不惜任何代價避免醜聞。

3 costs [plural] **a)** the money that you must regularly spend in order to continue having a home, car, business etc 費用; 花費; 成本: **increase costs** *Businesses protested that the new taxes would increase production costs unreasonably.* 商界抗議道, 新稅會不合理地增加生產成本。| **reduce/cut costs** *We've got to cut costs and we're starting with the phone bill.* 我們不得不削減成本, 先從電話費開始。| **cover costs** (=make enough money to pay for the things you have bought) 支付花費 *At this rate we'll barely cover our costs.* 照這樣下去我們剛剛能支付花費。| **running costs** (=the cost of owning and using a car or machine)〔汽車或機器的〕運轉費用 *Because of the engine's efficiency the car has very low running costs.* 由於引擎的高效率, 這輛汽車的運轉費用很低。**b) costs** also 又作 **court costs** *AmE* the money that you must pay to lawyers etc if you are involved in a legal case in court, especially if you are guilty【美】訴訟費用: *Bellisario won the case and was awarded costs.* 貝利撒里奧贏了官司, 訴訟費被判由敗訴方支付。

4 ►PRICE PAID 支付的價格◄ [singular] *especially AmE* the price that someone pays for something that they are going to sell; COST PRICE【尤美】成本價格: **at cost** *His uncle's a car dealer and let him buy the car at cost.* 他的叔叔是汽車銷售商, 因此讓他按成本價格購買汽車。

5 find/know/learn etc sth to your cost to realize something is true because you have had a very unpleasant experience 從不愉快的經歷中得知某事: *Driving fast in wet conditions is dangerous, as my brother discovered to his cost!* 我兄弟從自己的痛苦經歷中知道, 雨天快速駕車是危險的! —see also 另見 **count the cost** (COUNT¹ (9))

This graph shows some of the words most commonly used with the noun **cost**. 本圖表所示為含有名詞 cost 的一些最常用的詞組。

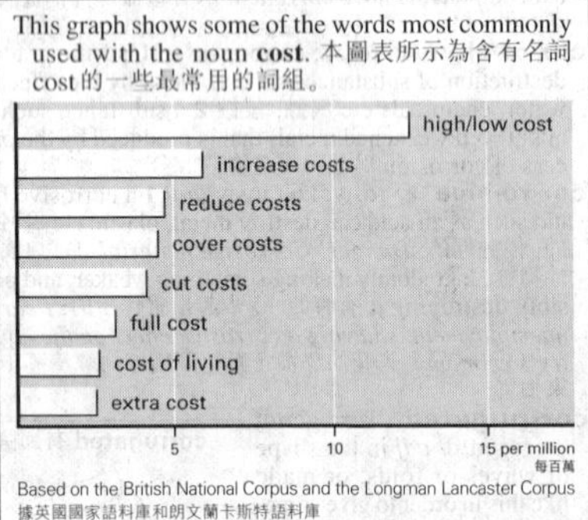

Based on the British National Corpus and the Longman Lancaster Corpus
據英國國家語料庫和朗文蘭卡斯特語料庫

USAGE NOTE 用法說明: COST

WORD CHOICE 詞語辨析: **price, cost, charge, fare, fees, rent, rental**

When you are talking about the money you need to buy a particular thing, the usual word is **price**. 談到購買某一特定物品需用的錢時一般用 price: *the price of a CD/piece of land/packet of cigarettes/cauliflower* 一張雷射唱片/一塊地/一包香煙/花椰菜的價格

Cost (*n*) is like **price**, but is used less for objects, and more for services or activities. 名詞 cost 和 price 相似, 但較少用於物品, 較多用於服務或活動: *the*

cost of having the house painted/going on holiday 粉刷房子的費用/度假的花費。It is also used for general things. 也用於一般費用: *the cost of living* (NOT 不用 *of life*) 生活費用 | *the cost of food* 食品費用 | *the cost of production/postage* (NOT 不用 … *for postage*) 生產費用/郵費。The **cost** of something may be *high* or *low* but not *free* or *expensive*. 形容物品的費用可用 high (高) 或 low (低), 但是不能用 free (免費) 或 expensive (昂貴)。

The amount of money you pay for something is what it **costs** (*v*) you. 你買某物花錢, 動詞是 cost: *How much did this CD cost you?* 這張雷射唱片你花了多少錢? | *It cost £1000 to have the house painted.* 粉刷房子花了 1000 英鎊。Things may **cost** *a lot* but not *cost high/expensive*. 物品可能會 cost a lot (昂貴), 但是不能說 cost high/expensive。

The person who is selling goods or services to you **charges** you for them. 賣東西或提供服務的人索價, 動詞是 charge: *How much did he charge you for mending the car/for that CD?* 修理汽車/買那張雷射唱片他要了你多少錢? A **charge** (*n*) is a sum of money asked, especially for allowing someone to do something or for a service. 名詞 charge 意指要支付的一筆錢, 尤指准許某人做某事或為獲得服務所需支付的錢: *There will be a small charge for admission to the museum/for reconnecting your gas supply.* 參觀博物館/重新開通煤氣要付少量的錢。

A charge for travelling on a plane, train, bus etc. is the **fare**. The charge for professional services, for a course etc is the **fees** (plural). The charge for living in someone else's room or house for some time is the **rent**. In a hotel, however, you pay the **price** of the room. The charge when you rent/hire a car etc is the **rental**. 乘飛機、火車、公共汽車等旅行的費用是 fare。專業服務、課程等的費用是 fees〔複數〕。房租是 rent, 但是酒店的房租是 price。租/雇用汽車的費用是 rental。

GRAMMAR 語法

Remember that the past tense and past participle of **cost** is **cost**, not *costed.* 記住 cost 的過去式和過去分詞是 cost, 而不是 costed。*This trip has cost her a fortune.* 這次旅行花了她一大筆錢。

1 2 **cost²** *v*

1 ►PRICE 價錢◄ *past tense and past participle* **cost** [linking verb 連繫動詞] to have a particular price 價錢為; 使付出〔金錢〕: *Buy one of your own – they don't cost much.* 你自己也買一個吧, 花不了多少錢。| **cost (sb) sth** *How much did the work cost you?* 這件成品花了你多少錢? | **cost a (small) fortune/the earth** (=cost a lot of money) 價錢昂貴 *The meal cost a small fortune, but it was well worth it.* 這頓飯價錢昂貴但是很值。| **cost a bomb** *BrE* (=cost a lot of money)【英】昂貴 *What a fantastic dress. It must have cost a bomb!* 這件衣服真漂亮, 一定很昂貴!

2 cost sb their job/life/marriage etc to do something that makes you lose your job etc 以工作/生命/婚姻等為代價: *Joe's brave action cost him his life.* 喬的英勇行為讓他犧牲了生命。

3 it will cost you *spoken* used to say that something will be expensive【口】你得花大錢: *Tickets are still available, but they'll cost you!* 票仍然能買到, 但是你得花大價錢!

4 ►CALCULATE COST 計算成本◄ *past tense and past participle* **costed** [T usually passive 一般用被動態] to calculate the cost of something or decide how much something should cost 計算…的成本; 估計…的花費: *We'll get the plan costed before presenting it to the board.* 在提交董事會以前, 我們要估計一下該計劃的成本。

5 cost an arm and a leg/cost a pretty penny to have a price that is too high 昂貴: *We'd like to send the children to private school but it would cost us an arm and a leg.* 我們想把孩子送到私立學校去, 但是學費非常昂貴。

6 cost sb dear/dearly to make someone suffer a lot 使某人付出沉重代價: *The delay in sending our report cost us dearly because it meant we lost the contract.* 我們的報告延誤了, 因此我們損失很大, 因為那意味着我們失去了合同。

7 sth costs money *spoken* used to remind or warn someone that they should be careful because something is expensive【口】某物很貴的〔提醒或警告某人小心〕: *Don't leave your sneakers in the rain! Shoes cost money, you know.* 不要讓雨水淋濕你的運動鞋! 你知道鞋子很貴的。

co-star¹ /ˋko ˋstɑr; ˈkəʊ stɑː/ *n* [C] one of two or more famous actors that work together in a film or play 合演者; 聯合主演者

co-star² *v* [I+**with**] to be working in a film or play with other famous actors 合演, 聯袂出演

cost-ben·e·fit a·nal·y·sis /ˌ· ˈ··· ·ˌ···/ *n* [C] *technical* a way of calculating the methods or plans that will bring you the most benefits for the smallest cost【術語】成本效益分析

cost ef·fec·tive /ˌ· ·ˈ··◂/ *adj* bringing the best possible profits or advantages for the lowest possible costs 低成本高利潤的; 有成本效益的: *Recruitment and training have to be planned in the most cost effective way.* 招聘和培訓必須要以最經濟的方式來進行。—**cost effectively** *adv* —**cost effectiveness** *n* [U]

cos·ter·mon·ger /ˋkɑstɚˌmʌŋgɚ; ˈkɒstəˌmʌŋgə/ *n* [C] *BrE old use* someone who sells fruit and vegetables in the street【英舊】〔在街上賣水果和蔬菜的〕小販

cost·ing /ˋkɔstɪŋ; ˈkɒstɪŋ/ *n* [C,U] the process of calculating the cost of a future business activity, product etc, or the calculation itself 成本估算: *Have we got the costings through yet?* 我們完成成本估算了嗎?

cost·ly /ˋkɔstlɪ; ˈkɒstli/ *adj* **1** too expensive and wasting a lot of money 太昂貴的, 花太多錢的: *Replacing all the windows would be too costly.* 更換所有的窗戶要花很多錢。**2** something that is costly causes a lot of problems or trouble 代價高的; 損失大的: *Hawksworth letting that goal in proved a costly mistake.* 霍克沃斯讓球進了, 這是一個代價高昂的錯誤。—**costliness** *n* [U]

cost-plus /ˌ· ˈ·◂/ *adj technical* a cost-plus contract gives the person selling all of their costs (COST¹ (3)) and part of the profit as well【術語】〔合同〕成本加成的, 成本加利潤的

cost price /ˌ· ˈ·◂/ *n* [U] the price that someone pays for something that they are going to sell 成本價格; COST¹ (4) *especially AmE*【尤美】

cos·tume /ˋkɑstum; ˈkɒstjʊm/ *n* **1** [C,U] a set of clothes that are typical of a particular place or historical period of time〔代表某一特定地方或歷史時期的〕服裝: *The dancers were all in national costume.* 跳舞的人都穿着民族服裝。**2** [C] a set of clothes worn to make you look like something such as an animal, GHOST¹ (1) etc or to hide who you are 化裝服; 戲裝: *Hallowe'en costumes* 萬聖節化裝服 **3** [C] *BrE* a SWIMMING COSTUME【英】游泳衣, 泳裝

costume dra·ma /ˈ·· ˌ··/ *n* [C] a play that is about a particular time in history, in which people wear costumes from that time 古裝劇

costume jew·elle·ry /ˈ·· ˌ···/ *n* [U] cheap jewellery that is often designed to look expensive〔便宜但貌似昂貴的〕人造珠寶飾物

co·sy¹ *especially BrE*【尤英】, **cozy** *AmE*【美】/ˋkozɪ; ˈkəʊzi/ *adj* **1** a place that is cosy is small, comfortable, and warm 小而溫暖舒適的: *a cosy room* 溫暖舒適的小房間 **2** a situation that is cosy is comfortable and friendly 友好的, 融洽的: *a cosy chat* 友好的談話 **3** having a close connection or relationship, especially one you do not approve of 密切的; 互相勾結的: *cosy deals with local councils* 與幾個地方議會的默契交易 —**cosily** *adv* —**cosiness** *n* [U]

cosy² *n* [C] a covering for a teapot etc that keeps the tea inside from getting cold too quickly〔茶壺的〕保暖罩: *a tea cosy* 茶壺保暖罩

cot /kɑt; kɒt/ *n* [C] **1** *BrE* a small bed with high sides for a young child【英】〔有欄杆的〕嬰兒牀; CRIB¹ (1) *AmE*【美】—see picture at 參見 BED¹ 圖 **2** *AmE* a CAMP BED【美】行軍牀, 摺疊牀

co·tan·gent /koˋtændʒənt; kəʊˈtændʒənt/ *n* [C] *technical* the measurement of an angle in a TRIANGLE (1) with a RIGHT ANGLE that is calculated by dividing the length of the side next to it by the length of the side opposite it【術語】〔數學的〕餘切 —compare 比較 TANGENT (3)

cot death /ˈ· ,·/ *n* [C] *BrE* the sudden and unexpected death of a healthy baby while it is sleeping【英】嬰兒猝死; CRIB DEATH *AmE*【美】

co·te·rie /ˋkotərɪ; ˈkəʊtəri/ *n* [C] a small group of people who enjoy doing the same things together, and do not like including others〔有共同興趣、嗜好的排外〕小團體, 小圈子

co·ter·mi·nous /koˋtɝmənəs; kəʊˈtɜːmɪnəs/ *adj formal* coterminous countries share the same border【正式】〔國家〕有共同邊界的; 毗鄰的

co·til·lion /koˋtɪljən; kəˈtɪljən/ *n* [C] a formal occasion when people dance; BALL¹ (11) 正式舞會

S2 W3 **cot·tage** /ˋkɑtɪdʒ; ˈkɒtɪdʒ/ *n* [C] *especially BrE* a small house in the country【尤英】小屋; 村舍: *We're staying in a holiday cottage in Dorset.* 我們在多塞特的村舍裡度假。

cottage cheese /,·· ˈ·/ *n* [U] soft white cheese made from sour milk 農家乾酪〔一種白色軟乾酪, 用酸奶製成〕

cottage hos·pi·tal /,·· ˈ···/ *n BrE* a small hospital, usually in a country area【英】〔鄉村的〕小醫院

cottage in·dus·try /,·· ˈ···/ *n* [C] an industry that consists of people working at home 家庭小工業: *a programme to promote cottage industry in rural areas* 促進農村地區家庭小工業發展的項目

cot·tag·er /ˋkɑtɪdʒɚ; ˈkɒtɪdʒə/ *n* [C] *BrE slang* a man who looks for HOMOSEXUAL partners in a public place such as a toilet【英俚】〔在公共場所〕尋找同性戀伴侶的男子

cot·tag·ing /ˋkɑtɪdʒɪŋ; ˈkɒtɪdʒɪŋ/ *n* [U] *BrE slang* the practice of looking for male HOMOSEXUAL partners in a public place such as a toilet【英俚】在公共場所尋找男同性戀伴侶

cot·ton¹ /ˋkɑtn̩; ˈkɒtn/ *n* [U] **1** cloth or thread made from the white hair of the cotton plant 棉布; 棉紗: *a crisp cotton shirt* 清爽的棉襯衫 **2** a plant with white hairs on its seeds that are used for making cotton cloth and thread 棉〔植物〕 **3** *BrE* thread used for sewing【英】〔縫紉用的〕線 **4** *AmE* COTTON WOOL【美】藥棉

cotton² *v*

cotton on *phr v* [I] *informal* to begin to understand something【非正式】開始明白, 領會: *I dropped about six hints before he cottoned on.* 我暗示了大約六次他才開始醒悟。

cotton to *phr v* [T] *AmE informal* to begin to like a person, idea etc【美, 非正式】開始喜歡: *I didn't cotton to her at first, but she's really nice.* 我一開始並不喜歡她, 但是她真的很好。

cotton bud /,·· ˈ·/ *n* [C] *BrE* a small thin stick with COTTON WOOL at each end, used for cleaning places that are hard to reach, such as inside your ears【英】棉籤; Q-TIP *AmE*【美】

cotton can·dy /,·· ˈ··/ *n* [U] *AmE* CANDYFLOSS【美】棉花糖

cotton gin /ˈ·· ·/ *n* [C] a machine that separates the seeds of a cotton plant from the cotton 軋棉機, 軋花機

cotton pick·ing /ˈ·· ,··/ *adj* [only before noun 僅用於名詞前] *AmE spoken* used to emphasize that you are annoyed or surprised【美口】該死的, 糟糕透頂的〔感嘆語〕: *Mind your own cotton picking business!* 別多管老子的閒事!

cotton reel /ˈ·· ·/ *n* [C] *BrE* the small object that cotton thread is wound around【英】線軸; SPOOL (2) *AmE*【美】

cot·ton·tail /ˋkɑtn̩,tel; ˈkɒtnteɪl/ *n* [C] *AmE* a small rabbit with a white tail【美】棉尾兔, 白尾兔

cot·ton·wood /ˋkɑtn̩,wʊd; ˈkɒtnwʊd/ *n* [C,U] a North American tree with seeds that look like white cotton 棉白楊, 三角葉楊

cotton wool /,·· ˈ·◂/ *n* [U] *BrE*【英】**1** a soft mass of cotton that you use especially for cleaning and protecting wounds 藥棉, 脫脂棉: *Cotton wool pads are good for removing make-up.* 脫脂棉墊用來抹去化妝品很好。 **2 wrap sb in cotton wool** to protect someone completely from the dangers, difficulties etc of life 保護某人使其完全免於〔危險、困難等〕: *You can't wrap those kids in cotton wool all their lives.* 你不可能保護那些孩子一輩子。

cot·y·le·don /,kɑtl̩ˋidn̩; ,kɒtɪˈliːdn/ *n* [C] *technical* the first leaf that grows from a seed【術語】子葉

couch¹ /kaʊtʃ; kaʊtʃ/ *n* [C] **1** a comfortable piece of furniture for two or three people to sit on, or for one person to lie down on; SOFA 長沙發 **2** *literary* a bed【文】臥榻

couch² *v* **be couched in** *formal* to be expressed in a particular way【正式】以〔特定方式〕表達, 措辭: *The offer was couched in obscure legal jargon.* 那份提議用晦澀的法律用語寫成。

cou·chette /kuˋʃɛt; kuːˈʃet/ *n* [C] **1** a narrow bed that folds down from the wall in a train〔火車上的〕可摺疊臥鋪 **2** a comfortable seat on a night boat or train〔夜航船隻、火車的〕軟席 —compare 比較 SLEEPING CAR

couch po·ta·to /ˈ· ·,··/ *n* [C] *informal* someone who spends a lot of time sitting and watching television【非正式】老泡在電視機前的人

cou·gar /ˋkugɚ; ˈkuːgə/ *n* [C] a large brown wild cat from the mountains of Western North America and South America; MOUNTAIN LION 美洲獅

cough¹ /kɔf; kɒf/ *v* **1** [I] to suddenly push air out of your throat with a short sound 咳嗽, 咳: *coughing from smoking too many cigarettes* 抽煙太多而咳嗽 **2** also 又作 **cough up** [T] to get something out of your throat or lungs by coughing 咳出: *You must go to the doctor if you're coughing up blood.* 如果咳血的話你必須去看醫生。 **3** [I] to make a coughing sound 發出咳嗽般的聲音: *The engine coughed once or twice but wouldn't start.* 發動機喀喀地響了一兩聲, 但是發動不起來。

cough up *phr v* [I,T **cough** sth ↔ **up**] *informal* to unwillingly give someone money, information etc【非正式】勉強給以〔錢、信息等〕: *Dad's finally coughed up for the stereo I wanted.* 爸爸終於勉強出錢買了我想要的立體聲音響。

cough² *n* **1** [C] the action or sound made when you cough 咳嗽; 咳嗽聲 **2** [U] a medical condition that makes you cough a lot 咳嗽病: *She's got a terrible smoker's cough.* 她由於抽煙而得了嚴重的咳嗽病。

cough drop /ˈ· ·/ *n* [C] *especially AmE* a cough sweet【尤美】潤喉糖, 止咳糖

cough mix·ture /ˈ· ,··/ also 又作 **cough syrup** *BrE*【英】*n* [U] a thick liquid containing medicine that helps you to stop coughing 止咳藥水

cough sweet /ˈ· ·/ *n* [C] *BrE* a sweet containing medicine that you suck when you have a sore throat【英】潤喉糖, 止咳糖; COUGH DROP *especially AmE*【尤美】

could /kəd; kəd; *strong* 強讀 kud; kʊd/ *modal verb 3rd person singular* 第三人稱單數 **could** *negative short form* 否定縮略式為 **couldn't** **1** the past tense of 'can' can 的過去式: *Could you hear that all right?* 你能聽清楚嗎? | *I couldn't get tickets after all, they were sold out.* 我終於沒買到票, 票都賣完了。| *Marcia said we could smoke, it was okay with her.* 馬西婭說我們可以抽煙, 她不介意的。—see 見 CAN¹ (USAGE) **2** used to ask if someone is able or allowed to do something〔用於問某人是否能或被允許做某事〕: *Could I ask you a couple of questions?*

我能問你幾個問題嗎? | *What about Sam? Could he come along too?* 薩姆怎麼樣?他也能來嗎? **3** used to express something that might be possible or might happen, when it is not certain that it will happen or be possible〔用於表示某事有可能發生〕: *Most accidents in the home could be easily prevented.* 大多數家庭事故都是可以輕易避免的。| *It could be weeks before the construction is actually finished.* 建築工程真正完成可能還要幾個星期。| *If you're not careful, you could find yourself without enough stock to fill the order.* 如果你不仔細的話, 可能會沒有足夠的存貨來應付訂單。**4** used to be polite when you are asking someone to do something〔用於禮貌地請某人做某事〕: *Could you pay this check into the bank for me tomorrow?* 明天你能替我把支票存進銀行嗎? | *Yeah, there are a couple of things you could do for me if you're going into town.* 是的, 如果你要進城的話, 或許可以替我辦幾件事。**5** used to suggest what you think someone should do or might be able to do〔用於表示你認為某人應當做或可能做某事〕: *We could get the bus instead.* 我們可以改乘公共汽車。| *You could always try phoning her at the office.* 你甚麼時候都可以試着打她辦公室的電話找她。| *If you could let us know your decision as soon as possible, it would be a great help.* 如果你能儘快通知我們你的決定, 那會有很大的幫助。**6** used to show that you are annoyed about something〔用於表示懊惱〕: *You could have told me you were going to be late!* 你應當告訴我你會遲到的! | *I'm sure John could be more careful when he's washing up.* 我確信約翰洗餐具的時候可以更細心。| *How could you say such an insulting thing to her! She's my best friend!* 你怎麼能對她說那種侮辱性的話呢! 她是我最好的朋友! **7 I couldn't care less** used when you are not at all interested in or concerned about something 一點也不關心, 不在乎: *I said I couldn't care less if I got paid triple time, I'm not coming in on a Sunday.* 我說我不在乎得三倍的酬金, 星期天我是不會來的。| *A lot of the students just couldn't care less about learning anything.* 很多學生對學習漠不關心。**8 I couldn't agree more** used when you completely agree with someone 完全同意: *I couldn't agree more. There's just far too much sex and violence on TV.* 我完全同意, 電視上確實有太多的色情和暴力。**9 I could have strangled/hit/killed etc sb** used to emphasize that you were very angry with someone 對某人氣憤得真恨不得扼死/打/殺死他〔用於加強語氣〕: *I could have murdered Ryan for telling Jason that!* 瑞安居然把那件事告訴了賈森, 我真恨不得殺了他! **10 couldn't be more wonderful/exciting/boring etc** also 又作 **couldn't be better/prettier/worse etc** used to emphasize how good, exciting etc something is 非常好/令人激動/無聊等: *It couldn't have been a more restful vacation.* 那是一個非常舒心的假期。| *Things couldn't be worse, everything seems to be going wrong at once.* 事情非常糟, 好像一切都同時出毛病了。**11 I couldn't** used to politely say that you do not want any more food or drink 不需要了〔用於禮貌地表示你不再需要食物或飲料〕: *"Would you like another piece of pie?" "Oh, no thanks, I couldn't."* "你再來一塊餡餅好嗎?" "哦, 不, 謝謝, 我吃不下了。"

couldst /kʊdst; kʊdst/ *v* **thou couldst** *old use* you could【舊】你能

cou·lee /ˈkulɪ; ˈkuːli/ *n* [C] *AmE* a small valley with steep sides【美】斜壁小峽谷

coun·cil /ˈkaʊnsḷ; ˈkaʊnsəl/ *n* [C] **1** a group of people that are chosen to make rules, laws or decisions, or to give advice 委員會; 理事會: *the council for civil liberties* 民權委員會 **2** the organization that is responsible for local government in a particular region in Britain〔英國地方政府的〕政務委員會; 地方議會: *Bob Jones has been on the Borough Council for years.* 鮑勃·瓊斯已在自治市議會待了很多年。| **council offices/housing/worker etc** *BrE* (=owned, employed etc by local government)【英】地方政府辦公室/建的住房/工作人員等 *Dave's got his name down for a council flat.* 戴夫已經申請了地方政府建的公寓, 正在等候。**3** a group of people elected to the government of a city in the US〔美國的〕地方議會: *the Los Angeles city council* 洛杉磯市議會 **4 council of war** *humorous* a meeting to decide how to deal with a particular problem【幽默】緊急會議

council es·tate /ˈ·· ·,·/ *n* [C] *BrE* an area consisting of streets of council houses【英】地方政府建的住房群

council house /ˈ·· ·/ *n* [C] a house or flat in Britain that is provided by the local council for a very low rent〔英國地方議會提供的〕市[郡]建住房

coun·cil·lor *BrE*【英】, **councilor** *AmE*【美】/ˈkaunslə; ˈkaʊnsələ/ *n* [C] a member of a council 委員; 理事; 市政議員; 議員: *Write to your local councilor to complain.* 寫信給你當地的市政議員來投訴。

coun·cil·man /ˈkaunsḷmən; ˈkaʊnsəlmən/ *n* [C] a man who is a member of the government of a city in the US〔美國的〕男市議會議員

coun·cil·wom·an /ˈkaunsḷˌwumən; ˈkaʊnsəlˌwʊmən/ *n* [C] a woman who is a member of the government of a city in the US〔美國的〕女市議會議員

coun·sel¹ /ˈkaunsḷ; ˈkaʊnsəl/ *n technical*【術語】**1** [singular] a type of lawyer who represents you in court 訟務律師: *The judge asked counsel for the defence to explain.* 法官要求被告的辯護律師作出解釋。**2 keep your own counsel** to keep your plans, opinions etc secret 不透露自己的計劃[觀點等] **3** [U] *literary* advice【文】忠告

counsel² *v* [T] **1** *formal* to advise someone【正式】建議: **counsel sb to do sth** *She counselled them not to accept this settlement.* 她建議他們不要接受這解決方案。**2** to listen and give support to someone with problems 忠告; 輔導: *a new unit to counsel alcoholics* 一個輔導酗酒者的新機構

coun·sel·ling *BrE*【英】, **counseling** *AmE*【美】/ˈkaunsḷɪŋ; ˈkaʊnsəlɪŋ/ *n* [U] the act of listening to people and giving them support with their problems, especially as your job 輔導〔尤指職業性的〕: *She's been undergoing counseling for depression.* 她由於精神沮喪而在接受輔導。

coun·sel·lor *BrE*【英】, **counselor** *AmE*【美】/ˈkaunslə; ˈkaʊnsələ/ *n* [C] someone whose job is to help and support people with problems 顧問: *Have you thought of seeing a counsellor?* 你想過要去找顧問嗎? —see 見 LAWYER (USAGE)

count¹ /kaunt; kaʊnt/ *v*

1 ►SAY NUMBERS 數數◄ also 又作 **count up** [I] to say numbers in their correct order〔按順序〕數: [+to] *Sarah can count up to five now.* 莎拉現在能數到五。| *Try to count to ten before you lose your temper.* 你要發脾氣時先數到十。

2 ►FIND THE TOTAL 得出總數◄ also 又作 **count up** [T] to count the people, objects, numbers etc in a group in order to find a total 計數; 點數目: *The teacher was counting the children as they got on the bus.* 在上公共汽車的時候, 老師清點學生的數目。| **count sheep** (=count imaginary sheep as a way of getting to sleep) 數羊〔睡前數數字幫助入睡的一種方法〕

3 ►INCLUDE 包括◄ [T] to include someone or something in a total 把…計算在內; 包括: *There are five people in the family counting my parents.* 我家有五口人, 包括我父母在內。| **count sb/sth among** *I count Jules and Ady among my closest friends.* 我把朱爾斯和埃迪算作我最親密的朋友。

4 ►BE ALLOWED 得到許可◄ [I,T] to be officially allowed or accepted; VALID 正式被允許, 被接受; 有效: *Illegible entries do not count.* 不清晰的參賽品無效。

5 count yourself lucky/fortunate etc to feel that you are lucky etc 認為自己是幸運的等: *After the avalanche we counted ourselves lucky to be alive.* 我們經歷了雪崩後還能活着真幸運。

6 ►IMPORTANT 重要的◄ [I not in progressive 不用進行式] to be a very important or valuable thing 重要: *First impressions really do count.* 第一印象真的很重要。| **count for something/anything/more etc** *His promises* *don't count for much.* 他的承諾算不了甚麼。

7 be able to count sb/sth on (the fingers of) one hand *spoken* used to emphasize how small the number of something is【口】屈指可數: *You could have counted the number of people in the theater on one hand.* 劇院中的人很少, 你用指頭就可以數過來。

8 don't count your chickens (before they're hatched) *especially spoken* used to say that you should not make plans because you hope something good will happen【尤口】不要指望過早: *It should be worth a few million, but I don't like to count my chickens.* 那應該會值幾百萬, 但是我不想打如意算盤。

9 count the cost to start having problems as a result of your earlier decisions or mistakes 開始嘗惡果: *We're now counting the cost of not taking out medical insurance.* 我們現在嘗到沒有買醫療保險的後果。

10 who's counting? used to say that you are not worried about the number of times something happens 不在乎, 不擔心〔某事發生的次數〕: *"But I always smoke your cigarettes." "No problem, who's counting?"* "但是我總是抽你的香煙。" "沒問題, 我不在乎。" —see also 另見 **stand up and be counted** (STAND[1]), **it's the thought that counts** (THOUGHT[2] (12))

count sb/sth **as** *phr v* [I] to consider or regard someone or something in a particular way 認為, 看作: *For tax purposes this counts as unearned income.* 報稅時這被視為非工資收入。

count down *phr v* [I] to record the time passing until an important event happens〔重要事情發生前的〕倒數: *We're counting down to our holiday.* 我們在倒數計時, 等待假期來臨。

count sb **in** *phr v* [T] *informal* to include someone in a planned activity【非正式】把…計算在內: *Mark, can we count you in for the cricket team?* 馬克, 我們能把你算在板球隊裡嗎?

count on/upon sb/sth *phr v* [T] **1** to depend on or be certain of someone or something 依靠; 指望: *You can count on my vote.* 我準會投你一票。| *If I got into trouble I could always count on Rusty.* 如果我有麻煩, 總可以依靠拉斯蒂幫忙。| **count on doing sth** *We're all counting on winning this contract.* 我們都指望爭取到這份合同。| **count on sb/sth doing sth** *Just don't count on Bev being too thrilled about the news.* 不要指望貝夫會對這個消息很高興。| **count on sb/sth to do sth** *You can count on Dean to ruin any party.* 迪安去甚麼聚會都會令人掃興。**2** to plan or expect to do something 期望, 指望, 料想: **count on (sb/sth) doing sth** *We didn't count on so many people being on vacation.* 我們沒有想到會有那麼多人度假。

count sb/sth **out** *phr v* [T] **1** to lay things down one by one as you count them 數, 數出: *The teller counted out ten $50 bills.* 出納點出十張 50 美元面額的鈔票。**2** *informal* to not include someone or something【非正式】不包括, 不算: *If you're looking for trouble you can count me out.* 如果你要找麻煩, 別把我拉進去。

S2 W3 **count²** *n* [C]

1 ▶TOTAL 合計◀ the total that you get by counting a particular set of things, or the process of doing this 總數; 計算: *The vote was so close that we had to have several counts.* 選票數如此接近, 我們不得不計算好幾次。

2 ▶MEASUREMENT 計算◀ a measurement that shows how much of a substance is present in the area or thing being examined〔某物存在或經計算得出的〕數字, 數目: *The pollen count is high today.* 今天的花粉數很高。| *a low sperm count* 精子數量不多

3 at the last count used to give the latest information about a particular situation 據最新的信息: *At the last count, 46 students were interested in the trip.* 根據最新統計, 有 46 個學生對這次旅行感興趣。

4 on all/several etc counts in every way, in several ways etc 方方面面/在某些方面等: *Their education policy has failed on several counts.* 他們的教育政策在幾個方面失敗了。

5 keep count to keep a record of the changing total of something over a period of time〔在一段時間內〕記錄變化的數字: *I never manage to keep count of what I spend on the credit card.* 我從來弄不清用信用卡花了多少錢。

6 lose count to forget a number you were calculating or a total you were trying to count 計不清數字: *Shut up – you've made me lost count now!* 閉嘴! 我都被你吵得忘記數到幾了!

7 be out for the count a) to be in a deep sleep 沉睡中: *There's no point in asking George – he's out for the count.* 問喬治根本沒用, 他正在酣睡。**b)** if a BOXER (1) is out for the count, he has been knocked down for ten seconds or more〔拳擊比賽中〕被擊倒地十秒

8 ▶LAW 法律◀ *technical* one of the crimes that someone is charged with【術語】被指控的罪狀: *Davis was found not guilty on all counts.* 指控戴維斯的各項罪狀都不能成立。

9 ▶RANK/TITLE 等級/頭銜◀ a European NOBLEMAN whose rank is similar to a British EARL 伯爵〔歐洲貴族的稱號〕: *the Count of Monte Cristo* 基度山伯爵

count·a·ble /ˈkaʊntəbl; ˈkaʊntəbəl/ *adj* a countable noun has both a singular and a plural form 可數的: *Countable nouns like 'table' or 'tables' are marked [C] in this book.* 可數名詞如 table 或 tables 在本書中用 [C] 標示。—see also 另見 COUNT NOUN —compare 比較 UNCOUNTABLE

coun·te·nance¹ /ˈkaʊntənəns; ˈkaʊntn̩əns/ *n formal*【正式】**1** [C] your face or your expression 面部表情, 面容: *the gloomy countenance of a disappointed child* 一個失望孩子的憂鬱面容 **2** [U] support or approval 支持; 贊成

countenance² *v* [T] to accept, support, or approve of something 支持; 贊同; 認可: **countenance doing sth** *Her father won't countenance her getting married so young.* 她父親不贊同她那麼年輕就結婚。

counter- /kaʊntə; kaʊntə/ *prefix* **1** the opposite of something〔與…〕相反: *a counterproductive thing to do* (=producing results opposite to what you wanted) 適得其反的行為 **2** matching something 對應, 對等, 相當: *my counterpart in the American system* (=someone who has the same job as mine) 美國體制中與我地位相當的人 **3** done or given as a reaction to something, especially to oppose it 反, 逆: *proposals and counter-proposals* 建議和反建議 **4** acting to prevent something 反, 防, 抗: *a counterinsurgency strategy* (=to prevent INSURGENTS) 反叛亂策略

coun·ter¹ /ˈkaʊntə; ˈkaʊntə/ *n* [C]

1 ▶SHOP 商店◀ the place where you pay or are served in a shop, bank, restaurant etc 櫃台

2 over the counter drugs, medicines etc that are bought over the counter are ones that you can buy in a shop without a PRESCRIPTION (1) from a doctor〔買藥〕不用處方

3 under the counter if you buy something under the counter, you buy it secretly and usually illegally 祕密地, 暗地裡〔通常違法地〕: *It's risky, but you can get alcohol under the counter.* 那是危險的, 但是你可以暗地裡買酒。

4 ▶KITCHEN 廚房◀ *AmE* a flat surface on top of a piece of furniture, especially in a kitchen, used for working on, preparing food etc【美】〔尤指廚房中的〕操作台面, 工作台; WORK-SURFACE *BrE*【英】: *Just leave my keys on the kitchen counter.* 把我的鑰匙放在廚房的台面就行了。—see picture on page A10 參見 A10 頁圖

5 ▶GAME 遊戲◀ a small round object that you use in some games that are played on a board 籌碼

6 ▶EQUIPMENT 裝備◀ a piece of electrical equipment that counts something 計算器, 計數器: *Set the video counter to zero before you press play.* 在你按播放鍵之前把錄像機上的計數器撥到零。—see also 另見 GEIGER COUNTER

7 ▶ACTION AGAINST STH 反對◀ an action that is

used to try to prevent something bad from happening, or an argument used to prove that something is wrong 制止; 反駁: [+to] *Britain began its pro-Japanese policy as a counter to Russian advances in Asia.* 英國開始執行親日政策以對抗俄羅斯在亞洲的擴張。

counter[2] *v* **1** [I,T] to say something in order to try to prove that what someone said was not true 反駁, 反對: [+that] *"That's not what James told me," he countered.* "詹姆斯不是這樣告訴我的。"他反駁道。| **counter an argument/allegation etc** *He was determined to counter the bribery allegations.* 他決心要反駁受賄的指控。**2** [T] to do something in order to reduce the bad effects of something, or to defend yourself against them 抵消; 對抗; 制止: *One way of countering these problems would be to redistribute wealth among the poor.* 制止這類問題的一種方法是在窮人中間重新分配財富。

counter[3] *adv* [not before noun 不用於名詞前] in a way that is opposite to something 相反地: **run counter to** *The child is asked to behave in ways which run counter to his natural desires.* 孩子被要求做違背他意願的事。—**counter** *adj*: *To publicize this revolting film is counter to the standards of your newspaper.* 宣傳這部令人反感的電影有悖貴報的標準。

coun·ter·act /ˌkaʊntɚˋækt; ˌkaʊntərˈækt/ *v* [T] to reduce or prevent the bad effect of something, by doing something that has the opposite effect 抵消; 對抗: *a drug that counteracts the poison* 解毒藥 —**counteraction** /-ˋækʃən; -ˈækʃən/ *n* [C,U]

coun·ter·at·tack /ˋkaʊntərəˌtæk; ˈkaʊntərəˌtæk/ *n* [C] an attack that you make against someone who has attacked you, in a war, sport, or an argument 反攻, 反擊: *I decided on a swift counterattack.* 我決定迅速反擊。—**counterattack** *v* [I,T] —**counterattacker** *n* [C]

coun·ter·bal·ance /ˌkaʊntɚˋbæləns; ˌkaʊntəˈbæləns/ *v* [T] to have an equal and opposite effect to something such as a change, feeling etc 使平衡; 抵消: *His fear of his father is counterbalanced by a genuine respect.* 他對父親的畏懼被發自內心的尊敬抵消了。—**counterbalance** /ˋkaʊntɚˌbæləns; ˈkaʊntəˌbæləns/ *n* [C]

coun·ter·clock·wise /ˌkaʊntɚˋklɑkˌwaɪz; ˌkaʊntəˈklɒkwaɪz◂/ *adv AmE* moving in the opposite direction to the hands of a clock【美】逆時針方向地; ANTICLOCKWISE *BrE*【英】: *To remove the lid, turn it counterclockwise.* 要打開蓋子, 請把它按逆時針方向轉。—opposite 反義詞 CLOCKWISE

coun·ter·feit[1] /ˋkaʊntɚfɪt; ˈkaʊntəfɪt/ *adj* made to look exactly like something else 偽造的; 仿造的: *The task force were looking for counterfeit money.* 特警隊在尋找偽幣。

counterfeit[2] *v* [T] to copy something exactly in order to deceive people 偽造; 仿造

coun·ter·foil /ˋkaʊntɚˌfɔɪl; ˈkaʊntəfɔɪl/ *n* [C] the part of something such as a cheque that you keep so that you can remember how much money you have spent〔支票等的〕存根

coun·ter·in·sur·gen·cy /ˌkaʊntərɪnˋsɝdʒənsɪ; ˌkaʊntərɪnˈsɜːdʒənsi/ *n* [U] military action against people who are fighting against their own country's government 反暴動; 反叛亂

coun·ter·in·tel·li·gence /ˌkaʊntərɪnˋtɛlədʒəns; ˌkaʊntərɪnˈteləˌdʒəns/ *n* [U] action that a country takes in order to stop other countries discovering their secrets 反情報[反間諜]活動

coun·ter·mand /ˌkaʊntɚˋmænd; ˌkaʊntəˈmɑːnd/ *v* [T] to officially tell people to ignore an order, especially by giving them a different one 撤回[更改]〔命令〕: *Senior officers persuaded the general to countermand the order.* 高級軍官們說服將軍撤回命令。

coun·ter·mea·sure /ˋkaʊntɚˌmɛʒɚ; ˈkaʊntəmeʒə/ *n* [C usually plural 一般用複數] an action taken to prevent another action from having a harmful effect 對策; 對付措施: *new countermeasures against terrorism* 對抗恐怖主義的新措施

coun·ter·pane /ˋkaʊntɚˌpen; ˈkaʊntəpeɪn/ *n* [C] *old-fashioned* a thick cover that you put over all the other covers on a bed; BEDSPREAD【過時】牀罩

coun·ter·part /ˋkaʊntɚˌpɑrt; ˈkaʊntəpɑːt/ *n* [C] someone or something that has the same job or purpose as someone or something else in a different place 與另一方面地位職務相當的人[物]: *Belgian officials are discussing this with their French counterparts.* 比利時官員與法國同級官員正在討論這個問題。

coun·ter·point /ˋkaʊntɚˌpɔɪnt; ˈkaʊntəpɔɪnt/ *n* **1** [U] a combination of two or more tunes that are played together to sound like one tune 對位法〔音樂中結合兩個或兩個以上旋律的方法〕**2** [C] a tune that is one part of counterpoint 對位旋律

coun·ter·pro·duc·tive /ˌkaʊntɚprəˋdʌktɪv; ˌkaʊntəprəˈdʌktɪv◂/ *adj* achieving the opposite result to the one that you want 產生相反效果的: *Sending young offenders to prison can be counterproductive.* 把少年犯送進監獄會產生適得其反的效果。

counter-rev·o·lu·tion /ˌ·· ··ˈ··/ *n* [C,U] political or military actions taken to get rid of a government that is in power because of a previous REVOLUTION (2) 反革命 —**counter-revolutionary** *adj*

counter-rev·o·lu·tion·a·ry /ˌ·· ··ˈ····/ *n* [C] someone who is involved in a counter-revolution 反革命分子

coun·ter·sign /ˋkaʊntɚˌsaɪn; ˈkaʊntəsaɪn/ *v* [T] to sign a paper that has already been signed by someone else 連署, 副署: *The note must be countersigned by a doctor.* 這張便條必須有一個醫生連署。

coun·ter·ten·or /ˋkaʊntɚˌtɛnɚ; ˌkaʊntəˈtenə/ *n* [C] a man who is trained to sing with a very high voice 男音最高音歌手

counter-ter·ror·ist /ˈ·· ˌ···/ *adj* **counter-terrorist operation/team/unit etc** a plan or group that tries to prevent the violent activities of political groups who use force 反恐怖主義行動/隊伍/小組等 —**counter-terrorist** *n* [C]

coun·ter·vail·ing /ˋkaʊntɚˌvelɪŋ; ˌkaʊntəˈveɪlɪŋ◂/ *adj formal* with an equally strong but opposite effect【正式】抗衡的, 制衡的; 抵消的: *the need for countervailing forces to that of the state* 抗衡國家權力的需要

coun·tess /ˋkaʊntɪs; ˈkaʊntəs/ *n* [C] a woman with the same rank as an EARL or a COUNT[2] (9) 伯爵夫人; 女伯爵

counting house /ˈ·· ·/ *n* [C] an office where accounts and money were kept in former times〔舊時的〕賬房

count·less /ˋkaʊntlɪs; ˈkaʊntləs/ *adj* too many to be counted 無數的, 數不盡的: *It has saved my life, and the lives of countless others.* 它救了我的命, 也救了無數其他人的生命。| *I spent countless hours on trains and buses.* 我坐了很長很長時間的火車和公共汽車。

count noun /ˈ· ·/ *n* [C] *technical* a noun that has both singular and plural forms, can be used with numbers and with words such as many, few etc, or can be used with a or an【術語】可數名詞 —see also 另見 NOUN

coun·tri·fied /ˋkʌntrɪˌfaɪd; ˈkʌntrifaɪd/ *adj* typical of the countryside, or made to seem typical of the countryside 鄉村的, 土裡土氣的: *the countrified existence of the newly rich* 暴發戶土裡土氣的生活方式

coun·try[1] /ˋkʌntrɪ; ˈkʌntri/ *n* **1** [C] an area of land that is controlled by its own government, president, king etc 國家: *Pakistan became a fully independent country shortly after the Second World War.* 第二次世界大戰後不久巴基斯坦就成為一個完全獨立的國家。—compare 比較 NATION (1) —see also 另見 MOTHER COUNTRY —see 見 LAND[1] (USAGE) **2 the country a)** land that is outside towns and cities, including land used for farming; the countryside 郊外; 鄉村: *I've always wanted to live in the country.* 我一直想住在鄉下。**b)** all the people who live in a particular country 全國人民; 全體國民: *The President has the support of over 50 per cent of the country.* 總統獲得全體國民 50% 以上的支持。**3 farm-**

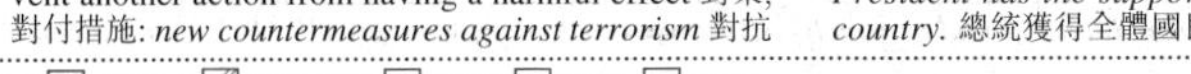

ing country/walking country etc land that is suitable for a particular activity 農業用地/散步場所等: *The Peak District is good walking country.* 峯區是散步的好場所。
4 go to the country *BrE* if a Prime Minister goes to the country, they ask for a GENERAL ELECTION to be held 【英】舉行大選

country² *adj* [only before noun 僅用於名詞前] belonging to or connected with the countryside 鄉下的, 農村的: *They much preferred country life to life in the city.* 比起城市生活來他們更喜歡農村生活。

country and west·ern /,‥ ·ˈ‥/ *n* [U] popular music in the style of music from the southern and western US 〔美國的〕鄉村與西部音樂

C

country bump·kin /,‥ ˈ‥/ *n* [C] someone from the countryside who seems stupid 鄉巴佬

country club /ˈ‥ ,·/ *n* [C] a sports and social club in the countryside, especially one for rich people 鄉村俱樂部

country danc·ing /,‥ ˈ‥/ *n* [U] a traditional form of dance in which pairs of dancers move in rows and circles 鄉村舞; 土風舞

country house /,‥ ˈ·/ *n* [C] *BrE* a large house in the countryside, especially one that is of historical interest 【英】鄉間邸宅[別墅]

coun·try·man /ˈkʌntrɪmən; ˈkʌntrimən/ *n plural* **countrymen** /-mən; -mən/ [C] **1** someone from your own country; COMPATRIOT 同胞; 同國人: *During the war, the loyalty of fellow countrymen was all-important.* 戰爭期間, 國民的忠誠是很重要的。**2** a man who lives in the country rather than a town or city 鄉下人

country mu·sic /ˈ‥ ,‥/ *n* [U] COUNTRY AND WESTERN 〔美國的〕鄉村與西部音樂

country seat /,‥ ˈ·/ *n* [C] *BrE* the countryside house of someone who is rich and owns land 【英】鄉紳的住宅; 莊園宅第

2 3 **coun·try·side** /ˈkʌntrɪˌsaɪd; ˈkʌntrisaɪd/ *n* [U] land that is outside cities and towns 郊外; 鄉下, 農村: *Our new house is surrounded by the most beautiful countryside.* 我們的新房子四周是非常美麗的鄉村。

coun·try·wom·an /ˈkʌntrɪˌwʊmən; ˈkʌntriˌwʊmən/ *n plural* **countrywomen** /-ˌwɪmɪn; -ˌwɪmɪn/ [C] a woman who lives in the country rather than a town or city 鄉村婦女

1 2 **coun·ty¹** /ˈkauntɪ; ˈkaʊnti/ *n* [C] an area of Great Britain, the US and some other countries that contains several towns that are governed together 〔英國的〕郡; 〔美國等國家的〕縣

county² *adj BrE informal* belonging to or typical of people from the upper classes in Britain 【英, 非正式】〔英國〕上流階層的

county coun·cil /,‥ ˈ‥/ *n* [C] an organization consisting of a group of people who are elected to organize schools, HOUSING etc, in a county in Britain 〔英國的〕郡政務委員會; 郡議會

county court /,‥ ˈ·/ *n* [C] *BrE* a local court of law that deals with private quarrels between people rather than with serious crimes 【英】〔英國的〕郡法院

county fair /,‥ ˈ·/ *n* [C] *AmE* an event that happens each year in a particular county, with games and competitions for the best farm animals, cooking etc 【美】〔農、畜產品的〕縣集市

county town /,‥ ˈ·/ *BrE* 【英】, **county seat** *AmE* 【美】 *n* [C] the town in a COUNTY¹ where its government is 郡[縣]首府

coup /ku; kuː/ *n* [C] **1** a sudden and sometimes violent attempt by citizens or the army to take control of the government; coup d'état (軍事)政變: *There were rumours of a coup in Moscow before Gorbachev was actually overthrown.* 在戈爾巴喬夫被真正推翻以前莫斯科有謠言說會發生政變。**2** an achievement that is extremely impressive because it was very difficult 成功之舉; 漂亮之舉: *Getting a former International as coach was a real coup for the club.* 俱樂部得到一個前國家隊隊員作教練確實是一個漂亮之舉。

coup de grâce /ku də ˋgrɑs; ˌkuː də ˈgrɑːs/ *n* [singular] *French* 【法】 **1** an action or event that ends or destroys something that has gradually been getting weaker 致命的打擊〔比喻〕: *The nuclear atoms delivered the coup de grâce to classical physics.* 核原子給予傳統物理學致命的打擊。**2** a hit or shot that kills someone or something 致命的一擊

coup d'état /ku deˋtɑ; ˌkuː deɪˈtɑː/ *n plural* **coups d'état** (*same pronunciation* 讀音相同) [C] *French* a COUP (1) 【法】(軍事)政變

cou·pé /kuˋpe; ˈkuːpeɪ/ *n* [C] *especially BrE* a car with two doors and a sloping back 【尤英】雙門小轎車

cou·ple¹ /ˋkʌpḷ; ˈkʌpəl/ *n* **1 a couple a)** two things or people of the same kind 一對, 一雙: *We just need a couple more chairs so everyone can sit down.* 我們只要再有兩把椅子就可以讓每人都能坐下。| [+of] *There's a couple of girls waiting for you outside.* 外面有兩個女孩子在等你。**b)** a small number of things 一些, 幾個: [+of] *I don't know why I feel so bad, I only had a couple of drinks.* 我不知道為甚麼感覺不舒服, 我只喝了幾杯酒。—see 見 PAIR¹ (USAGE) **2** [C] two people who are married or having a sexual or romantic relationship 一對夫婦; 一對情侶: *This hotel is a favourite with young honeymoon couples.* 這家酒店特別受度蜜月的年輕夫婦所喜愛。| *the couple next door* 隔壁的夫婦

couple² *v* **1** [T] to join or fasten two things together, especially two vehicles 結合, 連接〔尤指把兩輛汽車拴在一起〕 **2** [I] *formal* to have sex 【正式】性交
couple with *phr v* [T usually passive 一般用被動態] if one thing is coupled with another, they happen or exist together and produce a particular result 加上: *Lack of rain coupled with high temperatures caused the crops to fail.* 雨量少加上高温導致農作物歉收。

coup·let /ˋkʌplɪt; ˈkʌplǀt/ *n* [C] two lines of poetry, one following the other, that are the same length 〔同長度的〕兩行詩; 對句; 對聯: *rhyming couplets* 押韻的兩行詩

coup·ling /ˋkʌplɪŋ; ˈkʌplɪŋ/ *n* [C] **1** something that connects two things together, especially two vehicles 〔尤指連接兩輛汽車的〕掛鈎; 連接裝置 **2** *formal* an act of coming together to have sex 【正式】性交

cou·pon /ˋkupɑn; ˈkuːpɒn/ *n* [C] **1** a small piece of printed paper that gives you the right to pay less for something or get something free 優待券; 贈貨券: *The coupon entitles you to 10 cents off your next purchase.* 你在下次購買時使用這張優待券可以節省十分錢。**2** a printed form, that you write your name and address on, in order to send for information or enter a competition 查詢表格; 參賽表格

cour·age /ˋkɝɪdʒ; ˈkʌrɪdʒ/ *n* [U] **1** the ability to be brave when you are in danger, in pain, in a difficult situation etc 勇氣, 膽量, 勇敢: *Sue showed great courage throughout her illness.* 蘇在生病期間表現出了巨大的勇氣。| **summon up the courage/pluck up the courage** (=try to make yourself be brave enough) 鼓起勇氣 *Liz was trying to summon up the courage to tell Paul it was all over between them.* 莉茲試圖鼓起勇氣告訴保羅他們之間完了。| **take courage** (=need courage) 需要勇氣 *Driving again after his accident must have taken a lot of courage.* 他出事以後再駕車一定是鼓了很大的勇氣。**2 have the courage of your (own) convictions** to be brave enough to say or do what you think is right even though other people may not agree or approve 有勇氣去說[做]自己認為正確的事 —see also 另見 DUTCH COURAGE

cou·ra·geous /kəˋredʒəs; kəˈreɪdʒəs/ *adj* brave 勇敢的, 有膽量的: *a courageous and independent woman* 勇敢且獨立的女人 | *a courageous decision* 勇敢的決定 —**courageously** *adv* —**courageousness** *n* [U]

cour·gette /kurˋʒɛt; kʊəˈʒet/ *n* [C] *BrE* a long vegetable with a dark green skin【英】小胡瓜, 密生西葫蘆; ZUCCHINI *AmE*【美】—see picture on page A9 參見 A9 頁圖

cou·ri·er¹ /ˈkʊriɚ; ˈkʊriə/ *n* [C] **1** someone who is employed to take a package, documents etc somewhere〔遞送包裹或文件的〕信使; 快遞員 **2** *BrE* someone who is employed by a travel company to help people on holiday, by giving them information, helping them with problems etc【英】旅遊團領隊, 導遊

courier² *v* [T] to send something somewhere by using a courier 由快遞員[信使]遞送

1 1 **course¹** /kors; kɔːs/ *n*

1 of course a) used when you are mentioning something that you think other people already know, or should know 當然, 自然〔用於提及你認為別人已經知道或應當知道的某事〕: *Your car insurance must, of course, be renewed every year.* 你的汽車保險當然必須要每年更新。 **b)** used to say that what you or someone else has just said is not surprising 自然〔用於表示你或別人說的話不令人吃驚〕: *Hannah applied for the job and got it, of course.* 漢娜申請這份工作自然就得到了。 **c)** *spoken*【口】also 又作 **course** *informal*【非正式】used to agree with someone, or to give permission to someone 當然〔用於同意某人或允許某人〕: *"Can I borrow the car tonight?" – "Yeah, course you can."* "今天晚上我能借用一下汽車嗎?" "可以, 當然可以。" **d)** also 又作 **course** *spoken* used to emphasize that what you are saying is true or correct【口】當然〔用於強調你所說的是真的或正確的〕: *"You promise you won't forget?" "Of course I won't!"* "你保證不會忘記?" "我當然不會忘記!" —see 見 OF COURSE (USAGE)

2 of course not/course not *spoken* used to emphasize that you are saying no to something, or that something is not true or correct【口】當然不; 決不: *"Do you think they'll mind if I arrive late?" "No, of course not."* "你認為如果我遲到的話他們會介意嗎?" "不, 當然不會。"

3 ►LESSONS 課◄ [C] *especially BrE* a series of lessons, or studies in a particular subject【尤英】課程: *Andy's doing a one-year journalism course.* 安迪正在修讀為期一年的新聞課程。| **[+on]** *a course on the French Revolution* 法國革命課 | **[+in]** *She's taking a course in flower arranging.* 她正在學習插花。—see also 另見 CORRESPONDENCE COURSE, CRASH COURSE, REFRESHER COURSE, SANDWICH COURSE

4 in the course of/during the course of *formal* during a process or period of time【正式】在...過程中; 在...時期中: *During the course of our conversation it emerged that Bob had been in prison.* 在我們的談話過程中得知鮑勃已經入獄了。

5 ►ACTIONS 行動◄ [C] an action or series of actions that you could take in order to deal with a particular situation〔處理事件的〕行動; 一系列行動: *In this case, the best course would be to avoid talking about it altogether.* 在這種情況下, 最好是根本不要談論這件事。| **course of action** *One possible course of action would be to increase tax on alcohol.* 一個可能的舉措是提高酒稅。

6 ►USUAL/NATURAL 通常的/自然的◄ [C] the usual or natural way that something happens, develops, or is done 自然的進展; 通常的過程: *Once the story is begun, it must follow its course.* 一旦故事開始了, 就應該順其自然地發展下去。| **course of history/nature etc** *When he met Sally it changed the whole course of his life.* 遇到莎莉以後, 他的一生改變了。| **in the normal course of events** *In the normal course of events a son would take over the farm from his father.* 在正常情況下, 兒子應該繼承父親的農場。

7 let sth take its course to wait for something to develop in the usual way 讓某事按正常途徑發展: *Just relax and let nature take its course.* 放鬆些順其自然吧。

8 run its course to develop in the usual way and come to a natural end 自然發展直到終結: *The illness has run its course.* 這病自然發展下去, 終於痊癒了。

9 ►PLANE/BOAT 飛機/船◄ [C] the planned direction that a boat or plane takes to go somewhere〔船或飛機的〕航向: **on/off course** (=going in the right or wrong direction) 航向正確/錯誤 *The ship had been blown off course in the storm.* 這艘船在暴風雨中被颳得偏離了航向。

10 ►PART OF A MEAL 一餐的部分◄ [C] one of the separate parts of a meal 一道菜: **3-course meal/5-course meal etc** *That restaurant has excellent 3-course meals for very reasonable prices.* 那家餐館的三道菜的套餐非常好而且價錢很公道。| **first/second/main course etc** *We're having fish for the main course.* 我們的主菜是魚。

11 be on course to be likely to achieve something because you have already had some success 可能成就〔某事〕: **[+for]** *The company is on course for record profits this year.* 這家公司有可能在今年取得歷史上最高利潤。| **be on course to do sth** *Brazil are on course to win the World Cup.* 巴西有可能贏得世界杯。

12 ►RACE 比賽◄ [C] an area of land or water where races happen 競賽場地; 跑道: *The course is a particularly difficult one.* 這跑道非常難跑。—see also 另見 ASSAULT COURSE, OBSTACLE COURSE

13 golf course [C] an area of land that is designed for you to play golf on 高爾夫球場

14 ►MEDICAL TREATMENT 醫治◄ [C] *especially BrE* an amount of medicine or medical treatment given or taken regularly for a fixed period of time【尤英】療程: *If your doctor prescribes antibiotics, you should finish the course.* 如果醫生開了抗生素藥, 你要吃完一個療程。| **course of injections/drugs/treatment etc** *a course of injections for weight loss* 減肥的注射療程

15 in (the) course of time after some or enough time has passed 終於; 總有一天: *She'll get used to school in the course of time.* 她會逐漸適應學校生活的。

16 ►RIVER 河流◄ [C] the direction a river moves in 河水的流向: *The course of the water was shown by a line of willow trees.* 一行柳樹顯示出水流的方向。

17 ►BRICKS/STONE 磚/石◄ [C] a layer of bricks, stone etc 一層磚[石] —see also 另見 **in due course** (DUE[1] (6)), **as a matter of course** (MATTER[1] (18)), **par for the course** (PAR (3)), **stay the course** (STAY[1] (7))

course² *v* **1** [I always+adv/prep] *literary* if a liquid courses somewhere, it flows rapidly【文】奔流; 快速流動: **[+down/along/through etc]** *He could not stop the tears coursing down his cheeks.* 他的眼淚止不住地沿着臉頰流下來。**2** [I always+adv/prep] *literary* if a feeling or thought courses through your body or mind, you feel it very strongly, or think it quickly【文】〔感情、思想〕湧動: **[+down/through]** *The shock was so great, it coursed down every nerve in Sam's body.* 那打擊非常大, 它迅速傳遍薩姆的每一根神經。**3** [I,T] to chase a rabbit with dogs as a sport〔用獵犬〕追獵〔兔子〕

coursebook /ˈ· ·/ *n* [C] *BrE* a book that you use regularly during a set of lessons on a particular subject; TEXTBOOK[1]【英】課本

court¹ /kort; kɔːt/ *n* 1 1

1 ►LAW 法律◄ [C,U] a building or room where all the information concerning a crime is given so that it can be judged 法院; 法庭: *There was a large crowd of reporters gathered outside the court.* 法庭外聚集了一大羣記者。| **in court** *He was summoned to appear in court as a witness.* 他被傳喚出庭作證。| **go to court** (=start the legal process to have a case dealt with in a court) 打官司; 起訴 *She was prepared to go to court to get compensation if necessary.* 如果需要, 她準備提出起訴, 要求賠償。| **take sb to court** (=make someone be judged in a court) 控告某人 *Davis was taken to court for assaulting a policeman.* 戴維斯被控告毆打警察。| **settle out of court** (=agree without being judged in a court) 庭外和解 *We decided to settle the matter out of court.* 我們決定庭外和解。| **court case/appearance/judge etc** *The*

court case lasted six weeks. 這場訴訟持續了六個星期。
2 the court [U] the people in a court, especially the judge and the JURY (1) 全體出庭人員,〔尤指〕法官和陪審團: *The defendant told the court that he was in Newcastle at the time of the alleged rape.* 被告對法官和陪審團說, 所述的強姦案發生時他在紐卡素。
3 ►SPORT 體育◄ an area that has been specially made for playing games such as tennis on 球場: *There are three squash courts available this evening.* 今天晚上有三個壁球場可用。| **on/off court** (=playing or not playing) 上場/不上場 *Becker and Edberg are due on court in an hour.* 碧加和艾保該一小時後上場。—see picture at 參見 TENNIS 圖
4 ►KING/QUEEN ETC 國王/王后等◄ [C] **a)** the official place where a king or queen lives and works 宮廷: *This was one of the most splendid of the royal courts of Europe.* 這是歐洲最金碧輝煌的宮廷之一。| **court painter/jester/adviser etc** (=someone who is employed by the court to paint etc) 宮廷畫師/宮廷弄臣/皇室顧問等 **b)** the royal people and the people who work for them or advise them 皇室成員、侍臣等的統稱; 朝廷; 朝臣: *Several members of the court were under suspicion.* 皇室的幾個成員有嫌疑。
5 hold court to speak in an interesting and amusing way so that people gather to listen to you 說笑話吸引人圍觀: *Gary was holding court in the pub last night.* 加里昨晚在酒館裡大說笑話。
6 pay court to *old-fashioned* to give a lot of your attention to someone in order to impress them【過時】討好: *Stefan was dancing with everyone and paying court to all the girls.* 史蒂文與每個人都跳舞, 向每個女孩子獻殷勤。
7 ►CASTLE/LARGE HOUSE 城堡/大型房屋◄ [C] an open space that is completely or partly surrounded by buildings, especially one that is part of a castle or large house; COURTYARD 庭院, 院子
8 Court *especially BrE* used as part of the name of a short street or of an apartment building【尤英】...大院, ...大樓〔用作短街道或公寓建築的名稱〕—see also 另見 **the ball is in your court** (BALL¹ (10)), **be laughed out of court** (LAUGH¹ (7))

court² *v* **1** [T] *old-fashioned* if a man courts a woman, he visits her, takes her to restaurants etc because he hopes to marry her【過時】〔男子向女子〕求愛, 追求: *Richard courted Lindsay for years before she agreed to marry him.* 理查德追了林賽多年後, 她才同意嫁給他。**2** [I,T] *old-fashioned* if a man and a woman are courting, they are having a romantic relationship and may get married【過時】〔男女〕戀愛: *We were courting for two years before we even got engaged.* 我們在訂婚以前就交往了兩年。**3 court danger/death/punishment etc** to behave in a way that makes danger etc more likely 招惹危險/找死/招惹懲罰等: *You realize you're simply courting danger by driving that old car?* 你知道你駕駛那輛舊車是在惹危險嗎? **4** [T] to try to get something you want, especially support from other people, by doing something to please them 奉承, 討好: *The directors are courting the support of the shareholders.* 董事由於需要支持而討好股東。

court card /ˈ· ·/ *n* [C] *BrE* the king, queen or JACK¹ (2) in a set of playing cards【英】〔撲克中的〕花牌; FACE CARD *AmE*【美】

cour·te·ous /ˈkɝtɪəs; ˈkɜːtiəs/ *adj* having good manners and respect for other people 有禮貌的: *The staff are always courteous and helpful.* 職員們總是彬彬有禮、樂於助人。| *I received a courteous reply from the manager.* 我從經理那裡得到了禮貌的回覆。—opposite 反義詞 DISCOURTEOUS —**courteously** *adv* —**courteousness** *n* [U]

cour·te·san /ˈkɔrtəzn̩; ˌkɔːtʃˈzæn/ *n* [C] a woman in former times who had sex with rich or important men for money〔昔日與貴族或要人周旋的〕高級妓女, 交際花

cour·te·sy /ˈkɝtəsɪ; ˈkɜːtʃsi/ *n* **1** [U] polite behaviour that shows that you have respect for other people 有禮的舉止, 禮貌: *Lack of courtesy is sometimes seen as a disease of modern day society.* 缺少禮貌有時被看作是現代社會的一種病。—opposite 反義詞 DISCOURTESY **2** [C] something you do or say in order to be polite 禮貌的行為[話]: *The managers exchanged courtesies before getting down to business.* 經理們談正事前寒暄一番。**3 by courtesy of/courtesy of** by the permission or kindness of someone rather than by paying them 由於...的好意; 承蒙...的允許〔而不是由於付了錢〕: *Paul had his own flat and sports car courtesy of his celebrity father.* 因為有個名流父親, 所以保羅擁有自己的房子和跑車。

courtesy bus /ˈ··· ˌ·/ *n* [C] a bus provided by a hotel near an airport that their guests can use to travel to and from the airport〔由機場附近的酒店提供給客人往返機場的〕免費公共汽車

courtesy call /ˈ··· ˌ·/ *n* [C] a visit to someone that you make to be polite or to show your respect for them 禮節性訪問

courtesy car /ˈ··· ˌ·/ *n* [C] a car that a garage, hotel etc lends to its customers while they are having their own car fixed, are staying at the hotel etc〔修車場在客人的汽車修理期間或酒店在客人住宿時提供給客人的〕方便用車

court·house /ˈkɔrtˌhaus; ˈkɔːthaʊs/ *n* [C] *especially AmE* a building containing courts of law【尤美】法院(大樓)

court·ier /ˈkɔrtɪə; ˈkɔːtiə/ *n* [C] someone in former times who had an important position in the COURT¹ (4b)〔昔日的〕朝臣

court·ly /ˈkɔrtlɪ; ˈkɔːtli/ *adj* graceful and polite 彬彬有禮的; 優雅的: *He answered with a courtly bow.* 他禮貌地鞠一個躬作答。—**courtliness** *n* [U]

court-mar·tial¹ /ˌ· ˈ··/ *n* [C] **1** a military court that deals with people who break military law 軍事法庭: *A court-martial found him guilty of assaulting an officer.* 他襲擊軍官, 被軍事法庭定罪。**2** an occasion on which someone is judged by one of these courts 軍事法庭的審判

court-martial² *v past tense and past participle* **court-martialled** *BrE*【英】, **court-martialed** *AmE*【美】[T] to hear and judge someone's case in a military court 以軍法審判: *Soldiers were often court-martialled for cowardice.* 士兵常常由於膽怯行為而被軍事法庭審判。

Court of Ap·peal /ˌ· · ˈ··/ *n* [singular] the highest court of law in Britain apart from the HOUSE OF LORDS〔英國的〕上訴法院

Court of Ap·peals /ˌ· · ˈ··/ *n* [singular] one of 12 law courts in the US that deals with cases when people are not satisfied with the judgment given by a lower court〔美國的〕上訴法院 —see also 另見 APPELLATE COURT

court of en·quir·y, court of inquiry /ˌ· · · ˈ··/ *n* [C] *BrE* a group of people chosen to discover the facts about something or the causes of something, for example a serious accident【英】調查法庭 —compare 比較 GRAND JURY

court of law /ˌ· · ˈ·/ *n* [C] a place where law cases are judged; COURT¹ (1) 法院, 法庭

court or·der /ˌ· ˈ··/ *n* [C] an order given by a court of law that someone must do or must not do something 法院指令, 庭諭

court re·port·er /ˌ· · ˈ··/ *n* [C] someone who works in a court and records everything that is said during a case, on a special machine similar to a TYPEWRITER〔法院的〕書記官, 證言速記員; 法庭記錄員

court·room /ˈkɔrtˌrum; ˈkɔːtruːm/ *n* [C] a room in a law court where cases are judged 審判室, 法庭

court·ship /ˈkɔrt·ʃɪp; ˈkɔːt-ʃɪp/ *n* **1** [C,U] the period of time during which a man and woman have a romantic relationship before getting married 求愛期, 戀愛期 **2** [U] special behaviour used by animals to attract each other for sex〔動物的〕求偶

court shoe /ˈ· ·/ *n* [C] *BrE* a type of woman's formal shoe that is very plain and has no fastening【英】〔半高跟無鞋帶的〕淺幫鞋; PUMP¹ (3) *AmE*【美】—see picture at 參見 SHOE¹ 圖

court·yard /ˈkɔrtˌjɑrd; ˈkɔːtjɑːd/ *n* [C] an open space that is completely or partly surrounded by buildings, especially one that is part of a castle or large house 庭院, 院子

cous·cous /ˈkuskus; ˈkuːskuːs/ *n* [U] a North African dish made of crushed wheat, served with meat and vegetables 蒸粗麥粉〔北非的一道菜, 與蔬菜和肉一齊吃〕

3 **cous·in** /ˈkʌzn̩; ˈkʌzən/ *n* [C] **1** the child of your UNCLE or AUNT 堂[表]兄弟; 堂[表]姐妹 —see also 另見 FIRST COUSIN, SECOND COUSIN, KISSING COUSIN —see picture at 參見 FAMILY 圖 **2** *rare* someone who is similar to you, or something that is similar to something else【罕】同性質的人[物]; 類似之物

cou·ture /kuˈtur; kuːˈtjʊə/ *n* [U] *French* expensive and fashionable clothes【法】昂貴的時裝

cove /kov; kəʊv/ *n* [C] **1** part of the coast where the land bends around, partly enclosing the sea so the shore is protected from the wind, rain etc 小海灣 **2** *BrE old-fashioned* a man【英, 過時】漢子, 傢伙: *He's an odd cove.* 他是個怪人。

cov·en /ˈkʌvn̩; ˈkʌvən/ *n* [C] a meeting of witches (WITCH (1)) 女巫的集會

cov·e·nant /ˈkʌvənənt; ˈkʌvənənt/ *n* a formal agreement between two or more people 盟約, 契約 —**covenant** *v* [T]

Cov·en·try /ˈkɑvəntrɪ; ˈkɒvəntri/ *n* **send sb to Coventry** *BrE informal* to refuse to speak to someone in order to punish them or show disapproval【英, 非正式】不理某人〔作為懲罰或表示不滿〕

1 **cov·er¹** /ˈkʌvɚ; ˈkʌvə/ *v* [T]

1 **1 ▶PUT STH OVER STH** 用某物覆蓋…◀ also 又作 **cover up** to put something over the top of something in order to hide or protect it 遮蓋, 遮蔽: *Cover the pan when the sauce boils and let it simmer.* 調味汁煮沸時把鍋蓋起來慢慢燉。| **cover sth with sth** *They covered the tables with clean white cloths.* 他們在桌上都鋪上乾淨的白桌布。

2 ▶BE OVER STH 在…之上◀ to be on top of something or spread over something 覆蓋: *Colourful pictures covered the walls.* 牆上掛着五顏六色的圖畫。| **be covered with sth** *If it carries on snowing the ground will be covered by morning.* 如果雪不停地下, 到早上地面就會被雪覆蓋。| **be covered in sth** *The children were covered in paint.* 這些孩子身上滿是顏料。

3 ▶AN AREA 面積◀ to spread over an area 包含, 包括: *The city covers 25 square miles.* 這個城市佔地 25 平方英里。

4 ▶DISTANCE 距離◀ to travel a particular distance 走完〔一段路程〕: *They were hoping to cover 40 miles yesterday.* 他們昨天計劃走 40 英里。| **cover a lot of ground** (=travel a long way) 走很長的路 *We covered a lot of ground during those two weeks in Spain.* 在西班牙的兩週間我們到了很多地方。

5 ▶DEAL WITH/INCLUDE 處理/包括◀ to include or deal with something 涉及, 處理; 包括: *The course covers all aspects of business and law.* 這門課程包括商業和法律的各方面。| *Most of the key points are covered in this book.* 這本書談到了大部分的要點。| *This scheme would cover only a few of the three million people without jobs.* 這個計劃只能為三百萬失業者中的一小部分解決問題。| *development officers whose work would cover a local area* 負責一地區的開發官員

6 ▶RULES 規則◀ to deal with a particular situation 處理, 對待, 應付: *The rules, while they cover a wide range of issues, do not cover every possible situation.* 雖然這些規定涉及廣泛的問題, 但是沒有包含一切可能的情況。

7 ▶NEWS 新聞◀ to report the details of an event for a newspaper, television, or radio 報道: *Simonson was sent to Switzerland to cover the Winter Olympics.* 西蒙森被派遣到瑞士去報道冬季奧運會。

8 ▶PAY FOR STH 支付◀ money that covers a cost is enough to pay for it 夠支付: *He should get enough money from the council to cover his rent.* 他應當從市政務委員會得到足夠的錢來支付他的房租。| **cover the cost of sth** *You will have to pay an extra amount to cover the cost of insurance.* 你要另外付一筆錢支付保險費用。

9 ▶INSURANCE 保險◀ if an insurance agreement covers someone or something, it states that money will be given to the person if they are injured, if something is damaged etc 給…保險, 承保: *The policy will cover any medical expenses that you incur while you are abroad.* 這份保單承保你在國外的醫療費用。| **cover sb against sth** *We're not covered against theft.* 我們的保險不理賠失竊損失。

C

10 ▶GUNS 槍砲◀ **a)** to protect someone by being ready to shoot anyone who attacks them 掩護: *We'll cover you while you run for it.* 你跑過去的時候我們會掩護你。**b)** to aim a gun at a person, or the door of a building with people in it, so that they cannot escape 用槍瞄準〔使人無法逃走〕: *Don't move – we've got you covered.* 不許動, 我們瞄準你了。| *The police had the back entrance covered.* 警察持槍封鎖了後面的出口。

11 ▶SPORT 體育◀ to stay close to a member of the opposing team or a part of the field in a game, in order to prevent your opponents from gaining points〔體育〕盯防, 防守: *Who's covering second base?* 誰防守第二壘?

12 cover (all) the bases *AmE* to be prepared to deal with any situation, and be sure that nothing bad will happen and no one can criticize you【美】準備好應付各種情況; 面面俱到: *Just be sure to cover all your bases if you join in their business venture.* 如果你要加入他們的企業, 一定要準備好應對各種情況。

13 cover your back *BrE spoken* to be careful to do nothing that would make people criticize you【英口】不讓別人抓住辮子

cover for sb *phr v* **a)** to do the work that someone else usually does because they are ill or not present 代替〔某人工作〕: *Who's going to cover for you when you're on holiday?* 你度假期間誰接替你的工作? **b)** to prevent someone from getting into trouble by lying, especially about where they are or what they are doing 替…打掩護, 替…找藉口: *Cover for me, will you? Just say I'm at the dentist's.* 替我搪塞一下, 就說我在看牙醫, 好嗎?

cover up *phr v* **1** [T **cover** sth ↔ **up**] to put something over the top of something in order to hide it or protect it 遮蓋, 覆蓋: *She put a cloth over the floor to cover up the mess.* 她用一塊布鋪在地板上蓋住髒東西。**2** [T **cover** sth ↔ **up**] to prevent mistakes or unpleasant facts from being known about 掩飾, 隱瞞: *The whole thing was very well covered up and never reached the newspapers.* 整個事情都被巧妙地隱瞞起來, 始終沒有在報紙上曝光。—see also 另見 COVER-UP **3 cover up for sb** to protect someone by hiding unpleasant facts about them 為…掩蓋錯誤; 包庇: *They covered up for Kirk by refusing to answer any of the questions.* 為了袒護柯克, 他們拒絕回答任何問題。**4** [I] to put clothes on in order to keep warm or to prevent people from seeing your body 穿上衣服: *Cover up well against the cold.* 穿暖和些以禦寒。**5 cover yourself up** to put clothes, sheets etc over yourself so that your body is covered 用〔衣服、牀單等〕遮蓋身體: *Some religions require that women cover themselves up completely.* 有些宗教要求婦女要用服飾把自己嚴嚴實實地包起來。

cover² *n* 1

1 ▶STH THAT PROTECTS STH 保護物◀ [C] something that is put over or onto something to protect it or keep dirt etc out 覆蓋物, 遮蓋物: *a cushion cover* 墊子套 | *Put a cover over the bowl.* 用蓋子蓋住碗。 2

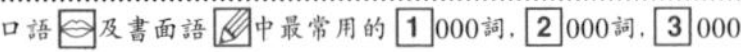

2 ►BOOKS 書◄ [C] the outer front or back page of a magazine, book etc 封面; 封底: *a picture of President Clinton on the cover of Newsweek*《新聞週刊》封面上的克林頓總統的照片 | **read sth from cover to cover** (=read everything in a book, magazine etc) 從頭讀到尾

3 ►SHELTER/PROTECTION 遮蔽/保護◄ [U] shelter or protection from bad weather or attack 掩蔽處, 掩蔽工事: *The soldiers ran for cover when the shooting began.* 射擊開始後士兵跑向掩蔽工事。| **take cover** (=find shelter or protection) 找到掩護處 *Come on, we can take cover in that barn over there!* 快點, 我們可以到那邊的穀倉中躲避一下! | **break cover** (=come out from the place where you have been sheltered or protected) 從掩蔽處中出來

C

4 covers [plural] the sheets, blankets etc on a bed 牀罩; 牀毯: *The covers had slipped off the bed during the night.* 夜裡牀罩從牀上滑了下來。

5 ►INSURANCE 保險◄ [U] insurance against injury, damage etc 保險: *The policy gives you temporary medical cover for your holiday.* 這份保單為你提供假期期間臨時醫療保險。| **[+against]** *cover against fire and theft* 火險和盜竊險

6 a cover for a business that seems normal and honest, but is really used to hide illegal activities〔非法活動的〕掩飾; 掩蓋: *He used the shop as a cover for various illegal activities.* 他用該商店掩護各種各樣的非法活動。

7 under cover pretending to be someone else in order to do something without being noticed 隱匿地, 暗地裡: *She was working under cover to get information on the drug dealers.* 她祕密地打聽毒販的情況。

8 under cover of darkness hidden by darkness 在夜幕的掩護下: *They escaped under cover of darkness.* 他們在夜幕的掩護下逃跑了。

9 under plain cover/under separate cover if a letter etc is sent under plain cover or under separate cover, it is sent in a plain envelope or a separate envelope 在未寫明寄件人、內容等的信封內; 在另函內: *The bill will be sent to you later under separate cover.* 賬單稍後將以另函寄上。

cov·er·age /ˈkʌvərɪdʒ; ˈkʌvərɪdʒ/ *n* [U] **1** the way in which a subject or event is reported on television or radio, or in newspapers 新聞報道: *ABC gave the story extensive coverage in the evening news.* 美國廣播公司在晚間新聞中對該事件進行了廣泛的報道。**2** the amount of protection given to you by an insurance agreement 保險範圍, 保險項目: *Make sure your policy will give you adequate coverage in case of a break-in.* 務必使你的保單能在遭到入室盜竊時也提供充分保障。**3** the range of subjects and facts included in a course, class etc 課程內容; 一堂課的內容: *The syllabus includes coverage of all the outdoor skills.* 教學大綱的內容包含所有的戶外技巧。

cov·er·alls /ˈkʌvəˌrɔlz; ˈkʌvərɔːlz/ *n* [plural] *AmE* a piece of clothing that you wear over all your clothes to protect them【美】〔穿在最外面衣褲相連的〕工作服; overalls (OVERALL[3] (3)) *BrE*【英】

cover charge /ˈ·· ·/ *n* [C] money that you have to pay in a restaurant in addition to the cost of the food and drinks〔飯店等的〕服務費

covered wag·on /ˌ·· ˈ··/ *n* [C] a large vehicle with a curved cloth top that is pulled by horses, used in former times in North America〔從前北美的〕有篷大馬車, 大篷車

cover girl /ˈ·· ·/ *n* [C] a young attractive woman whose photograph is on the front cover of a magazine〔雜誌的〕封面女郎

cov·er·ing /ˈkʌvərɪŋ; ˈkʌvərɪŋ/ *n* [singular] something that covers or hides something 覆蓋物: *a light covering of snow* 薄薄的一層雪

covering let·ter /ˌ··· ˈ··/ *n* [C] *BrE* a letter that you send with documents or a package explaining what it is or giving additional information【英】〔文件或包裹的〕附函; COVER LETTER *AmE*【美】

cov·er·let /ˈkʌvəlɪt; ˈkʌvəlɪ̵t/ *n* [C] a cloth cover for a bed; BEDSPREAD 牀罩

cover let·ter /ˈ·· ˌ··/ *n* [C] *AmE* a covering letter【美】附函

cover note /ˈ·· ·/ *n* [C] *BrE* a document that proves that you have car insurance【英】汽車保單

cover sto·ry /ˈ·· ˌ··/ *n* [C] the story that goes with a picture on the cover of a magazine 封面故事〔雜誌中與封面圖片有關的主要文章〕

cov·ert[1] /ˈkovərt; ˈkʌvət/ *adj* secret or hidden 祕密的; 隱藏的: *illegal, covert actions of enemy agents* 敵人間諜的非法祕密活動 —opposite 反義詞 OVERT —**covertly** *adv*

covert[2] *n* [C] a group of small bushes growing close together in which animals can hide〔動物藏身的〕樹叢

cover-up /ˈ·· ·/ *n* [C] an attempt to prevent the public from discovering the truth about something 掩飾; 隱瞞 —see also 另見 **cover up** (COVER[1])

cov·et /ˈkʌvɪt; ˈkʌvɪ̵t/ *v* [T] *formal* to have a very strong desire to have something that someone else has【正式】貪求; 垂涎, 覬覦: *He possessed rare and much coveted works of art.* 他擁有非常令人垂涎的稀世藝術珍品。

cov·et·ous /ˈkʌvɪtəs; ˈkʌvɪ̵təs/ *adj* having a very strong desire to have something that someone else has, especially wealth 貪婪的; 垂涎的: *They began to cast covetous eyes on their neighbours' fields.* 他們開始覬覦鄰居的土地。—**covetously** *adv* —**covetousness** *n* [U]

cow[1] /kau; kaʊ/ *n* [C] **1** a large female animal that is kept on farms and produces milk 奶牛 —compare 比較 BULL[1] (1) **2** a male or female animal of this type 牛 **3** the female of some large land and sea animals, such as the ELEPHANT or the WHALE 大型雌性動物〈如象、鯨等〉**4** *BrE spoken* an impolite way of saying that a woman is stupid or very unpleasant【英口】蠢女人; 潑婦〔不禮貌用語〕: *Linda's a silly cow – just ignore her!* 琳達是個蠢女人, 不要理她! **5 have a cow** *AmE informal* to be very angry or surprised about something【美, 非正式】非常生氣; 非常吃驚 **6 till the cows come home** *informal* for a very long time, or for ever【非正式】長時間地; 無限期地; 永遠

cow[2] *v* [T] to make someone behave in the way you want them to by using violence or threats 恐嚇, 威脅: *I was determined not to be cowed by their threats.* 我決心不被他們的威脅嚇住。

cow·ard /ˈkauərd; ˈkaʊəd/ *n* [C] someone who is not at all brave 膽小鬼; 懦夫: *He called me a coward because I would not fight.* 因為我不肯打架, 他就叫我懦夫。

cow·ard·ice /ˈkauərdɪs; ˈkaʊədɪ̵s/ also 又作 **cow·ard·li·ness** /ˈkauərdlɪnəs; ˈkaʊədlɪnɪ̵s/ *n* [U] lack of courage 膽小; 怯懦: *cowardice in the face of danger* 在危險面前的怯懦

cow·ard·ly /ˈkauərdlɪ; ˈkaʊədli/ *adj* behaving in a way that shows that you are not brave 膽小的, 懦弱的: *That was a very cowardly thing to do.* 那樣做非常懦弱。| *a cowardly attack on a defenceless man* 對無自衛能力的人懦弱的攻擊

cow·bell /ˈkauˌbɛl; ˈkaʊbel/ *n* [C] a bell that is put around a cow's neck so that it can be found easily 牛頸鈴

cow·boy /ˈkauˌbɔɪ; ˈkaʊbɔɪ/ *n* [C] **1** a man who rides a horse and is employed to look after cattle in North America〔北美的〕騎馬牧人; 牛仔 **2** *BrE informal* someone who is dishonest in business, or who produces very bad quality work【英, 非正式】不誠實的商人, 低劣產品的製造商: *a firm of cowboy builders* 一家不誠實的建築商 **3 cowboys and Indians** a game played by children who pretend to be cowboys and Native Americans, fighting each other (NATIVE AMERICAN) 牛仔與印第安人〔一種兒童遊戲〕

cowboy hat /ˈ·· ˌ·/ *n* [C] a hat with a wide circular edge and a soft round top; STETSON 牛仔帽

cow·catch·er /ˈkauˌkætʃər; ˈkaʊˌkætʃə/ *n* [C] a piece of metal on the front of a train used to push things off the track〔火車機車前的〕排障裝置

cow chip /ˈ· ·/ *n* [C] *AmE* a round flat mass of dry solid waste from a cow【美】乾牛糞塊

cow·er /ˈkauə; ˈkauə/ *v* [I] to bend low and move back, especially because you are frightened 退縮, 畏縮; 蜷縮: *They were cowering in the cellars, trapped by the shelling.* 他們蜷縮在地窖裡, 因遭受砲擊而出不去。| *He cowered against the wall.* 他蜷縮在牆根。

cow·girl /ˈkau͵gɜl; ˈkaugɜːl/ *n* [C] a woman who rides a horse and is employed to look after cattle in North America〔北美的〕牧牛女工

cow·hand /ˈkau͵hænd; ˈkauhænd/ *n* [C] someone who is employed to look after cattle 牧場工人, 牧牛工

cow·hide /ˈkau͵haɪd; ˈkauhaɪd/ *n* [C,U] the skin of a cow or the leather that is made from this 牛皮

cowl /kaul; kaul/ *n* [C] **1** a very large hood that covers your head and shoulders, especially worn by MONKS (修道士等戴的) 蒙頭斗篷, 風帽 **2** a cover for a chimney that protects it from wind and rain; HOOD (4)〔用於擋風雨的〕煙囪帽, 通風帽

cow·lick /ˈkau͵lɪk; ˈkau͵lɪk/ *n* [C] hair that sticks up on top of your head 翹起的一綹頭髮

cow·ling /ˈkaulɪŋ; ˈkaulɪŋ/ *n* [C] a metal cover for an aircraft engine〔飛機的〕發動機外罩, 整流罩 —see picture at 參見 AIRCRAFT 圖

cowl neck /͵· ˈ·/ *n* [C] the neck on a piece of clothing that falls in folds at the front 胸前皺領

co-work·er /ˈko ͵wɜkə; ͵kəu ˈwɜːkə/ *n* [C] someone who works with you and has a similar position 同事, 同僚

cow·pat /ˈkau͵pæt; ˈkaupæt/ *n* [C] *BrE* a round flat mass of solid waste from a cow【英】〔一團〕牛糞

cow pie /͵· ˈ·/ *n* [C] *AmE* a COW CHIP【美】乾牛糞塊

cow·poke /ˈkau͵pok; ˈkaupəuk/ *n* [C] *AmE old-fashioned* a COWBOY (1)【美, 過時】牛仔, 騎馬牧人

cow·pox /ˈkau͵pɑks; ˈkaupɒks/ *n* [U] a disease that cows suffer from and that can be given to humans to protect them from SMALLPOX 牛痘

cow·rie /ˈkaurɪ; ˈkauri/ *n* [C] a shiny brightly-coloured tropical shell, used in former times as money in parts of Africa and Asia〔古時亞非一些地區用作貨幣的〕寶螺

cow·shed /ˈkau͵ʃɛd; ˈkauʃed/ *n* [C] a building where cows live in the winter, or where their milk is taken from them 牛棚, 牛舍

cow·slip /ˈkau͵slɪp; ˈkau͵slɪp/ *n* [U] a small European wild plant with sweet smelling yellow flowers 黃花九輪草, 野櫻草

cox /kɑks; kɒks/ *n* [C] someone who controls the direction of a rowing boat, especially in races〔賽艇的〕舵手 —**cox** *v* [T]

cox·comb /ˈkɑks͵kom; ˈkɒkskəum/ *n* [C] *old use* a stupid man who spends too much time and money on his clothes and appearance【舊】〔特別注意衣着的〕花花公子

cox·swain /ˈkɑksn̩; ˈkɒksən/ *n* [C] a cox〔賽艇的〕舵手

coy /kɔɪ; kɔɪ/ *adj* **1** pretending to be shy in order to attract interest, or to avoid dealing with something difficult〔為了引人注目或逃避困難而〕裝作害羞的, 故作忸怩的: *She gave him a coy smile.* 她對他含羞一笑。**2** unwilling to give information about something 含糊其詞的, 不肯表態的: **[+about]** *Tania was always coy about her age.* 塔尼亞對自己的年齡總是含糊其詞。—**coyly** *adv* —**coyness** *n* [U]

coy·ote /ˈkaɪot; ˈkɔɪ-əut/ *n* [C] a small wild dog that lives in North West America and Mexico〔北美西部和墨西哥的〕郊狼

coy·pu /ˈkɔɪpu; ˈkɔɪpuː/ *n* [C] an animal like a BEAVER, kept on farms for its fur; NUTRIA 河狸鼠

coz /kʌz; kʌz/ *n old use* a way of addressing a cousin【舊】堂[表]兄弟[姐妹]〔稱呼〕

co·zy /ˈkozɪ; ˈkəuzi/ *adj* the American spelling of COSY cosy 的美式拼法 —**cozily** *adv* —**coziness** *n* [U]

CPA /͵si pi ˈe; ͵siː piː ˈeɪ/ *n* [C] *AmE* Certified Public Accountant; an ACCOUNTANT who has passed all their examinations【美】特許會計師; CHARTERED ACCOUNTANT *BrE*【英】

CPR /͵si pi ˈɑr; ͵siː piː ˈɑː/ *n* [C] cardiopulmonary resuscitation; a method of helping someone who has stopped breathing and whose heart has stopped beating 心肺復蘇

CPU /͵si pi ˈju; ͵siː piː ˈjuː/ *n* the part of a computer that controls and organizes all its activities; CENTRAL PROCESSING UNIT〔電腦的〕中央處理器

crab¹ /kræb; kræb/ *n* **1** [C] a sea animal whose body is covered with a shell and that has five legs on each side and two large CLAWS on the front legs 蟹 **2** [U] the flesh of this animal that you can cook and eat as food 蟹肉 **3 crabs** [plural] a medical condition in which a kind of LOUSE is in the hair around the sexual organs 生陰蝨; 陰蝨病 **4** [singular] *AmE informal* someone who easily becomes annoyed about unimportant things【美, 非正式】脾氣乖戾的人, 易怒的人: *He's a real crab – always finding fault with everything.* 他真是一個脾氣乖戾的人, 總是到處挑刺。

crab 蟹

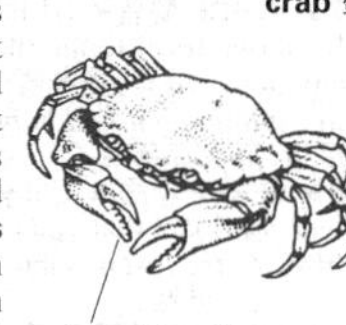

crab² *v* **crabbed, crabbing** [I] *informal* to complain about something in an annoyed way; GRUMBLE¹ (1)【非正式】抱怨, 發牢騷

crab ap·ple /ˈ· ͵··/ *n* [C] a small apple that tastes sour, or the tree that it grows on 沙果(樹), 花紅(樹)

crab·bed /ˈkræbɪd; ˈkræbɨd/ *adj* **1** writing which is crabbed is difficult to read because the letters are small and untidy〔字跡〕潦草的, 難認的 **2** *old-fashioned* someone who is crabbed always behaves as if they are annoyed; BAD-TEMPERED【過時】乖戾的

crab·by /ˈkræbɪ; ˈkræbi/ *adj informal* someone who is crabby easily becomes annoyed about unimportant things; BAD-TEMPERED【非正式】脾氣壞的, 易怒的: *a rather crabby old man* 脾氣很壞的老人 | *I was feeling crabby.* 我心情不好, 很暴躁。

crab·grass /ˈkræb͵græs; ˈkræbgrɑːs/ *n* [U] a kind of rough grass 馬唐〔一種野草〕

crab·wise /ˈkræbwaɪz; ˈkræbwaɪz/ also 又作 **crabways** /-wez; -weɪz/ *adv* sideways, especially in a way that seems difficult 橫向地〔尤指行動不靈活〕; 蟹行地: *I moved crabwise along the edge of the cliff.* 我側身沿着懸崖邊挪動。

crack¹ /kræk; kræk/ *v* [S3]

1 ►BREAK 斷裂◄ [I,T] to break or make something break so that it gets one or more lines on its surface (使)破裂; (使)裂開: *Don't put that delicate china in the dishwasher – it may crack.* 不要把那件易碎的瓷器放入洗碗機, 會碎的。| *She fell off her bike and cracked a bone in her leg.* 她從自行車上摔了下來, 摔斷了一根腿骨。

2 ►LOUD SOUND 響聲◄ [I,T] to make a sudden quick sound like the sound of something breaking, or to make something do this (使)發爆裂聲: *The branch cracked loudly and broke off.* 樹枝啪的一聲斷了。| *He had a habit of cracking his knuckles.* 他有扣響指節的習慣。

3 ►HIT STH 擊撞某物◄ [I always+adv/prep, T always+adv/prep] to hit something hard but not deliberately, especially part of your body 重擊: **[+against/on]** *The rock cracked against my shoulder.* 石頭重重地砸在我的肩膀上。| **crack sth against/on** *He fell, cracking his head on the wall.* 他摔倒了, 頭撞到牆上。

4 ►HIT SB 擊打某人◄ [T] to hit someone hard and deliberately on part of their body 重擊〔某人〕: **crack sb over/in/on** *He cracked the burglar over the head with a vase.* 他把花瓶重重地砸在竊賊的頭上。

5 ►LOSE CONTROL 失控◄ also 又作 **crack up** [I] to be unable to continue doing something or working well because of great pressure〔因受大壓力而〕失去控制; 崩潰: *We're hoping the prisoner will crack under interrogation.* 我們希望審訊時能夠使囚犯屈服招供。| *The whole political system is beginning to crack up.* 整個政治制度開始崩潰。

6 ▶MENTALLY ILL 精神病◀ also 又作 **crack up** [I] to become mentally ill because of too much pressure (使) 發瘋, (使) 神經錯亂: *Many of the soldiers cracked up on returning from the war.* 很多士兵打仗歸來就精神失常了。

7 ▶VOICE 聲音◀ [I] if your voice cracks, it changes from one level to another suddenly because of strong emotions〔聲音〕變嘶啞: *Her voice cracked as she tried to explain what had happened.* 她設法解釋發生了甚麼事情, 聲音都嘶啞了。

8 ▶NERVE 神經◀ [I] if your nerve cracks, you no longer feel confident that you can do something difficult 失去勇氣: *At the last moment his nerve cracked.* 在最後時刻他失去了勇氣。

9 ▶EGG/NUT 蛋/堅果◀ [T] to break the outside part of something, such as an egg or a nut, in order to get what is inside it 打開, 砸開〔雞蛋、堅果等的〕殼: *The foxes crack the eggs, and suck out the yolk.* 狐狸敲破蛋殼, 把蛋黃吸出來。

10 ▶STEAL 偷◀ [T] to open a SAFE[2] illegally, in order to steal what is inside 非法地打開; 撬開〔保險櫃盜竊〕

11 ▶SOLVE 解決◀ [T] to find the answer to a problem or find how to use a CODE[1] (4) 解決〔難題〕; 破解〔密碼〕: *His skill at cracking codes proved invaluable during the war.* 他能破解密碼, 這種技能證明在戰爭中無比重要。| *This is a national problem, we're not going to crack it here this afternoon.* 這是一個全國性問題, 今天下午我們不會在這裡解決它。

12 ▶STOP CRIME/ENEMY 制止犯罪/敵人◀ [T] to find a way of destroying an enemy or stopping something they are doing 消滅〔敵人〕; 制止〔敵人做的事〕: *Police are hoping to crack the drug-smuggling ring.* 警方希望能剷除這個毒品走私團夥。

13 crack it *BrE* to succeed in some way【英】成功

14 crack a deal *AmE informal* to succeed in making a business deal, especially when this has been difficult【美, 非正式】〔尤指費力地〕達成協議; 做成買賣: *We finally managed to crack that deal with the Japanese.* 我們終於設法與日本人談成了那筆交易。

15 crack a joke *informal* to tell a joke【非正式】說笑話: *He kept cracking jokes about my appearance.* 他老是拿我的長相開玩笑。

16 crack a smile *AmE informal* to smile when you have been serious, sad, or angry【美, 非正式】轉怒為喜; 破涕為笑: *She finally cracked a smile, although she had tears in her eyes.* 她雖然眼中含着淚花, 終於還是破涕為笑。

17 crack open a bottle *informal* to open a bottle of alcohol for drinking【非正式】打開一瓶酒: *Let's crack open a bottle to celebrate!* 讓我們打開一瓶酒慶祝一下!

18 not all/everything it's cracked up to be *informal* not as good as people say it is【非正式】不如人們所說的那樣好; 名不副實: *The film wasn't all it's cracked up to be – I was quite bored in parts.* 這部電影不像人們所說的那樣好, 我覺得其中有些部分非常沉悶。

19 get cracking *informal* to start doing something or going somewhere as quickly as possible【非正式】抓緊時間: *The train goes at ten so let's get cracking.* 火車十點鐘開, 我們得趕快點。

20 crack the whip *informal* to make people you have control over work very hard【非正式】逼手下人努力工作

crack down *phr v* [I] to become more strict in dealing with a problem and punishing the people involved〔對…〕採取嚴厲措施; 制裁; 鎮壓: **[+on]** *The police are cracking down on illegal parking.* 警方在嚴厲打擊非法停車。—see also 另見 CRACKDOWN

crack on *phr v* [I] *BrE informal* to continue working hard at something in order to try to finish it【英, 非正式】繼續努力: **[+with]** *I'm hoping to crack on with that translation this weekend.* 我想這個週末繼續盡力翻譯。

crack up *phr v informal*【非正式】**1** [I,T] to laugh a lot at something, or to make someone laugh a lot (使) 捧腹大笑: *Everyone in the class just cracked up.* 班上所有的人都大笑起來。| **crack sb up** *She's so funny. She cracks me up.* 她非常滑稽, 逗得我捧腹大笑。**2** [I] to become unable to think or behave sensibly because you have too many problems, too much work etc 吃不消, 精神垮掉: *I must be cracking up – I've lost those papers again!* 我一定昏了頭了, 又把那些文件弄丢了! —see also 另見 CRACK-UP

crack² *n* [C]

1 ▶THIN SPACE 狹窄的空間◀ a very narrow space between two things or two parts of something 裂縫, 縫隙: **[+in]** *A thin ray of light shone through a crack in the curtains.* 一縷光線透過窗簾上的縫隙照射進來。| **[+between]** *The children carefully avoided the cracks between the paving stones.* 孩子們小心地躲過砌路石間的縫隙。| **open sth a crack** (=open something very slightly) 稍稍打開 *She opened the door a crack and peeped out.* 她把門打開一條縫, 向外瞟了一眼。

2 ▶BREAK 斷裂◀ a thin line on the surface of something when it is broken but has not actually come apart 裂痕, 裂口: **[+in]** *There were several cracks in the glass.* 玻璃上有幾條裂紋。

3 ▶PROBLEM 問題◀ a fault in an idea, system, or organization 瑕疵, 缺點: **[+in]** *Cracks were appearing in the government's economic policy.* 政府的經濟政策出現了漏洞。

4 ▶SOUND 聲音◀ a sudden loud very sharp sound like the sound of a stick being broken 爆裂聲, 劈啪聲: *There was a loud crack as the wood finally broke in two.* 木頭最後在爆裂聲中斷成兩半。—see picture on page A19 參見A19頁圖

5 ▶JOKE/REMARK 玩笑/話語◀ a clever joke or rude remark 俏皮話; 粗魯的話: **[+about]** *I've had enough of your cracks about my weight.* 我聽夠了你對我的體重的挖苦。| **make a crack** *I wish I hadn't made that crack about lawyers.* 我不該說那些俏皮話挖苦律師。

6 ▶CHANCE TO DO STH 機遇◀ *informal* an opportunity or attempt to achieve something, especially for the first time【非正式】試圖, 嘗試: **[+at]** *I'd like a crack at climbing that mountain.* 我想試試爬那座山。| **have/take a crack at sth** *Why don't you have a crack at that competition – you might win!* 為甚麼你不嘗試參加那個競賽, 說不定你會贏的! | **a (fair) crack of the whip** *BrE* (=a chance to do something or be in control)【英】〔做事或管事的〕機會 *They'll do well if we give them a fair crack of the whip.* 如果我們給他們一個公平的機會, 他們會做得很好的。

7 a crack on the head what you feel when you are hit on the head, usually not deliberately 腦袋上挨了一下: *I got a nasty crack on the head as I went through the low doorway.* 我通過那低矮的門道時, 把頭撞了一下。

8 a crack in sb's voice a sudden change in the level of someone's voice, especially because they are very upset〔尤指因情緒激動而引起的〕嗓音的變化: *He noticed the crack in her voice as she tried to continue.* 他注意到她想繼續說下去的時候聲音都變了。

9 crack of dawn very early in the morning 大清早, 黎明: *We'll have to get up at the crack of dawn tomorrow.* 我們明天得起個大早。

10 ▶DRUG 毒品◀ [U] a very pure form of the drug COCAINE that some people take illegally for pleasure 強效可卡因

11 good crack *IrE, BrE spoken* friendly, enjoyable talk in a group【愛爾蘭, 英, 口】一羣人友好的交談; 盡興的談話: *We go there for the crack.* 我們到那裡去聊天。

12 what's the crack? *BrE spoken* used to ask someone what is happening, or what has been happening recently

【英口】發生甚麼事了? 最近發生了甚麼事? —see also 另見 **paper over the cracks** (PAPER[3] (2))

crack³ *adj* [only before noun 僅用於名詞前] **1** having a very high level of quality or skill, or being very highly trained 第一流的; 受過良好訓練的: *A crack regiment was sent in to deal with the situation.* 一團精兵被派去處理這種局勢。**2 crack shot** someone who always hits what they shoot at 神槍手

crack·down /ˈkrækˌdaʊn; ˈkrækdaʊn/ *n* [C usually singular 一般用單數] severe action that is taken in order to deal with a problem 取締; 制裁; 鎮壓: [+on] *They're having a crackdown on drunk driving.* 他們正在嚴厲查處酒後駕車。—see also 另見 **crack down** (CRACK[1])

cracked /krækt; krækt/ *adj* **1** something that is cracked has been damaged and has one or more lines on its surface 有裂縫的; 破裂的: *cracked cups and saucers* 破裂的杯子和杯托 | *Her skin was cracked and dry.* 她的皮膚龜裂且乾燥。—see picture on page A18 參見A18頁圖**2** [not before noun 不用於名詞前] *informal* someone who is cracked is slightly crazy【非正式】有點瘋的 **3** someone's voice that is cracked sounds rough and uncontrolled because they are upset〔因激動而嗓音〕嘶啞的

crack·er /ˈkrækɚ; ˈkrækə/ *n* [C] **1** a small thin BISCUIT often eaten with cheese 薄脆餅乾 **2** also 又作 **Christmas cracker** a brightly coloured paper tube that makes a small exploding sound when you pull it apart, and that usually contains a small gift and a joke, used at Christmas in Britain 聖誕彩包爆竹 **3** a FIRECRACKER 爆竹 **4** *BrE spoken* something that is very good or very funny【英口】好東西; 有趣的事物: *Did you hear his joke? It was a real cracker!* 你聽了他講的笑話嗎? 真有意思! **5** *BrE old-fashioned* a very attractive woman【英, 過時】迷人的女子

crack·ers /ˈkrækɚz; ˈkrækəz/ *adj* [not before noun 不用於名詞前] *BrE informal* crazy【英, 非正式】瘋狂的; 精神失常的: *You lent him all that money? You must be crackers!* 你把那筆錢都借給他了? 你一定是瘋了!

crack·ing /ˈkrækɪŋ; ˈkrækɪŋ/ *adj* [only before noun 僅用於名詞前] **1** very fast 快速的, 飛快的: *We set off at a cracking pace.* 我們快步出發。**2** *BrE spoken* very good【英口】極好的, 出色的: *It's going to be a cracking good race.* 會是一場精彩的比賽。

crack·le /ˈkrækḷ; ˈkrækəl/ *v* [I] to make a repeated short sharp sound like something burning in a fire 發劈啪聲: *The dry sticks crackled as they caught fire.* 乾枝條着火時發出劈劈啪啪的聲響。| *The radio crackled so much we could hardly hear what was said.* 收音機老是劈啪作響, 我們幾乎聽不清說的是甚麼。—**crackle** *n* [C] —**crackly** *adj* —see picture on page A19 參見A19頁圖

crack·ling /ˈkræklɪŋ; ˈkræklɪŋ/ *n* **1** [singular] the sound made by something when it crackles 劈啪聲; 爆裂聲: *There was a silence after that , except for the crackling of the fire.* 隨後, 除了火的劈啪聲, 一片沉寂。**2** *BrE*【英】**cracklings** *AmE*【美】[U] the hard skin of a pig when it has been cooked and is easily broken〔烤豬肉的〕脆皮

crack·pot /ˈkrækˌpɑt; ˈkrækpɒt/ *n* [C] *humorous* someone who is slightly crazy【幽默】有點精神失常的人; 有點發瘋的人 —**crackpot** *adj*

crack-up /ˈ· ·/ *n* [C] *AmE informal*【美, 非正式】**1** a NERVOUS BREAKDOWN 精神崩潰 **2** a car accident 車禍 —see also 另見 **crack up** (CRACK[1])

-cracy /krəsɪ; krəsi/ *suffix* [in nouns 構成名詞] another form of the suffix -OCRACY 後綴 -ocracy 的另一種形式: *bureaucracy* (=government by officials who are not elected) 官僚政治

cra·dle¹ /ˈkredḷ; ˈkreɪdl/ *n* [C]

1 ▶BED 牀◀ a small bed for a baby, especially one that you can move gently from side to side 搖籃: *She rocked the cradle to quieten the child.* 她搖動搖籃, 讓寶寶安靜下來。—see picture at 參見 BED[1] 圖

2 the cradle of the place where something important began …的發源地; …的策源地: *Athens is often regarded as the cradle of democracy.* 雅典通常被認為是民主的發源地。

3 from/in the cradle from or in the earliest years of your life 從/在嬰兒[幼年]時期: *Sara had learned that language from the cradle.* 莎拉在幼年就學會了那門語言。

4 from the cradle to the grave all through your life 一輩子, 從生到死: *a promise of security from the cradle to the grave* 保證終身安穩的許諾

5 *BrE* a structure that people working on the sides of high buildings stand in which can be moved up and down【英】〔空中作業用的〕吊架, 吊籃: *a window-cleaner's cradle* 窗戶清潔工的吊籃

6 the part of a telephone where the part that you hold in your hand is put when it is not being used〔電話的〕聽筒架, 叉簧 —see also 另見 CAT'S CRADLE, **rob the cradle** (ROB (5))

cradle² *v* [T] to hold something gently in your hands or arms, as if to protect it 輕輕地抱着: *John cradled the baby in his arms.* 約翰把寶寶抱在懷裡。| *The wine-glass looked tiny cradled in his big hands.* 酒杯握在他的大手裡看上去很小。

cradle-snatch·er *BrE*【英】, **cradle-robber** *AmE*【美】/ˈ·· ,··/ *n* [C] someone who has a romantic relationship with someone much younger than they are 和比自己年輕很多的人談戀愛的人 —**cradle-snatch** *v* [I]

-craft /kræft; krɑːft/ *suffix* [in nouns 構成名詞] **1** a vehicle of a particular kind 運載工具: *a spacecraft* 航天器 | *a hovercraft* 氣墊船 | *several aircraft* 幾架飛機 **2** skill of a particular kind 技藝: *statecraft* (=skill in government) 政治手腕 | *stagecraft* (=skill in acting or directing plays) 演技; 舞台經驗; 戲劇導演技巧 3

craft¹ /kræft; krɑːft/ *n* **1** *plural* **craft** [C] **a)** a small boat 小船: *I steered the craft carefully round the rocks.* 我小心駕船繞過岩石。**b)** an aircraft or SPACECRAFT 飛機, 飛行器, 航空器; 航天器 **2** *plural* **crafts** [C] an activity, especially a traditional one that needs a lot of skill, in which you make something with your hands〔尤指傳統的手工〕工藝; 手藝: *a craft such as needlework* 針線活一類的手藝 **3** [C] a profession, especially one needing a special skill 行業, 職業: *The anthropologist takes years to learn his craft.* 人類學家要花多年時間來學習自己的專業。**4** [U] skill in deceiving people 詭計, 手腕: *Craft and cunning were necessary for the scheme to work.* 實施陰謀需要詭計和狡猾。—see also 另見 LANDING CRAFT

craft² *v* [T usually passive 一般用被動態] to make something using a special skill, especially with your hands 手工製作, 精製: *Each doll will be crafted individually by specialists.* 每個娃娃都要由專門人員來單獨手工製作。| **hand-crafted** (=made by hand, not by machine) 手工製作的 *a hand-crafted silver cigarette case* 手工製作的銀煙盒

craft knife /ˈ· ·/ *n* [C] *BrE* a very sharp knife used for cutting paper, thin wood etc, when the cutting needs to be exact【英】工藝刀

crafts·man /ˈkræftsmən; ˈkrɑːftsmən/ *n* [C] someone who is very skilled at a particular CRAFT[1] (2) 工匠; 手藝人

crafts·man·ship /ˈkræftsmənˌʃɪp; ˈkrɑːftsmənʃɪp/ *n* [U] **1** the special skill that someone uses to make something beautiful with their hands 手藝; 工藝, 技藝: *These works of art combine precious materials with exquisite craftsmanship.* 這些藝術品用料珍貴, 工藝精湛。**2** very detailed work that has been done using a lot of skill, so that the result is beautiful 手工藝品: *the fine craftsmanship of the carved Georgian table* 喬治時代精工雕刻的桌子

crafts·wom·an /ˈkræftsˌwʊmən; ˈkrɑːftsˌwʊmən/ *n* [C] a woman who is very skilled at a particular CRAFT[1] (2) 女工匠, 女手藝人

craft·y /ˈkræftɪ; ˈkrɑːfti/ *adj* good at getting what you 3 want by clever planning and secretly deceiving people; CUNNING[1] (1,2) 詭計多端的, 狡猾的: *You crafty devil, you!* 你這個詭計多端的傢伙! —**craftily** *adv* —**craftiness** *n* [U]

crag /kræg; kræg/ *n* [C] a high and very steep rough rock or mass of rocks 險崖, 峭壁

crag·gy /ˈkrægɪ; ˈkrægi/ *adj* **1** a mountain that is craggy is very steep and covered in rough rocks 陡峭的; 多岩石的 **2** having a face with many deep lines on it 〔臉〕滿是皺紋的: *craggy good looks* 佈滿皺紋的俊美容貌

cram /kræm; kræm/ *v* **crammed, cramming 1** [T always+adv/prep] to force something into a small space 把…塞入〔小空間〕: **cram sth into/onto/down etc** *Jessica crammed her clothes into the bag.* 傑西卡把她的衣服塞入袋子。**2 cram into sth** if people cram into a place, they fill it 〔人〕擠進某地, 擠滿某地: *Thousands of people crammed into the stadium to see the final game.* 成千上萬的人擠進體育場看決賽。**3 a)** [I] to prepare yourself for an examination by learning a lot of information very quickly 〔為考試而〕死記硬背, 臨時抱佛腳; SWOT[2] *BrE* 【英】: *I've been cramming hard all week.* 我整個星期都在刻苦準備考試。| [+for] *He'd crammed for the test until four in the morning.* 他為準備考試臨急抱佛腳地一直複習到凌晨四點。**b)** [T] *BrE* to help someone prepare for an examination by cramming 【英】〔為考試而〕填鴨式地教〔某人〕: *The college is cramming the students hard for the summer exams.* 該學院填鴨式地給學生拚命灌輸知識, 準備夏季考試。

crammed /kræmd; kræmd/ *adj* **crammed with/crammed full of** completely full of things or people 填滿的, 塞滿的: *monthly reports crammed full of information* 信息豐富的每月報告

cram·mer /ˈkræmɚ; ˈkræmə/ *n* [C] *BrE* a special school that prepares people quickly for examinations 【英】〔為應付考試而〕給學生灌注知識的補習學校

cramp[1] /kræmp; kræmp/ *n* **1** [C,U] a severe pain that you get in part of your body when a muscle becomes too tight, making it difficult for you to move that part of your body 痙攣; 痛性痙攣, 抽筋: *I woke up in the middle of the night with cramp in my leg.* 因為腿抽筋我半夜醒了。| **have/get cramp** *BrE* 【英】 **have/get a cramp** *AmE* 【美】 *The swimmer got a cramp and had to quit the race.* 該游泳運動員因抽筋不得不退出比賽。—see also 另見 WRITER'S CRAMP **2 cramps** [plural] *especially AmE* severe pains in the stomach, especially the ones that women get during MENSTRUATION 【尤美】(腹) 絞痛〔尤指婦女痛經〕

cramp[2] *v* [T] **1** to prevent the development of someone's ability to do something 限制〔某人的能力〕; 約束: *Her education was cramped by lack of money.* 由於缺錢她沒受過良好教育。**2 cramp sb's style** to prevent someone from doing something they want to do, especially by going with them when they do not want you 不讓某人做某事: *He left Helen in the ski lodge. He didn't want anyone cramping his style on the slopes.* 他把海倫留在滑雪區旅館內, 因為他不想有人在斜坡地上妨礙他。

cramped /kræmpt; kræmpt/ *adj* **1** a cramped room, building etc does not have enough space for the people in it 狹窄的: *I couldn't sleep on the plane, it was too cramped.* 我在飛機上睡不着, 座位之間太狹窄了。| *cramped living conditions* 擁擠的居住條件 | *cramped offices* 狹小的辦公室 **2** also 又作 **cramped up** unable to move properly and uncomfortable because there is not enough space 〔活動〕受限制的; 擁擠的: *We all felt stiff from having been cramped up in the back of the car for so long.* 擠在汽車的後面老半天, 我們都感到渾身僵硬了。**3** writing that is cramped is very small and difficult to read 〔字跡〕擠在一起難辨認的

cram·pon /ˈkræmpɑn; ˈkræmpɒn/ *n* [C usually plural 一般用複數] a piece of metal with sharp points on the bottom that you fasten onto your boots to help in mountain climbing in the snow 〔登山鞋底上的〕防滑鐵釘

cran·ber·ry /ˈkrænˌbɛrɪ; ˈkrænbəri/ *n* [C] a small red sour fruit 越橘: *cranberry sauce* 越橘醬 —see picture on page A8 參見 A8 頁圖

crane[1] /kren; kreɪn/ *n* [C] **1** a large tall machine used by builders for lifting heavy things 起重機, 吊車 **2** a tall water bird with very long legs 鶴

crane[2] *v* [I always+adv/prep, T] to look around or over something by stretching or leaning 伸長〔脖子〕看; 探頭看: *The children craned forward to see what was happening.* 孩子們伸長脖子向前看發生了甚麼事。| **crane your neck** *Everyone on the bus craned their necks out of the windows and stared at them.* 公共汽車上的所有的人都從車窗裡面伸出脖子盯着他們看。

crane fly /ˈ· ·/ *n* [C] a flying insect with long legs 大蚊; DADDY LONGLEGS (1) *BrE* 【英】

cra·ni·um /ˈkrenɪəm; ˈkreɪniəm/ *n* [C] *technical* the part of your head that is made of bone and covers your brain 【術語】頭蓋骨, 顱骨

crank[1] /kræŋk; kræŋk/ *n* [C] **1** *informal* someone who has unusual ideas and behaves strangely 【非正式】怪人: *I was treated like a troublemaker and a crank.* 我被看成是個惹事生非、想法古怪的人。| **crank caller/letters** *We get quite a few crank phone calls.* 我們接到很多古怪的電話。**2** *AmE informal* someone who easily gets angry or annoyed with people 【美, 非正式】脾氣壞的人 **3** a piece of equipment with a handle that you can turn in order to move something 曲柄, 曲軸

crank[2] also 又作 **crank up** *v* [T] **1** to make something move by turning a crank 用曲柄啟動[轉動]: *crank an engine* 用曲柄發動引擎 **2** *informal* to make music louder 【非正式】增加〔音量〕: *Crank up the volume!* 把音量放大些!

crank sth ↔ **out** *phr v* [T] *informal especially AmE* to produce a lot of something very quickly 【非正式, 尤美】快速大量地製造: *He cranks out detective novels at the rate of three a year.* 他每年能寫出三部偵探小說。

crank·shaft /ˈkræŋkˌʃæft; ˈkræŋkʃɑːft/ *n* [C] a long piece of metal in a vehicle that is connected to the engine and helps to turn the wheels 〔汽車中與引擎連接的〕曲軸

crank·y /ˈkræŋkɪ; ˈkræŋki/ *adj* **1** bad-tempered 脾氣壞的: *The baby's a little cranky this morning.* 今天早上寶寶脾氣有點壞。**2** *BrE* having very strange ideas, or behaving strangely; ECCENTRIC[1] (1) 【英】〔想法或行為〕古怪的: *She's just a cranky old woman.* 她是一個古怪的老太太。—**crankiness** *n* [U]

cran·ny /ˈkrænɪ; ˈkræni/ *n* [C] a small narrow hole in a wall or rock 〔牆上或岩石上的〕裂縫, 縫隙: *The toad hid itself in a cranny in the wall.* 蟾蜍躲藏在牆縫裡。—see also 另見 **nook and cranny** (NOOK (3)) —**crannied** *adj*

crap[1] /kræp; kræp/ *n slang* 【俚】 **1** [U] something someone says that you think is completely wrong or untrue 廢話, 胡扯: *Jane doesn't really think we believe all that crap, does she?* 簡不是真的認為我們會相信那些廢話, 對嗎? | **be full of crap** (=often say things that are untrue or completely wrong) 滿口謊言, 全是廢話 *We all knew Mark was full of crap, but we still had to listen to him.* 我們都知道馬克說的全是廢話, 但是仍不得不聽他說話。| **cut the crap** (=used to tell someone to stop saying things that are completely wrong or untrue) 別說廢話了 **2 be a load of crap** also 又作 **be a bunch of crap** *AmE* 【美】 to be very bad, or completely untrue 糟透了; 一派胡言: *That new comedy last night was a load of crap, I thought.* 我認為昨晚的新喜劇全是胡鬧。**3** [U] things that are useless or unimportant 廢物: *What is all this crap doing on my desk?* 我桌上的這些破玩意都是些甚麼? **4** [singular] solid waste that is passed from your bowels 排泄物, 糞便, 屎: **have/take a crap** (=to pass solid waste from the BOWELS) 排便 **5 not take crap from someone** to refuse to allow someone to treat you badly or to say something unfair to you 不允許某人待自己不好[對自己說不公正的話]: *I don't have to take that crap* *from her – I'm leaving!* 我不必受她的氣，我要走了！**6 I don't need this (kind of) crap** used when you are angry at the way someone is talking or behaving to you 少來這一套 **7 craps** [plural] *AmE* a game played for money in the US, using two DICE[1] (1)【美】雙骰子賭博遊戲: **shoot craps** (=play this game) 玩雙骰子賭博遊戲

crap² *adj slang* of very bad quality【俚】質量極糟的: *Everyone knows those cars are crap!* 大家都知道那些汽車都是蹩腳貨！

crap³ *v* **crapped, crapping** [I] *spoken taboo* to pass waste matter from the bowels【口諱】拉屎

crape /krep; kreɪp/ *n* [U] **1** CREPE (1) 縐紗，縐綢，縐呢 **2** black material that people wore in former times as a sign of their sadness when someone died〔舊時〕表示哀悼的黑紗

crap·per /ˋkræpɚ; ˈkræpə/ *n* **the crapper** *BrE slang* a rude word meaning the toilet【英俚】廁所

crap·py /ˋkræpɪ; ˈkræpi/ *adj spoken slang* not very good【口俚】差的，不好的: *We arrived late and ended up staying in a crappy hotel.* 我們來晚了，到頭來只能住在一家很差的旅館裡。

crash¹ /kræʃ; kræʃ/ *v*

1 ►CAR/PLANE ETC 汽車/飛機等◄ [I,T] to have an accident in a car, plane etc by violently hitting another vehicle or something such as a wall or tree（使）〔飛機、汽車等〕墜毀；撞壞: *The DC10 crashed shortly after take-off.* 那架DC10飛機起飛後不久就墜毀了。| **[+into/onto etc]** *The car crashed straight into a tree.* 這輛車直撞到了樹上。| **crash a car/bus/plane etc** *Rick crashed his bike before he'd finished paying for it.* 里克還沒有付清買那輛自行車的錢就把它撞壞了。

2 ►HIT STH/SB HARD 重擊某物/某人◄ [I always+adv/prep, T always +adv/prep] to hit something or someone extremely hard while you are moving, causing a lot of damage, or making a lot of noise〔嘩啦啦地〕猛撞，猛擊: **[+into/through etc]** *The ladder came crashing through the window.* 梯子嘩啦一聲就把玻璃窗撞碎了。| **crash sth down** *Rod's face went bright red and he crashed his fist down on the table.* 羅德的臉漲得通紅，啪的一聲一拳打在桌子上。| **go crashing into** *He lost his balance on the ice and went crashing into the crowd.* 他在冰上失去平衡，撞入人羣。| **come crashing down** *A branch came crashing down onto the greenhouse.* 一根樹枝嘩啦一聲掉在温室上。

3 ►MAKE A LOUD NOISE 發出巨響◄ [I] to make a sudden, loud noise 發出巨響: *The cymbals crashed, and the symphony came to an end.* 鐃鈸發出巨響，交響曲結束了。—see picture on page A19 參見A19頁圖

4 ►SLEEP 睡覺◄ also 又作 **crash out** [I] *spoken*【口】**a)** to go to bed, or go to sleep very quickly, especially because you are very tired〔尤指由於很疲倦〕很快入睡: *I was so tired last night, I got home and just crashed out on the sofa.* 昨天晚上我太累了，回到家在沙發上就很快睡着了。**b)** to stay at someone's house for the night, especially when you have not planned to〔尤指事先沒有準備而留在別人家裡〕過夜: *Can I crash at your place on Saturday night?* 星期六晚上我能在你那兒過夜嗎？

5 ►COMPUTER 電腦◄ [I,T] if a computer crashes or you crash the computer, it suddenly stops working〔電腦〕癱瘓: *The system crashed at nine this morning, so we haven't been able to do anything.* 今天上午九點系統癱瘓了，因此我們甚麼也做不了。

6 ►FINANCIAL 金融◄ [I] if a STOCK MARKET crashes, the stocks (STOCK[1] (3a)) suddenly lose a lot of value〔股票〕狂跌

7 ►PARTY 聚會◄ [T] *informal* to go to a party that you have not been invited to【非正式】不請自來〔參加聚會〕: *She crashes parties all the time even though she always gets thrown out.* 儘管總是被趕出去，她還是常常不請自來地參加聚會。

8 crashing bore *BrE old-fashioned* someone who is very boring【英，過時】令人厭煩的人

crash² *n* [C] **1** a violent accident involving one or more vehicles〔汽車的〕撞車事故；〔飛機的〕失事: **plane/car etc crash** *41 people were killed in a plane crash in the Himalayas last week.* 上週喜馬拉雅山的飛機失事中有41人喪生。**2** a sudden loud noise made by something falling, breaking etc 突然發出的巨響；〔東西倒下、打破等時發出的〕碰撞聲: **[+of]** *Jessica heard the crash of breaking glass behind her.* 傑西卡聽到身後有玻璃被打碎的聲音。| **with a crash** *There was a loud crack and the branch came down with a crash.* 伴隨着巨大的斷裂聲，樹枝啪的一聲掉下來。**3** a sudden, unexpected failing of a computer or computer system〔電腦或電腦系統的〕癱瘓，失效，死機 **4** an occasion on which the stocks (STOCK[1] (3a)) in a STOCK MARKET suddenly lose a lot of value〔股票的〕狂跌: *Nobody was prepared for the crash on Black Monday in 1987.* 1987年黑色星期一的股票狂跌使所有的人都措手不及。 3

crash bar·ri·er /ˈ· ˌ··/ *n* [C] *BrE* a strong fence or wall built to keep cars apart or to keep them away from people, in order to prevent an accident【英】防撞護欄

crash course /ˈ· ·/ *n* [C] a course in which you learn the most important things about a particular subject in a very short period of time 速成班: **[+in]** *a crash course in Spanish* 西班牙語速成班

crash di·et /ˈ· ˌ··/ *n* [C] an attempt that someone makes to lose a lot of weight in a very short period of time 快速減肥

crash-dive /ˈ· ·/ *v* [I] if a SUBMARINE[1] crash-dives, it sinks quickly to a great depth〔潛水艇〕緊急下潛

crash hel·met /ˈ· ˌ··/ *n* [C] a very strong hat that covers your whole head, worn by racing car drivers, motorcyclists etc〔賽車手、摩托車手等戴的〕防護頭盔，安全帽 —see picture at 參見 HELMET 圖

crash-land /ˈ· ·/ *v* [I,T] to crash a plane in a controlled way because it is damaged and cannot be flown any more（使）〔飛機〕強行着陸；緊急降落

crass /kræs; kræs/ *adj* behaving in a way that shows you do not understand other people's feelings, or care about them 愚笨的，粗魯的；冷酷的: *crass stupidity* 極端愚蠢的 | *a crass commercial adventure* 愚蠢的商業冒險 —**crassly** *adv*

-crat /kræt; kræt/ *suffix* [in nouns 構成名詞] another form of the suffix -OCRAT 後綴 -ocrat 的另一種形式

crate¹ /kret; kreɪt/ also 又作 **crate up** *v* [T] to pack things into a crate 把…裝入貨箱

crate² *n* [C] **1** a box made of wood or plastic that is used for carrying fruit, bottles etc 板條箱；裝貨箱: *They lifted the crates onto the wagon.* 他們把箱子搬到運貨車上。—see picture at 參見 CONTAINER 圖 **2** *old-fashioned* a very old car or plane that does not work very well【過時】破舊的汽車[飛機]

cra·ter /ˋkretɚ; ˈkreɪtə/ *n* [C] **1** the round open part of a VOLCANO 火山口 **2** a round hole in the ground, especially made by an explosion or by something that has fallen from the sky〔尤指炸彈爆炸、流星墜落等在地上造成的〕坑: *the craters on the moon* 月球上的環形山

cra·vat /krəˋvæt; krəˈvæt/ *n* [C] a wide piece of loosely folded material that men wear around their necks〔男人戴的〕領巾 —compare 比較 TIE[2] (1)

crave /krev; kreɪv/ *v* **1** [T] to have an extremely strong desire for something, especially a drug 渴望，熱望: *She's an insecure child who craves attention.* 她是患得患失的孩子，渴望受到關注。**2** *formal* to ask seriously for something【正式】懇求；請求: *May I crave your pardon?* 你能原諒我嗎？

cra·ven /ˋkrevən; ˈkreɪvən/ *adj formal* completely lacking courage; COWARDLY【正式】懦弱的，膽小的: *You craven coward.* 你這個膽小鬼。—**cravenly** *adv* —**cravenness** *n* [U]

crav·ing /ˋkrevɪŋ; ˈkreɪvɪŋ/ *n* [C] an extremely strong desire for something 渴望，熱望: **[+for]** *a craving for some chocolate* 想吃巧克力的渴望

C

craw /krɔ; krɔ:/ *n* [C] *AmE*【美】—see 見 **stick in your craw** (STICK[1] (12))

craw·dad /ˋkrɔˏdæd; ˈkrɔ:dæd/ *n* [C] *AmE informal* a small animal like a LOBSTER that lives in rivers and streams; CRAYFISH【美, 非正式】淡水螯蝦

crawl[1] /krɔl; krɔ:l/ *v* [I]
1 ►MOVE ON HANDS AND KNEES 爬行◄ to move along on your hands and knees with your body close to the ground 爬, 爬行: **[+along/across etc]** *She suddenly got down and crawled along behind the wall so that Carl wouldn't see her.* 她突然趴下來, 在牆後爬行, 這樣卡爾就看不到她了。| *Is your baby crawling yet?* 你的寶寶會爬了嗎? —see picture at 參見 KNEEL 圖
2 ►INSECT 昆蟲◄ if an insect crawls, it moves using its legs〔昆蟲〕爬: **[+over/up etc]** *Watch out! There's a wasp crawling up your leg.* 小心! 你的腿上有一隻黃蜂在往上爬。
3 ►CARS ETC 汽車等◄ if a vehicle crawls, it moves forward very slowly〔汽車〕緩慢移動: **[+by/along etc]** *The traffic was crawling by at 5 miles an hour.* 路上的車以每小時五英里的速度緩慢行駛。
4 ►TOO HELPFUL 奉承的◄ to be too pleasant or helpful to someone in authority, especially because you want them to help you 巴結, 奉承: **crawl to sb** *Just look at Janice – crawling to the director of studies again!* 看看賈妮斯, 她又在討好教學主任了!
5 be crawling with to be completely covered with insects, people etc 爬滿〔蟲子〕; 擠滿〔人〕: *Eugh! This floor is crawling with ants.* 哎喲! 地板上爬滿了螞蟻。
6 make your skin crawl if something or someone makes your skin crawl, you think they are extremely unpleasant 使感覺不舒服; 使噁心: *The way Jonathan looks at her really makes my skin crawl.* 喬納森看她的樣子真使我噁心。

crawl[2] *n* [singular] **1** a very slow speed 緩慢移動, 徐行: *The traffic had slowed down to a crawl.* 車輛慢了下來, 成了爬行。**2** a fast way of swimming in which you lie on your stomach and move one arm and then the other over your head 自由泳; 爬泳

crawler lane /ˈ·· ˌ·/ *n* [C] *BrE* a special part of a road that can be used by slow vehicles so that other vehicles can go past【英】〔車輛的〕慢行道

cray·fish /ˋkreˏfɪʃ; ˈkreɪˌfɪʃ/ *n* [C,U] a small animal like a LOBSTER that lives in rivers and streams, or the flesh of this animal eaten as food 淡水螯蝦(肉)

cray·on[1] /ˋkreən; ˈkreɪən/ *n* [C] a stick of coloured WAX[1] (1) or CHALK[1] (2) used for writing or drawing, especially on paper 彩色蠟筆[粉筆]: *children's crayons* 兒童彩色蠟筆

crayon[2] *v* [I,T] to draw with a crayon 用彩色蠟筆[粉筆]畫畫

craze /krez; kreɪz/ *n* [C] a fashion, game, type of music etc that suddenly becomes very popular but usually only remains popular for a very short time 時尚; 時髦的東西: *This computer game is the latest craze.* 這種電腦遊戲是最新時尚。

crazed /krezd; kreɪzd/ *adj* behaving in a wild and uncontrolled way as if you are crazy 瘋狂的, 狂野的: *a crazed expression* 瘋狂的表情 | **[+with]** *He was crazed with grief.* 他傷心得發瘋。

cra·zy[1] /ˋkrezɪ; ˈkreɪzi/ *adj informal*【非正式】
1 ►STRANGE 奇怪的◄ behaving in a way that is very strange〔行為〕古怪的: *Don't mind her, she's crazy.* 不要管她, 她很古怪。| *The neighbours must think we're crazy.* 鄰居們一定會認為我們很古怪。| *You have some crazy friends.* 你有些古怪的朋友。
2 ►NOT SENSIBLE 不理智的◄ an action or behaviour that is crazy is not sensible and likely to cause problems〔行動或行為〕愚蠢的, 愚笨的: **it's crazy** *spoken*【口】: *I get more money if I don't work – it's crazy.* 不工作時我會得到更多的錢——這個想法真荒唐。| *That's the craziest idea I've ever heard.* 這是我所聽到的最荒謬的想法。| **be crazy to do sth** *It'd be crazy to try and drive home in this weather.* 這種天氣要想駕車回家簡直是發瘋。
3 ►ANGRY 生氣的◄ angry or annoyed 生氣的; 煩惱的: **drive sb crazy** (=make sb angry or annoyed) 讓人生氣[煩惱]: *Turn that music down, it's driving me crazy!* 把音樂調輕點, 實在叫我心煩!
4 be crazy about sb/sth to like someone very much, or be very interested in something 對〔某人〕着迷; 醉心於〔某物〕: *Frank is just crazy about you!* 弗蘭克對你很着迷!
5 like crazy very quickly or very hard 極快地; 拚命地: *We're going to have to work like crazy to get this finished on time.* 為了按時完成工作我們要拚命幹。
6 ►ILL 生病的◄ mentally ill 瘋狂的, 發瘋的: *He lived alone and they were sure he was crazy.* 他一人獨居, 他們確信他已經瘋了。| **go crazy** *Kurtz had gone crazy, alone in the jungle.* 庫爾茨發瘋了, 獨自一人在叢林裡。
7 crazy as a loon *AmE informal* very strange and possibly mentally ill【美, 非正式】想法怪異的, 瘋瘋顛顛的 —**crazily** *adv* —**craziness** *n* [U]

crazy[2] *n* [C] *AmE informal* someone who is crazy【美, 非正式】瘋子

crazy golf /ˌ·· ˈ·/ *n* [U] *BrE* a game like GOLF in which the players hit the ball through various amusing OBSTACLES【英】小型高爾夫球運動; MINIATURE GOLF *AmE*【美】

crazy pav·ing /ˌ·· ˈ··/ *n* [U] *especially BrE* pieces of stone of different shapes fitted together to make a path or flat place【尤英】〔用形狀不規則的石塊拼鋪的〕碎紋石路

crazy quilt /ˌ·· ˈ·/ *n* [C] *AmE* a cover for a bed made from small pieces of cloth of different shapes that have been sewn together【美】百衲被, 碎布牀單

creak[1] /krik; kri:k/ *v* [I] if something such as a door, bed, stair etc creaks, it makes a long high noise when someone opens it, sits on it, walks on it etc〔門、牀、樓梯等〕嘎吱作響: *The window shutters creaked in the wind.* 百葉窗在風中嘎吱作響。

creak[2] *n* [C] the sound made by something when it creaks 吱吱嘎嘎的聲音: **[+of]** *the creak of a door* 門的吱吱嘎聲

creak·y /ˋkrikɪ; ˈkri:ki/ *adj* something such as a chair, bed etc that is creaky creaks when you sit on it, stand on it etc〔椅子、牀等〕嘎吱作響的 —**creakily** *adv* —**creakiness** *n* [U]

cream[1] /krim; kri:m/ *n* [U] **1** a thick yellowish-white liquid that rises to the top of milk 奶油; 乳脂: *Have some cream in your coffee.* 在你的咖啡中加些奶油吧。| *strawberries and cream* 澆奶油的草莓 **2** [C,U] a food containing this 含奶油食品: *cream of chicken soup* 奶油雞湯 | *cream cakes* 奶油蛋糕 **3** [C,U] a thick soft substance that you put on your skin in order to make it soft, treat a medical condition etc 護膚霜; 雪花膏: *Put some sun cream on before you go out.* 出去以前塗上一些防曬霜。**4 the cream of** the cream of a group of people are the best people in that group 精華, 精英: *a team representing the cream of Britain's young athletes* 代表英國年輕優秀運動員的運動隊

cream[2] *adj* yellowish-white in colour 奶油色的, 淡黃色的: *a cream coloured carpet* 奶黃色的地毯 —**cream** *n* [U] —see picture on page A5 參見 A5 頁圖

cream[3] *v* [T] **1** to make something into a thick soft mixture 使成奶油狀: *Cream the butter and sugar together.* 把黃油和糖調成奶油狀。| *creamed potatoes* 馬鈴薯泥 **2** to take cream from the surface of milk 從牛奶中提取奶油 **3** *AmE informal* to defeat someone completely【美, 非正式】徹底打敗

cream sb/sth **off** *phr v* [T] to choose the best people or things from a group, especially so that you can use them for your own advantage 提取〔精華〕: *We cream off the best athletes and put them into a special squad.* 我們挑選最好的運動員送到特殊訓練隊去。

cream cheese /ˌ· ˈ·/ *n* [U] a type of soft white smooth cheese 奶油乾酪

cream crack·er /ˌ· ˈ··/ *n* [C] *BrE* a light BISCUIT (1) often eaten with cheese【英】奶油薄脆餅乾

cream·er /ˈkrimɚ; ˈkriːmə/ *n* **1** [U] a liquid that you can use instead of cream in drinks 代奶油, 植脂末 **2** [C] a small container for holding cream 小奶油壺

cream·e·ry /ˈkrimərɪ; ˈkriːməri/ *n* [C] *old-fashioned* a place where milk, butter, cream, and cheese are produced or sold【過時】乳製品廠; 乳製品商店

cream·y /ˈkrimɪ; ˈkriːmi/ *adj* **1** containing cream 含乳脂的; 含奶油的: *creamy milk* 含脂牛奶 **2** thick smooth and soft like cream 似奶油的; 軟厚平滑的, 光滑細軟的: *This make-up has a lovely creamy consistency.* 這種化妝品的質地像奶油一樣柔滑。**3** yellowish-white in colour 奶油色的, 淡黃色的

crease¹ /kris; kriːs/ *n* **1** [C] a line on cloth, paper etc, made by folding, crushing or pressing it〔衣服、紙等的〕褶痕; 皺褶: *You've got a crease in your dress where you've been sitting.* 你的連衣裙坐過的地方起皺了。| *I can never get the creases straight in these trousers.* 我怎麼也無法把褲子上的皺褶燙直。**2** [singular] the line where the player has to stand to hit the ball in CRICKET (2)〔板球場上擊球手站在上面的〕區域線, 擊球線

crease² *v* [I,T] to become marked with a line or lines, or to make a line appear on cloth, paper etc by folding or crushing it 使起皺褶; 使起皺: *Don't sit on my paper, you'll crease it!* 不要坐在我的卷子上, 你會把它弄皺的! | *This material creases really easily.* 這種材料很容易起皺。

crease (sb) up *phr v* [I,T] *BrE spoken* to laugh or make someone laugh a lot【英口】(使)〔某人〕大笑: *That guy really creases me up!* 那個人使我笑得直不起腰!

creased /krist; kriːst/ *adj* cloth or paper that is creased has a line or lines on it because it has been folded or crushed 有皺的, 有皺褶的: *She wanted to wear her black dress but it was too creased.* 她想穿她那件黑色連衣裙, 但是皺得太厲害。

1 1 **cre·ate** /krɪˈet; kriˈeɪt/ *v* **1** [T] to make something exist that did not exist before 創造; 創建: *Her behaviour is creating a lot of problems.* 她的行為引起了很多的麻煩。| *Government promises to create more public sector jobs.* 政府承諾在公共部門創造更多的職位。**2** [T] to invent something 發明; 創作: *The writer creates his own special language.* 這個作家創作出自己獨特的語言。| [**+by**] *This dish was created by our chef Jean Richard.* 這道菜是由我們的廚師吉恩·理查德創製的。**3 create sb/sth** *BrE* to officially give someone special rank or title【英】封爵; 任命; 授予: *James I created him Duke of Buckingham.* 詹姆士一世封他為白金漢公爵。**4** [I] *BrE old-fashioned* to be noisily angry【英, 過時】大喊大叫; 大發雷霆: *Don't tell Grandad – he'll only start creating.* 不要告訴爺爺, 他只會大發雷霆。

3 2 **cre·a·tion** /krɪˈeʃən; kriˈeɪʃən/ *n* **1** [U] the act of creating something 創造; 創建: [**+of**] *The report proposed the creation of an independent Scottish parliament.* 該報告建議成立一個獨立的蘇格蘭議會。| *a job-creation scheme* 創造就業機會的計劃 **2** [C] something that has been created 創造物; 作品; 產物: *The story was a fanciful creation.* 該故事是個富有想像力的作品。| *this year's new fashion creations from Paris* 今年來自巴黎的新時裝 **3** [U] the whole universe, and all living things 宇宙; 世界; 天地萬物: *Are we the only thinking species in creation?* 我們是萬物中惟一有思想的物種嗎? **4 the Creation** the act by God, according to the Bible, of making the universe, including the world and everything in it (神) 創造天地

cre·a·tion·ist /krɪˈeʃənɪst; kriˈeɪʃənɪ̆st/ *n* [C] someone who believes that God created the universe in the way described in the Bible 神造天地論者 —**creationism** *n* [U]

3 3 **cre·a·tive** /krɪˈetɪv; kriˈeɪtɪv/ *adj* **1** producing or using new and effective ideas, results etc 創造(性)的: *He came up with a really creative solution to the problem.* 他想出了一個解決這個問題的方案, 很有創造性。| *I enjoy my job, but I'd like to do something more creative.* 我很喜歡我的工作, 但我想做些更具創造性的工作。**2** someone who is creative is very imaginative and good at making things, painting etc〔人〕有創造力的: *You're so creative! – I could never make my own clothes.* 你真有創造力! 我從來不會給自己做衣服。—**creatively** *adv* —**creativeness** *n* [U] —**creativity** /ˌkrieˈtɪvətɪ; ˌkriːeɪˈtɪvɪ̆ti/ *n* [U]

creative ac·count·ing /ˌ·· ·ˈ··/ *n* [U] the act of changing business accounts to achieve the result you want in a way that hides the truth but is not illegal〔不違法的〕改造賬目

cre·a·tor /krɪˈetɚ; kriˈeɪtə/ *n* [C] **1** someone who made or invented a particular thing 創作者; 創造者: *Walt Disney, the creator of Mickey Mouse* 米老鼠的創造者和路迪士尼 **2 the Creator** God 上帝, 造物主

crea·ture /ˈkritʃɚ; ˈkriːtʃə/ *n* [C] 3

1 ▶LIVING THING 生物◀ anything that is living, but not a plant 動物: *The crocodile is a strange-looking creature.* 鱷魚是一種樣子古怪的動物。| **living creature** *He has great respect for all living creatures.* 他對所有的生物都很尊重。

2 ▶STRANGE 奇怪的◀ a strange and sometimes frightening living thing 不可名狀的生物, 怪物: *creatures from outer space* 來自外太空的怪物

3 stupid/adorable/horrid etc creature someone who has a particular character or quality 愚蠢/可愛/可怕等的人: *"Lady Jones is a charming creature", he sighed.* "瓊斯夫人是個尤物。" 他讚嘆說。

4 ▶SB CONTROLLED BY STH 受某物控制的某人◀ someone who is controlled by, or completely in the power of a particular person or organization 受支配的人, 傀儡, 奴才: [**+of**] *He was a creature of the military government.* 他是軍政府的傀儡。

5 a creature of habit someone who always does things in the same way or at the same times 墨守成規的人

6 ▶STH MADE OR INVENTED 製造或發明的東西◀ something, especially something bad, that has been made or invented by a particular person or organization 創造物〔尤指不好的東西〕; 產物

creature com·forts /ˌ·· ˈ··/ *n* [plural] all the things that make life more comfortable and enjoyable such as good food, a warm house etc 給肉體舒適感的東西; 物質享受

crè·che /kreʃ; kreʃ/ *n* [C] **1** *BrE* a place where babies are looked after while their parents are at work【英】托兒所, 日托中心 —compare 比較 DAY CARE CENTRE (1) *AmE*【美】**2** *AmE* a model of the scene of Jesus' birth, often placed in churches and homes at Christmas【美】基督誕生情景的模型〔聖誕節時在教堂或家裡陳列〕; CRIB¹(3) *BrE*【英】

cre·dence /ˈkridn̩s; ˈkriːdəns/ *n* [U] *formal* the acceptance of something as true【正式】相信; 信任: *The amount of credence accorded to written records will undoubtedly vary.* 對書面記錄的信任度肯定會不一樣。| **gain credence** (=to become more widely accepted or believed) 得到認可; 獲得信任 *This doctrine gained credence in academic circles over the next few decades.* 在接下來的幾十年裡這一學說得到了學術界的認可。| **give credence to sth** (=to believe or accept something as true) 相信某事 *I don't give any credence to these rumors.* 我不相信這些謠言。| **lend credence to sth** (=to make something more believable)〔提供佐證〕使某事更可信

cre·den·tials /krɪˈdɛnʃəlz; krɪˈdenʃəlz/ *n* [plural] **1** the things that show people that you have the ability to do something, are suitable for something etc, such as your education, experience, and achievements 資格; 資格的證明: *He spent the first hour trying to establish his credentials as a financial expert.* 第一個小時他設法證明自己是金融專家。**2** a letter or other document which

proves your good character or your right to have a particular position 資格證書;〔品格的〕證明信, 推薦書: *The commissioner presented his credentials to the State Department.* 委員向國務院遞交了資格證書。

cred·i·bil·i·ty /ˌkrɛdəˈbɪlətɪ; ˌkredʒˈbɪlʒti/ *n* [U] **1** the quality of deserving to be believed and trusted 可靠性; 可信性: *This latest scandal has damaged his credibility as a leader.* 最近的醜聞破壞了他作為領導人的可信性。| **[+of]** *There are serious questions about the credibility of these reports.* 這些報告的可靠性有很多重大疑問。| **gain/lose credibility** *Predictions of economic recovery have now lost all credibility.* 經濟復蘇的預言現在已完全不可信。**2 credibility gap** the difference between what someone, especially a politician, says and what people can believe 信用差距〔尤指政治家的言論和公眾對他的信任的差距〕

cred·i·ble /ˈkrɛdəbḷ; ˈkredʒbəl/ *adj* deserving or able to be believed or trusted 可信的, 可靠的: *a credible witness* 可信的目擊者 —**credibly** *adv*

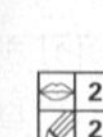

cred·it¹ /ˈkrɛdɪt; ˈkredʒt/ *n*

1 ▶DELAYED PAYMENT 推遲付款◀ [U] an arrangement with a shop, bank etc that makes it possible for you to buy something and pay for it later 賒購: **on credit** (=bought using this arrangement) 賒購, 記賬 *stores that sell goods on credit* 可賒購商品的商店 | **interest-free credit** (=credit with no additional charge) 無息賒購 —compare 比較 DEBIT¹ (2)

2 ▶PRAISE 讚揚◀ [U] approval or praise that you give to someone for something they have done 讚揚; 讚許: **give (sb) credit (for sth)** *You could at least give him some credit for all the effort he's put in.* 你至少應該對他所作的所有努力給予讚揚。| **take/claim/deserve etc (the) credit** *Sam never once accepted all the credit for himself.* 薩姆從來沒有把一切歸功於自己。| **to sb's credit** (=making someone deserve praise or admiration) 值得讚揚[欽佩] *It is much to her credit that Joy persevered in spite of all the difficulties.* 儘管有那麼多的困難, 喬伊還是挺住了, 值得讚揚。

3 be a credit to sb/sth also 又作 **do sb/sth credit** to behave so well or be so successful that everyone who is connected with you can be proud of you 為…增光: *She's a credit to the team.* 她為隊裡增了光。| *Your children really do you credit.* 你的孩子真為你增光了。

4 have sth to your credit to have achieved something 成功: *She already has two successful novels to her credit.* 她已經寫了兩部很成功的小說。

5 be in credit to have money in your bank account〔銀行賬戶中〕有存款: *There are no bank charges if you stay in credit.* 只要你賬戶裡有錢, 銀行就不收費。

6 ▶FILM 電影◀ the credits [plural] the list of names of actors and other people involved shown at the beginning or end of a film or television programme〔影片或電視節目的〕演員和攝製人員名單

7 on the credit side used to say that the things you are going to mention are the good or positive things about someone or something 好的方面; 正面: *On the credit side, the school has considerable success in sport and music.* 從好的方面來講, 這所學校培養了很多體育和音樂人材。

8 ▶UNIVERSITY 大學◀ [C] a successfully completed part of a course at a university or college 學分: *The drama course should give me enough credits to finish my degree.* 戲劇課應該給我足夠的學分使我能夠獲得學位。

9 ▶TRUE/CORRECT 真的/正確的◀ [U] the belief that something is true or correct 信任

credit² *v* [T not in progressive 不用進行式] **1** to believe that something is true 信任; 相信: *He told me he'd just won first prize – would you credit it?* 他告訴我他剛得了頭獎, 你信嗎? | *I find that statement rather hard to credit.* 我覺得很難相信那個說法。**2** to add money to a bank account 把錢存入〔賬戶〕: **[+to]** *The cheque has been credited to your account.* 支票已轉進你的賬戶了。—compare 比較 DEBIT² (1) **3 credit sb with sth** to believe that someone has a quality, or has done something good 相信某人有優點[做了好事]: *Do credit me with a little intelligence!* 我還是有點小聰明的, 請相信我! | *This symbol was credited with magical powers.* 這個符號被認為有魔力。**4 be credited to** if something is credited to someone or something, they have achieved it or are the reason for it 歸功於…; …是某事發生的原因: *Much of their success can be credited to Wilson – an expert.* 他們的成功很大程度上歸功於威爾遜——一位專家。

cred·i·ta·ble /ˈkrɛdɪtəbḷ; ˈkredʒtəbəl/ *adj* deserving praise or approval 值得讚揚的; 該稱譽的: *a creditable piece of factual research* 值得稱道的實況調查 | **a creditable performance** *Sue gave a very creditable performance as Lady Macbeth.* 蘇演麥克白夫人演得很出色。—**creditably** *adv*

credit ac·count /ˈ·· ˌ·ˌ·/ *n* [C] *BrE* an account with a shop which allows you to take goods and pay for them later【英】信用賬戶; 賒購賬戶; CHARGE ACCOUNT *AmE*【美】

credit card /ˈ·· ·/ *n* [C] a small plastic card that you use to buy goods or services 信用卡: *We accept all major credit cards.* 我們接受所有主要的信用卡。—compare 比較 CASH CARD, CHEQUE CARD, DEBIT CARD

credit freeze /ˈ·· ˌ·/ *n* [C] a period during which the government makes it more difficult for people to borrow money, to reduce the amount of money people spend 信用凍結

credit note /ˈ·· ·/ *n* [C] a document which a shop gives you when you return goods allowing you to exchange them for goods of the same value 換貨憑證〔商店發出的憑證, 顧客可以據此把貨物換作等價貨物〕

cred·i·tor /ˈkrɛdɪtɚ; ˈkredʒtə/ *n* [C] someone who money is owed to 債權人; 債主 —compare 比較 DEBTOR

credit rat·ing /ˈ·· ˌ··/ *n* [C] a judgement made by a financial institution about how likely a person or business is to pay their debts 信用等級, 信用評價

credit voucher /ˈ·· ˌ··/ *n* [C] *AmE* a credit note【美】換貨憑證

cred·it·wor·thy /ˈkrɛdɪtˌwɝθɪ; ˈkredʒtˌwɜːθi/ *adj* considered to be able to repay debts 信用可靠的, 有還款能力的 —**creditworthiness** *n* [U]

cre·do /ˈkrido; ˈkriːdəʊ/ *n* [C] a formal statement of the beliefs of a religion etc 教義; 信條

cre·du·li·ty /krəˈdulətɪ; krɪˈdjuːlʒti/ *n* [U] willingness or ability to believe that something is true 輕信, 易信: *childish credulity* 幼稚的輕信 | **strain/stretch credulity** *This explanation strained my credulity too far.* 我覺得這個解釋太離譜。

cred·u·lous /ˈkrɛdʒələs; ˈkredjʒləs/ *adj* always believing what you are told, and therefore easily deceived 輕信的, 易上當的: *This man has coaxed millions of pounds from a credulous public.* 這個人從輕信的公眾那裡騙取了幾百萬英鎊。—**credulously** *adv* —**credulousness** *n* [U]

creed /krid; kriːd/ *n* [C] **1** a set of beliefs or principles 信條, 教條: *the Marxist-Leninist creed* 馬列主義信條 | *people of every creed* (=all different religious beliefs) 各種教派的人 **2 the Creed** a formal statement of belief spoken in certain Christian churches〔在某些基督教會中宣講的〕教義

creek /krik; kriːk/ *n* [C] **1** *BrE* a long narrow area of water that flows from the sea, a river, or a lake into the land【英】〔通海、河或湖的〕小灣, 小港 **2** *AmE, AusE* a small narrow stream or river【美, 澳】小溪, 小河 **3 be up the creek** *spoken* to be in a difficult situation【口】處於困境: *If I don't get my passport by Friday, I'll be completely up the creek.* 如果到星期五還拿不到護照, 我就慘了。**4 be up shit creek (without a paddle)** *slang* an impolite way of saying that you are in serious trouble【俚】陷入嚴重困境, 倒了邪霉

creel /kril; kriːl/ *n* [C] a fisherman's basket for carrying fish 魚簍, 魚籃

creep¹ /krip; kriːp/ *v past tense and past participle* **crept** /krɛpt; krept/ [I always+adv/prep] **1** to move in a quiet, careful way, especially to avoid attracting attention 悄悄地小心行進: **[+into/over/around etc]** *Johann would creep into the gallery to listen to the singers.* 約翰會悄悄溜進樓座去聽歌手唱歌。| *He crept back up the stairs, trying to avoid the ones that creaked.* 他躡手躡腳地回到樓上, 盡量避開會嘎吱嘎吱響的那幾級樓梯。—see picture on page A24 參見A24頁圖 **2** if something such as an insect, small animal, or car creeps, it moves slowly and quietly 爬行, 匍匐: **[+down/along/away etc]** *a caterpillar creeping down my arm* 順着我的胳膊慢慢爬下的毛毛蟲 **3** to gradually enter something and change it 漸漸侵入, 逐漸融進: **[+in/into/over etc]** *Funny how religion is creeping into the environmental debate.* 很奇怪宗教怎麼會融進環境辯論中去。**4** if a plant creeps it grows or climbs up or along a particular place〔植物〕攀緣, 蔓生: **[+up/over/around etc]** *ivy creeping up the walls of the building* 爬滿了建築物各面牆的常春藤 **5** if mist, clouds etc creep, they gradually fill or cover a place〔霧、雲等〕彌漫: **[+into/over etc]** *Fog was creeping into the valley.* 霧飄進山谷。**6** *BrE informal* to be insincerely nice to someone, especially someone in authority, in order to gain an advantage for yourself【英, 非正式】卑躬屈膝, 巴結奉承: **creep (up) to sb** *I'm not the kind of person to creep to anybody.* 我不是那種巴結別人的人。**7 sb/sth makes my flesh creep** used to say that someone or something makes you feel strong dislike or fear 某人/某事物使我不舒服[恐懼]: *His glassy stare made my flesh creep.* 他那呆滯的凝視使我毛骨悚然。

creep up on sb/sth *phr v* [T] **1** to surprise someone by walking up behind them silently 躡手躡腳在後面走〔而嚇人一跳〕: *Don't yell – let's creep up on them and scare them.* 別喊, 讓我們悄悄從他們後面走過去嚇他們一跳。**2** if a feeling or idea creeps up on you, it gradually increases〔感情或觀點〕漸漸變強: *The feeling she had for Malcolm had crept up on her and taken her by surprise.* 她慢慢對馬爾科姆產生了感情, 她自己也感到吃驚。**3** to seem to come sooner than you expect 不知不覺中到來: *Somehow, the end of term had crept up on us.* 不知不覺又到期末了。

creep² *n* **1** *informal especially AmE* someone who you dislike extremely【非正式, 尤美】極討厭的人: *Get lost, you little creep!* 走開, 你這個討厭鬼! **2** [C] *BrE informal* someone who tries to make you like them or do things for them by being insincerely nice to you【英, 非正式】獻媚者; 奴顏婢膝的人: *Don't try and flatter her – she doesn't approve of creeps.* 別去奉承她, 她不喜歡拍馬屁的傢伙。**3 give sb the creeps** if a person or place gives you the creeps, they make you feel nervous and a little frightened, especially because they are strange〔人或地方〕使某人毛骨悚然[緊張]: *That house gives me the creeps.* 那棟房子使我毛骨悚然。

creep·er /ˋkripɚ; ˈkriːpə/ *n* [U] a plant that grows up trees or walls or along the ground 攀緣[匍匐]植物

creep·y /ˋkripɪ; ˈkriːpi/ *adj* making you feel nervous and slightly frightened 使人緊張的; 令人毛骨悚然的: *There's something creepy about the way he looks at me.* 他看我的樣子使我有點緊張。| *a creepy old house* 令人毛骨悚然的老房子

creepy-crawl·y /ˌ·· ˈ··/ *n* [C] *spoken especially BrE* an insect, especially one that you are frightened of【口, 尤英】令人討厭的昆蟲

cre·mate /ˋkrimet; krɪ̈ˈmeɪt/ *v* [T] to burn the body of a dead person at a funeral ceremony 火葬, 火化 —**cremation** /krɪˋmeʃən; krɪˈmeɪʃən/ *n* [C,U]

crem·a·to·ri·um /ˌkriməˋtorɪəm; ˌkreməˈtɔːriəm/ **crem·a·to·ry** /ˋkriməˌtorɪ; ˈkremətəri/ *especially AmE*【尤美】*n* [C] a building in which the bodies of dead people are burned at a funeral ceremony 火葬場

crème car·a·mel /ˌkrɛm ˋkærəməl; ˌkrem ˈkærəməl/ *n* [C] a sweet food made from milk, eggs, and sugar 焦糖蛋奶

crème de la crème /ˌkrɛm də lɑ ˋkrɛm; ˌkrem də lɑː ˈkrem/ *n* [singular] *French* the very best of a kind of thing or group of people【法】精華; 最優秀分子, 精英: *The chefs there are the crème de la crème of the culinary world.* 那裡的廚師是廚藝界裡最好的。

crème de menthe /ˌkrɛm də ˋmɑnθ; ˌkrem də ˈmɒnθ/ *n* [U] a strong, sweet, green alcoholic drink 薄荷甜酒〔一種綠色的甜味烈酒〕

cren·el·lat·ed *BrE*【英】, **crenelated** *AmE*【美】/ˋkrɛnl̩ˌetɪd; ˈkrenəleɪtɪ̈d/ *adj technical* a wall or tower that is crenellated has BATTLEMENTS【術語】〔圍牆或塔樓〕有雉堞的

cre·ole /ˋkriol; ˈkriːəʊl/ *n* **1** [C,U] a language that is a combination of a European language with one or more other languages 克里奧耳語〔一種歐洲語言和其他語言的混合語〕—compare 比較 PIDGIN **2** [C] someone descended from both Europeans and Africans 克里奧耳人〔歐洲和非洲的混血兒〕**3** [C] a white person born in the West Indies or parts of Spanish America, or descended from the original French settlers in the southern US 克里奧耳白人〔出生於西印度羣島或拉丁美洲一部分地區的白人或美國南部法國移民的後裔〕**4** [U] food prepared in the hot strong-tasting style of the southern US〔美國南部的〕克里奧耳式辣味食品: *shrimp creole* 克里奧耳辣蝦 —**creole** *adj*

cre·o·sote /ˋkriəˌsot; ˈkriːəsəʊt/ *n* [U] a thick, brown, oily liquid used for preserving wood 雜酚油〔用於木材防護處理〕—**creosote** *v* [T]

crepe, crêpe /krep; kreɪp/ *n* **1** also 又作 **crape** [U] light, soft, thin cloth, with very small folded lines on the surface, made from cotton, silk, wool, etc. 縐紗, 縐綢, 縐呢 **2** [U] tightly pressed rubber used especially for making the bottoms of shoes〔尤用以製鞋底的〕縐橡膠: *crepe-soled shoes* 有縐膠底的鞋 **3** [C] a very thin PANCAKE (1) 薄煎餅

crepe pa·per /ˌ· ˈ··/ *n* [U] thin, brightly coloured paper with very small folded lines on the surface, especially used as decorations〔尤用於裝飾的〕縐紙

crept /krɛpt; krept/ the past tense and past participle of CREEP¹

cre·scen·do /krəˋʃɛndo; krɪ̈ˈʃendəʊ/ *n* [C] **1** a sound or a piece of music that becomes gradually louder〔聲音或音樂的〕漸強: **rise to/reach a crescendo** (=to gradually become louder) 逐漸變響 *The violins had reached a crescendo.* 小提琴奏到了強音。| *Her voice rose to a crescendo.* 她的嗓音越來越響。—opposite 反義詞 DIMINUENDO **2** a time when people are becoming more and more excited, anxious, or angry 高潮, 頂點: *A crescendo of resentment built up between the two women.* 這兩個女人之間的憤恨達到了極點。| **rise to/reach a crescendo** *the clamour of telephones as the working day reached its crescendo of activity* 一天中工作最忙時的電話嘈雜聲 —**crescendo** *adj*

cres·cent /ˋkrɛsn̩t; ˈkresənt/ *n* [C] **1** a curved shape, wider in the middle and pointed at the ends 新月形: **crescent moon/knife/biscuit etc** *A new crescent moon rose above the town.* 一彎新月升起在市鎮上空。—see picture at 參見 SHAPE¹ 圖 **2** the curved shape as a sign of the Muslim religion 新月〔伊斯蘭教的象徵〕**3** a word meaning a street with a curved shape, often used in the street's name 彎曲的街道〔常用作街名〕: *Turn left into Badgerly Crescent.* 向左拐進巴傑里曲街。

cress /krɛs; kres/ *n* [U] a small plant with round green leaves that can be eaten and has a slightly hot taste 水芹: *egg and cress sandwiches* 水芹雞蛋三明治

crest¹ /krɛst; krest/ *n* **1** [C usually singular 一般用單數] the top or highest point of something such as a hill or a wave〔山〕頂;〔浪〕峯: **[+of]** *He climbed over the crest of the hill.* 他翻過了山頂。—see picture on page A12 參

見A12頁圖 **2** [C] a special picture used as a sign of a family, town, school etc 徽章: *the school colours and crest* 學校的旗幟和徽章 | *the family crest on his notepaper* 他信箋上的家族飾章 **3** [C] a pointed group of feathers on top of a bird's head, or a raised area on the body of an animal 羽冠; 肉冠: *the dramatic feathery crest of the cockatoo* 白鸚漂亮的羽冠 **4** [C] a decoration of bright feathers, worn, especially in former times, on top of soldiers' helmets (HELMET)〔昔日士兵的頭盔上的〕羽飾 **5 be riding the crest of a wave** to be very successful, happy etc 走運; 無往不利: *The President is currently riding the crest of a wave of popularity.* 總統的聲望目前已達到頂點。

C

crest² *v* **1** [T] to reach the top of a hill, mountain etc 到達〔山頂〕; 達到…的頂點: *They'd crested another ridge by the afternoon.* 到下午時他們爬上了另一個山頂。**2** [I] if a wave crests it reaches its highest point before it falls 形成波峯

crest·ed /ˋkrɛstɪd; ˈkrestɪ̣d/ *adj* **1** having a crest 有羽冠的; 有羽飾的: *crested birds* 有羽冠的鳥 **2** marked by a crest 有徽章的: *the Duke's crested notepaper* 公爵有徽章的信紙

crest·fal·len /ˋkrɛst,fɔlən; ˈkrest,fɔːlən/ *adj* disappointed especially because you have failed to do something 沮喪的, 垂頭喪氣的: *The kids came back from the game looking crestfallen.* 孩子們比賽歸來滿臉沮喪。

cre·ta·ceous /krɪˋteʃəs; krɪ̣ˈteɪʃəs/ *adj technical*【術語】**1** similar to CHALK¹ (1) or containing chalk 似白堊的; 含白堊的 **2 the Cretaceous period** the time when rocks containing chalk were formed 白堊紀

cret·in /ˋkritɪn; ˈkretɪ̣n/ *n* [C] *especially spoken* someone who is extremely stupid【尤口】笨蛋, 白痴: *Don't be such a cretin! Don't you know anything?* 不要那麼傻了! 你甚麼也不知道嗎? **—cretinous** *adj*

cre·vasse /krəˋvæs; krɪˈvæs/ *n* [C] a deep open crack in thick ice, especially in a GLACIER〔尤指冰川的〕裂縫, 缺口 —see picture on page A12 參見A12頁圖

crev·ice /ˋkrɛvɪs; ˈkrevɪ̣s/ *n* [C] a narrow crack, especially in rock〔尤指岩石的〕裂縫, 缺口: *He climbed the cliff, finding footholds in the crevices.* 他攀登懸崖, 在岩石裂縫裡尋找踩腳的地方。

S3 W3 **crew¹** /kru; kruː/ *n* **1** [C] all the people working on a ship, plane etc 全體船員;〔飛機上〕全體機組人員: *These planes carry over 300 passengers and crew.* 這些飛機載有三百多名乘客和機組人員。**2** [C] all the people working on a ship, plane etc except the most important officers〔除船長外的〕船員;〔除機長外的〕機組人員: *How many crew does he need to sail his yacht?* 他需要多少船員開動他的遊艇? **3** [C] a group of people working together with special skills for a particular purpose 一隊工作人員: *a TV camera crew* 電視攝影隊 —see also 另見 GROUND CREW **4** [singular] a group of people 一羣人: *We found a happy crew of foreign students in the hostel.* 在旅舍裡我們發現一羣快樂的外國學生。| **motley crew** (=a group of people who are a strange mixture of types) 三教九流的一羣人 *My son came home from college with this motley crew.* 我兒子從大學回到家, 帶了一羣亂七八糟的朋友。**5** [C] a team of people who compete in rowing (ROW³) races〔划船比賽中的〕全體划船隊員; 划船隊: *Who will be on the college crew?* 大學划船隊會有誰?

crew² *v* [I,T] to be part of the crew on a boat 當船員: *He asked me to crew for him in the sailing races.* 他要求我當他的划船比賽隊員。

crew³ *old use*【舊】the past tense of CROW²

crew cut /ˈ· ·/ *n* [C] a very short hair style for men〔男子的〕平頭髮型, 板刷頭 —see picture at 參見 HAIRSTYLE 圖

crew·man /ˋkrumən; ˈkruːmən/ *n plural* **crewmen** /-mən; -mən/ [C] a member, especially a male member, of a CREW¹ (2)〔尤指男的〕水手; 機組人員

crew mem·ber /ˈ· ˌ··/ *n* [C] a member of a CREW¹ (2) 一名船員; 一名機組人員

crew neck /ˈ· ·/ *n* [C] a plain, round neck on a SWEATER 圓式衣領 —see picture on page A17 參見A17頁圖 —compare 比較 V-NECK

crib¹ /krɪb; krɪb/ *n especially AmE*【尤美】**1** [C] a bed for a baby or young child, especially one with bars to keep the baby from falling out〔有圍欄的〕嬰兒牀; COT (1) *BrE*【英】—see picture at 參見 BED¹ 圖 **2** [C] an open box or wooden frame holding food for animals; MANGER 飼料槽; 秣槽 **3** [C] *BrE* a model of the scene of Jesus's birth, often placed in churches and homes at Christmas【英】〔聖誕節時教堂或家中陳列的〕耶穌誕生情景的模型; CRÈCHE *AmE*【美】**4** [C] *informal*【非正式】**a)** something copied dishonestly from someone else's work, especially at school〔尤指在學校的〕抄襲, 剽竊 **b)** a book giving a translation or answers to questions, often used dishonestly by students〔學生用於作弊的〕對照本 **5** [U] the card game of cribbage 克里比奇紙牌戲

crib² *v* **cribbed, cribbing** [I,T] to copy school or college work dishonestly from someone else 抄襲, 剽竊: **crib sth off/from sb** *He cribbed the answers off his friend.* 他抄襲朋友的答案。

crib·bage /ˋkrɪbɪdʒ; ˈkrɪbɪdʒ/ also 又作 **crib** *informal*【非正式】*n* [U] a card game in which points are shown by putting small pieces of wood in holes in a small board 克里比奇紙牌戲〔用木釘插入木板上的小孔計分的一種紙牌戲〕

crib death /ˈ· ·/ *n* [C] *AmE*【美】COT DEATH *BrE*【英】嬰兒猝死

crick¹ /krɪk; krɪk/ *n* [C] a sudden, painful stiffening of the muscles, especially in the back or the neck〔尤指背或頸的〕痛性痙攣: **[+in]** *Reading over your shoulder gives me a crick in my neck.* 隔着你的肩膀看書使我脖子都痙攣了。

crick² *v* [T] to do something that produces a crick in your back or neck 引起〔背或頸〕的痛性痙攣: *He bent to lift the case and cricked his back.* 他彎腰提箱子, 扭傷了背部。

crick·et /ˋkrɪkɪt; ˈkrɪkɪ̣t/ *n* **1** [C] a small brown jumping insect, which makes a noise by rubbing its wings together 蟋蟀 **2** [U] an outdoor game between two teams of 11 players in which players try to get points by hitting a ball and running between two sets of STUMPS (=special sticks) 板球(運動)

crick·et·er /ˋkrɪkɪtɚ; ˈkrɪkɪ̣tə/ *n* [C] someone who plays CRICKET (2) 板球運動員

cri·er /ˋkraɪɚ; ˈkraɪə/ *n* [C] a TOWN CRIER〔昔日〕沿街呼喚傳報消息的人

cri·key /ˋkraɪkɪ; ˈkraɪki/ *interjection BrE informal* used to show that you are surprised or annoyed【英, 非正式】哎呀〔表示驚訝或心煩〕: *Oh crikey, I'm going to miss the bus!* 哎呀, 我要趕不上公共汽車了!

crime /kraɪm; kraɪm/ *n*

1 ►CRIME IN GENERAL 犯罪◄ [U] illegal activities in general〔泛指〕違法犯罪活動: *We moved here ten years ago because there was very little crime.* 我們十年前搬來這裡, 因為這裡的犯罪活動很少。| **crime prevention** (=work done to stop crime from happening) 防止犯罪的措施 *Neighborhood watch groups have been a very effective means of crime prevention.* 組織鄰里巡邏組已成為防止犯罪的一種十分有效的方法。| **serious crime** *Police need more personnel to tackle serious crime in the inner cities.* 警方需要更多的人員對付舊城區嚴重的犯罪。| **crime rate** (=the amount of crime in society) 犯罪率 *Voters are becoming frustrated with the growing crime rate.* 選民對上升的犯罪率感到沮喪。| **violent crime** *a worrying increase in violent crime* 暴力犯罪率令人不安的上升 | **petty crime** (=crime that is not very serious) 輕度犯罪 *Kids living on the streets are likely to be involved in petty crime.* 無家可歸的孩子很容易捲入輕度犯罪。| **crime wave** (=a sudden increase in the amount of crime) 犯罪案件的突然上升 | **turn to crime** (=start doing illegal things) 走上犯罪道路 *Rich kids don't generally need to turn to crime.* 富有人家的

孩子通常不需要去走犯罪道路。| **a life of crime** (=a way of living and getting money by doing illegal activities) 犯罪生涯 | **white-collar crime** (=crimes done by professional people that involve clever and complicated ways of illegally getting money) 白領罪行

2 ▶A PARTICULAR CRIME 罪行◀ [C] a dishonest, violent, or immoral action that can be punished by law 罪, 罪行: *A thirty-four year old man was charged with the crime after the murder weapon was found in his home.* 在一名三十四歲的男子家中發現兇器後, 他被指控犯有謀殺罪。| **[+against]** *Crimes against the elderly are becoming more common.* 針對老人的犯罪活動越來越普遍。| **commit a crime** (=do something illegal) 犯罪 *Most crimes are committed by males under the age of 30.* 大部分案件的作案者是30歲以下的男子。| **scene of the crime** (=place where a particular crime happened) 犯罪現場 *They say a murderer always returns to the scene of the crime.* 據説殺人兇手老是會回到犯罪現場的。

3 it's a crime *spoken* used to say that you think something is completely immoral【口】(這麼做是) 不道德的: *It's a crime to waste all that good food.* 浪費那些美味的食物真是罪過。

4 crime against humanity a cruel crime against a lot of ordinary people, that is considered unacceptable in any situation, even a war 違反人性的罪行: *The commandant of the prison camp was found guilty of crimes against humanity.* 戰俘集中營的司令官被判犯了違反人性的罪行。

5 crime of passion a crime, usually murder, that happens as a result of someone's sexual jealousy 情殺罪; 桃色案件

6 crime doesn't pay used to say that it is wrong to think that being involved in crime will bring you any advantage, because you will probably be caught and punished for it 違法犯罪是沒有好處的 —see also 另見 ORGANIZED CRIME, **partners in crime** (PARTNER[1] (5)), WAR CRIME, **white-collar crime** (WHITE-COLLAR (2))

This graph shows some of the words most commonly used with the noun **crime**. 本圖表所示為含有名詞 crime 的一些最常用的詞組。

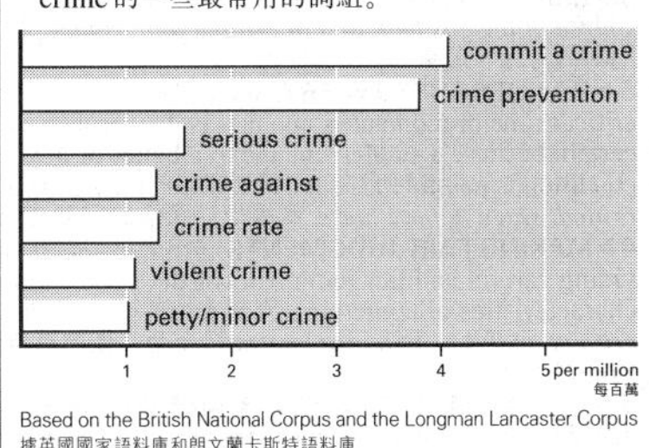

Based on the British National Corpus and the Longman Lancaster Corpus
據英國國家語料庫和朗文蘭卡斯特語料庫

3 **crim·i·nal¹** /ˈkrɪmənl; ˈkrɪmɪ̵nəl/ *adj* **1** related to or con-
2 nected with crime 犯罪的, 犯法的: *criminal behaviour* 犯罪行為 | *The boy had shown criminal tendencies since early adolescence.* 這個男孩在青春期初期就表現出了犯罪的傾向。| **a criminal offence** (=a crime that can be punished by law) 刑事犯罪 | **criminal element** (=people within a particular group who are known to be involved in crime) 犯罪團夥成員 *Ray got mixed up with the local criminal element.* 雷與當地的犯罪團夥混到了一起。| **criminal negligence** (=the illegal act of not doing something you should do, with the result that someone is hurt) 刑事疏忽, 過失犯罪 | **criminal damage** (=the illegal act of damaging someone else's property) 刑事毀壞, 破壞罪 **2** [no comparative 無比較級] related to the part of the legal system that is concerned with crime 與犯罪有關的; 刑事的: *criminal court* 刑事法庭 | *criminal case* 刑事案件 | *criminal attorney* 刑事律師 | **criminal charges** (=official statements saying that someone has done something illegal) 刑事控告 *Wharton faces criminal charges and will be tried in May.* 沃頓面臨着刑事控告, 將在五月受審。—compare 比較 CIVIL (3) **3** wrong, dishonest, and unacceptable 罪過的; 錯誤的; 奸詐的; 無法容忍的: *There was a criminal lack of foresight in the planning of this venture.* 這個風險投資計劃缺少遠見, 使人難以接受。—**criminally** *adv*

criminal² *n* [C] someone who is involved in illegal activities or has been proved guilty of a crime 罪犯: *The man is a criminal. How could the people elect him to office?* 這個人是個罪犯, 人們怎麼能選他當官呢? | **hardened criminal** (=someone who has been involved in crime for a long time) 慣犯 *Teenagers should not be sent to prison with hardened criminals.* 少年犯不應當與慣犯關在同一個監獄。

crim·i·nal·ize also 又作 **-ise** *BrE*【英】/ˈkrɪmənl̩ˌaɪz; ˈkrɪmɪ̵nəl-aɪz/ *v* [T] to make something illegal 立法禁止, 使…為犯罪: *The police have tried in the past to criminalize hitchhiking.* 警方曾經嘗試立法禁止搭便車。

criminal law /ˌ··· ˈ·/ *n* [U] laws or the study of laws concerning crimes and their punishments 刑法 (學) —see also 另見 CANON LAW, CIVIL LAW, COMMON LAW²

criminal rec·ord /ˌ··· ˈ··/ also 又作 **record** *n* [C] an official record kept by the police of any crimes a person has committed 犯罪記錄, 前科: *The defendant has no previous criminal record.* 該被告沒有犯罪前科。

crim·i·nol·o·gy /ˌkrɪməˈnɑlədʒɪ; ˌkrɪmɪ̵ˈnɒlədʒi/ *n* [U] the scientific study of crime and criminals 犯罪學 —**criminologist** *n* [C]

crimp /krɪmp; krɪmp/ *v* [T] **1** to press something, especially cloth, paper etc into small regular folds 在〔布、紙〕上壓小褶子 **2** to make your hair slightly curly by using a special heated tool 使〔頭髮〕輕微捲曲

crim·son¹ /ˈkrɪmzn̩; ˈkrɪmzən/ *adj* having a deep purplish red colour 深紅色的: *a crimson sky* 深紅色的天空 | *She turned crimson when he made the remark.* 他説這些話的時候她的臉變得通紅。—**crimson** *n* [C] —see picture on page A5 參見A5頁圖

crimson² *v* [I] if your face crimsons, it becomes red because you are embarrassed〔臉〕變深紅色

cringe /krɪndʒ; krɪndʒ/ *v* [I] **1** to move back or away from someone or something, especially because you are afraid or in pain 畏縮, 退縮: *The dog cringed and whimpered when the tall man appeared.* 那高個男子出現時, 狗一邊後退一邊發出哀鳴。**2** to feel embarrassed by something that seems stupid 感到難堪: *I cringe when I think what I used to wear in the Sixties.* 一想到我在20世紀60年代穿的衣服我就覺得很傻。| *They sing this song that makes me cringe.* 他們唱這首使我難為情的歌曲。—**cringe** *n* [C]

crin·kle¹ /ˈkrɪŋkl̩; ˈkrɪŋkəl/ *v* [I,T] also 又作 **crinkle up** to become covered with small folds, or make something do this (使) 起皺: *The heat was beginning to make the cellophane crinkle.* 高温使玻璃紙開始起皺。—compare 比較 WRINKLE² —**crinkled** *adj*

crinkle² *n* [C usually singular 一般用單數] a thin fold, especially in your skin or on cloth, paper etc〔尤指皮膚、衣服、紙等上的〕細皺紋 —compare 比較 WRINKLE¹ (1,2)

crin·kly /ˈkrɪŋklɪ; ˈkrɪŋkli/ *adj* **1** having many thin folds 多皺紋的: *Andrew stared at the old man's crinkly face.* 安德魯盯着老人佈滿皺紋的臉。**2** hair that is crinkly is stiff and curly〔頭髮〕硬而鬈曲的 —**crinkliness** *n* [U]

crin·o·line /ˈkrɪnl̩ɪn; ˈkrɪnəlɪ̵n/ *n* [C] a round frame worn under a woman's skirt in former times to support it and give it shape〔舊時支撐女裙的〕裙撐; 圈環裙

cripes /kraɪps; kraɪps/ *interjection old-fashioned* used to express surprise or annoyance【過時】天哪! 啊!〔表示驚訝或煩惱〕

crip·ple¹ /ˋkrɪpḷ; ˈkrɪpəl/ *n* [C] **1** an offensive word for someone who is physically unable to use their arms or their legs properly 跛子; 手臂殘廢者〔侮辱用語〕**2 emotional cripple** *informal* someone who is not able to deal with their own or other people's feelings【非正式】感情殘廢〔不能處理自己或他人的感情的人〕—compare 比較 DISABLED

cripple² *v* [T] **1** to hurt or wound someone so that they cannot use their arms or legs properly 使〔手臂或腿〕受傷致殘: *The accident crippled her for life.* 這次事故使她終生殘廢。**2** to seriously damage or weaken something 嚴重損壞[削弱]: *The incident could easily cripple the peace talks.* 這一事件很可能使和平談判破裂。—**crippled** *adj* —**crippling** *adj*

2 2 **cri·sis** /ˋkraɪsɪs; ˈkraɪsəs/ *n plural* **crises** /-siz; -siːz/ [C, U] **1** a period or moment of great danger, difficulty, or uncertainty, especially in politics or economics〔尤指政治、經濟等〕危機; 緊要關頭: *the energy crisis of 1972* 1972年的能源危機 | *the Cuban missile crisis* 古巴導彈危機 **2** a time when a personal emotional problem or situation has reached its worst point〔個人的〕危急之際: *In times of crisis you find out who your real friends are.* 危急時刻你就會發現誰是你真正的朋友了。| **be at a crisis point** (=be in a condition that cannot get any worse) 處於危機時刻 *I think Paul and Lucinda are at a crisis point in their marriage.* 我認為保羅和露辛達的婚姻處於危機時刻。**3** the time during a serious illness when it could get either better or worse〔重病的〕轉折點: *The crisis came that night.* 病情的轉折點出現在那天晚上。**4 crisis management** the skill or process of dealing with unusually dangerous or difficult situations 應付危機[困境]的技巧; 危機[困境]處理過程 **5 crisis of confidence** a situation in which people no longer believe a government, economy, system etc is working properly, and will no longer support it, work with it etc 信任危機: **[+in]** *a crisis of confidence in the foreign exchange when interest rates were cut* 利率下調後出現的對外匯市場的信任危機 —see also 另見 MIDLIFE CRISIS

crisp¹ /krɪsp; krɪsp/ *n* [C] *BrE* a very thin, flat round piece of potato cooked in oil and eaten cold【英】油炸〔馬鈴〕薯片; CHIP¹ (3b) *AmE*【美】—see also 另見 **burn sth to a crisp** (BURN¹ (4))

crisp² *adj* **1** pleasantly dry, hard, and easily broken 乾而脆的; 易碎的: *crisp bacon* 鬆脆的熏豬肉 | *His feet broke through the crisp outer layer of snow.* 他的雙腳踩碎了雪脆弱的表面。**2** a fruit, vegetable, or plant that is crisp is firm and fresh〔水果、蔬菜或植物〕新鮮而爽口的: *a crisp apple* 鮮脆的蘋果 | *a crisp salad* 爽口的沙拉 **3** paper or cloth that is crisp is fresh, clean, and new〔紙或布〕清新的; 乾淨的; 新的: *a crisp, new five dollar bill* 簇新的五元鈔票 **4** weather that is crisp is cold and dry〔天氣〕乾而冷的; 清爽的: *a crisp winter day* 乾冷的冬日 **5** someone's behaviour or manner that is crisp is quick, confident, and shows no doubts or slowness; BRISK (1,2)〔行為、態度〕乾脆利落的, 利索的: *The general's voice was crisp and clear as he addressed the meeting.* 將軍在會上發言的時候聲音清晰洪亮。—**crisply** *adv* —**crispness** *n* [U]

crisp³ *v* [T] to make something become crisp, especially by cooking or heating it〔尤指通過烹調或加熱〕使變脆

crisp·bread /ˋkrɪsp͵brɛd; ˈkrɪspbred/ *n* [C,U] a thin dry biscuit that is not sweet 薄脆餅乾

crisp·y /ˋkrɪspɪ; ˈkrɪspi/ *adj* a word meaning CRISP² (1) used especially to talk about food〔尤指食物〕鬆脆的: *crispy bacon* 脆熏豬肉

criss·cross¹, criss-cross /ˋkrɪs͵krɔs; ˈkrɪskrɒs/ *n* [C] a pattern made up of straight lines, usually a lot of them, that cross each other 線條縱橫交錯的圖案: *the crisscross of scars on his back* 他背上縱橫交錯的傷疤 —**crisscross** *adj*: *trees planted in a crisscross pattern* 縱橫交錯種植的樹木

crisscross², criss-cross *v* [I,T] to make a regularly repeated pattern of straight lines that cross each other, or to make this pattern on something (在…上) 畫交錯的直線; 畫十字圖案: *The flyovers crisscross the city above the congested streets.* 立交橋縱橫交錯於城市擁擠的街道上方。

cri·te·ri·on /kraɪˋtɪrɪən; kraɪˈtɪəriən/ *n plural* **criteria** /-rɪə; -riə/ [C often plural 常用複數] a standard which is established so that a judgment or decision, especially a scientific one, can be made〔判斷、決定的〕標準, 準則: *More detailed criteria are necessary before a logical decision can be reached.* 需要更詳細的標準才能作出合乎邏輯的決定。| **[+for]** *What are your criteria for judging a bottle of wine?* 你用甚麼標準判斷一瓶酒的好壞?

crit·ic /ˋkrɪtɪk; ˈkrɪtɪk/ *n* [C] **1** someone whose job is to make judgments about the good and bad qualities of something, especially art, music, films etc〔尤指藝術、音樂、電影等的〕評論家, 批評家: *The jazz critic for the Times panned the show, calling it 'a joke'.*《泰晤士報》的爵士樂評論家嚴厲批評該演出, 稱之為"一個玩笑"。**2** someone who expresses strong disapproval or dislike of a person, idea, organization etc 反對[憎惡]…的人: **[+of]** *He became an outspoken critic of the country's educational policies.* 他成了對該國教育政策直言不諱的批評者。**3 armchair critic** someone who does nothing themselves but criticizes others for what they do 空頭批評家; 只說不做的批評家

crit·i·cal /ˋkrɪtɪkḷ; ˈkrɪtɪkəl/ *adj*

1 ►MAKING SEVERE JUDGMENTS 作出嚴厲的判斷◄ someone who is critical makes severe and often unfair judgments of people or things 批評的, 批判的; 吹毛求疵的, 愛挑剔的: *I don't mean to be over critical, but isn't all of this completely unnecessary?* 我不是想過多地挑剔, 但是所有這些不都是完全多餘的嗎? | **[+of]** *Pat is always very critical of her son's appearance.* 帕特對兒子的外表總是很挑剔。

2 ►IMPORTANT 重要的◄ very important because what happens in the future depends on it 緊要的, 關鍵性的: *We need an immediate decision on this critical issue.* 我們需要立即對這個關鍵問題作出決定。| **be critical to** *Parental attention is critical to the child's socialization.* 父母的關注對孩子適應社會是很重要的。| **of critical importance** (=very important) 至關重要的 *Finding the source of the gas leak was of critical importance.* 找到漏氣的源頭至關重要。

3 ►DANGEROUS/UNCERTAIN 危險的/不確定的◄ a critical time or moment is one that is dangerous or uncertain because a sudden change to a better or a worse condition is possible 危急的, 緊要關頭的: *David is at a critical stage in the illness.* 戴維處於病情的關鍵時期。

4 ►MAKING FAIR JUDGMENTS 作出公正判斷◄ providing careful and fair judgments of the good and bad characteristics of something 判斷審慎的; 評判性的: *a critical analysis of Stevens' poem* 對斯蒂文斯的詩所作的評判性分析

5 ►ART/FILM/BOOKS ETC 藝術/電影/書等◄ produced by or resulting from the work of CRITICS 評論: *'The Piano' got a lot of critical acclaim, but I didn't like the music in it.* 電影《鋼琴別戀》得到了很多好評, 但是我不喜歡其中的音樂。| *a critical success* (=the critics liked it) 受到評論家的好評

6 in a critical condition *BrE*【英】, **in critical condition** *AmE*【美】so ill that you could die 病情危急: *The patient is in critical condition at Bellvue Hospital tonight.* 今天晚上病人在貝爾維尤醫院治療, 病情危急。

7 the critical list a list of people in hospital who are so ill that they could die 病危病人名單: *He was taken off the critical list last night, so we're very relieved.* 他的名字昨晚從病危病人名單上除掉了, 因此我們大大地鬆了口氣。

8 with a critical eye if you look at or examine something with a critical eye, you examine it carefully in order to judge its good and bad qualities 以評判[鑑別]的眼光

critically /ˋkrɪtɪkl̩ɪ; ˈkrɪtɪkli/ *adv* **1 critically ill/injured/important etc** very seriously ill, very important etc 病情嚴重/傷得很重/極端重要等: *10 people died and 30 were critically injured in a rail crash yesterday.* 在昨天的火車相撞事故中有10人死亡30人重傷。**2** in a way that shows you have thought about the good and bad qualities of something 批評性地, 批判性地: *You need to critically assess your lifestyle.* 你應該全面地評價你的生活方式。

critical mass /ˌ··· ˈ·/ *n* [C,U] *technical* the amount of a substance necessary for an ATOMIC CHAIN REACTION to start【術語】〔核連鎖反應的〕臨界質量

critical path a·nal·y·sis /ˌ··· ˌ· ·ˈ···/ *n plural* **critical path analyses** [C] *technical* a method of planning a large piece of work so that there will be few delays and the cost will be as low as possible【術語】關鍵途徑分析法〔制定一項大型工作計劃時為減少耽擱和降低花費的規劃方式〕

2 2 **crit·i·cis·m** /ˋkrɪtəˌsɪzəm; ˈkrɪtɪsɪzəm/ *n* **1** [C,U] the act of giving your opinion or judgment about the good and bad qualities of someone or something 評論, 批評: *Kate doesn't take any kind of criticism very well.* 凱特從來不好好接受批評。| **constructive criticism** (=intended to help someone or something improve) 建設性評論 **2** [C,U] written or spoken remarks that express your disapproval or bad opinion of someone or something 批評, 指責; 批評文: *We all felt that Wanda's criticism was unjustified.* 我們都認為溫達的批評沒有道理。| **[+of]** *My only criticism of the book is that it's a little too academic.* 我對這本書的唯一批評是學術氣重了一點。**3 a)** [U] the activity of forming and expressing judgments about the good or bad qualities of books, films, music etc〔書、電影、音樂等〕評論: *literary criticism* 文藝評論 **b)** [C,U] the written work that results from this activity 評論文, 批評文

3 3 **crit·i·cize** also 又作 **-ise** *BrE*【英】/ˋkrɪtəˌsaɪz; ˈkrɪtɪsaɪz/ *v* **1** [I,T] to express your disapproval of someone or something, or to talk about their faults 批評; 指責: *Ron does nothing but criticize and complain all the time.* 羅恩甚麼也不幹, 只是一味指責和抱怨。| **criticize sb for (doing) sth** *The report strongly criticizes the police for failing to deal with the problem quickly.* 該報告強烈指責警方沒有儘快處理這個問題。**2** [T] to express judgments about the good and bad qualities of something 評論: *Criticizing your own work is very difficult.* 評論自己的作品是非常困難的。

cri·tique¹ /krɪˋtik; krɪˈtiːk/ *n* [C,U] an article, book etc expressing judgments about the good and bad qualities of something such as the work of a writer or artist 評論〔文章、書刊等〕: **[+of]** *The final article is a critique of John Updike's latest novel.* 最後一篇文章是評論約翰·厄普代克的最新小說的。

critique² *v* [I,T] *AmE* to make remarks about the good and bad qualities of something, especially artistic or literary work【美】評論〔文藝作品等〕: *I asked my professor to critique the paper before I turned it in to the examining board.* 我請教授先對我的論文評判一番再交給審查委員會。

crit·ter /ˋkrɪtɚ; ˈkrɪtə/ *n* [C] *AmE spoken* a creature, especially an animal【美口】生物; 動物: *Be careful, that horse is a mean critter!* 小心, 那匹馬碰不得!

croak¹ /krok; krəʊk/ *v* **1** [I] to make a deep low sound like the sound a FROG makes 作蛙鳴聲 **2** [I,T] to speak in a low, rough voice as if you have a sore throat 用低沉沙啞的聲音說話: *He was shivering and croaking in a voice they barely recognized as his.* 他渾身發抖, 聲音嘶啞, 他們簡直辨認不出是他的聲音。**3** [I] *slang* to die【俚】死亡

croak² *n* [C] a low sound made in an animal's or person's throat, like one that a FROG makes〔動物或人發出的〕類似蛙鳴的聲音

cro·chet /kroˋʃe; ˈkrəʊʃeɪ/ *v* [I,T] to make clothes, blankets etc from wool using a special needle with a hook at one end 用鉤針編織 —compare 比較 KNIT (1) —**crochet** *n* [U] —**crotcheting** *n* [U]

crock /krɑk; krɒk/ *n* [C] **1** *old use* a clay pot【舊】瓦罐 **2 crocks** [plural] **a)** *BrE old-fashioned* plates, cups etc, especially made of baked clay【英, 過時】陶[瓦]器 **b)** pieces of broken EARTHENWARE (=baked clay) 碎瓦片 **3** *spoken*【口】**a crock of shit** *AmE taboo* something that is unbelievable, unfair, untrue etc【美諱】屁話; 騙人的東西: *You can't expect me to believe that! What a crock of shit!* 你別指望我會相信那種事! 簡直是屁話! **4 old crock** *BrE slang*【英俚】**a)** an old car 舊汽車 **b)** an old person 老人: *We old crocks can't run like you.* 我們老傢伙不能像你那樣跑了。

crocked /krɑkt; krɒkt/ *adj* [never before noun 不用於名詞前] **1** *BrE old-fashioned* injured or broken【英, 過時】受傷的; 破碎的 **2** *AmE spoken* drunk【美口】喝醉了的: *Don't mind Roger. He's always crocked by noon.* 不要介意羅傑, 中午他總是醉醺醺的。

crock·e·ry /ˋkrɑkərɪ; ˈkrɒkəri/ *n* [U] *especially BrE* cups, plates etc, especially made of CHINA【尤英】陶器, 瓦器

crocodile 鱷魚

croc·o·dile /ˋkrɑkəˌdaɪl; ˈkrɒkədaɪl/ *n* **1** [C] a large REPTILE (1) with a long mouth and many sharp teeth that lives in lakes and rivers in hot wet parts of the world 鱷魚 **2** [U] the skin of this animal, used for making things such as shoes 鱷魚皮 **3** [singular] *BrE* a long line of people, especially school children, walking in pairs【英】兩人一排成縱隊行進的一長隊人〔尤指小學生〕**4 shed crocodile tears** to pretend you feel sad, sorry, or upset when you do not really feel that way 掉鱷魚眼淚; 假慈悲

cro·cus /ˋkrokəs; ˈkrəʊkəs/ *n* [C] a small purple, yellow, or white flower that comes up in early spring 番紅花, 藏紅花

croft /krɔft; krɒft/ *n* [C] a very small farm in Scotland〔蘇格蘭的〕小農場

croft·er /ˋkrɔftɚ; ˈkrɒftə/ *n* [C] someone who lives and works on a croft〔蘇格蘭的〕佃農; 小農場主

croft·ing /ˋkrɔftɪŋ; ˈkrɒftɪŋ/ *n* [U] the system of farming on crofts in Scotland〔蘇格蘭的〕佃農制度

croissant 牛角麵包

crois·sant /krwɑˋsɑn; ˈkwɑːsɒŋ/ *n* [C] *French* a piece of bread, shaped in a curve and usually eaten for breakfast【法】羊角麵包; 新月形麵包; 牛角麵包

crone /kron; krəʊn/ *n* [C] an ugly or unpleasant old woman 討厭的醜老太婆

cro·ny /ˋkronɪ; ˈkrəʊni/ *n* [C usually plural 一般用複數] one of a group of people, who spend a lot of time with each other and will usually help each other, even if this involves dishonesty 密友, 老朋友: *Nixon gave positions of power to many of his political cronies.* 尼克遜把許多有權力的職位給了他政治上的老朋友。

crook¹ /krʊk; krʊk/ *n* [C] **1** *informal* someone who is dishonest【非正式】騙子, 無賴: *I wouldn't buy a car from them – they're a bunch of crooks.* 我不會從他們那裡買汽車的, 他們是一夥騙子。**2** a long stick with a curved end, used by people who look after sheep〔牧羊人的〕曲手杖 —see picture at 參見 STICK² 圖 **3 the crook of your arm** the part of your arm where it bends, used for holding things 臂彎: *She cradled the little dog in the crook of her arm.* 她彎着手臂輕輕地抱着小狗。—see picture at 參見 BODY 圖

crook² *v* [T] if you crook your finger or your arm, you bend it 使〔手指、手臂〕彎曲: *She beckoned me, crooking her finger.* 她勾了勾手指招呼我過去。

crook³ *adj* [never before noun 不用於名詞前] *informal AustrE* ill【非正式，澳】有病的，生病的

crook·ed /ˈkrukɪd; ˈkrʊkɨd/ *adj* **1** dishonest 不誠實的；狡詐的：*a crooked cop* 行為不端的警察 **2** bent, twisted, or not in a straight line 彎曲的；不直的：*Her teeth were all crooked.* 她的牙齒歪歪扭扭的。—**crookedly** *adv* —**crookedness** *n* [U]

croon /krun; kruːn/ *v* [I,T] to sing or speak in a soft gentle voice, especially about love 柔聲唱〔尤指情歌〕；柔聲說〔尤指談情說愛〕：*Sinatra crooning mellow tunes* 仙納杜拉柔聲哼唱着甜美的調子

3 **crop¹** /krɑp; krɒp/ *n* [C] **1** a plant such as wheat, rice, or fruit that is grown by farmers, especially in order to be eaten 莊稼；作物：*The main crop in China is rice.* 中國的主要作物是水稻。| *Most of the land is used for growing crops.* 這片土地大部分用以種植莊稼。| *crops being harvested in September* 九月份收穫的莊稼 **2** the amount of wheat, rice, fruit etc that is produced in a season 一季的收成，收穫：*Wheat farmers have had a record crop this year.* 種植小麥的農民今年的收成創記錄。| **bumper crop** (=a very large amount of wheat, rice etc produced in a season) 大豐收 **3 a crop of** a group of people that arrive or things that happen at the same time 一羣〔同時到達的人〕；一批〔同時發生的事〕：*There was the usual crop of problems to deal with when I got back to the office.* 我回到辦公室時如常有一大堆問題等着處理。| *this season's crop of young players* 本賽季的年輕選手們 **4** a short whip used in horse riding 短馬鞭 —see picture at 參見 WHIP¹ 圖 **5** the part under a bird's throat where food is stored〔鳥的〕嗉囊 **6** a very short hairstyle 平頭髮型 **7 a crop of dark hair/blonde curls etc** hair that is short, thick, and attractive 一頭漂亮的粗短黑髮/金色鬈髮等

crop² *v* [T] **1** to cut someone's hair short 剪短〔頭髮〕**2** to cut a part off a photograph or picture so that it is a particular size or shape 裁切〔照片、圖畫〕**3** if an animal crops grass or other plants, it makes them short by eating them〔牲畜〕啃吃〔草〕**4** if a plant crops, it produces fruit, grain etc 結果；結穗：*The apple trees cropped well that year.* 那年蘋果樹收成好。

crop up *phr v* [I] **1** if something, especially a problem, crops up, it happens or appears suddenly and unexpectedly〔問題等〕突然發生[出現]：*Please let me know if anything crops up while I'm away.* 我不在的時候如果發生了甚麼事，請通知我。—see 見 OCCUR (USAGE) **2** if something such as a name or a subject crops up, it appears in something you read or hear〔名字、話題等〕被提到：*Your name kept cropping up in conversation.* 你的名字在談話中一再被提到。

crop cir·cle /ˈ· ˌ··/ *n* [C] a CORN CIRCLE 農田圈

crop-dust·ing /ˈ· ˌ··/ *n* [U] *AmE*【美】CROP-SPRAYING 對作物噴灑殺蟲劑

crop·per /ˈkrɑpɚ; ˈkrɒpə/ **come a cropper** *BrE informal*【英，非正式】**a)** to fail in something, especially unexpectedly（意外）失敗：*I came a cropper on the last question in the test.* 考試中最後一個問題我意外地沒有回答上來。**b)** to accidentally fall onto the ground from a horse or bicycle〔從馬或自行車上〕摔下來：*Jimmy came a cropper as he turned the corner.* 吉米拐彎的時候摔了一跤。

crop ro·ta·tion /ˈ· ·ˌ··/ *n* [U] the practice of changing the crops that you grow in a field each year to preserve the good qualities in the soil 莊稼輪作

crop-spray·ing /ˈ· ˌ··/ *n* [U] the practice of spreading crops with chemicals that kill insects 對作物噴灑殺蟲劑；CROP-DUSTING *AmE*【美】

cro·quet /kroˈke; ˈkrəʊkeɪ/ *n* [U] a game played on grass in which players hit balls with wooden MALLETs (=long-handled hammers) so that they roll under curved wires 槌球遊戲〔在草地上用木槌擊球使之穿過彎曲的金屬絲〕

cro·quette /kroˈkɛt; krəʊˈket/ *n* [C] a piece of crushed meat, fish, potato etc that is made into a small round piece, covered in BREADCRUMBs, fried (FRY¹ (1)) and eaten〔外面裹麵包屑做成的〕炸肉[魚、馬鈴薯]丸

cro·sier, crozier /ˈkroʒɚ; ˈkrəʊʒə/ *n* [C] a CROZIER 主教的權杖

cross- /krɔs; krɒs/ *prefix* **1** going from one side to the other; across 橫穿，橫跨，穿越：*a cross-Channel ferry* (=sailing from Britain to France) 橫渡英吉利海峽的渡船 **2** going between two things and joining them 交叉，關聯：*cross-cultural influences* 交叉文化的影響

cross out 劃掉，刪去

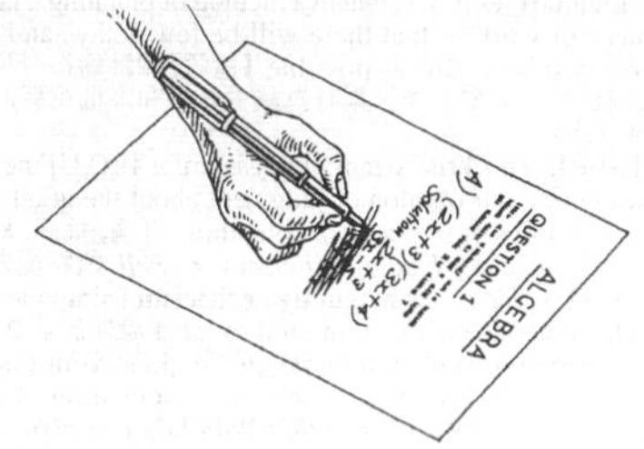

cross¹ /krɔs; krɒs/ *v*

1 ►GO FROM ONE SIDE TO ANOTHER 從一邊到另一邊◄ [I,T] to go or stretch from one side of something such as a road, river, room etc to the other 橫穿，橫渡，橫跨：*It took them four weeks to cross the desert.* 他們花了四個星期橫穿沙漠。| *Look both ways before you cross the road.* 過馬路前要左右看看。| *The railway line from Leeds to Manchester crosses the Pennines.* 從利茲到曼徹斯特的鐵路穿過奔寧山脈。

2 ►CROSS A LINE ETC 穿過界線等◄ [T] if you cross a line, track etc you go over and beyond it 穿過，越過，跑過〔終點線等〕：*Two cyclists crossed the finish line together in first place.* 兩名自行車選手同時越過終點線，並列第一。

3 ►TWO ROADS/LINES ETC 兩條路/線等◄ [T] if two or more roads, lines, etc cross, they go across each other 交叉，相交：*There's a shopping mall near where Ventura Boulevard crosses Sepulveda.* 在凡圖拉大道和塞普爾維達大街交叉處附近有一個商場。| **cross sth** *Station Avenue crosses East Street about a mile down the road.* 車站大道在這條路往前約一英里處與東街相交。

4 ►LEGS/ARMS 腿/臂◄ [T] if you cross your legs or arms, you put one on top of the other 交叉，疊放：*She was sitting on the floor with her legs crossed.* 她蹺着腿坐在地上。

5 cross your fingers used to say that you hope something will happen in the way you want 希望如願，但願，祈求：*Cross your fingers that I get the job.* 為我祈求能得到那份工作。

6 cross sb's mind if an idea, thought etc crosses someone's mind, it comes into their mind for a short time〔想法、思想等〕掠過，一閃而過：*It never crossed my mind to check whether the deal was genuine.* 我從來沒想過去核實一下這項交易是不是真的。| **the thought has crossed my mind** (=used to tell someone you have thought of the thing they are suggesting) 我有過這個念頭

7 cross sb's face if an expression crosses someone's face, it appears on their face 臉上浮現出〔某種表情〕：*A look of horror crossed Ken's face when he realized what he had done.* 意識到他做的事時，肯的臉上露出恐懼的神情。

8 cross that bridge when you come to it used to say that you will not think or worry about something until it actually happens 船到橋頭自然直；不用為未發生之事擔

心; 問題發生了再考慮解決: *Don't worry about running out of money. We'll cross that bridge when we come to it.* 別擔心錢會用完。船到橋頭自然直。

9 ►BREED OF PLANT/ANIMAL 種植植物/繁殖動物◄ [T] to mix two or more different breeds of animal or plant to form a new breed 雜交: *This flower has been produced by crossing several different varieties.* 這種花是由幾種不同的品種雜交而成的。| **[+with]** *If you cross a horse with a donkey, you get a mule.* 馬與驢雜交的後代是騾子。—see also 另見 CROSS[2] (3), CROSSBREED[1]

10 cross my heart (and hope to die) *spoken informal* used to say that you promise that you will do something or that what you are saying is true【口, 非正式】〔在胸口畫十字〕答應要做某事; 發誓所說屬實: *I didn't take it, cross my heart!* 我發誓我沒有拿!

11 sb's paths cross if two people's paths cross they meet, usually unexpectedly 不期而遇, 偶然遇見: *I know Irving quite well – our paths first crossed when we were at Yale.* 我和歐文很熟 —— 我們第一次見面是在耶魯大學。

12 ►MAKE SB ANGRY 使某人生氣◄ [T] to make someone angry by opposing their plans or orders 惹…生氣: *Anyone who dares to cross me will find themselves in serious trouble.* 誰膽敢惹我生氣, 一定會給自己惹來大麻煩。

13 ►SPORT 體育◄ [I,T] to kick, throw, or hit the ball across the playing area in a sport such as football, HOCKEY etc〔在足球、曲棍球等運動中〕橫傳 (球)

14 ►CHEQUE 支票◄ [T] *BrE* to draw two lines across a cheque to show that it must be paid into a bank account【英】〔在支票上〕劃兩條平行線〔則支票只能轉入銀行賬戶而不能支取現金〕

15 cross swords (with) to argue with someone 與…爭論[辯論]; 交鋒: *He has crossed swords with the District Attorney several times.* 他已經和地方檢察官爭論過數次。

16 cross yourself to move your hand across your upper body in the shape of a cross, especially as a sign of the Roman Catholic faith 用手在胸前劃十字〔尤為羅馬天主教信仰的象徵〕

17 cross sb's palm with silver *especially BrE* to give money to someone【尤英】給…錢 —see also 另見 **dot the i's and cross the t's** (DOT[2] (4)), **keep your fingers crossed** (FINGER[1] (3)), **cross the Rubicon** (RUBICON)

cross sth ↔ **off** *phr v* [T] to draw a line through one or more things on a list because you have dealt with them or they are not needed any more 劃掉, 刪去〔已經處理或無用的東西〕: *As you do each job, cross it off the list.* 每做完一件事, 就把它從清單上劃掉。

cross sth ↔ **out** *phr v* [T] to draw a line or lines through something you have written or drawn, usually because it is wrong 劃掉, 刪去〔錯誤的內容〕

cross over *phr v* [I] **1** if an entertainer crosses over from one area of entertainment to another, they become successful in the second one as well as the first〔娛樂界人士〕轉型成功 **2** *BrE old use* to die【英舊】死

3 **cross²** *n* [C]

3 **1 ►CHRISTIAN SIGN 基督教的標記◄ a)** an upright post of wood with another crossing it, that people were nailed to and left to die on as a punishment in the past 十字架: *Christians believe that Jesus Christ died on a cross.* 基督徒相信耶穌基督死在十字架上。**b)** an object or picture in the shape of a cross used as a sign of the Christian faith or for decoration 十字形物體[圖畫]〔以示信仰或裝飾〕: *Pauline wore a tiny gold cross around her neck.* 葆琳脖子上戴着一個小小的金十字架。| **the Cross** (=cross that Christ died on, used as a sign of Christian faith) 十字架〔基督被釘死之處, 基督教信仰的標記〕

2 ►A MARK ON PAPER 紙上的記號◄ *especially BrE*【尤英】**a)** a mark (x or +) used on paper, to represent where something is, or where something should be〔在紙上標出所在位置的〕十字標記〈如 x 或 +〉: *I've put a cross on the map to mark where our house is.* 我已在地圖上用十字標出我們的房子所在的位置。| *Please sign your name by the cross, to give your consent.* 請在十字標記旁邊簽名, 以示同意。**b)** a mark (x) used on paper to show that something that has been written or printed is not correct 叉號〔以示錯處〕: *There were more crosses than ticks on Mark's French homework.* 馬克的法語家庭作業上叉號比勾號多。**c)** a mark (x or +) used by someone who cannot write to write their name〔不識字的人簽名時畫的〕十字押

3 a mixture of two things, breeds, or qualities 混合物; 雜交; 雜種: *Their dog is a Jack Russell cross.* 他們的狗是傑克·拉塞爾種雜交犬。| **[+between]** *He seems to think his girlfriend is a cross between Naomi Campbell and Tina Turner.* 他好像認為他的女朋友是內奧米·堪貝爾和天娜·端納的結合體。

4 ►MILITARY AWARD 軍事獎賞◄ a decoration in the shape of a cross worn as an honour, especially for military bravery 十字勳章: *He was awarded the George Cross.* 他被授予喬治十字勳章。

5 ►SPORT 體育◄ a) a kick or hit of the ball in a sport such as football, HOCKEY etc that goes across the field〔將球〕踢[擊]過場地 **b)** a way of hitting someone in the sport of BOXING in which your arm goes over theirs as they try to hit you〔拳擊中〕鉤拳迎擊

6 a (heavy) cross to bear a problem that makes you very unhappy or worried, often one that continues for a long time〔尤指長期的〕心理負擔, 心病; 煩惱: *His mother's illness has been a very heavy cross to bear.* 母親的病一直是他的一大心理負擔。—see also 另見 **the sign of the Cross** (SIGN[1] (10))

cross³ *adj especially BrE* angry or annoyed【尤英】生氣的; 惱怒的: **get cross** *Charlotte, Mummy will get very cross if you do it again.* 夏洛特, 你再這樣做, 媽媽會很生氣的。| **get/be cross with sb** *Alright you two, don't get cross with each other!* 好了, 你們兩個不要互相生怨氣啦! —see also 另見 CROSSWIND 2

cross·bar /ˈkrɔsˌbɑr; ˈkrɒsbɑː/ *n* [C] **1** a bar that joins two upright posts especially two GOALPOSTS〔連接兩個立柱, 尤指球門的〕橫木 **2** the metal bar between the seat and the HANDLEBARS on a man's bicycle〔自行車的〕橫梁 —see picture at 參見 BICYCLE[1] 圖

cross·bones /ˈkrɔsˌbonz; ˈkrɒsbəʊnz/ *n* —see 見 SKULL AND CROSSBONES

cross·bow /ˈkrɔsˌbo; ˈkrɒsbəʊ/ *n* [C] a weapon like a small BOW[3](1) fixed onto a longer piece of wood, used for shooting bolts (=short, heavy sticks) 十字弓, 弩

cross·breed¹ /ˈkrɔsˌbrid; ˈkrɒsbriːd/ *v* [I,T] **a)** to make one kind of a plant or animal breed with a different breed (使) 雜交 **b)** if a plant or animal crossbreeds it breeds with one of a different breed〔動植物的〕雜交繁殖 —**crossbred** /ˈkrɔsˌbrɛd; ˈkrɒsbred/ *adj*

crossbreed² *n* [C] an animal or plant that is a mixture of breeds〔動植物的〕雜交品種 —compare 比較 INTERBREED

cross-Chan·nel /ˌ· ˈ··◂/ *adj* travelling across the English Channel 橫渡英吉利海峽的: *There are several cross-Channel ferries from Dover every day.* 每天有好幾班從多佛出發橫渡英吉利海峽的渡船。

cross·check /ˌkrɔsˈtʃɛk; ˌkrɒsˈtʃek/ *v* [T] to make certain that results or calculations are correct by using a different method of calculation from the one you first used〔用不同的計算方法〕反覆核對, 核實 —**crosscheck** *n* [C]

cross-coun·try¹ /ˌ· ˈ··◂/ *adj* across fields or open country 越野的: *Duncan prefers cross-country skiing to downhill.* 比起滑降滑雪, 鄧肯更喜歡越野滑雪。—**cross-country** *adv*: *travelling cross-country* 越野旅行

cross-country² *n* [C,U] *BrE* a race that is run across countryside and fields, not on a track【英】越野賽跑

cross-cul·tur·al /ˌ· ˈ···◂/ *adj* belonging to or involving two or more different societies, countries or cultures

(CULTURE (1)) 跨文化的, 交叉文化間的

cross·cur·rent /ˈkrɔsˌkɝənt; ˈkrɒsˌkʌrənt/ *n* [C] a current in the sea, a river etc that moves across the general direction of the main current〔海、河等中的〕交叉水流, 逆流

cross-dress·ing /ˌ· ˈ··/ *n* [U] *AmE* the practice of wearing the clothes of the opposite sex, especially for sexual pleasure【美】穿異性服裝 —**cross-dresser** *n* [C]

crossed /krɔst; krɒst/ *adj* if a telephone line is crossed, it is connected by mistake to two or more telephones, so that you can hear other people's conversations〔電話〕串線的

crossed cheque /ˌ· ˈ·/ *n* [C] a cheque in Britain that has two lines across it showing that it must be paid into a bank account 劃線支票〔英國的一種支票, 劃有兩條平行線, 只能入銀行賬戶〕

cross-ex·am·ine /ˌ· ·ˈ··/ *v* [T] to question someone very thoroughly, especially a WITNESS in a law court 盤問〔尤指法庭上詰問證人〕—**cross-examination** /ˌ· ···ˈ··/ *n* [C, U] —**cross-examiner** /ˌ· ·ˈ···/ *n* [C]

cross-eyed /ˌ· ˈ·◂/ *adj* having eyes that look in towards the nose 內斜視的, 鬥雞眼的; BOSS-EYED *BrE*【英】

cross-fer·ti·lize also 又作 **-ise** *BrE*【英】/ˌ· ˈ···/ *v* [T] **1** to combine the male sex cells from one type of plant with female sex cells from another 使〔植物〕異體受精 **2** [often passive 常用被動態] to influence someone or something with ideas from other areas〔與不同地區的思想接觸〕(使) 相互影響: *Europe has been cross-fertilized by contact with many other societies.* 歐洲因與其他許多社會接觸而受影響。—**cross-fertilization** /ˌ· ····ˈ··/ *n* [U]

cross·fire /ˈkrɔsˌfaɪr; ˈkrɒsfaɪə/ *n* [U] **1 be caught in the crossfire** to be involved in a situation in which other people are arguing, when you do not want to be 被捲入〔不想參與的他人的〕爭辯中: *I left the room to avoid being caught in the crossfire between Dad and William.* 我離開房間, 以免被捲入爸爸和威廉的爭辯中。**2** two or more lines of bullets being fired across a particular point 交叉火力

cross-grained /ˌ· ˈ·◂/ *adj* wood that is cross-grained has lines that go across it instead of along it〔木材〕橫紋的, 斜紋的

cross-hatch·ing /ˈ· ˌ··/ *n* [U] lines drawn across part of a picture, DIAGRAM etc to show that something is made of different material, or to produce the effect of shade〔圖畫、圖表等中表明不同材料或陰影的〕交叉影線

cross·ing /ˈkrɔsɪŋ; ˈkrɒsɪŋ/ *n* [C] **1** a marked place where you can safely cross a road, railway, river etc〔道路、鐵路的〕(人行) 橫道;〔河流的〕渡口 —see also 另見 LEVEL CROSSING, PEDESTRIAN CROSSING, PELICAN CROSSING, ZEBRA CROSSING **2** a place where two lines, roads, tracks etc cross 十字路口, 交叉口 **3** a journey across the sea 橫渡海洋的旅程, 跨海旅程: *The crossing was rough and lots of people were seasick.* 這次渡海風急浪大, 許多人都暈船了。

cross-legged 盤着腿

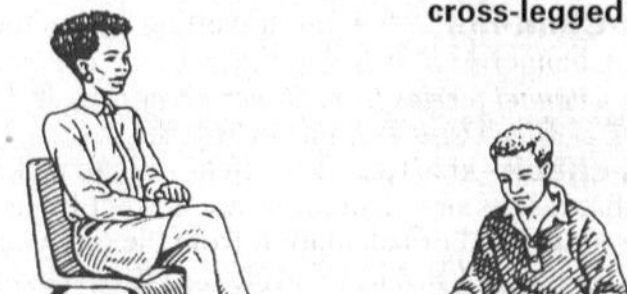

She sat with her legs crossed. 她蹺着腿坐着。

Paul is sitting cross-legged. 保爾盤腿坐着。

cross-legged /ˌkrɔs ˈlɛgɪd; ˌkrɒs ˈlegd◂/ *adv* in a sitting position with your knees wide apart and ankles crossed 盤着腿: *children sitting cross-legged on the floor* 盤腿坐在地上的孩子們 —**cross-legged** *adj*

cross·o·ver /ˈkrɔsˌovɚ; ˈkrɒsəʊvə/ *n* [C] the change a popular performer makes from working in one area of entertainment to another〔娛樂圈人士的〕轉型, 轉向: [+from] *Madonna has made a crossover from rock music to the movies.* 麥當娜從搖滾樂轉向電影發展。—see also 另見 **cross over** (CROSS[1])

crossover pri·ma·ry /ˈ··· ˌ···/ *n* [C] *AmE* an OPEN PRIMARY【美】開放預選

cross·patch /ˈkrɔsˌpætʃ; ˈkrɒspætʃ/ *n* [C] *old-fashioned* someone who is bad-tempered【過時】脾氣暴躁的人

cross·piece /ˈkrɔsˌpis; ˈkrɒspiːs/ *n* [C] something that lies across another thing, especially in a building, railway track etc〔尤指建築物、鐵軌等的〕橫木, 橫杆, 橫檔

cross·ply /ˈkrɔsˌplaɪ; ˈkrɒsplaɪ/ *adj* RADIAL 輻射狀的

cross-pur·pos·es /ˌ· ˈ···/ *n* **at cross-purposes** two people who are at cross-purposes do not understand each other, because they are talking about different things but do not realize it〔因未意識到而〕互相誤解

cross-ques·tion /ˌ· ˈ··/ *v* [T] to CROSS-EXAMINE someone 盤問, 反詰 —**cross-questioner** *n*

cross-re·fer /ˌ· ·ˈ·/ *v* [I,T] to tell a reader to look in another place in the book they are reading so that they can get further information〔書中〕互見, 相互參照: [+to/from] *The author cross-refers you to Chapter 10 for more details.* 作者建議你參考第十章以了解更多細節。

cross-ref·er·ence /ˌ· ˈ···/ *n* [C] a note that tells the reader of a book to go to another place in the book, to get further information〔書中的〕互見, 相互參照

cross·roads /ˈkrɔsˌrodz; ˈkrɒsrəʊdz/ *n plural* **crossroads 1** a place where two roads meet and cross each other 十字路口, 交叉路口 **2** a time in your life when you have to make a very important decision that will affect your future〔人生作出重大決定的〕關鍵時期, 轉折點: *When my marriage ended, I felt as if I had reached a crossroads in my life.* 當我的婚姻結束時, 我覺得好像處於人生的十字路口。

cross-sec·tion /ˈ· ˌ··/ *n* [C] **1** something that has been cut in half so that you can look at the inside, or a drawing of this 橫截面 (圖), 剖面 (圖): *cross-section of a plant stem* 植物莖的橫截面 (圖) **2** a group of people or things that is typical of a much larger group 典型; 有代表性的一羣: *a cross-section of the American public* 美國公眾的典型代表

cross-stitch /ˈ· ·/ *n* [C,U] a stitch in a cross shape used in decorative sewing 十字形針法〔用於裝飾的縫法〕

cross street /ˈ· ·/ *n* [C] *AmE* a smaller street that crosses the street you are on【美】〔穿過所處大街的〕小街道

cross·town /ˈkrɔsˌtaun; ˈkrɒstaʊn/ *adj* [only before noun 僅用於名詞前] *AmE* moving in a direction across a town or city【美】穿過城鎮的: *the crosstown bus* 穿越本市的公共汽車

cross trees /ˈ· ·/ *n* [plural] *technical* two beams fastened across the top of a ship's MAST (1)【術語】桅頂橫桁

cross·walk /ˈkrɔsˌwɔk; ˈkrɒswɔːk/ *n* [C] *AmE* a special place for people to cross the road【美】人行橫道; PEDESTRIAN CROSSING *BrE*【英】

cross·wind /ˈkrɔsˌwɪnd; ˈkrɒsˌwɪnd/ *n* [C] a wind that blows across the direction that you are moving in 側風

cross·wise /ˈkrɔsˌwaɪz; ˈkrɒsˌwaɪz/ *adv* **1 lay/cut sth crosswise** to lay etc something from one corner of something to the opposite corner 斜對角地放/切某物 **2** two things that are placed crosswise are arranged to form the shape of an 'x'〔兩樣東西呈 X 形〕交叉疊放地

cross·word /ˈkrɔsˌwɝd; ˈkrɒsˌwɜːd/ also 又作 **crossword puz·zle** /ˈ·· ˌ··/ *n* [C] a word game in which you write the answers to questions in a pattern of numbered boxes 縱橫填字謎, 縱橫填字 (遊戲)

crotch /krɑtʃ; krɒtʃ/ also 又作 **crutch** *BrE*【英】*n* [C] the part of your body between the tops of your legs, or the part of a piece of clothing that covers this 胯部; 褲襠 —see picture at 參見 BODY 圖

crotch·et /ˈkrɑtʃɪt; ˈkrɒtʃə̇t/ *n* [C] *BrE* a musical note which continues for a quarter of the length of a SEMIBREVE【英】四分音符; QUARTER NOTE *AmE*【美】—see picture at 參見 MUSIC 圖

crotch·et·y /ˈkrɑtʃətɪ; ˈkrɒtʃə̇ti/ *adj* often slightly angry or annoyed 脾氣壞的; 愛發牢騷的: *a crotchety old man* 脾氣壞的老人

crouch 蹲下, 蹲伏

squat 蹲(坐) crouch/squat 蹲下 crouch 蹲伏

crouch /krautʃ; kraʊtʃ/ *v* [I] **1** also 又作 **crouch down** to lower your body close to the ground by bending your knees completely 蹲下: *My legs began to ache from crouching for so long.* 蹲了那麼久我的腿開始痛了。| *The boy crouched down to fix his sandal.* 那個男孩蹲下來繫涼鞋。**2** if an animal crouches it sits as low as possible, often because it is frightened or is going to attack something〔動物因為害怕或準備攻擊而〕蹲伏: *The cat crouched, its eyes following the mouse as it scurried away.* 貓蹲伏着, 兩眼盯着要匆匆跑開的老鼠。

croup /krup; kruːp/ *n* [U] an illness in children which makes them cough and have difficulty breathing 格魯布, 哮吼〔發生於兒童的一種疾病, 患者咳嗽, 呼吸困難〕

crou·pi·er /ˈkrupɪɚ; ˈkruːpiə/ *n* [C] someone whose job is to collect and pay out money where people play cards, ROULETTE etc for money〔賭場上的〕賭資收付人

crou·ton /kruˈtɑn; ˈkruːtɒn/ *n* [C usually plural 一般用複數] a small square piece of bread cooked in fat and served with soup or on salad 油炸麵包丁〔與湯一起吃或放在沙拉上〕

crow¹ /kro; krəʊ/ *n* **1** [C] a large shiny black bird with a loud cry 烏鴉 **2** [singular] the loud sound a COCK¹ (1) makes 公雞的鳴叫聲 **3 as the crow flies** in a straight line 筆直地, 直線地: *ten miles from here as the crow flies* 離這裡直線距離十英里 —see also 另見 **eat crow** (EAT (5))

crow² *v* [I] **1** if a COCK¹ (1) crows, it makes a loud high sound〔雄雞〕啼叫 **2** if a baby crows, it makes a noise that shows it is happy〔嬰兒〕歡叫: *The baby crowed with delight at the toy.* 嬰兒看到玩具高興得叫起來。**3** [+over/about] to talk about what you have done in a very proud way 得意洋洋地談論

crow·bar /ˈkroˌbɑr; ˈkrəʊbɑː/ *n* [C] a heavy iron bar used to lift or open things 鐵撬棍

crowd¹ /kraud; kraʊd/ *n* **1** [C] a large group of people in a public place 人羣: *A vast crowd had assembled in the main square.* 主要廣場上聚集了一大羣人。**2** [C] a large number of a particular kind of people or things 一羣; 一堆: **[+of]** *a crowd of supporters* 一羣支持者 | *Kemp stepped out to face a crowd of cameras.* 肯普走出去面對一大堆攝影機。| **crowds of** *streets filled with crowds of people* 擠滿了人的街道 **3** [singular] *informal* a group of people who know each other, work together etc【非正式】〔互相認識、一起工作等的〕一羣人; 一夥人; 一幫人: *"Who'll be at the party?" "Oh, the usual crowd – Maura, Tom, Joe, Jen, Turi..."* "誰會出席晚會?" "哦, 平時的那一夥人, 莫拉、湯姆、喬、詹、圖里…" **4 follow the crowd/go with the crowd** to always do what other people do, without thinking for yourself 隨大流, 人云亦云

crowd² *v* **1** [I,T] to gather together in large numbers, filling a particular place, or moving in a particular direction 羣集, 聚集; 擁擠: *Supporters crowded the stadium.* 支持者羣集在體育場裡。| **[+around/into etc]** *We all crowded around the speaker.* 我們都聚集在演講者周圍。**2** [T] if thoughts or ideas crowd your brain, mind, head etc, they fill it〔想法或觀點〕塞滿〔腦子〕: *A jumble of confused thoughts crowded my brain.* 一堆雜亂無章的想法塞滿了我的腦袋。**3** [T] **a)** to make someone angry by moving too close to them 擠, 逼近〔因而激怒〕: *The guy standing behind me was crowding me, so I poked him in the ribs.* 站在我後面的那個人擠我, 所以我戳了一下他的肋骨。**b)** *especially AmE* to make someone angry or upset by making too many unfair demands on them【尤美】催促; 催逼〔因而激怒煩擾〕: *Stop crowding me! I need time to make this decision.* 不要再催我了! 我需要時間來作決定。

crowd sb/sth ↔ **out** *phr v* [T] to force someone or something out of a place or situation 把…擠出, 排擠: *The bigger software firms are crowding small businesses out.* 較大的軟件公司正在將小公司排擠出局。

crowd·ed /ˈkraudɪd; ˈkraʊdə̇d/ *adj* too full of people or things 擠滿人[物]的; 擁擠的: *Sometimes the classes were very crowded.* 有時課堂上非常擁擠。| *a crowded street* 擁擠的街道 | **[+with]** *It was two weeks before Christmas and the mall was crowded with shoppers.* 離聖誕節還有兩個星期, 商場擠滿了購物者。

crown¹ /kraun; kraʊn/ *n* **1** [C] **a)** a circle made of gold and decorated with jewels, worn by kings and queens on their heads 皇冠, 冕 **b)** a similar circle, sometimes made of other things such as leaves or flowers, worn by someone who has won a special honour〔象徵特殊榮譽的〕冠帽 **2 the crown a)** the position of being king or queen 王位: *when the crown passed to George the Third...* 當王位傳給喬治三世的時候… **b)** the government of a country such as Britain that is officially led by a king or queen 王國政府: *The islands are possessions of the Crown.* 這些島嶼是王國政府的。**3** [usually singular 一般用單數] the top part of a hat, head, or hill〔帽子、頭或山的〕頂部: *a hat with a high crown* 高帽子 —see picture at 參見 HAT 圖 **4 a)** a unit of money in several European countries 克朗〔歐洲有些國家的貨幣單位〕: *Swedish crowns* 瑞典克朗 **b)** an old British coin, four of which made a pound〔英國舊幣的〕四分之一鎊硬幣 **5** [C] an artificial top for a damaged tooth 假齒冠 **6** a mark, sign, BADGE etc in the shape of a crown, used especially to show rank or quality 冠狀物〔用於表示等級或質量〕 **7** *informal* the fact of winning an important sports competition【非正式】獲得冠軍: *Can she retain her Wimbledon crown?* 她能保住她的温布頓冠軍地位嗎?

crown² *v* [T] **1** to place a crown on someone's head as a sign of royal power 為…加冕, 立…為王: *The Empress was crowned ten years ago.* 女皇是在十年前加冕的。| **crown sb king/queen** *Henry was crowned king.* 亨利加冕為王。**2** to make something complete or perfect by adding success, beauty, happiness etc to it 使圓滿成功; 完善: **crown sth with** *All their efforts have been crowned with success.* 他們的一切努力以圓滿成功告終。**3 crowned with** *literary* having something on top【文】給…加頂, 覆蓋…的頂端: *mountain peaks crowned with snow* 白雪覆蓋的山峯 **4** to put a protective top on a damaged tooth 鑲假牙冠 **5** *slang* to hit someone on the head【俚】打〔某人〕的頭部 **6 to crown it all** *informal* used to say that the next thing that happened was the worst in a series of bad things【非正式】最糟糕的是: *And then, to crown it all, I lost my purse.* 然後, 最糟糕的是, 我丟了錢包。

crown col·o·ny /ˌ· ˈ···/ *n* [C] a COLONY¹ controlled by the British government〔英國政府的〕直轄殖民地

crown court /ˈ· ·/ *n* [C,U] a court of law in Britain that deals with serious criminal cases and is higher than a Magistrates' Court〔英國的〕刑事法庭

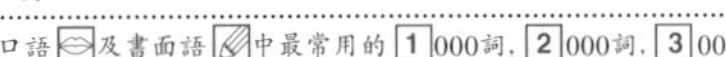

crowned head /ˌ· ˈ·/ *n* [C usually plural 一般用複數] a king or queen 國王; 女王: *All the crowned heads of Europe were present at the funeral.* 歐洲所有的君主都出席了葬禮。

crown·ing glory /ˋkraʊnɪŋ ˋglorɪ; ˈkraʊnɪŋ ɡlɔːri/ *n* [singular] **1** something that is more valuable, beautiful, or important than anything else you have or do 無上光榮; 最有價值[最漂亮; 最重要]的東西: *The hotel's crowning glory was a stunning roof garden with a panoramic view.* 這家酒店最精彩的是一個令人驚嘆的屋頂花園, 在那裡周圍的景物一覽無遺。**2** *humorous* your hair【幽默】頭髮

C

crown jew·els /ˌ· ˈ··/ *n* [plural] the crown, sword, jewels etc worn by a king or queen for ceremonies 御寶〔國王或王后參加典禮時佩戴的王冠、寶劍、珠寶等〕

crown prince /ˌ· ˈ·◂/ *n* [C] the boy or man who is expected to become the next king 王太子, 王儲: *Crown Prince Frederick* 弗雷德里克王儲

crown prin·cess /ˌ· ˈ··◂/ *n* [C] the girl or woman who is expected to become queen 將繼承王位的公主, 女王儲: *the Crown Princess of Prussia* 普魯士的女王儲

crow's feet /ˈ· ·/ *n* [plural] very small lines in the skin near your eyes〔眼角外的〕魚尾紋

crow's nest /ˈ· ·/ *n* [C] a small box at the top of a ship's MAST (1) from which someone can watch for danger, land etc 桅杆瞭望台

cro·zier, crosier /ˋkroʒɚ; ˈkrəʊʒə/ *n* [C] a long stick with a decorative curved end carried by a BISHOP (1) 主教的權杖

CRT /ˌsi ɑ ˋti; ˌsiː ɑː ˈtiː/ *n* [C] the abbreviation of 縮寫 = CATHODE RAY TUBE

3 2 **cru·cial** /ˋkruʃəl; ˈkruːʃəl/ *adj* **1** something that is crucial is extremely important because everything else depends on it 決定性的, 緊要關頭的: *crucial decisions involving millions of dollars* 事關幾百萬美元的重要決定 **2** *slang* excellent【俚】極好的, 非常好的 —**crucially** *adv*

cru·ci·ble /ˋkrusəbḷ; ˈkruːsɪ̈bəl/ *n* [C] a container in which substances are heated to very high temperatures 坩堝

cru·ci·fix /ˋkrusəˌfɪks; ˈkruːsɪ̈fɪks/ *n* [C] a cross with a figure of Christ on it 有耶穌像的十字架

cru·ci·fix·ion /ˌkrusəˋfɪkʃən; ˌkruːsɪ̈ˈfɪkʃən/ *n* **1** [C,U] the act of killing someone by fastening them to a cross and leaving them to die 釘死在十字架上 **2 the Crucifixion** the death of Christ in this way 耶穌受難〔被釘死在十字架上〕**3** [C] also 又作 **Crucifixion** a picture or other object representing Christ on the cross 耶穌受難像

cru·ci·form /ˋkrusəˌfɔrm; ˈkruːsɪ̈fɔːm/ *adj* shaped like a cross 十字形的

cru·ci·fy /ˋkrusəˌfaɪ; ˈkruːsɪ̈faɪ/ *v* [T] **1** to kill someone by fastening them to a cross 把…釘在十字架上處死 **2** to criticize someone severely and cruelly for something they have done, especially in public〔尤指當眾〕狠狠批評, 嚴厲指責: *If the newspapers find out you'll be crucified.* 如果報界發現的話, 你會受到嚴厲的指責。

crud /krʌd; krʌd/ *n* [U] *informal* something unpleasant to look at, smell, taste etc【非正式】〔難聞、難吃等〕令人厭惡的事物: *I can't eat this crud!* 我沒法吃這破玩意兒! —**cruddy** *adj*

crude[1] /krud; kruːd/ *adj* **1** offensive or rude, especially in a sexual way; VULGAR (1) 粗俗的, 粗野的; 粗魯的: *a crude gesture* 粗魯的手勢 | *crude jokes* 粗俗的笑話 **2** not developed to a high standard or made with great skill 粗製的: *crude tools made of stone* 粗製的石頭工具 **3** crude oil, rubber etc is in its natural or raw condition before it is treated with chemicals〔石油、橡膠等〕天然的, 未加提煉的 **4** done without attention to detail 粗糙的; 未加修飾的; 簡陋的: *a crude comparison of different engines* 不同引擎間的粗略比較 **5 in crude terms** expressed in a simple way 簡單地說: *In crude terms, the gulf between wealth and poverty is growing wider each year.* 簡單地說, 貧富之間的差距每年都在擴大。—**crudely** *adv*: *crudely built shacks* 粗糙建造的棚屋 —**crudity** also 又作 **crudeness** *n* [C,U]

crude[2] also 又作 **crude oil** /ˌ· ˈ·/ *n* [U] the oil that comes out of OIL WELLS, before it is separated into different products 原油: *1000 barrels of crude* 1,000桶原油

cru·dit·és /ˌkrudəˋte; ˈkruːdɪ̈teɪ/ *n* [plural] *French* pieces of raw vegetable served before a meal【法】〔飯前吃的〕生拌涼菜 —see picture on page A15 參見A15頁圖

cru·el /ˋkruəl; ˈkruːəl/ *adj* **1** causing unfair or unnecessary pain or suffering 殘忍的, 殘酷的: *a cruel twist of fate* 命運的殘酷轉折 | **a cruel blow** (=a sudden event that is painful and unfair) 殘酷的打擊 *My brother's death was a cruel blow.* 我兄弟的去世是個無情的打擊。**2** deliberately making people or animals suffer 有意傷害的: *The older kids played cruel jokes on her little brother.* 大孩子們開她小弟弟惡毒的玩笑。| **cruel look/smile/laugh etc** *Cilla gave a cruel laugh and left him standing there alone.* 西莉亞冷酷地笑了笑, 留下他獨自一人站在那裡。**3 be cruel to be kind** to do something to someone that will make them upset or unhappy in order to help them in another way 為使人今後受益而讓其先吃苦頭 —**cruelly** *adv*: *cruelly neglected by his parents* 父母任由他自生自滅, 十分殘酷 

cru·el·ty /ˋkruəltɪ; ˈkruːəlti/ *n* **1** [U] a willingness or desire to make people or animals suffer 殘忍, 殘酷: *There was a hint of cruelty in Brian's smile.* 布賴恩的微笑流露出一絲殘忍。**2** [U] behaviour that deliberately causes pain to people or animals 殘忍的行為: *The children had suffered cruelty and neglect.* 這些孩子受了虐待, 根本沒有人管。| [+**to**] *cruelty to animals* 對動物的殘忍 **3** [C] a cruel action 殘忍的行動: *horrifying cruelties that occur in wartime* 戰爭時期令人髮指的暴行 **4** [U] the unfairness of something that happens 不公平, 不公正: *Ruth's eyes filled with tears at life's cruelty.* 魯思由於生活的不公而雙眼含滿了淚水。

cru·et /ˋkruɪt; ˈkruːɪ̈t/ *n* [C] a thing that holds the containers for salt, pepper etc on a table 放調味品小瓶的小架

cruise[1] /kruz; kruːz/ *v* **1** [I] to sail along slowly, especially for pleasure〔尤指為了娛樂〕乘船巡遊: *cruising in the Mediterranean* 乘船在地中海游弋 **2** [I] to move at a steady speed in a car, aircraft etc〔飛機〕巡航,〔汽車〕以快而平穩的速度行駛: *cruising at 50 miles per hour* 以每小時50英里的穩定速度行駛 **3** [I,T] to drive a car slowly through a place with no particular purpose 開車兜風: *We were out cruising Friday night, and I saw Jerry with Kimberly.* 星期五晚上我們開車兜風時, 我看到傑里和金芭莉在一起。**4** [I,T] *slang* to look in a public place for a sexual partner【俚】〔在公共場所〕尋覓性伴侶: *cruising the singles bars* 在單身酒吧尋覓性伴侶

cruise[2] *n* [C] **1** a holiday on a large ship 在大船上度假: *a Caribbean cruise* 乘船在加勒比海度假 **2** a journey by boat for pleasure 乘船遊覽

cruise con·trol /ˈ· ·ˌ·/ *n* [C] a piece of equipment in a car that makes it go at a steady speed〔汽車的〕勻速控制器

cruise li·ner /ˈ· ˌ··/ *n* [C] a large ship for cruising 遊覽班輪

cruise mis·sile /ˌ· ˈ··/ *n* [C] a large explosive weapon that flies close to the ground and can be aimed at an exact point hundreds of kilometres away 巡航導彈

cruis·er /ˋkruzɚ; ˈkruːzə/ *n* [C] **1** a large fast warship 巡洋艦: *a battle cruiser* 戰列巡洋艦 **2** a boat used for pleasure 遊艇 **3** *AmE* a police car【美】警車

cruise ship /ˈ· ·/ *n* [C] a large ship with restaurants, bars etc that people have holidays on〔設有餐館、酒吧等供度假的〕大型郵輪

crul·ler /ˋkrʌlɚ; ˈkrʌlə/ *n* [C] *AmE* a small piece of sweet bread with a twisted shape【美】炸麵圈, 炸麻花

crumb /krʌm; krʌm/ *n* [C] **1** a very small piece of dry food, especially bread or cake 食品屑; 麵包[蛋糕]屑: *Brush the crumbs off the table.* 把桌上的麵包屑拭掉。—see picture on page A7 參見A7頁圖 **2 crumb of**

comfort/hope etc a very small amount of comfort, hope etc 少許的安慰/希望等: *Marie's offer of help was our only crumb of comfort.* 瑪麗提出幫助我們是我們唯一的小小安慰。**3** *AmE old-fashioned* someone who has done something unpleasant 【美, 過時】討厭的人

crum·ble¹ /ˋkrʌmbḷ; ˈkrʌmbəl/ *v* **1** [I,T] also 又作 **crumble away** to break apart into little pieces, or make something do this 把…弄碎, (使)碎成細屑: *Billy crumbled the bread in his fingers.* 比利用手指把麵包捻碎。**2** [I] if a building crumbles, it is old and starting to fall down 〔建築物〕破舊: *Britain's crumbling schools* 英國的破舊學校 **3** [I] also 又作 **crumble away** if your determination, courage etc crumbles, it becomes weak or fails 〔決心、勇氣等〕減弱, 崩潰: *Brigg's resolve crumbled and he reached for the whisky bottle.* 布里格的決心動搖了, 伸手去拿威士忌瓶子。**4** [I] if a military operation, government etc crumbles, it loses its power and its effectiveness 〔軍事行動〕挫敗; 〔政府〕敗落, 衰敗: *a crumbling empire* 敗落的帝國

crumble² *n* [U] a cooked dish of fruit covered with a dry mixture of flour, butter, and sugar 酥皮水果甜點心: *apple crumble* 酥皮蘋果甜點心

crum·bly /ˋkrʌmblɪ; ˈkrʌmbli/ *adj* something such as food or soil that is crumbly breaks easily into small pieces 〔食物、土壤等〕易碎的, 脆的: *a nice, crumbly cheese* 鬆脆可口的乾酪

crumbs /krʌmz; krʌmz/ *interjection BrE informal* used to express surprise 【英, 非正式】喔喲, 哎呀〔用於表示驚訝〕

crum·my /ˋkrʌmɪ; ˈkrʌmi/ *adj informal* 【非正式】**1** of bad quality 劣質的: *a crummy book* 糟糕的書 | *What a crummy idea!* 真是個餿主意! **2** ill or upset 生病的, 身體不舒服的: *I felt pretty crummy the next morning.* 第二天早上我感覺相當不舒服。

crum·pet /ˋkrʌmpɪt; ˈkrʌmpḷt/ *n* **1** [C] a small round bread with holes in one side, eaten hot with butter 小圓烤餅 **2** [U] *BrE slang* an offensive word for a sexually attractive woman 【英俚】騷貨〔對性感的女人的冒犯用語〕

crum·ple /ˋkrʌmpḷ; ˈkrʌmpəl/ *v* **1** [I,T] also 又作 **crumple up** to crush something so that it becomes smaller and bent, or to be crushed in this way (使)皺; 扭曲: *I had crumpled up about ten sheets, trying to write the letter.* 為了寫這封信, 我已經把十張紙揉成一團了。**2** [I] if your face crumples you suddenly look sad or disappointed, as if you might cry 〔臉容〕扭曲 **3** [I] if your body crumples, you fall in an uncontrolled way because you are unconscious, drunk etc 〔身體因失去知覺、醉酒而〕倒下: *Watkins crumpled in a heap and the referee stopped the fight.* 沃特金斯倒下來, 蜷作一團, 裁判便終止了拳賽。

crum·pled /ˋkrʌmpḷd; ˈkrʌmpəld/ *adj* **1** also 又作 **crumpled up** crushed into a smaller bent shape 皺的; 扭曲的: *a crumpled banknote* 皺巴巴的鈔票 —see picture on page A18 參見A18頁圖 **2** cloth or clothes that are crumpled have a lot of lines or folds in them 〔布、衣服〕有褶皺的: *Don't sit around in your suit. It'll get crumpled.* 不要穿着西服到處亂坐, 會起皺的。**3** someone who is crumpled somewhere, is lying still in a strange position after they have fallen 〔人〕歪歪扭扭地倒地不起

crumple zone /ˈ·· ·/ *n* [C] part of a car that crumples easily in an accident to protect the people inside 〔汽車為發生事故時保護乘客的〕防撞壓損區

crunch¹ /krʌntʃ; krʌntʃ/ *n* [singular] **1** a noise like the sound of something being crushed 嘎吱嘎吱的聲音: *the crunch of footsteps on gravel* 砂礫上嘎吱嘎吱的腳步聲 | *a horrible crunch* 令人恐懼的嘎吱聲 —see picture on page A19 參見A19頁圖 **2** *AmE* a difficult situation caused by a lack of money 【美】經濟困境: *The company's in a crunch right now.* 這家公司現在資金窘迫。| **feel the crunch** (=not have enough money) 手頭緊, 資金不足 **3 when/if it comes to the crunch** used to say what you will do when something important happens or when a difficult decision has to be made 當關鍵時刻到來時, 需要作出困難決定時: *If it comes to the crunch, whose side will you take?* 在關鍵時刻, 你會站在哪一邊?

crunch² *v* **1** [I] to make a sound like something being crushed 發嘎吱嘎吱聲: *Our feet crunched on the frozen snow.* 我們的腳踩在冰上發出嘎吱嘎吱的聲音。**2** [I always+adv/prep, T] to eat hard food in a way that makes a noise 嘎吱嘎吱地咬嚼: **[+on]** *The dog was crunching on a bone.* 這條狗在嘎吱嘎吱地啃骨頭。| **crunch sth** *crunching a biscuit* 嘎吱嘎吱地咬餅乾

crunch·y /ˋkrʌntʃɪ; ˈkrʌntʃi/ *adj* food that is crunchy is firm and fresh, and makes a noise when you bite it 脆的: *a crunchy apple* 鮮脆的蘋果 —**crunchiness** *n* [U]

cru·sade¹ /kruˋsed; kruːˈseɪd/ *n* [C] **1** one of a series of wars fought in the 11th, 12th, and 13th centuries by Christian armies trying to take Palestine from the Muslims 〔發生於11、12、13世紀的〕十字軍東征 **2** a determined attempt to change something because you think you are morally right 改革運動: **[+against/for]** *He seems to be running a one-man crusade against cigarette smoking.* 他像是在單槍匹馬進行反對吸煙的運動。

crusade² *v* [I] to take part in a CRUSADE¹ 加入十字軍; 從事改革運動: **[+against/for]** *crusading against nuclear weapons* 開展反對核武器的運動 —**crusader** *n* [C]

cruse /kruz; kruːz/ *n* [C] *old use* a small pot for oil, wine etc 【舊】罐, 壺, 罈

crush¹ /krʌʃ; krʌʃ/ *v* [T] **1** to press something so hard that it breaks or is damaged 壓碎, 壓壞, 壓扁: *His leg was crushed in the accident.* 他的腿在事故中被壓斷了。| **be crushed to death** (=die by being crushed) 被壓死 *Two people were crushed to death in the rush to escape.* 在匆忙逃跑中有兩個人被壓死。**2** to press something in order to break it into very small pieces, or into a powder 搗碎, 弄碎, 粉碎: *Crush two cloves of garlic.* 弄碎兩瓣大蒜。—see picture on page A11 參見A11頁圖 **3 crush a rebellion/uprising/revolt etc** to use severe methods to stop people from fighting you or opposing you 平定叛亂/起義/反叛等: *The revolution was crushed within days.* 幾天之內革命就被鎮壓了。**4 crush sb's hopes/enthusiasm/confidence etc** to make someone lose all hope, confidence etc 毀滅某人的希望/熱情/信心等 **5** to make someone feel extremely upset or shocked 使非常傷心; 使震驚: *Sara was crushed by their insults.* 莎拉因他們的侮辱而非常傷心。

crush up *phr v* [I] *BrE informal* if people crush up, they fit into a small space by moving closer to each other 【英, 非正式】擠, 塞, 擠入: *"Is there room for one more in your car?" "Yes, but you'll have to crush up."* "你車裡還能再坐一個人嗎?" "可以, 但是你要擠一擠。"

crush² *n* **1** [singular] a crowd of people pressed so close together that it is difficult for them to move 擁擠的人羣: *There's always such a crush on the train in the mornings.* 早晨火車上總是那麼擁擠。**2** [C] an uncontrollable feeling of love for someone, especially that a young person has for someone older 〔尤指對年齡比自己大者的〕迷戀: **have a crush on** *Did you have a crush on one of your teachers when you were at school?* 你上學時迷戀過某位教師嗎? **3 orange/lemon etc crush** a drink made by crushing the juice out of a fruit 橙汁/檸檬汁等

crush bar·ri·er /ˈ· ˌ···/ *n* [C] a fence used to control crowds at football matches, public events etc 〔足球賽或公共活動等中的〕防擠欄杆

crush·ing /ˋkrʌʃɪŋ; ˈkrʌʃɪŋ/ *adj* **1** very hard to deal with, and making you lose hope and confidence 難以應付的, 使人受不了的: *the crushing burden of debt* 使人難以承受的債務負擔 | **crushing blow** (=something that makes you lose hope and confidence) 沉重的打擊 *Failing his final exams was a crushing blow.* 期末考試不及格對他是個沉重的打擊。| **crushing defeat** *his party's crushing defeat in the local elections* 他的黨在地方選舉中慘敗 **2** a crushing remark, reply etc contains a very strong

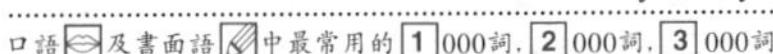

criticism〔評論、回答等〕帶有強烈批評的 **—crushingly** *adv*: *"That's fairly obvious," she replied crushingly.* "那非常明顯。"她很不滿地回答。

crust /krʌst; krʌst/ *n* [C,U] **1** the hard brown outer surface of bread 麵包皮: *cucumber sandwiches with the crusts cut off* 去掉皮的麵包做的黃瓜三明治 **2** the baked pastry on a PIE (1,2) 點心的酥皮 **3** a thin hard dry layer on the surface of something〔某物的〕硬薄外層: *the Earth's crust* 地殼

crus·ta·cean /krʌsˈteʃən; krʌˈsteɪʃən/ *n* [C] *technical* an animal such as a LOBSTER or a CRAB that has a hard outer shell and several pairs of legs, and usually lives in water【術語】甲殼綱動物〈如龍蝦、螃蟹〉**—crustacean** *adj*

C

crust·ed /ˈkrʌstɪd; ˈkrʌstɪ̵d/ *adj* **[+with]** having a thin hard dry layer on the surface 有硬薄外層的: *old boots crusted with mud* 黏滿泥的舊靴子

crust·y /ˈkrʌstɪ; ˈkrʌsti/ *adj* **1** bread that is crusty is pleasant to eat because it has a hard crust〔麵包〕脆皮的 **2** *informal* someone who is crusty is bad-tempered【非正式】愛發脾氣的, 暴躁的: *crusty old ladies in big hats* 戴着大帽子、脾氣暴躁的老婦人 **3** having a thin dry hard layer of something on the surface 有薄硬外層的: *walls crusty with dirt* 覆蓋着一層薄薄硬污垢的牆壁 **—crustiness** *n* [U]

crutch /krʌtʃ; krʌtʃ/ *n* [C] **1** [usually plural 一般用複數] one of a pair of long sticks that you put under your arms to help you walk when you have hurt your leg 拐杖: *walking on crutches* 拄拐杖走路 **2** something that gives you support or help 支撐物: *Joan's religion was a crutch to her when her husband died.* 瓊的丈夫去世後, 她信仰的宗教對她是一種精神支柱。**3** *BrE* the part of your body between the tops of your legs【英】胯部

crux /krʌks; krʌks/ *n* **the crux** the most important part of a problem, question, argument etc〔問題、論據等的〕核心, 中心; 癥結: *The crux of the play is his inability to accept his wife as an equal.* 這齣戲的中心是他不能平等看待他的妻子。| *The crux of the matter is whether or not he'd intended to commit a crime.* 問題的核心在於他是不是故意犯罪。

2 2 **cry**[1] /kraɪ; kraɪ/ *v past tense and past participle* **cried** /kraɪd; kraɪd/ *present participle* **crying**

1 ►PRODUCE TEARS 流淚◄ [I] to produce tears from your eyes, usually because you are unhappy or hurt 哭: *Don't cry, Laura. It's OK.* 不要哭, 勞拉, 沒事的! | *I always cry at weddings.* 參加婚禮時我老是要哭。| **[+over/about]** *I know it's stupid to cry over something so unimportant.* 我知道為如此無關緊要的事哭泣是愚蠢的。| **[+with/in]** *Zack began to cry with frustration.* 扎卡由於失望而哭了起來。| **[+for]** *The baby was crying for attention.* 寶寶哭了, 要人關注。| **cry your eyes out/cry your heart out** *informal* (=be extremely sad and cry a lot)【非正式】哭得死去活來 | **cry yourself to sleep** (=cry until you fall asleep) 哭到睡着

2 ►SAY LOUDLY 大聲説◄ [T] to shout something loudly 喊叫: *"Stop!" she cried.* "停下!"她喊道。

3 ►ANIMALS/BIRDS 動物/鳥類◄ [I] if animals and birds cry they make a loud sound 鳥鳴, 鳥叫;〔動物〕大聲叫: *seagulls on the cliffs crying loudly* 在懸崖上大聲鳴叫的海鷗

4 cry on sb's shoulder *informal* to tell someone why you are unhappy or worried【非正式】告訴某人自己的苦衷: *I've had Glen crying on my shoulder all afternoon about his love life.* 整個下午我已讓格倫訴説他愛情生活中的苦楚。

5 cry over spilt milk to waste time feeling sorry about an earlier mistake or problem that cannot be changed 作無益的悔恨: *It's no use crying over spilt milk.* 牛奶灑了, 哭也無用。

6 cry into your beer *informal* to feel too much pity for yourself, especially because you think you have been treated unfairly【非正式】〔尤因受不公正待遇而〕感到十分委屈

7 cry wolf to ask for help when you do not need it, so that people do not believe you when you really need help 謊報險情; 發假警報

8 for crying out loud *spoken* used when you feel annoyed or impatient with someone【口】豈有此理; 天哪〔用於感到厭煩或不耐煩時〕: *For crying out loud, stop nagging me about it!* 豈有此理, 別再嘀咕個沒完!

9 [T] *literary* to make something known to the public by shouting【文】當眾大聲宣布: **cry your wares** *market traders crying their wares* 市場上大聲叫賣的小販 —see also 另見 **cry for the moon** (MOON[1] (4))

cry off *phr v* [I] *BrE* to say that you will not do something that you have already promised to do【英】取消承諾: *Paul tried to cry off at the last moment saying he had to work late.* 保羅在最後時刻想反悔, 説他得工作到很晚。

cry out *phr v* **1** [I] to make a loud sound of fear, shock, pain etc〔由於害怕、震驚、疼痛等而〕大聲喊叫, 哼: *He was in a lot of pain, but he didn't cry out.* 他痛得很厲害, 但是一聲也沒有喊。| **[+in/with]** *Even the smallest movement made him cry out in pain.* 哪怕最輕微的動作也會使他痛得直叫。**2** [I,T] to shout something loudly 大聲喊叫: *Maria cried out sharply, "Don't touch it!"* 瑪麗亞厲聲喊道:"別碰它!" | **[+for]** *I was so scared, I couldn't even cry out for help.* 我害怕極了, 連喊救命都喊不出來。**3 be crying out for** *informal* to need something urgently【非正式】迫切需要: *The kitchen is crying out for a coat of paint.* 廚房急需油漆一遍。**4 cry out against** to complain strongly or protest strongly about something 強烈抱怨; 強烈抗議

cry[2] *n plural* **cries** 3

1 ►SOUND EXPRESSING FEELING 表達感情的聲音◄ [C] a loud sound showing fear, pain, shock etc〔因驚恐、疼痛、震驚等而發出的〕叫喊聲: *a baby's cry* 嬰兒的叫喊聲 | **a cry of alarm/anger/despair etc** *A cry of protest rose from the crowd.* 人羣中發出抗議的呼喊聲。| *a cry of delight* 一聲歡呼 | **give a cry/let out a cry** *Hugh let out a startled cry as he fell into the water.* 休在掉到水裡的時候發出驚恐的喊叫聲。

2 ►SHOUT 喊叫◄ [C] a loud shout 呼喊聲: **[+of]** *As they left the stage there were cries of "More! More!"* 他們離開舞台的時候, 人們喊道:"再來一個! 再來一個!"

3 ►ANIMAL/BIRD 動物/鳥◄ [C] a sound made by a particular animal〔某種動物的〕鳴叫; 吠; 嗥叫: *the cries of seagulls wheeling over the docks* 在碼頭上方盤旋的海鷗發出的鳴叫聲

4 ►TIME WHEN SB CRIES 某人哭喊的時候◄ [singular] *especially BrE* a period of time during which you cry【尤英】哭喊時: **have a cry** *You'll feel better after you've had a good cry.* 痛哭一場後你會感覺好受些。

5 be a far cry from *informal* to be very different from something else【非正式】與…大不相同: *It was a far cry from the leafy suburbs she was used to.* 這裡和她所習慣的樹木茂密的郊區大不相同。

6 cry for help something someone says or does that shows that they are very unhappy and need help〔某人的所言所行表示其〕需要幫助: *Janie's suicide attempt was obviously a cry for help.* 詹妮的自殺企圖顯然表示她需要人幫助。

7 ►PHRASE 片[短]語◄ [C] a phrase that is used to unite people in support of a particular action or idea; SLOGAN 口號: **war/battle cry** (=a phrase shouted at the enemy in a fight) 打仗[打鬥]時的吶喊, 喊殺聲

8 in full cry a) if someone is in full cry they are strongly or loudly criticizing someone or something 強烈譴責; 大聲譴責: *The Democrats were in full cry over Reagan's defence spending plans.* 民主黨人大聲譴責列根的國防開支計劃。**b)** if a group of dogs is in full cry, they are making loud noises as they hunt an animal〔一羣獵犬〕吠叫着追趕 —see also 另見 HUE AND CRY

cry·ing /ˈkraɪɪŋ; ˈkraɪ-ɪŋ/ *adj* **1 a crying need for sth** a serious need for something 迫切需要某事物: *There is a* *crying need for improvements to our public transport system.* 我們的公共交通系統迫切需要改善。**2 it's a crying shame** *spoken* used to say you are angry and upset about something【口】真令人生氣[傷心]: *It's a crying shame the way she works so hard to have Ken waste it all gambling.* 她辛辛苦苦掙的錢都讓肯賭掉了, 真令人生氣。

crypt /krɪpt; krɪpt/ *n* [C] a room under a church, used in former times for burying people〔舊時用作墓地的〕教堂地下室

cryp·tic /ˋkrɪptɪk; ˈkrɪptɪk/ *adj* deliberately mysterious, or having a secret meaning 故作神祕的; 有隱義的: **cryptic remark/comment/statement etc** *What are we supposed to understand from a cryptic remark like that?* 我們到底該如何理解那種含義隱晦的話呢? —**cryptically** /-klɪ; -kli/ *adv*

crypto- /krɪpto; krɪptəʊ/ *prefix formal* secret or hidden【正式】祕密的, 隱蔽的: *a crypto-Communist* 祕密共產黨員

cryp·to·gram /ˋkrɪptəˌgræm; ˈkrɪptəgræm/ *n* [C] a message written in code (CODE[1] (4)) 密碼文, 暗碼文

cryp·to·gra·phy /krɪpˋtɑgrəfɪ; krɪpˈtɒgrəfi/ *n* [U] the study of secret writing and codes (CODE[1] (4)) 密碼學 —**cryptographer** *n* [C]

crys·tal /ˋkrɪstḷ; ˈkrɪstl/ *n* **1** [C,U] rock that is transparent like ice, or a piece of this 水晶 **2** [U] very high quality transparent glass 水晶玻璃: *On the sideboard was his mother's collection of crystal and cut-glass.* 餐具櫃上是他母親收集的水晶玻璃和雕花玻璃器皿。**3** [C] a small regular shaped piece of a substance, formed naturally when this substance becomes solid 結晶(體): *crystals of ice* 冰晶 | *copper sulphate crystals* 硫酸銅結晶 **4** [C] *AmE* the transparent cover on a clock or watch【美】〔鐘面或錶面的透明〕蓋片

crystal ball /ˌ·· ˈ·/ *n* [C] a glass ball that you can look into to magically see what is going to happen in the future〔占卜用的〕水晶球

crystal clear /ˌ·· ˈ·◂/ *adj* very clearly stated, easy to understand 明白的, 無疑問的, 非常清楚的: *I want to make one thing crystal clear – I do not agree with these proposals.* 有一件事我要說清楚, 我不同意這些提議。

crys·tal·line /ˋkrɪstḷˌaɪn; ˈkrɪstəlaɪn/ *adj* **1** very clear or transparent, like crystal 清澈透明的; 水晶般的 **2** made of crystals 水晶[結晶體]構成的

crys·tal·lize also 又作 **-ise** *BrE*【英】/ˋkrɪstḷˌaɪz; ˈkrɪstəlaɪz/ *v* **1** [I,T] if a liquid crystallizes, it forms crystals (CRYSTAL (3)) (使) 結晶: *The liquid will crystallize at 50 degrees centigrade.* 這種液體在攝氏 50 度時結晶。**2** [I,T] if an idea, plan etc crystallizes or if you crystallize it, it becomes very clear in your mind (使) 變得明朗而具體: *a number of related ideas that gradually crystallized into a practical plan* 逐漸具體化為實際計劃的若干有關聯的想法 —**crystallization** /ˌkrɪstḷaɪˋzeʃən; ˌkrɪstəlaɪˈzeɪʃən/ *n* [U]

crys·tal·lized /ˋkrɪstəlaɪzd; ˈkrɪstəlaɪzd/ *adj* crystallized fruit is made by a special process which covers it with sugar〔水果等〕裹糖的: *crystallized ginger* 蜜餞薑

crystal set /ˈ·· ·/ *n* [C] a very simple old-fashioned radio 晶體管收音機

CSE /ˌsi ɛs ˋi; ˌsiː es ˈiː/ *n* [C] Certificate of Secondary Education; an examination taken at the age of 16 in schools in Britain before 1988〔英國〕中等教育證書考試

C-section /ˋsi ˌsɛkʃən; ˈsiː ˌsekʃən/ *n* [C] *AmE informal* a CAESAREAN【美, 非正式】剖腹產

CS gas /ˌsi ɛs ˋgæs; ˌsiː es ˈgæs/ *n* [U] *BrE* TEAR GAS【英】催淚瓦斯

ct 1 the written abbreviation of 縮寫= CARAT: *a 24ct gold necklace* 一條 24 開的金項鏈 **2** a written abbreviation for 縮寫= CENT: *These cost 75 cts.* 這些花費了 75 美分。

cu the written abbreviation of 縮寫= CUBIC: *40 cu m of rock* 40 立方米石頭

cub /kʌb; kʌb/ *n* [C] **1** a young lion, bear etc 幼獸: *a lion cub* 小獅子 | *A fox and her cubs were crossing the field.* 一隻狐狸與幼狐正在穿過田野。**2 the Cubs** *BrE* the CUB SCOUT organization【英】幼年童子軍 **3** a member of the CUB SCOUT organization 幼年童子軍成員

cub·by·hole /ˋkʌbɪˌhol; ˈkʌbihəʊl/ *n* [C] a very small space in a house, used for storing things or hiding in〔房屋內用於儲藏的〕窄小的地方

cube[1] /kjub; kjuːb/ *n* [C] **1** a solid object with six equal square sides 立方形的東西; 立方體: *a sugar cube* 一塊方糖 | *an ice cube* 一小方塊冰 | *Cut the meat into small cubes.* 把肉切成丁。—see picture at 參見 SHAPE[1] 圖 **2 the cube of sth** the number you get when you multiply a number by itself twice, so for example 4×4×4=64 so the cube of 4 is 64 三次方, 立方

cube[2] *v* [T] **1** to multiply a number by itself twice 自乘兩次: *4 cubed is 64.* 4 的立方是 64。**2** to cut food into cubes; DICE[2] (1) 將〔食物〕切成小方塊

cube root /ˌ· ˈ·/ *n* [C] *technical* the cube root of a particular number is the number that when multiplied by itself twice will give that number【術語】立方根: *4 is the cube root of 64.* 4 是 64 的立方根。

cu·bic /ˋkjubɪk; ˈkjuːbɪk/ *adj* **cubic centimetre/metre/inch etc** a measurement of space which is calculated by multiplying the length of something by its width and height 立方厘米/米/英寸等: *What's the cubic capacity of this engine?* 這台機器的容積是多少?

cu·bi·cle /ˋkjubɪkḷ; ˈkjuːbɪkəl/ *n* [C] a small part of a room that is separated from the rest of the room so that you cannot be seen by other people, cannot hear any noise etc 小室, 小房間

cub·is·m /ˋkjubɪzəm; ˈkjuːbɪzəm/ *n* [U] a 20th century style of art, in which objects and people are represented by GEOMETRIC shapes 立體派[主義]〔20 世紀的一種藝術流派, 以幾何圖形來表現主題〕—**cubist** *adj*: *cubist paintings* 立體派油畫 —**cubist** *n* [C]

cu·bit /ˋkjubɪt; ˈkjuːbḷt/ *n* [C] *biblical* an ancient measure of length equal to the length of your arm between your wrist and your elbow【聖經】腕尺, 肘尺〔古代長度單位, 相當於手腕到肘的長度〕

Cub Scout /ˈ· ˌ·/ *n* [C] *BrE*【英】**1 the Cub Scouts** the part of the SCOUT[1] (1a) organization for younger boys 幼年童子軍 **2** a young boy who is a member of this organization 幼年童子軍成員

cuck·old[1] /ˋkʌkḷd; ˈkʌkəld/ *n old-fashioned* an insulting name for a man whose wife has deceived him by having sex with another man【過時】"烏龜"〔妻子與人通姦的人, 侮辱用語〕

cuckold[2] *v* [T] *old-fashioned* if a wife or her LOVER cuckold her husband, they deceive him by having sex with each other【過時】給…戴綠帽子;〔妻子〕與人通姦, 與…的妻子通姦

cuck·oo[1] /ˋkuku; ˈkʊkuː/ *n* [C] a grey European bird that puts its eggs in other birds' NESTs and that makes a sound that sounds like its name 杜鵑, 布穀鳥

cuckoo[2] *adj* [not before noun 不用於名詞前] *informal* crazy or silly【非正式】瘋瘋癲癲的, 傻的: *You're completely cuckoo!* 你真是個傻子!

cuckoo clock /ˈ·· ·/ *n* [C] a clock with a wooden bird inside that comes out every hour and makes the sound of a cuckoo to show what time it is 杜鵑自鳴鐘

cu·cum·ber /ˋkjukʌmbɚ; ˈkjuːkʌmbə/ *n* [C,U] a long thin round vegetable with a dark green skin and a light green inside usually eaten raw 黃瓜: *tomato and cucumber salad* 番茄黃瓜色拉 —see picture on page A9 參見 A9 頁圖

cud /kʌd; kʌd/ *n* [U] **1** food that a cow has eaten, swallowed, and brought back into its mouth to eat a second time 反芻的食物 **2 chew the cud a)** *informal* to think very hard about something before making a decision【非正式】反覆思考 **b)** if a cow chews the cud, it eats cud 吃反芻的食物

cud·dle[1] /ˋkʌdḷ; ˈkʌdl/ *v* [I,T] to hold someone or something very close to you with your arms around them, especially to show that you love them〔尤指表示喜愛

C

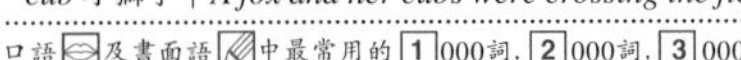

而)抱，擁抱，摟抱：*Dawn and her boyfriend were cuddling on the sofa.* 道恩和她的男朋友在沙發上摟摟抱抱。—see picture on page A21 參見A21頁圖

cuddle up *phr v* [I] to lie or sit very close to someone or something 緊貼着身子躺[坐]，依偎：**[+to/together]** *The children cuddled up to each other for warmth.* 孩子們互相依偎在一起取暖。

cuddle² *n* [singular] an act of cuddling someone 擁抱，緊貼着身子躺：**give sb a cuddle** *Come over here and let me give you a cuddle.* 過來，讓我擁抱你一下。

cud·dly /ˋkʌdlı; ˈkʌdli/ *adj* someone or something that is cuddly makes you want to cuddle them 可愛的，值得擁抱的：*a cuddly little baby* 逗人愛的小寶寶

C

cud·gel¹ /ˋkʌdʒəl; ˈkʌdʒəl/ *n* **1** [C] a short thick stick used as a weapon (用作武器的)短粗棍[棒] **2 take up the cudgels** to start to fight for an idea that you believe in 努力為…奮鬥，奮起捍衛

cudgel² *v* [T] **1** to hit someone with a cudgel 用棍棒打 **2 cudgel your brains** to think very hard about something 絞盡腦汁

cue¹ /kju; kjuː/ *n* [C] **1** an action or event that provides a signal 提示，暗示：*The fall in interest rates may be a cue for an upturn in consumer spending.* 利率的降低可能暗示消費的上升。**2** a word, phrase, or action in a play that is a signal for the next person to speak or act (戲劇中暗示下一位演員接言或出場的)尾白，提示：*She stood nervously in the wings waiting for her cue.* 她緊張地站在台側等該她上場的尾白。| **miss your cue** (=not speak or act when you are supposed to) 漏説台詞[該説的話]；該行動時沒行動 **3 (right) on cue** happening or done at exactly the right moment 恰好，正好：*I had just suggested Philip's name when he walked in, right on cue.* 我剛提到菲利普的名字時他就走了進來，真是湊巧。**4 take your cue from** to copy what someone else does, especially in order to behave in the right way 學別人的樣：*With interest rates, the smaller banks will take their cue from the Federal Bank.* 調整利率時，小銀行會仿效聯邦銀行。**5** a long straight wooden stick used for hitting the ball in games such as BILLIARDS and SNOOKER¹ (枱球等的)球杆

cue² *v* [T] to give someone a sign that it is the right moment for them to speak or do something especially during a performance (尤指在表演中)提示：*The studio manager will cue you when it's your turn to come on.* 該你上場的時候，錄製室監督會提示你的。

cue ball /ˈ· ·/ *n* [C] the ball which a player hits with the CUE in a game such as BILLIARDS (枱球等的)主球

cuff¹ /kʌf; kʌf/ *n* [C] **1** the end of a SLEEVE (=the arm of a shirt, dress etc) 袖口 —see picture on page A17 參見A17頁圖 **2** *AmE* a narrow piece of cloth turned upwards at the bottom of a trouser leg【美】(褲腳的)翻邊；TURN-UP *BrE*【英】**3** an action in which you hit someone lightly on the head with your hand open 用手掌輕拍(某人頭部) **4 cuffs** [plural] HANDCUFFS 手銬 —see also 另見 OFF-THE-CUFF

cuff² *v* [T] **1** to hit someone lightly, especially in a friendly way (尤指友好地)用掌輕拍：*She cuffed him playfully on the side of the head.* 她開玩笑地拍拍他的腦袋。**2** to put HANDCUFFS on someone 給…戴手銬

cuff link /ˈ· ·/ *n* [C] one of a pair of small round objects used for fastening shirt cuffs (襯衫袖口的)鏈扣，袖扣 —see picture on page A17 參見A17頁圖

cui·rass /kwıˋræs; kwıˈræs/ *n* [C] a piece of metal or leather that covers a soldier's chest and back, worn for protection in battle in former times (舊時戰爭中士兵穿的)護胸背鐵甲，胸甲

cui·sine /kwıˋzin; kwıˈziːn/ *n* [U] *French*【法】**1** a particular style of cooking 烹飪(法)：*French cuisine* 法式烹飪 | *vegetarian cuisine* 素食烹飪 **2** the food cooked in a particular restaurant or hotel, especially when it is very good 特製飯菜：*Enjoy the delicious cuisine created by our award-winning chef.* 請享用我們的獲獎廚師精製的可口飯菜。

cul-de-sac /ˋkʌl də ˌsæk; ˈkʌl də ˌsæk/ *n* [C] **1** a road which is closed at one end so that there is only one way in and out 死胡同，死巷 **2** an unhelpful situation in which you cannot make any more progress 困境，死路；僵局：*These ideas lead us into a philosophical cul-de-sac.* 這些觀點把我們領進了一個哲學上的死胡同。

cul·i·na·ry /ˋkjuləˌnɛrı; ˈkʌlənəri/ *adj* [only before noun 僅用於名詞前] *formal* connected with cooking【正式】烹飪(用)的：*culinary herbs* 調味香料 | *culinary skills* 烹飪技術 | **culinary delights** (=food that tastes very good) 美味佳餚 *the region's culinary delights* 本地區的美味佳餚

cull¹ /kʌl; kʌl/ *v* **1** [T] *formal* to find or choose information from many different places【正式】挑選，收集，選用(信息)：**cull sth from** *photographs culled from various sources* 從各種來源中挑選出的照片 **2** [I,T] to kill the weakest animals in a group so that the size of the group does not increase too much 從(一羣動物中)剔出，殺掉(最弱者) **3** [T] *literary* to gather flowers or fruit【文】採摘(花或水果)

cull² *n* [C] the act of killing the weakest animals in a group so that the size of the group does not increase too much 宰殺(一羣動物中最弱者)

cul·len·der /ˋkʌləndə; ˈkʌləndə/ another spelling of COLANDER colander的另一種拼法

cul·mi·nate /ˋkʌlməˌnet; ˈkʌlməneıt/

culminate in sth *phr v* [T] if a process culminates in something, it finally reaches the highest point of development or the most important result 達到…高峯[頂點]；最終達到：*a series of minor clashes culminating in a full scale war* 最終導致全面戰爭的一系列小衝突

cul·mi·na·tion /ˌkʌlməˋneʃən; ˌkʌlməˈneıʃən/ *n* [U] **the culmination of** the final or highest point that is reached after a long period of effort or development 頂點，極點：*This little book represented the culmination of 15 year's work.* 這本小書是15年工作的結果。

cu·lottes /kjuˋlɑts; kjuːˈlɒts/ *n* [plural] women's trousers which stop at the knee and are shaped to look like a skirt (女用的)裙褲

cul·pa·ble /ˋkʌlpəbl; ˈkʌlpəbəl/ *adj* **1** *formal* deserving blame【正式】應受譴責[處罰]的：*Both parties were held to be to some extent culpable.* 雙方都應受某種程度的譴責。**2** *technical* an action that is criminal【術語】(行動)有罪的：**culpable homicide/negligence etc** *He pleaded guilty to culpable homicide.* 他承認犯了殺人罪。—**culpably** *adv* —**culpability** /ˌkʌlpəˋbılətı; ˌkʌlpəˈbıləti/ *n* [U]

cul·prit /ˋkʌlprıt; ˈkʌlprət/ *n* [C] **1** the person who is guilty of a crime, or responsible for damage, a problem etc 罪犯；造成破壞[問題]的人：*Police finally managed to catch the culprit.* 警察最終抓住了罪犯。**2** *informal* the reason for a particular problem or difficulty【非正式】問題的起因；困難的起源：**the main culprit** *High production costs are the main culprit.* 高生產成本是主要原因。

cult /kʌlt; kʌlt/ *n* **1** [C] an extreme religious group that is not part of an established religion 異教，邪教：*Anyone who betrayed the cult could be punished by death.* 任何背叛邪教的人都可能會被處死。**2 cult film/figure/TV show etc** a film, music group etc that has become very popular but only among a particular group of people 某一羣人熱愛的電影/人物/電視節目等：*a cult band* 有一羣狂熱樂迷的樂隊 | *James Dean acquired the status of a cult hero.* 占士甸成了某些人崇拜的英雄偶像。**3** [C] a fashionable belief, idea, or attitude that influences people's lives (影響人們生活的)時尚信仰[觀點，態度]：*Diet, therapy, exercise ... It's all part of this cult of self-improvement.* 節食、治療法、鍛鍊身體…這些都是自我改善的時尚做法。**4** [C,U] *formal* a system of religious beliefs and practices【正式】宗教信仰體系[慣例]

cul·ti·va·ble /ˋkʌltəvəbl; ˈkʌltəvəbəl/ *adj* land which is cultivable can be used to grow crops (土地)可耕作的

cul·ti·vate /ˋkʌltə͵vet; ˈkʌltɪ̇veɪt/ *v* **1** [T] to prepare and use land for growing crops and plants 耕, 耕作: *Some of the land would be impossible to cultivate.* 有些地無法耕作。**2** to develop a particular skill or quality in yourself 培養, 養成: *The company have been successful in cultivating a very professional image.* 該公司在建立專業形象方面非常成功。**3** to make an effort to develop a friendly relationship with someone because you want something from them〔為了利益〕與...交往, 結交〔朋友〕: *Professor Gladwyn would be an acquaintance worth cultivating.* 格拉德溫教授是值得結交的朋友。

cul·ti·vat·ed /ˋkʌltə͵vetɪd; ˈkʌltɪ̇veɪtɪ̇d/ *adj* **1** someone who is cultivated is intelligent and knows a lot about music, art, literature etc 有素養的, 有教養的: *It was a pleasure to talk to such a cultivated audience.* 與這麼有教養的觀眾談話非常高興。**2** land that is cultivated is used for growing crops or plants〔土地〕耕作的: *cultivated fields* 耕地 **3** crops or plants that are cultivated are grown in order to be sold〔作物等〕栽培的

cul·ti·va·tion /͵kʌltəˋveʃən; ͵kʌltɪ̇ˈveɪʃən/ *n* [U] **1** the preparation and use of land for growing crops 耕作: *different methods of soil cultivation* 不同的土地耕作法 | **under cultivation** (=used for growing crops and plants) 耕作中的 *These fields have been under cultivation for years.* 這些土地已耕作很多年了。**2** the planting and growing of plants and crops 栽培, 種植: *Terraces for rice cultivation covered the hillsides.* 山坡上全是種植水稻的梯田。| **[+of]** *the successful cultivation of tobacco* 煙草的成功種植 **3** the deliberate development of a particular quality or skill 培養〔特性〕; 學習〔技能〕

cul·ti·va·tor /ˋkʌltə͵vetɚ; ˈkʌltɪ̇veɪtə/ *n* [C] **1** *formal* someone who grows crops or plants, especially a farmer【正式】耕種者〔尤指農民〕**2** a tool or machine that is used to prepare land for growing crops 中耕機; 耕耘機

2 **cul·tu·ral** /ˋkʌltʃərəl; ˈkʌltʃərəl/ *adj* **1** belonging to or connected with a particular society and its way of life 某個社會的; 文化上的: *a wide range of cultural influences* 廣泛的文化影響 | **cultural heritage/traditions etc** (=ideas, customs etc that have existed in a particular society for a long time) 文化遺產/文化傳統等 **2** related to art, literature, music etc 與文藝有關的, 文化的: **cultural activity** *They enjoy cultural activities like going to the theatre and the opera.* 他們喜歡看戲劇看歌劇等文化活動。| **cultural centre** (=a place, usually a big city, where a lot of artistic and musical events happen) 文化中心 *Vienna is a real cultural centre for music lovers.* 維也納確實是音樂愛好者的文化中心。| **cultural desert** *informal* (=a place such as a small town where there are no cultural activities)【非正式】文化沙漠

cul·tu·ral·ly /ˋkʌltʃərəlɪ; ˈkʌltʃərəli/ *adv* **1** in a way that is related to the ideas, beliefs, or customs of a society 社會地; 人文地: *culturally approved patterns of behaviour* 社會認可的行為方式 **2** in a way that is related to art, music, literature etc 與文藝有關: *The French are a culturally sophisticated people.* 法國人民是文化底蘊很深的民族。| [sentence adverb 句子副詞] *Culturally, the city has a lot to offer.* 從文藝角度看, 這座城市可提供的東西很多。

2 1 **cul·ture** /ˋkʌltʃɚ; ˈkʌltʃə/ *n*

1 ▶IN A SOCIETY 在社會中◀ [C,U] the ideas, beliefs, and customs that are shared and accepted by people in a society 文化: *Our culture teaches us to hide a lot of our true feelings.* 我們的文化教我們要把許多真實情感隱藏起來。| *black culture* 黑人文化 | **Western/British/Japanese etc culture** *Western culture places a high value on material acquisition.* 西方文化很看重物質的獲得。

2 culture shock the feelings of shock and anxiety that someone has when they visit a foreign country or a new place for the first time 文化衝擊〔指首次去國外或一個新地方的人感受到的震驚和焦慮〕: *John found life in London a bit of a culture shock at first.* 最初約翰覺得在倫敦的生活是一種文化衝擊。

3 ▶IN A GROUP 在一組人中◀ [C,U] the attitudes and beliefs about something that are shared by a particular group of people or in a particular organization〔團體或組織中共同的〕態度, 信仰, 習俗: *Working late hours for very little money seems part of the company culture.* 工作時間長而薪酬低看來是該公司的慣例。| **drug/computer etc culture** *90's rave culture* 90 年代的狂歡聚會文化 | *youth culture* 年輕人的文化 —see also 另見 SUBCULTURE

4 ▶ART/MUSIC/LITERATURE ETC 藝術/音樂/文學等◀ [U] activities that are related to art, music, literature etc 文化活動: *If it's culture you're looking for, the city has plenty of museums and art galleries.* 如果你要尋找文化, 這個城市有很多博物館和美術館。| **popular culture** (=the music, books, films etc that are liked by most people in a society) 流行文化

5 ▶SOCIETY 社會◀ [C] a society that existed at a particular time in history〔處於歷史上特定時期的〕社會: *primitive cultures* 原始社會 | *the Ancient Greek and Roman cultures* 古希臘和羅馬社會 —see also 另見 CIVILIZATION

6 ▶CROPS 作物◀ [U] *technical* the practice of growing crops【術語】栽培: *strawberry culture* 草莓的種植

7 ▶SCIENCE 科學◀ [C,U] the process of growing BACTERIA for scientific use, or the bacteria produced by this 細菌培養; 培養出的細菌

cul·tured /ˋkʌltʃɚd; ˈkʌltʃəd/ *adj* having had a good education so that you are interested in art, literature, music etc 有文化的, 有修養的: *a well-read and cultured woman* 博覽羣書有教養的女人

cultured pearl /͵.. ˈ./ *n* [C] a PEARL (1) that has been grown artificially 人工養殖珍珠

cul·vert /ˋkʌlvɚt; ˈkʌlvət/ *n* [C] a pipe that takes a stream under a road, railway line etc 排水渠, 陰溝, 涵洞

cum /kʌm; kʊm/ *prep* used between two nouns to show that something or someone has two purposes 兼, ...兩用: *a kitchen-cum-dining room* 廚房兼飯廳 | *a lunch-cum-business meeting* 工作午餐會

cum·ber·some /ˋkʌmbɚsəm; ˈkʌmbəsəm/ *adj* **1** a process or system that is cumbersome is slow and difficult〔過程或系統〕慢的, 累贅的: *The technique was cumbersome and created problems with sound reproduction.* 這項技術不是很靈活, 而且聲音失真。**2** heavy and difficult to move 笨重的: *cumbersome equipment that slowed us down considerably* 大大降低了我們的速度的笨重設備 **3** words or phrases that are cumbersome are long or complicated〔話或措辭〕冗長的; 晦澀的

cum·in /ˋkʌmɪn; ˈkʌmɪ̇n/ *n* [U] the seeds of a plant that have a sweet smell and are used in cooking, or the plant that they grow on 小茴香; 蒔蘿

cum lau·de /kum ˋlaudɪ; kʌm ˈlɔːdi/ *adv AmE* if you GRADUATE[3] (1) cum laude, you finish a university degree in the US and are given official praise for special achievement【美】以優等成績〔畢業於大學〕

cum·mer·bund /ˋkʌmɚ͵bʌnd; ˈkʌməbʌnd/ *n* [C] a wide piece of cloth that a man wears around his waist as part of a suit worn to very formal occasions〔男子在正式場合穿的〕寬腰帶

cum·quat, kumquat /ˋkʌmkwɑt; ˈkʌmkwɒt/ *n* [C] a fruit that looks like a very small orange 金橘

cu·mu·la·tive /ˋkjumjə͵letɪv; ˈkjuːmjʊ̇lətɪv/ *adj* increasing gradually as more of something is added or happens 積累的, 漸增的: *Learning is a cumulative process.* 學習是個逐漸積累的過程。| **cumulative effect (of)** *Depression is often caused by the cumulative effects of stress and over-work.* 抑鬱症通常是由壓力和過度工作逐漸積累引起的。

cu·mu·lus /ˋkjumjələs; ˈkjuːmjʊ̇ləs/ *n* [C,U] a thick white cloud with a flat bottom edge 積雲

cu·nei·form /kjuˋnɪə͵fɔrm; ˈkjuːnɪ̇fɔːm/ *adj* connected with the writing used by the people of ancient Mesopotamia〔古代美索不達米亞人使用的〕楔形文字的 —**cuneiform** *n* [U]

cun·ni·lin·gus /ˌkʌnəˈlɪŋgəs; ˌkʌnɪˈlɪŋgəs/ *n* [U] the act of touching the female sex organs with the lips and tongue in order to give sexual pleasure 舔陰〔用唇和舌頭刺激女性生殖器的性行為〕—compare 比較 FELLATIO

cun·ning¹ /ˈkʌnɪŋ; ˈkʌnɪŋ/ *adj* **1** someone who is cunning is good at deceiving people in order to get what they want〔人〕狡猾的, 狡詐的: *She can be very cunning when she wants to be.* 只要她願意, 她會非常狡猾。**2** behaviour or actions that are cunning are dishonest and unfair, and are used to get what you want〔行為或動作〕狡詐的, 狡猾的: *That was a cunning trick!* 那是一個狡猾的騙局! **3** a cunning object or piece of equipment is clever and unusual〔物體或設備〕巧妙的, 不同尋常的: *a cunning little device for keeping out draughts* 防風用的巧妙小裝置 **4** *AmE old-fashioned* attractive【美, 過時】可愛的, 吸引人的: *That's a cunning little dress you're wearing.* 你穿的衣服真精緻。—**cunningly** *adv*: *There was a microphone cunningly placed behind the picture.* 畫的後面非常巧妙地裝了麥克風。

cunning² *n* [U] the ability to achieve what you want by deceiving people in a clever way 狡猾, 狡詐: *the tiger's ferocity and cunning* 老虎的兇猛和狡詐 | **low cunning** (=unpleasant dishonest methods) 令人討厭而不誠實的方法, 花招 *She would use low cunning in order to win people's sympathy.* 她會為了贏得人們的同情耍花招。

cunt /kʌnt; kʌnt/ *n* [C] *spoken taboo*【口諱】**1** a stupid or unpleasant person 蠢人, 使人討厭的人: *Shut up, you stupid cunt!* 閉嘴, 你這個蠢貨! **2** a woman's VAGINA (=sex organ)〔女人的〕陰部, 陰道

cups 杯子

cup 杯子 | mug 大杯 | espresso cup 咖啡杯 | tankard *BrE*【英】/ stein *AmE*【美】啤酒杯

1 1 **cup¹** /kʌp; kʌp/ *n*

1 ▶FOR DRINKING FROM 飲具◀ [C] a small round container with a handle, that you use to drink tea, coffee etc 杯子: *a cup and saucer* 一副杯碟 | **tea cup/coffee cup** *a beautiful set of tea cups* 一套漂亮的茶杯 —compare 比較 MUG¹ (1)

2 ▶DRINK 飲料◀ [C] the liquid contained inside a cup〔杯中的〕液體: *Would you like another cup?* 要再來一杯嗎? | **[+of]** *a nice hot cup of coffee* 一杯美味的熱咖啡

3 ▶AMOUNT OF LIQUID 液體的量◀ [C] **a)** also 又作 **cupful** the amount of liquid a cup can hold 一杯的容量: *She came round to borrow a cupful of sugar.* 她過來借一杯糖。**b)** *AmE* an exact measure of quantity used in cooking in the US, Canada, and New Zealand【美】〔美國、加拿大、新西蘭烹飪計量的〕一杯: *Stir half a cup of sugar and one cup of flour into the batter.* 將半杯糖和一杯麵粉拌入麵糊裡攪拌。

4 ▶ROUND THING 圓形物◀ [C] something round and hollow that is shaped like a cup 杯狀物: *acorn cups* 橡碗〔橡果的殼斗〕| **[+of]** *the cup of a flower* 花萼 | *She held it in the cup of her hand.* 她把它捧在手裡。

5 ▶SPORT 體育運動◀ **a)** [C] a specially shaped silver container that is given as a prize in a competition, especially a sports competition 獎杯: *The president of the club came to present the cup to the winners.* 俱樂部的總裁給勝者頒發獎杯。**b)** [singular] *especially BrE* a sports competition【尤英】體育比賽: *She's been picked to play in the Wightman Cup.* 她入選參加懷特曼杯比賽。**c)** *AmE* a hole in the ground that you have to try to get the ball into in the game of GOLF【美】〔高爾夫球的〕球洞 —see picture on page A23 參見 A23 頁圖

6 ▶CLOTHING 衣服◀ [C] the part of a BRA that covers a woman's breast 乳罩窩

7 ▶MIXED DRINK 混合飲料◀ [C,U] *BrE* a mixed alcoholic drink【英】含酒精的混合飲料: *cider cup* 蘋果酒 | *a glass of champagne-cup* 一杯香檳混合飲料

8 not be your cup of tea *spoken* to not be the sort of thing that you like【口】不感興趣的東西, 不對胃口的事物: *Jazz just isn't my cup of tea – I prefer classical music.* 我不喜歡爵士樂, 我喜歡古典音樂。

9 in your cups *BrE old-fashioned* drunk, or when drunk【英, 過時】喝醉了; 在喝醉時: *He sometimes attempted to speak French, in his cups.* 他有時想藉着酒勁說法語。—see also 另見 EGGCUP, LOVING CUP

cup² *v* **cupped, cupping** [T] **1** to hold something in your hands, so that your hands form part of a circle around it 捧: *Phil cupped her face in his hands and kissed her.* 菲爾用手捧着她的臉親吻。**2 cup your hand(s)** to make a shape like a cup with your hand or hands 用手作杯狀: *He cupped his hands and I poured some water into them.* 他把雙手合成杯狀, 我便給他倒了些水。

cup·bear·er /ˈ· ˌ··/ *n* [C] someone in a royal court who serves wine on official occasions〔宮中〕在正式場合專司斟酒的侍酒官

cup·board /ˈkʌbəd; ˈkʌbəd/ *n* [C] a piece of furniture with doors, and sometimes shelves, used for storing clothes, plates, food etc 櫥櫃, 衣櫃; 碗櫃, 食品櫃: *It's in the kitchen cupboard.* 在廚房的碗櫃裡。| *The cupboard doors were open.* 櫥櫃的門開着。—see also 另見 AIRING CUPBOARD, **skeleton in the cupboard** (SKELETON (4)) —see picture on page A10 參見 A10 頁圖

cup·cake /ˈkʌpˌkek; ˈkʌpkeɪk/ *n* [C] a small round cake 杯形蛋糕

cup fi·nal /ˈ· ˌ··/ *n* [C] *BrE* the last and most important game in a competition, especially a football competition【英】〔尤指足球的〕決賽

cup·ful /ˈkʌpfʊl; ˈkʌpfʊl/ *n* [C] the amount that a cup can hold 一杯的容量 —see 見 CUP¹ (3)

cu·pid /ˈkjupɪd; ˈkjuːpɪd/ *n* **1** the Roman god of sexual love, represented as a beautiful boy with wings who is carrying a BOW³ (1) and ARROW (1) 丘比特〔愛神〕: *a sentimental picture with cupids around the edge* 一幅感傷的圖畫, 畫面周圍畫着丘比特 **2 play cupid** to try to arrange for two people to fall in love with each other 當月老, 做媒人: *She vowed never to play cupid again.* 她發誓再也不做紅娘。

cu·pid·i·ty /kjuˈpɪdətɪ; kjʊˈpɪdəti/ *n* [U] *formal* very strong desire for something, especially money or property; GREED (2)【正式】貪心, 貪財, 貪婪: *We were astounded by the young man's cupidity.* 這個年輕人的貪婪使我們震驚。

cu·po·la /ˈkjupələ; ˈkjuːpələ/ *n* [C] a small round part on top of a building 穹頂, 圓屋頂: *a golden edifice with an onion-shaped cupola* 一幢有洋葱形屋頂的金色大樓

cup·pa /ˈkʌpə; ˈkʌpə/ *n* [C] *BrE spoken* a cup of tea【英口】一杯茶: *I'm dying for a cuppa!* 我非常想喝一杯茶!

cu·pric /ˈkjuprɪk; ˈkjuːprɪk/ *adj technical* containing COPPER (1)【術語】含銅的

cup tie /ˈ· ·/ *n* [C] *BrE* a game between two teams in a competition in which only the winning team will play any more games【英】淘汰賽: *Saturday's FA Cup tie against Spurs* 星期六對熱刺隊的英國足總杯比賽

cur /kɝ; kɜː/ *n* [C] **1** *old-fashioned* an unfriendly dog, especially a MONGREL【過時】惡狗, 雜種狗 **2** *old use* an unpleasant person【舊】卑劣可鄙的人

cu·ra·ble /ˈkjurəbl; ˈkjʊərəbəl/ *adj* an illness that is curable can be cured〔病〕可醫好的 —opposite 反義詞 INCURABLE (1)

cu·ra·çao /ˌkjurəˈsau; ˈkjʊərəsəʊ/ *n* [U] a strong thick alcoholic drink that tastes of oranges 庫拉索酒〔一種帶有橙子味的醇酒〕

cu·ra·cy /ˈkjurəsɪ; ˈkjʊərəsi/ *n* [U] the job or position of curate or the period of time that someone has this position 助理牧師的工作[身分, 任期]: *My first curacy was in St Luke's.* 我第一次當助理牧師是在聖路加。

cu·rate /ˋkjʊrɪt; ˈkjʊərɪ̥t/ *n* [C] **1** a priest of the lowest rank, whose job is to help the priest who is in charge of an area 助理牧師 **2 curate's egg** something that has good and bad parts 質量優劣兼備的東西: *The book is something of a curate's egg.* 這本書的質量不好也不壞。

cu·ra·tive /ˋkjʊrətɪv; ˈkjʊərətɪv/ *adj* able to, or intended to cure illness 有療效的: *the curative effects of lemon juice on scurvy victims* 檸檬汁對壞血病人的治療效果 — **curative** *n* [C]: *This herb was once thought to be a curative.* 這種草藥曾被認為能治病。

cu·ra·tor /kjuˋretə; kjʊˈreɪtə/ *n* [C] someone who is in charge of a MUSEUM 博物館館長: *He's Curator of Prints at the Metropolitan.* 他是大都會藝術博物館版畫部館長。

curb¹ /kɝb; kɜːb/ *v* [T] to control or limit something in order to prevent it from having a harmful effect 控制, 抑制, 約束: *measures to curb the spread of the virus* 抑制病毒擴散的措施

curb² *n* [C] **1** an influence which helps to control or limit something 控制, 約束, 抑制: **[+on]** *We are trying to keep a curb on their activities.* 我們正設法控制他們的活動。 **2** *AmE* the edge of the part of a road where people can walk【美】路緣; KERB *BrE*【英】

curb crawler /ˈ· ˌ··/ *n* [C] the American spelling of KERB CRAWLER kerb crawler 的美式拼法

curd /kɝd; kɜːd/ *n* [U] also 又作 **curds** *plural* the thick substance that forms in milk when it becomes sour 凝乳

cur·dle /ˋkɝdl̩; ˈkɜːdl/ *v* [I,T] **1** to become thicker or form curd, or to make a liquid do this (使)變稠; (使)凝結: *Milk may curdle in warm weather.* 天暖時牛奶會凝結。 **2 make your blood curdle** to make you very frightened 使極度驚恐 —see also 另見 BLOODCURDLING

cu·r·é /kjuˋre; ˈkjʊəreɪ/ *n* [C] a PARISH (1) priest in France 〔法國的〕教區神父

cure¹ /kjur; kjʊə/ *v* [T] **1** to make someone who is ill well again 治癒〔病人〕: *The doctors did everything they could to cure her, but she died three months later.* 儘管醫生盡了一切努力來治她的病, 但三個月後她還是死了。| *When I left hospital I was completely cured.* 出院時我已痊癒了。**2** to make an illness disappear completely, usually by medical treatment 治癒, 治好〔疾病〕: *an operation to cure a hernia problem* 治療疝氣的手術 **3** to remove a problem, or improve a bad situation 解決〔問題〕; 改善〔困境〕: *Attempts to cure unemployment have so far failed.* 到目前為止, 解決失業問題的種種努力都失敗了。| **cure sb of** *Even whisky could not cure him of his anxieties.* 連威士忌也不能消除他的憂慮。**4** to preserve food, tobacco etc by drying it, hanging it in smoke, or covering it with salt 〔用曬、熏、醃等方法〕保存〔食品、煙草等〕: *cured ham* 醃製的火腿

cure² *n* [C] **1** a medicine or medical treatment that can cure an illness 藥, 藥劑; 療法: **[+for]** *a cure for cancer* 治癌法 **2** something that removes a problem, or improves a bad situation 對策: *a cure for inflation* 解決通貨膨脹的對策 **3** the act of making someone well again after an illness 治癒: *The new treatment effected a miraculous cure.* 這種新療法產生了奇跡般的療效。**4 take the cure** the practice in former times of going to a SPA (1) in order to improve your health 〔舊時〕進行礦泉治療

cure-all /ˈ· ·/ *n* [C] something that people think will cure any problem 萬應靈藥, 靈丹妙藥: *Privatisation is seen as a cure-all.* 私有化被視作靈丹妙藥。

cu·ret·tage /kjuˋrɛtɪdʒ; kjʊəˈretɪdʒ/ *n* [U] *technical* medical treatment to remove unhealthy flesh or skin【術語】刮除術

cur·few /ˋkɝfju; ˈkɜːfjuː/ *n* **1** [C] a law forcing everyone to stay indoors from a particular time in the evening until a particular time in the morning 宵禁: *The military regime decided to impose a curfew.* 軍政府決定實行宵禁。**2** [singular, not with *the* 不與 the 連用] the time after which everyone must stay indoors, according to this law 宵禁時間: *Anyone found in the streets after curfew will be shot.* 違反宵禁者格殺勿論。

cu·ri·o /ˋkjurɪˌo; ˈkjʊəriəʊ/ *n plural* **curios** [C] a small object that is valuable because it is old, beautiful, or rare 古物, 古董; 珍品: *Sue came across a shop selling curios and antiques.* 蘇正好碰到一家賣古董文物的商店。

cu·ri·os·i·ty /ˌkjurɪˋɑsətɪ; ˌkjʊəriˈɒsɪ̥ti/ *n* **1** [singular, U] the desire to know about something, or to know about a lot of different things 好奇心, 求知慾: **[+about]** *Children have a natural curiosity about the world around them.* 兒童對周圍的世界有天然的好奇心。| **out of curiosity** *Just out of curiosity, how old are you?* 只是出於好奇, 請問你多大? | **burning/bursting with curiosity** (=having an extremely strong desire to know something) 非常好奇 | **idle curiosity** (=the desire to know something that you do not need to know) 無謂的好奇, 多餘的好奇 *It's not just idle curiosity.* 這並非只是無謂的好奇心。| **satisfy your curiosity** (=find out what you want to know) 滿足自己的好奇心 *I just had to satisfy my curiosity, so I opened the parcel.* 我只是想滿足自己的好奇心, 於是打開了包裹。**2** [C] something that is interesting because it is unusual or strange 奇品, 珍品: *His house was full of old maps and other curiosities.* 他的房子裡裝滿了舊地圖和其他珍品。**3 curiosity killed the cat** an expression used to tell someone not to ask questions about something that does not concern them 過於好奇會惹禍上身; 不關自己的事不要打聽

cu·ri·ous /ˋkjurɪəs; ˈkjʊəriəs/ *adj* **1** wanting to know about something 好奇的, 好打聽的: *When I mentioned her name everyone was very curious.* 我提到她的名字時, 大家都很好奇。| **[+about]** *I'm curious about this book she's supposed to be writing.* 我對她據說在寫的那本書感到好奇。| **curious to see/hear/know etc** *Mandy was curious to hear what Peter had to say for himself.* 曼蒂很想知道彼得自己怎麼說。—opposite 反義詞 INCURIOUS **2** strange or unusual 稀奇古怪的: *a curious noise coming from the cellar* 地窖裡傳來的怪聲 | **curious that** *It's very curious that she left without saying goodbye.* 她沒道別就離開了, 真奇怪。—**curiously** *adv*: *She watched curiously as I opened the box.* 她好奇地看着我打開盒子。 S3

curl¹ /kɝl; kɜːl/ *n* **1** [C] a small mass of hair that hangs in a curving shape 鬈髮: *a little boy with beautiful blonde curls* 有漂亮的金黃色鬈髮的小男孩 **2** [C] something that forms a curved shape 卷曲物, 螺旋狀物: *A curl of smoke rose from her cigarette.* 她的香煙冒出一縷青煙。**3 a curl of your lip/mouth** a sideways and upwards movement of your lip or mouth, showing that you disapprove of someone or something 撇嘴〔表示不贊同〕

curl² *v* [I,T] **1** to form a twisted or curved shape or to make something do this 盤繞, 纏繞: *Ivy curled round the trunk of the tree.* 常春藤纏繞着樹幹。| **curl sth** *Maria used to curl her hair each week.* 瑪麗亞過去每週燙一次髮。**2** [I always+adv/prep T, always+adv/prep] to move, forming a twisted or curved shape, or to make something do this (使)彎曲: **[+across/along etc]** *Morning mists curled across the surface of the river.* 晨霧在河面繚繞瀰漫。| **curl sth around/round/over etc** *The baby curled his fingers around my thumb.* 寶寶用手指攥着我的大拇指。**3** if you curl your lip, or if your lip curls, you move it upwards and sideways, to show that you disapprove of someone or something 〔表示反對〕撇〔嘴〕: *Her lip curled in contempt.* 她輕蔑地撇撇嘴。**4 make your hair curl** *spoken* if a story, experience etc would make your hair curl it is very surprising, frightening, or shocking【口】〔故事、經歷等〕使人毛骨悚然, 使…戰慄: *The stories they tell about him would make your hair curl.* 他們講的有關他的事會使你毛骨悚然。—see also 另見 **make sb's toes curl** (TOE¹ (5))

curl up *phr v* [I] **1** to lie or sit with your arms and legs bent close to your body 蜷縮: *I just wanted to curl up*

C

and go to sleep. 我只想蜷着身體睡覺。**2** if something flat curls up, its edges start to become curved and point upwards 捲曲: *The letter was now yellow and beginning to curl up.* 現在, 這信已發黃並開始捲曲。**3** to move upwards in the form of a curl or curls 彎曲着上升, 螺旋着上升: *Wisps of smoke were already curling up from the fireplace.* 壁爐裡已裊裊升起一縷縷煙。

curl·er /ˋkɝlɚ; ˈkɜːlə/ *n* [C] [usually plural 一般用複數] a small plastic or metal tube used for making hair curl 捲髮夾: *Edith came to the door with her hair in curlers.* 伊迪絲帶着滿頭髮捲走到門口。

cur·lew /ˋkɝlu; ˈkɜːljuː/ *n* [C] a brown and grey bird with long legs and a curved beak, that lives near water or damp areas of land〔生活在水邊或濕地的〕鷸

cur·li·cue, curlycue /ˋkɝlɪˌkju; ˈkɜːlɪkjuː/ *n* [C] a decorative twisted pattern 花體, 卷曲裝飾物

curl·ing /ˋkɝlɪŋ; ˈkɜːlɪŋ/ *n* [U] a winter sport played on ice by sliding flat heavy stones towards a marked point 冰上溜石遊戲〔一種冬季運動〕

curling tongs /ˈ·· ˌ·/ *BrE*【英】also 又作 **curling i·rons** /ˈ·· ˌ··/ *especially AmE*【尤美】*n* [plural] a piece of electrical equipment that you heat and use to put curls in your hair 燙髮鉗, 捲髮鉗

3 **curl·y** /ˋkɝlɪ; ˈkɜːli/ *adj* having a lot of curls 彎彎曲曲的: *long dark curly hair* 又長又黑的鬈髮 —**curliness** *n* [U]

cur·mud·geon /kɚˋmʌdʒən; kɜːˈmʌdʒən/ *n* [C] *old-fashioned* an old person who is often angry or annoyed【過時】脾氣壞的老人 —**curmudgeonly** *adj*

cur·rant /ˋkɝənt; ˈkʌrənt/ *n* [C] a small dried GRAPE used especially in baking cakes〔尤用於製糕點的〕葡萄乾: *currant bun* 有葡萄乾的小圓麵包

2 **cur·ren·cy** /ˋkɝənsɪ; ˈkʌrənsi/ *n* **1** [C,U] the system or type of money that a particular country uses 貨幣, 通貨: *The stronger currencies are under pressure in the world markets.* 強勢貨幣在國際市場上受到壓力。| *decimal currencies* 十進制貨幣 | **local currency** *The local currency is francs.* 當地貨幣是法郎。—see also 另見 HARD CURRENCY, SINGLE CURRENCY **2** [U] the state of being generally accepted or used 流傳, 流通; 被接受, 傳播: **wide currency** (=accepted by many people) 廣泛傳播 *The idea enjoys wide currency in 20th century fiction.* 這種觀點在20世紀的小說裡得到廣泛傳播。| **gain currency** (=become accepted) 被接受 *Marxism began to gain currency.* 馬克思主義開始被人們所接受。

1 1 **cur·rent¹** /ˋkɝənt; ˈkʌrənt/ *adj* [only before noun 僅用於名詞前] happening or existing now but not expected to last for a long time 現時的, 當前的, 現行的: *her current boyfriend* 她的現任男友 —**currently** *adv*: *Sir Ranulph is currently occupied writing a book about his Antarctic expedition.* 雷納夫爵士目前正忙於寫一本關於他在南極探險的書。

current² *n* [C] **1** a continuous movement of water in a particular direction in the sea or in a river 流; 水流: *The current was very strong.* 水流很急。**2** a flow of electricity through a wire 電流

current ac·count /ˈ·· ·ˌ·/ *n* [C] *BrE* a bank account that you can take money out of at any time【英】活期存款賬戶; CHECKING ACCOUNT *AmE*【美】—compare 比較 DEPOSIT ACCOUNT

current af·fairs /ˌ·· ·ˈ·/ *n* [U] important political events or other events in society that are happening now 時事

2 2 **currently** /ˋkɝəntlɪ; ˈkʌrəntli/ *adv* at the present time 現時, 當前: *Two major changes are currently being considered.* 當前正在考慮兩個主要的變化。| *They need more help than is currently available.* 他們對幫助的需求比當前能得到的要多。—see 見 ACTUALLY (USAGE)

2 **cur·ric·u·lum** /kəˋrɪkjələm; kəˈrɪkjʊləm/ *n plural* **curricula** /-lə; -lə/ or **curriculums** [C] the subjects that are taught by a school, college etc, or the things that are studied in a particular subject 課程: *Has computer studies been introduced into the school curriculum?* 電腦科列入學校課程了嗎? —compare 比較 SYLLABUS

curriculum vi·tae /kəˌrɪkjələm ˋvitaɪ; kəˌrɪkjʊləm ˈviːtaɪ/ *n* [C] **1** *BrE* a CV【英】簡歷; RESUMÉ² (2) *AmE*【美】**2** *AmE* a document on which a university teacher writes a list of their teaching experience and articles, books etc they have written when they are applying for a job【美】〔大學教師求職的〕簡歷, 個人履歷

cur·ry¹ /ˋkɝɪ; ˈkʌri/ *n* [C,U] a type of food from India consisting of meat or vegetables covered in a thick liquid with a hot taste 咖喱食品

curry² *v* [T] **1** to make meat or vegetables into curry 把〔肉、蔬菜〕做成咖喱食品 **2 curry favour with** to try to make someone like you or notice you in order to get something that you want 討好, 奉承, 拍馬屁: *currying favour with the teachers* 討好老師

curry pow·der /ˈ·· ˌ··/ *n* [U] a mixture of SPICES (=dried vegetable parts with a hot taste) crushed into a fine powder, used in cooking 咖喱粉

curse¹ /kɝs; kɜːs/ *v* **1** [I] to swear 咒罵: *You should have heard him cursing when he tripped over the cat.* 你真該聽聽他被貓絆倒時是如何咒罵的。**2** [T] to say or think bad things about someone or something because they have made you angry〔嘴上或心裡〕臭罵: **curse sb/sth for (doing) sth** *I cursed myself for not buying a phrase book.* 我因沒買一本片語書而咒罵自己。**3** [T] to ask God or a magical power to harm someone 詛咒: *The man had been cursed by a witch doctor and was in despair.* 那男人因受巫醫的詛咒而感到絕望。

curse² *n* [C] **1** a word or words that you use when you swear or when you express anger etc 罵人話: *The convict screamed out curses at them.* 囚犯吼着髒話來罵他們。**2** a word or sentence used to ask God or a magical power to make something happen to someone or something 詛咒, 咒語: **put a curse on** *The witch doctor put a curse on him.* 巫醫詛咒他。**3** something that causes trouble, harm etc 禍因, 禍根: **[+to]** *Foxes can be a curse to farmers.* 狐狸可能成為農民的一大禍害。**4 the curse** *old-fashioned* an expression meaning MENSTRUATION【過時】月經

curs·ed /ˋkɝsɪd; ˈkɜːsɪ̆d/ *adj* **1 be cursed with** to suffer because of a problem that you have 受折磨的, 痛苦的: *She had always been cursed with ill-health.* 她總是受疾病的折磨。**2** [only before noun 僅用於名詞前] *old-fashioned* unpleasant or annoying【過時】討厭的; 煩人的: *I'm sick to death of being stuck in this cursed place.* 被困在這個討厭的地方, 我簡直煩死了。**3** *literary* suffering as a result of a punishment by God or a god【文】被詛咒的 —**cursedly** *adv*

cur·sive /ˋkɝsɪv; ˈkɜːsɪv/ *adj* written in a flowing rounded style of writing with the letters joined together〔字跡〕草寫的,〔字母間〕連筆的: *cursive script* 草體 —**cursively** *adv*

cur·sor /ˋkɝsɚ; ˈkɜːsə/ *n* [C] a mark or a small light which can be moved around a computer screen to show where you are working〔電腦的〕光標

cur·so·ry /ˋkɝsərɪ; ˈkɜːsəri/ *adj* quick and done without enough attention to details 粗略的, 草率的, 倉促的: *After only a cursory glance he tore up the note.* 他粗略看了一下紙條便將它撕掉了。—**cursorily** *adv*

curt /kɝt; kɜːt/ *adj* replying with very few words in a way that does not seem polite〔人言語舉止〕簡慢無禮的, 唐突的: *With a curt nod, he turned away and sat down.* 他匆匆點了下頭, 轉身坐下。—**curtly** *adv* —**curtness** *n* [U]

cur·tail /kɚˋtel; kɜːˈteɪl/ *v* [T] *formal* to reduce something such as the amount of money you spend【正式】減少, 縮減, 削減: *The Government wants private firms to curtail wage rises.* 政府希望私營公司縮減工資增幅。| *Our evening's enjoyment was curtailed when Alfred became ill.* 阿爾弗雷德病了, 我們的晚間娛樂活動便減少了。—**curtailment** *n* [C,U]

cur·tain /ˋkɝtn̩; ˈkɜːtn/ *n* [C] **1** a piece of hanging cloth that can be pulled across to cover a window, door etc to divide a room etc 窗簾; 門簾; 簾子: **draw the curtains** (=close the curtains) 拉上簾子 **2** a sheet of heavy material that can be made to come down across the front of the stage in a theatre〔舞台上的〕幕 —see picture at 參見 THEATRE 圖 **3** a thick layer of something that stops anything behind it from being seen 幕狀物, 簾狀物: *a thick curtain of smoke* 濃厚的煙幕 | *a curtain of trailing branches* 下垂的枝條形成的幕 **4 the curtain falls on** *literary* if the curtain falls on an event or period of history, it ends【文】〔事件〕落幕;〔時代〕結束 **5 it'll be curtains for sb/sth** *informal* used to say that someone will die, or that something will end【非正式】該完蛋了: *It'll be curtains for you if they find you here!* 如果他們發現你在這兒, 你就完蛋了!

curtain call /ˈ·· ·/ *n* [C] the time at the end of a performance when the actors come out to receive APPLAUSE〔演員的〕謝幕

curtain hook /ˈ·· ·/ *n* [C] a small hook which is joined to the top of a curtain so that you can hang it up 窗簾鉤, 門簾鉤

curtain rail /ˈ·· ·/ *n* [C] a long piece of plastic or metal that you hang a curtain on 窗簾杆, 門簾杆

curtain rais·er /ˈ·· ˌ··/ *n* [C] **1** a short play, film etc that is performed or shown before the main one〔正戲前的〕開場小戲;〔電影的〕開場短片 **2** a small thing that happens or is done just before something more important 前奏, 引子: *a curtain raiser for the main programme of research* 主要研究項目的前奏

curt·sy, curtsey /ˈkɝtsɪ; ˈkɜːtsi/ *n* [C] a sign of respect that a woman makes to a more important person by bending her knees with one foot behind the other〔女子行的〕屈膝禮 —**curtsy** *v* [I] —compare 比較 BOW² (1)

cur·va·ceous, curvacious /kɝˋveʃəs; kɜːˈveɪʃəs/ *adj* having an attractively curved body shape 有曲線美的, 豐滿而勻稱的: *curvacious female models* 身材優美的女模特兒 —**curvaceousness** *n* [U]

cur·va·ture /ˈkɝvətʃɚ; ˈkɜːvətʃə/ *n* [C,U] *technical*【術語】**1** the state of being curved, or the degree to which something is curved 彎曲(的形態); 曲率: *the curvature of the Earth's surface* 地表的曲率 **2** a medical condition in which part of someone's body curves in a way that is not natural〔人體病態的〕彎曲: *curvature of the spine* 脊柱彎曲

3 3 **curve¹** /kɝv; kɜːv/ *n* [C] **1** a line which gradually bends like part of a circle 曲線, 弧線: *a curve on a graph* 圖表上的曲線 | *the curve of her hips* 她的臀部曲線 **2** a rounded bend in a road, river etc〔道路、河流等的〕彎曲處: *The car took the curve much too quickly.* 那輛汽車拐彎太快了。**3 curve ball** a throw in BASEBALL in which the ball spins so that it curves suddenly and is difficult to hit〔棒球的〕曲線球 **4** *AmE*【美】**throw sb a curve** to surprise someone with a question or problem that is difficult to deal with〔提出疑問或問題〕使…感到突然[棘手]; 戲弄: *They threw us a curve and asked us about Longfellow when we were ready for a question on Thoreau.* 我們準備好了回答有關梭羅的問題, 他們卻問我們有關朗費羅的問題, 這讓我們措手不及。

curve² *v* [I,T] to bend or move in the shape of a curve, or to make something do this 弄彎, (使)彎曲: *The track curved into the woods.* 小路彎彎曲曲地拐進森林裡。

curved /kɝvd; kɜːvd/ *adj* having a shape that is rounded and not straight 彎曲的: *a sword with a curved blade* 彎刀

curv·y /ˈkɝvɪ; ˈkɜːvi/ *adj* having a shape with several curves 弧形的, 有曲線的: *her curvy red lips* 她弧形的紅嘴唇 | *Eileen has a curvy figure.* 艾琳的身材曲線玲瓏。

3 **cush·ion¹** /ˈkʊʃən; ˈkʊʃən/ *n* [C] **1** a cloth bag filled with soft material that you put on a chair to make it more comfortable 墊子 —compare 比較 PILLOW¹ (1) **2** something that stops one thing from hitting another thing 墊形物, 起墊子作用的東西; 緩衝物: *The hovercraft rides on a cushion of air.* 氣墊船行駛在空氣墊子上。**3** something, especially money, that prevents you from being affected by a situation immediately〔尤指金錢〕起緩解作用的東西; 防備不時之需的積蓄: *I have some savings – hopefully they'll act as a cushion while I'm looking for a job.* 我有一些積蓄, 希望能幫助我度過找工作的那段日子。**4** the soft rubber edge of the table that is used for playing BILLIARDS or SNOOKER¹〔枱球桌的〕橡皮邊, 彈性襯邊

cushion² *v* [T] **1** to make a fall or knock less painful, for example by having something soft in the way 緩衝: *They had put mattresses on the ground to cushion his fall.* 他們已在地上鋪好褥墊, 以緩解他落地時的衝擊。**2** to reduce the effects of something unpleasant 減輕〔令人不愉快的〕效果: **cushion the blow** *generous leaving allowances to help cushion the blow of redundancy* 慷慨的離職補貼以減輕裁員所帶來的打擊 | **be cushioned against** (=be protected from something unpleasant) 使…免遭困苦衝擊 *The rich are cushioned against the effects of the recession.* 富人能應付經濟不景氣的衝擊。

cush·y /ˈkʊʃɪ; ˈkʊʃi/ *adj* **cushier, cushiest** *informal* very easy【非正式】輕鬆的, 容易的: *I wish I had a nice cushy job like her.* 我希望有份像她那樣輕鬆的好工作。| **a cushy number** *BrE* (=an easy job)【英】輕鬆的工作

cusp /kʌsp; kʌsp/ *n* [C] **1** *technical* the point formed by two curves meeting【術語】尖(角); 兩條曲線的交點 **2 on the cusp** someone who was born on the cusp was born near the time when one STAR SIGN ends and another one begins〔占星術〕兩宮會切時段

cus·pi·dor /ˈkʌspəˌdɔr; ˈkʌspɪdɔː/ *n* [C] *AmE* a container for people to SPIT¹ (1,2) in; SPITTOON【美】痰盂

cuss¹ /kʌs; kʌs/ *v* [I,T] *AmE informal, BrE old-fashioned* to use rude words because you are annoyed by something【美, 非正式; 英, 過時】詛咒, 咒罵: *It does a fella good to cuss if he wants to.* 如果他想罵, 罵一通對他是有好處的。

cuss sb **out** *phr v* [T] *AmE spoken* to swear and shout at someone because you are angry【美口】咒罵: *My Mom cussed me out for breaking the lamp.* 我打碎了燈, 媽媽因此而大罵我。

cuss² *n* [C] *AmE old-fashioned* **stubborn/stupid/ornery etc cuss** a very annoying person【美, 過時】討厭的傢伙, 賤骨頭

cuss·ed /ˈkʌsɪd; ˈkʌsɪd/ *adj* behaving in a deliberately unhelpful way 彆扭的, 頑固的 —**cussedness** *n* [U]

cuss word /ˈ· ·/ *n* [C] *AmE* a SWEAR WORD【美】詛咒, 罵人話

cus·tard /ˈkʌstɚd; ˈkʌstəd/ *n* **1** [U] *especially BrE* a yellow liquid that is eaten with sweet dishes, made with milk, sugar, eggs, and flour【尤英】牛奶蛋糊, 蛋奶甜羹 **2** [C,U] a soft baked mixture of milk, sugar, and eggs 乳蛋糕

custard pie /ˌ·· ˈ·/ *n* [C] a PIE filled with custard, which people throw at each other as a joke in films etc〔電影中當作玩笑相互扔的〕蛋奶餡餅

cus·to·di·al /kʌsˋtodɪəl; kʌˈstəʊdiəl/ *adj formal* connected with the custody of someone【正式】監護的, 看守的, 監禁的: *custodial care* 看護

custodial sen·tence /ˌ···· ˈ··/ *n* [C] *law* a period of time that someone has to spend in prison as a punishment【法律】刑期

cus·to·di·an /kʌsˋtodɪən; kʌˈstəʊdiən/ *n* [C] **1** someone who is responsible for looking after a public building or a collection of valuable objects〔公共建築或貴重物品的〕監護人, 看守人, 保管人 **2 custodian of tradition/moral values etc** someone who tries to protect a traditional set of beliefs, attitudes etc〔傳統價值、道德等的〕捍衛者

cus·to·dy /ˈkʌstədɪ; ˈkʌstədi/ *n* [U] **1** the right to take care of a child, especially when the child's parents are legally separating from each other 監護權〔尤指父母離異後對孩子的監護〕: **[+of]** *In most divorce cases the mother is awarded custody of the children.* 大部分離婚案中, 孩子的監護權判歸母親。| **have custody** *a dispute over who should have custody* 關於監護權歸屬問題的

C

爭執 **2 in custody** being kept in prison by the police until you go to court, because the police think you are guilty 拘留, 監禁〔警方認定有罪, 庭審前的羈押〕: **hold/keep sb in custody** *A man is being held in police custody in connection with the murder.* 一名男子因涉及此樁謀殺案而被警方拘留。| **take sb into custody** (=catch someone and keep them in custody) 拘捕監禁某人 **3 in sb's custody** *formal* being kept and looked after by someone【正式】由…保管: *The silver seal was placed in the custody of the mayor.* 這枚銀圖章由市長保管。

3 **cus·tom** /ˈkʌstəm; ˈkʌstəm/ *n* **1** [C,U] something that is done by people in a particular society because it is traditional 風俗, 習慣, 傳統: **local/tribal/ancient/Swedish etc custom** *"Why the pile of salt?" "It's an old Japanese custom."* "那個鹽堆是甚麼意思?" "那是古老的日本習俗。" | **it is the custom (for sb) to do sth** *It's the custom for the bride's father to pay for the wedding.* 根據傳統, 由新娘父親支付婚禮費用。| **the custom of doing sth** *the old French custom of serving the vegetables separate from the meat* 蔬菜與肉類分開端上桌的法國舊俗 | **by custom/according to the custom** *By custom we had to stop and speak to every person we met.* 按照習俗, 我們必須停下和遇到的每個人說幾句。**2** [singular] *especially literary* something that you usually do every day, or in a particular situation【尤文】日常習慣: *He awoke early, as was his custom.* 他每天醒得很早, 這是他的習慣。—see 見 HABIT (USAGE) **3** [U] *formal* the practice of regularly using a particular shop or business【正式】〔經常性的〕惠顧, 光顧 **4 customs** [plural] the place where your bag is checked for illegal drugs, guns etc when you go into a country 海關: *She was stopped at customs and questioned.* 她在海關被攔下來接受問話。| **clear customs** (=be allowed through customs after being checked) 清關, 海關檢查後放行

cus·tom·a·ry /ˈkʌstəmˌɛrɪ; ˈkʌstəməri/ *adj* **1** something that is customary is normal because it is the way something is usually done 風俗的, 慣例的: **it is customary (for sb) to do sth** *It is customary for the most important person to sit at the end of the table.* 按慣例, 最重要的人坐首席。**2** someone's customary behaviour is the way they usually do things〔人〕習慣性的: *Barbara answered with her customary frankness.* 巴巴拉以慣有的坦率回答。—**customarily** /ˌkʌstəˈmɛrɪlɪ; ˈkʌstəmərəli/ *adv*

custom-built /ˌ·· ˈ·◂/ *adj* a custom-built car, house etc has been specially designed and made for a particular person〔汽車、房子等〕定製的, 定做的

1 1 **cus·tom·er** /ˈkʌstəmɚ; ˈkʌstəmə/ *n* [C] **1** someone who buys goods or services from a shop, company etc 顧客, 客戶: *Next customer please!* 請下一位顧客! | *the customer complaints department* 客戶投訴部 | **regular customer** *keeping the shop's regular customers happy* 讓老客戶滿意 | **sb's biggest/best customer** (=someone who buys the most goods or services) 最大/最佳客戶 *We don't want to lose them – they're one of our biggest customers.* 他們是我們最大的客戶之一, 我們不想失去。—compare 比較 PATRON (2) —see picture on page A15 參見A15頁圖 **2 a cool customer** *informal* someone who is always calm and very confident but in an unpleasant way【非正式】冷靜但討厭的人 **3 awkward/tricky etc customer** someone who is difficult to deal with because they behave in a deliberately unhelpful way 難對付的/詭計多端的傢伙

cus·tom·ize also 又作 **-ise** *BrE*【英】/ˈkʌstəmˌaɪz; ˈkʌstəmaɪz/ *v* [T] to change something to make it more suitable for you, or to make it look special or unusual 定做, 定製; 按規格改製: *The program allows computer users to customize the menu.* 該程序允許電腦用戶自定項目單。| *a customized car* 定製的汽車

custom-made /ˌ·· ˈ·◂/ *adj* a custom-made pair of shoes, shirt etc is specially made for a particular person〔鞋、襯衫等〕定製的, 定做的

Customs and Ex·cise /ˌ·· · ˈ··/ *n* [singular] the department of the British government that is responsible for collecting the tax on goods that are being bought or sold or have been brought into the country〔英國的〕關稅及消費稅務局

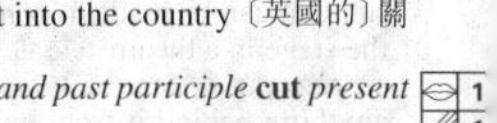

cut¹ /kʌt; kʌt/ *v past tense and past participle* **cut** *present participle* **cutting** 1 1

1 ►DIVIDE WITH KNIFE ETC 用刀等分開◄ [T] to divide something into two or more pieces using a sharp tool such as a knife 切, 割: *Do you want me to cut the cake?* 要我切蛋糕嗎? | *The thieves had cut the phone wires.* 小偷把電話線割斷了。| **cut sth in half/in two** *cut the orange in half* 將橙子對半切開 | **cut sth into quarters/pieces/four** *Cut each one into about 6 pieces.* 把每一個切成六塊左右。

2 ►REMOVE A PIECE OF 去掉某個部分◄ [T] to use a knife to remove a piece from the main part of something 切除, 割下, 削掉: **cut sth** *I cut another slice of bread.* 我又切下一片麵包。| **cut sb sth** *Cut me a big slice of that lemon cake, will you?* 把那個檸檬蛋糕切一大塊給我, 好嗎?

3 ►MAKE A SHAPE 做成某形狀◄ [T] to make something into a particular shape by using a sharp tool such as a knife 雕鑿, 剪[割, 削, 砍]成: **cut sth into chunks/rings etc** *Cut the carrots into small cubes.* 把胡蘿蔔切成小方塊。

4 ►MAKE A HOLE 鑽洞[孔]◄ [I,T] to make a hole in the surface of something, or to open it by using a sharp tool such as a knife 鑿[挖]〔洞〕: **[+into/through etc]** *a knife that will cut through glass* 可以劃開玻璃的刀 | **cut a hole in sth** *Firefighters had to cut a hole in the car roof.* 消防員不得不在車頂開個洞。| **cut sth open** *Ben cut the sack open in a great hurry to see what was inside.* 本匆忙割開袋子, 看看裡面有甚麼。

5 ►GRASS/HAIR ETC 草/毛髮等◄ [T] to make something shorter with a knife, scissors etc in order to improve its appearance 修理, 修剪: **cut the lawn/the grass/the hedge** *I think I'll cut the grass this afternoon if it doesn't rain.* 如果不下雨, 我想下午修剪草地。| **have/get your hair cut** (=pay someone to cut your hair) 理髮 *Where do you have your hair cut?* 你在哪兒理髮?

6 cut sb free/loose to allow someone to escape by using a knife to cut the rope that they are tied by〔割斷繩索〕讓…逃走, 放走

7 ►CROPS 農作物◄ [T] to take the top part off crops such as wheat before gathering them 收割〔莊稼〕: *cutting corn* 收割玉米

8 ►WOUND 傷害◄ [T] to injure yourself when a sharp object or surface breaks open your skin so that you start bleeding 劃破, 劃傷, 割傷: **cut your finger/knee/hand etc** *Be careful not to cut your fingers with that knife – it's very sharp.* 小心, 別割破手指 —— 那把刀很鋒利。| **cut yourself (on sth)** *I cut myself quite badly on a piece of glass.* 我被一塊玻璃嚴重劃傷。| **cut sth open** (=injure part of your body by cutting it on something) 把…割傷 *He fell and cut his head open.* 他跌倒了, 把頭割破了。

9 ►REDUCE PRICES/TIME/MONEY ETC 縮減價格/時間/錢等◄ [T] to reduce something a lot, especially prices, time, or money 削減, 裁減, 減少: *A secure home will cut the risk of burglary.* 有安全防護設備的家可減少被盜的危險。| **cut sth by a quarter/25% etc** *Marston's is to cut its workforce by 20%.* 馬斯頓公司將裁員20%。| **cut sth off/from/to etc** *The new direct service will cut 2 hours off the flying time between London and Seoul.* 新的直航將使倫敦與漢城間的航程縮短兩個小時。

10 ►FILM/SPEECH 影片/演講◄ [T] **a)** to reduce the length of a film, speech etc 刪剪, 縮短: *The original version was cut by more than 30 minutes.* 原版被刪去了三十多分鐘。**b)** to remove part of a film, speech, or piece of writing, for example because it might offend people 刪節〔影片、演講、文字等以免冒犯人〕, 剪掉 **c)** to put the parts of a film together so that they make a continuous story and get rid of the parts you do not want 剪輯〔影片〕 **d) Cut!** *spoken* said by the director of a film to tell everyone to stop acting, stop filming etc【口】停!〔導演口令〕

11 ▶DIVIDE AN AREA 劃分區域◀ [T] to divide an area into two or more parts 劃分〔區域〕: **cut sth in/into** *The river cuts the valley in two.* 那條河將山谷一分為二。

12 ▶PLAYING CARDS 打牌◀ [I,T] to divide a pack of cards into two 切(牌), 倒(牌)

13 ▶MUSIC/RECORD 音樂/唱片◀ [T] if a musician cuts a record, they make a record of their music 灌製唱片

14 ▶LINE 線條◀ [T] if a line cuts another line, they cross each other at a particular point〔一條線〕與〔另一條線〕相交

15 ▶TOOTH 牙齒◀ if a baby cuts a tooth, the tooth starts to grow 長新牙

16 cut your teeth on sth to get your first experience of doing something by practising on something simple 從〔簡單的情況〕獲得初步經驗

17 cut in line *AmE* to unfairly go in front of other people who are waiting to buy or do something【美】插隊, 不按次序排隊; **jump the queue** (JUMP¹ (17)) *BrE*【英】

18 cut class *AmE informal* to deliberately not go to a class that you should go to【美, 非正式】逃課: *I cut class to go hang out in the bar.* 我逃課去泡酒吧。

19 cut corners to do something in a way that is not perfect, in order to save time, effort, or money〔做事〕抄近路, 走捷徑

20 cut sth short to stop doing something earlier than was planned 縮短, 中斷: *She had to cut short her vacation when she heard that her mother was ill.* 聽說母親病了後, 她不得不中斷假期。

21 cut sb short to stop someone from finishing what they wanted to say 打斷, 插嘴: *I tried to explain, but he cut me short.* 我想解釋, 他卻打斷了我。

22 cut the crap *spoken* an impolite way of telling someone to deal only with the most important things without wasting time on unimportant details【口】閒話少說, 不要瞎折騰: *I wish they'd cut the crap and get on with this meeting!* 我希望他們別糾纏瑣事, 快點開會!

23 cut sb dead to deliberately ignore someone when you meet them 不理睬, 裝作沒看見: *I saw Ian in town but he just cut me dead!* 我在鎮上看見了伊恩, 他卻沒理睬我!

24 cut sb to the quick to upset someone very much by saying something cruel 出口傷人, 說話損人

25 cut the ground from under sb's feet to make someone or their ideas seem less impressive by having better ideas yourself, doing something before they do etc 把某人的計劃比下去, 先發制人

26 cut your own throat to behave in a way that will harm you, especially because you are proud or angry 自取其辱, 自取滅亡: *He'd just be cutting his own throat if he left now.* 他如果現在離開就等於毀了自己。

27 cut a fine figure/cut an odd figure etc *literary* to have an impressive, strange, etc appearance【文】惹人注目/怪模怪樣等: *Steve cut an odd figure in his cloak and Spanish riding hat.* 斯蒂夫穿着那件斗篷, 戴着那頂西班牙式騎士帽, 非常惹眼。

28 it cuts both ways *informal* used to say that something has advantages but also disadvantages【非正式】有利有弊, 有正反兩種效果

29 cut the cord to stop depending on someone, especially your parents 擺脫〔尤指對父母的〕依賴,〔生活上〕獨立

30 cut and run *informal* to leave a situation suddenly when it becomes too difficult, especially when you should have stayed【非正式】開溜, 臨陣脫逃: *Don't worry. He won't cut and run.* 別擔心。他不會見難而逃的。

31 cut your losses to stop trying to do something that is already failing in order to prevent the situation becoming even worse 及早放棄無利可圖的事

32 not cut the mustard *AmE informal* to not be good enough【美, 非正式】不符合要求: *Lawrence tries really hard but his work just doesn't cut the mustard.* 儘管勞倫斯工作很盡力, 但仍不如人意。

33 ▶ILLEGAL DRUG 非法毒品◀ [T usually passive 一般用被動態] to mix an illegal drug such as HEROIN with some other substance 混合〔毒品和其他物質〕

34 cut your coat according to your cloth to spend only as much money as you can afford 量入為出

35 cut no ice/not cut much ice if something cuts no ice with someone, it will not persuade them to change their mind 不起作用, 不產生影響: *I don't expect anything I say will cut much ice with him.* 我不指望我的話能影響他。—see also 另見 **cut a long story short** (STORY (11)), **cut a swathe through** (SWATHE¹ (4)), **cut it fine** (FINE³ (5))

cut across *phr v* [T] **1** to go across an area of land instead of going around it, in order to save time 抄近路穿過, 橫越: *Come on, if we cut across the field we'll get there before Frank.* 快點, 如果從田裡穿過去, 我們就能趕在弗蘭克之前到那兒。**2** if a problem or feeling cuts across different groups of people, they are all affected by it〔問題、看法等〕影響〔不同羣體的人〕: *The drug problem cuts across all social classes.* 在社會各階層中都存在毒品問題。

cut sth ↔ **away** *phr v* [T] to remove the unwanted or unnecessary parts from something 去掉; 切掉; 砍掉: *Cut away all the dead wood.* 把枯木都砍掉。

cut back *phr v* **1** [I, T **cut back** sth] to reduce the numbers of something, or the time or money that is spent on something, especially because you do not have enough money 削減, 縮減: *Defence spending is to be cut back.* 國防開支將被削減。| **[+on]** *Many schools are cutting back on staff at the moment.* 目前許多學校在裁員。**2** [T **cut** sth ↔ **back**] to remove the top part of a plant in order to help it to grow 修剪〔植物〕, 打頂: *I must cut that holly bush back a bit.* 我必須修剪那冬青樹叢了。—see also 另見 CUTBACK

cut down *phr v*

1 ▶REDUCE 減少◀ [I,T] to reduce the amount of something that you eat, buy, use etc 減少, 縮減: *You smoke too much – you should try to cut down.* 你抽煙太兇了, 該少抽點。| **cut sth ↔ down** *The coal industry was cut down to half its former size.* 煤炭業規模縮小了一半。| **[+on]** *My doctor's told me to cut down on carbohydrates.* 我的醫生告訴我要減少碳水化合物的攝入量。

2 ▶TREE 樹◀ [T **cut** sth ↔ **down**] to cut through the trunk of a tree so that it falls on the ground 砍倒〔樹〕

3 ▶KILL/INJURE 殺死/傷害◀ *literary*【文】[T **cut** sb ↔ **down**] to kill or injure someone with a sword or gun〔用劍或槍〕殺傷, 砍倒, 擊倒: *Our men were cut down by a hail of machine-gun fire.* 我們的人被一陣機槍掃射擊倒了。

4 ▶MAKE SHORTER 使縮短◀ [T **cut** sth ↔ **down**] to reduce the length of something such as a piece of writing 縮短, 剪短〈如文章〉: *The essay's too long – it needs cutting down a little.* 這篇文章太長了, 需要縮短一些。

5 cut sb down to size to make someone realize that they are not as important, successful etc as they think they are 使有自知之明

cut in *phr v* **1** [I] to interrupt someone who is speaking by saying something 插嘴, 打斷別人說話: **[+on]** *I wish Marie would stop cutting in on our conversation all the time.* 我希望瑪麗在我們談話時別老插嘴。**2** [I] to suddenly drive into the space between two moving cars in a dangerous way 強行超車: *This idiot cut in right in front of me.* 這個傻瓜把車強行插到我的正前方。**3** [I] if a part of a machine cuts in, it starts to operate when it is needed〔機器的一部分在有需要時〕開動; 接通: *The safety device cuts in automatically when needed.* 安全裝置在需要時會自動接通。**4 cut sb in on** *informal* to allow someone to take part in a secret plan to make money【非正式】讓〔某人〕加入祕密賺錢計劃: *Come on, Joey, you said you were going to cut me in on this one!* 得了, 喬伊, 你說過這次也算我一份的!

cut off *phr v*
1 ►PIECE OF STH 一片◄ [T **cut** sth ↔ **off**] to separate something by cutting it from the main part 切掉; 分割開: *She cut off a big piece of meat.* 她切下一大塊肉。| *One of his fingers was cut off in the accident.* 他的一根手指在事故中被切斷了。
2 ►STOP THE SUPPLY 停止供應◄ [T **cut** sth ↔ **off**] to stop the supply of something such as electricity, gas, water etc 中斷, 切斷〔電、煤氣、水等的〕供應: *The electricity company are threatening to cut us off.* 電力公司以停電威脅我們。| *The US has cut off aid to Cambodia.* 美國已中斷對柬埔寨的援助。
3 get cut off to suddenly not be able to hear someone that you were speaking to on the telephone 〔電話〕中斷, 掉線: *I don't know what happened – we just got cut off.* 不知出了甚麼事, 我們的通話無緣無故中斷了。
4 ►PLACE/PEOPLE 地方/人們◄ [T **cut** sb/sth ↔ **off**] to surround a place so that the people there are completely separated from other places or people 隔斷; 包圍; 隔絕: *In winter the town is often cut off by snow.* 冬天時, 這座小鎮常因大雪與外界隔斷聯繫。| *They were cut off by the Russian army and forced to surrender.* 他們徹底被俄軍包圍, 被迫投降。
5 ►STOP BEING FRIENDLY 不再友好◄ [T **cut** sb **off**] to stop having a friendly relationship with someone 中止關係: *Julia had been completely cut off by all her family and friends.* 朱莉婭的家人與朋友都與她脱離了關係。| **cut yourself off (from)** (=avoid people) 躲開所有人 *After his wife died he cut himself off completely from the rest of the world.* 妻子去世後, 他徹底與外界隔絕。
6 ►MONEY/PROPERTY 金錢/財產◄ [T **cut** sb ↔ **off**] to take away someone's right to receive your money or property, especially when you die 剝奪〔某人的〕財產繼承權: **cut sb off without a penny** *My parents have threatened to cut me off without a penny if I marry him.* 我父母威脅説如果我嫁給他, 我就別想繼承一分錢。
7 ►STOP SB TALKING 打斷某人談話◄ [T **cut** sb **off**] to prevent someone from finishing what they are saying 打斷〔某人的談話〕: *She cut me off in mid sentence.* 我剛説了半句就被她打斷了。
8 be cut off a) if a place is cut off, it is difficult to get to and is a long way from any other place 〔地方〕被隔絕的: *The village is so cut off from civilization that it receives almost no visitors.* 這個村莊與文明如此隔絕, 幾乎沒有外人去。**b)** if someone is cut off they are lonely because they are not able to meet people 〔人〕被隔絕[隔離]: **[+from]** *Mothers with very young children often feel cut off from the rest of the community.* 有小兒女的母親常感覺與街坊們隔離。
9 cut off your nose to spite your face to do something because you are angry even though it will harm you 拿自己出氣; 賭氣做出不顧後果的事

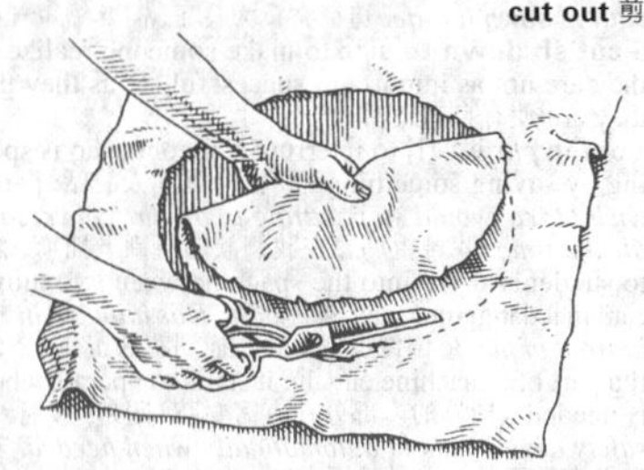
cut out 剪下

cut out *phr v*
1 ►REMOVE STH 去掉某物◄ [T **cut** sth ↔ **out**] to remove something by cutting 割掉, 剪下: *I cut the advertisement out of the newspaper.* 我從報紙上剪下這則廣告。| *The surgeon cut out the tumour.* 外科醫生切除了腫瘤。
2 ►MAKE STH INTO A SHAPE 將某物弄成某形狀◄ [T **cut** sth ↔ **out**] to cut a piece of paper, cloth etc so that it becomes a particular shape 把〔紙、布等〕剪[切]成某形狀: *The children were cutting out squares from the scraps of material.* 孩子們正用零碎材料剪出方塊。
3 ►PIECE OF WRITING/NEWS REPORT ETC 文章/新聞報道等◄ [T **cut** sth ↔ **out**] to take out part of a piece of writing, a news report etc, especially because it might offend people 截短, 刪節
4 ►STOP DOING STH 停止做某事◄ [T **cut** sth ↔ **out**] to stop doing or eating something, especially because it is harmful to you 〔尤指某事有害而〕戒除, 改掉: *If you cut out the drink you'd feel much healthier.* 如果你戒酒, 就會覺得身體好得多。
5 cut it/that out *spoken* used to tell someone to stop doing something because it is annoying you【口】停止〔做某事〕: *Hey, you guys, cut it out – Mom's trying to get some sleep.* 喂, 你們別鬧了, 媽媽要睡一會兒。
6 ►STOP SB FROM DOING STH 阻止某人做某事◄ [T **cut** sb **out**] to stop someone from doing something or taking part in something 阻止, 制止: *Todd's injuries cut him out of being selected for the team.* 陶德的傷勢讓他不能入選球隊。
7 ►MOTOR 發動機◄ [I] if a motor cuts out, it suddenly stops working 突然熄火: *The engine cut out halfway across the lake.* 開到湖中間發動機便熄了火。
8 ►STOP STH BEING SEEN 阻止被看見◄ [T] to prevent light from reaching somewhere, or prevent a particular view from being seen 隔斷〔光線或某種景色〕: *The tinted windows help cut out the glare from the sun.* 窗戶的染色玻璃阻擋了耀眼的陽光。
9 cut sb out of your will to remove someone's name from the list of people who will receive your money or property when you die 取消某人的遺產繼承權
10 be cut out for/cut out to be [usually in questions and negatives 一般用於疑問句和否定句] to have the qualities that you need for a particular job or activity 適合於...: *In the end I decided I wasn't cut out for the army.* 我最後得出結論, 自己不是當兵的料。| *Are you sure you're really cut out to be a teacher?* 你確定你真的適合做教師嗎? —see also 另見 **have his/her work cut out** (WORK² (13))

cut up *phr v* **1** [T **cut** sth ↔ **up**] to cut something into small pieces 切碎, 割碎: *His mother has to cut up all his food for him.* 他媽媽不得不為他將所有的食品切碎。**2** [I] *AmE informal* if a class cuts up, the students in it behave badly【美, 非正式】〔上課時學生〕惡作劇, 胡鬧 **3 be badly cut up** to have a lot of injuries because you have been in an accident or fight 〔因事故或打架〕多處受傷 **4 cut up (about sth)** *informal* very upset because something bad has happened to you【非正式】傷心, 難受: *She still seems very cut up about it.* 她似乎仍為那件事感到十分傷心。**5 cut up rough** *BrE informal* to react in an angry or violent way【英, 非正式】發脾氣, 發怒

cut² *n* [C]
1 ►WOUND 傷◄ a wound that is caused when something sharp cuts your skin 傷口: *The driver escaped with a few cuts and bruises.* 司機逃過了一劫, 只割破了幾處, 並有一些瘀傷。
2 ►HOLE/MARK 洞/記號◄ a hole in something, or a mark in the surface of something, made by something sharp 切口; 切痕: *The kitchen counter is covered with cuts.* 廚房的台面上全是刀口。
3 ►REDUCTION 減少◄ [often plural 常用複數] a planned reduction in the size or amount of something 〔尺寸、數量的〕削減, 縮短: **job cuts/wage cuts/tax cuts etc** *A shorter working week will mean pay cuts for millions of workers.* 較短的工作週將意味着幾百萬工人的工資要降低。| **[+in]** *a massive cut in public spending*

公共開支的大幅削減
4 ►HAIR 毛髮◄ [usually singular 一般用單數] **a)** the act of cutting someone's hair 剪髮, 理髮: *How much do they charge for a cut and blow-dry?* 理髮加吹乾他們要收多少錢? **b)** the style in which your hair has been cut 髮式
5 ►CLOTHES 衣服◄ [usually singular 一般用單數] the style in which your clothes have been made〔衣服的〕款式, 剪裁, 式樣: *From the cut of his suit, I'd say he was pretty wealthy.* 從他的服裝式樣來看, 我敢說他相當富有。
6 ►MONEY 錢◄ [singular] *informal* someone's share of something, especially money【非正式】份額〔尤指分配的金錢〕: *Investigators found that her cut of the profits amounted to more than 25%.* 調查人員發現她所佔的利潤份額超過25%。
7 make a cut to remove part of a speech, piece of writing etc 刪節〔演說、文章等〕: *The censors made several cuts.* 審查官做了幾處刪節。
8 ►FILM 電影◄ the process of putting together the different parts of a film and removing the parts that will not be shown 剪輯: *Spielberg himself oversaw the final cut.* 史匹堡親自監督了影片的最後剪輯。
9 the cut and thrust of the violent or unpleasant way in which a particular activity is done 激烈的爭鬥; 交鋒: *the cut and thrust of international politics* 國際政治的激烈鬥爭
10 be a cut above to be much better than someone else or something else 高人一等, 比別人高明: **a cut above the rest** *Just because she went to a private school, Jayne seems to think she's a cut above the rest of us.* 傑恩僅僅因為自己上過私立學校, 便認為自己比我們都高明。
11 ►MEAT 肉◄ a piece of meat that has been cut so that you can cook it 切下的一塊: *cuts of fresh lamb* 幾塊新鮮的羔羊肉
12 ►ROAD 路◄ *AmE* a road that has been made through a hill【美】〔在山中開出的〕通道 —see also 另見 POWER CUT

cut and dried /ˌ· · ˈ·◄/ *adj* a decision or result that is cut and dried cannot now be changed 已成定局的; 不可改變的: *I think we can say that the result of the election is now cut and dried.* 我想我們可以說現在的選舉結果已成定局。

cut·a·way /ˈkʌtəˌwe; ˈkʌtəweɪ/ *adj* a cutaway model, drawing etc is open on one side so that you can see the details inside it〔模型、圖等〕剖面的

cut·back /ˈkʌtˌbæk; ˈkʌtbæk/ *n* [C usually plural 一般用複數] a reduction in something, such as the number of workers in an organization, the amount of money spent by the government etc 削減, 裁減〔員工或政府開支等〕: [+in] *recommended cutbacks in social programmes* 建議減少的社會福利項目 —see also 另見 **cut back** (CUT¹)

3 **cute** /kjut; kjuːt/ *adj informal*【非正式】**1** very pretty or attractive 漂亮的, 逗人喜愛的: *Jenny's such a cute little girl.* 珍妮真是一個可愛的小女孩。**2** attractive in a sexual way 性感迷人的: *an all-American type – cute, blonde and vivacious* 一個十足的美國類型: 性感、金髮、活潑 **3** *especially AmE* clever and practical when dealing with people, sometimes in an unpleasant way【尤美】機靈的, 精明的〔有時貶〕: *He's one cute lawyer!* 他可是個精明的律師! | **get cute with** (=try to deceive someone) 設法欺騙〔某人〕*Don't get cute with me – I know what those tires cost.* 別騙我了, 我知道那些輪胎值多少錢。—**cutely** *adv* —**cuteness** *n* [U]

cute·sy /ˈkjutsɪ; ˈkjuːtsi/ *adj AmE*【美】**1** something that is cutesy is too pretty or clever in a way you think is annoying 矯揉造作的, 忸怩作態的: *That greeting card is too cutesy.* 那張賀卡太肉麻了。

cute·y /ˈkjutɪ; ˈkjuːti/ *n* [C] *spoken* someone who is attractive, kind, and helpful【口】迷人、友善、樂於幫助別人的人: *He's such a cutey!* 他真是一個熱心人!

cut glass /ˌ· ˈ·◄/ *n* [U] glass that has patterns cut into its surface 雕花玻璃

cut-glass *adj* **1** made of cut glass 雕花玻璃(製品)的: *a cut-glass decanter* 雕花玻璃盛酒瓶 **2 cut-glass accent/vowel** an accent or vowel that is typical of someone from a high social class 上層社會的口音/上流社會的發音

cu·ti·cle /ˈkjutɪkl̩; ˈkjuːtɪkəl/ *n* [C] an outer layer of hard skin, especially around the base of your nails〔尤指指甲根部的〕角質層

cut·lass /ˈkʌtləs; ˈkʌtləs/ *n* [C] a short sword with a curved blade, used by sailors or PIRATES in former times〔舊時水手和海盜使用的〕短劍, 短彎刀 —see picture at 參見 SWORD 圖

cut·ler /ˈkʌtlɚ; ˈkʌtlə/ *n* [C] someone who makes or sells cutlery 刀剪匠, 刀具工人; 刀具商

cut·le·ry /ˈkʌtlərɪ; ˈkʌtləri/ *n* [U] knives, forks, spoons, and other things used for eating with 刀叉等餐具; SILVERWARE *AmE*【美】: *Can you put the cutlery on the table?* 你能將刀叉擺在餐桌上嗎? —see pictures on pages A10 and A15 參見A10頁和A15頁圖

cut·let /ˈkʌtlɪt; ˈkʌtl̩t/ *n* [C] **1** a small flat piece of meat on a bone, usually LAMB¹ (2) or VEAL 肉排〔通常為羔羊排或小牛肉〕: *a grilled lamb cutlet* 烤羊排 **2 vegetable/nut/prawn cutlet** a flat mass of vegetables, nuts etc covered with egg and BREADCRUMBS and cooked in hot fat 炸蔬菜餅/炸乾果餅/炸蝦餅

cut·off also 又作 **cut-off** *BrE*【英】/ˈkʌtˌɔf; ˈkʌtɒf/ *n* **1** [C] a fixed limit or level at which you decide to or have to stop doing something 停止點; 截止點: **cutoff date/score/point** (=the date etc when you stop doing something) 截止日期/底線分數/截止點 *The cutoff point for this sample was a score of 50% or more.* 這個樣品的最低分數不低於50%。**2 cutoffs** [plural] short trousers that you make by cutting off the bottom part of a pair of trousers〔用長褲裁剪成的〕短褲 **3** [C] a part of a pipe that you open and shut to control the flow of gas or liquid〔氣體或液體流動的〕截斷裝置, 截止閥

cut·out /ˈkʌtˌaut; ˈkʌtaʊt/ *n* [C] **1** the shape of a person, object etc that has been cut out of wood or paper 紙剪〔木刻〕的圖形: *a life-size cardboard cutout of Margaret Thatcher* 一幅和戴卓爾夫人一樣大小的硬紙剪影 **2** a piece of equipment that stops a machine when something is not working properly 切斷裝置, 保險裝置

cut-price /ˌ· ˈ·◄/ *adj* **1** sold at less than the usual price 減價的, 削價的: *cut-price petrol* 減價汽油 **2** a cut-price shop, supermarket etc sells goods at reduced prices 廉價的〔商店等〕: *a cut-price garage* 廉價汽車修理站

cut·purse /ˈkʌtˌpɝs; ˈkʌtpɜːs/ *n* [C] *old use* a PICKPOCKET【舊】扒手

cut-rate /ˈ· ·/ *adj* sold at less than the usual price 減價銷售的

cut·ter /ˈkʌtɚ; ˈkʌtə/ *n* [C] **1** a small ship 小艇 **2** [often plural 常用複數] a tool that is used for cutting 切割器具, 刀具: *wire cutters* 鋼絲鉗, 鐵絲剪

cut·throat¹ /ˈkʌtˌθrot; ˈkʌtθrəʊt/ *adj* [only before noun 僅用於名詞前] a cutthroat activity involves people who are all trying to get the same thing, often behaving badly or unfairly to each other 競爭激烈的, 無情的: *Cutthroat competition led to a lot of bankruptcies and mergers.* 無情的競爭導致許多公司倒閉和被合併。

cut·throat² *n* [C] *old use* a murderer【舊】兇手, 謀殺者

cut-throat ra·zor /ˌ· · ˈ··/ *n* [C] a RAZOR with a very long sharp blade 剃刀 —see picture at 參見 RAZOR 圖

cut·ting¹ /ˈkʌtɪŋ; ˈkʌtɪŋ/ *n* [C] **1** a stem or leaf that is cut from a plant and put in soil or water to grow into a new plant〔用來插種的〕插枝, 插條 **2** *BrE* a piece of writing that is cut from a newspaper, magazine etc【英】剪報; 剪下來的材料; CLIPPING (1) *AmE*【美】: **press/newspaper cuttings** *Margot had sent him a bunch of press cuttings about the wedding.* 瑪戈給他寄去了許多有關那次婚禮的剪報。**3** *BrE* something that is produced by cutting, especially a passage cut through a hill for a road or railway【英】〔在山中〕開鑿出來的通道; CUT² (12) *AmE*【美】

cutting² *adj* **1** very unkind and intended to upset someone 尖刻的, 傷人感情的: *Danny can be so cutting at times.* 丹尼有時特別刻薄。| *Sue made a cutting remark about my clothes.* 蘇對我的衣服作了刻薄的評論。**2** a cutting wind is very cold and you can feel it through your clothes〔風〕刺骨的 **3 be (at) the cutting edge of sth** to be the most advanced form of an activity, in which the newest methods, systems, equipment etc are developed and used 為…最先進的, 處於…的領先地位: *The information highway is the cutting edge of the electronic revolution.* 信息高速公路處於電子革命的先鋒地位。

cutting board /ˈ‧‧ ‧/ *n* [C] *AmE* a large piece of wood or plastic used for cutting meat or vegetables on【美】砧板; CHOPPING BOARD *BrE*【英】

C

cutting room /ˈ‧‧ ‧/ *n* [C] a room where the final form of a film is prepared by cutting and putting the different parts into the correct order〔影片的〕剪輯室

CV /ˌsi ˋvi; ˌsiː ˈviː/ also 又作 **curriculum vitae** *n* [C] *BrE* a short written document giving your education and past employment, used when you are looking for a job【英】簡歷(書); RESUME[2] (2) *AmE*【美】: *Please send a CV and brief letter to the address below.* 請按以下地址郵寄一份簡歷和簡短的應徵信。

cwt the written abbreviation of 縮寫 = HUNDREDWEIGHT

-cy /sɪ; si/ *suffix* [in nouns 構成名詞] **1** the state or quality of being something 表示某種狀態或性質: *privacy* (=state of being private) 隱私 | *accuracy* 精確 | *bankruptcy* 破產 **2** a particular rank or position 表示某種職位、職別: *a baronetcy* (=the rank of a BARONET) 男爵爵位

cy·an /ˋsaɪæn; ˈsaɪən/ *adj* dark greenish blue 帶綠的深藍色的, 青色的 —**cyan** *n* [U]

cy·a·nide /ˋsaɪəˌnaɪd; ˈsaɪənaɪd/ *n* [U] a very strong poison 氰化物

cyber- /saɪbɚ; saɪbə/ *prefix* connected with computers, especially with the sending of messages on the INTERNET 與電腦有關的, 與互聯網上的信息傳遞有關的

cy·ber·net·ics /ˌsaɪbɚˋnɛtɪks; ˌsaɪbəˈnetɪks/ *n* [U] the scientific study of the way in which information is moved about and controlled in machines, the brain and the NERVOUS SYSTEM 控制論 —**cybernetic** *adj*

cy·ber·punk /ˋsaɪbɚˌpʌŋk; ˈsaɪbəpʌŋk/ *n* [U] stories about imaginary events connected with computer science 電腦幻想故事: *cyberpunk fiction* 電腦幻想小說

cy·ber·space /ˋsaɪbɚˌspes; ˈsaɪbəspeɪs/ *n* [U] a word from SCIENCE FICTION, used to mean the place where electronic messages, information, pictures etc exist when they are sent from one computer to another 電子空間〔語出科幻小說, 指信息、圖像等在電腦之間傳遞時所處的空間〕: *We didn't meet in San Francisco – we met in cyberspace!* 我們並不是在三藩市相遇的, 我們是在電子空間裡認識的!

cy·borg /ˋsaɪbɔrg; ˈsaɪbɔːg/ *n* [C] a creature that is partly human and partly machine 電子人, 半機械人

cyc·la·men /ˋsɪkləmən; ˈsɪkləmən/ *n* [C] a plant with pink, red, or white flowers 仙客來〔一種植物〕

3 3 **cy·cle**[1] /ˋsaɪkḷ; ˈsaɪkəl/ *n* [C] **1** a number of events happening in a regularly repeated order 循環: [+of] *the cycle of the seasons* 四季的周而復始 | *the endless cycle of violence in this part of the world* 世界上這一地區永無休止的暴力事件 —see also 另見 LIFE CYCLE **2** a bicycle or MOTORCYCLE 自行車; 摩托車 **3** the period of time needed for a machine to finish a process 週期: *This washing machine has a 50 minute cycle.* 這台洗衣機完成洗衣的全部程序要 50 分鐘。**4** a group of songs, poems etc that are all about a particular important event〔表現同一重大事件的〕組歌, 組詩

cycle[2] *v* [I] *especially BrE* to travel by bicycle【尤英】騎自行車: *Do you cycle to work?* 你騎自行車上班嗎?

cy·clic /ˋsaɪklɪk; ˈsaɪklɪk/ also 又作 **cyc·li·cal** /ˋsaɪklɪkḷ; ˈsɪklɪkəl/ *adj* happening in cycles (CYCLE[1] (1)) 循環的, 週期的: *the cyclical nature of history* 歷史的循環本質 —**cyclically** /-klɪ; -kli/ *adv*

cy·clist /ˋsaɪklɪst; ˈsaɪklɪst/ *n* [C] someone who rides a bicycle 騎自行車的人: *Andrew and Merv are very keen cyclists.* 安德魯和默夫熱衷於騎自行車。

cy·clone /ˋsaɪklon; ˈsaɪkləʊn/ *n* [C] a very violent storm that moves very rapidly in a circle 旋風, 龍捲風: *Darwin was flattened by Cyclone Tracy in 1974.* 旋風特蕾西於 1974 年將達爾文夷為平地。—compare 比較 HURRICANE, TYPHOON

cy·clops /ˋsaɪklɑps; ˈsaɪklɒps/ *n* [singular] a very big man in ancient Greek stories who only had one eye in the middle of his forehead〔希臘神話中的〕獨眼巨人

cy·der /ˋsaɪdɚ; ˈsaɪdə/ *n* [U] *BrE*【英】another spelling of CIDER cider 的另一種拼法

cyg·net /ˋsɪgnɪt; ˈsɪgnɪt/ *n* [C] a young SWAN[1] 幼天鵝

cyl·in·der /ˋsɪlɪndɚ; ˈsɪlɪndə/ *n* [C] **1** a shape, object, or container with circular ends and long straight sides 圓柱體; 圓筒: *The gases are stored under pressure in separate cylinders.* 氣體被壓縮分裝在幾個圓筒裡。—see picture at 參見 SHAPE[1] 圖 **2** the tube within which a PISTON moves forwards and backwards in an engine〔引擎的〕汽缸: *a four cylinder engine* 四汽缸引擎

cy·lin·dri·cal /sɪˋlɪndrɪkḷ; sɪˈlɪndrɪkəl/ *adj* in the shape of a cylinder 圓柱體的: *A huge cylindrical oil tank stood beside the engine.* 發動機旁邊有一個大的圓筒形油箱。

cym·bal /ˋsɪmbḷ; ˈsɪmbəl/ *n* [C] a musical instrument made of a thin round metal plate that you play by hitting it with a stick, or by hitting two of them together 鐃鈸, 鈒鈸: *the sudden clash of cymbals* 突然的鐃鈸響聲

cyn·ic /ˋsɪnɪk; ˈsɪnɪk/ *n* [C] someone who is not willing to believe that people have good, honest, or sincere reasons for doing something 憤世嫉俗的人; 諷世者; 認為人的動機皆自私者: *Even the most hardened cynic must agree that charity does some good.* 即使最頑固的憤世嫉俗者也必須承認慈善活動有一定的益處。—**cynicism** *n* [U]

cyn·i·cal /ˋsɪnɪkḷ; ˈsɪnɪkəl/ *adj* unwilling to believe that people have good, honest, or sincere reasons for doing something 憤世嫉俗的, 冷嘲熱諷的: *You're just so cynical, Dave! Don't you believe in anything?* 你太憤世嫉俗了, 戴夫! 你難道甚麼也不信嗎? | **[+about]** *Since her divorce she's become very cynical about men.* 離婚後, 她懷疑所有的男人。—**cynically** /-klɪ; -kli/ *adv*

cy·no·sure /ˋsaɪnəˌʃʊr; ˈsɪnəzjʊə/ *n* [usually singular 一般用單數] *formal* someone or something that everyone is interested in or attracted to【正式】引人興趣[注目]的人[事物]

cy·pher /ˋsaɪfɚ; ˈsaɪfə/ *n* [C] another spelling of CIPHER cipher 的另一種拼法

cy·press /ˋsaɪprəs; ˈsaɪprɪs/ *n* [C] a tree with dark green leaves and hard wood, that does not lose its leaves in winter 柏樹; 柏屬植物

Cy·ril·lic /sɪˋrɪlɪk; sɪˈrɪlɪk/ *adj* Cyrillic writing is written in the alphabet used for Russian, Bulgarian, and other Slavonic languages 西里爾字母〔俄語、保加利亞語和其他斯拉夫語字母〕的: *a Cyrillic typewriter* 西里爾字母打字機

cyst /sɪst; sɪst/ *n* [C] a mass containing liquid that grows in your body or under your skin 囊腫: *an ovarian cyst* 卵巢囊腫

cystic fi·bro·sis /ˌsɪstɪk faɪˋbrosəs; ˌsɪstɪk faɪˈbrəʊsɪs/ *n* [U] a serious medical condition, especially in children, in which breathing and digesting (DIGEST[1] (1)) food is very difficult 囊性纖維變性〔一種嚴重疾病〕

cyst·i·tis /sɪsˋtaɪtɪs; sɪˈstaɪtɪs/ *n* [U] an infection of the BLADDER[1] (1), especially in women〔尤指婦女的〕膀胱炎

cy·tol·o·gy /saɪˋtɑlədʒɪ; saɪˈtɒlədʒi/ *n* [U] the scientific study of cells from living things 細胞學 —**cytologist** *n* [C]

czar /zɑr; zɑː/ *n* [C] **1** another spelling of TSAR tsar 的另一種拼法 **2 banking/drug/health etc czar** *AmE* someone who is very powerful in a particular job or activity【美】銀行業大王/毒品大王/衛生權威

cza·ri·na /zɑˋrinə; zɑːˈriːnə/ *n* [C] another spelling of TSARINA tsarina 的另一種拼法

D,d

D /di; diː/ **d** *plural* **D's, d's** *n* [C] **1** the fourth letter of the English alphabet 英語字母表的第四個字母 **2** the number 500 in the system of ROMAN NUMERALS 羅馬數字 500

D 1 the second note in the SCALE[1] (8) of C major, or the musical KEY[2] (4) based on this note D 音〔C 大調音階中的第二個音〕**2** a mark that a teacher gives to a student's work, showing that it is not very good D 級, 丁級, 丁等〔表示學業成績不太好〕—see also 另見 D AND C, D-DAY

d 1 the written abbreviation of 縮寫= died 死於: *John Keats d 1821* 約翰·濟慈死於 1821 年 **2** the abbreviation of 縮寫= PENNY (4) in the system of money used in Britain before 1971 便士〔1971 年前用於英國的貨幣體系〕

d' *spoken*【口】the short form of 縮略式= do: *D'you know how many people are going to be there?* 你知道有多少人要去那兒嗎?

-'d 1 the short form of 縮略式= would: *I asked if she'd be willing to help.* 我問她是否願意幫忙。**2** the short form of 縮略式= had: *Nobody knew where he'd gone.* 沒有人知道他去了哪裡。

-d /d, t; d, t/ *suffix* the form used for -ED after 'e'〔用於 e 之後代替 -ed 的後綴形式〕: *baked* 烘[烤]過的

DA /ˌdi ˋe; ˌdiː ˈeɪ/ *n* [C] the abbreviation of 縮寫= DISTRICT ATTORNEY

dab[1] /dæb; dæb/ *n* [C] **1** a small amount of something that you put onto a surface with your hand, a cloth etc 少量, 少許〔用手、布等放在物體表面的某物〕: **[+of]** *Add a dab of butter and some parsley.* 加少許牛油和西芹。**2** a light touch with your hand, a cloth etc〔用手、布等的〕輕敷, 輕觸: *She wiped her tears away with a dab of her handkerchief.* 她用手絹輕輕地擦掉眼淚。**3** a small flat fish 比目魚; 孫鰈屬的魚, 孫鰈 **4 dabs** [plural] *BrE old-fashioned* your FINGERPRINTs[1]【英, 過時】指紋

dab[2] *v* **dabbed, dabbing 1** [I,T] to touch something lightly, usually several times 輕觸, 輕拍〔多次〕: **[+at]** *He dabbed at his bleeding lip.* 他輕輕地揩拭流血的嘴唇。**2** [T] to put a substance onto something with quick, light movements of your hand〔輕而快地〕敷, 搽: **dab sth on/onto etc** *She hastily dabbed some cream on her face.* 她匆忙地往臉上搽了些面霜。

dab·ble /ˋdæbḷ; ˈdæbəl/ *v* **1** [I] to do something or be involved in something in a way that is not very serious 涉獵, 涉足, 淺嘗: **[+at/in]** *James dabbles in politics.* 詹姆斯淺涉政治。**2** [T+in] to move your hands, feet etc about in water〔用手、腳等〕玩水, 嬉水: *children dabbling their feet in the sea* 孩子們把雙腳浸在海裡玩水

dab hand /ˌ· ˈ·/ *n* **be a dab hand at** *BrE informal* to be very good at a particular activity【英, 非正式】擅長於〔某種活動〕

dachs·hund /ˋdɑksˌhʊnd; ˈdækshʊnd/ *n* [C] a type of small dog with short legs and a long body 獵獾狗, 臘腸狗〔一種身長腿短的狗〕—see picture at 參見 DOG[1] 圖

Dac·ron /ˋdeˌkrɑn; ˈdækrɒn/ *n* [U] *trademark AmE* a kind of cloth that is not made from natural materials【商標, 美】滌綸, 的確涼, 達克龍

dac·tyl /ˋdæktḷ; ˈdæktɪl/ *n* [C] *technical* a repeated sound pattern in poetry, consisting of one long sound followed by two short sounds as in the word 'carefully'【術語】揚抑抑格〔即一長音後接兩個短音, 如 carefully〕—**dactylic** /dækˋtɪlɪk; dækˈtɪlɪk/ *adj*

1 2 **dad** /dæd; dæd/ *n* [C] *informal* father【非正式】爸爸, 爹爹: *She lives with her Mom and Dad.* 她和爸爸媽媽一起生活。

1 **dad·dy** /ˋdædɪ; ˈdædi/ *n* [C] a word meaning father, used especially by or to young children 爸爸, 爹爹〔尤用於兒語〕: *Look, Daddy's home!* 看, 爸爸回家啦! —see also 另見 SUGAR DADDY

daddy long·legs /ˌdædɪ ˋlɔŋlɛgz; ˌdædi ˈlɒŋlegz/ *n* [C] **1** *BrE* a flying insect with long legs; CRANE FLY【英】長腳飛蟲; 大蚊 **2** *AmE* an insect with long legs that is similar to a SPIDER【美】盲蛛〔類似蜘蛛的長腳昆蟲〕

da·do /ˋdedo; ˈdeɪdəʊ/ *n plural* **dadoes** [C] the lower part of a wall in a room, especially when it is decorated differently to the upper part of the wall 護壁板, 牆裙〔房間牆壁下面與牆身其他部分裝飾不同的部分〕

dae·mon /ˋdimən; ˈdiːmən/ *n* [C] a spirit in ancient Greek stories that is half a god and half a man〔古希臘神話中的〕半人半神的精靈, 半神 —compare 比較 DEMON

daf·fo·dil /ˋdæfədɪl; ˈdæfədɪl/ *n* [C] a tall yellow spring flower with a central tube-shaped part 水仙(花), 黃水仙

daft /dæft; dɑːft/ *adj BrE informal*【英, 非正式】**1** silly or not very sensible 傻的; 不明智的: *What a daft thing to say!* 真是蠢話! | **don't be daft** *spoken* (=used to tell someone not to be silly)【口】別傻了 | **as daft as a brush** (=extremely silly) 蠢透了 *Jay's a nice bloke but he's as daft as a brush.* 傑伊是個好人, 只是他太傻了。**2 be daft about** to be extremely interested in 對…着迷: *Tony's still daft about cars!* 東尼對汽車還是那麼着迷! —**daftness** *n* [U]

dag /dæg; dæg/ *n* [C] *AustrE spoken* a strange or stupid person【澳口】怪人; 笨蛋

dag·ger /ˋdægɚ; ˈdægə/ *n* [C] **1** a short pointed knife used as a weapon 匕首, 短劍 —see picture at 參見 KNIFE[1] 圖 **2 look daggers at** *BrE* to look at someone angrily【英】對〔某人〕怒目而視 —see also 另見 CLOAK-AND-DAGGER **3 be at daggers drawn** if two people are at daggers drawn, they are extremely angry with each other 拔刀相向, 勢不兩立, 劍拔弩張

da·go /ˋdego; ˈdeɪgəʊ/ *n* [C] an extremely offensive word for someone from Spain, Italy, Portugal etc 拉丁佬, 外國佬〔對西班牙人、意大利人、葡萄牙人等的極端冒犯用語〕

da·guer·reo·type /dəˋgɛrəˌtaɪp; dəˈgerəʊtaɪp/ *n* [C, U] an old type of photograph〔老式的〕銀版照相 (法)

dahl /dɑl; dɑːl/ *n* [C,U] an Indian dish with a hot taste, made with beans, PEAs, or LENTILs 一道印度菜〔味辣, 用蠶豆、豌豆或小扁豆煮成〕

dah·li·a /ˋdæljə; ˈdeɪliə/ *n* [C] a large garden flower with a bright colour 大麗花, 大麗菊

dai·ly[1] /ˋdelɪ; ˈdeɪli/ *adj* [only before noun 僅用於名詞前] 3 **1** happening or done every day 每日的, 每天的: *daily flights to Miami* 每天飛往邁阿密的航班 **2 daily life** the ordinary things that you usually do or experience 日常生活 **3** connected with a single day 一天的; 按天計算的: *a daily rate of pay* 日工資 2

daily[2] *adv* done or happening every day 每日, 天天: *The zoo is open daily, from 9 am to 5 pm.* 動物園每天上午 9 點到下午 5 點開放。

daily[3] *n* **1** [C usually plural 一般用複數] a DAILY PAPER 日報 **2** [C] *BrE old-fashioned* a DAILY HELP【英, 過時】日工 **3 dailies** [plural] *AmE* the first prints of a film before it has been edited (EDIT (1))【美】〔未經剪輯的〕電影毛片; rushes (RUSH[2] (7)) *BrE*【英】

daily help /ˌ·· ˈ·/ *n* [C] *BrE old-fashioned* someone, especially a woman, who is employed to clean someone's house【英, 過時】日工, 女傭

daily pa·per /ˌ·· ˈ··/ *n* [C] a newspaper that is printed and sold every day except Sunday〔除星期日外每天都發行的〕日報

dain·ty[1] /ˋdentɪ; ˈdeɪnti/ *adj* **daintier, daintiest 1** small, pretty, and delicate 小巧的, 精緻的: *a dainty white hand-*

kerchief 一條精緻的白手帕 **2** dainty movements are small and careful〔舉止〕輕巧而優雅的 **—daintily** *adv* **—daintiness** *n* [U]

dainty² *n* [C] something small that is good to eat such as a sweet cake 精美可口的小點心, 珍饈〈如甜蛋糕〉

dai·qui·ri /ˈdaɪkərɪ; ˈdaɪkəri/ *n* [C, U] a sweet alcoholic drink made with RUM¹ and fruit juice 代基里酒〔一種由朗姆酒與果汁製成的甜味酒類飲品〕

dai·ry /ˈdɛrɪ; ˈdeəri/ *n* [C] **1** a place on a farm where milk is kept and butter and cheese are made 乳品場; 牛奶場; 製酪場 **2** a company which sells milk and makes other dairy products 牛奶公司; 乳品公司

dairy cat·tle /ˈ·· ˌ··/ *n* [plural] cattle that are kept to produce milk rather than for their meat 奶牛, 乳牛

dairy farm /ˈ·· ˌ·/ *n* [C] a farm that has cows and produces milk 牛奶場

dai·ry·maid /ˈdɛrɪˌmed; ˈdeərimeɪd/ *n* [C] a woman who worked in a dairy in the past 牛奶場女工

dai·ry·man /ˈdɛrɪmən; ˈdeərimən/ *n* [C] a man who works in a dairy 牛奶場男工

da·is /ˈdeɪs; ˈdeɪəs/ *n* [singular] a low stage that you stand on when you are making a speech or performing, so that people can see and hear you 講台

dai·sy /ˈdezɪ; ˈdeɪzi/ *n* [C] **1** a white flower with a yellow centre 雛菊(花) **2 pushing up the daisies** *humorous* someone who is pushing up the daisies is dead【幽默】死 —see also 另見 **fresh as a daisy** (FRESH (12))

daisy chain /ˈ·· ·/ *n* [C] daisies tied together into a string to wear around your neck or wrist 雛菊花環

dai·sy·wheel print·er /ˈdezɪhwil ˌprɪntə; ˈdeɪziwiːl ˌprɪntə/ *n* [C] a type of PRINTER (1) that produces good quality writing〔打印效果很好的〕菊花輪式打印機

Dal·ai La·ma /ˌdɑlaɪ ˈlɑmə; ˌdælaɪ ˈlɑːmə/ *n* [C] **the Dalai Lama** the leader of the Tibetan Buddhist religion 達賴喇嘛〔西藏佛教領袖〕

dale /del; deɪl/ *n* [C] a word meaning valley, used in former times or in the names of places, especially in the North of England 山谷〔過去或在地名中使用, 尤指英格蘭北部的山谷〕

dal·li·ance /ˈdælɪəns; ˈdæliəns/ *n* [U] *old-fashioned* the behaviour of two people who are dallying with each other【過時】調戲; 調情

dal·ly /ˈdælɪ; ˈdæli/ *v* [I] *old-fashioned* to waste time, or do something very slowly【過時】浪費時間, 慢吞吞做事: *Don't dally along the way!* 別在路上磨磨蹭蹭的!

dally with sb/sth *phr v* [T] **1** to think about something but not in a very serious way〔不十分認真地〕考慮〔某事〕: *They'd dallied with the idea of going on a world tour many times.* 他們多次想着要周遊世界。**2** *old-fashioned* to start a romantic relationship with someone but not in a serious way【過時】〔與某人〕調情, 玩弄〔某人的〕感情

dal·ma·tian /dælˈmeʃən; dælˈmeɪʃən/ *n* [C] a large dog with short white hair and black or brown spots 大麥町犬, 斑點狗〔一種白毛大狗, 毛短, 帶有黑色或棕色斑點〕—see picture at 參見 DOG¹ 圖

dam 堤壩

dam¹ /dæm; dæm/ *n* [C] **1** a special wall built across a river, stream etc to stop the water from flowing, especially to make a lake or produce electricity 水壩, 水堤, 堤壩: *the Aswan dam in Egypt* 埃及的阿斯旺大壩 **2** *technical* the mother of a four-legged animal, especially a horse【術語】母獸〔尤指母馬〕—compare 比較 SIRE¹ (2)

dam² *v* **dammed, damming** [T] to stop the water in a river, stream etc from flowing by building a special wall across it 築壩攔〔水〕, 在...中築提

dam sth ↔ **up** *phr v* [T] to dam a river, stream etc 建水壩於〔江、河等〕: *The stream had been dammed up.* 這條河上已築壩攔水。

dam·age¹ /ˈdæmɪdʒ; ˈdæmɪdʒ/ *n* [U]

1 ►PHYSICAL HARM 對物體或身體的損害◄ physical harm caused to something or someone〔對某物、某人造成的〕損害: **[+to]** *damage to property* 對財產造成的破壞 | **serious/severe/extensive damage** (=very bad damage) 嚴重損害 *The earthquake caused extensive structural damage.* 地震造成大面積的建築物毀壞。| **minor/superficial damage** (=damage that is not very serious) 輕微損害 | **do/cause damage** *Don't you realize the damage these chemicals are doing to our environment?* 你難道沒意識到這些化學物質正在破壞我們的環境嗎? | **brain/liver/lung etc damage** (=damage caused to someone's brain etc) 腦/肝/肺等的損傷 *permanent brain damage from the accident* 事故造成的永久性腦損傷 | **irreparable/irreversible damage** (=damage that cannot be repaired) 無法修復的/無法挽回的損害 | **water/storm/flood etc damage** (=damage caused by water, a storm etc) 水/暴風雨/洪水等造成的損害

2 ►EMOTIONAL HARM 情感上受到的傷害◄ harm caused to someone's emotions or mind〔對一個人感情或心理造成的〕傷害: *Such a traumatic childhood experience can cause terrible emotional damage.* 這樣創深痛巨的童年經歷容易造成極大的感情創傷。

3 ►BAD EFFECT 不好的影響◄ a bad effect on something 壞影響: **[+to]** *The damage to his reputation was considerable.* 對他名譽造成的損害是巨大的。

4 ►MONEY 錢◄ **damages** [plural] *law* money that a court orders someone to pay to someone else for harming them or their property【法律】損害賠償金: *The court awarded him £15000 in damages.* 法院裁定給他 15,000 英鎊損害賠償金。

5 the damage is done used to say that something bad has happened which makes it impossible to go back to the way things were before it happened 已造成的傷害無法挽回: *She immediately regretted her outburst, but the damage was done.* 她發作之後立刻就後悔了, 但是傷害已造成, 無法挽回。

6 what's the damage? *spoken* used humorously to ask how much you have to pay【口】要花多少錢?〔幽默問法〕

7 damage limitation an attempt to limit the damage to something 損失控制, 降低損失: *a damage limitation exercise to save the Prime Minister* 一項為挽救首相而採取的損失控制舉措

This graph shows some of the words most commonly used with the noun **damage**. 本圖表所示為含有名詞 damage 的一些最常用詞組。

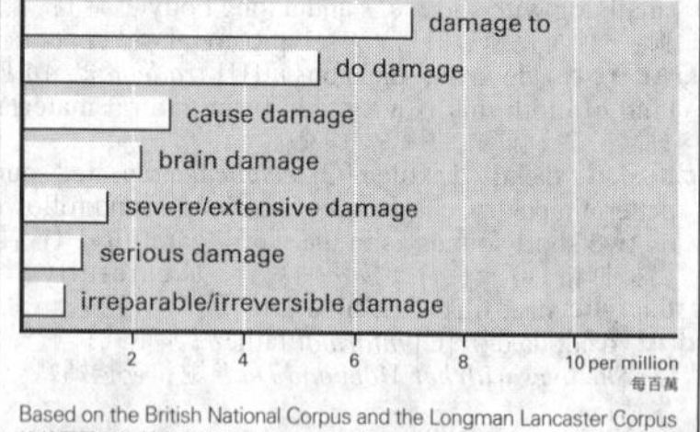

Based on the British National Corpus and the Longman Lancaster Corpus
據英國國家語料庫和朗文蘭卡斯特語料庫

3 3 **damage[2]** *v* [T] **1** to cause physical harm to something or to part of someone's body 損害, 損壞, 損傷〔某物或某人的身體部位〕: *Take care not to damage the timer mechanism.* 當心別弄壞計時器的機械裝置。| *I've damaged a knee ligament.* 我拉傷了膝蓋的韌帶。**2** to have a bad effect on something or someone in a way that makes them weaker or less successful〔對某物或某人〕有不好的影響: *Taylor felt her reputation had been damaged by the newspaper article.* 泰勒覺得她的名譽已經因為報紙上的這篇報道而受到損害。—**damaging** *adj*: *Unemployment has had a damaging effect on morale.* 失業損害了士氣。

dam·ask[1] /ˈdæməsk; ˈdæməsk/ *n* [U] a type of cloth with a pattern in it, often used to cover furniture〔經常用來鋪在家具上的〕緞子, 錦緞

damask[2] *adj* **1** made of damask 緞子的, 錦緞的: *a damask tablecloth* 一塊織花桌布 **2** *literary* pink【文】粉紅色的: *her damask cheek* 她粉紅色的面頰

damask rose /ˈ·· ,·/ *n* [C] a pink rose with a beautiful smell 大馬士革薔薇〔一種粉紅色, 有香味的玫瑰〕

Dame /dem; deɪm/ *n* a British title of honour given to a woman as a reward for the good things she has done 女爵士, 貴夫人〔英國的榮譽頭銜〕

dame *n* [C] **1** *AmE old-fashioned* a woman【美, 過時】女人 **2** a character in a PANTOMIME (=a special play at Christmas) dressed as an ugly old woman but acted by a man〔聖誕節期間演出的童話劇中常由男性扮演的〕醜老太婆 **3** a woman who has been given the British title Dame〔被授予英國女爵士頭銜的〕貴夫人: *Dame Edith Evans* 伊迪絲·埃文斯(女)爵士

dam·mit /ˈdæmɪt; ˈdæmɨt/ *interjection* used to show that you are annoyed 該死, 他媽的〔表示生氣〕: *Hurry up, dammit!* 快點, 該死!

2 **damn[1]** /dæm; dæm/ *adj* [only before noun 僅用於名詞前] *spoken* used to show that you are angry or annoyed with someone or something【口】該死的〔表示由於某人或某事很生氣〕: *I can't get this damn button undone!* 我解不開這該死的鈕扣!

damn[2] *adv* [+adj/adv] *spoken*【口】**1** used to emphasize how good something is, how bad something is etc; very 非常, 很: *We've been so damn busy all day, I'm shattered!* 我們一整天忙透了, 我要累垮了! | *It's damn cold in here.* 這兒真冷。| **damn good/fine etc** *He was damn lucky he didn't have an accident.* 他還真幸運, 沒出事。**2 damn well** used to emphasize how determined or sure you are about something 肯定地, 無疑地: *I damn well will go, and I'd like to see anyone try and stop me!* 我去定了, 看誰敢攔我! **3 know damn well** used to say that someone definitely knows something, especially when you are angry 清清楚楚地知道〔表示某人肯定知道某事, 尤用在說話人發火的時候〕: *Chris knew damn well we wanted to leave at 8. Where the hell is he?* 克里斯明明知道我們要在8點出發。他死到哪裡去了? **4 damn all** *especially BrE* nothing at all【尤英】完全沒有: *Make him wash the dishes, there's damn all else he's good for.* 讓他洗盤子, 別的他根本做不來。

damn[3] *interjection* used to show that you are very annoyed or disappointed 該死, 倒霉〔表示煩惱或失望〕: *Damn! I've forgotten the keys.* 該死!我忘記帶鑰匙了。

damn[4] *n spoken*【口】**1 not give a damn** used to show that you do not care about something 毫不在乎: *I don't give a damn about her.* 我一點也不在乎她。**2 not worth a damn** used to say that you think something has no value at all 毫無價值: *Her promise isn't worth a damn.* 她的承諾分文不值。

damn[5] *v* [T] **1 damn you/them/it etc** *spoken* used to show that you are extremely angry with someone or something【口】該死的, 見鬼的, 他媽的〔表示極度氣憤〕: *Damn you! If you think you can do this to me, you're wrong!* 該死的!你如果以為可以這麼對待我, 你就錯了! **2** to state that something is very bad 貶斥; 把…說得很糟糕: *The critics damned the play on the first night.* 這齣戲在首演之夜就被評論家批評得一無是處。| **damn with faint praise** (=show that you think someone or something is very bad by only praising them a little) 名褒實貶 —see also 另見 **(as) near as damn it** (NEAR[1] (5))

dam·na·ble /ˈdæmnəbl̩; ˈdæmnəbəl/ *adj old-fashioned* very bad or annoying【過時】極壞的; 討厭的: *This damnable heat!* 這該死的高温! —**damnably** *adv*

dam·na·tion[1] /dæmˋneʃən; dæmˈneɪʃən/ *n* [U] the act of deciding to punish someone by sending them to HELL[1] (3) for ever, or the state of being in hell for ever 遭天罰; 下地獄

damnation[2] *interjection old-fashioned* used to show that you are very angry or annoyed【過時】該死〔表示憤怒或厭煩〕

damned[1] /dæmd; dæmd/ *adj* **1** [only before noun 僅用於名詞前] *spoken* used to show that you are angry or annoyed with something【口】該死的, 討厭的〔表示某物惹人生氣或厭煩〕: *a damned nuisance* 討厭的東西 **2 be damned** be sent by God to punishment without end after death 下地獄 **3 I'll be damned** *spoken* used as a strong expression of surprise【口】真沒想到〔表示極度驚奇〕**4 I'm damned if/I'll be damned if** *spoken* used to emphasize that you do not want something to happen, or that you do not know something【口】〔強調某人絕不會讓某事發生或某人根本不知道某事〕: *I'll be damned if I let her come into my house.* 我絕不讓她進我家。| *I'm damned if I know.* 我根本就不知道。**5 damned if you do, damned if you don't** used to mean that whatever you say or do will be considered to be wrong 做也不對, 不做也不對; 左右都不是〔無論某人說甚麼或做甚麼都會被認為是錯的〕

damned[2] *adv* [+adj/adv] *spoken* used to say how good something is, how bad something is etc【口】極, 非常: *War is a damned expensive business.* 戰爭是極其耗費錢財的事情。—see also 另見 DAMN[2] (1)

damned[3] *n* **the damned** the people who God will send to HELL[1] (3) when they die because they have been so bad〔由於做壞事而〕該下地獄的人

damned·est /ˈdæmdɪst; ˈdæmdɨst/ *adj informal especially AmE*【非正式, 尤美】**1 the damnedest thing/luck etc** the most unusual or surprising thing etc 最非凡[驚人]的東西/運氣等: *That machine was the damnedest thing you ever saw!* 那台機器是你見過的最奇妙的玩意兒! **2 do your damnedest** to try very hard to make something work or succeed 盡最大努力: *I'll do my damnedest to fix it, but I can't promise anything.* 我會盡全力, 但是我不能保證修好它。

damn-fool /ˈ· ·/ *adj* [only before noun 僅用於名詞前] *spoken* very stupid【口】非常愚蠢的: *That was the biggest damn-fool mistake I ever made.* 那是我犯過的最最愚蠢的錯誤。

damn·ing /ˈdæmɪŋ; ˈdæmɪŋ/ *adj* **damning indictment/comment/account** something that shows someone or something is very bad 極為不利的控告/評論/敘述: *a damning indictment of the government's economic record* 對政府經濟記錄的強烈指責

Dam·o·cles /ˈdæmə,kliz; ˈdæməkliːz/ —see 見 **sword of Damocles** (SWORD (3))

damp[1] /dæmp; dæmp/ *adj* **1** slightly wet, often in an unpleasant way 潮濕的: *Wipe the leather with a damp cloth.* 用塊濕布把皮革擦一擦。**2 damp squib** *BrE informal* something that is intended to be exciting, effective etc, but which is disappointing【英, 非正式】未達到預期效果而使人失望的事; 濕水爆竹 —**damply** *adv*

USAGE NOTE 用法說明: DAMP

WORD CHOICE 詞語辨析: **damp, moist, humid**

Damp is often used about something you would prefer to be dry. damp 通常用於最好是乾爽的東西: *damp clothes/weather* 潮濕的衣服/天氣 | *a damp bed/wall/room* 潮濕的牀鋪/牆壁/房間 | *In the* *rainy season everything gets damp I'm afraid.* 雨季的時候恐怕甚麼東西都會變潮濕的。

Moist is used especially when something is not too wet and not too dry. moist 尤其用於説明某物不太濕也不太乾: *a moist ginger cake* 一塊鬆軟的薑汁蛋糕 | *Keep houseplant soil moist – don't let it dry out.* 保持室內盆栽植物的土壤濕潤, 別讓土乾透了。

Humid is a more technical word used mainly to describe the climate or weather, or air that feels wet. humid 較術語化一些, 主要指氣候、天氣或空氣的濕潤: *It gets very humid here in the summer* (=the air is hot and damp). 這個地方的夏天非常濕熱。

You do not usually use these words to talk about people who get wet. 這三個詞通常不用來表示被水弄濕的人。

D

damp² *n* [U] *BrE* a part or area that is slightly wet【英】潮濕的部分[地方]: *There's a patch of damp on my bedroom wall.* 我臥室的牆上有一塊潮濕的地方。

damp³ *v* [T] to make a sound less loud 減低〔聲響〕: *Damp the sound with the pedal after each beat.* 每拍之後用踏板來減弱音量。

damp sth ↔ **down** *phr v* [T] **1** to make a fire burn more slowly, often by covering it with ash〔常指用蓋灰的方法〕封〔火〕, 減弱〔火勢〕**2** to control, reduce or limit something, especially a feeling 抑制〔感情〕: *damping down a child's high spirits* 打擊孩子的高漲熱情

damp course /ˈ· ·/ *n* [C] *BrE* a layer of material which is put into the bottom of a wall to prevent water rising through it【英】防潮層

damp·en /ˈdæmpən; ˈdæmpən/ *v* [T] **1** to make something slightly wet 使…潮濕 **2 dampen sb's enthusiasm/spirits** to make people feel less confident, happy, or ENTHUSIASTIC 打擊某人的熱情/情緒: *The accident had done nothing to dampen his competitive spirit.* 這次事故絲毫沒有挫傷他的競爭熱情。

dampen sth ↔ **down** *phr v* [T] to damp something down 減弱; 控制

damp·er /ˈdæmpɚ; ˈdæmpə/ *n* [C] **1** a piece of equipment that stops a piano string from making a sound〔終止鋼琴弦發出聲音的〕制音器 **2** a piece of metal that is opened or closed to control how strongly a fire burns〔控制火勢的〕擋板, 氣門, 氣閘 **3 put a damper on** to affect something in a way that makes people sad, disappointed, or less hopeful 使掃興: *This unwelcome news put a damper on the celebrations.* 這個不受歡迎的消息使慶祝會頗為掃興。

damp·ness /ˈdæmpnɪs; ˈdæmpnəs/ *n* [U] the state or condition of being slightly wet 微濕, 潮濕

dam·sel /ˈdæmzl̩; ˈdæmzəl/ *n* [C] **1** *old use* a young woman who is not married【舊】未婚的少女 **2 damsel in distress** *humorous* a young woman who needs help or protection【幽默】需要幫助[保護]的年輕女子

dam·son /ˈdæmzn̩; ˈdæmzən/ *n* [C] a small bitter dark purple PLUM¹ (1) 西洋李子

dan /dæn; dæn/ *n* [C, singular] a level of skill in a fighting sport such as JUDO, including a BLACK BELT 段〔柔道等競技運動的技藝等級〕

S2 W3 **dance¹** /dæns; dɑːns/ *n* **1** [C] an act of dancing 舞蹈, 舞: **have a dance** *Let's have one more dance before we go home.* 讓我們回家之前再跳支舞吧。| **do a dance** (=move as if you are dancing) 跳躍, 雀躍 *When Claire heard the news she did a little dance of excitement.* 克萊爾聽到這個消息時, 激動得跳了起來。**2** [C] a particular set of movements performed to music 舞蹈, 舞步: *The waltz is an easy dance to learn.* 華爾茲這種舞很容易學。**3** [C] a social meeting or party for dancing 舞會: *Are you going to the dance this weekend?* 這個週末你去參加舞會嗎? **4** [C] a piece of music which you can dance to 舞曲: *The band was playing a slow dance.* 樂隊正在演奏一支慢舞曲。**5** [U] the activity or art of dancing 舞蹈活動; 舞蹈藝術: *a course in dance and movement* 舞蹈與形體課 —see also 另見 **song and dance about** (SONG (4)), **lead sb a dance** (LEAD¹ (17))

dance² *v* **1** [I] to move your feet and body in a way that matches the style and speed of music 跳舞: *She danced with me until 3 am at a bar downtown.* 她和我在市中心的一個酒吧裡跳舞一直跳到凌晨3點。**2 dance a waltz/rumba/tango etc** to do a particular type of dance 跳華爾兹/倫巴/探戈等 **3** [I] to move up, down, and around quickly in a way that looks like dancing 跳躍, 雀躍: *Moths danced around the porch light.* 蛾子繞着門廊的燈亂舞。**4** [T always+adv/prep] to make someone or something move as if they were dancing 使…上下擺動, 使…輕快移動: *She danced the baby up and down on her knee.* 她把嬰兒放在膝上顛着。**5 dance attendance on** to do everything possible in order to please someone 奉承〔某人〕, 討〔某人〕歡心: *a movie star with several young men dancing attendance on her* 被好幾個年輕男子前呼後擁獻殷勤的女電影明星 **6 dance to sb's tune** to do what someone wants you to do in a way that shows complete obedience〔完全〕聽從某人指揮, 服從某人差遣: *They control all the funding so we have to dance to their tune.* 他們控制着所有的資金, 所以我們得聽他們指揮。—**dancing** *n* [U]: *her love of dancing* 她對舞蹈的熱愛

dance-band /ˈ· ·/ *n* [C] a group of musicians who play music that you dance to 伴舞樂隊

dance floor /ˈ· ·/ *n* [C] a special floor in a restaurant, hotel etc for people to dance on 舞池

dance hall /ˈ· ·/ *n* [C] a large public room where people used to pay to go and dance 舞廳

danc·er /ˈdænsɚ; ˈdɑːnsə/ *n* [C] **1** someone who dances as a profession 舞蹈演員, 舞蹈家: **ballet/ballroom etc dancer** *I want to be a ballet dancer when I grow up.* 我長大後想當一名芭蕾舞演員。**2 good/bad etc dancer** someone who dances well, badly etc 跳舞跳得好/差等的人

D and C /ˌdi ənd ˈsi; ˌdiː ənd ˈsiː/ *n* [C] a medical operation to clean out the inside of a woman's WOMB 刮宮術

dan·de·li·on /ˈdændɪˌlaɪən; ˈdændəlaɪən/ *n* [C] a wild plant with yellow flowers, and white balls of seeds that travel a long way in the air 蒲公英

dandelion clock /ˈ···· ˌ·/ *n* [C] the soft ball of white seeds that grows on the dandelion plant 蒲公英上的白色絨球

dan·der /ˈdændɚ; ˈdændə/ *n* **get sb's dander up** *old-fashioned* to make someone angry【過時】惹某人生氣, 使某人發火

dan·di·fied /ˈdændɪˌfaɪd; ˈdændɪfaɪd/ *adj old-fashioned* a man who is dandified wears very fashionable clothes in a way that shows he cares too much about his appearance【過時】〔男子〕穿着非常時髦的, 過分注重外表的

dan·dle /ˈdændl; ˈdændl/ *v* [T] *old-fashioned* to play with a baby or small child by moving them up and down in your arms or on your knee【過時】〔在懷中或在膝上顛着〕逗孩子玩

dan·druff /ˈdændrəf; ˈdændrəf/ *n* [U] pieces of dead skin from your head that can be seen as a white dust in your hair and on your shoulders 頭皮屑

dan·dy¹ /ˈdændɪ; ˈdændi/ *n* [C] *old-fashioned* a man who spends a lot of time and money on his clothes and appearance【過時】過分注重穿着打扮的男子, 花花公子

dandy² *adj old-fashioned especially AmE* very good【過時, 尤美】很好的: *"Let's go to the movies." "That'll be dandy."* "我們去看電影吧。" "那太好了。"

Dane /den; deɪn/ *n* [C] someone from Denmark 丹麥人

dang /dæŋ; dæŋ/ *interjection AmE spoken* a less offensive word for DAMN【美口】該死的〔damn 的委婉詞〕

dan·ger /ˈdendʒɚ; ˈdeɪndʒə/ *n* **1** [U] the possibility that someone or something will be harmed or killed 危險: *Danger! High Voltage.* 高壓! 危險! | [+of] *Is there any* danger of infection, doctor? 醫生, 有感染的危險嗎? | [+from] *danger from radioactive sources* 來自放射源的危險 | **in danger** (=in a situation in which you may be harmed or killed) 處在危險中 *I had a sudden feeling that Petra was in danger.* 我忽然預感到彼得拉有危險。| **out of danger** (=not in danger any more) 脫離危險 *The patient is now out of danger.* 病人現在已經脫離危險。**2** [C often plural 常用複數] something or someone that may harm or kill you 威脅, 危害: *I think he enjoys the dangers of rock climbing.* 我想他喜歡攀岩過程中的種種危險。| **face dangers** (=do something that involves dangers) 面對[應付]危險的事物 *All boxers are well aware of the dangers they face in the ring.* 所有的拳擊手都十分清楚, 他們在拳擊場中會遇到種種危險。| **be a danger to** *The wreck is a danger to other ships.* 沉船對其他船隻構成威脅。**3** [C,U] the possibility that something unpleasant will happen〔不愉快事情可能發生的〕危險: **danger that** *There is always the danger that Elizabeth will go back on her promise.* 伊麗莎白違背諾言的危險總是存在的。| [+of] *Is there much danger of losing money?* 賠錢的危險是不是很大? | **be in danger of** (=be in a situation in which something unpleasant may happen) 有〔不好事情發生的〕危險 *Carlos is in danger of losing his job.* 卡洛斯有丟掉工作的危險。**4 be on the danger list** to be so ill that you may die 病危 **5 there's no danger of that** used to mean that something bad will not happen 沒有發生壞事的危險

danger mon·ey /ˈ·· ˌ··/ *n* [U] *especially BrE* additional money that you are paid for doing dangerous work【尤英】危險工作津貼; DANGER PAY *AmE*【美】

2 **dan·ger·ous** /ˈdendʒərəs; ˈdeɪndʒərəs/ *adj* **1** able or
2 likely to harm or kill you 危險的, 有危害的: *dangerous animals* 危險動物 | *Neil thought the man looked dangerous.* 尼爾認為那個男子看起來很危險。| **it is dangerous (for sb) to do sth** *It's dangerous for women to walk alone at night.* 女子晚上一個人走路有危險。| **highly/very dangerous** *It would be highly dangerous to attempt to cross the river just here.* 想從這兒過河會非常危險。**2** a belief, situation, or action that is dangerous involves a lot of risk, or is likely to cause problems〔信念、形勢或行動〕充滿風險的, 有危險的: *The business is in a dangerous financial position.* 公司的財政狀況非常危急。**3 dangerous ground/territory** a situation or subject that could make someone very angry or upset 危險地帶〔指能惹某人生氣或不安的情形或話題〕: *You're on dangerous ground when you talk politics with Ed.* 你一和艾德談政治, 就步入了危險境地。—**dangerously** *adv*: *driving dangerously* 危險駕駛 | *dangerously high temperatures* 危險的高溫

danger pay /ˈ·· ˌ·/ *n* [U] *AmE*【美】= DANGER MONEY *BrE*【英】

dan·gle /ˈdæŋgl̩; ˈdæŋgəl/ *v* **1** [I,T] to hang or swing loosely, or make something do this 懸吊, 晃動不定; 使…懸吊[晃動]: *a leather purse dangled from his belt* 他皮帶上懸吊着的一個皮包 | **dangle sth** *I dangled my feet in the clear blue water.* 我把腳放到清澈碧藍的水中搖晃着。**2 dangle sth in front of sb** to offer something good to someone in order to persuade them to do something〔為讓某人做某事〕用某物誘惑某人, 用某物引誘某人: *The promise of an ice-cream cone was dangled in front of us, as a reward for washing the car.* 用吃甜筒冰淇淋的許諾來誘惑我們洗車。

Da·nish¹ /ˈdenɪʃ; ˈdeɪnɪʃ/ *n* [U] **1** the language of Denmark 丹麥語 **2** [C] *AmE* a Danish pastry【美】丹麥甜酥皮糕餅

Danish² *adj* connected with the people or language of Denmark 丹麥人的; 丹麥語的

Danish pas·try /ˌ·· ˈ··/ *n* [C] a very sweet cake made of light PASTRY (1) 丹麥甜酥皮糕餅

dank /dæŋk; dæŋk/ *adj* unpleasantly wet and cold 濕冷的, 陰冷的: *a dank prison cell* 陰冷的牢房 —**dankness** *n* [U]

dap·per /ˈdæpɚ; ˈdæpə/ *adj* **1** a man who is dapper is small and has a neat appearance〔指男人〕短小精悍的: *He was small, dapper, and wore a green bow tie.* 他長得短小精悍, 繫着綠色的蝶形領結。**2** nicely dressed 衣冠楚楚的: *You're looking very dapper in your new suit!* 你穿着新西裝真精神!

dap·ple /ˈdæpl̩; ˈdæpəl/ *v* [T] *literary* to mark something with spots of colour, light, or shade【文】使〔某物〕有斑點, 使〔某物〕斑駁

dap·pled /ˈdæpl̩d; ˈdæpəld/ *adj* marked with spots of colour, light, or shade 有花斑的, 有亮斑的, 斑駁的: *a sky dappled with clouds* 點綴着朵朵白雲的天空

dapple-grey /ˌ·· ˈ· ◂/ *n* [C] a horse that is grey with spots of darker grey 灰色帶黑斑的馬

Dar·by and Joan /ˈdɑrbɪ ən ˈdʒon; ˌdɑːbi ən ˈdʒəʊn/ *n* **be like Darby and Joan** *BrE humorous* used when talking about an old husband and wife who live very happily together【英, 幽默】是一對恩愛的老夫婦

dare¹ /dɛr; deə/ *v* 3

1 ►DO STH DANGEROUS 做危險的事◄ [I not in progressive 不用進行式] to be brave enough to do something dangerous or that you are afraid to do 膽敢, 敢於〔做危險的或一般人害怕做的事情〕: *The others used to steal things from stores, but I would never dare.* 其他人曾經偷過商店的東西, 我可從來不敢。| **dare (to) do sth** *Would you dare to do a parachute jump?* 你敢跳傘嗎?

2 ►DO STH RUDE/SHOCKING ETC 做無禮的/令人震驚的事情等◄ [I] to be confident enough, rude enough, or dishonest enough to do something that is very rude, shocking, or wrong 膽敢, 竟敢〔做特別無禮的、令人震驚的或錯誤的事情〕: *Tell her what I really think? I wouldn't dare!* 告訴她我的真實想法? 我可不敢!

3 how dare you *spoken* used to show that you are very angry and shocked about what someone has done or said【口】你竟敢, 你怎麼敢〔表示對他人行為、言辭的憤怒和震驚〕: *How dare you accuse me of lying!* 你竟敢指責我撒謊!

4 don't you dare! *spoken* used to warn someone not to do something because it makes you angry【口】你敢!〔用於警告某人不要做某事以免惹你生氣〕: *Don't you dare talk to me like that!* 少跟我這樣講話!

5 ►PERSUADE SB TO DO STH 激某人做某事◄ [T] to try to persuade someone to do something dangerous or embarrassing as a way of proving that they are brave 激將, 激: **dare sb to do sth** *They dared Lenny to climb to the very top branch.* 他們挑激倫尼, 看他敢不敢爬到最高的樹杈上去。| **I dare you!** *spoken*【口】*Go on! Ask her for her telephone number. I dare you!* 去呀! 問她要電話號碼。我量你不敢!

6 dare I say/suggest *formal spoken* used when adding information that you think people may not accept or believe【正式, 口】我可以說〔用於添加可能不被承認或相信的信息〕: *I found him intelligent, observant, and, dare I say it, a sparkling wit!* 我認為他這個人聰明、機警, 或許我可以說他非常風趣!

7 I dare say *spoken especially BrE* used when saying or agreeing that something may perhaps be true【口, 尤英】我相信; 可能: *I dare say things will improve.* 我想事情會好起來的。

dare² *n* [C] something dangerous that you have dared someone to do 激將, 挑戰: *a dare to run through the field with the bull in it* 跑過公牛所在的田地的挑戰 | **for a dare** (=because someone has dared you to) 因受到激將 *I only did it for a dare.* 我受到激將才這麼做的。

dare·dev·il /ˈdɛrˌdɛvl̩; ˈdeədevəl/ *n* [C] someone who likes doing dangerous things 喜歡冒險的人: *a daredevil motorcyclist* 一個膽子很大的摩托車手 —**daredevil** *adj*

daren't /dɛrnt; deənt/ *spoken*【口】the short form of 縮略式 = 'dare not' (DARE¹ (1))

dare·say /ˌdɛrˈse; ˌdeəˈseɪ◂/ *v* **I daresay** *especially BrE* used when saying or agreeing that something may perhaps be true【尤英】我想, 也許: *I daresay you're right.*

也許你是對的。

dar·ing¹ /ˈdɛrɪŋ; ˈdeərɪŋ/ *adj* **1** willing to do something that is dangerous or that involves a lot of risk 勇敢的, 英勇的: *the daring lifeboatmen* 勇敢的救生艇水手 | *a daring rescue attempt* 英勇的救援努力 **2** new or unusual in a way that is sometimes shocking 大膽的, 別出心裁的: *a daring film* 一部大膽的電影 | *Sometimes her outfits were more daring than usual.* 有時候, 她的衣着比平時更大膽出奇。—**daringly** *adv*: *daringly close to the edge* 離懸崖邊緣非常近

daring² *n* [U] courage that makes you willing to take risks 勇氣, 膽量: *a plan of great daring* 大膽創新的計劃

dark¹ /dɑrk; dɑːk/ *adj*

1 ►PLACE 地方◄ a dark place is one where there is little or no light〔指某個地方〕黑暗的, 昏暗的, 無光的: *The church was dark and quiet.* 教堂裡黑黑的、靜靜的。| *I waited for them in a dark alley.* 我在昏暗的小巷裡等他們。| **go dark** (=become dark) 變暗 *Suddenly, the room went dark and somebody screamed.* 忽然, 屋裡的燈滅了, 有人尖叫起來。—opposite 反義詞 LIGHT² (3)

2 ►COLOUR 顏色◄ not light or pale in colour 暗色的, 深色的: **dark blue/green/pink etc** *a dark blue dress* 一件深藍色的衣服 —opposite 反義詞 LIGHT² (1)

3 it gets dark when it gets dark in the evening the light disappears and night begins 天黑了, 天晚了: *Come on, let's go in, it's getting dark.* 快點, 我們進去吧, 天快黑了。

4 ►HAIR/EYES 頭髮/眼睛◄ someone who is dark has hair and eyes that are black or brown〔頭髮和眼睛〕黑色的; 褐色的: *a tall, dark man* 黑眼睛黑頭髮的高個子男人 —opposite 反義詞 FAIR¹ (5)

5 ►THREATENING/MYSTERIOUS ETC 陰險的/神祕的等◄ threatening, mysterious, or evil 陰險的, 神祕的, 邪惡的: *the dark forces of the night* 夜晚的神祕力量 | *There was a darker side to his character.* 他性格有着邪惡的一面。

6 ►FEELINGS/THOUGHTS 情感/思想◄ dark thoughts are sad and show that you think something very bad may happen 憂愁的, 憂鬱的: *I sat there gloomily, thinking dark thoughts.* 我憂鬱地坐在那兒, 想着一些不愉快的事。

7 keep sth dark *informal* to keep something secret【非正式】對某事保密: *You're getting married! You kept that dark!* 你要結婚了! 但你卻守口如瓶!

8 ►UNHAPPY TIME 不快樂的時光◄ a dark time is unhappy or without hope 無望的, 希望渺茫的: *in the dark days of the war* 在那段黑暗的戰爭日子裡 | *Even in the darkest moments, I still had you, my love.* 即使在最無望的日子裡我還有你, 親愛的。

9 dark horse a) someone who people do not know much about who surprises everyone by winning a competition 黑馬〔競爭中出乎意料獲勝的人〕 **b)** *BrE* someone who does not tell people much and who has surprising qualities or abilities【英】深藏不露的人: *She's a dark horse. I didn't know she'd written a novel.* 她深藏不露。我不知道她寫過小說。

10 darkest Africa/South America etc *old-fashioned* the parts of Africa etc about which we know very little【過時】鮮為人知的非洲/南美地區等 —see also 另見 PITCH-BLACK

dark² *n* [U] **1 the dark** a situation in which there is no light 黑暗, 無光: *Children are sometimes afraid of the dark.* 孩子們有時怕黑。| **in the dark** *Be careful if you're walking home in the dark.* 晚上走路回家時小心點。**2 after dark** at night 天黑以後: *Some of my friends won't go out after dark.* 我的一些朋友天黑以後不願外出。**3 before dark** before the time when it gets dark at night 天黑以前: *You can go out, but make sure you come home before dark.* 你可以出去, 但是你必須天黑以前回家。**4 be in the dark** *informal* to know nothing about something important because you have not been told about it【非正式】不知, 無知: *Well, I'm afraid we're in the dark as much as you are.* 恐怕我們和你們一樣都被蒙在鼓裡。| **keep sb in the dark** *The public was kept in the dark about the assassination attempt.* 公眾對這次暗殺行動一無所知。—see also 另見 **a shot in the dark** (SHOT¹ (13))

Dark Ag·es /ˈ· ˌ··/ *n* **the Dark Ages** the period in European history from 476 AD to about 1000 AD 黑暗時代〔歐洲歷史上從公元476年到公元1000年的一段時期〕

dark·en /ˈdɑrkən; ˈdɑːkən/ *v* [I, T] **1** to become dark, or make something dark (使…) 變暗: *the skies darkened* 天空暗了下來 | *The sun had darkened his skin.* 太陽曬黑了他的皮膚。**2** to become less happy or positive or make someone feel this way (使) 變得不樂觀; (使) 不快: *The news darkened their view of the situation.* 這個消息使他們對形勢的看法悲觀起來。**3 never darken my door again** *old-fashioned humorous* used to tell someone that you do not want them in your house again【過時, 幽默】別再來我家了

dark glass·es /ˌ· ˈ··/ *n* [plural] glasses with dark glass in them, that you wear to protect your eyes from the sun or to hide your eyes 墨鏡, 太陽眼鏡

dark·ie /ˈdɑrkɪ; ˈdɑːki/ *n* [C] *old-fashioned* an offensive word for a black person【過時】黑鬼〔對黑人的冒犯用語〕

dark·ly /ˈdɑrklɪ; ˈdɑːkli/ *adv* **1** in an unpleasant or threatening way 不快地, 威脅地: *'Don't you be too sure,' said Marcus darkly.* "你別那麼肯定。"馬庫斯臉色陰沉地說。**2** with a dark colour 深色地: *Philip flushed darkly.* 菲利普臉漲得通紅。

dark·ness /ˈdɑrknɪs; ˈdɑːknɪs/ *n* [U] **1** a place or time when there is no light 黑暗: *Beyond the glittering street was darkness.* 燈火通明的街道盡頭是一片黑暗。| **total darkness** (=complete darkness) 一片漆黑 *The clouds moved across the moon, leaving us in total darkness.* 雲把月亮遮住了, 我們被籠罩在黑暗之中。| **darkness falls** (=it becomes night) 天色黑下來 **2 forces/powers of darkness** evil or the devil 黑勢力, 惡勢力 **3** the dark quality of a colour〔一種顏色的〕深, 暗

dark·room /ˈdɑrkˌrum; ˈdɑːkruːm/ *n* [C] a dark room where film is taken out of a camera and made into a photograph〔沖洗膠卷的〕暗室, 暗房, 黑房

dar·ling¹ /ˈdɑrlɪŋ; ˈdɑːlɪŋ/ *n* [C] **1** a way of speaking to someone that you love 親愛的, 寶貝〔稱呼心愛的人〕: *Hurry up, darling.* 快點, 親愛的。**2** someone who seems very nice, generous, friendly etc 好人, 樂於助人的人: *He's such a darling.* 他真是個好人。**3 the darling of** the most popular person in a particular group or area of activity 紅人, 寵兒〔某一羣體或領域中最受歡迎的人〕: *She's the darling of the fashion world.* 她是時裝界的紅人。

darling² *adj* [only before noun 僅用於名詞前] *spoken* used when you love someone or something very much, or when you think something is very attractive【口】心愛的, 惹人喜愛的: *my two darling daughters* 我的兩個可愛的女兒 | *What a darling little house!* 多麼討人喜歡的小屋啊!

darn¹ /dɑrn; dɑːn/ *v* [T] **1** to repair a hole in a piece of clothing by stitching wool over it 織補, 縫補: *darning socks* 縫補襪子 **2 darn it!** *spoken* used when you are annoyed about something【口】討厭! 可惡! 倒霉!〔用於某人生氣、厭煩的時候〕: *Darn it! I'll have to do it all myself!* 討厭! 都得由我一個人來做! **3 I'll be darned!** *spoken* used when you are surprised about something【口】真沒想到!〔表示驚訝〕: *Did they really? Well, I'll be darned!* 他們真的嗎? 哎, 真沒想到!

darn² *n* [C] a place where a hole in a piece of clothing has been repaired neatly with wool 縫補之處

darn³ also 又作 **darned** /dɑrnd; dɑːnd/ *adj spoken* used to emphasize how bad, stupid, unfair etc someone or something is【口】極, 非常〔強調某人或某物是多麼糟糕、愚蠢、不公平等〕: *The darn fool got lost on the way.* 這個十足的傻瓜竟然迷了路。—**darn** also 又作 **darned**

adv: *It was a darned good movie.* 這是一部極好的電影。

darn·ing /ˋdarnɪŋ; ˈdɑːnɪŋ/ *n* [U] the practice of repairing holes in clothing by using wool 織補, 織補工作

dart¹ /dart; dɑːt/ *v* **1** [I always+adv/prep] to move suddenly and quickly in a particular direction 突進, 猛衝: **[+forward/across/off etc]** *Jill darted forward and pulled him away from the fire.* 吉爾衝上前把他從火邊拉開。**2 dart a glance/look** to look at someone or something very quickly and suddenly 瞥一眼/掃一眼: *Tom darted a terrified glance over his shoulder.* 湯姆驚恐地回頭瞥了一眼。

dart² *n* **1** [C] a small pointed object that is thrown or shot as a weapon or thrown in the game of darts 鏢, 飛鏢: *a poisoned dart* 毒鏢 **2 darts** a game in which darts are thrown at a round board with numbers on it 擲鏢遊戲 **3** [singular] a sudden, quick movement in a particular direction 猛衝, 突進: **make a dart at/for** *The prisoner made a dart for the door.* 犯人猛地朝門口衝去。**4** [C] a small fold put into a piece of clothing to make it fit better〔衣服上的〕縫褶

dart·board /ˋdartˌbɔrd; ˈdɑːtbɔːd/ *n* [C] a round board used in the game of darts〔擲鏢遊戲中的〕圓靶

dash¹ /dæʃ; dæʃ/ *v* **1** [I] to go or run somewhere very quickly 猛衝: **[+into/across/behind etc]** *Olive dashed into the room, grabbed her bag and ran out again.* 奧利芙衝進屋, 抓起她的手提袋又跑了出來。**2** [T always+adv/prep] to make something move violently against a surface, usually so that it breaks 猛擊, 撞擊: **dash sth against/onto/to etc** *The ship was dashed against the rocks.* 船猛撞在礁石上。**3 dash sb's hopes** to disappoint someone by telling them that what they want is not possible 使某人的希望破滅, 讓某人失望: *Budget cuts dashed hopes for several plans proposed by NASA.* 削減預算使幾個由美國太空總署提出的計劃落了空。**4 (I) must dash/(I) have to dash** *BrE spoken* used to tell someone that you must leave quickly【英口】(我) 得趕緊走了: *I must dash – I said I'd meet Daniel at eight o'clock.* 我得趕緊走了, 我説好和丹尼爾 8 點鐘見面。**5 dash it (all)!** *BrE spoken* used to show that you are slightly annoyed or angry about something【英口】〔表示有些厭煩、生氣〕討厭!: *Dash it! I can't find my scissors!* 討厭!我找不着剪刀了! **6** [I always+adv/prep] if a wave or rain dashes against something it hits it hard〔波浪或大雨猛烈地〕撞擊, 沖擊: *Stormy waves dashed against the shore.* 洶湧的海浪沖擊着海岸。

dash off *phr v* **1** [I] to leave somewhere very quickly 匆匆地離開: *Harry dashed off before she had a chance to thank him.* 她還沒來得及説聲謝謝, 哈里就匆匆地跑開了。**2** [T **dash** sth ↔ **off**] to write or draw something very quickly 匆匆地寫[畫]〔某物〕: *She dashed off a quick letter excusing him from school that day.* 她匆匆地寫了封信, 為他那天沒有到校上學開脱。

dash² *n*

1 ►LINE 線條◄ [C] a line [–] used in writing and printing, for example in the sentence "Go home – they're waiting for you." 破折號 —compare 比較 HYPHEN

2 make a dash for to run very quickly in order to get away from something or in order to reach something 猛衝, 飛奔: **make a dash for cover/freedom etc** *The prisoners made a dash for freedom.* 犯人們猛跑, 想逃出去獲得自由。| **make a dash for it** *It's pouring with rain – we'll have to make a dash for it.* 下大雨了 — 我們得趕緊跑去找個避雨的地方。

3 ►SMALL AMOUNT 少量◄ [singular] a very small amount of a liquid or other substance 少許, 少量〔液體或其他物質〕: **[+of]** *Add salt, pepper and a dash of vinegar.* 加點鹽、胡椒, 再加少許醋。—see picture on page A7 參見 A7 頁圖

4 a mad dash *informal* an attempt to get somewhere or do something extremely quickly【非正式】急奔, 狂衝: *When the alarm went there was a mad dash for the exit.* 警報一響, 人們都朝着出口處猛衝。

5 ►SOUND 聲音◄ [C] a long sound or flash of light used for sending messages in MORSE CODE〔用莫爾斯電碼發報時用的〕長音; 光的一長閃 —compare 比較 DOT¹ (4)

6 ►CAR 汽車◄ [C] *AmE informal* DASHBOARD【美, 非正式】〔汽車的〕儀表板

7 ►STYLE 風範◄ [U] *old-fashioned* style, energy, and courage in someone such as a soldier【過時】〔如士兵般的〕帥勁, 精力, 幹勁; 勇氣

8 cut a dash to look very impressive and attractive in particular clothes〔尤指穿着〕有氣派, 精神, 漂亮: *Edmond really cut a dash in that white linen suit.* 艾德蒙穿着那套白色亞麻西裝真是帥氣。

dash·board /ˋdæʃˌbɔrd; ˈdæʃbɔːd/ *n* [C] the board at the front of a car that has the controls on it〔汽車的〕儀表板 —see picture on page A2 參見 A2 頁圖

dashed /dæʃt; dæʃt/ *adj* [only before noun 僅用於名詞前] *BrE old-fashioned* used to emphasize what you are saying【英, 過時】該死的, 討厭的〔強調所說的話〕: *Harry talked dashed nonsense all evening.* 哈里整個晚上講的全都是大廢話。

dash·ing /ˋdæʃɪŋ; ˈdæʃɪŋ/ *adj* a man who is dashing is very attractive, fashionable, and confident〔指人〕精神抖擻的; 時髦的; 有自信的 —**dashingly** *adv*

dast·ard·ly /ˋdæstədlɪ; ˈdæstədli/ *adj old-fashioned* very cruel or evil【過時】殘酷的, 邪惡的: *a dastardly plot* 陰險惡毒的陰謀

DAT /ˌdi e ˋti; ˌdiː eɪ ˈtiː/ *n* [U] digital audio tape; a system used to record music, sound, or information in DIGITAL form〔用數碼形式錄製音樂、聲音或信息的〕數碼錄音磁帶

da·ta /ˋdetə; ˈdeɪtə/ *n* [U, plural] **1** information or facts 資料: *We cannot tell you the results until we have looked at all the data.* 我們看過所有的資料之後才能告訴你結果。**2** information in a form that can be stored and used 數據, 資料: *data retrieval system* 數據檢索系統 [S1] [W1]

data bank /ˈ‥ ˌ·/ *n* [C] a place, especially a computer, where information on a particular subject is stored 數據庫, 資料庫: *a missing persons data bank* 失蹤人員的數據庫

da·ta·base /ˋdetəˌbes; ˈdeɪtəˌbeɪs/ *n* [C] a large amount of data stored in a computer system so that you can find and use it easily〔存入電腦系統中的可供隨時檢索、使用的〕資料庫, 數據庫: *Put the new customers on the database.* 把新客戶的資料輸入數據庫。[S2] [W2]

data bus /ˈ‥ ·/ *n* [C] *technical* an electronic path along which DATA travels from one part of a computer to another【術語】〔資料從電腦的一個部分到另一個部分的〕數據總線

data pro·cess·ing /ˌ‥ ˈ‥·/ *n* [U] the use of computers to store and organize data, especially in business 數據處理

date¹ /det; deɪt/ *n* [C] **1** the numbers or words you use to talk about a particular day, month, and year 日期, 日子: *The date on the letter was the 30th August 1962.* 這封信上的日期是 1962 年 8 月 30 日。| **date of birth** (=the day you were born) 出生日期 *Please write your name, address, and date of birth on the form.* 請在表格裡填上你的姓名、地址和出生日期。**2** a particular day 日子〔特定的某一天〕: *a date for the next meeting* 下一次會議的日期 | **set a date** (=choose a particular date) 選定一個日子 *Have you set a date for the wedding?* 婚禮的日子定下來了嗎? **3 at a later date** *formal* at some time in the future【正式】晚些時候〔將來的某個時間〕: *We'll deal with this problem at a later date.* 我們晚些時候再處理這個問題。**4 to date** up to now 迄今, 至今, 到目前為止: *To date there has been no improvement in his condition.* 到現在為止, 他的狀況還是沒有改善。**5 a)** an occasion when you arrange to meet someone that you like in a romantic way〔戀人之間的〕約會: *Do you have a date tonight?* 今晚你有約會嗎? | **go (out) on a date** *"So, what did he say?" "Well, we're going on a date* [S1] [W1]

Friday night." "他怎麼說?" "嗯, 我們星期五晚上去約會。" —see also 另見 BLIND DATE **b)** *AmE* someone that you have a date with【美】約會對象: *Can I bring my date to the party?* 我可以帶約會對象來參加派對嗎? **6 make a date** to agree on a time to meet someone socially 約好時間: *Let's make a date to go and see 'Arcadia' one day next week.* 讓我們約個時間下個星期去看"阿卡迪亞"。**7** a sweet sticky brown fruit with a long hard seed inside 椰棗, 海棗 —see also 另見 CLOSING DATE, **expiry date** (EXPIRY (2)), SELL-BY DATE, OUT-OF-DATE, UP-TO-DATE

date² *v* **1** [T] to write or print the date on something〔在某物上〕寫上[印上]日期: *a newspaper dated November 23, 1963* 一份日期為 1963 年 11 月 23 日的報紙 **2** [T] to find out when something old such as a book, painting, building etc was made 鑑定〔古書、古畫、古建築等的〕年代: *The rocks are dated by examining the fossils found in the same layer.* 通過查看在同一岩層裡發現的化石來鑑定岩石的年代。**3** [I] if clothing, art etc dates, it looks old-fashioned〔衣物、藝術等〕過時: *His designs are so successful, they've hardly dated at all.* 他的設計太成功了, 現在看起來都幾乎一點也不過時。**4** [T] *AmE* to have a romantic relationship with someone【美】〔談戀愛〕與…約會: **be dating sb** *Is he still dating Sarah?* 他還和莎拉好嗎? **5** [T] if something that you say, do, or wear dates you, it shows that you are fairly old 顯示〔某人〕老了: *Yes, I remember the moon landings – that dates me doesn't it?* 是的, 我記得登月的事 —— 這說明我老了, 是不是?

date from also 又作 **date back to** *phr v* [I] to have existed since a particular time in the past 自…存在至今, 追溯到…年代: *This church dates from the 13th century.* 這座教堂的歷史可以追溯到 13 世紀。

dat·ed /ˋdetɪd; ˈdeɪtɪ̈d/ *adj* old-fashioned 過時的: *That dress looks dated now.* 那件衣服現在看起來過時了。—compare 比較 OUT-OF-DATE

date·line /ˋdetˌlaɪn; ˈdeɪtlaɪn/ *n* [singular] the INTERNATIONAL DATE LINE〔國際〕日界線, 國際日期變更線

date rape /ˈ· ·/ *n* [C, U] a RAPE that is done by someone the woman has met in a social situation 約會強姦

date stamp /ˈ· ·/ *n* [C] **a)** a piece of equipment used for printing the date on letters, documents etc 日期戳 **b)** the mark that it makes 日期戳印

dating a·gen·cy /ˈ·· ˌ···/ *n* [C] a business that helps people to meet other people, to have a romantic relationship 婚姻介紹所

da·tive /ˋdetɪv; ˈdeɪtɪv/ *n* [C] *technical* a particular form of a noun in some languages such as Latin and German, which shows that the noun is the INDIRECT OBJECT of a verb【術語】與格〔拉丁語和德語等語言中名詞的特殊形式, 表示這個名詞是某個動詞的間接賓語〕—**dative** *adj*

daub¹ /dɔb; dɔːb/ *v* [T] to paint or cover something with a soft substance, without being very careful〔胡亂〕塗抹, 玷污: *faces daubed with black mud* 抹上黑泥的臉

daub² *n* **1** [U] *technical* mud or clay used for making walls【術語】〔抹牆的〕塗料 —see also 另見 **wattle and daub** (WATTLE (2)) **2** a small amount of a soft or sticky substance 少量軟而黏的物質: **[+of]** *a daub of paint* 少量的塗料

daugh·ter /ˋdɔtɚ; ˈdɔːtə/ *n* [C] **1** someone's female child 女兒: *My daughter's at university now.* 我女兒現在正在讀大學。—see picture at 參見 FAMILY 圖 **2** *technical* something new that forms or develops when something else divides or ends【術語】產物: *a daughter language* 子語言

daughter-in-law /ˈ·· ·ˌ·/ *n plural* **daughters-in-law** [C] your son's wife 兒媳婦 —compare 比較 SON-IN-LAW —see picture at 參見 FAMILY 圖

daugh·ter·ly /ˋdɔtɚlɪ; ˈdɔːtəli/ *adj old-fashioned* behaving in a way that a daughter is supposed to behave【過時】女兒般的; 盡女兒之道的

daunt /dɔnt; dɔːnt/ *v* [T usually passive 一般用被動態] **1** to make someone feel afraid or less confident 使〔某人〕害怕, 使減少信心: *He felt utterly daunted by the prospect of moving to another country.* 他一想到要移居到別的國家就感到十分害怕。**2 nothing daunted** *formal* not at all discouraged【正式】毫不氣餒, 並不畏難: *It was steep but, nothing daunted, he started climbing.* 路很陡峭, 但是他還是毫不畏懼, 開始向上攀登。

daunt·ing /ˋdɔntɪŋ; ˈdɔːntɪŋ/ *adj* frightening in a way that makes you feel less confident 使人氣餒的: *It's a daunting task, but we're optimistic.* 這是一項艱巨的任務, 但是我們很樂觀。| **daunting prospect** (=something daunting that you are going to do) 嚇人[令人畏懼]的前景 *the daunting prospect of asking for a loan* 令人發怵的借貸一事

daunt·less /ˋdɔntlɪs; ˈdɔːntləs/ *adj literary* confident and not easily frightened【文】勇敢的, 無畏的: *dauntless optimism* 無所畏懼的樂觀精神 —**dauntlessly** *adv*

dau·phin /ˋdɔfɪn; ˈdɔːfɪn/ *n* [C] the oldest son of a King of France 法國王儲, 王太子

dau·phine /dɔˋfin; ˈdɔːfiːn/ *n* [C] the wife of the oldest son of a King of France 法國王太子妃

dav·en·port /ˋdævənˌport; ˈdævənpɔːt/ *n* [C] *AmE* a large SOFA, especially one that can be made into a bed【美】〔尤指可以作牀用的〕大沙發

dav·it /ˋdævɪt; ˈdævɪ̈t/ *n* [C] one of a pair of long curved poles that sailors swing out over the side of a ship in order to lower a boat into the water〔輪船上的〕吊艇柱, 吊艇架, 吊艇杆

daw·dle /ˋdɔdl̩; ˈdɔːdl/ *v* [I] to take a long time to do something or go somewhere〔做事等〕磨蹭, 緩慢地做: *Don't dawdle – we're late already!* 別磨蹭了 —— 我們已經晚了! | **[+over]** *I dawdled over a second cup of coffee.* 我慢吞吞地啜飲着第二杯咖啡。—**dawdler** *n* [C]

dawn¹ /dɔn; dɔːn/ *n* [C, U] **1** the time at the beginning of the day when light first appears 黎明, 破曉: *We talked almost until dawn.* 我們幾乎一直談到天亮。| **at dawn** *The first boats set off at dawn.* 第一批船天一亮就出發了。| **dawn breaks** (=the first light of the day appears) 破曉 *When dawn broke we were still 50 miles from Calcutta.* 破曉的時候, 我們離加爾各答還有 50 英里。| **at the crack of dawn** (=very early in the morning) 黎明, 破曉 *I was up at the crack of dawn to get the plane.* 我一大早就起來趕飛機。—compare 比較 DUSK **2 the dawn of civilization/time etc** the time when something began or first appeared 文明/時代等的開端: *People have been falling in love since the dawn of time.* 自先民伊始, 人們就一直在墜入愛河。**3 a false dawn** something that seems positive or hopeful but really is not 假曙光〔指虛幻的好跡象〕: *another false dawn on the road to recovery* 康復路上的又一線假曙光

dawn² *v* [I] **1** if day or morning dawns, it begins 破曉, 天亮: *The morning dawned fresh and clear after the storm.* 暴雨過後的清晨, 天一破曉就晴空萬里, 空氣清新。**2** *literary* if a period of time or situation dawns, it begins【文】開始: *The age of Darwin had dawned.* 達爾文時代開始了。**3** *formal* if a feeling or idea dawns, you think of it for the first time【正式】開始明白, 第一次想起〔某種感覺或想法〕

dawn on sb *phr v* [T not in passive 不用被動態] if a fact dawns on you, you realize it for the first time 開始明白〔某個事實〕, 醒悟: *Then the ghastly truth dawned on me.* 接着我突然明白了可怕的真相。| **it dawns on sb that** *It dawned on me that Joanna had been right all along.* 我突然意識到喬安娜一直都是對的。

dawn cho·rus /ˌ· ˈ··/ *n* [singular] *especially BrE* the sound of many birds singing at dawn【尤英】〔清晨〕百鳥齊鳴

dawn raid /ˌ· ˈ·/ *n* [C] an attack or operation that happens very early in the morning, especially involving the police〔尤指警方的〕淩晨突襲; 拂曉襲擊

day /de; deɪ/ *n*

① PERIOD OF TIME 一段時間
② THE TIME YOU ARE AWAKE 白天
③ FUTURE 將來
④ PAST 過去
⑤ SB'S LIFE/STH'S EXISTENCE 一個人的一生/一件東西的壽命
⑥ WORK 工作
⑦ EACH DAY/EVERY DAY 每天
⑧ NOW 現在
⑨ BAD THINGS HAPPEN 壞事發生
⑩ GOOD THINGS HAPPEN 好事發生
⑪ PLEASURE 快樂
⑫ SUCCESS/FAME 成功/出名
⑬ SPOKEN PHRASES 口語片語
⑭ OTHER MEANINGS 其他意思

D

① PERIOD OF TIME 一段時間

1 [C] a period of 24 hours〔二十四小時長的〕一天, 一日: *We spent three days in Paris then went south.* 我們在巴黎度過三天, 然後到南方去了。| *What day is it today – Tuesday?* 今天星期幾——星期二? | **the day before yesterday** *I just saw Pat the day before yesterday.* 我前天剛剛見到過帕特。| **the day after tomorrow** *We're leaving for LA the day after tomorrow.* 後天我們將出發去洛杉磯。

2 [C,U] the period of time between when it becomes light in the morning and the time it becomes dark 白天, 日間: *I'm usually out during the day.* 白天我通常出門。| *It rained all day.* 一整天都下着雨。| **by day** (=during the day) 在白天 *Owls usually sleep by day and hunt by night.* 貓頭鷹通常白天睡覺, 夜晚獵食。

day 日, 天

Monday 星期一	the day before yesterday 前天
Tuesday 星期二	yesterday 昨天
Wednesday 星期三	TODAY 今天
Thursday 星期四	tomorrow 明天
Friday 星期五	the day after tomorrow 後天
Saturday 星期六	
Sunday 星期天	

② THE TIME YOU ARE AWAKE 白天

3 [C usually singular 一般用單數] the time during the day when you are awake 白天: *His day begins at six.* 他的一天從六點開始。| **long day** (=a day when you had to get up early and were busy all day) 漫長的一天〔指早上起得很早而且一整天都十分忙碌〕*It's been a very long day.* 真是漫長的一天。| **all day (long)** (=during the whole time you are awake) 一天到晚, 一整天 *I've been studying all day. I'm beat!* 我一整天都在學習, 我都筋疲力盡了。

③ FUTURE 將來

4 one day also 又作 **some day** at an unknown time in the future 將來有一天, 有朝一日: *One day I'll buy a boat and sail around the world.* 有朝一日我要買艘船周遊世界。

5 one of these days *informal* at some time in the future【非正式】這幾天〔將來的某個時候〕: *I might find the time to paint the bedroom one of these days.* 這幾天我或許能找到時間把臥室粉刷一下。

6 any day (now) *spoken* very soon【口】不久, 很快: *She's expecting the baby any day now.* 她的孩子這幾天就要出生了。

7 the day will come (when) used to emphasize that something will definitely happen at some time in the future 終有一天〔強調某事必定在將來某個時間發生〕: *The day will come when he loses his eyesight completely.* 總有一天他會完全失明。

④ PAST 過去

8 one day on a particular day in the past 有一天〔過去的某一天〕: *One day, she just didn't turn up for work, and we never saw her again.* 有一天, 她沒來上班, 從此我們再也沒見過她。

9 childhood/student/army days the time when you were a child, student, soldier etc 兒童/學生/參軍時代

10 the good old days time in the past that you think was better than the present time 過去的好時光〔認為過去的時光較現在的好〕: *In the good old days people never had to lock their doors.* 在過去的好日子裡, 人們從來不用鎖門。

11 those were the days *spoken* used to say that a time in the past was better than the present time【口】那才叫好日子〔表示過去的日子比現在好〕

12 the other day a few days ago; recently 前幾天, 最近: *We had a letter from Kim the other day.* 前幾天我們收到了金姆的來信。

13 in those days during a period of time in the past 那時〔過去的一段時間〕: *Women wore long skirts in those days.* 那時婦女都穿長裙。

14 in my day used to describe what things were like when you were young 我年輕的時候: *In my day we used to have to get up at six o'clock.* 我年輕時, 我們常常得六點起牀。

15 in his or her day during the most successful part of someone's life 鼎盛時期, 當紅時期, 〔某人的〕當年: *Your grandfather was a famous radio personality in his day.* 你祖父當年是個廣播界名人。

16 the standards/fashion/wages etc of the day the standards etc that existed in a particular period of time in the past 過去某一時期的標準/時尚/工資等

17 five/three/nine years to the day exactly five years, three years, etc ago 正好五年/三年/九年前: *It's two years to the day since we moved here.* 我們搬到這裡整整兩年了。

⑤ SB'S LIFE/STH'S EXISTENCE 一個人的一生/一件東西的壽命

18 sb's days someone's life 某人的一生: *She ended her days in poverty.* 她在貧困中度過了餘生。

19 sb's/sth's days are numbered someone or something will not continue to exist or be effective 某人將不久人世, 活不了多長時間; 某物將不再有效, 支撐不了多久: *The days of the vinyl record are numbered.* 塑膠唱片的日子已屈指可數了。

⑥ WORK 工作

20 [C] the time spent working during a 24-hour period 工作日: *I work an eight-hour day.* 我一天工作八個小時。| *Did you have a good day at the office?* 你在辦公室工作得愉快嗎? —see also 另見 WORKING DAY

21 day off a day when you do not have to work 休息日; 休假日: *I'm taking a day off next week.* 我下個禮拜將休一天假。

22 be on days *spoken* to be working during the day doing a job that you often have to do at night, for example, if you work in a hospital【口】值日班〔通常夜班的工作暫時挪到白天做〕: *I'm on days this week.* 這個星期我值日班。

⑦ EACH DAY/EVERY DAY 每天

23 day after day happening continuously for a long time so that you become annoyed or bored 日復一日, 天天地: *I couldn't stand sitting at a desk day after day.* 我忍受不了日復一日地坐在桌旁。

24 from day to day if something changes from day to day it changes often 天天; 每天; 日益 —compare 比較 DAY-TO-DAY

25 day by day slowly and gradually 一天天, 逐日, 漸漸地, 慢慢地: *Her health was improving day by day.* 她的身體一天天好起來了。

26 day in, day out every day for a long time 一天接一天地, 日復一日, 天天: *She cooked and cleaned day in, day out for forty years.* 她四十年來日復一日地做飯、清掃。

27 night and day also 又作 **day and night** all the time; continuously 日日夜夜, 夜以繼日: *He was attended by nurses night and day.* 他有護士夜以繼日地看護。

⑧ NOW 現在

28 these days used to talk about your situation, behaviour, feelings etc now, especially if they used to be different 如今, 現今, 當今, 這年頭, 眼下〔尤指現在的情形、行為、感覺等和以前有所不同〕: *I don't go out much these days – once or twice a month at the most.* 如今我不太出去 —— 至多一個月一兩次。

29 in this day and age used when you are surprised or annoyed that something still happens 時至如今, 在我們這個年代〔指一些令人驚訝或生氣的事情仍然在發生〕: *I find it incredible that such punishments still exist in this day and age.* 這樣的懲罰方式現在還有, 真是難以置信。

30 to this day even now, after so much time has passed 至今: *To this day I don't know who told Katy about Duncan.* 到現在我也不知道誰把鄧肯的事告訴了凱蒂。

31 up to/until/to the present day from a time in the past until now〔從過去的某一時間〕直到現在: *This tradition has continued right up until the present day.* 這種傳統一直延續至今。

⑨ BAD THINGS HAPPEN 壞事發生

32 it's not my/your/his day *spoken* used when several unpleasant things have happened to someone in one day【口】我/你/他倒霉的一天〔表示一天中不愉快的事接連發生〕: *It's really not Chris's day – he overslept, his car broke down, and he spilt coffee on his new pants.* 這一天克里斯真不走運 —— 睡過了頭, 車拋了錨, 還把咖啡灑到了新褲子上。

33 have an off day to be less successful or happy than usual, for no particular reason 不順利, 不順心: *His work isn't usually this bad – he must have had an off day.* 他的工作通常沒這麼糟 —— 今天他一定是狀態不佳。

34 it's (just) one of those days *spoken* used when everything seems to be going wrong【口】〔諸事出錯的〕不幸的一天: *It's just been one of those days.* 今天真倒霉。

⑩ GOOD THINGS HAPPEN 好事發生

35 make sb's day to make someone very happy 使某人非常高興: *Hearing her voice on the phone really made my day.* 在電話裡聽到她的聲音真令我高興。

36 it's your/his/my lucky day! used when something very good happens to someone 你/他/我幸運的日子!: *Ruth just found a ten pound note in the street. It must be her lucky day!* 魯思剛在街上拾到一張十英鎊的鈔票。今天一定是她的幸運日!

⑪ PLEASURE 快樂

37 make a day of it *spoken* to choose to spend all day doing something, usually for pleasure, when you could have spent only part of the day doing it【口】好好玩它一整天: *We were going into New York for the concert anyway, so we decided to make a day of it.* 反正我們要去紐約聽音樂會, 於是我們決定好好玩它一整天。

38 day out *especially BrE* a day spent at the beach, in the countryside, at the zoo etc【尤英】〔到海灘、鄉村、動物園等〕外出遊玩的一天, 出遊的一天

⑫ SUCCESS/FAME 成功/出名

39 sb's day will come used to say that someone will have a chance to succeed in the future, even if they are not successful now 某人的好日子〔將來成功的日子〕將會到來

40 have had your day to be no longer successful, powerful, or famous 不再成功[強大, 有名]: *It seems as if typewriter has had its day.* 打字機的鼎盛時期似乎已經過去了。

⑬ SPOKEN PHRASES 口語片語

41 that'll be the day *spoken* used to say that you think something is very unlikely to happen【口】不太可能: *"Bill says he'll wash the dishes tonight." "That'll be the day!"* "比爾說今晚他洗碗。" "不太可能!"

⑭ OTHER MEANINGS 其他意思

42 not have all day *spoken* to not have much time available【口】時間不多了: *Hurry up, we don't have all day!* 快點, 我們沒那麼多時間了!

43 it's not every day (that) *spoken* used to say that something does not happen often and is therefore very special【口】並不是每天都...: *Let's go out and celebrate. After all, it's not every day you get a new job.* 我們出去慶祝一下吧。畢竟並不是每天都能找到新工作。

44 (live to) see the day *spoken* to experience something that you thought would never happen【口】看到那一天: *I never thought I'd live to see the day when women became priests.* 我怎麼也想不到婦女還有當上神父這一天。

45 40/50/60 etc if she's a day *spoken* used to emphasize that someone is at least as old as you are saying【口】她至少有 40/50/60 歲等: *She's ninety if she's a day.* 她至少有 90 歲。

46 from one day to the next if something changes from one day to the next, it does not stay the same for very long 從一天到下一天: *I never know where he'll be from one day to the next.* 他天天換地方, 我從來不知道他會在哪兒。

47 soup/dish/fish of the day the special soup etc that a restaurant serves on a particular day〔餐廳〕某一天的特色湯/特色菜/特色魚

48 day of action *BrE* a day when the workers in a particular place stop working for one day, to protest about something; a STRIKE[2] (1)【英】罷工日

49 the day of reckoning the time when you are punished or made to suffer for the things you have done wrong〔做壞事的人〕受到懲罰[報應]的日子 —see also 另見 **call it a day** (CALL[1] (22)), **carry the day** (CARRY[1] (23)), **every dog (has) its day** (DOG[1] (11)), **have a field day** (FIELD DAY (1)), HALF-DAY, **it's early days** (EARLY[1] (5)), **it's (a little) late in the day** (LATE[1] (9)), OPEN DAY, **save the day** (SAVE[1] (11)), SPEECH DAY, SPORTS DAY

USAGE NOTE 用法說明: DAY

WORD CHOICE 詞語辨析: **from day to day, day by day, day after day**

Something that changes or goes on **day by day** or **from day to day** is a continuous action. day by day或者 from day to day 用來表示一個連續的動作, 如事情一天天地進行或變化: *The problem is getting worse day by day.* 這個問題變得一天比一天嚴重。| *We just muddle along from day to day.* 我們只是一天天地混日子。

Separate events that are repeated happen **day after day**. day after day用來表示一天天地重複某一事情: *Day after day he tramps the streets looking for work* (=he does the same thing every day). 他成天走街串巷找工作。

GRAMMAR 語法

Remember that *on* is used with days and the word **day** itself. 記住: 表示某一天或者和 day 這個詞本身連用的時候要用介詞 on: *on Thursday/on that day/on the same day/on the second day* (NOT 不用 **in** or **at**) 在星期四/在那一天/在同一天/在第二天

On is never used with the phrase **the other day**, when you do not say the exact day when something happened. 用 the other day 表示某事發生在不確定的某一天時, 前面不用 on: *I saw Joey in Dick's Bar the other day* (=a few days ago). 前幾天我在狄克酒吧看見喬伊了。Compare 比較: *We spent two days in the mountains – on one day we went hiking and on the other we went fishing.* 我們在山裡度過了兩天 — 一天我們去遠足, 另一天我們去釣魚。

Note that you say **in those days** but **these days** (NOT 不用 **in these days**). 注意可以說 in those days, 但是在these days前面不加in: *In those days not many people had TVs, but these days a lot of households have more than one.* 那時候有電視機的人家很少, 但是如今許多家庭都不只擁有一台電視機。

Remember that the phrase is **during the day**. 記住: 詞組是 during the day: *I couldn't get much work done during the day* (NOT 不用 *during day* or 或 *in the day*, though you can say 然而可以說 *in the daytime*). 白天我做不了太多工作。

You do not use **the** with **all day**. all day 前面不能加the。

SPELLING 拼法

Remember that **today** is one word. 記住: today 是一個詞。

day boy /ˈ· ·/ *n* [C] *BrE* a boy DAY PUPIL【英】走讀男生

day·break /ˈdeˌbrek; ˈdeɪbreɪk/ *n* [U] the time of day when light first appears 黎明, 破曉: *We arrived in Cairo at daybreak.* 天剛亮我們就到了開羅。

day camp /ˈ· ·/ *n* [C] *AmE* a place where children can go in the day during the school holidays to do sports, art etc【美】日間夏令營〔學校放假時, 孩子們白天可去的地方, 可以做體育運動、進行藝術活動等〕

day care centre *BrE*【英】, **day care center** *AmE*【美】*n* /ˈ·· ˌ··/ [C] **1** *AmE* a place where babies are looked after while their parents are at work【美】日間托兒所; CRÈCHE *BrE*【英】**2** a place in Britain where people who are old or ill can be looked after during the day〔英國日間照顧老人或病人的〕日間看護所

day·dream[1] /ˈdeˌdrim; ˈdeɪdriːm/ *v* [I] to think about something pleasant, especially when this makes you forget what you should be doing 做白日夢, 幻想, 夢想: *Stop daydreaming! You were meant to finish that hours ago.* 別做白日夢了!你本來幾個小時前就該做完的。—**daydreamer** *n* [C]

daydream[2] *n* [C] pleasant thoughts you have while you are awake, that make you forget what you are doing 白日夢

day girl /ˈ· ·/ *n* [C] *BrE* a girl DAY PUPIL【英】走讀女生

Day-Glo /ˈdeglo; ˈdeɪgləʊ/ *adj trademark* having a very bright orange, green, yellow, or pink colour【商標】含"狄格洛"熒光加色劑的: *Dayglo socks* 熒光襪子

day·light /ˈdeˌlaɪt; ˈdeɪlaɪt/ *n* [U] **1** the light produced by the sun during the day 日光, 白晝, 白天: *We'll keep working while there's still enough daylight.* 趁着天還不太黑, 我們將繼續工作。**2 daylight robbery** *BrE informal* a situation in which something costs you a lot more than it should【英, 非正式】明目張膽地索取高價, 敲竹槓: *£2.50 for a cup of coffee? It's daylight robbery!* 一杯咖啡要 2.5 英鎊? 這簡直是公開搶劫! **3 see daylight** *informal* to begin to understand something that you have found difficult to understand before【非正式】開始理解, 明白〔以前不懂的事情〕: *Joan explained it again, and at last I began to see daylight.* 瓊又解釋了一遍, 我終於開始明白了。**4 scare/frighten the (living) daylights out of** *informal* to frighten someone a lot【非正式】使〔某人〕非常害怕, 驚恐: *It scared the living daylights out of me when the flames shot out.* 火焰向外噴射的時候, 我嚇壞了。**5 beat/knock the (living) daylights out of** *informal* to hit someone a lot and seriously hurt them【非正式】狠打〔某人〕致重傷 —see also 另見 **in broad daylight** (BROAD[1] (6))

daylight sav·ing time /ˌ·· ˈ·· ˌ·/ also 又作 **daylight savings** /ˌ·· ˈ··/ *n* [U] *AmE* the time during the summer when clocks are one hour ahead of standard time【美】夏令時〔計時器比標準時間提早一小時〕—compare 比較 BRITISH SUMMER TIME

day nur·se·ry /ˈ· ˌ···/ *n* [C] *BrE* a place where small children can be left while their parents are at work【英】日間托兒所

day of judge·ment /ˌ· · ˈ··/ *n* [singular] JUDGMENT DAY 最後審判日, 世界末日

day pu·pil /ˈ· ˌ··/ *n* [C] *BrE* a pupil who goes to a BOARDING SCHOOL but who lives at home【英】〔寄宿學校的〕走讀學生

day re·lease /ˌ· · ˈ·/ *n* [U] *BrE* a system that allows workers to spend one day a week studying a subject at a college【英】〔准許工人一個星期有一天的時間到大學學習的〕每週一天獲准請假進修制度

day re·turn /ˌ· · ˈ·/ *n* [C] *BrE* a train or bus ticket that lets you go somewhere at a cheaper price than usual, if you go there and back on the same day【英】〔火車或公共汽車的〕當日來回票〔票價較低〕

day room /ˈ· ·/ *n* [C] a room in a hospital where patients can go to read, watch television etc〔醫院裡供病人去看書、看電視的〕康樂室; 閱覽室

day school /ˈ· ·/ *n* [C, U] a school where the students go home in the evening rather than one where they live 日校, 走讀學校 —compare 比較 BOARDING SCHOOL

day·time /ˈdeˌtaɪm; ˈdeɪtaɪm/ *n* [U] the time during the day between the time when it gets light and the time when it gets dark; DAY (2) 白天, 日間: *I can't sleep in the daytime.* 我白天睡不着覺。

day-to-day /ˌ· · ˈ·◂/ *adj* **day-to-day management/running/administration etc** work that is done as a normal part of your life, your job etc 日常[常規]的管理/運營/行政工作等: *The manager is responsible for the day-to-day running of the hotel.* 經理負責酒店的日常管理工作。

day trip /ˈ· ·/ *n* [C] a visit to the beach, the zoo etc when you go there and come back the same day 當天往返的旅行; 一日遊

day-trip·per /ˈ· ˌ··/ *n* [C] *BrE* someone who visits a place for pleasure but spends only one day there【英】當天往返的遊客; 一日遊的遊客: *Yarmouth is crowded with day-trippers at this time of year.* 每年的這個時候雅茅斯都會擠滿一日遊的遊客。

dazed /dezd; deɪzd/ *adj* **1** unable to think clearly, especially because of a shock, accident etc〔由於震驚、意外事故等而〕茫然的, 迷亂的, 恍惚的: *Dazed survivors* *staggered from the wreckage.* 嚇呆了的倖存者踉蹌着走出廢墟。**2 in a daze** unable to think clearly 處於茫然狀態: *I've been wandering around in a daze all day.* 我一整天都在迷迷糊糊地四處遊蕩。

daz·zle /ˋdæzḷ; ˈdæzəl/ *v* [T often passive 常用被動態] **1** if a very bright light dazzles you it stops you from seeing properly for a short time〔強光等〕使〔某人〕目眩, 眼花繚亂: *a deer dazzled by the headlights* 被車燈燈光照得看不清東西的鹿 **2** to make someone feel strong admiration 使〔某人〕傾倒: *As children, we were dazzled by my uncle's good looks and charm.* 小時候我們都被叔叔的英俊外表和魅力所傾倒。—**dazzle** *n* [U] *BrE*【英】

daz·zling /ˋdæzlɪŋ; ˈdæzəlɪŋ/ *adj* **1** a light that is dazzling makes you unable to see properly for a short time 使人目眩的, 令人眼花繚亂的 **2** very impressive and attractive 給人印象深刻的; 特別吸引人的: *a dazzling display of football skills* 讓人眼花繚亂的足球技巧表演

dbl the written abbreviation of 縮寫= double

DC /ˌdi ˋsi; ˌdiː ˈsiː/ **1** direct current; electric current that always flows in one direction 直流電 —compare 比較 AC **2** the abbreviation of 縮寫= District of Columbia, in the US〔美國的〕哥倫比亞特區: *Washington, DC* 哥倫比亞特區華盛頓

D-Day /ˋdi ˌde; ˈdiː deɪ/ *n* [singular] **1** 6th June 1944; the day the British, Americans, and other armies landed in France during the Second World War 第二次世界大戰盟軍在法國登陸的日子〔即 1944 年 6 月 6 日〕**2** *informal* a day on which an important action is planned to happen or begin【非正式】重大行動要開始的日子: *So Friday is D-Day, then?* 那麼星期五是開始行動的日子啦?

DDT /ˌdi di ˋti; ˌdiː diː ˈtiː/ *n* [U] a chemical used to kill insects that harm crops 滴滴涕〔用來殺滅危害莊稼的害蟲的一種化學製品〕

de- /di; diː/ *prefix* **1** in some verbs and nouns, shows an opposite〔構成某些動詞和名詞, 表示"否定"、"與...相反"之意〕: *a depopulated area* (=which all or most of the population has left)〔由於大部分人口已經離開而〕人口減少的地區 | *deindustrialization* (=becoming less industrial) 非工業化 **2** in some verbs, means to remove something or remove things from something 除去, (使) 脱離〔用於構成動詞〕: *to debone the fish* (=remove its bones) 剔掉魚刺 | *The king was dethroned.* (=removed from power) 國王被廢黜了。**3** in some verbs, means to make something less; reduce 降低, 貶低〔用於構成動詞〕: *to devalue the currency* 使貨幣貶值

dea·con /ˋdikən; ˈdiːkən/ *n* [C] a religious official, in some Christian churches, who is just below the rank of a priest 執事; 會吏〔基督教會中比牧師低一級的神職人員〕

dead[1] /dɛd; ded/ *adj* [no comparative 無比較級]

① NO LONGER ALIVE OR EXISTING 死去的, 不復存在的
② HAVING NO POWER/NOT WORKING 沒電的/不運作的
③ HAVING NO FEELING OR ENERGY 沒有知覺的, 沒有精力的
④ NOT INTERESTING, USEFUL, OR IMPORTANT 沒有意思的, 無用的, 不重要的
⑤ SPOKEN PHRASES 口語片語
⑥ OTHER MEANINGS 其他意思

① NO LONGER ALIVE OR EXISTING 死去的, 不復存在的

1 no longer alive 死的, 逝世的: *Her mother had been dead for ten years.* 她媽媽已經去世十年了。| *dead leaves* 枯葉 | **dead body** (=the body of a person who has died) 死屍 | **dead as a doornail/stone dead** *informal* (=completely dead with no signs of life at all)【非正式】完全死了的 | **drop dead** (=die suddenly when no-one expects it) 猝死, 暴斃 *37 years old, no health problems, and he just dropped dead at work!* 他 37 歲, 沒有健康問題, 而就在工作的時候忽然那麼死了! —compare 比較 LIVE[2] (1)

2 the dead people who have died, especially people who have been killed 已死的人, 死者〔尤指被害的人〕: *There wasn't even time to bury the dead.* 甚至沒有時間埋葬死去的人。

3 rise from the dead/come back from the dead according to Christian beliefs, to become alive again after dying〔根據基督教的信仰〕死後重生, 再生, 復活

② HAVING NO POWER/NOT WORKING 沒電的/不運作的

4 dead battery/engine etc an engine etc that no longer works because it has no electricity 沒電的電池/熄火的引擎等

5 ►TELEPHONES ETC 電話等◄ a telephone line, radio etc that is dead is not working and makes no sound when you try to use it〔電話線路、收音機等〕停止運作的, 沒有聲音的: *All the lines out of town are dead.* 城外所有的電話線路都沒有聲音了。| **go dead** *Suddenly the radio went dead.* 收音機忽然一下子沒有聲音了。

③ HAVING NO FEELING OR ENERGY 沒有知覺的, 沒有精力的

6 arm/leg etc a part of your body that is dead has no feeling in it〔胳膊、腿等身體部位〕失去知覺的, 麻木的: **go dead** *When I got up my leg had gone totally dead.* 我起來的時候腿完全麻了。

7 ►NO EMOTION 沒有感情◄ showing no emotion or sympathy 沒有感情[同情心]的: *Jennie's eyes were cold and dead.* 珍妮的眼神冷酷而麻木。| **[+to]** *dead to all feelings of compassion* 毫無同情心

8 ►TIRED 疲勞的◄ *spoken* very tired【口】十分疲勞的: *I can't go out tonight. I'm absolutely dead!* 今晚我不能出去了, 我累死了!

9 dead to the world very deeply asleep or unconscious 熟睡的; 失去知覺的: *Better leave Craig – he's dead to the world.* 最好別打擾克雷格 —— 他睡得正熟。

④ NOT INTERESTING, USEFUL, OR IMPORTANT 沒有意思的, 無用的, 不重要的

10 ►BORING 乏味的◄ a town that is dead is boring because nothing interesting or exciting happens there, and there is nothing interesting to do 沒趣的, 死氣沉沉的: *This place is dead after nine o'clock.* 這個地方九點之後就變得死寂一片。

11 ►IDEA/SUBJECT 想法/話題◄ **dead and buried** an argument, problem, plan etc that is dead and buried is not worth considering again〔論點、問題、計劃等〕不值得再考慮的: *You're talking as if the issue of low pay is dead and buried.* 你說話的意思好像是工資低的問題不值得再提了。

12 a dead duck *informal* a plan, idea etc that is not worth considering because it is very likely to fail【非正

式】注定失敗的計劃[想法]等
13 be a dead loss *informal* to be completely useless【非正式】完全沒用的: *That building firm's a dead loss.* 那家建築公司完全垮了。
14 dead as a dodo no longer important or useful, and no longer having any influence 不再重要的, 已失效的, 不再有影響力的: *The extreme Right of this country is as dead as a dodo.* 這個國家的極右黨派已經完全失去了影響力。

⑤ **SPOKEN PHRASES** 口語片語
15 drop dead *spoken* used to rudely and angrily tell someone to go away and leave you alone【口】滾開〔用於語氣粗魯、無禮地叫某人離開, 不許來打擾你〕
16 over my dead body *spoken* used to say that you are determined not to allow something to happen【口】除非我死了〔表示堅決不讓某事發生〕: *You'll marry him over my dead body!* 我死也不讓你和他結婚!
17 I wouldn't be seen/caught dead *spoken* used to say that you would never wear particular clothes, go to particular places, or do particular things, because you would feel embarrassed【口】我決不; 我死也不〔堅決不穿某種衣服、不去某些地方或不做某事〕: **[+in/on/with etc]** *I wouldn't be seen dead in a dress like that!* 我死也不穿那樣的衣服!
18 be in dead trouble *BrE spoken* to be in serious trouble【英口】陷入大麻煩: *You'll be in dead trouble if your Dad finds out.* 你爸爸要是發現了, 你的麻煩就大了。
19 dead from the neck up *BrE spoken* very stupid【英口】沒頭腦的, 笨極了的

⑥ **OTHER MEANINGS** 其他意思
20 ▶LANGUAGE 語言◀ a dead language is no longer used by ordinary people〔某種語言〕不再被使用的: *What's the point of learning a dead language like Latin?* 學習像拉丁語那樣已經死亡的語言有甚麼意義呢? —opposite 反義詞 LIVING[1] (6)
21 the dead centre the exact centre 正中心
22 ▶GLASS/BOTTLE 玻璃杯/瓶子◀ *BrE informal* a glass etc that is dead is no longer being used【英, 非正式】〔表示杯子等〕不再被使用的
23 dead silence complete silence 死一般的沉寂, 死寂: *Everyone stood and waited in dead silence.* 每個人都在死一般的沉寂中站着等待。
24 ▶PLANET 行星◀ a dead PLANET (1) has no life on it〔某個行星〕沒有生命存在的
25 ▶IN SPORT 在體育運動中◀ when the ball is dead in some games it is no longer on the playing area〔體育比賽中的球〕界外的
26 a dead cert *BrE spoken* something that is definitely going to happen or is definitely going to win a race【英口】必然發生的事; 贏定[穩贏]的比賽
27 in a dead faint completely unconscious 完全失去知覺的
28 dead ringer someone who looks exactly like someone else 外貌酷似的人: *Dave's a dead ringer for Paul McCartney.* 戴夫和保羅·麥卡特尼長得一模一樣。
29 dead weight something that is very heavy and difficult to carry〔很難搬動的〕重物: *The boy was unconscious, a dead weight.* 這個男孩失去了知覺, 死沉死沉的。
30 dead wood the people or things within an organization that are useless or no longer needed〔一個組織內〕無用的人[物]
31 more dead than alive in a very weak physical condition 身體特別虛弱的: *They were more dead than alive when they were airlifted off the ice.* 他們被空運離開冰面的時候, 身體極度虛弱。—**deadness** *n* [U]

3 **dead**[2] *adv* **1** *BrE informal* completely【英, 非正式】完全地: *Ben's dead against coming with us.* 班恩堅決反對和我們一起去。**2** *BrE spoken* very【英口】非常, 十分: *He was dead good-looking.* 他長得極為英俊。**3** [+adj/adv] *informal* directly or exactly【非正式】直接地, 正對着地: **dead ahead/in front/at etc** *I stared dead ahead at the doorway.* 我直盯着前面的門口看。| **dead on time** *informal* (=exactly at a particular time or the arranged time)【非正式】十分準時地 *The bus arrived dead on time.* 公共汽車準時到達。**4 dead beat** *informal* very tired【非正式】筋疲力盡的: *I can't go any further – I'm dead beat.* 我再也走不動了 — 我都累死了。

dead[3] *n* **the dead of night/winter** the middle of the night or the middle of the winter 在夜深人靜的時候/在隆冬

dead beat /ˈ· ˌ·◂/ *n* [C] *AmE informal*【美, 非正式】**1** someone who is lazy and who has no plans in life 懶鬼; 庸庸碌碌的人 **2** someone who avoids paying their debts 賴賬的人

dead bolt /ˈ· ·/ *n* [C] *AmE* a strong lock often used on doors【美】〔常用於門上的〕插鎖, 嵌鎖; MORTICE LOCK *BrE*【英】

dead·en /ˈdɛdn̩; ˈdedn/ *v* [T] to make a feeling or sound less strong 減輕〔某種感覺〕; 降低〔聲響〕: *medicine to deaden the pain* 鎮痛藥

dead end /ˌ· ˈ·◂/ *n* [C] **1** a street with no way out at one end 死巷, 死胡同 **2** a situation from which no more progress is possible 僵局: **come to/reach a dead end** *The negotiations have reached a dead end.* 談判陷入了僵局。**3 dead-end job** a job with low wages and no chance of progress 低工資且無晉升機會的工作

dead·head[1] /ˈdɛdˌhɛd; ˈdedhed/ *v* **1** [T] *BrE* to remove the dead flowers from a plant【英】摘去〔植物的〕枯花 **2** [I] *AmE* to drive a train, bus, or TRUCK[1] (1) with no passengers or goods【美】放空車〔火車、公共汽車或卡車在沒有乘客或貨物的情況下駕駛〕

deadhead[2] *n* [C] *AmE* a vehicle that has no passengers or goods【美】不載乘客[貨物]的空車

dead heat /ˌ· ˈ·/ *n* [C] the result of a race in which two or more competitors finish at exactly the same time 兩個[多個]競賽者同時到達終點的比賽成績

dead let·ter /ˌ· ˈ··/ *n* [C] **1** a law, idea that still exists but that people no longer obey, or are not interested in 形同虛設的法規, 空文; 過時的想法: *An arts education is a dead letter as far as many students are concerned.* 就許多學生而言, 藝術教育已形同虛設。**2** a letter that cannot be delivered or returned 無法投遞[退回]的信, 死信

dead·line /ˈdɛdˌlaɪn; ˈdedlaɪn/ *n* [C] a date or time by which you have to do or complete something 截止時間; 最後期限: *The deadline is May 27th.* 截止時間是5月27日。| **work to a deadline** (=plan your work so that it can be finished by the deadline) 計劃如期完成 | **meet a deadline** (=finish by the deadline) 如期完成 *The deadlines are very short and difficult to meet.* 時間非常短, 很難如期完成任務。| **tight deadline** (=a deadline that is difficult) 時間緊促〔難以如期完成任務的期限〕

dead·lock /ˈdɛdˌlɑk; ˈdedlɒk/ *n* [singular,U] a situation in which a disagreement cannot be settled; STALEMATE (1) 僵局: *The talks have reached a complete deadlock.* 商談完全陷入僵局。| **break the deadlock** (=end the deadlock) 打破僵局 —**deadlock** *v* [I,T] —**deadlocked** *adj*

dead·ly[1] /ˈdɛdlɪ; ˈdedli/ *adj*
1 ▶VERY DANGEROUS 非常危險的◀ likely to cause death 致命的: *a deadly poison* 致命的毒藥
2 deadly enemy someone who will always be your enemy and will try to harm you as much as possible 不共戴天的敵人, 死敵: *The inhabitants soon came to regard the white settlers as their deadly enemy.* 居民們不久就把白人定居者視為死敵。
3 ▶COMPLETE 完全的◀ complete or total 完完全全

D

的: *We sat in deadly silence.* 我們在死一般的寂靜中坐着。

4 ►VERY EFFECTIVE 非常有效的◄ causing harm in a very effective way 極有效的; 極精確的: *She hit the target with deadly accuracy.* 她準確無誤地射中目標。

5 ►LIKE DEATH 死一樣的◄ [only before noun 僅用於名詞前] like death in appearance 如死一樣的: *His face had a deadly paleness.* 他的臉死一般的蒼白。

6 ►BORING 無聊的◄ *spoken* not at all interesting or exciting【口】沒趣的, 乏味的: *"How was the party?" "Pretty deadly."* "派對開得怎麼樣?" "沒勁透了。"

deadly² *adv* **deadly serious/dull/boring etc** very serious, dull etc 非常嚴肅/沉悶/乏味等: *I'm deadly serious, this isn't a game!* 我是非常認真的, 這不是遊戲!

deadly night·shade /ˌ.. ˈ../ *n* [C,U] a poisonous European plant; BELLADONNA 顛茄〔一種有毒的歐洲植物〕

dead-man's float /ˌ. . ˈ./ *n* [singular] *AmE* a way of floating in water with your body and face turned downwards【美】〔身體和臉部朝下的〕俯臥漂浮姿勢

dead·pan /ˈdɛdˌpæn; ˈdedpæn/ *adj* sounding and looking completely serious when you are not really 故作嚴肅的: *telling a joke in a deadpan voice* 不動聲色地講笑話; 冷面孔地講笑話 —**deadpan** *adv*

dead reck·on·ing /ˌ. ˈ.../ *n* [U] the practice of calculating the position of a ship or aircraft without using the sun, moon, or stars〔不依靠太陽、月亮或星星測定船隻或飛機位置的〕航位推測法

3 **deaf** /dɛf; def/ *adj* **1** physically unable to hear anything or unable to hear well 耳聾的, 失聰的: *He's quite deaf and needs a hearing aid.* 他有些耳聾, 需要用助聽器。| **stone deaf/deaf as a post** *informal* (=completely deaf)【非正式】完全耳聾的 —see also 另見 TONE-DEAF **2 the deaf** people who are deaf 耳聾的人: *a school for the deaf* 聾人學校 **3 deaf to** *literary* unwilling to hear or listen to something【文】不願聽, 不肯聽取: *She was deaf to his pleas.* 她對他的懇求充耳不聞。**4 turn a deaf ear** be unwilling to listen to what someone is saying or asking 對...充耳不聞[置若罔聞]: *The factory owners turned a deaf ear to the demands of the workers.* 工廠廠主對工人們提出的要求充耳不聞。**5 fall on deaf ears** if advice or a warning falls on deaf ears, everyone ignores it〔建議、警告等〕被別人忽視; 不受注意 —**deafness** *n* [U]

deaf-aid /ˈ. ./ *n* [C] *BrE informal* a small electric machine, worn near your ear, that helps you to hear better; HEARING AID【英, 非正式】助聽器

deaf-and-dumb /ˌ. . ˈ.◄/ *adj* unable to hear or speak 聾啞的, 又聾又啞的 —**the deaf and dumb** *n* [plural]

deaf·en /ˈdɛfən; ˈdefən/ *v* [T usually passive 一般用被動態] **1** if a noise deafens you, it is so loud that you cannot hear anything else 使〔某人〕感到震耳欲聾: *deafened by the roar of the engine* 發動機的轟鳴聲震耳欲聾 **2** to make someone unable to hear 使〔某人〕耳聾

deaf·en·ing /ˈdɛfənɪŋ; ˈdefənɪŋ/ *adj* noise or music that is deafening is very loud〔噪聲或音樂〕震耳欲聾的

deaf-mute /ˌ. ˈ./ *n* [C] someone who is unable to hear or speak 聾啞人

1 1 **deal¹** /dil; diːl/ *v past tense and past participle* **dealt** /dɛlt; delt/ **1** also 又作 **deal out** [I,T] to give playing cards to each of the players in a game〔紙牌遊戲中的〕發(牌): **deal sth (out) to sb** *Deal out three cards to each player.* 給每個玩牌的人發三張牌。**2** [I] *informal* to buy and sell illegal drugs【非正式】買賣非法毒品: *Many users end up dealing to support their habit.* 許多吸毒的人結果是做起非法毒品買賣來維持他們吸毒。**3 deal a blow** *literary*【文】**a)** to cause harm to someone or something 給〔某人或某物〕造成損失, 傷害; 打擊: **deal a crippling/decisive etc blow** (=cause very serious harm) 給予...致命的打擊[傷害] *The recession dealt many small businesses a fatal blow.* 經濟衰退給予許多小型企業致命的打擊。**b)** to hit someone 打〔某人〕

deal in sth *phr v* [T] **1** to buy and sell a particular type of product 經營, 買賣〔某種產品〕: *dealing in 19th century watercolours* 從事買賣 19 世紀水彩畫 —see also 另見 DEALER (1) **2** to have a particular attitude to your work〔對工作〕持有〔某種態度〕: *As a scientist, I do not deal in speculation.* 作為科學家, 我不相信猜測。

deal out sth *phr v* [T] **1** to give playing cards to each of the players in a game 發〔牌〕 **2** to decide what kind of punishment someone will get 決定給予〔某人某種處罰〕

deal with sb/sth *phr v* [T] **1** to take the correct action for a piece of work, type of work etc 處理〔某項工作等〕: *Who's dealing with the Glaxo account?* 是誰在負責與葛蘭素公司的業務往來? **2** to succeed in solving a problem 解決〔問題〕: *Don't worry, Mr Symes, it's already been dealt with.* 別擔心, 賽姆斯先生, 問題已經解決了。**3** to succeed in controlling an emotional problem so that it does not affect your life 控制〔感情〕: *It's OK, I'm dealing with it so far.* 還可以, 到現在我還能應付得了它。**4** to do business with someone or have a business connection with someone 和〔某人〕做生意: *I've dealt with them for a long time.* 我和他們已經打了很長時間的交道了。**5** if a book, speech, work of art etc deals with a particular subject, it is about that subject 涉及, 論及, 探討〔某個主題〕: *These ideas are dealt with more fully in Chapter Four.* 這些觀點在第四章中有較全面的闡述。

deal² *n*

1 a great deal also 又作 **a good deal** a large quantity of something 很多的, 大量的: **[+of]** *A great deal of their work is unpaid.* 他們很多工作都是沒有報酬的。| **a great deal more/a great deal longer etc** (=a lot more, longer etc) 多許多/長許多等 *He knew a good deal more than I did.* 他懂得比我多很多。

2 ►AGREEMENT 協議, 買賣, 交易◄ [C] an agreement or arrangement, especially in business or politics, that helps both sides involved〔尤指生意或政治上雙方的〕協議: *The band has negotiated a new deal with their record company.* 樂隊和唱片公司達成了一項新的協議。| **get a good deal** (=buy something at a good price)〔買東西〕價格便宜 *You can get some really good deals from travel agents right now.* 現在找旅行社(代辦旅遊)價格可以非常合算。| **strike/make/cut/do a deal** (=produce or make an agreement) 達成一項協議 *The two teams did a deal and Robson was traded.* 兩隊達成了羅布森轉隊的協議。

3 it's a deal *spoken* used to say that you agree to do something【口】成交〔同意做某事〕: *"OK, $500, but that's my last offer." "OK, it's a deal."* "好, 500 美元, 但這是我最後的價格。" "好, 成交。"

4 ►TREATMENT 待遇◄ [C usually singular 一般用單數] treatment of a particular type that is given or received 待遇: **a better/fairer deal** *a better deal for nurses* 給護士更好的待遇 | **a new deal** (=a new and fairer system of social or political treatment) 新政(策) *The prime minister promised a new deal for farmers.* 首相許諾為農民制定新的政策。| **a rough/raw deal** (=unfair treatment) 不公平的待遇 *Women tend to get a raw deal from employers.* 婦女往往受到雇主的不公平對待。

5 ►GAME 遊戲◄ [singular] the process of giving out cards to players in a card game〔紙牌遊戲中的〕發牌: *It's your deal, Alison.* 該你發牌了, 艾利森。—see also 另見 DEALER (3)

6 ►WOOD 木材, 木頭◄ [U] *BrE* FIR or PINE¹ (2) wood used for making things【英】冷杉木; 松木: *a deal table* 冷杉[松]木桌子

7 a deal of *old-fashioned* a large quantity of something【過時】大量的 —see also 另見 **big deal** (BIG (7))

USAGE NOTE 用法說明: DEAL
GRAMMAR 語法
A great/good deal of... is usually only used with

uncountable nouns. a great/good deal of 通常只用來修飾不可數名詞: *a great deal of time/money/difficulty/pressure/interest* 大量時間/大量金錢/許多困難/巨大壓力/很多興趣。Compare 比較以下兩個句子: *There's been a good deal of change/There have been a good many changes.* 出現了很多變化。

deal·er /ˈdilɚ; ˈdiːlə/ *n* [C] **1** someone who buys and sells a particular product, especially an expensive one〔尤指買賣貴重商品的〕商人: *a car dealer* 汽車經銷商 **2** someone who sells illegal drugs 毒品販子 **3** someone who gives out playing cards in a game〔紙牌遊戲的〕發牌人 —see also 另見 DOUBLE-DEALER

deal·er·ship /ˈdilɚʃɪp; ˈdiːləʃɪp/ *n* [C] a business that sells a particular company's product, especially cars〔尤指汽車的〕特許經銷商[店]: *Nissan dealerships* 日產汽車經銷商[店]

deal·ing /ˈdilɪŋ; ˈdiːlɪŋ/ *n* **1 dealings** [plural] the business activities or relationships that you have been involved in 商業活動; 商業往來: *The secret dealings of his department were made public.* 他所在部門進行的祕密交易被曝了光。| **have dealings with** (=have a business relationship with someone) 和...有生意上的交往 *We've had dealings with ITBF for the past few years.* 我們在過去的幾年中一直和ITBF公司有業務往來。**2 plain dealing/honest dealing etc** a particular way of doing business with people 樸實/誠實的經營方式

dealt /dɛlt; delt/ *v* the past tense and past participle of DEAL[1]

dean /din; diːn/ *n* [C] **1** a priest of high rank, especially in the Anglican church, who is in charge of several priests or churches〔尤指英國國教中的〕高職牧師; 教長; 主任牧師 **2** someone in a university who is in charge of an area of study, or in charge of students and their behaviour〔大學的〕學院院長; 系主任; 學監

dean·e·ry /ˈdinərɪ; ˈdiːnəri/ *n* [C,U] the area controlled by a dean or the place where a dean lives 高職牧師[主任牧師]所管轄的教區

dean's list /ˈ· ·/ *n* [C] *AmE* a list of the best students at a university【美】〔大學裡〕優秀學生名單

1 **dear¹** /dɪr; dɪə/ *interjection* The phrases 'oh dear', 'dear oh dear', 'dear dear', and 'dear me' are all used to show that you are surprised, upset, or annoyed because you have done something wrong, because something bad has happened etc. 'Oh dear' is much more common than the others. 'Dear oh dear' and 'dear dear' are used to emphasize how surprised, upset, or annoyed you are. 'Dear me' is a little old-fashioned. 天哪, 天啊〔oh dear, dear oh dear, dear dear, dear me 都用來表示驚訝、不安或惱怒的情緒, 因為自己做錯事或者因為糟糕的事情已經發生等等。oh dear 比其他詞組較為常見。dear oh dear 和 dear dear 用來強調一個人感到太驚訝、太不安或者太生氣了。dear me 有點兒過時〕: *Oh dear I've broken the lamp.* 天啊, 我把燈打破了。| *"He's been taken into hospital." "Oh dear!"* "他被送進了醫院。" "我的天哪!" | *Dear oh dear, that's terrible news.* 天哪, 天哪, 那真是個可怕的消息。| *Dear, dear, I am sorry. Hope I didn't hurt you.* 天哪, 天哪, 太抱歉了。希望沒弄痛你。| *Dear me! I forgot to call Kathy and now it's too late.* 糟糕! 我忘了給凱西打電話, 現在太晚了。

2 **dear²** *n* [C] **1** used when speaking to someone you love 親愛的〔用於和自己愛的人說話〕: *How did the interview go, dear?* 面試進行得怎麼樣, 親愛的? **2** *spoken* a friendly way of speaking to someone you do not know, for example, to a customer in a shop【口】〔用於和不認識的人講話, 表示友好〕: *Can I help you, dear?* 請問, 我能為您做些甚麼嗎? **3** *spoken especially BrE* someone who is very kind and helpful【口, 尤英】好人, 可愛的人: *Be a dear and make me some coffee.* 做個好人, 給我弄點咖啡來。**4 old dear** *BrE* a fairly rude expression meaning an old woman【英】老太婆〔相當不禮貌的用法〕

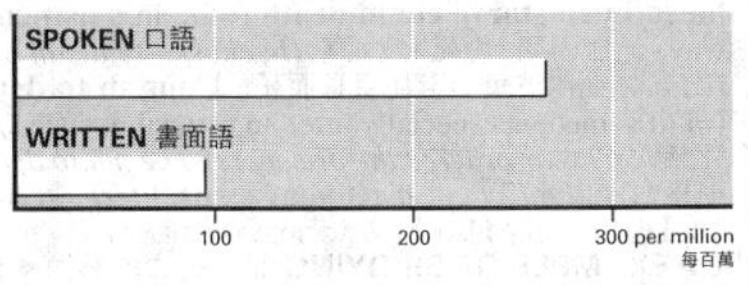

Based on the British National Corpus and the Longman Lancaster Corpus 據英國國家語料庫和朗文蘭卡斯特語料庫

This graph shows that the word **dear** is much more common in spoken English than in written English. This is because it has some special uses in spoken English and is used in some common spoken phrases. 本圖表顯示, 單詞 dear 在英語口語中的使用頻率遠遠高於書面語, 因為它在英語口語中有一些特殊的用法, 而且口語中一些常用片語是由 dear 構成的。

dear³ *adj* **1 Dear** used before someone's name or title when you begin a letter〔用在信函的開頭, 放在上款的人名、稱謂或頭銜前面〕: *Dear Madam* 尊敬的女士 | *Dear Meg* 親愛的梅格 **2** *BrE* expensive【英】貴的, 昂貴的: *I didn't buy it because it was too dear.* 我沒買它, 因為價格太貴。**3** *formal* a dear friend or relative is very important to you and you love them a lot【正式】珍貴的, 鍾愛的: *Mark had become a dear friend.* 馬克已成為一個親密的朋友。| **be dear to sb** *His sister was very dear to him.* 他的妹妹是他非常鍾愛的。**4 for dear life** if you run, fight, climb etc for dear life, you do it as fast or as well as you can because you are afraid 拚命地〔譬如拚命地跑、打、爬等, 用來表示因為恐懼而盡可能最快地或最好地做某事〕 2 2

dear⁴ *adv* **cost sb dear** to cause a lot of trouble and suffering for someone 使某人損失慘重; 給某人帶來許多麻煩和痛苦: *Carolyn's marriage to Pete cost her dear.* 與彼得的婚姻使卡羅琳痛苦不堪。

dear·est /ˈdɪrəst; ˈdɪərɪ̵st/ *n* [C] used when speaking to someone you love〔用以稱呼所愛的人〕: *Well, dearest, I was a little worried.* 我最親愛的, 我有些擔心。

dear·ie /ˈdɪrɪ; ˈdɪəri/ *n* [C] another spelling of DEARY deary 的另一種拼法

dear John let·ter /ˌ· ˈ· ˌ··/ *n* [C] a letter to a man from his wife or GIRLFRIEND, saying that she no longer loves him〔妻子或女朋友寫給男子的〕絕交信

dear·ly /ˈdɪrlɪ; ˈdɪəli/ *adv* **1** if you love someone dearly, want something dearly etc, you do so with strong emotions 由衷地, 深情地: *James loved his sister dearly.* 詹姆斯非常疼愛他的妹妹。**2 cost sb dearly** to cause a lot of trouble or suffering 給某人帶來很多麻煩和痛苦: *Vandalism costs schools dearly.* 恣意破壞公物的行為使學校損失慘重。**3 pay dearly** to suffer a lot for something that you have done 付出沉重的代價: *They've paid dearly for not explaining beforehand.* 他們因為沒有事先解釋清楚而付出了沉重的代價。**4 dearly beloved** used by a priest or minister at the beginning of a Christian marriage or funeral 親愛的兄弟姐妹〔牧師在主持基督徒的婚禮或葬禮時用的開場語〕

dearth /dɝθ; dɜːθ/ *n* [singular] *formal* a lack of something【正式】缺乏: **[+of]** *problems owing to the dearth of experienced personnel* 缺少富有經驗的職員而引發的問題

dear·y, dearie /ˈdɪrɪ; ˈdɪəri/ *n* [C] *old-fashioned*【過時】**1** used as a way of speaking to someone you love 親愛的〔用於稱呼所愛的人〕**2 dearie me** *old-fashioned* used when you are surprised or sad about something【過時】呵, 哎呀〔用於表示驚訝或不快之情〕

death /dɛθ; deθ/ *n* 1 1

1 ►THE END OF SB'S LIFE 某人生命的結束◄ [U] the end of the life of a person or animal〔人或動物的〕死, 死亡: **[+of]** *The death of his mother was a great shock* *to him.* 他媽媽的死給他打擊很大。| *shortly after Lenin's death in 1924* 列寧1924年去世後不久 | *the risk of death or serious injury at work* 工作中死亡或受重傷的危險 | **bleed/burn/starve etc to death** (=die in a particular way) 流血而死/燒死/餓死等 *He choked to death on a fishbone.* 他被魚刺卡住窒息而死。| **put sb to death** (=kill someone, especially after an official decision) 處死某人 *Caesar ordered the prisoners to be put to death.* 凱撒命令處死犯人。| **meet your death** *literary* (=die)【文】逝世 —see also 另見 ACCIDENTAL DEATH

2 ►EXAMPLE OF SB DYING 某人死亡的事例◄ [C] an example of someone dying 死亡的事例: *a campaign to reduce the number of deaths on Britain's roads* 降低英國交通事故死亡人數的宣傳運動 | [+**from**] *deaths from lung cancer* 肺癌導致的死亡

3 die a horrible/terrible etc death to die in a terrible etc way 死得很慘等: *The animals in the traps can die a slow and agonizing death.* 落入陷阱的動物可能會死得很慢、很痛苦。

4 ►IN ART 在藝術中◄ Death [singular] a creature that looks like a SKELETON (1a), used in paintings, stories etc as a sign of death and destruction 死神〔被畫成或被描述成一個骷髏, 作為死亡和毀滅的象徵〕

5 scared/bored to death *informal* extremely frightened or bored【非正式】嚇得/厭煩得要死

6 sick to death of very unhappy with something because it has been annoying you for a long time 對…厭煩, 厭倦, 厭惡: *I am sick to death of your complaining!* 你老是抱怨, 我都煩透了!

7 you'll catch your death (of cold) *spoken* used as a warning to someone when you think they are likely to become ill because it is wet or cold【口】你會得重傷風; 你會得致命的感冒〔用於警告某人由於天氣潮濕或寒冷, 有可能得病〕: *Don't go out without a coat! You'll catch your death of cold!* 穿上大衣再出去! 否則你會得重感冒的!

8 at death's door be very ill and likely to die 病入膏肓; 危在旦夕; 行將就木

9 like death warmed up/warmed over *informal* if someone looks or feels like death warmed up, they look or feel very ill or tired【非正式】病得不輕; 累得要命

10 ►THE END 終止◄ [singular] the permanent end of an idea, custom etc〔觀點、習俗等的〕終結: *an article lamenting the death of classical music* 一篇哀嘆古典音樂衰亡的文章

11 you'll/he'll be the death of me! *spoken* used, especially humorously, when someone makes you very worried and anxious【口】你/他會讓我擔心死!〔尤作幽默用法, 表示某人帶來極大的憂慮〕: *That boy is going to be the death of me!* 那個男孩早晚會讓我擔心死!

12 fight to the death a) to fight until one person is killed 力拚到底, 戰鬥到死; 拚個你死我活 **b)** to fight very hard to achieve something even if it means that you suffer〔為了達到某個目標而〕拚命奮鬥

13 death blow an action or event that makes something fail or end 致命的打擊: *The new evidence dealt a death blow to the prosecution case.* 新的證據給予這件公訴案件致命的打擊。—see also 另見 BLACK DEATH, **kiss of death** (KISS[2] (2)), **a matter of life and death** (LIFE (11))

death·bed /ˈdɛθˌbɛd; ˈdeθbed/ *n* **1 on your deathbed** just before you die 臨終前 **2 deathbed confession/conversion/reconciliation** something that you admit or do just before you die 臨終前的懺悔/信仰改變/和解: *a deathbed conversion to Catholicism* 臨終前皈依天主教 **3 be on your deathbed a)** to be close to death 臨終, 生命垂危 **b)** *humorous* to be feeling very ill【幽默】病入膏肓

death camp /ˈ· ·/ *n* [C] a place where large numbers of prisoners are killed or die, usually in a war〔一般指戰爭中〕死亡集中營

death cer·tif·i·cate /ˈ· ·,···/ *n* [C] a legal document, signed by a doctor, that states the time and cause of someone's death 死亡證明書

death du·ty /ˈ· ,··/ *n* [U] *BrE law* tax on the money or property that you give to someone else after you die; INHERITANCE TAX【英, 法律】遺產稅, 繼承稅

death knell /ˈ· ·/ *n* [singular] **sound the death knell** to be a sign that something will soon stop existing or stop being used 敲響喪鐘〔某事即將終結或停止使用的信號〕: *Plans to build a bridge across the river sounded the death knell for the ferry.* 在這條河上建橋的計劃敲響了渡船的喪鐘。

death·less /ˈdɛθləs; ˈdeθləs/ *adj* **deathless prose/verse/lines etc** *humorous* writing that is very bad or boring【幽默】不朽[永恆]的散文/詩篇/詩行等〔指非常差勁或乏味的作品〕

death·ly /ˈdɛθlɪ; ˈdeθli/ *adj* reminding you of death or of a dead body 死一般的: *Rachel felt deathly cold.* 雷切爾感到死一般的冰冷。| **a deathly hush** (=complete silence) 一片死寂 *A deathly hush fell over the room when the manager walked in.* 經理進屋的時候, 屋裡一片死寂。—**deathly** *adv*

death mask /ˈ· ·/ *n* [C] a model of a dead person's face, made by pressing a soft substance over their face and letting it become hard 死人面具〔在死人的面部壓上一種柔軟的物質, 讓它變硬而製成的模型〕

death pen·al·ty /ˈ· ,···/ *n* [singular] punishment by killing, used in some countries for serious crimes 死刑

death rate /ˈ· ·/ *n* [C] the number of deaths for every 100 or every 1,000 people in a particular year and in a particular place 死亡率 —compare 比較 BIRTHRATE

death rat·tle /ˈ· ,··/ *n* [C] a strange noise sometimes heard from the throat or chest of someone who is dying 臨終時的喉鳴〔臨死的人喉頭或胸中有時發出的奇怪的聲響〕

death row /ˌdɛθ ˈro; ˌdeθ ˈrəʊ/ *n* [U] the part of a prison where prisoners are kept while waiting to be punished by being killed〔監獄的〕死囚區: **on death row** *a murderer on death row* 等待處決的謀殺犯

death sen·tence /ˈ· ,··/ *n* [C] the punishment of death given by a judge〔由法官判處的〕死刑: *Gilmore received a death sentence.* 吉爾摩被判處死刑。

death's head /ˈ· ·/ *n* [C] a human SKULL used as a sign of death〔象徵死亡的〕骷髏頭

death squad /ˈ· ·/ *n* [C] a group of people who kill their political opponents, often because they have been ordered to by a political party〔常指受命於某一政黨去謀殺政治對手的〕死亡小分隊

death throes /ˈ· ·/ *n* [plural] **1** the final stages before something fails or ends〔某事失敗或終結前的〕最後階段: *The coalition seems to be in its death throes.* 這個聯盟似乎正處在解體的最後階段。**2** sudden violent movements sometimes made by someone who is dying 臨終前的痛苦掙扎

death toll /ˈ· ·/ *n* [C] the total number of people who die in a particular accident, war etc〔在意外事故或戰爭中的〕死亡總數, 死亡人數: *As the civil unrest continued, the death toll rose.* 隨着內亂的持續, 死亡人數在上升。

death trap /ˈ· ·/ *n* [C] *informal* a vehicle or building that is in dangerously bad condition【非正式】死亡陷阱〔指狀況十分糟糕、危險的車輛或建築物〕: *Some of those secondhand cars are real death traps.* 那些二手車中有一部分實在是死亡陷阱〔安全隱患特別大〕。

death war·rant /ˈ· ,··/ *n* [C] **1** an official document stating that someone is to be killed as a punishment for their crimes 死刑執行令 **2 sign your own death warrant** to do something that seems likely to cause you very serious trouble 做出可能給自己帶來極大麻煩的事

death wish /ˈ· ·/ *n* [singular] a desire to die 死亡願望: *He's going out with Debbie; What does he have, a death wish?* 他正在和黛比約會; 他難道想找死嗎?

deb /dɛb; deb/ *n* [C] *informal* a DEBUTANTE【非正式】初次參加社交的上流社會年輕女子

de·ba·cle, débâcle /deˋbɑkl; deɪˈbɑːkəl/ *n* [C] an event or situation that is a complete failure because plans have failed〔由於計劃無法實現而導致的〕慘敗

de·bar /dɪˋbɑr; dɪˈbɑː/ *v* **debarred, debarring** [T] to officially prevent someone from doing something〔正式地〕阻止，禁止: **[+from]** *He was debarred from the golf club for stealing club funds.* 由於盜用俱樂部資金，他被趕出了高爾夫俱樂部。—compare 比較 DISBAR

de·base /dɪˋbes; dɪˈbeɪs/ *v* [T] **1** *informal* to reduce the quality or value of something【非正式】降低〔某物的品質或價值〕: *a once rational society debased by war and corruption* 一個曾經理性的社會由於戰爭和腐敗而嚴重地降低了水平 **2 debase yourself** to do something that makes other people have less respect for you 降低[貶損]你的聲望[身分]: *women forced to debase themselves by selling their bodies* 被迫賣身而貶低自己人格的婦女 —**debasement** *n* [C,U]

de·ba·ta·ble /dɪˋbetəbḷ; dɪˈbeɪtəbəl/ *adj* a question or opinion that is debatable is not clear because different people express different views about it 有爭議的，可爭議的: *That is a highly debatable point.* 那是個有嚴重爭議的觀點。| **it is debatable whether/how long etc** *It is debatable whether nuclear weapons actually prevent war.* 核武器是否能夠真正防止戰爭是有爭議的。

1 2 **de·bate¹** /dɪˋbet; dɪˈbeɪt/ *n* **1** [C,U] discussion or argument on a subject that people have different opinions about 討論，辯論: **[+on/over/about]** *As yet there has been little public debate on these issues.* 到目前為止，對於這些問題幾乎還沒有進行過公眾討論。| **fierce/heated/intense debate** (=discussion involving very strong opinions) 激烈的/熱烈的辯論 | **the welfare/abortion etc debate** *the gun control debate in the US* 美國的槍支管制大討論 **2** [C] a formal discussion on a subject〔就某一個話題進行的〕正式討論: **[+about/on]** *a lively debate on the relevance of Marx today* 關於馬克思主義對現今社會相關性問題的熱烈辯論 **3 be open to debate** also 又作 **be a matter for debate** if an idea is open to debate no-one has proved yet whether it is true or false〔某種觀點〕可以進行討論的: *Whether that would have made any difference is open to debate.* 當時要是那樣做是否會有作用尚待商榷。**4 under debate** being discussed 正在討論[辯論]中: *The whole question of compensation is still under debate.* 整個賠償問題還在討論之中。

debate² *v* [I,T] **1** to discuss a subject formally when you are trying to make a decision or find a solution〔正式地〕討論，辯論: *We debated for several hours before taking a vote.* 我們辯論了好幾個小時才投票。| **debate whether/what/how etc** *debating whether to raise the price of school meals* 討論是否提高學校用餐價格 | **hotly debated** (=argued about strongly) 熱烈地辯論 *His conclusions are hotly debated among academics.* 他的結論在學術界引起了熱烈的辯論。**2** to consider something in your own mind before reaching a decision〔作出決定前〕反覆考慮，斟酌: **debate with yourself** *He debated with himself for a moment then replied.* 他反覆考慮後才作出回答。| **debate who/what/how etc** *I wasn't feeling well and was debating whether to go to work.* 那時我身體不太舒服，所以正琢磨着去不去上班。—**debater** *n* [C]

de·bauch /dɪˋbɔtʃ; dɪˈbɔːtʃ/ *v* [T] *formal* to make someone behave in an immoral way, especially with alcohol, drugs, or sex【正式】〔尤指用酒、毒品或色情〕使〔某人〕墮落，使放蕩

de·bauched /dɪˋbɔtʃt; dɪˈbɔːtʃt/ *adj* someone who is debauched is immoral because they drink a lot of alcohol, take drugs, or have an immoral attitude to sex〔因為酗酒、吸毒或者持有不健康的性觀念而〕不道德的，道德敗壞的，放蕩的，墮落的

de·bauch·e·ry /dɪˋbɔtʃərɪ; dɪˈbɔːtʃəri/ *n* **1** [U] immoral behaviour involving drugs, alcohol, sex etc 道德敗壞: *a life of total debauchery* 放蕩淫逸的生活 **2** [C] an occasion when someone behaves in this way 放蕩

de·ben·ture /dɪˋbɛntʃɚ; dɪˈbentʃə/ *n* [C] *technical* an official document given by a company, showing that it has borrowed money and that it will pay a fixed rate of INTEREST¹ (4), whether or not it makes a profit【術語】債券

de·bil·i·tate /dɪˋbɪlə,tet; dɪˈbɪlɪ̈teɪt/ *v* [T] **1** if illness, heat, hunger etc debilitates someone, it makes their body or mind weak 使虛弱，使衰弱: *debilitated by fever* 因發燒身體虛弱 **2** if an action debilitates an organization or structure, it weakens its authority or effectiveness 削弱〔權威性或有效性〕

de·bil·it·at·ing /dɪˋbɪlə,tetɪŋ; dɪˈbɪlɪ̈teɪtɪŋ/ *adj* **1** a debilitating disease or condition makes your body or mind weak 使〔身體或精神〕虛弱的: *debilitating heat* 使人虛弱的高溫天氣 **2** a debilitating action, result etc weakens an organization, structure etc 使〔組織、機構等〕削弱的: *the debilitating effect of economic decline* 經濟衰退造成的削弱性後果

de·bil·i·ty /dɪˋbɪlətɪ; dɪˈbɪlɪ̈ti/ *n* [C,U] *formal* weakness, especially as the result of illness【正式】〔尤指疾病造成的〕虛弱，衰弱

deb·it¹ /ˋdɛbɪt; ˈdebɪ̈t/ *n* [C] *technical*【術語】**1** something in a book of accounts that shows money spent or owed〔賬本中的〕收方，借方，借入 **2** a sum of money taken out of a bank account 從銀行賬戶中提取的款項 —compare 比較 CREDIT¹ (1) —see also 另見 DIRECT DEBIT

debit² *v* [T] *technical*【術語】**1** to take money out of a bank account〔從銀行賬戶中〕取〔款〕: *the sum of £25 debited from your account* 從你的賬戶中劃出的25英鎊的款項 **2 [+against]** to record the amount of money taken from a bank account〔將取出的金額〕記入…的借方賬中 —compare 比較 CREDIT² (2)

debit card /ˈ·· ,·/ *n* [C] a special plastic card that you can use to pay for things directly from your bank account 借記卡，借方卡 —compare 比較 CASH CARD, CHEQUE CARD, CREDIT CARD

debit note /ˈ·· ·/ *n* [C] a document sent by a company to a customer telling them how much money they owe〔公司發給顧客的〕借項清單，借項賬單，借方報單，借方票，借方通知

deb·o·nair /,dɛbəˋnɛr; ,debəˈneə◂/ *adj* a man who is debonair is fashionable and well dressed and behaves in an attractively confident way〔通常指男士〕溫文爾雅的，穿着入時的: *a stylish, debonair young man* 一個穿着時髦、溫文爾雅的青年男子

de·bouch /dɪˋbuʃ; dɪˈbaʊtʃ/ *v* [I always+adv/prep] **1** *technical* if a river, road etc debouches somewhere, it comes out from a narrow place into a wider place【術語】〔河流〕流至較大區域；〔道路〕延伸至開闊地區 **2** *formal* if people debouch from one place to another, they move out of one place into somewhere larger【正式】〔人〕進入較開闊地方

de·brief /,diˋbrif; ,diːˈbriːf/ *v* [T] to talk to someone to get information from them after they have done a job that you told them to do 詢問〔任務完成者〕執行情況，聽取〔任務完成者〕匯報情況: *The returning bomber crews were debriefed.* 聽取返回的轟炸機機組人員匯報情況。—compare 比較 BRIEF³ —**debriefing** *n* [U]

deb·ris /dəˋbri; ˈdebriː/ *n* [U] all the pieces that are left after something has been destroyed in an accident, explosion etc 碎片；殘骸: *The beach was littered with debris.* 海灘上到處都是散落的殘骸。

debt /dɛt; det/ *n* **1** [C] a sum of money that you owe 債務，欠款: **pay off/repay/clear your debts** *He now had enough money to pay off his father's outstanding debts.* 他現在有足夠的錢來償還他父親尚未清還的債務。| 2 2 **[+of]** *The company has debts of around $1,000,000.* 該公司負債大約100萬美元。| **run up a debt** (=borrow money without paying it back on time) 積欠債務 *students running up massive credit card debts* 積欠大量信用卡債務的學生 **2** [U] the state of owing money 欠債，負債: *He was imprisoned for debt.* 他由於欠債而入獄。| **be in debt** (=owe money) 欠債，負債 | **£200/$1000 etc in debt** *She was still $600 in debt.* 她還欠600美元。| **go/get/run/slip etc into debt** (=spend so much money that you need to borrow money) 陷入債務之中，負債

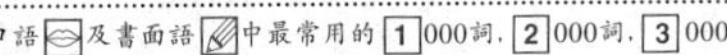

Malone was sinking hopelessly into debt. 馬隆無可救藥地陷入債務之中。| **be heavily/deeply/up to your ears in debt** (=owe a lot of money) 債台高築 **3 your debt to sb** the degree to which you have learned from or been influenced by someone else 受某人的影響, 受某人的恩惠: *Marx's debt to earlier thinkers such as Hegel* 馬克思從黑格爾等早期思想家受益的地方 **4 be in debt** also 又作 **owe a debt of gratitude to sb** to be very grateful to someone for what they have done for you 感激某人, 欠某人的情 —see also 另見 BAD DEBT, NATIONAL DEBT

debt col·lect·or /ˈ· ·,··/ *n* [C] someone who is employed to get back the money that people owe 收債人

debt·or /ˋdɛtɚ; ˈdetə/ *n* [C] a person, group, or organization that owes money 債務人 —compare 比較 CREDITOR

de·bug /diˋbʌg; ˌdiːˈbʌg/ *v* **debugged, debugging** [T] **1** to take the mistakes out of a computer's PROGRAM (=set of instructions) 排除〔電腦程式中的錯誤、故障〕 **2** to find and remove secret listening equipment in a room or building 從…拆除竊聽器

D

de·bunk /diˋbʌŋk; ˌdiːˈbʌŋk/ *v* [T] to show that an idea or belief is false 證明〔觀點或觀念〕錯誤: *debunking the myth that British cuisine is bad* 證明英國烹調很差勁這種沒有根據的觀念是錯誤的 —**debunker** *n* [C]

de·but /deˋbju; ˈdeɪbjuː/ *n* [C] the first public appearance of someone such as an entertainer or a sports player or of something new and important〔演員或運動員等的〕首次公開露面, 首次登台: *Their debut album was recorded in 1991.* 他們的首張唱片錄製於 1991 年。| **make your debut** *a young actress making her debut on Broadway* 在百老匯首次登台演出的年輕女演員

deb·u·tante /ˌdɛbjʊˋtɑnt; ˈdebjʊtɑːnt/ *n* [C] a young UPPER CLASS woman who goes to special parties as a way of being formally introduced to upper-class society 初次參加社交的上流社會年輕女子

Dec the written abbreviation of 縮寫= DECEMBER

deca- /dɛkə; dekə/ *prefix* ten 十: *decalitre* (=ten litres) 十升 | *the decathlon* (=a sports competition with 10 different events) 十項全能運動 —see table on page C4 參見 C4 頁附錄

3 2 **dec·ade** /ˋdɛked; ˈdekeɪd/ *n* [C] a period of ten years 十年; 十年期間

dec·a·dence /ˋdɛkədṇs; ˈdekədəns/ *n* [U] the state of having low moral standards and being more concerned with pleasure than with serious matters 墮落, 頹廢: *the corruption and decadence of the nobility* 貴族的腐敗和頹廢

dec·a·dent /ˋdɛkədṇt; ˈdekədənt/ *adj* having low moral standards and being more concerned with your own pleasure than serious matters 墮落的, 頹廢的: *Pop music was condemned as decadent and crude.* 流行音樂被指責為墮落、粗俗的音樂。—**decadently** *adv*

de·caf /ˋdikæf; ˈdiːkæf/ *n* [U] *spoken* decaffeinated coffee or tea【口】去掉咖啡因的咖啡[茶]

de·caf·fein·a·ted /diˋkæfəˌnetɪd; diːˈkæfɪ̍neɪtɪ̍d/ *adj* coffee or tea that is decaffeinated has had CAFFEINE (=a drug that keeps you awake) removed〔咖啡或茶〕除去咖啡因的

de·cal /ˋdikæl; ˈdiːkæl/ *n* [C] *AmE* a piece of paper with a pattern or picture on it that you stick onto another surface【美】貼花紙; TRANSFER² (3) *BrE*【英】

Dec·a·logue /ˋdɛkəˌlɔg; ˈdekəlɒg/ *n* [singular] the Ten Commandments〔《聖經》的〕十誡

de·camp /dɪˋkæmp; dɪˈkæmp/ *v* [I] to leave a place quickly and usually secretly 逃走, 潛逃: *The secretary decamped with the members' money.* 那個祕書帶着會員們的錢逃跑了。

de·cant /dɪˋkænt; dɪˈkænt/ *v* [T] to pour liquid, especially wine, from one container into another 將〔液體, 尤指酒〕從一個容器倒入另一個容器

de·cant·er /dɪˋkæntɚ; dɪˈkæntə/ *n* [C] a glass container for holding alcoholic drinks〔用來裝酒的〕帶塞玻璃瓶

de·cap·i·tate /dɪˋkæpəˌtet; dɪˈkæpɪ̍teɪt/ *v* [T] to cut off someone's head 砍…的頭, 把…斬首 —**decapitation** /dɪˌkæpəˋteʃən; dɪˌkæpɪ̍ˈteɪʃən/ *n* [C,U]

de·cath·lon /dɪˋkæθlɑn; dɪˈkæθlɒn/ *n* [singular] a competition including ten different sports 十項全能運動 —compare 比較 PENTATHLON

de·cay¹ /dɪˋke; dɪˈkeɪ/ *v* **1** [I,T] to be slowly destroyed by a natural chemical process, or to make something do this (使)腐爛; (使)變壞: *The carcass was already starting to decay.*〔動物的〕屍體已經開始腐爛。**2** [I often in progressive 常用進行式] if buildings, structures, or areas decay, their condition gradually becomes worse〔可以指建築物、結構或地區等的狀況〕變壞, 破敗: *The Metropole Hotel was now decaying after years of neglect.* 都會大酒店由於長年失修, 已經十分破敗。**3** [I often in progressive 常用進行式] if traditional beliefs, morals, standards etc decay, people do not believe in them or support them any more〔傳統觀念、道德、標準等〕失去影響力, 衰敗, 衰落: *Educational standards have decayed.* 教育標準已大幅度降低。

decay² *n* **1** [U] the natural chemical change that causes the slow destruction of something 腐爛, 朽爛: *The house had stood empty for years and smelled of decay.* 這座房子已經空了好多年, 有股朽爛的氣味。| **tooth decay** *Use a fluoride toothpaste to fight tooth decay.* 使用含氟的牙膏預防蛀牙。**2** [singular] the part of something that has been destroyed in this way 腐爛部分, 腐蝕部分: *The dentist used a drill to remove the decay.* 牙醫用牙鑽除去牙齒的蛀蝕部分。**3** [U] the gradual destruction of ideas, beliefs, social or political organizations etc〔觀念、信仰、社會組織或政治組織等的〕衰退, 衰敗: *moral and spiritual decay* 道德和精神的頹廢 **4** [U] the change from economic success to a state of being poor〔經濟上的〕成功到貧窮的轉變, 衰退: *urban decay* 市區的衰敗 **5** [U] the gradual destruction of buildings and structures caused by a lack of care〔疏於管理而造成建築物和大樓的〕逐漸毀壞: **fall into decay/fall into a state of decay** *the old fortress falling into a state of decay* 那個慢慢頹塌的要塞

de·cease /dɪˋsis; dɪˈsiːs/ *n* [U] *formal* death【正式】死亡: *Upon your decease the house will pass to your wife.* 你去世後, 這座房子將由你妻子繼承。

de·ceased /dɪˋsist; dɪˈsiːst/ *n* **the deceased** *formal* someone who has died, especially recently【正式】死者, 已故之人〔尤指最近剛去世的人〕: *The deceased left a large sum of money to his children.* 死者留給他的孩子們一大筆錢。—**deceased** *adj*

de·ceit /dɪˋsit; dɪˈsiːt/ *n* [C,U] behaviour that is intended to make someone believe something that is not true, or an example of this behaviour 欺騙, 欺詐: *hypocrisy and deceit* 虛偽與欺騙

de·ceit·ful /dɪˋsitfəl; dɪˈsiːtfəl/ *adj* someone who is deceitful tells lies in order to get what they want 欺騙的, 撒謊的 —**deceitfully** *adv* —**deceitfulness** *n* [U]

de·ceive /dɪˋsiv; dɪˈsiːv/ *v* [T] **1** to make someone believe something that is not true in order to get what you want 欺騙: *You deceived me, and I can't forgive you.* 你欺騙了我, 我不能原諒你。| **deceive sb into doing sth** *They deceived the old man into signing the papers.* 他們騙那個老人在文件上簽了字。**2 deceive yourself** to pretend to yourself that something is not true, because the truth is unpleasant 自欺欺人: *I thought she loved me, but really I was deceiving myself.* 我以為她是愛我的, 但事實上, 我是在欺騙自己。**3 are my eyes deceiving me?** *spoken* used when you see someone or something that you are very surprised to see【口】我是不是看錯了? 是不是我眼花了?〔表示非常驚訝〕: *Are my eyes deceiving me, or is that a genuine Persian carpet.* 我沒眼花吧, 那不是正宗的波斯地毯嗎。—**deceiver** *n* [C]

de·cel·e·rate /diˋsɛləˌret; ˌdiːˈseləreɪt/ *v* [I] *technical* to go slower, especially in a vehicle【術語】〔尤指車輛〕減速: *Decelerate when approaching a corner.* 駛到路口處要減速。—opposite 反義詞 ACCELERATE —**decelera-**

tion /di͵sɛləˋreʃən; ͵diːseləˈreɪʃən/ *n* [U]

De·cem·ber /dɪˋsɛmbɚ; dɪˈsembə/ written abbreviation 縮寫為 **Dec** *n* [C,U] the 12th and last month of the year, between November and January 十二月: **in December** *The course starts in December.* 課程十二月開課。| **last/next December** *I arrived here last December.* 我是去年十二月份到這兒的。| **on December 6th** (also 又作 **on 6th December** *BrE*【英】) *The meeting will be on December 6th* (spoken as 讀作 *on the sixth of December* or *on December the sixth* or *AmE*【美】 *on December 6th*). 會議將於12月6日舉行。

de·cen·cy /ˋdisn̩sɪ; ˈdiːsənsi/ *n* [U] **1** a quality in someone's character that makes them honest and polite and makes them have respect for other people 正派, 端莊, 體面: *a judgement that reflects the decency and good sense of the American people* 反映美國人民寬容和智慧的評價 **2** acceptable behaviour, especially moral and sexual behaviour 合乎禮儀〔尤指道德和性方面的行為〕: **sense of decency** *They have no sense of honour or decency.* 他們沒有榮譽感或體面感。| **common decency** (=basic standards of behaviour that everyone should follow) 基本行為標準 *It's common decency to let someone know if you are going to arrive late.* 如果你要遲到, 最好通知別人, 這是最起碼的禮貌。| **have the decency to do sth** (=behave in a way that follows the basic standards of acceptable behaviour) 按禮節行事 *You could have had the decency to ask me before you invited all your friends to stay!* 你應該懂點道理, 在把你所有的朋友請來住之前, 先問問我的意見。**3 decencies** *old-fashioned* standards of behaviour that people think are acceptable【過時】文雅的行為標準

2 **de·cent** /ˋdisn̩t; ˈdiːsənt/ *adj* **1** acceptable and good enough 可接受的, 相當好的, 像樣的: *Haven't you got a decent pair of shoes?* 你難道沒有一雙像樣的鞋? | *a house with a decent sized yard* 院子還算大的房子 **2** treating people in a fair and kind way〔待人〕公平的; 和善的: *I decided her father was a decent guy, after all.* 畢竟, 我覺得她父親是個還不錯的人。| **be decent of sb to do sth** *It was decent of him to offer to help us paint the house.* 他真好, 主動提出幫助我們粉刷房子。| **be decent about something** *especially BrE* (=treat someone fairly and sympathetically when they have done something wrong)【尤英】公正的; 寬容的 *The lecturers were really decent about my absences.* 授課老師們對於我的缺課真的很寬容。**3** following the standards of moral behaviour accepted by most people 正派的, 規矩的: *Decent citizens have nothing to fear from this legislation.* 規矩的公民無需害怕這項法規。| **do the decent thing** (=do something because you feel you ought to) 做該做的事 *When Tom found out that his girlfriend was pregnant, he did the decent thing and married her.* 湯姆發現他的女朋友懷孕時, 做了該做的事, 和她結了婚。**4** *usually humorous* wearing enough clothes to not show too much of your body【一般幽默】穿着得體的, 不暴露太多的: *Don't come in – I'm not decent!* 別進來 —— 我還沒穿好衣服! —opposite 反義詞 INDECENT (1) **5 a decent burial/funeral** if someone is given a decent burial, they are buried in an acceptable way 體面的葬禮 —**decently** *adv*

de·cen·tral·ize also 又作 **-ise** *BrE*【英】/diˋsɛntrəl͵aɪz; ͵diːˈsentrəlaɪz/ *v* [T] to move parts of a government, organization etc from one central place to several different smaller ones 分散, 下放〔權力〕: *Many firms are decentralizing parts of their operations.* 許多公司正分散部分經營活動。—**decentralized** *adj*: *a decentralized economy* 分散經濟 —**decentralization** /͵disɛntrələˋzeʃən; ͵diːsentrəlaɪˈzeɪʃən/ *n* [U]

de·cep·tion /dɪˋsɛpʃən; dɪˈsepʃən/ *n* [C,U] the act of deliberately making someone believe something that is not true 欺騙(行為): *outrage at the government's deception* 對政府欺騙行徑的憤怒

de·cep·tive /dɪˋsɛptɪv; dɪˈseptɪv/ *adj* **1** something that is deceptive seems to be one thing but is in fact very different 造成假象的, 似是而非的: *A boa constrictor can move with deceptive speed.* 蟒蛇能以令人難料的速度爬行。**2** deliberately intended to make someone believe something that is not true 欺騙的, 欺詐的: *deceptive behavior* 欺騙行為 —**deceptively** *adj* —**deceptiveness** *n* [U]

deci- /dɛsɪ; desɪ/ *prefix* a 10th part of a unit 十分之一: *a decilitre* (=0.1 litres) 分升〔1/10 升〕—see table on page C4 參見C4頁附錄

dec·i·bel /ˋdɛsə͵bɛl; ˈdesɪbel/ *n* [C] *technical* a unit of measurement for the loudness of sound【術語】分貝〔衡量聲音強度的單位〕: *The noise level in factories must not exceed 85 decibels.* 工廠的噪聲水平不得超過85分貝。

This graph shows how common the different grammar patterns of the verb **decide** are. 本圖表所示為動詞 decide 構成的不同語法模式的使用頻率。

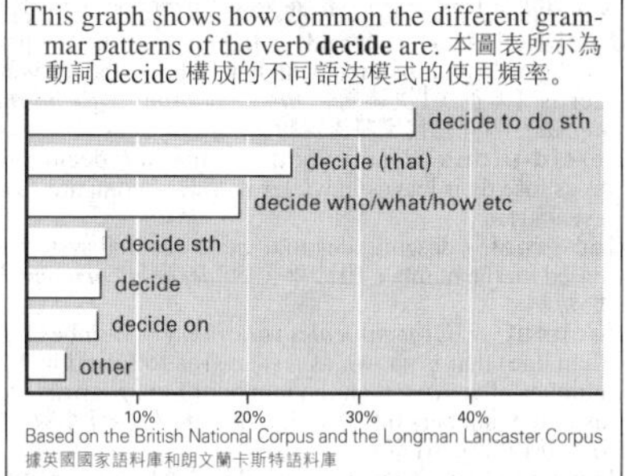

Based on the British National Corpus and the Longman Lancaster Corpus
據英國國家語料庫和朗文蘭卡斯特語料庫

de·cide /dɪˋsaɪd; dɪˈsaɪd/ *v* **1** [I,T] to make a choice or judgment about something, especially after a period of not knowing what to do or in a way that ends disagreement 決定, 決斷, 判斷: **decide to do sth** *Tina's decided to go to Prague for her holidays.* 蒂娜已決定到布拉格去度假。| **decide that** *It was eventually decided that four London hospitals should be closed.* 最後決定關閉四家倫敦醫院。| **decide who/what/how etc** *I can't decide what to do.* 我不知道該做甚麼。| **decide whether/if** *Women now have greater freedom to decide whether or not to get married.* 婦女現在擁有較大的自由來決定自己是否結婚。| **[+between]** *I'm trying to decide between the green and the blue for the bathroom.* 我正在考慮把浴室刷成綠色的好還是藍色的好。| **decide sth** *I'm eighteen now – I have a right to decide my own future.* 我現在十八歲了 —— 有權決定自己的未來。| **decide for yourself** (=make your own choice or judgment, without asking anyone else to do it for you) 自己決定 *You must decide for yourself whether to leave college.* 你必須自己決定是否退學。—see also 另見 DECISION (1) **2** [T] to be the reason for someone making a particular judgment or choice 使決定, 使下決心: **decide sb to do sth** *What was it that finally decided you to give up your job?* 甚麼使你最終決定放棄你的工作? | **deciding factor** (=a very strong reason that forces you to make a particular decision) 決定性因素 *Money should not be the deciding factor over who runs a TV station.* 錢不應該成為選擇電視台管理者的決定性因素。**3** [T] if an event, action etc decides something, it influences events so that one particular result will happen 決定〔事件的結果〕: *A goal in the last minute decided the match.* 最後一分鐘的一個進球決定了比賽的勝負。| **the deciding vote** (=the person who has the deciding vote makes the final decision, because all the other votes are equally divided) 決定性一票 **4 decide in favour of/decide against a)** to choose or not choose someone or something 選擇/不選擇〔某人或某物〕: *After long discussion they decided in favour of the younger candidate.* 經過長時間的討論, 他們決定選那個年輕些的候選人。**b)** if a judge or JURY (1) decides in favour of someone or against someone, they say in court that someone is guilty or not guilty 作出有利於/不利於〔某人的〕裁決: *The jury decided in*

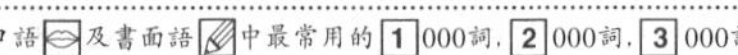

favour of the plaintiff. 陪審團作出了有利於原告的裁決。

decide on sth *phr v* [T] to choose one thing from many possible choices 選定: *Have you decided on a date for your wedding?* 你結婚的日子選好沒有?

de·cid·ed /dɪˋsaɪdɪd; dɪˈsaɪdᵻd/ *adj* definite and easily noticed 清楚的, 明確的; 明顯的: *a decided change for the better* 明顯的好轉

de·cid·ed·ly /dɪˋsaɪdɪdlɪ; dɪˈsaɪdᵻdli/ *adv* **1** [+adj/adv] *especially BrE* definitely or in a way that is easily noticed【尤英】肯定地, 無疑地; 明顯地: *The man was decidedly drunk.* 這個男人肯定是喝多了。**2** in a way that shows that you are very sure and determined about what you want to do 堅決地, 堅定地: *"I'm not going to do it," said Margaret decidedly.* "這件事, 我不做。"瑪嘉烈堅決地說。

de·cid·er /dɪˋsaɪdɚ; dɪˈsaɪdə/ *n* [C] *informal* the last part of a game or competition, which will show who the winner is【非正式】決勝局: *This next round will be the decider.* 下一輪比賽將決定勝負。

D

de·cid·u·ous /dɪˋsɪdʒuəs; dɪˈsɪdʒuəs/ *adj* deciduous trees lose their leaves in winter 落葉的 —compare 比較 EVERGREEN[2]

dec·i·mal[1] /ˋdɛsəml̩; ˈdesᵻməl/ *adj* a decimal system is based on the number 10 十進位的: *decimal currency* 十進幣制

decimal[2] *n* [C] *technical* a FRACTION (=a number less than one) that is shown as a FULL STOP followed by the number of TENTHS, then the number of HUNDREDTHS etc, as in the numbers 0.5, 0.175, 0.661 etc【術語】小數〈如 0.5, 0.175, 0.661 等〉

dec·i·mal·ize also 又作 **-ise** *BrE*【英】/ˋdɛsəml̩ˌaɪz; ˈdesᵻməlaɪz/ *v* [I,T] to change to a decimal system of money or measurements (將)〔幣制或度量衡〕改為十進制 —**decimalization** /ˌdɛsəməlɪˋzeʃən; ˌdesᵻməlaɪˈzeɪʃən/ *n* [U]

decimal place /ˌ··· ˈ·/ *n* [C] *technical* one of the positions after a FULL STOP in a decimal【術語】小數點後的位數: *measurements accurate to three decimal places* 精確到小數點後三位的測量結果

decimal point /ˌ··· ˈ·/ *n* [C] *technical* the FULL STOP in a decimal, used to separate whole numbers from TENTHS, HUNDREDTHS, etc【術語】小數點

decimal sys·tem /ˈ··· ˌ··/ *n* [singular] a system of counting that is based on the number 10 十進制

dec·i·mate /ˋdɛsəˌmet; ˈdesᵻmeɪt/ *v* [T usually passive 一般用被動態] to destroy a large part of something 大量毀滅: *The population has been decimated by disease.* 疾病導致大批的人死亡。—**decimation** /ˌdɛsəˋmeʃən; ˌdesᵻˈmeɪʃən/ *n* [U]

de·ci·pher /dɪˋsaɪfɚ; dɪˈsaɪfə/ *v* [T] to find the meaning of something that is difficult to read or understand 辨認; 解釋: *I can't decipher his handwriting.* 我辨認不出他寫的是甚麼。—see also 另見 INDECIPHERABLE

This graph shows some of the words most commonly used with the noun **decision**. 本圖表所示為含有名詞 decision 的一些最常用詞組。

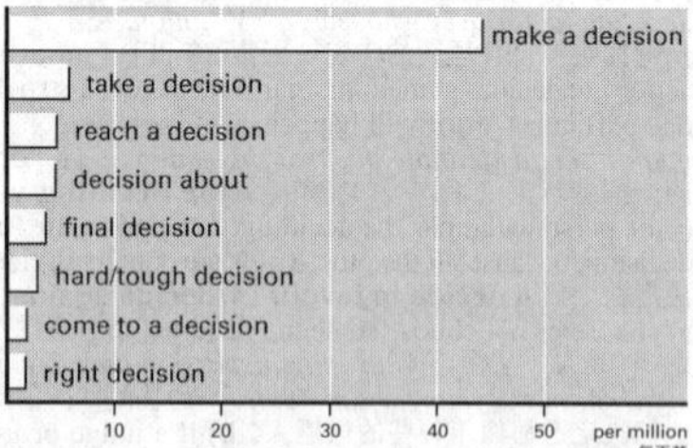

make a decision
take a decision
reach a decision
decision about
final decision
hard/tough decision
come to a decision
right decision

10 20 30 40 50 per million 每百萬

Based on the British National Corpus and the Longman Lancaster Corpus
據英國國家語料庫和朗文蘭卡斯特語料庫

de·ci·sion /dɪˋsɪʒən; dɪˈsɪʒən/ *n* **1** [C] a choice or judgment that you make after a period of discussion or thought 決定, 抉擇: *The judges' decision is final.* 裁判們的決定是不可更改的。| **decision to do sth** *his wife's decision to leave him* 他妻子離開他的決定 | **make/take a decision** (=decide) 作出決定 *The committee is due to make its decision this week.* 委員會預期本週作出決定。| **come to/reach a decision** (=finally decide) 作出決定 *We finally came to a firm decision.* 我們最終果斷地作出了決定。| **[+about]** *a decision about whether to expand the business* 關於是否擴展業務的決定 | **final decision** (=a decision that will not be changed) 最後決定 *I'm afraid I don't have the final decision in these matters.* 在這些事情上恐怕我還無法作出最終的決定。| **big decision** (=an important decision) 重大決定 | **difficult/hard/tough decision** *It was a tough decision, but I decided to leave my job.* 這是個艱難的抉擇, 但我還是決定辭職。**2** [U] the quality someone has that makes them able to make choices or judgments quickly and confidently 果斷, 堅定, 決斷: *This job requires the ability to act with speed and decision.* 這個工作需要迅速、果斷行事的能力。—opposite 反義詞 INDECISION **3** [U] the act of deciding something 判決, 裁決: *The burden of decision rests with the Supreme Court.* 裁定的責任在最高法院。

decision-mak·ing /ˈ·· ˌ··/ *n* [U] the process of thinking about a problem, idea etc, and then making a choice or judgment 決策: *an attempt to make workers more involved in decision-making* 讓工人們更多地參與決策的嘗試

de·ci·sive /dɪˋsaɪsɪv; dɪˈsaɪsɪv/ *adj* **1 a decisive step/role/battle etc** an action, event etc that has a powerful effect on the final result of something 決定性的一步/角色/戰役等: *Waterloo was the decisive battle of the entire war.* 滑鐵盧戰役在整個戰爭中起了決定性作用。**2** good at making decisions quickly and with confidence 果斷的, 堅決的, 決斷的: *a decisive leader* 果斷的領袖 | **decisive action** (=action taken quickly and confidently in order to solve a problem) 果斷的行動 *She demonstrated a talent for quick, decisive action.* 她表現出做事迅速、果斷的素質。**3** leading to a clear result and ending doubt 決定性的, 確定的: *a decisive election victory* 一次決定性的選舉勝利 **4 play a decisive role (in sth)** to be one of the most important causes of something (在某事中)起着至關重要的作用: *a decisive role in the recent peace process* 在最近的和平進程中起着決定性作用 **5 a decisive step** something that results in important change 決定性的一步: *The covenant at Sinai was the decisive step in the creation of Israel.* 在西奈簽訂的決議是創建以色列國的決定性一步。**6** definite and not able to be doubted 確定的, 明確的: *The answer was a decisive no.* 回答是非常明確的不。—**decisively** *adv*

de·ci·sive·ness /dɪˋsaɪsɪvnɪs; dɪˈsaɪsɪvnᵻs/ *n* [U] the ability to make decisions quickly with confidence and determination 果斷, 決斷: *David acted with speed and decisiveness.* 大衛辦事迅速、果斷。

deck[1] /dɛk; dek/ *n* [C] **1** the outside top level of a ship that you can walk on 甲板: **on deck** *Let's go up on deck and sit in the sun.* 讓我們上去到甲板上坐坐, 曬曬太陽。| **above/below deck(s)** *Peter stayed below decks.* 彼得留在下面, 沒到甲板上面來。—see picture at 參見 YACHT 圖 **2** one of the levels on a ship or bus〔船或公共汽車的〕一層: **lower/upper deck** (=on a ship) 船的下層/上層 *Our cabin is on the lower deck.* 我們的船艙在下層。| **top/bottom deck** (=on a bus) 公共汽車的頂層/底層 *The kids love riding on the top deck.* 孩子們喜歡到公共汽車的頂層上坐。**3** *AmE* a wooden floor built out from the back of a house, used for relaxing on【美】〔房屋後面延伸搭建供休息用的〕木製平台 **4** *especially AmE* a set of playing cards【尤美】一副紙牌; PACK[2] (8) *BrE*【英】**5 all hands on deck** *informal* used when everyone must work together to do something as quickly as possible【非正式】齊心合力 —see also 另見 **clear the decks** (CLEAR² (14)), **hit the deck** (HIT¹ (21)), FLIGHT DECK, TAPE DECK

deck² *v* [T] **1** also 又作 **deck sth out** to decorate something with flowers, flags etc, especially for a special occasion〔用花、旗幟等〕裝飾: **[+with]** *The street was decked with flags for the royal wedding.* 為了慶祝皇家婚禮, 人們用旗子裝飾街道。**2** *slang* to hit someone so hard that they fall over【俚】將〔某人〕擊倒: *Gerry just swung round and decked him.* 格里迅速轉過身把他一下子打倒在地。

deck·chair /ˋdɛkˌtʃɛr; ˈdektʃeə/ *n* [C] a folding chair with a long seat made of cloth, used especially on the beach〔尤指在海灘上使用的〕摺疊躺椅 —see picture at 參見 CHAIR¹ 圖

deck·hand /ˋdɛkˌhænd; ˈdekhænd/ *n* [C] someone who does unskilled work on a ship 艙面水手, 普通水手

deck shoe /ˋ· ·/ *n* [C] a flat shoe made of CANVAS (=heavy cloth) 平底帆布鞋 —see picture at 參見 SHOE¹ 圖

de·claim /dɪˋklem; dɪˈkleɪm/ *v* **[I+against/about;T]** to speak loudly, sometimes with actions, so that people will notice you 慷慨陳詞 —**declamation** /ˌdɛkləˋmeʃən; ˌdekləˈmeɪʃən/ *n* [C,U]

de·clam·a·to·ry /dɪˋklæməˌtorɪ; dɪˈklæmətəri/ *adj* a declamatory speech or piece of writing expresses your feelings and opinions very strongly 激昂的, 強烈的

3 **dec·la·ra·tion** /ˌdɛkləˋreʃən; ˌdekləˈreɪʃən/ *n* [C,U] **1** an important statement saying that something such as a war, peace etc has officially begun 重要聲明; 宣言: *a ceasefire declaration* 停火聲明 | **[+of]** *issue a declaration of war* 宣戰 **2** an official or serious statement of what someone believes〔官方或正式的〕宣言, 公告: **[+of]** *the United Nations Declaration of Human Rights* 聯合國人權宣言 **3** a statement in which you officially give information, especially about yourself 聲明, 申報: *a declaration of taxable earnings* 一份應納稅收入的申報

de·clar·a·tive /dɪˋklærətɪv; dɪˈklærətɪv/ *adj technical* a declarative sentence has the form of a statement【術語】陳述的, 敘述的

2 **de·clare** /dɪˋklɛr; dɪˈkleə/ *v*

1 ►STATE OFFICIALLY 正式宣布◄ [T] to state officially and publicly that a particular situation exists or that something is true 宣布, 聲明: **declare that** *The doctor finally declared that the man was dead.* 醫生最終宣布該男子死亡。| **declare sth (to be) sth** *The government of New South Wales declared 8000 hectares of forest a national park.* 新南威爾斯政府宣布 8000 公頃的森林為國家公園。| **declare sth open** *I declare this exhibition open.* 我宣布展覽開幕。| **declare sth unsafe/a failure/a success etc** *The use of certain chemicals has now been declared illegal.* 某些化學物質的使用現已被宣布為非法。| **declare sb insane/unfit/a traitor etc** (=state officially that someone is crazy etc) 正式宣布某人瘋了/不合適/是叛徒等 | **declare sb the winner/the champion etc** *Ali was declared the winner of the fight.* 阿里被宣布為這場比賽的獲勝者。

2 declare war (on sb) a) to decide and state officially that you will begin fighting another country 對〔某國〕宣戰 **b)** *informal* to say that something is wrong and that you will do everything you can to stop it【非正式】向〔不好的事〕宣戰: *Police have now declared war on drug dealers in the area.* 警方現在已經對這個地區的毒販宣戰了。

3 ►SAY WHAT YOU THINK/FEEL 說出所想/感覺到的◄ [T] to say very clearly and publicly what you think or feel 聲稱, 宣稱: *"On that point, I cannot agree with you," he declared.* "在那一點上我無法同意你的觀點。" 他宣稱。| **declare that** *Jane declared that she would rather resign than change her decision.* 珍宣稱她寧可辭職也不改變決定。| **declare sth** *The opposition declared their support for the bill.* 反對黨表示將支持這個法案。| **declare yourself (to be) sth** *She had publicly declared herself a lesbian.* 她公開聲明自己是同性戀。

4 ►MONEY/PROPERTY ETC 金錢/財產等◄ [T] to make an official statement saying how much money you have earned, what property you own etc 申報〔收入、財產等〕: *All investment income must also be declared.* 所有的投資收益也必須申報。

5 declare an interest to tell people that you are connected with something that is being discussed 宣布和…有關係: *I should declare an interest here; Mr Hackett used to work for me.* 我宣布與此事有關; 哈克特先生曾經為我工作過。

6 declare bankruptcy to state officially that you are unable to pay your debts 宣告破產

7 ►SURPRISE 驚奇◄ (Well) I declare! *spoken old-fashioned* used as an expression of surprise【口, 過時】嘿! 真怪了!〔用於表示驚奇〕: *Well I declare! What a pretty little village.* 我的天!多美的小村莊啊。—**declarable** *adj*

declare against sb/sth *phr v* [T] to state that you oppose someone or something 聲明反對

declare for sb/sth *phr v* [T] to state that you support someone or something 聲明贊成: *Paredes decided to declare for federation.* 帕雷德斯決定聲明支持聯邦政府。

de·clared /dɪˋklɛrd; dɪˈkleəd/ *adj* **declared wish/intention/policy etc** a wish, intention etc that you state publicly 公開表明的願望/打算/政策等: *It is their declared intention to increase taxes.* 他們公開宣稱有意增稅。

de·clas·si·fied /diˋklæsəˌfaɪd; diːˈklæsɪfaɪd/ *adj* official information that is declassified was secret but is not secret any more〔官方信息〕不再保密的, 解除保密的

de·clen·sion /dɪˋklɛnʃən; dɪˈklenʃən/ *n* [C] *technical*【術語】**1** the set of various forms that a noun, PRONOUN, or adjective can have according to whether it is the SUBJECT¹ (5), OBJECT¹ (6) etc of a sentence in a language such as Latin or German 詞形變化(表)〔在某種語言中如拉丁語或德語中, 一個名詞、代名詞或形容詞根據它們在句子中是主詞還是受詞等可以有的一系列不同的形式〕**2** a particular set of nouns etc that all have the same type of these forms 詞形變化相同的一組詞

de·cline¹ /dɪˋklaɪn; dɪˈklaɪn/ *n* [singular,U] a gradual decrease in the quality, quantity, or importance of something 減少, 削減: **[+in]** *a sharp decline in profits* 利潤的急劇下降 | **economic/moral etc decline** *Economic decline is often tangled up with political turmoil.* 經濟衰退經常和政治動盪有關。| **fall/go into decline** (=start to decrease) 開始衰退 *The activities of Welsh mines went into decline after about 1880.* 從 1880 年前後起, 威爾斯煤礦的開採活動開始減少。 

decline² *v* 

1 ►BECOME LESS 變少◄ [I] to decrease in quantity or importance 減少, 下降, 衰退: *In regions such as New England textile industries had declined and unemployment was high.* 新英格蘭等地區的紡織工業已經衰退, 失業率很高。| *declining prices* 下降的價格

2 ►BECOME WORSE 變糟◄ [I] to become gradually worse in quality〔質量〕越來越差: *Do you think standards of education have declined in recent years?* 你是否覺得最近幾年教育水準下降了? | *declining health* 每況愈下的健康狀況

3 ►SAY NO 說不◄ [I,T] to say no when someone invites you somewhere or offers you something 拒絕, 謝絕: *Talbot had been invited but declined on the grounds that he was too busy.* 塔爾博特獲邀請, 但他以太忙為由拒絕了。| **decline an offer/proposal etc** *We declined their offer of financial help.* 我們謝絕了他們提供的經濟援助。

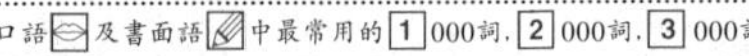

4 ►REFUSE 拒絕◄ to refuse to do something 拒絕〔做某事〕: **decline to do sth** *Allen angrily declined to discuss the matter.* 艾倫氣憤地拒絕談論此事。—see 見 REFUSE[1] (USAGE)

5 **sb's declining years** *formal* the last years of someone's life【正式】某人的晚年, 殘生

6 ►GRAMMAR 語法◄ *technical*【術語】**a)** [I] if a noun, PRONOUN, or adjective declines, its form changes according to whether it is the SUBJECT[1] (5), OBJECT[1] (6) etc of a sentence〔根據名詞、代名詞或形容詞在句中的作用, 作主詞、受詞或是其他成分〕變格, 詞形變化 **b)** [T] if you decline a noun etc, you show these various forms that it can take 使〔名詞等〕詞形變化, 使變格

de·code /ˌdiˋkod; ˌdiːˈkəʊd/ *v* [T] **1** to discover the meaning of a secret or complicated message 譯〔碼〕, 解〔碼〕: *a computer that can decode and implement complex instructions* 能夠解碼和執行複雜指令的電腦 **2** *technical* to understand the meaning of a word rather than use a word to express meaning【術語】解讀, 解釋 —opposite 反義詞 ENCODE

D

dé·colle·tage /deˌkɑləˋtɑʒ; ˌdeɪkɒlˈtɑːʒ/ *n* [U] *French* the top edge of a woman's dress that is cut very low to show part of her shoulders and breasts【法】〔袒胸露肩的女裝的〕低領 —**décolleté** /ˌdekɑləˋte; deɪˈkɒlteɪ/ *adj*: *a satin dress, high-waisted and decolleté* 高腰低領的緞子禮服

de·col·o·nize also 又作 **-ise** *BrE*【英】/diˋkɑləˌnaɪz; ˌdiːˈkɒlənaɪz/ *v* [T] to make a former COLONY politically independent 使〔以前的殖民地〕政治獨立; 使非殖民〔地〕化 —**decolonization** /diˌkɑlənəˋzeʃən; diːˌkɒlənaɪˈzeɪʃən/ *n* [U]

de·com·mis·sion /ˌdikəˋmɪʃən; ˌdiːkəˈmɪʃən/ *v* [T] to stop using a NUCLEAR weapon or REACTOR and prepare to take it to pieces 廢棄〔核武器〕; 關閉〔核電站〕

de·com·pose /ˌdikəmˋpoz; ˌdiːkəmˈpəʊz/ *v* [I,T] **1** to decay or make something decay (使) 變壞, (使) 腐爛: *a partially-decomposed body* 部分腐爛的屍體 **2** *technical* to divide into smaller parts or to make something do this【術語】(使) 分解 —**decomposition** /ˌdikɑmpəˋzɪʃən; ˌdiːkɒmpəˈzɪʃən/ *n* [U]

de·com·press /ˌdikəmˋprɛs; ˌdiːkəmˈpres/ *v* [T] to reduce the pressure of air on something 使減壓, 減少…的氣壓

de·com·pres·sion cham·ber /ˌdikəmˋprɛʃən ˌtʃembɚ; ˌdiːkəmˈpreʃən ˌtʃeɪmbə/ *n* [C] a special room where people go after they have been deep under the sea, in order to slowly return to normal air pressure〔幫助從深海返回的潛水者慢慢地恢復到正常壓力的〕減壓室

decompression sick·ness /ˌdikəmˋprɛʃən ˌsɪknɪs; ˌdiːkəmˈpreʃən ˌsɪknɪs/ *n* [U] a dangerous medical condition that people get when they come up from deep under the sea too quickly; bends (BEND[2] (3))〔因深海潛水員浮出水面太急而造成的〕潛函病, 減壓病

de·con·gest·ant /ˌdikənˋdʒɛstənt; ˌdiːkənˈdʒestənt◄/ *n* [C,U] medicine that you can take if you have a cold to help you breathe more easily〔鼻〕減充血劑

de·con·struc·tion /ˌdikənˋstrʌkʃən; ˌdiːkənˈstrʌkʃən/ *n* [U] *technical* a method used in the criticism of literature which claims that there is no single explanation of the meaning of a piece of writing【術語】解構, 拆析〔認為一部文學作品不僅僅有一種解釋的文學評論方法〕

de·con·tam·i·nate /ˌdikənˋtæməˌnet; ˌdiːkənˈtæmɪneɪt/ *v* [T] to remove a dangerous substance from somewhere 消除…的污染, 淨化: *It may cost over $5 million to decontaminate the whole site.* 對這個地方全面消除污染可能要花費超過五百萬美元。—**decontamination** /ˌdikənˌtæməˋneʃən; ˌdiːkəntæmɪˈneɪʃən/ *n* [U]

de·cor /deˋkɔr; ˈdeɪkɔː/ *n* [C,U] the way that the inside of a building is decorated 佈置, 裝飾, 裝修: *tacky furniture and tasteless decor* 俗氣的家具和毫無品味的裝修

decorate 裝修; 裝飾

dec·o·rate /ˋdɛkəˌret; ˈdekəreɪt/ *v especially BrE*【尤英】**1** [I,T] to make the inside of a building look more attractive by painting it, putting paper on the walls etc 裝修: *I'm going to decorate the bathroom next.* 接下來我要裝修浴室。**2** [T] to make something look more attractive by putting something pretty on it 裝飾, 佈置, 美化: **decorate sth with** *We decorated the Christmas tree with tinsel and lights.* 我們用金屬箔和燈來裝飾聖誕樹。**3** [T+for] to give someone a MEDAL as an official sign of honour 授予…勳章[獎章] —**decorating** *n* [U] 3

dec·o·ra·tion /ˌdɛkəˋreʃən; ˌdekəˈreɪʃən/ *n* **1** [C often plural 常用複數] something pretty that you put onto something else in order to make it more attractive 裝飾物: *Christmas decorations* 聖誕節裝飾物 **2** [U] the way in which something is decorated 裝飾方式: *The Rococo decoration inside the palace is delightful.* 宮殿內部的洛可可式裝飾風格賞心悅目。**3** [C,U] *especially BrE* the act or process of decorating【尤英】裝飾: *The decoration of the house had taken months to complete.* 裝修這所房子花了好幾個月的時間。**4** [C] something such as a MEDAL that is given to someone as an official sign of honour 獎章, 勳章 3

dec·o·ra·tive /ˋdɛkəˌretɪv; ˈdekərətɪv/ *adj* pretty or attractive, but not always necessary or useful 裝飾(性)的, 作裝飾用的: *a decorative panel above the door* 門楣上方裝飾性的鑲板 —**decoratively** *adv*

dec·o·ra·tor /ˋdɛkəˌretɚ; ˈdekəreɪtə/ *n* [C] someone who paints houses and puts paper on the walls as their job 油漆匠; 裱糊匠

dec·o·rous /ˋdɛkərəs; ˈdekərəs/ *adj formal* having the correct appearance or behaviour for a particular occasion【正式】〔外表或行為〕端莊得體的 —**decorously** *adv*: *A servant was hovering decorously behind them.* 一名僕人莊重地跟在他們身後。

de·co·rum /dɪˋkorəm; dɪˈkɔːrəm/ *n* [U] *formal* correct behaviour that shows respect【正式】端莊得體, 有禮: *I hope you will behave with suitable decorum at the prize-giving tomorrow.* 我希望你在明天的頒獎會上能表現得有禮得體。

de·coy /ˋdikɔɪ; ˈdiːkɔɪ/ *n* [C] **1** someone or something used to trick someone into going where you want them to go so that you can catch them, attack them etc 誘餌, 誘惑物: *Police have been using mocked-up patrol cars as decoys to make drivers slow down.* 警方一直使用模擬的巡邏車作偽裝, 讓司機減慢車速。**2** a model of a bird used to attract wild birds so that you can watch them or shoot them〔觀鳥或獵鳥時用以引誘鳥羣的〕假鳥 —**decoy** /dɪˋkɔɪ; dɪˈkɔɪ/ *v* [T]

de·crease[1] /dɪˋkris; dɪˈkriːs/ *v* [I,T] to go down to a lower level, or to make something do this (使) 變小, (使) 減少: *In the last ten years cars have generally decreased in size.* 過去十年裡, 汽車總的說來變小了。| *making further efforts to decrease military spending* 作進一步的努力以削減軍費開支 —opposite 反義詞 INCREASE[1] —**decreasing** *adj*

de·crease[2] /ˋdikris; ˈdiːkriːs/ *n* [C,U] the process of reducing something, or the amount by which it reduces 減少; 減少的數量: **[+in]** *There has been a decrease in the annual birth rate for the last twenty years.* 過去二十年裡年出生率一直在下降。| **[+of]** *He refused to accept a decrease of 20% to his salary.* 他拒絕接受把自己的工資調降20%。

de·cree[1] /dɪˋkri; dɪˈkriː/ *n* [C] **1** an official command or decision, especially one made by the ruler of a country〔尤指由國家統治者頒布的〕命令, 法令: *On 13 November the Emperor issued the decree.* 11月13日皇帝頒布了敕令。**2** a judgment in a court of law〔法院的〕判決, 裁定

decree[2] *v* [T] to make an official judgment or give an official command 下令, 頒布命令: **decree that** *The King decreed that there should be an end to the fighting.* 國王下令結束戰鬥。

decree ab·sol·ute /·,· ˈ···/ *n* [C] *BrE law* an order by a court of law which officially ends a marriage【英, 法律】〔法院作出的〕離婚判決

decree ni·si /dɪ,kri ˋnaɪsaɪ; dɪ,kriː ˈnaɪsaɪ/ *n* [C] *BrE law* an order by a court of law that a marriage will end at a particular time in the future unless there is a good reason not to end it【英, 法律】〔除非有正當理由, 否則在指定日期即生效的〕法院離婚判決令

de·crep·it /dɪˋkrɛpɪt; dɪˈkrepɨt/ *adj* old and in bad condition 衰老的, 破舊的: *The buildings were in a decrepit state.* 這些建築物已經破舊不堪。—**decrepitude** *n* [U]

de·crim·in·a·lize also 又作 **-ise** *BrE*【英】/diˋkrɪmɪnə,laɪz; diːˈkrɪmɨnəlaɪz/ *v* [T] to state officially that something is not illegal any more 使〔原屬非法的東西〕合法化: *the campaign to decriminalize cannabis* 使大麻合法化的運動 —**decriminalization** *n* [U]

de·cry /dɪˋkraɪ; dɪˈkraɪ/ *v* **decried, decrying** [T] *formal* to state publicly that you do not approve of something【正式】〔公開〕反對, 譴責

ded·i·cate /ˋdɛdə,ket; ˈdedɨkeɪt/ *v* [T] **1 a)** to say that something such as a book or film has been written, made, or sung to express love, respect etc for someone 把〔作品等〕獻給〔某人〕: **dedicate sth to sb** *I'd like to dedicate this song to my wife.* 我想把這首歌獻給我的妻子。**b)** to state in an official ceremony that a building will be given someone's name in order to show respect for them 用...命名〔建築物, 以表達崇敬之情〕: **dedicate sth to sb** *a chapel dedicated to St Francis* 以聖弗朗西斯命名的教堂 **2 dedicate yourself/your life to sth** to decide to spend all your time on and put all your efforts into one particular thing 獻身於/把一生獻給某事: *Sheila dedicated herself to a life of religion.* 希拉獻身於宗教事業。

ded·i·cat·ed /ˋdɛdə,ketɪd; ˈdedɨkeɪtɨd/ *adj* **1** someone who is dedicated works very hard at what they do because they care a lot about it 敬業的, 有奉獻精神的, 有獻身精神的: *He's certainly dedicated but really not very talented.* 他確實敬業, 但是實在不大有天賦。| **[+to]** *dedicated to one's art* 獻身於藝術 | **dedicated sportsman/musician/Marxist etc** *Simon has been a dedicated Marxist all his life.* 西門一生都是虔誠的馬克思主義者。**2** made for or used for only one particular purpose 專用的: *the transmission of software code through dedicated satellite channels* 通過專用衛星頻道進行的軟件密碼傳送 **3** *technical* a dedicated computer, computer system etc is only used for one particular job, such as controlling a machine【術語】〔電腦、電腦系統等〕專用的 —**dedicatedly** *adv*

ded·i·ca·tion /,dɛdəˋkeʃən; ,dedɨˈkeɪʃən/ *n* **1** [U] hard work or effort that someone puts into a particular activity because they care about it a lot 奉獻(精神), 敬業: *The success of the festival is a tribute to the dedication of one man.* 這個慶祝活動的成功充分說明了一個人的奉獻精神。| **[+to]** *singleminded dedication to her art* 她對藝術執着的奉獻精神 **2** [C] an act of dedicating something to someone 奉獻, 敬獻 **3** [C] a ceremony in which a building is given someone's name in order to show respect for them〔以某人的名字命名某個建築物以表達對此人的尊敬的〕命名典禮

de·duce /dɪˋdus; dɪˈdjuːs/ *v* [T] *formal* to make a judgment about something, based on the information that you have【正式】推理, 推斷, 演繹: **deduce that** *I deduced that she was married by the ring on her finger.* 我從她手指上戴的戒指推斷出她已結婚。| **[+from]** *What did Darwin deduce from the presence of these species?* 達爾文從這些物種的存在推斷出了甚麼? —**deducible** *adj*

de·duct /dɪˋdʌkt; dɪˈdʌkt/ *v* [T] to take away an amount or part from a total; subtract 減去, 扣除: **deduct sth from** *The dues will be deducted from his weekly pay-cheques.* 會費將從他週薪中扣除。—**deductible** *adj*

de·duc·tion /dɪˋdʌkʃən; dɪˈdʌkʃən/ *n* [C,U] **1** the process of making a judgment about something, based on the information that you have〔根據已知資料進行的〕推理, 推斷, 演繹: *His powers of deduction were impressive.* 他的推理能力令人驚嘆。**2** the process of taking away an amount from a total, or the amount that is taken away 扣除; 扣除額: *After deductions for tax etc your salary is about £700 a month.* 扣除稅款等之後, 你的月薪大約有700英鎊。

de·duc·tive /dɪˋdʌktɪv; dɪˈdʌktɪv/ *adj* using the knowledge that you have to make a judgment about a fact or situation 推理的, 演繹的: *deductive reasoning* 演繹推理

deed /did; diːd/ *n* [C] **1** *literary* something someone does that is very good or very bad【文】行為, 行動: *heroic deeds in battle* 戰場上的英雄事跡 **2** *law* an official paper that is a record of an agreement, especially an agreement concerning who owns property【法律】〔尤指關於財產所有人的〕契約, 證書 **3 your good deed for the day** *humorous* something kind or helpful that you do【幽默】你當天做的好事

deed poll /ˈ· ·/ *n* [C] a legal document signed by only one person, for example in order to officially change your name 單邊契約, 片務契約〈如為正式改名而單方簽的契約〉

deem /dim; diːm/ *v* [T not in progressive 不用進行式] *formal* to think of something in a particular way; consider【正式】認為, 視為: **deem that** *They deemed that he was no longer capable of managing the business.* 他們認為他沒有能力再管理這個企業了。| **deem sth necessary/appropriate etc** *They were told to take whatever action they deemed necessary.* 他們被告知可採取任何他們認為必需的行動。

deep[1] /dip; diːp/ *adj*

1 ►GOING FAR DOWN 往下很深◄ going far down from the top or from the surface 深的〔從頂部或表面向下延伸〕: *a deep hole in the ground* 地底下的一個深洞 | *Come on, get in! The water's not very deep here.* 快點, 進來呀! 這兒的水不太深。| **2 metres/6 feet etc deep** *At this point the lake is ninety metres deep.* 此處湖水深達九十米。

2 knee-deep/ankle-deep etc deep enough to come up to your knees etc 齊膝深/深到腳踝等: *Soon they were in waist-deep mud.* 不一會他們就陷入齊腰深的泥中。

3 ►GOING FAR IN 往裡很深◄ going far in from the outside or from the front edge of something 深處的, 縱深的〔從某物的外部或前緣往裡延伸〕: *He had a deep wound on his forehead.* 他額頭上有道很深的傷口。| **deep in the forest/mountains etc** (=far from the edge of the forest etc) 森林/山等的深處 *The path led them deep into the forest.* 小徑把他們帶到森林深處。

4 ►FEELING/BELIEF 感覺/信念◄ a deep feeling or belief is very strong and sincere〔感情或信念等〕強烈的, 深厚的: *Even Rob's parents regarded him with deep suspicion.* 連羅伯的父母都對他深表懷疑。

5 run/go deep if a feeling such as hatred or anger runs deep in someone, they feel it very strongly, especially because of things that have happened in the past〔仇恨或憤怒〕非常強烈: *Resentment against the police runs deep in the community.* 這個社區對警察的怨恨十分強烈。—see also 另見 **still waters run deep** (STILL[2] (5))

6 ►SOUND 聲音◄ a deep sound is very low 低沉的: *his deep voice* 他低沉的嗓音 | *There was a flash and a deep roar.* 電光一閃, 緊接着聽到一種沉悶的隆隆聲。
7 ►COLOUR 顏色◄ a deep colour is dark and strong 暗的, 濃重的: *the deep blue sky* 深藍色的天空 —compare 比較 LIGHT² (1), PALE¹ (2)
8 ►BREATH ETC 呼吸等◄ a deep SIGH², GULP² etc involves taking a lot of air into your lungs before letting it out again with a loud sound 深深的: *He took a deep breath and began to sing.* 他深深地吸了口氣, 然後開始演唱。
9 ►SERIOUS 嚴肅的◄ **a)** someone who is deep or has deep thoughts thinks very hard about things, often in a way that other people find difficult to understand 深邃的, 難以理解的: *Hal seems to me to be a very deep, sensitive type of person.* 哈爾在我看來好像是個非常深沉、敏感的人。**b)** a deep book, conversation, thought etc involves serious, complicated, or mysterious subjects that are often difficult to understand 深奧的, 神祕的: *a deep conversation about the meaning of life* 關於生命意義的深奧談話

D

10 deep in debt owing a lot of money 負債纍纍; 債台高築
11 deep sleep if someone is in a deep sleep it is difficult to wake them 酣睡的
12 be in deep trouble also 又作 **be in deep shit** *slang* to be in a bad situation because you have done something wrong or stupid 【俚】惹上大麻煩: *Don't say another word. You're in deep shit already.* 別再說了, 你已經麻煩大了。
13 in deep water in trouble or in a difficult or serious situation 處於嚴重困境: *He had an uneasy feeling he was getting into deep water.* 他有種不安的感覺, 覺得自己正陷入嚴重困境中。
14 to be in deep *informal* to be very involved in a situation, especially one that causes you problems 【非正式】深深捲入, 深深陷入
15 deep in thought/conversation etc thinking so hard, or paying attention to something so much that you do not notice anything else that is happening around you 陷入沉思/專注於談話等
16 jump/be thrown in at the deep end to choose to do or be made to do a very difficult job without having prepared for it 〔在沒有準備的情況下〕做困難的事: *Our policy is to throw trainee representatives right in at the deep end.* 我們的培訓方式是把受訓的代表置於困境中, 讓他們自己應付。
17 go off at the deep end *informal* to become angry suddenly and violently, usually without good reason 【非正式】〔通常是莫名其妙地〕勃然大怒 —**deepness** *n* [U]

3 **deep²** *adv* **1** [always+adv/prep] a long way into or below the surface of something; deeply 深入地, 深深地: **[+down/below etc]** *He pushed his stick deep down into the mud.* 他把手杖深深地插進泥裡。| *Carl was looking deep into her eyes.* 卡爾深情地望着她的眼睛。**2 deep down a)** if you know or feel something deep down, you are sure about it even though you do not admit it 心底, 內心: *I knew deep down that I would probably never see Marie again.* 我心裡知道我也許再也看不到瑪麗了。**b)** if someone is good, evil etc deep down, that is what they are really like even though they usually hide it 實際上: *She may seem unfriendly, but deep down she's very nice.* 她或許看起來不太友好, 但是實際上她人很好。**3 deep into the night** until very late 一直到深夜: *They talked deep into the night.* 他們一直談到深夜。**4 two/three etc deep** if things or people are two deep, there are two rows or layers of things or people 二/三等排, 二/三等層: *People were standing three deep at the bar.* 人們在酒吧台前站了三圈。

deep³ *n* **the deep** *poetical* the sea 【詩】海洋

deep·en /ˋdipən; ˈdiːpən/ *v* **1** [I,T] if a feeling such as love or sadness deepens, it gradually becomes stronger (使)〔感情〕加深, (使) 變深: *Enid's sorrow deepened as she thought of the long years ahead without him.* 伊妮德想到未來漫長歲月中將沒有他的陪伴, 便愈發傷心。**2** [I] if a serious situation deepens, it gets worse 〔局勢、情形〕惡化: *a deepening recession* 日益嚴重的衰退 **3** [I, T] if you deepen your knowledge or understanding of something, you learn more about it and understand it better (使)〔理解〕加深: *an opportunity for young people to deepen their understanding of the world* 一個讓年輕人加深對世界了解的機會 **4** [I] if water deepens, it becomes deeper 〔水〕變深 **5** [I] if a colour deepens, it becomes darker 〔顏色〕變暗 **6** [I] if a sound deepens, it becomes lower 〔聲音〕變低

deep freeze /ˌ· ˈ·/ *n* [C] a large metal box in which food can be stored at very low temperatures for a long time; FREEZER (1) 冰櫃, 冷藏箱

deep fry /ˈ· ·/ *v* [T] to cook food under the surface of hot fat or oil 油炸, 油煎

deep·ly /ˋdiplɪ; ˈdiːpli/ *adv* **1** a long way into something 很深地: *The parrot dug its claws deeply into my hand.* 鸚鵡把爪子深深地摳進我的手裡。**2 deeply embarrassing/worrying/involved etc** extremely or very much 令人極其尷尬的/令人十分憂慮的/深陷其中的等: *His remarks were deeply embarrassing.* 他的話令人非常尷尬。**3** if you breathe deeply you completely fill your lungs with air 〔呼吸〕深深地 **4 deeply held** a deeply held belief or opinion is one that you are very sure about and feel very strongly about 〔信仰、觀念等〕堅信的 **5 deeply rooted** a deeply rooted belief, opinion etc is difficult to change 〔信仰、觀念等〕根深蒂固的, 難以消除的: *These traditions were deeply rooted in local custom.* 這些傳統深深地扎根於當地風俗之中。  3

deep-root·ed /ˌ· ˈ··◄/ also 又作 **deeply rooted** /ˌ·· ˈ··◄/ *adj* a deep-rooted habit, idea, belief etc is so fixed in a person or society that it is very difficult to change or destroy it 〔習慣、觀念、信仰等〕根深蒂固的: *a deep-rooted suspicion of lawyers* 對律師根深蒂固的不信任

deep-seat·ed /ˌ· ˈ··◄/ *adj* a deep-seated attitude, feeling, or idea is strong and is very difficult to change 〔態度、感情、觀念等〕不易改變的, 頑固的: *a deep-seated fear of failure* 對失敗難以消除的恐懼感

deep-set /ˌ· ˈ·◄/ *adj* deep-set eyes seem to be further back into the face than most people's 〔眼睛〕深陷的, 瞘眼的

deep six /ˌ· ˈ·/ *v* [T] *AmE informal* to decide not to use something such as a plan 【美, 非正式】棄用, 拋棄: *We decided to deep six the whole project.* 我們決定把整個計劃擱置一邊, 不予採用。

Deep South /ˌ· ˈ·/ *n* [singular] the most southern states of the US 南方腹地〔指美國最南部諸州〕

deer /dɪr; dɪə/ *n plural* **deer** or **deers** [C] a large grass eating wild animal that can run very fast and has wide branching horns 鹿

deer·stalk·er /ˋdɪrˌstɔkɚ; ˈdɪəˌstɔːkə/ *n* [C] a type of soft hat with pieces of cloth that cover your ears 獵鹿帽〔軟質、有遮耳〕

de·face /dɪˋfes; dɪˈfeɪs/ *v* [T] to spoil the surface or appearance of something, especially by writing or making marks on it 損壞〔某物的〕表面[外觀], 塗污: *Most of the monuments had been broken or defaced.* 大多數紀念碑都被打碎或者遭到破壞。—**defacement** *n* [U]

de fac·to /dɪ ˋfækto; ˌdeɪ ˈfæktəʊ/ *adj Latin* really existing although not legally stated to exist 【拉丁】〔法律未作規定但〕實際上存在的: *a de facto state of war* 實際上存在的戰爭狀態 —**de facto** *adv*

def·a·ma·tion /ˌdɛfəˋmeʃən; ˌdefəˈmeɪʃən/ *n* [U] *formal* the act of defaming someone 【正式】誹謗: **defamation of character** *Chambers sued the newspaper for defamation of character.* 錢伯斯指控這家報紙誹謗人格。

de·fame /dɪˋfem; dɪˈfeɪm/ *v* [T] *formal* to write or say something that makes people have an unfairly bad opinion of someone or something 【正式】誹謗, 中傷 —**defa-**

matory /dɪˋfæməˏtorɪ; dɪˈfæmətəri/ *adj*

de·fault¹ /dɪˋfɔlt; dɪˈfɒlt/ *n* **1 by default** if you win a game, competition etc by default, you win it because your opponent did not play or because there were no other competitors 因對手棄權〔而獲勝〕**2** [U] *formal* failure to do something that you are supposed to do according to the law or because it is your duty【正式】違約, 未履行職責: *the risk of default by borrowers* 借方不償還的風險 **3 in default of** *formal* because of the lack or absence of something【正式】因缺乏, 因缺席 **4** [C usually singular 一般用單數] *technical* the way in which things will be arranged on a computer screen unless you decide to change them【術語】預設值, 預置值

default² *v* [I] to not do something that you are legally suposed to, especially not to pay money you are supposed to pay 不履行, 拖欠: **[+on]** *He defaulted on his child support payments.* 他未付孩子撫養費。—**defaulter** *n* [C]

3 **de·feat¹** /dɪˋfit; dɪˈfiːt/ *n* **1** [C,U] failure to win or succeed 失敗: *an election defeat* 競選失敗 | **serious defeat** *The government has suffered a serious defeat.* 政府嚴重受挫。| **admit defeat** (=stop trying to succeed) 認輸 *She's told him she won't marry him, but he'll never admit defeat.* 她已經告訴他她是不會嫁給他的, 但是他永遠不會放棄。**2** [U] victory over someone or something 戰勝, 擊敗: **[+of]** *We made the defeat of fascism our major priority.* 我們把戰勝法西斯作為首要任務。

defeat² *v* [T] **1** to win a victory over someone in a war, competition, game etc; BEAT¹ (1)〔在戰爭、競爭、比賽等中〕戰勝, 打敗: *After a long campaign Wellington's army finally defeated Napoleon.* 經過長時間的戰役, 威靈頓的軍隊最終打敗了拿破崙。| **defeat sb by 10 points/by 3 goals to 2 etc** *We defeated the other team by six runs.* 我們以六分的優勢擊敗對手。—see 見 WIN (USAGE) **2** if something defeats you, you cannot understand it and therefore cannot answer or deal with it 把〔某人〕難住: *It was the last question on the paper that defeated me.* 考卷上的最後一個問題把我難住了。**3** to make something fail 使…失敗: *It was a lack of money, not effort, that defeated their plan.* 導致他們計劃失敗的不是不夠努力而是因為缺錢。

de·feat·ist /dɪˋfitɪst; dɪˈfiːtɪ̣st/ *n* [C] someone who believes that they will not succeed 失敗主義者 —**defeatist** *adj*: *a defeatist attitude* 失敗主義的態度 — **defeatism** *n* [U]

def·e·cate /ˋdɛfəˏket; ˈdefɪ̣keɪt/ *v* [I] *formal* to get rid of waste matter from your BOWELS【正式】排便 —**defecation** /ˏdɛfəˋkeʃən; ˌdefɪ̣ˈkeɪʃən/ *n* [U]

de·fect¹ /ˋdifɛkt; dɪˈfekt/ *n* [C] a fault or a lack of something that means that something is not perfect 缺陷, 瑕疵: *All the cars are tested for defects before they leave the factory.* 所有的汽車在出廠之前都要檢查有無缺陷。

de·fect² /dɪˋfɛkt; dɪˈfekt/ *v* [I] to leave your own country or a group in order to go to or join an opposing one 背叛, 叛變, 投敵, 變節: *a talented Russian actor who defected to the West* 一位投靠西方的、有才華的俄羅斯演員 —**defector** *n* [C] —**defection** /dɪˋfɛkʃən; dɪˈfekʃən/ *n* [C,U]

de·fec·tive /dɪˋfɛktɪv; dɪˈfektɪv/ *adj* **1** not made properly, or not working properly 有問題的, 有毛病的, 有缺陷的: *defective components* 有毛病的部件 **2** *technical*【術語】**defective verb** a verb such as 'must' or 'can' that cannot be used in all the forms that a verb can usually be used in 不完全變化動詞〔如 must 或 can, 不能有其他動詞的各種變化形式〕—**defectively** *adv* —**defectiveness** *n* [U]

2 1 **de·fence** *BrE*【英】, **defense** *AmE*【美】/dɪˋfɛns; dɪˈfens/ *n*

1 ►PROTECTING 保護◄ [U] the act of protecting something or someone from attack 防禦, 防護: **come to sb's defence** (=help someone by protecting them from attack) 幫助某人; 保護某人 *Several people witnessed the attack, but no one came to her defence.* 有好幾個人目睹了這次襲擊事件, 但是沒人站出來幫助她。| **in defence of** *Hundreds gave their lives in defence of freedom.* 數以百計的人為了捍衛自由而獻出了自己的生命。—see also 另見 SELF-DEFENCE

2 ►PROTECT A COUNTRY 保衛國家◄ [U] all the systems, people, materials etc that a country uses to protect itself from attack 國防: *He's one of the President's top advisors on defense.* 他是總統的高級國防顧問之一。| **defence cuts/spending/budget etc** *There are plans to increase defence spending by 6%.* 有計劃將國防支出提高 6%。

3 defences *BrE*【英】, **defenses** *AmE*【美】all the armies and weapons that are available to defend a place 防禦力量: *The city's defenses were not strong enough to withstand the attack.* 這個城市的防禦力量不夠強, 不能抵擋這次攻擊。

4 ►AGAINST CRITICISM 抵制批評◄ [C,U] something that you say or do in order to protect someone or something from criticism〔為保護某人或某物不受批評而做的〕辯護, 答辯: **in sb's/sth's defence** *Speaking in defence of the proposal, he pointed out how much cheaper it would be.* 在替這項提議辯護發言時, 他指出這項提議實施起來將更省錢。

5 ►IN A LAW COURT 在法庭上◄ **a)** [C] the things that are said in a court of law to prove that someone is not guilty of a crime〔為了證明某人沒犯罪而做的〕辯護, 辯詞, 答辯: *Our defense looked pretty solid.* 我們的辯護詞看起來相當有力。**b) the defence** all the people who are concerned with showing in a court of law that someone is not guilty of a crime 辯方: *The defense's case is strong.* 辯方的陳述非常有說服力。—compare 比較 PROSECUTION (2)

6 ►AGAINST ILLNESS 抵禦疾病◄ [C] something that your body produces naturally as a way of preventing illness〔人體對疾病的〕抵抗力, 防禦能力: *The body's immune system is its defence against infection.* 身體的免疫系統是抵禦感染的武器。

7 ►EMOTIONS 感情◄ [C] something you do or a way of behaving that prevents you from being upset or seeming weak 自我防衛: **[+against]** *Dean's aggressive behaviour is his defence against depression.* 迪安好鬥的行為是為了防止陷入沮喪。

8 ►SPORT 體育◄ [C] *BrE* the players in a game of football etc whose main job is to try to prevent the other team from getting points【英】防守隊員, 後衛: *Barnaby cut through the heart of Arsenal's defence.* 班納比切入阿仙奴隊的防守腹地。

de·fence·less *BrE*【英】, **defenseless** *AmE*【美】/dɪˋfɛnsləs; dɪˈfensləs/ *adj* weak and unable to protect yourself from attack or harm 沒有防衛能力的: *a defenceless old lady* 沒有自衛能力的老太太

defence mech·a·nis·m *BrE*【英】, **defense mechanism** *AmE*【美】/ˑ·ˋ· ˏ···/ *n* [C] **1** a process in your brain that makes you forget things that are painful for you to think about 防衛機制〔人腦忘掉痛苦事情的機制〕**2** a reaction in your body that protects you from an illness or danger 防禦機制〔身體抵制疾病或危險的反應〕

de·fend /dɪˋfɛnd; dɪˈfend/ *v* **1** [T] to do something in order to protect someone or something from being attacked 保護, 保衛: **defend sth against/from** *They needed more troops to defend the border against possible attack.* 他們需要更多的部隊來保衛邊境地區免受可能的攻擊。| **defend yourself** *I picked a stick up to defend myself.* 我拿起一根棍子進行自衛。**2** to do something in order to stop something being taken away or in order to make it possible for something to continue 捍衛, 維護: *The union said they would take action to defend their members' jobs.* 工會稱他們將採取行動來維護會員們的工作權益。**3** [T] to use arguments to protect something or someone from criticism, or to prove that something is right 為…辯護, 為…辯白, 為…辯解: *How can you de-* 3 3 *fend the torture of animals for scientific research?* 你怎能用科學研究的理由為折磨動物這件事辯解呢？| **defend sb against/from** *He had to defend himself against their charges.* 他必須對他們的指控為自己辯解。| **defend yourself** *As a politician, you have to be able to defend yourself when things get tough.* 作為政界人物，在形勢嚴峻時你必須能為自己辯解。**4** [I,T] to protect your own team's end of the field in a game such as football, to prevent your opponents from getting points〔在比賽中〕防守，防衛 **5 defend a title/championship** to take part in a regular competition that you won the last time it was held〔冠軍〕衛冕 **6** [T] to be a lawyer for someone who has been charged with a crime〔律師〕為〔被指控犯罪者〕辯護: *Who is defending the case?* 誰在為這個案子辯護？—compare 比較 PROSECUTE (2)

2 **de·fen·dant** /dɪˈfɛndənt; dɪˈfendənt/ *n* [C] *law* the person in a court of law who has been accused (ACCUSE) of doing something illegal【法律】被告: *We find the defendant not guilty.* 我們認為被告無罪。—compare 比較 PLAINTIFF

de·fend·er /dɪˈfɛndə; dɪˈfendə/ *n* [C] **1** one of the players in a game such as football who have to defend their team's GOAL (3) from the opposing team 防守隊員，後衛 **2 a defender of the poor/liberty/privilege etc** someone who defends a particular idea, belief, person etc 窮人/自由/特權等的守護者

de·fense¹ /dɪˈfɛns; dɪˈfens/ *n* the American spelling of DEFENCE defence 的美式拼法

de·fense² /ˈdifɛns; dɪˈfens/ *n* [C,U] *AmE* the players in a game of football etc whose main job is to try to prevent the other team from getting points【美】防守隊員，後衛: *He plays defense for the New York Giants.* 他為紐約巨人隊打後衛。—opposite 反義詞 OFFENSE²

de·fen·si·ble /dɪˈfɛnsəbl; dɪˈfensəbəl/ *adj* **1** a defensible opinion or idea seems reasonable and you can easily support it〔意見或觀點〕正當有理的，可辯解的: *Richmond's theories are not morally defensible.* 從道德上講，里奇蒙的理論是站不住腳的。**2** a defensible building or area is easy to protect against attack〔建築物、地區等〕能防禦進攻的，可防衛的 **—defensibly** *adv*

de·fen·sive¹ /dɪˈfɛnsɪv; dɪˈfensɪv/ *adj* **1** used or intended to protect people against attack 防禦用的，防禦性的: *The rockets are a purely defensive measure against nuclear attack.* 火箭純粹是防止核進攻的防禦性措施。—opposite 反義詞 OFFENSIVE¹ (3) **2** behaving in a way that shows you think someone is criticizing you even if they are not 防備批評的，自衛的，有戒心的: *There's no need to be so defensive, I just asked how old you are!* 你沒有必要這麼戒備，我只是問你多大年齡！**3** *AmE* concerned with stopping the other team from getting points in a game【美】〔比賽中〕防守的，防禦的: *defensive play* 防守型打法 | *the defensive coach* 防守型教練 **—defensively** *adv* **—defensiveness** *n* [U]

defensive² *n* **on the defensive** behaving in a way that shows that you think that someone is criticizing you even if they are not 處於防禦姿態，採取守勢，存有戒心

de·fer /dɪˈfɝ; dɪˈfɜː/ *v* **deferred, deferring** [T] to delay something until a later date 延期，推遲: *Let's defer the decision for a few weeks.* 我們推遲幾週再作決定吧。

defer to sb/sth *phr v* [T] *formal* to agree to accept someone's opinion or decision because you have respect for that person【正式】服從，遵從，聽從

def·er·ence /ˈdɛfərəns; ˈdefərəns/ *n* [U] *formal* behaviour that shows that you respect someone and are therefore willing to accept their opinions or judgment【正式】尊敬，敬重；服從: *He had the arrogance of someone who had always been accustomed to deference.* 他為人傲慢，一向習慣於別人對他尊敬和服從。| **in/out of deference to** (=done because you respect someone's beliefs, opinions etc) 出於對…的尊敬 *They were married in church out of deference to their parents' wishes.* 出於對雙方父母意願的尊重，他們在教堂結婚。**—deferential** /ˌdɛfəˈrɛnʃəl; ˌdefəˈrenʃəl◂/ *adj* **—deferentially** *adv*

de·fi·ance /dɪˈfaɪəns; dɪˈfaɪəns/ *n* [U] behaviour that shows you clearly refuse to do what someone tells you to do 違抗，挑釁的態度: *The boy gave me a look of hatred and defiance as he slammed the door.* 那個男孩砰的一聲關上門時，用仇恨和挑釁的目光看了我一眼。| **in defiance of** *The company had been dumping their waste into the sea, in defiance of government regulations.* 這家公司一直無視政府的規定，往海裡傾倒垃圾。

de·fi·ant /dɪˈfaɪənt; dɪˈfaɪənt/ *adj* refusing clearly to do what someone tells you to do 違抗的，挑釁的: *He gave a short, defiant laugh.* 他挑釁地笑了一聲。**—defiantly** *adv*

de·fi·cien·cy /dɪˈfɪʃənsɪ; dɪˈfɪʃənsi/ *n* [C,U] **1** a lack of something that is necessary 不足，缺乏: *The disease is caused by a vitamin deficiency.* 這種疾病是由於缺少某種維生素而引起的。**2** a weakness or fault in something 缺點，毛病

deficiency dis·ease /·ˈ··· ·,·/ *n* [C,U] a disease caused by a lack of a food substance that is necessary for good health 營養缺乏症: *deficiency diseases such as rickets* 如佝僂病之類的營養缺乏症

de·fi·cient /dɪˈfɪʃənt; dɪˈfɪʃənt/ *adj* **1** not containing or having enough of something 缺乏的，不足的: *zinc deficient plants* 缺鋅的植物 | **[+in]** *a diet deficient in calcium* 缺鈣的飲食 **2** not good enough 不完美的: *Some of the methods used were deficient.* 所使用的方法有一些還不夠完善。

def·i·cit /ˈdɛfəsɪt; ˈdefəsət/ *n* [C] the difference between the amount of something that you have and the higher amount that you need 差額，逆差，虧損，赤字: **[+of]** *The directors have reported a deficit of £2.5 million.* 董事們報告說虧損250萬英鎊。| **[+in]** *a deficit in magnesium* 缺鎂

de·file¹ /dɪˈfaɪl; dɪˈfaɪl/ *v* [T] *formal* to make something less pure or good【正式】污損，污染，褻瀆: *These disgusting videos defile and corrupt the minds of the young.* 這些令人噁心的錄影帶污染並腐蝕了年輕人的思想。

de·file² /ˈdifaɪl; dɪˈfaɪl/ *n* [C] *formal* a narrow passage, especially through mountains【正式】〔尤指山中的〕小路，狹道，隘路

de·fine /dɪˈfaɪn; dɪˈfaɪn/ *v* [T] **1** to describe something correctly and thoroughly 闡明，說明: *the ability to define clients' needs* 說明顧客需求的能力 | **define sth clearly/precisely** *The powers of the President are clearly defined in the Constitution.* 總統的權力在憲法中有明確規定。**2** to explain exactly the meaning of a particular word or idea 給…下定義，解釋: *Each of us might define the concept of freedom in a very different way.* 我們每個人可能會以極不同的方式來定義自由這個概念。| **define sth as** *The dictionary defines it as 'a narrow passage'.* 字典把它解釋為"狹窄的通道"。| **define sth loosely/broadly** (=define something in a way that is less exact) 籠統地/大體上解釋某事 **3** to show the edge or shape of something clearly 標明…界限，顯出…輪廓: **sharply/clearly defined** *sharply defined footprints in the fresh snow* 新雪裡輪廓清晰的腳印 **4** to have particular features or qualities that make you different or separate from other people or things 是…的特徵，界定: **define sth as** *Which qualities define us as human?* 是甚麼特徵界定了我們是人？**—definable** *adj*

def·i·nite /ˈdɛfənɪt; ˈdefənət/ *adj* **1** clearly known, seen, or stated 清楚的，明確的: *Amanda saw a definite change in her son that year.* 那一年阿曼達在她兒子身上發現了明顯的變化。**2** a definite arrangement, promise etc will happen in the way that someone has said〔安排、許諾等〕確切的，確定的: *We have to set a definite date for the concert.* 我們得為音樂會定下一個確切的日期。**3 be definite (about)** to say something very firmly so that people understand exactly what you mean（對…）有把握，肯定: *She was very definite about how she felt.* 她對自己的感覺很有把握。

definite ar·ti·cle /,··· '···/ *n* [C usually singular 一般用單數] **1** the word 'the' in English〔英語中的〕定冠詞〔即 the〕 **2** a word in another language that is like 'the'〔其他語言中的〕定冠詞 —compare 比較 INDEFINITE ARTICLE —see also 另見 ARTICLE (4)

1 **def·i·nite·ly** /ˈdɛfənɪtlɪ; ˈdefɪn $\frac{1}{2}$tli/ *adv* with no chance of being wrong; certainly 確切地, 肯定地: *Max knew that he had definitely been wrong about Diana.* 馬克斯知道他在戴安娜的問題上肯定是錯了。| *"It's not worth that much, is it?" "No, definitely not!"* "不值那麼多, 對不對?" "對, 肯定不值!" —see 見 OF COURSE (USAGE), SURELY (USAGE)

3 **def·i·ni·tion** /ˌdɛfəˈnɪʃən; ˌdefɪˈnɪʃən/ *n* **1** [C] a phrase
2 or sentence that says exactly what a word, phrase, or idea means 定義, 釋義: *a definition in a dictionary* 字典裡的定義 | [+of] *No one has yet come up with a satisfactory definition of terrorism.* 關於恐怖主義還沒有人想出一個令人滿意的定義。**2 by definition** if something has a particular quality by definition, it must have that quality because all things of that type have it 從定義上講, 根據其定義: *A message that cannot be seen or heard is, by definition, not effective.* 一個看不見、聽不着的信息, 根據定義來説是無效的。**3** [U] the degree to which something such as a picture, sound etc is clear〔相片、聲音等的〕清晰度, 鮮明度: **lack definition** *The photograph lacks definition.* 這張照片清晰度不夠。

de·fin·i·tive /dɪˈfɪnətɪv; dɪˈfɪnɪtɪv/ *adj* **1** [usually before noun 一般用於名詞前] a definitive book, study of something etc is considered to be the best ever produced and cannot be improved 最具權威的, 最可靠的: *She has written the definitive book on the poet Wordsworth.* 她寫的關於詩人華茲華斯的書是最具權威性的。**2** a definitive statement, VERDICT etc will not be changed〔陳述、裁決等〕最終的, 決定性的 —**definitively** *adv*

de·flate /dɪˈflet; ˌdiːˈfleɪt/ *v* **1** [I,T] if a tyre, BALLOON[1] (1, 2) etc deflates, or if you deflate it, it gets smaller because the gas inside it comes out (使) 放氣, (使) 漏氣 **2** [T] to make someone feel less important or less confident 使〔某人〕泄氣: *I'd love to deflate that ego of his!* 我想挫一挫他的鋭氣! **3** [T] to show that a statement, argument etc is wrong 揭破 **4** [T] *technical* to change economic rules or conditions in a country so that prices fall or stop rising【術語】緊縮〔通貨〕—**deflation** /dɪˈfleʃən; ˌdiːˈfleɪʃən/ *n* [U]

de·flat·ed /dɪˈfletɪd; ˌdiːˈfleɪtɪd/ *adj* feeling less cheerful or confident than before 氣餒的, 泄氣的, 灰心的: *I felt utterly deflated and let down.* 我覺得非常灰心失望。

de·fla·tion·a·ry /dɪˈfleʃənˌɛrɪ; ˌdiːˈfleɪʃənəri/ *adj technical* causing a situation in which prices fall or stop rising【術語】通貨緊縮的: *deflationary policies* 緊縮通貨的政策

de·flect /dɪˈflɛkt; dɪˈflekt/ *v* **1** [I,T] to turn in a different direction, especially after hitting something else, or to make something do this (使) 轉向, (使) 偏斜: *The waves are deflected by the lifeboat's high narrow bows.* 救生船的又高又尖的船頭使海浪改變方向。**2 deflect attention/criticism/anger etc** to stop people criticizing something, getting angry about it etc 轉移注意力/批評/憤怒等: *a transparent attempt to deflect public criticism* 明顯的轉移公眾批評的企圖 **3** [T] if something deflects you from what you are doing, it takes your attention away from it 把〔某人的注意力從某事〕移開: *Nothing could deflect him from his goal.* 沒有甚麼能使他改變目標。

de·flec·tion /dɪˈflɛkʃən; dɪˈflekʃən/ *n* [C,U] **1** the action of making something change its direction 轉向, 偏差: *the deflection of the bullet* 子彈的轉向 **2** *technical* the degree to which the moving part on a measuring instrument moves away from zero【術語】〔計量儀器的〕偏差 (度)

de·flow·er /diˈflauɚ; ˌdiːˈflaʊə/ *v* [T] *literary* to have sex with a woman who has never had sex before【文】使〔女子〕失去童貞

de·fog /diˈfɑg; diːˈfɒg/ *v* **defogged, defogging** [T] *AmE* to remove the CONDENSATION from the window inside a car, by using heat or warm air【美】除去〔汽車擋風玻璃上的〕霧水; DEMIST *BrE*【英】

de·fo·li·ant /diˈfolɪənt; diːˈfəʊliənt/ *n* [C,U] a chemical substance used on plants to make their leaves drop off 脱葉劑

de·fo·li·ate /diˈfolɪˌet; diːˈfəʊlieɪt/ *v* [T] to use defoliant on a plant or tree 使落葉

de·for·es·ta·tion /dɪˌfɔrəsˈteʃən; diːˌfɒrɪˈsteɪʃən/ *n* [U] the cutting or burning down of all the trees in an area 砍伐樹林, 毀林 —**deforest** /diˈfɔrɪst; diːˈfɒrɪst/ *v* [T usually passive 一般用被動態]

de·form /dɪˈfɔrm; dɪˈfɔːm/ *v* [T] to change the usual shape of something so that its usefulness or appearance is spoiled 使變形; 毀壞…的外觀: *The heat had deformed the plastic.* 高温使得塑料變形。

de·for·ma·tion /ˌdifɔrˈmeʃən; ˌdiːfɔːˈmeɪʃən/ *n* **1** [C,U] a change in the usual shape of something, especially one that makes it worse 走樣, 畸形: *deformation of the telescope's mirror* 望遠鏡鏡片的變形 **2** [U] the process of changing the shape of something in a way that spoils its usefulness or appearance 變形

de·formed /dɪˈfɔrmd; dɪˈfɔːmd/ *adj* something that is deformed has the wrong shape, especially because it has grown or developed wrongly〔尤指發育、生長不良而〕畸形的: *a deformed foot* 一隻畸形的腳

de·for·mi·ty /dɪˈfɔrmətɪ; dɪˈfɔːmɪti/ *n* [C,U] a condition in which part of someone's body is not the normal shape〔人體某部分的〕變形, 畸形

de·fraud /dɪˈfrɔd; dɪˈfrɔːd/ *v* [T] to trick a person or organization in order to get money from them 欺騙, 騙取〔金錢〕: **defraud sb of** *She defrauded her employers of thousands of pounds.* 她從雇主那兒騙取了數千英鎊。

de·fray /dɪˈfre; dɪˈfreɪ/ *v* [T] **defray costs/expenses** *formal* to pay someone's costs etc【正式】支付費用: *The company will defray any expenses you have on the journey.* 公司將為你支付旅程中的所有費用。

de·frock /diˈfrɑk; ˌdiːˈfrɒk/ *v* [T] to officially remove a priest from his job because he has done something wrong 免去〔行為不檢的牧師、神父的〕聖職 —**defrocked** *adj*

de·frost /diˈfrɔst; ˌdiːˈfrɒst/ *v* **1** [I,T] if frozen food defrosts, or if you defrost it, it gets warmer until it is not frozen (使) 解凍 **2** [I,T] if a FREEZER or REFRIGERATOR defrosts, or if you defrost it, it is turned off so that the ice inside it melts (給)〔冰箱、冰櫃等〕除霜 **3** [T] *AmE* to remove ice from inside the windows of a car by using heat or warm air【美】除去〔汽車玻璃上的〕霜[冰] —compare 比較 DEFOG

deft /dɛft; deft/ *adj* **1** a deft movement is skilful, and often quick〔行動〕敏捷的, 靈巧的: *With one deft movement, she flipped the pancake over.* 她敏捷地一動, 把煎餅翻了過來。**2** skilful at doing something〔做某事〕在行的, 熟練的: *a deft political operator* 手腕嫻熟的政治高手 —**deftly** *adv* —**deftness** *n* [U]

de·funct /dɪˈfʌŋkt; dɪˈfʌŋkt/ *adj formal* not existing any more, or not useful any more【正式】不再存在的, 不再使用的

de·fuse /diˈfjuz; ˌdiːˈfjuːz/ *v* [T] **1** to improve a difficult or dangerous situation, for example by making people less angry or by dealing with the causes of a problem 緩和, 改善〔困難或危險局面〕: *We believe that greater economic stability might defuse the current crisis.* 我們相信較為穩定的經濟或許能緩和當前的危機。| **defuse tension/anger/fears etc** *In an attempt to defuse the tension, Rob put some music on.* 為了緩和緊張的氣氛, 羅伯放了些音樂。**2** to remove the FUSE[1] (2) from a bomb in order to stop it exploding 拆除〔炸彈的〕引信

de·fy /dɪˈfaɪ; dɪˈfaɪ/ *v* **defied, defying** [T] **1** to refuse to obey a law or rule, or refuse to do what someone in authority tells you to do 違抗〔法律或規則〕, 公然蔑視, 拒不服從: *He defied his father's wishes and married Agnes.*

他違抗父親的意願，和阿格妮斯結了婚。**2 defy description/analysis/imagination etc** to be so extreme or unusual that it is almost impossible to describe or understand 無法描述/分析/想像等: *The beauty of the scene defies description.* 這裡風景的優美無法用語言描述。**3 I defy you (to)** *spoken formal* used when asking someone to do something that you think is impossible, in order to prove that you are right【口，正式】我倒要看看…〔用於激某人做某事〕: *I defy you to think of one way in which this government has helped the poor.* 我倒要看看你能否想出這個政府為窮人做的一件好事。

de·gen·e·rate[1] /dɪˋdʒɛnəˌret; dɪˈdʒenəreɪt/ *v* [I] to become worse 惡化，墮落，退化: [+into] *The debate soon degenerated into petty squabbling.* 爭論不多久就演變成無聊的爭吵。—**degeneration** /dɪˌdʒɛnəˋreʃən; dɪˌdʒenəˈreɪʃən/ *n* [U]

de·gen·e·rate[2] /dɪˋdʒɛnərɪt; dɪˈdʒenərɪ̵t/ *adj* **1** *formal* having become worse in character or quality than before【正式】〔性格、品質上〕墮落的，沒落的，腐化的，退化的: *the last degenerate member of a noble family* 貴族家庭最後一個沒落的成員 **2** having very low standards or moral behaviour〔道德〕敗壞的，腐敗的: *The Emperor was denounced as a degenerate debauchee.* 這個皇帝被指責是個道德敗壞的浪蕩子。

degenerate[3] *n* [C] someone whose behaviour is considered to be morally unacceptable 墮落的人

de·gen·era·tive /dɪˋdʒɛnərətɪv; dɪˈdʒenərətɪv/ *adj* a degenerative illness gradually gets worse and cannot be stopped〔疾病〕不斷惡化的

de·grad·a·tion /ˌdɛgrəˋdeʃən; ˌdegrəˈdeɪʃən/ *n* **1** [singular,U] an experience that makes you feel ashamed and angry 落魄，丟臉: *a life of poverty and degradation* 窮困潦倒的生活 **2** [U] the process by which something changes to a worse condition 退化，惡化

de·grade /dɪˋgred; dɪˈgreɪd/ *v* **1** [T] to treat someone without respect or make people lose their respect for someone; DEBASE 貶低〔某人〕，使〔某人〕丟臉: *a movie that degrades women* 侮辱婦女人格的影片 | **degrade yourself** *How can you degrade yourself by writing such trash?* 你怎麼能寫這種垃圾作品來降低自己的身分呢? **2** [T] to make a situation or the condition of something worse 使〔局面或情況〕惡化 **3** [I,T] *technical* to change a substance, chemical etc to a simpler form【術語】(使)〔物質、化學製品等〕分解，降解

de·grad·ing /dɪˋgredɪŋ; dɪˈgreɪdɪŋ/ *adj* a degrading experience, event etc makes you lose respect for yourself 丟臉的，降低身分的，有辱人格的: *We oppose flogging and other cruel, inhuman, or degrading punishments.* 我們反對鞭笞和其他殘酷的、野蠻的或者羞辱性的懲罰方式。

de·gree /dɪˋgri; dɪˈgriː/ *n*

1 ►ANGLES/TEMPERATURE 角度/溫度◄ [C] a unit of measurement, especially for temperature or angles 度，度數〔尤作溫度或角度的度量單位〕—see table on page C4 參見C4頁附錄

2 ►AMOUNT 數量◄ [C,U] the amount of a quality that exists or how much something happens 程度: [+of] *People will choose the party that offers some degree of social change.* 人們將選擇提出某種程度社會變革的政黨。| *There are different views about the degree to which unemployment is society's fault.* 對於失業在多大程度上是社會的過錯，有着不同的觀點。

3 to a degree also 又作 **to some degree/to a certain degree** partly 在某種程度上: *I think that's true to a degree, but the situation isn't quite as simple as that.* 我認為在某種程度上説那是對的，但是情形並沒有那麼簡單。

4 ►UNIVERSITY 大學◄ [C] **a)** a course of study at a university or college〔大學的〕學位課程; 學位: *a law degree* 法律課程 | *a degree course* 學位課程 | [+in] *a degree in Economics* 經濟學學位 | **take/do a degree** *Isabelle's doing her degree at the Sorbonne.* 伊莎貝爾正在巴黎大學文理學院攻讀學位。**b)** a QUALIFICATION (1) given to someone who has successfully completed this course of study〔授予成功完成學業者的〕學位資格: **have/hold a degree** *Lori has a degree in Chemistry from Harvard.* 洛麗擁有哈佛大學化學學位。

5 by degrees very slowly; gradually 慢慢地; 逐漸地: *By degrees, the music drove all thoughts from his head.* 慢慢地，音樂驅散了他腦子裡的種種雜念。

6 ►POSITION IN SOCIETY 社會地位◄ [U] *old use* your position in society【舊】(社會) 地位

de·hu·man·ize also 又作 **-ise** *BrE*【英】/diˋhjuməˌnaɪz; ˌdiːˈhjuːmənaɪz/ *v* [T often passive 常用被動態] to treat people so badly that they lose their good human qualities such as kindness etc 使〔某人〕喪失人性: *War dehumanizes people.* 戰爭使人們喪失人性。—**dehumanizing** *adj* —**dehumanization** /dɪˌhjumənəˋzeʃən; diːˌhjuːmənaɪˈzeɪʃən/ *n* [U]

de·hy·drate /diˋhaɪdret; ˌdiːhaɪˈdreɪt/ *v* **1** [T] to remove the liquid from a substance such as food or chemicals 使脱水，使乾燥: *The substance is dehydrated and stored as powder.* 該物質被脱水並以粉末形式儲存。**2** [I] to lose too much water from your body〔人體〕脱水 —**dehydrated** *adj* —**dehydration** /ˌdihaɪˋdreʃən; ˌdiːhaɪˈdreɪʃən/ *n* [U]

de-ice /ˌdiˋaɪs; ˌdiːˈaɪs/ *v* [T] to remove the ice from something 除冰; 化凍

de·i·fy /ˋdiəˌfaɪ; ˈdiːɪ̵faɪ/ *v* **deified, deifying** [T] *formal* to treat someone or something with far too much respect and admiration【正式】崇拜; 神化; 奉若神明 —**deification** /ˌdiəfəˋkeʃən; ˌdiːɪ̵fɪ̵ˈkeɪʃən/ *n* [U]

deign /den; deɪn/ *v* **deign to do something** an expression meaning to agree to do something, often used jokingly when you think someone should do that thing all the time 俯就[屈尊]做某事〔常為玩笑用法，尤用於認為某人本來就應該那麼做〕: *Ah, so you've deigned to grace us with your presence I see!* 啊，你還是屈尊光臨，我們不勝榮幸!

de·is·m /ˋdiɪzəm; ˈdiːɪzəm/ *n* [U] the belief in a God who made the world but has no influence on human lives 自然神論，理神論〔認為上帝創造世界，但是不影響人們的生活〕—compare 比較 THEISM

De·i·ty /ˋdiətɪ; ˈdiːɪ̵ti/ *n formal*【正式】**the Deity** God 上帝

deity *n* [C] a god or GODDESS 神; 女神: *the deities of ancient Greece* 古希臘諸神

déjà vu /ˌdeʒɑ ˋvju; ˌdeɪʒɑː ˈvjuː/ *n* [U] *French* the feeling that you have previously experienced exactly the same thing as you are experiencing now【法】似曾經歷的感覺，似曾相識的感覺: *Madeleine felt a strange sense of déjà vu as she walked into the room.* 馬德琳走進房間時，有一種似曾來過的奇怪感覺。

de·jec·ted /dɪˋdʒɛktɪd; dɪˈdʒektɪ̵d/ *adj* unhappy, disappointed, or sad 抑鬱的，失望的，沮喪的 —**dejectedly** /dɪˋdʒɛktɪdlɪ; dɪˈdʒektɪ̵dli/ *adv* —**dejection** /dɪˋdʒɛkʃən; dɪˈdʒekʃən/ *n* [U]

de ju·re /di ˋdʒurɪ; ˌdiː ˈdʒʊəri/ *adj law* true or right because of a law【法律】法律上的，合法的

de·lay[1] /dɪˋle; dɪˈleɪ/ *n* **1** [C usually singular 一般用單數] the length of time between the moment when something should start and the moment it actually does start 延誤的時間，耽擱的時間: *Sorry for the delay, Mr Weaver.* 對不起，韋弗先生，耽擱了一些時間。| [+of] *a delay of twenty minutes* 二十分鐘的延誤 | **short/long etc delay** *There was a slight delay before the show.* 演出推遲了一小會兒。| **without delay** (=immediately) 立即，立刻，毫不耽擱 **2** [C] a situation in which someone or something is made to wait 延誤，耽擱: **severe delays** *There are severe delays on Route 95 this morning because of an accident.* 由於交通事故，今天早晨95號公路上嚴重塞車。| [+in] *delays in transporting the goods to London* 貨物運往倫敦過程中的延誤 **3** [U] the situation in which something does not happen or start when it should do 推遲〔某事沒有按時發生或開始〕: **be subject to delay** (=likely to be delayed) 可能推遲

3 **delay²** *v* **1** [I,T] to wait until a later time to do something 推遲, 延期〔做某事〕: *She delayed for months before deciding.* 她拖延了好幾個月才作決定。| **delay sth until** *Ralph decided to delay his trip until April or May.* 拉爾夫決定把他的旅行推遲到四月或五月。| **delay doing sth** *Don't delay claiming or you may lose benefit.* 索賠萬勿延遲, 否則你會吃虧。**2** [T often passive 常用被動態] to make someone or something late 耽誤, 耽擱: *The plane was badly delayed by fog.* 由於有霧, 飛機嚴重誤點。—**delayed** *adj*

delayed-ac·tion /ˌ·ˌ· ˈ··◂/ *adj* designed to work or start only after a fixed period of time has passed 延遲的; 定時的: *a delayed-action bomb* 定時炸彈

delaying tac·tic /ˈ··· ˌ··/ *n* [C usually plural 一般用複數] something you do deliberately in order to delay something so that you gain an advantage for yourself 拖延策略〔故意拖延某事以便為自己爭得優勢〕

de·lec·ta·ble /dɪˋlɛktəbl̩; dɪˈlektəbəl/ *adj literary* extremely pleasant to taste, smell etc【文】美味的; 好聞的: *a delectable mixture of flavours* 各種味道集於一身的美味組合 —**delectably** *adv*

de·lec·ta·tion /ˌdilɛkˋteʃən; ˌdiːlekˈteɪʃən/ *n* [U] *formal* enjoyment, pleasure, or amusement【正式】享受, 愉快; 娛樂

del·e·gate¹ /ˋdɛlɪgət; ˈdeləgət/ *n* [C] someone who has been elected or chosen to speak, vote, or take decisions for a group 代表: *We sent five delegates to the conference.* 我們派了五個代表參加會議。

de·le·gate² /ˋdɛləˌget; ˈdeləgeɪt/ *v* **1** [I,T] to give part of your power or work to someone in a lower position than you 授權, 委託權限: *A good manager knows when to delegate.* 一個好的經理知道何時該把權限下放。| **delegate sth to sb** *Minor tasks should be delegated to your assistant.* 不太重要的工作應交給你的助手去做。**2** [T] to choose someone to do a particular job, or to be a representative of a group, organization etc 委派〔某人〕做〔某項工作〕; 委任〔某人〕做代表: **delegate sb to do sth** *I've been delegated to organize the weekly meetings.* 我被指派組織每週的會議。

del·e·ga·tion /ˌdɛləˋgeʃən; ˌdeləˈgeɪʃən/ *n* **1** [C] a group of people who represent a company, organization etc 代表團: *A small delegation had been sent to address the UN.* 一個小型代表團被派往聯合國會議上發言。**2** [U] the process of giving power or work to someone else so that they are responsible for part of what you normally do 授權, 委派, 委託

de·lete /dɪˋlit; dɪˈliːt/ *v* [T] to remove a letter, word etc from a piece of writing 刪除, 刪掉: *His name was deleted from the list.* 他的名字被從名單上刪掉了。

del·e·ter·i·ous /ˌdɛləˋtɪrɪəs; ˌdeləˈtɪəriəs◂/ *adj formal* damaging or harmful【正式】有害的: *the deleterious effects of smoking* 吸煙的害處

de·le·tion /dɪˋliʃən; dɪˈliːʃən/ *n* **1** [U] the act or process of removing something from a piece of writing 刪除 **2** [C] a letter or word that has been removed from a piece of writing 刪掉的字母[詞]

del·i /ˋdɛlɪ; ˈdeli/ *n* [C] *informal* a DELICATESSEN【非正式】熟食店

de·lib·e·rate¹ /dɪˋlɪbərɪt; dɪˈlɪbərət/ *adj* **1** intended or planned, and not happening accidentally 故意的, 有意的, 蓄意的: *a deliberate act of disobedience* 故意的違抗行為 **2** deliberate speech, thought, or movement is slow and careful〔講話、思想或行動〕沉着的, 從容不迫的: *He began working in his usual deliberate and meticulous manner.* 他開始以他那種慣有的審慎精細的方式工作起來。—**deliberateness** *n* [U]

de·lib·e·rate² /dɪˋlɪbəˌret; dɪˈlɪbəreɪt/ *v* [I] to think about something very carefully 仔細考慮: *We really can't afford to deliberate any longer.* 我們真的沒有時間再仔細考慮了。| [+on/about] *They met to deliberate on possible solutions to the problem.* 他們聚在一起仔細商討關於問題可能的解決方法。

de·lib·er·ate·ly /dɪˋlɪbərɪtlɪ; dɪˈlɪbərətli/ *adv* **1** done in a way that is intended or planned 故意地, 蓄意地: *I don't think he deliberately tried to shove you.* 我想他不是故意推你的。| *They're deliberately choosing a cautious policy.* 他們有意地選擇了一項謹慎的政策。**2** done or said in a slow, careful way〔做事、說話〕慎重地, 從容不迫地, 不慌不忙地 3 3

de·lib·e·ra·tion /dɪˌlɪbəˋreʃən; dɪˌlɪbəˈreɪʃən/ *n* **1** [C often plural 常用複數;U] careful consideration or discussion of something 仔細考慮; 商議; 討論: *Their deliberations went on for hours.* 他們商量了好幾個小時。**2** [U] if you speak or move with deliberation, you speak or move slowly and carefully〔說話、行動〕從容, 謹慎

de·lib·e·ra·tive /dɪˋlɪbəˌretɪv; dɪˈlɪbərətɪv/ *adj* existing for the purpose of discussing or planning something 審議的; 商議的

del·i·ca·cy /ˋdɛlɪkəsɪ; ˈdelɪkəsi/ *n* **1** [C] something good to eat that is expensive or rare 珍饈, 佳餚: *Snails are considered a delicacy in France.* 在法國, 蝸牛被認為是一種美味佳餚。**2** [U] a careful and sensitive way of speaking or behaving so that you do not upset anyone; TACT〔說話、做事的〕謹慎; 敏感; 技巧 **3** [U] the quality of being easy to harm, damage, or break 脆弱

del·i·cate /ˋdɛləkət; ˈdelɪkət/ *adj*

1 ▶EASILY DAMAGED 容易受損的◀ easily damaged or broken; FRAGILE (1) 易壞的, 易碎的, 脆弱的: *a delicate bubble of Venetian glass* 易碎的威尼斯玻璃泡

2 ▶NEEDING SENSITIVITY 需要敏感性的◀ needing to be dealt with carefully or sensitively in order to avoid problems or failure 微妙的, 需要謹慎處理的: *The negotiations are at a delicate stage.* 談判正處於微妙階段。

3 ▶PERSON 人◀ someone who is delicate is hurt easily or easily becomes ill〔人〕容易生病的; 嬌弱的: *a delicate child* 身體嬌弱的孩子

4 ▶PART OF THE BODY 身體的一部分◀ a part of the body that is delicate is attractive and graceful 優美的, 優雅的: *He looked down at his long white delicate fingers.* 他低頭看着自己修長、白皙、纖細的手指。

5 ▶SKILFULLY MADE 製作精巧的◀ made skilfully and with attention to the smallest details 精巧的, 精緻的, 精美的: *a delicate pattern of butterflies and leaves* 蝴蝶和樹葉構成的精美圖案

6 ▶TASTE/SMELL/COLOUR 味道/氣味/顏色◀ a taste, smell, or colour that is delicate is pleasant and not strong 柔和的, 清淡的, 淡雅的: *a delicate shade of blue* 一抹淡藍 —compare 比較 INDELICATE —**delicately** *adv*

del·i·cates /ˋdɛləkəts; ˈdelɪkəts/ *n* [plural] clothes that are made from material that needs careful treatment 質地柔軟的服裝

del·i·ca·tes·sen /ˌdɛlɪkəˋtɛsn̩; ˌdelɪkəˈtesən/ *n* [C] a shop that sells high quality cheeses, SALADS, cooked meats etc〔出售高品質乳酪、沙拉、熟肉等的〕熟食店

de·li·cious /dɪˋlɪʃəs; dɪˈlɪʃəs/ *adj* **1** very pleasant to taste or smell 美味的, 可口的; 芳香的: *This cake is absolutely delicious!* 這蛋糕絕對好吃! **2** *literary* extremely pleasant or enjoyable【文】宜人的, 令人愉快的: *It was a delicious but unlikely fantasy.* 那是個美妙的幻想, 但不太可能實現。

de·light¹ /dɪˋlaɪt; dɪˈlaɪt/ *n* **1** [U] feelings of great pleasure and satisfaction 高興, 快樂: **with/in delight** *The kids rushed down to the beach, shrieking with delight.* 孩子們高興地尖叫着衝向海灘。| **to sb's delight** *To my secret delight, Sarah announced that she was leaving.* 令我暗喜的是莎拉宣布她要走了。| **scream/gasp etc of delight** *With a cry of delight he ran towards Jen.* 他歡呼一聲跑向珍。**2** [C] something that makes you feel very happy or satisfied 使人高興[滿意]的事: **the delights of** *the delights of owning your own home* 擁有自己的家的

種種喜悅 **3 take delight in (doing) sth** to enjoy something very much, especially something you should not do 以(做)某事為樂〔尤指做不該做的事〕: *Chris takes great delight in teasing his sister.* 克里斯特別喜歡戲弄他妹妹。

delight² *v* [T] to give someone great satisfaction and enjoyment 使愉快, 使高興: *a book that is certain to delight any reader* 一本肯定會讓所有讀者喜歡的書 | **delight sb with sth** *He delighted them with his charm and sparkling wit.* 他用自己的魅力和機智詼諧讓他們感到愉快。

delight in sth *phr v* [T not in passive 不用被動態] to enjoy something very much, especially something unpleasant 以…為樂, 喜歡…〔尤指不好的事〕

2 **de·light·ed** /dɪˈlaɪtɪd; dɪˈlaɪtɨd/ *adj* very pleased and happy 愉快的, 高興的: *The puppies ran around the delighted children.* 小狗們圍着歡樂的孩子們跑來跑去。| **be delighted to do sth** *Thanks for the invitation. I'd be delighted to come!* 謝謝你的邀請。我很樂意前來! | **delighted (that)** *We're delighted that you'll be there.* 你能去, 我們很高興。| **[+at/by]** *Tom was delighted at the sensation he was creating.* 湯姆對他製造出來的轟動效應感到非常高興。—**delightedly** *adv*

de·light·ful /dɪˈlaɪtfəl; dɪˈlaɪtfəl/ *adj* very pleasant 令人愉快的, 討人喜歡的: *a delightful young man* 惹人喜愛的年輕人 —**delightfully** *adv*

de·lim·it /dɪˈlɪmɪt; dɪˈlɪmɨt/ *v* [T] *formal* to fix or say exactly what the limits of something are【正式】確定…界線, 界定, 限定 —**delimitation** /dɪˌlɪmɪˈteʃən; dɪˌlɪmɨˈteɪʃən/ *n* [C]

de·lin·e·ate /dɪˈlɪnɪˌet; dɪˈlɪnieɪt/ *v* [T] *formal* to describe or draw something carefully so that people can understand it【正式】描寫, 描繪: *Make sure your ideas are clearly delineated in your speech.* 要確保在演講中能夠清楚地闡述你的觀點。—**delineation** /dɪˌlɪnɪˈeʃən; dɪˌlɪniˈeɪʃən/ *n* [U]

de·lin·quen·cy /dɪˈlɪŋkwənsɪ; dɪˈlɪŋkwənsi/ *n* **1** [U] illegal or immoral behaviour, especially by young people 青少年犯罪 **2** [C] *formal* an action that is illegal or immoral【正式】違法[不道德]的行為

de·lin·quent¹ /dɪˈlɪŋkwənt; dɪˈlɪŋkwənt/ *adj* **1** behaving in a way that is illegal or that society does not approve of 違法的, 有過失的: *delinquent behaviour* 違法行為 **2** *technical* a delinquent debt, account etc has not been paid on time【術語】〔債務、賬目等〕到期未付的

delinquent² *n* [C] someone, especially a young person, who breaks the law or behaves in ways their society does not approve of 違法的人〔尤指青少年〕: *juvenile delinquents vandalizing telephones* 恣意破壞公用電話的少年犯

del·i·ques·cent /ˌdɛləˈkwɛsn̩t; ˌdelɨˈkwesənt◂/ *adj technical* a deliquescent substance becomes a liquid because of water in the air【術語】潮解的, 因受潮而溶化的

de·lir·i·ous /dɪˈlɪrɪəs; dɪˈlɪriəs/ *adj* **1** talking continuously in an excited or anxious way, especially because you are ill〔尤指由於有病而〕神智混亂的; 語無倫次的; 囈語的: *One patient had been babbling all night, delirious with a high fever.* 一個病人高燒燒得神志不清, 整個晚上都在說胡話。**2** extremely excited or happy 特別激動的, 特別高興的 —**deliriously** *adv*

de·lir·i·um /dɪˈlɪrɪəm; dɪˈlɪriəm/ *n* **1** [C,U] a state in which someone is delirious, especially because they are very ill 精神錯亂, 胡言亂語, 譫妄〔尤指由於生病〕: *High doses of certain drugs produce delirium.* 某些藥物大劑量服用會導致精神錯亂。**2** [singular] extreme excitement 狂喜

delirium tre·mens /dɪˌlɪrɪəm ˈtrimənz; dɪˌlɪriəm ˈtremənz/ *n* [U] *technical* a medical condition, caused especially by drinking too much alcohol, in which someone's body shakes and they see things that are not there【術語】〔尤指由於飲酒過度引起的〕震顫性譫妄

de·liv·er /dɪˈlɪvɚ; dɪˈlɪvə/ *v*

1 ►TAKE STH SOMEWHERE 把某物帶到某處◄ [I,T] to take goods, letters etc to the place where they have been sent 把〔貨物、信件等〕送往〔某處〕: *Do you deliver on Saturdays?* 星期六你們送貨嗎? | **deliver sth to** *Could you deliver this letter to the accounts department?* 你能把這封信送到會計部嗎? | **have sth delivered** *I'm having some flowers delivered for her birthday.* 我要派人送花給她祝賀生日。

2 deliver a speech/lecture/talk etc to make a speech etc to a lot of people 發言/授課/講話等: *The President, as was customary, delivered the opening address.* 按照慣例, 總統致開幕辭。

3 ►DO STH YOU SHOULD DO 做應該做的事◄ [I,T] to do or provide the things you are expected to, because you are responsible for them or they are part of your job 不負所望, 做該做的事: *Local councils are responsible for delivering most basic services.* 地方議會負責提供大部分基本服務。| **deliver the goods** (=do or provide what you are expected to) 履行承諾, 說到做到 *They made all kinds of promises before the election, but have since failed to deliver the goods.* 他們選舉前作出各種許諾, 但是後來卻一直沒有兌現。| **deliver on a promise** *AmE* (=do what you promised to do)【美】履行諾言

4 ►BABY 嬰兒◄ [T] to help a woman give birth to a baby 給…接生; 幫助〔產婦〕分娩: *Traditionally, local midwives would deliver all the babies in the area.* 過去的習俗是, 當地接生婆會給該地區所有的嬰兒接生。| **deliver sb of** *formal*【正式】: *On May 14th, she was safely delivered of a daughter.* 5月14日, 她平安地產下一個女嬰。

5 deliver a blow/shock etc to to hit someone, give them a shock etc 給予〔某人〕打擊/使〔某人〕震驚等: *He delivered a wild, desperate blow to Derek's jaw.* 他猛烈地、狠狠地往德里克下巴打了一拳。

6 deliver a verdict/judgment/ruling etc to officially state a formal decision or judgment 作出裁決/判斷/裁定等

7 ►PERSON 人◄ [T always+adv/prep] to put someone into someone else's control 把〔某人〕交出; 把〔某人〕送到…手中: **deliver sb to** *Sharett had betrayed him and delivered him to the enemy.* 沙雷特出賣了他, 並把他交給了敵人。

8 ►VOTES 投票◄ [T] *especially AmE* to get the votes or support of a particular group of people in an election【尤美】〔在競選中〕為…拉票: *We're counting on you to deliver the blue collar vote.* 我們指望你拉到藍領選票。

9 ►MAKE SB FREE OF 解脫某人◄ [T] *literary or Biblical* to help someone escape from something bad or evil【文或聖經】解救, 解脫〔某人〕: **deliver sb from** *Deliver us from temptation.* 讓我們免受誘惑。—**deliverer** *n* [C]

deliver sth **up** *phr v* [T often passive 常用被動態] *formal* to give something to someone else【正式】把〔某物〕移交給〔某人〕: **[+to]** *All documents must be delivered up to the trustee.* 所有的文件必須交付給委託人。

de·liv·er·a·ble /dɪˈlɪvərəbl̩; dɪˈlɪvərəbəl/ *n* [C usually plural 一般用複數] something that a company has promised to have ready for a customer, especially parts of computer systems 備送貨物〔尤指電腦部件〕: *a list of software deliverables* 軟件備送貨清單

de·liv·er·ance /dɪˈlɪvərəns; dɪˈlɪvərəns/ *n* [U+**from**] *formal* the state of being saved from harm or danger【正式】拯救, 解救

de·liv·er·y /dɪˈlɪvərɪ; dɪˈlɪvəri/ *n* **1** [C,U] the act or process of bringing goods, letters etc to the person or place they have been sent to 送貨, 送信: *postal deliveries* 郵件遞送 | *a delivery charge* 送貨費用 | **take delivery of** (=officially accept something that has been brought or sent to you) 正式接收 **2** [C] something that is delivered 發送的東西: *Deliveries to the restaurant should be made at the back entrance.* 貨物應該送到餐廳後門口。**3** [C] the process of giving birth to a child 分娩, 生產: *Mrs Howell had an easy delivery.* 豪威爾太太順產。| **deliv-**

ery room/ward etc (=a room in a hospital for births) 產房 **4** [singular] the way in which someone speaks or performs in public〔在公共場合〕講話方式, 演說風格: *You'll have to work on your delivery.* 你還得在演說技巧上下功夫。

de·liv·er·y·man /dɪˈlɪvərɪmən; dɪˈlɪvərimən/ *n* [C] someone who delivers goods to people 送貨員

dell /dɛl; del/ *n* [C] *literary* a small valley with grass and trees【文】〔有草有樹的〕小山谷, 幽谷

de·louse /diˈlaʊs; ˌdiːˈlaʊs/ *v* [T] to remove lice (LOUSE[1] (1)) or similar animals from someone's hair, clothes etc 除去〔頭髮上、衣服上等〕的虱子

del·phin·i·um /dɛlˈfɪnɪəm; delˈfɪniəm/ *n* [C] a tall garden plant with many blue flowers along its stem〔沿莖部長許多藍花的〕飛燕草

del·ta /ˈdɛltə; ˈdeltə/ *n* [C] **1** the fourth letter of the Greek alphabet 希臘字母表的第四個字母 **2** an area of low land where a river spreads into many smaller rivers near the sea〔河口的〕三角洲: *the Nile delta* 尼羅河三角洲 —see picture on page A12 參見A12頁圖

de·lude /dɪˈlud; dɪˈluːd/ *v* [T] to make someone believe something that is not true; deceive 欺騙, 哄騙: **delude sb/yourself** *You're deluding yourself if you think you'll change Rob's mind.* 如果你認為能使羅伯改變主意, 你就是自欺欺人。| **delude sb into doing sth** *That new job title is just a way of deluding her into thinking she's been promoted.* 那個新的工作頭銜只是騙她相信自己已被提升的一種方法而已。

del·uge[1] /ˈdɛljudʒ; ˈdeljuːdʒ/ *n* **1** [C usually singular 一般用單數] a large flood, or period when there is a lot of rain 洪水; 暴雨期 **2 deluge of letters/questions etc** a lot of letters, questions etc that all come at the same time 同時湧來的大量信件/問題等: *a deluge of complaints about the show* 對那場演出的大量抗議

deluge[2] *v* [T] **1** [usually passive 一般用被動態] to send a very large number of letters, questions etc to someone all at the same time〔大量的信件、問題等同時〕湧向〔某人〕; …如雪片飛來: **be deluged with/by** *The response has been great – we've been deluged with new orders.* 反應特別大 —— 我們收到的新訂單不計其數。**2** *formal* to cover something with a lot of water【正式】用水淹沒 —see also 另見 INUNDATE

de·lu·sion /dɪˈluʒən; dɪˈluːʒən/ *n* **1** [C,U] a false belief about yourself or the situation you are in 錯覺; 妄想: **be under the delusion that** (=wrongly believe that) 有…的錯覺 *I was still under the naive delusion that everyone was good at heart.* 我還天真地認為每個人內心都是善良的。**2 delusions of grandeur** the belief that you are much more important or powerful than you really are 妄自尊大, 誇大妄想 —**delusive** /-sɪv; -sɪv/ *adj* —**delusively** *adv*

de·luxe /dɪˈlʊks; dʒˈlʌks/ *adj* [usually before noun 一般用於名詞前] something that is of better quality than other things of the same type〔比同類事物〕質量高的; 豪華的: *The deluxe model costs a lot more.* 豪華型要貴很多。

delve /dɛlv; delv/ *v* [I] **1** [always+adv/prep] to search for something by putting your hand deeply into a bag, container etc〔把手伸到手提袋、容器等的深處〕搜尋, 翻找: **delve in/among/between etc** *Hank delved in his pockets for some change.* 漢克在口袋裡翻找一些零錢。**2** *poetic* to dig【詩】挖掘

delve into *phr v* [T] to try to find more information about someone or something 探究, 探索, 鑽研: *I wouldn't delve too deeply into his past if I were you.* 如果我是你的話, 我不會深究他的過去。

Dem /dɛm; dem/ the written abbreviation of 縮寫= Democrat or Democratic

de·mag·ne·tize also 又作 **-ise** *BrE*【英】/diˈmægnəˌtaɪz; ˌdiːˈmægnətaɪz/ *v* [T] **1** to take away the MAGNETIC qualities of something 除去〔某物的〕磁性, 使消磁 **2** *technical* to remove sounds from a MAGNETIC TAPE【術語】除去〔磁帶的〕聲音 —**demagnetization** /ˌdimægnətəˈzeʃən; ˌdiːmægnətaɪˈzeɪʃən/ *n* [U]

dem·a·gogue also 又作 **demagog** *AmE*【美】/ˈdɛməˌgɑg; ˈdeməgɒg/ *n* [C] someone who gives political speeches that try to persuade people by using emotional language rather than reason 蠱惑民心者, 煽動民眾的政客 —**demagogy, demagogery** *n* [U] —**demagogic** /ˌdɛməˈgɑgɪk; ˌdeməˈgɒgɪk◂/ *adj* —**demagogically** /-klɪ; -kli/ *adv*

de·mand[1] /dɪˈmænd; dɪˈmɑːnd/ *n* S1 W1

1 ►FIRM REQUEST 堅決要求◄ [C] a very firm request for something that you think someone should give you, or think you have a right to 要求, 請求: *The government refused to give in to the demands of the terrorists.* 政府拒絕對恐怖分子提出的要求作出讓步。| **[+for]** *a demand for a 10% pay increase* 提高工資10%的要求 —see 見 REQUEST[2] (USAGE)

2 demands [plural] the difficult, annoying, or tiring things that someone or something makes you do 困難的[煩人的、累人的]事情: **the demands of** *the pace and demands of modern life* 現代生活的節奏和煩心事 | **make demands (on)** *The job makes great demands on my time.* 這項工作需要我花很多時間。

3 ►GOODS/SERVICES 貨物/服務◄ [singular,U] people's need or desire to buy or use particular goods and services 需求: **[+for]** *There's not much demand for oil heaters any more.* 現在燃油加熱器的需求不大了。| **meet demand** (=supply or sell enough goods etc for people to buy) 滿足需求 *Ford have increased production in order to meet demand.* 福特公司為了滿足需求, 已提高了產量。| **be in demand** (=be wanted by a lot of people) 廣受歡迎 *Her books are in great demand at the moment.* 目前, 她的書非常暢銷。—see also 另見 **supply and demand** (SUPPLY[1] (5))

4 by popular demand because a lot of people have asked for something to be done, performed etc 應公眾要求: *Here they are, back by popular demand, The Wild Ones!* 根據公眾的要求,《野蠻人》〔馬龍白蘭度50年代的電影〕又回來了!

5 on demand *formal* done or given whenever someone asks【正式】見票即付: *This note entitles the bearer to $20 on demand.* 這張票據的持有者隨時有權領取20美元。

demand[2] *v* **1** [T] to ask for something very firmly, especially something that someone does not want to give you〔堅決〕要求〔尤其是別人不想給的東西〕: *The Governor has demanded your resignation.* 州長已經要求你辭職。| **demand to know/see etc** *I demand to know what's going on!* 我要求了解正在發生甚麼事情! | **demand that** *Protesters went on hunger strike to demand that all political prisoners be freed.* 抗議者絕食示威, 要求釋放所有政治犯。**2** [I,T] to ask a question or order something to be done very firmly 詢問, 質問; 命令: *"Did you do this?" Kathryn demanded angrily.* "這是你做的嗎?" 凱思琳氣憤地質問道。| **demand sth of sb** (=ask someone for something) 向某人要某物 **3** [T] to need someone's time, energy, skill etc 需要〔時間、精力、技能等〕: *There are just too many things all demanding my attention at once.* 有太多事情需要我立即處理。 W2

de·mand·ing /dɪˈmændɪŋ; dɪˈmɑːndɪŋ/ *adj* **1** needing a lot of ability, effort, or skill 費力的: *a demanding job* 高要求的工作 **2** expecting a lot of attention, especially in a way that is not fair 苛求的, 要求過高的: *Her mother could be very demanding at times.* 她媽媽有時會變得十分難伺候。 S3

de·mar·cate /dɪˈmɑrket; ˈdiːmɑːkeɪt/ *v* [T] *formal* to state or fix the limits of an area, system etc【正式】標明〔一個地區、系統等〕的界線: *The development of clearly demarcated territories is fairly recent in history.* 界線分明的版圖是在近代歷史方才出現的。

de·mar·ca·tion /ˌdimɑrˈkeʃən; ˌdiːmɑːˈkeɪʃən/ *n* [U] **1** the point at which one person's area of work, respon-

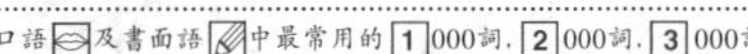

sibility etc ends and someone else's begins〔工作範圍、職權範圍等的〕界限, 分界線: *There is no clear demarcation between the responsibilities of our two departments.* 我們兩個部門的職責沒有明顯的劃分。**2** a way of separating one area of land from another〔地區的〕劃分, 劃定, 定界

de·mean /dɪˋmin; dɪˈmiːn/ *v* [T] *formal* to do something that you think you are too good for【正式】降低…的身分, 貶低, 貶損: *Don't demean yourself by taking that job.* 不要降低你的身分去接受那份工作。—**demeaning** *adj*: *Cleaning the toilets was the most demeaning task at the camp.* 在營地, 清洗廁所是最有失身分的差事。

de·mea·nour *BrE*【英】, **demeanor** *AmE*【美】/dɪˋminɚ; dɪˈmiːnə/ *n* [singular,U] the way someone behaves or looks that gives you a general idea of their character〔能讓人看出大致性格特點的〕舉止, 外表, 風度: *There was certainly a large element of irony in his demeanour.* 他的舉止中確實有很大的嘲諷成分。

D

de·men·ted /dɪˋmɛntɪd; dɪˈmentɨd/ *adj* **1** behaving as if you are crazy, especially because of an upsetting experience〔由於痛苦的經歷而〕瘋狂的: *The woman was almost demented with grief.* 那個婦女悲痛得幾乎瘋掉。**2** *old-fashioned* suffering from a mental illness【過時】精神錯亂的

de·men·tia /dɪˋmɛnʃə; dɪˈmenʃə/ *n* [U] *technical* an illness that affects the brain and memory, and makes you gradually lose the ability to think and behave normally【術語】痴呆

dem·e·ra·ra sug·ar /ˌdɛmərɛrə ˋʃugɚ; ˌdeməreərə ˈʃugə/ *n* [U] a type of rough brown sugar 德麥拉拉蔗糖〔一種褐色粗蔗糖〕

de·mer·it /diˋmɛrɪt; diːˈmerɨt/ *n* [C] **1 the merits and demerits of** *formal* the good and bad qualities or features of something【正式】…的長處和短處, …的優缺點 **2** *AmE* a mark showing that a student has done something wrong at school【美】記過

de·mesne /dɪˋmen; dɪˈmeɪn/ *n* [C] *old use or law* a very big house and all the land that belongs to it, especially in former times【舊或法律】〔尤指過去〕莊園的大片房地產

demi- /dɛmɪ; demɪ/ *prefix* **1** half 一半: *a demisemiquaver* (=very short musical note) 32分音符 **2** partly something 部分: *a demigod* (=partly human and partly a god) 半人半神

dem·i·god /ˋdɛməˌgɑd; ˈdemigɒd/ *n* [C] **1** someone who is so important and powerful that they are treated like a god 被人像神一樣崇拜的人物: *a dictator with demigod status* 享有像神一樣地位的獨裁者 **2** a man in ancient stories, who is half god and half human〔古典神話中的〕半人半神

dem·i·john /ˋdɛməˌdʒɑn; ˈdemidʒɒn/ *n* [C] a large bottle with a short narrow neck, often used for making wine 細頸大瓶〔常用於釀酒〕

de·mil·i·ta·rize also 又作 **-ise** *BrE*【英】/diˋmɪlətəˌraɪz; ˌdiːˈmɪlɨtəraɪz/ *v* [T usually passive 一般用被動態] to remove the weapons, soldiers etc from a country or area so that there can be no fighting there 使非軍事化, 使解除武裝 —**demilitarization** /diˌmɪlətərəˋzeʃən; diːˌmɪlɨtəraɪˈzeɪʃən/ *n* [U]

de·mise /dɪˋmaɪz; dɪˈmaɪz/ *n* [U] **1** *formal* the end of something that used to exist【正式】〔曾經存在的某物的〕終止, 結束: [+of] *the sad demise of the local newspaper* 地方報紙的令人惋惜的停刊 **2** *formal or law* death【正式或法律】死亡 —**demise** *v* [I] *especially AmE*【尤美】: *The sport has continued to demise over the years.* 這些年來, 這項體育運動在繼續衰退。

de·mist /diˋmɪst; ˌdiːˈmɪst/ *v* [T] *BrE* to remove mist from a car window using heat【英】除去〔汽車玻璃上的〕霧水; DEFROST (3) *AmE*【美】—**demister** *n* [C]

dem·o /ˋdɛmo; ˈdeməʊ/ *n* [C] *informal*【非正式】**1** an event at which a large group of people publicly protest about something〔為抗議某事而舉行的〕遊行, 示威 **2 give sb a demo** to show someone how something works or is done 給某人示範 **3** a piece of recorded music that is sent to a record company so that they can decide whether to sell it or not 錄音樣帶, 試樣唱片: *a demo tape* 錄音樣帶 —compare 比較 DEMONSTRATION (2)

de·mob /diˋmɑb; diːˈmɒb/ *v* **demobbed, demobbing** [T] *BrE informal* to demobilize【英, 非正式】遣散〔軍隊〕, 使〔軍人〕復員

de·mo·bi·lize also 又作 **-ise** *BrE*【英】/diˋmoblˌaɪz; diːˈməʊbɨlaɪz/ *v* [T usually passive 一般用被動態] to send home the members of an army, navy etc, especially at the end of a war〔尤指戰爭結束時〕使〔陸軍、海軍等的成員〕復員回家: *Unemployed demobilized soldiers drifted toward the cities.* 失業的復員士兵漫無目的地流向各個城市。—**demobilization** /diˌmobələˋzeʃən; diːˌməʊbɨlaɪˈzeɪʃən/ *n* [U]

de·moc·ra·cy /dɪˋmɑkrəsɪ; dɪˈmɒkrəsi/ *n* **1** [U] a system of government in which everyone in the country can vote to elect its members 民主政體 **2** [C] a country that has a government which has been elected by the people of the country 民主國家 **3** [U] a situation or system in which everyone is equal and has the right to vote, make decisions etc 民主作風, 民主精神

dem·o·crat /ˋdɛməˌkræt; ˈdeməkræt/ *n* [C] **1** someone who believes in, or works to achieve democracy 民主主義者, 民主人士 **2 Democrat** a member or supporter of the Democratic party of the US 美國民主黨黨員; 美國民主黨支持者

dem·o·crat·ic /ˌdɛməˋkrætɪk; ˌdeməˈkrætɪk◂/ *adj* **1** controlled by representatives who are elected by the people of a country 民主的, 民主政體的: *a democratic government* 民主政府 **2** organized according to the principle that everyone has a right to be involved in making decisions 民主制的, 民主管理的: *a democratic management style* 民主的管理風格 —**democratically** /-klɪ; -kli/ *adv*: *democratically-elected councils* 民主選舉出來的委員會

de·moc·ra·tize also 又作 **-ise** *BrE*【英】/dɪˋmɑkrəˌtaɪz; dɪˈmɒkrətaɪz/ *v* [T] to change the way in which a government, company etc is organized, so that the people in it have more power 使〔政府、公司等〕民主化 —**democratization** /dɪˌmɑkrətəˋzeʃən; dɪˌmɒkrətaɪˈzeɪʃən/ *n* [U]

dé·mo·dé /ˌdemoˋde; ˌdeɪˈməʊdeɪ/ *adj formal* not fashionable any more【正式】過時的, 不再時髦的

de·mog·ra·phy /dɪˋmɑgrəfɪ; dɪˈmɒgrəfi/ *n* [U] the study of human populations and the ways in which they change 人口學, 人口統計學 —**demographer** *n* [C] —**demographic** /ˌdɛməˋgræfɪk; ˌdeməˈgræfɪk◂/ *adj*

de·mol·ish /dɪˋmɑlɪʃ; dɪˈmɒlɪʃ/ *v* [T] **1** to completely destroy a building, especially so that the land it is on can be used for something else 拆毀, 拆除〔建築物〕: *Several houses were demolished to make way for the new road.* 好幾所房子都被拆掉以便騰出地方修新公路。**2** to prove that an idea or opinion is completely wrong 推翻, 駁倒〔想法、觀點〕: *He demolished my argument in minutes.* 他幾分鐘內就把我的論點給駁倒了。**3** *informal especially BrE* to eat all of something very quickly【非正式, 尤英】吃光, 吞掉

dem·o·li·tion /ˌdɛməˋlɪʃən; ˌdeməˈlɪʃən/ *n* [C,U] the act, or process of demolishing a building〔房屋的〕拆除

de·mon /ˋdimən; ˈdiːmən/ *n* [C] **1** an evil spirit 魔鬼 **2** *humorous* someone who is very good at a game, especially cards【幽默】〔玩遊戲尤指玩紙牌的〕高手: *Pete is a demon poker player.* 彼得是撲克牌高手。**3 the demon drink** *humorous* alcoholic drink【幽默】含酒精的飲料 —compare 比較 DAEMON

de·mo·ni·a·cal /ˌdiməˋnaɪəkl; ˌdiːməˈnaɪəkəl◂/ also 又作 **de·mo·ni·ac** /diˋmonɪˌæk; dɪˈməʊniæk/ *adj formal* wild, uncontrolled, and evil【正式】狂野的; 邪惡的: *demoniacal cruelty* 充滿邪惡的兇殘 —**demoniacally** /-klɪ; -kli/ *adv*

de·mon·ic /dɪˋmɑnɪk; dɪˈmɒnɪk/ *adj* **1** wild and cruel 瘋狂的, 殘忍的: *demonic laughter* 狂笑 **2** like a demon

魔鬼般的: *demonic possession* 魔鬼附身 **—demonically** /-klɪ; -kli/ *adv*

de·mon·stra·ble /dɪˋmɑnstrəbḷ; dɪˋmɒnstrəbəl/ *adj formal* able to be shown or proved【正式】可表明的, 可證實的 **—demonstrably** *adv*: *These conclusions are demonstrably wrong.* 這些結論可以證明是錯誤的。**—demonstrability** /dɪˏmɑnstrəˋbɪlətɪ; dɪˌmɒnstrəˈbɪlɪ̣ti/ *n* [U]

2 **dem·on·strate** /ˋdɛmənˏstret; ˈdemənstreɪt/ *v* **1** [T] to show or prove something clearly 證明, 論證, 證實: *These findings clearly demonstrate the fact that unemployment leads to poor health.* 這些發現清楚證明失業導致健康不佳這個事實。| **demonstrate that** *Edwin Hubble demonstrated that ours was not the only galaxy.* 艾德温·哈勃證實了我們所在的星系並不是唯一的星系。**2** [T] to show or describe how something works or is done 示範, 演示 **3** [I] to march through the streets with a large group of people in order to publicly protest about something〔為公開抗議某事〕遊行示威: *Supporters demonstrated outside the courtroom during the trial.* 在審訊期間, 支持者們在法庭外遊行示威。| **demonstrate against** *What are they demonstrating against?* 他們示威抗議甚麼? **4** [T] to show that you have a particular skill, quality, or ability 展示, 表露出〔某種技能、品質或能力〕: *At last she had the chance to demonstrate her musical talents.* 最後, 她終於得到了機會一展自己的音樂才華。

demonstration 遊行示威

3
3 **dem·on·stra·tion** /ˏdɛmənˋstreʃən; ˌdemənˈstreɪʃən/ *n* **1** [C] an event at which a large group of people march through the streets, in order to publicly protest about something〔為抗議某事而進行的〕遊行, 示威: *The new tax proposals sparked mass demonstrations.* 新的税收提議引發了大規模示威遊行。| **[+against]** *a demonstration against the war* 反戰遊行 | **stage/hold a demonstration** *Students staged a demonstration to protest about the rises in tuition fees.* 學生們舉行了示威遊行抗議學費上漲。| **break up a demonstration** *Police used tear gas to break up the demonstration.* 警察使用催淚彈來驅散示威者。**2** [C,U] an act of explaining and showing how something works or is done 示範, 演示: **give a demonstration** *He gave a demonstration of how the program works.* 他作示範來説明這個程式是如何運作的。**3** [C] *formal* the expression of a feeling【正式】〔感情的〕表示, 表露: *a demonstration of her love* 她愛的表示

de·mon·stra·tive /dɪˋmɑnstrətɪv; dɪˈmɒnstrətɪv/ *adj* willing to show loving feelings towards people 感情外露的: *Dave's not very demonstrative, but I know he loves me.* 戴夫不太善於表露感情, 但是我知道他愛我。**—demonstratively** *adv*

demonstrative pro·noun /·ˏ··· ˋ··/ *n* [C] *technical* a PRONOUN such as 'that' or 'this' that shows which person or thing is meant, and separates it from others【術語】指示代(名)詞〈如 that 或 this〉

dem·on·stra·tor /ˋdɛmənˏstretɚ; ˈdemənstreɪtə/ *n* [C] **1** someone who takes part in a DEMONSTRATION 遊行者, 示威者: *Thousands of demonstrators gathered outside the Capitol building.* 數以千計的示威遊行者聚集在國會大廈外面。**2** someone who shows people how something works or is done 示範人員

de·mor·al·ize also 又作 **-ise** *BrE*【英】/dɪˋmɑrəlˏaɪz; dɪˈmɒrəlaɪz/ *v* [T] to reduce or destroy someone's courage or confidence 削弱〔勇氣〕, 摧毀〔自信〕: *Such a move would undermine standards in schools and demoralize teachers.* 這樣的舉措會降低學校的標準, 削弱教師的信心。**—demoralized** *adj*: *Defeated and demoralized, the protesters made their way home.* 抗議者受挫後垂頭喪氣地打道回府了。**—demoralizing** *adj*: *a series of demoralizing failures* 一連串令人泄氣的失敗 **—demoralization** /dɪˏmɔrələˋzeʃən; dɪˌmɒrəlaɪˈzeɪʃən/ *n* [U]: *widespread demoralization in the police force* 在警察隊伍中普遍存在的士氣低落

de·mote /dɪˋmot; dɪˈməʊt/ *v* [T often passive 常用被動態] to make someone's rank or position lower or less important 將〔某人〕降職 —opposite 反義詞 PROMOTE (2) **—demotion** /-ˋmoʃən; -ˈməʊʃən/ *n* [C,U]

de·mot·ic /dɪˋmɑtɪk; dɪˈmɒtɪk/ *adj formal* used by or popular with most ordinary people【正式】大眾的, 通俗的

de·mo·ti·vate /diˋmotəˏvet; ˌdiːˈməʊtɪ̣veɪt/ *v* [T] to make someone less eager or willing to do their job 使〔某人〕失去動力, 使〔某人〕不願〔工作〕**—demotivating** *adj*: *Lack of sufficient challenge at work can be very demotivating.* 工作中缺乏足夠的挑戰會使人變得非常消極。**—demotivation** /ˏdimotəˋveʃən; ˌdiːməʊtɪ̣ˈveɪʃən/ *n* [U]

de·mur[1] /dɪˋmɝ; dɪˈmɜː/ *v* **demurred, demurring** [I] *formal* to express doubt about or opposition to a plan or suggestion【正式】〔對計劃或建議〕表示懷疑, 表示反對: *They demurred at the idea of working on a Sunday.* 他們對星期天上班的主意表示反對。

demur[2] *n* [U] *formal* disagreement or disapproval【正式】反對, 異議, 不贊成: **without demur** *I agreed to this without demur.* 我毫無異議地贊同此事。

de·mure /dɪˋmjur; dɪˈmjʊə/ *adj* a word meaning quiet, serious, and always behaving well, used especially about women in former times〔尤指舊時的婦女〕嫻靜的, 莊重的, 舉止得體的 **—demurely** *adv*: *She lowered her eyes demurely.* 她羞怯地垂下雙眼。**—demureness** *n* [U]

de·mys·ti·fy /diˋmɪstəˏfaɪ; ˌdiːˈmɪstɪ̣faɪ/ *v* [T] to make a subject that seems difficult or complicated easier to understand, especially by explaining it in simpler language〔尤指通過較簡單的語言解釋〕使〔似乎困難或複雜的問題〕容易理解: *This book attempts to demystify the whole subject of computers.* 這本書試圖使電腦這門學科變得不再神祕。**—demystification** /diˏmɪstəfəˋkeʃən; diːˌmɪstɪ̣fɪ̣ˈkeɪʃən/ *n* [U]

den /dɛn; den/ *n* [C] **1** the home of some types of animal, for example lions or foxes (FOX[1] (1))〔某些動物的〕穴, 窩, 窟 **2** a place where secret or illegal activities take place〔進行祕密或非法活動的〕巢穴, 老窩: *a gambler's den* 賭窩 | *a den of thieves* 賊窩 **3** an enclosed and secret place where children play〔孩子們玩耍的封閉祕密的〕集合地 **4** *especially AmE* a room in someone's house where they can relax, watch television etc【尤美】〔家中休息、看電視以及進行其他活動的〕私室 **5** *AmE* a group of CUB SCOUTS【美】幼年童子軍小隊 **6** *BrE old-fashioned* a small room in someone's house where they can work, read, etc without being disturbed【英, 過時】〔家中的〕書齋: *Father retreated to his den.* 爸爸躲入了自己的書房。**7 den of iniquity** *often humorous* a place where activities that you think are immoral or evil happen【常幽默】污穢之地: *Her mother saw the city as a den of iniquity.* 她媽媽把這座城市看成是個藏污納垢之處。

de·na·tion·al·ize also 又作 **-ise** *BrE*【英】/di`næʃənḷ,aɪz; diː'næʃənəlaɪz/ *v* [T] to sell a business or industry that is owned by the state, so that it is then owned privately; PRIVATIZE 使非國有化, 使私營化 —**denationalization** /di,næʃənələ`zeʃən; diː,næʃənəlaɪ'zeɪʃən/ *n* [U]

de·ni·a·ble /dɪ`naɪəbḷ; dɪ'naɪəbəl/ *adj* something that is deniable can be proved not to be true 可否定的, 可證明是錯誤的 —opposite 反義詞 UNDENIABLE

de·ni·al /dɪ`naɪəl; dɪ'naɪəl/ *n* **1** [C,U] a statement saying that something is not true 否認, 否定: [+of] *The government issued a firm denial of the rumour.* 政府對謠言予以堅決否認。**2 denial of justice/humanity/rights etc** a situation in which someone is not allowed to have justice, their rights etc 拒絕給予公平處理/人道對待/權利等: *protests against the denial of human rights* 對剝奪人權的抗議 **3** [U] *technical* a condition in which someone cannot or will not admit what they are really feeling【術語】〔對真實想法的〕拒絕承認

D

den·i·er /`dɛnɪɚ; 'deniə/ *n* [U] *BrE* a measure of how thin NYLON or silk threads are【英】旦尼爾, 旦〔尼龍或絲的纖度單位〕: *a pair of 15-denier tights* 一條 15 旦纖度的緊身褲襪

den·i·grate /`dɛnə,gret; 'denɪ̸,greɪt/ *v* [T] to say that something or someone is not good or important 貶低, 詆毀, 誹謗: *men who denigrate the status of women* 貶低婦女地位的男人們 —**denigration** /dɛnə`greʃən; ,denɪ̸'greɪʃən/ *n* [U]

den·im /`dɛnəm; 'denɪ̸m/ *n* **1** [U] a type of strong cotton cloth, used especially to make JEANS〔尤指用於製作牛仔褲的〕粗棉布, 勞動布 —see picture on page A16 參見 A16 頁圖 **2 denims** [plural] *old-fashioned* a pair of trousers made of this material; JEANS【過時】牛仔褲

den·i·zen /`dɛnəzṇ; 'denɪ̸zən/ *n* [C+of] *literary* an animal, plant, or person that lives or is found in a particular place【文】〔特定地區的〕棲息者, 居住者〔指動物、植物或人〕

den moth·er /'· ,··/ *n* [C] *AmE* a woman who leads a group of CUB SCOUTS【美】美國幼年童子軍小隊的女訓導

de·nom·i·nate /dɪ`nɑmə,net; dɪ'nɒmɪ̸neɪt/ *v* [T] *formal* to give a name to something; DESIGNATE[1] (2)【正式】給〔某物〕命名

de·nom·i·na·tion /dɪ,nɑmə`neʃən; dɪ,nɒmɪ̸'neɪʃən/ *n* [C] **1** a religious group that is part of a larger religious organization 宗教派別: *Christians of all denominations* 各種教派的基督徒 **2** *technical* the value of a coin or NOTE[1] (5)【術語】貨幣面值[單位] **3** *formal* a name for a group or type【正式】〔一組或一類事物的〕名稱, 種類名

de·nom·i·na·tion·al /dɪ,nɑmə`neʃənḷ; dɪ,nɒmɪ̸'neɪʃənəl/ *adj* connected with or belonging to a particular religious denomination 教派的

de·nom·i·na·tor /dɪ`nɑmə,netɚ; dɪ'nɒmɪ̸neɪtə/ *n* [C] *technical* the number below the line in a FRACTION (2)【術語】〔分數的〕分母 —compare 比較 NUMERATOR —see also 另見 LOWEST COMMON DENOMINATOR

de·no·ta·tion /,dino`teʃən; ,diːnəʊ'teɪʃən/ *n* [C] *technical* the thing that is actually described by a word rather than the feelings or ideas it suggests【術語】〔詞的〕指示意義, 本義〔而非隱含意義〕—compare 比較 CONNOTATION

de·note /dɪ`not; dɪ'nəʊt/ *v* [T] *formal*【正式】**1** to mean 意思是…: *The word 'family' is used here to denote the members of a household, whether or not they are related.* "家庭"這個詞在這裡用來指一戶人家的所有成員, 而不論他們是否有親戚關係。**2** to be a sign of something; INDICATE (4) 是…的標記; 表示…: *Crosses on the map denote villages and hamlets.* 地圖上的十字表示村莊和小村子。—**denotative** *adj*

de·noue·ment /,denu`mã; deɪ'nuːmɒŋ/ *n* [C] the explanation at the end of a story or play〔小說或戲劇等的〕結局, 收場; 結局[收場]的段落

de·nounce /dɪ`naʊns; dɪ'naʊns/ *v* [T] **1** to express strong disapproval of someone or something, especially in public 譴責, 指責, 斥責: *The President's statement was denounced by all parties.* 總統的聲明遭到了各黨派的指責。| **denounce sb/sth as** *He denounced the waste of public money as 'criminally negligent'.* 他譴責浪費公款是"構成犯罪的玩忽職守"。**2** to give information to the police or other authority about someone's illegal political activities 告發, 檢舉, 舉報: **denounce sb to sb** *She eventually denounced him to the secret police.* 她終於向祕密警察告發了他。—see also 另見 DENUNCIATION

dense /dɛns; dens/ *adj*

1 ►CLOSE TOGETHER 挨在一起◄ made of several things that are closely packed together 茂密的, 密集的, 稠密的: *He forced his way through the dense crowd.* 他從密集的人羣中擠過。| *Dense jungle covered the whole area.* 茂密的熱帶叢林覆蓋了整個地區。

2 ►SMOKE/MIST 煙/霧◄ difficult to see through or breathe in 濃密的, 不易看透[呼吸]的: *dense fog* 濃霧 | *a dense black cloud* 密密的烏雲

3 ►STUPID 愚蠢的◄ *informal* not able to understand things easily; stupid【非正式】遲鈍的, 愚蠢的: *Oh, don't be so dense!* 天啊, 別那麼笨!

4 ►WRITING 寫作◄ a dense piece of writing is difficult to understand because it contains a lot of information or uses complicated language〔寫的東西〕不易懂的

5 ►SUBSTANCE 物質◄ *technical* a substance that is dense has a lot of MASS[1] (6) in relation to its size【術語】密度大的: *Water is eight hundred times denser than air.* 水的密度是空氣密度的八百倍。—**densely** *adv*: *a densely populated area* 人口稠密的地區 —**denseness** *n* [U]

den·si·ty /`dɛnsətɪ; 'densɪ̸ti/ *n* [U] **1** the degree to which an area is filled with things or people 密度: *population density* 人口密度 **2** *technical* the relationship between something's MASS[1] (5) and its size【術語】密度〔質量與體積的關係〕

dent[1] /dɛnt; dent/ *n* [C] **1** a hollow area in the surface of something, usually made by something hitting it〔通常由於碰撞而造成的〕凹痕, 凹坑: [+in] *There was a dent in the door where he'd kicked it.* 他踢門的地方陷了一塊。**2** a reduction in the amount of something, especially money or supplies〔尤指金錢或供應〕減少, 削減, 耗減: *The trip made a big dent in our savings.* 這次旅行花掉了我們很多積蓄。

dent 凹痕, 凹坑

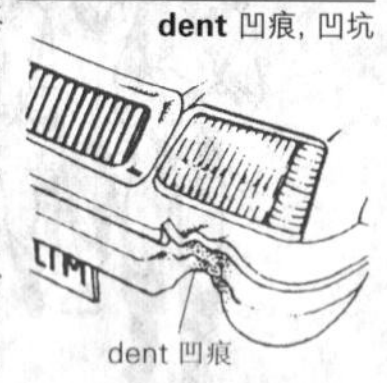

dent 凹痕

dent[2] *v* [T] **1** to make a hollow area in the surface of something, usually by hitting it 使造成凹痕: *I'm afraid I've dented the car.* 恐怕我把汽車撞出了凹痕。**2** to damage or harm something 損害, 破壞: *Diesel sales have been badly dented by environmental concerns.* 由於對環保問題的關注, 柴油的銷售受到了嚴重影響。

den·tal /`dɛntḷ; 'dentl/ *adj* connected with your teeth 牙齒的: *dental treatment* 牙齒的治療

dental floss /,·· '·/ *n* [U] a kind of thin string that you use for cleaning between your teeth 潔牙線〔用以清潔牙縫的細線〕

dental hy·gien·ist /,·· '···/ *n* [C] someone who works with a dentist and cleans people's teeth, or gives them advice about how to look after their teeth 牙科保健員, 牙科清潔員, 牙醫助手

dental nurse /'·· ·/ *n* [C] someone whose job is to help a dentist 牙科護士

dental sur·geon /,·· '··/ *n* [C] *formal* a dentist【正式】牙科醫生

den·tine /`dɛntin; 'dentiːn/ also 又作 **den·tin** /`dɛntɪn; 'dentɪn/ *AmE*【美】*n* [U] the type of bone that your teeth are made of 牙質, 齒質 —see picture at 參見 TEETH 圖

den·tist /`dɛntɪst; 'dentɪ̸st/ *n* [C] someone whose job is to treat people's teeth 牙科醫生: *I'm going to the dentist's this afternoon.* 今天下午我要去看牙醫。

den·tis·try /ˋdɛntɪstrɪ; ˈdentɪ̤stri/ *n* [U] the medical study of the mouth and teeth, or the work of a dentist 牙科學; 牙醫術; 牙醫業

den·tures /ˋdɛntʃɚz; ˈdentʃəz/ *n* [plural] a set of artificial teeth worn by someone who does not have their own teeth any more; FALSE TEETH (一副)假牙

de·nude /dɪˋnud; dɪˈnjuːd/ *v* [T] *formal* to remove a natural layer or part of something【正式】使〔自然層〕剝光: **denude sth of** *The trees were now denuded of their leaves.* 樹木的葉子已經落光。—**denudation** /ˌdinuˋdeʃən; ˌdiːnjuːˈdeɪʃən/ *n* [U]

de·nun·ci·a·tion /dɪˌnʌnsɪˋeʃən; dɪˌnʌnsiˈeɪʃən/ *n* [C] a public statement that someone or something is wrong or bad 譴責, 斥責, 控訴

Den·ver boot /ˌdɛnvɚ ˋbut; ˌdenvə ˈbuːt/ *n* [C] *AmE informal* a metal object that the police fasten to an illegally parked car so that it cannot be moved; WHEEL CLAMP【美, 非正式】丹佛扣鎖, 車輪固定夾〔警察用來夾住非法停靠的汽車〕

2 2 **de·ny** /dɪˋnaɪ; dɪˈnaɪ/ *v* [T]

1 ▶SAY STH IS UNTRUE 說某事不是事實◀ to say that something someone has said about you is not true 否認, 否定: *I saw you, so don't try to deny it!* 我看見你了, 所以別想否認了! | **deny (that)** *Do you deny that this is your writing?* 你否認這是你的筆跡嗎? | *I can't deny her remarks hurt me.* 我不能否認她的話傷害了我。| **deny doing sth** *He denied ever having been there.* 他否認曾經去了那個地方。| **flatly/categorically deny** (=deny very strongly) 堅決/斷然否認 *Jackson categorically denied any involvement in the affair.* 傑克遜斷然否認與此事有任何關聯。

2 ▶NOT ALLOW 不允許◀ [often passive 常用被動態] to refuse to allow someone to have or do something 不允許〔某人擁有某物或做某事〕: *Permission was denied.* 沒有得到准許。| **deny sb sth** *She could deny her son nothing.* 她對她兒子有求必應。| **deny sth to sb** *The campaign aims to deny contraceptive advice to girls under sixteen.* 活動旨在不許十六歲以下的女孩獲得有關避孕的諮詢。—see 見 REFUSE[1] (USAGE)

3 there's no denying *spoken* used to say that it is very clear that something is true【口】無可否認, 不容否認: *There's no denying that this is a serious blow.* 無可否認這是個嚴重的打擊。

4 ▶PRINCIPLES/BELIEFS 原則/信仰◀ *formal* to do something that is the opposite of something you strongly believe in【正式】背棄, 拋棄

5 ▶FEELINGS 感情◀ to refuse to admit that you are feeling something 拒絕承認: *I realized I'd been denying a lot of angry feelings towards my mother.* 我意識到自己一直在否認對母親有許多憤怒的情緒。

6 deny yourself to decide not to have something that you would like, especially for moral or religious reasons〔尤指出於道德或宗教原因〕克制自己, 自制

de·o·do·rant /diˋodərənt; diːˈəʊdərənt/ *n* [C,U] a chemical substance that you put on your skin to hide or destroy unpleasant smells〔除體臭的〕防臭劑, 除臭劑

de·o·do·rize also 又作 **-ise** *BrE*【英】/diˋodəˌraɪz; diːˈəʊdəraɪz/ *v* [T] to remove or hide the unpleasant smell of something 除去…的臭氣

dep the written abbreviation of 縮寫= DEPART or 或 DEPARTURE

de·part /dɪˋpɑrt; dɪˈpɑːt/ *v* **1** [I] to leave, especially when you are starting a journey 離開〔尤指動身去旅行〕, 啟程, 上路: *The train for Edinburgh will depart from platform 5.* 開往愛丁堡的火車將從5號月台出發。**2 depart this life** *formal* to die【正式】去世, 故去, 離開人間 —see also 另見 DEPARTURE

depart from sth *phr v* [T] to start to do something differently from the usual, traditional, or expected way 背離, 違反, 不同於〔常規等〕: *Her approach departs radically from normal educational practices.* 她的方法與通常的教育慣例大相徑庭。

de·part·ed /dɪˋpɑrtɪd; dɪˈpɑːtɪ̤d/ *adj* [only before noun 僅用於名詞前] **1** a word meaning dead, used to avoid saying this directly 已故的, 去世的〔委婉說法〕: *our dear departed father* 我們摯愛的已故的父親 **2** *literary* a period of time that is departed has gone for ever【文】過去的, 不復再來的: *departed youth* 逝去的青春

de·part·ment /dɪˋpɑrtmənt; dɪˈpɑːtmənt/ *n* [C] **1** one of the groups of people working together to form part of a large organization such as a hospital, university, or company〔醫院、大學或公司等大機構的〕科, 系, 處, 部門: **the English/sales etc department** *She's in charge of the personnel department.* 她主管人事部門。| **[+of]** *the Department of Genetic Research* 基因研究部門 **2** one of the parts that the government is divided into which is responsible for a particular problem or part of people's lives〔政府的〕院, 部, 司: *the State Department* 國務院 | *the Department of Transport* 交通部 **3** [C] one of the areas that sells a particular type of product in a large shop〔大商店的〕部: *the toy department* 玩具部 **4** one of the separate areas that some countries are divided into, for example in France〔法國等國家的〕行政區, 省 **5 be sb's department** *spoken* to be something that a particular person is responsible for【口】某人負責的事, 某人的職責範圍: *Don't ask me – cooking's John's department.* 別問我 —— 做飯是約翰的事。—see also 另見 FIRE DEPARTMENT, POLICE DEPARTMENT —**departmental** /ˌdɪpɑrtˋmɛntl̩; ˌdiːpɑːtˈmentl◂/ *adj*: *a departmental meeting* 部門會議 3 1

de·part·men·ta·lize also 又作 **-ise** *BrE*【英】/ˌdipɑrtˋmɛntl̩ˌaɪz; ˌdiːpɑːtˈmentl-aɪz/ *v* [T] to divide something into different departments 把〔某機構〕分成不同的部門: *Most large organizations are departmentalized.* 大多數大機構都被劃分成不同的部門。

department store /-ˈ-- ˌ-/ *n* [C] a large shop that is divided into separate departments, each selling a different type of goods 百貨商店, 百貨公司

de·par·ture /dɪˋpɑrtʃɚ; dɪˈpɑːtʃə/ *n* **1** [C,U] an act of leaving a place, especially at the start of a journey 離開, 起程: **[+for]** *I saw Simon shortly before his departure for Russia.* 在西門離開這兒去俄羅斯前不久我見過他。**2** [C,U] an act of leaving an organization or position 離職: *His sudden departure from the political scene took everyone by surprise.* 他從政治舞台上突然引退, 使每個人深感驚訝。**3** [C] a flight, train etc that leaves at a particular time〔航班、火車等的〕出發: *There are several departures for New York every day.* 每天有好幾個班次開往紐約。**4** [C] a way of doing something that is different from the usual, traditional, expected way〔對一般傳統的〕背離, 違反: **new/fresh/radical etc departure** (=a completely new and usually better way of doing something) 新的嘗試/根本上的不同〔通常指全新及較好的做事方式〕 *This approach represents a radical departure from previous policy.* 這種方法與以往的策略有着根本區別。—opposite 反義詞 ARRIVAL 3

departure lounge /-ˈ-- ˌ-/ *n* [C] the place at an airport where people wait until their plane is ready to leave〔飛機場的〕候機室

departures board /-ˈ-- ˌ-/ *n* [C] a board in an airport or station that shows the times at which planes or trains leave〔火車站的〕車次告示板; 〔飛機場的〕航班告示板

de·pend /dɪˋpɛnd; dɪˈpend/ *v* **it/that depends** *spoken* used to say that you cannot give a definite answer to something, because the answer could change according to what happens【口】那得看情況: *"Are you going to visit him?" "Well, it depends."* "你要去看他嗎?" "哦, 這要看情況。"

depend on/upon *phr v* [T] **1** to need the support, help, or existence of someone or something else 依靠, 依賴: *The country depends heavily on its tourist trade.* 這個國家在很大程度上依靠旅遊業。| *We depend en-*

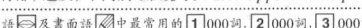

tirely on donations from the public. 我們完全依賴公眾的捐助。| **depend on sb/sth for** *Children depend on their parents for all of their material needs.* 孩子們依靠父母為他們提供所有的物質需要。| **depend on sb/sth to do sth** *I'm depending on you to get this done.* 我指望着你把這件事給辦了。| **depend on sb/sth doing sth** *We're depending on him finishing the job by Friday.* 我們指望着他在星期五前完成這項工作。**2** to trust or have confidence in someone or something 信賴, 相信: *You can depend on Jane – she always keeps her promises.* 你可以相信珍 —— 她一向都是信守諾言的。| **depend upon it** *spoken* (=you can be sure) 【口】請放心 *Depend upon it, he'll turn up.* 請放心, 他一定會來的。**3** [not in progressive 不用進行式] to change according to what else happens or whether something else changes 取決於..., 視...而定: *The length of the treatment depends on the severity of the illness.* 治療時間的長短取決於病情的嚴重程度。| **depending on** *The plant may grow to a height of several meters, depending on soil conditions.* 這種植物可以長到好幾米高, 視土壤條件而定。| **depend on who/what/how etc** *The amount you pay depends on where you live.* 付款多少取決於你居住的地區。

de·pen·da·ble /dɪˋpɛndəbl; dɪˈpendəbəl/ *adj* someone or something that is dependable can be trusted to do what you need or expect 可靠的, 可信賴的: *Ed Duncan was a dependable, hardworking detective.* 艾德·鄧肯是個可信賴的、勤奮的偵探。| *a dependable source of income* 可靠的收入來源 —**dependably** *adv* —**dependability** /dɪ,pɛndəˋbɪlətɪ; dɪ,pendəˈbɪləti/ *n* [U]

de·pen·dant /dɪˋpɛndənt; dɪˈpendənt/ *n* [C] someone, especially a child, who depends on you for food, clothes, money etc 依賴他人供養的人〔尤指孩子〕

de·pen·dence /dɪˋpɛndəns; dɪˈpendəns/ *n* [U] **1** a situation in which you depend on the help and support of someone or something else in order to exist or be successful 依賴, 依靠: **[+on/upon]** *We need to reduce our dependence on oil as a source of energy.* 我們需要減少對石油這種能源的依賴。—opposite 反義詞 INDEPENDENCE **2 drug/alcohol dependence** the state of being ADDICTED (1) to drugs or alcohol 毒癮/酒癮 **3** *formal* trust; RELIANCE 【正式】信任, 信賴: *I always place a lot of dependence on what she says.* 我總是很信賴她說的話。

de·pen·den·cy /dɪˋpɛndənsɪ; dɪˈpendənsi/ *n* **1** [U] a state of dependence 依靠, 依賴 **2** [C] a country that is controlled by another country 附屬國, 屬地

de·pen·dent /dɪˋpɛndənt; dɪˈpendənt/ *adj* **1** needing someone or something else in order to exist, be successful, be healthy etc 依賴的, 依靠的: *Do you have any dependent children?* 你有沒有需要扶養的孩子? | **be dependent on/upon sth (for)** *The young are totally dependent on their parents for food and shelter.* 小孩子完全依賴父母提供食宿。**2 drug/alcohol etc dependent** ADDICTED (1) to drugs, alcohol etc 有毒癮的/有酒癮的等 **3 be dependent on/upon** *formal* to change according to what else happens or whether something else changes 【正式】取決於: *How much you get paid is dependent on how much you produce.* 你賺多少錢取決於你產出多少。

dependent clause /.,.. ˈ./ *n* [C] a CLAUSE (2) in a sentence that gives information related to the main clause, but cannot exist alone 〔不能單獨存在的〕從屬子句, 從句

de·pict /dɪˋpɪkt; dɪˈpɪkt/ *v* [T] to describe something, especially in writing or pictures, in a way that gives a clear idea of a real situation 描寫, 描述, 描繪: *a book that depicts life in pre-revolutionary Russia* 描寫革命前俄國生活的一本書 —**depiction** /dɪˋpɪkʃən; dɪˈpɪkʃən/ *n* [C,U]

de·pil·a·to·ry /dɪˋpɪlə,torɪ; dɪˈpɪlətəri/ *n* [C] a substance that gets rid of unwanted hair from your body 脫毛劑 —**depilatory** *adj* [only before noun 僅用於名詞前] *Try one of our depilatory creams.* 試用一下我們的脫毛霜。

de·plete /dɪˋplit; dɪˈpliːt/ *v* [T usually passive 一般用被動態] to reduce the amount of something that is available 削減, 損耗: *Our food reserves had been severely depleted over the winter.* 經過了冬天, 我們的食物儲備已經消耗得差不多了。—**depletion** /dɪˋpliʃən; dɪˈpliːʃən/ *n* [U]: *the depletion of the ozone layer* 臭氧層的損耗

de·plor·a·ble /dɪˋplɔrəbl; dɪˈplɔːrəbəl/ *adj formal* very bad, unpleasant, and shocking 【正式】糟透的, 可悲的, 極可哀嘆的: *Conditions in the prison were deplorable.* 監獄的狀況糟透了。| *a deplorable waste of tax-payers' money* 對納稅人錢財的隨便浪費 —**deplorably** *adv*

de·plore /dɪˋplɔr; dɪˈplɔː/ *v* [T] to disapprove very strongly of something and criticize it severely, especially publicly 〔尤指公開地〕強烈反對; 譴責: *The UN deplored the invasion as a 'violation of international law'.* 聯合國譴責這次侵略行為“違反了國際法”。

de·ploy /dɪˋplɔɪ; dɪˈplɔɪ/ *v* [T] to organize people or things, especially soldiers, military equipment etc, so that they are in the right place and ready to be used 部署, 調度〔尤指士兵、軍事裝備等〕: *They decided it was time to deploy more troops.* 他們認為該是部署更多部隊的時候了。—**deployment** *n* [C,U]

de·pop·u·late /diˋpɑpjə,let; ,diːˈpɒpjʊleɪt/ *v* [T usually passive 一般用被動態] to greatly reduce the number of people living in a particular area 減少〔某一地區〕的人口: *Many rural areas were completely depopulated by the end of the century.* 到世紀末, 許多農村地區不再有人居住了。—**depopulation** /,dipɑpjəˋleʃən; diː,pɒpjʊˈleɪʃən/ *n* [U]

de·port /dɪˋport; dɪˈpɔːt/ *v* [T] **1** to make someone who is not a citizen of a particular country leave that country, especially because they do not have a legal right to stay 將〔尤其是沒有合法居住權的外國人〕驅逐出境 **2 deport yourself** *formal* to behave in a particular way, especially in the proper or correct way 【正式】表現得體

de·por·ta·tion /,diporˋteʃən; ,diːpɔːˈteɪʃən/ *n* [C,U] the act of deporting someone 驅逐出境: *a deportation order* 驅逐出境令

de·por·tee /,diporˋti; ,diːpɔːˈtiː/ *n* [C] someone who has been deported or is going to be deported 〔將要〕被驅逐出境的人

de·port·ment /dɪˋportmənt; dɪˈpɔːtmənt/ *n* [U] **1** *especially BrE* the way that someone stands and walks 【尤英】舉止, 儀態, 風度: *As a girl, she had lessons in elocution and deportment.* 她小時候曾上過言談技巧課和儀態課。**2** *old-fashioned especially AmE* the way that a person, especially a young woman, behaves in public 【過時, 尤美】〔尤指女孩在公共場合的〕行為, 舉止

de·pose /dɪˋpoz; dɪˈpəʊz/ *v* [T] **1** to remove a king, queen, or ruler from a position of power 罷免, 廢黜〔國王、王后或統治者〕: *The army was threatening to depose him.* 軍隊威脅說要罷黜他。**2** *law* to officially give information about something, after you have promised to tell the truth 【法律】宣誓作證

de·pos·it[1] /dɪˋpɑzɪt; dɪˈpɒzɪt/ *n* [C]

1 ►SUM OF MONEY 金額◄ the first part of the money for a house, car, holiday etc, that you pay so that it will be kept for you 〔購屋、買車、度假等的〕定金, 頭款, 首期: **put down a deposit (on)** (=pay a deposit) 付定金 *We put down a deposit on a house last week.* 上週我們付了房子的定金。

2 ►RENT 租用◄ money that you pay when you rent or HIRE something, which will be given back if you do not damage the thing you are renting or hiring 〔租用東西的〕押金, 保證金: *You will have to pay one month's rent in advance, plus a deposit of $500.* 你得預付一個月的租金, 外加500美元的押金。

3 ►BANK 銀行◄ an amount of money that is paid into a bank account 存款: **make a deposit** *I'd like to make a deposit, please.* 我想辦理一下存款。

4 ►SOIL/MINERALS 土壤/礦物質◄ a layer of a

mineral, metal etc that is left in soil or rocks through a natural process 礦牀: *rich deposits of gold in the hills* 山裡豐富的金礦牀
5 ►LAYER 層◄ an amount or layer of a substance that gradually develops in a particular place 沉積物, 沉積層: *fatty deposits on the heart* 心臟上澱積的油脂層
6 ►ELECTION 選舉◄ money paid by someone who is a CANDIDATE (1) in a political election in Britain, that will be returned to them if they get enough votes 選舉保證金〔在英國參加政治選舉的候選人付的保證金, 如果候選人得到足夠的選票, 保證金將發還給他〕: **lose your deposit** (=not get enough votes)〔因選票不夠而〕失去保證金

deposit² *v* **1** [T always+adv/prep] *formal* to put something down in a particular place【正式】把〔某物〕放在〔某地〕: **[+on/in/by etc]** *The female deposits her eggs directly into the water.* 這種雌性動物把卵直接產在水中。**2** [T] to leave a layer of a substance on the surface of something 沉積: *As the river slows down, it deposits a layer of soil.* 河流流速變慢時, 一層泥沙便沉積下來。**3** [T] to put money or something valuable in a bank or other place where it will be safe 將〔錢等貴重物品〕存入〔銀行或其他安全的地方〕: *You are advised to deposit your valuables in the hotel safe.* 建議您把貴重物品存到旅館的保險箱裡。

deposit ac·count /ˈ·· ·,·/ *n* [C] *especially BrE* a bank account that pays INTEREST¹ (4) on condition that you keep money there for a particular length of time【尤英】定期存款賬戶 —compare 比較 CHECKING ACCOUNT, CURRENT ACCOUNT

dep·o·si·tion /ˌdɛpəˋzɪʃən; ˌdepəˈzɪʃən/ *n* **1** [C] *law* a statement written for a court of law, by someone who has promised to tell the truth【法律】〔經宣誓為真實的〕證詞 **2** [U] *technical* the natural process of depositing a substance in rocks or soil【術語】沉澱, 沉積 **3** [C,U] the act of removing someone from a position of power 罷免, 廢黜

de·pos·i·tor /dɪˋpɑzɪtɚ; dɪˈpɒzɪ̈tə/ *n* [C] someone who puts money in a bank or other financial organization 存款人, 存戶

de·pos·i·to·ry /dɪˋpɑzəˌtorɪ; dɪˈpɒzɪ̈təri/ *n* [C] a place where something can be safely kept〔可以安全存放物品的〕貯藏室, 倉庫 —**depository** *adj*

deposit slip /·ˈ·· ·/ *n* [C] *AmE* a form that you use to pay money into your bank account【美】存款單; PAYING-IN SLIP *BrE*【英】

dep·ot /ˋdipo; ˈdepəʊ/ *n* [C] **1** a place where goods are stored until they are needed 倉庫, 儲存處, 貨場 **2** a place where buses are kept and repaired〔公共汽車的〕車庫; 修車場 **3** *AmE* a railway station or bus station, especially a small one【美】〔尤指小規模的〕火車站; 公共汽車站

de·prave /dɪˋprev; dɪˈpreɪv/ *v* [T] *formal* to be an evil influence on someone, especially someone who is young or not very experienced【正式】使道德敗壞〔尤指對年青人或缺乏經驗者的不良影響〕—**depravity** /dɪˋprævətɪ; dɪˈprævɪ̈ti/ *n* [U]: *scenes of depravity* 腐化墮落的場面 —**depravation** /ˌdɛprəˋveʃən; ˌdeprəˈveɪʃən/ *n* [U]

de·praved /dɪˋprevd; dɪˈpreɪvd/ *adj* completely evil or morally unacceptable 墮落的, 腐化的, 道德敗壞的: *a vicious and depraved man* 一個惡毒、墮落的人

dep·re·cate /ˋdɛprəˌket; ˈdeprɪ̈keɪt/ *v* [T] *formal* to strongly disapprove of or criticize something【正式】堅決反對; 強烈批評 —**deprecation** /ˌdɛprəˋkeʃən; ˌdeprɪ̈ˈkeɪʃən/ *n* [U]

dep·re·cat·ing /ˋdɛprəˌketɪŋ; ˈdeprɪ̈keɪtɪŋ/ also 又作 **dep·re·ca·to·ry** /ˋdɛprəkəˌtorɪ; ˈdeprɪ̈keɪtəri/ *adj* **1** expressing criticism or disapproval 批評的; 反對的, 不贊成的: *She made several deprecating remarks about my dress sense.* 她好幾次對我的穿着品味頗有微詞。**2** words or actions that are deprecating are intended to make someone feel less annoyed or disapproving〔話語、行動〕意在使人不那麼生氣的; 抱歉的; 求恕的: *"He's not here at the moment," She said with a deprecating smile.* "他現在不在這兒。"她抱歉地笑一笑說。—see also 另見 SELF-DEPRECATING —**deprecatingly** *adv*

de·pre·ci·ate /dɪˋpriʃɪˌet; dɪˈpriːʃieɪt/ *v* **1** [I] to decrease in value or price 貶值, 跌價: *A new car will depreciate quite fast.* 新車往往很快就跌價。—opposite 反義詞 APPRECIATE (4) **2** [T] *formal* to make something seem unimportant【正式】貶低〔重要性〕

de·pre·ci·a·tion /dɪˌpriʃɪˋeʃən; dɪˌpriːʃiˈeɪʃən/ *n* [U] a reduction in the value or price of something 貶值, 跌價: *the depreciation of the dollar* 美元的貶值 —**depreciatory** /dɪˋpriʃɪəˌtorɪ; dɪˈpriːʃiətəri/ *adj*

dep·re·da·tion /ˌdɛprɪˋdeʃən; ˌdeprɪ̈ˈdeɪʃən/ *n* [C often plural 常用複數] *formal* an act of cruelty, violence, or destruction【正式】蹂躪, 破壞

de·press /dɪˋprɛs; dɪˈpres/ *v* [T] **1** to make someone feel very unhappy 使憂愁, 使抑鬱: *The thought of having to take the exam again depressed him.* 想到又要參加考試讓他心情沮喪。**2** to prevent something from working properly or being as active as it usually is 使不能正常運轉, 使不活躍, 使不景氣: *Several factors combined to depress the American economy.* 幾個因素合在一起使美國的經濟不景氣。**3** *formal* to press something down, especially a part of a machine【正式】按下, 壓下, 推下〔尤指機器的一部分〕: *Depress the clutch fully.* 把離合器踩到底。**4** *formal* to reduce the value of prices or wages【正式】減少, 降低〔價格或工資〕: *Competition between workers will depress wage levels.* 工人們之間的競爭將會降低工資水平。

de·press·ant /dɪˋprɛsn̩t; dɪˈpresənt/ *n* [C] a substance or drug that makes your body's processes slower and makes you feel very relaxed or sleepy 抑制劑, 抑制藥 —compare 比較 STIMULANT —**depressant** *adj*

de·pressed /dɪˋprɛst; dɪˈprest/ *adj* **1 a)** feeling very unhappy 憂愁的, 消沉的, 沮喪的: *She felt lonely and depressed.* 她感到孤獨和沮喪。| **[+about/at]** *Carter seemed depressed about the situation.* 卡特似乎對形勢感到憂慮。**b)** suffering from a medical condition in which you are so unhappy that you cannot live a normal life 患抑鬱症的 **2** an area, industry etc that is depressed does not have enough economic or business activity〔地區、工業等〕不景氣的, 蕭條的, 經濟困難的 **3** a depressed level or amount is lower than normal 低於一般水準的: *During the illness certain hormone levels are depressed.* 患病期間, 某些荷爾蒙水平低於一般水準。

de·press·ing /dɪˋprɛsɪŋ; dɪˈpresɪŋ/ *adj* making you feel very sad 令人憂愁的, 令人沮喪的: *I found the whole experience very depressing.* 我覺得這整個經歷非常令人沮喪。| *It's a depressing thought.* 這是個令人沮喪的想法。—**depressingly** *adv*: *a depressingly familiar story* 令人憂傷的熟悉故事

de·pres·sion /dɪˋprɛʃən; dɪˈpreʃən/ *n* **1** [C,U] **a)** a feeling of sadness that makes you think there is no hope for the future 憂傷, 沮喪, 消沉: *She was overcome by depression.* 她抑鬱成疾。| **deep/severe depression** *Peter fell into a deep depression on hearing the news.* 彼得聽到這個消息後極度沮喪。**b)** a medical condition that makes you so unhappy and anxious you cannot live a normal life 抑鬱症 **2 a)** [C,U] a long period during which there is very little business activity and lots of people do not have jobs 經濟蕭條期, 不景氣時期: *the long years of economic depression* 多年的經濟蕭條 —compare 比較 RECESSION **3 the Depression** the period when there was not much business activity and not many jobs in the 1930s 大蕭條〔20世紀30年代的經濟不景氣〕**4** [C] a part of a surface that is lower than the other parts 窪地, 坑: *The rain had collected in several depressions on the ground.* 地面上的幾處窪地都積了雨水。**5** [C] *technical* a mass of air that has a low pressure and usually causes rain【術語】低氣壓〔通常會導致下雨〕 3 3

de·press·ive¹ /dɪˋprɛsɪv; dɪˈpresɪv/ *adj* often feeling

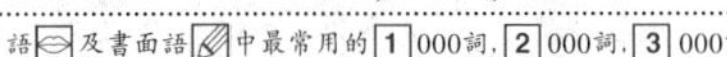
口語 及書面語 中最常用的 1 000詞, 2 000詞, 3 000詞

DEPRESSED 抑鬱的, 沮喪的

depressive² *n* [C] someone who suffers from DEPRESSION 抑鬱症患者

dep·ri·va·tion /ˌdɛprɪˋveʃən; ˌdeprɨˈveɪʃən/ *n* **1** [C usually plural 一般用複數] something you need or usually have that you are prevented from having 喪失, 剝奪: *People suffered terrible deprivations during the war.* 戰爭期間, 人們遭受了嚴重的損失。**2** [U] a lack of something that you need or want 缺少, 缺乏: *Sleep deprivation can result in mental disorders.* 睡眠不足會導致精神疾病。

de·prive /dɪˋpraɪv; dɪˈpaɪv/ *v*

deprive sb **of** sth *phr v* [T often passive 常用被動態] to take something from someone, especially something that they need or want 剝奪: *A lot of these children have been deprived of a normal home life.* 這些孩子中有許多人被剝奪了正常的家庭生活。

de·prived /dɪˋpraɪvd; dɪˈpraɪvd/ *adj* not having the things that are considered to be necessary for a comfortable or happy life 貧困的, 窮苦的: *a deprived childhood* 貧苦的童年

de·pro·gram /diˋprogræm; ˌdiːˈprəʊgræm/ *v* [T] to help someone who has been involved in a religious CULT to stop obeying its orders and to start thinking for themselves again 使被洗腦者覺醒, 反洗腦〔旨在消除宗教崇拜〕

dept the written abbreviation of 縮寫= DEPARTMENT

3 3 **depth** /dɛpθ; depθ/ *n*

1 ►DISTANCE 距離◄ [C usually singular 一般用單數, U] **a)** the distance down from the top surface to the bottom of something〔從頂部到底部的〕深, 深度: *What depth is the lake?* 這湖水有多深? | **to/at a depth of** *Plant the seeds at a depth of ten centimetres.* 把種子種到十厘米深的地方。| **a metre/foot etc in depth** *The pond is no more than a metre in depth.* 這個池塘最多一米深。**b)** the distance from the front to the back of an object〔從前端到後端的〕深度, 縱深: *The depth of the shelves is about 35cm.* 擱板大約有35厘米寬。

2 ►EMOTION/SITUATION 情感/形勢◄ [U] how strong an emotion is or how serious a situation is〔表明情感的〕強烈程度,〔情形的〕嚴重程度: *Lawmakers underestimated the depth of public feeling on this issue.* 立法人員低估了公眾在這個問題上的敏感程度。

3 ►KNOWLEDGE 知識◄ [U] *approving* the quality of knowing or giving a lot of details about a subject【褒】深度: *I was impressed by the depth and complexity of the book.* 這本書的深度和複雜性給我印象很深。| *The network's news coverage lacks depth.* 網絡上的新聞報道缺乏深度。| **in depth** (=considering all the details) 完全地, 徹底地, 深入地 *We'll need to study the report in some depth.* 我們需要比較深入地研究這個報告。—see also 另見 IN-DEPTH

4 be out of your depth a) to be involved in a situation or activity that is too difficult for you to understand 非…所能理解, 非…力所能及: *I felt completely out of my depth when they started discussing philosophy.* 他們一討論哲學, 我就感到一竅不通了。**b)** to be in water that is too deep for you to stand in and be able to breathe 在深得不能站立並呼吸的水中

5 be in the depths of despair/depression etc to feel very unhappy 深感絕望/沮喪等

6 the depths of the countryside/forest etc the middle of a place where there are not many people 偏遠的鄉村/森林深處等

7 the depths of winter the middle of winter, especially when it is very cold 隆冬

8 hidden depths a part of someone's character that you do not notice when you first meet them 深藏不露: *I didn't know she wrote poems – she obviously has hidden depths.* 我不知道她會寫詩——很顯然她是深藏不露。

9 ►SEA 大海◄ **the depths** *literary* the deepest parts of the sea【文】深海

depth charge /ˈ· ·/ *n* [C] a bomb that explodes at a particular depth under water 深水炸彈

dep·u·ta·tion /ˌdɛpjəˋteʃən; ˌdepjʊˈteɪʃən/ *n* [C] a group of people who are sent to talk to someone in authority, as representatives of a larger group〔較大的羣體推選出來與當權者談判的〕代表團

de·pute /dɪˋpjut; dɪˈpjuːt/ *v* [T] **depute sb to do sth** *formal* to tell or allow someone to do something instead of you【正式】委派某人做某事, 委派某人為代表

dep·u·tize also 又作 **-ise** *BrE*【英】/ˋdɛpjəˌtaɪz; ˈdepjʊtaɪz/ *v* [I] to do the work of someone of a higher rank than you for a short time because they are unable to do it 充當〔職位比自己高的人的〕代表: **[+for]** *Who's going to deputize for Liam while he's away?* 利亞姆不在的時候, 將由誰代理他的工作?

dep·u·ty /ˋdɛpjətɪ; ˈdepjʊti/ *n* [C] **1** someone who is directly below a manager in rank, and who is officially in 2
charge when the manager is not there〔經理的〕副手;〔經理不在時負責工作的〕代理人 **2** a member of the LOWER HOUSE of parliament in some countries, for example France〔某些國家如法國的〕下議院議員 **3** someone whose job is to help a SHERIFF (1) in the US 美國縣治安官的助理: *On the third day, a deputy unlocked my cell.* 第三天的時候, 治安官的助手打開了我住的牢房。

de·rail /dɪˋrel; ˌdiːˈreɪl/ *v* **1** [usually passive 一般用被動態] to make a train go off the railway line 使〔火車〕出軌 **2** [T] to spoil or interrupt a plan, agreement etc 破壞, 干擾〔計劃、協議等〕: *The dispute has temporarily derailed the arms control agreement.* 這項爭端暫時破壞了軍備控制協議。—**derailment** *n* [C,U]

de·ranged /dɪˋrendʒd; dɪˈreɪndʒd/ *adj* behaving in a crazy or dangerous way 精神失常的, 瘋狂的 —**derangement** *n* [C,U]

der·by /ˋdɝbɪ; ˈdɑːbi/ *n* [C] **1** *AmE* a man's round hard hat that is usually black【美】常禮帽〔一種男用硬質圓頂帽, 通常為黑色〕; **bowler hat** (BOWLER (2)) *BrE*【英】—see picture at 參見 HAT 圖 **2** *BrE* a sports match between two teams from the same area or city【英】〔同一地區或城市的兩隊之間進行的〕體育比賽 **3** a race that anyone can enter 賽跑, 競賽: *a donkey derby* 騎驢大賽 **4** *AmE* a type of horse race【美】賽馬

de·reg·u·late /diˋrɛgjəˌlet; ˌdiːˈregjʊleɪt/ *v* [T] to remove government rules and controls from some types of business activity 撤銷政府對…的管制: *Data communications have largely been deregulated in Europe.* 在歐洲已經廣泛解除對數據交流的管制。—**deregulation** /diˌrɛgjəˋleʃən; diːˌregjʊˈleɪʃən/ *n* [U]

der·e·lict¹ /ˋdɛrəˌlɪkt; ˈderɨlɪkt/ *adj* a building or piece of land that is derelict is in very bad condition because it has not been used for a long time〔建築物、土地〕破舊的, 棄置的

derelict² *n* [C] someone who has no money or home and who has to live on the streets 無家可歸的窮人, 流浪者, 遊民

der·e·lic·tion /ˌdɛrəˋlɪkʃən; ˌderɨˈlɪkʃən/ *n* **1 dereliction of duty** *formal* failure to do what you should do as part of your job【正式】失職, 玩忽職守, 瀆職 **2** [U] the state of being derelict 破舊, 棄置

de·ride /dɪˋraɪd; dɪˈraɪd/ *v* [T] *formal* to make remarks or jokes that show you think someone or something is silly or useless【正式】嘲笑, 嘲弄, 譏諷: *You shouldn't deride their efforts.* 你不應該嘲笑他們的努力。| **deride sb as sth** *Wayne was derided as a mere playboy.* 人們嘲笑韋恩, 說他只不過是個花花公子。

de ri·gueur /də riˋgɝ; də riːˈgɜː/ *adj* [not before noun 不用於名詞前] *French* considered to be necessary if you want to be fashionable【法】〔按照禮節、時尚等〕要求的, 必需的; 符合時尚的: *Hats are de rigueur at society weddings.* 在上流社會的婚禮上一定要戴禮帽。

de·ri·sion /dɪˋrɪʒən; dɪˈrɪʒən/ *n* [U] remarks that show you think someone or something is stupid or silly 嘲笑, 嘲弄: *There was a note of derision in his voice.* 他的聲

音裡有一種嘲弄的語氣。

de·ri·sive /dɪˋraɪsɪv; dɪˈraɪsɪv/ *adj* showing that you think someone or something is stupid or silly 嘲笑的, 嘲弄的: *derisive laughter* 嘲弄的笑聲 —**derisively** *adv*

de·ri·so·ry /dɪˋraɪsərɪ; dɪˈraɪsəri/ *adj* **1** an amount of money that is derisory is so small that it is not worth considering seriously〔錢〕微不足道的, 少得可憐的: *Unions described the pay offer as derisory.* 工會稱工資開價低得可憐。**2** derisive 嘲笑的, 嘲弄的: *derisory comments* 嘲弄的評論 —**derisorily** *adv*

de·riv·able /dɪˋraɪvəbḷ; dɪˈraɪvəbəl/ *adj formal* something that is derivable can be calculated from something else【正式】可派生的, 可推論出的

der·i·va·tion /ˌdɛrəˋveʃən; ˌderɪ̸ˈveɪʃən/ *n* **1** [C,U] the origin of something, especially a word〔尤指詞語的〕起源, 出處: *the derivation of place names* 地名的起源 **2** [C] a word that comes from another word or language 派生詞

de·riv·a·tive¹ /dɪˋrɪvətɪv; dɪˈrɪvətɪv/ *n* [C] something that has developed or been produced from something else 派生物, 提取物, 製成物: **[+of]** *Heroin is a derivative of morphine.* 海洛因是嗎啡的提取物。

derivative² *adj* not new or invented, but copied or taken from something else 非獨創的, 模仿他人的: *a largely derivative text* 大部分蹈襲他人的文章

de·rive /dɪˋraɪv; dɪˈraɪv/ *v* **1** [T] to get something, usually a pleasant feeling, from something or someone 得到, 獲得〔通常是愉快的感受〕: **derive sth from** *He derived some comfort from the fact that he wasn't the only one to fail the exam.* 得知自己並不是唯一沒通過考試的人時他得到了一些安慰。**2** [I] to develop or come from something else 源自, 源於: **[+from]** *This word is derived from Latin.* 這個詞來源於拉丁文。**3** [T] *technical* to get a chemical substance from another substance【術語】提取〔化學物質〕

der·ma·ti·tis /ˌdɝməˋtaɪtɪs; ˌdɜːməˈtaɪtɪ̸s/ *n* [U] a disease of the skin that causes redness, swelling, and pain 皮(膚)炎

der·ma·tol·o·gy /ˌdɝməˋtɑlədʒɪ; ˌdɜːməˈtɒlədʒi/ *n* [U] the part of medical science that deals with the skin, its diseases, and their treatment 皮膚學, 皮膚病學 —**dermatologist** *n* [C]

de·rog·ate /ˋdɛrəˌget; ˈderəgeɪt/ *v*

derogate from sth *phr v* [T] *formal* to make something seem less important or less good【正式】貶低, 貶損

de·rog·a·to·ry /dɪˋrɑgəˌtorɪ; dɪˈrɒgətəri/ *adj* insulting and disapproving 侮辱的, 貶義的: **derogatory remark/comment/term etc** *Many gay men still regard 'queer' as a very derogatory term.* 許多男同性戀者仍然認為 queer 是個極具侮辱性的詞語。—**derogatorily** *adv*

der·rick /ˋdɛrɪk; ˈderɪk/ *n* [C] **1** a tall machine used for lifting heavy weights, used especially on ships〔尤指輪船上的〕桅杆起重機 **2** a tall tower built over an oil well to raise and lower the DRILL¹ (1) 油井架, 鑽塔

der·riè·re /ˌdɛrɪˋɛr; ˈderieə/ *n* [C] *humorous* your bottom【幽默】臀部: *sitting around on your derriere* 閒坐着

der·ring-do /ˋdɛrɪŋ ˋdu; ˌderɪŋ ˈduː/ *n* [U] **deeds/acts etc of derring-do** *humorous* very brave actions like the ones that happen in adventure stories【幽默】英勇事蹟

derv /dɝv; dɜːv/ *n* [U] *trademark BrE* an oil product like petrol that is used in DIESEL ENGINES【商標, 英】柴油, 重油

der·vish /ˋdɝvɪʃ; ˈdɜːvɪʃ/ *n* [C] a member of a Muslim religious group, some of whom dance fast and spin around as part of a religious ceremony〔伊斯蘭教的〕托鉢僧, 苦行僧〔有些在宗教儀式上跳快速旋轉舞〕

de·sal·i·nate /diˋsæləˌnet; diːˈsælɪ̸neɪt/ *v* [T] to remove the salt from sea water so that it can be used in homes and factories 使〔海水〕脫鹽 —**desalination** /diˌsæləˋneʃən; diːˌsælɪ̸ˈneɪʃən/ *n* [U]

de·scale /diˋskel; ˌdiːˈskeɪl/ *v* [T] to remove the white substance that forms on the inside of pipes, KETTLES etc 除去〔管道和水壺等內壁上的〕水垢[水鏽]

des·cant /ˋdɛskænt; ˈdeskænt/ *n* [C,U] a tune that is played or sung above the main tune in a piece of music 高音部, 上方聲部

de·scend /dɪˋsɛnd; dɪˈsend/ *v* **1** [I,T] *formal* to move from a higher level to a lower one【正式】下來, 下降: *The plane started to descend.* 飛機開始降落。| **[+from]** *He descended slowly from the railway carriage.* 他慢慢地從火車車廂中走下來。| **descend sth** *Mrs Danvers descended the stairs.* 丹弗斯太太走下樓梯。—opposite 反義詞 ASCEND **2** [I] *literary* if darkness, night etc descends, it begins to get dark【文】〔黑暗、夜幕等〕降臨 **3 in descending order** numbers, choices etc that are in descending order are arranged from the highest or most important to the lowest or least important 降序排列〔按照從大到小或從最重要的到最次要的順序排列〕

descend from sth *phr v* [T] **1** to have developed from something that existed in the past 從〔過去的東西〕繼承下來, 傳下來: *These ideas descend from those of the ancient philosophers.* 這些觀點是從古代哲學家的觀點中傳承下來的。**2 be descended from sb** to be related to someone who lived a long time ago 為某人的後裔: *My mother claims she is descended from Abraham Lincoln.* 媽媽聲稱自己是亞伯拉罕·林肯的後代。

descend on/upon sb/sth *phr v* [T] **1** if a feeling descends on someone, they begin to feel it 使感覺到: *Gloom descended on the office when we heard the news.* 我們聽到這個消息時, 辦公室裡立即愁雲籠罩。**2** *informal* if a large number of people descend on you, they come to your home【非正式】突然造訪: *My in-laws are descending on us this weekend.* 我的親家們忽然這個週末要來我們家。

descend to sth *phr v* [T] to behave or speak in an unpleasant way that is not what people expect from you 自降身分到…, 墮落到…: **descend to (doing) sth** *I refused to descend to petty personal attacks.* 我拒絕降低身分去進行卑劣的人身攻擊。| **descend to sb's level** (=behave or speak in the same unpleasant way as someone else) 墮落到和某人一樣的水平

de·scen·dant /dɪˋsɛndənt; dɪˈsendənt/ *n* [C] someone who is related to a person who lived a long time ago 後代, 後裔: **direct descendant** (=from one father or mother to the next) 直系後代 *He reckons he's a direct descendant of Napoleon Bonaparte.* 他推算自己是拿破侖·波拿巴的嫡系後代。—compare 比較 ANCESTOR (1)

de·scent /dɪˋsɛnt; dɪˈsent/ *n* **1** [C,U] *formal* the process of going down【正式】下降, 降落: *Passengers must fasten their seat belts prior to descent.* 乘客在飛機降落之前必須繫好安全帶。**2** [C] a path or road that goes steeply downwards〔陡峭下行的〕下坡路: *a slippery descent* 滑溜的下坡路 **3** [U] your family origins, especially in connection with the country that you come from 出身, 血統: **by descent** *They're Irish by descent.* 他們祖籍是愛爾蘭。| **be of Russian/Chinese etc descent** *She's of German descent.* 她祖籍德國。**4** [singular] a gradual change towards behaviour that is wrong or not acceptable 淪落, 墮落: **[+into]** *her descent into a life of crime* 她墮入犯罪生涯 **5** [singular] a sudden unwanted visit or attack〔不受歡迎的〕突然到訪, 突襲: *the descent on the town by a motorcycle gang* 一羣摩托車幫夥對城鎮的突襲

de·scribe /dɪˋskraɪb; dɪˈskraɪb/ *v* [T] **1** to say what something or someone is like by giving details about them 描述, 描寫, 敍述, 形容: *The police asked her to describe the two men.* 警察叫她描述一下那兩個人。| *An alternative approach to the problem is described in Chapter 3.* 這個問題的另一種解決方法在第3章有所闡述。| **describe how/why/what etc** *It's difficult to describe how I feel.* 很難形容我的感受。| **describe sb/sth as** *Sarah described him as shy.* 莎拉説他很害羞。| **describe sb/** [1] [1]

sth to sb *So describe this new boyfriend to me!* 那麼，和我詳細說說你的新男朋友吧！| **describe doing sth** *He described going downstairs and finding his mother lying on the floor.* 他描述下樓時發現他媽媽躺在地板上。—see 見 SPEAK (USAGE) **2** *formal* to make a shape in the air by moving your hands in a particular way【正式】〔用手在空中〕劃出〔某種形狀〕: *Her hand described a circle in the air.* 她用手在空中劃了一個圓圈。

2 **de·scrip·tion** /dɪˋskrɪpʃən; dɪˈskrɪpʃən/ *n* **1** [C,U] a
2 piece of writing or speech that says what someone or something is like 描述, 描寫, 敍述, 形容: *Berlin sounds fascinating from your description.* 從你的敍述來看, 柏林好像是個迷人的城市。| **detailed/accurate description** *The police have issued a detailed description of the missing woman.* 警察已經發布了這個失蹤婦女的詳細描述資料。| **give a description** *I gave them a description of my car.* 我給他們形容了一下我的汽車。| **brief/general description** *a brief description of what the job involves* 對這項工作內容的簡要說明 | **full/complete description** *I'll need a full description of the stolen property.* 我需要一份被竊財產的完整描述資料。| **answer/fit a description** (=be like the person or thing described) 和所描述的相吻合 *A man fitting that description was seen outside the bank.* 有人在銀行外面看到一名與所描述特徵相符的男子。**2 be beyond/past description** to be too good, bad, big etc to be described easily 無法形容, 難以描述: *I found the play boring beyond description.* 我覺得這部戲乏味得無法形容。**3** [C] a type of thing, person etc 種類, 類型: **of every/some/that etc description** *flowers and plants of every description* 各種各樣的花和植物 | **of all descriptions** *People of all descriptions came to see the show.* 形形色色的人都來觀看演出。

D

This graph shows some of the words most commonly used with the noun **description**. 本圖表所示為含有名詞 description 的一些最常用詞組。

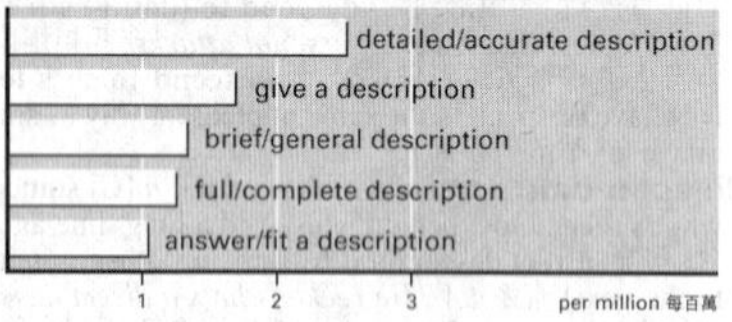

detailed/accurate description
give a description
brief/general description
full/complete description
answer/fit a description
1 2 3 per million 每百萬

Based on the British National Corpus and the Longman Lancaster Corpus
據英國國家語料庫和朗文蘭卡斯特語料庫

de·scrip·tive /dɪˋskrɪptɪv; dɪˈskrɪptɪv/ *adj* **1** giving a description of something in words or pictures 描寫的, 描繪的: *The book is full of descriptive passages.* 這本書中有許多描寫的段落。**2** *technical* describing how the words of a language are actually used, rather than saying how they ought to be used【術語】描寫性的〔描述詞語的使用情況而不規定它們該如何使用〕—**descriptively** *adv* —**descriptiveness** *n* [U]

de·scry /dɪˋskraɪ; dɪˈskraɪ/ *v* [T] *literary* to notice or see something, especially when it is a long way away【文】〔尤指從遠處〕遙望到, 眺望到

des·e·crate /ˋdɛsɪˌkret; ˈdesɪkreɪt/ *v* [T] to spoil or damage something holy 褻瀆〔聖物〕—**desecration** /ˌdɛsɪˋkreʃən; ˌdesɪˈkreɪʃən/ *n* [U]

de·seg·re·gate /diˋsɛgrɪˌget; diːˈsegrɪgeɪt/ *v* [T] to end a system by which people of different races are kept separate 廢除…的種族隔離制度 —**desegregation** /diˌsɛgrəˋgeʃən; ˌdiːsegrɪˈgeɪʃən/ *n* [U]

de·se·lect /ˌdisəˋlɛkt; ˌdiːsəˈlekt/ *v* [T] **1** to remove something from a list of choices on a computer〔在電腦上〕刪除 **2** *BrE* to refuse to choose an existing Member of Parliament as a CANDIDATE (1) at the next election【英】否決〔現任議員〕擔任下屆候選人 —**deselection** /-ˋlɛkʃən; -ˈlekʃən/ *n* [U]

de·sen·si·tize also 又作 **-ise** *BrE*【英】/diˋsɛnsəˌtaɪz; diːˈsensɪtaɪz/ *v* [T] **1** to make someone react less strongly to something by making them become used to it〔通過使之習慣於某事物〕使〔某人〕變得不敏感: **[+to]** *Many children have become desensitized to violence.* 許多孩子對暴力已變得麻木了。**2** *technical* to make photographic material less sensitive to light【術語】使減少感光度 —**desensitization** /diˌsɛnsətəˋzeʃən; diːˌsensɪtaɪˈzeɪʃən/ *n* [U]

des·ert¹ /ˋdɛzɚt; ˈdezət/ *n* **1** [C,U] a large area of sand where it is always very hot and dry 沙漠, 荒漠: *the Sahara Desert* 撒哈拉沙漠 **2** [C] a place where there is no activity or where nothing interesting happens 荒涼的地方: *a cultural desert* 文化沙漠

de·sert² /dɪˋzɝt; dɪˈzɜːt/ *v* **1** [T] to leave someone alone and refuse to help or support them any more 遺棄, 拋棄, 離棄: *Mike just deserted her when she got pregnant.* 她懷孕後, 邁克就乾脆拋棄了她。**2** [T] to leave a place so that it is completely empty 捨棄, 離開〔某地〕: *They deserted their homes and fled to the hills.* 他們捨棄家園, 逃到山上。**3** [T] if a feeling or quality deserts you, you no longer have it, especially at a time when you need it 喪失, 失去〔感覺、品質〕: *Mike's confidence seemed to have deserted him.* 邁克似乎喪失了信心。**4** [I+**from**] to leave the army without permission 擅自離開〔軍隊〕

de·sert·er /dɪˋzɝtɚ; dɪˈzɜːtə/ *n* [C] a soldier who leaves the army without permission 逃兵

de·ser·tion /dɪˋzɝʃən; dɪˈzɜːʃən/ *n* **1** [C,U] the act of leaving the army without permission 開小差, 擅離軍隊 **2** [U] *law* the act of leaving your wife or husband because you do not want to live with them any longer【法律】遺棄

desert is·land /ˌ‥ ˈ‥/ *n* [C] a small tropical island far from other places with no people living on it〔熱帶地區的〕荒島

deserts /dɪˋzɝts; dɪˈzɜːts/ *n* **get your just deserts** to be punished in a way that you deserve 得到應得的懲罰, 罪有應得

de·serve /dɪˋzɝv; dɪˈzɜːv/ *v* [T] **1** to have earned something by good or bad actions or behaviour 應得, 應受到〔獎賞或懲罰〕: *You've been working all morning – I think you deserve a rest.* 你已經工作了一早上——我想你該歇歇了。| **deserve to do sth** *The team deserves to win.* 這個隊該贏。| **deserve it** *Yeah, I hit him but he deserved it.* 對, 我打了他, 但是他該打。| **get what you deserve** (=be punished or have something unpleasant happen in a way that you deserve) 罪有應得 | **deserve all you get** (=deserve any unpleasant things that may happen to you) 受到這一切是理所應當的 | **deserve better** (=deserve more pleasant treatment or situations than you are getting) 該得到更好一些的待遇 **2 deserve consideration/attention etc** if a suggestion, idea, or plan deserves consideration etc, it is good or sensible enough to be considered〔建議、觀點、計劃〕值得考慮/注意等: *These proposals deserve serious consideration.* 這些建議值得認真考慮。**3 deserve a medal** *spoken* used to say that you admire the way someone dealt with a situation or problem【口】該賞一枚勳章〔表示欣賞某人應付某種局面或處理某個問題的方式〕: *You deserve a medal for putting up with Phil for so long!* 你能忍耐菲爾這麼久, 真應該賞你一枚勳章！

de·served /dɪˋzɝvd; dɪˈzɜːvd/ *adj* earned because of good or bad behaviour, skill, work etc 應得的, 理所當然的; 該受的: *a well-deserved result* 完全應得的結果

de·serv·ed·ly /dɪˋzɝvɪdlɪ; dɪˈzɜːvɪdli/ *adv* **1** in a way that is right or deserved 正當地, 應得地, 理所當然地: *Her novels have been, quite deservedly, very successful.* 她的小說一直非常成功, 她受之無愧。**2 deservedly so** used to show that you agree that something is right and deserved 理應如此: *She is widely respected in the music world, and deservedly so.* 她在音樂

圈子裡廣受尊敬, 也理應如此。

de·serv·ing /dɪˋzɝvɪŋ; dɪˈzɜːvɪŋ/ *adj* **1** needing help and support, especially financial support〔尤指經濟上的支持〕應得的, 值得的: *Grants will only be awarded to deserving applicants.* 補助金只能發給那些真正需要的申請者。| **deserving case** (=someone or something which deserves help, especially financial help) 值得幫助的人[事] **2 be deserving of** *formal* to deserve something【正式】值得..., 該得...: *This stupid-looking hat is deserving of ridicule!* 這頂樣子很傻的帽子應該受到嘲笑。

de·sex·u·al·ize also 又作 **-ise** *BrE*【英】/diˋsɛkʃuəl͵aɪz; diːˈsekʃuəlaɪz/ *v* [T] to remove the sexual quality from something 除去〔某物〕的性特徵, 閹割 —**desexualization** /di͵sɛkʃuələˋzeʃən; diː͵sekʃuəlaɪˈzeɪʃən/ *n* [C,U]: *desexualization of the body* 除去身體的性特徵

dés·ha·bil·lé /͵dɛzəˋbil; ͵deɪzæˈbiːeɪ/ also 又作 **dishabille** *AmE*【美】—*n* [U] *literary or humorous* the state of being only partly dressed, used especially of a woman【文或幽默】〔尤指女性〕衣着僅部分遮體, 衣衫不整

des·ic·cant /ˋdɛsəkənt; ˈdesɪ̥kənt/ *n* [C,U] *technical* a substance that takes water from the air so that it keeps other things dry【術語】乾燥劑

des·ic·cate /ˋdɛsə͵ket; ˈdesɪ̥keɪt/ *v* [T] *formal* to remove all the water from something【正式】除去...水分, 使脱水, 使乾燥 —**desiccation** /͵dɛsəˋkeʃən; ͵desɪ̥ˈkeɪʃən/ *n* [U]

des·ic·cat·ed /ˋdɛsə͵ketɪd; ˈdesɪ̥keɪtɪ̥d/ *adj* **1** dessicated food has been dried in order to preserve it〔食物〕脱水的, 乾燥的: *desiccated coconut* 椰子乾 **2** *formal* completely dry【正式】乾透的, 脱水的

de·sid·e·ra·tum /dɪ͵sɪdəˋretəm; dɪ͵zɪdəˈreɪtəm/ *n plural* **desiderata** /-tə; -tə/ [C] *Latin formal* something that is wanted or needed【拉丁, 正式】需要的東西

3 **de·sign¹** /dɪˋzaɪn; dɪˈzaɪn/ *n*

1 **1 ▶ARRANGEMENT OF PARTS** 各部分的安排◀ [U] the way that something has been planned and made, including its appearance, how it works etc 設計〔包括其外觀及運作方式等〕: *One or two changes have been made to the computer's basic design.* 對電腦的基本設計已作了一兩處改動。| *the importance of good design* 良好設計的重要性

2 ▶PATTERN 圖案◀ [C] a decorative pattern on something 裝飾圖案: *wallpaper with a floral design* 帶花圖案的牆紙

3 ▶DRAWING PLANS 繪製圖表◀ [U] the art or process of making a drawing of something to show how you will make it or what it will look like 設計術, 製圖術: *graphic design* 平面造型設計, 版面設計

4 ▶DRAWN PLAN 繪製的圖紙◀ [C] a drawing showing how something will be made or what it will look like 設計圖, 圖樣, 圖紙: [**+for**] *The Council has just approved the design for the new sports centre.* 市議會剛剛通過新體育中心的草圖。

5 ▶INTENTION 意圖◀ [C] a plan that someone has in their mind〔頭腦中的〕計劃: *Did he have some sinister design in doing this?* 他做這事是不是有邪惡的企圖? | **by design** (=intentionally) 有意地, 故意地 *Whether this happened by design or not we shall never know.* 這事的發生是否有意安排的, 我們將永遠無法得知。

6 have designs on sb to want a sexual relationship with someone 對某人居心不良〔想和某人發生性關係〕: *It soon became obvious that he had designs on her.* 不久, 他對她存有不良居心就變得非常明顯了。

7 have designs on sth to be interested in something because you want it for yourself, especially if it will bring you money 企圖將某物據為己有〔尤指可以帶來錢財的東西〕: *I reckon they have designs on their uncle's business.* 我看他們打算把他們叔叔的生意據為己有。

3 **design²** *v* **1** [I,T] to make a drawing or plan of something that will be made or built 設計: *A local architect designed the theatre.* 一名當地的建築師設計了這座劇院。| **well/badly etc designed** *a well designed office* 設計不錯的辦公室 **2** [T usually passive 一般用被動態] to plan or develop something for a specific purpose〔為某種特定目的〕計劃, 設計: **design sth to do sth** *These exercises are designed to develop and strengthen muscles.* 這些練習是為了增強肌肉力量而設計的。| **be designed for** *coursebooks designed for intermediate students* 為中級水平學生設計的教科書 | **be designed as** *a short film designed as an introduction to road safety* 為介紹道路安全知識而編製的電影短片 —see also 另見 DESIGNER¹

des·ig·nate¹ /ˋdɛzɪg͵net; ˈdezɪgneɪt/ *v* [T] **1** to choose someone or something for a particular job or purpose〔為某項工作或目的〕任命, 選定, 指派: **designate sth as/for** *We're going to designate this room as a no-smoking area.* 我們準備把這個房間指定為禁煙區。| **designate sb to do sth** *She has been designated to take over the position of treasurer.* 她被選派接任財務主管的職位。**2** to show or mean something, especially by using a special name or sign〔用特殊的名字或符號〕表明, 標明, 表示: *Buildings are designated by red squares on the map.* 在地圖上建築物是用紅色方塊來標明的。

des·ig·nate² /ˋdɛzɪgnɪt; ˈdezɪgnɪ̥t/ *adj* [only after noun 僅用於名詞後] *formal* a word used after the name of an official job showing that someone has been chosen for that job but has not yet officially started work【正式】候任的〔用在官職名稱的後面〕: *the ambassador designate* 候任大使

designated dri·ver /͵.... ˈ../ *n* [C] *AmE informal* someone who agrees to drive their friends and not drink alcohol when they go out together to a party, bar etc【美, 非正式】指定的司機〔指外出聚會、上酒吧等時同意開車送朋友因而不飲酒的人〕

designated hit·ter /͵.... ˈ../ *n* [C] *AmE*【美】**1** someone in the game of BASEBALL whose job is usually to hit the ball, but who replaces the PITCHER (=person who throws the ball) when it is their turn to hit 指定擊球手〔棒球比賽中在賽前指定的只執行進攻任務的擊球員〕**2** *informal* someone who does a job for someone else, especially in politics or business【非正式】〔尤指在政界或生意場上〕執行指定任務的下屬

des·ig·na·tion /͵dɛzɪgˋneʃən; ͵dezɪgˈneɪʃən/ *n* **1** [U] the act of choosing someone or something for a particular purpose, or of giving them a particular description 任命, 委派: *the designation of a student library assistant* 圖書館學生管理員的委派 **2** [C] *formal* a name or title【正式】名稱, 稱號: *Her official designation is Systems Manager.* 她的正式職稱是系統經理。

de·sign·ed·ly /dɪˋzaɪnɪdlɪ; dɪˈzaɪnɪ̥dli/ *adv formal* on purpose; intentionally【正式】故意地, 蓄意地, 有計劃地

de·sign·er¹ /dɪˋzaɪnɚ; dɪˈzaɪnə/ *n* [C] someone whose job is to make plans or patterns for clothes, furniture, equipment etc〔服裝、家具、設備等的〕設計師, 設計者: *a dress designer* 服裝設計師 ✎ 3

designer² *adj* [only before noun 僅用於名詞前] **1** made by a well-known and fashionable designer 由〔著名的、時尚的〕設計師設計的: *designer jeans* 設計師品牌牛仔褲 **2** *not technical* changed by GENETIC ENGINEERING【非術語】經基因工程而改變的: *a designer virus* 一種基因被改變的病毒

designer drug /.͵.. ˈ./ *n* [C] a drug similar to COCAINE or HEROIN that is produced artificially but is not illegal itself 化合致幻藥〔類似於可卡因或海洛因的人工合成藥品, 但本身並不屬於違禁藥品〕

de·sign·ing¹ /dɪˋzaɪnɪŋ; dɪˈzaɪnɪŋ/ *adj* someone who is designing tries to deceive people in order to get what they want 工於心計的, 別有用心的, 狡猾的

designing² *n* [U] DESIGN¹ (1) 設計

de·sir·a·ble /dɪˋzaɪrəbl; dɪˈzaɪərəbəl/ *adj formal*【正式】**1** something that is desirable is worth having or doing because it is useful or popular 值得擁有的; 值得做的: **highly desirable** (=very desirable) 非常想要的, 很可取的 | **it is desirable that** *It is desirable that you should have some familiarity with computers.* 你應該對電腦知

識有所熟悉, 這是很有益處的。—compare 比較 UNDESIRABLE **2** someone who is desirable is very sexually attractive 性感的, 引起性慾的 —**desirably** *adv* —**desirability** /dɪˌzaɪrəˈbɪlətɪ; dɪˌzaɪərəˈbɪlɪ̈ti/ *n* [U]

2 **de·sire[1]** /dɪˋzaɪr; dɪˈzaɪə/ *v* [T not in progressive 不用進行式] **1** *formal* to want or hope for something very much【正式】想要, 希望: *the qualities we desire in our employees* 我們希望雇員擁有的各種素質 | **desire to do sth** *Anyone desiring to vote must come to the meeting.* 凡想投票的人都必須來參加會議。| **desire sb to do sth** *The prince desired her to be his queen.* 王子希望她能成為自己的王后。**2 leave a lot to be desired** *especially spoken* used to say that something is not as good as you think it should be【尤口】不夠好, 仍有許多有待提高之處〔表明某事做得不如期望的好〕: *The standard of cooking here leaves a lot to be desired.* 這兒的烹飪水平遠不夠好。**3** *old-fashioned* to want to have sex with someone【過時】想和〔某人〕發生性關係 —**desired** *adj*: *My remarks had the desired effect.* 我的話取得了預期的效果。

D

desire[2] *n* **1** [C,U] a strong hope or wish 渴望; 慾望: **[+for]** *a desire for knowledge* 對知識的渴望 | **desire to do sth** *Anna has a great desire to travel.* 安娜非常嚮往旅遊。| **desire that** *a desire that his books should reach as many people as possible* 希望他的書能夠被盡可能多的人閱讀的願望 | **show/express a desire** *They did not show the slightest desire to accompany us.* 他們絲毫沒有表現出陪我們的意願。| **overwhelming/burning desire** (=very strong desire) 無法遏制的/迫切的願望 *He fought a burning desire to break into the conversation.* 他極力遏制着想插話的強烈衝動。| **have no desire to do sth** (=used to emphasize that you do not want to do something) 不想做某事 *I have no desire to see him hurt, I assure you.* 我向你保證, 我不想看見他受到傷害。**2 sb's heart's desire** a very strong wish that someone has 某人內心的渴望 **3** [U+for] *formal* a strong wish to have sex with someone【正式】肉慾, 性慾

de·sir·ous /dɪˋzaɪrəs; dɪˈzaɪərəs/ *adj formal* wanting something very much【正式】希望的, 渴望的: **[+of]** *No one had ever been so openly desirous of my attention.* 從未有人如此公開地表示過渴望引起我的注意。

de·sist /dɪˋzɪst; dɪˈzɪst/ *v* [I] *formal* to stop doing something【正式】停止, 中止; 斷念: **[+from]** *You are ordered to desist from such behaviour.* 命令你不得再有這種行為。

2
2 **desk** /dɛsk; desk/ *n* [C] **1** a piece of furniture like a table, usually with drawers in it, that you sit at to write and work 書桌, 辦公桌, 寫字枱 **2** a place where you can get information in a hotel, airport etc〔酒店、機場等的〕詢問處: *the check-in desk* 登記處 **3** an office that deals with a particular subject, especially in newspapers or television〔尤指報社或電視台負責某方面題材的〕部, 司, 組, 室: *Lloyd is running the sports desk.* 勞伊德現在負責體育新聞組。

desk clerk /ˈ· ·/ *n* [C] *AmE* someone who works at the main desk in a hotel【美】〔旅館的〕服務台接待員

de·skill /diˋskɪl; ˌdiːˈskɪl/ *v* [T] to remove or reduce the need for skill in a job, usually by changing to machinery〔通常指通過轉為機器操作而〕降低…的技術含量

desk job /ˈ· ·/ *n* [C] a job that involves working mostly at a desk in an office 文案工作, 案頭工作

desk ti·dy /ˈ· ˌ··/ *n* [C] *BrE* a container for putting pens, pencils etc in, that you keep on your desk【英】筆筒

desk·top /ˋdɛsktɑp; ˈdesktɒp/ *adj* **1 desktop computer** a computer that is small enough to be used on a desk 枱式電腦, 桌上型電腦 —see picture on page A14 參見A14頁圖 **2 desktop publishing** the work of getting a magazine, small book etc ready to be produced, using a small computer 桌面出版〔用微型電腦工作, 把雜誌、小型書籍等準備好等待出版〕

des·o·late[1] /ˋdɛslɪt; ˈdesələt/ *adj* **1** a place that is desolate is empty and looks sad because there are no people there and not much activity 荒涼的, 荒蕪的, 無人煙的: *desolate moorland* 荒涼的高沼地 **2** someone who is desolate feels very sad and lonely〔人〕淒涼的; 孤獨的 —**desolately** *adv* —**desolation** /ˌdɛslˋeʃən; ˌdesəˈleɪʃən/ *n* [U]

des·o·late[2] /ˋdɛslˌet; ˈdesəleɪt/ *v* [T usually passive 一般用被動態] *literary*【文】**1** to make someone feel very sad and lonely 使悲傷, 使孤獨: *Martin was desolated by his wife's death.* 妻子的死使馬丁悲痛欲絕。**2** to make a place seem empty and sad 使荒涼, 使荒無人煙: *He returned to the desolated camp.* 他返回到空無一人的營地。

de·spair[1] /dɪˋspɛr; dɪˈspeə/ *n* [U] **1** a feeling that you have no hope at all for the future 絕望: **in despair** *I spent ages trying to fix it, but gave up in despair.* 我花了很長時間想把它修好, 但還是絕望地放棄了。| **the depths of despair** (=very strong feelings of despair) 絕望的深淵 | **drive sb to despair** *Norman's constant drinking drives his family to despair.* 諾曼沒完沒了地喝酒, 讓他的家人陷入絕望。**2 the despair of sb** someone or something that makes someone feel very worried, upset, or unhappy 令某人絕望的人[事]: *That Jones girl is the despair of her teachers.* 那個叫瓊斯的女孩在她老師們的心目中已經無可救藥了。

despair[2] *v* [I] to feel that there is no hope that a situation will improve 絕望, 感到無望: *Dirk came close to despairing in those months of unemployment.* 在失業的那幾個月中, 德克近乎絕望。| **despair of (doing) sth** *They despaired of finding the children alive.* 他們對能找到生還的孩子不抱任何希望了。

de·spair·ing /dɪˋspɛrɪŋ; dɪˈspeərɪŋ/ *adj* showing a feeling of despair 絕望的: *He raised his eyes in a despairing gesture.* 他絕望地抬起眼睛。—**despairingly** *adv*: *Don was shaking his head despairingly.* 唐恩絕望地搖着頭。

de·spatch /dɪˋspætʃ; dɪˈspætʃ/ another spelling of DISPATCH dispatch 的另一種拼法

des·pe·ra·do /ˌdɛspəˋrɑdo; ˌdespəˈrɑːdəʊ/ *n* [C] *old-fashioned* a violent criminal who is not afraid of danger【過時】亡命之徒, 暴徒

des·per·ate /ˋdɛspərɪt; ˈdespərɪ̈t/ *adj* **1** willing to do anything and not caring about danger, because you are in a very bad situation〔由於處在絕境而〕拚命的, 不顧一切的: *We had no food left at all and were getting desperate.* 我們一點食物都沒剩, 十分絕望。| *an appeal from the teenager's desperate parents* 少年絕望的父母的懇求 **2** [not before noun 不用於名詞前] needing or wanting something very much 非常需要的, 極其需要的: **[+for]** *By then I was desperate for a holiday.* 到那時候, 我已特別渴望休假了。| **desperate to do sth** *Ben was desperate to get a job.* 班恩急切地想找到一份工作。| **in desperate need** *We're in desperate need of help.* 我們極其需要幫助。**3** a desperate situation is very bad or serious〔局勢、情形等〕危急的, 嚴峻的: *There was a desperate shortage of doctors.* 醫生人數嚴重不足。**4** a desperate action is something that you only do because you are in a very bad situation〔在危急時刻〕孤注一擲的: **desperate attempt/effort/measures** *The victim had made a desperate attempt to escape.* 受害者曾經孤注一擲, 企圖逃跑。

des·per·ate·ly /ˋdɛspərɪtlɪ; ˈdespərɪ̈tli/ *adv* **1** in a desperate way 絕望地; 拚命地, 不顧一切地: *He looked round desperately for someone to help him.* 他絕望地四處張望, 希望有人能來幫他。| **try desperately** *The doctors were trying desperately to save her life.* 醫生們正拚命努力, 試圖挽救她的生命。**2** very much 非常地: *Joe's work is desperately important to him.* 喬的工作對他來說非常重要。| **desperately need** *He desperately needs reassurance.* 他極需安慰。

des·per·a·tion /ˌdɛspəˋreʃən; ˌdespəˈreɪʃən/ *n* [U] the state of being desperate 絕望; 拚命, 不顧一切: *a look of desperation in his eyes* 他眼中絕望的眼神 | **in desperation** *Finally, in desperation, we went to a pawnbroker.*

最後我們實在走投無路, 就去了當鋪。

des·pic·a·ble /ˈdɛspɪkəbl; dɪˈspɪkəbəl/ *adj* extremely unpleasant 卑鄙的: *a despicable liar* 卑鄙的撒謊者 | *It's despicable the way he treats those kids.* 他那樣對待那些孩子, 真是卑鄙。—**despicably** *adv*: *grinning despicably* 無恥地咧嘴笑着

de·spise /dɪˈspaɪz; dɪˈspaɪz/ *v* [T not in progressive 不用進行式] to dislike someone or something very much 鄙視, 看不起, 藐視: *Mrs Morel had come to despise her husband.* 莫雷爾太太漸漸開始瞧不起她的丈夫。

S2 W1 **de·spite** /dɪˈspaɪt; dɪˈspaɪt/ *prep* **1** in spite of something 儘管, 不管, 任憑: *Despite all our efforts to save the school, the County decided to close it.* 儘管我們竭盡全力想保住這所學校, 郡議會還是決定把它關閉。| **despite the fact that** *She went to Spain despite the fact the doctor had told her to rest.* 儘管醫生告訴她應該休息, 她還是去了西班牙。**2 despite yourself** if you do something despite yourself, you do it although you did not intend to 儘管並非某人的本意〔但仍被迫去做〕: *Despite herself, she found his attention rather enjoyable.* 儘管她不願承認, 她還是喜歡他來獻殷勤。

de·spoil /dɪˈspɔɪl; dɪˈspɔɪl/ *v* [T] *literary*【文】**1** to make a place much less attractive by removing or damaging things 劫掠; 破壞 **2** to steal from a place using force, especially in a war〔尤指戰爭中用暴力〕掠奪, 搶劫

de·spon·dent /dɪˈspɑndənt; dɪˈspɒndənt/ *adj* unhappy and not hopeful 沮喪的, 失望的: *Gill had been out of work for a year and was getting very despondent.* 吉爾失業有一年的時間了, 他變得非常消沉。—**despondency** *n* [U] —**despondently** *adv*: *He was staring despondently into the distance.* 他正沮喪地盯着遠處。

des·pot /ˈdɛspət; ˈdespɒt/ *n* [C] someone such as a ruler who used power in a cruel and unfair way 專制統治者; 暴君 —**despotic** /dɪˈspɑtɪk; dɪˈspɒtɪk/ *adj* —**despotically** /-klɪ; -kli/ *adv*

des·pot·is·m /ˈdɛspətˌɪzəm; ˈdespətɪzəm/ *n* [U] rule by a despot 暴政, 專制

des res /ˌdɛz ˈrɛz; ˌdez ˈrez/ *n* [C] *BrE informal* a house that a lot of people admire and would like to live in【英, 非正式】〔許多人嚮往並希望入住的〕理想住宅

des·sert /dɪˈzɝt; dɪˈzɜːt/ *n* [C,U] sweet food served after the main part of a meal〔飯後的〕甜食, 甜品, 甜點: *There's ice-cream for dessert.* 甜品是冰淇淋。

des·sert·spoon /dɪˈzɝtˌspun; dɪˈzɜːtspuːn/ *n* [C] **1** *especially BrE* a spoon that is between the sizes of a TEASPOON and a TABLESPOON【尤英】點心匙, 中型匙 —see picture at 參見 SPOON 圖 **2** also 又作 **dessertspoonful** /-ˌful; -fʊl/ the amount held by a dessertspoon 一中匙的量

dessert wine /-ˈ· ·/ *n* [C,U] a sweet wine served with dessert〔吃甜品時飲用的〕餐末甜酒

de·sta·bil·ize also 又作 **-ise** *BrE*【英】/diˈstebḷˌaɪz; diːˈsteɪbəlaɪz/ *v* [T] to make something less likely to remain politically successful 使〔政治〕不穩定, 破壞〔政治〕穩定: *an attempt to destabilize the government* 旨在破壞政府穩定的企圖 —**destabilization** /diˌstebələˈzeʃən; ˌdiːsteɪbəlaɪˈzeɪʃən/ *n* [U]

des·ti·na·tion /ˌdɛstəˈneʃən; ˌdestəˈneɪʃən/ *n* [C] the place that someone or something is going to 目的地, 終點: *holiday destinations* 度假目的地

des·tined /ˈdɛstɪnd; ˈdestənd/ *adj* **1** [not before noun 不用於名詞前] certain to have something or do something at some time in the future 命中注定的; 預定的: [+for] *She seemed destined for a long and successful career.* 她似乎注定能擁有一份持久且成功的事業。| **destined to do sth** *We were destined never to meet again.* 我們命中注定無緣再相見。**2 be destined for** to be travelling towards a particular place 去, 赴〔某地〕: *a flight destined for Cairo* 飛往開羅的航班 **3 destined lover/profession etc** *literary* the person, thing etc that you will have in the future【文】命中注定的情人/職業等

des·ti·ny /ˈdɛstənɪ; ˈdestəni/ *n* **1** [C usually singular 一般用單數] the things that will happen to someone in the future, especially those that cannot be changed or controlled; FATE (1) 命運, 天命, 定數: **your/my/his etc destiny** *Juan accepted his destiny without complaint.* 胡安毫無怨言地認命了。**2** [U] the power that some people believe decides what will happen to them in the future 天意; 命運之神: *I'm a great believer in destiny.* 我特別相信命運。

des·ti·tute /ˈdɛstəˌtut; ˈdestətjuːt/ *adj* **1** having no money, no food, and nowhere to live 窮困的, 貧困的: *Many people were so destitute they lived out of garbage cans.* 許多人貧困得靠撿垃圾箱裡的東西來過活。**2 be destitute of** *formal* to be completely without something【正式】完全沒有…的, 毫無…的: *a man destitute of all compassion* 毫無同情心的人 —**destitution** *n* [U]

de·stroy /dɪˈstrɔɪ; dɪˈstrɔɪ/ *v* [T] **1** to damage something so badly that it cannot be repaired or so that it no longer exists 破壞, 毀掉, 摧毀: *The school was completely destroyed by fire.* 學校被大火徹底燒毀了。| *an accident that destroyed her ballet career* 一次毀掉她芭蕾生涯的意外事故 **2** to kill an animal, especially because it is sick, or dangerous 殺死〔動物, 尤因其生病或產生危險〕 **3 destroy sb** to ruin someone's life completely so that they have no hope for the future 毀掉某人 —see also 另見 DESTRUCTION S2 W2

USAGE NOTE 用法說明: DESTROY

WORD CHOICE 詞語辨析: **destroy, ruin, spoil**

Destroy means to damage something so badly that it no longer exists or cannot be repaired. destroy 表示嚴重毀壞某物, 結果使之不復存在或無法修復: *Whole areas of the city were destroyed.* 整座城市被徹底摧毀了。| *a drug to destroy cancer cells* 殺滅癌細胞的藥物 | *Their traditional way of life has been destroyed.* 他們傳統的生活方式已經被破壞。

You **ruin** or (less strong) **spoil** something good or useful. It then usually still exists, but no longer has its good qualities or features. spoil 語氣比 ruin 稍輕一些, 這兩個詞都可以用來表示毀壞某種好的或者有用的東西, 事後此物雖仍然存在, 卻已失去其優良的特性或特徵: *Too much sugar can ruin your teeth.* 吃糖太多能毀掉你的牙齒。| *You've completely spoiled my day.* 你把我的一天徹底地毀掉了。

de·stroy·er /dɪˈstrɔɪə; dɪˈstrɔɪə/ *n* [C] **1** a small fast military ship with guns 驅逐艦 **2** someone or something that destroys things or people 破壞者: *They feared photography would be the destroyer of art.* 他們擔心攝影會毀掉藝術。

de·struc·tion /dɪˈstrʌkʃən; dɪˈstrʌkʃən/ *n* [U] **1** the act or process of destroying something 破壞, 摧毀, 毀壞, 消滅: *the threat of nuclear destruction* 核毀滅的威脅 **2 be sb's destruction** *formal* to be the thing that completely ruins someone's life【正式】是某人毀掉的原因: *Gambling was his destruction.* 賭博把他徹底給毀了。—see also 另見 DESTROY W3

de·struc·tive /dɪˈstrʌktɪv; dɪˈstrʌktɪv/ *adj* causing damage to people or things 毀滅性的, 造成破壞的: *Jealousy is a very destructive emotion.* 嫉妒是一種破壞性很強的情感。—**destructively** *adv* —**destructiveness** *n* [U]

des·ul·to·ry /ˈdɛsəlˌtorɪ; ˈdesəltəri/ *adj formal* done without any particular plan or purpose【正式】漫無目的的, 毫無計劃的, 散漫的: *They talked in a desultory manner for a few minutes.* 他們漫無邊際地談了幾分鐘。—**desultorily** /ˈdɛsəlˌtorɪlɪ; ˈdesəltərəli/ *adv*

Det the written abbreviation of 縮寫 = DETECTIVE

de·tach /dɪˈtætʃ; dɪˈtætʃ/ *v* [T] **1** to remove a piece or part of something that is designed to be removed 拆下, 分開, 拆開, 卸下: *If you are interested in the course, detach and fill out the application form.* 如果你對這個課程感興趣, 把申請表撕下並填好。| **detach sth from** *You can detach the hood from the jacket.* 你可以把帽子

從夾克上拆下來。**2 detach yourself** to try to be less involved in, or less concerned about a situation 使自己超然物外: *I try to detach myself from my patients.* 我盡量和我的病人保持距離。

de·tach·a·ble /dɪˋtætʃəbl̩; dɪˈtætʃəbəl/ *adj* able to be removed and put back 可拆卸的: *a detachable handle* 可拆卸的把手

de·tached /dɪˋtætʃt; dɪˈtætʃt/ *adj* **1** not reacting in an emotional way, so that you can do your job properly or make the right decisions 冷靜的, 不動感情的, 客觀的: *Try to take a more detached view.* 盡量採取更為客觀的態度。**2** *BrE* a detached house or garage is not joined to another building on any side【英】〔房子或車庫〕單幢的, 獨立的: *a large detached house on the outskirts of the town* 在城郊的一所獨立式的大房子 —compare 比較 SEMIDETACHED, TERRACED HOUSE —see picture on page A4 參見A4頁圖

de·tach·ment /dɪˋtætʃmənt; dɪˈtætʃmənt/ *n* **1** [U] the state of not reacting in an emotional way, so that you can do your job properly or make the right decisions 冷靜, 超然, 客觀: *Doctors need to have some degree of emotional detachment.* 醫生在情緒上需要有幾分冷靜。**2** [C] a group of soldiers who are sent away from the main group to do a special job 分遣隊, 支隊

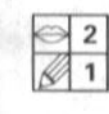
2 1 **de·tail¹** /dɪˋtel; ˈdiːteɪl/ *n* **1** [C,U] a single feature, fact, or piece of information, or many small features considered together 細節, 詳情: *Todd had planned the journey down to the smallest detail.* 托德把這次旅行都規劃好了, 直到最小的細節。| *We need to discuss a few details before you start.* 在你開始之前, 我們需要討論一些細節問題。| **attention to detail** *Editing requires great attention to detail.* 編輯工作需要格外注重細節部分。| **go into detail/details** (=include a lot of details when describing or explaining something) 敍述詳情 | **read/describe etc sth in detail** (=pay attention to all the details) 詳細地閱讀/描述某物等 *Study the contract in detail before signing.* 簽字之前要先詳細地研究一下合同。| **have an eye for detail** (=be skilled at noticing details) 善於注意到細微之處 **2 details** [plural] all the additional information you need about something you already know a little about 詳細情況, 詳細資料: **[+of]** *Send for details of the course.* 請來函索取有關課程的詳細資料。| **full/further details** *For further details, contact the personnel department.* 欲知詳情, 請與人事部聯繫。**3** [singular, U] *technical* a specific duty in the army, or the person or group who have that duty【術語】〔軍隊中的〕特遣隊, 小分隊: *the security detail* 安全小分隊

detail² *v* [T] **1** to give all the facts or information about something 詳述: *The paper then goes on to detail a number of joint initiatives.* 接着, 報紙詳細列舉了一些合作的初步行動。**2 detail sb to do sth** to officially order someone, especially soldiers, to do a particular job 指派某人〔尤指士兵〕做某事: *Vance, you're detailed to the night watch.* 萬斯, 派你去值夜。

2 **de·tailed** /dɪˋteld; ˈdiːteɪld/ *adj* including a lot of information and detail 詳細的, 詳盡的: *a detailed account of the development of the atom bomb* 一份研製原子彈的詳盡報告

de·tail·ing /dɪˋtelɪŋ; ˈdiːteɪlɪŋ/ *n* [U] decorations that are added to something such as a car or piece of clothing〔汽車上或衣服上的〕裝飾物

de·tain /dɪˋten; dɪˈteɪn/ *v* [T] **1** to officially prevent someone from leaving a place 拘留, 扣押, 羈押: *Police detained the terrorists.* 警察拘留了恐怖分子。**2** to delay someone who wants to leave, by talking to them, asking them to do something etc〔通過與對方談話或讓其做某事等〕耽擱, 延誤, 留住: *I want a quick word, but I won't detain you long.* 我想和你說句話, 不會耽擱你很久的。

de·tain·ee /dɪˌteˋni; ˌdiːteɪˈniː/ *n* [C] someone who is officially kept in a prison, usually because of their political views〔通常由於所持政治觀點〕被拘留者

de·tan·gle /diˋtæŋgl; ˌdiːˈtæŋgəl/ *v* [I,T] *especially AmE* to remove the knots in hair【尤美】(使)〔頭髮〕不打結, (使)〔頭髮〕不絞在一塊兒

de·tect /dɪˋtɛkt; dɪˈtekt/ *v* [T] to notice or discover something, especially something that is not easy to see, hear etc 發現, 察覺〔尤指不易察覺到的事物〕: *Many forms of cancer can be cured if detected early.* 如果發現得早, 許多種癌症都是可以治癒的。| *Do I detect a note of sarcasm in your voice?* 我怎麼聽得出你話語裡有種諷刺的意味呢? —**detectable** *adj* 3

de·tec·tion /dɪˋtɛkʃən; dɪˈtekʃən/ *n* [U] the process of detecting, or the fact of being detected 發現, 覺察: *the early detection of cancer* 癌症的早期發現

de·tec·tive /dɪˋtɛktɪv; dɪˈtektɪv/ *n* [C] **1** a police officer whose job is to discover information that will result in criminals being caught 偵探, 警探 —see also 另見 STORE DETECTIVE **2** someone who is paid to discover information about someone or something 私家偵探: *She hired a detective to find out where her husband was going after work.* 她雇了一個私人偵探調查她丈夫下班後的去處。**3 detective story/novel etc** a story about a crime, often a murder, and a detective who tries to find out who did it 偵探故事/小說等 3

de·tec·tor /dɪˋtɛktɚ; dɪˈtektə/ *n* [C] a piece of equipment that makes a signal if it discovers something 探測器: *smoke detectors* 煙塵探測器; 煙霧報警器 | *a metal detector* 金屬探測器 —see also 另見 LIE DETECTOR

dé·tente /deˋtɑ̃t; deɪˈtɑːnt/ *n* [C,U] a state of more friendly political relations between countries that have previously been unfriendly〔國家間緊張關係的〕緩和

de·ten·tion /dɪˋtɛnʃən; dɪˈtenʃən/ *n* **1** [U] the state of being kept somewhere by the police, because they think you have done something illegal 拘留, 扣留: *Willis spent over 100 days in detention.* 威利斯被扣押了一百多天。**2** [C,U] a punishment in which children who have behaved badly are forced to stay at school for a short time after the others have gone home〔放學後〕留校懲罰; 留堂; 留課

detention cen·tre *BrE*【英】, **detention center** *AmE*【美】/·ˋ·· ˌ··/ *n* [C] a place where young people who have done something illegal are kept, because they are too young to go to prison 青少年管教所; 感化中心; 羈留中心

de·ter /dɪˋtɝ; dɪˈtɜː/ *v* **deterred, deterring** [T] to persuade someone not to do something, by making them realize it will be difficult or will have unpleasant results〔通過讓對方意識到做此事會有困難或會有不太好的結果〕勸說〔某人〕不做〔某事〕, 制止: *security measures aimed at deterring shoplifters* 意在防止店鋪遭竊的安全措施 | **deter sb from doing sth** *a new program designed to deter kids from experimenting with drugs* 為防止孩子嘗試毒品而制定的新計劃 —see also 另見 DETERRENT

de·ter·gent /dɪˋtɝdʒənt; dɪˈtɜːdʒənt/ *n* [C,U] a liquid or powder that contains soap used for washing clothes, dishes etc 洗滌劑; 洗衣粉; 洗潔精; 去污劑

de·te·ri·o·rate /dɪˋtɪrɪəˌret; dɪˈtɪəriəreɪt/ *v* [I] **1** to become worse 惡化: *deteriorating health* 不斷惡化的健康狀況 | *Relations between the two countries have since deteriorated.* 從此, 兩國的關係開始惡化。**2** **[+into]** to develop into a bad or unpleasant situation 演變成; 惡化成: *The meeting soon deteriorated into a fight.* 這次會議不久就演變成一場鬥毆。—**deterioration** /dɪˌtɪrɪəˋreʃən; dɪˌtɪəriəˈreɪʃən/ *n* [U]: *environmental deterioration* 環境的惡化

de·ter·mi·nant /dɪˋtɝmənənt; dɪˈtɜːmɪnənt/ *n* [C] *formal* something that strongly influences what you do or how you behave【正式】決定性因素: **[+of]** *Social class is a major determinant of consumer spending patterns.* 社會等級是消費者消費模式的主要決定因素。

de·ter·mi·nate /dɪˋtɝmənɪt; dɪˈtɜːmɪnət/ *adj formal* strictly controlled or limited【正式】嚴格控制的, 限定的: *A firm will act in a determinate way to maximize its* *profits.* 一家公司將會按嚴格控制的方式運作, 以求利潤最大化。

3 **de·ter·mi·na·tion** /dɪˌtɝməˈneʃən; dɪˌtɜːmɪ̵ˈneɪʃən/ *n* **1** [U] the ability to continue trying to achieve what you have decided to do even when this is difficult 決心, 堅韌, 毅力: **determination to do sth** *Her determination to do well made her keep on studying.* 她想取得好成績的決心使得她堅持學習下去。| **dogged determination** (=very strong determination) 堅定不移的決心 *They were admired for their dogged determination to learn the language.* 人們欽佩他們學習語言堅定不移的決心。**2** [U] *formal* the act of deciding something officially【正式】〔官方的〕決定, 規定: *the determination of government policy* 政府政策的確定 **3** [C] *technical* the act of finding the exact level, amount, or causes of something【術語】〔對水平、數量或原因的〕測定, 確定: *determination of the cause of death* 死亡原因的確定 —see also 另見 SELF-DETERMINATION

1 **de·ter·mine** /dɪˈtɝmɪn; dɪˈtɜːmɪ̵n/ *v* [T] **1** to find out the exact details or facts about something 找出, 測定, 確定: *Your parents' income is used to determine your level of financial aid.* 你父母的收入情況被用來決定你所得的經濟援助水平。| **[+how/what/who etc]** *The purpose of the exercise is to determine where we want to go from here.* 這次練習的目的是決定我們該何去何從。**2** to have a strong influence or effect on something 決定, 支配: *Usually the size of the practice will determine the number of doctors.* 通常醫務所規模的大小決定醫生的人數。**3** to officially decide something〔官方的〕確定, 規定: *The date of the court case was yet to be determined.* 開庭的日期還沒有確定下來。**4** *formal* to form a firm intention to do something【正式】決心〔做某事〕: **determine to do sth** *We determined to leave at once.* 我們決心立即離開。

3 **de·ter·mined** /dɪˈtɝmɪnd; dɪˈtɜːmɪ̵nd/ *adj* **1** having a strong desire to do something, so that you will not let anyone stop you 有決心的, 意志堅定的: *a determined young woman* 一位下定決心的年輕女士 | **determined to do sth** *I am determined to find out who is responsible for this.* 我決意要弄清楚誰該對此事負責任。| **determined that** *Determined that his son would do well, Eliot sent him to a private school.* 艾略特堅信兒子會學業優異, 因此把他送到私立學校學習。**2** showing determination, especially in a difficult situation〔尤指在困境中〕堅決的, 堅定的: **determined attempts/opposition etc** *The library was closed down despite determined opposition.* 儘管受到堅決的反對, 圖書館還是被關閉了。

de·ter·min·er /dɪˈtɝmɪnɚ; dɪˈtɜːmɪ̵nə/ *n* [C] *technical* a word that comes before an adjective that describes a noun, for example 'his' in 'his new car' or 'that' in 'that big tree'【術語】限定詞〔置於修飾名詞的形容詞前, 如 his new car 中的 his 或 that big tree 中的 that 都是限定詞〕

de·ter·min·is·m /dɪˈtɝmənˌɪzəm; dɪˈtɜːmɪ̵nɪzəm/ *n* [U] the belief that what you do and what happens to you are caused by things that you cannot control 決定論〔相信某人所做的事或發生在某人身上的事是由他無法控制的力量決定的〕—**deterministic** /dɪˌtɝmɪˈnɪstɪk; dɪˌtɜːmɪ̵ˈnɪstɪk◂/ *adj*

de·ter·rent /dɪˈtɝənt; dɪˈterənt/ *n* [C] **1** something that makes someone less likely to do something 制止物, 威懾物, 威懾力量: **be a deterrent to sb** *Window locks are an effective deterrent to potential burglars.* 窗上的鎖可以有效地防止竊賊從窗戶潛入屋內。**2 nuclear deterrent** NUCLEAR weapons that a country has, that are supposed to prevent other countries from attacking 核威懾力量 —**deterrence** *n* [U]

de·test /dɪˈtɛst; dɪˈtest/ *v* [T not in progressive 不用進行式] to hate something or someone very much 憎惡, 憎恨, 嫌惡: *I detest computers.* 我討厭電腦。—**detestation** /ˌditɛˈsteʃən; ˌdiːteˈsteɪʃən/ *n* [U]

de·test·able /dɪˈtɛstəbḷ; dɪˈtestəbəl/ *adj* very bad, and deserving to be criticized or hated 令人憎恨的, 可惡的, 討厭的: *a detestable little man* 一個討厭的小個子男人 —**detestably** *adv*

de·throne /dɪˈθron; dɪˈθrəʊn/ *v* [T] **1** to remove a king or queen from power 廢黜〔君主〕**2** to remove someone from a position of authority or importance 撵〔某人〕下台, 使〔某人〕失去重要地位 —**dethronement** *n* [U]

det·o·nate /ˈdɛtəˌnet; ˈdetəneɪt/ *v* [I,T] to explode or make something explode, using special equipment 引爆, (使) 爆炸

det·o·na·tion /ˌdɛtəˈneʃən; ˌdetəˈneɪʃən/ *n* [C,U] an explosion, or the action of making a bomb etc explode 爆炸; 引爆

det·o·na·tor /ˈdɛtəˌnetɚ; ˈdetəneɪtə/ *n* [C] a piece of equipment that is used to start an explosion 引爆裝置, 雷管

de·tour¹ /ˈditur; ˈdiːtʊə/ *n* [C] a way of going from one place to another that is longer than the usual way, for example because you want to avoid traffic problems or to visit something〔為避開交通問題或為參觀某處等而走的〕繞行路線, 迂迴路線: **make/take a detour** *BrE*【英】: *We took a detour to avoid the town centre.* 我們繞道而行, 避開了市中心。

detour² *v* [I,T] *especially AmE* to make a detour【尤美】繞道而行; 繞過…

de·tox /ˈditɑks; ˈdiːtɒks/ *n* [U] special treatment at a hospital to help people stop drinking alcohol or taking drugs 戒酒 (治療); 戒毒 (治療)

de·tox·i·fi·ca·tion /diˌtɑksəfəˈkeʃən; diːˌtɒksɪ̵fɪ̵ˈkeɪʃən/ *n* [U] **1** the process of removing harmful chemicals or poison from something 解毒, 清毒 **2** detox 戒酒; 戒毒: *detoxification unit* 戒毒[戒酒]中心 —**detoxify** /diˈtɑksəˌfaɪ; diːˈtɒksɪ̵faɪ/ *v* [T]

de·tract /dɪˈtrækt; dɪˈtrækt/ *v*

detract from sth *phr v* [T not in progressive 不用進行式] to make something seem less good than it really is 貶損, 詆毀: *One mistake is not going to detract from your achievement.* 一個錯誤不會抹殺你的成就。—**detraction** /dɪˈtrækʃən; dɪˈtrækʃən/ *n* [C,U]

de·trac·tor /dɪˈtræktɚ; dɪˈtræktə/ *n* [C] someone who says bad things about someone or something, in order to make them seem less good than they really are 詆毀者, 貶低者: *The President's detractors expressed their usual low expectations of his policies.* 貶低總統的人照例對總統的政策表示不抱很高的期望。

det·ri·ment /ˈdɛtrəmənt; ˈdetrɪ̵mənt/ *n* [U] *formal* the state of being harmed or damaged by something【正式】損害, 傷害, 不利: **to the detriment of** (=resulting in harm or damage to something) 有害於…, 有損於…, 不利於… *He worked longer and longer hours, to the detriment of his marriage.* 他工作的時間越來越長, 這不利於他的婚姻。

det·ri·men·tal /ˌdɛtrəˈmɛntḷ; ˌdetrɪ̵ˈmentl◂/ *adj formal* causing harm or damage【正式】有害的, 不利的: **[+to]** *Smoking is detrimental to health.* 吸煙有害健康。—**detrimentally** *adv*

de·tri·tus /dɪˈtraɪtəs; dɪˈtraɪtəs/ *n* [U] *technical* pieces of waste that remain after something has been broken up or used【術語】〔某物被打碎或使用後留下的〕碎塊, 碎屑

de trop /də ˈtro; də ˈtrəʊ/ *adj* [not before noun 不用於名詞前] *French* a word meaning too much or not necessary, used when you are trying too hard to sound important or educated【法】過多的, 多餘的, 不必要的〔用於表示裝腔作勢, 以使自己顯得很重要或很有文化的樣子〕

deuce /dus; djuːs/ *n* **1** the situation in tennis when both players have 40 points, after which the next player must win two points to win the game〔網球賽中〕局末平分; 盤末平局, 賽末點〔其後一方須連勝兩分方可獲勝〕**2 what/where/who etc the deuce?** *spoken old-fashioned* used to add force to a question【口, 過時】到底是甚麼鬼東西/到底在甚麼鬼地方/到底是哪個傢伙等〔用於加強語

氣〕: *What the deuce is going on?* 到底發生甚麼事了? **3 a deuce of** *old-fashioned* a very severe example or case of something【過時】極其糟糕的; 非常嚴重的: *She had a deuce of a row with her father.* 她和她爸爸大吵了一場。

deuc·ed /ˋdusɪd; ˈdjuːsɪ̇d/ *adj, adv old-fashioned* very or very great【過時】很, 非常: *I'm deuced glad you turned up when you did.* 看見你出現的時候, 我都快高興死了。

Deutsch·mark /ˋdɔɪtʃˏmɑrk; ˈdɔɪtʃmɑːk/ *n* [C] the former standard unit of money in Germany; MARK[2] (8) 馬克〔原德國貨幣單位〕

de·val·ue /diˋvælju; diːˈvæljuː/ *v* **1** [I,T] to reduce the value that the money of one country has when it is exchanged for the money of another country (使)〔貨幣〕貶值 **2** [T] to make someone or something seem less important or valuable than they really are 降低〔某人的或某物的〕價值, 貶低: *The skills of women were not recognized and often devalued.* 婦女的技能過去並沒有得到承認, 而且其價值還經常被貶低。—**devaluation** /diˏvæljuˋeʃən; diːˌvæljuˈeɪʃən/ *n* [C,U]

dev·a·state /ˋdɛvəsˏtet; ˈdevəsteɪt/ *v* [T usually passive 一般用被動態] **1** to cause so much damage to a place or area that most of it is destroyed 毀壞, 摧毀, 毀滅: *The bomb devastated the city centre.* 炸彈炸毀了市中心地區。**2** to make someone feel extremely shocked and sad 令〔某人〕極度震驚, 使〔某人〕傷心欲絕: *Rob was devastated by the news of her death.* 羅伯聽到她死去的消息, 悲痛欲絕。| *a country devastated by war* 被戰爭摧毀的國家 —**devastation** /ˏdɛvəsˋteʃən; ˌdevəˈsteɪʃən/ *n* [U]: *A cyclone came over the island, causing complete devastation.* 龍捲風襲擊了這個島嶼, 造成了徹底的破壞。

dev·a·stat·ing /ˋdɛvəsˏtetɪŋ; ˈdevəsteɪtɪŋ/ *adj* **1** destroying or badly damaging something 毀滅性的, 破壞力極強的: *Acid rain has a devastating effect on the environment.* 酸雨對環境的破壞力極大。**2** shocking and upsetting 令人震驚的: *the devastating news of a plane crash* 令人震驚的飛機失事的消息 **3** almost impossible to argue against or deal with 難以反駁的, 無法應付的: *a devastating argument in favour of legalization* 贊成合法化的強有力論點 **4** *old-fashioned* extremely attractive【過時】極富吸引力的, 極漂亮的 —**devastatingly** *adv*: *Mathew looked devastatingly handsome in his white linen suit.* 馬修穿上他那套白色的亞麻西裝看上去帥極了。

de·vel·op /dɪˋvɛləp; dɪˈveləp/ *v*

1 ►GROW 生長◄ [I,T] to grow or gradually change into a larger, stronger, or more advanced state, or to make someone or something do this (使)成長, (使)發展: *Children develop very rapidly.* 兒童成長得很快。| **[+into]** *James has developed into a charming young man.* 詹姆斯已經長成為一個富有魅力的年輕人。| **[+from]** *In less than ten years it develops from a seed into a full-grown tree.* 不到十年的時間, 它就從一粒種子長成一棵大樹。| **develop sth** *exercises designed to develop your muscles* 為使肌肉發達而設計的鍛鍊

2 ►PLAN/PRODUCT 計劃/產品◄ [T] to make a new idea, plan, or product become successful over a period of time 形成〔觀點〕; 制訂〔計劃〕; 研製〔產品〕: *Scientists are developing new drugs to treat arthritis.* 科學家們正在研製治療關節炎的新藥。

3 ►START TO HAVE 開始有◄ [I,T] to gradually begin to have a quality, illness, problem etc 逐漸形成〔某種品質、疾病、問題等〕: *Some alcoholics develop liver disease.* 一些酗酒的人會得肝病。

4 ►BECOME MORE ACTIVE 變得更加活躍◄ [I] to become more active or more of a problem, and therefore become more noticeable〔問題等〕變得活躍、顯現: *Trouble is developing in the cities.* 一些城市裡正在醞釀事端。

5 ►IDEA/ARGUMENT 觀點/論點◄ [T] to make an argument or idea clearer, by studying it more or by speaking or writing about it in more detail 詳細闡述〔論點、觀點〕: *We will develop a few of these points in the seminar.* 在研討會上我們將詳細闡述其中的一些觀點。

6 ►LAND 土地◄ [T] to use land for the things that people need, for example by taking minerals out of it or by building on it 開發〔土地, 如開採礦藏或修蓋建築等〕: *We're waiting to hear if permission to develop the land will be granted.* 我們正等着看能否得到批准開發這塊土地。

7 ►PHOTOGRAPHY 攝影◄ [I,T] to make a photograph out of a photographic film, using chemicals 沖印, 使〔底片〕顯影

de·vel·oped /dɪˋvɛləpt; dɪˈveləpt/ *adj* **1 developed country/nation/society** a rich industrial country, nation etc with a lot of business activity 發達國家/社會: *a study of farming methods used in developed countries* 對發達國家農耕方法的研究 —compare 比較 DEVELOPING, UNDERDEVELOPED **2** in a larger or more advanced state 先進的, 發達的

de·vel·op·er /dɪˋvɛləpɚ; dɪˈveləpə/ *n* **1** [C] a person or company that buys land or buildings and hopes to make a profit by building new houses, roads etc〔土地、房產等的〕開發商, 發展商: *an industrial developer* 工業用地開發公司 **2** [C,U] *technical* a chemical substance used for developing photographs【術語】〔沖印底片的〕顯影劑 **3 late developer** a child whose mental or physical growth happens more slowly than other children of the same age 智力[身體]發育得比較慢的孩子

de·vel·op·ing /dɪˋvɛləpɪŋ; dɪˈveləpɪŋ/ *adj* **developing country/nation** a poor country that is trying to increase its industry and improve trade 發展中國家: *One of the basic needs in many developing countries is water.* 在許多發展中國家, 最基本的需求之一就是水。—compare 比較 DEVELOPED, UNDERDEVELOPED

de·vel·op·ment /dɪˋvɛləpmənt; dɪˈveləpmənt/ *n* **1** [U] the gradual growth of something, so that it becomes bigger or more advanced 發育, 成長: *an expert in child development* 兒童成長問題的專家 | **[+of]** *a course on the development of Greek thought* 關於古希臘思想發展的課程 **2** [C] a new event or piece of news that is likely to have an effect on the present situation 事態發展, 新情況: *recent political developments in the former Soviet Union* 前蘇聯的最新政治動態 **3** [C] the act or result of making a product or design better and more advanced〔產品或設計的〕發展, 進展, 進步: *There have been significant computer developments during the last decade.* 在過去的十年內, 電腦有了顯著的發展。**4** [U] the process of planning and building new houses, offices etc on a piece of land〔土地的〕開發: *The land was sold for development.* 這塊土地被出售供開發之用。**5** [C] a group of new buildings that have all been planned and built together on the same piece of land〔在同一塊土地上建造的〕新開發的房產; 新建住宅區, 新社區: *a new housing development* 新建住宅區 —**developmental** /dɪˏvɛləpˋmɛntl; dɪˌveləpˈmentl◄/ *adj* —**developmentally** *adv*

de·vi·ance /ˋdivɪəns; ˈdiːviəns/ also 又作 **de·vi·an·cy** /ˋdivɪənsɪ; ˈdiːviənsi/ *n* [U] deviant behaviour 反常的行為, 不正常之處: *sexual deviance* 性變態

de·vi·ant /ˋdivɪənt; ˈdiːviənt/ *adj* deviant behaviour, especially sexual behaviour, is considered to be strange and morally unacceptable〔尤指性行為〕怪異的, 道德上難以接受的: *Many formerly deviant activities have gradually become accepted forms of behaviour.* 許多以前被認為是離經叛道的行為方式, 已慢慢地變得可以讓人接受。—**deviant** *n* [C] —**deviance, deviancy** *n* [U]

de·vi·ate[1] /ˋdivɪˏet; ˈdiːvieɪt/ *v* [I] *formal* to change what you are doing so that you are not following an expected plan, idea, or type of behaviour【正式】背離, 偏離〔原定計劃、觀點或行為〕: **[+from]** *The plane had to deviate from its normal flight path.* 飛機不得不偏離正常的航線。

de·vi·ate² /ˈdiviɪt; ˈdiːviɪ̮t/ *adj AmE formal* deviant【美, 正式】怪異的, 離經叛道的

de·vi·a·tion /ˌdivɪˈeʃən; ˌdiːviˈeɪʃən/ *n* **1** [C,U] a noticeable difference from what is expected or acceptable 偏離, 背離, 越軌: **[+from]** *deviation from the norm* 背離正常的標準 **2** [C] *technical* a difference between a number or measurement in a set and the average of all the numbers or measurements in that set【術語】偏差, 誤差 —see also 另見 STANDARD DEVIATION

de·vi·a·tion·ist /ˌdivɪˈeʃənɪst; ˌdiːviˈeɪʃənɪ̮st/ *n* [C] a word for someone who disagrees with some parts of a system of political beliefs, used to show disapproval 背離某種政治信仰的人 —**deviationism** *n* [U]

2 **de·vice** /dɪˈvaɪs; dɪˈvaɪs/ *n* [C]

1 ►PIECE OF EQUIPMENT 裝置◄ a piece of equipment intended for a particular purpose, for example for recording or measuring something〔用於專門用途的〕裝置, 器具: **[+for]** *a useful device for detecting electrical activity* 用於探測電流活動的有用儀器 | *modern labour-saving devices* 節省勞力的現代化裝置 —see 見 MACHINE¹ (USAGE)

2 leave sb to their own devices to leave someone alone to do whatever they want 聽任某人自便, 讓某人自行做想做的事情: *I just gave her a brush and paints, and left her to her own devices.* 我只給了她一枝畫筆和一些顏料, 就讓她自己發揮了。

3 ►PLAN/TRICK 計劃/策略◄ a plan or trick, especially for a dishonest purpose〔尤指為不正當目的而採用的〕計劃, 詭計: *Their proposal was only a device to confuse the opposition.* 他們的建議只是為迷惑反對派而使用的花招而已。

4 ►SPECIAL METHOD 特殊方法◄ a special way of doing something that makes it easier to do〔使做某事更容易一些的〕特殊方法, 手段: *Testing yourself with information on cards is a useful device for studying.* 用卡片上的內容測試自己是一種有效的學習方法。

5 ►BOMB 炸彈◄ a bomb or other explosive weapon 炸彈, 爆破裝置: *an explosive device* 一個爆破裝置

6 ►LITERATURE/THEATRE 文學/戲劇◄ the special use of words in literature, or of words, lights etc in a play, to achieve an effect〔文學作品中的〕手法, 修辭手段;〔戲劇中燈光使用的〕技巧: *Metaphor is a common literary device.* 隱喻是一種常用的文學手法。

7 ►PICTURE 圖形◄ *technical* a picture or design used by a NOBLE¹ (3) family as their sign【術語】〔貴族用作家族標誌的〕族徽, 紋章: *the device on his shield* 他盾上的族徽

dev·il /ˈdɛvl̩; ˈdevəl/ *n*

1 ►EVIL 邪惡◄ **a) the Devil** the most powerful evil spirit in Christianity; SATAN〔基督教中的〕惡魔, 撒旦 **b)** [C] any evil spirit 魔鬼: *The villagers believed a devil had taken control of his body.* 村裡的人相信他已魔鬼附身了。

2 ►PERSON 人◄ [C] *informal* someone who behaves very badly, especially a child【非正式】調皮鬼, 淘氣鬼〔尤指孩子〕: *Tommy's a little devil!* 湯米是個小淘氣鬼!

3 speak/talk of the devil *spoken* used when someone you have just been talking about walks into the room where you are【口】說某人某人就到; 說到曹操, 曹操就到

4 play/be devil's advocate to pretend that you disagree with something so that there will be a discussion about it 假裝不同意以促成一場討論

5 be a devil *BrE spoken* used to persuade someone to do something they are not sure they should do【英口】〔用來說服某人做猶豫不決的事〕: *Go on, be a devil, have another gin and tonic.* 來, 膽子大一點, 再來一杯摻奎寧水的杜松子酒。

6 lucky/poor/silly etc devil *spoken* someone who is lucky, unlucky, silly etc【口】幸運/可憐/愚蠢等的傢伙

7 what/who/why etc the devil? *spoken old-fashioned* used to show that you are surprised or annoyed【口, 過時】究竟是甚麼鬼名堂/哪個鬼傢伙/為甚麼等?〔表示驚訝或惱怒〕: *What the devil d'you think you're doing?* 你到底在搞甚麼鬼名堂?

8 a devil of a job/mess etc *old-fashioned* a very unpleasant job, mess etc【過時】糟糕透頂的工作/爛攤子等: *We had a devil of a job trying to get the carpet clean again.* 我們要把地毯再弄乾淨, 真是麻煩極了。

9 go to the devil! *spoken* used to tell someone rudely to go away or stop annoying you【口】滾開! 見鬼去吧!

10 have the luck of the devil to be very lucky 運氣極佳, 鴻運當頭

11 better the devil you know (than the devil you don't) used to say that it is better to deal with someone or something you know, even if you do not like them, than to deal with someone or something new that might be worse 兩害相權取其輕; 寧跟認識的魔鬼打交道〔比跟不認識的魔鬼打交道為好〕

12 be between the devil and the deep blue sea to be in a difficult situation in which you have to choose between two unpleasant things 進退維谷, 左右為難

13 do sth like the devil *old-fashioned* to do something very fast or using a lot of force【過時】迅速地做某事, 賣力地做某事: *They rang the bell and ran like the devil.* 他們按了門鈴, 之後就拚命地跑開了。

14 devil take the hindmost used to describe a situation in which people think about their own success and do not care what happens to anyone else 魔鬼專抓落後者; 要鬼捉不到, 搶在人前逃〔形容只顧及自己的成功而不管別人的死活〕

dev·il·ish /ˈdɛvəlɪʃ; ˈdevəlɪʃ/ *adj* very bad, difficult, or unpleasant 極壞的; 惡毒的: *devilish schemes* 陰謀詭計

dev·il·ish·ly /ˈdɛvəlɪʃlɪ; ˈdevəlɪʃli/ *adv old-fashioned* [+adj/adv] a word meaning very, used to show annoyance【過時】非常, 極其〔表示惱怒〕: *The collector was a devilishly hard fellow to talk to.* 這個收賬人是個極難說話的傢伙。

dev·illed *BrE*【英】, **deviled** *AmE*【美】/ˈdɛvl̩d; ˈdevəld/ *adj* devilled food is cooked in or mixed with very hot pepper〔食物〕辣味的

devil-may-care /ˌ‥ · ˈ·◂/ *adj* cheerful, careless, and willing to take risks 無憂無慮的, 滿不在乎的, 不顧一切的: *a devil-may-care attitude to life* 天塌了也不管的生活態度

dev·il·ment /ˈdɛvl̩mənt; ˈdevəlmənt/ *n* [U] *literary* wild or bad behaviour that causes trouble【文】惡作劇, 搗蛋: *eyes blazing with devilment* 透着狡獪的眼睛

dev·il·ry /ˈdɛvl̩rɪ; ˈdevəlri/ *n* [U] devilment 惡作劇, 搗蛋

devil's food cake /ˈ‥ · ˌ·/ *n* [C,U] an American chocolate cake 美式巧克力蛋糕

de·vi·ous /ˈdiviəs; ˈdiːviəs/ *adj* **1** using dishonest tricks and deceiving people in order to get what you want 欺詐的, 不誠實的: *I wouldn't trust him – he's devious.* 我不會相信他的 —— 他很狡詐。**2** *formal* not going in the most direct way to get to a place【正式】〔路線〕迂迴的, 繞彎的: *a devious route* 迂迴的路線 —**deviously** *adv* —**deviousness** *n* [U]

de·vise /dɪˈvaɪz; dɪˈvaɪz/ *v* [T] to plan or invent a way of doing something, especially something complicated and clever 想出, 設計, 發明: *She devised a method for quicker communications between offices.* 她發明出一種加快辦公室之間互相交流的方法。

de·vi·tal·ize also 又作 **-ise** *BrE*【英】/diˈvaɪtl̩ˌaɪz; ˌdiːˈvaɪtl-aɪz/ *v* [T] to take the power or strength away from something 使失去活力, 使失去生命力 —**devitalization** /diˌvaɪtl̩əˈzeʃən; diːˌvaɪtl-aɪˈzeɪʃən/ *n* [U]

de·void /dɪˈvɔɪd; dɪˈvɔɪd/ *adj* **be devoid of** to be completely lacking in something 毫無…, 完全沒有…: *That man is totally devoid of all humour.* 那個人毫無幽默感。

de·vo·lu·tion /ˌdɛvəˈluʃən; ˌdiːvəˈluːʃən/ *n* [U] the act of giving power from a national government to a group or organization at a lower or more local level〔中央政府向地方政府或下級組織的〕權力下放 —**devolutionary** *adj* —**devolutionist** *n* [C]

de·volve /dɪ`vɑlv; dɪ'vɒlv/ *v*
devolve on/upon sb *phr v* [T not in passive 不用被動態] *formal* to give work, responsibility etc to someone at a lower level【正式】〔工作、職責等〕下放給〔下級〕, 委派給〔下級〕: **devolve sth on/upon sb** *The Governor devolved the choice upon the committee.* 州長把選擇權下放給了委員會。| **it devolves on/upon sb** *It devolved upon the deputy to make a speech.* 發表講話的任務落在了副手的頭上。
devolve to sb *phr v* [T not in passive 不用被動態] *formal*【正式】**1** to give work, responsibility etc to someone at a lower level 把〔工作、職責等〕移交給〔下級〕 **2** if land, goods etc devolve to someone they become the property of that person when their owner dies〔指定在自己死後〕轉讓〔土地、物品等〕給〔某人〕, 讓〔某人〕繼承〔土地、物品等〕

de·vote /dɪ`vot; dɪ'vəʊt/ *v.* **1 devote time/effort/money etc to** to use your time, effort etc in order to do something or help something be successful 為…付出時間/努力/金錢等: *I'm devoting all my time and energy to being a mom right now.* 目前我把所有時間和精力都放在當媽媽這件事上。**2 devote yourself to** to do everything you can to achieve something or help someone 獻身於…, 專心致力於…: *Mother Teresa has devoted herself to caring for the poor.* 德蘭修女把自己的全部身心都傾注在照顧窮苦人之上。

de·vot·ed /dɪ`votɪd; dɪ'vəʊtɪ̈d/ *adj* showing great love and loyalty for someone or something 摯愛的, 忠誠的: *a devoted father* 慈愛的父親 | **[+to]** *Kiko is devoted to her music.* 基科熱愛她的音樂。—**devotedly** *adv*

dev·o·tee /ˌdɛvə`ti; ˌdevə'tiː/ *n* [C] **1** someone who admires someone or something very much 仰慕者, 敬仰者, 愛好者: **[+of]** *a devotee of 1930s films* 一個迷戀20世紀30年代電影的人 **2** a very religious person 虔誠的宗教信徒: *a Sikh devotee* 一個虔誠的錫克教徒

de·vo·tion /dɪ`voʃən; dɪ'vəʊʃən/ *n* **1** [U] great love or loyalty 深愛, 摯愛, 忠心: **[+to]** *Alanna has always shown intense devotion to her children.* 阿蘭娜一直非常鍾愛她的孩子們。**2** [U] the act of spending a lot of time and energy on something 奉獻, 獻身: **[+to]** *her total devotion to her job* 她對工作全心全意的投入 **3** [U] great loyalty to a religion〔對宗教的〕虔誠, 忠信 **4 devotions** [plural] prayers and other religious acts 祈禱等宗教行為

de·vo·tion·al /dɪ`voʃənl̩; dɪ'vəʊʃənəl/ *adj* related to or used in religious services 和宗教儀式有關的, 用於宗教儀式上的: *devotional music* 宗教儀式上使用的音樂

de·vour /dɪ`vaʊr; dɪ'vaʊə/ *v* [T] **1** to eat something quickly because you are very hungry 吞食; 狼吞虎咽地吃: *The boys devoured their pancakes with great joy.* 男孩子們高興地大口吃着餅。**2** to read something quickly and eagerly 快速地閱讀, 貪婪地閱讀: *Joseph devoured the contents of the book avidly.* 約瑟夫如飢似渴地讀着書的內容。**3 be devoured by** to be filled with a strong feeling that seems to control you 充滿〔強烈的, 無法擺脫的情感〕: *Cindy felt devoured by jealousy.* 辛迪心裡充滿了妒忌。**4** to destroy someone or something 毀滅〔某人或某物〕: *beams devoured by rot* 朽爛的梁木 **5 devour sb/sth with your eyes** to look eagerly at someone or something and notice everything about them 貪婪地看某人/某物

de·vout /dɪ`vaʊt; dɪ'vaʊt/ *adj* **1** someone who is devout has a very strong belief in a religion 虔誠的, 篤信宗教的: *a devout Catholic* 虔誠的天主教徒 **2** *formal* a devout hope or wish is one that you feel very strongly【正式】〔希望或願望〕真誠的, 衷心的, 誠摯的: *It is my devout hope that we can work together in peace.* 我衷心希望我們能和睦地在一起工作。—**devoutly** *adv* —**devoutness** *n* [U]

dew /du; djuː/ *n* [U] the small drops of water that form on outdoor surfaces during the night 露珠, 露水

dew·drop /`duˌdrɑp; 'djuːdrɒp/ *n* [C] a small drop of dew 露珠: *dewdrops sparkling in the morning sunlight* 晨光中閃爍的露珠

dew·fall /`duˌfɔl; 'djuːfɔːl/ *n* [U] *literary* the forming of dew or the time when dew begins to appear【文】結露; 開始結露的時候

dew·lap /`duˌlæp; 'djuːlæp/ *n* [C] a hanging fold of loose skin under the throat of a cow, dog etc〔牛、狗等〕喉部垂下的鬆皮, 垂皮, 垂肉

dew·y /`duɪ; 'djuːi/ *adj* wet with drops of DEW 被露水所濕的, 帶露水的: *The dewy woodland was solitary and still.* 露濕的林地一片孤寂和靜謐。

dewy-eyed /ˌ·· `·◂/ *adj* having eyes that are slightly wet with tears 眼睛微濕的, 眼睛含淚的

dex·ter·i·ty /dɛks`tɛrətɪ; dek'sterɪ̈ti/ *n* [U] the ability to be very quick and skilful with your hands〔手的〕敏捷, 靈巧, 熟練: *He used his knife with speed and dexterity.* 他使刀又快又嫻熟。

dex·ter·ous /`dɛkstərəs; 'dekstərəs/ also 又作 **dextrous** /`dɛkstrəs; 'dekstrəs/ *adj* able to use your hands in a skilful way 用手靈活的, 靈巧的, 熟練的: *dextrous use of the needle* 靈巧的針法 —**dexterously, destrously** *adv*

dex·trose /`dɛkstros; 'dekstrəʊz/ *n* [U] a type of sugar that is in many sweet fruits 葡萄糖, 右旋糖

dex·trous /`dɛkstrəs; 'dekstrəs/ *adj* another spelling of DEXTEROUS dexterous 的另一種拼法

dho·ti /`dotɪ; 'dəʊti/ *n* [C] a piece of clothing worn by some Hindu men, consisting of a piece of cloth that is wrapped around the waist and between the legs〔印度男子用的〕纏腰布

dhow /daʊ; daʊ/ *n* [C] an Arab ship with one large sail 單桅阿拉伯帆船

DI /ˌdi `aɪ; ˌdiː 'aɪ/ *n* [C] Detective Inspector; a middle rank in the British police 刑事偵緝督察〔英國的中級警銜〕

di- /daɪ, dɪ; daɪ, dɪ/ *prefix* two; twice; double 二; 兩倍; 雙重: *A dipthong is a vowel made up of two sounds.* 雙元音是由兩個音組成的元音。—compare 比較 SEMI —see also 另見 BI-, TRI-

di·a·be·tes /ˌdaɪə`bitɪs; ˌdaɪə'biːtiːz/ *n* [U] a serious disease in which there is too much sugar in your blood 糖尿病

di·a·bet·ic[1] /ˌdaɪə`bɛtɪk; ˌdaɪə'betɪk◂/ *adj* **1** having diabetes 患糖尿病的: *Sarah is diabetic.* 莎拉患有糖尿病。**2** caused by diabetes 由糖尿病引起的: *a diabetic coma* 由糖尿病引起的昏迷 **3** produced for people who have diabetes 為糖尿病患者專門製作的: *diabetic chocolate* 供糖尿病患者食用的巧克力

diabetic[2] *n* [C] someone who has diabetes 糖尿病患者

di·a·bol·i·cal /ˌdaɪə`bɑlɪkl̩; ˌdaɪə'bɒlɪkəl◂/ *adj* **1** also 又作 **diabolic** /ˌdaɪə`bɑlɪk; ˌdaɪə'bɒlɪk◂/ evil or cruel 邪惡的, 毒辣的: *diabolical abuse* 殘酷的虐待 | *a diabolical plan to destroy him* 一個要毀掉他的惡毒計劃 **2** *informal especially BrE* extremely unpleasant or bad【非正式, 尤英】很壞的, 糟透的: *The toilets were in a diabolical state.* 廁所的情況糟透了。—**diabolically** /-kl̩ɪ; -kli/ *adv*

di·achron·ic /ˌdaɪə`krɑnɪk; ˌdaɪə'krɒnɪk◂/ *adj technical* dealing with something such as a language as it changes over time【術語】歷時的〔研究某物如語言長時間以來的發展情況〕: *a diachronic study* 歷時的研究 —**diachronically** /-kl̩ɪ; -kli/ *adv*

di·a·crit·ic /ˌdaɪə`krɪtɪk; ˌdaɪə'krɪtɪk/ *n* [C] a mark placed over, under, or through a letter in some languages, to show that the letter should be pronounced differently from the letter without a mark〔標於某些語言中的某些字母上方、下方或中間, 表示其發音與無此標誌的字母有所不同的〕變音符號 —**diacritical** *adj*

di·a·dem /`daɪəˌdɛm; 'daɪədem/ *n* [C] *literary* a circle of jewels, flowers etc that you wear on your head【文】鑲有珠寶的環狀頭飾; 花冠

di·ae·re·sis, dieresis /daɪ`ɛrəsɪs; daɪ'ɪərɪ̈sɪ̈s/ *n plural* diaereses /-siz; -siːz/ [C] *technical* a sign (¨) put over the second of two VOWEL*s* to show that it is pronounced separately from the first 分音符, 隔音符〔即"¨",置於兩個元音中的第二個元音之上, 表示此元音與前一元音分開發音〕

di·ag·nose /ˌdaɪəgˋnos; ˈdaɪəgnəʊz/ *v* [T] to find out what is wrong with someone or something, especially what illness someone has, by examining them carefully 判斷; 診斷: *diagnosing computer faults* 找出電腦的毛病 | **diagnose sth as** *The illness was diagnosed as mumps.* 所患疾病被診斷為腮腺炎。

di·ag·no·sis /ˌdaɪəgˋnosɪs; ˌdaɪəgˈnəʊsɪs/ *n plural* **diagnoses** /-siz; -siːz/ [C,U] the discovery of exactly what is wrong with someone or something, by examining them closely 診斷, 判斷: **[+of]** *diagnosis of kidney disease* 腎病的診斷 | **make/give a diagnosis** *An exact diagnosis can only be made by obtaining a blood sample.* 只有採血樣才能作出準確的診斷。—compare 比較 PROGNOSIS

di·ag·nos·tic /ˌdaɪəgˋnɑstɪk; ˌdaɪəgˈnɒstɪk◂/ *adj* related to or used for diagnosis 診斷的, 判斷的: *diagnostic tests* 診斷化驗

di·ag·o·nal /daɪˋægənḷ; daɪˈægənəl/ *adj* **1** a diagonal line is straight and joins two opposite corners of a flat shape, usually a square 對角的, 對角線的 —compare 比較 HORIZONTAL[1] —see picture at 參見 VERTICAL 圖 **2** a diagonal pattern follows a sloping direction 斜的 —**diagonal** *n* [C] —**diagonally** *adv*: *The path goes diagonally across the field.* 這條小徑斜穿過田地。

di·a·gram /ˋdaɪəˌgræm; ˈdaɪəgræm/ *n* [C] a drawing or plan that shows exactly where something is, what something looks like, or how something works 圖解, 圖表, 示意圖: *a diagram of the human body* 人體示意圖 —**diagrammatic** /ˌdaɪəgrəˋmætɪk; ˌdaɪəgrəˈmætɪk◂/ *adj* —**diagrammatically** /-kḷɪ; -kli/ *adv*

dial¹ /ˋdaɪəl; ˈdaɪəl/ *n* [C] **1** the part of a machine or piece of equipment such as a watch, that is usually covered in glass and shows the time or a measurement 儀表盤, 刻度盤; 鐘面, 錶面: *She looked at the dial to check her speed.* 她看了看儀表, 檢查一下自己的速度。**2** the wheel on a telephone with numbered holes for your fingers, that you move around in order to make a call〔電話的〕撥號盤 **3** part of a piece of equipment such as a radio, that you turn around to listen to different radio stations〔收音機等的〕調諧指示板, 調諧度盤

dial² *v* **dialled, dialling** *BrE*【英】, **dialed, dialing** *AmE*【美】[I,T] to move the numbered wheel or press the buttons on a telephone in order to make a telephone call 撥〔電話號碼〕

di·a·lect /ˋdaɪəˌlɛkt; ˈdaɪəlekt/ *n* [C,U] a variety of a language spoken only in one area, in which words or grammar are slightly different from other forms of the same language 方言, 地方話, 土語 —compare 比較 ACCENT¹ (1), IDIOLECT

di·a·lec·tic /ˌdaɪəˋlɛktɪk; ˌdaɪəˈlektɪk/ also 又作 **dialectics** *n* [U] a method of examining and discussing ideas in order to find the truth, that follows rules developed by Socrates, Plato and Hegel〔遵循由蘇格拉底, 柏拉圖以及黑格爾提出的原則研究並討論觀點以發現真理的〕辯證法 —**dialectical** /ˌdaɪəˋlɛktɪkḷ; ˌdaɪəˈlektɪkəl◂/ *adj*

dialling code /ˋ·· ·/ *n* [C] *BrE* the numbers at the beginning of a telephone number that represent a specific area of a city or country【英】電話區域號碼; AREA CODE *AmE*【美】

dialling tone /ˋ·· ·/ *n* [C] *BrE* the sound you hear when you pick up the telephone that lets you know that you can make a call【英】〔電話的〕撥號音; DIAL TONE *AmE*【美】

di·a·logue *BrE*【英】, **dialog** *AmE*【美】/ˋdaɪəˌlɔg; ˈdaɪəlɒg/ *n* [C,U] **1** a conversation in a book, play, or film〔書、戲劇、電影中的〕對話, 對白: *a boring movie full of bad dialog* 充滿差勁對白的乏味電影 **2** *formal* a discussion between two groups, countries etc【正式】〔兩個組織或國家等之間的〕討論, 對話, 意見交換: *There is a need for constructive dialogue between leaders.* 領導人之間需要進行建設性的對話。—compare 比較 MONOLOGUE

dial tone /ˋ· ·/ *n* [C] *AmE* the sound you hear when you pick up the telephone that lets you know that you can make a call【美】〔電話的〕撥號音; DIALLING TONE *BrE*【英】

di·al·y·sis /daɪˋæləsɪs; daɪˈælɪsɪs/ *n* [U] the process of taking harmful substances out of someone's blood using a special machine, because their KIDNEY*s* do not work properly 透析, 滲析〔使用一種特殊的儀器除去腎功能不正常的病人血液中的有害物質〕

di·a·mant·é /ˌdiəmɑnˋte; ˌdiːəˈmɒnteɪ◂/ *adj* decorated with artificial diamonds 飾有人造鑽石的: *a diamanté necklace* 人造鑽石項鏈

di·am·e·ter /daɪˋæmətə; daɪˈæmɪtə/ *n* [C] a straight line going from one side of a circle to the other side, passing through the centre of the circle 直徑: **3 inches/1 metre etc in diameter** *Draw a circle six centimetres in diameter.* 畫一個直徑為六厘米的圓。—see picture at 參見 CIRCLE 圖

di·a·met·ri·cally /ˌdaɪəˋmɛtrɪkḷɪ; ˌdaɪəˈmetrɪkli/ *adv* **diametrically opposed/opposite** completely different and opposite 截然不同的, 截然相反的: *The two ideas are diametrically opposed.* 兩個觀點截然相反。

di·a·mond /ˋdaɪəmənd; ˈdaɪəmənd/ *n*
1 ►**STONE** 寶石◄ [C,U] a very hard valuable stone, that usually has no colour and is used in jewellery 鑽石: *Did you see the size of that diamond engagement ring?* 你有沒有看到那枚訂婚鑽戒有多大?
2 ►**SHAPE** 形狀◄ [C] a shape with four straight sides of equal length that stands on one of its points 菱形 —see picture at 參見 SHAPE¹ 圖
3 ►**ON A PLAYING CARD** 在紙牌上◄ [C] **a)** a diamond shape printed in red on a playing card 紅方塊 **b)** [C] one of the cards in the set that are printed in this way 紅方塊花色的紙牌: *the queen of diamonds* 紅方塊Q, 方塊王后
4 ►**SPORTS FIELD** 體育場地◄ [C] **a)** the area in a BASEBALL field within the diamond shape formed by the four bases (BASE² (8))〔棒球賽場的〕內場〔四壘連線內呈菱形的場地〕**b)** the whole playing field used in BASEBALL 棒球場 —see picture on page A22 參見 A22 頁圖

diamond an·ni·ver·sa·ry /ˌ··· ··ˈ···/ *n* [C] *especially AmE* the date that is exactly 60 years after the date when two people were married【尤美】鑽石婚〔結婚 60 年紀念〕; DIAMOND WEDDING *BrE*【英】

diamond in the rough /ˌ··· · ·ˈ·/ *n* [C] *AmE informal* someone who behaves in a slightly rude way, but is really kind and generous【美, 非正式】外粗內秀的人; ROUGH DIAMOND *BrE*【英】

diamond ju·bi·lee /ˌ··· ˈ···/ *n* [C] the date that is exactly 60 years after the date of an important event, especially of someone becoming a king or queen〔尤指國王或女王加冕的〕60 週年紀念, 60 週年慶典 —compare 比較 GOLDEN JUBILEE, SILVER JUBILEE

diamond wed·ding /ˌ··· ˈ··/ *n BrE* the date that is exactly 60 years after the date when two people were married【英】鑽石婚〔結婚 60 年紀念〕; DIAMOND ANNIVERSARY *AmE*【美】—compare 比較 GOLDEN WEDDING, SILVER WEDDING ANNIVERSARY

di·a·per /ˋdaɪpə; ˈdaɪəpə/ *n* [C] *AmE* a piece of soft cloth that is put between a baby's legs and fastened around its waist to hold liquid and solid waste【美】尿布, 尿片; NAPPY *BrE*【英】 S3

diaper rash /ˋ··· ˌ·/ *n* [U] *AmE* sore skin between a baby's legs and on its BUTTOCK*s*, caused by a wet diaper【美】尿布疹; NAPPY RASH *BrE*【英】

di·aph·a·nous /daɪˋæfənəs; daɪˈæfənəs/ *adj* diaphanous cloth is so fine and thin that you can almost see through it〔布料〕半透明的, 極薄的

di·a·phragm /ˋdaɪəˌfræm; ˈdaɪəfræm/ *n* [C] **1** the muscle

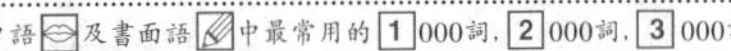

that separates your lungs from your stomach 膈膜, 橫膈膜 **2** a round rubber object that some women wear inside their VAGINA so that they can have sex without having children; DUTCH CAP〔避孕用的〕子宮帽 **3** *technical* any thin piece of stretched material that is moved by sound【術語】振動膜, 膜片

di·a·rist /ˋdaɪərɪst; ˈdaɪərɪst/ *n* [C] someone who keeps a diary and later sells this as a book 日記作者〔尤指日後發表日記的人〕

di·ar·rhoea, diarrhea /ˌdaɪəˋriə; ˌdaɪəˈrɪə/ *n* [U] a medical condition that makes you empty your BOWELS very often and in a very liquid form 腹瀉

di·a·ry /ˋdaɪərɪ; ˈdaɪəri/ *n* [C] **1** a book in which you write down the things that happen to you each day; JOURNAL (2) 日記, 日誌, 日記簿: **keep a diary** (=write things in a diary regularly) 記日記 **2** *BrE* a book with marked separate spaces for each day of the year, in which you write down the meetings, events etc that are planned for each day【英】〔可登記工作日程的〕日程簿, 記事簿; CALENDAR (2a) *AmE*【美】: *Did you put the meeting date in your diary?* 你把開會日期寫在工作記事簿上了嗎?

di·as·po·ra /daɪˋæspərə; daɪˈæspərə/ *n* [C] *formal*【正式】**1 the Diaspora** the movement of the Jewish people away from ancient Palestine, to settle in other countries 大流散〔古代巴比倫人佔領巴勒斯坦後把猶太人趕走, 迫使他們在其他國家定居〕**2** the spreading of people from a national group or culture to other areas〔某一國家或文化的人羣〕流散〔到其他地區〕

di·a·ton·ic scale /ˌdaɪətɑnɪk ˋskel; ˌdaɪətɒnɪk ˈskeɪl/ *n* **the diatonic scale** a set of eight musical notes that uses a fixed pattern of spaces between the notes 自然音音階, 全音階

di·a·tribe /ˋdaɪəˌtraɪb; ˈdaɪətraɪb/ *n* [C] a long speech or piece of writing that criticizes someone or something very severely 長篇抨擊: **[+against]** *a diatribe against contemporary American civilization* 對當代美國文明的長篇抨擊

dibs /dɪbz; dɪbz/ *n* **dibs on sth** *AmE spoken* an expression used especially by children in order to claim a right to something【美口】…歸我所有〔尤指孩子們用來聲明自己有權使用或擁有某物〕: *Dibs on the seat near the window!* 靠窗的位子歸我!

dice¹ /daɪs; daɪs/ *n plural* **dice 1** [C usually plural 一般用複數] a small block of wood, plastic etc that has six sides with a different number of spots on each side, used in games of chance 骰子, 色子: **throw/roll the dice** *She threw the dice and moved her counter across the board.* 她擲了骰子, 然後把籌碼移到賭枱的另一邊。**2** [U] any game of chance that is played with dice 擲骰子遊戲 **3 no dice** *especially AmE spoken* used to refuse to do something or to say that something is not possible【尤美口】沒門兒, 不行〔表示拒絕做某事或說某事是不可能的〕: *"Can I borrow some cash?" "Sorry, no dice."* "我能借些錢嗎?" "對不起, 不行。"

dice 骰子

dice² *v* **1** also 又作 **dice up** [T] to cut food into small square pieces 把〔食物〕切成小方塊[丁]: *diced carrots* 切成丁的胡蘿蔔 —see picture on page A11 參見 A11 頁圖 **2 dice with death** to put yourself in a very dangerous situation 冒險, 玩命 **3** [I+for] *literary* to play dice with someone, for money, possessions etc【文】〔為了錢或財產等〕擲骰子賭博

dic·ey /ˋdaɪsɪ; ˈdaɪsi/ *adj informal* slightly dangerous and uncertain【非正式】稍有危險的; 不肯定的; 無法預計的: *The future looks pretty dicey for small businesses.* 小型企業的前途相當難以預料。

di·chot·o·my /daɪˋkɑtəmɪ; daɪˈkɒtəmi/ *n* [C] *formal* a separation between two things or ideas that are completely opposite【正式】一分為二; 二分法: **[+between]** *a dichotomy between his public and private lives* 他公眾生活和私人生活的兩面性

dick /dɪk; dɪk/ *n* [C] **1** *slang* a PENIS【俚】陰莖 **2** *slang* a stupid annoying person, especially a man【俚】笨蛋, 討厭鬼〔尤指男人〕: *He's acting like a complete dick.* 他表現得就像個大混蛋。**3** *AmE old-fashioned* a PRIVATE DETECTIVE【美, 過時】私人偵探 —see also 另見 **clever dick** (CLEVER (6)), SPOTTED DICK

dick·ens /ˋdɪkɪnz; ˈdɪkənz/ *n* **1 what/who/where the dickens** *spoken* used when asking a question to show that you are very surprised or angry【口】到底是甚麼/誰/在哪兒〔表示非常驚訝或憤怒〕: *What the dickens is the matter with her?* 她到底怎麼回事? **2 as pretty/smart etc as the dickens** *AmE informal* very pretty, clever etc【美, 非正式】非常漂亮/聰明等: *Isn't she as cute as the dickens!* 她多麼可愛啊!

Dic·ken·si·an /dɪˋkɛnzɪən; dɪˈkenziən/ *adj* Dickensian buildings, living conditions etc are poor, dirty, and unpleasant 像狄更斯描繪的, 狄更斯筆下的〔建築物、生活條件等貧困、骯亂、令人不愉快的〕: *a single mother living in a Dickensian block of flats* 住在像狄更斯筆下的公寓房子裡的單身母親

dick·ey /ˋdɪkɪ; ˈdɪki/ *n* another spelling of DICKY² dicky² 的另一種拼法

dick·head /ˋdɪkˌhɛd; ˈdɪkhed/ *n* [C] *slang* a stupid annoying person, especially a man【俚】笨蛋, 討厭鬼〔尤指男人〕: *Don't be such a dickhead!* 別那麼討人厭!

dick·y¹ /ˋdɪkɪ; ˈdɪki/ *adj BrE informal* weak, and likely to break or not work properly【英, 非正式】虛弱的; 不結實的, 易破的, 易壞的: **dicky heart/ticker** (=a heart that is weak and not very healthy) 虛弱的心臟

dicky², dickey *n* [C] a false shirt front sometimes worn by a man under a jacket〔男子穿在上衣裡面的〕只有前襟的假襯衫

dick·y·bird /ˋdɪkɪˌbɝd; ˈdɪkibɜːd/ *n* [C] *BrE*【英】**1** a word meaning any small bird, used by or to children 小鳥〔兒語〕**2 not hear a dickybird** *informal* to not hear any news about someone or something【非正式】杳無音信: *"Have you heard from them since they moved?" "No, not a dickybird."* "他們搬走後你聽到過他們的消息了嗎?" "沒有, 一點也沒有。"

dicky bow /ˋdɪkɪ ˌbo; ˈdɪki bəʊ/ *n* [C] *informal* a BOW TIE【非正式】〔蝶形〕領結

dic·ta /ˋdɪktə; ˈdɪktə/ the plural of DICTUM

Dic·ta·phone /ˋdɪktəˌfon; ˈdɪktəfəʊn/ *n* [C] *trademark* an office machine on which you can record speech so that someone can listen to it and TYPE² (1) it later【商標】口述錄音機〔可錄下講話然後播出給人聽或供人打印出來〕

dic·tate¹ /ˋdɪktet; dɪkˈteɪt/ *v* **1** [I,T] to say words for someone else to write down 口授, 讓〔某人〕聽寫: **dictate sth to sb** *She's dictating a letter to her secretary right now.* 她現在正在給祕書口述一封信。**2** [I,T] to tell someone exactly what they must do or how they must behave 命令, 強制規定, 指定: **[+to]** *I refuse to be dictated to by some mindless bureaucrat!* 我拒絕聽從一些毫無頭腦的官僚的指使! | **dictate who/what/how etc** *Can they dictate how the money will be spent?* 他們能強行規定如何花這些錢嗎? | **as dictated by** (=according to what someone said) 如〔某人〕所指定的那樣 *Federal funds have to be used as dictated by Washington.* 聯邦款項得按照華盛頓規定的方法使用。| **dictate that** *The custom dictates that men should be clean-shaven.* 這兒的習俗規定男士必須把鬍子刮乾淨。**3** [T] to control or influence something; DETERMINE (2) 支配; 影響; 決定: *Funds dictate what we can do.* 資金的多少決定我們能做些甚麼。

dic·tate² /ˋdɪktet; ˈdɪkteɪt/ *n* [C] *formal* an order, rule, or principle that you have to obey【正式】命令, 規定, 指示

dic·ta·tion /dɪkˋteʃən; dɪkˈteɪʃən/ *n* **1** [U] the act of saying words for someone to write down 口授, 口述, 聽寫: **take dictation** (=write down words that someone else is saying) 做聽寫 **2** [C] a piece of writing that a teacher reads out to test your ability to hear and write the words correctly 聽寫的文章〔老師讀出來以測驗學生聽力和寫字是否正確〕: *I hate doing French dictations.* 我討厭做法文聽寫。

dic·ta·tor /ˋdɪktetɚ; dɪkˈteɪtə/ *n* [C] **1** a ruler who has complete power over a country, especially when their power has been gained by force〔尤指通過武力獲取政權的〕獨裁者: *the downfall of the hated dictator* 令人憎恨的獨裁者的垮台 **2** someone who tells other people what they should do, in a way that seems unreasonable 霸道的人: *a real little dictator* 一個十足的小獨裁者

dic·ta·to·ri·al /ˌdɪktəˋtorɪəl; ˌdɪktəˈtɔːriəl◂/ *adj* **1** a dictatorial government or ruler has complete power over a country〔政府或統治者〕獨裁的 **2** a dictatorial person tells other people what to do in an unreasonable way 專橫的, 霸道的: *Professor Clement's dictatorial attitude* 克萊門特教授盛氣凌人的態度 **—dictatorially** *adv*

dic·ta·tor·ship /dɪkˋtetɚˌʃɪp; dɪkˈteɪtəʃɪp/ *n* **1** [C,U] government by a ruler who has complete power 獨裁政府, 獨裁制度, 專政 **2** [C] a country that is ruled by one person who has complete power 獨裁國家

dic·tion /ˋdɪkʃən; ˈdɪkʃən/ *n* [U] **1** the way in which someone pronounces words 發音法: *Actors have training in diction.* 演員接受發音法訓練。**2** the choice and use of words and phrases to express meaning, especially in literature or poetry〔尤指文學或詩歌中的〕措詞, 遣詞用字

dic·tion·a·ry /ˋdɪkʃənˌɛrɪ; ˈdɪkʃənəri/ *n* [C] **1** a book that gives a list of words in alphabetical order and explains their meanings in the same or another language 詞典, 字典: *a German-English dictionary* 一本德英詞典 **2** a book like this that deals with the words and phrases used in a particular subject 專業詞典: *a science dictionary* 科學詞典

dic·tum /ˋdɪktəm; ˈdɪktəm/ *n plural* **dicta** /-tə; -tə/ *or* **dictums** [C] **1** a formal statement of opinion by someone who is respected or has authority〔由受人尊敬的、有權威的人士正式發表的〕意見, 宣言 **2** a short phrase that expresses a general rule or truth 名言, 格言: *He followed the age-old dictum of 'age before beauty'.* 他遵循着"老人優先"這句古老的箴言。

did /dɪd; dɪd/ the past tense of DO¹

di·dac·tic /daɪˋdæktɪk; daɪˈdæktɪk/ *adj formal*【正式】**1** speech or writing that is didactic is intended to teach people a moral lesson 說教的: *His novel has a didactic tone.* 他的小說有一種道德說教的語氣。**2** someone who is didactic is too eager to teach people things or give instructions 好說教的, 喜歡教訓人的 **—didactically** /-klɪ; -kli/ *adv*

did·dle /ˋdɪdl̩; ˈdɪdl/ *v* [T] **diddle sb (out of sth)** *informal* to get money from someone by deceiving them【非正式】從某人處騙得(某物): *They'll diddle you out of your last penny if you give them the chance.* 如果你給他們機會, 他們會把你的錢騙得一分不剩。

did·dly /ˋdɪdlɪ; ˈdɪdli/ also 又作 **diddly-squat** /ˈ·· ·/ *n* **not know/mean diddly** *AmE informal* to know or mean nothing at all【美, 非正式】一無所知/毫無意義: *Brad? He doesn't know diddly about baseball.* 布拉德? 他對棒球一無所知。

did·dums /ˋdɪdəmz; ˈdɪdəmz/ *interjection BrE* a word used to someone who is upset or annoyed in a way you think seems childish【英】〔用於說某人孩子氣地發火、無理取鬧的感嘆詞〕

did·ge·ri·doo /ˌdɪdʒərɪˋdu; ˌdɪdʒəriˈduː/ *n* [C] a long wooden musical instrument, played especially in Australia 狄潔里都號角〔尤指在澳大利亞演奏用的一種長形木管樂器〕

did·n't /ˋdɪdn̩t; ˈdɪdnt/ the short form of 縮略式= 'did not': *You saw him, didn't you?* 你看到他了, 不是嗎?

didst /dɪdst; dɪdst/ **thou didst** *old use*【舊】= you did

1 **die¹** /daɪ; daɪ/ *v past tense and past participle* **died** *present*
1 *participle* **dying** [I]

1 ▶BECOME DEAD 死◀ to stop living and become dead 死去, 死亡: *He was very sick and we knew he might die.* 他病得很重, 我們知道他或許會死。| **of/from** *The animals died of starvation in the snow.* 這些動物在雪中餓死了。| *My grandfather died from a heart attack.* 我爺爺死於心臟病發作。| **[+for]** *Do you believe in anything enough to die for it?* 有沒有甚麼東西讓你相信到能夠為它獻出生命的地步? | **die happy/poor/young etc** *He died young, at the age of 27.* 他英年早逝, 年僅27歲。| **die a hero/martyr/rich man etc** *Van Gogh died a broken man.* 梵谷死時窮困潦倒。| **die a natural/horrible etc death** (=die in a particular way) 自然死亡/死得很慘等 | **to your dying day** (=until you die) 直到你死的那一天 | **die by your own hand** *literary* (=kill yourself)【文】自殺 | **die in your sleep** *She died peacefully in her sleep at the age of 98.* 她在睡眠中安然辭世, 享年98歲。

2 ▶DISAPPEAR 消失◀ to disappear or stop existing 消失, 不復存在: *Our love will never die.* 我們的愛始終不渝。| **die with sb** (=disappear or be finished when someone dies) 隨某人一起消失 *The family name will die with him.* 他去世的時候, 家族的姓氏也隨之消失。

3 ▶MACHINES 機器◀ *informal* to stop working【非正式】停止運作: *The car's engine spluttered and died.* 汽車的引擎發出劈啪聲, 隨後就熄火了。| **die on sb** (=stop working while they are using it) 某人正在使用時突然壞了 *The mower just died on me.* 我正除着草, 忽然割草機壞了。

4 be dying for *spoken* to want something very much【口】極想要, 渴望〔某物〕: *I'm dying for a cup of coffee.* 我真想喝一杯咖啡。

5 be dying to do sth *spoken* to want to do something very much, so that it is difficult to wait【口】迫不及待地想做某事, 渴望做某事: *We're dying to get started.* 我們迫不及待地想開始。

6 be dying of hunger/thirst *spoken* to be very hungry or thirsty【口】都要餓死了/渴死了

7 I nearly died/I could have died *spoken* used to say that you felt very surprised or embarrassed【口】我太驚訝了/我尷尬極了: *I nearly died when my ex-husband walked into the room!* 我的前夫走進屋裡的時候, 我尷尬極了!

8 I'd rather die *spoken* used to say very strongly that you do not want to do something【口】我寧願死〔用來強烈表示某人不想做某事〕: *I'd rather die than work for him!* 我寧願死也不替他工作!

9 old habits die hard used to say that it takes a long time to change to a new way of doing something 積習難改

10 never say die *spoken* used to encourage someone to continue doing something that is difficult【口】別放棄〔用於鼓勵某人繼續做困難的事〕

11 die laughing *spoken* to laugh a lot【口】笑死了: *I nearly died laughing when I saw him with that ridiculous haircut.* 看到他那滑稽的髮型我都要笑死了。

12 die the death *informal* to gradually fail or be destroyed【非正式】慢慢消亡, 壽終正寢: *Eventually the photography club died the death.* 終於, 這個攝影會無疾而終了。

13 dying breath/wish someone's very last breath or wish before they die 最後一口氣/最後一個願望: *No matter what you think, say nothing about it to your dying breath.* 不管你是怎麼想的, 至死都要守口如瓶。

14 die on the vine *literary* to fail, especially at an early stage, because of a lack of support【文】〔由於缺少支持而〕夭折

15 sth to die for something that is so nice or attractive that you would do anything to have it 特別想得到的東西: *cream cakes to die for* 特別想要的奶油蛋糕

die away *phr v* [I] if sound, wind, or light dies away, it becomes gradually weaker and finally stops〔聲音、風、光等〕慢慢變弱, 漸漸消失: *The strange noise died*

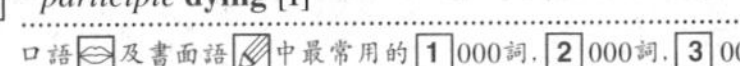

away and an absolute silence closed in upon us. 那種奇怪的聲音慢慢消失了，我們漸漸被一片寂靜所籠罩。

die back *phr v* [I] if a plant dies back, it dies above the ground but remains alive at its roots〔植物〕頂死，回枯，假死〔地面以上部分枯萎，根部卻仍活着〕

die down *phr v* [I] if something dies down, it becomes less strong, active, or violent 減弱，平息: *Don't worry, the gossip will soon die down.* 別擔心，流言蜚語不久就會消失的。

die off *phr v* [I] if a group of people, animals etc die off, they die one by one until there are no more of them 相繼死去，死亡殆盡

die out *phr v* [I] to disappear or stop existing completely 滅絕，絕跡: *Smallpox has completely died out in this country.* 天花在這個國家已經絕跡了。

die² *n* [C] **1** a metal block used to press or cut something into a particular shape 金屬模具，鑄模，壓模 **2** a DICE¹ (1) 骰子 **3 the die is cast** used to say that a decision has been taken and cannot now be changed 木已成舟，事情已成定局

die cast·ing /ˈ· ˌ··/ *n* [U] the process of making metal objects by forcing liquid metal into a hollow container with a particular shape, and then allowing it to become hard 壓鑄〔將液態金屬注入特定形狀的空心容器使其成形〕

die·hard /ˈdaɪˌhɑrd; ˈdaɪhɑːd/ *n* [C] someone who opposes change and refuses to accept new ideas 頑固分子，死硬派〔反對變化、拒絕新觀點的人〕—see also 另見 **old habits die hard** (DIE¹ (9)) —**diehard** *adj*: *a diehard bigot* 老頑固

di·e·re·sis /daɪˈɛrəsɪs; daɪˈɪərɪ̇sɪ̇s/ *n plural* **diereses** /-siz; -siːz/ [C] another spelling of DIAERESIS diaeresis 的另一種拼法

die·sel /ˈdizl; ˈdiːzəl/ *n* **1** [U] a type of heavy oil used instead of petrol in diesel engines 柴油 **2** [C] *informal especially AmE* a vehicle that uses diesel【非正式，尤美】內燃機車；柴油車；柴油船

diesel en·gine /ˈ·· ˌ··/ *n* [C] an engine that burns diesel instead of petrol used especially for buses, trains, and goods vehicles 柴油機，內燃機

diesel fu·el /ˈ·· ˌ··/ also 又作 **diesel oil** /ˈ·· ·/ *n* [U] DIESEL (1) 柴油

3 2 **di·et¹** /ˈdaɪət; ˈdaɪət/ *n*

1 ▶KIND OF FOOD 食物種類◀ [C,U] the kind of food that someone eats each day 日常飲食: *It is important to have a balanced, healthy diet.* 均衡、健康的日常飲食很重要。| *a vegetarian diet* 素食食譜 | **[+of]** *They exist on a diet of fish.* 他們以吃魚為生。

2 ▶TO GET THIN 減肥◀ [C] a limited range and amount of food that you eat when you want to get thinner 節食: **go/be on a diet** *Lyn always seems to be on a diet.* 林恩似乎總是在節食。

3 ▶FOR HEALTH 為了健康◀ [C] a limited type of food and drink that someone is allowed because they have a health problem〔基於健康考慮的〕飲食限制，規定飲食: *a salt-free diet* 無鹽飲食

4 a diet of too much of an activity that you think is boring or has bad effects 多得令人生厭的: *Kids today are raised on a constant diet of pop music and television.* 今天的孩子在成長過程中不斷地被灌輸過多的流行音樂和電視。

5 ▶MEETING 會議◀ [C] *old use* an official meeting to discuss political or church matters【舊】〔討論政治或宗教問題的正式〕會議

diet² *v* [I] to limit the amount and type of food that you eat in order to become thinner〔為減肥而〕節食，限食，按規定進食

di·e·ta·ry /ˈdaɪəˌtɛrɪ; ˈdaɪətəri/ *adj* related to someone's diet 與(規定)飲食有關的: *special dietary requirements* 特殊的飲食要求

di·e·tet·ics /ˌdaɪəˈtɛtɪks; ˌdaɪəˈtetɪks/ *n* [U] the science that is concerned with what people eat and drink and how this affects their health 飲食學，營養學

di·e·ti·cian, dietitian /ˌdaɪəˈtɪʃən; ˌdaɪəˈtɪʃən/ *n* [C] someone who is specially trained in dietetics 飲食學家，營養學家

dif·fer /ˈdɪfɚ; ˈdɪfə/ *v* **1** [I] to be different from something in quality, features etc〔在質量、特徵等上〕不同於，不一樣，有區別: **[+from]** *Humans differ from other mammals in their ability to speak.* 人和其他哺乳動物之不同在於人能說話。| **differ widely/greatly** *Opinions on the subject differ widely.* 在這個問題上意見分歧很大。**2** [I] if two people or groups differ about something, they have opposite opinions 有異議，〔意見〕有分歧: **[+about/on/over]** *The two lawyers differed about how to present the case.* 兩個律師在如何為該案件辯護方面意見不同。**3 agree to differ** to stop arguing with someone and accept that you will never agree 承認意見分歧，保留不同意見 **4 I beg to differ** *spoken formal* used to say that you disagree with someone【口，正式】恕我不能同意，恕我不能贊同

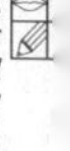

dif·fe·rence /ˈdɪfərəns; ˈdɪfərəns/ *n* **1** [C] something that makes one thing or person different from another thing or person 差異，不同之處: **[+between]** *It's hard to see many differences between the centrist political parties.* 在各中央集權政黨之間很難看出有多少差別。**2** [singular,U] the fact of being different, or an amount by which one thing is different from another 不同，差別；差額: **difference in age/size etc** *There's not much difference in price.* 價格上沒有太大的區別。| **tell the difference** (=recognize that two similar things are different) 辨認出兩個相似事物之間的區別 *The twins are so alike, it's difficult to tell the difference.* 這對雙胞胎長得太像了，很難分出誰是誰。| **a world of difference** (=a big difference) 天壤之別 *There's a world of difference between going abroad on holiday and going there to live.* 出國旅遊和到國外生活有着天壤之別。**3 your/their etc differences** the disagreements that people have 你們/他們等之間的分歧: **have your differences** *We've had our differences in the past, but we get on OK now.* 過去我們有過分歧，但是現在我們相處得不錯。| **settle your differences** (=agree not to argue any more) 消除分歧 **4 difference of opinion** a slight disagreement 意見稍有不一致: *The two sides have a difference of opinion over aims and methods.* 雙方在目的和方法上有些意見不一致。**5 make a (big) difference/make all the difference** to have an important effect on a thing or a situation 有(很大)影響/使大不相同: *Having a good teacher has made all the difference for Alex.* 亞歷克斯有個好老師後情況完全不一樣了。**6 make no difference a)** to have no effect at all on something〔對某事〕根本沒有影響: *Even if you'd tried to help, it wouldn't have made the slightest difference.* 即使你設法幫忙，結果也不會有絲毫不同。**b)** to be unimportant to someone〔對某人〕不重要，無所謂: *It doesn't make any difference to me whether you go or stay.* 你是去是留對我都無所謂。**7 with a difference** used to express approval about something that is different and better 與眾不同: *That was a meal with a difference!* 那頓飯就是不一樣啊！—see also 另見 **split the difference** (SPLIT¹ (8))

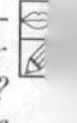

dif·fe·rent /ˈdɪfərənt; ˈdɪfərənt/ *adj* **1** not like something or someone else, or not like before 不同的，不一樣的: *You look different. Have you had your hair cut?* 你樣子變了。你剪髮了嗎？| **[+from]** *Our two sons are very different from each other.* 我們的兩個兒子彼此間一點也不像。| **[+to]** *Her jacket's a bit different to mine.* 她的上衣和我的有點不一樣。| **[+than]** (*AmE* 美) *The estimate is different than we expected.* 這個估價和我們預期的有所不同。**2** [only before noun 僅用於名詞前] separate; DISTINCT 分別的，各不相同的: *He took the photo from three different angles.* 他從三個不同的角度拍照。| *There are many different types of fabric.* 有許多不同種類的布料。**3** [only before noun 僅用於名詞前] another 另外的: *I think she's moved to a different job now.* 我想

她現在已經改做另一份工作去了。| [+from] *This is a different girl from the one he used to go out with.* 這個女孩不是他以前約會的那個。**4** various; several 各種不同的, 幾種的: *There are several different books on the subject.* 有好幾本書都是關於那個主題的。**5** *spoken* unusual, often in a way that you do not like【口】與眾不同的〔常指不是自己喜歡的那種類型〕: *His new jacket is certainly different, but I can't imagine wearing it myself!* 他的新夾克的確很特別, 但是我自己是無論如何也不會穿那樣的衣服的! —**differently** *adv*: *The two words sound the same but they're spelled differently.* 這兩個詞聽起來一樣, 但是拼寫卻不同。

USAGE NOTE 用法說明: DIFFERENT
GRAMMAR 語法
Teachers often prefer **different(ly) from**, but **different(ly) to** is equally common in spoken British English (though not usual in American English). **Different(ly) than** is also used, especially in American English. Note that you never say **different of**. 老師通常喜歡用 different(ly) from, 但是在英國英語口語中 different(ly) to 也同樣常用 (儘管在美語中並不常用)。different(ly) than 也很常用, 尤其是在美語中。注意: 絕對不能說 different of。
SPELLING 拼寫
The noun is **difference**. 名詞是 difference: *the difference between your country and mine* (NOT 不用 *the different*) 你我兩國之間的區別

dif·fe·ren·tial¹ /ˌdɪfəˋrɛnʃəl; ˌdɪfəˈrenʃəl◂/ *n* [C] **1** an amount or degree of difference between things, especially difference in the wages of people doing different types of jobs in the same industry or profession〔尤指同行業不同工作之間的〕工資差額, 差別: *pay differentials* 工資差額 **2** a differential gear 差速器, 差動齒輪

differential² *adj* based on or depending on a difference 基於差別的, 依差別而定的: *differential rates of pay for skilled and unskilled workers* 熟練工人和非熟練工人間不同的工資額

differential cal·cu·lus /ˌ····ˈ···/ *n* [U] *technical* a way of measuring the speed at which an object is moving at a particular moment【術語】微分 (學)

differential gear /ˌ····ˈ·/ *n* [C] an arrangement of gears (GEAR¹ (1)) that allows one back wheel of a car to turn faster than the other when the car goes around a corner〔車輛轉彎時使車的一個後輪轉動得比另一個後輪快的〕差速器, 差動齒輪

dif·fe·ren·ti·ate /ˌdɪfəˋrɛnʃɪet; ˌdɪfəˈrenʃieɪt/ *v* **1** [I,T] to recognize or express the difference between things or people 辨別, 區別: [+between] *The reviews don't even differentiate between good books and bad books.* 這些評論文章甚至連好書和壞書都不加區分。| **differentiate sb/sth from** *It's sometimes hard to differentiate one sample from another.* 有時候很難把一個樣品和另一個樣品區分開來。**2** [T] to be the quality, condition etc that shows the difference between things or people〔特徵或條件等〕構成…間的差別, 使有不同: **differentiate sth/sb from** *Its unusual nesting habits differentiate this bird from others.* 這種鳥獨特的築巢習慣使牠不同於其他的鳥。| **differentiate sth** *What differentiates these two periods of history?* 是甚麼使這兩段歷史時期有所不同? **3** [I] to behave differently towards someone or something, especially in an unfair way; DISCRIMINATE (2) 區別對待〔尤指不公平對待〕: [+between] *He shouldn't differentiate between the quiet and the talkative children.* 他不應該區別對待安靜的孩子和愛講話的孩子。—**differentiation** /ˌdɪfəˌrɛnʃɪˋeʃən; ˌdɪfərenʃiˈeɪʃən/ *n* [U]: *socio-economic differentiation* 社會經濟的區分

1 1 **dif·fi·cult** /ˋdɪfəˌkʌlt; ˈdɪfɪkəlt/ *adj* **1** very hard to do, understand, or deal with; not easy 困難的; 不易的: *Was the exam very difficult?* 考試很難嗎? | *a difficult job* 一份艱難的工作 | **difficult to do** *She finds it difficult to climb stairs.* 她發現爬樓梯很費勁。**2** someone who is difficult never seems pleased or satisfied 難以取悅的, 不易相處的, 不易滿足的: *Don't be so difficult!* 別這麼難纏! **3** involving a lot of problems and causing a lot of trouble or worry 有困難的, 有問題的, 有麻煩的: *Things are a bit difficult at home at the moment.* 目前家裡遇到了些麻煩。| **make life difficult for sb** (=cause problems for someone) 讓某人不好過; 給某人製造麻煩 *They've done everything in their power to make life difficult for me.* 他們用盡一切辦法來讓我的日子不好過。

dif·fi·cul·ty /ˋdɪfəˌkʌltɪ; ˈdɪfɪkəlti/ *n* **1** [U] the state of being hard to do, understand or deal with 困難, 艱難: 1 1
have difficulty doing sth *We have enough difficulty paying the rent as it is!* 目前我們連付租金都很困難! | **with difficulty** *With difficulty, we hauled it up the stairs.* 我們費力地把它拖上了樓梯。| **be in difficulty** (=be having problems) 有困難 *The business is in financial difficulty.* 公司陷入了財務困境。| **get/run into difficulty** (=get into a difficult situation) 陷入困境 *I had to sell my sewing machine when we got into difficulty with an electric bill.* 我們付不起電費時, 我不得不把縫紉機賣掉。**2** [C] a problem or something that causes trouble 難題, 難事: *If you have any difficulties, give me a shout.* 如果你有甚麼困難就喊我一聲。**3** [U] how difficult something is〔某事的〕難度: *The tests vary in difficulty.* 考試的難易程度有所不同。

D

dif·fi·dent /ˋdɪfədənt; ˈdɪfɪdənt/ *adj* shy and unwilling to make people notice you or talk about you 膽怯的, 羞怯的: *He suddenly felt diffident in the presence of these people.* 在這些人面前他忽然感到膽怯。| [+about] *She was diffident about her prize.* 她對自己獲得獎項還不大好意思。—**diffidently** *adv* —**diffidence** *n* [U]

dif·fract /dɪˋfrækt; dɪˈfrækt/ *v* [T] *technical* to divide light into coloured bands or into light and dark bands【術語】使〔光〕衍射, 繞射〔即將光分解成有色光帶或明暗有別的光帶〕—**diffraction** /dɪˋfrækʃən; dɪˈfrækʃən/ *n* [U]

diffuse 擴散

The colour diffused throughout the water.
顏料在水中擴散開來。

dif·fuse¹ /dɪˋfjuz; dɪˈfjuːz/ *v* [I,T] *formal*【正式】**1** to make heat, a gas etc spread so that it mixes with the surrounding air or water (使)〔熱量、氣體等〕擴散, (使) 瀰漫: *The kitchen stove diffused its warmth all over the house.* 廚房的爐子把熱氣擴散到房子的每個角落。**2** to spread ideas, information etc among a lot of people 把〔觀點、信息等〕傳播, (使) 散佈: *Their ideas diffused quickly across Europe.* 他們的觀點很快在歐洲傳播開來。—**diffusion** /dɪˋfjuʒən; dɪˈfjuːʒən/ *n* [U]

dif·fuse² /dɪˋfjus; dɪˈfjuːs/ *adj* **1** scattered over a large area 散開的, 分散的: *The organization is large and diffuse.* 這個組織規模龐大且分佈各地。**2** using a lot of words and not explaining things clearly and directly 堆砌詞藻的, 囉嗦的: *His writing is diffuse and difficult to understand.* 他寫的東西行文冗贅, 晦澀難懂。—**diffusely** *adv* —**diffuseness** *n* [U]

dig¹ /dɪg; dɪg/ *v* past tense and past participle **dug** /dʌg; 3
dʌg/ *present participle* **digging** **1** [I,T] to move earth or make a hole in it using a SPADE or your hands 挖〔土〕, 掘〔洞〕: *They escaped by digging an underground tunnel.* 他們挖個地道逃走了。| **dig for sth** (=dig in or-

der to find something) 挖尋某物 *They're digging for treasure.* 他們在挖掘寶藏。**2** [T] to remove vegetables from under the earth using a SPADE 挖〔菜〕: *She's digging potatoes at the moment.* 這時候她正在挖馬鈴薯。**3** [T] *old-fashioned* to like something【過時】喜歡: *I really dig that dress!* 我真喜歡那件衣服！**4 dig your own grave** to do something that will cause serious problems for you in the future 自掘墳墓, 自取滅亡, 自討苦吃 **5 dig sb in the ribs** to touch someone with your elbow, especially because you want them to notice something amusing 用肘碰某人的肋部〔讓某人注意好笑的事〕

dig in *phr v* **1** [T **dig** sth ↔ **in**] to mix something into soil by digging 翻地把〔某物〕摻入土壤裡: *I need to dig some manure in before I plant the potatoes.* 在種馬鈴薯之前我需要翻土埋進肥料。**2 dig your heels in** to refuse to do something in spite of other people's efforts to persuade you〔儘管別人苦苦相勸〕堅決不做〔某事〕, 固執己見 **3** [I] *informal* to start eating food that is in front of you【非正式】開始吃: *Dig in! There's plenty for everyone!* 盡量吃吧！足夠大家吃的！**4** [I,T] if soldiers dig in or dig themselves in, they make a protected place for themselves by digging〔士兵〕挖壕溝等掩體以隱蔽自己

dig into *phr v* **1** [T **dig** sth **into** sth] to mix something into soil by digging 翻土把〔某物〕混在土壤中: *Dig some fertilizer into the soil first.* 先在翻地時把一些肥料摻到土壤裡。**2** [I,T **dig** sth **into** sth] to push hard into something, or to make something do this（使）推入,（使）戳進: *Her nails were digging into his arm.* 她的指甲正往他的胳膊裡摳。**3** [T **dig into** sth] to start using a supply of something, especially money 開始使用儲備的東西〔尤指錢〕: *I'm going to have to dig into my savings again.* 我又得動用我的存款了。

dig sth ↔ **out** *phr v* [T] **1** to get something out of a place, using a SPADE or your hands 把〔某物〕挖出來: *We had to dig the car out of a snow drift.* 我們得把汽車從雪堆裡挖出來。**2** to find something you have not seen for a long time, or that is not easy to find 找到, 翻出〔很久沒看到的或很難找到的東西〕: *I must remember to dig out that book for you.* 我必須記着把那本書給你找出來。

dig sth ↔ **up** *phr v* [T] **1** to remove something from under the earth using a SPADE〔從地裡〕挖出, 掘起: *I'll dig up that plant and move it.* 我要把那棵植物挖出來, 把它挪個地方。**2** to find hidden or forgotten information by careful searching〔通過仔細搜索、查詢〕找出, 揭露: *They tried to dig up something from his past to spoil his chances of being elected.* 他們試圖從他的過去挖出些東西來破壞他當選的機會。

dig² *n* **1 give sb a dig** to push someone quickly and lightly with your finger or elbow〔用手指或肘部〕觸某人, 碰某人, 戳某人: *John's falling asleep – give him a dig will you?* 約翰要睡着了 —— 捅他一下好嗎？**2** [C] a joke or remark that you make to annoy or criticize someone 挖苦, 嘲諷: **[+at]** *I thought that last comment was a dig at the boss.* 我認為最後的那句話是挖苦老闆的。**3** [C] the process of digging in an ancient place in order to find objects for study〔為找到可供研究的東西在遺址上〕發掘: *an archaeological dig* 考古發掘 **4 digs** [plural] *BrE old-fashioned* a room that you pay rent to live in【英, 過時】租住的房間

di·gest¹ /daɪˋdʒɛst; daɪˈdʒest/ *v* [T] **1** to change food that you have just eaten into substances that your body can use 消化〔食物〕: *Most babies can digest a wide range of food easily.* 大多數嬰兒能容易地消化多種食物。—compare 比較 INGEST **2** to understand new information, especially when there is a lot of it or it is difficult to understand 理解, 領悟, 消化〔尤指大量新資訊或難以理解的資訊〕: *I struggled to digest the news.* 我費力地琢磨着那條新聞的意思。

di·gest² /ˋdaɪdʒɛst; ˈdaɪdʒest/ *n* [C] a short piece of writing that gives the most important facts from a book, report etc 摘要, 概要, 文摘

di·gest·i·ble /daɪˋdʒɛstəbḷ; daɪˈdʒestɨbəl/ *adj* food that is digestible can be easily digested 容易消化的, 易吸收的 —opposite 反義詞 INDIGESTIBLE

di·ges·tion /dəˋdʒɛstʃən; daɪˈdʒestʃən/ *n* **1** [U] the process of digesting food 消化 **2** [C] your ability to digest food easily 消化能力: **a good/poor etc digestion** *I've always had a poor digestion.* 我一直消化不好。

di·ges·tive /daɪˋdʒɛstɪv; daɪˈdʒestɪv/ *adj* [only before noun 僅用於名詞前] connected with the process of digestion 消化的: *the digestive system* 消化系統

digestive bis·cuit /ˌ.ˌ.. ˈ../ *n* [C] a type of plain, slightly sweet BISCUIT (1) that is popular in Britain 消化餅乾〔一種在英國很受歡迎的、味道微甜的餅乾〕

digestive system 消化系統

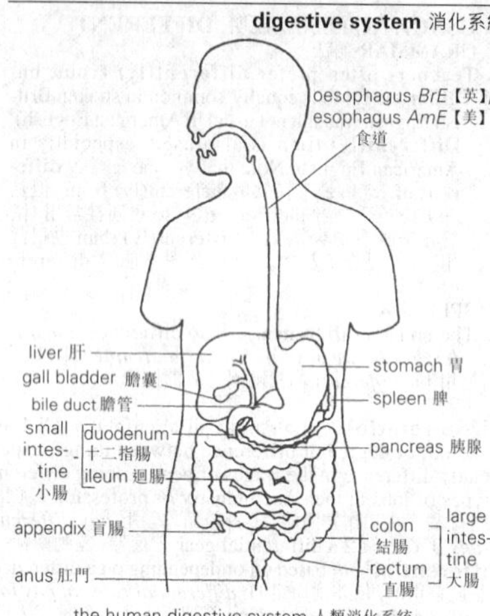

the human digestive system 人類消化系統

digestive sys·tem /ˈ... ˌ../ *n* [C] the system of organs in which your body digests (DIGEST¹ (1)) food 消化系統

dig·ger /ˋdɪgɚ; ˈdɪgə/ *n* [C] a large machine that digs and moves earth 挖掘機 —see also 另見 **gold digger**

dig·gings /ˋdɪgɪŋz; ˈdɪgɪŋz/ *n* [plural] a place where people are digging for metal, especially gold〔尤指開採黃金的〕礦區, 礦場

di·git /ˋdɪdʒɪt; ˈdɪdʒɨt/ *n* [C] **1** one of the written signs that represent the numbers 0 to 9〔0 到 9 的任何一個〕數字: **three-digit/four-digit etc number** *4305 is a four-digit number.* 4305 是個四位數。**2** *technical* a finger or toe【術語】手指; 腳趾

di·gi·tal /ˋdɪdʒətḷ; ˈdɪdʒɨtl/ *adj* **1** using a system in which information is represented in the form of changing electrical signals 數字的, 數碼的: **digital cassette/compact disc/audio-tape etc** *recorded on digital audiotape* 在數碼錄音磁帶上錄音的 **2** giving information in the form of numbers 數字顯示的: *a digital watch* 一個數字顯示式電子手錶 **3** *formal* of the fingers and toes【正式】手指的; 腳趾的

digital com·put·er /ˌ.... ˈ../ *n* [C] a type of computer that uses a BINARY (1) system〔使用二進制系統的〕數字計算機; 數位電腦

digital re·cord·ing /ˌ.... ˈ../ *n* [C,U] a high quality recording of sound made by changing information about the sound into the binary system (BINARY (1)) 數碼錄音〔把音頻信息轉化成二進制系統的高質量錄音方式〕

di·gi·tize also 又作 **-ise** *BrE*【英】/ˋdɪdʒəˌtaɪz; ˈdɪdʒɨtaɪz/ *v* [T] to put information into a digital form 把〔信息〕轉變成數字形式, 使〔信息〕數字化

dig·ni·fied /ˋdɪgnəˌfaɪd; ˈdɪgnɨfaɪd/ *adj* behaving in a calm and serious way, even in a difficult situation, which makes people respect you〔舉止〕莊重的, 有尊嚴的: *a dignified old lady* 頗有威嚴的老太太 | *She made a dignified departure.* 她不失尊嚴地離去。

dig·ni·fy /ˋdɪgnə,faɪ; ˈdɪgnɪ̈faɪ/ *v* [T] to make something or someone seem better or more important than they really are by using a particular word to describe them 抬高…的身價: **dignify sb/sth with** *I cannot dignify him with the name 'physician'.* 我不能用"醫生"這個稱呼來高抬他。

dig·ni·ta·ry /ˋdɪgnə,tɛrɪ; ˈdɪgnɪ̈təri/ *n* [C] someone who has an important official position 顯要人物, 權貴: *Flowers were presented to visiting dignitaries.* 向到訪的達官貴人獻上了鮮花。

dig·ni·ty /ˋdɪgnətɪ; ˈdɪgnɪ̈ti/ *n* **1** [U] the ability to behave in a way that shows you respect yourself and stay calm, even in a very difficult situation 莊重, 尊貴, 尊嚴, 體面: *The family faced their ordeal with dignity and courage.* 這一家人以尊嚴和勇氣面對磨難。| **human dignity** *Even in the prison camp we tried to retain some human dignity.* 即使在戰俘營裡我們也盡力保留一些做人的尊嚴。**2** [U] a calm and serious manner or quality 莊嚴, 端莊: *The dignity of the occasion was spoilt when she fell down the steps.* 她從台階上摔下來, 破壞了這個場合的莊嚴氣氛。**3 be beneath your dignity** if something is beneath your dignity, you think you are too good or important to do it 有失身分, 有失體面: *Such arguing was beneath her dignity.* 這樣的爭吵有失她的身分。**4 stand on your dignity** to demand to be treated with proper respect 要求受到禮遇, 擺架子: *He stood on his dignity, insisting that the car be brought to the door.* 他擺起架子, 堅持讓人把車開到門口。**5** [C] a high social position, rank, or title 高位, 顯職

di·graph /ˋdaɪgræf; ˈdaɪgrɑːf/ *n* [C] *technical* a pair of letters that represent one sound, such as 'ea' in 'head' and 'ph' in 'phrase'【術語】〔代表一個音的〕二合字母, 單音雙字母〈如 head 中的 ea, phrase 中的 ph〉

di·gress /daɪˋgrɛs; daɪˈgres/ *v* [I] *formal* to move away from the main subject that you are talking or writing about【正式】〔說話或寫作時〕偏離主題, 轉移話題: *Do you mind if I digress for a moment?* 我說些題外話, 你不介意吧? —**digression** /daɪˋgrɛʃən; daɪˈgreʃən/ *n* [C, U]: *After several long digressions he finally reached the interesting part of the story.* 說了好幾番長時間的題外話之後, 他終於開始講故事的有趣部分。

dike /daɪk; daɪk/ *n* [C] another spelling of DYKE dyke 的另一種拼法

dik·tat /dɪkˋtɑt; dɪkˈtæt/ *n* [C,U] an order that is forced on people by a ruler or government〔統治者或政府強加在人民身上的〕強制命令, 勒令: *government by diktat* 用專橫手段統治〔人民〕的政府

di·lap·i·dat·ed /dəˋlæpə,detɪd; dɪ̈ˈlæpɪ̈deɪtɪ̈d/ *adj* a dilapidated building, vehicle etc is old and in very bad condition〔建築物、車輛等〕破爛不堪的

di·lap·i·da·tion /də,læpəˋdeʃən; dɪ̈,læpɪ̈ˈdeɪʃən/ *n* **1** [U] the state of an old building when it is in very bad condition and beginning to fall down 破舊; 坍塌 **2 dilapidations** [plural] *BrE law* money that you have to pay if you damage a house that you are renting【英, 法律】〔租用期間損壞房子而應支付的〕賠償金

di·late /daɪˋlet; daɪˈleɪt/ *v* [I,T] if a part of your body dilates or if something dilates it, it becomes wider 擴張, 張大, 膨大: *dilated pupils* 擴大的瞳孔 —**dilation** /daɪˋleʃən; daɪˈleɪʃən/ *n* [U]: *pupil dilation during sexual arousal* 性興奮時的瞳孔擴大

dilate on/upon sth *phr v* [T] *formal* to speak or write a lot about something【正式】詳述某事, 鋪敘某事: *He dilated upon their piety and heroism.* 他詳盡地敘述了他們的虔誠和英雄主義行為。

dil·a·to·ry /ˋdɪlə,torɪ; ˈdɪlətəri/ *adj formal* slow and tending to delay decisions or actions【正式】拖延的, 拖拉的, 遲緩的: *dilatory attempts to reach an agreement* 試圖拖延達成協議

dil·do /ˋdɪldo; ˈdɪldəʊ/ *n* [C] an object shaped like a male sex organ that some women put inside their VAGINA for sexual pleasure 假陰莖〔一種性用具〕, 人造男性生殖器

di·lem·ma /dəˋlɛmə; dɪ̈ˈlemə/ *n* [C] a situation in which it is very difficult to decide what to do, because all the choices seem equally good or equally bad 進退兩難的境地, 困境: *a moral dilemma* 道德上進退兩難的窘境 | **be in a dilemma** *I'm in a dilemma about this job offer.* 對於提供的這份工作我不知道是接受還是不接受。| **be on the horns of a dilemma** (=be unable to decide between two unpleasant choices) 左右為難

dil·et·tan·te /,dɪləˋtæntɪ; ,dɪlɪ̈ˈtænti/ *n* [C] someone who seems or pretends to be interested in a subject but is not seriously interested and does not know very much about it 半瓶醋的涉獵者, 玩票式的愛好者, 假行家, 半吊子〔看似或假裝對某個科目感興趣, 但實際上對此並非真正感興趣或對此所知不多〕—**dilettante** *adj*

dil·i·gent /ˋdɪlədʒənt; ˈdɪlɪ̈dʒənt/ *adj* someone who is diligent works hard and is careful and thorough 勤奮的, 勤勉的: *Philip is a diligent worker and should do well in the examinations.* 菲利普是個勤奮的學生, 他會考出好成績的。—**diligently** *adv*: *They worked diligently all morning.* 他們整個上午工作都很勤奮。—**diligence** *n* [U]

dill /dɪl; dɪl/ *n* [U] a garden plant used to give a special taste to food 蒔蘿, 小茴香〔用於給食物調味〕

dill pick·le /,· ˈ··/ *n* [C] a whole CUCUMBER which has been preserved in vinegar 酸黃瓜

dil·ly /ˋdɪlɪ; ˈdɪli/ *n* [C] *AmE old-fashioned* something or someone exciting or special【美, 過時】驚人的人[物]; 精彩的事物: *That's a dilly of a rollercoaster!* 過山車可真是驚險啊!

dilly-dal·ly /ˈ·· ,··/ *v* [I] *informal* to waste time, because you cannot decide about something【非正式】〔由於對某事猶豫不決而〕浪費時間, 猶猶豫豫: *Don't dilly-dally, just get on with it!* 別磨磨蹭蹭的, 繼續做下去吧!

di·lute¹ /dɪˋlut; daɪˈluːt/ *v* [T] **1** to make a liquid weaker by adding water or another liquid 把〔液體〕稀釋, 使〔液體〕變淡: *Give the baby diluted fruit juice.* 給嬰兒喝稀釋的果汁。| **dilute sth with sth** *Dilute the paint with a little oil.* 用少量汽油把油漆稀釋一下。**2** to make a quality, belief etc weaker or less effective 降低〔質量〕, 削弱〔信念〕: *Opening NATO to new members may dilute its strength.* 把北大西洋公約組織向新成員國開放可能會削弱它的力量。—**dilution** /dɪˋluʃən; daɪˈluːʃən/ *n* [U]: *Any dilution of academic standards must be resisted.* 任何降低學術水平的行為都必須加以抵制。

dilute² /dɪˋlut; ,daɪˈluːt◂/ *adj* a dilute liquid has been made weaker by the addition of water or another substance 稀釋的, 沖淡的: *dilute hydrochloric acid* 稀釋的鹽酸

dim¹ /dɪm; dɪm/ *adj* **dimmer, dimmest**

1 ►DARK 暗◄ fairly dark or not giving much light, so that you cannot see well 陰暗的, 昏暗的: *in the dim light of the early dawn* 在破曉的微曦下

2 ►SHAPE 形狀◄ a dim shape is one which is not easy to see because it is too far away, or there is not enough light 朦朧的, 隱約的: *The dim outline of a large building loomed up out of the mist.* 一座龐大建築物朦朧的輪廓在霧靄中隱現出來。

3 ►EYES 眼睛◄ *literary* dim eyes are weak and cannot see well【文】視力不好的, 弱視的: *The dim eyes of the old woman were surprisingly attractive.* 那位老太太矇朧的雙目出奇地迷人。

4 dim recollection/awareness etc a memory or understanding of something that is not clear in you mind; VAGUE (2) 模糊的記憶/意識等: *Laura had a dim recollection of someone telling her this before.* 勞拉隱約記得以前曾有人告訴過她這事。

5 ►FUTURE CHANCES 未來的機會◄ if your chances of success in the future are dim, they are not good〔未來成功的機會或可能〕暗淡的, 不樂觀的: *Prospects for an*

D

early settlement of the dispute are dim. 爭端得到早日解決的希望渺茫。

6 in the dim and distant past *humorous* a very long time ago【幽默】很久以前

7 take a dim view of to disapprove of something 不贊成〔某事〕: *We took a dim view of his disobedience.* 我們不喜歡他的違命。

8 ►UNINTELLIGENT 不聰明的◄ *informal especially BrE* not intelligent【非正式, 尤英】愚笨的: *You can be really dim sometimes!* 有時候你是真笨啊! —**dimly** *adv*: *a dimly lit room* 燈光暗淡的房間 | *She was only dimly aware of the risk.* 她只是隱隱約約意識到有危險。—**dimness** *n* [U]

dim² *v* **dimmed, dimming 1** [I,T] if a light dims, or if you dim it, it becomes less bright (使)變暗淡, (使)變得不亮: *The lights in the theatre began to dim.* 劇院裡的燈光開始暗下來。**2** [I,T] if a feeling or quality dims or is dimmed, it grows weaker〔感覺等〕變弱, 〔質量等〕下降: *Her beauty had not dimmed over the years.* 過了這麼多年她的美貌依舊。| *His words dimmed our hopes of a peaceful settlement.* 他的話削弱了我們和平解決問題的希望。**3 dim your headlights/lights** *AmE* to lower the angle of the front lights of your car, especially when someone is driving towards you【美】〔尤其當對面有車開來的時候〕使汽車前燈燈光變暗; DIP¹ (3) *BrE*【英】

D

dime /daɪm; daɪm/ *n* [C] **1** a coin of the US and Canada, worth one tenth of a dollar〔美國、加拿大的〕十分硬幣 —compare 比較 CENT **2 a dime a dozen** *AmE informal* very common and not valuable【美, 非正式】不值錢的, 稀鬆平常的: *PhDs are a dime a dozen nowadays.* 如今, 博士學位一文不值。

dime nov·el /'· ,··/ *n* [C] *AmE* a cheap book with a story that contains a lot of exciting events【美】廉價小説〔其中包含許多令人興奮的故事情節〕

3 **di·men·sion** /də`mɛnʃən; daɪ'menʃən/ *n* **1** [C] a part of a situation that makes you regard the situation in a particular way; ASPECT (1)〔形勢的〕方面, 部分: **new/different dimension** *The baby has added a new dimension to their lives.* 嬰兒給他們的生活增添了新的一面。| **political/social/spiritual dimension** *We should not forget that education has an important spiritual dimension.* 我們不應該忘記精神教育是教育的一個重要部分。**2** [C] a measurement in space, for example length, height etc〔空間的〕量度, 維度〔如長度、高度等〕: *A diagram represents things in only two dimensions.* 示意圖是以二維的〔平面的〕方式展現事物的。—see also 另見 FOURTH DIMENSION **3 dimensions** [plural] **a)** the size of something, especially when this is given as its length, height, and width 大小, 尺寸, 規模〔尤指某物的長、寬、高〕: *What are the room's dimensions?* 這個房間面積多少? **b)** how great or serious a problem is〔問題的〕嚴重程度: *We're heading for a catastrophe of enormous dimensions.* 我們正走向極其嚴重的災難。

dime store /'· ·/ *n* [C] *AmE* a shop that sells many different kinds of cheap goods, especially for the house【美】廉價〔家用品〕雜貨店

di·min·ish /də`mɪnɪʃ; dɪ̵'mɪnɪʃ/ *v* **1** [I,T] to become or make something become smaller or less important (使)減少, (使)減小: *The party's share of the electorate has diminished steadily.* 這個政黨擁有的選民數量正持續下降。| **diminish sth** *These drugs diminish blood flow to the brain.* 這些藥物減少流向大腦的血液量。**2** [T] to deliberately make someone or something appear less important or valuable than they really are 削弱, 貶低〔重要性、價值〕: *Don't let him diminish your achievements.* 別讓他貶低你的成就。**3 diminishing returns** the idea that a point can be reached at which the profits or advantages you are getting stop increasing in relation to the effort you are making 收益遞減, 報酬遞減

diminished re·spon·si·bil·i·ty /·'·· ···'···/ *n* [U] *law* a state in which someone is not considered to be responsible for their actions because they are mentally ill【法律】〔由於某人精神失常而〕減輕的刑事責任

di·min·u·en·do /də,mɪnju`ɛndo; dɪ̵,mɪnju'endəʊ/ *n* [C] *technical* a part in a piece of music where it becomes gradually quieter【術語】〔音樂的〕逐漸減弱, 漸弱 —opposite 反義詞 CRESCENDO —**diminuendo** *adj adv*

dim·i·nu·tion /,dɪmə`nuʃən; ,dɪmɪ̵'nju:ʃən/ *n* [C,U] a reduction in the size, number, or amount of something〔大小、數目、數量的〕變小, 縮小, 減少: [+of/in] *a diminution in value* 價值的減少

di·min·u·tive¹ /də`mɪnjətɪv; dɪ̵'mɪnjʊ̵tɪv/ *adj formal* small or short【正式】個子矮小的: *a shy diminutive man* 一個腼腆的矮個子男人

diminutive² *n* [C] a word formed by adding a diminutive suffix 由表示"小"的後綴構成的詞

diminutive suf·fix /·,··· '··/ *n* [C] *technical* an ending that is added to a word to express smallness, for example 'ling' added to 'duck' to make 'duckling'【術語】〔加在某詞後面的〕表示"小"的後綴[詞尾]〈如 ling, 它加在 duck (鴨子) 後面便變成了duckling (小鴨子)〉

dim·i·ty /`dɪmətɪ; 'dɪmɪ̵ti/ *n* [U] a strong cotton cloth with a slightly raised pattern on it 提花棉布, 凸紋棉布

dim·mer /`dɪmə; 'dɪmə/ also 又作 **dimmer switch** *n* [C] **1** an electric light SWITCH² (1) that can change the brightness of the light 調光器; 變光器 **2** a SWITCH for lowering the beam of a car's front lights 調節汽車前燈燈光角度的開關 —DIPSWITCH *BrE*【英】

dim·ple /`dɪmpl; 'dɪmpəl/ *n* [C] a small hollow place on your cheek or chin, especially one that forms when you smile〔臉頰上的〕酒窩; 〔下巴上的〕凹痕 —see picture on page A6 參見A6頁圖

dim·pled /`dɪmpḷd; 'dɪmpəld/ *adj* having dimples 有酒窩的: *her dimpled cheeks* 她帶着酒窩的雙頰

dim·wit /`dɪm,wɪt; 'dɪmwɪt/ *n* [C] *spoken* a stupid person【口】笨人, 傻子: *dimwits not worthy of our attention* 不值得我們關心的傻人 —**dim-witted** /,· '··◂/ *adj*

din¹ /dɪn; dɪn/ *n* [singular] a loud unpleasant noise that continues for a long time〔持續很久的〕嘈雜聲, 喧鬧聲: *The kids were making a horrendous din.* 孩子們吵得厲害。

din² *v* **dinned, dinning**

din sth into sb *phr v* [T] to make someone learn and remember something by repeating it to them again and again 再三叮囑, 反覆告誡: *Respect for our elders was dinned into us at school.* 在學校裡我們被反覆教導要尊敬長者。

di·nar /dɪ`nɑr; 'di:nɑ:/ *n* [C] the standard unit of money used in the former Yugoslavia and in several muslim countries 第納爾〔前南斯拉夫和一些穆斯林國家的貨幣單位〕

dine /daɪn; daɪn/ *v* [I] *formal* to eat dinner【正式】進餐: *We dined at the Ritz.* 我們在里兹大酒店用了餐。—see also 另見 **wine and dine** (WINE²)

dine on/off sth *phr v* [T] *formal* to eat a particular kind of food for dinner, especially expensive food【正式】吃〔尤指昂貴的食物〕當正餐: *We dined on lobster and strawberries.* 我們正餐吃的是龍蝦和草莓。

dine out *phr v* [I] **1** *formal* to eat dinner in a restaurant or in someone else's house【正式】外出用餐〔指在餐廳或別人家吃飯〕: *They would dine out together once a month.* 他們每月一起出去吃一次飯。—see also 另見 **eat out** (EAT (1b)) **2 dine out on** *BrE humorous* to keep using a story about something that has happened to you in order to entertain people at meals【英, 幽默】〔吃飯時〕總用〔發生在自己身上的某一件事〕來逗樂

din·er /`daɪnə; 'daɪnə/ *n* [C] **1** someone who is eating dinner in a restaurant〔在餐廳〕用餐者 **2** *AmE* a small restaurant that serves cheap meals【美】〔價格便宜的〕小餐館, 小飯店: *She's a waitress in an all-night diner in North Vegas.* 她在北維加斯的一個通宵營業的小餐館裡當侍應。**3** *AmE* a DINING CAR【美】餐車

di·nette /daɪ`nɛt; daɪ'net/ *n* [C] *AmE* a small area, usually in or near the kitchen, where people eat meals【美】〔廚房裡或靠近廚房供人們吃飯用的〕小飯廳

dinette set /ˈ‥ ˌ·/ *n* [C] *AmE* a table and matching chairs【美】配套的餐桌椅

ding-a-ling /ˋdɪŋ ə lɪŋ; ˈdɪŋ ə lɪŋ/ also 又作 **ding·bat** /ˋdɪŋbæt; ˈdɪŋbæt/ *n* [C] *AmE spoken* a stupid person【美口】傻瓜, 笨蛋: *Who's that fat dingbat over there?* 那邊那個肥胖的傻瓜是誰?

ding-dong /ˋdɪŋ ˌdɔŋ; ˈdɪŋ dɒŋ/ *n* **1** [U] the noise made by a bell 鈴聲; 叮噹聲 **2** [singular] *BrE informal* a noisy argument【英, 非正式】喧鬧的爭吵, 爭辯: *They were having a real ding-dong in the kitchen.* 他們在廚房爭吵得正兇呢。

din·ghy /ˋdɪŋgɪ; ˈdɪŋgi/ *n* [C] **1** a small open sailing boat used especially for racing 無篷小帆船〔尤指用作比賽的小帆船〕 **2** a small open boat used for pleasure or for taking people between a ship and the shore 〔娛樂用的〕小遊艇;〔載人往返於大船與岸邊的〕小艇 —see also 另見 RUBBER DINGHY

din·gle /ˋdɪŋgḷ; ˈdɪŋgəl/ *n* [C] *literary* a small valley with trees in it【文】〔長滿樹木的〕小山谷, 幽谷: *He went alone to the dingle to clear his thoughts.* 他獨自去了小幽谷整理思緒。

din·go /ˋdɪŋgo; ˈdɪŋgəʊ/ *n plural* **dingoes** [C] an Australian wild dog 澳洲野犬

din·gy /ˋdɪndʒɪ; ˈdɪndʒi/ *adj* a dingy room, street, or place is dark, dirty, and in bad condition 骯髒的, 邋遢的: *a dingy back street* 又黑又髒的後街 —**dingily** *adv*: *dingily furnished* 裝飾暗淡、破舊的 —**dinginess** *n* [U]

din·ing car /ˈ‥ ·/ *n* [C] a carriage on a train where meals are served; RESTAURANT CAR 〔火車上的〕餐車

dining room /ˈ‥ ·/ *n* [C] a room where you eat meals in a house, hotel etc 〔家裡的〕飯廳;〔旅館的〕餐廳

dining ta·ble /ˈ‥ ˌ‥/ *n* [C] a table for having meals on 餐桌 —compare 比較 DINNER TABLE

dink /dɪŋk; dɪŋk/ *n* [C] *informal* Double Income No Kids; one of two young people who are married to each other and who both earn a lot of money, but who have no children【非正式】〔夫妻雙方都有收入但並未生育孩子的〕頂客族; DINKY² *BrE*【英】

din·kum /ˋdɪŋkəm; ˈdɪŋkəm/ *adj* —see 見 FAIR DINKUM

din·ky¹ /ˋdɪŋkɪ; ˈdɪŋki/ *adj* **1** *BrE informal* small and attractive【英, 非正式】小巧的; 精緻的: *What a dinky little cottage!* 多漂亮的小村舍啊! **2** *AmE* small and not very nice【美】狹小的, 簡陋的: *It was a really dinky hotel room.* 那家旅館房間真是簡陋!

dinky² *n* [C] *BrE* a dink【英】頂客族〔雙收入沒有孩子的年輕夫妻〕

1 2 **din·ner** /ˋdɪnɚ; ˈdɪnə/ *n* **1** [C,U] the main meal of the day, eaten in the middle of the day or the evening 〔中午或晚上吃的〕正餐, 主餐: *Would you like to come over for dinner on Friday?* 星期五過來吃晚飯好嗎? | *We're having fish for dinner tonight.* 今天晚餐我們吃魚。| **Sunday/Christmas/Thanksgiving dinner etc** (=a special meal eaten on Sunday, at Christmas, at Thanksgiving, etc) 星期日/聖誕節/感恩節等的盛餐 | **school dinner** (=a meal provided at school in the middle of the day) 學校午餐 **2** [C] a formal occasion when an evening meal is eaten, often to celebrate something 〔為了慶祝某事而舉行的〕晚宴: *They're giving a dinner in honour of her retirement.* 為了慶祝她退休, 他們將舉行一個晚宴。**3 had more ... than you've had hot dinners** *BrE spoken humorous* used to say that someone has had a lot of experience of something and has done it many times【英口, 幽默】做過的…比你吃的飯還多〔用來說明某人做某事已許多次, 有着豐富的經驗〕: *She's nursed more babies than you've had hot dinners.* 她哺育過的孩子比你吃過的飯還多。—see also 另見 TV DINNER, **be dressed up like a dog's dinner** (DOG¹ (9))

dinner dance /ˈ‥ ˌ·/ *n* [C] a social event in the evening, that includes a formal meal and music for dancing 晚宴舞會: *the annual dinner dance* 一年一度的晚宴舞會

dinner jack·et /ˈ‥ ˌ‥/ *n* [C] *BrE* a black or white JACKET (1) worn by men on very formal occasions, usually with a BOW TIE【英】男子晚禮服〔正式場合穿着, 黑色或白色, 通常打蝶形領結〕; TUXEDO *AmE*【美】

dinner la·dy /ˈ‥ ˌ‥/ *n* [C] *BrE* a woman who serves meals to children at school【英】在學校午餐時為孩子們端飯菜的婦女

dinner par·ty /ˈ‥ ˌ‥/ *n* [C] a social event when people are invited to someone's house for an evening meal 〔人們被邀請到某人家裡吃的〕社交晚宴

dinner ser·vice /ˈ‥ ˌ‥/ also 又作 **dinner set** /ˈ‥ ·/ *n* [C] a complete set of plates, dishes etc, used for serving a meal 成套餐具

dinner ta·ble /ˈ‥ ˌ‥/ *n* **the dinner table a)** an occasion when people are eating dinner together 人們聚餐的場合: *That's not a very pleasant topic for the dinner table.* 這個話題不太適合在進餐時討論。**b)** the table at which people eat dinner 餐桌 —compare 比較 DINING TABLE

dinner thea·ter /ˈ‥ ˌ‥/ *n* [C] *AmE* a restaurant in which you see a play after your meal【美】餐後可以觀劇的餐廳劇院

din·ner·time /ˋdɪnɚˌtaɪm; ˈdɪnətaɪm/ *n* [singular] the time when you usually have dinner, especially in the middle of the day 用餐時間〔尤指午餐時間〕: *He always seems to call me at dinnertime.* 他似乎總是在吃飯時間打電話給我。

di·no·saur /ˋdaɪnəˌsɔr; ˈdaɪnəsɔː/ *n* [C] **1** one of a group of REPTILES that lived about 200 million years ago 恐龍 **2** *informal* something very large and old-fashioned that no longer works well or effectively【非正式】龐大而過時的東西: *one of the dinosaurs of the computer industry* 電腦工業中那種體積笨重的落後型號之一

dint /dɪnt; dɪnt/ *n* **1 by dint of** by using a particular method 通過使用…方法: *By dint of persistent questioning, I finally got to the truth.* 在不斷追問後, 我終於得到真相。**2** a small hollow in the surface of something made by hitting it 〔因受擊打而留下的〕凹陷, 凹坑: *a dint in the car door* 車門上的凹痕

di·o·cese /ˋdaɪəˌsɪs; ˈdaɪəsɪs/ *n* [C] the area under the control of a BISHOP (1), in the Christian church 〔基督教的〕主教轄區, 教區 —**diocesan** /daɪˋɑsəsṇ; daɪˈɒsɪsən/ *adj*

di·ox·ide /daɪˋɑksaɪd; daɪˈɒksaɪd/ *n* [C,U] *technical* a chemical compound containing two atoms of oxygen to every atom of another ELEMENT (=simple substance)【術語】二氧化物 —see also 另見 CARBON DIOXIDE

di·ox·in /daɪˋɑksɪn; daɪˈɒksɪn/ *n* [C,U] a very poisonous chemical used for killing plants 二惡英〔一種極毒的化學物質, 用於殺滅植物〕

Dip the written abbreviation of 縮寫= DIPLOMA

dip¹ /dɪp; dɪp/ *v* **dipped, dipping 1** [T] to put something into a liquid and quickly lift it out again 蘸, 浸: *Dip your finger in the batter and taste it.* 用手指蘸一點麵糊, 嚐一下。—see picture on page A11 參見 A11 頁圖 **2** [I] to go downwards 下降, 下落: *We watched the sun dip below the horizon.* 我們看見太陽落到地平線下。**3 dip your headlights/lights** *BrE* to lower the angle of the front lights of your car, especially when someone is driving towards you【英】降低汽車前燈角度〔尤其當對面有車開來時〕; DIM² (3) *AmE*【美】**4** [T] to make animals go through a bath containing a chemical that kills insects on their skin 讓〔動物〕洗藥浴〔滅蟲〕—see also 另見 SKINNY-DIPPING

dip into sth *phr v* [T] **1** to read short parts of a book, magazine etc, but not the whole thing 翻閱, 瀏覽〔書或雜誌等〕: *It's the kind of book you can dip into now and again.* 這是可以有時翻閱一下的那種書。**2** to use some of an amount of money that you have 動用〔存款〕: **dip into your savings** *Medical bills forced her to dip into her savings.* 為了付醫藥費, 她不得不動用存款。| **dip**

into your pocket (=pay for something with your own money)〔為買某物〕花你自己的錢 *Parents are being asked to dip into their pockets for new school books.* 父母得自掏腰包〔為孩子〕買新課本。**3** to put your hand into a bag or box in order to take out one of the things inside 把手伸進〔袋裡或盒子裡, 為了把裡面的東西掏出來〕: *On her lap was a bag of candy which she kept dipping into.* 她不斷地從腿上放着的一袋糖果裡面摸出糖來吃。

dip² *n*

1 ►SWIM 游泳◄ [C] *informal* a quick swim【非正式】〔為時較短的〕游泳: *Are you coming in for a dip?* 你來游一會兒嗎? | **have/take a dip** *They've decided to take a dip in the lake before lunch.* 他們已經決定午餐前到湖裡游一小會兒泳。

2 ►DECREASE 下降◄ [C] a slight decrease in the amount of something〔某物數量上輕微的〕減少下降: *an unexpected dip in profits* 出乎意料的利潤下降

3 ►IN A SURFACE 在表面◄ [C] a place where the surface of something goes down suddenly, then goes up again 凹陷: *a dip in the road* 路上的凹陷處

4 ►FOOD 食物◄ [C,U] a thick mixture that you can dip food into before you eat it〔用來蘸食物吃的〕調味醬汁: *sour cream and onion dip* 酸奶油和洋葱醬汁 —see picture on page A15 參見 A15 頁圖

5 ►FOR ANIMALS 動物用的◄ [C,U] a liquid that contains a chemical which kills insects on sheep and other animals〔給動物洗浴用的〕藥浴液〔以便殺蟲〕

6 ►PERSON 人◄ [C] *AmE spoken* a stupid person【美口】傻瓜, 笨蛋 —see also 另見 LUCKY DIP

diph·ther·i·a /dɪf`θɪrɪə; dɪf'θɪəriə/ *n* [U] a serious infectious throat disease that makes breathing difficult 白喉

diph·thong /`dɪfθɔŋ; 'dɪfθɒŋ/ *n* [C] *technical*【術語】 **1** a compound vowel sound made by pronouncing two vowels quickly one after the other. For example, the vowel sound in 'my' is a diphthong. 複合元音, 雙母音〈如 my 中的元音便是雙母音〉—see also 另見 GLIDE² (3) **2** a DIGRAPH 二合字母

di·plo·ma /dɪ`plomə; dʒ̍'pləʊmə/ *n* [C] **1** *BrE* a document showing that someone has successfully completed a course of study or passed an examination【英】結業證書: *I'm hoping to get my teaching diploma this year.* 我希望今年能拿到教師證書。| **[+in]** *a diploma in catering* 承辦酒席的資格證書 **2** *AmE* a document showing that a student has successfully completed their HIGH SCHOOL, college, or university education【美】畢業文憑, 學位證書: *a master's diploma* 碩士文憑

di·plo·ma·cy /dɪ`ploməsɪ; dʒ̍'pləʊməsi/ *n* [U] **1** the work of managing the relationships between countries 外交: *a major player in post-war diplomacy* 戰後外交的主要活動家 **2** skill in dealing with people and persuading them to agree to something without upsetting them 處世之道, 交際手段: *The job requires tact and diplomacy.* 這個工作需要策略以及外交手腕。—see also 另見 **gunboat diplomacy** (GUNBOAT (2))

dip·lo·mat /`dɪplə͵mæt; 'dɪpləmæt/ *n* [C] **1** someone who officially represents their government in a foreign country 外交官; 外交家 **2** someone who is good at dealing with people without upsetting them 有手腕的人; 善於處理人際關係的人: *As a natural diplomat, Baxter found it easy to placate the two sides.* 作為一個天生的交際能手, 巴克斯特覺得不難安撫雙方。

dip·lo·mat·ic /͵dɪplə`mætɪk; ͵dɪplə'mætɪk◂/ *adj* **1** concerning or involving the work of diplomats 外交的: *She was hoping for a diplomatic post in the Middle East.* 她盼望着能獲得一個在中東工作的外交職位。**2** dealing with people politely and skilfully without upsetting them 世故的, 圓滑的: *They were always very diplomatic with awkward clients.* 他們與難纏的客戶打交道一向很有策略。| *a diplomatic answer* 很圓滑的回答 **—diplomatically** /-klɪ; -kli/ *adv*: *Maria handled the situation very diplomatically.* 瑪麗亞非常老道得體地處理了這個情況。

diplomatic corps /··'·· ͵·/ *n* [U] all the diplomats working in a particular country〔駐某國的〕外交(使節)團

diplomatic im·mu·ni·ty /͵···· ·'···/ *n* [U] *law* a diplomat's special rights in the country where they are working, which protect them from local taxes and PROSECUTION (1)【法律】外交特權, 外交豁免權

diplomatic re·la·tions /͵···· ·'··/ *n* [plural] the arrangement between two countries that each should keep representatives at an EMBASSY in the other country 外交關係: **break off diplomatic relations** *Britain broke off diplomatic relations after the crisis of 1982.* 1982年的危機之後, 英國中斷了(與該國的)外交關係。

Diplomatic Ser·vice /··'·· ͵··/ *n* [singular] all the people who work for their government abroad in an EMBASSY or a CONSULATE 外交部門, 外交系統

di·plo·ma·tist /dɪ`plomətɪst; dʒ̍'pləʊmətʒ̍st/ *n* [C] a DIPLOMAT 外交官; 外交家

dip·per /`dɪpɚ; 'dɪpə/ *n* [C] **1** a large spoon with a long handle used for taking liquid out of a container 長柄杓 **2** a small bird that feeds in mountain streams 河鳥〔在山中小溪覓食的一種小鳥〕—see also 另見 BIG DIPPER

dip·py /`dɪpɪ; 'dɪpi/ *adj informal* silly or crazy【非正式】笨的, 愚蠢的; 瘋狂的

dip·shit /`dɪpʃɪt; 'dɪpʃɪt/ *n* [C] *AmE spoken* an impolite word meaning a stupid person【美口】笨蛋, 傻瓜〔不禮貌用語〕

dip·so /`dɪpso; 'dɪpsəʊ/ *n* [C] *slang* a dipsomaniac【俚】嗜酒狂患者, 間發性酒狂患者

dip·so·ma·ni·ac /͵dɪpsə`menɪ͵æk; ͵dɪpsə'meɪniæk/ *n* [C] someone who has a very strong desire for alcoholic drinks, which they cannot control 嗜酒狂患者, 間發性酒狂患者 **—dipsomania** /-nɪə; -niə/ *n* [U]

dip·stick /`dɪp͵stɪk; 'dɪp͵stɪk/ *n* [C] **1** a stick for measuring the amount of liquid in a container, especially the amount of oil in a car's engine〔尤指測量汽車引擎中油量的〕浸量尺, 測深尺, 量油尺 —see picture at 參見 ENGINE 圖 **2** *spoken* a stupid person【口】傻瓜, 笨蛋

dip switch /'· ·/ *n* [C] *BrE* a SWITCH² (1) for lowering the beam of a car's front lights【英】汽車前燈變光開關; DIMMER (2) *AmE*【美】

dip·tych /`dɪptɪk; 'dɪptɪk/ *n* [C] a picture made in two parts which can be closed like a book 摺合式雙連畫 —compare 比較 TRIPTYCH

dire /daɪr; daɪə/ *adj* **1** extremely serious, bad or terrible 極其嚴重的; 極糟糕的; 極可怕的人: *He was in dire trouble and he knew it.* 他麻煩大了, 他自己也知道這一點。| *That makes the situation sound dire.* 那使得局勢聽起來非常嚴峻。| **in dire need/poverty** *The country was in dire need of financial aid.* 這個國家亟需經濟援助。| **dire consequences** *Increasing fuel prices will have dire consequences for the poor.* 提高燃料價格將給窮人帶來嚴重後果。| **be in dire straits** (=be in an extremely difficult or serious situation) 處於岌岌可危的境地 **2 dire warning/threat** a dire warning or threat warns people about something terrible that will happen in the future 大難臨頭的警告/威脅

di·rect¹ /də`rɛkt; dʒ̍'rekt/ *adj*

1 ►WITHOUT ANYTHING BETWEEN 沒有東西介入的◄ done without any other people, actions, processes etc coming between 直接的〔沒有其他人、行動或過程介入〕: *Can we have direct access to the information on file?* 我們能直接獲得存檔的資料嗎? | *She has direct control over the business.* 她直接控制這個企業。| *I'm not in direct contact with them.* 我和他們沒有直接的聯繫。

2 ►FROM ONE PLACE TO ANOTHER 從一個地方到另一個地方◄ going straight from one place to another without stopping or changing direction 筆直的, 逕直的〔中間不停的, 不改變方向的〕: *Which is the most direct route to London?* 哪條是最直接到倫敦的路線? | *We can get a direct flight to New York.* 我們可以乘直達班機去紐約。

3 ►EFFECT 效果, 結果◄ likely to change something immediately 直接的〔可能立即發生改變〕: *The change in the law will have a direct bearing on the way benefits are calculated.* 法律的變動將對利潤的計算方式產生直接影響。

4 ►EXACT 恰好的◄ [only before noun 僅用於名詞前] exact or total 恰好的, 截然的: *Weight increases in direct proportion to mass.* 重量的增長和質量的增長成正比。| *These ideas are in direct contrast with the themes of her earlier essays.* 這些觀點與她早期文章中的主旨截然相反。| **direct quote** (=what someone said in their exact words) 直接引用, 直接引語

5 ►BEHAVIOUR/ATTITUDE 行為/態度◄ saying exactly what you mean in an honest clear way 率直的, 坦率的, 直言的: *If only she'd been less direct in her approach, he might have helped.* 如果她當時的方式不那麼直截了當, 他或許會幫忙的。

6 direct descendant someone who is related to someone else through their parents and grandparents, not through their AUNTS, UNCLES, brothers, sisters etc 直系的後裔: *She claimed to be a direct descendant of Wordsworth.* 她聲稱是華兹華斯的直系後裔。

7 direct result/consequence something that happens only because of one particular thing 直接後果: *They were suffering from stress, and their physical symptoms were a direct result.* 他們正承受着精神壓力, 他們身體上出現的症狀便是其直接後果。

8 direct question/answer a question that asks for information exactly and specifically, with no possibility of misunderstanding, or an answer that gives information in this way 直截了當的問題/回答: *Now, let me ask you a direct question, and I expect a direct answer.* 現在, 讓我問你一個直截了當的問題, 希望你能直截了當地回答。

9 direct heat/sunlight strong heat or sunlight that someone or something is not protected from〔沒有任何防護的〕直接受熱/日照: *Never change the film in direct sunlight.* 千萬不要在陽光下換膠卷。—opposite 反義詞 INDIRECT

2 2 **direct²** *v* [T]

1 ►AIM 瞄準◄ [always+adv/prep] to aim something in a particular direction or at a particular person, group etc 把〔某物〕對準, 針對: **[+at/towards/away from etc]** *The machine directs an X-ray beam at the patient's body.* 機器把X光射線對準病人的身體。| *For once her sarcasm was not directed at us.* 難得這一次她的諷刺不是針對我們的。| *Environmental policy was traditionally directed at pollution control.* 環保政策一向是着眼於控制污染的。| **direct your efforts towards sth** (=try hard to do one particular thing) 把精力投入到某事中〔努力做某事〕 *I want to direct my efforts more towards my own projects.* 我想把精力更多地投入到自己的項目中去。| **direct your attention towards sth** *None of them had ever directed serious attention to the problem.* 他們中間從來沒有人認真地注意過這個問題。

2 ►BE IN CHARGE 負責◄ to be in charge of something or control it 負責, 管理, 指導, 監督: *Stella had been asked to direct a research project.* 斯特拉被任命負責一個研究項目。

3 to tell someone how to get to a place 給〔某人〕指路, 指揮: *A policeman stood in the middle of the road, directing the traffic.* 一名警察站在路中央指揮交通。| **[+to]** *Could you direct me to Trafalgar Square, please?* 你能告訴我去特拉法爾加廣場怎麼走嗎? —see 見 LEAD[1] (USAGE)

4 *formal* to tell someone what they should do【正式】指示, 命令: *We were directed to hand over our passports.* 我們被指示把護照交過去。| **direct that** *Judge Rice directed that a verdict of 'not guilty' be entered.* 賴斯法官命令把"無罪"的判決記錄入冊。

5 ►ACTING 表演◄ to give the actors in a play, film, or television programme instructions about what they should do 擔任〔戲劇、電影、電視節目等〕的導演: *Who directed that movie we saw last week?* 我們上週看的那部電影是誰導演的?

direct³ *adv* **1** without stopping or changing direction 中途不停地; 逕直地: *Can we fly direct to Chicago, or do we stop in Salt Lake City first?* 我們能否直飛芝加哥, 還是要先在鹽湖城停一下? **2** without dealing with anyone else first 直接地〔和某人打交道〕: *Esther decided to contact the manager direct.* 艾絲特決定直接和經理聯繫。| *It is usually cheaper to buy the goods direct from the wholesaler.* 直接從批發商那裡買東西通常比較便宜。

direct cur·rent /ˌ·ˌ· ˈ··/ *n* [U] a flow of electricity that moves in one direction only 直流電 —compare 比較 ALTERNATING CURRENT

direct deb·it /ˌ·ˌ· ˈ··/ *n* [C,U] *especially BrE* an instruction you give your bank to pay money directly out of your account regularly to a particular person or organization【尤英】直接借記, 直接付款 —compare 比較 STANDING ORDER

direct de·pos·it /ˌ·ˌ· ·ˈ··/ *n* [U] *AmE* a method of paying someone's wages directly into their bank account【美】直接存款付薪〔把某人的工資直接打入此人的帳戶〕

direct dis·course /ˌ·ˌ· ˈ··/ *n* [U] an American form of the expression DIRECT SPEECH direct speech 的美式說法

direct hit /ˌ·ˌ· ˈ·/ *n* [C] an occasion when something thrown or dropped, for example a bomb, exactly hits the object it was aimed at 直接命中〔指投射的某物, 如炸彈, 正好擊中目標〕: *The railway station suffered two direct hits that night.* 那天晚上, 火車站遭兩次直接擊中。

di·rec·tion /dəˈrɛkʃən; dʒˈrekʃən/ *n* 1 1

1 [C] the way something or someone moves, faces, or is aimed 方向: **in the direction of** (=towards) 朝着…的方向 *The suspects were last seen heading in the direction of Miami.* 嫌疑犯最後一次被看見向邁阿密方向跑了。| **in sb's direction** (=towards someone) 朝着某人的方向 *Tristram glanced in her direction and their eyes met.* 特里斯坦朝着她的方向瞥了一眼, 結果他們四目相對。| **in the opposite direction** *The girls giggled and pointed in the opposite direction.* 女孩子們咯咯地笑着, 指向相反的方向。| **change direction** *On seeing me, Maurice changed direction and went along the wharf instead.* 莫里斯看見我便調轉方向, 沿着碼頭走去。| **in a southerly/easterly etc direction** *Continue in a southerly direction until you reach the road.* 繼續往南走直到走到大路上。| **in all directions** *As shots rang out, the crowd ran screaming in all directions.* 槍聲響起的時候, 人羣尖叫着向四面八方逃散。

2 directions [plural] instructions about how to get from one place to another, or about what to do 指示, 〔行路的〕指引, 〔用法、操作的〕說明: *A very helpful woman gave me directions to the police station.* 一個非常肯幫忙的婦女告訴我到警察局怎麼走。

3 ►WAY STH DEVELOPS 事情發展的趨勢◄ [C] the general way in which someone or something changes or develops 趨向, 趨勢: **take a direction** *Drayson was surprised at the direction his career had taken.* 德雷森對於他事業發展的趨向感到驚訝。| *The company is hoping to extend its operations in this direction.* 公司正盼望着朝這個方向擴充經營。

4 ►WHERE FROM OR WHERE TO 從哪兒來或到哪兒去◄ [C] where something comes from or where something leads 方向: *The evidence all points in this direction.* 所有證據都指向這個方向。| *Help came from a wholly unexpected direction.* 援助來自一個完全沒有預料到的地方。

5 ►CONTROL 管理◄ [U] control, management, or advice 控制, 監控, 管理, 指點: **under sb's direction** *The project progressed well, under the capable direction of Magnus Armstrong.* 由於馬格努斯·阿姆斯特朗指導有方, 這個項目進展順利。

6 ▶FILM 電影◀ [U] the instructions and advice given by a film DIRECTOR (2)〔電影導演的〕指導, 指示
7 ▶PURPOSE 目的◀ [U] a general purpose or aim〔總體〕目標: *Her mother felt that Rachel's life lacked direction.* 雷切爾的媽媽覺得雷切爾的生活缺少目標。
8 **sense of direction a)** the ability to know which way you should be going in a place you do not know well 方向感, 方位感: *"Are we going north?" "Don't ask me! I've got no sense of direction at all."* "我們是在朝北走嗎?" "別問我!我根本沒有方向感。" **b)** an idea about what your aims in life are〔生活的〕目標: *Doing the course gave her more sense of direction.* 修這門課程使得她感到更有目標了。

di·rec·tion·al /dəˋrɛkʃənḷ; dʒ̍ˈrekʃənəl/ *adj technical*【術語】**1** pointing in a particular direction 方向的 **2** a directional piece of equipment receives or gives out radio signals from some directions more strongly than others 定向的〔定向儀器發出或接收的無線電信號在某些方向上比其他方向強〕

D

di·rec·tive¹ /dəˋrɛktɪv; dʒ̍ˈrektɪv/ *n* [C] an official order or instruction 正式命令, 指示: *the EU directive on paternity leave* 歐盟關於陪產假的指示

directive² *adj* giving instructions 指示的, 指導的: *It is important in these cases that doctors take a less directive approach.* 在這些情況下, 重要的是醫生應該採取指令性不太強的態度。

S2 W2 **di·rect·ly¹** /dəˋrɛktlɪ; dʒ̍ˈrektli/ *adv* **1** with no other person, action, process etc between 直接地: *The new law won't directly affect us.* 新的法律不會直接影響到我們。| *I know where you can get that directly from the manufacturers.* 我知道在甚麼地方你可以直接從製造商那兒買到那種東西。**2** exactly 恰好, 正好: *Have you noticed how he never looks directly at you?* 你有沒有注意到他從未正視過你? | *Her practical ideas seemed directly opposed to the department's academic style.* 她實用的想法似乎和這個系的學術風格正好背道而馳。**3 speak/ask/answer etc directly** to say exactly what you mean without trying to hide anything 坦率地, 直截了當地說/問/回答等: *Cindy has a job in mind, but refuses to say directly what it is.* 辛迪心裡想着一種工作, 但是她不肯直截了當地說那是甚麼工作。**4** *BrE old-fashioned* very soon【英, 過時】很快地: *He should be here directly, if you don't mind waiting.* 如果你不介意多等一會兒, 他應該很快就會到的。**5** *BrE old-fashioned* immediately【英, 過時】立即

directly² *conjunction BrE* as soon as【英】一…就…: *I came directly I got your message.* 我一接到你的消息就來了。

direct mail /ˌ·ˌ ˈ·/ *n* [U] advertisements that are sent by post to many people 郵遞廣告

direct meth·od /ˌ·ˌ ˈ··/ *n* [singular,U] a method of teaching a foreign language without using the student's own language 外語直接教學法〔不使用學生的本國語〕

direct ob·ject /ˌ·ˌ ˈ··/ *n* [C] *technical* the noun, noun phrase, or PRONOUN that you need to complete the meaning of a statement using a TRANSITIVE verb, for example 'Mary' in the statement 'I saw Mary'【術語】直接受詞, 直接賓語〔指接在及物動詞後面的名詞、名詞詞組或代詞, 如在I saw Mary這句話中, Mary便是直接受詞〕—compare 比較 INDIRECT OBJECT

W1 **di·rec·tor** /dəˋrɛktɚ; dʒ̍ˈrektə/ *n* [C] **1** one of the committee of top managers who control a company 董事; 理事: *a former director of Gartmore Pensions Ltd* 加特莫爾退休基金有限公司的前任董事 | **board of directors** (=the committee of directors) 董事會; 理事會 **2** the person who gives instructions to the actors, CAMERAMAN etc in a film or play 導演 —compare 比較 PRODUCER (2) **3** someone who is in charge of a particular activity or organization 負責人, 主管: *the director of transport operations* 運輸業務的主管 | *Greta has been appointed project director.* 嘉烈塔被任命為項目主管。| **financial/sales/personnel director** (=a director in charge of the financial department etc) 財務部/銷售部/人事部主任—see also 另見 MANAGING DIRECTOR, NON-EXECUTIVE DIRECTOR

di·rec·tor·ate /dəˋrɛktərɪt; dʒ̍ˈrektərʒ̍t/ *n* [C] **1** the BOARD (=committee) of directors of a company 董事會; 理事會 **2** a directorship 董事[主任; 主管]職位

Director of Stud·ies /ˌ·ˌ·· · ˈ··/ *n* [singular] a teacher in a British university or language school who is in charge of organizing the students' programmes of study〔英國大學或語言學校的〕負責編製學生學習大綱的老師, 教務長

di·rec·tor·ship /dəˋrɛktɚˌʃɪp; dʒ̍ˈrektəʃɪp/ *n* [C] the position of being a director of a company 董事[主管]職位

di·rec·to·ry /dəˋrɛktərɪ; daɪˈrektəri/ *n* [C] a book or list of names, facts etc, usually arranged in alphabetical order〔通常按字母順序排列的〕姓名地址錄; 工商人名錄; 電話簿等: *I couldn't find your number in the telephone directory.* 我在電話簿裡找不到你的號碼。| *a new business directory* 新的商行名錄

directory en·qui·ries /ˌ·ˌ··· ·ˈ··/ *BrE*【英】, **directory assistance** /ˌ·ˌ··· ˈ··/ *AmE*【美】*n* [U] a service on the British telephone network that you can use to find out someone's telephone number〔英國的〕電話查號台

direct speech /ˌ·ˌ ˈ·/ *n* [U] *technical* the style used to report what someone says by giving their actual words, for example 'I don't want to go,' said Julie.【術語】直接引語〔指直接引用某人說的原話, 如 'I don't want to go,' said Julie. 這裡 I don't want to go 便是直接引語〕; DIRECT DISCOURSE *AmE*【美】—compare 比較 INDIRECT SPEECH, REPORTED SPEECH

direct tax /ˌ·ˌ ˈ·/ *n* [C,U] *technical* a tax, such as income tax, which is actually collected from the person who pays it, as opposed to a tax on goods or services【術語】直接稅〔直接從納稅人徵收, 如所得稅; 它不同於商品稅或服務稅等間接稅〕—opposite 反義詞 **indirect tax** —**direct taxation** /ˌ·ˌ ·ˈ··/ *n* [U]

dirge /dɝdʒ; dɜːdʒ/ *n* [C] **1** a slow sad song sung at a funeral 輓歌, 哀歌: *When I die, I don't want any of those awful dirges.* 我死後可不想要那種討厭的輓歌。**2** a song or piece of music that is too slow and boring 緩慢乏味的音樂

dir·i·gi·ble /ˋdɪrədʒəbḷ; ˈdɪrʒ̍dʒʒ̍bəl/ *n* [C] an AIRSHIP 飛艇; 飛船

dirk /dɝk; dɜːk/ *n* [C] a heavy pointed knife used as a weapon in Scotland in the past〔舊時蘇格蘭人當作武器使用的一種沉重的〕尖刀, 短劍, 匕首

dirt /dɝt; dɜːt/ *n* [U] **1** any substance that makes things dirty, such as mud or dust 灰塵, 塵土, 髒土: *You should have seen the dirt on that car!* 可惜你沒有看見那車上沾了多少泥! | **dog dirt** *especially AmE* (=waste from a dog's BOWELS (1))【尤美】狗屎 **2** loose earth or soil 鬆土, 泥土: *Michael threw his handful of dirt onto the coffin.* 米克撒了一把土到棺材上。**3** *informal* information about someone's private life or activities which could give people a bad opinion of them if it became known【非正式】〔某人私生活的〕醜事; 醜行: *Apparently, confidential files were combed for dirt on the candidates.* 很顯然, 為了找出候選人的醜行, 機密檔案被仔細翻查過。**4** talk, writing, films etc that are considered unpleasant or immoral because they are about sex 下流話; 下流文章; 色情電影 —see also 另見 **dish the dirt** (DISH² (1)), **hit the dirt** (HIT¹ (21)), **treat sb like dirt** (TREAT¹ (1))

dirt bike /ˈ· ˌ·/ *n* [C] a small MOTORCYCLE for young people, usually ridden on rough paths or fields 輕型摩托車〔通常適合在粗糙的小路上或田野中行駛〕

dirt cheap /ˌ· ˈ·◂/ *adj, adv informal* extremely cheap【非正式】非常便宜的: *We got the cow dirt cheap because the Parsons sold off their farm.* 因為帕森一家廉價出售他們的農場, 所以我們沒花幾個錢就買下了這頭牛。

dirt farm·er /ˈ· ˌ··/ *n* [C] *AmE* a poor farmer who works to feed himself and his family, without paying anyone else to help【美】自耕農

dirt poor /ˌ· ˈ·◂/ *adj AmE informal* extremely poor【美, 非正式】極貧困的, 赤貧的

dirt road /ˈ· ·/ *n* [C] a road made of hard earth 泥路, 土路

dirt track /ˈ· ·/ *n* [C] a track used for MOTORCYCLE races〔用於摩托車比賽的〕賽道

2 3 **dirt·y¹** /ˋdɝtɪ; ˈdɜːti/ *adj* **dirtier, dirtiest**
1 ▶NOT CLEAN 不乾淨的◀ covered in dirt or marked with dirt 有灰塵的, 骯髒的: *Just stack the dirty dishes in the sink.* 把髒盤子堆放在水槽裡就行了。| *Look how dirty your hands are! Go wash them right now!* 看看你的手有多髒!馬上去洗洗!
2 ▶IMMORAL 不道德的◀ connected with sex in a way that is considered immoral or unpleasant 下流的, 黃色的, 色情的, 猥褻的: *Mick's always telling dirty jokes.* 米克總是講下流的笑話。| *There were a bunch of dirty magazines under his bed.* 他牀底下有一堆色情雜誌。| **a dirty mind** (=a mind that often thinks about sex) 經常想下流事的腦子 | **dirty weekend** *humorous* (=a weekend when a man and woman who are not married to each other go away to have sex)【幽默】風流週末〔非夫妻關係的男女週末外出過性生活〕
3 ▶UNPLEASANT 令人討厭的◀ *spoken* used to emphasize that you think someone or something is very bad【口】可惡的, 可恨的〔強調某人或某事非常糟糕、差勁〕: *You're a dirty liar!* 你是個卑鄙的騙子! | *Yeah, they gave us all the dirty jobs.* 對, 他們把最難搞的差使都分給我們。
4 ▶DISHONEST 不誠實的◀ unfair or dishonest 不公正的, 不誠實的: *a dirty fighter* 競爭時用不公平手段的人 | *There's been some dirty business over these contracts.* 圍繞這些合同有着一些不可告人的勾當。| **dirty trick** (=an unkind dishonest way of treating someone)〔對待某人的〕卑鄙手段 *I'm so sorry anyone should play such a dirty trick!* 很遺憾, 竟然有人使用這麼卑劣的手段! | **do the dirty on sb** *BrE* (=treat someone in a way that is unfair or dishonest)【英】以卑劣手段耍弄某人 | **dirty pool** *AmE* (=unfair or dishonest behaviour)【美】不正當行為; 欺詐行為
5 be a dirty word if something is a dirty word, people believe it is a bad thing even if they do not know or think much about it 是不好聽的字眼: *Nowadays power tends to be a slightly dirty word as far as organizations are concerned.* 如今, 就組織而言, 權力往往被看作是不太好聽的字眼。
6 give sb a dirty look to look at someone in a very disapproving way 厭惡地看某人一眼: *When I went in there she gave me a dirty look and told me to take a seat.* 我進去的時候她厭惡地看了我一眼, 叫我坐下。
7 do sb's dirty work to do an unpleasant or dishonest job for someone so that they do not have to do it themselves 替某人幹骯髒的工作: *I told them to do their own dirty work.* 我告訴他們自己去幹自己的骯髒工作。
8 ▶DRUGS 毒品◀ *AmE slang* containing or possessing illegal drugs【美俚】含有[擁有]毒品的 —see also 另見 **wash your dirty linen in public** (WASH¹ (6)) —**dirtily** *adv*

dirty² *adv* [I,T] **1 dirty rotten** *spoken* extremely nasty【口】極討厭的: *the dirty rotten bastard!* 這個特別令人厭惡的傢伙! | *What a dirty rotten trick!* 多麼卑劣的伎倆啊! **2 play dirty a)** to behave in a very unfair and dishonest way 耍花招, 使用卑鄙手段 **b)** to cheat in a game〔比賽中〕作弊 **3 talk dirty** to talk rudely about sex 說髒話, 說下流話 **4 dirty great/dirty big** *BrE spoken* extremely big【英口】特別大的: *We suddenly saw this dirty great truck coming towards us.* 忽然我們看到這輛龐然大物的卡車朝我們開過來。

dirty³ *v* **dirtied, dirtying** [I,T] **1** to put or leave marks on something and make it no longer clean 弄髒: *Max wiped his dirtied hands on his thighs.* 馬克斯把髒手在大腿上擦了擦。**2 dirty your hands on sth** to become involved in something bad that will affect people's opinion of you 因某事弄髒自己的手〔因捲入不好的事情當中而影響自己的名聲〕

dirty old man /ˌ·· · ˈ·/ *n* [C] *informal* an older man who is too sexually interested in younger women【非正式】老色鬼, 老淫棍

dirty tricks /ˌ·· ˈ·/ *n* [plural] secret, dishonest, and often criminal activities by a government, political group, or company, for example spreading false information about their competitors or opponents 卑鄙手段, 卑劣伎倆: **dirty tricks campaign** (=a planned series of dirty tricks) 一系列有計劃的卑劣活動 *The airline was accused of a dirty tricks campaign against their rivals.* 這家航空公司被指控對競爭對手使用一系列有預謀的卑鄙手段。

dis- /dɪs; dɪs/ *prefix* **1** shows an opposite or negative〔表示相反或否定〕: *I disapprove* (=do not approve) 我不贊成 | *his dishonesty* (=lack of honesty) 他的不誠實 | *a discontented look* 不滿意的表情 **2** shows the stopping or removing of a condition〔表示停止或除去〕: *Disconnect the machine from the electricity supply.* (=so that it is no longer connected) 把機器的電源斷開。| *Disinfect the wound first.* 首先要給傷口消毒。**3** [in verbs 構成動詞] to remove something〔表示除掉某物〕: *a dismasted ship* 一艘折斷了桅杆的船

dis·a·bil·i·ty /ˌdɪsəˋbɪlətɪ; ˌdɪsəˈbɪlə̥ti/ *n* **1** [C] a physical problem that makes someone unable to use a part of their body properly〔身體上的〕傷殘; 殘障: *She manages to lead a normal life in spite of her disabilities.* 儘管她有殘疾, 她仍努力過着正常人的生活。**2** [U] the state of not being able to use parts of your body properly 喪失能力: *learning to cope with disability* 學會應付生理上的缺陷

dis·a·ble /dɪsˋebḷ; dɪsˈeɪbəl/ *v* [T] **1** [often passive 常用被動態] to make someone unable to use a part of their body properly 使喪失能力, 使殘廢: *Carter was permanently disabled in the war.* 卡特在戰爭中變成終生殘廢。**2** to deliberately make a machine or piece of equipment impossible to use 故意毀壞〔機器設備〕, 使無法使用: *This system is designed to destroy or disable enemy ballistic missiles.* 這個系統是為摧毀敵人的彈道導彈或者使之癱瘓而設計的。—**disablement** *n* [C,U]

dis·a·bled /dɪsˋebḷd; dɪsˈeɪbəld/ *adj* **1** someone who is disabled cannot use a part of their body properly 殘障的, 殘疾的: **severely disabled** (=unable to use most of your body) 有嚴重殘疾的 | **disabled parking/toilet/entrance** (=for disabled people) 為傷殘人士設置的停車場/廁所/入口 **2 the disabled** people who are disabled 傷殘人士: *The theatre has good access for the disabled.* 這家劇院為傷殘人士準備了很方便的通道。—compare 比較 CRIPPLE¹ (1), HANDICAPPED 3

dis·a·buse /ˌdɪsəˋbjuz; ˌdɪsəˈbjuːz/ *v* [T] *formal* to persuade someone that what they believe is untrue【正式】糾正, 使…消除錯誤觀點: **[+of]** *I never did anything to disabuse him of that idea.* 我從沒做過任何事使他打消那個念頭。

dis·ad·van·tage /ˌdɪsədˋvæntɪdʒ; ˌdɪsədˈvɑːntɪdʒ/ *n* [C, U] an unfavourable condition or quality that makes someone or something less likely to be successful or effective 不利條件, 劣勢: **[+of]** *The main disadvantage of the project is the cost.* 這個項目最主要的缺點便是費用太大。| **[+to]** *There are some disadvantages to his proposal.* 他的建議有幾處弱點。| **be at a disadvantage** (=have a disadvantage) 處於不利境地 *I was at a disadvantage because I didn't speak French.* 我不會說法語, 所以處於劣勢。| **put sb at a disadvantage/be to sb's disadvantage** (=give someone a disadvantage) 置某人於不利境地/使某人處於劣勢 *Her height will be very much to her disadvantage if she wants to be a dancer.* 她如果想當舞蹈演員的話, 她的身高將對她很不利。

dis·ad·van·taged /ˌdɪsədˋvæntɪdʒd; ˌdɪsədˈvɑːntɪdʒd◂/ *adj* having social disadvantages, such as a lack of money or education, which make it difficult for you to succeed 社會地位低下的, 處於不利社會經濟地位的〔如缺錢或教

育程度不夠等〕: *disadvantaged kids from the ghetto* 來自貧民區的貧賤孩子

dis·ad·van·ta·geous /dɪsˌædvænˋtedʒəs; ˌdɪsædvən-ˈteɪdʒəs/ *adj* [+to/for] unfavourable and likely to cause problems for you 不利的, 引發問題的 —**disadvantageously** *adv*

dis·af·fec·ted /ˌdɪsəˋfɛktɪd; ˌdɪsəˈfektɪ̣d◂/ *adj* no longer loyal because you are not at all satisfied with your leader, ruler etc 不忠的, 疏遠的〔由於對領導者、統治者等不滿〕: *Some of the government's most loyal supporters are now becoming disaffected.* 政府一些最忠實的支持者現在變得越來越心懷不滿了。—**disaffection** /-ˋfɛkʃən; -ˈfekʃən/ *n* [U]

dis·af·fil·i·ate /ˌdɪsəˋfɪlɪˌet; ˌdɪsəˈfɪlieɪt/ *v* [I,T+**from**] if an organization disaffiliates from another organization or is disaffiliated from it, it breaks the official connection it has with it 脫離, 正式退出〔某個組織〕, 割斷關係 —compare 比較 AFFILIATE[1]

2 **dis·a·gree** /ˌdɪsəˋgri; ˌdɪsəˈgriː/ *v* [T] **1** to have or express a different opinion from someone else 不同意, 有分歧: **[+with]** *Peter may disagree with this, but I don't really care.* 彼得或許不贊成此事, 但是我並不真的在乎。| **[+about/on]** *We often disagree about politics.* 我們經常對政治問題有不同的見解。| **I disagree** *spoken* 【口】 *I disagree; I think it's a bad idea.* 我反對; 我認為那是個壞主意。**2** if statements or reports about the same event or situation disagree, they are different from each other〔對於同個事件或形勢的幾個陳述或報道〕互不相符, 不一致, 互不相同

disagree with sb *phr v* [T] if something such as food or weather disagrees with you, it has a bad effect on you or makes you ill〔食物、氣候〕對〔某人〕有不良影響; 使〔某人〕身體不適: *Seafood always disagrees with me.* 我吃海鮮總是感到不舒服。

This graph shows how common the different grammar patterns of the verb **disagree** are. 本圖表所示為動詞 disagree 構成的不同語法模式的使用頻率。

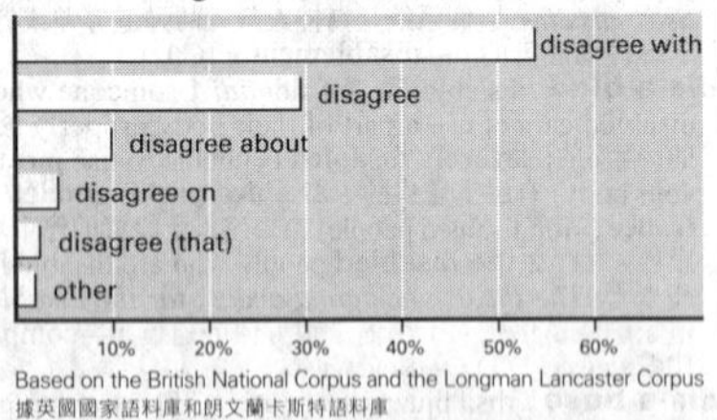

Based on the British National Corpus and the Longman Lancaster Corpus 據英國國家語料庫和朗文蘭卡斯特語料庫

dis·a·gree·a·ble /ˌdɪsəˋgriəbḷ; ˌdɪsəˈgriːəbəl◂/ *adj* **1** not at all enjoyable or pleasant 令人不快的; 不合意的; 討厭的: *a disagreeable experience* 一次令人不愉快的經歷 **2** unfriendly and bad-tempered 不友好的; 脾氣壞的: *a rude, disagreeable woman* 一個不懂禮數、難相處的女人 —**disagreeably** *adv*

dis·a·gree·ment /ˌdɪsəˋgrimənt; ˌdɪsəˈgriːmənt/ *n* **1** [C, U] a situation in which people express different opinions about something and sometimes quarrel 意見不合, 分歧, 爭論: *Just because we've had a few disagreements, it doesn't mean we aren't still friends.* 僅僅是我們有過幾次意見不合並不說明我們不再是朋友。| **[+about/over/as to]** *There is some disagreement as to whether the disease is curable.* 關於這種疾病是否可以治癒, 意見有些分歧。| **[+among/between]** *There is a lot of disagreement among doctors about this.* 關於此事, 醫生之間有着許多不同的意見。| **be in disagreement** (=disagree) 有分歧 **2** [U] differences between two statements, reports etc that ought to be similar〔兩個本該相似的陳述或報道〕互不相符, 不一致: **[+between]** *There is considerable disagreement between these two estimates.* 這兩種估計很不一致。

dis·al·low /ˌdɪsəˋlaʊ; ˌdɪsəˈlaʊ/ *v* [T] to officially refuse to allow something such as a claim, because a rule has been broken〔由於違反了規則〕不准許, 駁回: *Leeds had a goal disallowed for being offside.* 利茲隊由於越位被判進球無效。

dis·ap·pear /ˌdɪsəˋpɪr; ˌdɪsəˈpɪə/ *v* [I] **1** to become impossible to see or find 消失, 失蹤: *Where are my keys? They seem to have disappeared.* 我的鑰匙哪兒去了? 好像失蹤了。| **disappear behind/under/into etc** *Grab the cat quick! Before he disappears out the door!* 快把貓抓住! 趁牠還沒溜出門去! | **disappear from view/sight** *David watched her car until it disappeared from view.* 大衛一直望着她的車, 直到看不見為止。**2** to stop existing 不復存在: *So what happens when the rain forest disappears for ever?* 那麼, 熱帶雨林若永遠消失了會怎樣呢? —**disappearance** *n* [C,U]: *Her sudden disappearance was very worrying.* 她忽然失蹤, 很令人擔憂。 

dis·ap·point /ˌdɪsəˋpɔɪnt; ˌdɪsəˈpɔɪnt/ *v* [T] **1** to make someone feel sad because something they hoped for or expected did not happen 使〔某人〕失望: *I'm sorry to disappoint you, but I can't come after all.* 我很抱歉讓你失望, 但是我還是來不了。| *You disappoint me, Eric. I expected better.* 你令我失望, 艾里克。我期望於你的要好些。**2 disappoint sb's hopes/expectations** to prevent something from happening that someone hoped for or expected 讓某人的希望/期望破滅

dis·ap·point·ed /ˌdɪsəˋpɔɪntɪd; ˌdɪsəˈpɔɪntɪ̣d◂/ *adj* **1** sad because something you hoped for did not happen, or because someone or something was not as good as you expected 失望的、沮喪的: *Dad seemed more disappointed than angry.* 與其說爸爸很生氣, 倒不如說他很失望。| **[+about]** *Nathan's really disappointed about not being able to go.* 納森對於自己去不了着實感到失望。| **disappointed in sb** *I'm disappointed in you! How could you have lied like that?* 你真讓我失望! 你怎麼能那樣撒謊呢? | **disappointed (that)** *Of course I'm disappointed I didn't get an invitation.* 我沒有受到邀請, 當然感到很失望。| **[+with]** *I have to say we're disappointed with your work.* 我不得不說你們的工作讓我們很失望。| **[+at]** *Are you disappointed at not being chosen?* 你沒被選中, 是不是很失望? | **disappointed to hear/see/find** *We were disappointed to find the museum closed.* 看到博物館已經關門, 我們感到很沮喪。| **bitterly/terribly disappointed** *Gordon was bitterly disappointed when he failed that course.* 高登那門課沒及格, 他非常灰心。**2 disappointed hope/plan/expectation** something you hope for, plan, or expect that does not happen or is not as good as you expected 破滅的希望/計劃/期望

dis·ap·point·ing /ˌdɪsəˋpɔɪntɪŋ; ˌdɪsəˈpɔɪntɪŋ◂/ *adj* not as good as you hoped or expected 令人失望[沮喪、掃興]的: *disappointing profit figures* 令人失望的盈利數字 | *Well, Bill was really negative about it, which was pretty disappointing.* 嗯, 比爾對此事的態度很消極, 這很讓人掃興。—**disappointingly** *adv*

dis·ap·point·ment /ˌdɪsəˋpɔɪntmənt; ˌdɪsəˈpɔɪntmənt/ *n* **1** [U] sadness that something is not as good as you expected it to be, or has not happened in the way you hoped it would 失望; 沮喪: **to sb's (great) disappointment** *To her great disappointment none of her tomatoes grew well.* 令她十分沮喪的是, 她種的番茄長得都不好。**2** [C] someone or something that is not as good as you hoped or expected 令人失望的人[事物]: *The movie was kind of a disappointment.* 那部電影有些讓人失望。| **be a disappointment to sb** *Frankly, I've been a disappointment to my father; he wanted me to be a lawyer.* 說實話, 我很叫我父親失望; 他本想讓我成為一名律師。

dis·ap·pro·ba·tion /ˌdɪsæprəˋbeʃən; ˌdɪsæprəˈbeɪʃən/ *n* [U] *formal* disapproval of someone or something because you think they are morally wrong 【正式】〔認為某人或某事道德上不正確而〕反對, 不贊成; 責難

dis·ap·prov·al /ˌdɪsəˋpruvl̩; ˌdɪsəˈpruːvəl/ *n* [U] an attitude that shows you think that someone or their behaviour, ideas etc are bad or unsuitable 不贊同, 反對; 責難; 不許可: **[+of]** *We intend to express our disapproval of the marriage.* 我們打算反對這門婚事。| **with disapproval** *Baxter eyed our dirty clothes with obvious disapproval.* 巴克斯特打量着我們的髒衣服, 很明顯是不滿意。| **in disapproval** *Aunt Clarissa snorted in disapproval.* 克拉麗莎姨媽不以為然地哼了一聲。

dis·ap·prove /ˌdɪsəˋpruv; ˌdɪsəˈpruːv/ *v* [I] to think that someone or their behaviour, ideas etc are bad or unsuitable 不贊成, 反對; 認為不好; 非難: **[+of]** *Mother disapproves of every boyfriend I bring home.* 媽媽對我帶回家的每一個男朋友都不滿意。| **strongly disapprove** *I strongly disapprove of couples living together before marriage.* 我堅決反對兩個人未結婚便住在一起。

dis·ap·prov·ing /ˌdɪsəˋpruvɪŋ; ˌdɪsəˈpruːvɪŋ◂/ *adj* showing that you think someone or something is bad or unsuitable 不贊成的, 表示反對的: *a disapproving frown* 不滿地皺着眉頭 —**disapprovingly** *adv*: *Tyler shook his head disapprovingly.* 泰勒不滿地搖了搖頭。

dis·arm /dɪsˋɑrm; dɪsˈɑːm/ *v* **1** [I] to reduce the size of your armed forces and the number of weapons 裁軍; 裁減軍備: *Getting the rebels to disarm will not be easy.* 要讓叛亂分子解除武裝並非易事。**2** [T] to take away someone's weapons 繳〔某人的〕械, 解除〔某人的〕武裝: *Captured soldiers were disarmed and put into camps.* 被俘獲的士兵被繳了械, 然後關進戰俘營。**3** [T] if your manner or behaviour disarms someone, it is so pleasant that it makes them stop feeling angry or disapproving towards you 消除〔某人的〕怒氣[不滿]: *That charm of hers can disarm even her sternest critics.* 她的那種魅力甚至可以使得對她最為苛刻的批評者也火不起來。—see also 另見 DISARMING **4** [T] to take the explosives out of a bomb, MISSILE (1) etc 拆除, 取出〔炸彈、導彈等〕的引信

dis·ar·ma·ment /dɪsˋɑrməmənt; dɪsˈɑːməmənt/ *n* [U] the reduction of the size of a country's military forces and the number of weapons that it has 裁軍; 裁減軍備: **nuclear disarmament** (=reduction in the number of atomic weapons) 核裁軍, 核武器的裁減

dis·arm·ing /dɪsˋɑrmɪŋ; dɪsˈɑːmɪŋ/ *adj* making you trust someone or feel less angry with them than before 使人消氣的, 消除敵意的, 使人不存戒心的: *Kenneth has such a disarming smile!* 肯尼思的微笑真讓人傾倒! —**disarmingly** *adv*

dis·ar·range /ˌdɪsəˋrendʒ; ˌdɪsəˈreɪndʒ/ *v* [T] *formal* to make something untidy【正式】使不整齊, 弄亂 —**disarrangement** *n* [U]

dis·ar·ray /ˌdɪsəˋre; ˌdɪsəˈreɪ/ *n* [U] *formal* the state of being completely confused or untidy【正式】混亂, 凌亂: **in disarray** *Troops retreated in disarray under heavy gunfire.* 軍隊在猛烈的砲火下倉皇撤退。| *Manuscripts lay in wild disarray on the side table.* 手稿凌亂地放在邊桌上。| **throw sth into disarray/fall into disarray** *Gray's plans have been thrown into disarray because of injuries.* 由於發生傷人事故, 格雷的計劃全被打亂了。

dis·as·so·ci·ate /ˌdɪsəˋsoʃɪˌet; ˌdɪsəˈsəʊʃieɪt/ *v* [T] another form of DISSOCIATE dissociate 的另一種拼法

2 3 **di·sas·ter** /dɪˋzæstɚ; dɪˈzɑːstə/ *n* [C,U] **1** a sudden event such as a flood, storm, or accident which causes great damage or suffering 災難, 災禍〈如水災、暴風雨、意外事故等〉: *108 people died in the mining disaster.* 在這次礦山慘禍中, 有 108 人喪生。| **natural disaster** (=caused by nature, not by an accident) 自然災害 *The 1987 hurricane was the worst natural disaster to hit England for decades.* 1987 年的颶風是數十年來襲擊英格蘭的最為嚴重的自然災害。| **disaster area** (=a place where a disaster has happened) 災區 | **disaster strikes** *Disaster struck on the first day, when all our equipment was stolen.* 災難頭一天就降臨了, 我們所有的裝備都被偷盜一空。**2** a complete failure 徹底的失敗: *The party was a total disaster – half the guests didn't even turn up!* 晚會真是失敗——竟有一半的客人沒有來!

di·sas·trous /dɪzˋæstrəs; dɪˈzɑːstrəs/ *adj* very bad, or ending in failure 災難性的; 以失敗告終的: *Warrington's disastrous early marriage* 沃林頓以失敗告終的早婚 | *Chemical leaks have had a disastrous effect on wildlife.* 化學物質泄漏對野生生物造成了災難性的影響。—**disastrously** *adv*

dis·a·vow /ˌdɪsəˋvau; ˌdɪsəˈvaʊ/ *v* [T] *formal* to state that you are not responsible for something, or that you have no knowledge of it【正式】否認, 不承認: *He later disavowed any connection with the Fascist collaborators.* 他後來否認與法西斯通敵分子有任何關係。—**disavowal** *n* [C,U]

dis·band /dɪsˋbænd; dɪsˈbænd/ *v* [I,T] if a club or organization disbands or is disbanded, its activities are officially stopped, and it no longer exists〔俱樂部或組織等〕解體; 解散

dis·bar /dɪsˋbɑr; dɪsˈbɑː/ *v* **disbarred, disbarring** [T] to make a lawyer leave the bar (BAR[1] (8)) or the legal profession 取消〔某人的〕律師資格, 使〔某人〕退出律師行業 —compare 比較 DEBAR —**disbarment** *n* [U]

dis·be·lief /ˌdɪsbəˋlif; ˌdɪsbl̩ˈliːf/ *n* [U] a feeling that something is not true or does not exist 不相信, 懷疑: *My initial response was one of utter disbelief.* 我最初的反應便是根本不相信。| **stare/gasp/blink etc in disbelief** *Marta shook her head in disbelief, shocked by the damage.* 瑪爾塔不相信地搖着頭, 被造成的損失給嚇呆了。—compare 比較 UNBELIEF, BELIEF

dis·be·lieve /ˌdɪsbəˋliv; ˌdɪsbl̩ˈliːv/ *v* [I+in,T] *formal* to not believe something or someone【正式】不相信, 懷疑〔某人或某事〕: *I see no reason to disbelieve him.* 我看沒有甚麼理由不相信他。—**disbelieving** *adj*: *disbelieving laughter* 懷疑的笑聲

dis·burse /dɪsˋbɝs; dɪsˈbɜːs/ *v* [T] *formal* to pay out money, especially from a large sum that is available for a special purpose【正式】〔從一大筆專用資金中拿出錢來〕支付; 支出: *Over $25 million has been disbursed from the fund.* 已從這項資金中支付兩千五百多萬美元。—**disbursement** *n* [C,U]

disc also 又作 **disk** *AmE*【美】/dɪsk; dɪsk/ *n* [C] **1** a round, flat shape or object〔扁平的〕圓盤狀物; 圓盤形狀: *a revolving metal disc* 一個旋轉的金屬圓盤 **2** a COMPACT DISC 雷射[激光]唱片 **3** a record that you play on a RECORD PLAYER 唱片 **4** *BrE* a computer DISK【英】電腦磁盤, 磁碟 **5** a flat piece of CARTILAGE between the bones of your back 椎間盤: **slipped disc** (=one that has slipped out of its correct place) 突出的椎間盤 3

dis·card[1] /dɪsˋkɑrd; dɪsˈkɑːd/ *v* **1** [T] to get rid of something because it is useless 扔掉, 棄置: *What was more worrying was a box of used syringes that hadn't been properly discarded.* 更令人擔憂的是一盒用過的注射器沒有得到妥善棄置。**2** [I,T] to put down unwanted cards in a card game〔在牌戲中〕打出 (不想要的牌) —**discarded** *adj*: *old discarded clothes* 不要的舊衣服

discard[2] /ˋdɪskɑrd; ˈdɪskɑːd/ *n* [C] an unwanted card that is put down in a card game〔在牌戲中〕因不要而打出的牌

disc brakes /ˋ· ·/ *n* [plural] BRAKES[1] that work by means of a pair of hard surfaces pressing against a DISC (1) in the centre of a car wheel〔汽車的〕盤式制動器, 圓盤煞車

di·scern /dɪˋsɝn; dɪˈsɜːn/ *v* [T not in progressive 不用進行式] *formal* to see, notice, or understand something only after looking at it or thinking about it carefully; PERCEIVE (2)【正式】〔仔細地看過或想過之後才〕覺察出, 弄清楚, 辨明: *In the distance I could just discern the hills near Tendaho.* 在遠處我只能望見滕達霍附近的羣山。| **discern who/what/how etc** *It was difficult to discern which of them was telling the truth.* 很難弄清楚他們之中誰說的是實話。—**discernible** *adj*: *There is still no discernible improvement in the economic situation.* 經濟形勢

D

仍然看不出明顯的好轉。—**discernibly** *adv*

di·scern·ing /dɪˋsɝnɪŋ; dɪˈsɜːnɪŋ/ *adj* showing the ability to make good judgments, especially about art, music, style etc〔尤指藝術、音樂、時尚等方面〕有鑑賞力的, 有品味的, 識別能力好的: *Amanda liked to think she was discerning in her tastes.* 阿曼達自以為很有鑑賞力。| *With prices down by a third, there are many bargains around for the discerning buyer.* 價格降了三分之一, 對於那些識貨的人來說, 有許多便宜貨可買。

di·scern·ment /dɪˋsɝnmənt; dɪˈsɜːnmənt/ *n* [U] *formal* the ability to make good judgments about people or about art, music, style etc【正式】〔在對人或藝術、音樂、時尚等方面的〕鑑賞力, 識別能力, 品味: *I hope Pam shows more taste and discernment in choosing a husband.* 我希望帕姆選擇丈夫時能更有品味和識別能力。

dis·charge¹ /dɪsˋtʃardʒ; dɪsˈtʃɑːdʒ/ *v*

1 ►SEND SB AWAY 讓某人走◄ [T] to officially allow a person to go or send them away, especially after being ill in hospital or working in the army, navy etc 正式准許〔某人〕離開〔尤指讓住院的病人出院或讓服役的人退伍等〕: **[+from]** *I think Oliver gets discharged from the RAF in August.* 我想奧利弗將於今年八月從皇家空軍退役。| **discharge yourself** (=leave hospital before your treatment is complete) 擅自出院

2 ►LET STH OUT 排出某物◄ [I always+adv/prep,T] to send out gas, liquid, smoke etc, or allow it to escape 放出〔氣體、液體、煙等〕: **[+into]** *pollutants being discharged into the atmosphere* 被排放到大氣中的污染物

3 ►SHOOT 射出◄ [T] to fire a gun or shoot an ARROW (1) etc 開〔槍、砲〕; 射〔箭〕

4 discharge a duty/promise/responsibility etc *formal* to do properly everything that is part of a particular duty etc【正式】盡職責/履行諾言/承擔責任等: *the failure of the council to discharge its duty* 市議會未能履行其職責

5 discharge a debt *formal* to pay a debt【正式】清償債務

6 ►GOODS/PASSENGERS 貨物/乘客◄ [T] to unload goods or passengers from a ship, plane etc 卸〔貨〕; 讓〔乘客〕下船[下飛機]

7 ►ELECTRICITY 電◄ [I,T] if a piece of electrical equipment discharges or is discharged, it sends out electricity 放〔電〕

8 ►A WOUND 傷口◄ [I,T] to send out PUS (=infected liquid) 流〔膿〕, 出〔水〕

discharge² /ˋdɪstʃardʒ; ˈdɪstʃɑːdʒ/ *n* **1** [U] the action of allowing someone to go away, especially someone who has been ill in hospital or working in the army, navy etc 准許離開〔尤指病人出院, 服役的人退伍等〕: **[+from]** *Patients' needs after discharge from hospital will be monitored.* 出院後病人的需求將得到監控。—see also 另見 DISHONOURABLE DISCHARGE **2** [C,U] the act of sending out gas, liquid, smoke etc, or the substance that is sent out〔氣體、液體、煙等的〕排放; 排放的物質: **[+of]** *the discharge of toxic waste into the sea* 有毒廢物向海裡的排放 | **nasal/vaginal discharge** (=a thick liquid that comes out of someone's nose or VAGINA because of illness) 鼻腔/陰道分泌物 **3** [C,U] electricity that is sent out by a piece of equipment, a storm etc〔儀器、雷暴等釋放出來的〕電 **4** [U+of] the act of doing a duty or paying a debt〔職責的〕履行; 〔債務的〕清償: *the discharge of the college's legal responsibilities* 學院法律責任的履行

discharged bank·rupt /ˌ·ˌ· ˈ··/ *n* [C] someone who cannot pay their debts but who has obeyed the orders of the court and can do business again 免除債務的破產者〔已執行法庭規定, 可以再做生意的破產者〕

di·sci·ple /dɪˋsaɪpl̩; dɪˈsaɪpəl/ *n* [C] **1** someone who believes in the ideas of a great teacher, especially a religious one, and tries to follow them〔尤指宗教導師的〕追隨者, 門徒, 信徒: *Dian Fossey, the American disciple of Louis Leakey who studied gorillas in Rwanda* 迪昂·福塞, 在盧旺達研究大猩猩的路易斯·利基的美國弟子 **2** one of the first twelve men to follow Christ 耶穌最初的十二門徒之一

di·sci·ple·ship /dɪˋsaɪpl̩ˌʃɪp; dɪˈsaɪpəlʃɪp/ *n* [U] the period of time when someone is a disciple, or the state of being one 當信徒期間; 信徒身分

dis·ci·pli·nar·i·an /ˌdɪsəplɪnˋɛrɪən; ˌdɪsəpləˈneəriən/ *n* [C] someone who believes people should obey orders and rules, and who makes them do this 執行紀律者: *a strict disciplinarian* 一個嚴格執行紀律的人

dis·ci·pli·na·ry /ˋdɪsəplɪnˌɛrɪ; ˈdɪsəplɪnəri/ *adj* connected with the punishment of someone who has not obeyed rules, or with trying to make people obey rules 有關紀律的, 執行紀律的, 懲處的: **disciplinary action/measures** (=things you do to punish someone) 懲戒行動/措施 *The investigation led to disciplinary action against several officers.* 調查引發了對幾名軍官採取紀律行動。| **disciplinary hearing/committee** (=to decide if someone should be punished) 懲戒聆訊會/委員會〔決定某人是否應受到處罰〕

dis·ci·pline¹ /ˋdɪsəplɪn; ˈdɪsəplən/ *n* **1** [U] the practice of making people obey rules and orders, or the controlled situation that results from this practice 紀律, 紀律狀況: *We have high standards of discipline at this school that must be maintained.* 在這所學校裡, 我們有很高的紀律標準, 必須遵守。| *strict military discipline* 嚴格的軍紀 | **keep discipline** *teachers who can't keep discipline in the classroom* 無法維持課堂紀律的老師們 **2** [C,U] a method of training your mind or learning to control your behaviour〔思想或行為的〕訓練, 磨練: *Learning poetry is a good discipline for the memory.* 背詩是訓練記憶力的一種好方法。**3** [U] the ability to control your own behaviour and way of working 克制能力: *He'll never finish that course – he's got no discipline!* 他永遠也修不完那門課程 — 他一點克制能力都沒有! —see also 另見 SELF-DISCIPLINE **4** [U] punishment for not obeying rules 處罰, 懲處, 處分: *That child needs discipline.* 那個孩子需要受到處罰。**5** [C] an area of knowledge such as history, chemistry, mathematics etc that is studied at a university〔大學裡學習的〕專業, 科目

discipline² *v* [T] **1** to teach someone to obey rules and control their own behaviour 訓練, 管教: *At least I'm not afraid of disciplining my kids!* 至少我不害怕管教自己的孩子! **2 discipline yourself (to do sth)** to control the way you work, how regularly you do something etc, because you know it is good for you 嚴格要求自己, 約束自己〔去做某事〕: *It's a question of disciplining yourself to write every day.* 這是個約束你自己每天堅持寫作的問題。**3** to punish someone in order to keep order and control 懲處〔某人〕: *One director left today and two others have been disciplined.* 一名主管今天離了職, 另外兩名也已經受到了懲處。

dis·ci·plined /ˋdɪsəplɪnd; ˈdɪsəplənd/ *adj* behaving in a controlled way according to strict rules 遵守紀律的: *the most disciplined, effective army in the world* 世界上最具有紀律性、效率最高的一支軍隊 | *a disciplined approach* 嚴謹有序的方法

disc jock·ey /ˈ· ˌ··/ *n* [C] someone who introduces and plays records of popular music on a radio show or at a dance club〔電台〕音樂唱片節目主持人;〔夜總會〕舞曲唱片播放員, 唱片騎師

dis·claim /dɪsˋklem; dɪsˈkleɪm/ *v* [T] **disclaim responsibility/knowledge etc** *formal* to state that you are not responsible for something, that you do not know anything about it, etc【正式】否認[不承認]〔對某事〕有責任/知情等: *I can't believe the insurance company disclaimed liability for the accident.* 我無法相信保險公司竟然拒絕對此意外事故負賠償責任。

dis·claim·er /dɪsˋklemɚ; dɪsˈkleɪmə/ *n* [C] a statement that you are not responsible for something, that you are not connected with it etc 不承擔責任的聲明, 與某事沒有關聯的聲明

dis·close /dɪsˋkloz; dɪsˈkləʊz/ *v* [T] **1** to make something publicly known, especially after it has been kept secret from the public〔尤指在被隱瞞後〕透露, 揭露, 泄露; 公開〔某事〕: *The Security Service is unlikely to disclose any information.* 保安部門不可能透露任何消息。| **disclose that** *It has recently been disclosed that 30% of donations are spent on publicity.* 據最新消息透露, 30% 的捐款被用於宣傳。**2** to show something by removing the thing that covers it〔把蓋在某物上的東西去掉以〕顯露; 揭開: *The curtains rose, disclosing a stage bathed in red light.* 帷幕升起, 顯露出籠罩在一片紅光之中的舞台。

dis·clo·sure /dɪsˋkloʒɚ; dɪsˈkləʊʒə/ *n* **1** [U] the act of telling or showing something that has been kept secret 公開; 透露; 披露: *MPs called for public disclosure of the committee's findings.* 議員要求公開委員會的調查結果。**2** [C] a fact which is made known after being kept secret 被公開的祕聞, 被透露的事實: *Following sensational disclosures concerning his personal life, he has offered to resign.* 在他的私生活被大肆披露之後, 他主動提出辭職。

dis·co /ˋdɪsko; ˈdɪskəʊ/ *n* [C] a club or social event at which people dance to recorded popular music 的士高[迪斯科]舞廳, 的士高[迪斯科]舞會

dis·cog·ra·phy /dɪˋskɑgrəfɪ; dɪˈskɒgrəfi/ *n* [C] a list of the music and songs recorded by a musician or musical group〔音樂家或音樂團體的〕錄音作品目錄

dis·col·or /dɪsˋkʌlɚ; dɪsˈkʌlə/ *v* [T] the American spelling of DISCOLOUR discolour 的美式拼法

dis·col·o·ra·tion /dɪsˌkʌləˋreʃən; dɪsˌkʌləˈreɪʃən/ *n* **1** [U] the process of becoming discoloured 變色; 褪色 **2** [C] a place on the surface of something where it has become discoloured 變色點, 褪色處

dis·col·our *BrE*【英】, **discolor** *AmE*【美】/dɪsˋkʌlɚ; dɪsˈkʌlə/ *v* [I,T] if something is discoloured or if it discolours, its colour changes, making it look dirty or unattractive (使) 變色, 褪色: *Sprinkle the apple slices with lemon juice to prevent them from discolouring.* 在蘋果片上灑些檸檬汁, 防止它們變色。

dis·com·bob·u·late /ˌdɪskəmˋbɑbjəˌlet; ˌdɪskəmˈbɒbjʊleɪt/ *v* [T] *humorous* to make someone feel completely confused or upset【幽默】使〔某人〕感到困惑, 使〔某人〕極度不安

dis·com·fit /dɪsˋkʌmfɪt; dɪsˈkʌmfɪt/ *v* [T] *formal* to make someone feel slightly uncomfortable, annoyed, or embarrassed【正式】使〔某人〕窘迫, 使〔某人〕尷尬: *Expecting a handshake, Jenny was discomfited by his kiss.* 珍妮只是期待着和他握握手, 因而對於他的親吻感到有些無所適從。—**discomfiture** *n* [U]

dis·com·fort /dɪsˋkʌmfɚt; dɪsˈkʌmfət/ *n* **1** [U] a feeling of slight pain or of being physically uncomfortable 不舒服, 不適: *You may experience some discomfort for a few days after the operation.* 手術後幾天內你可能會感到有些不舒服。**2** [U] a feeling of embarrassment, shame, or slight worry 尷尬, 慚愧, 窘迫: **[+at]** *Paul's discomfort at facing criticism tends to make him too defensive.* 受到批評時保羅時常感到彆扭, 這往往使他為自己辯解得太多。**3** [C] something that makes you uncomfortable 使人感到不舒服的事情: *the discomforts of travel* 旅途中的不適

dis·com·mode /ˌdɪskəˋmod; ˌdɪskəˈməʊd/ *v* [T] *formal* to cause trouble or difficulties for someone; INCOMMODE【正式】給〔某人〕帶來麻煩, 給〔某人〕添麻煩

dis·com·pose /ˌdɪskəmˋpoz; ˌdɪskəmˈpəʊz/ *v* [T] *formal* to make someone feel worried and no longer calm【正式】使〔某人〕焦慮, 使〔某人〕不安 —**discomposure** /-ˋpoʒɚ; -ˈpəʊʒə/ *n* [U]

dis·con·cert /ˌdɪskənˋsɝt; ˌdɪskənˈsɜːt/ *v* [T often passive 常用被動態] to make someone feel slightly confused or worried 使〔某人〕困惑; 使不安: *It was that cold, steady gaze of his that disconcerted her most.* 最讓她感到不安的是他那冷漠的、目不轉睛的凝視。

dis·con·cert·ing /ˌdɪskənˋsɝtɪŋ; ˌdɪskənˈsɜːtɪŋ◂/ *adj* making you feel slightly confused or worried 令人困惑的, 令人擔憂的 —**disconcertingly** *adv*: *It all seemed disconcertingly familiar.* 這一切似乎熟悉得令人感到疑惑。

dis·con·nect /ˌdɪskəˋnɛkt; ˌdɪskəˈnekt/ *v* [T] **1** to take out the wire, pipe etc that connects a machine or piece of equipment to something 斷開, 切斷: *Disconnect the cables before you try to move the computer.* 在你挪動電腦之前, 先把連接電纜拔下來。**2** to remove the supply of power from a machine or building 切斷〔電力供應〕: *You realize if we don't pay that bill soon they'll disconnect our gas?* 你有沒有意識到如果我們不付煤氣費, 他們很快就會切斷對我們的煤氣供應? **3** to break the telephone connection between two people 掛斷〔電話〕: *Operator? We've been disconnected.* 是接線員嗎? 我們的電話被中斷了。—**disconnection** /-ˋnɛkʃən; -ˈnekʃən/ *n* [C,U]

dis·con·nect·ed /ˌdɪskəˋnɛktɪd; ˌdɪskəˈnektɪd◂/ *adj* disconnected thoughts or ideas do not seem to be related to each other〔思想或想法等〕不連貫的, 無關聯的

dis·con·so·late /dɪsˋkɑnsl̩ɪt; dɪsˈkɒnsəlɪt/ *adj* feeling extremely sad and hopeless 極度憂鬱的, 絕望的: *A few disconsolate men sat in the foyer with their hats in their hands.* 幾個面色憂鬱的男子坐在休息廳裡, 手裡拿着他們的帽子。—**disconsolately** *adv*: *O'Grady trudged disconsolately back home.* 奧格雷迪神情沮喪地邁着沉重的步子走回家。

dis·con·tent[1] /ˌdɪskənˋtɛnt; ˌdɪskənˈtent/ *n* [U] a feeling of being unhappy and not satisfied with the situation you are in 不愉快; 不滿足; 不滿意: **[+with]** *There is no evidence whatsoever of customer discontent with our credit terms.* 沒有任何證據顯示顧客對於我們的信貸條件有不滿之意。—opposite 反義詞 CONTENTMENT

discontent[2] *v* [T] to make someone feel discontented 使不愉快; 使不滿

dis·con·tent·ed /ˌdɪskənˋtɛntɪd; ˌdɪskənˈtentɪd◂/ *adj* unhappy or not satisfied with the situation you are in 不愉快的, 不滿的, 不滿足的: **[+with]** *Eva was ambitious and was discontented with her job at the post office.* 伊娃很有志向, 她對自己在郵局的工作並不滿足。—**discontentedly** *adv*

dis·con·tin·ue /ˌdɪskənˋtɪnju; ˌdɪskənˈtɪnjuː/ *v* [T] to stop doing or providing something that you have regularly done or provided until now 中止, 中斷, 終止: *Bus Route 51 is being discontinued as of March 1st.* 51路公共汽車將從3月1日起停止運營。| *a discontinued china pattern* 不再使用的瓷器圖案 | **discontinued line** (=a type of product that is no longer being produced) 已停止生產的產品 —**discontinuation** /ˌdɪskəntɪnjuˋeʃən; ˌdɪskəntɪnjuˈeɪʃən/ *n* [U] —**discontinuance** /ˌdɪskənˋtɪnjuəns; ˌdɪskənˈtɪnjuəns/ *n* [U]

dis·con·ti·nu·i·ty /ˌdɪskɑntəˋnuətɪ; ˌdɪskɒntɪˈnjuːɪti/ *n* **1** [U] the fact of a process not being continuous 不連續性, 間斷性 **2** [C] a sudden change or pause in a process 中斷, 間斷

dis·con·tin·u·ous /ˌdɪskənˋtɪnjʊəs; ˌdɪskənˈtɪnjuəs◂/ *adj* not continuous 不連續的, 斷續的: *Women are particularly affected because of their discontinuous employment patterns.* 婦女尤其受到影響, 因為她們的就業模式是不連續的。—**discontinuously** *adv*

dis·cord /ˋdɪskɔrd; ˈdɪskɔːd/ *n* **1** [U] *formal* disagreement or quarrelling between people【正式】不和, 紛爭: *marital discord* 婚姻的不和 | *discord within NATO* 北約內部的不和 **2** [C,U] an unpleasant sound made by a group of musical notes that do not go together well 不和諧的音調, 刺耳的聲音 —compare 比較 HARMONY

dis·cord·ant /dɪsˋkɔrdn̩t; dɪsˈkɔːdənt/ *adj* **1** **strike/sound a discordant note** *literary* to seem strange and unsuitable in relation to everything around【文】顯得不諧調/聽起來突兀: *The modern decor strikes a discordant note in this 17th century building.* 這座17世紀建築上面的現代裝飾顯得很不和諧。**2** a discordant sound is unpleasant because it is made up of musical notes that do not go together well〔聲音〕刺耳的, 嘈雜的 **3** not in agreement 不一致的, 相互衝突的: *discordant results from the experiment* 不一致的實驗結果

dis·co·theque /ˌdɪskəˋtɛk; ˈdɪskətek/ *n* [C] a DISCO 的士高[迪斯科]舞廳; 的士高[迪斯科]舞會

3 **dis·count¹** /ˋdɪskaunt; ˈdɪskaʊnt/ *n* [C] **1** a reduction in the cost of goods that you are buying 減價, 折扣: *Do I get a discount if I buy a whole case of wine?* 如果我買一整箱酒, 能給我打折扣嗎? | **discount price/fare** (=cheaper than the usual price) 折扣價 | **discount store/shop/warehouse** (=where you can buy goods cheaply) 廉價商店/貨倉 **2 at a discount a)** bought or sold for less than the usual price〔買賣〕低於正常價, 打折 **b)** *informal* not wanted or not regarded as valuable【非正式】不受歡迎的, 不值錢的, 受輕視的: *a ridiculous place where intelligence is at a discount* 一個聰明才智不受重視的可笑的地方

discount² /ˋdɪskaunt; dɪsˈkaʊnt/ *v* [T] to regard an idea, opinion, or piece of news as unimportant or unlikely to be true 不理會, 不重視〔觀點、意見、消息〕: *Larry tends to discount any suggestion I make in meetings.* 拉里往往不理會我在會上提出的任何建議。| **discount the possibility of** (=think that something is very unlikely to happen) 認為〔某事〕很不可能發生 *General Hausken had not discounted the possibility of aerial attack.* 豪斯肯將軍並非認為空襲完全沒有可能。

dis·coun·te·nance /dɪsˋkauntənəns; dɪsˈkaʊntɪ̣nəns/ *v* [T] *formal* to stop someone from doing something by showing that you disapprove of their behaviour【正式】不贊成, 阻止〔某人的行為〕

dis·cour·age /dɪsˋkɝɪdʒ; dɪsˈkʌrɪdʒ/ *v* [T] **1** to prevent or try to prevent someone from doing something by making the action difficult or unpleasant, or by showing them that it would not be a good thing to do (設法)阻止, 打消…的念頭: *You should install locks on all your windows to discourage burglars.* 你應該在所有的窗戶上都安上鎖, 以防竊賊入屋。| **discourage sb from doing sth** *We ought to be focusing on discouraging kids from smoking.* 我們應把重點集中在勸阻孩子們不要吸煙。**2** to make someone think that they will not be able to succeed in doing something so that they no longer want to continue doing it 使灰心, 使泄氣: *Students soon get discouraged if you criticize them too often.* 如果你批評學生次數太多, 他們很快就會泄氣的。—opposite 反義詞 ENCOURAGE

dis·cour·age·ment /dɪsˋkɝɪdʒmənt; dɪsˈkʌrɪdʒmənt/ *n* **1** [U] a feeling that you have lost confidence or determination and no longer want to continue doing something 氣餒, 泄氣, 失去信心 **2** [U] the act of trying to discourage someone from doing something 勸阻, 阻止 **3** [C] something that discourages you 使某人氣餒的事情, 挫折

dis·cour·a·ging /dɪsˋkɝɪdʒɪŋ; dɪsˈkʌrɪdʒɪŋ/ *adj* making you lose the confidence or determination you need to continue doing something 令人失去信心的, 使人氣餒的, 使人泄氣的: *The test results so far encountered have been very discouraging.* 目前所看到的考試結果讓人非常泄氣。—**discouragingly** *adv*

3 **dis·course¹** /ˋdɪskɔrs; ˈdɪskɔːs/ *n* **1** [C] a serious speech or piece of writing on a particular subject〔就某個題目的〕演講, 論述, 著述: **[+on/upon]** *Professor Grant delivered a long discourse on aspects of moral theology.* 格蘭特教授就道德神學的幾個方面發表了長篇的演講。**2** [U] serious conversation between people〔嚴肅的〕談話, 交談: *You can't expect meaningful discourse when you two disagree so violently.* 既然你們兩位的意見分歧這麼大, 別指望進行甚麼有意義的交談。**3** [U] the language used in particular kinds of speech or writing〔在特定類型的講述或論著中使用的〕語言, 話語: *scientific discourse* 科學話語

discourse² /dɪˋskɔrs; dɪsˈkɔːs/ *v*

discourse on/upon sth *phr v* [T] to make a long formal speech about something〔關於某事作長篇的、正式的〕講述, 論說: *Mrs Hitchins discoursed at length on the ignorance of the frontier people.* 希欽斯夫人詳細地講述了邊疆居民的無知。

dis·cour·te·ous /dɪsˋkɝtɪəs; dɪsˈkɜːtiəs/ *adj formal* not polite, and not showing respect for other people【正式】不講禮貌的; 失禮的: *Cameron was not really interested, but it would be discourteous to say so.* 卡梅倫並不真正感興趣, 但是若這麼說會很不禮貌。—**discourteously** *adv* —**discourteousness** *n* [U]

dis·cour·te·sy /dɪsˋkɝtəsɪ; dɪsˈkɜːtəsi/ *n* [C,U] *formal* an action or behaviour that is not polite【正式】粗魯的舉動

dis·cov·er /dɪsˋkʌvɚ; dɪsˈkʌvə/ *v* [T] **1** to find something that was hidden or that people did not know about before 發現〔隱藏的東西或以前不知道的事物〕: *I've just discovered a secret drawer in my old desk.* 我剛剛在我的舊書桌上發現了一個祕密抽屜。| *The Curies are best known for discovering radium.* 居里夫婦最為出名的是發現了鐳。—see 見 INVENT (USAGE) **2** to find out something yourself, without being told about it〔自己〕發現; 查出; 發覺: **discover that** *Police discovered that Kim's son was dealing in drugs.* 警方發現金的兒子在做毒品買賣。| **[+who/what/how etc]** *Emily's not even two, but she's discovered how to open doors.* 艾米莉還不到兩歲, 但她已經弄清怎麼開門了。**3** to notice someone who is very good at something and help them to become successful and well-known 發現〔某人有某方面的才能, 並幫助他成功、出名〕—**discoverer** *n* [C]

dis·cov·e·ry /dɪsˋkʌvərɪ; dɪsˈkʌvəri/ *n* **1** [C] a fact or thing that someone discovers that was hidden or not known about before 被發現的事實[事物]: *recent archaeological discoveries* 最近的考古發現 | **make a discovery** *Astronomers have made significant discoveries about our galaxy.* 天文學家對於我們的星系已作出了重大的發現。**2** [C] something that you learn or find out yourself, without being told about it〔自己〕發現, 發覺: **[+that]** *The discovery that her assistant had lied made Patty decide to fire him.* 帕蒂發現她的助手撒了謊, 這使得她決定解雇他。**3** [U] the act of discovering something 發現: **[+of]** *The discovery of oil in Alaska was a boon to the economy.* 在阿拉斯加找到石油對經濟是件大好事。

dis·cred·it¹ /dɪsˋkrɛdɪt; dɪsˈkredɪ̣t/ *v* [T] **1** to make people stop respecting or trusting someone or something 損壞〔某人或某物〕的名聲: *Black's remarks were taken out of context in an effort to discredit him.* 布萊克的話被斷章取義, 他們是想破壞他的名聲。**2** to make people stop believing in a particular idea 使〔人們〕不再相信〔某種觀點〕: *Some of Freud's theories have now been discredited.* 弗洛伊德的一些理論現在已經不為人們所相信了。

discredit² *n* loss of other people's respect or trust 喪失名譽, 喪失信用: **to sb's discredit** *I know enough to her discredit* (=enough bad things about her) *not to vote for her.* 我知道很多關於她的不光彩的事情, 這足以讓我不投她的票。| **bring discredit on/to** (=make people stop respecting someone or something) 讓〔某人或某物〕蒙羞; 給〔某人或某物〕帶來恥辱 *Their outrageous behaviour has brought discredit on English football.* 他們的可恥行為已經損害了英國足球的名譽。

dis·cred·i·ta·ble /dɪsˋkrɛdɪtəbḷ; dɪsˈkredɪ̣təbəl/ *adj* bad or wrong, and making people lose respect for you or trust in you 敗壞名譽的; 丟臉的: *a discreditable secret* 有損名譽的祕密 —**discreditably** *adv*

di·screet /dɪˋskrit; dɪˈskriːt/ *adj* **1** done or said in a careful way so that you do not offend, upset, or embarrass people 言行審慎的; 謹慎小心的: *It wasn't very discreet of you to ring me up at the office.* 你往辦公室給我打電話是有失謹慎的。| *That morning I began making discreet inquiries.* 那天早上我開始進行審慎的查詢。**2** careful not to talk about things that other people want to keep secret 小心謹慎的〔不會泄露別人的祕密〕: *Don't worry about my secretary hearing us; he's very discreet.* 別擔心我的祕書聽我們的談話; 他非常小心謹慎。—opposite 反義詞 INDISCREET —compare 比較 DISCRETE —**discreetly** *adv*

di·screp·an·cy /dɪˋskrɛpənsɪ; dɪˈskrepənsi/ *n* [C,U] a difference between two amounts, details, reports etc that ought to be the same〔兩個本該一樣的數目、細節、報告等的〕不一致; 不符; 差異; 出入: **[+in]** *How do you explain these discrepancies in the accounts?* 你如何解釋賬目中這些不相符的地方? | **[+between]** *There are big discrepancies between what Margaret says and what you say.* 瑪嘉烈所説的和你所説的有着很大出入。

di·screte /dɪˋskrit; dɪˈskriːt/ *adj formal* separate【正式】分開的; 各別的; 互不相關的: *There are two discrete breeding groups on the island.* 島上有兩個互不相關的繁殖羣體。—compare 比較 DISCREET —**discretely** *adv* —**discreteness** *n* [U]

di·scre·tion /dɪˋskrɛʃən; dɪˈskreʃən/ *n* [U] **1** the ability and right to decide exactly what should be done in a particular situation 決斷能力; 處理權; 酌情決定權: *Promotions are left to the discretion of the supervisor.* 提升事宜由主管決定。| **at sb's discretion** (=according to someone's decision or wishes) 根據某人的決定[意願] *The size of your payment may be changed at your discretion.* 你的付款定額可以隨你的意願而改變。**2** the ability to deal with situations in a way that does not offend or embarrass people, especially by keeping other people's secrets 謹慎; 慎重: *It's a delicate matter, Mr Nagel, that must be handled with the utmost discretion.* 這是件微妙的事情, 納格爾先生, 處理起來必須格外謹慎。| **be the soul of discretion** (=be extremely discreet) 極為謹慎的 **3 discretion is the better part of valour** used to say that it is better to be careful than to take unnecessary risks 不知進退非真勇〔謹慎要比無謂冒險強得多〕

di·scre·tion·a·ry /dɪˋskrɛʃənˌɛrɪ; dɪˈskreʃənəri/ *adj* not controlled by strict rules, but left for someone to make a decision about in each particular situation 不受嚴格規定控制的; 自由決定的; 酌情決定的: *the court's discretionary powers* 法庭酌情決定權

di·scrim·i·nate /dɪˋskrɪməˌnet; dɪˈskrɪmɪ̠neɪt/ *v* **1** [I, T] to recognize a difference between things 區別, 辨別: **[+between]** *It's sometimes difficult to discriminate between edible and poisonous mushrooms.* 可食用的蘑菇和毒蘑菇有時候很難區分。| **discriminate sth from** *You must learn to discriminate fact from opinion.* 你必須學會把事實和看法區分開來。**2** [I] to treat people differently from each other in an unfair way 不公正地區別對待; 歧視: **[+against]** *Are you saying the law discriminates against the disabled?* 你是説法律歧視傷殘人士嗎? | **discriminate in favour of** *As an employer, she always discriminates in favour of women.* 作為雇主, 她總是優待婦女。

di·scrim·i·nat·ing /dɪˋskrɪməˌnetɪŋ; dɪˈskrɪmɪ̠neɪtɪŋ/ *adj* able to judge what is of good quality and what is not 有鑑別能力的; 有鑑賞能力的; 識別能力強的: *We have a large wine list for those of discriminating taste.* 我們擁有種類繁多的酒可供那些有鑑賞能力的人選擇。

di·scrim·i·na·tion /dɪˌskrɪməˋneʃən; dɪˌskrɪmɪ̠ˈneɪʃən/ *n* [U] **1** the practice of treating one particular group in society in an unfair way 歧視: **[+against]** *Laws have got to be tougher to stop discrimination against the disabled.* 法律應該再強硬一些以制止對傷殘人士的歧視。| **[+in favour of]** *discrimination in favour of university graduates* 對大學畢業生的優待 | **racial discrimination** (=discrimination against someone who is of another race or colour) 種族歧視 | **sex discrimination** (=discrimination against women)〔對婦女的〕性別歧視 —see also 另見 POSITIVE DISCRIMINATION, REVERSE DISCRIMINATION **2** the ability to judge what is of good quality and what is not 鑑別力; 識別力; 鑑賞力

di·scur·sive /dɪˋskɝsɪv; dɪˈskɜːsɪv/ *adj* changing from one subject to another without any clear plan 東拉西扯的; 漫無邊際的: *a discursive style of writing* 東拉西扯的寫作風格 —**discursively** *adv* —**discursiveness** *n* [U]

dis·cus /ˋdɪskəs; ˈdɪskəs/ *n* [C] a heavy plate-shaped object which is thrown as far as possible as a sport 鐵餅

di·scuss /dɪˋskʌs; dɪˈskʌs/ *v* [T] **1** to talk about something with another person or a group in order to exchange ideas or decide something 商討, 談論, 討論: *Sandy won't ever discuss money.* 桑迪從不肯談論錢。| **discuss sth with sb** *I'd like to discuss my contract with you.* 我想和你談一下我的合同。| **discuss what/who/where etc** *We're here to discuss what we can do to prevent crime.* 我們來到這裡是為了討論我們能做些甚麼以防止犯罪。—see 見 SPEAK (USAGE) **2** to talk or write about something in detail and consider different ideas or opinions about it 詳細闡述; 論說: *Chapter One discusses the rise of the city-state on the European continent.* 第一章詳細論述了歐洲大陸上城邦的興起。 S3 W1

di·scus·sion /dɪˋskʌʃən; dɪˈskʌʃən/ *n* [C,U] **1** the act of discussing something, or a conversation in which people discuss something 討論; 談論; 商討: **have a discussion (about)** *Yes, on Friday we had a long discussion about the wording of the proposal.* 是的, 週五我們曾就這份建議的措辭進行了長時間的討論。| **under discussion** (=being discussed) 在討論中 *The section now under discussion focuses on tenants' rights.* 目前正在討論的這部分集中探討房客的權利問題。| **be up for discussion** (=be something that can be discussed and possibly changed) 可以討論的; 可能改變的 *Joe, I'm sorry, but item three is not up for discussion.* 喬, 對不起, 第三條是不予討論的。**2** something that is written about a subject that considers different ideas or opinions about it〔對某一話題的〕論述, 闡述: *the report's discussion of the legislation* 該報告對立法的論述 W1

dis·dain¹ /dɪsˋden; dɪsˈdeɪn/ *n* [U] a complete lack of respect that you show for someone or something because you think they are not at all worth paying attention to 鄙視; 輕視; 藐視; 不屑的態度: **[+for]** *He maintained an obvious disdain for the customs of the local people.* 他對當地人的習俗持有明顯的鄙視態度。| **treat sb/sth with disdain** *Mrs Strachan's evidence was treated with disdain by the prosecution.* 斯特羅恩夫人的證據被控方所輕視。

disdain² *v* **1** [T] to have no respect for someone or something, and believe they are unimportant 鄙視; 輕視; 藐視 **2 disdain to do sth** to refuse to do something because you are too proud to do it 不屑於做某事: *Tom Butler disdained to reply to such a trivial question.* 湯姆·巴特勒不屑於回答這麼一個瑣碎的問題。

dis·dain·ful /dɪsˋdenfəl; dɪsˈdeɪnfəl/ *adj* showing that you do not respect someone or something and think that they are unimportant 鄙視的; 輕視的; 藐視的; 不屑的: *a long disdainful look* 輕蔑的注視 | **[+of]** *There are some in the sport who are disdainful of amateurs.* 體育界中有些人瞧不起業餘運動員。—**disdainfully** *adv*

dis·ease /dɪˋziz; dɪˈziːz/ *n* **1** [C,U] an illness or unhealthy condition in your body, especially one caused by infection〔尤指感染而得的〕疾病; 病: **eye/liver/kidney etc disease** *Heart disease runs in our family.* 我們的家族有心臟病病史。| **cause disease** *filthy insanitary conditions that cause disease* 導致疾病的骯髒而不衛生的環境 | **infectious/contagious disease** (=easily passed from one person to another) 傳染病 *vaccination against infectious diseases such as typhoid* 預防如傷寒等傳染性疾病的疫苗接種 | **suffer from a disease** (=have a disease) 患某種疾病 *She suffers from a rare disease of the central nervous system.* 她得了一種罕見的中樞神經系統疾病。| **catch/contract a disease** (=get a disease by being infected) 感染上疾病 **2** [C] something that is seriously wrong with society or with someone's mind, behaviour etc〔社會的〕嚴重弊病;〔某人頭腦、行為的〕病態, 不健全: *Loneliness is a disease of our urban communities.* S3 W1

寂寞是我們都市人羣的一種精神疾病。—see also 另見 HEART DISEASE, SOCIAL DISEASE —**diseased** *adj*: *diseased muscles* 有病的肌肉 | *a diseased plant* 有病害的植物

USAGE NOTE 用法說明: DISEASE
WORD CHOICE 詞語辨析: **disease, illness**
Though **illness** and **disease** are often used in the same way and are equally common in spoken English, **illness** is really the state, or length of time, of being unwell (usually caused by some **disease**). 儘管 illness 和 disease 兩個詞通常用法相同, 而且在口語中同樣常用, 但 illness 真正指的是身體不舒服的狀態或者身體不舒服的時間〔通常由某種 disease 引起〕: *She died after a long illness.* 她久病之後死了。| *How many working days have you missed through illness?* 你因病誤了多少個工作日了?
It is **diseases** that have medical names, are related to parts of the body, and can be caught, carried and passed on if they are infectious. disease 均有醫學名稱, 與身體的部位有關。如果是傳染性疾病的話, 能被傳染、攜帶並且傳播: *a kidney/sexually-transmitted disease/infectious disease/Alzheimer's disease* 腎病/性傳播疾病/傳染性疾病/早年性痴呆病。However, you would usually talk about *mental illness* or a *terminal/critical illness.* 然而, 在談論精神病或晚期疾病/重病時通常用 illness。

This graph shows some of the words most commonly used with the noun **disease**. 本圖表所示為含有名詞 disease 的一些最常用詞組。

heart/lung/kidney disease
cause disease
infectious/contagious disease
suffer from a disease
catch/contract a disease
1 2 3 4 5 per million 每百萬
Based on the British National Corpus and the Longman Lancaster Corpus
據英國國家語料庫和朗文蘭卡斯特語料庫

dis·em·bark /ˌdɪsɪmˋbɑrk; ˌdɪsɪ̵mˈbɑːk/ *v* **1** [I] to get off a ship or aircraft 下船; 下飛機 —opposite 反義詞 EMBARK **2** [T] to put people or goods onto the shore from a ship 使上岸, 使登陸; 卸(貨) —**disembarkation** /ˌdɪsɛmbɑrˋkeʃən; ˌdɪsembɑːˈkeɪʃən/ *n* [U]

dis·em·bod·ied /ˌdɪsɪmˋbɑdɪd; ˌdɪsɪ̵mˈbɒdid◂/ *adj* **1** existing without a body or separated from a body 無軀體而存在的; 脱離軀體的: *disembodied spirits* 遊魂 **2** a disembodied sound or voice comes from someone who cannot be seen〔指聲響、聲音〕不知道來源的, 看不見來源的

dis·em·bow·el /ˌdɪsɪmˋbauəl; ˌdɪsɪ̵mˈbaʊəl/ *v* **disembowelled, disembowelling** *BrE*【英】, **disemboweled, disemboweling** *AmE*【美】[T] to remove someone's bowels (BOWEL (1)) 取出〔某人〕的腸子 —**disembowelment** *n* [U]

dis·en·chant·ed /ˌdɪsɪnˋtʃæntɪd; ˌdɪsɪ̵nˈtʃɑːntɪ̵d/ *adj* disappointed with someone or something, and no longer believing that they are good, exciting, or right 對〔某人或某事物〕失望的; 已醒悟的; 不再着迷的; 不再抱有幻想的: [+with] *By that time I was becoming disenchanted with the whole idea.* 到那個時候, 我對那種想法不再迷戀了。—**disenchantment** *n* [U]

dis·en·fran·chise /ˌdɪsɪnˋfræntʃaɪz; ˌdɪsɪnˈfræntʃaɪz/ *v* [T] to take away from someone their right to vote 剝奪〔某人〕的選舉權 —**disenfranchisement** /-tʃaɪzmənt; -tʃɪzmənt/ *n* [U]

dis·en·gage /ˌdɪsɪnˋgedʒ; ˌdɪsɪ̵nˈgeɪdʒ/ *v* **1** [T] to separate something from something else that is fastened to it or holding it 使脱離, 使分開: **disengage yourself** *Sally found it difficult to disengage herself from his embrace.* 莎莉發現很難從他的懷裡掙脱開。**2** [I,T] if you disengage part of a machine or if it disengages, you make it move away from another part that it was connected to (使)〔機器的某一部分與另一相連部分〕分離開, 移開, 鬆開: *Disengage the gears when you park the car.* 你泊車時要鬆開排擋。**3** [I] if two armies disengage, they stop fighting〔兩軍〕停止交戰 —**disengagement** *n* [U]

dis·en·tan·gle /ˌdɪsɪnˋtæŋgl; ˌdɪsɪ̵nˈtæŋgəl/ *v* [T] **1** **disentangle yourself (from)** to escape from a difficult situation that you are involved in 從〔陷入的困境中〕解脱出來 **2** to remove knots from ropes, strings etc that have become twisted or tied together 解開〔繩子等上面〕的結 **3** to separate different ideas or pieces of information that have become confused together 理順; 分清〔混雜的不同觀念或信息〕: *It's very difficult to disentangle fact from fiction in what she's saying.* 很難分清她説的話哪些是真的, 哪些是虛構的。—**disentanglement** *n* [U]

dis·e·qui·lib·ri·um /dɪsˌikwəˋlɪbrɪəm; ˌdɪsekwɪ̵ˈlɪbriəm/ *n* [U] *formal* a lack of balance in something【正式】失衡, 不平衡; 失調

dis·es·tab·lish /ˌdɪsəˋstæblɪʃ; ˌdɪsɪ̵ˈstæblɪʃ/ *v* [T] *formal* to officially decide that a particular church is no longer the official church of your country【正式】廢除〔教會〕的國教地位

dis·fa·vour *BrE*【英】, **disfavor** *AmE*【美】/dɪsˋfevɚ; dɪsˈfeɪvə/ *n* [U] *formal* a feeling of dislike and disapproval【正式】不喜歡; 不贊成; 冷淡; 疏遠: **look with disfavour on/upon** *The job creation program is looked upon with disfavor by the local community.* 當地社區並不贊同那個創造就業機會的計劃。

dis·fig·ure /dɪsˋfɪgjɚ; dɪsˈfɪgə/ *v* [T] to spoil the beauty that something naturally has 毀壞〔某事物〕天生具有的美麗: *good looks marred by a disfiguring scar* 被一處醜陋的疤痕破壞了的美麗外貌 —**disfigured** *adj* —**disfigurement** *n* [C,U]

dis·fran·chise /dɪsˋfræntʃaɪz; dɪsˈfræntʃaɪz/ *v* [T] *especially AmE* to DISENFRANCHISE someone【尤美】剝奪〔某人〕的選舉權

dis·gorge /dɪsˋgɔrdʒ; dɪsˈgɔːdʒ/ *v* **1** [T] *literary* if a vehicle or building disgorges people, they come out of it in a large group【文】〔車輛〕下(客);〔建築物〕使〔人流〕湧出 **2** [T] if something disgorges what was inside it, it lets it pour out 使〔某物〕大量流出, 冒出, 吐出: *Chimneys in the valley were disgorging smoke into the air.* 山谷裡的煙囱正在往空中噴吐煙霧。**3** [I,T] if a river disgorges, it flows into the sea〔指河流〕流入(大海等): *The Mississippi disgorges its waters into the Gulf of Mexico.* 密西西比河水匯入墨西哥灣。**4** [T] to give back something that you have taken illegally 交還, 交出, 吐出〔非法所得〕**5** [T] to bring food back up from your stomach through your mouth 嘔吐出〔食物等〕

dis·grace[1] /dɪsˋgres; dɪsˈgreɪs/ *n* **1** [U] the complete loss of other people's respect because you have done something they strongly disapprove of 丟臉; 恥辱; 出醜: *Smith faced total public disgrace after the incident.* 該事件發生之後, 史密斯面對着在公眾中名譽掃地的局面。| **in disgrace** *Toranaga's father sent my mother away in disgrace.* 寅壽的父親把我的母親不體面地打發走了。**2** **sth is a disgrace** used to say that something should not be allowed to happen because it is very wrong or unfair 某事是一種恥辱: **it's an absolute/utter disgrace** *It's an absolute disgrace, the way he treats his wife.* 他那樣對待他的妻子, 簡直太可恥了。**3** **be a disgrace to** to have a very bad effect on people's opinion of the family or other group that you belong to 給〔某人的家庭或所屬的團體〕帶來恥辱: *Your conduct is a disgrace to the medical profession, and I'll see your licence is revoked.* 你的行為給醫學界帶來了恥辱, 我一定要讓人吊銷你的行醫執照。

disgrace[2] *v* [T] to do something so bad that people lose respect for your family or for the group you belong to

給…丟臉; 給…帶來恥辱: *How could you disgrace us all like that?* 你怎麼能這樣地讓我們都丟臉呢? | **disgrace yourself** *Well, I'm not the one who disgraced herself at a friend's wedding!* 噢, 我可不是那個在朋友的婚禮上出洋相的女人! | **be (publicly) disgraced** (=be made to feel ashamed, especially in public) 被(公開)羞辱

dis·grace·ful /dɪsˋgresfəl; dɪsˈgreɪsfəl/ *adj* extremely bad or unacceptable 可恥的; 丟臉的; 很差勁的: *It's a disgraceful state of affairs when decent folk are afraid to leave their homes.* 正經人都害怕出門, 這種情形真是丟人啊。—**disgracefully** *adv*

dis·grun·tled /dɪsˋgrʌntḷd; dɪsˈgrʌntld/ *adj* annoyed, unhappy, and disappointed, especially because things have not happened in the way that you wanted〔尤因事情未像自己所想要的那樣發生而〕惱火的; 不高興的; 失望的; 不滿的: *a disgruntled client* 不滿的客戶

dis·guise[1] /dɪsˋgaɪz; dɪsˈgaɪz/ *v* [T] **1** to change someone's appearance so that they look like someone else and people cannot recognize them 裝扮; 假扮: **disguise yourself as** *Maybe you could disguise yourself as a waiter and sneak in there.* 或許你可以假扮成一個侍應, 混進去。| **be disguised as** *He escaped across the border disguised as a priest.* 他裝扮成神父越境逃走了。**2** to change the appearance, sound, taste etc of something so that people do not recognize it〔為不讓別人認出來而〕改變〔某物的外表、聲音、口味等〕: *There's no way you can disguise that southern accent.* 你是無法掩蓋南方口音的。**3** to hide something so that people will not notice it〔為不讓別人發現而〕隱瞞, 掩蓋, 偽裝〔某事物〕: *Try as he might, Dan couldn't disguise his feelings for Katie.* 不管丹恩多麼努力, 他都無法掩蓋自己對凱蒂的感情。| **disguise the fact (that)** *There's no disguising the fact that business is bad.* 生意不好, 這是無法掩蓋的事實。| **thinly disguised** (=only slightly disguised) 略加掩飾的 *The speech was seen by many as a thinly disguised attack on the president.* 許多人認為這場演說是對總統稍加掩飾的攻擊。

disguise[2] *n* **1** [C,U] something that you wear to change your appearance and hide who you are, or the act of wearing this 偽裝物; 假扮; 偽裝: *The beard, the glasses, and the German accent were all part of his disguise.* 鬍子、眼鏡和德國口音都是他偽裝的一部分。**2 in disguise a)** wearing a disguise 穿戴偽裝的物品; 化了裝的; 假扮過的: *I kept forgetting I was in disguise, and got a lot of funny looks.* 我總是忘記我是化了裝的, 所以多次有人異樣地看我。**b)** made to seem like something else that is better 經過偽裝的〔使看起來似乎更好〕: *'Tax reform' is just a tax increase in disguise.* "稅務改革"只不過是喬裝改扮後的增稅。—see also 另見 **blessing in disguise** (BLESSING (3))

dis·gust[1] /dɪsˋgʌst; dɪsˈgʌst/ *n* [U] **1** a very strong feeling of dislike that almost makes you sick, caused by something unpleasant 嫌惡, 厭惡; 反感; 作嘔; 噁心: **with disgust** *Everybody except Joe looked at me with disgust.* 除了喬以外, 大家都反感地看着我。**2** a feeling of annoyance and disappointment because of someone's unacceptable behaviour, the bad quality of something etc 氣憤; 失望: **in disgust** *Sam threw his books down in disgust and stormed out of the room.* 山姆憤憤地把書扔下, 氣沖沖地衝出房間。| **much to sb's disgust** *Much to my disgust I found that there were no toilets for the disabled.* 令我非常氣憤的是, 我發現沒有供傷殘人士使用的廁所。

disgust[2] *v* [T] **1** to make someone feel very annoyed and disappointed about something unacceptable 使〔某人〕反感, 厭惡, 氣憤, 失望: *Enid said she was disgusted by the sex in the film.* 伊妮德說她對該影片中的性行為鏡頭感到噁心。| **be disgusted to find/hear/see etc** *Dear Sir: I was disgusted to see the picture on page one of Sunday's feature section.* 親愛的先生: 看到週日的特寫專欄第一頁上的照片, 我感到很氣憤。**2** to make someone feel almost sick because of something unpleasant 使〔人〕感到噁心, 作嘔: *The thought of dissecting a frog disgusts me.* 一想起解剖青蛙就讓我感到噁心。

dis·gust·ing /dɪsˋgʌstɪŋ; dɪsˈgʌstɪŋ/ *adj* **1** extremely unpleasant and making you feel sick 令人噁心的; 使人極其反感的; 令人厭惡的: *"Here, hold this a minute." "Yuck! It's disgusting!"* "來, 把這個東西給我拿一會兒。" "呸! 真噁心!" **2** shocking and unacceptable 令人吃驚的; 無法接受的: *Sixty pounds for a thirty-minute consultation. I think that's disgusting!* 諮詢三十分鐘就要六十英鎊, 我看這也太離譜了! | *Man, do you have a disgusting imagination.* 老兄, 你的想像力是不是豐富得令人作嘔。—compare 比較 NAUSEATING —**disgustingly** *adv*: *They're disgustingly rich.* 他們富得令人反感。 S2

dish[1] /dɪʃ; dɪʃ/ *n* [C] **1** a flat round container with not very high sides, from which food is served on the table 盤子, 碟子: *a serving dish* 上菜用的盤子 | *a vegetable dish* 盛蔬菜用的盤子 —compare 比較 BOWL[1] (1) **2 the dishes** all the plates, cups, bowls etc that have been used to eat a meal and need to be washed〔用餐時用過的、需要清洗的〕所有餐具〔包括盤子、杯子、碗等〕: **do/wash the dishes** *I'll just do the dishes before we go.* 我們走之前我會把碗洗好的。—see picture at 參見 CLEAN[2] 圖 **3** food cooked or prepared in a particular way as a meal 烹製好的菜餚, 食品, 一道菜: *a wonderful pasta dish* 很棒的意大利麵食 **4 be a dish** *informal* to be sexually attractive【非正式】有吸引力的, 性感的, 漂亮的 —see also 另見 SIDE DISH, SATELLITE DISH S3

dish[2] *v* [T] *old-fashioned*【過時】**1 dish the dirt** *informal* to spend time talking about other people's private lives and saying unkind or shocking things about them【非正式】談論別人的私生活並說他們的壞話; 揭短 **2 dish sb's hopes/chances** *especially BrE* to prevent someone from doing something that they hoped to do【尤英】使某人的希望/機會破滅; 使某人不能做想做的事

dish sth ↔ **out** *phr v* [T] *informal*【非正式】**1** to give something to various people in a careless way〔隨意地〕分發; 提供: *We'll probably dish out some leaflets there too.* 我們很可能也上那兒分發些傳單。| *Portnoy still tends to dish out unwanted advice.* 波特諾伊仍然喜歡隨意地拋出人家根本不愛聽的建議。**2** to serve food to people 給〔人們〕上菜, 分菜: *Sam's dishing out sandwiches if you want one.* 如果你想要三明治, 山姆正在分呢。**3 sb can dish it out but they can't take it** used to say that someone is quick to criticize others but does not accept criticism well 某人很會批評別人, 但自己卻不能接受批評

dish up *phr v* [I,T] to put food for a meal into dishes, ready to be eaten 把(食物)盛到盤裡〔準備讓人食用〕: **dish sth ↔ up** *Could you dish up the vegetables? They're there, on the sideboard.* 請你把蔬菜盛到盤子裡, 好嗎? 蔬菜在那兒, 餐具櫃上。

dis·ha·bille /ˏdɪsəˋbil; ˏdɪsəˈbiːl/ *n* [U] *AmE*【美】the usual American form of DÉSHABILLÉ déshabillé的一般美式形式

dis·har·mo·ny /dɪsˋharmənɪ; dɪsˈhɑːməni/ *n* [U] *formal* disagreement about important things that makes people be unfriendly to each other【正式】〔在重要事情上的〕分歧, 不一致; 不和諧的事 —**disharmonious** /ˏdɪsharˋmonɪəs; ˏdɪshɑːˈməʊniəs/ *adj*

dish·cloth /ˋdɪʃˏklɑθ; ˈdɪʃklɒθ/ *n* [C] a cloth used for washing dishes 洗碗布 —see picture on page A10 參見A10頁圖

dis·heart·ened /dɪsˋhartṇd; dɪsˈhɑːtnd/ *adj* disappointed so that you lose hope and the determination to continue doing something 沮喪的; 氣餒的; 灰心的: *If young children don't see quick results they grow disheartened.* 如果小孩子不能很快地看到結果, 他們會變得灰心的。—**dishearten** *v* [T]

dis·heart·en·ing /dɪsˋhartṇɪŋ; dɪsˈhɑːtn-ɪŋ/ *adj* making you lose hope and determination 令人灰心的, 令人氣餒的: **be disheartening to hear/see etc sth** *It's dis-*

heartening to see what little progress has been made. 看到只有少得可憐的一點進展, 令人感到灰心喪氣。—**dishearteningly** *adv*

di·shev·elled *BrE*【英】, **disheveled** *AmE*【美】/dɪˋʃɛvl̩d; dɪˈʃevəld/ *adj* dishevelled clothes, hair etc are very untidy〔衣服、頭髮等〕不整齊的, 凌亂的: *Pam arrived late, dishevelled and out of breath.* 帕姆衣冠不整, 上氣不接下氣地遲到了。

dis·hon·est /dɪsˋɑnɪst; dɪsˈɒnɪ̣st/ *adj* not honest 不老實的; 不誠實的: *Unfortunately there are dishonest traders about.* 不幸的是, 到處都有奸商。—**dishonestly** *adv*

dis·hon·est·y /dɪsˋɑnɪstɪ; dɪsˈɒnɪ̣sti/ *n* [U] dishonest behaviour 不誠實的行為

dis·hon·our¹ *BrE*【英】, **dishonor** *AmE*【美】/dɪsˋɑnɚ; dɪsˈɒnə/ *n* [U] *formal* loss of respect from other people because you have behaved in a morally unacceptable way【正式】不名譽; 恥辱; 丟臉: **bring dishonour on** *You've brought enough dishonour on your family already without causing any more trouble.* 你已經給你的家庭帶來了很多恥辱, 不再惹麻煩也夠瞧的了。

dishonour² *BrE*【英】, **dishonor** *AmE*【美】*v* [T] **1** *formal* to make your family, country, profession etc lose the respect of other people【正式】敗壞〔家庭、國家、行業等〕的名譽 **2** if a bank dishonours a cheque, it refuses to pay out money for it〔指銀行等〕拒付, 拒絕承兑〔支票等〕, 使〔票據〕退票

dis·hon·ou·ra·ble *BrE*【英】, **dishonorable** *AmE*【美】/dɪsˋɑnɚəbl̩; dɪsˈɒnərəbəl/ *adj* not morally correct or acceptable 不名譽的; 不光彩的; 可恥的: *There's nothing dishonourable in charging for advice.* 收取諮詢費並沒有甚麼不光彩的。

dishonourable dis·charge /ˌ·.··· ˈ··/ *n* [C,U] an order to someone to leave the army because they have behaved in a morally unacceptable way〔因做了不光彩的事〕被開除軍籍

dish·pan /ˋdɪʃˌpæn; ˈdɪʃpæn/ *n* [C] *AmE* a large bowl which you use for washing dishes in【美】洗碗碟用的大盆

dish tow·el /ˈ· ˌ··/ *n* [C] *AmE* a cloth used for drying dishes【美】〔把碗碟等擦乾用的〕擦碗布; TEA TOWEL *BrE*【英】

dish·wash·er /ˋdɪʃˌwɔʃɚ; ˈdɪʃˌwɒʃə/ *n* [C] a machine that washes dishes 洗碗機 —see picture on page A10 參見A10頁圖

dish·wash·ing liq·uid /ˋdɪʃwɔʃɪŋ ˌlɪkwɪd; ˈdɪʃwɒʃɪŋ ˌlɪkwɪ̣d/ *n* [U] *AmE* liquid soap used to wash dishes【美】洗滌液; 洗潔精; WASHING-UP LIQUID *BrE*【英】—see picture on page A10 參見A10頁圖

dish·wa·ter /ˋdɪʃˌwɔtɚ; ˈdɪʃˌwɔːtə/ *n* [U] **1** dirty water that dishes have been washed in 洗過碗碟的水 **2 like dishwater** *informal* tea or coffee that tastes like dishwater tastes unpleasantly weak【非正式】〔茶或咖啡等〕淡而無味

dishwater blond /ˌ··· ˈ·/ *adj AmE old-fashioned* dishwater blond hair is a dull brown colour【美, 過時】〔指頭髮〕暗無光彩的褐色的

dish·y /ˋdɪʃɪ; ˈdɪʃi/ *adj old-fashioned* sexually attractive【過時】性感的, 迷人的

dis·il·lu·sion /ˌdɪsɪˋluʒən; ˌdɪsɪ̣ˈluːʒən/ *v* [T] to make someone realize that something which they thought was true or good is not really true or good 使醒悟; 使不再抱幻想: *I hate to disillusion you, but you're unlikely to learn any more than I've told you already.* 我真不願意讓你失望, 但你不可能了解到比我已經告訴你的更多的信息。—**disillusionment** *n* [U]

dis·il·lu·sioned /ˌdɪsɪˋluʒənd; ˌdɪsɪ̣ˈluːʒənd◂/ *adj* disappointed because you have lost your belief that someone is good, or that an idea is right 不抱幻想的; 失望的; 幻滅的; 理想破滅的: **[+by/with]** *As she grew older, Laura grew increasingly disillusioned with politics.* 隨着年齡的增長, 勞拉對政治越來越不抱幻想了。

dis·in·cen·tive /ˌdɪsɪnˋsɛntɪv; ˌdɪsɪ̣nˈsentɪv/ *n* [C] something that tries to stop people from doing something 抑制因素; 限制因素: **[+to]** *The biggest disincentive to spend is the fear of debt.* 遏制消費的最大因素是害怕負債。

dis·in·cli·na·tion /ˌdɪsɪnkləˋneʃən; ˌdɪsɪŋklɪ̣ˈneɪʃən/ *n* [U] *formal* a lack of willingness to do something【正式】不情願; 厭惡: *Very naturally there has been a disinclination to face up to these issues.* 很自然, 人們不願意正視這些問題。

dis·in·clined /ˌdɪsɪnˋklaɪnd; ˌdɪsɪnˈklaɪnd/ *adj* **be/feel disinclined to do sth** *formal* to be unwilling to do something【正式】不願意做某事: *In the present case I feel disinclined to interfere in the matter.* 在目前情況下我不願意介入此事。

dis·in·fect /ˌdɪsɪnˋfɛkt; ˌdɪsɪ̣nˈfekt/ *v* [T] to clean something with a chemical that destroys BACTERIA 為〔某物〕消毒, 給…殺菌: *First use some iodine to disinfect the wound.* 首先, 用碘酒把傷口消消毒。| *Disinfect the area thoroughly.* 把這個區域徹底消毒。

dis·in·fec·tant /ˌdɪsɪnˋfɛktənt; ˌdɪsɪ̣nˈfektənt/ *n* [C,U] a chemical that destroys BACTERIA, or a cleaning product that does this 殺菌劑; 消毒劑

dis·in·for·ma·tion /ˌdɪsɪnfɚˋmeʃən; ˌdɪsɪnfəˈmeɪʃən/ *n* [U] false information which is given intentionally in order to hide the truth or confuse people, especially in political situations〔尤指在政治形勢下故意透露的〕假消息, 假情報: *government disinformation about the effects of nuclear testing* 政府透露的關於核試驗結果的假消息 —compare 比較 MISINFORMATION

dis·in·gen·u·ous /ˌdɪsɪnˋdʒɛnjuəs; ˌdɪsɪ̣nˈdʒenjuəs◂/ *adj* not sincere and slightly dishonest 不真誠的; 略有些不誠實的; 不坦率的: *McEwan's claims about the incident strike me as disingenuous.* 麥克尤恩關於那個事件的聲明給我的印象是不夠坦誠。—**disingenuously** *adv*

dis·in·her·it /ˌdɪsɪnˋhɛrɪt; ˌdɪsɪ̣nˈherɪ̣t/ *v* [T] to take away from someone, especially your son or daughter, their legal right to receive your money or property after your death 剝奪〔尤指子女〕的繼承權 —**disinheritance** *n* [U]

dis·in·te·grate /dɪsˋɪntəˌgret; dɪsˈɪntɪ̣greɪt/ *v* [I,T] **1** to break up or make something break up into very small pieces (使) 粉碎; 崩裂; 分崩離析: *The whole plane just disintegrated in mid-air.* 整架飛機在半空中就解體了。**2** to become weaker or less united and be gradually destroyed 衰弱; 瓦解; 解體: *a society disintegrating under economic pressures* 在經濟壓力下正在瓦解中的社會 —**disintegration** /dɪsˌɪntəˋgreʃən; dɪsˌɪntɪ̣ˈgreɪʃən/ *n* [U]

dis·in·ter /ˌdɪsɪnˋtɝ; ˌdɪsɪnˈtɜː/ *v* **disinterred, disinterring** [T] *formal* to dig a dead body from a grave【正式】把〔屍體〕從墳墓中掘出 —opposite 反義詞 INTER —**disinterment** *n* [U]

dis·in·terest /dɪsˋɪntrɪst; dɪsˈɪntrɪ̣st/ *n* [U] a lack of interest 無興趣: **[+in]** *The exception to Balfour's disinterest in social issues was education.* 貝爾弗對除教育以外的社會問題都不感興趣。

dis·in·terest·ed /dɪsˋɪntrɪstɪd; dɪsˈɪntrɪ̣stɪ̣d/ *adj* **1** able to judge a situation fairly because you are not concerned with gaining any personal advantage from it; OBJECTIVE² (1) 公正無私的; 無利害關係影響的; 客觀的: *disinterested advice* 客觀的忠告 **2** sometimes used to mean 'uninterested', although many people think this is wrong〔有時用於表示〕無興趣的; 不關心的 —**disinterestedly** *adv* —**disinterestedness** *n* [U]

USAGE NOTE 用法說明: DISINTERESTED

WORD CHOICE 詞語辨析: **uninterested (in), disinterested (in)**

Uninterested (**in** something) means not interested in it. uninterested 表示對某事物不感興趣: *I'm completely uninterested in football.* 我對足球完全不感興趣。| *an uninterested student* (=bored) 一個提

不起興趣的學生

If someone is **disinterested** they are able to be fair because they are not involved in a situation where other people are fighting, disagreeing etc, and not expecting to gain anything themselves from it. disinterested用於表示某人公正無私, 因為此人並沒有捲入到他人的爭鬥或分歧中去, 而且此人並沒有期望從中賺取個人利益: *We need the advice of a disinterested party* (=someone who is not directly involved). 我們需要一個(與此事)沒有利害關係的人給我們一些建議。

Native speakers of English also sometimes say that people are **disinterested in** things, meaning the same as **uninterested in**, though is usually considered to be incorrect. 以英語為母語的人有時也用disinterested來表示uninterested (不感興趣), 儘管這種用法通常被認為是錯誤的: *I'm completely disinterested in football.* 我對足球毫無興趣。

dis·in·vest·ment /ˌdɪsɪnˋvɛstmənt; ˌdɪsɨnˈvestmənt/ *n* [U] *BrE technical* the act of taking your money out of a company, by selling your shares (SHARE[2] (5)) in it【英, 術語】投資收回〔通過賣掉股份〕; 減資; 投資停止; DIVESTMENT *AmE*【美】

dis·joint·ed /dɪsˋdʒɔɪntɪd; dɪsˈdʒɔɪntɨd/ *adj* a disjointed speech or piece of writing is one in which the words or ideas are not well connected together or arranged in a resonable order〔講話、文章等〕不連貫的; 表達混亂的; 支離破碎的 —**disjointedly** *adv* —**disjointedness** *n* [U]

dis·junc·tive /dɪsˋdʒʌŋktɪv; dɪsˈdʒʌŋktɪv/ *adj technical* a disjunctive CONJUNCTION (3) expresses a choice or opposition between two ideas. For example, 'or' is a disjunctive conjunction【術語】轉折的, 反意的

dis·junc·ture /dɪsˋdʒʌŋktʃɚ; dɪsˈdʒʌŋktʃə/ *n* [C,U] a difference between two things that you would expect to be in agreement〔兩個事物之間的〕不同; 不一致; 相悖: *a disjuncture between his private and public life* 他的私生活和公眾生活的不一致

2 3 **disk** /dɪsk; dɪsk/ *n* [C] **1** a flat circular piece of plastic or metal used for storing computer information〔電腦的〕磁盤, 磁碟 —see picture on page A14 參見A14頁圖 **2** the usual American spelling of DISC disc的一般美式拼法 —see also 另見 COMPACT DISC, FLOPPY DISK, HARD DISK, LASER DISK

disk drive /ˈ· ·/ *n* [C] a piece of equipment in a computer system that is used to pass information to or from a disk 磁盤[碟]驅動器, 磁碟機

dis·kette /dɪsˋkɛt; dɪsˈket/ *n* [C] *AmE* a FLOPPY DISK【美】軟磁盤[碟]

dis·like[1] /dɪsˈlaɪk; dɪsˈlaɪk/ *v* [T, not in progressive 不用進行式] to think someone or something is unpleasant and not like them 不喜歡; 討厭: *Why do you dislike her so much?* 你為甚麼那麼討厭她? | **dislike doing sth** *Tom dislikes going to the dentist, that's why he's crabby.* 湯姆不喜歡去看牙醫, 所以他脾氣那麼壞。

dislike[2] *n* **1** [C,U] a feeling of not liking someone or something 不喜歡; 討厭: **[+of/for]** *She shared her mother's dislike of housework.* 她和她媽媽一樣, 不愛做家務。| **intense dislike** (=very strong dislike) 極不喜歡, 強烈的反感 *His colleagues regarded him with intense dislike.* 他的同事們特別討厭他。| **take a dislike to** (=decide that you dislike someone) 開始不喜歡〔某人〕*When the two men met, they took an instant dislike to each other.* 這兩個人見面伊始就彼此討厭對方。**2 dislikes** [plural] the things that you do not like 不喜歡的東西: **likes and dislikes** *A good hotel manager should know his regular guests' likes and dislikes.* 一個稱職的酒店經理應該知道老主顧的好惡。

dis·lo·cate /ˋdɪsloˌket; ˈdɪsləkeɪt/ *v* [T] **1** to injure a joint so that the two bones at the joint are moved out of their normal position 使〔關節〕脫位, 使脫臼: *I dislocated my shoulder playing football.* 踢足球時我的肩膀脫了臼。**2** to spoil the way in which a plan, system, or service is arranged, so that it cannot work normally; DISRUPT 擾亂, 破壞〔計劃、制度、服務等的正常安排〕—**dislocated** *adj*: *a dislocated shoulder* 脫了臼的肩膀 —**dislocation** /ˌdɪsloˋkeʃən; ˌdɪsləˈkeɪʃən/ *n* [C,U]: *The storm caused considerable dislocation of air traffic.* 這場暴風雨極大地擾亂了空中交通。

dis·lodge /dɪsˋlɑdʒ; dɪsˈlɒdʒ/ *v* [T] **1** to force or knock something out of its position 將〔某物〕逐出或移開: *Ian dislodged a few stones as he climbed up the rock.* 伊恩攀岩的時候碰掉了幾塊石頭。**2** to make someone leave a place or lose a position of power 使〔某人〕離開某地; 使〔某人〕失去權勢: *the revolution that failed to dislodge the British in 1919* 未能推翻英國統治的1919年革命 —compare 比較 LODGE[1] (3) —**dislodgement** *n* [U]

dis·loy·al /dɪsˋlɔɪəl; dɪsˈlɔɪəl/ *adj* unfaithful to your friends, your country, or the group you belong to 不忠實的; 不忠誠的: **[+to]** *He felt he had been disloyal to his friends.* 他覺得自己對朋友們不忠誠。—**disloyally** *adv* —**disloyalty** *n* [C,U]

dis·mal /ˋdɪzml; ˈdɪzməl/ *adj* **1** a dismal place, situation, thought etc has nothing pleasant in it and makes it difficult for you to feel happy and hopeful〔指某個地方、某種形勢、想法等〕沉悶的; 陰鬱的; 令人憂鬱的; 沮喪的: *The future looks pretty dismal right now.* 現在看來, 前景相當暗淡。| *a dismal, grey November afternoon* 十一月份一個陰沉、灰暗的下午 **2** bad and unsuccessful 差勁的, 不成功的, 糟糕的: *Your record so far is pretty dismal.* 你迄今為止的記錄相當差。| **be a dismal failure** *His scheme was a dismal failure.* 他的計劃失敗得很慘。—**dismally** *adv*

dis·man·tle /dɪsˋmæntl; dɪsˈmæntl/ *v* **1** [T] to take a machine or piece of equipment apart so that it is in separate pieces 拆開; 拆卸〔機器、設備等〕: *Chris dismantled the bike in five minutes.* 克里斯五分鐘內就把腳踏車給拆了。**2** [T] to gradually get rid of a system or organization〔逐漸地〕廢除〔某種制度或組織等〕: *an election promise to dismantle the existing tax legislation* 將廢除現有稅收法規的競選許諾

dis·may[1] /dɪsˋme; dɪsˈmeɪ/ *n* [U] the worry, disappointment, and unhappiness you feel when something unpleasant happens 憂慮; 失望; 沮喪; 恐慌: **with/in dismay** *Amanda read her exam results with dismay.* 阿曼達看到自己的考試成績, 感到十分傷心。| *They stared at each other in dismay.* 他們沮喪地互相凝視着對方。| **to sb's dismay** *I found to my dismay that I had left my notes behind.* 令我沮喪的是, 我發現我忘了拿筆記了。| **fill sb with dismay** *The thought of making the journey filled him with dismay.* 一想到要出門旅行, 他就感到十分擔憂。

dismay[2] *v* [T] to make someone feel worried, disappointed, and upset 使〔某人〕擔憂[失望、傷心]: **be dismayed to see/hear etc** *Brenda was dismayed to find that work on the roof had not even begun.* 布倫達失望地發現屋頂的工作竟然還沒開始。| **be dismayed at** *We were dismayed at the cost of the repairs.* 修理費這麼貴, 令我們十分沮喪。

dis·mem·ber /dɪsˋmɛmbɚ; dɪsˈmembə/ *v* [T] **1** to cut a body into pieces or tear it apart 肢解 **2** to divide a country, area, or organization into smaller parts 瓜分, 分割〔某個國家、地區或組織〕—**dismemberment** *n* [U]

dis·miss /dɪsˋmɪs; dɪsˈmɪs/ *v* [T] 3

1 ▶IDEA 觀點◀ to refuse to consider someone's idea, opinion etc, without thinking carefully about it 拒絕考慮〔某人的觀點、意見等〕: **dismiss sth as** *He just laughed and dismissed my suggestion as unrealistic.* 他只是笑笑, 就以不實際為由拒絕了我的建議。| **dismiss sth out of hand** (=dismiss something completely) 全然拒絕某事物

2 ▶JOB 工作◀ to remove someone from their job 解

雇, 開除: **dismiss sb for** *Will they dismiss Woods for stealing the money?* 他們會因伍兹偷了錢而解雇他嗎? | **dismiss sb from** *Bryant was dismissed from his post.* 布賴恩特被免職了。
3 ►SEND AWAY 打發走◄ to send someone away or allow them to go 把〔某人〕打發走; 讓〔某人〕離開; 解散: *The teacher might dismiss the class early today because of the snow.* 由於下雪, 今天老師或許會提早下課。
4 ►IN A COURT 在法庭上◄ if a judge dismisses a court CASE[1] (9a), they stop it before a result is reached 駁回, 不受理〔案子〕: *The case was dismissed owing to lack of evidence.* 由於證據不足, 案子被駁回了。
5 ►SPORT 體育運動◄ to end the INNINGS of a player or a team in the game of CRICKET (2)〔板球比賽中〕迫使〔對方擊球員或球隊〕退場

dis·miss·al /dɪsˋmɪsl; dɪsˈmɪsəl/ *n* **1** [C,U] an act of removing someone from their job 解雇; 開除: **unfair dismissal** *Wilson was claiming compensation for unfair dismissal.* 威爾遜要求得到被無理解雇的賠償金。**2** [U] a refusal to consider something seriously 不予理會; 拒絕考慮

dis·miss·ive /dɪsˋmɪsɪv; dɪsˈmɪsɪv/ *adj* refusing to consider someone or something seriously 不予理會的; 拒絕考慮的: [+of] *Why, I wonder, is Mr Sykes so dismissive of the protesters?* 我想知道, 為甚麼賽克斯先生對抗議者如此地不予理會? —**dismissively** *adv*

dis·mount /dɪsˋmaunt; dɪsˈmaʊnt/ *v* **1** [I +from] to get off a horse, bicycle, or MOTORCYCLE〔從馬背、腳踏車、摩托車上〕下來 **2** [T] to take something, especially a gun, down from its base or support〔把某物, 尤指槍砲, 從底座或支架上〕取下, 卸下

dis·o·be·di·ent /ˌdɪsəˋbidɪənt; ˌdɪsəˈbiːdiənt/ *adj* deliberately not doing what you are told to do by your parents, teacher, employer etc 不順從的; 不服從的; 違抗的 —**disobediently** *adv* —**disobedience** *n* [U] —see also 另見 CIVIL DISOBEDIENCE

dis·o·bey /ˌdɪsəˋbe; ˌdɪsəˈbeɪ/ *v* [I,T] to refuse to do what someone with authority tells you to do, or refuse to obey a rule or law 不服從〔上級的命令〕; 不遵守〔規定或法律等〕: *Remember you're in the army; if you disobey orders you'll get a court martial.* 記住, 你是在軍隊裡; 如果你不服從命令, 就會被送上軍事法庭。

dis·o·bli·ging /ˌdɪsəˋblaɪdʒɪŋ; ˌdɪsəˈblaɪdʒɪŋ/ *adj formal* unwilling to help someone or do what they want【正式】不願幫忙的; 不肯通融的 —**disoblige** *v* [T]

3 **dis·or·der** /dɪsˋɔrdɚ; dɪsˈɔːdə/ *n* **1** [U] a situation in which things or people are very untidy or disorganized 混亂; 凌亂; 雜亂; 無秩序: **in disorder** *Everything was in disorder, but nothing seemed to be stolen.* 一切都凌亂不堪, 但好像沒有甚麼東西被偷。**2** [C,U] a situation in which many people disobey the law, especially in a violent way, and are impossible to control 動亂; 暴亂; 騷亂: **civil/public disorder** *a campaign of civil disorder* 一系列的社會騷亂 **3** [C] an illness which prevents part of your body from working properly〔身體機能的〕失調; 功能紊亂: **skin/stomach/liver etc disorder** *a rare genetic disorder* 一種罕見的基因疾病

dis·or·dered /dɪsˋɔrdɚd; dɪsˈɔːdəd/ *adj* **1** untidy or not arranged, planned, or done in a clear order 不整潔的; 雜亂的; 沒有秩序的 **2** if someone is mentally disordered, their mind is not working in a normal and healthy way 精神失常的, 精神錯亂的

dis·or·der·ly /dɪsˋɔrdɚlɪ; dɪsˈɔːdəli/ *adj* **1** untidy or lacking order 凌亂的; 無秩序的: *Joe left his clothes in a disorderly heap.* 喬把他的衣服亂七八糟地放成一堆。**2** behaving in a noisy violent way and causing trouble in a public place 喧鬧的; 擾亂治安的; 破壞公共秩序的: **drunk and disorderly** (=behaving very badly in a public place because you have drunk too much alcohol) 酗酒後擾亂治安; 酒後失態; 發酒瘋 —**disorderliness** *n* [U]

disorderly house /ˌ·ˈ··· ˈ·/ *n* [C] *BrE law* a place where men pay to have sex; BROTHEL【英, 法律】妓院

dis·or·gan·ized also 又作 **-ised** *BrE*【英】/dɪsˋɔrgəˌnaɪzd; dɪsˈɔːgənaɪzd/ *adj* not arranged or planned in a clear order, or lacking any kind of plan or system 雜亂無章的; 組織不善的; 計劃不周的: *The conference arrangements were completely disorganized.* 會議的安排毫無條理, 一片混亂。| *The whole thing's being run by a bunch of disorganized amateurs.* 整個事情正由一羣組織不善的外行人在打理。—compare 比較 UNORGANIZED

dis·or·i·en·tate /dɪsˋɔrɪɛnˌtet; dɪsˈɔːrienteɪt/ also 又作 **dis·or·i·ent** /dɪsˋɔrɪˌɛnt; dɪsˈɔːriənt/ *AmE*【美】*v* [T] **1** to make someone not know which direction they have come from or are going in 使〔某人〕迷失方向 **2** to make someone uncertain about what is happening around them and unable to think clearly 使迷惑, 使暈頭轉向 —**disorientating, disorienting** *adj* —**disorientation** /dɪsˌɔrɪɛnˋteʃən; dɪsˌɔːrienˈteɪʃən/ *n* [U]

dis·or·i·en·tat·ed /dɪsˋɔrɪɛnˌtetɪd; dɪsˈɔːrienteɪtɪ̮d/ also 又作 **dis·or·i·ent·ed** /dɪsˋɔrɪˌɛntɪd; dɪsˈɔːriəntɪ̮d/ *adj, adv* **1** confused and not understanding what is happening around you 迷惑的; 頭腦混亂的: *His wife said he was disoriented and begged to be allowed to sleep.* 他妻子說, 他昏沉沉的, 懇求獲准睡覺。**2** confused about which direction you are facing or which direction you should go 迷失方向的

dis·own /dɪsˋon; dɪsˈəʊn/ *v* [T not in progressive 不用進行式] to say that you no longer have any connection with someone or something; REPUDIATE (3) 聲明與…斷絕關係 *Frankly, I'm not surprised her family disowned her.* 老實說, 她的家人和她斷絕關係, 我並不感到意外。

di·spar·age /dɪˋspærɪdʒ; dɪˈspærɪdʒ/ *v* [T] *formal* to criticize someone or something in a way that shows you do not think they are very good or important【正式】貶低, 詆毀: *Matcham's theatres were widely disparaged by architects.* 馬切姆設計的劇院廣遭建築師的詆毀。—**disparagement** *n* [C,U]

di·spar·a·ging /dɪˋspærədʒɪŋ; dɪˈspærədʒɪŋ/ *adj* disparaging remarks criticize someone or something and show that you do not think they are very good〔言語等〕貶低的; 輕視的; 詆毀的; 損害名聲的 —**disparagingly** *adv*

dis·pa·rate /ˋdɪspərɪt; ˈdɪspərɪ̮t/ *adj formal* very different and not connected with each other【正式】迥然不同的; 不相干的; 全異的; 無法相比較的: *The challenge is to make disparate computer systems work together.* 難題是讓迥然相異的電腦系統一起工作。—**disparately** *adv*

di·spar·i·ty /dɪsˋpærətɪ; dɪˈspærɪ̮ti/ *n* [C,U] *formal* a difference between two or more things, especially an unfair one【正式】〔兩個或兩個以上事物之間的〕不同; 不平等; 差異; 懸殊: [+in/between] *We are still seeing a disparity between the rates of pay for men and women.* 我們仍然可以看到男女的工資之間有着差異。—see also 另見 PARITY

dis·pas·sion·ate /dɪsˋpæʃənɪt; dɪsˈpæʃənɪ̮t/ *adj* not influenced by emotion and therefore able to make fair decisions 不為感情所左右的; 不動感情的; 公正的: *a dispassionate view* 客觀公正的見解 —**dispassionately** *adv*

di·spatch[1] also 又作 **despatch** *BrE*【英】/dɪsˋpætʃ; dɪˈspætʃ/ *v* [T] **1** *formal* to send someone or something somewhere for a particular purpose【正式】派遣; 發送: **dispatch sb/sth to** *A reporter was dispatched to Naples to cover the riot.* 一名記者被派往那不勒斯去報道暴亂之事。**2** *old-fashioned* to deliberately kill a person or animal【過時】故意殺死〔人或動物〕**3** *old-fashioned* to finish all of something【過時】辦完〔全部事情〕

dispatch[2] also 又作 **despatch** *BrE*【英】*n* **1** [C] a message sent between military or government officials〔在軍官或政府官員之間傳遞的〕公文, 急件: *a dispatch from headquarters* 從總部發來的電文 **2** [C] a report sent to a newspaper from one of its writers who is in another town or country〔由身在另一城市或國家的記者發給報刊的〕報道, 電訊 **3 with dispatch** *formal* if you do something with dispatch, you do it well and quickly【正式】利落

地，迅速地 **4** [singular] the act of sending people or things to a particular place 派遣，發送 —see also 另見 **mentioned in dispatches** (MENTION[1] (6))

dispatch box /ˈ·· ·/ *n* **1** [C] a box for holding official papers〔裝文件用的〕公文遞送箱 **2 the dispatch box** a box on a central table in the British Parliament next to which important members of parliament stand to make speeches 英國議會中央桌上的箱子〔重要議員在發言時便站在該箱子旁〕

dispatch rid·er /ˈ·· ˌ··/ *n* [C] someone whose job is to take messages or packages by MOTORCYCLE or bicycle 騎摩托車[腳踏車]的通信員

di·spel /dɪˋspɛl; dɪˈspel/ *v* **dispelled, dispelling** [T] to stop someone believing or feeling something, especially because it is wrong or harmful 驅散，消除：*The film aims to dispel the notion that AIDS only affects gay men.* 這部電影意在消除只有同性戀男子才會得愛滋病的錯誤觀念。

di·spen·sa·ble /dɪˋspɛnsəbḷ; dɪˈspensəbəl/ *adj* easy to get rid of because not really needed〔因並不真正需要而〕可省去的；可以丟棄的；可有可無的：*Part-time workers are considered dispensable in times of recession.* 在經濟蕭條時期，兼職工人被認為是可以不要的。—opposite 反義詞 INDISPENSABLE

di·spen·sa·ry /dɪˋspɛnsərɪ; dɪˈspensəri/ *n* [C] a place where medicines are prepared and given out, especially in a hospital〔尤指醫院的〕配藥處，藥房 —compare 比較 PHARMACY

dis·pen·sa·tion /ˌdɪspənˋseʃən; ˌdɪspənˈseɪʃən/ *n* **1** [C, U] special permission from someone in authority or a religious leader to do something that is not usually allowed〔當權者或宗教領袖給予的〕特許：**special dispensation** *Caroline's marriage was annulled by special dispensation from the Church.* 嘉羅琳的婚約是在教會的特許之下解除的。**2** [C] *formal* a religious or political system that has control over people's lives at a particular time【正式】〔某一時期控制人們生活的〕宗教[政治]制度；教規 **3** [U] *formal* the act of providing people with something as part of an official process【正式】正式的施予，提供，分配：*the dispensation of justice* 正義的實施

di·spense /dɪˋspɛns; dɪˈspens/ *v* [T] **1** *formal* to give something to people, especially in fixed amounts【正式】〔尤指以固定數額〕施予；分配〔某物〕：*Villagers dispensed tea to people involved in the accident.* 村民們送茶給遭遇這場意外事故的人們。**2** to prepare and give medicines to people 配藥，發藥〔給人們〕**3** to officially provide something for people in a society〔以官方身分〕正式提供〔某物〕；分配，分發；施予：**dispense justice/punishments** (=decide whether or not someone is guilty of a crime and what punishment they should receive) 主持正義；實施懲罰〔決定某人是否有罪，應該得到怎樣的懲罰〕

dispense with sb/sth *phr v* [T] *formal* to not use or do something that you usually use or do, because it is no longer necessary【正式】〔因已無必要〕不再使用：**can dispense with** *I think we can dispense with a translator.* 我想我們可以不用翻譯人員。| **dispense with the formalities** (=not use very polite behaviour, such as introducing people to each other) 不必拘禮，免去客套

di·spens·er /dɪˋspɛnsə; dɪˈspensə/ *n* [C] a machine in a public place which gives you things such as drinks or money when you press a button 自動售貨機；自動櫃員機 — see also 另見 CASH DISPENSER

dispensing chem·ist /ˈ·· ˌ··/ *n* [C] *BrE* someone who is trained to sell medicines and advise people about them; PHARMACIST【英】配藥者，藥劑師

di·sper·sal /dɪˋspɝsḷ; dɪˈspɜːsəl/ *n* [U] the act of spreading things over a wide area 散發，散布；傳播：*the dispersal of information* 散布消息

di·sperse /dɪˋspɝs; dɪˈspɜːs/ *v* [I,T] **1** if a group of people disperses or is dispersed, they separate and go away in different directions（使）〔人羣〕分散，散開：*The police used tear gas to disperse the crowd.* 警察用催淚彈驅散人羣。**2** if something disperses or is dispersed, it spreads over a wide area（使）〔某物〕消散：*The clouds dispersed as quickly as they had gathered.* 雲聚集得快，散得也快。—**dispersal** *n* [U]

Dis·per·sion /dɪˋspɝʒən; dɪˈspɜːʃən/ *n* **the Dispersion** the DIASPORA 大流散

dispersion *n* [U] *technical* dispersal【術語】色散；彌散；頻散

di·spir·it·ed /dɪˋspɪrɪtɪd; dɪˈspɪrɪtɪd/ *adj* discouraged or without hope 灰心的；沮喪的；絕望的：*After six hours, dispirited and weary, they gave up the search.* 六個小時後，他們又絕望又疲勞，於是就放棄了搜尋。—**dispiritedly** *adv*

dis·place /dɪsˋples; dɪsˈpleɪs/ *v* [T] **1** to take the place of someone or something 取代，替代：*Coal is being displaced by natural gas as a major source of energy.* 作為一種主要能源的煤正為天然氣所取代。**2** to make a group of people or animals have to leave the place where they normally live 使〔人或動物的羣體〕離開原來的生活之地；使流離失所；迫使流亡 —**displaced** *adj*

displaced per·son /ˌ·· ˈ··/ *n plural* **displaced persons** [C] *technical* someone who has been forced to leave their country because of war or cruel treatment; REFUGEE【術語】〔因戰爭或迫害而被迫離開本土的〕流亡者；難民

dis·place·ment /dɪsˋplesmənt; dɪsˈpleɪsmənt/ *n* **1** [U] the act of forcing a group of people or animals to leave the place where they usually live〔人或動物羣體的〕被迫遷徙，流亡 **2** [singular] *technical* the weight or VOLUME (1) of liquid that something such as a ship floating on it takes the place of【術語】排水量

displacement ac·tiv·i·ty /ˈ··· ˌ···/ *n* [C,U] *technical* something that is done in order to avoid doing something else that you do not want to think about【術語】替換活動，轉移活動〔為避免做不想做的事而做的另外一件事〕

di·splay¹ /dɪˋsple; dɪˈspleɪ/ *n* [W2]

1 ► ATTRACTIVE ARRANGEMENT 吸引人的佈置 ◄ [C,U] an attractive arrangement of objects for people to look at or buy〔物品的〕展示，陳列：[+of] *a display of African tribal masks* 非洲部落面具展覽

2 ► PERFORMANCE 表演 ◄ [C] a public performance of something that is intended to entertain people〔為了娛樂人們而進行的〕公開表演：*a fireworks display* 煙花[煙火]匯演 | [+of] *a display of juggling* 雜耍表演

3 be on display something that is on display is in a public place where people can look at it 被展示，被陳列：**put sth on display** *Mapplethorpe's photographs were first put on display in New York.* 梅普爾索普所拍攝的照片首先在紐約展出。

4 display of affection/temper/loyalty etc an occasion when someone clearly shows a particular feeling, attitude, or quality 愛慕/脾氣/忠誠等的流露

5 ► EQUIPMENT 設備 ◄ [C] a piece of equipment that can show changing information, for example the screen of a computer 顯示器

display² *v* [T] [W2] **1** to show goods for sale in a shop, or paintings, historical objects etc in a public place 展示，陳列：*shop windows displaying the latest fashions* 展示最新時裝的商店櫥窗 **2** to clearly show a feeling, attitude, or quality by what you do or say 顯示，顯露〔某種情感、態度、才能等〕：*All the musicians displayed considerable skill.* 所有的音樂家都展示出相當高的技藝。**3** if a computer or notice displays information, it shows information in a way that can be clearly seen 顯示〔信息等〕：*Local train and bus times are displayed on the noticeboard.* 佈告牌上張貼着當地火車和公共汽車的時間表。

dis·pleased /dɪsˋplizd; dɪsˈpliːzd/ *adj formal* not satisfied and annoyed【正式】不滿意的；不高興的：*"We are most displeased," said the Queen.* "我們非常不滿意。" 女王說道。—**displease** *v* [T]

dis·plea·sure /dɪsˋplɛʒə; dɪsˈpleʒə/ *n* [U] *formal* the feeling of being annoyed with someone because you do not approve of their behaviour【正式】不悦; 不滿; 惱火: **incur sb's displeasure** (=make someone displeased) 惹某人生氣

dis·port /dɪˋspɔrt; dɪˈspɔːt/ *v* [T] **disport yourself** *old-fashioned* to amuse yourself by doing active enjoyable things【過時】自娛; 嬉戲; 玩樂: *a charming painting of lords and ladies disporting themselves by a lake* 一幅王孫小姐在湖邊嬉戲的美好畫作

dis·po·sa·ble /dɪˋspozəbḷ; dɪˈspəʊzəbəl/ *adj* **1** intended to be used once or for a short time and then thrown away 一次性的; 用完即可丟棄的: *disposable nappies* 一次性尿布 **2** available to be used 可使用的, 可支配的: *disposable resources* 可支配的資源

disposable in·come /ˌ···ˈ··/ *n* [U] the amount of money you have left to spend after you have paid your taxes, bills etc 可支配收入〔完稅並付清各種賬款等之後所剩的錢〕

D

dis·pos·al /dɪˋspozḷ; dɪˈspəʊzəl/ *n* **1** [U] the act of getting rid of something 丟棄; 處理: **[+of]** *the safe disposal of radioactive waste* 放射性廢料的安全處理 **2 at sb's disposal** available for someone to use 供某人使用, 支配: *Tanner had a considerable amount of cash at his disposal.* 坦納手頭有很多現金可以支配。| **sb is at your (complete) disposal** (=someone is ready to help you in any way) 某人可隨時為您效勞 **3** [C] *AmE informal* a small machine under the kitchen SINK[2] which breaks vegetable waste into small pieces【美, 非正式】污物碾碎器〔裝在廚房洗滌槽下面、把菜葉果皮等弄碎的機器〕; WASTE DISPOSAL *BrE*【英】**4** [U] *formal* the act of putting people or things in a particular place or in a particular order【正式】〔人或事物的〕安排, 編排

dis·pose /dɪˋspoz; dɪˈspəʊz/ *v* [T] *formal* to arrange things or put them in their places【正式】安排, 編排, 處理, 支配〔事物〕

dispose of sth *phr v* [T] **1** to get rid of something, especially something that is difficult to get rid of 處置, 處理〔尤指難以處理的東西〕: *How did Dahmers dispose of his victims' bodies?* 達默斯是怎樣將被他殺害的人毀屍滅跡的? **2** to deal with something such as a problem or question successfully 成功地處理問題, 解決問題 **3** to defeat an opponent 戰勝, 打敗〔對手〕

dispose sb **to** sth *phr v* [T usually in passive 一般用於被動態] to make someone more likely to feel or think a particular way about something 使〔某人〕較傾向於

dis·posed /dɪˋspozd; dɪˈspəʊzd/ *adj* [not before noun 不用於名詞前] **1 well/favourably/kindly disposed (to)** liking or approving of someone or something such as an idea or plan 很贊成...: *Management is favourably disposed to the idea of job-sharing.* 管理層很贊成"一工分做制"這一主張。**2 be disposed to do sth** *formal* feel willing to do something or behave in a particular way【正式】願意做某事: *Johnson disagreed, but did not feel disposed to argue.* 約翰遜不贊成, 但他並不想爭辯。**3 be disposed to sth** *formal* to have a tendency towards something【正式】傾向於某事物: *a man disposed to depression* 一個趨於沮喪的人

dis·po·si·tion /ˌdɪspəˋzɪʃən; ˌdɪspəˈzɪʃən/ *n formal*【正式】**1** [C] a particular type of character which makes someone more likely to behave or react in a certain way; TEMPERAMENT 性情; 性格: **have a cheerful/sunny disposition** (=have a happy character and behave in a happy way) 性格開朗、活躍 | **people of a nervous disposition** *The film is not suitable for people of a nervous disposition.* 這部電影不適合神經質的人觀看。**2** [U] a tendency to behave in a particular way 意向; 傾向: **have/show a disposition to do sth** *Neither side shows the slightest disposition to compromise.* 雙方都絲毫沒有表露出妥協的意思。**3** [C] the position or arrangement of something in a particular place 安排; 佈置: **[+of]** *a map showing the disposition of the American forces* 展示美軍部署的地圖 **4** [C,U] *law* the act of formally giving property to someone【法律】〔財產的〕贈予, 給予, 處置

dis·pos·sess /ˌdɪspəˋzɛs; ˌdɪspəˈzes/ *v* [T, usually passive 一般用被動態] *formal* to take property or land away from someone【正式】剝奪〔某人的財產、土地等〕: **be dispossessed of sth** *black South Africans who had been dispossessed of their homes* 被攆出家園的南非黑人 —**dispossession** /-ˋzɛʃən; -ˈzeʃən/ *n* [U]

dis·pos·sessed /ˌdɪspəˋzɛst; ˌdɪspəˈzest◂/ *adj* **1** having had property or land taken away 被奪走財產[土地等]的 **2 the dispossessed** [plural] people who are dispossessed 被剝奪財產[土地]的人

dis·proof /dɪsˋpruf; dɪsˈpruːf/ *n* [C,U] *formal* a fact, argument etc that proves that something is wrong or false, or the act of proving that something is wrong or false【正式】反證; 反駁; 反證物; 反駁的證據

dis·pro·por·tion /ˌdɪsprəˋpɔrʃən; ˌdɪsprəˈpɔːʃən/ *n* [C, U] *formal* the lack of a suitable or equal relation between two or more things【正式】不均衡; 不相稱; 不成比例

dis·pro·por·tion·ate /ˌdɪsprəˋpɔrʃənɪt; ˌdɪsprəˈpɔːʃənɪ̈t◂/ *adj* too much or too little in relation to something else 不相稱的; 不勻稱的; 不成比例的: *the disproportionate amount of money being spent on defence projects* 花在防禦計劃上的錢與其他支出相比不成比例 —**disproportionately** *adv*

dis·prove /dɪsˋpruv; dɪsˈpruːv/ *v* [T] to prove something false or wrong 證明〔某事〕是虛假的或錯誤的; 給予...反證: *She was able to quote figures that disproved Smith's argument.* 她引用了一些數據, 證明史密斯的論點是錯誤的。

dis·pu·ta·ble /dɪˋspjutəbḷ; dɪˈspjuːtəbəl/ *adj* something that is disputable is not definitely true or right and therefore is something that you can argue about; DEBATABLE 有爭議的; 可商榷的; 未確定的 —opposite 反義詞 INDISPUTABLE —**disputably** *adv*

dis·pu·ta·tion /ˌdɪspjuˋteʃən; ˌdɪspjʊ̈ˈteɪʃən/ *n* [C,U] *formal* a formal discussion about a subject which people cannot agree on【正式】討論; 辯論, 爭論

dis·pu·ta·tious /ˌdɪspjuˋteʃəs; ˌdɪspjʊ̈ˈteɪʃəs/ *adj formal* tending to argue; ARGUMENTATIVE【正式】愛爭論的, 好爭辯的; 爭論性的 —**disputatiously** *adv*

dis·pute¹ /dɪˋspjut; dɪˈspjuːt/ *n* [C,U]

1 ▶SERIOUS DISAGREEMENT 嚴重分歧◀ a situation in which two countries or groups of people quarrel or disagree with each other 爭吵; 爭端: *a border dispute* 邊界爭端 | *A prolonged labor dispute disrupted rail services.* 久延未決的勞資爭端使鐵路的營運陷入混亂。

2 be beyond dispute if something is beyond dispute, everyone agrees that it is true or that it really happened 無可爭辯; 確定無疑: *It is beyond dispute that advances in medicine have enabled people to live longer.* 醫學的發展使得人們更加長壽了, 這是無可置疑的。

3 be in/under dispute if facts are in or under dispute, people do not agree about them 處在爭論中; 有爭議

4 be in dispute (with sb) to disagree publicly with another person or group〔與某人或某個羣體〕有分歧: *The miners were in dispute with their employers over pay.* 礦工們與雇主在工資問題上發生了糾紛。

5 be open to dispute if something is open to dispute, it is not completely certain and not everyone agrees about it 不確定的; 有爭議的: *His interpretation of the poem is open to dispute.* 他對這首詩的詮釋是有爭議的。

dis·pute² /dɪˋspjut; dɪˈspjuːt/ *v* **1** [T] to say that you think something such as a fact or idea is not correct or true 對〔某事〕表示異議; 辯駁: *Few would dispute that travel broadens the mind.* 旅行能夠開闊視野, 幾乎沒有人會對此提出異議。**2** [I,T] to argue or disagree with someone 與〔某人〕爭辯, 爭論, 爭執; 有分歧: **hotly disputed** (=argued about with strong feelings or with anger) 激烈地爭辯 **3** [T] to argue with another country, group etc about who owns a piece of land〔與其他國家、羣體等〕爭奪〔土地〕: *The defending army disputed every inch of* *ground.* 防禦一方的軍隊寸土必爭。

disputed ter·ri·to·ry /ˌ··ˈ····/ *n* [C,U] an area of land that is claimed by two or more countries 有爭議的領土

dis·qual·i·fi·ca·tion /dɪsˌkwɑləfəˈkeʃən; dɪsˌkwɒlɪ̇fɪ̇ˈkeɪʃən/ *n* [C,U] a situation in which someone is stopped from doing an activity or taking part in a competition because they have broken a rule 取消〔參賽〕資格: *Drug-taking is punished by instant disqualification from the game.* 服食(違禁)藥物者會立即被取消參賽資格作為懲罰。

dis·qual·i·fy /dɪsˈkwɑləˌfaɪ; dɪsˈkwɒlɪ̇faɪ/ *v* [T] **1** to stop someone taking part in a competition because they have broken a rule 取消…的參賽資格: **[+from]** *Schumacher was disqualified from the race for ignoring a black flag.* 由於無視黑旗, 舒馬赫被取消參賽資格。**2** to prevent someone from doing a job or taking part in an activity, often unfairly〔通常不公正地〕阻止〔某人〕做某項工作[參加某項活動]; 剝奪…資格[權利]: **[+from]** *women in their 50's who are disqualified from working simply because of their age* 僅因年齡關係而被剝奪工作權利的五十來歲的婦女

dis·qui·et /dɪsˈkwaɪət; dɪsˈkwaɪət/ *n* [U] *formal* feelings of being anxious or not satisfied about something【正式】憂慮; 不滿: **[+over]** *Growing disquiet was voiced over police handling of terrorist investigations.* 在警察處理對恐怖分子的調查問題上, 不滿言論越來越多。

dis·qui·si·tion /ˌdɪskwəˈzɪʃən; ˌdɪskwɪ̇ˈzɪʃən/ *n* [C] *formal* a long speech or written report【正式】長篇演講; 論文

dis·re·gard¹ /ˌdɪsrɪˈgɑrd; ˌdɪsrɪˈgɑːd/ *v* [T] to ignore something or treat it as unimportant 忽視; 輕視; 無視; 不顧: *The judge ordered the jury to disregard the witness's last statement.* 法官命令陪審團不要理會證人的最後陳述。

disregard² *n* [U] the act of ignoring something that other people think is important 忽視; 輕視; 無視: **complete/total/blatant disregard for** *Rudi drove with blatant disregard for his passengers' safety.* 魯迪駕車時公然不顧乘客的安全。

dis·re·pair /ˌdɪsrɪˈpɛr; ˌdɪsrɪˈpeə/ *n* [U] buildings, roads etc that are in disrepair are in bad condition because they have not been repaired or looked after〔建築物、道路等的〕破損; 失修: **be in disrepair/fall into disrepair** *a fine Georgian mansion that had been allowed to fall into disrepair* 一座年久失修的喬治王朝風格的精美宅第

dis·rep·u·ta·ble /dɪsˈrɛpjətəbl̩; dɪsˈrepjʊ̈təbəl/ *adj* a disreputable person or organization is not respected because they are thought to be involved in dishonest or illegal activities〔人或組織〕名聲不好的; 不受尊敬的 —**disreputably** *adv* —**disreputableness** *n* [U]

dis·re·pute /ˌdɪsrɪˈpjut; ˌdɪsrɪˈpjuːt/ *n* [U] **bring sb/sth into disrepute** to make people stop trusting or having a good opinion of an activity, idea, organization etc 使某人/某事物喪失名譽[蒙羞]: *When one policeman is convicted of corruption, it brings the whole system into disrepute.* 如果一個警察被判犯有貪污罪, 這將使得整個警方系統都蒙受恥辱。

dis·re·spect /ˌdɪsrɪˈspɛkt; ˌdɪsrɪˈspekt/ *n* [U] **1** lack of respect for someone or for something such as the law 不尊敬, 失禮, 無禮 **2 no disrespect (to)** *spoken* used when you are criticizing someone or something to say that you do not want to seem rude【口】並不想無禮, 並無不敬〔用在批評某人或某事物的時候〕: *No disrespect to Adrian, but he's not very experienced.* 我說這話不是不尊重他, 不過艾德里安並不是很有經驗的。—**disrespectful** *adj* —**disrespectfully** *adv*

dis·robe /dɪsˈrob; dɪsˈrəʊb/ *v* [I] *formal or humorous* to take off your clothes【正式或幽默】寬衣; 脱衣服

dis·rupt /dɪsˈrʌpt; dɪsˈrʌpt/ *v* [T] to prevent a situation, event, system etc from continuing in its usual way by causing problems 擾亂; 使混亂: *We hope the move to Kansas won't disrupt the kids' schooling too much.* 我們希望我們搬家到堪薩斯州不會過多地耽誤孩子們上學。

dis·rup·tion /dɪsˈrʌpʃən; dɪsˈrʌpʃən/ *n* [C,U] a situation in which something is prevented from continuing in its normal way because of problems and difficulties 中斷; 擾亂: *The strike caused widespread disruption to train services.* 罷工使鐵路服務普遍陷入混亂。

dis·rup·tive /dɪsˈrʌptɪv; dɪsˈrʌptɪv/ *adj* disruptive behaviour prevents something from continuing in its usual way and causes trouble〔指行為等〕擾亂性的; 搗亂的: *a child who was disruptive in class* 一個破壞課堂秩序的孩子 —**disruptively** *adv*

diss /dɪs; dɪs/ *v* [T] *AmE slang* to make unfair and unkind remarks about someone【美俚】説〔某人的〕壞話

dis·sat·is·fac·tion /ˌdɪssætɪsˈfækʃən; dɪˌsætɪ̇sˈfækʃən/ *n* [U] a feeling of not being satisfied 不滿意; 不滿足

dis·sat·is·fied /dɪsˈsætɪsˌfaɪd; dɪˈsætɪ̇sfaɪd/ *adj* not satisfied because something is not as good as you had expected 不滿意的; 不滿足的: **[+with]** *If for any reason you are dissatisfied with this product, please return it to the address below.* 對產品如有任何不滿, 請將其退回下列地址。

dis·sat·is·fy /dɪsˈsætɪsˌfaɪ; dɪˈsætɪ̇sfaɪ/ *v* [T] to fail to satisfy someone or something 使不滿

dis·sect /dɪˈsɛkt; dɪˈsekt/ *v* [T] **1** to cut up the body of a dead person or animal in order to study it 解剖〔人或動物的屍體〕**2** to examine something in great detail so that you discover its faults or understand it better 剖析〔某事物〕

dis·sec·tion /dɪˈsɛkʃən; dɪˈsekʃən/ *n* [C,U] the act of cutting up the body of a dead person or animal to study it 解剖

dis·sem·ble /dɪˈsɛmbl̩; dɪˈsembəl/ *v* [I,T] *formal* to hide your true feelings, ideas, desires etc【正式】掩飾, 掩藏〔真實的情感、觀點、願望等〕

dis·sem·i·nate /dɪˈsɛməˌnet; dɪˈsemɪ̇neɪt/ *v* [T] *formal* to spread information, ideas etc to as many people as possible, especially in order to influence them【正式】散布, 廣泛傳播〔消息、觀點等〕—**dissemination** /dɪˌsɛməˈneʃən; dɪˌsemɪ̇ˈneɪʃən/ *n* [U]: *the dissemination of information about new tax rules* 關於新稅務條例的消息的傳播

dis·sen·sion /dɪˈsɛnʃən; dɪˈsenʃən/ *n* [C,U] disagreement and argument among a group of people〔某一團體內部的〕爭執, 分歧: *On the issue of the single market, there was little dissension.* 在單一市場這一問題上幾乎沒有甚麼不同的意見。

dis·sent¹ /dɪˈsɛnt; dɪˈsent/ *n* **1** [U] refusal to accept an official opinion or an opinion that most people accept〔尤指對某種官方意見或多數人所持意見的〕異議; 意見的分歧: *political dissent* 不同政見 **2** [C] *AmE* a judge's written statement giving their reasons for disagreeing with the other judges in a law case【美】〔某法官表示與其他法官在某一案件中持不同見解的理由的〕書面陳述 **3** [U] *old use* a disagreement with accepted religious beliefs, especially one that makes someone leave an established church【舊】〔對公認的宗教教義的〕不贊成, 反對; 不信奉國教 —see also 另見 CONSENT¹, ASSENT¹

dissent² *v* [I] to say that you strongly disagree with an official opinion or decision, or one that is accepted by most people 強烈反對〔官方的觀點、決定或多數人所接受的意見〕; 持異議 —**dissenter** *n* [C]

dis·ser·ta·tion /ˌdɪsəˈteʃən; ˌdɪsəˈteɪʃən/ *n* [C] a long piece of writing about a subject, especially one that you write as part of a university degree 專題論文〔尤指大學學位論文〕

dis·ser·vice /dɪsˈsɝvɪs; dɪˈsɜːvɪ̇s/ *n* **do a disservice to** to do something that harms someone or something, especially by giving other people a bad opinion about them 對…造成損害[危害, 傷害]: *The fans' behaviour has done the game a great disservice.* 球迷們的行為對這項運動造成了很大的損害。

dis·si·dent /ˈdɪsədənt; ˈdɪsɪ̇dənt/ *n* [C] someone who publicly criticizes a government or political party, es-

D

pecially in a country where this is not allowed 持不同政見者 —**dissident** *adj*: *a group of dissident writers* 一羣持不同政見的作家 —**dissidence** *n* [U]

dis·sim·i·lar /dɪˋsɪmələ; dɪˈsɪmɪ̡lə/ *adj* not the same 不相同的; 不相似的 —**dissimilarity** /dɪˌsɪməˋlærətɪ; dɪˌsɪmɪ̡ˈlærɪ̡ti/ *n* [C,U]

dis·sim·u·late /dɪˋsɪmjəˌlet; dɪˈsɪmjʊ̡leɪt/ *v* [I,T] *formal* to hide your true feelings or intentions, especially by lying to people【正式】〔尤指通過撒謊〕隱藏, 掩飾〔真實的感情或意圖〕

dis·si·pate /ˋdɪsəˌpet; ˈdɪsɪ̡peɪt/ *v formal*【正式】**1** [I,T] to scatter or disappear, or make something do this (使)〔某事物〕消散, 消失: *England's arrogance was dissipated by a 1–0 defeat by the United States.* 英格蘭隊被美國隊以 1–0 打敗後, 其傲慢氣焰消失殆盡。**2** [T] to gradually waste something such as money or energy by trying to do a lot of different or unnecessary things 揮霍〔金錢〕; 耗費〔精力〕; 消耗

dis·si·pat·ed /ˋdɪsəˌpetɪd; ˈdɪsɪ̡peɪtɪ̡d/ *adj* spending too much time on physical pleasures such as drinking alcohol, in a way that is harmful to your health 放蕩的, 浪蕩的, 無節制的, 奢糜的

dis·si·pa·tion /ˌdɪsəˋpeʃən; ˌdɪsɪ̡ˈpeɪʃən/ *n* [U] *formal*【正式】**1** the process of making something disappear or scatter 消失, 驅散, 耗盡: **[+of]** *the dissipation of heat* 熱量的消散 **2** the enjoyment of physical pleasures such as drinking too much alcohol, that are harmful to your health 放蕩; 花天酒地: *a life of luxury and dissipation* 奢侈而放蕩的生活 **3** the act of wasting money, time, energy etc〔金錢、時間、精力等的〕浪費

dis·so·ci·ate /dɪˋsoʃɪˌet; dɪˈsəʊʃieɪt/ *v* [T] **1 dissociate yourself from** to do or say something to show that you do not agree with a person or organization, especially so that you avoid being criticized for their behaviour or views〔尤指為避免受到牽連或遭到批評而〕表示與…沒有關係: *I wish to dissociate myself from the views expressed by Mr Irving.* 我想表明我不贊同歐文先生的觀點。**2 dissociate sb/sth from** to regard two things or people as separate and not connected to each other 把某人/某物與…分開 —**dissociation** /dɪˌsoʃɪˋeʃən; dɪˌsəʊʃiˈeɪʃən/ *n* [U]

dis·so·lute /ˋdɪsəˌlut; ˈdɪsəluːt/ *adj* having an immoral way of life, for example drinking too much alcohol, having sex with many people etc〔生活〕放蕩的; 道德淪喪的: *Dylan Thomas, then an intensely romantic, though dissolute figure* 迪倫·湯馬斯那時候是個非常浪漫但又放蕩的人物 —**dissolutely** *adv* —**dissoluteness** *n* [U]

dis·so·lu·tion /ˌdɪsəˋluʃən; ˌdɪsəˈluːʃən/ *n* [U] **1** the act of formally ending a parliament〔議會的〕解散 **2** the act of formally ending a marriage or business arrangement〔婚姻關係、商務安排的〕正式解除 **3** the process by which something gradually becomes weaker and disappears〔某事物的〕衰敗; 消亡: *the dissolution of the Roman Empire* 羅馬帝國的衰亡

dissolve (使)溶解

dis·solve /dɪˋzalv; dɪˈzɒlv/ *v*

1 ►STH SOLID 固體物◄ a) [I] if a solid dissolves, it mixes with a liquid and becomes part of it〔固體〕溶解: **[+in]** *Sugar dissolves in water.* 糖能溶解於水。**b)** [T] to make something solid become part of a liquid by putting it in a liquid and mixing it 使〔固體〕溶解: **dissolve sth in** *Dissolve the tablets in water.* 把藥片溶於水中。

2 dissolve into laughter/tears start to laugh or cry 開始哈哈大笑/淚流滿面

3 ►BECOME WEAKER 變弱◄ [I] to become weaker and disappear 變弱, 消失: *Her objections to the plan began to dissolve.* 漸漸地, 她對這項計劃不再持反對意見了。

4 ►PARLIAMENT 議會◄ [T] to formally end a parliament before an election〔在大選前〕正式解散〔議會〕

5 ►MARRIAGE/BUSINESS/ORGANIZATION 婚姻/商務/組織◄ [T usually passive 一般用被動態] to formally end a marriage, business arrangement, or organization 解除〔婚姻關係〕; 取消〔商務安排〕; 解散〔組織〕

dis·so·nance /ˋdɪsənəns; ˈdɪsənəns/ *n* **1** [C,U] a combination of musical notes that have a strange sound because they are not in HARMONY (1)〔樂聲的〕不和諧音 **2** [U] *formal* a lack of agreement between different ideas or opinions【正式】〔觀點、意見的〕不一致 —**dissonant** *adj*

dis·suade /dɪˋswed; dɪˈsweɪd/ *v* [T] to persuade somebody not to do something 勸〔某人〕不要做某事; 勸阻: **dissuade sb from doing sth** *a campaign to dissuade young people from smoking* 勸年輕人不要吸煙的活動 | —compare 比較 PERSUADE —**dissuasion** /dɪˋsweʒən; dɪˈsweɪʒən/ *n* [U]

dis·tance¹ /ˋdɪstəns; ˈdɪstəns/ *n* [C,U]

1 ►HOW FAR 有多遠◄ the amount of space between two places or things 距離, 間距: **short/long distance** *Sylvia could only run a short distance without getting out of breath.* 西爾維亞只能跑較短的距離, 跑遠了就會氣喘吁吁。| **[+from]** *What's the distance from Chicago to Detroit?* 芝加哥離底特律有多遠? | **at a distance of 5 metres/2 miles etc** (=5 metres etc away) 相隔 5 米/2 英里等 *Place the rod at a distance of 40mm from the light source.* 把棒放在離光源 40 毫米的地方。| **some distance from/a good distance away from** (=a fairly long distance from) 離…有一段距離/很遠 *Gareth's cottage is some distance from the road.* 加雷思的小屋離公路有一段距離。

2 in the distance in a place that is far away, but close enough to be seen or heard 在遠處〔但可以看到或聽到〕: *That's Long Island in the distance over there.* 那邊遠處是長島。

3 at/from a distance a) from a place that is not very close 在遠處/從不太近的地方: **follow sb from a distance** (=follow them by walking a long way behind them) 遠遠地跟着某人 *The detective followed him at a distance.* 偵探遠遠地跟着他。**b)** a long time after something happened〔時間〕相隔很久: *It's difficult to remember exactly what they looked like at this distance in time.* 時間隔了這麼久, 很難確切地記清楚他們到底長得甚麼樣。

4 within walking/driving distance near enough to walk or drive to 走路/開車去很近: **[+of]** *There are two good Chinese restaurants within walking distance of my house.* 從我家走過去不遠處有兩家很好的中國餐廳。

5 within spitting distance of *informal* very near【非正式】非常近

6 keep your distance a) to avoid becoming too friendly with someone or too closely involved in something 避免〔和某人〕太親近; 避免過多地捲入〔某事〕**b)** to not go too close to someone or to another car〔與某人或其他車輛〕保持距離

7 keep sb at a distance to not become too friendly with someone 不與某人太親近: *Ann likes to keep people at a distance.* 安喜歡與人保持一段距離。

8 ►UNFRIENDLY FEELING 不友好的感情◄ a situation in which two people do not tell each other what they really think or feel, in a way that seems unfriendly〔兩個人之間的〕疏遠: [+between] *There was still a certain distance between me and my father.* 我和父親之間仍然有些疏遠。

9 go the distance *informal* if you go the distance in a sport or competition, you continue playing or competing until the end【非正式】〔在體育比賽或其他競賽中〕繼續比賽直到最後 —see also 另見 LONG-DISTANCE, MIDDLE DISTANCE

distance² *v* **distance yourself** to say that you are not involved with someone or something, or try to become less involved, especially to avoid being connected with them 使自己與…保持距離; 疏遠〔某人〕; 不介入〔某事〕: *The Soviet Union distanced itself from the US position.* 蘇聯對美國的立場保持了距離。

distance learn·ing /ˈ·· ,··/ *n* [U] *BrE* a method of study that involves watching television programmes and sending work to teachers instead of going to a school【英】遙距教學, 遠程學習〔通過收看電視節目並把作業寄給老師的學習方式〕

3 **dis·tant** /ˋdɪstənt; ˈdɪstənt/ *adj*

1 ▶FAR AWAY 遠處的◀ far from where you are now 遠處的, 遠方的: *the distant sound of traffic* 遠處往來的車輛聲 | *Nora gazed at the distant hills.* 諾拉凝視着遠山。

2 ▶UNFRIENDLY 不友好的◀ unfriendly and showing no emotion 不友好的; 冷淡的: *After the quarrel Susan remained cold and distant.* 那次爭吵之後, 蘇珊一直非常冷淡疏遠。

3 ▶RELATIVE 親屬◀ [only before noun 僅用於名詞前] not very closely related to you 遠親的: *a distant cousin* 一位遠房表[堂]親

4 in the (dim and) distant past a long time ago 很久以前, 在遙遠的過去

5 in the not too distant future used when talking about what will happen in a few months or years from now 在不遠的將來: *The President hopes to visit Ireland in the not too distant future.* 總統希望在不遠的將來訪問愛爾蘭。—**distantly** *adv*

dis·taste /dɪsˋtest; dɪsˈteɪst/ *n* [U] a feeling of dislike for someone or something that you think is unpleasant or morally offensive 不喜歡, 厭惡, 反感: [+for] *her distaste for any form of compromise* 她對任何形式的妥協的反感

dis·taste·ful /dɪsˋtestfəl; dɪsˈteɪstfəl/ *adj* very unpleasant or morally offensive 令人生厭的; 令人反感的: *What follows is John's story. Parts of it may seem distasteful, even shocking.* 下面是約翰講的故事, 其中有些部分也許聽起來令人生厭, 甚至令人震驚。—**distastefully** *adv* —**distastefulness** *n* [U]

dis·tem·per /dɪsˋtɛmpɚ; dɪˈstempə/ *n* [U] **1** an infectious disease that affects dogs and cats 瘟熱〔貓、狗所得的一種傳染性疾病〕**2** *BrE* a type of paint that you mix with water used for painting walls【英】〔刷牆用的〕水漿塗料

dis·tend /dɪˋstɛnd; dɪˈstend/ *v* [I,T] to swell or make something swell because of pressure from inside〔因來自內部的壓力〕(使) 膨脹, (使) 腫脹 —**distended** *adj*: *a distended stomach* 胃脹 —**distension** /-ˋtɛnʃən; -ˈtenʃən/ *n* [U] *technical*【術語】

dis·til also 又作 **distill** *AmE*【美】/dɪˋstɪl; dɪˈstɪl/ *v* **distilled, distilling** [T] **1** to make a liquid such as water or alcohol more pure by heating it so that it becomes a gas and then letting it cool 蒸餾 **2** to make a strong alcoholic drink such as WHISKY by this method 採用蒸餾法製造〔烈性酒, 如威士忌〕**3** to get ideas, information etc from a large amount of knowledge or experience〔從大量的知識或經驗中〕提取, 提煉〔觀念或資訊等〕—**distillation** /ˌdɪstəˋleʃən; ˌdɪstɪˈleɪʃən/ *n* [C,U]

dis·til·ler /dɪˋstɪlɚ; dɪˈstɪlə/ *n* [C] a person or company that makes strong alcoholic drinks such as WHISKY 製酒商; 釀酒廠

dis·til·le·ry /dɪˋstɪlərɪ; dɪˈstɪləri/ *n* [C] a factory where strong alcoholic drink is produced by distilling〔採用蒸餾法的〕釀酒廠

dis·tinct /dɪˋstɪŋkt; dɪˈstɪŋkt/ *adj* **1** clearly different or belonging to a different type 明顯不同的; 不同種類的: 3 **quite/entirely distinct** (=completely distinct) 截然不同的, 完全不同的 *two entirely distinct languages* 兩種完全不同的語言 | [+from] *The behavior of men as individuals is distinct from their behavior in a group.* 人在獨處時的行為與在羣體中的行為是不一樣的。**2 as distinct from** used when emphasizing that you are talking about a particular kind of thing and not something else 與…有所區別〔用於表示強調你在談論的是某一事物〕: *childhood as distinct from adolescence* 有別於青春期的童年時期 **3** something that is distinct can clearly be seen, heard, smelled etc 清晰的, 清楚的, 明顯的: *The outline of the ship became more distinct.* 船的輪廓變得更加清晰了。**4** [only before noun 僅用於名詞前] a distinct possibility, feeling, quality etc definitely exists or is definitely important and cannot be ignored〔指可能性、感覺、特徵等〕確實存在的; 確實重要的; 不容忽視的: *a distinct lack of interest among the general public* 在普通大眾之間明顯存在的漠不關心的情況 | **have a distinct advantage** *Oxbridge graduates have a distinct advantage when applying for jobs in the civil service.* 牛津大學和劍橋大學的畢業生在申請公務員職務時有明顯的優勢。

D

dis·tinc·tion /dɪˋstɪŋkʃən; dɪˈstɪŋkʃən/ *n* **1** [C] a clear difference between two similar things 差別, 不同: 3 2 [+between] *the distinction between formal and informal language* 正式與非正式語言之間的差別 **2 make/draw a distinction** to say that two things or groups are different or treat them in a different way 區分開來〔指區別對待〕: *The school makes no distinction between male and female students.* 學校並沒有對男女學生區別對待。**3** [U] the quality of being excellent and important 優秀; 卓越, 傑出: *No one today doubts Eliot's distinction as a poet.* 如今沒有人懷疑艾略特是位傑出的詩人。| **of (great) distinction** (=very good and very important) 卓越的 *Collingwood was a scholar of great distinction.* 科林伍德是位卓越的學者。**4** [C] a special honour given to someone to show them respect or to reward their achievements 榮譽; 殊榮: **have the distinction of doing sth** *Dinah had the great distinction of being invited to meet the Prime Minister.* 黛娜獲得殊榮, 被邀請與首相見面。**5** [C] a special mark given to a student who has done very well 授予優秀學生的特殊分數: *Bianca got a distinction in her chemistry exam.* 畢安卡的化學考試得到了優異的等級。

dis·tinc·tive /dɪˋstɪŋktɪv; dɪˈstɪŋktɪv/ *adj* having a special quality, character, or appearance that is different and easy to recognize〔特徵、性格、外表等〕與眾不同的: *a rock band with a distinctive sound* 聲音很有特色的搖滾樂隊 —**distinctively** *adv* —**distinctiveness** *n* [U]

dis·tinct·ly /dɪˋstɪŋktlɪ; dɪˈstɪŋktli/ *adv* **1** clearly 清楚地; 明白地: *I distinctly heard him say my name.* 我清楚地聽見他說我的名字。**2** used when saying that someone or something has a particular quality, character etc that is easy to recognize 明顯地〔用於表示某人或某物具有某種易辨認的特徵、特點等〕: *The rest of the passengers had distinctly Indian names.* 其他乘客的名字都具有明顯的印度人的特徵。**3** used when emphasizing an adjective that you are using to describe something or someone 非常, 特別〔用來強調某個形容詞〕: *Paul was feeling distinctly foolish.* 保羅感到非常愚蠢。**4 distinctly remember doing sth** used to say that you definitely remember details about something very clearly 清清楚楚地記得做過某事

dis·tin·guish /dɪˋstɪŋgwɪʃ; dɪˈstɪŋgwɪʃ/ *v* **1** [I,T] to be able to recognize and understand the difference between two similar things or people 區別, 辨別: *Dogs can distinguish a greater range of sounds than humans.* 狗能辨別的音域較人類為大。| [+between] *It's important to* *distinguish between tax avoidance and tax evasion.* 把避税和逃税區別開是很重要的。| **distinguish sb/sth from** *The twins are so alike it's difficult to distinguish one from the other.* 這對孿生兒長得太像了，很難分辨誰是誰。**2** [T not in progressive 不用進行式] to be able to see the shape of something or hear a particular sound 辨清〔某物的輪廓〕; 分清〔某種聲音〕: *The light was too dim for me to distinguish anything clearly.* 光線太暗了，我甚麼也看不清楚。**3** [T not in progressive 不用進行式] *formal* to be the thing that makes someone or something different from other people or things【正式】使有別於; 使有特色: **distinguish sb/sth from** *There's not much to distinguish her from the other candidates.* 她沒有太多有別於其他候選人的特點。| **distinguishing feature/mark** (=a feature or mark that makes someone or something look different) 與眾不同的特徵/標記 **4 distinguish yourself** to do something so well that people notice you and remember you 表現突出: *McEnroe first distinguished himself by winning a junior tournament at Wimbledon.* 麥肯羅最初因在一次温布頓少年網球賽中獲勝而受人注目。

D

dis·tin·guish·a·ble /dɪ`stɪŋgwɪʃəbḷ; dɪˈstɪŋgwɪʃəbəl/ *adj* easily recognized as being different from other things or people 能分辨出來的，區別得出的: **[+from]** *The copy was barely distinguishable from the original painting.* 這摹本幾乎可以亂真。

dis·tin·guished /dɪ`stɪŋgwɪʃt; dɪˈstɪŋgwɪʃt/ *adj* **1** very successful and therefore respected and admired 受人尊敬的，令人欽佩的: *a school with a distinguished academic record* 一所教學成績超羣的學校 —see 見 FAMOUS (USAGE) **2** someone who has a distinguished appearance looks important in a way that makes you respect and admire them〔指某人的外表〕氣度不凡的，高雅的: *a tall, distinguished-looking man* 一位儀表出眾的高個男士

dis·tort /dɪ`stɔrt; dɪˈstɔːt/ *v* [T] **1** to explain a fact, statement, idea etc in a way that changes its real meaning 歪曲〔事實、陳述、觀點等〕: *The journalist was accused of distorting the facts.* 該記者被指責歪曲事實。**2** to change the appearance, sound, or shape of something so that it is strange or unclear 使變形; 使失真; 使反常: *Tall buildings can distort radio signals.* 高大的建築物會使無線電信號失真。—**distorted** *adj* —**distortion** /dɪs`tɔrʃən; dɪˈstɔːʃən/ *n* [U]

dis·tract /dɪ`strækt; dɪˈstrækt/ *v* [T] to make someone who is working, studying etc unable to continue what they are doing by making them look at or listen to something else 分散〔某人〕的注意力; 使〔某人〕分心: *Try not to distract the other students.* 盡量不要讓其他學生分心。| **distract sb from** *Meg was distracted from her work by the noise outside.* 外面的嘈雜聲使得梅格不能專心工作。| **distract sb's attention** (=deliberately stop someone paying attention to what they are doing) 分散某人的注意力 —**distracting** *adj*

dis·tract·ed /dɪ`stræktɪd; dɪˈstræktɪ̵d/ *adj* anxious and unable to think clearly 心神不定的，心煩意亂的，精神無法集中的: *After the argument, Kathryn felt too distracted to work.* 爭吵之後，凱思琳感到心神不定，無法工作。—**distractedly** *adv*

dis·trac·tion /dɪ`strækʃən; dɪˈstrækʃən/ *n* **1** [C,U] something that makes you stop paying attention to what you are doing 使人分心的事物: *I have to study in the library – there are too many distractions at home.* 我得在圖書館學習 —— 家裡分心的事太多。**2** [C] a pleasant and not very serious activity that you do for amusement 消遣，娛樂 **3 drive sb to distraction** to annoy someone so much, that they become angry, upset, and no longer able to think clearly 讓某人煩得要命; 把某人逼瘋: *The baby's constant crying was driving me to distraction.* 嬰兒不停地哭，真要把我給弄瘋了。

dis·trait /dɪ`stre; dɪˈstreɪ/ *adj French* distracted【法】心神不定的，精神無法集中的

dis·traught /dɪ`strɔt; dɪˈstrɔːt/ *adj* so upset and worried that you cannot think clearly 憂心如焚的，心神不定的，憂慮欲狂的: *The distraught woman was yesterday giving police a description of her attacker.* 昨天，那個心慌意亂的婦女向警察描述了那個襲擊者的情況。

dis·tress[1] /dɪ`strɛs; dɪˈstres/ *n* [U]

1 ►EXTREME WORRY 極度憂慮◄ a feeling of extreme worry and unhappiness 極度憂慮; 苦惱: *Luke's destructive behaviour caused his parents great distress.* 盧克的破壞行為使他的父母深感憂慮。| **in distress** *The girl was crying and clearly in distress.* 那個女孩哭了，顯然是很痛苦。

2 ►PAIN 疼痛◄ *formal* great physical pain【正式】身體上的痛苦，劇痛

3 ►LACK OF MONEY/FOOD 缺少錢/食物◄ a situation in which you suffer or have great problems because you have no money, food etc 貧困; 困苦: **in distress** *charities that aid families in distress* 救助貧困家庭的慈善機構 | *acute financial distress* 嚴重的財務困難

4 distress signal a message sent from a ship, aircraft etc asking for help 求救信號

5 be in distress if a ship, aircraft etc is in distress, it is in danger of sinking or crashing〔船隻、飛機等〕處於險境，遇險

distress[2] *v* [T] to make someone feel extremely upset and worried 使傷心，使不安，使憂慮

dis·tressed /dɪ`strɛst; dɪˈstrest/ *adj* **1** extremely upset and shocked 極為難過的，十分不安的: **deeply distressed** *Hannah was deeply distressed by the news about her father.* 漢納得知她父親的消息，深感悲痛。**2** experiencing a lot of pain 十分痛苦的: *The animal was clearly distressed.* 那動物顯然很痛苦。**3** *formal* having very little money【正式】貧困的: *a family living in distressed circumstances* 生活在貧困中的一家人

dis·tress·ing /dɪ`strɛsɪŋ; dɪˈstresɪŋ/ also 又作 **distressful** *adj* making you feel extremely upset and anxious 令人不安的，使人憂慮的: *a distressing experience* 一次痛苦的經歷 —**distressingly** *adv*

dis·trib·ute /dɪ`strɪbjut; dɪˈstrɪbjuːt/ *v* [T] **1** to give something such as food, medicine, books etc to a large group of people, especially in a planned way〔尤指有計劃地〕分發，分配，分送: **distribute sth among/to** *Clothes and blankets have been distributed among the refugees.* 已經向難民分發了衣服和毯子。| *a man distributing leaflets to passers-by* 一個派發傳單給路人的男子 **2** to supply goods to shops and companies in a particular area 提供，配送〔貨物〕: *Milk is distributed to the local shops by Herald's Dairies.* 牛奶是由赫拉德牛奶場提供給當地商店的。**3** to share something such as wealth or power among different people or organizations 分享〔財富或權力〕 **4** to spread something over a large area 散佈; 分佈; 撒; 播: *The flowers rely on the wind to distribute their pollen.* 這些花靠風來傳播花粉。

dis·tri·bu·tion /ˌdɪstrə`bjuʃən; ˌdɪstrɪ̵ˈbjuːʃən/ *n* **1** [U] the act of giving things to a large group of people or delivering goods to companies, shops etc 分發，分配; 發送: **[+of]** *the distribution of aid supplies* 救濟物資的分發 **2** [C,U] the way in which people, buildings etc are arranged over a large area〔人口、建築物等的〕分佈: *population distribution* 人口分佈 **3** [U] *technical* the way in which wealth, property etc is shared among the members of a society【術語】〔財富、財產等的〕分配

dis·trib·u·tive /dɪ`strɪbjətɪv; dɪˈstrɪbjʊ̈tɪv/ *adj* **1** connected with distribution 分發的，分配的; 分佈的: *distributive costs* 配送費用 **2** *technical* referring to each single member of a group; distributing words in English include 'each', 'every' and 'either'.【術語】〔詞〕個體的，個別的; 分配的〔英語中的個體[分配]詞包括 each, every 和 either〕

dis·trib·u·tor /dɪ`strɪbjətɚ; dɪˈstrɪbjʊ̈tə/ *n* [C] **1** a company or person that supplies shops and companies with goods 銷售者; 批發商; 分銷商 **2** the part of a car's engine that sends an electric current to the SPARK PLUGS 配電器; 配電盤 —see picture at 參見 ENGINE 圖

3 2 **dis·trict** /ˋdɪstrɪkt; ˈdɪstrɪkt/ *n* [C] **1** a particular area of a town or the countryside 地區; 區域: *a semi-detached house in a pleasant suburban district* 處在景色宜人的郊區的半獨立式房子 —see 見 AREA (USAGE) **2** an area of a country, city etc that has official borders 行政區: *a postal district* 郵政區

district at·tor·ney /,·· ·ˋ··/ *n* [C] a lawyer in the US who is responsible for bringing legal charges against criminals in a particular area〔美國〕地方檢察官

district coun·cil /,·· ˋ··/ *n* [C] a group of people elected in Britain to organize local services such as education, cleaning the streets etc in a particular area〔英國〕區議會〔負責組織當地事務如教育、清掃街道等〕

district court /,·· ˋ·/ *n* [C] a local court in the US where people are judged in cases involving national rather than state law〔美國〕地方法院〔審理涉及聯邦法律而非州法律的案子〕

district nurse /,·· ˋ·/ *n* [C] a nurse who visits and treats people in their own homes in Britain〔英國〕社區護士〔上門為病人護理的護士〕

dis·trust[1] /dɪsˋtrʌst; dɪsˈtrʌst/ *n* [U] a feeling that you cannot trust someone 不信任: *The local people regard the police with suspicion and distrust.* 當地人以一種懷疑及不信任的眼光看待警察。| **[+of]** *Dylan's distrust of journalists makes him difficult to interview.* 迪倫對記者的不信任使他們很難採訪他。—**distrustful** *adj* —**distrustfully** *adv* —compare 比較 MISTRUST[1]

distrust[2] *v* [T] to not trust someone or something 不信任, 懷疑

dis·turb /dɪˋstɝb; dɪˈstɜːb/ *v* [T]

1 ►INTERRUPT 打擾◄ to interrupt someone so that they cannot continue what they are doing by asking a question, making a noise etc 干擾, 打擾, 使中斷: *Sorry to disturb you, but I have an urgent message from your husband.* 對不起打擾一下, 我這兒有你丈夫的一份急電。

2 ►WORRY 憂慮◄ to make someone feel worried or slightly shocked 使焦慮, 使驚訝: *What disturbs me most is his total lack of remorse.* 最令我不安的是他完全不感到後悔。

3 ►MOVE 移動◄ to move something or change its position 挪動, 移動, 改變〔某物的〕位置: *If you find a bird's nest, never disturb the eggs.* 如果你發現鳥巢, 千萬別動那些鳥蛋。

4 do not disturb a sign that you put on a door when you do not want anyone to interrupt you 請勿打擾〔掛在門上的牌子〕

5 disturb the peace *law* to behave in a noisy and unpleasant way in public【法律】擾亂治安

dis·turb·ance /dɪˋstɝbəns; dɪˈstɜːbəns/ *n* **1** [C,U] something that stops you from being able to continue doing something, or the act of stopping someone from being able to continue doing something 造成干擾的事物; 干擾, 擾亂: *The noise of the traffic is a continual disturbance.* 交通噪音是一種持續性的干擾。| *I need a place where I can work without disturbance.* 我需要一個可以靜心工作的地方。**2** [C] a situation in which people fight or behave violently in public 騷亂, 混亂: *There were disturbances in the crowd as fans left the stadium.* 在球迷們離開運動場時, 人羣中發生了騷亂。**3** [U] a state in which someone is emotionally upset and does not behave normally 情緒困擾, 精神失常: *a long history of mental disturbance* 長期的精神失常病史

dis·turbed /dɪˋstɝbd; dɪˈstɜːbd/ *adj* someone who is disturbed does not behave in a normal way, because they have had very shocking or upsetting experiences 心理不正常的, 精神失常的

dis·turb·ing /dɪˋstɝbɪŋ; dɪˈstɜːbɪŋ/ *adj* making you feel worried or shocked 令人不安的, 使人震驚的: *a disturbing increase in the crime rate* 令人不安的犯罪率的增長

dis·u·nite /ˌdɪsjuˋnaɪt; ˌdɪsjuːˈnaɪt/ *v* [T] *formal* to prevent people from agreeing with each other and working together【正式】使分裂, 使不和 —**disunited** *adj*

dis·u·ni·ty /dɪsˋjunɪtɪ; dɪsˈjuːnɪ̥ti/ *n* [U] a situation in which a group of people cannot agree with each other or work together 不和; 分裂; 紛爭

dis·use /dɪsˋjus; dɪsˈjuːs/ *n* [U] a situation in which something is no longer used 廢棄, 不用, 棄置: **fall into disuse** (=stop being used) 廢棄不用 *The building eventually fell into disuse.* 該建築物最終被廢棄不用了。

dis·used /ˌdɪsˋjuzd; ˌdɪsˈjuːzd◄/ *adj* no longer used 不再使用的: *a disused mine* 廢棄的礦井

di·syl·lab·ic /ˌdaɪsəˋlæbɪk; ˌdaɪsɪ̥ˈlæbɪk◄/ *adj technical* having two SYLLABLES【術語】雙音節的

ditch[1] /dɪtʃ; dɪtʃ/ *n* [C] a long narrow hole cut into the ground at the side of a field, road etc, especially for water to flow through〔挖在田邊、路邊等處的〕溝, 渠〔尤用於排水〕—see also 另見 LAST-DITCH

ditch[2] *v* **1** [T] to get rid of something because you no longer need it 扔掉, 拋棄, 甩掉 **2** [T] *informal* to end a romantic relationship with someone【非正式】與〔某人〕斷絕戀愛關係; 拋棄〔某人〕: *Julie's ditched her boyfriend.* 朱莉把她的男朋友甩了。**3** [I,T] to deliberately crash an aircraft into the sea 使〔飛機〕在海上降落; 海上迫降

ditch·wa·ter /ˋdɪtʃˌwɔtɚ; ˈdɪtʃwɔːtə/ *n* **as dull as ditchwater** *BrE* very boring【英】極其乏味的

dith·er[1] /ˋdɪðɚ; ˈdɪðə/ *v* [I] to not do something because you are unable to decide what to do 猶豫不決: *Stop dithering, Linda, and get on with it!* 別猶豫了, 琳達, 快繼續幹啊! —**ditherer** *n* [C]

dither[2] *n* **be (all) in a dither** *BrE informal* to be nervous and confused because you cannot decide what to do【英, 非正式】緊張; 茫然不知所措

di·tran·si·tive /ˌdaɪˋtrænsətɪv; ˌdaɪˈtrænsɪ̥tɪv/ *adj technical* a ditransitive verb has an INDIRECT OBJECT and a DIRECT OBJECT. 'Give' in the sentence 'Give me the book.' is ditransitive【術語】〔動詞〕帶雙賓語的〔即帶直接賓語和間接賓語, 如 give 在句子 Give me the book 中便是個帶雙賓語的動詞〕—compare 比較 INTRANSITIVE, TRANSITIVE —**ditransitive** *n* [C]

dit·to[1] /ˋdɪto; ˈdɪtəʊ/ *adv spoken* used to say that something is the same as something else, or that you think the same as someone else【口】我也一樣: *"I'm absolutely fed up with this job." "Ditto."* "我真是煩透了這個工作。" "我也一樣。"

ditto[2] *n plural* **dittos** [C] a mark (") you use instead of repeating what you have already written, usually immediately above in a list 表示"同上"或"同前"的符號 (")

dit·ty /ˋdɪtɪ; ˈdɪti/ *n* [C] *humorous* a short simple poem or song【幽默】小詩; 短歌謠

di·u·ret·ic /ˌdaɪjuˋrɛtɪk; ˌdaɪjʊˈretɪk◄/ *n* [C] a substance that increases the flow of URINE 利尿劑 —**diuretic** *adj*

di·ur·nal /daɪˋɝnl̩; daɪˈɜːnəl/ *adj technical*【術語】**1** happening in the daytime 白天的, 白晝的 **2** happening every day 每日的, 每天的

Div *n* the written abbreviation of 縮寫= DIVISION

di·van /ˋdaɪvæn; dɪˈvæn/ *n* [C] **1** a bed with a thick base 底部很厚的矮牀 **2** a long low soft seat that has no back or arms〔無靠背或扶手的〕長沙發

dive[1] /daɪv; daɪv/ *v past tense* **dived** also 又作 **dove** /dov; dəʊv/ *AmE*【美】[I]

1 ►JUMP INTO WATER 跳入水中◄ to jump into water with your head and arms first〔頭和胳膊先入水地〕跳水: **[+into/off etc]** *Sally dived expertly into the pool.* 莎莉熟練地跳入水池。| *Diving off the cliffs is very dangerous.* 從懸崖上向下跳水是很危險的。

2 ►GO DEEPER 進入深處◄ to go deeper under water 下潛: *The submarine began to dive.* 潛水艇開始下潛。

3 ►SWIM UNDER WATER 潛水◄ to swim under water using special breathing equipment〔使用特殊呼吸器〕潛水: *frogmen diving for sunken treasure* 在水底潛游尋找沉沒的寶藏的蛙人

4 ►BIRD/AIRCRAFT 鳥/飛行器◄ if a bird or an air-

craft dives, it goes down through the air very quickly and steeply, head first〔指鳥、飛行器〕俯衝
5►JUMP FORWARDS 向前蹦跳◄ [always+adv/prep] to jump forwards or to one side in order to catch something or to avoid something〔為抓到或躲開某物〕跳躍: [**+after/towards/aside etc**] *Jackson dived after the ball.* 傑克遜撲過去搶球。
6►INTO BUILDING/CROWD 進入建築物/人羣中◄ to quickly go into a building or a crowd of people 衝進去: [**+into**] *We dived into a coffee shop to avoid the rain.* 我們衝進一家咖啡廳躲雨。
7 dive into your bag/pockets etc to put your hand into your bag, pockets etc so that you can get something out 把手伸入提包/衣袋等〔取出東西〕

dive in *phr v* [I] **1** to start doing something eagerly and energetically 熱切地開始做某事: *Harvey dived in with several questions.* 哈維開始投入到討論中來，問了幾個問題。**2 dive in!** *spoken* used to invite people to start eating a meal【口】開飯啦!〔用於邀請某人開始用餐〕

D

dive² *n* [C] **1** a jump into the water with your head and arms first 跳水 **2 make a dive for** to move quickly and suddenly towards something 撲向，衝向 **3** *informal* a place such as a bar or club that is cheap and dirty【非正式】廉價而低級的酒吧[俱樂部]: *I've heard the new club's a bit of a dive.* 我聽說新開的那家俱樂部有些低級。

dive-bomb /'· ·/ *v* [I,T] to attack someone or something by flying down towards them from the air 俯衝轟炸

dive bomb·er /'· ,· ·/ *n* [C] a type of military plane that flies low over a place and drops bombs on it 俯衝轟炸機

div·er /ˋdaɪvɚ; 'daɪvə/ *n* [C] **1** someone who swims or works underwater using special breathing equipment 潛水員: *a deep sea diver* 深海潛水員 **2** someone who jumps into water with their head and arms first 跳水者

di·verge /daɪˋvɝdʒ; daɪ'vɜːdʒ/ *v* [I] **1** if two lines or paths diverge, they go in different directions 岔開，分開 **2** if two things diverge, they become different although they used to be the same 開始有分歧，出現不一致: *Our business interests diverged and we had to sell the company.* 我們的商業利益出現了分歧，我們不得不賣掉公司。—opposite 反義詞 CONVERGE

di·ver·gence /daɪˋvɝdʒəns; daɪ'vɜːdʒəns/ *n* [C, U+**between/of**] a difference between two or more things such as opinions or interests〔看法或興趣等的〕差異；分歧

di·ver·gent /daɪˋvɝdʒənt; daɪ'vɜːdʒənt/ *adj* divergent opinions, interests etc are very different from each other〔指看法或興趣等〕不同的，有差異的

di·vers /ˋdaɪvɚz; 'daɪvəz/ *adj* [only before noun 僅用於名詞前] *old-fashioned* of many different kinds【過時】各種各樣的

di·verse /dəˋvɝs; daɪ'vɜːs/ *adj* very different from each other 各不相同的: *subjects as diverse as pop music and archeology* 如流行音樂和考古學一樣完全不同的科目—**diversely** *adv*

di·ver·si·fy /dəˋvɝsə,faɪ; daɪ'vɜːsǐfaɪ/ *v* **1** [I] if a business or a country's ECONOMY¹ (1) diversifies, it starts to produce a range of different products and services, instead of just one or two〔指某企業或國家的經濟〕多元化；從事多種經營: *a publishing company that is diversifying into the software market* 一家正向兼營軟件方面發展的出版公司 **2** [T] to make a business or ECONOMY¹ (1) start to produce a range of different products or services 使〔企業或經濟〕多元化，使開始多種經營 **3** [I,T] to change something so that there is more variety 多元化，使…多樣化—**diversification** /də,vɝsəfəˋkeʃən; də,vɜːsǐfǐ'keɪʃən/ *n* [U]

di·ver·sion /daɪˋvɝʒən; daɪ'vɜːʃən/ *n* **1** [C] something that stops you from paying attention to what you are doing or what is happening 分散注意力的事物；聲東擊西的手段: **create a diversion** (=deliberately take someone's attention away from something else) 轉移注意力 *Some of the prisoners created a diversion while Riggs climbed the wall.* 在里格斯爬牆的時候，一些囚犯故意製造事端以轉移注意力。**2** [C,U] a change in the direction or purpose of something 轉向；改變〔某事物的〕用途: [**+of**] *the massive diversion of resources into the military budget* 把財力大量轉入軍事預算 **3** [C] *formal* an activity that you do for pleasure【正式】消遣；娛樂: *The cinema is always a pleasant diversion.* 看電影一直是非常好的消遣方式。**4** [C] *especially BrE* a different road for traffic to travel on when the usual road cannot be used【尤英】〔正常道路不能使用時的〕臨時支路

di·ver·sion·a·ry /daɪˋvɝʒən,ɛrɪ; daɪ'vɜːʃənəri/ *adj* intended to take someone's attention away from something 轉移注意力的；聲東擊西的

di·ver·si·ty /daɪˋvɝsətɪ; daɪ'vɜːsǐti/ *n* [singular] **1** a range of different people or things; variety〔人或事物的〕多種多樣: *the cultural diversity of the United States* 美國文化的多樣性 | *a diversity of opinion* 眾說紛紜的看法 **2** [U] the quality of having variety and including a wide range of different people or things 多樣性

di·vert /daɪˋvɝt; daɪ'vɜːt/ *v* [T] **1** to change the direction or purpose of something 轉變〔方向或用途〕: *diverted traffic* 改道行駛的車輛 | **divert sth into** *The company should divert more resources into research.* 該公司應該把更多的資源轉用在研究上面。**2 divert attention/criticism etc** to stop people from paying attention to something or criticizing it 轉移注意力/批評等: *The tax cuts diverted attention from the real economic problems.* 減稅把（人們的）注意力從真實存在的經濟問題上轉移了。**3** *formal* to entertain someone【正式】使消遣；使歡娛；使解悶

di·vert·ing /daɪˋvɝtɪŋ; daɪ'vɜːtɪŋ/ *adj formal* entertaining and amusing【正式】有趣的；逗樂的: *a mildly diverting film comedy* 一部略帶逗笑性質的喜劇片

di·vest /daɪˋvɛst; daɪ'vest/ *v*

divest sb **of** sth *phr v* [T] *formal*【正式】**1 divest yourself of** to take off something you are wearing or carrying 脫下〔所穿的衣服等〕；放下〔所拿的東西〕: *Pedro divested himself of his overcoat and boots.* 佩德羅脫下大衣和靴子。**2** to get rid of something that you own 擺脫〔擁有的東西〕: **divest yourself of** *A new minister must divest himself of his business interests.* 一個新任部長必須脫離他的商業利益。**3** to take away someone's power, rights, etc 剝奪〔某人的權力、權利等〕: *The king was divested of all his wealth and power.* 國王被剝奪了一切財富與權力。

di·vest·ment /daɪˋvɛstmənt; daɪ'vestmənt/ *n* [U] *AmE technical* the act of taking your money out of a company or place where you had put it in order to make a profit【美，術語】〔在某公司或某地的〕投資收回; DISINVESTMENT *BrE*【英】

di·vide¹ /dəˋvaɪd; dǐ'vaɪd/ *v*
1►SEPARATE 分開◄ **a)** [T] to separate something such as an area, group, or object into two or more parts 把…分成〔若干部分〕: **divide sth into** *Take the orange and divide it into quarters.* 把橘子拿去，分成四份。| *The USA is divided into 50 states.* 美國分為50個州。| **divide sth between** *He divides his time between his house in Connecticut and New York.* 他一部分時間留在康涅狄格州家裡，另一部分時間留在紐約。**b)** [I] to become separated into two or more different parts 分開，分成幾部分: [**+in/into**] *The cell quickly divides in two.* 該細胞很快分裂成兩個。
2►KEEP SEPARATE 分隔◄ also 又作 **divide off** [T] to keep two areas separate from each other 把〔兩個地區〕隔開: *The Berlin Wall used to divide East and West Berlin.* 過去有柏林牆把東、西柏林給分隔開來。| **divide sth from** *The chapel is divided from the rest of the church by a screen.* 一個圍屏把私人祈禱室和教堂的其他部分分隔開來。
3►SHARE 分享◄ also 又作 **divide up** [T] to separate something into two or more parts and share them be-

tween two or more people 分配, 分享, 共用: **divide sth between/among** *The money is to be divided up equally among the six grandchildren.* 這筆錢將被平分給六個孫兒、孫女。

4 ▶MATHEMATICS 數學◀**a)** [T] to find out how many times one number is contained in another larger number 除, 除以: **divide sth by sth** *Divide 21 by 3.* 21除以3。| **divided by sth** *6 divided by 3 is 2.* 6除以3等於2。**b)** [I] to be contained in another, usually larger, number one or more times 除盡〔一個更大的數〕: [**+into**] *8 divides into 64.* 64可用8除盡。—compare 比較 MULTIPLY (2)

5 ▶DISAGREE 分歧◀[T] to make people disagree with each other and form groups with opposing views 使〔人〕對立, 產生分歧: **be divided over/about** (=disagree about something) 在…上有分歧 *Voters are bitterly divided over the issue of gun control.* 選民在槍支管制問題上有嚴重的分歧。

6 dividing line the difference between two types or groups of similar things 分界線〔指兩種或兩組相似事物之間的區別〕: [**+between**] *There's a thin dividing line between genius and madness.* 在天才與瘋狂之間只有很細微的差別。

7 divide and rule to control people by making them argue or fight with each other instead of opposing you 分而治之〔讓人們相互爭吵或爭鬥而不反對自己, 從而控制他們〕—**divided** *adj*

divide[2] *n* [C usually singular 一般用單數] **1** a difference between two groups of people, especially in their beliefs or way of life, that makes them seem separate from each other〔尤指兩個羣體在信仰或生活方式上的〕差異, 差別: *two politicians on either side of a political divide* 兩個政治立場截然相反的政治家 **2** *AmE* a line of high ground between two river systems; WATERSHED (3)【美】分水嶺; 分水線

divided high·way /ˌ.ˌ.. ˈ../ *n* [C] *AmE* a main road on which the traffic travelling in opposite directions is kept apart by a piece of land or a low fence【美】有分隔帶的雙向公路; 上下行雙線車道; DUAL CARRIAGEWAY *BrE*【英】

3 **div·i·dend** /ˋdɪvəˌdɛnt; ˈdɪvɪ̇dənd/ *n* [C] **1** a part of a company's profit that is divided among the people who have shares (SHARE[2] (5)) in the company 股息, 紅利 **2 pay dividends** if something you do pays dividends, you get an advantage from it later 產生效益; 有好處; 有回報: *All Ken's hard work eventually paid dividends.* 肯恩所付出的極大努力最終有了回報。**3** *BrE* the money you can win in a national competition that involves guessing the results of football games【英】〔猜中足球比賽結果可贏得的〕彩金 **4** *technical* a number that is to be divided by another number【術語】被除數

di·vid·er /dəˋvaɪdɚ; dɪ̇ˈvaɪdə/ *n* [C] **1** something that divides something else into parts〔把某物分成幾部分的〕分隔物; 劃分者; 區劃線 **2** a piece of card that separates pages in a FILE[1] (2)〔用於分隔檔案中文件的〕分隔卡 **3 dividers** [plural] an instrument used for measuring or marking lines or angles, that consists of two pointed pieces of metal joined together at the top 兩腳規; 分線規

div·i·na·tion /ˌdɪvəˋneʃən; ˌdɪvɪ̇ˈneɪʃən/ *n* [U] the act of finding out what will happen in the future by means of special powers, or the ability to do this 占卜(術), 預測; 預言

di·vine[1] /dəˋvaɪn; dɪ̇ˈvaɪn/ *adj* **1** having the qualities of a god or connected with, or coming from God 神的, 上帝的; 神或上帝賦予的: *the authority of divine law* 神的法律的權威 | **divine service** (=a formal ceremony involving prayers etc to God) 向上帝祈禱的儀式; 禮拜 **2 divine help/intervention/inspiration/retribution** help etc from God 上帝[神]的幫助/干預/啟示/懲罰 **3** *old-fashioned* very pleasant or good; WONDERFUL【過時】極好的, 極妙的: *You look simply divine!* 你看起來簡直美極了!

divine[2] *v* **1** [T] *literary* to discover or guess something【文】發現; 猜出: *He must have divined from my expression that I was angry.* 他必定是從我的表情猜出我生氣了。**2** [I] to search for underground water or minerals using a special Y-shaped stick〔用一丫形卜棒〕探測〔地下水、礦牀〕

divine[3] *n* [C] *old use* a priest【舊】牧師, 神父

di·vin·er /dəˋvaɪnɚ; dɪ̇ˈvaɪnə/ *n* [C] someone who searches for underground water or minerals using a special Y-shaped stick〔用一丫形卜棒〕探測地下水[礦牀]者

divine right /.ˌ. ˈ./ *n* **1** [singular] the right given to a king or queen by God to rule a country, that in former times could not be questioned or opposed〔國王或女王統治一個國家的〕神授王權 **2 have a divine right to do sth** *informal* to be able to do what you want without having to ask permission【非正式】有神授之權〔想做甚麼就可做甚麼而不必經人允許〕: *You don't have a divine right to open all my mail, you know.* 你要知道, 你無權隨便拆開我所有的信件。

div·ing /ˋdaɪvɪŋ; ˈdaɪvɪŋ/ *n* [U] **1** the activity of swimming under water using special breathing equipment 潛水 **2** the activity of jumping into water with your head and arms first 跳水: *a diving competition* 跳水比賽

diving bell /ˈ.. ./ *n* [C] a metal container shaped like a bell, in which people can work under water 潛水鐘〔鐘形金屬罩, 人在其中可進行水下工作〕

diving board /ˈ.. ./ *n* [C] a board fixed above a SWIMMING POOL and used for diving〔安裝在游泳池上方的〕跳(水)板

diving suit /ˈ.. ./ *n* [C] a special protective suit worn when swimming deep under water 潛水服

di·vin·ing rod /.ˈ.. ˌ./ *n* [C] a special Y-shaped stick used to search for underground water or minerals〔用於探測地下水或礦牀的〕丫形卜棒

di·vin·i·ty /dəˋvɪnətɪ; dɪ̇ˈvɪnɪ̇ti/ *n* **1** [U] the study of God and religious beliefs; THEOLOGY 神學 **2** [U] the quality or state of being like God or a god 神性; 神力; 神威 **3** [C] God or a god 上帝; 神

divinity school /.ˈ... ˌ./ *n* [C] *AmE* a college where students study to become priests【美】神學院

di·vis·i·ble /dəˋvɪzəbḷ; dɪ̇ˈvɪzɪ̇bəl/ *adj* able to be divided, especially by another number 可分的; 可除盡的: *6 is divisible by 3.* 6可被3除盡。

di·vi·sion /dəˋvɪʒən; dɪ̇ˈvɪʒən/ *n* 3 1

1 ▶SEPARATING 分開◀[C,U] the act of dividing something into different parts or the way it is divided 分開; 分割: [**+between**] *the division between public and private life* 把公眾生活和私生活分開 | [**+of sth into**] *the division of people into winners and losers* 把人分成成功者和失敗者

2 ▶SHARING 分擔◀[C,U] the act of dividing something so that it can be shared or the way it is divided 分配; 分擔; 分享: [**+of sth between**] *the division of power between church and state* 教會與國家之間的權力分配

3 ▶DISAGREEMENT 分歧◀[C,U] a disagreement among the members of a group, especially one that makes them form smaller groups 分歧; 分裂: *There are deep divisions in the party over Europe.* 該黨派在歐洲問題上有嚴重分歧。

4 ▶MATHEMATICS 數學◀[U] the process of finding out how many times one number is contained in another 除; 除法 —compare 比較 MULTIPLICATION (1) —see also 另見 LONG DIVISION

5 ▶PART OF AN ORGANIZATION 某組織的一部分◀[C] a large part of an organization, company etc, consisting of several smaller parts〔機構、公司等的〕部, 部門: *I work in the Computer Services Division.* 我在電腦維修部門工作。

6 ▶SPORT 體育◀[C] *BrE* one of the groups of teams that a sports competition, especially football, is divided into【英】〔尤指足球比賽中球隊被分成的〕級: **the First/Second Division** *Brighton play in the Second Division.* 布賴頓隊參加乙級隊比賽。

7 ▶ARMY 軍隊◀[C] a part of an army larger than a

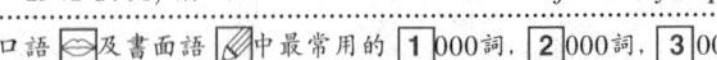

BRIGADE (1) 師: *the Guards Division* 近衛師
8 ►IN PARLIAMENT 在議會◄ [C] *technical* a process in which members of the British parliament vote for something by dividing into groups【術語】〔英國議會議員進行的〕分組表決: *MP's forced a division on the bill.* 下議院議員強行將該議案進行分組表決。

di·vi·sion·al /dəˋvɪʒənḷ; dɪ̵ˈvɪʒənəl/ *adj* connected with a DIVISION (=one of the parts into which a large organization or army is divided) 部門的; 師的: *divisional headquarters* 師指揮部

division bell /·ˈ··· ·/ *n* [C] a bell that is rung to tell members of the British parliament to vote 英國議會告知議員即將進行分組表決的通知鈴

division lob·by /·ˈ·· ˌ··/ *n* [C] one of the two places to which a British Member of Parliament must go to vote 投票廳〔英國議會議員進行分組投票的兩個地點之一〕

division of la·bour /·ˌ·· · ˈ··/ *n* [C,U] a way of organizing work in which each member of a group has a particular job to do 分工

D

di·vi·sive /dəˋvaɪsɪv; dɪ̵ˈvaɪsɪv/ *adj* having the effect of dividing people into groups with opposing opinions 造成不和的, 導致分裂的: *Religious schools were seen as socially divisive.* 宗教派別曾被認為是導致社會分裂的一個因素。

di·vi·sor /dəˋvaɪzɚ; dɪ̵ˈvaɪzə/ *n* [C] *technical* the number by which another number is to be divided【術語】除數

3 **di·vorce¹** /dəˋvɔrs; dɪ̵ˈvɔːs/ *n* **1** [C,U] the legal ending of a marriage 離婚: *In Britain, one in three marriages ends in divorce.* 在英國, 三分之一的婚姻以離婚告終。| **get a divorce** *Why doesn't she get a divorce?* 她為甚麼不離婚呢? | **divorce case** (=the legal process of divorce) 離婚訴訟 | **divorce proceedings** (=the official actions to legally end your marriage) 離婚訴訟; 離婚手續 | **divorce rate** (=the number of divorces each year) 離婚率 | **divorce settlement** (=the legal decision about how much money, property etc you get after a divorce) 離婚財產協議 —compare 比較 SEPARATION (2) **2** [C] a separation of ideas, subjects, values etc〔觀念、主題、價值觀等的〕分歧, 脱離: **[+between]** *the divorce between power and ideology* 權力與思想意識的分離

divorce² *v* **1** [I,T] if someone divorces their husband or wife, or if two people divorce, they legally end their marriage (與...) 離婚: *David's parents divorced when he was six.* 大衛的父母在他六歲時就離婚了。**2** [T] to separate two ideas, subjects, values etc completely 把...完全分開; 徹底區分: **divorce sth from** *It is difficult to divorce sport from politics.* 把體育與政治完全分開是很困難的。| **be divorced from reality** (=not based on real things or sensible thinking) 脱離現實 *Some of his ideas are completely divorced from reality.* 他的一些想法完全脱離實際。

di·vorced /dəˋvɔrst; dɪ̵ˈvɔːst/ *adj* no longer married to your former wife or husband 已離婚的: *75% of divorced women remarry.* 75% 的離婚婦女再婚。| **get divorced** (=legally end your marriage) 離婚 *My parents are getting divorced.* 我父母正在辦離婚。

di·vor·cee /dəˌvɔrˋsi; dɪ̵ˌvɔːˈsiː/ *n* someone who is no longer legally married to their former wife or husband 離了婚的人

div·ot /ˋdɪvət; ˈdɪvət/ *n* [C] a small piece of earth and grass that you dig out accidentally while playing sport〔體育運動時無意間〕削起的一小塊泥土[草皮]

di·vulge /dəˋvʌldʒ; daɪˈvʌldʒ/ *v* [T] to give someone information, especially about something secret 泄露; 透露〔祕密〕: *Staff may not divulge confidential information.* 員工不能泄露機密資料。| **divulge sth to sb** *Do not divulge the conclusions of the report to anyone.* 不要向任何人泄露這份報告的結論。| **divulge what/where etc** *Adams refused to divulge what he had done with the money.* 亞當斯拒絕透露他是如何處理那筆錢的。| **divulge your sources** (=say who told you) 泄露消息的來源

div·vy /ˋdɪvɪ; ˈdɪvi/ *n* [C] *BrE slang* a stupid person【英俚】傻瓜

Di·wa·li /dɪˋwɑlɪ; dɪˈwɑːli/ *n* an important Hindu FESTIVAL (2) that is celebrated in the autumn 排燈節〔在秋季舉行的印度的重大節日〕

Dix·ie /ˋdɪksɪ; ˈdɪksi/ *n* [singular] *AmE informal* the southern states of the US【美, 非正式】美國南部各州

dix·ie·land /ˋdɪksɪˌlænd; ˈdɪksilænd/ *n* [U] a type of JAZZ (1) with a strong rhythm 迪克西蘭爵士樂

DIY /ˌdi aɪ ˋwaɪ; ˌdiː aɪ ˈwaɪ/ *n* [U] *especially BrE* do-it-yourself; the activity of making or repairing things yourself instead of buying them or paying someone else to do it【尤英】自己動手〔do-it-yourself的縮寫, 指自己動手做東西或修理東西〕

dizzy 頭暈目眩的

diz·zy /ˋdɪzɪ; ˈdɪzi/ *adj* **1** feeling unable to balance, especially after spinning around or because you feel ill〔因旋轉或生病而〕頭暈目眩的: *Greg felt sick and dizzy in the hot sun.* 格雷格在大太陽底下曬得噁心頭暈。| **dizzy spell** (=a short period when you feel dizzy) 一陣頭暈 **2 the dizzy heights** *humorous* an important position【幽默】令人眩暈的高處〔指重要的職位〕: *Naomi had reached the dizzy heights of manageress.* 納奧米已經高居經理的寶座。**3** *informal* careless and forgetful【非正式】粗心大意的; 心不在焉的; 糊塗健忘的: *A dizzy blonde works at the front desk.* 一個糊裡糊塗的金髮女郎在前台工作。**4 dizzy height/peak** *literary* a dizzy height or peak is very high【文】令人頭暈的高度/頂峯 —**dizzily** *adv* —**dizziness** *n* [U]

DJ /ˌdi ˋdʒe; ˌdiː ˈdʒeɪ◂/ *n* [C] a disc jockey; someone who plays records on a radio show or in a club〔電台〕音樂唱片節目主持人;〔夜總會〕舞曲唱片播放員, 唱片騎師

djinn /dʒɪn; dʒɪn/ *n* [C] a magical spirit in Arab fairy stories; GENIE〔阿拉伯童話故事中的〕精靈; 神怪

DNA /ˌdi ɛn ˋe; ˌdiː en ˈeɪ/ *n* [U] an acid that carries GENETIC information in a cell 脱氧核糖核酸

do¹ /du; duː/ *auxiliary verb past tense* **did** /dɪd; dɪd/ *past participle* **done** /dʌn; dʌn/ *3rd person singular present tense* **does** /dəz; dəz *strong* 強讀 dʌz; dʌz/
1 ►IN QUESTIONS/NEGATIVES 在疑問句/否定句中◄ **a)** used with another verb to form questions or negatives〔與另一動詞連用, 構成疑問句或否定句〕: *Do you like bananas?* 你喜歡吃香蕉嗎? | *I don't feel like going out tonight.* 我今天晚上不想出門。| *Ian didn't answer.* 伊恩沒有回答。| *Where do you live?* 你住在哪兒? | *Doesn't Rosie look wonderful?* 羅茜看上去是不是特別精神? | *Don't just stand there – do something!* 別光站在那兒——想點辦法! | *Why don't you come for the weekend?* (=please come) 你來我們這兒度週末好不好? | *Don't let's invite her.* (=let's not invite her) 我們別邀請她。**b)** *especially spoken* used to form QUESTION TAGS【尤口】〔用於構成附加疑問句〕: *You know Tony, don't you?* 你認識東尼, 是不是? | *She didn't pay cash, did she?* 她沒付現金, 對不對?
2 ►FOR EMPHASIS 表示強調◄ used to give emphasis to the main verb〔用於強調主要動詞〕: *Do take care!* 一定要小心! | *"Why didn't you tell me?" "I did tell you."* "你怎麼不告訴我呢?" "我確實告訴你了。" | *He owns, or did own, a yacht.* 他擁有, 或者說曾經擁有, 一艘遊艇。
3 ►IN POLITE REQUESTS 用於禮貌的請求◄ used as a polite way of offering someone something〔用於在給某人某物時表示禮貌〕: *Do have a cup of tea.* 來, 請喝一杯茶。
4 ►INSTEAD OF VERB 代替動詞◄ used to avoid repeating another verb〔用於避免重複某一動詞〕: *Omar speaks English better than he did.* (=better than he used to speak it) 奧馬爾的英語說得比以前好了。| *"You broke my pencil!" "No I didn't!"* "你弄斷了我的鉛筆!" "我沒

有！" | *"You left the door open." "So I did."* (=you are right) "你沒關門。" "沒錯。" | *"Will Kay come?" "She may do."* "凱能來嗎?" "或許能來。" | *"You ought to phone your mother." "I have done."* "你應該給你媽打個電話。" "我已經打過了。" | *So he plays the piano, does he?* 那麼他會彈鋼琴, 對吧? | **so do I** *Emma loves chocolate, and so do I.* 艾瑪愛吃巧克力, 我也愛吃。| **neither do I** *"I don't want any more." "Neither do I."* "我不想再要了。" "我也不想。"
5 what is sb/sth doing? used to ask why someone or something is in a particular place, when you think they should not be there 某人/某物怎麼會在這[那]裡?〔你認為不該在那兒〕: *What's this cake doing on the floor?* 蛋糕怎麼會在地板上? | *What was that man doing in our garden anyway?* 那個人到我們的花園來幹甚麼?
6 ►WITH ADVERB 與副詞連用◄ used to reverse the order of the subject and the verb when an adverb or adverbial phrase starts a sentence〔以副詞或副詞詞組引出句子時用以調換主語和動詞的語序〕: *Not only did I see him, I spoke to him, too.* 我不僅見到了他, 還和他說話了。

Frequencies of the verb **do** in spoken and written English 動詞 do 在英語口語和書面語中的使用頻率

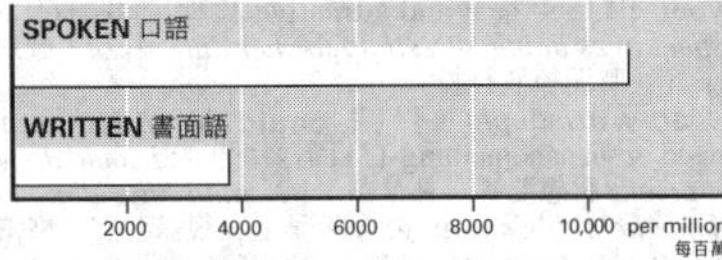

Based on the British National Corpus and the Longman Lancaster Corpus
據英國國家語料庫和朗文蘭卡斯特語料庫

This graph shows that the verb **do** is much more common in spoken English than in written English. This is because it is used to form questions and negatives and is used in some common spoken phrases. 本圖表顯示, 動詞 do 在英語口語中的使用頻率遠遠高於書面語。因為該詞用以形成疑問句和否定句, 而且一些常用片語是由 do 構成的。

do up 繫上, 扣上

She's doing up her blouse. 她在扣上襯衫。

She's undoing her blouse. 她在解開襯衫。

1 1 **do²** *v*
1 ►ACTIVITY/JOB 活動/工作◄ [T] to PERFORM (2) and finish a particular activity or job 做, 幹; 履行; 完成: *Have you done your homework yet?* 你做完家庭作業了嗎? | *Jo does aerobics three times a week.* 喬每星期做三次增氧健身操。| *It's a pleasure doing business with you.* 很高興跟你做生意。| **do the dishes/washing up/laundry etc** *It's your turn to do the washing.* 輪到你洗衣服了。—see 見 JOB (USAGE), MAKE[1] (USAGE)
2 do your hair/teeth/nails to spend time making your hair look nice, brushing your teeth etc 做頭髮/刷牙/修剪指甲: *Jan spends ages doing her hair in the mornings.* 簡早上會花很長時間做頭髮。
3 what do you do (for a living)? *spoken* used to ask someone what their job is【口】你是做甚麼工作的?
4 ►SUCCEED/FAIL 成功/失敗◄ [I] used to ask or say whether someone is being successful〔用於詢問或講述某人目前是否很成功〕: *How are you doing?* 你幹得怎麼樣? | **[+with/in etc]** *How are you doing in your new job?* 你的新工作幹得怎麼樣? | **do well/badly** *The children are doing very well at school.* 孩子們在學校學得很好。
5 do nothing for/do a lot for etc [T] to have a particular effect on something or someone 對…沒有效果/有很大效果等: **do nothing for sb** (=not improve someone's appearance) 沒有改善某人的外貌 *That colour does nothing for her.* 那種顏色並沒有讓她好看一些。| **do a lot for** (=have a good effect on) 對…有好的效果 *Getting the job has done a lot for her self-esteem.* 得到這份工作對她的自尊心很有好處。| **do wonders for** (=have a very good effect on) 對…有極好的效果 *Moving to the city has done wonders for my social life.* 搬到城市裡極大地改善了我的社交生活。
6 ►SPEND TIME 花時間◄ [T] *informal* to spend a period of time doing something difficult or something that you have to do【非正式】度過〔一段時間, 做某種困難的或不得不做的事情〕: *I did two years of teaching before that.* 在那以前我教了兩年書。
7 ►FOOD 食物◄ [T] *informal* to make a particular kind of food【非正式】做〔某種食品〕: *I was thinking of doing a casserole tonight.* 我正考慮着晚上弄一個砂鍋來吃。
8 ►A SERVICE 某項服務◄ [T] to provide a particular service 提供〔某項服務〕: *Do you do theatre bookings here?* 你們這裡能訂戲票嗎? | *We don't do food after 2 o'clock.* 我們兩點以後就不供應食物了。
9 ►COPY 模仿◄ [T] *informal* to copy someone's behaviour, in order to entertain people【非正式】模仿〔某人的舉止來逗樂〕: *He does Clinton very well.* 他模仿克林頓像極了。
10 ►STUDY 學習◄ [T not in passive 不用被動態] *BrE* to study a particular subject in a school or university【英】〔在學校或大學裡〕學習, 攻讀, 研究〔某門課程〕: *I did French for 5 years.* 我學了5年法語。
11 do sb good to make someone feel better, more cheerful etc 對某人有好處: *A break will do you good.* 休息一下會對你有好處。
12 do 10 miles/do 20 kms etc to achieve a particular speed, distance etc 走完 10 英里/20 公里等: *We did 300 miles on the first day.* 第一天我們走了 300 英里的路程。| *The car can do 120 mph.* 這車能達到 120 英里的時速。
13 ►VISIT 參觀◄ [T] to visit a particular place, especially when you are going to see a lot of other places 參觀, 遊覽〔某一個地方, 尤指還要參觀其他許多地方時〕: *Let's do the Eiffel Tower today and the Pompidou Centre tomorrow.* 咱們今天去參觀埃菲爾鐵塔, 明天遊覽龐比杜中心。
14 ►ENOUGH/SUITABLE 足夠的/合適的◄ *especially spoken* [I,T not in progressive 不用進行式] used to say that something will be enough or be suitable【尤口】〔某物〕足夠; 合適: **[+for]** *Ten bottles of wine should do for the party.* 為派對準備十瓶酒應該足夠了。| *That vase would do for your Mum's birthday present.* 買那個花瓶給你媽媽作生日禮物很合適。| *"I've got a saucepan." "That'll do."* "我有一個平底鍋。" "那就可以了。" |

should/will do sb *Here's £20 – that should do you.* 這裡有20英鎊，應該夠你花的了。| **should/will do sb for** *A few sandwiches will do us for lunch.* 幾塊三明治就夠我們午餐吃的了。

15 that will do! *spoken* used to tell a child that you want them to stop behaving in the way they are behaving【口】夠了!〔用於命令孩子停止某種行為〕

16 do as you're told *spoken* used to tell a child to behave in the way you tell them to【口】告訴你怎麼做，你就怎麼做〔用於告誡孩子聽從吩咐〕

17 would do well to do sth used to advise someone that they should do something〔建議某人〕最好做某事: *You'd do well to avoid that restaurant.* 你最好別去那家餐廳。

18 ►CHEAT 欺騙◄ [T] *BrE spoken* to cheat someone【英口】欺騙〔某人〕: *That painting's a fake. You've been done.* 那幅畫是贋品，你上當了。

19 ►PUNISH 懲罰◄ [T] *BrE spoken* to punish someone【英口】懲罰〔某人〕: *Your Dad'll do you when he finds out.* 要是你爸知道了，他會揍你的。| **get done** *I got done for speeding yesterday.* 我昨天因超速行駛被罰了。

20 do it *informal* to have sex【非正式】性交

21 ►HAPPEN 發生◄ [I] *spoken* to happen【口】發生: *What's doing at your place tonight?* 你們那兒今晚有甚麼活動?

22 do sth to death to talk about or do something so often that it becomes boring 頻繁地談論[做]某事而讓人厭煩: *That joke has been done to death.* 那個笑話人人在說，真是聽得膩死人了。

23 do well by sb to treat someone well 善待某人: *He's left home, but he still does well by his kids.* 他已經離開家另外過了，但他仍然對孩子們很好。—see also 另見 **do your bit** (BIT¹ (15)), **how do you do** (HOW¹ (10)), **nothing doing** (NOTHING¹ (13)), **do sb proud** (PROUD (4))

do away with sb/sth *phr v* [T] **1** to get rid of something so that it does not exist any longer 擺脫，廢除: *The government has done away with free eye tests for everyone.* 政府已不再為大家提供免費眼科檢查。**2** *informal* to kill someone【非正式】殺死，除掉〔某人〕

do sb **down** *phr v* [T] *BrE informal* to criticize someone, especially when they are not there【英，非正式】〔尤指背後〕批評〔某人〕，中傷

do for sb/sth *phr v* [T] **1 what will you do for sth?** *spoken* used to ask someone what arrangements they have made for a particular thing【口】〔用於詢問某人為某事做了甚麼安排?〕: *What will you do for transport tonight?* 今天晚上的車你是怎麼安排的? **2** *BrE slang* to kill someone【英俚】除掉，殺死〔某人〕**3** *old-fashioned* to make someone feel so tired that they cannot do anything【過時】使感到疲憊不堪；使累得動不了: *All that travelling around really did for me.* 到處旅行真把我給累死了。| **be done for** *I'm going to bed, I'm done for.* 我要上牀睡覺去，我都累死了。**4** *BrE old-fashioned* to have a job cleaning someone else's house, cooking for them etc【英，過時】〔替別人〕料理家務

do in *phr v* [T] **1** [**do** sb ↔ **in**] *informal* to kill someone【非正式】殺死〔某人〕: *They say Bates did his wife in.* 他們說貝茨把他妻子給殺了。**2** [**do** sb **in**] to make someone feel extremely tired 使〔某人〕筋疲力盡: *That walk really did me in.* 走了那麼多路真是把我累壞了。

do sth ↔ **out** *phr v* [T] **1** to make a room look nice by decorating it 裝飾〔房間〕: *The room was beautifully done out in pastel colours.* 這個房間用柔和的色彩粉刷過。**2** *informal especially BrE* to clean a room or cupboard thoroughly【非正式，尤英】徹底清掃，清理〔房間或櫥櫃〕: *I'll do out the kitchen cupboards tonight.* 今晚我要把廚房的碗櫥清理一下。

do sb **out of** sth *phr v* [T often passive 常用被動態] *informal* to cheat someone by not giving them something that they deserve, or something that they are owed【非正式】剝奪〔某人應得的東西〕；騙取〔某人的東西〕: *I was done out of £10 in the shop this morning.* 今天早上我在商店裡被騙走了10英鎊。

do over *phr v* [T] **1** [**do** sth ↔ **over**] to decorate a room, wall etc 裝飾〔房間、牆壁等〕**2** [**do** sth **over**] *AmE* to do something again because you did it wrong the first time【美】把〔某事〕重新做一遍: *Your homework's full of mistakes, you'd better do it over.* 你的家庭作業錯誤連篇，你最好重做一遍。**3** [**do** sth ↔ **over**] *slang* to steal things from a place【俚】偷〔某處〕的東西: *The factory was done over last night.* 這家工廠昨夜被盜了。**4** [**do** sb ↔ **over**] *BrE slang* to attack and injure someone【英俚】襲擊，傷害〔某人〕

do up *phr v* **1** [I,T] to fasten or tie 繫上，扣上: *This skirt does up at the back.* 這條裙子在後面繫扣。| **do** sth ↔ **up** *I can't do my shoelaces up.* 我鞋帶繫不上了。| *Do up your coat or you'll be cold.* 把大衣扣好，不然你會凍着的。—see 見 OPEN² (USAGE) **2** [T **do** sth ↔ **up**] to repair or redecorate a building or old car, so that it looks much better 修理〔汽車〕；重新裝修〔房子〕: *They did up the house and sold it for a vast profit.* 他們把房子重新裝修後賣出去，賺了不少錢。**3 do yourself up** to make yourself look neat and attractive 梳妝，打扮自己: *Sue spent ages doing herself up for her date.* 蘇為了赴約花了好長時間梳妝打扮。

do with sth *phr v* [T] **1 could do with** *spoken* to need or want something【口】需要，想要: *I could do with a drink.* 我想要喝一杯飲料。| *I could have done with some help this morning.* 今天早上我很需要有人來幫幫忙。**2 what you do with yourself** what you spend your time doing 怎樣過的，如何打發時間的: *What do you do with yourself when you're not working?* 你不工作的時候幹些甚麼? | **not know what to do with yourself** *June didn't know what to do with herself after she retired.* 茱恩退休後不知道該如何打發時間。**3 what shall we do with?/what have you done with?** *spoken* used to ask someone about arrangements that have been made or something that has been done【口】做了甚麼安排?/做了甚麼事?: *What shall we do with the kids while you're working?* 你上班的時候，孩子們怎麼辦? | *I can't find my pen, what have you done with it?* 我找不到鋼筆，你把它弄哪去了? **4 have/be to do with** to have a connection with something 與…有關: *The programme is to do with mental illness.* 這個計劃與精神病有關。| **be nothing to do with you** (=used to say that someone should not ask about something) 與某人無關 *What I do when you're out is nothing to do with you.* 你不在時我做了些甚麼與你無關。| **not have anything to do with** (=not have any connection with) 與…沒有任何關係 *This question doesn't have anything to do with the main topic of the survey.* 這個問題與調查的主題沒有任何關係。| **be something to do with** (=having some connection, but you are not sure what) 似乎與…有關 *Judy's job is something to do with marketing.* 朱迪的工作好像與市場銷售有關。**5 what is someone doing with?** used to ask why someone has something 為甚麼某人拿某物?: *What are you doing with my diary?* 你拿我的日記幹甚麼?

do without *phr v* **1** [I,T] to manage to live without something or someone 沒有…也行；將就: *I can't afford a car, so I guess I'll just have to do without.* 我買不起汽車，所以也就只好將就着不用了。| **do without sth** *You'll have to do without your dinner if you don't get back in time.* 你如果不準時回來就別吃飯了。**2 can do without** used to say that you prefer not to have something 寧可沒有…: *"Oh shut up, I can do without all this hassle."* "噢，閉嘴，別跟我吵了。"

do³ *n* [C] *informal*【非正式】**1** a party or other social event 聚會；其他社交活動: *Are you going to this do at John's tonight?* 約翰家今晚舉辦的晚會你去嗎? **2 dos and don'ts** things that you must and must not do in a particular situation 該做的和不該做的事情

do⁴, doh /do; dəʊ/ *n* [singular,U] the first or eighth note in a musical SCALE[1] (8) according to the SOL-FA system 全音階中的第一[第八]音

D.O.A. /ˌdi o ˋe; ˌdiː əʊ ˈeɪ/ *adj AmE* dead on arrival; someone who is dead on arrival is declared to be dead as soon as they are brought to a hospital【美】〔指某人〕送到醫院時已經死亡

d.o.b. the written abbreviation of 縮寫= date of birth 出生日期

doc /dɑk; dɒk/ *n* [C] *spoken* a doctor【口】醫生, 大夫

do·cent /doˋsɛnt; dəʊˈsent/ *n* [C] *AmE*【美】**1** a university teacher 大學老師 **2** someone who guides visitors through a MUSEUM, etc〔博物館等的〕嚮導; 講解員

do·cile /ˋdɑsḷ; ˈdəʊsaɪl/ *adj* quiet and easily controlled 安靜的; 容易控制的; 溫順的: *a docile child* 溫順的孩子 —**docilely** *adv*—**docility** /doˋsɪlətɪ; dəʊˈsɪlʒti/ *n* [U]

dock¹ /dɑk; dɒk/ *n* **1** [C] a place in a port where ships are loaded and unloaded 碼頭: *A crowd was waiting at the dock to greet them.* 一羣人在碼頭等着迎接他們。| **in dock** *The ship is now in dock for repairs.* 這艘船目前正在船塢裡等待修理。—see also 另見 DRY DOCK **2** [C] the part of a law court where the person being tried (TRY[1] (6)) stands 被告席 **3** [C,U] a plant with thick green leaves that grows wild in Britain〔英國的〕厚葉野草; 酸模

dock² *v* **1** [I,T] if a ship docks or you dock a ship, it sails into a dock (使)〔船〕進港[進碼頭]: *We'll be docking in about half an hour.* 大約半小時後我們就要進港了。**2** **dock sb's wages/pay** to reduce the amount of money you pay someone 扣某人的工資/薪酬: *Your wages will be docked if you're away for too long.* 如果你出去太久就會被扣工資。**3** [I] if two spaceships dock, they join together in space〔指宇宙飛船在太空〕對接 **4** [T] to cut an animal's tail short 剪短〔動物的尾巴〕

dock·er /ˋdɑkɚ; ˈdɒkə/ *n* [C] *BrE* someone whose job is loading and unloading ships; LONGSHORE-MAN, STEVEDORE【英】碼頭工人

dock·et /ˋdɑkɪt; ˈdɒkʒt/ *n* [C] **1** *technical* a short document used in business that shows what is in a package or describes goods that are being delivered【術語】包裝單據〈如包裹單或送貨單〉; 貨物標籤 **2** *AmE law* a list of legal cases (CASE[1] (9a)) that will take place in a particular court【美, 法律】備審案件目錄表

dock·land /ˋdɑklənd; ˈdɒklənd/ [U] also 又作 **docklands** *plural n* [U] *BrE* the area surrounding the place where ships are loaded and unloaded in a large port【英】港區; 碼頭區

dock·side /ˋdɑkˌsaɪd; ˈdɒksaɪd/ *n* [singular] the area around the place in a port where ships are loaded and unloaded 碼頭鄰區; 碼頭邊

dock·yard /ˋdɑkˌjɑrd; ˈdɒkjɑːd/ *n* [C] a place where ships are repaired or built 船塢; 修船廠; 造船廠

2 **doc·tor¹** /ˋdɑktɚ; ˈdɒktə/ *n* [C] **1** someone who is trained
1 to treat people who are ill 醫生, 大夫: **go to a doctor/see a doctor** *I think you'd better go to the doctor about your chest.* 我想你最好找個醫生看看你的胸部。| **Doctor Smith/Brown etc** *I'd like to make an appointment to see Doctor Pugh.* 我想預約皮尤醫生看病。**2** someone who holds the highest level of degree given by a university 博士: *a Doctor of Law* 法學博士 **3** *AmE* a way of addressing or referring to a DENTIST【美】〔用於稱呼或指牙醫〕

doctor² *v* [T] **1** to dishonestly change something in order to make it seem better 竄改, 偽造: *The figure had been doctored to read $5,000 instead of $500.* 數字經竄改從500元變成了5,000元。**2** to add a substance, especially a drug or poison, to food or drink 將某物質〔尤指藥物或毒藥〕放入〔食物或飲料中〕: *Paul suspected that his drink had been doctored.* 保羅懷疑他的飲料被人做了手腳。**3** to remove the sex organs of an animal, especially a cat or dog, so that it cannot produce babies 閹割〔貓、狗等〕

doc·tor·al /ˋdɑktərəl; ˈdɒktərəl/ *adj* [only before noun 僅用於名詞前] done as part of work for the university degree of DOCTOR[1] (2) 博士(學位)的: *a doctoral thesis on Kant* 一篇關於康德的博士論文

doc·tor·ate /ˋdɑktərɪt; ˈdɒktərʒt/ *n* [C] a university degree of the highest level 博士學位

Doctor of Phi·los·o·phy /ˌ..·..ˈ.../ *n* [C] a PHD 哲學博士

doc·tri·naire /ˌdɑktrɪˋnɛr; ˌdɒktrʒˈneə/ *adj formal* certain that your beliefs or opinions are completely correct and unable to consider the practical problems involved in making them work【正式】教條主義的; 空談理論的; 脫離實際的: *a facile doctrinaire argument* 膚淺的、純理論的論點

doc·trine /ˋdɑktrɪn; ˈdɒktrʒn/ *n* [C] a belief or set of beliefs that form the main part of a religion or system of ideas 信條; 教義; 主義; 學說: *the doctrine of predestination* 宿命論的學說—**doctrinal** /ˋdɑktrɪnḷ; dɒkˈtraɪnl/ *adj*

doc·u·dra·ma /ˋdɑkjuˌdrɑmə; ˈdɒkjʊˌdrɑːmə/ *n* [C] *AmE* a film, usually for television, that presents a true story as a play【美】文獻(電視)片, 紀實片

doc·u·ment¹ /ˋdɑkjəmənt; ˈdɒkjʒmənt/ *n* [C] a piece 2
of paper that gives official written information about something 文件; 公文: *legal documents* 法律文件

doc·u·ment² /ˋdɑkjəˌmɛnt; ˈdɒkjʒment/ *v* [T] to write about something, film it, or take photographs of it, in order to record information about it〔通過記述、拍電影或拍照片的方式來〕記載: *photographs documenting the early history of the motor car* 記錄汽車早期歷史的照片

doc·u·men·ta·ry¹ /ˌdɑkjəˋmɛntərɪ; ˌdɒkjʒˈmentəri◂/ *n* [C] a film or television programme that gives facts and information about something 紀錄片: [+**on/about**] *a documentary about volcanoes* 關於火山的記錄片

documentary² *adj* **1** **documentary film/programme** a film or television programme that gives facts and information about something 紀錄片/紀實(電視)節目 **2** [only before noun 僅用於名詞前] documentary proof or evidence is proof in the form of documents〔證據等〕書面的; 文件形式的

doc·u·men·ta·tion /ˌdɑkjəmɛnˋteʃən; ˌdɒkjʒmənˈteɪʃən/ *n* [U] official documents that are used to prove that something is true or correct〔用於引證的〕文件證據; 證件

DOD the written abbreviation of 縮寫= the US Department of Defence 美國國防部

dod·der /ˋdɑdɚ; ˈdɒdə/ *v* [I] to walk in an unsteady way shaking slightly, especially because you are very old〔尤指因年老〕步履不穩; 走路搖晃

dod·der·ing /ˋdɑdərɪŋ; ˈdɒdərɪŋ/ *adj informal* shaking slightly and unable to walk properly because you are old or ill【非正式】〔因年老體病而〕顫抖的, 蹣跚而行的

dod·dery /ˋdɑdərɪ; ˈdɒdəri/ *adj informal* weak and unable to walk properly or do things quickly because you are old or ill【非正式】〔因年老或生病而〕虛弱的; 步履蹣跚的; 做事緩慢的: *Some of the patients are a bit doddery.* 有些病人有點虛弱。

dod·dle /ˋdɑdḷ; ˈdɒdl/ *n* **be a doddle** *BrE informal* to be extremely easy【英, 非正式】...是輕而易舉的事情: *The exam was a doddle!* 這次考試太簡單了!

dodge¹ /dɑdʒ; dɒdʒ/ *v* **1** [T] to move quickly in order to avoid being hit by someone or something〔快速〕躲開, 避開, 閃開: *I managed to dodge the shot that came flying through the air.* 我設法避開了飛來的一球。—see picture on page A22 參見A22頁圖 **2** [I always+adv/prep] to move quickly in a particular direction to avoid someone or something 快速朝某方向移動; 躲閃: [+**into/out/behind**] *He dodged in and out of the traffic.* 他在車流中東躲西閃。**3** [T] to avoid a law or unpleasant duty in a dishonest way 逃避〔法律制裁或令人不快的責任〕: *Senator O'Brian skillfully dodged the crucial question.* 奧布賴恩參議員巧妙地迴避了這一關鍵問題。**4** **dodge the issue** to avoid considering or discussing something that needs to be dealt with 迴避問題〔對需要處理的事情不予考慮或討論〕

dodge² *n* [C] **1** *informal* something dishonest you do in order to avoid a responsibility or law【非正式】〔為逃避法律或責任而使用的〕伎倆, 詭計: *Jake was full of clever dodges to avoid paying his debts.* 傑克有的是逃債的詭計。| **tax dodge** *He'll claim the car was a present as a tax dodge.* 為了逃稅, 他將聲稱這輛車是別人送的禮物。 **2 make a dodge** to make a sudden forward or sideways movement to avoid something 躲閃, 避開

dodge ball /ˈ· ·/ *n* [U] a game played by children in which you try to avoid being hit by a large rubber ball thrown by the other players〔兒童玩的〕躲球遊戲〔盡量躲開別的孩子投過來的大橡膠球〕

dodg·em car /ˈdɑdʒəm ˌkɑr; ˈdɒdʒəm kɑː/ *n* [C] *BrE* a small electric car that people drive around an enclosed area at a FUNFAIR【英】〔遊樂場中的〕碰碰車; BUMPER CAR *AmE*【美】

dodg·ems /ˈdɑdʒəmz; ˈdɒdʒəmz/ *n* **the dodgems** a form of entertainment at a FUNFAIR in which people drive small electric cars around an enclosed space, chasing and hitting other cars〔遊樂場中的〕碰碰車遊戲: *Let's go on the dodgems.* 我們去玩碰碰車吧。

D

dodg·er /ˈdɑdʒɚ; ˈdɒdʒə/ *n* [C] **tax/draft dodger** someone who uses dishonest methods to avoid paying taxes or serving in the army 逃稅/逃兵役的人

dodg·y /ˈdɑdʒɪ; ˈdɒdʒi/ *adj BrE informal*【英, 非正式】 **1** containing false information, often for a dishonest purpose 含虛假資料的; 不可靠的: *dodgy accounts* 假賬 **2** uncertain or difficult 不確定的; 困難的: *It's a dodgy situation.* 這是個困難的局面。 **3** not working properly 不好使的; 壞了的: *The gears in the car are a bit dodgy.* 這輛車的排擋有些不好使。 **4** dishonest or not to be trusted 不誠實的; 不可信的: *a dodgy character* 一個不可信的傢伙 —**dodginess** *n* [U]

do·do /ˈdodo; ˈdəʊdəʊ/ *n* [C] **1** a large bird that no longer exists and was unable to fly 渡渡鳥〔一種已經滅絕的、不能飛行的大鳥〕 **2** *AmE* a stupid person【美】愚蠢的人, 傻瓜 —see also 另見 **dead as a dodo** (DEAD¹ (14))

doe /do; dəʊ/ *n* [C] a female rabbit, DEER, etc 雌兔; 雌鹿 —compare 比較 BUCK¹ (4)

do·er /ˈduɚ; ˈduːə/ *n* [C] **1** someone who does things instead of just thinking or talking about them 實幹家: *She's a doer, not a thinker.* 她不是個思想家, 而是個實幹家。 **2 evildoer/wrongdoer** someone who does evil or wrong 作惡的人/做錯事的人

does /dəz; dəz; *strong* 強讀 dʌz; dʌz/ the 3rd person singular of the present tense of DO¹ do¹ 的第三人稱單數現在式

does·n't /ˈdʌzn̩t; ˈdʌzənt/ the short form of 縮略式= 'does not'

doff /dɑf; dɒf/ *v* [T] *old-fashioned* to take off a piece of clothing, especially your hat【過時】脫〔衣物, 尤指脫帽〕: *Everyone called him 'Sir' and doffed their hats.* 大家都稱呼他"先生", 並向他脫帽致意。—opposite 反義詞 DON²

dog¹ /dɔg; dɒg/ *n* [C]

1 ►ANIMAL 動物◄ a very common animal that people keep as a pet or to guard a building 狗: *I could hear a dog barking.* 我能聽見狗吠聲。

2 ►MALE ANIMAL 雄性動物◄ a male dog, FOX¹ (1) etc 公狗; 雄狐等 —compare 比較 BITCH¹ (1)

3 be going to the dogs *informal* if an organization is going to the dogs, it is getting much worse and will be difficult to improve【非正式】〔組織〕每況愈下, 趨於衰敗; 一蹶不振: *This country's really going to the dogs!* 這個國家確實在走向崩潰!

4 ►WOMAN 婦女◄ *slang* an offensive word used by men meaning an unattractive woman【俚】醜婆娘, 醜女人〔冒犯用詞〕

5 it's dog eat dog an expression used to describe a situation in which people compete strongly and will do anything to get what they want 殘酷無情的競爭: *Show business isn't all glamour, it's dog eat dog out there.* 娛樂業並不是光有迷人的一面, 其中的競爭十分殘酷。| *Advertising is a dog-eat-dog business.* 廣告業的競爭十分殘酷。

dogs 狗

poodle 長毛狗, 貴婦狗

pekinese 北京狗, 獅子狗, 哈巴狗

dachshund 獵獾狗, 臘腸狗

spaniel 西班牙獵狗

collie 柯利牧羊犬

greyhound 靈缇

Afghan 阿富汗獵犬

German shepherd 德國牧羊犬/ Alsatian *BrE*【英】阿爾薩斯狼狗

Labrador 拉布拉多獵犬

pit bull terrier 鬥牛㹴

dalmatian 大麥町犬, 斑點狗

6 it's a dog's life *spoken* used to say that life is difficult and full of hard work and worry, with very little pleasure【口】苦難的生活

7 not have a dog's chance *informal* to have no chance of being successful【非正式】毫無成功的機會; 毫無希望

8 make a dog's breakfast of sth *BrE informal* to do something very badly【英, 非正式】把某事弄得一團糟: *You've made a real dog's breakfast of putting those shelves up.* 你把那些書架做得太差勁了。

9 be dressed up like a dog's dinner *BrE informal* to be wearing expensive clothes that you think are suitable for a social event, but that other people think are silly【英, 非正式】穿得花裡胡哨; 打扮炫麗

10 dog in the manger someone who will not let other people use or have something, even though they do not need it themselves 狗佔馬槽, 佔着茅坑不拉屎的人

11 every dog has its day an expression used to mean that even the most unimportant person has a time in their life when they are successful and noticed 凡人皆有得意時

12 sth is a dog *AmE informal* used to say that something is very poor quality【美, 非正式】某物質量低劣: *This radio is a dog.* 這個收音機質量很差。

13 the dogs *BrE informal* a sports event which consists of a series of races for dogs【英, 非正式】跑狗比賽

14 put on the dog *AmE old-fashioned* to pretend to be richer than you really are or to know more than you really do【美, 過時】擺闊氣; 擺架子; 裝腔作勢 —see also 另見 DOGHOUSE, **the hair of the dog** (HAIR (10)), SHAGGY DOG STORY, **as sick as a dog** (SICK¹ (1)), **let sleeping dogs lie** (SLEEP¹ (6)), **the tail wagging the dog** (TAIL¹ (11)), **top dog** (TOP² (7)), **treat someone like a dog** (TREAT¹ (1))

dog² *v* **dogged, dogging** [T] **1** if a problem or bad luck dogs you, it causes trouble for a long time〔問題或噩運〕緊隨〔某人〕: *Maradona had been dogged by injury all season.* 馬拉多納整個賽季不斷受傷。**2** to follow close behind someone 跟蹤, 緊跟〔某人〕: *A mob of youths had been dogging us for some time.* 一羣年輕人已經跟着我們好一段時間了。

dog bis·cuit /ˈ· ˌ··/ *n* [C] a small dry hard BISCUIT for dogs〔餵狗的〕小塊硬餅乾

dog·cart /ˈdɔgˌkɑrt; ˈdɒgkɑːt/ *n* [C] **1** a vehicle pulled by a horse, that has two wheels and two seats〔雙輪雙座的〕馬車 **2** a small vehicle pulled by a large dog 狗拉小車

dog·catch·er /ˈdɔgˌkætʃɚ; ˈdɒgˌkætʃə/ *n* [C] *AmE* someone whose job is to collect dogs without owners【美】捕狗員〔專職捕捉沒有主人的狗〕; DOG WARDEN *BrE*【英】

dog col·lar /ˈ· ˌ··/ *n* [C] **1** a collar worn by dogs, onto which a LEAD (=length of leather, rope, chain etc) can be fastened 狗項圈〔可以繫拴狗繩〕**2** a stiff round white collar worn by priests 牧師戴的白色硬圓領, 牧師領

dog days /ˈ· ·/ *n* [plural] *literary* the hottest days of the year【文】盛夏, 三伏天, 酷暑期: *the dog days of summer* 盛夏的日子; 夏三伏

doge /dodʒ; dəʊdʒ/ *n* [C] the highest government official in Venice and in Genoa in the past〔舊時威尼斯和熱那亞的〕總督; 首長

dog-eared /ˈ· ·/ *adj* dog-eared books or papers have been used so much that the corners are turned over or torn〔書或紙等因翻得多而形成〕摺角的: *a dog-eared novel* 一本翻得捲了角的小說 —see picture on page A18 參見A18頁圖

dog-end /ˈ· ·/ *n* [C] **1** *BrE informal* the small part of a cigarette that is left after it has been smoked【英, 非正式】煙蒂, 煙頭 **2** something left over and not considered to be worth very much〔不值錢的〕剩餘物品

dog·fight /ˈdɔgˌfaɪt; ˈdɒgfaɪt/ *n* [C] **1** an organized fight between dogs 鬥狗 **2** a fight between armed aircraft〔戰鬥機的〕空戰

dog·fish /ˈdɔgˌfɪʃ; ˈdɒgˌfɪʃ/ *n* [C] *plural* **dogfish** a kind of small SHARK (1) 角鯊, 星鯊

dog·ged /ˈdɔgɪd; ˈdɒgɪ̇d/ *adj* dogged actions or behaviour show that you are very determined to continue doing something 堅持不懈的, 頑強的, 不屈不撓的: *her dogged determination to succeed* 她那不屈不撓務要成功的決心 —**doggedly** *adv* —**doggedness** *n* [U]

dog·ge·rel /ˈdɔgərəl; ˈdɒgərəl/ *n* [U] poetry that is silly or funny and not intended to be serious 打油詩, 蹩腳詩

dog·gie /ˈdɔgɪ; ˈdɒgi/ *n* [C] another spelling of DOGGY doggy 的另一種拼法

dog·go /ˈdɔgo; ˈdɒgəʊ/ *adv* **lie doggo** *old-fashioned* to stay quiet and still so that people will not notice you or find you【過時】悄悄隱蔽着; 隱伏不動

dog·gone /ˈdɔgˌgɔn; ˈdɒgɒn/ *v* [T] **doggone it** *AmE old-fashioned spoken* used when you are slightly annoyed that something has happened【美, 過時, 口】該死的; 討厭的; 去他的〔用於表示對發生的事有些生氣〕: *The door blew open and, doggone it, if the chickens didn't get loose!* 門被風吹開了, 該死, 雞都跑了! —**doggone, doggoned** *adj*: *That doggone cat!* 那隻討厭的貓!

dog·gy, doggie /ˈdɔgɪ; ˈdɒgi/ *n* [C] **1** a word meaning dog, used especially by or to young children 小狗〔尤為兒語〕**2 doggy style/fashion** a position in which two people have sex that is similar to the position that dogs or other animals use〔指人像狗或其他動物那樣的〕做愛方式

doggy bag /ˈ·· ˌ·/ *n* [C] a small bag for taking home food that is left over from a meal, especially from a restaurant 狗食袋〔顧客把在餐廳吃剩的食品打包帶走的小袋子〕

doggy pad·dle /ˈ·· ˌ··/ *n* DOG PADDLE 狗爬式游泳(法)

dog han·dler /ˈ· ˌ··/ *n* [C] a police officer who works with a trained dog 攜帶警犬值勤的警察

dog·house /ˈdɔgˌhaʊs; ˈdɒghaʊs/ *n* **be in the doghouse** *informal* to be in a situation in which someone is annoyed with you because you have done something wrong【非正式】〔因做錯事而〕惹得某人生氣: *I'm in the doghouse because I forgot Sam's birthday.* 由於我把山姆的生日給忘了, 所以很受埋怨。

do·gie /ˈdogɪ; ˈdəʊgi/ *n* [C] *AmE* a baby cow without a mother【美】〔無母牛的〕牛犢

dog·leg /ˈdɔgˌlɛg; ˈdɒgleg/ *n* [C] a place in a road, path etc where it changes direction suddenly〔道路等的〕急轉彎

dog·like /ˈ· ·/ *adj* faithful and loving without asking for anything for yourself〔像狗一樣〕忠誠的, 無私的: *doglike fidelity* 像狗一樣的忠誠

dog·ma /ˈdɔgmə; ˈdɒgmə/ *n* [C,U] a fixed belief, or set of beliefs that people are expected to accept without question 教條; 教義; 教理: *party dogma* 黨派的信條

dog·mat·ic /dɔgˈmætɪk; dɒgˈmætɪk/ *adj* having ideas or beliefs that you are completely certain about and expect other people to accept without question 自以為是的; 固執己見的; 武斷的: *Her staff find her bossy and dogmatic.* 她的員工發現她是個愛指揮別人、自以為是的人。—**dogmatically** /-klɪ; -kli/ *adv*

dog·ma·tise /ˈdɔgməˌtaɪz; ˈdɒgmətaɪz/ *v* a British spelling of DOGMATIZE dogmatize 的英式拼法

dog·ma·tis·m /ˈdɔgməˌtɪzəm; ˈdɒgmətɪzəm/ [U] attitudes or behaviour that are dogmatic 教條主義; 武斷 —**dogmatist** *n* [C]

dog·ma·tize /ˈdɔgməˌtaɪz; ˈdɒgmətaɪz/ *v* also 又作 **-ise** *BrE*【英】[I+**about**] to speak, write, or act in a dogmatic way 教條式地說[寫]; 武斷地行事

do-good·er /ˌ· ˈ··/ *n* [C] someone who thinks they are being helpful but who annoys other people because they get involved in situations where they are not wanted〔自以為〕專做好事的人〔其實是多管閒事〕

dog pad·dle /ˈ· ˌ··/ also 又作 **doggy paddle** *informal n* [singular] a simple way of swimming by moving your legs and arms like a swimming dog【非正式】狗爬式游泳(法)

dogs·bod·y /ˈdɔgzˌbɑdɪ; ˈdɒgzˌbɒdi/ *n* [C] *BrE* someone who has to do all the jobs that nobody else wants to do【英】勤雜工, 打雜的人: *I'm just the general dogsbody around here.* 我只不過是這裡的普通雜工罷了。

dog·sled /ˈdɔgˌslɛd; ˈdɒgsled/ *n* [C] a SLEDGE (=low flat vehicle on metal blades) pulled by dogs over snow 狗拉雪橇

dog tag /ˈ· ˌ·/ *n* [C] *AmE* a small piece of metal that soldiers wear around their necks with their name, blood type, and number written on it【美】身分識別牌〔士兵掛在頸部標有名字、血型和部隊番號的牌子〕

dog-tired /ˌ· ˈ·◂/ *adj informal* extremely tired【非正式】筋疲力盡的

dog war·den /ˈ· ˌ··/ *n* [C] *BrE* someone whose job is to collect dogs without owners【英】捕狗員〔專職捕捉沒有主人的狗的人〕; DOGCATCHER *AmE*【美】

dog·wood /ˈdɔgˌwʊd; ˈdɒgwʊd/ *n* [C,U] a tree or bush with red or pink berries (BERRY) and red stems 狗木〔一種紅莖、長着紅色或粉紅色漿果的樹木或灌木〕

DoH /ˌdi o ˈetʃ; ˌdiː əʊ ˈeɪtʃ/ *n* the abbreviation of 縮寫= the Department of Health 衛生部

doh, do /do; dəʊ/ *n* [singular, U] the first or eighth note in the SOL-FA musical SCALE[1] (8) 全音階中的第一[第八]音

doi·ly /ˈdɔɪlɪ; ˈdɔɪli/ *n* [C] a circle of paper or cloth with a pattern cut into it that you put on a plate before putting cakes etc on it〔襯在盤中蛋糕等點心下面的刻花紙或布做的〕圓形墊子

do·ing /ˈduɪŋ; ˈduːɪŋ/ *n* **1 be sb's doing** if something bad is someone's doing, they did it 是某人幹的壞事: *This mess is all your doing.* 這一團糟全都是你搞的。**2 take some doing** to be hard work 費點勁, 得花些功夫: *Sorting this lot out is going to take some doing.* 把這些東西

D

都整理好得費些功夫。**3 doings** *BrE*【英】**a)** [plural] things that someone does〔某人〕做的事情 **b)** [C] *informal* a small thing whose name you have forgotten or do not know【非正式】那東西〔指忘了或叫不出名稱的小東西〕: *Pass me that doings.* 把那個東西遞給我。

do-it-your·self /ˌ‚ · ·ˈ·◂/ *n* [U] DIY 自己動手(做)

Dol·by /ˈdolbɪ; ˈdɒlbi/ *n* [U] *trademark* a system for reducing unwanted noise when you record music or sounds【商標】杜比[道爾貝](降噪)系統

dol·drums /ˈdɑldrəmz; ˈdɒldrəmz/ *n* **1 be in the doldrums** *informal*【非正式】**a)** to be feeling sad 無精打采; 傷心; 鬱悶: *Fay's really in the doldrums today.* 費伊今天心情實在不佳。**b)** to not be growing or improving 沒發展, 無進展, 停滯: *The car industry has been in the doldrums for several years.* 數年來汽車工業一直停滯不前。**2 the doldrums** an area in the ocean just north of the EQUATOR where the weather can be so calm that sailing ships cannot move 赤道以北海域的無風帶〔帆船無法行駛〕

D

dole¹ /dol; dəʊl/ *n* [U] *BrE*【英】**1** money given by the government in Britain to people who are unemployed〔英國政府發放給失業人士的〕失業救濟金: **be/go on the dole** (=be or become unemployed and receive money from the government) 領取政府失業救濟金 *Kevin was on the dole for a year before he got a job.* 凱文領了一年的失業救濟金才又找到工作。**2 the dole queue a)** the line of people waiting to claim this money each week 每週等待領取失業救濟金的隊伍 **b)** the number of people who are unemployed and claiming money from the state 向政府領取救濟金的失業人口: *As two factories closed today, 500 people joined the dole queue.* 隨着今天兩家工廠的倒閉, 又有500人加入了領取失業救濟金的行列。

dole² *v*

dole sth ↔ **out** *phr v* [T] *informal* to give money or food to more than one person【非正式】發放, 分發〔錢、食物等〕: **[+to]** *Vera was doling out candy to all the kids.* 維拉正在給所有的孩子派發糖果。

dole·ful /ˈdolfəl; ˈdəʊlfəl/ *adj* very sad 哀傷的: *a doleful song about lost love* 一首關於失去愛情的哀傷歌曲 —**dolefully** *adv* —**dolefulness** *n* [U]

S3 **doll¹** /dɑl; dɒl/ *n* **1** [C] a child's toy that looks like a small person 玩偶, 玩具娃娃 **2** [C] *slang* a word meaning an attractive young woman, that is now usually considered offensive【俚】漂亮的年輕女子〔現通常被視為具有冒犯之意〕**3** [singular] *AmE informal* a very nice person【美, 非正式】大好人: *Jim's a real doll – he let me borrow his car.* 吉姆真是個大好人——他讓我用他的車。

doll² *v*

doll sb **up** *phr v* [T] *informal* if a woman dolls herself up, she gets ready for a social occasion by putting on attractive clothes and MAKE-UP (1)【非正式】〔指婦女為參加某個社交活動而〕把…打扮起來: **doll yourself up** *I can't be bothered to doll myself up tonight.* 今晚我懶得打扮自己。| **be/get dolled up** *The girls were all dolled up for a party.* 女孩子們都打扮得漂漂亮亮的去參加派對。

S1 W3 **dol·lar** /ˈdɑlɚ; ˈdɒlə/ *n* [C] **1** the standard unit of money in the US, Australia, Canada, and other countries, for which the sign is $ 元, 圓〔美國、澳大利亞、加拿大等國的貨幣單位, 符號為$〕: *This book costs ten dollars.* 買這本書得花十元。**2** a piece of paper or coin worth this amount of money 一元的紙幣[硬幣] **3 the dollar** the value of US money in relation to the money of other countries〔和其他國家貨幣相關的〕美元價值: *The pound has risen against the dollar.* 英鎊對美元的比價上升了。—see also 另見 **you can bet your bottom dollar** (BET¹ (4)), **feel/look like a million dollars** (MILLION (4))

dollars-and-cents /ˌ‚· · ˈ·/ *adj AmE* considered in a financial way【美】金錢的; 經濟的: *It's an interesting idea, but from a dollars-and-cents point of view it just won't work.* 這是個有趣的想法, 但是從金錢的角度來看並不可行。

doll house /ˈ· ·/ *n* [C] *AmE*【美】= a DOLL'S HOUSE *BrE*【英】

dol·lop¹ /ˈdɑləp; ˈdɒləp/ *n* [C] a mass of soft food, usually dropped from a spoon 一團, 一塊〔軟質食物〕: **[+of]** *a large dollop of cream* 一大團奶油 —see picture on page A7 參見A7頁圖

dollop² *v* [T always+adv/prep] *informal* to drop a mass of soft food onto a surface【非正式】把〔一團軟質食物〕舀到…上: **dollop sth onto/into** *May dolloped the mixture into the frying pan.* 梅把混合物舀到煎鍋裡。

doll's house /ˈ· ·/ *n* [C] *BrE* a child's toy house with small furniture in it【英】玩具房子; DOLL HOUSE *AmE*【美】

dol·ly /ˈdɑlɪ; ˈdɒli/ *n* [C] **1** another word for a DOLL¹, used by and to children 玩具娃娃〔兒語〕**2** *technical* a flat frame on wheels used for moving heavy objects【術語】〔用來移動重物的〕手推車

dolly bird /ˈ· · ·/ *n* [C] *BrE old-fashioned* a pretty young woman, especially one who wears fashionable clothes【英, 過時】〔尤指身穿時髦衣服的〕漂亮的年輕女子

dol·men /ˈdɑlmɛn; ˈdɒlmen/ *n* [C] *technical* two or more large upright stones supporting a large flat piece of stone, built in ancient times【術語】〔古時建造的〕石桌墳〔由兩塊或多塊豎立的石頭支撐起大塊扁平的石板構成〕

dol·our *BrE*【英】, **dolor** *AmE*【美】/ˈdolɚ; ˈdɒlə/ *n* [U] *literary* great sadness【文】哀傷, 悲痛 —**dolorous** *adj*

dol·phin /ˈdɑlfɪn; ˈdɒlfɪn/ *n* [C] a very intelligent sea animal like a fish with a long grey pointed nose 海豚

dolphin 海豚

dol·phi·na·ri·um /ˌdɑlfɪˈnɛrɪəm; ˌdɒlfɪˈneəriəm/ *n* [C] a pool where dolphins are kept and people can go to see them 海豚館, 海豚池

dolt /dolt; dəʊlt/ *n* [C] *old-fashioned* a silly or stupid person【過時】愚蠢的人, 傻瓜, 笨蛋 —**doltish** *adj* —**doltishly** *adv*

-dom /dəm; dəm/ *suffix* [in U nouns 構成不可數名詞] **1** the state of being something 作為某事物的狀態: *freedom* 自由 **2 a)** [in C nouns 構成可數名詞] a particular rank 職位: *He was rewarded with a dukedom.* (=was made a DUKE) 他被封為公爵。**b)** an area ruled by a particular type of person 某種人所管轄的區域: *kingdom* 王國 **3** [in U nouns 構成不可數名詞] *informal* all the people who share the same set of interests, have the same job, etc【非正式】擁有同樣利益、工作等的羣體: *officialdom* (=all officials) 官員〔總稱〕| *yuppiedom*〔全體〕雅皮士

do·main /doˈmen; dəˈmeɪn/ *n* [C] *formal*【正式】

1 ▶ACTIVITY/KNOWLEDGE 活動/知識◀ an area of activity, interest, or knowledge〔活動、興趣、知識的〕領域, 範圍, 範疇: *This problem lies outside the domain of medical science.* 這個問題不屬於醫學範疇。

2 sb/sth's domain an area of activity controlled by someone 由某人/某事物控制的領地: *Mortgages were until recently the domain of building societies.* 直到最近抵押貸款還是由房屋互助會經管的。

3 ▶LAND 土地◀ an area of land owned and controlled by one person or government 領地; 領土; 版圖: *feudal domains* 封建領地

4 in the public domain if information is in the public domain, it is not kept secret 屬公共所有的; 為公眾所知曉的: *Details of the arms deals must be brought into the public domain.* 武器交易的細節必須公諸於眾。

5 ▶QUANTITIES 數量◀ *technical* the set of possible quantities by which something can vary【術語】〔數學的〕域; 整環

dome /dom; dəʊm/ *n* [C] **1** a round roof on a base like a circle 穹頂; 圓屋頂; 拱頂 **2** a shape like a ball cut in half

半球形狀: *the dome of his bald head* 他那圓圓的光頭頂

domed /domd; dəʊmd/ *adj* covered with a dome or shaped like a dome 有穹頂的; 半球形的: *a high domed ceiling* 高高的穹形屋頂

2 **do·mes·tic¹** /dəˋmɛstɪk; dəˈmestɪk/ *adj*
1 ▶WITHIN ONE COUNTRY 國內的◀ happening within a country and not involving any other countries 國內的; 本國的: *the domestic market* 國內市場 | *Domestic flights go from Terminal 1.* 國內航班從一號航站樓出發。
2 ▶USED AT HOME 家用的◀ used in the house or home 家中使用的, 家用的: **domestic appliance/equipment etc** *Electricity charges can be at business or domestic rate.* 電費可分為企業用電和家庭用電兩種費率。
3 ▶ABOUT FAMILY AND HOME 關於家庭的◀ [only before noun 僅用於名詞前] concerning family relationships and life at home 涉及家庭關係和生活的; 家事的: **domestic life** *I suspect Tony's domestic life isn't very happy.* 我懷疑東尼的家庭生活不是很幸福。| **domestic violence/problem/trouble etc** (=violence etc between members of the same family)家庭暴力/問題/麻煩等
4 ▶PERSON 人◀ someone who is domestic enjoys spending time at home and is good at cooking, cleaning etc 喜愛操持家務的, 善於烹飪、清潔等家務的
5 ▶ANIMAL 動物◀ a domestic animal lives on a farm or in someone's home 馴養的; 家養的 —**domestically** /-kḷɪ; -kli/ *adv*

domestic² *n* [C] a servant who works in a large house 僕人, 傭人

do·mes·ti·cate /dəˋmɛstəˏket; dəˈmestɨkeɪt/ *v* [T] to make an animal able to live with people as a pet or work for them on a farm 馴養〔動物〕—compare 比較 TAME² (2) —**domestication** /dəˏmɛstəˋkeʃən; dəˌmestɨˈkeɪʃən/ *n* [U]

do·mes·ti·cat·ed /dəˋmɛstəˏketɪd; dəˈmestɨˈkeɪtɨd/ *adj* someone who is domesticated enjoys spending time at home and doing work in the home 喜愛操持家務的: *Ray's very domesticated – he loves cooking.* 雷伊很喜歡做家務——他喜愛烹飪。

do·mes·tic·i·ty /ˏdomɛsˋtɪsətɪ; ˌdəʊmesˈtɪsɨti/ *n* [U] life at home with your family 家庭生活; 家庭小天地: *a scene of happy domesticity* 一派幸福家庭的景象

domestic sci·ence /·ˏ·· ˋ··/ *n* [U] *BrE old-fashioned* the study in schools of cooking, SEWING etc【英, 過時】家政學〔學習烹飪、縫紉等〕

domestic ser·vice /·ˏ·· ˋ··/ *n* [U] the work of a servant in a large house〔傭人做的〕家務

dom·i·cile /ˋdɑməsḷ; ˈdɒmɨsaɪl/ *n* [C] *law* a place where someone lives【法律】住處, 住所: *His last known domicile was 11 Park Road, London, N8.* 他最後一處為人所知的住所是在倫敦N8區, 公園路11號。

dom·i·ciled /ˋdɑməsḷd; ˈdɒmɨsaɪld/ *adj law*【法律】**be domiciled in** to live in a particular place 在…居住的

dom·i·cil·i·a·ry /ˏdɑməˋsɪlɪˏɛrɪ; ˌdɒmɨˈsɪliəri/ *adj law*【法律】**domiciliary services/care/visits etc** care or services at someone's home 上門服務/護理/拜訪等

dom·i·nance /ˋdɑmənəns; ˈdɒmɨnəns/ *n* [U] the fact of being more powerful, more important, or more noticeable than other people or things 優勢; 顯要; 突出: *military dominance* 軍事上的優勢 | [+of] *Japan's dominance of the market* 日本在市場的獨霸地位

3 **dom·i·nant¹** /ˋdɑmənənt; ˈdɒmɨnənt/ *adj* **1** stronger, more powerful, or more noticeable than other people or things 強大的; 有優勢的; 突出的: *The dominant male gorilla is the largest in the group.* 這隻佔支配地位的雄性大猩猩是這羣大猩猩中個頭最大的。| *a dominant personality* 霸道的性格 **2** *technical* a dominant physical feature can appear in a child even if it has been passed on from only one parent【術語】〔遺傳特性〕顯性的: *Brown eyes are dominant.* 棕色眼睛是顯性的。—compare 比較 RECESSIVE **3** high and easily seen 高聳的; 顯眼的: *The castle was built in a dominant position on a hill.* 城堡建在山上一處居高臨下的地方。

dominant² *n* [singular] the fifth note of a musical SCALE¹ (8) of eight notes 全音階的第五音

dom·i·nate /ˋdɑməˏnet; ˈdɒmɨneɪt/ *v* **1** [I,T] to have 3
power and control over someone or something 支配, 控制: *a society in which males dominate* 一個由男性支配一切的社會 | **dominate sth** *Sue's very nice, but she does tend to dominate the conversation.* 蘇的人品很好, 但喜歡在談話中佔上風。**2** [I,T] to be the most important feature of something 成為 (…的) 最主要特徵; (在…中) 佔最重要的地位: *Education issues dominated the election campaign.* 教育問題成為競選活動中的主題。**3** [T] to be very large and easily noticed 聳立於; 比…高, 俯視: *The cathedral dominates the city.* 大教堂高高矗立, 俯瞰整個城市。—**domination** /ˏdɑməˋneʃən; ˌdɒmɪˈneɪʃən/ *n* [U]: *a fight to free the country from foreign domination* 為把國家從外國統治下解放出來而進行的鬥爭

dom·i·na·trix /ˏdɑməˋnetrɪks; ˌdɒmɨˈneɪtrɪks/ *n* [C] a woman who is the stronger partner in a sado-masochistic (SADO-MASOCHISM) sexual relationship〔在性關係上的〕女性施虐狂; 母夜叉

dom·i·neer·ing /ˏdɑməˋnɪrɪŋ; dɒmɨˈnɪərɪŋ◂/ *adj* someone who is domineering tries to control other people without considering how they feel or what they want 專橫的, 霸道的: *a domineering mother* 專橫的母親 —**domineer** *v* [I]

Do·min·i·can /dəˋmɪnɪkən; dəˈmɪnɪkən/ [C] a member of a Christian religious group who leads a holy life〔基督教〕多明我會修道士[修女] —**Dominican** *adj*

do·min·ion /dəˋmɪnjən; dəˈmɪnjən/ *n* **1** [U] *literary* the power or right to rule people【文】統治權; 管轄權: **have/hold dominion over** *Alexander the Great held dominion over a vast area.* 亞歷山大大帝曾統治過遼闊的疆域。**2** [C] *formal* the land owned or controlled by one person or a government【正式】領地; 領土; 版圖: *the king's dominion* 國王的領地 **3** [C] one of the countries that was a member of the British COMMONWEALTH in the past〔舊時〕英聯邦的自治領 —see also 另見 COLONY (1), PROTECTORATE

dom·i·no /ˋdɑməno; ˈdɒmɨnəʊ/ *n plural* **dominoes 1** [C] one of a set of small flat pieces of wood, plastic etc, with different numbers of spots on, used for playing a game 多米諾骨牌 **2 dominoes** [U] the game played using dominoes 多米諾骨牌遊戲 **3 the domino effect** a situation in which one event or action causes several other things to happen one after the other 多米諾 (骨牌) 效應〔指一個事件或行動導致其他事情接連發生〕

don¹ /dɑn; dɒn/ *n* [C] *BrE* a university teacher, especially one who teaches at the universities of Oxford or Cambridge【英】〔尤指牛津大學或劍橋大學的〕大學教師

don² *v* **donned, donning** [T] *formal* to put on a hat, coat etc【正式】戴上〔帽子〕; 穿上〔衣服等〕—opposite 反義詞 DOFF

do·nate /ˋdonet; dəʊˈneɪt/ *v* [I,T] **1** to give something, especially money, to a person or an organization in order to help them 捐贈, 捐獻〔尤指錢〕: **donate sth to sb/sth** *Last year he donated $1,000 to cancer research.* 去年他捐了1,000美元支持癌症研究。**2 donate blood** to allow some blood to be removed from your body so that it can be used in a hospital to help someone who is ill or injured 捐血, 獻血

do·na·tion /doˋneʃən; dəʊˈneɪʃən/ *n* **1** [C] something, especially money, that you give to a person or an organization in order to help them 捐贈物〔尤指捐款〕: *All donations will be gratefully received.* 我們將十分感激地接受所有的捐贈。| **make a donation** (=give money) 捐款 **2** [U] the act of giving something, especially money, to help a person or an organization 捐助〔尤指錢〕

done¹ /dʌn; dʌn/ the past participle of DO¹

done² *adj* [not before noun 不用於名詞前, no comparative 無比較級]
1 ▶FINISHED 完成的◀ finished or completed 完成的,

終了的: *The job's nearly done.* 工作快做完了。| *As soon as I'm done I'll give you a call.* 我一忙完就給你打電話。| **over and done with** (=completely finished) 結束, 了結 *I'll be glad when this wedding is over and done with!* 等婚禮辦完, 一切都了結了, 我就高興了!

2 ►COOKED 煮熟的◄ cooked enough to eat 煮熟的, 煮好的: *Is the pasta done yet?* 意大利麵食做好了沒有? —compare 比較 OVERDONE, UNDERDONE

3 be done for *informal* to be in serious trouble or likely to fail【非正式】遭殃了; 完蛋了: *If we're caught we're done for.* 要是被抓住, 我們就完了。

4 done in *informal* extremely tired【非正式】累壞了的; 筋疲力盡的: *I've got to sit down – I'm done in.* 我得坐下來 — 我太累了。

5 be done/be the done thing to be socially acceptable 得體的, 合乎禮儀的: *It just isn't the done thing to call teachers by their first names.* 直呼老師的名字是不禮貌的。

6 be/have done with it to finish dealing with something or someone, and never deal with them again 與某事[某人]了結關係: *I know it's unfair but let's just pay the fine and have done with it.* 我知道這不公平, 但是我們就交一下罰款, 把這事給了結掉算了。

7 be done *BrE informal* to be deceived or cheated【英, 非正式】上當, 受騙: *You paid £50 for that! You were done mate!* 你買那東西竟然花了50英鎊! 你上當了, 老兄!

8 be/get done *BrE informal* to be caught by the police for doing something illegal, but usually not too serious【英, 非正式】〔因做不太嚴重的違法事情而〕被警察逮着: **[+for]** *I got done for speeding on the M1 last night.* 我昨晚由於在一號高速公路上超速行駛被警察逮住了。—see also 另見 **be hard done by** (HARD[2] (5))

done³ *interjection* used to agree to and accept the conditions of a deal 好, 行, 成交〔用於表示同意或接受某交易的條件〕: *"I'll give you $90 a day for the job." "Done!"* "這項工作我一天給你90美元。" "行!"

dong /dɑŋ; dɒŋ/ *n* [C] *taboo slang* the male sex organ【諱, 俚】男性性器官

don·jon /ˋdɑndʒən; ˈdɒndʒən/ *n* [C] the strong main tower of a MEDIEVAL castle〔中世紀〕堅固的城堡主塔

Don Ju·an /ˌdɑn ˋdʒuən; ˌdɒn ˈhwɑːn/ *n* [C] a man who is good at persuading women to have sex with him 唐璜; 善於勾引女性的人, 風流浪蕩子, 花花公子

don·key /ˋdɑŋkɪ; ˈdɒŋki/ *n* [C] **1** a grey or brown animal like a horse, but smaller and with long ears 驢 **2** a stupid person 蠢人, 笨蛋 **3 donkey's years** *BrE informal* a very long time【英, 非正式】很久, 多年: *It's donkey's years since I went to the pictures.* 我已經很久沒看電影了。

donkey der·by /ˋ·· ˌ··/ *n* [C] *BrE* a race on donkeys done for amusement or to raise money【英】〔為娛樂或籌款而舉辦的〕騎驢大賽

donkey en·gine /ˋ·· ˌ··/ *n* [C] a small additional engine used for special jobs, especially on a ship〔尤指船上的〕輔助發動機

donkey jack·et /ˋ·· ˌ··/ *n* [C] *BrE* a short thick coat, usually very dark blue, that has a piece of leather or plastic across the shoulders【英】厚實的短大衣〔通常為深藍色, 肩部有一塊皮革或塑料〕—see picture at 參見 COAT[1] 圖

don·key·work /ˋdɑŋkɪˌwɝk; ˈdɒŋkiwɜːk/ *n* [U] *informal* hard boring work【非正式】艱苦而乏味的工作; GRUNT WORK *AmE*【美】: *Why do I always have to do the donkeywork?* 為甚麼那些沒意思的苦差事老是得由我來幹?

don·nish /ˋdɑnɪʃ; ˈdɒnɪʃ/ *adj especially BrE* clever, serious, and more interested in ideas than real life【尤英】聰明而嚴肅的; 學究式的 —**donnishly** *adv*

do·nor /ˋdonɚ; ˈdəʊnə/ *n* [C] **1** a person, group etc that gives something, especially money, to an organization in order to help people 捐贈者: *Funding for the clinic has come mostly from private donors.* 診所的資金大多來自私人捐贈者。**2** someone who gives a part of their body so that it can be used in the medical treatment of someone else 捐獻器官者: *The search is under way for a suitable donor.* 正在尋找一個合適的器官捐獻者。**3 donor card** a card that you carry to show that when you die, a doctor can take parts of your body to use in the medical treatment of someone else 器官捐贈卡〔隨身攜帶, 上面寫明死後器官可捐贈〕

do-noth·ing /ˋ· ˌ··/ *n* [C] *informal* a lazy person【非正式】懶人; 無所事事者

Don Quix·ote /ˌdɑn ˋkwɪksət; ˌdɒn ˈkwɪksət/ *n* [singular] someone who is determined to change what is wrong, but who does it in a way that is silly or not practical 唐吉訶德似的人物; 不切實際的理想主義者 —see also 另見 QUIXOTIC

don't /dont; dəʊnt/ **1** the short form of 縮略式= 'do not': *Don't worry!* 別擔心! | *You know him, don't you?* 你認識他, 對不對? —see also 另見 **dos and don'ts** (DO[3] (2)) **2** *spoken* an incorrect short form of 'does not'【口】〔does not 不正確的縮略式〕: *She don't like it.* 她不喜歡它。

do·nut /ˋdonʌt; ˈdəʊnʌt/ *n* [C] an American spelling of DOUGHNUT doughnut 的美式拼法

doo·dah /ˋduˌdɑ; ˈduːdɑː/ *BrE*【英】, **doo·dad** /ˋduˌdæd; ˈduːdæd/ *AmE*【美】*n* [C] *informal* a small object whose name you have forgotten or do not know【非正式】〔忘記或不知名稱的〕小東西, 小玩意兒: *Where's the control doodah for the TV?* 控制電視的那玩意哪去了?

doo·dle /ˋdudl̩; ˈduːdl/ *v* [I] to draw shapes, lines, or patterns without really thinking about what you are doing〔心不在焉地〕亂塗, 亂畫: *I always doodle when I'm on the phone.* 我在講電話時總喜歡隨手亂畫點甚麼。—**doodle** *n* [C]

doo·dle·bug /ˋdudl̩ˌbʌg; ˈduːdlbʌg/ *n* [C] a flying bomb used by the Germans in World War II〔德軍在第二次世界大戰中使用的〕V 型飛彈

doo-doo /ˋdudu; ˈduːduː/ *n* [U] *informal* a word for solid waste from your body, used by or to children【非正式】〔兒語〕屉屉〔指糞便〕—**doo-doo** *v* [I]

doo·fer /ˋdufɚ; ˈduːfə/ also 又作 **doo·fah** /ˋdufə; ˈduːfə/ *n* [C] *informal* a small object whose name you have forgotten or do not know【非正式】〔忘記或不知名稱的〕小東西, 小玩意兒

doo·fus /ˋdufəs; ˈduːfəs/ *n* [C] *AmE informal* a silly or stupid person【美, 非正式】蠢人; 笨蛋

doo·hick·ey /ˋduˌhɪkɪ; ˈduːˌhɪki/ *n* [C] *AmE informal* a small object whose name you have forgotten or do not know, especially a part of a machine【美, 非正式】〔忘記或不知其名稱的〕小物件〔尤指機器的小部件〕

doo·lal·ly /duˋlælɪ; duːˈlæli/ *adj informal* crazy【非正式】瘋狂的

doom¹ /dum; duːm/ *v* [T usually passive 一般用被動態] to make someone or something certain to fail, die, be destroyed etc 注定〔失敗、死亡、毀滅等〕: **doom sth to sth** *The species is doomed to extinction.* 這一物種注定要滅絕。| **doom sb/sth to do sth** *Marx's theory was that capitalist economies are eventually doomed to collapse.* 根據馬克思的理論, 資本主義的經濟體系最終注定會崩潰。| **doomed to failure** *The marriage seems doomed to failure.* 這場婚姻似乎注定長不了。—**doomed** *adj*

doom² *n* [U] the end of something especially by destruction or death, that will soon come and that you cannot avoid〔不可避免的〕毀滅; 死亡; 終結; 劫數: *a terrible sense of impending doom* 一種末日即將來臨的駭人感覺 | **meet your doom** *Thousands of soldiers met their doom on this very field.* 數以千計的士兵就是在這個戰場上喪生的。| **spell doom for** (=mean that something will end) 意味着〔某事〕將終結 *The budget cuts spelled doom for the mining community.* 縮減預算意味着這個礦區要完結了。| **doom and gloom** (=a feeling that the future will be terrible) 悲觀情緒

Dooms·day /ˋdumzˌde; ˈduːmzdeɪ/ *n* [singular] **1 till/**

until Doomsday *informal* forever【非正式】直到永遠: *You could wait till Doomsday and he'd never show up.* 你可以永遠等下去，但他是不會出現的。**2** the last day of the Earth's existence 世界末日

doom·ster /ˈdumstɚ; ˈduːmstə/ *n* [C] *informal* someone who always thinks something bad is going to happen【非正式】預言災難者，末日論者

1 1 **door** /dɔr; dɔː/ *n* [C] **1** the large flat object that you open and close at the entrance to a building, room, vehicle etc 門: **open/close/shut/slam the door** *Could you open the door for me?* 請你幫我開門好嗎? | *Close the door behind you.* 進來時把門關上。| **knock on/at the door** *Knock on the door and see if they're home.* 敲一下門看他們在不在家。| **kitchen/bathroom/bedroom etc door** *Don't forget to lock the office door.* 別忘了把辦公室的門鎖上。| **front/back/side door** *Is the front door open?* 前門是開着的嗎? | **revolving/sliding/swing doors** *Nathan got stuck in the revolving doors!* 納森被卡在旋轉門裡了! —compare 比較 GATE¹ (1) —see picture on page A4 參見A4頁圖 **2** the space made by an open door; DOORWAY 門口，出入口，門道: *Rick turned around and ran out of the door.* 里克一轉身跑出了門。| *I glanced through the open door.* 我從敞開的門往外望了一眼。**3 at the door** if someone is at the door they are waiting for you to open it so they can come inside 在門口，在門外: *There's somebody at the door.* 門外有人。**4 answer the door** to open the door to see who is there 應門 **5 show/see sb to the door** to take someone to the main way out of a building 把某人送到門口: *Good-bye, Mr Carter. My secretary will show you to the door.* 再見，卡特先生。我的祕書會送你到門口。**6 two/three doors down etc** a place that is a particular number of houses or buildings away from where you are 再走兩/三個門面等: *The Rigbys live two doors down from us.* 里格比家住的地方和我們家隔兩個門面。**7 (from) door to door a)** between one place and another 兩地之間: *My commute takes forty minutes, door to door.* 從我家到工作的地方需要四十分鐘。**b)** going to each house in a street or area to sell something, collect money or ask for votes 挨家挨戶〔推銷東西、籌錢或拉選票〕: *Joe sold vacuum cleaners door to door for years.* 喬多年來一直挨家挨戶推銷吸塵器。—see also 另見 DOOR-TO-DOOR **8 out of doors** outside; OUTDOORS 外面，戶外，室外 **9 behind closed doors** where other people cannot see you; secretly 祕密地，不讓別人看見地: *The meeting took place behind closed doors.* 會議是祕密舉行的。**10 show sb the door** to make it clear to someone that you want them to leave 下逐客令: *I'm warning you, if he gets drunk I'll show him the door.* 我警告你，如果他喝醉了，我就攆他走。**11 lay sth at sb's door** to say that something is someone's fault 把某事歸咎於某人 **12 be on the door** to work at the entrance to a theatre, club, etc collecting tickets 在〔劇院、俱樂部等〕門口把門〔收票〕**13 an open door policy** willingness to allow people to come in 開放政策〔允許人們進來〕: *an open door policy for immigration* 對移民的開放政策 **14 open doors for sb** to give someone an opportunity they would not have had otherwise 給某人提供不易得到的機會: *I think your new job will really open doors for you.* 我認為你的新工作確實會為你提供機會。**15 open the door to** to make something possible 使…有可能發生: *You're opening the door to trouble by hitchhiking.* 你搭便車會惹麻煩上身的。**16 shut/close the door on** to make something impossible 使…不可能發生: *Sasha's accident shut the door on her ballet career.* 莎莎所遭遇的事故使她的芭蕾舞事業永遠完結了。—see also 另見 BACK DOOR, FRONT DOOR, NEXT DOOR, **at death's door** (DEATH (8))

door·bell /ˈdorˌbɛl; ˈdɔːbel/ *n* [C] a button outside a house that you push to make a sound so that people inside know you are there 門鈴: **ring the doorbell** (=push the button) 按門鈴

do-or-die /ˌ· · ˈ·/ *adj* very determined 拚死的: *a do-or-die attitude* 破釜沉舟的態度

door·jamb /ˈdɔrˌdʒæm; ˈdɔːdʒæm/ *n* [C] one of two upright posts on either side of a doorway; DOORPOST 門柱; 門側柱

door·keep·er /ˈdɔrˌkipɚ; ˈdɔːˌkiːpə/ *n* [C] someone who guards the main door of a large building and lets people in and out 看門人，守門人，門衛

door·knob /ˈdɔrˌnɑb; ˈdɔːnɒb/ *n* [C] a round handle that you turn to open a door 球形門把手

door·knock·er /ˈdɔrˌnɑkɚ; ˈdɔːˌnɒkə/ *n* [C] a heavy metal ring or bar on a door that visitors use to knock with 門環; 敲門器

door·man /ˈdɔrˌmæn; ˈdɔːmæn/ *n plural* **doormen** /-mɛn; -men/ [C] a man in a hotel or theatre who watches the door, helps people find taxis, and usually wears a uniform〔酒店、劇院的〕門衛，門僮 —compare 比較 PORTER (2)

door·mat /ˈdɔrˌmæt; ˈdɔːmæt/ *n* [C] **1** a piece of material just inside a door for you to clean your shoes on〔門口的〕擦鞋墊 **2** *informal* someone who lets other people treat them badly and never complains【非正式】逆來順受的人，甘受屈辱的人: *Ted lets Tracy treat him like a doormat.* 泰德甘心忍受崔茜的欺侮。

door·nail /ˈdɔrˌnel; ˈdɔːneɪl/ *n* [singular] —see 見 **dead as a doornail** (DEAD¹ (1))

door·plate /ˈdɔrˌplet; ˈdɔːpleɪt/ *n* [C] a flat piece of metal fixed to the door of a house or building showing the name of the person or company that works inside〔釘在門上的金屬〕門牌，戶名牌

door·post /ˈdɔrˌpost; ˈdɔːpəʊst/ *n* [C] one of two upright posts on either side of a doorway; DOORJAMB 門柱，門側柱

door prize /ˈ· ·/ *n* [C] *AmE* a prize given to someone who has the winning number on their ticket for a show, dance, or party【美】〔演出、舞會、晚會的〕門票對號獎

door·sill /ˈdɔrˌsɪl; ˈdɔːˌsɪl/ *n* [C] the part of a door frame that you step across when you go through a doorway 門檻

door·step¹ /ˈdɔrˌstɛp; ˈdɔːstep/ *n* [C] **1** a step just outside a door to a house or building 門階 **2 on your doorstep** very near to where you live or are staying 在某人住所[逗留處]近旁: *Wow! You've got the beach right on your doorstep!* 哇! 你住的地方離海灘這麼近! **3** *BrE informal* a very thick piece of bread cut from a loaf【英，非正式】厚麵包片

doorstep² *v* [I] if politicians wanting votes or JOURNALISTS looking for a news story go doorstepping, they visit people who do not want to see them〔政客〕上門〔拉選票〕;〔記者〕造訪〔找新聞等〕

door·stop /ˈdɔrˌstɑp; ˈdɔːstɒp/ also 又作 **door·stop·per** /-ˌstɑpɚ; -ˌstɒpə/ *n* [C] **1** something you put under or against a door to keep it open〔讓門保持敞開的〕制門器 **2** a rubber object fixed to a wall to stop a door hitting it when it is opened〔防止門撞牆的〕門碰頭

door-to-door /ˌ· · ˈ·◂/ *adj* visiting each house in a street or area, usually to sell something, collect money, or ask for votes 挨家挨戶的

door·way /ˈdɔrˌwe; ˈdɔːweɪ/ *n* [C] the space where the door opens into a room or building 門口，出入口: *I looked up and there was Paolo, standing in the doorway.* 我一抬頭，看見保羅站在門口。

door·yard /ˈdɔrˌjɑrd; ˈdɔːjɑːd/ *n* [C] *AmE* an area in front of the door of a house【美】門前庭院

doo·zy, doozie /ˈduzi; ˈduːzi/ *n* [C] *AmE informal* something that is so good, bad, strange etc that you can hardly believe it【美，非正式】極好[極壞、極奇怪]的東西: *I've heard lies before, but that one was a real doozy!* 以前我也聽到過各種謊言，但那個謊言才真叫離譜!

dope¹ /dop; dəʊp/ *n informal*【非正式】**1** [U] a drug that is not legal, especially MARIJUANA 毒品〔尤指大麻〕: *a dope dealer* 毒品販子 **2** [C] someone who is stupid 蠢人，傻瓜: *Pam, you dope!* 帕姆，你這個傻瓜! **3 the dope**

on new information about someone or something, especially information that not many people know 有關…的內幕消息: *Give me all the dope on the new teacher.* 給我講講那個新老師的所有情況。**4** [U] medicine, especially medicine that makes you sleep easily〔尤指使人易入睡的〕藥物

dope² *v* [T] *informal*【非正式】**1** also 又作 **dope up** to give someone a drug, often in their food or drink, to make them sleep or feel better 使服麻醉品[藥品]〔通常放在食物或飲料中〕: *They dope the elephants in order to tag them.* 他們把大象麻醉了, 以便為牠們掛上標籤。| *If we dope you up enough you'll still be able to sing with a cold.* 如果我們給你服用足量的藥劑, 即使你感冒了, 仍然可以唱歌。**2** to give an animal a drug that makes it perform better in a race or competition 給〔動物〕服用興奮劑

dope·head /ˈdopˌhɛd; ˈdəʊphed/ *n* [C] *slang* someone who takes a lot of drugs【俚】吸毒鬼; 白面客

dop·ey, dopy /ˈdopɪ; ˈdəʊpi/ *adj informal*【非正式】**1** slow to react mentally or physically, as if you have taken a drug 昏昏沉沉的, 迷迷糊糊的: *I'm still a little dopey from the anesthetic.* 由於麻醉藥的作用, 我還有點昏昏沉沉的。**2** slightly stupid 有些愚笨的: *Dan gave me a dopey grin.* 丹恩向我咧嘴傻笑了一下。

dop·pel·gang·er /ˈdɑplˌgæŋə; ˈdɒpəlgæŋə/ *n* [C] *German*【德】**1** a spirit that looks exactly like a living person〔外形和活人一樣的〕幽靈 **2** someone who looks exactly like someone else〔與另一人〕外貌極相似的人

do·py /ˈdopɪ; ˈdəʊpi/ *adj* another spelling of DOPEY dopey 的另一種拼法

Dor·ic /ˈdɔrɪk; ˈdɒrɪk/ *adj* in the oldest and most simple of the Greek building styles 陶立克式的〔古希臘建築中最古老的、最簡單的式樣〕: *a Doric column* 陶立克式圓柱 —compare 比較 CORINTHIAN, IONIC

dork /dɔrk; dɔːk/ *n* [C] *AmE informal* someone who you think is stupid, because they behave strangely or wear strange clothes【美, 非正式】傻瓜, 呆子: *You look a real dork in that outfit.* 你穿上那套衣服看起來傻透了。—**dorky** *adj*

dorm /dɔrm; dɔːm/ *n* [C] *informal* a dormitory【非正式】寢室; 宿舍

dor·mant /ˈdɔrmənt; ˈdɔːmənt/ *adj* not active or not growing at the present time but able to be active later 蟄伏的, 休眠的: *The seeds remain dormant in the soil all winter.* 整個冬天種子在土壤裡呈休眠狀態。| **lie dormant** *Stress may activate the virus which has lain dormant in the blood.* 緊張有可能激活潛伏在血液中的病毒。—**dormancy** *n* [U]

dor·mer /ˈdɔrmə; ˈdɔːmə/ also 又作 **dormer win·dow** /ˈ·· ˌ··/ *n* [C] a window built upright in the slope of a roof〔建在斜屋頂上的〕豎天窗; 老虎窗; 屋頂窗

dor·mi·to·ry¹ /ˈdɔrməˌtɔrɪ; ˈdɔːmə̩təri/ *n* [C] **1** a large room in a BOARDING SCHOOL or HOSTEL for several people to sleep in 宿舍; 寢室 **2** *AmE* a large building in a college or university where students live【美】〔大學裡的〕學生宿舍樓; HALL OF RESIDENCE *BrE*【英】

dormitory² *adj* [only before noun 僅用於名詞前] *especially BrE* a dormitory town is a place from which people travel into a city to work every day【尤英】〔指每天去市區工作的人的〕郊外住宅區的

dor·mo·bile /ˈdɔrməˌbil; ˈdɔːməbiːl/ *n* [C] *trademark BrE* a vehicle big enough to live in when you travel, with cooking equipment and beds in it【商標, 英】野營車〔旅行時供居住用, 內有烹飪用具、牀〕

dor·mouse /ˈdɔrˌmaus; ˈdɔːmaʊs/ *n* [C] a small European forest animal with a long furry tail 榛睡鼠〔一種歐洲森林小動物, 長有毛茸茸的長尾巴〕

dor·sal /ˈdɔrsl; ˈdɔːsəl/ *adj* [only before noun 僅用於名詞前] *technical* on or related to the back of an animal or fish【術語】〔動物或魚〕背部的: *a shark's dorsal fin* 鯊魚的背鰭 —see picture at 參見 FISH¹ 圖

do·ry /ˈdɔrɪ; ˈdɔːri/ *n* **1** [C] a rowing boat that has a flat bottom and is used for fishing 平底小漁船 **2** [C,U] a flat sea fish that can be eaten, or the flesh of this fish 海魴; 海魴肉

DOS /dɑs; dɒs/ *n* [U] *trademark* Disk Operating System; SOFTWARE that is loaded onto a computer system to make all the different parts work together【商標】磁盤操作系統

dos·age /ˈdosɪdʒ; ˈdəʊsɪdʒ/ *n* [C usually singular 一般用單數] the amount of medicine that you should take at one time〔一次用藥的〕劑量, 服用量: *Do not exceed the recommended dosage.* 不要超過規定的劑量。

dose¹ /dos; dəʊs/ *n* [C] **1** a measured amount of a medicine〔藥物的〕一劑, 一服; 一次服用量: **[+of]** *a dose of antibiotics* 一劑抗生素藥物 **2** an amount of something unpleasant that you experience at one time 一次; 一番; 一回〔指不愉快的經歷〕: **[+of]** *Workers were exposed to a large dose of radiation.* 工人們暴露在大劑量的輻射之下。| *a bad dose of flu* 一次嚴重的流感 | **in small doses** (=for a short time) 一小會兒, 短時間地 *I can only tolerate Joseph in small doses.* 我只能容忍約瑟夫一小會兒。**3 like a dose of salts** *BrE informal* very quickly and easily【英, 非正式】很快且很輕易地: *The new owners went through the company like a dose of salts, stripping it of its assets.* 那些新來的老闆們很快就把公司的財產侵吞一空。**4 have a dose** *slang* to be infected with VENEREAL DISEASE【俚】得性病, 染上花柳病

dose² also 又作 **dose up** *v* [T] to give someone medicine 給〔某人〕服藥: **dose sb with** *Sumi dosed herself with aspirin and went to bed.* 舒米自己服用了阿士匹靈, 然後就上牀睡覺了。

dosh /dɑʃ; dɒʃ/ *n* [U] *BrE spoken* money【英口】鈔票, 錢

do-si-do /ˌdo sɪ ˋdo; ˌdəʊ si ˈdəʊ/ *n* [singular] an action in COUNTRY DANCING in which partners pass each other sideways〔鄉村舞蹈中〕舞伴互從身側背對背交換位置的舞步 —**do-si-do** *v* [I]

doss¹ /dɑs; dɒs/ *v*

doss around/about *phr v* [I] *BrE informal* to do very little【英, 非正式】幾乎不做甚麼事; 閒混: *We just dossed around all day Saturday.* 星期六一整天我們是在閒散中度過的。

doss down *phr v* [I] *BrE informal* to sleep somewhere that is not your usual place or not a real bed【英, 非正式】〔在別處〕過夜; 將就着睡: *Hundreds dossed down in the theatre because of the blizzards.* 由於暴風雪, 數百人只好在劇院裡將就着過夜。

doss² *n* **a doss** *BrE informal* work that does not need much effort【英, 非正式】不費力的工作: *This job's a real doss.* 這份工作真是輕鬆得很。

doss·er /ˈdɑsə; ˈdɒsə/ *n* [C] *BrE informal* someone who has nowhere to live and sleeps in the street or in cheap HOSTELs【英, 非正式】居無定所的人, 露宿街頭者; 住廉價客棧的人

doss-house /ˈ· ·/ *n* [C] *BrE slang* a place where people who have nowhere to live can stay cheaply【英俚】〔供居無定所者居住的〕廉價客棧; FLOPHOUSE *AmE*【美】

dos·si·er /ˈdɑsɪˌe; ˈdɒsieɪ/ *n* [C] a set of papers containing detailed information on a person or subject; FILE¹ (1)〔有關一人或一事的〕檔案, 卷宗: **keep a dossier on** *The secret police kept dossiers on all opponents of the regime.* 祕密警察對所有反對當局的人都存有檔案。

dost /dʌst; dʌst/ *v* **thou dost** *old use or biblical*【舊或聖經】= you do

dot¹ /dɑt; dɒt/ *n* [C] **1** a small round mark or spot 點, 小圓點 **2 on the dot** *informal* exactly at a particular time【非正式】正好在某一時間: **on the dot of five (o'clock)/at five (o'clock) on the dot** *Mr Green arrived at six on the dot.* 格林先生正好在六點鐘到達。**3** something that looks like a small spot because it is so far away〔因相距很遠〕看似一個小點的物體: *The plane was just a dot in the sky.* 飛機當時只是天空中的一個小點。**4** a short sound or flash of light used when sending messages by MORSE CODE 摩爾斯電碼的點 —compare 比較 DASH[2] —see also 另見 **the year dot** (YEAR (11))

dot[2] *v* **dotted, dotting** [T] **1** to mark something by putting a dot on it or above it 在〔某物上面或上方〕加點: *She never dots her i's.* 她從來不在 i 上面加點。—see picture on page A16 參見A16頁圖 **2** [often passive 常用被動態] to spread things over a wide area and quite far apart〔星羅棋佈地〕佈滿; 分佈: **be dotted with** *The lake was dotted with sailboats.* 湖面上星星點點地密佈着帆船。| **be dotted about/around etc** *The company now has over 20 stores dotted around the country.* 該公司現擁有二十多家商店遍佈全國。**3** to put a very small amount of something on a surface or in several places on a surface 點; 點綴: *Dot some rouge on your cheeks, then blend carefully.* 往你的臉頰上點些胭脂, 然後再仔細抹勻。**4 dot the i's and cross the t's** *informal* to pay attention to all the details when you are finishing something【非正式】〔即將完成某事情時〕注意完成所有的細節: *Well, we haven't dotted the i's and crossed the t's, but the contract's nearly ready.* 我們還沒有把合同的細節弄好, 但已經快擬好了。—see also 另見 DOTTED LINE

do·tage /ˈdotɪdʒ; ˈdəʊtɪdʒ/ *n* **in your dotage** in your old age 在某人之老年, 年邁昏聵

dote /dot; dəʊt/ *v*

dote on/upon sb *phr v* [T] to love someone and to show this by your actions 溺愛, 寵愛: *I can't help doting on my granddaughter.* 我不免寵愛我的孫女。—**doting** *adj* [only before noun 僅用於名詞前]: *a doting parent* 溺愛孩子的父親[母親] —**dotingly** *adv*

doth /dʌθ; dʌθ/ *old use or biblical*【舊或聖經】= does

dot-ma·trix print·er /ˈ··· ˌ·· ˈ··/ *n* [C] a machine connected to a computer that prints letters, numbers etc using many small dots 點陣式打印機

dot·ted line /ˌ·· ˈ·/ *n* [C] **1** a series of printed or drawn DOTS that form a line 虛線, 點線: *Cut along the dotted lines.* 沿虛線剪下。**2 sign on the dotted line** *informal* to officially agree to something, especially by signing a contract【非正式】正式同意〔尤指在合同上簽字〕

dot·ty /ˈdɑtɪ; ˈdɒti/ *adj informal especially BrE*【非正式, 尤英】**1** slightly crazy or likely to behave strangely 瘋瘋癲癲的;〔行為〕古怪的 **2 dotty about sb/sth** very fond of or interested in someone or something 對某人/某物喜愛的[感興趣的, 着迷的]: *Gemma's dotty about horses.* 傑瑪非常喜歡馬。

1 **dou·ble[1]** /ˈdʌbl; ˈdʌbəl/ *adj*
2 **1 ▶OF TWO PARTS** 兩部分的◀ consisting of two parts that are similar or exactly the same 成對的, 成雙的: *You can't park on double yellow lines.* 你不可以在雙黃線上泊車。

2 double l/s/9 etc *BrE spoken* used when you are spelling a word or telling someone a number, to show that a letter or number is repeated【英口】兩個 l/s/9 等〔用在拼寫單詞或告訴某人某個數字時, 表示應該重複某個字母或數字〕: *My number is 869 34 double 2.* 我的號碼是8693422。| *That's Robbins with a double 'b'.* 是有兩個"b"的 Robbins。

3 ▶TWICE AS BIG 兩倍大◀ twice as big, twice as much, or twice as many as usual, or twice as big, much, or many as something else 雙倍的, 兩倍的: *Leave the dough in a warm place to rise until it is double in bulk.* 把濕麵團放在暖和的地方發酵, 一直發到以前兩倍那麼大。| *I'll have a double whisky please.* 我要一杯雙份威士忌。

4 ▶FOR TWO PEOPLE 雙人的◀ made to be used by two people 供兩人使用的: *a double room* 雙人房間 —compare 比較 SINGLE[1] (4)

5 ▶WITH TWO DIFFERENT USES 雙重用途的◀ combining two different uses or qualities; DUAL 有兩種用途的, 雙重的: *a double-action corkscrew* 雙重功能的瓶塞鑽 | *the double advantage of money and a good education* 既有錢又受過良好教育的雙重優勢

6 ▶DECEIVING 欺詐的◀ seeming to be one thing while actually being another; deceiving 兩面派的, 表裡不一的; 欺詐的: *There was a double meaning in Sybil's words.* 西比爾的話口不對心。| **lead a double life** (=pretend to be one type of person but really be another) 過着雙重人格的生活

7 ▶FLOWER 花◀ a double flower has more than the usual number of PETALS 雙瓣的; 重瓣的 —see also 另見 DOUBLY, **double figures** (FIGURE[1] (1b))

double[2] *n*

1 ▶TWICE THE SIZE 兩倍◀ [C,U] something that is twice the size, quantity, value, or strength of something else 兩倍, 雙倍(的量、數): *Scotch and water, please – make it a double.* 請來蘇格蘭威士忌加水 —— 要雙份的。| *"What did they offer you?" "Ten thousand." "I'll give you double."* "他們給你甚麼?" "一萬塊錢。" "我給你這個數的兩倍。"

2 ▶SIMILAR PERSON 相似的人◀ [C] someone who looks very much like someone else 極為相似的人: *Caroline's her mother's double.* 嘉羅琳和她母親長得一模一樣。

3 ▶IN FILMS 在電影中◀ [C] an actor who takes the place of another actor in a film because the acting involves something very dangerous 替身演員: *a stunt double* 特技替身演員

4 at the double *BrE*【英】, **on the double** *AmE*【美】very quickly and without any delay 飛快地, 快步地: *The firemen came around on the double.* 消防人員快速趕來。

5 ▶TENNIS 網球◀ **doubles** [U] a game played between two pairs of players 雙打: *the men's doubles* 男子雙打 —compare 比較 **singles** (SINGLE[2] (3)) —see also 另見 MIXED DOUBLES

6 double or nothing *AmE*【美】, **double or quits** *BrE*【英】a decision in a game when you must decide to do something that will either win you twice as much money or make you lose it all〔下注的一種方式〕要麼贏雙倍, 要麼輸得精光; 一賭決輸贏

7 ▶IN RACING 在比賽中◀ [C] a BET[2] (1) on the results of two races in which any money won on the first race is risked on the second 複式押注〔下注於兩場比賽, 第一場若贏將自動轉押到第二場上〕

8 ▶A THROW 投擲◀ [C] a throw in the game of darts (DART[2] (2)) that hits a point between the two outer circles on the board, and has twice the usual value〔投鏢遊戲中的〕投中加倍記分圈

9 ▶A HIT 擊打◀ [C] a hit which allows the BATTER[2] (3) in BASEBALL to reach second BASE[1] (8)〔棒球的〕二壘打

double[3] *v* **1** [I,T] to become twice as much or as many, or to make something twice as big (使) 加倍: *Unemployment more than doubled in 1921.* 失業率在1921年增加了一倍多。| *The Federal government has doubled its tax on liquor.* 聯邦政府把酒稅提高了一倍。**2** also 又作 **double sth over** [T] to fold something in half 把某物對摺: *Take a sheet of paper and double it.* 拿一張紙, 然後把它對摺。**3** [I] if a BATTER[2] (3) in a game of BASEBALL doubles, he hits the ball far enough to get to second BASE[1] (8)〔棒球比賽中〕擊出二壘打 **4 double your fists** *AmE* to curl your fingers tightly to make FISTS ready to fight【美】握緊拳頭〔準備打鬥〕

double as sb/sth *phr v* [T] to have a second use, job, or purpose as something else 兼任, 兼作: *Our local police chief doubles as the fire chief.* 我們當地的警察局長兼任消防隊長。

double back *phr v* [I] to turn around and go back the way you have come 原路折回: *I doubled back along the main highway to LA.* 我沿着去洛杉磯的主要公路折回。

double up *phr v* **1** also 又作 **double over** [I,T **double sb up**] to suddenly bend at the waist because you are laughing too much or are in pain and cannot stand up〔笑、痛得〕彎下腰; 使…直不起身: *Emilio doubled over, grabbing his leg.* 艾米利奧彎下身, 抱住自己的腿。| **be doubled up/over with** *We leant against the table,*

D

doubled over with laughter. 我們靠在桌邊，笑得直不起身。**2** [I] to share something, especially a bedroom〔尤指臥室的〕共用: *There aren't enough textbooks. Can you double up?* 課本不夠了，你們能合着用嗎？| **[+with sb]** *You'll have to double up with Susie while Aunt Clara is visiting.* 克萊拉姨媽來的時候你得和蘇茜同住一屋。

double⁴ *adv* **1 see double** to have something wrong with your eyes so that you see two things instead of one〔因眼睛有問題〕看到重影: *I was feeling dizzy and seeing double.* 我感到頭暈，看東西都是雙的。**2 be bent double** to be bent over a long way 彎得很厲害: *The trees were almost bent double in the wind.* 樹木被風吹得快要折斷了。**3 fold sth double** to fold something in half to make it twice as thick 將某物對摺〔使其比以前厚一倍〕

double⁵ *predeterminer* twice as much or twice as many 是…兩倍那麼多: *It's worth double the amount I paid for it.* 這東西值我所付價錢的兩倍。

D

double-act /ˈ·· ·/ *n* [C] two actors, especially COMEDIANS, who perform together 一起演出的兩個演員〔尤指滑稽演員〕

double a·gent /ˌ·· ˈ··/ *n* [C] someone who finds out an enemy country's secrets for their own country but who also gives secrets to the enemy 雙重間諜 —compare 比較 SPY[1]

double-bar·relled *BrE*【英】, **double-barreled** *AmE*【美】/ˌ·· ˈ··◂/ *adj* **1** a double-barrelelled gun has two places where the BULLETs come out〔槍、砲〕雙管的 **2** *BrE* a double-barrelled family name has two parts【英】〔姓氏〕由兩個姓組成的; 複姓的 **3** *AmE* with two purposes【美】雙重目的的: *a double-barreled plan* 雙重目的的計劃 **4** *AmE* very strong or using a lot of force【美】強有力的; 使用大量武力的: *a double-barreled attack* 猛烈的進攻[抨擊]

double bass /ˌdʌbl̩ ˋbes; ˌdʌbəl ˈbeɪs/ also 又作 **bass** *n* [C] a very large musical instrument shaped like a VIOLIN that the musician plays standing up 低音提琴

double bed /ˌ·· ˈ·/ *n* [C] a bed made for two people to sleep in 雙人牀 —see picture at 參見 BED[1] 圖

double bill /ˌ·· ˈ·/ *n* [C] a cinema or theatre performance in which two films or plays are shown one after the other 兩部電影[戲劇]連續放映[演出]; DOUBLE FEATURE *AmE*【美】

double bind /ˌ·· ˈ·/ *n* [C usually singular 一般用單數] a situation in which any choice you make will have unpleasant results 進退兩難的困境

double-blind /ˌ·· ˈ·◂/ *adj technical* a double-blind EXPERIMENT[1] (1) or study compares two or more groups in which neither the scientists nor the people being studied know which group is being tested and which group is not【術語】〔兩組或多組進行比較的試驗或研究中〕雙盲的〔指科學家和被試驗者均不知道哪一組正接受測試〕

double bluff /ˌ·· ˈ·/ *n* [C] an attempt to deceive someone by telling them the truth, hoping that they will think you are lying 虛實並用的詐騙術〔告訴某人實情並希望此人以為有詐〕

double boil·er /ˌ·· ˈ··/ *n* [C] a pot for cooking food, consisting of one pan resting on top of another pan with hot water in it 雙層蒸鍋

double-book /ˌ·· ˈ·/ *v* [I,T] to promise the same seat in a theatre, on a plane, etc to more than one person 重複預訂〔同一座位等〕—**double-booking** *n* [U]

double-breast·ed /ˌ·· ˈ··◂/ *adj* a double-breasted jacket, coat etc has two sets of buttons〔夾克、大衣等〕雙排鈕扣的, 對襟的 —compare 比較 SINGLE-BREASTED —see picture on page A17 參見 A17 頁圖

double-check /ˌ·· ˈ·/ *v* [I,T] to check something again so that you are completely sure 複查, 複核

double chin /ˌ·· ˈ·/ *n* [C] a fold of loose skin under someone's chin that looks like a second chin 雙下巴 —see picture on page A6 參見 A6 頁圖

double cream /ˌ·· ˈ·/ *n* [U] *BrE* very thick cream【英】高脂濃[厚]奶油 —compare 比較 SINGLE CREAM

double-cross /ˌ·· ˈ·/ *v* [T] to cheat someone, especially after you have already agreed to do something dishonest with them〔尤指在已答應和某人一起幹不誠實之事後〕出賣, 欺騙〔某人〕: *Shorty's murder was blamed on a gang he'd double-crossed in the past.* 矮子的被害歸咎於他以前出賣過的一個幫夥。—**double cross** *n* [C] —**double-crosser** *n* [C]

double date /ˌ·· ˈ·/ *n* [C] *especially AmE* an arranged social meeting for two couples (COUPLE[1](2))【尤美】為兩對男女安排的社交約會 —**double-date** *v* [I,T]

double-deal·er /ˌ·· ˈ··/ *n* [C] *informal* someone who deceives other people【非正式】表裡不一的人, 奸詐之徒 —**double-dealing** *n* [U]

double-deck·er /ˌ·· ˈ··◂/ *n* [C] **1** a bus with two levels 雙層公共汽車 **2** a SANDWICH[1] (1) made with three pieces of bread leaving two spaces to be filled with food〔三層麵包夾兩層菜或肉的〕雙層三明[文]治

double-di·git /ˌ·· ˈ··/ *adj AmE* related to the numbers 10 to 99, especially as a PERCENTAGE【美】兩位數的〔尤指百分比〕: *double-digit inflation* 兩位數的通貨膨脹率 —see also 另見 DOUBLE FIGURES

double-dip¹ /ˌ·· ˈ·/ *n* [C] *AmE* an ice-cream CONE[1] (4) with two balls of ice-cream【美】雙球冰淇淋甜筒

double-dip² *v* [I] *AmE* to collect pay or money from two places at once, usually in a way that is not legal or not approved of; MOONLIGHT[2] (2)【美】同時從兩處領取報酬〔通常以非法或不為人所贊同的方式〕

double-dutch /ˌ·· ˈ··/ *n* [U] **1** *informal* speech or writing that you cannot understand; nonsense【非正式】難懂的言語[文章]; 莫名其妙的話 **2** *AmE* a skipping (SKIP[1] (1)) game using two long ropes【美】〔使用兩條長繩的〕跳繩遊戲

double du·ty /ˌ·· ˈ··/ *n* [U] *AmE*【美】**do double duty** to do more than one job or be used for more than one thing at the same time 有雙重作用, 可以兩用: *The lids on the camping pans do double duty as plates.* 野營鍋的蓋子又可作盤子用。

double-edged /ˌ·· ˈ·◂/ *adj* **1** with two very different meanings 有兩種不同含義的, 模棱兩可的: *a double-edged remark* 模棱兩可的話 **2** with two cutting edges 雙刃的: *a double-edged sword* 雙刃劍

double en·ten·dre /ˌdubl̩ ɑnˋtɑndrə; ˌduːbl ɒnˈtɒndrə/ *n* [C] *French* a word or phrase that may be understood in two different ways, one of which is often sexual【法】〔常帶有猥褻含意的〕雙關語

double fault /ˌ·· ˈ··/ *n* [C] two mistakes, one after another, when you are serving (SERVE[1] (10)) in tennis, that make you lose a point 雙誤〔網球連續兩次發球失誤〕

double fea·ture /ˌ·· ˈ··/ *n* [C] *AmE* a cinema performance in which two films are shown one after the other; DOUBLE BILL【美】兩部影片連續放映

double fig·ures /ˌ·· ˈ··/ *n* [plural] *BrE* the numbers from 10 to 99【英】兩位數: *The death toll is thought to have reached double figures.* 據信, 死亡人數達到了兩位數。—see also 另見 DOUBLE-DIGIT

double first /ˌ·· ˈ·/ *n* [C] a British university degree in which a student reaches the highest standard in two subjects〔英國大學中的〕雙優學位〔兩門學科獲得優等成績〕

double-glaz·ing /ˌ·· ˈ··/ *n* [U] *especially BrE* glass on a window or door in two separate sheets with a space between them, in order to keep noise out and heat in【尤英】〔窗或門的〕雙層玻璃 —**double-glaze** *v* [T]

double-head·er /ˌ·· ˈ··/ *n* [C] *AmE* two BASEBALL games played one after the other【美】連續舉行的兩場棒球賽

double he·lix /ˌ·· ˈ··/ *n* [C] *technical* a shape consisting of two parallel spirals (SPIRAL[2] (1)) that twist around the same centre, found especially in the structure of DNA

【術語】雙螺旋〔尤指脫氧核糖核酸結構中的雙螺旋結構〕

double in·dem·ni·ty /,·· ·'···/ *n* [U] *AmE law* a feature of a life insurance POLICY that allows double the value of the contract to be paid in the case of death by accident【美, 法律】〔人壽保險的〕雙倍賠償〔如遇意外死亡〕

double jeop·ar·dy /,·· '···/ *n* [C] *AmE law* the act of taking someone to court a second time for the same offence, in some rare situations【美, 法律】〔在極個別情況下〕同一罪行的兩次審理

double-joint·ed /,·· '··◂/ *adj* able to move the joints in your fingers, arms etc backwards as well as forwards〔手指、手臂等關節〕可前後彎曲的; 可反彎的

double neg·a·tive /,·· '···/ *n* [C] a sentence in which two negatives (NEGATIVE² (1)) are used when only one is needed in correct English grammar, for example in the sentence 'I don't want nobody to help me!' 雙重否定〔一個句子中帶有兩個否定詞, 而其實正確的英語語法只需要一個, 如 I don't want nobody to help me! 便是雙重否定句〕

double-park /,·· '·/ *v* [I,T] to leave a vehicle on a road beside another vehicle that is already parked there 並排停放(汽車)〔把車並排停放在另一輛已停在路邊的車旁〕

double play /,·· '·/ *n* [C] *AmE* the action of making two runners in a game of BASEBALL have to leave the field by throwing the ball quickly from one BASE¹ (8) to another before the runners reach either one【美】〔棒球〕雙殺

double-quick /,·· '·◂/ *adv BrE informal* as quickly as possible【英, 非正式】快速地, 極快地: *Call an ambulance double-quick!* 快叫救護車!

double stand·ard /,·· '··/ *n* [C] a rule, principle etc that is unfair because it treats one group or type of people more severely than another in the same situation〔帶有歧視性的〕雙重標準

doub·let /ˈdʌblɪt; ˈdʌbl̩ɪt/ *n* [C] a man's shirt, worn in Europe from about 1400 to the middle 1600s〔15到17世紀中期歐洲的一種〕男用襯衫

double take /,·· '·/ *n* [C] **do a double take** to react to something after a short delay because you are surprised 先怔後悟; 慢半拍才恍然大悟

double-talk /'·· ·/ *n* [U] *informal* speech that seems to be serious and sincere, but has another meaning or is a mixture of sense and nonsense【非正式】不知所云的空話: *legal double-talk* 空洞的法律辭令 —**double-talk** *v* [I,T] —**double-talker** *n* [C]

double·think /ˈdʌbl̩ˌθɪŋk; ˈdʌbəlˌθɪŋk/ *n* [U] a dishonest belief in two opposing ideas at the same time〔同時接受兩種矛盾觀念的、不誠實的〕雙重信念; 雙重思想

double time /,·· '·/ *n* [U] **1** double wages paid to someone when they work on a day or at a time when people do not normally work〔付給加班者的〕雙倍工資 —compare 比較 **time and a half** (TIME¹ (89)) **2** *AmE* a fast military march【美】快步行進; 快步走

double-time *adv AmE informal* as quickly as possible【美, 非正式】以最快的速度: *C'mon get upstairs and clean your room – double-time!* 上樓打掃你的房間——越快越好!

double vi·sion /,·· '··/ *n* [U] a medical condition in which you see two of everything, for example after hitting your head or drinking too much alcohol 複視〔碰撞頭部或喝酒過多後會出現的一種情況〕

double wham·my /,·· '··/ *n* [C] *informal* two bad things that happen together, or one after the other【非正式】壞事成雙; 禍不單行: *the double whammy of higher prices and more taxes* 物價上漲與加稅的雙重打擊

double whole note /,·· '· ·/ *n* [C] *AmE* a musical note that continues for twice the length of a WHOLE NOTE【美】倍全音符; 二全音符; BREVE *BrE*【英】

dou·bloon /dʌˈblun; dʌˈbluːn/ *n* [C] a gold coin used in the past in Spain and Spanish America 達布隆〔舊時西班牙以及西班牙屬美洲國家使用的金幣〕

doub·ly /ˈdʌblɪ; ˈdʌbli/ *adv* **1** by twice the amount, or to twice the degree 加倍地: *Be doubly careful when driving in fog.* 在霧中開車要加倍小心。**2** in two ways or for two reasons 在兩個方面; 由於雙重原因造成: *You are doubly mistaken.* 你有兩個方面的錯誤。

doubt¹ /daut; daʊt/ *n* S1 W1

1 ►UNCERTAIN FEELING 不確定的感覺◄ [C,U] a feeling or feelings of being uncertain about something 不確定, 懷疑: **[+about/as to]** *Maisie expressed private doubts about Lawrence's sanity.* 梅西對勞倫斯的神志正常與否在私下裡表示懷疑。| **[+whether/who/what etc]** *There's no doubt who was responsible for this outrage.* 誰該對這項惡事負責, 已無疑問。| **[+(that)]** *I have little doubt that the coup will succeed.* 這次突然行動將取得成功, 對此我毫不懷疑。| **cast doubt(s) on sth/raise doubts about sth** (=say that something may not be true or real) 對某事提出懷疑 *The new evidence cast some doubt on his reliability as a witness.* 新的證據令人懷疑他作為證人的可靠性。| **an element of doubt** (=a slight doubt) 少許懷疑 | **without a shadow of a doubt** (=there is no doubt at all) 絲毫沒有懷疑

2 no doubt used when you are saying that you think something is probably true 多半, 很可能: *No doubt she was disturbed by the noise.* 多半是噪音驚擾了她。| **no doubt about it** (=it is certainly true) 確實無疑 *Someone had been eavesdropping, no doubt about it.* 確實無疑, 有人一直在偷聽。

3 have your doubts (about) used to say that you have reasons for not feeling certain about something or someone (對…) 持有懷疑: *"Don't you think she'd be a good candidate?" "Well, I have my doubts."* "難道你不認為她會是一個不錯的候選人嗎?" "嗯, 我有懷疑。"

4 if/when in doubt used when advising someone what to do 如無把握; 如有懷疑〔用於建議〕: *If in doubt, don't eat it.* 如果有懷疑, 就別吃它。

5 be in doubt if someone's or something's future or success is in doubt, they may not be able to continue or succeed〔對…的將來或成功等〕不太有把握: *The future of the public library is in doubt.* 公共圖書館的前途難以預料。

6 be in doubt about to not be certain about something 對…不確定: *He's still in some doubt about what to do.* 他對該如何行事還是猶豫不決。

7 be beyond doubt if something is beyond doubt, it is completely certain 確實無疑: *Patel's integrity is beyond doubt.* 帕特爾的誠實是確實無疑的。| **beyond reasonable doubt** *law*【法律】*Her guilt was established beyond reasonable doubt.* 她被確實證明有罪。

8 without/beyond doubt *formal* used to emphasize an opinion【正式】確實〔用於強調某個觀點〕: *Sally was without doubt one of the finest swimmers in the school.* 莎莉確實是學校最優秀的游泳能手之一。

9 open to doubt something that is open to doubt has not been proved to be definitely true or real 有待證明的: *The authenticity of the relics is open to doubt.* 這些遺骸的真假有待考證。—see also 另見 SELF-DOUBT, **give sb/sth the benefit of the doubt** (BENEFIT¹ (4))

doubt² *v* [T not in progressive 不用進行式] S2 **1** to think that something may not be true 懷疑, 不確信: *Kim never doubted his story.* 金對於他講的事情從不懷疑。| **doubt (that)** *I don't doubt that he's a brilliant scientist, but can he teach?* 我不懷疑他是個出色的科學家, 但他會教書嗎? **2** *especially spoken* to think that something is unlikely【尤口】認為〔某事〕未必可能: **doubt if/whether** *You can complain, but I doubt if it'll make any difference.* 你可以抱怨, 但是我看抱怨也未必有用。| **doubt sth** *"Do you think there'll be any tickets left?" "I very much doubt it."* "你認為還會有餘票嗎?" "我認為很可能沒有了。" | **doubt (that)** *I doubt that we'll ever see George again.* 我懷疑我們可能再也不會見到喬治了。**3** to not trust or have confidence in someone 不信任〔某人〕; 對〔某人〕沒有信心: *If anyone doubts my ability to handle this, they should say so.* 如果有人懷疑我處理此事的能力, 他應該說出來。| **doubt sb's word** (=think that someone may not be telling the truth) 懷疑某人說的話 —**doubter** *n* [C]

doubt·ful /ˈdaʊtfəl; ˈdaʊtfəl/ *adj* **1** having doubts about something 有疑問的, 感到懷疑的: *The journalist looked doubtful when he heard her story.* 記者聽她講事情經過時面有疑色。| **[+if/whether]** *I'm still doubtful whether I should accept this job.* 我還是拿不定主意該不該接受這份工作。| **doubtful about (doing) sth** *At first we were doubtful about employing Charlie.* 起初我們拿不定主意是否應該雇用查理。**2** something that is doubtful may not be true or may not happen in the way you want 難以預料的, 未定的: *The company's prospects are starting to look more doubtful.* 公司的前景看起來開始更難以預料了。| **[+if/whether]** *It was doubtful whether the patient would survive the operation.* 病人是否能熬過這次手術還很難說。**3** unlikely 不大可能的: **[+that]** *It now seems doubtful that the missing airmen will ever be found.* 要找到那個失蹤的飛行員現在看來是不大可能了。**4** probably false or of no value; DUBIOUS 有可能是假的[沒價值的]: *Pringle was given the doubtful privilege of leading the troops.* 普林格爾受命統率部隊, 這對他是否是件好事還不好說。—**doubtfully** *adv*

doubt·ing Thom·as /ˌdaʊtɪŋ ˈtɑməs; ˌdaʊtɪŋ ˈtɒməs/ *n* [singular] *humorous* someone who tends to doubt things if they have not seen proof of them【幽默】懷疑主義者; 有真憑實據才肯相信的人

doubt·less /ˈdaʊtləs; ˈdaʊtləs/ *adv formal* used when saying something that you believe to be true although you have no proof【正式】無疑地, 肯定地: *Renee was doubtless reassured by the news.* 蕾妮聽到這個消息確實感到放心了。

douche /duʃ; duːʃ/ *n* [C usually singular 一般用單數] **1** a mixture of water and something such as VINEGAR, that a woman puts into her VAGINA to wash it 沖洗液, 灌洗液〔水與某物如醋的混合液, 供婦女清洗下體之用〕**2** water that is poured over part of someone's body 沖向身體某部位的水 —**douche** *v* [I,T]

dough /do; dəʊ/ *n* **1** [singular, U] a mixture of flour and water ready to be baked into bread, PASTRY etc〔做麵包、糕點等用的〕生麵團, 濕麵團 **2** [U] *informal* money【非正式】錢

dough·nut /ˈdonət; ˈdəʊnʌt/ *n* [C] **1** a small round cake, often in the form of a ring 炸麵圈; 多福餅 **2 do doughnuts** *AmE informal* to make a car spin around in circles【美, 非正式】讓汽車轉圈

dough·ty /ˈdaʊtɪ; ˈdaʊti/ *adj* [only before noun 僅用於名詞前] *literary* brave and determined【文】勇敢的, 堅決的: *a doughty fighter* 勇猛的鬥士

dough·y /ˈdoɪ; ˈdəʊi/ *adj* **1** looking and feeling like DOUGH (1) 像麵團的 **2** doughy skin is unhealthily pale and soft〔皮膚〕蒼白的, 柔軟的

dour /dʊr; dʊə/ *adj* **1** severe and never smiling 嚴厲的; 臉色陰沉的 **2** making you feel anxious or afraid; GRIM (1) 令人憂慮[恐懼]的: *a dour reminder* 嚴峻的提示 —**dourly** *adv*

douse, dowse /daʊs; daʊs/ *v* [T] **1** to put out a fire by pouring water on it 用水澆滅〔火〕**2** **[+with/in]** to cover something in water or other liquid 用水[其他液體]浸沒〔某物〕

dove¹ /dʌv; dʌv/ *n* [C] **1** a kind of small PIGEON (=bird) often used as a sign of peace 鴿子〔常用作和平的象徵〕**2** someone in politics who prefers peace and discussion to war〔政治上的〕鴿派人物〔指主張和平與對話、反對戰爭的人〕—opposite 反義詞 HAWK¹ (2)

dove² /dov; dəʊv/ *especially AmE*【尤美】a past tense of DIVE¹

dove·cot /ˈdʌvˌkɑt; ˈdʌvkɒt/ also 又作 **dove·cote** /ˈdʌvˌkot; ˈdʌvkəʊt/ *n* [C] a small house built for doves to live in 鴿舍, 鴿房

dove·tail¹ /ˈdʌvˌtel; ˈdʌvteɪl/ *v* **1** [I,T] to fit perfectly together or to make two plans, ideas etc fit together perfectly 吻合; 使〔兩個計劃、觀點等〕吻合: **[+with]** *My vacation plans dovetail nicely with Joyce's.* 我的度假計劃與喬伊絲的度假計劃完全一致。**2** **[T+together]** to join two pieces of wood by means of dovetail joints 用鳩尾榫接合〔兩塊木頭〕

dovetail² also 又作 **dovetail joint** /ˌ.. ˈ./ *n* [C] a type of JOINT² (3) fastening two pieces of wood together 鳩尾榫

dov·ish /ˈdʌvɪʃ; ˈdʌvɪʃ/ *adj* preferring peace and discussion to war 鴿派的, 愛好和平的

dow·a·ger /ˈdaʊədʒɚ; ˈdaʊədʒə/ *n* [C] **1** a woman from a high social class who has land or a title from her dead husband〔承襲亡夫土地或封號的〕孀居貴婦: *the dowager Duchess of Devonshire* 德文郡公爵的遺孀 **2** *informal* a respected and impressive old lady【非正式】受人欽敬的老婦人

dow·dy /ˈdaʊdɪ; ˈdaʊdi/ *adj* **1** unattractive or unfashionable 不漂亮的; 過時的: *a dowdy frock* 款式陳舊的衣裙 **2** a dowdy woman wears dull or unfashionable clothes〔指婦女〕穿着單調[過時]的 —**dowdily** *adv* —**dowdiness** *n* [U]

dow·el /ˈdaʊəl; ˈdaʊəl/ *n* [C] a wooden pin for holding two pieces of wood, metal, or stone together 木釘, 暗榫

Dow Jones Av·e·rage /ˌdaʊ dʒonz ˈævərɪdʒ; ˌdaʊ dʒəʊnz ˈævərɪdʒ/ *n* [singular] a daily list of prices of shares (SHARE² (5)) on the American STOCK EXCHANGE, based on the daily average prices of 30 industrial shares 道瓊斯(工業)平均指數〔指在美國證券交易所中, 以特定的30種工業股票的日平均價格為依據的股票相對價格指數〕

down- /daʊn; daʊn/ *prefix* **1** to a lower position 向下: *to downgrade a job* (=make it lower in importance) 降低某工作的重要性 | *a downpour* (=heavy rain) 傾盆大雨 **2** in some adverbs and adjectives, means at or towards the bottom or end of something〔構成某些副詞和形容詞〕在[接近]某事物的底部[一端]: *downstairs* 在樓下; 往樓下 | *downriver* (=nearer to its mouth) 近河口的; 下游的 **3** in some adverbs and adjectives, means at or towards the lower or worst part of something〔構成某些副詞和形容詞〕在[面向]某事物的低層的[最差的]部分: *down-market* (=meeting the demand of the lower social groups) 面向社會低層市場的 —compare 比較 UP-

down¹ /daʊn; daʊn/ *adv* **1** from above towards a lower place or position 從上到下, 從高到低, 朝下: *David bent down to tie his shoelace.* 大衛彎下身繫鞋帶。| *The sun beat down on their heads all day long.* 太陽一整天火辣辣地照在他們頭上。**2** at a lower place or position than usual 處在比通常更低的地方[位置]: *You can't cross here, the bridge is down.* 你無法在這兒過河, 橋在下游。**3** at or towards a lower position or floor 位於[朝向]低處[低層]: *We heard the sound of laughter down below.* 我們聽到樓下的笑聲。| *Let's go down to the kitchen.* 我們下去到廚房吧。**4** into a sitting or lying position (坐)下, (躺)下: *Please sit down.* 請坐。| *I think I'll go and lie down for a while.* 我想去躺一小會兒。**5** firmly and tightly into place or position 牢固地固定好, 緊緊地附着: *Have you stuck down the envelope?* 你把信封粘牢了嗎? **6** towards the south 朝南, 向南方: *They drove all the way down from Boston to Miami.* 他們開車南下從波士頓一直到邁阿密。—opposite 反義詞 UP¹ (4) **7** *BrE* away from a university at the end of a period of study【英】〔學習期滿〕離開大學, 畢業: *Sarah went down from Oxford in 1966.* 莎拉在1966年從牛津大學畢業。**8** at or towards a lower level in price or amount〔價格或數量〕處於低水平, 減少: *Keep your speed down.* 保持低速度。| *House prices have come down in recent months.* 最近幾個月屋價降下來了。**9** into a weaker, smaller, or quieter state 變弱; 變小; 變安靜: *Would you mind turning the radio down?* 你把收音機音量調小些好嗎? | *The heels of his shoes had worn down.* 他的鞋跟已經磨薄了。| **[+to]** *Sharif cut his report down to only three pages.* 沙里夫把他的報告刪減到只有三頁。**10 be down to your last pound/dollar/litre** to be left with only a small amount of something 只剩下最後一鎊/一元/一升: *We're down to our last five dollars.* 我們只剩下最後五塊錢了。**11 write/note/jot/take down** to write something on paper 記下, 寫下: *I'll write down the address for you.* 我替你把地址寫下來。**12 pass/hand down** to give or tell something to people in the next GENERATION (1) 把〔某物〕傳給[告知]〔下一代〕: *The jewels were passed down through the family.* 這些珠寶是家傳的。**13** paid to someone immediately in CASH[1] (1) 首付現金: *A top quality freezer for only £20 down and £5 a week for a year.* 品質最佳的冰櫃只需先付20英鎊現金, 餘額每週付5英鎊, 一年內付清。**14** from top to bottom 從頂部到底部: *I want you to wash my car down.* 請你把我的車徹底沖洗乾淨。**15** in or into the body as a result of swallowing 咽下, 吞下: *Meg's been very ill and can't keep her food down.* 梅格病得很重, 吃不下東西。**16 be down to sb** if something is down to someone they are responsible for it or must make a decision about it 該由某人負責; 該由某人作出決定: *It's down to Tom to decide whether to pay it or not.* 是否付款應該由湯姆來決定。—see also 另見 **be up to sb** (UP[1] (16)) **17 be/come down to sth** to be mainly the result of one particular thing 是由於某事物的原因/歸結為某事物: *Most of the problems came down to bad management.* 多數問題是由於管理不善造成的。**18 Down!** *spoken* used to tell a jumping dog to get down【口】趴下!〔用於命令跳躍的狗〕**19 down to** including something or someone at a low level or rank 下至〔等級低或職位低的物或人〕: *Everyone uses the cafeteria, from the managing director down to the office boy.* 上至經理下到辦公室的工友, 大家都在食堂用餐。**20 down under** *informal* in or to Australia or New Zealand【非正式】位於[前往]澳大利亞[澳洲]或新西蘭[紐西蘭] **21 Down with...** *spoken* used to express opposition and a wish for someone or something to go【口】打倒...: *Down with the government!* 打倒政府! **22 be/go down with sth** to have a particular illness 患某種疾病: *Jane's down with flu.* 珍得了流感。

1 **down²** *prep* **1** towards the ground or a lower point, or in a lower position 向[位於]較低處: *The bathroom is down those stairs.* 浴室順着樓梯往下走便是。**2** along 沿着, 順着: *The wind raced down the alley.* 風順着胡同颼過去。**3 down the river** in the direction of the river's current 順流: *We sailed down the river.* 我們沿河向下游航行。**4 down the shops/park/market etc** *BrE informal* an expression meaning to or at the shops etc, that some people think is not correct【英, 非正式】前往[位於]商店/公園/市場等〔有人認為這種表達法不正確〕: *Bob's just gone down the pub.* 鮑伯剛去了酒吧。**5 down the road/pike/line etc** *AmE* at some time in the future【美】在未來的某個時間: *You'll understand better a few years down the line when you've had some experience.* 過幾年你有了經驗時會更加明白的。

down³ *adj*

1 ►SAD 傷心的◄ [not before noun 不用於名詞前] sad and discouraged 傷心的; 沮喪的: *Andy's been feeling down lately.* 安迪最近情緒很低落。

2 ►IN A GAME 在比賽中◄ [not before noun 不用於名詞前] behind an opponent by a certain number of points〔比分〕落後的: *Agassi was down by two sets to one.* 阿加西以1:2落後於對手。

3 ►COMPLETED 完成的◄ [not before noun 不用於名詞前] *informal* done or finished【非正式】完成的, 做完的: *Three exercises down and two to go.* 完成了三個練習, 還剩下兩個。

4 be down on sb/sth *informal* to have a low opinion of someone or something【非正式】看不上[不齒]某人/某物: *Why is Mark so down on her at the moment?* 為甚麼現在馬克這麼嫌惡她?

5 ►COMPUTER 電腦◄ [not before noun 不用於名詞前] if a computer is down, it is not working 停止工作的, 停機的, 不運行的 —opposite 反義詞 UP[3] (3)

6 have/put sb down for sth to have or put someone's name on a list of people who want to do something 把某人的名字寫在想做某事者的名單上: *Put me down to bring the desserts.* 把我登記上, 我要帶甜品來。

7 down escalator/staircase an ESCALATOR (=moving stairs) or stairs which take you down to a lower level 下行的自動扶梯/樓梯 — see also 另見 **be down on your luck** (LUCK[1] (14))

down⁴ *v* [T] **1** to drink or eat something quickly 很快吃下, 喝下: *Jack downed three beers with his steak and fries.* 傑克就着牛排和炸薯條喝下了三杯啤酒。**2** to knock or force someone to the ground 將〔某人〕打倒在地: *O'Malley downed his opponent in the first round.* 奧馬利第一回合就把對手擊倒。**3 down tools** *BrE* to stop working at the end of a day or to STRIKE (=protest about conditions by stopping work)【英】停工; 罷工〔抗議惡劣的工作條件〕

down⁵ *n* **1** [U] soft hair like a baby's 柔毛, 絨毛 **2** [U] the soft fine feathers of a bird 小鳥的絨羽 **3** [C] one of the four chances that an American football team has to move forward when it is their turn to have the ball〔美式足球〕10碼進攻 **4 the downs** low round hills covered with grass, as in the south of England 草木覆蓋的低圓山丘〈如英格蘭南部的山丘〉**5 have a down on sb** *BrE informal* to dislike or have a bad opinion of someone【英, 非正式】討厭某人; 看不上某人: *Mark had a down on Utopians.* 馬克討厭所有烏托邦式的空想主義者。—see also 另見 **ups and downs** (UP[4] (2))

down-and-out /ˌ· · ˈ·◂/ *n* [C] *informal* someone who has no job, no money, and nowhere to live【非正式】窮困潦倒的人 —**down-and-out** *adj*

down-at-heel /ˌ· · ˈ·◂/ *adj especially BrE* dressed in old clothes and looking as if you do not have much money【尤英】穿着破舊的, 衣衫襤褸的, 看似貧窮的

down·beat¹ /ˈdaunˌbit; ˈdaʊnbiːt/ *n* [C] **1** the first note in a BAR[1] (6) of music〔樂譜上的〕強拍 **2** the movement a CONDUCTOR makes to show when this note is to be played or sung 下拍〔樂隊指揮表示要演奏或唱出某個音符時向下的手勢〕

downbeat² *adj informal* not showing any strong feelings, especially not happy ones【非正式】無激情的; 憂鬱的: *Al was surprisingly downbeat about the party.* 奇怪的是, 阿爾對那個聚會一點也不熱心。—compare 比較 UPBEAT

down·cast /ˈdaunˌkæst; ˈdaʊnkɑːst/ *adj* **1** sad or upset because of something bad that has happened〔因發生了壞事而〕悲哀的, 不安的: *Keith is very downcast at the moment – he misses his wife terribly.* 基思現在非常沮喪 —— 他極度想念他的妻子。**2** downcast eyes are looking down〔指眼睛〕目光向下的, 低垂的

down·er /ˈdaunɚ; ˈdaʊnə/ *n informal*【非正式】**1** [C] a drug that makes you feel very relaxed or sleepy 鎮靜藥; 安眠藥 —compare 比較 UPPER[2] (2) **2** [singular] a person or situation that stops you feeling cheerful or happy 令人沮喪的人[情況]: *"Nick can't come." "What a downer."* "尼克來不了啦。" "真掃興。" **3 be on a downer** *BrE* to be sad or experiencing a series of sad events【英】沮喪; 經歷一連串傷心事: *What's up with Ruth? She's been on a downer all week.* 魯思怎麼啦? 她整個星期心情都不好。

down·fall /ˈdaunˌfɔl; ˈdaʊnfɔːl/ *n* [singular] complete loss of your money, moral standards, social position etc, or the sudden failure of an organization 衰落; 墮落; 垮台: *The scandal led to the family's downfall.* 醜聞導致了那個家族的敗落。| **be sb's downfall** *That one error of judgment was his downfall.* 那一次判斷錯誤是他失敗的原因。

down·grade /ˈdaunˌgred; ˈdaʊngreɪd/ *v* [T] **1** to make a job less important or move someone to a less important job 降低〔某職位〕的重要性; 降〔某人〕的職: **downgrade sb/sth to sth** *Harris was downgraded to Assistant Manager.* 哈里斯被降為助理經理。—opposite 反義詞 UPGRADE **2** to make something seem less important or valuable than it is 貶低, 輕視

down·heart·ed /ˌdaun`hɑrtɪd; ˌdaʊnˈhɑːtɪ̍d◂/ *adj* discouraged or made sad by something 情緒低落的, 沮喪的: *When no replies came, I began to feel downhearted.* 因為沒有收到答覆, 我開始感到沮喪。

down·hill¹ /`daun,hɪl; ˌdaʊnˈhɪl◂/ *adv* [only after verb 僅用於動詞後] **1** towards the bottom of a hill or lower land 向山下: *I had to run downhill as fast as I could.* 我得盡快往山下跑。**2 go downhill** to become worse 走下坡路, 每況愈下: *They won the first game but after that things went downhill.* 他們打贏了第一場比賽, 但此後便每況愈下。

downhill² *adj* **1** on a slope that goes down to a lower point 下坡的: *downhill skiing* 下坡滑雪 | *The path was all downhill.* 小路全程都是下坡。**2** [not before noun 不用於名詞前] easy to do, especially after you have been doing something difficult 容易做的〔尤指在做過困難的事情之後〕; 一帆風順的: **all downhill/downhill all the way** *The worst is over — it's all downhill from here.* 最困難的已經過去了 —— 從此一切都將是一帆風順了。

D

down·home /`daun,hom; ˈdaʊnhəʊm/ *adj AmE* related to the values and customs of people who live in the countryside【美】鄉村的; 有鄉村人特點的

Dow·ning Street /`daunɪŋ ,strit; ˈdaʊnɪŋ striːt/ *n* [not with *the* 不與 the 連用] the government or PRIME MINISTER of Great Britain 唐寧街, 英國政府; 英國首相: *Downing Street declined to comment on the allegations.* 英國政府拒絕就那些說法置論。

down·load /ˌdaun`lod; ˌdaʊnˈləʊd/ *v* [T] to move information or PROGRAMs from one part of a computer system to another 下載〔資訊或程式〕

down·mar·ket /ˌdaun`mɑrkɪt; ˌdaʊnˈmɑːkɪ̍t◂/ *adj BrE* downmarket goods or services are cheap and not of very good quality【英】〔指商品、服務等〕低檔的, 廉價的; 質量不好的: *a downmarket magazine aimed at working mums* 針對有工作的母親的低檔雜誌 —compare 比較 UPMARKET —**downmarket** *adv*

down pay·ment /ˌ· ˈ··/ *n* [C] a payment you make when you buy something that is only part of the full price, with the rest to be paid later〔分期付款購物的〕首次付款; 定金: **make a down payment** *We've made a down payment on a washing machine.* 我們買洗衣機的首期付款已經交了。—compare 比較 DEPOSIT¹

down·play /ˌdaun`ple; ˌdaʊnˈpleɪ/ *v* [T] to make something seem less important than it really is; play down (PLAY¹) 貶低; 輕視: *Officials are downplaying last month's drop in exports.* 官員們對上月出口額的下降輕描淡寫。

down·pour /`daun,pɔr; ˈdaʊnpɔː/ *n* [C often singular 常用單數] a lot of rain that falls in a short time 傾盆大雨 —see picture on page A13 參見 A13 頁圖

down·right¹ /`daun,raɪt; ˈdaʊnraɪt/ *adj* [only before noun 僅用於名詞前] used to emphasize that someone or something is completely bad, false, or unpleasant 徹頭徹尾的, 全然的〔用於強調某人或某事物極差、極假、極討厭〕: *That's a downright lie!* 那是徹頭徹尾的謊言!

downright² *adv* [+adj/adv] used to emphasize that someone or something is completely bad, untrue, unpleasant etc 十足地, 徹底地〔用來強調某人或某事物極差、極假或極討厭等〕: *Jed's just downright lazy.* 傑德簡直是懶透了。

down·riv·er /ˌdaun`rɪvɚ; daʊnˈrɪvə/ *adv* in the direction that the water in a river is flowing 順流地: *The bridge was another mile downriver.* 橋在往下游再走一英里處。—compare 比較 DOWNSTREAM

down·side /`daun,saɪd; ˈdaʊnsaɪd/ *n* **the downside** the negative side of something〔某事物〕消極的一面, 負面, 反面: *The downside of the plan is that we lose a lot of time.* 這項計劃的缺點是我們失去很多時間。

down·size /`daun,saɪz; ˈdaʊnsaɪz/ *v* [I,T] if a company or organization downsizes, or downsizes its operations, it reduces the number of people it employs in order to reduce costs〔指公司、機構為縮減開支而〕裁(員); 緊縮(編制) —**downsizing** *n* [U]

down·spout /`daun,spaut; ˈdaʊnspaʊt/ *n* [C] *AmE* a pipe that carries water away from the roof of a building【美】水落管, 屋頂排水管; DRAINPIPE *BrE*【英】

Down's syn·drome /ˈ· ,··/ *n* [U] a condition that someone is born with, that stops them from developing in a normal way, both mentally and physically 唐氏綜合徵, 先天愚型

down·stage /`daun`stedʒ; ˌdaʊnˈsteɪdʒ◂/ *adv* towards or near the front of the stage in a theatre 向[接近]舞台前部 —**downstage** *adj* —opposite 反義詞 UPSTAGE²

down·stairs /`daun`stɛrz; ˌdaʊnˈsteəz◂/ *adv* **1** towards or on a lower floor of a building, especially a house 往樓下; 在樓下: *Rosie ran downstairs.* 羅茜跑下樓去。**2 the downstairs** the rooms on the ground floor in a house 房屋中第一層樓的房間: *We have still got to paint the downstairs.* 我們還得把底層的房間粉刷一下。—compare 比較 UPSTAIRS —**downstairs** *adj*: *a downstairs room* 樓下的房間

down·stream /`daun`strim; ˌdaʊnˈstriːm◂/ *adv* in the direction the water in a river or stream is flowing 順流而下; 向下游方向: *a boat drifting downstream* 順水漂流而下的小船 —compare 比較 DOWNRIVER, UPSTREAM

down·time /`daun,taɪm; ˈdaʊntaɪm/ *n* [U] the time when a computer is not working〔電腦的〕停機時間

down-to-earth /ˌ· · ˈ·◂/ *adj* practical and direct in a sensible honest way 實事求是的, 實際的, 切實的, 務實的, 腳踏實地的: *a down-to-earth approach to health care* 切實可行的衛生保健方法

down·town /`daun`taun; ˌdaʊnˈtaʊn◂/ *adv especially AmE* towards or in the centre or main business area of a town or city【尤美】向[在]城鎮商業中心區, 向[在]市中心; CITY CENTRE *BrE*【英】: **go downtown** *I have to go downtown later.* 過一會兒我得到市中心去。—**downtown** *adj* [only before noun 僅用於名詞前]: *downtown restaurants* 位於鬧市區的餐廳 —compare 比較 UPTOWN

down·trod·den /`daun`trɑdn̩; ˈdaʊn,trɒdn/ *adj* downtrodden people, workers etc are treated badly and without respect by people who have power over them 被〔有權勢者〕踐踏的, 受壓迫的

down·turn /`dauntɝn; ˈdaʊntɜːn/ *n* [C usually singular 一般用單數] a period or process in which business activity, production etc is reduced and conditions become worse〔指經濟活動、生產等的〕下降趨勢; 衰退: *a sharp economic downturn* 經濟的急劇下滑 | **[+in]** *a downturn in shipbuilding orders* 造船訂單數量的減少 —opposite 反義詞 UPTURN

down·ward /`daunwɚd; ˈdaʊnwəd/ *adj* [only before noun 僅用於名詞前] going down to a lower level or place 向下的, 向低處的: *a gentle downward slope* 平緩往下的坡 | *Share prices continued their downward trend.* 股價持續其下跌的趨勢。—opposite 反義詞 UPWARD

down·ward·ly mo·bile /ˌ··· ˈ··/ *adj* someone who is downwardly mobile is becoming poorer〔指人〕越來越窮的; 趨向貧困的

down·wards /`daunwɚdz; ˈdaʊnwədz/ also 又作 **downward** *adv* **1** towards a lower level or position 向下: *Nina glanced downwards.* 妮娜向下瞥了一眼。| **face downwards** (=with the front towards the ground) 臉朝下 *The body lay face downwards on the rug.* 屍體臉朝下伏在地毯上。—opposite 反義詞 UPWARDS (1) **2** down to and including the lowest position in a set 一整體中下至及包括最低的職位: *Everyone from the chairman downwards is taking a pay cut.* 每個人, 上至總裁下至職位最低的人都將減薪。—opposite 反義詞 UPWARDS (1)

down·wind /ˌdaun`wɪnd; ˌdaʊnˈwɪnd/ *adv* in the direction that the wind is moving 順風地

down·y /`daunɪ; ˈdaʊni/ *adj* covered in or filled with soft fine hair or feathers 被絨羽覆蓋的; 充滿絨毛的: *the baby's downy head* 嬰兒毛茸茸的腦袋

dow·ry /ˋdaʊri; ˈdaʊəri/ *n* [C] property and money that a woman gives to her husband when they marry in some societies〔新娘的〕嫁妝

dowse[1] /dauz; daʊz/ *v* [I+for] to look for water or minerals under the ground using a special stick that points to where they are; DIVINE[2] (2) 用一種特殊的枝椏探水[探礦]

dowse[2] /daus; daʊs/ *v* [T] another spelling of DOUSE douse 的另一種拼法

dow·ser /ˋdauzɚ; ˈdaʊzə/ *n* [C] someone who dowses for water or minerals 用枝椏探水[探礦]者

dows·ing rod /ˈ·· ·/ *n* [C] a special stick in the shape of a Y used by a dowser 探測水源[礦牀]者使用的丫形卜棒

doy·en /ˋdɔɪən; ˈdɔɪən/ *n* [C] the oldest, most respected, or most experienced member of a group〔某團體中的〕資深者; 老前輩; 元老: **the doyen of** *the doyen of sports commentators* 體育評論員中的元老

doy·enne /dɔɪˋɛn; dɔɪˈen/ *n* [C] the oldest, most respected, or most experienced woman in a group〔某團體中的〕女老前輩: **the doyenne of** *the doyenne of gossip columnists* 漫談專欄作家中的女元老

doz *n* the written abbreviation of 縮寫= DOZEN

doze /doz; dəʊz/ *v* [I] to sleep lightly for a short time 小睡, 打瞌睡, 打盹兒: *Pam often dozes in her chair after lunch.* 帕姆經常在午飯後坐在椅子上打盹。—**doze** *n* [singular] *especially BrE*【尤英】: *having a doze in front of the telly* 坐在電視機前打個盹兒

doze off *phr v* [I] to go to sleep, especially when you did not intend to; **drop off** (DROP[1]), **nod off** (NOD[1])〔尤指在無意的情況下〕打盹, 打瞌睡: *I was just dozing off when the phone rang.* 我剛打盹, 電話就響了。

2 3 **doz·en** /ˋdʌzn̩; ˈdʌzən/ written abbreviation 縮寫為 **doz** *determiner plural* **dozen** *or* **dozens 1 a dozen/two dozen/three dozen** a group of twelve 一打/兩打/三打〔每打為12個〕: *a dozen eggs* 一打雞蛋 | *half a dozen* 半打; 六個 **2 dozens (of)** *informal* a lot of【非正式】許多; 數十個; 幾打: *I've been there dozens of times.* 我到過那兒很多次了。| **dozens and dozens** *They collected dozens and dozens of shells on the beach.* 他們在海灘上撿了很多很多的貝殼。—see also 另見 BAKER'S DOZEN, **a dime a dozen** (DIME (2)), **nineteen to the dozen** (NINETEEN (2)), **six of one and half a dozen of the other** (SIX (2))

doz·y /ˋdozɪ; ˈdəʊzi/ *adj* **1** not feeling very awake 昏昏欲睡的; 睏倦的: *I was feeling dozy after lunch.* 吃過午餐後我覺得有點睏。**2** *BrE informal* slow to understand things; stupid【英, 非正式】遲鈍的, 愚蠢的: *Those kids are really dozy!* 那些孩子們真是笨啊! —**dozily** *adv* —**doziness** *n* [U]

DP /ˌdi ˋpi; ˌdiː ˈpiː/ the abbreviation of 縮寫= DATA PROCESSING

D Phil /ˌdi ˋfɪl; ˌdiː ˈfɪl/ the abbreviation of 縮寫= Doctor of Philosophy

Dr 1 the written abbreviation of 縮寫= DOCTOR **2** the written abbreviation of 縮寫= DRIVE[2] (7): *88 Park Dr* 公園大道88號

drab[1] /dræb; dræb/ *adj* not bright in colour or not interesting〔色彩〕暗淡的, 單調的; 乏味的: *The city looked drab and colourless to me.* 那座城市在我看來枯燥乏味。

drab[2] *n* [C] *old use* a dirty, untidy, and perhaps immoral woman【舊】邋遢的女人; 不規矩的女人 —see also 另見 DRIBS AND DRABS

drach·ma /ˋdrækmə; ˈdrækmə/ *n* [C] *plural* **drachmas** *or* **drachmae** /-mi; -miː/ **1** the unit of money in modern Greece 德拉克馬〔現代希臘貨幣單位〕 **2** an ancient Greek silver coin and weight 古希臘銀幣; 古希臘重量單位

dra·co·ni·an /drəˋkonɪən; drəˈkəʊniən/ *adj* very strict and cruel 嚴厲的, 殘酷的: **draconian laws/measures/methods etc** *draconian measures to control population growth* 控制人口增長的嚴厲措施

2 3 **draft[1]** /dræft; drɑːft/ *n*

1 ▶UNFINISHED FORM 未完成的形式◀ [C] a piece of writing, a drawing, or a plan that is not yet in its finished form 草稿; 草圖; 草案: **make a draft** *Let's make a rough draft of the letter.* 我們寫一下信的草稿吧。| **first/final draft** *the first draft of a poem* 詩的初稿 | **draft proposal/copy/version etc** *a draft copy of a newspaper article* 報紙文章的稿樣

2 ▶ARMY 軍隊◀ **the draft** *AmE*【美】**a)** *informal* a system in which people are ordered to fight for their country when it is involved in a war; CONSCRIPTION【非正式】徵兵, 徵募 **b)** the group of people who are ordered to do this 被徵入伍者

3 ▶MONEY 錢◀ [C] *especially BrE* a written order for money to be paid by a bank, especially from one bank to another【尤英】匯票: **by draft** *Payment must be made by bank draft.* 必須以銀行匯票付款。

4 ▶SPORTS 體育運動◀ [C] a system in some American sports in which PROFESSIONAL[1] (3) teams pick players from colleges for their teams〔美國一些職業球隊〕從大學選拔隊員的制度

5 ▶COLD AIR/DRINKS 冷空氣/飲料◀ [C] the American spelling of DRAUGHT draught 的美式拼法

draft[2] *v* [T] **1** to write a plan, letter, report etc that will need to be changed before it is in its finished form 起草, 草擬〔計劃、信件、報告等〕: *Eva's busy drafting her speech for the conference.* 伊娃正忙着起草她在大會發言的講演稿。**2** *AmE* to order someone to serve in their country's military during a war; CONSCRIPT[1] (1)【美】〔戰時〕徵召〔某人〕入伍; 徵募; CALL-UP *BrE*【英】: **be drafted into sth** *Joe's been drafted into the army.* 喬已經應徵入伍。

draft board /ˈ· ·/ *n* [C] *AmE* the committee that decides who will be drafted into the military【美】徵兵局

draft card /ˈ· ·/ *n* [C] *AmE* a card sent to someone telling them they have been drafted【美】服兵役通知卡

draft dod·ger /ˈ· ˌ··/ *n* [C] *AmE* someone who illegally avoids joining the military even though they have been drafted【美】逃避兵役者

draft·ee /dræfˋti; drɑːfˈtiː/ *n* [C] *AmE* someone who has been drafted【美】應徵入伍者

drafts·man /ˋdræftsmən; ˈdrɑːftsmən/ *n plural* **draftsmen** /-mən; -mən/ [C] **1** someone who puts a suggested law or a new law into the proper words 法案[新法律]的起草人 **2** the American spelling of DRAUGHTSMAN draughtsman 的美式拼法

draft·y /ˋdræftɪ; ˈdrɑːfti/ *adj* the American spelling of DRAUGHTY draughty 的美式拼法

drag[1] /dræg; dræg/ *v* **dragged, dragging** 3 3

1 ▶PULL ALONG THE GROUND 在地面上拖◀ [T] to pull someone or something along the ground, often because they are too heavy to carry 拖, 拉: **drag sth away/along/through etc** *Inge managed to drag the table into the kitchen.* 英奇費了很大勁把桌子拖到廚房裡。| *Angry protesters were dragged away by the police.* 憤怒的抗議者被警察拖走了。| **drag a leg/foot etc** (=let it touch the ground as you move) 拖着腿/腳等〔挪動〕 *a bird dragging its broken wing* 一隻拖着斷翅的鳥 —see picture on page A21 參見A21頁圖

2 ▶NOT GENTLY 粗魯地◀ [T always+adv/prep] to pull someone or something somewhere in a way that hurts or damages them 硬拉, 硬拖, 硬拽: **drag sth up/over etc** *The plants had been dragged out by the roots.* 這些植物已被連根拔了起來。| *Harvey dragged her over to the window.* 哈維粗魯地把她拖到窗前。| **drag sb to the ground** (=pull someone down to the ground) 將某人拖倒在地

3 drag yourself up/down/into etc *informal* to move somewhere with difficulty【非正式】吃力地挪上/挪下/挪進等: *Jacob could hardly drag himself up the stairs.* 雅各布上樓時幾乎挪不動腳。

4 ▶PERSUADE SB TO COME 勸某人來◀ [T always+adv/prep] *informal* if you drag someone somewhere, you persuade or force them to come when they do not want to【非正式】硬拉某人去某處: **drag sb along/away etc**

Try and drag her along to the meeting tonight. 盡量把她也拉來參加今晚的聚會。| *Carla can't drag him away from the football on TV.* 卡拉無法把他拉開不看電視上的足球賽。

5 drag yourself away (from) to leave someone or something, or stop doing something, although you do not want to 戀戀不捨地離開〔某人或某物〕; 不情願地停止〔做某事〕: *It's well worth a visit if you can drag yourself away from the pool.* 這個地方很值得看一看, 如果你能離得開撞球桌的話。

6 ►TIME 時間◄ [I] if time or an event drags, it seems to go very slowly because nothing interesting is happening〔指時間、事情〕進行得緩慢: *Friday afternoons always drag.* 星期五下午總是過得那麼慢。

7 ►TOUCH THE GROUND 拖在地上◄ [I] if something is dragging along the ground, in the mud etc, part of it is touching the ground, the mud etc as you move〔指某物〕拖着地; 拖到泥上: **[+along/in]** *Your coat's dragging in the mud.* 你的大衣拖着泥了。

8 drag your feet/heels *informal* to take too much time to do something because you do not want to do it【非正式】做事拖拉; 遲遲不做: *The authorities are dragging their feet over banning cigarette advertising.* 當局在禁止香煙廣告一事上遲遲不採取行動。

9 drag sb's name through the mud/mire to tell people about the bad things that someone has done, so that they will have a bad opinion of them 公開某人的壞事, 使某人出醜

10 drag (along) behind sb to go more slowly than someone so that you are always behind them〔放慢腳步以便始終〕跟在某人後面

11 ►COMPUTER 電腦◄ [T always+adv/prep] to move something on a computer screen by pulling it along with the MOUSE (2)〔在電腦屏幕上〕用鼠標器拖動〔某物〕

12 drag a pond/river etc to look for something in a lake, river etc by pulling a heavy net along the bottom 拖着重網在池底/河底等搜尋〔某物〕: *They dragged the lake for the missing girl's body.* 他們用拖網在湖底搜尋失蹤女孩的屍體。

13 ►BOAT 船◄ [T] if a boat drags its ANCHOR[1] (1), it pulls the anchor away from its place on the sea bottom 把〔錨〕拖離海底

drag sb ↔ **down** *phr v* [T] **1** to make someone feel unhappy or discouraged 使〔某人〕感到不愉快[沮喪]: *All these criticisms were dragging her down.* 所有這些批評使她情緒低落。**2 drag sb down to your level** *informal often humorous* to make someone behave like you, in a worse way than they would usually behave【非正式, 常幽默】把某人帶壞; 讓某人行為標準下降: *"Look at this mess – it's not like you!" "I know – Ken's dragged me down to his level."* "看看這亂糟糟的樣子 —— 你以前可不這樣啊!" "我知道 —— 肯恩把我帶壞了。"

drag sb/sth ↔ **in** *phr v* [T] to start to talk about someone or something that is not connected with what you are talking or arguing about 把〔不相干的人或事〕扯進談話[爭論]中: *Why drag Jules in? He has nothing to do with it.* 為甚麼把朱爾斯扯進來? 他與此事無關。

drag sb/sth **into** sth *phr v* [T] to make someone get involved in a particular situation, discussion etc even though they do not want to 把…硬扯進〔某個情況、討論等〕之中: *I'm sorry to drag you into this mess.* 很抱歉, 把你扯進這爛攤子中來。

drag on *phr v* [I] if an event drags on, it seems to continue for longer than is necessary, often because you are bored〔指事情〕拖延地進行: **[+for]** *The meeting dragged on for hours.* 會議拖拖拉拉地開了好幾個小時。

drag sth ↔ **out** *phr v* [T] to make a meeting, an argument etc last longer than is necessary 使〔會議、爭論等〕不必要地拖長時間: *"How long can she drag this argument out?" Calvin wondered.* "她會把這場爭論拖到甚麼時候?" 卡爾文想。

drag sth **out of** sb *phr v* [T] to make someone tell you something when they had not intended to or were not supposed to do so 迫使〔某人〕說出〔某事〕: *He'll tell me, even if I have to drag it out of him!* 他必須告訴我, 即使是逼他, 也要他說出來!

drag sb/sth ↔ **up** *phr v* [T] **1** to mention an unpleasant subject or event, even though it is not necessary and it upsets the people who were involved in it 提起令人不愉快的話題[事情]: *The newspapers are dragging up her alleged affair again.* 報紙又把她所謂的風流韻事抖了出來。**2** *BrE informal often humorous* to RAISE[1] (4) a child so badly that when they are adult they behave badly, have bad manners etc【英, 非正式, 常幽默】不加管教地把〔孩子〕養大: *That child must have been dragged up.* 那孩子一定是沒受到良好的家庭教育。

drag² *n*

1 ►SB/STH BORING 乏味的人/事◄ **a drag** *informal* something or someone that is unexciting or boring【非正式】乏味無聊的人[事物]: *The party was a real drag.* 那晚會真是乏味。| *Don't be such a drag! Come out with us.* 別掃大家的興了! 跟我們一起去吧。

2 be a drag on a person or thing that is a drag on someone makes it hard for them to make progress towards what they want 是…的累贅: *Marriage would be a drag on my career.* 婚姻會成為我事業的累贅。

3 ►ON CIGARETTE 關於香煙◄ [C] the act of breathing in smoke from your cigarette 吸入一口煙: **take a drag on** *Pran took a deep drag on his cigarette.* 普蘭深深地吸了一口香煙。

4 ►CLOTHES 衣服◄ [U] women's clothes worn by a man, or men's clothes worn by a woman 男子穿的女服; 女子穿的男服: **in drag** *The whole performance is done in drag.* 在整場演出中, 演員們都穿着異性的服裝。

5 ►FORCE 力◄ [singular,U] the force of air that pushes against an aircraft or a vehicle that is moving forward〔作用於行進中的飛行器或車輛的〕空氣阻力: *Increasing the car's height increases aerodynamic drag.* 增加汽車的高度會增加空氣阻力。

6 ►BORING JOURNEY 乏味的旅程◄ [U] *BrE informal* a long and boring journey【英, 非正式】漫長而乏味的旅程: *It's a terrible drag all the way from Tijuana.* 從蒂華納出發的這段旅途太漫長乏味了。

7 the main drag *AmE informal* the biggest or longest street that goes through a town【美, 非正式】〔橫穿城鎮的〕主要街道, 主馬路: *We passed the last buildings on the main drag of Encino.* 我們走過了恩西諾市主馬路的最後幾座樓宇。

8 ►STH THAT IS PULLED 拖[拉]之物◄ [C] something that is made to be pulled along 用於拖[拉]的東西: *a drag harrow* 拖耙

drag·gled /ˈdrægld; ˈdrægəld/ *adj literary* BEDRAGGLED【文】弄濕的, 弄髒的

drag·gy /ˈdrægɪ; ˈdrægi/ *adj informal* boring or unpleasant【非正式】乏味的, 令人不愉快的

drag·net /ˈdrægˌnɛt; ˈdrægnet/ *n* [C] **1** a net that is pulled along the bottom of a river or lake, to bring up things that may be there 拖網 **2** a system in which the police look for criminals, using very thorough methods〔警察搜尋罪犯的〕法網, 羅網; 拉網搜捕: *a police dragnet* 警察的搜捕網

drag·on /ˈdrægən; ˈdrægən/ *n* [C] **1** a large imaginary animal that has wings and a long tail and can breathe out fire 龍 **2** *informal* a woman who behaves in an angry, unfriendly way【非正式】兇狠的婦女, 悍婦: *Casey's new teacher's a real dragon.* 凱西的新老師真是個母老虎。—see also 另見 **chase the dragon** (CHASE[1] (6))

dragon 龍

drag·on·fly /ˈdrægənˌflaɪ;

'drægənflaɪ/ *n* [C] a brightly coloured insect with a long thin, often coloured body and transparent wings 蜻蜓

dra·goon¹ /drə`gun; drə'guːn/ *n* [C] a soldier in past times who rode a horse and carried a gun and sword〔舊時騎馬、佩槍劍的〕重騎兵; 龍騎兵

dragoon² *v*

dragoon sb **into** sth *phr v* [T] to force someone to do something they do not want to do 強迫〔某人〕做〔某事〕: **dragoon sb into doing sth** *Monica was dragooned into being on the management committee.* 莫妮卡被迫加入管理委員會。

drag queen /'· ·/ *n* [C] *slang* a HOMOSEXUAL man who dresses as a woman【俚】着女裝的同性戀男子

drag race /'· ·/ *n* [C] *AmE* a car race that is won by the car that can increase its speed fastest over a very short distance【美】短程汽車加速賽 —**drag racing** *n* [U]

drag·ster /`drægstɚ; 'drægstə/ *n* [C] a car used in drag races that is long, narrow, and low 短程汽車加速賽賽車

drain¹ /dren; dreɪn/ *v*

1 ▶LIQUID 液體◀ a) [T] to make the water or liquid flow away from something 使流走; 使排出: *Can you drain the spaghetti, please?* 請把意大利麵條的水瀝乾, 好嗎? | *Deep ditches were dug to drain the fields.* 挖了深溝以排乾田裡的水。| **drain sth from sth** *Brad drained all the oil from the engine.* 布拉德將引擎中的機油全部放了出去。| **well/poorly etc drained** *Carrots grow best in a well drained soil.* 胡蘿蔔在排水性能良好的土壤中長得最好。—see picture on page A11 參見A11頁圖 **b)** [I] if liquid drains, it flows away〔液體〕流走; 流失: **[+away]** *I watched the bath water drain away.* 我看着浴缸裡的水漫慢流光。**c)** [I] if something drains, the liquid that is in it or on it flows away and it becomes dry 流乾; 瀝乾: *Open ditches drain very efficiently.* 明溝排水效果非常好。

2 drain a glass/cup etc to drink all the liquid in a glass, cup etc 喝乾玻璃杯/茶杯等中的飲料: *Hannah drained her mug in one gulp.* 漢娜一口氣就把她大杯子中的飲料喝光了。

3 ▶USE TOO MUCH 消耗過多◀ [T] to use too much of something so that there is not enough left 消耗太多, 耗盡: *Huge imports were draining the country's currency reserves.* 大量的進口正在耗竭國家的貨幣儲備。| **drain sb/sth of sth** *Our country is being drained of many of its best scientsists.* 我們國家許多最優秀的科學家正在流失。

4 ▶MAKE TIRED 使疲勞◀ [T] to make someone feel very tired and without any energy 使〔某人〕疲勞, 使筋疲力盡: *Working with sick children every day really drains you.* 每天和病童們打交道確實讓人非常疲勞。

5 ▶COLOUR 顏色◀ [I always+adv/prep] if the colour drains from your face, your skin becomes very pale usually because you are frightened or shocked〔因恐懼或震驚而〕臉色煞白, 面無血色: **[+from/away etc]** *All the colour had drained from Zelda's cheeks.* 澤爾達面如死灰。

6 ▶BE REDUCED 減少◀ [I always+adv/prep] to gradually be reduced 慢慢減少: **[+away/out of etc]** *The family's wealth has slowly drained away.* 家裡的財產已逐漸減少。

drain sth ↔ **off** *phr v* [T] to make water or a liquid flow off something, leaving it dry 使流走, 使變乾: *Leave to simmer for 40 minutes then drain off the stock.* 煨40分鐘, 之後把湯瀝掉。

drain² *n* [C] **1** *especially BrE* a pipe that carries water or waste liquids away【尤英】下水管, 下水道, 排[廢]水管: **blocked drains** *The drains were blocked and the streets were full of water.* 下水道堵塞了, 街道上到處是水。**2** the frame of metal bars over a drain where water etc can flow into it〔下水道開口上面的〕排水格柵: *Clear the leaves out of the drain.* 把排水格柵上的樹葉清除掉。**3 a drain on sth** something that continuously uses time, money, strength etc 消耗〔時間、金錢、體力等〕的事物: *Not having anybody to rent my room is a serious drain on my financial resources.* 沒有人租我的房子, 這對我的財源是嚴重的損耗。**4 down the drain** *informal* wasted or having no result【非正式】被浪費掉; 沒有結果: *The fire meant two years' hard work down the drain.* 那場火災意味着兩年的辛勞都付諸東流了。—see also 另見 BRAIN DRAIN

drain·age /`drenɪdʒ; 'dreɪnɪdʒ/ *n* [U] **1** a system of pipes or passages in the ground for carrying away water or waste liquids 排水系統; 排水管; 排水溝; 下水道: *drainage channels* 排水溝渠 **2** the process by which water or waste liquid flows away through this system 排水, 排污

drained /drend; dreɪnd/ *adj* very tired and without any energy 精疲力盡的: *Steve felt so drained he could hardly make it to the car.* 史提夫覺得精疲力盡, 幾乎走不到汽車邊上。

drain·ing board /'·· ·/ *n* [C] a slightly sloping area next to the kitchen SINK² where you put wet dishes to dry〔廚房洗碗槽邊略呈傾斜的、可放置濕碗碟的〕滴水板 —see picture on page A10 參見A10頁圖

drain·pipe /`dren͵paɪp; 'dreɪnpaɪp/ *n* [C] **1** *BrE* a pipe that carries rain water away from the roof of a building【英】〔排除屋頂雨水的〕排水管; 落水管 **2** *BrE* a pipe that carries waste water away from buildings【英】〔把廢水排出建築物的〕排水管; 下水道的管子; DOWNSPOUT *AmE*【美】—see picture on page A4 參見A4頁圖

drainpipe trou·sers /͵·· '··/ *n* [plural] *BrE* trousers with narrow legs【英】瘦腿褲, 緊身褲

drake /drek; dreɪk/ *n* [C] a male duck 公鴨 —see also 另見 DUCKS AND DRAKES

dram /dræm; dræm/ *n* [C] **1** also 又作 **drachm** a small unit of weight or of liquid 打蘭〔重量單位或液量單位〕—see table on page C4 參見C4頁附錄 **2** a small alcoholic drink, especially WHISKY 少量的酒〔尤指威士忌〕: *Would you like a wee dram before you go?* 你走之前想喝點酒嗎?

dra·ma /`drɑmə; 'drɑːmə/ *n* **1** [C] a play for the theatre, television, radio etc 戲劇; 電視劇; 廣播劇 **2** [U] plays considered as a form of literature 劇本; 戲劇作品; 戲劇學: *drama classes* 戲劇課 | **drama school** (=place for students to study drama) 戲劇學校; 戲劇學院 **3** [C,U] an exciting and unusual situation or set of events 戲劇性場面; (一連串)戲劇性事件: *Maggie's life is always full of drama.* 瑪姬的生活總是充滿了戲劇性的事件。| **the drama of** *We all shared in the drama of the rescue.* 我們共同經歷了驚險的救援工作。**4 make a drama out of sth** to make things seem worse than they really are 對某事大驚小怪, 對某事小題大作: *We won't make a drama out of a crisis.* 我們不會把危機誇大其詞。 W3

dra·mat·ic /drə`mætɪk; drə'mætɪk/ *adj* **1** impressive, sudden, and often surprising 給人深刻印象的; 突然的; 驚人的: *the dramatic changes taking place in Eastern Europe* 發生在東歐的巨變 **2** exciting 激動人心的: *a dramatic point in the story* 故事的一處高潮 **3** connected with drama or the theatre 戲劇的: *a dramatic production* 戲劇演出 **4** in a way that you intend to be impressive and exciting 誇張的; 像演戲似的: *Tristan immediately threw up his hands in a dramatic gesture.* 特里斯丹立即像演戲一樣把雙手向上甩了一下。—**dramatically** /-klɪ; -kli/ *adv*: *Output has increased dramatically.* 產量已大幅度提高。

dramatic i·ron·y /·͵·· '···/ *n* [U] a special effect in a play in which the people watching know something that the characters in the play do not, and can understand the real importance or meaning of what is happening 戲劇性諷示〔一種特殊的戲劇效果, 觀眾知道劇中人所不知道的某些情況, 因而能理解劇中正在發生之事真正的重要性或含義〕

dra·mat·ics /drə`mætɪks; drə'mætɪks/ *n* **1** [U] the study or practice of skills used in drama, such as acting 戲劇表演藝術[研究]; 演技; 演戲: *amateur dramatics* 業餘戲劇活動 **2** [plural] behaviour that shows too much feeling, and that is often insincere; HISTRIONICS

誇張做作的行為

dram·a·tis per·so·nae /ˌdræmətɪs pə`soni; ˌdræmətɪs pɜːˈsəʊnaɪ/ *n* [plural] *Latin* the characters in a play【拉丁】劇中人物

dram·a·tist /ˈdræmətɪst; ˈdræmətɪst/ *n* [C] someone who writes plays, especially serious ones; PLAYWRIGHT〔尤指嚴肅的〕劇作家, 編劇

dram·a·tize also 又作 **-ise** *BrE*【英】/ˈdræməˌtaɪz; ˈdræmətaɪz/ *v* **1** [T] to change a story so that it can be performed as a play 把〔小說、故事等〕改編為劇本: *a novel dramatized for television* 改編成電視劇的一部小說 **2** [I,T] to make a situation seem more exciting, terrible etc than it really is (使)戲劇化; 戲劇性地表現: *Why do you have to dramatize everything?* 你為甚麼一定要把每件事都戲劇化呢? —**dramatization** /ˌdræmətə`zeʃən; ˌdræmətaɪˈzeɪʃən/ *n* [C,U]

drank /dræŋk; dræŋk/ the past tense of DRINK[1]

drape[1] /drep; dreɪp/ *v* [T] **1** to cover or decorate something with folds of cloth〔用打褶的布〕披, 蓋; 裝飾: **drape sth over/around etc sth** *Jack emerged with a towel draped around him.* 傑克身上圍了一條浴巾走了出來。| **drape sth with/in etc sth** *a coffin draped in the national flag* 覆蓋着國旗的靈柩 **2** to let something hang or lie somewhere loosely 將〔某物〕隨便地掛[放]在〔某處〕: **drape sth over/around sth** *Mina lay back, her arms draped lazily over the cushions.* 米娜向後靠了靠, 胳膊懶散地搭在靠墊上。

drape[2] *n* **drapes** [plural] *especially AmE* curtains, especially long thick curtains【尤美】〔尤指長而厚重的〕窗簾, 布簾

drap·er /ˈdrepə; ˈdreɪpə/ *n* [C] *BrE old-fashioned* someone who sells cloth, curtains, etc【英, 過時】布商; 紡織品商

drap·er·y /ˈdrepərɪ; ˈdreɪpəri/ *n* **1** [C,U] cloth arranged in folds 打褶的布: *a casket covered with embroidered silk drapery* 蓋有繡花絲質罩布的小箱子 **2** [U] *BrE* cloth and other goods sold by a draper【英】布料, 布匹; 紡織品; DRY GOODS (2) *AmE*【美】**3** [U] *BrE* the trade of selling cloth, curtains, etc【英】布業; 簾幕業

dras·tic /ˈdræstɪk; ˈdræstɪk/ *adj* strong, sudden, and often severe 激烈的; 突然的; 嚴厲的: *NATO threatened more drastic action if its terms were not met.* 如果條款得不到履行, 北約威脅將要採取更為嚴厲的行動。—**drastically** /-klɪ; -kli/ *adv*: *The size of the army was drastically cut.* 軍隊被大幅裁減。

drat /dræt; dræt/ *interjection old-fashioned* used to show you are annoyed【過時】見鬼〔用來表示氣憤〕: *Drat! The car won't start!* 見鬼! 車發動不起來了! —**dratted** *adj*: *Where are my dratted keys?* 該死的鑰匙在哪兒?

draught[1] *BrE*【英】, **draft** *AmE*【美】/dræft; drɑːft/ *n* [C]

1 ►COLD AIR 冷空氣◄ a current of cold air flowing through a room〔穿過房間的〕一股冷風, 穿堂風: *Shut the window – there's a draught in here!* 把窗戶關上 — 有穿堂風!

2 ►GAME 遊戲◄ **draughts** [plural] *BrE*【英】**a)** a game played by two people, each with 12 round pieces, on a board of 64 squares 國際跳棋; CHECKERS (2) *AmE*【美】**b)** the pieces used in a game of draughts 國際跳棋的棋子

3 ►SWALLOW 吞◄ the act of swallowing liquid, or the amount of liquid swallowed at one time 一飲; 一口之量: *Mick took a long draught of lager.* 米克喝了一大口淡啤酒。

4 on draught *especially BrE* a beer that is on draught is served from a large container rather than a bottle; on tap (TAP[1] (4b))【尤英】〔啤酒〕從大的容器中汲取的, 散裝的

5 ►MEDICINE 藥◄ *literary* a medicine that you drink【文】〔藥的〕飲劑: *a sleeping draught* 一劑安眠藥水

6 ►FIRE 火◄ the flow of air to a fire〔爐子的〕通風氣流

7 ►SHIP 船◄ the depth of water needed by a ship so that it will not touch the bottom of the sea, a river etc〔船的〕吃水深度

draught[2] *BrE*【英】, **draft** *AmE*【美】*adj* [only before noun 僅用於名詞前] **1** a draught animal is used for pulling heavy loads〔牲畜〕負重的, 役用的 **2** a draught beer is served from a large container, not a bottle〔啤酒〕從桶中汲取的, 桶裝的

draught·board /ˈdræftˌbɔrd; ˈdrɑːftbɔːd/ *n* [C] *BrE* a board with 64 squares on which the game of draughts (DRAUGHT[1] (2)) is played【英】國際跳棋棋盤; CHECKERBOARD *AmE*【美】

draughts·man *BrE*【英】, **draftsman** *AmE*【美】/ˈdræftsmən; ˈdrɑːftsmən/ *n* [C] **1** someone who draws all the parts of a new building or machine that is being planned 繪圖員, 製圖員 **2** someone who draws well 善於繪畫的人

draugh·ty *BrE*【英】, **drafty** *AmE*【美】/ˈdræftɪ; ˈdrɑːfti/ *adj* with currents of air blowing through it 通風的; 有過堂風的: *a draughty old house* 四面通風的老房子

draw[1] /drɔ; drɔː/ *v past tense* **drew** /dru; druː/ *past participle* **drawn** /drɔn; drɔːn/

① PICTURE/DESCRIPTION 圖畫/描繪
② MOVE 移動
③ GET/CAUSE STH 得到某物/引起某事
④ MAKE COMPARISON/JUDGMENT 進行比較/評判
⑤ MAKE SB NOTICE 引起某人注意
⑥ MONEY 錢
⑦ AIR/WATER 空氣/水
⑧ BY CHANCE 碰巧
⑨ STOP/END 停止/結束
⑩ SPORT 體育運動
⑪ OTHER MEANINGS 其他意思

① **PICTURE/DESCRIPTION 圖畫/描繪**

1 ►WITH PENCIL 用鉛筆◄ [I,T] to make a picture of something with a pencil or pen〔用鉛筆或鋼筆〕畫, 繪畫: *Can I draw your portrait?* 我能給你畫張肖像嗎? | *I've never been able to draw well.* 我總是畫不好。| **draw sb sth/draw sth for sb** *Hans drew her a map showing her how to get there.* 漢斯給她畫了張圖, 告訴她怎樣去那兒。

2 ►DESCRIBE 描繪◄ [T] to describe something in speech or writing〔用語言或文字〕描寫, 刻畫: *the vividly drawn character of Heathcliff* 刻畫得惟妙惟肖的希思克利夫這個人物

② **MOVE 移動**

3 ►MOVE IN ONE DIRECTION 往一個方向移動◄ [I always+adv/prep] to move steadily in a particular direction〔往某個方向〕穩步移動: **draw towards/past etc** *We watched from the deck as their boat drew*

alongside. 我們在甲板上看着他們的船開過來與我們的船平行。
4 draw near/close to move closer in time or space〔時間、空間的〕臨近: *Maria grew anxious as the men drew closer.* 當那些男人靠近的時候, 瑪麗亞變得很着急。| *Christmas is drawing near.* 聖誕節即將來臨。
5 draw level to move into a position where you are equal to someone else in a race, game, or competition〔在比賽、競賽中與某人〕拉平: *Black drew level with the other runners.* 布萊克和其他賽跑選手拉平了。
6 ►PULL 拉◄ [T always+adv/prep] to make someone or something move by pulling them gently〔輕拉〕使移動: **draw aside/up/across etc** *Drawing the covers around her, Zoe curled up in bed.* 佐伊拉過被子蓋在身上, 在牀上蜷成一團。| *Hussain drew me aside to whisper in my ear.* 侯賽因把我拉到一邊, 在我耳邊私語。
7 draw the curtains to open or close the curtains 拉開[上]窗簾
8 ►PULL A VEHICLE 拉車◄ [T] if an animal draws a vehicle, it pulls it along〔指動物〕拉〔車〕: *a carriage drawn by six horses* 六匹馬拉的車
9 ►TAKE OUT 拿出來◄ [T always+adv/prep] to take something out of a container, cover etc〔從容器、覆蓋物等中〕拿出來: **draw sth out/from etc** *Smedley drew some papers from his pocket.* 斯梅德利從口袋中掏出一些文件來。
10 draw a gun/pistol/sword etc to take a weapon from its container or from your pocket 拔出槍/手槍/劍等: *Jack drew his knife with a flourish.* 傑克揮手拔出刀來。
11 draw a tooth/cork/nail to pull a tooth etc out 拔牙/瓶塞/釘子

③ **GET/CAUSE STH 得到某物/引起某事**
12 ►GET STH IMPORTANT 得到重要之物◄ [T] to get something that you need or that is important from someone or something 得到, 獲取〔所需要的或重要的東西〕: *I drew a lot of comfort from her kind words.* 從她體貼的話語中我得到了許多安慰。| *Plants draw nourishment from the soil.* 植物從土壤中汲取營養。
13 ►GET A REACTION 引起反應◄ to get a particular kind of reaction from someone because of something you have said or done〔因言行〕引起〔某種反應〕: **draw praise/criticism etc (from)** *Reagan's remarks drew an angry response from the Democrats.* 列根的話引起了民主黨人憤怒的反應。| **draw fire (from)** (=be criticized) (從...) 招致批評 *The new proposals drew fire from all sides for being elitist.* 新的提議由於主張精英主義而遭到了各方的批評。

④ **MAKE COMPARISON/JUDGMENT 進行比較/評判**
14 draw a comparison/analogy etc to compare two things, people, ideas etc 進行對照/類比等: *Do you think we can draw a parallel between the two novels?* 你認為我們能把這兩部小説相比較嗎?
15 draw a distinction/line etc to say that you think two things are different and show why you think so 區分/劃分等: *We have to draw a line between fantasy and reality.* 我們必須劃清幻想與現實的界線。
16 draw a conclusion/moral etc (from sth) to decide that a particular fact or principle is true after thinking carefully about it (從某事物中) 得出結論/獲得教益等: *Now that you've heard the evidence, you can draw your own conclusions.* 既然你們已經聽過了證詞, 你們就可以自己得出結論了。

⑤ **MAKE SB NOTICE 引起某人注意**
17 draw sb's attention (to sth) to deliberately make someone notice something 有意使某人注意 (某事物): *I'd like to draw your attention to the no smoking rule.* 我希望你們注意禁止吸煙的規定。
18 draw sb's eye if something draws your eye, it is so interesting that you notice it 吸引某人的目光: *The intentness of his gaze drew all eyes towards him.* 他目不轉睛的凝視把所有人的目光都吸引到他身上了。

⑥ **MONEY 錢**
19 ►FROM YOUR BANK ACCOUNT 從銀行賬戶◄ also 又作 **draw out** [T] to take money from your bank account〔從銀行賬戶中〕取〔錢〕: *Hughes had drawn $8,000 in cash from a bank in Toronto.* 休斯從多倫多的一家銀行中提走了8,000美元現金。
20 ►BE PAID 領錢◄ [T] to receive an amount of money regularly from your employer or from the government〔從雇主或政府那裡〕定期領取〔一定數量的錢〕: *How long have you been drawing unemployment benefit?* 你領取失業救濟金有多久了?
21 draw a cheque (on sth) *BrE*【英】, **draw a check (on sth)** *AmE*【美】to write a cheque for taking money out of a bank 開〔從某銀行取款的〕支票: *a check drawn on a Swiss bank* 由一家瑞士銀行支付的支票

⑦ **AIR/WATER 空氣/水**
22 ►LIQUID 液體◄ [T] to take water, beer etc from a well or container〔從井裡或容器中〕抽出, 打出〔水、啤酒等〕
23 ►INTO YOUR LUNGS 進入肺裡◄ [T] to take air or smoke into your lungs 吸入〔空氣或煙〕: **draw breath** *I was having trouble just drawing breath, but Meg ran on up the hill.* 我連喘氣都有困難, 但麥格卻一直跑着上了山。
24 ►FIRE/CHIMNEY 火/煙囱◄ [I] if a fire or CHIMNEY draws, it lets the air flow through to make the fire burn well〔火或煙囱〕通風好; 通氣〔使火燒得旺〕

⑧ **BY CHANCE 碰巧**
25 ►PLAYING CARD/TICKET 抓牌/抽籤◄ [I,T] to choose a card, ticket etc by chance 隨意抽牌, 抽籤: *I drew the ace of spades.* 我抽到了黑桃A。
26 draw the short straw used to say that someone has been unlucky because they were chosen by chance to do an unpleasant job 運氣不佳: *I'm only here because I drew the short straw.* 我全是因為運氣不好才到這兒來的。
27 draw lots to decide who will do something by taking pieces of paper etc out of a container 抓鬮; 抽籤〔以決定誰來做某事〕: *We drew lots to see who would go first.* 我們抽籤決定誰先去。
28 be drawn against sb *BrE* to be chosen by chance to play or compete against someone【英】抓鬮決定與某人競賽

⑨ **STOP/END 停止/結束**
29 draw to a halt/stop if a vehicle draws to a halt, it slows down and stops〔車輛等〕慢慢停下來
30 draw to a close/end if an event or a period of time draws to a close etc, it ends or finishes〔某事件或一段時間等〕結束, 終止
31 draw a line under sth to say that something is completely finished 某事已徹底結束: *The agreement draws a line under the recent rail dispute.* 這一協議結束了最近的鐵路糾紛。

⑩ **SPORT 體育運動**
32 ►GAME 比賽◄ [I,T] *especially BrE* to end a game or match without either side winning【尤英】(使)〔比賽〕打成平局, 不分勝負: *They drew 3-3.* 他們打成三平。| *Inter drew with Juventus last night.* 昨晚國際米蘭隊和祖雲達斯隊打平了。
33 draw a bow to bend a BOW³ (1) by pulling back the string in order to shoot an ARROW (1) 拉弓

⑪ OTHER MEANINGS 其他意思

34 [T] to attract someone 吸引〔某人〕: *Beth felt drawn to this gentle stranger.* 貝思被這個溫文爾雅的陌生人吸引住了。| **draw a crowd** *The festival is likely to draw huge crowds.* 這個節日有可能吸引大羣大羣的人。

35 draw the line (at sth) to refuse to do something because you disapprove of it〔因不贊同而〕拒絕〈做某事〉: *I'd really like to help you, but I draw the line at lying.* 我確實想幫助你, 但撒謊的事我不幹。

36 draw a blank *informal* to be unsuccessful, especially when you have been trying to find information or the answer to a problem【非正式】〔尤指在尋求消息或問題的答案時〕不成功, 無結果: *Detectives hunting the missing girl have drawn a blank.* 偵探們對尋找那個失蹤的女孩毫無所獲。

37 ►PERSUADE SB 勸說某人◄ [T usually passive 一般用被動態] to persuade someone to talk about something 說服某人談論某事: *She refused to be drawn on the subject of her divorce.* 她拒絕談論她離婚的話題。

38 draw blood to make someone BLEED 使〔某人〕流血

39 draw breath to find time to have a rest when you are busy〔在忙碌時〕喘口氣, 歇一下: *I didn't have time to draw breath this morning.* 今天早上我連喘口氣的時間都沒有。

40 draw a veil over sth to deliberately keep something unpleasant or embarrassing from being known 隱瞞某事; 避而不談某事〔指不愉快或尷尬的事〕: *It might be best to draw a veil over Peter's past for now.* 現在或許最好別談彼得的過去。

41 ►SHIP 船◄ *technical* if a ship draws a certain depth, it needs that depth of water to float in【術語】吃水 —see also 另見 be at daggers drawn (DAGGER (3))

draw back *phr v* [T] **1** to move yourself away from something 閃避, 後退: *He drew back in horror when he saw the cuts on her face.* 當他看到她臉上的傷口時, 他嚇得直往後退。**2** to be afraid or unwilling to do something 害怕[不願]做〔某事〕: **[+from]** *The company drew back from making a firm commitment.* 該公司不肯作出肯定的承諾。

draw in *phr v* **1** [I] if the days or nights draw in, it gets dark earlier in the evening and so there are fewer hours of daylight〔白晝〕變短: *In October the nights start drawing in.* 十月裡天黑得越來越早了。**2** [T usually passive 一般用被動態] to involve someone in something, often when they do not really want to take part 使〔某人〕捲入〔某事〕〔通常在其不情願的情況下〕: **draw sb in** *We invited Al along to our meetings but he was wary of getting drawn in.* 我們邀請阿爾一起來參加我們的會議, 但他不想被扯進來。**3 draw your horns in** *BrE* to spend less money because you have financial problems【英】緊縮開支

draw sb into sth *phr v* [T] to involve someone in something, often when they do not really want to take part 將〔某人〕扯入〔某事中〕: *Homeless children often get drawn into crime.* 無家可歸的兒童經常被扯進犯罪活動中。

draw sth ↔ off *phr v* [T] to remove some liquid from a larger supply 使流走, 排掉: *We had to draw off some water from the radiator.* 我們得從散熱器中放掉一些水。

draw on *phr v* **1 draw on a cigarette/cigar etc** to breathe in smoke from a cigarette etc 吸香煙/雪茄等 **2** [T] to use money, experiences etc for a particular purpose〔為某種目的〕利用, 動用〔錢、經驗等〕: **draw on/upon sth** *It was a challenge but luckily we had the expertise to draw on.* 這是個挑戰, 但幸運的是, 我們可以利用我們的專長。| **draw on your savings** *I had to draw on my savings to pay for the repairs.* 我得動用存款來支付修理費。**3** [I] if a period of time draws on, it comes nearer〔指時間〕臨近: *Winter is drawing on.* 冬天快到了。

draw out *phr v* **1** [T] to make someone feel less nervous and more willing to talk 使〔某人〕不緊張, 使〔某人〕願意說話: **draw sb out** *Try to draw the new boy out a bit if you can.* 可能的話, 盡量哄這個新來的男孩說上一點話。**2** [T] to make an event last longer than usual 拖延: **draw sth ↔ out** *The final questions drew the meeting out for another hour.* 最後幾個問題使會議又延長了一個小時。**3** [I] if the days draw out, it stays light until later in the evening and so there are more hours of daylight〔白晝〕變長: *It's nice when the days start drawing out again.* 白天又開始變長時真好。

draw up *phr v*

1 ►LIST/CONTRACT ETC 名單/合同等◄ [T] to prepare a written document 起草, 草擬〔文件〕: **draw sth ↔ up** *They drew up a list of candidates.* 他們草擬了一份候選人的名單。

2 ►VEHICLE 車輛◄ [I] to arrive somewhere and stop 到達某處停下: *The taxi drew up at the gate.* 計程車在大門口停了下來。

3 draw up a chair [T] to bring a chair closer to someone or something 把椅子拉近〔某人或某物〕: *Ben drew his chair up to the fireplace.* 班恩把他的椅子拉到壁爐旁。

4 draw yourself up (to your full height) to stand up very straight because you are angry or determined about something〔因生氣或下決心而〕挺直身體站立: *Drawing himself up to his full height, he ordered me out of the room.* 他挺直身體, 命令我出去。

5 draw up your knees to bring your legs closer to your body 蜷起雙膝〔讓腿靠緊身體〕: *I found him rolling on the floor in pain, with his knees drawn up to his chest.* 我看見他痛得雙膝蜷在胸前在地板上打滾。

6 ►SOLDIERS 士兵◄ [T usually passive 一般用被動態] to arrange people in a special order 使排好隊形; 使列陣: **draw sth up** *troops drawn up in ranks* 排好隊列的部隊

draw² *n* [C] **1** *especially BrE* a game that ends with both teams having the same number of points【尤英】平局, 不分勝負 **2** the act of choosing a winning number, ticket etc in a LOTTERY (1) 抽獎; 抓鬮; 抽籤: *Bill picked the winning number on the first draw.* 比爾第一次抽獎就抽中了獲獎號碼。**3** a performer, show, sports team etc that a lot of people are willing to pay to see 有吸引力的表演者[演出, 球隊]等: *Whitney Houston is always a big draw.* 〔美國歌手〕惠特尼·休斯頓總是很叫座。**4 quick/fast on the draw a)** able to pull a gun out quickly in order to shoot 出槍快速 **b)** good at reacting quickly and intelligently to difficult questions or in difficult situations〔對困難形勢或問題〕反應機敏: *Amit was very quick on the draw in his interview.* 在面試中, 阿米特反應非常迅速。—see also 另見 **the luck of the draw** (LUCK¹ (15))

draw·back /ˈdrɔˌbæk; ˈdrɔːbæk/ *n* [C] a disadvantage of a situation, product etc 缺點, 毛病; 不利因素: **[+of/to (doing sth)]** *One drawback of New York in the summer is the heat.* 紐約夏天的一個缺點就是炎熱。

draw·bridge /ˈdrɔˌbrɪdʒ; ˈdrɔːbrɪdʒ/ *n* [C] a bridge that can be pulled up to let ships pass, or to stop people from entering or attacking a castle 吊橋; 開合橋

drawer /drɔr; drɔː/ *n* **1** [C] part of a piece of furniture, such as a desk, that you pull out and push in and use to keep things in 抽屜: *The scissors are in the kitchen drawer.* 剪刀在廚房抽屜裡。—see also 另見 BOTTOM DRAWER, TOP-DRAWER —see picture on page A10 參見 A10 頁圖 **2 drawers** [plural] *old-fashioned* underwear that women and girls wear between their waist and the tops of their legs; KNICKERS【過時】女用短襯褲

draw·ing /ˈdrɔɪŋ; ˈdrɔːɪŋ/ *n* **1** [C] a picture that you draw with a pencil, pen etc 圖畫: *She's done some beautiful charcoal drawings.* 她畫了一些漂亮的炭筆畫。**2** [U] the art of making pictures, plans etc with a pen or pencil

〔用筆進行的〕繪畫; 製圖: *Drawing has never been my strong point.* 畫圖從來都不是我的強項。

drawing board /'·· ·/ *n* **1** [C] a large flat board that artists and DESIGNERS work on 畫板 **2 (go) back to the drawing board** to start working on a plan or idea again after something that you have tried has failed 失敗後從頭做起: *We didn't raise enough money so it's back to the drawing board.* 我們沒有籌集到足夠的錢, 因此又得從頭開始了。

drawing pin /'·· ·/ *n* [C] *BrE* a short pin with a round flat head, used especially for putting notices on boards or walls【英】圖釘; THUMBTACK *AmE*【美】—see picture at 參見 PIN[1] 圖

drawing room /'·· ·/ *n* [C] *old-fashioned* a room, especially in a large house, where you can entertain guests or relax【過時】客廳, 起居室

drawl /drɔl; drɔːl/ *v* [I,T] to speak in a slow unclear way with vowel sounds that are longer than normal 拉長腔調慢吞吞地說話 —**drawl** *n* [singular]: *a Southern drawl* 〔美國〕南方拉長調的說話方式

drawn[1] /drɔn; drɔːn/ the past participle of DRAW[1]

drawn[2] *adj* someone who looks drawn has a thin pale face, usually because they are ill or worried 臉色蒼白的, 憔悴的, 愁眉苦臉的

drawn-out /,· '·◂/ *adj* taking more time than usual or more time than you would like 拖長了的, 冗長的: **long drawn-out** *a long drawn-out dispute* 冗長的爭論

draw·string /'drɔ,strɪŋ; 'drɔːstrɪŋ/ *n* [C] a string through the top of a bag, piece of clothing etc that you can pull tight or make loose〔袋口、衣服的〕束帶, 拉繩 —see picture on page A17 參見 A17 頁圖

dray /dre; dreɪ/ *n* [C] a flat CART[1] (1) with four wheels that was used in the past for carrying heavy loads, especially BARRELs of beer〔舊時用於裝運大桶啤酒的〕四輪平板車

dread[1] /drɛd; dred/ *v* **1** [T] to feel anxious or worried about something that is going to happen or you think will happen in the future 畏懼, 懼怕; 擔心: *I've got an interview tomorrow and I'm dreading it.* 明天我要去面試, 我正為此擔驚受怕呢。| **dread doing sth** *I'm dreading going back to work.* 我害怕回去工作。| **dread sb doing sth** *Tim dreaded his parents finding out.* 提姆惟恐他父母發現這事。| **dread (that)** *I'm dreading that I'll be asked to help on Sunday.* 我擔心會要我星期天幫忙做事。**2 I dread to think** *spoken* used to show that you think a situation is very worrying【口】我不敢去想〔用於表示對某事十分擔憂〕: *I dread to think what the children will get up to when I'm away.* 我真不敢想我不在家的時候孩子們會幹出些甚麼事來。

dread[2] *n* **1** [U] a fear of something in the future 恐懼, 害怕; 擔心: *The prospect of meeting Mark's relatives filled her with dread.* 要見馬克的親屬使她充滿了恐慌。| **a dread of** *a dread of the unknown* 對未知事物的恐懼 **2 be/live in dread of** to continuously be very anxious or afraid of what may happen 處於對…的恐懼之中: *The people of the war-torn city live in dread of further shelling.* 飽受戰爭破壞的城市中的居民生活在再次遭到轟炸的恐懼中。

dread·ed /'drɛdɪd; 'dredɨd/ also 又作 **dread** *literary*【文】*adj* [only before noun 僅用於名詞前] *sometimes humorous* making you feel afraid or anxious【有時幽默】可怕的, 嚇人的: *I hear the dreaded Miss Jones is going to be at the meeting.* 我聽說令人生畏的鍾斯小姐也將出席那個會議。

dread·ful /'drɛdfəl; 'dredfəl/ *adj especially BrE*【尤英】**1** extremely unpleasant 糟糕的, 令人極討厭的: *We've had some dreadful weather lately.* 最近天氣糟透了。**2** [only before noun 僅用於名詞前] used to emphasize how bad something or someone is 極糟的〔用於強調〕: *It's a dreadful waste of money.* 那真是太浪費錢了。

dread·ful·ly /'drɛdfəlɪ; 'dredfəli/ *adv especially BrE*【尤英】**1** [+adj/adv] extremely 非常, 極其: *They're dreadfully busy at the moment.* 此刻他們非常忙。**2** very badly 糟糕地: *The team played dreadfully.* 那個球隊表現得太差勁了。**3** very much 十分, 很: *Would you mind dreadfully if I didn't come?* 我不來你會很不高興嗎?

dread·locks /'drɛd,lɑks; 'dredlɒks/ *n* [plural] a way of arranging your hair, popular with RASTAFARIANs, in which it hangs in thick lengths like pieces of rope〔常見於牙買加拉斯塔法里教信徒的〕"駭人"長髮綹; 拉斯塔法里髮綹 —see picture at 參見 HAIRSTYLE 圖

dread·nought /'drɛd,nɔt; 'drednɔːt/ *n* [C] a type of WARSHIP used at the beginning of the 20th century 無畏戰艦, 弩級戰艦〔20 世紀初使用的一種戰艦〕

dream[1] /drim; driːm/ *n* 

1 ▶ASLEEP 睡着的◀ [C] a series of thoughts, images, and feelings that you experience when you are asleep 夢: *In my dream, I was playing football with the children.* 在夢裡, 我在和孩子們踢足球。| **have a dream** *I had a really weird dream last night.* 昨晚, 我做了個特別怪異的夢。| **bad dream** (=frightening or unpleasant) 噩夢 *He claims that eating cheese late at night gives him bad dreams.* 他聲稱在夜裡吃乳酪會讓他做噩夢。| **recurring dream** (=a dream you have again and again) 反覆出現的夢境

2 ▶WISH 願望◀ [C] something you hope for and want to happen very much 夢想; 願望; 理想: *Mike's big dream was to be a professional racing driver.* 邁克的最大夢想就是成為一名職業賽車手。| **[+of]** *a dream of becoming rich* 發財的夢想 | **dream house/car etc** (=the house, car etc you really want) 夢寐以求的房子/汽車等 *Three weeks in Barbados is my idea of a dream holiday.* 在巴巴多斯停留三個星期是我夢寐以求的絕好假期。| **the house/job of your dreams** *I have just met the man of my dreams!* 我剛剛遇到了我夢中的白馬王子! | **beyond your wildest dreams** (=better than anything you ever imagined or hoped for) 做夢也想不到

3 ▶UNREAL SITUATION 不真實的情景◀ [singular] a situation that does not seem real or part of normal life 像夢一樣的情景, 夢境: **be/seem like a dream** *After a few weeks back at work our vacation seems like a dream.* 回來工作了幾個星期之後, 我們的假期彷彿發生在夢裡一樣。

4 ▶PLEASANT THOUGHTS 遐想◀ [C usually singular 一般用單數] a set of pleasant thoughts that make you forget about what is really happening; DAYDREAM[2] 幻想, 遐想, 白日夢: *Peter's lost in a dream again.* 彼得又陷入幻想之中。

5 a dream come true something that you wanted to happen for a long time 夢想成真: *Finding my real mother after all these years was a dream come true.* 這麼多年後終於找到我的親生母親, 我的夢想成真了。

6 like a dream *usually spoken* extremely well or effectively【一般口】好極了; 非常有效: *The plan worked like a dream.* 這個計劃進行得非常順利。| **go like a dream** (=work perfectly) 用起來極好; 性能極佳 *The new motorbike goes like a dream.* 這輛新摩托車開起來特別得心應手。

7 a dream *usually spoken* a very attractive person or thing【一般口】非常漂亮的人[物]: *Her latest boyfriend is an absolute dream.* 她的新任男友絕對夠帥。

8 be/live in a dream world to have ideas or hopes that are not practical or likely to happen 生活在夢幻世界: *If you think he'll change, you're living in a dream world.* 如果你認為他會改變, 你就太不實際了。

9 in your dreams *spoken* used to say that something is not likely to happen【口】妄想; 在做夢〔表示某事不可能發生〕: *"I'm going to ask her to go out with me." "In your dreams!"* "我要約她出來。" "你做夢吧!"

dream[2] *v past tense and past participle* **dreamed** or **dreamt** /dɛmt; dremt/ 3

1 ▶THINK ABOUT 夢想◀ [I,T] to think about something that you would like to happen 夢想, 幻想, 嚮往: **[+of]** *We dream of buying our own house.* 我們嚮往着

D

買自己的房子。| **dream (that)** *She dreamed that one day she would be famous.* 她夢想有朝一日會成名。| **[+about]** *We used to dream about living abroad.* 過去我們常常夢想去國外生活。

2 ►WHILE SLEEPING 睡覺時◄ [I,T] to have a dream while you are asleep 做夢; 夢見: **[+about]** *I dreamt about you last night.* 我昨晚夢到你了。| **dream (that)** *It's quite common to dream that you're falling.* 做夢夢到自己在往下掉落是件常有的事。

3 ►IMAGINE 想像◄ [I,T] to imagine that you have done, seen, or heard something that you have not 想像着做過[見過; 聽到]〔某事〕: *I was sure I posted the letter but I must have dreamt it.* 我確信自己已經把信寄出去了, 但我一定是在憑空想像。

4 wouldn't dream of (doing) sth *spoken* used to say that you would never do something because you do not approve of it or think it is unpleasant【口】無論如何也不會做某事: *We wouldn't dream of letting our daughter go out on her own at night.* 我們無論如何也不會讓女兒晚上獨自出門。

5 who would have dreamt it? *spoken* used to express surprise about something that has happened【口】誰能料到會這樣呢?〔表示驚訝、驚奇〕: *"Did you hear that Bruno's been made Managing Director?" "Yes, who would have dreamt it?"* "你聽説布魯諾被任命為總經理這件事了嗎?" "聽説了, 誰也想不到啊!"

dream sth ↔ **away** *phr v* [T] to waste time by thinking about what may happen〔在空想中〕虛度〔光陰〕: *She would just sit in her room dreaming away the hours.* 她常常會在自己房間裡坐着幻想上數小時。

dream on *phr v* [I] *spoken*【口】**dream on!** used to tell someone that they are hoping for something that will not happen 別做夢了!〔用於告訴某人希望的事情不可能發生〕: *You think I'm going to help you move house? Dream on!* 你以為我會幫你搬家? 別做夢了!

dream sth ↔ **up** [T] to think of a plan or idea, especially an unusual one 虛構出, 憑空想出〔不同尋常的計劃、主意等〕: *Who on earth dreams up the plots for these soap operas?* 這些肥皂劇的情節到底是誰想出來的?

dream·boat /ˈdrimˌbot; ˈdriːmbəʊt/ *n* [C] *old-fashioned* someone who is very good-looking and attractive【過時】好看而有吸引力的人; 夢中人

dream·er /ˈdrimɚ; ˈdriːmə/ *n* [C] **1** someone who has ideas or plans that are not practical 空想家 **2** someone who dreams while they are asleep 做夢的人

dream·i·ly /ˈdrimɪlɪ; ˈdriːmə̩li/ *adv* thinking about pleasant things and not about what is actually happening 神情恍惚地; 心不在焉地: *"I'm coming," he replied dreamily, without moving.* "我來了。" 他心不在焉地回答道, 動都沒有動一下。

dream·land /ˈdrimˌlænd; ˈdriːmlænd/ *n* [U] a happy place or situation that exists only in your imagination 夢境; 夢鄉; 理想世界

dream·less /ˈdrimlɪs; ˈdriːmləs/ *adj* dreamless sleep is very deep and peaceful〔睡眠〕無夢的; 安寧的

dream·like /ˈdrimˌlaɪk; ˈdriːmlaɪk/ *adj* as if happening in a dream; unreal 如夢的, 虛幻的, 夢幻般的: *There was a dreamlike quality about the film.* 這部電影有一種夢幻般的情調。

dreamt /drɛmt; dremt/ a past tense and past participle of DREAM[2]

dream tick·et /ˈ· ˌ··/ *n* [C] a combination of people who you think will be sure to win an election for a political party〔被認為一定會為某政黨贏得選舉的候選人的〕夢幻組合: *Clinton and Gore were the Democrats' dream ticket.* 克林頓和戈爾是民主黨的理想候選班子。

dream·y /ˈdrimɪ; ˈdriːmi/ *adj* **1** someone who is dreamy has a good imagination but is not very practical〔指人〕愛幻想的: *a bright, but dreamy child* 一個聰明但愛幻想的孩子 **2** looking as though you are thinking about something pleasant rather than things happening around you 神情恍惚的, 心不在焉的: *a dreamy look* 恍惚的神情 **3** a dreamy sight, sound etc is peaceful and relaxing〔景色、聲音等〕恬靜的, 悠閒的: *She loved the dreamy music of those old songs.* 她喜歡那些老歌優美的曲調。**4** *informal* very attractive and desirable【非正式】極富吸引力的; 理想的; 極好的: *a dreamy new sports car* 一輛極漂亮的新跑車 **—dreaminess** *n* [U]

drear·y /ˈdrɪrɪ; ˈdrɪəri/ also 又作 **drear** /drɪr; drɪə/ *poetical adj* not interesting or cheerful【詩】乏味的; 沉悶的: *the same old dreary routine* 枯燥的老一套例行公事 | *a dreary winter's day* 沉悶的冬日

dredge /drɛdʒ; dredʒ/ *v* **1** [T] to remove mud or sand from the bottom of a river, HARBOUR[1] etc 疏浚, 給…清淤 **2** [I,T] to search for something on the bottom of a river, lake, etc with a dredge〔用挖泥船、疏浚機在河底、湖底等處〕尋找, 打撈 **3** [T] to cover food lightly with flour, sugar etc〔在食物上〕撒上〔麵粉、糖等〕

dredge sth ↔ **up** *phr v* [T] **1** *informal* to start talking again about something that happened a long time ago【非正式】重提〔舊事〕: *Come on now, let's not dredge up old quarrels.* 好了, 我們不要再提以前的爭吵了。**2** to pull something up from the bottom of a river〔從河底〕撈取; 打撈

dredg·er /ˈdrɛdʒɚ; ˈdredʒə/ also 又作 **dredge** *n* [C] a machine or ship used for digging or removing mud and sand from the bottom of a river, HARBOUR[1] etc 挖泥船; 疏浚機

dregs /drɛgz; dregz/ *n* **1** [plural] small pieces that sink to the bottom of wine, coffee etc〔沉入酒、咖啡等物中的〕渣滓, 沉澱物 —compare 比較 LEES (3) **2 the dregs of society/humanity** an offensive expression used to describe the people that you consider are the least important or useful 社會/人類渣滓

drench /drɛntʃ; drentʃ/ *v* [T] to make something or someone extremely wet 使濕透; 淋透; 澆透 **—drenching** *adj*

drenched /drɛntʃt; drentʃt/ *adj* **1** extremely wet 濕透的: *Come on in – you're drenched!* 快進來——你都淋透了! | **[+with/in]** *I came back from aerobics drenched in sweat.* 我練完健身操回來, 渾身都讓汗給濕透了。| **drenched to the skin** (=wearing completely wet clothes) 渾身濕透 **2** covered in something〔以某物〕覆蓋着的: **[+in]** *women drenched in cheap perfume* 全身噴滿廉價香水的女人 | **rain-drenched/sun-drenched etc** (=covered in rain, or in the effects of something such as the sun) 被雨水浸泡的/沐浴在陽光裡的 *sun-drenched deserts* 沐浴在陽光裡的沙漠

dress[1] /drɛs; dres/ *n* **1** [C] a piece of clothing worn by a woman or girl that covers her body from her shoulder to somewhere on her leg 連衣裙, 套裙: *Sheila wore a long red dress.* 希拉穿了一條長的紅色連衣裙。—compare 比較 SKIRT[1] (1) **2** [U] the way someone dresses 穿着, 着裝: *His dress is always very formal.* 他的衣着總是很正式。**3 dress code** a standard of what you should wear for a particular situation〔某種特定場合的〕衣着標準: *This restaurant has a strict dress code – no tie, no service.* 這家餐廳有嚴格的衣着標準——不繫領帶, 恕不招待。**4 evening/national/battle etc dress** a special set of clothes that you wear for a particular occasion 晚禮服/民族服裝/野戰服裝等 —see also 另見 DRESS SENSE, CLOTHES (USAGE)

dress[2] *v*

1 ►PUT ON CLOTHES 穿上衣服◄ **a)** [I] to put on clothes, etc, especially before a special occasion〔尤指為某種特殊場合〕穿好衣服: *I've got to go home to dress.* 我得回家去更衣打扮一下。| **dress for** (=put on clothes you wear for a particular activity) 為…穿好衣服 *How do you normally dress for work?* 你通常穿甚麼衣服上班? | **dress for dinner** (=put on formal clothes for your evening meal) 為晚餐而穿上正式的服裝 **b)** [T] to put clothes on yourself or someone else 給…穿衣: *I dress the kids before I go to work.* 我給孩子們穿好衣服, 然後上班。—see also 另見 DRESSED

dress 穿衣服

He got dressed. 他穿上了衣服。

He put on a jacket. 他穿上外衣。

He wore a dark suit. 他穿着黑色西裝。

dress up 裝扮; 打扮

The kids are dressing up in their room. 孩子們在自己的房間裡裝扮。

Jill's getting dressed up for the dinner party. 吉爾在為晚宴打扮。

2 ►WEAR CLOTHES 穿着衣服◄ [I] to wear a particular kind of clothes 穿衣: *Dress warmly if you're going out for a walk.* 如果你出去散步就穿得暖和些。

3 dress a wound/cut etc to clean and cover a wound etc 清洗並包紮傷口/刀口等

4 dress a salad to put a mixture of oil, VINEGAR, salt etc onto a SALAD (=cold vegetables) 給沙拉[沙律]加〔油、醋、鹽等〕調味品 *Don't dress the salad until just before you're ready to eat.* 沙拉要在準備吃的時候才加調味品。

5 dress poultry/crab etc to clean and prepare meat or fish so that it is ready to cook or eat 清洗並加工禽肉/螃蟹等〔以備烹飪或食用〕

6 ►MAKE CLOTHES 製作服裝◄ [T] to make or choose clothes for someone 為〔某人〕製作[選擇]服裝: *The Princess is dressed by one of Britain's most famous designers.* 王妃的服裝是由英國最著名的設計師之一設計的。

7 ►HAIR 頭髮◄ [T] *formal* to arrange someone's hair into a special style【正式】做〔頭髮〕

8 ►HORSE 馬◄ [T] to brush a horse in order to make it clean 梳刷〔馬的毛〕

9 dress wood/metal/leather etc *technical* to polish or put a special surface onto wood etc【術語】對木材/金屬/皮革等做表面處理

10 dress stone *technical* to cut and shape stone so that it can be used in building【術語】加工石料

11 ►SOLDIERS 士兵◄ [I,T] *technical* a word used in the army to tell soldiers to form a straight line【術語】看齊; (使) 排列整齊

dress down *phr v* **1** [I] to wear clothes that are more informal than you would usually wear〔比平時〕穿着隨便 **2** [T **dress sb ↔ down**] to speak angrily or severely to someone about something they have done wrong 訓斥, 怒斥〔某人〕—see also 另見 DRESSING-DOWN

dress up *phr v* **1** [I,T] to wear special clothes, MAKE-UP (1), etc for fun〔鬧着玩地〕裝扮: **[+as]** *He went to the party dressed up as a Chicago gangster.* 他裝扮成一個芝加哥歹徒去參加晚會。| **[+in]** *I keep a box of old clothes for the children to dress up in.* 我保存着一箱舊衣服讓孩子們穿着玩。| **[dress sb ↔ up]** *We dressed him up as a gorilla.* 我們把他裝扮成大猩猩。**2** [I] to wear clothes that are more formal than you would usually wear〔比平時〕穿着正式: *It's a small informal party – you don't have to dress up.* 這是個非正式的小型聚會 —— 你不用穿得那麼正式。**3** [T **dress sth ↔ up**] to make something sound more interesting or attractive than it really is 對…加以修飾, 美化: *It was the old offer dressed up as something new.* 這只不過是原來的那個提議, 改頭換面像新的罷了。

USAGE NOTE 用法説明: DRESS

WORD CHOICE 詞語辨析: **dress, get dressed, put on, dress up, dress yourself, have on, wear, dress in, be in**

If you **dress** (slightly formal) or **get dressed** you **put on** all your clothes. But you usually use **put on** if you are talking about just one piece of clothing or things like glasses and jewellery. dress〔稍正式〕或 get dressed 表示穿上所有的衣服。但是 put on 則通常表示穿上一件衣服或戴上眼鏡或首飾等物品: *It's ten o'clock – isn't time you got dressed?* 十點鐘了 —— 你是不是該穿好衣服了? | *We had to wash and dress in a freezing bathroom.* 我們只得在冰冷的浴室裡洗臉並穿好衣服。| *OK, you can put your shirt back on.* 好了, 你可以把襯衫重新穿上了。| *Wait a moment while I put my shoes on.* 等一會兒, 我把鞋穿上。

You **dress up** only in special clothes or for a special occasion. These may be particularly good or formal ones. dress up 表示為參加某個特殊的場合而穿着特殊的服裝, 可以是特別好的衣服或正式的衣服: *What kind of party is it? Will we have to dress up?* 那是個甚麼樣的聚會? 我們要不要穿得正式些? Or they may be unusual clothes that make you look like someone else, for example if you are acting in a play. dress up 還可以表示穿上不同尋常的衣服，以使你看起來像另外一個人，如當你在演戲時：*He had to dress up as a clown.* 他不得不裝扮成小丑。

You only talk about someone **dressing themselves** if a special effort is involved. 只在談論某人穿衣需要特別費力時，才使用 dressing oneself: *Can Tara dress herself yet?* (=Tara is a small child) 塔拉能自己穿衣服嗎？〔塔拉是個小孩兒〕| *Since the accident he can't feed or dress himself.* 自從發生那次事故之後，他無法自己吃飯、穿衣。

After you have **put on** your clothes etc, you **have** them **on**. put on 表示穿戴衣物等的動作，而 have ... on 表示已穿戴上之後的狀態：*They all had dark glasses on.* 他們都戴着墨鏡。

Wear means to **have** clothes, jewellery etc **on** and is often used to describe someone's usual style of dressing. wear 表示穿着衣服或佩戴着珠寶，而且還經常用來描述一個人平時慣常的穿着風格：*She always wears earrings/casual clothes/black.* 她總是佩戴着耳環/穿着休閒服裝/穿着黑色衣服。| *I'll be wearing a red coat.* 我將會穿着一件紅外套。| *All visitors to the site must wear a protective helmet.* 所有參觀現場的人都必須戴防護頭盔。You can also use **dress (in)** and **be (dressed) in** to talk about what clothes someone is wearing, or their style of clothes. dress (in) 和 be (dressed) in 也可以用來表示某人正穿戴着甚麼服飾或表示某人的穿戴風格：*She always dresses casually/in black.* 她總是穿得很隨便/身穿黑色衣服。| *The band were all (dressed) in green and red jackets.* 樂隊裡的人都穿着紅綠相間的短上衣。

GRAMMAR 語法

You **dress in** clothes, or **dress** someone **in** them. You cannot *dress clothes* or *dress with clothes.* 穿衣服用 dress in clothes 表示，給某人穿衣服用 dress someone in clothes。不能用 dress clothes 或 dress with clothes 表示穿衣服。

dres·sage /drɛˋsɑʒ; ˈdresɑːʒ/ *n* [U] a competition in which a horse performs a complicated series of actions in answer to signals from its rider 花式騎術比賽，馬術比賽

dress cir·cle /ˈ· ˌ··/ *n* [C] the lowest of the curved rows of seats upstairs in a theatre 戲院樓上最低層前排座位

dressed /drɛst; drest/ *adj* **1 get dressed** to put your clothes on 穿上[穿好]衣服：*Go and get dressed!* 趕快把衣服穿好！**2** having your clothes on 穿好衣服的：*Aren't you dressed yet?* 你還沒有穿好衣服嗎？| **fully dressed** (=with all your clothes on) 穿戴齊備的 **3** wearing a particular type of clothes 穿某種類型衣服的：**[+in/as]** *The older woman was dressed in a suit.* 那位年長些的婦女穿着套裝。| **well/neatly/badly etc dressed** *a very well-dressed young man* 穿着很體面的小夥子 **4 dressed to kill** *informal* wearing very attractive clothes so that everyone notices you【非正式】穿着非常漂亮的 **5 dressed (up) to the nines** *informal* wearing your best or most formal clothes【非正式】穿着盛裝；衣飾華麗：*Where on earth's he going dressed up to the nines like that?* 他穿得那麼考究到底要去哪兒？

dress·er /ˋdrɛsɚ; ˈdresə/ *n* [C] **1** *BrE* a large piece of furniture with open shelves for storing plates, dishes etc; WELSH DRESSER【英】碗櫃，碗櫥 **2** *AmE* a piece of furniture with drawers for storing clothes, sometimes with a mirror on top; CHEST OF DRAWERS【美】衣櫥 **3 a fashionable/stylish/sloppy etc dresser** someone who dresses in a fashionable etc way 穿着新潮者/時髦者/邋遢者等：*Stanley was an impeccable dresser, with plenty of money.* 史丹利很有錢，穿得特別講究，無可挑剔。**4** someone who looks after an actor's clothes in the theatre and helps them to dress for a play〔劇團的〕服裝師

dress·ing /ˋdrɛsɪŋ; ˈdresɪŋ/ *n* **1** [C,U] a mixture of liquids, usually made from oil and VINEGAR, that you put on raw vegetables〔放在生的蔬菜上面的〕調料，調味醬：*a vinaigrette dressing* 香醋沙拉[沙律]調料 —see also 另見 FRENCH DRESSING, SALAD DRESSING **2** [C,U] *AmE* a mixture of food that you put inside a piece of meat, for example a chicken, before you cook it; STUFFING (1)【美】調味餡料，填料 **3** [C] a special piece of material used to cover and protect a wound〔包紮、護理傷口的〕敷料；繃帶：*Put the soiled dressings in this bin.* 把用過的髒繃帶放到這個箱子裡。—see also 另見 CROSS-DRESSING, POWER DRESSING, WINDOW DRESSING

dressing-down /ˌ·· ˈ·/ *n* **give sb a dressing-down** to talk to someone angrily because they have done something wrong 狠狠地訓斥某人：*He gave the children a good dressing-down.* 他狠狠地訓斥了孩子們一頓。

dressing gown /ˈ·· ·/ *n* [C] *especially BrE* a piece of clothing like a long loose coat that you wear inside the house; BATHROBE【尤英】〔室內穿的長而寬鬆的〕晨衣；睡袍；浴袍

dressing room /ˈ·· ·/ *n* [C] **1** a room where an actor or performer can get ready, before going on stage, appearing on television etc〔演員的〕化妝室 **2** a small room next to a BEDROOM〔臥室旁邊的〕小梳妝室

dressing ta·ble /ˈ·· ˌ··/ *n* [C] *BrE* a piece of furniture like a table with a mirror on top, sometimes with drawers, that you use when you are doing your hair, putting on MAKE-UP (1) etc【英】梳妝台；VANITY TABLE *AmE*【美】

dressing-up /ˌ·· ˈ·/ *n* [U] a children's game in which they put on special clothes and MAKE-UP (1) and pretend that they are someone else〔兒童的〕化裝遊戲：*a box of dressing-up clothes* 一箱化裝用的衣服

dress·mak·er /ˋdrɛsˌmekɚ; ˈdresˌmeɪkə/ *n* [C] someone who makes their own clothes, or makes clothes for other people as a job 給自己做衣服的人；裁縫 —**dressmaking** *n* [U]

dress re·hears·al /ˈ· ·ˌ··/ *n* [C] the final practice of a play, OPERA etc, using all the clothes that will be worn for the actual performance 彩排

dress sense /ˈ· ·/ *n* [U] the ability to choose clothes that make you look attractive 衣着品位

dress shirt /ˈ· ·/ *n* [C] a formal shirt, sometimes with a special decoration at the front, that you wear under a DINNER JACKET〔前襟有特殊裝飾的〕晚禮服襯衫

dress u·ni·form /ˈ· ˌ···/ *n* [C,U] a uniform that officers in the army, navy etc wear for formal occasions or ceremonies 軍禮服

dress·y /ˋdrɛsɪ; ˈdresi/ *adj* **1** dressy clothes are suitable for formal occasions〔服裝〕適合正式場合穿的，講究的：*Her outfit was just right for a summer evening – smart, but not too dressy.* 她的套裝很適合夏日的傍晚穿——時尚但又不過於正式。**2** someone who is dressy likes to wear very fashionable or formal clothes〔指人〕愛穿時髦[正式]服裝的：*Mr Menendez is a very dressy sort of person.* 梅嫩德斯先生是一位很講究穿着的人。

drew /dru; druː/ the past tense of DRAW[1]

drib·ble[1] /ˋdrɪbḷ; ˈdrɪbəl/ *v* **1** [I] *BrE* to let SALIVA (=natural liquid in your mouth) flow out of your mouth onto your chin【英】流口水；垂涎；DROOL (1) *AmE*【美】：*Watch out, the baby is dribbling on your shirt!* 小心，嬰兒的口水淌到你的襯衫上了！**2** [I always+adv/prep] if a liquid dribbles, it flows very slowly in small irregular drops〔指液體〕慢慢滴淌：**[+down/from/out etc]** *There was a tiny hole in the pipe and water was dribbling out.* 管子上有個小洞，水正慢慢地往外滴。**3** [T] to pour something out slowly in an irregular way 使〔慢而不規則地〕往外傾注：*This artist works by dribbling paint straight from the tube.* 這位美術家直接把顏料從管子裡擠出作畫。**4** [I,T] to move the ball along with you, by short kicks, BOUNCE*s*, or hits, in a game of football, BASKETBALL etc〔足球、籃球等運動中的〕運（球），帶（球）：*We've been learning how to dribble the ball.* 我們一直在學習如何運球。—see picture on page A23 參見 A23 頁圖

dribble² *n* **1** [U] *BrE* a flow of SALIVA (=natural liquid in your mouth) from your mouth【英】流淌的口水; SALIVA *AmE*【美】**2 a dribble of sth** a small amount of liquid 少量某物〔指液體〕: *He wiped a dribble of ice-cream from his chin.* 他擦掉下巴上的一小塊冰淇淋。**3** [C] the way in which you move the ball along with you in football, BASKETBALL etc 運球, 帶球

drib·let /ˋdrɪblɪt; ˈdrɪblɪ̵t/ *n* [C] a very small amount of something 少量, 一丁點

dribs and drabs /ˌdrɪbz ən ˋdræbz; ˌdrɪbz ən ˈdræbz/ *n* [plural] **in dribs and drabs** in small irregular amounts or numbers over a period of time 少量地, 零星地: *The guests arrived in dribs and drabs.* 客人們三三兩兩地到了。

dried /draɪd; draɪd/ *adj* dried substances, such as food or flowers, have had the water removed〔食物、花等〕乾的, 除去水分的, 脱水的

dried fruit /ˌ· ˈ·/ *n* [C,U] fruit that has been dried and is used in cooking or eaten on its own 果脯, 乾果

dried milk /ˌ· ˈ·/ *n* [U] milk that is made into a powder and can be used by adding water 奶粉

dri·er /ˋdraɪɚ; ˈdraɪə/ *n* [C] another spelling of DRYER dryer 的另一種拼法

drift¹ /drɪft; drɪft/ *v* [I] **1** to move slowly on water or in the air 飄移; 漂流: **[+out/towards etc]** *The rubber raft drifted out to sea.* 橡皮筏子漂向大海。**2** [always+adv/prep] to move or go somewhere without any plan or purpose〔毫無計劃或漫無目的地〕漂泊: **[+around/along etc]** *Jenni spent the year drifting around Europe.* 珍妮這一年來一直在歐洲各地漂泊。| **drift from sth to sth** *The conversation drifted from one topic to another.* 談話從一個話題轉到另一個話題。**3 drift into sth** to go from one situation or condition to another without realizing it 不知不覺進入某種狀況: *She was just drifting into sleep when the alarm went off.* 她迷迷糊糊地剛要睡着鬧鐘就響了。**4** if snow, sand etc drifts, the wind blows it into large piles〔指雪、沙等受風〕吹積: *The snow was drifting in great piles against the house.* 雪被風吹到屋旁, 積成了好幾大堆。**5 let sth drift** to allow something to continue in the same way 聽任某事發展下去, 聽之任之: *He couldn't let the matter drift for much longer.* 他不會聽任這種事情持續很久的。

drift apart *phr v* [I] if people drift apart, their relationship gradually ends〔人們之間的關係逐漸地〕疏遠: *Over the years my college friends and I have drifted apart.* 這些年來, 我和大學時期的朋友們已經疏遠了。

drift off *phr v* [I] to gradually fall asleep 慢慢入睡: *I was just drifting off when the phone rang.* 我迷迷糊糊地剛要睡着, 電話鈴就響了。

drift² *n*

1 ►SNOW 雪◄ [C] a large pile of snow, sand etc that has been blown by the wind〔風吹積成的〕雪堆, 沙堆: **[+of]** *The road is blocked with massive drifts of snow.* 大堆大堆的積雪把路給堵死了。

2 ►SHIP 船◄ [U] the degree to which a ship or plane changes its direction because of the movement of the wind or water 偏移, 偏離

3 ►GENERAL MEANING 大意◄ **the drift** the general meaning of what someone is saying〔話語的〕大意, 要旨: **[+of]** *So what's the drift of the argument?* 那麼論點的要義是甚麼? | **follow/get/catch sb's drift** (=understand the general meaning) 明白[了解]某人的意思 *I didn't hear every word of her speech, but I got the drift.* 我沒有聽到她講話的全部, 但是我知道了她的意思。

4 ►CHANGE 變化◄ [singular] a slow change or development from one situation, opinion etc to another〔情形、意見等的〕漸變; 趨勢: *the drift of public opinion towards the political left* 公共輿論轉向左派政黨的趨勢 | **the broad/whole/general drift** (=the general change in direction) 總的趨勢, 動向 *A general drift towards anarchy must be prevented at all costs.* 無論花任何代價都要制止住朝無政府狀態發展的總趨勢。

5 ►MOVEMENT OF PEOPLE 人口流動◄ a slow and unplanned movement of large numbers of people〔大量人口緩慢、無計劃的〕流動: **[+from/to/into]** *the drift from the countryside to the cities* 從鄉村往城市的人口流動

drift·er /ˋdrɪftɚ; ˈdrɪftə/ *n* [C] **1** someone who is always moving from one job or place to another 漂泊者, 流浪者, 遊民 **2** a fishing boat that uses a floating net 拖網[飄網]漁船

drift-ice /ˈ· ·/ *n* [U] pieces of broken ice floating in a sea, river etc 流冰, 浮冰

drift·net /ˋdrɪftˌnɛt; ˈdrɪftnet/ *n* [C] a large net behind a boat, used to catch fish 流網, 飄網

drift·wood /ˋdrɪftˌwʊd; ˈdrɪftwʊd/ *n* [U] wood floating in the sea or left on the shore 漂流木, 浮木〔在海上漂流或被海水沖上岸的木頭〕

drills 鑽

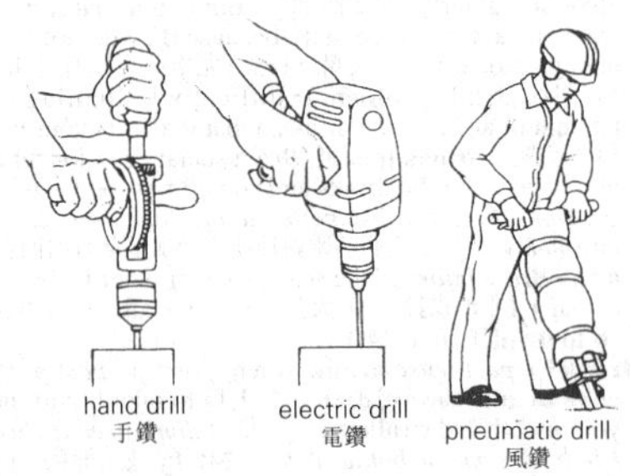

drill¹ /drɪl; drɪl/ *n*

1 ►TOOL 工具◄ [C] a tool or machine used for making holes in something 鑽; 鑽牀; 鑽機: *an electric drill* 電鑽

2 ►WAY OF LEARNING 學習方法◄ [U] a way of learning something by repeating it many times 練習; 訓練: *a pronunciation drill* 發音練習

3 fire/emergency drill a practice of the things you should do in a dangerous situation such as a fire 消防/應急演習

4 ►MILITARY TRAINING 軍事訓練◄ [U] military training in which soldiers practice marching and other actions 軍事操練: *rifle drill* 步槍操練

5 ►CLOTH 布◄ [U] a type of strong cotton cloth 粗斜紋布

6 the drill *BrE old-fashioned* the correct way of doing something【英, 過時】正確的步驟; 程序: *What's the drill for getting money after four o'clock?* 四點鐘之後領錢的手續是怎樣的?

7 ►SEEDS 種子◄ **a)** [C] a machine for planting seeds in rows 條播機 **b)** a row of seeds planted by machine 條播的一排種子

drill² *v* **1** [I,T] to make a hole in something using a drill〔用鑽〕鑽孔, 打眼: *You need to drill holes for the fittings.* 安裝這些設備需要鑽孔。| **drill for oil/water/gas etc** *The Saudi government has announced plans to drill for water in the desert.* 沙特政府已經宣布在沙漠鑽井探水的計劃。**2** [T] to teach someone by making them repeat something many times 教〔某人〕反覆練習: *She was drilling the class in the forms of the past tense.* 她指導全班學生反覆練習過去式的各種形式。| **well-drilled** *The well-drilled cabin crew evacuated the passengers in minutes.* 訓練有素的機組人員在幾分鐘內就疏散了乘客。**3** [I,T] to practice marching and other military actions, or to train soldiers to do this 訓練, 操練 **4** [T] to plant seeds in rows 條播〔種子〕

drill sth **into sb** *phr v* [T] to keep telling someone something until they know it very well 向某人灌輸〔某事〕: *Mother had drilled it into me not to talk to strangers.*

媽媽跟我講了一遍又一遍，叫我不要和陌生人說話。

drilling plat·form /ˈ·· ˌ·/ *n* [C] a large structure in the sea used for drilling for oil, gas etc 鑽井平台

dri·ly /ˈdraɪlɪ; ˈdraɪli/ *adv* another spelling of DRYLY dryly 的另一種拼法

drink¹ /drɪŋk; drɪŋk/ *n* **1** [C] an amount of liquid that you drink 一杯[份]飲料: *Can I have a drink of water, please?* 我能喝杯水嗎？| **soft drink** (=a non-alcoholic drink) 非酒精飲料，軟性飲料 *They sell ice-cream and soft drinks.* 他們賣冰淇淋和軟飲料。**2** [C,U] alcohol, or a glass or bottle of alcohol 酒；一杯[瓶]酒: *Have another drink.* 再喝一杯。| *There were lots of food and drink left over from the party.* 晚會過後剩了許多食物和酒。| **a stiff drink** (=very strong alcohol) 烈性酒 *After that news I need a stiff drink!* 聽到那則消息後我需要喝一杯烈酒！| **go out for a drink** *BrE* (=go to a PUB)【英】去酒館喝一杯 | **take to drink** (=start drinking a lot of alcohol regularly) 開始酗酒 | **stand sb a drink**(=buy someone a drink, especially because they do not have enough money) 請某人喝一杯酒〔尤指此人沒有足夠的錢〕| **a drink problem** (=difficulty in limiting the amount of alcohol you drink so that it affects your life) 酗酒問題 **3 drinks** [plural] *BrE* a social occasion when you have alcoholic drinks and sometimes food【英】酒會: *Don't forget we're invited to the Jones' for drinks on Sunday.* 別忘了我們應邀到鍾斯家參加星期日的酒會。**4 the drink** *informal* the sea, a lake, or other large area of water【非正式】海；湖；大片水域 —see also 另見 **drive sb to drink** (DRIVE¹ (4))

drink² *v past tense* **drank** /dræŋk; dræŋk/ *past participle* **drunk** /drʌŋk; drʌŋk/ **1** [I,T] to take liquid into your mouth and swallow it 喝，飲: *I don't need a glass, I'll drink from the bottle.* 我不需要杯子，我用瓶喝。| *If you have a fever, drink plenty of water.* 如果你發燒的話要多喝水。| *What would you like to drink?* 你想喝點甚麼？**2** [I] to drink alcohol, especially regularly or too much 酗酒，縱酒: *He's been drinking heavily since his wife died.* 自他妻子死後，他一直酗酒無度。| **don't/doesn't drink** (=never drink alcohol) 從不喝酒 *Whisky? No thanks, I don't drink.* 要威士忌嗎？不，謝謝，我從不喝酒。| **drink and drive** (=driving after you have drunk too much alcohol) 酒後駕車 *a new campaign to stop drinking and driving at Christmas* 旨在制止聖誕節期間酒後駕車的一場新的運動 | **drink like a fish** (=regularly drink a lot of alcohol) 經常狂飲 | **drink yourself unconscious/silly etc** (=drink so much alcohol that you become unconscious etc) 喝得失去知覺/暈頭轉向等 *If he goes on this way he'll drink himself to death.* 如果他這麼喝下去，會喝死的。| **drink sb under the table** (=drink more alcohol than someone else but not be as ill as them)〔比酒量〕喝到使某人醉倒 **3 what are you drinking?** *spoken* used to offer to buy someone a drink, especially in a PUB【口】你想喝點甚麼？〔用於表示主動給某人買酒，尤指在酒館中〕

drink sth ↔ **in** *phr v* [T] to look at or listen to something carefully and enjoy it 入迷地看[聽]，欣賞: *We spent the day drinking in the sights and sounds of Paris.* 這一天我們盡情地享受巴黎的景色和喧囂。

drink to sth *phr v* [T] **1** to wish someone success, good luck, good health etc before having an alcoholic drink 為〔某人的成功、好運、健康等〕祝酒，乾杯: *Let's drink to your success in your new job.* 讓我們為你在新的工作中取得成功而乾杯。**2 I'll drink to that!** *spoken* used to agree with what someone has said【口】我為這乾一杯！〔用於表示贊同某人的話〕

drink sth ↔ **up** *phr v* [T] to drink all of something 喝光，喝乾: *Come on, drink up your milk.* 快，把牛奶都喝了。

drin·ka·ble /ˈdrɪŋkəbḷ; ˈdrɪŋkəbəl/ *adj* **1** water that is drinkable is safe to drink〔水〕可飲用的，適合飲用的 **2** wine, beer etc that is drinkable is of good quality and tastes pleasant〔葡萄酒、啤酒等〕質量好的，口感好的

drink-dri·ving /ˌ· ˈ··/ *n* [U] *BrE* driving a car after having drunk too much alcohol【英】酒後駕駛；DRUNK-DRIVING *AmE*【美】

drink·er /ˈdrɪŋkɚ; ˈdrɪŋkə/ *n* [C] **1** someone who regularly drinks alcohol 酒徒: *Dave has always been a bit of a drinker.* 戴夫一直是個小酒鬼。| **hard/heavy drinker** (=someone who drinks a lot) 狂飲者，酗酒者 **2 coffee/wine/champagne etc drinker** someone who regularly drinks coffee etc 習慣喝咖啡/葡萄酒/香檳等的人: *There's no wine – we're all beer drinkers, I'm afraid.* 沒有準備葡萄酒 —— 恐怕我們都習慣於喝啤酒。

drink·ing foun·tain /ˈ·· ˌ··/ *n* [C] a piece of equipment in a public place that produces a stream of water for you to drink from〔公共場所的〕噴泉式飲水器；WATER FOUNTAIN *AmE*【美】

drinking-up time /ˌ·· ˈ· ·/ *n* [U] *BrE* the time, after a PUB has closed, when people are allowed to finish their drinks【英】〔酒館關門後〕允許顧客把酒喝完的時間

drinking wa·ter /ˈ·· ˌ··/ *n* [U] water that is pure enough for you to drink 飲用水

drinks ma·chine /ˈ· ·ˌ·/ *n* [C] a machine that serves hot and cold drinks when you put money into it 自動飲料售賣機

drinks par·ty /ˈ· ˌ··/ *n* [C] *BrE* a party where you mainly talk to people and have alcoholic drinks; COCKTAIL PARTY【英】酒會

drip¹ /drɪp; drɪp/ *v* **dripped, dripping 1** [I] to produce small drops of liquid 滴水，漏水: *The tap's dripping.* 水龍頭在滴水。| *Be careful – your paintbrush is dripping.* 小心 —— 你的漆刷在往下滴漆。**2** [I,T] to fall or let something fall in very small drops (使) 滴下；瀝下: [**+down/from etc**] *Sweat dripped from his body.* 汗從他身上滴落下來。| *Water was dripping through the ceiling.* 水正透過天花板往下滴。| **drip water/blood etc** *John came in, his arm dripping blood.* 約翰進來了，他的手臂在滴着血。| **be dripping with sth** *It's so hot, I'm dripping with sweat.* 天太熱了，我渾身都在滴着汗。**3 be dripping with jewels/diamonds etc** to be wearing too much jewellery etc 渾身戴滿了珠寶/鑽石等

drip² *n* **1** [singular,U] the sound or action of a liquid falling in very small drops 滴水聲；滴落: *There was no noise except for the drip drip drip of water.* 除了滴滴答答的水聲以外，沒有別的聲音。**2** [C] one of the very small drops of liquid that falls from something 液滴: *I put some plastic on the floor to catch the drips.* 我把一些塑料鋪在地板上接滴下來的水。**3** [C] a piece of equipment used in hospitals for putting liquids directly into your blood 滴注器；IV *AmE*【美】: *They put her on a drip to speed up the contractions.* 他們給她輸液來加快子宮收縮。**4** [C] *informal* someone who is boring and has a weak character【非正式】怯懦無趣的人，平庸乏味者

drip-dry /ˌ· ˈ·◂/ *adj* drip-dry clothing does not need ironing (IRON²)〔衣服〕滴乾免燙的 —**drip-dry** *v* [I,T]

drip·ping¹ /ˈdrɪpɪŋ; ˈdrɪpɪŋ/ *n* [U] *BrE* the oily substance that comes out of meat when you cook it【英】〔烤肉時滴下的〕油滴

dripping² *adj* extremely wet 濕淋淋的: **dripping wet** *Take off that jacket, you're dripping wet.* 把上衣脱下來，你都濕透了。

drip·py /ˈdrɪpɪ; ˈdrɪpi/ *adj* very emotional and weak 易動感情而軟弱的: *Don't be so drippy, just call Kate and ask her out!* 別當窩囊情種了，給凱特打電話約她出來！

drive¹ /draɪv; draɪv/ *v past tense* **drove** /drov; drəʊv/ *past participle* **driven** /ˈdrɪvən; ˈdrɪvən/

1 ►OPERATE A VEHICLE 開車◄ [I,T] to sit in a car, bus etc and make it travel from one place to another 開車；駕駛〔轎車、公共汽車等〕: *Do you drive?* 你會開車嗎？| *She drove the pick-up and got our supplies.* 她開着小貨車給我們買來了日用必需品。—see picture on page A3 參見A3頁圖

2 ►TRAVEL SOMEWHERE 去某處◄ [I,T] to travel in a car 開車去〔某處〕: *Shall we drive or take the bus?* 我

們開車去還是坐公共汽車去?

3 ▶TAKE SB SOMEWHERE 送某人去某處◀ [T] to take someone somewhere in a car 開車送某人去某處: *Just tell us when you have to go, and Jim will drive you.* 你甚麼時候走告訴我們一聲, 吉姆會開車送你。| **drive sb back/down/over etc** *Can I drive you home?* 我能開車送你回家嗎?

4 ▶FEELING 感覺◀ [T] to make someone feel or do something bad or unpleasant 使〔某人〕感覺不悦; 迫使〔某人〕做壞事: **drive sb to sth** *The children are driving me to despair.* 孩子們逼得我束手無策。| **drive sb to do sth** *It was hunger that drove them to steal the bread.* 他們是為飢餓所迫才去偷麵包的。| **be driven by sth** (=be encouraged to do something by an unpleasant feeling or quality) 受某種不悦的感覺[品性]所驅使 *Phil, driven by jealousy, started spying on his wife.* 受嫉妒心的驅使, 菲爾開始監視他的妻子。| **drive sb to drink** (=upset someone very much) 把某人逼得借酒澆愁 *This job's enough to drive anyone to drink!* 這項工作足以把任何人逼得借酒澆愁! | **drive sb mad/crazy etc** *The noise from the neighbours is driving me mad.* 鄰居家的噪音快要把我逼瘋了。

5 ▶FORCE SB/STH 逼迫某人/某物◀ [T] to force someone or something to go somewhere 驅趕; 驅使; 迫使…去某處: *Tourists were driven indoors by the rain.* 雨迫使遊客進入室內。| *Cowhands drove the cattle into the corral.* 牧牛人把牛趕進了牛欄。

6 ▶PROVIDE POWER 提供動力◀ [T] to provide the power for something 為〔某物〕提供動力: *a steam-driven generator* 以蒸汽為動力的發電機

7 ▶HIT STH INTO STH 把某物釘入某物◀ [T] to hit something, such as a nail, into something else 將〔釘子等〕敲[砸]入: *We watched Dad drive the posts into the ground.* 我們看着爸爸把木樁打入地裡。

8 ▶SPORT 體育運動◀ [I,T] to move a ball in a game of football, GOLF etc by kicking, hitting, or bouncing (BOUNCE¹ (1)) it hard and fast 〔在足球、高爾夫球等運動中〕猛踢, 猛抽, 猛擊 (球): *Bonds drove the ball to center field.* 邦兹猛地把球踢到中場。—see picture on page A23 參見 A23 頁圖

9 drive a hard bargain to make an agreement difficult by demanding a lot or refusing to give too much 極力討價還價; 狠狠殺價

10 drive sb out of their mind to do something that makes someone feel as if they are crazy 使某人喪失理智

11 drive a coach and horses through sth to destroy an argument, plan etc completely 徹底推翻某事, 摧毀某事〔指論點、計劃等〕: *The new bill will drive a coach and horses through recent trade agreements.* 這項新法案將徹底推翻最近達成的貿易協定。

12 ▶MAKE A HOLE 鑽洞◀ [T] to make a large hole in something using heavy equipment or machinery 〔用重型設備或機器〕鑽 (洞): *They're planning to drive a tunnel through the mountains.* 他們計劃在山裡開出一條隧道。

13 drive home a point to make something completely clear to someone 使清楚無誤地理解: *I tried to drive home the point that we need extra people, but the boss wasn't interested.* 我盡力想説明白我們需要額外的人員, 但老闆對此不感興趣。

14 drive a wedge between to do something that makes people disagree or start to dislike each other 挑撥〔人們的關係〕, 使不和[互相厭惡]: *Lisa's lies drove a wedge between the couple.* 莉莎的謊言挑起了那對夫婦的不和。

15 drive yourself too hard to force yourself to work too hard, because you want to be successful 〔因為想成功而〕逼迫自己過分努力地工作

drive at sth *phr v* [T] **what sb is driving at** the thing someone is really trying to say 某人説話的真正意圖: *He didn't mention the word 'redundancy' but I knew what he was driving at.* 他沒有提"裁員"這個詞, 但我知道他話裡的意思。

drive sb ↔ **away** *phr v* [T] to behave in a way that forces someone to leave 趕跑〔某人〕: *Your possessiveness will drive Liz away if you're not careful.* 如果你不小心, 你的佔有慾會把莉兹嚇跑的。

drive off *phr v* **1** [I] if a car, driver etc drives off, they leave 〔指汽車、駕駛人員等〕開走; 駕車離開: *After the accident the other car just drove off.* 車禍之後, 另外那輛車徑自揚長而去了。**2** [T **drive** sb/sth ↔ **off**] to force someone or something that is attacking or threatening you to go away 趕跑, 擊退〔正在威脅或攻擊你的某人或某物〕: *We keep dogs in the yard to drive off intruders.* 我們在院子裡養着幾隻狗以趕走闖入者。**3** [I] to hit the first ball in a game of GOLF 〔高爾夫球運動中的〕發球

drive sb/sth ↔ **out** *phr v* [T] to force someone or something to leave 迫使〔某人或某物〕離開: *Downtown stores are being driven out by crime.* 犯罪活動使得市中心的商店人去店空。

drive sth ↔ **up** *phr v* [T] to force prices, costs etc to rise quickly 迫使〔價格、成本等〕快速上升: *The oil shortage drove gas prices up by 20 cents a gallon.* 石油短缺使得每加侖油價上漲了 20 美分。

D

drive² *n*

1 ▶IN A CAR 乘車◀ [C] a trip in a car 驅車出行: *It's a four day drive to Prague.* 開車到布拉格需要四天。| **go for a drive** *Let's go for a drive along the coast.* 我們開車到海岸邊去兜兜風吧。

2 ▶OUTSIDE YOUR HOUSE 在房屋外邊◀ [C] the area or road between your house and the street; DRIVEWAY 〔房屋與街道之間的〕私家車道: *He parked his car in the drive.* 他把車停在私家車道上。—see picture on page A3 參見 A3 頁圖

3 ▶SPORT 體育運動◀ [C] an act of hitting a ball hard, especially in tennis or GOLF 〔尤指網球或高爾夫球的〕猛擊, 猛抽: *He hit a long, high drive to right field.* 他打了個高遠球到右場。

4 ▶A FIGHT FOR STH 爭取某事物的運動◀ [C] a planned effort by an organization or government to achieve a change that will improve people's lives 〔某個組織或政府為改善人民生活而作的〕有計劃的努力; 運動: *a big anti-smoking drive* 大規模的反吸煙運動 | **economy drive** (=effort to reduce spending) 節約運動

5 ▶NATURAL NEED 自然需求◀ [C] a strong natural need which must be satisfied 基本慾求, 本能的需求: *Hunger is a human drive.* 飢餓是人類的一種原始驅動力。| *sex drive* 性慾

6 ▶SB'S ENERGY 某人的活力◀ [U] determination and energy that make you successfully achieve something 幹勁, 魄力: *Brian has got tremendous drive.* 布賴恩幹勁十足。

7 Drive used in the names of roads 路, 大道〔用於路名〕: *They live at 141 Park Drive.* 他們住在公園路 141 號。

8 ▶POWER 動力◀ [singular] the power from an engine that makes the wheels of a vehicle go round 驅動力, 傳動力: *four wheel drive* 四輪驅動

9 ▶MILITARY ATTACK 軍事進攻◀ [C] several military attacks 大規模強攻〔包括數次軍事進攻〕: *a drive deep into enemy territory* 深入敵人領土的強攻戰役 —see also 另見 DISK DRIVE, WHIST DRIVE

drive-by /ˈ· ·/ *adj* **drive-by shooting/killing** the act of shooting someone from a moving car 從行駛的車上射擊/殺人

drive-in /ˈ· ·/ *adj* [only before noun 僅用於名詞前] a drive-in restaurant, cinema etc allows you to buy food or watch a film without leaving your car 〔餐廳、電影院等〕可駕車進去的, 可坐在車上享用的 —**drive-in** *n* [C]

driv·el¹ /ˈdrɪvl; ˈdrɪvəl/ *n* [U] something that is said or written that is silly or does not mean anything 廢話, 蠢話, 無聊話: *Don't talk such drivel!* 別説這樣的廢話!

drivel² *v* **drivelled, drivelling** [I] *BrE*【英】**drivel on/away** to speak continuously without saying anything

important〔喋喋不休地〕說廢話 —**drivelling** *adj*: *a drivelling idiot* 嘮叨些廢話的白痴

driv·en¹ /ˈdrɪvən; ˈdrɪvən/ the past participle of DRIVE¹

driven² *adj* trying extremely hard to achieve what you want 有緊迫感的; 迫切的 —see also 另見 **as pure as the driven snow** (PURE (8))

driv·er /ˈdraɪvɚ; ˈdraɪvə/ *n* [C] **1** someone who drives a car, bus etc 司機, 駕駛員; 開車的人 **2** a GOLF CLUB (2) with a wooden head〔有木製槌頭的〕高爾夫球桿, 發球桿 —see also 另見 **back seat driver** (BACK SEAT (2)), **Sunday driver** (SUNDAY (3))

driv·er's ed·u·ca·tion /ˌ‥ ‥ˈ‥/ *n* [U] *AmE* a course that you usually take at school, that teaches you how to drive a car【美】〔中學的〕駕駛課程

driver's lic·ense /ˈ‥ ˌ‥/ *n* [C] *AmE* an official document that allows you to drive on public roads【美】〔汽車〕駕駛執照; DRIVING LICENCE *BrE*【英】

drive shaft /ˈ· ·/ *n* [C] *technical* a part of a vehicle that takes power from the GEARBOX to the wheels【術語】〔車輛的〕主動軸, 驅動軸

drive-through /ˈ· ·/ *n* [singular] *especially AmE* a restaurant, bank etc where you can buy food or do business without getting out of your car【尤美】〔不必下車就可購買食物或做生意的〕汽車餐廳; 汽車銀行

drive·way /ˈdraɪvˌwe; ˈdraɪvweɪ/ *n* [C] the area or road between your house and the street; DRIVE² (2)〔房子與街道之間的〕私家車道 —see picture on page A3 參見 A3 頁圖

driv·ing /ˈdraɪvɪŋ; ˈdraɪvɪŋ/ *adj* **1 driving rain/snow** rain or snow that falls very hard and fast 暴雨; 大雪 **2 driving force/ambition/politician** someone or something that produces a strong effect on people or situations 驅動力/激勵向上的抱負/強有力的政治家: *Hawksworth was the driving force behind the project.* 霍克斯沃思是推動該項目的主要人物。

driving li·cence /ˈ‥ ˌ‥/ *n* [C] *BrE* an official document that allows you to drive on public roads【英】〔汽車〕駕駛執照; DRIVER'S LICENSE *AmE*【美】

driving range /ˈ‥ ·/ *n* [C] an open outdoor area where people practice hitting GOLF balls 室外高爾夫球練習場

driving school /ˈ‥ ·/ *n* [C] an organization that teaches you how to drive a car 駕駛學校

driving seat /ˈ‥ ·/ *n* **be in the driving seat** *BrE*【英】**be in the driver's seat** *AmE*【美】to be the person who is in control of a situation 掌控局面; 處於主管地位: *Fiona led the meeting but Marie was the one in the driving seat.* 菲奧娜主持會議, 但瑪麗卻是真正掌控會議的人。

driving test /ˈ‥ ·/ *n* [C] the official test that you must pass in order to drive a car on public roads 駕駛考試

driving un·der the in·flu·ence /ˌ‥ ‥ ˈ‥/ *n* [U] *AmE* DUI【美】酒後駕駛

driz·zle¹ /ˈdrɪzl; ˈdrɪzəl/ *v* [I] to rain slightly 下濛濛細雨, 下毛毛雨: *The rain isn't too bad – it's only drizzling.* 雨下得不太大 —— 只是毛毛雨而已。

drizzle² *n* [singular,U] weather that is between mist and rain 濛濛細雨, 毛毛雨: *A light drizzle had started by the time we left.* 我們離開的時候, 天已經開始下毛毛雨了。 —**drizzly** *adj*

droll /drol; drəʊl/ *adj old-fashioned or humorous* amusing【過時或幽默】逗樂的, 有趣的: *Oh! Very droll!* 噢! 太好玩了!

droll·e·ry /ˈdrolərɪ; ˈdrəʊləri/ *n* [C,U] *old-fashioned* humour【過時】幽默, 詼諧

-drome /drom; drəʊm/ *suffix* [in nouns 構成名詞] *old-fashioned* a large place for a particular purpose【過時】〔作某種用途的〕大地方, 大場地: *an aerodrome* (=an airport) 飛機場

drom·e·da·ry /ˈdrɑməˌdɛrɪ; ˈdrɒmədəri/ *n plural* **dromedaries** [C] a CAMEL with one raised part on its back 單峯駱駝

drone¹ /dron; drəʊn/ *v* [I] to make a continuous low dull sound 發出持續的嗡嗡聲, 嗡嗡作響: *An airplane droned overhead.* 一架飛機在頭頂上嗡嗡地飛過。

drone on *phr v* [I] to speak in a boring way, usually for a long time 令人厭煩地嘮叨: **[+about]** *Tom was droning on about work.* 湯姆在沒完沒了地談工作。

drone² *n* [C] **1 the drone (of)** a continuous low dull sound (…的) 持續而單調的低沉聲音; (…的) 嗡嗡聲: *the steady drone of traffic* 來往車輛發出的持續而低沉的聲音 **2** a male BEE that does no work 雄蜂, 公蜂 **3** someone who does a lot of dull work without many rewards 從事大量乏味工作而報酬很少的人 **4** someone who has a good life but does not work to earn it 遊手好閒者: *idle drones living at the expense of society* 靠社會養活的遊手好閒者

dron·go /ˈdrɑŋgo; ˈdrɒŋgəʊ/ *n* [C] *informal, especially AustrE* a boring and stupid person【非正式, 尤澳】乏味的人; 蠢人, 笨人

drool /drul; druːl/ *v* [I] **1** to let SALIVA (=the liquid in your mouth) flow from your mouth 流口水, 垂涎; DRIBBLE¹ (1) *BrE*【英】**2** to show great pleasure in looking at someone or something 痴迷地看〔某人或某物〕: **[+over]** *Janet was drooling over the two little kittens.* 珍妮特痴迷地看着那兩隻小貓咪。—compare 比較 SLOBBER

droop¹ /drup; druːp/ *v* [I] **1** to hang or bend downwards 低垂, 下垂: *The plant needs some water – it's starting to droop.* 植物需要澆些水 —— 它開始萎垂了。**2** to become sad or weak 情緒低落; 喪失活力: *Our spirits drooped as we faced the long trip home.* 我們在面臨着回家的漫長路程時就無精打采了。

droop² *n* [singular] **1** an act of drooping 低垂, 下垂 **2 brewer's/drinker's droop** *humorous* a condition in which a man cannot get an ERECTION (1) because he has drunk too much alcohol【幽默】男子因飲酒過多而無法勃起

drop¹ /drɑp; drɒp/ *v*

① FALL/ALLOW TO FALL 掉落/使落下
② DECREASE 下降, 減少
③ STOP (DOING STH) 停止 (做某事)
④ NOT USE 不使用
⑤ GO SOMEWHERE 去某處
⑥ OTHER MEANINGS 其他意思

① FALL/ALLOW TO FALL 掉落/使落下

1 [T] to stop holding or carrying something so that it falls 讓〔某物〕落下: *I must have dropped my scarf on the bus.* 我一定是把圍巾掉落在公共汽車上了。| *The dog dropped a stick at George's feet.* 狗啣來一根木棍放在喬治的腳邊。

2 ►FALL 落下◄ [I] to fall suddenly, especially from a high place〔尤指從高處〕忽然落下: *A bottle rolled across the table, dropped onto the floor and smashed.* 一個瓶子從桌上滾落到地板上, 摔得粉碎。| *Your button has dropped off.* 你的鈕扣掉了。

3 ►LOWER YOUR BODY 坐下; 倒下◄ [I always+adv/prep,T] to lower yourself or part of your body suddenly (使) 忽然倒下, 坐下: **[+to/into/down etc]** *He dropped into a chair with a sigh.* 他嘆了一口氣, 一屁股坐在椅子上。

4 ►GROUND 地面◄ [I always+adv/prep] if a path, land etc drops it goes down suddenly, forming a steep slope〔指小徑、地面等〕陡降: *At that point the path dropped sharply to the right.* 在那個地方，小徑忽然向右急轉直下。| **[+away]** *The cliff dropped away to the sea.* 懸崖陡然直下到海裡。
5 drop anchor to lower a boat's ANCHOR[1] (1) to the bottom of the sea, lake etc so that the boat stays in the same place 拋錨〔停船〕
6 ►HIT 擊◄ [T] to hit someone so hard that they fall down 擊倒〔某人〕: *Ali dropped him with one punch.* 阿里一拳就將他擊倒了。

② DECREASE 下降，減少
7 ►LEVEL/AMOUNT 水平/數量◄ [I] to fall to a lower level or amount〔水平〕降低；〔數量〕減少: *The town's population is expected to drop in the next decade.* 預計該城鎮的人口在未來十年內將會減少。| **[+to/from]** *The number of people out of work has dropped to 2 million.* 失業人數已經降低到 200 萬。| **drop sharply** *House prices have dropped sharply in the recession.* 屋價在經濟衰退時期已經急劇下降。
8 ►TEMPERATURE 氣溫◄ [I] to become colder quite quickly 驟然降溫: *The temperature dropped below zero.* 氣溫一下子降到了零下。
9 ►LOWER A LEVEL/AMOUNT 降低水平/數量◄ [T] to lower the level or amount of something 降低〔水平〕；減少〔數量〕: *Drop your speed as you approach the bend.* 接近彎道時要減速。
10 drop your voice/let your voice drop to speak more quietly 壓低/放低聲音: *Barbara saw the manager coming and dropped her voice to a whisper.* 芭芭拉看見經理走過來，就把聲音壓低成耳語。

③ STOP (DOING STH) 停止(做某事)
11 ►STOP DOING STH 停止做某事◄ [T] to stop doing something or planning to do something 停止；擱置；放棄: *Plans for a new swimming pool were dropped due to lack of funding.* 由於資金短缺，建造新游泳池的計劃被擱置了。
12 ►TO STOP TALKING 停止談論◄ to stop talking about something because it upsets people〔因某事讓人不安而〕停止談論: **drop it/drop the subject** *spoken*【口】*Just drop it can't you? I'm tired of arguing.* 就此打住，行不行？我不想再爭論了。| **let the matter drop** *I wish you'd let the matter drop.* 我希望你不要再提這件事。
13 drop everything to stop what you are doing in order to do something else 放下手頭所有的工作〔去做別的事〕: *I can't just drop everything and go, I've got far too much work.* 我不能放下手中的工作就去，我有很多事情要做。
14 ►RELATIONSHIP 關係◄ [T] to end a relationship with someone, usually without thinking about how the other person will feel 終止與〔某人〕的關係，將〔某人〕給甩了: *Sally drops her boyfriends as soon as she gets bored.* 莎莉一覺得厭煩就會甩了男朋友。
15 drop history/physics/German etc to decide to stop studying history etc at school or university 放棄學習歷史/物理/德語等: *I wish I hadn't dropped French, it would've been useful for this job.* 我當初沒有放棄學法語就好了，現在做這個工作法語會很有用。

④ NOT USE 不使用
16 ►NOT USE 不使用◄ [T] to decide not to use something that you had planned to use 決定不使用〔原計劃要用的東西〕: *This article won't be of interest to our readers. Let's drop it.* 讀者不會對這篇文章感興趣的，我們不要採用了。
17 ►NOT INCLUDE 不包括在內◄ [T] to no longer include someone in a team or group 將〔某人〕除名，開除；使離隊: **[+from]** *Jeff's been dropped from the team for Saturday's game.* 傑夫被隊裡排除在外，不參加星期六的比賽。
18 ►WORD OR LETTER 詞或字母◄ [T] to not use a particular word or letter 刪掉；遺漏；略去〔某詞或字母〕: *He often drops his 'h's' when he talks.* 他說話時經常不發 h 音。| *Oh, drop the 'senator', just call me Gordon.* 噢，去掉"參議員"，就叫我戈登吧。

⑤ GO SOMEWHERE 去某處
19 ►VISIT 拜訪◄ [I always+adv/prep] to visit someone informally without arranging a particular time 順便造訪，臨時拜訪: **[+in/over/round/by]** *Drop by whenever you're in the area.* 你不管甚麼時候來這地方，都到我這裡坐坐。| **drop in on sb** *I think I'll drop in on Jill on my way home.* 我想我回家時會順路看望一下吉爾。
20 ►TAKE SB SOMEWHERE 送某人到某處◄ [T always+adv/prep] to take someone by car to a particular place that you are driving past〔用汽車〕順路送某人到某處: **drop sb off/at etc** *She usually drops the kids off at school on her way to work.* 她通常在開車上班時順路把孩子們送到學校。
21 ►TAKE STH SOMEWHERE 把某物送到某處◄ [T always+adv/prep] to take something to a particular place and leave it there 順便把〔某物〕送至〔某處〕: **drop sth off/at/in etc** *I'll drop the books off at your place after my class.* 上完課我會順便把書送到你那兒。
22 drop behind/back to move slowly so that you get separated from the group you are with 落後；掉隊: *Don't drop behind the others on the trail in case you get lost.* 路上別掉隊，以免迷路。

⑥ OTHER MEANINGS 其他意思
23 drop sb a line/note to write a short letter to someone 給某人寫短信/便條: *Drop me a line when you get to Hawaii.* 到了夏威夷給我寫封短信。
24 ►BE TIRED 疲勞◄ [I] to be extremely tired 累趴下，累倒: *They worked until they dropped.* 他們一直工作到都累趴下了。
25 (let) drop a hint/suggestion/remark etc to say something informally and without emphasizing it 無意中暗示/隨口建議/漏出話語等: *He let drop a remark about his childhood which quite surprised me.* 他無意間談起他的童年，這使我相當吃驚。
26 drop your eyes/gaze to stop looking at someone and look down, usually because you feel embarrassed or uncomfortable 垂下眼睛/目光〔通常因為尷尬〕: *She blushed and dropped her gaze.* 她臉紅了，垂下目光。
27 drop dead a) to die suddenly and unexpectedly without having previously been ill 猝死，暴斃: *One day he just dropped dead in the street.* 一天，他就那樣猝死在街上。**b)** *spoken* used angrily to tell someone to be quiet, stop annoying you etc【口】去你的〔用於氣憤地叫某人保持安靜、別再打擾等〕
28 ►MONEY 錢◄ [T] *informal* to lose money in business, a game etc【非正式】〔做生意、玩遊戲時〕輸〔錢〕: *Phil dropped $200 playing poker yesterday.* 菲爾昨天玩撲克牌輸了 200 美元。
29 ►NOT CATCH 未接住◄ [T] to fail to catch a ball hit by a BATSMAN in the game of CRICKET (2)〔板球比賽中〕沒接住〔擊球手擊來的球〕
30 ►LOSE 失掉◄ [T] to lose a point, game etc in a sports competition〔體育比賽中〕失〔分〕，丟〔分〕: *Davison has dropped three points in the fourth round.* 戴維森在第四局比賽中丟了三分。
31 ►DRUGS 毒品◄ [T] *informal* to swallow an illegal drug【非正式】吞服〔毒品〕: *She dropped acid in the 60s.* 她在 60 年代曾經服用過迷幻藥。
32 drop names to use the names of famous or important

people in conversations to make yourself seem important 把重要人物的名字掛在嘴邊來炫耀自己
33 drop a stitch to let the wool fall off the needle when you are knitting (KNIT[1] (1))〔編織時〕掉一針，漏一針
34 drop a clanger/brick *BrE* to say something socially embarrassing【英】說出令人發窘的話；失言；說話失態
35 drop a bombshell *informal* to suddenly tell someone a shocking piece of news【非正式】突然告訴某人一則驚人的消息：*Then she dropped a bombshell and told me she wanted a divorce.* 接着她告訴我一個爆炸性的新聞：她要離婚。

drop away *phr v* [I] to become lower in level or amount 逐漸減少，下降：*Sales have dropped away in recent months.* 近幾個月來，銷售量有所下降。

drop off *phr v* [I] **1** to begin to sleep 入睡，睡着：*Just as I was dropping off, I heard a noise in the house.* 我剛要睡着，就聽見屋子裡有動靜。**2** to become lower in level or amount 下降；減少：*Interest in the game has dropped off recently.* 人們對這項運動的興趣近來減退了。

drop out *phr v* [I] **1** to leave an activity, course etc before it has finished 中途退出，輟學：**[+of]** *He dropped out of college.* 他從大學輟學了。| *Dwyer had to drop out of the race because of injury.* 德懷爾由於受傷不得不退出比賽。**2** to move away from or refuse to take part in society because you do not agree with its principles〔因反對當前社會的道德標準而〕脫離社會；逃避現實而隱退，遁世 —see also 另見 DROPOUT (2) **3** if a word or expression drops out of a language, it is no longer used〔指某單詞或表達法〕不再被使用，過時

drop² *n*
1 ►LIQUID 液體◄ [C] a very small amount of liquid that falls in a round shape 珠，滴：**[+of]** *Big drops of rain rolled down the window.* 大滴的雨水從窗上滾落下去。| *a tear drop* 淚珠，淚滴 —see picture on page A7 參見 A7 頁圖
2 ►A SMALL AMOUNT 少量◄ a drop *informal*【非正式】**a)** a small amount of liquid that you drink〔液體的〕少量，一丁點：*I like my whisky with just a drop of soda.* 我喜歡在威士忌酒中稍加點蘇打水。**b)** a small amount of something〔某物的〕少量，少許：*He hasn't a drop of sense in his head.* 他毫無頭腦。
3 ►DISTANCE 距離◄ [singular] a distance from something down to the ground 下落距離；落差：*a path that ended in a vertical drop of fifty feet* 盡頭是直落五十英尺的陡峭山崖的一條小徑
4 ►LESS IN AMOUNT 數量的減少◄ [singular] if there is a drop in the amount, level, or number of something, it goes down or becomes less〔水平的〕下降；〔數量的〕減少：*a drop in interest rates* 利率的下降 | *a sudden drop in air pressure* 氣壓的驟然下降
5 at the drop of a hat used to say that you would do something immediately if you had the opportunity〔一有機會〕立刻，立即：*I'd go to the Far East at the drop of a hat.* 如有機會我會立刻去遠東。
6 ►DELIVER 運送◄ [C] an act of dropping or leaving something, such as food or medical supplies, especially from an aircraft 運貨；空投：*an air drop to the war-torn region* 給受戰爭侵害地區的空投物資 —see also 另見 MAIL DROP
7 lemon/fruit/chocolate etc drop a sweet that tastes of LEMON etc 檸檬/水果/巧克力等味的糖球 —see also 另見 COUGH DROP
8 a drop in the ocean *BrE*【英】, **a drop in the bucket** *AmE*【美】a very small amount of something compared to what is actually needed or wanted 滄海一粟；杯水車薪：*The fund raising is going well, but it's really only a drop in the ocean.* 資金籌集進展順利，但這只不過是杯水車薪罷了。
9 eye/ear etc drops a type of medicine that you put in your eye etc, one drop at a time 滴眼液/滴耳液等
10 not touched a drop used to say that you have not drunk any alcohol at all 滴酒未沾

drop cloth /ˈ· ·/ *n* [C] *AmE* a large cloth for covering furniture, floors, etc in order to protect them from dust or paint【美】〔防止家具、地板等落灰或弄上油漆而使用的〕罩單，罩布；DUSTSHEET *BrE*【英】

drop-dead gor·geous /ˌ· · ˈ··/ *adj BrE spoken* very attractive【英口】極其引人注目的

drop goal /ˈ· ·/ *n* [C] a GOAL in RUGBY football made with a dropkick〔英式橄欖球〕以拋踢法射中球門得分

drop-in cent·re /ˈ· · ˌ··/ *n* [C] *BrE* a place where people who have no job, nowhere to live etc can get information, relax, and talk【英】失業者活動中心

drop·kick /ˈdrɑpˌkɪk; ˈdrɒpkɪk/ *n* [C] a kick in a game such as RUGBY football, made by dropping the ball and kicking it immediately〔英式橄欖球等中的〕拋踢球 —see picture on page A22 參見 A22 頁圖

drop·let /ˈdrɑplɪt; ˈdrɒplɪ̣t/ *n* [C] a very small drop of liquid〔液體的〕小滴

drop·out /ˈdrɑpˌaʊt; ˈdrɒpaʊt/ *n* **1** [C] someone who leaves school or college before they have finished 中途輟學的學生：*a high school dropout* 中學退學生 **2** [C] someone who refuses to join ordinary society because they do not agree with its social practices, moral standards etc〔因不贊同社會習俗、道德標準等而〕逃避傳統社會的人，遁世者 **3** [C,U] *technical* a short loss of signal when an electronic machine is working【術語】〔電子器件運作時的〕短時間信號漏失

drop·per /ˈdrɑpɚ; ˈdrɒpə/ *n* [C] a short glass tube with a hollow rubber part at one end, that you use to measure out liquid one drop at a time 滴管

drop·pings /ˈdrɑpɪŋz; ˈdrɒpɪŋz/ *n* [plural] solid waste from animals or birds〔鳥獸的〕糞便

drop scone /ˈ· ·/ *n* [C] a small flat plain cake 麵餅，烙餅

drop shot /ˈ· ·/ *n* [C] a shot in a game such as tennis in which the ball falls quickly at the front of the court〔網球等的〕網前球，短吊，短球

drop·sy /ˈdrɑpsɪ; ˈdrɒpsi/ *n* [U] a medical condition in which liquid forms in parts of your body 水腫；浮腫(症)

dross /drɔs; drɒs/ *n* [U] **1** *BrE* something that is of very low quality【英】質量低劣之物：*That film was utter dross!* 那部電影簡直是垃圾片子！**2** waste or useless substances 廢料，渣滓：*gold with impurities or dross* 含雜質的金子

drought /draʊt; draʊt/ *n* [C,U] a long period of dry weather when there is not enough water for plants and animals to live 乾旱，久旱，旱災

drove¹ /drov; drəʊv/ the past tense of DRIVE¹

drove² *n* [C] **1** a group of animals that are being moved together〔被驅趕着走的〕畜羣：*a drove of cattle* 被驅趕的一羣牛 **2 droves** [plural] a crowd of people 人羣：**in droves** *Tourists come in droves to see the White House.* 遊客們成羣結隊地來參觀白宮。

drov·er /ˈdrovɚ; ˈdrəʊvə/ *n* [C] someone who moves cattle or sheep from one place to another in groups 趕牛羊牲畜者

drown /draʊn; draʊn/ *v* **1** [I,T] to die from being under water for too long or to kill someone in this way (使)淹死，(使)溺斃：*The woman drowned while swimming in the sea.* 那個女人在海裡游泳時淹死了。**2** also 又作 **drown out** [T] to prevent a sound from being heard by making a loud noise〔用聲音〕淹沒：*His voice was drowned out by the traffic.* 他的聲音被來往的車輛聲淹沒了。**3** [T] to cover something completely with liquid 把〔某物〕浸泡在〔液體〕中：**drown sth with/in** *Grant drowned his pancakes in syrup.* 格蘭特把煎餅浸泡在糖漿裡。**4 drown your sorrows** to drink a lot of alcohol in order to forget your problems 借酒澆愁

drowse /draʊz; draʊz/ *v* [I] to be in a light sleep or feel pleasantly as though you are almost asleep 打瞌睡, 半睡半醒, 假寐: *I was drowsing in front of the television when you called.* 我正坐在電視機前打瞌睡, 忽然你打來了電話。

drow·sy /ˈdraʊzɪ; ˈdraʊzi/ *adj* **1** tired and almost asleep, usually because of food, drugs, or because you are in a warm place 昏昏欲睡的, 昏昏沉沉的: *The cat lay drowsy and content in the sunshine.* 貓迷迷糊糊地在陽光下滿足地躺着。**2** so peaceful that you feel relaxed and tired〔安靜得讓人〕放鬆的, 睏倦的: *a drowsy summer afternoon* 一個令人昏昏欲睡的夏日午後 —**drowsily** *adv* —**drowsiness** *n* [U]: *The tablets may cause drowsiness.* 這種藥片可能會引起睏倦。

drub·bing /ˈdrʌbɪŋ; ˈdrʌbɪŋ/ *n* [C] *informal* an occasion when one team easily beats another team in sport【非正式】〔體育運動中的〕輕易取勝: **give sb a drubbing** *We gave the other team a good drubbing.* 我們把另一隊打得落花流水。

drudge /drʌdʒ; drʌdʒ/ *n* [C] someone who does hard boring work 做苦工者, 幹乏味工作的人 —**drudge** *v* [I]

drudg·e·ry /ˈdrʌdʒərɪ; ˈdrʌdʒəri/ *n* [U] hard boring work 苦工, 賤役, 辛苦乏味的工作

2 **drug¹** /drʌg; drʌg/ *n* [C] **1** an illegal substance that people
1 smoke, INJECT (1) etc to make them feel happy or excited 毒品: *He was arrested for selling drugs.* 他因販賣毒品而被捕了。| **take/use drugs** *My cousin has been taking drugs for years.* 我表哥已經吸毒多年了。| **do drugs** *slang* (=take drugs habitually)【俚】習慣性吸毒 *Has she been doing drugs, or does she always act like this?* 她是在吸毒呢, 還是一向就這副樣子? | **be on drugs** (=use drugs regularly) 經常吸毒 *My grandfather thinks all kids these days are on drugs.* 我爺爺認為現在所有的孩子都吸毒。| **illegal drugs** *They test their employees for traces of illegal drugs.* 他們對自己的雇員進行體檢, 看看有沒有使用毒品的跡象。| **drug abuse** (=the use of illegal drugs) 濫用毒品 *the problem of drug abuse in the inner city* 舊城區居民的濫用毒品問題 | **hard drug** (=a dangerous drug such as HEROIN, COCAINE etc) 硬毒品〈如海洛因、可卡因等危險麻醉品〉| **soft drug** (=one that is not considered very harmful such as MARIJUANA) 軟毒品〈如大麻等危害性較小的麻醉品〉| **dangerous drugs** *a well-known expert on the abuse of dangerous drugs* 研究濫用危險毒品問題的著名專家 **2** a medicine or a substance for making medicines 藥物; 藥材: *a drug used in the treatment of cancer* 用於治療癌症的一種藥物 | **prescribe a drug** *Doctors should only prescribe drugs when it's really necessary.* 醫生應該在確實必要時才開藥。**3 a drug on the market** something that cannot be sold because there is too much of it available 市場上的滯銷品[滯銷貨] —see also 另見 **miracle drug** (MIRACLE (3)), DESIGNER DRUG

This graph shows some of the words most commonly used with the noun **drug**. 本圖表所示為含有名詞 drug 的一些最常用詞組。

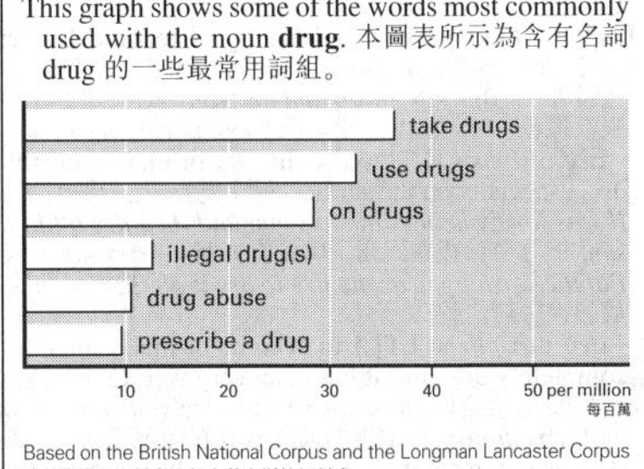

Based on the British National Corpus and the Longman Lancaster Corpus
據英國國家語料庫和朗文蘭卡斯特語料庫

drug² *v* **drugged, drugging** [T] **1** to give someone a drug, especially in order to make them feel tired or go to sleep 使服用麻醉藥; 用藥麻醉: *They had to drug the lion before they transported it.* 他們在運送獅子之前得先用藥將牠麻醉。**2** to add drugs to someone's food or drink to make them feel tired or go to sleep 在〔某人的食物或飲品中〕投放麻醉藥, 在…中下麻醉藥 **3 be drugged up (to the eyeballs)** *especially BrE* to have been given a lot of drugs by a doctor【尤英】被〔醫生〕用大量麻醉藥麻醉: *I tried to speak to her after the operation, but she was drugged up to the eyeballs.* 她手術後我想和她說話, 但她被麻醉得很厲害(還沒有醒)。**4 drugged out** *AmE* always taking and influenced by drugs【美】經常吸毒並處於毒品的影響下: *Greg's a real smart guy, it's too bad he's drugged out all the time.* 格雷格是個非常精明的人, 真可惜他總是吸毒, 沒有清醒的時候。—**drugged** *adj*

drug ad·dict /ˈ· ˌ··/ *n* [C] someone who cannot stop taking drugs, such as HEROIN or COCAINE 吸毒者, 吸毒成癮的人 —**drug addiction** /ˈ· ·ˌ··/ *n* [U]

drug bar·on /ˈ· ˌ··/ *n* [C] someone who leads an organization that deals in large quantities of illegal drugs 大毒梟

drug czar /ˈ· ·/ *n* [C] an official employed by the US government to try to stop the trade of illegal drugs〔受雇於美國政府力圖制止非法毒品交易的〕毒品緝查官; 首席禁毒官員

drug deal·er /ˈ· ˌ··/ *n* [C] someone who sells illegal drugs 毒品販子, 販毒者

drug·get /ˈdrʌgɪt; ˈdrʌgɨt/ *n* [C,U] rough heavy cloth used especially as a floor covering, or a piece of this material 粗毛織物;〔尤指〕粗毛地毯

drug·gie /ˈdrʌgɪ; ˈdrʌgi/ *n* [C] *informal* someone who often takes illegal drugs【非正式】吸毒者, 癮君子

drug·gist /ˈdrʌgɪst; ˈdrʌgɨst/ *n* [C] *AmE old-fashioned* someone who is trained to prepare drugs and medicines, and works in a shop【美, 過時】藥劑師; CHEMIST (2) *BrE*【英】—compare 比較 PHARMACIST

drug mis·use /ˈ· ·ˌ·/ *n* [U] *BrE* the practice of using drugs for pleasure rather than for medical reasons【英】濫用藥物〔不為治病而為享樂〕

drug re·hab·il·i·ta·tion /ˌ· ····ˈ··/ also 又作 **drug rehab** /ˌdrʌg ˋrihæb; ˌdrʌg ˈriːhæb/ *AmE*【美】*n* [U] the process of helping someone to live without drugs after they have been ADDICTED to them 幫助吸毒者戒毒; 吸毒康復工作

drug run·ner /ˈ· ˌ··/ *n* [C] someone who brings illegal drugs from one country to another 運毒犯

drug·store /ˈdrʌgˌstɔr; ˈdrʌgstɔː/ *n* [C] *AmE* a shop where you can buy medicines, beauty products etc【美】藥店, 藥房; 雜貨店; PHARMACY, CHEMIST'*s BrE*【英】

dru·id /ˈdruɪd; ˈdruːɨd/ *n* [C] a member of an ancient Celtic group of priests, in Britain, Ireland, and France, before the Christian religion〔在基督教之前, 古代不列顛、愛爾蘭和法蘭西等境內凱爾特人信仰的〕德魯伊特教的祭司

drum¹ /drʌm; drʌm/ *n* [C] **1** a musical instrument made of skin stretched over a circular frame that you hit with your hand or a stick 鼓: *the steady rhythmic beating of the drums* 節奏分明、連續不斷的擊鼓聲 **2** something that looks like a drum, especially part of a machine 鼓狀物;〔尤指機器的〕鼓輪; 滾筒: *The brake drums are gone on my car.* 我車上的制動鼓壞了。**3** a large round container for storing liquids such as oil, chemicals etc〔裝有如油、化學物質等液體的〕大桶: *dirty, green oil drums at the back of the yard* 在院子後面那些骯髒的綠色油桶 —see picture at 參見 CONTAINER 圖 **4 the drum of** a sound like the sound a drum makes …擊鼓似的聲音: *the steady drum of the rain on the window* 雨打在窗戶上不斷發出的滴答聲 **5 bang/beat the drum for sb/sth** to speak eagerly in support of someone or something 竭力支持某人/某事: *He's always banging the drum for better schools.* 他總是極力主張要創建更好的學校。

drum² *v* **drummed, drumming 1** [I] to play a drum 擊鼓, 打鼓 **2** [I,T] to make a sound similar to a drum by hitting a surface again and again 有節奏地擊打〔使發出打鼓似的聲音〕: *Rain drummed on the windows.* 雨水嗒嗒地敲着窗戶。| **drum your fingers** *Drumming your fingers can be a sign of anxiety.* 用手指不斷扣擊東西可能是一種焦慮的表現。

drum sth **into** sb *phr v* [T] to keep telling someone something until they cannot forget it 向〔某人〕灌輸〔某種觀點, 直到記住為止〕: *It was drummed into me to never borrow money.* 我一向被灌輸不可向人借錢這一觀點, 已經牢記不忘了。

drum sb **out of** sth *phr v* [T] to force someone to leave an organization 迫使〔某人〕離開〔某個組織、團體等〕; 開除, 逐出: *He was drummed out of the army.* 他被逐出軍隊。

D

drum sth ↔ **up** *phr v* [T] to obtain something by asking a lot of people for help, information etc 竭力爭取; 招徠; 兜攬: *We managed to drum up support for the idea.* 我們盡力爭取到了人們對這一主張的支持。

drum·beat /ˈdrʌmˌbit; ˈdrʌmbiːt/ *n* [C] a sound of someone hitting a drum 擊鼓聲

drum kit /ˈ· ·/ *n* [C] a set of drums used especially by professional musicians〔尤指專業音樂人使用的〕成套的鼓

drum ma·jor /ˌ· ˈ··/ *n* [C] the male leader of a BAND (=a group of marching musicians), especially in the army 軍樂隊的男指揮

drum ma·jor·ette /ˌ· ··ˈ·/ *n* [C] a MAJORETTE〔在跟隨樂隊行進時轉動着指揮棒的〕女指揮, 女領隊

drum·mer /ˈdrʌmɚ; ˈdrʌmə/ *n* [C] someone who plays drums 鼓手

drum·ming /ˈdrʌmɪŋ; ˈdrʌmɪŋ/ *n* [U] the act of playing a drum or the sound a drum makes 擊鼓; 鼓聲

drum-roll /ˈ· ·/ *n* [C] a quick continuous beating of a drum, usually used to introduce an important event 一串連續快節奏的擊鼓聲; 一通鼓聲〔通常用於宣告某重大事件時作為開始〕

drum·stick /ˈdrʌmˌstɪk; ˈdrʌmˌstɪk/ *n* [C] **1** the lower part of the leg of a chicken or other bird, cooked as food〔煮熟的雞或其他禽類的〕小腿部 **2** a stick that you use to hit a drum 鼓槌 —see picture at 參見 STICK² 圖

drunk¹ /drʌŋk; drʌŋk/ the past participle of DRINK¹

drunk² *adj* **1** [not before noun 不用於名詞前] unable to control your behaviour, speech etc because you have drunk too much alcohol 喝醉的: *Graham was too drunk to remember what happened last night.* 格雷厄姆醉得太厲害了, 都不記得昨晚發生了甚麼事。| **get drunk (on)** *As students we used to go out and get drunk most nights.* 當學生時, 我們差不多每晚都出去喝得爛醉。| *I got hideously drunk on tequila last night.* 昨晚我喝龍舌蘭酒喝得爛醉。| **blind drunk** (=very drunk) 醉得厲害 *I'm fed up of you coming home blind drunk.* 你常常喝得爛醉回家, 真讓我無法忍受。| **drunk as a skunk/lord** (=very drunk) 酩酊大醉 **2 drunk and disorderly** *law* the crime of behaving in a violent noisy way in a public place when you are drunk【法律】醉酒並擾亂治安 **3 drunk with power/happiness etc** so excited by a feeling of power etc that you behave in a strange way 為擁有權勢而飄飄然/高興得忘乎所以等 —see also 另見 **roaring drunk** (ROARING (5)), PUNCH-DRUNK —compare 比較 SOBER¹ (1)

drunk³ also 又作 **drunkard** /ˈdrʌŋkɚd; ˈdrʌŋkəd/ *n* [C] someone who is drunk or often gets drunk 醉鬼, 酒鬼 —compare 比較 ALCOHOLIC

drunk-driv·ing /ˌ·ˈ··/ *n* [U] driving a car after having drunk too much alcohol 酒後駕駛; DRINK-DRIVING *BrE*【英】

drunk·en /ˈdrʌŋkən; ˈdrʌŋkən/ *adj* [only before noun 僅用於名詞前] **1** drunk or showing that you are drunk 酒醉的, 有醉態的: *drunken shouting* 酒後大喊大叫 | **be in a drunken stupor** (=almost asleep because you are so drunk) 醉得神志不清, 酒醉昏迷 **2 drunken party/orgy etc** a party etc where people are drunk 縱酒宴樂 —**drunkenly** *adv* —**drunkenness** *n* [U]

drunk tank /ˈ· ·/ *n* [C] *AmE informal* a cell in a prison for people who have drunk too much alcohol【美, 非正式】〔監獄中的〕酒鬼監禁室

dry¹ /draɪ; draɪ/ *adj comparative* 比較級 **drier** *superlative* 最高級 **driest**

1 ▶NOT WET 不濕的◀ without water or liquid inside or on the surface 乾的, 乾燥的: *The floor was made of hard dry earth.* 地面是乾硬的泥地。| *The paint isn't dry yet – be careful!* 油漆還沒乾 —— 小心! | *Can you check if the washing's dry?* 你能去看看洗的東西乾了沒有嗎? | **shake/rub/wipe sth dry** *Give it to me and I'll wipe it dry.* 把它給我, 我會把它擦乾的。| **as dry as a bone** (=very dry) 乾透的, 十分乾燥的

2 ▶WEATHER 天氣◀ having very little rain or MOISTURE 乾旱的, 乾燥的: *The air was dry, and the sun beat down fiercely.* 空氣十分乾燥, 太陽毒辣辣地照着。| *the dry season*〔熱帶的〕旱季

3 run/go dry if a lake, river etc runs dry, all the water gradually disappears, especially because there has been no rain〔湖泊、河流等〕乾涸

4 ▶HUMOUR 幽默◀ someone with a dry sense of humour pretends to be serious when they are really joking〔指某人説笑話時〕冷面滑稽的

5 ▶THIRSTY 口渴的◀ *informal* thirsty【非正式】口乾的, 口渴的: *I'm really dry – do you have any orange juice?* 我很口渴 —— 你有沒有橙汁?

6 dry mouth/skin/lips etc without enough of the liquid that is normally in your mouth etc 口/皮膚/嘴唇等發乾: *I felt nervous and dizzy and my mouth was dry.* 我感覺緊張, 頭暈, 口發乾。

7 dry cough a cough which does not produce any PHLEGM (1) 乾咳

8 ▶SPEECH/WRITING 講話/文章◀ boring 乏味的; 無趣的: *I found the lecture dry and uninspired.* 我覺得那個講座枯燥無味。| **as dry as dust** (=very boring) 十分乏味的

9 dry wine/sherry etc wine etc that is not sweet 無甜味的果酒/雪利酒等: *dry white wine* 乾白葡萄酒

10 dry bread bread eaten on its own without butter, JAM¹ (1) etc 未塗奶油、果醬等的麵包

11 ▶TOWN/COUNTRY 城鎮/國家◀ not allowing any alcohol to be sold there 禁酒的: *There are still some dry states in the US.* 在美國仍然有一些州實行禁酒。

12 ▶VOICE 聲音◀ showing no emotion 冷漠的, 沒有感情的

13 not a dry eye in the house *often humorous* used to say that everyone was crying because something was very sad【常幽默】〔因傷心之事〕在場眾人無不淚汪汪的 —see also 另見 DRIP-DRY —**dryly, drily** *adv* —**dryness** *n* [U]

dry² *v* [I,T] to make something dry or become dry (使)變乾, 把…弄乾: *My boots haven't dried yet.* 我的靴子還沒乾。| **dry sth** *Sit up and dry your eyes.* 坐起來, 把眼淚擦乾。—see also 另見 CUT AND DRIED, DRIED

dry off *phr v* [I,T] to become dry or make something dry, especially on the surface (使)變乾, 把〔某物〕弄乾: *It was lovely being able to swim and then dry off in the sun.* 能夠游泳後在太陽下曬乾真好呀。| **dry sth ↔ off** *Put the washing near the fire to dry it off.* 把洗好的衣服放到火旁烤烤乾。

dry out *phr v* [I,T] **1** to become or make something completely dry after it has been very wet (使)乾透; 使〔某物〕完全變乾: **dry sth ↔ out** *Dry your anorak out on the radiator.* 把帶風帽的外套放在暖氣上烤乾。**2** to stop drinking alcohol after you have become an ALCOHOLIC〔喝酒上癮後〕戒酒

dry up *phr v*
1 ►RIVER/LAKE ETC 河流/湖泊等◄ [I,T] if something such as a river dries up, the water in it disappears (使)乾涸: *During the drought all the reservoirs dried up.* 在乾旱時期, 所有的水庫都乾涸了。| **dry sth ↔ up** *The sun has completely dried up the soil and the crops are dying.* 太陽把土地都烤乾了, 莊稼即將枯死。
2 ►SUPPLY OF STH 供應某物◄ [I] to come to an end and have no more available 耗盡, 枯竭: *The research is finishing because the money's dried up.* 研究要停止了, 因為錢已用完。
3 ►PLATES/DISHES ETC 盤子/碟子等◄ [I,T] to rub dry with a cloth 用布擦乾: **dry sth ↔ up** *Would you mind drying up the supper things?* 你把晚飯的碗盤擦乾好嗎?
4 dry up! *spoken* used to angrily tell someone to be quiet, especially when they are complaining about something【口】住口! 住嘴! : *Just dry up! I'm enjoying the film even if you're not!* 別說話了! 你不愛看這部電影我還愛看呢!
5 ►STOP TALKING 停止說話◄ [I] to stop talking because you have forgotten what you were going to say or what you should say when speaking or acting 忘記台詞

dry·ad /ˋdraɪæd; ˈdraɪæd/ *n* [C] a female spirit in ancient Greek stories who lived in a tree 林中女仙〔古希臘神話中的樹神〕

dry bat·te·ry /ˋ· ˌ···/ also 又作 **dry cell** /ˋ· ·/ *n* [C] an electric BATTERY (1) containing chemicals that are not in a liquid form 乾電池

dry-clean /ˌ· ˋ·/ *v* [T] to clean clothes etc with chemicals instead of water 乾洗〔衣服等〕

dry clean·er's /ˌ· ˋ··/ *n plural* **dry cleaner's** [C] a shop where you can take clothes etc to be dry-cleaned 乾洗店

dry dock /ˋ· ·/ *n* [C] a place where a ship can be taken out of the water for repairs 乾船塢

dry·er /ˋdraɪɚ; ˈdraɪə/ *n* [C] **hairdryer/spin-dryer** a machine that dries things〔吹乾頭髮用的〕吹風機[筒]/旋轉式脫水機

dry-eyed /ˌ· ˋ·◄/ *adj* not crying 不哭的; 無淚的

dry ginger /ˌ· ˋ··/ *n* [U] a drink that tastes of GINGER and can be mixed with WHISKY or other alcoholic drinks 薑味飲品〔可與威士忌或其他酒類飲品摻在一起飲用〕

dry goods /ˋ· ·/ *n* [plural] **1** goods such as tobacco, tea, coffee 乾貨〈如煙草、茶葉、咖啡等〉 **2** *AmE* things that are made from cloth such as clothes, sheets, and curtains【美】紡織品〈如衣服、牀單、窗簾等〉: *a dry goods store* 紡織品商店

dry ice /ˌ· ˋ·/ *n* [U] mist produced by a machine that is used as a special effect in the theatre, DISCOs etc 固體二氧化碳, 乾冰〔用機器製造乾冰噴霧, 用於劇院、的士高[迪斯科]舞廳的舞台效果〕

dry land /ˌ· ˋ·/ *n* [U] land rather than water 陸地: *After three weeks at sea we were glad to be back on dry land again.* 在海上航行三個星期後再回到陸地, 我們很高興。

dry·ly /ˋdraɪlɪ; ˈdraɪli/ *adv* if you say something dryly, you do not put any emotion in your voice, especially in order to sound funny〔指說話〕乾巴巴地, 冷冰冰地〔尤指為達到幽默的效果〕: *"If you're lucky," said Harrison dryly, "they'll only hang you."* "如果你們走運的話," 哈里森冷冰冰地說, "他們只不過會處你們絞刑。"

dry rot /ˌ· ˋ·/ *n* [U] a disease in wood, that turns it into powder〔木材的〕乾腐, 乾朽

dry run /ˌ· ˋ·/ *n* [C] an event that you use as a way of practising for a more important event 演習, 排練: *Both the parties are treating the local elections as a dry run.* 兩黨都把在地方的選舉當成了一種預演。

dry-shod /ˌ· ˋ·/ *adv literary* without getting your feet wet【文】不濕腳地

dry-stone wall /ˌ· · ˋ·/ *n* [C] a wall built with pieces of stone that fit closely together and no cement〔不用水泥砌成的〕乾砌牆

dry wall /ˌ· ˋ·/ *n* [U] *AmE* a hard substance used as the inside wall of a house【美】板壁牆 —**dry-wall** *v* [I,T]

DTI /ˌdi ti ˋaɪ; ˌdiː tiː ˈaɪ/ *n* **the DTI** the abbreviation of 縮寫= the Department of Trade and Industry 貿易工業部

DTP /ˌdi ti ˋpi; ˌdiː tiː ˈpiː/ *n* [U] DESKTOP PUBLISHING; the production of books, newspapers etc using computers 桌面出版〔利用電腦出版書、報紙等〕

DT's /ˌdi ˋtiz; ˌdiː ˈtiːz/ *n* **the DT's** *humorous* a condition caused by drinking too much alcohol in which your body shakes, and you see imaginary things【幽默】〔長期酗酒造成的〕震顫性譫妄(症)

du·al /ˋduəl; ˈdjuːəl/ *adj* [only before noun 僅用於名詞前] **dual nationality/controls/purpose etc** having two nationalities, sets of controls etc 雙重國籍/控制/目的等 —**duality** /duˋælətɪ; djuˈælɜti/ *n* [U]

dual car·riage·way /ˌ·· ˋ···/ *n* [C] *BrE* a main road that has two lines of traffic travelling in each direction and has a strip of land in the centre【英】〔中間有分隔帶、上下行各有兩線的〕雙向公路, 雙線車道, 複式車道; DIVIDED HIGHWAY *AmE*【美】

dual cit·i·zen·ship /ˌ·· ˋ····/ *n* [U] the state of being a citizen of two countries 雙重國籍

dub¹ /dʌb; dʌb/ *v* **dubbed, dubbing** [T] **1** [usually passive 一般用被動態] to give something or someone a humorous name that describes their character 把…詼諧地稱為; 給…起綽號: *Mrs Thatcher was dubbed 'The Iron Lady'.* 戴卓爾夫人被稱為"鐵娘子"。**2** to change the original spoken language of a film or television programme into another language 為〔電影或電視節目〕配音: **dub sth into sth** *It's a Swedish film dubbed into English.* 這是一部用英語配音的瑞典影片。**3** *especially BrE* to make a record out of two or more different pieces of music or sound mixed together【尤英】混合錄音 **4** *literary* if a king or queen dubs someone, they give the title of KNIGHT¹ (2) to that person in a special ceremony【文】封…為爵士

dub² *n* [U] a style of poetry or music from the West Indies with a strong regular beat〔西印度羣島式〕說唱詩[樂]

dub·bin /ˋdʌbɪn; ˈdʌbɜn/ *n* [U] a thick oily substance used to make leather softer and to stop water going through it 皮革軟化防水油

du·bi·e·ty /duˋbaɪətɪ; djuːˈbaɪəti/ *n* [U] *formal* doubt【正式】疑念, 疑惑

du·bi·ous /ˋdubɪəs; ˈdjuːbiəs/ *adj* **1 be dubious** to not be sure whether something is good or true〔好壞〕不能確定的; 疑惑的: **[+about]** *I'm a bit dubious about the idea of lending Jim my car.* 我有點拿不定主意是不是該把車借給吉姆。**2** making you doubt whether someone or something is honest, safe etc 不大可靠的, 令人生疑的: *He looks like a dubious character.* 他看起來像是個不大可靠的人。| **highly dubious** *This deal sounds highly dubious to me.* 這筆交易在我看來十分靠不住。—**dubiously** *adv* —**dubiousness** *n* [U]

du·cal /ˋdukl; ˈdjuːkəl/ *adj* like a DUKE (1) or belonging to a duke 公爵(似)的

duc·at /ˋdʌkət; ˈdʌkət/ *n* [C] a gold coin that was used in several European countries in the past 達克特〔舊時歐洲一些國家通用的金幣〕

duch·ess /ˋdʌtʃɪs; ˈdʌtʃɜs/ *n* [C] a woman with the highest social rank outside the royal family, or the wife of a DUKE (1) 女公爵; 公爵夫人: *the Duchess of York* 約克公爵夫人

duch·y /ˋdʌtʃɪ; ˈdʌtʃi/ *n* [C] the land and property of a DUKE (1) or DUCHESS (1); DUKEDOM (2) 公爵[女公爵]領地

duck¹ /dʌk; dʌk/ *n* 3
1 ►BIRD 禽鳥◄ [C] a very common water bird with short legs and a wide beak that is used for its meat, eggs, and soft feathers 鴨子; 野鴨
2 ►FEMALE BIRD 雌性禽鳥◄ [C] a female duck 母鴨
3 ►MEAT 肉◄ [U] the meat of this bird used as food 鴨肉: *roast duck with orange sauce* 配橘子醬的烤鴨(肉)
4 take to something like a duck to water to learn

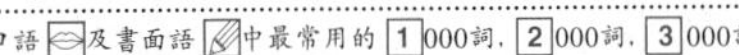

how to do something very easily 輕而易舉地學會做某事: *Don't worry, you'll take to it like a duck to water.* 別擔心, 你會很快學會的。
5 ►PERSON 人◄ also 又作 **ducks** *BrE spoken* a friendly way of speaking to someone, especially a woman or child【英口】親愛的, 寶貝兒〔尤用於對婦女、小孩友善的稱呼〕: *What can I get you, ducks?* 我能給你們弄點甚麼, 寶貝們?
6 ►PERSON 人◄ [C] a SCORE[1] (1) of zero by a BATSMAN in a game of CRICKET (2)〔板球中擊球手〕未得分; 零分
7 duck shoot *AmE slang* a very easy job or piece of work【美俚】輕而易舉的工作 —see also 另見 **a dead duck** (DEAD[1] (12)), **lame duck** (LAME[1] (3)), **like water off a duck's back** (WATER[1] (5)), DUCKS AND DRAKES

duck² *v* **1** [I,T] to lower your head or body very quickly, especially to avoid being seen or hit 迅速低下頭[身體]: *He saw a policeman coming, and ducked behind a car.* 他看見一個警察走過來, 趕緊彎腰躲在一輛汽車後面。| **duck sth** *We had to duck our heads to get through the doorway.* 我們不得不低頭才能穿過那門道。**2** [T] to push someone under water for a short time as a joke 把〔某人〕猛地按入水中片刻: *The children were busy ducking each other in the swimming pool.* 孩子們在游泳池中玩得正起勁, 互相把對方按入水中。**3** [T] *informal* to try to avoid something, especially a difficult or unpleasant duty; DODGE[1] (1,2)【非正式】躲避, 推諉〔責任等〕: *His speech ducked all the major issues.* 他的講話迴避了所有主要的問題。

duck 低頭躲避

duck out of sth *phr v* [T] *informal* to avoid doing something that you have to do or have promised to do【非正式】躲避, 逃避〔應該做或答應做的事情〕: **duck out of doing sth** *Don't try and duck out of cleaning the kitchen!* 別想逃避收拾廚房!

duck·billed plat·y·pus /ˌdʌkbɪld ˋplætəpəs; ˌdʌkbɪld ˈplætɪ̣pəs/ *n* [C] a PLATYPUS 鴨嘴獸

duck·boards /ˋdʌkˌbɔrdz; ˈdʌkbɔːdz/ *n* [plural] long narrow boards that you use to make a path over muddy ground〔在泥地上鋪的〕木板道; 鋪道板

duck·ing stool /ˈ·· ·/ *n* [C] a seat on the end of a long pole, used to DUCK² (2) a woman in water as a punishment in the past 浸刑椅〔舊時縛在長杆一端用以懲罰婦女的一種刑具, 被罰者被綑於椅上浸入水中〕

duck·ling /ˋdʌklɪŋ; ˈdʌklɪŋ/ *n* [C] a small young duck 小鴨, 幼鴨

ducks and drakes /ˌ· · ˈ·/ *n* [U] a children's game in which you make flat stones jump across the surface of water〔兒童玩的〕打水漂遊戲

duck·weed /ˋdʌkˌwid; ˈdʌkwiːd/ *n* [U] a plant that grows on the surface of fresh water 浮萍; 浮萍屬植物

duck·y¹ /ˋdʌkɪ; ˈdʌki/ *n BrE spoken* a friendly way of speaking to someone, especially a woman or child【英口】親愛的, 寶貝兒〔尤用於對婦女、小孩的友善稱呼〕

ducky² *adj AmE old-fashioned*【美, 過時】**1** perfect or satisfactory 極好的, 令人滿意的: *That's just ducky!* 那真是好極了! **2** attractive in an amusing or interesting way; CUTE (1) 可愛的, 漂亮的: *That's a ducky dress you're wearing!* 你穿的衣服真可愛!

duct /dʌkt; dʌkt/ *n* [C] **1** a pipe or tube for carrying liquids, air, cables (CABLE[1] (1)) etc〔輸送液體、氣體、電纜等的〕管道, 槽: *the air duct* 輸氣管 **2** a thin narrow tube that carries air, liquid etc inside your body, in a plant etc〔人體或植物中輸送氣體、液體等的〕細管; 導管: *a tear duct* 淚腺管

duc·tile /ˋdʌktl̩; ˈdʌktaɪl/ *adj* **1** ductile metals can be pressed or pulled into shape without needing to be heated〔指金屬〕可鍛壓的, 可拉長的, 易塑的, 柔軟的 **2** *formal* someone who is ductile can be easily influenced or controlled【正式】〔指人〕易受影響[控制]的, 柔順的 —**ductility** /dʌkˋtɪlətɪ; dʌkˈtɪlɪ̣ti/ *n* [U]

duct·less gland /ˌdʌktlɪs ˋglænd; ˌdʌktləs ˈglænd/ *n* [C] an ENDOCRINE GLAND 無管腺, 內分泌腺

dud /dʌd; dʌd/ *n* [C] *informal*【非正式】**1** something that is useless, especially because it does not work correctly 無用的東西〔尤指不能正常起作用的東西〕; 廢品: *Several of the fireworks were duds.* 煙火中有幾個是啞砲。**2 duds** [plural] *slang* clothes【俚】衣服 —**dud** *adj*: *a dud light bulb* 壞燈泡

dud cheque /ˌ· ˈ·/ *n* [C] a cheque that is useless because the person who writes it has no money in their bank account 空頭支票

dude /dud; djuːd/ *n* [C] **1** *slang especially AmE* a man【俚, 尤美】男人: *a real cool dude* 一位很帥的男士 **2** *AmE old-fashioned* an American man from a city, who is living in or visiting the countryside【美, 過時】〔指住在鄉村或去鄉村遊覽的〕城裡人

dude ranch /ˈ· ·/ *n* [C] a holiday place in the US where you can ride horses and live like a COWBOY (1)〔美國西部供遊客騎馬和像牛仔一樣生活的〕度假牧場

dud·geon /ˋdʌdʒən; ˈdʌdʒən/ *n* **in high dudgeon** *formal* angry because someone has treated you badly【正式】極為憤怒, 非常生氣: *She slammed the door and flounced out in high dudgeon.* 她砰地一聲關上門, 氣沖沖地大步走了出去。

due¹ /du; djuː/ *adj*
1 be due to be expected to happen or arrive at a particular time 預定, 預期: *When is your baby due?* 你的預產期是甚麼時候? | **be due at five o'clock/thirteen hundred hours etc** *The flight from Boston is due at 9:30.* 從波士頓飛來的航班應於9點30分到達。| **be due in an hour/two days etc** *The bus is due any minute now.* 公共汽車隨時都可能到來。| **be due to do sth** *The meeting isn't due to start until three.* 會議預定要到三點鐘才開始。| **be due for sth** (=expect to get something) 期望應得到某事物 *I'm due for a pay rise soon.* 不久就該給我加工資了。| **due back/out/in etc** *You were due back an hour ago.* 你本該一小時前回來。
2 due to because of 由於, 因為: *The company's problems are due to a mixture of bad luck and poor management.* 該公司的問題出在運氣不佳以及管理不善兩個方面。| *The 15:30 train to Sheffield has been cancelled due to circumstances beyond our control.* 由於一些我們不能控制的情況, 15點30分開往謝菲爾德鎮的火車已經被取消了。—see 見 OWING (USAGE)
3 ►OWED 欠下◄ owed to someone either as a debt or because they have a right to it 欠下的, 應給的: *You're due three weeks holiday this year.* 今年你應該有三個星期的假期。| **be due to** *Treat him with the respect that is due to a world champion.* 要以一個世界冠軍應得的尊重去對待他。
4 ►MONEY 錢◄ [not before noun 不用於名詞前] an amount of money that is due is the amount that should be paid now 應付的, 到期的: *The first interest payments will be due in August.* 首筆利息將在八月份支付。
5 with (all) due respect *spoken* used when you disagree with someone or criticize them in a polite way【口】恕我冒昧〔用以禮貌地反對某人或批評某人〕: *With all due respect, you don't have as much experience as she does.* 恕我冒昧, 你不如她有經驗。
6 in due course at some time in the future when it is the right time, but not before 在適當[一定]的時候: *The committee will consider your application in due course.* 委員會將在適當的時候考慮你的申請。
7 ►PROPER 適當的◄ [only before noun 僅用於名詞前] *formal* proper or suitable【正式】適當的, 適宜的: *She was convicted of driving without due care and attention.*

她被判為駕車不慎。—see also 另見 DULY

due² *n* **1 give sb his/her due** used when criticizing someone to admit that not all the things they did were bad, wrong, unpleasant etc 給予某人應有的承認〔用於批評某人時〕: *John was a lousy teacher, but to give him his due he tried hard.* 約翰是個很糟的老師, 但應當承認, 他已非常努力。**2 dues** [plural] regular payments you make to an organization of which you are a member 會(員)費: **pay your dues** *All the union members have already paid their dues.* 所有工會會員都已繳納了會費。**3 your/his etc due** the amount of money someone is owed, or something they have a right to 某人應得的錢物[權益]: *Gwen never takes more than her due.* 格溫從來都只拿自己應得的那份。

due³ *adv* **due north/south/east/west** directly or exactly north etc 正北/正南/正東/正西

due date /ˌ· ˈ·/ *n* [usually singular 一般用單數] the date on which something is supposed to happen, especially when money must be paid 預期某事應發生的日子〔尤指該付款的日子〕; 到期日

du·el¹ /ˈduəl; ˈdjuːəl/ *n* [C] **1** a fight with weapons between two people, used in the past to settle a quarrel〔舊時兩男子使用武器以解決爭執的〕(雙人) 決鬥: *The officer challenged him to a duel.* 那軍官向他提出決鬥。**2** a situation in which two people or groups are involved in an angry disagreement〔雙方進行的〕鬥爭; 對抗

duel² *v* **duelling, duelled** *BrE*【英】, **dueling, dueled** *AmE*【美】[I+with] to fight a duel 進行決鬥

du·en·na /duˋɛnə; djuˈenə/ *n* [C] an older woman whose job was to look after the daughters in a Spanish or Portuguese family in former times; CHAPERON〔舊時西班牙人或葡萄牙人家庭中照料女孩子的〕年長保姆, 陪媪

due pro·cess /ˌ· ˈ··/ *n* [U] *AmE law* the correct process that should be followed in law and is designed to protect someone's legal rights【美, 法律】合法 (訴訟) 程序

du·et /duˋɛt; djuˈet/ *n* [C] a piece of music for two performers 二重奏 (曲); 二重唱 (曲) —compare 比較 QUARTET (2), SOLO² (1), TRIO (3)

duff¹ /dʌf; dʌf/ *n* **1 up the duff** *slang* PREGNANT (=with a baby growing inside you)【俚】懷孕的; 有身孕的 **2** [U] a type of cake 水果布丁: *plum duff* 葡萄乾布丁

duff² *adj BrE informal* useless and broken【英, 非正式】無用的; 壞了的

duff³ *v*

duff sb ↔ **up** also 又作 **duff** sb ↔ **in** *phr v* [T] *BrE slang* to fight someone and injure them【英俚】痛打, 毆傷某人: *Let's go and duff him up!* 讓我們去揍他一頓!

duf·fel bag /ˈdʌfl̩ bæg; ˈdʌfəl bæg/ *n* [C] a bag made of strong cloth, with a round bottom and a string around the top〔圓筒狀〕旅行袋, 帆布袋 —see picture at 參見 BAG¹ 圖

duffel coat, duffle coat /ˈdʌfl̩ kot; ˈdʌfəl kəʊt/ *n* [C] *especially BrE* a coat made of rough heavy cloth, usually with a HOOD (1) and TOGGLES (=buttons shaped like tubes)【尤英】連帽粗呢外套〔通常有棒形鈕扣〕—see picture at 參見 COAT 圖

duf·fer /ˈdʌfɚ; ˈdʌfə/ *n* [C] *old-fashioned* someone who is stupid or not very good at something【過時】笨蛋, 無能的人

dug /dʌg; dʌg/ the past tense and past participle of DIG

dug·out /ˈdʌgˌaut; ˈdʌgaʊt/ *n* [C] **1** a small boat made by cutting out a hollow space in a tree trunk〔挖空樹幹做成的〕獨木舟: *a dugout canoe* 獨木小舟 **2** a shelter dug into the ground for soldiers to use〔供士兵使用的〕地下掩體; 防空洞 —compare 比較 TRENCH (2) **3** a low shelter at the side of a sports field, where players and team officials sit〔設在運動場邊供運動員和教練用的〕休息棚

DUI /ˌdi ju ˋaɪ; ˌdiː juː ˈaɪ/ *n* [U] *AmE* driving under the influence; the crime of driving when you have had too much alcohol to drink【美】酒後駕駛: *a large number of DUI arrests on New Year's Eve* 新年前夜許多因酒後駕駛而被逮捕的人

duke /duk; djuːk/ *n* [C] **1** a man with the highest social rank outside the royal family 公爵: *the Duke of Norfolk* 諾福克公爵 —see also 另見 DUCHESS **2 dukes** [plural] *old-fashioned* FISTS【過時】拳頭: *Put up your dukes and fight!* 舉起拳頭打吧!

duke·dom /ˈdukdəm; ˈdjuːkdəm/ *n* [C] **1** the rank of a duke 公爵爵位 **2** the land and property belonging to a duke; DUCHY 公爵的領地, 財產

dul·cet /ˈdʌlsɪt; ˈdʌlsɪ̮t/ *adj* **1 sb's dulcet tones** *humorous* someone's voice【幽默】某人的嗓音: *Is the boss in yet? I thought I heard his dulcet tones.* 老闆回來了嗎? 我好像聽到他的嗓音了。**2** *literary* dulcet sounds are soft and pleasant to hear【文】〔聲音〕悅耳的, 輕柔的, 動聽的

dul·ci·mer /ˈdʌlsəmɚ; ˈdʌlsɪ̮mə/ *n* [C] **1** a musical instrument with up to 100 strings, played with light hammers 揚琴 **2** a small instrument with strings that is popular in American FOLK MUSIC, and is played across your knees 杜西莫琴〔美國的一種民間樂器〕

dull¹ /dʌl; dʌl/ *adj* S3

1 ►BORING 乏味的◄ not interesting or exciting 無趣的, 枯燥的; 沉悶的; 無聊的: *Bill's friends are a pretty dull bunch.* 比爾的朋友都是一羣乏味無趣的傢伙。| *the dull routine of the office* 辦公室裡單調枯燥的例行公事 | **as dull as ditchwater** *BrE informal* (=very boring)【英, 非正式】非常枯燥乏味的

2 never a dull moment *often humorous* used to say that a lot of interesting things are happening or that you are very busy【常幽默】絕不會有沉悶無聊之時

3 ►COLOUR/LIGHT 顏色/光◄ not bright or shiny 暗淡的, 不鮮明的: *Nina's hair was a dull, darkish brown.* 尼娜的頭髮是暗褐色的。

4 ►SOUND 聲音◄ not clear or loud 不清楚的, 沉悶的: *The sack hit the floor with a dull thud.* 袋子落在地上發出沉悶的響聲。

5 ►PAIN 疼痛◄ a dull pain is not severe but does not stop 隱約的, 不明顯的: *a dull throbbing at the base of the spine* 脊柱底部的一陣隱痛 —see graph at 參見 PAIN¹ 圖表

6 ►WEATHER 天氣◄ not bright and with lots of clouds 陰沉的, 昏暗的: *It'll be dry but dull today, with outbreaks of rain this evening.* 今天白天天陰無雨, 傍晚將有陣雨。

7 ►NOT INTELLIGENT 不聰明的◄ not able to think quickly or understand things easily 遲鈍的; 愚笨的

8 ►KNIFE/BLADE 刀/刃◄ not sharp; BLUNT¹ (1) 不鋒利的, 鈍的

9 ►TRADE 貿易◄ if business on the Stock Exchange is dull, few people are buying and selling 蕭條的, 不景氣的 —**dully** *adv* —**dullness** *n* [U]

dull² *v* [T] to make something such as pain or a feeling become less sharp, less clear etc 使〔疼痛、感覺等〕不明顯, 使不清楚: *tranquillizers to dull the pain* 用於減輕疼痛的安定藥 —see graph at 參見 PAIN¹ 圖表

dull·ard /ˈdʌlɚd; ˈdʌləd/ *n* [C] *old-fashioned* someone who is stupid and has no imagination【過時】愚笨的人, 無想像力的人

du·ly /ˈdulɪ; ˈdjuːli/ *adv* **1** in the proper or expected way 適當地, 恰當地, 應當地: *Here are your travel documents, all duly signed.* 這是你的旅遊證件, 都簽好了。**2** at the proper time or as expected 準時地, 按時地: *The Queen duly appeared on the balcony to wave to the crowds.* 女王準時出現在陽台上, 向人羣招手。

dumb /dʌm; dʌm/ *adj* S3 **1** *not technical* a word used to describe someone who is permanently unable to speak, which some people find offensive【非術語】〔指人〕啞巴的, 不能說話的〔有些人認為此詞具有冒犯性〕: **deaf and dumb** (=unable to hear or speak) 聾啞的 *She's been deaf and dumb since birth.* 她生下來就又聾又啞。**2** *informal especially AmE* stupid【非正式, 尤美】愚蠢的: *What a dumb question.* 多麼愚蠢的問題。| *That was a* *dumb thing to do!* 那件事幹得真愚蠢！| **play dumb** (=pretend to be stupid) 裝傻 | **dumb blonde** (=a woman who is sexually attractive, but seems stupid) 性感、漂亮但沒有頭腦的金髮女郎 **3** unable to speak, because you are angry, surprised, shocked etc〔因憤怒、驚訝、震驚等而〕說不出話的: *He stared in dumb misery at the wreckage of the car.* 他痛苦地呆望着被撞得不像樣的汽車, 說不出話來。| **be struck dumb** (=be so shocked that you cannot speak) 震驚得說不出話來 **4 dumb animals/beasts** used to emphasize that animals cannot speak and that people often treat them badly 不會說話的動物, 啞巴牲口〔用於強調動物不會說話, 但人們常虐待它們〕: *It's cruel to bait dumb animals.* 折磨不會說話的動物是殘忍的。—**dumbly** *adv*: *They all stood dumbly staring at the coffin.* 他們全部站在那兒, 木然地看着棺材。—**dumbness** *n* [U]

dumb·bell /ˋdʌm͵bɛl; ˈdʌmbel/ *n* [C] **1** two weights connected by a short bar, that you can lift in each hand to strengthen your arms and shoulders 啞鈴 **2** *informal especially AmE* someone who is stupid【非正式, 尤美】笨蛋, 傻瓜

D

dumb·found /dʌmˋfaʊnd; dʌmˈfaʊnd/ *v* [T] to shock or surprise someone so much that they are very confused 使驚呆, 使發愣: *Pollini's piano playing continues to dumbfound the critics.* 波利尼〔意大利鋼琴家〕的鋼琴演奏仍然使評論家們驚羨得說不出話來。

dumb·found·ed /dʌmˋfaʊndɪd; dʌmˈfaʊndᵻd/ *adj* so surprised that you are confused and cannot speak 驚得目瞪口呆的: *Victor stared dumbfounded as the woman continued to scream abuse at him.* 當那個婦女不斷地尖聲辱罵維克托時, 他呆呆地瞪眼看着, 說不出話來。

dum·bo /ˋdʌmbo; ˈdʌmbəʊ/ *n* [C] *informal* someone who is stupid【非正式】傻瓜, 蠢蛋

dumb show /ˈ· ·/ *n* [C,U] a performance or action in which you do not say anything, but instead use movements to express your meaning 啞劇, 默劇; 手勢

dumb·struck /ˋdʌm͵strʌk; ˈdʌmstrʌk/ *adj* so shocked or surprised that you cannot speak 被嚇呆的; 被驚呆的

dumb wait·er /͵· ˈ··/ *n* [C] **1** a small LIFT² (1) used to move food, plates etc from one level in a restaurant, hotel etc to another〔餐廳、酒店中在樓層間運送食物、餐具等的〕小型升降機 **2** a small table that turns around on a base, used for serving food〔餐桌上便於上菜的〕圓轉台[盤]

dum-dum /ˋdʌm dʌm; ˈdʌm dʌm/ *n* [C] a soft bullet that causes serious wounds because it breaks into pieces when it hits you 達姆彈〔一種會炸成碎片、殺傷力很強的軟頭子彈〕

dum·my¹ /ˋdʌmɪ; ˈdʌmi/ *n* [C]

1 ▶COPY 仿製◀ an object that is made to look like a tool, weapon, vehicle etc but which you cannot use〔工具、武器、車輛等的〕仿製品; 仿真物品: *Don't worry about the gun, it's a dummy.* 別擔心這槍, 它是假的。

2 ▶FOR CLOTHES 用於服裝◀ a large model in the shape of a person, especially used when you are making clothes or to show them in a shop〔製作或陳列服裝用的〕人體模型: *a dressmaker's dummy* 服裝師用的人體模型

3 ▶FOR BABIES 用於嬰兒◀ *BrE* a specially shaped rubber object that you put in a baby's mouth for it to suck【英】橡皮奶嘴; PACIFIER (1) *AmE*【美】

4 ▶STUPID PERSON 笨蛋◀ *informal especially AmE* someone who is stupid【非正式, 尤美】傻瓜; 蠢貨

5 ▶IN CARD GAME 在撲克牌遊戲中◀ cards that are placed on the table by one player for all the other players to see in a game of BRIDGE¹ (4)〔橋牌中的〕明手牌

dummy² *adj* [only before noun 僅用於名詞前] a dummy tool, weapon, vehicle etc is made to look like a real one but you cannot use it 假的, 仿真的: *a dummy rifle* 仿製步槍

dummy³ *v*

dummy up *phr v* [I] *AmE slang* to stay silent and not speak【美俚】閉口不說, 默不吭聲: *When I asked her name she just dummied up.* 我問她叫甚麼名字, 她就是不吭聲。

dummy run /͵·· ˈ·/ *n* [C] an occasion when you practise doing something in complete detail to see if it works 演習, 預演

dump¹ /dʌmp; dʌmp/ *v*

1 ▶PUT STH SOMEWHERE 將某物放置某處◀ [T always +adv/prep] to put something such as a load, bag etc somewhere in a careless, untidy way 亂放, 亂堆, 亂扔: **dump sth in/on/there etc** *Who dumped all these books on my desk?* 誰把這些書亂堆在我的書桌上?

2 ▶GET RID OF 丟棄◀ [T] to get rid of someone or something that you do not want 拋棄〔某人〕; 丟棄, 扔掉〔某物〕: *I hear Lucy has dumped her boyfriend.* 我聽說露西已經把她的男朋友甩了。| *Let's dump the car and walk the rest of the way.* 讓我們把車丟在這兒, 剩下的路走着去。

3 ▶SELL GOODS 出售貨物◀ [T] to get rid of goods by selling them in a foreign country at a much lower price〔向國外〕廉價傾銷〔貨物〕

4 ▶COPY INFORMATION 複製資訊◀ [T] *technical* to copy information stored in a computer's memory on to something else such as a DISK or MAGNETIC TAPE【術語】轉儲; 轉存; 轉出〔將存儲在電腦中的資料轉存到磁碟或磁帶中〕

5 dumping ground a place where you send people or things that you want to get rid of 把想擺脫掉的人送往的地方; 垃圾傾倒場: *The estate is a dumping ground for problem tenants.* 那個住宅區是個打發難纏租客的地方。

dump on sb *phr v* [T] *AmE informal*【美, 非正式】**1** to criticize someone very strongly and often unfairly〔不公正地〕詆毀, 貶低: *Don't dump on the teachers we've got, they're doing a good job.* 別詆毀我們的老師們, 他們工作得很好。**2** to tell someone all your problems 向〔某人〕傾訴〔所有的問題〕: *Sorry to dump on you like that, I was feeling kind of low.* 我這樣把所有的煩惱都傾訴給你聽, 很對不起, 我心情有些不好。

dump² *n* [C]

1 ▶WASTE 廢品◀ a place where unwanted waste is taken and left 垃圾堆, 垃圾場, 廢品堆: *the town rubbish dump* 該城鎮的垃圾場

2 ▶WEAPONS 武器◀ a place where military supplies are stored, or the supplies themselves 軍需品存放處; 軍需品: *an ammunition dump* 軍火(臨時)存放處

3 ▶UNPLEASANT PLACE 討厭的地方◀ *informal* a place that is unpleasant to live in because it is dirty, ugly, untidy etc【非正式】髒亂的居住之地: *Do something about your room, it's a dump.* 收拾收拾你的房間, 簡直像個垃圾堆。

4 down in the dumps *informal* very sad and without much interest in life【非正式】傷心的, 對生活失去興趣的: *I've been feeling a bit down in the dumps lately.* 最近我感到生活有些沒勁。

5 ▶COMPUTER 電腦◀ *technical* the act of copying the information stored in a computer's memory onto something else, such as a DISK【術語】轉儲, 轉存, 轉出

dump·er truck /ˈ·· ·/ *n* [C] *BrE* a vehicle with a large open container at the back that can move up to pour sand, soil etc onto the ground【英】自動卸貨車, 翻斗車; DUMP TRUCK *AmE*【美】

dump·ling /ˋdʌmplɪŋ; ˈdʌmplɪŋ/ *n* [C] **1** a round lump of flour and fat mixed with water, cooked in boiling liquid and served with meat〔水煮的〕肉餡麵團子, 水餃: *mince and dumplings* 肉餡餃子 **2** a sweet dish made of PASTRY filled with fruit 水果餡點心, 水果布丁: *apple dumplings* 蘋果布丁

Dump·ster /ˋdʌmpstɚ; ˈdʌmpstə/ *n* [C] *trademark AmE* a large metal container used for waste in the US【商標, 美】置垃圾的大鐵桶; SKIP² (2) *BrE*【英】

dump truck /ˈ· ·/ *n* [C] *AmE*【美】= a DUMPER TRUCK *BrE*【英】

dump·y /ˋdʌmpɪ; ˈdʌmpi/ *adj informal* someone who is dumpy is fat, short, and unattractive【非正式】矮胖而醜陋的: *a dumpy little man* 矮墩墩的小個子男人

dun /dʌn; dʌn/ *n* [C,U] a dull brownish-grey colour 暗褐色, 棕灰色 —**dun** *adj*

dunce /dʌns; dʌns/ *n* [C] *old-fashioned* someone who is slow at learning things【過時】〔學習〕遲鈍的人, 愚笨的人: *the dunce of the class* 這個班上的笨學生

dunce's cap /ˈ‥ ·/ *n* [C] a tall pointed hat that a stupid student had to wear in school in the past 笨蛋帽〔舊時劣等生必須在學校戴的尖頂高帽〕

Dun·dee cake /dʌnˋdi ˌkek; dʌnˈdiː ˌkeɪk/ *n* [C,U] a British cake made with fruit and nuts 敦提蛋糕〔英國的一種水果果仁蛋糕〕

dun·der·head /ˋdʌndɚˌhɛd; ˈdʌndəhed/ *n* [C] *old-fashioned* someone who is stupid【過時】笨蛋, 蠢人

dune /dun; djuːn/ also 又作 **sand dune** *n* [C] a hill made of sand near the sea or in the desert〔海邊或沙漠中的〕沙丘

dune bug·gy /ˈ· ˌ··/ *n* [C] *AmE* a car with big wheels and no roof that you can drive across sand; BEACH BUGGY【美】〔裝有大號輪胎適合在沙地行駛的〕沙地汽車

dung /dʌŋ; dʌŋ/ *n* [U] solid waste from animals, especially cows 動物糞;〔尤指牛的〕糞便

dun·ga·rees /ˌdʌŋgəˋriz; ˌdʌŋgəˈriːz/ *n* [plural] **1** *BrE* loose trousers that have a square piece of cloth that covers your chest, and long thin pieces that fasten over your shoulders【英】工裝褲; OVERALL[3] (2) *AmE*【美】**2** *AmE* heavy cotton trousers used for working in【美】粗棉布工作褲

dun·geon /ˋdʌndʒən; ˈdʌndʒən/ *n* [C] a dark underground prison used in the past, especially under a castle〔尤指舊時城堡下面的〕地牢

dunk /dʌŋk; dʌŋk/ *v* [T] **1** to dip something that you are eating into coffee, tea etc 將〔正在吃的東西〕浸入〔咖啡、茶等中〕: *Don't dunk your biscuit in your tea!* 別把餅乾往茶裡蘸! **2** *AmE* to push someone under water for a short time as a joke; DUCK[2] (2)【美】〔玩時〕將〔某人〕按到水裡片刻 **3** to throw the ball downwards into the basket in BASKETBALL〔籃球賽中〕扣籃 —see also 另見 **dunk for apples** (APPLE (3)), SLAM DUNK —**dunk** *n* [C] —see picture on page A22 參見 A22 頁圖

dun·no /ˋdʌno; ˈdʌnəʊ/ *spoken* a way of saying 'I don't know', that some people think is incorrect【口】我不知道〔I don't know 的一種說法, 有些人認為這種說法不正確〕: *"Do you want to come?" "I dunno, I might."* "你想來嗎?" "我不知道, 也許吧。"

du·o /ˋduo; ˈdjuːəʊ/ *n* [C] **1** a piece of music for two performers 二重奏(曲); 二重唱(曲) **2** two people who perform together or are often seen together〔在一起表演的〕一對藝人, 兩人的搭檔: *comedy duo Reeves and Mortimer* 一對喜劇搭檔里夫斯和莫蒂默

du·o·dec·i·mal /ˌduəˋdɛsəml; ˌdjuːəˈdesə̇məl◂/ *adj technical* a duodecimal system of numbers is based on the number 12, instead of the usual system based on ten【術語】十二進制的

du·o·de·num /ˌduəˋdinəm; ˌdjuːəˈdiːnəm/ *n* [C] *technical* the top part of your BOWEL, below your stomach【術語】十二指腸 —**duodenal** /ˌduəˋdinl; ˌdjuːəˈdiːnl◂/ *adj*: *a duodenal ulcer* 十二指腸潰瘍 —see picture at 參見 DIGESTIVE SYSTEM 圖

du·o·logue /ˋduəˌlɔg; ˈdjuːəlɒg/ *n* [C] *formal* a conversation or discussion between two people, especially in a play【正式】〔尤指戲劇中二人的〕對話; 商談

dupe[1] /dup; djuːp/ *n* [C] someone who is tricked, especially into becoming involved in something illegal 受騙[上當]者〔尤指受騙參與違法之事的人〕

dupe[2] *v* [T usually passive 一般用被動態] to trick or deceive someone 欺騙, 哄騙: **dupe sb into doing sth** *Consumers are being duped into buying faulty electronic goods.* 消費者經常受騙購買有毛病的電子產品。

du·plex /ˋduplɛks; ˈdjuːpleks/ *n* [C] *AmE*【美】**1** a type of house divided into two parts, with two separate homes in it 毗聯式住宅〔並排住兩家人〕—see picture on page A4 參見 A4 頁圖 **2** an apartment with rooms on two levels 佔兩層樓的公寓; 上下兩層的公寓套房

du·pli·cate[1] /ˋdupləkɪt; ˈdjuːplə̇kə̇t/ *n* [C] **1** an exact copy of something that you can use in the same way 複製品: *If you've lost your key I can give you a duplicate.* 如果你把鑰匙丟了, 我可以給你一把配製的。**2 in duplicate** if something is written in duplicate, there are two copies of it 一式兩份 —**duplicate** *adj*: *a duplicate copy* 副本

duplicate[2] /ˋdjupləˌket; ˈdjuːplə̇keɪt/ *v* [T] **1** to copy something exactly 複製: *It can duplicate the movements of the human hand.* 它能模仿人手的活動。| *piles of duplicated notes* 一疊疊複製的說明文稿 **2** *formal* to succeed in repeating something【正式】〔成功地〕重複: *Scientists were not able to duplicate the effect under laboratory conditions.* 科學家們無法在實驗室條件下重現那種效果。—**duplication** /ˌdupləˋkeʃən; ˌdjuːplə̇ˈkeɪʃən/ *n* [U]

du·pli·ca·tor /ˋdupləˌketɚ; ˈdjuːplə̇keɪtə/ *n* [C] *BrE old-fashioned* a machine used to make copies of written pages【英, 過時】複印機

du·plic·i·ty /duˋplɪsətɪ; djuːˈplɪsə̇ti/ *n* [U] *formal* dishonest behaviour that is intended to deceive someone【正式】欺騙行為, 奸詐行徑 —**duplicitous** *adj*

dur·a·ble /ˋdurəbl; ˈdjʊərəbəl/ *adj* **1** staying in good condition for a long time even if used a lot 耐用的: *Plastic window frames are more durable than wood.* 塑料窗框比木質窗框耐用。**2** continuing for a long time 持久的: *a durable peace between France and Germany* 法、德兩國間持久的和平 —see also 另見 CONSUMER DURABLES —**durably** *adv* —**durability** /ˌdurəˋbɪlətɪ; ˌdjʊərəˈbɪlə̇ti/ *n* [U]

durable goods /ˈ‥ ˌ·/ *n* [plural] *AmE* large things such as cars, televisions, and furniture, that you do not buy often【美】〔大件〕耐用消費品〈如汽車、電視、家具等〉; CONSUMER DURABLES *BrE*【英】

du·ra·tion /duˋreʃən; djʊˈreɪʃən/ *n* [U] *formal* the length of time that something continues【正式】持續時間: *an illness of relatively short duration* 持續時間較短的疾病 | **for the duration (of)** *He was interned and had to stay in the US for the duration of the war.* 他遭到扣押, 在戰爭期間不得不留在美國。

du·ress /djuˋrɛs; djʊˈres/ *n* [U] *formal* illegal or unfair threats【正式】脅迫; 威逼: **under duress** (=using unfair threats) 在威逼下 *The confession was obtained under duress.* 供詞是在逼供之下取得的。

dur·ex /ˋdurɛks; ˈdjʊəreks/ *n trademark*【商標】**1** [C] *BrE* a rubber CONTRACEPTIVE that a man wears over his PENIS during sex【英】〔"杜蕾斯"牌〕避孕套, 保險套 **2** [U] *AustrE* clear narrow plastic that is sticky on one side and is used for fastening paper【澳】透明膠帶

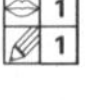

dur·ing /ˋdurɪŋ; ˈdjʊərɪŋ/ *prep* **1** all through a length of time 在…期間: *We didn't see a soul during the holidays.* 假期裡我們一個人影也沒見到。| *Children were evacuated to the country during the war.* 戰爭期間, 孩子們都被疏散到鄉間。**2** at some point in a period of time 在〔一段時間中的〕某一時候: *Henry died during the night.* 亨利是在夜間死去的。| *There will be one ten-minute interval during the performance.* 在演出期間會有一次十分鐘的休息。

USAGE NOTE 用法說明: DURING
WORD CHOICE 詞語辨析: **during, for**
If someone asks you a question beginning with *When...?*, you can answer with **during** but not **for**. 如果某人問你一個以 when 開頭的問題, 你可以用 during 來回答, 但不能用 for 回答: *"When did he get those scars?" "During the last war."* "他那些疤是甚麼時候弄的?" "在上次戰爭期間。" If someone asks you a question beginning with *How long...?*

you can answer with **for** but not with **during**. 如果某人問你一個以 how long 開頭的問題, 你可以用 for 來回答, 但不能用 during: *"How long did you stay in Mexico City?" "For about three months."* "你在墨西哥城停留了多長時間?" "大約有三個月。"

When you want to talk about the time within which something happens, you use **during**. 談論在某一時期內發生某事要用 during: *Call me sometime during the vacation.* 假期裡甚麼時候給我打個電話吧。| *Thieves broke in during the night.* 盜賊在夜間闖了進來。

When you are talking about how long something lasts, you use **for**. 談論某事持續多長時間要用 for: *I was only out of the room for a few minutes.* 我離開房間只有幾分鐘。| *They were married for 20 years.* 他們結婚有 20 年了。

During is common with words for something that continues for a length of time. during 經常和表示持續一段時間的詞連用: *during the program/the semester/the war/a conversation* 在節目中/這學期中/戰爭期間/談話過程中。You also use it to talk about specific periods of time. during 還可以用於表示具體的某段時間: *during office hours/the day/last week/that year/the 80s* 在辦公時間/白天/上個星期/那一年/〔20 世紀〕80 年代。**For** is more usual with phrases used to measure length of time. for 多與計量時間長度的詞組連用: *for two hours/a week/many years/a long period* 兩小時/一星期/許多年/很長一段時間

GRAMMAR 語法

During is never used with a clause like a **while** clause. during 從來不能引導從句, while 可以: *While I was at home, I met a nice boy* (NOT 不用 *During I was...*, but you can say 但可以說 *During my time at home,...*). 我在家時, 遇上了一個很好的男孩。Also, you would say 再舉一例, 通常說: *I did the dishes while you were asleep* (NOT 不用 *during you were asleep*). 你睡覺的時候我把碗碟洗了。

durst /dɜːst; dɜːst/ *old use* 【舊】the past tense of DARE

dusk /dʌsk; dʌsk/ *n* [U] the time before it gets dark when the sky is becoming less bright 黃昏, 傍晚: **at dusk** *The street lights go on at dusk.* 街燈在黃昏時亮起來。—compare 比較 DAWN[1]

dusk·y /ˈdʌskɪ; ˈdʌski/ *adj* dark or not very bright in colour 昏暗的, 暗淡的, 朦朧的: *The room was filled with dusky shadows.* 房間裡到處都是朦朧的影子。| **dusky pink/orange/blue etc** *a dusky pink room* 暗粉色色調的房間

dust[1] /dʌst; dʌst/ *n* **1** [U] dry powder consisting of extremely small bits of earth or sand 沙塵; 塵土: *The truck drove off in a cloud of dust.* 卡車開走了, 揚起一片塵土。| *the heat and dust of an Indian town* 一個印度小城的炎熱和塵土 **2** [U] dry powder consisting of extremely small bits of dirt which you find in buildings on furniture, floors etc 灰塵, 塵埃: *The table was covered with a layer of dust.* 桌子上覆蓋了一層灰塵。**3 coal dust/gold dust/wood dust etc** [U] powder consisting of extremely small bits of coal or gold etc 煤灰/金粉/木屑等 **4 a dust** the act of dusting something 撣灰, 去塵: *Can you give the room a quick dust?* 你能把這個房間的灰塵快速清掃一遍嗎? **5 let the dust settle/wait for the dust to settle** to allow or wait for a confused situation to become clear 讓塵埃落定/等待煙消雲散 **6 not see sb for dust** *BrE informal* if you do not see someone for dust, they leave a place very quickly in order to avoid something 【英, 非正式】不見某人的蹤影〔指某人為逃避某事而迅速離開某處〕: *Tell him it's his turn to pay for the drinks and you won't see him for dust.* 如果你告訴他這次該他付酒錢了, 他一定會逃得無影無蹤的。—see also 另見 **bite the dust** (BITE[1] (7)), DUSTY

dust[2] *v* **1** [I,T] to clean the dust from a surface by moving something such as a soft cloth across it 擦去...的灰塵, 打掃: *Could you dust the dining room?* 你能把飯廳的灰塵打掃一下嗎? —see picture at 參見 CLEAN 圖 **2** also 又作 **dust off** [T] to remove something such as dust or dirt from your clothes by brushing them with your hands 〔用手〕撣灰: *Jim got to his feet and dusted the knees of his trousers.* 吉姆站起身, 撣了撣褲子的膝蓋部位。**3** [T] to shake a fine powder over something 將〔粉狀物〕撒於: *Dust icing sugar over the pastry.* 將糖粉撒在點心上面。

dust sth ↔ **down** *phr v* [T] to remove something such as dirt or dust from your clothes by brushing them with your hands 將〔衣服上〕的灰塵撣[拂]去: *Burt stood there dusting down his overalls.* 伯特站在那兒, 在撣工裝褲上的灰塵。| **dust yourself down** *The horse threw him, but Joe just laughed, picked himself up and dusted himself down.* 喬被馬甩了下來, 但他只是笑笑, 站起來拂去身上的塵土。

dust sth ↔ **off** *phr v* [T] **1** to clean something by brushing it or wiping it with a cloth 撣〔灰〕, 擦〔灰〕: *She dusted the snow off Billy's coat.* 她把比利大衣上的雪撣去。**2** to get something ready in order to use it again after not using it for a long time 把〔長期不用的東西〕備好待用, 重新採用: *Investors are at last dusting off their cheque books as the economy recovers.* 隨着經濟的復蘇, 投資者終於又要把支票簿備好待用了。

dust·bin /ˈdʌstˌbɪn; ˈdʌstbɪn/ *n* [C] *BrE* a large container outside your house, used for holding food waste, empty containers etc 【英】〔家庭用的〕垃圾箱; 垃圾桶; GARBAGE CAN *AmE* 【美】—see picture on page A4 參見 A4 頁圖 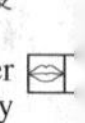

dustbin man /ˈ.. ˌ./ *n* [C] *BrE informal* a DUSTMAN 【英, 非正式】清理垃圾的工人

dust bowl /ˈ. ./ *n* [C] an area of land that has DUST STORMS and very long periods without rain 乾旱塵暴區〔長期乾旱而多塵暴的地帶〕

dust cart /ˈ. ./ *n* [C] *BrE* a large vehicle that goes from house to house to collect waste from dustbins 【英】垃圾車; GARBAGE TRUCK *AmE* 【美】

dust cov·er /ˈ. ˌ../ *n* [C] *AmE* a dust jacket 【美】〔書籍的〕護封, 書套

dust·er /ˈdʌstɚ; ˈdʌstə/ *n* [C] **1** a cloth for removing dust from furniture 抹布; 塵拂, 撣子 **2** *AmE* a light coat that you wear to protect your clothes while you are cleaning the house 【美】〔清掃房子時穿的〕防塵罩衫 **3** *AmE informal* a DUST STORM 【美, 非正式】沙塵暴

dust jack·et /ˈ. ˌ../ *n* [C] a paper cover of a book, which you can remove 〔書籍的〕護封, 書套; DUST COVER *AmE* 【美】

dust·man /ˈdʌstmən; ˈdʌstmən/ *n* [C] *BrE* someone whose job is to remove waste from DUSTBINS 【英】清理垃圾的工人, 收垃圾的清潔工; GARBAGE COLLECTOR *AmE* 【美】

dust·pan /ˈdʌstˌpæn; ˈdʌstpæn/ *n* [C] a flat container with a handle that you use with a brush to remove dust and waste from the floor 畚箕 —see picture at 參見 BRUSH[1] 圖

dust·sheet /ˈdʌstˌʃit; ˈdʌst-ʃiːt/ *n* [C] *BrE* a large sheet of cloth used to protect furniture from dust or paint 【英】〔防塵用的〕家具罩單, 罩布; DROP CLOTH *AmE* 【美】

dust storm /ˈ. ./ *n* [C] a storm with strong winds that carries large amounts of dust 沙塵暴

dust-up /ˈdʌstˌʌp; ˈdʌst-ʌp/ *n* [C] *BrE slang* a fight 【英俚】打架; 鬥毆

dust·y /ˈdʌstɪ; ˈdʌsti/ *adj* **1** covered with dust 佈滿灰塵的: *a dusty road* 滿是塵土的道路 | *The shelves are really dusty.* 架子上灰塵真多。—see picture on page A18 參見 A18 頁圖 **2 dusty blue/pink etc** blue etc that is not bright but is slightly grey 灰藍色/暗粉紅色等: *The curtains had faded to a dusty pink.* 窗簾的顏色已經褪成了暗粉紅色。**3** *literary* subjects, facts etc that are dusty are not interesting 【文】〔話題、情況等〕乏味的, 枯燥的

Dutch[1] /dʌtʃ; dʌtʃ/ *n* **1** [U] the language of the Netherlands 荷蘭語 **2 the Dutch** [plural] people from the Netherlands 荷蘭人 —see also 另見 DOUBLE-DUTCH

Dutch[2] *adj* **1** from or connected with the Netherlands 荷蘭的 **2 go Dutch (with sb)** to share the cost of a meal in a restaurant〔在餐廳用餐時〕(和某人) 平攤費用, 各付各的賬 **3 talk (to sb) like a Dutch uncle** to tell someone severely that you disapprove of what they have done 嚴厲地批評〔某人〕, 訓斥〔某人〕 **4 Dutch treat** *AmE* an occasion when you share the cost of something such as a meal in a restaurant【美】分擔費用, 各付各的賬〈如在餐廳的用餐費用〉

Dutch auc·tion /ˌ· ˈ··/ *n* [C,U] a public sale at which the price is gradually reduced until someone will pay it〔逐漸降低價格直到有人買為止的〕荷蘭式拍賣, 降價式拍賣

Dutch barn /ˌ· ˈ·/ *n* [C] a farm building with a curved roof on a frame that has no walls, used for storing HAY〔無牆、僅以支架支撐弧形屋頂的〕荷蘭式乾草棚

Dutch cap /ˌ· ˈ·/ *n* [C] *informal* a round rubber CONTRACEPTIVE, that a woman wears inside her VAGINA during sex; DIAPHRAGM (2)【非正式】〔避孕用的〕子宮帽

Dutch cour·age /ˌ· ˈ··/ *n* [U] courage or confidence that you get when you drink alcohol 酒後之勇

Dutch elm dis·ease /ˌ· ˈ· ·ˌ·/ *n* [U] a disease that affects and kills ELM trees 荷蘭榆樹病

Dutch·man /ˈdʌtʃmən; ˈdʌtʃmən/ *n* [C] **1** someone from the Netherlands 荷蘭人 **2 and I'm a Dutchman** *BrE spoken* used when someone has just said something you do not believe is true【英口】必無其事〔用於表示不相信某人剛說過的話〕: *"I've got a date with Cindy." "Oh yeah, and I'm a Dutchman!"* "我和辛迪有個約會。" "是嗎? 鬼才相信呢!"

Dutch ov·en /ˌ· ˈ··/ *n* [C] *old-fashioned* a kind of container used for cooking【過時】荷蘭燉鍋[烘箱, 磚灶]

du·ti·able /ˈdutɪəbl; ˈdjuːtiəbəl/ *adj* dutiable goods are those that you must pay DUTY (4) on〔貨物〕應納稅的

du·ti·ful /ˈdutɪfəl; ˈdjuːtɪfəl/ *adj* always doing what you are expected to do and always behaving in a loyal and obedient way 盡職盡責的; 順從的, 恭敬的: *I'm not going to play the dutiful little housewife any more!* 我再也不想當賢惠的家庭小主婦了!

dut·i·ful·ly /ˈdutɪfəlɪ; ˈdjuːtɪfəli/ *adv* if you do something dutifully you do it because you think it is the correct way to behave 盡職盡責地: *I dutifully wrote down every word.* 我盡職地記下了每一個字。

1 1 **du·ty** /ˈdutɪ; ˈdjuːti/ *n*

1 ▶STH YOU HAVE TO DO 應做的事情◀ [C,U] something that you have to do because it is morally or legally right〔道德上或法律上的〕義務, 責任: **[+to/towards]** *Ian felt a sense of duty towards his parents.* 伊恩對他的父母有一種責任感。| **have a duty to do sth/be your duty to do sth** *The company has a duty to its shareholders to accept the highest bid.* 公司應對其股東負責, 接受最高的投標價格。| *As Christians it's our duty to help the less fortunate.* 作為基督徒, 幫助不幸的人是我們的責任。| **do your duty** *You must do your duty and report him to the police.* 你必須履行義務, 向警方舉報他。| **be (in) duty bound to do sth** (=have a duty to do something) 某事義不容辭

2 ▶PART OF YOUR JOB 職責的一部分◀ [C usually plural 一般用複數,U] something you have to do as part of your job or because of your social position〔工作或社會方面的〕職責, 義務: *Your duties will also include coordinating secretarial support to the Head of Planning.* 你的職責還包括協調祕書對計劃部主任工作的支持。| **medical/official etc duties** *Illness prevented her from carrying out her official duties.* 由於生病, 她不能履行她的公務職責。| **report for duty** (=go somewhere and officially say you are ready to work) 報到 *Private Jones reporting for duty, Sir.* 長官, 列兵鍾斯向您報到。

3 be on/off duty to be working or not working at a particular time, especially doing a job which people take turns to do so that someone is always doing it 值班[勤]/下班[不值勤]: *It was the same nurse who was on duty when you had your accident.* 你出事故時就是這個護士在值班。| **be on night duty** *Helen is on night duty all next week.* 下個星期海倫全都是值夜班。

4 ▶TAX 稅◀ [C,U] a tax you pay on something you buy〔購物繳納的〕稅: *The duty on wine has gone up.* 葡萄酒稅已經上調。| **customs duty** (=tax paid on goods coming into the country) 關稅 —see also 另見 DEATH DUTY, STAMP DUTY, TAX (USAGE)

5 do duty as/for sth to be used as something 用以充當/代替某物

duty-free[1] /ˌ·· ˈ·◂/ *adj* duty-free goods can be brought into a country without paying tax on them〔貨物入境〕免稅的: *duty-free cigarettes* 免稅香煙 | *the duty-free shop* 免稅商店 —**duty-free** *adv*

duty-free[2] *n* [C,U] *informal* alcohol, cigarettes etc that you can bring into a country without paying tax on them【非正式】〔酒、香煙等〕免稅商品

du·vet /duˈve; ˈduːveɪ/ *n* [C] *especially BrE* a large cloth bag filled with feathers or similar material that you use to cover yourself in bed【尤英】羽絨被; 纖維棉被; COMFORTER (2) *AmE*【美】

dwarf[1] /dwɔrf; dwɔːf/ *n plural* **dwarves** /dwɔrvz; dwɔːvz/ or **dwarfs** [C] **1** an imaginary creature that looks like a small man〔虛構的人物〕小矮人: *Snow White and the Seven Dwarfs* 白雪公主和七個小矮人; 雪姑七友 **2** a word that some people find offensive, for someone who does not continue growing to the normal height but stays very short 矮子, 侏儒〔一些人認為此詞對身材矮小者帶有侮辱性〕

dwarf[2] *adj* [only before noun 僅用於名詞前] a dwarf plant or animal is much smaller than the usual size〔植物或動物等〕矮小的: *a dwarf conifer* 矮小的針葉樹

dwarf[3] *v* [T usually passive 一般用被動態] to be so big that other things are made to seem very small〔因自身巨大而〕使…顯得矮小; 使…相形見絀: *The cathedral is dwarfed by its surrounding skyscrapers.* 這座大教堂與其周圍的摩天大樓相比顯得格外矮小。

dwell /dwɛl; dwel/ *v past tense and past participle* **dwelt** /dwɛlt; dwelt/ or **dwelled** [I] *literary* to live in a particular place【文】〔在某一地方〕居住: *A woodsman and his family dwelt in the middle of the forest.* 一個伐木工和他的家人居住在森林的中央地帶。

dwell on/upon sth *phr v* [T] to think or talk for too long about something, especially something unpleasant 老是想着; 嘮叨〔令人不愉快的事情〕: *Don't dwell on the past – try and be more positive.* 別老想着過去 —— 盡量樂觀一些。

dwel·ler /ˈdwɛlɚ; ˈdwelə/ *n* [C] **city/town/cave/forest dweller** a person or animal that lives in a particular place 居住在城裡/鎮上/山洞/森林中的人[動物]: *City-dwellers suffer higher pollution levels.* 城市居民所遭受的污染程度較為嚴重。

dwell·ing /ˈdwɛlɪŋ; ˈdwelɪŋ/ *n* [C] *formal* a house, apartment etc where people live【正式】住宅, 寓所, 住處 2

dwelling house /ˈ·· ·/ *n* [C] *law* a house that people live in, not one that is being used as a shop, office etc【法律】〔與商店、辦公室等相對而言的〕住宅房屋

dwelt /dwɛlt; dwelt/ a past tense and past participle of DWELL

dwin·dle /ˈdwɪndl; ˈdwɪndl/ *v* [I] also 又作 **dwindle away** to gradually become less and less or smaller and smaller 逐漸變小; 縮小; 減少: *The workforce has dwindled since its pre-war heyday.* 勞動大軍在戰前人數最多, 其後已日益減少。| **dwindle (away) to nothing/one/two etc** *Their supply of food had dwindled to almost nothing.* 他們的食物供應已經減少到接近於無。—**dwindling** *adj*: *a dwindling population* 逐漸減少的人口

dye[1] /daɪ; daɪ/ *n* [C,U] **1** a substance you use to change the colour of your clothes, hair etc 染料: *hair dye* 染髮劑 **2 dye job** *informal* someone who has had a dye job has used a substance to change the colour of their hair【非正式】〔用染料〕染髮

dye² *v* **dyes, dyed, dyeing** [T] to give something a different colour using a dye〔用染料〕染: **dye sth black/blue/blonde etc** *Priscilla's hair was dyed jet black.* 普里希拉的頭髮染成了烏黑色。—**dyed** *adj*

dyed-in-the-wool /ˌ· · · ˈ·◂/ *adj* having strong beliefs or opinions that will never change〔在信仰或主張等方面〕根深蒂固的, 頑固不化的: *Even dyed-in-the-wool republicans admitted he had talent.* 甚至頑固的共和黨人都承認他有才能。

dy·ing /ˋdaɪ·ɪŋ; ˈdaɪ-ɪŋ/ the present participle of die

dyke, dike /daɪk; daɪk/ *n* [C] **1** a wall or bank built to keep back water and prevent flooding 堤; 壩; 堰 **2** an offensive word for a LESBIAN (=woman who is sexually attracted to women) 搞同性戀的女子〔冒犯用詞〕 **3** *especially BrE* a narrow passage to carry water away【尤英】排水溝, 排水渠

D

dy·nam·ic¹ /daɪˋnæmɪk; daɪˈnæmɪk/ *adj* **1** full of energy and new ideas, and determined to succeed 精力充沛的; 有創新思想的; 志在成功的: *a dynamic young businesswoman* 一位精力旺盛的年輕女實業家 **2** *technical* continuously moving or changing【術語】不斷移動的; 不斷變化的: *Markets are dynamic and a company must learn to adapt.* 市場千變萬化, 因此一個公司必須學會適應變化。**3** *technical* connected with a force or power that causes movement【術語】(動)力的; 動力(學)的 **4** *technical* a dynamic verb describes an action or event, not a state【術語】〔動詞〕動態的 —**dynamically** /-kḷɪ; -kli/ *adv*

dynamic² *n* [singular] **1 dynamics a)** [plural] the way in which things or people behave, react, and affect each other 動態: *the dynamics of capitalist economies* 資本主義經濟的動態 | **group dynamics** (=the way in which the members of a group behave towards each other) 羣體動態〔指某一團體成員之間的相互行為和態度〕 **b)** [U] the science concerned with the movement of objects and with the forces related to movement 動力學, 力學 **c)** [plural] changes of loudness in music〔音樂的〕力度, 力度變化 **2** *formal* something that causes action or change【正式】〔導致某種行動或變化的〕動力, 活力: *Feminism is seen as a dynamic of social change.* 女權運動被視為促進社會變革的一種動力。

dy·na·mis·m /ˋdaɪnəˌmɪzəm; ˈdaɪnəmɪzəm/ *n* [U] energy and determination to succeed 精力, 活力; 成功志向: *entrepreneurial dynamism* 企業家的志向

dy·na·mite¹ /ˋdaɪnəˌmaɪt; ˈdaɪnəmaɪt/ *n* [U] **1** a powerful explosive used especially for breaking rock〔尤指用於炸石頭的〕達納炸藥, 黃色炸藥 **2** something or someone that is very exciting or is likely to cause a lot of trouble 很刺激的人[事物]; 易惹出許多麻煩的人[事物]: *They've only been playing together for six months but they're dynamite.* 他們在一起演奏只有六個月, 但已很轟動。

dynamite² *v* [T] to damage or destroy something with dynamite〔用炸藥〕炸毀

dy·na·mo /ˋdaɪnəˌmo; ˈdaɪnəməʊ/ *n plural* **dynamos** [C] **1** a machine that changes some other form of power directly into electricity〔尤指直流〕發電機: *bicycle lights powered by a dynamo* 以小發電機供電的腳踏車車燈 **2** someone who is very keen and energetic 精力充沛的人: *Gordon Strachan, Leeds midfield dynamo* 戈登·斯特羅恩, 利兹隊的中場幹將

dyn·a·sty /ˋdaɪnəstɪ; ˈdɪnəsti/ *n* [C] **1** a family of kings or other rulers whose parents, grandparents etc have ruled the country for many years 王朝: *The Habsburg dynasty ruled in Austria from 1278 to 1918.* 哈布斯堡王朝在1278年至1918年期間統治奧地利。**2** a period of time when a particular family ruled a country or area 某一王朝的統治期間, 朝, 代: *Shang dynasty* 商朝

d'you /dʒə; djʊ/ *spoken*【口】the short form of 縮略式= 'do you': *D'you know what I mean?* 你知道我的意思嗎?

dys·en·te·ry /ˋdɪsṇˌtɛrɪ; ˈdɪsəntəri/ *n* [U] a serious disease of your BOWELS (1) that makes them bleed and pass much more waste than usual 痢疾

dys·func·tion·al /dɪsˋfʌŋkʃənḷ; dɪsˈfʌŋkʃənəl/ *adj technical*【術語】**1** not following the normal patterns of social behaviour, especially with the result that someone cannot behave in a normal way or have a satisfactory life 與社會規範相悖的: *dysfunctional family relationships* 有問題的家庭關係 **2** not working properly or normally 不能正常運作[工作]的; 機能不良的; 有故障的

dys·lex·i·a /dɪsˋlɛksɪə; dɪsˈleksiə/ *n* [U] *technical* a difficulty with reading and writing because you are unable to see the difference between the shapes of letters; WORD BLINDNESS【術語】〔因無法分清字形而造成的〕誦讀困難症 —**dyslexic** *adj*: *Two of the children in the class are dyslexic.* 班上有兩個孩子患有誦讀困難症。

dys·pep·si·a /dɪsˋpɛpʃə; dɪsˈpepsiə/ *n* [U] *technical* a problem that your body has in dealing with the food you eat; INDIGESTION【術語】消化不良

dys·pep·tic /dɪsˋpɛptɪk; dɪsˈpeptɪk/ *adj* **1** suffering from dyspepsia 消化不良的 **2** *old-fashioned* bad-tempered【過時】脾氣壞的

E,e

E, e /iː; iː/ *plural* **E's, e's** *n* [C] the fifth letter of the English alphabet 英語字母表的第五個字母

E¹ *n* **a)** the third note in the musical SCALE[1] (8) of C major E音〔C大調音階中的第三個音〕**b)** the musical KEY[2] (4) based on this note E調〔基於E音的音調〕

E² **1** the written abbreviation of 縮寫= east or 或 eastern **2** *BrE technical* the written abbreviation of 縮寫= earth, a connection between a piece of electrical equipment and the ground【英, 術語】地線〔電器與地連接的導線〕 **3** *slang* the abbreviation of 縮寫= ECSTASY (2), an illegal drug【俚】"狂喜"〔一種非法的迷幻藥〕 **4** short for 縮略式= E NUMBER **5** a very low mark for an exam or piece of school work E級, 及格〔表示學業成績較差〕

1 1 **each¹** /iːtʃ; iːtʃ/ *determiner, pronoun* **1** every single one of two or more things or people considered separately〔兩個或兩個以上物、人中的〕每個, 各: *Jane had a blister on each foot.* 簡每隻腳上都有一個水疱。| *There are four bedrooms, each with its own shower.* 共有四間臥室, 每間都有淋浴器。| *The price is $60 for a week, then $10 for each extra day.* 一個星期的價格60美元, 此後每加一天10美元。| *My sister's got two boys and I've got one of each.* (=one son and one daughter) 我姐姐有兩個兒子, 我則兒女各一個。| [+of] *I gave a piece of cake to each of the children.* 我給孩子們每人一塊蛋糕。| **we/you/they each** *My wife and I each have our own bank accounts.* 我和妻子各有各的銀行賬戶。| **one/half/a piece etc each** *Biscuits! Can we have two each, Mum?* 餅乾! 媽媽, 我們每人兩塊行嗎? **2 each and every one** an expression used to emphasize that you are talking about every single person or thing in a group 每一個, 無例外〔用於加強語氣〕: *These are issues that affect each and every one of us.* 這些問題影響到我們每一個人。**3 each to his own** *old-fashioned* used to mean that we all have different ideas about how to do things, what we like etc【過時】人各不同〔人們各有不同的做事方法和愛好等〕—see also 另見 ALL, EVERY

USAGE NOTE 用法説明: EACH

WORD CHOICE 詞語辨析: **each, every, both, everybody/everyone, nobody/no one, neither**

Each is used for any number of people or things considered separately, **every** for any number considered together. each 是指任何數量的人或物中的各個, every 則將任何數量的人或物當作整體來看: *Each item is carefully checked* (=probably one by one). 逐一仔細檢查各項。| *Every item has been carefully checked* (=all of them). 所有各項都仔細檢查過了。| *Each child was given a small gift* (=a gift of their own). 每個孩子都得到一件小禮物。| *Every child was given a small gift* (=they were all given one). 所有的孩子都得到了一件小禮物。

Both is used for two things taken together. both 是指兩者都: *Both my children* (= I have two children) *go to the same school.* 我的兩個孩子〔我有兩個孩子〕上同一所學校。| *Each of my children* (=I have two or more children) *goes to a different school.* 我的孩子們〔我有兩個或更多的孩子〕各上各的學校。

You usually use **everyone** or **everybody** rather than *every person*, though in a formal report you might read 一般情況下使用everyone 或everybody 而不用every person, 不過在正式的報告中也會看到後者: *The document was signed by every person present* (NEVER 永不用 *every persons/people*). 在場的所有人都在文件上簽了名。

You do not usually use **everyone** or **everybody** followed by **not**. Instead you say **not everybody/everyone...** or **no one/nobody...**, depending on which you mean. everyone 或everybody 後通常不接not, 而是依説話人想表達的意思使用not everybody/everyone... 或no one/nobody...: *Not everybody here is a vegetarian* (=some people are but not all). 這兒並非所有人都是素食者。| *No one here is a vegetarian* (=none of the people here is a vegetarian). 這兒沒有人是素食者。You would almost NEVER say 幾乎從來不説: *Everyone here isn't a vegetarian.*

Similarly instead of using **both...** followed by **not...** you would say **only one...** or **neither...** 同樣, 不用 both 後接 not, 而用 only one 或 neither: *Only one of them knows the answer.* 他們中僅一人知道答案。| *Neither of them knows the answer.* 他倆誰也不知道答案。You would not usually say 通常不説: *Both of them don't know the answer.*

GRAMMAR 語法

Both is always plural. both 總是表示複數: *Both these books are mine.* 這兩本書都是我的。A noun immediately after **each** or **every** is always singular. 緊跟在each 或every 後的名詞總是單數: *each/every area of the country* (NOT 不用 *areas*) 該國的每個地區

Every, everyone, everything etc always take a singular verb. every, everyone 和 everything 等後的動詞總用單數: *Every state elects its own governor.* 所有各州均選舉自己的州長。

Each takes a singular verb except when it comes after a plural word. each 後面用單數動詞, 除非它位於複數名詞之後: *Each of them won $50.* 他們各贏了50美元。| *They each won/have each won $50.* 他們各贏了50美元。However in informal spoken English people sometimes use a plural verb, especially when there are a lot of words between **each of** and the verb. 但在非正式英語口語中, 人們有時使用動詞複數形式, 尤其是在 each of 和動詞之間存在很多詞的情況下: *Each of the kids arriving for the first time are shown around the school.* 每個第一次來的孩子都被帶着參觀學校。However, some people think only the singular verb is correct. 但是一些人認為只有動詞單數形式才是正確的。

Each and **every** may be followed by a plural pronoun, especially when you are talking about both males and females. each 和 every 可後跟複數代名詞, 尤其在被提及者有男也有女的時候: *Each girl must make up her own mind.* 每個女孩都必須自己拿主意。| *Each person must make up their own mind.* 每個人都必須自己拿主意。It sounds a little formal to say 這一説法顯得略微正式: *Each person must make up his or her own mind* 每個人都必須自己拿主意 and it is considered sexist to use *he* unless you are only talking about men or boys 除非僅僅談及男性, 否則只用 he 被看作是性別歧視。

In a similar way plural pronouns (but not plural verbs) can go with **everyone, everybody, anyone, no one, someone** etc. 同樣, 複數代名詞〔但不是複數動詞〕可與 everyone, everybody, anyone, no one 和

E

someone 等連用: *Has everyone finished their drinks?* 大家酒都喝光了嗎? | *Somebody's left their umbrella behind.* 有人忘了拿走雨傘了。| *No one here seems to know what they are doing.* 這兒的人似乎都不知道自己在做甚麼。

each² *adv* for or to every one 每, 每個地: *The tickets are $5 each.* 每張票五美元。

each oth·er /·ˈ··/ *pron* [not used as the subject of a sentence 不用作句子主詞] used to show that each of two or more people does something to the other or others 互相, 彼此: *Susan and Robert kissed each other passionately.* 蘇珊和羅伯特深情地親吻。| *They were holding each other's hands.* 他們彼此手拉着手。| *We had a lot to tell each other about our trip.* 關於我們的旅行我們有許多話要告訴對方。| *Stop arguing with each other.* 別再互相爭吵了。—see also 另見 **be at each other's throats** (THROAT (5)) —compare 比較 ONE ANOTHER

each way /,· ˈ·/ *adv* if you BET (=try to win money by guessing the winner of a race) money each way, you will win if the horse or dog you choose comes first, second, or third 一注三贏〔下注之馬或狗獲得前三名便贏〕—**each way** *adj*: *a £10 each way bet* 十英鎊的一注三贏賭注

ea·ger /ˈigɚ; ˈiːgə/ *adj* **1** very keen and excited about something that is going to happen or about something you want to do 熱切的, 渴望的: *There was a queue of eager schoolchildren outside the theatre.* 劇院外排着一隊急切的學童。| **eager to do sth** *Clara was eager to tell her side of the story.* 克萊拉急於訴說她對於那件事的體會。| **eager for** (=eager to get or have) 急於得到 *fans eager for a glimpse of the singer* 急於見到歌手的歌迷們 **2 eager to please** willing to do anything to be helpful to people 樂於助人: *She's a very hard worker and very eager to please.* 她工作很勤奮, 且非常樂於助人。**3 eager beaver** *informal* someone who is too keen and works harder than they should【非正式】過分熱心的人; 過於勤奮的人 —**eagerly** *adv*: *the eagerly awaited sequel to 'Star Wars'* 觀眾翹首企盼的《星球大戰》續集 —**eagerness** *n* [U] *In his eagerness to secure peace Roosevelt was duped, it was said, by Stalin.* 據說羅斯福因為渴望和平, 上了史太林的當。

ea·gle /ˈigḷ; ˈiːgəl/ *n* [C] a very large strong bird with a beak like a hook that eats small animals, birds etc 鷹

eagle-eyed /,·· ˈ·◂/ *adj* very good at seeing or noticing things 目光鋭利的; 觀察敏鋭的: *One eagle-eyed passer-by noticed that the window was slightly open.* 一位觀察敏鋭的過路人注意到窗戶是微微開着的。

ea·glet /ˈiglɪt; ˈiːglɪ̆t/ *n* [C] a young EAGLE 小鷹

-ean /ɪən; iən/ *suffix* [in adjectives and nouns 構成形容詞和名詞] another form of the suffix -AN 後綴 -an 的另一種形式: Mozartean (=of or like Mozart) 莫扎特的; 像莫扎特的

ear /ɪr; ɪə/ *n*

1 ►PART OF YOUR BODY 身體部位◄ [C] one of the organs on either side of your head that you hear with 耳, 耳朵: *Lou turned to Mark and whispered something in his ear.* 盧轉向馬克, 貼着他的耳朵小聲嘀咕了幾句。—see picture at 參見 HEAD¹ 圖

2 ►HEARING 聽覺◄ [U] the ability to hear sounds 聽力: *too high-pitched to be heard by the human ear* 音調太高, 人耳聽不到 | **have good ears** (=be able to hear quiet noises) 聽覺靈敏, 聽力極佳

3 ►GRAIN 穀物◄ [C] the top part of plants, such as wheat, that produces grain 穗: *an ear of corn* 玉米穗

4 long-eared/short-eared etc having long etc ears 長耳/短耳的: *a long-eared rabbit* 長耳兔

5 be all ears *informal* to be very keen to hear what someone is going to tell you【非正式】全神貫注地聽, 洗耳恭聽: *As soon as I mentioned money, Karen was all ears.* 我一提到錢, 卡倫就馬上豎起了耳朵。

6 be out on your ear *informal* to be forced to leave a job, organization etc, especially because you have done something wrong【非正式】〔尤指因犯錯〕被迫離職[退出某組織]: *You'd better start working harder, or you'll be out on your ear.* 你最好開始加把勁, 否則將被開除。

7 be up to your ears in work/debt/problems etc to have a lot of work etc 工作/債務/問題等很多: *I'm up to my ears in work at the moment. Can we discuss this later?* 我現在忙得團團轉, 我們能以後討論這事嗎?

8 close/shut your ears to to refuse to listen to bad or unpleasant news 拒不聽〔壞消息或令人討厭的消息〕

9 smile/grin etc from ear to ear to show that you are very happy or pleased by smiling so much 咧着嘴笑, 眉開眼笑: *She came out of his office, grinning from ear to ear. 'I've been promoted.'* 她走出他的辦公室, 眉開眼笑地說: "我升職了。"

10 give sb a thick ear *BrE informal* to hit someone【英, 非正式】打某人: *Behave yourself or I'll give you a thick ear!* 規矩點, 要不我揍你了!

11 go in (at) one ear and out (at) the other *informal* if information goes in one ear and out the other, you forget it as soon as you have heard it【非正式】左耳進, 右耳出: *I don't know why I tell her anything. It just goes in one ear and out the other.* 我不知道我為甚麼告訴她, 我的話她只是當作耳邊風。

12 have an ear for music/languages etc to be very good at learning music, copying sounds etc 善於學音樂/語言等: *She has no ear for languages at all.* 她對學語言一點也不在行。| *a good ear for dialogue* 善於聽別人交談

13 have sb's ear to be trusted by someone so that they will listen to your advice, opinions etc 獲得某人信任, 忠告[意見等]被某人接納: *While Ross Perot had the ear of the nation, he did spout a number of home truths.* 當羅斯·佩羅特獲得國人信任時, 他的確道出了一些令人不快的事實。

14 keep your/an ear to the ground to make sure that you always know what is happening in a situation 保持關注〔以確保知曉某事態的發展動向〕: *I haven't heard any more news but I'll keep my ear to the ground.* 我還未聽到更多的消息, 但我將對此繼續關注。

15 lend an ear to listen to what someone is saying sympathetically 同情地傾聽: *I'm always ready to lend an ear, if you need to talk.* 如果你需要找人談, 我隨時都願傾聽。

16 play sth by ear to play music without having to read written music 不看樂譜演奏樂曲 —see also 另見 **play it by ear** (PLAY¹ (6))

17 sb's ears are burning used to say that someone thinks that people are talking about them 有人耳朵在發燒〔認為背後有人在議論時說〕

18 sb's ears are flapping *BrE* used to say that someone is trying to listen to your private conversation【英】有人在設法偷聽 —see also 另見 **bend sb's ear** (BEND¹ (5)), **send sb off with a flea in their ear** (FLEA (2)), **make a pig's ear of** (PIG¹ (5)), **prick (up) your ears** (PRICK¹ (5)), **turn a deaf ear** (DEAF¹ (4)), **wet behind the ears** (WET¹ (6))

ear·ache /ˈɪr,ek; ˈɪəreɪk/ *n* [singular, U] a pain inside your ear (內) 耳痛

ear drops /ˈ· ·/ *n* [plural] medicine to put in your ear 滴耳藥水

ear·drum /ˈ· ·/ *n* [C] a tight thin skin over the inside of your ear which allows you to hear sound 鼓膜, 耳膜

ear·ful /ˈɪrfʊl; ˈɪəfʊl/ *n* **give sb an earful** *informal* to tell someone how angry you are about something they have done【非正式】斥責某人; 抱怨某人: *He gave me a real earful about being late so often.* 他着實抱怨了我一頓, 說我經常遲到。

earhole /ˈɪr,hol; ˈɪəhəʊl/ *n* [C] *BrE informal* your ear【英, 非正式】耳朵: *If you don't shut up I'll give you a clip round the earhole!* (=hit you) 如果你不住嘴, 我就

抽你一個耳光!

earl /ɝl; ɜːl/ *n* [C] a man with a high social rank 伯爵: *the Earl of Warwick* 沃里克伯爵

earl·dom /ˈɝldəm; ˈɜːldəm/ *n* [C] **1** the rank of an earl 伯爵爵位 **2** the land or property belonging to an earl 伯爵的領地[財產]

ear·li·est /ˈɝlɪəst; ˈɜːliəst/ *n* **at the earliest** no earlier than the time or date mentioned 最早, 至早: *Work will begin in October at the very earliest.* 最早在十月開始工作。

ear lobe /ˈ· ·/ *n* [C] the soft piece of flesh at the bottom of your ear 耳垂 —see picture at 參見 HEAD[1] 圖

1 1 **ear·ly**[1] /ˈɝlɪ; ˈɜːli/ *adj*

1 ►NEAR THE BEGINNING 接近開始時◄ near to the beginning of a day, year, someone's life etc 早期的, 初期的: *We've booked two weeks' holiday in early May.* 我們已定好五月初度假兩週的安排。| *Her early life was miserably unhappy.* 她的早年生活十分悲慘。| **in the early days** (=at the beginning of a process, project etc) 最初, 開始時 *In the early days we used to work Saturdays as well.* 最初我們週六也上班。

2 ►BEFORE THE USUAL TIME 通常時間之前◄ arriving or happening before the usual or expected time 提早的, 提前的: *Hey, you're early! It's only five o'clock!* 嘿, 你真早! 現在只有五點鐘! | *The rains are early this year.* 今年雨水來得早。| **five minutes early/three hours early etc** *The bus was ten minutes early.* 公共汽車提前了十分鐘到達[開出]。| **an early grave** (=dying too soon) 過早去世

3 ►NOT TOO LATE 不太晚◄ near enough to the beginning of a process to prevent something bad from happening 及早的: *There is far less risk with cancer if it is detected early.* 如及早發現, 癌症的危險會大大降低。

4 ►FIRST 最初的◄ [only before noun 僅用於名詞前] being one of the first people, events, machines etc 最初的, 第一批的: *Early motor cars had very poor brakes.* 早期的汽車剎車裝置很差。| *early man* 原始人類

5 it's early days *spoken* used to say that it is too soon to be sure about what the result of something will be 【口】為時還過早: *She's having a few problems with the coursework at school but it's early days yet.* 她在學業上有些困難, 但最終成績如何現在還言之過早。

6 at/from an early age at or since a time when you were very young 年少[早年]時/自年少[早年]時起: *At an early age she decided she wanted to be a surgeon.* 她年少時就立志當外科醫生。

7 make an early start to start an activity, journey etc very early in the day because you have a lot to do, far to go etc 一大早就開始[出發]〔因為工作繁重、路途遙遠等〕

8 the early hours the time between MIDNIGHT and morning 凌晨: *Order was restored in the prison in the early hours of Saturday morning.* 週六凌晨, 監獄恢復了秩序。

9 early night if you have an early night you go to bed earlier than usual 〔某晚〕比平時睡得早: *I could really do with an early night!* 我真需要早點睡了!

10 early bird someone who always gets up very early in the morning 早起者: *Seven? No problem! I'm a real early bird!* 七點? 沒問題! 我起牀早得很!

11 the early bird catches the worm used to say that someone is successful because they were the first to do something 捷足先登

12 early riser someone who always gets up early in the morning 慣於早起的人

13 early potatoes/lettuces/avocados etc potatoes etc that are ready to be picked before any others 早熟的馬鈴薯/萵苣/鱷梨等

1 1 **early**[2] *adv* **1** before the usual, arranged, or expected time 提早, 提前: *I arrived early, to make sure of a seat.* 我提前到了, 以確保有座位。| *The play ended early so we still had time for a drink.* 劇提早結束了, 因此我們還有時間喝點甚麼。**2** near the beginning of a day, week, or other period of time 在早期, 在初期: *Early the following day he phoned to apologize.* 第二天一早他就打電話道歉。**3** near the beginning of an event, story, process etc 在開展階段, 在早期部分: *Early in the film we see Paul's violent temper.* 在電影開頭部分, 我們見識了保羅暴躁的脾氣。**4 early on** at an early stage in a relationship, process etc 在初期, 開始不久: *I realized early on I'd never pass the exam.* 開始不久我便意識到, 我絕對通不過考試。

early warn·ing sys·tem /ˌ·· ˈ·· ˌ··/ *n* [C] a series of RADAR stations that give a warning when enemy aircraft are going to attack 〔能及早發現敵方空襲的雷達〕預警系統

ear·mark /ˈɪrˌmɑrk; ˈɪəmɑːk/ *v* [T usually passive 一般用被動態] to decide that someone or something will be used for a particular purpose in the future 指定…的用途: **earmark sb/sth for** *80% of the funds have been earmarked for education.* 80% 的資金已被指定用於教育。| *schools earmarked for closure* 被指定關閉的學校 | **earmark sb/sth as** *The building has been earmarked as a new treatment center.* 那幢建築已被定為用作新的治療中心。

ear·muffs /ˈɪrˌmʌfs; ˈɪəmʌfs/ *n* [plural] two pieces of material joined by a band over the top of your head, that you wear to keep your ears warm 〔保暖用的〕耳套

earn /ɝn; ɜːn/ *v* 2 2

1 ►GET MONEY 賺錢◄ [I,T] to receive a particular amount of money for the work that you do 掙(錢): *He earns nearly £20,000 a year.* 他每年掙約 20,000 英鎊。| *If you aren't earning you simply can't afford a holiday.* 你如果不掙錢, 就當然沒錢去度假。| **earn a fortune** (=earn a lot of money) 掙大錢 —see 見 GAIN[1] (USAGE)

2 ►MAKE A PROFIT 獲利◄ [T] to make a profit from business or from putting money in a bank, lending it to a company etc 獲得〔利潤〕: *'Dracula' earned £7 million on its first day.* 《德拉庫拉》〔根據寫吸血鬼的同名小說改編的恐怖電影〕第一天上映便獲利 700 萬英鎊。

3 ►GET STH YOU DESERVE 獲得所值◄ [T] to get something that you deserve, because of your qualities or actions 應獲得; 博得: *I think you should have a rest. You've certainly earned it.* 我想你該休息一下, 這是你應得的。

4 earn sb praise/a reputation etc if something earns you praise, a name etc it makes other people think of you in a particular way 為某人贏得讚揚/名聲等: *Her perfectionism earned her a reputation as a 'difficult' star.* 她力求完美的勁頭給她帶來了"難纏"明星的名聲。

5 earn a living to make money in order to pay for the things you need 謀生: *I earned my living mainly from teaching.* 我主要以教書為生。

6 earn your keep to do jobs etc as a way of paying the owner of the place where you live〔為房東做工以〕掙生活費: *Harry is unemployed at the moment but he does lots of jobs around the house to earn his keep.* 哈里目前正失業, 但他靠在房前屋後做雜活來賺取食宿。

earn·er /ˈɝnɚ; ˈɜːnə/ *n* **1** [C] someone who earns money for the job that they do 掙工薪者: **high earner/low earner etc** *Private childcare is still too expensive for the average earner.* 對普通工薪階層來說, 雇家庭保姆照顧孩子還是太貴。| **wage earner** *Most wage earners are paid by cheque.* 大多數掙工資的人發工資時拿的是支票。**2 a nice little earner** *BrE informal* something that earns you a lot of money 【英, 非正式】使人賺大錢的東西, 搖錢樹: *They're onto a nice little earner with that roadside café.* 他們的路邊餐館帶來了滾滾財源。

ear·nest[1] /ˈɝnɪst; ˈɜːnɪ̣st/ *adj* **1** very serious and believing that what you say is very important 認真的; 鄭重其事的: *such an earnest young man* 如此認真的一名男青年 **2 in earnest** if something starts happening in earnest, it begins properly or as it was planned to happen 正確地; 按照計劃地: *On Monday your training begins in earnest!* 星期一你的訓練就真正開始了! **3 be in earnest** to really mean what you are saying, especially when expressing an intention or wish 是認真的, 是誠摯的: *I'm* *sure he was in earnest when he said he wanted to marry her.* 我確信當他說想娶她時, 他是認真的。| **be in dead/deadly/complete earnest** *I couldn't believe what he was telling me but he was in deadly earnest.* 我難以相信他對我說的話, 但他卻是十分誠摯的。—**earnestly** *adv* —**earnestness** *n* [U]

earnest² *n* [singular] **an earnest of** *formal* something that you do or give someone to show that you will do what you have promised to do【正式】…的保證

earn·ings /ˈɝnɪŋz; ˈɜːnɪŋz/ *n* [plural] **1** the money that you receive for the work that you do 薪水, 工資: *He has had to pay tax on his earnings since he started at the firm.* 自進公司上班以來, 他就得繳納所得稅。**2** the profit that a company makes 利潤: *The company's earnings have dropped by 5% in the first quarter.* 公司第一季度的利潤下降了5%。

earnings-re·lat·ed /ˌ‥ ·ˈ‥◂/ *adj* connected with the amount of money that you earn 與收入掛鈎的: *an earnings-related pension scheme* 與收入掛鈎的退休金計劃

ear·phones /ˈɪrˌfonz; ˈɪəfəʊnz/ *n* [plural] electrical equipment that you put over your ears to listen to a radio, RECORD PLAYER etc 耳機 —see picture at 參見 PERSONAL STEREO 圖

ear·piece /ˈɪrˌpis; ˈɪəpiːs/ *n* [C] **1** a piece of electrical equipment that you put into your ear to hear a recording, message etc〔錄音機等的〕耳塞: *Translations are heard through an earpiece.* 通過耳塞收聽翻譯。**2** [usually plural 一般用複數] one of the two pieces at the side of a pair of glasses that go round your ears 眼鏡腳 —see picture at 參見 GLASS¹ 圖 **3** the part of a telephone that you listen through 電話機聽筒

ear·plug /ˈɪrˌplʌg; ˈɪəplʌg/ *n* [C usually plural 一般用複數] a small piece of rubber put inside your ear to keep out noise etc〔擋噪音等的〕耳塞

ear·ring /ˈɪrˌrɪŋ; ˈɪərɪŋ/ *n* [C] a piece of jewellery that you fasten to your ear 耳環; 耳飾 —see picture at 參見 JEWELLERY 圖

ear·shot /ˈɪrˌʃɑt; ˈɪəʃɒt/ *n* **1 within earshot** near enough to hear what someone is saying 在聽力所及範圍內: *Everyone within earshot soon knew her opinion of Reggie.* 能聽到她說話的人很快就知道了她對雷吉的看法。**2 out of earshot** not near enough to hear what someone is saying 在聽力所及範圍之外: *I waited for her to get out of earshot before laughing.* 等她走遠到聽不見我的聲音, 我才笑起來。

ear-split·ting /ˈ· ‥/ *adj* very loud 震耳欲聾的, 極響的: *Suddenly an ear-splitting shriek came from behind the door.* 突然門後傳來一聲刺耳的尖叫。

earth 地球

axis 地軸
Arctic Circle 北極圈
line of longitude 經線
North Pole 北極
line of latitude 緯線
northern hemisphere 北半球
tropic of Cancer 北回歸線
southern hemisphere 南半球
equator 赤道
tropic of Capricorn 南回歸線
South Pole 南極
Antarctic Circle 南極圈

 2 2 **earth¹** /ɝθ; ɜːθ/ *n*

1 ▶WORLD 世界◀ [singular] also 又作 **the Earth** the world that we live in 地球: *the planet Earth* 地球 | *The earth revolves around the sun.* 地球繞着太陽公轉。| *The space shuttle is returning to earth.* 航天飛機正返回地球。—see 見 LAND¹ (USAGE) —see picture at 參見 SOLAR SYSTEM 圖

2 ▶SOIL 土壤◀ [U] substance that plants, trees etc grow in 泥土, 土壤: *footprints in the wet earth* 濕土中的腳印 | *a lump of earth* 一團泥土

3 ▶LAND 陸地◀ [singular] the hard surface of the world, as opposed to the sea 陸地; 地面: *After six months at sea, it was good to feel the earth beneath my feet again.* 在海上過了六個月後, 再次踏上陸地的感覺真好。—see 見 LAND¹ (USAGE)

4 what/why/how etc on earth...? *spoken* used when you are asking a question about something that you are very surprised or annoyed about【口】究竟, 到底〔用於詢問令人驚訝或厭煩的事〕: *What on earth did you do that for?* 你做那事究竟為了甚麼?

5 cost/pay/charge the earth *informal* to cost etc a very large amount of money【非正式】花費/支付/收取一大筆錢: *What a beautiful necklace! It must have cost the earth!* 多漂亮的一串項鏈啊! 一定很值錢了!

6 the biggest/tallest/most expensive etc on earth the biggest etc example of something that exists 世界上最大的/最高的/最貴的

7 come back/down to earth (with a bump) to stop behaving or living in a way that is not practical 回到現實, 覺悟前非: *When he realized he'd spent all the money he really came back to earth with a bump.* 當他意識到錢都花光了時, 才猛然醒悟。

8 ▶ELECTRICITY 電◀ [C usually singular 一般用單數] *BrE* a wire that makes a piece of electrical equipment safe by connecting it with the ground【英】地線; GROUND¹ (30) *AmE*【美】

9 ▶ANIMAL'S HOME 動物居所◀ [C] the hole where a wild animal such as a FOX lives〔狐狸等野獸的〕洞穴

10 go to earth *BrE* to hide in order to escape from someone who is chasing you【英】躲藏起來

11 nothing on earth a strong way of saying 'nothing' 絕對沒有甚麼〔用於加強語氣〕: *Nothing on earth would persuade me to repeat the experience of marriage.* 絕對沒甚麼能說服我重蹈婚姻的覆轍。

12 look/feel etc like nothing on earth *BrE* to look or feel very strange【英】看上去/摸起來非常奇怪: *It looks like smoked salmon, but tastes like nothing on earth.* 它看着像熏鮭魚, 但吃起來味道怪極了。

13 run sb/sth to earth *BrE* to find someone, especially by looking in many places【英】〔四處搜尋後終於〕找到某人/某物: *I finally ran him to earth in the stockroom.* 我最終在貯藏室找到了他。—see also 另見 DOWN-TO-EARTH, **move heaven and earth** (HEAVEN (10)), **hell on earth** (HELL¹ (1)), **promise sb the moon/the earth** (PROMISE¹ (3)), **the salt of the earth** (SALT¹ (2))

earth² *v* [T] *BrE* to make electrical equipment safe by connecting it to the ground with a wire【英】把〔電器〕接地; GROUND² (5) *AmE*【美】: *The amplifier wasn't properly earthed.* 擴音器沒有妥善接地。

earth·bound /ˈɝθˌbaund; ˈɜːθbaʊnd/ *adj* **1** unable to move away from the surface of the Earth 不能離開地球表面的; 附着於土地的 **2** having very little imagination, thinking too much about practical things 缺乏想像力的; 太實際的

earth·en /ˈɝθən; ˈɜːθən/ *adj* [only before noun 僅用於名詞前] **1** an earthen pot, VASE etc is made of baked clay 陶製的 **2** an earthen floor or wall is made of earth 泥土(製)的

earth·en·ware /ˈɝθənˌwɛr; ˈɜːθənweə/ *adj* an earthenware cup, plate etc is made of very hard baked clay 硬陶的 —**earthenware** *n* [U]

earth·ling /ˈɝθlɪŋ; ˈɜːθlɪŋ/ *n* [C] a word used, in SCIENCE FICTION stories, by a creature from another world talking about a human 地球人〔科幻小說中外星人對地球人類的稱法〕

earthly /ˈɝθlɪ; ˈɜːθli/ *adj* **1 no earthly reason/use/solution etc** no reason, use etc at all 毫無緣由/用處/

辦法等: *There seemed to be no earthly reason for his strange behaviour.* 他奇怪的舉止看起來毫無來由。**2** [only before noun 僅用於名詞前] *literary* connected with life on Earth rather than in heaven【文】塵世的, 人間的: *our earthly pleasures* 我們塵世間的歡樂

earth·quake /ˈɝθˌkwek; ˈɜːθkweɪk/ *n* [C] a sudden shaking of the earth's surface that often causes a lot of damage 地震: *Mexico City was badly hit in the 1985 earthquake.* 1985年墨西哥城因地震嚴重受損。

earth-shat·ter·ing /ˈ· ˌ···/ *adj* surprising or shocking and very important 驚天動地的, 震驚世界的: *the day we heard the earth-shattering news of Kennedy's assassination* 我們驚聞甘迺迪遇刺消息的那天

earth·wards /ˈɝθwɚdz; ˈɜːθwədz/ also 又作 **earth·ward** /-wɚd; -wəd/ *adv* in a direction towards the earth's surface 向地面: *The missile fell earthwards.* 導彈落向地面。—**earthward** *adj*

earth·work /ˈɝθˌwɝk; ˈɜːθwɜːk/ *n* [C usually plural 一般用複數] a large long pile of earth used to stop attacks in the past〔昔日的〕土壘防禦工事

earth·worm /ˈɝθˌwɝm; ˈɜːθwɜːm/ *n* [C] a common type of long thin brown worm that lives in soil 蚯蚓

earth·y /ˈɝθɪ; ˈɜːθi/ *adj* **1** talking about sex and the human body in a direct and impolite way 粗俗的, 粗鄙的: *Simon has a very earthy sense of humour.* 西蒙的幽默感很粗俗。**2** tasting, smelling, or looking like earth or soil 泥土味的; 似泥土的: *a strong earthy smell* 一股很重的泥土味 —**earthiness** *n* [U]

ear trum·pet /ˈ· ˌ··/ *n* [C] a type of tube that is wide at one end, used by old people in the past to help them hear〔昔時老年人用的〕號角狀助聽器

ear·wig /ˈɪrˌwɪg; ˈɪəˌwɪg/ *n* [C] a long brown insect with two curved pointed parts at the back of its body 蠼螋

ease[1] /iz; iːz/ *n* [U] **1 with ease** if you do something with ease, it is very easy for you to do it 輕易, 毫不費勁: *The car travelled smoothly up the hillside, taking the bends with ease.* 小汽車順利地爬上山, 轉彎輕松自如。| *It was the ease with which the burglars got into the house that worried her.* 使她擔憂的是, 盜賊竟能如此輕而易舉地進入屋內。| **with consummate ease** (=easily and gracefully) 巧妙地 **2 at ease** feeling relaxed in a situation in which most people might feel a little nervous 不拘束; 放鬆: **feel/look at ease** *Nurses do all they can to make patients feel at ease.* 護士盡力使病人心情舒緩。| **put/set sb at their ease** (=try to make someone feel relaxed) 使某人放鬆, 使某人鬆弛下來 | **ill at ease** (=not relaxed) 不自在, 侷促不安 *You always look ill at ease in a suit.* 你穿套裝看上去總有些不自然。**3** the ability to feel or behave in a natural or relaxed way 優雅自在: *He had a natural ease which made him very popular.* 他優雅自在的風度使他深受歡迎。**4 for ease of application/use etc** *formal* if something is done for ease of use, APPLICATION etc, it is done to make that process easier【正式】為使用方便: *For ease of application there is a special nozzle attached to the tube.* 為使用方便, 管子上裝有專用噴嘴。**5 a life of ease** a comfortable life, without problems or worries 安逸的生活: *She had a life of ease, having married her boss.* 嫁給老闆後, 她的生活安逸舒適。**6 stand at ease** used to tell soldiers to stand in a relaxed way with their feet apart〔軍事口令〕稍息

ease[2] *v*

1 ►MAKE EASIER 使較容易◄ [T] to make something, especially a process, happen more easily 使容易; 使順利: *a new drug designed to ease childbirth for women everywhere* 用於各地婦女助產的一種新藥

2 ►MOVE STH 移動某物◄ [T always + adv/prep] to move something slowly and carefully into another place 小心緩慢地移動; 挪動: **ease sth in/onto etc** *Ease the patients slowly onto the bed.* 將病人慢慢挪到牀上去。| *She eased the binoculars out of the box.* 她小心地從盒子中取出雙筒望遠鏡。

3 ►GET BETTER 變得較好◄ [I,T] if something unpleasant eases or you ease it, it gradually gets better 改善: *When the storm eases a little, we'll be able to go out.* 暴風雨減弱點後, 我們就能外出了。| **ease the pain/pressure/stress/tension** *The cream should help ease the pain.* 這種油膏可以幫助減輕疼痛。| *an out-of-town shopping project to ease congestion in the city* 旨在改善城市擁塞狀況的城外購物場所的計劃

4 ►MAKE BETTER 使變得較好◄ [T] to reduce the amount or the bad effect of something 減少〔數量〕; 減輕〔壞影響〕: *a plan designed to ease housing shortages* 旨在緩解住房短缺狀況的計劃

5 ease your grip to hold something less tightly 放鬆〔對某物的〕把持

6 ease your mind to make you feel less worried or nervous about something 寬慰: *It would ease my mind to know you had arrived safely.* 知道你已安全到達我就安心了。

ease out *phr v* [I] if a vehicle eases out, it slowly moves forward into the traffic〔汽車〕緩慢駛入車道, 慢慢上路: *Take your time, ease out slowly and ignore the cars waiting behind you.* 別急, 看準空當駛入車流, 別管你後面等着的車。

ease sb **↔ out** *phr v* [T] to deliberately try to make someone leave a job, a position of authority etc without officially saying anything 悄然使…自動離職

ease off also 又作 **ease up** *phr v* [I] **1** if something, especially something that annoys you, eases off or eases up, it gets less or better〔煩惱等〕減緩: *The noise didn't ease up for some time.* 有一陣兒噪音並未減弱。| *Why don't you wait until the traffic eases off a little?* 為甚麼不等到路上車少一些再走? **2 ease off on sb** to stop being unpleasant to someone, especially because they do not deserve to be treated like this 不再為難某人〔尤其是因為該人不應遭此等對待〕: *Ease off on Roger will you, he's not that bad.* 你別再為難羅傑了好嗎, 他沒有那麼壞。

ease up *phr v* [I] **1** to do something more slowly than before, especially because you have been going too fast, working too hard etc 放慢; 鬆弛: *Dan should ease up or he'll have a nervous breakdown.* 丹該鬆弛一下了, 否則會精神崩潰的。**2** [+on] to ease off 減緩, 緩解

ea·sel /ˈizl; ˈiːzəl/ *n* [C] a wooden frame that you put a painting on while you paint it 畫架

eas·i·ly /ˈizɪlɪ; ˈiːzəli/ *adv* S1 W1 **1** without problems or difficulties 容易地, 輕易地: *This recipe can be made quickly and easily.* 這道菜做起來又快又容易。| *I'll be able to finish that easily by tonight.* 今晚我就能把它輕鬆完成。**2 easily the best/biggest/most stupid etc** definitely the best etc 絕對最好/最大/最蠢: *She is easily the most intelligent person in the class.* 她絕對是班上最聰明的。**3 could/can/might easily** used to say that something is possible or is very likely to happen 可能, 極有可能: *I don't think we should tell her. She could easily forget and say something to Mum.* 我認為不應該告訴她, 她極可能會忘記並且對媽媽說些甚麼。| **all too easily** (=used to say that a bad event is definitely possible) 極其容易〔指壞事完全可能發生〕*The friendly crowd can degenerate, all too easily, into an unruly mob.* 友善的人羣很容易變成為難以駕馭的暴徒。**4** in a relaxed way 輕鬆地; 鬆弛地: *His son grinned easily back at him.* 他的兒子向他輕鬆地咧着嘴回笑。

eas·i·ness /ˈizɪnɪs; ˈiːzinəs/ *n* [U] **1** lack of difficulty 容易, 無困難 **2** a feeling of being relaxed and comfortable with someone 自在; 自如; 無拘束

East /ist; iːst/ *n* **1 the East a)** the countries in Asia, especially China and Japan 亞洲國家; 東方國家〔尤指中國和日本〕: *The martial arts originated in the East.* 武術起源於東方國家。**b)** the countries in the eastern part of Europe, especially the ones that had communist governments 東歐國家〔尤指該地區的前社會主義國家〕: *American relations with the East were at their worst in* *the late 1950s.* 美國與東歐國家的關係在20世紀50年代末降到了最低點。**c)** *AmE* the part of the US east of the Mississippi River, especially the states north of Washington DC【美】美國東部地區〔密西西比河以東的地區, 尤指華盛頓特區以北的各州〕: *She was born in the East but now lives in Atlanta.* 她生於美國東部, 但現在住在亞特蘭大。| **back East** *He was born in Minneapolis but he went to college back East.* 他生在美國明尼阿波利斯, 但在東部上大學。**2 East-West relations/trade etc** political relations etc between countries in eastern Europe and those in Europe and North America 東西方關係/貿易等〔指東歐國家與西歐和北美洲國家之間的政治關係等〕—compare 比較 FAR EAST, MIDDLE EAST, NEAR EAST

2 2 **east¹** /ist; iːst/ abbreviation 縮寫為 **E** *n* **1** [singular, U] the direction from which the sun rises, that is on the right of a person facing north 東, 東方: *The mountains in the east get a lot of snow.* 東邊的山上經常下雪。| *Which way is east?* 哪邊是東? | **to the east (of)** *The sky to the east of the town was already lightening.* 鎮子東面的天空已開始變亮。**2 the east** the eastern part of a country 〔一個國家的〕東部地區: *The rain will spread later to the east.* 雨帶將向東部移動。**3 in the east** if there is wind, rain etc in the east, it is coming from the east〔風、雨等〕來自東方, 從東邊來

E

east² *adj* **1** in the east or facing the east 在東方的, 東部的; 向東方的: *We sailed down the east coast of the island.* 我們沿着島嶼的東海岸向南航行。**2 east wind** an east wind comes from the east 東風: *a bitterly cold east wind* 刺骨的東風

east³ *adv* towards the east 向東方, 朝東面: *We zigzagged through the trees, moving east all the time.* 我們曲折行進穿過樹林, 一直向東前進。| *The road runs east to west.* 這條路東西向。

east·bound /ˈistˌbaund; ˈiːstbaʊnd/ *adj* travelling or leading towards the east 向東行的, 朝東駛的: *A crash on the eastbound side of the freeway is blocking traffic.* 高速公路朝東方向的一側發生的車禍正阻礙着交通。

East Coast /ˌ· ˈ·◂/ *n* **the East Coast** the part of the US that is next to the Atlantic Ocean, especially those states north of Washington DC 美國東海岸地區〔尤指華盛頓特區以北各州〕

East End /ˌ· ˈ·◂/ *n* **the East End** the eastern part of London, north of the River Thames〔泰晤士河以北的〕倫敦東區 —**East Ender** *n* [C]

Eas·ter /ˈistə; ˈiːstə/ *n* [C,U] **1** a Christian holy day in March or April when Christians remember the death of Christ and his return to life 復活節 **2** the period of time just before and after this 復活節期間: *We spent the Easter holidays in Wales.* 我們在威爾斯度過了復活節假期。

Easter Bun·ny /ˌ·· ˈ··/ *n* [singular] an imaginary rabbit that children believe brings chocolate eggs at Easter 復活節兔子〔小孩子認為該虛構的兔子會在復活節時給他們帶來巧克力蛋〕

Easter egg /ˈ·· ·/ *n* [C] **1** *BrE* a chocolate egg usually given as a present at Easter【英】〔通常作禮物用的〕復活節巧克力蛋 **2** *AmE* an egg that has been coloured and decorated, usually by a child【美】〔通常由小孩子裝飾的〕復活節彩蛋

eas·ter·ly¹ /ˈistəlɪ; ˈiːstəli/ *adj* **1** towards or in the east 向東方的; 在東方的: *an easterly course across the Pacific ocean* 向東穿過太平洋的航線 **2** easterly winds come from the east〔風〕來自東方的: *an easterly breeze* 微微的東風

easterly² *n* [C] a wind that blows from the east 東風

2 **east·ern** /ˈistən; ˈiːstən/ *adj* **1** in or from the east of a country or area 在〔某國家或地區〕東部的; 來自東部的: *There were heavy snows in eastern Minnesota.* 明尼蘇達州東部下了大雪。| *The eastern sky was just turning pink.* 東邊的天空剛剛泛紅。**2** in or from the countries in Asia, especially China and Japan 在東方國家的; 來自東方國家的〔尤指中國和日本〕: *Eastern religions* 東方宗教 **3** in or from the countries in the east part of Europe, especially the countries that used to have Communist governments 在東歐國家的; 來自東歐國家的〔尤指東歐前社會主義國家〕: *the Eastern bloc* 東歐集團

East·ern·er /ˈistənə; ˈiːstənə/ *n* [C] *AmE* someone who lives in or comes from the eastern US【美】美國東部人

east·ern·most /ˈistənˌmost; ˈiːstənməʊst/ *adj* furthest east 最東的; 極東的: *the easternmost part of the island* 島嶼的最東端

East Side /ˌ· ˈ·◂/ *n* **the East Side** the south-eastern part of Manhattan in New York, lived in mostly by poor people who have come to the US from other countries 東區〔紐約市曼哈頓東南部地區, 多為貧困移民居住〕

east·ward /ˈistwəd; ˈiːstwəd/ *adj, adv* going or facing towards the east 向東的[地], 朝東的[地]: *The eastward view toward the mountains was spectacular.* 向東望去, 羣山景色壯美。

east·wards /ˈistwədz; ˈiːstwədz/ also 又作 **eastward** *adv* towards the east 向東, 朝東: *We sailed eastwards.* 我們向東航行。

eas·y¹ /ˈizɪ; ˈiːzi/ *adj*

1 ►NOT DIFFICULT 不困難◄ not difficult, and not needing much physical or mental effort 容易的, 不費力的: *The easiest way to get there is through the park.* 去那兒的捷徑是穿過公園。| *It can't have been easy raising three children all by herself.* 她一個人撫養三個孩子一定不容易。| **easy to make/build/do etc** *Are the instructions easy to follow?* 這些用法説明容易理解嗎? | **make things easy (for sb)** *Having a computer will definitely make things a lot easier.* 有台電腦做起事情來無疑會容易得多。| **easy as pie** (=very easy) 易如反掌, 極其容易 | **within easy (walking) distance** (=near enough to walk to) 離得很近〔步行便可到達〕

2 ►NOT WORRIED 不擔心的◄ not feeling worried or anxious 不擔心的; 不緊張的: *Would it make you feel easier if I phoned when I got there?* 如果我到那兒便給你打電話, 這會讓你放心些嗎? | **with an easy mind** *I can't go to bed with an easy mind until I know she's safe.* 在知道她安然無恙之前, 我不可能安心地去睡覺。—opposite 反義詞 UNEASY

3 easy victim/prey etc someone who cannot easily defend themselves against bad treatment, attack etc 易受虐待[攻擊]的人: *Elderly and frail, she was easy prey for muggers.* 她年紀大身體又弱, 很容易成為搶劫犯的目標。

4 easy on the eye/ear pleasant to look at or listen to 好看的/悦耳的: *Choose colours that are soft and easy on the eye.* 選擇柔和悦目的顏色。

5 have an easy time of it to have no problems or difficulties 沒有問題; 很順心: *She hasn't had an easy time of it since Jack left.* 傑克離開後她沒有過過舒適的日子。

6 take the easy way out to end a difficult situation in a way that seems easy, but is not the best or most sensible way 採取省事的做法〔但不是最佳或最明智的做法〕以擺脱困境: *She took the easy way out, and told him she had to visit her mother that afternoon.* 她想了個簡單的辦法, 對他説那天下午要去看望母親。

7 get off easy *informal* to escape severe punishment for something that you have done wrong【非正式】逃脱重懲: *I thought I was in deep trouble, but I got off easy.* 我以為有大麻煩了, 但還是逃過了。

8 easy money money that you do not have to work hard to get 來得容易的錢

9 I'm easy *spoken* used to say that you do not mind what choice is made【口】我隨便, 我無所謂〔即無論哪種選擇都可以〕: *"Would you rather go out for a Chinese or an Indian meal?" "Oh, I'm easy."* "你想去吃中國菜還是印度菜?" "噢, 我無所謂。"

10 that's easy for you to say *spoken* used when someone has given you some advice that would be difficult for you to follow【口】你説得倒容易

11 be on easy street *informal, especially AmE* to be in a situation in which you have plenty of money【非正式, 尤美】手頭很寬裕, 生活優裕: *They're on easy street now that he's inherited his aunt's money.* 由於他繼承了姑媽的財產, 他們日子好過了。

12 on easy terms *BrE* if you buy something on easy terms, you pay for it with several small payments instead of paying the whole amount at once【英】〔購物〕分期付款

13 ►SEX 性◄ *informal* someone, especially a woman, who is easy has a lot of sexual partners【非正式】淫蕩的〔尤指女性〕

14 a woman of easy virtue *old-fashioned* a woman who has sex with a lot of men【過時】水性楊花的女人

15 eggs over easy *AmE* eggs cooked on a hot surface and turned over quickly before serving【美】嫩煎蛋 — see also 另見 EASE, EASILY

2 **easy**² *adv* **1 take it easy a)** also 又作 **take things easy** to relax and not do very much 放鬆; 悠着點: *The doctor says I'm going to have to take it easy for a few weeks.* 醫生說我得休息幾個星期。 **b)** *spoken* used to tell someone to become less upset or angry【口】〔勸人〕別煩惱; 不要生氣: *Just take it easy and tell us what happened.* 別急, 告訴我們發生了甚麼事。 **2 go easy on/with sth** to not use too much of something 節省使用…, 對…節制: *Go easy on that whiskey if you're driving!* 如果你要開車, 威士忌少喝點! **3 go easy on sb** to be more gentle and less strict or angry with someone 溫和對待某人; 對某人寬容: *Go easy on Peter for a while – he's having a hard time at school.* 對彼得寬容一陣兒吧, 他現在在學校功課正忙。 **4 rest/breathe easy** to stop worrying 不再擔心, 停止憂慮: *You can rest easy now – they've gone.* 他們已經走了, 你現在不用擔心了。 **5 easy does it** *spoken* used to tell someone to be careful, especially when they are moving something【口】〔告訴別人, 尤其是搬東西的人〕小心點 **6 easier said than done** *especially spoken* used when it would be difficult to actually do what someone has suggested【尤口】說來容易做來難: *I should treat Jim like any other client, but that's easier said than done.* 我應當像對待其他客戶那樣對待吉姆, 但這說起來容易做起來難。 **7 stand easy** a command telling soldiers who are already standing at ease (EASE¹ (6)) to relax more〔軍事口令〕稍息〔比 stand at ease 更隨便自由些〕 **8 easy come, easy go** *spoken* used when something, especially money, was easily obtained and is quickly used or spent【口】來得容易, 去得快〔尤指錢財〕

easy chair /ˌ·· ˈ·/ *n* [C] a large comfortable chair 安樂椅

easy-go·ing /ˌ·· ˈ··◂/ *adj* not easily upset, annoyed, or worried 脾氣隨和的, 溫和的: *Her easy-going nature made her popular.* 她生性隨和, 受人歡迎。

easy lis·ten·ing /ˌ·· ˈ···/ *n* [U] music that is relaxing to listen to and has nice tunes, but is not very unusual 悠揚悅耳的〔但風格並不獨特的〕音樂

easy-pea·sy /ˌizɪ ˈpizɪ; ˌiːzi ˈpiːzi◂/ *adj BrE* a word meaning very easy, used especially by children【英】極容易的〔尤為兒童用語〕

1 1 **eat** /it; iːt/ *v past tense* **ate** /et; eɪt/ *past participle* **eaten** /ˈitn̩; ˈiːtn/

1 ►FOOD 食物◄ **a)** [I,T] to put food in your mouth and swallow it 吃: *Vegetarians don't eat meat.* 素食者不吃肉。| **something to eat** (=some food) 一些食物 *Would you like something to eat?* 想吃點甚麼嗎? | **eat like a bird** (=eat very little) 吃得很少 | **eat like a horse** (=eat a lot) 吃得很多 | **eat right** *AmE* (=eat food that keeps you healthy)【美】保持健康的飲食習慣 | **I couldn't eat another thing** *spoken* (=I am full)【口】我飽了, 我再也吃不下了 **b)** [I,T] to have a meal 吃飯, 就餐: *We usually eat at seven.* 通常我們七點吃飯。| *Do you want to eat at Musso's Restaurant before the movie?* 看電影前你想去墨索餐廳吃飯嗎? | **eat out** (=have a meal in a restaurant, not at home) 下館子, 出去吃飯 *Do you fancy eating out tonight?* 今晚你想出去吃飯嗎?

2 eat your heart out a) used to compare two things and say that one is much better 強多了: *He's the new teen idol – eat your heart out, Michael Jackson!* 他是少年的新偶像, 你去嫉妒吧 —— 米高積遜! **b)** *BrE* to be unhappy about something or to want someone or something very much【英】沮喪; 渴求〔某人或某物〕: *She's not coming back so it's no use lying here eating your heart out.* 她不會回來了, 因此你躺在這裡苦苦想她也沒用。

3 eat sb alive/eat sb for breakfast to be very angry with someone, especially someone that you have power over 對某人大發脾氣: *You can't tell him that – he'll eat you alive!* 你不能告訴他那件事, 他會氣得活吞了你!

4 eat sb out of house and home *humorous* to eat a lot of someone's supply of food, so that they have to buy more【幽默】把某人吃窮

5 eat crow *AmE*【美】also 又作 **eat humble pie** to be forced to admit that you were wrong and say that you are sorry 被迫認錯

6 have sb eating out of your hand to have made someone very willing to believe you or do what you want 使某人俯首聽命, 使某人百依百順: *The clients were suspicious at first, but he soon had them eating out of his hand.* 客戶們開始有些懷疑, 但很快他就使他們言聽計從了。

7 what's eating him/her/you? *spoken* used to ask why someone seems annoyed or upset【口】是甚麼讓他/她/你煩心?: *What's eating Sally today? She just yelled at me.* 今天莎莉為甚麼心煩呀? 她對我大喊大叫的。

8 eat your words to admit that what you said was wrong 承認自己說錯了話: *I had to eat my words when he turned up on time after all.* 他還是準時到了, 我只好承認說錯了話。

9 I could eat a horse *spoken* used to say you are very hungry【口】我餓極了

10 I'll eat my hat *spoken old-fashioned* used to say that you think something is not true or will not happen【口, 過時】我敢打賭〔表示認為某事不是真的或不可能發生〕: *If the Democrats win the election, I'll eat my hat!* 如果民主黨選舉贏了, 我把腦袋給你!

11 ►USE/DAMAGE 使用/損壞◄ [I always+adv/prep, T] to damage, destroy, or use a lot of something 損壞; 毀壞; 大量消耗: *Work alone ate 72 hours of my week.* 每週光工作就佔了我72個小時。—see also 另見 EATS

eat sth ↔ **away** *phr v* [T] to gradually remove or reduce the amount of something 侵蝕; 消耗: *The wooden parts had been eaten away by damp.* 木製部件已被濕氣侵蝕殆盡。

eat away at sth/sb *phr v* [T] **1** to gradually remove or reduce the amount of something 侵蝕; 消耗: *Rust had eaten away at the metal frame.* 金屬框架已鏽蝕了。 **2** to make someone feel very worried over a long period of time 困擾, 煩擾: *The thought of mother alone like that was eating away at her.* 一想起母親孤身一人的情景, 她心裡就不好受。

eat into sth *phr v* [T] **1** to gradually reduce the amount of time, money etc that is available 消耗〔時間、金錢等〕: *All these car expenses are eating into our savings.* 花在汽車上的這些錢都在逐步耗去我們的積蓄。 **2** to damage or destroy something 侵蝕; 腐蝕: *Acid eats into the metal, damaging its surface.* 酸腐蝕金屬, 損壞其表面。

eat up *phr v* **1** [I,T **eat** sth ↔ **up**] *especially spoken* to eat all of something【尤口】吃完, 吃光: *Come on, eat it up, there's a good girl.* 乖, 把它吃光, 這才是好女孩。 **2** [T **eat** sth ↔ **up**] *informal* to use all of something until it is gone【非正式】用光; 耗盡: *A big car just eats up money.* 開輛大汽車只會耗光你的錢。 **3 be eaten up with jealousy/anger/curiosity etc** to be very jealous, angry etc, so that you cannot think about anything else 嫉妒/憤怒/好奇之極

eat·able /ˈitəbḷ; ˈiːtəbəl/ *adj* in a good enough condition to be eaten 能食用的, 可吃的 —see also 另見 EDIBLE

eat·er /ˋitɚ; ˈiːtə/ *n* [C] **big/light/fussy etc eater** someone who eats a lot, not much, only particular things etc 食量大/食量不大/挑食的人: *I've never been a big eater.* 我向來吃得不多。

eat·e·ry /ˋitərɪ; ˈiːtəri/ *n* [C] *informal especially AmE* a restaurant or other place to eat【非正式, 尤美】餐館; 飲食店: *one of the best Knoxville eateries* 諾克斯維爾最好的餐館之一

eating ap·ple /ˈ·· ˌ··/ *n* [C] an apple that you eat raw rather than cooked 生吃的蘋果

eating dis·or·der /ˈ·· ·ˌ··/ *n* [C] a medical condition in which you do not eat normal amounts or at normal times 飲食失調症

eats /its; iːts/ *n* [plural] *informal* food, especially for a party【非正式】〔尤指用於聚會的〕食品, 吃食: *You get the drink, and I'll organize the eats.* 你搞喝的, 我弄吃的。

eau-de-co·logne /ˌo də kəˋlon; ˌəʊ də kəˈləʊn/ *n* [U] a sweet-smelling liquid used to make you feel fresh and smell nice 科隆香水, 古龍香水

eaves /ivz; iːvz/ *n* [plural] the edges of a roof that stick out beyond the walls 屋簷: *Birds had nested under the eaves.* 鳥兒在屋簷下築了巢。

E

eaves·drop /ˋivzˌdrɑp; ˈiːvzdrɒp/ *v* **eavesdropped, eavesdropping** [I] to listen secretly to other people's conversations 偷聽〔別人的談話〕: *There was Helena eavesdropping outside the door.* 當時海倫娜正在門外偷聽。—compare 比較 OVERHEAR —**eavesdropper** *n* [C]

eavesdrop 偷聽

ebb¹ /ɛb; eb/ *n* **1** [singular] also 又作 **ebb tide** the flow of the sea away from the shore, when the TIDE¹ (1) goes out 落潮, 退潮 —opposite 反義詞 FLOOD TIDE **2 be at a low ebb** to be in a bad state or condition 處於低潮; 處於衰退狀態: *By March 1933, the economy was at its lowest ebb.* 到 1933年3月, 經濟衰退至最低點。**3 ebb and flow** a situation or state in which something increases and decreases in a kind of pattern〔有規律的〕漲落, 起伏: *I relaxed into the ebb and flow of the music.* 我隨着起伏的音樂鬆弛下來。

ebb² *v* [I] **1** if the TIDE ebbs, it flows away from the shore〔潮水〕落, 退 **2** also 又作 **ebb away** to gradually decrease 衰退; 逐漸減少: *Linda's enthusiasm began to ebb away.* 琳達的熱情開始減退。

eb·o·ny¹ /ˋɛbənɪ; ˈebəni/ *n* [U] a hard black wood 烏木; 黑檀

ebony² *adj literary* black【文】烏黑的: *Sunlight glinted on her ebony hair.* 太陽光把她烏黑的頭髮照得油光閃亮。

e·bul·li·ent /ɪˋbʌljənt; ɪˈbʌliənt/ *adj formal* very happy and excited【正式】興高采烈的: *An ebullient three-year-old bounced around the room.* 一個三歲大的孩子在房間裡高興地跑來跑去。—**ebullience** *n* [U]

EC /ˌi ˋsi; ˌiː ˈsiː◂/ *n* **the EC** the European Community; the former name for the EU 歐洲共同體〔歐盟的舊稱〕

ec·cen·tric¹ /ɪkˋsɛntrɪk; ɪkˈsentrɪk/ *adj* **1** behaving or appearing in a way that is unusual and different from most people〔行為或裝束〕怪異的, 古怪的: *students dressed in eccentric clothing* 衣着怪異的學生 | *an eccentric old woman* 一個古怪的老婦人 **2** *technical* eccentric circles do not have the same centre point【術語】不同圓心的 —compare 比較 CONCENTRIC —**eccentrically** /-klɪ; -kli/ *adv* —see picture at 參見 CONCENTRIC 圖

eccentric² *n* [C] someone who behaves in a way that is different from what is usual or socially accepted 行為古怪的人: *I was regarded as something of an eccentric.* 那時人們認為我有點古怪。

ec·cen·tri·ci·ty /ˌɛksənˋtrɪsətɪ; ˌeksenˈtrɪsəti/ *n* **1** [U] strange or unusual behaviour 古怪行為; 反常行為: *Kate's mother had a reputation for eccentricity.* 凱特的媽媽是個出了名的怪人。**2** [C] an opinion or action that is strange or unusual 古怪的想法; 怪異的動作: *I found his eccentricities amusing rather than irritating.* 我覺得他的怪癖挺好笑, 並不煩人。

Ec·cles cake /ˋɛklz ˌkek; ˈekəlz keɪk/ *n* [C] *BrE* a round cake filled with CURRANTS (=type of dried fruit)【英】葡萄乾餡餅

ec·cle·si·as·tic /ɪˌklizɪˋæstɪk; ɪˌkliːziˈæstɪk◂/ *n* [C] *formal* a priest, usually in the Christian church【正式】〔常指基督教的〕牧師, 神父

ec·cle·si·as·ti·cal /ɪˌklizɪˋæstɪkḷ; ɪˌkliːziˈæstɪkəl/ also 又作 **ecclesiastic** *adj* connected with the Christian church or its priests 基督教的; 基督教士的: *ecclesiastical history* 基督教教會歷史

ECG /ˌi si ˋdʒi; ˌiː siː ˈdʒiː/ *n* [C] *especially BrE*【尤英】**1** an electrocardiograph; a piece of equipment that records electrical changes in your heart 心電圖儀 **2** an electrocardiogram; a drawing produced by an electrocardiograph 心電圖

ech·e·lon /ˋɛʃəˌlɑn; ˈeʃəlɒn/ *n* [C] **1** also 又作 **echelons** a rank or level of responsibility in an organization, business etc, or the people at that level〔組織、企業等的〕梯隊; 階層: *the upper echelons of government* 政府高層 **2** *technical* a line of ships, soldiers, planes etc arranged in a pattern that looks like a series of steps【術語】〔船隻、士兵和飛機等的〕梯形編隊

ech·o¹ /ˋɛko; ˈekəʊ/ *v present tense* **echoes** *past tense and past participle* **echoed** **1** [I often+adv/prep] if a sound echoes, you hear it again because it was made near something such as a wall or hill〔聲音〕回響, 發出回聲: *The thunder echoed over the mountains.* 雷聲在山巒間回響。| *Our shouts echoed through the silent streets.* 我們的喊聲在寂靜的大街上發出回聲。**2** [I] if a place echoes, it is filled with sounds that are repeated or are similar to each other〔場所〕充滿回聲: [+**with**] *The hall echoed with laughter and stamping feet.* 大廳內回蕩着笑聲和跺腳聲。**3** [T] *literary* to repeat what someone else has just said【文】重複〔別人的話〕: *"Paula's dead!" "Dead?" echoed Teri, stunned.* "葆拉死了!" "死了?" 特里重複道, 滿臉驚異。**4** [T] to repeat an idea or opinion because you agree with it 附和: *The article simply echoed the NRA's arguments against gun control.* 這篇文章只是附和了全國步槍射擊運動協會反對槍支控制的觀點。

echo² *n plural* **echoes** [C] **1** a sound that you hear again after a loud noise, because it was made near something such as a wall 回聲, 回音: *The echo of the bells died away, and the valley was quiet again.* 鐘聲的回音逐漸消失, 山谷又恢復了寧靜。**2** something that is very similar to something that has happened or been said before 十分相似的東西, 如出一轍的事物: [+**of**] *This crash has chilling echoes of the Lockerbie disaster.* 這次失事與洛克比空難有驚人的相似之處。

éclair /eˋklɛr; ɪˈkleə/ *n* [C] a long cake covered with chocolate and filled with cream〔外塗巧克力內填奶油的〕長條酥卷

é·clat /eˋklɑ; eɪˈklɑː/ *n* [U] *literary*【文】**1** praise and admiration 讚揚, 喝采: *Miller's new play has been greeted with great éclat.* 米勒的新劇贏得一片喝采。**2** a way of doing something with a lot of style, especially in order to attract attention〔尤指為吸引注意的〕炫耀

e·clec·tic¹ /ɪkˋlɛktɪk; ɪˈklektɪk/ *adj* including a mixture of many different things or people, especially so that you can use the best of all of them 兼收並蓄的; 博採眾長的: *galleries with an eclectic range of styles and artists* 收藏各個流派和藝術家作品的美術館 —**eclectically**

/-klɪ; -kli/ *adv* —**eclecticism**/-tɪˌsɪzəm; -tɪsɪzəm/ *n* [U]

eclectic² *n* [C] *formal* someone who chooses the best or most useful parts from many different ideas, methods etc【正式】博採眾長的人

e·clipse¹/ɪ`klɪps; ɪ'klɪps/ *n* **1** [C] an occasion when the sun or the moon seems to disappear, because one of them is passing between the other one and the Earth 日蝕; 月蝕 **2** [singular] a situation in which someone loses their power or fame, because someone else has become more powerful or famous〔與他人相比之下權力或名望的〕黯然失色: *New movie studios in Hollywood soon led to the eclipse of New York as a film-making center.* 在荷里活出現的新製片廠很快就使作為電影製作中心的紐約黯然失色。**3 in/into eclipse** *formal* less famous or powerful than you should be【正式】被埋沒, 湮沒無聞: *Mary Shelley, the author of Frankenstein, has been too long in eclipse.*《科學怪人》的作者瑪麗·雪萊 (1797-1851, 英國女作家, 詩人雪萊的第二個妻子) 的地位長久以來得不到公正評價。

eclipse² *v* [T] **1** if the moon eclipses the sun or the earth eclipses the moon, it makes it seem to disappear, by passing in front of it 日[月]蝕 **2** [often passive 常用被動態] to become more important, powerful, famous etc than someone or something else, so that they are no longer noticed 使失色, 蓋過: *She felt totally eclipsed by her prettier, brighter, younger sister.* 她的妹妹比她漂亮、聰明, 她覺得自己黯然失色。

e·clip·tic/ɪ`klɪptɪk; ɪ'klɪptɪk/ *n* [singular] *technical* the path along which the sun seems to move【術語】黃道

eco-/iko; iːkəʊ/ *prefix* concerned with the environment 與環境相關的, 生態的: *eco-warriors* (=people who try to stop damage to the environment) 環境衛士 (指盡力保護環境的人)

e·co-friend·ly/`iko ˌfrɛndlɪ; 'iːkəʊ ˌfrendli/ *adj* not harmful to the environment 不損害環境的: *eco-friendly products* 對環境無害的產品

e·co·lo·gi·cal/ˌikə`lɑdʒɪkl; ˌiːkə'lɒdʒɪkəl◂/ *adj* [only before noun 僅用於名詞前] **1** connected with the way plants, animals, and people are related to each other and to their environment 生態的: *an ecological disaster* 生態災難 **2** interested in preserving the environment 主張生態保護的: *ecological groups* 生態保護組織 —**ecologically**/-klɪ; -kli/ *adv*: *an ecologically-sound production process* 一種對生態無害的生產過程

e·col·o·gist/ɪ`kɑlədʒɪst; ɪ'kɒlədʒɨst/ *n* [C] a scientist who studies ecology 生態學家

e·col·o·gy/ɪ`kɑlədʒɪ; ɪ'kɒlədʒi/ *n* [singular U] the way in which plants, animals, and people are related to each other and to their environment, or the scientific study of this 生態; 生態學: *the fragile ecology of the tundra* 凍原地帶脆弱的生態

3 1 **ec·o·nom·ic**/ˌikə`nɑmɪk; ˌekə'nɒmɪk◂/ *adj* **1** [only before noun 僅用於名詞前] connected with trade, industry, and the management of money 經濟(上)的: *strategies to promote economic growth* 促進經濟增長的策略 | *It makes no economic sense at all!* 經濟上這絕不明智! | **economic climate**(=conditions affecting trade, industry, and business) 經濟氣候〔指影響貿易、工業和商業發展的條件〕**2** an economic process, activity etc produces enough profit for it to continue; PROFITABLE 產生經濟效益的; 合算的: *It is no longer economic for us to run the service.* 經營這項服務不再賺錢了。| *an economic price* 合算的價格 —see 見 ECONOMIC (USAGE)

USAGE NOTE 用法說明: ECONOMIC

WORD CHOICE 詞語辨析: **economy, economic, economics, economical, cheap, economically**

The adjective of the word **economy** [C], meaning the economy of a country is **economic**. economy (指一國的經濟) 的形容詞是 economic: *government measures to boost the economy* 政府促進經濟發展的措施 | *the various economies of South America* 南美洲各經濟體 | *We are faced with a deepening economic crisis* (NOT 不用 *economical*). 我們面臨日益嚴重的經濟危機。| *economic growth/benefits/problems/policy* 經濟增長/收益/問題/政策

The study of economies and their money systems is called **economics** (singular 單數形式). 對各類經濟體及其貨幣體系的研究被稱為 economics (經濟學): *He's got a degree in Modern History and Economics* (NOT 不用 *economic* or 或 *economy*). 他有現代史和經濟學的學位。| *Economics is my favorite subject* (NOT 不用 *are my favorite subject*). 經濟學是我最喜歡的學科。

The adjective **economical** relates to the word **economy** (sense 2 [U]) meaning the careful use of money, a supply of something, effort etc that avoids any waste. economical 是 economy (名詞釋義 2) 的形容詞, 意為"省錢的, 節約的": *My new car is quite economical* (=cheap to run). 我的新車很省油。| *She was brought up to be economical with the housekeeping money* (=spend it carefully). 她從小就養成了節儉持家的習慣。

Something that is **economical** is not necessarily cheap. For example it may be more economical to buy a packet of soap powder that is twice the usual size, because even though it costs more than the small packet, it does not cost twice the amount. However, sometimes people who sell things call **cheap** things **economical** simply because this word sounds better. 經濟 (economical) 的東西並不一定便宜 (cheap)。例如, 買雙量包裝的洗衣粉會較經濟, 因為雖然它的價格比標準包裝的高, 卻低於兩袋標準包裝的價格之和。但是銷售商有時會把cheap的商品說成是economical, 只是因為後者好聽些。

The adverb of both **economic** and **economical** is **economically**. economic 和 economical 兩個詞的副詞形式都是 economically: *The country is not economically stable.* 這個國家的經濟不穩定。| *You can live here quite economically.* 你可以很經濟地生活在這兒。

ec·o·nom·i·cal/ˌikə`nɑmɪkl; ˌekə'nɒmɪkəl/ *adj* using money, time, goods etc carefully and without wasting any 經濟的, 節約的: *an economical method of heating* 一種經濟的供暖方法

ec·o·nom·i·cally/ˌikə`nɑmɪklɪ; ˌekə'nɒmɪkli/ *adv* **1** in a way that is related to systems of money, trade, or business 在經濟上: *In economically advanced countries, childbearing typically begins later in life.* 在經濟發達國家, 人們一般比較晚才要孩子。[sentence adverb 句子副詞] *Economically and politically, they've been disenfranchised.* 他們被剝奪了經濟上和政治上的權利。**2** in a way that uses money, goods, time etc without wasting any 經濟地, 節約地: *We'll just have to shop as economically as we can from now on.* 從現在開始, 我們買東西得盡可能節省。

ec·o·nom·ics/ˌikə`nɑmɪks; ˌekə'nɒmɪks/ *n* **1** [U] the 3
study of the way in which money and goods are produced and used 經濟學 **2** [plural] the way in which money influences whether a plan, business etc will work effectively 經濟情況, 經濟因素; 經濟意義: *The economics of the scheme will have to be looked at very carefully.* 這項計劃的經濟因素須認真考慮。—see also 另見 HOME ECONOMICS

e·con·o·mist/ɪ`kɑnəmɪst; ɪ'kɒnəmɨst/ *n* [C] someone who studies the way in which money and goods are produced and used and the systems of business and trade 經濟學家

e·con·o·mize also 又作 **-ise** *BrE*【英】/ɪ`kɑnəˌmaɪz;

ɪˋkɒnəmaɪz/ *v* [I] to reduce the amount of money, time, goods etc that you use 削減; 節省: [+on] *We can't economize on the central heating because the baby needs a warm house.* 我們不能減少中央供暖, 因為嬰兒需要一個暖和的家。

e·con·o·my¹ /ɪˋkɑnəmɪ; ɪˋkɒnəmi/ *n* **1** [C] the system by which a country's money and goods are produced and used, or a country considered in this way 經濟; 經濟情況; 經濟制度: *a capitalist economy* 資本主義經濟 | *the burgeoning economies of the Pacific rim* 太平洋周邊迅速發展的經濟體 **2** [U] the careful use of money, time, goods etc so that nothing is wasted 節約; 節儉: *For the sake of economy, I hadn't yet turned on the heating.* 為了省錢, 我還未打開供暖系統。| **economy drive** (=a period of time during which you try to spend less money than usual) 節約運動; 節省開支的一段日子 **3** [C] something that you do in order to spend less money 節約措施, 省錢辦法: *One economy would be to take sandwiches instead.* 一種省錢的辦法就是改吃三明治。| **make economies** *We're trying to make a few economies this month.* 這個月我們盡力節省一點。| **false economy** (=something that seems cheaper but costs more in the end) 虛假節約 (看上去省錢, 實際上費錢) *Buying cheap tyres is a false eonomy – they wear out much more quickly.* 買便宜的輪胎表面上省錢, 實際上並不劃算 — 因為它們磨損快得多。**4 economies of scale** *technical* the financial advantages of producing something in very large quantities【術語】規模經濟 —see also 另見 BLACK ECONOMY, MARKET ECONOMY, MIXED ECONOMY

economy² *adj* [only before noun 僅用於名詞前] **economy size/pack** a product that is cheaper, usually because you are buying a larger amount〔產品的〕經濟裝〔一般指比標準包裝量大而便宜的包裝〕

economy class /ˈ·ˈ·· ˌ·/ *n* [U] the cheapest type of seats in a plane〔飛機的〕經濟艙 —**economy class** *adv*: *We flew economy class.* 我們乘坐的是經濟艙。

e·co·sys·tem /ˋikoˌsɪstəm; ˈiːkəʊˌsɪstəm/ *n* [C] all the animals and plants in a particular area, and the way in which they are related to each other and to their environment 生態系統

ec·sta·sy/ˋɛkstəsɪ; ˈekstəsi/ *n* **1** [C,U] a feeling of extreme happiness 狂喜, 欣喜若狂: *His expression was one of pure ecstasy.* 他的表情是一種完完全全的欣喜若狂。| **in ecstasy/ecstasies** (=feeling extremely happy) 處於狂喜之中 | **go into ecstasies** (=become very happy and excited) 變得欣喜若狂 **2** [U] a state in which you cannot see or hear what is happening around you, because you are having a powerful religious experience 出神〔指一種宗教體驗〕

Ecstacy *n* [U] an illegal drug used especially by young people to give a feeling of happiness and energy at parties "狂喜"迷幻藥

ec·stat·ic /ɪkˋstætɪk; ɪkˈstætɪk/ *adj* **1** feeling extremely happy and excited 狂喜的, 欣喜若狂的: *an ecstatic welcome from the thousands who lined the streets* 數千人狂熱的夾道歡迎 **2** in a state in which you are having a powerful religious experience〔指處於一種宗教體驗時〕出神的 —**ecstatically** /-klɪ; -kli/ *adv*

ECT /ˌi si ˋti; ˌiː siː ˈtiː/ *n* [U] electro-convulsive therapy; another word for ELECTRIC SHOCK THERAPY 電擊療法

-ectomy /ɛktəmɪ; ektəmi/ *suffix* [in nouns 構成名詞] *technical* the removing of a particular part of someone's body by an operation【術語】切除術, 摘除術: *an appendectomy* (=removing the APPENDIX) 闌尾切除手術

ECU /eˋku; ˈekjuː/ *n* [C] European Currency Unit; the official unit of money of the former EC〔舊時歐洲共同體的〕歐洲通貨單位

e·cu·men·i·cal /ˌɛkjuˋmɛnɪkl; ˌiːkjʊˈmenɪkəl◂/ *adj* supporting the idea of uniting the different branches of the Christian religion 支持基督教 (不同教派) 大聯合的 —**ecumenically** /-klɪ; -kli/ *adv*

ec·ze·ma /ˋɛksɪmə; ˈeksɪmə/ *n* [U] a condition in which your skin becomes dry, red, and swollen 濕疹

ed 1 an abbreviation for 縮寫= EDITOR **2** an abbreviation for 縮寫= EDITION

-ed /d, ɪd, t; d, ɪd, t/ *suffix* **1** forms the regular past tense and past participle of verbs. The past participle form is often used as an adjective〔構成規則動詞的過去式和過去分詞, 其中過去分詞常被用作形容詞〕: *I want, I wanted, I have wanted* 我想 | *I show, I showed, I have shown* 我出示 | *He walked away.* 他走開了。| *a sound that echoed through the room* 在房中回蕩過的聲音 | *a wanted criminal* 通緝犯 **2** [in adjectives 構成形容詞] having a particular thing 有某種特徵的: *a bearded man* (=a man with a beard) 留着鬍子的男人 | *a kind-hearted woman* 好心的婦女

E·dam /ˋidəm; ˈiːdəm/ *n* [U] a type of yellow cheese from the Netherlands 伊頓乾酪〔荷蘭球形奶酪, Edam是荷蘭一村名〕

ed·dy¹ /ˋɛdɪ; ˈedi/ *n* [C] a circular movement of water, wind, dust etc〔水、風、塵土等的〕旋渦: *The racing river caused swirling eddies.* 湍急的河水形成了許多旋渦。

eddy² *v* [I] if water, wind, dust etc eddies, it moves around with a circular movement〔水、風、塵土等〕起旋渦: *The mist eddied round the old house.* 霧旋繞在舊房子周圍。

E·den /ˋidn; ˈiːdn/ also 又作 **the Garden of Eden** *n* [singular] in the Bible story, the garden where Adam and Eve, the first humans lived, often seen as a place of happiness and INNOCENCE 伊甸園〔《聖經》故事中人類始祖亞當和夏娃最初居住的園子, 常被認為是樂土和純潔清淨的地方〕

edge 邊緣

on the edge of a cliff 在懸崖邊緣

at the water's edge 在水邊

edge¹/ɛdʒ; edʒ/ *n* [C] **1** the part of an object that is furthest from its centre 邊緣: *Just leave it on the edge of your plate.* 把它放在你盤子邊上就行了。| *Suli stood at the water's edge.* 蘇利站在水邊上。**2** the thin sharp part of a blade or tool that cuts 刀口; 刃: *Careful – that knife has a very sharp edge!* 小心點, 那把刀很鋒利! **3 have the edge on/over** to be slightly better than someone or something, because you have an advantage that they do not have 稍微勝過…: *Marcia has the edge over the other students, having spent a year in England.* 瑪西婭在英國待過一年, 所以比其他學生稍好一些。**4 be on edge** to be nervous, especially because you are expecting something unpleasant to happen 惴惴不安; 煩躁: *I've been on edge ever since I got her letter.* 收到她的信以後我就惴惴不安。**5 be on the edge** *informal* to be behaving in a way that makes it seem as if you are going crazy【非正式】舉止瘋癲; 行為幾近瘋狂 **6 take the edge off** to make something less bad, good, strong etc 削弱; 減輕: *Try this. It should take the edge off the* pain. 試試這個, 它會緩解疼痛。—see also 另見 **the cutting edge of** (CUTTING[2] (3))

edge[2] *v* **1** [I always+adv/prep, T always+adv/prep] to move gradually with several small movements, or to make something do this (使) 徐徐移動: *The car edged forwards at walking pace.* 汽車以行人步行的速度徐徐挪動。| **edge sth in/across/towards etc** *Hetty edged her chair closer to mine.* 赫蒂把椅子向我挪近一些。| **edge your way in/through/towards etc** (=move somewhere carefully with small movements) 緩慢而小心地進入/穿過/移向等 *Slowly, we edge our way towards the front of the crowd.* 我們慢慢地向人羣前面移動。—see picture on page A24 參見 A24 頁圖 **2** [T] to put something on the edge or border of something 加邊於; 在...的邊上鑲: **edge sth with** *The sleeves were edged with lace.* 袖子上鑲了網眼花邊。**3** [I always+adv/prep, T always+adv/prep] to develop gradually, or to make something do this (使) 緩慢發展: **edge (sth) in/up/towards** *Prices have been static for months, but are now beginning to edge up.* 物價穩定了幾個月, 但現在開始慢慢上漲了。**4** [T] to cut the edges of an area of grass so that they are tidy and straight 修剪〔草地邊緣〕

edge·ways /ˋɛdʒˌwez; ˈedʒweɪz/ also 又作 **edge·wise** /-ˌwaɪz; -waɪz/ *adv* sideways 側着; 斜着 —see also 另見 **get a word in edgeways** (WORD[1] (31))

edg·ing /ˋɛdʒɪŋ; ˈedʒɪŋ/ *n* [C,U] something that forms an edge or border 邊緣; 飾邊: *a white handkerchief with blue edging* 鑲藍邊的白手帕

edg·y /ˋɛdʒɪ; ˈedʒi/ *adj* nervous and worried 緊張不安的: *She's been edgy lately, waiting for the test results.* 她最近一直心緒不寧, 在等測驗結果。

ed·i·ble /ˋɛdəbl̩; ˈedɪ̈bəl/ *adj* something that is edible can be eaten 可以食用的: *These berries are edible, but those are poisonous.* 這些漿果可以吃, 但那些有毒。

e·dict /ˋidɪkt; ˈiːdɪkt/ *n* [C] *formal*【正式】**1** an official public order made by someone in a position of power 法令, 敕令: *The emperor issued an edict forbidding anyone to leave the city.* 皇帝下令禁止任何人出城。**2** *especially humorous* any order or command【尤幽默】命令

ed·i·fice /ˋɛdəfɪs; ˈedɪ̈fɪ̈s/ *n* [C] *formal* a building, especially a large one【正式】建築〔尤指宏偉的建築〕: *Their head office was an imposing edifice in Millbank.* 他們的總部大樓是位於梅爾班克的一幢宏偉建築。

ed·i·fy /ˋɛdəˌfaɪ; ˈedɪ̈faɪ/ *v* [T] *formal* to improve someone's mind or character by teaching them something【正式】教誨, 教導 —**edification** /ˌɛdəfəˋkeʃən; ˌedɪ̈fɪˈkeɪʃən/ *n* [U] *For our edification, the preacher reminded us what 'duty' meant.* 教士教導我們, 提醒我們"責任"的意義。

ed·i·fy·ing /ˋɛdəˌfaɪɪŋ; ˈedɪ̈faɪ-ɪŋ/ *adj formal or humorous* an edifying speech, book etc improves your mind or moral character by teaching you something【正式或幽默】教誨的; 啟迪的; 陶冶情操的: *No one would claim that the film is morally edifying.* 沒有人會認為那部電影有教育意義。

ed·it /ˋɛdɪt; ˈedɪ̈t/ *v* **1** [I,T] to prepare a book, piece of film etc for printing or broadcasting by deciding what to include, and making sure there are no mistakes 編輯; 剪輯: *hours and hours spent editing text* 花在編輯文本上的大量時間 **2** [T] to work as the editor of a newspaper, magazine etc 任〔報紙、雜誌等〕的編輯: *She used to edit the Washington Post.* 她曾編過《華盛頓郵報》。—**edit** *n* [C]

edit sth ↔ out *phr v* [T] to remove something when you are preparing a book, piece of film etc for printing or broadcasting〔在編輯、剪輯等過程中〕刪除, 去掉: *All the swear words were edited out before the film was broadcast.* 在電影播映之前所有的髒話都被去掉了。

e·di·tion /ɪˋdɪʃən; ɪˈdɪʃən/ *n* [C] the copies of a book, newspaper etc that are produced and printed at the same time〔書、報等的〕版次; 版本: *Is there a paperback edition?* 有平裝本嗎? | **first edition** (=the first copies of a particular book, that are often valuable) 初版

ed·i·tor /ˋɛdɪtɚ; ˈedɪ̈tə/ *n* [C] **1** the person who decides what should be included in a newspaper, magazine etc〔報紙、雜誌等的〕主編: *the editor of the Daily Telegraph*《每日電訊報》的主編 **2** someone who prepares a book, film etc for printing or broadcasting by deciding what to include and checking for any mistakes 編輯, 剪輯者: *a TV script editor* 電視劇本編輯 —**editorial** /ˌɛdəˋtorɪəl; ˌedɪ̈ˈtɔːriəl◂/ *adj*: *Not screening the program was an editorial decision.* 不播映這個節目是編輯上的決定。 W2

ed·i·to·ri·al /ˌɛdəˋtorɪəl; ˈedɪ̈ˈtɔːriəl◂/ *n* [C] a piece of writing in a newspaper that gives the editor's opinion about something, rather than reporting facts〔報紙的〕社論, 社評

ed·i·tor·ship /ˋɛdɪtɚˌʃɪp; ˈedɪ̈təʃɪp/ *n* [U] the position of being the editor of a newspaper or magazine〔報紙、雜誌的〕主編職位

ed·u·cate /ˋɛdʒəˌket; ˈedjʊkeɪt/ *v* [T] to teach or train someone, especially at a school, college, or university〔尤指學校〕教育; 訓練: *How can our children be educated if schools are not properly funded?* 如果學校沒有足夠的經費, 我們的孩子怎麼能得到好的教育呢? | **educate sb about/on** *a campaign to educate teenagers about the dangers of smoking* 教育青少年認識吸煙危害的運動 —see 見 TEACH (USAGE)

ed·u·cat·ed /ˋɛdʒəˌketɪd; ˈedjʊkeɪtɪ̈d/ *adj* **1** intelligent because you have been taught or trained somewhere 受過教育的; 受過訓練的: *an educated and sensitive woman* 有教養、感覺敏銳的女人 | **Harvard-educated/Oxford-educated etc** *a Harvard-educated lawyer* 在哈佛大學受過教育[畢業]的律師 **2** having a high standard of judgement about art, literature etc〔在藝術、文學等方面〕很有修養的: *She has very educated tastes.* 她很有修養。**3** **educated guess** a guess that is likely to be correct because you have enough information 有根據的猜測

ed·u·ca·tion /ˌɛdʒəˋkeʃən; ˌedjʊˈkeɪʃən/ *n* **1** [singular, U] the process by which your mind develops through learning at a school, college, or university 教育; 培養: *They had worked hard to give their son a good education.* 他們勤奮工作以便兒子能受到良好的教育。| *adult education classes* 成人教育課程 **2** [singular, U] the knowledge and skills that you gain from being taught〔通過接受教育而獲得的〕知識; 技能: *a college education* 大學教育 **3** the general area of work or study connected with teaching 教育體系; 教育學: *a lecturer in higher education* 高等教育講師 —see also 另見 FURTHER EDUCATION, HIGHER EDUCATION S1 W1

ed·u·ca·tion·al /ˌɛdʒəˋkeʃənl; ˌedjʊˈkeɪʃənəl◂/ *adj* **1** connected with education 教育的; 與教育有關的: *a fall in educational standards* 教育水平下降 **2** teaching you something you did not know before 有教育意義的: *Work experience is an important educational experience for young people.* 工作經歷對於年輕人有重要的教育意義。 S2 W2

ed·u·ca·tion·al·ist /ˌɛdʒəˋkeʃənlɪst; ˌedjʊˈkeɪʃənəlɪ̈st/ also 又作 **ed·u·ca·tion·ist** /-ʃənɪst; -ʃənɪ̈st/ *n* [C] *formal* someone who knows a lot about methods of education【正式】教育家; 教育學家

ed·u·ca·tor /ˋɛdʒəˌketɚ; ˈedjʊkeɪtə/ *n* [C] *formal especially AmE* a teacher【正式, 尤美】教師, 教育工作者

ed·u·tain·ment /ˌɛdʒəˋtenmənt; ˌedjʊˈteɪnmənt/ *n* [U] films, television programmes, or computer SOFTWARE that educate and entertain at the same time 寓教於樂的影片[電視節目, 電腦軟件]

Ed·ward·i·an /ɛdˋwɔrdɪən; edˈwɔːdiən/ *adj* connected with or coming from the time of King Edward VII of Britain (1901-1910) 英王愛德華七世(1901-1910)的; 英王愛德華七世時代的: *Edwardian furniture* 英王愛德華七世時代的家具

-ee /i; iː/ *suffix* [in nouns 構成名詞] **1** someone who is being treated in a particular way 受動者: *the payee* (=someone who is paid) 受款人, 收款人 | *a trainee* 受訓者 | *an employee* 雇員 **2** someone who is in a particular state or who is doing something 處於某種情況下的人; 行動者: *an absentee* (=someone who is absent) 缺席者 | *an escapee* 逃亡者

EEC /ˌi i ˋsi; ˌiː iː ˈsiː/ *n* [singular] the European Economic Community; the former name for the EC 歐洲經濟共同體〔歐洲共同體的前稱〕

EEG /ˌi i ˋdʒi; ˌiː iː ˈdʒiː/ *n* **1** electroencephalograph; a piece of equipment that records the electrical activity of your brain 腦電圖儀 **2** electroencephalogram; a drawing made by an electroencephalograph 腦電圖

eek /ik; iːk/ *interjection* an expression of sudden fear and surprise 唷, 呀〔表示突然的驚嚇〕: *Eek! A mouse!* 呀! 一隻老鼠!

eel /il; iːl/ *n* [C] a long thin fish that looks like a snake and can be eaten 鰻; 鱔: *He wriggled like an eel to get free.* 他像鰻魚似地扭動身體試圖逃脫。

e'en /in; iːn/ *adv poetic*【詩】the short form of 縮略式= EVEN[1]

e'er /ɛr; eə/ *adv poetic*【詩】the short form of 縮略式= EVER

-eer /ɪr; ɪə/ *suffix* [in nouns 構成名詞] someone who does or makes a particular thing, often something bad 從事[做出]某事〔常為壞事〕的人: *an auctioneer* (=someone who runs AUCTION sales) 拍賣商 | *a profiteer* (=someone who makes unfair profits) 牟取暴利的商人

E

ee·rie /ˋɪrɪ; ˈɪəri/ *adj* strange and frightening 怪異而令人恐懼的: *the eerie sound of an owl hooting in the forest at night* 夜間森林裡貓頭鷹那怪異恐怖的叫聲

eff /ɛf; ef/ *v* [I] *BrE*【英】**1 effing and blinding** *slang* swearing【俚】詛咒: *You should have heard him effing and blinding when he hit his thumb with the hammer.* 你真該聽聽錘子砸到拇指時他的叫罵聲。**2 eff off!** *taboo* used to tell someone to go away instead of saying **fuck off** (FUCK[1] (1))【諱】滾蛋! —see also 另見 EFFING

ef·face /ɪˋfes; ɪˈfeɪs/ *v* [T] *formal*【正式】**1** to prevent you from remembering an unpleasant experience 使忘記〔不愉快的經歷〕: *Nothing could efface the indignity of being publicly criticized.* 沒有甚麼能讓人忘記當眾挨批評的恥辱。**2** to remove a mark or sign, especially by rubbing it 抹去; 擦除 **3 efface yourself** to behave in a way that does not make people notice you or look at you (使)不引人注目; 不露鋒芒 —see also 另見 SELF-EFFACING

1 1 **ef·fect[1]** /əˋfɛkt; ɪˈfekt/ *n*

1 ►CHANGE/RESULT 改變/結果◄ [C,U] the way in which an event, action, or person changes someone or something 效應; 作用; 結果: [+**of**] *the harmful effects of smoking* 吸煙的壞處 | **have an effect on** *Inflation is having a disastrous effect on the economy.* 通貨膨脹給經濟帶來災難性的影響。| **have/achieve the desired effect** (=produce the result you wanted) 取得所期望的成果 *The plan failed to achieve the desired effect of diverting traffic from the city.* 該計劃未能如期望的那樣分流城裡的車輛。| **cause and effect** (=something that happens, and the other things that happen as a result of this) 因果 —see 見 AFFECT (USAGE)

2 put/bring sth into effect to make a plan or idea happen 實施計劃; 落實想法: *It won't be easy to put the changes into effect.* 把這些變化落到實處不會是件容易的事。

3 come into effect/take effect if a new law, rule, or system comes into effect, it officially starts〔法律、規則或系統〕生效: *The new tax rates come into effect from April.* 新的稅率從4月起生效。

4 take effect to start to produce results 開始起作用; 開始產生效果: *The morphine was starting to take effect and the pain eased.* 嗎啡開始起作用, 疼痛減輕了。

5 in effect used when you are describing what the real situation is, especially when it is different from the way that it seems to be 實際上; 事實上: *In effect, our wages will fall by 2%.* 實際上, 我們的工資將下降2%。

6 to good/little effect if you do something to good effect, it is successful and does what you want it to 產生好的/差的效果: *Pat rubbed the stain frantically with a cloth, but to little effect.* 帕特用布發瘋似的擦着污跡, 但收效甚微。

7 to this/that effect used when you are giving the general meaning of what someone says, rather than the exact words 有這樣/那樣的意思[內容]: *I thought he was wrong and said something to that effect at dinner.* 我認為他錯了, 吃晚飯時我大概表達了這個意思。| **words to that effect** *Jim said he was unhappy at work, or words to that effect.* 吉姆說了些工作不順心之類的話。| **to the effect that** *Karl's memo was to the effect that we all needed to think more about marketing possibilities.* 卡爾的便箋的大意是說, 我們都需要多考慮營銷機會。

8 with immediate effect/with effect from starting to happen immediately, or from a particular date 立即生效/自…起開始實行: *Hoskins is appointed manager, with immediate effect.* 霍斯金斯被任命為經理, 立即上任。

9 ►IDEA/FEELING 想法/感受◄ [C usually singular 一般用單數] an idea or feeling that an artist, speaker, book etc tries to make you think of or feel〔藝術家、演講者或書等給人的〕感受, 印象: *Turner's paintings give an effect of light.* 透納的畫表現出光的效果。| **do sth for effect** (=do something deliberately to shock or surprise people) 譁眾取寵

10 ►PERSONAL THINGS 私人物品◄ **effects** [plural] *formal* the things that someone owns; BELONGINGS【正式】私人物品; 個人財產: *Don's few personal effects were in a suitcase under the bed.* 唐的幾件個人物品在牀下的箱子裡。

11 ►FILM 電影◄ **effects** [plural] unusual or impressive sounds or images that are artificially produced for a film, play, or radio programme 效果 —see also 另見 SOUND EFFECTS, SPECIAL EFFECT

effect[2] *v* [T] *formal* to make something happen【正式】引起; 使發生: *efforts to effect a reconciliation between the warring factions* 使交戰各派達成和解的努力

ef·fec·tive /əˋfɛktɪv; ɪˈfektɪv/ *adj* **1** producing the result that was wanted or intended 產生預期效果的; 有效的: *The ads were simple, but remarkably effective.* 這些廣告很簡單, 但效果出奇地好。**2** impressive or interesting enough to be noticed 引人注意的; 醒目的: *an effective use of colour* 使用引人注目的顏色 **3** [no comparative 無比較級] if a law, agreement, or system becomes effective, it officially starts〔法律、協議或制度等〕生效的: *The cut in interest rates is effective from Monday.* 從星期一起利率下調正式生效。**4** [no comparative 無比較級] real rather than what is officially intended or generally believed 實際的, 事實上的: *The rebels are in effective control of the city.* 反叛者實際上已控制了城市。—**effectiveness** *n* [U]

ef·fec·tive·ly /əˋfɛktɪvlɪ; ɪˈfektɪvli/ *adv* **1** in a way that produces the result that was intended 有效地: *Children have to learn to communicate effectively.* 小孩子應該學會有效地交流。**2** [sentence adverb 句子副詞] used to describe what the real situation is, especially when it is different from the way that it seems to be 實際上, 事實上: *Effectively, it has become impossible for us to help.* 事實上, 我們已不可能幫忙了。

ef·fec·tu·al /əˋfɛktʃuəl; ɪˈfektʃuəl/ *adj formal* producing the result that was wanted or intended; EFFECTIVE (1)【正式】有效的, 奏效的 —opposite 反義詞 INEFFECTUAL —**effectually** *adv*

ef·fec·tu·ate /əˋfɛktʃuˌet; ɪˈfektʃueɪt/ *v* [T] *formal* to make something happen【正式】引起; 使發生

ef·fem·i·nate /əˋfɛmənɪt; ɪˈfemənət/ *adj* a man who is effeminate looks or behaves like a woman〔男人〕女人氣的, 女性化的: *very young and handsome in an effeminate way* 非常年輕英俊又帶陰柔氣質 —**effeminacy** *n* [U] —**effeminately** *adv*

ef·fer·vesce /ˌɛfəˋvɛs; ˌefəˈves/ *v* [I] *technical* a liquid that effervesces produces small bubbles (BUBBLE[1] (1)) of gas【術語】〔液體〕冒氣泡, 起沫

ef·fer·vesc·ent /ˌɛfɚˋvɛsn̩t; ˌefəˈvesənt◂/ *adj* **1** someone who is effervescent is very cheerful and active 興高采烈的; 充滿活力的, 活潑的: *an effervescent personality* 活潑樂觀的個性 **2** a liquid that is effervescent produces small bubbles (BUBBLE[1] (1)) of gas〔液體〕冒泡的, 起沫的 —**effervescence** *n* [U]

ef·fete /ɛˋfit; ɪˈfiːt/ *adj formal*【正式】**1** weak and powerless in a way that you dislike 軟弱的, 懦弱的: *an attack against effete intellectuals* 對軟弱的知識分子的攻擊 **2** looking or behaving like a woman 女人氣的, 女性化的: *an effete, languid young man* 充滿女人氣又無精打采的年輕男子 —**effetely** *adv*

ef·fi·ca·cious /ˌɛfəˋkeʃəs; ˌefɪ̵ˈkeɪʃəs◂/ *adj formal* producing the result that was intended, especially when dealing with an illness or a problem【正式】〔尤指在治病或處理問題方面〕有效的: *an equally efficacious method of treatment* 同樣有效的治療方法 —**efficaciously** *adv*

ef·fi·ca·cy /ˋɛfəkəsɪ; ˈefɪ̵kəsi/ *n* [U] *formal* the quality of being able to produce the result that was intended【正式】有效性; 功效

3 3 **ef·fi·cien·cy** /əˋfɪʃənsɪ; ɪˈfɪʃənsi/ *n* [U] the quality of doing something well and effectively, without wasting time, money, or energy 效率; 效能: *The improvements in efficiency have been staggering.* 效率大大提高, 使人震驚。

2 3 **ef·fi·cient** /əˋfɪʃənt; ɪˈfɪʃənt/ *adj* a person, machine, or organization that is efficient works well and effectively without wasting time, money, or energy 有效率的; 高效能的: *an efficient heating system* 高效能的供暖系統 | *a very efficient secretary* 高效率的祕書 —**efficiently** *adv*

ef·fi·gy /ˋɛfədʒɪ; ˈefɪ̵dʒi/ *n* [C] **1** a figure made of wood, paper, stone etc, that looks like a person, especially one that makes the person look ugly or funny〔尤指醜化本人的木[紙, 石等]質〕雕像; 肖像; 模擬像: **[+of]** *an effigy of the prime minister* 首相的模擬像 **2 burn/hang sb in effigy** to burn or hang a figure of someone at a political DEMONSTRATION (1) because you hate them〔在政治示威中〕焚燒某人的模擬像; 對某人的模擬像處以絞刑

ef·fing /ˋɛfɪŋ; ˈefɪŋ/ *adj* [only before noun 僅用於名詞前] *BrE spoken* a rude word used to emphasize that you are angry【英口】該死的〔表達說話者的憤怒〕: *She's gone to effing bingo again.* 她又去玩該死的賓戈遊戲了。 —**effing** *adv* —see also 另見 **effing and blinding** (EFF (1))

ef·flo·res·cence /ˌɛfloˋrɛsn̩s; ˌefləˈresəns/ *n* [U] *technical* the action of flowers, art etc forming and developing, or the period of time when this happens【術語】開花 (期); 〔藝術等〕發展 (期), 全盛期: *His work represents the efflorescence of a dying culture.* 他的作品代表着一種行將消失的文化的發展。

ef·flu·ent /ˋɛfluənt; ˈefluənt/ *n* [C,U] liquid waste, especially chemicals or SEWAGE 廢液; 污水: *The effluent was being discharged straight into the sea.* 廢水被直接排放到海裡。

ef·flux /ˋɛflʌks; ˈeflʌks/ *n* [U] *technical* an outward flow of gas or liquid【術語】〔氣體或液體的〕流出; 外流

1 1 **ef·fort** /ˋɛfɚt; ˈefət/ *n*

1 ▶PHYSICAL/MENTAL ENERGY 體力/精力◀ [U] the physical or mental energy that is needed to do something 力氣, 精力: *Lou lifted the box without any apparent effort.* 盧毫不費力地把箱子搬起來。| **take/require effort** *It takes a lot of time and effort to get an exhibition ready.* 準備一次展覽要花費很多時間和精力。| **take all the effort out of** (=make something much easier) 使…變得容易多了 | **put a lot of effort into** (=work very hard at something) 投入很多精力 *Frank put a lot of effort into the preparations for the party.* 弗蘭克花了很大力氣來準備這次聚會。

2 ▶ATTEMPT 努力◀ [C,U] an attempt to do something, especially when this involves a lot of hard work or determination 努力: **effort to do sth** *My efforts to convince Lucy to return failed.* 我試圖說服露西回來但未成功。| **[+at]** *Further efforts at negotiation have broken down.* 為談判所作的進一步努力已經失敗了。| **concerted effort** (=a strong sincere attempt) 全力 *Jack has made a concerted effort to improve his behaviour.* 傑克盡全力改進自己的行為。| **through sb's efforts** (=because of what someone did) 通過某人的努力 *It's only through your efforts that we have managed to raise the money.* 全靠你的努力我們才籌到這筆錢。| **in an effort to do sth** (=in order to achieve something) 為做成某事 *They've been working night and day in an effort to get the bridge ready on time.* 為了使橋能準時完工, 他們一直夜以繼日地工作。

3 make an effort (to do sth) to try hard to do something, especially something you do not want to do 盡力 (做某事); 勉為其難 (做某事): *I know you don't like her, but you could make an effort to be polite.* 我知道你不喜歡她, 但你要盡量禮貌些。| **make every effort** (=use a lot of effort and try different ways) 盡一切努力 *Every effort is being made to deal with the issues you raised at the last meeting.* 正盡一切努力處理你在上次會議上提出的問題。

4 an effort of will/imagination/concentration the determination needed to do something〔做某事所需的〕毅力/想像力/專心: *She dismissed the painful memory with a deliberate effort of will.* 她竭力從痛苦的回憶中掙脫出來。

5 be an effort to be difficult or painful to do 費力, 痛苦: *I was so weak that even standing up was an effort.* 我太虛弱了, 站起來都很費力。| *Would it be too much effort to get it yourself?* 你自己去拿會不會太費勁呢?

6 a good/bad/poor etc effort something that has been done well, badly etc 幹得好/不好/差勁等: *Not a bad effort for a beginner!* 對一個新手來說不錯了!

ef·fort·less /ˋɛfɚtlɪs; ˈefətləs/ *adj* something that is effortless is done in a very skilful way that makes it seem easy 不費力的, 輕鬆的: *a smooth, effortless volley* 輕鬆自如的空中截擊 —**effortlessly** *adv*: *Her fingers darted effortlessly over the keys.* 她的手指在鍵上輕巧地敲擊。

ef·fron·te·ry /əˋfrʌntərɪ; ɪˈfrʌntəri/ *n* [U] *formal* behaviour that you think someone should be ashamed of, although they do not seem to be【正式】厚顏無恥: *You have the effrontery to ask for a loan!* 你還有臉要借錢!

ef·ful·gence /ɛˋfʌldʒəns; ɪˈfʌldʒəns/ *n* [U] *literary* brightness of light【文】光輝, 燦爛 —**effulgent** *adj*

ef·fu·sion /əˋfjuʒən; ɪˈfjuːʒən/ *n* [C,U] *formal* an uncontrolled expression of strong feelings【正式】〔強烈感情的〕迸發: **[+of]** *effusions of gratitude* 感激之情的迸發

ef·fu·sive /ɛˋfjusɪv; ɪˈfjuːsɪv/ *adj* showing strong excited feelings 熱情的, 感情洋溢的: *Our host gave us an effusive welcome.* 主人熱情地歡迎我們。—**effusively** *adv*: *"How lovely to see you," she said effusively.* "見到你太好了," 她熱切地說。—**effusiveness** *n* [U]

EFL /ˌi ɛf ˋɛl; ˌiː ef ˈel/ *n* [U] English as a Foreign Language; the way English is taught to people who do not speak it as their first language 作為外語的英語 (教學)

eg, e.g. /ˌi ˋdʒi; ˌiː ˈdʒiː/ an abbreviation for 縮寫= 'for example' 例如: *citrus fruits, e.g. oranges and grapefruit* 柑橘屬水果, 例如橙和葡萄柚

e·gal·i·tar·i·an /ɪˌgæləˋtɛrɪən; ɪˌgælɪ̵ˈteəriən/ *adj* believing that everyone is equal and should have equal rights 平等主義的: *an egalitarian society* 一個人人平等的社會 —**egalitarianism** *n* [U]

egg[1] /ɛg; eg/ *n* 1 2

1 ▶BIRDS 鳥類◀ [C] a round object with a hard surface, that contains a baby bird, snake, insect etc and which is made by a female bird, snake, or insect 蛋: *Blackbirds usually lay their eggs in March.* 烏鶇通常在三月產蛋。| *an ostrich egg* 鴕鳥蛋

2 ▶FOOD 食物◀ [C,U] an egg, especially one from a chicken, that is used for food〔作食物的〕蛋; 雞蛋: *fried eggs* 煎蛋
3 ▶ANIMALS/PEOPLE 動物/人類◀ [C] a cell produced by a woman or female animal that combines with SPERM (=male cell) to make a baby 卵, 卵細胞
4 have egg on your face if someone, especially someone in authority, has egg on their face, they look silly because something embarrassing has happened〔尤指有權威的人〕丟臉, 出醜: *The Pentagon's been left with egg on its face.* 五角大樓丟盡了臉。
5 put all your eggs in one basket to depend completely on one thing or one course of action in order to get success 孤注一擲
6 lay an egg *AmE informal* to fail or be unsuccessful at something that you are trying to do【美, 非正式】失敗, 未成功
7 as sure as eggs is eggs *BrE old-fashioned* used to tell someone that you are sure that something will happen【英, 過時】毫無疑問, 確定無疑
8 good egg *old-fashioned* someone who you can depend on to be honest, kind etc【過時】好人

egg² *v*
egg sb ↔ **on** *phr v* [T] to encourage someone to do something, especially something that they should not do 慫恿; 鼓動: *Joe didn't want to jump but his friends kept egging him on.* 喬不想跳, 可他的朋友們一個勁地鼓動他。

egg·cup /ˋɛg,kʌp; ˈeg-kʌp/ *n* [C] a small container that holds a boiled egg while you eat it〔吃蛋時用的〕蛋杯

egg·head /ˋɛg,hɛd; ˈeghed/ *n* [C] *informal*【非正式】**1** someone who is very intelligent, and only interested in theories and books 學究; 學問家 **2** *AmE* someone who has no hair【美】禿頭者

egg·plant /ˋɛg,plænt; ˈegplɑːnt/ *n* [C] *especially AmE* a large vegetable with smooth purple skin【尤美】茄子; AUBERGINE *BrE*【英】—see picture on page A9 參見 A9 頁圖

egg roll /ˌ· ˈ·/ *n* [C] *AmE* a SPRING ROLL【美】春卷

egg·shell /ˋɛg,ʃɛl; ˈegʃel/ *n* [C,U] **1** the hard outside part of a bird's egg 蛋殼 **2 eggshell china/paint** a type of CHINA or paint that is thin and hard, like the shell of an egg〔薄而硬的〕蛋殼細薄瓷器/蛋殼漆

egg-tim·er /ˈ· ,··/ *n* [C] a small glass container with sand in it that runs from one part to the other, used for measuring the time it takes to boil an egg 煮蛋計時器〔用於計量煮蛋時間的小沙漏〕

e·go /ˋigo; ˈiːgəʊ/ *n* [C] **1** the opinion that you have about yourself 自我, 自我意識: *That promotion was a real boost for her ego.* 這次升職大大地增強了她的自信心。| **have a big ego** (=think that you are very clever or important) 自高自大 *big bikes and equally outsized Hollywood egos* 大型摩托車和同樣大號的荷里活自大心態 **2 ego trip** *informal* something that you do because it makes you feel important【非正式】自我表現: *This DJ work is just a big ego trip for him!* 這份當音樂節目主持人的工作對他是自我展現的好機會! **3** the part of your mind with which you think and take action, according to Freudian PSYCHOLOGY〔弗洛伊德心理學中的〕自我 —compare 比較 ID, SUPEREGO

e·go·cen·tric /ˌigoˋsɛntrɪk; ˌiːgəʊˈsentrɪk◂/ *adj* thinking only about yourself and not thinking about what other people might need or want 自我中心的; 自私自利的 —**egocentrically** /-klɪ; -kli/ *adv* —**egocentricity** /ˌigosɛnˋtrɪsətɪ; ˌiːgəʊsenˈtrɪsəti/ *n* [U]

e·go·is·m /ˋigo,ɪzəm; ˈiːgəʊɪzəm/ *n* [U] egotism 自我主義; 自大的行為 —**egoist** *n* [C] —**egoistic** /ˌigoˋɪstɪk; ˌiːgəʊˈɪstɪk◂/ *adj*

e·go·ma·ni·ac /ˌigoˋmenɪæk; ˌiːgəʊˈmeɪniæk/ *n* [C] someone who thinks that they are very important, and tries to get advantages for themselves without caring about how this affects other people 利己主義者; 自大狂 —**egomania** /-nɪə; -niə/ *n* [U]

e·go·tis·m /ˋigətɪzəm; ˈiːgətɪzəm/ *n* [U] the belief that you are much better or more important than other people, or behaviour that shows this 自我主義; 自大的行為

e·go·tis·tic·al /ˌigəˋtɪstɪkl; ˌiːgəˈtɪstɪkəl/ *adj* believing that you are much better or more important than other people 自大的; 自負的: *He's the most selfish, egotistical individual I have ever met!* 他是我見過的最自私、最狂妄自大的人! —**egotistically** /-klɪ; -kli/ *adv* —**egotist** /ˋigə,tɪst; ˈiːgətɪst/ *n* [C]

e·gre·gious /ɪˋgridʒəs; ɪˈgriːdʒəs/ *adj formal* an egregious ERROR, failure, problem etc is extremely bad and noticeable【正式】〔錯誤、失敗、問題等〕極其嚴重的; 令人震驚的: a *most egregious error of judgement* 極其嚴重的誤判 —**egregiously** *adv*

e·gress /ˋigrɛs; ˈiːgres/ *n* [U] *formal or law* the act of leaving a building or place, or the right to do this【正式或法律】外出; 出外權

e·gret /ˋigrɪt; ˈiːgrɪt/ *n* [C] a bird that lives near water and has long legs and long white tail feathers 白鷺

E·gyp·tian¹ /ɪˋdʒɪpʃən; ɪˈdʒɪpʃən/ *n* [C] someone from Egypt 埃及人

Egyptian² *adj* from or connected with Egypt 埃及的; 與埃及有關的

eh /e; eɪ/ *interjection spoken BrE, CanE*【口, 英, 加】**1** used when you want someone to repeat something because you did not hear it 嗯; 啊〔表示未聽清, 請對方重複一遍〕: *Eh? She's got how many?* 嗯? 她有多少? **2** used when you want someone to reply to you or agree with something you have said 是嗎; 好嗎〔表示請對方應答或同意〕: *Look at these. Smart, eh?* 看看這些。真棒, 是嗎? **3** used when you are surprised by something that someone has said 啊; 嗯〔表示對對方的話感到驚訝〕

ei·der·down /ˋaɪdɚ,daun; ˈaɪdədaʊn/ *n* [C] a thick warm cover for a bed, filled with duck feathers 鴨絨被

eight /et; eɪt/ *number* **1** 8 八 **2** a team of eight people who row a racing boat〔划船比賽中的〕八人划船隊 **3 have had one over the eight** *BrE old-fashioned* to be drunk【英, 過時】喝醉 —**eighth** *number*

eigh·teen /eˋtin; ˌeɪˈtiːn◂/ *number* 18 十八

eighth /etθ; eɪtθ/ *n* [C] one of eight equal parts of something 八分之一

eighth note /ˈ· ·/ *n* [C] *AmE* a musical note that continues for an eighth of the length of a WHOLE NOTE【美】八分音符; QUAVER² (1) *BrE*【英】—see picture at 參見 MUSIC 圖

eigh·ty /ˋetɪ; ˈeɪti/ *number* 80 八十

ei·stedd·fod /eˋstɛðvɑd; aɪˈstedfəd/ *n* [C] a special meeting in Wales at which there are competitions in singing, poetry, and music 威爾斯詩歌音樂比賽大會

ei·ther¹ /ˋiðɚ; ˈaɪðə/ *conjunction* **1** used to begin a list of two or more possibilities separated by 'or' 或是, 或者〔用以引出兩個或多個可能的事物, 用 or 隔開〕: *You add either one or two stock cubes.* 你加入一兩塊濃縮固體湯料。| *She's the kind of person you either love or hate.* 她是那種叫你不是愛就是恨的人。| *It was either pink, red, or orange.* 不是粉紅色的, 就是紅色的, 要不就是橙色的。—compare 比較 OR (1) **2** used to say that if one thing does not happen then something else will have to 要麼〔表示非此即彼〕: *It's your choice! Either she leaves or I will!* 你看着辦吧! 要麼她走, 要麼我走! | *£75 seems a lot to pay for a starter motor but it's either that or a new car!* 花 75 英鎊換一個發動機起動裝置似乎很貴, 但是不換起動裝置就得換輛新車!

either² *determiner* **1** one or the other of two things or people〔兩物或兩人中〕任一的: *I've lived in New York and Chicago but don't like either city very much.* 我在紐約和芝加哥住過, 但兩個城市我都不是很喜歡。| **either way** (=in one way or the other)〔兩種方式中的〕任一種方式 *You can get to Edinburgh by train or plane but either way it's very expensive.* 你可以坐火車或飛機去愛丁堡, 但兩種方式都很貴。| *"Shall we have Indian* or Chinese?" "I don't mind either way really." "我們去吃印度菜還是中國菜?" "哪種都行, 我真的不介意。" | The baby's due on the 10th but the doctor said it could be a fortnight either way. (=it could be born two weeks early or two weeks late) 嬰兒應該是10號出生, 但醫生說提前或推遲兩週都有可能。—compare 比較 ANY, NEITHER[1] **2** one and the other of two things or people; each 〔兩物或兩人中〕各一的; 每一的: *He sat in the back of the car with a policeman on either side.* 他坐在汽車後座上, 左右各坐一名警察。| *There are shops at either end of the street.* 街的兩端都有商店。—compare 比較 BOTH **3 an either-or situation** a situation in which you cannot avoid having to make a decision or choice 必須作出決定[選擇]的處境 —see 見 ALSO (USAGE)

either[3] *pron* one or the other of two things or people 〔兩者中〕任一個: *There's tea or coffee – you can have either.* 有茶和咖啡, 你可任選一種。| *Do either of you know where I can buy a zip round here?* 你倆誰知道附近哪兒能買到拉鏈?

either[4] *adv* **1** [only in negatives 僅用於否定句] also 也: *I haven't seen the movie and my brother hasn't either.* (=both haven't seen it) 我沒看過這部電影, 我弟弟也沒看過。| *"I can't swim." "I can't, either."* "我不會游泳。" "我也不會。" **2 me either** *AmE spoken* used to say that something is also true about you【美口】我也是: *"I don't have any money right now." "Me either."* "我現在沒錢。" "我也沒有。" —compare 比較 NEITHER[3], TOO (2)

e·jac·u·late /ɪˋdʒækjəˏlet; ɪˈdʒækjʊleɪt/ *v* [I,T] **1** when a man ejaculates, SPERM comes out of his PENIS 射精 **2** *old-fashioned* to suddenly shout or say something, especially because you are surprised【過時】〔尤指因驚奇而〕喊出; 突然說出 —**ejaculation** /ɪˏdʒækjəˋleʃən; ɪˌdʒækjʊˈleɪʃən/ *n* [C,U]

e·ject /ɪˋdʒɛkt; ɪˈdʒekt/ *v* **1** [T] to make someone leave a place or building by using force 〔用武力〕驅逐; 趕出: **eject sb from** *The demonstrators were ejected from the hall.* 示威者被趕出大廳。**2** [T] to suddenly send something out 噴射; 射出: *Ants eject formic acid when another insect tries to attack them.* 當受到其他昆蟲攻擊時, 螞蟻就噴出蟻酸。**3** [I] to jump out of a plane because it is going to crash 〔從要墜毀的飛機中〕彈射出來 **4** [I,T] to make something come out of a machine by pressing a button 〔按按鈕將某物從機器中〕彈出 —**ejection** /ɪˋdʒɛkʃən; ɪˈdʒekʃən/ *n* [C,U]

e·jec·tor seat /·ˈ·· ˏ·/ also 又作 **ejection seat** *AmE*【美】*n* [C] a special seat that throws the pilot out of a plane when it is going to crash 〔飛機上的〕彈射座椅

eke /ik; iːk/ *v*

eke sth ↔ **out** *phr v* [T] *literary*【文】**1** to make a small supply of something such as food or money last longer by carefully only using small amounts of it 精打細算地維持; 盡量節省使用: *Today's retired home-owner has to eke out his pension as best he can.* 如今自己擁有住房的已退休人士必須盡量節省使用退休金了。**2 eke out a living/existence** to succeed in getting the things you need to live, even though you have very little money or food 勉強度日, 竭力維持生計: *They eke out a miserable existence in cardboard shacks.* 他們在紙板屋中淒慘度日。

EKG /ˏi ke ˋdʒi; ˌiː keɪ ˈdʒiː/ *n* [C] an American form of ECG ECG的美語形式

e·lab·o·rate[1] /ɪˋlæbərɪt; ɪˈlæbərɪ̣t/ *adj* containing a lot of small details or parts that are connected with each other in a complicated way 精心製作的; 複雜的: *an elaborate mosaic consisting of thousands of tiny pieces* 由數千小塊拼成的精美的鑲嵌圖 | **elaborate plan/notes/excuses etc** (=carefully produced and full of details) 詳盡的計劃/詳細的筆記/精心編造的藉口等 —**elaborately** *adv*: *an elaborately carved wooden statue* 做工精美的木雕 —**elaborateness** *n* [U]

e·lab·o·rate[2] /ɪˋlæbəˏret; ɪˈlæbəreɪt/ *v* [I,T] to give more details or new information about something 詳盡說明; 闡述: *He said he had new evidence, but refused to elaborate any further.* 他聲稱有新證據, 但拒絕進一步詳細說明。| **[+on]** *Later chapters simply elaborate on her original theses.* 後面的章節只是對她最初的論點進行詳述。—**elaboration** /ɪˏlæbəˋreʃən; ɪˌlæbəˈreɪʃən/ *n* [U]

é·lan /eˋlɑ̃; ˈeɪlɒn/ *n* [U] *literary* a style that is full of energy and determination【文】熱忱; 活力; 銳氣: *The attack was planned and led with great élan.* 進攻計劃制定得雄心勃勃, 將帥領軍作戰異常勇猛。

e·lapse /ɪˋlæps; ɪˈlæps/ *v* [I not in progressive 不用進行式] *formal* if a particular period of time elapses, it passes【正式】〔時間〕流逝, 過去: *Several months were to elapse before his case was brought to trial.* 幾個月過去了, 他的案子才開審。

e·las·tic[1] /ɪˋlæstɪk; ɪˈlæstɪk/ *n* [U] a type of rubber material that can stretch and then return to its usual length or size 〔橡皮〕彈力材料: *The ball was attached to the bat with a piece of elastic.* 球用一根橡皮帶連在球拍上。

elastic[2] *adj* **1** made of elastic 彈力材料製成的: *elastic stockings* 彈力長筒襪 **2** a material that is elastic can stretch and then go back to its usual length or size 有彈性的: *Children's bones are far more elastic.* 兒童的骨骼彈性要大得多。**3** a system or plan that is elastic can change or be changed easily 〔系統或計劃〕靈活的, 有伸縮性的: *Language usage is too elastic to be described using just a few simple rules.* 語言的運用靈活性太大, 僅用幾條簡單的規則難以描述。—**elasticity** /ɪˏlæsˋtɪsətɪ; ˌiːlæˈstɪsɪ̣ti/ *n* [U]

elastic band /·ˏ·· ˈ·/ *n* [C] *BrE* a thin circular piece of stretchy rubber used for fastening things together; RUBBER BAND【英】橡皮筋

E·las·to·plast /ɪˋlæstəˏplæst; ɪˈlæstəplɑːst/ *n* [C,U] *BrE trademark* a sticky bandage used to cover small cuts【英, 商標】創口貼; BAND-AID *AmE*【美】

e·lat·ed /ɪˋletɪd; ɪˈleɪtɪ̣d/ *adj* extremely happy and excited, especially because you have been successful 〔尤指因成功〕興高采烈的, 歡欣鼓舞的: *Elated by our victory, we sang all the way home.* 我們因勝利而歡欣鼓舞, 一路唱着歌回家。

e·la·tion /ɪˋleʃən; ɪˈleɪʃən/ *n* [U] a feeling of extreme happiness and excitement 興高采烈, 得意洋洋

el·bow[1] /ˋɛlˏbo; ˈelbəʊ/ *n* [C] **1** the joint where your arm bends 肘 —see picture at 參見 BODY 圖 **2** the part of a shirt etc that covers your elbow 〔襯衫等的〕肘部 **3 elbow grease** *informal* hard work and effort, especially when cleaning or polishing something【非正式】費力的工作〔尤指擦洗等勞動〕**4 give sb the elbow** *BrE informal* to tell someone that you no longer like them or want them to work for you and that they should leave【英, 非正式】讓某人離開〔或是不再喜歡他, 或是不再需要他工作〕**5** a curved part of a pipe or CHIMNEY, that is shaped like an elbow 〔管子或煙囱的〕肘狀彎

elbow[2] *v* [T] to push someone with your elbows, especially in order to move past them 用肘擠開〔某人〕: **elbow your way through** (=move through a group of people by pushing past them) 擠過〔人羣〕*I began elbowing my way through the crowd.* 我開始奮力擠過人羣。—see picture on page A21 參見A21頁圖

elbow-room /ˈ·· ·/ *n* [U] enough space in which to move easily 自由活動的空間: *There's less elbow room in the Ford.* 福特汽車內身體活動空間較小。

el·der[1] /ˋɛldɚ; ˈeldə/ *adj* **1 elder brother/daughter/sister etc** [only before noun 僅用於名詞前] a brother etc who is older than other brothers etc 哥哥/大女兒/姐姐等: *My elder brother looks nothing like me.* 我哥哥一點都不像我。—see 見 OLD (USAGE) **2 the elder a)** the older one of two people 〔兩人當中的〕年長者: *Sarah is the elder of the two.* 兩人當中莎拉年齡大。**b)** used after someone's name to show that they are the older of two people with the same name, usually a father and son 大, 老〔用於人名後表示兩個同名者中的年長者, 二人通常為父子〕: *Pitt the elder* 老皮特 —compare 比較 YOUNGER

E

elder² *n* [C] **1** a member of a tribe or other social group who is important and respected because they are old 長者, 長輩: *a meeting of the village elders* 村裡長輩們的集會 **2** someone who has an official position of responsibility in some Christian churches〔基督教某些教會中的〕長老 **3** a small wild tree with white flowers and black berries 接骨木 **4 your elders (and betters)** people who are older than you and who you should respect 你的長輩

el·der·ber·ry /ˋɛldɚˌbɛrɪ; ˈeldəbəri/ *n* [C] the fruit of the elder tree 接骨木果

2 2 **el·der·ly** /ˋɛldɚlɪ; ˈeldəli/ *adj* **1** old or becoming old 年老的; 漸老的: *an elderly lady with white hair* 白髮的老婦人 —see 見 OLD (USAGE) **2 the elderly** people who are old, especially people who are too old to look after themselves and need special help 老人, 上了年紀的人

elder states·man /ˌ·· ˈ··/ *n* [C] someone old and respected, especially a politician, who people ask for advice because of their knowledge and experience 年高德劭的人〔尤指政界元老〕

el·dest /ˋɛldɪst; ˈeldʒst/ *adj* **1 eldest son/sister/child etc** the oldest son, etc among a group of people, especially brothers and sisters 長子/大姐/年齡最大的孩子等: *Her eldest child is at university now.* 她最大的孩子已經上大學了。**2 the eldest** the oldest one in a group of people, especially brothers and sisters〔尤指兄弟姐妹中〕年齡最大者: *I have two brothers – I'm the eldest.* 我有兩個兄弟, 我是老大。

2 3 **e·lect¹** /ɪˋlɛkt; ɪˈlekt/ *v* **1** [T] to choose someone for an official position by voting 選舉, 推選: *the country's first democratically elected government* 該國第一個民主選舉的政府 | **elect sb to** *She was elected to Parliament in 1978.* 她於1978 年入選議會。| **elect sb president/mayor etc** *Ronald Reagan was first elected President in 1980.* 朗奴·列根於1980年首次當選總統。**2 elect to do sth** *formal* to choose to do something【正式】選擇做某事: *Purchasers can elect to pay in monthly instalments.* 購買者可選擇逐月分期付款。

elect² *adj* **president/governor/prime minister elect** the person who has been elected as president etc, but who has not yet officially started their job 候任總統/已當選尚未就任的州長/候任首相

2 1 **e·lec·tion** /ɪˋlɛkʃən; ɪˈlekʃən/ *n* **1** [C] an occasion when people vote to choose someone for an official position 選舉: *The Socialists won the 1948 election by a huge majority.* 社會黨在1948年選舉中以很大的優勢獲勝。**2** [singular] the fact of being elected to an official position 當選: *Within three months of his election he was forced to resign.* 當選後不到三個月他就被迫辭職。—see also 另見 GENERAL ELECTION

e·lec·tion·eer·ing /ɪˌlɛkʃənˋɪrɪŋ; ɪˌlekʃəˈnɪərɪŋ/ *n* [U] speeches and other activities intended to persuade people to vote for a particular person or political party 競選活動, 拉票活動

e·lec·tive¹ /ɪˋlɛktɪv; ɪˈlektɪv/ *adj formal*【正式】**1** an elective position or organization is one for which there is an election〔職位或組織〕由選舉產生的 **2** elective medical treatment is treatment that you choose to have, although you do not have to〔治療〕非必須的

elective² *n* [C] *AmE* a course that you can choose to study because you are interested in it, while you are studying for a degree in a different subject【美】選修課

e·lec·tor /ɪˋlɛktɚ; ɪˈlektə/ *n* [C] someone who has the right to vote in an election 選民, 有選舉權的人: *gradually losing the support of the electors* 逐漸失去選民的支持

e·lec·to·ral /ɪˋlɛktərəl; ɪˈlektərəl/ *adj* [only before noun 僅用於名詞前] connected with elections and voting 選舉的, 與選舉有關的: a *campaign for electoral reform* 倡導改革選舉制度的運動

electoral col·lege /·ˌ··· ˈ··/ *n* [singular] a group of people chosen by the votes of the people in each US state, who come together to elect the President〔由美國各州人民選舉組成的〕總統選舉團

electoral re·gis·ter /·ˌ··· ˈ···/ also 又作 **electoral roll** /·ˌ··· ˈ·/ *n* [C] an official list of the people who are allowed to vote in a particular area 選民名冊

e·lec·to·rate /ɪˋlɛktərɪt; ɪˈlektərʒt/ *n* [singular] all the people in a country who have the right to vote〔一個國家的〕全體選民

E·lec·tra com·plex /ɪˋlɛktrə ˌkɑmplɛks; ɪˈlektrə ˌkɒmpleks/ *n* [C usually singular 一般用單數] *technical* the unconscious sexual feelings that a girl is supposed to have towards her father【術語】戀父情結 —compare 比較 OEDIPUS COMPLEX

e·lec·tric /ɪˋlɛktrɪk; ɪˈlektrɪk/ *adj* **1** an electric machine, light etc works using electricity 用電的, 電動的: *an electric heater* 電熱器 **2 electric current** a flow of electricity 電流 **3** an electric wire, PLUG¹ (1) etc is used for carrying electricity 用來導電的; 帶電的 **4** an electric situation is one in which people are very excited because something important is going to happen 扣人心弦的, 高度刺激的: *The atmosphere in the courtroom was electric.* 法庭上的氣氛十分緊張。

e·lec·tri·cal /ɪˋlɛktrɪkḷ; ɪˈlektrɪkəl/ *adj* related to or connected with electricity 電的, 與電有關的: *I think there's an electrical fault.* 我認為電力出了故障。| *an electrical engineer* 電機工程師 —**electrically** /-kḷɪ; -kli/ *adv*

electrical storm /·ˌ··· ˈ·/ also 又作 **electric storm** /·ˌ·· ˈ·/ *n* [C] a violent storm in which electricity is produced 電暴, 雷暴

electric blan·ket /·ˌ·· ˈ··/ *n* [C] a special BLANKET (=large cloth on a bed) with electric wires in it, used for making the bed warm 電熱毯

electric chair /·ˌ·· ˈ·/ *n* [C usually singular 一般用單數] a chair in which criminals are killed using electricity, in order to punish them for crimes such as murder; used in the US etc 電椅

electric eel /·ˌ·· ˈ·/ *n* [C] a large South American fish that looks like a snake, and can give an electric shock 電鰻

electric eye /·ˌ·· ˈ·/ *n* [C] *informal* a PHOTOELECTRIC CELL【非正式】光電池

el·ec·tri·cian /ɪˌlɛkˋtrɪʃən; ɪˌlekˈtrɪʃən/ *n* [C] someone whose job is to deal with or repair electrical equipment 電工, 電氣技師

e·lec·tri·ci·ty /ɪˌlɛkˋtrɪsətɪ; ɪˌlekˈtrɪsʒti/ *n* [U] **1** the power that is usually used in modern buildings to provide light and to make machines work 電 **2** the supply of electricity to a particular place 電力供應: *The electricity was cut off when we didn't pay the bill.* 我們未付電費, 電力供應被切斷。**3** a feeling of excitement 激情, 強烈感情: *The electricity seemed to have gone out of their relationship.* 他們之間似乎已激情不再。

e·lec·trics /ɪˋlɛktrɪks; ɪˈlektrɪks/ *n* [plural] *BrE* the parts of a machine that use electrical power【英】〔設備中的〕電動部分; 電路: *The car won't start – I think there's something wrong with the electrics.* 汽車發動不起來, 我認為是電路出了問題。

electric shock /·ˌ·· ˈ·/ *n* [C] a sudden shock to your body, caused by electricity 觸電; 電擊

electric shock ther·a·py /·ˌ·· ˈ· ˌ···/ *n* [U] a method of treatment for mental illness that involves sending electricity through someone's brain〔醫治精神病的〕電擊療法

e·lec·tri·fi·ca·tion /ɪˌlɛktrəfəˋkeʃən; ɪˌlektrʒfʒˈkeɪʃən/ *n* [U] the process of changing a railway so that it uses electrical power, or making electricity available in a particular area〔鐵路的〕電氣化;〔向某一地區的〕供電

e·lec·tri·fy /ɪˋlɛktrəˌfaɪ; ɪˈlektrʒfaɪ/ *v* [T] **1** to change a railway so that it uses electrical power, or to make electricity available in a particular area 使〔鐵路〕電氣化; 向〔某一地區〕供電 **2** if a performance or a speech electrifies the people who are watching it, it makes them feel very interested or excited〔表演或演講〕使激動; 使興奮: *Her words had an electrifying effect.* 她的話激動人心。—**electrifying** *adj* —**electrified** *adj*: *electrified fences* 通電的籬笆

electro- /ɪlɛktro; ɪlektrəʊ/ *prefix technical*【術語】**1** concerning or worked by electricity 電的; 與電有關的; 用電的: *to electrocute* (=kill by electricity) 電死; 用電刑處死 | *an electromagnet* 電磁鐵, 電磁體 **2** electric and 電與…的: *electro-chemical* 電化(學)的

e·lec·tro·car·di·o·gram /ɪˌlɛktroˋkɑrdɪəˌgræm; ɪˌlektrəʊˈkɑːdiəgræm/ *n* [C] *technical* an ECG (2)【術語】心電圖

e·lec·tro·car·di·o·graph /ɪˌlɛktroˋkɑrdɪəˌgræf; ɪˌlektrəʊˈkɑːdiəgrɑːf/ *n* [C] *technical* an ECG (1)【術語】心電圖儀

electro-con·vuls·ive ther·a·py /ˌ‚·· ·ˌ·· ˈ···/ *n* [U] ELECTRIC SHOCK THERAPY 電擊療法

e·lec·tro·cute /ɪˋlɛktrəˌkjut; ɪˈlektrəkjuːt/ *v* [T usually passive 一般用被動態] to injure or kill someone by passing electricity through their body 使觸電受傷[身亡]; 用電擊傷[處死]: *An employee was electrocuted on the new equipment.* 一名員工被新設備電死了。—**electrocution** /ɪˌlɛktrəˋkjuʃən; ɪˌlektrəˈkjuːʃən/ *n* [U]

e·lec·trode /ɪˋlɛktrod; ɪˈlektrəʊd/ *n* [C] one of the two points at which electricity enters or leaves a BATTERY (1) or other piece of electrical equipment 電極: *fuel cells with two electrodes* 帶兩個電極的燃料電池

e·lec·tro·en·ceph·a·lo·gram /ɪˌlɛktroɛnˋsɛfələgræm; ɪˌlektrəʊɪnˈsefələgræm/ *n* [C] *technical* an EEG (2)【術語】腦電圖

e·lec·tro·en·ceph·a·lo·graph /ɪˌlɛktroɛnˋsɛfələˌgræf; ɪˌlektrəʊɪnˈsefələgrɑːf/ *n* [C] *technical* an EEG (1)【術語】腦電圖儀

e·lec·trol·y·sis /ɪˌlɛkˋtrɑləsɪs; ɪˌlekˈtrɒlɪ̣sɪ̣s/ *n* [U] **1** *technical* the process of separating a liquid into its chemical parts by passing an electric current through it【術語】電解 **2** the process of using electricity to destroy hair roots and to remove unwanted hairs from your face etc 電蝕除毛

e·lec·tro·lyte /ɪˋlɛktrəˌlaɪt; ɪˈlektrəlaɪt/ *n* [C] a liquid that can be separated into different chemical parts by passing electricity through it 電解液

e·lec·tro·mag·net /ɪˌlɛktroˋmægnɪt; ɪˌlektrəʊˈmægnɪ̣t/ *n* [C] a piece of metal that becomes MAGNETIC (=able to attract metal objects) when an electric current is turned on 電磁體, 電磁鐵 —**electromagnetic** /ɪˌlɛktromægˋnɛtɪk; ɪˌlektrəʊmægˈnetɪk◂/ *adj*

e·lec·tro·mag·ne·tis·m /ɪˌlɛktroˋmægnəˌtɪzəm; ɪˌlektrəʊˈmægnətɪzəm/ *n* [U] *technical* a force caused by the movement and exchange of positively and negatively charged PARTICLES (=bits of material) in atoms【術語】電磁

e·lec·tron /ɪˋlɛktrɑn; ɪˈlektrɒn/ *n* [C] a very small piece of matter that moves around the NUCLEUS (=central part) of an atom 電子: *an electron microscope* 電子顯微鏡

e·lec·tron·ic /ɪˌlɛkˋtrɑnɪk; ɪˌlekˈtrɒnɪk/ *adj* **1** electronic equipment uses things such as chips (CHIP[1] (4a)), TRANSISTORS, or valves (VALVE (3)) that have an effect on the electricity going through a piece of equipment such as a television or computer 電子的, 用電子操作的; 電子器件的: *'smart' electronic car alarms* "智能"汽車電子報警系統 **2** using electronic equipment 使用電子設備的: *electronic music* 電子音樂 —**electronically** /-klɪ; -kli/ *adv*

electronic mail /ˌ····ˈ·/ *n* [U] E-MAIL 電子郵件(系統)

e·lec·tron·ics /ɪˌlɛkˋtrɑnɪks; ɪˌlekˈtrɒnɪks/ *n* [U] **1** the study of making equipment that works electronically 電子學 **2** the industry connected with making electronic equipment 電子工業

e·lec·tro·plate /ɪˋlɛktroˌplet; ɪˈlektrəʊpleɪt/ *v* [T usually passive 一般用被動態] to put a very thin layer of metal onto the surface of an object, using ELECTROLYSIS 電鍍

el·e·gant /ˋɛləgənt; ˈelɪ̣gənt/ *adj* **1** very beautiful and graceful 高雅的, 優美的: *a tall, elegant woman* 身材修長, 舉止優雅的女子 | *elegant handwriting* 優美的書法 **2** an idea or a plan that is elegant is very clever and simple〔想法或計劃〕巧妙的, 簡潔的: *an elegant solution to a problem* 解決問題的簡捷方法 —**elegantly** *adv* —**elegance** *n* [U]

el·e·gi·ac /ɪˋlidʒɪˌæk; ˌelɪ̣ˈdʒaɪək◂/ *adj literary*【文】**1** showing that you feel upset about someone or something that no longer exists 哀悼的; 悲傷的: *He spoke of his childhood in elegiac tones.* 他以悲傷的口吻談他的童年。**2** connected with elegies (ELEGY) 輓歌(體)的: *elegiac verse* 輓詩

el·e·gy /ˋɛlədʒɪ; ˈelɪ̣dʒi/ *n* [C] a poem or song written to show sadness for someone or something that no longer exists 輓歌; 輓詩: *an elegy to Lenny's memory* 緬懷列尼的輓歌

el·e·ment /ˋɛləmənt; ˈelɪ̣mənt/ *n* [C] S2 W1

1 ►CHEMISTRY 化學◄ a simple chemical substance such as CARBON or oxygen that consists of atoms of only one kind 元素 —compare 比較 COMPOUND[1] (1)

2 an element of surprise/danger/doubt etc a small amount of a quality or feeling 少許驚奇/危險/懷疑等: *There's always an element of risk in this kind of investment.* 這類投資中總有點風險。

3 ►PEOPLE 人羣◄ a group of people who form part of a larger group, especially when the rest of the group does not approve of them〔尤指遭團體中他人非議的〕一夥人: *There is a strong right-wing element in the organization.* 該組織中右翼分子眾多。

4 ►PART 部分◄ one part of a whole system, plan, piece of writing etc 部分; 部件: *Rhyme is just one of the elements of his poetry.* 押韻只是他的詩歌特色的一部分。

5 ►WEATHER 天氣◄ the elements [plural] the weather, especially bad weather 天氣〔尤指壞天氣〕: *battling against the elements* 與惡劣天氣搏鬥

6 ►HEATING 加熱◄ the heating part of a piece of electrical equipment such as a KETTLE 電熱元件

7 the elements of sth the most simple things that you have to learn first about a subject 基礎原理; 綱要: *I never managed to understand even the elements of calculus.* 我連微積分的基礎原理也未能掌握。

8 ►EARTH/AIR/FIRE/WATER 土/風/火/水◄ one of the four substances (earth, air, fire, and water) from which people used to believe that everything was made 四元素〔舊時人們認為土、風、火、水是構成一切物質的四大元素〕

9 be in your element to be in a situation that you enjoy, because you are good at it 適得其所, 得心應手: *He's in his element when he's talking to large groups of people.* 面對大羣人講話他很拿手。

10 be out of your element to be in a situation that makes you uncomfortable or unhappy 不得其所, 處於不相宜的環境: *I felt out of my element surrounded by so much finery.* 身處這麼多衣着華麗的人之間, 我感到很不自在。

el·e·men·tal /ˌɛləˋmɛntḷ; ˌelɪ̣ˈmentl◂/ *adj* **1** an elemental feeling exists at the simplest and most basic level〔情感〕固有的, 最基本的: *Love and fear are two of the most elemental human emotions.* 愛和恐懼是人類最基本的兩種情感。**2** *technical* existing as a simple chemical element that has not been combined with anything else【術語】元素的

el·e·men·ta·ry /ˌɛləˋmɛntərɪ; ˌelɪ̣ˈmentəri◂/ *adj* **1** simple or basic 簡單的; 基本的: *You made a very elementary mistake.* 你犯了一個非常簡單的錯誤。**2** [only before noun 僅用於名詞前] concerning the first and easiest part of a subject 基礎的, 初級的: *an elementary coursebook for learners of English* 針對英語初學者的初級課本 **3** [only before noun 僅用於名詞前] *AmE* elementary education is for children between 5 and 11 years old【美】小學的; PRIMARY[1] (2) *BrE*【英】

elementary par·ti·cle /ˌ····· '···/ *n* [C] *technical* one of the types of pieces of matter including ELECTRONS, PROTONS, and NEUTRONS that make up atoms【術語】基本粒子

elementary school /··'··· ˌ·/ *n* [C] **1** a school in the US where basic subjects are taught for the first six years of a child's education〔美國的〕小學 **2** a state school in England or Wales during the late 19th and early 20th century for children aged 5 to 13〔19 世紀後期和 20 世紀初期英格蘭或威爾斯的〕公立小學

el·e·phant /ˋɛləfənt; 'eləfənt/ *n* [C] a very large grey animal with four legs, two TUSKS (=long curved teeth) and a TRUNK (=long nose) that it can use to pick things up 象 —see also 另見 WHITE ELEPHANT

el·e·phan·tine /ˌɛləˋfæntin; ˌeləˈfæntaɪn◂/ *adj formal* slow, heavy, and awkward, like an elephant【正式】〔似象一樣〕遲緩的, 笨重的, 笨拙的: *She climbed the steps with heavy elephantine movements.* 她笨拙地爬上台階。

el·e·vate /ˋɛləˌvet; 'eləveɪt/ *v* [T] **1** *formal* to give someone or something a more important rank or position than they had before【正式】提拔, 晉升: **[+to]** *Both were later elevated to positions of authority.* 兩人後來都被提拔做了領導。**2** *formal* to make someone feel happier and more sensitive【正式】使高興; 使情緒高昂: *The beautiful countryside was enough to elevate her spirits.* 美麗的鄉間景色足以讓她精神煥發。**3** to improve something or make it more important 改進; 提升: *in Japan, where just-in-time delivery has been elevated to an art form* 在日本, 及時送貨已經上升為一種藝術 **4** *technical* to lift someone or something to a higher position【術語】抬高, 舉高: *Elevate the leg.* 抬腿。**5** *technical* to increase the amount, temperature, pressure etc of something【術語】增加[提高]〔數量、溫度、壓力等〕: *These drugs may elevate acid levels in the blood.* 這些藥可能增加血液酸度。

el·e·vat·ed /ˋɛləˌvetɪd; 'eləveɪtəd/ *adj* **1** elevated thoughts, words etc seem to be intelligent or of high moral standard〔思想、話語等〕智慧的; 高尚的: *elevated philosophical language* 充滿智慧的哲學語言 **2** [only before noun 僅用於名詞前] an elevated position or rank is very important〔地位或級別〕高級的; 重要的 **3** higher up than other things 比〔他物〕高的: *From our elevated vantage point we could see the castle.* 從我們這個制高點可以看見城堡。**4** *formal* elevated levels, temperatures etc are higher than normal【正式】〔水平、溫度等〕偏高的

elevated rail·way /ˌ···· '··/ *BrE*【英】, **elevated railroad** *AmE*【美】*n* [C] a railway that runs on a kind of continuous bridge above the streets in a town〔城市裡的〕高架鐵路

el·e·vat·ing /ˋɛləˌvetɪŋ; 'eləveɪtɪŋ/ *adj formal or humorous* making you feel interested in intelligent or moral subjects【正式或幽默】〔使人〕增長知識的, 提高品格的: *beach holiday that you would hardly call an elevating experience* 很難稱得上對加強修養有裨益的海灘度假

el·e·va·tion /ˌɛləˋveʃən; ˌeləˈveɪʃən/ *n* **1** [singular] a height above the level of the sea 海拔: **[+of]** *The observatory is located on Mt Hopkins at an elevation of 2,600m.* 氣象台位於霍普金斯山上, 海拔 2,600 米。**2** [U] *formal* a situation in which someone is given a more important rank or position【正式】提升, 晉升: *His sudden elevation to the Council surprised everyone.* 他突然晉升入理事會使大家都很吃驚。**3** [C,U] *formal* an increase in the amount or level of something【正式】〔數量、水平的〕增加, 升高: *a sudden elevation of blood pressure* 血壓突然升高 **4** [C] *technical* an upright side of a building, as shown in a drawing done by an ARCHITECT (=person who plans buildings)【術語】〔建築的〕立面〔圖〕; 立視圖 *the front elevation of a house* 房子的正面外觀 **5** [C] *technical* the angle made with the HORIZON by pointing a gun【術語】〔槍砲的〕射角, 仰角: *The cannon was fired at an elevation of 60 degrees.* 大砲以 60 度仰角射擊。

el·e·va·tor /ˋɛləˌvetɚ; 'eləveɪtə/ *n* [C] **1** *AmE* a machine that takes people and goods from one level to another in a building【美】電梯; LIFT[2] (1) *BrE*【英】**2** a machine with a moving belt and containers, used for lifting grain and liquids, or for taking things off ships〔運送糧食、液體或卸船的〕升降機, 起卸機

elevator mu·sic /'···· ˌ··/ *n* [U] *AmE informal* the type of music that is played in shops and public places, and is usually thought to be boring【美, 非正式】背景音樂〔在商店等公共場所播放的音樂, 通常被認為很乏味〕

e·lev·en /ɪˋlɛvən; ɪˈlevən/ *number* **1** 11 十一 **2** a team of eleven players in football or CRICKET (2)〔由十一名球員組成的〕足球隊; 板球隊 —**eleventh** *number*

eleven-plus /·ˌ·· '·/ *n* **the eleven-plus** an examination which children in Britain aged 11 took in the past in order to decide what type of education they would have〔英國過去 11 歲兒童參加的〕升中學甄別考試

e·lev·en·ses /ɪˋlɛvənzɪz; ɪˈlevənzəz/ *n* [U] *BrE informal* a cup of coffee or tea and a BISCUIT (1), that you have in the middle of the morning【英, 非正式】上午茶點

e·lev·enth /ɪˋlɛvənθ; ɪˈlevənθ/ *n* [C] **1** one of eleven equal parts of something 十一分之一 **2 the eleventh hour** the last moment before something important happens〔重大事件即將發生前的〕最後一刻, 最後時刻: *War was averted at the eleventh hour.* 戰爭在最後時刻得以避免。

elf /ɛlf; elf/ *n plural* **elves** /ɛlvz; elvz/ [C] an imaginary creature like a small person with pointed ears 小精靈〔傳說中的精靈, 形似小人, 耳尖〕

el·fin /ˋɛlfɪn; 'elfən/ *adj* someone who looks elfin is small and delicate〔指人〕小巧的: *dark hair and a white elfin face* 黑頭髮和白皙的小臉

e·li·cit /ɪˋlɪsɪt; ɪˈlɪsət/ *v* [T] to succeed in getting information or a reaction from someone, especially when this is difficult〔從某人處〕套出〔信息〕; 引起〔某人的反應〕: *My attempts at conversation didn't elicit much response.* 我試圖跟他搭訕, 但他愛理不理的。| **elicit sth from sb** *By patient questioning we managed to elicit enough information from the witnesses.* 經耐心盤問, 我們從目擊者處探得了足夠的信息。—**elicitation** /ɪˌlɪsəˋteʃən; ɪˌlɪsəˈteɪʃən/ *n* [U]

e·lide /ɪˋlaɪd; ɪˈlaɪd/ *v* [T] to leave out the sound of a letter or of a part of a word 省略〔一個字母或音節的〕發音 —**elision** /ɪˋlɪʒən; ɪˈlɪʒən/ *n* [C,U]

el·i·gi·ble /ˋɛlɪdʒəbl̩; 'elədʒəbəl/ *adj* **1** someone who is eligible for something is able or allowed to do it, for example because they are the right age 合格的; 有資格的: **[+for]** *Are you eligible for social security benefits?* 你有資格享受社會福利了嗎? | **eligible to do sth** *Anyone over the age of 18 is eligible to vote.* 超過 18 歲就有選舉資格。**2** rich, attractive, and not married, and therefore desirable for marriage〔作為婚姻對象〕理想的, 合適的: *a rich eligible bachelor* 一個富有的合意的單身漢 —**eligibility** /ˌɛlədʒəˋbɪlɪtɪ; ˌelədʒəˈbɪləti/ *n* [U]

e·lim·i·nate /ɪˋlɪməˌnet; ɪˈlɪməneɪt/ *v* [T] **1** to completely get rid of something that is unnecessary or unwanted 消除, 根除: *Under the agreement, all trade barriers will be eliminated.* 根據該協議, 所有的貿易壁壘都將被消除。| **eliminate sth from** *Police have eliminated Morris from their enquiries.* 警察已將莫里斯排除在調查對象之外。**2** [usually passive 一般用被動態] to defeat a team or person in a competition, so that they no longer take part in it 淘汰: *Our team was eliminated in the first round.* 我們隊第一輪就被淘汰了。**3** to kill someone in order to prevent them from causing trouble 消滅; 鏟除: *a ruthless dictator who eliminated all his rivals* 鏟除所有異己的殘酷的獨裁者

e·lim·i·na·tion /ɪˌlɪməˋneʃən; ɪˌlɪməˈneɪʃən/ *n* [U] **1 ►REMOVAL OF STH 除掉某物◄** the removal or destruction of something 消除, 根除: **[+of]** *the elimination of smallpox with worldwide vaccination* 通過世界範圍

內的接種疫苗消除天花
2 process of elimination a way of discovering the cause of something by carefully examining each possibility until only one is left 排除法: *The identity of the murderer was arrived at by a process of elimination.* 通過排除法, 殺人兇手的身分最終被確定。
3 ▶DEFEAT 失敗◀ the defeat of a team or player in a competition, so that they may no longer take part 淘汰
4 ▶KILLING 殺害◀ a situation in which someone is killed in order to prevent them from causing trouble 消滅, 鏟除: [+of] *the elimination of dissidents* 鏟除持不同政見者
5 ▶BODY PROCESS 身體機能◀ *technical* the process of getting rid of substances that your body no longer needs【術語】排泄

e·lite /ɪˋlit; eɪˈliːt/ *n* [C] **1** a group of people who have a lot of power and influence because they have money, knowledge, or special skills (社會) 精英; 上層人士: *a small privileged elite* 少數特權階層 **2 elite corps/squad/college etc** a group of people that contains the best, most educated etc people of a larger group 精銳軍團; 精英小組/大學等: *an elite corps of officers* 軍官中的精英小組

e·lit·ist /eˋlitɪst; eɪˈliːtɪst/ *adj* based on a system in which small groups of people have a lot of power or advantages 精英統治的: *an elitist education system* 精英教育體制 —**elitism** *n* [U] —**elitist** *n* [C]

e·lix·ir /ɪˋlɪksɚ; ɪˈlɪksə/ *n* **1** [C] *literary* a magical liquid that is supposed to cure people of illness, make them younger etc【文】靈丹妙藥; 不老藥 **2** [C] something that is supposed to solve problems as if by magic〔解決問題的〕靈丹妙藥: *Don't imagine that lowering inflation is an elixir for all our economic ills.* 不要以為降低通貨膨脹是醫治我們所有經濟弊病的靈丹妙藥。

E·liz·a·be·than /ɪˌlɪzəˋbiθən; ɪˌlɪzəˈbiːθən◀/ *adj* connected to the period 1558-1603 when Elizabeth I was queen of England〔英國女王〕伊麗莎白一世時代的: *Elizabethan drama* 伊麗莎白一世時代的戲劇 —**Elizabethan** *n* [C]: *The Earl of Essex was a famous Elizabethan.* 埃塞克斯伯爵是伊麗莎白一世時代的一位名流。

elk /ɛlk; elk/ *n* [C] a very large European and Asian DEER with big flat horns 駝鹿; 麋

el·lipse /ɪˋlɪps; ɪˈlɪps/ *n* [C] a curved shape like a circle, but with two slightly longer and flatter sides 橢圓

el·lip·sis /ɪˋlɪpsɪs; ɪˈlɪpsɪs/ *n plural* **ellipses** /-siz; -siːz/ [C,U] an occasion when words are deliberately left out of a sentence, though the meaning can still be understood〔不影響意義的句子成分的〕省略

el·lip·ti·cal /ɪˋlɪptɪkḷ; ɪˈlɪptɪkəl/ also 又作 **el·lip·tic** /-tɪk; -tɪk/ *adj* **1** having the shape of an ellipse 橢圓的; 橢圓形的: *The earth's orbit is elliptical.* 地球的軌道是橢圓形的。**2** elliptical speech or writing is difficult to understand because more is meant than is actually said〔言辭或文章〕晦澀的, 隱晦的: *an elliptical remark* 隱晦的評論

elm /ɛlm; elm/ *n* [C,U] a type of large tree with broad leaves, or the wood from this tree 榆樹; 榆木

el·o·cu·tion /ˌɛləˋkjuʃən; ˌeləˈkjuːʃən/ *n* [U] good clear speaking in public, involving voice control, pronunciation etc 口齒清晰的演講; 演講術: *elocution lessons* 演講技巧課程 —**elocutionary** *adj* —**elocutionist** *n* [C]

e·lon·gate /ɪˋlɔŋget; ˈiːlɒŋgeɪt/ *v* [I,T] to become longer, or make something longer than normal (使) 拉長 —**elongation** /ɪˌlɔŋˋgeʃən; ˌiːlɒŋˈgeɪʃən/ *n* [C,U]

e·lon·gat·ed /ɪˋlɔŋgetɪd; ˈiːlɒŋgeɪtɪd/ *adj* longer than normal 拉長的, 偏長的: *tribeswomen with rings around their elongated necks* 拉長的脖子上戴着項圈的部落婦女

e·lope /ɪˋlop; ɪˈləʊp/ *v* [I] to leave your home secretly in order to get married 私奔 —**elopement** *n* [C,U]

el·o·quent /ˋɛləkwənt; ˈeləkwənt/ *adj* **1** able to express your ideas and opinions well, especially in a way that influences people 雄辯的, 能言善辯的: *an eloquent appeal for support* 能打動人心的求助呼籲 **2** showing a feeling or meaning without using words 清楚表明的; 形象地顯示的: *The photographs are an eloquent reminder of the horrors of war.* 這些照片形象地提醒人們不要忘記戰爭的恐怖。—**eloquently** *adv* —**eloquence** *n* [U]

else /ɛls; els/ *adv* **1 who/what/why etc else** or **anything/ someone/anywhere etc else a)** besides or in addition to someone, something etc 另外, 其他: *I've said I'm sorry. What else can I do?* 我已經說過對不起了, 我還能做甚麼呢? | *Who else was at the party?* 出席晚會的還有甚麼人? | *Do you want anything else to eat?* 你還要吃點別的嗎? **b)** apart from or instead of something, someone etc 除去; 其他: *Everyone else but me was invited.* 除我之外, 其他人都被邀請了。| *In the end she married somebody else.* 結果她嫁給了別人。| *It's not in my drawer, where else could it be?* 它不在我的抽屜裡, 可又能在哪兒呢? **2 or else** or otherwise 否則, 要不: *You must pay £100 or else go to prison.* 你必須付 100英鎊, 否則就得入獄。| *Your book must be here, or else you've lost it.* 你的書應該在這裡, 要不就是你弄丢了。 1 1

Frequencies of the word **else** in spoken and written English 單詞else在英語口語和書面語中的使用頻率

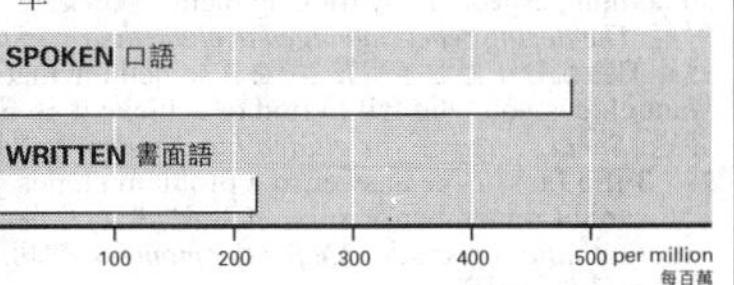

Based on the British National Corpus and the Longman Lancaster Corpus
據英國國家語料庫和朗文蘭卡斯特語料庫

This graph shows that the word **else** is much more common in spoken English than in written English. This is because it is used a lot in questions and is used in some common spoken phrases. 本圖表顯示, else 一詞在英語口語中使用的頻率要大大高於書面語, 因為它大量用於疑問句和一些常見口語片語中。

else (*adv*) **SPOKEN PHRASES**
含 else 的口語片語

3 anything else? used to ask someone if they want to buy another thing, say another thing etc 還要別的嗎; 還有別的嗎?: *"Twenty Marlborough and a box of matches please." "Anything else?" "No, thanks."* "請來一包二十支裝的萬寶路煙和一包火柴。" "還要別的嗎?" "不要了, 謝謝。" **4 there's nothing else** used to say that the thing you have mentioned is the only one that exists, is possible etc 沒有別的; 沒有其他可能〔用來表示你剛才所提的是唯一存在或可能的〕: *You'll have to have bread and cheese. There's nothing else, I'm afraid.* 你只好吃麵包和乾酪, 恐怕別的甚麼也沒有。| *The club was closed, so we just went home. There was nothing else to do.* 俱樂部關門了, 所以我們只好回家, 因為別無他事可做。 **5 what else?/who else?/where else? etc** used to say that it is obvious that the thing, person, place etc that has been mentioned is the only one possible 還能有別的甚麼/甚麼人/甚麼地方?〔用來表示你剛才提及的事物、人、地方等是顯而易見的唯一可能〕: *"Are you giving him computer games for his birthday?" "Of course, what else?"* "你準備送他電腦遊戲作生日禮物嗎?" "當然, 要不還能送甚麼?" **6 what else can you do/say?** used to say that it is impossible to do or say anything apart from what you have mentioned 你還能做/說甚麼?: *I had to give it to her. What else could I do?* 我只能把那給她, 還能怎麼辦呢? **7 or else** used to threaten someone 要不然〔用

於表示威脅〕: *You'd better do it, or else!* 你最好去做，要不然夠你受的！**8 if nothing else** used to say that something is worth doing, good for you etc for one reason, even if there are no other reasons 起碼，即使不是出於別的原因〔表示某事值得做或有好處〕: *He said that if nothing else, teaching taught him how to deal with people.* 他說教書起碼讓他學會了如何與人打交道。

2 2 **else·where** /ˋɛlsˏhwɛr; elsˈweə/ *adv* in or to another place 在別處; 去別處: *outbreaks of rioting elsewhere in the region* 該地區別處爆發的騷亂

ELT /ˏi ɛl ˋti; ˌiː el ˈtiː/ *n* [U] *especially BrE* English Language Teaching; the teaching of the English language to people whose first language is not English【尤英】英語（語言）教學;〔英語並非母語的〕英語教學

e·lu·ci·date /ɪˋlusəˏdet; ɪˈluːsɪ̈deɪt/ *v* [I,T] *formal* to explain something that is difficult to understand very clearly, by providing more information【正式】闡明，解釋: *His theory is further elucidated in a series of articles published between 1976 and 1980.* 他的理論在1976年至1980年發表的一系列文章中得到了進一步闡述。—**elucidation** /ɪˏlusəˋdeʃən; ɪˌluːsɪ̈ˈdeɪʃən/ *n* [C,U] **elucidatory** /ɪˋlusədəˏtorɪ; ɪˈluːsɪ̈deɪtəri/ *adj*

e·lude /ɪˋlud; ɪˈluːd/ *v* [T] **1** to escape from someone or something, especially by tricking them〔機敏地〕逃避，躲避: *The fleeing rebels managed to elude their pursuers.* 逃跑的叛亂分子擺脫了追蹤者。**2** if something that you want eludes you, you fail to find or achieve it 找不到，錯過: *Success had so far eluded him.* 成功至今與他無緣。**3** if a fact or the answer to a problem eludes you, you cannot remember or solve it 忘記; 把...難倒: *The exact terminology eludes me for the moment.* 確切的術語我一時想不起來。

e·lu·sive /ɪˋlusɪv; ɪˈluːsɪv/ *adj* **1** an elusive person or animal is difficult to find or not often seen〔人或動物〕難找的; 常見不到的: *an elusive man who was never in his office* 從來不在辦公室的一個難找的人 **2** an elusive result is difficult to achieve 困難的，難實現的: *Success in the business world has so far proved elusive.* 到目前為止，想在商界獲得成功仍是困難重重。**3** an elusive idea or quality is difficult to describe or understand 難以表述的; 難懂的: *The meaning of the poem was somewhat elusive.* 這首詩的含義有點難以捉摸。—**elusively** *adv* —**elusiveness** *n* [U]

elves /ɛlvz; elvz/ *n* the plural of ELF

'em /əm; əm/ *pron spoken* sometimes used as a short form of 'them'【口】有時用作 them 的縮約形式: *Go on, Bill, you tell 'em!* 你說吧，比爾，告訴他們！

em- /ɪm; ɪm/ *prefix* the form used for EN- before b, m, or p en- 的變體，用在字母 b, m, p 之前: *an embittered man* (=made bitter) 一個痛苦的男人 | *empowerment* 授權

e·ma·ci·a·ted /ɪˋmeʃɪˏetɪd; ɪˈmeɪʃieɪtɪ̈d/ *adj* extremely thin from lack of food or illness〔因飢餓或疾病〕極其消瘦的，憔悴的: *The prisoners were ill and emaciated.* 囚犯們疾病纏身，骨瘦如柴。—**emaciation** /ɪˏmeʃɪˋeʃən; ɪˌmeɪʃiˈeɪʃən/ *n* [U]: *in an advanced state of emaciation* 處於極其瘦弱的狀態

e-mail /ˋi mel; ˈiː meɪl/ *n* [U] a system that allows people to send messages to each other by computer; ELECTRONIC MAIL 電子郵件系統; 電子郵件 —**e-mail** *v* [T] *Will you e-mail me about it?* 你能就此事給我發個電子郵件嗎? —see picture on page A14 參見A14頁圖

em·a·nate /ˋɛməˏnet; ˈeməneɪt/ *v*

emanate from sth *phr v* [T not in passive 不用被動態] to flow or come from 散發自; 來自: *Delicious smells emanated from the kitchen.* 從廚房散發出誘人的香味。—**emanation** /ˏɛməˋneʃən; ˌeməˈneɪʃən/ *n* [C,U]

e·man·ci·pate /ɪˋmænsəˏpet; ɪˈmænsɪ̈peɪt/ *v* [T] *formal* to make someone free from social, political, or legal restrictions that limit what they can do【正式】解放，使不受〔社會、政治或法律的〕束縛: *Learning will emancipate the oppressed and engender social change.* 知識可以解放受壓迫者，引發社會變革。—**emancipation** /ɪˏmænsəˋpeʃən; ɪˌmænsɪ̈ˈpeɪʃən/ *n* [U] *the emancipation of slaves* 奴隸的解放

e·man·ci·pat·ed /ɪˋmænsəˏpetɪd; ɪˈmænsɪ̈peɪtɪ̈d/ *adj* **1** socially, politically, or legally free 解放了的; 不受束縛的 **2** an emancipated woman is not influenced by old-fashioned ideas about how women should behave〔婦女〕思想解放的，不受傳統觀念束縛的

e·mas·cu·late /ɪˋmæskjəˏlet; ɪˈmæskjɪ̈leɪt/ *v* [T often passive 常用被動態] **1** to make someone or something weaker or less effective 使衰弱; 使效力減弱: *The bill has been emasculated by Congress.* 國會削弱了這個法案的效力。**2** to make a man feel less male 使缺少男子氣: *Some men feel emasculated if they work for a woman.* 在女人手下工作，有些男人會覺得沒有男子氣。**3** *technical* to remove all or part of a male's sex organs; CASTRATE【術語】閹割; 去勢 —**emasculation** /ɪˏmæskjəˋleʃən; ɪˌmæskjɪ̈ˈleɪʃən/ *n* [U]

em·balm /ɪmˋbɑm; ɪmˈbɑːm/ *v* [T] to treat a dead body with chemicals, oils etc to prevent it from decaying〔用藥物、油等對屍體〕進行防腐處理: *ancient Egyptian embalming techniques* 古埃及防腐術 —**embalmer** *n* [C]

em·bank·ment /ɪmˋbæŋkmənt; ɪmˈbæŋkmənt/ *n* [C] **1** a wide wall of stones or earth built to keep the water in a river from flowing over its banks, or to support a road or railway over low ground 河堤; 路堤 **2** a slope of earth, stone etc that rises from either side of a railway or road〔鐵路、公路的〕堤坡

em·bar·go¹ /ɪmˋbɑrgo; ɪmˈbɑːgəʊ/ *n plural* **embargoes** [C] an official order stopping trade with another country 貿易禁令; 禁運: **put/impose an embargo on** *an embargo imposed on wheat exports* 小麥出口禁令 | **trade/oil/arms etc embargo** *They're accused of trying to break the oil embargo.* 他們被指控試圖違反石油禁運的規定。| **[+on]** *an embargo on wheat exports* 小麥出口禁運

embargo² *v* [T] to stop trade with another country by an official order 禁止〔與另一國家〕通商; 下令禁運: *a decision to embargo the Southern States* 對南方各州實行禁運的決定

em·bark /ɪmˋbɑrk; ɪmˈbɑːk/ *v* [I,T] to get onto a ship or put or take something onto a ship 上船; 裝船; 使上船; 裝載 —opposite 反義詞 DISEMBARK —**embarkation** /ˏɛmbɑrˋkeʃən; ˌembɑːˈkeɪʃən/ *n* [C,U]

embark on/upon sth *phr v* [T] to start something, especially something new and difficult that will take a long time 開始，着手〔尤指新的、有難度且費時的事〕: *In the 1950s China embarked on a major program of industrialization.* 20世紀50年代，中國開始實施工業化的一項重大計劃。

em·bar·rass /ɪmˋbærəs; ɪmˈbærəs/ *v* [T] **1** to make someone feel anxious, ashamed, or uncomfortable, especially in a social situation〔尤指在社交場合〕使尷尬，使窘迫: *The old woman's blunt questions embarrassed her, making her momentarily tongue-tied.* 老婦人不客氣地提出一些問題，使她尷尬，一時語塞。**2** to do something that causes problems for a government, political organization, or politician 為〔政府、政治組織或政治人物〕出難題; 使...陷入困境: *a series of revelations that has embarrassed the government* 使政府難堪的一系列曝光事件

em·bar·rassed /ɪmˋbærəst; ɪmˈbærəst/ *adj* **1** ashamed, nervous, or uncomfortable in a social situation 難堪的，尷尬的: *I managed to spill water on one of the guests – I was so embarrassed!* 我竟把水灑到一名客人身上，我難堪極了！| *an embarrassed smile* 尷尬的笑 | **[+about]** *At about the age of twelve, girls start feeling acutely embarrassed about changing their clothes in front of other people.* 大約到十二歲時，女孩子便開始對當着別人的面換衣服感到極不自在。—see 見 SHAME¹ (USAGE) **2 financially embarrassed** having no money or having debts 拮据的, 負債的

em·bar·ras·sing /ɪmˋbærəsɪŋ; ɪm'bærəsɪŋ/ *adj* making you feel ashamed, nervous, or uncomfortable 令人尷尬的, 使人難堪的: *The firm wants to avoid any embarrassing questions about its finances.* 這家公司力圖迴避有關財務方面的任何難堪問題。—**embarrassingly** *adv*

em·bar·rass·ment /ɪmˋbærəsmənt; ɪm'bærəsmənt/ *n* **1** [U] the feeling you have when you are embarrassed 窘迫; 尷尬: **[+at]** *He could not hide his embarrassment at his children's rudeness.* 他無法掩飾孩子們的無禮給他帶來的難堪。**2** [C] an event that causes a government, political organization etc problems 使〔政府或政治機構等〕為難的事: *The allegations have been an embarrassment to the administration.* 指控令當局頭痛。**3** [C] someone who behaves in a way that makes you feel ashamed and uncomfortable 使人難堪的人, 令人不快的人: **[+to]** *His mother's boasting was an embarrassment to him.* 母親的吹嘘令他無地自容。**4 financial embarrassment** debts or a lack of money that causes problems for you 欠賬, 拮据 **5 embarrassment of riches** so many good things that it is difficult to decide which one you want 〔好東西〕多得不知道選哪個好

em·bas·sy /ˋɛmbəsɪ; 'embəsi/ *n* [C] **1** a group of officials who represent their government in a foreign country 大使館全體外交官員 **2** the official building used by these officials 大使館: *the American Embassy in Paris* 巴黎的美國大使館

em·bat·tled /ɪmˋbætḷd; ɪm'bætld/ *adj formal*【正式】**1** surrounded by enemies, especially in war or fighting〔尤指在戰爭或打鬥中〕被敵人包圍的: *Their embattled army finally surrendered.* 他們那陷入包圍的軍隊最終投降了。**2** an embattled person, organization, etc has many problems or difficulties 問題纏身的; 困難重重的: *embattled companies fighting off takeover bids* 抵制競價收購的內外交困的公司

em·bed /ɪmˋbɛd; ɪm'bed/ *v* **embedded, embedding** [T usually passive 一般用被動態] **1** to fix something firmly and deeply in a surface or solid object 把…嵌入; 把…插入: **[+in]** *Small stones were embedded in the ice.* 冰裡嵌了許多小石子。**2** if ideas, attitudes, or feelings etc are embedded, you believe or feel them very strongly 深信, 強烈感受〔思想、態度、感情等〕: *deeply embedded feelings of shame* 揮之不去的羞愧感

em·bel·lish /ɪmˋbɛlɪʃ; ɪm'belɪʃ/ *v* [T] **1** to make a story or statement more interesting by adding details that are not true 給〔故事或敘述〕添枝加葉; 對…加以渲染: *She gave an embellished account of what had happened.* 她添油加醋地把發生的事描述了一番。**2** to make something more beautiful by adding decorations 裝飾, 修飾: **[+with]** *The ceiling was embellished with cherubs.* 天花板上裝飾着小天使的圖案。—**embellishment** *n* [C,U]

em·ber /ˋɛmbɚ; 'embə/ *n* [C usually plural 一般用複數] a piece of wood or coal in a fire that is no longer burning but is still red and very hot〔木塊或煤塊的〕餘燼: *glowing embers* 發光的餘燼

em·bez·zle /ɪmˋbɛzḷ; ɪm'bezəl/ *v* [I,T] to steal money from the place where you work 貪污; 侵吞: *She had embezzled $10,000 by falsifying the accounts.* 她通過做假賬侵吞了一萬美元。—**embezzlement** *n* [U] —**embezzler** *n* [C]

em·bit·ter /ɪmˋbɪtɚ; ɪm'bɪtə/ *v* [T] to make someone feel hate and anger for a long time because they think they have been treated unfairly 使怨恨, 使怨憤: *The incident had embittered relations between the two countries.* 該事件使兩國失和。—**embittered** *adj*

em·bla·zon /ɛmˋblezn̩; ɪm'bleɪzən/ *v* [T] **1** to put a name, design etc on something so that it can easily be seen 在…上明顯地刻上名字[標記等]: *The manufacturer's name was emblazoned on the packet.* 包裝上明顯標有生產廠家的名字。**2** to decorate a SHIELD[1] (2) or flag with a COAT OF ARMS 用紋章裝飾〔盾形紋徽、旗〕

em·blem /ˋɛmbləm; 'embləm/ *n* [C] **1** a picture or shape that is used to represent a country, group etc〔用來代表國家或團體等的〕標誌, 徽章; 紋章: **[+of]** *The national emblem of England is a rose.* 英格蘭的標誌是一朵玫瑰花。—see picture at 參見 SIGN[1] 圖 **2** something that represents an idea or principle〔代表一種觀念或原則的〕標誌; 象徵: **[+of]** *Expensive cars are seen as an emblem of success.* 豪華汽車被看成是成功的標誌。—compare 比較 SYMBOL (3)

em·ble·mat·ic /ˌɛmbləˋmætɪk; ˌembləˈmætɪk◂/ *adj formal* seeming to represent or be a sign of something【正式】象徵性的; 標誌性的—**emblematically** /-kḷɪ; -kli/ *adv*

em·bod·i·ment /ɪmˋbɑdɪmənt; ɪm'bɒdɪmənt/ *n* **the embodiment of** someone or something that represents or is very typical of an idea or quality 化身, 體現: *He is the embodiment of evil.* 他是邪惡的化身。

em·bod·y /ɪmˋbɑdɪ; ɪm'bɒdi/ *v* [T] **1** if a person, thing, or organization embodies an idea or principle it clearly expresses it and shows its importance by the way it behaves or affects behaviour 體現〔思想、原則〕: *The country's constitution embodies the ideals of equality and freedom.* 這個國家的憲法體現了平等和自由的理想。**2** *formal* to include something【正式】包括, 收錄: *Their latest car model embodies many new improvements.* 他們的最新一款車型包含了許多新的改進。

em·bold·en /ɪmˋboldn̩; ɪm'bəʊldən/ *v* [T] *formal* to give someone more courage【正式】使有膽量, 使(較)勇敢: *Emboldened by her smile, he asked her to dance.* 她的微笑給他壯了膽, 於是他邀請她跳舞。

em·bo·lis·m /ˋɛmbəˌlɪzəm; 'embəlɪzəm/ *n* [C] *technical* something such as a hard mass of blood or a small amount of air that blocks a tube carrying blood through the body【術語】〔血管的〕栓塞, 血栓: *a coronary embolism* 冠狀動脈血栓

em·boss /ɪmˋbɔs; ɪm'bɒs/ *v* [T usually passive 一般用被動態] to make a raised pattern on the surface of metal, paper, leather etc 在〔金屬、紙或皮革等〕表面上用浮雕圖案裝飾: **emboss sth with** *The firm's paper is embossed with its name and address.* 公司的信紙上凸印有公司的名稱和地址。—**embossed** *adj*

em·brace[1] /ɪmˋbres; ɪm'breɪs/ *v* **1** [I,T] to put your arms around someone and hold them in a friendly or loving way 抱, 擁抱: *She embraced her son tenderly.* 她溫柔地擁抱着兒子。**2** [T] *formal* to include something as part of a subject, discussion etc【正式】包括, 涉及: *This course embraces several different aspects of psychology.* 這門課程涉及心理學的幾個不同方面。**3** [T] *formal* to accept and use new ideas, opinions etc eagerly【正式】欣然接受, 採納 **4** [T] *formal* to start to believe in a religion or political system【正式】〔開始〕信奉; 皈依: *She embraced the Muslim faith.* 她皈依伊斯蘭教。—see also 另見 ALL-EMBRACING

embrace[2] *n* [C] the act of holding someone close to you as a sign of love 擁抱: *The lovers were in a close embrace.* 這對情人緊緊擁抱在一起。

em·bro·ca·tion /ˌɛmbroˋkeʃən; ˌembrəˈkeɪʃən/ *n* [C,U] *formal* a liquid medicine that you rub on a part of your body that is stiff or ACHING after too much exercise【正式】擦劑〔用於揉搓因運動過度導致的僵硬或脹疼部位〕

em·broi·der /ɪmˋbrɔɪdɚ; ɪm'brɔɪdə/ *v* **1** [I,T] to make a pattern of stitches on cloth with coloured cotton or silk threads 刺繡, 在…上刺繡: *The dress was embroidered with flowers.* 那件裙子上繡着花。—see picture on page A16 參見A16頁圖 **2** [T] to make a story or report of events more interesting or exciting by adding details, that you have invented; EMBELLISH (1) 對〔故事或報道〕加以渲染 —**embroidered** *adj*: *richly embroidered* 大加渲染的

em·broi·der·y /ɪmˋbrɔɪdərɪ; ɪm'brɔɪdəri/ *n* **1** [C,U] a decoration or pattern made by sewing onto cloth, or the act of making this 刺繡(法) **2** [U] imaginary details that are added to make a story seem more interesting or exciting 誇張之詞; 渲染成分: *I just want the truth from*

E

you, with no embroidery. 我只想你告訴我真相，不要添枝加葉。

embroidery hoop *n* [C] a circular wooden frame used to hold cloth firmly in place while patterns are being SEWN into it; TAMBOUR〔刺繡用的〕綳圈

em·broil /ɛmˋbrɔɪl; ɪmˈbrɔɪl/ *v* [T usually passive 一般用被動態] to involve someone in a difficult situation 使〔某人〕捲入〔困境〕: **embroil sb/sth in** *Soon they were embroiled in a fierce argument.* 很快他們就捲入了一場激烈的爭論。

em·bry·o /ˋɛmbrɪˌo; ˈembriəʊ/ *n plural* **embryos** [C] **1** an animal or human that has not yet been born, and is in its first state of development in the mother's body 胚，胚胎 —compare 比較 FOETUS **2 in embryo** not yet complete, but still developing 在胚胎階段; 萌芽的, 未成熟的: *His plans were still in embryo.* 他的計劃仍在醞釀中。

em·bry·ol·o·gy /ˌɛmbrɪˋɑlədʒɪ; ˌembriˈɒlədʒi/ *n* [U] the scientific study of embryos 胚胎學 —**embryologist** *n* [C]

em·bry·on·ic /ˌɛmbrɪˋɑnɪk; ˌembriˈɒnɪk◂/ *adj* in an undeveloped or very early stage of growth 萌芽階段的, 剛起步的: *Britain's embryonic wind energy industry* 英國剛剛起步的利用風能的工業

em·cee, MC /ˌɛmˋsi; ˌemˈsiː/ *n* [C] *AmE* someone who is in charge of a social event or programme and introduces various people or performers; MASTER OF CEREMONIES【美】司儀; 節目主持人: *She's emcee of her radio show.* 她為自己的廣播節目擔任主持。—**emcee** *v* [I,T]

e·mend /ɪˋmɛnd; ɪˈmend/ *v* [T] to take the mistakes out of something that has been written, before it is printed〔付印前〕校訂〔文稿〕, 修改〔作品〕—compare 比較 AMEND —**emendation** /ˌimɛnˋdeʃən; ˌiːmenˈdeɪʃən/ *n* [C, U]

em·e·rald¹ /ˋɛmərəld; ˈemərəld/ *n* [C] a bright green stone that is valuable and often used in jewellery 翡翠, 綠寶石

2 **emerald²** *adj* bright green 翠綠色的 —see picture on page A5 參見 A5 頁圖

e·merge /ɪˋmɝdʒ; ɪˈmɜːdʒ/ *v* [I] **1** to appear or come out from somewhere 浮現, 出現: **[+from]** *The sun emerged from behind the clouds.* 太陽從雲層後露了出來。**2** if facts emerge, they become known after being hidden or secret 顯露, 暴露: *Eventually the truth emerged.* 終於真相大白。| **it emerged that** *Later it emerged that the judge had been employing an illegal immigrant.* 後來情況明朗了, 那個法官一直雇用着一名非法移民。**3** to come to the end of a difficult experience〔從困境中〕擺脫出來, 出頭: **[+from]** *She emerged from the divorce a stronger person.* 她走出離婚的陰影, 變得更堅強了。**4** to begin to be known or noticed 開始被人所知; 興起: *a religious sect that emerged in the 1830s* 興起於 19 世紀 30 年代的一個宗教派別 —**emergence** *n* [U]: *Japan's emergence as a world leader* 日本漸成世界大國

2 3 **e·mer·gen·cy** /ɪˋmɝdʒənsɪ; ɪˈmɜːdʒənsi/ *n* [C] an unexpected and dangerous situation that must be dealt with immediately 緊急情況, 不測事件: *Lifeguards are trained to deal with emergencies.* 救生員接受過處理緊急情況的訓練。| **emergency meeting/repairs/exit etc** (=needed to deal with an urgent and unexpected problem) 緊急會議/搶修/太平門 *He called an emergency meeting of the governors.* 他召集州長召開緊急會議。| *Emergency exits are clearly marked.* 太平門的標誌很明顯。—see also 另見 STATE OF EMERGENCY

emergency brake /-ˈ··· ˌ·/ *n* [C] *AmE* a piece of equipment in a car that you pull up with your hand to stop the car from moving【美】〔汽車〕手閘; HANDBRAKE *especially BrE*【尤英】

emergency cord /-ˈ··· ·/ *n* [C] *AmE* a chain that a passenger pulls to stop a train in an emergency【美】〔火車上的〕緊急制動索; COMMUNICATION CORD *BrE*【英】

emergency room /-ˈ··· ˌ·/ *n* [C] *AmE* a place in a hospital where people who have been hurt in accidents are taken for treatment【美】〔醫院的〕急救室, 急症室; CASUALTY (3) *BrE*【英】

emergency services /-ˈ··· ˌ···/ [plural] *BrE* the official organizations, for example the police, that deal with crime, fires, and injuries【英】〔警方等處理犯罪、火災、傷害的〕緊急應變機構

e·mer·gent /ɪˋmɝdʒənt; ɪˈmɜːdʒənt/ *adj* [only before noun 僅用於名詞前] in the early stages of existence or development 新出現的; 處於萌芽階段的: *the emergent nations of the world* 世界上新近建立的國家

e·mer·ging /ɪˋmɝdʒɪŋ; ɪˈmɜːdʒɪŋ/ *adj* [only before noun 僅用於名詞前] in an early state of development 新興的, 發展初期的: *the emerging Thai auto industry* 新興的泰國汽車工業

e·mer·i·tus /ɪˋmɛrətəs; ɪˈmerɪtəs/ *adj* an emeritus PROFESSOR (=university teacher) is no longer working but still has an official title〔大學教師〕退休後仍保留頭銜的, 榮譽退休的

em·e·ry /ˋɛmərɪ; ˈeməri/ *n* [U] a very hard mineral that is used for polishing things and making them smooth 金剛砂

emery board /ˈ··· ·/ *n* [C] a long narrow piece of stiff paper with emery on it, used for shaping your nails 指甲砂銼

e·met·ic /ɪˋmɛtɪk; ɪˈmetɪk/ *n* [C] *technical* something that you eat or drink in order to make yourself VOMIT (=bring up food from your stomach)【術語】催吐劑

em·i·grant /ˋɛməgrənt; ˈemɪgrənt/ *n* [C] someone who leaves their own country to live in another〔移居外國的〕移民 —compare 比較 IMMIGRANT

em·i·grate /ˋɛməˌgret; ˈemɨgreɪt/ *v* [I] to leave your own country in order to live in another 移居外國: *Her family emigrated to America in the 1850s.* 她的家人於 19 世紀 50 年代移居美國。—**emigration** /ˌɛməˋgreʃən; ˌemɨˈgreɪʃən/ *n* [C,U]

ém·i·gré /ˋɛməˌgre; ˈemɪgreɪ/ *n* [C] *French* someone who leaves their own country to live in another, usually for political reasons【法】〔通常指因政治原因移居國外的〕流亡者: *Russian émigrés living in Paris* 住在巴黎的俄國流亡者

em·i·nence /ˋɛmənəns; ˈemɪnəns/ *n* **1** [U] the quality of being famous and important 傑出, 卓越: *a scientist of great eminence* 出類拔萃的科學家 **2** [C] *formal* a hill or area of high ground【正式】山丘; 高地 **3 Eminence** a title used when talking to or about a CARDINAL (=priest of high rank in the Roman Catholic Church) 閣下, 大人〔對天主教紅衣主教的尊稱〕: *Their Eminences are discussing the matter.* 主教大人們正在討論那件事。

em·i·nent /ˋɛmənənt; ˈemɪnənt/ *adj* an eminent person is famous and admired by many people〔指人〕傑出的, 顯赫的: *an eminent lawyer* 傑出的律師 —see 見 FAMOUS (USAGE)

eminent do·main /ˌ··· ·ˈ·/ *n* [U] *technical* the right of the US government to take private land for public use【術語】〔美國政府對私有土地的〕徵用權

em·i·nent·ly /ˋɛmənəntlɪ; ˈemɪnəntli/ *adv formal approving* to a very high degree; perfectly【正式, 褒】非常; 完全: *eminently qualified for the job* 完全有資格做這項工作

e·mir /əˋmɪr; eˈmɪə/ *n* [C] a Muslim ruler, especially in Asia and parts of Africa 埃米爾〔尤指亞洲和非洲部分地區的穆斯林統治者〕: *the emir of Kano in Nigeria* 尼日利亞卡諾的埃米爾

e·mir·ate /əˋmɪrɪt; ˈemɪrɨt/ *n* [C] the position or country of an emir 埃米爾的職位; 酋長國

em·is·sa·ry /ˋɛməˌsɛrɪ; ˈemɨsəri/ *n* [C] someone who is sent with an official message or to do special work, often secretly 使者; 特使; 密使: *a special emissary of the ayatollah*〔伊斯蘭教什葉派領袖〕阿亞圖拉的特使

e·mis·sion /ɪˋmɪʃən; ɪˈmɪʃən/ *n* **1** [C] an amount of gas or other substance that a machine or factory produces and sends into the air〔機器或工廠的〕排氣; 排放物: *Britain has agreed to cut emissions of nitrogen oxide from power stations.* 英國同意減少發電站一氧化氮的排放量。| *emissions of CFCs* 含氯氟烴的排放物 **2** [U] the sending out of light, heat, gas etc〔光、熱、氣等的〕散發

e·mit /ɪˋmɪt; ɪ'mɪt/ *v* **emitted, emitting** [T] **1** to send out heat, light, gas etc 散發〔熱、光、氣等〕: *The chimney emitted clouds of smoke.* 煙囱裡冒出一團團的煙霧。**2** to make a particular kind of sound 發出〔聲響〕: *recording the whistles emitted by dolphins* 記錄海豚發出的叫聲

e·mol·li·ent /ɪˋmɑljənt; ɪ'mɒliənt/ *n* [C] *formal*【正式】**1** a substance that makes your skin softer and reduces pain 潤膚劑, 護膚劑: *This is a powerful emollient against sunburn.* 這是防止曬傷的有效護膚劑。**2 emollient words/phrases etc** emollient words etc make you feel calmer when you have been angry 安撫的話語等

e·mol·u·ment /ɪˋmɑljəmənt; ɪ'mɒljᵿmənt/ *n* [C] *formal* money or another form of payment for work you have done【正式】酬金; 酬勞

3 **e·mo·tion** /ɪˋmoʃən; ɪ'məʊʃən/ *n* [C,U] a strong human feeling such as love, hate, anger etc 強烈的情感; 激情: *A mixture of emotions welled up inside him as she spoke.* 當她講話時, 他百感交集。| *The accused man showed little sign of emotion as he was sentenced.* 宣判時被告並沒有多少表情。

3 **e·mo·tion·al** /ɪˋmoʃənḷ; ɪ'məʊʃənəl/ *adj* **1** making people have strong feelings or opinions 令人激動的; 敏感
3 的: *Abortion is a very emotional issue.* 墮胎是個非常敏感的問題。**2** showing your feelings to other people, especially by crying when you are upset 情緒激動的〔尤指傷心哭泣〕: *He became very emotional when we had to leave.* 當我們不得不離開時, 他非常傷感。**3** [only before noun 僅用於名詞前] connected with your feelings and the way you control them 情緒(上)的, 情感(上)的: *We monitor the physical and emotional development of the children.* 我們監測孩子們生理和情緒的變化。**4** influenced by your feelings rather than by your thoughts or knowledge 感情用事的; 憑感情的: *an emotional response to the problem* 對問題的感性反應 —**emotionally** *adv*

e·mo·tion·al·is·m /ɪˋmoʃənḷˌɪzəm; ɪ'məʊʃənəlɪzəm/ *n* [U] a tendency to show or feel too much emotion 易露感情; 易動感情, 感情用事

e·mo·tive /ɪˋmotɪv; ɪ'məʊtɪv/ *adj* making people have strong feelings 使情緒激動的: **emotive issue/area/word etc** *Child abuse is an emotive subject.* 虐待兒童是一個易引發強烈感情的問題。—**emotively** *adv*

em·pan·el /ɪmˋpænḷ; ɪm'pænl/ *v* [T] to choose the people to serve on a JURY 挑選〔陪審團成員〕

em·pa·thize also 又作 **-ise** *BrE*【英】/ˋɛmpəˌθaɪz; 'empəθaɪz/ *v* [I] to be able to understand someone else's feelings, problems etc, especially because you have had similar experiences 移情, 有同感; 同情: [**+with**] *A founder member of the Gay Rights Movement, Mr Smith ensures that the reader empathizes with him.* 同性戀權益運動的創始人之一史密斯先生確保讀者會跟他有同感。—compare 比較 SYMPATHIZE

em·pa·thy /ˋɛmpəθɪ; 'empəθi/ *n* [U] the ability to understand other people's feelings and problems 同情; 同感: [**+with**] *a doctor who had great empathy with her patients* 對病人充滿同情的醫生 —compare 比較 SYMPATHY

em·pe·ror /ˋɛmpərə; 'empərə/ *n* [C] the ruler of an EMPIRE 皇帝

3 **em·pha·sis** /ˋɛmfəsɪs; 'emfəsᵻs/ *n plural* **emphases**
2 /-siz; -siːz/ [C,U] **1** special importance that is given to one part of something 重要性, 重點: *In Japan there is a lot of emphasis on politeness.* 在日本人們非常注重禮節。| **place/put emphasis on** *The course puts an emphasis on practical work.* 這門課程重視實踐。**2** [C, U] if you put emphasis on a particular word or phrase, you say it slightly louder in order to make it more important〔單詞、短語的〕重音, 強調音: *The emphasis should be on the first syllable.* 重音應落在第一個音節。

em·pha·size also 又作 **-ise** *BrE*【英】/ˋɛmfəˌsaɪz; 2
'emfəsaɪz/ *v* [T] to give special or additional importance 2
to something 強調, 着重: *Logan made a speech emphasizing the need for more volunteers.* 羅根發表了談話, 強調需要更多的志願者。| **emphasize that** *It should be emphasized that flying is a very safe way to travel.* 應該着重指出的是, 坐飛機旅行十分安全。

em·phat·ic /ɪmˋfætɪk; ɪm'fætɪk/ *adj* **1** an emphatic remark, opinion etc is expressed in a clear, strong way to show its importance 強調的; 有力的; 堅決的: *an emphatic denial* 斷然否認 **2** clear and undoubted 明顯的, 突出的: *an emphatic victory* 大勝 —**emphatically** /-kḷɪ; -kli/ *adv*

em·phy·se·ma /ˌɛmfɪˋsimə; ˌemfᵻ'siːmə/ *n* [U] *technical* a disease that affects the lungs, making it difficult to breathe【術語】肺氣腫

em·pire /ˋɛmpaɪr; 'empaɪə/ *n* [C] **1** a group of countries 3
that are all controlled by the ruler or government of one country 帝國: *the Roman empire* 羅馬帝國 **2** a group of organizations controlled by one powerful company or person 大企業; 大集團: *an enormous business empire* 巨大的商業集團

E

em·pir·i·cal /ɛmˋpɪrɪkḷ; ɪm'pɪrɪkəl/ *adj* [only before noun 僅用於名詞前] based on scientific testing or practical experience, not on ideas from books 以科學實驗[經驗]為依據的; 經驗主義的: *Scientists are hoping to find empirical evidence to confirm their theories.* 科學家希望能找到實驗證據證明自己的理論。—**empirically** /-kḷɪ; -kli/ *adv*

em·pir·i·cis·m /ɛmˋpɪrəˌsɪzəm; ɪm'pɪrᵻsɪzəm/ *n* [U] the belief in basing your ideas on practical experience 經驗主義, 經驗論 —**empiricist** *n* [C]

em·place·ment /ɪmˋplesmənt; ɪm'pleɪsmənt/ *n* [C] a special position prepared for a gun or other large piece of military equipment 砲位, 砲台; 安置軍事裝備的陣地: *a gun emplacement* 砲台

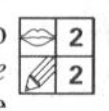

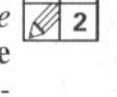

em·ploy[1] /ɪmˋplɔɪ; ɪm'plɔɪ/ *v* [T] **1** to pay someone to 2
work for you 雇用: *The company employs 2000 people* 2
worldwide. 這家公司在全世界雇用了2000名員工。| **be employed as sth** *Dave is employed as a baggage handler at the airport.* 戴夫受雇在機場做行李搬運工。| **employ sb to do sth** *Freelance consultants have been employed to look at ways of reducing waste.* 獨立顧問們受雇研究減少浪費的辦法。—see also 另見 SELF-EMPLOYED, UNEMPLOYED **2** to use a particular method or skill in order to do something 使用, 運用: *The report examines teaching methods employed in the classroom.* 這個報告考查了課堂教學方法。**3 be employed in doing sth** to spend your time doing something 花時間做某事; 忙於做某事: *Her days are employed in gardening and voluntary work.* 她的時間全花在搞園藝和做義工上。

employ[2] *n* [U] **in sb's employ** *formal* if you are in someone's employ, you work for them【正式】受雇於某人, 為某人工作: *in the Prince's employ* 為王子工作

em·ploy·a·ble /ɪmˋplɔɪəbḷ; ɪm'plɔɪəbəl/ *adj* suitable to be employed 適合雇用的; 可供使用的

em·ploy·ee /ɪmˋplɔɪ·i; ɪm'plɔɪ-iː/ *n* [C] someone who 2
is paid to work for someone else 受雇者, 雇員: *bad em-* 2
ployee relations 很差的雇員間的關係

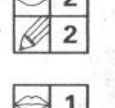

em·ploy·er /ɪmˋplɔɪə; ɪm'plɔɪə/ *n* [C] a person, 1
company, or organization that employs people 雇用者, 2
雇主: *The clothing industry is a large-scale employer of women.* 服裝業雇用大量女工。| *a fair employer* 公平的雇主

em·ploy·ment /ɪmˋplɔɪmənt; ɪm'plɔɪmənt/ *n* **1** [U] work 1
that you do to earn money 職業, 工作: *students seeking* 1
employment after college 畢業後求職的大學生 | *Are you in full-time employment?* 你是在全職工作嗎? | **in employment** (=doing a job) 在業, 有工作 **2** [U] the situ-

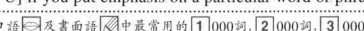

ation or condition in which people are employed 就業(環境), 雇用(條件): *a government inquiry into employment and training* 政府對就業和培訓情況的調查 | **full employment** (=a situation in which everyone in society has a job) 充分就業 —opposite 反義詞 UNEMPLOYMENT **3** [U] *formal* the use of a particular method or skill to achieve something【正式】使用, 運用: [+of] *Was the employment of force justified?* 使用武力是正當的嗎? **4** [C] *formal* a useful activity【正式】有益的活動: *Knitting is a pleasant evening employment.* 晚上做些編織活很舒心。

employment a·gen·cy /-ˈ···ˌ···/ *n* [C] a business that makes money by finding jobs for people 職業介紹所

em·po·ri·um /ɛmˋpɔrɪəm; ɪmˈpɔːriəm/ *n plural* **emporiums** *or* **emporia** [C] *old-fashioned* a large shop【過時】大商店; 大百貨商場

em·pow·er /ɪmˋpauɚ; ɪmˈpaʊə/ *v* [T] **1** to give someone more control over their own life or situation 使能夠; 使自主: *The aim of the course is to empower women.* 這門課程的目的是教婦女如何做自己的主人。**2** *formal* to give an organization the power or legal right to do something【正式】授權〔某組織做某事〕: **be empowered to do sth** *The college is empowered to grant degrees.* 這所學院有權授與學位。—**empowerment** *n* [U]

em·press /ˋɛmprɪs; ˈemprɪ̵s/ *n* [C] a female ruler of an EMPIRE, or the wife of an EMPEROR 女皇; 皇后: *the empress Josephine* 約瑟芬皇后

emp·ties /ˋɛmptɪz; ˈemptiz/ *n* [plural] bottles or glasses that are empty 空瓶子; 空杯子: *We can take the empties to be recycled.* 我們可以把這些空瓶子拿去回收利用。

emp·ti·ness /ˋɛmptɪnɪs; ˈemptinɪ̵s/ *n* [U] **1** a feeling of great unhappiness and loneliness 空虛; 寂寥: *She felt an emptiness in her heart when he left.* 他走後她心裡感到空虛。**2** the state of having nothing in an area or space〔地區或空間的〕空, 無: [+of] *the silence and emptiness of the desert* 沙漠的寂靜和空曠

emp·ty¹ /ˋɛmptɪ; ˈempti/ *adj*

1 ▶CONTAINER 容器◀ having nothing inside 空的: *an empty box* 空盒子 | *Your glass is empty – can I fill it up?* 你的杯子空了, 我給你倒一杯吧?

2 ▶ROOM/BUILDING 房間/建築物◀ an empty room, building etc does not have any people in it 無人的; 無人居住的: *The house had been empty for six months before we moved in.* 在我們搬進去之前, 這房子有六個月沒人住了。| *The hall was half-empty.* 大廳有一半是空的。

3 ▶NOT USED 沒人用的◀ not being used by anyone 無人用的: *I spotted an empty table in the corner.* 我發現角落裡有一張桌子沒人。| **be empty of** *The roads were almost empty of traffic.* 路上幾乎沒有車輛。

4 ▶PERSON/LIFE 人/生活◀ unhappy because nothing interesting or important happens or because you feel your life has no purpose 寂寥的; 空虛的: *His early death left her empty and despairing.* 他的早逝使她陷入空虛和絕望。| *Her days were empty.* 她的日子過得很無聊。

5 empty words/gestures/promises etc empty words etc are not sincere or have no effect 空話/做樣子/空頭許諾等: *She knew her protest would be nothing more than an empty gesture.* 她知道她的抗議只是做做樣子而已。

6 do sth on an empty stomach to do something without having eaten any food first 空肚子做某事: *Children shouldn't go to school on an empty stomach.* 小孩子不該空着肚子上學。

7 empty nest *AmE* the situation that parents are in when all their children have left home【美】空巢〔指子女都已長大離家〕—**emptily** *adv*

empty² *v* **1** [T] also 又作 **empty out** if you empty a container, you remove everything that is in it 倒空, 傾空: *I had to completely empty out my bag to find my keys.* 我得把包中所有東西都倒出來找我的鑰匙。**2** [T] if you empty the things that are in a container, you take or pour them out of it 把…拿出來; 傾倒: *It's your turn to empty the garbage.* 該你倒垃圾了。| **empty sth onto/into etc** *Kim emptied the candies into a glass jar.* 金把糖果倒入一個玻璃罐。**3** [I] if a place empties, everyone leaves it〔場所〕變空, 人全走光: *The stores were closing, and the streets began to empty.* 商鋪陸續關門, 街道開始變得空空蕩蕩的。**4** [I+(out) into] if a river empties into a larger area of water, it flows into it〔河流〕流入, 注入: *The Elbe empties out into the North Sea.* 易北河注入北海。

empty-hand·ed /ˌ··ˈ··◂/ *adj* without getting what you hoped or expected to get 一無所獲的, 空手的: *I spent all morning looking for a suitable present, but came home empty-handed.* 我整個上午都在尋找一件合適的禮物, 但最後還是空手回家了。

empty-head·ed /ˌ··ˈ··◂/ *adj informal* silly, and unable to think or behave seriously【非正式】傻的; 無頭腦的: *an empty-headed blonde* 頭腦簡單的金髮女孩

EMS /ˌi ɛm ˋɛs; ˌiː em ˈes/ *n* [singular] European Monetary System; a system for limiting how much the different currencies (CURRENCY) of countries within the European Union can go up and down in value in relation to each other before the euro was adopted 歐洲貨幣體系

e·mu /ˋimju; ˈiːmjuː/ *n plural* **emus** *or* **emu** [C] a large Australian bird that can run very fast but cannot fly〔澳大利亞產的跑得很快卻不會飛的〕鴯鶓

em·u·late /ˋɛmjəˌlet; ˈemjʊ̵leɪt/ *v* [T] **1** to try to be like someone else, because you admire them 效仿, 模仿: *The local khans tried to emulate the art, culture, and pageantry of the Persian courts.* 當地的可汗們努力效仿波斯宮廷的藝術、文化和奢華。**2** if one computer or piece of electronic equipment emulates another, they both perform in the same way〔電腦等電子儀器的〕仿真 —**emulation** /ˌɛmjəˋleʃən; ˌemjʊ̵ˈleɪʃən/ *n* [U]

e·mul·si·fi·er /ɪˋmʌlsəˌfaɪɚ; ɪˈmʌlsɪ̵faɪə/ *n* [C] something that is added, especially to food, to prevent liquids and solids from separating 乳化劑: *contains sunflower oil, emulsifiers, and lecithin* 含有葵花子油、乳化劑和卵磷脂

e·mul·si·fy /ɪˋmʌlsəˌfaɪ; ɪˈmʌlsɪ̵faɪ/ *v* [I,T] if two liquids emulsify, they combine to become a smooth mixture (使)〔液體〕乳化

e·mul·sion /ɪˋmʌlʃən; ɪˈmʌlʃən/ *n* [C,U] **1** a mixture of liquids that do not completely combine, such as oil and water 乳濁液, 乳狀液 **2** a type of paint used inside buildings on walls or ceilings, that is not shiny when it dries 乳化漆 —compare 比較 GLOSS PAINT **3** *technical* the substance on the surface of photographic film that makes it react to light【術語】〔照相膠片上的〕感光乳劑

en- /ɪn; ɪn/ *prefix* **1** to cause to become; make 使成為, 使: *enlarge* 擴大 **2** to put into a particular condition 使處於…狀態: *endanger* 使處於危險 | *enriched* 濃縮的, 強化的

-en /ən; ən/ *suffix* **1** [in adjectives 構成形容詞] made of something 由…製成的: *a golden crown* 金冠 | *wooden seats* 木頭座位 **2** [in verbs 構成動詞] to make something, have a particular quality 使具有某種特性: *to darken* (=make or become dark) (使)變黑 | *ripening fruit* 即將成熟的水果 | *This strengthened his resolve.* (=made it stronger) 這增強了他的決心。

en·a·ble /ɪnˋebl̩; ɪˈneɪbəl/ *v* [T] **1** to give someone the ability or opportunity to do something 使能夠; 使有機會: **enable sb to do sth** *Money from her aunt enabled Jan to buy the house.* 嬸嬸給簡的錢使她有能力買下那幢房子。**2** *formal* to make something possible【正式】使可能: *a policy designed to enable the introduction of flexible working hours* 為引進浮動工作時間而制定的政策

en·a·bling /ɪnˋeblɪŋ; ɪˈneɪblɪŋ/ *adj* [only before noun 僅用於名詞前] *technical* an enabling law is one that makes something possible or gives someone special legal powers【術語】〔指法律〕使可能的; 授予權力的

en·act /ɪnˋækt; ɪˈnækt/ *v* [T] **1** to make a proposal into law 將…制定成法律: *Congress refused to enact the bill.* 國會拒絕通過該法案。**2** *formal* to act in a play, story etc【正式】上演; 扮演: *a drama enacted on a darkened stage* 在燈光暗淡的舞台上上演的戲劇 —**enactment** *n* [C,U]

e·nam·el¹ /ɪˋnæml̩; ɪˈnæməl/ *n* [U] **1** a glass-like substance that is put onto metal, clay etc for decoration or protection 瓷釉; 搪瓷; 珐瑯 **2** the hard, smooth outer surface of your teeth〔牙齒的〕珐瑯質, 釉質 —see picture at 參見 TEETH 圖 **3** paint that is usually used on wood, and that produces a shiny surface 亮漆, 光漆, 瓷漆 —**enamel** *adj*

enamel² *v* [T] to cover or decorate something with enamel 給…上瓷漆[搪瓷]

en·am·oured *BrE*【英】, **enamored** *AmE*【美】/ɪnˋæmɚd; ɪˈnæməd/ *adj* [not before noun 不用於名詞前] **1** liking something very much〔對某物〕喜愛的, 迷戀的: **[+of/with]** *You don't seem very enamoured with your job.* 看起來你不太喜歡你的工作。**2** *formal* in love with, or very fond of someone【正式】〔對某人〕傾心的, 迷戀的: **[+of/with]** *He was greatly enamoured of Elizabeth.* 他十分傾心於伊莉莎白。

en bloc /ɛn ˋblɑk; ɒn ˈblɒk/ *adv* all together as a single unit, rather than separately 整個, 全部, 一起: *You cannot dismiss these stories en bloc.* 你不能把這些説法一股腦兒全給否定了。

en·camp /ɪnˋkæmp; ɪnˈkæmp/ *v* [I,T] *formal* to make a camp or put someone in a camp【正式】紮營, 宿營: *The soldiers were encamped near Damascus.* 士兵們在大馬士革附近安營。

en·camp·ment /ɪnˋkæmpmənt; ɪnˈkæmpmənt/ *n* [C] a large temporary camp, especially of soldiers〔尤指軍隊的〕臨時營地: *a military encampment* 軍營

en·cap·su·late /ɛnˋkæpsəˌlet; ɪnˈkæpsjʊleɪt/ *v* [T] to put the main facts or ideas of something in a short form or a small space 壓縮, 概括: **[+in]** *Her whole philosophy can be encapsulated in this one sentence.* 她的全部哲學理論可以概括成這一句話。—**encapsulation** /ɛnˌkæpsəˋleʃən; ɪnˌkæpsjʊˈleɪʃən/ *n* [C,U]

en·case /ɪnˋkes; ɪnˈkeɪs/ *v* [T often passive 常用被動態] to cover or surround something completely 把…包住; 把…圍住: **[+in]** *His broken leg was encased in plaster.* 他的斷腿打着石膏。| *her sleek legs encased in sheer black stockings* 她那雙裹在透明黑色長統襪中的秀腿

-ence /əns; əns/ *suffix* [in nouns 構成名詞] another form of the suffix -ANCE 後綴 -ance 的另一種形式: *its existence* (=the fact that it exists) 它的存在 | *reference* 參考 | *occurrence* 發生

en·chant /ɪnˋtʃænt; ɪnˈtʃɑːnt/ *v* [T often passive 常用被動態] **1** to make someone feel very interested, happy, and excited 使陶醉, 使入迷: **[+by/with]** *Venice enchanted me instantly.* 我一下子就被威尼斯迷住了。**2** *literary* to use magic on something【文】對…用魔法

en·chant·ed /ɪnˋtʃæntɪd; ɪnˈtʃɑːntɪd/ *adj* an enchanted object or place has been changed by magic, so that it has special powers〔物體或場所〕施了魔法的: *an enchanted castle* 施了魔法的城堡 —see also 另見 DISENCHANTED

en·chant·er /ɪnˋtʃæntɚ; ɪnˈtʃɑːntə/ *n* [C] *literary* someone who uses magic on people and things【文】魔法師

en·chant·ing /ɪnˋtʃæntɪŋ; ɪnˈtʃɑːntɪŋ/ *adj* very attractive 可愛的; 令人着迷的: *The child looked enchanting in a pale blue dress.* 那個孩子穿着淺藍色連衣裙, 十分可愛。| *an enchanting romantic comedy* 引人入勝的浪漫喜劇 —**enchantingly** *adj*

en·chant·ment /ɪnˋtʃæntmənt; ɪnˈtʃɑːntmənt/ *n* **1** [C,U] a feeling of mystery that strongly interests or attracts you 着迷; 陶醉: *The forest had an air of enchantment.* 森林散發着迷人的氣息。**2** [C] *literary* a change caused by magic; SPELL² (1)【文】着魔, (被施)魔法, 咒語

en·chant·ress /ɪnˋtʃæntrɪs; ɪnˈtʃɑːntrɪs/ *n* [C] *literary*【文】**1** a woman that men find very attractive and interesting 迷人的女子 **2** a woman who uses magic on people and things 女巫, 女魔法師

en·chi·la·da /ˌɛntʃɪˋlɑdə; ˌentʃɪˈlɑːdə/ *n* [C] **1** a Mexican food consisting of a flat piece of bread rolled around meat and covered with a hot-tasting thick liquid〔墨西哥式〕肉餡卷餅 **2 the whole enchilada** *AmE informal* the whole situation; everything【美, 非正式】全部事情, 整樁事情: *Come on. Let's hear it – the whole enchilada.* 來, 讓我們聽一聽整個事情的經過。

en·cir·cle /ɪnˋsɝkl̩; ɪnˈsɜːkəl/ *v* [T] to surround someone or something completely 圍繞, 環繞: *a luscious garden, encircled by walled parkland* 四周有圍墻的邸園中賞心悦目的花園 —**encirclement** *n* [U]

en·clave /ˋɛnklev; ˈenkleɪv/ *n* [C] a place or a group of people that is surrounded by people or areas that are different 聚居地; 身處異地的一羣人: *the Italian-American enclave in New York* 紐約的意大利裔美國人聚居地

en·close /ɪnˋkloz; ɪnˈkləʊz/ *v* [T] **1** to put something inside an envelope as well as a letter 隨信附上, 隨信裝入: *Please enclose a cheque with your order.* 請您隨定單附上支票。| **please find enclosed** (=used in business letters to say that you are sending something as well as a letter) 兹附上… *Please find enclosed an agenda for the meeting.* 兹附上會議議程表。**2** [often passive 常用被動態] to surround something, especially with a fence or wall, in order to make it separate〔用籬笆或圍牆〕圍起來: *A high wall enclosed the courtyard.* 一堵高牆圍着院子。

en·clo·sure /ɪnˋkloʒɚ; ɪnˈkləʊʒə/ *n* **1** [C] an area surrounded by a wall or fence, and used for a particular purpose〔用於特定目的的〕圍地, 圍場: *the bear enclosure at the zoo* 動物園中的熊園 **2** [U] the act of making an area separate by putting a wall or fence around it 圍住; 圈起來: *the enclosure of arable land for pasture* 將可耕地圈起來用作牧場 **3** [C] something that is put inside an envelope as well as a letter〔信中的〕附件, 裝入物

en·code /ɪnˋkod; ɪnˈkəʊd/ *v* [T] to put a message or other information into a CODE¹ (4) 把…譯成電碼[密碼] —opposite 反義詞 DECODE

en·com·pass /ɪnˋkʌmpəs; ɪnˈkʌmpəs/ *v* [T] **1** to include a wide range of ideas, subjects, etc 包含, 包括: *The study encompasses social, political, and economic aspects of the situation.* 這項研究包含了該情況的社會、政治和經濟等方方面面。**2** to completely cover or surround something 覆蓋; 圍住: *The houses encompassed about one hundred square metres.* 房子佔地約一百平方米。

en·core¹ /ˋɑŋkor; ˈɒŋkɔː/ *n* [C] an additional or repeated part of a performance, especially a musical one 加演節目; 重演[奏, 唱]: *The audience demanded an encore.* 聽眾要求再來一個。

encore² *interjection* used when you have enjoyed a musical performance very much and want the performer to sing or play more 再唱一首; 再來一個: *Pavarotti's performance, greeted by roars of 'Encore!'* 帕伐洛蒂的演唱會, 聽眾要求再來一個的聲音如潮

en·coun·ter¹ /ɪnˋkauntɚ; ɪnˈkaʊntə/ *v* [T] **1** to experience problems, difficulties, or opposition when you are trying to do something 遇到, 遭遇〔問題、困難、反對〕: *We encountered a serious setback when two members of the expedition were injured.* 兩名遠征隊員受傷了, 我們嚴重受挫。**2** to meet someone or experience something unexpectedly 偶然碰到〔某人〕; 突然遇到〔某事〕: *I first encountered him at summer school.* 我第一次遇到他是在暑期班裡。 W3

encounter² *n* [C] **1** an occasion when you meet someone, especially in an unplanned or unexpected way 相遇, 邂逅: *She didn't remember our encounter last summer.* 她記不起我們去年夏天那次相遇了。| **chance encounter** (=a meeting caused by luck or chance) 巧遇 **2** a short dangerous struggle or meeting between two people or groups 遭遇戰; 衝突: *one of the bloodiest encounters of the American Civil War* 美國南北戰爭期間

最慘烈的遭遇戰之一 | **close encounter** (=situation that could have been dangerous or unpleasant) 差一點釀成禍事; 幾乎導致不愉快 *a close encounter with a poisonous snake* 險遇一條毒蛇

2 1 **en·cour·age** /ɪn`kɝɪdʒ; ɪn'kʌrɪdʒ/ *v* [T] **1** to say or do something that helps someone have the courage or confidence to do something 鼓勵, 激勵: *Haldene encouraged him in his work.* 哈爾登鼓勵他好好工作。| **encourage sb to do sth** *Patricia encouraged me to apply for the job.* 帕特里夏鼓勵我申請那份工作。**2** to make something more likely to happen or make people more likely to do something 促進, 激發: *a meeting format that will encourage debate* 鼓勵辯論的會議安排 | **encourage sb to do sth** *A good public transport encourages people to leave their cars at home.* 良好的公共交通會促使人們將汽車留在家中。—opposite 反義詞 DISCOURAGE —**encouragement** *n* [C,U]

en·cour·aged /ɪn`kɝɪdʒd; ɪn'kʌrɪdʒd/ *adj* [not before noun 不用於名詞前] feeling more hopeful and confident 受到鼓舞的, 更有信心的: *She felt encouraged by the many letters of support.* 許多支持信使她很受鼓舞。

3 **en·cour·ag·ing** /ɪn`kɝɪdʒɪŋ; ɪn'kʌrɪdʒɪŋ/ *adj* giving you hope and confidence 令人鼓舞的, 振奮人心的: *The results of the survey have been very encouraging.* 調查結果非常令人鼓舞。—**encouragingly** *adv*

en·croach /ɪn`krotʃ; ɪn'krəʊtʃ/ *v*

encroach on/upon sth *phr v* [T] **1** to gradually take more control of someone's time, possessions, rights etc than you should 逐步侵佔[侵犯]; 蠶食: *a government that is encroaching on the rights of individuals* 正逐步侵犯公民個人權利的政府 **2** to gradually cover more and more land 侵佔〔土地〕: *houses encroaching upon farmland* 正漸漸侵佔耕地的住房 —**encroachment** *n* [C,U]

en·crust·ed /ɪn`krʌstɪd; ɪn'krʌstɪd/ *adj* covered with a thin hard layer of something 覆有薄薄一層硬外層的, 結外殼的: [+**with/in**] *boots thickly encrusted with mud* 外面沾了厚厚一層泥的靴子 —**encrustation** /ˌɪnkrʌs`teʃən; ˌɪnkrʌ'steɪʃən/ *n* [C,U]

en·cum·ber /ɪn`kʌmbɚ; ɪn'kʌmbə/ *v* [T] *formal* to make it difficult for someone to move easily or for something to happen in the usual way【正式】妨礙, 阻礙: [+**by/with**] *I was too encumbered by suitcases to run.* 我提着手提箱, 跑不動。—**encumbrance** *n* [C]

-ency /ənsɪ; ənsi/ *suffix* [in nouns 構成名詞] another form of the suffix -ANCY 後綴 -ancy 的另一種形式: *a tendency* 趨勢

en·cyc·li·cal /ɛn`sɪklɪkl; ɪn'sɪklɪkəl/ *n* [C] *technical* a letter sent by the Pope to all Roman Catholic BISHOPS or to members of the Roman Catholic Church【術語】羅馬教皇〔給全體主教或教徒〕的通諭

en·cy·clo·pe·di·a also 又作 **encyclopaedia** *BrE*【英】/ɪnˌsaɪklə`pidɪə; ɪnˌsaɪklə'piːdiə/ *n* [C] a book or set of books containing facts about many different subjects, or about one particular subject 百科全書; 〔某一學科的〕專科全書, 大全

en·cy·clo·pe·dic also 又作 **encyclopaedic** *BrE*【英】/ɪnˌsaɪklə`pidɪk; ɪnˌsaɪklə'piːdɪk◂/ *adj* encyclopedic knowledge, memory etc has a very large amount of information in it〔知識、記憶等〕百科全書式的, 淵博的

1 1 **end**[1] /ɛnd; end/ *n* [C]

1 ►LAST PART 最後部分◄ the last part of something such as a period of time, activity, book, or film 最後部分; 末尾: *He's leaving at the end of October.* 他計劃於十月底離開。| *I found the end of the movie very disappointing.* 我覺得電影的結尾部分十分令人失望。| **from beginning to end** *Her story was a pack of lies from beginning to end.* 她的故事徹頭徹尾都是謊言。

2 ►FURTHEST POINT 最遠端◄ the furthest point of a place or object 端; 盡頭: *He sat at one end of the table and I sat at the other.* 他坐在桌子的一端, 我坐在另一端。| *The street is closed off at both ends.* 街道兩頭都被封鎖了。| *a long pole with a hole at one end* 一端有個洞的長杆 | **end to end** (=in a line with the ends touching) 首尾相接地; 頭對頭地 *Put the two tables end to end.* 把兩張桌子拼接在一起。

3 ►FINISHED 結束◄ a situation in which something is finished or no longer exists 結束; 結局; 完結: *the end of all my dreams* 我所有夢想的完結 | **be at an end** (=finished) 結束了 *The long hot summer was at last at an end.* 漫長的酷暑終於過去了。| **come to an end** (=finished and no longer continuing) 完結 *That job came to an end last month.* 那項工作上個月完成了。| **put an end to** *Winning the competition put an end to his financial problems.* 在比賽中獲勝使他的財政問題隨之消失。| **to the end of time** *literary* (=for ever)【文】永遠

4 ►AIM 目的◄ [usually plural 一般用複數] the result that you hope to achieve 目的, 目標: *She'll stop at nothing to achieve her own ends.* 為達到個人目的, 她不會被任何事物阻止。| **to that end** *formal*【正式】*Joel wants to buy a car and is saving money to that end.* 喬爾想買一輛汽車, 並正為此攢錢。| **an end in itself** (=something you aim to do because you want to, not in order to get other advantages) 自發想做的事情, 本身就是目的 *Learning to play the piano was an end in itself for me.* 我學鋼琴不是為了別的目的, 只是因為想學。| **the end justifies the means** (=the result you want makes acceptable the bad things you do in order to get it) 只要能達到目的, 可以採取任何手段

5 in the end after a period of time; finally 後來; 終於: *In the end, I decided that I wouldn't go after all.* 最終我決定還是不去。—see 見 LASTLY (USAGE)

6 days/hours/weeks etc on end for many days, hours etc without stopping 連續數天/數小時/數週等: *It snowed for days on end.* 雪一連下了好幾天。

7 no end *spoken* very much【口】非常: *Thanks for the letter – it cheered me up no end.* 謝謝來信, 這我非常高興。

8 no end of *spoken* a lot of something【口】大量的, 許多: *We've had no end of problems with the house since we moved.* 我們搬進去以後, 房子的麻煩不斷。

9 put/stand sth on end to put something in a position so that its longest edge is upright 把…豎起來 —see also 另見 **make sb's hair stand on end** (HAIR (6))

10 ►PART OF AN ACTIVITY 活動的一部分◄ *informal* the particular part of a job, activity, place etc that you are involved in, or that affects you【非正式】〔工作、活動、場所等相關的〕部分; 方面: *She works in the sales end of things.* 她做銷售方面的工作。| *Let's hope they keep their end of the bargain.* 希望他們能信守協議。| **at your end** *spoken* (=where you are)【口】在你(們)那兒 *What's the weather like at your end?* 你們那裡天氣如何?

11 ►SPORT 體育◄ one of the two halves of a sports field that a team defends or attacks 半邊球場, 半場: *The teams change ends at half-time.* 中場時兩隊交換場地。

12 ►DEATH 死亡◄ [C usually singular 一般用單數] a word meaning death, used because you want to avoid saying this directly 生命的盡頭〔死亡的委婉說法〕: *James was with his father at the end.* 父親臨終時詹姆斯陪在身邊。

13 at the end of the day *spoken* used to give your opinion after you have discussed all the possibilities of a situation or problem【口】最終; 到頭來; 不管怎麼說: *At the end of the day, it's his responsibility, and there's nothing you can do.* 不管怎麼說這是他的責任, 你幫不了甚麼。

14 be at the end of your tether/rope to have no more PATIENCE or strength to deal with something 忍無可忍; 無能為力: *I'm at the end of my tether with their constant arguing.* 他們沒完沒了地爭吵, 我已忍無可忍。

15 it's not the end of the world *spoken* used to say that a possible problem is not too serious or bad【口】還未到世界末日〔表示事情並不那麼可怕〕: *After all, it's not the end of the world if you fail this test.* 不管怎麼

說，就算你這次考試不及格，那也不是甚麼世界末日。

16 hold/keep your end up *BrE informal* to continue to be brave or act effectively in a difficult situation【英，非正式】堅持，不泄氣

17 make (both) ends meet to have just enough money to buy what you need 收支僅能相抵: *Since Mike lost his job, we can hardly make ends meet.* 自從邁克失業以後，我們簡直難以維持生計。

18 the end of the road/line the end of a process or activity 進程的盡頭/活動的結局: *I tried to tell him that this defeat was not the end of the road, that football was only a game.* 我盡量對他講，這次失敗並不代表一切，畢竟足球比賽只是一種遊戲。

19 the (absolute) end *BrE spoken* used to show disapproval of someone or something in an amused way【英口】〔用於表示好笑的責難〕糟糕透了的人[物]: *Look at this untidy room – you're the absolute end!* 看看這亂七八糟的屋子，你簡直糟透了！

20 living end *AmE spoken* used as an expression of strong approval or disapproval【美口】頂呱呱；十足的混蛋: *What will she do next? She's the living end!* 她下一步要幹甚麼？她這混蛋！

21 do sth to the bitter end to keep doing something until you have tried every possible method 盡一切努力做某事: *We'll fight this decision to the bitter end.* 這個決定我們要反對到底。

22 go to the ends of the earth to do everything you can, even if it is very difficult, in order to have or achieve something 竭盡所能: *I'd go to the ends of the earth to be with him.* 哪怕走到天涯地角我也要和他在一起。

23 get/have your end away *BrE slang* to have sex【英俚】性交 —see also 另見 **be-all and end all** (BE² (10)), DEAD END, **go off at the deep end** (DEEP¹ (17)), **be at a loose end** (LOOSE¹ (14)), ODDS AND ENDS, **be on the sharp end of** (SHARP¹ (21)), **come to a sticky end** (STICKY (8)), **the tail end of a queue/meeting etc** (TAIL¹ (9)), **jump/be thrown in at the deep end** (DEEP¹ (16)), **get the wrong end of the stick** (WRONG¹ (12)), **at your wit's end** (WIT (6))

1 **end²** *v* **1** [I] to finish or stop 結束；停止: *World War II*
1 *ended in 1945.* 第二次世界大戰於 1945 年結束。| *The film ended with the heroine dying.* 在電影結束時，女主角去世了。**2** [T] to make something finish or stop 使結束；使停止: *Jane decided it was time to end the relationship with Bob.* 簡決定該結束與鮑勃的關係了。**3 end your days/life** if you end your days in a particular place or doing a particular thing, you spend the last part of your life there or doing that〔在某處或在進行某種活動過程中〕度過餘生 **4 end it all** to kill yourself 自殺

end in sth *phr v* [T not in passive 不用被動態] to have in a particular result, or finish in a particular way 結果為…；以…結束[告終]: *Their marriage ended in divorce.* 他們的婚姻以離婚告終。| **it'll all end in tears** *BrE spoken* (=used to warn that a situation will end in an unpleasant or unhappy way)【英口】將以不快[悲劇]收場 *This game will end in tears. I know it.* 這場比賽將以悲劇收場，我確信。

end up *phr v* [I] *informal*【非正式】**1** to come to be in a particular situation or state, especially when you did not plan it 結果為…；以…結束〔尤指意料之外的〕: *He'll end up in prison if he's not careful.* 如果他不小心，最後可能會鋃鐺入獄。| **end up doing sth** *We were going to go out, but ended up watching videos.* 我們原計劃外出，但結果卻是在家看錄像。**2** to arrive in a place you did not plan to go to 意外到達〔某處〕: *We got to Rome okay, but our luggage ended up in Paris.* 我們順利到達羅馬，但我們的行李卻被送到了巴黎。

en·dan·ger /ɪn`dendʒɚ; ɪn'deɪndʒə/ *v* [T] to put someone or something in a dangerous situation where they can be hurt, damaged, or destroyed 使處於險境；危及: *Smoking during pregnancy can endanger your baby's health.* 懷孕期間吸煙會危及胎兒的健康。| *If unemployment continues to rise, social stability may be endangered.* 失業率持續上升將會危及社會安定。

endangered spe·cies /·,·· '··/ *n* [C] a type of animal or plant that may soon no longer exist 瀕於滅絕的物種: *The whale is an endangered species.* 鯨魚是一種瀕於滅絕的動物。

en·dear /ɪn`dɪr; ɪn'dɪə/ *v*

endear sb **to** sb *phr v* [T] to make someone popular and liked 使受歡迎，使被喜愛: *Diana's friendly disposition endears her to everyone she meets.* 戴安娜性情友善，因而人緣很好。

en·dear·ing /ɪn`dɪrɪŋ; ɪn'dɪərɪŋ/ *adj* making someone love or like you 惹人喜愛的，引人愛慕的: *an endearing smile* 可愛的微笑 —**endearingly** *adv*

en·dear·ment /ɪn`dɪrmənt; ɪn'dɪəmənt/ *n* [C] an action or word that expresses your love for someone 表示愛慕的舉動[言語]: *whispering endearments to her* 向她悄悄說着情話 | **term of endearment** (=a way you address someone you love) 愛稱

en·deav·our¹ *BrE*【英】, **endeavor** *AmE*【美】/ɪn`dɛvɚ; ɪn'devə/ *v* [I] *formal* to try very hard【正式】努力；奮力: **endeavour to do sth** *We always endeavor to give our customers excellent service.* 我們總是竭盡全力向顧客提供優質的服務。

endeavour² *BrE*【英】, **endeavor** *AmE*【美】*n* [C,U] *formal* an attempt or effort, especially to do something new or difficult【正式】嘗試；努力: *The expedition was an outstanding example of human endeavour.* 這次遠征是人類奮勇進取的突出例證。| **best endeavours** *Despite our best endeavours, we couldn't get the machine started.* 我們雖然盡了最大努力，但還是無法開動機器。

en·dem·ic /ɛn`dɛmɪk; en'demɪk/ *adj* an endemic disease is always present in a particular place, or among a particular group of people〔疾病〕地方性的；某些人常有的: *Violent crime is now endemic in parts of Chicago.* 暴力犯罪現在成了芝加哥一些地區的問題，無法根除。—compare 比較 PANDEMIC

end game /'· ·/ *n* [C] *technical* something that happens at the end of an activity, especially a game of CHESS【術語】〔尤指棋賽的〕殘局；結束階段；尾聲

end·ing /`ɛndɪŋ; 'endɪŋ/ *n* [C] **1** the way in which of a story, film, etc finishes〔故事、電影等的〕結局，結尾: *The story has a happy ending.* 這個故事結局美滿。**2** the last part of a word〔單詞的〕詞尾: *Verbal nouns have the ending -ing.* 動名詞以 -ing 結尾。

en·dive /`ɛndaɪv; 'endɪv/ *n* [C,U] **1** a plant with curly green leaves that you eat raw 苣蕒菜 **2** *AmE* a plant with bitter tasting leaves that is eaten raw【美】菊苣; CHICORY *BrE*【英】

end·less /`ɛndlɪs; 'endləs/ *adj* **1** something unpleasant that is endless continues, or seems to continue, for a long time〔不愉快的事情〕永無休止的，無窮盡的: *the endless round of meetings and interviews* 沒完沒了的會議和採訪 **2** *technical* an endless belt, chain etc is circular with the ends joined【術語】〔帶、鏈等〕環狀的，兩端連接的 —**endlessly** *adv*: *Sue was endlessly patient.* 蘇是個極度耐心的人。

en·do·crine gland /`ɛndo,kraɪn `glænd; 'endəʊkrɪn ,glænd/ *n* [C] *technical* an organ of your body that puts HORMONES into your blood【術語】內分泌腺

en·dorse /ɪn`dɔrs; ɪn'dɔːs/ *v* [T] **1** to express formal support or approval for someone or something〔正式〕贊同；認可；支持: *The committee has endorsed our proposals.* 委員會已經表態支持我們的建議。**2** to sign your name on the back of a cheque〔在支票背面〕簽名，背書 **3** to say in an advertisement that you use a particular product and like it〔在廣告中〕聲稱使用〔這種產品〕: *big names who endorsed American Express* 為美國運通信用卡做廣告的名人 **4** [usually passive 一般用被動態] *BrE* to write a driving offence on someone's DRIVING LICENCE【英】〔在駕駛執照上〕註明司機違章: *His licence was endorsed for speeding.* 他因超速駕駛，執照被註上

違章記錄。—**endorsement** *n* [C,U]

en·dow /ɪnˋdau; ɪnˈdaʊ/ *v* [T] to give a college, hospital etc a large sum of money that will provide it with an income〔向院校、醫院等〕捐款, 資助

endow sb **with** sth *phr v* [T] **1 be endowed with** to naturally have a good feature or quality 天生賦有: *She was endowed with both looks and brains.* 她天生漂亮又聰明。**2** *formal* to give someone something【正式】給予, 賦予 —see also 另見 WELL-ENDOWED

en·dow·ment /ɪnˋdaumənt; ɪnˈdaʊmənt/ *n* **1** [C,U] a sum of money that is given to a place such as a college or hospital to give it an income, or the giving of this money 捐贈的款項; 捐款(的行為), 資助: *an endowment of land and investments given to the college* 給該大學的土地捐贈和投資 **2** [C] a quality or ability that someone has naturally 天賦, 天資: *Man has already changed dogs' genetic endowments by breeding them selectively.* 人類已通過選擇性育種的方式改變了狗的基因品質。

endowment pol·i·cy /·ˈ·· ˌ···/ *n* [C] *technical* an insurance arrangement that pays you an agreed sum of money after a period of time【術語】養老保險〔指保險公司應允在一段時間後支付一筆約定的錢款〕

end prod·uct /ˈ· ˌ··/ *n* [C usually singular 一般用單數] something that is produced by an industrial process, or by a particular activity 最終產品, 製成品: *Desktop publishing can produce a very high quality end product.* 桌面出版可以製作出高質量的產品。—compare 比較 BY-PRODUCT

end re·sult /ˌ· ·ˈ·/ *n* [C usually singular 一般用單數] the final result of a process or activity 最終結果: *If present trends continue, the end result will inevitably be socialized medicine.* 如果現在的趨勢持續下去, 最終將不可避免地導致公費醫療。

en·due /ɪnˋdju; ɪnˈdjuː/ *v* [T] *formal*【正式】

endue sb **with** sth *phr v* [T] to make someone have a lot of a good quality 大量賦予〔某人〕以〔某種優良的品質〕: *endued with a spirit of public service* 極富公共服務精神

en·dur·ance /ɪnˋdjurəns; ɪnˈdjʊərəns/ *n* [U] the ability to suffer difficulties or pain with strength and patience (忍)耐力: *The marathon really tested his endurance.* 馬拉松賽跑真正考驗了他的耐力。

en·dure /ɪnˋdjur; ɪnˈdjʊə/ *v* **1** [T] to suffer something painful or deal with a very unpleasant situation for a long time with strength and patience 忍耐; 容忍; 堅持: *There are limits to what the human body can endure.* 人體的耐力是有限度的。| *Bosnians have now endured several years of war.* 波斯尼亞人已忍受了數年的戰爭。—see graph at 參見 BEAR 圖表 **2** [I] to remain alive or continue to exist 生活下去; 持續存在: *a city built to endure* 建築牢固、歷世長存的城市 —**endurable** *adj*

en·dur·ing /ɪnˋdjurɪŋ; ɪnˈdjʊərɪŋ/ *adj* continuing to exist for a long time 持久的, 持續的: *the enduring appeal of the short story* 短篇小說經久不衰的感染力

end us·er /ˈ· ˌ··/ *n* [C] the person who actually uses a particular product〔產品的〕最終使用者: *researching end-users' preferences* 調查終端用戶的喜好

end·ways /ˋɛndˌwez; ˈendweɪz/ also 又作 **end·wise** /-ˌwaɪz; -waɪz/ *adv AmE*【美】**1** with the end forward 末端朝前: *The box looks narrow when you look at it endways.* 這盒子從末端看較窄。**2** with the ends touching each other 兩端相接: *Put the tables together endways.* 把桌子接排成一行。

end zone /ˈ· ·/ *n* [C] the place at the end of an American football field where you take the ball to get points〔美式足球的〕球門區 —see picture on page A22 參見 A22 頁圖

en·e·ma /ˋɛnəmə; ˈenɪ̣mə/ *n* [C] a liquid that is put into someone's RECTUM in order to make them empty their BOWELS 灌腸劑

2 **en·e·my** /ˋɛnəmɪ; ˈenəmi/ *n* [C] **1** someone who hates you and wants to harm you 敵人, 仇敵: *She's a dangerous enemy to have.* 有她這樣的敵人是很危險的。| **be enemies** (=hate and oppose each other) 互為仇敵, 互相敵視 *Jake and Paul have been enemies for years.* 傑克和保羅已是多年的宿敵了。| **make an enemy (of sb)** *He's a ruthless businessman and has made a lot of enemies.* 他是個無情的商人, 樹敵很多。| **sworn enemies** (=enemies determined never to end their quarrel) 死敵, 不共戴天的仇敵 **2** someone who opposes you and wants to prevent you doing something 反對者: *political enemies* 政敵 | *Greenpeace, an enemy of the chemical industry, is pressing for more environmental legislation.* 綠色和平組織是化學工業的反對者, 正敦促更多的環保立法。**3** someone you are fighting in a war 敵兵, 敵軍: *Our enemies were hidden in the trenches.* 敵軍躲在戰壕裡。| **enemy forces** (=the army, navy etc of the country that you are fighting) 敵國的軍隊 | **enemy soldiers/aircraft** *Enemy aircraft were spotted overhead.* 發現了空中的敵機。**4 be your own worst enemy** to behave in a way that causes problems for yourself 自作自受, 自己害自己 **5** *literary* something that changes something else or makes it weaker【文】改變物; 危害物: *Jealousy is the enemy of love.* 妒忌是愛情的大敵。

en·er·get·ic /ˌɛnəˋdʒɛtɪk; ˌenəˈdʒetɪk◂/ *adj* very active because you have a lot of energy 充滿活力的, 精力充沛的: *an able and energetic politician* 能幹又充滿活力的政治家 —**energetically** /-klɪ; -kli/ *adv*: *He fought energetically against apartheid.* 他積極地與種族隔離進行鬥爭。

en·er·gize also 又作 **-ise** *BrE*【英】/ˋɛnəˌdʒaɪz; ˈenədʒaɪz/ *v* [T] **1** to make someone feel more determined and energetic 使增強決心, 使充滿活力 **2** [usually passive 一般用被動態] to make a machine work 使〔機器〕運轉: *electric motors energized by solar cells* 使用太陽能電池的電動機 —**energizing** *adj*

en·er·gy /ˋɛnədʒɪ; ˈenədʒi/ *n* [C,U] **1** the physical and mental strength that makes you able to be active 力量, 活力: *The task will take an enormous amount of time and energy.* 完成那項任務需要大量時間和精力。| **be full of energy** *She came back full of energy after her vacation.* 度假歸來後她精力充沛。| **nervous energy** (=energy that you have because you feel nervous) 亢奮; 興奮不安 **2** power that is used to provide heat, drive machines etc such as oil and coal 能, 能量; 能源: *the world's energy resources* 世界能源 **3 energies** the effort that you use to do things 精力: **apply/devote your energies to** *She's devoting all her energies to the wedding preparations.* 她把所有精力都花在準備婚禮上了。

en·er·vat·ed /ˋɛnəˌvetɪd; ˈenəveɪtɪ̣d/ *adj formal* having lost energy and feeling weak【正式】無力的; 沒精打采的: *I was utterly enervated by the argument.* 我被這場爭論搞得精疲力竭。| *reclining on the chaise longue, languid and enervated* 靠在躺椅上, 倦怠無力

en·er·vat·ing /ˋɛnəˌvetɪŋ; ˈenəveɪtɪŋ/ *adj* making you feel weak 使無力的, 使沒精打采的: *Extreme heat can be very enervating.* 酷熱會使人渾身乏力。

en·fant ter·ri·ble /ˌɑnfɑn tɛˋribl̩; ˌɒnfɒn teˈriːblə/ *n* [C] *French* someone who behaves in a way that shocks and amuses other people【法】莽撞而令人發笑的人: *Ken Russell, the enfant terrible of the British film industry* 肯·羅素, 英國電影界中那個常有驚人之舉的人

en·fee·ble /ɪnˋfibl̩; ɪnˈfiːbəl/ *v* [T] *formal* to make someone weak【正式】使衰弱, 使無力 —**enfeebled** *adj*

en·fold /ɪnˋfold; ɪnˈfəʊld/ *v* [T] *formal* to enclose or surround something【正式】圍住, 包住: *He enfolded her in his arms.* 他摟住她。

en·force /ɪnˋfɔrs; ɪnˈfɔːs/ *v* [T] **1** to make people obey a rule or law 執行〔法律〕, 實施: *Governments make laws and the police enforce them.* 政府制定法律, 警察負責執行。**2** to make something happen, especially by threats or force; IMPOSE〔強迫〕實行; 把…強加於: *The unions hope to enforce a closed shop.* 工會希望實行只雇用工會會員的制度。—**enforceable** *adj* —**enforcement** *n* [U]

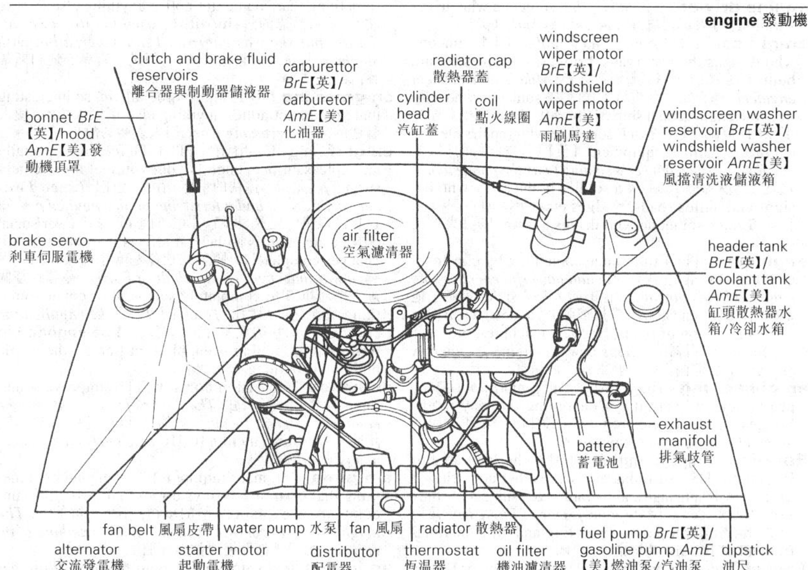

law enforcement agencies in the US 美國的執法機構

en·forced /ɪnˋfɔrst; ɪnˈfɔːst/ *adj* made to happen or exist by law, or by conditions that you cannot control 依法強制的; 強迫的: *a period of enforced isolation* 強制隔離期

en·fran·chise /ɛnˋfræntʃaɪz; ɪnˈfræntʃaɪz/ *v* [T] **1** to give a group of people the right to vote 給予…選舉權 —opposite 反義詞 DISENFRANCHISE **2** to free a slave 解放〔奴隸〕—**enfranchisement** /-tʃɪz-; -tʃɪz-/ *n* [U]

3 **en·gage** /ɪnˋgedʒ; ɪnˈgeɪdʒ/ *v formal*【正式】**1** [T] to attract someone and keep their interest 吸引〔某人的興趣〕: *The new toy didn't engage the child's interest for long.* 這個新玩具對孩子的吸引力沒有維持多久。**2** [T] to arrange to employ someone 安排雇用, 聘請: **engage sb to do sth** *His father engaged a private tutor to improve his maths.* 他爸爸請了一位家庭教師給他補習數學。**3** [I,T] to make one part fit into another part of a machine (使)〔機器〕嚙合, 接合: *She engaged the clutch and the car moved forwards.* 她踩下離合器, 汽車便朝前開了。| **[+with]** *The wheel engages with the cog and turns it.* 輪子咬住輪齒並帶動它轉動。—opposite 反義詞 DISENGAGE (2) **4** [T] to begin to fight with an enemy 開始與〔敵人〕交戰: *The two armies engaged at dawn.* 兩軍在拂曉時分開始交火。

engage in *formal*【正式】*phr v* [T] **1** to take part or become involved in an activity 參加; 參與: *a politician engaged in various business activities* 參與各種商業活動的政治家 **2 engage sb in conversation** to start talking to someone and involve them in a conversation 與某人攀談; 使某人加入談話中

en·gaged /ɪnˋgedʒd; ɪnˈgeɪdʒd/ *adj* **1** having agreed to get married 已訂婚的: *They've been engaged for six months.* 他們訂婚已經六個月了。| **[+to]** *Have you met the man she's engaged to?* 你見過她的未婚夫嗎? | **get engaged** (=agree to marry someone) 訂婚 *Siobhan and Ray have just got engaged.* 西沃恩和雷剛剛訂婚。**2** *BrE* an engaged telephone is being used【英】電話佔線的; BUSY[1] (7) *AmE*【美】: **engaged line/number** *I can't get through – her line's engaged.* 我打不通, 她的電話佔線。| **engaged tone** (=the sound you hear when the telephone is engaged)〔電話佔線的〕忙音 **3** a public toilet that is engaged is being used〔公共廁所〕使用中的 —opposite 反義詞 VACANT (1) **4 be otherwise engaged** *formal* to be unable to do something because you have arranged to do something else【正式】另外有約, 另外有事

en·gage·ment /ɪnˋgedʒmənt; ɪnˈgeɪdʒmənt/ *n* **1** [C] an agreement to marry someone 訂婚, 婚約: *They've officially announced their engagement.* 他們已正式宣布訂婚。| **break off your engagement** (=say you no longer want to marry someone) 解除婚約 **2** [C] an arrangement to do something or meet someone 約定; 約會: *He has engagements this month at various clubs.* 他本月與數家俱樂部有約。| **prior/previous engagement** (=an arrangement you have already made) 已定好的約會 *I won't be able to make it – I have a prior engagement.* 我不能去了, 我已另有約在先。**3** [C] *technical* a battle between armies, navies etc【術語】〔陸軍、海軍等的〕戰鬥, 交火 **4** [U] the fitting together of the working parts of a machine〔機器部件的〕嚙合, 銜接

engagement ring /ˈ·· ·/ *n* [C] a ring that a man gives to a woman when they decide to marry〔男方給女方的〕訂婚戒指

en·gag·ing /ɪnˋgedʒɪŋ; ɪnˈgeɪdʒɪŋ/ *adj* attracting someone's attention and interest 動人的, 迷人的: *an engaging smile* 迷人的微笑 —**engagingly** *adv*

en·gen·der /ɪnˋdʒɛndɚ; ɪnˈdʒendə/ *v* [T] *formal* to be the cause of a situation or feeling【正式】導致〔某種情形或感覺〕: *Racial inequality engenders conflict.* 種族不平等導致衝突。

en·gine /ˋɛndʒən; ˈendʒɪn/ *n* [C] **1** a piece of machinery with moving parts that changes power from steam, electricity, oil etc, into movement 發動機, 引擎: *the engine of a car* 汽車發動機 | *a jet engine* 噴氣發動機 **2** a vehicle that pulls a railway train 火車頭, 機車 **3 engine of change/destruction etc** *formal* something that causes change etc【正式】變革/毀滅等的原動力: *a newspaper that was the engine of cultural change* 推動文化變革的一家報紙 —see also 另見 FIRE ENGINE

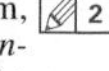
S1 W2

engine driv·er /ˈ‥ ˌ‥/ *n* [C] *BrE* someone who drives a train【英】火車司機; ENGINEER[1] (5) *AmE*【美】

3 3 **en·gi·neer[1]** /ˌɛndʒəˈnɪr; ˌendʒəˈnɪə/ *n* [C] **1** someone who designs the way roads, bridges, machines etc are built 工程師, 工程[機械]設計人員: *Mike's an electrical engineer.* 邁克是一名電氣工程師。**2** someone who controls the engines on a ship or aircraft〔船或飛機上控制引擎的〕機師, 機工 **3** *BrE* someone who repairs electrical or mechanical equipment【英】〔負責維修的〕機械師, 修理工: *The engineer's coming to fix the phone today.* 修理工今天來修電話。**4** a soldier in the army who designs and builds roads, bridges etc〔軍隊的〕工兵, 工程兵 **5** *AmE* someone who drives a train【美】火車司機

engineer[2] *v* [T] **1** to arrange something by clever secret planning 策劃; 謀劃: *He had powerful enemies who engineered his downfall.* 他的敵人勢力強大, 策劃了他的垮台。**2** [often passive 常用被動態] to design and plan the construction of roads, bridges, machines, etc 設計〔公路、橋梁、機器等〕: *This new jet engine is superbly engineered.* 這個新噴氣發動機設計精良。

2 **en·gi·neer·ing** /ˌɛndʒəˈnɪrɪŋ; ˌendʒəˈnɪərɪŋ/ *n* [U] the profession and activity of designing the way roads, bridges, machines etc are built 工程師行業; 工程設計 —see also 另見 CIVIL ENGINEERING

E

En·glish[1] /ˈɪŋglɪʃ; ˈɪŋglɪʃ/ *n* [U] **1** the language of Britain, the US, Australia, and some other countries 英語 **2** English language and literature as a subject of study 英語語言和文學(課程): *a professor of English* 英語教授 **3 the English** people from England, or sometimes from all of Britain 英格蘭人; 英國人

English[2] *adj* from or connected with England or Britain 英格蘭的; 英國的

English break·fast /ˌ‥ ˈ‥/ *n* [C] *BrE* a large cooked breakfast consisting of BACON, eggs, TOAST[1] (1) etc【英】英國式早餐〔包括熏肉、蛋和烤麵包等〕—compare 比較 CONTINENTAL BREAKFAST

English horn /ˌ‥ ˈ‥/ *especially AmE* COR ANGLAIS【尤美】英國管

En·glish·man /ˈɪŋglɪʃmən; ˈɪŋglɪʃmən/ *n* [C] a man from England 英格蘭男人; 英國男人

English muf·fin /ˌ‥ ˈ‥/ *n* [C] *AmE* a round flat piece of bread that you TOAST[2] (2) before eating it【美】英式鬆餅; MUFFIN *BrE*【英】

En·glish·wom·an /ˈɪŋglɪʃˌwʊmən; ˈɪŋglɪʃˌwʊmən/ *n* [C] a woman from England 英格蘭女人; 英國女人

en·grave /ɪnˈgrev; ɪnˈgreɪv/ *v* [T] **1** to cut words or pictures on metal, wood, glass etc〔在金屬、木、玻璃等上〕雕刻〔文字或圖案〕: **engrave sth on** *a silver pocket watch with the initials HTS engraved on the back* 背面刻着 HTS 三個首字母的銀製懷錶 | **engrave sth with** *a pendant engraved with a simple geometric design* 雕刻有簡單幾何圖案的項鏈墜 **2 be engraved in your memory/mind/heart** *formal* to be impossible to forget【正式】銘刻在記憶裡/腦海中/心中: *That day would be engraved in his memory for ever.* 那一天將永遠銘刻在他的記憶裡。**3** to prepare a special metal plate for printing〔為印刷而〕鐫版, 製版 **4** to print something using a specially prepared metal plate 用鐫版印 —**engraver** *n* [C]

en·grav·ing /ɪnˈgrevɪŋ; ɪnˈgreɪvɪŋ/ *n* **1** [C] a picture printed from an engraved metal plate 金屬版畫: *an old engraving of London Bridge* 一幅倫敦大橋的舊金屬版畫 **2** [U] the art or work of engraving things 雕刻術; 雕刻工作; 鐫版術; 鐫版工作

en·gross /ɪnˈgros; ɪnˈgrəʊs/ *v* [T] **1** if something engrosses you, you are extremely interested in it 使非常感興趣; 使全神貫注: *Their revolutionary talk engrossed him, and he listened intently.* 他們的革命性的談話使他着迷, 他入神地聽着。**2 engross yourself in/with** to become very interested in something and spend a lot of time doing it 專注於, 專心致志於

en·grossed /ɪnˈgrost; ɪnˈgrəʊst/ *adj* so interested in something that you do not notice anything else 全神貫注的, 專心致志的: **[+in/with]** *I tried to attract her attention but she was engrossed in conversation with Stephen.* 我試圖引起她的注意, 但她一直專心地和斯蒂芬說話。

en·gross·ing /ɪnˈgrosɪŋ; ɪŋˈgrəʊsɪŋ/ *adj* so interesting that you do not notice anything else 引人入勝的; 使人着迷的: *an engrossing story* 引人入勝的故事

en·gulf /ɪnˈgʌlf; ɪnˈgʌlf/ *v* [T] **1** if a feeling, especially an unpleasant one, engulfs you, you feel it extremely strongly〔尤指不愉快的情感〕吞沒; 包圍: *I knew I was very near death, and a terrifying panic engulfed me.* 知道自己很快要死了, 我陷入極大的恐慌。**2** if a war/social change etc engulfs a place, it affects it so much that it changes completely〔戰爭或社會變革等〕徹底改變; 吞噬: *a war that engulfed the whole of Europe* 蔓延到整個歐洲的戰爭 **3** to completely surround or cover something 完全包圍; 遮住: *Thick white smoke engulfed the courtyard.* 白色的濃煙吞沒了庭院。**4 be engulfed in flames** if a building is engulfed in flames, the whole building is burning 被大火吞沒

en·hance /ɪnˈhæns; ɪnˈhɑːns/ *v* [T] to improve something 提高; 改進; 增強: *The flavor of most foods can be enhanced by good cooking.* 好的烹飪可以使大多數食物增味。—**enhancement** *n* [C,U]: *much needed enhancements* 亟須的改進 3

e·nig·ma /ɪˈnɪgmə; ɪˈnɪgmə/ *n* [C] someone or something that is strange or mysterious and difficult to understand or explain 費解的事物; 不可理解的人: *The neighbours had come to regard him as something of an enigma.* 鄰居們都已把他當作一個謎一樣的人。

en·ig·mat·ic /ˌɛnɪgˈmætɪk; ˌenɪgˈmætɪk◂/ *adj* rather mysterious and difficult to understand or explain 費解的; 難捉摸的: *an enigmatic smile* 令人難以捉摸的微笑 —**enigmatically** /-klɪ; -kli/ *adv*: *"You'll find out soon enough," she said enigmatically.* "你很快就會發現的。" 她神秘地說。

en·join /ɪnˈdʒɔɪn; ɪnˈdʒɔɪn/ *v* [T] **1** *formal* to order someone to do something【正式】命令, 責令 **2** *AmE law* to legally prevent someone from going near a person or place【美, 法律】依法阻止〔某人〕接近〔某人或某地〕

en·joy /ɪnˈdʒɔɪ; ɪnˈdʒɔɪ/ *v* [T] **1** to get pleasure from something 喜歡; 享受…的樂趣: *Did you enjoy the movie?* 你喜歡那部電影嗎? | **enjoy doing sth** *Young children enjoy helping with household tasks.* 小孩子們喜歡幫着做家務。**2** to have something good such as success or a particular ability or advantage 享有; 擁有: *These workers enjoy a high level of job security.* 這些工人的工作非常穩定。**3 enjoy yourself** to be happy and experience pleasure in a particular situation 過得愉快; 感到快樂: *She was determined to enjoy herself at the party, even though her ex-boyfriend would be there.* 儘管她從前的男朋友會來, 她還是決心在晚會上痛痛快快地玩。**4 enjoy!** *AmE spoken* used when you give someone something and you want them to get pleasure from it【美口】好好享用吧!: *Here's your steak – enjoy!* 你的牛排來了, 好好享用吧!

USAGE NOTE 用法說明: ENJOY

GRAMMAR 語法

Enjoy is nearly always followed by a noun phrase, a pronoun, or by a verb with *-ing*. 絕大多數情況下, enjoy 後跟名詞片語、代名詞或是加 ing 的動詞: *Did you enjoy the movie? Yes, I enjoyed it a lot* (NOT 不用 *I enjoyed with/of it.*) 你喜歡那電影嗎? 是的, 我非常喜歡。| *I really enjoyed myself last night at the theater* (NOT 不用 *I enjoyed at the theater*). 我昨晚看戲看得很開心。| *He enjoys travelling very much* (NOT 不用 *He enjoys very much travelling* or *He enjoys to travel*). 他非常喜歡旅行。

3 **en·joy·a·ble** /ɪnˋdʒɔɪəbḷ; ɪnˈdʒɔɪəbəl/ *adj* something enjoyable gives you pleasure 使人愉快的, 令人快樂的: *games to make learning more enjoyable* 寓教於樂的遊戲 —**enjoyably** *adv*

en·joy·ment /ɪnˋdʒɔɪmənt; ɪnˈdʒɔɪmənt/ *n* **1** [U] the pleasure that you get from something 愉快, 樂趣: *Acting has brought me enormous enjoyment.* 演戲給我帶來巨大的快樂。**2** [C] something that you enjoy doing; AMUSEMENT (2) 樂事, 消遣, 娛樂: *Golf and bridge were just some of his enjoyments.* 打高爾夫球和打橋牌僅是他消遣方式的一部分。**3** [U] *formal* the fact of having something【正式】擁有, 享有

en·large /ɪnˋlɑrdʒ; ɪnˈlɑːdʒ/ *v* [I,T] to become bigger or to make something bigger (使) 增大, 擴大: *We're planning to enlarge the garden.* 我們正打算擴大花園。| *Travel enlarges the mind.* 旅遊使人心胸開闊。

enlarge on/upon sth *phr v* [T] to provide more facts or details about something you have already mentioned 詳述; 詳細說明: *Mrs Maughan did not enlarge on what she meant by 'unsuitable'.* 莫恩夫人並未具體講她所謂的"不合適"是甚麼意思。

en·large·ment /ɪnˋlɑrdʒmənt; ɪnˈlɑːdʒmənt/ *n* **1** [C] a photograph that has been printed again in a larger size 放大的照片 **2** [C,U] an increase in size or amount 擴大, 增大

en·lar·ger /ɪnˋlɑrdʒɚ; ɪnˈlɑːdʒə/ *n* [C] a piece of equipment for making photographs larger〔照片〕放大機

en·light·en /ɪnˋlaɪtṇ; ɪnˈlaɪtn/ *v* [T] *formal* to explain something to someone【正式】指導, 教導; 啟迪: *Baldwin enlightened her as to the nature of the experiment.* 鮑德溫給她講解了這個實驗的性質。—**enlightening** *adj*: *an enlightening explanation* 啟發性的解釋

en·light·ened /ɪnˋlaɪtṇd; ɪnˈlaɪtənd/ *adj* **1** treating people in a kind and sensible way and understanding their needs and problems 開明的: *The more enlightened factory owners built homes for their workers in Britain in the 19th century.* 在19世紀的英國, 較開明的工廠主為工人建造住所。**2** showing a good understanding of something and not believing things about it that are false 有見識的: *enlightened opinions* 明智的意見

En·light·en·ment /ɪnˋlaɪtṇmənt; ɪnˈlaɪtnmənt/ *n* **the Enlightenment** a period in the eighteenth century when many writers and scientists believed that science and knowledge, not religion, could improve people's lives〔18世紀的〕啟蒙運動

enlightenment *n* [U] **1** *formal* the state of understanding something clearly or the act of making someone understand something clearly【正式】領悟; 啟發, 開導 **2** the state in the BUDDHIST and HINDU religions, of no longer having any human desires, so that you are united spiritually with the universe〔佛教或印度教的〕覺悟, 般若〔指擺脫慾望達到最高的精神境界〕

en·list /ɪnˋlɪst; ɪnˈlɪst/ *v* **1 enlist sb's help** to persuade someone to help you 請求某人的幫助: *I enlisted the help of a local artist to do a painting for her birthday.* 我請一名當地畫家幫忙, 為她生日畫幅畫。**2** [I] to join the army, navy etc 參軍, 入伍: *In the first year of the war a million men enlisted voluntarily.* 戰爭的第一年, 有一百萬男人自願參軍。—see 見 JOIN¹ (USAGE) **3** [T+in/into] to persuade people to join your organisation 勸說某人加入〔組織〕—**enlistment** *n* [C,U]

enlisted man /ˌ·ˈ·· ·/ *n* [C] *AmE*【美】**enlisted man/woman** someone in the army, navy etc whose rank is below that of an officer 士兵/女兵

en·liv·en /ɪnˋlaɪvən; ɪnˈlaɪvən/ *v* [T] to make something more interesting or amusing 使…較生動活潑, 使…較有趣: *a talk enlivened by photos* 因有照片而生色的演說

en masse /ˌɑn ˋmæs; ˌɒn ˈmæs/ *adv French* if a group of people do something en masse, they all do it together【法】一起, 全體: *The senior management resigned en masse.* 高級管理人員全體辭職。

en·meshed /ɛnˋmɛʃt; ɪnˈmeʃt/ *adj* [not before noun 不用於名詞前] very involved in an unpleasant or complicated situation 陷入; 捲入: *Congress worried about becoming enmeshed in a foreign war.* 國會擔心會陷入一場外國戰爭。

en·mi·ty /ˋɛnmətɪ; ˈenmɨti/ *n* [C,U] *formal* the feeling of hatred or anger towards someone【正式】仇恨; 怨恨; 憤怒: *We must try to remove the causes of distrust and enmity between the two communities.* 我們必須設法消除兩個團體彼此不信任和敵視的根源。

en·no·ble /ɪˋnobḷ; ɪˈnəʊbəl/ *v* [T] *formal*【正式】**1** if something ennobles you it improves your character 使〔某人〕高尚; 使〔某人〕崇高 **2** to make someone a NOBLEMAN (=a member of the part of society that includes princes, DUKES) etc 封〔某人〕為貴族 —**ennoblement** *n* [U]

en·nui /ˋɑnwi; ɒnˈwiː/ *n* [U] *French formal* a feeling of being tired and bored, especially as a result of having nothing to do【法, 正式】〔尤指因無所事事引起的〕倦怠, 無聊

e·nor·mi·ty /ɪˋnɔrmətɪ; ɪˈnɔːmɨti/ *n* **1** [singular] the enormity of a situation, event etc is how serious it is or how big an effect it will have 嚴重(性);〔後果的〕深遠: *the enormity of his crimes* 他的罪行的嚴重性 **2** [U] the enormity of a problem, subject, job etc is how large or difficult it is〔問題、主題、工作等〕巨大; 艱巨: *Don't be put off by the enormity of the task.* 不要被任務的艱巨所嚇倒。**3** [C] an extremely serious and cruel act 極其兇殘的暴行

e·nor·mous /ɪˋnɔrməs; ɪˈnɔːməs/ *adj* extremely large in size or in amount〔尺寸、數量〕巨大的, 龐大的: *an enormous bouquet of flowers* 巨大的花束 | *The amount of paperwork involved is enormous.* 需要做的文書工作量非常大。—**enormously** *adv*: *enormously fat* 極其肥胖 —**enormousness** *n* [U] 2 3

enough 足夠

Joel wasn't tall enough to play.
喬爾不夠高不適合打球。

There wasn't enough cake for everyone.
蛋糕不夠分給每個人吃。

e·nough¹ /əˋnʌf; ɪˈnʌf/ *adv* **1** to the necessary degree 足夠(地): *Her sentence was light because the judge said she had suffered enough already.* 她的刑罰輕, 因為法官說她已經吃夠苦頭了。| *Are the carrots cooked enough?* 胡蘿蔔煮熟了嗎? **2 tall/kind/fast etc enough** as tall, kind, fast etc as is necessary 足夠高/友好/快等: *I didn't bring a big enough bag.* 我帶來的包不夠大。| *Is your tea sweet enough?* 你的茶夠甜嗎? | **[+for]** *Is it warm enough for you?* 你覺得夠暖和嗎? | **mad/tall/** 1 1 silly etc enough to do sth *Is the water hot enough for a bath?* 這水用來洗澡夠熱嗎? | *He said he would never see her again and I was gullible enough to believe him.* 他說他再也不會見她, 而我竟輕信了。| *Would you be kind enough to let us know when you are arriving?* 請你通知我們你到達的時間, 好嗎? | **not good enough** (=not satisfactory or acceptable) 不令人滿意; 不夠好 *I'm going to go up to that school and tell them it's just not good enough.* 我要到那個學校去, 告訴他們這樣讓人無法接受。**3 difficult/happy/busy etc enough** rather difficult, happy etc 相當困難/高興/忙碌等: *I was happy enough in Bordeaux, but I missed my family.* 我在波爾多過得不錯, 但還是想家。| *It's bad enough doing this without you giving me orders all the time.* 且不說你沒完沒了地指揮我, 做這件事本身就夠難為人。| *It was natural enough that she should be annoyed.* 她感到厭煩, 這再正常不過了。**4 strangely/oddly/curiously enough** although this is strange, odd etc 令人奇怪的是, 說來奇怪: *Funnily enough, I bumped into her only yesterday.* 說來好笑, 我昨天剛好碰見她。**5 near enough** *BrE spoken* nearly【英口】幾乎; 差不多: *Your jacket's near enough dry now.* 你的夾克現在差不多乾了。| *This bottle's near enough finished.* 這瓶酒快喝完了。| *That's £3000 near enough, isn't it?* 那大約是3000英鎊, 是不是? —see also 另見 **fair enough** (FAIR¹ (17)), **sure enough** (SURE² (2))

enough² *determiner, pron* **1** as much or as many as may be necessary 充分, 足夠: *Move over, I don't have enough room.* 挪一挪, 我的地方不夠大。| *Not enough is known about what really happened.* 究竟發生了甚麼事還沒有弄清楚。| *Leave the potatoes if you've had enough.* 如果你吃飽了, 就把馬鈴薯剩下吧。| **[+for]** *There aren't enough chairs for everyone.* 椅子不夠每人一把。| **enough to do/eat etc** *Erica was worried that the children weren't getting enough to eat.* 埃里卡擔心孩子們吃不飽。| **enough sth to do sth** *There's enough material left to make matching pillows.* 剩下的材料做配套的枕頭足夠了。| **more than enough** (=too much) 太多, 過多 *No, thank you, I've had more than enough.* 不, 謝謝, 我已經吃太多了。| **not nearly enough/nowhere near enough** (=much less than enough) 太少; 差得太遠 *There was nowhere near enough wine to go round.* 酒太少, 根本不夠大家喝。| **that's enough** *spoken* (=stop behaving like that)【口】不要那樣 *Now, David, that's quite enough – be a good boy.* 噢, 戴維, 行了, 乖點兒吧。| **enough is enough** *spoken* (=there is no need to say or do any more)【口】適可而止; 不必再… *I could lend him another $20 but, really, enough's enough.* 我可以再借給他 20 美元, 但凡事皆應適可而止。| **time/food etc enough** *There'll be time enough to get to know each other later on.* 以後會有足夠的時間相互了解。**2 have had enough (of sth)** *spoken* to be thoroughly tired or sick of something and want it to stop【口】受夠了: *When I got in from work I just sat down and cried. I'd had enough.* 下班後回到家, 我就坐下哭了起來。我受夠了。| *I've just about had enough of your sass.* 你的無禮我已經快要受夠了。**3 enough said** *spoken* there is no need to say any more, I understand everything【口】不用再說了〔我都明白了〕: *"I saw her coming out of his room at 6 o'clock this morning." "Enough said."* "今早6點鐘我看見她從他房間出來。" "不用再說了。" —see 見 ADEQUATE (USAGE)

USAGE NOTE 用法說明: ENOUGH

GRAMMAR 語法

Enough comes after adjectives and adverbs. enough 用在形容詞和副詞之後: *She's not old enough* (NOT 不用 *She's not enough old*). 她年紀不夠大。| *He didn't pack the bowls carefully enough and they broke.* 他在包裝碗的時候不夠小心, 結果碗都碎了。| *Well I've done my best, and I hope it's good enough.* 我已經盡力了, 我希望結果會令人滿意。

Enough usually comes before a plural or uncountable noun. enough 通常用在複數名詞或不可數名詞前: *enough people/money* 足夠的人/錢。It is only used after the noun in slightly formal or old-fashioned English. 只有在稍正式或過時的英語中, 才用於名詞後面: *There was money enough for all.* 錢足夠所有人花。However, *time enough* is still fairly common 但是, time enough 的用法還很常見: *There'll be time enough for that later.* 以後會有足夠的時間做那件事。

en pas·sant /ˌɑn pɑˋsɑn; ˌɒn ˈpæsɒn/ *adv French formal* if you say or mention something en passant, you say a few words about it while you are talking about something else【法, 正式】順便提到: *She happened to mention en passant, that she'd seen Joan.* 她順便提到她見過瓊。

en·quire /ɪnˋkwaɪr; ɪnˈkwaɪə/ *v* [I,T] *especially BrE*【尤英】another spelling of INQUIRE inquire 的另一種拼法

en·qui·ry /ɪnˋkwaɪrɪ; ɪnˈkwaɪəri/ *n* [C,U] *especially BrE*【尤英】another spelling of INQUIRY inquiry 的另一種拼法

en·rage /ɪnˋredʒ; ɪnˈreɪdʒ/ *v* [T] to make someone extremely angry 使〔某人〕非常憤怒; 激怒: *She asked him to leave, enraged by his sexist comments.* 他帶有性別歧視的言論激怒了她, 她叫他離開。

en·rap·tured /ɪnˋræptʃɚd; ɪnˈræptʃəd/ *adj formal* feeling such pleasure and happiness that you can think of nothing else【正式】着迷的; 心花怒放的: *The orchestra played before an enraptured audience.* 管弦樂隊的演奏使聽眾如醉如痴。

en·rich /ɪnˋrɪtʃ; ɪnˈrɪtʃ/ *v* [T] **1** to improve the quality of something, especially by adding things to it 使豐富, 充實; 富集, 強化: *a fertilizer that enriches the soil* 使土壤肥沃的肥料 | *Education can enrich your life.* 教育可以使生活充實。**2** to make someone richer 使〔某人〕更富裕 —**enrichment** *n* [U]

en·rol *BrE*【英】, **enroll** *AmE*【美】/ɪnˋrol; ɪnˈrəʊl/ *v* **enrolled, enrolling** [I,T] to officially arrange to join a school, university or course, or arrange for someone else to 招 (生), 吸收 (成員); 註冊 (學習): **[+on** *BrE* 英, **+in** *AmE* 美**]** *There were 500 people enrolled in the Western Civilization class.* 有 500 人註冊學習西方文明課。—see 見 JOIN¹ (USAGE) —**enrolment** *n* [C,U]

Enrolled Nurse /·,· ˈ·/ *n* [C] a nurse who has passed an examination in England, Scotland, or Wales〔英國的〕登記護士

en route /ˌɑn ˋrut; ˌɒn ˈruːt/ *adv French* on the way【法】在路上; 在途中: *We were going to the Florida Keys but we stopped en route to visit Miami.* 我們計劃到佛羅里達羣島去, 途中順道遊覽了邁阿密。| **[+from/for/to]** *a boat en route to the Bahamas* 去巴哈馬羣島途中的一艘船

en·sconce /ɛnˋskɑns; ɪnˈskɒns/ *v* [T] to put yourself in a comfortable and safe place 安頓: **ensconce yourself** *He ensconced himself in an armchair in front of the fire.* 他安坐於爐火前的扶手椅裡。| *safely ensconced in the penthouse suite* 安全地在頂樓套房安頓下來

en·sem·ble /ɑnˋsɑmbḷ; ɒnˈsɒmbəl/ *n* **1** [C] a small group of musicians who play together regularly〔經常在一起演奏的〕小樂隊, 合奏組: *The ensemble will play an all-Bach program tonight.* 合奏組今晚要演奏清一色的巴赫曲目。**2** [C usually singular 一般用單數] a set of clothes that are worn together 套服: *The leggings combined with a long black tunic made an attractive ensemble.* 黑色的長緊身外衣配上綁腿精神極了。**3** [C usually singular 一般用單數] a set of things that go together to form a whole 成套的東西

en·shrine /ɪnˋʃraɪn; ɪnˈʃraɪn/ *v* [T usually passive 一般用被動態] *formal* if something such as a law, tradition, or right is enshrined in something, it is preserved, especially in written form, so that people will remember and respect it【正式】銘記; 珍藏〔指法律、傳統或權利保存下來, 尤指用書面形式保存以使人銘記、珍視〕: **enshrine sth in** *Ancient practices and customs are enshrined in local folk literature.* 古代的風俗習慣傳承於當地的民間文學之中。| *inalienable rights enshrined in the Constitution* 神聖地記載在憲法中的不可剝奪的權利

en·shroud /ɪn`ʃraʊd; ɪn'ʃraʊd/ *v* [T] *formal*【正式】**1** if something such as mystery enshrouds something, it makes it difficult to understand or explain 使有神祕色彩; 使費解: *corn circles and the mystery that enshrouds them* 麥田怪圈以及這一現象所籠罩的神祕色彩 **2** to cover or hide something 遮蓋; 遮掩: *hills enshrouded in mist* 霧氣籠罩的羣山

en·sign /`ɛnsaɪn; 'ensaɪn/ *n* [C] **1** a flag on a ship that shows what country the ship belongs to〔表示船隻國籍的〕旗 **2** a low rank in the US navy, or an officer who has this rank〔美國〕海軍少尉 —see table on page C6 參見 C6 頁附錄 **3** an officer of low rank in the British army in the past〔英國舊時〕步兵少尉 **4** *AmE* a small piece of metal on your uniform that shows your rank【美】〔軍裝上表示等級的〕徽章, 標誌

en·slave /ɪn`slev; ɪn'sleɪv/ *v* [T usually passive 一般用被動態] **1** *formal* to trap someone in a situation that they cannot easily escape from【正式】束縛; 制約: *enslaved by marriage and trapped by taboos and prejudice* 受到婚姻約束並陷於禁忌和偏見之中 **2** to make someone into a slave 使成為奴隸, 奴役 —**enslavement** *n* [U]

en·snare /ɛn`snɛr; ɪn'sneə/ *v* [T] *formal* to force or trick someone into doing something that they do not want to do【正式】強迫[欺騙]〔某人做某事〕, 使入圈套: *ensnared into a loveless relationship* 受了騙陷入一種沒有愛的關係之中

en·sue /ɪn`su; ɪn'sjuː/ *v* [I] to happen as a result of something 因而發生, 繼而發生: *Serious problems will ensue if something is not done about gang rivalry now.* 如果不採取措施制止幫派爭鬥, 會發生嚴重的問題。

en·su·ing /ɪn`suɪŋ; ɪn'sjuːɪŋ/ *adj* [only before noun 僅用於名詞前] happening after a particular action or event, especially as a result of it 隨後的; 因而發生的: **the ensuing battle/argument/panic etc** *Japan attacked Port Arthur and in the ensuing Russo-Japanese war the Russians were defeated.* 日本襲擊了旅順口, 在接下來的日俄戰爭中俄國人打敗了。| **the ensuing year/six months/weeks etc** (=the time after an event) 隨後的一年/半年/幾星期等

en suite /ˌɑn `swit; ˌɒn 'swiːt◂/ *adj BrE* an en suite bathroom is joined onto a bedroom【英】〔浴室和臥室〕成套的, 構成一體的: *four bedrooms, two with en suite bathrooms* 四間臥室, 兩間帶浴室

3 **en·sure** *especially BrE*【尤英】/ɪn`ʃʊr; ɪn'ʃʊə/ *v* [T] to
1 make it certain that something will happen 確保, 保證: *All the necessary steps had been taken to ensure their safety.* 已採取所有必要措施以確保他們的安全。| [**+that**] *His wife ensured that he took all his pills every day.* 他妻子確保他每天都服下所有該服的藥片。—compare 比較 INSURE —see 見 INSURE (USAGE)

-ent /ənt; ənt/ *suffix* [in adjectives and nouns 構成形容詞和名詞] another form of the suffix -ANT 後綴 -ant 的另一種形式: *different* 不同的 | *residents* 居民

en·tail /ɪn`tel; ɪn'teɪl/ *v* [T] **1** to make it necessary to do something 使必須〔做某事〕; 需要: *Changing the computer system would entail substantial periods of retraining.* 改換電腦系統就需要進行相當長時間的再培訓。| **entail doing sth** *My job entailed being on call 24 hours a day.* 我的工作需要我一天 24 小時隨叫隨到。**2** *old use* to arrange for your property to become the property of a particular person, especially your son, after your death【舊】遺贈〔財產〕; 限定繼承

en·tan·gle /ɪn`tæŋgḷ; ɪn'tæŋgəl/ *v* [T always+adv/prep] to make something become twisted or caught in a rope, net etc〔用繩、網等〕纏住; 套住

en·tan·gled /ɪn`tæŋgḷd; ɪn'tæŋgəld/ *adj* **1** involved in an argument, or a situation that is difficult to escape from, or a relationship that causes problems etc 捲入…的; 陷於…的: [**+in**] *Military observers fear that the US could get entangled in another Vietnam.* 軍事觀察員們擔心美國會陷入另一場越南戰爭。| [**+with**] *Sue became romantically entangled with a work colleague.* 蘇與一個同事陷入感情糾葛中。**2** twisted or caught in something such as a rope or net 被纏住的, 被繞住的: [**+in/with**] *Penguins and seals have been found entangled in lengths of fishing net.* 發現企鵝和海豹纏在一段段的漁網裡。

en·tan·gle·ment /ɪn`tæŋgḷmənt; ɪn'tæŋgəlmənt/ *n* [C] **1** a difficult situation or relationship that is hard to escape from 糾纏; 糾葛: *emotional entanglements* 情感糾葛 **2** [C often plural 常用複數] a fence made of BARBED WIRE that prevents enemy soldiers from getting too close〔阻止敵人接近的〕帶刺鐵絲網圍欄

entendre *n* —see 見 DOUBLE ENTENDRE

en·tente /ɑn`tɑnt; ɒn'tɒnt/ *n* [C,U] *French* a situation in which two countries have friendly relations with each other【法】〔兩國間的〕友好關係, 和解

en·ter /`ɛntɚ; 'entə/ *v* 1

1 ►GO INTO 進入◄ **a)** [I,T] to go or come into a place 1
進入〔某處〕: *Silence fell as I entered the room.* 我一進屋大家就安靜下來。| *Adie was one of the few reporters who had dared to enter the war zone.* 埃迪是僅有的幾個敢於進入交戰區的記者之一。**b)** [T] if an object enters part of something, it goes inside it 進入〔某物中〕: *The bullet had entered his brain through the back of his skull.* 子彈穿過他的顱骨後部進入大腦。

2 ►START WORKING 開始工作◄ [I,T] to start working in a particular profession or organization 開始從事〔某職業〕; 加入〔某組織〕: *Andrea is studying law as a preparation for entering politics.* 安德烈婭正在學習法律為以後從政作準備。| *He entered the Church as a young man.* 他加入教會時很年輕。

3 ►START TO TAKE PART IN 開始參加◄ [T] to start to take part in an activity, for example a course or a game 開始參加〔活動〕: *Her doctor recommended that she enter a drug treatment program.* 她的醫生建議她接受戒毒治療。

4 ►COMPUTER 電腦◄ [T] **a)** to put information into a computer by pressing the keys 輸入〔信息〕: *If a command is entered incorrectly, the machine will not recognize it.* 如果命令輸入不正確, 機器就不能辨別。**b)** if you enter a computer system, you are given permission to use it by the computer 進入〔電腦系統〕

5 ►WRITE INFORMATION 寫下信息◄ [T] to write information on a particular part of a form, document etc〔在表格、文件等中〕寫下, 填上: *Enter your name in the space provided.* 在空白處填上你的姓名。

6 ►COMPETITION/EXAMINATION 競賽/考試◄ [I,T] to arrange to take part in a race, competition, examination etc, or to arrange for someone else to take part 報名參加〔賽跑、競賽、考試等〕; 安排〔某人〕參加: *I've entered you and Dan in the sack race.* 我已經安排你和丹參加套袋賽跑。

7 ►PERIOD OF TIME 時期◄ [T] **a)** to begin a period of time when something happens 進入…時期: *The economy entered a period of recession in the mid 1980s.* 20 世紀 80 年代中期, 經濟步入衰退時期。**b) enter its third week/sixth day/second year etc** if something enters its third week, its sixth day etc, it continues for a third week, a sixth day etc 進入第三週/第六天/第二年等: *The talks have now entered their third week.* 會談已進入第三週。

8 it never entered my mind/head *spoken* used when you are very surprised by what has happened【口】我從未想到: *It never entered my head that he would have a gun.* 我從未想到他會有槍。

9 ►CHANGE 改變◄ [T] if a particular quality enters something, it starts to exist in it and change it, especially suddenly〔尤指突然〕具有某種特質: *A note of panic entered her voice.* 她的聲音突然透出一絲恐慌。
10 enter sb's life if someone or something enters your life, you start to know them or be affected by them 進入某人的生活: *By the time Angie entered his life, he was almost 30.* 安吉走進他的生活時, 他已差不多30歲了。
11 ►START DISCUSSING 開始討論◄ [T] to start to discuss or study a particular subject 開始討論; 開始研究: *Here we enter a disputed and delicate area of the law.* 這裡我們開始研究法律當中一個充滿爭議且十分微妙的領域。
12 enter a plea of guilty/not guilty *law* to say that you are guilty or not guilty of a particular crime in a court【法律】〔在法庭上〕承認/否認有罪
13 enter an offer/complaint/objection etc *formal* to officially make an offer, complaint etc【正式】正式提出建議/申訴/反對等

enter into sth *phr v* [T] **1** to start doing something, especially discussing or studying something 開始做某事〔尤指討論或研究某事〕: *This is not the place to enter into a detailed discussion of economic policy.* 這裡不是詳細討論經濟政策的地方。**2** to affect a situation and be something that you must consider when you make a choice 十分有影響; 干係重大: *Money doesn't enter into it – it's the principle I object to.* 錢在這件事上無關緊要, 我反對的是原則。**3 enter into an agreement/contract etc** *formal* to officially make an agreement to do something【正式】達成協議/合同等 **4 enter into the spirit of it/things** to take part in a game, party etc in an eager way 急切地參加, 興致勃勃地參與; 進入角色

enter upon sth *phr v* [T] *formal* to start doing something or being involved in it【正式】開始做某事; 開始參與某事

Frequencies of **enter** and **go/come in** in spoken and written English 在英語口語和書面語中 enter和 go/come in的使用頻率

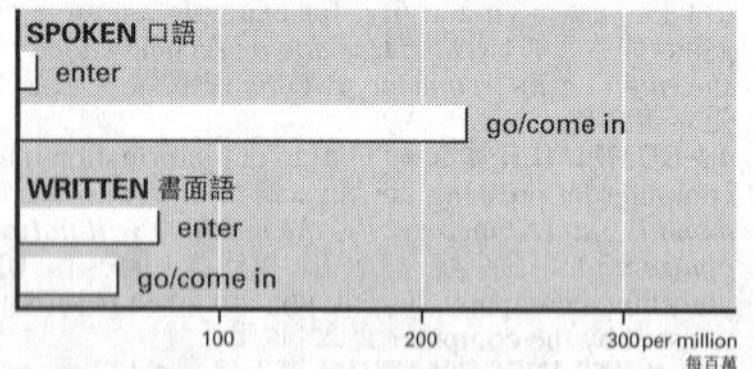

Based on the British National Corpus and the Longman Lancaster Corpus
據英國國家語料庫和朗文蘭卡斯特語料庫

This graph shows that it is much more usual in spoken English to use the expressions **go in** and **come in**, rather than the word **enter**. This is because **enter** is a formal word when used in this meaning and is more common in written English. 本圖表顯示, 在英語口語中 go in 和 come in 的使用頻率要遠遠高於 enter, 這是因為 enter 用於此意時是一個較正式的詞, 所以它更常見於英語書面語中。

en·te·ri·tis /ˌɛntəˋraɪtɪs; ˌentəˈraɪtɪ̈s/ *n* [U] a painful infection in your INTESTINES 腸炎

2 **en·ter·prise** /ˋɛntɚˌpraɪz; ˈentəpraɪz/ *n* **1** [C] a large and complicated piece of work, especially one that is done with a group of other people〔尤指與人合作的〕大型而複雜的工作: *a joint scientific enterprise* 聯合科學事業 **2** [U] the ability to think of new activities or ideas and make them work 創業能力, 開創能力: *a woman with enterprise and creativity* 富有開創精神的婦女 **3** [C] a company, organization, or business 企業, 公司; 組織: *state-owned enterprises* 國有企業 **4** [U] the practice of starting and running small companies 創立和經營小企業(的行為): *a knowledge of American capitalist enterprise* 美國資本主義企業經營之道 —see also 另見 FREE ENTERPRISE, PRIVATE ENTERPRISE

enterprise cul·ture /ˈ··· ˌ··/ *n* [C,U] a society or attitude in which starting successful businesses is believed to be very important 創業文化〔高度重視開創成功企業的社會或態度〕

en·ter·pris·ing /ˋɛntɚˌpraɪzɪŋ; ˈentəpraɪzɪŋ/ *adj* showing the ability to think of new activities or ideas and make them work 富於創業精神的; 具有開創能力的: *An enterprising young student was selling copies of the answers to the test.* 一名別出心裁的年輕學生正在出售測驗答案的複印件。—**enterprisingly** *adv*

en·ter·tain /ˌɛntɚˋten; ˌentəˈteɪn/ *v* **1** [I,T] to invite people to your home for a meal or party or take your company's customers to have a meal, drinks etc 招待, 款待, 請客: *The restaurant is mainly used by executives entertaining clients.* 這家飯店主要是公司老總們用來宴請客戶的地方。**2** [T] to do something that amuses or interests people 使〔某人〕快樂; 使〔某人〕有興趣: **entertain sb with** *He entertained us with a stream of anecdotes about the Yukon.* 他講了一連串有關育空地區的趣事引我們開心。**3 entertain an idea/hope/doubt etc** to think that something might be true, even for a short period of time 懷有想法/希望/疑惑等

en·ter·tain·er /ˌɛntɚˋtenɚ; ˌentəˈteɪnə/ *n* [C] someone who tells jokes, sings etc to amuse people〔以講笑話、唱歌等來逗樂的〕表演者, 藝人: *street entertainers* 街頭藝人

en·ter·tain·ing[1] /ˌɛntɚˋtenɪŋ; ˌentəˈteɪnɪŋ◂/ *adj* amusing and interesting 使人愉快的, 有趣的: *very entertaining storyteller* 妙趣橫生的説書人 | *an entertaining evening* 一個令人開心的夜晚

entertaining[2] *n* [U] the practice of inviting people for meals or to parties, especially for business reasons〔尤指出於生意原因的〕宴請; 招待客戶

en·ter·tain·ment /ˌɛntɚˋtenmənt; ˌentəˈteɪnmənt/ *n* **1** [U] things such as films, television, performances etc that amuse or interest people 娛樂節目: *providing entertainment for tourists* 為遊客提供娛樂節目 **2** [C] a performance or show 娛樂表演: *a musical entertainment* 音樂演出

en·thral also 又作 **enthrall** *especially AmE*【尤美】/ɛnˋθrɔl; ɪnˈθrɔːl/ *v* [T] to make someone so interested and excited that they listen or watch something very carefully 迷住〔某人〕, 使〔某人〕着迷

en·thralled /ɛnˋθrɔld; ɪnˈθrɔːld/ *adj* so interested that you pay a lot of attention to what you are seeing or hearing 着迷的, 被強烈吸引的: *Richard listened, enthralled by the Captain's stories.* 理查德聽着, 完全被船長的故事吸引住了。

en·thrall·ing /ɛnˋθrɔlɪŋ; ɪnˈθrɔːlɪŋ/ *adj* extremely interesting 迷人的, 非常有趣的

en·throne /ɪnˋθron; ɪnˈθrəʊn/ *v* [T usually passive 一般用被動態] to have a ceremony to show that a new king or queen is beginning to rule 為…舉行登基儀式 —**enthronement** *n* [C,U]

en·thuse /ɪnˋθjuz; ɪnˈθjuːz/ *v* **1** [I] to talk about something in a very interested or excited way 津津樂道地講述, 興奮地説: **[+about/over]** *Jenny spent the entire evening enthusing about her new car.* 詹妮整個晚上都在津津樂道地大談她的新汽車。**2** [T] to make someone interested in something or excited by it 使〔某人〕對…感興趣, 激起〔某人〕熱情

en·thu·si·as·m /ɪnˋθjuzɪˌæzəm; ɪnˈθjuːziæzəm/ *n* **1** [U] a strong feeling of interest and enjoyment about something and an eagerness to be involved in it 熱情, 熱忱: *Although she's a beginner, she played with great enthusiasm.* 雖然她是個新手, 但演奏時卻充滿了激情。| **[+for]** *He shares your enthusiasm for jazz.* 他與你一樣愛好爵士樂。| **lack of enthusiasm** *the government's lack of enthusiasm for women's rights* 政府對維護婦女

權益的不熱心 **2** [C] *formal* an activity or subject that someone is very interested in【正式】熱衷的活動; 熱愛的事物

en·thu·si·ast /ɪn`θjuzɪˌæst; ɪn'θjuːziæst/ *n* [C] someone who is very interested in a particular activity or subject 熱衷者, 熱心的人: *a golfing enthusiast* 高爾夫球迷

3 **en·thu·si·as·tic** /ɪnˌθjuzɪ`æstɪk; ɪnˌθjuːzi'æstɪk◂/ *adj* showing a lot of interest and excitement about something〔對某事物〕熱心的, 熱衷的: *The singer got an enthusiastic reception.* 那個歌手受到了熱情歡迎。| **[+about]** *I was less than enthusiastic about the idea of Bob coming to visit.* 我對鮑勃來訪的事一點都不起勁。—**enthusiastically** /-klɪ; -kli/ *adv*

en·tice /ɪn`taɪs; ɪn'taɪs/ *v* [T] to persuade someone to do something by offering them something if they will do it 誘惑; 誘使: **entice sb away/across/down etc** *He tried to entice the dog away from its post by the door.* 那條狗守在門旁, 他試圖誘使牠離開。| **entice sb** *Banks are offering low interest rates in an attempt to entice new customers.* 銀行在降低利率以吸引新客戶。—**enticement** *n* [C,U]

en·ti·cing /ɪn`taɪsɪŋ; ɪn'taɪsɪŋ/ *adj* very pleasant or interesting so that you feel strongly attracted 有吸引力的; 迷人的; 有誘惑力的: *It was a hot day and the water looked enticing.* 天氣熱, 水看起來十分誘人。—**enticingly** *adv*

3 **en·tire** /ɪn`taɪr; ɪn'taɪə/ *adj* [only before noun 僅用於名
2 詞前] the entire group, amount, period of time etc is used when you want to emphasize what you are saying 全部的, 整個的: *the entire staff* 所有職員 | *We spent the entire afternoon gossiping.* 我們整個下午都在聊天。

2 **en·tire·ly** /ɪn`taɪrlɪ; ɪn'taɪəli/ *adv* completely and in ev-
2 ery possible way 完全地, 徹底地: *an entirely different matter* 完全不同的事 | *She devoted herself entirely to her research.* 她全心全意地投入到研究當中。| **consist/depend entirely etc** *The programme consists entirely of taped interviews with survivors of the Holocaust.* 這個節目全部由猶太人大屠殺的倖存者的訪談錄音組成。

en·tir·e·ty /ɪn`taɪrtɪ; ɪn'taɪərəti/ *n* [U] **in its/their entirety** *formal* as a whole and including every part【正式】整體, 全部: *The correspondence has been published in its entirety for the first time.* 那些信件第一次被全文發表。

2 **en·ti·tle** /ɪn`taɪtl̩; ɪn'taɪtl/ *v* [T] **1** if something entitles
2 you to something, it gives you the official right to have or do it 給予〔某人獲得某物或做某事的〕權利: **be entitled to sth** *Mothers under 16 were entitled to a maternity grant of £25 a week.* 不滿16歲的母親有資格每週領取25英鎊的育兒補貼。**2 be entitled sth** if a book, play etc is entitled something, that is its name 給〔書、劇等〕命名, 起名: *an autobiography entitled "Myself, My Two Countries"* 一本名為《我自己, 我的兩個祖國》的自傳 **3 be entitled to do something** *Ricardo believes his daughter is perfectly entitled to marry whoever she chooses.* 里卡爾多相信他的女兒完全有權選擇要嫁給誰。

en·ti·tle·ment /ɪn`taɪtl̩mənt; ɪn'taɪtlmənt/ *n* [C,U] the official right to have or receive something, or the amount that you receive〔擁有或獲得某物的〕權利; 津貼: *welfare entitlements* 福利待遇 | **[+to]** *The amount of money you earn does not affect your entitlement to child benefit.* 你掙的錢並不影響你可以領取的子女津貼。

en·ti·ty /`ɛntətɪ; 'entəti/ *n* [C] *formal* something that exists as a single and complete unit【正式】實體: *The mind and body are seen as separate entities.* 心靈和身體被看成是各自獨立的實體。

en·tomb /ɪn`tum; ɪn'tuːm/ *v* [T often in passive 常用被動態] *formal* to bury or trap someone under the ground【正式】埋葬, 掩埋

en·to·mol·o·gy /ˌɛntə`mɑlədʒɪ; ˌentə'mɒlədʒi/ *n* [U] the scientific study of insects 昆蟲學 —**entomologist** *n* [C] —**entomological** /ˌɛntəmə`lɑdʒɪkl̩; ˌentəmə'lɒdʒɪkəl◂/ *adj*

en·tou·rage /ˌɑntu`rɑʒ; 'ɒntʊrɑːʒ/ *n* [C usually singular 一般用單數, also+plural verb *BrE* 英] a group of people who travel with an important person 隨從, 隨行人員: *the popstar and her entourage* 流行歌星和她的隨行人員

en·trails /`ɛntrəlz; 'entreɪlz/ *n* [plural] the inside parts of an animal or person's body, especially their BOWELs 內臟〔尤指腸〕

en·trance /`ɛntrəns; 'entrəns/ *n* **1** [C] a door, gate etc that you go through to enter a place〔門等的〕入口, 通道: **[+to/of]** *the main entrance to the school* 學校的大門 —opposite 反義詞 EXIT[1] **2** [C usually singular 一般用單數] the act of entering a place or room 進入, 進門: *Their conversation was interrupted by the entrance of four visitors.* 他們的談話因進來了四個來訪者而被打斷。**3** [U] permission to become a member of or become involved in a profession, university, society etc〔某行業、大學、社團等的〕進入許可: *entrance examinations* 入學考試 | **gain entrance to** *By some chance he gained entrance to the Indian Civil Service.* 機緣湊巧, 他加入了(殖民時代的)印度文職部門。**4** [U] the right or ability to go into a place〔某場所的〕進入權; 進入〔某場所的〕本領: *entrance fees* 入場費 | **gain entrance to** *No one is sure how the men gained entrance to the factory.* 沒人確切知道那些人是怎麼進入工廠的。**5 make your/an entrance a)** to come on to the stage in a play 登台, 出場〔表演戲劇〕: *The hero doesn't make his entrance until Act II, Scene 2.* 男主角直到第二幕第二場才出台。**b)** to enter a room, especially in a way that makes everyone notice you 進入房間〔尤指以引人注目的方式進入〕: *Lady Elizabeth made a noisy entrance.* 伊莉莎白小姐進屋時動靜很大。

en·tranced /ɪn`trænst; ɪn'trɑːnst/ *adj* very interested in and pleased with something so that you pay a lot of attention to it 着迷的, 非常喜愛的: *entranced by the sweetness of her voice* 被她甜美的聲音迷住了 —**entrance** *v* [T]

en·tran·cing /ɪn`trænsɪŋ; ɪn'trɑːnsɪŋ/ *adj* very interesting and attractive 使人着迷的, 迷人的

en·trant /`ɛntrənt; 'entrənt/ *n* [C] *formal* someone entering a competition, university, or profession【正式】參賽者; 大學新生; 新成員: *The winning entrant will receive a £500 scholarship.* 比賽獲勝者將獲得500英鎊的獎學金。

en·trap /ɪn`træp; ɪn'træp/ *v* [T] *formal* to trap someone, especially by tricking or deceiving them【正式】使〔某人〕陷入圈套; 誘捕: *cunning and devious questions intended to entrap her* 旨在讓她上當的狡詐問題

en·trap·ment /ɪn`træpmənt; ɪn'træpmənt/ *n* [U] the practice of trapping someone by tricking them, especially to show that they are guilty of a crime 誘捕

en·treat /ɪn`trit; ɪn'triːt/ *v* [T] *formal* to ask someone to do something for you in a way that shows you are very upset【正式】懇求; 乞求

en·trea·ty /ɪn`tritɪ; ɪn'triːti/ *n* [C,U] *formal* a serious request in which you ask someone to do something for you【正式】懇求; 乞求

en·trée /`ɑntre; 'ɒntreɪ/ *n French*【法】**1** [C] the main dish of a meal 主菜, 正菜 **2** [C,U] *formal* the right or freedom to enter a place or to join a group of people【正式】進入權: **[+to/into]** *The letter provided an easy entrée to the court at Turin.* 憑這封信容易覲見都靈的王族。

en·trenched /ɪn`trɛntʃt; ɪn'trentʃt/ *adj* strongly established and not likely to change 牢固的: **entrenched attitudes/habits/positions etc** *The government's attitude now seems less entrenched.* 政府的態度現在似乎不那麼強硬了。| **deeply/firmly entrenched** *deeply entrenched racial views* 頑固的種族偏見

en·trench·ment /ɪn`trɛntʃmənt; ɪn'trentʃmənt/ *n* **1** [U] the process in which an attitude, belief etc becomes firmly established〔態度、信念等的〕牢固確立 **2** [C] a system of TRENCHes (=long deep holes) dug by soldiers for defence or protection 塹壕

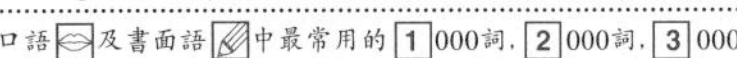

口語 及書面語 中最常用的 1 000詞, 2 000詞, 3 000詞

en·tre nous /ˌɑntrə `nu; ˌɒntrə 'nuː/ *adv French spoken* an expression used to tell someone that what you are going to say is secret and they must not tell anyone else【法口】你知我知, 不得外傳

en·tre·pre·neur /ˌɑntrəprə`nɝ; ˌɒntrəprə'nɜː/ *n* [C] someone who starts a company, arranges business deals, and takes risks in order to make a profit 企業家 —**entrepreneurial** *adj*: *entrepreneurial skills* 企業家的技能

en·tro·py /`ɛntrəpɪ; 'entrəpi/ *n* [U] *technical* a measure of the lack of order in a system, that includes the idea that the lack of order increases over a period of time【術語】熵

en·trust, intrust /ɪn`trʌst; ɪn'trʌst/ *v* [T] to make someone responsible for doing something important 委託, 交代: **entrust sb with sth** *I was entrusted with the task of looking after the money.* 我受委託負責保管錢。| **entrust sth to sb** *The infant Prince was entrusted to an English nurse, Miss Shaw.* 年幼的王子被託付給一位姓蕭英國護士照料。

en·try /`ɛntrɪ; 'entri/ *n*

1 ►COMPETITION 競賽◄ [C] **a)** a set of answers, a song or picture etc that is intended to win a competition 參賽的事物[作品]: *Over a thousand entries were received within the first week of the competition.* 競賽第一週內就收到了一千多件參賽作品。**b)** [usually singular 一般用單數] the number of people or things taking part in a competition 參賽者[物]的數量: *We've attracted a record entry this year.* 今年我們吸引到的參賽者數量創造了紀錄。

2 ►BECOMING INVOLVED 參與◄ [C,U] a situation in which someone starts to take part in a system, a particular kind of work etc, or joins a group of people 參加, 加入: *the entry of women into the paid labour force* 婦女加入有償勞動者隊伍 | **gain entry** (=become involved) 加入, 參與 *More Eastern European countries hope to gain entry to the European Union in the next few years.* 更多的東歐國家希望在今後幾年內加入歐盟。

3 ►RIGHT TO ENTER 進入權◄ [U] the right to enter a place, building etc 進入某地[樓房等]的權利: *an entry visa* 入境簽證 | **no entry** (=a phrase written on signs to show that you are not allowed to go into a place or through a particular door) 禁止入內

4 ►ACT OF ENTERING 進入的動作◄ [C,U] the act of going into something 進入〔的動作〕: **[+into]** *the triumphal entry of the Russian army into the city* 俄國軍隊的勝利進城 | **gain entry** (=get into a place, especially when this is difficult or illegal)〔尤指克服困難或非法地〕進入 *The thieves gained entry through an open kitchen window.* 竊賊是從廚房一扇開着的窗戶進來的。

5 ►DOOR 門◄ [C] a door, gate, or passage that you go through to enter a place 門; 入口; 通道 —see also 另見 ENTRANCE[1] (1)

6 ►STH WRITTEN 文字◄ [C] a short piece of writing in an ENCYCLOPAEDIA, DIARY etc〔百科全書〕條目;〔日記的〕一則: *The journal's last few entries described the events vividly.* 日記最後幾天的記錄生動描述了所發生的事。

7 ►COMPUTER 電腦◄ [U] the act of writing of information onto a computer 輸入, 錄入: *data entry* 數據輸入

en·try·phone /`ɛntrɪˌfon; 'entrifəʊn/ *n* [C] a type of telephone outside a building that allows visitors to ask someone inside to open the door〔樓房外讓訪客叫樓內的人開門的〕對講機

en·try·way /`ɛntrɪˌwe; 'entriweɪ/ *n* [C] *AmE* a passage or small room you go through to enter a place【美】〔作為入口的〕通道; 小房間

en·twine /ɪn`twaɪn; ɪn'twaɪn/ *v* [I,T often passive 常用被動態] **1** to twist two things together or to wind one thing around another (使) 交錯; (使) 纏繞: *They walked together with their arms entwined.* 他們挽着胳膊一起走。**2 be entwined** to be closely connected with each other in a complicated way 緊密聯繫在一起: *The meaning of art and the meaning of life are almost inextricably entwined.* 藝術和生活的含義幾乎是密不可分的。

E num·ber /`i ˌnʌmbɚ; 'iː ˌnʌmbə/ *n* [C] *BrE* a number representing a chemical that has been added to a food, shown on the outside of a container【英】〔容器上標明食品所含特定化學品的〕E 數

e·nu·me·rate /ɪ`njuməˌret; ɪ'njuːməreɪt/ *v* [T] *formal* to name a list of things one by one【正式】數, 點; 列舉

e·nun·ci·ate /ɪ`nʌnsɪˌet; ɪ'nʌnsieɪt/ *v* **1** [I,T] to pronounce words clearly and carefully〔清晰仔細地〕發(音); 唸(字) —see also 另見 ARTICULATE[2] (2) **2** [T] *formal* to express an idea clearly and exactly【正式】〔清楚準確地〕闡明; 闡述: *the theory Darwin was to enunciate decades later* 數十年後達爾文將會闡述的理論 —**enunciation** /ɪˌnʌnsɪ`eʃən; ɪˌnʌnsi'eɪʃən/ *n* [U]

e·nure /ɪ`njur; ɪ'njʊə/ *v* [T] another spelling of INURE inure 的另一種拼法

en·vel·op /ɪn`vɛləp; ɪn'veləp/ *v* [T] to wrap something up or cover it completely 包住; 覆蓋: *mountain peaks enveloped in thick mist* 隱沒在濃霧中的羣峰 —**enveloping** *adj* —**envelopment** *n* [U]

en·ve·lope /`ɛnvəˌlop; 'envələʊp/ *n* [C] **1** a thin paper cover in which you put a letter 信封 **2** a layer of something that surrounds something else 外裹物; 外層: **[+of]** *an envelope of gases around the planet* 包圍着行星的大氣層

en·vi·a·ble /`ɛnvɪəbl̩; 'enviəbəl/ *adj* an enviable quality, position, or possession is good and other people would like to have it 令人羨慕的: *Now he was in the enviable position of not having to work for a living.* 現在他已不必為生計而工作, 着實令人羨慕。—**enviably** *adv*

en·vi·ous /`ɛnvɪəs; 'enviəs/ *adj* wanting something that someone else has 妒忌的; 羡慕的: *an envious look* 妒忌的神色 | **[+of]** *Her colleagues were envious of her success.* 她的同事都羡慕她的成功。—see also 另見 JEALOUS —**enviously** *adv*

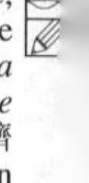

en·vi·ron·ment /ɪn`vaɪrənmənt; ɪn'vaɪərənmənt/ *n* [C, U] **1** all the situations, events, people etc that influence the way in which people live or work 環境, 周圍狀況: *a helpful learning environment* 有益的學習環境 | *a more competitive economic environment* 競爭更激烈的經濟環境 **2 the environment** the air, water, and land in which people, animals, and plants live 自然環境: *More legislation is needed to protect the environment.* 需要制定更多法律來保護環境。—see also 另見 ECOLOGY

en·vi·ron·ment·al /ɪnˌvaɪrən`mɛntl̩; ɪnˌvaɪərən'mentl◄/ *adj* concerning or affecting the air, land, or water on Earth 自然環境的; 影響自然環境的: *the environmental damage caused by the chemical industry* 化學工業對環境造成的危害 —**environmentally** *adv*

en·vi·ron·men·tal·ist /ɪnˌvaɪrən`mɛntl̩ɪst; ɪnˌvaɪərən'mentəl-ɪst/ *n* [C] someone who is concerned about protecting the environment 環境保護主義者, 環境保護論者 —**environmentalism** *n* [U]

environmentally friend·ly /ˌ···· `··◄/ also 又作 **environment friendly** /ˌ··· `··/ *adj* soaps, containers etc that are environmentally friendly do not harm the environment〔肥皂、容器等〕對環境無害的, 不損害環境的

en·vi·rons /ɪn`vaɪrənz; 'envɪrənz/ *n* [plural] *formal* the area surrounding a place【正式】附近的地方; 周圍環境: *Geneva and its immediate environs* 日內瓦及其近郊

en·vis·age /ɛn`vɪzɪdʒ; ɪn'vɪzɪdʒ/ also 又作 **en·vi·sion** *AmE*【美】/ɛn`vɪʒən; ɪn'vɪʒən/ *v* [T] to imagine that something will happen in the future 展望; 設想: *I don't envisage any major problems.* 我想不會有甚麼大問題。

en·voy /`ɛnvɔɪ; 'envɔɪ/ *n* [C] someone who is sent to another country as an official representative 使者, 代表; 外交官: *A special envoy was sent to try to secure the release of the hostages.* 派了一名特使以設法確保人質獲釋。

en·vy[1] /`ɛnvɪ; 'envi/ *v* **envied, envying** [T] to wish that you had someone else's possessions, abilities etc 忌妒;

羡慕: *Evelyn was good-looking, rich, and intelligent – all the girls envied her.* 伊夫琳漂亮、富有而且聰明, 所有的女孩都羡慕她。| **envy sb (for) sth** *He envied Rosalind for her youth and strength.* 他羡慕羅莎琳德的青春和活力。—compare 比較 JEALOUS

envy² *n* [U] **1** the feeling of wanting something that someone else has 忌妒; 羡慕: *He stared with envy at Robert's new car.* 他羡慕地盯着羅伯特的新汽車。| **green with envy** (=envying someone a lot) 忌妒極了; 羡慕極了 **2 be the envy of** to be something that other people admire and want to have very much 是令人羡慕[忌妒]的事物: *Britain's National Health Service was once the envy of the world.* 英國的國民保健制度曾一度為世人所羡慕。—compare 比較 JEALOUSY

en·zyme /ˋɛnzaɪm; ˈenzaɪm/ *n* [C] *technical* a chemical substance produced by living cells in plants and animals, that causes changes in other chemical substances without being changed itself【術語】酶: *the digestive enzymes in your stomach* 胃中的消化酶

e·on /ˋiən; ˈiːən/ *n* [C] another spelling of AEON aeon 的另一種拼法

ep·au·let, epaulette /ˋɛpə,lɛt; ˌepəˈlet/ *n* [C] a small piece of cloth decorating the shoulder of a coat or shirt, especially on a uniform〔尤指制服上的〕肩飾, 肩章

é·pée /eˋpe; ˈepeɪ/ *n* [C] *French* a narrow sword with a sharp point, used in the sport of FENCING (1)【法】〔擊劍用的〕重劍

e·phem·e·ra /əˋfɛmərə; ɪˈfemərə/ *n* [plural] things that are only popular or important for a short time 短暫流行的事物; 僅在短期內重要的事物: *records, pictures of popstars, and other such ephemera* 唱片、流行歌星照片以及諸如此類只會短暫流行的東西

e·phem·e·ral /əˋfɛmərəl; ɪˈfemərəl/ *adj* popular or important for only a short time 短暫流行的; 只重要一時的: *Fashions are by nature fickle and ephemeral.* 在本質上, 時裝式樣變化無常, 流行時間短暫。—**ephemerally** *adv*

ep·ic¹ /ˋɛpɪk; ˈepɪk/ *n* [C] **1** a book, poem, or film that tells a long story 長篇敍事性小說、詩歌、電影等作品; 史詩般的作品: *Universal Pictures' dinosaur epic "Jurassic Park"*〔美國〕環球影片公司講述恐龍的史詩般作品《侏羅紀公園》**2** a long poem that tells the story of what gods or important people did in ancient times〔講述神仙或古代重要人物的故事的〕史詩: *Homer's epic "Iliad"* 荷馬的史詩《伊利亞特》

epic² *adj* **1** epic stories or poems are full of brave actions and events 英雄的, 英勇的: *Phileas Fogg's epic journey around the world* 菲萊亞斯·弗格勇敢的環球旅行 **2** very big or impressive 巨大的, 宏偉的: **of epic proportions** *They organized a banquet of epic proportions.* 他們組織了盛大的宴會。

ep·i·cen·tre *BrE*【英】, **epicenter** *AmE*【美】/ˋɛpɪ,sɛntɚ; ˈepɪˌsentə/ *n* [C] a place on the surface of the Earth that is above the point where an EARTHQUAKE begins inside the Earth 震中, 震央

ep·i·cure /ˋɛpɪ,kjʊr; ˈepɪkjʊə/ *n* [C] *formal* someone who enjoys good food and drink; GOURMET【正式】美食家

ep·i·cu·re·an /,ɛpɪkjʊˋriən; ˌepɪkjʊˈriːən◂/ *adj formal* gaining pleasure from the senses, especially through good food and drink【正式】〔尤指在吃喝上〕愛奢侈享受的 —**epicurean** *n* [C]

ep·i·dem·ic /,ɛpəˋdɛmɪk; ˌepɪ̈ˈdemɪk◂/ *n* [C] **1** a large number of cases of a particular infectious disease occuring at the same time 流行病, 傳染病: *a flu epidemic* 流行性感冒 **2** a sudden increase in the amount of times that something bad happens〔壞事的〕發生次數陡增; 頻率突增: *the recent epidemic of car thefts* 近來頻繁發生的汽車被盜案件 —**epidemic** *adj*: *Violence is reaching epidemic proportions in the inner cities.* 市中心貧民區的暴力事件幾近泛濫。

ep·i·der·mis /,ɛpəˋdɝmɪs; ˌepɪ̈ˈdɜːmɪ̈s/ *n* [C,U] *technical* the outside layer of your skin【術語】表皮

ep·i·dur·al /,ɛpəˋdjurəl; ˌepɪˈdjuːrəl◂/ *n* [C] a medical process in which a drug is put into your lower back to prevent you feeling pain, especially when you are having a baby 硬脊膜外注射 (麻醉)

ep·i·glot·tis /,ɛpəˋglɑtɪs; ˌepɪ̈ˈglɒtɪ̈s/ *n* [C] a thin piece of flesh at the back of your throat〔喉後部的〕會厭 —see picture at 參見 RESPIRATORY 圖

ep·i·gram /ˋɛpə,græm; ˈepɪ̈græm/ *n* [C] a short sentence that expresses an idea in a clever or amusing way 警句, 雋語

ep·i·gram·mat·ic /,ɛpəgrəˋmætɪk; ˌepɪ̈grəˈmætɪk◂/ *adj* expressed in a way that is short, clever, and amusing 雋語式的, 簡練幽默的 —**epigrammatically** /-klɪ; -kli/ *adv*

ep·i·lep·sy /ˋɛpə,lɛpsɪ; ˈepɪ̈lepsi/ *n* [U] a medical condition in the brain that can suddenly make you become unconscious or unable to control your movements 癲癇, 羊癇瘋

ep·i·lep·tic¹ /,ɛpəˋlɛptɪk; ˌepɪ̈ˈleptɪk◂/ *adj* caused by epilepsy 癲癇的: *an epileptic fit* 癲癇發作

epileptic² *n* [C] someone who has epilepsy 癲癇患者

ep·i·logue also 又作 **epilog** *AmE*【美】/ˋɛpə,lɔg; ˈepɪ̈lɒg/ *n* **1** [C] a speech or piece of writing added to the end of a book, film, or play〔書的〕跋, 後記;〔電影、戲劇的〕收場白 **2** [singular] *literary* something that happens at the end of a series of events【文】〔一系列事件的〕尾聲, 結尾 —compare 比較 PROLOGUE

E·piph·a·ny /ɪˋpɪfənɪ; ɪˈpɪfəni/ *n* [not with *the* 不與 the 連用] a Christian holy day on January 6th that celebrates the Three Kings coming to see the baby Jesus〔基督教 1 月 6 日的〕主顯節〔為紀念三博士拜見聖嬰耶穌的節日〕

epiphany *n* [C] *literary* a moment of sudden very strong emotions【文】一陣突發的強烈情感

e·pis·co·pa·cy /ɪˋpɪskəpəsɪ; ɪˈpɪskəpəsi/ also 又作 **e·pis·co·pate** /ɪˋpɪskəpɪt; ɪˈpɪskəpət/ *n* [U] *technical*【術語】**1** the rank of a BISHOP (=a priest of high rank in charge of a large area), or the time during which someone is bishop 主教職位; 主教任期 **2** all the bishops, or the system of the church government by bishops 全體主教; 主教統轄制度

e·pis·co·pal /ɪˋpɪskəpḷ; ɪˈpɪskəpəl/ *adj* **1** connected with a BISHOP 主教的 **2** an episcopal church is governed by BISHOPS〔教會由〕主教管轄的

Episcopal Church /.,··· ˈ·/ *n* [singular] a PROTESTANT church in the US that developed from the Anglican Church 美國 (新教) 聖公會

E·pis·co·pa·li·an /ɪ,pɪskəˋpelɪən; ɪˌpɪskəˈpeɪliən◂/ *n* [C] a member of an episcopal church 美國新教聖公會教徒 —**Episcopalian** *adj*

ep·i·sode /ˋɛpə,sod; ˈepɪ̈səʊd/ *n* [C] **1** an event or a short period of time during which something specific happened 一段經歷; 一段時期: *one of the saddest episodes in his tormented life* 他苦難一生中最悲傷的時期之一 **2** a television or radio programme that is one of a series of programmes telling one story〔電視連續劇或廣播連載節目中的〕一集, 一節: *Watch next week's thrilling episode!* 請於下週收看精彩的一集!

ep·i·sod·ic /,ɛpɪˋsɑdɪk; ˌepɪ̈ˈsɒdɪk◂/ *adj formal*【正式】**1** happening at times that are not regular 不定期〔發生〕的: *episodic headaches* 陣發性頭痛 **2** consisting of many different parts when different things happen 由許多片斷組成的: *an episodic account of how a group of humble people are affected by the war* 對一羣卑微的人如何受戰爭影響的片段式的描述 —**episodically** /-klɪ; -kli/ *adv*

E·pis·tle /ɪˋpɪsḷ; ɪˈpɪsəl/ *n* [C] one of the letters written by the first Christians which are in the New Testament of the Bible〔聖經《新約全書》中的〕使徒書信

epistle *n* [C] *formal* a long or important letter【正式】〔長或重要的〕書信

e·pis·to·la·ry /ɪˋpɪstə,lɛrɪ; ɪˈpɪstələri/ *adj formal* written in the form of a series of letters【正式】書信體的: *an epistolay novel* 書信體小說

ep·i·taph /ˋɛpə͵tæf; ˈepɪ̵tɑːf/ *n* [C] a short piece of writing on the stone over someone's grave 墓誌銘

ep·i·thet /ˋɛpə͵θɛt; ˈepɪ̵θet/ *n* [C] an adjective or short phrase used to describe someone, especially when praising or blaming them〔尤其是褒貶人時使用的〕表述詞語: *He hardly deserves the epithet 'fascist'.* 用"法西斯分子"這個詞來形容他並不恰當。

e·pit·o·me /ɪˋpɪtəmɪ; ɪˈpɪtəmi/ *n* **the epitome of** the best possible example of something …的典型[典範]: *Jan's behaviour seemed to me to be the very epitome of selfishness.* 在我看來, 簡的所作所為是自私自利的典型。

e·pit·o·mize also 又作 **-ise** *BrE*【英】/ɪˋpɪtə͵maɪz; ɪˈpɪtəmaɪz/ *v* [T] to be a very typical example of something 成為…的典型: *This fiasco epitomizes the lack of regulation in the industry.* 這次困局突顯了該行業缺乏管制的問題。

e·poch /ˋɛpək; ˈiːpɒk/ *n* [C] a period of history, especially one in which important events take place〔尤指重要事件發生的〕時代, 紀元: *the beginning of a new epoch in the history of mankind* 人類歷史新紀元的開始

epoch-mak·ing /ˈ·· ͵··/ *adj* very important in changing or developing people's lives 劃時代的, 開創新紀元的

e·pon·y·mous /ɛˋpɑnəməs; ɪˈpɒnɪ̵məs/ *adj technical* the eponymous character in a book, film, or play is the character whose name forms its title【術語】〔以作品中的人物〕使〔書、電影或戲劇〕得名的;〔人物與作品〕同名的: *Hester, the book's eponymous heroine* 與本書同名的女主人公赫斯特 —**eponymously** *adv*

e·pox·y res·in /ɛpˋɑksɪ ˋrɛzn̩; ɪ͵pɒksi ˈrezɪ̵n/ *n* [U] a type of RESIN used as a glue 環氧樹脂

Ep·som salts /͵ɛpsəm ˋsɔlts; ͵epsəm ˈsɔːlts/ *n* [plural, U] a white powder that can be mixed with water and used as a kind of medicine 瀉鹽

Ep·stein-Barr vi·rus /͵ɛpstaɪn ˋbɑr ͵vaɪrəs; ͵epstaɪn ˈbɑː ͵vaɪərəs/ also 又作 **EBV** *n* [U] *AmE* an illness that makes you feel very tired and weak and can last for a long period of time【美】愛潑斯坦－巴爾病毒; ME *BrE*【英】

eq·ua·ble /ˋɛkwəbl̩; ˈekwəbəl/ *adj* **1** *formal* calm and not easily annoyed【正式】平和的, 性情溫和的: *Mary's equable temperament made her easy to work with.* 瑪麗性情溫和, 很容易共事。**2** *technical* having weather or conditions that are neither too hot nor too cold【術語】天氣冷熱適中的: *an equable climate* 溫和的氣候 —**equably** *adv* —**equability** /͵ɛkwəˋbɪlətɪ; ͵ekwəˈbɪlɪ̵ti/ *n* [U]

e·qual¹ /ˋikwəl; ˈiːkwəl/ *adj*

1 ▶SAME 相同◀ the same in size, value, amount, number etc as something else〔在大小、價值、數量、數字等方面〕相等的: *Jennifer cut the cake into six equal pieces.* 珍妮弗將蛋糕切成六等份。| [+to] *A pound is roughly equal to 500 grams.* 一磅約等於 500 克。| **of equal power/strength/weight** *Choose two stones of roughly equal weight and size.* 選兩塊重量和大小都差不多的石頭。

2 ▶SAME RIGHTS/CHANCES 同等權利/機會◀ having the same rights, opportunities etc as everyone else, whatever your race, religion, or sex 平等的: *Our constitution states that all men are equal.* 我們的憲法規定人人平等。| **equal opportunities** (=the same chances of employment, pay etc for everyone) 平等的機會 *This company is an equal opportunity employer.* 這家公司平等地對待員工。| **equal rights** (=the same rights for everyone) 平等權利 *a clear statement guaranteeing equal rights for women* 確保婦女享有平等權利的明確聲明

3 ▶BE ABLE 能夠◀ be equal to to have the ability to deal with a problem, piece of work etc successfully 勝任的, 能應付的: *I'm sure Barbara's quite equal to the task.* 我確信芭芭拉完全有能力承擔這項任務。

4 ▶AS GOOD AS 同等出色◀ having as high a standard or quality as something else 同樣出色的, 水平[質量]一樣高的: *religious architecture equal to any in the world* 堪與世界上任何同類建築媲美的宗教建築

5 on equal terms with neither side having any advantage over the other 地位平等, 互不佔優: *a new law to enable small businesses to compete on equal terms with large multinational corporations* 確保小公司能與跨國大公司平等競爭的新法律

6 all (other) things being equal *spoken* used when saying what you would normally choose, unless there were special facts to consider【口】假若所有(其他)情況相同: *I'd rather go by train, all other things being equal.* 如果其他一切情況都一樣, 我寧願坐火車去。

equal² *v* **equalled, equalling** *BrE*【英】, **equaled, equaling** *AmE*【美】**1** [linking verb 連繫動詞] to be exactly the same in size, number, or amount as something else〔大小、數字、數量等上〕等於, 與…相同: *Two plus two equals four.* 二加二等於四。| *Trade should balance when supply equals demand.* 供需相當時貿易便達到平衡。**2** [T] to be as good as or get to the same standard as someone or something else 比得上, 達到: *Thompson equalled the world record.* 湯普森平了世界紀錄。**3** [T] to produce a particular result or effect 產生, 得出〔特定結果或效果〕: *A highly-trained workforce equals high productivity.* 高素質的勞動力創造高生產力。

equal³ *n* [C] **1** someone who is as important, intelligent etc as you are, or who has the same rights and opportunities as you do 同等的人: *It's a relief to find a boss who treats employees as equals.* 能碰到一個平等對待員工的老闆真是令人寬慰。**2 be without equal** also 又作 **have no equal** *formal* to be better than everyone or everything else of the same type【正式】最傑出, 首屈一指: *His paintings are without equal in the Western world.* 他的畫在西方世界無與倫比。

e·qual·i·ty /ɪˋkwɑlətɪ; ɪˈkwɒlɪ̵ti/ *n* [U] a position or situation in which people have the same rights, advantages etc 平等: *Women have yet to achieve full equality with men in the work-place.* 婦女仍需爭取與男人在職業方面完全平等。| **racial/sexual equality** (=equality between all races or between men and women) 種族/男女平等

e·qual·ize also 又作 **-ise** *BrE*【英】/ˋikwəl͵aɪz; ˈiːkwəlaɪz/ *v* **1** [T] to make two or more things the same in size, value, amount etc〔大小、價值、數量等上〕使相等; 使平等 **2** [I] *BrE* to get a point in a game, especially football, so that you have the same number of points as your opponent【英】〔尤指足球〕打成平局, 扳平比分; TIE¹ (2) *AmE*【美】: *England equalized a few minutes before the end of the game.* 英格蘭隊在比賽結束前幾分鐘時將比分扳平。—**equalization** /͵ikwələˋzeʃən; ͵iːkwəlaɪˈzeɪʃən/ *n* [U]

e·qual·iz·er /ˋikwəl͵aɪzɚ; ˈiːkwəlaɪzə/ *n* [C] **1** *BrE* a GOAL (2) that makes the points of each team in a game equal【英】〔足球賽中〕扳平比分的一個進球 **2** *AmE slang* a gun【美俚】槍

eq·ual·ly /ˋikwəlɪ; ˈiːkwəli/ *adv* **1** [+adj/adv] to the same degree or amount 相等地, 相同地: *An equally acceptable solution could surely be found elsewhere.* 在別處肯定能找到同樣可以接受的解決方案。**2** in equal parts or amounts 均等地, 平均地: *We try to divide the work equally.* 我們盡量平分工作。**3** [sentence adverb 句子副詞] used when introducing a second idea or statement that is as important as your first one 同樣〔重要〕地: *I want to encourage her to do well, but equally I don't want to make her feel pressurized.* 我想鼓勵她好好幹, 但同時我也不想讓她有太大壓力。

equals sign /ˈ·· ·/ *BrE*【英】, **equal sign** *AmE*【美】*n* [C] a sign used in mathematics to show that two things are the same size, number, or amount〔數學中的〕等號: *In the equation x=y, x is to the left of the equals sign.* 在等式 x=y 中, x 在等號的左側。

eq·ua·nim·i·ty /͵ikwəˋnɪmətɪ; ͵iːkwəˈnɪmɪ̵ti/ *n* [U] *formal* calmness, especially in the way that you react to things【正式】〔尤指對某事的反應〕平和, 鎮靜, 沉着: *He received the news with surprising equanimity.* 他接到消息時顯得異常鎮靜。

e·quate /ɪˈkwet; ɪˈkweɪt/ *v* [T] to consider that two or more things are similar or connected 等同: **equate sth with** *Some people equate nationalism with fascism.* 有些人將民族主義和法西斯主義等同起來。

3 **e·qua·tion** /ɪˈkweʒən; ɪˈkweɪʒən/ *n* **1** [C] a statement in mathematics, showing that two quantities are equal 等式, 方程式: *In the equation 2x + 1 = 7, what is x?* 在2x+1=7這個方程式中, x是多少? **2** [C] **enter into the equation/be part of the equation** to be a fact that affects a particular problem, situation, idea etc 成為影響因素: *We hadn't realized that cost would enter into the equation at all.* 我們壓根兒未曾想到成本會成為影響因素。**3** [singular] the act of equating two things 將兩事物等同

e·qua·tor, Equator /ɪˈkwetɚ; ɪˈkweɪtə/ *n* [singular, U] an imaginary line drawn around the middle of the Earth that is exactly the same distance from the North Pole and the South Pole 赤道 —see picture at 參見 EARTH[1] 圖

eq·ua·to·ri·al /ˌikwəˈtɔrɪəl; ˌekwəˈtɔːriəl◂/ *adj* **1** connected with or near the equator 赤道的; 赤道附近的: *the equatorial rainforest* 赤道雨林 **2** very hot and wet 非常濕熱的: *an equatorial climate* 又濕又熱的氣候

e·quer·ry /ˈɛkwərɪ; ɪˈkweri/ *n* [C] a male official in a royal court, who serves a member of the royal family 王宮侍衛官

e·ques·tri·an /ɪˈkwɛstrɪən; ɪˈkwestriən/ *adj* connected with horse riding 騎馬的, 騎術的: *equestrian events* 馬術比賽項目 —**equestrian** *n* [C]

equi- /ikwə; ekwɪ̈/ *prefix* equal or equally 相等的; 相等地: *equidistant* 等距離的 | *an equilateral triangle* (=with equal sides) 等邊三角形

e·qui·dis·tant /ˌikwəˈdɪstənt; ˌiːkwɪ̈ˈdɪstənt◂/ *adj* at an equal distance from or between two places 等距離的

e·qui·lat·e·ral tri·an·gle /ˌikwəlætərəl ˈtraɪæŋgl; ˌiːkwɪ̈lætərəl ˈtraɪæŋgəl/ *n* [C] *technical* a TRIANGLE (1) whose three sides are all the same length【術語】等邊三角形 —see picture at 參見 SHAPE[1] 圖

e·qui·lib·ri·um /ˌikwəˈlɪbrɪəm; ˌiːkwɪ̈ˈlɪbriəm/ *n* [singular,U] **1** a balance between opposing forces or influences〔相反的力量或影響〕平衡, 均衡: *They were anxious not to upset the trading equilibrium.* 他們小心地維持貿易均衡。**2** a calm balance of emotions, attitudes, feelings etc〔情緒、態度、感情等的〕平靜, 安寧: *Setting up a home helped to re-establish some kind of equilibrium in her life.* 建立家庭有助於使她的生活恢復了一些平靜。

eq·uine /ˈikwaɪn; ˈekwaɪn/ *adj* connected with horses, or looking like a horse 馬的; 像馬的

eq·ui·noc·tial /ˌikwəˈnɑkʃəl; ˌiːkwɪ̈ˈnɒkʃəl◂/ *adj* connected with the equinox 春分的; 秋分的

eq·ui·nox /ˈikwəˌnɑks; ˈiːkwɪ̈nɒks/ *n* [C] one of the two times in a year when all places in the world have a day and night of equal length 春分; 秋分 —compare 比較 SOLSTICE

e·quip /ɪˈkwɪp; ɪˈkwɪp/ *v* **equipped, equipping** [T] **1** to provide a person, group, building etc with the things that are needed for a particular kind of activity or work 裝備, 配備: **equip sb with** *The boys equipped themselves with torches and rope, and set off.* 男孩們帶上火把和繩索就出發了。| **be equipped to do sth** *The emergency services are equipped to deal with disasters of this kind.* 應變人員配有裝備, 可處理此類災難事件。| **equip sb/sth** *It cost $100,000 to equip the gym.* 裝備體育館花費了10萬美元。| **well/ poorly/fully etc equipped** *It was a modern, bright, well equipped hospital.* 那是一家現代化、明亮且設備精良的醫院。**2** if education or training equips you to do something, it prepares you and makes you able to do it 使有準備, 使能夠〔做某事〕: **equip sb for** *We want our son to have an education that will equip him for later life.* 我們想讓兒子接受能為他今後生活打基礎的教育。

e·quip·ment /ɪˈkwɪpmənt; ɪˈkwɪpmənt/ *n* **1** [U] all the special tools, machines, clothes etc that you need for a particular activity 裝備, 設備, 用具: *Dentists must take great care in sterilizing all their equipment.* 牙醫在給其所有用具消毒時必須十分仔細。| **office/video/sports etc equipment** *fire-fighting equipment* 消防設備 | **piece of equipment** *a very delicate piece of equipment* 一件非常精密的設備 **2** [singular] the process of equipping someone or something 裝備〔某人或物的〕過程 2 2

eq·ui·poise /ˈɛkwəˌpɔɪz; ˈekwɪ̈pɔɪz/ *n* [U] *formal* a balance between different influences, especially mental or emotional influences【正式】平衡; 均勢〔尤指思想或情感上的影響〕

eq·ui·ta·ble /ˈɛkwɪtəbl; ˈekwɪ̈təbəl/ *adj formal* an equitable action, process etc treats everyone in an equal way; fair【正式】公平合理的; 公正的: *an equitable division of wealth* 財富的合理分配 —**equitably** *adv*

eq·ui·ty /ˈɛkwətɪ; ˈekwɪ̈ti/ *n* **1** [U] *formal* a situation in which no one has an unfair advantage; fairness【正式】公平; 公正: *a society run on the principles of equity and justice* 以公平、正義為原則的社會 **2** [U] *technical* the value of a piece of property or of a company's shares (SHARE[2] (5)) after debts have been paid【術語】〔付清債務後的〕財產淨值; 股本值 **3 equities** [plural] *technical* business shares (SHARE[2] (5)) that give you some of the company's profits rather than a fixed regular payment【術語】〔分享紅利而非固定股息的〕股票 **4** [U] *law* the principle that a fair judgement must be made in a situation where the existing laws do not provide an answer【法律】衡平法〔一種原則, 指現存法律不適用時, 應當作出公正的裁決〕

e·quiv·a·lent¹ /ɪˈkwɪvələnt; ɪˈkwɪvələnt/ *adj* having the same value, purpose, job etc as a person or thing of a different kind 等同的, 等價的, 相當的: **[+to]** *It's equivalent to the rank of captain in our army.* 這相當於我們軍隊中的上尉軍銜。| *Alternatively, we could give you an equivalent amount in company shares.* 或者我們可以給你等價的公司股票。—**equivalently** *adv* —**equivalence** *n* [U] 3

equivalent² *n* [C] something that is equivalent to something else 等同物; 等價物; 對應物: *Some Japanese words have no English equivalents.* 一些日語詞在英語中沒有對應的詞。| *It's the French equivalent of the IRS.* 這是法國相當於美國國內稅務局的機構。

e·quiv·o·cal /ɪˈkwɪvəkḷ; ɪˈkwɪvəkəl/ *adj* **1** words or statements that are equivocal have more than one possible meaning and are deliberately unclear; AMBIGUOUS〔詞語、聲明故意〕模棱兩可的; 含糊的: *His answer was evasive and equivocal.* 他的回答含糊其辭, 模棱兩可。**2** equivocal actions or behaviour are mysterious or difficult to understand〔行為〕神祕的; 費解的 —**equivocally** /-kḷɪ; -kli/ *adv*

e·quiv·o·cate /ɪˈkwɪvəˌket; ɪˈkwɪvəkeɪt/ *v* [I] *formal* to say something that has more than one possible meaning, in order to avoid giving a clear or direct answer【正式】含糊其辭, 說模棱兩可的話 —**equivocation** /ɪˌkwɪvəˈkeʃən; ɪˌkwɪvəˈkeɪʃən/ *n* [C,U]

er /ɝ; ɜː/ *interjection* a sound you make when you do not know exactly what to say next 嗯, 哦〔表示猶豫、遲疑〕: *Well, er – I'm not really sure.* 嗯, 哦 —— 我不太有把握。

-er¹ /ɚ; ə/ *suffix* forms the comparative of many short adjectives and adverbs〔附在許多短小的形容詞或副詞後, 構成比較級〕: *hot, hotter* 熱, 較熱 | *dry, drier* 乾燥, 較乾燥 | *My car is fast, but hers is faster.* 我的汽車很快, 但她的汽車更快。| *Her car goes faster than mine.* 她的汽車跑得比我的快。—see also 另見 -EST

-er² *suffix* [in nouns 構成名詞] **1** someone who does something or who is doing something（正在）做某事的人: *a dancer* (=someone who dances or is dancing) 舞蹈演員;

跳舞的人 | *the diners* (=people having dinner) 就餐者 **2** something that does something 用於做某事的器械: *a screwdriver* (=tool for driving in screws) 螺絲刀 **3** someone who makes a particular kind of thing 專做某種物品的人: *a hatter* (=someone who makes hats) 製帽匠 **4** someone who lives in or comes from a particular place 住在[來自]某地的人: *a Londoner* (=someone from London) 倫敦人 | *the villagers* (=people who live in the village) 村民 **5** someone skilled in or studying a particular subject 精於[研究]某學科的人: *a geographer* (=someone who studies GEOGRAPHY) 地理學家 **6** something that has something 擁有某物的東西: *a three-wheeler car* (=with three wheels) 三輪汽車 —see also 另見 -AR, -OR

e·ra /ˋɪrə; ˈɪərə/ *n* [C] a long period of time in history that is different in some way from other periods 時代, 年代: *In the Victorian era such behaviour was socially unacceptable.* 在維多利亞時代, 這種行為是不為社會所接受的。

e·rad·i·cate /ɪˋrædɪˌket; ɪˈrædɪ̣keɪt/ *v* [T] to completely get rid of something such as a disease or a social problem 根除; 消滅: **[+from]** *Smallpox has now been eradicated from the world.* 天花已經在世界上根除了。—**eradication** /ɪˌrædɪˋkeʃən; ɪˌrædɪ̣ˈkeɪʃən/ *n* [U]

3 **e·rase** /ɪˋres; ɪˈreɪz/ *v* [T] **1** to remove information from a computer memory or recorded sounds from a tape 刪除〔電腦文件〕; 抹去〔磁帶錄音〕: *Unfortunately, the tape has been erased.* 不幸的是, 磁帶錄音已被抹掉了。**2** to remove marks or writing so that they can no longer be seen 擦掉; 抹去〔痕跡或文字〕 **3** *formal* to get rid of or destroy something so that it no longer exists【正式】消除, 消滅: *The World Bank has agreed to erase the debt.* 世界銀行已同意免除這筆債務。| *the 163 villages erased by the eruption of Krakatoa* 被喀拉喀托火山噴發所毀滅的163個村莊 **4 erase sth from your mind/memory** to make yourself forget something bad that has happened 忘卻〔壞事〕

e·ras·er /ɪˋresɚ; ɪˈreɪzə/ *n* [C] *especially AmE*【尤美】**1** a rubber object used to remove pencil or pen marks from paper 橡皮; RUBBER (2a) *BrE*【英】**2** a thing you use for cleaning marks from a BLACKBOARD 黑板擦

e·ra·sure /ɪˋreʒɚ; ɪˈreɪʒə/ *n formal*【正式】**1** [C] a mark that is left when words or letters are removed with an eraser〔用橡皮擦去字後留下的〕痕跡, 字印 **2** [U] the act of completely removing or destroying something 根除, 消除

ere /ɛr; eə/ *preposition, conjunction, old use or poetic* before【舊或詩】在…之前: **ere long** (=soon) 不久, 很快

e·rect¹ /ɪˋrɛkt; ɪˈrekt/ *adj* **1** in a straight upright position 直立的, 垂直的: *She held her head erect.* 她昂着頭。**2** an erect PENIS or NIPPLE is stiff and bigger than it usually is〔陰莖〕勃起的;〔乳頭〕挺起的 —**erectly** *adv* —**erectness** *n* [U]

erect² *v* [T] **1** *formal* to build a building, wall, STATUE etc【正式】建造, 建立: *an imposing town hall, erected in 1892* 建於1892年的氣勢宏偉的市政廳 **2** to fix all the pieces of something together, and put it in an upright position 搭建, 豎起: *We had to sleep in hastily erected bunk beds.* 我們只能睡在匆匆搭成的雙層牀上。**3** to establish something such as a system or institution 創建, 確立〔體系或制度〕

e·rec·tile /ɪˋrɛktl; ɪˈrektaɪl/ *adj technical* connected with a man's erection【術語】〔陰莖〕勃起的

e·rec·tion /ɪˋrɛkʃən; ɪˈrekʃən/ *n* **1** [C] if a man has an erection, his PENIS increases in size and becomes stiff and upright because he is sexually excited〔陰莖〕勃起 **2** [U] the act of building something or putting it in an upright position 建造, 建立; 豎立: *the erection of a new temple* 建造新寺廟 **3** [C] *formal* something that has been built, especially a large structure【正式】豎立物; 建築物〔尤指結構龐大者〕

erg /ɝg; ɜːg/ *n* [C] *technical* a unit used to measure work or energy【術語】爾格〔功或能量單位〕

er·go /ˋɝgo; ˈɜːgəʊ/ *adv Latin formal* [sentence adverb 句子副詞] therefore【拉丁, 正式】因此, 所以

er·go·nom·ics /ˌɝgəˋnɑmɪks; ˌɜːgəˈnɒmɪks/ *n* [U] the study of how the design of equipment affects how well people can do their work 工效學, 人類工程學: *the ergonomics of computer hardware* 電腦硬件設計中的人類工程學 —**ergonomic** *adj* —**ergonomically** /-klɪ̣; -kli/ *adv*

ERM /ˌi ɑr ˋɛm; ˌiː ɑːr ˈem/ *n* **1** [U] the abbreviation of 縮寫= EXCHANGE RATE MECHANISM **2** [singular] the abbreviation of 縮寫= the EUROPEAN EXCHANGE RATE MECHANISM

er·mine /ˋɝmɪn; ˈɜːmɪ̣n/ *n* **1** [U] an expensive white fur, used especially for the clothes of judges, kings, and queens 白鼬皮〔尤用於法官、國王和女王的服飾中〕**2** [C] a small thin animal of the WEASEL¹ family whose fur is white in winter 白鼬

e·rode /ɪˋrod; ɪˈrəʊd/ *v* also 又作 **erode away 1** [I,T] if the wind, rain etc erodes something such as rock or soil, or if they erode, their surface is gradually destroyed〔風、雨等〕侵蝕, 腐蝕: *East-facing cliffs are being constantly eroded by heavy seas.* 朝東的懸崖正不斷受到洶湧海浪的侵蝕。**2** [I,T] to gradually destroy or reduce something such as somone's power, rights or confidence 逐步損害, 削弱〔權力、權利或信心〕: *She feels that her personal authority has been eroded.* 她覺得自己的威信已被削弱。

e·ro·ge·nous zone /ɪˌrɑdʒənəs ˋzon; ɪˌrɒdʒənəs ˈzəʊn/ *n* [C] a part of your body that gives you sexual pleasure when it is touched 性敏感區

e·ro·sion /ɪˋroʒən; ɪˈrəʊʒən/ *n* [U] **1** the process of being gradually destroyed by rain, wind, the sea etc〔風、雨、海水等的〕侵蝕, 腐蝕: *soil erosion* 土壤(受到的)侵蝕 | *the erosion of the coastline* 海岸線(遭受的)侵蝕 **2** the process of gradually destroying or reducing something 逐步毀壞, 削弱: *the erosion of civil liberties* 公民自由的逐漸削弱 —**erosive** /ɪˋrosɪv; ɪˈrəʊsɪv/ *adj*

e·rot·ic /ɪˋrɑtɪk; ɪˈrɒtɪk/ *adj* **1** an erotic book, film etc shows people having sex, and is often intended to make people reading or looking at it have feelings of sexual pleasure 色情的 **2** erotic dreams, experiences, or activities involve feelings of sexual excitement (引起)性慾的 —**erotically** /-klɪ̣; -kli/ *adv*

e·rot·i·ca /ɪˋrɑtɪkə; ɪˈrɒtɪkə/ *n* [plural] erotic writing, drawings etc 色情文學, 色情藝術 —compare 比較 PORNOGRAPHY

e·rot·i·cis·m /ɪˋrɑtəˌsɪzəm; ɪˈrɒtɪ̣sɪzəm/ *n* [U] a style or quality that expresses strong feelings of sexual love and desire, especially in works of art 色情; 性慾〔尤指文藝作品的〕: *the eroticism of Donne's early love poems*〔英國玄學派詩人〕多恩早期愛情詩中展現的色情

err /ɝ; ɜː/ *v* [I] **1 err on the side of caution** to be too careful rather than risk making mistakes 寧願過於謹慎也不要冒險犯錯 **2** *formal or old use* a word meaning to make a mistake【正式或舊】犯錯誤

er·rand /ˋɛrənd; ˈerənd/ *n* [C] **1** a short journey in order to do something for someone, for example delivering or getting something for them〔短程〕差事; 跑腿: *I have a couple of errands for you.* 我有幾件差事要你去辦一下。| **send sb on an errand** *His mother sent him on an errand.* 他媽媽讓他出去辦件事。| **run an errand** *Uncle Pio has made me run errands for him all morning.* 皮奧叔叔整個上午都在讓我為他跑腿。**2 errand of mercy** *literary or humorous* a journey made in order to help someone who is in a very difficult or dangerous situation【文或幽默】幫助受困者之行; 雪中送炭之行 —see also 另見 **(send sb on) a fool's errand** (FOOL¹ (10))

er·rant /ˋɛrənt; ˈerənt/ *adj* [only before noun 僅用於名詞前] *usually humorous* an errant husband, wife, son etc has done something wrong【一般幽默】〔家庭成員等〕犯錯的; 迷途的 —see also 另見 KNIGHT-ERRANT

er·rat·ic /ə`rætɪk; ɪ'rætɪk/ *adj* erractic actions, movements etc seem to have no pattern or plan〔行為、動作等〕不規則的; 不確定的; 無計劃的: *The bus service into town was highly erratic.* 駛往市區的公共汽車班次極不固定。—**erratically** /-klɪ; -kli/ *adv*: *The car was weaving erratically across the road.* 汽車左拐右拐地穿過馬路。

er·ra·tum /ɪ'retəm; e'rɑːtəm/ *n plural* **errata** /-tə; -tə/ [C] *Latin technical* a mistake in a book, shown in a list added after it is printed【拉丁, 術語】〔書中勘誤表列出的〕錯誤

er·ro·ne·ous /ə`ronɪəs; ɪ'rəʊniəs/ *adj formal* erroneous ideas, statements etc are wrong because they are based on information that is not correct【正式】〔想法、聲明等〕錯誤的, 不正確的 —**erroneously** *adv*

2 2 **er·ror** /'ɛrɚ; 'erə/ *n* **1** [C,U] a mistake, especially a mistake in speaking or writing or a mistake that causes serious problems 錯誤, 謬誤〔尤指口誤、筆誤或重大過失〕: *an essay full of spelling errors* 滿是拼寫錯誤的文章 | *Heath committed a grave error by making concessions to the right wing of the party.* 希斯向黨內右翼勢力妥協, 犯了一個嚴重的錯誤。| **computer/driver etc error** *Mrs Leigh's huge phone bill was the result of a computer error.* 利夫人的巨額電話賬單是由於電腦出錯造成的。| **human error** (=made by a person rather than a machine) 人為錯誤〔而非機器出錯〕| **commit an error** (=make a mistake) 犯錯誤 *Heath committed an error by making concessions to extremists.* 希斯向極端分子作出了讓步, 犯了個錯誤。| **a grave error** (=a serious mistake) 嚴重的失誤 **2 error of judgment** a mistake in the way that you examine a situation and decide what to do 判斷失誤 **3 see the error of your ways** *literary or humorous* to realize that you have been behaving badly and decide to stop【文或幽默】意識到自己的過失準備改正, 知錯即改 **4 be in error** to have made a mistake, especially when making an official decision〔尤指在作正式決定時〕犯錯, 失誤: *The company has admitted that they were in error.* 這家公司承認他們犯錯誤了。**5 in error** if you do something in error, it is wrong but you did not intend to do it 失誤: *The letter was opened in error.* 信被誤拆了。—compare 比較 MISTAKE —see also 另見 **trial and error** (TRIAL[1] (3))

Frequencies of the nouns **error** and **mistake** in spoken and written English 名詞 error 和 mistake 在英語口語和書面語中的使用頻率

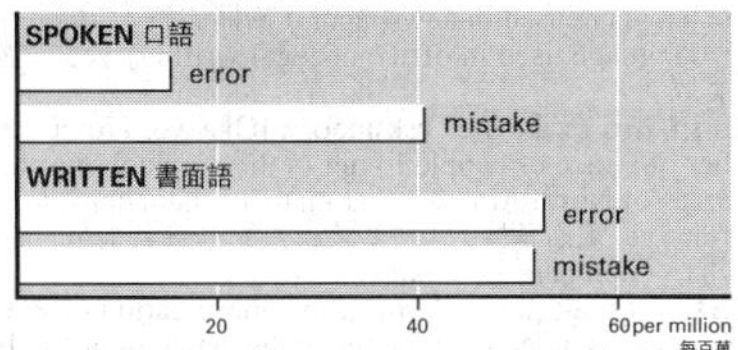

Based on the British National Corpus and the Longman Lancaster Corpus
據英國國家語料庫和朗文蘭卡斯特語料庫

This graph shows that the adverb **mistake** is more common in spoken English than the word **error**. This is because **error** is not used in a very general way. It is used when describing particular types of mistake, for example in the expressions **computer error** or **error of judgement**, and sounds formal when used on its own. It is therefore more common in written English. 本圖表顯示, 在英語口語中 mistake 比 error 常用, 這是因為 error 並不是很通用。當描述某些類型的錯誤時才使用 error, 如電腦錯誤或判斷失誤等, 單獨使用時顯得較正式, 因此它更常用於書面語。

er·satz /ɛr`zɑts; 'eəzæts/ *adj* [usually before noun 一般用於名詞前] artificial, and not as good as the real thing 代用的, 人造的: *ersatz coffee* 代用咖啡

Erse /ɝs; ɜːs/ *n* [U] a GAELIC language spoken in Ireland〔愛爾蘭口頭使用的〕蓋耳語

erst·while /`ɝstˌhwaɪl; 'ɜːstwaɪl/ *adj* [only before noun 僅用於名詞前] your erstwhile friends, supporters, enemies etc were your friends etc until recently 從前的; 過去的〔指不久以前〕: *He has won over many of his erstwhile critics.* 他把許多不久以前還批評他的人爭取到自己一邊。

er·u·dite /`ɛruˌdaɪt; 'erʊdaɪt/ *adj* showing a lot of knowledge based on careful study 博學的, 學問精深的 —**eruditely** *adv* —**erudition** /ˌɛru`dɪʃən; ˌerʊ'dɪʃən/ *n* [U]

e·rupt /ɪ`rʌpt; ɪ'rʌpt/ *v* [I] **1** if a VOLCANO erupts, it explodes and sends smoke, fire, and rock into the sky〔火山〕爆發, 噴發 **2** if fighting, violence, loud noises etc erupt, they start suddenly〔搏鬥、暴力事件、噪音等〕突然發生; 爆發: *Gang violence can erupt for no apparent reason.* 有時沒有甚麼明顯的原因也會爆發犯罪集團之間的暴力事件。**3 erupt into laughter/shouting etc** to suddenly start laughing or shouting 突然大笑/叫起來等 **4** if spots erupt on your body, they suddenly appear on your skin〔皮膚丘疹等〕突然大片出現, 冒出 —**eruption** /ɪ`rʌpʃən; ɪ'rʌpʃən/ *n* [C,U]

-ery /ərɪ; əri/ *suffix* also 又作 **-ry** [in nouns 構成名詞] **1 a)** the art, behaviour, or condition of something or of being something 技藝; 行為; 狀態: *slavery* (=being a slave) 奴隸身分 | *bravery* (=being brave) 勇氣 **b)** a collection of things of a particular kind 某類事物: *modern machinery* (=machines) 現代機械 | *in all her finery* (=fine clothes) 穿着她所有的好衣服 **2** a place where a particular thing lives or is done, made, or sold 場所: *a rookery* (=where birds called ROOKs live) 禿鼻烏鴉結巢處 | *a bakery* (=where bread is baked) 麵包房 | *an oil refinery* 煉油廠

-es /əz; ɪz/ *suffix* the form used for -s when it is added to a word ending with s, z, ch, sh, or y 後綴 -s 的變體〔加在以字母 s, z, ch, sh 或 y 結尾的詞後面〕: *glasses* 玻璃杯 | *buzzes* 嗡嗡聲 | *watches* 手錶 | *ladies* 女士們

es·ca·late /`ɛskəˌlet; 'eskəleɪt/ *v* **1** [I,T] if fighting, violence, or an unpleasant situation escalates, or if someone escalates it, it becomes much worse (使)〔戰鬥、暴力或不好的情況等〕升級; (使) 惡化: *They don't want the fighting to escalate into a full-scale war.* 他們不想讓這場戰鬥升級為全面戰爭。**2** [I] if prices or costs escalate, they become much higher〔價格或成本〕大量增加, 升高 —**escalation** /ˌɛskə`leʃən; ˌeskə'leɪʃən/ *n* [C,U]

es·ca·la·tor /`ɛskəˌletɚ; 'eskəleɪtə/ *n* [C] a set of stairs that move and carry people from one level within a building to another 自動扶梯

escalator 自動扶梯

es·ca·lope /ɛ`skɑləp; 'eskəlɒp/ *n* [C] *BrE* a thin piece of meat, especially VEAL (=meat from a young cow), cooked in hot fat【英】油煎薄〔尤指小牛肉〕肉片

es·ca·pade /`ɛskəˌped; 'eskəpeɪd/ *n* [C] an adventure or series of events that are exciting or contain some risk 冒險行為, 越軌行為: *Have you heard about Jane's latest escapade?* 你聽說過簡最近胡鬧的事兒了嗎?

es·cape[1] /ə`skep; ɪ'skeɪp/ *v* 3 2
1 ►PERSON/PLACE 人/地點◄ [I,T] to get away from a place when someone is trying to catch you or stop you leaving 逃走; 逃離〔某地〕; 逃脱〔某人的追捕或阻攔〕: *Anyone trying to escape will be shot!* 誰想逃走就把他斃了! | **[+from/through/over etc]** *Two men have escaped from Durham jail.* 兩名男子從達勒姆監獄逃脱。| **escape sb's clutches** (=escape from them) 從某人手中逃脱 *They managed to escape the clutches of the enemy*

soldiers and flee to Switzerland. 他們設法從敵兵手中逃了出來，跑到了瑞士。

2 ►DANGER 危險◄ [I,T] to get away from a dangerous situation that is likely to harm you if you do not leave 逃離〔險境〕: *Only four people managed to escape before the roof collapsed.* 只有四個人搶在屋頂塌下來之前逃了出來。| **escape from/through/into etc** *The dog escaped through the back window of the bus.* 狗從公共汽車的後窗戶逃走了。| **escape sth** *refugees escaping war and famine* 躲避戰爭和饑荒的難民

3 ►GAS/LIQUID ETC 氣體/液體等◄ [I] if gas, liquid, light, heat etc escapes from somewhere, it comes out when you do not want it to 〔氣體、液體、光、熱等〕泄漏，逸出: *Screw the top back firmly to prevent any fumes escaping.* 將蓋子往回擰緊以防漏氣。

4 ►AVOID 避免◄ [I,T] to succeed in avoiding being involved in an unpleasant, difficult, or dangerous situation 逃避，避開: *The back seat passengers escaped death by inches.* 後座的乘客死裡逃生。

5 ►SOUND 聲音◄ [I,T] if a sound escapes from someone's mouth, they accidentally make that sound 意外發出〔聲音〕

6 escape sb's attention/notice if something escapes your attention or notice, you do not see it or realize that it is there 逃過某人的注意; 被某人忽視

7 the name/date/title escapes me *spoken* used when you cannot remember something【口】我記不起這個名字/日期/題目: *I've met him before, but his name escapes me.* 我以前見過他，但想不起他的名字了。

8 there's no escaping (the fact) used to emphasize that something is definitely important or will definitely happen 不可否認的是; 毫無疑問: *There's no escaping the fact that she did actually lie to you.* 不可否認的是，她的確對你撒了謊。—**escaped** *adj* [only before noun 僅用於名詞前]: *escaped prisoners* 越獄犯

3 **escape[2]** *n* **1** [C,U] the act of getting away from a place where you do not want to be, or from an unpleasant or dangerous situation 逃離，逃脫: *They had been planning their escape for months.* 為逃跑他們已計劃數月了。| [+**from**] *the story of Papillon's daring escape from Devil's Island* 帕皮倫從魔鬼島英勇逃脫的故事 | **make your escape** *The party was boring – we couldn't wait to make our escape.* 晚會很無聊，我們迫不及待要逃走。| **a lucky escape** (=a situation in which you were lucky to have avoided something unpleasant) 幸運逃脫 **2** [singular, U] a way of getting away from an unpleasant situation, especially by doing something else to avoid thinking about it 逃避〔現實〕，迴避: *Teenagers turn to drugs as a form of escape.* 青少年使用毒品以逃避現實。 **3 an escape of gas/liquid etc** an amount of gas, liquid etc that comes out of the place where it is being kept as a result of an accident 氣體/液體等泄漏: *escapes of radiation from the generating plant* 發電廠的輻射泄漏 —see also 另見 FIRE ESCAPE

es·cap·ee /ɪˌske`pi; ˌeskeɪˈpiː/ *n* [C] *literary* someone who has escaped from somewhere【文】逃離者，逃脫者

escape ve·lo·ci·ty /ˈ·ˌ··/ *n* [C,U] the speed that a ROCKET[1] (1) must travel at in order to get into space 逃逸速度〔火箭進入太空所需的速度〕

es·cap·is·m /ɪ`skepɪzəm; ɪˈskeɪpɪzəm/ *n* [U] something that helps you to forget about your normal life and think of more pleasant things 幫助人逃避現實的事物: *It's not intended to be a serious movie – it's sheer escapism.* 這部電影本來就不嚴肅，純粹是為了讓人逃避現實。—**escapist** *adj*

es·ca·pol·o·gy /ˌɛskə`pɑlədʒɪ; ˌeskəˈpɒlədʒi/ *n* [U] the skill of escaping from ropes, chains etc as part of a performance 脫逃術，脫身術 —**escapologist** *n* [C]

e·scarp·ment /ɛ`skɑrpmənt; ɪˈskɑːpmənt/ *n* [C] a high steep slope or cliff that joins two levels on a hill or mountain 陡坡; 峭壁

es·chew /ɛs`tʃu; ɪsˈtʃuː/ *v* [T] *formal* to deliberately avoid doing or using something, usually for moral, religious, or practical reasons【正式】〔通常為道德、宗教或實際原因而〕迴避，避開: *a meek, lamb-like saviour who eschews violence* 迴避衝突、溫順如羔羊般的救世主

es·cort[1] /`ɛskɔrt; ˈeskɔːt/ *n* [C] **1** a person or a group of people or vehicles that go with someone in order to protect or guard them 護衛者; 護送車輛: *a motorcycle escort* 摩托車護衛隊 | **under escort** (=protected or guarded by an escort) 在護送[押送]下 *The suspects arrived under armed escort.* 嫌疑犯們在武裝人員的押送下到達。**2** someone, especially a man, who takes someone to a formal social event 陪伴別人出席正式社交場合的人〔尤指男性〕: *Her escort was a handsome young officer.* 陪她一起來的是一名英俊的年輕軍官。**3** someone who is paid to go out with someone socially 受雇陪同某人參加社交的人: *She works for an escort agency.* 她在一家社交陪伴服務社工作。

e·scort[2] /ɪ`skɔrt; ɪˈskɔːt/ *v* [T] **1** to go with someone to protect or guard them 護送，護衛: *The visitors were escorted by marine guards to the airport.* 來訪者由海軍陸戰隊隊員護送到機場。**2** to go with someone and show them a place 引導某人遊覽，導遊: **escort sb round** *BrE*【英】**/around** *The Queen was escorted round the factory by two of the managers.* 女王在兩名經理的陪同下參觀了工廠。

es·cri·toire /ˌɛskrɪ`twɑr; ˌeskrḷˈtwɑː/ *n* [C] *French* a small writing desk【法】小寫字枱

es·crow /`ɛskro; ˈeskrəʊ/ *n* [U] *law* an object such as a written contract, money etc that is held by someone while an agreement is being fulfilled【法律】履行協議期間交由某人保管的物品〔如合同、錢款等〕

e·scutch·eon /ɪ`skʌtʃən; ɪˈskʌtʃən/ *n* [C] *formal* a SHIELD[1] (2) on which someone's COAT OF ARMS (=FAMILY SIGN) is painted【正式】飾有紋章的盾，形紋徽

-ese /iz; iːz/ *suffix* **1** [in nouns 構成名詞] the people or language of a particular country or place 某國[地方]的人[語言]: *The Viennese* (=people from Vienna) *are so charming.* 維也納人非常可愛。| *learning Japanese* (=the language of Japan) 學習日語 **2** [in adjectives 構成形容詞] belonging to a particular country or place 屬於某國[地方]的: *Chinese music* 中國音樂 **3** [in nouns 構成名詞] language or words used by a particular group, especially when it sounds ugly or is difficult to understand 特定人羣的語言[用詞]〔尤指難聽或難懂〕: *journalese* (=language used in newspapers) 新聞文體 | *officialese* (=language used in office or legal writing) 公文文體，官腔

Es·ki·mo /`ɛskəˌmo; ˈeskḷməʊ/ *n* [C] a word for a member of a race of people living in the very cold northern areas of North America that many of them consider offensive 愛斯基摩人〔許多該族人認為該名稱是冒犯用語〕—compare 比較 INUIT

ESL /ˌi ɛs `ɛl; ˌiː es ˈel/ *n* [U] the abbreviation of 縮寫= English as a Second Language; the teaching of English to students living in an English-speaking country 作為第二語言的英語（課程）

ESOL /`isɔl; ˈiːsɒl/ the abbreviation of 縮寫= English for Speakers of Other Languages 操其他語種者的英語（課程）

e·soph·a·gus /ɪ`sɑfəgəs; ɪˈsɒfəgəs/ *n* [C] the American spelling of OESOPHAGUS oesophagus 的美式拼法

es·o·ter·ic /ˌɛsə`tɛrɪk; ˌesəˈterɪk◂/ *adj* known and understood by only a few people who have special knowledge about something 深奧的，只有內行才懂的: *an esoteric form of Buddhism* 一種深奧的佛法 —**esoterically** /-klɪ; -kli/ *adv*

ESP /ˌi ɛs `pi; ˌiː es ˈpiː/ *n* [U] **1** the abbreviation of 縮寫= extra-sensory perception; the ability to know what will happen in the future, or to know what another person is thinking 超感知覺〔即可預知未來或感知他人所思的能力〕**2** the abbreviation of 縮寫= English for special purposes; the teaching of English to business people, scientists etc 專業英語課程〔即針對商業人士、科學家等專業人員的課程〕

esp the written abbreviation of 縮寫= especially

es·pa·drille /ˌɛspəˋdrɪl; ˌespəˈdrɪl/ *n* [C] *French* a light shoe that is made of cloth and rope【法】用布和繩帶製成的輕便鞋, 帆布便鞋 —see picture on page A17 參見 A17 頁圖

es·pe·cial /əˋspɛʃəl; ɪˈspeʃəl/ *adj formal*【正式】= SPECIAL

1 1 **es·pe·cial·ly** /əˋspɛʃəlɪ; ɪˈspeʃəli/ also 又作 **specially** *spoken*【口】*adv* **1** [sentence adverb 句子副詞] used to emphasize that something is more important or happens more with one particular thing than with others 尤其: *Crime is growing at a rapid rate, especially in urban areas.* 犯罪率正迅速上升, 尤其是在城市裡。**2** [+adj/adv] to a particularly high degree or much more than usual 特別, 格外: *I was feeling especially tired that evening.* 那天晚上我感到特別累。| *"Do you feel like going out for a drink?" "Not especially, no."* "你想出去喝一杯嗎?" "不, 不是特別想。" **3** for a particular person, purpose etc 專門(地): [+ **for**] *I bought these chocolates especially for you.* 這些巧克力是我專門為你買的。

USAGE NOTE 用法說明: ESPECIALLY

WORD CHOICE 詞語辨析: **especially, specially, special**

Especially is most often used to emphasize something, or to say that something is more worth mentioning or more important than the other things you are talking about. especially 通常用於強調某事物, 或表示該事物比其他被談論的事物更值得一提或更重要: *It can be especially difficult for drivers to see cyclists at night.* 汽車司機夜間特別不容易看見騎車人。| *The town is especially crowded in the summer* (=much more than in winter). 這個城鎮夏天時人格外多(比冬天時多許多)。| *I hate interruptions, especially when I'm trying to work* (=I do not mind as much at other times). 我不喜歡被打斷, 尤其是在工作時間。

Specially is usually used when you do something that is different from what you usually do for a particular purpose. It is often used with the passive form of a verb. specially 通常用於表示因為某個特殊目的, 所做之事異於平常。它常與被動態的動詞連用: *a specially made/designed/adapted etc car* 特別製造/設計/改裝等的汽車 | *I bought it specially for you.* 這是我特地為你買的。

Special is the adjective for both **specially** and **especially**. special 是 specially 和 especially 兩個詞的形容詞形式。

SPELLING 拼法

In spoken English **especially** is often shortened to **specially**, but it is usually written in full. 在英語口語中, especially 常簡化為 specially, 但書寫時通常不簡化。

Specially may be written (and heard) as **especially** in slightly formal English. **Special** is hardly ever written **especial**, which is very formal. 在稍正式的英語口語和書面語中, specially 可以說成或寫作 especially。special 幾乎從不寫作 especial, 因為 especial 是非常正式的用語。

GRAMMAR 語法

Specially and **especially** are not common at the start of a sentence or clause. specially 和 especially 兩詞通常不用於句子或分句的開頭。You would usually say 一般都說: *I especially like New York* (NOT 不用 *especially I like New York*). 我特別喜歡紐約。

Es·pe·ran·to /ˌɛspəˋrɑnto; ˌespəˈræntəʊ/ *n* [U] an artificial language invented in 1871 to help people from different countries in the world speak to each other 世界語

es·pi·o·nage /ˋɛspɪənɑdʒ; ˈespiənɑːʒ/ *n* [U] the activity of secretly finding out a country's or company's secrets 諜報活動, 間諜行為: *Some of the embassy staff were certainly involved in espionage.* 使館中的一些人肯定參與了諜報活動。

es·pla·nade /ˌɛspləˋned; ˌespləˈneɪd/ *n* [C] *especially BrE* a wide street next to the sea in a town【尤英】濱海大街

es·pouse /ɪˋspaʊz; ɪˈspaʊz/ *v* [T] *formal* to support an idea, belief etc especially a political one【正式】支持, 擁護〔某觀點、信仰, 尤指政治主張〕: *This government claims to espouse the principle of freedom of choice.* 該政府聲稱支持自由選擇原則。—**espousal** *n* [singular, U]

es·pres·so /ɛsˋprɛso; eˈspresəʊ/ *n* [C,U] a strong black Italian coffee 蒸餾咖啡〔一種意大利濃咖啡, 不加牛奶〕

esprit de corps /ɛˋspri də ˋkɔr; eˌspriː də ˈkɔː/ *n* [U] *French* feelings of loyalty towards people who are all involved in the same activity as you【法】團隊精神, 集體成員之間的團結

es·py /əˋspaɪ; ɪˈspaɪ/ *v* [T] *literary* to suddenly see someone or something【文】突然看見

Esq *especially BrE*【尤英】a written abbreviation of 縮寫= esquire

-esque /ɛsk; esk/ *suffix* [in adjectives 構成形容詞] **1** in the manner or style of a particular person, group, or place …式樣[風格]的: *Kafkaesque* (=in the style of the writer Franz Kafka, or like the situations or characters in his books) 卡夫卡式的〔指奧地利小說家卡夫卡的風格或與他小說中的情景或人物相似的〕**2** like something 似…般的: *picturesque* (=pleasant to look at) (風景)如畫的

es·quire /ˋɛsˌkwaɪr; ɪˈskwaɪə/ *n* a title that can be written after a man's name, especially on the address of an official letter …先生〔寫在男子姓名後的尊稱, 尤用於正式信件的地址中〕

-ess /ɛs; es/ *suffix* [in nouns 構成名詞] a female 女性; 雌性: *an actress* (=a female actor) 女演員 | *a waitress* 女侍者 | *two lionesses* 兩頭母獅子

es·say[1] /ˋɛse; ˈeseɪ/ *n* [C] **1** a short piece of writing by a student as part of a course of study〔學生為某門課程所寫的〕短文, 論說文: [**+on/about**] *an essay on the causes of the French Revolution* 關於法國大革命的起因的一篇短文 **2** a short piece of writing giving someone's ideas about politics, society etc〔關於政治、社會等的〕小品文, 散文 **3** *formal* an attempt to do something【正式】嘗試; 企圖 2

essay[2] *v* [T] *formal* to attempt to do something【正式】試圖; 企圖

es·say·ist /ˋɛseɪst; ˈeseɪ-ɪst/ *n* [C] someone who writes essays, especially as a form of literature 散文家

es·sence /ˋɛsṇs; ˈesəns/ *n* **1** [singular] the most basic and important quality of something 本質, 實質; 要素: [**+of**] *In his paintings Picasso tries to capture the essence of his subjects.* 畢加索在畫中努力抓住所選對象的實質。**2** [U]a liquid obtained from a plant, flower etc that has a strong smell or taste and is used especially in cooking 香精, 精油: *vanilla essence* 香草香精 **3 in essence** used when talking about the most basic and important part of something, especially an idea, belief, or argument 本質上, 實質上: *In essence, you are saying that people do not really have free will.* 實質上你是在說, 人們並不真正擁有自由意志。**4 speed/time is of the essence** used to say that it is important to do something as quickly as possible 速度/時間是至關重要的

es·sen·tial[1] /əˋsɛnʃəl; ɪˈsenʃəl/ *adj* **1** extremely important and necessary in order to do something correctly or successfully 絕對重要的; 必不可少的: *If you're going walking in the mountains, strong boots are essential.* 在山間行走, 結實的靴子是必不可少的。| [**+for/to**] *Good food and plenty of exercise are essential for a healthy life.* 要健康地生活, 吃得好並做大量的鍛鍊是最重要的。| **it is essential (that)** *It is essential that the oil is checked every 10,000 km.* 每行駛 10,000 公里就必須 2 2

檢查一下潤滑油。| **it is essential to do sth** *It's essential to read the small print at the bottom of any document.* 閱讀任何文件時, 看清楚頁腳處的小字非常重要。**2** the essential parts, qualities, or features of something are the most important, typical, or noticeable ones 最重要的; 最典型的; 最顯著的: *The essential character of the village has not changed in over 300 years.* 這個村莊最顯著的特徵三百多年來一直未變。| **essential difference/feature/point etc** *The essential difference between man and apes is intelligence.* 人和猿最根本的區別在於智力。

essential² *n* **1** [C usually plural 一般用複數] something that is important because it is necessary for life or for doing something 必需品; 不可缺的東西: *The charity provides homeless people with essentials like food and clothing.* 慈善機構為無家可歸者提供了食品和衣物等生活必需品。| **bare essentials** (=the most necessary things) 最必要的東西 *We don't have much room for luggage so we're only taking the bare essentials.* 我們沒有多少地方放行李, 所以只帶最要緊的東西。**2 the essentials** [plural] the basic and most important information or facts about a particular subject 要點, 要素: *the essentials of English grammar* 英語語法的要點

es·sen·tial·ly /ə`sɛnʃəlı; ɪ'senʃəli/ *adv* used when stating the most basic facts about something 本質上, 根本上: *Eisenhower was essentially a moderate in politics.* 艾森豪威爾基本上屬於政治上的溫和派。| [sentence adverb 句子副詞] *Essentially, the plan is worthwhile, but some changes will have to be made.* 從根本上講, 這個計劃值得做, 但必須做些修改。

essential oil /·,·· '·/ *n* [C] an oil from a plant that has a strong smell and is used for making PERFUME¹ (1) or in AROMATHERAPY (香) 精油〔用於香水製造或芳香療法〕

est **1** the written abbreviation of 縮寫= established: *H. Perkins and Company, est. 1869* H·珀金斯公司, 成立於1869年 **2** the written abbreviation for 縮寫= ESTIMATED

-est /ɪst; ɨst/ *suffix* **1** forms the SUPERLATIVE of many shorter adjectives and adverbs〔附在許多較短小的形容詞和副詞後面, 構成最高級〕: *cold, colder, coldest* 冷, 更冷, 最冷 | *dry, drier, driest* 乾燥, 更乾燥, 最乾燥 | *Our soap washes whitest.* 我們的肥皂洗起東西來最乾淨。—see also 另見 -ER **2** also 又作 **-st** *old use or Biblical* forms the second person singular of verbs【舊或聖經】〔用以構成動詞的第二人稱單數〕: *thou goest* 你走

es·tab·lish /ə`stæblɪʃ; ɪ'stæblɪʃ/ *v* [T] **1** to start a company, organization, system, situation etc that is intended to exist or continue for a long time 建立, 設立: *My grandfather established the family business in 1938.* 我的祖父於1938年創立了這個家族企業。**2** to find out facts that will prove that something is true 證實, 確定: *Attorneys are trying to establish the validity of his claim.* 律師們正努力證實他的說法是正確的。| **establish that** *It has been firmly established that she was not there at the time of the crime.* 有確鑿的證據證明案發時她不在場。| **establish a link/connection** *establishing a link between ozone depletion and the use of CFC gases* 確定臭氧層遭破壞和使用含氯氟烴二者之間有關聯 **3** to make people accept that you can do something, or that you have a particular quality 使被接受; 使得到承認: **establish yourself as/in** *They have established themselves as the most powerful political party in the country.* 他們已經在國內確立了最有影響力的政黨的地位。**4 establish links/contacts/trust etc** to start having a relationship with someone or to start discussions with them 建立關係/聯繫/信任等: *We decided to try and establish contacts with similar groups in the US.* 我們決定設法與美國的同類團體建立聯繫。

es·tab·lished /ə`stæblɪʃt; ɪ'stæblɪʃt/ *adj* [only before noun 僅用於名詞前] **1** already in use or existing for a long period of time 早已確立的; 早已投入使用的: *established anti-cancer drugs* 已投入使用的抗癌藥物 | **well established** *well-established teaching methods* 被廣泛採用的教學方法 **2** known to do a particular job well, because you have done it for a long time 資深的: *an established political figure* 資深政界人物

es·tab·lish·ment /ə`stæblɪʃmənt; ɪ'stæblɪʃmənt/ *n* **1** [C] *formal* an institution, especially a business, shop etc【正式】機構; 單位〔尤指企業、商店等〕: *The hotel is a well-run establishment.* 這家旅館經營良好。**2 the Establishment** the group of people in a society who have a lot of power and influence and are often opposed to any kind of change or new ideas 統治集團, 權勢集團: *It's no good fighting the Establishment; it will always win in the end.* 同當權者鬥沒有用, 到頭來贏的總是他們。**3 the medical/legal/military etc establishment** a powerful controlling group within a particular type of activity 醫學界/法律界/軍界等的當權派 **4** [U] the act of establishing an organization, relationship, or system 建立, 設立: **[+of]** *Since the establishment of the club three years ago, membership has doubled.* 自從三年前該俱樂部成立起來, 會員數已增加了一倍。

es·tate /ə`stet; ɪ'steɪt/ *n* **1** [C] *BrE* an area where houses or buildings of a similar type have all been built together in a planned way【英】有計劃地建有同類建築物的地區: **council/industrial/housing etc estate** *Rachel was brought up on a bleak post-war council estate in Liverpool.* 雷切爾在利物浦一個破舊的二戰後市建住宅區內長大。**2** [singular] *law* all of someone's property and money, especially everything that is left after they die【法律】個人全部財產〔尤指遺產〕: *She left her estate to her husband.* 她把財產留給了丈夫。**3** [C] a large area of land in the country, usually with one large house on it and one owner 在鄉村附近有宅邸的一大片私有土地, 莊園: *workers on the Osborne estate* 奧斯本莊園的雇工 **4** [singular] *old-fashioned* a condition or state of life【過時】〔人生的〕狀況, 狀態: *the holy estate of matrimony* 神聖的婚姻狀況 —see also 另見 FOURTH ESTATE, REAL ESTATE

estate a·gent /·'· ,··/ *n* [C] *BrE* someone whose business is to buy and sell houses or land for people【英】房地產經紀人; REAL ESTATE AGENT or REALTOR *AmE*【美】—**estate agency** *n* [C]

estate car /·'· ·/ *n* [C] *BrE* a car with a door at the back, folding back seats, and a lot of room for boxes, cases etc【英】旅行車, 客貨兩用車; STATION WAGON *AmE*【美】

estate tax /·'· ·/ *n* [C,U] a tax in the US on the money and possessions of a dead person〔美國的〕遺產稅 —see also 另見 INHERITANCE TAX

es·teem¹ /ə`stim; ɪ'stiːm/ *n* [U] a feeling of respect and admiration for someone 尊敬, 敬重: **hold sb in high/great esteem** *She was an actress who was held in high esteem by everyone who knew her.* 她是一名讓所有認識她的人都十分尊重的演員。| **a token of sb's esteem** (=a sign of their esteem) 某人表達敬意的象徵 *Please accept this gift as a small token of our affection and esteem.* 區區小禮, 聊表心意, 請笑納。—see also 另見 SELF-ESTEEM

esteem² *v* [T] **1** to respect and admire someone 尊敬, 尊重: **highly esteemed** (=greatly respected) 極受尊重的 *a highly esteemed artist and critic* 極受尊重的藝術家兼批評家 **2 esteem it an honour/ favour/pleasure etc** *old-fashioned* used as a very polite way of saying you think something is an honour etc【過時】將某事物看作一種榮耀/恩惠/樂趣等 **3 esteem someone worthy/reliable etc** *old-fashioned* to believe that someone has a particular quality【過時】認為某人值得信賴/可靠等: *He esteemed the assistant trustworthy enough to look after the shop.* 他認為可以信賴這個助手, 託付其照看店鋪。

es·thete /`ɛsθit; 'iːsθiːt/ *n* [C] an American spelling of AESTHETE aesthete 的美式拼法 —**esthetic** /ˌɛs`θɛtɪk; iːs'θetɪk/ *adj* —**esthetical** *adj* —**esthetically** /-klɪ; -kli/ *adv* —**esthetics** *n* [U]

es·ti·ma·ble /`ɛstəməbl̩; 'estɨməbəl/ *adj formal* deserving respect and admiration【正式】值得尊敬的

3 2 **es·ti·mate¹** /ˈɛstəmɪt; ˈestɪ̣mɪ̣t/ *n* [C] **1** a calculation of the value, size, amount etc of something 估計, 估算: **a rough estimate** (=not very exact) 粗略估計 *At a rough estimate I'd say it's about 150 miles.* 粗略估計, 我覺得約有150英里。| **a conservative estimate** (=deliberately rather low) 保守的估計 *That seems a conservative estimate to me.* 我覺得那是一個保守的估計。—see also 另見 GUESSTIMATE **2** a statement of how much it will probably cost to build or repair something 估價, 報價: *We got two or three estimates so we could pick the cheapest.* 我們收到兩三家的報價, 因此可以選擇最低的一家。

3 3 **estimate²** /ˈɛstəˌmet; ˈestɪ̣meɪt/ *v* [T] to try to judge the value, size, speed, cost etc of something, partly by calculating and partly by guessing 估計, 估算: *The mechanic estimated the cost of repairs at $150.* 修理工估計維修費用為150美元。| *Iraq is estimated to have over 100 such weapons.* 估計伊拉克有一百多件這樣的武器。| **estimate that** *It is estimated that between 70 and 90 per cent of car crimes occur in the daytime.* 據估計, 70%到90%的汽車犯罪發生在白天。| **estimate how many/what etc** *It is difficult to estimate how many deaths are caused by passive smoking each year.* 很難估算每年有多少人死於被動吸煙。—**estimated** *adj* an estimated number, cost etc has been partly calculated and partly guessed 估計的, 估算的: *The concert was watched on TV by an estimated one billion people.* 估計有十億人通過電視收看了這場音樂會。—**estimator** *n* [C]

es·ti·ma·tion /ˌɛstəˈmeʃən; ˌestɪ̣ˈmeɪʃən/ *n* [U] **1** your opinion of the value, nature etc of someone or something 判斷, 看法: **in my/your etc estimation** *This will simply lead, in our estimation, to further problems.* 根據我們判斷, 這樣只會引發更多的問題。**2** respect or admiration for someone; ESTEEM¹ 尊敬, 尊重: **go up/come down in sb's estimation** (=be respected more or less by someone) 在某人心目中的地位升高/下降

es·tranged /ɪˈstrendʒd; ɪˈstreɪndʒd/ *adj* **1** an expression used especially in newspaper reports meaning no longer living with your husband or wife〔與配偶〕分居的〔尤用於新聞報道中〕: **estranged husband/wife** *She was shot in bed by her estranged husband.* 她被已分居的丈夫槍殺在牀上。**2** no longer having any connection with a relative or good friend, because of an argument〔因爭吵而與親戚或好朋友〕疏遠的, 不再聯繫的: **[+from]** *Mollie became increasingly estranged from her son.* 莫莉與兒子越來越疏遠。**3** no longer feeling any connection with something that used to be important in your life 與〔曾經重要的事物〕遠離的, 決裂的: **[+from]** *estranged from their religious traditions* 背離了他們的宗教傳統 —**estrangement** /əˈstrendʒmənt; ɪˈstreɪndʒmənt/ *n* [C,U]

es·tro·gen /ˈɛstrədʒən; ˈiːstrədʒən/ *n* [U] the usual American spelling of OESTROGEN oestrogen 的一般美式拼法

es·tu·a·ry /ˈɛstʃʊˌɛrɪ; ˈestʃuəri/ *n* [C] the wide part of a river where it goes into the sea 河口: *the Thames estuary* 泰晤士河河口

Estuary En·glish /ˈ···· ˌ··/ *n* [U] a way of speaking English that is common in the London area and is now starting to spread to other areas of England. In Estuary English the letters 't', 'l', and 'h' are often pronounced as a GLOTTAL STOP, and /l/ like /w/. 河口英語〔在倫敦地區流行, 現已開始傳至英格蘭其他地區, 其特點是字母t, l和h常發聲門閉塞音; /l/的發音和/w/相似〕

ETA /ˌi ti ˈe; ˌiː tiː ˈeɪ/ *n* the abbreviation for 縮寫= estimated time of arrival; the time when a plane, ship etc is expected to arrive〔飛機或船等〕估計到達時間: *What's our ETA?* 估計我們甚麼時候到?

et al /ˌɛt ˈæl; ˌet ˈæl/ *adv Latin* written after a list of names to mean that other people are also involved in something【拉丁】以及其他〔有關的〕人; 等人: *'The Human Embryo' by Brodsky, Rosenblum, et al* 布羅德斯基和羅森布拉姆等人所著的《人體胚胎》

etc /ˌɛt ˈsɛtərə; et ˈsetərə/ *adv Latin* the written abbreviation for 縮寫= et cetera, used after a list to show that there are many other similar things or people that you could have added【拉丁】等等; 以及其他〔類似的〕事物〔人〕: *loans taken out to cover the cost of repairs, new equipment etc* 支付修理、購置新設備等等費用的貸款 | **etc etc** (=used when you are rather bored or annoyed by the list you are giving) 等等, 等等〔用於表示對所列出的事物感到厭煩〕*The letter says pay at once, they've reminded us before etc etc.* 信中說了些要立刻付款、他們以前已提醒過我們等等等等的話。

et cet·e·ra /ˌɛt ˈsɛtərə; et ˈsetərə/ *adv Latin* the full form of etc【拉丁】etc 的全拼形式

etch /ɛtʃ; etʃ/ *v* **1** [I,T] to cut lines on a metal plate, piece of glass, stone etc to form a picture 蝕刻; 鑿刻 **2 be etched on your memory/mind** *literary* if an experience, name etc is etched on your memory or mind, you cannot forget it and you think of it often【文】〔經歷、姓名等〕銘刻在記憶中/腦海裡: *a terrible event that is etched forever on my memory* 永遠留在我記憶裡的可怕事件 **3** [T usually passive 一般用被動態] if someone's face is etched with pain, sadness etc you can see these feelings from their expression〔臉上〕刻着〔痛苦、悲傷等〕**4** [T] to make lines or patterns appear on something very clearly 使〔線條或圖案〕清晰: *deep furrows etched in the sand* 沙地上清晰的深溝 —**etched** *adj*: *etched glass* 刻有圖案的玻璃 —**etcher** *n* [C,U]

etch·ing /ˈɛtʃɪŋ; ˈetʃɪŋ/ *n* [C] a picture made by printing from an etched metal plate 刻版畫; 蝕刻畫

e·ter·nal /ɪˈtɝnl; ɪˈtɜːnəl/ *adj* **1** continuing for ever and having no end 永遠的; 永恆的: *the Christian promise of eternal life* 基督教承諾的永生 **2** *informal* seeming to continue for ever, especially because of being boring or annoying【非正式】似乎無休無止的; 沒完沒了的: *Why can't you stop your eternal complaining!* 你為甚麼就不能停止你那沒完沒了的抱怨呢! **3 eternal truths** principles that are always true 永恆的真理

e·ter·nal·ly /ɪˈtɝnḷɪ; ɪˈtɜːnəl-i/ *adv* **1** for ever 永遠, 永久地 **2 eternally grateful** used to say that you are very grateful 感激不盡的 **3** *informal* very often【非正式】頻繁地, 不斷地: *She seems to be eternally asking me for help.* 她似乎總是在向我求助。

eternal tri·an·gle /ˌ·ˌ·· ˈ···/ *n* [singular] the difficult situation that occurs when two people have a sexual relationship with the same person 三角性關係, 三角戀愛

e·ter·ni·ty /ɪˈtɝnətɪ; ɪˈtɜːnɪ̣ti/ *n* **1 an eternity** a period of time that seems very long because you are annoyed, anxious etc 似乎很漫長的一段時間: *Every moment seemed like an eternity.* 每一瞬間都似乎無窮無盡。**2** [U] the whole of time without any end 永恆: **for all eternity** *a little animal preserved for all eternity as a fossil* 作為化石得以永遠保存下來的小動物 **3** [U] the state of existence after death that some people believe continues for ever 永生

-eth /ɪθ; ɪ̣θ/ *suffix* also 又作 **-th** *old use or Biblical* forms the third person singular of verbs【舊或聖經】〔構成動詞的第三人稱單數〕: *he goeth* 他走

eth·a·nol /ˈɛθəˌnol; ˈeθənɒl/ *n* [U] *technical* ETHYL ALCOHOL【術語】乙醇

e·ther /ˈiθɚ; ˈiːθə/ *n* **1** [U] a clear liquid used in the past as an ANAESTHETIC to make people sleep before an operation 醚; 乙醚 **2 the ether** *BrE*【英】**a)** the air through which radio waves travel 以太, 能媒: *Messages are flying through the ether.* 信息在以太空間中傳輸。**b)** also 又作 **aether** *poetic* the upper part of the sky【詩】蒼天, 蒼穹

e·the·re·al /ɪˈθɪrɪəl; ɪˈθɪəriəl/ *adj* very delicate and light, in a way that does not seem real 縹緲的; 超凡的: *ethereal beauty* 超凡的美麗 —**ethereally** *adv*

e·ther·net /ˈiθɚˌnɛt; ˈiːθənet/ *n* [U] a special system of wires used for connecting computer networks around the world 以太網

eth·ic /ˋɛθɪk; ˈeθɪk/ *n* **1** [C] a general idea or belief that influences people's behaviour and attitudes 倫理; 道德體系: *The modern ethic seems to be to get as much money as you can without worrying how you get it.* 現代的道德觀似乎是不擇手段盡量弄錢。—see also 另見 WORK ETHIC **2 ethics** [plural] moral rules or principles of behaviour for deciding what is right and wrong 道德標準, 道德規範: *The ethics of his actions are suspect, but technically he is within the law.* 他的行為是否合乎道德規範值得懷疑, 但從嚴格的法律意義上講他並沒有違法。| **professional ethics** (=the moral rules relating to a particular profession) 職業道德 | **a code of ethics** (=a set of moral rules) 道德準則

eth·i·cal /ˋɛθɪkḷ; ˈeθɪkəl/ *adj* [no comparative 無比較級] **1** connected with principles of what is right and wrong 關於倫理的: *The use of animals in scientific tests raises some difficult ethical questions.* 用動物做科學實驗引發了一些棘手的道德問題。**2** morally good or correct 合乎道德的; 正確的: *Is it ethical to use drugs to control prisoners' behaviour?* 用藥物來控制犯人的行為合乎道德嗎? —opposite 反義詞 UNETHICAL —**ethically** /-kḷɪ; -kli/ *adv*

3 **eth·nic**[1] /ˋɛθnɪk; ˈeθnɪk/ *adj* **1** connected with a particular race, nation, or tribe and their customs and traditions 種族[民族, 部落]的; 具有種族[民族, 部落]特色的: *The city's population includes a wide range of different ethnic groups.* 這座城市居住着許多不同種族的人。| *ethnic Turks living in Bulgaria* 居住在保加利亞的土耳其人 | **ethnic violence/divisions/unrest** (=violence etc between people from different races, tribes etc) 種族[部落]衝突/分裂/騷亂 **2 ethnic cooking/fashion/design etc** cooking, fashion etc from countries that are a long way from Britain or the US, which seems very different and unusual〔對英國或美國來說具有〕異國風情的烹調/時尚/設計等: *the delights of ethnic cooking* 品嘗外國菜餚的樂趣 **3 ethnic cleansing** the action of forcing people to leave their homes because of their RACIAL or national group 種族清洗 —**ethnically** /-kḷɪ; -kli/ *adv*

ethnic[2] *n* [C] *AmE* someone who belongs to a different race from the main group living in a particular country【美】少數民族的一員

ethnic mi·nor·i·ty /,‥ ·ˋ‥/ *n* [C] a group of people of a different race from the main group in a country 少數民族

eth·no·cen·tric /ˌɛθnoˋsɛntrɪk; ˌeθnəʊˈsentrɪk◂/ *adj* based on the idea that your own race, nation, group etc is better than any other 種族[民族、集團]優越感的: *ethnocentric insensitivity* 種族優越感導致的麻木 —**ethnocentrism** *n* [U] —**ethnocentricity** /ˌɛθnosɛnˋtrɪsətɪ; ˌeθnəʊsenˈtrɪsɪ̵ti/ *n* [U]

eth·nog·ra·pher /ɛθˋnɑgrəfɚ; eθˈnɒgrəfə/ *n* [C] someone who studies ethnography 人種學家

eth·nog·ra·phy /ɛθˋnɑgrəfɪ; eθˈnɒgrəfi/ *n* [U] the scientific study of different races of people 人種誌, 人種論 —**ethnographic** /ˌɛθnəˋgræfɪk; ˌeθnəˈgræfɪk◂/ *adj* —**ethnographically** /-kḷɪ; -kli/ *adv*

eth·nol·o·gy /ɛθˋnɑlədʒɪ; eθˈnɒlədʒi/ *n* [U] the scientific study and comparison of the origins and organization of different races of people 人種學, 民族學 —compare 比較 ANTHROPOLOGY, SOCIOLOGY —**ethnologist** *n* [C] —**ethnological** /ˌɛθnəˋlɑdʒɪkḷ; ˌeθnəˈlɒdʒɪkəl◂/ *adj* —**ethnologically** /-kḷɪ; -kli/ *adv*

e·thos /ˋiθɑs; ˈiːθɒs/ *n* [singular] the set of ideas and moral attitudes belonging to a person or group〔個人或團體的〕精神特質: *the competitive spirit in the American ethos* 美國精神中的競爭意識

eth·yl al·co·hol /ˌiθaɪl ˋælkəhɔl; ˌeθəl ˈælkəhɒl/ *n* [U] *technical* the type of alcohol in alcoholic drinks【術語】食用酒精

e·ti·o·lat·ed /ˋitɪəˌletɪd; ˈiːtiəleɪtɪ̵d/ *adj* **1** *literary* pale and weak【文】蒼白無力的 **2** *technical* a plant that is etiolated is white because it has not received enough light【術語】〔植物因缺乏陽光而〕發黃的, 變白的 —**etiolation** /ˌitɪəˋleʃən; ˌiːtiəˈleɪʃən/ *n* [U]

et·i·ol·o·gy /ˌitɪˋɑlədʒɪ; ˌetiˈɒlədʒi/ *n* [C,U] *technical* the cause of a disease or the scientific study of this【術語】病因(學), 病源(學) —**etiological** /ˌitɪəˋlɑdʒɪkḷ; ˌetiəˈlɒdʒɪkəl◂/ *adj* —**etiologically** /-kḷɪ; -kli/ *adv*

et·i·quette /ˋɛtɪkɛt; ˈetɪket/ *n* [U] the formal rules for polite behaviour in society or in a particular group 禮儀, 禮節: *a breach of professional etiquette* 違反職業禮儀規範

-ette /ɛt; et/ *suffix* [in nouns 構成名詞] **1** a small thing of a particular type 小: *a kitchenette* (=small kitchen) 小廚房 | *a snackette* (=a very small meal) 小吃 **2** a woman who is doing a particular job〔做某種工作的〕女(性): *an usherette* (=female USHER) 女引座員 **3** something that is not real, but is IMITATION (2) 仿(製)〔的東西〕: *flannelette* 棉法蘭絨 | *chairs covered with leatherette* 鋪有人造革的椅子

et·y·mol·o·gy /ˌɛtəˋmɑlədʒɪ; ˌetɪ̵ˈmɒlədʒi/ *n* **1** [U] the study of the origins, history, and changing meanings of words 詞源學 **2** [C] a description of the history of a particular word 詞源 —**etymologist** *n* [C] —**etymological** /ˌɛtəməˋlɑdʒɪkḷ; ˌetɪ̵məˈlɒdʒɪkəl◂/ *adj* —**etymologically** /-kḷɪ; -kli/ *adv*

EU /ˌi ˋju; ˌiː ˈjuː/ *n* [singular] the abbreviation of 縮寫= the EUROPEAN UNION

eu·ca·lyp·tus /ˌjukəˋlɪptəs; ˌjuːkəˈlɪptəs/ *n* [C,U] a tall tree that produces an oil with a strong smell, used in medicines 桉樹

Eu·cha·rist /ˋjukərɪst; ˈjuːkərɪ̵st/ *n* **the Eucharist** the holy bread and wine, representing Christ's body and blood, used during a Christian ceremony, or the ceremony itself〔基督教〕聖餐中的麵包和葡萄酒; 聖餐儀式 —**Eucharistic** /ˌjukəˋrɪstɪk; ˌjuːkəˈrɪstɪk◂/ *adj*

eu·clid·e·an, Euclidean /juˋklɪdɪən; juːˈklɪdiən/ *adj* related to the GEOMETRY described by Euclid〔希臘數學家〕歐幾里得幾何的

eu·gen·ics /juˋdʒɛnɪks; juːˈdʒenɪks/ *n* [plural] the study of methods to improve the mental and physical abilities of human beings by choosing who should become parents 優生學; 人種改良學

eu·lo·gize also 又作 **-ise** *BrE*【英】/ˋjuləˌdʒaɪz; ˈjuːlədʒaɪz/ *v* [I,T] to praise someone or something very much 歌頌, 讚美: *a poem eulogizing the bravery of the nation's warriors* 歌頌民族戰士英勇事跡的詩 —**eulogist** *n* [C] —**eulogistic** /ˌjuləˋdʒɪstɪk; ˌjuːləˈdʒɪstɪk◂/ *adj* —**eulogistically** /-kḷɪ; -kli/ *adv*

eu·lo·gy /ˋjulədʒɪ; ˈjuːlədʒi/ *n* [C, U] a speech or piece of writing in which you praise someone or something very much, especially at a funeral 頌詞; 頌文〔尤指葬禮上的悼詞或悼文〕

eu·nuch /ˋjunək; ˈjuːnək/ *n* [C] a man who has had his TESTICLES removed, especially someone who guarded a king's wives in some Eastern countries in the past 閹人〔尤指過去的宦官〕

eu·phe·mis·m /ˋjufəˌmɪzəm; ˈjuːfɪ̵mɪzəm/ *n* [C] a polite word or expression that you use instead of a more direct one to avoid shocking or upsetting someone 委婉語; 委婉說法: *'Pass away' is a euphemism for 'die'.* "過去"是"死"的委婉說法。

eu·phe·mis·tic /ˌjufəˋmɪstɪk; ˌjuːfɪ̵ˈmɪstɪk◂/ *adj* euphemistic language uses polite words and expressions to avoid shocking or upsetting people〔言語〕委婉的; 婉言的: *a euphemistic expression such as 'powder room' for 'toilet'* 例如將"廁所"說成"化妝間"的委婉說法 —**euphemistically** /-kḷɪ; -kli/ *adv*

eu·pho·ni·ous /juˋfonɪəs; juːˈfəʊniəs/ *adj formal* words or sounds that are euphonious are pleasant to listen to【正式】悅耳的, 動聽的

eu·pho·ri·a /juˋfɔrɪə; juːˈfɔːriə/ *n* [U] a short but extremely strong feeling of happiness and excitement 狂喜; 興奮異常: *the current state of euphoria after*

Ireland's amazing victory over England last Saturday 上週六愛爾蘭隊奇跡般戰勝英格蘭隊後引發的狂喜

eu·phor·ic /ju`fɑrɪk; juː'fɒrɪk/ *adj* feeling very happy and excited 非常高興的; 極其興奮的 —**euphorically** /-klɪ; -kli/ *adv*

Eu·ra·sian[1] /ju`reʒən; jʊ'reɪʒən/ *adj* concerned with both Europe and Asia 歐亞大陸的; 與歐洲和亞洲有關的

Eurasian[2] *n* [C] *old-fashioned* someone who has one European parent and one Asian parent【過時】歐亞混血兒

Eu·re·ka /ju`rikə; jʊ'riːkə/ *interjection often humorous* used to show how happy you are that you have discovered the answer to a problem, found something etc【常幽默】我發現了〔因找到問題的解決方法或發現某物等時而發出的歡呼〕

Eu·ro /`jʊro; 'jʊərəʊ/ *adj* [only before noun 僅用於名詞前] European, especially connected with the European Union 歐洲的〔尤指歐盟的〕: *There's some new Euro directive on import regulations.* 歐盟對進口制度有了一些新指示。

Euro- /jʊro; jʊərəʊ/ *prefix* **1 a)** European, especially western European 歐洲的〔尤指西歐的〕: *Eurocommunism* 歐洲共產主義 **b)** European and 歐洲和…的: *Euro-American relations* 歐美關係 **2** of the European Union 歐盟的: *the Europarliament* 歐洲議會

Eu·ro·cheque /`jʊrotʃɛk; 'jʊərəʊtʃek/ *n* [C] *trademark* a special cheque that can be used in different banks or shops, especially in Europe【商標】〔尤指歐洲的〕通用支票

Eu·ro·crat /`jʊrəkræt; 'jʊərəʊkræt/ *n* [C] *informal* a government official of the European Union, especially one who makes decisions you do not like【非正式】歐盟官員〔尤指所作決定不受歡迎的官員〕

Eu·ro·dol·lar /`jʊro,dɑlə; 'jʊərəʊ,dɒlə/ *n* [C usually plural 一般用複數] *technical* a US dollar that has been put in a European bank or lent to a European customer to help trade and provide an international money system【術語】歐洲美元〔指存於歐洲銀行或借給歐洲客戶以幫助促進貿易和建立國際貨幣體系的美元〕

Eu·rope /`jʊrəp; 'jʊərəp/ *n* **1** the large land mass that lies north of the Mediterranean and goes as far east as the Ural Mountains 歐洲 **2** the European Union 歐盟: *Britain's future lies in Europe.* 英國的未來繫於歐盟。**3** *BrE* the CONTINENT[1] (1) of Europe not including Britain【英】〔不包括英國在內的〕歐洲大陸: *a rail link to Europe through the Channel Tunnel* 通過(英吉利海峽)海底隧道與歐洲大陸連接的鐵路

Eu·ro·pe·an[1] /,jʊrə`piən; ,jʊərə'piːən◂/ *n* [C] someone from Europe 歐洲人

European[2] *adj* from or connected with Europe 歐洲的: *European law* 歐洲的法律

European Cur·ren·cy Unit /,···· '··· ,··/ *n* [C] an ECU〔歐洲共同體的〕歐洲通貨單位

European Ex·change Rate Mech·a·nis·m /,···· ·'·· · ,····/ *n* [singular] the ERM; a system for controlling the EXCHANGE RATE between the money of the different countries of the European Union 歐洲匯率機制

European Mon·e·ta·ry Sys·tem /,···· '···· ,··/ *n* [singular] the EMS; a system for limiting how much the different currencies (CURRENCY (1)) of countries within the European Union can go up or down in value in relation to each other 歐洲貨幣體系〔限制在歐盟範圍內不同貨幣彼此之間匯率升降幅度的體系〕

European U·nion /,···· '··/ *n* [singular] a European political and economic organization that encourages trade and friendship between the countries that are members 歐洲聯盟

Eu·sta·chian tube /jus`teʃən ,tub; juː'steɪʃən ,tjuːb/ *n* [C] one of the pair of tubes that join your ears to your throat 耳咽管, 歐氏管〔連接咽喉與耳朵的管〕

eu·tha·na·si·a /,juθə`neʒə; ,juːθə'neɪziə/ *n* [U] the painless killing of people who are very ill or very old in order to stop them suffering; MERCY KILLING 安樂死

e·vac·u·ate /ɪ`vækju,et; ɪ'vækjueɪt/ *v* **1** [T] to send people to a safe place from a dangerous place 撤離, 撤出: **evacuate sb from/to** *The villagers were evacuated to the countryside.* 村民們被撤到郊區。**2** [I,T] to empty a place by making all the people leave 撤空〔某地〕, 讓所有人撤離〔某地〕: *The whole building has been evacuated.* 整幢大樓裡的人已被疏散。**3** *formal* to empty your BOWELS【正式】大便 —**evacuation** /ɪ,vækju`eʃən; ɪ,vækju'eɪʃən/ *n* [C,U]

e·vac·u·ee /ɪ`vækju,i; ɪ,vækju'iː/ *n* [C] someone who is sent away from a place because it is dangerous, for example because there is a war 被撤離者, 被疏散者

e·vade /ɪ`ved; ɪ'veɪd/ *v* [T] **1 evade the subject/question/issue etc** to avoid talking about something, especially because you are trying to hide something 迴避主題/問題/議題等: *Stop trying to evade the issue.* 不要再試圖迴避這個問題了。**2** to find a way of not doing something you should do 逃避〔該做的事〕: **evade your responsibilities/duty/problems** *You can't go on evading your responsibilities forever.* 你不能永遠都逃避責任。**3** to avoid doing something that you should do according to the law such as paying tax 規避, 逃避〔依法該做的事〕: *If you try to evade paying taxes you risk going to prison.* 如果你試圖逃税, 你就有坐牢的危險。**4** to escape from someone who is trying to catch you 躲避〔某人的追捕〕: *Williams succeeded in evading capture for several days.* 威廉姆斯好幾天都躲過了追捕。**5** *formal* if success, the truth etc evades you, you cannot achieve it or understand it【正式】難倒; 使困惑

e·val·u·ate /ɪ`vælju,et; ɪ'væljueɪt/ *v* [T] to carefully consider something to see how useful or valuable it is 評估, 評價: *evaluating the success of the training scheme* 評估訓練計劃的成果

e·val·u·a·tion /ɪ,vælju`eʃən; ɪ,vælju'eɪʃən/ *n* [C,U] the act of considering something to decide how useful or valuable it is, or a document in which this is done 評估, 評價; 評估報告: *an intensive evaluation of the health care program* 對醫療保健制度深入仔細的評估 W3

e·van·gel·i·cal /,ivæn`dʒɛlɪkḷ; ,iːvæn'dʒelɪkəl◂/ *adj* **1** evangelical Christians believe that they should persuade as many people as possible to become Christians 福音傳道者的, 基督教福音派的 **2** very eager to persuade people to accept your ideas and beliefs 狂熱宣傳自己的主張和信仰的: *Andrew talks about green issues with almost evangelical fervour.* 安德魯在談到環保問題時近乎狂熱。

e·van·ge·list /ɪ`vændʒəlɪst; ɪ'vændʒəlɪst/ *n* [C] **1** someone who travels around speaking at meeting to persuade people to become Christians 巡迴布道者 **2 Evangelist** one of the four writers of the books in the Bible called the Gospels《聖經》福音書的四位作者之一 —**evangelism** /ɪ`vændʒəlɪzəm; ɪ'vændʒəlɪzəm/ *n*[U] —**evangelistic** /ɪ,vændʒə`lɪstɪk; ɪ,vændʒə'lɪstɪk◂/ *adj*

e·van·ge·lize also 又作 **-ise** *BrE*【英】/ɪ`vændʒə,laɪz; ɪ'vændʒəlaɪz/ *v* [I,T] to try to persuade people to become Christians 勸(人)皈依基督教

e·vap·o·rate /ɪ`væpə,ret; ɪ'væpəreɪt/ *v* **1** [I,T] if a liquid evaporates or if something evaporates it, it changes into steam (使)〔液體〕汽化, (使)蒸發 **2** [I] if a feeling evaporates, it slowly disappears〔感覺〕逐漸消逝: *Hopes of reaching an agreement are beginning to evaporate.* 達成協議的希望開始逝去。—**evaporation** /ɪ,væpə`reʃən; ɪ,væpə'reɪʃən/ *n* [U]

evaporated milk /·,···· '·/ *n* [U] milk which has been made thicker by removing some of the water 淡煉乳

e·va·sion /ɪ`veʒən; ɪ'veɪʒən/ *n* [C, U] **1** the act of avoiding doing something that you should do, or an example of this behaviour 迴避; 逃避: *tax evasion* 逃税 **2** an act of deliberately avoiding talking about something or dealing with something 遁辭; 藉口: *His speech was full of lies and evasions.* 他的演講充滿了謊言和遁辭。

e·va·sive /ɪ`vesɪv; ɪ'veɪsɪv/ *adj* **1** not willing to answer questions directly 模棱兩可的, 推託的, 迴避的: *Paul's* *being very evasive about the new contract.* 保羅對新合同含糊其辭。**2 evasive action** action to avoid being injured or harmed〔為免受傷害而採取的〕規避動作 —**evasively** *adv* —**evasiveness** *n* [U]

eve /iv; iːv/ *n* **1** [C usually singular 一般用單數] the night or day before an important religious day or holiday 前夕; 前一天: **Christmas Eve** (=24th December) 聖誕節前夕 | **New Year's Eve** (=31st December) 除夕 **2 the eve of** the time just before an important event〔重大事件的〕前夕, 前一刻: *on the eve of the election* 在選舉前夕 **3** [C] *poetic* evening【詩】傍晚: *one summer's eve* 夏日傍晚

e·ven¹ /ˈivən; ˈiːvən/ *adv* **1** used to emphasize something that is unexpected or surprising in what you are saying 甚至; 即使: *Even the younger children enjoyed the concert.* 連較小的孩子也喜歡這場音樂會。| *We've all been naughty sometimes – even Mummy!* 我們都有頑皮的時候, 甚至媽媽也這樣! | **not even** *Henry's a strict vegetarian – he doesn't even eat cheese.* 亨利是個嚴格的素食者——甚至連乾酪都不吃。| *I never even saw the kid until I hit him.* 我在撞到那個小孩前甚至都未曾看見他。**2 even bigger/better/brighter etc** used to emphasize that someone or something is bigger, better etc than before, or than someone or something else you have just mentioned〔比從前或剛才提到的其他人或事物〕更大/好/明亮等: *New Jet now washes even whiter.* 現在用新耶特洗得更乾淨。| *Diane knows even less about it than I do.* 關於此事黛安娜知道的甚至比我還少。**3** used to add a stronger, more exact word to what you are saying 甚至可以説; 更確切地説: *Molly looked depressed, even suicidal.* 莫莉看上去情緒低落, 甚至可以説是有些自殺傾向。| *The bride looked beautiful, radiant even.* 新娘非常漂亮, 更確切地説是光彩照人。**4 even so** *spoken* used to introduce something that is the opposite or very different from what you have been saying【口】即使如此, 即使這樣: *I myself don't believe in ghosts. Even so, I wouldn't like to be alone in that room at night.* 我並不相信鬼神。即便如此, 我也不願意夜裡一個人待在那個房間裡。**5 even if** no matter if 即便, 縱然: *Charlie's going to have problems finding a job even if she gets her A levels.* 即便查莉通過了高級程度考試, 她以後找工作也成問題。**6 even though** used to emphasize that although something happens or is true, something else also happens or is true 雖然, 儘管: *Even though they loved each other, they decided to part.* 他們雖愛對方, 但還是決定分手。| *I can still remember, even though it was so long ago.* 雖然這是很久以前的事, 我還是記得。**7 even now/then** in spite of what has happened, what you have done, or what is true 即使到這/那時; 即使這/那樣: *I explained it all to him again, but even then he didn't understand.* 我又全部給他解釋了一遍, 可即使那樣他還是不懂。| *Even now I find it hard to believe her story.* 即使到現在我還是難以相信她的説法。**8 even as** used to emphasize that something happens at the same moment as something else 正當, 恰好在…時候: *I tried to phone her, but even as I was phoning she was leaving the building.* 我試圖打電話給她, 但我打電話的時候, 她正離開大樓。| *Even as we watched the car skidded out of control.* 就在我們看着的時候, 汽車打滑失去了控制。

even² *adj*

1 ►SURFACE 表面◄ completely flat with all parts at the same height 平的, 平坦的: *The floor must be completely even before we lay the tiles.* 先要把地面弄得十分平坦才能鋪地磚。| *an even stretch of road* 一段平坦的道路

2 ►NOT CHANGING 無變化◄ an even rate, temperature etc is steady and does not change much〔比率、溫度等〕平穩的, 無大波動的: *We were travelling at an even speed.* 我們以勻速行駛。| *an even rhythm* 平穩的節奏

3 ►DIVIDED EQUALLY 均分◄ divided equally, so that there is the same amount of something in each place, for each person etc 平分的, 均分的: *an even distribution of wealth* 財富均分

4 even number a number that can be divided exactly by two 偶數: *2, 4, 6 and 8 are even numbers.* 2, 4, 6, 8 是偶數。—opposite 反義詞 **odd number** (ODD (6))

5 ►COMPETITION 競賽◄ having teams or competitors that are equally good so that everyone has a chance of winning 勢均力敵的, 水平相當的: *This year's Superbowl was a very even contest.* 今年的〔美式足球〕超級盃賽兩隊水平非常接近。

6 ►LINE OF THINGS 物品排列◄ regularly spaced and neat-looking 排列整齊的, 擺放均勻的: *even rows of gleaming white teeth* 整齊的兩排閃亮潔白的牙齒

7 be even *informal* to no longer owe someone something, especially money【非正式】互不欠〔錢〕的, 兩訖的: *If you give me $5 for the ticket, we'll be even.* 如果你給我5塊錢票錢, 我們就兩訖了。

8 have an even chance (of) to be just as likely to happen as to not happen 有一半機會…, …的可能性有一半: *Derek has an even chance of getting the job.* 德里克有一半的可能得到那份工作。

9 get even with *informal* to harm someone just as much as they have harmed you【非正式】對…進行(同等)報復; 以眼還眼, 以牙還牙: *He's not getting away with this, I'll get even with him one day.* 不能就這樣放他過去, 總有一天我會找他算賬。—compare 比較 UNEVEN —see also 另見 EVEN-TEMPERED, **break even** (BREAK¹ (9)) —**evenness** *n* [U]

even³ *v*

even out *phr v* [I,T] if two amounts, levels etc even out, or if you even them out, the differences between them become smaller (使)相等; (使)平均: *You have to wait until the water level in the pipes evens out.* 你得等一等, 直到每根管子中的水位一樣高。| **even sth ↔ out** *They even out your payments over the whole year.* 他們將你的付款分攤到全年各個月。

even up *phr v* [T **even sth ↔ up**] to make a situation or competition more equal 拉平; 使平衡

even⁴ *n* [U] *poetic* evening【詩】傍晚

even-hand·ed /ˌ.. ˈ..◄/ *adj* giving fair and equal treatment to everyone; IMPARTIAL 公正的; 不偏不倚的: *even handed justice* 公正無私 —**even-handedly** *adv*

eve·ning¹ /ˈivnɪŋ; ˈiːvnɪŋ/ *n* **1** [C,U] the early part of the night between the end of the day and the time you go to bed 傍晚; 晚上: *We always go swimming on Friday evenings.* 週五晚上我們總是去游泳。| **in the evening** *Mick often goes to the pub in the evening.* 米克晚上常去酒吧。| **for the evening** *I'm going out for the evening.* 我今晚要出去。| **early/late evening** *It happened in the early evening, around half past six.* 事情發生在傍晚時分, 大約六點半左右。**2 a musical/poetry etc evening** an event involving music, poetry etc that takes place in the evening 音樂/詩歌等晚會 **3 the evening of your life** *literary* the last part of your life【文】晚年

evening² *interjection informal* used to greet someone when you meet them in the evening【非正式】晚上好: *Evening Joe, everything all right?* 晚上好, 喬, 一切都好嗎?

evening class /ˈ.. ./ *n* [C] a course of study for adults in the evening〔成人參加的〕夜校, 夜間課程

evening dress /ˈ.. ./ *n* **1** [U] special clothes worn for formal meals, parties etc in the evening 晚禮服 **2** also 又作 **evening gown** *especially AmE*【尤美】[C] a dress worn by women to formal meals, parties etc in the evening 女士晚禮服

eve·nings /ˈivnɪŋz; ˈiːvnɪŋz/ *adv especially AmE* during the evening【尤美】在晚上: *I'm always at home evenings.* 晚上我一定在家。

evening star /ˌ.. ˈ./ *n* [singular] the PLANET Venus, seen as a bright star in the western sky in the evening 黃昏星〔指金星〕

e·ven·ly /ˋivənlɪ; ˈiːvənli/ *adv* **1** with equal amounts or numbers of something in every part of a particular area, or divided equally among a group of people 平均地, 均匀地: *Support for the Liberals is fairly evenly spread across the country.* 自由黨的支持者在全國分佈較平均。| *Spread the butter evenly over the toast.* 將黃油均匀地塗在烤麵包上。**2** in a steady or regular way 平穩地; 有規律地: *breathing deeply and evenly* 呼吸又深又平穩 | **evenly spaced** *rows of evenly spaced desks* 一排排擺放整齊的桌子 **3** dealing with or affecting all parts of something in the same way 均匀地: *Cook the meat quickly for about 3 minutes, until evenly browned.* 將肉炒約三分鐘, 直至其變成均匀褐色。**4 evenly matched** if two competitors are evenly matched, they have an equal chance of winning 勢均力敵的: *The two wrestlers were very evenly matched.* 兩名摔跤選手實力非常接近。**5** if you say something evenly, you say it in a calm way without getting angry or upset 心平氣和地: *"You can do whatever you like," she said evenly.* "你想做甚麼就可以做甚麼," 她心平氣和地說。

e·vens /ˋivənz; ˈiːvənz/ *adj technical* if the ODDS (=probability that a horse will win a race) of a horse in a race are evens, then it is equally likely that it will win or lose【術語】〔賽馬〕輸贏機會相等的: *Black Flag is the evens favourite.* 名為"黑旗"的賽馬是熱門, 賠率大約是一比一。

e·ven·song /ˋivən͵sɔŋ; ˈiːvənsɒŋ/ *n* [U] the evening religious ceremony in the Church of England〔英國國教的〕晚禱

1 1 **e·vent** /ɪˋvɛnt; ɪˈvent/ *n*

1 ▶INTERESTING/EXCITING 有趣的/令人興奮的◀ [C] something that happens, especially something important, interesting or unusual〔尤指重要、有意思或不尋常的〕事件: *the most important events of 1994* 1994年最重大的事件 | *The article discusses the events which led up to the prime minister's resignation.* 這篇文章討論了導致首相辭職的一系列事件。| **sequence of events** (=the order in which events happened) 事件發生的順序 *reconstructing the sequence of events on the night of the murder* 再現謀殺案發當晚事件的全過程 | **course of events** (=the way that each event caused the next one, without being planned)〔未經計劃的〕事件發展的過程 *Nothing you could have done would have changed the course of events.* 不管你曾做過甚麼, 也無法改變事件的進程。

2 ▶COMPETITION/PERFORMANCE/PARTY 競賽/演出/聚會◀ [C] an important performance, sports competition, party etc which has been arranged for a particular date and time〔事先安排好的〕演出; 賽事; 聚會: *the biggest event of the racing season* 本賽季最大的一場賽事 | **social/sporting/fund-raising etc event** *The Christie Ball soon became the social event of the year.* 克里斯蒂舞會很快就成了一年中最重大的社會活動。

3 ▶IN A SPORTS COMPETITION 在體育比賽中◀ [C] any of the races, competitions etc arranged as part of a day's sports 運動項目: *The next event will be the 100 metres.* 下一個比賽項目將是100米跑。—see also 另見 FIELD EVENT, THREE-DAY EVENT

4 in any/either event also 又作 **at all events** used just before or after a statement to emphasize that it will happen in spite of anything else that may happen 不管是哪種情況, 無論如何: *I'll probably see you tomorrow but I'll phone in any event.* 我明天可能會與你見面, 但無論如何我都會給你打電話。

5 in the event used to emphasize what actually happened in a situation as opposed to what you thought might happen 結果, 到頭來: *We were afraid he would be nervous on stage, but in the event he sang beautifully.* 我們擔心他在台上會怯場, 結果他唱得好極了。

6 in the event of rain/fire/an accident etc also 又作 **in the event that** used to tell people what they should do or what will happen if something else happens 萬一下雨/起火/發生意外等; 假若發生…的情況: *Britain agreed to support the US in the event of war.* 英國同意, 一旦發生戰爭將支持美國。

7 in the normal course of events if things happen in the normal way 如果一切正常: *In the normal course of events, John will inherit the money from his uncle.* 如果一切正常, 約翰將繼承他叔叔的財產。

even-tem·pered /͵.. ˈ..◂/ *adj* not becoming angry easily; calm 性情平和的; 沉着的

e·vent·ful /ɪˋvɛntfəl; ɪˈventfəl/ *adj* full of interesting or important events 充滿大事的; 多變故的: *She's led quite an eventful life.* 她一生歷盡滄桑。| *an eventful holiday* 不平凡的假期 —**eventfully** *adv*

e·ven·tide /ˋivən͵taɪd; ˈiːvəntaɪd/ *n* [U] *poetic* evening【詩】傍晚

e·ven·tu·al /ɪˋvɛntʃuəl; ɪˈventʃuəl/ *adj* [only before noun 僅用於名詞前] happening or achieving something at the end of a process 最終發生的; 最後獲得的: *Sweden were the eventual winners of the tournament.* 瑞典是錦標賽的最後贏家。| *the eventual outcome* 最後結果

e·ven·tu·al·i·ty /ɪ͵vɛntʃuˋælətɪ; ɪ͵ventʃuˈæləti/ *n* [C] *formal* a possible event or result, especially an unpleasant one【正式】可能發生的事件[結果]〔尤指不愉快的事件〕: *We must be prepared for every eventuality.* 我們必須作好應付各種情況的準備。

e·ven·tu·al·ly /ɪˋvɛntʃuəlɪ; ɪˈventʃuəli/ *adv* after a long time, especially after a long delay or a lot of problems 終於, 最終: *He worked so hard that eventually he made himself ill.* 他工作太努力, 終於病倒了。| *She eventually passed her driving test.* 她終於通過了駕駛考試。| *"Did you manage to contact Roger?" "Well yes, eventually."* "你與羅傑聯繫上了嗎?" "噢, 是的, 最終聯繫上了。" 1 2

e·ven·tu·ate /ɪˋvɛntʃu͵et; ɪˈventʃueɪt/ *v formal* to happen as a result of something【正式】終於發生; 因而發生

eventuate in sth *phr v* [T] *formal* to be the final cause of something【正式】最終導致: *The scandal finally eventuated in the resignation of the prime minister.* 該醜聞最終導致首相辭職。

ev·er /ˋɛvɚ; ˈevə/ *adv* **1** a word meaning at any time; used mostly in questions, negatives, comparisons, or sentences with 'if'〔一般用於疑問句、否定句、比較結構或帶 if 的句子中〕在任何時候: *Nothing ever makes Ted angry.* 從來沒有甚麼事情會使特德生氣。| *"Do you ever get to the theatre?" "No, never."* "你有時會去看話劇嗎?" "不, 從來不會。" | *I don't remember ever seeing him before.* 我不記得以前見過他。| *If you're ever in Seattle, come and see me.* 如果你到西雅圖, 來看我吧。| **have you ever** *"Have you ever been to Paris?" "Yes, I have."* "你去過巴黎嗎?" "是的, 我去過。" | *That's the biggest fish I've ever seen.* 那是我見過的最大的魚。| **hotter/thinner/taller etc than ever** (=hotter, thinner etc than before) 比以前任何時候都熱/瘦/高等 *It's colder than ever today.* 天氣從沒有像今天這樣冷過。| **as friendly/cheerful/boring etc as ever** (=as friendly, cheerful etc as in the past) 與往常一樣友好/快活/煩人等 *Magda was pale and thin, but her eyes were as bright as ever.* 瑪格達蒼白消瘦, 但她的眼睛和往常一樣明亮。| **hardly ever** (=almost never) 幾乎從來不 *I hardly ever see Sara these days.* 最近我幾乎沒有見過莎拉。| **never ever** *spoken* (=used to emphasize that something has never happened or someone has never done something)【口】從不, 決不, 永不: *I never ever said anything like that!* 我從未說過那樣的話! | **rarely, if ever** (=probably never) 幾乎從不, 極少 *Brian rarely, if ever, gets to bed before 3 am.* 布萊恩難得在淩晨3點鐘以前上牀睡覺。| **if ever there was one** *spoken* (=used when saying that someone or something is a typical example of something)【口】非常典型〔用於強調某人或某物是典型〕 *Joe's great, a real Northern comic if ever there was one.* 喬是個偉大的、真正的北方喜劇演員, 非常典型。**2** a word 1 1 meaning always; used especially with expressions of time 總是〔尤用於表示時間的用語中〕: *Ever optimistic, Gemma decided to give him another chance.* 一向樂觀的傑瑪決定再給他一次機會。| *His company is making ever larger profits.* 他的公司的利潤一直在增加。| **ever since** (=continuously since) 從那以後一直 *Paul came here for a holiday several years ago and he's been here ever since.* 保羅幾年前來這裡度假, 從那以後他就一直待在這個地方。| **for ever** *He said he would love her for ever.* 他說會永遠愛她。| **for ever and ever** (=always, used especially in children's stories) 永遠, 一直〔尤用於童話故事中〕| **happily ever after** (=used at the end of children's stories) 從此一直幸福地...〔用於童話故事的結尾〕*The prince and princess got married and lived happily ever after.* 王子和公主結了婚, 從此一直過着幸福的生活。| **as ever** *especially BrE* (=as usually happens)【尤英】同往常一樣 *As ever, Kim refused to admit she was wrong.* 同往常一樣, 金拒絕承認她犯了錯誤。| **ever-growing/ever-increasing/ever-present etc** (=always growing etc) 不斷增長的/不斷增加的/始終存在的等 *the ever-increasing problems of our inner cities* 我們舊城區不斷增加的問題 **3 how/what/who etc ever** *BrE old-fashioned* used to add force to a question【英, 過時】究竟如何/甚麼/誰等〔用於加強問句的語氣〕: *How ever shall we get there?* 我們到底怎樣才能到達那裡? | *Whatever are you doing?* 你到底在幹甚麼? **4 did you ever!** *old-fashioned* used to show your surprise, disbelief etc【過時】你看到過[聽到過]〔這種事〕嗎!: *Did you ever hear of such a thing!* 你聽到過這種事嗎! **5 ever so cold/wet/nice etc** *BrE spoken* very cold, wet etc【英口】非常冷/濕/好等: *The assistant was ever so helpful.* 這個助手幫了大忙。| *Thanks ever so much.* 非常感謝。**6 ever such a nice boy/cold day/pretty colour etc** *BrE* a very nice, cold etc person or thing【英】如此可愛的男孩/非常冷的一天/十分漂亮的顏色等: *You'll like her, she's ever such a nice girl.* 你會喜歡她的, 她是一個如此可愛的姑娘。**7 Was sb ever** *AmE spoken* used to add force to a statement【美口】非常〔用於加強語氣〕: *Was he ever mad!* (=he was very angry) 他氣瘋了! **8 Yours ever/Ever yours** *informal* used at the end of a letter above the signature【非正式】你的永久的朋友〔信尾簽名前的套語〕**9 ever and anon** *poetical* from time to time【詩】時而, 不時地

ev·er·green[1] /ˈɛvɚˌgrin; ˈevəgriːn/ *n* [C] a tree or bush that does not lose its leaves in winter 常青樹, 常綠樹

evergreen[2] *adj* **1** an evergreen tree or bush does not lose its leaves in winter〔樹木或灌木〕常青的, 常綠的 **2** an evergreen sportsman, singer etc is very good even though they are fairly old〔運動員、歌手等〕永葆青春的; 持久的; 經久不衰的: *the evergreen Perry Como* 事業常青的〔美國歌手〕佩里·科莫

ev·er·last·ing /ˌɛvɚˈlæstɪŋ; ˌevəˈlɑːstɪŋ◂/ *adj* a word used especially in religious writing, meaning continuing to exist for ever; ETERNAL (1) 永久的, 永恆的〔尤用於宗教文章中〕: *life everlasting* 永生 | *the Buddhist's search for everlasting peace* 佛教徒對永恆寧靜的追尋 —**everlastingly** *adv*

ev·er·more /ˌɛvɚˈmɔr; ˌevəˈmɔː/ *adv* **for evermore** *literary* if you do something for evermore you continue to do it for ever【文】永遠, 始終: *I will love you for evermore.* 我將永遠愛你。

S1 W1 **ev·ery** /ˈɛvrɪ; ˈevri/ *determiner* **1** each one of a group of things or people that make a group or set 每個, 所有的: *Every student has to fill in a questionnaire.* (=all the students) 每個學生都得填寫一份問卷。| **every single** *Unfortunately the President disagreed with every single thing his aides said.* 不幸的是, 總統對助手們所說的每一件事都不同意。**2** used to emphasize that you are talking about the whole of something 全部, 整體〔用於強調〕: *Victor ate every bit of his meal.* 維克多把飯菜全吃光了。| *What a wonderful movie! I enjoyed every minute of it.* 多棒的一部電影! 我覺得每一分鐘都很精彩。| **every word** (=everything someone says or writes) 每一句話 *I know every word of his songs by heart.* 我對他的歌中的每一句歌詞都了熟於胸。**3 every time** each time; WHENEVER (1) 每次; 無論何時: *Every time I see him, he looks miserable.* 每次我看見他, 他都是一副愁眉苦臉的樣子。**4 every day/every 3 weeks/every 10 years etc** used to say that something happens at regular periods of time, after a certain distance etc 每天/每三個星期/每十年等〔用於表示事物按一定的時間或距離間隔發生〕: *Richard visits his mother every week.* 理查德每週都去看望媽媽。| *You should change the oil every 5,000 miles.* 你應該每行 5,000 英里換一次油。| *Freda had to stop to rest every hundred yards or so.* 弗雷達不得不每走一百碼左右就停下來休息一次。**5 one in every hundred/two in every thousand etc** used when saying how often something affects a particular group of people or things 每百個中的一個/每千個中兩個等: *Thirty children in every hundred born in Mali will die before the age of five.* 馬里兒童每百人中有三十個在五歲前夭折。**6 in every way** in all ways 在各個方面, 在所有方面: *My new job's better than my old one in every way.* 我的新工作在各方面都比舊工作要好。**7 every other** the first, third, fifth etc or the second, fourth, sixth etc of things that can be counted 每隔一...: *Apply the ointment every other day.* 藥膏每隔一天塗一次。| *I see Harold every other Friday.* 每隔一週的週五我都見到哈羅德。**8 every bit as** used when saying strongly that someone is just as good, important as someone else 完全同樣地: *She was every bit as rude as her sister.* 她和她妹妹一樣無禮。**9 every Tom, Dick, and Harry** *spoken* an expression meaning eveyone or anyone used especially when talking about people you don't approve of【口】所有人; 任何人〔尤指說話者不滿意的人〕: *She didn't want every Tom, Dick, and Harry knowing about her private affairs.* 她不想讓張三、李四等所有不相干的人知道她的私事。**10 every hope/chance/reason etc** as much hope, chance, reason etc as possible 一切希望; 所有機會; 充分理由: *There is every chance that you will succeed.* (=you probably will) 你完全有機會取得成功。| *We have every reason to believe that Hodges is telling the truth.* 我們有充分理由相信霍奇斯講的是真話。| *The airline takes every possible precaution to ensure the safety of its passengers.* 航空公司採取一切可能措施確保旅客的安全。**11 every last drop/bit/scrap etc** *informal* every single drop, piece etc【非正式】每一滴/每一點/每一片等: *Robert had to pick up every last bit of paper from the floor.* 羅伯特不得不把地上的所有紙屑都撿起來。**12 every now and then/again** also 又作 **every so often** sometimes but not often 偶爾, 有時: *I still see her every now and then.* 我仍偶爾能看見她。**13 every which way** *AmE informal* in every direction【美, 非正式】朝各個方向: *The rain came down and the crowd in the field ran every which way.* 下雨了, 田地裡的人四散避雨。—see 見 EACH[1] (USAGE)

USAGE NOTE 用法說明: EVERY

SPELLING 拼法

Everyone written as one word is only used about people and can never be followed by **of. Every one** can be used about anything and is always used with an *of* phrase either stated or suggested. 寫作單詞的 everyone 僅用於人, 後面不能接 of; every one 可用於表示人或物, 後面總是跟 of 短語, 有時 of 短語省略: *Every one of your tires needs replacing.* 你汽車的所有輪胎都需要換了。| *There are five thousand people living here and almost every one (of them) has their own car* (=every one of the group mentioned has a car). 有五千人居住在這兒, 幾乎每個人都有汽車。

Everybody is written as one word. **Every body** would mean 'every dead body'. everybody 是一個

單詞; 分開寫成 every body 意為“每一具屍體”。

Every day is spelled as two words as an adverb but only one word as an adjective. every day 用作副詞, 如果合在一起寫成 everyday, 就變成了形容詞: *She swims every day.* 她每天游泳。| *the everyday life of Scottish Highlanders* 蘇格蘭高地人的日常生活。Note that you never say **every days**. 注意, 永遠不要說 every days。

Everything and **everywhere** are single words; **every time** is two words. everything 和 everywhere 都是單詞, 而 every time 由兩個單詞組成。

ev·ery·bod·y /ˋɛvrɪˏbɑdɪ; ˈevribɒdi/ *pron* everyone 每個人, 人人

ev·ery·day /ˋɛvrɪˋde; ˈevrideɪ/ *adj* [only before noun 僅用於名詞前] ordinary, usual, or happening every day 日常的; 通常的; 每天的: *The book is written in simple everyday language.* 這本書用簡單的日常用語寫成。| **everyday life** *Stress is just part of everyday life.* 壓力是日常生活的一部分。

Ev·ery·man /ˋɛvrɪˏmæn; ˈevrimæn/ *n* [singular] *literary* a typical, ordinary person【文】普通人, 凡夫俗子: *This character is a symbol for Everyman.* 這個角色是普通人的代表。

ev·ery·one /ˋɛvrɪˏwʌn; ˈevriwʌn/ *pron* every person; everybody 每個人, 人人: *If everyone is ready, I'll begin.* 如果大家都準備好了, 我就開始。| *They gave a prize to everyone who passed the exam.* 他們給每個考試及格的人發了獎。| *Has everyone finished their drinks?* 大家都把酒喝光了嗎? | *The canteen's almost empty. Where is everyone?* (=the people who are usually here) 食堂幾乎沒有人, 人都去哪兒了? | **everyone else** (=all the other people) 所有其他人 *I usually stay up after everyone else has gone to bed.* 在別人都上牀睡覺後, 我一般仍不休息。| **everyone but Ann/Mark/me etc** (=all of the people except Ann, Mark etc) 除安/馬克/我等之外的所有人 *Everyone but Peter got there on time.* 除了彼得, 所有人都準時到達那裡。—see 見 EACH¹ (USAGE)

ev·ery·place /ˋɛvrɪˏples; ˈevripleɪs/ *adv AmE* in, at, or to every place; everywhere【美】在各個地方; 到各個地方; 處處

ev·ery·thing /ˋɛvrɪˏθɪŋ; ˈevriθɪŋ/ *pron* **1** each thing or all things 每件事物; 所有事物: *Everything is ready for the party.* 聚會的準備工作已全部就緒。| *I've forgotten everything I learned at school.* 學校裡學的東西我全忘光了。| **everything else** (=all the other things) 其他所有事物 *There's only bread left; they've eaten everything else.* 只剩麵包了, 他們吃光了其餘所有東西。**2** used when talking in general about your life or about a situation 一切, 所有事物: *I'm OK – how's everything with you?* 我還行, 你一切都好嗎? | *Everything's much better now we're allowed to work at home.* 現在我們可以在家工作, 一切都好多了。**3 be/mean everything (to sb)** to be the thing that is most important to you and that you care about the most (對某人來說)是/意味着最重要的: *Money isn't everything.* 金錢不是最重要的。| *Her daughter means everything to her now.* 現在女兒對她來說比甚麼都重要。**4 and everything** *spoken* and so on【口】等等, 以及其他: *Tina's worried about her work and everything.* 蒂娜擔心她的工作以及其他情況。**5 have everything going for you** to have all the qualities that are likely to give you an advantage over other people and make you succeed 擁有一切有利條件: *You shouldn't worry so much – you've got everything going for you.* 你不必這麼擔心, 一切都對你有利。**6 everything but the kitchen sink** *informal* all the equipment that you need and also a lot of things that you do not need【非正式】需要的一切設備和許多不需要的東西: *"What's he got in that bag?" "Everything but the kitchen sink!"* “他那個包裡裝着甚麼?” “甚麼都有!”

ev·ery·where /ˋɛvrɪˏhwɛr; ˈevriweə/ also 又作 **everyplace** *AmE*【美】*adv* **1** in, at, or to every place 在各個地方; 到各個地方; 處處: *I've looked everywhere but I can't find it.* 我到處都找過了, 但就是找不到。| *His dog used to follow him everywhere.* 過去他走到哪裡, 他的狗就跟到哪裡。| *It must have rained overnight – there are puddles everywhere.* 夜裡一定下過雨, 到處都是小水坑。| **everywhere else** (=in, at, or to every other place) 在其他所有地方; 到其他所有地方 *It must be in here – I've looked everywhere else.* 它一定在這裡, 別的地方我都找過了。**2 be everywhere** to be very common 非常普遍, 到處都是: *Girls with long straight hair were everywhere in the 1960s.* 在20世紀60年代, 到處可見留着長長直髮的女孩子。 

e·vict /ɪˋvɪkt; ɪˈvɪkt/ *v* [T] to legally force someone to leave the house they are living in〔依法從房屋裡〕驅逐, 趕走: *We were evicted for non-payment of rent.* 我們未付房租, 被趕出來了。—**eviction** /ɪˋvɪkʃən; ɪˈvɪkʃən/ *n* [C,U]

ev·i·dence¹ /ˋɛvədəns; ˈevɪ̈dəns/ *n* **1** [U] facts, objects, or signs that make you believe that something exists or is true 證據, 證明: [+of/for] *evidence of life on other planets* 其他行星上有生命的證據 | **evidence that** *There's some evidence that a small amount of alcohol is good for you.* 有證據顯示, 少量飲酒有益健康。| **medical/scientific/archaeological etc evidence** *Medical evidence shows that men are more likely to have heart attacks than women.* 醫學證據表明男人比女人更容易患心臟病。| **not a shred of evidence** (=no evidence at all) 毫無依據, 沒有任何證據 *There is not a shred of evidence in support of these outrageous claims.* 這些蠻橫的說法毫無根據。**2** [U] information given in a court of law in order to prove that someone is guilty〔法庭上證明某人有罪的〕證據; 證詞: *Murrow's evidence was enough to convict Hayes of murder.* 默羅的證詞足以證明海斯犯了謀殺罪。| **give evidence** *Carol was called upon to give evidence.* 卡羅爾被傳喚出庭作證。**3 be in evidence** *formal* to be present and easily seen or noticed【正式】顯眼, 引人矚目: *The army is more in evidence in the cities than in rural areas.* 軍隊在城市中比在鄉村裡更顯眼。—see also 另見 KING'S EVIDENCE, QUEEN'S EVIDENCE, STATE'S EVIDENCE 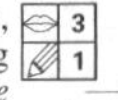

evidence² *v* [T usually passive 一般用被動態] *formal* to show that something exists or is true【正式】證明: *The volcano is still active, as evidenced by the recent eruption.* 最近的爆發證明, 這座火山依然活躍。

ev·i·dent /ˋɛvədənt; ˈevɪ̈dənt/ *adj* easily noticed or understood; OBVIOUS 明顯的; 明白的: *Bob began eating his lunch with evident enjoyment.* 鮑勃開始顯得津津有味地吃午餐。| **it is evident that** *From the look on Joe's face it was evident that the news came as a complete shock.* 從喬的表情可以明顯看出, 他被這個消息驚呆了。—see also 另見 SELF-EVIDENT 

ev·i·dent·ly /ˋɛvədəntlɪ; ˈevɪ̈dəntli/ *adv* **1** [sentence adverb 句子副詞] used when saying that something seems likely, based on the information that you have 從現有證據來看, 看來: *Evidently she's been bullied at work and is very unhappy.* 看來她在工作中被欺侮了, 非常難過。**2** [+adj/adv] in a way that is very easy to see and understand 顯然, 明顯地: *Mary was evidently upset when she heard about Irene's death.* 聽到艾琳的死訊, 瑪麗顯然十分難過。

e·vil¹ /ˋivḷ; ˈiːvəl/ *adj* **1** someone who is evil deliberately does very cruel things to harm other people 邪惡的; 危害他人的: *an evil dictator responsible for the deaths of millions* 應為幾百萬人的死亡負責的邪惡獨裁者 | *An evil glint came into her eye when she picked up the knife.* 當她拾起刀時, 眼中閃過一絲惡毒的光。**2** very unpleasant 令人極不舒服的: *There's an evil smell coming from the drains.* 排水溝發出很難聞的氣味。**3** 

connected with the Devil or having special powers to harm people 惡魔的; 有害人魔力的: *evil spirits* 惡鬼 **4** having a very harmful influence on people 造成巨大傷害的, 帶來很壞影響的: *the evil effects of materialism* 物質主義的惡劣影響 **5 the evil eye** the power, which some people believe exists, to harm people by looking at them〔據説可以傷害人的〕邪毒眼光: *traditional symbols to ward off the evil eye*（阻擋邪毒眼光的）避邪符號 **6 the evil hour/day etc** a time when you expect something unpleasant or difficult to happen 不祥的時刻; 倒霉的時候: *the evil hour when he would have to face his uncle's anger* 他不得不面對憤怒的叔叔的不幸時刻 —**evilly** *adv*

evil² *n* **1** [C] a very harmful or unpleasant influence or effect 極壞影響[後果]: *the evils of capitalism* 資本主義的種種禍害 **2** [U] a powerful force that makes people behave in a cruel way, or wicked behaviour in general 邪惡; 惡行: *the eternal struggle between good and evil* 善與惡的永恆鬥爭 —see also 另見 **the lesser of two evils** (LESSER (2)), **necessary evil** (NECESSARY¹ (3))

evil-do·er /ˌ·· ˈ··/ *n* [C] *old-fashioned* someone who does evil things【過時】惡人, 壞人

e·vince /ɪˋvɪns; ɪˈvɪns/ *v* [T] *formal* to show a feeling or quality very clearly in what you do or say【正式】〔行為或言語〕表明, 表露: *His remarks evinced a strong interest in my daughter's financial position.* 他的話表明他對我女兒的財政狀況很感興趣。

e·vis·ce·rate /ɪˋvɪsəˌret; ɪˈvɪsəreɪt/ *v* [T] *formal or technical* to cut the BOWELS or other organs out of a body【正式或術語】從…切除腸子; 從…切除內臟

e·voc·a·tive /ɪˋvɑkətɪv; ɪˈvɒkətɪv/ *adj* making people remember something by producing a feeling or memory in them 使想起〔某事〕的; 喚起記憶的: **[+of]** *a huge scrubbed kitchen evocative of the sun and bright colours of Provence* 一個寬敞而擦洗乾淨的廚房, 讓人想起（法國）普羅旺斯地區的太陽和明亮色彩

e·voke /ɪˋvok; ɪˈvəʊk/ *v* [T] to produce a strong feeling or memory in someone 引起, 喚起〔某人強烈的感情或回憶〕: *a stage set intended to evoke the mood of a brothel* 意圖讓人產生妓院感覺的舞台佈景 —**evocation** /ˌɛvoˋkeʃən; ˌevəˈkeɪʃən/ *n* [C,U]

3 **ev·o·lu·tion** /ˌɛvəˋluʃən; ˌiːvəˈluːʃən/ *n* [U] **1** the scientific idea that plants and animals develop gradually from simpler to more complicated forms 進化（論）**2** the gradual change and development of an idea, situation, or object 演變, 逐步發展: *the evolution of the computer over the past 30 years* 過去30年電腦的發展

ev·o·lu·tion·a·ry /ˌɛvəˋluʃənˌɛrɪ; ˌiːvəˈluːʃənəri◂/ *adj* **1** connected with scientific evolution 進化的; 進化論的: *evolutionary biology* 進化生物學 **2** connected with gradual change and development 演變的, 逐步發展的: *an evolutionary process* 演化過程

e·volve /ɪˋvɑlv; ɪˈvɒlv/ *v* [I,T] to develop or make something develop by gradually changing（使）逐步發展;（使）逐漸演變: **[+from/out of etc]** *Darwin believed that we evolved from apes.* 達爾文認為人類是由猿進化而來。| **evolve sth** *evolving a new management style* 形成新的管理風格

ewe /ju; juː/ *n* [C] a female sheep 母羊

ew·er /ˋjuɚ; ˈjuːə/ *n* [C] a large container for water used in the past〔過去使用的〕水罐, 大口水壺

ex /ɛks; eks/ *n* [C usually singular 一般用單數] *informal* someone's former wife, husband, GIRLFRIEND, or BOYFRIEND【非正式】前妻; 前夫; 前女友; 前男友: *Unfortunately, my ex showed up at the dance.* 不幸的是, 我的前妻出現在舞會上。

ex- /ɛks; eks/ *prefix* former and still living 以前的, 前任的〔仍然在世的〕: *my ex-wife* 我的前妻 | *an ex-England cricketer* 前英格蘭板球運動員 —compare 比較 LATE¹ (7)

ex·a·cer·bate /ɪgˋzæsɚˌbet; ɪgˈzæsəbeɪt/ *v* [T] to make a bad situation worse 使惡化; 使加重: *Reilly's crass comments just exacerbated the tension.* 賴利的蠢話使局勢更加緊張。—**exacerbation** /ɪgˋzæsɚˌbeʃən; ɪgˌzæsəˈbeɪʃən/ *n* [U]

ex·act¹ /ɪgˋzækt; ɪgˈzækt/ *adj* **1** correct and including all the necessary details 確切的, 精確的: *exact description of the assassin* 對刺客的精確描述 | *I don't know the exact terms of the agreement.* 我不知道該協議的確切條款。| **exact replica/copy etc** *They built an exact replica of the opera house in Naples.* 他們仿照那不勒斯的歌劇院建造了一座一模一樣的複製品。| **to be exact** *spoken* (=used when giving an exact answer, statement etc)【口】確切地説 *It was more than 20 years ago – to be exact!* 確切地説, 是在二十多年以前! **2 the exact colour/moment/type etc** used to emphasize how similar or close two things are 一樣的顏色/時間/類型等: *the exact colour I was looking for* 正是我要找的那種顏色 | *He came into the room at the exact moment I mentioned his name.* 就在我提到他的名字時他進入房間。**3** someone who is exact is very careful and thorough in what they do〔人〕嚴格的; 嚴謹的 **4 the exact opposite** someone or something that is as different as possible from another person or thing 正好相反: *Gina's the exact opposite of her sister in character.* 吉娜和她妹妹的性格完全相反。**5** an exact science is based on calculating and measuring things rather than on opinions, guessing etc〔科學〕嚴密的, 精密的 3

exact² *v* [T] *formal* to demand and get something from someone by using threats, force etc【正式】強要, 勒索: *exacting payment* 索款

ex·act·ing /ɪgˋzæktɪŋ; ɪgˈzæktɪŋ/ *adj* exacting work is hard and involves a high level of skill〔工作〕嚴格的, 要求高的: *exacting but stimulating work* 要求很高但激勵人心的工作 | *exacting scrutiny of the texts* 對文本的嚴格審讀 —**exactingly** *adv*

ex·act·i·tude /ɪgˋzæktəˌtjud; ɪgˈzæktɪtjuːd/ *n* [U] *formal* the state of being exact【正式】精確, 確切

ex·act·ly /ɪgˋzæktlɪ; ɪgˈzæktli/ *adv* **1** used to emphasize that a particular number, amount, or piece of information is completely correct 精確地, 確切地: *We were wearing exactly the same clothes.* 我們穿着一模一樣的衣服。| *It's exactly half past five.* 一分不差正好五點半。| **exactly where/what/when etc** *Tell me exactly what he said.* 確切地告訴我他是怎麼説的。| *Exactly where does Petra live?* 彼得拉到底住在哪裡? **2** used to emphasize a statement 恰好, 正好〔用於加強語氣〕: *He gave exactly the reply they wanted to hear.* 他的答覆恰好是他們想聽的。| *That's exactly what we've been trying to tell you.* 那正是我們一直想告訴你的。 1 2

Frequencies of the adverb **exactly** in spoken and written English 副詞 exactly 在英語口語和書面語中的使用頻率

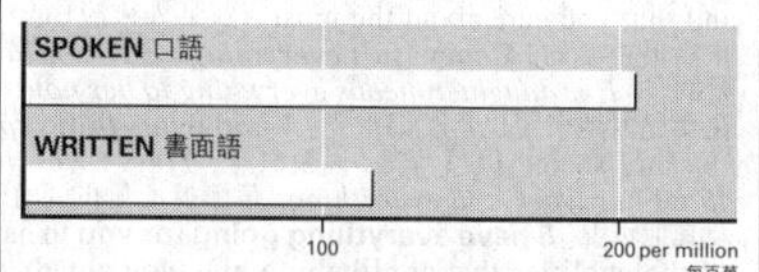

Based on the British National Corpus and the Longman Lancaster Corpus
據英國國家語料庫和朗文蘭卡斯特語料庫

This graph shows that the adverb **exactly** is much more common in spoken English than in written English. This is because it is used in some common spoken phrases. 本圖表顯示, 副詞 exactly 在英語口語中的使用頻率遠遠高於書面語, 因為一些常用的口語片語是由 exactly 構成的。

exactly (*adv*) **SPOKEN PHRASES**
含 exactly 的口語片語

3 exactly used as a reply to show that you think what someone has said is completely correct or true 正是, 不錯: *"So you think we should sell the house and move to the country?" "Exactly."* "這麼說你認為我們應該賣掉房子搬到鄉下去?" "正是。" **4 not exactly a)** used as a reply to show that you think that what someone has said is not completely correct or true 不完全如此: *"You hate Lee, don't you?" "Not exactly. I just think he's a bit annoying that's all."* "你恨李, 是不是?" "不完全是這樣。我只是覺得他有一點討厭, 如此而已。" **b)** used when you say the opposite of what you mean, either as a humorous remark, or to show that you are annoyed 並不是, 可不是〔表示幽默或厭煩〕: *Imagine calling me fat! I mean, she's not exactly thin herself, is she?* 居然說我胖! 我的意思是, 她自己並不見得瘦啊, 不是嗎? | *I wouldn't bother asking Dave, he's not exactly Einstein, is he?* 我不想問戴夫, 他又不是愛因斯坦, 對吧? **5 why/what/where etc exactly...?** used when asking someone to tell you the exact place, reason, thing etc 確切地說為甚麼/甚麼/何處等...?: *Where exactly did you stay in Portugal?* 確切地說, 你待在葡萄牙甚麼地方? **6 I don't know exactly/I don't exactly know** used to say that you are not sure about something 我不十分清楚: *"What does he want?" "I don't know exactly, but he said it's really urgent."* "他想要甚麼?" "我不十分清楚, 但他說真的很緊急。" **7 that's exactly what...** used to say that what someone has said, done etc is exactly the same as what you or another person said, did etc 那恰恰是...: *"I don't think he should leave his job." "That's exactly what I told him yesterday."* "我認為他不該離職。" "我昨天也正是這樣對他說的。"

ex·ag·ge·rate /ɪg`zædʒəˌret; ɪgˈzædʒəreɪt/ *v* [I,T] to make something seem better, more important etc than it really is 誇張, 言過其實: *Sue says she's seen Jurassic Park twenty times, but I'm sure she's exaggerating.* 蘇說《侏羅紀公園》她已看過二十遍了, 但我肯定她在說大話。| **exaggerate sth** *exaggerating the pain to get our sympathy* 誇大疼痛以博取我們的同情 | **greatly exaggerate** *The extent of the damage was greatly exaggerated by the press.* 損害程度被媒體極力誇大了。—**exaggeratedly** /ɪg`zædʒəˌretɪdlɪ; ɪgˈzædʒəreɪtɪ̣dli/ *adv*

ex·ag·ge·rat·ed /ɪg`zædʒəretɪd; ɪgˈzædʒəreɪtɪ̣d/ *adj* **1** described as better, more important etc than is really true 誇大的, 言過其實的: *exaggerated reports of the army's gains* 對軍隊戰果的誇大報告 **2** an exaggerated sound or movement is emphasized to make people notice〔聲音或動作〕強調的; 誇張的; 引人注目的: *exaggerated movements of his arms* 他手臂幅度很大的動作

ex·ag·ge·ra·tion /ɪgˌzædʒə`reʃən; ɪgˌzædʒəˈreɪʃən/ *n* [C,U] a statement or way of saying something that makes something seem better, more important etc than it really is 誇張, 誇大, 言過其實: *I can say without exaggeration he's the best operator in the business.* 我可以毫不誇張地說, 他是整個行業中最好的管理人員。| **it is no exaggeration** *It is no exaggeration to say your life will be changed forever.* 說你的生活將被永遠改變, 這一點也不誇張。

ex·alt /ɪg`zɔlt; ɪgˈzɔːlt/ *v* [T] *formal*【正式】**1** to put someone or something into a high rank or position 提升, 提拔 **2** to praise someone, especially God 讚揚; 歌頌〔尤指歌頌上帝〕: *Exalt ye the Lord.* 讚美你, 我的主。

ex·al·ta·tion /ˌɪgzɔl`teʃən; ˌegzɔːlˈteɪʃən/ *n formal*【正式】**1** [C,U] a very strong feeling of happiness, power etc 異常興奮; 洋洋得意 **2** [U] the state of being put into a high rank or position 晉升, 被提拔

ex·alt·ed /ɪg`zɔltɪd; ɪgˈzɔːltɪ̣d/ *adj* **1** having a very high rank and highly respected 顯貴的, 高貴的: *I felt shy in such exalted company.* 我與如此顯貴的人在一起, 覺得不好意思。**2** *formal* filled with a great feeling of joy【正式】異常興奮的, 興高采烈的

ex·am /ɪg`zæm; ɪgˈzæm/ *n* [C] **1** a spoken or written test of knowledge, especially an important one 考試〔尤指重要考試〕: *How did you do in your exams?* 你考試考得怎麼樣? | *an oral exam* 口試 | **pass/fail an exam** (=succeed/not succeed) 考試通過/未通過 *Did you pass the exam?* 你考試通過了嗎? | **chemistry/French etc exam** (=an exam in a particular subject) 化學/法語等科目的考試 | **take/sit an exam** *He failed his English exam and had to take it again.* 他英語考試不及格, 只好再考一次。**2** *AmE* a set of medical tests【美】醫學檢查: *an eye exam* 眼睛檢查 **3** *AmE* the paper on which the questions for an exam are written【美】考試卷: *Do not open your exams until I tell you.* 在未聽到指令前請勿打開試卷。 S1

ex·am·i·na·tion /ɪgˌzæmə`neʃən; ɪgˌzæmɪ̣ˈneɪʃən/ *n* **1** [C] *formal* a spoken or written test of knowledge【正式】考試: *The examination results will be announced in September.* 考試成績將於九月公佈。**2** [C,U] the process of looking at something carefully in order to see what it is like 檢查, 審查: *a detailed examination of population statistics* 對人口統計數字的詳細審查 | **be under examination** *The proposals are still under examination.* 那些建議還在審查之中。| **on closer examination** *On closer examination the vases were seen to be cracked in several places.* 經進一步檢查發現, 這些花瓶上有幾處裂紋。**3** a set of medical tests 醫學檢查 **4** [C,U] the process of asking questions to get specific information, especially in a court of law 查問〔尤指法庭訊問〕—see also 另見 CROSS-EXAMINE S3 W2

examine 檢查

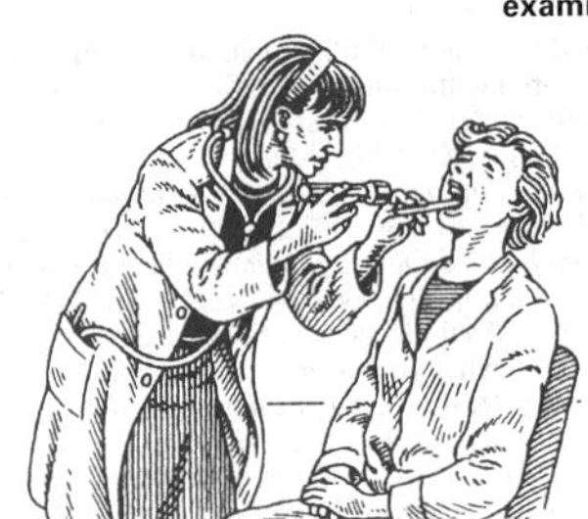

examining a patient 為病人作檢查

ex·am·ine /ɪg`zæmɪn; ɪgˈzæmɪ̣n/ *v* [T] **1** to look at something carefully, in order to make a decision, find something, check something etc〔仔細地〕檢查, 審查: *After examining the evidence, I can find no truth in these claims.* 檢查過證據後, 我發現這些說法都不成立。| **examine sth for** *The police will have to examine the weapon for fingerprints.* 警察得檢查兇器看有沒有指紋。**2** if a doctor examines you, they look at your body to check that you are healthy 檢查〔身體〕**3** *formal* to ask someone questions to test their knowledge of a subject【正式】考核, 對...進行考試: **examine sb on** *You will be examined on American history.* 你將接受美國歷史的考試。**4** *technical* to officially ask someone questions in a law court【術語】〔在法庭上〕查問, 訊問 S3 W2

Frequencies of the verbs **examine, take/have a look at** and **inspect** in spoken and written English 動詞（片語）examine, take/have a look at 和 inspect 在英語口語和書面語中的使用頻率

SPOKEN 口語
examine
take/have a look at
inspect
WRITTEN 書面語
examine
take/have a look at
inspect
100 200 300 400 500 per million 每百萬

Based on the British National Corpus and the Longman Lancaster Corpus
據英國國家語料庫和朗文蘭卡斯特語料庫

This graph shows that the expressions **have a look at** and **take a look at** are much more common in spoken English than the words **examine** or **inspect**. This is because **have a look at** and **take a look at** are much more general than **examine** or **inspect**, which mean to look at something carefully in order to find out about it or check if it is satisfactory. They are more common in written English. 本圖表顯示, 在英語口語中動詞片語 have a look at 和 take a look at 的使用頻率遠遠高於 examine 及 inspect, 因為 have a look at 和 take a look at 的含義更廣。而 examine 和 inspect 側重於表示仔細檢查某事物以找出信息或決定其是否令人滿意。因此這兩個詞在書面語中更常用些。

ex·am·in·er /ɪg`zæmɪnɚ; ɪg'zæmɨnə/ *n* [C] someone from a university, college, or professional institution who tests students' knowledge or ability 考官, 主考人

exam pa·per /·'· ˌ··/ *n* [C] **1** *BrE* the paper on which the questions for an EXAM are written【英】考卷 **2** *AmE* the papers on which you write the answers to a test or exam【美】答題紙, 答卷

1 1 **ex·am·ple** /ɪg`zæmpḷ; ɪg'zɑːmpəl/ *n* [C] **1 for example** used before mentioning a specific thing, person, place etc in order to explain what you mean or to support an argument 例如, 舉例來說: *Many countries, for example, Mexico and Japan, have a lot of earthquakes.* 許多國家, 例如墨西哥和日本, 經常發生地震。| *Look at John, for example, now there's someone who's overcome his physical disabilities.* 例如約翰, 就是一個已經戰勝了自身殘疾的人。**2** a thing, person, situation etc that you mention to show what you mean or to show that something is true 例子, 例證: *The two examples on this page show the behaviour patterns of severely depressed patients.* 本頁的兩個例子顯示了情緒極度低落的病人的行為方式。| **[+of]** *a wonderful example of High Gothic architecture* 哥特式建築風格的極好實例 | **give an example** *I don't really understand what you mean, could you give me an example?* 我不大明白你的意思, 你能舉例説明一下嗎? | **good example** (=example that shows something clearly)〔將事情説清楚的〕好例子; 恰當的例子 | **classic/typical example** *a classic example of what not to do* 不當行為的典型實例 | **prime example** (=example of something you do not like or do not approve of)〔壞的〕典型,〔不好方面的〕代表 *Franco, a prime example of a man hungry for power* 佛朗哥, 權慾熏心者的典型 **3 set an example** to behave in a sensible way so that other people will copy you 樹立榜樣: *It's my duty as an officer to set an example to the troops.* 作為軍官, 我有責任為士兵樹立好榜樣。**4 be an example to** if someone's behaviour is an example to you, it is so good that you should copy it 是…效仿的好榜樣: *Her courage is an example to us all.* 她的勇氣是我們所有人的榜樣。**5 follow sb's example** to copy someone's be-haviour yourself 效仿某人, 學某人的樣子: *I suggest you follow Rosie's example and start doing regular exercise.* 我建議你效仿羅西, 經常鍛鍊身體。**6 make an example of** to punish someone so that other people are afraid to do the same thing 懲罰某人以儆戒他人, 殺雞嚇猴

This graph shows some of the words most commonly used with the noun **example**. 本圖表所示為幾個與名詞 example 構成的最常見搭配詞的使用頻率。

for example
example of
give an example
good example
set an example
classic example
typical example
prime example
50 100 150 per million 每百萬

Based on the British National Corpus and the Longman Lancaster Corpus
據英國國家語料庫和朗文蘭卡斯特語料庫

ex·as·pe·rate /ɛg`zæspəˌret; ɪg'zɑːspəreɪt/ *v* [T usually passive 一般用被動態] to make someone very annoyed by continuing to do something that upsets them 使惱怒; 使煩惱

ex·as·pe·rat·ed /ɛg`zæspəˌretɪd; ɪg'zɑːspəreɪtɨd/ *adj* very annoyed and upset 惱怒的; 極厭煩的: *He gave an exasperated snort.* 他惱怒地哼了一聲。—**exasperatedly** *adv* —**exasperation** /ɪgˌzæspə`reʃən; ɪgˌzɑːspə'reɪʃən/ *n* [U]

ex·as·pe·rat·ing /ɪg`zæspəˌretɪŋ; ɪg'zɑːspəreɪtɪŋ/ *adj* extremely annoying 令人極其厭煩的, 使人惱怒的: *You have this exasperating habit of never looking at me!* 你從來不看着我, 我對你這個習慣十分不滿! —**exasperatingly** *adv*

ex·ca·vate /`ɛkskəˌvet; 'ekskəveɪt/ *v* [I,T] **1** to make a hole in the ground by digging up soil etc 挖掘; 開鑿 **2** discover something that was buried in the earth in an earlier time by digging for it 挖出; 發掘: *Schliemann excavated the ancient city of Troy.* 謝里曼發掘出特洛伊古城。—**excavation** /ˌɛkskə`veʃən; ˌekskə'veɪʃən/ *n* [C,U]

ex·ca·va·tor /`ɛkskəˌvetɚ; 'ekskəveɪtə/ *n* [C] **1** a large machine that digs and moves earth and soil 挖土機, 電鏟; STEAM SHOVEL *AmE*【美】**2** someone who digs to find things that have been buried under the ground for a long time 發掘者

ex·ceed /ɪk`sid; ɪk'siːd/ *v* [T] **1** to be more than a number or amount, especially a fixed number 超過, 超出〔尤指超過一固定值〕: *Working hours must not exceed 42 hours a week.* 工作時間每週不得超過 42 小時。**2** to go beyond an official or legal limit 超越〔政府或法律規定的範圍〕: *He was fined for exceeding the speed limit.* 他因超速行駛而被罰款。 3

ex·ceed·ing·ly /ɪk`sidɪŋlɪ; ɪk'siːdɪŋli/ *adv* extremely 非常, 極其: *I'd like to say thank you. You've been exceedingly kind.* 我想説聲謝謝, 你真是太好了。

ex·cel /ɪk`sɛl; ɪk'sel/ *v* **excelled, excelling** [I, not in progressive 不用進行式] to do something very well, or much better than most people 優於, 擅長, 勝過他人: **[+at/in]** *I never excelled at sport.* 我從來不擅長體育運動。| **excel yourself** (=do better than you usually do) 比平常做得好, 超水平發揮 *Dinner was fantastic! Joe's really excelled himself this time.* 晚飯好吃極了! 喬這頓飯做得特別出色。

ex·cel·lence /`ɛksləns; 'eksələns/ *n* [U] the quality of being excellent 卓越, 傑出

Ex·cel·len·cy /ˋɛkslənsɪ; ˈeksələnsi/ *n* **Your Excellency/His Excellency** a way of talking to or about people who hold high positions in the state or the church 閣下: *His Excellency the Spanish ambassador* 西班牙大使閣下

1 2 **ex·cel·lent** /ˋɛkslənt; ˈeksələnt/ *adj* extremely good or of very high quality 卓越的; 極好的: *Edward made an excellent speech.* 愛德華的演講十分精彩。| *You've got some excellent CDs here.* 你這裡有些非常棒的激光唱片。—**excellently** *adv*

2 2 **ex·cept**[1] /ɪkˋsɛpt; ɪkˈsept/ *conjunction* **1 except for a)** apart from 除...之外: *Except for one old lady, the bus was empty.* 除了一位老婦人, 公共汽車上沒有別的乘客。| *The roads were clear except for a few cars.* 除了幾輛汽車之外, 馬路上空蕩蕩的。**b) except for John/her/me etc** leaving out or not including John, her etc 除了約翰/她/我等之外: *The children are all asleep except for Lorna.* 除了洛娜, 孩子們都睡着了。**c)** if someone or something had not happened or existed 要不是由於: *Nina would have left him years ago except for the children.* 要不是為了孩子們, 尼娜幾年前就離開他了。**2 except do sth** apart from doing something 除了做某事: *Tom does everything around the house except cook.* 除了做飯之外, 屋裡屋外的活湯姆都幹。| *a computer that can do everything except talk* 除了不會講話別的甚麼都能做的電腦 **3** *spoken* but【口】但是, 只是: *I'd love to go, except it's too expensive.* 我很想去, 但那太貴了。| *It doesn't matter that I had to wait, except you did say four o'clock.* 我不介意等, 但你講好是四點鐘。

except[2] *prep* used to introduce the only thing or person in a group about which a statement is not true 除...之外: *Everyone except Adam went to the concert.* 除了亞當, 大家都去聽音樂會了。| *You can have any of the cakes except this one.* 你可以拿任何一塊蛋糕, 但這塊除外。| *We're open every day except Monday.* 除了週一, 我們天天開門。| **[+in/to/up etc]** *I can take my vacation at any time except in August.* 我可以在八月之外的任何時間休假。| *Peter's not going anywhere except to work.* 彼得除了上班之外哪兒也不去。| **[+(that)]** *The house was just as I left it except that everything was covered with dust.* 除了積滿灰塵之外, 這房子與我離開時沒甚麼兩樣。| *I've got one exactly the same except it's silver.* 我有一個一模一樣的, 但我的這個是銀的。| **[+what/how/why etc]** *I don't know anything about the case except what I read in the newspaper.* 除了在報紙上讀到的報道之外, 我對這個案子一無所知。| **except by doing sth** *You can't get credit except by making special arrangements with the management.* 不與管理部門作出特殊安排就得不到信貸。

except[3] *v* [T+from] *formal* to not include something when you are talking about or considering a number or group of things【正式】把...排除在外, 不計

ex·cept·ed /ɪkˋsɛptɪd; ɪkˈseptɨd/ *adj* **Paul/football/biology excepted** used to say that you are not including a particular person, subject, or thing in a statement about something 除了保羅/足球/生物學之外: *We want every one at the meeting, David and Steven excepted of course.* 我們希望每個人都出席會議, 當然大衛和史蒂文除外。| *History excepted, Peter has made good progress in all subjects this term.* 除了歷史之外, 彼得這學期在所有學科中都有很大進步。—see also 另見 **present company excepted** (PRESENT[1] (5))

ex·cept·ing /ɪkˋsɛptɪŋ; ɪkˈseptɪŋ/ *prep* used to introduce the only thing or person in a group about which a statement is not true 除...之外: *O'Rourke answered all the questions excepting the last one.* 除了最後一個問題外, 奧羅克回答了所有問題。| **always excepting** *Dogs are not allowed in here, always excepting guide dogs.* 狗不得入內, 但導盲犬例外。

2 2 **ex·cep·tion** /ɪkˋsɛpʃən; ɪkˈsepʃən/ *n* [C,U] **1** something or someone that is not included in a rule, does not follow the expected pattern etc 例外, 除外: *With one or two notable exceptions, there are few women conductors.* 除了一兩個明顯的例子之外, 幾乎沒有女指揮。| **no exception** (=used to emphasize that a law or rule concerns someone or something) 無例外 *The law applies to all European countries, Britain is no exception.* 這項法律適用於所有歐洲國家, 英國也不例外。| **minor exception** (=one that is not very important) 不太重要的例外 | **exception to a rule** *The spelling of this word is an interesting exception to the rule.* 這個單詞的拼法是該規則一個有趣的例外。| **the exception that proves the rule** (=used to say that the fact that something is not true or does not exist in one situation emphasizes the fact that it is true or exists in general) 證明普通規律的例外〔雖然是例外, 但反過來證明了一個普遍存在的規律或現象〕*Most people here are very dedicated; I'm afraid Rhea's the exception that proves the rule.* 這裡的大多數人都十分投入, 恐怕雷亞是個例外, 但也反過來證明了其他人的專注精神。**2 make an exception** used to say that on one particular occasion the normal rules or standards do not have to be obeyed 按例外處理, 作為例外: *We don't usually give credit, but as you're a regular customer we'll make an exception this time.* 我們一般不賒賬, 但因為你是老顧客, 這次我們就破個例。**3 take exception to sth** to be angry or upset because of something 因某事而生氣[煩惱]: *Tom took great exception to my remark about Americans.* 湯姆對我有關美國人的評論極為不滿。**4 without exception** used to say that something is true of all the people or things in a group 毫無例外: *Every type of plant, without exception, contains some kind of salt.* 所有植物都毫無例外地含有某種鹽分。**5 with the exception of** used to introduce the only thing, person, or place about which a statement is not true 除...之外: *I think everyone, with the possible exception of Fauzi, will pass the exam.* 我想或許除了福齊之外, 所有人都會通過考試。

ex·cep·tion·a·ble /ɪkˋsɛpʃənəbl; ɪkˈsepʃənəbəl/ *adj formal* making you feel offended and angry【正式】引起反感的; 令人氣憤的: *a highly exceptionable remark* 令人異常氣憤的話

ex·cep·tion·al /ɪkˋsɛpʃənl; ɪkˈsepʃənəl/ *adj* **1** unusually good 非常好的, 傑出的: *Richard is an exceptional student.* 理查德是個出類拔萃的學生。| *exceptional bravery* 非凡的勇氣 **2** unusual and likely not to happen often 罕見的, 不尋常的: *This is an exceptional case; I've never seen anything like it before.* 這是一個不尋常的案例, 我從沒見過這樣的事。| **in exceptional circumstances** *Promotion in the first year is only given in exceptional circumstances.* 只有在特殊情況下, 第一年才會得到提升。

ex·cep·tion·al·ly /ɪkˋsɛpʃənlɪ; ɪkˈsepʃənəli/ *adv* [+adj/adv] used to emphasize a quality that you are describing 特別, 非常: *She defended her position exceptionally well.* 她出色地捍衛了自己的立場。| *an exceptionally talented player* 一名極有天分的選手

ex·cerpt /ˋɛksɝpt; ˈeksɜːpt/ *n* [C+from] a short piece taken from a book, poem, piece of music etc〔書籍、詩歌、音樂等的〕摘錄, 節錄

ex·cess[1] /ɪkˋsɛs; ɪkˈses/ *n* **1** [singular, U] a larger amount of something than is allowed or needed 過多, 過量: *Scrape any excess off with a spatula.* 用鏟子將多餘的部分刮去。| **an excess of** *It was an excess of enthusiasm that caused the problem.* 是過度熱情導致了問題。**2 in excess of** more than a particular amount 超過, 多於: *The car reached speeds in excess of 100 miles per hour.* 這輛汽車的時速超過了 100 英里。**3 do sth to excess** to do something too much or too often, so that it may harm you 做某事過度[過分]: *Drinking is OK as long as you don't do it to excess.* 飲酒可以, 但不要過量。**4 excesses** [plural] harmful or thoughtless actions that are socially or morally unacceptable 過分的行為; 過激行為: *The government was unable to curb the excesses of the secret police.* 政府無法約束祕密警察過分的行為。

5 [U] behaviour which is not acceptable because it is too harmful or extreme 有害的行為；極端行徑：*The minister preached a long sermon against the dangers of excess.* 牧師長篇佈道，告誡極端行為的危害。

ex·cess² /ˋɛksɛs; ˈekses/ *adj* [only before noun 僅用於名詞前] **1** additional and not wanted or needed because there is already enough of something 過多的，不要的：*Cut any excess fat from the meat.* 將肉中不要的肥肉切掉。**2 excess baggage/luggage** bags or cases that weigh more than the legal limit that you can take on a plane 超重行李

ex·ces·sive /ɪkˋsɛsɪv; ɪkˈsesɪv/ *adj* much more than is reasonable or necessary 過度的；過多的：*Boyd's wife left him because of his excessive drinking.* 博伊德的妻子因為他酗酒而離開了他。| *$15 for two cokes seems a little excessive.* 兩杯可樂就要 15 美元，似乎有點過分。

ex·change¹ /ɪksˋtʃendʒ; ɪksˈtʃeɪndʒ/ *n*

1 ►GIVING/RECEIVING 給予/接受◄ [C,U] the act of exchanging one thing for another or doing something to someone at the same time as they do it to you 交換，互換：*an exchange of political prisoners* 互換政治犯 | *an honest exchange of information* 坦誠的信息交換 | **fair exchange** (=an exchange in which the things given and received are of equal value) 公平的交換，等價交換 *Four of my cassettes for your Madonna CD is a fair exchange.* 我用四盒磁帶換你的麥當娜激光唱片很公平。—see also 另見 PART-EXCHANGE

2 in exchange if you do or give something in exchange for something else, you do it or give it in order to get that thing 作為交換：*They have offered to release the hostages, but what do they want in exchange?* 他們提出可以釋放人質，但他們想要甚麼作為交換？| **[+for]** *I've offered to paint the kitchen in exchange for a week's accommodation.* 我提出願意粉刷廚房，條件是讓我免費住一週。

3 ►ARGUMENT 爭論◄ [C] a short conversation, usually between two people who are angry with each other 短時間的交談〔通常指兩人相互生氣時〕：*a quiet exchange between the judge and the clerk* 法官和書記員之間平心靜氣地交換意見 | **heated exchange** (=a very angry conversation) 激烈爭吵 *The DJ was fired after a heated exchange on air with a call-in listener.* 在和一名打進電話的收聽者大吵一頓之後，音樂節目主持人被解雇了。

4 ►MONEY 錢◄ [U] **a)** a process in which you change money from one CURRENCY to another〔貨幣的〕兑換：*Most capital cities have extensive exchange facilities.* 大部分首都城市都有大量外匯兑換處。**b)** [C] the EXCHANGE RATE 匯率，兑換率

5 ►BETWEEN FAMILIES/SCHOOLS 家庭/學校間◄ [C] an arrangement in which someone changes their job, home etc with someone else usually for a short period of time, or in which students from different countries visit each other〔通常指短期的〕交換工作；交換住所；交換學生：*I'm only here for one term. I'm on an exchange with Dr Fisher.* 我只在這兒待一個學期，是與費舍爾教授交換工作。

6 ►WAR 戰爭◄ [C,U] an event during a war when armies use weapons against each other 交火，交戰：*an exchange of fire* 交火

7 corn/wool/cotton etc exchange a large building in a town, that was used in the past for buying and selling corn, wool etc 玉米/羊毛/棉花等交易所 —see also 另見 LABOUR EXCHANGE, STOCK EXCHANGE

8 ►SCIENCE 科學◄ [U] *technical* the movement of one substance into the place where another substance was【術語】〔物質的〕交換

ex·change² *v* [T] **1** to give someone something and receive the same kind of thing from them at the same time 交換，交易：*We still exchange gifts at Christmas.* 我們依然在聖誕節時交換禮物。| *At the end of the game players traditionally exchange shirts with each other.* 按照傳統，比賽結束時兩隊隊員互換球衣。| **exchange addresses/telephone numbers** (=give someone your address or telephone number and take theirs) 互換地址/電話號碼 *Did you exchange phone numbers with the guy that hit you?* 你和那個撞你車的傢伙互換電話號碼了嗎？**2** to give someone something so that they will give you something that is better, more suitable, or more useful for you 調換〔指換取更好、更適合或更有用的東西〕：*The store will not exchange goods without a receipt.* 這家商店沒有發票不予調換商品。| **exchange sth for** *Where can I exchange my dollars for pounds?* 我在哪可以用美元兑換英鎊？**3** if two people exchange something, they do something to each other 相互做某事：**exchange looks/glances** (=look at each other) 對視；互瞥 *Sally and I exchange amused glances when we heard this.* 聽到這話時，我與莎莉開心地交換了一下眼色。| **exchange greetings/insults** (=greet or insult each other) 互打招呼；相互謾罵 | **exchange words** (=talk to someone) 交談 *Until this evening I had never so much as exchanged a word with him.* 在今天晚上之前，我甚至連一句話都未跟他說過。| **exchange blows** (=fight) 打架 *Students exchanged blows with locals, and police were called in.* 學生與當地居民打了起來，叫來了警察。**4 exchange information/ideas** if two people or a group of people exchange information, ideas etc they discuss something 交流信息/想法：*We envision an artistic community where people are free to exchange ideas.* 我們設想着一個人們可以自由交流思想的藝術團體。**5 exchange houses** to go and live in someone else's house while they come and live in yours, usually for a holiday〔通常指為度假〕交換住所：*We exchanged houses with an American family for three weeks.* 我們與一個美國家庭互換住處，住了三個星期。**6 exchange contracts** *especially BrE* to complete the final stage of buying a house by signing a contract with the person you are buying it from【尤英】〔與賣方簽署並〕交換購房契約 —**exchangeable** *adj*

exchange rate /ˈ· ·/ *n* [C] the value of the money of one country compared to the money of another country 匯率，兑換率：*a more favourable exchange rate in the bank than in the hotel* 銀行匯率高於酒店提供的匯率

exchange rate mech·a·nis·m /ˈ· · ,···/ *n* [U] a system for controlling the exchange rate between the money of one country and that of another; ERM 匯率機制

Ex·cheq·uer /ɪksˋtʃɛkɚ; ɪksˈtʃekə/ *n* **the Exchequer** the British government department that is responsible for collecting taxes and paying out public money; TREASURY (1) 英國財政部

ex·cise¹ /ɪkˋsaɪz; ˈeksaɪz/ *n* [C,U] the government tax that is put on the goods that are produced and used inside a country 國內貨物稅；消費稅：*excises on gasoline and cigarettes* 汽油和香煙稅 | **excise officer** (=someone who collects excise) 消費稅稅務官 | **excise duty** (=the money paid as excise) 消費稅金 —see also 另見 CUSTOMS AND EXCISE

ex·cise² /ɪkˋsaɪz; ɪkˈsaɪz/ *v* [T] *formal* to remove or get rid of something, especially by cutting it out【正式】切除；去除：*The tumour was excised.* 腫瘤被切除了。—**excision** /ɪkˋsɪʒən; ɪkˈsɪʒən/ *n* [C,U]

ex·ci·ta·ble /ɪkˋsaɪtəbl̩; ɪkˈsaɪtəbəl/ *adj* becoming excited too easily 易激動的：*A puppy is naturally affectionate and excitable.* 小狗生性親熱好動。—**excitability** /ɪk,saɪtəˋbɪlətɪ; ɪk,saɪtəˈbɪlɪ̈ti/ *n* [U]

ex·cite /ɪkˋsaɪt; ɪkˈsaɪt/ *v* [T] **1 excite interest/suspicion/jealousy etc** to make someone feel a particular emotion 引起[激起]興趣/懷疑/忌妒等：*The court case has excited a lot of public interest.* 這場官司引起了公眾的極大興趣。**2 excite comment/rumour etc** if something excites comment etc, it makes people talk about it 引發評論/謠言等：*The book excited very little comment on this side of the Atlantic.* 這本書在大西洋這一邊並未引起多大反響。**3** [not in progressive or passive 不用進行式或被動態] to make someone feel happy, interested, or hopeful because something good has happened or is going to happen 使興奮, 使激動: *His playing is technically brilliant, but it doesn't excite me.* 他的演奏技巧嫻熟, 但無法讓我興奮起來。**4** [not in progressive 不用進行式] to make someone feel nervous so that they cannot relax 刺激, 使緊張: *The doctor warned us not to excite Douglas, who had been very ill.* 醫生警告我們不要刺激道格拉斯, 他的病很重。**5** to make someone feel sexual desire 使產生性慾 **6** *technical* to make an organ, nerve etc in your body react or increase its activity【術語】刺激〔身體某器官或神經等〕

ex·cit·ed /ɪk`saɪtɪd; ɪk'saɪtɪ̵d/ *adj* **1** happy, interested, or hopeful because something good has happened or will happen 興奮的, 激動的: *Steve's flying home tomorrow – we're all really excited.* 史蒂夫明天就坐飛機回家了——我們都非常激動。| *excited crowds of shoppers* 興奮的購物人羣 | **[+about]** *The kids are so excited about Christmas.* 要到聖誕節了, 孩子們十分激動。| **[+by]** *We were all excited by the prospect of a party.* 想到要舉行一場晚會, 我們都很興奮。| **[+at]** *He got very excited at finding such perfect specimens.* 能找到這樣完美的標本, 他感到異常高興。| **get/feel/look etc excited** *Maria's starting to get pretty excited about the wedding.* 瑪利亞開始變得對婚禮十分熱心。**2** very nervous and upset about something so that you cannot relax 緊張不安的: *When Thierry gets excited he starts to stutter.* 蒂里一緊張就口吃。| **[+about]** *There's no point getting excited about it. We can't change things.* 沒必要緊張, 我們改變不了甚麼。**3** feeling sexual desire 性衝動的, 有性慾的 **4 nothing to get excited about** *spoken* used to say that a film, book etc is not very good or enjoyable and rather disappointing【口】〔電影、書等〕不帶勁的, 令人失望的: *Unfortunately Doyle's latest novel is nothing to get excited about.* 遺憾的是, 多伊爾的新小說一點都不帶勁兒。—**excitedly** *adv*: *Squirrels chattering excitedly in the branches above.* 松鼠們在上面的樹枝上吱吱叫個不休。

3 3 **ex·cite·ment** /ɪk`saɪtmənt; ɪk'saɪtmənt/ *n* **1** [U] the feeling of being excited 興奮; 激動: *squeals of excitement* 因興奮而發出的尖叫聲 | **[+of]** *The new job held none of the excitement of her career in the police.* 與她原來的警察工作相比, 新工作一點也不令人興奮。| **[+at]** *their excitement at the discovery* 他們發現（某事物）時的興奮心情 | *The news that Ms Street had eloped with Jean caused great excitement.* 斯特里特女士與讓私奔的消息引起一片譁然。| *his eyes shining with excitement* 他的目光閃爍着興奮 | **in (sb's) excitement** *In my excitement, I had forgotten to turn off the taps.* 由於激動, 我忘了關水龍頭。| **mounting excitement** (=a feeling of excitement that increases) 越來越激動[興奮] **2** [C] an exciting event or situation 令人興奮的事[情況]: *I found it difficult to sleep after the excitements of the day.* 興奮了一整天後, 我發現晚上很難入睡。

2 3 **ex·cit·ing** /ɪk`saɪtɪŋ; ɪk'saɪtɪŋ/ *adj* making you feel excited 令人興奮的; 使人激動的; 刺激的: *an exciting discovery* 激動人心的發現 | **find sth exciting** *Stuart found the atmosphere of the college enormously exciting.* 斯圖爾特發現該大學的氛圍很讓人興奮。—**excitingly** *adv*: *excitingly different band* 卓爾不羣的樂隊

ex·claim /ɪk`sklem; ɪk'skleɪm/ *v* [I,T] to say something suddenly and loudly because you are surprised, angry, or excited〔因驚訝、憤怒或興奮而〕呼喊; 驚叫: *"Look at you!" she exclaimed when we came in, covered in mud.* 我們渾身是泥地走進來時, 她驚呼道: "瞧瞧你們這樣子!" | **[+at/over]** *They all exclaimed at his ignorance.* 他們都猛烈譴責他的無知。

ex·cla·ma·tion /ˌɛksklə`meʃən; ˌekskləˈmeɪʃən/ *n* [C] a sound, word, or short sentence that you say suddenly and loudly because you are surprised, excited, or angry 驚叫, 呼喊: **[+of]** *horrified exclamations of disgust* 厭惡的驚叫

exclamation mark /ˌ··ˈ·· ·/ *BrE*【英】, **exclamation point** *AmE*【美】 *n* [C] the mark '!' that you write after a sentence or word that expresses surprise, anger, or excitement 感嘆號, 驚嘆號 —see picture at 參見 PUNCTUATION MARK 圖

ex·clude /ɪk`sklud; ɪk'skluːd/ *v* [T] **1** to deliberately not include something, especially a particular group of people or things〔故意〕不包括; 把…排除在外: *a special diet that excludes dairy products* 不包含奶製品的特別食譜 | **exclude sb/sth from sth** *If we exclude uncompleted projects from the calculations, the total spent is still more than $15 billion.* 即使我們在計算中除去未完成的項目, 總支出還是超過150億美元。| **specifically/explicitly exclude sth** *The provisions of the Act specifically excluded minors.* 這項法律的條款明確將未成年人排除在外。**2** to not allow someone to take part in something or not allow them to enter a place 不准…參與〔某事〕; 不准…進入: **exclude sb from (doing) sth** *navigation laws to exclude foreign vessels from trading in English ports* 禁止外國船隻在英國港口進行交易的航海法 **3** to deliberately not pay attention to someone so that they feel lonely or unwanted 排斥〔某人〕; 不理睬〔某人〕: *We're not trying to exclude her, it's just that we have nothing in common with her.* 我們並非想排斥她, 只是我們與她毫無共同語言。**4** to decide that something is not a possibility 認為…不可能; 排除…的可能性: *Social workers have excluded sexual abuse as a reason for the child's disappearance.* 社工人員排除了這個孩子失蹤是因為遭受性虐待的可能性。| **exclude the possibility of/that** *At this stage we cannot entirely exclude the possibility of staff cuts.* 在這個階段, 我們不能完全排除裁員的可能性。—opposite 反義詞 INCLUDE 2 3

ex·clud·ing /ɪk`skludɪŋ; ɪk'skluːdɪŋ/ *prep* a word meaning not including, used especially when you are making a list or calculating a total 不包括, 除去: *Television is watched in 97 per cent of American homes (excluding Alaska and Hawaii).* 在美國, 97%的家庭收看電視（不包括阿拉斯加和夏威夷兩個州）。

ex·clu·sion /ɪk`skluʒən; ɪk'skluːʒən/ *n* [U] **1** a situation in which someone or something is not allowed to take part in an activity, be a member of an organization etc 被排除在外[被拒絕]的狀態: *China's exclusion from the United Nations* 中國被排除在聯合國之外 **2 to the exclusion of** if you do something to the exclusion of something else, you only do the first thing and do not do the second thing at all 排除掉, 不涉及: *Your essays tend to concentrate on one theme to the exclusion of everything else.* 你的文章往往會集中於一個主題, 而不提別的。**3 exclusion zone** an area that the government does not allow people to enter, because it is dangerous or because secret things happen there 禁區: *the military exclusion zone* 軍事禁區

ex·clu·sive[1] /ɪk`sklusɪv; ɪk'skluːsɪv/ *adj* **1** exclusive places, organizations, clothes etc are so expensive that not many people can afford to use or buy them 高級的; 昂貴的: *Bel Air is an exclusive suburb of Los Angeles.* 貝萊爾是洛杉磯郊外一處高級住宅區。| *an exclusive girls' school* 貴族女子學校 **2** available only to particular people, so that only they can have, do, or use something 獨有的; 獨做的; 獨享的: **be exclusive to sb** *This offer is exclusive to readers of The Sun.* 只有《太陽報》的讀者才能獲此優待。| **exclusive access/rights/use etc** *Rafferty managed to gain exclusive control of the company.* 拉弗蒂設法取得了對那個公司的專控權。**3 exclusive report/interview/coverage** a report, interview etc which is only printed in one newspaper or broadcast by one television programme 獨家報道/採訪/披露: *Tune in to our exclusive coverage of Wimbledon.* 請收看我們對溫布頓網球賽的獨家報道。**4 mutually exclusive** if two things are mutually exclusive, you cannot have or do both of them 相互排斥的, 互不相容的: *Lesbianism and motherhood are not mutually exclusive.*

女性的同性戀傾向和母親身分並不是相互排斥的。**5 exclusive of** not including 不包括, 排除…在外: *Our prices are exclusive of sales tax.* 我們的價格不包括銷售稅。—**exclusively** *adv* —**exclusiveness** *n* [U]

exclusive² *n* [C] an important or exciting story that is printed in only one newspaper, because that newspaper was the first to find out about it 獨家新聞, 獨家報道: *a New York Post exclusive about the Kennedy marriage* 《紐約郵報》有關甘迺迪婚姻的獨家新聞

ex·com·mu·ni·cate /ˌɛkskəˋmjunəˌket; ˌekskəˈmjuːnɪ̥keɪt/ *v* [T] to punish someone by no longer allowing them to be a member of the Roman Catholic church 開除…的〔羅馬天主教〕教籍 —**excommunication** /ˌɛkskəˌmjunəˋkeʃən; ˌekskəmjuːnɪ̥ˈkeɪʃən/ *n* [C,U]

ex·co·ri·ate /ɪkˋskorɪˌet; ɪkˈskɔːrieɪt/ *v* [T] *formal* to express a very bad opinion of a book, play etc【正式】嚴厲批評; 痛斥〔書、戲劇等〕: *an excoriating review in the Times* 《泰晤士報》刊登的一篇措辭嚴厲的評論 —**excoriation** /ɪksˌkorɪˋeʃən; ekˌskɔːriˈeɪʃən/ *n* [C,U]

ex·cre·ment /ˋɛkskrɪmənt; ˈekskrɪ̥mənt/ *n* [U] *formal* the solid waste material that you get rid of through your BOWELS【正式】糞; 大便

ex·cres·cence /ɪkˋskrɛsn̩s; ɪkˈskresəns/ *n* [C] *formal*【正式】**1** something such as an ugly building that makes the surrounding area seem less attractive 破壞周圍景致的東西〈如醜陋的建築〉: *The new museum is nothing but an excrescence on the urban landscape.* 新博物館破壞了市區的景色。**2** an ugly growth on an animal or plant 瘤; 贅生物

ex·cre·ta /ɛkˋskritə; ɪkˈskriːtə/ *n* [plural] *formal* the solid or liquid waste material that people and animals produce and get rid of from their bodies【正式】排泄物

ex·crete /ɛkˋskrit; ɪkˈskriːt/ *v* [I,T] *formal* to get rid of waste material from your body through your BOWELS, your skin etc【正式】排泄 —compare 比較 SECRETE (1)

ex·cre·tion /ɪkˋskriʃən; ɪkˈskriːʃən/ *n* **1** [U] the process of getting rid of waste material from your body 排泄 **2** [C,U] the waste material that people or animals get rid of from their bodies 排泄物

ex·cru·ci·at·ing /ɪkˋskruʃɪˌetɪŋ; ɪkˈskruːʃieɪtɪŋ/ *adj* **1** extremely painful, so that you are unable to move or do something 使人極疼痛的: *When I bend my arm the pain is excruciating.* 彎胳膊的時候, 我疼得簡直受不了。**2** extremely unpleasant, because it is boring, embarrassing, or sad 令人難以忍受的: *Helena described the events of the night before in excruciating detail.* 海倫娜詳細地描述了頭天晚上發生的那些極令人不愉快的事。—**excruciatingly** *adv*

ex·cul·pate /ˋɛkskʌlˌpet; ˈekskʌlpeɪt/ *v* [T] *formal* to prove that someone is not guilty of something【正式】證明〔某人〕無罪; 為…開脫 —**exculpation** /ˌɛkskʌlˋpeʃən; ˌekskʌlˈpeɪʃən/ *n* [U]

ex·cur·sion /ɪkˋskɝʒən; ɪkˈskɜːʃən/ *n* [C] **1** a short journey arranged so that a group of people can visit a place, especially while they are on holiday〔尤指一羣人度假時的〕短途旅行: *a day's excursion to the island* 去島上的一天旅行 **2** a short journey made for a particular purpose〔有特定目的的〕短途出行: *a shopping excursion* 購物遊 **3 excursion into sth** *formal* an attempt to experience or learn about something that is new to you【正式】嘗試[涉獵]某事: *Neither of his brief excursions into marriage had been a success.* 他的兩次短暫婚姻嘗試均以失敗告終。

ex·cu·sa·ble /ɪkˋskjuzəbl̩; ɪkˈskjuːzəbəl/ *adj* behaviour that is excusable can be forgiven〔行為〕可原諒的: *an excusable reaction of anger* 可以原諒的生氣的反應

S2 **ex·cuse¹** /ɪkˋskjuz; ɪkˈskjuːz/ *v* [T] **1 excuse me** *spoken*【口】**a)** used when you want to get someone's attention politely, especially when you want to ask a question 勞駕〔用於禮貌地引起人注意, 尤其是發問時〕: *Excuse me, can you tell me the way to the museum please?* 勞駕, 你能告訴我去博物館怎麼走嗎? **b)** used to say that you are sorry for doing something rude or embarrassing 對不起: *Oh, excuse me. I didn't know anyone was in here.* 噢, 對不起, 我不知道裡面有人。**c)** used to ask someone politely to move so that you can walk past 借光: *Excuse me, could I just squeeze past you?* 借光, 能讓我從你這兒過去嗎? **d)** used when you want to politely tell someone that you are leaving a place 抱歉〔用於禮貌地表示要離開〕: *Excuse me a moment, Mr Jonson. I'll be right back.* 抱歉, 瓊森先生, 我離開一下, 馬上就回來。**e)** used when you disagree with someone but want to be polite about it 請原諒〔用於禮貌地表示反對〕: *Excuse me, but I don't think that's what he meant at all.* 請原諒, 不過我認為他絕對不是這個意思。**f)** *AmE* used to say you are sorry when you hit someone accidentally, make a small mistake etc【美】對不起〔用於意外撞到某人或犯小錯誤等時表示歉意〕: *Oh, excuse me, did I spell your name wrong?* 啊, 對不起, 我是不是把你的名字拼寫錯了? **g)** *especially AmE* used to ask someone to repeat something that they have just said【尤美】請再說一遍: *"What time is it?" "Excuse me?" "I asked you what time it is."* "現在幾點了?" "對不起, 你說甚麼?" "我問你現在幾點了。" **2** to forgive someone for doing something that is not seriously wrong, such as being rude or careless 原諒〔某人的小錯〕: *I'll excuse you this time, but try and be prompt in the future.* 這次我原諒你, 但你以後要麻利些。| *Please excuse my bad handwriting.* 請原諒我的字寫得不好。| **excuse sb for (doing) sth** *I cannot excuse them for treating their animals so badly.* 他們這樣虐待自己的動物, 我不能原諒他們。**3** to allow someone not to do something that they are supposed to do 免除〔某人〕的職責: *Ball was excused guard duty that night.* 保爾被免除了那天夜裡的警衛任務。| **excuse sb from (doing) sth** *Can I be excused from swimming today? I have a cold.* 我今天能不去游泳嗎? 我感冒了。**4** to give reasons for someone's careless or offensive behaviour in order to make it seem more acceptable 為…開脫; 給…找理由: *Nothing can excuse that kind of rudeness.* 甚麼也無法為那種粗魯行為開脫。| **sb can be excused for doing sth** (=used to say that you understand why someone has done something and think they should not be blamed for it) 某人做某事情有可原 *His poetry means a lot to him, so perhaps he can be excused for neglecting his work in order to write.* 詩歌對他極為重要, 所以他因為寫詩而疏忽了工作或許也是情有可原的。**5** to give someone permission to leave a place 准許…離開: *May I please be excused from the table?* 我可以離開飯桌了嗎? | **excuse yourself** *Richard politely excused himself, claiming he had too much work to do.* 理查德禮貌地告辭, 說他有太多的工作要做。**6 excuse me for living!** *spoken* used when someone has offended you or told you that you have done something wrong【口】實在對不住了!

USAGE NOTE 用法說明: EXCUSE

WORD CHOICE 詞語辨析: **excuse me, I'm sorry, I beg your pardon, pardon me**

In British English, you say **(I'm) sorry** to a person if you accidentally touch them, or push against them, or get in their way (for example, if you step on someone's foot). You might also hear the rather old-fashioned expression **I beg your pardon**. 如果你無意間碰到或擠到別人, 或是擋了他們的路(如踩了他們的腳), 英國英語說 (I'm) sorry, 也有人使用相當過時的說法 I beg your pardon。

In American English you say **Excuse me** or **Pardon me**. 在同樣情況下, 美國英語說 Excuse me 或 Pardon me。

ex·cuse² /ɪkˋskjus; ɪkˈskjuːs/ *n* [C] **1** a reason that you give to explain careless or offensive behaviour〔辯解的〕理由: **[+for]** *What's your excuse for being late this time?* 你遲到了, 這次還有甚麼理由? | **there is no excuse for sth** *There is no excuse for such rudeness.* 這種

無禮行為怎麼說都不對。| **make an excuse** *Fay's always making excuses for his erratic moods.* 費伊總是為他的情緒起伏不定找藉口。| **have an excuse** *I'm sure Mike has a good excuse for not repaying the money.* 我確信邁克不還錢一定有充足的理由。**2** a false reason that you give to explain why you are doing something or not doing something 虛假的理由; 託辭; 藉口: **excuse to do sth** *She wanted an excuse to be at the bus stop when Billy got off.* 她想找個理由, 使比利下車時自己正好在公共汽車站。| **[+for]** *The conference is an excellent excuse for a few days' holiday by the sea.* 參加這個會議為在海邊度幾天假提供了絕好的藉口。| **find/have an excuse** *Now at last I had an excuse to call him.* 現在我終於有藉口給他打電話了。| **make an excuse** *I made an excuse at the first possible moment, and got up to leave.* 一有機會我就找了個藉口起身離開了。| **give sb an excuse** *The arrival of the doctor gave them an excuse to leave.* 醫生的到來使他們有藉口離開。**3 make your excuses** to explain why you are not able to do something 解釋為何不能做某事: *Please make my excuses at the meeting tomorrow. I have an appointment with an important client.* 請在明天的會上替我解釋一下不能到會的原因, 我與一個重要客戶有個約會。**4 a poor/rotten etc excuse for sth** used when you think someone is very bad at something they are doing or at their job 做事極差; 極不稱職: *Derico is a rotten excuse for a lawyer, why on earth did you hire him?* 德里克是個極糟糕的律師, 你幹嘛雇用他? **5** *AmE* a note written by your doctor or one of your parents saying that you were ill on a particular day【美】病假條; SICK NOTE *BrE*【英】

USAGE NOTE 用法說明: EXCUSE

WORD CHOICE 詞語辨析: **reason, explanation, excuse, pretext**

If you call something a **reason**, either you believe it, or you are just repeating what someone else has said. 所謂 reason (原因), 可以是你自己相信確有其事, 也可以只是重複別人的話: *His reason for being late was that his car broke down* (=either you know the car did break down which made him late, or that was simply the reason he gave you). 他遲到的原因是汽車拋錨了〔也許你知道他的汽車的確拋錨了才遲到的, 也許拋錨之說只是他告訴你的話而已〕。

If you call something an **explanation**, you are just repeating what someone else has said. 所謂 explanation (解釋), 只是在重複別人的話: *His explanation for being late was that his car broke down* (=that was the reason he gave – it may or may not be true). 他遲到了, 他的解釋是汽車拋錨了〔這是他給你的原因, 可能是真的也可能是假的〕。An **explanation** often sounds more like a personal opinion, a **reason** more like a fact. 通常, explanation 聽起來更像是個人見解, 而 reason 更像是事實。

If you call something an **excuse** it suggests that you may not believe it is true or, if it is true, you do not believe that it really explains what happened. 所謂 excuse (藉口) 暗指你可能並不相信那是真的; 即使是真的, 也不相信足以解釋所發生的事: *His excuse for being late was that his car broke down* (=perhaps the car broke down, or perhaps it did not OR you think it did break down, but that is not really a good enough reason for being late). 他遲到的藉口是汽車拋錨了〔也許汽車真的拋錨了, 也許沒有。或者你相信汽車的確拋錨了, 但認為這並不構成他遲到的充足理由〕。If you say *My excuse is ...,* you are giving a reason that you know is not really good enough to explain what you did. 如果你說 My excuse is ..., 你知道你所給的理由其實並不足以解釋自己的行為。

If you call something a **pretext**, you definitely do not think that it is true or the real reason. 所謂 pretext (託辭), 表明你絕對不相信真有其事或者認為那絕對不是真正的原因: *His pretext for being late was that his car broke down* (=you do not believe it broke down OR it did, but you know there was another reason why he was really late). 他遲到了, 他託辭說是汽車拋錨了〔你不相信他的汽車真的拋錨了, 或者你相信汽車拋錨了, 但你相信他之所以遲到肯定另有原因〕。

ex·di·rec·to·ry /ˌ· ·ˈ···◂/ *adj BrE* deliberately not given in the public telephone book【英】〔故意〕使電話號碼不列入電話簿的; UNLISTED (2) *AmE*【美】: **go ex-directory** *After a number of threatening calls, Amy went ex-directory.* 接到數個威脅電話後, 埃米不再將自己的電話號碼列入電話簿了。

ex·ec /ɪgˈzɛk; ɪgˈzek/ *n* [C] *informal* an EXECUTIVE¹ (1)【非正式】主管

ex·e·cra·ble /ˈɛksɪkrəbl; ˈeksəkrəbəl/ *adj formal* extremely bad【正式】極壞的, 極差的: *execrable handwriting* 極差勁的書法 —**execrably** *adv*: *execrably bad* 極差的

ex·e·crate /ˈɛksɪˌkret; ˈeksəkreɪt/ *v* [T] *literary* to express strong disapproval or hatred for someone or something.【文】憎惡; 詛咒

ex·e·cute /ˈɛksɪˌkjut; ˈeksəkjuːt/ *v* [T] **1** to kill someone, especially legally as a punishment for a serious crime〔尤指依法〕將…處死: **be executed for sth** *He was executed for treason.* 他因叛國罪被處死。—see 見 KILL¹ (USAGE) **2** *formal* to do something that you have carefully planned or that you have agreed to do【正式】實行; 執行; 履行: *The directors make the decisions, but the managers have to execute them.* 董事們作出決定, 但要由經理們來執行。**3** *formal* to perform a difficult action or movement【正式】完成, 表演〔高難動作〕: *The skaters' routine was perfectly executed.* 那些滑冰選手把整套動作完成得非常出色。**4** *law* to make sure that the instructions in someone's WILL² (2) are followed【法律】確保〔遺囑〕得到執行 **5** *formal* to make a work of art such as a painting【正式】創作〔繪畫等藝術作品〕

ex·e·cu·tion /ˌɛksɪˈkjuʃən; ˌeksəˈkjuːʃən/ *n* **1** [C,U] the act of killing someone, especially as a legal punishment for a serious crime (依法) 處死[處決]: *a public execution* 當眾處死 **2** [U] *formal* a process in which you do something that has been carefully planned or agreed【正式】實施; 執行: **[+of]** *the formulation and execution of urban policy* 城市政策的制定與實施 **3** [U] *formal* the performance of a difficult action or movement【正式】〔高難動作的〕表演 **4** [U] *formal* the act of making a work of art such as a painting【正式】〔繪畫等藝術作品的〕創作, 製作

ex·e·cu·tion·er /ˌɛksɪˈkjuʃənɚ; ˌeksəˈkjuːʃənə/ *n* [C] someone who legally kills someone else as a punishment for a serious crime 死刑執行人, 行刑人: *a public executioner, also called at that time, the hangman* 公共行刑人, 那時又被稱作絞刑劊子手

ex·ec·u·tive¹ /ɪgˈzɛkjʊtɪv; ɪgˈzekjətɪv/ *n* **1** [C] someone who has an important job as a manager in a company or business〔公司或商業機構中的〕主管, 行政人員: *a publishing executive* 一個出版業的主管人員 **2 the executive** the part of a government that is responsible for making sure that new laws and other decisions are done in the way they have been planned〔政府的〕行政部門 —compare 比較 JUDICIARY, LEGISLATURE **3** [C] the group of people in a political organization, society etc that makes the rules and makes sure that they work in the way they were planned〔政治組織、團體等的〕執行委員會: *the executive of the union* 工會的執行委員會 S3 W2

executive² *adj* [only before noun 僅用於名詞前] **1** connected with making decisions and organizing, especially within a company or a government〔尤指公司或政府〕行政的, 管理的: *Clancy has been given full executive powers on this matter.* 在這方面克蘭西已被授予絕對執行權。| **executive body/committee** (=a group of people who make decisions etc) 主管機構/委員會 **2** for the use of people who have important jobs in the management of a company or business 供〔公司或商業機構〕主管人員使用的: *the executive dining-room* 經理人員飯廳 **3** expensive and of high quality, so that only someone with a good job can afford it 高檔的; 經理級的: *an executive car* 高檔汽車

executive priv·i·lege /·,··· '···/ *n* [C] *AmE* the right of a president or other government leader to keep official records and papers secret【美】行政豁免權〔指總統或其他政府領導人保守官方機密不向外透露的權力〕

ex·ec·u·tor /ɪg`zɛkjətɚ; ɪg'zekjʊ̈tə/ *n* [C] a person, lawyer, or bank that deals with the instructions in someone's WILL[2] (2) 遺囑執行人[律師、銀行]

ex·e·ge·sis /,ɛksə`dʒisɪs; ,eksʒ̍'dʒiːsʒ̍s/ *n* [C,U] *formal* a detailed explanation of a piece of writing, especially one from the Bible【正式】〔尤指對《聖經》內容的〕詳細解釋; 詮釋

ex·em·plar /ɪg`zɛmplɚ; ɪg'zemplə/ *n* [C] *formal* a good or typical example【正式】模範; 典型

ex·em·pla·ry /ɪg`zɛmplərɪ; ɪg'zempləri/ *adj* **1** excellent and providing a good example for people to follow 模範的, (可作) 楷模的: *praised for their exemplary behaviour* 他們的模範行為受到表揚 **2** [only before noun 僅用於名詞前] severe and intended to be a warning 儆戒性的, 懲戒性的: *an exemplary punishment* 儆戒性的懲罰

ex·em·pli·fy /ɪg`zɛmplə,faɪ; ɪg'zemplʒ̍faɪ/ *v* [T] **1** to be a very typical example of something 是…的範例: *Los Angeles exemplifies America's diversity.* 洛杉磯是美國 (文化) 多元性的典範。**2** to give an example of something 舉例説明 —**exemplification** /ɪg,zɛmpləfə`keʃən; ɪg,zemplʒ̍fɪ'keɪʃən/ *n* [C,U]

ex·empt[1] /ɪg`zɛmpt; ɪg'zempt/ *v* [T] to give someone special permission not to do something that they would normally have to do 免除, 豁免: *a special clause exempting children* 將兒童免除在外的特殊條款 | **exempt sb from** *Marty's bad health exempts him from military service.* 馬蒂因身體差而豁免服兵役。

exempt[2] *adj* having special permission not to do something you would normally have to do 被免除 (義務) 的, 被豁免的: [**+from**] *The interest is exempt from income tax.* 利息收入免徵所得税。

ex·emp·tion /ɪg`zɛmpʃən; ɪg'zempʃən/ *n* **1** [C] *AmE* the amount of money that you are allowed to earn each year before you start to pay tax【美】〔年收入中的〕免税額, 可免税部分; PERSONAL ALLOWANCE *BrE*【英】**2** [C, U] permission not to do something you would normally have to do 免除, 豁免

ex·er·cise[1] /`ɛksɚ,saɪz; 'eksəsaɪz/ *n*

1 ►FOR HEALTH 為了健康◄ [U] physical activities that you do in order to stay healthy and become stronger 運動, 鍛鍊: *I could use some exercise – let's go for a swim.* 我想鍛鍊一下身體 —— 咱們去游泳吧。| **do/take exercise** (=exercise regularly) 經常性地鍛鍊[運動] *Do at least fifteen minutes exercise each day.* 每天至少鍛鍊十五分鐘。| **get exercise** (=do exercise as part of your daily life) 身體得到鍛鍊〔作為日常生活的一部分〕*You don't get much exercise sitting at a desk all day like this.* 像這樣整天坐在桌子前, 你的身體就得不到多少鍛鍊。

2 ►MOVEMENT 動作◄ [C] a movement or set of movements that you do regularly in order to keep a particular part of your body strong and healthy 練習, 體操: *The doctor gave me some exercises to help with my back.* 醫生教我做一些練習來增強背部力量。| **do exercises** *Jan does her exercises every morning.* 簡每天都做早操。

3 ►FOR A SKILL 為獲得技能◄ [C usually plural 一般用複數] an activity or process that helps you practise a particular skill such as playing a musical instrument or singing 練習, 訓練

4 ►IN A BOOK 在書中◄ [C] a set of questions in a book which test a student's skill or knowledge 練習, 習題: *Do Exercises 3 and 4 on page 51 for homework.* 家庭作業是51頁上的練習3和4。

5 ►ARMY/NAVY ETC 陸軍/海軍等◄ [C] an activity that trains soldiers, pilots etc for war when there is still peace 訓練, 演練: *a naval exercise* 海軍演練

6 ►FOR A RESULT 為達到某結果◄ [singular] an activity that is intended to have a particular result 活動; 任務: *Getting everyone to agree was quite a difficult exercise.* 要讓大家都同意是一項困難的任務。| **an exercise in awareness/self-control etc** (=something that you do in order to gain or develop a particular quality) 提高認識/增強自制力等的活動 *The ceremony was an exercise in self-congratulation for a leader desperate to regain popularity.* 這個儀式是一個急於重獲民眾支持的領導人自吹自擂之舉。

7 the exercise of power/influence/authority etc *formal* the use of power, influence etc in order to achieve something【正式】運用權力/施加影響/行使權威等

exercise[2] *v* **1** [I] to walk, do sports etc in order to stay healthy and become stronger 運動, 鍛鍊〔身體〕: *It's important to exercise regularly.* 經常鍛鍊身體十分重要。**2** [T] to make a particular part of your body move in order to make it stronger 鍛鍊〔身體某一部分〕: *Swimming exercises all the major muscle groups.* 游泳能使身體所有的主要肌羣得到鍛鍊。**3 exercise power/influence/caution etc** *formal* to use power, influence etc【正式】運用權力/施加影響/小心謹慎等: *I intend to exercise my right to vote.* 我打算行使我的選舉權。**4** [T] to make an animal walk or run in order to keep it healthy and strong 遛〔動物〕: *Don's out exercising the horses.* 唐出去遛馬了。**5** [T often passive 常用被動態] *formal* to make someone think about a subject or problem and consider how to deal with it【正式】使關注; 使致力於〔解決問題〕: *Scientists continue to be exercised about the ethics of genetic engineering.* 科學家們持續關注基因工程的倫理問題。

exercise bike /'··· ,·/ *n* [C] a bicycle that does not move and is used for indoor exercise 自行車式健身器

exercise book /'··· ,·/ *n* [C] a small book that students write their work in 練習本[簿]

ex·ert /ɪg`zɝt; ɪg'zɜːt/ *v* [T] **1 exert pressure/control/influence** to use your power, influence etc in order to have a particular effect 施加壓力/控制/影響: *Photography has exerted a profound influence on art in this century.* 在本世紀, 攝影術對藝術產生了重大影響。**2 exert yourself** to make a strong physical or mental effort 盡力, 努力: *He won both games without even seeming to exert himself.* 他毫不費力地贏得了那兩場比賽。

ex·er·tion /ɪg`zɝʃən; ɪg'zɜːʃən/ *n* [C,U] strong physical or mental effort 用力氣, 花心思: *The afternoon's exertions had left us feeling exhausted.* 下午太用勁, 我們感到精疲力竭。| *mental exertion* 費心思

ex·e·unt /`ɛksɪənt; 'eksiʌnt/ *v Latin* a word written in the instructions of a play to tell two or more actors to leave the stage【拉丁】〔舞台指示〕至少兩個角色退場, 下場

ex gra·tia /,ɛks `greʃə; ,eks 'greɪʃə/ *adj Latin* an ex gratia payment is one made to help someone or as a gift, not because you have a legal duty to do it【拉丁】出於幫助的; 作為優惠的〔非出於法律義務的〕: *an ex gratia payment of £15,000* 15,000 鎊的補助款項

ex·hale /ɛks`hel; eks'heɪl/ *v* [I,T] to breathe air, smoke etc out of your mouth 呼出: *Take a deep breath, then exhale slowly.* 深深吸一口氣, 然後慢慢呼出。—**exhalation** /,ɛksə`leʃən; ,ekshə'leɪʃən/ *n* [U]

ex·haust[1] /ɪg`zɔst; ɪg'zɔːst/ *v* [T] **1** to make someone extremely tired so that they have no energy left 使精疲

力竭: *I find a full day's teaching exhausts me.* 我講了一整天課, 覺得精疲力竭。| **exhaust sb to do sth** *It exhausted him even to talk very long.* 講話時間長一些他都會感到沒有力氣。**2** to use all of something 用完, 耗盡: *We've nearly exhausted our coal reserves.* 我們儲備的煤快要用完了。**3 exhaust a subject/topic etc** to talk about something so much that you have nothing more to say about it 詳盡無遺地論述某主題/話題等: *Once we'd exhausted the subject of Jill's wedding, we had nothing to say to each other.* 談完吉爾的婚禮以後, 我們彼此就無話可説了。

exhaust² *n* **1** [C] a pipe on a car or machine through which gas or steam passes; EXHAUST PIPE 排氣管 **2** [U] the gas or steam produced when an engine is working〔引擎排出的〕廢氣

ex·haust·ed /ɪgˋzɔstɪd; ɪgˈzɔːstɪ̈d/ *adj* **1** extremely tired and having no energy 筋疲力盡的; 疲憊不堪的: *Man, I'm exhausted!* 老兄, 我實在太累了! | **[+from/by]** *Jill lay on the grass, exhausted by her long run.* 吉爾躺在草地上, 長跑使她精疲力竭。| *What's wrong? You look absolutely exhausted.* 怎麼了? 你一副疲憊不堪的樣子。**2** having or containing no more of a particular thing or substance 耗盡的; 枯竭的: *an exhausted coal mine* 礦源枯竭的煤礦

ex·haust·ing /ɪgˋzɔstɪŋ; ɪgˈzɔːstɪŋ/ *adj* making you feel extremely tired 使人精疲力竭的: *an exhausting journey* 令人疲憊不堪的旅程

ex·haus·tion /ɪgˋzɔstʃən; ɪgˈzɔːstʃən/ *n* [U] **1** extreme tiredness 精疲力竭: **nervous exhaustion** (=a medical condition in which you feel very sad or anxious because you have been working too hard or have been very worried) 神經衰弱 **2** the act of using all the available substances, materials etc so that there are none left 用光, 耗盡: **[+of]** *the exhaustion of oil supplies* 石油供應的耗盡

ex·haus·tive /ɪgˋzɔstɪv; ɪgˈzɔːstɪv/ *adj* extremely thorough 全面的, 徹底的: *an exhaustive search for the missing boy* 對失蹤男孩展開的徹底搜尋 —**exhaustively** *adv*: *examined the issue exhaustively without result* 對問題進行了徹底調查卻毫無結果

exhaust pipe /ˈ· · ·/ *n* [C] a pipe on a car or a machine through which gas or steam passes 排氣管 —see picture on page A2 參見 A2 頁圖

ex·hib·it¹ /ɪgˋzɪbɪt; ɪgˈzɪbɪ̈t/ *v* **1** [I,T] to put something in a public place so that people can go to see it 展出, 展覽: *David's going to exhibit his roses at the flower show.* 戴維準備將自己的玫瑰花在花展中展出。**2** [T] *formal* to show a particular quality, emotion, or ability so that people notice it easily【正式】展示〔氣質、情感或能力〕: *Moira's exhibiting classic signs of depression.* 莫伊拉表現出典型的抑鬱跡象。**3** [T] *formal* to show someone something【正式】出示, 展示出: *He rolled up his trouser leg to exhibit his wounded knee.* 他捲起褲腿露出受傷的膝蓋。

exhibit² *n* [C] **1** something, for example a painting, that you put in a public place so that people can go to see it 展品, 展出物: *Many exhibits were donated by local millionaire John Severi.* 許多展品都是由當地的百萬富翁約翰·塞弗里捐贈的。**2** an object, piece of clothing etc that is used in a court of law to prove that someone is guilty or not guilty〔法庭上出示的〕證物: *Exhibit A is the blood-stained hammer found next to the victim's body.* 證物 A 是在受害者身邊發現的一把帶血跡的錘子。**3** an EXHIBITION (1) 展覽會: *a big exhibit in Milan* 在米蘭舉行的大型展覽

2 **ex·hi·bi·tion** /ˌɛksəˋbɪʃən; ˌeksɪ̈ˈbɪʃən/ *n* **1** [C] a public show where you put things so that people can go to see them 展覽(會): **[+of]** *an exhibition of black and white photographs* 黑白照片展覽 **2** [U] the act of showing something such as a painting in a public place 展出, 展覽: **[+of]** *She never agreed to the public exhibition of her sculptures while she was still alive.* 她從未同意在生前公開展出自己的雕塑作品。| **on exhibition** also 又作 **on exhibit** (=being shown) 展出中 *A collection of paintings by David Hockney is on exhibition at the Museum of Contemporary Art.* 大衛·赫克內的一批繪畫作品正在當代藝術館展出。**3 an exhibition of rudeness/jealousy/temper etc** very rude, embarrassing, or offensive behaviour 顯露出無禮/嫉妒/壞脾氣等: *I've never seen such an exhibition of jealousy in my entire life.* 我一生中從未見過如此嫉妒的表現。**4 make an exhibition of yourself** behave in a silly or embarrassing way 出洋相, 出醜: *Sam made a real exhibition of himself, getting drunk and then taking all his clothes off.* 山姆喝醉了酒後又脱掉所有的衣服, 出盡了洋相。**5** [C] *BrE* a small amount of money given as a prize to a student【英】〔小額〕獎學金: *Michael won an exhibition at Cambridge.* 邁克爾在劍橋大學獲得了一小筆獎學金。

ex·hi·bi·tion·is·m /ˌɛksəˋbɪʃənˌɪzəm; ˌeksɪ̈ˈbɪʃənɪzəm/ *n* [U] **1** behaviour that is intended to make people notice or admire you, but which most people think is silly 表現癖: *Look at those idiots standing on the statue. It's just pure exhibitionism.* 看看那些站在雕像上的笨蛋, 純粹是表現癖。**2** behaviour in which someone shows their PENIS or breasts to people in a public place because they have mental problems 露陰癖; 露乳癖 —**exhibitionist** *n* [C] —**exhibitionistic** /ˌɛksəbɪʃəˋnɪstɪk; ˌeksɪ̈bɪʃəˈnɪstɪk/ *adj*

ex·hib·i·tor /ɪgˋzɪbɪtɚ; ɪgˈzɪbɪ̈tə/ *n* [C] someone who is showing something, for example a painting, in a public place so that people can go to see it 參展者, 展出者: *a book exhibitor at TESOL* 在英語外語教學大會上參展的書商

ex·hil·a·rate /ɪgˋzɪləˌret; ɪgˈzɪləreɪt/ *v* [T] to make someone feel very excited and happy 使興高采烈, 使感到激動 —**exhilaration** /ɪgˌzɪləˋreʃən; ɪgˌzɪləˈreɪʃən/ *n* [U]

ex·hil·a·rat·ed /ɪgˋzɪləˌretɪd; ɪgˈzɪləreɪtɪ̈d/ *adj* feeling extremely happy and excited 興高采烈的, 異常興奮的: *I am always exhilarated by the bustle and noise of New York.* 紐約的繁華喧鬧總令我興奮。

ex·hil·a·rat·ing /ɪgˋzɪləˌretɪŋ; ɪgˈzɪləreɪtɪŋ/ *adj* making you feel very excited and happy 使人興高采烈的, 令人極度興奮的: *Racing down the ski slope for the first time was an exhilarating experience.* 第一次急速滑下雪坡真是萬分刺激。—**exhilaratingly** *adv*

ex·hort /ɪgˋzɔrt; ɪgˈzɔːt/ *v* [T] *formal* to try very hard to persuade someone to do something【正式】規勸; 懇請; 激勵: **exhort sb to do sth** *He exhorted the troops to prepare for battle.* 他激勵軍隊做好戰鬥準備。—**exhortation** /ˌɛgzɚˋteʃən; ˌeksɔːˈteɪʃən/ *n* [C,U]

ex·hume /ɪgˋzjum; ɪgˈzjuːm/ *v* [T usually passive 一般用被動態] *formal* to remove a dead body from a grave, especially in order to check the cause of death【正式】〔尤指為驗屍而從墓內〕掘出〔屍體〕—**exhumation** /ˌɛkshjuˋmeʃən; ˌekshjʊˈmeɪʃən/ *n* [C,U]

ex·i·gen·cy /ˋɛksədʒənsɪ; ˈeksɪ̈dʒənsi/ also 又作 **ex·i·gence** /ˋɛksədʒəns; ˈeksɪ̈dʒəns/ *n* [C usually plural 一般用複數] *formal* something that you must do to deal with an urgent situation【正式】應急措施; 應急情況: *the exigencies of war* 戰時急需

ex·i·gent /ˋɛksədʒənt; ˈeksɪ̈dʒənt/ *adj formal*【正式】**1** demanding a lot of attention from other people in a way that is unreasonable 苛求的, 要求過多的 **2** an exigent situation is urgent, so that you must deal with it very quickly〔情況〕緊急的, 急迫的

ex·ig·u·ous /ɪgˋzɪgjuəs; ɪgˈzɪguəs/ *adj formal* very small in amount【正式】極少的; 微薄的: *exiguous earnings* 微薄的收入

ex·ile¹ /ˋɛgzaɪl; ˈeksaɪl/ *n* **1** [singular, U] a situation in which you are forced to leave your country to live in another country, especially for political reasons〔尤指因政治原因的〕流放, 流亡: *After a long period of enforced exile he returned to rule his country again.* 被迫流亡國外很長一段時間後, 他回國再次執政。| **be in**

exile *Some of her best works were written while she was in exile.* 她的一些最好的作品是在她流亡期間寫的。| **go into exile** *He was forced to go into exile to escape imprisonment after the coup.* 政變後為逃避拘捕，他被迫流亡國外。| **send sb into exile** (=force someone to leave) 放逐某人 **2** [C] someone who has been forced to live in exile 被流放者；流亡者 —see also 另見 TAX EXILE

exile² *v* [T usually passive 一般用被動態] to force someone to leave their country, especially for political reasons〔尤指因政治原因而〕放逐，流放〔某人〕: *After the war he was exiled and the other leaders imprisoned.* 戰後他被流放國外，其他領導人則被捕入獄。| **exile sb to** *After publishing the novel he was arrested and exiled to Siberia.* 小說發表後他被捕並被流放至西伯利亞。—**exiled** *adj* [only before noun 僅用於名詞前]

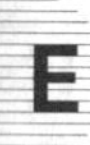

ex·ist /ɪg`zɪst; ɪg'zɪst/ *v* [I not in progressive 不用進行式] **1** if someone or something exists, that person or thing is real and has not been imagined by someone 存在；實際上有: *Do fairies really exist?* 真的有神仙嗎？| *Stop pretending the problem doesn't exist.* 別再假裝不存在這個問題了。| *Tom acts as if I don't exist at times.* 有時湯姆表現得就像我不存在一樣。**2** to happen or be present in a particular situation or place 出現，發生；在場，存在: *The custom of arranged marriages still exists in many countries.* 許多國家仍然存在着包辦婚姻的習俗。**3** to stay alive, especially in a difficult situation when you do not have enough money, food etc 維持生存〔尤指勉強餬口〕: **[+on]** *The hostages existed on bread and water for over 5 months.* 人質靠麵包和水生存了五個多月。

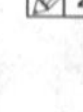

ex·ist·ence /ɪg`zɪstəns; ɪg'zɪstəns/ *n* **1** [U] the state of existing 存在；實有: *It is impossible to prove the existence of God.* 無法證明上帝的存在。| **be in existence** (=exist at a particular time)〔在某一時間〕存在 *There are three different versions of his health record currently in existence.* 目前他有三份不同的健康記錄。| **come into existence** (=start to exist) 產生，出現，開始存在 *Scientists have many theories about how the universe first came into existence.* 關於宇宙是如何產生的，科學家們有許多種理論。**2** [C usually singular 一般用單數] the type of life that someone has, especially when it is bad or unhappy 生活，生活方式〔尤指不幸的生活〕: *Pablo led a lonely existence when he first moved to San Juan.* 巴勃羅剛搬到聖胡安時，生活很孤獨。| *I don't call this a life, it's an existence.* 我認為這不叫生活，這只是勉強維生。| **eke out an existence** (=get just enough food or money to live on) 勉強餬口 *Farmers eked out a primitive existence on the dry, stony land.* 農民們在乾旱多石的土地上勉強維持簡單原始的生活。| **sb's/sth's very existence** (=the fact that something exists at all, especially when something could prevent it from existing) 某人的生命；某物的存在〔尤指當生命、存在成問題時〕*a drug on which his very existence depended* 維繫他生命的藥物

ex·ist·ent /ɪg`zɪstənt; ɪg'zɪstənt/ *adj formal* existing now【正式】現存的，現有的: *The existent pension scheme will not change.* 現有的退休金制度不會改變。—opposite 反義詞 NONEXISTENT

ex·is·ten·tial /ˌɛgzɪs`tɛnʃəl; ˌegzɪ'stenʃəl◂/ *adj* [only before noun 僅用於名詞前] connected with the existence of humans or existentialism 關於（人類）存在的；存在主義的: *the existential notion that man is in control of his own life* 認為人能主宰自己生命的存在主義觀點

ex·is·ten·tial·is·m /ˌɛgzɪs`tɛnʃəlɪzm; ˌegzɪ'stenʃəlɪzəm/ *n* [U] the modern belief that people are responsible for their own actions and experiences 存在主義: *Sartre, the high priest of French existentialism* 法國存在主義的宗師薩特 —**existentialist** *adj* —**existentialist** *n* [C]

ex·ist·ing /ɪg`zɪstɪŋ; ɪg'zɪstɪŋ/ *adj* [only before noun 僅用於名詞前] existing systems, situations etc are the present ones being used now 正在使用的；現存的: *Changes will be made to the existing laws.* 將對現有的法律進行修改。

ex·it¹ /`ɛgzɪt; 'egzɪ̵t/ *n* [C] **1** a door or space through which you can leave a place, especially a room in a big building 出口〔尤指大建築物的出口〕: *We made for the nearest exit.* 我們走向最近的出口。| *an exit sign* 出口通道標誌 | **emergency/fire exit** (=a special door used only when there is a fire etc) 太平門；緊急出口；失火通道出口 **2** [usually singular 一般用單數] the act of leaving a place, especially a room 離去〔尤指離開房間〕: **make an exit** (=go out) 出去，離開 *They made a swift exit when they saw the police approaching.* 看見警察來了，他們便迅速離去。**3** a place on a MOTORWAY or FREEWAY where vehicles can leave it 高速公路出口: *Take exit 13 into Lynchburg.* 從13號出口開出到林奇堡。**4** [usually singular 一般用單數] an occasion when someone stops being involved in a situation, event, etc, often because they have not been successful or have done something wrong 退出〔常指因未成功或做錯事而停止參與某局勢或事件〕: *Manchester United's early exit from the championship* 曼聯隊早早退出冠軍的爭奪

exit² *v* **1** [I] to leave a place 離去，離開〔某處〕: **[+from/through]** *I exited through a side window.* 我從側面的一扇窗戶離開。**2** [I,T] to stop using a computer PROGRAM¹ (1) 退出（軟件）: *You exit the system by pressing the F3 button.* 你按F3鍵就能退出系統。**3** [I,T] *Latin* a word used in the instructions of a play to tell an actor to leave the stage【拉丁】退場，下場〔劇本裡的舞台指示〕: *Exit Hamlet, bearing the body of Polonius.* 哈姆雷特扛着波洛尼厄斯的屍體退場。

exit poll /ˈ· ·/ *n* [C] a process of asking people how they have voted in an election in order to discover the likely result of the election〔投票場所之外的〕投票後民意調查

ex·o·dus /`ɛksədəs; 'eksədəs/ *n* [singular] a situation in which a lot of people leave a particular place at the same time〔大批人同時〕離開；湧離: **[+from/to]** *the exodus of Jews from Eastern Europe* 猶太人大批湧離東歐 | **mass exodus** *often humorous* (=when everybody goes somewhere)【常幽默】全體出動，所有人都去〔某處〕*I joined in the mass exodus to the bar every lunchtime.* 每天午飯時間我都加入湧向酒吧的人羣。

ex·of·fi·ci·o /ˌɛks ə`fɪʃɪˌo; ˌeks ə'fɪʃiəʊ/ *adj Latin formal* an ex-officio member of an organization is only a member because of their rank or position【拉丁，正式】〔因級別或職位而成為某組織〕當然成員的: *The Mayor is an ex-officio member of the Parish Council.* 市長是教區議會的當然成員。—**ex officio** *adv*

ex·on·e·rate /ɪg`zɑnəˌret; ɪg'zɒnəreɪt/ *v* [T] to state officially that someone who has been blamed for something is not responsible for it 免除對…的指控[責備]: *The report did not exonerate the social workers involved in the Cleveland child abuse case.* 這份報告並未替克利夫蘭虐待兒童案件涉及的社工洗脫干係。| **exonerate sb from/of** *Recent medical evidence has exonerated Dr Lamont from all blame.* 最近的醫學證據表明對拉蒙特醫生的所有責難都不成立。—**exoneration** /ɪgˌzɑnə`reʃən; ɪgˌzɒnə'reɪʃən/ *n* [U]

ex·or·bi·tant /ɪg`zɔrbətənt; ɪg'zɔːbɪ̵tənt/ *adj* an exorbitant price, rate, demand etc is much higher than is reasonable or usual〔價格、費用、要求等〕過高的；過分的: *It's a good restaurant but the prices are exorbitant.* 這家飯店不錯，但價格實在太高了。—**exorbitance** *n* [U] —**exorbitantly** *adv*

ex·or·cis·m /`ɛksɔrˌsɪzəm; 'eksɔːsɪzəm/ *n* [C,U] **1** a process during which someone forces evil spirits to leave a place or someone's body by using special words and ceremonies 驅邪，驅魔 **2** the act of making yourself forget a bad memory or experience〔對不好的回憶或經歷的〕設法忘卻，淡忘

ex·or·cist /`ɛksɔrˌsɪst; 'eksɔːsɪ̵st/ *n* [C] someone who forces evil spirits to leave a place or someone's body 驅魔師

ex·or·cize also 又作 **-ise** *BrE*【英】/`ɛksɔrˌsaɪz; 'eksɔːsaɪz/

v [T] to force evil spirits to leave a place or someone's body by using special words and ceremonies〔通過念咒語或做法事〕驅除〔邪魔〕: *prayers to exorcize ghosts* 驅鬼的禱詞

ex·ot·ic /ɪg`zɑtɪk; ɪg'zɒtɪk/ *adj approving* seeming unusual and exciting because of being connected with a foreign country【褒】異國風情的, 外國情調的: *exotic birds* 外國的奇異鳥類 | *Zara is an exotic name. Where's she from?* 扎拉是一個頗具外國味的名字, 她是哪國人? —**exotically** /-kḷɪ; -kli/ *adv*

ex·ot·ic·a /ɪg`zɑtɪkə; ɪg'zɒtɪkə/ *n* [plural] unusual and exciting things that come from foreign countries〔來自外國的〕奇異事物

exotic danc·er /·,·· '··/ *n* [C] a dancer who takes off their clothes while dancing 脫衣舞蹈員; 跳豔舞者 —see also 另見 STRIPTEASE

2 3 **ex·pand** /ɪk`spænd; ɪk'spænd/ *v* **1** [I,T] to become larger in size, number, or amount, or to make something become larger (使) 擴大; 增加: *Water expands as it freezes.* 水結冰時會膨脹。| *The population of the town expanded rapidly in the 1960s.* 20世紀60年代, 這個鎮子的人口迅速增加。| **expand sth** *exercises designed to expand the chest muscles* 為擴展胸肌而設計的練習 —opposite 反義詞 CONTRACT[2] (1) **2** [T] to increase the amount or range of an activity 增加〔活動量〕; 擴展〔活動範圍〕: *As children grow older they expand their interests and become more confident.* 兒童在成長過程中興趣會變廣, 人也會變得更自信。**3** [I,T] if a company, business etc expands or if someone expands it, they open new shops, factories etc 擴展 (業務) **4** [I] to become more confident or friendly 變得更自信[友善]: *After a few whiskies he started to expand a little.* 幾杯威士忌下肚, 他開始多了些信心。

expand on/upon sth *phr v* [T] to add more details or information to something that you have already said 詳述, 進一步說明: *Payne later expanded on his initial statement, saying he hadn't meant it the way it sounded.* 佩恩後來對他最初的聲明解釋稱, 那句話表面的意思並非他的本意。

ex·pand·a·ble /ɪk`spændəbḷ; ɪk'spændəbəl/ *adj* able to be made larger 可擴大的, 可放大的: *an expandable waistband* 能放寬的腰帶

ex·panse /ɪk`spæns; ɪk'spæns/ *n* [C] a very large area of water, sky, land etc 寬廣的空間: [+of] *Vast expanses of sand stretched out in front of us.* 在我們面前是廣袤的沙地。

3 **ex·pan·sion** /ɪk`spænʃən; ɪk'spænʃən/ *n* **1** [U] the act or process of increasing in size, range, amount etc〔尺寸、範圍、數量等的〕擴大; 增加: *the expansion of gases* 氣體的膨脹 **2** [U] the act or process of making a company or business larger by opening new shops, factories etc〔公司或企業的〕擴張: *The industry has just undergone a period of rapid expansion.* 該產業剛經歷了一輪快速擴張。**3** [C] a detailed idea, story etc that is based on one that is simpler or more general 詳述, 展開, 擴充: *The novel is an expansion of a short story he wrote about forty years ago.* 這部小說由他大約四十年前寫的一篇短篇小說擴展而成。

ex·pan·sion·is·m /ɪks`pænʃənɪzm; ɪk'spænʃənɪzəm/ *n* [U] a process in which the amount of land and power that a country has increases 擴張 (主義) —**expansionary** *adj* —**expansionist** *adj* —**expansionist** *n* [C]

ex·pan·sive /ɪk`spænsɪv; ɪk'spænsɪv/ *adj* **1** very friendly and willing to talk a lot 友善健談的: *After a couple of drinks she suddenly became more expansive.* 喝了幾杯酒後她突然變得友好健談起來。**2** very large and wide in area〔面積〕廣闊的, 遼闊的: *a broad expansive valley* 寬廣的山谷 **3** expansive behaviour or ideas are confident but not always practical〔行為或想法〕自信但不一定實在的: *He made an expansive gesture and said, "Who cares anyway?"* 他做了個有些輕浮的手勢說: "誰會在乎呢?" —**expansively** *adv* —**expansiveness** *n* [U]

ex·pat /,ɛks`pæt; ,eks'pæt/ *n* [C] *informal* an expatriate【非正式】居住國外的人; 僑民

ex·pa·ti·ate /ɪk`speʃɪ,et; ɪk'speɪʃieɪt/ *v*

expatiate on/upon sth *phr v* [T] *formal* to speak or write in detail about a particular subject【正式】詳述, 闡述: *He began to expatiate on the topic of the free market economy.* 他就自由市場經濟的題目開始詳細論述。

ex·pat·ri·ate¹ /ɛks`petrɪ,et; eks'pætriət/ *n* [C] someone who lives in a foreign country 居住國外的人; 僑民: *British expatriates living in Spain* 在西班牙的英國僑民 —**expatriate** *adj* [only before noun 僅用於名詞前]

ex·pat·ri·ate² /ɛks`petrɪ,et; eks'pætrieɪt/ *v* [T] to force someone to leave their own country and go to live in another country, especially because they have broken the law〔尤指依法〕使移居國外, 把...逐出本國 —compare 比較 EXILE[2]

ex·pect /ɪk`spɛkt; ɪk'spekt/ *v* [T] 1 1

1 ►THINK STH WILL HAPPEN 認為某事會發生◄ to think that something will happen because it seems likely or has been planned 預料, 預期: **expect (that)** *The troops expect the attack will come at dawn.* 部隊預料進攻將於拂曉發起。| **expect to do sth** *The rent was much more than we had expected to pay.* 租金比我們預計要付的多得多。| **expect sb/sth to do sth** *He'd been out celebrating and expected his girlfriend to drive him home.* 他出去慶祝, 以為女朋友會開車送他回家。| **fully expect** (=be completely sure something will happen) 完全相信, 確信〔某事會發生〕*Smedley fully expected to be paid for giving me this information.* 斯梅德利確信向我提供這個信息會得到報酬。| **half expect** (=think it is possible that something will happen) 認為 (某事) 有可能 *I half expected to see her at the party.* 我覺得可能會在晚會上看見她。| **as expected** (=in the way that was planned) 按計劃進行 *The ascent of the mountain is proceeding as expected.* 登山活動正在按計劃進行。| **is (only) to be expected** (=used to say that you are not surprised that an unpleasant situation or remark etc has happened or been said) 在預料之中, 並不意外 *Some resentment of the new baby was only to be expected.* 新生嬰兒的哥哥、姐姐有點吃醋不足為奇。

2 ►BE WAITING FOR 等待◄ to believe that someone or something is going to arrive 期待, 預料: *We're expecting Alison home any minute now.* 我們想艾利森現在隨時會到家。| *Snow is expected by the weekend.* 預計週末會下雪。

3 ►DEMAND 要求◄ to demand that someone does something because it is a duty or seems reasonable 要求; 期望〔某人做某事〕: *The officer expects complete obedience from his troops.* 這位軍官要求部下絕對服從。| **expect sb to do sth** *You can't expect kids to be quiet all the time.* 你不能指望孩子們一直保持安靜。| **expect a lot/too much of sb** (=think someone can do more than perhaps is possible) 對某人要求很高/過高 *The school expects a lot of its students.* 這所學校對學生要求很高。

4 ►WANT STH TO HAPPEN 想要某事發生◄ to think it is reasonable that something should happen or exist 期待, 期望〔某事發生或某物存在〕: *A job and somewhere to live – is that too much to expect?* 有份工作, 有地方住 —— 這是不是期望過多了? | *We had expected to be consulted at the very least.* 我們原本料想起碼會與我們商量商量。

5 be expecting if a woman is expecting, she is going to have a baby 懷孕

6 What else can/do you expect? *spoken* used to say that you are not surprised by something unpleasant or disappointing because it has happened before【口】這不奇怪? 你還能指望怎麼樣?: *Tracey didn't leave a forwarding address, but then what can you expect?* 特蕾西沒留下轉寄地址, 你又能指望甚麼呢?

7 I expect *spoken especially BrE* used to introduce or

E

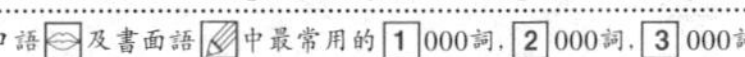

agree with a statement that you think is probably true【口, 尤英】我覺得, 依我看: *I expect Mum will phone tonight.* 我覺得媽媽今晚會打電話。| **I expect so** *"Do you think Ruth will get to art college?" "Yes, I expect so."* "你覺得魯思能進藝術學院嗎?" "我看會。"

This graph shows how common the different grammar patterns of the verb **expect** are. 本圖表所示為動詞 expect 構成的不同語法模式的使用頻率。

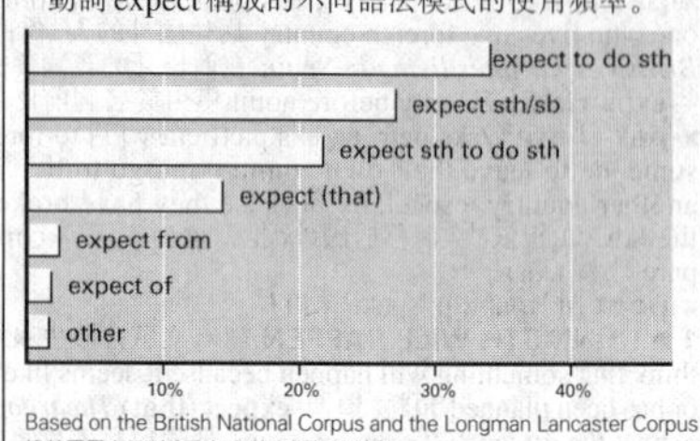

Based on the British National Corpus and the Longman Lancaster Corpus
據英國國家語料庫和朗文蘭卡斯特語料庫

ex·pec·tan·cy /ɪk`spɛktənsɪ; ɪk'spektənsi/ *n* [U] the feeling that something pleasant or exciting is going to happen 期待, 期望: *I saw the look of expectancy in the children's eyes.* 我從孩子們眼中看到了期待的神情。—see also 另見 LIFE EXPECTANCY

ex·pec·tant /ɪk`spɛktənt; ɪk'spektənt/ *adj* [usually before noun 一般用於名詞前] **1** hopeful that something good or exciting will happen 期待的, 期望的: *a row of expectant faces* 一張張滿懷期待的面孔 **2 expectant mother** a woman who is going to have a baby 孕婦 —**expectantly** *adv*

2 2 **ex·pec·ta·tion** /ˌɛkspɛk`teʃən; ˌekspek'teɪʃən/ *n* [C,U] **1** the belief that something will happen because it is likely or planned 預料, 預期: **your expectation is that** *My expectation is that interest rates will go up.* 我預料利率將上調。| **against/contrary to (all) expectations** *Against all expectations, Mike finished high school with top grades.* 出乎所有人的預料, 邁克中學畢業時成績優異。| **in expectation of** (=thinking that something will happen) 預計 *They closed the windows in expectation of rain.* 他們預計天會下雨, 把窗都關上了。**2** [usually plural 一般用複數] a belief that something good will happen in the future 期待, 期望: **have high expectations** (=believe that something good will happen or that someone will be successful in the future) 懷有很高的期望 *The school has high expectations for his future career.* 學校對他未來事業成功懷有很高的期望。| **beyond (your) expectations** (=better than you expected) 沒有想到; 比預期的更好 *Paulito has succeeded beyond our expectations.* 保利托取得的成就比我們預期的還要高。| **fall short of/not come up to sb's expectations** (=not be as good or as successful as you expected) 未達到期望, 沒有預期的那樣好 *If profits fall short of expectations, how will you repay your loan?* 如果利潤少於預期, 你怎麼還貸款呢? | *The film just didn't come up to our expectations.* 這部電影沒我們想像的那麼好。| **(not) live up to sb's expectations** (=(not) be as good as people expected) (未) 達到期望 *The show lived up to all our expectations – it was wonderful!* 這場演出不負眾望——精彩極了! | **arouse expectations** (=make you think that something good is going to happen) 引起期望, 使充滿期望 *The ceasefire has aroused expectations of an end to the war.* 停火使人們對結束戰爭充滿了希望。**3** the belief that something ought to happen or that someone should behave in a particular way 期待; 希望: *Some have totally unrealistic expectations of both medical and nursing staff.* 有些人對醫護人員的期望完全不切實際。**4 expectation of life** the number of years that someone is likely to live; LIFE EXPECTANCY 預期壽命

3 2 **ex·pec·ted** /ɪk`spɛktɪd; ɪk'spektɨd/ *adj* [only before noun 僅用於名詞前] an event or person that is expected is one you think will happen or are waiting for 預料中的; 被等待的: *The expected storm never occurred so we had the barbecue after all.* 預料中的暴風雨沒有來, 所以我們最終還是舉行了燒烤野餐。

ex·pec·to·rant /ɪk`spɛktərənt; ɪk'spektərənt/ *n* [U] *formal* a type of cough medicine that you take to help get rid of PHLEGM (=a sticky substance) in your lungs【正式】祛痰劑

ex·pec·to·rate /ɪk`spɛktəˌret; ɪk'spektəreɪt/ *v* [I] *formal* to force liquid out of your mouth; SPIT[1] (1)【正式】咳出; 吐出

ex·pe·di·en·cy /ɪk`spidɪənsɪ; ɪk'spi:diənsi/ also 又作 **ex·pe·di·ence** /-dɪəns; -diəns/ *n* [C,U] what it is useful or necessary to do in a particular situation, even if it is morally wrong 不得已而做的事; 權宜之計: *Not burying the dead soldiers was unfortunately a matter of expediency.* 不掩埋死亡士兵的屍體也是不得已的事。

ex·pe·di·ent[1] /ɪk`spidɪənt; ɪk'spi:diənt/ *n* [C] a clever and effective way of dealing with a problem, even though it may be morally wrong 應急對策; 權宜之計: **by the expedient of** *Moore escaped by the simple expedient of lying down in a clump of grass.* 穆爾急中生智, 躺倒在草叢中得以脱身。

expedient[2] *adj* helping you to deal with a problem quickly and effectively, although sometimes in a way that is morally wrong 權宜之計的: **be expedient to do sth** *We have decided it would be expedient to appoint a committee to investigate the problem.* 我們認為指定一個委員會來調查這個問題是權宜之計。—opposite 反義詞 INEXPEDIENT —**expediently** *adv*

ex·pe·dite /`ɛkspɪˌdaɪt; 'ekspɨdaɪt/ *v* [T] to make a process happen more quickly 促進, 加快〔進程〕: *strategies to expedite the decision-making process* 加快決策進程的策略

ex·pe·di·tion /ˌɛkspɪ`dɪʃən; ˌekspɨ'dɪʃən/ *n* **1** [C] a long journey, especially one made by a group of people, to a place that is dangerous or that has not been visited before〔尤指一隊人的〕遠征; 探險: *Brown led an expedition to the top of Kilimanjaro.* 布朗帶隊赴乞力馬扎羅山頂探險。**2** [C] the group of people that make this journey 遠征隊; 探險隊: *He was the youngest member of the British Everest expedition in 1974.* 他是 1974 年英國珠穆朗瑪峯探險隊中最年輕的成員。**3** [C] *often humorous* a short journey, usually made for a particular purpose【常幽默】〔有特定目的的〕短途出行: **a shopping expedition** *a shopping expedition to the mall* 去購物中心買東西 **4** [U] the act of doing something more quickly than you would usually〔與平時相比的〕快速行事, 動作敏捷

ex·pe·di·tion·a·ry /ˌɛkspɪ`dɪʃənˌɛrɪ; ˌekspɨ'dɪʃənəri◂/ *adj* **expeditionary army/force etc** an army etc that is sent to a battle in another country 遠征軍/部隊等

ex·pe·di·tious /ˌɛkspɪ`dɪʃəs; ˌekspɨ'dɪʃəs◂/ *adj formal* quick and effective【正式】迅速而有效的 —**expeditiously** *adv*: *Complaints must be dealt with expeditiously.* 一定要迅速有效地處理投訴事件。

ex·pel /ɪk`spɛl; ɪk'spel/ *v* **expelled, expelling** [T] **1** to dismiss someone officially from a school or organization〔從學校或組織中正式〕開除: **expel sb from** *I was expelled from school when I was fourteen.* 我在十四歲時被學校開除了。| **expel sb for doing sth** *Three party members were expelled for accepting bribes.* 三名政黨成員因受賄而被開除。| **get expelled** *You can get expelled for smoking.* 你會因吸煙而被開除。**2** to force a foreigner to leave a country, especially because they have broken the law or for political reasons〔尤指因犯法或政治原因〕驅逐〔外國人〕: *The government is trying to expel all journalists.* 政府正試圖驅逐所有外國記者。**3** to force air, water, or gas etc out of your body or out of a container 排出〔空氣、水或氣體等〕

—see also 另見 EXPULSION

ex·pend /ɪkˋspɛnd; ɪk'spend/ *v* [T] **expend time/money/resources etc** to use or spend a lot of time etc in order to do something 耗費時間／金錢／資源等: *Try not to expend more energy than necessary.* 盡量不要耗費不必要的精力。| **expend sth in/on (doing) sth** *A great deal of time and money has been expended on creating a pleasant office atmosphere.* 為創造舒心的辦公環境已花費了大量的時間和金錢。

ex·pen·da·ble /ɪkˋspɛndəbḷ; ɪk'spendəbəl/ *adj* **1** no longer useful or important so that you can get rid of it 可扔掉的, 可廢棄的: *This government seems to think skilled shipyard workers are expendable.* 該政府似乎認為熟練的造船工人是可有可無的。**2** a soldier who is expendable could be allowed to die〔士兵〕可犧牲的

2 **ex·pen·di·ture** /ɪkˋspɛndɪtʃɚ; ɪk'spendɪtʃə/ *n* **1** [C,U] the total amount of money that a government, organization, or person spends during a particular period of time 開支(額), 支出(額): *welfare expenditures* 福利開支 | **[+on]** *The total expenditure on defence has dropped since 1989.* 1989 年以來國防總開支已有所下降。| **public expenditure** (=the amount of money a government spends on services for the public) 公共開支 —compare 比較 INCOME **2** [U] the act of spending or using time, money, energy etc〔時間、金錢、能量等的〕耗費, 花費: *The work should be produced with minimum expenditure of time and money.* 這項工作應以最少的時間和金錢來完成。

3 2 **ex·pense** /ɪkˋspɛns; ɪk'spens/ *n* [C,U] **1** the amount of money that you have to spend on something 花銷, 花費: **household/medical/living etc expenses** (=the money that you spend for a particular purpose) 家庭／醫療／生活等的支出 *The students share all the household expenses.* 學生們分擔所有的日用開支。| **go to great expense** also 又作 **go to a lot of expense** (=spend a lot of money on something) 花大價錢〔在某事物上〕*We went to a lot of expense to provide the safety equipment so please take care of it.* 我們在安全設施上花了很多錢, 所以請好好照管。| **spare no expense** (=spend as much money as is necessary to get the best or most expensive things) 不惜費用, 不惜代價 *Julie's parents had spared no expense for her wedding.* 朱莉的父母不惜金錢, 就是要把她的婚禮辦好。| **at great/little/no expense** *We were wined and dined at great expense.* 花大錢設了酒宴款待我們。| **think of the expense** (=it's too expensive) 想想要花的錢〔太貴了〕*I'd love to go to the Caribbean but think of the expense!* 我非常想去加勒比海度假, 但那得多少錢呀! **2 expenses** [plural] money that you spend while you are doing your job on things such as travel and food, and which your employer then pays to you 業務費用: **be on expenses** (=if the cost of something is on expenses, the person that you work for pays for it rather than you) 可以報銷 *Come on, have another drink. It's all on expenses, you know.* 來吧, 再喝一杯, 反正能報銷, 你知道。| **all expenses paid** (=something, especially a holiday or journey that is all paid for by someone else)〔尤指度假或旅行〕免費的, 別人支付的 *The prize is an all expenses paid trip to Rio.* 獎品為全程免費到里約熱內盧度假。**3 at sb's expense a)** if you do something at someone's expense, they pay for you to do it 由某人付費: *Bill's just been on a computing course, all at the company's expense.* 比爾剛開始學習一個電腦課程, 費用全部由公司支付。**b)** if you make jokes at someone's expense, you laugh about them 嘲笑某人: *Louis kept making jokes at his wife's expense.* 路易斯不斷地嘲笑妻子。**4 at the expense of** if something is done at the expense of something else, it is only achieved by harming the other thing 以(損害)…為代價: *High production rates are often achieved at the expense of quality of work.* 高產出率常常是以產品質量下降為代價的。

expense ac·count /·ˈ· ·,·/ *n* [C] a system that allows someone who works for a company to spend the company's money rather than their own on hotels, meals etc 費用賬戶〔由公司支付食宿費等〕

ex·pen·sive /ɪkˋspɛnsɪv; ɪk'spensɪv/ *adj* **1** costing a lot of money 昂貴的, 花錢多的: *That's a very expensive camera. Is it insured?* 那台照相機非常貴, 買保險了嗎? | *the most expensive restaurant in town* 城裡最貴的餐館 | **expensive to produce/run/buy etc** *Cadillacs are beautiful cars but expensive to run.* 卡迪拉克牌汽車很漂亮, 但用起來很費錢。| **prohibitively expensive** (=so expensive that most people cannot afford it) 極昂貴的, 大多數人不敢問津的 **2 expensive mistake** a mistake that puts you in a very bad situation 代價昂貴的錯誤: *Losing your temper with the client was a very expensive mistake; we've lost the contract.* 你對客戶發脾氣是個代價昂貴的錯誤, 我們的合同簽不成了。—**expensively** *adv* 1 2

ex·pe·ri·ence¹ /ɪkˋspɪrɪəns; ɪk'spɪəriəns/ *n* 1 1

1 ►KNOWLEDGE/SKILL 知識/技能◄ [U] knowledge or skill gained while doing a job 經驗: **[+in]** *Karl has considerable experience in modern methods of diagnosis.* 卡爾在現代診斷方法方面非常有經驗。| **political/teaching/computing etc experience** *The job requires no secretarial experience.* 這個職位無需祕書工作的經驗。| **previous experience** *The interviewer asked if I had any previous experience.* 面試考官問我以前是否做過這方面的工作。| **lack of experience** *He didn't get the post, due to lack of experience.* 他因缺乏工作經驗而未能獲得那個職位。| **get/gain experience** *Fran is gaining valuable experience working for her father's firm.* 弗蘭在她父親的公司上班, 正在積累寶貴的工作經驗。| **practical experience** (=experience gained by actually doing something, rather than knowledge from books etc) 實踐經驗 *good judgements based on sound practical experience* 以充足的實際經驗為基礎的良好判斷 | **have experience on your side** (=have an advantage over other people because you know more about a particular thing than they do or have been doing it for longer) 比別人更有經驗 *Sampras is a skilful player, but Becker has experience on his side.* 森柏斯是一名技術出色的球員, 但貝克爾經驗豐富些。| **first-hand experience of** (=experience gained by actually doing something) …的第一手經驗; …的親身體驗 *Kevin has first-hand experience of living in Italy.* 凱文對意大利的生活有親身體驗。

2 ►OF LIFE 關於生活◄ [U] the state of knowing, or having learnt a lot, about life and the world from events that have happened to you and people you have met 經歷; 閱歷: **in your experience** *In my experience, these things never last very long.* 從我的經驗來看, 這些事情從未長久過。| **past/personal experience** *Past experience told her that none of the students would have prepared the lesson.* 過去的經驗告訴她, 沒有一個學生會預習功課。| **know from bitter experience** (=know what is likely to happen in a particular situation because you have learned from unpleasant or difficult experiences) 有過經驗教訓 *Rita knew from bitter experience not to rely on Martin in a crisis.* 慘痛的教訓告訴麗塔, 危難時刻不能依賴馬丁。| **learn from (your) experience** *There's no point telling teenagers anything – you just have to let them learn from their experience.* 教導青少年該如何做毫無意義 —— 你只能讓他們從實踐中學習。| **experience shows that...** *Experience shows that staff respond very well to a more consultative approach.* 經驗表明, 員工們會非常歡迎更具協商性的方式。

3 ►STH THAT HAPPENS 發生的事◄ [C] something that happens to you or something you do, especially when this affects or influences you in some way 往事, 經歷; 感受: *childhood experiences* 兒時的經歷 | **[+of/with]** *This was my first experience of living with other people.* 這是我第一次與別人住在一起的經歷。| **[+for]** *Failing an exam was a new experience for me.* 考試不過關對我來說還是第一次。| **a bad/strange/dreadful**

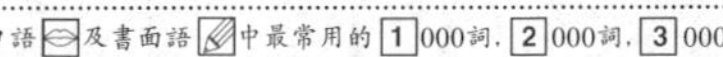

experience *It was a strange experience to see my father being taken to hospital on a stretcher.* 對我來說，看見父親被擔架抬到醫院去是一次奇怪的感受。| **a memorable/unforgettable etc experience** *Reaching the top of Mt Whitney was an unforgettable experience.* 登上惠特尼峯是一次難忘的經歷。| **quite an experience** (=very interesting, exciting etc) 非常帶勁兒[刺激]的事 *Parachuting is quite an experience, let me tell you.* 聽我說，跳傘是件非常刺激的事。| **religious experience** (=a situation in which you feel, hear, or see something that affects you strongly and makes you believe in God) 宗教體驗〔使人信仰上帝的體驗〕*She claimed to have had some sort of religious experience while in Africa.* 她聲稱在非洲期間感受到某種宗教體驗。

4 the black/female/Russian etc experience [U] events or knowledge shared by the members of a particular society or group of people 黑人/女性/俄羅斯人等的經驗[體驗]: *No writer has ever expressed the black experience with such passion as Toni Morisson.* 沒有作家像托尼·莫里森那樣以充滿激情的筆調描述了黑人社會的體驗。

5 work experience a) a system in which a student can work for a company in order to learn about a job〔學生到公司進行的〕工作實習 **b)** the period of time during which a student does this 實習期: *Ella is about to do work experience with a clothing manufacturer.* 埃拉將去一家服裝生產企業進行實習。

experience² *v* [T] **1** if you experience a problem or situation, it happens to you or affects you 經歷; 體驗: *Children need to experience things for themselves in order to learn from them.* 兒童需要自己經歷事情以便從中學習。| *Germany experienced a period of enormous growth in the 60s.* 西德在60年代經歷了一段時間的經濟騰飛。| **experience sth at first hand** (=know about something because it has affected you directly, rather than just reading or hearing about it) 親身經歷[體驗] *During the war they experienced at first hand the horror of night bombing raids.* 在戰爭期間，他們親身體驗了夜間空襲的恐懼。**2** to feel a particular emotion or physical sensation 體會到; 感受到: *Many women experience feelings of nausea during pregnancy.* 許多婦女在懷孕期間會有噁心想吐的感覺。

ex·pe·ri·enced /ɪk`spɪrɪənst; ɪk'spɪəriənst/ *adj* possessing skills or knowledge because you have done something often or for a long time 經驗豐富的, 有經驗的: *an experienced pilot* 經驗豐富的飛行員 | **[+in]** *Blake's very experienced in microsurgery.* 布萊克在顯微外科方面極富經驗。

ex·per·i·en·tial /ɪk͵spɪrɪ`ɛnʃəl; ɪk͵spɪəri'enʃəl◂/ *adj* based on or connected with experience 由經驗得來的; 與經驗相關的: *experiential approaches to learning* 學習上的經驗方法

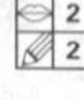

ex·per·i·ment¹ /ɪk`spɛrəmənt; ɪk'sperɪ̇mənt/ *n* [C,U] **1** a thorough test using scientific methods to discover how someone or something reacts under certain conditions 實驗: **[+in/on/with]** *experiments on sleep deprivation* 剝奪睡眠實驗 | **do/conduct/carry out/perform an experiment** (=do an experiment) 做實驗 *Joule carried out a series of simple experiments to test his theory.* 焦耳做了一系列簡單的實驗來驗證他的理論。**2** a process in which a new idea or method is tested to see if it is useful or effective 試驗: *an experiment in private enterprise* 私有制企業的試驗 | **by experiment** *Find out by experiment what foods the baby likes.* 通過試驗來弄清楚嬰兒喜歡吃甚麼。

ex·per·i·ment² /ɪk`spɛrəmɛnt; ɪk'sperɪ̇ment/ *v* [I] **1** to try various ideas, methods etc to see whether they will work or what effect they will have 試驗; 試用: **[+with/on]** *I'm seeing children of 6 experiment with drugs.* 我看見六歲大的孩子在試吸毒品。**2** to test something using scientific methods to see if it is true or to obtain more information about it 用…做實驗: **[+with/on]** *activists protesting against experimenting on animals* 抗議用動物做實驗的積極分子 —**experimenter** *n* [C]

ex·per·i·men·tal /ɪk͵spɛrə`mɛntl; ɪk͵sperɪ̇'mentl◂/ *adj* **1** used for, connected with, or resulting from experiments 用於做實驗的; 實驗的; 實驗得出的: *experimental animals* 用於實驗的動物 | *experimental data* 實驗數據 **2** using new ideas or methods 試驗(性)的: *experimental teaching techniques* 試驗性的教學技巧

ex·per·i·men·tal·ly /ɪk͵spɛrə`mɛntḷɪ; ɪk͵sperɪ̇'mentli/ *adv* **1** in a way that is connected with experiments 實驗地: *data obtained experimentally* 實驗獲得的數據 **2** in a way that involves using new ideas or methods 作為試驗地: *The Americans experimentally exploded the first nuclear weapon in the history of mankind.* 美國人試爆了人類歷史上第一件核武器。**3** if you do something experimentally you do it in order to see or feel what something is like 試探(性)地: *He ran his fingers experimentally over the animal's back.* 他試探着用手指撫摸那動物的後背。

ex·pe·ri·men·ta·tion /ɪk͵spɛrəmɛn`teʃən; ɪk͵sperɪ̇men'teɪʃən/ *n* [U] the process of testing various ideas, methods etc to see whether they will work or what effect they have 試驗: *There is often a period of sexual experimentation during adolescence.* 人在青春期常會經歷一個性體驗階段。| **[+with/in]** *experimentation with different combinations of chemicals* 試驗不同的化學物質組合

ex·pert¹ /`ɛkspɝt; 'ekspɜːt/ *n* [C] someone who has a special skill or special knowledge of a subject 專家, 內行: **[+on/in/at]** *He's an expert in electronic music.* 他是電子音樂方面的行家。

expert² *adj* having a special skill or special knowledge of a subject 專家的, 內行的: *Ministers depend on civil servants for expert advice.* 部長需要公務員提供內行的意見。—**expertly** *adv* —**expertness** *n* [U]

ex·per·tise /͵ɛkspɚ`tiz; ͵ekspɜː'tiːz/ *n* [U] special skills or knowledge in a particular subject 專門技能[知識]: *trainee engineers with varying degrees of computer expertise* 電腦專業技能參差不齊的受訓工程師 | **[+in]** *expertise in the field of literary criticism* 文學批評方面的專業知識

expert sys·tem /͵.. '../ *n* [C] a computer system containing a lot of information about one particular subject, so that it can help someone find an answer to a problem 專家系統〔指儲存大量某方面的信息以便幫人解決問題的電腦系統〕

ex·pi·ate /`ɛkspɪ͵et; 'ekspieɪt/ *v* [T] *formal* to be sorry for something you have done wrong and accept your punishment willingly, or try to do something to improve what you did【正式】為〔做錯事而〕甘願受罰; 補償 —**expiation** /͵ɛkspɪ`eʃən; ͵ekspi'eɪʃən/ *n*: *the expiation of your sins* 贖罪

ex·pir·a·tion /͵ɛkspə`reʃən; ͵ekspɪ̇'reɪʃən/ *n* [U] the American form of EXPIRY expiry 的美語形式

expiration date /..`.. ͵./ *n* [C] *AmE* the date on which something can no longer be used or is no longer safe to eat【美】(開始)失效日期 —see also 另見 **expiry date** (EXPIRY (2)), SELL-BY DATE

ex·pire /ɪk`spaɪr; ɪk'spaɪə/ *v* [I] **1** if an official document expires, the period of time during which it can be used ends〔正式文件等〕到期, 過期, 失效: *My passport expires next week.* 我的護照下週就過期了。| **[+on/in/at]** *Our contracts are due to expire on 20 June.* 我們的合同6月20日到期。**2** if a period of time when someone has a particular position of authority expires, it ends〔任期〕屆滿: *The chairman's term of office expires at the end of March.* 主席的任期3月底屆滿。**3** *literary* if someone expires, they die【文】死亡: *Ophelia expires in Act IV of Hamlet.* 奧菲莉婭在《哈姆雷特》第四幕中死去。

ex·pir·y /ɪk`spaɪrɪ; ɪk'spaɪəri/ *n* [U] *BrE*【英】**1** the end of a period of time during which an official document can be used, or of a period of authority〔正式文件〕到期;〔任期〕屆滿; EXPIRATION *AmE*【美】**2 expiry date** the date on which something can no longer be used（開始）失效日期: *Check the expiry date on your passport.* 看一下你的護照甚麼時候到期。

1 1 **ex·plain** /ɪk`splen; ɪk'spleɪn/ *v* [I,T] **1** to make something clear or easy to understand 解釋, 說明: *Our lawyer carefully explained the procedure.* 我們的律師仔細解釋了程序。| **explain (to sb) why/how/where etc** *The librarian will explain how to use the catalogue system.* 圖書館管理員將說明如何使用目錄系統。| **explain that** *I explained that I was really a police officer.* 我解釋說我的確是警察。| **explain (sth) to sb** *He briefly explained the situation to them.* 他向他們簡要介紹了一下情況。**2** to give or be a reason for something 說明[是]…的原因: *Wait! I can explain everything.* 等一下！我可以解釋一切。| **explain that** *She explained that she had been ill.* 她解釋說她病了。| **explain why/how etc** *Perhaps genetic differences can explain why some women develop breast cancer and others do not.* 也許基因差異可以解釋為甚麼有些婦女患乳腺癌, 另一些婦女卻沒有。**3 explain yourself a)** to tell someone who is angry or upset with you the reasons why you did something 作出解釋; 表白: *Mr Hennessey tells me you haven't been to school for the last few days; I think you'd better explain yourself.* 赫尼西先生告訴我你有好幾天沒上學了, 你最好解釋一下為甚麼。**b)** to say clearly what you mean 把自己的意思說清楚: *No, I didn't mean that. I guess I haven't explained myself very well.* 不, 我不是那個意思, 我想我是沒說清楚。

explain sth ↔ **away** *phr v* [T] to tell someone the reason why you did something or why something happened in order to make it seem less important or not your fault 通過解釋消除〔某事的影響〕; 辯解: *That woman finds more ways to explain away her failures than anyone I've ever met!* 那個女人是我見過的最能找辦法為自己的失敗開脫的人！

3 2 **ex·pla·na·tion** /ˌɛksplə`neʃən; ˌekspləˈneɪʃən/ *n* **1** [C,U] the reasons given for why something happened or why you did something 解釋, 給出的原因: *I'm waiting to hear your explanation.* 我在等着聽你的解釋。| **[+for]** *He'd better have a good explanation for his behaviour!* 他真該好好解釋一下自己的行為！| **[+of]** *Did Valerie give any explanation of why she was late?* 瓦萊麗有沒有解釋她為甚麼遲到？| **in explanation of** (=as a reason for) 作為解釋 *In explanation of the job cuts, the firm said that orders had been much lower than expected.* 在解釋裁員的原因時, 公司說定貨量比預期要少得多。| **provide/come up with an explanation** *After failing to come up with an adequate explanation, Smith was arrested for robbery.* 由於未能給出充分的解釋, 史密斯因搶劫罪被捕了。—see 見 EXCUSE² (USAGE) **2** [C] a statement or piece of writing intended to describe how something works or make something easier to understand 解釋, 說明: *Each of the diagrams was accompanied by a simple explanation.* 每一張圖表都附有簡單的說明。| **[+of]** *I'll try and give you a quick explanation of how the machine works.* 我爭取快速地給你解釋一下機器的工作原理。

ex·plan·a·to·ry /ɪk`splænəˌtorɪ; ɪkˈsplænətəri/ *adj* intended to describe how something works or make something easier to understand 解釋的, 說明的: *explanatory notes at the end of each chapter* 每一章後的註釋 —see also 另見 SELF-EXPLANATORY

ex·ple·tive /`ɛksplətɪv; ɪkˈspliːtɪv/ *n* [C] *formal* a rude word that you use when you are angry or in pain【正式】咒罵語: *a mild expletive such as 'damn'* 像"該死"之類較輕的咒罵語

ex·pli·ca·ble /`ɛksplɪkəbḷ; ekˈsplɪkəbəl/ *adj* [often in negatives 常用於否定句] able to be easily understood or explained 易於理解的; 容易解釋的: *for no explicable reason* 原因不明 —opposite 反義詞 INEXPLICABLE

ex·pli·cate /`ɛksplɪˌket; ˈekspləkeɪt/ *v* [T] *formal* to explain a work of literature, an idea etc in detail【正式】詳細解釋〔文學作品、主張等〕—**explication** /ˌɛksplɪ`keʃən; ˌeksplə̇ˈkeɪʃən/ *n* [C,U]

ex·pli·cit /ɪk`splɪsɪt; ɪkˈsplɪsə̇t/ *adj* **1 explicit instructions/warnings etc** an explicit instruction etc is expressed in a way that is very clear 清楚明確的指示/警告等: *There was no explicit mention in the report of Capt Kirk's involvement.* 報告中並未明確提及如何牽連到柯克上尉。| **make something explicit** *The contrast could not have been made more explicit.* 這個對比再清楚不過了。**2 be explicit** to say something very clearly and directly 直截了當: *I don't quite understand your plan. Could you be a little more explicit, please?* 對你的計劃我不太明白, 你能直截了當說清楚嗎？| **[+about]** *Sadie was very explicit about her reasons for wanting a divorce.* 薩迪清楚地表明了她想離婚的理由。**3** language or pictures that are explicit describe or show sex or violence very clearly〔描繪性行為或暴力時〕清晰露骨的: *The film contains some very explicit love scenes.* 這部影片含有一些露骨的性行為鏡頭。—compare 比較 IMPLICIT —**explicitly** *adv* **explicitness** *n* [U]

ex·plode /ɪk`splod; ɪkˈspləʊd/ *v*

1 ►BURST 爆炸◄ [I,T] to burst, or to make something burst, into small pieces, usually with a loud noise and in a way that causes damage（使）爆炸: *We sat in the bombshelter listening to the enemy shells exploding.* 我們坐在防空洞裡, 聽見敵人砲彈的陣陣爆炸聲。—compare 比較 IMPLODE

2 ►GET ANGRY 發怒◄ [I] to suddenly become angry or dangerous 勃然大怒; 變得危險: *These guys tend to explode at any moment over the least thing.* 這些傢伙隨時都會因微不足道的事而大發雷霆。| **[+in/with/into]** *Tensions are running high and police are afraid the situation may explode into violence.* 局勢越來越緊張, 警方擔心會爆發暴力行為。

3 ►PROVE FALSE 證明錯誤◄ [T] to prove that something that many people think or believe, is wrong or not true 戳穿, 破除: **explode a myth/rumour etc** *The book explodes many myths about rape.* 這本書推翻了許多有關強姦的錯誤觀點。

4 ►GET BIGGER 變大◄ [I] to increase greatly in numbers or amount 急劇增長, 激增: *The population exploded in the early 1970s.* 20世紀70年代初期, 人口急劇增長。

5 ►MAKE A LOUD NOISE 發出巨響◄ [I] to make a very loud noise 爆響, 發出巨大聲音: *A clap of thunder exploded overhead.* 一聲驚雷在頭頂爆響。

6 ►MOVE SUDDENLY 突然移動◄ [I] to suddenly begin moving or doing something very quickly 迸發, 突發: **[+into]** *Nancy exploded into action.* 南希突發行動。| *The engine suddenly exploded into life.* 發動機突然開動了。

ex·plod·ed /ɪk`splodɪd; ɪkˈspləʊdə̇d/ *adj technical* an exploded drawing, model etc shows the parts of something separately but in a way that shows how they are related or put together【術語】〔圖或模型〕分解的: *an exploded diagram of an engine* 發動機的分解圖

ex·ploit¹ /ɪk`splɔɪt; ɪkˈsplɔɪt/ *v* [T] **1** to treat someone unfairly in order to get money or an advantage for yourself 剝削, 利用〔某人為自己服務〕: *People who work at home are more easily exploited by employers.* 在家工作的人更容易受雇主的剝削。**2** to use something fully and effectively in order to gain an advantage or profit 充分利用; 開發〔某物〕: *Casey founded a company to exploit the mineral resources in the area.* 卡塞伊創立了一家公司來開發當地的礦產資源。—**exploitable** *adj* —**exploiter** *n* [C] 3

ex·ploit² /`ɛksplɔɪt; ˈeksplɔɪt/ *n* [C usually plural 一般用複數] brave and exciting actions that people admire 英雄業績; 英勇行為: *the exploits of the early explorers of the Canadian forests* 加拿大森林早期拓荒者的業績

ex·ploi·ta·tion /ˌɛksplɔɪ`teʃən; ˌeksplɔɪˈteɪʃən/ *n* [U] **1** a situation in which someone treats someone else unfairly in order to get money or an advantage for themselves 剝削: *the exploitation of children in factories in* *the 1900's* 20世紀最初的幾年中工廠對童工的剝削 **2** a process in which materials or someone's skills are used effectively in order to gain an advantage or profit 開發, 充分利用: *guidelines on the controlled exploitation of ocean resources* 關於有節制地開發海洋資源的指導方針

ex·ploit·a·tive /ɛk`splɔɪtətɪv; ɪk'splɔɪtətɪv/ *adj* treating people unfairly to get money or an advantage 剝削的: *exploitative employers* 剝削(雇工)的雇主

ex·plo·ra·tion /ˌɛksplə'reʃən; ˌeksplə'reɪʃən/ *n* [C,U] **1** an examination of an area or journey through it in order to find out what is there or what it is like〔對某地區的〕勘查, 考察: *The North Sea has been an important centre for oil exploration.* 北海已成為重要的石油勘探中心。| **[+of]** *the exploration of space* 宇宙空間探索 **2** an examination or discussion of something to find out more about it 研究, 探究: **[+into]** *an exploration into the local records* 研究當地記錄

ex·plo·ra·to·ry /ɪk`splorəˌtorɪ; ɪk'splɒrətəri/ *adj* done in order to find out more about something 探索的, 考察的: *exploratory surgery* 診察性外科手術

3 2 **ex·plore** /ɪk`splɔr; ɪk'splɔː/ *v* **1** [I,T] to travel through or examine an area in order to find out what is there or what it is like 勘查, 考察〔某地區〕: *Lewis and Clark explored the territory from St Louis to the Pacific.* 劉易斯和克拉克勘查了從聖路易斯到太平洋海岸之間的地區。| *exploring for gold* 勘探金礦 **2** [T] to examine or discuss something carefully in order to find out more about it 檢查, 探討: *a theme explored by Mrs. Gaskell in her later novels*〔英國作家〕蓋斯凱爾夫人後期小說探討的主題

ex·plo·rer /ɪk`splɔrɚ; ɪk'splɔːrə/ *n* [C] someone who travels through an area about which little is known or which has not been visited before 探險者; 勘查者

ex·plo·sion /ɪk`sploʒən; ɪk'spləʊʒən/ *n* **1** [C] a loud sound caused by something such as a bomb bursting into small pieces 爆炸(聲): *a nuclear explosion* 核爆炸 | **[+of]** *The explosion of the space shuttle Challenger shocked the nation.* "挑戰者"號航天飛機的爆炸震驚了整個國家。**2** [C,U] a process in which something such as a bomb is deliberately made to explode 引爆: *controlled explosion of the device* 裝置的控制引爆 **3** [C] a sudden or rapid increase in the number or amount of something 激增, 急劇膨脹: *The population explosion in India caused famine and poverty.* 印度人口激增導致了饑荒和貧困。**4** [C] a sudden expression of emotion, especially anger〔感情的, 尤指憤怒的〕爆發, 迸發: *His frustration grew, and I expected an explosion at any minute.* 他越來越沮喪, 我感到他隨時會爆發。**5** [C] a sudden very loud noise 突然發出的響聲: *an explosion of laughter* 迸發的一陣笑聲

ex·plo·sive¹ /ɪk`splosɪv; ɪk'spləʊsɪv/ *adj* **1** able or likely to explode 會爆炸的: *At high temperatures this gas is explosive.* 這種氣體在高溫時會爆炸。| **explosive device** (=a bomb) 爆炸裝置, 炸彈 **2** an explosive situation is violent or dangerous〔形勢〕爆炸性的, 一觸即發的: *the explosive atmosphere of the inner cities* 市中心貧民區內一觸即發的氣氛 **3** increasing suddenly or rapidly in amount or number〔數量或數字〕激增的: *the computer industry's explosive growth* 電腦產業的迅猛發展 **4** tending to show angry violent feelings suddenly 暴躁的: *an explosive temperament* 暴躁的脾氣 **5** having great force or power, usually as the result of an explosion〔通常指因爆炸而〕力量巨大的: *The bullet hit its target with explosive force.* 子彈猛烈地擊中了目標。**6** an explosive sound is sudden and loud 轟響的 —**explosively** *adv* —**explosiveness** *n* [U]

explosive² *n* [C] a substance that can cause an explosion 炸藥, 爆炸物質: *Semtex, the explosive used in the Lockerbie airplane disaster* 森泰克斯, 洛克比空難中使用的炸藥 —see also 另見 HIGH EXPLOSIVE, PLASTIC EXPLOSIVE

ex·po /`ɛkspo; 'ekspəʊ/ *n* [C] *informal* an EXPOSITION (2)【非正式】展覽會, 博覽會

ex·po·nent /ɪk`sponənt; ɪk'spəʊnənt/ *n* [C] **1** someone who supports an idea, belief etc and who tries to explain it and persuade others that it is good or useful〔想法、信仰的〕倡導者, 鼓吹者, 說明者: **[+of]** *a leading exponent of Jungian psychology*〔瑞士精神病學家〕榮格精神分析法的主要倡導者 **2** someone whose work or methods provide a good example of a particular skill, idea, or activity 典型代表: **[+of]** *The poet Goethe is a supreme exponent of the Romantic response to nature.* 詩人歌德的作品代表了浪漫主義文學對大自然的回應, 成就最高。**3** *technical* a sign written above and to the right of a number or letter to show how many times that quantity is to be multiplied by itself, for example 2^3【術語】指數, 冪

ex·po·nen·tial /ˌɛkspo`nɛnʃəl; ˌekspə'nenʃəl◂/ *adj* **1** **exponential growth/increase** *technical* a rate of growth that becomes faster as the amount of the thing that is growing increases【術語】指數增長 **2** *technical* using a sign that shows how many times a number is to be multiplied by itself【術語】指數的, 含有指數的: *y^n is an exponential expression.* y^n是一個指數式。—**exponentially** *adv*

ex·port¹ /`ɛkspɔrt; 'ekspɔːt/ *n* **1** [U] the sale of goods to another country 出口: **[+of]** *The export of electronic equipment has risen sharply.* 電子設備出口已大幅增加。| **export market/industry/licence etc** *Export licences for arms are strictly controlled.* 武器出口許可證受到嚴格限制。**2** [C usually plural 一般用複數] a product that is sold to another country 出口商品: *Wheat is one of Alberta's chief exports.* 小麥是〔加拿大〕艾伯塔省的主要出口商品之一。| **invisible export** (=something that is sold to another country which is not an industrial product, food etc) 無形出口商品〔指非實物的出口〕*Selling insurance overseas is Britain's largest invisible export.* 在海外銷售保險是英國最大的無形出口。—opposite 反義詞 IMPORT¹ (1,2) 2

ex·port² /ɪks`pɔrt; ɪk'spɔːt/ *v* **1** [I,T] to sell goods to another country 出口: **export sth to sb** *In 1986 the company exported about 210,000 cases of wine to the UK.* 1986年該公司向英國出口了約21萬箱葡萄酒。**2** [T] to introduce an activity, idea etc to another place or country 傳播, 輸送〔到另一國家或地區〕: *The influence of African music has been exported to many parts of the western world.* 非洲音樂的影響已傳播到西方世界的許多地方。—opposite 反義詞 IMPORT¹ —**exportation** /ˌɛkspor`teʃən; ˌekspɔː'teɪʃən/ *n* [U]

ex·port·er /ɪk`spɔrtɚ; ɪk'spɔːtə/ *n* [C] a person, company, or country that sells goods to another country 出口者〔包括個人、公司或國家〕: **[+of]** *Saudi Arabia, a leading exporter of oil* 沙特阿拉伯, 主要石油輸出國 —opposite 反義詞 IMPORTER

ex·pose /ɪk`spoz; ɪk'spəʊz/ *v* [T] 3

1 ►SHOW 顯示◄ to show something that is usually covered 顯露, 暴露: *The wolf opened its mouth to expose a row of sharp white teeth.* 狼張開嘴, 露出一排白色的尖牙。| **expose sth to sth** *Wounds that are exposed to the air heal more quickly.* 傷口暴露在空氣中癒合得更快。

2 ►TO STH DANGEROUS 遇到危險之物◄ to put someone in a harmful situation, position etc, where they have no protection against something dangerous 使暴露於〔險境〕, 使置身於〔危險〕當中: **expose sb to sth** *The report revealed that workers had been exposed to unacceptably high levels of radiation.* 報告披露了工人們受到有害的高強度輻射。| **expose yourself to ridicule/criticism etc** (=say or do something that may make people laugh at you, criticize you etc) 使自己被取笑/批評等

3 ►TELL THE TRUTH 講真話◄ to tell the truth about something, or show what it is really like, especially because you think it is harmful, illegal etc 揭露, 揭發: *a radical group that works to expose and condemn racism* 專門揭發和譴責種族主義的激進團體 | **expose sb**

as sth *Klaus von Bulow was exposed as a liar and a cheat.* 揭發出來克勞斯·馮·布洛是一個說謊者和騙子。
4 ►SEE/EXPERIENCE 看/體驗◄ to learn about beliefs, ideas etc, especially by seeing things or having new experiences 使接觸〔學習新事物〕: **expose sb to sth** *Travel abroad exposes children to different languages and cultures.* 去國外旅行使孩子們接觸到不同的語言和文化。
5 ►PHOTOGRAPH 照片◄ to allow light onto a piece of film in a camera in order to take a photograph 使曝光
6 ►FEELINGS 感受◄ to show other people feelings that you usually hide, especially by behaving in a particular way 顯露〔情感〕: *Eric broke down and wept, exposing the vulnerable side of his nature.* 埃里克失聲痛哭，顯露出他個性中脆弱的一面。
7 expose yourself if a man exposes himself, he shows his sexual organs to someone he does not know in a public place, usually because he is mentally ill〔由於病態心理而在公共場所〕裸露性器官

ex·po·sé /ˌɛkspəˋze; ekˈspəʊzeɪ/ *n* [C] a story in a newspaper or on television that shows people the truth about something, especially something dishonest or illegal〔報紙、電視節目等〕揭露: **[+of]** *an exposé of corrupt practices by lawyers* 對律師們腐敗行為的揭露

ex·posed /ɪkˋspozd; ɪkˈspəʊzd/ *adj* **1** not protected from the weather 無遮蔽的，暴露（於風雨中）的: *an exposed coastline* 裸露的海岸線 **2** not protected from attack; VULNERABLE 無保護的，易受攻擊的: *Fiorentina's defence looked very exposed in the second half.* 在下半場，科倫天拿隊的防守名存實亡。

ex·po·si·tion /ˌɛkspəˋzɪʃən; ˌekspəˈzɪʃən/ *n* **1** [C,U] a clear and detailed explanation 明確細緻的解釋，詳細闡述: **[+of]** *a lucid exposition of educational theories* 對教育理論的明白闡述 **2** [C] an important event at which industrial goods are shown 展覽會，博覽會

ex post fac·to law /ˌɛks post ˋfækto ˌlɔ; ˌeks pəʊst ˈfæktəʊ ˌlɔː/ *n* [C] *law* a law that makes a particular action into a crime, and then punishes people who took that action before it had legally become a crime【法律】有追溯效力的法律

ex·pos·tu·late /ɪkˋspɑstʃəˌlet; ɪkˈspɒstʃʊleɪt/ *v* [I] *formal* to express strong disapproval, disagreement, or annoyance【正式】反對；抗議；反駁: **expostulate (that)** *"But that's the equivalent of saying that you drank beer but didn't swallow it," expostulated one reporter.* "但那等於是說，你喝了啤酒但未咽下去。"一名記者反駁說。 —**expostulation** /ɪkˌspɑstʃəˋleʃən; ɪkˌspɒstʃʊˈleɪʃən/ *n* [C,U]

W3 **ex·po·sure** /ɪkˋspoʒɚ; ɪkˈspəʊʒə/ *n*
1 ►TO DANGER 受危害◄ [C,U] the state of being put into a situation that is harmful because you have no protection from something that is dangerous 暴露: **[+to]** *Skin cancer can be caused by prolonged exposure to the sun.* 長時間曬太陽會導致皮膚癌。| *Through TV, kids have regular exposure to sex and violence.* 兒童在電視中時常看到性和暴力鏡頭。
2 ►TRUTH 真相◄ [C,U] something that is said or written in order to tell people the truth about something illegal, dishonest, or harmful 揭發，披露: *The exposure of George Davis' illicit financial dealings provoked a public outcry.* 喬治·戴維斯的非法金融交易被揭露後，公眾為之譁然。
3 ►MAKE FACTS KNOWN 使事實被知曉◄ [U] things that are said and written on television and in newspapers that make a person or event known to a lot of people 報道，曝光: *The failure of their marriage has received a lot of exposure in the press recently.* 他們婚姻失敗一事近來被媒體頻頻曝光。
4 ►BE VERY COLD 感覺非常冷◄ [U] if you have exposure you are extremely cold and ill, especially because you have been outside in very cold weather for too long without protection 受凍: *We nearly died of exposure on the mountainside.* 我們在山腰差點凍死。
5 ►PHOTOGRAPHY 攝影◄ [C] **a)** a length of film in a camera that is used to take a photograph 底片中的一張: *I have three exposures left on this roll.* 我這卷膠卷還剩三張。**b)** the amount of time a piece of film is exposed (EXPOSE (5)) to the light when making a photograph 曝光時間
6 ►SHOW 顯示◄ [C] the act of showing something that is usually hidden 顯露，暴露
7 ►DIRECTION 方向◄ [singular] the direction in which a building, hill etc faces〔建築、山等的〕朝向: *My bedroom has a southern exposure.* 我的臥室朝南。—see also 另見 INDECENT EXPOSURE

ex·pound /ɪkˋspaund; ɪkˈspaʊnd/ *v* [I,T] *formal* to explain or talk about something in detail【正式】闡述；詳細解釋: **[+on]** *a philosopher expounding on the illusory nature of the world* 闡述世界虛幻本質的哲學家

S2 W1 **ex·press¹** /ɪkˋsprɛs; ɪkˈspres/ *v* [T]
1 ►IN WORDS 用話語◄ to tell people what you are feeling or thinking by using words 表達，陳述: *Bill's never been afraid to express his opinions.* 比爾從來不怕表達自己的觀點。| **express sympathy/fear/anger etc** *Parents have expressed their concerns about their children's safety.* 父母表達了對自己孩子安全的關切。| **express interest** (=say that you are interested in something) 表示有興趣 *The public are expressing an increasing interest in green issues.* 公眾對環保問題日益關注。| **express opposition to** (=say publicly that you do not agree with something) 對...表示反對 *Managers and players alike expressed opposition to the scheme.* 管理層和隊員都反對該計劃。| **express thanks/gratitude** (=thank someone in a speech or by writing a letter) 表示感謝/感激 *Finally, I'd like to express my sincere gratitude for your help in this matter.* 最後，我對你在此事中給予的幫助表示誠摯的感謝。| **express yourself** (=let people know your thoughts and feelings so that they can under-stand) 表達自己（的想法和感受）*Young children often have difficulty expressing themselves.* 幼兒常常很難清楚地表達自己。| **can't express** *Words can't express how angry we felt.* 言語無法表達我們心中的憤怒。
2 ►IN ART/MUSIC ETC 在藝術/音樂等方面◄ to show your feelings or thoughts using art, music, films etc 描繪，表達: *Many of Munch's paintings express a deep feeling of despair.* 蒙克的許多畫作都表達一種深深的絕望。| **express yourself by/through etc** *Alain expresses himself best through his music.* 阿蘭最善於用音樂來表達自己的思想。
3 ►IN BEHAVIOUR/LOOK 在行為/表情方面◄ to let people know what you are feeling or thinking by the look on your face or by your behaviour〔以表情或行為來〕表現，顯示〔感受或想法〕: *The look on Paul's face expressed his total contempt for them.* 保羅臉上的表情顯示出對他們的徹底鄙視。
4 ►FEELING 感受◄ if a feeling expresses itself it can be clearly seen and understood 流露，表露: *Major Hall's frustration expressed itself in occasional bouts of rage.* 豪爾少校偶爾發火，表露出他的沮喪。
5 ►LETTER/PACKAGE 信件/包裹◄ *BrE* to send a letter or package using a special post system so that it arrives very quickly【英】用快郵寄出
6 ►MATHEMATICS 數學◄ *technical* to show a mathematical idea in a particular form【術語】〔用某種形式〕表示: *Express three-quarters as a decimal.* 用小數來表示四分之三。

express² *adj* [only before noun 僅用於名詞前] **1** an express command, desire, or aim is deliberately stated for a particular reason 專門表示的，特別指出的: *Matthew left express instructions to keep all doors locked.* 馬修特別指示要把門都鎖好。| *I came here with the express purpose of seeing you.* 我來這裡就是為了看你。**2 express train/coach/service** a train or bus that travels very quickly 快速列車/長途汽車/（客運）服務:

There's an express service between London and Glasgow twice daily. 倫敦和格拉斯哥之間每天有兩班快車。**3 express post/mail/delivery** a system within the Post Office that delivers letters and packages very quickly 特快郵遞 **4 express lane** *AmE* a LANE (2) on a FREEWAY used by vehicles that are travelling fast【美】〔高速公路上的〕快車道

express³ *n* **1** [C usually singular 一般用單數] a train or bus that travels from one place to another very quickly 〔火車或公共汽車的〕快車: **London-Gatwick Express/Orient Express** (=a fast train or bus which does a particular journey regularly) 倫敦－蓋特威克快車/東方快車 **2** [U] a post service that delivers letters and packages very quickly 郵件快遞: *Send these books by express.* 把這些書用快件寄出去。

express⁴ *adv* **send/deliver sth express** to send or deliver a letter, parcel etc quickly using a special post service 用快遞寄/送某物

S2 W2 **ex·pres·sion** /ɪk`sprɛʃən; ɪk'spreʃən/ *n*

1 ►WORDS 言語◄ [C] a word or group of words with a particular meaning 詞; 詞組; 措辭: *The expression 'in the family way' means 'pregnant'.* 詞組 in the family way 的意思是"懷孕的"。| **pardon/forgive/excuse the expression** (=used when you have used a word that you think may offend someone) 原諒出言冒犯 *He doesn't know his ass from a hole in the ground if you'll pardon the expression.* 請原諒我出言冒犯, 不過他真是狗屁不懂。

2 ►ON SB'S FACE 在某人臉上◄ [C] a look on someone's face that shows what they are thinking or feeling 表情: *a thoughtful expression* 若有所思的表情 | **an expression of surprise/fear/amusement** *Petra looked at her plate with an expression of disgust.* 彼得拉看着自己盤子裡的食物, 臉上露出厭惡的表情。

3 ►SAY/WRITE 說/寫◄ [C,U] something you say or write that shows what you think or feel 〔口頭或書面形式的〕表達, 表示: **an expression of sympathy/thanks etc** *Mrs Mayer received their expressions of sympathy with great dignity.* 邁耶夫人接受了他們所表達的同情, 神態極其莊重。| **give expression to sth** *The minister gave expression to his anger in an attack on the government last night.* 這位部長昨晚對政府進行攻擊, 表達了他的憤怒。| **freedom of expression** (=the right to express your opinions freely) 言論自由

4 ►ACTIONS/BEHAVIOUR 行動/行為◄ [C,U] something you do or make that shows what you think or feel 表露, 展現: **[+of]** *The recent strikes are an expression of the worker's discontent.* 最近的罷工顯示出工人的不滿情緒。| **give expression to** *John gave expression to his love of nature in his paintings.* 約翰的畫展現了他對自然的熱愛。| **find expression** *Pam's latent artistic talents found their expression in music.* 帕姆的藝術潛能在音樂中得以體現。

5 ►EVENTS 事件◄ [C,U] the way in which feelings and ideas are shown in particular events 體現, 展現: **find expression in sth** *The fiscal crisis has found its clearest expression in the poverty of the inner cities.* 市中心貧民區的貧困狀況最清楚地顯露了財政危機。

6 ►MUSIC 音樂◄ [U] the quality of singing or playing a musical instrument with feeling 〔唱歌或演奏時的〕感情: *Try to put a bit more expression into the slow passage.* 在演奏緩慢的段落時要盡量多投入一點的感情。

7 ►MATHEMATICS 數學◄ [C] *technical* a sign or group of signs that show a mathematical idea in a particular form【術語】表達式: *x^2+4 is an algebraic expression.* x^2+4是一個代數式。

ex·pres·sion·is·m /ɪk`sprɛʃən,ɪzəm; ɪk'spreʃənɪzəm/ *n* [U] a style of painting, writing, or music that expresses feelings rather than describing objects and experiences 〔繪畫、文學或音樂的〕表現主義 —**expressionist** *n* [C] —**expressionist** *adj*

ex·pres·sion·less /ɪk`sprɛʃənlɪs; ɪk'spreʃənləs/ *adj* an expressionless face or voice does not show what someone thinks or feels 無表情的, 無感情的: *a blank expressionless stare* 毫無表情的盯視 —**expressionlessly** *adv*

ex·pres·sive /ɪk`sprɛsɪv; ɪk'spresɪv/ *adj* **1** showing very clearly what someone thinks or feels 富於感情的; 明確表露想法的: *Cath threw up her arms in an expressive gesture.* 卡斯富於表情地張開雙臂。**2 be expressive of sth** showing a particular feeling or influence 體現出某種感情[影響]: *The sculpture is expressive of Michelangelo's spiritual aspirations.* 這座雕塑體現了米開朗基羅的心靈追求。—**expressively** *adv* —**expressiveness** *n* [U]

ex·press·ly /ɪk`sprɛslɪ; ɪk'spresli/ *adv formal*【正式】**1** if you say something expressly, you say it very clearly and firmly 明確地, 確切地: *I expressly forbade them to bring animals into the house.* 我明確禁止他們將動物帶進屋。**2** deliberately 特意地, 故意地: *The building is expressly designed to conserve energy.* 這座建築經特意設計以節約能源。

express post /·,· '·/ *BrE*【英】, **express mail** *AmE*【美】 *n* [U] a post service that delivers letters and parcels very quickly 快郵

ex·press·way /ɪk`sprɛs,we; ɪk'spresweɪ/ *n* [C] *AmE* a very wide road, usually in a city, on which cars can travel very quickly without stopping【美】〔通常指城市內的〕快速幹道, 高速公路 —see also 另見 FREEWAY, MOTORWAY

ex·pro·pri·ate /ɛks`proprɪ,et; ɪk'sprəʊprieɪt/ *v* [T] *formal*【正式】**1** to take away private property for public use 徵用, 沒收〔私人財產〕**2** to take something from someone illegally in order to use it 侵佔〔他人財物〕, 把…據為己有 —**expropriator** *n* [C] —**expropriation** /ɛks,proprɪ`eʃən; ɪk,sprəʊpri'eɪʃən/ *n* [C,U]

ex·pul·sion /ɪk`spʌlʃən; ɪk'spʌlʃən/ *n* [C,U] **1** the process of sending a person or group of people away from a place often by using force 驅逐, 趕走: *the expulsion of rebel forces* 驅逐叛軍 **2** the act of sending someone away from a school or organization so that they can no longer go there or be a member 開除, 除名: *Tina's anti-social behaviour eventually led to her expulsion.* 蒂娜的反社會行為最終導致自己被開除。**3** the act of getting rid of a substance from your body or from a container 排出 —see also 另見 EXPEL

ex·punge /ɪk`spʌndʒ; ɪk'spʌndʒ/ *v* [T] *formal*【正式】**1** to remove a name from a list, piece of information, or book 刪去, 勾銷 **2** to make someone forget something unpleasant 使淡忘, 抹掉: *I tried to expunge the whole episode from my memory.* 我努力想把整件事從記憶中抹掉。

ex·pur·gat·ed /`ɛkspɚ,getɪd; 'ekspəgeɪtɨd/ *adj* an expurgated book, play etc has had some parts removed because they are considered harmful or offensive 被刪節的, 經刪改的: *an expurgated version of the writings of de Sade* 薩德作品的刪節本 —**expurgate** *v* [T] —**expurgation** /,ɛkspɚ`geʃən; ,ekspə'geɪʃən/ *n* [C, U]

ex·qui·site /`ɛkskwɪzɪt; ɪk'skwɪzɨt/ *adj* **1** extremely beautiful and very delicately made 精美的, 精緻的: *exquisite craftsmanship* 精美的工藝 **2** very sensitive and delicate in the way you behave or do things 細緻的, 敏感的: *Darling, you have exquisite taste.* 親愛的, 你的情趣很高雅。**3** *literary* exquisite pain or pleasure is felt very strongly【文】〔疼痛或快樂〕強烈的 —**exquisitely** *adv* —**exquisiteness** *n* [U]

ex-ser·vice·man /,· '··/ *n plural* **ex-servicemen** [C] *especially BrE* a man who used to be in the army, navy, or AIRFORCE【尤英】退役[退伍]男軍人

ex-ser·vice·wom·an /,· '···/ *n plural* **ex-servicewomen** [C] *especially BrE* a woman who used to be in the army, navy, or AIRFORCE【尤英】退役[退伍]女軍人

ext. the written abbreviation of 縮寫= EXTENSION (2): *Contact Alison Lever on Ext. 3945.* 請與3945分機的艾利森·利弗聯繫。

ex·tant /ɪk`stænt; ɪk'stænt/ *adj formal* still existing in spite of being very old【正式】尚存的, 現存的: *Few of the manuscripts are extant.* 手稿大都散逸無存。

ex·tem·po·ra·ne·ous /ɪk͵stɛmpə`renɪəs; ɪk͵stempə'reɪnɪəs◂/ *adj* spoken or done without any preparation or practice 即興的, 無準備的: *an extemporaneous speech* 即席演講 —**extemporaneously** *adv* —**extemporaneousness** *n* [U]

ex·tem·po·re /ɪk`stɛmpərɪ; ɪk'stempəri/ *adj* spoken or done without any preparation or practice 即興的, 無準備的: *an extempore speech* 即席演講 —**extempore** *adv*

ex·tem·po·rize also 又作 **-ise** *BrE*【英】/ɪk`stɛmpə͵raɪz; ɪk'stempəraɪz/ *v* [I] *formal* to speak without preparation, especially during a performance; AD-LIB【正式】臨場講話; 臨時編詞 —**extemporization** /ɪk͵stɛmpərə`zeʃən; ɪk͵stempəraɪ'zeɪʃən/ *n* [C,U]

3 2 **ex·tend** /ɪk`stɛnd; ɪk'stend/ *v*

1 ▸CONTINUE 繼續◂ [I always+adv/prep] to continue for a particular distance or over a particular area 延伸, 伸展: **[+across/over/through etc]** *The River Nile extends as far as Lake Victoria.* 尼羅河一直延伸至維多利亞湖。| **extend 100 km/30 yards etc** *Smith Point extends a hundred yards or so into the water.* 史密斯角向水中伸出約一百碼。| *The forest extended in all directions as far as the eye could see.* 森林向四面伸展, 一望無際。

2 ▸MAKE STH BIGGER 使某物增大◂ [T] to make a building, road etc bigger or longer 擴大; 延長〔建築或道路等〕: *We extended the kitchen by six feet.* 我們把廚房擴大了六英尺。

3 ▸HAPPEN/EXIST 發生/存在◂ [I always+adv/prep] to continue to happen or exist for a certain period of time 延續, 持續: **[+for/into/over etc]** *The hot weather extended well into October.* 炎熱的天氣一直持續到10月。

4 ▸TIME 時間◂ [T] to increase a period of time that has been agreed, especially in order to finish a job or pay money that you owe 延長, 推延〔期限〕: *Management have agreed to extend the deadline.* 資方已同意延長最後期限。

5 ▸CONTROL/INFLUENCE 控制/影響◂ [I always+adv/prep, T] if you extend your control, influence etc or if it extends over something, it becomes more powerful 延伸, 擴大: *We hope to extend the effects of sanctions against the regime.* 我們希望加大對該政權的制裁力度。| **[+into/over/beyond etc]** *My duties at the school extend beyond just teaching.* 我在學校的職責不只是教書。| *The regulations do not extend to foreign visitors.* 這些規定不適用於外國遊客。

6 ▸OFFER HELP/THANKS 提供幫助/表示感謝◂ [T] *formal* to offer someone help, sympathy, thanks etc【正式】提供, 給予, 表示: **extend a welcome/greeting/invitation etc** *We'd like to extend a warm welcome to our French visitors.* 我們對法國朋友的到來表示熱烈歡迎。| **extend thanks to sb** (=thank someone officially)〔正式地〕向某人致謝 | **extend condolences/sympathies** (=offer sympathy to someone when someone they know or love dies) 致哀/慰唁 | **extend credit to sb** (=if a bank extends credit to someone it lends them money) 向某人提供貸款

7 ▸ARMS/LEGS ETC 手臂/腿等◂ [T] to stretch out a part of your body 伸開, 舒展: *a bird soaring on extended wings* 展翅高飛的鳥

8 ▸STRENGTH/INTELLIGENCE 力量/智力◂ [T] to make someone use all their strength, intelligence etc, in order to achieve good results 使竭盡全力: *Olympiakos won the match without ever being fully extended.* 奧林比亞高斯未用全力便輕鬆獲勝。

extended fam·i·ly /͵.. '.../ *n* [C] a family group that consists not only of parents and children but also of grandparents, AUNTs etc 大家庭〔指包括(外)祖父母、姑(姨)等在內的親屬〕

ex·ten·sion /ɪk`stɛnʃən; ɪk'stenʃən/ *n* 2 3

1 ▸EXTRA ROOMS 額外房間◂ [C] another room or rooms which are added to a building〔建築的〕擴建部分: *The extension to the National Museum houses the Picasso collection.* 國家美術館收藏的畢加索作品在擴建的展廳展出。

2 ▸TELEPHONE 電話◂ [C] **a)** one of many telephone lines in a large building which all have different numbers 分機: **extension number** *My extension number is 3821.* 我的分機號碼是3821。**b)** one of two or more telephones, usually in someone's house, which all have the same number〔共用一個號碼的〕分機: *Can you put an extension in the bedroom?* 你能在臥室裡安一部分機嗎?

3 ▸EXTRA TIME 額外時間◂ [C usually singular 一般用單數] an additional period of time given to someone in order to finish a job, pay money that they owe etc 展期, 延期: *Donald's been given an extension to finish his thesis.* 唐納德得到寬限期以完成他的論文。| *The pub's got an extension tonight.* (=it will stay open longer than usual) 酒館今晚延時關門。

4 ▸ELECTRIC WIRE 電線◂ [C] also 又作 **extension lead** *BrE*【英】, **extension cord** *AmE*【美】an additional piece of electric wire used when the wire you already have is not long enough 延長線路, 電線延長部分: *Use the extension when you cut the grass.* 割草時請使用外接電源線。

5 ▸CONTROL/INFLUENCE 控制/影響◂ [singular U] a process in which someone's or something's influence or control increases 擴大, 延伸: **[+of]** *the extension of the copyright laws to cover recorded material* 版權法範圍擴大到涵蓋錄製的音像材料

6 ▸MAKING STH BIGGER 使某物變大◂ [singular U] the process of making a road, building etc bigger or longer〔道路、建築等的〕擴建; 延長: **[+of]** *the proposed extension of the London–Cambridge motorway* 延長倫敦—劍橋高速公路的建議

7 by extension used before mentioning something that is naturally connected to or is a natural result of something else 自然地, 當然地: *My primary responsibility is to the company, and by extension to the people who work for it.* 我主要是對公司負責, 當然也就對公司的員工負責。

8 ▸UNIVERSITY/COLLEGE 大學/學院◂ [U] part of a British university or college that offers courses to people who are not full time students〔為非全日制學生開設的〕大學附設部分: **extension course** (=a course done by people who cannot study full time) 大學附設部分的課程

9 ▸STRETCH ARM/LEG 伸展手臂/腿◂ [U] **a)** a process in which you stretch a part of the body 伸展, 舒展: *I had physiotherapy to improve the extension of my right hand.* 我做物理療法來幫助伸展右手。**b)** the position of a part of the body when it is stretched〔身體部分〕伸展開的狀態: *Your leg should now be at full extension.* 你的腿現在應該完全伸直。

ex·ten·sive /ɪk`stɛnsɪv; ɪk'stensɪv/ *adj* **1** covering a large area 廣闊的, 大面積的: *The house stands in extensive grounds.* 這棟房子佔地很大。| **extensive damage/repairs etc** *The storm caused extensive damage.* 暴風雨造成了大範圍的破壞。**2** containing or dealing with a lot of information and details 廣泛的, 全面的: *The abortion issue has been the subject of extensive debate.* 墮胎一直是備受爭議的話題。—**extensively** *adv*: *Despite reading extensively, I still failed the exam.* 雖然進行了廣泛閱讀, 但我考試仍不及格。—**extensiveness** *n* [U] 3

ex·tent /ɪk`stɛnt; ɪk'stent/ *n* **1** [singular] the limit or degree of something's influence etc 限度; 程度: *The success of a marriage depends on the extent to which you are prepared to work at it.* 婚姻的成功取決於你們努力的程度。| **to a certain extent/to some extent** (=used to say that something is partly, but not completely, true) 在某種程度上 *To a certain extent it was my fault that* 

we lost the contract. 我們丢掉合同在某種程度上是我的錯。| **to a great/large extent** (=used to say that something is mainly true) 在很大程度上 *These policies are to a large extent responsible for the region's economic decline.* 這些政策是該地區經濟衰退的主要原因。| **to a lesser/greater extent** (=used when comparing two things to say that one thing has less or more influence) 在較輕/更大程度上 *These changes will affect all managers and to a lesser extent some shop-floor workers.* 這些變化將影響到所有的管理人員，也將在較輕程度上影響到一些車間工人。| **to such an extent/to the extent that** (=used to say that something has affected or influenced something so much that it causes something else to happen) 達到如此程度/達到…的程度 *Violence increased to the extent that residents were afraid to leave their homes.* 暴力事件多到了令居民不敢出門的程度。| **to what extent...?** (=used to ask how big an amount or influence is) 在多大程度上…? *To what extent can we blame the government for this lack of information?* 對於這種信息缺乏，我們能在多大程度上指責政府呢? **2** [U] the size of a large area 方圓，範圍: **full extent of** *From the top window we could see the full extent of the park.* 透過最高的窗戶我們可以看見公園的全景。| **in extent** *The region is over 10,000 square kilometres in extent.* 這個地區的面積超過 10,000 平方公里。**3** [U] the size or degree of something dangerous or difficult, such as an injury or a problem〔傷勢或問題等的〕嚴重性;〔困難的〕程度: *Considering the extent of his injuries he's lucky to be alive.* 就他的傷勢來說，他能活下來真是夠幸運的。| *It would be foolish to underestimate the extent of the problem.* 低估該問題的困難程度是愚蠢的。

ex·ten·u·ate /ɪk`stɛnjʊˏet; ɪk'stenjueɪt/ *v* [T] *formal* to make an action, especially a crime, seem less bad or harmful by suggesting reasons for it【正式】為〔某行為，尤指犯罪行為〕辯解: **extenuating circumstances** (=facts which explain bad or criminal behaviour) 情有可原的具體情況 —**extenuation** /ɪkˏstɛnjʊ`eʃən; ɪkˌstenju'eɪʃən/ *n* [U]

ex·te·ri·or¹ /ɪk`stɪrɪɚ; ɪk'stɪəriə/ *n* [C] **1** [usually singular 一般用單數] the appearance or outside surface of something 外觀; 外表: *Sun, rain and frost had damaged the exterior of the building.* 陽光、雨水和霜侵蝕了該建築的外表。**2 a cool/sullen etc exterior** behaviour that seems calm, unfriendly etc but which often hides a different feeling or attitude 表面上鎮定/陰沉等: *Karl hid his nervousness behind a calm exterior.* 卡爾強作鎮定以掩蓋內心的緊張。**3** a picture, film etc of an outdoor scene 風景畫; 戶外景色畫;(電影) 外景 —opposite 反義詞 INTERIOR¹

exterior² *adj* **1** on the outside or outside surface of something 外部的; 外面的: *The exterior walls need a new coat of paint.* 外牆需要刷新漆了。**2 exterior to** separate or divided from something 與…分離[分開]的 —opposite 反義詞 INTERIOR²

ex·ter·mi·nate /ɪk`stɝməˏnet; ɪk'stɜːmɨneɪt/ *v* [T] to kill large numbers of people or animals of a particular type so that they no longer exist 滅絕，根除 —**exterminator** *n* [C] —**extermination** /ɪkˏstɝmə`neʃən; ɪkˌstɜːmɨ'neɪʃən/ *n* [C,U]

2 **ex·ter·nal** /ɪk`stɝnl; ɪk'stɜːnl/ *adj* **1** connected with the outside of a surface or body 外面的; 外部的: *The external walls were in need of repair.* 外牆需要修補。| **for external use** (=medicine that is for external use must be put on your skin and not swallowed)〔藥〕外用的 **2** coming from outside a particular place or organization 來自外部的，外來的: *Considerable external pressure was put on Congress to override the veto.* 要求國會推翻該否決的外界壓力相當大。| *information from external sources* 來自外部的信息 **3** connected with foreign countries 外國的: *China will not tolerate any external interference in its affairs.* 中國不會容忍任何國家干涉其內政。**4** *BrE* coming from outside a particular school or university【英】來自學校[大學]之外的，外來的: **external examination** (=not arranged by your own school or university) 校外(主持的)考試 | **external examiner** (=someone from outside a particular school or university who examines its students) 校外考官 **5 external ear/gill/genitals etc** *technical* a part of an animal's body that is on the outer surface of the body rather than inside it【術語】〔動物長在身體〕外部的耳朵/鰓/生殖器等 —opposite 反義詞 INTERNAL —**externally** *adv*

ex·ter·nal·ize also 又作 **-ise** *BrE*【英】/ɪk`stɝnlˏaɪz; ɪk'stɜːnəlaɪz/ *v* [T] to express inner feelings 表露〔內心感受〕—**externalization** /ɪkˏstɝnlə`zeʃən; ɪkˌstɜːnəlaɪ'zeɪʃən/ *n* [C,U]

ex·ter·nals /ɪk`stɝnlz; ɪk'stɜːnlz/ *n* [plural] the outer appearance of a situation 外觀，外表; 外在形式

ex·tinct /ɪk`stɪŋkt; ɪk'stɪŋkt/ *adj* **1** an extinct animal, plant, language etc no longer exists 滅絕的，絕種的: *Dinosaurs have been extinct for millions of years.* 恐龍已滅絕數千萬年了。**2** an extinct belief or custom no longer exists〔信仰或風俗〕已廢棄的 **3** an extinct VOLCANO no longer erupts (ERUPT (1))〔火山〕死的，不再活躍的

ex·tinc·tion /ɪk`stɪŋkʃən; ɪk'stɪŋkʃən/ *n* [U] **1** a situation in which a particular kind of animal, plant etc no longer exists 滅絕，絕種: *Conservationists are trying to save the whale from extinction.* 生態環境保護主義者正努力挽救鯨類以防止其滅絕。| **face extinction/be threatened with extinction** *Many endangered species now face extinction.* 許多瀕危物種現已面臨滅絕。**2** a process in which a belief, way of life, feeling etc is destroyed or stops existing〔信仰、生活方式或感情等〕遭毀滅; 消亡: *Their traditional way of life seems doomed to extinction.* 他們的傳統生活方式似乎注定要消亡。

ex·tin·guish /ɪk`stɪŋgwɪʃ; ɪk'stɪŋgwɪʃ/ *v* [T] *formal*【正式】**1** to make a fire or light stop burning or shining 熄滅〔火、光〕: *Please extinguish all cigarettes.* 請把所有的香煙都熄滅。**2** to destroy an idea or feeling or make it stop existing 使〔想法或感情〕破滅; 使消亡: *All hope was almost extinguished.* 幾乎所有的希望都破滅了。

ex·tin·guish·er /ɪk`stɪŋgwɪʃɚ; ɪk'stɪŋgwɪʃə/ *n* [C] *informal* a FIRE EXTINGUISHER【非正式】滅火器

ex·tir·pate /`ɛkstɚˏpet; 'ekstɜːpeɪt/ *v* [T] *formal* to completely destroy something that is unpleasant or unwanted【正式】消滅，根除 —**extirpation** /ˏɛkstɚ`peʃən; ˌekstɜː'peɪʃən/ [U]

ex·tol /ɪk`stol; ɪk'stəʊl/ *v* [T] *formal* to praise something very much【正式】讚美，頌揚: **extol the virtues/merits of** *a speech extolling the merits of free enterprise* 讚頌自由企業制的講話

ex·tort /ɪk`stɔrt; ɪk'stɔːt/ *v* [T] to illegally force someone to give you money by threatening them 敲詐，勒索〔錢財〕: **extort money from/out of sb** *Landlords tried to cover their losses by extorting high rents from tenants.* 地主向佃戶勒索租金以彌補自己的損失。—**extortion** /ɪk`stɔrʃən; ɪk'stɔːʃən/ *n* [U]: *Confessions were obtained by extortion.* 招供是逼出來的。—**extortioner** *n* [C] —**extortionist** *n* [C]

ex·tor·tion·ate /ɪk`stɔrʃənɪt; ɪk'stɔːʃənɨt/ *adj* an extortionate price, demand, etc is extremely high〔價格、要求等〕過分的，過高的: *Most drivers under 25 can only get insurance at extortionate rates.* 大多數 25 歲以下的司機要想獲得保險需交付極高的保費。—**extortionately** *adv*

extra- /ɛkstrə; ekstrə/ *prefix* outside; beyond 在…之外; 超出: *extragalactic* (=outside our GALAXY) 銀河系外的 | *extramarital sex* (=between people who are not married to each other) 婚外性行為

ex·tra¹ /`ɛkstrə; 'ekstrə/ *adj* more of something, in addition to the usual or standard amount or number 額外的，另外的: *Could you get an extra loaf of bread?* 你能多拿一條麵包嗎? | *Alan had taken extra care with his appearance that evening.* 艾倫那天晚上格外注重

儀表。| *Residents can use the gym at no extra cost.* 居民使用體育館可不必另外付費。| **extra ten minutes/three metres/five kilos etc** *I asked for an extra day to finish the work.* 我要求額外再加一天來完成工作。

extra² *adv* **1 cost/earn/pay extra** to cost, earn, or pay more money than the usual amount 額外花費/掙得/支付: *I earn extra for working on Sunday.* 我星期天工作獲取額外收入。| **be extra** (=cost an additional amount of money) 額外付費, 另外收費 *Dinner costs $15 but wine is extra.* 晚餐費為15美元, 但酒水另算。| **ten minutes/three metres/five kilos extra** *I got 2 metres extra to make the curtains.* 我還有兩米布可以做簾子。**2** [+adj/adv] used to emphasize an adjective or adverb 特別地, 非常: *You're going to have to work extra hard to pass the exam.* 你要格外用功才能通過考試。

extra³ *n* [C] **1** something which is added to a basic product or service which improves it and also costs more 另外計價的項目: **optional extra** (=something attractive or comfortable that you can choose to have or not) 可選擇的額外事物 *Tinted windows and a sunroof are optional extras.* 帶色玻璃窗和活動車頂是可選的額外配件。**2** something attractive or helpful that you do not get more money for 不另收費的好東西: *Lena did a lot of little extras for him that weren't part of her job description.* 莉娜在職責範圍之外為他義務提供了許多幫助。**3** an actor in a film who does not say anything but is part of a crowd〔電影中的〕臨時演員 **4** a special EDITION of a newspaper containing important news〔報紙的〕號外: *Extra! Extra! Read all about it!* 號外!號外!來看哪!

ex·tract¹ /ɪk`strækt; ɪk'strækt/ *v* [T] **1** to remove an object from somewhere, especially by pulling it 取出, 拔出: *You'll have to have that wisdom tooth extracted.* 你得把那顆智齒拔掉。| **extract sth from sth** *Prue managed to extract the stopper from the bottle.* 普呂設法把瓶塞拔了出來。**2** to carefully remove a substance from another substance which contains it, using a machine, chemical process etc 採掘; 提煉: *47 tonnes of gold have been extracted at the mine.* 這座礦已採掘了47公噸黃金。| **extract sth from sth** *The nuts are crushed to extract the oil from them.* 這些堅果被碾碎後用來榨油。**3** to skilfully remove something which is among a lot of other objects or inside something 靈巧地取出, 抽出: **extract sth from sth** *James slowly extracted a £5 note from his wallet.* 詹姆斯慢慢從錢包裡抽出一張五英鎊的紙幣。**4** to find out information or get money from someone who does not want to give it by asking questions or using physical force 套出〔信息〕; 逼問; 索得〔錢財〕: **extract sth from sb** *I finally managed to extract the truth from her.* 我最終設法從她嘴裡套出了事實真相。

ex·tract² /`ɛkstrækt; 'ekstrækt/ *n* **1** [C] a short piece of writing, music etc taken from a particular book, piece of music etc, especially in order to show what it is like 摘錄; 選段: **[+from]** *I've only seen short extracts from the film.* 我只是看過那部電影的部分片斷。**2** [C,U] a substance taken from another substance by using a special process 提煉物, 提取物: **vanilla/malt/yeast extract** *Add one teaspoon of vanilla extract.* 加入一茶匙香草精。

ex·trac·tion /ɪk`strækʃən; ɪk'strækʃən/ *n* **1** [C,U] the process of removing an object or substance from inside something else 取出; 提煉: **[+of]** *the extraction of uranium from uranium ore* 從鈾礦石中提取鈾 **2 be of French/Russian/Italian etc extraction** to be from a French, Russian etc family even though you were not born in that country 祖籍法國/俄羅斯/意大利等

ex·trac·tor /ɛk`stræktɚ; ɪk'stræktə/ also 又作 **extractor fan** /·'·· ·/ *n* [C] a machine for removing air that is hot or smells unpleasant from a kitchen, factory etc 排氣扇; 抽油煙機

ex·tra·cur·ric·u·lar /ˌɛkstrəkə`rɪkjələ; ˌekstrəkə'rɪkjələ◂/ *adj* extracurricular activities are not part of the course that a student is doing 課外的

ex·tra·di·ta·ble /`ɛkstrəˌdaɪtəbl; 'ekstrədaɪtəbəl/ *adj* an extraditable crime is one for which someone can be sent back to the country where the crime happened to be judged in a court of law〔罪犯〕可引渡的: *Terrorism is an extraditable offense.* 恐怖主義罪犯可以被引渡。

ex·tra·dite /`ɛkstrəˌdaɪt; 'ekstrədaɪt/ *v* [T+from/to] to use a legal process to send someone who may be guilty of a crime back to the country where the crime happened in order to judge them in a court of law 引渡 —**extradition** /ˌɛkstrə`dɪʃən; ˌekstrə'dɪʃən/ *n* [C,U]: *an extradition order* 引渡命令

ex·tra·ju·di·cial /ˌɛkstrədʒu`dɪʃəl; ˌekstrədʒuː'dɪʃəl◂/ *adj* beyond or outside the ordinary powers of the law 法律制裁範圍以外的; 法律管轄以外的

ex·tra·mar·i·tal /ˌɛkstrə`mærətḷ; ˌekstrə'mærḷtl◂/ *adj* an extramarital sexual relationship is one that someone has with a person who is not their husband or wife 婚外(性關係)的

ex·tra·mu·ral /ˌɛkstrə`mjurəl; ˌekstrə'mjʊərəl◂/ *adj* **1** connected with a place or organization but happening or done outside it 某地點以外的; 機構以外的: *extramural activities* 機構外的活動 **2** *especially BrE* extramural courses, studies etc involve students from outside a particular college or university【尤英】校外的, 校外學生參與的 —opposite 反義詞 INTRAMURAL

ex·tra·ne·ous /ɪk`strenɪəs; ɪk'streɪnɪəs/ *adj* **1** not belonging to or directly connected with a particular subject or problem; IRRELEVANT 外部的; 無直接關係的: **[+to]** *Such details are extraneous to the matter in hand.* 這些細節與手頭這件事沒有直接關係。**2** coming from outside 外來的: *extraneous noises* 外部的噪聲 —**extraneously** *adv*

ex·tra·or·di·na·ri·ly /ɪk`strɔrdṇˌɛrɪlɪ; ɪk'strɔːdənərḷli/ *adv especially BrE*【尤英】**1** [+adj/adv] extremely 極其, 極端地: **extraordinarily beautiful/difficult/successful etc** *an extraordinarily beautiful young boy* 很好看的小男孩 **2** in a way that seems strange 奇怪地: *I'm afraid Jane can behave quite extraordinarily at times.* 恐怕簡有時行為頗為古怪。

ex·tra·or·di·na·ry /ɪk`strɔrdṇˌɛrɪ; ɪk'strɔːdənəri/ *adj* **1** very much better, more beautiful, or more impressive than usual 非凡的, 出色的: *a woman of extraordinary beauty* 容貌出眾的女子 **2** very unusual or surprising because it would normally be very unlikely to happen or exist 令人驚嘆的, 極不尋常的: *the extraordinary landscapes of Cappodocia* 卡帕多基亞奇特的地貌景觀 | **quite/most extraordinary** *BrE* (=very unusual)【英】非常奇怪的, 令人驚奇的 *Chris's behaviour that morning was quite extraordinary.* 克里斯那天上午的行為非常奇怪。| **extraordinary thing to do/say/happen** *What an extraordinary thing to do!* 做這件事多奇怪呀! | **how extraordinary!** *BrE spoken* (=used to express surprise)【英口】太奇怪了! *"Well then Jim got down on all fours and started barking like a dog." "How extraordinary!"* "然後吉姆就手腳同時着地像狗一樣叫了起來。""太奇怪了!" **3 extraordinary meeting/session etc** a meeting which takes place in addition to the usual ones 特別會議 **4 envoy/ambassador/minister extraordinary** an official employed for a special purpose, in addition to the usual officials 特使; 特命公使

S3 W3

ex·trap·o·late /ɪks`træpəˌlet; ɪk'stræpəleɪt/ *v* [I,T] **1** to make a guess about something in the future from facts that you already know 推斷, 推知: **extrapolate sth from sth** *It's my job to extrapolate future developments from contemporary trends.* 我的工作是依據現時的趨勢推斷未來的發展。**2** *technical* to guess a value that you do not know by continuing a curve which is based on values that you already know【術語】外推 —**extrapolation** /ɛkˌstræpo`leʃən; ɪkˌstræpə'leɪʃən/ *n* [C,U]

extra sen·so·ry per·cep·tion /ˌ·· ···· ·'··/ *n* [U] ESP (1) 超感知覺

ex·tra·ter·res·tri·al¹ /ˌɛkstrətə`restrɪəl; ˌekstrətə-

E

'restriəl◂/ *n* [C] a living creature that people think may exist on another PLANET 外星生物

extraterrestrial² *adj* connected with things that exist outside the Earth 地球外的; 宇宙的

ex·tra·ter·ri·to·ri·al /ˌɛkstrəˌtɛrəˋtɔrɪəl; ˌekstrəterɜ-'tɔːriəl◂/ *adj* **1** *formal* outside a particular country【正式】境外的, 疆界以外的 **2** *law* extra-territorial rights, powers etc are governed from outside a country or area【法律】治外法權的, 不受當地法律限制的: *an extraterritorial jurisdiction treaty* 治外法權司法協議 —**extraterritoriality** /ˌɛkstrəˌtɛrətorɪˋæləti; ˌekstrə-terɜˌtɔːri'ælɜti/ *n* [U]

extra time /ˌ·· '·/ *n* [U] *especially BrE* a period of usually thirty minutes added to the end of football games to give one of the two teams a chance to win【尤英】〔足球〕加時賽; OVERTIME (4) *AmE*【美】

ex·trav·a·gant /ɪkˋstrævəgənt; ɪk'strævəgənt/ *adj* **1** spending a lot of money on things that are not necessary〔花錢〕浪費的, 無必要的: *It was very extravagant of you to spend £500 on a dress.* 花 500 英鎊去買一件衣服, 那太奢侈了。**2 extravagant with sth** using too much of something or wasting it 大手大腳, 過度使用[浪費]某物: *We mustn't be too extravagant with the electricity.* 我們決不能濫用電力。**3** very impressive because of being very expensive, beautiful etc 豪華的; 鋪張的: *Myra and Paul decided to give an extravagant dinner party.* 邁拉和保羅決定舉行一次豪華晚宴。**4** ideas or behaviour that are extravagant are too extreme and are not sensible 過度的; 越軌的: *extravagant claims about the effectiveness of the system* 對系統有效性的誇大言辭 —**extravagantly** *adv* —**extravagance** *n* [C,U]

ex·trav·a·gan·za /ɪkˌstrævəˋgænzə; ɪkˌstrævə'gænzə/ *n* [C] a very large and expensive entertainment 鋪張華麗的娛樂表演

ex·tra·vert /ˋɛkstrəˌvɝt; 'ekstrəvɜːt/ *n* [C] another spelling of EXTROVERT extrovert 的另一種拼法

ex·treme¹ /ɪkˋstrim; ɪk'striːm/ *adj* **1** [only before noun 僅用於名詞前] very great in degree 極大的; 極度的: *Extreme poverty still exists in many rural areas.* 農村許多地區仍處於赤貧狀態。**2 extreme south/point/end/limit etc** the extreme south etc is the place furthest towards the south etc 最南端/端點/盡頭/極限等 **3** extreme opinions, beliefs, or organizations, especially political ones, are considered by most people to be unacceptable and unreasonable 極端的, 偏激的: *extreme right-wing nationalists* 極右翼的民族主義分子 **4** very unusual and severe 極為異常的, 極嚴厲的: *Her ideas about raising kids have always been a little extreme.* 她關於教養孩子的主意總是有點怪僻。| **extreme example/case** *Social workers were horrified by this extreme case of cruelty.* 社會工作者們被這一極其殘酷的事例驚呆了。

extreme² *n* [C] **1** something that goes beyond normal limits, so that it seems very unusual and unacceptable 極端: *We had every extreme of weather that weekend – gales, snow, and sunshine.* 那個週末天氣經歷了劇烈的變化, 一會兒颶大風, 一會兒下雪, 一會兒又陽光燦爛。| **be driven to extremes** *Driven to extremes by the rioting, the government imposed a six pm curfew.* 為對付騷亂, 政府被迫採取了下午六點開始宵禁的極端做法。| **go to extremes/take sth to extremes** (=behave in a way that goes beyond normal limits, especially in order to achieve something) 走極端 | **go to the opposite extreme/go from one extreme to the other** (=change from being extreme in one way to being extreme in a completely different way) 走到另一個極端/從一個極端走到另一個極端 **2 in the extreme** to a very great degree 極度, 非常: *My great-aunt had been generous in the extreme over the years.* 我的姨婆這些年來一直極為慷慨。

ex·treme·ly /ɪkˋstrimlɪ; ɪk'striːmli/ *adv* to a very great degree 極度, 極其: *I'm extremely sorry to have troubled you.* 給你添了麻煩, 我實在是很抱歉。

extremis *n* —see 見 IN EXTREMIS

ex·trem·is·m /ɪkˋstrimɪzəm; ɪk'striːmɪzəm/ *n* [U] opinions, ideas, and actions, especially political or religious ones, that most people think are unreasonable and unacceptable 極端主義, 極端性

ex·trem·ist /ɪkˋstrimɪst; ɪk'striːmɜst/ *n* [C] someone who has extreme political opinions and aims, and who is willing to do unusual or illegal things in order to achieve them 極端主義者, 過激分子: *The bomb was planted by right-wing extremists.* 炸彈是右翼極端分子放置的。—**extremist** *adj*

ex·trem·i·ty /ɪkˋstrɛmətɪ; ɪk'stremɜti/ *n* **1** [C often plural 常用複數] one of the parts of your body that is furthest away from the centre, for example your fingers and toes 人體離中心最遠的部位〈如手指、腳趾〉**2** [U] the degree to which a belief, opinion, situation, or action goes beyond what is usually thought to be acceptable 極端性, 偏激: *The committee was uncomfortable about the extremity of the proposal.* 委員會因該建議太極端而感到不安。**3** [C] the part that is furthest away from the centre of something 末端, 端點: *A land-locked stretch of water formed the western extremity of the Gulf of Tajura.* 一片內陸水域構成了塔朱拉灣的最西端。

ex·tri·cate /ˋɛkstrɪˌket; 'ekstrɜkeɪt/ *v* [T] **1** to escape from a difficult or embarrassing situation 使擺脫, 使脫離: **[+from]** *By 1897 his lawyers had managed to extricate him from the contract.* 到 1897 年時, 他的律師幫他擺脫了那份合約的束縛。| **extricate yourself** *I desperately tried to think of a way to extricate myself from Mrs. Bedford's questioning.* 我拚命想辦法要擺脫貝德福德夫人的追問。**2** to remove someone or something from a place in which they are trapped 解救, 救出: *Firemen had to extricate the driver from the wreckage.* 消防隊員得把司機從殘骸中救出來。—**extrication** /ˌɛkstrəˋkeʃən; ˌekstrɜ'keɪʃən/ *n* [U]

ex·tro·vert, extravert /ˋɛkstroˌvɝt; 'ekstrəvɜːt/ *n* [C] someone who is active and confident, and who enjoys spending time with other people 性格外向的人: *Gini was an extrovert and loved to perform to a crowd.* 吉尼性格外向, 愛在眾人面前表演。—**extrovert** *adj* —opposite 反義詞 INTROVERT

ex·tro·vert·ed /ˋɛkstroˌvɝtɪd; 'ekstrəvɜːtɜd/ *adj* having a confident character and enjoying the company of other people 性格外向的 —**extroversion** /ˌɛkstroˋvɝʃən; ˌekstrə'vɜːʃən/ *n* [U] —opposite 反義詞 INTROVERTED

ex·trude /ɪkˋstrud; ɪk'struːd/ *v* [T] *formal*【正式】**1** to push or force something out through a hole 擠出 **2** *technical* to force plastic or metal through a hole so that it has a particular shape【術語】擠壓成形 —**extrusion** /ɪkˋstruʒən; ɪk'struːʒən/ *n* [C,U]

ex·u·be·rant /ɪgˋzjubərənt; ɪg'zjuːbərənt/ *adj* **1** happy and cheerful, and full of energy and excitement 興高采烈的, 精神煥發的 **2** plants that are exuberant are healthy and growing very quickly〔植物〕茁壯的; 茂盛的 —**exuberance** *n* [U] —**exuberantly** *adv*

ex·ude /ɪgˋzjud; ɪg'zjuːd/ *v* **1 exude confidence/sympathy etc** if you exude a particular quality, it is easy to see that you have a lot of it 充分顯露信心/同情等 **2** [I, T] to flow out slowly and steadily, or to make something do this (使) 滲出; (使) 緩慢流出: *Trunkfishes exude a poisonous liquid that can kill other fish.* 箱鲀分泌一種毒液, 可以毒殺其他魚類。

ex·ult /ɪgˋzʌlt; ɪg'zʌlt/ *v* [I] *formal* to show that you are very happy and proud, especially because you have succeeded in doing something【正式】歡欣鼓舞; 洋洋得意: **[+at/in]** *They exulted at their victory.* 他們為勝利而興高采烈。| **[+over]** *The people exulted over their fallen enemies.* 人們為擊敗敵人而歡欣鼓舞。—**exultation** /ˌɛgzʌlˋteʃən; ˌegzʌl'teɪʃən/ *n* [U]

ex·ul·tant /ɪgˋzʌltn̩t; ɪg'zʌltənt/ *adj formal* very happy or proud, especially because you have succeeded in doing something【正式】歡欣鼓舞的; 洋洋得意的: *Exultant crowds were dancing in the streets.* 歡騰的人羣在

街上跳舞。—**exultantly** *adv*

-ey /ɪ; i/ *suffix* [in adjectives 構成形容詞] the form used for -Y especially after y -y 的變體〔尤用於以 y 結尾的詞後面〕: *clayey soil* 黏質土壤

1 1 **eye[1]** /aɪ; aɪ/ *n* [C]

① **BODY PART** 身體部位
② **WATCH/SEE** 注視/看見
③ **LOOK AT** 看
④ **LOOK AFTER** 照顧
⑤ **WATCH FOR** 小心留意
⑥ **NOTICE** 注意
⑦ **DISAGREE/DISBELIEVE** 不贊成/不相信
⑧ **SURPRISE** 驚奇
⑨ **LOVE/SEXUAL ATTRACTION** 愛/性吸引力
⑩ **JUDGE** 判斷
⑪ **SPOKEN PHRASES** 口語片語
⑫ **PURPOSE** 目的
⑬ **OTHER MEANINGS** 其他意思

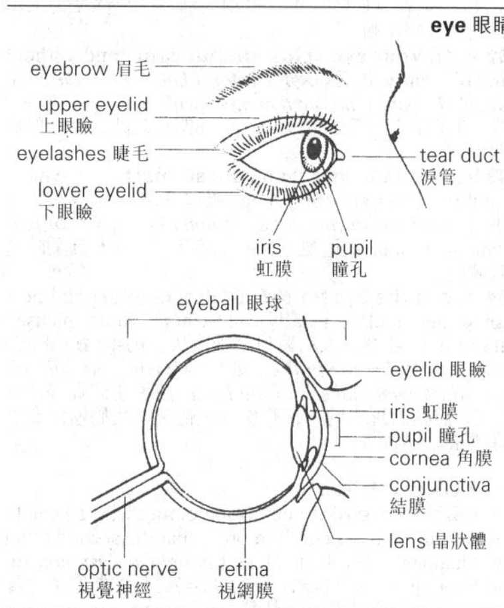

① **BODY PART** 身體部位

1 one of the two parts of the body that people and animals use to see 眼睛: *Annie has blue eyes.* 安妮的眼睛是藍色的。| *Close your eyes and count to ten.* 閉上你的眼睛, 數到十。

2 blue-eyed/one-eyed/bright-eyed/wide-eyed etc having blue eyes, one eye, bright eyes, eyes that are wide open etc 藍眼睛的/一隻眼睛的/眼睛明亮的/雙目圓睜的等

② **WATCH/SEE** 注視/看見

3 have/keep your eye on sb to be carefully watching everything that someone does, especially because you do not trust them to do things properly 注視[密切注意]某人(的舉動): *I've got my eye on you now, so you do as you're told!* 我盯着你呢, 所以你要按吩咐的去做!

4 clap/lay/set eyes on sb/sth *spoken* an expression meaning to see someone or something, used especially when you are surprised or shocked【口】看見[注意到]某人/某事物〔尤用於感到驚訝時〕: *I'd never clapped eyes on him before in my life!* 我以前從沒見過他!

5 the naked eye if you can see something with the naked eye, you can see it without using any artificial help such as a TELESCOPE or microscope 肉眼: *On a clear night these stars can be seen with the naked eye.* 在天氣晴朗的夜晚, 憑肉眼就可以看到這些星星。| **invisible to the naked eye** (=cannot be seen without artificial help) 肉眼看不到的

6 be all eyes *especially spoken* to watch carefully what is happening or what someone is doing【尤口】全神貫注地看: *We were all eyes as he slowly drew back the curtain.* 當他慢慢拉開幕布時, 我們都目不轉睛地看着。

7 in front of/before your (very) eyes *especially spoken* an expression meaning happening so that you can clearly see it, used especially when what you see is surprising or shocking【尤口】就在你眼前, 當着某人的面: *Ladies and gentlemen, before your very eyes I will now make this rabbit disappear.* 女士們, 先生們, 我現在要當着諸位的面讓這隻兔子消失。

③ **LOOK AT** 看

8 catch sb's eye a) to attract someone's attention and make them look at something 引起某人注目, 吸引某人的目光: *All of a sudden something red caught his eye.* 突然, 一個紅色的東西引起了他的注意。**b)** to look at someone at the same moment that they are looking at you 碰到某人的目光: *I caught Ben's eye in the rear-view mirror and knew what he was thinking.* 我從後視鏡裡看到本的目光, 明白了他在想甚麼。

9 eye contact if you have eye contact with someone, you look directly at them and they look directly at you 對視, 相互直視: *Always establish eye contact with the customer – it inspires confidence.* 要與客戶保持目光交流, 這樣能增強他對你的信任。

10 cannot take your eyes off sb/sth to be unable to stop looking at someone or something, especially because they are very attractive or interesting 無法將目光從某人身上/某物上挪開: *She was so beautiful I simply couldn't take my eyes off her.* 她太漂亮了, 我簡直無法將目光從她身上挪開。

11 look sb in the eye [usually in negatives 一般用於否定句] to look directly and steadily at someone because you are not embarrassed or ashamed 直視[正視]某人: *I couldn't look him in the eye afterwards, knowing that I had lost all that money.* 我無法再正視他的目光, 我已把那筆錢全丢了。

12 run/cast your eye over sth to look at something quickly without reading it in detail 匆匆看[瀏覽]某物: *Could you just cast your eye over this report before I hand it in?* 我把報告上交之前你能過目一下嗎?

④ **LOOK AFTER** 照顧

13 keep your eye on sth/sb to look after someone or something and make sure that they are safe 照看[照料]某物/某人: *Mary offered to keep an eye on the baby while I went out.* 瑪麗提出可以在我外出期間照看嬰兒。

⑤ **WATCH FOR** 小心留意

14 keep an eye out for sth to hope to notice or find something 留意[想找到]某物: *Could you keep an eye out for my red pen? I seem to have mislaid it.* 你能留意一下我的那支紅鋼筆嗎? 我不知道放哪兒了。

E

15 keep your eyes open/peeled *spoken* to watch carefully for something【口】密切注意, 留神: *Keep your eyes peeled for a campsite.* 留神找一塊營地。

⑥ **NOTICE** 注意

16 have eyes in the back of your head to know what is happening all around you, even when this might seem impossible 腦後長眼睛〔知道身邊發生的一切〕: *You need to have eyes in the back of your head to be a teacher.* 作為教師, 你需要能眼觀六路。

17 have eyes like a hawk to notice every small detail or everything that is happening, and therefore to be difficult to deceive 有鷹一樣的眼睛; 目光犀利: *We never got away with anything in Mrs. Podell's class – she had eyes like a hawk.* 在波德爾夫人的課上, 我們幹甚麼都瞞不過她 —— 她眼睛尖着呢。

18 have your eye on sth to have noticed something that you want to buy or have 看中某物: *I've got my eye on a nice little sports car that I'm saving up for.* 我看中了一輛漂亮的小跑車, 現在正攢錢呢。

⑦ **DISAGREE/DISBELIEVE** 不贊成/不相信

19 not see eye to eye to always disagree with someone 一向〔與某人〕看法不一致: *Liz never saw eye to eye with her daughter-in-law.* 利茲與她的兒媳總想不到一塊兒。

20 my eye! *spoken* used to express surprise or disagreement【口】天哪! 胡說!〔用於表示驚奇或不同意〕: *A diamond necklace my eye! That was glass!* 一串鑽石項鏈, 不對! 那項鏈是玻璃的!

21 in a pig's eye! *AmE spoken* used to show that you do not believe what someone is saying【美口】不可能!〔表示不相信〕: *Dan said he got up early to do all his chores. In a pig's eye he did!* 丹說他早早起來把他所有的家務活都做了。才沒那回事呢!

⑧ **SURPRISE** 驚奇

22 not be able to believe your eyes *spoken* used when you see something very surprising【口】難以相信自己的眼睛: *I couldn't believe my eyes – there she was, stark naked!* 我簡直不敢相信自己的眼睛 —— 她就在那裡, 渾身一絲不掛!

23 eyes popping out of your head also 又作 **eyes out on stalks** *BrE especially spoken* used when you are very surprised or shocked by something you see【英, 尤口】雙目圓睜

⑨ **LOVE/SEXUAL ATTRACTION** 愛/性吸引力

24 make eyes at sb/give sb the eye to look at someone in a way that shows you find them sexually attractive 眉目傳情; 向某人送秋波: *Janet spent the whole evening making eyes at other men.* 珍妮特整個晚上都在向別的男人擠眉弄眼, 傳送秋波。

25 only have eyes for sb if someone only has eyes for someone else, they only love and are interested in that one person 只愛某人一個; 對某人情有獨鍾: *I knew it was hopeless – Mark only had eyes for his wife.* 我知道那是毫無希望的 —— 馬克只愛他妻子一個人。

26 have your eye on sb to notice someone, especially because you think they are attractive 注意到某人〔尤指看中某人〕: *Mark's got his eye on that new girl in the accounts department.* 馬克看中了會計部那個新來的女孩。| *I hear you've got your eye on a new player for the team.* 我聽說你已經相中了一名新選手想讓他加入球隊。

⑩ **JUDGE** 判斷

27 have a (good) eye for sth to be good at noticing and recognizing what is attractive, valuable, of good quality etc 對某事物有鑑賞眼光: *Gail has a good eye for colour.* 蓋爾對色彩頗具眼光。

28 in the eyes of the law/the world/the police etc in the opinion or judgment of the law, the world, the police etc 從法律/世界/警察等的角度來看: *In the eyes of the law stealing is an offence, no matter what your motives.* 從法律的角度來看, 偷竊是一種犯罪行為, 無論其動機是甚麼。

29 to my eye *spoken* used when you want to give your opinion about the way something looks【口】我覺得, 在我看來: *To my eye the paint seemed darker than it had done in the shop.* 我覺得這漆比店中刷的要暗一些。

30 get/keep your eye in *BrE* to begin to practise or to continue practising your ability to judge the speed and direction of the ball in games such as CRICKET (2) and tennis【英】〔板球或網球等運動中〕訓練判斷球的速度和運動方向的眼力

⑪ **SPOKEN PHRASES** 口語片語

31 be up to your eyes in sth to be very busy doing something 十分忙碌地做某事: *I really can't take on anything else just now – I'm up to my eyes in paperwork as it is.* 我現在真的無法再承擔別的活 —— 這些文書工作讓我忙得團團轉。

32 with your eyes closed/shut easily and without any difficulty 輕而易舉地: *I don't know why you're so worried – you could run that place with your eyes closed!* 我不明白你為甚麼這麼擔心 —— 你閉着眼睛也能管理那個地方!

33 have eyes bigger than your stomach to take more food than you are able to eat 眼饞肚飽; 眼睛大, 肚子小: *I can't finish this cake – I must have eyes bigger than my stomach!* 這塊蛋糕我吃不下了 —— 我真是眼饞肚飽啊!

34 one in the eye for *BrE* a defeat or disappointment for someone else, usually used when you are pleased about it【英】令某人高興但令他人失望的事: *If we win the cup it'll be one in the eye for Martin – he said we wouldn't even make it to the final.* 如果我們贏得杯賽冠軍, 將是對馬丁的一個打擊 —— 他曾說我們連決賽也進不去。

⑫ **PURPOSE** 目的

35 with an eye to if you do something with an eye to something else, you do it in order that the second thing will happen 指望, 期待: *Davies bought several houses, with an eye to making a quick profit.* 戴維斯買了好幾幢房子, 指望着能賺一筆快錢。

36 with an eye to the main chance an expression meaning wanting to take advantage of any possible chance to succeed, usually used in a disapproving way〔為成功而〕不錯過任何機會, 不惜利用任何機會〔通常含貶義〕

⑬ **OTHER MEANINGS** 其他意思

37 more to sth/sb than meets the eye if there is more to a situation, problem, or person than meets the eye, they are more complicated than they seem to be at first 某事/某人比(外表)看起來要複雜: *I reckon there's more to this 'relocation' business than meets the eye.* 我覺得"重新安置"這件事並不像看起來那樣簡單。

38 with your eyes open knowing fully what the problems, difficulties, results etc of a situation might be 心知肚明: *You went into this with your eyes open, so it's no use complaining now!* 在做這件事之前你很清楚它可能有甚麼後果, 所以現在抱怨沒有用!

39 close/shut your eyes to sth to ignore something or pretend that you do not know it is happening 不理會[假裝不知道]某事: *I closed my eyes to the fact that she wasn't supposed to be there, and bought her a drink.* 她不應該在那裡, 但我不管這些, 還是給她買了杯酒喝。

40 drop/lower your eyes to move your eyes so that you are looking at a point lower than where you were looking before, especially because you are shy 往下看; 垂下眼簾〔尤指因為害羞〕: *Melissa lowered her eyes demurely as he came into the room.* 他走進房間時, 梅

利莎羞澀地垂下眼簾。
41 for your eyes only used to say that something is secret and must only be seen by one particular person〔密件〕只供某人親閱
42 an eye for an eye a system in which you punish someone by hurting them in the same way as they hurt someone else 以眼還眼，以牙還牙：*An eye for an eye is no way to run a civilized justice system.* 文明的司法系統不允許以眼還眼、以牙還牙的行為。
43 ►NEEDLE 針◄ the hole in a needle that you put the thread through 針眼 —see picture at 參見 NEEDLE[1] 圖
44 ►CLOTHING 服裝◄ a small circle or U-shaped piece of metal used together with a hook for fastening clothes (鈎)扣，(鈎)環
45 ►STORM 暴風雨◄ the calm centre of a storm, especially a CYCLONE 風眼〔尤指氣旋的中心〕
46 ►POTATO 馬鈴薯◄ a dark spot on a potato from which a new plant can grow 芽眼 —see also 另見 BLACK EYE, CAT'S EYE, PRIVATE EYE, RED EYE, **the apple of sb's eye** (APPLE (2)), **not bat an eye/eyelid** (BAT[2] (2)), BIRD'S-EYE VIEW, **turn a blind eye (to)** (BLIND[1] (2b)), **see sth out of the corner of your eye** (CORNER[1] (8)), **cry your eyes out** (CRY[1] (1)), **the evil eye** (EVIL[1] (5)), **give sb the glad eye** (GLAD (8)), **in your mind's eye** (MIND[1] (43)), **here's mud in your eye** (MUD (4)), **open sb's eyes (to)** (OPEN[2] (3b)), **in the public eye** (PUBLIC[1] (4)), **make sheep's eyes at** (SHEEP (4)), **a sight for sore eyes** (SIGHT[1] (11)), **in the twinkling of an eye** (TWINKLE[1] (3)), **keep a weather eye on** (WEATHER[1] (5)), **pull the wool over sb's eyes** (WOOL (4))

eye² *present participle* **eyeing** *or* **eying** *v* [T] to look at someone or something with interest, especially because you do not trust them or because you want something 審視，盯着看：*The child eyed me with curiosity.* 那個小孩好奇地看着我。| *Julian sat there eyeing my brandy.* 朱利安坐在那裡，眼睛盯着我的白蘭地。

eye sb ↔ **up** *phr v* [T] *informal* to look at someone in a way that shows you think they are sexually attractive【非正式】〔因認為某人很性感而〕盯着看，眼睛在某人身上打轉：*They all stood in a corner, eyeing up the local girls.* 他們都站在角落裡，眼睛在那些本地女孩身上轉來轉去。

eye·ball¹ /ˈaɪˌbɔl; ˈaɪbɔːl/ *n* [C] **1** the round ball that forms the whole of your eye, including the part inside your head 眼球 —see picture at 參見 EYE[1] 圖 **2 eyeball to eyeball** if two people are eyeball to eyeball, they are directly facing each other, especially in an angry or threatening way 面對面〔尤指怒目相視〕：*an eyeball-to-eyeball confrontation* 怒目相視的對抗

eyeball² *v* [T] *informal* to look directly and closely at something【非正式】盯住；打量：*They eyeballed us suspiciously before speaking.* 在開口之前，他們懷疑地打量了我們一番。

eye·brow /ˈaɪˌbraʊ; ˈaɪbraʊ/ *n* [C] **1** the line of hair above your eye 眉(毛) —see picture at 參見 EYE[1] 圖 **2 raise your eyebrows** to move your eyebrows upwards in order to show surprise or disapproval 揚起眉毛〔表示驚訝或反對〕：*"Really?" she said, raising one eyebrow slightly.* "真的嗎?"她說，一道眉微微揚起。**3 be up to your eyebrows in sth** *spoken* to be very busy doing something【口】埋頭於…；非常忙：*I'm sorry I can't come, but I'm up to my eyebrows in marking exams.* 很抱歉我不能來，我批改試卷忙得不可開交。

eyebrow pen·cil /ˈ·· ˌ··/ *n* [C,U] a special pencil you can use to make your eyebrows darker 描眉筆

eye-catch·ing /ˈ· ˌ··/ *adj* something eye-catching is unusual or attractive in a way that makes you notice it 惹人注意的，搶眼的：*an eye-catching new outfit* 搶眼的新衣服 —**eye-catchingly** *adv*

eye·ful /ˈaɪˌful; ˈaɪfʊl/ *n* [C] **1** an amount of liquid, dust, or sand that has got into someone's eye 滿眼〔的液體、灰塵或沙子〕**2** *slang* something or someone, especially a woman, who is very attractive to look at【俚】引人注目的東西或人〔尤指美女〕：*She's quite an eyeful!* 她可是個美人兒！**3 get an eyeful of this/that!** *spoken especially BrE* used to tell someone to look at something because it is interesting or unusual【口，尤英】好好看一下這個/那個！

eye·glass /ˈaɪˌglæs; ˈaɪglɑːs/ *n* [C] **1** a LENS (1) for one eye, worn to help you see better with that eye; MONOCLE 單眼鏡 **2 eyeglasses** *BrE old-fashioned or AmE* a pair of glasses (GLASS[1] (3))【英，過時或美】一副眼鏡

eye·lash /ˈaɪˌlæʃ; ˈaɪlæʃ/ *n* [C] **1** one of the small hairs that grow along the edge of your EYELIDS 睫(毛) —see picture at 參見 EYE[1] 圖 **2 flutter your eyelashes** if a woman flutters her eyelashes, she moves them up and down very quickly, especially in order to look sexually attractive〔女人〕閃動睫毛〔尤指為了吸引異性〕

eye·less /ˈaɪləs; ˈaɪləs/ *adj* having no eyes 無眼的

eye·let /ˈaɪlɪt; ˈaɪlɨt/ *n* [C] a hole surrounded by a metal ring that is put in leather or cloth so that a string can be passed through it〔皮革或布上供穿線繩用的〕孔眼 —see picture at 參見 SHOE[1] 圖

eye lev·el /ˈ· ˌ··/ *n* [singular] a height equal to the level of your eyes 齊眼的高度：*Pictures should be hung at eye level.* 畫應掛在與眼睛同高的位置上。

eye·lid /ˈaɪlɪd; ˈaɪlɪd/ *n* [C] the two pieces of skin that cover your eye when it is closed 眼皮，眼瞼 —see also 另見 **not bat an eyelid** (BAT[2] (2)), —see picture at 參見 EYE[1] 圖

eye·lin·er /ˈaɪˌlaɪnɚ; ˈaɪˌlaɪnə/ *n* [C,U] a coloured substance that you put along the edges of your eyelids to make your eyes look bigger or more noticeable〔化妝用的〕眼線膏[粉，筆] —see picture at 參見 MAKE-UP 圖

eye-o·pen·er /ˈ· ˌ···/ *n* [C] a situation, event etc from which you learn something surprising, or something that you did not know before 使人大開眼界的事物 —see also 另見 **open sb's eyes (to)** (OPEN[2] (3b))

eye patch /ˈ· ·/ *n* [C] a piece of material worn over one eye, usually because that eye has been damaged 眼罩〔通常在眼睛受傷時使用〕

eye pen·cil /ˈ· ˌ··/ *n* [C,U] an eyeliner 眼線筆

eye·piece /ˈaɪˌpis; ˈaɪpiːs/ *n* [C] the glass piece that you look through in a MICROSCOPE or TELESCOPE〔顯微鏡或望遠鏡的〕(接)目鏡

eye shad·ow /ˈ· ˌ··/ *n* [C,U] a coloured substance that you put on your EYELIDS to make your eyes look more attractive 眼瞼膏[粉]，眼影 —see picture at 參見 MAKE-UP 圖

eye·sight /ˈaɪˌsaɪt; ˈaɪsaɪt/ *n* [U] your ability to see 視力

eye·sore /ˈaɪˌsɔr; ˈaɪsɔː/ *n* [C] something that is very ugly, especially a building surrounded by other things that are not ugly 不順眼的事物，難看的東西：*The tower block was an obvious eyesore in such a rural area.* 在這樣一處鄉村，這座高樓實在有礙觀瞻。

eye strain /ˈ· ·/ *n* [U] a pain you feel in your eyes, for example because you are tired or have been reading a lot 眼痛；眼疲勞

eye tooth /ˈ· ·/ *n* [C] **1** one of the long pointed teeth at the corner of your mouth; CANINE TOOTH 上尖牙，上犬牙 **2 give your eye teeth for sth** *spoken* used when you want something very much【口】非常希望得到某事物：*I'd give my eye teeth to be able to play the piano like that.* 要是我能像那樣演奏鋼琴，我願意付出任何代價。

eye wash /ˈ· ·/ *n* [U] **1** a special liquid used for washing your eyes when they are sore 洗眼劑，洗眼藥水 **2** *BrE spoken old-fashioned* something that you do not believe is true【英口，過時】把戲，騙局〔表示不相信〕：*Don't talk such eyewash!* 別再這麼胡扯了！

eye·wit·ness /ˈaɪˌwɪtnɪs; ˈaɪˌwɪtnɨs/ *n* [C] someone who has seen something such as a crime happen, and is able to describe it afterwards 目擊者；見證人：*According to* *an eyewitness, the bomb went off at exactly three o'clock.* 一名目擊者說, 炸彈是在三點正時爆炸的。

ey·ing /ˈaɪ-ɪŋ; ˈaɪ-ɪŋ/ the present participle of EYE[2]

eyot /ˈaɪət; eɪt/ *n* [C] *BrE* a small island in a river【英】河中的小島

ey·rie also 又作 **eyry** *BrE*【英】/ˈɛrɪ; ˈɪəri/ *n* [C] **1** the NEST of a large bird, especially an EAGLE, that is usually built high up in rocks or trees〔築於岩石或樹上等高處的〕猛禽巢〔尤指鷹巢〕**2** *informal* a room or building that is very high up【非正式】極高處的房間[建築物]

E

F,f

F, f /ɛf; ef/ *plural* **F's, f's** *n* [C] the sixth letter of the English alphabet 英語字母表的第六個字母

f 1 the written abbreviation of 縮寫= FORTE[2] **2** [plural] **ff** the written abbreviation of 縮寫= 'following', used in a book 其後的〔用於書中〕: *see pages 54ff* 見第 54 頁及其後幾頁

F[1] /ɛf; ef/ *n* **1** also 又作 **f** [C,U] the fourth note in the musical scale (SCALE[1] (8)) of C major or the musical key (KEY[2] (4)) based on this note F 音〔C 大調音階中的第四個音〕; F 調 **2** a mark given to a student whose work is not good enough〔學業成績〕F 級, 不及格

F[2] 1 the written abbreviation of 縮寫= FAHRENHEIT: *Water boils at 212°F.* 水在華氏 212 度時沸騰。**2** the written abbreviation of 縮寫= FEMALE **3** the written abbreviation of 縮寫= FALSE

FA /ˌɛf ˋe; ˌef ˈeɪ◂/ *n* **1** the Football Association; the organization that is in charge of professional football in England〔英國職業足球的〕足球協會: *the FA Cup* 足(球) 協 (會) 盃 **2 sweet FA** *BrE slang* nothing【英俚】甚麼都沒有, 無

fa /fɑ; fɑː/ *n* [singular] the fourth note in a musical SCALE[1] (8) according to the SOL-FA system〔首調唱名法的〕全音階中的第四音

fab /fæb; fæb/ *adj informal* a word meaning extremely good, used especially in the 1960s【非正式】極好的; 極妙的〔尤用於 20 世紀 60 年代〕

Fa·bi·an /ˋfebɪən; ˈfeɪbiən/ *adj* [only before noun 僅用於名詞前] connected with, or based on, the ideas of a British political group that has SOCIALIST[2] ideas and aims〔具有社會主義思想和目標的英國政治團體〕費邊社的 — **Fabian** *n* [C]

fa·ble /ˋfebl̩; ˈfeɪbəl/ *n* **1** [C] a traditional short story that teaches a moral lesson, especially a story about animals 寓言: *the fable of the fox and the crow* 狐狸和烏鴉的寓言故事 **2** [U] such stories considered as a group; LEGEND (2) 神話傳說〔總稱〕: *monsters of fable and legend* 神話和傳奇作品中的怪物

fa·bled /ˋfebl̩d; ˈfeɪbəld/ *adj especially literary* famous and often mentioned in traditional stories; LEGENDARY【尤文】寓言[傳奇]中著名的; 寓言[傳奇]中的: **[+for]** *a city fabled for its wealth* 傳說中以財富聞名的城市

3 **fab·ric** /ˋfæbrɪk; ˈfæbrɪk/ *n* **1** [C,U] cloth used to make clothes, curtains etc; material 織物; 衣料: *man-made fabrics* 人造織物 —see 見 CLOTHES (USAGE) **2** [singular] the basic structure of a society, way of life etc and its relationships and traditions〔社會〕結構: *The family is the most important unit in the social fabric.* 家庭是社會結構中最重要的單位。**3 the fabric of** the basic structure of a building including the walls and the roof〔建築物的〕基本結構〔包括牆和屋頂〕

fab·ri·cate /ˋfæbrɪˌket; ˈfæbrɪkeɪt/ *v* [T] **1** to invent a story, piece of information etc in order to deceive someone 編造, 捏造: *The police were accused of fabricating evidence.* 警方被控捏造證據。**2** *technical* to make or produce goods or equipment; MANUFACTURE[1] (1)【術語】製造, 生產: *The discs are expensive to fabricate.* 這些磁盤製造成本很昂貴。

fab·ri·ca·tion /ˌfæbrɪˋkeʃən; ˌfæbrɪˈkeɪʃən/ *n* **1** [C,U] a piece of information or story that someone has invented in order to deceive people 捏造的信息[說法]: *Officer, can't you see their story is a complete fabrication?* 長官, 你看不出他們說的事完全是捏造的嗎? **2** [U] *technical* the process of making or producing something【術語】製造, 生產

fabric con·di·tion·er /ˋ·· ·ˌ···/ *BrE*【英】, **fabric soft·en·er** *AmE*【美】/ˋ·· ˌ···/ *n* [C,U] a chemical that you put in water when washing clothes in order to make them feel softer〔洗衣時用的〕織物柔軟劑

fab·u·lous /ˋfæbjələs; ˈfæbjᵊləs/ *adj* **1** extremely good or impressive 極好的; 絕妙的: *You look fabulous!* 你看上去多美啊! | *a fabulous goal by Maradona* 馬勒當拿射中的絕妙一球 **2** [only before noun 僅用於名詞前] very large in amount or size 巨額的; 巨大的: *The painting was sold for a fabulous sum.* 那幅油畫以天價賣出。**3** [only before noun 僅用於名詞前] fabulous creatures, places etc are mentioned in traditional stories, but do not really exist 神話寓言中的, 傳說中的: *dragons and other fabulous creatures* 龍和其他傳說中的生物

fab·u·lous·ly /ˋfæbjələslɪ; ˈfæbjᵊləsli/ *adv* **fabulously expensive/rich/successful etc** extremely expensive etc 極其昂貴/富有/成功等

fa·cade, façade /fəˋsɑd; fəˈsɑːd/ *n* [C] **1** the front of a building, especially a large and important one〔尤指大型或重要建築物的〕正面: *A gang of stonemasons were restoring the facade of the cathedral.* 一羣石匠正在修復大教堂的正面。**2** [usually singular 一般用單數] a way of behaving that hides your real feelings〔掩蓋真實感情的〕表面: *the unpleasant reality lurking behind that facade of respectability* 隱藏在假裝體面背後的令人不快的現實

face[1] /fes; feɪs/ *n* [C] 1 1

1 ►FRONT OF YOUR HEAD 頭部的正面◄ the front part of the head from the chin to the forehead 臉, 面部: *She has such a pretty face.* 她有那麼美的一張臉。| *Bob's face was covered in cuts and bruises.* 鮑勃的臉上滿是劃痕與擦傷。| **a sea of faces** (=a lot of faces seen together) 許許多多的臉 *The Principal looked down from the platform at the sea of faces below.* 校長從講台上看着下面數不清的臉。—see picture at 參見 HEAD[1] 圖

2 ►EXPRESSION 表情◄ an expression on someone's face 面部表情; 臉色: *the children's happy faces* 孩子們歡快的表情 | **make/pull a face** (=change your expression to make people laugh, or to show that you are angry, disappointed etc) 做鬼臉 *Emma was making faces at me through the window.* 愛瑪隔着窗子朝我做鬼臉。| **you should have seen his/her face** *spoken* (=used to say how angry, surprised etc someone looked) 你該看到他/她的神色〔用來說明某人看上去是何等生氣、驚訝等〕*You should have seen Steve's face when I told him I was resigning.* 我告訴史蒂夫我要辭職時, 你該看得到他臉上的表情。| **sb's face was a picture** *spoken* (=used to say that they looked very angry, surprised etc) 某人當時的表情極為可觀〔用來說明某人看上去十分生氣、驚訝等〕| **sb's face brightened/lit up** (=they started to smile and look happy) 某人面露喜色 *David's face lit up when I mentioned her name.* 我提到她的名字時, 大衞面露喜色。| **sb's face fell** (=they started to look disappointed or upset) 某人的臉色沉下來 *His face fell when I told him the news.* 我告訴他這一消息時, 他的臉色一沉。| **a face like thunder** (=a very angry expression) 震怒的表情 *Mr Neeson came striding towards us with a face like thunder.* 尼森先生怒氣沖沖地大步朝我們走來。| **a long face** (=an unhappy or worried expression) 鬱悶[憂慮]的表情; 愁眉苦臉

3 ►PERSON 人◄ **a) a famous/well-known face** someone who is famous from television, magazines, films etc〔因出現在電視、雜誌、電影等中而出名的〕名人 **b) new/different face** someone who you have not seen before 新人/不同的人: *There are a few new faces in class this year.* 今年班上有幾張新面孔。**c) the same old faces** people that you see often, especially too often 經常看到的人; 看厭了的老面孔: *It's the same old faces at our meetings every week.* 每星期出席我們會議的老是那些人。

4 pale-faced/round-faced etc having a face that has a particular shape or colour 臉色蒼白的/圓臉的等: *a pale-faced youth* 臉色蒼白的青年 —see also 另見 RED-FACED

5 serious-faced/grim-faced etc showing a particular expression on your face 表情嚴肅的/表情嚴峻的等: *Negotiators emerged grim-faced after the day's talks.* 經過一天的談判之後, 談判者表情嚴峻地走了出來。—see also 另見 BAREFACED, PO-FACED, POKER-FACED, STONY-FACED

6 face to face a) if two people are face to face, they are very close and in front of each other 面對面地: **meet sb face to face** *I've never met her face to face. We've only talked on the phone.* 我從來沒有當面見過她。我們只在電話中交談過話。| **come face to face with** (=suddenly meet someone who makes you very frightened, surprised etc) 突然面對面地遇見〔使你害怕、驚訝等的人〕 *At that moment he came face to face with Sergeant Burke.* 那時他突然面對面地遇見了伯克中士。**b)** in a situation where you have to accept or deal with something unpleasant 面臨着, 面對着〔令人不愉快的事〕: **bring sb face to face with** *He was brought face to face with the truth about his daughter's disappearance.* 他不得不面對女兒失蹤的事實。| **come face to face with** *This was the first time I'd ever come face to face with poverty.* 這是我第一次面對貧窮。—see also 另見 FACE-TO-FACE

7 to sb's face if you say something unpleasant to someone's face you say it to them directly 當着某人的面; 坦率地: *I told him to his face just what I thought.* 我當面把我的想法告訴了他。

8 face down/downwards with the face or front towards the ground 臉朝下, 面朝下: *The body was lying face down on the carpet.* 屍體臉朝下趴在地毯上。

9 face up/upwards with the face or front towards the sky 臉朝上, 面朝上: *She laid the cards out face upwards.* 她把紙牌面朝上攤開了。

10 in the face of in a situation where there are many problems, difficulties, or dangers 面對〔問題、困難或危險〕: *bravery in the face of danger* 面對危險時的勇氣

11 on the face of it used to say that something seems true but that you think there may be other facts about it which are not yet clear 從表面上看; 乍看起來〔實情可能不同〕: *It looks, on the face of it, like a minor change in the regulations.* 這表面上看好像是對規定作了一點小變動。| *On the face of it, Norman seems the ideal man for the job.* 乍看起來, 諾曼似乎是這份工作的理想人選。

12 the face of a) the way in which an organization, system etc appears to people〔組織、體制等的〕面貌: *recent events that changed the face of the British monarchy* 改變英國君主制面貌的一些最新事件 **b)** the general appearance of a particular place〔某個地方的〕外觀, 景觀: *the changing face of the landscape* 不斷變化的地貌景色

13 lose face to make other people lose their respect for you 丟臉: *He doesn't want to back down and risk losing face.* 他不想打退堂鼓, 怕會丟臉。

14 save face if you do something to save face, you do it so that people will not lose their respect for you 保全面子: *Rather than admit defeat, Franklin compromised in order to save face.* 富蘭克林為了保全面子沒有承認失敗, 而是作了妥協。

15 blow up/go up in sb's face if a situation blows up or goes up in your face, it goes wrong, especially in an embarrassing way 當場出醜, 當眾丟臉

16 disappear/vanish off the face of the earth to suddenly disappear 從地球上消失, 突然消失: *I haven't seen Paul in ages, he seems to have vanished off the face of the earth.* 我很久沒見到保羅了, 他好像已經從地球上消失。

17 sb's face doesn't fit used to say that someone is not the right kind of person for a particular group, organization etc 某人不適合〔某個羣體、組織等〕

18 put a brave face (on) to make an effort to behave in a happy cheerful way when you are upset or disappointed〔雖然煩惱、失望等但〕裝作若無其事的樣子: *He was shattered, though he put on a brave face.* 他大為震驚, 儘管他裝作若無其事的樣子。

19 set your face against *especially BrE* to be very determined that something should not happen【尤英】沉下臉反對, 堅決反對

20 ►MOUNTAIN/CLIFF 山/懸崖◄ a steep, high side of a mountain, cliff etc〔山、懸崖等的〕正面; 坡面: *The cliff face was starting to crumble into the sea.* 懸崖的正面開始崩裂並墜入大海。

21 ►CLOCK 鐘◄ the front of a clock 鐘面

22 ►MINE 礦井◄ the part of a mine from which coal, stone etc is cut〔礦井的〕採掘面

23 ►OUTSIDE SURFACE 表面◄ one of the outside surfaces of an object or building〔物體或建築物的〕面, 表面: *A cube has six faces.* 立方體有六個面。

24 ►SPORT 體育運動◄ the part of a bat (BAT¹ (2)) or racket (RACKET¹ (3)) that you use to hit the ball〔球棒或球拍的〕擊球面

25 in your face/in yer face *slang* behaviour, criticisms, remarks etc that are in your face are very direct and often shocking or surprising【俚】〔行為、批評、評論等〕當着你的面, 直截了當地, 不留情面地: *Parson's 'in your face' style of interviewing* 帕森的那種當面直言不諱的面談方式

26 what's his face/what's her face *spoken* used as a way of talking about someone when you cannot remember their name【口】那個叫甚麼名字的人: *I saw old what's his face in school yesterday.* 我昨天在學校裡見到了那個叫甚麼名字的老相識。

27 put your face on *informal humorous* to put MAKE-UP on【非正式, 幽默】〔面部〕化妝 —see also 另見 **have egg on your face** (EGG¹ (4)), **fly in the face of** (FLY¹ (28)), **a straight face** (STRAIGHT² (11)), **laugh in sb's face** (LAUGH¹ (12)), **not just a pretty face** (PRETTY² (5)), **show your face** (SHOW¹ (12)), **shut your face** (SHUT¹ (3)), **a slap in the face** (SLAP² (2)), **be staring sb in the face** (STARE¹ (2)), **do sth till you're blue in the face** (BLUE¹ (6)), **wipe the smile/grin off sb's face** (WIPE¹ (7)), **have sth written all over your face** (WRITE (5))

face² *v* [T]

1 ►DIFFICULT SITUATION 困難的局面◄ if you face a difficult situation or if it faces you, you must deal with it 面臨, 面對: *The President faces the difficult task of putting the economy back on its feet.* 總統面對着恢復經濟的艱巨任務。| *McManus is facing the biggest challenge of his career.* 麥克馬納斯正面臨着畢生事業中的最大挑戰。| **be faced with/by** *I was faced with the awful job of breaking the news to the girl's family.* 我面臨着要向女孩的家人報告這一消息的可怕任務。

2 ►ADMIT A PROBLEM EXISTS 承認問題的存在◄ to accept that a difficult situation or problem exists, even though you would prefer to ignore it 正視, 面對: **face the fact that** *Many couples refuse to face the fact that they have problems with their marriage.* 許多夫婦拒絕面對自己的婚姻出現問題這一事實。| **face facts** *It's time that we started to face a few hard facts.* 我們是時候開始面對一些鐵一般的事實了。| **face the truth** *He had to face the awful truth that she no longer loved him.* 他不得不正視她不再愛他這一可怕的事實。| **(let's) face it** *spoken* (=used when saying something that someone may find difficult to accept or admit)【口】(讓我們) 面對現實吧〔用於說別人難以接受或承認的話時〕: *Face it kid, you're never gonna be a rock star.* 孩子, 面對現實吧, 你永遠也成不了搖滾樂歌星的。

3 can't face if you cannot face something, you feel unable to do it because it seems too unpleasant or difficult 無法面對, 無法正視: *I don't want to go back to school again – I just can't face it.* 我不想再回到學校去 —— 我無法面對這事。| **can't face doing sth** *He couldn't face driving all the way to Los Angeles.* 他受不了一直開車到洛杉磯。

4 ►BE OPPOSITE 在對面◄ to be opposite a person, building etc so that you are pointing towards them, or to point in a particular direction 面向, 面朝: *They stood facing each other for a few minutes.* 他們面對面站了好幾分鐘。| *Rita's apartment faces the harbor.* 麗塔的房間面朝海港。| **face north/east etc** (=point towards the north, east etc) 朝北/東等 *My bedroom faces south.* 我的臥室朝南。| **south-facing/west-facing etc** *a south-facing garden* 朝南的花園 —see 見 FRONT[1] (USAGE)

5 ►UNPLEASANT POSSIBILITY 可能發生的不愉快的事◄ to have the possibility that something bad or unpleasant might happen to you 面臨〔可能發生到自己頭上的壞事或不愉快的事〕: *If he can't pay up, he's faced with losing his home.* 他如果無法付款, 將面臨失去家園的後果。| *Evans could face the electric chair.* 埃文斯可能面臨坐電椅的判決。

6 ►TEAM/OPPONENT 團隊/對手◄ to play against an opponent or team in a game or competition 與…比賽[競賽]: *Martinez will face Robertson in tomorrow's final.* 馬丁尼茲將在明天的決賽中和羅伯遜較量。

7 ►DIFFICULT PERSON 難相處的人◄ to deal with someone who is difficult to deal with, or talk to someone who you do not want to talk to 對付, 應付〔難對付的人或不願意答理的人〕: *You're going to have to face him sooner or later.* 你遲早得對付他。

8 face the music *informal* to accept criticism or punishment for something you have done【非正式】〔為自己的行為〕接受批評[懲罰]; 承擔後果

9 ►BUILDING 建築物◄ **be faced with stone/concrete etc** to be covered in stone, CONCRETE[2] etc 以石頭/混凝土等砌面[抹面; 覆蓋]的

face sb ↔ **down** *phr v* [T] to deal with someone in a strong and confident way〔用堅定和自信的方式〕壓倒, 挫敗, 懾服: *The police chief faced down reporters who were calling for his resignation.* 警察局長懾服了要求他辭職的記者們。

face up to sth *phr v* [T] to accept and deal with an unpleasant fact or problem 勇於接受並處理〔不愉快的事實或問題〕: *They'll never offer you another job; you might as well face up to it.* 他們決不會再給你一份工作, 你還是接受事實吧。

face sb **with** sth *phr v* [T often passive 常用被動態] to show someone evidence that proves they have done something wrong 向某人出示〔其做了錯事的證據〕; 把〔證據〕擺在〔某人〕面前

face card /ˈ· ·/ *n* [C] *AmE* the king, queen, or jack (JACK[1] (2)) in a set of playing cards【美】〔紙牌戲中的〕花牌, 人頭牌〔紙牌中的 K, Q, J〕; COURT CARD *BrE*【英】

face·cloth /ˈ· ·/ *n* [C] *BrE* a small piece of rough cloth used to wash the face or hands【英】〔小塊圓布做的〕洗臉巾; 洗手巾; WASHCLOTH *AmE*【美】

face cream /ˈ· ·/ *n* [C,U] a thick cream used to clean the face or to keep it soft and smooth 洗面乳; 潤膚霜; 面霜

face·less /ˈfeslɪs; ˈfeɪsləs/ *adj* a faceless person, organization etc consists of a lot of people who you do not know, and who do not seem interested in or to have sympathy for ordinary people〔人或機構等〕冷漠的; 沒有人情味的: *faceless bureaucrats* 無人情味的官僚

face·lift /ˈfesˌlɪft; ˈfeɪslɪft/ *n* [C] **1** a medical operation in which doctors remove loose skin on someone's face in order to make them look younger 整容術; 面部拉皮手術 **2** work or repairs that make a place or object look newer or better 翻新; 整修: **give sth a facelift** *The new owner had given the pub a face-lift.* 新業主對酒吧進行了翻修。

face-off /ˈ· ·/ *n* [C] **1** *AmE informal* a fight or argument【美, 非正式】對抗, 對峙; 爭吵: *a face-off between police and rioters* 警察與騷亂者的對抗 **2** a way of starting a game of ICE HOCKEY〔冰球比賽的〕開球 —**faceoff** *phr v* [T]

face pack /ˈ· ·/ *n* [C] a thick cream that you spread over your face in order to clean and improve your skin 美容潔膚膏; 面霜

face pow·der /ˈ· ˌ··/ *n* [U] powder that you put on your face in order to make it look smoother and give it more colour 撲面粉 —see picture at 參見 MAKE-UP 圖

face sav·er /ˈ· ˌ··/ *n* [C] something that helps you not to lose other people's respect 保全面子的事物

face-sav·ing /ˈ· ˌ··/ *adj* [only before noun 僅用於名詞前] a face-saving action or arrangement helps you not to lose other people's respect〔行為或安排〕保全面子的: *a face-saving compromise* 保全面子的妥協

fac·et /ˈfæsɪt; ˈfæsɨt/ *n* [C] **1** one of several parts of someone's character, a situation etc; ASPECT (1)〔性格、情況等的〕(一個) 方面: **[+of]** *discussing the many facets of the problem* 討論這個問題的許多方面 **2 multi-faceted/many faceted** consisting of many different parts 多方面的: *a multi-faceted issue* 涉及多方面的問題 **3** one of the flat sides of a jewel〔寶石的〕(一個) 琢面, 刻面, 小平面

facet 刻面

fa·ce·tious /fəˈsiʃəs; fəˈsiːʃəs/ *adj* saying things that are intended to be clever and funny but are really silly and annoying 好亂開玩笑的, 故作詼諧的, 不正經的: *Don't be so facetious!* 別這麼沒正經的! | *facetious comments* 故作詼諧的評論 —**facetiously** *adv* —**facetiousness** *n* [U]

face-to-face /ˌ· · ˈ·◂/ *adj* [only before noun 僅用於名詞前] a face-to-face meeting, conversation etc is one where you are actually with another person and talking to them〔指會晤、談話等〕面對面的

face val·ue /ˌ· ˈ··/ *n* [U] **1 take sth at face value** to accept a situation or accept what someone says, without thinking there may be a hidden meaning 對〔某一情況或別人的話〕信以為真: *You shouldn't always take his remarks at face value.* 你不該總是拿他的話當真。**2** [C,U] the value or cost shown on the front of something such as a stamp or coin〔郵票或錢幣等的〕面額, 票面價值

fa·cial[1] /ˈfeʃəl; ˈfeɪʃəl/ *adj* on your face or connected with your face 臉上的; 面部的: *a slight facial resemblance between the two men* 兩個男子的容貌有點相似 | *facial hair* 臉上的汗毛、鬍鬚等 —**facially** *adv*: *Facially the two sisters are very similar.* 這兩姐妹長相十分相似。

facial[2] *n* [C] a process in which creams are rubbed into the skin of your face in order to clean and improve your skin 面部美容

facial scrub /ˌ·· ˈ·/ *n* [C] a thick substance which you use to clean the skin on your face thoroughly 面部磨砂膏, 磨砂潔面霜

fa·cile /ˈfæsl̩; ˈfæsaɪl/ *adj* **1** a facile remark, argument etc is too simple and shows a lack of careful thought or understanding〔指話語、論點等〕膚淺的, 未認真思考[理解]的: *facile logic* 膚淺的道理 **2** [only before noun 僅用於名詞前] *formal* a facile achievement or success has been obtained too easily【正式】〔指成就或成功〕太容易得到的: *a facile victory* 輕易取得的勝利 —**facilely** *adv* —**facileness** *n* [U]

fa·cil·i·tate /fəˈsɪləˌtet; fəˈsɪlɨteɪt/ *v* [T] *formal* to make it easier for a process or activity to happen【正式】使容易, 使便利; 有助於: *Computers can be used to facilitate language learning.* 使用電腦能為語言學習帶來方便。—**facilitation** /fəˌsɪləˈteʃən; fəˌsɪlɨˈteɪʃən/ *n* [U]

fa·cil·i·tat·or /fəˈsɪləˌtetɚ; fəˈsɪlɨteɪtə/ *n* [C] **1** someone who helps a group of people discuss things with each other or do something effectively 促進者，推動者；協調人 **2** *technical* something that helps a process to take place【術語】促進[方便]某過程的事物

3 1 **fa·cil·i·ty** /fəˋsɪlətɪ; fəˈsɪlɪ̥ti/ *n* **1 facilities** [plural] rooms, equipment, or services that are provided for a particular purpose〔為某種目的而提供的〕設施〈如房屋、設備、服務等〉: *a 5-star hotel with fantastic facilities* 設施完善的五星級酒店 | *child-care facilities* 兒童保育設施 | *toilet facilities* 衛生間設備 **2** [usually singular 一般用單數] a special part of a piece of equipment or a system which makes it possible to do something〔使某事得以進行的〕安排，設備，裝置: *Is there a call-back facility on this phone?* 這台電話有回話裝置嗎? | *a bank account with an overdraft facility* 可以透支的銀行賬戶 **3** [singular] a natural ability to do something easily and well 天賦；才能: [+**for**] *She has an amazing facility for mental arithmetic.* 她的心算技能令人驚嘆。**4** [C] a place or building used for a particular activity or industry, or for providing a particular type of service〔特定用途的〕場所；建築: *a chlorine-production facility* 生產氯的工廠 **5 with great facility** *formal* very easily【正式】十分容易地，毫不費力地

fac·ing /ˋfesɪŋ; ˈfeɪsɪŋ/ *n* [C,U] **1** an outer surface of a wall or building made of a different material from the rest in order to make it look attractive〔牆或建築的〕飾面；面層 **2** material fastened to the inside of a piece of clothing to strengthen it〔衣服的〕襯裡 **3 facings** parts of a jacket, coat etc around the neck and wrists which have a different colour from the rest〔領口或袖口的〕鑲邊；飾邊；貼邊

fac·sim·i·le /fækˋsɪməlɪ; fækˈsɪmɪ̥li/ *n* [C] **1** an exact copy of a picture, piece of writing etc〔圖片、文字作品等的〕摹本，精確的複製品 **2** *formal* a FAX[1](1)【正式】傳真 —**facsimile** *adj*

1 1 **fact** /fækt; fækt/ *n*

1 ►TRUE INFORMATION 真實信息◄ [C] a piece of information that is known to be true 事實；真相: *First of all, we need to establish the facts of the case.* 首先，我們需要確定案子的事實真相。| [+**about**] *The book is full of interesting facts about the World Cup.* 這本書滿是有關世界盃的有趣事實。| **facts and figures** (=the basic details, numbers etc concerning a particular situation or subject) 確切情況，詳細的資料 | **it's a fact/that's a fact** (=used to emphasize that something is definitely true or that something definitely happened) 事實就是如此〔用於強調〕*The divorce rate in the US is now twice as high as in the 1950s – that's a fact.* 美國現在的離婚率是20世紀50年代的兩倍。事實就是如此。| **it's a fact that** *It's a fact that most deaths from lung cancer are caused by smoking.* 事實是，大部分因肺癌而導致的死亡是由吸煙引起的。| **I know for a fact that** *spoken* (=used to say that you definitely know that something is true)【口】我確實知道 *I know for a fact that she earns more than I do.* 我確實知道她掙錢比我多。| **get your facts right/wrong** (=be right or wrong about something) 弄對/錯事實 *We need to be sure we've got our facts right before making wild accusations.* 我們先要確保掌握的事實準確無誤，不要胡亂指責人。| **stick/keep to the facts** (=only say what you know is true) 實事求是，只說確實知道的事實 *Let's just stick to the facts and not jump to any conclusions.* 我們還是實事求是吧，不要貿然下結論。| **the bare facts** (=the basic details of a situation or story) 基本情況，赤裸裸的事實 | **hard facts** (=details or pieces of information that can be proved to be true) 鐵一般的事實，真實情況 *We need some hard facts not just theories and suppositions.* 我們需要一些確鑿的事實，而不僅僅是理論和推測。| **the facts speak for themselves** (=they show clearly that something is true) 事實不言自明 *She obviously knows what she's doing–the facts speak for themselves.* 她顯然知道自己在做甚麼——事實已經不言而喻。

2 the fact (that) used when talking about a situation and saying that it is true ...的事實〔用於談論某個情況並說明它是真實的〕: *He refused to help me, despite the fact that I asked him several times.* 儘管我確實求了他好幾次，他還是拒絕幫助我。| **given the fact (that)/in view of the fact (that)** (=used when saying that a particular fact influences your judgement about something or someone) 鑑於，考慮到〔用於說明某一事實影響自己對某人或某事的看法〕*Given the fact that this is their first game, I think they did pretty well.* 考慮到這是他們的首次比賽，我認為他們打得很好了。| **owing to the fact (that)/due to the fact (that)** (=because) 由於，因為 *The school's poor exam record is largely due to the fact that it is chronically underfunded.* 這所學校考試成績差，主要是由於長期以來資金不足。

3 ►REAL EVENTS/NOT A STORY 真實事件/非虛構的故事◄ [U] situations, events etc that really happened and have not been invented 事實，實情: *Much of the novel is based on fact.* 這部小說大部分內容都是以事實為依據的。

4 in fact/in actual fact a) used to say what the real truth of a situation is, especially when this is different from what people think or say it is 事實上/實際上: *They told me it would be cheap but in fact it cost me nearly $500.* 他們對我說那是便宜貨，但實際上我花了差不多500美元。| *Her teachers said she was a slow learner, whereas in actual fact she was partially deaf.* 她的老師都說她學習反應慢，然而實際上她是局部失聰的。**b)** used when you are adding something, especially something surprising, to emphasize what you have just said 其實；事實上: *We live very close to Lesley's parents, in the same road in actual fact.* 我們住得離萊斯利的父母家很近，其實就在同一條路上。

5 as a matter of fact *spoken*【口】**a)** used when you are answering someone and telling them what you really think or what the real situation is 實際上；其實〔用於回覆並告訴某人你的真實想法或實際情況〕: *"I didn't think you'd mind me using your office." "Well as a matter of fact I do mind."* "我原以為你不會介意我用一下你的辦公室。""哦，其實我很介意。" **b)** used to add an important fact that increases the effect of what you are saying 事實上〔用於加插某一重要情況，以增強所說話語的效果〕: *Our ELT department is doing really well. As a matter of fact we've just signed a big new contract in China.* 我們的英語教學部成績真不錯，事實上我們剛剛在中國簽訂了一份新的大合同。

6 in point of fact *spoken* an expression used in discussions and speeches to add another piece of information or disagree with what someone else has said【口】事實上，實際上〔用於商談或演講中需增添另一事實或反駁對方的一種表達法〕

7 the fact is/the fact of the matter is *spoken* used when you are telling someone what is actually true in a particular situation, especially when this is different from what people believe【口】事實是/實際情況是: *The fact of the matter is that the company is unlikely to survive the recession.* 實際情況是這家公司不大可能渡過這場經濟衰退。

8 the fact remains used to emphasize that a situation is true and people must realize this 事實是，真實的情況是〔用於強調某一情況為事實，人們必須對其有認識〕: *The fact remains that the number of homeless people is rising daily.* 實際情況是無家可歸者的人數每天都在增加。

9 sth is a fact of life used to say that a situation exists and must be accepted（某事）已成為必須面對的事實: *Mass unemployment seems to be a fact of life nowadays.* 大規模失業似乎已成為當今無法避免的事實。

10 the facts of life a) the details about sex and how babies are born 性知識 **b)** the way life really is, with all its problems and difficulties 嚴酷的生活現實；現實生活

11 after the fact after something has happened or been

done, especially after a mistake has been made 情況發生後; 錯誤發生後 —see also 另見 **as a matter of fact** (MATTER[1] (16))

fact-find·ing /ˈ· ˌ··/ *adj* **fact-finding trip/tour/mission etc** a trip during which you try to find out facts and information about something for your organization, government etc 實地調查[為弄清楚事實真相的]旅行/旅遊/任務等

fac·tion /ˋfækʃən; ˈfækʃən/ *n* **1** [C] a small group of people within a larger group, who have different ideas from the other members〔團體中的〕派別, 派系, 小集團: *warring factions* 敵對的派系 **2** [U] *formal* disagreement or fighting within a group or a political party【正式】〔團體或政黨內部的〕派系鬥爭, 派系糾紛 **3** [C,U] a story in a film or television programme that is based on real events but is not completely true〔以真實事件為依據但又加入虛構內容的〕紀實小說; 紀實電影[電視節目] —**factional** *adj*

fac·ti·tious /fækˋtɪʃəs; fækˈtɪʃəs/ *adj formal* made to happen artificially by people rather than happening naturally【正式】做作的, 不自然的; 虛假的

3 1 **fac·tor¹** /ˋfæktɚ; ˈfæktə/ *n* [C]

1 ►CAUSE/INFLUENCE 原因/影響◄ one of several things that influence or cause a situation 因素, 要素: *The rise in crime is mainly due to social and economic factors.* 犯罪率上升主要是由社會及經濟因素造成的。| [+in] *The vaccination program has been a major factor in the improvement of health standards.* 接種疫苗計劃是人類健康水平得以提高的一個主要因素。| **key/crucial factor** *The weather could be a crucial factor in tomorrow's game.* 天氣情況會是明天比賽的一個至關重要的因素。| **the deciding factor** (=the most important factor) 決定性因素 *We liked both houses, but in the end the deciding factor was the location.* 這兩幢房子我們都挺喜歡, 但歸根結底地段的好壞才是決定性因素。

2 by a factor of five/ten etc if something increases or decreases by a factor of five, ten etc it increases or decreases by five times, ten times etc 以五倍/十倍等係數(增加或減少)

3 ►LEVEL ON A SCALE 等級標準◄ a particular level on a scale of measurement of the force or effectiveness of something〔某物的〕效力等級係數: *factor 15 suntan oil* 防曬係數為15的防曬油 | *a wind chill factor of -20* 風寒指數為 -20

4 ►MATHEMATICS 數學◄ a number that divides into another number exactly 因子, 商(數), 因數: *3 is a factor of 15.* 3是15的因數。

5 ►LAND 土地◄ *ScotE* someone who looks after another person's land【蘇格蘭】代人管理土地者, 地產管理人

factor² *v* [T] *AmE technical* to divide a number into factors【美, 術語】將…分解為因子, 把…化為因數

factor sth ↔ **in** *phr v* [T] to include a particular thing in your calculations about how long something will take, how much it will cost etc 將…計入; 把…考慮在內

fac·to·ri·al /fækˋtɔrɪəl; fækˈtɔːriəl/ *n* [C] *technical* the result when you multiply a whole number by all the numbers below it【術語】階乘, 階乘積: *factorial 3 = 3 × 2 × 1* 3的階乘=3×2×1

fac·tor·ize also 又作 **-ise** *BrE*【英】/ˋfæktəˌraɪz; ˈfæktəraɪz/ *v* [T] *technical* to divide a number into factors【術語】把…分解成因子, 把…化為因數 —**factorization** /ˌfæktərəˋzeʃən; ˌfæktəraɪˈzeɪʃən/ *n* [U]

2 2 **fac·to·ry** /ˋfæktərɪ; ˈfæktəri/ *n* [C] **1** a building or group of buildings in which goods are produced in large quantities, using machines 工廠, 製造廠: *a car factory* 汽車製造廠 | *factory workers* 工廠工人 **2 on the factory floor** among the ordinary workers in a company 在工人[員工]當中

factory farm /ˈ··· ˌ·/ *n* [C] *BrE* a farm where animals are kept inside, in small spaces or small CAGEs, and made to grow or produce eggs very quickly【英】〔以現代化方式飼養禽畜, 以迅速提高肉、蛋產量的〕工廠化農場 —**factory farming** *n* [U]

fac·to·tum /fækˋtotəm; fækˈtəʊtəm/ *n* [C] *formal* a servant or worker who has to do many different kinds of jobs for someone【正式】勤雜工, 雜務工, 雜役: *He's our general factotum.* 他是我們的雜務總管。

fact sheet /ˈ· ·/ *n* [C] a piece of paper giving all the most important information about something 情況簡報, 資料摘要

fac·tu·al /ˋfæktʃuəl; ˈfæktʃuəl/ *adj* based on facts (基於)事實的, 真實的: *factual information* 真實信息 | *Try to keep your account of events as factual as possible.* 你對事件的敘述要盡量以事實為根據。—**factually** *adv*: *The document is factually correct.* 這份文件在事實上是準確的。

fac·ul·ty /ˋfækl̩tɪ; ˈfækəlti/ *n plural* **faculties** [C] **1** a natural ability, such as the ability to see, hear, or think clearly 天賦, 能力: [+of] *the faculty of reason* 推理能力 | **in full possession of all your faculties** (=able to see, hear, think etc in the normal way) 心智健全的 **2** a particular skill that someone has 才能, 技能: [+for] *She had a great faculty for absorbing information.* 她十分擅長汲取信息。**3** a department within a university〔大學的〕系, 部, 院: *the Faculty of Engineering* 工程學院 **4 the faculty** *AmE* all the teachers in a university【美】〔大學的〕全體教員: *There was a mixed reaction to the proposal among the faculty.* 教員們對這項建議的反應不一。

fad /fæd; fæd/ *n* [C] something that someone likes or does for a short time, or that is fashionable for a short time 一時的狂熱; 時尚, 風尚: *The break-dancing craze soon passed, as most fads do.* 跟大多數流行時尚一樣, 這一陣霹靂舞熱很快就過去了。—**faddy, faddish** *adj*: *She keeps trying all these faddy diets.* 她不停地嘗試各種流行的節食法。—**faddiness, faddishness** *n* [U]

fade /fed; feɪd/ *v* **1** also 又作 **fade away** [I] to gradually disappear 逐漸消失: *Hopes of a peace settlement are beginning to fade.* 和平解決的希望正開始消失。| *Over the years her beauty had faded a little.* 過去幾年裡, 她的美貌已有點失色。**2** [I, T] to lose colour and brightness, or to make something do this (使)褪色; (使)失去光澤: *the fading evening light* 逐漸蒼茫的暮色 | **fade sth** *The sun had faded the curtains.* 太陽把窗簾曬得褪了色。—see picture on page A18 參見A18頁圖 **3** also 又作 **fade away** [I] to become weaker physically, especially so that you become very ill or die〔身體〕變得虛弱 **4** [I] if a team fades, it stops playing as well as it did before〔運動隊〕水準下降: *The Broncos faded in the second half.* 野馬隊下半場打得較差。

fade sth ↔ **in** *phr v* [T] to make a picture or sound appear or be heard gradually 使〔畫面〕淡入, 漸顯; 使〔聲音〕漸強 —**fade-in** /ˈ· ·/ *n* [C]

fade sth ↔ **out** *phr v* [T] to make a picture or sound disappear slowly or become quieter 使〔畫面〕淡出, 漸隱; 使〔聲音〕漸弱 —**fade-out** /ˈ· ·/ *n* [C]

fae·ces also 又作 **feces** *AmE*【美】/ˋfisiz; ˈfiːsiːz/ *n* [plural] *formal* solid waste material from the BOWELs【正式】糞便 —**faecal** /ˋfikl̩; ˈfiːkəl/ *adj*

fae·ry, faerie /ˋfɛrɪ; ˈfeəri/ *n* [C] *old-use* a FAIRY(1)【舊】仙子, 小精靈

faff /fæf; fæf/ *v*

faff about/around *phr v* [I] *BrE informal* to waste time doing unnecessary things【英, 非正式】無事瞎忙: *I wish you'd stop faffing around!* 我希望你不要再無事瞎忙了。

fag¹ /fæg; fæg/ *n* [C] **1** *BrE slang* a cigarette【英俚】香煙 **2** *AmE slang* an offensive word for a HOMOSEXUAL【美俚】男同性戀者〔冒犯用語〕**3 be a fag** *BrE informal* to be a boring or difficult thing to do【英, 非正式】煩人的活, 苦差事: *I hate ironing – it's such a fag.* 我討厭熨衣服——這是件苦差事。**4** a young student in some British PUBLIC SCHOOLs who has to do jobs for an older student〔英國一些私立中學裡〕受高年級學生使喚的低年級學生

fag² *v* [I+for] to do jobs for an older student at a British

PUBLIC SCHOOL〔英國私立中學裡的低年級學生〕聽高年級學生使喚 —**fagging** *n* [U]

fag end /,· '·◂/ *n* [C] *informal*【非正式】**1** *BrE* the end of a cigarette that someone has finished smoking【英】(香) 煙蒂 **2 the fag end of** *especially BrE* the last part of something, especially when it is not as good or interesting as the rest【尤英】...的末尾, 末端; 無味[沒趣]的剩餘部分

fagged /fægd; fægd/ *adj BrE informal*【英, 非正式】**1** also 又作 **fagged out** [not before noun 不用於名詞前] extremely tired 疲憊不堪的: *I was fagged out after the journey.* 旅行後我累極了。**2 I can't be fagged** used to say that you are too tired or bored to do something 我不願幹那種累事〔用於表示自己太累或太厭煩不願去做某事〕

fag·got /ˈfægət; ˈfægət/ *n* [C] **1** *BrE* a ball made of meat mixed with bread, which is cooked【英】〔由碎肉和麵包屑做成並煮熟的〕肉丸子 **2** *AmE slang* an offensive word for a HOMOSEXUAL【美俚】男同性戀者〔冒犯用語〕**3** a collection of small sticks for burning on a fire 柴捆, 柴把 **4** *BrE informal* an impolite word for someone you do not like, especially a woman【英, 非正式】討厭的人〔非禮貌用語, 尤指女人〕

fag-hag /ˈ· ·/ *n* [C] *slang especially AmE* an offensive word for a woman who spends time with HOMOSEXUAL men【俚, 尤美】與男同性戀者在一起的女人〔冒犯用語〕

Fah·ren·heit /ˈfærənˌhaɪt; ˈfærənhaɪt/ *n* [U] a scale of temperature in which water freezes at 32° and boils at 212° 華氏溫度

2 **fail¹** /fel; feɪl/ *v*

1 **1 ▶TRY BUT FAIL** 嘗試但失敗◀ [I] to be unsuccessful in something that you want to do 失敗, 未成功: *Peace talks between the two countries have failed.* 兩國間的和談已經失敗。| **fail to do sth** *Doctors failed to save the girl's life.* 醫生們未能保住這女孩的性命。| **fail miserably** (=be completely unsuccessful in a way that it is embarrassing) 完全失敗, 慘敗: *Millions of people have tried to quit smoking and failed miserably.* 千百萬人試圖戒煙, 但完全失敗。

2 ▶NOT DO WHAT IS EXPECTED 沒做應做的事◀ [I] to not do what is expected, needed, or wanted: **fail to do sth** *The letter failed to arrive.* 信沒有寄到。| *The report cleverly fails to mention the real cost of this experiment.* 報告巧妙地不提這項試驗的實際費用。| **fail in your duty/responsibility** *I would be failing in my duty if I didn't warn you of the consequences of your actions.* 如果我對你的行動將產生的後果不提出告誡, 那我就是失職。

3 ▶EXAM/TEST 考試/測驗◀ **a)** [I,T] to not pass a test or examination 不及格; 未能通過: *I failed my driving test the first time I took it.* 我第一次參加駕駛執照考試時沒過關。| **[+on]** *I passed the written paper but failed on my oral.* 我通過了筆試, 但口試不及格。**b)** [T] to decide that someone has not passed a test or examination 評定〔某人〕不及格

4 I fail to see/understand *formal* used to show that you are annoyed by something that you do not accept or understand【正式】我搞不清楚/明白〔用於表示生氣〕: *I fail to see why you find it so amusing.* 我不明白你為甚麼會覺得這很有趣。

5 ▶COMPANY/BUSINESS 公司/商號◀ [I] to be unable to continue because of a lack of money〔因缺錢而〕倒閉, 破產: *A large number of small businesses failed in the recession.* 許多小型企業在經濟衰退中倒閉了。

6 ▶MACHINE/BODY PART 機器部件/身體部位◀ [I] if a part of a machine or an organ in your body fails, it stops working〔機件、人體器官〕失靈; 出毛病: *The rocket's engine failed a few seconds after take-off.* 火箭發射幾秒鐘後, 發動機便失靈了。| *My uncle's kidneys failed two days after the operation.* 我叔叔的兩個腎在手術後兩天便功能全失了。

7 never fail to do sth to do something so regularly that people are sure that you will do it 從來不會忘記做某事: *My grandson never fails to phone me on my birthday.* 我的孫兒從來不會忘記在我生日時打電話給我。

8 your courage/will/nerve fails (you) if your courage etc fails, or fails you, you suddenly do not have it when you need it 你的勇氣/意志/膽量消失: *At the last moment my nerve failed. I walked away from her door without knocking.* 最後一刻我失去了膽量, 我沒敲門就從她的門口走開了。

9 fail sb to not do what someone has trusted you to do 使某人失望: *I feel I've failed my children by not spending more time with them.* 我覺得我使孩子們失望了, 因為我沒能多花些時間陪伴他們。—see also 另見 **words fail me** (WORD¹ (25))

10 ▶CROPS 作物◀ [I] to not grow or produce food 歉收: *If the crops fail again this year, people will starve.* 如果今年莊稼再歉收, 人們就會挨餓。

11 ▶RAINS 雨水◀ [I] to not come at the usual time of year〔在該下雨的季節〕無雨, 不下雨

12 failing sight/health sight or health that is becoming worse 衰退的視力/健康

fail² *n* **1 without fail a)** if you do something without fail, you always do it 必定, 總是: *Tim visits his mother every day without fail.* 蒂姆每天必去看望他的母親。**b)** used to tell someone very firmly that they must do something 務必, 一定〔用於告誡別人定要做某事〕: *I want that work finished by tomorrow, without fail!* 我要求那項工作必須在明天前完成, 不得有誤! **2** [C] an unsuccessful result in a test or examination〔考試〕不及格: *I got a fail in history.* 我歷史考試不及格。

failed /feld; feɪld/ *adj* [only before noun 僅用於名詞前] **a failed actor/writer etc** someone who wanted to be an actor etc but was unsuccessful 不成功[失敗]的演員/作家等

fail·ing¹ /ˈfelɪŋ; ˈfeɪlɪŋ/ *n* [C] a fault or weakness 缺點, 弱點: *I love him, despite his failings.* 儘管他有種種缺點, 我還是愛他。

failing² *prep* used to say that if your first suggestion is not successful or possible, there is another possibility that you could try 如果不行〔用於說明如果第一個建議行不通時, 還可能做的另一件事〕: *There are two cheap hotels, but failing either of these, you may as well go back to where you were before.* 有兩家廉價的旅館; 但如果兩家都不行的話, 你不妨回到你以前住的地方。| **failing that** *Try to get them to pay for the damage, or failing that, claim on their insurance.* 力爭讓他們賠償損失。如果不行的話, 就要求從他們的保險賠款中賠付。

fail-safe /ˈ· ·/ *adj* **1** a fail-safe machine, piece of equipment etc contains a system that makes the machine stop working if one part of it fails〔機器、設備等〕有自動防止故障裝置的; 有安全保障裝置的 **2** a fail-safe plan is certain to succeed 萬無一失的, 萬全的

fail·ure /ˈfeljə; ˈfeɪljə/ *n*

1 ▶LACK OF SUCCESS 不成功◀ [C,U] a lack of success in achieving or doing something 失敗: *How can we account for the failure of the League of Nations to achieve peace in Europe?* 我們怎麼解釋國際聯盟為何無法在歐洲實現和平呢? | **end/result in failure** *Harry's ambitious plans ended in failure.* 哈里雄心勃勃的計劃以失敗告終。

2 ▶UNSUCCESSFUL PERSON/THING 失敗的人/事◀ [C] someone or something that is not successful 失敗的人[事]: *I always felt a bit of a failure at school.* 我上學時總覺得自己多少是個失敗者。| **a total/complete failure** *The whole thing was a total failure from start to finish.* 這件事從頭到尾都是個失敗。| **crop failure** *a series of crop failures* 連年莊稼歉收

3 failure to do sth an act of not doing something which should be done or which people expect you to do 未能做〔應做到的〕某事: *Failure to produce proof of identity could result in prosecution.* 未能出示身分證明可能會被起訴。

4 ▶MACHINE/BODY PART 機器部件/人體部分◀ [C,

U] an occasion when a machine or part of your body stops working properly 故障, 失靈; 衰竭: *engine failure* 發動機故障 | **[+in]** *a failure in the computer system caused by a mechanical fault* 因機械故障引起的電腦系統失靈 | **heart/kidney/liver failure** *The disease can result in terminal kidney failure.* 這種病會引起腎衰竭而不治。
5 ▶BUSINESS 企業◀ [C,U] a situation in which a business has to close because of a lack of money 倒閉, 關閉: *The number of small business failures is growing each year.* 破產的小型企業數量每年都在增加。

fain /fen; feɪn/ *adv old use* 【舊】 **would fain do sth** *old use* if you would fain do something, you would like to do it 【舊】樂意地

faint¹ /fent; feɪnt/ *adj* **1** difficult to see, hear, smell etc〔指看、聽、嗅等〕不清楚的, 模糊的: *a faint noise* 微弱的響聲 | *the faint outline of the cliffs* 懸崖的模糊輪廓 **2 a faint hope/chance/feeling etc** a very small or slight chance etc 很小的希望/機會/感覺等: *There's still a faint hope that they might be alive.* 還有一線希望, 他們可能還活着。| *There was a faint edge of menace in his voice.* 他的聲音中帶有一點威脅的味道。**3** feeling weak because you are very ill, tired, or hungry〔因生病、疲倦或飢餓而〕虛弱的: **[+with]** *feeling faint with hunger and fatigue* 又餓又累, 感到虛弱 **4 not have the faintest idea** to not know anything at all about something〔對某事〕根本不知道, 一無所知: *They didn't seem to have the faintest idea what I was talking about.* 他們好像一點也不明白我在說甚麼。—see also 另見 **damn sb/sth with faint praise** (DAMN⁵ (2)) —**faintly** *adv*: *Her name sounds faintly familiar.* 她的名字聽起來有一點點耳熟。| *The sun shone faintly through the clouds.* 陽光透過雲層微弱地照射着。—**faintness** *n* [U]

faint² *v* [I] **1** to suddenly become unconscious for a short time 暈倒, 昏厥: *Several fans fainted in the blazing heat.* 幾個球迷在炙熱的氣温下暈過去了。**2 I nearly/almost fainted** *spoken* used to say that you were very surprised by something 【口】我差點昏過去〔表示很驚訝〕: *I nearly fainted when they told me the price.* 他們告訴我價格時, 我差點昏過去。

faint³ *n* [C] an act of becoming unconscious 昏厥: **in a (dead) faint** *She fell down in a faint.* 她昏倒了。

faint-heart·ed /,· '··◂/ *adj* **1** not trying very hard, because you do not want to do something, or you are not confident that you can succeed 沒有勇氣的, 缺乏信心的, 怯懦的: *She made a rather faint-hearted attempt to stop him from leaving.* 她有點膽怯地試圖阻止他離開。**2 not for the faint-hearted** *humorous* used to say that something is difficult and needs a lot of effort 【幽默】不是懦夫所能幹的

1 **fair¹** /fɛr; feə/ *adj*
2 **1 ▶REASONABLE AND ACCEPTABLE** 合理並可接受的◀ a situation, system, or way of treating people that is fair seems reasonable and acceptable 公平的, 合理的: *a fair wage for the job* 為這份工作提供的合理工資 | *Who said life was fair?* 誰說生活是公平的? | *Everyone should have the right to a fair trial.* 每個人都應有權得到公平的審訊。| **it is fair to do sth** *It seems fair to give them their money back.* 把錢還給他們, 這似乎是應該的。| **it's fair to say that** (=used to say that a judgement about something seems reasonable) 說句公道話…; 說…才是公平的 *I think it's fair to say that she was not to blame for the accident.* 我認為, 公正地說, 這次事故不該怪她。
2 ▶TREATING EVERYONE EQUALLY 一視同仁◀ a fair situation, judgement, description etc is one in which everyone is treated equally 公正的, 公平的: *Why do you let her stay out late and not me? It's not fair!* 你為甚麼允許她晚回家而不讓我這樣做? 這不公平! | **fair to** *The old law wasn't fair to women.* 那條舊的法律對婦女不公平。| **it's only fair (that)** *You pay him $10 an hour – it's only fair that I should get the same.* 既然你給他每小時10美元, 我也該得到同樣的工資, 這才是公平的。
3 ▶FAIR PERSON 公正的人◀ someone who treats everyone in a reasonable, equal way〔指人〕公平合理的, 公正的, 正直的: *The boss is a hard man – hard but fair.* 老闆是個嚴厲的人 —— 嚴厲但公正。
4 ▶QUITE BIG/FAR/A LOT 很大/遠/多◀ **a fair size/number/amount/distance etc** *especially BrE* a fairly large size, number etc 【尤英】相當大的尺寸/數目/數量/距離等: *There's a fair amount of unemployment around here.* 這附近失業的人相當多。| *We had travelled a fair way by lunch time.* 到午飯時, 我們已走了相當遠的一段路。
5 ▶SKIN/HAIR 皮膚/頭髮◀ light in colour 白皙的; 金色的: *He had blue eyes and fair hair.* 他長着藍眼睛和金色頭髮。| *Both her children are very fair.* 她的兩個孩子皮膚都很白皙。—opposite 反義詞 DARK¹ (4) —see picture on page A6 參見A6頁圖
6 ▶LEVEL OF ABILITY 能力水平◀ neither particularly good nor particularly bad; average 中等的, 普通的: *Her written work is excellent but her practical work is only fair.* 她的文字功夫極佳, 但實際工作卻很一般。
7 ▶ACCORDING TO THE RULES 根據規則◀ a fair fight, game, or election is one that is played or done according to the rules〔拳擊、比賽、選舉等〕根據規則進行的: *free and fair elections* 自由公正的選舉
8 ▶WEATHER 天氣◀ pleasant and not windy, rainy etc 晴朗的: *That morning the weather was fair, and the air was warm.* 那天上午天氣晴朗暖和。
9 have a fair idea of to know quite a lot about what something is like 對…相當了解: *I think I have a fair idea of what the job involves.* 我想我對這項工作包含的內容有相當的了解。
10 have had more than your fair share of to have had more of something, especially something unpleasant, than seems reasonable or fair 受夠了〔尤指不愉快之事〕: *Poor old Alan! He's had more than his fair share of bad luck recently.* 可憐的老阿倫!他最近遇到的倒霉事太多了。
11 give sb a fair crack of the whip *BrE informal* to give someone the chance to do something especially to show that they are able to do it 【英, 非正式】給某人均等的機會〔以證明他能做好某事〕
12 a fair shake *AmE informal* fair treatment that allows someone the same chances as everyone else 【美, 非正式】公平的待遇; 均等的機會: *Inner city kids aren't getting a fair shake in the schools.* 市中心貧民區的孩子在學校裡得不到公平的待遇。
13 by fair means or foul using any method to get what you want, including dishonest or illegal methods 不擇手段, 千方百計
14 fair-to-middling not feeling very well 差強人意
15 all's fair in love and war used to say that in some situations any method of getting what you want is acceptable 情場和戰場, 兩者皆不厭詐〔指在某些情況下為達目的不擇手段是可以接受的〕
16 ▶PLEASANT/ATTRACTIVE 悅人的/吸引人的◀ *old use* pleasant and attractive 【舊】漂亮的, 迷人的: *The fair city of Rome.* 美麗的羅馬城 | *a fair maiden* 美麗的少女 —see also 另見 FAIRLY, FAIRNESS

Frequencies of the adjective **fair** in spoken and written English. 形容詞 fair 在英語口語和書面語中的使用頻率

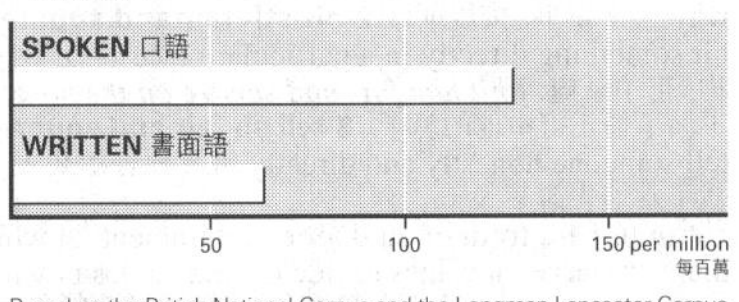

Based on the British National Corpus and the Longman Lancaster Corpus 據英國國家語料庫和朗文蘭卡斯特語料庫

This graph shows that the adjective **fair** is much more common in spoken English than in written English. This is because it is used in a lot of common spoken phrases. 本圖表顯示, 形容詞 fair 在英語口語中的使用頻率遠遠高於書面語, 因為口語中很多常用片語是由 fair 構成的。

fair (*adj*) SPOKEN PHRASES
含 fair 的口語片語

17 fair enough *especially BrE* used to say that you agree with someone's suggestion or that something seems reasonable【尤英】說得對, 有道理: *"See you on Tuesday at 8." "Fair enough."* "星期二八點見。" "行。" | *Well, if you want to go on your own that's fair enough.* 好吧, 如果你要自己去, 那也可以。

18 it's/that's not fair used when you think that what is happening is unfair 這/那不公平: *It's not fair, you never let me borrow your clothes.* 這不公平, 你從來不借給我你的衣服。| **It's/that's not fair on sb** *You can't just give the clever kids attention because that's not fair on the rest of the class.* 你不能只注意那些聰明的孩子, 因為那對班上的其他學生是不公平的。

19 to be fair used when adding something after someone has been criticized, which helps to explain or excuse what they did 說句公道話: *She should have phoned to tell us what her plans were although, to be fair, she's been very busy.* 她早該打電話將她的計劃告訴我們。不過, 說句公道話, 她一直很忙。

20 fair comment *BrE* used to say that a remark or criticism seems fair【英】合理的話; 公正的評論: *"I don't mind doing the work, but you should have asked me." "Fair comment."* "我不介意做那項工作, 但你應該先問我一下。" "此言有理。"

21 be fair! used to tell someone not to be unreasonable or criticize someone too much 要公道些!: *Come on, be fair, the poor girl's trying her hardest!* 算了吧, 要公道些! 這可憐的女孩正盡力而為!

22 fair's fair used when you think it is fair that someone should do something, especially because of something that has happened earlier 應當公道才是: *Come on, fair's fair – I paid last time so it's your turn.* 得啦, 應當公平才是 —— 上次我付錢, 所以這次輪到你了。

23 you can't say fairer than that *BrE* used to say that an offer you are making to someone is the best, fairest offer they can possibly get【英】這是再公道不過了, 無法比這再合理了: *I'll give you £25 for it – you can't say fairer than that, can you?* 這東西我給你 25 英鎊 —— 這是再公道不過了, 不是嗎?

24 it's a fair cop *BrE* used in a joking way when someone catches you doing something that you should not be doing【英】抓個正着, 當場抓住〔用於被人發現做不該做之事時的玩笑說法〕: *"I saw you, now give me that back." "All right, it's a fair cop."* "我看見你了, 把那東西還給我。" "好吧, 被你抓個正着。"

25 with your own fair hands *BrE humorous* used to say that you did something by yourself without any help【英, 幽默】用自己的雙手, 親自: *"Did you do all the decorating yourself?" "Yes, it's all been done with my own fair hands."* "所有的裝飾都是你自己做的嗎?" "是的, 都是我親手做的。"

S2 W3 **fair²** *adv* **1 play fair** to do something in a fair and honest way 公平辦事, 按規則做 **2 hit sth fair and square** to hit something directly in a particular place 直接擊中某物; 正中某處: *I hit him fair and square on the nose.* 我不偏不倚正打中他的鼻子。**3 tell sb fair and square** to tell someone honestly and directly 誠實地告訴某人; 直截了當地告訴某人

fair³ *n* [C] **1** a form of outdoor entertainment, at which there are large machines to ride on and games in which you can win prizes 露天遊樂場〔有大型機動遊戲和有獎遊戲的戶外活動〕; CARNIVAL (2) *AmE*【美】—see also 另見 FUNFAIR **2** *BrE* a market where animals and farm products are sold【英】〔出售動物和農產品的〕市場; 集市: *a cattle fair* 牛市場 **3** an event at which farm products and equipment are shown and entered in competitions, and where there are often games and large machines to ride on〔有農產品和農業設備展出、有競賽, 並常有娛樂活動和大型機動遊戲的〕農牧集市: **state/county fair** (=a fair for the whole state or county) 州/縣物產集市 **4** a regular occasion when companies show their newest products in order to advertise them〔商品〕博覽會, 展銷會, 展覽會: *a trade fair* 商品交易會 | *The Frankfurt Book Fair* 法蘭克福書展 **5** an outdoor event with games and things to buy, organized to get money 義賣會; FETE¹(1) *BrE*【英】

fair cop·y /ˌ· ˈ··/ *n* [C] a neat copy of a piece of writing 謄清本, 清稿

fair din·kum /ˌfɛr ˈdɪŋkəm; ˌfeə ˈdɪŋkəm/ *adj AustrE spoken* real or true【澳口】真正的; 真實的

fair game /ˌ· ˈ·/ *n* [U] someone or something that is easy to criticize or deserves to be criticized 易受批評的人[物]; 該受批評的人[物]: *The behaviour of the younger royals made them fair game for the tabloid press.* 年輕的王室成員的行為使他們成了小報的批評對象。

fair·ground /ˈfɛrˌgraund; ˈfeəgraʊnd/ *n* [C] an open space on which a fair (FAIR³ (1)) takes place 露天遊樂場(會場)

fair-haired boy /ˌ·· ˈ·/ *n* [C] *AmE informal* someone who is likely to succeed because someone in authority likes them【美, 非正式】得寵的人; BLUE-EYED BOY *especially BrE*【尤英】: *the boss's fair-haired boy* 老闆的寵兒

fair·ly /ˈfɛrlɪ; ˈfeəli/ *adv* **1** more than a little, but much less than very 相當, 頗: *The house had a fairly large garden.* 那幢房子有個相當大的花園。| *She speaks English fairly well.* 她英語講得相當好。—see 見 RATHER (USAGE) **2** in a way that is fair and not dishonest, unreasonable etc 公正地; 誠實地: *I felt I hadn't been treated fairly.* 我覺得我沒受到公正的待遇。**3** *BrE* used to say that someone did something quickly or a lot【英】迅速地; 大量地: *He fairly raced past us on his motorcycle.* 他騎着摩托車飛快地從我們身邊駛過。

fair-mind·ed /ˌ· ˈ··◂/ *adj* able to understand and judge situations fairly and always considering other people's opinions 公正的, 不偏不倚的: *He's a fair-minded man – I'm sure he'll listen to what you have to say.* 他是個公正的人 —— 我確信他會傾聽你說的話。

fair·ness /ˈfɛrnɪs; ˈfeərn̩s/ *n* [U] **1** the quality of being fair 公平, 公正 **2 in fairness (to)** used after you have just criticized someone to add something more favourable which explains their behaviour 說句公道話, 公正地說〔用於在批評某人後說一些有利於他的話〕: *Tardelli had a poor match, although in fairness he was playing with a knee injury.* 塔德利在場上表現很差, 但說句公道話, 他是膝部帶傷參加比賽的。

fair play /ˌ· ˈ·/ *n* [U] **1** playing according to the rules of a game without cheating〔按規則進行的〕公平比賽 **2** *BrE* fair treatment of people without cheating or dishonesty【英】公正處理; 公平對待 —see also 另見 **turnabout is fair play** (TURNABOUT (2))

fair sex /ˌ· ˈ·/ *n* **the fair sex** *old-fashioned* women【過時】婦女, 女性

fair·way /ˈfɛrˌwe; ˈfeəweɪ/ *n* [C] the part of a GOLF COURSE that you hit the ball along towards the hole〔高爾夫球場上的〕平坦球道, 無障礙區 —see picture on page A23 參見 A23 頁圖

fair-weath·er friend /ˌ· ·· ˈ·/ *n* [C] someone who only wants to be your friend when you are successful 不能共患難的朋友

fai·ry /ˈfɛrɪ; ˈfeəri/ *n* [C] **1** a small imaginary creature with magic powers, which looks like a very small person 仙子, 小精靈 **2** an offensive word for a HOMOSEXUAL man 男同性戀者〔冒犯用語〕

fairy god·moth·er /ˌ·· ˈ···/ *n* [C] a woman with magic

powers who saves people from trouble, especially in children's stories〔尤指童話中幫助人的〕仙姑, 仙女

fai·ry·land /ˈfɛrɪˌlænd; ˈfeərilænd/ *n* **1** [U] an imaginary place where fairies live 仙鄉, 仙界 **2** [singular] a place that looks very beautiful and special 仙境, 幻境, 美麗神奇的地方: *At night, the harbor is a fairyland.* 夜晚, 港口美如仙境。

fairy lights /ˈ·· ·/ *n* [plural] *BrE* small coloured lights used especially to decorate a Christmas tree【英】〔裝飾聖誕樹的〕小彩燈

fairy tale /ˈ·· ·/ also 又作 **fairy sto·ry** /ˈ·· ˌ··/ *BrE*【英】*n* [C] **1** a children's story in which magical things happen 童話; 神話; 神仙故事 **2** a story that someone has invented and is difficult to believe 謊言; 騙人話; 不可信的事

fai·ry·tale /ˈfɛrɪˌtel; ˈfeəriteɪl/ *adj* [only before noun 僅用於名詞前] extremely happy, lucky etc in a way that usually only happens in children's stories 童話裡才有的; 童話般的; 極其美滿幸福的: *a fairytale romance* 童話般的愛情故事

fait ac·com·pli /ˌfet ˌækɑmˈpli; ˌfeɪt əˈkɒmpliː/ *n* [singular] *French* something that has already happened or been done and cannot be changed【法】既成事實

2 **faith** /feθ; feɪθ/ *n*

1 ►TRUST/BELIEF IN SB/STH 信任/相信某人/某物◄ [U] a strong belief that someone or something can be trusted to be right or to do the right thing 信念; 信任; 信心: **have faith in** *I have great faith in her, she won't let me down.* 我對她很有信心, 她不會讓我失望的。| **destroy/restore sb's faith in** (=take away or give back their faith) 毀滅/恢復某人對...的信念[信心] *It's really restored my faith in human nature.* 此事確實恢復了我對人性的信念。| **lose faith in** *The public has quite simply lost faith in the government.* 公眾已完全對政府失去信心。

2 ►RELIGION 宗教◄ **a)** [U] belief and trust in God 對上帝的信仰; 宗教信仰: *deep religious faith* 堅定的宗教信仰 | **[+in]** *my faith in God* 我對上帝的信仰 **b)** [C] one of the main religions in the world 宗教: *people from all faiths* 各種宗教信仰的人 | *the Jewish faith* 猶太教

3 break faith with to stop supporting or believing in a person, organization, or idea 背棄; 背信, 不信守; 脫離: *How could he tell them the truth without breaking faith with the Party?* 他不脫黨怎麼能跟他們說明事實真相呢?

4 keep faith with to continue to support or believe in a person, organization, or idea 恪守對...的信仰; 信守; 不背棄

5 good faith honest and sincere intentions 真誠, 誠意, 誠信: *He proposed a second meeting as a sign of his good faith.* 他建議再舉行一次會議, 以表示他的誠意。| **in good faith** (=without intending to deceive someone) 真誠地, 善意地 *The woman who sold me the car claimed she had acted in good faith.* 那個賣車給我的女人聲稱她是誠意出售的。

6 an act of faith something you do that shows you trust someone completely 信賴某人的行為[表示]: *Letting Sammy borrow my new camera was a real act of faith.* 讓薩米借走我的新相機確實是出於對他的信任。

faith·ful[1] /ˈfeθfəl; ˈfeɪθfəl/ *adj* **1** remaining loyal to a person, belief, political party etc and continuing to support them〔對人、信念、政黨等〕忠誠的, 忠實的; 守信的: *years of faithful service* 多年忠誠的服務 | **[+to]** *Russell remained faithful to his principles to the last.* 羅素至死忠於自己的原則。**2** representing an event or an image in a way that is exactly true or that looks exactly the same 如實的, 準確可靠的; 忠於原事[物]的: *a faithful account of what had happened* 對所發生之事的如實報道 | *a faithful reproduction of the original picture* 忠於原圖的複製品 **3** loyal to your wife, boyfriend etc by not having a sexual relationship with anyone else〔愛情上〕忠貞的: **[+to]** *Do you think Bob's always been faithful to you?* 你認為鮑勃一直對你忠誠嗎? —**faithfulness** *n* [U]

faithful[2] *n* **1 the faithful a)** the people who are very loyal to a leader, political party etc and continue to support them〔領袖、政黨等的〕忠實信徒 **b)** the people who believe in a religion〔宗教〕教徒; 信眾 **2** [C] a loyal follower, supporter, or member 忠實的追隨者[支持者; 成員]: *a handful of old faithfuls at the meeting* 會上的一些多年的忠實追隨者

faith·ful·ly /ˈfeθfəlɪ; ˈfeɪθfəl-i/ *adv* **1** in a faithful way 忠誠地, 忠實地; 如實地: *He had served the family faithfully for 40 years.* 他已忠心耿耿為這一家人服務了40年。**2 promise faithfully** to promise that you will definitely do something 真心實意地答應: *Ann promised faithfully that she would never tell.* 安真心實意地答應說她決不會說出去。**3 Yours faithfully** *especially BrE* the usual polite way of ending a formal letter, which you have begun with Dear Sir or Dear Madam【尤英】忠實於您的〔正式信件結尾所用的客套話, 信的開端用 Dear Sir 或 Dear Madam 時用〕—compare 比較 **Yours sincerely** (SINCERELY (2))

faith heal·ing /ˈ· ˌ··/ *n* [U] a method of treating illnesses by praying〔通過祈禱來治病的〕信仰療法 —**faith healer** *n* [C]

faith·less /ˈfeθlɪs; ˈfeɪθləs/ *adj formal* someone who is faithless cannot be trusted【正式】不忠實的, 不能信賴的, 背信棄義的, 不守信義的: *a faithless friend* 不能信賴[不忠誠]的朋友 —**faithlessly** *adv* —**faithlessness** *n* [U]

fake[1] /fek; feɪk/ *n* [C] **1** a copy of a valuable object, painting etc that is intended to deceive people 贗品, 假貨: *We thought it was a genuine antique, but it was only a fake.* 我們以為那是真古董, 可實際上只是一件贗品。**2** someone who is not what they claim to be or does not have the skills they say they have 騙子, 冒充者, 假冒者: *He claimed to have natural healing powers, but he turned out to be a fake.* 他聲稱擁有自然治病的本領, 結果發現他只是個騙子。

F

fake[2] *adj* [usually before noun 一般用於名詞前] **1** made to look like a real material or object in order to deceive people 偽造的, 假的: *fake fur* 假毛皮 **2** pretending to be something you are not in order to deceive people 冒充的, 假冒的: *A fake doctor tricked his way into a hospital last night.* 昨晚有位冒牌醫生用計混進了醫院。

fake[3] *v* **1** [T] to make an exact copy of something, or invent figures or results, in order to deceive people 仿造; 捏造, 偽造: *He faked his father's signature on the cheque.* 他在支票上偽造父親的簽名。| *The results of these experiments were faked.* 這些實驗的結果都是捏造的。**2** [I,T] to pretend to be ill, interested etc when you are not 假裝, 偽裝: **fake it** *I thought he was really hurt but he was faking it.* 我以為他真的受傷了, 可他是裝出來的。**3** [I,T] to pretend to move in one direction, but then move in another, especially when playing sport〔比賽中〕做(...的)假動作: *He faked a pass and then handed the ball off to Perry.* 他做了個傳球的假動作, 然後把球傳給佩里。

fake sb **out** *phr v* [T] *AmE* to deceive someone by making them think you are planning to do something when you are really planning to do something else【美】故意欺騙〔某人〕

fa·kir /fəˈkɪr; ˈfeɪkɪə/ *n* [C] a travelling Hindu or Muslim holy man〔印度教的〕苦行者;〔伊斯蘭教的〕托鉢僧

fa·laf·el /ˌfəˈlæfəl; ˌfəˈlæfəl/ *n* [C,U] fried balls of an Arabic food made with CHICKPEAS 炸豆丸子, 炸豆泥

fal·con /ˈfɔlkən; ˈfɔːlkən/ *n* [C] a bird that kills and eats other animals and can be trained to hunt 獵鷹

fal·con·er /ˈfɔlkənə; ˈfɔːlkənə/ *n* [C] someone who trains falcons to hunt 放鷹狩獵者; 訓練獵鷹的人, 獵鷹師

fal·con·ry /ˈfɔlkənrɪ; ˈfɔːlkənri/ *n* [U] the skill or sport of using falcons to hunt 獵鷹訓練術; 放鷹狩獵運動, 鷹獵

fall[1] *v* /fɔl; fɔːl/ *past tense* **fell** /fɛl; fel/ *past participle* **fallen** /ˈfɔlən; ˈfɔːlən/ 

1 ►MOVE DOWNWARDS 向下移動◄ [I] to move downwards from a higher position to a lower position 落下, 降落; 跌落: *The rain had started falling again.* 雨

又開始下了。| **[+out of/from/on etc]** *Wyatt fell from a second floor window.* 懷亞特從二樓的窗子摔下來。| **[+down]** *I'm always worried that one of the kids will fall down the stairs.* 我總是擔心其中一個小孩會從樓梯上摔下來。| **sb's trousers/socks etc are falling down** *His shirt was all dirty and his trousers were falling down.* 他的襯衫很髒, 褲子也快掉下了。| **rise and fall** *The little boat rose and fell with the movement of the waves.* 小船隨着波浪起伏。

2 ►GO DOWN ONTO THE GROUND 落到地上◄ [I] to suddenly go down onto the ground after you have been standing, walking, or running, especially without intending to 摔倒, 跌倒: *I fell and hit my head.* 我跌倒, 撞到了頭。| *Careful you don't fall – the path's very icy.* 小心別摔倒 —— 路上結了很多冰。| **[+on/into etc]** *One of the horses slipped and fell into a ditch.* 有一匹馬滑倒, 掉進了溝裡。| **fall flat on your face** (=fall so that you are lying facing the ground) 摔了個嘴啃地 *She fell flat on her face in the mud.* 她在爛泥裡摔了個嘴啃地。| **fall to your knees** (=move down from a standing position so that your body is resting on your knees) 跪下, 下跪

3 ►TO A LOWER AMOUNT ETC 數量等下降◄ [I] to go down to a lower price, amount, level etc, especially a much lower one〔價格、數量、水平等較大幅度地〕下跌, 下降, 降低: *In winter the temperature often falls below zero.* 冬天溫度經常跌到零度以下。| **fall steeply/sharply** (= by a large amount) 急劇下降 *Interest rates fell sharply.* 利率暴跌。| *falling income levels* 不斷下降的收入水平

4 fall asleep/ill/silent/pregnant to become asleep, ill etc 睡着/病倒/安靜下來/懷孕: *I fell asleep halfway through the film.* 電影放映了一半我就睡着了。

5 fall in love to start to love someone or something very much 愛[戀]上: **[+with]** *As soon as we met, we fell in love with each other.* 我們彼此一見鍾情。| *Primmie fell in love with California on sight.* 普里米一眼就愛上了加利福尼亞。

6 fall to pieces/bits a) to break into many pieces 碎成許多片: *The vase fell to bits as soon as it hit the floor.* 花瓶一摔到地板上就碎了。**b)** if something such as a plan or a relationship falls to pieces, it stops working properly〔計劃〕失敗;〔關係〕破裂

7 be falling to pieces/bits to be in very bad condition, especially because of being very old〔尤因年久而〕快要垮掉, 快要崩潰: *The walls were all dirty and the furniture was falling to pieces.* 牆壁很髒, 家具也都快散架了。

8 fall into/out of to go into or out of a place very quickly because you are in a hurry or very tired〔因匆忙或疲倦而〕迅速進入/離開: *As soon as she got home she fell into bed.* 她一到家便一頭倒到牀上。

9 fall into decay/disrepair/disrepute etc to become decayed, in bad condition, no longer respected etc 朽壞/失修/名聲掃地: *Over the years the old palace had fallen into decay.* 多年以來這座古老的宮殿已破爛不堪。

10 fall flat if a joke, remark, or performance falls flat, it fails to interest or amuse people〔笑話、說話或表演〕達不到預期效果; 無法逗人笑

11 fall short of to be less than the amount or standard that is needed or that you want 未達到…; 不足…; 未滿…: *Unfortunately, the course fell far short of our expectations.* 不幸的是, 這個課程沒有達到我們的期望。

12 fall out of fashion/favour to stop being popular or fashionable 不再時髦; 不再受歡迎

13 fall from grace/favour to stop being liked by people in authority 失寵〔於權勢者〕: *I don't think she'll get promotion – she's rather fallen from grace recently.* 我認為她不會得到提升 —— 她近來已經失寵。

14 fall into the hands of/clutches of if something or someone falls into the hands of an enemy or dangerous person, the enemy etc gets control or possession of them 落入…的手中/控制中: *The documents fell into the hands of the KGB.* 這些文件落入克格勃的手中。

15 fall victim/prey to to get a very serious illness or be attacked or deceived by someone 得〔重病〕; 受到…的攻擊[欺騙]: *While in Africa she fell victim to a rare blood disorder.* 在非洲的時候, 她得了一種罕見的血液病。

16 fall into the habit of to start doing something, especially something that you should not do 沾染[養成]…的習慣: *He soon fell into the habit of having a drink on the way home from work.* 他很快沾染上了在下班回家的路上去喝酒的習慣。

17 fall into a trap/pitfall to make a mistake that many people make 犯許多人會犯的錯誤: *It's easy to fall into the trap of believing that the threat of nuclear war is over.* 人們很容易犯錯, 認為核戰爭的威脅已不存在。

18 fall back into your old ways to start doing things or behaving in the way that you used to, especially in a way that other people disapprove of 回到過去的壞習慣; 重犯已改掉的壞習慣: *I expect she'll soon fall back into her old ways.* 我想她很快就會重蹈過去的惡習。

19 fall into a category/group etc also 又作 **fall under a heading** to be part of a group of things or people that are similar in some way 屬於某一類: *A lot of my friends fall into the same category.* 我的許多朋友都屬於這一類人。

20 fall into place a) if parts of a situation that you have been trying to understand fall into place, you start to understand how they are connected with each other 變得一清二楚; 變得條理清楚; 變得明朗: *Gradually the clues started falling into place and it became clear who the murderer was.* 這些線索使情況逐漸明朗, 兇手是誰就一清二楚了。**b)** if the parts of something that you want to happen fall into place, they start to happen in the way that you want〔事情〕按照意願[設想]發生; 互相符合; 有條有理: *We've found someone who'll lend us the money, and it looks as if things are finally falling into place.* 我們已找到願意借錢給我們的人, 看起來一切終將按部就班地實現了。

21 fall into line to obey someone or do what other people want you to do, especially when you do not want to do it at first 聽從, 服從; 取得一致: *If you can persuade her, the others will soon fall into line.* 如果你能說服她, 其他人很快就會一致跟上。

22 fall into step with a) to start doing something in the same way as the other members of a group 與…步調一致; 與…方式一樣: *The other countries on the Security Council are expected to fall into step with the US.* 預計安理會的其他成員國會與美國步調一致。**b)** to start to walk next to someone else, at the same speed as them 與…齊步行走

23 fall by the wayside a) to become unsuccessful after being successful at first 半途失敗: *A lot of marriages fall by the wayside because couples cannot talk to each other.* 許多婚姻因夫妻倆無法交流而中途破裂。**b)** to stop being important and therefore be forgotten about〔因失去重要性〕被人遺忘, 被忽視: *With so many domestic problems, foreign policy issues tended to fall by the wayside.* 由於出現這麼多的國內問題, 外交政策問題就容易被人忽視了。

24 night/darkness/dusk falls *literary* used to say that the night begins and that it starts to become dark【文】夜幕降臨: *We arrived at the village just as night was falling.* 夜幕降臨時, 我們到達了這座村子。

25 ►LIGHT/SHADOW 光線/陰影◄ [I always+adv/prep] to shine on a surface or go onto a surface 照射(到): *The last rays of sunlight were falling on the fields.* 夕陽的餘暉照射在田野上。

26 fall down on the job *informal* to not do your work or duties as well as you should【非正式】工作做得不理想: *I'd be falling down on my job if I didn't take an interest in the welfare of my staff.* 如果我不關心員工的福利, 我就是沒有做好我的工作。

27 it fell off the back of a lorry *BrE humorous* used to say that something was stolen【英, 幽默】被偷走了

28 fall foul of to do something which makes someone angry, or which breaks a rule with the result that you are punished 激怒…; 同…爭吵; 違反（法規）〔從而受到懲處〕: *Edwards fell foul of the authorities and was ordered to leave the country.* 愛德華兹同當局發生糾紛後被勒令離境。
29 it's as easy as falling off a log *spoken* used to say that something is very easy to do【口】這極其簡單容易
30 fall on deaf ears if someone's words fall on deaf ears, no-one pays any attention to them 未受到注意; 被置若罔聞: *His pleas fell on deaf ears.* 他的請求未受到注意。
31 fall on hard times to have problems because you do not have enough money 陷入貧困, 境遇艱難: *middle-class families that have fallen on hard times* 生活陷入困境的中產階級家庭
32 ►LOSE POWER 失去權力◄ [I] if a leader or a government falls, they lose their position of power〔領導人或政府〕垮台; 失勢: *The previous administration fell after only 6 months in office.* 上屆政府僅執政六個月便垮台了。
33 ►BE TAKEN BY AN ENEMY 被敵人佔領◄ [I] if a place falls in a war or an election, a group of soldiers or a political party takes control of it 陷落; 被攻佔; 被打敗: **[+to]** *The city fell to the advancing Russian armies.* 這座城市被挺進中的俄軍攻克了。
34 ►BE KILLED 被殺死◄ [I] *literary* to be killed in a war【文】陣亡, 戰死
35 ►HIT 打中, 擊中◄ [I always+adv/prep] to hit a particular place or a particular part of someone's body 打中, 擊中; 撞到: **[+on]** *The first punch fell on his nose.* 第一拳打到他的鼻子上。
36 ►HANG DOWN 下垂◄ [I always+adv/prep] to hang down loosely 下垂: **[+to/over]** *Her hair fell to her shoulders.* 她的長髮垂在肩上。
37 ►VOICE/SOUND 嗓音/聲音◄ [I] if someone's voice or a sound falls, it becomes quieter or lower〔嗓音〕變小;〔聲音〕放低
38 fall from sb's lips *literary* if words fall from someone's lips, they say them【文】從某人的口中說出
39 silence/sadness/calm etc falls *literary* used to say that a group of people or a place becomes quiet, sad etc【文】安靜下來/變得傷心/冷靜下來: **[+on/upon]** *As she entered the ballroom a great silence fell on the assembled guests.* 她進入舞廳時, 聚在一起的客人突然鴉雀無聲了。
40 ►SPECIAL EVENT/CELEBRATION 特殊事件/慶典◄ **fall on** to happen on a particular day or date 落在〔某一天〕: *Christmas falls on a Saturday this year.* 今年聖誕節在星期六。
41 sb's eyes/gaze/glance fell on used to say that someone saw something when they were looking at something else 某人的目光落在…上;〔在看別的東西時〕瞥見: *He was going through some old papers when his eyes fell on a photo of his mother.* 他正瀏覽一些舊文件, 突然看到他母親的一張照片。
42 the stress/accent/beat falls on used to say that a particular part of a word, phrase, or piece of music is emphasized or is played more loudly than the rest 重讀/重音/節拍落在…: *In the word 'report', the stress falls on the second syllable.* 在 report 這個詞裡, 重音落在第二個音節上。
43 fall at sb's feet to kneel in front of someone, especially to ask them to do something or to show your respect 跪在某人面前〔乞求或表示敬仰〕
44 fall between two stools to be neither one type of thing nor another, or be unable to choose between two ways of doing something〔因舉棋不定而〕兩頭落空: *The movie falls between two stools – it's neither a thriller nor a comedy.* 這部電影兩頭都不是 —— 既不是驚險片也不是喜劇片。
45 I almost fell off my chair *spoken* used to say that you were very surprised when something happened【口】我驚訝極了 —see also 另見 **fall/land on your feet** (FOOT[1] (18)), **let drop/fall** (LET[1] (17)), **sb's face fell** (FACE[1](2)), **stand or fall by/on** (STAND[1] (46))

fall about *phr v* [I] *BrE* to laugh a lot about something【英】放聲大笑: **fall about laughing** *The moment she started speaking everyone fell about laughing.* 她一開始說話, 大家就放聲大笑。

fall apart *phr v* [I] **1** if an organization, system etc falls apart, it stops working effectively and has a lot of problems〔組織、制度等〕崩潰, 瓦解: **be falling apart at the seams** *The Health Service is falling apart at the seams.* 醫療保健制度正在開始瓦解。**2 be falling apart** to be in very bad condition 快散架的, 破舊不堪的: *I'm not riding in your old car – it's falling apart.* 我才不坐你的舊車 —— 它都快散架了。**3** if your life, your world etc falls apart, you suddenly have a lot of personal problems〔生活、個人小天地等〕垮掉, 崩潰: *When his wife left him his world just fell apart.* 他的妻子離開他時, 他的世界就垮了。**4** to break into pieces 破碎, 斷裂, 散開: *The book fell apart in my hands as soon as I tried to pick it up.* 我剛要把書拿起來, 書就在我手裡散架了。

fall away *phr v* [I] **1** if something such as a feeling, a quality, or a noise falls away, it gradually becomes weaker or quieter and disappears〔逐漸〕衰落, 減少; 消失: *As confidence fell away consumers kept more of their cash in their pockets.* 隨着信心逐漸消失, 消費者把更多的現金留在口袋裡。**2** to slope downwards 向下傾斜: *After that the road falls away to the city of Odawara.* 在那以後路就朝着小田原市的方向傾斜。**3** to become separated from something after being fixed to it 脱落, 掉出: *A piece of wood had fallen away from the foot of the door.* 一塊木頭已從門腳下掉了出來。**4** to stop being able to be seen as you move through an area 從〔移動着的觀察者的〕視野裡消失: *An hour out of London the rows of houses started to fall away and we were surrounded by beautiful countryside.* 驅車出倫敦一小時後, 一排排的房子開始從視野裡消失, 我們的四周全是美麗的鄉村了。

fall back *phr v* [I] **1** if soldiers fall back, they move back because they are being attacked 撤退, 退後: *He ordered the men to fall back.* 他命令士兵後撤。**2** to move backwards because you are very surprised, frightened etc〔因驚奇、驚慌等而〕後退, 退卻: *They fell back in horror.* 他們嚇得往後退。

fall back on *phr v* [I] **1** to use something or depend on someone's help when dealing with a difficult situation, especially after you have tried using other methods or tried to deal with it yourself（轉而）依靠: **have sb/sth to fall back on** *Diana always had her father's money to fall back on.* 黛安娜總是還有她父親的錢可依靠。| *In that case we'll have to fall back on our original plan.* 這麼說, 我們得退而依靠我們原來的計劃。**2** to use a particular method, argument etc because it seems simple and easy, not because it is the best one to use〔退而求其次地〕使用〔簡單易行的方法、論點等〕: *They tend to fall back on the same tired old arguments.* 他們傾向於退而使用同樣的老一套的陳腐論點。

fall behind *phr v* [I,T] **1** to go more slowly than other people so that they gradually move further ahead of you 落在（…的）後面: *The older walkers soon fell behind.* 年紀大一些的步行者很快就落在後面了。**2** to become less successful than someone else 落後（於）: *The Eisenhower administration allowed the US to fall behind the Soviet Union in the production of nuclear arms.* 艾森豪威爾政府容許美國在核武器生產方面落後於蘇聯。| **[+with]** *In secondary school she started falling behind with her schoolwork.* 上中學時, 她的功課開始落後了。**3** to fail to finish a piece of work or to pay someone money that you owe them at the right time 拖欠（還款）, 不能按時完成（工作）: **[+with/on]** *We fell behind with the payments on the car and it was repossessed.* 我們拖欠分期付款買車的錢, 結果車子被收回去了。| **fall**

F

behind schedule *Preparations for the festival have fallen behind schedule because of technical difficulties.* 由於技術上的困難，節日的準備工作已落後於原定日程。

fall down *phr v* [I] **1** if someone falls down, they fall onto the ground 跌倒，摔倒: *Margo fell down and twisted her ankle.* 瑪果跌倒了，扭傷了踝關節。**2** if something such as a wall, building, tree etc falls down, it falls onto the ground〔牆、建築物、樹等〕倒下，倒塌，掉到地上: *The bridge fell down with an enormous crash.* 大橋倒塌了，發出一聲巨響。**3 be falling down** if a building is falling down, it is in very bad condition 快要塌下來，搖搖欲墜 **4** if an argument, plan, system etc falls down, it fails to work because of a particular weakness〔因缺陷而〕失敗；不起作用: *That's where the whole argument falls down.* 那就是整個論點站不住腳的地方。

fall for *phr v* [T] *informal*【非正式】**1** to be tricked into believing something that is not true 上…的當，受…的騙: *She'll never fall for that one!* 她永遠也不會上那樣的當！| **fall for sth hook, line, and sinker** (=to be completely deceived by a trick) 完全受騙，完全上當 **2** to start to love someone 愛上〔某人〕: *That was the summer I worked at the fairground, and met and fell for Lucy.* 那年夏天我在露天遊樂場工作，遇到了露茜並愛上了她。

fall in *phr v* [I] **1** if the roof, ceiling etc falls in, it falls onto the ground〔屋頂、天花板等〕坍倒，塌下，垮掉 **2** if a group of soldiers fall in, they form neat lines behind each other so that an officer can check them〔士兵〕列隊，集合

fall in behind sb *phr v* [T] to form a line behind someone 在…後面排成一行；以…為排頭列隊

fall into sth *phr v* **1 fall into conversation/a discussion/an argument** to start talking or arguing with someone 開始交談/討論/爭論: *I fell into conversation with a visiting Japanese professor.* 我開始和一位來訪的日本教授交談。**2** to start to have a particular mood, especially suddenly〔尤指突然〕陷入〔某種心境〕: *She's liable to fall into sudden fits of rage.* 她很容易會突然間勃然大怒。**3** to contain two or more different parts 可分為〔若干部分〕: *The agreement falls into two distinct sections.* 協議書分為兩個不同的部分。

fall in with *phr v* [T] to accept someone's suggestions, decisions etc and not disagree with them 贊同，接受〔建議、決定等〕: *I'm quite happy to fall in with whatever you decide.* 我很樂意接受你作出的任何決定。

fall off *phr v* **1** [I,T] if part of something falls off, it becomes separated from the main part 掉下，脫落: *The door handle keeps falling off.* 門把手老是掉下來。**2** [I] if the amount, rate, or quality of something falls off, it becomes less〔數量、比率、質量〕下降；減少: *Rising prices have caused demand for household goods to fall off dramatically.* 價格不斷上漲導致家用商品的需求大幅度減少。

fall on/upon *phr v* [I] **1** *literary* to suddenly attack or get hold of someone【文】突然攻擊；抓住: *The samurai fell on him and pinned his arms tight.* 那個日本武士突然撲向他，緊緊抓住他的雙臂。**2** *literary* to eagerly start eating or using something【文】急着開始吃[用]: *The kids fell on the pizzas as if they hadn't eaten for weeks.* 孩子們撲向比薩餅大吃起來，好像他們好幾週沒吃東西似的。**3** if a duty or responsibility falls on you, you are given that duty or responsibility〔責任等〕落在…的身上: *an obligation which may fall upon any citizen* 可能落到任何一位公民身上的義務

fall out *phr v* [I] **1** to have a quarrel 爭吵: **[+with]** *She's fallen out with her boyfriend.* 她和男朋友吵嘴了。**2** if a group of soldiers who are standing together fall out, they leave and go to different places〔士兵〕離開隊列，解散 **3** if something such as a tooth or your hair falls out, it comes out〔牙齒或頭髮〕掉下，脫落: *My dad's hair fell out when he was only 30.* 我爸爸才30歲的時候就開始掉頭髮了。

fall over *phr v* [I] **1** [I,T] if someone falls over or if they fall over something, they fall onto the ground 跌倒，摔倒: *Mind you don't fall over.* 當心，別摔倒。| *Tommy fell over one of the electric cables.* 湯米被一根電纜絆倒了。**2** if something falls over, it falls from an upright position onto its side 倒下: *The fence fell over in the wind.* 籬笆被風颳倒了。**3 be falling over yourself to do sth** to be very eager to do something, especially something you do not usually do 忙不迭地做某事，急着做某事，渴望做某事〔尤指一般不做的事〕: *Sylvia was falling over herself to be nice to me.* 西爾維婭急着要顯出對我好。

fall through *phr v* [I] if an agreement, plan etc falls through, it is not completed successfully〔協議、計劃等〕失敗，化為泡影: *The deal fell through at the last minute.* 這筆交易在最後一刻落空了。

fall to *phr v* [T] **1** if a duty falls to someone, especially an unpleasant one, it is their responsibility to do it〔責任等〕落在…的身上: **it fell to sb to do sth** *It fell to me to give her the bad news.* 這個壞消息由我負責告訴她。**2** to start doing something with a lot of effort〔用力地〕開始: *They fell to work with a will.* 他們起勁地開始幹起來。**3 fall to doing something** *especially literary* to start doing something【尤文】開始做某事: *When things really started to go wrong, they fell to arguing among themselves.* 當真的開始出現問題時，他們便互相爭吵起來。**4 fall to sb's lot** *literary* to be something that someone has or must deal with【文】命定應由某人〔做某事〕；成為某人的任務[責任]

fall² *n*

1 ►MOVEMENT DOWNWARDS 向下移動◄ [C, singular] movement downwards towards the ground or towards a lower position 下跌；跌落；跌倒: *the constant fall of the rain* 下個不停的雨 | **break sb's fall** (=prevent someone from falling too quickly and hurting themselves badly) 阻止某人下跌，減弱跌勢 *Luckily there were some bushes next to the house and they broke my fall.* 幸運的是，房子旁有些灌木，我跌落時把我擋了一下。

2 have a fall to fall onto the ground and hurt yourself 摔傷，跌傷: *Grandma had a bad fall and broke her hip.* 祖母摔得很重，髖部骨折了。

3 ►REDUCTION 減少◄ [C] a reduction in the amount, level, price etc of something〔數量、水平、價格等的〕下降，降低，減少: **[+in]** *the recent fall in house prices* 房價最近的下跌 | *a fall in coal output* 煤產量的減少

4 ►AUTUMN 秋天◄ [singular] *AmE* autumn【美】秋天，秋季: **the fall** *We met in the fall of '88.* 我們是在1988年秋天初次見面的。

5 ►LOSE POWER/BECOME UNSUCCESSFUL 失去權力/失敗◄ [singular] a situation in which someone or something loses their position of power or becomes unsuccessful 垮台，崩潰；滅亡: **[+from]** *Until his fall from power in 1978, the Shah remained a firm ally of the Americans.* 伊朗國王直到1978年倒台之前一直是美國人的堅定盟友。| **rise and fall** (=period of success and then failure) 興衰 *the rise and fall of the British motorcycle industry* 英國摩托車工業的興衰

6 fall from grace a situation in which someone stops being respected by other people or loses their position of authority, especially because they have done something wrong〔尤指做錯事後〕失寵，墮落；不再受人尊敬；失去權威性: *Jackson's spectacular fall from grace* 傑克遜令人吃驚的墮落

7 ►DEFEAT 戰敗，毀滅◄ [singular] a situation in which a country, city etc is defeated by an enemy〔國家、城市等的〕陷落，淪陷；戰敗，敗亡: *the fall of France in 1940* 1940年法國的淪陷

8 falls [plural] a place where a river suddenly goes straight down over a cliff 瀑布: *Niagara Falls* 尼亞加拉大瀑布 | **the falls** *We went to see the falls.* 我們去看瀑布。

9 ►SPORT 體育運動◄ [C] an act of forcing your opponent onto the ground in WRESTLING or JUDO〔摔跤或柔道中的〕壓倒，按倒

10 ►AMOUNT OF SNOW ETC 降雪量等◄ [C] an amount of snow, rocks etc that has fallen onto the ground〔雪、岩石等的〕降落量: *a heavy fall of snow* 降大雪

11 the fall the occasion in the Bible when God punished Adam and Eve by making them leave the Garden of Eden〔《聖經》中亞當與夏娃的〕墮落

fal·la·cious /fəˋleʃəs; fəˈleɪʃəs/ *adj formal* containing or based on false ideas 謬誤的, 虛妄的: *Such an argument is misleading, if not wholly fallacious.* 這種論點如果不全是謬誤的, 也是誤導人的。—**fallaciously** *adv*

fal·la·cy /ˋfæləsɪ; ˈfæləsi/ *n* **1** [C] a false idea or belief, especially one that a lot of people believe is true 謬論; 謬見: *It's a common fallacy to think that crime is caused by poverty.* 認為犯罪是由貧窮引起的, 這是一種常見的謬論。**2** [C, U] *formal* a weakness in someone's argument or ideas which is caused by a mistake in their thinking【正式】錯誤的推理[推論] —see also 另見 PATHETIC FALLACY

fall·back /ˋfɔlˌbæk; ˈfɔːlbæk/ *n* [C] something that can be used if the usual supply, method etc fails 儲備物, 備用物; 退路; 可依靠的人[物]: *It's wise to have an extra video player as a fallback.* 最好準備另一台錄像播放機作為備用。

fall·en¹ /ˋfɔlən; ˈfɔːlən/ past participle of FALL[1]

fallen² *adj* **1** on the ground after falling down 倒下的, 落下的, 倒在地上的: *The road was blocked by a fallen tree.* 路被倒下的一棵樹堵塞了。**2 a fallen woman** *old-fashioned* a woman who has had a sexual relationship with someone she is not married to【過時】〔女子〕已失身的, 墮落的 **3 the fallen** *formal* soldiers who have been killed in a war【正式】陣亡者

fall guy /ˋ· ·/ *n* [C] *informal, especially AmE*【非正式, 尤美】**1** someone who is punished for someone else's crime or mistake; SCAPEGOAT 替罪羊, 替死鬼, 代罪羔羊, 代人受過者: *I knew what he had in mind. He'd kill Barak and set me up as the fall guy.* 我知道他的想法。他將會殺死巴拉克, 然後陷害我, 拿我當替罪羊。**2** someone who is easily tricked or made to seem stupid 易受騙上當的人, 易被愚弄的人

fal·li·ble /ˋfæləbl̩; ˈfælɪ̈bəl/ *adj* able to make mistakes or be wrong 易犯錯誤的; 會做錯事的: *Parents are fallible, Susie, just like everyone else.* 蘇西, 父母親跟其他人一樣都是會做錯事的。| *These surveys are often a rather fallible guide to public opinion.* 這些調查作為衡量民意的指標經常都不太可靠。—**fallibility** /ˌfæləˋbɪlətɪ; ˌfælɪ̈ˈbɪlɪ̈ti/ *n* [U] —opposite 反義詞 INFALLIBLE

falling-out /ˌ·· ˋ·/ *n* **have a falling-out (with)** *informal* to have a bad quarrel with someone【非正式】與…爭吵, 不和

falling star /ˌ·· ˋ·/ *n* [C] a SHOOTING STAR 流星

fall line /ˋ· ·/ *n* [C] the natural slope of a hill straight down from top to bottom〔小山的〕斜坡

fal·lo·pi·an tube /fəˋlopɪən ˋtub; fəˌləʊpiən ˈtjuːb/ *n* [C] one of the two tubes in a female through which eggs move to the UTERUS 輸卵管

fall·out /ˋfɔlˋaʊt; ˈfɔːlaʊt/ *n* [U] **1** the dangerous RADIOACTIVE dust which is left in the air after a NUCLEAR (3) explosion and which slowly falls to earth〔核爆炸後的〕放射性墜塵; 沉降物; 輻射性塵埃: *There can be little lasting protection against the effects of radioactive fallout.* 幾乎沒有持久性的保護能夠抵禦放射性墜塵的影響。**2** the results or effects of a particular event, especially when they are unexpected〔尤指預料不到的〕附帶影響, 附帶結果: *The political fallout of the Iran-Contra affair cost him his job.* 伊朗叛軍事件附帶的政治影響使他失去了工作。

fallout shel·ter /ˋ·· ˌ··/ *n* [C] a building under the ground in which people can shelter from a NUCLEAR (3) attack〔地下〕輻射塵掩蔽所

fal·low /ˋfælo; ˈfæləʊ/ *adj* fallow land is dug or ploughed (PLOUGH[2] (1)) but is not used for growing crops〔土地〕犁過而不播種的, 休閒的: *Dig over the plot in autumn and let it lie fallow over winter.* 秋天把這塊地的土翻一翻, 讓它休閒過冬。

fallow deer /ˋ·· ·/ *n* [C] a small European DEER which is yellowish brown with white spots 黇鹿〔產於歐洲的一種小鹿, 毛皮淺黃棕色帶白斑〕

false /fɔls; fɔːls/ *adj* S3 W3

1 ►UNTRUE 不真實的◄ a statement, story, etc that is false is completely untrue 假的, 不真實的: *Please decide whether the following statements are true or false.* 請判斷下面的說法是真還是假。| *false accusations* 不實的控告

2 ►WRONG 錯誤的◄ based on incorrect information or ideas 不正確的, 錯的: *I don't want to give you any false hopes.* 我不想給你任何虛假的希望。| *We often make false assumptions about people of other cultures.* 我們經常對其他文化的人做出不正確的假設。| **a false sense of security** (=a feeling of being safe when you are not really safe) 虛假的安全感 *It's easy to feel a false sense of security if crime never touches you personally.* 如果自己沒有遇上過罪案, 就很容易產生虛假的安全感。

3 ►NOT REAL 不是真的◄ a) not real, but intended to seem real and deceive people 偽造的; 騙人的: *a suitcase with a false bottom* 帶夾層底的小提箱 | *The man had given a false name and address.* 那男子給了個假名和假地址。**b)** artificial 人造的: **false teeth/hair/eyelashes etc** *Oh no! Grandad's lost his false teeth again.* 啊, 不好! 爺爺又把假牙丟了。

4 ►NOT SINCERE 不真誠的◄ not sincere or honest, and pretending to have feelings that you do not really have 不真誠的, 不誠實的; 裝腔作勢的: *She's very false.* 她很會做作。| *a false laugh* 假笑 | **false modesty** *"You played brilliantly." "Not really," Ian replied with false modesty.* "你彈得真好。" "其實不太好。" 伊恩故作謙虛地答道。

5 one false move used when warning someone that if they disobey you, make a mistake, or move suddenly something very bad will happen to them 別亂動〔警告用語, 意為對方如果不聽從命令、做錯事或貿然行動, 就會遇到嚴懲〕: *One false move, and I'll shoot!* 如果亂動一下, 我就開槍!

6 under false pretences if you get something under false pretences, you get it by deceiving people 以欺詐手段, 靠欺騙: *He was accused of obtaining money under false pretences.* 他被指控以欺詐手段騙取錢財。

7 false imprisonment/arrest the illegal act of putting someone in prison or arresting (ARREST[1]) them for a crime they have not done〔在某人無罪情況下的〕非法監禁/拘留

8 false economy something that you think will save money but which will really cost you more 假省錢: *It's a false economy not to have travel insurance on your belongings.* 不給自己的財物辦理旅行保險是假省錢。

9 false friend a word in a foreign language that seems similar to one in your own, so that you wrongly think they both mean the same thing 假同源詞〔指外語中形似意異的詞〕

10 sail/fly under false colours to pretend to be something that you are not 冒充, 以假面目出現, 假裝

false a·larm /ˌ· ·ˋ·/ *n* [C] a situation in which people think that something bad is going to happen, but this is a mistake 虛驚, 假警報: *We all thought the building was about to go up in smoke, but it was a false alarm.* 我們都以為這幢樓要被燒毀, 但這只是一場虛驚。

false dawn /ˌ· ˋ·/ *n* [C] a situation in which something good seems likely to happen, but it does not 假曙光, 虛幻的希望; 令人空歡喜的事: *The ceasefire turned out to be another false dawn.* 這次停戰結果又是一場空歡喜。

false·hood /ˋfɔlshʊd; ˈfɔːlshʊd/ *n formal*【正式】**1** [C] a statement that is untrue 虛假的話, 謊言 **2** [U] the practice of telling lies 說謊

F

false start /ˌ· ˈ·/ *n* [C] **1** an unsuccessful attempt to begin a process or event 失敗的開端: *After several false starts, the concert finally began.* 音樂會在幾次延誤之後終於開始了。**2** a situation at the beginning of a race when one competitor starts too soon and the race has to start again〔賽跑開始時的〕搶跑, 起跑犯規

false teeth /ˌ· ˈ·/ *n* [plural] a set of artificial teeth worn by someone who has lost their natural teeth〔整副的〕假牙

fal·set·to /fɔlˋsɛto; fɔːlˈsetəʊ/ *n* [C] a very high male voice〔男高音的〕假聲, 假嗓 —**falsetto** *adv*

fals·ies /ˋfɔlsɪz; ˈfɔːlsiz/ *n* [plural] *informal* pieces of material inside a BRA used to make a woman's breasts look larger【非正式】〔墊在乳罩內側使乳房顯得豐滿的〕襯胸, 假乳房

fal·si·fy /ˋfɔlsəˌfaɪ; ˈfɔːlsɪfaɪ/ *v* **falsified, falsifying** [T] to change figures, records etc so that they contain false information 篡改; 偽造〔賬目、記錄等〕: *Somebody had been falsifying the accounts.* 有人篡改了賬目。—**falsification** /ˌfɔlsəfəˋkeʃən; ˌfɔːlsɪfɪˈkeɪʃən/ *n* [C, U]

fal·si·ty /ˋfɔlsətɪ; ˈfɔːlsɪti/ *n* [U] *formal* the quality of being false or not true【正式】虛假, 不(真)實

fal·ter /ˋfɔltɚ; ˈfɔːltə/ *v* [I] **1** to become weaker and unable to continue in an effective way 變弱, 衰退: *The economy is showing signs of faltering.* 經濟正出現衰退的跡象。| *My mother's iron grip upon the household never faltered.* 我母親牢牢地管着全家從不放鬆。**2** to speak in a voice that sounds weak and uncertain, and keeps stopping 結巴地說, 支支吾吾地說: *Laurie's voice faltered as she tried to thank him.* 勞麗結結巴巴地對他表示感謝。**3** to become less certain and determined that you want to do something 猶豫, 躊躇: *We must not falter in our resolve.* 我們切勿動搖決心。**4** to move unsteadily because you suddenly feel weak or afraid〔因虛弱或害怕而〕蹣跚, 踉蹌, 搖晃: *She faltered for a moment.* 她腳步踉蹌了一會兒。

fal·ter·ing /ˋfɔltərɪŋ; ˈfɔːltərɪŋ/ *adj* nervous and uncertain or unsteady 躊躇的, 猶豫的; 搖晃的: *a baby's first faltering steps* 嬰孩初學走路時搖搖晃晃的步子 —**falteringly** *adv*

fame /fem; feɪm/ *n* [U] the state of being known about by a lot of people because of your achievements 名聲, 名譽, 名氣: **win fame/rise to fame** *Streisand first won fame as a singer before she became an actress.* 史翠珊先作為歌手成名, 然後才成為演員。| **at the height of your fame** *The Beatles were at the height of their fame.* 披頭四樂隊當時正處於名氣最響的時候。| **claim to fame** (=the reason why someone or something is well known)〔某人或某物〕出名的原因 *The town's only claim to fame is that Queen Elizabeth I once visited it.* 該鎮出名的唯一原因是伊莉莎白女王一世曾來過這裡。| **fame and fortune** *He set off to find fame and fortune.* 他開始追名逐利。

famed /femd; feɪmd/ *adj especially literary* well-known【尤文】著名的, 出名的: **[+for]** *the island of Lontar, famed for its nutmeg and cloves* 以肉豆蔻和丁香聞名的隆塔爾島

fa·mil·i·al /fəˋmɪljəl; fəˈmɪliəl/ *adj* [only before noun 僅用於名詞前] *formal* connected with a family or typical of a family【正式】家庭的; 家庭成員特有的: *economic and familial relationships* 經濟關係和家庭關係

2 2 **fa·mil·i·ar¹** /fəˋmɪljɚ; fəˈmɪliə/ *adj*

1 ►EASY TO RECOGNIZE 容易辨認的◄ someone or something that is familiar is easy to recognize because you have seen or heard them many times before 熟悉的: *a familiar tune* 熟悉的曲調 | **vaguely familiar** (=a little familiar) 有點熟悉的 *Her face seems vaguely familiar, but I can't quite place her.* 她看起來有點面熟, 但我想不起她是誰。| **look/sound familiar (to sb)** *The voice on the phone sounded familiar to me.* 電話裡的聲音我聽起來很熟悉。

2 be familiar with to know something well because you have seen it, read it, or used it many times before 通曉, 熟悉: *Are you familiar with this type of machine?* 你熟悉這種機器嗎?

3 ►PLACE/SITUATION 地方/狀況◄ a familiar place, situation etc is one that you know well 熟悉的: *It was a relief to be back in familiar surroundings.* 回到熟悉的環境是令人寬慰的事。

4 ►COMMON 普通的◄ a familiar sight, problem, story etc is one that you see or hear about too often because it is part of a common social problem 常見的, 普通的: **all-too-familiar** *Beggars on the streets are becoming an all-too-familiar sight.* 街道上的乞丐正成為司空見慣的景象。

5 be on familiar terms with to know someone well and be able to talk to them in an informal way 和…交情很好, 和…關係友好: *He's on familiar terms with all the teachers.* 他和所有的教師關係都很好。

6 ►TOO FRIENDLY 過分友好的◄ talking to someone as if you know them well although you do not 故作親密的, 過分親暱的: **[+with]** *I thought he was being a bit familiar with my wife.* 我認為他對我妻子有點太親熱了。

7 ►INFORMAL STYLE 非正式文體◄ informal and friendly in speech, writing, etc 非正式的; 隨和的: *The novel is written in an easy, familiar style.* 這部小說是以相當輕鬆隨便的筆調寫成的。—see also 另見 FAMILIARLY

familiar² *n* [C] **1** a cat or other animal that lives with a WITCH and has magical powers〔與女巫共居的〕妖獸, 妖精 **2 familiars** *old use* close friends or companions【舊】密友, 伴侶

fa·mil·iar·ise /fəˋmɪljəˌraɪz; fəˈmɪliəraɪz/ *v* a British spelling of FAMILIARIZE familiarize 的英式拼法

fa·mil·i·ar·i·ty /fəˌmɪlɪˋærətɪ; fəˌmɪliˈærɪti/ *n* **1** [U] a good knowledge of a particular subject or place〔對某個領域或地方的〕精通, 通曉: **[+with]** *In fact his familiarity with the Bronx was pretty limited.* 事實上他對布朗克斯區的了解相當有限。**2** [U] a feeling of being relaxed and comfortable because you are in a place you know well or with people you know well 親切感: *I miss the familiarity of home.* 我懷念家中的那種親切感。**3 familiarity breeds contempt** an expression meaning that if you know someone too well, you find out their faults and respect them less 親密生嫌隙, 親暱生狎侮; 親不敬, 熟生蔑

fa·mil·i·ar·ize also 又作 **-ise** *BrE*【英】/fəˋmɪljəˌraɪz; fəˈmɪliəraɪz/ *v* **familiarize yourself with sth/familiarize sb with sth** to learn about something so that you understand it, or teach someone else about something so that they understand it 使熟悉, 使通曉: *Employees must familiarize themselves with the health and safety manual.* 雇員必須熟悉健康和安全手冊。—**familiarization** /fəˌmɪljərəˋzeʃən; fəˌmɪliəraɪˈzeɪʃən/ *n* [U]

fa·mil·i·ar·ly /fəˋmɪljɚlɪ; fəˈmɪliəli/ *adv* in an informal or friendly way 隨和地; 親密地: *Charles, familiarly known as Charlie* 查爾斯, 暱稱查利

fam·i·ly /ˋfæməlɪ; ˈfæməli/ *n plural* **families**

1 ►PEOPLE WHO ARE CLOSELY RELATED 關係密切的人◄ [U] a group of people who are related to each other, especially a mother, father, and their children〔由父母和孩子組成的〕家庭: *Ned comes from a big family of eight children.* 內德來自一個有八個小孩的大家庭。| *Do you know the family next door?* 你認識隔壁那家人嗎? | [also+plural verb] *BrE*【英】*The family now live in London.* 那家人現在住在倫敦。| **family home/business/holiday etc** *He grew up knowing that he would take over the family business one day.* 他從小就知道他有一天要接管家裡的生意的。| **nuclear family** (=a family consisting of mother, father, and their children) 核心家庭, 小家庭 | **extended family** (=all the people in a family including aunts, uncles, grandparents etc)〔包括姨嬸、伯叔、祖父母等的〕大家庭 | **one-parent family/single-parent family** (=a family in which there is only one parent) 單親家庭 | **family background** (=the sort of family you come from) 家庭背景 | **she's/he's family**

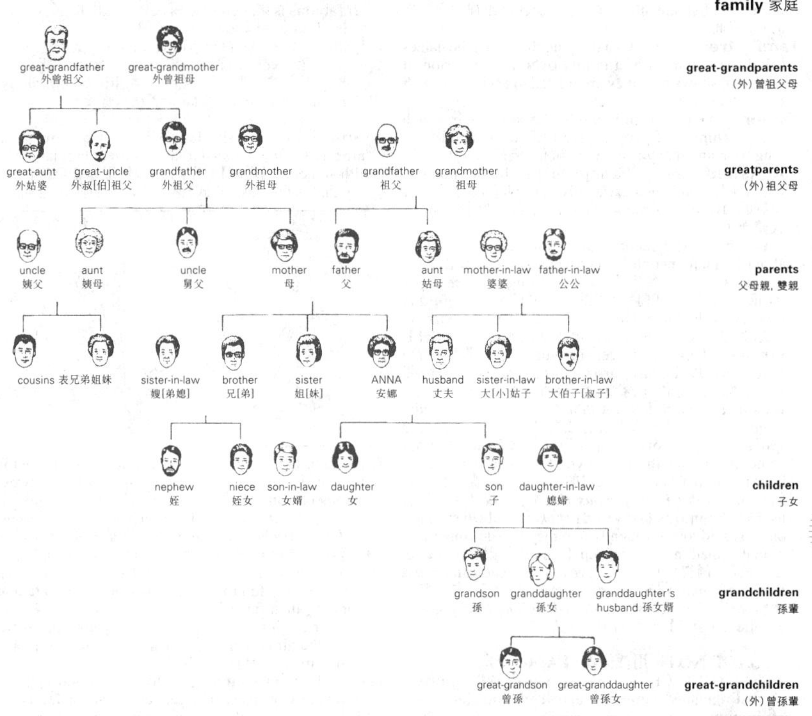

informal (=used to say that someone is related to you) 【非正式】她/他是我們的家人〔用於説明某人是自己的親屬〕

2 ▶ALL THE PEOPLE RELATED TO YOU 所有和你有親屬關係的人◀ [C,U] all the people you are related to, including those who are now dead 家族: *I'm moving to Detroit because I have some family there.* 我要搬到底特律, 因為我家族有一些人住在那兒。| [also+plural verb] *BrE*【英】*My family come from Scotland originally.* 我的祖籍是蘇格蘭。| **be in sb's family** (=be owned by someone's family, especially for a long time) 是屬於某人家族的 *That painting has been in our family for 200 years.* 那幅油畫屬於我們家族所有已有 200 年了。| **run in the family** (=be a common feature in a particular family) 是一家人共有的特徵, 家族世傳的 *Asthma runs in the family.* 這家人個個都有哮喘病。

3 ▶CHILDREN 孩子, 子女◀ [C] children 孩子, 子女: *Couples with young families wouldn't want to live here.* 子女年幼的夫妻不會願意住在這裡。| **start a family** (=have children) 開始生孩子, 生第一個孩子 *They're getting married next year, and hope to start a family straight away.* 他們準備明年結婚, 並希望馬上要孩子。| **bring up/raise a family** *the problems of bringing up a family on a very low income* 靠很低的收入養家糊口的問題 | **a family film/show etc** (=suitable for children as well as adults) 老少咸宜的電影/表演等

4 family size/pack/etc a product sold in a large container packet big enough for a whole family 家庭裝〔供全家人用的大包裝商品〕

5 ▶GROUP OF ANIMALS/THINGS 動物/事物的科、族、屬等◀ [C] *technical* a group of related animals, plants, languages etc【術語】〔動物、植物等的〕科;〔語言的〕語族, 語系: *The cat family includes lions and tigers.* 貓科動物包括獅子和老虎。| *Spanish and Italian are part of the Romance language family.* 西班牙語和意大利語屬於羅曼語系。

6 in the family way *old-fashioned* PREGNANT【過時】懷孕; 有身孕

family cred·it /,··· '··/ *n* [U] money given by the government in Britain to parents who do not earn much money〔英國政府發放的〕貧困家庭救濟金, 低收入家庭津貼〔發給低收入而有年幼子女的父母〕

family doc·tor /,··· '··/ *n* [C] a doctor trained in general medicine, who a family visits regularly 家庭醫生

family man /'··· ,·/ *n* [C] **1** a man who enjoys being at home with his wife and children 喜歡家庭生活的男人 **2** a man with a wife and children 有妻子兒女的男人

family name /'··· ,·/ *n* [C] the name someone shares with all the members of their family; SURNAME, LAST NAME 姓

family plan·ning /,··· '··/ *n* [U] the practice of controlling the number of children that are born using CONTRACEPTION 計劃生育; 家庭計劃: *a family planning clinic* 計劃生育門診部

family prac·tice /,·· '··/ *n* [U] *AmE* a part of medical practice in the US in which doctors learn to treat general health problems and problems connected with families and people of all ages【美】家庭保健, 普通醫療, 大眾醫療—**family practitioner** /,··· ·'···/ *n* [C]

family room /'··· ,·/ *n* [C] **1** *AmE* a room in a house where the family can play games, watch television etc

【美】家庭娛樂室; 起居室 **2** a room in a PUB in Britain where children are allowed to sit〔英國酒館裡讓兒童坐的〕家庭間

family tree /ˌ··· ˈ·/ *n* [C] a drawing that gives the names of all the members of a family over a long period of time, and shows how they are related to each other 家譜圖; 譜系圖

fam·ine /ˈfæmɪn; ˈfæmɪ̵n/ *n* [C, U] a situation in which a large number of people have little or no food for a long time and many people die 饑荒; 饑饉

fam·ished /ˈfæmɪʃt; ˈfæmɪʃt/ *adj* [not before noun 不用於名詞前] *informal* extremely hungry【非正式】極其飢餓的: *What's for supper? I'm famished.* 晚餐吃甚麼? 我餓極了。

fa·mous /ˈfeməs; ˈfeɪməs/ *adj* **1** known about and talked about by many people in many places 著名的, 出名的: *a famous actor* 著名演員 | **[+for]** *France is famous for its wine.* 法國以其葡萄酒而聞名。| **[+as]** *Virginia is famous as the birthplace of several US presidents.* 弗吉尼亞作為幾位美國總統的出生地而出名。| **world-famous** (=famous all over the world) 世界著名的 *Da Vinci's world-famous portrait of the Mona Lisa* 達·芬奇的那幅世界著名的《蒙娜·麗莎》肖像畫 | **the rich and famous** *a nightclub in LA that caters for the rich and famous* 洛杉磯的一家專為有錢的名人開設的夜總會 **2** *spoken* [only before noun 僅用於名詞前] used about someone or something who you have heard about but have never met【口】久聞大名的, 耳熟的〔但從未見過面的〕: *Ah, so this is the famous Jill.* 啊, 這就是大名鼎鼎的吉爾。**3 famous last words** *spoken* used when someone has said too confidently that they can do something or that something will happen【口】〔用於諷刺某人過分自信的話〕講得可真好聽: *"Even I can't get lost around there." "Famous last words."* "連我也不至於會在那兒迷路。""講得可真好聽。" **4** *old-fashioned* very good; excellent【過時】非常好的; 出色的

USAGE NOTE 用法說明: FAMOUS

WORD CHOICE 詞語辨析: **famous, well-known, distinguished, eminent, renowned, notorious, infamous**

Well-known is like **famous**, but if someone is well-known, it is often with a particular group of people, or for a particular skill, achievement etc. well-known和 famous 意思相似, 但如果說某人 well-known, 經常指他在某一羣人中著名, 或因某種技能、成就等著名: *She's very well-known in the literary world.* 她在文學界十分著名。If you are **famous**, most people have heard of you, and know who you are. 如果你是famous, 那麼大多數人聽說過你並知道你是甚麼人: *That big house in Malibu belongs to a famous movie star.* 馬里布的那幢大房子是一位著名影星的。

Distinguished and **eminent** are used especially of people who are famous for serious work in science, the arts etc. distinguished 和 eminent 專門用於指那些在科學、藝術等領域因作出重要貢獻而出名的人: *a distinguished writer* 著名作家 | *an eminent surgeon* 傑出的外科醫生

Places or people are **renowned** for a particular quality, characteristic, or skill. 地方或人因某種品質、特徵或技能而出名, 則用 renowned: *Florence is renowned for its beautiful buildings.* 佛羅倫斯因其漂亮的建築物而馳名。| *the renowned cellist, Jacqueline Du Pre* 著名大提琴家傑奎琳·杜·普雷。

If someone is **notorious** they are famous for something bad. 如果說某人notorious, 他是由於做壞事而聞名: *the notorious gangster Marco Fellini* 臭名遠揚的黑手黨魁費里尼 | *Many politicians are notorious hypocrites.* 許多政客都是臭名遠揚的偽君子。

Infamous is like **notorious** but slightly literary, and is often used about people, places, and events in the past or when they are a long way away. infamous 和notorious 相同, 但一般為書面語, 而且常與過去或遠處的人、地方和事件連用: *the infamous Bastille prison* 臭名昭著的巴士底監獄

fa·mous·ly /ˈfeməslɪ; ˈfeɪməsli/ *adv* **1 get on/along famously** *old-fashioned* to have a friendly relationship with someone【過時】〔與某人〕關係很好 **2** *formal* in a way that is famous【正式】著名地, 出名地; 出色地

fan 扇子; 風扇

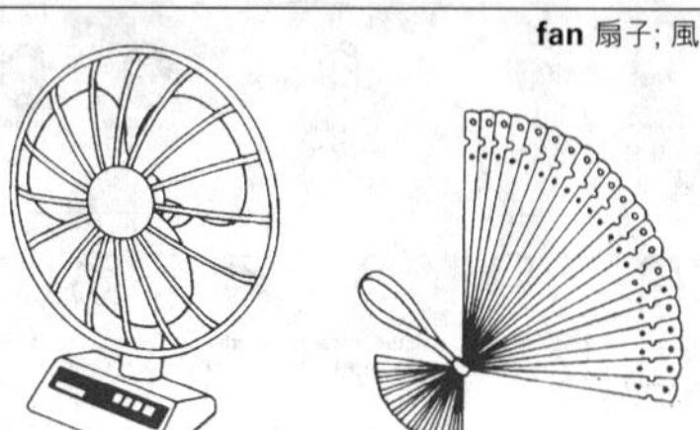

fan¹ /fæn; fæn/ *n* [C] **1** someone who likes a particular sport or performing art very much, or who admires a famous person〔運動、表演藝術、名人的〕熱烈崇拜者, ...迷: *a football fan* 足球迷 | **[+of]** *She's always been a big fan of Michael Jackson.* 她一直是米高積遜的熱烈追隨者。| **fan club** (=an organization for people who support a team, famous person etc) 名流[名隊]崇拜者俱樂部; ...迷會 | **fan mail/letters** (=letters sent to famous people by their fans) 球迷[歌迷、仰慕者]的來信 **2** a machine or a thing that you wave with your hand which makes the air cooler 扇子; 風扇: *a ceiling fan* 吊扇 —see picture at 參見 ENGINE 圖

fan² *v* [T] **fanned, fanning** *v* **1** to make air move around by waving a fan, piece of paper etc so that you feel cooler 搧(風): *People in the audience were fanning themselves with their programmes.* 觀眾中有人在用節目單給自己搧風。**2** to make someone feel an emotion more strongly 激起, 煽動: *Her resistance only fanned his desire.* 她的反抗只激起他的慾望。| **fan the flames** *A provocative article in The People's Daily only served to fan the flames of rebellion.*《人民日報》的一篇挑釁性的文章只會煽動起叛亂。**3 fan a fire/blaze** to make a fire burn more strongly, for example by blowing on it 把火搧得更旺, 把火吹得更旺: *The wind blew from the east, fanning the blaze.* 風從東邊吹來, 把火吹得更旺。

fan out *phr v* **1** [I] if a group of people fan out, they walk forwards while spreading over a wide area〔人羣〕成扇形散開前進 **2** [T **fan** sth ↔ **out**] to spread out a group of things that you are holding so that they make a half-circle 把〔一組東西〕展成扇形: *Fan the cards out, then pick one.* 將紙牌展成扇形, 然後選一張。

fa·nat·ic /fəˈnætɪk; fəˈnætɪk/ *n* [C] **1** someone who has extreme political or religious ideas and is often dangerous〔政治或宗教思想的〕狂熱者, 盲信者: *fanatics who represent a real danger to democracy* 成為民主真正威脅的狂熱者 **2** someone who likes a particular thing or activity very much〔對某種事物或活動〕入迷的人: *a health food fanatic* 極喜歡保健食品的人 —**fanatical** *adj* —**fanatically** /-klɪ; -kli/ *adv*

fa·nat·i·cis·m /fəˈnætəˌsɪzəm; fəˈnætɪ̵sɪzəm/ *n* [U] extreme political or religious beliefs〔對政治或宗教〕狂熱, 盲信

fan belt /ˈ· ·/ *n* [C] the belt that operates a fan (FAN¹ (2)) which keeps a car engine cool〔汽車發動機上的〕(冷卻) 風扇皮帶 —see picture at 參見 ENGINE 圖

fan·ci·a·ble /ˈfænsɪəbḷ; ˈfænsiəbəl/ *adj BrE* sexually

attractive【英】性感的; 誘惑人的

fan·ci·er /ˈfænsɪɚ; ˈfænsiə/ *n* [C] **pigeon/horse etc fancier** *especially BrE* someone who breeds and is interested in a particular kind of animal or plant【尤英】養鴿/馬等(馴養)愛好者

fan·ci·ful /ˈfænsɪfəl; ˈfænsɪfəl/ *adj* **1** imagined rather than based on facts 想像的, 空想的, 幻想的: *a fanciful story* 想像出來的故事 | *The suggestion that there was a conspiracy is not entirely fanciful.* 有人在搞陰謀這一看法不完全是空想出來的。**2** full of unusual and very detailed shapes or complicated designs 奇特的, 精細的, 花哨的: *fanciful decorations* 花哨的裝飾 —**fancifully** *adv*

3 **fan·cy**[1] /ˈfænsɪ; ˈfænsi/ *v* **fancied, fancying** [T]
1 ►LIKE/WANT 喜歡/想要◄ *especially BrE* to like or want something, or want to do something【尤英】喜歡, 想要: *Fancy a quick drink, Emma?* 想快快地喝一杯嗎, 愛瑪?
2 ►SEXUAL ATTRACTION 性吸引◄ *BrE informal* to feel sexually attracted to someone【英, 非正式】愛慕, 愛上: *All the girls fancied him like mad.* 所有的女孩子都瘋狂地愛他。
3 fancy yourself *BrE informal* to behave in a way that shows you think you are very attractive or clever【英, 非正式】自以為是, 自命不凡: *That bloke on the dance-floor really fancies himself.* 舞池裡的那傢伙真是自命不凡。
4 ►THINK STH WILL BE SUCCESSFUL 認為某事會成功◄ *BrE* to think someone or something is likely to be successful in something【英】認為, 相信〔某人或某事會成功〕: **fancy sb's chances** *I don't fancy our chances of getting a ticket this late.* 我不相信我們這麼晚還有機會弄到票子。
5 fancy!/fancy that! *BrE spoken* used to express your surprise or shock about something【英口】真想不到!/難以想像會有那種事!: *"The Petersons are getting divorced." "Fancy that!"* "彼德森夫婦要離婚了。" "這真難以想像!"
6 ►THINK/BELIEVE 想/相信◄ *literary* to think or believe something without being certain【文】〔不肯定地〕想; 以為: **fancy (that)** *She fancied she heard a noise downstairs.* 她覺得自己好像聽到樓下有聲音。

fancy[2] *n*
1 ►DESIRE FOR 對…的慾望◄ [singular] *especially BrE*【尤英】**a)** a feeling, especially one that is not particularly strong or urgent, that you would like something or someone 喜愛: **take a fancy to** (=decide that you like someone or want to have something) 愛上 *Mr Hill took a real fancy to Clara.* 希爾先生真的愛上了克拉拉。| **a passing fancy** (=one that does not last long) 一時的興致, 一時的愛好 *Wanting to go to Mexico was just a passing fancy.* 想去墨西哥只是一時的興致而已。**b) take your fancy** if something takes your fancy, you like it or want to have it〔某物〕讓你喜歡上, 讓你看中: *Did anything take your fancy?* 你看中了甚麼嗎?
2 tickle sb's fancy *informal* to seem attractive or amusing to someone【非正式】使某人喜歡, 吸引某人: *The idea of playing a joke on the Sergeant really tickled his fancy.* 跟中士開個玩笑的想法很使他感到有趣。
3 ►IDEA 想法, 主意◄ [C] *old-fashioned* an idea or opinion that is not based on fact【過時】〔無根據的〕想法, 空想, 猜想, 奇想: *Oh, that was a fancy of his.* 啊, 那是他的奇想。
4 ►IMAGINATION 想像◄ [U] *literary* imagination or something that you imagine【文】想像力; 想像出來的東西: **flight of fancy** (=when you let your imagination work in an uncontrolled way) 胡思亂想 *Pat went off on one of her flights of fancy.* 帕特又開始了胡思亂想。

fancy[3] *adj* **1** fancy hotels, restaurants, cars etc are expensive and fashionable〔旅館、餐廳、汽車等〕昂貴的, 豪華的: *Harry took me to a fancy restaurant for our anniversary.* 哈里帶我到一家豪華的餐廳吃飯, 慶祝我們的結婚紀念日。| **fancy prices** (=very high and often unreasonable prices) 十分昂貴的價格 **2** having a lot of decoration or bright colours, or made in a complicated way 有裝飾的, 花哨的, 別緻的: *fancy buttons* 花哨的鈕扣 | **nothing fancy** *I just want a basic sports coat – nothing fancy.* 我只要一件簡單的運動外衣 —— 不帶甚麼特別裝飾的。**3** complicated and needing a lot of skill 需要複雜技巧的, 高難度的: *I can't do all that fancy stuff on the computer.* 我無法在電腦上做那些高難度的操作。**4** [only before noun 僅用於名詞前] *AmE* fancy food is high quality【美】〔食品、菜餚等〕優質的, 特級的

fancy dress /ˌ.. ˈ./ *n* [U] *BrE* clothes that make you look like a famous person, a character from a story etc【英】化裝服: *a fancy-dress party* 化裝舞會

fancy-free /ˌ.. ˈ./ *adj* able to do anything you like because you do not have a family or other responsibilities〔因無家室或其他責任而〕無拘束的, 無憂無慮的: **footloose and fancy-free** *Ten years ago I was footloose and fancy-free.* 十年前我毫無牽累, 自由自在。

fancy man /ˈ.. ./ *n* [C] *old-fashioned* a man that a married woman has a sexual relationship with, who is not her husband【過時】情夫

fancy wom·an /ˈ.. ,../ *n* [C] *old-fashioned* a woman that a married man has a sexual relationship with, who is not his wife【過時】情婦

fan·cy·work /ˈfænsɪˌwɝk; ˈfænsiwɜːk/ *n* [U] decorative sewing; EMBROIDERY 刺繡, 刺繡品; 鉤編織品

fan·dan·go /fænˈdæŋgo; fænˈdæŋgəʊ/ *n* [C] a fast Spanish or South American dance, or the music for this dance 方丹戈舞〔一種西班牙或南美的快速舞〕; 方丹戈舞曲

fan·fare /ˈfænˌfɛr; ˈfænfeə/ *n* [C] a short, loud piece of music played on a TRUMPET[1] (1) to introduce an important person or event〔引導大人物進場或宣布重要事件時吹奏的〕一小段響亮的喇叭聲

fang /fæŋ; fæŋ/ *n* [C] a long sharp tooth of an animal such as a snake or wild dog〔蛇、野狗等的〕尖牙; 毒牙

fan·light /ˈfænˌlaɪt; ˈfænlaɪt/ *n* [C] **1** *especially BrE* a small window above a door or a larger window【尤英】〔門或大窗上方的〕楣窗, 氣窗; TRANSOM (3) *AmE*【美】**2** *AmE* a window shaped like a half circle【美】扇形窗

fan·ny /ˈfænɪ; ˈfæni/ *n* [C] **1** *AmE old-fashioned* the part of your body that you sit on; BOTTOM[1] (7)【美, 過時】屁股 **2** *BrE taboo* a woman's outer sex organs【英諱】女性陰部, 女性外生殖器

fan·ta·si·a /fænˈteʒə; fænˈteɪziə/ *n* [C] **1** a piece of music that does not have a regular form or style 幻想曲; 狂想曲 **2** a piece of music consisting of a collection of well known tunes〔名曲湊成的〕集成曲

fan·ta·size also 又作 **-ise** *BrE*【英】/ˈfæntəˌsaɪz; ˈfæntəsaɪz/ *v* [I,T] to imagine something strange, or very pleasant happening to you 想像, 幻想: **fantasize (that)** *I used to fantasize that my real parents were famous movie stars.* 我過去常幻想我真正的父母是著名的影星。| **[+about]** *She would fantasize about her future life with Kyle.* 她常想像自己將來與凱爾在一起的生活。

fan·tas·tic /fænˈtæstɪk; fænˈtæstɪk/ *adj* **1** extremely 3
good, attractive, enjoyable etc 極好的, 吸引人的, 有趣的: *You look fantastic!* 你的氣色好極了! | *Sounds like a fantastic idea to me.* 我覺得這主意太好了。**2** *spoken* used when someone has just told you something good【口】太好了: *"I've passed my driving test." "Fantastic!"* "我已通過駕駛考試。" "太好了!" **3** a fantastic amount is extremely large〔數量〕極大的: *Teenagers spend fantastic amounts of money on clothes.* 青少年在衣着方面花大筆的錢。**4** a plan, suggestion etc that is fantastic is not likely to be possible〔計劃、建議等〕不現實的, 異想天開的 **5** [only before noun 僅用於名詞前] a fantastic story, creature, or place is very strange or unreal〔故事、生物或場所等〕奇異的, 荒唐的, 古怪的: *fantastic tales of dragons and fairy queens* 龍和仙后的荒誕故事

—**fantastically** /-klɪ; -kli/ *adv*: *a fantastically expensive meal* 貴得嚇人的一餐

fan·tas·ti·cal /fæn`tæstɪkl; fæn'tæstɪkəl/ *adj* strange and unreal 奇異的, 荒唐的, 虛構的: *a fantastical tale* 荒誕故事

fan·ta·sy /`fæntəsɪ; 'fæntəsi/ *n plural* **fantasies 1** [C,U] an exciting and unusual experience or situation you imagine happening to you but which will probably never happen 幻想, 想像: *He used to indulge in fantasies about being a famous actor.* 他過去常沉溺於當一名名演員的幻想中。| *sexual fantasies* 性幻想 | *Young children sometimes can't distinguish between fantasy and reality.* 小孩子有時不能區分幻想與現實。| **live in a fantasy world** *He lived in a fantasy world and never faced up to his problems.* 他生活在一個幻想世界裡, 從來不敢直接面對自己的問題。**2** [singular, U] an idea or belief that is based only on imagination, not on real facts〔根據想像的〕空想, 怪念頭: *These claims about being 'the party of law and order' are pure fantasy.* 這些聲稱為"遵紀守法的黨"純粹是空想。

fan·zine /`fænzin; 'fænziːn/ *n* [C] a magazine written by and for people who admire and support a popular musician, a sports team etc〔仰慕和支持大眾喜愛的音樂家、運動隊等的〕愛好者雜誌; 影[球]迷雜誌

1 1

far[1] /fɑr; fɑː/ *adv comparative* 比較級 **farther** or **further** *superlative* 最高級 **farthest** or **furthest**

① A LONG DISTANCE 遠距離
② MUCH/VERY/A LOT ...得多, 很
③ GIVING YOUR OPINION 發表看法
④ NOT AT ALL 根本不
⑤ TO A PARTICULAR DEGREE 到某種程度
⑥ PROGRESS/SUCCEED 進展/成功

① A LONG DISTANCE 遠距離

1 ►LONG DISTANCE 遠距離◄ a long distance 遠: *Have you driven far?* 你駕車開了很遠的路嗎? | *We walked much further than we had intended.* 我們比原來計劃的走得遠多了。| **far away** *My parents don't live far away.* 我父母住在不遠的地方。| **far above/below/across etc** *The office blocks towered far above them.* 這些辦公大樓高高聳立在它們之上。| **far from/far away from** *We were sitting too far away from the stage to be able to see very much.* 我們坐的地方遠離舞台, 無法看清楚。

2 how far used when asking or mentioning the distance between two places or the distance someone has travelled 多遠: *How far is it to the station?* 到車站有多遠? | *I wonder how far we've walked today.* 我想知道今天我們已經走了多遠的路。

3 as far as up to a particular point or distance 遠至, 一直到: *The flood waters had come up as far as the house.* 洪水一直湧到那幢房子。

4 as far as the eye can see up to the longest distance away that you can see 在肉眼看得見的範圍內: *hills sweeping back as far as the eye could see* 從視野裡一掠而過的小山

5 far and wide over or from a large area 四處, 到處: **hunt/search far and wide** *He would hunt far and wide for rare medicinal herbs.* 他會到處尋找珍稀草藥。| **travel/wander/spread etc far and wide** *Since then I have travelled far and wide.* 從那時起我就到處旅行。

② MUCH/VERY/A LOT ...得多, 很

6 [+adj/adv] **far stronger/far more intelligent/far more quickly etc** much stronger, more intelligent etc 強壯得多/聰明得多/快得多等: *She works far longer hours than I do.* 她每天工作的時間比我長得多。| *You'll get there far more quickly by car.* 你坐車去那兒就快多了。

7 far too much/long/soon etc much too much, long, soon etc 太多/太久/太快等: *It costs far too much money.* 這要花太多的錢。| *It's far too early to tell if she'll be OK.* 現在談她是否安然無恙還為時過早。

8 to a great degree 很大程度上: **far above/below** *The increase in inflation is far below what experts predicted.* 通貨膨脹的增長遠遠低於專家的預測。| **far removed** (=very different) 大相徑庭的, 很不一樣的, 差得很遠的 *Life on the islands is far removed from the hustle and bustle of life in Manila.* 海島上的生活與馬尼拉熙熙攘攘的生活大不相同。

9 by far/far and away used to say that something is much better, worse etc than anything else 最; 無疑; 很: *The grass snake is by far the most common snake.* 這草蛇無疑是最常見的蛇。

③ GIVING YOUR OPINION 發表看法

10 as far as I'm/we're concerned *spoken* used to give your opinion about something【口】就我/我們而言: *As far as I'm concerned, it sounds like a great idea.* 就我而言, 這聽起來是個很好的主意。

11 as far as sth is concerned *spoken* used to give your opinion or to state facts about a particular thing【口】就某事而論, 至於某事: *This has been a difficult period as far as the German economy is concerned.* 就德國經濟而論, 這是一個很困難的時期。

12 as far as I know/as far as I can remember *spoken* used to say that you think that something is true, although you do not know all the facts, cannot remember completely etc【口】據我所知/據我所能記得的: *As far as I can tell, the whole thing should cost about £500.* 據我所知的情況來判斷, 整件事應該要花大約500英鎊。

13 I wouldn't go as far as to say *spoken* used to say that you think a particular idea or opinion is too extreme or unlikely to be true【口】我不願意把話說得這麼過分: *"Do you think they'll win?" "Oh I wouldn't go as far as to say that, but they're looking pretty good."* "你認為他們會贏嗎?" "啊, 我可不想這樣肯定, 不過他們看起來相當不錯。"

④ NOT AT ALL 根本不

14 far from used to say that the opposite of something is true, or the opposite of what you expect happens 遠遠不, 一點也不: **far from being** *Far from being a reactionary, he's actually quite liberal in his views.* 他根本不是反動分子, 實際上他的觀點相當開明。| **far from doing sth** *Far from helping the situation, you've just made it worse.* 你非但對情況沒甚麼幫助, 反而把它弄得更糟。| **far from pleased/happy etc** *Michael walked in, looking far from happy.* 邁克爾走了進來, 看上去一點也不快樂。

15 far from it *spoken* used to say that the opposite of what someone says is true; certainly not【口】遠遠不是: *"Is he a good driver?" "Far from it!"* "他是個好司機嗎?" "遠遠談不上!"

16 far be it from me to do sth *spoken* used when you are going to criticize someone or give them advice, and you want to pretend that you do not want to do this【口】我決不想做某事〔常用於批評人或向人提建議前, 表示這樣做並非情願〕: *Far be it from me to try and run your*

F

life, but I really think you should leave him. 我決不想控制你的生活，但我確實認為你應該離開他。

⑤ **TO A PARTICULAR DEGREE** 到某種程度

17 how far used to ask to what degree something is true 甚麼樣的程度: *How far is violence caused by society?* 暴力在多大程度上是由社會所引起的？ | *I'm not sure how far this will help the economy.* 這對經濟的幫助有多大，我沒把握。

18 as far as it goes used to say that an idea, suggestion, plan etc is satisfactory, but only to a limited degree 就其本身而言: *It's a perfectly good law as far as it goes, but it doesn't deal with the real problems.* 就其本身而言，這完全是一項好的法律，但它沒有涉及到實際的問題。

19 so far up to a particular point, degree, distance etc 到某一點／程度／距離為止: *You can only trust him so far.* 你只能信任他到這個程度。| **so far and no further** *They can extend the budget so far and no further.* 他們只能將預算增加到這個程度，不能再加了。

⑥ **PROGRESS/SUCCEED** 進展／成功

20 how far have you got? used when asking or talking about how much of something someone has done or how much they have achieved 你進展得怎麼樣?: [+**with**] *How far did you get with the cleaning?* 你打掃得怎麼樣了？

21 so far so good *spoken* used to say that things have been happening successfully until now【口】到目前為止一切都好

22 sb will/should go far used to say that you think someone will be successful in the future 某人會／準能成功: *She is an excellent musician and should go far.* 她是位優秀的音樂家，將來應該能大有作為。

23 ►LONG TIME 久遠◄ a long time in the past or the future, or a long time into a particular period 久，遠，久遠: **far back** (=a long time in the past) 久遠的過去 *The story takes us far back in the past, to the time of the Pharaohs.* 這個故事將我們帶到久遠的過去，到法老時代。| **far into** *We worked far into the night.* 我們工作到深夜。—see also 另見 FAR-OFF

24 so far until now 到目前為止，迄今為止: *We haven't had any trouble so far.* 迄今為止我們沒碰上麻煩。

25 as far as possible/so far as possible as much as possible 盡可能地: *We try to use local materials as far as possible.* 我們盡可能試着使用當地的材料。

26 go as far as to do sth to behave in a way that seems surprising or extreme 甚至做出某事: *She even went as far as to threaten to kill herself.* 她甚至威脅要自殺。

27 go too far also 又作 **take/carry sth too far** to do something too much or in an extreme way, especially so that people get angry〔將某事〕做得太過分: *That little brat has gone too far this time!* 那個小頑童這次做得太過分了！| *The general view was that the President had gone too far in his support for the Contras.* 人們普遍認為總統在支持反政府武裝人員一事上做得太過火了。

28 not go far a) if money does not go far you cannot buy very much with it〔錢〕買不了多少東西；用不多久就會完: *A dollar doesn't go very far these days.* 如今一美元買不了多少東西。**b)** if a supply of something does not go far, it is not enough 不夠用，不足: *That pot of coffee won't go far if everyone wants some.* 如果每個人都要一點，那壺咖啡就不夠了。

29 not be far off/out/wrong *informal* used to say that something is almost correct【非正式】基本上正確的；沒有大錯誤: *The weather forecast wasn't far off, just look at the rain.* 天氣預報基本上正確，瞧這雨。

30 in so far as/in as far as/insofar as *formal* to the degree that something affects another thing or is connected with it【非正式】到…的程度；在…的範圍內；就…而論: *The Committee's recommendations, in so far as they affect deaf people, are set out in this document.* 這份文件闡明了委員會那些會影響到聾人的建議。

1 **far²** *adj comparative* 比較級 **farther** /ˈfɑrðɚ; ˈfɑːðə/ *or* **fur-**
1 **ther** /ˈfɝðɚ; ˈfɜːðə/ *superlative* 最高級 **farthest** /ˈfɑrðɪst; ˈfɑːðɪ̣st/ *or* **furthest** /ˈfɝðɪst; ˈfɜːðɪ̣st/ **1** a long way away 遠的，遙遠的: *You can see my house from here; it isn't far.* 我的房子不遠，你從這裡可以看到。| *In the far distance she could see the outlines of tall, city buildings.* 她能看到遠處城市高樓的輪廓。**2 the far end/side etc** the end or side that is furthest from you 更遠的一端／一邊等: *She swam to the far side of the lake.* 她游向湖的另一邊。**3 the far north/south etc** the part of a country or area that is furthest in the direction of north, south etc 邊遠的北部／南部等: *the great plains in the far west of the country* 該國邊遠西部的大平原 **4 the far left/right** people who have extreme LEFT WING or RIGHT WING political opinions 極左／右分子 **5 be a far cry from** to be very different from something else 與…大不相同的: *The current economic situation is a far cry from what was predicted at the election.* 目前的經濟形勢與選舉時預計的大相徑庭。

far·a·way /ˈfɑrəˌwe; ˈfɑːrəweɪ/ *adj* **1** [only before noun 僅用於名詞前] distant 遙遠的: *She was lost and alone in a faraway place.* 她孤零零一個人在一個遙遠的地方迷了路。| *faraway noises* 遠處的喧囂聲 **2 a faraway look** an expression on your face which shows that you are not paying attention but thinking about something very different 心不在焉的神情；若有所思的神情

farce /fɑrs; fɑːs/ *n* **1** [singular] an event or a situation that is badly organized or that does not happen in the way that it should 鬧劇場面，一團糟的場面: *Blacks were completely shut out of the political process. For them, the right to vote was a farce.* 黑人完全被拒絕於政治進程之外。對他們來說，選舉權是一場鬧劇。**2** [C] a humorous play in which people are involved in silly situations 滑稽戲，笑劇，鬧劇 **3** [U] the style of writing or acting that is concerned with this kind of play 笑劇體裁；滑稽戲風格

far·ci·cal /ˈfɑrsɪkl̩; ˈfɑːsɪkəl/ *adj* extremely silly and badly organized 笑劇的，鬧劇性的，滑稽的: *the farcical effect of period costumes made with polyester fabrics* 聚酯纖維面料的舊時服裝所產生的滑稽效果 —**farcically** /-kl̩ɪ; -kli/ *adv*

fare¹ /fɛr; feə/ *n* **1** [C] the price you pay to travel by bus, train, plane etc〔公共汽車、火車、飛機等的〕票價: **bus/train/air fare** *Air fares have shot up by 20%.* 飛機票價已猛漲 20%。| **half-fare/full-fare** *Children under 4 travel half-fare.* 四歲以下兒童可半票旅行。—see 見 COST¹ (USAGE) **2 simple/wholesome/homely etc fare** *old-fashioned* good, healthy, simple food【過時】簡單／有益健康／家常的食品 **3** [C] a passenger in a taxi 計程車乘客

fare² *v* **fare well/badly/better etc** to be successful, unsuccessful etc 成功／失敗／更成功等: *Although Chicago has fared better than some cities, unemployment remains a problem.* 雖說芝加哥比其他一些城市情況好些，但失業仍是個問題。| **how did sb fare?** *He wondered how Paul had fared during the war.* 他想知道保羅在戰爭期間生活如何。

Far East /ˌ· ˈ·◄/ *n* **the Far East** the countries in the east of Asia, such as China, Japan etc 遠東地區 —compare 比較 MIDDLE EAST, NEAR EAST —**Far Eastern** *adj*

fare·well /ˈfɛrˈwɛl; feəˈwel/ *n* **1 farewell party/drink** a party or drink that you have because someone is leaving soon 告別會／告別酒 **2** [C,U] *old-fashioned* an act of saying goodbye to someone【過時】告別: **bid farewell to** (=say goodbye to someone) 向…告別，向…說再見 **3** *old-fashioned* used like 'goodbye' when leaving someone for a long time【過時】再見，再會〔舊時道別用語〕

F

far-fetched /ˌ· ˈ·◂/ *adj* extremely unlikely to be true or to happen 牽強的；不可信的；靠不住的：*His explanation sounds pretty far-fetched to me.* 我覺得他的解釋聽起來很牽強。

far-flung /ˌ· ˈ·◂/ *adj* **1** very distant 遙遠的：*some far-flung corner of Ontario* 安大略省的某個偏遠角落 **2** spread out over a very large area 分佈廣的；散至遠處的：*far-flung trading posts* 分佈廣的貿易站

far gone /ˌ· ˈ·/ *adj* [not before noun 不用於名詞前] *informal* very ill, drunk, crazy etc【非正式】〔生病、醉酒、瘋狂等〕(程度)嚴重的：*She's pretty far gone, can you drive her home?* 她醉得不行了，你能開車送她回家嗎？

3 2 **farm¹** /fɑrm; fɑːm/ *n* [C] **1** an area of land, used for growing crops or keeping animals 農場；養殖場：**live/work on a farm** *Joe had worked on the farm all his life.* 喬一輩子都在農場幹活。| **chicken/sheep/pig etc farm** *He runs a pig farm in Lincolnshire.* 他在林肯郡經營一個養豬場。**2** the main house on a farm where the farmer lives 農舍 —see also 另見 FACTORY FARM, FISH FARM, FUNNY FARM

farm² *v* [I,T] to use land for growing crops, keeping animals etc 經營農場；種植；養殖：*The family has farmed there for generations.* 這一家世代都在那兒經營農場。

farm sth ↔ **out** *phr v* [T] to send work to other people instead of doing it yourself 將〔工作〕包出去：*farming out work to freelancers* 把工作外包給自由職業者

farm belt /ˈ· ·/ *n* [C] an area where there are many farms 〔有許多農場的〕農場帶，農場區

3 2 **farm·er** /ˈfɑrmɚ; ˈfɑːmə/ *n* [C] someone who owns or manages a farm 農場主；養殖場主

farm·hand /ˈfɑrmhænd; ˈfɑːmhænd/ *n* [C] someone who works on a farm 農場工人

farm·house /ˈfɑrmˌhaus; ˈfɑːmhaʊs/ *n* [C] the main house on a farm, where the farmer lives 農舍〔指農場主住的主要住房〕

farm·ing /ˈfɑrmɪŋ; ˈfɑːmɪŋ/ *n* [U] the practice or business of growing crops or keeping animals on a farm 農場業；耕種；養殖(業)；畜牧(業)

farm·land /ˈfɑrmˌlænd; ˈfɑːmlænd/ *n* [U] land used for farming 農田，耕地；牧地

farm·stead /ˈfɑrmˌstɛd; ˈfɑːmsted/ *n* [C] *especially AmE* a farmhouse and the buildings around it【尤美】農場的主要住房和周圍建築物，農莊

farm·yard /ˈfɑrmˌjɑrd; ˈfɑːmjɑːd/ *n* [C] an area surrounded by farm buildings〔四周是農場建築物的〕農家宅院

far-off /ˌ· ˈ·◂/ *adj* **1** a long way from where you are 遙遠的：*a far-off country* 遙遠的國家 **2** a long time ago 很久以前的：*in those far-off days when we were young* 在很久以前我們尚年輕的歲月裡

far-out /ˌ· ˈ·◂/ *adj* **1** very strange or unusual 奇怪的，異乎尋常的：*far-out ideas* 古怪的想法 **2** *old-fashioned* extremely good【過時】極好的

far-reach·ing /ˌ· ˈ··◂/ *adj* having a great influence or effect〔影響〕深遠的：*far-reaching reforms* 影響深遠的改革

far·ri·er /ˈfærɪɚ; ˈfæriə/ *n* [C] someone who makes shoes (SHOE¹ (2)) for horses' feet 鍛製馬蹄鐵的鐵匠，蹄鐵工

Farsi /ˈfɑrzɪ; ˈfɑːzi/ *n* [U] the language of Iran; PERSIAN 現代伊朗語；現代波斯語；法爾西語

far-sight·ed /ˌ· ˈ··◂/ *adj* **1** able to realize what will happen in the future and make wise decisions【尤美】有遠見的，有先見之明的：*a far-sighted economic policy* 卓有遠見的經濟政策 **2** *especially AmE* able to see or read things clearly only when they are far away from you; LONGSIGHTED【尤美】遠視的 —opposite 反義詞 SHORT-SIGHTED —**farsightedly** *adv* —**farsightedness** *n* [U]

fart¹ /fɑrt; fɑːt/ *v* [I] *taboo* to make air come out of your BOWELS (1)【諱】放屁

fart about/around *phr v* [I] *informal* to waste time not doing very much【非正式】浪費時間；閒蕩

fart² *n* **1** *taboo* an act of making air come out of your BOWELS (1)【諱】放屁 **2** *slang* a stupid and uninteresting person【俚】愚蠢無聊的人：*a boring old fart* 令人討厭的無聊老傢伙

far·ther¹ /ˈfɑrðɚ; ˈfɑːðə/ *adv* **1** a greater distance than before or than something else; further 更遠地：*We'd better not go any farther today.* 今天我們最好不要再往前走了。| **farther away/apart etc** *The boats were drifting farther and farther apart.* 那些小船漂得越來越遠。| *He heard a voice farther down the track.* 他聽見小道的遠處有人說話。| **farther afield** (=at or to a greater distance away) 更遠處 | **farther south/north etc** *I think the state boundary is farther south than here.* 我想州界是在比這裡更南的地方。**2** if you do something farther, you do it more or to a greater degree; further 在更大程度上，更進一步：*We'd better investigate farther.* 我們最好作更進一步的調查。| **take sth farther** (=do more about it) 更進一步推進某事 *I don't think we should take this subject any farther or we'll be wasting time.* 我認為我們不應該再談這個問題，否則我們是在浪費時間。

farther² *adj* [only before noun 僅用於名詞前] more distant 更遠的：*A table was set at the farther end of the kitchen.* 廚房的那一頭放着一張桌子。

USAGE NOTE 用法說明：FARTHER

WORD CHOICE 詞語辨析：**farther, farthest, further, furthest**

When you are talking or writing about real places and distances you can use either **farther, farthest** or **further, furthest** (which are the most usual words in spoken English). 在談到實際地點和距離時，可以用 farther, farthest，也可以用 further, furthest〔這些都是英語口語中最常用的單詞〕：*farther/further down the road* 沿這條路繼續走下去 | *What's the farthest/furthest distance you've ever run?* 你最遠跑過多少距離？

Further (but not 但不用 **farther**) is also used with the meaning 'more', 'extra', 'additional' etc. further 也表示"更多的"、"額外的"、"附加的"等意思〔但 farther 不能〕：*a college of further education* 持續教育[進修]學院 | *For further information write to the above address.* 欲知詳情，請致函上述地址詢問。

far·thest¹ /ˈfɑrðɪst; ˈfɑːðɪst/ *adv* at or to the greatest distance away 最遠：*Who ran farthest?* 誰跑得最遠？| **farthest away/apart etc** *She lived farthest away from school of all of us.* 我們所有人裡，她住得離學校最遠。

farthest² *adj* the most distant 最遠的：*the farthest corners of the globe* 地球最偏遠的角落

far·thing /ˈfɑrðɪŋ; ˈfɑːðɪŋ/ *n* [C] an old British coin that was worth one quarter of a PENNY 法尋〔英國舊時值 1/4 便士的硬幣〕

fa·scia /ˈfeʃə; ˈfeɪʃə/ *n* [C] a long board above a shop with the shop's name on it〔掛在店門上的〕招牌；店門匾額

fas·ci·nate /ˈfæsnˌet; ˈfæsɪneɪt/ *v* [T not in progressive 不用進行式] if something fascinates you, it makes you think about it a lot, want to watch it a lot etc 迷住，吸引；使…着迷：*The idea of travelling through time fascinates me.* 穿越時間旅行的主意把我迷住。| **what fascinates sb is** *What fascinates me most about him is his accent. Where does it come from?* 他最使我感興趣的是他的口音。這口音是哪裡的？

fas·ci·nat·ed /ˈfæsnˌetɪd; ˈfæsɪneɪtɪd/ *adj* [not before noun 不用於名詞前] extremely interested by something or someone 被迷住的，被吸引住的；極感興趣的：**[+by]** *I was fascinated by her voice.* 我被她的嗓音迷住了。| **fascinated to discover/hear/learn etc** *Listeners will be fascinated to hear that Oprah has lost more than 50lbs.* 聽到奧普拉的體重減少了 50 多磅，聽眾會大感興趣的。

fas·ci·nat·ing /ˈfæsnˌetɪŋ; ˈfæsɪneɪtɪŋ/ *adj* extremely interesting 有極大吸引力的，迷人的：*a fascinating book* 引人入勝的書 | **find sb/sth fascinating** *I found his tale* *of a wild and lawless life fascinating.* 我覺得他說的那種放蕩不羈、無法無天的生活很吸引人。**—fascinatingly** *adv*

fas·ci·na·tion /ˌfæsn̩ˋeʃən; ˌfæsɪˈneɪʃən/ *n* **1** [singular, U] the state of being very interested in something, so that you want to look at it, learn about it etc 着迷, 迷戀: *The children looked on in fascination.* 孩子們入迷地觀看着。| **have a fascination for/with** (=be very interested in something) 對…十分感興趣, 酷愛 *Ken always had a fascination for stories about undersea exploration.* 肯一直特別喜歡有關海底探險的故事。**2** [C,U] something that interests you very much, or the quality of being very interesting 令人着迷的事物; 吸引力: *the fascinations of the busy street* 繁忙街道上的那些迷人事物 | **hold/have a fascination for sb** (=interest someone very much) 對某人很有吸引力 *India will always hold a great fascination for me.* 印度對我總會有非常大的吸引力。

fas·cis·m /ˋfæʃˌɪzəm; ˈfæʃɪzəm/ *n* [U] a RIGHT WING political system in which people's lives are completely controlled by the state and no political opposition is allowed, used in Germany and Italy in the 1930s and 40s 法西斯主義〔盛行於三、四十年代的德國和意大利〕

fas·cist /ˋfæʃɪst; ˈfæʃɪst/ *n* [C] **1** someone who supports fascism 法西斯主義支持者, 法西斯分子: *The fascists came to power in 1933.* 法西斯分子於 1933 年上台。**2** *informal* someone who is cruel and unfair and does not like people to argue with them【非正式】暴虐專橫的人: *My last boss was a real fascist.* 我的上一個老闆是個十足的法西斯。**3** *informal* someone who has extreme RIGHT WING opinions【非正式】極右分子: *They're just a bunch of fascists.* 他們只是一夥極右分子。**—fascist** *adj*: *fascist dictatorship* 法西斯專政

-fashion /fæʃən; fæʃən/ *suffix* [in adverbs 構成副詞] like something, or in the way that a particular group of people does something 像…樣子, 以…方式: *They ate Indian-fashion, using their fingers.* 他們像印度人那樣用手指抓東西吃。

2 2 **fash·ion¹** /ˋfæʃən; ˈfæʃən/ *n* **1** [singular, U] the popular style of clothes, hair, behaviour etc at a particular time, that is likely to change〔衣服、頭髮等的〕流行式樣;〔行為等的〕時髦; 時尚: **a/the fashion for** *a fashion for alternative therapies* 各種非傳統療法的盛行 | **be the fashion** *Eastern religions such as Buddhism used to be the fashion in the 60s.* 像佛教這一類的東方宗教曾在 60 年代很流行。| **be in fashion** *Hats are in fashion again this year.* 今年又流行戴帽子了。| **be out of fashion/go out of fashion** (=not be popular) 不流行 *Maxi skirts went out of fashion years ago.* 超長裙幾年前就不流行了。| **come into fashion** *His ideas are coming back into fashion these days.* 他的觀點近來又流行起來。| **be all the fashion** (=be very popular) 很流行, 風行一時 *Psychoanalysis now seems to be all the fashion.* 精神分析療法現在似乎很流行。| **fashion conscious** (=always wanting to wear the newest fashions) 熱衷於趕時髦 *Teenage girls are very fashion conscious.* 少女們都十分熱衷於趕時髦。**2** [C] a style of clothes, hair etc that is popular at a particular time 時裝; 時尚: *men's fashions* 男士時裝 | *This is a very popular fashion at the moment.* 這是目前十分流行的時裝樣式。| *High heels are this year's fashion.* 今年時興高跟鞋。| **the latest fashion** *They'll have all the latest fashions.* 他們將擁有所有最新的時裝樣式。| **a fashion for doing sth/the fashion of doing sth** *Camilla started the fashion of wearing odd socks.* 穿不成對短襪的時尚是卡米拉首先倡導起來的。**3** [U] the business or study of making and selling clothes, shoes etc in new and changing styles 時裝業; 時裝研究: *fashion magazines* 時裝雜誌 | **the fashion industry** *When I leave college I want to work in the fashion industry.* 離開大學後我想在時裝業工作。**4 in a... fashion** in a particular way 以…方式: *Leave the building in an orderly fashion.* 要有秩序地走出大樓去。**5 after a fashion** if you do something after a fashion, you can do it, but not very well 不很好, 馬馬虎虎, 勉強湊合: *"Can you speak Russian?" "After a fashion."* "你會說俄語嗎?" "勉強會一點。" **6 after the fashion of** in a style that is typical of a particular person 像〔某人〕的風格, 模仿: *Her early work is very much after the fashion of Picasso and Braque.* 她的早期作品風格很像畢加索和布拉克的。**7 like it's going out of fashion** *informal* if you eat, drink, or use something like it's going out of fashion, you eat, drink, or use a lot of it【非正式】大量地吃[喝, 用]: *Danny's been spending money like it's going out of fashion.* 丹尼在胡亂地花錢。**8 fashion victim** *BrE informal* someone who always wears or does what is fashionable, even if it does not look good on them【英, 非正式】盲目趕時髦的人; 穿戴只圖時髦而不管是否合適的人 —see also 另見 **parrot fashion** (PARROT¹ (2))

fashion² *v* [T] **1** to shape or make something, using your hands or only a few tools〔用手或幾件工具〕製作, 把…做成〔…形狀〕: **fashion sth from sth** *He fashioned a box from a few old pieces of wood.* 他用幾塊舊木板做成一個箱子。**2** [usually passive 一般用被動態] to influence and form someone's ideas and opinions 影響; 形成, 塑造: *Our attitudes to politics are fashioned by the media.* 我們對政治的態度是在傳媒影響下形成的。

fash·ion·a·ble /ˋfæʃənəbl; ˈfæʃənəbəl/ *adj* **1** popular, especially for a short period of time〔尤指短時期內〕時髦的, 流行的: *Pastel shades are very fashionable at the moment.* 柔和的色彩是目前最流行的。**2** popular with, or used by, rich people 受富人歡迎的, 上流人用的, 高級人士喜歡的: *She desperately wants to move to a more fashionable address.* 她不顧一切地想搬到更受上流社會歡迎的地址。**3** someone who is fashionable wears good clothes, goes to expensive restaurants etc 上流社會的; 時髦豪華的 —opposite 反義詞 UNFASHIONABLE **—fashionably** *adv*: *fashionably dressed* 穿着時髦

fashion house /ˋ‥ ˌ/ *n* [C] a company that produces new and expensive styles of clothes 時裝公司

fashion plate /ˋ‥ ˌ/ *n* [C] *AmE* someone who likes to wear very fashionable clothes【美】穿着很時髦的人

fashion show /ˋ‥ ˌ/ *n* [C] an event at which new styles of clothes are shown to the public 時裝表演

fast¹ /fæst; fɑːst/ *adj* 2 2

1 ►MOVING QUICKLY 快速移動的◄ a) moving or travelling quickly 快的, 快速的: *Burell is the fastest runner in the world.* 伯雷爾是世界上跑得最快的人。| *The first pitch was fast and hard.* 第一個投球又快又猛。**b)** able to travel or move very quickly 能非常快移動[行走]的; (動作) 敏捷的: *a fast car* 速度很快的車子 | *The horse was fast but not a good jumper.* 這匹馬跑得很快, 但跳躍不行。

2 ►IN A SHORT TIME 在短時間內◄ a) doing something or happening in a short time 做得很快的; 發生得很迅速的: *a fast journey* 行程緊湊的旅行 | *IBM is shedding labour at an alarmingly fast rate.* 國際商業機器公司正以令人憂慮的高速裁員。**b)** able to do something in a short time 能做得很快的: *Are you a fast reader?* 你看書很快嗎? **c)** happening without delay 沒有拖延的, 迅速的: *This time the response was much faster.* 這次反應迅速多了。

3 ►CLOCK 鐘◄ [not before noun 不用於名詞前] a clock that is fast shows a later time than the real time 偏快的, 走得快的: **five minutes/an hour etc fast** *That can't be the time – my watch must be fast.* 不可能是這個時間——我的錶一定是快了。

4 pull a fast one *informal* to deceive someone by using a clever trick【非正式】〔以巧妙手段〕欺騙, 詐騙: *Make sure he doesn't try and pull a fast one.* 弄清楚他不是想要詭計詐騙。

5 fast road a road on which vehicles can travel very quickly 快車道 —see also 另見 FAST LANE

6 fast film/lens a film or LENS (2) that can be used when there is little light, or when photographing something

that is moving very quickly 快速感光膠卷/快鏡頭
7 ►COLOUR 顏色◄ a colour that is fast will not change when clothes are washed 不褪色的 —see also 另見 COLOURFAST
8 ►SPORTS 體育運動◄ a fast surface is one on which a ball moves very quickly〔球在某一表面上滾動時〕速度快的
9 make sth fast an expression meaning to tie something firmly, used especially on ships 把某物拴牢: *He made the rope fast to the metal ring.* 他把繩子牢牢地拴在金屬環上。
10 fast and furious done very quickly with a lot of effort and energy, or happening very quickly with a lot of sudden changes 迅速而劇烈的, 迅速多變的: *Political developments in South Africa have been fast and furious.* 南非的政治發展迅速且多變。
11 He's/she's etc a fast worker *informal* used to say that someone can get what they want very quickly, especially in starting a sexual relationship with another person【非正式】能很快弄到自己想要之物的人;〔尤指在性關係方面〕進展神速的人
12 fast talker someone who talks quickly and easily but is often not honest or sincere 巧舌如簧的人, 油腔滑調的人: *Nixon quickly gained a reputation as a fast talker.* 尼克遜很快得到了一個口若懸河但不夠真誠的名聲。
13 the fast set *old-fashioned* a group of fashionable young people who spend their time doing exciting things【過時】〔進行富有刺激的各種活動以消磨時光的〕時髦[浪蕩]的年輕人

14 fast friends *literary* two people who are very friendly for a long time【文】摯友
15 ►WOMAN 女子◄ *old-fashioned* becoming involved quickly in sexual relationships with men【過時】〔女子在與男子的性關係上〕放蕩的 —see also 另見 FAST FOOD, FAST FORWARD, FAST LANE, **make a fast buck** (BUCK¹ (1))

2 3 **fast²** *adv*
1 ►QUICKLY 快速地◄ moving quickly〔移動〕快: *Slow down – you're going too fast.* 減速——你開得太快了。| *We ran back to the house as fast as we could.* 我們拚命跑回房子。| **as fast as his legs could carry him** (=running as quickly as he could) 盡快地跑
2 ►IN A SHORT TIME 在短時間內◄ **a)** in a short time 迅速地: *Young kids grow up fast these days.* 現在的小孩子長得快。| **fast becoming/disappearing/developing etc** *Britain is fast becoming a sweat-shop economy based on cheap labour.* 英國的經濟正迅速成為一種建立在廉價勞動力之上的血汗工廠經濟。**b)** soon and without delay 很快, 立即: *The survivors needed help fast.* 生還者需要馬上得到幫助。| *He wanted to know how fast we could get it done.* 他想知道我們多快能完成這件事。
3 fast asleep sleeping very deeply 熟睡的, 酣睡的: *Shh! The baby's fast asleep!* 噓! 寶寶睡得正香!
4 hold on fast to hold onto something very tightly 緊緊抓住: *She held on fast as they went round the bend.* 在他們繞過彎道處時, 她抓得很緊。
5 stick fast/be stuck fast to become or be firmly fixed and unable to move 緊緊夾住; 緊緊黏住; 被緊緊夾住, 被緊緊黏住: *My leg was stuck fast in the mud.* 我的腳深深地陷在泥裡。
6 hold fast to to continue to believe in or support an idea, principle etc 堅持〔主張、原則等〕: *Bonhoeffer held fast to his beliefs till the very end.* 邦霍弗堅持自己的信念直到最後。
7 be getting/be going nowhere fast *informal* to not succeed in making progress or achieving something【非正式】失敗; 不成功; 無成就: *I kept asking her the same question, but I was getting nowhere fast.* 我一直在問她同一個問題, 但總是沒有結果。
8 not so fast *spoken*【口】**a)** used to tell someone to do something more slowly or carefully 不要那麼快, 慢點: *Not so fast! You don't want to damage the engine.* 不要開得那麼快! 別把發動機弄壞了。**b)** used to say that something has not yet happened or is not yet true 不會那麼快吧: *"Henry will be manager soon." "Not so fast – he's only just been made a team leader."* "亨利很快就要當經理了。" "不會那麼快吧 —— 他才剛當上組長。"
9 fast by *literary* very close to something【文】緊挨着, 貼近: *fast by the river* 緊挨着河
10 play fast and loose with *old-fashioned* to treat a sexual partner in a careless way【過時】玩弄〔異性夥伴〕: *He felt that Lyn had played fast and loose with his emotions.* 他覺得琳玩弄了他的感情。—see also 另見 **stand fast** (STAND¹ (17)), **thick and fast** (THICK² (2))

fast³ *v* [I] to eat little or no food for a period of time, especially for religious reasons〔尤因宗教原因而〕禁食, 齋戒: *Muslims fast during Ramadan.* 穆斯林在齋月裡禁食。

fast⁴ *n* [C] a period during which someone does not eat for religious reasons 禁食期, 齋戒期: **break a fast** (=eat or drink something to end your fast) 開齋

fast·ball /ˈfæstˌbɔl; ˈfɑːstbɔːl/ *n* [C] a ball that is thrown very quickly towards the BATTER² (3) in a game of BASEBALL〔棒球賽中投向擊球手的〕快球

fast day /ˈ· ,·/ *n* [C] a day when you do not eat any food, especially for religious reasons〔尤因宗教原因而不吃東西的〕禁食日, 齋戒日

fas·ten /ˈfæsn̩; ˈfɑːsən/ *v*
1 ►CLOTHES/BAG ETC 衣服/袋子等◄ also 又作 **fasten up a)** [T] to join together the two sides of a coat, shirt, bag etc so that it is closed 扣牢; 繫牢, 縛緊; 把拉鏈拉好: *"I'm going now," she said, fastening her coat.* "現在我要走了。" 她一邊說, 一邊扣上大衣。| *Fasten your seatbelt!* 繫好你的安全帶! —opposite 反義詞 UNFASTEN **b)** [I] to become joined together with buttons, hooks etc 扣牢; 鉤住; 繫牢; 釘牢: *I was so fat that my skirt wouldn't fasten.* 我胖得連裙子都扣不上了。
2 ►WINDOW/GATE ETC 窗子/大門等◄ **a)** [T] to firmly close a window, gate etc so that it will not open 把〔窗、門等〕關住: *Make sure all the windows are securely fastened before you leave.* 離開前要確保所有的窗子都牢牢地關上。—opposite 反義詞 UNFASTEN **b)** [I] to become firmly closed 扣牢, 關緊: *This door won't fasten.* 這門閂不上。
3 ►FIX STH TO STH 將某物固定在某物上◄ [T] to fix something firmly to another object or surface, especially using tape, a metal pin etc〔尤指用膠帶、別針等〕貼; 固定; 釘: **fasten sth to sth** *Someone had fastened a notice to my door.* 有人將一張通知貼在我的門上。| *Chains were fastened round his ankles.* 鐵鏈拴在他的腳踝上。
4 fasten your teeth/legs/arms etc to hold something firmly with your teeth, legs, arms, etc 用你的牙齒咬住/用你的腿夾住/用你的雙臂抱住等: **[+around]** *She fastened her arms around his neck.* 她雙臂緊緊抱住他的脖子。| **[+onto/into]** *The snake had fastened its jaws onto his leg.* 蛇咬住他的腿。
5 fasten your eyes on to look at someone or something for a long time 注視着, 盯着: *He rose, his eyes still fastened on the piece of paper.* 他站起來, 眼睛仍緊盯着那張紙。
6 fasten your attention on to think a lot about one particular thing 集中注意力於; 認真地考慮
7 fasten blame on to blame someone or something, often unfairly 責怪, 指責, 怪罪〔常為不公正地〕

fasten on/upon sth *phr v* [T] to decide quickly and eagerly that an idea is the best one 迅速決定〔採用某一主意或方法〕: *American companies were quick to fasten on to Japanese business methods.* 美國各公司迅速決定採用日本的經營方式。

fasten onto sb *phr v* [T] to follow someone and stay with them, especially when they do not want you to 纏住, 糾纏

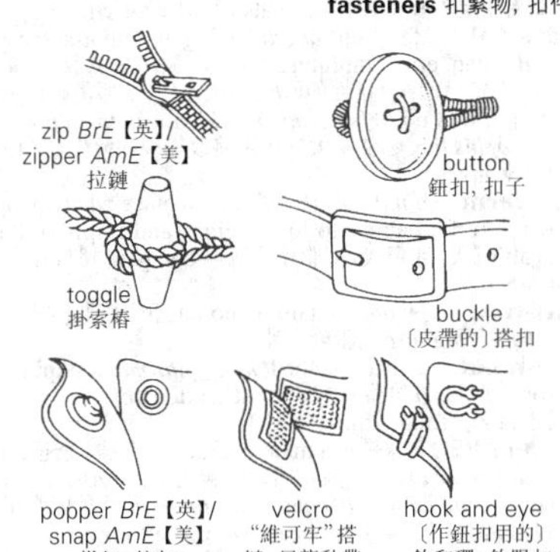

fas·ten·er /ˈfæsnə; ˈfɑːsənə/ *n* [C] *BrE* something such as a button, ZIP[1] (1) etc that you use to join something together, especially a piece of clothing【英】扣件; 扣緊物〈如鈕扣、拉鏈等〉

fas·ten·ing /ˈfæsṇɪŋ; ˈfɑːsənɪŋ/ *n* [C] something that you use to keep a door, window etc firmly shut〔門、窗等的〕緊固件, 扣件, 扣拴物, 插銷

fast food /ˌ· ˈ·/ *n* [U] food such as HAMBURGERS which is prepared quickly in a restaurant 快餐食品〈如漢堡包〉

fast for·ward /ˌ· ˈ··/ *n* [U] a process in which a TAPE or VIDEO is wound forward quickly without being played〔錄音帶或錄像帶的〕快進 —**fast-forward** *v* [I,T]

fas·tid·i·ous /fæsˈtɪdɪəs; fæˈstɪdiəs/ *adj* very careful about small details in your appearance, work etc 挑剔的, 過分講究的: *dressed with fastidious care* 穿戴得過分講究 —compare 比較 FUSSY (1) —**fastidiously** *adv* —**fastidiousness** *n* [U]

fast lane /ˈ· ·/ *n* **1** *BrE* the part of a big road that is used by fast vehicles【英】快車道, 快線 —see picture on page A3 參見 A3 頁圖 **2 life in the fast lane** *informal* an exciting way of living that involves dangerous and expensive activities【非正式】刺激的生活(方式)〔涉及危險而代價昂貴的活動〕

fast·ness /ˈfæstnɪs; ˈfɑːstnɪ̇s/ *n* [C] *literary* a safe place that is difficult to reach【文】堡壘, 要塞: *mountain fastnesses* 山間要塞, 山寨

fast-track /ˈ· ·/ *adj* [only before noun 僅用於名詞前] someone with a fast-track job will quickly become more important in an organisation〔工作上〕提升快的, 快速成功的, 青雲直上的

fat[1] /fæt; fæt/ *adj*

1 ▶FLESH 人身上的肉◀ having a lot of flesh on your body, especially too much flesh 肥胖的: *You'll get fat if you eat all that chocolate.* 如果你把那些巧克力都吃了, 你會變胖的。| *That big fat opera singer – what's his name?* 那位大胖子歌劇演員 ── 他叫甚麼名字? —opposite 反義詞 THIN[1] (2)

2 ▶THICK OR WIDE 厚或寬◀ thick or wide 厚的; 寬的: *Dobbs was smoking a fat cigar.* 多布斯正抽着一根粗大的雪茄。| *a big fat book* 又大又厚的書

3 ▶MONEY 錢◀ [only before noun 僅用於名詞前] *informal* containing or worth a large amount of money【非正式】巨額的: *a fat cheque* 巨額支票 | *a job in the City with a nice fat salary* 倫敦商業區裡的一份工資優厚的工作

4 fat chance *informal* used to say that something is very unlikely to happen【非正式】可能性極小: [+of] *What, John get a job? Fat chance of that!* 甚麼, 約翰找工作? 那是不可能的!

5 a fat lot of good/use *spoken* not at all useful or helpful【口】一點用處也沒有的, 全然沒有幫助的: *"I don't know much about cars." "Well you're a fat lot of use aren't you?"* "我對汽車不太了解。" "你真沒用, 不是嗎?"

6 fat cat *informal* someone who has too much money【非正式】闊佬, 富翁, 大亨

7 in fat city *AmE informal* having plenty of money【美, 非正式】很有錢的: *We'll be in fat city if this deal goes through.* 如果這筆生意做成功, 我們就發財了。

8 grow fat on sth to become rich because of something 靠某物致富, 因某事發財: *The finance men had grown fat on managing other people's money.* 金融理財業人士靠管理別人的錢發財致富。—**fatness** *n* [U]

USAGE NOTE 用法說明: FAT

WORD CHOICE 詞語辨析: **fat, overweight, large, heavy, plump, chubby, stout, tubby, obese**

If you want to be polite about someone, do not say that they are **fat. (A little) overweight** or just **large** is a more polite way of saying the same thing. In American English, you can also say that someone is **heavy** when you want to be polite. 如果你想對別人表示有禮貌, 就不能說他們 fat (肥胖的)。用 (a little) overweight (有點超重) 或 large 來表達同樣的意思較為禮貌。在美國英語中, 你想表示有禮貌時, 還可以說某人 heavy。

Plump is most often used of women and children and means slightly (and pleasantly) fat. plump 經常用來形容婦女和兒童, 意思為豐滿的、胖嘟嘟的。

Chubby is most often used of babies and children and also means pleasantly fat and healthy-looking. When you are describing adults, **stout** means slightly fat and heavy and **tubby** means short and fat, especially around the stomach. chubby 經常用來指嬰兒和兒童, 意思也是胖得可愛, 且看上去很健康。描述成人時, stout 表示稍胖而且略顯得粗壯; tubby 表示矮胖, 尤指大腹便便。

If someone is extremely fat and unhealthy they are **obese**. **Obese** is also the word used by doctors. 如果某人特別胖而且不健康, 那就是 obese。醫生也使用 obese 這個詞。

fat[2] *n*

1 ▶PERSON OR ANIMAL 人或動物◀ [U] a substance that is stored under the skin of people and animals, and helps to keep them warm〔人和動物皮下的〕脂肪; 肥肉: *Rolls of fat bulged over his collar.* 他的衣領上鼓出了一圈圈的胖肉來。| *I didn't like the meat – there was too much fat on it.* 我不喜歡那肉 ── 上面肥肉太多了。

2 ▶IN FOOD 食物中◀ [C,U] an oily substance contained in certain foods〔某些食物中所含的〕油(脂): *Try to reduce the amount of fat in your diet.* 要減少飲食中的油脂量。

3 ▶FOR COOKING 用於烹調◀ [C,U] an oily substance taken from animals or plants and used in cooking 食用油; 烹調用油: *Skim off all the fat, then add the vegetables.* 撇去所有的油, 然後加進蔬菜。

4 the fat is in the fire used to say that there will be trouble because of something that has happened 闖了禍; 將有麻煩

5 live off the fat of the land to get enough money to live comfortably without doing much work 過着養尊處優的生活

6 run to fat to start to become fat, especially because you are getting older or do not do much exercise〔尤因上年紀或不常運動而〕開始發胖 —see also 另見 **chew the fat** (CHEW[1] (4)), PUPPY FAT

fa·tal /ˈfetḷ; ˈfeɪtl/ *adj* **1** resulting in someone's death 致命的: *Meningitis is a serious illness, fatal in some cases.* 腦膜炎是一種嚴重疾病, 在有些情況下是致命的。| **fatal accident/illness/injury etc** *a fatal climbing accident* 致命的攀登事故 | **prove fatal** (=be fatal) 是致命的 *If it* *is not treated correctly, the condition can prove fatal.* 如果處理得不正確，這情況可能會是致命的。**2** having a very bad effect, especially making someone fail or stop what they are doing 災難性的，毀滅性的: **it is fatal to do sth** *It's always fatal to stay up late before an exam.* 考試前熬夜向來很有害。| **fatal mistake/error** *Graf made a fatal mistake halfway through the match.* 格拉芙在比賽中途犯了個致命的錯誤。| **fatal blow** *a fatal blow to the communist system in Eastern Europe* 對東歐共產主義制度的致命打擊 | **fatal flaw** (=a serious weakness in someone or something) 嚴重缺陷 *There was one fatal flaw in his argument.* 他的論據有一個致命的漏洞。

fa·tal·is·m /ˋfetḷˌɪzəm; ˈfeɪtl-ɪzəm/ *n* [U] the belief that there is nothing you can do to prevent events from happening 宿命論 —**fatalist** *n* [C]

fa·tal·is·tic /ˌfetḷˋɪstɪk; ˌfeɪtlˈɪstɪk◂/ *adj* believing that there is nothing you can do to prevent things from happening 宿命論的: *a fatalistic attitude towards death* 對死亡聽天由命的態度 —**fatalistically** /-klɪ; -kli/ *adv*

fa·tal·i·ty /fəˋtælətɪ; fəˈtæləti/ *n* **1** [C] a death in an accident or a violent attack〔事故、暴力襲擊中的〕死亡; 死亡者，死亡人數: *a 50% increase in the number of traffic fatalities* 交通事故死亡人數50%的增長率 **2** [U] the fact that a disease is certain to cause death〔疾病的〕致命性: *New drugs have reduced the fatality of the disease.* 新藥減少了這種疾病的致命性。**3** [U] the feeling that you cannot control what happens to you 不能控制自己命運的感覺; 無可奈何的感覺: *Gera looked on her future with a certain degree of fatality.* 傑拉對自己的未來在某種程度上持一種無可奈何的態度。

F

fa·tal·ly /ˋfetḷɪ; ˈfeɪtəl-i/ *adv* **1** in a way that causes death 致命地: **fatally injured/wounded/stabbed etc** *Two officers were fatally injured in the explosion.* 兩名軍官在爆炸中受了致命傷。**2** in a way that will make something fail or be unable to continue 災難性地，不幸地: **fatally flawed/weakened etc** *Bolton's idea was fatally flawed.* 博爾頓的想法存在致命的漏洞。

fate /fet; feɪt/ *n* **1** [C] the things that will happen to someone, especially unpleasant events〔尤指不好的〕命運，結局: *I wouldn't wish such a fate on my worst enemy.* 就算是我最壞的敵人，我也不希望他遇上這樣可怕的結局。| **sb's fate/the fate of sb** *No one knows what the fate of the hostages will be.* 沒有人知道這些人質的命運將會如何。| **seal/decide sb's fate** (=make it certain that something unpleasant will happen to someone) 決定某人的命運 *By then our fate had been sealed and we were doomed never to return home.* 到那時我們的命運已經成了定局，我們注定永遠回不了家。| **leave sb to their fate** (=leave someone when something terrible could happen to them) 讓某人聽從命運的擺佈 *He sailed away from the island, leaving the other men to their fate.* 他乘船離開了這個島，留下其他人聽從命運的擺佈。| **suffer a fate** *The rest of Europe was to suffer the same fate.* 歐洲的其他地方將遭受相同的命運。**2** [U] a power that is believed to control what happens in people's lives 天命，命運，運數: *Fate plays cruel tricks sometimes.* 命運有時會殘酷地捉弄人。| **by a twist of fate** (=in an unexpected way) 出乎意料地 *By a strange twist of fate, he died the day before Julia arrived.* 他在朱莉婭到達的前一天去世了，真是天意叵測。**3 a fate worse than death** *often humorous* something terrible that might happen to you【常幽默】比死還糟糕的事情，極可怕的事: *Toby saw marriage as a fate worse than death.* 托比把婚姻看成是比死還不如的事。**4 the Fates** the three goddesses who, according to the ancient Greeks, controlled what happened to people〔古希臘神話中的〕命運三女神 —see also 另見 **tempt fate** (TEMPT (3))

fat·ed /ˋfetɪd; ˈfeɪtəd/ *adj* [not before noun 不用於名詞前] something that is fated to happen seems certain to happen because mysterious force is controlling events 命運決定的，命中注定的: **to be fated to do sth** *She knew that their happiness was fated not to last.* 她知道他們的幸福注定不會長久。—see also 另見 ILL-FATED

fate·ful /ˋfetfəl; ˈfeɪtfəl/ *adj* having an important, especially bad, effect on future events〔對未來的發展〕重要的，決定性的; 災難性的: *that fateful day* 那災難性的一天 | *It was a fateful decision which was to change the rest of his life.* 這個重大的決定將改變他的餘生。—**fatefully** *adv*

fat farm /ˋ· ·/ *n* [C] *AmE informal* a place where people who are fat can go to lose weight and improve their health【美，非正式】減肥療養地 —compare 比較 HEALTH FARM

fat-free /ˌ·ˋ·◂/ *adj* containing no fat 不含脂肪[油脂]的: *fat-free yoghurt* 脱脂酸乳酪

fat·head /ˋfætˌhɛd; ˈfæthed/ *n* [C] *informal* a stupid person【非正式】笨蛋，傻瓜 —**fatheaded** *adj*

fa·ther[1] /ˋfɑðɚ; ˈfɑːðə/ *n* [C]

1 ▶PARENT 家長◀ a male parent 父，父親，爸爸: *Ask your father to help you.* 叫你父親幫你。| *Andrew was very excited about becoming a father.* 安德魯因當了父親而興奮不已。| **a father of two/three/four etc** (=a man with two, three etc children)兩個孩子/三個孩子/四個孩子等的父親 *The driver, a father of four, escaped uninjured.* 司機是位有四個孩子的父親，他沒有受傷，逃過了一劫。—see picture at 參見 FAMILY 圖

2 ▶PRIEST 神父◀ a priest, especially in the Roman Catholic church〔尤指天主教的〕神父: *I have sinned, Father.* 神父，我犯罪了。

3 fathers [plural] people related to you who lived a long time ago; ANCESTORS 祖先，先人，前輩: *We must honour the customs of our fathers.* 我們必須尊重我們祖先的風俗習慣。—see also 另見 FOREFATHERS

4 ▶GOD 上帝◀ **Father** a way of addressing or talking about God, used in the Christian religion〔用於基督教〕天父，上帝，聖父: *our Heavenly Father* 我們在天上的父

5 father figure an older man who you trust and respect〔受信任和尊敬的〕父親般的人物;〔男性〕長者

6 the father of sth the man who was responsible for starting something …的創始人，…之父: *Freud is the father of psychoanalysis.* 弗洛伊德是精神分析法之父。

7 like father like son used to say that a boy behaves like his father, especially when this behaviour is bad 有其父必有其子

8 a bit of how's your father *BrE informal humorous* the act of having sex【英，非正式，幽默】性交 —see also 另見 CITY FATHER, PILGRIM FATHERS

father[2] *v* [T] **1** to make a woman have a child〔作為父親〕生孩子，做…的父親: *It was rumoured that the bishop had fathered two children.* 謠傳主教是兩個孩子的父親。**2** to start an important new idea or system 首先提出; 創立: *Bevan fathered the concept of the National Health Service.* 比萬首先提出了國民保健制度的概念。

father sth **on** sb *phr v* [T] *especially BrE* to claim that someone is responsible for inventing or thinking of something【尤英】宣稱某事是某人發明的; 認為某事是某人提出的: *theories fathered on Freud by his critics* 被評論家説成是弗洛伊德首創的理論

Father Christ·mas /ˌ·· ˋ··/ *n* [singular] *BrE* an imaginary man who wears red clothes, has a long white beard, and is said to bring presents to children at Christmas; SANTA CLAUS【英】聖誕老人

fa·ther·hood /ˋfɑðɚˌhʊd; ˈfɑːðəhʊd/ *n* [U] the state of being a father 父親的身分; 父性

father-in-law /ˋ·· · ˌ·/ *n plural* **father-in-laws** or **fathers-in-law** [C] the father of your husband or wife 公公; 岳父 —see picture at 參見 FAMILY 圖

fa·ther·land /ˋfɑðɚˌlænd; ˈfɑːðəlænd/ *n* [singular] a word meaning the place where someone or their family was born, used especially about Germany 祖國〔尤用於指德國〕—see also 另見 MOTHER COUNTRY, MOTHERLAND

fa·ther·ly /ˋfɑðɚlɪ; ˈfɑːðəli/ *adj* kind and gentle in a way that is considered typical of a good father 父親般的, 慈父般的: *Howard put a fatherly arm around her.* 霍華德像慈父般地用胳膊摟着她。| *fatherly advice* 父親般的忠告

Fa·ther's Day /'·· ·/ *n* [C] a day on which people give cards and presents to their father 父親節

fath·om¹ /ˈfæðəm; ˈfæðəm/ *n* [C] a unit for measuring the depth of water, equal to 1.8 metres 英尋〔測水深的單位, 等於六英尺或 1.8 米〕

fathom² *v* [T] also 又作 **fathom out** to understand what something means after thinking about it carefully 弄清楚…的意思, 搞懂: *I still can't fathom out what she meant.* 我還是弄不清她的意思。

fath·om·less /ˈfæðəmlɪs; ˈfæðəmləs/ *adj literary*【文】**1** too deep to be measured 深不可測的: *the fathomless ocean* 深不可測的海洋 **2** too complicated to be understood 複雜難懂的: *a fathomless mystery* 難以理解的奧祕

fa·tigue¹ /fəˋtig; fəˈtiːg/ *n* **1** [U] very great tiredness 疲勞, 疲乏, 勞累: *Steve was pale with fatigue after two sleepless nights.* 史蒂夫兩晚沒睡, 累得臉色發白。**2** [U] a weakness in metal or wood, caused when it is bent or stretched many times, which is likely to make it break; METAL FATIGUE〔金屬或木頭材料的〕疲勞 **3 fatigues** [plural] **a)** loose-fitting army clothes〔士兵野外作業穿的〕寬鬆工作服 **b)** duties that a soldier has to do such as cleaning and cooking, especially as a punishment〔士兵的〕雜役, 勞動〔尤作為懲罰〕

fatigue² *v* [T] *formal* to make someone very tired【正式】使疲勞[勞累] —**fatigued** *adj*: *Fatigued after her long journey, Beth fell into a deep sleep.* 貝思在長途旅行之後感到極度疲勞, 倒頭大睡起來。

fat·so /ˈfætso; ˈfætsəʊ/ *n* [C] *informal* an insulting word for someone who is fat【非正式】胖子〔侮辱性用詞〕

fat·ted /ˈfætɪd; ˈfætɪ̈d/ *adj* —see 見 **kill the fatted calf** (KILL¹ (14))

fat·ten /ˈfætn̩; ˈfætn/ *v* [I,T] to make an animal become fatter so that it is ready to eat, or to become fat and ready to eat 餵肥, 養肥, (使) 變肥, 長肥

fatten sb/sth ↔ **up** *phr v* [T] *often humorous* to make a person or animal fatter【常幽默】使變肥, 使變胖, 餵肥: *He's too thin – you ought to try fattening him up a bit.* 他太瘦了 —— 你應該把他養胖一點。

fat·ten·ing /ˈfætn̩ɪŋ; ˈfætn-ɪŋ/ *adj* likely to make you fat 易使人發胖的: *I don't eat cake – it's far too fattening.* 我不吃蛋糕 —— 它太能使人發胖。

fat·ty¹ /ˈfætɪ; ˈfæti/ **fattier, fattiest** *adj* containing a lot of fat 含脂肪多的: *Avoid fatty foods.* 避免吃多脂肪的食品。| *fatty tissue* 脂肪組織

fatty² *n* [C] *informal* an insulting word for someone who is fat【非正式】胖子〔侮辱性用詞〕

fatty acid /,·· ˈ··/ *n* [C] an acid that a cell needs to use food effectively 脂肪酸

fat·u·ous /ˈfætʃuəs; ˈfætʃuəs/ *adj* very silly or stupid 愚昧的; 蠢的; 昏庸的: *fatuous comments* 愚昧的評論 —**fatuously** *adv* —**fatuousness** *n* [U]

fat·wa /ˈfætwɑ; ˈfætwɑː/ *n* [C] an official order made by an important Islamic religious leader〔伊斯蘭宗教領袖發出的〕指令

fau·cet /ˈfɔsɪt; ˈfɔːsɪ̈t/ *n* [C] *AmE* the thing that you turn on and off to control the flow of water from a pipe【美】水龍頭; 旋塞; TAP¹ (1) *BrE*【英】—see picture on page A10 參見 A10 頁圖

2 **fault¹** /fɔlt; fɔːlt/ *n* [C]

3 **1 ►RESPONSIBLE FOR MISTAKE** 對錯誤負責◄ **be sb's fault** if something bad that has happened is someone's fault, they should be blamed for it, because they made a mistake or failed to do something 是某人的錯: *I'm really sorry – it's all my fault.* 我真的很對不起 —— 都是我的錯。| **be sb's own fault** *She failed the test but it was her own fault, she didn't do any work.* 她測驗不及格, 但這是她自己的錯, 她不努力學習。| **be sb's fault (that)** *It's not my fault that the brakes didn't work properly.* 剎車不靈不是我的錯。| **be sb's fault for doing sth** *He lost his job, but it was his own fault for telling lies.* 他丟了工作, 但那是他自己撒謊的錯。

2 at fault if a particular person, organization, or system is at fault, they are responsible for something bad that has happened〔對某事〕有過錯; 應當負責: *The police said that the other driver was at fault – he should have slowed down.* 警方說錯在另一位司機 —— 他本來應該減速。

3 ►STH WRONG WITH STH 某事出毛病◄ **a)** something that is wrong with a machine, system, design etc, which prevents it from working properly 毛病; 錯誤; 過失: *a design fault* 設計上的錯誤 | **[+in]** *It sounds like there's a fault in one of the loudspeakers.* 聽起來好像其中一個喇叭有毛病。**b)** something that is wrong with something, which could be improved〔可以改進的〕缺點, 缺陷: *I suppose the book's worst fault is its total lack of good taste.* 我認為這本書的最大缺陷是毫無品味可言。| **for all its faults** (=in spite of its faults) 儘管有各種缺點 *The treaty was a great achievement for all its faults.* 條約儘管有缺點, 但它是一個很大的成就。**c)** a mistake in the way that something was made, which spoils its appearance〔有損外觀的〕瑕疵: **[+in]** *The sweater had a fault in it and I had to take it back.* 這件毛線衫有瑕疵, 我只好退貨。

4 ►SB'S CHARACTER 某人的性格◄ a bad or weak part of someone's character〔性格的〕缺點: *His worst fault is his arrogance.* 他的最大缺點是傲慢。| *I really like Sarah, but she does have her faults.* 我確實喜歡薩拉, 不過她有她的缺點。| **for all his/her etc faults** (=in spite of someone's faults) 儘管他/她等有缺點 *For all his faults he was a good father.* 儘管他有缺點, 他還算是個好父親。

5 find fault with to criticize someone or something and complain about them 找…的岔子, 對…吹毛求疵, 挑剔: *I wish you'd stop trying to find fault with everything I do.* 我希望你不要再對我做的事情百般挑剔。

6 through no fault of her/my etc own used to say that something bad that happened to someone was not caused by them 不是由於她/我等自己的錯: *Through no fault of her own, Lisa lost her job.* 麗莎不是由於她自己的錯而丟了工作。

7 ►CRACK 裂縫◄ a large crack in the rocks that form the Earth's surface〔地表岩石的〕斷層

8 generous/kind etc to a fault extremely generous, kind etc 過分大方/親切等: *Generous to a fault, Mr Samson agreed to provide the necessary equipment free of charge.* 薩姆森先生太大方了, 竟同意免費提供必需的設備。

9 ►TENNIS 網球◄ a mistake made when a player is serving (SERVE¹ (10)) 發球失誤

fault² *v* [T] to find a mistake in something 找…的缺點, 挑剔, 找毛病: **cannot fault sth** *Richards gave a superb performance which could not be faulted.* 理查茲做了一次精彩絕倫、無懈可擊的表演。| **be hard/difficult to fault** *His cooking's excellent – it's hard to fault.* 他的烹調太好了 —— 無可挑剔。

fault·less /ˈfɔltlɪs; ˈfɔːltləs/ *adj* having no mistakes; perfect 無錯誤的; 完美無缺的: *Yasmin spoke faultless French.* 耶斯明講一口完美的法語。—**faultlessly** *adv* —**faultlessness** *n* [U]

fault·y /ˈfɔltɪ; ˈfɔːlti/ *adj* **1** something such as a machine that is faulty has something wrong with it that stops it from working properly, or was not made properly 有毛病的; 有缺點的: *If the goods are faulty you are entitled to get your money back.* 如果貨物有瑕疵, 你有權退錢。**2** a way of thinking about something that is faulty contains a mistake which results in a wrong decision〔判斷〕錯誤的: *Through neglect or faulty judgment, Meredith had failed to take security measures.* 由於疏忽或判斷失誤, 梅雷迪思沒有採取安全措施。—**faultily** *adv*

F

faun /fɔn; fɔːn/ *n* [C] an ancient Roman god with the body of a man and the legs and horns of a goat 農牧神〔古羅馬神話中長有人身、羊角和羊腿的神〕

fau·na /ˈfɔnə; ˈfɔːnə/ *n* [C,U] *technical* all the animals living in a particular area or period in history【術語】〔某個地區或時期的〕動物羣 —compare 比較 FLORA

fauv·is·m /ˈfovɪzəm; ˈfəʊvɪzəm/ *n* [U] a style of painting that uses pure bright colours, which was developed in the early 20th century 野獸派, 野獸主義〔20世紀初出現的一種畫派, 使用鮮豔的色彩〕

faux /fo; fəʊ/ *adj* [only before noun 僅用於名詞前] *especially AmE* artificial【尤美】人造的; 假的: *a necklace of faux pearls* 人造珍珠項鏈

faux pas /ˈfo ˋpɑ; ˌfəʊ ˈpɑː/ *n* [C] *French* an embarrassing mistake in a social situation【法】失禮; 失言

fa·va bean /ˈfɑvə bin; ˈfɑːvə biːn/ *n* [C] *AmE* a large flat pale green bean【美】蠶豆; BROAD BEAN *BrE*【英】

fave /fev; feɪv/ *n* [C] *informal* a favourite person or thing【非正式】受喜愛的人[事物]: *Chocolate ice cream! That's my fave.* 巧克力冰淇淋! 那是我最喜歡吃的。— **fave** *adj*

fa·vor /ˈfevɚ; ˈfeɪvə/ *n,v* the American spelling of FAVOUR favour 的美式拼法

fa·vo·ra·ble /ˈfevərəbḷ; ˈfeɪvərəbəl/ *adj* the American spelling of FAVOURABLE favourable 的美式拼法

fa·vored /ˈfevɚd; ˈfeɪvəd/ *adj* the American spelling of FAVOURED favoured 的美式拼法

fa·vo·rite /ˈfevərɪt; ˈfeɪvər̩ɪt/ *adj,n* the American spelling of FAVOURITE favourite 的美式拼法

fa·vo·rit·is·m /ˈfevərɪtˌɪzəm; ˈfeɪvər̩ɪtɪzəm/ *n* [U] the American spelling of FAVOURITISM favouritism 的美式拼法

1 **fa·vour¹** *BrE*【英】, **favor** *AmE*【美】/ˈfevɚ; ˈfeɪvə/ *n*
2 **1 ►HELP** 幫助◄ [C] something that you do for someone in order to help them or be kind to them 恩惠; 善意的行為: **ask a favour (of sb)** *Can I ask a favor of you?* 請你幫個忙可以嗎? | **do sb a favour** *Could you do me a favour and turn off that light?* 勞您的駕, 請把那盞燈關掉好嗎? | **do sth as a favour** *I'm doing this as a favour, remember, it's not part of my job.* 記住, 我是為幫忙才做這件事的, 這不是我工作的一部分。| **owe sb a favour** (=feel that you should help someone because they have helped you) 欠某人的情 *Of course I'll help you move house; I owe you a favour anyway.* 我當然會幫你搬家; 說來我還欠你的情呢。| **return a favour** (=help someone because they have helped you) 還(某人的)情 *Thanks for looking after all my things – I'll return the favour sometime!* 謝謝你幫忙照看我這些東西 — 我改天會還你的情!

2 do me/us a favour! *BrE spoken* used when you are annoyed because someone has asked a silly question or done something to upset people【英口】幫幫我/我們的忙吧!〔因某人問了愚蠢的問題或做了令人厭煩的事而讓他停止時說的〕: *Do us a favour, Mike, and shut up!* 拜託你, 邁克, 別再說了! | *"Did you like it?" "Do me a favour!"* "你喜歡它嗎?" "饒了我吧!"

3 ►SUPPORT/APPROVAL 支持/讚許◄ [U] support or approval for something such as a plan, idea, or system 支持, 贊同, 讚許, 喜愛: **find/gain/win favour** (=be supported by a particular group of people) 受到讚許/得到贊同 *The idea may find favour with older people.* 這個想法也許會得到年紀較大的人的歡迎。| **lose favour** (=stop being supported by people) 不再受支持, 失去支持 *Plans to increase taxes have lost favour among party members.* 增稅計劃已失去黨派成員的支持。| **look with favour on** *formal* (=use your power to help something to succeed)【正式】支持; 受…青睞 *We're hoping the President will look with favour upon such a proposal.* 我們希望總統會支持這樣的建議。

4 in favour of if you are in favour of a plan, idea, or system, you agree with it and support it 同意, 支持〔計劃、主意或制度等〕: *Are you in favour of the death penalty?* 你贊同死刑嗎? | *Senior ministers spoke in favour of the bill.* 資歷較深的部長們發言支持這項議案。| **in sb's/sth's favour** *The vote was 60-59 in his favour.* 投票結果是 60 比 59, 他佔優勢。| **be all in favour of** (=completely approve of something) 完全同意, 完全支持 *I'm all in favour of people going out and enjoying themselves so long as they don't disturb other people.* 我完全支持人們出去好好玩一下, 只要他們不打擾其他人。| **come down in favour of** (=finally decide to support a plan or action) 終於決定支持 *The senate has come down in favour of the appointment of Judge Thomas.* 參議院終於決定同意對托馬斯法官的任命。| **vote/decide in favour of** (=vote or decide to support something) 投票/決定支持 | **find/rule in favour of sb** *formal* (=make a legal decision that supports someone)【正式】宣判/判決某人勝訴

5 ►CHOOSE STH INSTEAD 選擇其他事物代替◄ **in favour of** if you decide not to use one plan, idea, or system in favour of another, you choose the other one because you think it is better 寧願選擇, 選…而不選〔另外一個計劃、主意或系統〕: *Plans for a tunnel were rejected in favour of the bridge mainly because of the increased costs.* 修建隧道的計劃被否決而選擇了建橋, 主要是因為前者會使費用增加。

6 ►UNFAIR SUPPORT 偏袒◄ [U] support that is given to one person or group and not to others in a way that seems unfair 偏袒: **show favour to sb** *Judges have to be careful not to show favour to either party in a dispute.* 法官得小心謹慎, 不能偏袒糾紛中的任何一方。

7 ►POPULAR/LIKED 受歡迎/受喜愛◄ **in favour** if someone is in favour, people like them and approve of them at the present time 受喜愛, 受寵愛: **be in favour with** *She's very much in favour with the management at the moment.* 她目前在管理層中很得寵。| **back in favour** (=popular again) 重新受歡迎; 重新得寵 *Looks like her old boyfriend is back in favour.* 看來她以前的男朋友又得她歡心了。

8 ►UNPOPULAR/NOT LIKED 不受歡迎/不受喜愛◄ **out of favour a)** if someone is out of favour, they are no longer liked, for example by their employers, teachers, or voters 不受歡迎, 失寵: *The boss didn't say 'hello' this morning – I think I must be out of favour.* 老闆今天上午沒有跟我打招呼 — 我想我一定失寵了。| **fall out of favour** (=stop being liked) 不再受喜愛, 失寵 *Once a presidential candidate falls out of favour it is very difficult for them to regain popularity.* 總統候選人一旦不再受歡迎, 就很難重新獲得支持。**b)** methods, ideas etc that are out of favour are not fashionable or popular any more 不流行, 不時髦: **go out of favour** *Grammar-based teaching methods went out of favour in the 60s and 70s.* 以語法為基礎的教學方法在六、七十年代就不流行了。

9 ►ADVANTAGE 優勢◄ **in sb's favour** if something is in someone's favour, it gives them an advantage over someone else 對某人有利: *The fast surface at Wimbledon is very much in Becker's favour.* 溫布頓網球場的快速地面對貝克爾十分有利。| *The system operates in favour of the upper classes.* 這一制度的運作對上層階級有利。| **the odds are (stacked) in sb's favour** (=someone has a big advantage) 某人佔有很大的優勢

10 ►MONEY 錢◄ **in sb's favour** if a cheque is in someone's favour it should be paid to them〔支票〕開付給某人的: *He made out a cheque for £200 in her favour.* 他開了一張 200 英鎊的支票給她。

11 ►GIFT 禮物◄ [C] *AmE* a small gift given to guests at a party【美】〔聚會上分發給賓客的〕小禮物

12 ►STH YOU WEAR 佩戴之物◄ [C] something you wear to show that you support a particular political party, football team etc〔佩戴在身上表示支持某個政黨、足球隊等的〕緞帶; 徽章; 標誌

13 ►SEX 性◄ **favours** [plural] *old-fashioned* a sexual relationship that a woman agrees to have with a man【過時】〔女子同意與男子發生的〕性關係 —see also 另

見 **curry favour with** (CURRY[2] (2)), **without fear or favour** (FEAR[1] (6))

3 **favour[2]** *BrE*【英】, **favor** *AmE*【美】*v* [T]
1 ►PREFER 更喜歡◄ **a)** to think that a plan, idea etc is better than other plans, ideas etc 贊同, 支持〔計劃、想法等〕: *The president is believed to favour further tax cuts.* 大家認為總統會支持進一步減稅。**b)** to prefer something and choose it instead of something else 喜愛; 寧願選擇: *loose clothing of the type favoured in Arab countries* 阿拉伯國家中人們喜愛的那種寬鬆的衣服
2 ►GIVE AN ADVANTAGE 給予好處◄ to treat someone much better than someone else, in an unfair way 偏愛; 偏袒: *a tax cut that favours rich people* 偏袒富人的減稅
3 ►HELP 幫助◄ to provide suitable conditions for something to happen〔條件〕有利[有助]於: *The state of the economy does not favour the development of small businesses.* 這種經濟狀況不利於小企業的發展。
4 ►LOOK LIKE 看上去像◄ *especially AmE* to look like one of your parents or grandparents【尤美】容貌像, 酷似〔父母或(外)祖父母中的某一人〕: *She favours her Aunt Jen.* 她長得像她的簡姑姑。
favour sb **with** sth *phr v* [T] *formal* to give someone something such as a look or reply【正式】給予: *The Captain favoured her with a salute.* 船長向她敬禮。

fa·vou·ra·ble *BrE*【英】, **favorable** *AmE*【美】/ˋfevərəbḷ; ˈfeɪvərəbəl/ *adj* **1** a favourable report, comment, or reaction shows that you think that someone or something is good or that you agree with them 讚許的, 稱讚的; 同意的: *The film received favourable reviews.* 這部電影得到好評。| *Her ideas met with a favourable response.* 她的主張反應很好。**2** making people like or approve of someone or something 討人喜歡的; 贏得讚許的: **favourable impression** *The young girl made a most favourable impression on them.* 這位少女給他們留下了非常好的印象。**3** suitable and likely to make something happen or succeed 有利的: [+for/to] *The conditions are now favourable for economic recovery.* 情況現在對於經濟復蘇有利。**4** favourable conditions or terms are reasonable and not too expensive or difficult 優惠的: *The bank offered to lend us the money on very favourable terms.* 銀行提出以非常優惠的條件貸款給我們。—**favourably** *adv*

fa·voured *BrE*【英】, **favored** *AmE*【美】/ˋfevɚd; ˈfeɪvəd/ *adj* **1** receiving special attention, help, or treatment, especially in an unfair way 受到優待的; 受寵的, 得到偏愛的: *Foreign aid seems to go mostly to favoured governments who are supporters of the US.* 外援似乎大都是給支持美國的那些特別受到優待的政府。**2** chosen by many people 由許多人選中的; 受眾人喜愛的: *Brittany is a favoured holiday destination for families.* 布列塔尼是一個受人喜愛的家庭度假勝地。**3** having desirable qualities 稱心的, 合意的: *a house in a favoured position* 位於好地段的房子 —see also 另見 ILL-FAVOURED, WELL-FAVOURED

3 **fa·vou·rite[1]** *BrE*【英】, **favorite** *AmE*【美】/ˋfevərɪt;
3 ˈfeɪvərɨ̧t/ *adj* [only before noun 僅用於名詞前] **1** your favourite person or thing is the one that you like the most 最喜歡的: *Who's your favourite actor?* 誰是你最喜歡的演員? | *I'll take you to my favourite restaurant tomorrow.* 我明天帶你上我最喜歡的餐館。**2 favourite son** a politician, sports player etc who is popular with people in the area that they come from 受家鄉人歡迎的政治家、運動員等

favourite[2] *BrE*【英】, **favorite** *AmE*【美】*n* [C] **1** something that you like more than other things of the same kind 最喜愛的東西: **my/your etc favourite** *I like all her books but this one is my favourite.* 她所有的著作我都喜歡, 但這一本是我最喜歡的。| *Which one's your favourite?* 你最喜歡哪一個? | **an old favourite/a special favourite** *This dress is an old favourite of hers.* 這件衣服是她多年來最喜歡的。**2** someone who is liked and treated better than others by a teacher or parent 受寵的人, 寵兒: *You always were Dad's favourite.* 你總是最受爸爸的寵愛。—see also 另見 FAVOURITISM **3** the horse, runner etc that is expected to win a race or competition 最有希望獲勝的馬[選手等]; 最被看好的競賽者: *Italy were favourites to win the World Cup.* 意大利最有希望贏得世界盃。

fa·vou·ri·tis·m *BrE*【英】, **favoritism** *AmE*【美】/ˋfevərɪtˌɪzəm; ˈfeɪvərɨ̧tɪzəm/ *n* [U] the act of treating one person or group better than others in an unfair way 偏愛; 偏袒; 徇私: *If we give her the job we'll be accused of favouritism.* 如果我們給她這份工作, 我們就會被人指責為徇私。

fawn[1] /fɔn; fɔːn/ *n* [C] a young DEER 幼鹿

fawn[2] *adj* pale yellow-brown 淺黃褐色的 —**fawn** *n* [U]

fawn[3] *v*
fawn on/over sb to praise someone and be friendly to them in an insincere way, because you want them to like you or give you something 巴結, 討好: *When Madonna was in Paris she had the press fawning all over her.* 麥當娜在巴黎的時候, 傳媒都巴結她。

fax machine 傳真機

fax[1] /fæks; fæks/ *n* **1** [C] a letter or message that is sent in electronic form down a telephone line and then printed using a special machine 傳真件: *Did you get my fax?* 你收到我的傳真了嗎? **2** [C] also 又作 **fax machine** a machine used for sending and receiving faxes 傳真機: *What's your fax number?* 你的傳真號碼是多少? —see picture on page A14 參見 A14 頁圖 **3** [U] the system of sending letters and messages using a fax machine 傳真通信; 傳真: *Most of our business is done by fax these days.* 如今我們的大部分業務是透過傳真完成的。

fax[2] *v* [T] to send someone a letter or message using a fax machine 傳真傳輸: **fax sb sth** *They've agreed to fax us their proposals tomorrow.* 他們同意明天把他們的提議傳真給我們。| **fax sth (through) to sb** *The order will be faxed through to the manufacturer.* 訂單將傳真給廠家。

fay /fe; feɪ/ *n* [C] *poetic* a FAIRY (1)【詩】仙子, 小精靈

faze /fez; feɪz/ *v* [T] *informal* if you are fazed by a new or difficult situation, it makes you feel confused or shocked【非正式】使發窘, 使驚惶失措: *Ned seems rather fazed by the new computer system.* 內德好像被新的電腦系統嚇住了。

FBI /ˌɛf bi ˋaɪ; ˌef biː ˈaɪ/ *n* [U] Federal Bureau of Investigation; the police department in the US that is controlled by the central government, and is concerned with crimes in more than one state 美國聯邦調查局 —compare 比較 CIA

FC /ˌɛf ˋsi; ˌef ˈsiː/ an abbreviation of 縮寫= Football Club, used in names of football clubs 足球俱樂部: *Liverpool FC* 利物浦足球俱樂部

fe·al·ty /ˋfiəltɪ; ˈfiːəlti/ *n* [U] *old-fashioned* loyalty to a king, queen etc【過時】〔對國王、女王等的〕忠誠

fear[1] /fɪr; fɪə/ *n* [C,U] **1** an unpleasant feeling of being 3
frightened or worried that something bad is going to hap- 1
pen 害怕, 恐懼: *The boy's eyes were full of fear.* 這男孩的眼裡充滿着恐懼。| *McCarthy exploited deep-seated*

fears about communism among the American people. 麥卡錫利用了美國人對共產主義的那種根深蒂固的恐懼心理。| **[+of]** *fear of flying* 害怕飛行 | *My fear of dentists dates back to when I was a child.* 我對牙醫的恐懼可追溯到我小的時候。| **[+for]** *fears for the future* 對未來感到的恐懼 | **fear that** *fears that his wife might leave him* 害怕他的妻子會離開他 | **in fear** (=feeling afraid) 害怕地, 提心吊膽地 *He thought he heard something and glanced round in fear.* 他以為他聽到了甚麼, 於是提心吊膽地看了看周圍。| **live in fear of** (=always be afraid of) 活在恐懼中, 終日害怕 *Ordinary people live in fear of being arrested by the secret police.* 普通人終日害怕被祕密警察逮捕。| **in fear of your life** (=feeling afraid that you may be killed) 害怕會喪命 | **sb's fears are unfounded** (=there is no reason for someone to feel afraid or worried) 某人的恐懼是沒有根據的 *My fears for their safety proved unfounded.* 我擔心他們的安全結果證明是沒有根據的。**2 for fear of/for fear that** because you are worried that you will make something happen 因為怕…, 生怕…: *Helen didn't want to get out of bed, for fear of waking her husband.* 海倫不想起牀, 生怕會吵醒丈夫。**3 no fear!** *BrE informal often humorous* used to say that you are definitely not going to do something【英, 非正式, 常幽默】當然不! 絕不!〔用於説明自己絕不去做某事〕: *"Are you going to Bill's party tonight?" "No fear!"* "你今晚去參加比爾的聚會嗎?" "當然不去!" **4 put the fear of God into sb** *informal* to make someone feel that they must do something by telling them what will happen if they do not do it【非正式】使某人〔對不做某事的後果〕感到害怕: *The Italian manager must have put the fear of God into his team.* 這位意大利人領隊一定是恫嚇過他的隊員。**5 there's no fear of** used to say that something will definitely not happen 不會〔發生〕, 不可能〔有某種事〕: *There's no fear of him changing his mind.* 他不會改變主意。**6 without fear or favour** *formal* in a fair way【正式】公平的[地], 公正的[地], 不偏袒的[地]: *to enforce the law without fear or favour* 公正地執法

2 **fear²** *v* [T] **1** a word meaning to feel frightened or worried that something bad may happen 害怕, 恐懼; 擔心: *Fearing another earthquake, local officials ordered an evacuation.* 地方官員害怕再次發生地震, 於是命令人們疏散。| **fear that** *Einstein feared that other German scientists would build a nuclear bomb first.* 愛因斯坦擔心其他德國科學家會先造出原子彈。| **fear to do sth** *formal* (=be afraid to do something)【正式】害怕做某事 *Women feared to go out at night.* 婦女害怕晚上外出。**2 fear the worst** to think that the worst possible thing has happened or might happen 害怕(會)發生最壞的事: *When Tom heard about the accident he immediately feared the worst.* 湯姆聽説出了事故時, 立即就害怕會發生最壞的事。**3** to be afraid of someone and what they might do because they are very powerful 畏懼, 害怕〔某個有權勢的人〕: *The general manager was greatly feared by all his subordinates.* 總經理的所有下屬都很怕他。**4 fear for** to feel worried about someone because you think they might be in danger 為…擔憂: **fear for sb's safety/life** *Mary feared for her son's safety.* 瑪麗為兒子的安全擔憂。| **fear for sb** *He feared for his children.* 他為他的孩子擔憂。**5 I fear** *formal* used when telling someone that you think that something bad has happened or is true【正式】恐怕…, 很遺憾〔用於告知某種壞事已發生或成為事實〕: **I fear (that)** *I fear that we may be too late, Holmes.* 恐怕我們可能太遲了, 霍姆斯。| **I fear so/I fear not** *"Is she very ill?" "I fear so."* "她病得很重嗎?" "恐怕是的。" **6 fear not/never fear** *formal* used to tell someone not to worry【正式】不用怕, 別擔心〔用於使人安心〕: *Never fear, he'll be with us soon.* 別擔心, 他很快會和我們在一起的。—see also 另見 GOD-FEARING

fear·ful /ˋfɪrfəl; ˈfɪəfəl/ *adj* **1** *formal* frightened that something might happen【正式】擔心的, 害怕的: **[+of]** *The defenders are fearful of another attack.* 防守隊員擔心會遭到又一次進攻。| **fearful that** *fearful that the disease may strike again* 擔心這種疾病會再度爆發 **2** *BrE* extremely bad【英】極壞的: **be in a fearful state/condition/mess** *The room was in a fearful state.* 房間裡一片狼藉。**3** *old use* [only before noun 僅用於名詞前] frightening【舊】嚇人的, 可怕的: *fearful shapes in the darkness* 黑暗中嚇人的影子 —**fearfulness** *n* [U]

fear·ful·ly /ˋfɪrfəlɪ; ˈfɪəfəli/ *adv* **1** in a way that shows you are afraid 恐懼地, 害怕地: *She glanced fearfully over her shoulder.* 她提心吊膽地回頭看了一眼。**2** [+adj/adv] *old-fashioned* extremely【過時】極其, 非常: *She's fearfully clever.* 她非常聰明。

fear·less /ˋfɪrlɪs; ˈfɪələs/ *adj* not afraid of anything 無畏的, 不怕的: *a fearless warrior* 無畏的勇士 —**fearlessly** *adv* —**fearlessness** *n* [U]

fear·some /ˋfɪrsəm; ˈfɪəsəm/ *adj* very frightening to look at〔看上去〕可怕的, 嚇人的: *a woman of fearsome dimensions* 體形大得可怕的女人

fea·si·ble /ˋfizəbl̩; ˈfiːzəbəl/ *adj* a plan, idea, or method that is feasible is possible and is likely to work〔計劃、想法或方法〕可行的, 可實行的, 行得通的: *Your plan is not economically feasible.* 你的計劃從經濟上考慮是行不通的。—**feasibly** *adv* —**feasibility** /ˌfizəˋbɪlətɪ; ˌfiːzəˈbɪləti/ *n* [U]: *a feasibility study* 可行性研究

feast¹ /fist; fiːst/ *n* [C] **1** a large meal for a lot of people, to celebrate a special occasion 盛會, 宴會: *a wedding feast* 婚筵 | **hold a feast** *A great feast was held in Columbus's honour.* 為紀念哥倫布舉行了盛大的宴會。**2** a very good, large meal 美味的盛筵: *Jane's mother had cooked us a real feast.* 簡的母親為我們準備了一頓十分美味的盛筵。| **midnight feast** (=a meal eaten secretly at night by children)〔兒童在晚上偷偷吃的〕午夜宴會 **3** an occasion when there are a lot of enjoyable things to see or do 節日; 慶典日: **[+for]** *Next week's film festival should be a real feast for cinema-goers.* 下星期的電影節應該是電影迷的一個真正的盛大節日。**4** a day or period when there is a religious festival 宗教節日 —see also 另見 MOVABLE FEAST

feast² *v* **1 feast on/upon sth** to eat a lot of a particular food with great enjoyment 盡情地吃, 飽餐: *flies feasting on rotting flesh* 正飽餐着臭肉的蒼蠅 **2 feast your eyes on** to look at someone or something with great pleasure 盡情欣賞; 飽眼福: *Travellers came to feast their eyes on the natural beauty of the region.* 遊客們來盡情欣賞這個地區的自然美景。**3** [I] to eat and drink a lot to celebrate something 大吃大喝地慶祝 **4** [T usually passive 一般用被動態] to be honoured by a special meal 受到盛宴招待

feat /fit; fiːt/ *n* [C] something that someone does that is impressive because it needs a lot of skill, strength etc 業績, 功績, 壯舉: **[+of]** *a remarkable feat of engineering* 一項了不起的工程壯舉 | **perform/accomplish/achieve a feat** *How did they accomplish such an extraordinary feat?* 他們是怎樣作出如此非凡的業績的? | **sth is no mean feat** (=is difficult to do) 某事很難做; 某事是件了不起的成就 *Getting a degree is no mean feat!* 拿到學位可不是一件輕易可以做到的事!

fea·ther¹ /ˋfɛðɚ; ˈfeðə/ *n* [C] **1** one of the things that cover a bird's body, consisting of a stem with soft hairs growing on either side 羽毛, 翎: *an ostrich feather* 鴕鳥的羽毛 | **feather bed/pillow etc** (=a bed etc that is filled with feathers) 羽絨褥墊/枕頭等 **2 a feather in your cap** something you have done that you should be proud of 值得自豪的成就, 卓越的成就 —see also 另見 **light as a feather** (LIGHT² (4)), **birds of a feather** (BIRD (4)), **ruffle sb's feathers** (RUFFLE¹ (2))

feather 羽毛

feather² *v* [T] **1 feather your nest** to get money by dishonest methods 營私自肥, 中飽私囊 **2 feather the oars** to put the OARs flat on the surface of the water when you are rowing a boat 划平槳〔划船收槳時使槳葉與水面平行〕**3** to put feathers on an ARROW 為〔箭〕裝上翎 —see also 另見 **tar and feather sb** (TAR[2] (3))

feath·er bed·ding /ˌfɛðɚ ˋbɛdɪŋ; ˌfeðə ˈbedɪŋ/ *n* [U] the practice of letting workers keep their jobs even if they are not needed or do not work well〔即使不需要或工作不好也保留工人的〕超雇

feather bo·a /ˌ·· ˈ··/ *n* [C] a long SCARF[1] (1) made of feathers and worn around a woman's neck〔婦女的〕羽毛長圍巾

feath·er·brained /ˋfɛðɚˌbrend; ˈfeðəbreɪnd/ *adj* extremely silly 非常愚蠢的

feather dust·er /ˌ·· ˈ··/ *n* [C] a stick with feathers on the end used for removing dust 羽毛撣帚

feath·ered /ˋfɛðɚd; ˈfeðəd/ *adj* having feathers, or made from feathers 有羽毛的; 羽毛做的

feath·er·weight /ˋfɛðɚˌwet; ˈfeðəweɪt/ *n* [C] a BOXER (1) who is heavier than a BANTAMWEIGHT but lighter than a LIGHTWEIGHT[2] (2) 次輕量級拳擊運動員, 羽量級拳擊運動員

feath·er·y /ˋfɛðərɪ; ˈfeðəri/ *adj* **1** made of a lot of soft thin pieces〔輕柔的〕羽毛狀的: *The plant has feathery leaves.* 這種植物長着羽毛狀的葉子。**2** soft and light 輕柔的, 輕軟的

2 1 **fea·ture[1]** /ˋfitʃɚ; ˈfiːtʃə/ *n* [C] **1** a part of something that you notice because it seems important, interesting, or typical 特點, 特徵, 特色: *The house has many interesting features, including a large Victorian fireplace.* 這棟房子有許多有趣的特色, 包括一個維多利亞大壁爐。| **[+of]** *An important feature of Van Gogh's paintings is their bright colours.* 梵高的繪畫的一個重要特色是色彩鮮亮。| **common feature** *Mass unemployment is a common feature of industrialized societies.* 大量失業是各工業化社會的一個共同特徵。| **geographical feature** (=part of an area such as a hill, river etc) 地理特徵 **2** a piece of writing about a subject in a newspaper or a magazine〔報紙或雜誌上的〕特寫(報道): **[+on]** *There was a feature on Kevin Costner in last week's Sunday Times.* 上星期的《星期日泰晤士報》有一篇關於奇雲告士拿的特寫報道。**3** [usually plural 一般用複數] the parts of someone's face such as their eyes, nose etc 面貌的一部分〈如眼、鼻等〉; 面貌(特徵); 五官: *He had fine delicate features.* 他眉清目秀。**4** a film being shown at a cinema 影片, 故事片, 正片: *There were a couple of short cartoons before the main feature.* 正片前有一些卡通短片。

3 **feature[2]** *v* **1** [T] to show a particular person or thing in a film, magazine, show etc〔在電影、雜誌、表演等中〕介紹, 特載; 特別推出; 以…為主要內容: *an exhibition featuring paintings by contemporary artists* 展出當代藝術家繪畫作品的展覽 | **feature sb as** (=include a famous actor who plays a particular person) 由某人主演 *featuring Marlon Brando as the Godfather* 由馬龍·白蘭度主演教父 **2** [I] to be included in something and be an important part of it 是…的特色: **[+in]** *Violence seems to feature heavily in all of his books.* 暴力似乎是他所有作品中的主要特色。**3** [T] a word meaning to include something new or unusual, used especially in advertisements 以…為特色〔尤用於廣告〕: *The car features an anti-lock braking system.* 這種車裝有防鎖煞車系統。**4** [T] to show or advertise a particular kind of product 展示〔某種產品〕, 為…做廣告: *This week we're featuring a brand new range of frozen foods.* 這星期我們將推出一系列全新的冷凍食品。**5** to show a film, play etc 放映〔電影〕; 上演〔戲劇〕: *A popular Berkeley theater featured a porno movie called 'Slaves of Love'* 伯克萊一家大眾劇院放映了一部叫作《愛情奴隸》的色情影片。

feature film /ˈ·· ˌ·/ *n* [C] a full length film that has a story and is acted by professional actors 正片, 故事片

fea·ture·less /ˋfitʃɚlɪs; ˈfiːtʃələs/ *adj* a featureless place has no interesting parts〔地方〕無特色的, 平淡無奇的: *the flat and rather featureless plains in the south* 南方那單調而毫無特色的平原

Feb the written abbreviation of 縮寫= FEBRUARY

fe·brile /ˋfibrəl; ˈfiːbraɪl/ *adj* **1** *literary* full of nervous excitement or activity【文】興奮的, 激動的, 狂熱的: *a febrile imagination* 狂熱的想像 **2** *medical* concerned with or caused by a fever【醫】發熱的, 發熱引起的

Feb·ru·a·ry /ˋfɛbruˌɛrɪ; ˈfebruəri/ *n* [C,U] the second month of the year between January and March 二月: **in February** *The bridge will open in February 1998.* 這座橋將於 1998 年 2 月啟用。| **last/next February** *Mum died last February.* 媽媽去年2月去世了。| **on February 10th** (also 又作 **on 10th February** *BrE* 英) *The meeting will be on February 10th.* (spoken as 讀作 *on the tenth of February* or 或 *on February the tenth* or 或 (*AmE* 美) *on February tenth*) 會議將於 2 月 10 日舉行。

fe·ces /ˋfisiz; ˈfiːsiːz/ *n* [plural] the usual American spelling of FAECES faeces 的一般美式拼法 —**fecal** /ˋfikḷ; ˈfiːkəl/ *adj*

feck·less /ˋfɛklɪs; ˈfekləs/ *adj* lacking determination, and not achieving anything in your life 無能的, 窩囊的, 沒出息的: *a dull, rather feckless young man* 遲鈍呆笨、相當沒出息的年輕人 —**fecklessly** *adv* —**fecklessness** *n* [U]

fec·und /ˋfɛkənd; ˈfekənd/ *adj formal* able to produce many children, young animals, or crops; FERTILE 生殖力旺盛的; 多產的 —**fecundity** /fɪˋkʌndətɪ; fɪˈkʌndʒti/ *n* [U]

fed[1] /fɛd; fed/ the past tense and past participle of FEED[1] —see also 另見 FED UP

fed[2] *n* [C] *AmE informal* an agent of the FBI【美, 非正式】聯邦調查局探員[調查員]

fed·e·ral /ˋfɛdərəl; ˈfedərəl/ *adj* **1** a federal country or 3
system of government consists of a group of states which have their own government to decide their own affairs, and are controlled by a single national government which makes decisions on foreign affairs, defence etc 聯邦(制)的: *Switzerland is a federal republic.* 瑞士是一個聯邦共和國。**2** concerned with the central government of a country such as the US, rather than the government of one of its states〔美國等的〕聯邦政府的: *federal funding* 聯邦政府撥款

Federal Bu·reau of In·ves·ti·ga·tion /ˌ··· ˌ·· · ···ˈ··/ *n* the FBI (美國) 聯邦調查局

fed·e·ral·is·m /ˋfɛdərəlˌɪzəm; ˈfedərəlɪzəm/ *n* [U] belief in or support for a federal system of government 聯邦主義

federal tax /ˌ··· ˈ·/ *n* [C, U] *AmE* a tax in the US that is paid to the central government【美】〔美國〕聯邦稅

fed·e·rate /ˋfɛdəˌret; ˈfedəreɪt/ *v* **[I+with]** if a group of states federate, they join together to form a federation 結成聯邦[聯盟]

fed·e·ra·tion /ˌfɛdəˋreʃən; ˌfedəˈreɪʃən/ *n* **1** [C] a group of organizations, clubs, or people that have joined together to form a single group 聯合會; 聯盟: *the National Federation of Women's Institutes*〔英國及英聯邦國家〕婦女協會全國聯合會 **2** [C] a group of states that have joined together to form a single group 聯邦政府; 聯邦共和國: *the Russian Federation* 俄羅斯聯邦政府 **3** [U] the act of joining together to form a group 結成聯盟[聯邦]

fed up /ˌ· ˈ·/ *adj* [not before noun 不用於名詞前] *informal* annoyed or bored, and wanting something to change【非正式】厭煩的, 不滿的, 無法再忍受的: **[+with]** *I'm really fed up with this weather – why can't it be sunny for a change?* 我真的受夠了這種天氣 —— 為甚麼不變一下, 出出太陽? | *You look really fed up – what's the matter?* 你看來很不高興 —— 出了甚麼事? | **get fed up** *In the end she got fed up with waiting for him to decide.* 最後她等他作決定都等得不耐煩了。| *I'm getting fed up with your stupid comments.* 我聽膩了你那些愚蠢的評語。| **fed up to the back teeth** (=extremely annoyed) 極其厭煩的

USAGE NOTE 用法説明: FED UP
GRAMMAR 語法
In British English, you will often hear people say **fed up of,** as well as **fed up with.** 在英國英語裡, 經常會聽到人們既説 fed up of, 也説 fed up with: *I'm fed up of all this waiting around.* 我討厭這樣等待。But many people consider this to be wrong. 但許多人認為這種説法是錯誤的。

fee /fi; fiː/ *n* [C often plural 常用複數] **1** an amount of money that you pay to a professional person for their work〔付給專業人員的〕工作酬金; 服務費: **charge a fee** *Some lawyers charge exorbitant fees.* 有些律師收費高得嚇人。| **legal/medical fee** *The insurance company paid all my medical fees.* 保險公司支付了我的全部醫療費。**2** an amount of money that you pay to do something 費用: *school fees* 學費 | **entrance fee** *The entrance fees have gone up by 50%.* 入會[場]費已經上漲了 50%。—see 見 COST[1] (USAGE), PAY[2] (USAGE)

fee·ble /ˈfibḷ; ˈfiːbəl/ *adj* **1** extremely weak 非常虛弱的, 無力的: *My grandfather was too feeble to sit up in bed.* 我的祖父非常虛弱, 無法在牀上坐起來。| *a feeble attempt* 無力的嘗試 **2** a feeble joke, excuse, argument etc is not very good or effective〔笑話、藉口、論點等〕蹩腳的; 無效的, 站不住腳的: *people who come in late with feeble excuses* 帶着站不住腳的藉口晚進來的人 **3** a feeble manager, teacher etc cannot control the people they are in charge of〔經理、教師等〕軟弱的, 控制不住下屬的

feeble-mind·ed /ˌ‥ˈ‥◂/ *adj* **1** unable to think clearly and decide what to do 無決斷的, 動搖不定的, 思想糊塗的: *Her husband's so feeble-minded – he won't do a thing unless she tells him to.* 她的丈夫很優柔寡斷——除非她叫他做, 否則他甚麼事都不做。**2** *old use* having much less than average intelligence【舊】弱智的, 低能的 —**feeble-mindedly** *adv* —**feeble-mindedness** *n* [U]

feed[1] /fid; fiːd/ *past tense and past participle* **fed** /fɛd; fed/ *v*

1 ▶GIVE FOOD 給予食物◀ [T] **a)** to give food to a person or animal 餵養, 飼養, 為…提供食品: *Have you fed the cat?* 你餵貓了嗎? | *He's so old and ill he can't feed himself any more.* 他年老多病, 再也無法自己進食。| **feed sth to sb** *Feed the food to the baby in small pieces.* 用小塊的食品餵嬰兒。| **feed sb on sth** *Most people feed parrots on nuts.* 大多數人用乾果餵鸚鵡。**b)** to provide enough food for a group of people 養活〔一羣人, 一家人〕: *You can't feed a family of five on $100 a week.* 你無法靠每週 100 美元來養活一家五口。

2 ▶PLANT 植物◀ [T] to give a special substance to a plant which makes it grow 給…施肥: *Feed the tomatoes once a week.* 每週給番茄施一次肥。

3 ▶ANIMAL/BABY 動物/嬰兒◀ [I] if a baby or an animal feeds, they eat〔動物或嬰兒〕吃(東西): *Frogs generally feed at night.* 青蛙一般在晚上進食。—see also 另見 **feed on sth** (FEED[1])

4 ▶SUPPLY STH 供應某物◀ [T] to supply something such as FUEL[1] (1) or information to someone or something 給…供應(燃料); 給…提供〔信息〕: **feed sth with** *The carburettor has to keep feeding the cylinders with petrol.* 化油器得不停地向汽缸輸送汽油。| **feed sth into** *The data is then fed into a computer.* 數據隨後被輸入電腦。| **feed sth to sb** *US intelligence had been feeding false information to a KGB agent.* 美國情報機關過去一直在給一名克格勃間諜提供假情報。

5 ▶PUSH STH THROUGH 把某物導入◀ [T] to gradually push or put something such as a tube or a wire through a small hole〔由小孔逐漸地〕放入, 導入: **feed sth into/through** *The tube was fed down through the patient's throat into her stomach.* 軟管慢慢通過病人的喉嚨插入她的胃部。

6 [T] **feed sb's guilt/vanity/paranoia etc** to do something that makes someone feel more guilty etc 使某人更內疚/洋洋得意/偏執多疑等: *You shouldn't say that, you'll only feed his paranoia.* 你不該那樣説話, 這只會讓他更偏執猜疑。

7 feed lines/jokes to sb to say things to another performer so that they can make jokes 為某表演者提台詞〔以讓他作為笑料〕

8 well-fed/under-fed/poorly-fed having plenty of food or not enough food 吃得飽的/吃不飽的/吃得很差的: *exhausted, under-fed children* 疲憊不堪、食不果腹的兒童

9 feed your face *informal* to eat a lot of food【非正式】大吃一頓

10 feed sb a line *informal* to tell someone something which is not true so that they will do what you want【非正式】向某人虛報情況[撒謊]: *She tried to feed him a line about unexpected expenses.* 她企圖向他虛報情況, 來解釋那些意外的開支。

11 feed a meter to keep putting money into a machine so that you can have electricity, park your car etc〔為了供電或泊車等〕不斷往計時器投幣 —see also 另見 BREASTFEED, FORCE-FEED, SPOON-FEED, **mouth to feed** (MOUTH[1] (9))

feed off sth *phr v* [T] **1** if an animal feeds off something, it gets food from it〔動物〕從…取食: *The pigeons feed off our neighbour's crops.* 這些鴿子從我們鄰居的莊稼取食。**2** an insulting way of saying that someone uses something to continue their activities 亂用; 靠…過日子〔侮辱性説法〕: *The press feeds off gossip and tittle-tattle.* 新聞界靠搜集流言蜚語過活。

feed on sth *phr v* [T] **1** if an animal feeds on a particular food, it usually eats that food〔動物〕以…為食物: *Owls feed on mice and other small animals.* 貓頭鷹以老鼠和其他小動物為食。**2** if a feeling or process feeds on something, it becomes stronger because of it 使〔某種感覺或過程〕變得更強烈: *Prejudice feeds on mistrust and ignorance.* 懷疑和無知會助長偏見。

feed sb **up** *phr v* [T] to give someone a lot of food to make them more healthy〔用大量食物〕養肥, 養壯〔某人〕

feed[2] *n*

1 ▶BABY 嬰兒◀ [C] one of the times when you give milk to a small baby〔給嬰兒的〕一次餵奶: *Is it time for Zoe's feed yet?* 到了給佐伊餵奶的時間嗎?

2 ▶ANIMAL FOOD 動物的食物◀ [U] food for animals 飼料: *hen-feed* 雞飼料

3 ▶TUBE 管道◀ [C] a tube which supplies a machine with FUEL[1] (1) 進(燃)料管: *There's a blockage in the petrol feed.* 汽油的輸油管被阻塞了。

4 ▶MEAL 飯菜◀ [C] *old-fashioned* a big meal【過時】一頓飽餐

5 ▶PERFORMER 表演者◀ [C] *BrE* a performer who says things so that another performer can make jokes about them【英】〔喜劇演員的〕逗噱搭檔 —see also 另見 CHICKENFEED

feed·back /ˈfidˌbæk; ˈfiːdbæk/ *n* [U] **1** advice, criticism etc about how successful or useful something is 反饋意見: *Most of the feedback we've received so far has been positive.* 我們迄今收到的反饋意見大都是肯定的。**2** an unpleasant high noise heard when a MICROPHONE is too close to an AMPLIFIER〔話筒太靠近放大器而產生的〕噪聲

feed·bag /ˈfidbæg; ˈfiːdbæg/ *n* [C] *AmE* a bag put around a horse's head containing food; NOSEBAG【美】〔掛在馬頭上的〕飼料袋

feed·er /ˈfidɚ; ˈfiːdə/ *n* [C] **1 a slow/fussy etc feeder** a baby that eats it's food in a slow, FUSSY etc way 吃得慢的/挑食的嬰兒 **2** a small road or railway line that takes traffic onto a main road or railway line〔匯入主幹車道的〕支路; 公路[鐵路]支線 **3** a container with food for animals or birds〔餵鳥獸的〕飼料容器 **4** *old-fashioned* a piece of cloth put under a baby's chin when he or she is eating; BIB (1)【過時】〔嬰兒進食時放在下巴下的〕圍嘴

feeder school /'·· ,·/ *n* [C] a school from which many pupils go to a SECONDARY SCHOOL in the same area〔派學生到同一地區中學就讀的〕直屬學校

feed·ing-bot·tle /'·· ,··/ *n* [C] a plastic bottle used for giving milk to a baby or young animal（塑料）奶瓶

feeding ground /'·· ·/ *n* [C] a place where a group of animals or birds find food to eat〔動物或鳥類的〕聚食場

1 1 **feel**[1] /fil; fiːl/ *v past tense and past participle* **felt** /fɛlt; felt/

1 ►FEEL HAPPY/SICK ETC 感到愉快/不愉快等◄ [linking verb 連繫動詞, I] to experience a particular feeling or emotion 感受到, 覺得, 體會到: *You can never tell what he's feeling.* 你怎樣也無法明白他此刻的感覺。| **feel fine/sick/hungry/guilty etc** *I'm feeling a little better today.* 我今天覺得身體好了一點。| *I felt a bit awkward having to ask them for money.* 向他們要錢我覺得有點彆扭。| *We felt insulted by their offer.* 我們感到被他們的提議侮辱了。| **feel as if/as though** *I felt as though I'd won a million dollars.* 我覺得就像贏了一百萬美元似的。

2 ►NOTICE 注意到◄ [T not in progressive 不用進行式] to notice something that is happening to you 注意到, 感受到: *He loved feeling the sand between his toes.* 他喜歡腳趾踩在沙裡的感覺。| **feel sb/sth do sth** *Terry felt the snake touch his foot.* 特里感覺那條蛇觸到他的腳。| **feel yourself doing sth** *I felt myself blushing slightly.* 我覺得有點臉紅。

3 ►FEEL SMOOTH/DRY ETC 覺得光滑/乾燥等◄ [linking verb 連繫動詞] if something feels smooth, dry, cold etc, this is the feeling it gives you, especially when you touch it〔摸上去〕感覺是…: *Her skin felt cold and rough.* 她的皮膚摸上去又涼又粗糙。| **feel as if/as though** *My leg feels as if it's broken.* 我的一條腿好像斷了似的。

4 it feels good/strange etc if a situation, event etc feels good, strange etc, this is how it makes you feel〔情況、事件等使人〕覺得很好/感到奇怪等: *It felt wonderful to be wearing clean clothes again.* 再次穿上乾淨的衣服讓我感覺好極了。| *How does it feel to be 40?* 到了40歲有甚麼感受?

5 ►HAVE AN OPINION 有意見◄ [T not usually in progressive 一般不用進行式] to have a particular opinion, especially one that is based on your feelings, not on facts〔尤指根據感覺而不是事實〕以為, 認為: **feel (that)** *I can't help feeling that he deserved it.* 我不免認為他活該。| **[+about]** *How do you feel about all these changes in the curriculum?* 你認為課程的這些改動怎麼樣? | **feel sure/certain** (=think that something is definitely true) 確信/有把握 *She felt sure she'd made the right decision.* 她確信自己作了正確的決定。

6 feel like a) to want to have something or do something 想要: *I felt like another glass of wine.* 我想再喝一杯葡萄酒。| *He didn't feel like going to work.* 他不想去工作。**b)** to give you a particular feeling 感覺像, 摸上去像: *It's nice fabric – it feels like velvet.* 這布很好——摸上去像天鵝絨。| *I was only there two days but it felt like a week!* 我在那兒只有兩天, 但感覺像過了一個星期。**c)** to feel as if you are a particular kind of person 感覺自己是〔某一種人〕: *They made me feel like one of the family.* 他們使我覺得自己是他們家裡的一分子。

7 ►TOUCH 摸◄ [T] to touch something with your fingers to find out about it 觸摸: *She could feel a lump on her breast.* 她能摸到自己的乳房有一個腫塊。| *Feel the quality of this cloth.* 摸摸這布的質地吧。—see picture on page A21 參見A21頁圖

8 feel around/on etc sth (for sth) to search for something with your fingers〔用手指〕摸索〔某物〕: *She felt about in her bag for a pencil.* 她在袋子裡摸着找鉛筆。

9 feel the force/effects/benefits etc of sth to experience the good or bad results of something 感受某物的力量/受到某物的影響/感受某物的好處等: *The company is beginning to feel the effects of the strike.* 公司開始受到罷工的影響。

10 feel the need to do sth to feel that you need to do something 覺得需要做某事: *Sometimes we feel the need to get out of New York and take things easy.* 有時我們覺得需要離開紐約, 好好放鬆一下。

11 feel your way a) to move carefully, with your hands out in front of you because you cannot see properly〔因看不清楚而伸出手來〕摸索前進: *He felt his way across the room, and found the light switch.* 他摸着走到房間的另一頭, 找到電燈開關。**b)** to do things slowly and carefully, because you are unsure about a new situation〔由於對新情況無把握而〕謹慎行事; 摸索行進: *He hasn't been in the job long and he's still feeling his way.* 他做這個工作還不久, 所以仍然在摸索着幹。

12 feel free *spoken* used to tell someone that you are happy if they want to do something【口】儘管做, 沒問題: *"Could I use your phone for a minute?" "Feel free."* "我能用一下你的電話嗎?""請便。" | **feel free to do sth** *Please feel free to make suggestions.* 請隨便提建議, 不要拘束。

13 I know (just/exactly) how you feel *spoken* used to express sympathy with a remark someone has just made【口】我(十分)理解你的心情: *"Everything I do seems to go wrong!" "I know just how you feel!"* "我做的一切似乎都錯了!""我完全理解你的心情!"

14 not feel yourself *spoken* to not feel as healthy or happy as usual【口】身體不舒服; 心情不好: *Don't take any notice of her – she's not feeling quite herself today.* 別理睬她——她今天很不高興。

15 feel your age to realize that you are not as young or active as you used to be 感到老了: *It was only looking at his son that made him feel his age.* 他看着兒子才發現自己老了。

16 feel the cold to suffer because of cold weather 怕冷: *Old people tend to feel the cold more.* 老人往往更容易怕冷。

17 feel a death/a loss etc to react very strongly to a bad event, especially someone's death 對〔某人的〕死感覺到悲痛/對損失感到難過等: *Susan felt her grandmother's death more than the others.* 蘇珊對她祖母的死比別人更悲痛。

feel for sb *phr v* [T] to feel sympathy for someone 同情〔某人〕: *I really feel for the parents of that little boy who was killed.* 我實在同情那個被殺男孩的父母。

feel sb ↔ **out** *phr v* [T] *AmE informal* to ask someone's opinions or feelings【美, 非正式】徵求〔某人〕的看法: *Have you felt out your parents about using the cabin?* 你使用這小屋有沒有徵求過父母的看法?

feel sb ↔ **up** *phr v* [T] *informal* to touch someone sexually, without their permission【非正式】〔未得到允許而猥褻地〕摸弄〔某人〕

feel[2] *n* [singular] **1** the way that something feels when you touch it 感覺, 觸覺, 手感: *I like the feel of this cloth.* 我喜歡這塊布的手感。| *a soft feathery feel* 羽毛般的柔軟感覺 **2** a general idea about something〔對某事的〕一般印象, 大體感覺: *The weight adds a feel of quality to these plates.* 這些盤子的重量給它們增加了質感。**3 have a feel for** *informal* to have a natural understanding of something and skill in doing it【非正式】對…有天賦: *You've got to have a feel for the music.* 你得具備音樂天賦。 3

feel·er /'filɚ; 'fiːlə/ *n* [C usually plural 一般用複數] **1** one of the two long things on an insect's head which it uses to feel or touch things〔昆蟲頭部的〕觸角, 觸鬚 **2 put out feelers** to start to try to discover what people think about something that you want to do 試探〔別人對你想做的事怎麼想〕: *They seem to be interested in a peace settlement and have begun putting out feelers.* 他們似乎對和平解決感興趣, 已經開始進行試探。

feel-good /'· ·/ *adj* **feel-good film/programme/music etc** a film etc whose main purpose is to make you feel happy and cheerful 讓人感到愉悅的影片/節目/音樂等

feel good factor /'· · ,··/ *n* [U] *especially BrE* a feel-

F

ing among ordinary people that everything is going well, and they need not worry about spending money【尤英】〔普通人的〕快樂感; 快樂因子

feel·ing[1] /ˈfilɪŋ; ˈfiːlɪŋ/ *n*

1 ►ANGER/SADNESS/JOY ETC 憤怒/傷心/快樂等感覺◄ [C] something that you feel such as anger, sadness, or happiness〔憤怒、傷心、快樂等的〕感覺: **[+of]** *She suddenly had a great feeling of relief.* 她突然產生一種十分寬慰的感覺。| *Feelings of guilt are common in such cases.* 內疚感在這些情況下很常見。| *It's a wonderful feeling to be back home again.* 又回到家裡感覺太好了。| **the feeling's mutual** (=used to say that you have the same feeling about someone as they have about you) 這種感覺是我們彼此都有的 *"I don't ever want to see you again." "The feeling's mutual."* "我再也不想見到你。" "彼此彼此。" | **feelings are running high** (=people are very angry or excited) 人們情緒高漲; 人們十分生氣[興奮] *It was the last game of the season, and feelings were running high.* 這是這個賽季的最後一場比賽, 人們情緒高漲。

2 ►OPINION 看法◄ [C] what you think and feel about a situation〔對某一情況的〕感想, 看法, 想法: *My own personal feeling is that we should be very careful.* 我個人的看法是, 我們應當非常小心。| **[+on]** *What are your feelings on the issue of abortion?* 你對墮胎這一問題有甚麼看法? | **[+about]** *I think I've already made my feelings about this perfectly clear.* 我想我已經極其清楚地闡述了對這件事的感想。| **have mixed feelings** (=not be sure what you feel or think) 心裡矛盾, 感覺[想法]混亂 *Parents often have mixed feelings about their children leaving home.* 家長們對孩子長大離家一事心裡通常會很矛盾。

3 have/get the feeling (that) to think that something is probably true, or will probably happen 感覺〔某事可能是真的〕; 預感〔某事會發生〕: *Leslie suddenly got the feeling that somebody was watching her.* 萊斯莉突然感覺有人在看她。| *I've got a horrible feeling I forgot to turn off the cooker.* 我突然有一種可怕的感覺我忘了關爐灶了。

4 ►GENERAL ATTITUDE 普遍態度◄ [U] a general attitude among a group of people about a subject〔一羣人對某一問題的〕普遍情緒: **[+against/in favour of]** *Johnson underestimated the strength of public feeling against the war in Vietnam.* 約翰遜低估了公眾反對越戰情緒的強烈程度。

5 ►HEAT/COLD/PAIN ETC 熱/冷/痛等◄ [C] something that you feel in your body such as heat, cold, tiredness etc〔身體上的〕感覺: *I keep getting this funny feeling* (=a strange feeling) *in my neck* 我的脖子一直有這種奇怪的感覺。| *feelings of dizziness* 頭暈的感覺

6 ►ABILITY TO FEEL 感知能力◄ [U] the ability to feel pain, heat etc in part of your body〔身體部位疼痛、熱等的〕感覺, 知覺: *Herzog had lost all feeling in his toes.* 赫爾佐克的腳趾已經完全失去知覺。

7 ►EFFECT OF A PLACE/BOOK ETC 地方/書籍等給人的影響◄ [singular] the effect that a place, book, film etc has on people and the way it makes them feel〔地方、書籍、電影等的〕感染力: *Glastonbury has a great feeling of history about it.* 格拉斯頓伯里這地方有一種偉大的歷史感染力。

8 I know the feeling *spoken* used to say that you understand how someone feels because you have had the same experience【口】我知道那種感覺: *"It's so embarrassing when you can't remember someone's name." "I know the feeling."* "當你記不起別人的名字時是很尷尬的。" "我知道那種感覺。"

9 bad/ill feeling anger, lack of trust etc between people, especially after an argument or unfair decision〔尤指爭論或不公正的決定後人們之間的〕反感, 惡感; 不滿: *The recent rail strikes have caused a lot of ill feeling.* 最近的鐵路罷工引起了人們強烈的反感。

10 with feeling in a way that shows you feel very angry, happy etc 充滿感情地; 情緒激動地: *Chang spoke with feeling about the injustices of the regime.* 張情緒激憤地談論了這個政權的不公之處。

11 a feeling (for) a) an ability to do something or understand a subject, which you get from experience〔憑經驗〕做[理解]〔某事〕的能力: *It's difficult to explain – you just get this feeling for it.* 這很難解釋——這只是種感覺。**b)** a natural ability to do something 天分, 天賦: *She has a real feeling for the violin.* 她對小提琴真有天分。

12 ►EMOTIONS NOT THOUGHT 感情而非思想◄ [U] a way of reacting to things using your emotions, instead of thinking about them carefully 感情: *The Romantic writers valued feeling above all else.* 浪漫派作家重視感情超過其他一切。—see also 另見 **no hard feelings** (HARD[1] (26)), **hurt sb's feelings** (HURT[1] (5))

feeling[2] *adj* showing strong feelings 動人的, 多情的; 表現強烈感情的; 十分激動的: *a feeling look* 帶有感情的一瞥; 傳情的目光 —**feelingly** *adv*

fee-pay·ing /ˈ· ˌ··/ *adj BrE*【英】**1 fee-paying school** a school which you have to pay to go to 收費學校 **2 fee-paying student/patient** a student or PATIENT who pays for their education or medical treatment 繳費的學生/付費的病人

feet /fit; fiːt/ the plural of FOOT —see also 另見 **cold feet** (COLD[1] (7)), **feet of clay** (FOOT[1] (24)), **have itchy feet** (ITCHY (4))

feign /fen; feɪn/ *v* [T] *formal* to pretend to have a particular feeling or to be ill, asleep etc【正式】假裝〔某種感情〕、裝〔病、睡等〕: *Feigning a headache, I went upstairs to my room.* 我假裝頭痛, 上樓到房間去了。| *Mattie watched him approach with feigned indifference.* 馬蒂假裝冷漠地看着他走近。

feint[1] /fent; feɪnt/ *n* [C] a movement or an attack that is intended to deceive an opponent, especially in BOXING〔尤指拳擊中的〕佯攻, 虛晃一拳

feint[2] *v* [I,T] to pretend to hit someone in BOXING〔拳擊中〕佯攻, 虛擊

feist·y /ˈfaɪstɪ; ˈfaɪsti/ *adj approving* having a strong, determined character and being willing to argue with people【褒】頑強自信的; 好爭辯的: *She has the feisty image of the successful entrepreneur.* 她具有成功企業家自信好強的形象。

fe·la·fel /fəˈlɑfəl; fəˈlɑːfəl/ *n* [C] another spelling of FALAFEL falafel 的另一種拼法

feld·spar /ˈfɛldˌspɑr; ˈfeldspɑː/ also 又作 **felspar** *n* [U] a kind of grey or white mineral 長石〔一種灰色或白色的礦物〕

fe·li·ci·ta·tions /fəˌlɪsəˈteʃənz; fɪˌlɪsʒˈteɪʃənz/ *interjection formal* used to wish someone happiness【正式】〔用於祝願的〕祝賀; 祝辭

fe·li·ci·tous /fəˈlɪsətəs; fɪˈlɪsʒtəs/ *adj formal* well-chosen and suitable【正式】恰當的, 貼切的, 選得好的: *a felicitous choice of candidate* 候選人的恰當選擇 —**felicitously** *adv*

fe·li·ci·ty /fəˈlɪsətɪ; fɪˈlɪsʒti/ *n formal*【正式】**1** [U] happiness 幸福: *domestic felicity* 家庭幸福 **2** [U] the quality of being well-chosen or suitable 恰當, 巧妙: *the felicity of this arrangement* 這種安排的恰當 **3 felicities** [plural] suitable or well-chosen remarks or details 恰當[巧妙]的話[細節]

fe·line[1] /ˈfilaɪn; ˈfiːlaɪn/ *adj* **1** connected with cats or other members of the cat family such as lions 貓的; 貓科的 **2** looking like or moving like a cat 似貓的, 無聲潛行的: *She moves with feline grace.* 她輕柔無聲地行走, 姿態很美。

feline[2] *n* [C] *technical* a cat or a member of the cat family such as a tiger【術語】貓; 貓科動物〈如虎等〉

fell[1] /fɛl; fel/ the past tense of FALL[1]

fell[2] *n* [C] a mountain or hill in the north of England〔英格蘭北部的〕山, 山崗

fell[3] *v* [T] **1** to cut down a tree 砍伐〔樹木〕**2** to knock someone down with great force〔用力〕擊倒〔某人〕

fell⁴ *adj* **at/in one fell swoop** doing a lot of things at the same time, using only one action 一下子, 立即, 馬上: *I pressed the wrong button and deleted all the files in one fell swoop.* 我按錯了按鈕, 一下子把全部文檔都刪除了。

3 **fel·la** /ˋfɛlə; ˈfelə/ *n* [C] *spoken*【口】**1** a man 傢伙: *I was talking to this fella I work with.* 我正和這個一起工作的傢伙談話。**2** a boyfriend 男朋友: *She's fine. Her new fella's lovely.* 她很好, 她那新交的男朋友很可愛。

fel·la·ti·o /fəˋleʃio; fəˈleɪʃiəʊ/ *n* [U] *formal* the practice of touching a man's PENIS with the lips and tongue to give sexual pleasure【正式】吮吸陰莖; 口交 —compare 比較 CUNNILINGUS

fel·ler /ˋfɛlɚ; ˈfelə/ *n* [C] *informal* a man【非正式】人; 男人; 傢伙

fel·low¹ /ˋfɛlo; ˈfeləʊ/ *n* [C] **1** *old-fashioned* a man【過時】人; 男人: *Paul's an easy-going sort of fellow.* 保羅是個隨和的傢伙。**2** *old-fashioned* a friendly way of addressing a man【過時】朋友〔用於友好地稱呼男人〕: *Hello my dear fellow!* 你好, 親愛的朋友! **3** *old-fashioned*【過時】**your/his etc fellows** the people who you work with, go to school with etc 你的/他的夥伴們〔指工作的同事或學校的同學等〕: *He's much more serious than his school fellows.* 他比他的同學嚴肅多了。**4** *especially BrE* a member of an important society or a college【尤英】〔重要學會的〕會員;〔學院的〕董事; 研究員: *Fellow of the Royal College of Surgeons* 皇家外科醫學院院士

3 **fellow²** *adj* **1 fellow workers/students/countrymen etc** people who work, study etc with you 同事/同學/同胞等: *She ignored her fellow passengers throughout the whole journey.* 在整個旅程中她都不理睬同行的乘客。**2 our fellow man/men** other people in general 我們的同胞; 人類: *We all have obligations to our fellow men.* 我們大家對他人都負有義務。**3 fellow feeling** a feeling of sympathy and friendship towards someone because they are like you 同情, 同感; 情誼: *As an only child myself, I had a certain fellow feeling for Laura.* 我自己也是個獨生子, 因此與勞拉有某種同感。

fel·low·ship /ˋfɛlo͵ʃɪp; ˈfeləʊʃɪp/ *n* **1** [U] a feeling of friendship resulting from shared interests or experiences〔因共同的興趣或經歷而產生的〕友情, 友誼, 夥伴關係: *A close fellowship developed among them.* 他們之間產生了密切的夥伴情誼。**2** [C] a group of people who share an interest or belief, especially Christians who have religious ceremonies together〔具有共同興趣或信念的〕團體;〔基督教的〕團契 **3** [C] *BrE* a job at a university which involves making a detailed study of a particular subject【英】〔大學裡的〕研究員職位; 學院院士 **4** [C] *especially AmE* money given to a student to allow them to continue their studies at an advanced level【尤美】〔為讓學生能進一步深造而授予的〕獎學金 **5** [C] *AmE* a group of officials who decide which students will receive this money【美】〔決定獎學金人選的〕獎學金評選組

fellow trav·ell·er *BrE*【英】, **fellow traveler** *AmE*【美】/͵·· ˈ···/ *n* [C] someone you disapprove of because they agree with the aims of the Communist Party 同路人, 同情者〔指贊成共產黨的宗旨的人〕

fel·on /ˋfɛlən; ˈfelən/ *n* [C] *law* someone who is guilty of a serious crime【法律】重罪犯

fel·o·ny /ˋfɛlənɪ; ˈfeləni/ *n* [C,U] *law* a serious crime such as murder【法律】重罪〈如謀殺〉—compare 比較 MISDEMEANOUR (2)

fel·spar /ˋfɛl͵spar; ˈfelspɑː/ *n* [U] another spelling of FELDSPAR feldspar 的另一種拼法

felt¹ /fɛlt; felt/ the past tense and past participle of FEEL¹

felt² *n* [U] a thick soft material made of wool, hair, or fur that has been pressed flat 毛氈

felt-tip /ˋ· ·/ also 又作 **felt-tip pen** /͵· ·ˈ·/ *n* [C] a pen that has a hard piece of felt at the end that the ink comes through 氈頭筆, 氈尖筆 —see picture at 參見 PEN¹ 圖

fem a written abbreviation for 縮寫= FEMININE or FEMALE

fe·male¹ /ˋfi͵mel; ˈfiːmeɪl/ *adj* **1** belonging to the sex that can have babies or produce eggs 女(性)的; 雌(性)的; 母的: *a female spider* 雌蜘蛛, 母蜘蛛 **2** a female plant or flower produces fruit 雌性植物的, 雌蕊的 **3** *technical* a female part of a piece of equipment has a hole into which another part fits【術語】〔零件〕陰的, 內孔的, 凹的: *a female plug* 內孔式插頭 —**femaleness** *n* [U] 3 2

female² *n* [C] **1** a person or animal that belongs to the sex that can have babies or produce eggs 女性; 雌性動物 **2** a woman or girl 女人; 女孩: *the prettiest female in Savannah* 薩瓦納最漂亮的女人 3

Fem·i·dom /ˋfɛmɪdɑm; ˈfemɪdɒm/ *n* [C] *trademark* a loose rubber tube with one end closed that fits inside a woman's VAGINA when she is having sex, so that she will not have a baby【商標】女用避孕套

fem·i·nine /ˋfɛmənɪn; ˈfemɪ̣nɪ̣n/ *adj* **1** having qualities that are considered to be typical of women, especially by being gentle, delicate and pretty 女性的, 婦女的: *Dianne loved pretty feminine things.* 黛安娜喜愛漂亮的女性用品。| *his slim, feminine hand* 他的瘦長的女性般的手 **2** a feminine noun, PRONOUN etc belongs to a class of words that have different inflections (INFLECTION (2)) from MASCULINE (4) or NEUTER¹ (2) words〔名詞、代詞等〕陰性的

fem·i·nin·i·ty /͵fɛməˋnɪnətɪ; ͵femɪ̣ˈnɪnɪ̣ti/ *n* [U] qualities that are considered to be typical of women, especially qualities that are gentle, delicate, and pretty 女子氣質〔尤指溫柔、嬌小、美麗等〕: *Different cultures often have different concepts of femininity and masculinity.* 不同文化通常對女子氣質和男子氣概有不同的概念。

fem·i·nis·m /ˋfɛmə͵nɪzəm; ˈfemɪ̣nɪzəm/ *n* [U] the belief that women should have the same rights and opportunities as men 女權主義 —**feminist** *adj*: *feminist principles* 女權主義原則

fem·i·nist /ˋfɛmənɪst; ˈfemɪ̣nɪ̣st/ *n* [C] someone who supports the idea that women should have the same rights and opportunities as men 女權主義者: *If she's a sort of feminist, I can understand why she said that.* 如果她是某種女權主義者, 我會理解她為何那樣說。 3

femme fa·tale /͵fæm fəˋtɑl; ͵fæm fəˈtɑːl/ *n* [C] *French* a beautiful woman who men find very attractive, even though she may make them unhappy【法】引誘男子墮落的女子; 妖婦, 蕩婦

fe·mur /ˋfimɚ; ˈfiːmə/ *n* [C] the THIGH bone 股骨 —**femoral** /ˋfɛmərəl; ˈfemərəl/ *adj* —see picture at 參見 SKELETON 圖

fen /fɛn; fen/ *n* [C] an area of low flat wet land, especially in Eastern England〔尤指英格蘭東部的〕沼澤地帶; 濕地

fence¹ /fɛns; fens/ *n* [C] **1** a structure made of wood, metal etc that surrounds a piece of land〔木頭、金屬等做的〕柵欄, 圍欄, 籬笆 **2** a wall or other structure that horses jump over in a race or competition〔賽馬中的〕障礙物 **3** *slang* someone who buys and sells stolen goods【俚】買賣贓物的人 **4 sit on the fence** to avoid saying which side of an argument you support 保持中立, 抱騎牆態度: *The Liberals prefer to sit on the fence while the other parties fight it out.* 自由黨寧可抱騎牆態度, 坐待其他黨派去鬥爭到底。—see also 另見 **mend (your) fences** (MEND¹ (4)) 3

fence² *v* **1** [T] to put a fence around something 把…用欄柵[籬笆]圍起來 **2** [I] to fight with a long thin sword as a sport 擊劍 **3** [I+with] to answer someone's questions in a clever way in order to get an advantage in an argument 巧妙回答; 用言辭搪塞

fence sb/sth ↔ **in** *phr v* [T] **1** to surround a place with a fence 把〔某人/某物〕用欄柵[籬笆]圍住 **2** [often passive 常用被動態] to make someone feel that they cannot leave a place or do what they want 限制〔某人的〕自由, 束縛〔某人〕: *Mothers with young children often feel fenced in at home.* 有幼兒的母親們經常覺得被束縛在家裡。

fence sb/sth ↔ **off** *phr v* [T] to separate one area from

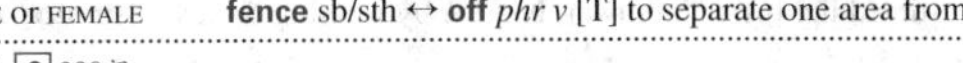

another area with a fence 用欄柵[籬笆]把…隔開: *a planting area fenced off from the main garden* 用欄柵與主花園隔開的種植區

fenc·er /ˈfɛnsɚ; ˈfensə/ *n* [C] someone who fights with a long thin sword as a sport 擊劍者, 擊劍運動員

fenc·ing /ˈfɛnsɪŋ; ˈfensɪŋ/ *n* [U] **1** the sport of fighting with a long thin sword 擊劍(運動) **2** fences or the pieces of wood, metal etc used to make them 築欄柵[籬笆]的材料

fend /fɛnd; fend/ *v* **fend for yourself** to look after yourself without needing help from other people 獨立生活; 照料自己: *The kids had to fend for themselves while their parents were away.* 父母不在家時, 孩子們只好自己照料自己。

fend sb/sth **off** *phr v* [T] **1** to defend yourself against someone who is attacking you 擋開〔某人/某物的攻擊〕: *A bag or briefcase can be used to fend off an attacker.* 提包或公文包可用來抵擋攻擊者。| *fending off the blows with his sword* 他用劍擋開攻擊 **2** to deal with difficult questions, especially by avoiding answering them directly 避開, 迴避〔難題〕: *I did my best to fend off his critical remarks.* 我盡力招架他的批評。

fend·er /ˈfɛndɚ; ˈfendə/ *n* [C] **1** *AmE* a bar fixed on the front or back of a car to protect it if it hits something【美】〔汽車前面或後面的〕保險槓; BUMPER¹ (1) *BrE*【英】—see picture on page A2 參見 A2 頁圖 **2** *AmE* the side part of a car that covers the wheels【美】〔汽車輪胎上的〕擋泥板; WING¹ (6) *BrE*【英】—see picture on page A2 參見 A2 頁圖 **3** a low metal wall around a FIREPLACE that prevents burning wood or coal from falling out 壁爐擋板 **4** *AmE* a curved piece of metal over the wheel of a bicycle that prevents water and mud from flying up【美】〔腳踏車上的〕擋泥板; MUDGUARD *BrE*【英】—see picture at 參見 BICYCLE¹ 圖 **5** an object such as an old tyre used to protect the side of a boat〔船的〕碰墊, 護舷木, 防擦墊

fender-bend·er /ˈ·· ,··/ *n* [C] *AmE informal* a car accident in which little damage is done【美, 非正式】〔損毀輕微的〕小車禍

fen·nel /ˈfɛnl; ˈfenl/ *n* [U] a pale green plant whose seeds are used to give a special taste to food and which is also used as a vegetable 茴香

fe·ral /ˈfɪrəl; ˈferəl/ *adj* feral animals used to live with humans but have become wild 未馴服的, 野的; 〔馴養後脫逃〕恢復野性的: *feral cats* 野貓

fer·ment¹ /fɚˈmɛnt; fəˈment/ *v* [I,T] if fruit, beer, wine etc ferments or if it is fermented, the sugar in it changes to alcohol, especially because of the action of YEAST〔水果、啤酒、葡萄酒等〕(使)發酵 —**fermented** *adj*: *fermented fruit* 發酵的水果 —**fermentation** /ˌfɝmɛnˈteʃən; ˌfɜːmenˈteɪʃən/ *n* [U]

fer·ment² /ˈfɝmɛnt; ˈfɜːment/ *n* [U] a situation of great excitement or trouble in a country, especially because people disagree strongly with the government 騷亂; 動亂; 激蕩: **be in (a state of) ferment** *The whole of Russia was in ferment.* 俄羅斯全國處於動亂之中。

fern /fɝn; fɜːn/ *n* [C] a type of plant which has feathery green leaves, but no flowers 蕨類植物, 羊齒植物 —**ferny** *adj*

fe·ro·cious /fəˈroʃəs; fəˈrəʊʃəs/ *adj* **1** violent, dangerous, and frightening 兇猛的, 兇殘的: *The battle was long and ferocious.* 戰鬥持久而且激烈。| *ferocious dogs* 兇猛的狗 **2** very strong, severe, and unpleasant 狂暴的; 猛烈的; 使人不舒服的: *a ferocious headache* 劇烈的頭痛 | *The heat was ferocious.* 那時熱得厲害。—**ferociously** *adv* —**ferociousness** *n* [U]

fe·ro·ci·ty /fəˈrɑsətɪ; fəˈrɒsəti/ *n* [U] violence and cruelty 兇暴, 殘暴, 兇猛

fer·ret¹ /ˈfɛrɪt; ˈferət/ *n* [C] a small animal with a pointed nose used to hunt rats and rabbits 雪貂, 白鼬

ferret² *v* [I] **1** [always+adv/prep] *informal* to search for something inside a drawer, box etc by pushing things about【非正式】〔在抽屜、箱子裡〕搜找, 翻尋: **[+about/around/for]** *She ferreted about in her desk for a pen.* 她在書桌抽屜裡翻找鋼筆。**2** to hunt rats and rabbits using a ferret 用雪貂獵鼠[獵兔]

ferret sth ↔ **out** *phr v* [T] to succeed in finding a piece of information that is difficult to find 查獲; 搜出: *She managed to ferret out the details of her husband's affair.* 她設法查悉丈夫婚外情的細節。

fer·ris wheel /ˈfɛrɪs ˌhwil; ˈferəs ˌwiːl/ *n* [C] *especially AmE* a large upright wheel with seats on it for people to ride on in an AMUSEMENT PARK【尤美】摩天輪, 大轉輪〔指遊樂園裡設有座位的直立巨輪〕; BIG WHEEL *BrE*【英】

fer·rous /ˈfɛrəs; ˈferəs/ *adj technical* containing or connected with iron【術語】含鐵的, 鐵的: *Ferrous metals are magnetic.* 含鐵[黑色]金屬有磁性。

fer·rule /ˈfɛrəl; ˈferuːl/ *n* [C] a piece of metal or rubber put on the end of a stick to make it stronger〔手杖末端的〕金屬箍; 橡皮箍

fer·ry¹ /ˈfɛrɪ; ˈferi/ *n* [C] a boat that carries people or goods across a river or a narrow part of a sea 渡船, 擺渡(船)

ferry² *v* [T always+adv/prep] to carry people or things a short distance from one place to another in a boat or other vehicle 渡運, 運送: **ferry sb/sth to/from etc** *The lifeboat ferried the crew and passengers to safety.* 救生艇把船員和乘客送到安全的地方。| *A small bus ferries tourists from their hotels to the beach.* 一輛小巴士將遊客從旅館送到海濱。

fer·ry·boat /ˈfɛrɪˌbot; ˈferibəʊt/ *n* [C] a FERRY¹ 渡船, 擺渡(船)

fer·ry·man /ˈfɛrɪmən; ˈferimən/ *n* [C] someone who guides a ferry across a river 渡船工人, 船夫

fer·tile /ˈfɝtl̩; ˈfɜːtaɪl/ *adj* **1** fertile land or soil produces good crops 肥沃的, 富饒的: *the fertile plains of western Canada* 加拿大西部肥沃的平原 **2** able to produce babies, young animals, or new plants 可繁殖的, 能生育的: *Most men remain fertile into old age.* 大多數男子直到老年還有生育能力。—opposite 反義詞 INFERTILE **3 fertile imagination/mind/brain** *often humorous* an imagination etc that is able to think of interesting and unusual ideas【常幽默】豐富的想像力, 主意多[有創造性]的頭腦 **4 fertile ground** a situation where new ideas, political groups etc can easily develop and succeed 有利於〔新思想、政治組織等〕發展的環境: *Poor areas of East London became fertile ground for Mosley's fascist movement.* 倫敦東部的貧民區成了有利於莫斯利的法西斯運動的溫牀。

fer·til·i·ty /fɝˈtɪlətɪ; fɜːˈtɪləti/ *n* [U] **1** the ability of the land or soil to produce good crops 肥沃; 肥力: *loss of soil fertility* 土壤肥力的流失 **2** the ability of a person, animal, or plant to produce babies, young animals, or seeds 生育能力, 繁殖力

fertility drug /·ˈ··· ,·/ *n* [C] a drug given to a woman to help her have a baby 助孕藥, 生育藥

fer·ti·lize also 又作 **-ise** *BrE*【英】/ˈfɝtl̩ˌaɪz; ˈfɜːtəlaɪz/ *v* [T] **1** to make SPERM join an egg so that a young baby or animal develops, or to join particles of POLLEN so that a new plant develops 使受精, 使受孕 **2** to put a substance on the soil which makes crops grow 施肥 —**fertilization** /ˌfɝtl̩əˈzeʃən; ˌfɜːtəlaɪˈzeɪʃən/ *n* [U]

fer·ti·liz·er /ˈfɝtl̩ˌaɪzɚ; ˈfɜːtəlaɪzə/ *n* [C,U] a substance that is put on the land to make crops grow 肥料

fer·vent /ˈfɝvənt; ˈfɜːvənt/ *adj* believing or feeling something very strongly and sincerely 熱情的; 熾熱的; 熱烈的; 強烈的: *a fervent appeal for peace* 對和平的強烈籲求 | **fervent admirer/believer/supporter etc** *Even her most fervent admirers admit that Thatcher had her faults.* 甚至連戴卓爾的最狂熱的傾慕者也承認她有過錯。—**fervency** *n* [U] —**fervently** *adv*

fer·vid /ˈfɝvɪd; ˈfɜːvəd/ *adj formal* believing or feeling something too strongly【正式】熱烈的; 激烈的; 熱情的 —**fervidly** *adv*

fer·vour *BrE*【英】, **fervor** *AmE*【美】/ˈfɝvɚ; ˈfɜːvə/ *n*

[U] very strong belief or feeling 狂熱, 熱誠: *religious fervour* 宗教熱情

fess /fɛs; fes/ *v*

fess up [I] *AmE informal* to admit that you have done something wrong but it is not very serious【美, 非正式】承認, 交代: *Come on, fess up! Who ate that last cookie?* 得了, 從實招來吧! 誰吃了最後那塊甜餅?

fes·ter /ˋfɛstɚ; ˈfestə/ *v* [I] **1** if an unpleasant feeling or problem festers, it gets more unpleasant〔不快的感覺或問題〕加劇, 惡化: *The insult festered in his mind.* 那次受辱使他心中的不快日益加深。**2** if a wound festers, it becomes infected〔傷口〕潰爛, 化膿: *festering sores* 潰爛的瘡 **3** if rubbish or dirty objects fester, they decay and smell bad〔垃圾等〕腐爛發臭

3 3 **fes·ti·val** /ˋfɛstəvl; ˈfestɪ̈vəl/ *n* [C] **1** an occasion when there are performances of many films, plays, pieces of music etc, which happens in the same place every year〔每年在同一地點舉行的〕節慶; 紀念活動: *the Newport Jazz festival* 紐波特爵士音樂節 **2** a special occasion when people celebrate something such as a religious event, and there is often a public holiday 節日, 喜慶日: *Christmas is one of the main festivals in the Christian Calendar.* 聖誕節是基督教曆法中的一個重要節日。

fes·tive /ˋfɛstɪv; ˈfestɪv/ *adj* **1** looking or feeling bright and cheerful in a way that seems suitable for celebrating something 歡樂的, 歡慶的: *There was a festive atmosphere in the city.* 城裡充滿歡樂的節日氣氛。| *John was obviously in a festive mood.* 約翰顯然心情十分愉快, 像在過節似的。**2 festive occasion** a day when you celebrate something special such as a birthday 節慶場合; 紀念活動 **3 the festive season** the period around CHRISTMAS 聖誕節期間, 節期

fes·tiv·i·ty /fɛsˋtɪvətɪ; feˈstɪvɪ̈ti/ *n* [U] **1 festivities** [plural] things that are done to celebrate a special occasion such as drinking, eating, dancing etc 慶祝活動, 慶典: *The festivities started with a procession through the town.* 慶祝活動以在城裡的巡遊開始。**2** a happy and cheerful atmosphere that exists when people celebrate something 歡樂, 歡慶: *There was an air of festivity in the village.* 村裡一片歡慶氣氛。

fes·toon[1] /fɛsˋtun; feˈstuːn/ *v* [T] to cover something with long pieces of material, especially for decoration 結彩於, 給…裝飾花彩: **be festooned with** *Malaga was festooned with banners and flags in honour of the king's visit.* 馬拉加彩旗飄揚, 歡迎國王到訪。

festoon[2] *n* [C] *formal* a long thin piece of material, used especially for decoration【正式】花彩, 花彩裝飾物

fet·a /ˋfɛtə; ˈfetə/ *n* [U] a white cheese from Greece made from sheep's milk〔希臘產的〕羊奶白乾酪

fe·tal /ˋfitḷ; ˈfiːtl/ *adj* the usual American spelling of foetal (FOETUS) foetal 的一般美式拼法

2 **fetch** /fɛtʃ; fetʃ/ *v* [T] **1** to go to the place where something or someone is and bring them back 拿來; 請來; 找來: *Quick! Go and fetch a doctor.* 快!快去請醫生來。| **fetch sth from** *Would you mind going to fetch the kids from school?* 你能去學校接孩子們嗎? | **fetch sb sth/fetch sth for sb** *Run upstairs and fetch me my glasses, will you?* 跑上樓替我拿眼鏡來, 好嗎? —see 見 BRING (USAGE) **2** to be sold for a particular amount of money, especially at a public sale 賣得, 售得: *The painting is expected to fetch at least $20 million.* 這幅畫預計至少能賣二千萬美元。**3 fetch sb a blow/clip etc** *BrE informal* to hit someone【英, 非正式】給某人一拳/一擊: *I fetched him a clip round the ear.* 我打了他一記耳光。**4 fetch and carry** to do simple and boring jobs for someone as if you were their servant 做雜務, 打雜: *Am I supposed to fetch and carry for him all day?* 難道要我整天替他打雜嗎? **5** *BrE* to make people react in a particular way【英】使做出某種反應; 吸引來; 引起: *This announcement fetched a huge cheer from the audience.* 這項通知博得聽眾一陣極其熱烈的歡呼聲。

fetch up *phr v BrE informal*【英, 非正式】**1** [I always+adv/prep] to arrive somewhere without intending to〔突然〕到達: **[+in/at etc]** *I fell asleep on the train and fetched up in Glasgow.* 我在火車上睡着了, 醒來時竟到了格拉斯哥。**2** [I,T] to VOMIT[1] 嘔吐: *She fetched up all over the blankets.* 她把毯子吐得一塌糊塗。

fetch·ing /ˋfɛtʃɪŋ; ˈfetʃɪŋ/ *adj* attractive, especially because the clothes you are wearing suit you〔尤指因衣着得體而〕動人的, 迷人的, 吸引人的: *Your sister looks very fetching in that dress.* 你妹妹穿那身衣服顯得格外動人。—**fetchingly** *adv*

fete[1] /fet; feɪt/ *n* [C] **1** *BrE* an outdoor event where there are competitions and things to eat and drink, usually organized to get money【英】〔尤指為募捐而組織的〕遊樂會: *the church fete* 教堂的遊樂會 **2** *AmE* a special occasion to celebrate something【美】慶祝活動, 盛會: *Prom Night is the fete of the year for high school students.* 班級舞會之夜對高中學生來說是一年裡最大的慶祝活動。

fete[2] *v* [T usually passive 一般用被動態] to honour someone by holding public celebrations for them〔通過舉行慶祝活動來〕款待, 向…致敬: *The team was feted from coast to coast.* 這個隊在全國所到之處都受到熱情款待。

fet·id /ˋfɛtɪd; ˈfiːtɪ̈d/ *adj formal* having a strong, bad smell【正式】惡臭的: *the black fetid water of the lake* 湖裡又黑又臭的水

fet·ish /ˋfɛtɪʃ; ˈfetɪʃ/ *n* [C] **1** something you are always thinking about or spending too much time doing 被狂熱崇拜之物, 迷戀物: *Physical exercise has become something of a fetish nowadays.* 如今體育鍛鍊已經成為一種狂熱。| **have a fetish about** *Sue has a real fetish about keeping everything tidy.* 蘇確有潔癖, 總是把一切弄得非常整潔。**2** an unusual object or activity which gives someone sexual pleasure〔能引起性快感的〕戀物: *a leather fetish* 皮具戀物狂 **3** an object that is treated like a god and is thought to have magical powers〔認為有魔力的〕神物, 崇拜物

fet·ish·ist /ˋfɛtɪʃɪst; ˈfetɪʃɪ̈st/ *n* [C] someone who gets sexual pleasure from unusual objects or activities 戀物癖者, 戀物狂者 —**fetishism** *n* [U] —**fetishistic** /ˌfɛtɪˋʃɪstɪk; ˌfetɪˈʃɪstɪk◂/ *adj*

fet·lock /ˋfɛtˌlɑk; ˈfetlɒk/ *n* [C] the back part of a horse's leg, just above the HOOF[1] (1)〔馬蹄後上部的〕球節, 肢關節 —see picture at 參見 HORSE[1] 圖

fet·ter[1] /ˋfɛtɚ; ˈfetə/ *n* **fetters** [plural] *literary*【文】**a)** the things that prevent someone from being free 桎梏, 羈絆, 束縛: *breaking the fetters of convention* 打破常規的束縛 **b)** chains that were put around a prisoner's feet in former times〔舊時的〕腳鐐

fetter[2] *v* [T] *literary*【文】**1** to restrict someone's freedom and prevent them from doing what they want 束縛: *fettered by family responsibilities* 被家庭責任所束縛 **2** to put chains on a prisoner's hands or feet 為…上腳鐐[手鐐]

fet·tle /ˋfɛtl; ˈfetl/ *n* **in fine fettle/in good fettle** *old-fashioned* healthy or working properly【過時】健康的, 強健的; 工作良好的

fet·tuc·ci·ne /ˌfɛtʊˋtʃinɪ; ˌfetʊˈtʃiːni/ *n* [U] *Italian* thin flat pieces of PASTA【意】寬麵條

fe·tus /ˋfitəs; ˈfiːtəs/ *n* [C] the usual American spelling of FOETUS foetus 的一般美式拼法

feud[1] /fjud; fjuːd/ *n* [C] an angry and often violent quarrel between two people or groups that lasts for a long time〔個人間或羣體間的〕長期不和, 長期爭鬥, 世仇: **[+over]** *a bitter feud over territory* 領土問題上的長期激烈爭執

feud[2] *v* [I] to continue quarrelling for a long time often in a violent way 長期爭鬥, 結仇, 結怨: **feud (with sb) over sth** *the bitter feuding over the leadership of the EC* 關於歐洲共同體領導權的長期激烈爭鬥

feud·al /ˋfjudl; ˈfjuːdl/ *adj* [only before noun 僅用於名詞前] connected with feudalism 封建的, 封建制度的: *the feudal system* 封建制度 | *feudal society* 封建社會

F

feu·dal·is·m /ˈfjudḷˌɪzəm; ˈfjuːdl-ɪzəm/ *n* [U] a system which existed in the Middle Ages, in which people received land and protection from a lord when they worked and fought for him 封建制度; 封建主義

feu·dal·is·tic /ˌfjudḷˈɪstɪk; ˌfjuːdl-ˈɪstɪk◂/ *adj* based on a system in which only a few people have all the power in a way that seems very old fashioned 封建制度的; 封建主義的

fe·ver /ˈfivɚ; ˈfiːvə/ *n* **1** [C,U] an illness or a medical condition in which you have a very high temperature 發燒, 發熱: *He's in bed with a fever.* 他因發燒而臥牀休息。| *Take some aspirin – it'll help the fever to go down.* 吃點阿斯匹林 —— 這有助於退燒。—see also 另見 HAY FEVER, SCARLET FEVER, YELLOW FEVER **2** [singular] a situation in which people feel very excited or feel very strongly about something 高度興奮, 狂熱, 極端活躍: *a fever of excitement on Wall Street* 華爾街上異常狂熱激動的氣氛 | **election/carnival fever etc** (=great interest or excitement about a particular activity or event) 選舉/狂歡節等的狂熱 **3 fever pitch/point/heat** if people's feelings are at fever pitch etc, they are extremely excited 狂熱, 異常激動, 高度活躍: *The children's excitement rose to fever pitch as Christmas approached.* 隨着聖誕節的臨近, 孩子們越來越激動。

fever blis·ter /ˈ·· ˌ··/ *n* [C] *AmE* a COLD SORE【美】〔發燒引起的〕唇疱疹

fe·vered /ˈfivɚd; ˈfiːvəd/ *adj* [only before noun 僅用於名詞前] *literary*【文】**1** extremely excited or worried; FEVERISH (2) 高度興奮的; 十分焦慮的: *fevered cries* 極其激動的喊叫聲 **2** suffering from a fever; FEVERISH (1) 發燒的, 發熱的: **fevered brow** (=a hot forehead caused by a fever) 發燒的額頭 *She wiped his fevered brow.* 她擦了擦他發燒的額頭。**3 a fevered imagination** someone who has a fevered imagination imagines strange things and cannot control their thoughts 狂想: *These stories are merely a product of her fevered imagination.* 這些故事只不過是她憑空臆想出來的東西。

fe·ver·ish /ˈfivərɪʃ; ˈfiːvərɪʃ/ *adj* **1** suffering from a fever 發燒的: *feeling feverish* 感到發燒 | *Her cheeks looked hot and feverish.* 她的臉頰看上去很熱, 有點發燒。**2** very excited or worried about something 狂熱的; 十分焦慮的: *They waited in a state of feverish anxiety for their mother to come home.* 他們焦躁不安地等着母親回家。| **feverish activity/preparations/haste** (=activities that are done very quickly because there is not much time) 忙亂的活動/忙亂的準備工作/匆匆忙忙 *The show was about to begin and there were signs of feverish activity backstage.* 表演快要開始了, 可以看出後台在緊張忙亂着。—**feverishly** *adv*

few /fju; fjuː/ *quantifier, n* [plural] **1 a few/the few** [no comparative 無比較級] a small number (of) 少數, 一些, 幾個: *I've got a few books on gardening.* 我有幾本園藝書。| *I'll pop into the supermarket and get a few bits and pieces.* 我得到超級市場去買幾樣零碎東西。| *only a few hundred yards past the crossroads* 過了十字路口才幾百碼 | *It's one of the few companies trying to tackle the problem.* 那是想解決這個問題的少數幾家公司之一。| **a few of** *I've read a few of her books.* 我讀過她的幾本著作。| **a few more** *There are a few more things I'd like to discuss.* 還有一些事我想討論一下。| **a few minutes/the last few days/the next few years etc** *George arrived a few minutes later.* 喬治幾分鐘後到了。| *Ignore this letter if you have paid in the last few days.* 如果你前幾天已經付款了, 請不用理會此信。| **a few people** *There were a few people sitting at the back of the hall.* 大廳後面坐着幾個人。| **only a very few** (=not many) 不多的, 很少的 **2 quite a few/a good few/not a few** a fairly large number 相當多, 不少: *She must have cooked a good few dinners over the years.* 這些年來, 她一定做過相當多的晚餐。**3** not many; not enough 很少, 不多; 不夠多的: *low-paid jobs that few people want* 沒有幾個人想要的低工資工作 | *There may be few options open to you.* 可供你選擇的辦法可能很少了。| *The meals are awful, but few complain.* 飯菜一塌糊塗, 但很少人抱怨。| *Which one has the fewest mistakes?* 哪個人差錯最少? | **few of** *Very few of the staff come from the local area.* 工作人員中幾乎沒有當地人。**4 no fewer than** used to emphasize how surprisingly large a number is; at least 至少, 不少於〔用於強調數目大得令人吃驚〕: *I tried to contact him no fewer than ten times.* 我至少有十次試圖與他聯絡。**5 as few as** used to emphasize how surprisingly small a number is 少到..., 只有〔用於強調數量出乎意料地小〕: *She can remember all the words accurately after reading it as few as three times.* 她只要看三遍就能準確記住所有的單詞。**6 to name but a few** used when you are mentioning only a small number of people or things as examples of a large group 列舉幾個, 略舉幾個例子: *I've visited many fascinating countries; Japan, India, Turkey, and Russia to name but a few.* 我遊覽過許多迷人的國家, 日本、印度、土耳其和俄羅斯, 就略舉這幾個吧。**7 the chosen few** the small number of people to be invited or selected 挑選出來[邀請]的少數幾個人: *Such information is made available only to the chosen few.* 這種信息只讓挑選出來的少數幾個人知道。**8 precious few (of)** a very small number 極少的: *Only a small percentage of the seeds germinated and precious few of those survived.* 只有少數的種子發芽, 其中存活下來的少得可憐。**9 few and far between** rare; not happening or available often 稀少的, 罕見的: *Jobs are few and far between at the moment.* 職位現在已經很少了。**10 have a few (too many)** *informal* to have too much alcohol to drink【非正式】喝太多酒, 喝醉, 喝多了: *He looks as if he's had a few!* 他看上去是喝多了! —opposite 反義詞 MANY

USAGE NOTE 用法說明: FEW

WORD CHOICE 詞語辨析: **a few, few, a little, little**

When talking about amounts, you use **(a) few** with plural countable nouns, and **(a) little** with uncountable nouns. 談論數量時, (a) few 與複數可數名詞連用, (a) little 與不可數名詞連用。

A few is positive and means a small number but not a lot. a few 表示肯定, 指少數幾個, 但不多: *Yes, I do know a few words of French.* 是的, 我確實懂幾個法語單詞。| *There are a few beers left in the fridge.* 冰箱裡還剩幾瓶啤酒。

Few is negative and means not many. few 表示否定, 指很少: *I'm afraid I know few words of French.* 對不起, 我懂的法語單詞很少。**Few** used alone is fairly formal, and you would most often use it with **very**. few 單獨使用時較正式, 經常在前面加上 very: *Very few people come here now.* 現在很少有人到這裡來。

With words for time, **a few** is almost always used. 後面帶有表示時間的單詞時, 常常用 a few: *after a few minutes* 幾分鐘後 | *a few years before* 幾年前

A little is positive and means some, but not a lot. a little 表示肯定, 指一些, 但不很多: *Fortunately he still had a little money left.* 幸運的是, 他還剩下點錢。In more informal British English, **a bit** means the same thing. 在更非正式的英國英語中, a bit 具有相同的意思: *Don't worry, you've got a bit more time to get the work done.* 別擔心, 你還有點時間可以把工作做完。

Little is negative and means 'not much'. little 表示否定, 指"很少": *Unfortunately he now had little money left.* 不幸的是, 他現在身邊沒有甚麼錢了。Again, this is fairly formal, and speakers often avoid using **little** on its own. You would normally say **very little**. 同樣, 這較為正式, 說話人常避免單獨使用little, 而通常用 very little。

fey /fe; feɪ/ *adj* very sensitive and behaving or talking in a strange way 瘋瘋癲癲的, 古怪的, 精神異常的: *a fey* *and delicate child* 一個古怪嬌弱的孩子

fez /fɛz; fez/ *n* [C] a round red hat with a flat top and no BRIM[1] 非斯帽, 土耳其紅色無邊圓筒帽

ff the written abbreviation for 縮寫= 'and following', meaning the pages after the one you have mentioned 及其後幾頁: *pages 17ff* 第17頁及其後幾頁

fi·an·cé /ˌfiɑnˋse; fiˈɒnseɪ/ *n* [C] the man who a woman is going to marry and who she is ENGAGED (1) to 未婚夫

fi·an·cée /ˌfiɑnˋse; fiˈɒnseɪ/ *n* [C] the woman who a man is going to marry and who he is ENGAGED (1) to 未婚妻

fi·as·co /fiˋæsko; fiˈæskəʊ/ *n* [C,U] an event that is completely unsuccessful, in a way that is very embarrassing or disappointing 慘敗, 徹底的失敗: *The first lecture I ever gave was a complete fiasco.* 我的第一次講課完全失敗了。

fi·at /ˋfaɪət; ˈfiːæt/ *n* [C] *formal* an official command given by someone in a position of authority, without considering what other people want【正式】〔當權者的〕命令; 法令, 諭旨: *The matter was settled by presidential fiat.* 這件事是根據總統的命令解決的。

fib¹ /fɪb; fɪb/ *n* [C] *spoken* a small unimportant lie【口】小謊, 無關緊要的謊言: **tell fibs** *Don't tell fibs!* 不要撒謊! [不要説瞎話!]

fib² *v* **fibbed, fibbing** [I] *spoken* to tell a small unimportant lie【口】撒小謊: *I think you're fibbing.* 我想你是在撒謊。—**fibber** *n* [C]

fi·ber /ˋfaɪbɚ; ˈfaɪbə/ *n* [C] the American spelling of FIBRE fibre 的美式拼法

fi·ber·board /ˋfaɪbɚˌbɔrd; ˈfaɪbəbɔːd/ *n* [U] the American spelling of FIBREBOARD fibreboard 的美式拼法

fi·ber·fill /ˋfaɪbɚˌfɪl; ˈfaɪbəfɪl/ *n* [U] an artificial substance used to fill PILLOWS[1] (1) and DUVETS〔填塞枕頭和絮被的〕合成纖維絮

fi·ber·glass /ˋfaɪbɚˌglæs; ˈfaɪbəglɑːs/ *n* [U] the American spelling of FIBREGLASS fibreglass 的美式拼法

fi·bre *BrE*【英】, **fiber** *AmE*【美】/ˋfaɪbɚ; ˈfaɪbə/ *n* **1** [U] parts of plants that you eat but cannot DIGEST[1] (1), which help food to move quickly through your body〔植物的〕纖維質, 食物纖維: *Fruit and vegetables are high in fibre content.* 水果和蔬菜的纖維含量很高。**2** [U] a mass of threads used to make rope, cloth etc〔用來做繩子、布等的〕纖維: *man-made/natural fibre* 人造/天然纖維 | *Nylon is a man-made fiber.* 尼龍是一種人造纖維。**3** [C] a thin thread, or one of the thin parts like threads that form natural materials such as wood〔構成天然材料, 如木材的〕(一根)纖維 **4 nerve/muscle fibres** [plural] the thin pieces of flesh that form the nerves or muscles in your body 神經/肌肉纖維 **5 with every fibre of your being/to the very fibre of your being** *literary* if you feel something with every fibre of your being, you feel it very strongly【文】竭盡全力地, 極其地, 全身心地: *He wanted her with every fibre of his being.* 他非常想要她。—see also 另見 **moral fibre** (MORAL[1] (2))

fi·bre·board *BrE*【英】, **fiberboard** *AmE*【美】/ˋfaɪbɚˌbɔrd; ˈfaɪbəbɔːd/ *n* [U] board made from wood fibres pressed together 纖維板

fi·bre·glass *BrE*【英】, **fiberglass** *AmE*【美】/ˋfaɪbɚˌglæs; ˈfaɪbəglɑːs/ *n* [U] a light material made from glass threads, used for making sports cars and small boats〔製造跑車和小船的〕玻璃纖維, 玻璃棉

fibre op·tics /ˌ·· ˋ··/ *n* [U] the process of using very thin threads of glass or plastic to carry information in the form of light, especially on telephone lines 光纖通訊 —**fibre optic** *adj*

fi·brous /ˋfaɪbrəs; ˈfaɪbrəs/ *adj* consisting of many fibres or looking like fibres 含纖維的; 纖維狀的: *The coconut has a fibrous outer covering.* 椰子有多纖維的外殼。

fib·u·la /ˋfɪbjələ; ˈfɪbjʊlə/ *n* [C] *technical* the outer bone of the two bones in your leg below your knee【術語】腓骨 —see picture at 參見 SKELETON[1] 圖

fiche /fiʃ; fiːʃ/ *n* [C,U] a MICROFICHE 縮微膠卷

fick·le /ˋfɪkl̩; ˈfɪkəl/ *adj* **1** someone who is fickle is always changing their mind about people or things that they like, so that you cannot depend on them 三心兩意的, 靠不住的, 變化無常的: *an unpredictable and fickle lover* 一個無法捉摸、三心兩意的情人 **2** something such as weather that is fickle often changes suddenly〔天氣等〕變幻莫測的 —**fickleness** *n* [U]: *the fickleness of fame* 名望的起落無常

fic·tion /ˋfɪkʃən; ˈfɪkʃən/ *n* **1** [U] books and stories about imaginary people and events 小説: *popular fiction* 通俗小説 —opposite 反義詞 NON-FICTION **2** [C] something that people want you to believe is true but which is not true 虛構的事, 想像的事: *preserving the fiction of his happy childhood* 保持他那快樂童年的幻象

fic·tion·al /ˋfɪkʃənl̩; ˈfɪkʃənəl/ *adj* fictional people or descriptions are imaginary and from a book or story 虛構的, 編造的, 小説的: *fictional characters* 虛構的人物 | *a fictional description of growing up in Detroit* 對在底特律成長的過程的虛構描寫

fic·tion·al·ize also 又作 **-ise** *BrE*【英】/ˋfɪkʃənl̩ˌaɪz; ˈfɪkʃənəlaɪz/ *v* [T] to make a film or story about a real event, changing some details and adding some imaginary characters 把…改編成電影, 把…編成小説, 使小説化: *a fictionalized account of his life in Berlin* 把他在柏林的生活用小説的筆法描述 —**fictionalization** /ˌfɪkʃənl̩əˋzeʃən; ˌfɪkʃənəlaɪˈzeɪʃən/ *n* [C,U]

fic·ti·tious /fɪkˋtɪʃəs; fɪkˈtɪʃəs/ *adj* invented by someone and not real 虛構的, 杜撰的, 捏造的: *a fictitious address* 杜撰[捏造]的地址 | *The author fills this real town with fictitious characters.* 作者給這座真實的城市裝滿了虛構的人物。

fic·tive /ˋfɪktɪv; ˈfɪktɪv/ *adj AmE* fictive events, people etc are imaginary and not real【美】〔事件、人等〕想像的, 虛構的, 非真實的: *the fictive world of James Bond* 占士邦的虛幻世界

fid·dle¹ /ˋfɪdl̩; ˈfɪdl/ *n* [C] *informal*【非正式】**1** *BrE* a dishonest way of getting money【英】欺詐, 欺騙行為: *a tax fiddle* 偷税行為 | **be on the fiddle** (=be getting money dishonestly or illegally) 搞欺詐勾當 *They suspected he was on the fiddle all along.* 他們懷疑他一直在搞欺詐勾當。**2** a VIOLIN 小提琴 **3 be a fiddle** to be difficult to do and involve complicated movements of your hands〔需要用手的〕細巧活, 難事: *This blouse is a bit of a fiddle to do up.* 扣上這件短上衣是一件比較難搞的事。—see also 另見 **fit as a fiddle** (FIT[2] (3)), **play second fiddle to sb** (PLAY[1] (15))

fiddle² *v* **1** [I] to keep moving something or touching it with your fingers, especially because you are bored or nervous〔尤指因厭煩或緊張而〕用手不停撥弄: **[+with]** *She sat for a time, fiddling with her glass.* 她坐了一些時候, 手不停地擺弄着玻璃杯。| *Stop fiddling will you!* 請你不要瞎撥弄了, 好不好! **2** [T] to give false information about something, in order to avoid paying money or to get extra money 篡改, 偽造〔賬目等〕: *Bert had been fiddling his income tax for years.* 伯特多年來都在虛報所得税。| **fiddle the books** (=give false figures in a company's financial records) 造假賬

fiddle around also 又作 **fiddle about** *BrE*【英】*phr v* [I] to waste time doing unimportant things 浪費時間, 虛度光陰: *We can't fiddle around here all day – let's move on.* 我們不能整天在這裡浪費時間了 —— 我們繼續前進吧。

fiddle around with sth also 又作 **fiddle about with** sth *BrE*【英】*phr v* [T] **1** to keep moving the parts of something or making changes to it, especially in a way that is stupid or dangerous 亂動, 瞎搞: *Why did you let her fiddle around with the remote control?* 你為甚麼讓她亂動遙控器呢? **2** to keep changing the positions of a group of things until you find the arrangement that you like 撥弄, 擺佈〔以求取得最佳位置〕: *Is it all right if I fiddle around with these figures?* 要是我把這些數字稍

作改動, 可以嗎?

fiddle with sth *phr v* [T] **1** to move part of a machine in order to make it work, without knowing exactly what you should do〔在不知如何操作的情況下〕撥弄, 瞎動: *After fiddling with the tuning I finally got JFM.* 我在瞎調了一會, 終於找到了 JFM 電台。**2** to move or touch something that does not belong to you, in an annoying way 亂動〔別人的東西〕: *Don't let him fiddle with my bag.* 別讓他亂動我的提包。

fiddle-fad·dle /ˈfɪdl̩ ˌfædl̩; ˈfɪdl ˌfædl/ *n* [U] *old-fashioned* nonsense【過時】無聊話, 廢話

fid·dler /ˈfɪdlɚ; ˈfɪdlə/ *n* [C] **1** someone who plays the VIOLIN, especially someone who plays FOLK MUSIC〔尤指演奏民間音樂的〕小提琴手 **2** someone who gives false information to the government or a company, to pay less money or get more than they should 騙子, 詐騙者: *tax fiddlers* 騙稅者

fid·dle·sticks /ˈfɪdl̩ˌstɪks; ˈfɪdlˌstɪks/ *interjection old-fashioned* nonsense【過時】廢話!胡說!

fid·dling /ˈfɪdlɪŋ; ˈfɪdlɪŋ/ *adj* [only before noun 僅用於名詞前] unimportant, and annoying 無足輕重的, 微不足道的; 令人厭煩的: *all these fiddling little jobs around the house* 家裡所有這些煩人的瑣碎活

fid·dly /ˈfɪdlɪ; ˈfɪdli/ *adj* **1** difficult to do because you have to deal with very small objects 精細而難做的: *He managed to fix the television, but it was a fiddly job.* 他設法修好了電視機, 這可是精細的工作。**2** unimportant, slightly difficult, and annoying 無足輕重的: *I can't be bothered with all the fiddly details.* 別拿這些瑣碎的細節來煩我!

fi·del·i·ty /faɪˋdɛlətɪ; fɪˈdeləti/ *n* [U] **1** loyalty to your husband, girlfriend etc, shown by having sex only with them〔對丈夫、女朋友等的〕忠貞, 忠實: **[+to]** *Tom's fidelity to his wife was never in question.* 湯姆對妻子的忠貞不二從來無需懷疑。**2** the quality of not changing something when you are producing it again in a different form, by recording, translating, making a film etc〔錄音、電影等的〕逼真, 不加改動;〔譯文等的〕確切, 忠實: **[+to]** *the new translation's fidelity to Proust's great work* 普魯斯特的傑作的新譯文忠於原作 **3** the quality of being faithful to your friends, or of not doing anything that is against your beliefs〔對朋友、信念等的〕忠貞, 忠誠 —see also 另見 HIGH FIDELITY, FAITHFUL[1]

fid·get[1] /ˈfɪdʒɪt; ˈfɪdʒɪt/ *v* [I] to keep moving your hands or feet, especially because you are bored or nervous〔因厭煩或緊張而〕坐立不安, 手足無措: *The teacher told them to stop fidgeting.* 老師叫他們別坐不住。| **fidget with sth** *Donna began fidgeting with her pencil.* 唐娜開始擺弄她的鉛筆。

fidget[2] *n* [C] *informal*【非正式】**1** someone who keeps moving and is unable to sit or stand still 坐立不安的人: *I wish you'd sit still for a change – you're such a fidget!* 我希望你能改改, 好好坐一會兒。你真是個坐不住的人! **2 get/have the fidgets** *BrE* to be unable to stop moving【英】煩躁不安: *He gets the fidgets if he has to sit in one place for more than ten minutes.* 他如果得在一個地方坐十分鐘以上, 就煩躁不安了。

fid·get·y /ˈfɪdʒɪtɪ; ˈfɪdʒɪti/ *adj informal* tending to fidget a lot【非正式】坐立不安的; 煩躁亂動的: *sitting with three bored, fidgety children* 與三個厭倦而煩躁的孩子同坐

fie /faɪ; faɪ/ *interjection, old use*【舊】**fie on sb** used to express anger or disapproval towards someone …真可恥〔表示生氣或不贊成〕

fief /fif; fiːf/ *n* [C] an area of land that belonged to a lord in former times〔昔日的〕采邑, 封地

field[1] /fild; fiːld/ *n* [C]

1 ▶FARM 農場◀ an area of land where crops are grown or animals feed on grass 田地, 田野: *a field of wheat* 一片麥地

2 ▶SUBJECT 學科◀ a subject that people study or are involved in as part of their work〔研究或工作的〕領域, 範圍: **[+of]** *He's well-known in the field of ancient history.* 他在古代史領域是很著名的。| *improvements in the field of health and safety* 衛生和安全領域中的改進 | **in his/her field** *Professor Marwick is one of the leading experts in her field.* 馬威克教授在她的研究領域裡是最傑出的專家之一。| **be outside your field** (=not be connected with your work or studies) 不屬於你的工作範圍[專業], 不是你的專長

3 ▶PRACTICAL WORK 實際工作◀ work or study that is done in the field is done in the real world rather than in a classroom or LABORATORY 現場, 實地: **in the field** *His theories haven't been tested in the field.* 他的理論還沒有在實地試驗過。| **field trials/testing** *field trials for an anti-cancer drug* 抗癌藥的臨牀試驗

4 baseball/soccer/sports etc field an area of ground where a sport is played 棒球場/英式足球場/運動場等

5 take the field to go onto the area where a sport is played so that you can take part in a game or competition〔運動員〕上場: *Supporters cheered as the team took the field.* 球隊上場時, 支持者都歡呼起來。

6 ▶COMPETITORS 競爭者◀ **the field a)** all the horses or runners in a race 所有參賽馬; 全體賽跑運動員: **lead/be ahead of the field** *Egyptian Prince is leading the field as they come round the final bend.* "埃及王子"在牠們繞過最後的彎道時處於領先地位。**b)** all the people, companies, or products who are competing against each other 全體競爭對手〔包括人、公司、產品等〕: **lead/be ahead of the field** *Microsoft is already way ahead of the rest of the field.* 微軟公司已經遙遙領先於其他同類公司。

7 snow/ice etc field a large area covered with snow etc 雪原/冰原等

8 coal/oil/gas field a large area where coal, oil, or gas is found 煤田/油田/天然氣田

9 magnetic/gravitational/force field the area in which a natural force is felt or has an effect 磁場/引力場/力場

10 field of vision/view the whole area that you are able to see without turning your head 視野: *The buildings obstructed our field of vision.* 那些建築物擋住了我們的視野。

11 the field (of battle) the time or place where there is fighting in a war 戰場, 戰地: **on the field of battle** *It is always better to negotiate than to settle disputes on the field of battle.* 談判總要比在戰場上解決爭端好。| **in the field** *The new tank has yet to be used in the field.* 新型坦克還沒有在戰場上使用過。

12 field of fire the area that you can hit by shooting from a particular position 射擊範圍; 火力範圍

13 ▶TEAM 隊◀ **the field** the team that is throwing and catching the ball in a game such as CRICKET (2) or BASEBALL, rather than the team that is hitting〔板球或棒球比賽中的〕防守隊; 全體外場隊員

14 ▶COMPUTERS 電腦◀ an amount of space made available for a particular type of information 字段, 信息組: *The field for the user's name is 25 characters.* 用戶名的字段是 25 個字符。—see also 另見 **play the field** (PLAY[1] (25))

field[2] *v* **1** [T] if you field a team, group of candidates, or an army, they represent you or fight for you in a competition, election, or war 派出〔運動隊、球隊、候選人或軍隊〕: *The Ecology Party fielded 109 candidates in the 1983 election.* 生態黨推舉 109 名候選人參加 1983 年的選舉。**2 be fielding** the team that is fielding in a game of CRICKET (2) or BASEBALL is the one that is throwing and catching the ball, rather than the one hitting it〔板球或棒球比賽中〕擔任防守隊員[外場員] **3** [T] if you field the ball in a game of CRICKET (2) or BASEBALL, you stop it after it has been hit〔板球或棒球比賽中〕截住, 接住〔對方擊出的球〕**4 field a question** to answer a difficult question 回答難對付的問題: *The Senator had to field some tricky questions from reporters.* 參議員不得不巧妙地回答記者們提出的一些刁鑽的問題。

field corn /ˈ· ·/ *n* [U] *AmE* MAIZE grown to use as grain or to feed to animals, rather than to be eaten【美】飼料玉米 —compare 比較 SWEET CORN

field day /ˈ· ·/ *n* [C] **1 have a field day** *informal* to have a chance to do what you want, especially a chance to criticize someone【非正式】得到好機會〔尤指去批評某人的機會〕: *When the scandal finally came out, the press had a field day.* 醜聞終於傳出來時, 新聞界便有機會大做文章。**2** *AmE* a day when pupils at a school have sports competitions and parents watch【美】〔有學生家長觀看的〕體育比賽日, 運動日; SPORTS DAY *BrE*【英】

field·er /ˈfildɚ; ˈfiːldə/ *n* [C] one of the players who tries to catch the ball in a game of CRICKET (2) or BASEBALL 〔板球或棒球比賽中〕守場員, 外野手

field e·vent /ˈ· ·,·/ *n* [C] a sport such as jumping or throwing the JAVELIN (1) in an ATHLETICS competition 田賽項目〈如跳高、跳遠或擲標槍等〉—compare 比較 TRACK EVENT

field glass·es /ˈ· ,··/ *n* [plural] BINOCULARS 雙筒望遠鏡

field goal /ˈ· ·/ *n* [C] **1** the act of kicking the ball over the bar of the GOAL (3) in American football〔美式足球中〕踢球越過球門橫木 **2** the act of putting the ball through the circle to get points in BASKETBALL〔籃球中的〕投球中籃得分

field hock·ey /ˈ· ,··/ *n* [U] *AmE* HOCKEY (1) played on grass【美】(草地) 曲棍球

field mar·shal /ˈ· ,··/ *n* [C] an officer of the highest rank in the British army 陸軍元師〔英國陸軍中的最高將領〕—see table on page C6 參見 C6 頁附錄

field·mouse /ˈfildmaus; ˈfiːldmaʊs/ *n* [C] a mouse that has a long tail and lives in fields 田鼠

fields·man /ˈfildzmən; ˈfiːldzmən/ *n* [C] *BrE* FIELDER【英】〔板球或棒球比賽中〕守場員, 外野手

field sports /ˈ· ,·/ *n* [plural] sports that happen in the countryside, such as hunting, shooting, and fishing 野外運動〈如打獵、射擊和釣魚等〉

field test /ˈ· ·/ *n* [C] a test of a new piece of equipment that is done in the place where it will be used rather than in a LABORATORY〔新儀器、設備等的〕現場試驗, 實地試驗 —**field-test** *v* [T]

field trip /ˈ· ·/ *n* [C] an occasion when students go somewhere to learn about a particular subject〔學生的〕校外旅行考察; 實地調查旅行: *a geography field trip* 地理旅行考察

field·work /ˈfild,wɝk; ˈfiːldwɜːk/ *n* [U] the study of scientific or social subjects that is done outside the classroom or LABORATORY〔科學或社會研究的〕實地考察; 野外考察 —**fieldworker** *n* [C]

fiend /find; fiːnd/ *n* [C] **1 television/fresh-air/sports fiend etc** someone who likes something much more than other people do 電視迷/最喜歡新鮮空氣的人/體育迷等 **2** a very cruel or wicked person 殘暴的人, 惡人, 惡魔般的人 **3** an evil spirit 惡魔, 魔鬼

fiend·ish /ˈfindɪʃ; ˈfiːndɪʃ/ *adj* **1** cruel and unpleasant 兇惡的; 殘酷的: *Philip had a fiendish instinct for discovering other people's weak spots.* 菲利普有專會找出別人弱點的壞本能。**2** very clever in an unpleasant way 刁鑽的, 棘手的: *a fiendish plan to take over the company* 接管公司的棘手計劃 **3** extremely difficult or unpleasant 極其困難的; 令人極不愉快的: *He set us some fiendish exam questions.* 他給我們出了一些刁鑽難解的考題。—**fiendishly** *adv*

fierce /fɪrs; fɪəs/ *adj* **1** a fierce person or animal is angry or ready to attack, and looks very frightening 兇猛的; 兇狠的: *armed guards accompanied by fierce dogs* 帶着惡狗的武裝衛兵 | *She turned round, looking fierce.* 她轉過身, 看上去很兇狠。**2** fierce emotions are very strong and often angry〔感情〕強烈的; 憤怒的: *Fierce resentment was aroused by this injustice.* 這種不公引起了強烈的不滿。**3** done with a lot of energy and strong feelings, and sometimes violent 猛烈的; 激烈的: *a fierce attack on government policy* 對政府政策的猛烈抨擊 | *Fighting was fiercest near the town centre.* 市中心附近的戰鬥最激烈。| **fierce competition** *There is fierce competition for those scholarships.* 那些獎學金的競爭很激烈。**4** fierce cold, heat, or weather is much colder, hotter etc than usual 極度的, 極端的: *a fierce wind* 一陣狂風 **5 something fierce** *AmE spoken* more loudly, strongly etc than usual【美口】極其強烈, 很厲害: *It was snowing something fierce yesterday.* 昨天雪下得非常大。—**fiercely** *adv* —**fierceness** *n* [U]

fi·er·y /ˈfaɪrɪ; ˈfaɪəri/ *adj* **1** containing or looking like fire 含有火的; 火一般的: *a fiery sunset* 火紅的落日 **2** bright red 鮮紅的: *a fiery blush* 滿臉通紅 **3** becoming angry very quickly 暴躁的, 易怒的: *He has a very fiery temper.* 他的脾氣很暴躁。**4** showing or encouraging anger 激昂的; 引人發怒的: *a fiery speech* 激昂的演說 **5** fiery foods taste very strong and hot〔食物〕辣的

fi·es·ta /fɪˈɛstə; fiˈestə/ *n* [C] *Spanish*【西】**1** a religious holiday with dancing, music etc, especially in Spain and South America〔尤指西班牙和南美洲以舞蹈、音樂等來慶祝的〕宗教節日 **2** a party 社交聚會

fife /faɪf; faɪf/ *n* [C] a small musical instrument like a FLUTE, often played in military bands〔軍樂隊中的〕橫笛

fif·teen /fɪfˈtin; ˌfɪfˈtiːn◂/ *number* 15 十五 —see table on page C1 參見 C1 頁附錄

fifth /fɪfθ; fɪfθ/ *n* [C] **1** one of five equal parts of something 五分之一 **2** *AmE* an amount of alcohol equal to 1/5 of an American GALLON (2), sold in bottles【美】〔瓶裝銷售的烈性酒〕五分之一加侖的: *a fifth of bourbon* 五分之一加侖的波旁威士忌酒 **3 fifth wheel** *AmE* someone who is with you when you do not want them to be there【美】多餘的人: *She said she didn't want to be the fifth wheel.* 她說她不想做多餘的人。

fifth col·umn /,· ˈ··/ *n* [C] a group of people who work secretly during a war to help the enemies of the country they live in〔戰時從事祕密活動、協助敵軍的〕第五縱隊 —**fifth columnist** *n* [C]

fif·ty /ˈfɪftɪ; ˈfɪfti/ *number* **1** 50 五十 —see table on page C1 參見 C1 頁附錄 **2 the fifties a)** the years between 1950 and 1959 20 世紀 50 年代: *Standards of living rose in the fifties.* 生活水平在 20 世紀 50 年代提高了。**b)** the numbers between 50 and 59, especially when used to measure temperature 50 至 59 之間的數字〔尤用於測量溫度〕: *sunny, with temperatures in the mid fifties* 晴天, 氣溫 55 度左右 **3 be in your fifties** to be aged between 50 and 59 在 50 到 59 歲之間; 50 多歲: **early/mid/late fifties** *He must be in his early fifties by now.* 他現在肯定有五十歲出頭了。**4** a piece of paper money equal to fifty dollars or fifty pounds 五十美元[英鎊]票面的紙幣

fifty-fif·ty /,·· ˈ··◂/ *adj spoken*【口】**1** divided or shared equally between two people〔兩人〕平分的; 對半的: *We should divide the profits on a fifty-fifty basis.* 我們應當平分利潤。| **go fifty-fifty (on sth)** (=share the cost of something equally) 均攤〔費用〕; 各出一半〔費用〕: *Let's go fifty-fifty on a new television set.* 我們一人出一半錢買一台新電視機吧。**2** having an equal chance of happening in one of two ways〔成敗、利弊〕各半的: *Do you reckon our chances of success are about fifty-fifty?* 你認為我們有一半的成功機會嗎?

fig¹ /fɪg; fɪg/ *n* [C] **1** a soft sweet fruit with a lot of small seeds, often eaten dried, or the tree on which this fruit grows 無花果 —see picture on page A8 參見 A8 頁圖 **2** *BrE* **not care/not give a fig (for sth)** to not be concerned or interested in something at all【英】(對某事) 毫不在乎 **3 not worth a fig** of no value 毫無價值, 不值一文

fig² **1** the written abbreviation of 縮寫= FIGURE **2** the written abbreviation of 縮寫= FIGURATIVE

fight¹ /faɪt; faɪt/ *past tense and past participle* **fought** /fɔt; fɔːt/ *v* [S1] [W1]

1 ►WAR 戰爭◄ [I,T] to take part in a war or battle 打仗, 作戰: *Did your Uncle fight in the last war?* 你叔叔參加了上一次戰爭嗎? | **fight sb** *Vietnam fought France and then the US over 30 years.* 越南先是跟法國, 後來跟美國, 共打了 30 多年的仗。| **[+against/with]** *He fought against the Russians on the Eastern Front.* 他在東線與俄國人作戰。| **[+about/over/for]** *Britain and Argentina fought for control of the islands.* 英國和阿根廷為爭奪這些島嶼的控制權而打仗。| **fight a war** *Neither country is capable of fighting a long war.* 這兩個國家都無法打持久戰。

2 ►HIT PEOPLE 打人◄ [I,T] if someone fights another person, or if two people fight, they hit and kick each other in order to hurt each other 打鬥, 打架, 鬥毆: *Two guys were fighting in the street outside the bar.* 有兩個傢伙在酒吧外的街道上打架。| **fight sb** *Grant has fought most of the boys in his street.* 格蘭特跟街上的大多數男孩子都打過架。| **[+with]** *Phil was fighting with Ryan in the playground.* 菲爾當時正在操場和瑞安打架。| **[+about/over/for]** *two dogs fighting over a bone* 為搶奪一塊骨頭而咬鬥的兩條狗

3 ►COMPETE 競爭◄ [I,T] to compete strongly for something, especially a job or political position or in a sport 爭奪, 爭鬥: **fight sb for sth** *Williams fought several rivals for the leadership of the party.* 威廉姆斯與幾個對手爭奪黨的領導權。| **[+for]** *If you want the job you'll have to fight for it.* 你如果想得到這份工作就得競爭。| **fight an election** *The mayor has decided against fighting another election.* 市長已經決定不參加另一次競選。

4 ►ARGUE 爭論◄ [I] to argue about something〔為…而〕爭吵, 爭論: *The kids fought in the back seat the whole trip.* 孩子們在整個車程中一直在後座上互相爭吵。| **[+about/over]** *They're fighting about whose turn it is to do the dishes.* 他們在為該輪到誰洗碗碟而爭吵。

5 ►SPORT 體育運動◄ [I,T] to hit someone as a sport 與…進行拳擊比賽: *Ali fought Foreman for the heavyweight title.* 阿里與福爾曼進行拳擊比賽, 爭奪最重量級冠軍。

6 ►EMOTION 感情◄ [T] also 又作 **fight back/down** to try very hard not to show your feelings or not to do something you want to do 克制, 忍住, 壓下去: *He fought the impulse to slap her.* 他盡力壓下了想打她一巴掌的念頭。

7 fight your way to push people away in order to go somewhere 打[擠; 推]出一條路; 用力開出一條路前進: *We fought our way through the crowd.* 我們從人羣中擠出一條路來。

8 fight a losing battle to work hard when you cannot succeed 進行肯定要失敗的鬥爭: *I think they're fighting a losing battle with that libel suit.* 我認為他們在那場誹謗官司中肯定會輸。

9 fight shy of doing sth to try to avoid doing something or being involved in something 避免做某事, 避免參與某事; 怕惹上某事: *Jane fought shy of participating in the discussions.* 簡躲閃着不參加討論。

10 fighting spirit/words the desire to fight or words which express that desire 鬥志 / 挑戰性的言詞: *The marches aroused their fighting spirit.* 行軍提高了他們的鬥志。

11 have a fighting chance to have a chance to do something or achieve something if you work very hard at it 經過很大努力有可能成功: *Lewis has a fighting chance to win the gold medal.* 劉易斯如果努力拚搏還會有得金牌的機會。

12 fight fire with fire to use the same methods as your opponents in an argument〔爭論中〕以火攻火, 以其人之道還治其人之身

fight back *phr v* **1** [I] to use violence against someone who has attacked you 還擊, 反攻: *The rebels are fighting back.* 叛軍正在還擊。**2** [I] to work hard to prevent something bad happening 制止, 抑制: *Victims of discrimination often don't have the power to fight back.* 受歧視的人經常沒有能力反擊。**3** [T **fight** sth ↔ **back**] to try hard not to show your feelings 克制, 忍住〔不使感情流露〕: **fight back tears** *She fought back the tears until she got home.* 她在到家前一直強忍住眼淚。

fight sb/sth ↔ **off** *phr v* [T] **1** to use violence to keep someone or something away 擊退, 竭力擺脱: *The stars had to fight off the crowds to get out of the auditorium.* 明星們得竭力擺脱人羣, 才能走出禮堂。**2** to try hard to get rid of something 盡力克服[去掉]: *Elaine's fighting off a cold.* 伊萊恩正在治療感冒。| *Bardot fought off the sex symbol image.* 芭鐸盡力擺脱掉自己的性感形象。

fight sth **out** *phr v* [T] to argue, or use violence until a disagreement is settled (通過爭鬥) 解決〔爭論〕, 平息〔不和〕: *We left them to fight it out.* 我們任由他們自行解決。

fight² *n*

1 ►HIT 打, 擊◄ [C] an act of fighting in which two people or groups hit, push etc each other 打鬥, 打架: **[+between]** *a fight between two gangs* 兩幫之間的打鬥 | **[+over]** *fights over territory* 爭奪領土的鬥爭 | **get into a fight** *He's always getting into fights with other boys.* 他老是和其他男孩打架。| **have a fight** *The cat had a fight last night.* 這隻貓昨晚打架了。| **start/pick a fight** *Are you trying to start a fight?* 你是在尋釁打架嗎?

2 ►BATTLE 戰鬥◄ [C] a battle between two armies, especially the fighting that happens at one particular place and time〔兩軍之間的〕戰鬥, 戰役: **[+for]** *the fight for Bunker Hill* 奪取邦克山的戰鬥

3 ►ARGUMENT 爭吵◄ [C] a quarrel or an argument 爭論; 爭吵: **have a fight** *They've had a fight with the neighbours.* 他們和鄰居爭吵了。

4 ►ACHIEVE/PREVENT STH 取得某物/防止某事◄ [singular] the work of trying to achieve something, change something, or prevent something 爭鬥, 鬥爭: **[+against]** *the fight against crime* 對犯罪行為所作的鬥爭 | **[+for]** *We will not give up the fight for better conditions.* 我們不會放棄為爭取更好條件而鬥爭。| **have a fight on your hands** (=have to oppose someone to achieve something) 要進行一場鬥爭〔方能達到目的〕 *He'll have a fight on his hands to get Malone acquitted.* 他將要進行艱巨的鬥爭, 以爭取馬隆無罪釋放。

5 ►SPORT 體育◄ [C] an act of fighting as a sport 拳擊(運動): *Are you going to watch the big fight tonight?* 你今晚打算去看拳擊大賽嗎?

6 ►ENERGY 精力◄ [U] the energy and desire to keep fighting for something you want to achieve 鬥志: *There's still plenty of fight left in your grandmother.* 你的祖母仍然鬥志旺盛。

7 put up a good fight to work very hard to fight or compete in a difficult situation〔在困難情況下〕英勇地鬥爭; 頑強地奮鬥: *Although our team didn't win, they put up a good fight.* 雖然我們隊沒有贏, 但隊員們打得很頑強。

8 a fight to the finish a fight that continues until one side is completely defeated 打到一方被完全擊敗為止; 打到分清勝負為止 —see also 另見 **pick a quarrel/fight** (PICK[1] (9))

fight·er /ˈfaɪtə; ˈfaɪtə/ *n* [C] **1** someone who fights 戰士, 士兵, 戰鬥者 **2** someone who keeps trying to achieve something in difficult situations 頑強拚搏者; 鬥士: *James is a fighter – he'll come through it all right.* 詹姆斯是個頑強拚搏的人 —— 他會順利渡過困境的。**3** also 又作 **fighter plane/aircraft** a small, fast military plane that can destroy other planes 戰鬥機; 殲擊機 —see also 另見 FREEDOM FIGHTER

fig leaf /ˈ· ·/ *n* [C] **1** the large leaf of the FIG[1] (1) tree, sometimes shown in paintings as covering people's sex organs〔有時在美術作品中用來遮蓋性器官的〕無花果樹葉 **2** something that is intended to hide embarrassing facts 遮羞物

fig·ment /ˈfɪgmənt; ˈfɪgmənt/ *n* [C] **a figment of sb's imagination** something that you imagine to be real, but does not exist 某人憑空想像的事物, 虛構的事物: *The sinister plot is just a figment of his imagination.* 這個陰謀只是他想像出來的。

fig·u·ra·tive /ˈfɪgjərətɪv; ˈfɪgjʊrətɪv/ *adj* **1** if a word or phrase is used in a figurative way, it is used about something different from what it normally refers to, to give you a picture in your mind 比喻的, 借喻的: *I was using the word 'battle' in its figurative sense.* 我在使用 battle (戰鬥) 這個詞的喻義。—compare 比較 LITERAL[1] (1) **2** *technical* figurative art shows objects, people, or the countryside in the way they really look【術語】象徵的 —compare 比較 ABSTRACT[1] (3) —**figuratively** *adv*: *He's up to his eyes in paperwork – figuratively speaking, of course.* 他都被案牘工作淹沒了 — 當然這是打個比方。

1 1 **fig·ure**[1] /ˈfɪgjɚ; ˈfɪgə/ *n* [C]

1 ►NUMBER 數字◄ **a)** a number representing an amount, especially an officially published number 數字〔尤指官方公佈的數字〕: *keeping unemployment figures down* 保持失業數字於低位 **b)** a number from 0 to 10, written as a sign rather than a word〔從 0 到 10 的〕數字符號, 位數: **a four/five/six figure number** (=a number in the thousands, ten thousands, hundred thousands etc) 四位數/五位數/六位數 | **double figures** (=numbers between 10 and 99) 兩位數〔從 10 到 99 的數字〕: *His score is now well into double figures.* 他的得分現在已成功地進入兩位數字了。

2 ►AMOUNT OF MONEY 錢的數目◄ a particular amount of money 金額, 價格: *an estimated figure of $200 million* 估計為二億美元的金額

3 father/mother/authority figure someone who is considered to be like a father etc, or to represent authority, because of their character or behaviour 父親/母親/權威人士形象: *He had always looked upon Sarah as a kind of mother figure.* 他一直把薩拉視為一個母親形象。

4 figures [plural] the activity of adding, multiplying etc numbers; ARITHMETIC 計算, 算術: **have a head for figures** (=be good at arithmetic) 擅長計算

5 put a figure on it/give an exact figure to say exactly how much something is worth, or how much or how many of something you are talking about 準確說出數額[數量]: *I know it's worth a lot of money but I couldn't put a figure on it.* 我知道這值很多錢, 但我說不出準確的金額。

6 ►WOMAN'S BODY 婦女的身體◄ the shape of someone's body, especially a woman's body〔尤指女人的〕體形, 體態: *She has a great figure.* 她有很優美的體態。| **keep your figure** (=keep your body in an attractive shape) 保持優美的身段: *How does she manage to keep her figure when she eats so much?* 她吃得這麼多, 究竟是怎樣保持優美的身段的?—see 見 BODY (USAGE)

7 ►KIND OF PERSON 人物類型◄ someone who has a particular type of character or appearance or who is important in a particular way〔具有某種性格特徵或外表的〕人物: *He was the outstanding political figure of his time.* 他是他那個時代的著名政治人物。| *She stood there, a frail but defiant figure.* 她就站在那兒, 人雖虛弱卻傲岸不屈。—see also 另見 **cult figure** (CULT (2))

8 a fine figure of a man/woman someone who is tall and has a good body 相貌堂堂的男子/身材優美的婦女

9 ►FAR AWAY/DIFFICULT TO SEE 在遠處/很難看清◄ the shape of a person, especially one that is far away or is difficult to see〔尤指遠處隱約可見的〕人影: *a dark figure in the distance* 遠處的一個黑色人影

10 ►PAINTING/MODEL 繪畫/模型◄ a person in a painting or model〔繪畫或模型中的〕人像; 人形: *an 18th century Maori figure* 一個 18 世紀的毛利人形象 —see also 另見 FIGURINE

11 ►DRAWING 圖◄ a numbered drawing or a DIAGRAM in a book〔書中有編號的〕圖, 圖表, 圖解

12 ►MATHEMATICAL SHAPE 數學中的圖形◄ a GEOMETRIC shape 幾何圖形, 幾何形狀: *A hexagon is a six-sided figure.* 六邊形是一個有六條邊的幾何圖形。

13 ►ON ICE 滑冰◄ a pattern formed in FIGURE SKATING〔花樣滑冰中的〕花樣, 花式

14 a figure of fun someone who people laugh at 被人嘲笑的人, 笑柄

figure[2] *v* **1** [I] to be important in a process, event, or 2 3
situation, and be noticed because of this (以重要地位) 出現: *Kennedy's descendants were to figure prominently in the country's history.* 甘迺迪的後代在其後的美國歷史上頗有名氣。**2** [T] *informal especially AmE* to form a particular opinion after thinking about a situation【非正式, 尤美】〔經過考慮後〕認為, 以為: **figure that** *I figured that he was drunk and shouldn't be allowed to drive.* 我認為他喝醉了, 不應該讓他開車。**3 that figures/it figures** *spoken especially AmE*【口, 尤美】**a)** used when something happens or someone behaves in a way that you expect, but do not like〔在預料中的不好的事發生時說的〕這是意料之中的事: *"It rained the whole weekend." "Oh, that figures."* "整個週末都下雨。" "噢, 這是意料之中的事。" **b)** used to say that something is reasonable or makes sense 這是合乎情理的: *If Terry has talked to Lennox, then he knows you are here. It figures.* 如果特里跟倫諾克斯說過話, 他就知道你在這裡。這是合乎情理的。**4** [T] *AmE* to calculate an amount【美】計算: *Larry figured his expenses for the past month.* 拉里計算他上個月的開支。

figure sth ↔ **out** *phr v* [T] to think about a problem or situation until you find the answer or understand what has happened 想出, 理解〔某事〕: **[+how/what]** *Can you figure out how to do it?* 你能想出這件事該怎麼做嗎? | **figure sth out** *It took me hours to figure those algebra problems out.* 我花了許多小時才推算出那些代數題。| **figure out that** *She figured out that he was leaving on Tuesday.* 她推斷他會在星期二離開。

figure sb **out** *phr v* [T] to understand why someone behaves in the way they do 弄明白, 看透, 理解〔某人〕: *Women. I just can't figure them out.* 女人。我就是捉摸不透她們。

fig·ured /ˈfɪgjɚd; ˈfɪgəd/ *adj* [only before noun 僅用於名詞前] decorated with a small pattern 飾有小圖案的; 有花紋的: *figured silk* 有花紋的絲綢

fig·ure·head /ˈfɪgjɚˌhɛd; ˈfɪgəhed/ *n* [C] **1** someone who seems to be the leader of a country or organization but who has no real power 有名無實的領導人, 掛名首腦, 傀儡: *The Queen is merely a figurehead.* 女王只不過是個掛名首腦。**2** a wooden model of a woman that used to be placed on the front of ships 船首飾像

figure of eight *BrE*【英】/**figure eight** *AmE*【美】8字形

figure of eight /ˌ‥ ˈ./ *BrE*【英】, **figure eight** *AmE*【美】*n* [C] the pattern or shape of a number eight, as seen in a knot, dance etc〔繩結、舞蹈等中的〕8 字形

figure of speech /ˌ‥ ˈ./ *n* [C] a word or expression that is used in a different way from the normal one, to give you a picture in your mind 比喻: *When I said it was a battle to the death it was just a figure of speech.* 我說

這是一場死亡之戰時，只是一種比喻。

figure skat·ing /ˈ·· ˌ··/ *n* [U] a kind of SKATING in which you cut patterns in the ice with your SKATES[1] (1) 花式溜冰，花樣滑冰 —**figure skater** *n* [C]

fig·u·rine /ˌfɪgjəˈrin; ˌfɪgjʊˈriːn/ *n* [C] a small model of a person made of CHINA (=baked clay), used as a decoration〔裝飾用的瓷製〕小塑像，小雕像

fil·a·ment /ˈfɪləmənt; ˈfɪləmənt/ *n* [C] a very thin thread, especially the thin wire in a LIGHT BULB 細絲；〔電燈泡內的〕燈絲

fil·bert /ˈfɪlbɚt; ˈfɪlbət/ *n* [C] *especially AmE* a HAZELNUT【尤美】榛子

filch /fɪltʃ; fɪltʃ/ *v* [T] *informal* to steal something, especially something small or not very expensive【非正式】偷〔不貴重的小東西〕: *He was sacked for filching food from the kitchen.* 他因偷廚房裡的食物而被開除。

1 2 **file**[1] /faɪl; faɪl/ *n* [C] **1** information about a particular person or subject that is kept by an official organization〔官方機構保存的〕檔案，卷宗: **[+on]** *Mendoza read over the file on the murders again.* 門多薩從頭到尾把謀殺案的文件檔案再閱一遍。| **keep a file on** (=collect and store information) 保存…的檔案 *The government keeps a file on known terrorists.* 政府保存着已知恐怖分子的檔案。**2** a box or folded piece of heavy paper that is used to store papers in the proper order 文件夾；文件箱: *Fran came in holding a blue file.* 弗蘭拿着一個藍色文件夾進來。**3** a collection of information on a computer that is stored under a particular name〔電腦分門別類儲存信息的〕檔案文件: *a spreadsheet file* 電子數據表檔案 **4 on file a)** kept in a file so that it can be used later 存檔: *We will keep your application on file.* 我們將把你的申請書存檔。**b)** officially recorded 登記在案: *The petition has to be on file by March 3rd.* 這份請願書須在3月3日前登記在案。**5** a metal tool with a rough surface used to smooth other surfaces or to cut through wood, metal etc 銼刀 —see also 另見 NAIL FILE —see picture at 參見 TOOL[1] 圖 **6** a line of people one behind the other 縱列: **in file** *walking in file* 排成縱隊行走；魚貫而行 —see also 另見 INDIAN FILE, SINGLE FILE, RANK AND FILE

3 **file**[2] *v* **1** [I always+adv/prep] to walk in a line of people, one behind the other 排成縱隊行走: **[+past/into/through etc]** *The mourners filed past the coffin.* 送葬者排成一列走過靈柩。**2** [I always+adv/prep,T] *law* to officially record something such as a complaint, law case, official document etc【法律】把〔投訴信、法律案件、正式文件等〕登記在案；正式提出: *Mr Genoa filed a formal complaint against the department.* 傑諾亞先生把對該部門的投訴正式登記在案。| **[+for]** *The Morrisons have filed for divorce.* 莫里森夫婦已經向法院正式申請離婚。**3** [T] to keep papers with information on them in a particular place so that you can find them easily 把…匯存起來，把…歸檔[存檔]: *Contributors' contracts are filed alphabetically.* 投稿人的合同按字母順序歸檔。| **file sth away** *The exam papers will be filed away in my office.* 試卷將歸檔存放在我的辦公室。**4** [I always+adv/prep,T] to cut or rub something or make something smooth, using a metal tool with a rough surface 銼，銼平，銼去: *She was filing her nails.* 她在銼指甲。| **[+through/away/down etc]** *I need to file down the sharp edges.* 我需要把尖利的邊緣銼平。

file cab·i·net /ˈ· ˌ···/ *n* [C] *AmE* a FILING CABINET【美】檔案櫃；文件櫃

fil·et[1] /fɪˈle; ˈfɪlʒt/ *n* [C] the usual American spelling of FILLET[1] fillet[1] 的一般美式拼法

filet[2] *v* [T] the usual American spelling of FILLET[2] fillet[2] 的一般美式拼法

fi·li·al /ˈfɪlɪəl; ˈfɪliəl/ *adj formal* concerning the way in which a son or daughter should behave towards their parents【正式】子女般的；孝順的: *her filial duty* 她作為子女的責任

fil·i·bus·ter /ˈfɪləˌbʌstɚ; ˈfɪlʒbʌstə/ *v* [I] *especially AmE* to try to delay action in Congress by making very long speeches【尤美】〔在美國國會中〕以冗長的發言阻撓議事 —**filibuster** *n* [C]

fil·i·gree /ˈfɪləˌgri; ˈfɪlʒgriː/ *n* [U] delicate work made of gold or silver wire, used to decorate things 金絲[銀絲]細工飾品: *silver filigree jewellery* 鑲銀絲的珠寶

filing cab·i·net /ˈ·· ˌ···/ *n* [C] *BrE* a piece of office furniture that has drawers for storing letters, reports etc【英】檔案櫃；文件櫃

fil·ings /ˈfaɪlɪŋz; ˈfaɪlɪŋz/ *n* [plural] very small sharp bits that come off a piece of metal when it is filed (FILE[2] (4)) 銼屑

fill in 填寫

APPLICATION FORM AF.002
Personal Details
Name ANTHONY JAMES WILLS
Address 487 VIRGINIA AVENUE SOUTHWOOD GROVE WETHERFIE
Code
Tel.No.
Signature

form 表格

fill[1] /fɪl; fɪl/ *v*

1 ►MAKE STH FULL 充滿◄ **a)** also 又作 **fill up** [T] to put the right amount of a liquid, substance, or material into a container, or put in enough to make it full 裝滿，注滿，填滿，充滿: *I filled a saucepan and put it on the stove.* 我把深平底鍋裝滿了，然後把它放在灶火上。| *You've filled the bath too full.* 你把浴缸灌得太滿了。| **fill sth with** *Fill the pots with earth.* 在花盆裡裝滿泥土。| **fill sth to the brim** (=fill something completely) 把某物裝得滿滿的 **b) be filled with** if a container is filled with something, it has had as much of something as possible put inside it 被裝滿: *The next drawer was filled with neat piles of shirts.* 下一個抽屜裝滿了疊放整齊的襯衫。

2 ►BECOME FULL 變滿◄ also 又作 **fill up** [I] if a place, building, or container fills, it gradually becomes full of people, things, or a particular substance〔地方、建築物或容器〕變滿: *They opened the doors and the hall quickly started to fill.* 他們開了門，大廳很快就開始擠滿了人。| **[+with]** *The trench is filling up with water.* 溝裡的水快要滿了。

3 ►NOT LEAVE ANY SPACE 不留下任何空間◄ [T] if a lot of people or things fill a place, there are so many of them that there seems to be no room for anyone or anything else 擠滿，佔滿，佈滿: *Piles of newspapers filled the garage.* 成堆的報紙佔滿了車庫。| **be filled with** *The streets were filled with cheering crowds.* 街道上擠滿了歡呼的人羣。

4 ►HOLE/CRACK 孔/縫隙◄ also 又作 **fill in** [T] to put a substance in a hole or crack in order to make a surface smooth again 填補: *Fill any cracks in the wall before you paint it.* 先把牆壁的裂縫填塞好再粉刷。

5 ►SOUND/SMELL/LIGHT 聲音/氣味/光線◄ [T] if a sound, smell, or light fills a place or space, you notice it because it is very loud or strong 遍佈，充滿: *The smell of freshly baked bread filled the room.* 房間充滿了剛出爐的麵包香味。| *The stage filled with light.* 舞台燈火通明。| **be filled with** *The air was filled with the sound of happy children.* 空氣中充滿着孩子們快樂的聲音。

6 ►EMOTIONS 感情◄ [T] if an emotion fills you, you feel it very strongly 充滿〔某種感情〕: *A feeling of bliss filled his body.* 他感到十分幸福。| **be filled with** *She was filled with a deep contentment.* 她感到極度心滿意足。

7 fill a need/demand to give people something they want but which they have not been able to have until now 滿足需要/要求: *The program helps fill a growing need among teenagers for practical advice about drugs.* 青少年需要得到有關毒品問題的切實可行的忠告, 而這項計劃有助於滿足他們在這方面不斷增長的需求。

8 [T] if you fill a period of time with a particular activity you use most of your time doing it 佔據〔時間〕: *Our days were filled with talk and music.* 我們以談話和聽音樂來打發日子。| **fill sth doing sth** *Harry filled his spare time reading and writing to friends.* 哈里把閒餘時間都用來看書和給朋友寫信。

9 fill yourself *informal* to eat so much food that you cannot eat any more【非正式】吃飽: **fill yourself with** *Don't fill yourself up with sweets, we're eating in an hour.* 別吃太多的糖果, 我們過一小時就要吃飯了。

10 fill a job/post/position a) to do a particular job 擔任工作/職位/職務: *Women fill 30% of the senior positions.* 婦女擔任了 30% 高級職位的工作。**b)** to accept someone's offer of a job 接受〔工作〕: *a shortage of trained secretaries willing to fill permanent office vacancies* 缺乏願意擔任辦公室長期工作的訓練有素的祕書

11 fill a role be a part of something 成為…的一部分; 起某種角色的作用: *Pop music undoubtedly fills an important role in teenagers' lives.* 流行音樂毫無疑問是青少年生活的一個重要部分。

12 fill an order *especially AmE* to supply the goods requested by a customer【尤美】供應訂單; 按單配足訂貨

13 fill the bill *AmE* to have exactly the right qualities; **fit the bill** (FIT[1] (7))【美】完全符合要求, 正合適: *We needed an experienced reporter and Willis fills the bill.* 我們需要一個經驗豐富的記者, 威利斯正合適。

14 ▶TEETH 牙齒◀ [T] to put a FILLING[2](1) in a tooth 補〔牙〕

15 ▶SAIL 帆◀ [I,T] if a sail fills or the wind fills a sail, the sail has a rounded shape rather than hanging down loosely〔帆〕張滿, 張開;〔風〕把〔帆〕張滿

fill in *phr v*

1 ▶DOCUMENT 文件◀ [T **fill** sth ↔ **in**] to write all the necessary information on an official document 填寫〔官方文件表格〕: *Don't forget to fill in your boarding cards.* 別忘了填寫你的登機證。

2 ▶TELL SB NEWS 告訴某人消息◀ [T **fill** sb ↔ **in**] to tell someone about things which have happened recently, especially because you have not seen them for a long time 向…提供最新消息: **fill sb in on sth** *Let me fill you in on what's been happening in the office over lunch.* 讓我告訴你午飯時辦公室裡發生的事。

3 ▶CRACK/HOLE 縫/孔◀ [T **fill** sth ↔ **in**] to put a substance in a hole or crack in order to make a surface smooth again 填平〔空洞或縫隙〕: *filling in the holes in the road* 填好路上的洞

4 fill in time to use your time doing something unimportant, especially when you are waiting for something to happen 消磨時間, 打發時間: *We've got some time to fill in before the show. Let's go for a drink.* 表演開始前我們有點時間要打發。我們去喝一杯吧。

5 ▶SPACE 空間◀ [T **fill** sth ↔ **in**] to paint or draw over the space inside a shape〔繪畫時〕在〔圖的輪廓線〕內填色: *Somebody had filled in all the 'o's' on the page.* 有人已經把這頁上所有的 o 字都填黑了。

6 ▶DO SB'S JOB 做某人的工作◀ [I] to do someone's job or work because they are unable to do it〔由於某人不能工作而〕臨時替代: **fill in for sb** *Sally's off sick. Can you fill in for her for a few days?* 薩莉因病請假。你能臨時替她幾天嗎?

7 ▶HIT SB 痛打某人◀ [T **fill** sb **in**] *BrE informal* to hit someone hard and repeatedly all over their body【英, 非正式】痛打: *One more crack like that and I'll fill you in.* 再開那樣的玩笑我就要好好收拾你一頓。

fill out *phr v* **1** [T **fill** sth ↔ **out**] to write all the necessary information on an official document 填寫: *You haven't filled out the counterfoil.* 你還沒填寫支票的存根。**2** [I] **a)** if your body fills out it becomes rounded or large in a way that is considered attractive〔身體〕變圓, 變豐滿, 變大: *Young Kevin has really filled out in the last six months.* 年輕的凱文最近六個月身體確實豐滿起來了。**b)** a phrase meaning to become fat, used when you do not want to offend someone 發福〔意為長胖, 當不想冒犯某人時用〕: *I think Eric is filling out around the waist.* 埃里克的腰部在發福。

fill up *phr v*

1 ▶MAKE STH FULL 將某物裝滿◀ [T **fill** sth ↔ **up**] to put the right amount of a liquid or substance in a container or enough to make it full 裝滿, 使充滿: *Brad just kept filling up everyone's glasses with champagne.* 布拉德不停地往大家的杯裡加滿香檳酒。

2 ▶BECOME FULL 變滿◀ [I] to gradually become full of people, things, or a substance〔慢慢〕充滿: *The church was filling up with people who had come to pay their respects.* 教堂坐滿了來表示敬意的人。

3 ▶DOCUMENT 文件◀ [T **fill** sth ↔ **up**] to write all the necessary information on an official document 填寫〔正式文件〕

4 fill (yourself) up *informal* to eat so much food that you cannot eat any more【非正式】吃飽: [+**with**] *Don't fill yourself up with too many cookies.* 別吃太多曲奇餅。

5 ▶STOP SB FEELING HUNGRY 使某人不覺得餓◀ [T **fill** sb **up**] *informal* food that fills you up makes you feel you have eaten a lot when you have only eaten a small amount【非正式】使…覺得飽〔實際只吃了很少的食物〕: *I used to just have a sandwich for lunch, but that doesn't fill me up anymore.* 我過去只吃一塊三明治當午餐, 但現在這樣吃不飽了。

fill[2] *n* **1 have your fill of sth** to no longer be able to accept an unpleasant situation 受夠了某物, 對某物忍無可忍: *I've had my fill of screaming kids for one day.* 聽了一天小孩的尖叫聲, 我已經受夠了。**2 eat/drink your fill** to eat or drink as much as you want or need 開懷大吃/開懷暢飲 **3 a fill of sth** the quantity you need to fill something 填滿某物所需的量

filled gold /ˌ· ˈ·◂/ *n* [U] *AmE* ROLLED GOLD【美】金箔, 包金

fill·er /ˈfɪlɚ; ˈfɪlə/ *n* [singular,U] **1** a substance used to fill cracks in wood, walls etc, especially before you paint them〔在木頭、牆壁等上用以填平裂縫的〕填料〔尤指油漆前使用〕; 填塞物 **2** *especially AmE* stories, information, drawings etc that are not important but are used to fill a page in a newspaper or magazine【尤美】〔報紙或雜誌上的〕補白; 補足版面用的文字[圖畫]

filler cap /ˈ·· ·/ *n* [C] *BrE* the lid that fits over the hole in a car that you pour petrol through【英】〔汽車的〕燃油箱蓋

fil·let[1] /ˈfɪlɪt; ˈfɪlʒt/ *n* [C] a piece of meat or fish without bones〔去骨的〕肉片; 魚片; FILET[1] *AmE*【美】: *a fillet of sole* 鰨魚片[柳]

fillet[2] *v* [T] to remove the bones from a piece of meat or fish 剔除〔肉或魚的〕骨頭; FILET[2] *AmE*【美】: *filleted sole* 去骨鰨魚片[柳]

fill-in /ˈ· ·/ *n* [singular] *BrE informal* someone who does someone else's job when they are unable to do it【英, 非正式】臨時替代的人, 替工: *I'm only here as a fill-in while Robert's away.* 我只是在羅伯特不在時來這裡臨時頂一會兒。

fill·ing[1] /ˈfɪlɪŋ; ˈfɪlɪŋ/ *adj* food that is filling makes your stomach feel full 耐飢的, 使人感到飽的: *That fruitcake is really filling stuff.* 那塊水果蛋糕真能果腹。

filling[2] *n* **1** [C] a small amount of metal that is put into your tooth to prevent it from decaying〔補牙用的〕金屬充填料 **2** [C,U] the food that is put inside a PIE, SANDWICH[1] etc〔餡餅、三明治等的〕餡: *cherry pie filling* 櫻桃餡餅的餡

filling sta·tion /ˈ·· ˌ··/ *n* [C] a place where you can

F

buy petrol for your car 汽車加油站; PETROL STATION *BrE* 【英】

fil·lip /ˋfɪləp; ˈfɪlɪ̥p/ *n* [singular] **give sb/sth a fillip** to do something that adds excitement or interest to something 激勵[刺激]某人/某物: *All these activities and parties have given a fillip to my self-esteem.* 這些活動和聚會都增強了我的自尊心。

fil·ly /ˋfɪlɪ; ˈfɪli/ *n* [C] a young female horse 小母馬

film¹ /fɪlm; fɪlm/ *n* **1** [C] *especially BrE* a story that is told using sound and moving pictures, shown at a cinema or on television for entertainment【尤英】〔電影院或電視上供娛樂的〕影片, 電影; MOVIE *AmE*【美】: *Have you seen any good films recently?* 你最近看過甚麼好的影片嗎? | *a French film* 法國影片 —see also 另見 **silent film** (SILENT (4)) **2** [U] the making of films considered as an art or a business 電影製作: *I'm interested in photography and film.* 我對攝影和電影製作感興趣。| *the film industry* 電影業 **3** [U] the material used in a camera for taking photographs or recording moving pictures for the cinema 膠片, 軟片: **roll of film** (=film in a metal container) (一卷) 膠卷 *I shot five rolls of film on vacation.* 我在度假時拍了五卷膠卷。| **on film** *The whole incident was recorded on film.* 事件的整個過程都被拍攝下來。**4** [C] *BrE* a metal container with film in it that you put inside a camera to take photographs【英】膠卷 **5** [singular,U] a very thin layer of something that appears on the surface of something else 薄層, 薄膜: *a film of oil on the surface of the water* 水面上的一層油 —see also 另見 CLINGFILM

film² *v* [I,T] to use a camera to record a story or real events so that it can be shown in the cinema or on television 把…拍成電影, 拍攝〔影片〕: *The explosion had been filmed by an amateur cameraman.* 爆炸被一位業餘攝影師拍攝下來了。| *filming on location in Prague* 在布拉格拍外景

film over *phr v* [I] if your eyes film over they become covered with a thin layer of liquid〔眼睛上〕蓋有薄薄一層液體: *The dog's eyes had filmed over, and it was breathing heavily.* 狗的眼睛有點模糊, 正氣喘吁吁。

film fes·ti·val /ˋ· ˌ···/ *n* [C] an event when a lot of films are shown, and sometimes prizes are given for the best ones 電影節

film star /ˋ· ·/ *n* [C] a famous actor or actress in cinema films 電影明星; MOVIE STAR *AmE*【美】

film·strip /ˋfɪlmˌstrɪp; ˈfɪlmˌstrɪp/ *n* [C] a photographic film that shows photographs, drawings etc, one at a time, not as moving pictures 幻燈片: *an educational filmstrip* 教學幻燈片

Fi·lo·fax /ˋfaɪləˌfæks; ˈfaɪləfæks/ *n* [C] *trademark* a small book in which you write addresses, things you must do etc, with pages you can add or take out【商標】活頁備忘記事本

fi·lo pas·try /ˌfilo ˋpestrɪ; ˌfiːləʊ ˈpeɪstri/ *n* [U] a type of PASTRY (2) with many very thin layers 薄片酥皮

fil·ter¹ /ˋfɪltɚ; ˈfɪltə/ *n* [C] **1** a piece of equipment or a substance that you pass gas or liquid through to remove unwanted substances 過濾器: *a water filter* 濾水器 **2** a piece of glass or plastic that changes the amount or colour of light allowed into a camera or TELESCOPE¹〔照相機或望遠鏡的〕濾光鏡, 濾色鏡 **3** a piece of equipment that only allows certain sounds to pass through it〔聲音的〕濾波器; 濾音器 **4** *BrE* a light used to tell drivers they can turn right or left【英】〔指示汽車司機左轉或右轉的〕限閾通行燈,〔綠色〕箭頭燈, 分流信號

filter² *v* **1** [T] to clean a liquid or gas by passing it through a special substance or piece of equipment〔用特別的物質或設備〕過濾: *You need to filter the drinking water.* 你需要把飲用水過濾一下。**2** [I always+adv/prep] if people filter somewhere, they move gradually in that direction through a door, passage etc〔人羣通過門、過道等〕逐漸移動; 逐漸走過: **[+in/out etc]** *Chattering noisily, the crowd began to filter into the auditorium.* 人羣嘰嘰喳喳說着話, 開始慢慢步入會堂。**3** [I always+adv/prep] if news or information filters somewhere, people gradually hear about it from each other〔消息或信息〕慢慢傳開, 走漏, 泄漏: **[+back/through etc]** *The news slowly filtered through to everyone in the office.* 這消息慢慢走漏出去, 結果辦公室裡每個人都知道了。**4** [I always+adv/prep] if light or sound filters into a place, it can be seen or heard only slightly〔光線或聲音〕隱約地透過; 隱約地傳入: **[+in/into/through]** *A few rays of sunshine filtered into the cave.* 幾縷陽光映進山洞。**5** [I] *BrE* if traffic filters, cars can turn left or right while other vehicles going straight ahead must wait【英】〔車輛〕轉彎〔直走的車輛必須等待〕

filter sth ↔ **out** *phr v* [T] to remove something by using a filter 濾除: *The machine filters out sediment.* 這台機器能濾除沉澱物。

filter tip /ˋ·· ·/ *n* [C] the special end of a cigarette that removes some of the harmful substances from the smoke〔香煙〕過濾嘴 —**filter tipped** *adj*

filth /fɪlθ; fɪlθ/ *n* [U] **1** an extremely dirty substance 污物, 污穢: *Go and wash that filth off your hands!* 去把你手上的髒東西洗掉吧! **2** very rude offensive language, stories, or pictures about sex 下流話; 淫穢故事; 淫穢圖片: *I don't know how you can read that filth!* 我不知道你怎麼會閱讀那種淫穢的東西!

filth·y¹ /ˋfɪlθɪ; ˈfɪlθi/ *adj* **filthier, filthiest 1** extremely dirty 十分骯髒的, 污穢的: *Simon never cleans his house – it's absolutely filthy!* 西蒙從來不打掃房子 —— 它髒極了! **2** showing or describing sexual acts in a very rude or offensive way 淫穢的, 下流的: *Mitch was just telling us a filthy joke when Kia walked in.* 基亞走進來時, 米奇正給我們講下流笑話。—**filthily** *adv* —**filthiness** *n* [U]

filthy² *adv* **1 filthy dirty** very dirty 十分骯髒 **2 filthy rich** *informal* an expression meaning extremely rich, used when you think someone has too much money【非正式】腰纏萬貫, 非常有錢

fil·tra·tion /fɪlˋtreʃən; fɪlˈtreɪʃən/ *n* [U] the process of being cleaned by passing through a FILTER¹ (1) 過濾

fin /fɪn; fɪn/ *n* [C] **1** one of the thin body parts that a fish uses to swim 魚鰭 **2** part of a plane that sticks up at the back and helps it to fly smoothly〔飛機的〕垂直尾翼 —see picture at 參見 AIRCRAFT 圖 **3** *BrE* a large flat rubber shoe that you wear to help you swim better【英】〔潛水、游泳用的〕腳蹼; FLIPPER (2) *AmE*【美】**4** a thin piece of metal that sticks out from something such as a car〔汽車等的〕鰭狀穩定板

fi·na·gle /fəˋnegl; fɪ̥ˈneɪgəl/ *v* [T] **finagled, finagling** *AmE informal*【美, 非正式】**1** to obtain something that is difficult to get, but not by using the usual or official methods 用欺詐手段得到; 耍花招弄到: *How he finagled four front row seats to the game I'll never know.* 他是怎樣弄到比賽的四張前排票子的, 我永遠不會知道。**2** to trick someone into giving you something, especially money 騙取〔尤指騙錢〕: **finagle sb out of sth** *He finagled me out of ten bucks.* 他騙去了我十塊錢。—**finagler** *n* [C]

fi·nal¹ /ˋfaɪnḷ; ˈfaɪnl/ *adj* **1** [only before noun 僅用於名詞前] last in a series of actions, events, parts of a story etc 最後的, 最終的: *The final episode of 'Prime Suspect' is on tonight.*《頭號嫌疑犯》的最後一集於今晚播出。| **final stage/moments etc** *They scored in the final minute of the game.* 他們在比賽的最後一分鐘得分。| **final demand** (=the last time you are sent a bill when you must pay)〔賬單的〕最後償付要求; 最終催付通知 **2** if a decision, offer, agreement etc is final, it cannot be changed〔決定、報價、協議等〕不可改變的, 決定性的, 最終的: **be final** *My decision is final. Do not ask me again!* 我的決定不變。不要再問我了! | **final decision/say/approval etc** *We recommended the plan to the chancellor, who had the final say.* 我們把計劃推薦給校長, 他有最後決定權。| **and that's final!** *spoken* (=used to say that a decision will not be changed)【口】就這麼定了! *No more money, and that's final!* 不能再多給錢了, 就這麼定了! **3** [only before noun 僅用於名詞前] happening at or near the end of an event or process 最後的: *They fought many battles before their final defeat.* 他們打了許多仗, 最後才被打敗。**4** [only before noun 僅用於名詞前] being the result at the end of a process 結果的, 最終的: *the differences between the original script and the final film* 原腳本和最終拍出來的影片之間的差別

final² *n* [C] **1 finals** *BrE* the set of examinations that university students take at the end of their time at university【英】〔大學期間〕最後一次考試, 畢業考試 **2** *AmE* an examination taken at the end of each class a student takes at university【美】〔大學〕期終考試 **3** the last and most important game, race etc in a set of games or races〔一場〕決賽: *He ran well in the heats but came in last in the final.* 他在分組預賽中跑得很好, 但在決賽中卻得了最後一名。| **the finals** (=the last few games or races in a competition)〔最後幾場〕決賽 *the 1994 World Cup finals* 1994年世界盃決賽

fi·na·le /fɪˋnælɪ; fɪˈnɑːli/ *n* [C] the last part of a piece of music or a show〔演出的〕終場, 最後一幕;〔音樂的〕終曲: *the finale of a Broadway show* 百老匯表演的終場 | **grand finale** (=very impressive end to a show)〔演出的〕大結局 *The fireworks were the grand finale of the closing ceremonies.* 閉幕儀式在煙火齊放中隆重結束。

fi·nal·ist /ˋfaɪnl̩ɪst; ˈfaɪnəl-ɪ̈st/ *n* [C] one of the people or teams that reaches the final game in a competition or set of sports matches〔競賽或體育比賽的〕決賽選手

fi·nal·i·ty /faɪˋnælətɪ; faɪˈnælɪ̈ti/ *n* [U] the quality or feeling that something has when you know it is over and cannot be changed 定局, 終結: *The word 'retirement' has a horrible air of finality about it.* "退休"這個詞蘊涵有終結的可怕意味。

fi·nal·ize also 又作 **-ise** *BrE*【英】/ˋfaɪnl̩ˌaɪz; ˈfaɪnəl-aɪz/ *v* [T] to finish the last part of a plan, business deal etc 最後定下, 使〔計劃、交易等〕確定: *Jo flew out to Thailand to finalize the details of the deal.* 喬乘飛機到泰國, 把這筆交易的細節定下來。—**finalization** /ˌfaɪnələˋzeʃən; ˌfaɪnəlaɪˈzeɪʃən/ *n* [U]

2 1 **fi·nal·ly** /ˋfaɪnl̩ɪ; ˈfaɪnəl-i/ *adv* **1** after a long time 最後, 終於: *After several delays we finally took off at six o'clock.* 幾經耽擱後, 我們終於在六點起飛了。| *Finally, to my relief, Garth brought up the subject of money.* 使我鬆了一口氣的是, 加思終於提出了錢的問題。**2** as the last of a series of things 最後(一點): [sentence adverb 句子副詞] *And finally, I'd like to thank the crew.* 最後, 我要感謝全體機組人員。**3** in a finished state 決定性地, 徹底地: *It's not finally settled yet.* 這件事還沒有徹底解決。—see 見 LASTLY (USAGE)

3 2 **fi·nance¹** /fəˋnæns; ˈfaɪnæns/ *n* **1** [U] the management of money, especially money controlled by a government, company, or large organization 財政, 金融: *the university's finance committee* 大學的財務委員會 | **high finance** (=financial activities involving countries or large companies)〔涉及國家或大公司的〕巨額資金活動 **2 finances a)** the money that a person, company, organization etc has available 資金, 財源, 財力: *The committee's finances are very limited.* 委員會的資金很有限。**b)** the way a person, company, organization etc manages their money 財務管理, 理財: *My finances are in a real mess.* 我的財務確實亂七八糟。**3** [U] money, especially money provided by a bank, to help run a business or buy something 資金: [+for] *We need to raise finance for further research.* 我們需要為進一步研究籌資。

3 **finance²** *v* [T] to provide money, especially a large amount of money, to pay for something 為…提供資金; 出資: *These concerts are financed by the Arts Council.* 這些音樂會是由藝術委員會資助的。

finance com·pa·ny /ˈ·· ˌ···/ *n* [C] *AmE* a company that lends money, especially to businesses【美】信貸公司, 金融公司, 財務公司

fi·nan·cial /fəˋnænʃəl; fɪ̈ˈnænʃəl/ *adj* connected with money or the management of money 財政的, 金融的: *New York is a great financial center.* 紐約是一個大金融中心。| *financial assistance for city schools* 對市立學校的資助 | **a financial success** (=something that makes a profit) 賺錢的事 *It was a wonderful film, but not exactly a financial success.* 這是一部很好的電影, 但不一定能賺錢。—**financially** *adv* 3 1

financial aid /·ˌ·· ˈ·/ *n* [U] *AmE* money given or lent to students at college or university to pay for their education【美】助學金, 助學貸款

financial in·cen·tive /·ˌ·· ·ˈ··/ *n* [C] money given to someone if they work harder or for special jobs 金錢鼓勵; 獎金

financial in·sti·tu·tion /·ˌ·· ··ˈ··/ *n* [C] *technical* a business organization that lends and borrows money, for example a bank【術語】金融機構〈如銀行〉: *All the big financial institutions cut their interest rates today.* 所有的大型金融機構今天都降低了利率。

financial mar·kets /·ˌ·· ˈ··/ *n* [plural] *technical* banks and other financial institutions that make business contracts with each other【術語】金融市場

financial year /·ˌ·· ˈ·/ *n* [singular] the period of a year over which a company's profits and losses are calculated 財政年度, 會計年度 —compare 比較 FISCAL YEAR

fi·nan·cier /ˌfɪnənˋsɪr; fɪ̈ˈnænsɪə/ *n* [C] someone who controls or lends large sums of money 財政家, 金融家

finch /fɪntʃ; fɪntʃ/ *n* [C] a small bird with a short beak 雀科鳴禽

find¹ /faɪnd; faɪnd/ *past tense and past participle* **found** /faund; faʊnd/ *v* [T] 1 1

1 ▶BY SEARCHING 通過搜尋◀ to discover or see something that you have been searching for 發現, 找到〔一直尋找的東西〕: *I can't find the car keys.* 我找不到汽車鑰匙。| *Let's hope we can find a parking space.* 但願我們能找到一個停車的地方。| *No-one has found a solution to this problem.* 還沒人找到解決這個問題的辦法。| **find sb sth** *I found him a nice second-hand car.* 我替他找了輛很好的二手車。—see 見 OBTAIN (USAGE)

2 ▶ARRIVE 到達◀ to discover that someone or something is in a particular condition or doing a particular thing when you arrive or first see them 發現, 發覺〔某人或某物處在某狀態或在做某事〕: *I'm sure we'll find her hard at work when we get home.* 我確信我們到家時會發現她還在努力工作。| *Michael woke up to find his bedroom ankle-deep in water.* 邁克爾醒來時發現他的臥室裡有齊踝深的水。| **find sb doing sth** *Carrie went into the kitchen, where she found them giggling together.* 卡麗走進廚房, 發現她們在那兒咯咯地笑着。| **[+(that)]** *When I got to school I found that class was cancelled.* 我到達學校時, 發現停課了。

3 ▶BY STUDY 通過研究◀ to discover or learn something by study, tests etc 找出, 查明: *Will we ever find a cure for the disease?* 我們究竟能找到治療這種病的藥嗎? | *The liquid was found to contain 7.4g of phenylamine.* 這種液體被發現含有7.4克苯胺。| **[+that]** *It was found that 80% of young people borrow money.* 調查發現80%的年輕人借錢。

4 ▶THINK/FEEL 認為/感覺◀ to have a particular feeling or idea about something 感到, 覺得, 認為: *I hate flying – I find it absolutely terrifying.* 我討厭坐飛機 —— 我覺得坐飛機非常可怕。| *Lots of women I know find him attractive.* 我認識的許多女子都覺得他很有魅力。

5 find sth easy/difficult/impossible if you find something difficult or easy it seems difficult or easy to you when you do it 覺得某事很容易/很難/是不可能的: *He said that, after Russian, I should find German easy.* 他說, 在學過俄語之後, 我應該覺得德語容易學。| **find it difficult/easy etc to do sth** *He found it almost impossible to express what he wanted to say.* 他覺得要表達他想說的話幾乎是不可能的。

6 ▶BY EXPERIENCE 通過經驗◀ to learn or know something by experience 學會; 知道; 發覺: [+(**that**)] *You might find that his work improves now he's going to a new school.* 你可能會發覺他因為上一所新學校, 學習有所進步。| *One thing I find about living in the big city is that people are more friendly than I expected.* 我發現生活在大城市的一個特點是, 那裡的人比我想像的要友好。| **find sb/sth doing sth** *You find more women entering the film business now.* 你會發現現在有越來越多的婦女進入電影業。

7 ►BY CHANCE 偶然發現◄ to discover something by chance, especially something useful or interesting 偶然發現, 碰上: *I found a purse in the street.* 我在街上撿到一個錢包。| *We found a really good bar near the hotel.* 我們在旅館附近發現一家非常好的酒吧。

8 ►STH YOU NEED 所需的東西◄ to achieve or get something that you need 獲得, 得到, 找到: *Finding accommodation in Berlin can be a nightmare.* 在柏林找地方住宿有時就像做惡夢一樣。| *two lonely people who managed to find happiness together* 設法一起尋找幸福的兩個孤獨的人

9 ►REALIZE 意識到◄ to notice or realize a fact, often a fact that is surprising 發覺, 發現: [+(**that**)] *He got up to leave and found that the door was jammed.* 他站起來要離開, 但發現門卡住了打不開。| *I found I was really looking forward to going back to work.* 我發覺我確實盼望回去工作。

10 ►ANIMALS/PLANTS 動物/植物◄ if something is found somewhere, it lives or exists there 發現…的存在〔指動植物自然地生長於某地〕: *This species is only found in West Africa.* 這物種只有西非才有。

11 ►MONEY/TIME/ENERGY 錢/時間/精力◄ to have enough money, time, energy etc to be able to do something you want to do 設法擁有, 努力獲得: *He has to find £1000 to repay the loan.* 他得去弄 1000 英鎊來償付貸款。| *I wouldn't mind learning a language, but I can't find the time right now.* 我不介意學一門語言, 但我現在擠不出時間來。| *David wanted to defend himself, but couldn't find the courage to speak up.* 大衛想為自己辯護, 但沒有勇氣說出來。

12 find your way to reach a place by discovering the right way to get there 設法到達: *Will you be able to find your way back to the house?* 你找得到回住所的路嗎?

13 find its way if something finds its way somewhere, it arrives or gets there after some time〔一段時間後〕(自然) 到達: *Only one of her inventions has found its way into the shops.* 她的發明只有一項最終進入了市場。

14 find yourself doing sth to gradually realize that you are doing something, although you had not intended or planned to do it 發現自己〔不知不覺地〕在做某事: *Peter, who was usually shy, found himself talking to the girls.* 彼得通常很怕羞, 但卻發現自己不知不覺中已在跟女孩子們說話。

15 find yourself in/at etc a) to realize that you are in a particular situation, especially a bad one, that you did not expect 發現自己處於某種狀態〔尤指沒預期的糟糕狀況〕: *If you find yourself worrying about things, call me.* 如果你覺得自己為甚麼事煩惱, 請打電話給我。| *They suddenly found themselves without a goalkeeper.* 他們突然發現己方沒有守門員。**b)** to realize that you have arrived somewhere without intending to 發現自己在不知不覺中到達: *After wandering around, we found ourselves back at the hotel.* 我們四處漫步後發現自己回到了酒店。

16 find yourself *often humorous* to discover what you are really like and what you want to do【常幽默】發現自己的真本質[真想做的事等]: *She went to India to find herself.* 她到印度去尋找真的自己。

17 find sb guilty/find sb not guilty to officially decide that someone is guilty or not guilty of something 判決某人有罪/判決某人無罪: *Galbraith was found not guilty and set free.* 加爾布雷思被判無罪而得到釋放。| [+**of**] *A clearly innocent man has been found guilty of a serious crime.* 一個明顯無辜的人被判決犯有重罪。

18 find comfort/pleasure/fulfilment in to experience a good feeling because of something 因…得到安慰/快樂/滿足: *He found great satisfaction in kneading the dough and baking the bread.* 他在揉麵團和烤麵包中得到很大滿足。

19 find fault with to criticize someone or something, often unfairly and frequently 批評, 挑剔, 找岔子: *The teacher would always find fault with our grammar.* 老師對我們的語法總是百般挑剔。

20 find favour (with) be liked or approved of by someone 得寵, 受青睞: *The recipes rapidly found favour with restaurant owners.* 這些食譜很快就受到餐館老闆的青睞。

21 find in sb's favour/find in favour of sb to judge that someone is right or not guilty 裁決〔某人〕正確; 判決〔某人〕無罪: *The Tribunal found in favour of the defendant.* 特別法庭判決被告無罪。

22 find your feet to get used to a new situation, especially one that is difficult at first 習慣新的環境〔尤指起初困難的環境〕: *Matt's only been at the school two weeks and he hasn't found his feet yet.* 馬特上這所學校才兩週, 還沒有習慣新的環境。

23 find its mark/target if an ARROW (1), bullet etc finds its target, it hits what it is supposed to〔箭、子彈等〕射中目標

24 find your tongue to manage to speak after being too nervous to say anything〔緊張得說不出話之後〕設法說話

25 be found wanting *formal* to not be good enough【正式】不夠格, 不令人滿意, 不合要求: *Ryan's proposals have been examined, and found wanting by the rest of the team.* 萊恩的提議得到審議, 隊裡的其他人認為不很滿意。

26 all found *BrE* used to mean that in addition to your wages you get food and a room【英】〔除工資外的〕膳宿供應: *The cook gets paid £90 a week all found.* 廚師每週工資 90 鎊並獲供應膳宿。

find against sb *phr v* [T not in passive 不用被動態] *law* to judge that someone is wrong or guilty【法律】作出不利於〔某人〕的判決; 判決〔某人〕有罪: *The judge found against the plaintiff.* 法官作出了不利於原告的判決。

find for sb *phr v* [T not in passive 不用被動態] *law* to judge that someone is right or not guilty【法律】作出有利於〔某人〕的判決; 判決〔某人〕無罪: *The judge found for the plaintiff.* 法官作出了有利於原告的判決。

find out *phr v* **1 find** sth ↔ **out** [I,T] to learn information, after trying to discover it or by chance 了解到, 找出: [+**who/what/how etc**] *He hurried off to find out what the problem was.* 他趕忙去弄明白問題何在。| **find out sth** *We never found out her real name.* 我們從來沒弄清楚她的真名。| [+**that**] *I found out that he was having an affair with another woman.* 我發現他與別的女人有染。| [+**about**] *I need to find out more about these night courses.* 我需要了解多一點這些夜間課程。| [+**if**] *A number of tests have been carried out to find out if these drugs have any effect.* 已經進行了一些測試來弄清楚這些藥品是否有療效。—see 見 KNOW¹ (USAGE) **2 find sb out** [T] to discover that someone has been doing something dishonest or illegal 發現〔某人〕不誠實或違法: *After years of defrauding the company, he was finally found out.* 他多年來一直詐取公司的錢財, 最後終於被揭發出來。

find² *n* **a find** something very good or valuable that you discover by chance〔偶然〕發現的好東西; 發現物: *That little Greek restaurant was a real find!* 找到那家希臘小餐館真是一項有價值的發現!

find·er /ˈfaɪndə; ˈfaɪndə/ *n* [C] someone who finds something 發現者, 發現的人

fin de siè·cle /ˌfæn də ˈsjɛkl; ˌfæn də ˈsjeklə◄/ *adj French* typical of the end of the 19th century, especially typical of the art, literature, and attitudes of the time【法】〔尤指藝術、文學和觀念〕具有19世紀末特徵的

2 **find·ing** /ˈfaɪndɪŋ; ˈfaɪndɪŋ/ *n* [C usually plural 一般用複數] **1** the information that someone has learnt as a result of their studies, work etc 研究[努力]的結果; 發現: *Surveys conducted in other countries reported similar findings.* 在其他國家進行的調查結果與此相似。**2** *law* a decision made by a judge or jury【法律】〔法官或陪審團的〕裁決, 判決

1 1 **fine¹** /faɪn; faɪn/ *adj*

1 ►ALL RIGHT 令人滿意的◄ *especially spoken*【尤口】**a)** good enough; all right 極好的, 令人滿意的: *"I could make you some dinner if you like." "It's okay, a sandwich is fine, thanks."* "如果你願意的話, 我可以給你弄點晚餐。" "好吧, 一塊三明治就挺不錯了, 謝謝。" | *This apartment is fine for two, but it gets very cramped with your mother here.* 這套公寓兩個人住很舒適, 但你母親住在這兒就會很擁擠。| **I'm fine** *"More coffee?" "No, I'm fine, thanks."* "再來點咖啡嗎?" "不用了, 很好了, 謝謝。" **b)** healthy 健康的: *"How are you?" "Fine, thanks."* "你身體好嗎?" "很好, 謝謝。" | *"Is your wife better now?" "Oh, she's fine."* "你太太現在身體好些嗎?" "噢, 她很好。"

2 ►VERY GOOD 很好的◄ of a very high quality or standard 優質的, 優秀的, 高級的: *Many people regard Beethoven's fifth symphony as his finest work.* 許多人把貝多芬的第五交響曲看成是他最優秀的作品。| *There is some fine architecture in the old city.* 老城區有些漂亮的建築。| *fine bone china* 高級骨灰瓷 | *fine wine* 優質葡萄酒

3 ►GRAND 華貴的◄ [usually before a noun 一般用於名詞前] grand, expensive, better than others of the same kind 華麗的, 豪華的, 高貴的: *A tall woman in fine clothes got out of the carriage.* 一位穿着華麗衣服的高個子女士從馬車裡走出來。| *the fine ladies and gentlemen who frequent the elegant restaurants of Paris* 經常光顧巴黎這些高雅餐館的上等男女

4 ►NOT GOOD 不好的◄ *informal* used when you really think that something is not good or satisfactory at all【非正式】糟透的, 十分令人失望的: *"Now's a fine time to tell me!" he fumed.* "現在告訴我很不是時候!" 他怒氣沖沖地說。| *That's a fine mess you've got us into!* 你使我們陷入糟糕的境地!

5 ►WEATHER 天氣◄ not raining, perhaps with the sun shining 晴朗的: *If it's fine tomorrow we'll go out.* 如果明天天氣晴朗, 我們就出門。| *It was a fine evening.* 這是個天朗氣清的傍晚。

6 ►THIN 細的◄ very thin 纖細的; 薄的: *This thread's very fine – it's difficult to see.* 這條線太纖細了 —— 很難看見。| *a fine coating of dust* 一層薄灰 —see picture at 參見 THIN 圖

7 ►SMALL 小的◄ **a)** involving differences, changes, or details that are difficult to understand or notice〔差別、改變或細節〕細微的: *the finer points of policy detail* 政策細節的細微之點 | *the fine tuning on the radio* 收音機上的微調鈕 | *Scientists are now able to measure fine distinctions between levels of sleep depth.* 科學家現在能夠測出不同睡眠深度的細微差別。**b)** in small grains, pieces, or drops〔顆粒〕細微的: *fine sugar* 精製食糖 | *fine drizzle* 濛濛細雨, 毛毛雨

8 ►NET 網[篩]◄ having small holes 有細微網孔的: *a fine mesh* 細網眼的網

9 ►IDEAS/SPEECHES 思想/演說◄ too grand and probably not true or unlikely to have any effect 過分誇飾的; 炫耀的: *It's all very well politicians making fine speeches, but they never get anything done.* 政客們的漂亮言辭雖然動聽, 但他們從來甚麼事都沒有做。

10 a fine woman/person a good person that you have a lot of respect for 優秀[傑出]的女性/人物: *Your father is a fine man, a real gentleman.* 你父親是個高尚的人, 一個真正的紳士。

11 that's/it's fine by me used to say that you agree to something 行, 可以, 我同意: *"I thought we could go out to eat." "That's fine by me."* "我想我們可以出外吃飯。" "我不反對。"

12 fine features someone with fine features has a small and attractively-shaped nose, mouth etc 俊秀的五官

13 finer feelings/qualities etc feelings, qualities etc such as love, honour, loyalty and kindness〔愛、榮譽、忠誠和仁慈等〕更高尚的感情/品質等

14 a fine figure of a man/woman someone who looks big, strong and physically attractive 身材好的男子/女子: *Vellios was a fine figure of a man.* 維利奧斯是個身材高大偉岸的男子漢。

15 a fine line if you say that there is a fine line between two different things, you mean that there is a point at which one can easily become the other 一線之隔; 極細微的分界線: *There's a fine line between bravery and recklessness.* 勇敢和魯莽只有一線之隔。

16 not to put too fine a point on it *often humorous* used when you are criticizing something in a plain and direct way【常幽默】說得不客氣一點: *That's a real yobs' pub – not to put too fine a point on it.* 說得不客氣一點, 那真是一家粗野人的酒吧。

17 sb's finest hour an occasion when someone is extremely successful and proud of their achievement 某人最感春風得意的時間[場合]

fine² *interjection* used to agree to a suggestion 好, 行, 可以: *"I'll see you at eight then." "Okay. Fine."* "那麼我們八點鐘見面。" "行, 好的。"

fine³ *adv* **1** *spoken* in a way that is satisfactory【口】很好: *"How's it going?" "Fine, thanks."* "你好嗎?" "很好, 謝謝。" | *The technician has been to fix it and it works fine now.* 技術員已經來修理過了, 現在它運轉得挺好的。**2** if you cut something fine, you cut it very thin or in very small pieces〔切得〕細小地 **3 do fine** *spoken*【口】**a)** to be good enough or be satisfactory 很好, 能行, 能令人滿意: *We don't need to get her anything expensive – a calendar will do fine.* 我們不需要買甚麼昂貴的東西給她 —— 一本日曆就可以了。**b)** to do something well or in a satisfactory way 很好地做, 令人滿意地做: *"I can't draw this." "You're doing fine! Don't give up now."* "我不會畫這個。" "你畫得很好! 現在別放棄。" **4 sth will do me/us fine** *BrE spoken* used to say that something is satisfactory or good enough【英口】某物對我/我們很適合[已經夠好了]: *Chips'll do me fine, darling.* 我吃炸薯條就好了, 親愛的。**5 cut it fine** *informal* to leave yourself only just enough time to do something【非正式】留出剛剛好的時間; 時間抓得很緊湊

fine⁴ *v* [T] to make someone pay money as a punishment 處…以罰金: **fine sb for doing sth** *She was fined $50 for passing a stopped school bus.* 她因超越一輛停住的校車而被罰款50美元。

fine sth ↔ **down** *BrE* to improve something by making it thinner, smaller, or more exact【英】使〔某物〕變細[小, 精確]

fine⁵ *n* [C] money that you have to pay as a punishment 罰金, 罰款: *I got a £40 fine for speeding* 我因超速駕車而被罰款40英鎊。| **heavy fine** (=a fine that costs you a lot of money) 一大筆罰金 *There's a heavy fine for driving drunk.* 酒醉開車的罰款很重。| **parking/library fines etc** *I forgot to return my books on time and paid $3 in library fines.* 我忘記按時還書, 被圖書館罰了3美元。

fine art /ˌ· ˈ·/ *n* [U] **1** paintings, drawings, music, SCULPTURE etc that is of very good quality 美術品〈如繪畫、音樂、雕刻等〉: *the question of whether photography should be considered fine art* 攝影是否應當被看成是美術品的問題 **2 have something down to a fine art** to be extremely good at something after having practised a lot〔經過大量實踐後〕對某事技術高超, 把某事學到家: *Chris and I have got the morning routine of showers, breakfast, kids to school down to a fine art.* 我和克里斯

F

都已經把每天早上的淋浴、早餐、送孩子上學這些事做得熟練無比了。**3 the fine arts** [plural] activities such as painting, music, and SCULPTURE that are concerned with producing beautiful rather than useful things 美藝術, 美術〈如繪畫、音樂、雕刻等〉: *a student of the fine arts* 美藝術學生

fine·ly /ˈfaɪnlɪ; ˈfaɪnli/ *adv* **1** into very thin or very small pieces 微小地, 細微地: *Add the finely chopped onion to the butter, and fry till golden.* 把剁得很細的洋蔥加到黃油裡, 然後煎到金黃色為止。**2** to a very exact degree 精確地: *These instruments are very finely tuned.* 這些儀器都調得十分精確。**3** beautifully and delicately 優雅地, 雅致地: *She had an oval face with finely formed features.* 她有一張眉清目秀的鵝蛋臉。

fine print /ˌ· ˈ·/ *n* [U] SMALL PRINT 附屬細則

fi·ne·ry /ˈfaɪnərɪ; ˈfaɪnəri/ *n* [U] clothes and jewellery that are beautiful or very expensive, and are worn for a special occasion 華麗的服飾: *The guests arrived in all their finery.* 客人們穿着極華麗的服飾到來。

fines herbes /ˌfin ˋɛrb; ˌfiːn ˈeəb/ *n* [U] *French* a mixture of thinly cut plants, added to food to improve its taste【法】〔切細混合製成的〕調味香菜

fi·nesse¹ /fəˋnɛs; fɪˈnes/ *n* [U] delicate and impressive skill 非凡[高超]的技巧: *Dario played the sonata with finesse.* 達里奧以非凡的技巧演奏了這支奏鳴曲。

finesse² *v* [T] **1** *AmE* to do something with style and delicate skill【美】巧妙地做: *The skier finessed the difficulties of the mountain.* 滑雪者巧妙地應付了在山上遇到的困難。**2** to handle a situation well, but in a way that is slightly deceitful 用巧妙的〔但略帶欺騙性的〕手段處理好: *He finessed the deal, using his charm to cover up his lack of knowledge.* 他施展手段, 用他的魅力來掩蓋他知識的貧乏, 完成了這筆交易。

F

fine-tooth comb /ˌ· ˈ· ·/ *n* [C] **go through/over sth with a fine-tooth comb** to examine something very carefully and thoroughly 仔細檢查; 徹底地查看: *going over the evidence with a fine-tooth comb* 仔細檢查證據

fine-tune /ˌ· ˈ·/ *v* [T] to make very small changes to something, especially a machine or system, so that it works as well as possible 對〔機器或系統〕進行微調, 精密調節 —**fine tuning** *n* [U]

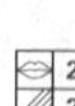

fin·ger¹ /ˈfɪŋgɚ; ˈfɪŋgə/ *n* [C]

1 ►PART OF YOUR HAND 手的部分◄ one of the four long thin parts on your hand, not including your thumb〔大拇指以外的〕手指: *She let sand run through her fingers.* 她讓沙子從手指縫裡滑落下去。| *Tim ran his finger along the windowsill.* 蒂姆用手指在窗台上抹了一下。—see also 另見 INDEX FINGER, LITTLE FINGER, MIDDLE FINGER, RING FINGER

finger 手指

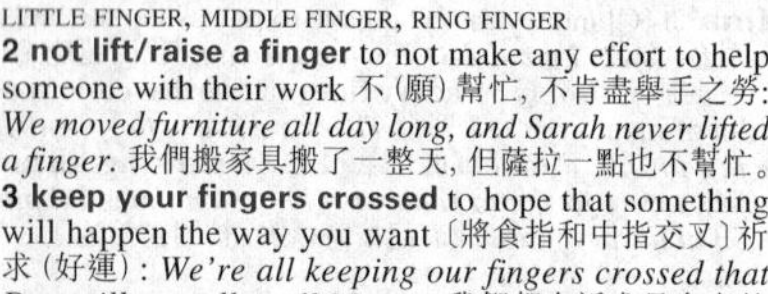

Keep your fingers crossed. 將食指與中指交叉。

2 not lift/raise a finger to not make any effort to help someone with their work 不(願)幫忙, 不肯盡舉手之勞: *We moved furniture all day long, and Sarah never lifted a finger.* 我們搬家具搬了一整天, 但薩拉一點也不幫忙。

3 keep your fingers crossed to hope that something will happen the way you want〔將食指和中指交叉〕祈求(好運): *We're all keeping our fingers crossed that Dan will actually call Megan.* 我們都在祈求丹會真的打電話給梅根。

4 put your finger on to realize exactly what is wrong, different, or unusual about a situation 確切地明白; 弄清; 準確地指出〔錯誤、不同、異常之處〕: *I couldn't quite put my finger on what was different about Simone.* 我無法確切地說出西蒙尼有甚麼兩樣。

5 not lay a finger on sb to not hurt someone at all, especially not to hit them 不傷害某人〔尤指不動手打人〕: *Don't you dare lay a finger on me, or I'll call the police!* 你要是敢碰我一根毫毛, 我就要報警了。

6 be all fingers and thumbs *BrE* to use your hands in an awkward or careless way, so that you drop or break things【英】笨手笨腳

7 pull/take/get your finger out *BrE spoken* used to tell someone to work harder【英口】更努力地工作, 加把勁幹〔用於告誡某人〕

8 be caught with your fingers in the till to be found stealing money from the place where you work 被發現在工作場所偷錢

9 ►SHAPED LIKE A FINGER 手指狀的◄ anything that is long and thin, like the shape of a finger, especially a piece of land, an area of water, or a piece of food 指狀物〔尤指土地、水域、食物等〕

10 ►DRINK 酒◄ an amount of an alcoholic drink that is as high in the glass as the width of someone's finger 一指寬, 一橫指〔指玻璃杯內酒的量度〕: *Gimme three fingers of whiskey, and make it quick!* 給我三橫指深的威士忌, 快點!

11 have a finger in every pie an expression meaning to be involved in many activities and have influence over them, used especially when you think someone has too much influence 多管閒事, 凡事插手

12 have/keep your finger on the pulse to always know about the most recent changes or developments in a situation or organization 了解最新變化[發展]

13 twist/wrap sb around your little finger to be able to persuade someone to do anything that you want 能任意擺佈某人, 能左右某人

14 put two fingers up at sb *BrE informal* to show someone you are angry with them in a very offensive way by holding up your first two fingers with the back of your hand facing them【英, 非正式】〔手背朝對方〕向某人豎起食指和中指〔表示對其生氣, 極具冒犯性〕

15 give sb the finger *AmE informal* to show someone you are angry with them in a very offensive way by holding up your middle finger with the back of your hand facing them【美, 非正式】〔手背朝對方〕向某人豎起中指〔表示對其生氣, 極具冒犯性〕

16 long-fingered/delicate-fingered etc having long fingers, delicate fingers etc 手指長的/手指纖細的等: *Lee rubbed his stubby-fingered hands together.* 李搓了搓他那雙手指短而粗的手。

17 two-fingered/three-fingered etc using two, three etc fingers to do something 用雙指的/用三指的等: *I've become pretty fast, even with my two-fingered typing.* 即使是用雙指打字, 我已經打得相當快了。—see also 另見 FISH FINGER, **have green fingers** (GREEN¹ (10)), **burn your fingers** (BURN¹ (18)), **point the finger at** (POINT² (7)), **let sth slip (through your fingers)** (SLIP¹ (7)), **snap your fingers** (SNAP¹ (6)), **have sticky fingers** (STICKY (7)), **work your fingers to the bone** (WORK¹ (26))

finger² *v* [T] **1** to touch or handle something with your fingers 用手指觸碰, 撥弄, 撫摸, 觸摸: *She fingered the beautiful cloth with envy.* 她羨慕地撫摸着這塊漂亮的布。**2** *informal especially AmE* if someone, especially a criminal, fingers another criminal, they tell the police what they have done【非正式, 尤美】〔尤指罪犯向警察〕告發〔另一個罪犯〕

finger bowl /ˈ·· ·/ *n* [C] a small bowl in which you wash your fingers during a meal〔進餐時〕洗手指用的碗

fin·ger·ing /ˈfɪŋgərɪŋ; ˈfɪŋgərɪŋ/ *n* [U] the positions in which a musician puts his fingers to play a piece of music, or the order in which he uses his fingers〔音樂家彈奏樂器的〕指法

fin·ger·mark /ˈfɪŋgɚˌmɑrk; ˈfɪŋgəmɑːk/ *n* [C] a mark made by dirty fingers on something clean〔髒手留下的〕指痕, 指跡

fin·ger·nail /ˈfɪŋɡɚˌnel; ˈfɪŋɡəneɪl/ *n* [C] the hard flat part that covers the top end of your finger 手指甲

finger-paints /ˈ·· ·/ *n* [plural] special paints that children use to paint with, using their fingers〔兒童〕作指畫用的水彩顏料 —**finger painting** *n* [U]

fin·ger·plate /ˈfɪŋɡɚˌplet; ˈfɪŋɡəpleɪt/ *n* [C] a metal or glass plate that is fastened to a door near the handle or key hole〔裝在門把手上或鎖眼附近的〕手污防護板

fin·ger·print¹ /ˈfɪŋɡɚˌprɪnt; ˈfɪŋɡəˌprɪnt/ *n* [C] a mark made by the pattern of lines at the end of a person's finger, which can be used by the police to help find criminals 指紋: *His fingerprints were all over the gun.* 槍上滿是他的指紋。| **leave (your) fingerprints** *He was careful not to leave any fingerprints.* 他小心翼翼, 避免留下指紋。| **take sb's fingerprints** (=make a picture of someone's fingerprints) 取某人的指紋 *The police questioned Beresford and took his fingerprints.* 警察審問了貝里斯福特, 並取了他的指紋。

fingerprint 指紋

fingerprint² *v* [T] to press someone's finger on ink and then press it on paper in order to make a pattern of the lines at the end of the finger 取〔某人的〕指紋

fin·ger·stall /ˈfɪŋɡɚˌstɔl; ˈfɪŋɡəstɔːl/ *n* [C] *BrE* a cover for your finger that protects it if it is injured【英】〔保護受傷手指的〕護指套

fin·ger·tip /ˈfɪŋɡɚˌtɪp; ˈfɪŋɡəˌtɪp/ *n* [C] **1** the end of a finger 指尖 **2 have sth at your/their fingertips** to have something, especially knowledge or information, ready and available to use very easily 手頭有某物〔隨時可供使用〕, 對某物瞭如指掌: *We have all the facts and figures at our fingertips.* 我們對所有的事實和數字瞭如指掌。**3 to your fingertips** *BrE* in all ways【英】完全地, 徹底地: *She's British to her fingertips.* 她是地道的英國人。

fin·i·cky /ˈfɪnɪkɪ; ˈfɪnɪki/ *adj* **1** too concerned with unimportant details and small things that you like or dislike; FUSSY 過分講究的, 愛挑剔的: *She's very finicky about what she eats.* 她太挑食了。**2** needing to be done very carefully, while paying attention to small details 需要細心做的, 細緻的: *It was a finicky job, trying to get the spring back into my watch.* 把彈簧裝回到我的手錶裡是個細緻活兒。

1 2 **fin·ish¹** /ˈfɪnɪʃ; ˈfɪnɪʃ/ *v*

1 ►STOP DOING STH 停止做某事◄ [I,T] to come to the end of doing or making something, so that it is complete 完成, 做完: **finish sth** *You can't go anywhere until you finish your homework.* 沒完成家庭作業前你哪兒也不能去。| **finish doing sth** *I finished typing the report just minutes before it was due.* 我在報告該交出前幾分鐘才打完它。| *"Are they still working on the road by you?" "No, they've finally finished."* "他們還在你家旁邊的路上幹活嗎?" "不, 他們終於完工了。"

2 ►STOP 停止◄ [I] *especially BrE* when an event, activity, or period of time finishes, it ends, especially at a particular time【尤英】〔事件、活動、時期〕結束, 終止: *The football season finishes in May.* 足球賽季在五月份結束。| *What time does school finish?* 學校甚麼時候放學?

3 ►EAT 吃◄ also 又作 **finish up/off** [T] to eat or drink all the rest of something, so there is none left 吃光, 喝光〔剩下的東西〕: *Finish up your peas or you won't get any dessert.* 把豌豆吃光, 不然就不給你吃甜點。| *Sylvia finished her cigarette.* 西爾維婭抽完了那支香煙。

4 ►END WITH/BY 以…結束, 以…告終◄ also 又作 **finish off** [I,T] to complete an event, performance, piece of work etc by doing one final thing 結束, 完成: **[+with]** *The party finished with a sing-song.* 聚會以唱一首歌結束。| **finish by doing sth** *She finished off her speech by thanking her sponsors.* 她以感謝贊助人結束了講話。

5 ►RACE 賽跑◄ [I,T] to be in a particular position at the end of a race, competition etc〔在賽跑、比賽等中〕獲得名次; 到達(終點): *I finished the 100 meters in sixth place.* 我在100米賽跑中得第六名。

6 ►SURFACE 表面◄ [T] to give the surface of something, especially wood, a smooth appearance by painting, polishing, or covering it〔用油漆、拋光或貼面等方法〕使光滑; 給…最後加工, 潤飾: *The furniture had been attractively finished in a walnut veneer.* 家具上貼了一層胡桃木飾面板, 十分漂亮。

7 ►ALL SB'S STRENGTH ETC 某人全部的力氣等◄ **finish sb** to take away all of someone's strength, energy etc 耗盡某人的精力, 使某人精疲力竭: *That last five-mile ride up the hill really finished me.* 騎車上山坡的那最後五英里路真把我累壞了。

8 ►USE ALL OF STH 用完某物◄ *BrE* to use up the entire supply of something, especially food【英】用完〔尤指吃光食物〕: *The ice cream's finished, can you get some more?* 冰淇淋吃完了, 你能再買一點嗎?

9 put/add the finishing touches to add the final detail or details that make your work complete 做最後的潤飾; 做完最後的細節工作

finish off *phr v* **1** [T **finish** sth ↔ **off**] to use or eat all of something, so there is none left 用完; 吃完: *Who finished off the cake?* 誰把蛋糕吃光了? **2** [T **finish** sb/sth ↔ **off**] to kill a person or animal when they are already weak or wounded 結束…的生命, 殺掉〔虛弱或已受傷的人或動物〕 **3** [T **finish** sb **off**] to take away all of someone's strength, energy etc 耗盡〔某人的〕精力, 使〔某人〕精疲力竭, 累垮〔某人〕: *It had already been an exhausting week, and that last argument just finished me off.* 這本來已經是令人精疲力竭的一個星期, 而最後那場爭論可真把我累垮了。**4** [I,T **finish** sth ↔ **off**] to end a performance, event etc by doing one final thing 結束〔演出、事件等〕: *We finished off the evening by going out for a drink.* 我們以出去喝一杯結束了那個晚上的活動。

finish up *phr v* **1** [linking verb 連繫動詞] *especially BrE* to finally be in a particular place, condition etc at the end of a situation or series of events; end up (END²)【尤英】最後到達; 最後處於: *We finished up in Rome after a three week tour.* 我們最後抵達羅馬, 結束了三星期的旅程。| *I finished up completely broke, tired, and hungry.* 我最後完全身無分文, 又累又餓。**2** [T **finish** sth ↔ **up**] to eat or drink all the rest of something 吃完, 喝完 **3** to end an event, situation etc by doing one final thing〔以做某件事來〕結束; 完成

finish with sth/sb *phr v* [T] **1** *especially BrE* to no longer need to use something【尤英】不再需要用〔某物〕: **be finished with** *Are you finished with the scissors?* 你用完剪刀了嗎? **2** *BrE* to end a relationship with someone【英】與〔某人〕斷絕關係: *Michael's finally finished with Teresa after all these years.* 邁克爾經過這些年之後, 最後與特麗薩斷絕了關係。

This graph shows how common the different grammar patterns of the verb **finish** are. 本圖表所示為動詞 finish 構成的不同語法模式的使用頻率。

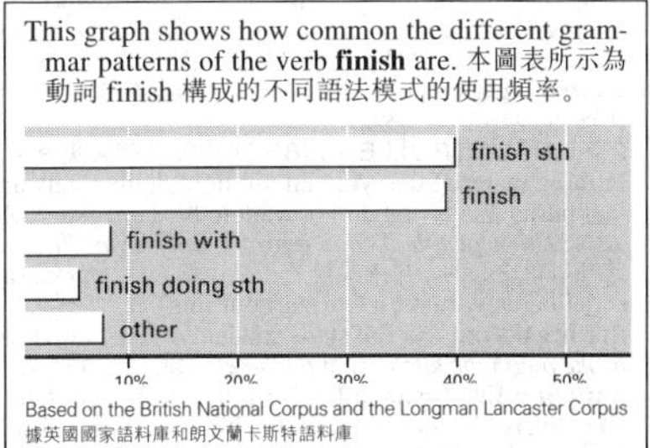

Based on the British National Corpus and the Longman Lancaster Corpus
據英國國家語料庫和朗文蘭卡斯特語料庫

finish² *n* **1** [C] the end or last part of something 終結, 最後部分: *I was watching the race but I didn't get to see the finish.* 我觀看了比賽, 但沒看到最後的結果。| 3

F

from start to finish (=from the beginning of something until the end) 自始至終, 從頭到尾 *The meeting was a disaster from start to finish.* 這次會議徹頭徹尾都一塌糊塗。| **a close finish** (=an end of a race where two competitors are very close to each other)〔兩名選手在比賽終結時〕不相上下, 成績接近 **2 fight to the finish** to fight until one side is completely defeated 戰鬥到底 **3** [C,U] the appearance of the surface of an object after it has been painted, polished etc 抛光; 光潔(度): *That table has a beautiful finish.* 那張桌子的表面光潔漂亮。

fin·ished /ˈfɪnɪʃt; ˈfɪnɪʃt/ *adj* **1** [only before noun 僅用於名詞前] fully and properly made or completed 完成了的, 結束了的: *It took a long time to do, but the finished product was worth it.* 幹那活花了很長時間, 但那件成品值得這樣去做。—opposite 反義詞 UNFINISHED **2** [not before noun 不用於名詞前] no longer able to do something successfully 沒有希望的, 完蛋了的: *If the bank refuses to give us money, we're finished!* 如果銀行拒絕借錢給我們, 我們就完蛋了!

finishing school /ˈ··· ·/ *n* [C] a private school where rich girls go to learn social skills 精修學校〔指富家女孩學習社交技能的一種私立學校〕

fi·nite /ˈfaɪnaɪt; ˈfaɪnaɪt/ *adj* [I] **1** having an end or a limit 有限的; 有限制的: *Earth's resources are finite.* 地球的資源是有限的。—opposite 反義詞 INFINITE **2** *technical* a finite verb form shows a particular tense or subject. 'Am', 'was', and 'are' are examples of finite verb forms, but 'being' and 'been' are non-finite【術語】限定的〔動詞的限定形式能顯示出具體的時態或主語, 例如 "am", "was"和"are", 但 "being" 和 "been" 是動詞的非限定形式〕

fink¹ /fɪŋk; fɪŋk/ *n* [C] *AmE informal old-fashioned*【美, 非正式, 過時】**1** someone who tells the police, a teacher, or a parent when someone else breaks a rule or a law 告發者, 告密者 **2** someone you dislike because they do cruel or unkind things 卑鄙的傢伙, 小人

fink² *v* [I] *AmE informal old-fashioned* to tell the police, a teacher, or a parent that someone has broken a rule or a law【美, 非正式, 過時】告發, 告密

fi·ord /ˈfjɔrd; ˈfiːɔːd/ *n* [C] another spelling of FJORD fjord 的另一種拼法

fir /fɝ; fɜː/ *n* [C] a tree with leaves like needles that it keeps in the winter 冷杉, 樅

1 1 **fire¹** /faɪr; faɪə/ *n*

1 ►BURNING 燃燒◄ [U] the flames, light and heat produced when something burns 火: *The warehouse was completely destroyed by fire.* 倉庫全部被火燒毀。| **be on fire** (=be burning) 在燃燒, 着火 *The house is on fire!* 房子着火了! | **catch fire/catch on fire** (=start to burn) 開始燃燒, 着火 *Mary knocked the candle over and the table cloth caught on fire.* 瑪麗打翻了蠟燭, 桌布開始燃燒起來。| **set sth on fire/set fire to sth** (=make something start burning) 使某物燃燒/放火燒某物 *Sparks from the fireplace could easily set the curtains on fire.* 壁爐裡爆出來的火花會很容易地使簾子燃燒起來。| *Rioters set fire to a whole row of stores.* 暴亂分子放火燒了一整排商店。

2 ►UNCONTROLLED FIRE 無法控制的火災◄ [C] burning material that you did not light deliberately and that burns things you do not want to be damaged 火災, 大火: *Thirty people died in a fire in downtown Chicago.* 芝加哥市中心的一場火災燒死了三十個人。| **start a fire** (=deliberately make a fire start burning) 放火, 縱火 | **a fire breaks out** (=a fire starts suddenly) 發生火災 *A fire broke out in the kitchens of the hotel.* 旅館的廚房失火。| **put out a fire** (=stop a fire burning) 滅火 *It took firemen several hours to put out the fire.* 消防隊員花了好幾個小時才把火撲滅。| **fight a fire** (=try to stop a fire burning) 撲滅火災 | **forest/brush fire** (=a very large fire in the forest or in an area of grass) 森林火災/灌木叢大火等

fire 火

Lisa lit the candle. 麗莎點燃蠟燭。

He set fire to the car. 他放火燒車。

The curtain caught fire. 窗簾着火了。

3 ►CONTROLLED FIRE 得到控制的火◄ [C] burning material that you have lit to provide heat, cook food etc〔為取暖、烹調等生的〕爐火, 灶火: *a cheerful fire crackling in the fireplace* 壁爐中噼啪燃燒的旺火 | **make/build/light a fire** (=start one burning) 生火, 點火 *You put up the tent and I'll start the fire.* 你們搭帳篷, 我來生火。| **put out the fire** (=stop it burning) 熄火 *It took fire fighters several hours to put out the fire.* 消防員花了數小時把火撲滅。

4 ►SHOOTING 射擊◄ [U] an act of shooting, especially of many guns at the same time 砲火, 火力, 射擊: *You will soon be facing enemy fire.* 你們很快會面臨敵人的砲火。| **be under fire** (=be shot at) 遭到射擊, 遭到砲火襲擊 *Our platoon was under fire from a machine gun position.* 我們排遭到來自一個機槍陣地的射擊。| **come under fire** (=be shot at) 遭到射擊, 遭到砲火襲擊 *The planes came under anti-aircraft fire.* 飛機遭到防空砲火射擊。| **open fire** (=start shooting) 開火, 開槍 *Troops opened fire on the rebels.* 部隊朝叛亂分子開槍。| **hold your fire** (=stop shooting) 停止射擊 | **be in the line of fire** (=be where you may be hit if someone shoots) 在火力線上; 首當其衝; 在射擊範圍之內

5 ►HEATING EQUIPMENT 供暖設備◄ [C] *BrE* a machine that produces heat to warm a room, using gas or electricity as power【英】煤氣取暖器; 電暖器: *Turn on the fire, I'm cold.* 打開電暖器吧, 我很冷。| *a gas fire* 煤氣取暖器

6 ►CRITICISM 批評◄ **under fire** being criticized very strongly for something you have done 受到抨擊, 遭到猛烈的批評: *The committee came under fire from fundamentalist church leaders.* 委員會遭到原教旨主義教會領導人的猛烈批評。

7 an open fire a fire that burns coal or wood in a FIREPLACE〔燒煤或木頭的〕壁爐裡的火

8 gas fired/coal fired etc *BrE* operated by burning gas, coal etc【英】燃氣的/燃煤的等: *a coal fired power station* 燃煤發電廠

9 light a fire under sb *AmE spoken* to do something that makes someone who is being lazy start doing their work【美口】激起〔偷懶的人〕的工作熱情

10 ►EMOTION 激情◄ [U] a very strong emotion that makes you want to think about nothing else 狂熱的情感, 激情: **[+of]** *the fire of religious fanaticism* 宗教狂熱的激情 | **be on fire with** *Harry was on fire with enthusiasm.* 哈里激情滿懷。

11 ►INJURY 傷痛◄ **be on fire** *literary* an injured part of your body that is on fire feels very painful【文】有劇痛感

12 go through fire (and water) (for sb) *old-fashioned* to do something very difficult and dangerous for someone【過時】(為某人) 赴湯蹈火

13 fire and brimstone a phrase describing Hell, used by some religious people〔一些宗教人士指的〕地獄 — see also 另見 CEASEFIRE, **add fuel to the fire/flames** (FUEL[1] (3)), **fight fire with fire** (FIGHT[1] (12)), **get on like a house on fire** (HOUSE[1] (8)), **hang fire** (HANG[1] (11)), **play with fire** (PLAY[1] (22)), **there's no smoke without fire** (SMOKE[1] (6))

USAGE NOTE 用法説明: FIRE

WORD CHOICE 詞語辨析: **light, set fire to, catch fire, put out, go out, extinguish**

If you want something to burn you usually **light** it. 使某物燃燒起來, 通常用 light: *She lit a cigarette/the stove/a match.* 她點燃香煙/爐火/火柴。

You can also **set fire to** things, especially things that are not supposed to be burnt. 放火燒不應該燒的東西, 通常用 set fire to: *Crowds rioted through the street, breaking windows and setting fire to cars.* 人羣在街道上鬧事, 打破窗子, 放火燒汽車。

When something begins to burn, especially by accident, it **catches fire**. 尤指某物出於意外開始燃燒時, 用 catch fire: *The blaze started when some oily rags caught fire.* 當一些碎油布着火時, 大火開始燒起來。

To stop a fire you **put** it **out**, or else it may **go out** on its own (NOT 不用 *go off*). 滅火用 put out, 火自動熄滅用 go out。

On official notices and instructions you may see **extinguish**. 正式通知和説明上有時用 extinguish: *Will passengers please extinguish all cigarettes.* 請乘客將香煙熄滅。

3 3 **fire²** *v*

1 ►SHOOT 射擊◄ [I,T] to shoot bullets from a gun, or to shoot small bombs 開槍, 開砲, 發射: *Roy took careful aim and fired.* 羅伊仔細瞄準, 然後開了槍。| **[+at/on/into]** *Police fired on the crowd.* 警察向人羣開槍。| **fire a gun/weapon etc** (=make it shoot) 開槍/發射武器 *The pistol has obviously been fired recently.* 很明顯, 這把手槍最近剛用過。| **fire a shot/bullet/round etc** *Who fired the bullet that killed the President?* 誰開了置總統於死地的那一槍? | **fire sth at sb** *The F16 fighter plane fired two missiles at the enemy aircraft.* F16 戰鬥機向敵機發射了兩枚導彈。

2 ►JOB 工作◄ *especially AmE* to force someone to leave their job【尤美】開除, 解雇; SACK² (1) *BrE*【英】: **fire sb for sth** *They fired her for stealing from the company.* 他們因她在公司偷竊而開除她。

3 ►EXCITE 激動◄ [T] also 又作 **fire up** to make someone feel very excited or interested in something; INSPIRE 使充滿熱情; 激發, 激勵: **be fired with ambition/longing etc** *After reading Steinbeck, Joel was fired with the ambition to become a writer.* 喬爾讀了斯坦貝克的小説後, 滿懷壯志想當作家。| **fire sb's imagination** *Jill's imagination was fired by Granny's stories.* 奶奶的故事激發了吉爾的想像力。

4 ►ENGINE 發動機◄ [I] if a vehicle's engine fires, the petrol is lit to make the engine work 點火; 引擎起動

5 ►CLAY 黏土◄ [T] to bake clay pots etc in a KILN〔在窯裡〕燒製: *fired earthenware* 燒製的陶器

6 fire questions (at) to ask someone a lot of questions quickly, often in order to criticize them (對...) 提出一連串問題

7 fire away also 又作 **fire ahead** *spoken* used when you are ready to answer questions【口】請説吧〔用於準備好回答問題時〕: *"I have a few questions." "Fire away."* "我有幾個問題。" "請提吧。"

8 not firing on all cylinders *informal* not thinking sensibly, or acting strangely【非正式】不明事理; 行為古怪

9 fired up *informal* excited and eager【非正式】情緒高昂的: *We've gotta get fired up for this game or we have no hope of winning!* 我們得鼓起勁頭來, 不然就沒有獲勝的希望了!

fire back sth *phr v* [T] to quickly and angrily answer a question or remark 快速而氣憤地回答[反駁]: *Claire fired back an angry response.* 克萊爾氣沖沖地作了反駁。

fire off *phr v* [T] **1** to shoot a weapon, often so that there are no bullets etc left 射光〔子彈〕: *Chuck reloaded and fired off both barrels.* 查克重新裝上子彈, 然後把兩根槍筒中的子彈都射了出去。**2** to quickly send an angry letter to someone 氣憤地匆忙寄發〔信件〕: *I fired off a furious letter to the editor.* 我向編輯發了一封信以示憤怒。

fire a·larm /ˈ· ·,·/ *n* [C] a piece of equipment that makes a loud noise to warn people of a fire in a building〔建築物裡的〕火警鐘, 火警報警器: *We were in the middle of an exam when the fire alarm went off.* 火警報警器響起的時候, 我們的考試正進行了一半。

fire·arm /ˈfaɪr,ɑrm; ˈfaɪərɑːm/ *n* [C] a small gun that can be carried 火器〔指可攜帶的步槍、手槍等小型槍支〕

fire·ball /ˈfaɪr,bɔl; ˈfaɪəbɔːl/ *n* [C] a large, hot fire, such as the very hot cloud of burning gases formed by an atomic explosion〔原子彈爆炸後氣體燃燒形成的〕火球

fire·bomb /ˈfaɪrbɑm; ˈfaɪəbɒm/ *n* [C] a bomb that makes a fire start burning when it explodes 燃燒彈

fire·brand /ˈfaɪr,brænd; ˈfaɪəbrænd/ *n* [C] **1** someone who tries to make people angry about a law, government etc so that they will try to change it 煽動暴亂者 **2** a large burning piece of wood 燃燒的大塊木頭

fire·break /ˈfaɪr,brek; ˈfaɪəbreɪk/ *n* [C] a narrow piece of land without any plants and trees on it, made to prevent fires from spreading 防火障, 防火線

fire·brick /ˈfaɪr,brɪk; ˈfaɪə,brɪk/ *n* [C] a brick that is not damaged by heat, used in chimneys 耐火磚

fire bri·gade /ˈ· ·,·/ *n* [C] **1** *BrE* an organization that works to prevent fires and stop them burning【英】消防隊; 消防署; FIRE DEPARTMENT *AmE*【美】**2** *AmE* a group of people who are not paid but who work together to stop fires burning【美】〔不領報酬的〕志願者消防隊

fire·bug /ˈfaɪr,bʌg; ˈfaɪəbʌg/ *n* [C] *informal* someone who deliberately starts fires to destroy property; arsonist (ARSON)【非正式】縱火者, 放火的人

fire chief /ˈ· ,·/ *n* [C] someone who is responsible for all the organizations that stop fires burning in a city or area 消防署署長; 消防隊隊長

fire·crack·er /ˈfaɪr,krækɚ; ˈfaɪə,krækə/ *n* [C] a small FIREWORK that explodes loudly 鞭炮, 爆竹

fire de·part·ment /ˈ· ·,··/ *n* [C] *AmE* the organization that works to prevent fires and stop them burning【美】消防署; 消防隊; FIRE SERVICE, FIRE BRIGADE *BrE*【英】

fire·dog /ˈfaɪr,dɔg; ˈfaɪədɒg/ *n* [C] *BrE* one of a pair of iron supports for burning logs in a FIREPLACE【英】〔壁爐裡的〕薪架

fire door /ˈ· ,·/ *n* [C] a heavy door in a building that is kept closed to help to prevent a fire from spreading 防火安全門

fire drill /ˈ· ·/ *n* [C,U] the act of practising what people must do to leave a burning building safely 消防演習

fire-eat·er /ˈ· ,··/ *n* [C] **1** an entertainer who puts burn-

F

ing sticks into his mouth 吞火魔術師 **2** *informal* someone who gets angry and quarrels very easily【非正式】動輒發火吵架的人, 脾氣暴躁的人

fire en·gine /ˈ· ,··/ *n* [C] a special large vehicle that carries people and equipment to stop fires burning, especially the equipment that shoots water at a fire 消防車, 救火車 —compare 比較 FIRE TRUCK *AmE*【美】

fire es·cape /ˈ· ·,·/ *n* [C] metal stairs or a metal LADDER on the outside of a tall building, that people can use to escape if there is a fire〔高樓的〕太平梯, 安全出口

fire ex·tin·guish·er /ˈ· ·,···/ *n* [C] a metal container with water or chemicals in it, used for stopping small fires 滅火器

fire extinguisher 滅火器

fire fight /ˈ· ·/ *n* [C] a short gun battle, involving soldiers or the police 交火, 砲戰

fire fight·er /ˈ· ,··/ *n* [C] someone who stops fires burning, either as their job or as a special helper during forest fires or wars 消防人員

fire fight·ing /ˈ· ,··/ *n* [U] **1** the work of preventing fires and stopping them burning 消防工作 **2** the actions that are taken to find out what has caused a sudden problem in an organization, machine etc, and to correct it 發現和糾正〔組織、機器等中的〕事故隱患的措施

fire·fly /ˈfaɪr,flaɪ; ˈfaɪəflaɪ/ *n plural* **fireflies** [C] an insect with a tail that shines in the dark; LIGHTNING BUG 螢火蟲

fire·guard /ˈfaɪr,gɑrd; ˈfaɪəgɑːd/ *n* [C] a large frame made of woven wire that is put in front of a FIREPLACE to protect people〔放在壁爐前保護人的〕爐欄, 擋火隔網; FIRESCREEN *AmE*【美】

fire·house /ˈfaɪr,haʊs; ˈfaɪəhaʊs/ *n* [C] *AmE* a small FIRE STATION, especially in a small town【美】〔尤指小城鎮的〕消防站

fire hy·drant /ˈ· ,··/ *n* [C] a water pipe in a street used to get water for stopping fires burning〔街道上的〕消防栓, 消防龍頭; FIREPLUG *AmE*【美】

fire i·rons /ˈ· ··/ *n* [plural] the metal tools used for looking after a fire in a FIREPLACE 火爐用具

fire·light /ˈfaɪr,laɪt; ˈfaɪəlaɪt/ *n* [U] the light produced by a small fire〔小火發出的〕火光: *The room glowed cozy and warm in the firelight.* 房間被爐火光照得紅通通的, 既舒適又暖和。

fire·light·er /ˈfaɪr,laɪtə; ˈfaɪə,laɪtə/ *n* [C] *BrE* a piece of a substance that burns easily and helps to light a coal fire【英】〔生煤火用的〕引火物

fire·man /ˈfaɪrmən; ˈfaɪəmən/ *n* [C] **1** a man whose job is to stop fires burning; FIREFIGHTER 消防人員 **2** someone who looks after the fire in a steam railway engine or a FURNACE〔負責火車的蒸汽爐或熔爐的〕司爐工

fire·place /ˈfaɪr,ples; ˈfaɪəpleɪs/ *n* [C] the opening in the wall of a room, used for a wood or coal fire to heat the room 壁爐

fire·plug /ˈfaɪr,plʌg; ˈfaɪəplʌg/ *n* [C] *AmE* a FIRE HYDRANT【美】消防栓, 消防龍頭

fire·pow·er /ˈfaɪr,paʊə; ˈfaɪə,paʊə/ *n* [U] *technical* the number of weapons that an army, military vehicle etc has available【術語】〔軍隊、軍用車輛等的〕火力

fire·proof /ˈfaɪr,pruf; ˈfaɪəpruːf/ *adj* a building, piece of cloth etc that is fireproof cannot be badly damaged by flames 防火的, 耐火的 —**fireproof** *v* [T]

fire-rais·ing /ˈ· ,··/ *n* [U] *BrE* the crime of starting a fire deliberately; ARSON【英】縱火(罪) —**fire-raiser** *n* [C]

fire sale /ˈ· ·/ *n* [C] a sale of goods that have been slightly damaged by a fire, or of goods that cannot be stored because of a fire 火災受損物品的拍賣

fire·screen /ˈfaɪr,skrin; ˈfaɪəskriːn/ *n* [C] *AmE* a large frame made of woven wire that is put in front of a FIREPLACE to protect people【美】〔壁爐前保護人的〕爐欄, 擋火隔網; FIREGUARD *BrE*【英】

fire ser·vice /ˈ· ,··/ *n* [singular] *BrE* the organization that works to prevent fires and stop them burning【英】消防署; 消防隊; FIRE DEPARTMENT *AmE*【美】

fire·side /ˈfaɪr,saɪd; ˈfaɪəsaɪd/ *n* [C usually singular 一般用單數] the area close to or around a small fire, especially in a home〔尤指家裡的〕爐邊: *a cat dozing in the broken armchair by the fireside* 一隻躺在爐邊破椅子裡打瞌睡的貓

fire sta·tion /ˈ· ,··/ *n* [C] a building where the equipment used to stop fires burning is kept, and where FIRE FIGHTERS stay until they are needed 消防站

fire·storm /ˈfaɪr,stɔrm; ˈfaɪəstɔːm/ *n* [C] a very large fire, usually started by bombs, that is kept burning by the high winds that it causes〔通常由炸彈等引起的〕風暴性大火

fire·trap /ˈfaɪr,træp; ˈfaɪətræp/ *n* [C] a building that would be very dangerous if a fire started there 無消防設施的建築物; 易引起火災的房子

fire truck /ˈ· ·/ *n* [C] *AmE* a special vehicle that carries people and special equipment to stop fires burning【美】救火車, 消防車 —compare 比較 FIRE ENGINE

fire·watch·er /ˈfaɪr,wɑtʃə; ˈfaɪəwɒtʃə/ *n* [C] *BrE* someone who watched for FIRE BOMBS in British cities during the Second World War【英】〔第二次世界大戰期間英國城市裡的〕火災警戒員

fire·wat·er /ˈfaɪr,wɔtə; ˈfaɪə,wɔːtə/ *n* [U] strong alcoholic drink, such as WHISKY 烈酒〈如威士忌〉

fire·wood /ˈfaɪr,wʊd; ˈfaɪəwʊd/ *n* [C] wood cut for burning on fires 柴火, 木柴

fire·work /ˈfaɪr,wɝk; ˈfaɪəwɜːk/ *n* [C usually plural 一般用複數] **1** a small container filled with powder that burns or explodes to produce coloured lights, noise, and smoke 煙火, 煙花, 焰火: *a New Year's Eve fireworks display* 除夕夜的煙火表演 **2 there will be fireworks** *spoken* used to say that someone will be angry【口】有人會發火的; 有人將會大怒的: *There'll be fireworks if I get home late again.* 如果我再遲回家, 有人會發火的。

firing line /ˈ·· ·/ *n* **be in the firing line** to be in a position or situation in which you can be attacked or blamed for something, often unfairly 首當其衝地受到攻擊[責備]

firing squad /ˈ·· ,·/ *n* [C] a group of soldiers with the duty of killing someone by shooting them as a punishment〔執行槍決的〕行刑隊

firm[1] /fɝm; fɜːm/ *n* [C] a business or company, especially a small one〔尤指較小的〕公司, 商行, 事務所: **electronics/advertising/law etc firm** *She works for an electronics firm.* 她在一家電子公司工作。| **a firm of accountants/solicitors etc** *Kevin is with a firm of accountants in Birmingham.* 凱文在伯明翰的一家會計師事務所工作。

firm[2] *adj*

1 ►HARD 硬的◄ not completely hard, but not soft and not easy to bend into a different shape 堅實的: *The sofa cushions are fairly firm.* 沙發的座墊相當硬。| *a firm green apple* 堅實的青蘋果

2 ►NOT LIKELY TO MOVE 不易移動的◄ strong or fixed in position, and not likely to move or break 牢固的, 穩固的: *The ladder felt strong and firm.* 梯子感覺很結實穩固。

3 ►NOT LIKELY TO CHANGE 不易變化的◄ firm decisions, beliefs etc are not likely to change, because you are sure about them〔決定、信念等〕堅定的, 不變的: *The client hasn't reached a firm decision on the matter yet.* 客戶對這件事還沒有做出肯定的決定。

4 ►STRONG AND IN CONTROL 堅決的◄ behaving or speaking in a way that is strong and that shows you are not likely to change your answer, belief etc 強有力的, 堅決的: *Cal replied with a polite but firm 'no'.* 卡爾用禮貌又堅決的"不"字作答。| *The country needs firm*

leadership. 國家需要強有力的領導。| **be firm with sb** *You need to be firm with her, or she'll try to take control.* 你需要對她強硬些，不然她會想控制一切。

5 a firm grip/hold/grasp if you have something in a firm hold you are holding it tightly and strongly 緊握，緊緊抓住，牢牢握住：*He took a firm grip of my arm and marched me towards the door.* 他緊緊抓着我的手臂，拉我往門口走去。| **a firm handshake** (=in which you hold the other person's hand strongly or tightly) 緊緊的握手

6 take a firm stand/line to state your opinion clearly and not be persuaded to change it 採取堅定立場；堅定不移地表態

7 stand/hold firm to not change your actions or opinions 堅持下去，堅定不移：*Gothard is urging Christians to stand firm against divorce.* 戈瑟德強烈要求基督教徒堅定不移地反對離婚。

8 ►MONEY 貨幣◄ not falling in value〔價格〕堅挺的：*The pound was still firm against the dollar this morning.* 今天上午英鎊對美元的匯價仍然很堅挺。—see also 另見 FIRM OFFER —**firmly** *adv* —**firmness** *n* [U]

firm³ *v* [T] to press down on soil to make it harder or more solid 使變硬；使堅固 3

firm sth ↔ up *phr v* [T] **1** to make arrangements, ideas etc more definite and exact 把〔安排、想法等〕確定下來：*We're hoping to firm up the deal later this month.* 我們希望能在這個月晚些時候把這筆買賣確定下來。**2** to make a part of your body have more muscle and less fat by exercising〔通過鍛鍊〕使〔身體〕結實

fir·ma·ment /ˈfɝməmənt; ˈfɜːməmənt/ *n* [singular] *literary* the sky or heaven【文】天空，蒼穹

firm of·fer /ˌ· ˈ··/ *n* [C] a price suggested for a service or for goods that becomes legally fixed if it is accepted〔價格、報價〕實盤，固定報價

firm·ware /ˈfɝmˌwɛr; ˈfɜːmweə/ *n* [U] *technical* instructions to computers that are stored on chips (CHIP¹ (4a)) so that they can be done much faster, and cannot be changed or lost【術語】〔電腦的〕固件 —compare 比較 HARDWARE, SOFTWARE

1 1

first /fɝst; fɜːst/ *number*

① BEFORE 在…前
② THE FIRST TIME STH HAPPENS OR IS DONE 某事首次發生或完成的時間
③ BEGINNING 最初，開始
④ MAIN/IMPORTANT 主要的/重要的
⑤ THE FIRST REASON/FACT ETC 首要原因/事實等
⑥ BEST 最好的
⑦ MORNING 早上，上午
⑧ NOT KNOW 不知道
⑨ OTHER MEANINGS 其他意思

① BEFORE 在…前

1 before anything or anyone else 最先，最早：*She reached the top of the hill first.* 她最先到達山頂。| *It's mine, I saw it first.* 這是我的，我先看到的。—see 見 FIRSTLY (USAGE)

2 the first someone or something that is before other people or things 第一個人[東西]；第一件事：**be (the) first to do sth** *My sister said I'd be first to get married, but she was wrong.* 妹妹說我會最先結婚，可她說錯了。| **come (in) first** (=win a race)〔比賽〕得第一名 *Lewis came first in the 100m race.* 劉易斯在100米比賽中得第一名。

3 before doing anything else, or before anything else happens 首先：*I always read the funnies first.* 我總是先看滑稽連環漫畫。| *First I have to clean up the house, then I'll come shopping with you.* 我得先打掃房子，然後和你去購物。| **first of all** *First of all we'd better make sure we have everything we need.* 首先我們最好確實弄清我們所需要的東西都有了。

4 make the first move to be the person who does something when everyone is nervous and uncomfortable about starting to do something〔當別人都緊張躊躇時〕首先採取行動，率先挺身而出：*Barney really likes Hannah, but he's too shy to make the first move.* 巴尼確實喜歡漢娜，但他太靦腆不敢採取主動。

5 do/say sth in the first place *spoken* used to say that someone said or did something before【口】起初就做/說某事：*I don't really want to go...." "Oh Well, why didn't you say so in the first place?"* "我確實不想去…" "嗬，那你為甚麼不早說呢？"

6 in the first instance *especially BrE* before you do anything else【尤英】首先，最初：*It is important in the first instance to be sure that there is a demand for the product you wish to sell.* 重要的是，要先確切地弄清楚你想出售的產品是有需求的。

② THE FIRST TIME STH HAPPENS OR IS DONE 某事首次發生或完成的時間

7 happening or done before other events or actions of the same kind 首次的，最早的，第一次的：*He made his first appearance on the stage in the 1950s.* 他在20世紀50年代首次登台演出。| *My first reaction was that the story couldn't possibly be true.* 我最初的反應是，這個說法不可能是真的。| **the first time** *The first time I flew in a plane I was really nervous.* 我第一次乘飛機時確實很緊張。

8 done for the first time 首次：*The book was first published in Australia last year.* 這本書去年在澳大利亞首次出版。

9 the first someone who does something that has never been done or happened before 第一個人：*No one had ever settled in the valley before; he was the first.* 以前沒有人在這個山谷住過，他是第一個。| **be the first to do sth** *She was the first to see the importance of the nineteenth century writers in this context.* 她是第一個看到19世紀作家在這方面的重要性的。

10 a first something that has never been done or happened before 先例，前所未有的事情：*Roger Bannister's four-minute mile was a notable first in the history of athletics.* 羅傑·班尼斯特四分鐘跑完一英里，這是田徑運動史上的傑出先例。

11 at first glance/sight the first time that you see something, before you notice much detail 乍一看，最初看到時：*At first glance the twins look identical.* 這對雙胞胎乍一看完全一樣。

12 first come, first served used to say that people who arrive, ask etc before other people, will be dealt with or given something before them 先到先得，先來先接待[供應]

③ BEGINNING 最初，開始

13 the first the people or things at the beginning of a row, line, series, period of time etc〔一行、一列、一系

列、一段時間等中〕第一個[批、件]: *the first Monday of every month* 每月的第一個星期一 | *for the first six months of my time in Nepal* 我在尼泊爾的頭六個月 | *the first chapter of the book* 本書的第一章

14 at the beginning of a situation or activity 最初時: *When we were first married, we lived in Toronto.* 我們剛結婚時住在多倫多。| *We first became friends when we were teenagers.* 我們早在十幾歲的時候就成了朋友。

15 at first in the beginning 開始時, 起先, 起初: *Alistair felt tired at first, but soon got used to the long working hours.* 阿利斯泰爾起先感到累, 但很快就適應了長時間的工作。—compare 比較 **at last** (LAST[3] (2)) —see 見 FIRSTLY (USAGE)

16 from the (very) first from the beginning 從一開始: *The relationship was doomed to failure from the first.* 這關係從一開始就注定是要失敗的。

④ **MAIN/IMPORTANT 主要的/重要的**

17 being the most important or main thing 首要的, 主要的: *The first priority is to maintain the standard of work.* 最優先的考慮是保持工作的水準。

18 first things first used to tell someone to deal with things in order of importance 要緊的事情應當先做; 凡事應有輕重緩急

19 put sth first to make something the most important thing 把某事擺在最重要的位置: *Rob seems to put money first, and happiness second in his life.* 羅布似乎把金錢放在人生的首位, 而把幸福放在第二位。

20 come first to be the most important thing to someone 成為〔某人〕最重要的東西: **[+with]** *Alma's family will always come first with her.* 在阿爾瑪的心中, 家庭總是放在第一位。

21 first and foremost as the main reason for or purpose of something 首要的: *The aim of the exercise was first and foremost to give confidence to the students.* 這個練習的目的最主要是給學生一點信心。

22 first among equals someone who leads a group of people but is not considered to be more important than them 一羣平等的人中的領導者

⑤ **THE FIRST REASON/FACT ETC 首要原因/事實等**

23 used to give an important fact or reason that will be followed by others 首先, 第一〔用於表達最重要的事實或原因〕: *Well, first, the building is too small, and second, it isn't in a very good location.* 嗯, 首先, 這座樓太小; 其次, 所處的位置不是很好。

24 first of all *spoken* used to introduce the first thing that you are going to talk about【口】首先, 第一〔用於引入要談論的第一件事〕: *First of all I'd like to welcome you to the meeting.* 首先, 我歡迎各位參加這次會議。

25 first off *spoken* used to introduce a fact, reason, or statement that will be followed by others, especially when you are annoyed with someone【口】首先〔尤用於表示對某人生氣時〕: *First off, you should have told me where you were going.* 首先, 你本該先告訴我你要去哪兒。

26 in the first place *spoken* used to give a fact or reason that proves what you are saying in an argument【口】首先, 第一〔用於舉出能證明自己論點的事實或理由〕: *Well, in the first place, Quinn would never say any such thing.* 嗯, 首先, 奎因是絕對不會說這種話的。—see 見 FIRSTLY (USAGE)

⑥ **BEST 最好的**

27 first choice the thing or person you like best 最好的選擇: *Frances was our first choice as a name for the baby.* "弗朗西絲"是我們給嬰兒起名字時的最佳選擇。

28 come first/win first prize to be the best in a competition 名列第一/獲一等獎: *My jam won first prize at the county fair.* 我的果醬在縣集市上獲一等獎。

29 a first the highest level of university degree you can get in Britain〔英國大學的〕一級榮譽學位: **get a first (in)** *Helen got a first in Law.* 海倫獲得法學的一級榮譽學位。

30 of the first water *old-fashioned* of the highest quality【過時】第一流的, 上等的, 質量最高的: *a jewel of the first water* 質量一流的寶石

⑦ **MORNING 早上, 上午**

31 first thing as soon as you get up in the morning, or as soon as you start work 早晨一醒來; 一上班: *The boss was here first thing, but he's gone to Newcastle now.* 老闆一上班就來這裡, 但現在他去了紐卡斯爾。| *I'll phone him first thing Monday.* 我星期一一起牀就打電話給他。

32 at first light very early in the morning 一大早; 天一亮: *They left at first light and were in the mountains by nightfall.* 他們一大早就啟程, 傍晚時分到了山裡。

⑧ **NOT KNOW 不知道**

33 not have the first idea about/not know the first thing about to not know anything about a subject, or not know how to do something 對…一竅不通/一無所知: *I wouldn't have the first idea about what to do in an emergency.* 發生緊急情況時該怎麼做, 我一無所知。| *I don't know the first thing about cars.* 我對汽車一竅不通。

34 the first I (have) heard/I knew etc of it *spoken* used when you have just found out about something that other people already know, and are slightly annoyed about it【口】我頭一次聽到/我頭一次知道〔表示不滿〕: *Andrew's been promoted? That's the first I've heard about it.* 安德魯升職了? 這事我頭一次聽到。

⑨ **OTHER MEANINGS 其他意思**

35 (at) first hand if you hear or experience something at first hand, you hear etc it directly, not through other people 第一手的, 直接的: *The school had to deal first hand with the social problems of the area.* 學校得直接應付該地區的社會問題。

36 first a) first gear; the lowest GEAR[1] (1) in a car, bicycle, or other vehicle, that you use to begin moving〔汽車、腳踏車或其他交通工具的〕第一擋, 頭擋, 最低擋: **be in first** *Put the car in first when you park on a hill.* 車停在坡道上時要調到第一擋。**b)** *AmE* FIRST BASE【美】一壘; 一壘手的防衛位置

37 I'd die/kill myself etc first *spoken* used to emphasize how strongly you do not want to do something【口】我就先死/自殺; 我寧可死也不…: *I'll never take him back. I'd die first!* 我寧可死也不會讓他回來!

first aid /ˌ· ˈ·/ *n* [U] simple medical treatment that is given as soon as possible to someone who is injured or who suddenly becomes ill 急救: **give first aid** *Being given first aid at the scene of the accident probably saved his life.* 他在事故現場得到了急救, 這可能救了他的命。

first aid·er /ˌ· ˈ··/ *n* [C] *BrE* someone who is trained to give first aid【英】急救員

first aid kit /ˌ· ˈ· ˌ·/ *n* [C] a special box containing BANDAGES and medicines to treat people who are injured or become ill suddenly 急救箱

first base /ˌ· ˈ·/ *n* [C] **1 a)** the first of the four places in a game of BASEBALL (1) that a player must touch before gaining a point〔棒球賽中的〕一壘 **b)** the position of a defending player near this place〔棒球賽中的〕一壘手的防衛位置: *He plays first base for the Red Sox.* 他在紅襪隊打一壘。**2** *AmE informal* the first stage of success in an attempt to achieve something【美, 非正式】成功的第一步, 初步成功: **get to/reach first base** 獲得初步

成功: *You've gotten to first base if you've landed an interview.* 如果你能得到面試機會, 那你就獲得了初步的成功。**3 get to first base** *AmE spoken* an expression meaning to kiss or hug someone in a sexual way, used especially by young men【美口】〔求愛方面〕跨出第一步〔尤為青年男子所使用〕

first·born /ˈfɝstˌbɔrn; ˈfɜːstbɔːn/ *n* [singular] *literary* your first child【文】頭胎的孩子 —**firstborn** *adj*: *her firstborn son* 她的頭一個兒子

first class /ˌ· ˈ·◂/ *n* **1** [U] the best and most expensive seats or rooms in a train, boat etc〔火車、船等的〕頭等艙位[車廂]: *We prefer to travel in first class.* 我們喜歡乘坐頭等艙[車廂]旅行。—compare 比較 BUSINESS CLASS, CABIN CLASS, ECONOMY CLASS, TOURIST CLASS **2** [U] **a)** a class of mail in Britain, used for letters and parcels, that is quicker and more expensive than second class mail〔英國的優先投遞的〕第一類郵件〔郵費比第二類郵件昂貴〕—compare 比較 SECOND CLASS (1) **b)** the class of mail used in the US for ordinary business and personal letters〔美國遞送普通商業和私人信函的〕第一類郵件; 普通平郵 **3** [C] the highest standard for a degree from a British university〔英國大學的〕學位考試第一等（成績）

first-class *adj* **1** of very good quality and much better than other things of the same type 第一流的, 優等的: *This is a first-class wine.* 這是一種第一流的葡萄酒。**2** using the first class of mail 優先投遞的, 第一類的; 平郵的 **3** using the first class of seats and rooms in a plane, train etc〔飛機艙位或火車車廂〕頭等的: *a first-class passenger* 頭等艙旅客 —**first class** *adv*: *If I send the letter first class it should arrive tomorrow.* 如果我把信作為第一類郵件投寄, 明天就會寄到。

first cous·in /ˌ· ˈ··/ *n* [C] a child of your AUNT or UNCLE; COUSIN (1) 堂兄弟[姐妹], 表兄弟[姐妹]

first-de·gree /ˌ· ·ˈ·◂/ *adj* [always before noun 總用於名詞前] **1 first-degree murder** *AmE* murder of the most serious type, in which someone deliberately kills someone else【美】一級謀殺罪; 最嚴重的兇殺 —compare 比較 MANSLAUGHTER **2 first-degree burn** a burn that is not very serious 一度燒傷, 第一度灼傷

first e·di·tion /ˌ· ·ˈ··/ *n* [C] one of the copies of a book that was produced the first time the book was printed〔書的〕第一版, 初版

first-ev·er /ˌ· ˈ··◂/ *adj* [always before noun 總用於名詞前] happening for the first time 第一次的: *It was the day that Michael Jackson gave his first-ever televised interview.* 就是在這一天, 米高積遜生平第一次接受了電視直播採訪。

first fam·i·ly /ˌ· ˈ···/ *n* [C usually singular 一般用單數] the family of the President of the US 第一家庭〔指美國總統的家庭〕

first floor /ˌ· ˈ·◂/ *n* [C] **1** *BrE* the floor of a building just above the one at the bottom level【英】二樓〔指底層上面的樓層〕**2** *AmE* the floor of a building at the bottom level【美】一樓, 底層 —compare 比較 GROUND FLOOR (1) *BrE*【英】—see 見 FLOOR[1] (USAGE)

first-foot·ing /ˌ· ˈ··/ *n* [U] *ScotE* the custom in Scotland of visiting people as soon as the New Year has begun【蘇格蘭】第一個登門拜年（的習俗）—**first-footer** *n* [C]

first fruits /ˌ· ˈ·/ *n* [plural] the first good result of something 最初成果: *One of the first fruits of Mao's visit to Moscow was a new treaty with the Russians.* 毛到莫斯科訪問的一項最初成果是與俄國人簽訂了一項新條約。

first gear /ˌ· ˈ·/ *n* [C] the lowest GEAR[1] (1) in a car or other motor vehicle, used when starting to move or when going up or down a very steep hill〔汽車或其他機動車輛的〕第一擋, 頭擋, 最低擋

first gen·e·ra·tion /ˌ· ··ˈ··◂/ *n* [singular] **1** the children of people who have moved to live in a new country 移民的第一代孩子 **2** the first type of a machine to be developed 第一代機器: *The first generation of computers were huge and slow.* 第一代電腦體積龐大, 而且速度慢。**3** the first people to do something 第一批人: *the first generation of environmentalists* 第一代環境保護主義者 —**first-generation** *adj*

first half /ˌ· ˈ·/ *n* [C] the first of two equal periods of time that a sports match is divided into〔體育比賽的〕上半場, 上半時

first-hand /ˌ· ˈ·◂/ *adj* **first-hand experience/knowledge/account** experience etc that has been learned or gained by doing something yourself 親身經驗/直接得來的知識/第一手報道: *journalists with first-hand experience of working in war zones* 具有戰地實際工作經驗的新聞記者 —compare 比較 SECOND-HAND —see also 另見 **(at) first hand** (FIRST[1] (35))

first la·dy /ˌ· ˈ··/ *n* [C usually singular 一般用單數] the wife of the President of the US, or of the GOVERNOR of a US state〔美國〕第一夫人, 總統夫人; 州長夫人

first lan·guage /ˌ· ˈ··/ *n* [C] the language that you first learn as a child 母語, 第一語言 —compare 比較 SECOND LANGUAGE

first lieu·ten·ant /ˌ· ·ˈ··◂/ *n* [C] a middle rank in the US army, Marines, or Air Force, or someone who has this rank〔美國陸軍、海軍陸戰隊或空軍的〕中尉 —see table on page C6 參見 C6 頁附錄

first·ly /ˈfɝstlɪ; ˈfɜːstli/ *adv* [sentence adverb 句子副詞] [S2] used to say that the fact or reason that you are going to mention is the first one and will be followed by others 第一, 首先: *Firstly, I would like to thank everyone who has contributed to this success.* 首先, 我要感謝對這次成功作出貢獻的每一個人。

USAGE NOTE 用法說明: FIRSTLY

WORD CHOICE 詞語辨析: **firstly, first (of all), in the first place, to start/begin with, at first, in the beginning**

Firstly/first (of all)/in the first place/to start with/to begin with are often used to introduce a series of reasons, ideas, remarks etc. firstly/first (of all)/in the first place/to start with/to begin with 常用於列舉一系列原因、看法、意見等: *There are three reasons why I don't like him: first(ly)/to start with he's rude, second(ly) he's a liar, and third(ly)/finally he owes me money.* 我不喜歡他有三個原因: 首先/第一, 他粗暴無禮; 第二, 他撒謊; 第三/最末, 他欠我錢不還。

You use **first (of all)** (NOT 不用 *firstly*) to introduce a series of actions, often in order of time. 人們常用first (of all)〔而不是 firstly〕並且往往根據時間順序依次列出一系列的動作: *First of all I get dressed, next I bring in the paper, then I fix breakfast.* 首先, 我穿上衣服, 接着把報紙拿進來, 然後做早餐。

At first can only be used for a period of time, often when you are comparing it with a later period. **To start/begin with** and **in the beginning** can be used in this way too. at first 只可用於表示一段時間, 常與稍後的一段時間作比較, to start/begin with和in the beginning 也可以這樣用: *You'll find it difficult at first/to begin with, but later/soon it'll get easier.* 起初/開始你會覺得很難, 但後來/很快就會感到容易起來。

first mate /ˌ· ˈ·/ *n* [C] the officer on a non-military ship who has the rank just below captain〔非軍用船隻上級別僅次於船長的〕大副

first name /ˈ· ·/ *n* [C] **1** the name or names that come before your family name 名字: *Her first name's Helen, but I don't know her surname.* 她的名字叫海倫, 但我不知道她姓甚麼。**2 be on first name terms (with sb)** *BrE*【英】, **be on a first name basis** *AmE*【美】to know someone well enough to call them by their first name〔因熟悉某人而〕直呼其名, 以名相稱 —compare 比較 SURNAME

first night /ˌ· ˈ·/ *n* [C] the evening when the first public

F

performance of a show, play etc is given〔演出、戲劇等的〕首演[首映]之夜

first of·fend·er /,· '··/ *n* [C] someone who is guilty of breaking the law for the first time 初次犯法者, 初犯

first of·fi·cer /,· '···◂/ *n* [C] FIRST MATE 大副

first per·son /,· '··◂/ *n* [singular] **1** *technical* a form of a verb or a pronoun that is used to show that you are the speaker. For example, 'I', 'me', 'we', and 'us' are first person pronouns, and 'I am' is the first person singular of the verb'to be'.【術語】第一人稱〈例如, I, me, we 和 us 都是第一人稱代詞, I am 是動詞 to be 的第一人稱單數形式〉 **2** a way of telling a story in which the writer or speaker tells it as though he were involved in the story〔敘述中的〕第一人稱: *a first person narrative* 第一人稱敘述 —compare 比較 SECOND PERSON, THIRD PERSON

first-rate /,· '·◂/ *adj* of the very best quality 第一流的, 極好的: *He's a first-rate surgeon.* 他是第一流的外科醫生。

first re·fus·al /,· '··/ *n* **have/give sb first refusal on sth** *BrE* to let someone decide whether to buy something before you offer to sell it to other people【英】讓某人對某物有優先購買權: *I'll let you have first refusal on the car.* 我會讓你優先決定是否買這輛車。

first strike /,· '·◂/ *n* [C] an attack made on your enemy before they attack you 先發制人的打擊

first-string /,· '·◂/ *adj* [only before noun 僅用於名詞前] a first-string player in a team plays when the game begins because they are the most skilled〔運動員〕主力的; 首發陣容的, 先上場的 —compare 比較 SECOND-STRING

first-time buy·er /,· · '··/ *n* [C] someone who is buying a house or an apartment for the first time〔房子或公寓的〕首次購買者; 首次置業者

First World /,· '·◂/ *n* [singular] the rich industrial countries of the world 第一世界〔指世界上富有的工業國家〕—compare 比較 THIRD WORLD —**first world** *adj* [always before noun 總用於名詞前]

First World War /,· · '·/ *n* [singular] the big war fought in Europe between 1914 and 1918 第一次世界大戰

firth /fɝθ; fɜːθ/ *n* [C] a narrow area of sea between two areas of land, or the place where a river flows into the sea, especially in Scotland〔尤指蘇格蘭的狹長的〕港灣, 河口灣: *the Firth of Forth* 福思灣

fis·cal¹ /ˈfɪskl; ˈfɪskəl/ *adj formal* connected with money, taxes, debts, etc owned and managed by the government【正式】(政府) 財政的, 公款的: *a fiscal crisis* 財政危機 —**fiscally** *adv*

fiscal² *n* [C] *informal* PROCURATOR FISCAL【非正式】(地方) 檢察官

fiscal year /,·· '·/ *n* [C] the period of a year which the government uses to calculate how much tax a person or business must pay 財政年度, 會計年度, 稅年 —compare 比較 FINANCIAL YEAR

fish 魚

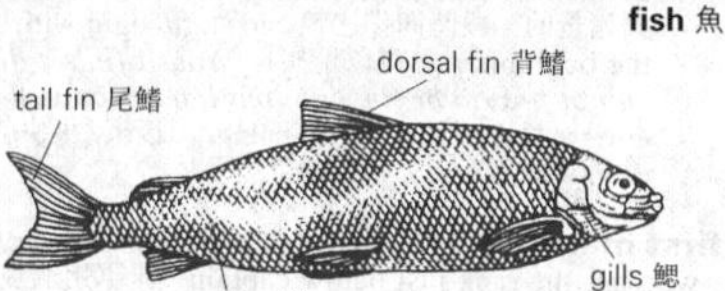

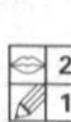

fish¹ /fɪʃ; fɪʃ/ *n plural* **fish** or **fishes** [C] **1** an animal that lives in water, and uses its FINS (1) and tail to swim 魚: *The lake is well stocked with fish.* 這個湖裡養了許多魚。| **catch a fish** *Ronny caught three huge fish this afternoon.* 羅尼今天下午捕到三條大魚。**2** [U] the flesh of a fish used as food 魚肉: *White wine is traditionally drunk with fish.* 在吃魚的時候照例是喝白葡萄酒的。**3 like a fish out of water** feeling uncomfortable because you are in an unfamiliar place or situation 如離水之魚, 感到生疏[不自在]: *I felt like a fish out of water in my new school.* 我在新學校裡感到很不適應。**4 there are plenty more fish in the sea** used to tell someone whose relationship has ended that there are other people they can have a relationship with 海裡的魚多得很〔用於告訴某人不必為結束同他人的某種關係而煩惱, 還可以同許多其他的人建立同樣的關係〕 **5 neither fish nor fowl** neither one thing nor another 不倫不類, 非驢非馬 **6 have other/bigger fish to fry** *informal* to have other things to do, especially more important things【非正式】另有更重要的事要做: *I can't deal with this now, I've got other fish to fry!* 我現在不能處理這件事, 我另有更重要的事要做! **7 an odd fish/a queer fish** *BrE old-fashioned* someone who is slightly strange or crazy【英, 過時】古怪的人 **8 a cold fish** an unfriendly person who seems to have no strong feelings 態度冷冰冰的人, 不熱情的人 **9 a big fish in a little pond** someone who is important or who has influence over a very small area 小塘中的大魚, 小地方的要人 —see also 另見 **drink like a fish** (DRINK² (2)), **a fine/pretty kettle of fish** (KETTLE (4))

fish² *v* **1** [I] to try to catch fish 捕魚, 釣魚: [+**for**] *We're fishing for trout.* 我們正在捕鱒魚。**2** [T always+adv/prep] also 又作 **fish out** to find something after searching through a bag, pocket etc, and take it out 掏出, 找出: **fish sth ↔ out** *Eric fished a peppermint out of the bag.* 埃里克從袋子裡掏出一塊薄荷糖。**3** [I always +adv/prep] *informal* to search for something in a bag, pocket etc【非正式】尋找, 摸索: [+**about/around**] *She fished around in her purse and pulled out a photo.* 她在錢包裡尋找着, 拿出了一張照片。| [+**for**] *Chris fished in his pocket for a coin.* 克里斯在口袋裡摸找硬幣。**4** [T] to try to catch fish in a particular area of water 在…中捕魚: *Other nations are forbidden to fish the waters within 200 miles of the coast.* 禁止其他國家在距海岸 200 海里的海域內捕魚。**5** [T] also 又作 **fish out** to pull someone or something out of water〔從水裡〕撈出, 拖出: **fish sb out** *Police frogmen fished the body out of the East River a week later.* 警方的蛙人一星期後從東河中打撈出屍體。**6 fish for compliments** to try to make someone say something nice about you, usually by asking a question〔一般通過提問〕討別人的恭維: *It's sickening the way he's always fishing for compliments when she's around.* 她在場的時候他總是討人恭維, 真噁心。**7 fish for information/news/gossip etc** to try to find out secret information 探聽消息/新聞/流言蜚語等: *Reporters were hanging around fishing for information on the Congressman's resignation.* 記者們都在附近徘徊, 探聽有關那位國會議員辭職的消息。**8 fish in troubled waters** to try to gain an advantage from other people's problems 趁火打劫, 混水摸魚 **9 fish or cut bait** *AmE spoken* used to tell someone to do what they say they will, or stop talking about it【美口】要麼說幹就幹, 要麼索性不要說

fish and chips /,· · '·/ *n* [U] a meal consisting of fish covered with a mixture of flour and milk and cooked in oil and long, thin pieces of potato cooked in oil 炸魚和炸馬鈴薯條

fish·cake /ˈfɪʃˌkek; ˈfɪʃkeɪk/ *n* [C] a small round flat food consisting of cooked fish mixed with cooked potato〔用魚和馬鈴薯做成的〕魚餅

fish·er·man /ˈfɪʃɚmən; ˈfɪʃəmən/ *n plural* **fishermen** /-mən; -mən/ [C] someone who catches fish as a sport or as a job 釣魚者; 漁民, 漁夫 —compare 比較 ANGLER

fish·e·ry /ˈfɪʃərɪ; ˈfɪʃəri/ *n* [C] a part of the sea where fish are caught as a business 漁場

fish-eye lens /,· · '·/ *n* [C] a type of curved LENS (=piece of glass on the front of a camera) that allows you to take photographs of a wide area 魚眼鏡頭, 超廣角鏡頭

fish farm /'· ,·/ *n* [C] an area of water used for breeding fish as a business 養魚場 —**fish farming** *n* [U]

fish fin·ger /,· '··/ *n* [C] *BrE* a long piece of fish covered with small pieces of dried bread and cooked【英】〔裹着麵包屑的〕魚條; FISH STICK *AmE*【美】

3 **fish·ing** /ˈfɪʃɪŋ; ˈfɪʃɪŋ/ *n* [U] **1** the sport or business of catching fish 釣魚; 捕魚: *Fishing is one of his hobbies.* 釣魚是他的一項業餘愛好。| **go fishing** *Terry's going fishing at Lake Arrowhead next weekend.* 特里下週末要到阿羅黑德湖釣魚。**2 be on a fishing expedition** *AmE* to try to find out secret information【美】在探聽祕密消息

fishing line /ˈ·· ·/ *n* [U] very long string made of strong material and used to catch fish 釣線, 釣絲

fishing rod /ˈ·· ·/ *n* [C] a long thin pole with a long string and a hook fixed to it, used for catching fish 釣竿

fishing tack·le /ˈ·· ˌ··/ *n* [U] equipment used for fishing 釣具; 捕魚索具

fish ket·tle /ˈ· ˌ··/ *n* [C] a long, deep dish used for cooking whole fish〔長而深的〕煮魚鍋

fish mar·ket /ˈ· ˌ··/ *n* [C] a special market that only sells fish 魚市場

fish meal /ˈ· ·/ *n* [U] dried fish crushed into a powder and put on the land to help plants grow〔用作肥料的〕魚粉

fish·mon·ger /ˈfɪʃˌmʌŋgə; ˈfɪʃmʌŋgə/ *n* [C] *especially BrE* someone who sells fish【尤英】魚商, 魚販

fish·net stock·ings /ˌfɪʃnɛt ˈstɑkɪŋz; ˌfɪʃnet ˈstɒkɪŋz/ also 又作 **fishnet tights** /ˌ·· ˈ·/ *BrE*【英】—*n* [plural] STOCKINGS with a pattern of small holes that make them look like a net 魚網絲襪, 網眼長襪

fish slice /ˈ· ·/ *n* [C] *BrE* a kitchen tool used especially for turning food when cooking, with a wide flat part and a handle【英】煎魚鏟, 鍋鏟, 炒勺 —see picture on page A10 參見A10頁圖

fish stick /ˈ· ·/ *n* [C] *AmE* a long piece of fish covered with small pieces of dried bread and cooked【美】〔裹麵包屑的〕魚條; FISH FINGER *BrE*【英】

fish·tail /ˈfɪʃˌtel; ˈfɪʃteɪl/ *v* [I] *AmE* if a vehicle or aircraft fishtails, it slides from side to side, usually because the tyres are sliding on water or ice【美】〔車〕擺尾行駛; 〔飛機〕擺尾飛行

fish·wife /ˈfɪʃˌwaɪf; ˈfɪʃwaɪf/ *plural* **fishwives** /-ˌwaɪvz; -waɪvz/ *n* [C] an insulting word for a woman with a loud voice 說話粗野的女人, 潑婦〔具冒犯性的詞語〕

fish·y /ˈfɪʃɪ; ˈfɪʃi/ *adj* **1** *informal* seeming bad or dishonest【非正式】可疑的, 靠不住的: *There's something very fishy about his business deals.* 他的商業交易很靠不住。**2** tasting or smelling of fish 魚的; 魚味的; 魚腥氣的

fis·sile /ˈfɪsl̩; ˈfɪsaɪl/ *adj* **1** *technical* able to be split by atomic fission【術語】〔原子〕可裂變的 **2** tending to split along natural lines of weakness 易裂開的, 可分裂的

fis·sion /ˈfɪʃən; ˈfɪʃən/ *n* [U] *technical*【術語】**1** the process of splitting an atom to produce large amounts of energy or an explosion〔原子的〕裂變 —compare 比較 FUSION (2) **2** the process of dividing a cell into two or more parts〔細胞的〕分裂

fis·sure /ˈfɪʃɚ; ˈfɪʃə/ *n* [C] a deep crack, especially in rock or earth〔尤指岩石或土地的〕裂縫, 裂隙

fist /fɪst; fɪst/ *n* [C] **1** the hand when the fingers are curled in towards the PALM, especially in order to express anger or hit someone 拳, 拳頭: *She held the money tightly in her fist.* 她緊緊把錢握在手中。| **clench your fist** (=hold your fist very tightly closed) 握緊拳頭 *Malcolm clenched his fists angrily.* 馬爾科姆憤怒地握緊拳頭。| **fist fight** (=a fight in which you use your bare hands to hit someone) 拳鬥, 鬥毆 *The argument quickly turned into an all-out fist fight.* 爭論很快變成一場激烈的拳鬥。—see also 另見 HAM-FISTED, TIGHT-FISTED, **hand over fist** (HAND¹ (37)) —see picture at 參見 BODY 圖 **2 make a good/bad fist of** *BrE informal* to make a successful or unsuccessful attempt to do something【英, 非正式】做成/做不成〔某事〕

fist·ful /ˈfɪstfʊl; ˈfɪstfʊl/ *n* [C] an amount that is as much as you can hold in your hand 一把, 一握: **[+of]** *a child clutching a fistful of toffees* 緊緊握着一把太妃糖的小孩

fis·ti·cuffs /ˈfɪstɪˌkʌfs; ˈfɪstɪkʌfs/ *n* [plural] *old-fashioned* a fight in which you use your bare hands to hit someone【過時】拳鬥, 鬥毆

fit¹ /fɪt; fɪt/ *v past tense* **fitted** also 又作 **fit** *AmE*【美】*past participle* **fit** S1 W2

1 ►RIGHT SIZE 合適的尺寸◄ [I,T not in progressive 不用進行式] to be the right size and shape for someone or something (使) 合適, 合身: *The dress fits perfectly.* 這件連衣裙十分合身。| **fit sb** *The jacket fitted me pretty well but the trousers were too small.* 我穿這件上衣很合身, 但褲子太小了。| **fit (sb) like a glove** (=fit the shape of sb's body perfectly) 非常合身 —see 見 CLOTHES (USAGE)

2 ►FIT A SPACE 容納於…◄ [I always+adv/prep, not in progressive 不用進行式] to be the right size and shape for a particular space, and not be too big 適合; 容得下: **[+in/into/under etc]** *Will my tennis racket fit in your bag?* 我的網球拍能裝進你的袋子嗎?

3 ►EQUIPMENT/PART 設備/部件◄ [T] to put a small piece of equipment into a place, or a new part onto a machine, so that it is ready to be used 安裝: **fit sth on/to etc** *Anti-theft devices are fitted to all our cars.* 我們所有的汽車上都安裝了防盜裝置。| **fit sth** *The plumber fit the sink this morning.* 管子工今天上午安裝了洗滌槽。

4 ►PUT IN PLACE 放在適當的位置◄ [I always+adv/prep,T always+adv/prep] to put or join something in a particular place where it is meant to go (把…) 放在適當的位置: **[+in/over/together]** *The plastic cover fits neatly over the frame.* 這塊塑料罩蓋在框架上正好合適。| **fit sth ↔ in/onto/together etc** *She fit a piece into the jigsaw puzzle.* 她在拼圖上拼進一塊。

5 ►FIND A PLACE FOR 為…找地方◄ [I always+adv/prep,T always+adv/prep] to find enough space for something in a room, vehicle, container etc〔房間、車輛、容器等〕裝得下: **fit sb/sth ↔ in** *Can you fit in another passenger?* 能容得下多一名乘客嗎?

6 ►MATCH 符合◄ [I,T not in progressive 不用進行式] if something fits a system, idea etc, it says the same thing or follows the same principles 符合, 適合: **fit in with** *Sonny's behaviour didn't fit in with what I knew of him.* 索尼的行為與我對他的了解不相符。| **[+in/into]** *educational videos designed to fit into the syllabus* 配合課程大綱而製作的教育錄像帶 | **fit sth** *a phenomenon that didn't fit the expected pattern* 與所預期的方式不相符的現象

7 ►SUITABLE 合適的◄ [T not in progressive 不用進行式] to have the qualities, experience etc that are suitable for a particular job, situation etc 適合〔某項工作、某情況等〕: *The punishment should fit the crime.* 應當按罪量刑。| *The music fits the words perfectly.* 音樂和歌詞配得很好。| **fit sb for sth** *Webb's negotiating skills fitted him for the task.* 韋布的談判技巧使他能勝任這項任務。| **fit the bill** (=have exactly the right qualities) 正合適; 正符合要求 *We wanted an experienced sportscaster, and Waggoner fit the bill.* 我們需要一名經驗豐富的體育節目主持人, 瓦根納正符合要求。

8 ►DESCRIPTION 描寫◄ [T not in progressive 不用進行式] if a description fits someone or something, it describes them exactly 與…完全吻合[相稱]: *Police said the car fits the description of the stolen vehicle.* 警方說這輛車與對那輛被盜的車的描述完全吻合。

9 ►DECIDE GROUP 判別羣體◄ [I,T] to belong to a particular group or set of ideas 屬於〔某個羣體或某種思想〕: **[+into]** *A lot of people didn't fit into the categories the researchers had devised.* 許多人無法歸納到研究人員所定的類別中去。—see also 另見 **sb's face doesn't fit** (FACE¹ (17)), **if the cap fits** (CAP¹ (4))

fit in *phr v* **1** [I] to be accepted by other people in a group because you have the same attitudes and interests〔因為有共同的看法、趣味等〕被他人接受, 相處融洽: *At first I felt awkward, but I soon learned to fit in.* 開頭我

F

感到不自在, 但很快就學會適應了。| **[+with]** *Larry doesn't seem to fit in with the other children.* 拉里好像和別的孩子們相處得不融洽。**2** [T **fit** sth/sb ↔ **in**] to manage to do something or see someone, even though you have a lot of other things to do 安排時間做〔某事〕, 安排時間見〔某人〕; 找出…的時間: *The doctor said he can fit me in at 4:30.* 醫生說他可以安排在4:30與我見面。**3** [T **fit** sth ↔ **in/into**] to find a time when something can happen without causing problems 安插〔時間〕: *How is the extra work going to fit into the schedule?* 額外的工作怎樣才能安插在時間表裡? | **[+with]** *Nancy tried to fit her holidays in with Alex's.* 南希試着把她的假期和亞歷克斯的假期配合起來。

fit sb/sth ↔ **out** *phr v* [T] **1** to provide a room or building with equipment or decorations 裝備, 配備; 佈置: *snug mountain cabins fitted out with pine furniture* 配有松木家具的整潔小巧的山間小屋 **2** to dress someone, especially in a particular type of clothing 給…穿衣〔尤指特定式樣的衣服〕: *Jennifer was fitted out like a Queen.* 詹妮弗穿得像女王。

fit sb/sth ↔ **up** *phr v* [T] **1** to provide a room or building with equipment or decorations 裝備, 配備; 佈置: *The bedroom is fitted up as an office.* 這間臥室被佈置成辦公室。**2** *BrE spoken* to make someone seem guilty of a crime they have not done; FRAME² (3)【英口】誣陷, 陷害: **fit sb up for sth** *Watson had been fitted up for the murder.* 沃森被誣害犯有謀殺罪。

USAGE NOTE 用法說明: FIT

WORD CHOICE 詞語辨析: **fit, suit, fit in, match, go together/with**

If something is not too big and not too small for a person or other thing, it **fits** (them). 如果某件東西對某人或其他東西 fits (正合適), 即這件東西對其來說不大也不小: *A size 12 dress should fit.* 12號的連衣裙應該會合身。| *You can't put those shelves in there, they won't fit.* 你不能把那些架子放在那兒, 它們的大小不合適。

If clothes or other personal things are the right style, colour etc for someone, you say they **suit** them. 如果衣服或其他個人物品的式樣、顏色等正適合某人, 可以說suit: *Casual clothes really don't suit her.* 她確實不適合穿休閒服。| *A green dress won't suit me.* 綠色連衣裙不適合我。| *That new haircut suits you!* 那種新髮式很適合你! Schools, places, times, situations etc may also **suit** people. 學校、地方、時間、情況等也可能suit (適合) 人: *A management position would suit him down to the ground.* 管理的職位會完全適合他。| *California doesn't suit everyone.* 加利福尼亞並不適合每個人。| *Will ten o'clock suit you?* 10點鐘你覺得合適嗎?

If people **fit in** they have a good social relationship with the other people in a group, and share the same attitudes, interests etc. 如果人們fit in (相處融洽), 是說他們在一起時關係很好, 有共同的看法、興趣等: *Laura fits in perfectly at the tennis club.* 勞拉在網球俱樂部與大家相處得十分融洽。

If things are almost the same in some way and look good together, they **match**. 如果事物很相似, 放在一起看上去很協調, 可以說它們match (相配): *The curtains don't match the carpet* (=they are not the same pattern/colour). 窗簾與地毯不相配 (=它們的花樣/顏色不一樣)。

If things look right together in style, colour etc, they **go together** or **go with** each other. 如果事物放在一起, 在式樣、顏色等方面看上去恰當, 可以說它們go together或go with (協調): *The curtains don't go with the carpet* (=they are not the same colour and do not look good together either). 窗簾與地毯不協調 (=它們顏色不一樣, 看上去也不相配)。Things can **go together** in other ways too. 事物也可以在其他方面go together (相配): *Fish and white wine go particularly well together.* 魚和白葡萄酒相配得特別好。

In British English the usual past form of **fit** is **fitted**, but in the first meaning you can also use **fit** in more informal English. 在英國英語中, fit通常的過去式是fitted, 但用作第一種意思時, 在較非正式的英語中也可以用fit: *Two years ago, these pants fit me perfectly.* 兩年前, 這褲子我穿着很合身。In American English, the usual past form is **fit**, but you can also use **fitted** for all the meanings. 在美國英語中, fit的過去式通常用fit, 但所有義項都可用fitted作為過去式。

fit² *adj* **fitter, fittest**

1 having the qualities that are suitable for a particular job, occasion, purpose etc 適合的, 合適的: **[+for]** *I don't think Carol is the fittest person for the job.* 我不認為卡羅爾是最適合這項工作的人。| **fit to do sth** *She's not fit to look after children.* 她不適合照看小孩。| **fit to eat/drink** *This food isn't fit to eat.* 這種食物不宜食用。| **be in a fit state** *We're trying to get the house into a fit state for visitors.* 我們正在把屋子弄得像樣些, 準備客人來訪。| **fit for a King** (=of the highest quality) 高質量的, 精美的, 最高級的 *food fit for a King* 精美的食品; 最高級的食品

2 ►STRONG 強壯的◄ *especially BrE* healthy and strong because you exercise regularly【尤英】〔因經常鍛鍊而〕健壯的: *Sandy's very fit – he runs almost 30 miles a week.* 桑迪十分健壯 — 他每星期跑差不多30英里。| **keep fit** (=exercise in order to stay strong)〔為了保持強壯而〕鍛鍊身體 *She keeps fit by swimming every morning.* 她每天上午游泳鍛鍊身體。| **physically fit** *AmE*【美】*Rowers have to be extremely physically fit.* 划船運動選手的身體必須特別健壯。—opposite 反義詞 UNFIT (1)

3 ►HEALTHY 健康的◄ *especially BrE* healthy after having been ill【尤英】〔病後〕健康的: *I'm glad to see you looking fit again.* 我很高興看到你氣色完全好了。| **fit as a fiddle** (=completely healthy) 身體非常好的 *She's 86, but as fit as a fiddle.* 她86歲, 但身體好極了。| **fighting fit** (=extremely healthy) 非常健康的 | **be in a fit state/condition** (=be healthy enough, after being ill or drunk, to be able to do something)〔生病或醉酒恢復後〕身體狀況良好 *Brog was in no fit state to drive when he left the party.* 布羅格離開聚會時情況欠佳(酒醉了), 不能開車。

4 fit to drop extremely tired after using a lot of effort or energy〔付出大量氣力、精力後〕累得快要癱倒在地上的: *We worked till we were fit to drop.* 我們一直工作, 直到累得快要癱倒在地上。

5 fit to be tied *spoken especially AmE* very angry, anxious, or upset【口, 尤美】十分惱火[着急, 煩惱]的: *The teacher will be fit to be tied when she sees the mess you've made.* 老師看到你們弄得這樣一團糟會非常生氣的。

6 fit to wake the dead a noise that is fit to wake the dead is extremely loud〔噪音〕非常大聲的: *They were screaming fit to wake the dead.* 他們高聲尖叫。

7 laughing/coughing fit to burst *informal* laughing or coughing a lot【非正式】笑破肚皮/使勁大聲咳嗽: *The girls were laughing fit to burst.* 女孩子們笑破了肚皮。

8 see/think fit (to do sth) an expression meaning to decide that it is right or suitable to do a particular thing, used especially when you do not agree with this decision 認為〔做某事〕恰當: *You know the situation best. Do whatever you think fit.* 你最了解情況。你認為怎麼恰當就怎麼幹。

fit³ *n*

1 ►EMOTION 情感◄ [C] a very strong and uncontrollable emotion〔感情〕衝動, 一陣發作: **[+of]** *In a fit of temper he slammed his hands down on the keyboard.* 他

突然發起脾氣，用雙手猛擊鍵盤。| *a fit of depression* 一陣沮喪
2 be a good/tight/close etc fit to fit a person or a particular space well, tightly, closely etc 非常適合/很緊/很密切: *This jacket is a beautiful fit.* 這件夾克衫非常合身。
3 ►LOSE CONSCIOUSNESS 失去知覺◄ [C] a short period of time when someone loses consciousness and cannot control their body because their brain is not working properly 昏厥; 一時失去知覺; 痙攣: *an epileptic fit* 癲癇發作 | **have a fit** *The baby's having a fit! Call the doctor!* 嬰兒痙攣了！叫醫生來！
4 ►SUITABLE 適合的◄ [singular] *formal* a relationship between two things or systems in which they match each other or are suitable for each other【正式】〔事物或制度之間〕相配合: **[+between]** *We must be sure that there's a fit between the needs of the children and the education they receive.* 我們必須確保兒童的需要和他們受到的教育相配合。
5 ►LAUGH/COUGH 笑/咳嗽◄ a period during which you laugh or cough a lot 一陣大笑; 一陣咳嗽: *a coughing fit* 一陣咳嗽 | **[+of]** *a fit of the giggles* 一陣咯咯笑 | **in fits (of laughter)** (=laughing a lot) 一陣陣大笑 *The show was hilarious – we were all in fits.* 表演十分滑稽——我們一陣陣地捧腹大笑。| **have sb in fits** (=make someone laugh a lot) 使某人一陣陣地大笑 *Cyril had us in fits from the minute we walked in the door.* 西里爾從我們一進門就開始把我們逗得一陣陣大笑。
6 in/by fits and starts repeatedly starting and stopping 一陣一陣地, 斷斷續續地: *The old car moved in fits and starts up the road.* 這輛舊車時走時停地在路上行駛。| *Beverley tends to do things in fits and starts.* 貝弗莉做事情往往是斷斷續續的。
7 have/throw a fit *informal* to be very angry or shocked【非正式】大發脾氣; 大吃一驚: *If your mother finds out about this she'll have a fit.* 如果你母親知道這事, 她會大發脾氣的。

fit·ful /ˈfɪtfəl; ˈfɪtfəl/ *adj* happening irregularly for short periods of time 不規則的, 間歇的, 一陣一陣的: *fitful showers of rain* 一陣一陣的大雨 —**fitfully** *adv*: *She slept fitfully.* 她睡睡醒醒。

fit·ment /ˈfɪtmənt; ˈfɪtmənt/ *n* [C] *BrE* a piece of furniture that is made especially for a particular space in a room【英】〔房間某個地方定製的〕家具, 設備: *bathroom fitments* 浴室設備

fit·ness /ˈfɪtnəs; ˈfɪtnɪ̵s/ *n* [U] **1** the state of being healthy and strong so that you are able to do hard work or sport 健壯; 健康: *She's following an exercise programme to improve her fitness.* 她按照鍛鍊計劃來增強體質。| **physical fitness** *Running marathons requires a high level of physical fitness.* 跑馬拉松需要有十分健壯的身體。**2** the degree to which someone or something is suitable or good enough for a particular situation or purpose 適合, 恰當: **[+for]** *We examine candidates' fitness for the job.* 我們考核應徵者是否勝任這項工作。| **fitness to do sth** *The police questioned his fitness to drive.* 警方懷疑他是否有資格開車。

fit·ted /ˈfɪtɪd; ˈfɪtɪ̵d/ *adj* **1 be fitted with** to have or include something as a permanent part 配備: *Is your car fitted with automatic locks?* 你的車子裝了自動鎖嗎? **2** [only before noun 僅用於名詞前] *BrE* made or cut to fit a particular space【英】按照特定空間做的, 配好大小的: *a fitted carpet* 定做的地毯 | *fitted cupboards* 定做的碗櫥 **3** having the right qualities or experience for a particular job 適合的, 稱職的: *Elinor is well fitted to be the sales manager.* 埃莉諾非常適合擔任銷售經理。

fitted kit·chen /ˌ·· ˈ··/ *n* [C] *BrE* a kitchen that has cupboards that fit exactly into a particular space【英】裝有定製家具的廚房, 碗櫥尺寸合適的廚房

fitted sheet /ˌ·· ˈ·/ *n* [C] a sheet that fits exactly over the MATTRESS on a bed 尺寸正好合適的牀單

fit·ter /ˈfɪtə; ˈfɪtə/ *n* [C] *BrE* someone who puts together or repairs machines or electrical equipment【英】裝配工, 修理工: *a gas fitter* 煤氣裝配工

fit·ting¹ /ˈfɪtɪŋ; ˈfɪtɪŋ/ *n* [C] **1** [usually plural 一般用複數] a piece of furniture that is usually included in a house but can be moved if necessary, such as a COOKER (1)〔房間內必要時可移動的〕設備, 家具〈如廚灶〉—compare 比較 FIXTURE (1) **2** [usually plural 一般用複數] a part of a piece of equipment that makes it possible for you to use it 配件, 裝置: *a sink with chrome fittings* (=handle and taps) 帶鍍鉻配件的洗碗槽 | *the light fittings* 電燈裝置 **3** an occasion when you put on a piece of clothing that is being made for you, to see if it fits properly 試穿, 試衣

fitting² *adj formal* right for a particular situation or occasion; APPROPRIATE¹【正式】合適的, 恰當的: *I thought the memorial was a fitting tribute to the President.* 我認為這座紀念碑表現了對總統的一種恰當的敬意。| **it is fitting that** *It was not fitting that he remarried so soon after his wife's death.* 他在妻子死後這麼快就再婚, 這是不合宜的。

fitting room /ˈ·· ·/ *n* [C] an area in a shop where you can put on clothes to see how they look〔商店裡的〕試衣室

five /faɪv; faɪv/ *number* **1** 5 五 —see table on page C1 參見 C1 頁附錄 **2** a piece of paper money worth $5 or £5 五美元鈔票; 五英鎊鈔票: *Do you have two fives for a ten?* 你有兩張五美元的鈔票來換一張十美元的嗎? —see also 另見 FIVER **3 give sb (a) five** to hit the inside of someone's hand with your hand to show that you are very pleased about something 用手掌拍打某人的手掌〔表示十分高興〕**4 take five** used to tell people to stop working for a few minutes 停下來休息幾分鐘 **5 five-day/five-month/five-year** happening or continuing for five days, months, or years 五天的/五個月的/五年的: *I've got a five-month contract in Bahrain.* 我在巴林有一項五個月的合同。**6 fives**[U] a British ball game in which the ball is hit with the hand against any of three walls〔英國的〕牆手球 —compare 比較 HANDBALL (1) —see also 另見 HIGH FIVE, NINE-TO-FIVE

five-and-ten /ˌ· · ˈ·/ also 又作 **five-and-dime** *n* [C] *AmE old-fashioned* a shop that sells many different types of inexpensive goods, especially for the house; DIME STORE【美, 過時】五分一角店, 出售廉價日用商品的雜貨店, 小零售店

five o'clock shad·ow /ˌ· ·· ˈ··/ *n* [singular] the dark colour on a man's chin where the hair has grown a little bit during the day（早上刮過後當天又長出的）短鬚子茬兒

fiv·er /ˈfaɪvə; ˈfaɪvə/ *n* [C] *BrE* £5 or a five pound note【英】五英鎊（鈔票）: *It's only a fiver to get in.* 只要五英鎊就可以進去。

five-spot /ˈ· ·/ *n* [C] *AmE old-fashioned* a piece of paper money worth $5【美, 過時】五美元鈔票: *It only costs a five-spot.* 這只需花費五美元。

five-star /ˈ· ·/ *adj* [only before noun 僅用於名詞前] a five-star hotel or restaurant is very good〔酒店或餐廳〕五星級的, 第一流的

five star gen·e·ral /ˈ· · ˈ···/ *n* [C] *AmE* a GENERAL who commands an army【美】五星上將

five-stones /ˈ· ·/ *n* [U] *BrE* a children's game in which the players try to pick up small objects between throwing one of them into the air and catching it【英】五石遊戲〔一種兒童玩的小物件拋接遊戲〕

fix¹ /fɪks; fɪks/ *v* [T] 
1 ►REPAIR 修理◄ to repair something that is broken or not working properly 修理; MEND¹ (1b) *BrE*【英】: *Dad's outside fixing the brakes on the Chevy.* 爸爸在外面修理那輛雪佛萊汽車的煞車。
2 ►LIMIT 限制◄ to decide on a limit for something, especially prices, costs etc, so that they do not change 確定, 決定〔價格、成本等〕: **[+at]** *The interest rate has been fixed at 6.5%.* 利率已經定為 6.5%。
3 fix a time/day/place etc to decide on a particular

F

time etc when something will happen 確定時間/日期/地點等: *Have you fixed a date for the wedding yet?* 你確定了婚禮的日期嗎?
4 ►ARRANGE 安排◄ also 又作 **fix up** to make arrangements for something 安排: *If you want to meet the big boss, I can fix it.* 如果你想見那位大老闆, 我可以安排一下。
5 ►FASTEN 使牢固◄ to fasten something firmly to something else, so that it stays there permanently 使固定[牢固]: **fix sth to/on** *We fixed the shelves to the wall using screws.* 我們用螺釘把架子裝在牆上。
6 ►MAKE FOOD 準備食物◄ *informal especially AmE* to prepare a meal or drinks【非正式, 尤美】準備〔食物或飲料〕: *I watched the kids while he fixed dinner.* 他做晚飯時我照看孩子。| **fix sb sth** *I'll fix you a whisky sour.* 我給你倒一杯威士忌酸味酒。
7 fix your attention/eyes/mind etc on to think about or look at someone or something carefully 把注意力/雙眼/思想等集中在…: *Aziz tried to fix his mind on the job at hand.* 阿齊斯努力想把思想集中在手頭的工作上。
8 ►HAIR ETC 頭髮等◄ *especially AmE* to make your hair or MAKE-UP look neat and attractive【尤美】使〔頭髮、化妝〕整潔[漂亮], 美容: *Who fixed your hair for the wedding?* 你婚禮時的髮式是誰給你梳的? | **fix your face** (=put make-up on your face) 化妝 *Hold on. Let me just fix my face before we go out.* 等等, 讓我在我們出去之前化一下妝。
9 ►CAT/DOG 貓/狗◄ *AmE informal* to do a medical operation on a cat or dog so that it cannot have babies; NEUTER²【美, 非正式】閹割〔貓、狗〕
10 ►RESULT OF COMPETITION 競賽的結果◄ to arrange an election, game etc dishonestly, so that you get the result you want 用不正當的手段操縱〔選舉、比賽等的〕結果: *The fight must have been fixed. Nobody goes down that easily!* 這場拳擊賽肯定是有人操縱的。沒有人會那麼容易倒下去的!
11 ►PUNISH 懲罰◄ *informal* to punish someone for something they have done【非正式】懲罰, 收拾: *I'll fix him for taking my car without my permission!* 他未經許可開我的車, 我得教訓教訓他!
12 fix sb with a stare/glare/look etc to look directly into someone's eyes for a long time 瞪眼看[凝視]某人: *Rachel fixed him with an icy stare.* 雷切爾冷冰冰地盯着他看了一會兒。
13 ►PAINTINGS/PHOTOGRAPHS 繪畫/照片◄ to use a chemical process on paintings, photographs etc that makes the colours or images permanent 定影〔使顏色或圖像持久〕
14 be fixing to do sth *AmE spoken* an expression meaning to prepare to do something, used in some parts of the US【美口】正準備[正打算]做某事: *I'm fixing to go to the store. Do you need anything?* 我正準備上商店去。你需要甚麼東西嗎?
15 ►CURE 治癒◄ *AmE informal* to make a part of the body that is damaged completely better【美, 非正式】治癒: *They'll fix your leg for you.* 他們會為你把腿治好的。

fix on sth/sb *phr v* [T] to choose a suitable thing or person especially after thinking about it carefully〔尤指經過認真考慮後〕選定, 確定: *We've finally fixed on a place to have the concert.* 我們最後確定了舉行音樂會的地點。

fix sb/sth ↔ **up** *phr v* [T] **1** to arrange a meeting, event etc, especially by persuading someone to agree to it〔尤指說服某人後〕安排: *We'll have to fix up a time to meet.* 我們得安排一個見面的時間。| **fix up to do sth** *BrE*【英】*I've fixed up to be in Toronto for the next conference.* 我已經安排好到多倫多參加下次會議。**2** to improve something or make it suitable 修理; 整理: *We fixed up the guest bedroom before my parents came to stay.* 我們在父母來住之前收拾了客房。**3** to provide someone with something they want 供給, 提供: **[+with]** *Can you fix me up with a bed for the night?* 你能弄張牀讓我過夜嗎? **4** to find a suitable romantic partner for someone 為〔某人〕找個浪漫伴侶: *Bring your brother too. I'm sure we can find someone to fix him up with.* 把你的兄弟也帶來吧。我確信我們能找個人陪他。

fix² *n* **1 be in a fix** to have a problem that is difficult to solve 處於困境, 遇到難題: *We were in a real fix. The car broke down and there wasn't a phone in sight.* 我們遇到大麻煩了。車子拋錨了, 而且看不到有電話。**2** [singular] an amount of something, especially an illegal drug, that you often use and badly want〔一劑〕上癮的東西, 毒品: *addicts looking for a fix* 尋找一劑毒品的癮君子 | *I need my fix of caffeine in the morning or I can't think.* 我清早需要一點咖啡因, 不然就無法思考問題。**3** [singular] something that has been dishonestly arranged 受操縱的事情: *The election was a fix!* 這次選舉是受人操縱的! **4 get a fix on sb/sth a)** to find out exactly where someone or something is 確定某人/某物的位置: *The search boat can't get a fix on the yacht's position.* 搜救船無法確定遊艇的位置。**b)** to understand what someone or something is really like 對某人/某事得出真確的看法: *I sat and stared for a while, trying to get a fix on the situation.* 我坐下來, 呆看了一會兒, 想弄清情況。

fix·a·ted /ˈfɪkˌsetɪd; fɪkˈseɪtɪ̈d/ *adj* **1** always thinking or talking about one particular thing〔思考或談話〕專注的; 依戀的: **[+on]** *Jeremy seems to be fixated on this idea of travelling around the world.* 傑里米似乎一心想要周遊世界。**2** *technical* having stopped developing emotionally or mentally【術語】〔情感或精神〕停止發展的, 固着的

fix·a·tion /fɪksˈeʃən; fɪkˈseɪʃən/ *n* [C] **1** an unnaturally strong interest in or love for someone or something 不正常的依戀, 固戀: **[+about/with]** *Trevor's got this fixation about cleanliness.* 特里弗有潔淨癖。**2** *technical* a kind of mental illness in which someone's mind or emotions stop developing, so that they are like a child【術語】〔心理或情感〕固着

fix·a·tive /ˈfɪksətɪv; ˈfɪksətɪv/ *n* [C,U] **1** a substance used to glue things together or to hold things such as hair or false teeth in place 固定劑 **2** a chemical used on a painting or photograph so that the colours do not change 定色劑, 定影劑

fixed /fɪkst; fɪkst/ *adj* **1** firmly fastened to a particular position 固定的: **be fixed to/in/on** *The tables are fixed to the floor.* 這些桌子都固定在地板上。**2** times, amounts, meanings etc that are fixed cannot be changed〔時間、數量、意思等〕確定的, 不變的: *The classes begin and end at fixed times.* 上下課的時間都是固定的。| *fixed prices* 固定價格 **3 have fixed ideas/opinions** to have very definite ideas or opinions which are often unreasonable 有固執的想法/看法: **[+about/on]** *He has very fixed ideas about how a wife should behave.* 他對一個妻子應如何表現有很固執的想法。**4 how are you fixed for** *spoken* used to ask someone how much of something they have【口】你有多少…?: *How are you fixed for cash?* 你有多少現金? **5 fixed expression/smile/frown etc** a fixed smile, expression etc does not change and does not seem to express real emotions 固定[僵化]的表情/微笑/皺眉等 **6 have no fixed abode/address** *law BrE* to not have a permanent place to live【法律, 英】無固定住所[住址], 居無定所

fixed as·sets /ˌ· ˈ··/ *n* [plural] *technical* land, buildings, or equipment that a business owns and uses【術語】固定資產

fixed cap·i·tal /ˌ· ˈ···/ *n* [U] *technical* buildings or machines that a business owns and that can be used for a long time to produce goods【術語】固定資本

fixed charge /ˌ· ˈ·/ *n* [C] a cost that does not change for a long time 固定費用, 固定收費

fixed costs /ˌ· ˈ·/ *n* [plural] *technical* costs, such as rent, that a business has to pay even when it is not producing anything【術語】固定成本

fix·ed·ly /ˈfɪksɪdlɪ; ˈfɪksɪ̈dli/ *adv* looking at, or thinking about only one thing 固定地; 專注地: *Anna stared fix-*

edly ahead, trying to concentrate on the road. 安娜凝視前方，力求把注意力集中在道路上。

fix·er /ˋfɪksɚ; ˈfɪksə/ *n* [C] someone who is good at arranging events, situations etc for other people so that they have the results they want, especially by using dishonest or illegal methods 代人行賄[疏通]者

fix·ings /ˋfɪksɪŋz; ˈfɪksɪŋz/ *n* **the fixings** *AmE* the vegetables, bread etc that are eaten with meat at a large meal【美】〔主菜以外的〕配菜; TRIMMINGS (3) *BrE*【英】: *turkey with all the fixings* 火雞肉加各種配菜

fix·i·ty /ˋfɪksətɪ; ˈfɪksɪ̵ti/ *n* [U] *formal* the state of not changing【正式】固定性, 穩定性: *fixity of purpose* 目標的固定性

fix·ture /ˋfɪkstʃɚ; ˈfɪkstʃə/ *n* [C] **1** [usually plural 一般用複數] a piece of equipment that is fixed inside a house or building and is sold as part of the house〔房屋或建築物內的〕固定裝修物; 固定附着物: **the fixtures and fittings** *BrE* (=all the pieces of equipment that are normally included as part of a house or building)【英】〔房屋的〕固定裝置和設備 **2 be a (permanent) fixture** to be always present and not likely to move or go away 是固定存在物; 是永不離去的人[物]: *The dog became a permanent fixture in our lives.* 這條狗成為我們生活中不可缺少的一部分。**3** *BrE* a sports match that has been arranged for a particular time and place【英】〔預定舉行的〕體育比賽: *a list of this season's fixtures* 本賽季各場比賽一覽表

fizz¹ /fɪz; fɪz/ *v* [I] if a liquid fizzes, it produces a lot of BUBBLE*s*¹ (1) and makes a continuous sound〔液體〕冒泡並嘶嘶作響: *champagne fizzing out of the bottle* 冒着氣泡嘶嘶地流出瓶子的香檳酒 —see picture on page A19 參見A19頁圖

fizz² *n* [singular,U] **1** the BUBBLE*s*¹ (1) of gas in some kinds of drinks or the sound that they make 飲料的泡沫; 嘶嘶聲 **2** *BrE informal* CHAMPAGNE【英, 非正式】香檳酒, 氣酒

fiz·zle /ˋfɪzḷ; ˈfɪzəl/ *v*

fizzle out *phr v* [I] *informal* to gradually stop happening, especially because people become less interested in something【非正式】〔因越來越不感興趣而〕終於失敗, 漸停; 夭折: *Their romance just fizzled out.* 他們的羅曼史逐漸結束了。

fiz·zy /ˋfɪzɪ; ˈfɪzi/ *adj* **1** a fizzy liquid contains BUBBLE*s*¹ (1) of gas〔液體〕起泡的 —opposite 反義詞 FLAT¹ (4) **2 fizzy drink** *BrE* a sweet, non-alcoholic drink with BUBBLE*s* of gas; SOFT DRINK【英】汽水

fjord, fiord /fjɔrd; ˈfiːɔːd/ *n* [C] a narrow area of sea between high cliffs on the coast of Norway〔挪威海岸邊的〕峽灣

flab /flæb; flæb/ *n* [U] *informal* soft, loose fat on a person's body【非正式】〔人體上〕鬆弛的脂肪[肌肉]

flab·ber·gas·ted /ˋflæbɚˌgæstɪd; ˈflæbəgɑːstɪ̵d/ *adj informal* extremely surprised or shocked【非正式】大吃一驚的, 目瞪口呆的: *Teachers were flabbergasted at the decision to close down the school.* 教師們對關閉學校的決定大吃一驚。

flab·by /ˋflæbɪ; ˈflæbi/ *adj informal*【非正式】**1** having soft, loose fat rather than strong muscles 鬆弛的, 鬆垂的: *She's getting old and flabby.* 她年紀大了, 肌肉鬆弛。**2** a flabby argument, excuse etc is weak and not effective〔論點、藉口等〕無力的 —**flabbiness** *n* [U]

flac·cid /ˋflæksɪd; ˈflæsɪ̵d/ *adj technical* soft and weak instead of firm【術語】軟弱的; 鬆垂的 —**flaccidity** /flækˋsɪdətɪ; flæˈsɪdɪ̵ti/ *n* [U]

flack /flæk; flæk/ *n* [U] another spelling of FLAK flak 的另一種拼法

flag¹ /flæg; flæg/ *n* [C] **1** a piece of cloth with a coloured pattern or picture on it that represents a country or organization 旗, 旗幟: *The children waved their flags as the Queen went by.* 女王走過時, 孩子們揮動着旗子。| *the flag of Texas* 得克薩斯州的州旗 | **a flag flies** (=a flag is shown on a pole) 掛起旗子 *Flags were flying at half-mast for the death of the Premier.* 為總理去世而下半旗致哀。**2** a coloured piece of cloth used as a signal 信號旗: *The flag went down, and the race began.* 信號旗一落下, 比賽便開始了。**3 under the flag of** if a group of people do something under the flag of a particular country or organization, they do it as representatives of that country or organization 在…的旗幟下; 代表… **4 the flag** an expression meaning a country or organization and its beliefs, values, and people 國家; 組織; 國家或組織代表的信仰、價值、人民等: *loyalty to the flag* 對國家的忠誠 **5 keep the flag flying** to achieve success on behalf of your country in a competition〔比賽中〕代表祖國獲勝 **6** a FLAGSTONE〔鋪地板或路的〕石板 —see also 另見 **fly the flag** (FLY¹(27))

flag² **flagged, flagging** *v* **1** [T] make a mark against something to show that it is important〔用特殊記號〕標示, 標出〔表示重要〕: *I've flagged the parts I want to comment on.* 我已經特別標示出我要評論的部分。**2** [I] to become tired or weak 疲倦; 變虛弱: *By ten o'clock I was beginning to flag and went up to bed.* 到十點鐘, 我開始感到疲倦, 就上牀睡覺去了。

flag sb/sth ↔ **down** *phr v* [T] to make the driver of a vehicle stop by waving at them 揮手[打信號]使〔某人〕停車: *I flagged down a taxi.* 我揮手招呼一輛計程車停下。

fla·gel·lant /ˋflædʒələnt; ˈflædʒɪ̵lənt/ *n* [C] *formal* someone who whips themselves as a religious punishment【正式】自行鞭笞以贖罪的宗教信仰者

fla·gel·late /ˋflædʒəˌlet; ˈflædʒɪ̵leɪt/ *v* [T] *formal* to whip yourself or someone else, especially as a religious punishment【正式】鞭打, 鞭笞〔尤作為宗教上的一種處罰〕

flag foot·ball /ˈ· ˌ··/ *n* [U] *AmE* a game like American football in which players tear off flags from around other players' waists instead of knocking them down【美】美式奪旗足球[橄欖球] —compare 比較 TOUCH FOOTBALL

flagged /flægd; flægd/ *adj* covered with FLAGSTONES〔指道路、地面等〕鋪石板的

flag·ging /ˋflægɪŋ; ˈflægɪŋ/ *adj* becoming tired, weaker, or less interested 疲倦的; 逐漸衰弱的; 失去興趣的: *concern for the United States' flagging economy* 對美國逐漸衰退的經濟的關注

flag·on /ˋflægən; ˈflægən/ *n* [C] a large container for liquids〔盛載液體的〕大肚壺

flag·pole /ˋflægˌpol; ˈflægpəʊl/ *n* [C] a tall pole on which a flag hangs; FLAGSTAFF 旗杆

fla·grant /ˋflegrənt; ˈfleɪgrənt/ *adj* **flagrant abuse/violation etc** a flagrant action is shocking because it is done in a way that is easily noticed and shows no respect for laws, truth etc 明目張膽的濫用/公然違反等: *flagrant disregard for human rights* 對人權的公然漠視 —**flagrantly** *adv*

flag·ship /ˋflægˌʃɪp; ˈflægʃɪp/ *n* [C] **1** the most important ship in a group of ships belonging to the navy, on which the ADMIRAL sails 旗艦 **2** the best and most important product, building etc that a company owns or produces〔某公司擁有或生產的產品、建築等中〕最重要者: *the flagship of the new Ford range* 新福特汽車系列中的旗艦產品

flag·staff /ˋflægˌstæf; ˈflægstɑːf/ *n* [C] a tall pole on which a flag hangs; FLAGPOLE 旗杆

flag·stone /ˋflægˌston; ˈflægstəʊn/ *n* [C] a smooth flat piece of stone used for floors, paths etc〔鋪地板或路等的〕石板

flag stop /ˈ· ·/ *n* [C] *AmE* a place where buses stop only if they are asked to do so【美】公共汽車招呼站

flag-wav·ing /ˈ· ˌ··/ *n* [U] the expression of strong national feelings, especially when these feelings seem too extreme 愛國情緒的強烈表現; 沙文主義表現

flail¹ /flel; fleɪl/ *v* **1** [I,T] to wave your arms or legs in an uncontrolled way 胡亂地揮動〔手臂或腿〕: *His arms flailed above the surface of the water.* 他的雙臂在水面上胡亂地揮動。**2** [T] to beat someone or something violently, usually with a stick〔用棍子〕敲打, 毆打 **3** [I, T] to beat grain with a flail 用連枷打〔穀〕

flail² *n* [C] a tool consisting of a stick that swings from a long handle, used in the past to separate grain from wheat by beating it 連枷〔舊時用作打穀的農具〕

flair/flɛr; fleə/ *n* **1** [singular] a natural ability to do something very well 天賦, 天分, 才能: **have a flair for** *Carla has an instinctive flair for business.* 卡拉有經商的天分。 **2** [U] a way of doing things that is interesting and shows imagination 獨特的處事風格; 時髦派頭; 新奇的創意: *Bates's advertising campaigns tended to lack flair.* 貝茨的廣告攻勢往往缺乏新意。

flak, flack/flæk; flæk/ *n* [U] **1** *informal* strong criticism【非正式】強烈的批評, 抨擊: **get/take flak** *The administration has taken a lot of flak over its decision to pull troops out of Somalia.* 政府從索馬里撤軍的決定遭到大量的批評。 **2** bullets or shells (SHELL¹ (3)) that are shot from guns on the ground at enemy aircraft 高射砲火 —see also 另見 FLAK JACKET

flake¹/flek; fleɪk/ *n* [C **+of**] **1** a very small flat thin piece that breaks away easily from something else 小薄片: *soap flakes* 肥皂片 —see also 另見 SNOWFLAKE —see picture on page A7 參見A7頁圖 **2** *AmE informal* someone who seems crazy【美, 非正式】古怪的人; 瘋瘋癲癲的人

flake² *v* **1** [I] also 又作 **flake off** to break off in small thin pieces (成片) 剝落: *The paint is beginning to flake off.* 油漆開始剝落了。 **2** [I,T] to break fish or another food into small thin pieces, or to break in this way (使) 碎裂成小薄片: *Poach the fish until it flakes easily.* 把魚加水煮到魚肉容易分成薄片為止。

flake out *phr v* [I] *informal* to fall asleep because you are extremely tired【非正式】(累得) 睡着: *Karl got home at eight o'clock and flaked out on the sofa.* 卡爾八點鐘回到家, 累得在沙發上睡着了。

flak jack·et/ˈ· ˌ··/ *n* [C] a special coat made of heavy material with metal inside it to protect soldiers and policemen from bullets〔有金屬片的〕防彈衣

flak·y/ˋflekɪ; ˈfleɪki/ *adj* **1** tending to break into small thin pieces 易碎裂成薄片的: *rich, flaky pastry* 重油酥餅 **2** *informal especially AmE* slightly crazy【非正式, 尤美】古怪的; 瘋瘋癲癲的: *Carrie's pretty flaky but she's fun to be with.* 卡麗相當古怪, 可是和她在一起很有趣。 —**flakiness** *n* [U]

flam·bé /flɑmˋbe; ˈflɒmbeɪ/ also 又作 **flam·béed** /flɑmˋbed; ˈflɒmbeɪd/ *adj French* food that is flambéed has an alcoholic drink such as BRANDY poured over it to produce flames【法】〔食物〕澆酒〈如白蘭地〉點燃後食用的 —see picture on page A15 參見A15頁圖

flam·boy·ant/flæmˋbɔɪənt; flæmˈbɔɪənt/ *adj* **1** behaving or dressing in a confident or surprising way that makes people notice you〔行為或衣着〕炫耀的, 浮誇的: *his flamboyant stage personality* 他那極為造作的舞台風格 | *flamboyant gestures* 浮誇的姿態 **2** brightly coloured and easily noticed 色彩豔麗的: *flamboyant clothes* 色彩豔麗的衣服 —**flamboyantly** *adv* —**flamboyance** *n* [U]

flame¹ /flem; fleɪm/ *n* [C,U] **1** hot bright burning gas that you see when something is on fire 火焰, 烈焰: *the flame of a candle* 燭火 | *Flames poured out of the windows of the building.* 火焰從大樓的窗戶裡不斷冒出。— see picture at 參見 CANDLE 圖 **2 in flames** burning strongly 熊熊燃燒: *The house was in flames by the time we arrived.* 我們到達時, 房子已在熊熊燃燒。 **3 go up in flames/burst into flames** to begin burning suddenly and strongly 突然着火/失火: *I was driving along and the engine just burst into flames.* 我正開着車, 發動機突然燃燒起來。 **4 a flame of passion/desire/vengeance etc** *literary* a strong feeling【文】激情/慾火/強烈的復仇心等 —see also 另見 **old flame** (OLD¹ (13)), **naked flame** (NAKED (3)), **fan the flames** (FAN² (2)), **add fuel to the fire/flames** (FUEL¹ (3))

flame² *v* [I] **1** *literary* to become suddenly bright with light or colour, especially red or orange【文】變成火紅色: *Her cheeks flamed for an instant.* 她的雙頰馬上通紅了。 **2** also 又作 **flame up** to suddenly burn more strongly or brightly 突然更熾烈地燃燒; (突然) 爆發

fla·men·co/fləˋmɛŋko; fləˈmeŋkəʊ/ *n* [C,U] a fast, exciting Spanish dance, or the GUITAR music that is played for this dance〔西班牙〕佛朗明哥舞[音樂]; 弗拉曼柯舞[音樂]

flamenco 佛朗明哥舞

flame·proof/ˋflemˌpruf; ˈfleɪmpruːf/ also 又作 **flame re·sist·ant**/ˈ· ·ˌ··/ *adj* specially made or treated with chemicals so it does not burn easily 防火的, 耐火的; 不易燃的

flame throw·er/ˈ· ˌ··/ *n* [C] a machine like a gun that shoots flames or burning liquid, used as a weapon or for clearing plants 噴火器; 火焰噴射器〔用作武器或清理植物〕

flam·ing/ˋflemɪŋ; ˈfleɪmɪŋ/ *adj* [only before noun 僅用於名詞前] **1 a flaming argument/row/temper** a very angry argument or temper 激烈的爭論/激烈的爭吵/火暴的脾氣: *He had had a flaming row with his wife earlier that evening.* 在那天傍晚時分, 他曾和妻子大吵了一場。 **2** *BrE informal* used to emphasize what you are saying, especially when you feel annoyed【英, 非正式】十足的, 該死的〔尤用於不耐煩時加強語氣〕: *You flaming idiot!* 你這十足的笨蛋! **3** covered with flames 燃燒着的, 被火焰吞噬的

fla·min·go/fləˋmɪŋgo; fləˈmɪŋgəʊ/ *n* [C] a tropical bird that has very long thin legs, pink feathers, and a long neck 紅鸛, 火烈鳥

flam·ma·ble/ˋflæməbl̩; ˈflæməbəl/ *adj* easily set on fire 易燃的: *Caution! Highly flammable chemicals.* 小心! 高度易燃化學品。—opposite 反義詞 NONFLAMMABLE

flan/flæn; flæn/ *n* [C] *especially BrE*【尤英】**1** a round PIE (1) or cake that is filled with fruit, cheese etc 果餡餅, 果醬餅 **2** *AmE* a sweet baked CUSTARD made with eggs【美】〔烤製的〕蛋奶糕 —compare 比較 PIE, QUICHE

flange/flændʒ; flændʒ/ *n* [C] the flat edge that stands out from the main surface of an object such as a railway wheel, to keep it in the right position 凸緣,〔火車的〕輪緣

flank¹/flæŋk; flæŋk/ *n* [C] **1** the side of an animal's or person's body, between the RIBS¹ (1) and the HIP¹ (1) 脇部, 脇腹 —see picture at 參見 HORSE¹ 圖 **2** the side of an army in a battle or war〔軍隊在戰役或戰爭中的〕側翼: *We were attacked on our left flank.* 我們的左翼受到攻擊。 **3** the side of a hill, mountain, or very large building〔山或大建築物的〕側面

flank² *v* **be flanked by** to have something or someone on both sides 兩側有…: *Yeltsin emerged, flanked by his bodyguards.* 葉利欽出現了, 兩側都有他的保鏢。

flan·nel¹/ˋflænl̩; ˈflænl/ *n* **1** [U] soft cloth, usually made of cotton or wool, used for making clothes〔製衣用的〕法蘭絨: *a flannel suit* 法蘭絨套裝 **2** [C] *BrE* a piece of cloth you use to wash yourself【英】〔洗澡用的〕法蘭絨布塊; WASHCLOTH *AmE*【美】**3** [U] *BrE informal* something that someone says that has no real meaning or is not sincere【英, 非正式】廢話, 胡說, 奉承話, 兜圈子的說話 **4 flannels** [plural] *especially BrE* men's trousers made of flannel【尤英】法蘭絨男裝褲子

flannel² *v* [I] *BrE* to say things that are not sincere to avoid answering a question directly【英】〔為避開直接回答而〕兜圈子說

flan·nel·ette /ˌflænl̩ˋɛt; ˌflænəlˈet/ *n* [U] soft cotton cloth used especially for night clothes, sheets etc〔尤用來做睡衣、被單等的〕絨布, 棉法蘭絨

flap¹/flæp; flæp/ *n* **1** [C] a thin flat piece of cloth, paper, skin etc that is fixed by one edge to a surface, which

F

you can lift up easily〔布、紙、皮等做的〕片狀垂懸物〈如口袋蓋等〉: *He lifted the tent flap slowly to see what was making the noise.* 他慢慢提起帳篷的布簾, 看看是甚麼在發出聲音。—see also 另見 CAT FLAP **2** [singular] the noisy movement of something such as cloth in the air 拍打聲: *the flap of the sails* 帆的拍動聲 **3** [singular] *informal* a situation in which people feel very excited, angry, or worried about something【非正式】慌亂, 激動; 生氣; 焦急: **be in a flap** *Rafi's in a bit of a flap over the wedding plans.* 拉菲對婚禮的安排略有點着急。—see also 另見 UNFLAPPABLE **4** [C] a part of the wing of an aircraft that can be raised or lowered to help the aircraft go up or down〔飛機的〕襟翼, 副翼

flap² *v* **1** [I] if a bird flaps its wings, it moves its wings up and down in order to fly〔鳥〕振翼, 撲動翅膀 **2** [I,T] if a piece of cloth, paper etc flaps it moves around quickly and noisily〔布、紙等〕呼啦呼啦地飄動, (使) 擺動: *The flags were flapping in the breeze.* 旗幟在微風中飄揚。**3** [I] *BrE informal* to behave in an excited, nervous, or angry way【英, 非正式】慌亂, 激動, 緊張; 生氣: *There's no need to flap!* 不必緊張! [不要生氣!]

flap·jack /ˈflæp,dʒæk; ˈflæpdʒæk/ *n* [C] **1** *BrE* a cake made of OATS, sugar, SYRUP, and butter【英】甜燕麥餅 **2** *AmE* a thick round unsweetened cake made of flour, milk, and eggs, cooked in a pan and eaten for breakfast; PANCAKE (2)【美】煎餅, 烙餅

flap·per /ˈflæpɚ; ˈflæpə/ *n* [C] a fashionable young woman in the late 1920s who wore short dresses, had short hair, and had ideas that were considered very modern〔20世紀20年代後期穿短裙、束短髮、思想被認為十分現代的〕時髦女子

flare¹ /flɛr; fleə/ *v* **1** also 又作 **flare up** [I] to suddenly begin to burn, or to burn more brightly for a short time 突然燒起來;〔短暫地〕燒旺: *The match flared in the darkness.* 火柴在黑暗中猛然一閃。**2** also 又作 **flare up** [I] if strong feelings flare or flare up, people suddenly become angry, violent etc 突然爆發: *Violence has flared up again in the Middle East.* 中東突然又爆發了暴力事件。**3** also 又作 **flare up** [I] if a disease or illness flares up, it suddenly becomes worse〔疾病〕突然加劇: *My asthma tends to flare up on smoggy days.* 在煙霧天我的氣喘就會加劇。**4** [I,T] to become wider towards the bottom end or edge, or to make something do this 張開, (使) 展開: **[+out]** *The dress flared out from the hips.* 這件連衣裙從腰下開始展寬。| *flared trousers* 喇叭褲 | *The bull flared its nostrils and charged.* 公牛張大了鼻孔向前衝去。—see picture on page A17 參見 A17 頁圖

flare out at sb *phr v* [T] *AmE* to say something suddenly in an angry way【美】突然痛斥: *I said something about the weather and he flared out at me for no reason.* 我談了談天氣, 他卻無緣無故地突然罵起我來。

flare² *n* **1** [C] a piece of equipment that produces a bright flame, or the flame itself, used outdoors as a signal 閃光信號, 信號燈, 信號彈: *Flares marked the landing site.* 信號彈標示了着陸地點。**2** [C usually singular 一般用單數] a sudden bright flame 閃光 **3 flares** [plural] trousers that become wide below the knee 喇叭褲

flare path /ˈ· ·/ *n* [C] a path for aircraft to land on that is lit with special lights〔指引飛機着陸的〕照明跑道

flare-up /ˈ· ·/ *n* [C] **1** a situation in which someone suddenly becomes angry or violent〔怒氣或暴力事件的〕突然爆發: *Apart from one or two flare-ups the match went fairly smoothly.* 除了出現一兩次爭吵外, 比賽進行得還很順利。**2** a situation in which someone suddenly has problems because of a disease or illness after not having any problems for a long time〔疾病的〕突然發作: *a flare-up of her arthritis* 她關節炎的突然發作

3 **flash¹** /flæʃ; flæʃ/ *v*

1 ►SHINE 發光◄ [I,T] to shine suddenly and brightly for a short time, or to make something shine in this way (使) 閃光, 閃亮: *The lightning flashed.* 閃電大作。| **flash sth into/at/towards** *Why is that guy flashing his headlights at me?* 那傢伙為甚麼朝我閃前燈呢? | **flash on and off** (=shine for a short time and then stop shining) 一亮一滅 *Red warning lights flashed on and off.* 紅色警告燈一閃一滅。

2 ►MOVE QUICKLY 迅速移動◄ [I always+adv/prep] to move very quickly 飛馳, 掠過: **[+by/past/through]** *A couple of police cars flashed past, sirens wailing.* 幾輛警車飛馳而過, 警笛聲呼嘯着。

3 ►SHOW STH QUICKLY 快速亮出某物◄ [T] to show something to someone for only a short time 亮出〔隨即收起〕: *He flashed his identification card.* 他出示了一下自己的身分證。

4 ►MEMORIES/IMAGES 記憶/印象◄ [I always+adv/prep] if thoughts, images, memories etc flash through your mind, you suddenly think of them or remember them 閃現: **[+across/through/into]** *The possibility that Frank was lying flashed through my mind.* 我腦中忽然閃過一個念頭, 弗蘭克可能是在撒謊。

5 ►TIME 時間◄ [I always+adv/prep] if a period of time flashes by, past etc, it seems to end very quickly 一閃而過, 飛逝: **[+by/past]** *Our vacation seemed to just flash by.* 我們的假期似乎只是一閃而過。

6 ►PICTURES 圖片◄ [I always+adv/prep] to be shown quickly on television or on a film〔在電視或電影中〕閃現: **[+across/onto/past etc]** *Images of the war flashed across the screen.* 戰爭的圖像在屏幕上閃現。

7 ►EYES 眼睛◄ [I] if your eyes flash, they seem to be very bright for a moment, especially because of a sudden emotion〔尤指由於突如其來的感情而〕閃耀, 發亮: **[+with]** *Janet's blue eyes flashed with anger.* 珍妮特的藍眼睛冒出了怒火。

8 ►NEWS/INFORMATION 新聞/消息◄ [T always+adv/prep] to send news or information somewhere quickly by radio, computer, or SATELLITE (1)〔通過收音機、電腦或衛星〕迅速播出; 傳送: **flash sth to/throughout/all over etc** *News can be flashed all over the world within seconds of its happening.* 新聞可以在事情發生後的幾秒鐘之內發送到世界各地。

9 flash a smile/glance/look etc at sb to smile or look at someone quickly and for a short time 對某人一笑/一瞥/一看等

10 ►SEX ORGANS 性器官◄ [I,T] if a man flashes, he shows his sexual organs in public〔男子〕當眾暴露性器官, 露陰

11 your life flashes before your eyes if your life flashes before your eyes, you suddenly remember many events from your life, especially because you are in great danger and might die〔尤指處於極度危險或臨終時〕平生之事都閃現在眼前

flash sth **around** *phr v* [T] to show people that you have a lot of money in order to try and make them admire you 炫耀〔金錢〕: *wealthy clients flashing their credit cards around and buying everything in sight* 炫耀着信用卡、見到甚麼買甚麼的富有顧客

flash² *n*

1 ►LIGHT 光◄ [C] a bright light that shines for a short time and then stops shining〔一閃而後消失的〕閃光: *flashes of lightning in the valley* 峽谷裡的閃電光

2 ►CAMERA 照相機◄ [C,U] a special bright light used when taking photographs indoors or when there is not much light 閃光燈: *Did the flash go off?* 閃光燈熄滅了嗎?

3 in a flash/like a flash/quick as a flash very quickly 一會兒, 馬上: *Just wait here. I'll be back in a flash.* 就在這裡等我。我馬上就回來。

4 flash of brilliance/inspiration/intuition/anger if someone has a flash of brilliance, anger etc, they suddenly have a clever idea or suddenly have a particular feeling 才華/靈感/直覺/怒氣的閃現: *Her essays show occasional flashes of brilliance.* 她的論文偶爾顯露出她的才華。

5 ►BRIGHT COLOUR/STH SHINY 豔麗的顏色/閃亮的東西◄ [C] if there is a flash of something brightly coloured or shiny, it appears suddenly for a short time 閃現物; 惹人注目的東西: [+of] *The bird stood watching for the underwater flash of a turning fish.* 那隻鳥站着, 注視着水中瞬間一閃轉身的一尾游魚。

6 ►LOOK 看◄ *BrE humorous* a quick look; GLIMPSE² (1)【英, 幽默】一瞥

7 ►SIGNAL 信號◄ the act of shining a light as a signal〔信號燈的〕閃亮: *Two flashes mean danger.* 兩閃表示危險。

8 a flash in the pan a sudden success that ends quickly and is unlikely to happen again 曇花一現: *Rival record companies assumed the group would be a flash in the pan.* 作為競爭對手的幾家唱片公司認為這個演唱組合只不過是曇花一現而已。

9 ►MILITARY 軍隊的◄ a small piece of coloured cloth worn on the shoulder of a military uniform〔軍裝上的〕肩章 —see also 另見 NEWSFLASH

flash³ *adj* **1** [only before noun 僅用於名詞前] happening very quickly or suddenly, and lasting for only a short time 閃現的, 突發的, 短暫的: *Flash fires swept through the Los Angeles foothills last night.* 昨晚瞬間出現的山火橫掃了洛杉磯的丘陵地帶。—see also 另見 FLASH FLOOD **2** *BrE informal* looking very new, bright, and expensive-looking【英, 非正式】奢華的, 華麗的: *a big flash car* 一輛奢華的大車子 **3** *informal* [not before noun 不用於名詞前] liking to have expensive clothes and possessions so that other people notice you【非正式】愛炫耀的: *Who was that flash geezer we saw you with last night?* 昨晚我們看見和你在一起的那個愛炫耀的傢伙是誰?

F

flash·back /ˈflæʃˌbæk; ˈflæʃbæk/ *n* **1** [C,U] a scene in a film, play, book etc that shows something that happened before that point in the story〔書中的〕倒敍;〔戲劇的〕閃回場景;〔電影的〕閃回鏡頭: *The events of the hero's childhood are shown as a series of flashbacks.* 主人公的童年往事用一連串閃回鏡頭展現出來。**2** [C] a sudden very clear memory of something that happened to you in the past〔往事〕突然記起 **3** [C] *technical* a burning gas or liquid that moves back into a tube or container【術語】火舌回閃; 回火〔指火循管道向氣瓶或油罐退回〕

flash bulb /ˈ· ·/ *n* [C] a small BULB (=a bright light) used when you take photographs indoors or when it is dark outside〔攝影用的〕閃光燈泡

flash burn /ˈ· ·/ *n* [C] a burn that you get from being near a sudden, very hot flame, for example an explosion〔爆炸造成的〕閃光燒傷

flash·card /ˈflæʃkard; ˈflæʃkɑːd/ *n* [C] a card with a word or picture on it, used in teaching〔上面有單詞或圖畫, 用於教學的〕抽示卡

flash·er /ˈflæʃɚ; ˈflæʃə/ *n* [C] a man who shows his sexual organs to women in public〔公開在女子前〕露陰的男子, 暴露狂

flash flood /ˌ· ˈ·/ *n* [C] a sudden flood that is caused by a lot of rain falling in a short period of time 暴洪, 驟發的洪水

flash freeze /ˌ· ˈ·/ *v* [T] to freeze food quickly so that the quality is not damaged 將〔食品〕速凍

flash·gun /ˈflæʃˌgʌn; ˈflæʃgʌn/ *n* [C] a piece of equipment that lights a special bright light when you press the button on a camera to take a photograph〔攝影用的〕閃光槍

flash·light /ˈflæʃˌlaɪt; ˈflæʃlaɪt/ *n* [C] a small electric light that you can carry in your hand 手電筒; TORCH¹ (1) *BrE*【英】

flash·point /ˈflæʃˌpɔɪnt; ˈflæʃpɔɪnt/ *n* [C] **1** a place where trouble or violence might easily develop suddenly and be hard to control〔動亂或暴力的〕爆發點, 一觸即發的地點: *Beirut is one of the flashpoints of the Middle East.* 貝魯特是中東的一個戰爭熱點。**2** [usually singular 一般用單數] *technical* the lowest temperature at which a liquid such as oil will produce enough gas to burn if a flame is put near it【術語】燃點, 閃點, 引火點

flash·y /ˈflæʃɪ; ˈflæʃi/ *adj informal* too big, bright, or expensive in a way that other people disapprove of【非正式】俗豔的, 華而不實的: *Marc always drove large flashy cars.* 馬克總是開豪華而俗氣的大車子。

flask /flæsk; flɑːsk/ *n* [C] **1** *BrE* a special type of bottle that you use to keep liquids either hot or cold, for example when travelling【英】保温瓶 **2** a flat bottle usually used to carry alcohol 扁酒瓶 **3** a glass bottle with a narrow top, used in a LABORATORY〔實驗室用的〕燒瓶

flasks 保温瓶; 瓶子

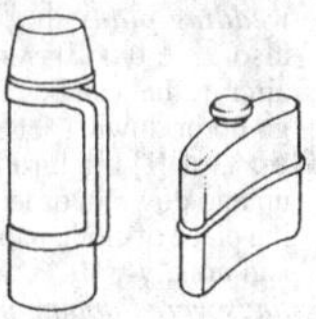

thermos flask 保温瓶 hip flask 扁酒瓶

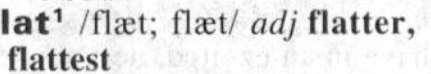

flat¹ /flæt; flæt/ *adj* **flatter, flattest**

1 ►SURFACE 表面◄ smooth and level, without raised or hollow areas, and not sloping or curving 平的, 平坦的: *a flat-bottomed boat* 平底船 | *a perfectly flat sandy beach* 十分平坦的沙灘 | **flat as a pancake** (=very flat) 非常平坦的 *The countryside near there is flat as a pancake.* 那兒附近的鄉間地勢非常平坦。

2 flat rate/price/fee etc a flat rate, price, amount of money etc is fixed and does not change or have anything added to it 統一[固定]的收費率/價格/費用等: *We charge a flat fee for car hire.* 我們的租車費是固定不變的。

3 ►TYRE/BALL 輪胎/球◄ having no air or not enough air in it 沒氣的, 氣不足的

4 ►DRINK 飲料◄ having lost its BUBBLES¹ (1) of gas and so not tasting fresh 走了氣的: *This Coke must have been opened ages ago – it's completely flat!* 這瓶可樂一定是老早就打開的——氣全跑光了!—opposite 反義詞 FIZZY (1)

5 ►NOT INTERESTING 沒有趣味的◄ [not before noun 不用於名詞前] a performance, book etc that is flat seems rather boring〔演出、書等〕沉悶乏味的, 平淡的

6 ►BATTERY 蓄電池◄ *BrE* a flat BATTERY (l) has lost its electrical power【英】電用完了的: **go flat** (=become flat) 電用完, 沒電了 *Have you checked that the batteries haven't gone flat?* 你檢查過電池裡有沒有電嗎?

7 ►BUSINESS/TRADE 生意/貿易◄ not busy 不景氣的, 不興旺的: *The building industry's been completely flat for several years.* 建築業已經蕭條了好幾年。

8 E flat/B flat/A flat etc a musical note that is one SEMITONE lower than the note E, B, A etc 降E調/降B調/降A調等〔音樂中降半音〕

9 ►MUSICAL SOUND 音樂聲◄ if a musical note is flat, it is played or sung at a slightly lower pitch (PITCH¹ (3)) than it should be 降音的; 偏低的: *The guitar was flat through the whole song.* 結他的音調在整首歌裡都偏低。

10 ►VOICE 嗓音◄ not showing much emotion, or not changing much in sound as you speak 平淡的, 無變化的: *"He's dead," she said in a flat voice.* "他死了。"她語調平淡地說道。

11 flat refusal/denial etc a refusal etc that is definite and which someone will definitely not change 斷然拒絕/否認等: *Our requests were met with a flat refusal.* 我們的要求遭到斷然拒絕。

12 and that's flat! *spoken* used to say that you will definitely not change what you have just said【口】絕無二話; 不必多說了: *I won't go, and that's flat!* 我不去, 絕無二話!

13 be flat on your back a) to be lying down so that all of your back is touching the floor 平躺在地上: *Arthur was flat on his back under the car.* 阿瑟平躺在車子下。**b)** to be very ill so that you have to stay in bed for a period of time 臥病在牀

14 ▶SHOES 鞋◀ flat shoes have very low heels〔鞋〕平底的, 無後跟的 —see picture on page A17 參見A17頁圖
15 ▶NOT DEEP 不深的◀ not very deep, thick, or high, especially in comparison to its width or length〔尤指與寬或長相比〕淺的; 薄的; 矮的: *a round, flat apple tart* 一塊又圓又薄的蘋果餅
16 ▶LIGHT 光◀ having little variety of light and dark 無深淺反差的, 無明暗的, 缺乏層次的: *Flat lighting is typical of Avedon's portraits.* 缺乏明暗層次變化是艾夫登拍攝的肖像照的典型特徵。—**flatness** *n* [U] —see also 另見 **fall/go into a flat spin** (SPIN² (4))

2 3 **flat²** *n* [C]
1 ▶PLACE TO LIVE 住的地方◀ *BrE* a place for people to live that consists of a set of rooms that are part of a larger building【英】一套住房; 一套公寓房; APARTMENT *AmE*【美】: *They have a flat in Crouch End.* 他們在克勞奇恩德有一套住房。| *a ground-floor flat* 底層的住房 | **a block of flats** (=a large building with many flats in it) 公寓樓
2 ▶TYRE 輪胎◀ *especially AmE* a tyre that does not have enough air inside【尤美】漏了氣的輪胎; PUNCTURE *BrE*【英】
3 ▶MUSIC 音樂◀ a) a musical note that is one SEMITONE lower than a particular note 降半音 **b)** the sign (♭) in written music that shows that a note is one SEMITONE lower than a particular note 降半音符號 —compare 比較 SHARP³, NATURAL² (2) —see picture at 參見 MUSIC 圖
4 ▶LAND 土地◀ flats [plural] an area of land that is at a low level, especially near water 低窪沼澤地; 淺灘: *mud flats* 淤泥灘
5 the flat of sb's hand/a knife/a sword etc the flat part or flat side of something 手掌/刀面/劍面等
6 on the flat *BrE* on ground that is level and does not slope【英】在平地上: *It's much easier walking on the flat.* 在平地上走路容易多了。

This graph shows how common the nouns **flat** and **apartment** are in British and American English. 本圖表所示為名詞 flat 和 apartment 在英國英語和美國英語中的使用頻率。

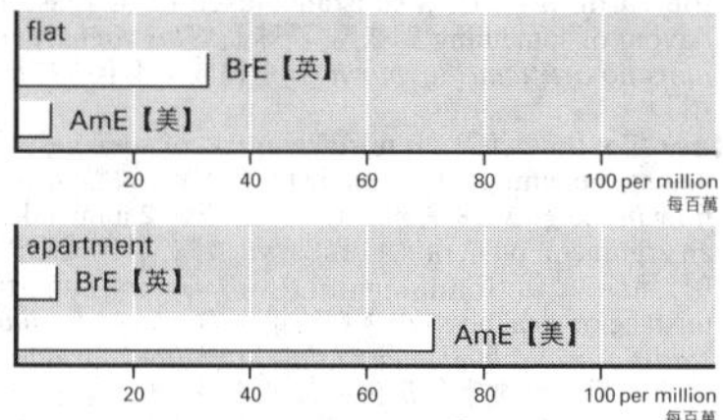

Based on the British National Corpus and the Longman Lancaster Corpus
據英國國家語料庫和朗文蘭卡斯特語料庫

In British English **flat** is used to mean a place where people live, which has a set of rooms including a kitchen and bathroom, and is part of a larger building. Americans use **apartment** for this meaning. In both British and American English **apartment** can be used to mean a large room with expensive furniture, decorations etc, used especially by an important person such as a president or prince. 在英國英語中, flat 用來表示屬於大樓一部分的一套房間(包括廚房和浴室), 作為人們的住所。美國人用 apartment 來表示這個意思。在英國英語和美國英語中, apartment 可用來指有昂貴家具、裝飾豪華的大房間, 特別是像總統或王子這樣的大人物使用的大房間。

flat³ *adv*
1 ▶FLAT POSITION 平直的姿勢◀ in a position in which the surface of something is against another surface without curving or sloping 平直地, 平坦地: **lie flat** *He lay flat on the floor to look for it under the bed.* 他平躺在地上, 向牀底下尋找它。
2 three minutes/10 seconds etc flat *informal* used to emphasize that something happens or is done very quickly【非正式】正好三分鐘/十秒鐘等〔用於強調事情發生的速度或做事的速度很快〕: *I was dressed in five minutes flat.* 我只用了五分鐘就穿好衣服了。
3 fall flat *informal*【非正式】**a)** if a joke or story falls flat, people are not amused by it〔笑話或故事〕不逗樂; 不好笑; 沒引人笑: *Oh Dear! My joke about fat people fell completely flat, didn't it?* 啊, 親愛的!我說的那些有關胖人的笑話一點都不好笑, 是嗎? **b)** if something you have planned falls flat it is unsuccessful〔計劃中所做的事〕完全失敗
4 ▶MUSIC 音樂◀ if you sing or play music flat, you sing or play slightly lower than the correct note so that the sound is unpleasant 降音[調]地, 音調偏低 —compare 比較 SHARP² (4)
5 fall flat on your face a) to fall so that you are lying on your front on the ground 摔趴在地上 **b)** *informal* to not have the result you wanted or expected, especially when this is embarrassing【非正式】達不到預期的效果〔尤指造成窘迫〕: *It is a wonderful theory, but falls flat on its face when put into practice.* 這是一種美妙的理論, 但付諸實行時卻完全行不通。
6 flat out a) *informal* as fast as possible【非正式】以最快速度, 以全速: *They were working flat out to get the job done on time.* 他們正以最快速度工作, 爭取按時完工。**b)** *AmE spoken* in a direct way【美口】坦率地, 直截了當地: **ask/tell sb flat out** *She asked him flat out whether he'd been seeing another woman.* 她直截了當地問他是否在跟另一個女人約會。
7 tell sb flat *BrE spoken* to tell someone something directly and definitely【英口】直截了當地告訴某人: *I told him flat that I didn't want to see him again.* 我直截了當地告訴他我不想再見到他了。
8 go flat against *BrE spoken* to directly disobey someone or ignore them【英口】公然不服從, 公然漠視: *I don't know why you bother to ask – you'll go flat against my advice anyway!* 我不知道你幹嘛還要問我 — 你反正根本不會聽我的話的! —see also 另見 **flat broke** (BROKE² (1))

flat cap /ˌ· ˈ·/ *n* [C] *BrE* a cap made of cloth, with a stiff piece that sticks out at the front【英】(低頂)鴨舌帽 —see picture at 參見 CAP 圖

flat·car /ˈflætˌkɑr; ˈflætkɑː/ *n* [C] *AmE* a railway carriage without a roof or sides, used for carrying goods【美】〔鐵路上運貨的〕平板車, 敞車

flat-chest·ed /ˌ· ˈ··◂/ *adj* a woman who is flat-chested has small breasts〔婦女〕乳房小的, 平胸的

flat feet /ˌ· ˈ·/ *n* [plural] a medical condition in which someone's feet rest flat on the ground because the middle of each foot is not as curved as it should be (扁)平足

flat·fish /ˈflætˌfɪʃ; ˈflætˌfɪʃ/ *n* [C] a type of sea fish with a thin flat body such as COD or PLAICE 比目魚〈如鱈、鰈〉

flat-foot·ed /ˌ· ˈ··◂/ *adj* **1** having flat feet (扁)平足的 **2** *informal* moving in an awkward way; CLUMSY (1)【非正式】拖着腳步走的, 蹣跚而行的 **3** *informal* dealing with situations in a way that is not sensitive to other people's thoughts or feelings【非正式】〔對別人的想法和感情〕不敏感的; 麻木漠然的: *Her husband's grasp on life is flat-footed and practical.* 她的丈夫對生活的看法是淡然的, 很注重實際。**4 catch sb flat-footed** *AmE old-fashioned* to find someone not working at a time when they should be【美, 過時】當場捉住某人〔發現他偷懶不工作〕

flat i·ron /ˈ· ˌ··/ *n* [C] a type of iron used in the past that was not heated by electricity〔舊時不用電的〕熨斗; 烙鐵

flat·let /ˈflætlɪt; ˈflætlət/ *n* [C] *BrE* a small apartment【英】一套小的住房

flat·ly /ˈflætlɪ; ˈflætli/ *adv* **1 flatly refuse/deny/oppose**

etc to say something in a direct and definite way that is not likely to change 斷然拒絕/否認/反對等: *She flatly refused to tell us where he was.* 她斷然拒絕告訴我們他在哪兒。**2** without showing any emotion 平淡地: *"Aunt Alicia has changed her will," she said flatly.* "阿莉西亞姑姑已經改了遺囑。" 她平淡地説道。

flat·mate /ˈflæt͵met; ˈflætmeɪt/ *n* [C] *BrE* someone who shares a flat with one or more other people【英】合住公寓套房者; ROOMMATE (2) *AmE*【美】

flat rac·ing /ˈ· ˌ··/ *n* [U] horse racing without any fences on flat ground (無障礙物的) 平地賽馬 —compare 比較 STEEPLECHASE (1)

flat share /ˈ· ·/ *n* [C] *BrE* an arrangement in which two or more people share an apartment【英】合住公寓套房

flat·ten /ˈflætn̩; ˈflætn/ *v* **1** [I,T] also 又作 **flatten out** to make something flat or flatter or to become flat or flatter (使) 變平: *Noah flattened the cardboard boxes before throwing them away.* 諾亞先把紙箱弄平後才扔掉。| *The land flattened out as we neared the coast.* 我們接近海岸時, 地勢變得低平了。**2** [T] to destroy a building or town by knocking it down, bombing it etc 夷平; 炸平: *Dresden was flattened in the war.* 德累斯頓在戰爭中被夷為平地。**3 flatten yourself against** to press your body against something 把身體緊貼在…: *I flattened myself against the wall.* 我把身體緊貼在牆上。**4** [T] *informal* to defeat someone completely and easily in a game, argument etc【非正式】〔在比賽、爭論中輕而易舉地〕擊敗, 擊倒, 駁倒: *We flattened them 6-0.* 我們以6-0徹底擊敗他們。**5** [T] *informal* to hit someone very hard【非正式】猛打〔某人〕; 毆擊〔某人〕

flat·tened /ˈflætn̩d; ˈflætnd/ *adj* [not before noun 不用於名詞前] unhappy and embarrassed because of what someone has said about you〔因某人説的有關自己的話而感到〕沮喪的; 丟臉的

flat·ter /ˈflætɚ; ˈflætə/ *v* [T] **1** to praise someone in an insincere way in order to please them or get something from them 奉承, 討好, 向…諂媚: *He flattered her, saying how beautiful her eyes were.* 他奉承她, 説她的眼睛有多美麗。**2 be flattered** to be pleased because someone has shown you that they like or admire you〔因被喜歡或看重而〕感到榮幸[高興]: *I was flattered to be asked to write an article for the magazine.* 我很高興獲邀為那本雜誌寫了一篇文章。**3** to make someone look more attractive, thinner, or younger than they really are 使形象勝過〔本人〕: *outfits designed to flatter the fuller figure* 使豐滿的身材更顯婀娜而設計的套裝 **4 flatter yourself** if you flatter yourself that something is true about your abilities or achievements, you make yourself believe it is true, although it is not 自以為是, 自鳴得意: **flatter yourself that** *She flatters herself that she could have been a model.* 她自以為本來是可以當上模特兒的。

flat·ter·er /ˈflætərɚ; ˈflætərə/ *n* [C] someone who flatters people 阿諛奉承者, 拍馬屁的人

flat·ter·ing /ˈflætərɪŋ; ˈflætərɪŋ/ *adj* clothes, pictures etc that are flattering make someone look more attractive than they really are〔衣服、照片等〕使比本人更漂亮的: *You look great! That colour is very flattering on you.* 你看上去太美了! 那種顏色讓你更加漂亮。

flat·ter·y /ˈflætərɪ; ˈflætəri/ *n* [U] insincere praise 奉承, 恭維: *She uses a mixture of charm and flattery to get what she wants.* 她用魅力加恭維來達到自己的目的。| **flattery will get you nowhere!** *humorous spoken* (=flattery will not help you get what you want from me)【幽默, 口】恭維話行不通!

flat·top /ˈflæt͵tɑp; ˈflæt-tɒp/ *n* [C] a type of hair style that is very short and looks flat on top〔指髮式〕平頭 —see picture at 參見 HAIRSTYLE 圖

flat·u·lence /ˈflætʃələns; ˈflætjʊləns/ *n* [U] too much gas in the stomach 腸胃氣脹 —**flatulent** *adj*

flat·ware /ˈflæt͵wɛr; ˈflætˌweə/ *n* [U] *AmE* a word for knives, forks, and spoons; CUTLERY【美】(扁平) 餐具〔指刀、叉和匙〕

flaunt /flɔnt; flɔːnt/ *v* [T] **1** to show your money, success, beauty etc so that other people notice it 誇耀, 炫耀: *In New York the rich flaunt their wealth while the poor starve on the streets.* 在紐約, 富人炫耀自己的財富, 而窮人則流落街頭挨餓。**2 if you've got it, flaunt it** *humorous spoken* used to tell someone not to hide their beauty, wealth, or abilities【幽默, 口】〔美麗、財富或能力〕如果擁有, 就要展示出來

flau·tist /ˈflɔtɪst; ˈflɔːtɪst/ *n* [C] *BrE* someone who plays the FLUTE【英】吹長笛的人; 長笛手; FLUTIST *AmE*【美】

fla·vor·ful /ˈflevɚful; ˈfleɪvəfʊl/ *adj AmE* having a strong pleasant taste【美】味濃而可口的: *a flavorful Mexican dish* 美味可口的墨西哥菜

fla·vour[1] *BrE*【英】, **flavor** *AmE*【美】/ˈflevɚ; ˈfleɪvə/ *n* **1** [C] the particular taste of a food or drink 味, 味道: *Which flavor do you want – chocolate or vanilla?* 你要哪種味道的, 巧克力味還是香草味? **2** [U] the quality of tasting good or pleasant 任何滋味, 味道: *A pinch of herbs will add flavour to any dish.* 一撮香草會給菜餚增添味道。**3** [singular] a quality or feature that makes something have a particular style or character 特色, 特點: *The stories have a strong regional flavour.* 這些故事有很強的地區特色。**4** [singular] an idea of what the typical qualities of something are 特色; 情調; 風味: *Marston's book gives you a flavour of life in the 16th century.* 馬斯頓的書讓你體會到16世紀的生活特色。**5 flavour of the month** the idea, person, style etc that is the most popular one for a short time 當前最受歡迎的思想[人物、風格等]: *Health care reform seems to be the political flavor of the month.* 保健改革似乎是本月最受歡迎的政治話題。

flavour[2] *BrE*【英】, **flavor** *AmE*【美】—*v* [T] to give something a particular taste or more taste 加味於…, 使更有…味道

fla·voured *BrE*【英】, **flavored** *AmE*【美】/ˈflevɚd; ˈfleɪvəd/ *adj* **1 strawberry-flavoured/chocolate-flavoured etc** tasting of strawberries, chocolate etc 草莓味的/巧克力味的等 **2** having had a flavour added 加味的, 調味的: *flavored milk* 加了味道的牛奶

fla·vour·ing *BrE*【英】, **flavoring** *AmE*【美】/ˈflevərɪŋ; ˈfleɪvərɪŋ/ *n* [C,U] a substance used to increase the flavour of something 調味劑; 調味品: *This yoghurt contains no artificial flavourings.* 這種酸奶不含人造調味劑。

flaw /flɔ; flɔː/ *n* [C] **1** a mistake, mark, or weakness that makes something imperfect; DEFECT[1] 瑕疵, 缺點: *a slight flaw in the glass* 玻璃杯上的一小點瑕疵 **2** a mistake in an argument, plan, or set of ideas〔論點、計劃或思想中的〕錯誤, 缺陷: **fundamental flaw** (=a very important mistake or weakness) 根本性的錯誤 *The lack of reliable statistics was a fundamental flaw in Walton's argument.* 缺乏可靠統計數字是沃爾頓論點的根本缺陷。| **fatal flaw** (=a very important weakness that makes something certain to fail) 致命的弱點 **3** a fault in someone's character〔性格上的〕缺點: *Jealousy is Othello's major flaw.* 妒忌是奧塞羅的主要缺點。

flawed /flɔd; flɔːd/ *adj* having a mistake or weakness 有缺點的, 有瑕疵的, 有錯誤的: *In many cases the data was incomplete or flawed.* 在許多情況下, 數據要麼不完整, 要麼有錯誤。

flaw·less /ˈflɔlɪs; ˈflɔːləs/ *adj* having no mistakes, marks, or weaknesses; PERFECT[1] (2) 無缺點的, 無痕的, 無瑕的: *Peterson's flawless performance as the hero* 扮演英雄的彼得森那完美的演出 —**flawlessly** *adv*

flax /flæks; flæks/ *n* [U] **1** a plant with blue flowers, used for making cloth and oil 亞麻 **2** the thread made from this plant, used for making LINEN (2) 亞麻纖維

flax·en /ˈflæksn̩; ˈflæksən/ *adj literary* flaxen hair is light in colour【文】〔頭髮〕亞麻色的, 淡黃色的

flay /fle; fleɪ/ *v* [T] **1** to criticize someone very severely 嚴厲批評, 痛斥: *I came out of the meeting feeling thor-*

oughly flayed and harassed. 我從會場走出來, 感覺受到徹底的嚴厲批評, 十分煩惱。**2** *literary* to whip or beat someone very severely 【文】鞭打, 猛擊

flea /fli; fliː/ *n* [C] **1** a very small insect without wings that jumps and bites animals and people to eat their blood 跳蚤 **2 send sb off with a flea in their ear** to talk angrily to someone, especially because they have done something you disapprove of〔尤指因某人做了你不贊成的事而〕用譏誚話氣走某人

flea·bag /ˈfli͵bæg; ˈfliːbæg/ *n* [C] **1** *BrE* a dirty animal or person that you dislike 【英】骯髒邋遢的動物[人] **2** *AmE* a cheap dirty hotel 【美】廉價但骯髒的旅館

flea·bite /ˈfli͵baɪt; ˈfliːbaɪt/ *n* [C] the bite of a flea 蚤咬

flea col·lar /ˈ· ͵··/ *n* [C] a special collar, worn by a dog or cat, that contains chemicals to keep fleas away from them〔給貓狗戴的含化學劑的〕滅蚤項圈

flea mar·ket /ˈ· ͵··/ *n* [C] a market where old or used goods are sold 跳蚤市場〔賣舊貨的市場〕

flea·pit /ˈfli͵pɪt; ˈfliː͵pɪt/ *n* [C] *old-fashioned humorous* a cheap dirty cinema or theatre 【過時, 幽默】蚤窩〔指廉價骯髒的電影院或劇院〕

fleck /flɛk; flek/ *n* [C] a small mark or spot 斑點; 微粒: [+of] *flecks of dust* 塵土粒

flecked /flɛkt; flekt/ *adj* having small marks or spots 有斑點的: *red cloth flecked with white* 有小白點的紅布

fledged /flɛdʒd; fledʒd/ *adj* —see 見 FULLY-FLEDGED

fledg·ling[1], **fledgeling** /ˈflɛdʒlɪŋ; ˈfledʒlɪŋ/ *n* [C] a young bird that is learning to fly 學飛的小鳥

fledgling[2], **fledgeling** *adj* [only before noun 僅用於名詞前] a fledgling state, or organization, has only recently been formed and is still developing〔國家或組織〕新形成的: *a fledgling republic* 新建立的共和國

flee /fli; fliː/ *past tense and past participle* **fled** /flɛd; fled/ *v* [I,T] to leave somewhere very quickly in order to escape from danger 逃, 逃走: *When they saw the police car, his attackers turned and fled.* 攻擊他的人看到警車時轉身就逃。| **flee the country/city** *We were forced to flee the country.* 我們被迫逃離這個國家。| [+from/to/into] *Many German artists fled to America at the beginning of World War II.* 第二次世界大戰初期, 許多德國藝術家逃到美國。

fleece[1] /flis; fliːs/ *n* [C] **1** the woolly coat of a sheep〔剪下而仍連在一起的〕羊毛 **2** an artificial soft material used to make warm coats〔用於製保暖衣服的〕人造柔軟面料

fleece[2] *v* [T] *informal* to charge someone too much money for something 【非正式】向...過多收費; 高價欺詐; 敲...的竹槓

flee·cy /ˈflisɪ; ˈfliːsi/ *adj* soft and woolly, or looking soft and woolly 羊毛的; 羊毛似的; 毛茸茸的: *fleecy white towels* 毛茸茸的白毛巾

fleet[1] /flit; fliːt/ *n* [C] **1** a group of ships, or all the ships in a navy 船隊; 艦隊: *the US seventh fleet* 美國第七艦隊 **2** a group of planes, cars etc that are controlled by one company〔某家公司控制的〕機羣, 車隊: *a fleet of taxis* 計程車隊

fleet[2] *adj literary* fast, quick 【文】快速的, 迅捷的: **fleet of foot** (=fast at running) 跑得快的, 飛毛腿 (的)

fleet ad·mi·ral /ˈ· ͵···/ *n* [C] the highest rank in the US navy, or someone who holds this rank〔美國的〕海軍五星上將 —see table on page C6 參見 C6 頁附錄

fleet·ing /ˈflitɪŋ; ˈfliːtɪŋ/ *adj* [usually before noun 一般用於名詞前] lasting for only a short time 短暫的, 飛逝的: **fleeting glimpse/impression/glance etc** *I caught a fleeting glimpse of them as they drove past.* 他們開車駛過時, 我飛快地看了他們一眼。| **fleeting moment** *For one fleeting moment, I thought I recognized her.* 剎那間我覺得我認出了她。—**fleetingly** *adv*

Fleet Street /ˈ· ·/ *n* [singular] a street in London where many important newspaper offices used to be, often used as a name for the British newspaper industry 艦隊街〔倫敦的一條街, 過去為大報館的辦公所在地, 常用來泛指英國報業界〕

Flem·ish /ˈflɛmɪʃ; ˈflemɪʃ/ *n* [U] a language like German spoken in northern Belgium 佛蘭芒語〔比利時北部地區使用, 近似德語〕

flesh[1] /flɛʃ; fleʃ/ *n* [U] **1** the soft part of the body of a person or animal that is between the skin and the bones〔人或動物的〕肉: **flesh wound** (=a slight injury from a knife or bullet) 皮肉之傷 **2** the soft part of a fruit or vegetable that can be eaten 果肉, 蔬菜的可食部分: *Cut the melon in half and scoop out the flesh.* 把瓜切成兩半, 然後挖出瓜肉。**3 in the flesh** if you see or meet someone in the flesh, you see or meet someone who you previously had only seen in pictures or films 本人: *Fans flocked to see their heroes in the flesh.* 影迷們成羣結隊去看他們的英雄本人。**4 make sb's flesh creep/crawl** to make someone feel frightened 使某人毛骨悚然[膽戰心驚]: *The way he always stared at her made her flesh creep.* 他總是盯着她看的樣子使她毛骨悚然。**5 your own flesh and blood** someone who is part of your family 親人, 親骨肉: *I couldn't see my own flesh and blood insulted in this way.* 我不能眼睜睜看着我的親人這樣受侮辱。**6 the spirit is willing but the flesh is weak** used to say that you would like to do something, but are not strong enough, either physically or mentally, to do it 心有餘而力不足, 力不從心 **7 the flesh** *literary* the physical human body, as opposed to the mind or spirit 【文】〔相對於靈魂或精神的〕肉體: **the pleasures of the flesh** (=things such as drinking, eating a lot, or having sex) 肉體上的享受 **8 put flesh on** to give more details about something to make it clear, more interesting etc 充實, 加細節於...: *I'll try to put some flesh on the plan Margaret has outlined.* 我將盡力使瑪格麗特勾畫的計劃更為充實。**9 more than flesh and blood can stand/bear** used to describe something that you find too unpleasant to think about 常人所忍受不了的 **10 go the way of all flesh** *literary* to die 【文】謝世, 去世 —see also 另見 **get your pound of flesh** (POUND[2] (6)), **press the flesh** (PRESS[2] (15)) 3

flesh[2] *v*

flesh sth ↔ out *phr v* [T] to add more details to something in order to improve it 使充實, 使完善: *You need to flesh out your argument with a few more examples.* 你需要再多用幾個案例來充實你的論點。

flesh-col·oured *BrE* 【英】, **flesh-colored** *AmE* 【美】 /ˈ· ͵··/ *adj* having a pinkish colour like that of white people's skin 肉色的, (白人) 膚色的: *flesh-coloured tights* 肉色緊身褲

flesh·ly /ˈflɛʃlɪ; ˈfleʃli/ *adj* [only before noun 僅用於名詞前] *literary* physical, especially sexual 【文】肉體的; 〔尤指〕肉慾的

flesh·pots /ˈflɛʃ͵pɑts; ˈfleʃpɒts/ *n* [plural] *humorous* areas where there are many places that people go to for pleasure, especially sexual pleasure 【幽默】滿足肉慾的場所; 尋歡作樂的地方

flesh·y /ˈflɛʃɪ; ˈfleʃi/ *adj* **1** having a lot of flesh 多肉的: *the fleshy part of your hand* 你手掌上肉多的部分 **2** having a soft, thick inner part 肉質的: *a plant with dark green fleshy leaves* 帶深綠色多肉質葉子的植物

flew /flu; fluː/ the past tense of FLY[1]

flex[1] /flɛks; fleks/ *v* [T] **1** to tighten your muscles or bend part of your body 收緊〔肌肉〕; 屈曲〔身體部位〕 **2 flex your muscles** to show your ability to do something, especially your skill or power 展示你的實力〔尤指技藝或權勢〕

flex[2] *n* [C] *BrE* an electrical wire covered with plastic, used to connect electrical equipment to an electricity supply 【英】〔電器用〕花線, 皮線; CORD[1] (3) *AmE* 【美】 —see also 另見 LEAD[2] (8)

flex·ib·il·i·ty /͵flɛksəˈbɪlətɪ; ͵fleksəˈbɪləti/ *n* [U] **1** the ability to change or be changed easily to suit a different situation 靈活性 **2** the ability to bend or be bent easily 彈性, 柔性

flex·i·ble /ˈflɛksəbl; ˈfleksəbəl/ *adj* **1** a person, plan etc that is flexible can change or be changed easily to suit

F

any new situation 靈活的, 可變通的: *We can be flexible about your starting date.* 我們對你開始的日期可靈活處理。—opposite 反義詞 INFLEXIBLE **2** something that is flexible can bend or be bent easily 易彎曲的, 有彈性的: *shoes with flexible rubber soles* 帶彈性橡膠底的鞋 —**flexibly** *adv*

flex·i·time /ˈflɛksɪtaɪm; ˈfleksitaɪm/ *BrE*【英】, **flex·time** /ˈflɛkstaɪm; ˈflekstaɪm/ *AmE*【美】—*n* [U] a system in which people work a fixed number of hours each week or month, but can change the times at which they start and finish each day 彈性工作時間制

flick¹ /flɪk; flɪk/ *v* **1** [T] to make something move away by hitting or pushing it suddenly or quickly, especially with your thumb and finger〔尤指用大拇指和另一手指〕彈去, 拂去: **flick sth from/off etc** *Papa flicked the ash from his cigar.* 爸爸彈去雪茄煙上的煙灰。| **flick sth ↔ away/off etc** *I flicked away the dandruff from his shoulders.* 我輕輕拂去他肩上的頭皮屑。—see picture on page A20 參見A20頁圖 **2** [I always+adv/prep,T] to move with a sudden, quick movement or to make something move in this way 晃動, 拍動; 抖掉: **[+from/up/down]** *The cow's tail flicked from side to side.* 母牛的尾巴左右甩動。**3** [T] to make a light, machine etc stop or start working by pressing or moving a button 按動鈕鍵啪地開動[關閉]: **flick sth ↔ on/off** *Sandra flicked the TV on.* 桑德拉啪地打開電視。**4** [T] if you flick something such as a whip or rope, you move it so that the end moves quickly away from you 用〔鞭或繩等〕輕拂, 輕快地甩打: *Ricky flicked a towel at his sister's bare legs.* 里基用毛巾輕輕拍打他妹妹赤裸的雙腿。

flick through sth *phr v* [T] to look at a book, magazine, set of photographs etc quickly 很快地瀏覽〔書、雜誌、照片等〕

flick² *n* **1** [C] a short, light, sudden movement or hit with a part of your body, whip etc 輕打, 輕彈; 抖動: *With a flick of the wrist, Frye sent the ball into the opposite court.* 弗萊伊一抖手腕, 把球打到對方的球場。**2 a flick of a switch** used to emphasize how easy it is to start a machine and use it (只要) 輕輕一撥開關 (就行了)〔用來強調開動和使用機器很容易〕: *All it takes is a flick of a switch.* 所需要做的只是輕輕一撥開關。**3** [C usually singular 一般用單數] *old-fashioned especially AmE* a film【過時, 尤美】電影 **4 the flicks** *BrE old-fashioned* the cinema【英, 過時】電影院 **5 have a flick through** to look at a book, magazine, set of pictures etc very quickly 很快瀏覽〔書、雜誌、照片等〕: *I had a quick flick through your report.* 我很快翻看了你的報告。

flick·er¹ /ˈflɪkɚ; ˈflɪkə/ *v* [I] **1** to burn or shine with an unsteady light that goes on and off quickly〔光〕閃爍, 搖曳: *The candle flickered.* 燭光搖曳着。**2** [always+adv/prep] if an emotion or expression flickers on someone's face or through their mind, it exists or is shown for only a short time〔感情或表情〕閃現: **[+across/through/on etc]** *A puzzled smile flickered across the lady's face.* 那位女士的臉上掠過一絲困惑的微笑。**3** to quickly make a sudden small movement or series of movements 抖動, 顫動: *Polly's eyelids flickered for a moment, then she slept.* 波莉的眼皮眨了一會兒, 然後她就睡了。

flicker² *n* [C] **1** an unsteady light that goes on and off quickly〔光的〕閃爍, 搖曳: *the flicker of the firelight* 火光的閃爍 **2 a flicker of interest/remorse/guilt etc** a feeling or expression that continues for a very short time 一時的興趣/悔恨/內疚等 **3** a quick sudden movement or series of movements〔一次或一系列的〕抖動, 顫動

flick knife /ˈ· ·/ *n* [C] *BrE* a knife with a blade inside the handle that moves quickly into position when you press a button【英】彈簧折刀; SWITCHBLADE *AmE*【美】

fli·er /ˈflaɪɚ; ˈflaɪə/ *n* another spelling of FLYER flyer 的另一種拼法

flies /flaɪz; flaɪz/ —see 見 FLY³

flight /flaɪt; flaɪt/ *n*

1 ►TRAVEL 旅行◄ [C] a journey in a plane or space vehicle〔乘坐飛機或太空飛船的〕飛行: *It's an hour's flight to Paris from here.* 從這裡坐飛機到巴黎要一小時。

2 ►PLANE 飛機◄ [C] a plane making a particular journey 班機, 航班: *TWA Flight 284* 環球航空公司284號航班 | **call a flight** (=tell people the plane is ready to leave)〔機場中的廣播系統〕通知旅客某班機即將起飛 *I've got to run – my flight's been called.* 我得快點走了——已經廣播我的班機即將起飛了。—see also 另見 CHARTER FLIGHT

3 ►FLYING 飛行◄ [U] the act of flying through the air 飛行, 飛翔: **in flight** *pelicans in flight* 飛翔中的鵜鶘

4 ►STAIRS 樓梯◄ [C] a set of stairs between one floor and the next〔兩個樓層間的〕一段樓梯: *Bert lives two flights down from here.* 伯特住在從這裡下兩層樓的地方。| **flight of stairs** *She tripped and fell down a whole flight of stairs.* 她絆了一跤, 從樓梯上摔下來, 摔了整整一段樓梯。

5 ►ESCAPE 逃跑◄ [U] the act of escaping from a dangerous situation or a difficult problem〔從險[困]境中的〕逃走, 逃跑: **[+from]** *Donald Wood's hasty flight from South Africa early in 1978* 1978年唐納德·伍德匆忙逃離南非

6 take (to) flight to run away in order to try and escape from someone 逃跑: *The rest of the gang took flight.* 其餘的幫匪逃跑了。

7 put sb to flight *old-fashioned* make someone run away in order to try and escape【過時】使某人潰逃; 把某人趕得倉遑逃命

8 flight of imagination/fancy/fantasy thoughts, ideas etc that are full of imagination but that are not practical or sensible 馳騁的想像/幻想

9 ►BIRDS 鳥類◄ [C] a group of birds all flying together 一羣飛鳥: *a flight of swallows* 一羣飛燕 —see also 另見 IN-FLIGHT, TOP-FLIGHT

flight at·tend·ant /ˈ· ·,··/ *n* [C] someone who looks after the comfort and safety of the passengers on a plane; STEWARD (1) or STEWARDESS 空中服務員

flight deck /ˈ· ·/ *n* [C] **1** the flat surface of a ship which military aircraft use to fly into the air from〔航空母艦的〕飛行甲板 **2** the room in a plane where the pilot sits to control the plane〔飛機的〕駕駛艙

flight·less /ˈflaɪtləs; ˈflaɪtləs/ *adj* unable to fly 不能飛的: *a flightless bird* 一種不能飛的鳥

flight lieu·ten·ant /,· ·ˈ··◂/ *n* [C] *BrE* a middle rank in the British air force, or someone who holds this rank【英】空軍上尉 —see table on page C7 參見C7頁附錄

flight path /ˈ· ·/ *n* [C] the course that a plane or space vehicle travels along〔飛機或太空飛船的〕飛行路線

flight re·cord·er /ˈ· ·,··/ *n* [C] a piece of equipment in an aircraft that records details such as the plane's speed and direction; BLACK BOX 飛行記錄儀, 黑匣子

flight ser·geant /ˈ· ,··/ *n* [C] *BrE* a middle rank in the British air force, or someone who holds this rank【英】空軍上士 —see table on page C7 參見C7頁附錄

flight sim·u·la·tor /ˈ· ,····/ *n* [C] a machine that imitates the movements of an aircraft, used to train pilots〔訓練飛行員的〕飛行模擬器

flight·y /ˈflaɪtɪ; ˈflaɪti/ *adj* a woman who is flighty changes her ideas or activities a lot without finishing them or being serious about them〔女子〕反覆無常的, 輕浮的, 見異思遷的 —**flightiness** *n* [U]

flim·flam /ˈflɪm,flæm; ˈflɪmflæm/ *n informal*【非正式】**1** [U] stories, information etc that do not seem serious or true 胡扯, 廢話, 鬼話, 怪談: *all this psychic flimflam* 所有這些有關通靈的鬼話 **2** [C usually singular 一般用單數] a trick intended to cheat someone 欺詐手段; 鬼把戲 —**flimflam** *v* [T]

flim·sy /ˈflɪmzɪ; ˈflɪmzi/ *adj* **1** flimsy cloth or clothing is light and thin, and can tear easily〔布或衣服〕輕而薄的, 易撕破的, 易磨損的: *a flimsy summer dress* 一件輕而薄的夏裝連衣裙 **2** flimsy equipment, buildings etc are not well-made and are easily broken〔設備、建築物等〕不結實的, 易損壞的 **3** a flimsy argument, excuse etc is not believable〔論點、藉口等〕不可信的: *The evidence against him is extremely flimsy.* 不利於他的那些證據十分不足信。—**flimsily** *adv* —**flimsiness** *n* [U]

flinch /flɪntʃ; flɪntʃ/ *v* [I] **1** to make a sudden small backward movement when you are shocked by pain or afraid of something〔因疼痛或害怕而〕退縮, 畏縮 **2 sb didn't (even) flinch** used to say that someone did not seem surprised about something 某人對某事絲毫不感到驚奇[不退縮] **3** to avoid doing something because you dislike it or are afraid of it〔因厭惡或害怕而〕迴避: **never flinch from doing sth** *He never flinched from doing his duty.* 他從來不逃避自己的責任。

fling¹ /flɪŋ; flɪŋ/ *v past tense and past participle* **flung** /flʌŋ; flʌŋ/ [T]

1 ►THROW 扔◄ [always+adv/prep] to throw something quickly with a lot of force〔用力地〕扔, 拋, 擲, 丟: **fling sth at/into/on etc** *Spectators flung bottles and cans at the marchers.* 觀眾向遊行者扔瓶子和罐子。| **fling sth ↔ down** *Sammy flings down his coat and stomps upstairs.* 薩米扔下大衣, 重步走到樓上去。

2 ►BODY 身體◄ [always+adv/prep] to move yourself or part of your body suddenly and with a lot of force〔突然〕撲向; 猛動, 急伸: **[+down/through/towards etc]** *Ian flung himself down on his bed.* 伊恩一下撲倒在牀上。| **fling sth around/towards etc** *Flinging his arms around her, he kissed her.* 他張開雙臂抱住她, 吻了她。| **fling sth ↔ back/out etc** *Katie flung back her head and laughed.* 凱蒂猛然仰起頭, 大笑起來。

3 fling yourself into to begin to do something using a lot of effort 全力投入, 投身於: *After the divorce he flung himself into his work and tried to forget her.* 他離婚後全力投入工作, 努力把她忘掉。

4 fling a door/window etc open to quickly and suddenly open a door, window etc 猛力打開門/窗等: *We flung open all the windows.* 我們猛地打開所有的窗。

5 fling sb in prison/jail to put someone in prison, often without having a good reason〔常指沒有充分理由而〕把某人投入監獄: *Opposition leaders were flung into jail.* 反對派領導人被投入監獄。

fling sth **↔ off** *phr v* to quickly remove a piece of clothing, a sheet, or a cover 匆忙地脫掉; 掀掉〔衣、被等〕: *Tom flung off his blanket in the middle of the night.* 湯姆在半夜一下扔開了毛毯。

fling sb/sth **↔ out** *phr v* [T] *especially BrE*【尤英】**1** to suddenly make someone leave an organization or place 突然趕走[開除] **2 [fling sth ↔ out]** to get rid of something you no longer want or need 丟棄, 甩掉〔不再需要的東西〕

fling² *n* [C usually singular 一般用單數] **1** a short and not very serious sexual relationship 一時的放縱[行樂]: **have a fling** *They had a brief fling years ago.* 他們幾年前有過一段很短暫的風流韻事。**2** a short period of time during which you enjoy yourself without worrying about anything 一陣的盡情享樂: **have your fling** *I'm going to have my fling first and see a bit of the world.* 我要先盡情玩一下, 見見世面。

flint /flɪnt; flɪnt/ *n* **1** [C,U] a type of smooth hard stone, usually black or grey in colour, or a piece of this stone 燧石, 火石 **2** [C] a piece of this stone or a small piece of metal that makes a small flame when you strike it with steel 打火石〔打火機用的電石〕

flint·lock /ˈflɪntˌlɑk; ˈflɪntlɒk/ *n* [C] a gun used in the past〔舊時用的〕燧發槍, 明火槍

flint·y /ˈflɪntɪ; ˈflɪnti/ *adj* a flinty expression or person does not show emotions 強硬的; 冷酷的; 鐵石心腸的: *Duvall gave him a flinty stare.* 杜瓦爾冷冷地瞪了他一眼。

flip¹ /flɪp; flɪp/ **flipped, flipping** *v* **1** [T] to turn something over or into a different position with a quick, sudden movement〔突然很快地〕翻倒, 翻動: **flip sth ↔ open** *Paula flipped the lid of the printer open.* 葆拉迅速翻開打印機的蓋。**2** [T] to make a flat object such as a coin go upwards and turn over in the air; TOSS¹ (4) 拋擲〔硬幣等〕: *We flipped a coin to see who would go first.* 我們拋擲硬幣, 看由誰先去。**3** [I] *informal* also 又作 **flip out** to suddenly become very angry or upset【非正式】大發雷霆; 心煩意亂: *Dad flipped when he found out I'd been skipping school.* 爸爸發現我在逃學, 頓時大發雷霆。| **flip your lid** (=suddenly become very angry) 大發雷霆, 暴跳如雷 **4** [I] *AmE informal* to feel very excited and like something very much【美, 非正式】着迷: **[+over]** *Krissy really flipped over our kitten.* 克里西對我們的小貓着了迷。**5** *especially AmE* [T] to quickly start or stop electrical equipment by pressing or moving a button【尤美】輕壓〔按鈕〕, 輕輕撥動〔按鈕〕: *Who flipped the switch?* 誰按動了開關? | **flip sth ↔ on/off** *Josie flipped on the radio.* 喬西啪地打開收音機。

flip sb **↔ off** *phr v* [T] *AmE* also 又作 **flip sb the bird** to make a rude sign at someone by raising your middle finger and keeping your other fingers down【美】〔朝某人〕伸出中指〔一種侮辱性的手勢〕

flip out *phr v* [I] *informal*【非正式】**1** to suddenly become very angry or upset 大發雷霆; 心煩意亂: *Francie will flip out if you get a scratch on her new car.* 要是你劃損了弗朗西的新車, 她會大發雷霆。**2** to suddenly start behaving in a crazy way 突然發瘋, 失去理智[自我控制]: *The paper says a veteran flipped out and gunned down a bunch of people.* 報上說一位老兵失去理智, 開槍打倒了一羣人。

flip over *phr v* [I,T] to turn something from one side onto the other 翻轉: *Larry flipped over onto his other side, trying to get comfortable.* 拉里把身體翻到另一側, 想讓自己舒服點。| **flip sth ↔ over** *Mary flipped over the cushions on the couch.* 瑪麗翻轉沙發上的坐墊。

flip through sth *phr v* [T] to look at a book, magazine etc quickly 快速瀏覽[翻閱]〔書、雜誌等〕

flip² *n* [C] **1** a quick, light hit with your thumb or finger, especially one that makes an object turn over in the air〔用拇指或別的手指〕輕拋, 輕彈: *a flip of the coin* 捻擲硬幣 **2** a movement in which you jump up and turn over in the air, so that your feet go over your head 筋斗, 空翻

flip³ *adj informal* FLIPPANT【非正式】輕率的, 輕浮的

flip chart /ˈ· ·/ *n* [C] large pieces of paper that are connected at the top so that the pages can be turned over to present information to groups of people〔頂部互相連着的〕翻頁掛圖

flip-flop¹ /ˈ· ·/ *n* [C] a type of open shoe, usually made of rubber, with only a V-shaped band across the front to hold your feet〔一般用橡膠製的〕平底人字拖鞋; THONGS (2) *AmE*【美】—see picture at 參見 SHOE¹ 圖

flip-flop² *v* [I] *AmE informal* to change your opinion about something【美, 非正式】改變觀點

flip·pant /ˈflɪpənt; ˈflɪpənt/ *adj* not being serious about something that other people think you should be serious about, so that they think you do not care 輕率的, 輕浮的: *A hospital is hardly the place for such flippant remarks.* 醫院決不是說這種輕率話的地方。—**flippantly** *adv* —**flippancy** *n* [U]

flip·per /ˈflɪpɚ; ˈflɪpə/ *n* [C] **1** a flat part on the body of some large sea animals such as SEALs, used for swimming〔海豹等的〕鰭狀肢, 鰭足 **2** a large flat rubber shoe worn to help you swim faster〔使人能游快些的〕腳蹼, 鴨腳板

flip·ping /ˈflɪpɪŋ; ˈflɪpɪŋ/ *adj BrE spoken* used to emphasize what you are saying when you are annoyed【英口】該死的, 討厭的〔用作強調〕: *I'm not flipping waiting any longer.* 見鬼的, 我不再等了。—**flipping** *adv*

flip side /ˈ· ·/ *n* [singular] **1** the side of a record that has

F

a song on it that is less popular than the one on the other side（唱片的）反面〔上面的歌曲不像正面的那麼流行〕**2** the bad effects of something, after you have just described the good effects 負面，反面，不好的方面〔用於對比剛描述過的好的方面〕: *The flip side is that it may cause more pollution.* 負面影響是這可能造成更多污染。

flirt[1] /flɝt; flɜːt/ *v* [I] to behave towards and talk to someone as though you are sexually attracted to them, but not in a very serious way 調情，打情罵俏: **[+with]** *Tony flirted with every woman at the party.* 托尼跟聚會上的每一個女人調情。

flirt with sth *phr v* [T not in passive 不用被動態] **1** to consider doing something, but not be very serious about it 不認真地考慮 **2** to take an unnecessary risk and not be worried about it 輕率從事，不認真對待: *The Prince has always enjoyed flirting with danger.* 王子總是喜歡不假思索便去冒險。

flirt[2] *n* [C] someone who often behaves towards and talks to people as though she or he is sexually attracted to them, but not in a very serious way 調情者

flir·ta·tion /flɝˋteʃən; flɜːˈteɪʃən/ *n* **1** [C] a short period of time during which you are interested in something 一時的興趣，一時的愛好: **[+with]** *a brief flirtation with Eastern religions* 對東方各種宗教的一時興趣 **2** [U] behaviour that shows a sexual attraction to someone, though not in a serious way 調情 **3** [C] a short sexual relationship which is not serious 短暫的風流韻事

flir·ta·tious /flɝˋteʃəs; flɜːˈteɪʃəs/ *adj* behaving in a way that deliberately tries to attract sexual attention, but not in a serious way（愛）調情的，賣弄風騷的: *a flirtatious young girl* 一位賣弄風騷的年輕姑娘 —**flirtatiously** *adv* —**flirtatiousness** *n* [U]

flit /flɪt; flɪt/ *v* **flitted, flitting** [I always+adv/prep] to move lightly or quickly and not stay in one place for very long 輕快地行進，掠過: *birds flitting about from branch to branch* 在樹枝間飛來飛去的鳥兒 —see also 另見 **do a moonlight flit** (MOONLIGHT[1] (2))

float[1] /flot; fləʊt/ *v*

1 ►ON WATER 在水上◄ [I] **a)** to stay or move on the surface of a liquid without sinking 浮；漂: *Wood usually floats.* 木頭通常會浮起來。| *Annie was floating on her back in the pool.* 安妮臉朝上地浮在池水上。| **[+along/down/past etc]** *The logs floated down the river.* 原木在河上順水漂流。**b)** [T] to put something on the surface of a liquid so that it does not sink 使浮起: *Pour the coffee and brandy into a mug, then float the cream on top.* 把咖啡和白蘭地倒入大杯，然後把奶油放進去，讓它浮在面上。

2 ►IN THE AIR 在空中◄ [I always+adv/prep] if something floats, especially something very light or filled with air, it moves slowly in the air or stays up in the air 飄浮: **[+up/down/through etc]** *He watched the balloon float up into the sky.* 他看着氣球升上天空。

3 ►MUSIC/SOUNDS/SMELLS ETC 音樂/聲音/氣味等◄ [I always+adv/prep] if sounds, smells etc float somewhere, people in another place can hear or smell them〔聲音、氣味等〕飄: **[+down/towards/into etc]** *The sound of her voice came floating down from an upstairs window.* 她的聲音從樓上的窗子裡飄下來。

4 ►MONEY 貨幣◄ [I,T] *technical* if a country floats its money or its money floats, the value of the money is allowed to change freely in relation to money from other countries【術語】(使) 浮動: *Russia floated the ruble on the foreign exchange market.* 俄羅斯讓盧布在外匯市場上自由浮動。

5 ►SUGGEST 建議◄ [T] to suggest an idea or plan, especially in order to find out what people think about it〔尤指為了解人們的想法而〕提出〔建議或計劃〕: *The idea was first floated in a speech given by the President a few months ago.* 這種想法是幾個月前總統在一次講話中首次提出來的。

6 ►COMPANY 公司◄ [T] to sell shares (SHARE[2] (5)) in a company or business to the public for the first time 首次發行〔股票〕—see also 另見 FLOTATION (1)

7 ►CHEQUE 支票◄ *AmE* [T] to write a cheque that you do not have enough money in the bank to pay【美】開〔空頭支票〕; BOUNCE[1] (3) *BrE*【英】

8 ►MOVE GRACEFULLY 優雅地走動◄ [I] to move gracefully and lightly 飄然移動: *Rachel floated around the bedroom in a lace nightgown.* 雷切爾穿着花邊睡衣在臥室裡飄然走動。

9 ►NO DEFINITE PURPOSE 無明確目的◄ [I always+adv/prep] to keep changing what you are doing without having any particular ideas or plans 不斷改變；遊蕩: *Dean seems to float from job to job, never getting anywhere.* 迪安似乎不斷地變換工作，一直是一事無成。—**floater** *n* [C]

float[2] *n* [C] **1** a large vehicle that is decorated to be part of a PARADE[1] (1)〔遊行時用的〕彩車: *a procession of Carnival floats* 狂歡節彩車的巡遊隊伍 —see also 另見 MILK FLOAT **2** *AmE* a SOFT DRINK[1] (1) that has ice cream floating in it【美】浮有冰淇淋的飲料 **3** a light object that floats on the surface of the water, used especially for catching fish〔尤指釣魚用的〕漂浮物；魚漂，浮子 **4** a light object used when swimming to support your body〔游泳時用的〕救生衣；救生圈 **5** a small amount of money that someone in a shop keeps so that they have enough money to give change to people〔商店的〕備用零錢

floa·ta·tion /floˋteʃən; fləʊˈteɪʃən/ *n* [C] a British spelling of FLOTATION flotation 的英式拼法

float·ing /ˋflotɪŋ; ˈfləʊtɪŋ/ *adj* **1 floating population** if a city has a floating population, the number of people who live there keeps changing because people move into and out of it 流動人口 **2** *technical* an organ or part of your body that is floating is not properly connected or is not in the usual place【術語】〔指身體器官〕浮游的，不在正常位置的

floating vot·er /ˌ‥ ˈ‥/ *n* [C] someone who is not sure which political party to vote for at an election 不固定投某一政黨票的投票人，無黨派投票人

flock[1] /flɑk; flɒk/ *n* **1** [C] a group of sheep, goats, or birds 畜羣；鳥羣 —compare 比較 HERD[1] (1) **2** [C usually singular 一般用單數] a large group of the same kind of people〔同類型的〕一大羣人: **[+of]** *a flock of tourists* 一大羣遊客 **3** [C usually singular 一般用單數] *formal or humorous* a priest's flock is the group of people who regularly attend his church【正式或幽默】〔經常到某位牧師所屬教堂禮拜的〕全體教徒[會眾] **4** [U] small pieces of wool, cotton etc used for filling CUSHIONS[1] (1)〔填充墊子的〕絮屑，毛棉填料 **5** also 又作 **flock·ing** /ˋflɑkɪŋ; ˈflɒkɪŋ/ *AmE* a soft substance used to make patterns on the surface of wallpaper, curtains, etc【美】〔供在牆紙、窗簾等表面製作圖案的〕植絨材料；柔軟貼料

flock[2] *v* [I always+adv/prep] to go to a place in large numbers because something interesting or exciting is happening there 成羣結隊；蜂擁而至: **flock to/into/around etc** *Californians are flocking to enrol in special aerobics classes.* 加利福尼亞州人正成羣結隊參加特別有氧健身操訓練班。

floe /flo; fləʊ/ *n* [C] —see 見 ICE FLOE

flog /flɑg; flɒg/ *v* **flogged, flogging** [T] **1** to beat a person or animal with a whip or stick 鞭打；棒打: *Thieves were flogged in public.* 小偷被當眾鞭打。**2** *especially BrE informal* to sell【尤英，非正式】出售，賣 **3 be flogging a dead horse** *spoken* to be wasting time or effort by trying to do something that is impossible【口】浪費時間，徒勞，白費勁 **4 flog sth to death** *especially BrE informal* to repeat a story, complaint, idea etc so often that people become bored with it【尤英，非正式】把某事反覆說得使人厭煩

flog·ging /ˋflɑgɪŋ; ˈflɒgɪŋ/ *n* [C] a punishment in which someone is severely beaten with a whip or stick〔作為懲罰的〕鞭笞

3 **flood**[1] /flʌd; flʌd/ *v*
1 ►COVER WITH WATER 被水淹◄ [I,T] to make a place become covered, or to become covered with water (被)淹沒: *Three days of heavy rain flooded many Eastern cities.* 三天的大雨淹了許多東部的城市。| *The basement flooded and everything got soaked.* 地下室被水淹了，所有的東西都濕透了。
2 ►GO/ARRIVE IN LARGE AMOUNTS/NUMBERS 大量/大批去/到達◄ [I] to arrive or go somewhere in large numbers〔大量地〕湧到，湧去: **[+in/into/out/across etc]** *Letters came flooding in from irate viewers.* 憤怒的觀眾的來信如潮水般湧至。| *Refugees flooded across the border.* 大批的難民湧過邊界。
3 be flooded with to receive so many things such as letters, complaints, or inquiries that you cannot deal with them 大量收到: *We've been flooded with offers of help.* 我們已經收到大量願意幫助的建議。
4 ►SEND LARGE AMOUNTS/NUMBERS 大量地發送◄ [T] to send a large number of things such as letters or complaints to an organization so that it is difficult for people there to deal with them 大量地寄送〔信件、投訴等〕: **flood sth with** *Campaigners flooded Congress with letters of protest.* 參加運動的人的抗議信如潮水般湧到國會。
5 flood the market to sell something in very large numbers or amounts, so that the price goes down〔用某物〕充斥市場〔以造成價格下跌〕: **[+with]** *Japanese companies were accused of flooding the market with cheap steel.* 日本公司因以廉價鋼材充斥市場而受指責。
6 ►RIVER 河流◄ [I,T] if a river floods, it is too full, and spreads water over the land around it (使)氾濫
7 ►ENGINE 發動機◄ [I,T] if an engine floods or you flood it, it has too much petrol in it, so that it will not start (使)溢油; (使)燃油過多
8 ►LIGHT 光線◄ [I,T] if light floods a place or floods into it, it makes it very light and bright 照亮，(使)明亮: *The sunset flooded the canyon with rose-colored light.* 落日那玫瑰色的光芒照遍峽谷。
9 ►FEELING 感覺◄ [I,T] if a feeling or memory floods over someone or floods back, they feel or remember it very strongly〔感情或回憶〕湧上心頭: **[+over/back]** *I felt happiness and relief flooding over me.* 我感到心裡充滿快樂和寬慰。
10 flood with tears if someone's face floods with tears, they cry a lot 淚流滿面
flood sb ↔ **out** *phr v* **be flooded out** to be forced to leave your home because of floods〔因洪水〕被迫離開家園

3 **flood**[2] *n* **1** [C,U] a very large amount of water that covers an area that is usually dry 洪水; 水災: *Floods in Bangladesh caused over 1000 deaths.* 孟加拉的洪水奪去一千多人的生命。—see picture on page A13 參見A13頁圖 **2 flood of** a very large number of things or people that arrive at the same time 大量的: *A TV show featuring sexy home videos was halted after a flood of complaints.* 在人們提出大量投訴之後，一個播放色情家庭錄像的電視節目被停播了。**3 in floods of tears** crying a lot 淚如雨下 **4 the Flood** the great flood described in the Bible story, that covered the world〔《聖經》故事中毀滅世界的〕大洪水: **before the Flood** (=a very long time ago) 很久很久以前，在大洪水以前 **5 be in flood** a river that is in flood has much more water in it than usual〔河水〕上漲，氾濫 —see also 另見 FLASH FLOOD

flood·gate /ˈflʌdˌget; ˈflʌdgeɪt/ *n* [C usually plural 一般用複數] **1 open the floodgates a)** to suddenly make it possible for a lot of people to do something by removing laws and rules which had previously prevented or controlled it 放開限制: *worries that a Labour government would open the floodgates to immigration* 對工黨政府會放開移民限制的憂慮 **b)** to make someone show their true feelings which they have been trying not to show 打開心扉 **2** a gate used to control the flow of water from a large lake, river etc 泄水閘; 防洪閘

flood·ing /ˈflʌdɪŋ; ˈflʌdɪŋ/ *n* [U] a situation in which an area of land becomes covered with water, for example because of heavy rain 水災，洪水氾濫

flood·light /ˈflʌdˌlaɪt; ˈflʌdlaɪt/ *n* [C usually plural 一般用複數] a very bright light, used to light the outside of buildings, sports grounds etc at night 泛光燈

flood·lit /ˈflʌdˌlɪt; ˈflʌdlɪt/ *adj* surrounded by floodlights so that people can see at night 泛光燈照明的

flood plain /ˈ· ·/ *n* [C] the large area of flat land on either side of a river that is sometimes covered with water〔河邊的〕洪氾區，氾濫平原

flood tide /ˈ· ·/ *n* [C] the flow of the TIDE[1] (1) in towards the land 漲潮，升潮 —opposite 反義詞 EBB[1] (1)

floor[1] /flɔr; flɔː/ *n* 1 1
1 ►FLAT SURFACE 平面◄ [C] the flat surface on which you stand indoors 地板; 室內的地面: *Amos ran inside, spreading mud all over the kitchen floor.* 阿莫斯跑進屋裡，把廚房的地板踩得都是泥漿。—see picture on page A10 參見A10頁圖 —see 見 LAND[1] (USAGE)
2 ►LEVEL IN BUILDING 建築物的樓層◄ [C] one of the levels in a building〔樓房的〕層: *Our office is on the top floor.* 我們的辦公室在最高一層樓。| *a two-bedroomed ground floor flat* 有兩個臥室的底層住房
3 ►OCEAN/FOREST/CAVE FLOOR ETC 海底/森林地面/山洞底等◄ [singular] the ground at the bottom of the ocean, the forest etc〔海洋等的〕底;〔森林等的〕地面: *creatures that live on the ocean floor* 生活在海底的生物
4 the floor a) the people attending a public meeting 全體與會者: *Are there any questions from the floor?* 與會者有問題要提嗎? **b)** the part of a parliament, public meeting place etc where people sit〔議會的〕議員席: *The delegates crowded the floor of the House.* 代表們擠滿了議院的議員席。
5 take the floor a) to begin speaking at an important public meeting〔在重要的公開會議上〕開始發言 **b)** to begin dancing〔在舞會上〕開始跳舞
6 have the floor to be speaking or have the right to speak at an important public meeting 發言; 有發言權: *The Senator from Wyoming had the floor.* 懷俄明州的參議員有發言權。
7 ►DANCE 跳舞◄ an area where people dance 舞池，舞場: **dance floor** *Couples were already gliding over the dance floor.* 一對對的舞伴已經在舞池中翩然起舞。
8 ►WHERE PEOPLE WORK 工作場所◄ [C] a large area in a building where a lot of people do their jobs〔工作場所的〕大廳: *The stock market floor was wildly busy.* 證券交易所的大廳裡忙得不可開交。| **shop floor** (=the area in a factory where people work using machines) 工廠的車間 *The manager's office is above the shop floor.* 經理辦公室在工作車間的上面。
9 ►CAR 汽車◄ [C] *BrE* the part of a car that forms its inside floor【英】〔汽車〕底板; FLOORBOARD (2) *AmE*【美】
10 go through the floor if a price, amount etc goes through the floor, it becomes very low〔價格、數量等〕降到很低的水平: *In the past few years share prices have gone through the floor.* 過去幾年來，股票價格已降到了很低的水平。
11 ►LIMIT 限度◄ [singular] an officially agreed limit so that something cannot go below a certain value 最低額，底限: **put a floor under** *The French government tried to put a floor under the value of the Franc.* 法國政府試圖限定法郎的最低價值。—see also 另見 **be/get in on the ground floor** (GROUND FLOOR (2)), **wipe the floor with** (WIPE[1] (5))
12 [C] *BrE* the area of the stock exchange where people buy and sell shares (SHARE[2] (5))【英】〔證券交易所的〕交易廳

F

USAGE NOTE 用法説明: FLOOR

In American English the bottom floor of a building (at ground level) is called the **first floor**. In British English this is called the **ground floor**. 建築物的最低層(地面的一層)在美國英語中叫作 first floor (一樓), 在英國英語中叫作 ground floor (底層)。

The next level up is called the **second floor** in American English and the **first floor** in British English. 再往上一層, 美國英語叫作 second floor (二樓), 英國英語叫作 first floor (一樓)。

GRAMMAR 語法

People say 人們説 *He lives on the second/ninth etc floor* (NOT 不用 *at/in the second/ninth etc floor*). 他住在二/九樓。

floor² *v* [T] **1** to surprise or shock someone so much that they do not know what to say or do 使驚訝得不知所措; 難倒: *Her last question completely floored me.* 她的最後一個問題完全把我難倒了。**2** to hit someone so hard that they fall down 把…打倒在地: *The Champion floored Watson with a single punch.* 冠軍一拳就把沃森打倒在地。**3 floor it** *AmE informal* to make a car go as fast as possible【美, 非正式】踩足油門, 全速行駛

floor·board /ˈflɔr,bɔrd; ˈflɔːbɔːd/ *n* [C] **1** [usually plural 一般用複數] a board in a wooden floor 一塊木地板 —see picture at 參見 BOARD 圖 **2** *AmE* the floor in a car【美】〔汽車〕底板

floor·ing /ˈflɔrɪŋ; ˈflɔːrɪŋ/ *n* [U] material used to make or cover floors 鋪地面的材料

floor lamp /ˈ· ·/ *n* [C] *AmE* a lamp at the top of a tall pole on a flat base that stands on the floor of a room【美】落地燈; STANDARD LAMP *BrE*【英】—see picture at 參見 LIGHT¹ 圖

floor-length /ˈ· ·/ *adj* long enough to reach the floor 〔衣裙〕拖到地的: *a floor-length evening gown* 長裙拖地的晚禮服

floor mod·el /ˈ· ˌ··/ *n* [C] *AmE* a piece of furniture or equipment for the home, such as a washing machine, that has been in a store for people to look at and is often sold at a cheaper price【美】〔售價較低的家具或家用設備的〕陳列樣品

floor plan /ˈ· ·/ *n* [C] a drawing of the shape of a room or area in a building and the position of things in it, as seen from above 樓層平面圖, 樓面佈置圖

floor show /ˈ· ·/ *n* [C] a performance by singers, dancers etc at a NIGHTCLUB〔夜總會舞池內的〕娛樂表演

floo·zy, floozie /ˈfluzɪ; ˈfluːzi/ *n* [C] *old-fashioned* a woman who is sexually immoral and who you disapprove of【過時】蕩婦, 不規矩的女子

flop¹ /flɑp; flɒp/ *v* **flopped, flopping** [I] **1** [always+adv/prep] also 又作 **flop down** to sit or lie down in a relaxed way, by letting all your weight fall heavily onto a chair etc 猛然坐下, 猛然躺下: **[+in/onto/across etc]** *"I'm exhausted," said Max, flopping into a chair.* "我累壞了。" 馬克斯説着, 一屁股坐在椅子上。**2** [always+adv/prep] to move or fall in an awkward, or uncontrolled way 笨拙地移動; 摔倒; 重重地落下: **[+around/along/onto etc]** *A bird with an injured wing flopped helplessly along the ground.* 一隻翅膀受傷的鳥無助地在地面上撲騰着。**3** *informal* if something such as a product, play, or plan flops, it is not successful because people do not like it【非正式】〔產品、戲劇或計劃等因無人喜歡而〕失敗, 砸鍋: *Despite all the media hype 'Heaven's Gate' flopped at the box office.* 儘管傳媒吹捧得天花亂墜,《天堂之門》的票房成績卻一塌糊塗。

flop² *n* **1** [C] *informal* a film, play, product etc that is not successful【非正式】〔電影、戲劇、產品等的〕失敗: *The show was a flop and lasted only one night.* 演出很失敗, 只演了一個晚上。**2** [singular] the movement or noise that something makes when it falls heavily 重墜; 重墜聲, 撲通聲: *He fell with a flop into the water.* 他撲通一聲掉進水裡。**3** *AmE* a flophouse【美】廉價旅館 —see also 另見 BELLY FLOP, FLIP-FLOP

flop·house /ˈflɑp,haus; ˈflɒphaus/ *n* [C] *AmE slang* a cheap hotel, that often has many beds in one room【美俚】廉價旅館; DOSS HOUSE *BrE*【英】

flop·py /ˈflɑpɪ; ˈflɒpi/ *adj* soft and often hanging loosely downwards 鬆軟的; 垂下的; 鬆垂的: *a dog with long, floppy ears* 耷拉着長耳朵的狗 —**floppiness** *n* [U]

floppy disk /ˌ·· ˈ·/ also 又作 **floppy** *n* [C] a square piece of plastic on which information for a computer is stored; DISKETTE 軟磁碟, 軟(磁)盤 —compare 比較 HARD DISK

flo·ra /ˈflɔrə; ˈflɔːrə/ *n* [U] all the plants of a particular place or country〔某個地方或國家的〕植物羣: *the flora of the Alps* 阿爾卑斯山脈的植物羣 —compare 比較 FAUNA

flo·ral /ˈflɔrəl; ˈflɔːrəl/ *adj* decorated with or made of flowers 花的; 用花裝飾的; 用花製作的: *floral dresses* 用花裝飾的連衣裙 | **floral tributes** (=flowers at a funeral)〔葬禮上〕敬獻的鮮花 —see picture on page A16 參見 A16 頁圖

flor·id /ˈflɔrɪd; ˈflɒrɪ̈d/ *adj literary*【文】**1** having a red face〔臉色〕紅潤的: *florid cheeks* 紅潤的臉頰 **2** having a lot of unnecessary decoration or detail 過分華麗的, 花哨的, 華而不實的: *florid language* 詞藻華麗的語言 —**floridly** *adv*

flor·in /ˈflɔrɪn; ˈflɒrɪ̈n/ *n* [C] a coin used in Britain before 1971, ten of which made one pound (£1) 弗羅林〔英國1971年以前使用的硬幣, 等於1/10英鎊〕

flor·ist /ˈflɔrɪst; ˈflɒrɪ̈st/ *n* [C] **1** someone who owns or works in a shop that sells flowers 花商; 花店主人[店員] **2** also 又作 **florist's** a shop that sells flowers 花店

floss¹ /flɔs; flɒs/ *n* [U] **1** thin silk used for sewing〔縫紉用的〕(繡花) 絲線 **2** DENTAL FLOSS 潔牙線 —see also 另見 CANDYFLOSS

floss² *v* [T] to clean between your teeth with DENTAL FLOSS 用潔牙線清潔〔牙縫〕

flo·ta·tion /floˈteʃən; fləʊˈteɪʃən/ *n* [C,U] **1** the act of offering shares (SHARE² (5)) in a company to the public for the first time〔公司股票的〕發行, 上市: *a massive flotation of government bonds* 政府債券的大量發行 **2 flotation chamber/compartment etc** a container filled with air or gas, fixed to something to make it float 浮室/浮艙等

flo·til·la /floˈtɪlə; fləˈtɪlə/ *n* [C] a group of small ships 小船隊; 小艦隊

flot·sam /ˈflɑtsəm; ˈflɒtsəm/ *n* [U] **1** broken pieces of wood, plastic etc from a wrecked ship floating in the sea or scattered on the shore〔遇難船隻的〕漂浮殘骸; 水面[海面]飄浮物 —compare 比較 JETSAM **2** also 又作 **flotsam and jet·sam** /ˌ·· · ˈ··/ people who do not have jobs or homes 流離失所的人; 流浪者; 無業游民; 失業者

flounce¹ /flauns; flaʊns/ *v* [I always+adv/prep] to move in a way that shows that you are angry 怒氣沖沖地走: **[+out/off/past etc]** *Sandra flounced out of the room.* 桑德拉怒沖沖地走出房間。

flounce² *n* **1** [C] a band of cloth on clothing that is stitched into folds as a decoration〔鑲在衣服上作裝飾的〕荷葉邊 **2** [singular] a sudden quick movement that shows people that you are annoyed〔表示生氣的〕驟動, 急動

flounced /flaunst; flaʊnst/ *adj* a flounced skirt or dress is one that is decorated with flounces〔裙子或連衣裙〕鑲荷葉邊的

floun·der¹ /ˈflaundɚ; ˈflaʊndə/ *v* [I] **1** [always+adv/prep] to move awkwardly or with difficulty, especially in water, mud etc〔尤指在水、泥等中〕掙扎, 踉蹌, 艱難地移動 **2** to be unable to decide what to say or do so that you find it difficult to continue 胡亂地[困難地]説話[做事]: *He left his interviewer floundering by answering every question with the word 'no'.* 他用"不"字來回答每個問題, 使採訪者難以繼續。**3** to have a lot of problems and have difficulty continuing 遇到許多問題[困難]: *Brando's career was floundering when he was offered the role.* 白蘭度被派演這個角色時, 他的事業正在困厄之中。

flounder² *n* [C] a small flat fish, used as food 鮃; 鰈

flour¹ /flaur; flaʊə/ *n* [U] a powder made by crushing grain, especially wheat, and used for making bread, cakes etc 麵粉; 穀物磨成的粉〔尤指小麥粉〕—see also 另見 PLAIN FLOUR, SELF-RAISING FLOUR

flour² *v* [T] to cover a surface with flour 在…上撒麵粉

flour·ish¹ /ˈflɝɪʃ; ˈflʌrɪʃ/ *v* **1** [I] to grow well and be very healthy; THRIVE 生長茂盛: *The plants flourished in the warm sun.* 這些植物在温暖的陽光下生長茂盛。**2** [I] to develop well and be successful 繁榮, 興旺, 成功: *Russia's flourishing black market economy* 俄羅斯繁榮的黑市經濟 **3** [T] to wave something in your hand in order to make people notice it〔為引起注意〕揮動〔手中的東西〕: *Ellie ran in, flourishing her acceptance letter.* 埃利揮動着錄取書跑進來。

flour·ish² *n* **1 with a flourish** with a large confident movement that makes people notice you 用引人注意的動作, 揮舞: *Mr Darcy swept back his hat with a flourish.* 達西先生用一個誇張的動作把帽子一揮放在背後。**2** [C] something such as a decoration or detail that is not necessary 不必要的裝飾; 過分華麗的詞藻: *His speech was full of rhetorical flourishes.* 他的講話充滿浮誇華麗的詞藻。**3** [C] a curved line when writing, which is done for decoration〔手寫花體字的〕花飾 **4** [C] a loud part of a piece of music, played especially when an important person enters〔尤指重要人物進場時演奏的〕響亮的樂曲: *a flourish of trumpets* 響亮的小號樂曲

flour·mill /ˈflaurˌmɪl; ˈflaʊəˌmɪl/ *n* [C] a place where flour is made from grain 麵粉廠

flour·y /ˈflaurɪ; ˈflaʊəri/ *adj* covered with or tasting of flour 蓋有麵粉的; (似) 麵粉味的

flout /flaut; flaʊt/ *v* [T] to deliberately disobey a law, rule etc 公然無視, 違抗〔法律、規定等〕: *Countries that flout the agreement will have sanctions imposed on them.* 違反協議的國家將受到制裁。

2 2 **flow¹** /flo; fləʊ/ *n*

1 ►MOVEMENT OF LIQUID 液體的流動◄ [C usually singular 一般用單數] a smooth steady movement or supply of liquid 流動: *Smoking affects the flow of blood to the brain.* 吸煙會影響血液往大腦的流動。

2 ►SUPPLY/MOVEMENT 供應/移動◄ [C usually singular 一般用單數] a continuous supply or movement of something from one place to another 不斷的供應[輸送]: **[+of]** *the flow of arms into Bosnia* 源源不斷地進入波斯尼亞的武器輸送

3 in full flow if someone is in full flow, they are busy talking about something and seem likely to continue for a long time 滔滔不絕; 口若懸河

4 ►WORDS/IDEAS 詞語/想法◄ [U] the continuous stream of words or ideas when someone is speaking, writing, or thinking about something 流暢, 連貫: **break/interrupt sb's flow** *You've interrupted my flow now – I don't know what I was going to say next.* 你現在已把我的話打斷了 —— 我不知我剛才接下去要説甚麼。

5 ►OF THE SEA 大海的◄ [singular] the movement of the TIDE¹ (1) towards the land 漲潮: *the ebb and flow of the tide* 潮水的漲落

6 go with the flow to decide to do the same thing as other people, and not ask if you can do something different 隨大流; 隨波逐流; 從眾: *I don't mind, I'll just go with the flow.* 我沒關係, 我隨大家好了。

7 go against the flow to do something very different from what other people are doing 逆潮流, 背道而馳 — see also 另見 CASH FLOW, **ebb and flow** (EBB¹ (3))

3 **flow²** *v* [I]

1 ►LIQUID 液體◄ if a liquid flows, it moves in a steady continuous stream 流動, 流淌: **[+over/down/through etc]** *A great river flowed along the valley.* 一條大河流過山谷。

2 ►GOODS/INFORMATION/PEOPLE ETC 商品/消息/人等◄ if goods, information, people etc flow, they move or are supplied continuously in large numbers from one place to another 流動; 流傳: **[+in/out/through/from etc]** *Money has been flowing into the country from Western aid agencies.* 錢源源不斷地從西方援助機構流進該國。

3 ►TRAFFIC 交通◄ if traffic flows, it moves easily from one place to another〔車輛〕暢通無阻

4 ►ALCOHOL 酒◄ if alcohol flows at a party, people drink a lot and there is a lot available 大量供應; 飲之不盡: **flow freely** *The champagne flowed freely and everyone had a good time.* 香檳酒大量供應, 大家玩得很開心。

5 ►WORDS/IDEAS 詞語/想法◄ if conversation or ideas flow, people talk or have ideas steadily and continuously, without anything stopping or interrupting them〔説話或思考〕流暢: **flow easily/freely** *The wine loosened our tongues, and conversation flowed freely.* 葡萄酒使我們打開了話匣子, 大家的話多了起來。

6 flow from to come from a particular idea, place, or person 來自, 產生於, 源於: *the political wrangle that has flowed from this decision* 這項決定所產生的政治爭論

7 ►FEELINGS 感情◄ if an emotion flows, someone feels it strongly 強烈地感到: **[+through/into/from etc]** *Compassion for Mattie flowed through her.* 她對馬蒂深感同情。

8 ►CLOTHES/HAIR 衣服/頭髮◄ if clothing, hair etc flows, it falls or hangs loosely and gracefully〔衣服、頭髮等〕飄垂, 飄拂

9 ►SEA 大海◄ if the TIDE¹ (1) flows, it moves towards the land〔潮〕漲 —compare 比較 EBB² (1)

flow chart /ˈ· ·/ also 又作 **flow di·a·gram** /ˈ· ˌ···/ *n* [C] a drawing that uses shapes and lines to show how a series of actions or parts of a system are connected with each other 流程圖; 作業圖: *a flow chart of the company's managerial structure* 公司的管理結構圖

flow·er¹ /ˈflauɚ; ˈflaʊə/ *n* **1** [C] the coloured part of a plant or tree that produces seeds or fruit 花, 花朵: *Fruit trees produce flowers in the spring.* 果樹在春天開花。**2** [C] a small plant that is grown for the beauty of this part 開花植物, 花卉: *He grows flowers in the front garden.* 他在前面的園子裡種花。**3 in flower** a plant or tree that is in flower has flowers on it 在開花: **come into flower** (=start to have flowers) 開始開花 *Roses usually come into flower in May or June.* 玫瑰通常在五、六月份開始開花。**4 the flower of** *literary* the best part or most perfect part of something【文】精華, 精英, 最好的部分: *The flower of the nation's youth was lost in the war.* 這個國家的青年精英在戰爭中損失殆盡。**5** *BrE old-fashioned* used to address someone in a friendly and informal way【英, 過時】花兒〔英國舊時一種友好的非正式稱呼語〕 2 2

flower² *v* [I] **1** to produce flowers 開花 **2** *formal* to develop and reach a high level of achievement【正式】繁榮, 興旺: *English painting flowered briefly during the Renaissance.* 英國繪畫藝術在文藝復興時期出現了短暫的繁榮。

flower ar·rang·ing /ˈ·· ·ˌ··/ *n* [U] the art of arranging flowers in an attractive way 插花 (藝術)

flow·er·bed /ˈflauɚˌbɛd; ˈflaʊəbed/ *n* [C] an area of ground in which flowers are grown 花壇

flower child /ˈ·· ·/ *n plural* **flower children** [C] a young person in the 1960s and 70s who was against war and wanted peace and love in society "花孩兒"; 執花嬉皮士〔指20世紀60年代和70年代反對戰爭、主張和平與愛的年輕人〕

flow·ered /ˈflauɚd; ˈflaʊəd/ *adj* decorated with pictures of flowers 用花卉圖案裝飾的: *flowered curtains* 有花卉圖案的窗簾

flower girl /ˈ·· ·/ *n* [C] **1** *BrE* a girl or woman who sells flowers in a street market【英】〔街市上的〕賣花女 **2** *AmE*

F

a young girl who carries flowers in a wedding ceremony【美】〔婚禮中的〕女花童 —compare 比較 BRIDESMAID

flow·er·ing /ˈflaʊərɪŋ; ˈflaʊərɪŋ/ *n* **the flowering of** a successful period in the development of something 頂峯時期, 繁榮時期

flow·er·less /ˈflaʊə·ləs; ˈflaʊələs/ *adj* not producing flowers 不開花的, 無花的

flower peo·ple /ˈ·· ,··/ *n* [plural] *BrE* young people in the 1960s and 70s who were against war and wanted peace and love in society【英】"花孩兒"; 執花嬉皮士〔指 20 世紀 60 年代和 70 年代反對戰爭、主張和平與愛的年輕人〕

flow·er·pot /ˈflaʊə,pɑt; ˈflaʊəpɒt/ *n* [C] a plastic or clay pot in which you grow plants〔塑料或陶瓷〕花盆

flower pow·er /ˈ·· ,··/ *n* [U] the ideas of young people in the 1960s and 70s who believed that peace and love were the most important things in life "權力歸花兒"〔指 20 世紀 60 年代和 70 年代年輕人的主張, 認為和平與愛是生活中最重要的東西〕

flower show /ˈ·· ,·/ *n* [C] a show at which people can look at different kinds of flowers and plants 花展

flow·er·y /ˈflaʊərɪ; ˈflaʊəri/ *adj* **1** decorated with pictures of flowers 用花卉圖案裝飾的: *a flowery pattern* 花卉圖案 **2** flowery speech or writing uses complicated and rare words instead of simple clear language〔演説或文章〕詞藻華麗的

flow·ing /ˈfloɪŋ; ˈfləʊɪŋ/ *adj* moving, curving, or hanging gracefully 流動的, 流暢的, 飄拂的: *long flowing white hair* 長長的飄拂的白髮

flown /flon; fləʊn/ the past participle of FLY[1]

flow sheet /ˈ· ·/ *n* [C] an American form of FLOW CHART flow chart 的美語形式

fl. oz. *n* the written abbreviation of 縮寫= FLUID OUNCE

flu /flu; fluː/ *n* [C,U] a common infectious disease which is like a bad COLD[2] (2) but is more serious; INFLUENZA 流行性感冒, 流感: **the flu** *Darby's been in bed with the flu.* 達比患流感, 臥牀休息了。| **flu** *BrE*【英】*Kate's got flu.* 凱特患了流感。

flub /flʌb; flʌb/ *v* [I,T] *AmE* to make a stupid mistake, or fail to do something by making a mistake【美】犯愚蠢的錯誤; 搞壞; 搞得一團糟: *He flubbed his first try at the SAT.* 他第一次考學業能力傾向測驗就不及格了。

fluc·tu·ate /ˈflʌktʃʊ,et; ˈflʌktʃueɪt/ *v* [I] if something such as a price or amount fluctuates, it changes very often from a high level to a low one and back again〔價格或數量〕波動, 上下變動, 漲落: **[+between]** *The present output of oil fluctuates between 3 and 5 million gallons per week.* 現在每週的石油產量在三百萬到五百萬加侖之間波動。| **fluctuate wildly** *House prices fluctuated wildly in the 80s.* 20 世紀 80 年代房價狂漲暴跌。

fluc·tu·a·tion /,flʌktʃʊˈeʃən; ,flʌktʃuˈeɪʃən/ *n* [C,U] sudden changes in something such as the price, amount, or level of something〔價格、數量或水平等的〕波動: *price fluctuations* 價格波動

flue /flu; fluː/ *n* [C] a metal pipe or tube, especially in a CHIMNEY, that lets smoke or heat from a fire out of a building〔尤指煙囱的〕煙道

flu·ent /ˈfluənt; ˈfluːənt/ *adj* **1** able to speak a language very well 熟練的, 流利的: *"Can she speak Arabic?" "Yes, she's fluent."* "她會講阿拉伯語嗎?" "會, 她説得很流利。" **2 fluent French/Japanese etc** someone who speaks fluent French etc speaks it like a person from that country 流利的法語/日語等 **3** speaking, writing, or playing a musical instrument confidently and without long pauses〔説話、寫作、演奏樂器等〕熟練的, 流暢的 —**fluently** *adv* —**fluency** *n* [U]

fluff[1] /flʌf; flʌf/ *n* [U] **1** soft, light bits of thread or wool that have come from wool, cotton, or other materials〔羊毛、棉或其他材料產生的〕絨毛; 蓬鬆毛; 碎絮 **2** soft light hair or feathers, especially from a young bird or animal〔尤指幼鳥或動物身上的〕絨毛, 軟毛 —compare 比較 DOWN[5] (2) —see also 另見 **bit of fluff** (BIT[1] (19))

fluff[2] *v* [T] **1** also 又作 **fluff up, fluff out** to make something soft appear larger by shaking or brushing it 抖開, 拍鬆: *Sue fluffed the pillows for me.* 蘇替我拍鬆了枕頭。**2** also 又作 **fluff up, fluff out** if a bird fluffs its feathers, it raises them and makes itself look bigger〔鳥類〕抖鬆〔羽毛〕**3** *informal* to make a mistake or do something badly【非正式】出錯, 把…搞糟: *Rupert fluffed the catch.* 魯珀特沒有接住球。| **fluff your lines** (=make a mistake when speaking in a play)〔演戲時〕唸錯台詞

fluff·y /ˈflʌfɪ; ˈflʌfi/ *adj* **1** made of or covered with something soft and light, such as wool, hair or feathers 絨毛的; 覆有絨毛的; 毛茸茸的: *a fluffy little kitten* 毛茸茸的小貓 **2** food that is fluffy is made soft and light by shaking, or beating so that air is mixed into it〔食物〕輕軟的, 鬆軟的: *Cream the butter and sugar until fluffy.* 將黃油和糖攪拌到鬆軟成奶油狀為止。—**fluffiness** *n* [U]

flu·id[1] /ˈfluɪd; ˈfluːɪd/ *n* [C,U] *technical* a liquid【術語】液(體): *The doctor told him to drink a litre of fluid a day.* 醫生告訴他每天喝一升液體。

fluid[2] *adj* **1** fluid movements are relaxed and graceful〔動作〕優美自然的; 優雅的; 流暢的: *fluid and expressive gestures* 流暢優美且富有表情的姿勢 **2** [not before noun 不用於名詞前] a situation or system that is fluid is likely to change often, or is able to change 不固定的, 易變的 —**fluidity** /fluˈɪdətɪ; fluˈɪdəti/ *n* [U]

fluid ounce /,·· ˈ·/ *n* [C] a unit for measuring liquids, equal to 0.0284 of a litre 液盎司, 液量盎司〔等於 0.0284 升〕—see table on page C5 參見 C5 頁附錄

fluke /fluk; fluːk/ *n* [C] *informal* something that is unlikely or surprising and only happens because of luck【非正式】僥倖, 偶然, 意外: *It was a complete fluke, meeting my sister at the airport.* 我在機場遇到妹妹, 這完全是偶然。—**fluky, flukey** *adj*

flum·moxed /ˈflʌməkst; ˈflʌməkst/ *adj* completely confused by something 弄得不知所措的: *I was totally flummoxed by his last question.* 我被他最後一個問題弄得暈頭轉向。—**flummox** *v* [T]

flung /flʌŋ; flʌŋ/ the past tense and past participle of FLING[1]

flunk /flʌŋk; flʌŋk/ *v informal especially AmE*【非正式, 尤美】**1** [I,T] to fail a test〔在考試中〕不及格: *Tony flunked chemistry last semester.* 托尼上學期化學考試不及格。**2** [T] to give someone low marks on a test so that they fail it 給…打不及格分數

flunk out *phr v* [I] *informal especially AmE* to be forced to leave a school or college because your work is not good enough【非正式, 尤美】〔因學業不好而〕被迫退學: *Ben messed around and flunked out of college.* 本在大學裡瞎混, 後來被迫退學了。

flun·key, flunky /ˈflʌŋkɪ; ˈflʌŋki/ *n* [C] someone who is always with an important person and treats them with too much respect 阿諛奉承的人, 馬屁精: *The Stones were surrounded by the usual flunkeys and hangers-on.* 斯通一家人的周圍常有一批阿諛奉承的人和馬屁精圍着。

flu·o·res·cent /,fluəˈrɛsn̩t; flʊəˈresənt/ *adj* **1** fluorescent colours are very bright and easy to see, even in the dark〔色彩〕熒光的: *a fluorescent pink T-shirt* 有熒光的粉紅色 T 恤衫 **2** a fluorescent substance produces a bright white light when electricity or other types of power pass through it〔物質〕發熒光的 —**fluorescence** *n* [U]

fluorescent light /·,·· ˈ·/ a fluorescent light produces light when electricity is passed through a gas-filled tube 熒光燈, 日光燈

flu·o·ri·date /ˈfluərə,det; ˈflʊərədeɪt/ *v* [T] to add fluoride to water in order to protect people's teeth〔為保護牙齒〕向〔水中〕加入氟化物 —**fluoridation** /,fluərəˈdeʃən; ,flʊərəˈdeɪʃən/ *n* [U]

flu·o·ride /ˈfluə,raɪd; ˈflʊəraɪd/ *n* [U] a chemical compound of fluorine, especially one that helps to protect teeth against decay〔尤指有助於防止齲齒的〕氟化物

flu·o·rine /ˈfluə,rin; ˈflʊəriːn/ *n* [U] a chemical substance

F

that is usually in the form of a poisonous gas 氟

fluo·ro·car·bon /ˌfluəroˋkarbən; ˌfluərəʊˈkɑːbən/ *n* [C] any chemical that contains the substances fluorine and CARBON (1) 碳氟化合物: *damage to the ozone layer caused by fluorocarbons* 碳氟化合物對臭氧層造成的破壞 —see also 另見 CFC

flur·ried /ˋflɝɪd; ˈflʌrid/ *adj* confused and nervous or excited 慌張的; 激動不安的: *the flurried activity surrounding the wedding* 圍繞這場婚禮的忙亂的活動

flur·ry /ˋflɝɪ; ˈflʌri/ *n* **1** [singular] an occasion when there is suddenly a lot of activity within a short period of time 緊張慌亂; 激動不安: **[+of]** *After a quiet spell there was a sudden flurry of phone calls.* 經過一段平靜之後, 電話突然響個不停。**2** [C] if there is a flurry of snow, rain, or wind, it suddenly starts snowing etc for a short time 陣雪; 陣雨; 陣風: *Snow flurries are expected overnight.* 整個晚上都可能有陣陣小雪。

flush[1] /flʌʃ; flʌʃ/ *n* **1** [singular] a red colour that appears on your face or body, especially because you are embarrassed, ill, or excited〔尤指因尷尬、生病或激動而引起的〕臉紅, 潮紅: *"How can you tell?" he said as a flush crept up his neck.* "你怎麼知道?"他説着, 脖子開始變得通紅。—see also 另見 HOT FLUSH **2 a flush of pride/embarrassment etc** a sudden feeling of pride, excitement, or another emotion 一陣自豪感/尷尬等 **3 the first flush of youth/success etc** the beginning of a period of time when you feel excited because you are young, successful etc 首次感到充滿青春活力的/首次感到成功的(一陣)喜悦 **4** [C] a set of cards that someone has in a card game that are all of the same suit (SUIT[1] (3))〔紙牌戲中的〕同花牌 **5** [C] the part of a toilet that cleans it with a sudden flow of water〔馬桶裡的〕沖洗裝置 **6** [C] the act of cleaning something by forcing water through it〔用水〕沖洗, 沖水

flush[2] *v* **1** [I,T] if you flush a toilet or if it flushes, you make water go through it to clean it〔用水〕沖洗〔馬桶〕;〔馬桶〕被沖洗: **flush sth down the toilet** *Mandy accidentally flushed her ring down the toilet.* 曼蒂不小心把戒指從馬桶裡沖下去了。**2** [I] to become red in the face 臉紅,〔臉〕發紅: *Flushing slightly, Lesley looked away.* 萊斯莉有點臉紅, 朝別處看去。**3** also 又作 **flush out** [T] to clean something by forcing water or another liquid through it〔用水或其他液體〕沖洗, 沖出: *Try flushing out the blockage with boiling water.* 試一試用沸水沖掉堵塞物。**4** [T always+adv/prep] to make someone leave the place where they are hiding 使〔某人〕離開隱蔽之處: **flush sb from/out of** *The police managed to flush the gang from their hideout.* 警方設法把這夥匪徒趕出躲藏處。

flush[3] *adj* **1** if two surfaces are flush they are at exactly the same level, so that the place where they meet is flat 在同一平面上的, 齊平的: **[+with]** *Make sure that the cupboard is flush with the wall.* 要確保碗櫥是嵌在牆中的。**2** [not before noun 不用於名詞前] *informal* if someone is flush they suddenly have plenty of money for a short time【非正式】突然很有錢的, 暴富的

flush[4] *adv* fitting together so that the place where two surfaces meet is flat 齊平地: *The door should fit flush into its frame.* 門應該剛好齊平地裝進門框內。

flushed /flʌʃt; flʌʃt/ *adj* **1** red in the face 臉紅的: *Nona was hot and flushed.* 諾娜身上發熱, 臉上發紅。| **[+with]** *Her face flushed with pride.* 她洋洋得意, 臉上發紅。**2 flushed with success/excitement** excited and eager because you have achieved something 因成功而滿臉喜色/因激動而滿臉通紅

flus·ter /ˋflʌstɚ; ˈflʌstə/ *v* [T] to make someone nervous and confused by making them hurry or interrupting them〔催促或打斷某人〕使緊張, 使困惑 —**fluster** *n* [singular] *BrE*【英】

flus·tered /ˋflʌstɚd; ˈflʌstəd/ *adj* confused and nervous 慌亂的, 緊張的: *Elijah got really flustered during the interview.* 伊萊賈在面試時確實十分緊張。

flute /flut; fluːt/ *n* [C] a musical instrument that you play by holding it across your lips, blowing into it, and pressing keys (KEY[2] (3)) with your fingers to change the notes 長笛

flut·ed /ˋflutɪd; ˈfluːtɪ̈d/ *adj* decorated with long narrow curves that curve inwards 飾有長凹槽的: *fluted columns* 刻有凹槽的柱子

flut·ist /ˋflutɪst; ˈfluːtɪ̈st/ *n* [C] *AmE* someone who plays the flute【美】吹長笛的人; 長笛手; FLAUTIST *BrE*【英】

flut·ter[1] /ˋflʌtɚ; ˈflʌtə/ *v* **1** [I,T] if a bird or insect flutters its wings or if its wings flutter, its wings move quickly and lightly up and down 振(翼), 拍打(翅膀): *butterflies fluttering from flower to flower* 在花叢中撲翅飛舞的蝴蝶 **2** [I] to wave or move gently in the air〔在空中〕飄揚, 飄動: *Dead leaves fluttered slowly to the ground.* 枯葉慢慢飄落到地上。**3** [I,T] if your heart or your stomach flutters, you feel very excited or nervous〔因激動或緊張〕(使)〔心臟或胃〕怦怦跳, 顫抖, 悸動 **4 flutter your eyelashes (at sb)** if a woman flutters her eyelashes at a man, she uses her sexual attractiveness to influence him〔女性〕(朝某人)眨眼, 拋媚眼

flutter[2] *n* **1** [singular] the state of being nervous, confused or excited 不安, 困惑, 激動: **in a flutter** *We're all in a flutter of excitement at the moment.* 我們此時此刻都興奮得心怦怦直跳。| **cause a flutter** (=make people excited or interested) 令人興奮; 引起興趣 *News of her arrest caused quite a flutter in the office.* 她被捕的消息在辦公室引起一陣不小的轟動。**2 have a flutter** *BrE informal* to risk a small amount of money on the result of a horse race; BET[2] (1)【英, 非正式】〔賽馬時〕下一筆小賭注 **3** [singular] a fluttering movement 拍動; 飄動: *a flutter of wings* 翅膀的拍動 **4** [C] *technical* an irregular heart beat【術語】〔心臟〕不規則的跳動, 振顫; 悸動 **5** [U] *technical* a shaking movement that stops a machine working properly【術語】〔機器的〕抖動, 顫動

flu·vi·al /ˋfluvɪəl; ˈfluːviəl/ *adj technical* relating to or produced by rivers【術語】河流的; 生長在河中的

flux /flʌks; flʌks/ *n* [U] **1 be in (a state of) flux** to be changing a lot so that you cannot be sure what will happen 處於不斷變化中: *The education system is in a state of flux, with new requirements constantly being added.* 教育體制處於不斷變化中, 人們不斷地增加新的要求。**2** a substance that is added to a metal to help it melt or when sticking two pieces of metal together; SOLDER[1] 助熔劑, 焊劑

2 2

fly[1] /flaɪ; flaɪ/ *v past tense* **flew** /flu; fluː/ *past participle* **flown** /flon; fləʊn/

① PLANE 飛機
② BIRDS/INSECTS ETC 鳥/昆蟲等
③ FLOAT 飄動
④ MOVE FREELY 自由活動
⑤ MOVE/GO FAST 迅速移動/迅速去
⑥ TIME GOES QUICKLY 時間過得很快
⑦ ANGRY 生氣的
⑧ ATTACK 攻擊
⑨ OTHER MEANINGS 其他意思

① **PLANE** 飛機

1 [I] to travel by plane 乘飛機: *You can fly direct from London to Tokyo in under 12 hours now.* 你現在可以在12小時內從倫敦直飛到東京。| **fly on** (=continue flying to another place) 繼續飛行 *The first stop is San Francisco, and from there we're flying on to Hawaii.* 第一站是三藩市，然後我們從那裡繼續飛到夏威夷。

2 [I] to move through the air in order to go from one place to another〔飛機〕飛行: *These planes can fly at incredibly high speeds.* 這些飛機能以難以置信的高速度飛行。

3 [T] to carry or send goods or people by plane 空運〔貨物或乘客〕: **fly sth into/out of** *US planes have been flying food and medical supplies into the area.* 美國飛機一直在把食品和藥品空運到該地區。

4 [I,T] to use a particular AIRLINE or use a particular type of ticket when flying 乘坐〔某家航空公司的〕飛機; 用〔某類票〕飛行: *We usually fly economy class.* 我們乘飛機通常坐經濟艙。

5 [I,T] to control a plane through the air 駕駛〔飛機〕: *The Prince has his own private jet which he flies himself.* 王子有私人噴氣式飛機，由他自己駕駛。

6 fly a mission to fly a plane in a war, especially in order to attack an enemy〔戰時〕駕機執行任務; 駕機出擊

7 [T] to cross an area of water in a plane（乘飛機）飛越〔水域〕: *the first woman to fly the Atlantic* 第一位飛越大西洋的女性

② **BIRDS/INSECTS ETC** 鳥/昆蟲等

8 [I] to move through the air using wings 飛: **[+up/into etc]** *a flock of seagulls flying overhead* 在頭上飛翔的一羣海鷗

③ **FLOAT** 飄動

9 [I always+adv/prep] to float high in the air 飄動: *I watched the balloons fly up into the sky.* 我看着氣球飄向空中。

④ **MOVE FREELY** 自由活動

10 [I] if your hair, coat etc is flying, it moves freely and loosely in the air〔頭髮、衣服等〕飄拂, 飛揚: *long hair flying in the wind* 在風中飄拂的長髮

⑤ **MOVE/GO FAST** 迅速移動/迅速去

11 [I always+adv/prep] to go somewhere very quickly 飛跑, 飛奔, 衝: **[+down/across/out of etc]** *She flew down the stairs to find out what had happened.* 她衝下樓去看看發生了甚麼事。

12 [I always+adv/prep] to move suddenly and very quickly 突然快速地移動: **[+open/shut/back etc]** *The door suddenly flew open.* 門突然打開了。| *Sparks were flying everywhere.* 火花四處飛濺。

13 send sb/sth flying to knock someone or something so that they fall through the air 使某人人仰馬翻; 把某物撞得飛散: *He crashed into the table and sent the glasses flying.* 他撞到桌子，把玻璃杯都撞飛了。

14 go flying to suddenly fall through the air after being knocked by something or someone〔被撞而〕飛落: *The boat rocked to the side and I went flying across the room.* 船搖擺得傾側了，我從房間的一邊飛落到另一邊。

15 I must fly *spoken* used to say that you must leave quickly【口】我得趕緊走了

⑥ **TIME GOES QUICKLY** 時間過得很快

16 time flies *spoken* used to say that a period of time passes or something happens in an unexpectedly short time【口】時間飛逝: *Is it August already? How time flies!* 已經八月了嗎? 時間過得多快! | **Time flies when you are having fun!** (=often used humorously to mean that something has been very boring) 人若快樂，時間就過得快!〔常幽默地用來表示厭煩某事〕

17 fly by/past if a period of time flies by or past, it passes very quickly without you noticing〔時間〕飛逝: *We've been so busy, the week has just flown by.* 我們很忙，整個星期就這麼飛逝而過。

⑦ **ANGRY** 生氣的

18 fly into a temper/rage to suddenly become extremely angry 勃然大怒: *My father flew into a rage and demanded his money back.* 我父親勃然大怒，要求取回他的錢。

19 fly off the handle *informal* to become very angry suddenly and unexpectedly about something that does not seem very important【非正式】〔為不太重要的事〕大發雷霆: *There's no need to fly off the handle like that.* 不必那樣大發雷霆。

20 let fly to suddenly start shouting at someone because you feel very angry about something 破口大罵: **[+at]** *The woman let fly a torrent of abuse at him.* 那個女人對他大罵一通。

21 go fly a kite *spoken* used to say that you think that someone is being very annoying【口】走開〔用於表示某人很煩時〕

⑧ **ATTACK** 攻擊

22 let fly to suddenly attack someone 突然攻擊, 突襲: **[+with]** *The soldiers let fly with a hail of machine-gun fire.* 士兵們突然用機關槍猛烈射擊。

⑨ **OTHER MEANINGS** 其他意思

23 ►ESCAPE 逃走◄ [T] to leave somewhere in order to escape 逃離: *They were forced to fly the country in 1939.* 1939年他們被迫逃到國外。

24 fly the coop *informal especially AmE* to leave or escape【非正式, 尤美】離開, 逃走, 離巢: *All my children have flown the coop now.* 我的所有孩子現在都離家走了。

25 fly by the seat of your pants *informal* to do something by guessing how to do it because you have very little knowledge or experience【非正式】憑猜測做事

26 ►FLAG 旗幟◄ [I,T] if a flag flies, or if you fly it, it is fixed to a pole or a building, ship etc 飄揚, 懸掛: *a ship flying the Dutch flag* 一艘掛着荷蘭國旗的船

27 fly the flag to behave in a way that shows that you are proud of your country, organization etc 揮舞旗幟〔以某種行動表明為自己的祖國、組織等而驕傲〕

28 fly in the face of to be the opposite of what most people think is reasonable, sensible, or normal 違反, 違抗: *Eysenck's claim flies in the face of all the evidence.* 艾森克的聲稱與所有的證據相違背。

29 rumours/accusations etc are flying if RUMOURS, ACCUSATIONS etc are flying about something, a lot of people are saying things about it 謠言四起/人人都在譴責等: *Rumours were flying round the capital about a possible military takeover.* 可能進行軍事接管的謠言在首都四處傳開。

30 ►PLAN 計劃◄ *AmE* [I] a plan that will fly is good or useful【美】〔計劃〕行得通 —see also 另見 **the bird has flown** (BIRD (7)), **as the crow flies** (CROW[1] (3)), **sparks fly** (SPARK[1] (6))

fly at sb also 又作 **fly into sb** *AmE phr v* [T] to suddenly rush towards someone because you are very angry with them【美】〔因生氣而〕衝向[撲向]某人: *The old man flew at her in rage.* 那位老人怒氣沖沖地衝向她。

fly² *v past tense and past participle* **flied** [I] *AmE* to hit a ball in BASEBALL high into the air, especially so that the ball is caught by the other team【美】〔棒球中〕擊騰空球, 擊高飛球〔尤指球被對方接住時〕

fly³ *n* [C]

1 ►INSECT 昆蟲◄ a small flying insect with two wings

蠅, 蒼蠅: *The flies kept buzzing around us.* 蒼蠅老在我們周圍嗡嗡叫。

2 ▶TROUSERS 褲子◀ also 又作 **flies** *BrE*【英】the part at the front of a pair of trousers which you can open and which consists of a ZIP[1] (1) or a row of buttons〔褲子前面的〕拉鎖蓋, 鈕扣蓋: *He did up his fly.* 他扣上了褲扣。

3 sb wouldn't hurt a fly/sb wouldn't harm a fly *spoken* used to say that someone is very gentle and is not likely to hurt anyone【口】某人不會傷害人, 某人心地善良

4 be going down like flies/be dropping like flies *informal* used to say that a lot of people are becoming ill with a particular disease【非正式】〔因患某種疾病許多人〕紛紛病倒

5 fly in the ointment *informal* the only thing that spoils something and prevents it from being successful【非正式】美中不足之處

6 be a fly on the wall to be able to watch what happens without other people knowing that you are there 做牆壁上的一隻蒼蠅, 做不被察覺的觀察者: *I wish I'd been a fly on the wall during that conversation.* 我真希望自己是牆壁上的一隻蒼蠅, 能聽到那次談話。—see also 另見 FLY-ON-THE-WALL

7 there are no flies on sb *BrE spoken* used to say that someone is not stupid and cannot be tricked【英口】某人很機靈, 某人不會上當受騙

8 ▶FISHING 釣魚◀ a hook that is made to look like a fly, used for catching fish 假蠅釣鉤

9 ▶BASEBALL 棒球◀ a flyball 騰空球, 高飛球

fly[4] *adj old-fashioned especially BrE* clever and not easily tricked【過時, 尤英】機靈的, 聰明的; 不易上當受騙的: *He's a fly old bird.* 他是個精明不易受騙的老傢伙。

fly·a·way /ˈflaɪəˌwe; ˈflaɪəweɪ/ *adj* **flyaway hair** hair that is soft and thin and becomes untidy easily〔頭髮〕飄拂的; 柔軟而纖細的; 易散開的

fly ball /ˈ· ·/ *n* [C] a ball that has been hit high into the air in a game of BASEBALL〔棒球中的〕騰空球, 高飛球

fly·blown /ˈflaɪˌblon; ˈflaɪbləʊn/ *adj* **1** *especially BrE* old, dirty, and in bad condition【尤英】骯髒破舊的 **2** *BrE* meat that is flyblown has flies' eggs in it and is not suitable for eating【尤英】〔肉類〕沾有蠅卵的

fly·boy /ˈflaɪˌbɔɪ; ˈflaɪbɔɪ/ *n* [C] *AmE informal* a pilot【美, 非正式】飛機駕駛員

fly·by /ˈflaɪˌbaɪ; ˈflaɪbaɪ/ *n* [C] *AmE* a group of planes that fly close together on a special occasion for people to watch【美】〔表演性的〕低空編隊飛行

fly-by-night /ˈ· · ˌ·/ *adj* [only before noun 僅用於名詞前] *informal* a fly-by-night company, businessman is not well established and may only be interested in making quick profits【非正式】〔只求迅速獲利而〕不講信用的; 不可靠的〔公司、商人等〕

fly·catch·er /ˈflaɪˌkætʃɚ; ˈflaɪˌkætʃə/ *n* [C] a small bird that catches flies in the air 鶲, 捕蠅鳥

fly-drive hol·i·day /ˈ· · ˌ···/ *n* [C] a holiday arranged at a fixed price that includes your flight, a car to drive, and a place to stay 空陸聯遊假期〔指包括機票、租汽車和住宿的全包度假旅遊〕

fly·er /ˈflaɪɚ; ˈflaɪə/ *n* [C] **1** a sheet of paper advertising something, which is given to people in the street or is pushed through their door〔廣告〕傳單 **2** *informal* a pilot【非正式】飛機駕駛員 **3** *informal* a FLYING START【非正式】快速起跑

fly·fish·ing /ˈflaɪˌfɪʃɪŋ; ˈflaɪˌfɪʃɪŋ/ *n* [U] the sport of fishing in a river or lake with special hooks that are made to look like flies 用假蠅鉤釣魚

fly half /ˌ· ˈ·/ *n* [C] a fast-running player in RUGBY whose job is to pass the ball to a line of players〔英式橄欖球賽中的〕外側前衛

fly·ing[1] /ˈflaɪɪŋ; ˈflaɪ-ɪŋ/ *adj* **1 with flying colours** if you pass a test with flying colours, you are very successful in it 出色地, 很成功地, 大獲全勝地〔通過考試〕 **2 a flying visit** a quick visit because you are in a hurry 短暫訪問: *They've been down here for a flying visit.* 他們到這裡進行短暫訪問。**3 a flying jump/leap** a long high jump made while you are running 急行起跳

flying[2] *n* [U] the activity of travelling by plane 乘飛機旅行; 飛行: *fear of flying* 害怕乘飛機旅行

flying but·tress /ˌ·· ˈ··/ *n* [C] a half ARCH[1] (1) joined to the top of the outside wall of a large building such as a church in order to support it 拱扶垛, 飛(扶)拱

flying doc·tor /ˌ·· ˈ··/ *n* [C] a doctor, especially in Australia, who goes by plane to visit sick people who live a long way from the nearest town〔尤指澳大利亞的〕飛行醫生〔乘飛機到偏遠地區出診的醫生〕

flying fish /ˌ·· ˈ·/ *n* [C] a tropical sea fish that can jump out of the water 飛魚〔熱帶海魚〕

flying fox /ˌ·· ˈ·/ *n* [C] a FRUIT BAT 狐蝠, 熱帶大蝙蝠

flying of·fic·er /ˈ·· ˌ···/ *n* [C] a rank in the British airforce〔英國的〕空軍中尉 —see table on page C7 參見C7頁附錄

flying pick·et /ˌ·· ˈ··/ *n* [C] someone who travels to different factories, mines etc during a strike (STRIKE[2] (1)) and tries to persuade workers to stop working, although they do not work there themselves〔罷工期間到各處工廠、礦山等勸說工人罷工的〕流動宣傳員

flying sau·cer /ˌ·· ˈ··/ *n* [C] a round-shaped SPACECRAFT carrying creatures from space; UFO 飛碟, 不明飛行物

flying squad /ˈ·· ·/ *n* [C] a special group of police officers in Britain whose job is to travel quickly to the place where there has been a serious crime〔英國的〕閃電行動隊, 快速特警隊

flying start /ˌ·· ˈ·/ *n* **1 get off to a flying start** *informal* to begin very well【非正式】開始時進展順利; 順利地開始: *He's got off to a flying start in his new job.* 他的新工作一開始就進展順利。**2** a start to a race in which the competitors are already moving very quickly 快速起跑

flying tack·le /ˌ·· ˈ··/ *n* [C] a way of stopping someone from running by putting your arms around their legs and making them fall over〔抱住對方的腿、使之摔倒的〕魚躍擒抱

fly leaf /ˈ· ·/ *n* [C] a page at the beginning or end of a book, on which there is usually no printing〔書籍前後的〕空白頁, 扉頁, 襯頁

fly-on-the-wall /ˌ· · · ˈ·◂/ *adj* [only before noun 僅用於名詞前] a fly-on-the-wall television programme shows people's daily lives in a very natural way, because they forget they are being filmed〔拍攝電視節目時〕不被覺察的; 隱祕拍攝的

fly·o·ver /ˈflaɪˌovɚ; ˈflaɪ-əʊvə/ *n* [C] **1** *BrE* a bridge that carries a road over another road【英】立交橋, 高架公路; OVERPASS *AmE*【美】—see picture on page A3 參見A3頁圖 **2** *AmE* a flypast【美】〔表演性的〕低空編隊飛行

fly·pa·per /ˈflaɪˌpepɚ; ˈflaɪˌpeɪpə/ *n* [C,U] paper covered with a sticky substance used to catch flies 黏蠅紙

fly·past /ˈflaɪˌpæst; ˈflaɪpɑːst/ *n* [C] *BrE* a group of planes that fly close together on a special occasion for people to watch【英】〔表演性的〕低空編隊飛行

fly·sheet /ˈflaɪˌʃit; ˈflaɪʃiːt/ also 又作 **fly** *n* [C] a sheet of material that is put over a tent to protect it from the rain〔帳篷上的〕防雨篷頂

fly·specked /ˈflaɪˌspɛkt; ˈflaɪspekt/ *adj especially AmE* covered with small spots of waste matter from flies【尤美】滿佈蠅屎的

fly·swat·ter /ˈflaɪˌswɑtɚ; ˈflaɪˌswɒtə/ *n* [C] a square net fixed to a handle and used for killing flies (蒼)蠅拍

fly·weight /ˈflaɪˌwet; ˈflaɪweɪt/ *n* [C] a BOXER (1) who belongs to the lightest class of boxers and weighs 51 kilos〔體重51公斤的〕次最輕量級拳擊手

fly·wheel /ˈflaɪˌhwil; ˈflaɪwiːl/ *n* [C] a heavy wheel that keeps a machine working at a steady speed because of its weight 飛輪, 慣性輪

fly·whisk /ˈflaɪˌhwɪsk; ˈflaɪˌwɪsk/ *n* [C] *BrE* a small brush, used in former times for keeping flies away【英】〔舊時驅蠅的〕撣子，蠅拂

FM /ˌɛfˋɛm; ˌef ˈem◂/ *n* [U] frequency modulation; a system used for broadcasting radio programmes which produces a very clear sound 調頻；調頻廣播系統 —compare 比較 AM

fnarr /fnɑr; fnɑː/ *interjection BrE spoken humorous* used to say that what has just been said also has a sexual meaning although this was not intended【英口，幽默】別說葷話: *"He's got a big one, hasn't he?" "Fnarr!"* "他的傢伙很大，不是嗎？""別說葷話！"

foal¹ /fol; fəʊl/ *n* [C] a very young horse 馬駒

foal² *v* [I] to give birth to a foal 產(駒)

foam¹ /fom; fəʊm/ *n* [U] **1** a mass of small BUBBLES¹ (1) on the surface of something, such as the sea or coffee, which are formed when air mixes with a liquid〔空氣與液體混合時產生的〕泡沫 **2** a substance used for cleaning or shaving (SHAVE¹ (1)) which consists of a mass of small BUBBLES¹ (1)〔清洗或剃鬚用的〕泡沫(劑) **3** foam rubber 泡沫橡膠，海綿橡膠: *a foam mattress* 海綿橡膠牀墊 —**foamy** *adj*

foam² *v* [I] **1** to produce foam 起泡沫: *When he opened the can it foamed all over his hand.* 他打開罐子時弄得滿手泡沫。**2 foam at the mouth** to make a mass of small BUBBLES¹ (1) come out of your mouth because you are very angry or ill〔發怒時〕唾沫四濺;〔生病時〕口吐白沫

foam rub·ber /ˌ· ˈ··◂/ *n* [U] soft rubber full of air bubbles used in PILLOWS, chair seats etc〔用在枕頭、椅座等中的〕泡沫橡膠，海綿橡膠

F

fob¹ /fɑb; fɒb/ *v* **fobbing, fobbed**

fob sb ↔ **off** [T] **1** to try to stop someone complaining or asking questions by giving them explanations, excuses etc that are obviously untrue〔用藉口等〕搪塞，哄騙: **fob sb off with** *He tried to fob her off with some story about losing her telephone number.* 他想用丟失電話號碼的假話來搪塞她。**2** to make someone accept something that is not as good as the thing they wanted 騙〔某人〕接受〔次貨、劣質品等〕: **fob sb off with** *Don't let them fob you off with some cheap imported brand.* 別讓他們用便宜的進口牌子貨色把你騙了。

fob sth ↔ **off on** sb [T] to persuade someone into accepting something by a trick or deceit 騙〔某人〕接受〔某事物〕: *You can't just fob all your difficult jobs off on to me!* 你不能騙我接受你的這些艱難的工作！

fob² *n* [C] **1** a small object fixed to a key ring as a decoration 鑰匙圈上的小飾物 **2** a short chain or piece of cloth to which a fob watch is fastened 懷錶短鏈；懷錶帶

fob watch /ˈ· ·/ *n* [C] a watch that fits into a pocket, or is pinned to a woman's dress 懷錶；掛錶

fo·cal /ˋfokḷ; ˈfəʊkəl/ *adj* [only before noun 僅用於名詞前] **1** the focal point, issue etc is the thing that people pay most attention to 焦點的 **2 focal attention/awareness** the main part of your attention when you are looking at or thinking about something 重點注意力；焦點意識

focal length /ˌ·· ˈ·/ *n* [C] *technical* the distance between the centre of a lens and the focal point【術語】焦距

focal point /ˈ·· ·/ *n* [C] **1** the person or thing that you pay most attention to〔注意力的〕焦點，重點: *The man on horseback acts as the focal point of the picture.* 騎在馬背上的那個人是那幅圖畫的焦點。**2** *technical* the point on a LENS or a mirror where light RAYS (1) meet【術語】聚焦點

fo'c'sle /ˋfoksḷ; ˈfəʊksəl/ *n* [C] *BrE* the front part of a ship, where the sailors live【英】〔船首的〕水手艙; FORECASTLE *AmE*【美】

2 **fo·cus¹** /ˋfokəs; ˈfəʊkəs/ *v* **focussing, focussed** or **focused 1** [I,T] to pay special attention to a particular person or thing instead of others (使)集中注意力於…: [+on] *Modern medicine has tended to focus too much on developing highly complicated surgical techniques.* 現代醫學常趨向於過分注意發展十分複雜的外科技術。| **focus attention on** *The recent wave of bombings has focussed public attention on the region.* 最近一連串的爆炸案把公眾的注意力集中到該地區。**2** [T] to change the position of the LENS (2) on a camera, TELESCOPE¹ etc, so that you can see something clearly 調節〔照相機、望遠鏡等〕的焦距: **focus sth on** *He focused his binoculars on the building opposite.* 他對準對面的建築物調節雙目望遠鏡的焦距。**3** [I,T] if your eyes focus, or if you focus your eyes, you gradually become able to see something clearly (使)逐漸看清 **4** [I,T] if you focus beams of light or if they focus, they pass through a LENS and meet at a point (使)〔光線〕聚焦；(使)集中

focus² *n* **1** [singular] the subject or situation that people pay special attention to〔話題或情況的〕焦點，重點: [+of] *The focus of the conference shifted from population growth to the education of women.* 會議的重點從人口增長轉移到婦女教育上。| **the focus is on sth** *The focus of recent legislation has been on environmental issues.* 最近立法的焦點是環境問題。| **the focus of attention** *The war in Bosnia had now become the focus of worldwide media attention.* 波斯尼亞的戰爭此時已成為全世界媒體關注的焦點。**2** [U] special attention that is given to one particular subject or situation〔注意力的〕集中點，中心點: [+on] *grammar based teaching, with its focus on accuracy rather than fluency* 以語法為基礎的教學法，其重點放在準確度而不是流利程度上 | **bring/throw sth into focus** (=make people notice something and pay special attention to it) 使明確，使清楚；使特別注意 *The case has brought the problem of child abuse sharply into focus.* 這個案例已經使虐待兒童的問題十分突出。**3 in focus/out of focus** if a photograph or an instrument such as a TELESCOPE¹ is in focus, the edges of the things you are looking at can be seen clearly, if it is out of focus they cannot be seen clearly〔照片或望遠鏡等〕焦點對準[沒有對準]的，清晰[不清晰]的 **4** [C] *technical plural* **foci** the point where beams of light or waves of sound meet after their direction has been changed【術語】聚光點；聚聲點 2

fo·cussed *BrE*【英】, **focused** *AmE*【美】/ˋfokəst; ˈfəʊkəst/ *adj* paying careful attention to what you are doing, in a way that shows you are determined to succeed 集中注意力的；聚精會神的: *This year she's a much more focused player.* 今年她更聚精會神地參加比賽。

fod·der /ˋfɑdɚ; ˈfɒdə/ *n* [C,U] food for farm animals 飼料，秣 —see also 另見 CANNON FODDER

foe /fo; fəʊ/ *n* [C] *literary* an enemy【文】敵人，仇敵

foe·tal, fetal /ˋfitḷ; ˈfiːtl/ *adj* [only before noun 僅用於名詞前] connected with a foetus 胎兒的，胚胎的: *foetal abnormalities* 胎兒的畸形

foetal po·si·tion /ˈ·· ·ˌ··/ *n* [C] the body position of an unborn child inside its mother, in which the body is curled, and the legs are pulled up against the chest 胎姿，胎位

foe·tus, fetus /ˋfitəs; ˈfiːtəs/ *n* [C] a young human or animal before birth 胎兒，胚胎 —compare 比較 EMBRYO (1)

fog¹ /fɑg; fɒg/ *n* [C,U] **1** cloudy air near the ground which is difficult to see through 霧: *Thick fog is making driving conditions hazardous.* 濃霧正使路面情況變得很危險。| **fog bank** (=a large area of fog) 霧陣，霧堤 —compare 比較 MIST¹ (1) **2 in a fog** *informal* confused and unable to think clearly【非正式】困惑的，迷惘的: *Sorry, what did you say? – My mind's in a fog at the moment.* 對不起，你說甚麼？——我的頭腦現在十分混亂。

fog² *v* **fogged, fogging 1** [I,T] if something made of glass fogs up or becomes fogged up, it becomes covered in small drops of water that make it difficult to see through〔玻璃製品因有微小水滴〕變得模糊 **2 fog the issue** to make a subject, problem etc become unclear and more complicated 使問題變得模糊不清: *I think we're just fogging the issue by looking at all these details.* 我認為我們察看這些細節只會使問題變得模糊不清。

fog·bound /ˈfɑg͵baund; ˈfɒgbaʊnd/ *adj* prevented from travelling or working normally because of fog 被霧所困的; 因霧受阻的: *Moscow airport was fogbound.* 莫斯科機場大霧瀰天, 不能使用。

fogey, fogy /ˈfogɪ; ˈfəʊgi/ *n plural* **fogeys** or **fogies** [C] someone who has old-fashioned ideas and dislikes change 守舊者: **old fogey** *Don't be such an old fogey!* 別這樣老頑固!

fog·gy /ˈfɑgɪ; ˈfɒgi/ *adj* **1** very misty because of fog 多霧的: *a foggy day in November* 十一月的一個多霧的日子 **2 not have the foggiest (idea)** *spoken* to not know at all【口】完全不知道; 全然不明白: *None of us had the foggiest idea about how to put the tent up.* 我們完全不知道怎樣搭帳篷。**3 a foggy memory/recollection** an unclear memory of something that happened in the past 模糊的記憶: *I only have a foggy recollection of my grandmother.* 我對祖母只有模糊的記憶。—**foggily** *adv* —**fogginess** *n* [U]

fog·horn /ˈfɑg͵hɔrn; ˈfɒghɔːn/ *n* [C] **1** a piece of equipment that makes a loud noise, which is used by ships in fog to warn other ships of their position〔霧天向其他船隻發出以示自己船隻方位的〕霧角, 霧笛 **2 a voice like a foghorn** *humorous* a very loud, unpleasant voice【幽默】響亮刺耳的嗓音

fog lamp /ˈ· ·/ *BrE*【英】, **fog light** /ˈ· ·/ *AmE*【美】—*n* [C] a strong light on the front of a car that helps drivers to see in fog 霧燈〔汽車在霧中使用的車前強光燈〕

foi·ble /ˈfɔɪbḷ; ˈfɔɪbəl/ *n* [C] a habit or feature of someone's character which is a little strange or silly 怪癖: *We all have our little foibles.* 我們大家都各有一些小怪癖。

foie gras /͵fwɑ ˈgrɑ; ͵fwɑː ˈgrɑː/ *n* [U] PATE DE FOIE GRAS (=type of food made from LIVER) 鵝肝醬

foil¹ /fɔɪl; fɔɪl/ *n* **1** [U] metal sheets that are as thin as paper, used for wrapping food〔包裹食品用的〕鋁箔, 金屬薄片: *Cover the chicken with silver foil and bake in a hot oven.* 用鋁箔把雞包起來, 放在熱爐裡烤。—see also 另見 TINFOIL **2** [U] paper that is covered with very thin sheets of metal 錫紙, 鋁箔紙: *Cigarettes are wrapped in foil to keep them fresh.* 香煙用鋁箔紙包裝以保持新鮮。**3 be a foil to** to emphasize another person or thing's good qualities, by being very different from them 襯托出…; 作為…的陪襯: *His quiet determination is a perfect foil to Eva's energetic enthusiasm.* 他那種不露聲色的決心正好襯托出伊娃的積極熱情。**4** [C] a light narrow sword used in FENCING (1)〔擊劍中的〕輕劍, 花劍

foil² *v* [T often passive 常用被動態] to prevent something bad that someone is planning to do 挫敗: *A massive arms-smuggling plan has been foiled by the CIA.* 一項大規模的武器走私計劃被中央情報局破獲了。

foist /fɔɪst; fɔɪst/ *v*

foist sth **on/upon** sb *phr v* [T] to force someone to accept or have to deal with something that they do not want 把…強加於, 把…硬塞給: *I keep getting work foisted on me at the last minute.* 我老是被人在最後一刻硬塞工作給我。

-fold /fold; fəʊld/ *suffix* **1** [in adjectives 構成形容詞] of a particular number of kinds …種的; …倍的: *A window has a twofold purpose – to allow light into the room and let people see out.* 窗戶有雙重用途——讓光線進入房間和讓人看到外面的東西。**2** [in adverbs 構成副詞] a particular number of times …倍: *The value of the house has increased fourfold.* (=it is now worth four times as much as before) 房子的價值已是原先的四倍。

fold¹ /fold; fəʊld/ *v*

1 ►BEND 摺疊◄ [T] to bend a piece of paper, cloth etc by laying or pressing one part over another 摺疊, 對摺: *Fold the paper along the dotted line.* 沿虛線將紙摺起來。| **fold sth in two/half** *The woman folded the tickets in two and tore them in half.* 那個女人把票對摺起來, 然後撕成兩半。

2 ►MAKE STH SMALLER/NEATER 使某物更小/更整齊◄ [T] also 又作 **fold up** to fold something several times so that it makes a small neat shape 摺起, 疊好: *I wish you kids would fold up your clothes!* 我希望你們這些孩子能把衣服疊好!

3 ►FURNITURE ETC 家具等◄ **a)** [I] if something such as a piece of furniture folds in a particular way, it is designed so that part of it can be folded to make it smaller 可摺疊: **[+away/up/down etc]** *a useful little bed that folds away when you don't need it* 一張有用的小牀, 不需要時可以摺好收起 **b)** [T] to fold or bend part of something such as a piece of furniture to make it smaller 摺疊, 摺起: **fold sth ↔ down/up/away etc** *Can you fold up these chairs while I clean the floor?* 你能在我刷洗地板時把這些椅子摺起來嗎?

4 fold your arms/legs etc to bend your arms or legs, especially so that they are resting against your body 交叉[交疊]雙臂/雙腿等: *George stood silently with his arms folded.* 喬治交叉着雙臂一言不發地站着。

5 ►BUSINESS 企業◄ [I] also 又作 **fold up** if an organization folds or folds up, it closes because it does not have enough money to continue 倒閉, 歇業

6 ►COVER 覆蓋◄ [T] to cover something, especially by wrapping it in material or putting your hand over it 包, 裹: **fold sth in sth** *a silver dagger folded in a piece of white cloth* 裹在一塊白布裡的一把銀色匕首

7 fold sb in your arms *especially literary* to hold someone closely by putting your arms around them【尤文】〔用雙臂〕抱住某人

fold sth **in** *phr v* [T] to gently mix another substance into a mixture when you are preparing food〔烹製食物時〕拌入, 把…調入: *Fold in the sugar and whisk until stiff.* 拌入糖, 攪拌到發稠為止。

fold² *n* [C]

1 ►LINE 線條◄ a line made in paper or material when you fold one part of it over another〔紙張或材料上的〕褶, 襉; 褶痕: *Bend back the card and cut along the fold.* 把摺疊的卡片恢復原狀, 然後沿褶痕剪開。

2 ►LOOSE SKIN/MATERIAL 鬆弛的皮膚/材料◄ [usually plural 一般用複數] **a)** a rounded shape made by folded material 材料的摺疊處, 褶子: *Ahmed had a dagger concealed in the folds of his robe.* 阿梅德在長袍的褶層裡藏着一把匕首。**b)** an area of loose folded skin 皺皮: *The old dog had thick folds of skin around its neck.* 那條老狗的脖子上有堆疊的皺皮。

3 the fold the group of people that you belong to and share the same beliefs and ideas as 同一羣體的人, 志同道合的人: **return/come back to the fold** *Many Democrats who voted Republican in the 80s have now returned to the fold.* 許多在20世紀80年代投共和黨票的民主黨人現在已經回頭了。| **stray from/leave the fold** *a former advocate of free market economics who had strayed from the fold* 以前提倡自由市場經濟而已經脫離這一學派的人

4 ►SHEEP 羊◄ a small area of a field surrounded by a wall or fence where sheep are kept for safety 羊欄

5 ►ROCK 岩石◄ *technical* a bend in layers of rock, caused by underground movements in the earth【術語】〔岩石的〕褶皺

6 ►VALLEY 山谷◄ *literary* a small narrow valley【文】小山谷

fold·a·way /ˈfoldə͵we; ˈfəʊldəweɪ/ *adj* [only before noun 僅用於名詞前] a foldaway bed, table etc can be folded up so it uses less space〔牀、桌等〕可摺疊 (存放) 的

fold·er /ˈfoldɚ; ˈfəʊldə/ *n* [C] **1** a container for keeping loose papers in, made of folded card 文件夾 **2** a picture of a folder on a computer screen, which shows you where information can be stored〔電腦屏幕上的圖示, 表示信息儲存位置的〕文件夾

F

fold·ing /ˈfoldɪŋ; ˈfəʊldɪŋ/ *adj* [only before noun 僅用於名詞前] a folding bicycle, bed, chair etc has parts that you can bend or fold together to make it easier to carry or store 可摺疊的; 摺疊式的

fo·li·age /ˈfolɪɪdʒ; ˈfəʊli-ɪdʒ/ *n* [U] the leaves of a plant〔植物的〕葉子, 葉

fo·li·o /ˈfolɪˌo; ˈfəʊliəʊ/ *n plural* **folios** *technical*【術語】**1** [C] a book made with very large sheets of paper 對開本 **2** [C] a single numbered sheet of paper from a book〔書本中有頁碼的〕一張

folk¹ /fok; fəʊk/ *n* **1 folks** [plural] **a)** *especially AmE* your parents and family【尤美】家人, 家屬, 親屬: *Is it OK if I call my folks?* 我打電話給家人可以嗎? | **the folks back home** *Wait till the folks back home hear about this!* 等到爸媽都得知此事就麻煩了! **b)** used when addressing a group of people in a friendly way 各位, 大夥兒: *That's all for now, folks.* 各位, 到此為止。**c)** *AmE* people【美】人, 人們: *Folks around here don't take too kindly to strangers.* 這裡的人對陌生人不太友好。**2 country folk/farming folk/fisher folk etc** [plural] *literary* people who live in a particular area or do a particular kind of work【文】鄉下人/農民/漁民等: *simple country folk* 純樸的鄉下人 **3** [plural] *BrE old-fashioned* people【英, 過時】人, 人們: **young folk/old folk** *Young folk these days don't know the meaning of work.* 當今的年輕人不懂得工作的意義。**4** [U] FOLK MUSIC 民間音樂

folk² *adj* [only before noun 僅用於名詞前] **1** folk art, stories, customs etc are traditional and typical of the ordinary people who live in a particular area 民間的, 民俗的: *folk tales* 民間故事, 民間傳說 | *an old Spanish folk song* 一首古老的西班牙民間歌曲 **2 folk science/psychology/wisdom etc** science etc that is based on simple ideas that ordinary people can understand and does not involve a high level of technical knowledge 民間科學/民間心理學/民間智慧等 **3 folk medicine/remedy** a traditional type of medical treatment that uses plants etc rather than modern scientific methods 民間傳統醫學/民間療法

folk dance /ˈ· ,·/ *n* [C] a traditional dance from a particular area, or a piece of music for this dance 民間舞蹈[舞曲]; 土風舞 —**folk dancer** *n* [C]

folk he·ro /ˈ· ,··/ *n* [C] someone who people in a particular place admire very much because of something they have done 民間英雄, 人們心目中的英雄; 百姓心裡的英雄: *Casey Jones is a well-known American folk hero.* 凱亞·瓊斯是美國人心目中的著名英雄。

folk·lore /ˈfokˌlɔr; ˈfəʊklɔː/ *n* [U] the traditional stories, customs etc of a particular area or country 民間傳說; 民俗: *According to local folklore, the cave was once occupied by a witch.* 根據當地的民間傳說, 一位女巫曾經住在這個山洞裡。

folk mu·sic /ˈ· ,··/ *n* [U] **1** traditional music that has been played by ordinary people in a particular area for a long time 民間音樂 **2** a style of popular music in which people sing and play GUITARS, without any electronic equipment〔用結他伴奏而無電子器材的〕仿民間音樂

folk·sy /ˈfoksɪ; ˈfəʊksi/ *adj informal*【非正式】**1** *especially AmE* friendly and informal【尤美】友好的, 隨和的, 無拘束的: *The town had a certain folksy charm.* 這個城鎮有種很吸引人的友好的氣氛。**2** in a style that is typical of traditional countryside styles or customs 民間風格的, 民俗風格的

fol·li·cle /ˈfɑlɪkḷ; ˈfɒlɪkəl/ *n* [C] one of the small holes in the skin that hairs grow from 小囊, 毛囊

fol·low /ˈfɑlo; ˈfɒləʊ/ *v*

① GO BEHIND 跟在後面
② AFTER/NEXT 在後面/接在後面的
③ OBEY RULES/TEACHINGS ETC 遵守規則/聽從教導等
④ UNDERSTAND 理解
⑤ DO THE SAME AS 仿效
⑥ BE INTERESTED IN 對…感興趣
⑦ OTHER MEANINGS 其他意思

① GO BEHIND 跟在後面

1 [I,T] to walk, drive, run etc behind someone else, going in the same direction as them 跟着, 跟隨: **follow sb/sth** *If you'll just follow me, I'll show you to the office.* 請跟我來, 我會帶你到辦公室。| *Tom Selleck walked in, followed by a crowd of photographers.* 湯姆·塞萊克走進來, 後面跟着一大羣攝影家。| **follow** *I knew the way, so I went first, and the others followed.* 我知道路, 所以我先走, 其他人隨後。

2 [T] to go closely behind someone in order to watch them and find out where they go 跟蹤: *Marlowe looked over his shoulder to make sure no-one was following him.* 馬洛回過頭看, 想確定沒有人在跟蹤他。

② AFTER/NEXT 在後面/接在後面的

3 [I,T] to happen directly after an event or period 接着…發生: *There was a major increase in immigration in the years that followed the First World War.* 第一次世界大戰後幾年, 移民人數大幅增加。| **be (closely) followed by** *The lightning was followed by a great crash of thunder.* 閃電之後緊接着是轟隆隆的一陣雷聲。| **in the days/weeks etc that followed** *We saw a lot of each other in the months that followed.* 此後的幾個月裡, 我們多次見面。| **there follows** (=after that there is) 隨後出現 *There followed a long and embarrassing silence.* 隨後出現長時間的令人尷尬的沉默。| **follow shortly** (=happen soon) 很快發生 *The late night movie will follow shortly.* 深夜電影馬上就要開始。—see also 另見 FOLLOWING[1]

4 [I,T] to come directly after something else, for example in a book or a series of things 緊隨…之後: *A full report of the results follows this chapter.* 本章之後是一份全面的結果報告。| **be followed by** *In English the letter 'Q' is always followed by a 'U'.* 在英語拼寫中, 字母Q後面總會有字母U。| **there follows** (=after that there is) 隨後是 *There follows a long description of the writer's early life.* 後面是對作家早年生活的詳盡描述。

5 [I,T] to do an important job after someone else 繼任〔重要職位〕: **be followed by** *Ivan was followed by a succession of weak rulers.* 伊凡的後繼者都是一個個懦弱昏庸的統治者。

6 a hard act to follow *spoken* someone who is so good at something that it will be difficult for the next person to be as good or as successful【口】難以再出現[仿效]的人

7 as follows used to introduce a list of names, things, instructions etc that come next 如下: *The results are as follows: First was Sweden, then Germany, then Ireland.* 結果如下: 第一名是瑞典, 第二名是德國, 然後是愛爾蘭。

8 to follow after the main part of a meal〔主菜後〕下一道菜: *We're having the poached salmon, with chocolate mousse to follow.* 我們正在吃水煮鮭魚, 下一道

菜吃巧克力奶油凍。

③ **OBEY RULES/TEACHINGS ETC** 遵守規則/聽從教導等

9 follow sb's orders/wishes/advice etc to do something in the way that someone has told you to do it, advised you to do it etc 服從某人的命令/遵照某人的願望/聽從某人的忠告等: *If you'd followed my advice, none of this would have happened.* 如果當初你聽從我的忠告, 這種事就不會發生了。| **follow sb's orders etc to the letter** (=do exactly what someone told you to do) 不折不扣地服從某人的命令

10 follow the instructions/a diagram etc to do something according to the rules or instructions that say how it should be done 按照使用説明/圖表去做等: *Did you follow the instructions on the package?* 你是按照包裝上的使用説明做的嗎?

11 follow the signs/sb's directions to go in the direction that the signs say you should go or that someone has told you to go 沿着標誌所指的方向行進/沿着某人指示的方向行進: *Follow the signs for the airport, then turn off when you see the hotel.* 沿着標誌指示向機場方向行進, 然後在看到旅館時拐上另一條路。

12 [T] to believe in and obey a particular set of religious or political ideas, or a leader who teaches these ideas 信奉, 追隨: *They still follow the teachings of Mahatma Gandhi.* 他們仍然信奉聖雄甘地的學説。

④ **UNDERSTAND** 理解

13 [I,T] to understand something such as an explanation or story 領會, 聽懂: *I didn't quite follow what he was saying.* 我不太明白他說的話。| **easy/hard to follow** *I must admit I found the plot a bit hard to follow.* 我必須承認我覺得情節有點難懂。

⑤ **DO THE SAME AS** 仿效

14 [I,T] to do the same thing as someone else after they have done it 仿效: *We all had to follow the teacher.* 我們都得仿效老師。| **follow sb into** (=do the same job as someone else especially a member of your family) 跟〔家中〕某人一樣從事〔某種行業〕*None of my children seem to want to follow me into journalism.* 我的孩子們似乎沒有一個想跟我一樣從事新聞工作。| **follow sb's example** (=do the same as them because it is a good thing to do) 以某人為榜樣 *They have an excellent childcare policy, and we're hoping other companies will follow their example.* 他們有一個很好的兒童保育政策, 我們希望其他公司能以他們為榜樣。

15 follow suit to do the same as someone else has just done 跟着做, 照着做, 仿效: *The Russian team pulled out of the Los Angeles Olympics, and several Eastern European countries followed suit.* 蘇聯隊退出洛杉磯奧運會, 幾個東歐國家也跟着退出了。

16 follow (in) sb's footsteps to do the same job as someone else who did it before you 步某人的後塵, 繼承某人的事業: *My father was a jazz player, and I wanted to follow in his footsteps.* 我父親是個爵士樂演奏家, 我想繼承他的事業。

17 follow the herd/crowd to do the same thing as other people, without really thinking about what you want to do 隨大流

⑥ **BE INTERESTED IN** 對…感興趣

18 [T] to be interested in a particular sports team, and be concerned about its performance and results 關注〔某一球隊〕; 擁護: *The President follows the Red Sox.* 總統擁護紅襪隊。

19 [T] to be interested in the way a situation or set of events develops, and try to find out the latest information about it 密切關注: *Have you been following that crime series on TV?* 你有一直留意着那部描寫犯罪的電視系列片嗎?

⑦ **OTHER MEANINGS** 其他意思

20 follow your instincts/feelings to do something in the way that you feel is best 憑本能行事/跟着感覺走

21 follow your nose a) to do something in the way that you feel is right, without asking or checking 憑直覺行事; 跟着感覺走 **b)** to go straight forward 朝…直走: *Turn left at the bank, then just follow your nose.* 在銀行處左拐, 然後一直往前走。

22 ►GO IN A PARTICULAR DIRECTION 朝某個方向行進◄ [T] **a)** to continue along a particular road, river etc 沿着…繼續行進: *Follow the main road until you get to the coast.* 沿着大路往前走到海岸。**b)** to go in the same direction as something else, especially something that is very close 順着…行進: *The railway follows the road for several miles, and then branches off.* 鐵路順着公路延伸好幾英里, 然後岔開。

23 follow a trend/pattern/course etc to continue to happen or develop in a particular way 按照某種趨勢/按照某一模式/遵循某一進程等: *In Australia, the weather follows a fairly predictable pattern.* 在澳大利亞, 天氣常按照基本上可預料的模式而變化。

24 it follows (that) [I] it must be true as a result of something else that is true 是…的必然結果: *Just because you're rich, it doesn't necessarily follow that you're happy.* 只是由於你很富有, 但你並不一定很幸福。

25 ►WATCH/LISTEN CAREFULLY 仔細觀察/仔細聽◄ [T] to carefully watch someone move or listen to them speaking 注視; 傾聽: **follow sb with your eyes** *The men all followed her with their eyes as she entered the bar.* 她進入酒吧時, 男人們都注視着她。

26 ►THINK ABOUT/STUDY 考慮/研究◄ [T] to study or think about a particular idea or subject and try to find out more about it 考慮, 研究: *It turned out we were both following the same line of research.* 原來我們倆考慮的是同樣的研究途徑。

27 ►BE ABOUT 關於◄ [T] to show or describe someone's life or a series of events, for example in a film or book 展現, 描寫: *The film follows Rocky's career as a boxer from his early days.* 這部電影描述了洛基從早期起當拳擊手的經歷。

28 follow a profession/trade/way of life *formal* to do a particular job or have a particular way of life【正式】從事某種職業/某種行業/遵循某種生活方式

follow sb around also 又作 **follow sb about** *BrE*【英】*phr v* [T] to keep following someone everywhere they go 到處跟隨: *I wish you'd stop following me around.* 我希望你不要到處跟着我。

follow through *phr v* **1** [I,T] to do what needs to be done after the main part of something is finished, in order to make sure it is complete or successful〔在把一件事基本上做完後〕進行到底; 執行: **follow sth ↔ through** *The success of any healthcare program depends on how it is followed through.* 任何一項保健計劃的成功均取決於它如何執行。**2** [I] to continue moving your arm after you have hit the ball in tennis, GOLF etc〔網球、高爾夫球等擊球後〕做隨球動作 —see also 另見 FOLLOW-THROUGH

follow up *phr v* **1** [T **follow** sth ↔ **up**] to do something as a result of something you have found out, someone has suggested etc 跟進〔線索、建議等〕: *The police were criticized for failing to follow up the complaint.* 警方因沒有對投訴進行追查而受到批評。**2 follow (sth) up with** to do something in addition to what you have already done in order to make sure of success 以…繼續做〔某事〕; 採取後續行動: *The train drivers have voted to follow up their one-day strike with a series of 48-hour stoppages.* 火車司機已經投票決定在罷工一天之後舉行一連串的48小時停工作為後續行動。—see also 另見 FOLLOW-UP[1]

F

fol·low·er /ˈfɑloɚ; ˈfɒləʊə/ *n* [C] someone who believes in a particular system of ideas, or who supports a leader who teaches these ideas 信徒, 追隨者, 支持者: *Marx and his followers were convinced that capitalism would destroy itself.* 馬克思及其支持者確信資本主義會自我毀滅。| [+of] *followers of Sun Myung Moon, better known as Moonies* 文鮮明的信徒, 更知名的稱呼是 Moonies —see also 另見 CAMP FOLLOWER

2 1 **fol·low·ing¹** /ˈfɑloɪŋ; ˈfɒləʊɪŋ/ *adj* **1 the following afternoon/month/page/chapter etc** the next afternoon, month etc 第二天下午/下個月/下頁/下章等: *He was sick in the evening, but the following day he was better.* 他晚上生病了, 但第二天就好一些了。**2 the following example/way etc** the example, way etc that will be mentioned next 以下的例子/方式等: *Payment may be made in any of the following ways: cheque, cash, or credit card.* 可用以下任何一種方式付款: 支票、現金或信用卡。**3 a following wind** a wind that is blowing in the same direction as a ship, and helps it to move faster 順風

following² *n* [C] **1** [usually singular 一般用單數] a group of people who support or admire someone 一批追隨者[支持者, 崇拜者]: *The band has a big following in Europe.* 這支樂隊在歐洲有一大批崇拜者。**2 the following** the people or things that you are going to mention 下列的人, 下列的事物: *The following have been selected to play in tomorrow's game: Louise Carus, Fiona Douglas...* 下列選手已被挑選參加明天的比賽: 路易斯·卡勒斯、菲奥娜·道格拉斯... —see also 另見 FOLLOWING¹

following³ *prep* after an event or as a result of it 在…以後; 由於: *Following the speech, there will be a few minutes for questions.* 演講後將留出幾分鐘時間讓大家提問。| *Thousands of refugees left the country following the outbreak of civil war.* 由於內戰爆發, 數以千計的難民逃到國外去。

follow-my-lead·er /ˌ·· ·ˈ··/ *BrE*【英】, **follow-the-leader** *AmE*【美】—*n* [U] a children's game in which one of the players does actions which all the other players must copy 跟領袖, 猴子學樣〔參加者要模仿領頭人做動作的兒童遊戲〕

follow-through /ˌ·· ˈ·/ *n* [singular] **1** movement of your arm after you have hit the ball in tennis, GOLF etc 隨球動作〔網球、高爾夫球等運動中擊球後的揮臂動作〕—see picture on page A23 參見 A23 頁圖 **2** the things that someone does in order to complete a plan〔計劃的〕貫徹(工作): *The budget has to cover not only the main project but the follow-through.* 預算不僅要包括主體工程, 還要包括貫徹的工作。

follow-up¹ /ˈ·· ·/ *adj* [only before noun 僅用於名詞前] a follow-up visit, examination, study etc is done to make sure that an earlier one was effective, or to continue a plan of action that was started earlier〔訪問、考試、研究等〕後續的; 跟進的; 隨訪的: *a follow-up story on the Watergate break-in* 有關水門入室安裝竊聽器事件的後續報道 —see also 另見 **follow up** (FOLLOW¹)

follow-up² *n* **1** [C,U] something that is done to make sure that earlier actions have been successful or effective 後續行動; 跟進行動; 隨訪: *preventative treatment and follow-up several weeks later* 預防性治療以及幾星期後的後續治療 **2** [C] a book, film, article etc that comes after another one that has the same subject or characters〔書、電影的〕續集;〔文章的〕續篇: *Spielberg says he's planning to do a follow-up next year.* 史匹堡說他打算明年拍一部續集。

fol·ly /ˈfɑlɪ; ˈfɒli/ *n* **1** [C,U] *formal* a very stupid thing to do, especially one that is likely to have serious results【正式】〔尤指可能導致嚴重後果的〕蠢事, 荒唐事: **it would be folly to do sth** *It would be sheer folly to reduce spending on health education.* 減少健康教育的開支全然是一件蠢事。| **the folly of** *a writer who satirized the follies of aristocratic society* 一位諷刺貴族社會荒唐事的作家 **2** [C] *BrE* an unusual building that was built in former times as a decoration, not to be used or lived in【英】〔古代不住人的〕怪異的裝飾性建築物

fo·ment /foˈmɛnt; fəʊˈment/ *v formal*【正式】**foment revolution/trouble/discord etc** to cause trouble and make people start fighting each other or opposing the government 挑起, 煽動: *They were accused of fomenting rebellion.* 他們被指控犯有煽動叛亂罪。—**fomentation** /ˌfomɛnˈteʃən; ˌfəʊmenˈteɪʃən/ *n* [U]

fond /fɑnd; fɒnd/ *adj* **1 be fond of sb** to like someone very much, especially when you have known them for a long time and almost feel love for them 喜歡某人: *Joe's quite fond of her, isn't he?* 喬很喜歡她, 是嗎? | **grow fond of** *Over the years we've grown very fond of each other.* 這些年來, 我們漸漸互相喜歡對方。**2 be fond of sth** to like something, especially something you have liked for a long time 喜歡某物, 愛好某物: *I'm not very fond of country music.* 我不太喜歡鄉村音樂。| **grow fond of** *I'd grown fond of the place and it was difficult to leave.* 我已愛上這個地方, 很難離開它。**3 be fond of doing sth a)** to enjoy doing something very much 喜歡做某事: *Jilly's very fond of drawing.* 吉利非常喜歡畫圖畫。**b)** to do something often, especially something that annoys other people 老愛做某事: *My Grandfather was very fond of handing out advice to all my friends.* 我的祖父很愛給我的朋友提出忠告。**4** [only before noun 僅用於名詞前] a fond look, smile, action etc shows you like someone very much 深情的, 柔情的: *He gave her a fond look.* 他深情地看了她一眼。| **a fond farewell** *As we parted we said a fond farewell.* 我們分手時深情地相互道別。**5 have fond memories of** to remember something with great pleasure 愉快地記着: *Marie still had fond memories of their time together.* 瑪麗仍愉快地記着他們在一起的時光。**6 a fond belief/hope** a belief or hope that something will happen, which seems silly because it is very unlikely to happen 輕信, 愚蠢的看法/痴心妄想: **in the fond hope/belief that** *They sent him to another school in the fond hope that his behaviour would improve.* 他們把他送到另一所學校, 天真地希望他的行為會有所改善。—see also 另見 FONDLY —**fondness** *n* [U]: *His wife had a great fondness for expensive clothes.* 他的妻子非常喜歡購買昂貴的衣服。

fon·dant /ˈfɑndənt; ˈfɒndənt/ *n* [C,U] a sweet made of small grains of sugar 糖霜糖, 方旦糖〔一種軟糖〕

fon·dle /ˈfɑndl; ˈfɒndl/ *v* [T] to gently touch and move your fingers over part of someone's body in a way that shows love 愛撫, 撫摸: *She fondled the puppy's neck.* 她愛撫着小狗的脖子。

fond·ly /ˈfɑndlɪ; ˈfɒndli/ *adv* **1 fondly imagine/believe/hope etc** to believe something that is untrue, hope for something that will probably not happen etc 天真地以為/盲目地相信/痴心地希望等: *Some people still fondly believe that modern science can solve all the world's problems.* 有些人仍然天真地相信現代科學能解決世界所有的問題。**2** in a way that shows you like someone very much 深情地, 柔情地: *He turned to see her smiling fondly at him.* 他轉過身, 看見她柔情地朝他微笑着。

fon·due /ˈfɑndu; ˈfɒndjuː/ *n* [C,U] a dish made of small

fondue 涮製菜餚, 火鍋

pieces of food that you put in melted cheese or chocolate〔放入融化的乳酪或巧克力的〕涮製菜餚，火鍋

font /fɑnt; fɒnt/ *n* [C] **1** a large stone container in a church, that holds the water used for the ceremony of BAPTISM (1)〔教堂裡的〕洗禮盆，聖水盂 **2** *technical* a set of letters of a particular size and type, used for printing books, newspapers etc【術語】〔用於印刷書籍、報紙等，同樣大小和式樣的〕一副鉛字

S1 W1 **food** /fud; fuːd/ *n* **1** [U] things that people and animals eat, such as vegetables or meat 食物: *The food's great and it's not that expensive.* 這裡的食物太好吃了，而且不是那麼貴。| *There are food shortages in many areas.* 許多地區出現食物短缺。**2** [C,U] a particular type of food〔某一種〕食品: **junk food/health food etc** *All he ever eats is junk food.* 他吃的都是"垃圾"食品〔即低營養高熱量的食品〕。| *Try to cut down on sweet and fatty foods.* 想辦法少吃甜食和脂肪多的食品。| **dog food/pet food/baby food** (=food for dogs etc) 狗食/寵物食品/嬰兒食品 | **be off your food** (=feel ill and not want to eat anything) 生病不想吃東西，沒有食慾 **3 food for thought** something that makes you think carefully 引人深思的事物: *The teacher's advice certainly gave me food for thought.* 老師的忠告啟發我深思。

food bank /ˈ· ·/ *n* [C] *AmE* a place that gives food to poor people【美】〔向窮人分發糧食的〕食物銀行

food chain /ˈ· ·/ *n* **the food chain** all animals and plants considered as a group in which one type of animal eats another and then is eaten by another animal 食物鏈: *Pollution is affecting many creatures lower down the food chain.* 污染正影響着在食物鏈下層的許多生物。

food cou·pon /ˈ· ˌ··/ *n* [C] a FOOD STAMP 食物券，糧食券

food·ie /ˈfudɪ; ˈfuːdi/ *n* [C] *informal* someone who is very interested in cooking and eating food【非正式】美食家；愛吃的人

food poi·son·ing /ˈ· ˌ···/ *n* [U] a painful stomach illness caused by eating food that contains harmful BACTERIA 食物中毒

food pro·cess·or /ˈ· ˌ···/ *n* [C] a piece of electrical equipment that helps to prepare food in various ways, such as cutting and mixing 食品加工器，多功能食品切碎攪拌機 —see picture on page A10 參見A10頁圖

food stamp /ˈ· ·/ *n* [C] an official piece of paper that the US government gives to poor people so they can buy food〔美國政府發給窮人的〕食物券，糧食券

food·stuff /ˈfudˌstʌf; ˈfuːdstʌf/ *n* [C usually plural 一般用複數,U] a word meaning food, used especially when talking about the business of producing or selling food〔尤指商業生產或銷售的〕食品: *A wide variety of foodstuffs is available in the local market.* 在當地市場可買到各式各樣的食品。

fool¹ /ful; fuːl/ *n*

1 ►STUPID PERSON 蠢人◄ [C] a stupid person or someone who has done something stupid 蠢人，傻子，笨蛋: *What a fool she had been to think that he would stay.* 她竟然那麼傻，以為他會留下來。

2 any fool can *spoken* used to say that it is very easy to do something or to see that something is true【口】任何人都會〔用於表示某事很簡單〕: *Any fool can see that the painting's a fake.* 任何人都能看出這張畫是贋品。

3 be no fool/nobody's fool to be difficult to trick or deceive, because you have a lot of experience and knowledge about something 不會輕易上當，為人精明；不是傻瓜: *Katherine was nobody's fool when it came to money.* 凱瑟琳在錢的問題上一點也不傻。

4 make a fool of yourself to do something stupid that you feel embarrassed about afterwards and that makes you seem silly 出醜，出洋相: *Sorry I made such a fool of myself last night. I must have been drunk.* 對不起，我昨天晚上出醜了。我一定是喝醉了。

5 ►FOOD 食品◄ **gooseberry fool/strawberry fool etc** *BrE* a sweet food made of soft cooked fruit mixed with cream【英】奶油醋栗泥/奶油草莓泥等

6 make a fool of sb to deliberately try to make someone seem stupid 愚弄某人，使某人顯得愚蠢: *I suddenly realised that I was being made a fool of.* 我突然意識到我正在被人愚弄。

7 more fool you/him etc *BrE spoken* used to say that you think someone was stupid to do something and it is their own fault if this causes trouble【英口】這是你自己傻/那是他自己傻等: *"Jim smashed up my car." "More fool you for letting him borrow it!"* "吉姆把我的車撞壞了。" "你真傻，竟讓他借你的車去開！"

8 be living in a fool's paradise to feel happy and satisfied, and believe there are no problems, when in fact this is not true 陶醉在幻想之中，黃粱美夢

9 play/act the fool to behave in a silly way, especially in order to make people laugh 裝傻；逗人笑: *Stop playing the fool! You'll fall.* 別逗人笑了！你會摔倒的。

10 (send sb on) a fool's errand to make someone go somewhere or do something for no good reason（派某人去做）徒勞無益的事

11 ►ENTERTAINER 表演者◄ [C] a man whose job was to entertain a king or other powerful person in former times, by doing tricks, singing funny songs etc〔古時候供國王或其他權勢人物娛樂的〕弄臣，小丑 —see also 另見 APRIL FOOL

fool² *v* **1** [T] to trick someone into believing something 欺騙: *You can't fool me with that old excuse.* 你那個老一套的藉口是騙不了我的。| **fool sb into doing sth** *Don't be fooled into believing their promises.* 別給騙得竟然相信他們的諾言。**2 you could have fooled me** *spoken* used to show that you do not believe what someone has told you【口】我不會相信你的話[上你的當]，我才不信你呢: *"Look, we're doing our best to fix it." "Well, you could have fooled me."* "看，我們正盡力修理它。" "嘿，我才不信你呢。" **3 sb is just fooling** *spoken* used to say that someone is not serious and is only pretending that something is true【口】某人只是在鬧着玩而已: *Don't pay any attention to Henry. He's just fooling.* 別理會亨利，他只是鬧着玩而已。

fool around also 又作 **fool about** *BrE*【英】*phr v* [I] **1** to waste time behaving in a silly way 閒蕩，遊手好閒: *He spent the whole afternoon just fooling around.* 他整個下午都在閒蕩。**2** to behave in a careless and irresponsible way 亂弄，瞎弄: **[+with]** *Some idiot's been fooling around with the electricity supply!* 不知道哪個傻子一直在亂弄電源！**3** to have a sexual relationship with someone else's wife, boyfriend etc 玩弄，搞不正當的性關係: *Anthony's been fooling around with one of the secretaries.* 安東尼一直在跟一個祕書鬼混。

fool³ *adj* [only before noun 僅用於名詞前] *AmE informal* silly or stupid【美，非正式】愚蠢的，傻的: *What did you say a fool thing like that for?* 你為甚麼要說那種蠢話？

fool·e·ry /ˈfulərɪ; ˈfuːləri/ *n* [C,U] *BrE old-fashioned* silly or stupid behaviour【英，過時】愚蠢的行為，蠢事

fool·har·dy /ˈfulˌhɑrdɪ; ˈfuːlhɑːdi/ *adj* taking stupid and unnecessary risks 魯莽的，蠻幹的: *a foolhardy attempt to capture more territory* 想佔領更多領土的魯莽企圖 —**foolhardiness** *n* [U]

fool·ish /ˈfulɪʃ; ˈfuːlɪʃ/ *adj* **1** a foolish action, remark etc is stupid and shows that someone is not thinking sensibly〔行為、評論等〕愚蠢的，傻的: *I've never heard anything so foolish in all my life.* 我這輩子從沒聽到過這麼愚蠢的話。| **it is foolish (of sb) to do sth** *It was foolish of them to expect the economy to recover so quickly.* 他們竟指望經濟會這麼快復蘇，真愚蠢。**2** a foolish person behaves in a silly way or looks silly〔人〕愚笨的，傻瓜似的: *I was young and foolish at the time.* 我當時年輕而且傻乎乎的。| *a foolish grin* 傻笑 —**foolishly** *adv*: *She foolishly agreed to go with them.* 她傻乎乎地同意跟他們去。—**foolishness** *n* [U]

fool·proof /ˈfulˌpruf; ˈfuːlpruːf/ *adj* a foolproof method, plan, system etc is certain to be successful〔方法、計

劃、系統等〕肯定成功的, 萬無一失的: *a foolproof way of preventing credit card fraud* 防止利用信用卡詐騙的一種萬無一失的方法

fools·cap /ˈfulˌskæp; ˈfu:lskæp/ *n* [U] a large size of paper, especially paper for writing on 大裁, 大頁紙〔尤指書寫用紙〕

fool's gold /ˌ· ˈ·/ *n* [U] **1** a kind of yellow metal that exists in some rocks and looks like gold 愚人金〔指一種存在於岩石中形似黃金的黃色金屬〕 **2** something that you think will be very exciting, very attractive etc but in fact is not 虛幻的東西, 華而不實的東西

foot[1] /fut; fʊt/ *n plural* feet /fit; fi:t/ [C]

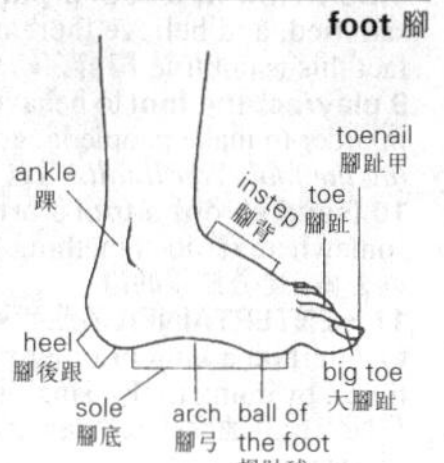

1 ►BODY PART 身體部位◄ the part of your body that you stand on and walk on 腳, 足: *I have a really bad pain in my foot.* 我的腳痛得很厲害。

2 on foot if you go somewhere on foot, you walk there 步行: *It takes about 30 minutes on foot, or 10 minutes if you go by car.* 步行去需要大約30分鐘, 如果坐車去, 則需要10分鐘。

3 ►MEASUREMENT 尺寸◄ *written abbreviation* 縮寫為 **ft** *plural* foot or feet a unit for measuring length, equal to 12 inches (INCH[1] (1)) or about 30 centimetres 英尺〔等於12英寸, 約30厘米〕: *He's six feet tall, with blonde hair and a moustache.* 他身高6英尺, 長着一頭金髮, 留着小鬍子。—see table on page C4 參見C4頁附錄

4 ►BOTTOM PART 底部◄ **the foot of** the lowest part of something such as a mountain, tree, or set of stairs, or the end of a bed where your feet go ...的底部, ...下端: *a stunningly beautiful lake at the foot of the mountain* 山腳下的一個極其美麗的湖

5 get/jump/rise to your feet etc to stand up after you have been sitting 站起身來/跳起身來/站起身來等: *Mike leapt to his feet and ran towards the window.* 邁克跳起身來, 向窗口跑去。

6 be on your feet a) to be standing for a long time without having time to sit down〔長時間〕站立着: *The worst thing about working in the shop is that you're on your feet all day.* 在商店裡工作最糟糕的事情是要整天站着。 **b)** to stand up 站起來: *As soon as the bell rang the class were on their feet and out of the door.* 鈴一響, 全班學生都站起來, 跑到門外去。 **c)** to feel better again after being ill and in bed〔生病臥牀後〕恢復健康: *We'll soon have you on your feet again.* 我們很快就會使你恢復健康。

7 be rushed off your feet/be run off your feet to be very busy 非常忙碌的, 忙得腳不沾地: *Just before Christmas, most of the salespeople are rushed off their feet.* 聖誕節前, 大多數售貨員都很忙碌。

8 set foot in to go to or enter a place 去; 進入, 踏進: *She swore she would never set foot in his house ever again.* 她發誓不再進入他的房子。

9 be/get under your feet to annoy you by always being in the same place as you and preventing you from doing what you want 妨礙着你, 阻礙着你: *I hate summer vacation. The kids are under my feet all day long.* 我不喜歡暑假。孩子們整天纏着我。

10 put your foot down a) to say very firmly that someone must do something or must stop doing something 果斷行事, 堅持立場; 堅決阻止: *You'll just have to put your foot down and tell him he can't stay out on school nights.* 你得果斷一點, 告訴他上課期間晚上不能在外面逗留。 **b)** *informal* to make a car go faster【非正式】加快車速; 踩下油門

11 put your feet up *informal* to relax, especially by sitting with your feet supported on something【非正式】擱起腳休息

12 put your foot in it *especially BrE*【尤英】, **put your foot in your mouth** *especially AmE*【尤美】to say something without thinking carefully, so that you embarrass or upset someone 失言, 講錯話,〔因說話隨便而〕招惹麻煩: *I've really put my foot in it this time. I didn't realize that was her husband!* 我這次確實講錯話了。我沒想到那人是她的丈夫!

13 have two left feet *informal* to be very CLUMSY (1)【非正式】笨拙的, 笨手笨腳的: *Dan's got two left feet when it comes to dancing.* 丹跳起舞來笨手笨腳的。

14 get off on the wrong foot to start a relationship badly, usually by having an argument〔關係〕開始得不好: *Simon and I got off on the wrong foot but we're good friends now.* 西蒙和我的關係開頭很不投機, 但現在我們是好朋友。

15 not put a foot wrong *especially BrE* to do everything right and make no mistakes, especially in your job【尤英】〔尤指工作中〕做事正確無誤

16 have/keep both feet on the ground to think in a sensible and practical way and not have ideas or aims that will be impossible to achieve 注重實際, 腳踏實地

17 put sth back on its feet to improve the situation of a country, organization etc 改善〔國家、組織等〕的狀況: *It was Larry who put the club back on its feet.* 是拉里使俱樂部有起色的。

18 fall/land on your feet to get into a good situation because you are lucky after being in a difficult situation 幸免於難, 化險為夷: *Don't worry about Nina, she always falls on her feet.* 別為尼娜擔心, 她總是能化險為夷的。

19 get your foot in the door to get your first opportunity to work in a particular organization or industry 獲得機會進入, 有幸加入

20 have a foot in both camps to be involved with or connected with two opposing groups of people 腳踏兩隻船, 騎牆

21 have one foot in the grave *humorous* to be very old or very ill【幽默】〔老得或病得〕一隻腳已踏進墳墓; 離死不遠

22 ...my foot! *BrE old-fashioned* used to show that you do not believe something that someone has just said【英, 過時】算了吧, 去你的, 得了〔表示不相信對方的話〕: *£50 my foot! It'll cost £200 at least.* 去你的50英鎊! 這至少值200英鎊。

23 leave feet first *humorous* to die before you leave a place or job【幽默】還沒離開〔某地或某工作〕就死去

24 feet of clay someone that you admire who has feet of clay has faults that you did not realize they had〔偶像的〕沒覺察到的弱點, 內在缺點

25 foot soldier/patrol a soldier or group of soldiers that walks and does not use a horse or a vehicle 步兵

26 foot passenger a passenger on a ship who has not brought a car with them〔汽車渡輪上的〕步行旅客, 無車旅客

27 -footed /futɪd; fʊtɪd/ **a) left-footed/right-footed** using your left foot or right foot when you kick the ball〔踢球時〕用左腳的/用右腳的 **b) flat-footed/four-footed** having a particular kind or number of feet 平足的/四足的

28 foot pedal/brake/pump etc a machine or control that you operate using your feet 踏板/腳剎車/腳踏泵等

29 ►SOCK 襪◄ **the foot** the part of a sock that covers your foot 襪底: *There's a hole in the foot of my stocking.* 我的襪底有個洞。

30 ►POETRY 詩◄ *technical* a part of a line of poetry in which there is one strong BEAT[2] (3) and one or two weaker ones【術語】音步 —see also 另見 **the boot is on the other foot** (BOOT[1] (6)), **get/have cold feet** (COLD[1] (7)), **drag your feet/heels** (DRAG[1] (8)), **find your feet** (FIND[1] (22)), **from head to foot** (HEAD[1] (2)), **stand on your own (two) feet** (STAND[1] (31)), **sweep sb off their feet** (SWEEP[1] (12))

foot² *v* **foot the bill** to pay for something, especially something expensive that you do not want to pay for 付賬〔尤指不情願為昂貴的東西支付時〕: *He ordered a load of drinks and then left me to foot the bill!* 他要了一大堆酒水, 然後讓我來付賬!

foot·age /ˈfutɪdʒ; ˈfʊtɪdʒ/ *n* [U] cinema film showing a particular event〔某個事件的〕影片: *old footage from the First World War* 第一次世界大戰的舊影片

foot and mouth dis·ease /ˌ· · ˈ· ·ˌ·/ *n* [U] a serious disease that kills cows and sheep 口蹄疫〔一種導致牛、羊死亡的嚴重傳染病〕

1 2 **foot·ball** /ˈfutˌbɔl; ˈfʊtbɔːl/ *n* **1** [U] *BrE* a game played by two teams of eleven players who try to kick a round ball into their opponents' GOAL (3); SOCCER【英】足球(比賽): *watching football on TV* 在電視上看足球比賽 | *a football club* 足球俱樂部 **2** [U] *AmE* a game played by two teams of eleven players who carry or kick an OVAL (=egg shaped) ball【美】(美式)足球, 橄欖球(比賽); AMERICAN FOOTBALL *BrE*【英】: *college football games* 大學橄欖球比賽 **3** [C] a ball used in these games 足球; 橄欖球 —see also 另見 FLAG FOOTBALL, **political football** (POLITICAL (5))

foot·bal·ler /ˈfutˌbɔlɚ; ˈfʊtbɔːlə/ *n* [C] *BrE* someone who plays football, especially a professional player【英】〔尤指職業的〕足球員; 橄欖球員

football pools /ˈ·· ˌ·/ *n* —see 見 **the pools** (POOL[1] (4))

foot·bridge /ˈfutˌbrɪdʒ; ˈfʊtˌbrɪdʒ/ *n* [C] a narrow bridge used by people who are walking 人行橋, 步行橋

foot·er /ˈfutɚ; ˈfʊtə/ *n* **1 six-footer/eighteen-footer etc** someone or something that measures six feet tall, eighteen feet long etc 六英尺高的人[東西]/十八英尺長的東西 **2** [U] *BrE* a game of football【英】(一場)足球[橄欖球]比賽

foot·fall /ˈfutˌfɔl; ˈfʊtfɔːl/ *n* [C,U] *literary* the sound of each step when someone is walking【文】腳步聲: *heavy footfalls* 沉重的腳步聲

foot fault /ˈ· ·/ *n* [C] a mistake in tennis when the person who is serving (SERVE[1] (10)) is not standing behind the line〔網球的〕腳步犯規〔發球踩線犯規〕

foot·hill /ˈfutˌhɪl; ˈfʊtˌhɪl/ *n* [C usually plural 一般用複數] one of the smaller hills below a group of high mountains 山麓丘陵: *the foothills of the Himalayas* 喜馬拉雅山脈的丘陵地帶

foot·hold /ˈfutˌhold; ˈfʊthəʊld/ *n* [C] **1** a position from which you can start to make progress and achieve your aims 穩固的基礎; 立足點: **gain/establish a foothold** *Extreme right wing parties gained a foothold in the latest European elections.* 極右黨派在最近的歐洲各國選舉中取得了穩固的基礎。**2** a small hole or crack where you can safely put your foot when climbing a steep rock〔攀登陡峭的岩石時的〕立腳點

footie /ˈfutɪ; fʊti/ *n* [U] *BrE* a game of football【英】足球運動

foot·ing /ˈfutɪŋ; ˈfʊtɪŋ/ *n* [U] **1** the conditions or arrangements under which something exists or operates 狀況; 基礎; 立足處: **on a legal/scientific/official etc footing** *The article attempts to put their work on a more scientific footing.* 這篇文章企圖把他們的工作置於更科學的基礎上。| **on a sound/firm/solid footing** *new reforms that will put the country back on a firm financial footing* 將使國家恢復到穩固的財政基礎上的新改革 | **on an equal footing/on the same footing** (=in the same situation or state as someone else) 以平等的地位/在相同的狀況下 *The new law puts women on an equal footing with men.* 新法律使婦女享有與男子平等的地位。| **on a war footing** (=ready to go to war at any time) 處於準備戰爭狀態 **2** the position of your feet when you are standing firmly on a SLIPPERY or dangerous surface〔在易滑或危險表面的〕立足處; 立足點: *struggling to keep her footing on the slippery path* 掙扎着在滑溜的小道上站穩 | **lose/miss your footing** (=fall because you are no longer balanced) 失足, 摔倒; 未能站穩

foo·tle /ˈfutl̩; ˈfuːtl/ *v* **footle around/about** to waste time doing unimportant things when you should be working 閒混

foot·lights /ˈfutˌlaɪts; ˈfʊtlaɪts/ *n* [plural] a row of lights along the front of the stage in a theatre〔劇場舞台前的〕腳燈 —see picture at 參見 THEATRE 圖

foot·ling /ˈfutlɪŋ; ˈfuːtlɪŋ/ *adj* [only before noun 僅用於名詞前] *old-fashioned* unimportant and annoying【過時】無足輕重的; 討厭的

foot lock·er /ˈ· ˌ··/ *n* [C] *AmE* a strong box that soldiers have at the end of their beds to keep their possessions in【美】〔士兵用來存放物品的〕牀腳櫃

foot·loose /ˈfutˌlus; ˈfʊtluːs/ *adj* **1** able to move around freely because you have no permanent work or home〔無固定工作或住所而〕可到處走動的: *footloose students traveling around Europe* 在歐洲到處遊逛的學生 **2 footloose and fancy free** able to do what you want and enjoy yourself because you have no responsibilities 自由自在的, 無拘無束的

foot·man /ˈfutmən; ˈfʊtmən/ *plural* **footmen** /-mən; -mən/ *n* [C] a male servant in former times who opened the front door, announced the names of visitors etc〔舊時的〕男僕

foot·mark /ˈfutˌmɑrk; ˈfʊtmɑːk/ *n* [C] a mark made by someone's shoe or foot 腳印, 足跡

foot·note /ˈfutˌnot; ˈfʊtnəʊt/ *n* [C] a note at the bottom of the page in a book, which gives more information about something 腳注

foot·path /ˈfutˌpæθ; ˈfʊtpɑːθ/ *n* [C] *especially BrE* a narrow path for people to walk along, especially in the countryside【尤英】〔尤指鄉間的〕人行小徑, 人行道; TRAIL² (4) *AmE*【美】

foot·print /ˈfutˌprɪnt; ˈfʊtˌprɪnt/ *n* [C] a mark made by a foot or shoe 腳印, 足跡: *the footprints of a deer* 鹿的足跡

footprint 腳印

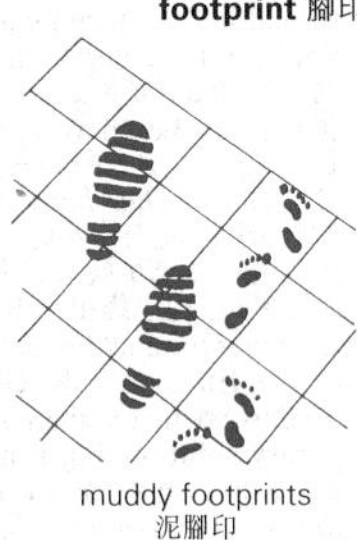

muddy footprints
泥腳印

foot·rest /ˈfutˌrɛst; ˈfʊt-rest/ *n* [C] a small piece of furniture that you can rest your feet on when you are sitting down 擱腳架; 腳櫈; 擱腳墊

foot·sie /ˈfutsɪ; ˈfʊtsi/ *n* **play footsie** *informal*【非正式】**a)** to secretly touch another person's feet with your feet under a table to show that you find them sexually attractive〔暗中在桌下〕碰腳調情 **b)** *AmE* to work together and help each other in a dishonest way【美】勾搭, 狼狽為奸: *politicians playing footsie with each other* 狼狽為奸的政客

foot·slog·ging /ˈfutˌslɑgɪŋ; ˈfʊtslɒgɪŋ/ *n* [U] *BrE informal* a lot of walking around, which makes you very tired【英, 非正式】長途費力的步行

foot·sore /ˈfutˌsɔr; ˈfʊtsɔː/ *adj* having feet that hurt because you have walked a long distance〔因走長路而〕腳痛的

foot·step /ˈfutˌstɛp; ˈfʊtstep/ *n* [C] the sound made when someone walks a single step 腳步聲: *heavy footsteps on the stairs* 樓梯上沉重的腳步聲 —see also 另見 **follow (in) sb's footsteps** (FOLLOW (16))

foot·stool /ˈfutˌstul; ˈfʊtstuːl/ *n* [C] a low piece of furniture used to support your feet when you are sitting down〔坐時擱腳的〕腳櫈

foot·wear /ˈfutˌwɛr; ˈfʊtweə/ *n* [U] things that people wear on their feet, such as shoes or boots 鞋類〈如鞋、靴等〉

foot·work /ˈfutˌwɝk; ˈfʊtwɜːk/ *n* [U] skilful use of your feet when dancing or playing a sport〔舞蹈、運動中的〕步法; 腿腳功夫

fop /fɑp; fɒp/ *n* [C] *old-fashioned* a man who is too interested in his clothes and appearance【過時】〔過分講

究衣着和外表的〕紈袴子弟 **—foppish** *adj* **—foppishness** *n* [U]

for¹ /fə; fə; *strong* 強讀 fɔr; fɔː/ *prep* **1** intended to be given to or belong to a particular person 給, 為: *I've got a present for you.* 我有一件禮物要送給你。| *Save some for Arthur.* 留一些給阿瑟吧。**2** intended to be used in a particular situation 適合於〔某一場合使用〕: *We've bought some new chairs for the office.* 我們買了一些辦公室用的新椅子。| *a name-plate for the door* 門上的名牌 **3** used to show the purpose of an object, action, etc 為了; 供: *a knife for cutting bread* 切麵包的刀子 | *What did you do that for?* 你為甚麼要那樣做? | *a space just large enough for a table and two chairs* 正好能擺一張桌子和兩把椅子的空間 | **for sale/hire/rent** (=available to be bought, hired) 供出售的/供出租的 *House for sale.* 有房屋出售。| *They have tools and garden equipment for hire.* 他們有工具和園藝設備出租。**4** if you do something for someone, you do it instead of them in order to help them 代替; 代表: *I looked after the kids for her.* 我替她照看小孩。| *Let me lift that for you.* 讓我替你提那個吧。**5** if something is done for someone, or if they are given something for a problem, they are helped or their situation is improved 為, 幫, 替: *The doctor knew that there was nothing he could do for her.* 醫生知道他無法為她做甚麼事了。| *I've found it for you.* 我已經幫你找到了它。| *I'll do what I can for you.* 我將盡力幫你。| *What can I do for you?* (=can I help you?) 我能幫你做點甚麼嗎?[可以為您效勞嗎?] **6** if something is arranged for a particular time, it is planned that it should happen then 在...〔時間〕: *I've invited them for 9 o'clock.* 我已經邀請他們九點來。| *I've made an appointment for 18th October.* 我已經約定了10月18日見面。| *It's time for supper.* 是吃晚飯的時候了。**7** if you buy someone something, or arrange an event for their birthday etc, you do it to celebrate that occasion 為〔慶祝一個日子〕而...: *What did you get for your birthday?* 你收到甚麼生日禮物? **8** used to express a length of time〔表示時間長度〕達, 計: *Bake the cake for 40 minutes.* 將蛋糕烤40分鐘。| *They had been walking for a good half hour.* 他們已步行了足有半小時。| *I've been meaning to ask you for ages.* 我老早就想問你了。| *He's been off work for a long time.* 他已經很久不工作了。| **for a while** *I'm borrowing it for a while.* 我借用它一會兒。—see 見 DURING (USAGE), SINCE³ (USAGE) **9 for now/for the moment** used to say that you are suggesting something as a temporary solution, but it may be changed later 暫時; 目前, 眼下: *I think for now we're just going to have to keep the cats in the house.* 我想暫時我們只能把貓留在房子裡。**10** used to express distance〔用於表示距離〕達, 計: *We walked for miles.* 我們已經走了好幾英里。| *Factories and warehouses stretched for quite a distance along the canal.* 沿着運河好一段距離都是工廠和倉庫。**11** used to state where a person, vehicle etc is going 往; 到...〔表示去向〕: *I set off for work.* 我動身上班去了。| *the night before leaving for New York* 去紐約之前的那個晚上 | *the train for Manchester* 開往曼徹斯特的火車 | **I'm for bed/home** *BrE* (=I'm going to bed/going home)【英】我打算去睡覺/我打算回家 **12** used to show a price or amount〔表示價格或數量〕達, 計: *a cheque for a hundred pounds* 一百英鎊的支票 | *The diamond was insured for two thousand dollars.* 這塊鑽石投保二千美元。**13** in order to have, do, get, or obtain something 為了要; 為了做; 為了得到: *She decided to look for a job.* 她決定找份工作。| *Mother was too ill to get up for dinner.* 母親病得無法起牀吃晚飯。| *the qualifications necessary for entry to university* 進入大學所必備的資格 | *I paid $3 for it.* 我付了三美元買這個東西。| *an expert whom you can rely on for advice* 一位可以信賴其忠告的專家 | *For further details, write to this address.* 欲了解進一步詳情, 請致函下列地址查詢。| *Let's go for a walk.* 我們去散步吧。| *We just did it for fun.* 我們做此事只是開玩笑而已。| *waiting for the bus* 等公共汽車 | *legislating for equality* 為平等而立法 | **run for your life** (=to save your life) 逃命 **14 now for** *spoken* used to say what you're going to have or do now【口】現在做吧: *Now for some fun!* 現在娛樂一下吧! **15** because of or as a result of something 由於, 因為: *if, for any reason, you cannot attend...* 如果由於某種原因你無法出席... | *a reward for bravery* 因英勇而得到的嘉獎 | *We could hardly see for the mist.* 由於起霧, 我們都看不清了。| *A certain amount must be deducted for depreciation.* 因有折舊, 必須扣除一些金額。| **for doing sth** *He got a ticket for driving through a red light.* 他因駕車闖紅燈而收到罰款通知單。**16** as to or concerning something 關於; 至於: *I felt sorry for him.* 我為他感到惋惜。| *He has a talent for upsetting people.* 他有使人生氣的本領。| *I'm sure she's the ideal person for the job.* 我確信她是做這項工作的理想人選。| *We had pasta for lunch.* 午餐我們吃了意大利麵食。| *Fortunately for him, he can swim.* 幸運的是, 他會游泳。| *The success rates for each task are given in Table 4.* 每項任務的成功率在表4中列出。| **too... for me/her etc** (=more than I can deal with) 對我/她來說太... *You're too quick for me!* 對我來說你太快了! | **he's a great one for** (=he always wants or is concerned with) 他總是想要; 他總是關心 *He's a great one for details.* 他是最喜歡關心細節的人。| **Are you all right for money?** (=do you have enough?) 你的錢夠用嗎? | **...is not for me** (=is not suitable or appropriate for me) ...不適合我 *City life is not for me.* 城市生活不適合我。**17** if you work for a company, play for a team etc, this is the one in which you work, play etc 為...〔工作、打球等〕: *surveyors working for property services* 在物業服務工作的測繪員 | *He writes for a weekly paper.* 他為一家週刊撰稿。| *She plays for the A team.* 她為A隊出賽。**18** in favour of, supporting, or in agreement with something 贊成; 支持; 同意: *discussing the case for and against nuclear energy* 討論支持和反對核能的理由 | *How many people voted for the proposal?* 多少人投票贊成這項提議? | *Three cheers for the captain.* 為隊長歡呼三聲吧。| **I'm all for** (=I approve of) 我完全同意; 我完全贊成 *I'm all for people enjoying themselves.* 我完全贊成人們多享樂。**19** representing, meaning, or as a sign of something 表示; 意思是; 是...的符號: *What's the word for 'happy' in French?* 法語中表示"happy"的單詞是甚麼? | *Red is for danger.* 紅色表示危險。**20** used after a comparative form to mean after, as a result of, or because of〔用於比較級後〕在...後; 作為...的結果; 由於, 因為: *You'll feel better for a break.* 你休息後就會感覺好一些。**21** used to say that a particular feature of someone or something is surprising when you consider what they are 就...而言〔表示在這種情況下, 所說的特點是令人驚訝的〕: *It's cold for the time of year.* 就這個季節來說, 天氣算是冷的。| *She looks young for her age.* 就她的年齡而言, 她看上去算是年輕的。**22 for sb/sth to do sth a)** used to introduce a phrase that is used instead of a CLAUSE (2)〔用於引出代替子句的片語〕: *It is really unusual for Michael to get cross.* 邁克爾發脾氣確實是不尋常的。| **I can't bear for sb/sth to** *I can't bear for you to be unhappy.* 看着你不高興我受不了。| **nothing worse/easier than for sb/sth to** *There's nothing worse than for a parent to ill treat a child.* 沒有甚麼比父母虐待小孩更惡劣的了。**b)** used when you are describing what someone should do, might do, or has done〔用於描寫某人應該做、可能做或已經做的事〕: *The plan is for us to leave in the morning.* 按照計劃是我們在上午離開。| **a need/desire/chance for sb/sth to** *There is an urgent need for someone to tackle this problem.* 急需有人來解決這個問題。| *There will be another opportunity for them to do it again.* 他們將有另一次機會再做這事。**c)** used when you are explaining a reason for something〔用來解釋理由〕由於, 為了: *He must have had some bad news for him to be so quiet.* (=as/since he is so quiet) 他這麼沉默不語, 一定是聽到了甚麼壞消息。| *I've sent off my coat for it to be cleaned.* (=in order that it may be cleaned) 我已經把大衣送去清洗了。**d)** used when you are saying what someone or something is able to do〔用來說明某人或某物能做某事〕: *It's easy for a computer to keep a record of this information.* 電腦保存這種資料的記錄很容易。| *It's impossible for me to get money out of Dorothy.* 要我從多蘿西那裡拿到錢是不可能的。| **large/difficult/near enough for sb/sth to** *The dolphin was near enough for me to reach out and touch it.* 海豚近得我伸手就可以摸到。| **too large/difficult/near for sb/sth to** *It's too difficult for me to explain.* 這太難了，我無法解釋。**23 for each/every** used to say that each of one kind of thing has or will have something of another kind 每…就有: *For each mistake, you'll lose half a point.* 你每犯一個錯誤，就要扣去半分。| *For every three people who agree, you'll find five who don't.* 每有三個人同意，就有五個人不同意。**24 for all a)** in spite of 雖然，儘管: *For all his efforts, he still came last.* 儘管他很努力，還是名落孫山。| *She still loves him for all that.* 儘管如此，她還是愛他。**b)** considering how little 儘管: *For all the success you've had, you might just as well have not bothered!* 儘管你已經獲得一點成功，你還是不去費事幹為好！**25 for all I know/care** *spoken* used to say that you do not really know or care【口】就我所知/我不介意: *For all I know, he could be dead.* 就我所知，他可能死了。| *He can jump into the river for all I care!* 他可以跳河，我才不管呢！**26 I wouldn't do it for anything** *informal* used to emphasize that you definitely would not do it【非正式】我決不做這事: *I would not go through that again for anything.* 我決不肯再經歷那樣的事了。**27 I for one believe/think that...** *spoken* this is my opinion, even if no one else agrees【口】我個人認為〔即使別人都不同意〕: *I for one believe that she's making a big mistake.* 我個人認為她正在犯一個大錯誤。**28 for one thing... (and for another)** used when you are giving reasons for a statement you have made〔用於說明理由〕一是…（二是…）: *No, I'm not going to buy it; for one thing I don't like the colour, and for another it's far too expensive.* 不，我不要買這東西；一是我不喜歡這顏色，二是太貴了。**29 if it weren't for/if it hadn't been for** if a particular thing had not happened, if someone had not done something, or if a situation was different 要不是: *If it hadn't been for you, I would not be alive now.* 要不是你，我早就死了。**30 (well,) that's/there's ... for you!** *spoken*【口】**a)** used to say that it is typical that something has been a disappointment; you cannot expect anything better of that type of thing 那正是…的特點！〔說明某物只可能是這麼差勁〕: *That's foreign hotels for you!* 外國旅館就是這份德行！**b)** used to say that something is the complete opposite of what you were saying 那還能算是…？那恰好跟…相反！: *I gave it to her and she just threw it away; there's gratitude for you!* 我把它給了她，她卻扔掉；這就是所謂的好心有好報！**31 be (in) for it** to be likely to be blamed or punished 要挨罵；要受罰: *You'll be in for it if she finds out what you've done!* 要是她發現你做了這種事，你就要挨罵了！

2 1 **for**[2] *conjunction formal* used to introduce the reason for something; because【正式】因為: *He found it increasingly difficult to read, for his eyes were failing.* 他覺得閱讀越來越費勁，因為他的視力越來越差。

for·age[1] /ˋfɔrɪdʒ; ˈfɒrɪdʒ/ *v* [I] **1** to go around searching for food or other supplies 四處搜尋〔食物、糧秣等〕: [+for] *The children are forced to forage for scraps in the streets.* 孩子們被迫在街上到處尋找殘羹剩飯。| **a foraging party** (=group of soldiers searching for food etc) 糧秣徵收隊 **2** to search for something with your hands in a bag, drawer etc〔用手在袋子、抽屜等〕搜尋；翻找: *She foraged around in her purse, and finally produced her ticket.* 她在錢包裡找來找去，最後拿出票來。—**forager** *n* [C]

forage[2] *n* **1** [singular] an act of searching for food 搜尋食物 **2** [U] food supplies for horses and cattle〔馬和牛的〕飼料

for·ay[1] /ˋfɔre; ˈfɒreɪ/ *n* [C] **1** a short attempt at doing a particular job or activity, especially one that is very different from what you usually do〔尤對某項非本行的艱難工作或活動的〕短暫嘗試: *After a brief unsuccessful foray into politics, he went back to his law practice.* 他短暫參政失敗之後，又回來做律師了。**2** a short sudden attack by a group of soldiers〔一隊士兵的〕突襲: *their nightly forays into enemy territory* 他們深入敵人領土的每夜突襲 **3** a short journey somewhere in order to get something or do something〔為得到某物或做某事而進行的〕短暫的旅行: *her twice-weekly foray to the shops* 她一週兩次到商店購物

foray[2] *v* [I+into] to go out and make a sudden attack against the enemy, especially in order to get food or supplies〔尤指為得到食品或糧秣〕進行突襲

for·bade /fəˋbed; fəˈbæd/ the past tense of FORBID

for·bear[1] /fɔrˋbɛr; fɔːˈbeə/ *past tense* **forbore** /-ˋbɔr; -ˈbɔː/ *past participle* **forborne** /-ˋbɔrn; -ˈbɔːn/ *v* [I] *formal* to not do something, even though you could do it if you wanted to【正式】克制；忍耐: [+from] *He forbore from making suggestions for fear of insulting her.* 他因怕侮辱她而克制住不提建議。| **forbear to do sth** *Clara forbore to mention that the result was likely to be the same.* 克萊拉抑制住自己，沒有說結果可能相同。

for·bear[2] /ˋfɔr͵bɛr; ˈfɔːbeə/ *n* [C] a FOREBEAR 祖先，祖宗

for·bear·ance /fɔrˋbɛrəns; fɔːˈbeərəns/ *n* [U] *formal* patience, self-control, and willingness to forgive someone【正式】忍耐，自制；寬容: *Higgins accepted the decision with commendable forbearance.* 希金斯以值得稱讚的寬大態度接受了這項決定。

for·bear·ing /fɔrˋbɛrɪŋ; fɔːˈbeərɪŋ/ *adj formal* patient and willing to forgive【正式】寬容的；有忍耐心的

for·bid /fəˋbɪd; fəˈbɪd/ *past tense* **forbade** /-ˋbed; -ˈbæd/ *past participle* **forbidden** /-ˋbɪdn̩; -ˈbɪdn/ *v* [T] **1** to tell someone that they definitely must not do something 不許，禁止: *You may not go to the party – I absolutely forbid it!* 你不可以去參加聚會——我絕對不許你去！| **forbid sb from doing sth** *Women are forbidden from going out without a veil.* 禁止婦女不披面紗外出。| **strictly forbid** *The law strictly forbids racial or sexual discrimination.* 這項法律嚴禁種族或性別歧視。| **forbid sb to do sth** *He was forbidden to leave the base as a punishment.* 他被禁止離開基地以作懲罰。**2 God/Heaven forbid** *spoken* used to emphasize that you hope that something will not happen【口】但願不會發生這樣的事: *Who would run the business if, God forbid, you were to die?* 如果你死了，但願不會發生這樣的事，誰來管理商行呢？**3** *formal* to make it impossible for someone to do something【正式】阻止；妨礙，使〔某人〕不可能做某事: *Lack of space forbids the listing of all those who contributed.* 篇幅不夠，無法列出所有捐款人的名字。

Frequencies of **forbid, say sb can't** and **not let/allow** in spoken and written English. forbid, say sb can't 和 not let/allow 在英語口語和書面語中的使用頻率

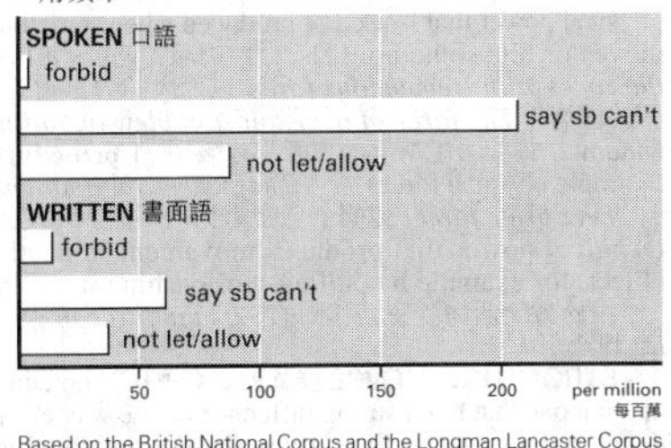

Based on the British National Corpus and the Longman Lancaster Corpus
據英國國家語料庫和朗文蘭卡斯特語料庫

This graph shows that it is much more usual in both spoken and written English to use the expressions **say sb can't** and **not let/allow**, rather than **forbid**. **Forbid** is less general. It is usually used when a government, law or person in authority orders someone not to do something. It is much more common in written English than in spoken English. 本圖表顯示, 在英語口語和書面語中更經常使用的是 say sb can't 和 not let/allow, 而不是 forbid。forbid 使用不太普遍。當政府、法律或權威人士命令某人不要做某事時, 則通常使用 forbid。forbid 在英語書面語中的使用頻率遠遠高於口語。

for·bid·den /fɚˋbɪdn̩; fəˈbɪdn/ *adj* **1** not allowed, especially because of an official rule〔尤指因官方規定而〕被禁止的: **strictly forbidden** *You can't smoke here – it's strictly forbidden.* 你不能在這裡吸煙 —— 這是嚴格禁止的。| **it is forbidden to do sth** *It is forbidden to marry someone who is not a member of the same faith.* 禁止與宗教信仰不同的人結婚。**2** a forbidden place is one that you are not allowed to go to〔地方〕禁止的: *the Great Mosque, whose precincts are forbidden to Christians* 禁止基督教徒進入其區域的大清真寺 **3** a forbidden activity, object etc is one that seems exciting because you are not allowed to do it or have it 禁戒的: *the forbidden sensual pleasures of the old city* 古城中的那些禁戒的肉慾快事 | **forbidden fruit** (=something forbidden that gives great pleasure) 禁果, 非法的歡樂

for·bid·ding /fɚˋbɪdɪŋ; fəˈbɪdɪŋ/ *adj* having a frightening or unfriendly appearance〔外表〕可怕的, 令人生畏的: *Despite her forbidding manner she's actually quite a kind person.* 雖然她的態度令人生畏, 但她實際上是個相當和藹的人。—**forbiddingly** *adv*

for·bore /fɔrˋbɔr; fɔːˈbɔː/ the past tense of FORBEAR

for·borne /fɔrˋbɔrn; fɔːˈbɔːn/ the past participle of FORBEAR

force¹ /fɔrs; fɔːs/ *n*

1 ►MILITARY 軍事◄ a) [C] a group of people who have been trained to fight in a war〔經訓練的〕戰鬥隊伍, 部隊: *forces loyal to President Aquino* 忠於阿基諾總統的部隊 | *a highly efficient fighting force* 一支效率十分高的戰鬥部隊 **b) the forces** the army, navy, and air force 陸海空三軍部隊; 軍隊: *Both her sons are in the forces.* 她的兩個兒子都在軍隊裡。**c)** [U] military action used as a way of achieving your aims 軍事行動; 武力: *After World War I the use of force to settle conflicts was prohibited.* 第一次世界大戰後禁止使用武力解決爭端。| **by force (of arms)** *The Serbs were accused of imposing these boundaries by force.* 塞爾維亞人被指責用武力強劃這些邊界。

2 ►VIOLENCE 暴力◄ [U] violent physical action used to get what you want〔為得到某物而使用的〕暴力, 武力: *The question is whether the police used reasonable force when arresting him.* 問題是警方在逮捕他時是否合理使用了武力。| **by force** *Her ex-husband tried to get the children back by force.* 她的前夫企圖強行要回孩子。

3 ►PHYSICAL POWER 體力◄ a) [U] the amount of physical power that is used or produced when something moves or hits something else 力, 力量: *waves hitting the rocks with tremendous force* 以巨大的力量拍擊岩石的波濤 | *The force of the explosion blew out all the windows.* 爆炸力把所有的窗子都炸破了。| **brute force** (=simple physical force) 蠻力 *They kicked the door open by sheer brute force.* 他們全憑蠻力把門踢開。**b)** [C,U] *technical* power that produces movement in another object, for example by pulling it or pushing it【術語】〔作用於另一個物體使其移動的〕力: *the force of gravity* 地心引力

4 ►STRONG INFLUENCE 強烈的影響◄ [C] something or someone that has a strong influence on the way events develop, on people's lives, or on the way people think〔對事件的發展、人們的生活或思維方式〕有影響力的人[事物]: *Mrs Thatcher is no longer the force she once was in British politics.* 戴卓爾夫人再也不像以前那樣對英國政界具有影響力了。| **driving force** (=person or thing that has the strongest influence on the way things happen) 推動力 *The need for short-term profits seems to be the driving force behind these mergers.* 對短期利潤的追求似乎是推動這些合併產生的力量。| **a force for peace/progress/good etc** (=someone whose actions make peace, progress etc more likely to happen) 和平/進步/正義的力量 | **a force to be reckoned with** (=a company, organization etc with a lot of power and influence) 需要認真對付的公司[組織] *Within just a few months, Microsoft became a force to be reckoned with in the global software market.* 僅在數月之內, 微軟便成為全球軟件市場中一股不可忽視的力量。| **forces beyond sb's control** *The fall in coffee prices was due to forces beyond their control.* 咖啡價格下降是由他們無法控制的力量引起的。| **the forces of evil/oppression** *the fight against the forces of oppression* 反抗壓迫勢力的鬥爭

5 ►POWERFUL EFFECT 威力◄ [U] the powerful effect of what someone says or does〔某人說的話或做的事產生的〕威力, 影響力: *Even after 30 years, the play has lost none of its force.* 甚至在30年之後, 這齣戲的影響力一點也沒有失去。| *the force of public opinion* 輿論的威力

6 ►ORGANIZED GROUP 有組織的羣體◄ [C] a group of people who have been trained and organized for a specific purpose〔為某個目的而訓練和組織的〕一羣人, 隊伍, 羣體: *the company's sales force* 公司的銷售隊伍

7 join/combine forces to join together so that you can deal with a problem, defend yourselves etc〔為解決問題、保護自己而〕聯合; 合作; 同心協力: *Local churches have joined forces to help the homeless.* 當地各個教堂聯合起來幫助無家可歸的人。| **[+with]** *The Nationalists joined forces with the Communists.* 國民黨人與共產黨人通力合作。

8 ►LAW/RULE 法律/規則◄ in force a) if a law or a rule is in force, it exists and must be obeyed 生效; 有效; 實施: **come into force** (=start to operate) 開始生效, 開始實施 *The new law on drink-driving comes into force next month.* 有關酒後駕車的新法律下月開始生效。**b)** in a large group, especially in order to protest about something 大批地, 成羣結隊地, 人數眾多地〔尤指為抗議某事〕: *Villagers turned out in force to protest about the new road.* 大批村民出動抗議修建這條新路。

9 by/from force of habit if you do something by force of habit, you do it because you have always done the same thing in the past 由於習慣, 因習慣的力量, 全因習慣

10 force of circumstance(s) the effect of a situation on what you do or decide 形勢的影響: *Force of circumstance compelled him to leave Italy.* 形勢迫使他離開意大利。

11 the forces of nature natural forces such as wind, rain, or EARTHQUAKEs 自然力〈如風、雨或地震〉

12 ►WIND 風◄ a) force 8/9/10 etc a unit for measuring the strength of the wind 風力8/9/10級 **b) gale/hurricane force wind** extremely strong wind that does a lot of damage〔能造成大量破壞的〕大風/颶風

13 ►POLICE 警察◄ the force a word meaning the police force, used especially by police officers 警察部隊: *He resigned after 17 years in the force.* 他在警察部門服務17年後辭職。—see also 另見 LABOUR FORCE, TASK FORCE, TOUR DE FORCE

force² *v* [T]

1 ►MAKE SB DO STH 迫使某人做某事◄ a) to make someone do something that they do not want to do, especially by threatening them〔尤指用威脅的手段〕強制, 逼迫, 迫使: **force sb to do sth** *Government troops have forced the rebels to surrender.* 政府軍已迫使叛亂分子投降。| **force sb** *Nobody forced me – it was my own decision.* 沒有人逼我 —— 這是我自己的決定。| **force sb/sth (into) doing sth** *These women are forced into* *accepting low-paid jobs.* 這些婦女被迫接受低工資的工作。**b)** if a situation forces you to do something, it makes you do it, even though you do not want to 迫使: **force sb to do sth** *The high cost of borrowing is forcing many companies to close.* 高昂的借貸成本正迫使許多公司倒閉。| **force sb into (doing) sth** *Bad health forced her into taking early retirement.* 她身體不好, 迫不得已要早早退休。

2 force yourself (to do sth) a) to make yourself do something that you do not want to do 勉強自己(做某事): *I forced myself to get out of bed.* 我強迫自己起牀。**b)** *BrE spoken* used when trying to persuade someone to do something that they seem unwilling to do, because you know they will enjoy it【英口】別客氣〔敦促某人做表面看來不願做的事〕: *"I couldn't eat another thing!" "Go on! Force yourself!"* "我不能再吃了!" "再吃點吧! 別客氣!"

3 ▶MAKE SB/STH MOVE 使某人/某物移動◀ to make someone or something move in a particular direction or into a different position, especially using physical force〔尤指用體力〕用力推動: **force sth into/out of** *Firemen attempted to enter the building but were forced back by the flames.* 消防隊員企圖進入大樓, 但被火焰頂了回來。

4 force your way in/out/through etc to push and use physical force to get into, out of, or through something 強行進入/擠出/通過等: *The doctor forced his way through the crowd.* 醫生擠過人羣。

5 ▶OPEN STH 打開某物◀ to use physical force to open something〔用體力〕砸開, 撬開: **force sth ↔ open** *Robbers forced open the safe in the manager's office.* 盜賊撬開了經理辦公室裡的保險箱。| **force the lock/window/door** (=open it using force, often causing damage) 撬開鎖/窗戶/門

6 force sb's hand to make someone do something unwillingly or earlier than they had intended 迫使某人採取行動; 迫使某人提前行動: *We didn't want to raise our prices but the fall in the dollar forced our hand.* 我們並不想提價, 但美元匯率下跌迫使我們不得不這樣做。

7 force the issue to do something that makes it necessary for someone to make decisions or take action, instead of waiting for the situation to develop 迫使〔不再觀望〕作出決定; 迫使採取行動: *Rather than trying to force the issue, we gave them another day to decide.* 我們沒有強迫他們立即採取行動, 而是再給他們一天的時間作決定。

8 force a smile/laugh etc to make yourself smile, laugh etc even though you feel upset or annoyed 強作笑顏/勉強一笑

9 force the pace to make the other runners in a race have to run faster by running ahead of them〔跑在前頭〕促使[催促]他人跑得更快

force sth ↔ **back** *phr v* [T] to try hard to stop yourself from showing your emotions 強忍住〔感情的流露〕: *Janet forced back her tears.* 珍妮特強忍住淚水。

force sth ↔ **down** *phr v* [T] **1** to make yourself swallow something that you do not want to eat or drink 強吞下: *I managed to force down a piece of stale bread.* 我勉強吞下一片不新鮮的麵包。**2** to make a plane have to land by threatening to attack it 迫使〔飛機〕降落

force sth **on/upon** sb *phr v* [T] to make someone accept something even though they do not want it 把〔某事〕強加於〔某人〕, 迫使〔某人〕接受: *children with piano lessons forced upon them* 被迫上鋼琴課的兒童

force sth ↔ **out of** sb *phr v* [T] to make someone tell you something by asking them many times, threatening them etc〔通過多次要求、威脅等〕強迫〔某人〕說出: *I wasn't going to tell him, but he forced it out of me.* 我不想告訴他, 但他逼我說了出來。

forced /forst; fɔːst/ *adj* **1** done unwillingly and with effort, not because of any sincere feeling 強迫的, 勉強的: *Their smiles seemed rather forced.* 他們的微笑似乎相當勉強。**2** done suddenly and quickly, because the situation makes it necessary 緊急的: *a forced march back to base* 返回基地的強行軍 | **a forced landing** (=when an aircraft has to land quickly because of an unexpected problem)〔飛機因出現意外的問題而〕迫降, 緊急降落

force-feed /ˈ· ·/ *v* [T] to force someone to eat by putting food or liquid down their throat 給…強灌〔食物〕, 強餵

force·ful /ˈforsfəl; ˈfɔːsfəl/ *adj* **1** a forceful person expresses their opinions very strongly and clearly and people are easily persuaded by them〔觀點〕有力的; 有說服力的: *She has a strong character, very forceful and determined.* 她個性堅強, 觀點非常鮮明有力, 態度堅決。**2** forceful arguments, reasons etc are strongly and clearly expressed, and help persuade you that something is true〔論據、理由等〕有力的; 有說服力的 —**forcefully** *adv*: *Dole spoke out forcefully against the plan.* 多爾大膽發言, 堅決反對這項計劃。—**forcefulness** *n* [U]

force ma·jeure /ˌfɔrs mɑˈʒɝ; ˌfɔːs mæˈʒɜː/ *n* [U] *French formal* unexpected events that prevent you from doing what you intended or promised【法, 正式】不可抗力: *The company tried to escape its obligations by claiming force majeure.* 公司企圖聲稱出現不可抗力來逃避責任。

for·ceps /ˈfɔrsəps; ˈfɔːseps/ *n* [plural] a medical instrument used for picking up and holding things〔醫用的〕鉗子, 鑷子

for·ci·ble /ˈfɔrsəbl̩; ˈfɔːsɪ̆bəl/ *adj* done using physical force, especially as a result of an official order〔尤指由於官方命令而〕強行的; 用暴力的: *forcible seizure of their assets* 強行沒收他們的財產 —**forcibly** *adv*: *Police threatened to have the protesters forcibly removed.* 警方威脅要強行帶走這些抗議者。

ford[1] /ford; fɔːd/ *n* [C] a place where a river is not deep, so that you can walk or drive across it〔河、川的〕可涉水而過之處, 淺灘

ford[2] *v* [T] to walk or drive across a river at a place where the water is not deep 涉水而過

fore- /fɔr; fɔː/ *prefix* **1** before 預先; 先, 前: *to forewarn* 預先警告 **2** placed at the front (在…) 前面的: *her forenames* 她的名字 | *a horse's forelegs* 馬的前腿 **3** the front part of something〔某物的〕前部: *his strong forearms* 他那強壯的前臂

fore[1] /fɔr; fɔː/ *n* **come to the fore** to become important or influential 變得重要; 嶄露頭角: *Yeltsin first came to the fore when he was the Party Chief in Moscow.* 葉利欽在莫斯科擔任黨的首腦時初次嶄露頭角。

fore[2] *adj* [only before noun 僅用於名詞前] *technical* the fore parts of a ship, plane, or animal are the parts at the front【術語】〔船、飛機或動物的〕前部〔即船頭、前艙、前腿等〕—opposite 反義詞 AFT

fore·arm /ˈfɔrˌɑrm; ˈfɔːrɑːm/ *n* [C] the lower part of the arm, between the hand and the elbow 前臂 —see also 另見 **forewarned is forearmed** (FOREWARN (2)) —see picture at 參見 BODY 圖

fore·bear /ˈfɔrˌbɛr; ˈfɔːbeə/ *n* [C usually plural 一般用複數] *formal* someone who was a member of your family a long time in the past【正式】祖先, 祖宗

fore·bod·ing /fɔrˋbodɪŋ; fɔːˈbəʊdɪŋ/ *n* [U] a feeling that something very unpleasant is going to happen soon〔對將發生不愉快事的〕預感: *She waited for news from the hospital with a grim sense of foreboding.* 她帶着一種可怕的預感, 等待醫院傳來的消息。

fore·cast[1] /ˈfɔrˌkæst; ˈfɔːkɑːst/ *n* [C] a description of what is likely to happen in the future, based on information that is available now 預測, 預報: *the company's annual sales forecast* 公司的年銷售預測 | *the weather forecast* 天氣預報

forecast[2] *past tense & past participle* **forecast** *or* **forecasted** *v* [T] to make a statement saying what is likely to happen in the future, based on information that is available now 預測, 預報: *Bad weather had been forecast for*

F

the day of the race. 預料比賽當天天氣不好。| **forecast (that)** *The Federal Reserve Bank has forecast that the economy will grow by 2% this year.* 聯邦儲備銀行預測今年的經濟會增長2%。—**forecaster** *n* [C]

fore·castle /ˋfoksḷ; ˈfəʊksəl/ *n* [C] *AmE* the front part of a ship, where the sailors live【美】〔船首的〕水手艙; FO'C'SLE *BrE*【英】

fore·close /fɔrˋkloz; fɔːˈkləʊz/ *v* [I+**on**,T] *technical* to take away someone's property because they have failed to pay back the money that they borrowed to buy it【術語】〔因抵押人無法償還貸款〕取消抵押品贖回權 —**foreclosure** /-ˋkloʒɚ; -ˈkləʊʒə/ *n* [U]

fore·court /ˋfɔr͵kort; ˈfɔːkɔːt/ *n* [C] a large open area in front of a building such as a garage, or hotel〔車庫、旅館等的〕前院; 前庭; 前場

fore·doomed /fɔrˋdumd; fɔːˈduːmd/ *adj formal* intended by FATE (2) to be unsuccessful or unhappy【正式】命中注定的, 注定失敗的

fore·fa·thers /ˋfɔr͵fɑðɚz; ˈfɔː͵fɑːðəz/ *n* [plural] the people, especially men, who were part of the same family as you a long time in the past 祖先, 祖宗〔尤指男性〕

fore·fin·ger /ˋfɔr͵fɪŋgɚ; ˈfɔː͵fɪŋgə/ *n* [C] the finger next to your thumb; INDEX FINGER 食指

fore·foot /ˋfɔr͵fʊt; ˈfɔːfʊt/ *n* [C] one of the two front feet of a four-legged animal〔四足動物的〕前足

fore·front /ˋfɔr͵frʌnt; ˈfɔːfrʌnt/ *n* **1 be in/at the forefront (of)** to have an important and leading position among a group of people, organizations etc that are trying to achieve something or are developing new ideas 位於最前列; 處於領先地位: *The Pasteur Institute has been at the forefront of research into the AIDS virus.* 巴斯德研究所在愛滋病病毒的研究上已經處於領先地位。**2 be in/at the forefront of sb's mind** to be thought about by someone and seem important to them 某人首先考慮的; 某人首先想到的

fore·gath·er /fɔrˋgæðɚ; fɔːˈgæðə/ *v* [I] to FORGATHER 聚會; 聚集

fore·go, forgo /fɔrˋgo; fɔːˈgəʊ/ *v past tense* **forewent** /-ˋwɛnt; -ˈwent/ *past participle* **foregone** /-ˋgɔn; -ˈgɒn/ [T] *formal* to decide to not do or have something, especially something enjoyable【正式】摒絕, 放棄: *The monks have to forego earthly pleasures.* 僧侶得摒棄俗世的樂趣。

fore·go·ing /fɔrˋgoɪŋ; fɔːˈgəʊɪŋ/ *adj* **the foregoing** *formal* the things that have just been mentioned【正式】剛提到的事物, 前面提到的事物, 上述事物

fore·gone con·clu·sion /͵.. .ˈ../ *n* **be a foregone conclusion** if something is a foregone conclusion, the result of it is certain, even though it has not yet happened or been decided 預料中的結論; (成為)定局: *The election result was a foregone conclusion.* 選舉結果已成定局。

fore·ground /ˋfɔr͵graʊnd; ˈfɔːgraʊnd/ *n* **1 the foreground** the nearest part of a scene in a picture or a photograph〔圖片或照片的〕前景 **2 be in the foreground** to be regarded as important and receive a lot of attention 處於最突出的地位; 成為眾所矚目的事[人]: *Education and health were very much in the foreground during the post-war years.* 教育和健康在戰後幾年是最受人關注的問題。

fore·hand /ˋfɔr͵hænd; ˈfɔːhænd/ *n* [singular] a way of hitting the ball in tennis, with the flat part of your hand facing the direction of the ball〔網球的〕正手擊球 —**forehand** *adj* —see picture on page A23 參見A23頁圖

fore·head /ˋfɔrɪd; ˈfɒrɨd/ *n* [C] the part of your face above your eyes and below your hair 額, 前額 —see picture at 參見 HEAD[1] 圖

S3 W1 **for·eign** /ˋfɔrɪn; ˈfɒrɨn/ *adj* **1** not from your own country or the country you are talking about 外國的, 國外的: *Can you speak any foreign languages?* 你會講外語嗎? | *foreign tourists* 外國遊客 | *I thought she sounded foreign.* 我認為她說話像外國人。**2** [only before noun 僅用於名詞前] involving or dealing with other countries 對外的, 涉外的, 外事的, 外交的: *America's foreign policy* 美國的對外政策 **3 foreign body/matter/object** *formal* something that has come into something else, and that should not be there【正式】異物, 外來物體: *Make sure you remove all foreign matter from the wound.* 要確保清除傷口裡的所有異物。**4 foreign to** *formal*【正式】**a)** not typical of someone's usual character 不相干的, 無關的; 不屬於本身的: *Any form of cruelty is foreign to his nature.* 任何形式的殘酷都與他的本性格格不入。**b)** seeming strange and unfamiliar 陌生的, 不熟悉的: *The idea of doing something just for pleasure is quite foreign to them.* 他們根本沒有純粹為了消遣而做一件事情的想法。—**foreignness** *n* [U]

foreign af·fairs /͵.. .ˈ./ *n* [plural] politics, business matters etc that affect or concern the relationship between your country and other countries 外交事務, 外事

for·eign·er /ˋfɔrɪnɚ; ˈfɒrɨnə/ *n* [C] someone who comes from a different country 外國人: *Foreigners are not allowed to own land.* 外國人不得擁有土地。

foreign ex·change /͵.. .ˈ./ *n* [U] **1** the system of buying and selling foreign money 國際匯兌; 外匯; 外匯兌換[交易]: *The foreign exchange markets reacted quickly to the cut in German interest rates.* 外匯市場對德國利率的下調反應迅速。**2** foreign money, especially money obtained by selling goods to a foreign country 外匯, 外幣: *Coffee is a valuable source of foreign exchange for Uganda.* 咖啡是烏干達寶貴的外匯來源。

Foreign Of·fice /ˈ.. ͵../ *n* the British government department that is responsible for dealing with foreign affairs〔英國〕外交部

fore·knowl·edge /ˋfɔr͵nɑlɪdʒ; fɔːˈnɒlɪdʒ/ *n* [U] *formal* knowledge that something is going to happen before it actually does【正式】預知, 事先知道: [+**of**] *The senator denied having any foreknowledge of the affair.* 這位參議員否認事先知道這件事。

fore·leg /ˋfɔr͵lɛg; ˈfɔːleg/ *n* [C] one of the two front legs of a four-legged animal〔四足動物的〕前腿

fore·lock /ˋfɔr͵lɑk; ˈfɔːlɒk/ *n* [C] **1** a piece of hair that falls over someone's forehead 額髮, 前髮;〔馬的〕額毛 —see picture at 參見 HORSE[1] 圖 **2 forelock-tugging/touching** *BrE* showing too much respect towards people in authority【英】對權勢人物表示過分敬意的

fore·man /ˋfɔrmən; ˈfɔːmən/ *n plural* **foremen** /-mən; -mən/ [C] **1** a skilled worker who is in charge of a group of builders or factory workers 工頭, 領班 **2** the leader of a JURY (=the group of 12 people who decide whether someone is guilty in a court of law) 陪審團團長

fore·most /ˋfɔr͵most; ˈfɔːməʊst/ *adj* **foremost scientist/expert/writer etc** the most important and respected scientist, writer etc 最傑出的科學家/專家/作家等: *one of Europe's foremost authorities on childhood diseases* 歐洲最傑出的兒科疾病權威之一 —see also 另見 **first and foremost** (FIRST (21))

fore·name /ˋfɔr͵nem; ˈfɔːneɪm/ *n* [C] *formal* someone's FIRST NAME【正式】名字

fo·ren·sic /fəˋrɛnsɪk; fəˈrensɪk/ *adj* [only before noun 僅用於名詞前] connected with the methods used for finding out who is guilty of a crime 法庭的; 用於法庭的: **forensic science/medicine etc** *A specialist in forensic science was called as a witness.* 一位法庭科學專家被傳召作證人。| **forensic evidence** (=blood, hair, FINGERPRINTS etc, used to prove that someone is guilty) 法庭證據

fore·or·dain /͵fɔrɔrˋden; ͵fɔːrɔːˈdeɪn/ *v* [T] *formal* to decide or arrange how something will happen before it actually happens【正式】預先決定, 預先安排, 注定: *Their love seemed foreordained.* 他們的愛情似乎是注定的。

fore·play /ˋfɔr͵ple; ˈfɔːpleɪ/ *n* [U] sexual activity, such as kissing and touching the sexual organs, done before having sex〔性交前的〕性愛撫; 前戲

fore·run·ner /ˋfɔr͵rʌnɚ; ˈfɔːˌrʌnə/ *n* [C] **1** a person, organization, machine etc which existed a long time before a similar one that exists now, and which the present one is based upon 先驅, 先導, 前鋒: **[+of]** *The suffragettes were forerunners of the modern women's movement.* 為婦女選舉權而鬥爭的女子是現代婦女運動的先驅。**2** a sign or warning that something is going to happen 預兆, 前兆, 徵兆

fore·see /fɔrˋsi; fɔːˈsiː/ *past tense* **foresaw** /-ˋsɔ; -ˈsɔː/ *past participle* **foreseen** /-ˋsin; -ˈsiːn/ *v* [T] to know that something is going to happen before it actually happens 預知; 預見, 預料: *The method was used in ways that could not have been foreseen by its inventors.* 這種方法以其發明者無從預見的各種方式得到使用。| **foresee that** *Few analysts foresaw that oil prices would rise so steeply.* 分析家中很少有人預料到油價會這麼飛漲。

fore·see·a·ble /fɔrˋsiəbḷ; fɔːˈsiːəbəl/ *adj* **1 in the foreseeable future** fairly soon 在可預見的將來; 相當快, 即將…: *There is a possibility of severe water shortages in the foreseeable future.* 在可預見的將來可能會出現嚴重的水資源短缺。**2 for the foreseeable future** continuing in the future for as long as you can imagine 在可預見的將來(裡): *Their dependence on oil exports is likely to continue for the foreseeable future.* 他們對石油出口的依賴在可預見的未來時日裡可能會持續下去。**3** foreseeable difficulties, events etc are ones that you can imagine happening in the future〔困難、事件等〕可預見到的: *planning for any foreseeable financial losses* 為應付任何可預見到的經濟損失而制定計劃

fore·shad·ow /fɔrˋʃædo; fɔːˈʃædəʊ/ *v* [T] to be a sign of something that will happen in the future 預示; 是…的預兆: *The events in Spain in the 1930s foreshadowed the rise of Nazi Germany.* 20世紀30年代西班牙發生的事件預示了納粹德國的興起。

fore·shore /ˋfɔr͵ʃɔr; ˈfɔːʃɔː/ *n* [singular] **1** the part of the shore between the highest and lowest levels that the sea reaches〔高潮線和低潮線之間的〕前灘, 前濱 **2** the part of the shore between the edge of the sea and the part of the land that has houses, grass etc 海灘

fore·short·ened /fɔrˋʃɔrtṇd; fɔːˈʃɔːtnd/ *adj* objects, places etc that are foreshortened appear to be smaller, shorter, or closer together than they really are〔事物、地方等顯得〕縮小的; 縮短的; 緊湊的: *Some of the figures are oddly foreshortened, giving the picture a disturbing quality.* 有些人物莫名其妙地縮小了, 給圖畫一種令人不安的感覺。—**foreshorten** *v* [T]

fore·sight /ˋfɔr͵saɪt; ˈfɔːsaɪt/ *n* [U] the ability to imagine what is likely to happen and to consider this when planning for the future 先見之明, 預見; 深謀遠慮: *The report blames the accident on lack of foresight by the original planners.* 該報告把這次事故歸咎於原設計者缺乏先見之明。| **have the foresight to do sth** *Luckily she had had the foresight to destroy the incriminating documents.* 幸運的是, 她有遠見地銷毀了可證明有罪的文件。

fore·skin /ˋfɔr͵skɪn; ˈfɔːˌskɪn/ *n* [C] a loose fold of skin covering the end of a man's PENIS〔陰莖的〕包皮

2 2 **for·est** /ˋfɔrɪst; ˈfɒrɪ̇st/ *n* [C] a large area of land that is thickly covered with trees 森林, 林區: *Much of Scandinavia is covered in dense pine forest.* 斯堪的納維亞許多地方都覆蓋着茂密的松林。| *a forest fire* 森林火災

fore·stall /fɔrˋstɔl; fɔːˈstɔːl/ *v* [T] to prevent something from happening or prevent someone from doing something by doing something first 預先阻止; 搶先: *Gero urged reforms in order to forestall trouble.* 傑羅敦促進行改革以防止出現麻煩。

for·est·er /ˋfɔrɪstɚ; ˈfɒrɪ̇stə/ *n* [C] someone who works in a forest taking care of, planting, and cutting down the trees 林務員; 林務官

for·est·ry /ˋfɔrɪstrɪ; ˈfɒrɪ̇stri/ *n* [U] the science or skill of looking after large areas of trees 林學; 林務

fore·taste /ˋfɔr͵test; ˈfɔːteɪst/ *n* **be a foretaste of** to be a sign of something more important, more impressive etc that will happen in the future 是…的前兆: *Two spectacular wins at the start of the season were a foretaste of things to come.* 該隊在賽季一開始就驚人地兩次獲勝, 預示着此後所要發生的事。

fore·tell /fɔrˋtɛl; fɔːˈtel/ *v past tense and past participle* **foretold** /-ˋtold; -ˈtəʊld/ [T] to say what will happen in the future, especially by using special magical powers〔尤指用超凡的能力〕預言; 預示: *the birth of Christ, foretold by prophets* 先知們所預言的基督的誕生

fore·thought /ˋfɔr͵θɔt; ˈfɔːθɔːt/ *n* [U] careful thought about what needs to be done in order to make sure things happen well in the future 事先的考慮, 事先的籌劃: *No one had had the forethought to bring a corkscrew.* 沒有一個人事先想到要帶開塞鑽來。

fore·told /fɔrˋtold; fɔːˈtəʊld/ the past tense and past participle of FORETELL

for·ev·er, for ever /fɚˋɛvɚ; fərˈevə/ *adv* **1** continuing or lasting for all future time 永遠: *Our love will last forever.* 我們的愛情將會直到永遠。| *These valuable works of art have been lost forever.* 這些珍貴的藝術品已經永遠丟失了。**2** *especially spoken* for a very long time【尤口】很長久地: *We'll be stuck here forever if the car won't start.* 如果車子發動不了, 我們就要在這裡被困到不知甚麼時候。| **take forever** (=take a long time) 花很長的時間 *It took forever to clean up after the party.* 聚會後收拾打掃花了很長時間。**3 be forever doing sth** *spoken* to do something many times, especially in a way that annoys people【口】老是做某事, 不斷做某事: *He's forever making comments about my weight.* 他老是在談論我的體重。**4 forever and a day** *spoken* a very long time【口】很長的時間: *It's going to take me forever and a day to pay for it.* 為此我要花很長的時間還清欠款。**5 forever and ever** a phrase meaning forever, used especially in stories 永遠, 永久〔尤用於故事〕 3

fore·warn /fɔrˋwɔrn; fɔːˈwɔːn/ *v* [T often passive 常用被動態] **1** to warn someone about something dangerous, unpleasant, or unexpected before it happens 預先警告; 事先告知: **[+of/about/against]** *She had been forewarned of the discomforts of travelling by train in the Soviet Union.* 她預先得到警告, 在蘇聯乘火車旅行是很不舒適的。**2 forewarned is forearmed** used to say that if you know about something in advance, you can be properly prepared for it 凡事預則立, 先知先戒備 —**forewarning** *n* [C,U]

fore·went, forwent /fɔrˋwɛnt; fɔːˈwent/ the past tense of FORGO

fore·wom·an /ˋfɔr͵wʊmən; ˈfɔːˌwʊmən/ *n* [C] **1** a female worker who is in charge of a group of other workers, especially in a factory〔尤指工廠裡的〕女工頭, 女領班 **2** a woman who is the leader of a JURY (=a group of 12 people who decide if someone is guilty in a court of law) 陪審團女團長

fore·word /ˋfɔr͵wɝd; ˈfɔːwɜːd/ *n* [C] a short piece of writing at the beginning of a book〔書的〕前言, 序言

for·feit¹ /ˋfɔrfɪt; ˈfɔːfɪ̇t/ *v* [T] to lose something valuable by having it taken away from you, either as a punishment or because of a law or rule〔作為懲罰或由於法律或規則而〕失去; 喪失; 被沒收: *By becoming a German citizen he forfeited his right to live in the US.* 由於成為德國公民, 他喪失了在美國的居住權。—**forfeiture** /-fɪtʃɚ; -fɪ̇tʃə/ *n* [U]

forfeit² *n* [C] something that is taken away from you or something that you have to do, because you have broken a rule or made a mistake 沒收物; 喪失的東西; 代價〔作為對某人違反規則或犯錯誤的懲罰〕

forfeit³ *adj* **be forfeit** *formal* to be legally or officially taken away from you as a punishment【正式】〔作為懲罰〕被沒收, 喪失: *Unless he returns with the prisoners as he promised, his life shall be forfeit.* 除非他按照自己的承諾把囚犯們帶回來, 不然他就要送命。

for·gath·er, foregather /fɔrˋgæðɚ; fɔːˈgæðə/ *v* [I]

F

formal to meet as a group【正式】聚會; 聚集

for·gave /fəˋgev; fəˈgeɪv/ the past tense of FORGIVE

forge¹ /fɔrdʒ; fɔːdʒ/ *v* [T] **1** to illegally copy something, especially something printed or written on paper, to make people think that it is real 偽造; 假冒〔尤指印或寫在紙上的事物〕: *Someone stole my credit card and forged my signature.* 有人偷了我的信用卡, 並假冒我的簽名。| *a forged passport* 假護照 **2 forge a relationship/alliance/links etc** to develop a strong relationship, with other groups or other countries〔與其他團體或國家〕建立關係/結盟/建立聯繫等: *Gorbachev was able to forge new links between Russia and the West.* 戈爾巴喬夫能建立俄羅斯和西方之間的新聯繫。**3** to make something from a piece of metal by heating the metal and shaping it 鍛造; 打〔鐵〕

forge ahead *phr v* [I] **1** to make progress and become more and more successful 穩步前進; 越來越成功: *individuals who have forged ahead in this competitive field* 在這個競爭性領域中領先的人 **2** to move forward in a strong and powerful way 突飛猛進, 奮力前進

forge² *n* [C] **1** a place where metal is heated and shaped into objects 鍛造車間; 鐵匠鋪 **2** a large piece of equipment that produces high temperatures and is used for heating and shaping metal objects 鍛鐵爐; 熔鐵爐

forg·er /ˋfɔrdʒɚ; ˈfɔːdʒə/ *n* [C] someone who illegally copies documents, money, paintings etc, to try to make people think they are real〔文件、錢幣、繪畫等的〕偽造者

for·ge·ry /ˋfɔrdʒəri; ˈfɔːdʒəri/ *n* **1** [C] a document, painting, or piece of paper money that has been forged〔文件、繪畫或紙幣的〕偽造品, 贋品: *The painting was actually a very clever forgery.* 實際上這幅畫是件很巧妙的贋品。**2** [U] the crime of forging official documents, money etc 偽造罪

for·get /fəˋgɛt; fəˈget/ *past tense* **forgot** /-ˋgɑt; -ˈgɒt/ *past participle* **forgotten** /-ˋgɑtn̩; -ˈgɒtn/ *v*

1 ►FACTS/INFORMATION 事實/信息◄ [I,T] to be unable to remember facts, information, or something that happened in the past 忘記, 遺忘: *I'm sorry, I've forgotten your name.* 對不起, 我忘了你的名字了。| **[+(that)]** *Don't forget that it's Sarah's birthday on Tuesday.* 別忘了星期二是薩拉的生日。| **[+about]** *Charles seems to have forgotten about what happened.* 查爾斯好像已忘了發生過的事。| **[+how/what/when/why etc]** *Natalie managed to forget where she'd parked the car.* 納塔莉竟然忘記她把車泊在哪裡了。

2 ►STH YOU MUST DO 你必須做的事◄ [I,T] to not remember to do something that you have to do 忘記, 忘掉〔做某件應當做的事〕: *"Did you remember to post that letter?" "Oh, sorry, I forgot."* "你記得要寄那封信嗎?" "哦, 對不起, 我忘了。" | **forget to do sth** *Someone's forgotten to turn off their headlights.* 有人忘記關汽車前燈了。| **forget (that)** *I forgot that I was supposed to come in early this morning.* 我忘記我今天上午應該早來。| **clean forget** (=completely forget) 忘得一乾二淨 *He meant to invite Monica to the party but he clean forgot.* 他本打算邀請蒙妮卡參加聚會, 但卻忘得一乾二淨。

3 ►NOT BRING 沒有帶◄ [I,T] to not bring something that you need, because you did not remember to bring it 忘記〔帶、拿〕: *Don't forget your passport.* 別忘了拿你的護照。| *I didn't forget the torch.* 我沒有忘記帶電筒。

4 ►STOP THINKING ABOUT 停止想◄ [I, T] to try to stop thinking and worrying about someone or something that makes you unhappy 忘掉〔令人不愉快的人或事〕, 不再去想: *Years after their divorce Olivia still could not forget John.* 奧莉維亞在他們離婚數年後仍忘不了約翰。| **[+about]** *I'd forget about it if I were you.* 如果我是你, 我就把它忘了。

5 ►NOT CARE ABOUT 對…不介意, 不關心◄ [I,T] to not care about or give attention to someone or something 不介意; 不關心; 忽視: **[+about]** *Don't go off to college and forget about your old friends, okay?* 不要上了大學就忘了老朋友, 好嗎?

6 ►STOP A PLAN 停止一項計劃◄ [I, T] to stop trying to do something because it no longer seems possible 不再打算做, 放棄: **[+about]** *We'll have to forget about going on holiday.* 我們將不得不放棄度假的計劃。| *If we can't get any funding we might as well forget the whole thing.* 如果我們不能得到資金, 那就不如乾脆別談這件事了。

7 not forgetting used to add something to a list of things 也包括…在內, 別忘了還有: *Bear in mind that we have to pay for all the packaging and transportation costs, not forgetting airport taxes.* 記住, 我們得支付所有的包裝和運輸費用, 還包括機場税。

8 forget yourself to do something stupid or embarrassing, especially by losing control of your emotions 忘乎所以; 失去理智; 行為或言談失態[不得體]

Frequencies of the verb **forget** in spoken and written English 動詞forget在英語口語和書面語中的使用頻率

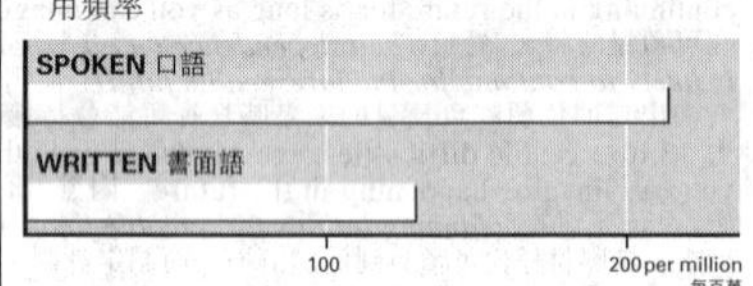

Based on the British National Corpus and the Longman Lancaster Corpus
據英國國家語料庫和朗文蘭卡斯特語料庫

This graph shows that the verb **forget** is much more common in spoken English than in written English. This is because it is used in a lot of common spoken phrases. 本圖表顯示, 動詞forget在英語口語中的使用頻率遠遠高於書面語, 因為口語中有很多常用片語是由forget構成的。

forget (*v*) **SPOKEN PHRASES**
含 forget 的口語片語

9 don't forget a) used to remind someone to do something 別忘了, 要記住〔做某事〕: *We need bread, milk, and eggs. Don't forget now, will you?* 我們需要麵包、牛奶和雞蛋。可別忘了, 好嗎? | **don't forget to do sth** *Don't forget to lock the place up when you leave.* 離開時別忘了把這個地方鎖好。**b)** used to remind someone about an important fact or detail that they should consider 別忘了〔某個重要事實或細節〕: *The kids won't be home until late, don't forget, so we'll be eating on our own.* 別忘了孩子們要很遲才回家, 所以我們自己吃飯吧。| **don't forget (that)** *But don't forget you have to pay interest on the loan.* 可是不要忘記你得為貸款付利息。

10 forget it a) used when someone asks you what you just said and you do not want to repeat it 別提它了〔用於不想重複剛才所說的話〕: *"What was that? I didn't hear." "Nothing, forget it."* "那是甚麼? 我沒聽見。" "沒甚麼, 別提它了[就當我沒說]。" **b)** used to tell someone that something is not important and they do not need to worry about it 沒關係, 別在意〔用於表示某物不重要〕: *"I'm really sorry, I'll get you another one." "Forget it, I've got lots of bowls."* "真的很對不起, 我買一個碗來賠你。" "沒關係, 我有很多碗。" **c)** used to tell someone that you refuse to do something or that it will be impossible for them to do something 休想, 不可能: *"Lend me $10." "Forget it, no way."* "借給我十美元。" "休想, 不可以。" | *If you're thinking of getting Roy to help, you can forget it!* 如果你想叫羅伊幫忙, 那還是算了吧! **d)** used to tell someone to stop asking or talking about something, because it is annoying you 別説了: *Look,* *just forget it will you. I'm not coming and that's that.* 瞧，你不要再説了。我不會來，就是這樣。

11 I'll never forget used to say that you will always remember something from the past, because it was sad, funny, enjoyable etc〔因某事可悲、滑稽、令人愉快等〕我永遠也忘不了：*I'll never forget the look on his face when I said I'd marry him.* 我永遠也忘不了我說要嫁給他時他臉上的神色。

12 I forget used to say that you cannot remember a particular detail about something you are talking about 我記不起來：**I forget what/where/how etc** *I forget what he said exactly, but it was very rude.* 我記不起他確切説過甚麼，不過他的話是很無禮的。| **I forget the name/details etc** *You go down Weir Road then turn left into, I forget the name of it, but it's first left after the bank.* 你沿着威爾路往前走，然後往左拐到，我記不起那條街的名字了，不過就是走過銀行後向左第一個拐彎。

13 forget that used to tell someone to ignore what you have just said because it is not correct, important etc 那不對，錯了：*Then mix the flour with 500 cls of milk, no, forget that, 50 cls of milk.* 然後將麵粉和500厘升牛奶攪和，不，不對，是50厘升牛奶。

14 and don't you forget it used to remind someone angrily about an important fact that should make them behave differently 可（千萬）別忘了：*Listen, I'm the boss around here, and don't you forget it!* 聽着，這裡我是老闆，可別忘了！

15 aren't you forgetting...?/haven't you forgotten...? used to tell someone that they have forgotten to consider something important 你是不是忘了...?：*"Wait a minute – aren't you forgetting something? No? Well what about saying 'thank you'?"* "等等——你是不是忘了一件事？沒有？嗯，是不是該説聲"謝謝"呢？"

for·get·ful /fɚˋgɛtfəl; fəˈgetfəl/ *adj* often forgetting things 健忘的，愛忘事的，不記事的，沒記性的 —**forgetfulness** *n* [U] —**forgetfully** *adv*

forget-me-not /·ˈ· · ,·/ *n* [C] a small plant with pale blue flowers 勿忘（我）草，毋忘我草〔一種開淡藍色小花的植物〕

for·get·ta·ble /fɚˋgɛtəbl̩; fəˈgetəbəl/ *adj often humorous* not very interesting or good【常幽默】易被忘記的，該置諸腦後的；無聊的，糟糕的：*a completely forgettable movie* 一部糟糕透頂、不值一提的影片

for·giv·a·ble /fɚˋgɪvəbl̩; fəˈgɪvəbəl/ *adj* bad behaviour that is forgivable is not seriously bad and you can easily forgive it〔糟糕的行為〕可寬恕的，可原諒的：*I suppose a little over-excitement is forgivable under the circumstances.* 我認為在那種情況下有點過分激動是可原諒的。

3 **for·give** /fɚˋgɪv; fəˈgɪv/ *v past tense* **forgave** /-ˋgev; -ˈgeɪv/ *past participle* **forgiven** /-ˋgɪvən; -ˈgɪvən/ [I,T] **1** to decide not to blame someone or be angry with them although they have done something wrong 原諒；寬恕；饒恕：*Can you ever forgive me?* 你能原諒我嗎？| **forgive sb for sth** *I can't forgive him for what he did to my sister.* 因為他對我妹妹所做的事，我無法原諒他。| **forgive sb sth** *forgive us our sins*〔請上帝〕赦免我們的罪 | **I'd never forgive myself** *If anything happened to the kids I'd never forgive myself.* 如果孩子們出了甚麼事，我永遠也不能原諒自己。| **forgive and forget** (=forgive someone for something and behave as if they had never done it) 寬大為懷，不念舊惡 **2 forgive me** *spoken* used when you are going to say something or ask something that might seem rude or offensive【口】請原諒，對不起：*Forgive me, Mr Lewis, but I don't think that is relevant.* 對不起，劉易斯先生，不過我認為那是不相干的。| **forgive me for asking/saying etc** *Forgive me for saying so, but I think that's nonsense.* 請原諒我這麼説，我認為那是胡説。**3 sb could be forgiven for thinking/wondering/believing etc sth** used to say that it is easy to understand why someone would think or believe something 某人認為.../想知道.../相信...等，那是可以理解的：*A foreign visitor could be forgiven for thinking football is a religion in this country.* 外國來訪者認為足球在這個國家是一種宗教，那是可以理解的。

for·give·ness /fɚˋgɪvnɪs; fəˈgɪvnə̇s/ *n* [U] the act of forgiving someone 原諒；寬恕：**ask for/beg for forgiveness** (=ask someone to forgive you) 請求原諒；懇求寬恕

for·giv·ing /fɚˋgɪvɪŋ; fəˈgɪvɪŋ/ *adj* willing to forgive 寬容的，寬大的：*My father was a kind and forgiving man.* 我父親是個善良寬容的人。

for·go /fɔrˋgo; fɔːˈgəʊ/ *v* [T] to FOREGO 摒絕，放棄

for·got /fɚˋgɑt; fəˈgɒt/ the past tense of FORGET

for·got·ten¹ /fɚˋgɑtn̩; fəˈgɒtn/ the past participle of FORGET

forgotten² *adj* [usually before noun 一般用於名詞前] that people have forgotten about or no longer pay much attention to 被遺忘的：*a rare plant growing in a forgotten corner of the churchyard* 生長在教堂墓地裡一個被人遺忘的角落裡的罕見植物

forks 叉子

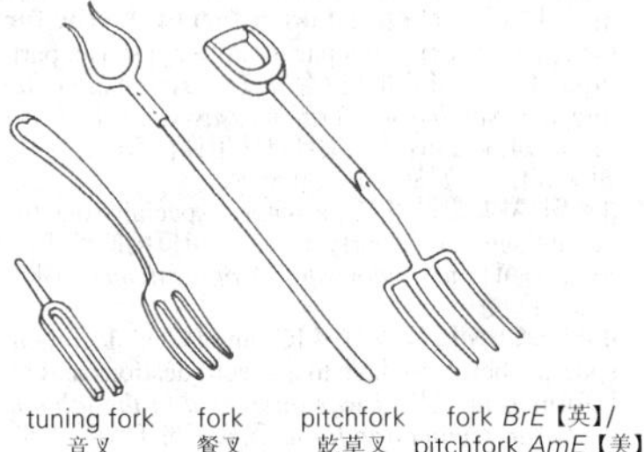

tuning fork 音叉 | fork 餐叉 | pitchfork 乾草叉 | fork *BrE*【英】/ pitchfork *AmE*【美】乾草叉

fork¹ /fɔrk; fɔːk/ *n* [C] **1** a tool used for picking up and eating food, with a handle and three or four points 餐叉，叉子：*knives and forks* 刀叉 **2** a garden tool used for digging, with a handle and three or four points 叉；耙 —compare 比較 PITCHFORK **3** a place where a road or river divides into two parts, or one of the parts it divides into 岔口；岔路；岔流：*Take the left fork then go straight on for two miles.* 走左邊的岔道，然後一直走兩英里。**4 the forks** the parallel metal bars between which the front wheel of a bicycle or MOTORCYCLE is fixed〔腳踏車或摩托車的〕前叉 —see also 另見 TUNING FORK —see picture at 參見 BICYCLE 圖

fork² *v* **1** [I] if a road, path, or river forks, it divides into two parts〔道路或河流〕分岔 **2 fork left/right** to travel towards the left or right part of a road when it divides into two parts 在岔口往左拐/往右拐：*Fork left at the bottom of the hill.* 在山底的岔口往左拐。**3** [T] to pick up, carry, or turn something over using a fork 叉起；〔用叉〕搬運；〔用叉〕翻耙：*He forked some bacon onto a piece of bread.* 他將一些鹹肉叉到一片麵包上。

fork out (sth) *phr v* [I,T] *informal* to spend a lot of money on something, not because you want to but because you have to【非正式】〔不情願地〕付錢，付出：**[+for/on]** *I had to fork out over £600 on my car when I had it serviced.* 我只好破費六百多英鎊請人修車。

forked /fɔrkt; fɔːkt/ *adj* having one end divided into two or more parts 叉狀的；分岔的；有叉的：*Snakes have forked tongues.* 蛇的舌頭是分叉的。

forked light·ning /,· ˈ··/ *n* [U] lightning that is in the form of a line of light that divides into several smaller lines near the bottom 叉狀閃電 —compare 比較 SHEET LIGHTNING —see picture on page A13 參見A13頁圖

fork-lift truck /ˌ· · ˈ·/ also 又作 **fork-lift** /ˈ· ·/ *n* [C] a small vehicle with special equipment on the front for lifting and moving heavy things 叉車, 鏟車, 叉式升降裝卸車

for·lorn /fəˈlɔrn; fəˈlɔːn/ *adj* **1** seeming lonely and unhappy 孤苦伶仃的, 愁苦的, 淒涼的: *a forlorn little figure sitting outside the station* 坐在車站外的一個可憐無依的小人影 **2** a place that is forlorn seems empty and sad, and is often in bad condition〔地方〕荒涼的: *The house looked old and forlorn.* 房子看上去破舊荒涼。**3 a forlorn hope** something you hope for that is very unlikely to happen 幾乎沒有成功希望的事物: *We continued negotiating in the forlorn hope of finding a peace formula.* 我們繼續談判, 十分渺茫地希望找到一個和平方案。

form¹ /fɔrm; fɔːm/ *n*
1 ►TYPE 種類, 形式◄ [C] a type of something, that exists in many different types 類型; 方式: [+of] *Trains are a very cost-effective form of transport.* 火車是一種成本效益很高的運輸方式。| *She dislikes any form of exercise.* 她不喜歡任何一種運動。
2 ►WAY STH IS/APPEARS 形式/外形◄ [C] the way in which something exists, is presented, or appears 形式, 方式: *We oppose racism in all its forms.* 我們反對所有形式的種族歧視。| **take a form/take the form of** (=happen or exist in a particular way or as a particular type) 以…的形式出現/存在 *The assignment can take any form you like – a written essay, a piece of recorded music, or whatever.* 作業可以使用你喜歡的任何方式——短文寫作、錄製的音樂或甚麼的。
3 ►SHAPE 形狀◄ [C] a shape, especially one that you cannot see very clearly 輪廓〔尤指模糊的形狀〕, 外形; 形狀: [+of] *the shadowy forms of the divers* 潛水員模糊不清的輪廓
4 ►DOCUMENT 文件◄ [C] an official document with spaces where you have to answer questions and provide information 表格: *I was interested in the job and sent off for an application form.* 我對這份工作感興趣, 便寄信去索取申請表。| **fill in/out a form** (=write the answers to the questions on a form) 填寫表格 *Fill in the form and send it back with your cheque.* 填好表格, 然後連同支票一起寄回來。—see picture at 參見 FILL 圖
5 in the form of a) having the shape of 呈…的形狀: *The main staircase was in the form of a big 'S'.* 主樓梯呈大S形。**b)** existing in a particular form 以…的形式: *People are bombarded with information in the form of magazines and TV advertising.* 人們受到以雜誌和電視廣告形式進行的信息轟炸。
6 ►ART/LITERATURE 藝術/文學◄ [U] the structure of a work of art or piece of writing, rather than the ideas it expresses, events it describes etc〔文藝作品的〕(表現)形式: *Writers like Henry James place a lot of emphasis on form as well as content.* 像亨利·詹姆斯這樣的作家對形式和內容都很強調。
7 ►LEVEL OR PERFORMANCE 水平或表現◄ [U] **a)** how well a sports person, team or race horse is performing, or has performed recently〔運動員、運動隊或賽馬的〕競技狀態: *Judging by her most recent form, she should easily win a medal at the Olympics.* 從她最近的競技狀態看, 她應當可以輕而易舉地在奧運會上獲得獎牌。**b) on present/current/past etc form** based on how well a person, team, organization etc is performing or achieving their aims 從目前的/當前的/過去的狀況看: *On current form, the Democrats could lose control of the Senate in the mid-term elections.* 從當前的狀況看, 民主黨可能會在中期選舉中失去對參議院的控制。
8 ►SCHOOL 學校◄ [C] *BrE* a class in a school【英】年級: *We stopped doing Art in the fourth form.* 我們在四年級停止上美術課。—see also 另見 SIXTH FORM, FORM TEACHER
9 ►GRAMMAR 語法◄ [C] a way of writing or saying a word, for example one that shows it is in the past or the plural（詞的）形式: *'Was' is a past form of the verb 'to be'.* was是動詞to be的過去式。
10 ►SEAT 座位◄ [C] a long low wooden seat without a back 長板櫈
11 bad form *BrE old-fashioned* behaviour that is considered to be socially unacceptable【英, 過時】不合禮節要求的行為, 不禮貌的行為: *It is considered rather bad form to arrive early at a dinner party.* 過早出席晚宴被認為是很不合禮節的行為。
12 be in good/great etc form also 又作 **be on good/great etc form** *BrE* to be full of confidence and energy, so that you do something well or talk in an interesting or amusing way etc【英】〔在社交場合〕情緒良好, 興高采烈: *Michelle was in great form at last week's conference.* 米雪兒在上星期的會議上狀態大好。

form² *v*
1 ►START TO EXIST 開始存在◄ [I,T often passive 常用被動態] to start to exist, or make something start to exist, especially as the result of a natural process〔尤指經過自然過程而〕形成; 產生: *The rocks were formed more than 4000 million years ago.* 這些岩石是四十多億年前形成的。| *Ice was beginning to form around the edges of the windows.* 窗子周圍開始結冰。
2 ►BE PART OF 成為…的一部分◄ [linking verb 連繫動詞] to be part of something, or be the thing that something is based on 成為…的一部分[基礎]: *Newton's theories form the basis of modern mathematics.* 牛頓的理論構成現代數學的基礎。
3 ►BE OR ACT AS STH 構成或充當某物◄ [linking verb 連繫動詞] if something forms something, it acts as or works in a particular way 成為; 充當: *The river formed a natural boundary between the two countries.* 這條河成為兩國的自然邊界。
4 ►MAKE/PRODUCE 製作/生產◄ [T] **a)** to make something, especially by combining two or more parts 構成: *In English the past tense is usually formed by adding 'ed'.* 在英語中, 過去式通常是通過加ed構成的。**b)** to make something so that it has a particular shape 形成; 塑造: *Cut off the corners of the square to form a diamond.* 切掉正方形的四角, 形成菱形。
5 ►ESTABLISH/MAKE 建立/製作◄ [T] **a)** to establish an organization, committee, government etc 建立, 組成〔組織、委員會、政府等〕: *The United Nations was formed in 1945.* 聯合國是1945年成立的。**b) form a relationship/alliance/attachment** to establish a relationship with someone 建立關係/結盟/建立感情: *She has difficulty forming long-term relationships with men.* 她難於與男子建立長期的關係。
6 form an opinion/impression/idea to use available information to develop or reach an opinion or idea 形成看法/印象/概念: *Police are trying to form an idea of what kind of person the killer is.* 警方正試圖構想出殺手是屬於哪一種類型的人。
7 ►DEVELOP 發展◄ [T] to make someone develop into a particular type of person 培養成: *Events in early childhood often help to form our personalities in later life.* 在幼年時發生的事常對形成我們日後的個性起着作用。
8 ►LINE 隊列◄ [I,T] to come together and make a group or a line（把…）編[排]成: *Film-goers began to form a line outside the cinema.* 來看電影的人開始在電影院外排成一行。

form·al¹ /ˈfɔrml; ˈfɔːməl/ *adj* **1** formal behaviour is very polite, and is used with people you do not know well, or in official situations or at important social occasions 拘謹的; 正式的: *Our boss is very formal, she doesn't call anyone by their first name.* 我們的老闆十分拘謹, 對任何人都不直呼其名。**2** formal language is used in speeches, in serious or official writing, or at official meetings or important social occasions〔語言〕規範的; 正式的; 公文的: *You shouldn't use 'Yours faithfully' in a letter to a friend – it sounds too formal.* 你在給朋友的信中不應該用 Yours faithfully —— 這聽起來太正式了。

3 a formal occasion is serious and important, and people who go to it wear good clothes and behave according to strict social rules〔場合〕正式的: *I only wear this suit for formal dinners.* 我只是在參加正式宴會時才穿這套衣服。**4** a formal decision or action is made or done officially or publicly〔決定或行動〕正式的; 官方的: *On July 19th a formal declaration of war was made in Berlin.* 7月19日柏林正式宣戰。**5 formal education/training/qualification** education etc in a subject or skill gained in a school, college etc rather than practical experience of it 正規教育/訓練/資格: *Many of the health workers had no formal medical training.* 許多衛生工作者沒有受過正規的醫學訓練。—see also 另見 FORMALLY

formal² *n* [C] *AmE*【美】**1** a formal social event such as a dance, at which you have to wear formal clothes 正式的場合〈如舞會〉**2** an expensive and usually long dress that women wear at a formal occasion〔女子的〕禮服

for·mal·de·hyde /fɔrˈmældəˌhaɪd; fɔːˈmældɪ̣haɪd/ *n* [U] a strong-smelling gas that can be mixed with water and used for preserving things 甲醛: *frogs preserved in formaldehyde* 保存在甲醛中的青蛙

formal dress /ˌ‥ ˈ·/ *n* [U] clothes worn for formal social occasions, especially a black JACKET (1), black trousers, and a BOW TIE for men, or a long dress for women〔正式社交場合穿的〕禮服

for·ma·lin /ˈfɔrməlɪn; ˈfɔːməlɪ̣n/ *n* [U] a liquid made by mixing formaldehyde and water, used for preserving things 甲醛水(溶液), 福爾馬林

for·ma·lise /ˈfɔrmḷˌaɪz; ˈfɔːməlaɪz/ *v* a British spelling of FORMALIZE formalize 的英式拼法

form·al·is·m /ˈfɔrmḷˌɪzəm; ˈfɔːməlɪzəm/ *n* [U] a style or method in art, religion, or science that pays too much attention to established rules〔藝術、宗教、科學等的〕形式主義 —**formalist** *n, adj*

for·mal·i·ty /fɔrˈmælətɪ; fɔːˈmælɪ̣ti/ *n* **1** [C usually plural 一般用複數] something that you must do as a formal or official part of an activity or process 正式手續: *There are a few formalities to settle before you become legal owner of the car.* 在成為合法車主之前, 要辦理一些正式手續。**2 be a formality** to be something that you must do even though it has no practical importance or effects 是一種俗套; 是一種形式: *The physical exam is just a formality.* 體格檢查只是例行公事而已。**3** [U] polite and formal behaviour 拘謹; 遵守禮節: *The following morning, Mr Harrison greeted her with stiff formality.* 第二天上午, 哈里森先生非常拘謹地和她打招呼。

for·mal·ize also 又作 **-ise** *BrE*【英】/ˈfɔrmḷˌaɪz; ˈfɔːməlaɪz/ *v* [T] to make a plan, decision, or idea official, especially by deciding and clearly describing all the details 使〔計劃、決定或想法〕正式化; 使定形; 使形式化: *Final arrangements for the takeover have yet to be formalized.* 這次接管的最後安排還沒有正式確定。—**formalization** /ˌfɔrmələˈzeʃən; ˌfɔːməlaɪˈzeɪʃən/ *n* [U]

for·mal·ly /ˈfɔrmḷɪ; ˈfɔːməli/ *adv* **1** officially 正式地: *Mr Wright has formally accepted the job.* 賴特先生已正式接受這項工作。**2** in a polite way 禮貌地: *He bowed formally to each guest in turn.* 他禮貌地依次向每個客人鞠躬。

3 **for·mat¹** /ˈfɔrmæt; ˈfɔːmæt/ *n* [C] **1** the way in which something is organized or arranged 方式, 樣式: *I'd like to change the format of the meetings a little.* 我想稍微改變一下會議的方式。**2** the size, shape, design etc, in which something such as a book or magazine is produced〔書、雜誌等的〕格式; 版式: *a travel show with a music video tape format* 以音樂錄像帶格式拍攝的旅遊節目

format² *v* **formatted, formatting** [T] **1** to arrange a book, page etc according to a particular design or plan〔根據設計或計劃〕為〔書刊等〕安排版式; 為…編排格式 **2** *technical* to organize the space on a computer DISK so that information can be stored on it【術語】使〔電腦磁盤〕格式化 —**formatting** *n* [U] —**formatted** *adj*

for·ma·tion /fɔrˈmeʃən; fɔːˈmeɪʃən/ *n* **1** [U] the process by which something develops into a particular thing 2
or shape 形成: *Damp conditions are needed for the formation of mould.* 黴菌的形成需要潮濕的環境。**2** the process of starting a new organization or group 構成, 組成: *the formation of a new government* 新政府的組成 **3** the way in which a group of things are arranged to form a pattern or shape 排列方式, 樣式: *The flowers had been planted in a star formation.* 這些花是排列成星形種植的。**4 in formation** if a group of planes, ships, soldiers etc are moving in formation, they are marching, flying etc in a particular order or pattern〔飛機、船隻、士兵等〕排列成隊, 列隊, 列陣 **5** [C,U] something, especially a rock or cloud, that is formed in a particular shape, or the shape in which it is formed〔某種形狀的〕形成物;〔尤指岩石或雲朵的〕形成方式, 結構: *rock formations* 岩層; 岩石結構

for·ma·tive /ˈfɔrmətɪv; ˈfɔːmətɪv/ *adj* [only before noun 僅用於名詞前] having an important influence on the way someone's character develops 影響性格形成的, 塑造性格的: **formative influence/effect etc** *Parents have the greatest formative effect on their childrens' behaviour.* 父母對孩子的行為有最深遠的影響。| **formative years/period/stages etc** (=the period when someone's character develops) 性格形成時期/階段等

for·mer¹ /ˈfɔrmɚ; ˈfɔːmə/ *adj* [only before noun 僅用於 2
名詞前] **1** happening or existing before, but not now 以 1
前的, 從前的: *The coal industry is now barely half its former size.* 煤炭業現在的規模幾乎不到以前的一半。| *civil war in the former Yugoslavia* 前南斯拉夫的內戰 | **former president/soldier/wife etc** (=someone who was a president etc, but who is not now) 前任總統/昔日的士兵/前妻等 *a former principal of the school* 學校的前任校長 **2 your former self** what you were like before you were changed by age, illness, trouble etc 以前的你〔指與現在經歷衰老、疾病、苦難等後對比〕: *She seems more like her former self.* 她似乎回到了以前的她的樣子。| **be a shadow of your former self** (=be much less confident, healthy, energetic etc than you used to be) 不像以前那樣自信, 遠不如以前自信[健康、有活力]

former² *n* **1 the former** *formal* the first of two people or things that you have just mentioned【正式】前者: *Of the two possibilities, the former seems more likely.* 在這兩種可能性中, 前者似乎更有可能。—opposite 反義詞 LATTER¹ **2 first/fourth/sixth former** *BrE* used in some schools to show which class a student is in, according to how many years they have been in school【英】一年級/四年級/六年級的學生

for·mer·ly /ˈfɔrmɚlɪ; ˈfɔːməli/ *adv* in earlier times 以前, 從前: *Peru was formerly ruled by the Spanish.* 祕魯從前受西班牙統治。—compare 比較 LATTERLY

for·mi·ca /fɔrˈmaɪkə; fɔːˈmaɪkə/ *n* [U] *trademark* strong plastic made in thin sheets, used especially for covering the surfaces of tables【商標】(福米加) 塑料貼面〔尤用於桌子表面〕: *formica tabletops* (福米加) 桌子塑料貼面

for·mic ac·id /ˌfɔrmɪk ˈæsɪd; ˌfɔːmɪk ˈæsɪ̣d/ *n* [U] an acid used especially for colouring cloth and in treating leather〔尤指用於染布或處理皮革的〕甲酸, 蟻酸

for·mi·da·ble /ˈfɔrmɪdəbl; ˈfɔːmɪ̣dəbəl/ *adj* **1** a formidable person etc is one that you feel respect for because they are very powerful, or impressive 令人敬畏的; 令人驚嘆的; 巨大的; 傑出的: *With her management skills and his marketing expertise, they make a formidable combination.* 她的管理能力和他的銷售專長使他們構成一個強大有力的組合。| *The Pentium machines have formidable processing power.* 奔騰機具有驚人的處理能力。**2** difficult to deal with and needing a lot of effort or skill 難對付的: *The rally is a formidable test of both car and driver.* 這次汽車會賽對車子和駕駛員來說都是一次艱巨的考驗。| **formidable problem/task** *the formidable task of creating a new filing system* 建立新

的文件歸檔系統的艱難任務 —**formidably** *adv*

form·less /ˋfɔrmlɪs; ˈfɔːmləs/ *adj* **1** without a definite shape 無形狀的, 無定形的: *Figures emerged out of the mist, dull and formless at first.* 人影從薄霧中出現, 開始時模糊不清而且無明確形狀。**2** ideas or feelings that are formless are not clear or definite〔思想或感情〕不清楚的, 不明確的; 雜亂的: *A formless melancholy overcame her.* 一種說不清的憂鬱壓倒了她。—**formlessly** *adv* —**formlessness** *n* [U]

form let·ter /ˋ· ˌ··/ *n* [C] a standard letter that is sent to a number of people〔寄給許多人的〕通函, 印刷函件, 打印信件

form teach·er /ˋ· ˌ··/ *n* [C] *BrE* the teacher who is responsible for all the students in the same class at a school【英】年級主任, 班主任

3 **for·mu·la** /ˋfɔrmjələ; ˈfɔːmjʊ̈lə/ *n plural* **formulas** *or* **formulae** /-li; -liː/ **1** [singular] a method or set of principles that you use to solve a problem or to make sure that something is successful 準則; 方案: *We're still searching for a peace formula.* 我們仍在尋找和平方案。| **[+for]** *The two sides worked out an acceptable formula for settling the strike.* 雙方制定了一套解決這場罷工的可接受的方案。| **magic formula** (=a method that is certain to be successful) 成功的魔法, 祕方妙法 *There's no magic formula for a happy marriage.* 幸福的婚姻沒有甚麼妙法。**2** [C] a series of numbers or letters that represent a mathematical or scientific rule 公式; 方程式; 分子式: *the formula for calculating distance* 計算距離的公式 **3** [C] a list of the substances used to make a medicine, FUEL[1] (1), drink etc, showing the amounts of each substance that should be used〔藥品、燃料、飲料等的〕配方: *Coca-Cola's patented formula* 可口可樂的專利配方 **4 Formula One/Two/Three etc** a type of car racing, in which the different types are based on the size of the cars' engines〔賽車的〕一級/二級/三級方程式等: *a Formula One car* 一級方程式賽車 **5** [C, U] *AmE* a type of liquid food for babies that is similar to milk【美】餵養嬰兒的配方奶 **6** [C] a fixed and familiar series of words that seems meaningless or insincere 俗套話; 慣用語句: *a speech full of the usual formulas and cliches* 充滿常用的套話和陳詞濫調的演說

for·mu·la·ic /ˌfɔrmjəˋleɪk; ˌfɔːmjʊ̈ˈleɪ-ɪk◂/ *adj formal* containing or made from ideas or expressions that have been used many times before and are therefore not very imaginative【正式】公式化的; 充滿俗套話的; 沒有獨創的: *formulaic verse* 公式化的詩節

for·mu·late /ˋfɔrmjəˌlet; ˈfɔːmjʊ̈leɪt/ *v* [T] **1 formulate a plan/policy/program etc** to develop a plan or proposal, and decide all the details of how it will be done 制定計劃/政策/方案等: *The government is formulating a new education policy.* 政府正制定新的教育政策。**2** to choose particular words to express your thoughts or feelings 確切地表達[闡述]: *He paused, trying to formulate an answer that would satisfy them.* 他停了一下, 力求作出一個令他們滿意的回答。—**formulation** /ˌfɔrmjəˋleʃən; ˌfɔːmjʊ̈ˈleɪʃən/ *n* [C,U]

for·ni·cate /ˋfɔrnəˌket; ˈfɔːnɪ̈keɪt/ *v* [I] a word meaning to have sex with someone who you are not married to, used to show strong disapproval 通姦, 私通 —**fornication** /ˌfɔrnɪˋkeʃən; ˌfɔːnɪ̈ˈkeɪʃən/ *n* [U]

for·sake /fɚˋsek; fəˈseɪk/ *v past tense* **forsook** /-ˋsʊk; -ˈsʊk/ *past participle* **forsaken** /-ˋsekən; -ˈseɪkən/ [T] *literary*【文】**1** to leave someone, especially when you should stay because they need you 遺棄, 拋棄, 棄之於不顧: *God will never forsake you.* 上帝永遠不會遺棄你的。**2** to stop doing or leave something that you have or enjoy 放棄, 摒棄; 戒掉: *We had to forsake the comfort of our hotel room and spend the night waiting at the airport.* 我們只好放棄旅館客房的舒適享受, 在機場等一晚。—see also 另見 GODFORSAKEN

for·sooth /fɚˋsuθ; fəˈsuːθ/ *adv old use* certainly【舊】確實地, 無疑地

for·swear /fɔrˋswɛr; fɔːˈsweə/ *v past tense* **forswore** /-ˋswɔr; -ˈswɔː/ *past participle* **forsworn** /-ˋswɔrn; -ˈswɔːn/ [T] *literary* to promise that you will not do or possess something【文】斷然放棄; 發誓放棄: *a monk forswearing all possessions* 發誓放棄所有私產的僧侶

for·sy·thi·a /fɚˋsɪθɪə; fɔːˈsaɪθiə/ *n* [C,U] a bush that is covered with bright yellow flowers in the spring 連翹〔一種在春天開鮮黃色花的灌木〕

fort /fɔrt; fɔːt/ *n* [C] a strong building or group of buildings used by soldiers or an army for defending an important place 堡壘, 城堡; 要塞 —see also 另見 **hold the fort** (HOLD[1] (19))

for·te[1] /fɔrt; ˈfɔːteɪ/ *n* **1 be your/their forte** to be something that you do well or are skilled at 是你/他們的專長: *Cooking has never been her forte.* 烹飪從來就不是她的強項。**2** [C] a note or line of music played or sung loudly 強音; 用強音演奏[唱出]的一段樂曲

for·te[2] /ˋfɔrte; ˈfɔːteɪ/ *adj, adv* music played or sung loudly【音樂】用強音的[地]; 響的[地]

forth /fɔrθ; fɔːθ/ *adv literary*【文】**1 and so forth** used to represent other things of the type you have already mentioned without actually naming them 等等: *She started telling me about her bad back, her migraines, and so forth.* 她開始告訴我她背痛、偏頭痛等等。**2 from that day/time/moment forth** *literary* beginning on that day or at that time【文】從那天起/從那個時候起/從那時起: *From that moment forth they became close friends.* 從那時起, 他們就成了親密的朋友。**3** [only after verb 僅用於動詞後] *literary* going out from a place or point, and moving forwards or outwards【文】向外, 往外: *factory chimneys that belched forth thick smoke* 噴吐着濃煙的工廠煙囱 **4** *literary* towards a place that is in front of you; forwards【文】向前: *She stretched forth her hand.* 她把手向前伸出。—see also 另見 **back and forth** (BACK[1] (11)), **hold forth** (HOLD[1]), **put forth** (PUT)

forth·com·ing /ˌfɔrθˋkʌmɪŋ; ˌfɔːθˈkʌmɪŋ◂/ *adj* **1** a forthcoming event, meeting etc is one that has been planned to happen soon 即將到來的; 即將出現的: *a potential vote-winner in the forthcoming election* 在即將舉行的選舉中很可能獲勝的人 **2 be forthcoming** to be willing to give information about something 樂於提供信息的: **[+about]** *Jarvis was never very forthcoming about his love life.* 賈維斯一直就很不願意透露他的愛情生活。**3** [not before noun 不用於名詞前] given or offered when needed 可得到的: *When no reply was forthcoming, she wrote again.* 她沒有得到答覆時, 就再寫了一封信去問。

forth·right /ˋfɔrθˌraɪt; ˈfɔːθraɪt/ *adj* saying honestly what you think, in a way that sometimes seems rude 直率的, 直截了當的: *She answered in her usual forthright manner.* 她和往常一樣, 直截了當地作出回答。

forth·with /fɔrθˋwɪθ; fɔːθˈwɪð/ *adv formal* immediately【正式】立即, 馬上: *These instructions must be carried out forthwith.* 這些指示必須立即執行。

for·ti·eth /ˋfɔrtɪɪθ; ˈfɔːtiəθ/ *n* [C] one of forty equal parts of something 第四十(個); 四十分之一

for·ti·fi·ca·tion /ˌfɔrtəfəˋkeʃən; ˌfɔːtɪ̈fɪ̈ˈkeɪʃən/ *n* [U] the process of making something stronger 強化, 加強

for·ti·fi·ca·tions /ˌfɔrtəfəˋkeʃənz; ˌfɔːtɪ̈fɪ̈ˈkeɪʃənz/ *n* [plural] towers, walls etc built around a place in order to protect it or defend it 防禦工事〈如堡壘、城垣等〉: *The army destroyed most of the town's fortifications.* 軍隊摧毀了該城的大部分防禦工事。

fortified wine /ˌ··· ˈ·/ *n* [C,U] wine such as SHERRY or PORT (3) that has strong alcohol added 加度葡萄酒

for·ti·fy /ˋfɔrtəˌfaɪ; ˈfɔːtɪ̈faɪ/ *v* [T] **1** to build towers, walls etc around an area or city in order to defend it 築防禦工事於; 築堡於: *a fortified city* 設防的城市 **2** to encourage an attitude or feeling and make it stronger 激勵, 鼓舞; 加強: *Recent successes had fortified the team spirit.* 最近獲得的成功鼓舞了這個隊的士氣。**3** [often passive 常用被動態] to make someone feel physically or mentally stronger 增強體質; 振奮精神: **fortify yourself** *We had some coffee to fortify ourselves for the journey.* 我們為了旅行，喝了些咖啡來提神。**4** [usually passive 一般用被動態] to make food or drinks more healthy by adding VITAMINS to them〔加維生素〕強化〔食品或飲料〕; 提高〔食品或飲料的〕營養價值: *fortified milk products* 強化奶產品

for·tis·si·mo /fɔrˋtɪsəˏmo; fɔːˈtɪsɪ̈məʊ/ *adj, adv music* played or sung very loudly【音樂】非常響的[地]; 極強的[地]; 用極強音的[地] —**fortissimo** *adj* —compare 比較 FORTE²

for·ti·tude /ˋfɔrtəˏtud; ˈfɔːtɪ̈tjuːd/ *n* [U] courage shown when you are in great pain or experiencing a lot of trouble 毅力, 堅忍, 剛毅, 毅勇: *She bore her illness with great fortitude.* 她以堅韌不拔的精神忍受着病痛。

3 **fort·night** /ˋfɔrtnaɪt; ˈfɔːtnaɪt/ *n* [C usually singular 一般用單數] *BrE* two weeks【英】兩星期, 十四天: *I'm going away for a fortnight's holiday.* 我要到外地度假兩週。

fort·night·ly /ˋfɔrtˏnaɪtlɪ; ˈfɔːtnaɪtli/ *adj, adv BrE* happening every fortnight or once a fortnight【英】兩星期一次的[地], 每兩週的[地]: *We used to dread my uncle's fortnightly visits.* 我們過去都很怕叔叔每兩週一次的到訪。

for·tress /ˋfɔrtrɪs; ˈfɔːtrɪ̈s/ *n* [C] a large, strong building used for defending an important place 堡壘; 要塞

for·tu·i·tous /fɔrˋtuətəs; fɔːˈtjuːɪ̈təs/ *adj formal* happening by chance, especially in a way that has a good result【正式】偶然（發生）的: *a fortuitous meeting* 邂逅, 幸遇 —**fortuitously** *adv*

3 **for·tu·nate** /ˋfɔrtʃənɪt; ˈfɔːtʃənət/ *adj* **1** someone who is fortunate has something good happen to them, or is in a good situation; lucky 幸運的: *Think of others less fortunate than yourselves.* 想想其他不如你那麼幸運的人。| **fortunate to do sth** *He was fortunate enough to escape unharmed.* 他真是幸運, 逃了出來, 沒有受傷。| **fortunate that** *You're fortunate that you've still got a job.* 你真幸運, 總算仍然有一份工作。| **fortunate in having** *I was fortunate in having such supportive parents.* 我有這樣支持我的父母, 真幸運。**2** a fortunate event is one in which something good happens by chance, especially when this saves you from trouble or danger 巧合的, 偶然發生的; 僥倖的: *By a fortunate coincidence, a passer-by heard her cries for help.* 真巧, 一位過路的人聽到她求助的呼叫。

for·tu·nate·ly /ˋfɔrtʃənɪtlɪ; ˈfɔːtʃənətli/ *adv* [sentence adverb 句子副詞] happening because of good luck 幸運地; 幸虧: *Fortunately the fire was discovered soon after it started.* 幸虧火剛着了不久就被發現了。

3 **for·tune** /ˋfɔrtʃən; ˈfɔːtʃən/ *n*

3 **1 ►MONEY 錢◄** [C] a very large amount of money 大筆的錢, 巨款: *He inherited his fortune from his father.* 他從父親那裡繼承了一大筆財產。| **cost/spend/be worth a fortune** *They must have spent a fortune on that house.* 他們買那棟房子肯定花了一大筆錢。| **a small fortune** (=a lot of money) 一大筆錢 *She won a small fortune on the horses.* 她在賽馬賭博中贏了一大筆錢。| **make a/your fortune** (=make a lot of money in business) 發財 *The guy who invented Post-It notes must have made a fortune by now.* 發明報事貼便條的那個人現在肯定已發財了。

2 ►CHANCE 機遇◄ [U] chance, and the good or bad influence that it has on your life 運氣; 機遇: *I felt it was useless to struggle against fortune.* 我覺得與運氣抗爭是無用的。| **ill-fortune** (=bad luck) 厄運, 壞運氣 *We were stoical, and did not complain of ill-fortune.* 我們處變不憂, 沒有怪運氣不好。| **have the good fortune to do sth** *I had the good fortune to be invited to stay in Rome.* 我運氣好, 獲邀請去羅馬小住。

3 ►WHAT HAPPENS TO YOU 發生在你身上的事◄ [C usually plural 一般用複數] the good or bad things that happen in life 時運; 命運: *This defeat marked a change in the team's fortunes.* 這次失敗使該隊的運氣發生轉變。| **the fortunes of war** (=things that can happen to people during a war) 戰爭中的命運

4 tell sb's fortune to tell someone what will happen to them in the future by looking at their hands, using cards etc 給某人算命: *She paid £5 to have her fortune told.* 她花了五英鎊找人算命。

5 fortune smiles on sth/sb *literary* used to say that someone or something is lucky【文】某物／某人的運氣很好 —see also 另見 SOLDIER OF FORTUNE, **fame and fortune** (FAME), **give hostages to fortune** (HOSTAGE (2)), **seek your fortune** (SEEK (4))

fortune cook·ie /ˈ·· ˏ··/ *n* [C] a Chinese BISCUIT that contains a piece of paper that says what will happen to you in the future 籤餅, 幸運曲奇〔據稱源於中國的一種小餅, 內有紙條, 寫着你的運氣〕

fortune hunt·er /ˈ·· ˏ··/ *n* [C] someone who wants to marry another person only to get their money 企圖通過結婚發財的人

fortune-tell·er /ˈ·· ˏ··/ *n* [C] someone who uses magical methods to tell people what will happen to them in the future 給人算命的人, 算命者 —**fortune telling** *n* [U]

for·ty /ˋfɔrtɪ; ˈfɔːti/ *number* 40 四十

forty-five /ˏ·· ˈ·◂/ *n* [C] *informal*【非正式】**1** also 又作 **45** a small record with one song on each side〔每面一首歌的〕每分鐘 45 轉的密紋唱片 **2** also 又作 **.45, Colt 45** *trademark* a small gun【商標】.45 口徑的（左輪）手槍〔一種槍管為 0.45 英寸口徑的手槍〕

forty winks /ˏ·· ˈ·/ *n* [U] *informal* a very short sleep【非正式】小睡, 打盹: *Mr. Carey lay down on the sofa for forty winks.* 凱里先生躺在沙發上打個盹。

for·um /ˋfɔrəm; ˈfɔːrəm/ *n* [C] **1** an organization, meeting, TV programme etc where people have a chance to publicly discuss an important subject〔人們能公開討論重要話題的〕論壇; 討論會; 電視專題討論節目: **[+for]** *The committee provided a useful forum for exposing the extent of discrimination.* 委員會提供了一個揭露歧視程度的有用的論壇。| **[+on]** *an international forum on the environment* 國際環境論壇 **2** a large outdoor public place in ancient Rome used for business and discussion〔古羅馬城市中用於商業和討論的〕廣場; 市場

F

for·ward¹ /ˋfɔrwəd; ˈfɔːwəd/ *adv* **1** also 又作 **forwards** 1
/-wədz; -wədz/ —towards a place or position that is in front of you 向前: *He leaned forward slightly to try and hear what they were saying.* 他稍微向前傾身, 想聽聽他們在說甚麼。| *The crowd surged forwards.* 人羣向前湧去。**2** towards greater progress, improvement, or development 大有進展[改善, 發展]地: *The building of the new sports stadium is going forward.* 新體育場的工程正在進行中。| *trying to find a way forward in the peace talks* 企圖找出一種推動和平談判的辦法 **3** towards the future in a way that is hopeful 向將來: *This is just the moment at which companies should be looking forward.* 這正是各家公司應該展望未來的時候。**4 from that day/time/moment etc forward** beginning on that day or at that time 從那天／那時／那刻等起: *They never met again from that day forward.* 他們從那天以後就再也沒見面了。**5** in or towards the front part of a ship 在船頭; 朝船頭 —compare 比較 AFT, BACKWARDS —see also 另見 FAST FORWARD, **look forward to** (LOOK¹), **backwards and forwards** (BACKWARDS (4))

forward² *adj* **1** [only before noun 僅用於名詞前] di- 2
rected towards a place or position that is in front of you 3
向前的: *Army roadblocks prevented any further forward movement.* 軍隊設下的路障阻止人們繼續前進。**2 forward planning/thinking** the act of making plans so that you will be prepared for what will happen in the future 預先計劃／提前考慮: *Forward planning is essential if you want the venture to succeed.* 如果想讓這個風險項目獲得成功, 預先計劃是必不可少的。**3 no further forward** not having made much progress, especially compared to what was expected 無進展: *We've been trying to find a solution for weeks but we're no further*

forward. 我們幾週來一直在設法尋覓解決辦法，但沒有甚麼進展。**4** [only before noun 僅用於名詞前] situated at or near the front of a ship, vehicle, building etc 在前部的；位於前面的：*We sat in one of the forward sections of the train.* 我們坐在火車前部的一節車廂裡。**5** *formal* too confident and friendly in dealing with people you do not know very well【正式】〔與不大熟悉的人交往時〕魯莽的；冒失的；過分主動的：*She was careful in what she said, having no wish to sound forward.* 她說話十分小心，不想讓人聽上去覺得她過分主動。—compare 比較 BACKWARD

forward³ *v* **1** [T] to send letters, goods etc to someone, especially when they have moved to a new address 寄發；轉寄；轉交；轉運：*We will forward the goods on receipt of your cheque.* 我們一收到貴方的支票便發貨。| **forward sth to sb** *Can you forward my mail to me, please?* 請把我的郵件轉寄給我，好嗎？**2** [T] *formal* to help something to develop so that it becomes successful【正式】助長，促進：*I see this new responsibility as a good chance to forward my career.* 我把這項新職責看作是促進自己事業發展的好機會。

forward⁴ *n* [C] an attacking player on a team in sports such as football, BASKETBALL etc〔足球、籃球等運動的〕前鋒

forwarding ad·dress /'··· ,·/ *n* [C] an address that you leave for someone when you move to a new place so that they can send your mail to you 轉遞地址

forward-look·ing /'·· ,··/ *adj* planning for and thinking about the future in a positive way, especially by being willing to use modern methods or ideas〔尤指樂意用現代方法或思想〕向前看的；有遠見的：*forward-looking companies able to spot the trends* 能認準潮流的有遠見的公司

forward mar·ket /'·· ,··/ *n* [C] *technical* a market on the STOCK EXCHANGE that buys and sells products at an agreed price on a fixed date in the future; FUTURES MARKET【術語】期貨市場

for·ward·ness /ˈfɔrwɚdnɪs; ˈfɔːwədnɪ̵s/ *n* [U] behaviour that is too confident or friendly 魯莽；冒失；過分主動

forward roll /,·· '·/ *n* [C] a movement in GYMNASTICS in which you roll over forwards onto your back so that your feet go over your head〔體操的〕前滾翻

for·wards /ˈfɔrwɚdz; ˈfɔːwədz/ *adv* FORWARD 向前

fos·sil /ˈfɑsl̩; ˈfɒsəl/ *n* [C] **1** an animal or plant that died many thousands of years ago and that has been preserved in rock 化石：*fossils of early reptiles* 早期爬行動物的化石 —see also 另見 LIVING FOSSIL **2** *informal* an insulting word for an old person【非正式】老頑固〔具侮辱性〕

fossil fu·el /'·· ,··/ *n* [C,U] a FUEL¹ (1) such as coal or oil that is produced by the very gradual decaying of animals or plants over millions of years 礦物燃料〈如煤、石油等〉：*Environmentalists would like to see fossil fuels replaced by renewable energy sources.* 環境保護主義者很希望看到可再生能源取代礦物燃料。

fos·sil·ize also 又作 **-ise** *BrE*【英】/ˈfɑsl̩,aɪz; ˈfɒsɪ̵laɪz/ *v* **1 be fossilized** people, ideas, systems etc that are fossilized are very old-fashioned and never change or develop〔人、思想、體制等〕石化；僵化；陳舊：*The valley's government was a fossilized specimen of feudal rule.* 這個山谷裡的政府是封建統治的化石標本。**2** [I,T] to become or form a FOSSIL by being preserved in rock 變成化石，使成化石 —**fossilization** /,fɑsl̩əˈzeʃən; ,fɒsɪ̵laɪˈzeɪʃən/ *n* [U]

foster- /fɔstɚ; fɒstə/ *prefix* giving or receiving parental care although not of the same family 收養的：*a foster-mother* 養母 | *a foster-son* 養子 | *a foster-home* 寄養家庭 | *Danny is my foster-brother.* (=we have different parents, but he is being brought up with me in my family) 丹尼是我的義兄弟。

fos·ter¹ /ˈfɔstɚ; ˈfɒstə/ *v* **1** [I,T] to take someone else's child into your family for a period of time but without becoming their legal parent〔在一定的時間內〕撫育，收養〔別人的孩子〕：*They fostered a little Romanian boy for a few months.* 他們收養一個羅馬尼亞男孩已有幾個月。—compare 比較 ADOPT (1) **2** [T] to help a skill, feeling, idea etc develop over a period of time 促進，培養，助長：*These sessions are designed to foster better working relationships.* 這些會議旨在培養更好的工作關係。

foster² *adj* **1 foster mother/father/parents** the people who foster a child 養母/養父/養父母：*It is sometimes difficult to find suitable foster parents.* 有時很難找到合適的養父母。**2 foster child** a child who is fostered 收養的孩子 **3 foster home** a private home where a child is fostered 寄養家庭

fought /fɔt; fɔːt/ the past tense and past participle of FIGHT¹

foul¹ /faul; faʊl/ *adj*

1 ►SMELL/TASTE 氣味/味道◄ a foul smell or taste is very unpleasant 難聞的，惡臭的；難吃的：*I gulped down some water to take the foul taste out of my mouth.* 我大口地喝點水來清除嘴裡的臭味。| **foul-tasting/foul-smelling** *The bags of garbage had been piled up in a foul-smelling heap.* 這一袋袋垃圾已堆成臭不可聞的一堆。

2 in a foul mood/temper *especially BrE* in a very bad mood and likely to get angry【尤英】情緒不好/發脾氣：*He's in a foul mood today, isn't he?* 他今天情緒不好，是不是？

3 ►UNPLEASANT 令人難受的◄ *especially BrE* very unpleasant【尤英】令人不快的；糟透的：*I've had an absolutely foul day.* 我今天過得很不愉快。

4 ►AIR/WATER 空氣/水◄ very dirty 骯髒的，污濁的：*The water in the harbour was foul with oil.* 海港的水上面浮着油，很髒。

5 foul language rude and offensive words 粗話，罵人話，髒話：*I've never heard such foul language in all my life!* 我這輩子還從來沒聽到過這樣的粗言穢語！

6 ►WEATHER 天氣◄ *especially BrE* if the weather is foul, it is stormy and windy, with a lot of rain or snow【尤英】惡劣的；有風雨的；有風雪的

7 ►EVIL 邪惡的◄ *especially literary* evil or cruel【尤文】罪惡的，邪惡的；殘酷的：*foul deeds* 殘酷的行為，惡行 —see also 另見 **by fair means or foul** (FAIR¹ (13)), **fall foul of** (FALL¹ (28)) —**foully** *adv* —**foulness** *n* [U]

foul² *v* **1** [I,T] **a)** if a player fouls in a game of sport, or fouls another player, they do something that is not allowed by the rules（對…）犯規，違例：*An Everton player had been fouled in the penalty area.* 有人在罰球區對一位埃弗頓隊的球員犯規。**b)** to hit a ball outside the limit of the playing area in BASEBALL〔棒球中〕擊〔球〕出界，打出壞球：*On average, most batters foul at least one ball in each at bat.* 大多數擊球員上場擊球時，平均每個人至少擊球出界一次。**2** *formal* to make something very dirty, especially with waste【正式】弄髒，玷污；污染：*A thick column of black smoke rose from the wreck, fouling the air.* 一股黑色的濃煙從失事的船隻升起，污染了空氣。**3** also 又作 **foul up** [I,T] if a rope, chain, or part of a machine fouls or if something fouls it, it twists or cannot move properly〔繩、鏈或機器部件〕纏住，纏結：*Check that nothing can foul the moving parts.* 檢查一下，不要讓任何東西纏住運轉的部件。

foul up *phr v informal*【非正式】**1** [T **foul** sth ↔ **up**] to spoil something 破壞，搞糟，弄亂：*The weather really fouled up our vacation plans.* 惡劣的天氣破壞了我們的度假計劃。**2** [I,T **foul** sth ↔ **up**] to do something wrong or spoil something by making mistakes〔因錯誤而〕搞亂，破壞：*Glen completely fouled up the seating arrangements.* 格倫把座位安排完全搞亂了。

foul³ *n* [C] an action in a sport that is against the rules〔體育比賽中的〕犯規（動作），違例（行動）：*That was a foul – he touched the ball with his hand!* 那是犯規——他用手觸了球！

foul line /'· ·/ *n* [C] a line marked on a sports field outside of which a ball cannot be legally played〔球場上

的〕邊線, 限制線

foul-mouthed /ˌ· ˈ·◂/ *adj* swearing too much 滿口髒話的, 惡語傷人的: *a foul-mouthed little boy* 一個口出惡言的小男孩 —**foul mouth** /ˈ· ·/ *n* [C]

foul play /ˌ· ˈ·/ *n* [U] **1** if the police think someone's death was caused by foul play, they think that person was murdered 謀殺: *The police said they had no reason to suspect foul play.* 警方說他們沒有理由懷疑是謀殺。 **2** actions that are dishonest or unfair 奸詐的行為, 犯罪行徑: *He will use any amount of foul play to get what he wants.* 他會使用各種奸詐的手段來得到自己想要的東西。

foul-up /ˈ· ·/ *n* [C] *informal* a problem caused by a stupid or careless mistake【非正式】〔因笨拙或疏忽引起的〕混亂, 一團糟: *There was a foul-up on my charter flight home and several people didn't get seats.* 我回家的包機上出了錯, 有幾個人沒有座位。

found¹ /faʊnd; faʊnd/ the past tense and past participle of FIND¹

3 **found²** *v* [T] **1** to start something such as an organization, company, or city 創立〔組織或公司〕; 創建〔城市〕: *Founded in 1935 in Ohio, Alcoholics Anonymous is now a world-wide organization.* 嗜酒者互誡協會於1935年在俄亥俄州創立, 現在是一個世界性的組織。 **2** to start something such as a school or hospital, by providing money for it〔提供資金〕創辦〔學校或醫院〕: *Eton College was founded by Henry VI in 1440.* 伊頓公學是1440年由亨利六世創辦的。 **3 be founded on a)** to be the main idea, belief etc that something else develops from 建立在…基礎上: *Racism is not founded on rational thought, but on fear.* 種族主義的基礎不是理性的思維而是恐懼。 **b)** to be the solid layer of cement, stones etc that a building is built on 成為〔建築物〕的基礎, 建基: *The castle is founded on solid rock.* 這座城堡建基在堅固的岩石上。 **4** *technical* to melt metal and pour it into a MOULD (=a hollow shape), to make things such as tools, parts for machines etc【術語】鑄造 —**founding** *n* [U]: *the founding of the University of Chicago* 芝加哥大學的創立 —see also 另見 FOUNDATION, WELL-FOUNDED

2 **foun·da·tion** /faʊnˋdeʃən; faʊnˈdeɪʃən/ *n*

1 ►BUILDING 建築物◄ [C] *AmE*【美】also 又作 **foundations** [plural] *especially BrE* the solid layer of cement, bricks, stones etc that is under a building to support it【尤英】地基, 基礎: **lay the foundations** (=build them) 打地基 *It should take us about three weeks to lay the foundations.* 我們需要大約三星期的時間打地基。

2 ►BASIC IDEA 基本的思想◄ [C] a basic idea, principle, situation etc that something develops from 基礎; 根據; 基本原理: **[+of]** *All theories should be built on a foundation of factual knowledge.* 一切理論應當建立在事實知識的基礎上。| **a solid/firm foundation** *He hoped that this job would serve as a firm foundation for his chosen career.* 他希望這份工作會成為他所選擇的職業的有力根基。

3 ►ORGANIZATION 組織◄ [C] an organization that gives money to a CHARITY (2), for research etc 基金會: *the Carnegie Foundation* 卡內基基金會

4 ►ESTABLISHMENT 建立◄ [C,U] the establishment of an organization, business, school etc 建立; 創辦: *Since its foundation in 1835, this school has served the community.* 這所學校自1835年創立以來, 就為這個社區服務。

5 lay/provide the foundation(s) for to provide the conditions that will make it possible for something to be successful 為…打下基礎: *Good planning after the war laid the foundations for the nation's economic miracle.* 戰後良好的計劃為這個國家的經濟奇蹟奠定了基礎。

6 be without foundation/have no foundation if a statement, idea etc is without foundation, there is no proof that it is true 沒有根據: *Your accusations are completely without foundation.* 你的指控完全沒有根據。

7 ►SKIN 皮膚◄ [U] a cream the same colour as your skin that you put on before the rest of your MAKE-UP〔與膚色相同的、化妝時打底用的〕粉底霜 —see picture at 參見 MAKE-UP 圖

8 shake/rock sth to its foundations to completely change the way something is done or the way people think by having a completely new idea 從根本上動搖某物; 動搖…的基礎: *Darwin's theory rocked the scientific establishment to its foundations.* 達爾文的理論從根本上動搖了科學界。

foundation course /ˈ·ˈ·· ˌ·/ *n* [C] *BrE* a course of study including several different subjects, taught in the first year at some universities in Britain【英】〔英國一些大學一年級的〕基礎課程

foundation gar·ment /·ˈ·· ˌ··/ *n* [C] a piece of clothing worn in the past by women under their clothes〔舊時婦女穿的〕緊身胸衣

foundation stone /·ˈ·· ·/ *n* [C] **1** a large stone placed at the bottom of an important building to show when it was built, usually as part of a ceremony〔建築物奠基典禮時放置的〕基石, 奠基石 **2** the facts, ideas, principles etc that form the base from which something else develops or begins 基礎; 根基; 基石: *Greek and Latin were once viewed as the foundation stones of a good education.* 希臘語和拉丁語曾經被看作是良好教育的基礎。

found·er¹ /ˈfaʊndɚ; ˈfaʊndə/ *n* [C] someone who establishes a business, organization, school etc〔公司、組織、學校等的〕創立者, 創辦人; 始創者

founder² *v* [I] *formal*【正式】**1** to fail after a period of time because something has gone wrong or a new problem has caused difficulties〔因出現問題於一段時間後〕失敗, 崩潰, 垮掉: *Their marriage began to founder soon after the honeymoon.* 他們的婚姻在蜜月之後不久便結束了。 **2** if a ship or boat founders, it fills with water and sinks〔船〕沉沒

founder mem·ber /ˌ·· ˈ··/ *n* [C] *BrE* someone who has helped to establish a new organization, club etc and is one of its first members【英】〔組織、俱樂部等的〕創立者之一, 創辦人之一; CHARTER MEMBER *AmE*【美】

founding fa·ther /ˌ·· ˈ··/ *n* [C often plural 常用複數] **1** someone who begins something such as a new way of thinking, or a new organization〔新思想或新組織的〕創立人, 開創者: *L. Threlkeld, one of the founding fathers of anthropology in Australia* 澳大利亞人類學創始人之一的斯雷爾凱爾德 **2 Founding Fathers** the group of men who wrote the American Constitution and Bill of Rights and started the US as a country〔創立美國並起草美國憲法和《人權法案》的〕制憲元勳, 開國元勳

found·ling /ˋfaʊndlɪŋ; ˈfaʊndlɪŋ/ *n* [C] *old use* a baby who has been left by its parents, and is found and looked after by other people【舊】棄嬰, 棄兒

foun·dry /ˋfaʊndrɪ; ˈfaʊndri/ *n* [C] a place where metals are melted and poured into MOULDS (=hollow shapes) to make parts for machines, tools etc 鑄造車間; 鑄造廠: *an iron foundry* 鑄鐵廠

fount /faʊnt; faʊnt/ *n* [C] **1 the fount of all knowledge/wisdom etc** *literary or humorous* the place, person, idea etc that all knowledge, WISDOM etc comes from; SOURCE¹ (1)【文或幽默】〔一切知識、智慧的〕源頭; 源泉 **2** *BrE technical* a complete set of letters of one kind and size used to print books, newspapers etc【英, 術語】〔相同字型和大小的〕一副鉛字; FONT (2) *AmE*【美】

foun·tain /ˋfaʊntn̩; ˈfaʊntɪn/ *n* [C] **1** a structure from which water is sent up into the air, which is often in a small pool (人造) 噴泉; 噴水池 **2** a flow of liquid, or of something bright and colourful that goes straight up into the air 噴水;〔明亮豔麗的〕噴出物: **[+of]** *A fountain of sparks shot high into the night sky.* 一股火花射向高高的夜空。—see also 另見 DRINKING FOUNTAIN, SODA FOUNTAIN

foun·tain·head /ˋfaʊntn̩ˌhɛd; ˈfaʊntɪnhed/ *n* [singular+of] the origin of something; SOURCE¹ (1) 源頭

fountain pen /ˈ·· ·/ *n* [C] a pen that you fill with ink 自

來水筆, 鋼筆 —see picture at 參見 PEN[1] 圖

four /fɔr; fɔː/ *number* **1** 4 四 **2** four o'clock 四點鐘: *I'll meet you just after four, okay?* 我就四點鐘後見你, 好嗎? **3** a group of four people or things〔人或物〕四個一組: *The boxes were stacked in fours.* 那些箱子四個一組地堆放着。| **make up a four** (=complete a group of 4 people) 構成四人一組 *Will you make up a four for a game of cards?* 你願意為四人牌戲湊足一組嗎? —compare 比較 FOURSOME **4 on all fours** supporting your body with your hands and knees 雙手雙腳着地地, 趴着: *Billy was down on all fours on the ice.* 比利摔得趴在冰上。**5 from the four corners of the earth/world** from places or countries that are very far away from each other 從世界各地: *People gathered from the four corners of the earth for the ecology convention.* 人們從世界各地前來參加這次生態會議。**6 four on the floor** *AmE* if a car has four on the floor, it has four GEARS worked by a GEAR LEVER【美】〔汽車〕四擋 **7** a long narrow boat rowed in races by four people 四人賽艇 **8 a coach and four** a carriage pulled by four horses 四馬馬車 —see also 另見 **four ply** (PLY[2]), **be scattered to the four winds** (SCATTER (3)) —**fourth** *number*

four-eyes /ˈ· ·/ *n* [singular] a rude way of addressing someone who wears glasses 四眼仔, 四眼兒〔對戴眼鏡者的不禮貌稱呼〕—**four-eyed** *adj*

four-flush·er /ˈ· ˌ··/ *n* [C] *AmE informal* someone who cheats or tries to deceive people【美, 非正式】騙子

four-leaved clo·ver /ˌ· · ˈ··/ also 又作 **four-leaf clo·ver** *n* [C] a CLOVER plant that has four leaves instead of the usual three, and is considered to be lucky 四葉苜蓿, 四葉草, 幸運草

four-let·ter word /ˌ· ·· ˈ·/ *n* [C] a word that is considered very rude and offensive〔由四個字母構成的〕粗俗下流詞: *complaints about the use of four-letter words on TV* 對電視上使用粗俗下流詞的投訴

four-post·er /ˌ· ˈ··/ also 又作 **four-poster bed** /ˌ· ·· ˈ·/ *n* [C] a bed with four tall posts at the corners, a cover fixed at the top of the posts, and curtains around the sides 有四根帷柱的牀, 四柱大牀

four·some /ˈfɔrsəm; ˈfɔːsəm/ *n* [C] a group of four people, especially two men and two women, who are together for a social occasion〔尤指社交場合二男二女的〕四人一組; 兩對: **make up a foursome** (=complete a group of four people) 組成四人一組 *make up a foursome for bridge* 組成四人一組打橋牌

four-square[1] /ˌ· ˈ·◂/ *adj* **1** a building that is foursquare is solidly and plainly built, and square in shape〔建築物〕方形的; 穩固的 **2** *especially BrE* firm and determined【尤英】堅決的, 堅定不移的

four-square[2] *adv* firmly 穩固地; 堅決地: *standing four-square in the hallway* 屹立在走廊裡

four-star[1] /ˈ· ·/ *n* [U] *BrE* a type of petrol with LEAD[3] (1) in it【英】〔含鉛的〕四星汽油

four-star[2] *adj* of a high standard or quality 高級的, 極好的, 四星級的: *four-star restaurants* 四星級的餐館

four-star gen·e·ral /ˌ· · ˈ···/ *n* [C] *AmE* a GENERAL[2] of a high rank in the US army【美】四星上將

four-stroke /ˈ· ·/ *adj* a four-stroke engine works with two up and down movements of a PISTON〔發動機〕四衝程的

four·teen /ˌfɔrˈtin; ˌfɔːˈtiːn◂/ *number* 14 十四 —**four·teenth** *n* [C]

fourth /fɔrθ; fɔːθ/ *number* [C] one of four equal parts of something; QUARTER[1] (1) 第四(個); 四分之一

fourth di·men·sion /ˌ· ·ˈ··/ *n* **the fourth dimension** **a)** an expression meaning time, used especially by scientists and writers of SCIENCE FICTION〔尤為科學家和科幻小說作家所用的〕時間, 第四維 **b)** a type of experience that is outside normal human experience 在一般人類體驗範圍以外的東西: *ghosts, ESP, and other aspects of the fourth dimension* 鬼魂、超感知覺和其他一般人體驗範圍以外的東西

fourth es·tate /ˌ· ·ˈ·/ *n* [singular] newspapers, news magazines, radio, and television, the people who work for them, and the political influence that they have; the PRESS[1] 新聞界, 報界; 新聞媒體

fourth-gen·e·ra·tion lan·guage /ˌ· ···· ˈ··/ also 又作 **4GL** /ˌfɔr dʒi ˋɛl; ˌfɔː dʒiː ˈel/ *n* [singular] a computer language that is easy to use, and contains easier and faster ways of doing things〔電腦〕第四代語言

Fourth of Ju·ly /ˌ· · · ˈ·/ *n* [singular] a national holiday in the US that celebrates the beginning of the United States as a nation; INDEPENDENCE DAY 美國獨立紀念日〔每年的7月4日〕: *a Fourth of July picnic* 美國獨立紀念日的郊遊野餐

four-wheel drive /ˌ· · ˈ·/ also 又作 **4WD** /ˈfɔr dʌbḷju ˋdi; ˈfɔː dʌbəljuː ˈdiː/ *n* [C,U] a system in a car or other vehicle by which the power of the engine is given to all four wheels to make it easier to drive 四輪驅動系統 —**four-wheel drive** *adj*: *a four-wheel drive Toyota* 一輛四輪驅動的豐田汽車

fowl /faul; faʊl/ *n plural* **fowls** *or* **fowl** [C] **1** a bird, especially a chicken, that is kept for its meat and eggs 家禽〔尤指養來食用或生蛋的雞〕**2** *old use* a bird【舊】鳥, 飛禽 —see also 另見 **neither fish nor fowl** (FISH[1] (5))

fowl pest /ˈ· ·/ *n* [U] an illness that spreads quickly among chickens and some other birds 雞瘟; 家禽疫病

fox[1] /fɑks; fɒks/ *n* **1** [C] a wild animal like a dog with reddish-brown fur, a pointed face, and a thick tail 狐狸 **2** [C] *informal* someone who is clever and deceitful【非正式】狡猾的人: *He was a sly old fox.* 他是狡猾的老狐狸。**3** [U] the skin and fur of a fox, used to make clothes〔用於做衣服的〕狐皮 **4** [C] *AmE informal* someone who is sexually attractive【美, 非正式】性感的人: *She's such a fox!* 她真迷人!

fox[2] *v* [T] **1** *BrE informal* to be too difficult for someone to do or understand【英, 非正式】把…難住; 使猜不透: *Those childproof containers always fox me.* 那些對小孩安全的容器總是把我難住。**2** *especially BrE* to confuse or deceive someone in a clever way【尤英】使迷惑; 欺騙

fox·glove /ˈfɑksˌglʌv; ˈfɒksglʌv/ *n* [C] a tall plant with many bell-shaped flowers 毛地黃

fox·hole /ˈfɑksˌhol; ˈfɒkshəʊl/ *n* [C] **1** a hole in the ground that soldiers use to fire from or hide from the enemy 散兵坑 **2** a hole in the ground where a fox lives〔地下的〕狐狸穴

fox·hound /ˈfɑksˌhaund; ˈfɒkshaʊnd/ *n* [C] a dog with a very good sense of smell, trained to hunt and kill foxes 獵狐狗, 狐猩

fox·hunt·er /ˈfɑksˌhʌntɚ; ˈfɒkshʌntə/ *n* [C] a horse used in the sport of foxhunting 獵狐時用的馬

fox·hunt·ing /ˈfɑksˌhʌntɪŋ; ˈfɒkshʌntɪŋ/ *n* [U] the sport of hunting foxes (FOX[1] (1)) with dogs while riding on a horse〔騎馬攜犬的〕獵狐(活動) —**fox-hunting** *adj* —**foxhunt** *n* [C]

fox ter·ri·er /ˌ· ˈ···/ *n* [C] a small dog with short hair 狐㹴

fox·trot /ˈfɑksˌtrɑt; ˈfɒkstrɒt/ *n* [C] a type of formal dance with short, quick steps, or a piece of music for this dance 狐步舞(曲) —**foxtrot** *v* [I]

fox·y /ˈfɑksɪ; ˈfɒksi/ *adj* **1** like a FOX[1] (1) in appearance〔外表〕似狐的: *He was a tall, thin man with a rather foxy face.* 他又高又瘦, 相貌有點像狐狸。**2** clever and deceitful 狡猾的: *That foxy bastard. How did he get away with it?* 那個狡猾的雜種。他怎麼蒙混過關的? **3** *AmE informal* sexually attractive【美, 非正式】性感的, 妖豔的: *a foxy lady* 妖豔媚人的女子

foy·er /ˈfɔɪɚ; ˈfɔɪeɪ/ *n* [C] **1** a room or hall at the entrance to a public building; LOBBY[1] (1)〔公共建築物入口處的〕休息廳, 門廳: *We met in the theatre foyer.* 我們是在劇院的門廳遇到的。**2** *AmE* a small room or hall at the entrance to a private house or flat【美】〔私人房子或公寓入口處的〕前廳, 門廳, 玄關

F

FPO /ˌɛf pi ˋo; ˌef piː ˈəʊ/ an abbreviation of 縮寫='fleet post office' or 'field post office', used as part of the address of someone in the American navy or army 艦隊郵局; 戰地郵局〔用於美國海軍或陸軍地址〕

Fr 1 a written abbreviation of 縮寫= Father, used in front of the name of a priest 神父〔用於教士的姓名前〕 **2** a written abbreviation of 縮寫= FRANC (=a unit of French money) 法郎 **3** a written abbreviation of 縮寫= French 或 France

frac·as /ˋfrekəs; ˈfrækɑː/ *n plural* **fracas** *or* **fracases** *AmE* [C] a short, noisy fight involving several people 【美】喧鬧的打架; 毆鬥騷亂: *There was a fracas outside the courtroom as the suspect emerged.* 嫌疑人出現時, 法庭外發生一陣騷亂。

frac·tion /ˋfrækʃən; ˈfrækʃən/ *n* [C] **1** a very small amount of something 少量; 一點兒: [+of] *Gwen carefully opened the door a fraction.* 格温小心地把門稍微打開了一點兒。**2** a division or a part of a whole number in mathematics 〔數學上的〕分數; 小數: *¾ and ½ are fractions.* ¾ 和 ½ 都是分數。—see also 另見 COMMON FRACTION, IMPROPER FRACTION, PROPER FRACTION, VULGAR FRACTION

frac·tion·al /ˋfrækʃənl̩; ˈfrækʃənəl/ *adj* **1** very small in amount 很少的, 少量的: *She made a fractional alteration to the floral centerpiece.* 她對餐桌中央的插花做了一點小改動。**2** connected with fractions, in mathematics 〔數學上〕分數的; 小數的 —**fractionally** *adv*

frac·tious /ˋfrækʃəs; ˈfrækʃəs/ *adj* if a baby or child is fractious, they are angry or upset 〔嬰兒或兒童〕煩躁的; 易怒的; 發脾氣的: *Babies tend to be fractious when they are teething.* 嬰兒在長乳牙時往往很易煩躁。—**fractiousness** *n* [U]

frac·ture[1] /ˋfræktʃɚ; ˈfræktʃə/ *v* [I,T] if a bone or other hard substance fractures or is fractured, it breaks or cracks (使) 斷裂; (使) 折斷: *He fractured a leg in preseason training.* 他在賽季前的訓練中摔斷了腿。| *Under such pressure, rock will begin to fracture.* 岩石在這樣的壓力下會開始斷裂。| *a fractured rib* 折斷的肋骨

fracture[2] *n* [C] a crack or broken part in a bone or other hard substance 骨折; 裂縫, 裂痕: *Check all the parts to be sure there are no fractures in the metal.* 請檢查所有的部件, 以確保金屬沒有裂縫。

fra·gile /ˋfrædʒəl; ˈfrædʒaɪl/ *adj* **1** not strong, and therefore easily broken or damaged 脆弱的, 易碎的, 易損壞的: *The parcel was marked FRAGILE–HANDLE WITH CARE.* 包裹上標着"易碎 —— 小心輕放"的字樣。**2** easily damaged, spoilt, or destroyed 纖弱的; 脆弱的: *The country's fragile economy is threatened by the continued drought.* 該國脆弱的經濟受到持續乾旱的威脅。**3** a fragile person looks thin and delicate and is often weak or likely to become ill 〔人〕瘦弱的, 弱不禁風的 **4** *BrE* if someone feels fragile they feel ill, especially because they have drunk too much alcohol 【英】〔尤指喝太多酒後〕有氣無力的; 虛弱的; 精神不振的 —**fragility** /frəˋdʒɪlətɪ; frəˈdʒɪləti/ *n* [U] —compare 比較 FRAIL

3 **frag·ment[1]** /ˋfrægmənt; ˈfrægmənt/ *n* [C] a small piece of something that has broken off or that comes from something larger 碎片, 碎塊; 片斷: *Roger examined the few words remaining on the charred fragment of paper.* 羅傑仔細地檢查燒焦的碎紙上留下來的那幾個詞。| *a fragment of poetry* 詩的殘篇斷簡

frag·ment[2] /frægˋmɛnt; frægˈment/ *v* [I,T often passive 常用被動態] to break something, or be broken into a lot of small, separate parts (使) 成碎片, 打碎; 分裂: *His day was fragmented by interruptions and phone calls.* 他一天中有各種事情干擾, 又有不斷的電話, 弄得時間支離破碎的。—**fragmented** *adj*: *a rapidly changing and fragmented society* 一個迅速變化、四分五裂的社會 —**fragmentation** /ˌfrægmɛnˋteʃən; ˌfrægmənˈteɪʃən/ *n* [U]

frag·ment·ary /ˋfrægmənˌtɛrɪ; ˈfrægməntəri/ *adj* made of many different pieces 碎片的; 片斷的; 不完整的: *We have received only fragmentary accounts of the incident.* 關於這事件, 我們只聽到了片言隻字。

fra·grance /ˋfregrəns; ˈfreɪgrəns/ *n* **1** [C,U] a pleasant smell 香氣, 香味, 芳香: *This soup has a delicate fragrance and a slightly sweet taste.* 這種湯聞起來有淡淡的香味, 吃起來略有點甜。—compare 比較 AROMA, SMELL[2] (1) **2** [C] a liquid that you put on your body to make it smell pleasant 香水: *They make soaps and fragrances based on natural ingredients.* 他們以天然配料製造肥皂和香水。

fra·grant /ˋfregrənt; ˈfreɪgrənt/ *adj* having a pleasant smell 香的, 芳香的: *The damask rose is extremely fragrant.* 大馬士革薔薇非常香。—**fragrantly** *adv*

fraid·y cat /ˋfredɪ kæt; ˈfreɪdi kæt/ *AmE informal n* [C] a word meaning someone who is too frightened to do something, used especially by children; SCAREDY-CAT 【美, 非正式】膽小鬼〔尤兒語〕

frail /frel; freɪl/ *adj* **1** someone who is frail is thin and weak, especially because they are old 〔尤因為年老而〕瘦弱的; 衰弱的: *He was a man of about sixty, frail and bent.* 他年紀大約六十歲, 瘦弱而且駝背。**2** not strongly made or built and therefore easily damaged 不堅實的, 不牢固的, 易損壞的: *It seemed impossible that these frail boats could survive in such a storm.* 這些不牢固的小船似乎不可能在這樣的暴風雨中幸免於難。—compare 比較 FRAGILE

frail·ty /ˋfreltɪ; ˈfreɪlti/ *n* **1** [U] lacking in strength or health 脆弱, 虛弱: *He noticed with shock the frailty of her thin body.* 他驚訝地注意到她那纖瘦的身體非常虛弱。| *the frailty of the urban economy* 城市經濟的脆弱 **2** [C] something bad or weak in your character 〔性格上的〕弱點, 缺點: *human frailties* 人類的弱點

frame[1] /frem; freɪm/ *n* 3 3

1 ►BORDER 邊框◄ [C] a firm structure that holds something such as a picture or window, and provides a border for it 框架, 邊框: *Stretch the embroidery on a frame before starting to sew.* 先把刺繡品緊繃在框架上, 然後開始縫製。| **door/window/picture frame** *He leaned against the door frame.* 他靠在門框上。

2 ►STRUCTURE 結構◄ [C] the structure or main supporting parts of a piece of furniture, vehicle, or other object 〔家具、車輛或其他物體的〕構架, 骨架, 支架: *a bicycle frame* 腳踏車車架 | *There was nothing wrong with the frame of the chair, just the upholstery.* 椅子的結構沒甚麼問題, 只是墊襯料有問題。

3 ►BODY 體格◄ [C] the structure formed by the bones of someone's body 體格; 身軀; 骨架: *Louise's slight frame* 路易斯瘦小的身軀

4 ►MAIN FACTS/IDEAS 主要的事實/想法◄ [singular] the main ideas, facts etc that something is based on 構想, 框架: *A clear explanation of the subject provides a frame on which a deeper understanding can be built.* 清晰地解釋主題能提供一個框架, 以便在此基礎上作更深刻的了解。

5 ►GLASSES 眼鏡◄ the metal or plastic part of a pair of glasses (GLASS[1] (3)) that holds the lenses (LENS (1)) 眼鏡框 —see picture at 參見 GLASS[1] 圖

6 be in a... frame of mind to have an attitude at a particular time that helps you to do something 處於…精神狀態[心情; 情緒]: *Philip, I don't think you're in a proper frame of mind to enter the House of God.* 菲利普, 我認為你的心情不適合進教堂。

7 ►BOX 箱◄ [C] a large wooden box covered with glass or plastic in which young plants are grown outdoors 〔木製〕温牀, 温箱: *cucumber frames* 黃瓜温箱

8 ►SPORT 體育◄ [C] a complete part in the games of SNOOKER or BOWLING 〔彩色桌球或保齡球的〕一輪, 一局, 一個回合: *I won the next three frames.* 我贏了接下去的三局。

9 ►PHOTOGRAPH 照片◄ [C] an area of a photographic film that contains one photograph, or many of these which together make a cinema or VIDEO film 〔影片的〕畫面, 畫格; 〔照片的〕幅, 幀 —see also 另見 CLIMBING FRAME, COLD FRAME

frame² *v* [T] **1** to surround something with a border so that it looks pleasant or so that you can see it clearly 給…形成框子, 框住: *Sarah's long, dark hair framed her face.* 薩拉的黑色長髮襯托着她的臉。| **be framed by** *a courtyard framed by a rectangle of tightly clipped grass* 被一圈修剪得很整潔的長方形草地圍住的庭院 **2** to put a picture in a structure that will hold it firmly 給〔畫等〕裝框 **3** to deliberately make someone seem guilty of a crime, by providing things that seem like proof 陷害, 誣告: *I'm convinced Murphy's been framed.* 我確信墨菲是被陷害了。| **frame sb for** *He told the court that the police had tried to frame him for assault.* 他告訴法庭警方想誣陷他襲擊他人。**4** to organize and develop a plan, system etc 制定, 構想〔計劃、系統等〕: *a theory originally framed by Marx* 馬克思最早構想的理論 **5 gilt-framed/wood-framed etc** having a frame or frames of a particular colour or material 鑲在鍍金架裡的/木框裡的等: *a red-framed mirror* 紅框的鏡子 | *wire-framed spectacles* 金屬絲框的眼鏡 —see also 另見 FRAME-UP

frame of ref·er·ence /ˌ· · ˈ···/ *n* [C usually singular 一般用單數] the knowledge, experiences, or beliefs that someone uses to understand something 參照依據; 參照標準; 準則

frame-up /ˈ· ·/ *n* [C] a plan to make someone seem guilty of a crime when they are not 陰謀, 陷害, 誣害

3 **frame·work** /ˈfremˌwɝk; ˈfreɪmwɜːk/ *n* [C] **1** the main supporting parts of a building, vehicle, or object〔建築物、車輛、物體的〕構架, 框架, 結構: *airships with a rigid metal framework* 有着堅硬的金屬框架的飛船 **2** a set of facts, ideas etc from which more complicated ideas are developed, or on which decisions are based 體系, 體制; 參照標準; 準則: **[+of]** *a framework of Marxist theory* 馬克思主義理論體系 | **[+for]** *This paper seeks to provide a framework for future research.* 這篇論文試圖為今後的研究提供一個框架。**3 social/political/legal etc framework** the structure of a society, a legal or political system etc 社會/政治/法律等的結構[制度]: *a legal and political framework favourable to trade* 有利於貿易的法律和政治制度

F

franc /fræŋk; fræŋk/ *n* [C] the standard unit of money in France and some other countries 法郎〔法國和其他一些國家的貨幣單位〕

fran·chise¹ /ˈfræntʃaɪz; ˈfræntʃaɪz/ *n* **1** [C] permission to sell a company's goods or service, that is given or sold to a business person〔經營某公司商品或服務的〕特許經營權: *a Benetton franchise* 貝納通集團的特許經營權 **2** [U] the legal right to vote in your country's elections 選舉權, 投票權: *universal franchise* 普選權

franchise² *v* [T] to give or sell a franchise to someone 給予〔某人〕特許權, 〔向某人〕出售特許權

fran·chi·see /ˌfræntʃaɪˈzi; ˌfræntʃaɪˈziː/ *n* [C] someone who is given or sold a franchise 特許經營人

Franco- /fræŋko; fræŋkəʊ/ *prefix* **1** of France 法國的: *a Francophile* (=someone who loves France) 親法分子, 愛法國事物的人 **2** French and 法國和…的: *the Franco-Belgian border* 法比邊界

fran·co·phone /ˈfræŋkəˌfon; ˈfræŋkəʊfəʊn/ *adj* **1** having a French-speaking population 講法語的: *francophone countries* 講法語的國家 **2** from a French-speaking country or population 來自講法語的國家的, 來自講法語人口的: *francophone African literature* 非洲法語國家文學

fran·glais /ˌfrɑŋˈgle; ˈfrɒŋgleɪ/ *n* [U] a mixture of the French and English languages 英語式法語

frank¹ /fræŋk; fræŋk/ *adj* **1** honest and truthful in what you say 坦率的, 坦誠的, 直言不諱的: *a frank exchange of ideas* 坦率的意見交換 | **be frank with sb** *He was completely frank with her about what happened.* 他完全坦率地告訴她所發生的事。**2 to be frank** used when you are saying something true that other people may not like 坦率地說: *To be perfectly frank, I think that's a crazy idea.* 坦白相告, 我認為那是個荒唐的主意。—**frankness** *n* [U]

frank² *v* [T] to print a sign on an envelope showing that the cost of sending it has been paid 在〔信封〕上蓋戳記〔表示郵資已付〕

frank·fur·ter /ˈfræŋkfɝtɚ; ˈfræŋkfɜːtə/ also 又作 **frank** *AmE*【美】—*n* [C] a long reddish smoked SAUSAGE; HOT DOG¹ *AmE*【美】熏肉香腸

frank·in·cense /ˈfræŋkɪnˌsɛns; ˈfræŋkɪ̣nsens/ *n* [U] a substance that is burnt to give a sweet smell, especially at religious ceremonies〔尤指宗教儀式上點燃的〕乳香

franking ma·chine /ˈ·· ·ˌ·/ *n* [C] a machine that prints signs on envelopes to show that the charge for sending them has been paid〔在信封上蓋戳記、表示郵資已付的〕郵資機

frank·ly /ˈfræŋklɪ; ˈfræŋkli/ *adv* **1** honestly and directly, especially in speech 坦率地, 坦誠地: *I stated my views frankly.* 我坦率地陳述了自己的觀點。**2** [sentence adverb 句子副詞] used to show that you are saying something direct and honest 坦率地說: *Frankly, I'm not very interested.* 坦率地說, 我不很感興趣。 3

fran·tic /ˈfræntɪk; ˈfræntɪk/ *adj* **1** extremely hurried and using a lot of energy but not very organized 緊張紛亂的: *I couldn't understand her frantic signalling.* 我無法理解她那緊張狂亂的示意手勢。| **frantic activity/search/rush etc** *Before the game there was a frantic rush to get the last few seats.* 比賽前, 人們急匆匆地趕去爭得最後的幾個座位。**2** extremely worried and frightened about a situation, so that you cannot control your feelings〔因極端焦急恐懼而〕發瘋似的; 情緒失控的: *A frantic note had crept into Jane's voice.* 簡的聲音開始帶有慌張急迫的味道。| **get/become/grow frantic** *There was still no news of Jill, and her parents were getting frantic.* 仍然沒有吉爾的消息, 她的父母急得要瘋了。| **frantic with worry/grief etc** *Your mother's been frantic with worry wondering where you've been.* 你的母親不知道你在哪裡, 已經擔心得要發瘋了。—**frantically** /-klɪ; -kli/ *adv* —see also 另見 FRENETIC

frap·pé /fræˋpe; ˈfræpeɪ/ *n* [C,U] **1** *AmE* a thick kind of MILK SHAKE【美】一種稠的奶昔 **2** a strong alcoholic drink poured over very thin pieces of ice 利口酒刨冰 —**frappé** *adj*

frat /fræt; fræt/ *n* [C] *AmE informal*【美, 非正式】= FRATERNITY (2)

fra·ter·nal /frəˋtɝnl; frəˈtɜːnl/ *adj* **1** showing a special friendliness to other people because you share interests or ideas with them〔對志同道合的人〕友好的, 親如手足的: *fraternal sympathy with the workers out on strike* 對罷工工人兄弟般的同情 **2** of or belonging to brothers 兄弟的; 兄弟般的: *fraternal loyalty* 兄弟般的忠誠 —**fraternally** *adv*

fra·ter·ni·ty /frəˋtɝnətɪ; frəˈtɜːnɪ̣ti/ *n* **1 the racing/teaching/scientific fraternity** all the people who work in a particular profession 賽馬界/教育界/科學界同人: *He's a member of the medical fraternity.* 他在醫務界工作。**2** [C] a club of male students at an American university, usually living in the same building〔美國大學裡的〕男生聯誼會, 兄弟會: *a fraternity brother*〔美國大學中〕兄弟會會員 —compare 比較 SORORITY **3** [U] a feeling of friendship between members of a group 友愛; 博愛; 兄弟情誼: *the Revolutionary ideas of fraternity and equality* 博愛和平等的革命思想

frat·er·nize also 又作 **-ise** *BrE*【英】/ˈfrætɚˌnaɪz; ˈfrætənaɪz/ *v* [I] to show friendliness towards people who you are not supposed to be friendly with 與敵人友好; 〔戰場上〕與敵軍友好交往: **[+with]** *The soldiers fraternized with the enemy on Christmas Day.* 這些士兵在聖誕節與敵人友善交往。—**fraternization** /ˌfrætɚnɪˋzeʃən; ˌfrætənaɪˈzeɪʃən/ *n* [U]

frat·ri·cide /ˈfrætrəˌsaɪd; ˈfrætrɪ̣saɪd/ *n* [C,U] **1** the crime of murdering your brother or sister 殺害兄弟姐妹的罪行 **2** the murder of people from your country or local area〔殺害本國人或本地人的〕自相殘殺

fraud /frɔd; frɔːd/ *n* **1** [C,U] a method of illegally getting money from someone, often by using clever and complicated methods 欺詐, 詐騙: *financial losses due to theft or fraud* 由盜竊或詐騙引起的錢財損失 | **tax/share/bankruptcy etc fraud** (=fraud in a particular financial area) 騙稅/股份詐欺/破產詐欺等 **2** [C] someone who deceives people to gain money, friendship etc 騙子: *She realized later that the insurance salesman had been a fraud.* 她後來意識到那個保險推銷員是個騙子。

Fraud Squad /ˈ· ·/ *n* [singular] the department in the British police force that examines fraud in business〔英國警察的〕反詐欺部門

fraud·u·lent /ˈfrɔdʒələnt; ˈfrɔːdjʊlənt/ *adj* fraudulent actions or words are intended to deceive〔行動或言語〕騙人的, 欺詐性的: *fraudulent banking practices* 欺詐性的銀行業務 | *fraudulent statements* 騙人的聲明 —**fraudulently** *adv* —**fraudulence** *n* [U]

fraught /frɔt; frɔːt/ *adj* **1** an activity or situation that is fraught is full of problems and is very difficult to deal with 充滿問題的; 難對付的: *After the argument, relations between them were fraught.* 這場爭論之後, 他們的關係很緊張。| **fraught with problems/difficulties/danger** *Any program of sudden change is likely to be fraught with pitfalls.* 任何突然改變的計劃都可能會有許多缺陷。**2** full of anxiety or worry 焦慮不安的; 非常緊張的: *Julie was unhappy, fraught and depressed.* 朱麗很不高興, 焦慮不安, 垂頭喪氣。**3 fraught with meaning** showing strong feelings that are not expressed in words 意味深長的: *She gave me a long look, fraught with meaning.* 她意味深長地朝我看了很久。

fray[1] /fre; freɪ/ *v* [I] **1** if cloth or other material frays, the threads become loose because the material is old〔布等〕磨損, 磨破; 磨散: *That sleeve will fray if you don't darn it.* 如果你不織補, 那個袖頭會散開的。—see picture on page A18 參見A18頁圖 **2** if someone's temper or nerves fray, they become annoyed 煩惱, 惱怒; 緊張: *It was only three o'clock and tempers were already beginning to fray.* 這時才三點鐘, 大家便已經開始發脾氣了。—**frayed** *adj*: *The carpet was badly frayed.* 地毯磨損得很厲害。

fray[2] *n* **the fray** a quarrel, argument, or fight 爭論; 吵架; 打架; 鬥毆: **join/enter the fray** *It wasn't long before all the demonstrators had joined in the fray.* 很快所有的遊行示威者都參加了鬥毆。

fraz·zle /ˈfræzl̩; ˈfræzəl/ *n* [singular] *BrE informal* **be burnt to a frazzle etc** to be so burnt that there is almost nothing left【英, 非正式】被燒個精光

fraz·zled /ˈfræzl̩d; ˈfræzəld/ *adj informal* annoyed and unable to deal with problems or difficulties, especially because you have been very busy【非正式】〔由於很忙〕疲憊躁怒的; 精疲力竭的: *I felt tired and frazzled.* 我感到精疲力竭, 煩躁不安。

freak[1] /frik; friːk/ *n* [C] **1 bike/fitness/film etc freak** *informal* someone who is so interested in bikes, fitness etc that other people think they are strange or unusual【非正式】腳踏車迷/健美迷/電影迷等: *Carrot juice is a favourite with health-food freaks.* 胡蘿蔔汁是健康食品迷最愛喝的。**2** someone who looks very strange or behaves in a very unusual way 怪異的人: *Women who were good at physics used to be considered freaks.* 擅長物理學的女性過去常被看作怪人。**3** something in nature, such as a strangely-shaped plant or animal, that is very unusual 畸形生物: *One of the lambs was a freak – it had two tails.* 其中一頭羔羊是畸形的——牠有兩條尾巴。| **a freak of nature** (=something physically strange or unusual) 畸形物; 怪異的事物 *By some freak of nature there was a snowstorm in June.* 天公作怪, 六月份竟然有暴風雪。**4 control freak** someone who always wants to control situations and other people 支配慾極強的人

freak[2] *adj* [only before noun 僅用於名詞前] **freak accident/storm/conditions etc** an accident, storm etc that is unexpected and very unusual 反常的事故/暴風雨/狀況等: *A freak wave wrecked most of the sea-front.* 一個異乎尋常的大浪損毀了大部分濱海區。

freak[3] *v* [I] *informal especially AmE* to become suddenly angry or frightened, especially so that you cannot control your behaviour【非正式, 尤美】突然發怒[害怕]: *She freaked when she heard he was coming to the party.* 她聽說他要來參加聚會時突然嚇得要死。

freak out *phr v* [I,T] *informal* to become very anxious, upset, or frightened, or make someone very anxious, upset or frightened【非正式】(使) 暴跳如雷; (使) 心煩意亂; (使) 嚇得要死: **freak sb out** *It freaked me out to see him so depressed.* 看到他這樣垂頭喪氣, 我心煩意亂。

freak·ish /ˈfrikɪʃ; ˈfriːkɪʃ/ *adj* very unusual and strange 反常的, 異乎尋常的: *freakish behaviour* 反常的行為 —**freakishly** *adv* —**freakishness** *n* [U]

freak·y /ˈfrikɪ; ˈfriːki/ *adj spoken* strange and slightly frightening【口】古怪嚇人的: *That science fiction film was really freaky!* 那部科幻影片真古怪嚇人!

freck·le /ˈfrɛkl̩; ˈfrekəl/ *n* [C usually plural 一般用複數] a small brown spot on your skin, caused by the sun〔日曬光引起的〕雀斑, 斑點 —see picture on page A6 參見A6頁圖

freck·led /ˈfrɛkl̩d; ˈfrekəld/ *adj* having freckles 長雀斑的, 長斑點的: *a lightly freckled face* 長了一些雀斑的臉

F

1 1

free[1] /fri; friː/ *adj*

① ALLOWED TO DO WHAT YOU WANT 能隨心所欲的
② COSTING NOTHING 免費的
③ NOT A PRISONER 不是囚犯
④ NOT BUSY 不忙的
⑤ NOT BEING USED 閒置的
⑥ WITHOUT/NOT HAVE 沒有
⑦ NOT FIXED/ABLE TO MOVE 未固定的/能移動的
⑧ OTHER MEANINGS 其他意思

① ALLOWED TO DO WHAT YOU WANT 能隨心所欲的

1 allowed to do whatever you want, without being controlled or restricted 自由的; 不受控制[約束]的: **free to do sth** *The children are free to decide which activity they would like to do.* 這些孩子能自由選擇喜歡做的活動。

2 feel free *spoken* used to tell someone that they can do something【口】隨便, 隨意: *Feel free to ask questions.* 請隨便提問吧。| *"Can I make myself some tea?" "Feel free."* "我可以自己泡點茶嗎?" "請隨便。"

3 without restrictions or controls 隨意的, 不受限制的: *We had a free and open discussion about religion.* 我們自由開放地討論了宗教。| *a free exchange of information* 隨意的信息交換 | **free access/passage/movement etc** *free movement of people and goods between the towns* 城鎮間人口和商品的自由流動 | **free speech** (=being able to say whatever you want) 言論自由

4 free election/society/press an election etc that is not controlled by the government so that people can vote, live etc how they want to 自由選舉/自由社會/新聞自由

5 give sb a free hand/rein to let someone do whatever they want or need to do in a particular situation 放

手讓某人幹: *She gave the producer a free rein with the script.* 她放手讓製片人處理劇本。
6 free and easy relaxed, friendly, and without many rules 無拘束的, 隨便的; 不拘禮節的: *a free and easy discussion* 無拘束的討論
7 a free spirit someone who lives as they want to rather than in the way that society considers normal 我行我素的人
8 free agent someone who can do what they want to, and who is not controlled by anyone else 有自主權的人, 行動自由的人: *You're a free agent – you don't owe them anything.* 你是自由人 —— 你不欠他們甚麼。

② **COSTING NOTHING** 免費的
9 costing nothing 免費的: *We were given a free lunch with lots of wine.* 我們吃了一頓免費的晚餐, 喝了許多葡萄酒。| *The soft drinks are free, but you have to pay for the beer.* 軟性飲料免費, 但啤酒你得付錢。| **a free gift** (=something you are given by a shop or company) 〔商店或公司的〕贈品
10 a free ride something that you do not have to pay for, because someone else is paying for it 白白得到的(由別人付款的)東西: *Government employees are getting a free ride on taxpayers' money.* 政府雇員正白白得到用納稅者的錢支付的東西。

③ **NOT A PRISONER** 不是囚犯
11 not a prisoner 不受監禁的, 自由的: *The rapist could be free in as little as three years.* 這個強姦犯甚至可能只服刑三年就可以獲得自由了。| **set sb free** (=give someone their freedom) 釋放某人 *Mandela was finally set free in 1993.* 曼德拉在1993年終於被釋放。| **a free man** (=a man who was a prisoner) 〔曾入獄的〕自由人

④ **NOT BUSY** 不忙的
12 if you are free, or have some free time, you have no work, and nothing else that you must do 空閒的; 不忙的: *Are you free next weekend?* 你下週末有空嗎? | **a free day/morning/half-hour etc** *If you have a free afternoon, go and see this movie.* 如果你哪個下午有空, 該去看這部影片。| **free time** *I don't have enough free time during the week.* 我這星期中沒有足夠的空閒時間。

⑤ **NOT BEING USED** 閒置的
13 something that you want to use is free if no one else is using it 閒置的, 空着的, 不在使用的: *There's a washing machine free, but you may have to wait for a dryer.* 有台洗衣機空着沒人用, 不過用烘乾機你可能得等着。

⑥ **WITHOUT/NOT HAVE** 沒有
14 tax-free/duty-free etc without tax etc 免稅的/免關稅的等: *duty-free wine* 免稅葡萄酒
15 lead-free/salt-free etc not containing lead, salt etc 無鉛的/無鹽的等: *lead-free petrol* 無鉛汽油
16 free from/of sth without something that you do not want to have 無〔某種不想要的事物〕的: *free of obligations* 無義務的 | *free from disease* 無病的
17 free of sth/sb away from something or someone you are glad to be without 擺脫某物/某人: *I'm free of that place at last.* 我終於擺脫掉那個地方了。

⑦ **NOT FIXED/ABLE TO MOVE** 未固定的/能移動的
18 an action or movement that is free is graceful and not restricted 優美自如的: *a free swing of the arm* 手臂優美自如的一擺
19 loose and not fixed to anything 鬆動的; 未固定的: *The free end of the flag has been torn by the wind.* 旗子未固定的一端被風颳破了。
20 free hand/arm/leg etc the arm, leg etc that you are not already using 空着的手/臂/腿等: *With her free hand, she clung to the rope.* 她用空着的手緊緊抓住繩子。
21 *technical* not combined with any other simple chemical substance; pure 【術語】游離的, 單體的: *free oxygen* 游離氧

⑧ **OTHER MEANINGS** 其他意思
22 *old-fashioned* too friendly, in a way that does not show enough respect 【過時】過分親近的; 不太有禮貌的; 過分隨便的: *Your son's manner is rather free.* 你兒子的舉止太隨便了。
23 be free with to be generous with something 慷慨使用; 隨意使用: *Mr. Leath is free with his money.* 利思先生花錢大手大腳。| *free with criticism* 隨意批評人的
24 make free with to use something that belongs to someone else when you should not 擅自使用〔他人的物品〕: *I wonder if he knows that Jenny is making free with his money?* 我弄不清楚他是否知道珍妮正擅自花他的錢。
25 a translation that is free gives a general idea of a piece of writing rather than exactly translating every word 〔翻譯〕根據大意的, 非逐字逐句的

3 **free²** *v* [T] **1** to allow someone to leave prison or somewhere they have been kept by force; RELEASE¹ (1) 釋放, 使自由: *Lincoln freed the slaves.* 林肯解放了奴隸。| *persuading the terrorists to free the hostages* 勸說恐怖分子釋放人質 **2** to move or loosen something or someone that is fixed or trapped 救出, 使解脫出來: *After three hours the firemen freed her from the wreckage.* 三小時後消防隊員把她從殘骸中救出來。**3** also 又作 **free up** to make something available so that it can be used 騰出; 使…可用: *This would free resources that are badly needed.* 這就會騰出急需的資源。**4** to help someone by removing something unpleasant 使〔某人〕解除; 使脫離: **[+from]** *They aim to free the country from its enormous debts.* 他們旨在解除這個國家的巨額債務。**5** to make someone no longer be restricted by unfair rules, a cruel government etc 解放: **[+from]** *marching to free the capital city from the rebels* 進軍去解放叛亂分子控制的首都 **6** to help someone to do something, by removing restrictions or making them responsible for fewer things 使脫身; 使有時間: **free sb to do sth** *freeing teachers to concentrate on particular subjects* 讓教師有時間專注某些科目 | **free sth** *Writing frees the imagination.* 寫作能發揮想像力。

free³ *adv* **1** without payment 免費地: *This card allows you to travel free for a month.* 這張卡能讓你免費旅遊一個月。| **for free** *They let me have these chillies for free.* 他們免費送我這些辣椒。| **free of charge** *You may park here free of charge after 6 p.m.* 下午六點後這裡可以免費泊車。**2** not fixed or held in a particular place or position 不固定地; 鬆脫地: *The window had swung free in the wind.* 窗子被風吹得來回擺動。| **pull/struggle free** (=move to get away from somewhere) 拉出來/掙脫開 *Ken grabbed her around the waist, but she managed to struggle free.* 肯抓住她的腰, 可她設法掙脫開了。**3 break free** to escape from a place or a situation 掙脫, 逃脫: *At last he's broken free and started a new life in New York.* 他終於逃離, 在紐約開始新的生活。**4 run free** if an animal runs free it is allowed to go where it wants to, without being controlled 〔動物〕亂跑, 自由走動: *a zoo where the animals can run free* 動物可以自由走動的動物園 **5 walk free** if a criminal walks free, they are not put in prison 〔罪犯〕不受監禁; 逍遙法外 **6 I'll tell you that for free** *spoken* used to emphasize what you are saying, in an angry way 【口】〔用於生氣地強調所說的話〕我坦白告訴你: *I'm not going to offer to help you out again, I'll tell you that for free!* 我再也不會主動幫你了, 我坦白告訴你! —compare 比較 FREELY —see also 另見 SCOT-FREE

-free /fri; friː/ *suffix* [in adjectives and adverbs 構成形容詞和副詞] without something that you do not want 無…的: *a salt-free diet* 無鹽飲食 | *a trouble-free journey* 無憂無慮的旅行 | *We bought the cigarettes duty-free.* 我們買了些免稅香煙。| *They live in the house rent-free.* 他們住在這棟房子裡, 免交房租。

free as·so·ci·a·tion /ˌ· ···ˈ··/ *n* [U] *technical* a method of finding out about someone's mind by asking them to say the first word they think of when you say a particular word【術語】自由聯想〔讓某人從聽到的某個詞中舉出第一個聯想到的詞來, 以測驗其心理活動〕

free·bie, freebee /ˈfribi; ˈfriːbiː/ *n* [C] *informal* something that you are given free, usually something small and not expensive【非正式】〔通常小而不值錢的〕免費物, 贈品

free·boot·er /ˈfriˌbutɚ; ˈfriːbuːtə/ *n* [C] someone who joins in a war in order to steal other people's goods and money〔參加戰爭的〕掠奪者; 海盜 —**freeboot** *v* [I]

free·born /ˈfriˌbɔrn; ˌfriːˈbɔːn◂/ *adj* not born as a slave 生來自由的, 自由民的

free col·lec·tive bar·gain·ing /ˌ· ··· ˈ···/ *n* [U] *BrE* talks between TRADE UNIONs and employers about pay or working conditions that are not controlled by law【英】勞資自由集體談判

2 2 **free·dom** /ˈfridəm; ˈfriːdəm/ *n* **1** [C,U] the right to do what you want without being controlled or restricted by anyone 自由權利: *The protest is about the infringement of our democratic freedoms.* 抗議是針對我們的民主自由權利受到侵犯而舉行的。| **freedom of speech/expression/choice etc** (=the legal right to choose, express yourself etc) 言論/表達/選擇等的自由權 *The journalists claimed they were being denied the right to freedom of expression.* 這些新聞記者聲稱他們正被剝奪自由表達的權利。**2** [U] the state of being free and allowed to do what you want 自由, 自主: *Kids have too much freedom these days.* 如今小孩子們太自由了。| **freedom to do sth** *Women have gained the freedom to decide whether or not to marry.* 女子已經能自主決定結婚還是不結婚。| **complete freedom** *The teachers are given complete freedom in their choice of teaching methods.* 教師可以完全自由地選擇教學方法。**3** [U] the state of being free because you are not in prison 未受監禁, 在獄外: *One of the escaped prisoners was arrested again after only 48 hours of freedom.* 其中一個逃犯在越獄只有48小時後又被捕了。**4 freedom from** the state of not being affected by something that makes you worried, unhappy, afraid etc 從…中擺脫, 不受…之苦: *The new supplies will ensure temporary freedom from starvation and disease.* 新的供應品將保證能暫時擺脫飢餓和疾病。| *freedom from worry* 無憂無慮 **5 freedom of information** the availability to everyone of information that a government has about people and organizations 資訊自由, 知情權 **6 freedom of the city** an honour in Britain that gives someone the right to be a full member of a city〔英國的〕榮譽市民權 —compare 比較 LIBERTY

freedom fight·er /ˈ·· ˌ··/ *n* [C] someone who fights in a war against an unfair or dishonest government, army etc〔反對不公平或不誠實政府的〕自由戰士 —compare 比較 GUERRILLA, TERRORIST

free en·ter·prise /ˌ· ˈ···/ *n* [U] the principle and practice of allowing private business to operate without much government control 自由企業制 —see also 另見 PRIVATE ENTERPRISE

free-fall /ˈ· ·/ *n* [U] **1** part of a jump or fall from an aircraft that is made before the PARACHUTE[1] is opened〔降落傘打開前的〕自由降落 **2** a very fast and uncontrolled fall in the value of something〔某物價值的〕暴跌: **in free-fall** *The pound sterling was in free fall.* 英鎊在暴跌。—**free-falling** *adj*

free-float·ing /ˌ· ˈ··◂/ *adj* not connected to or influenced by anything 自由浮動的, 無聯繫的, 不受影響的: *free-floating anxiety* 無緣無故的憂慮

free-for-all /ˈ· · ˌ·/ *n* [singular] *informal* a noisy quarrel or fight that a lot of people join【非正式】大吵大鬧; 羣架; 混戰: *Once a few people had been noticed stealing the supplies, there was a free-for-all.* 一發現有少數人在偷供應品, 便出現一場哄搶。

free·hand /ˈfriˌhænd; ˈfriːhænd/ *adj* drawn with your hand and a pen or pencil 徒手畫的: *a freehand sketch* 徒手畫的草圖 —**freehand** *adv*

free·hold /ˈfriˌhold; ˈfriːhəʊld/ *n* [C,U] complete ownership of a building for an unlimited time〔土地或房產的〕終身保有權: *They've bought the freehold of their house.* 他們買下了房子的終身保有權。—**freehold** *adj*: *The flat is a freehold property.* 這套公寓是終身保有財產。—**freehold** *adv* —compare 比較 LEASEHOLD

free·hold·er /ˈfriˌholdɚ; ˈfriːhəʊldə/ *n* [C] an owner of freehold land or property〔土地或房產的〕終身保有者

free house /ˌ· ˈ·/ *n* [C] *BrE* a PUB that can buy beer from different companies, rather than being controlled by one company【英】可出售各種牌子啤酒的酒館 —compare 比較 TIED HOUSE *BrE*【英】

free kick /ˌ· ˈ·/ *n* [C] a chance for one football team to kick the ball, when the other team has done something wrong〔足球的〕任意球, 自由球

free·lance /ˈfriˌlæns; ˈfriːlɑːns/ *adj, adv* working independently for several different companies or organizations rather than being directly employed by one 獨立的[地]; 做自由職業者的[地]: *a freelance journalist* 自由記者 | *She's working freelance.* 她現在是自由職業者。—**freelance** *v* [I]: *He's freelancing for the BBC.* 他是英國廣播公司的自由撰稿人。—**freelance** also 又作 **freelancer** *n* [C]

free·loader /ˈfriˌlodɚ; ˈfriːləʊdər/ *n* [C] *informal* someone who takes food, drink, etc from other people, without giving anything in return【非正式】白吃白喝的人; 佔便宜的人 —**freeload** *v* [I]

free love /ˌ· ˈ·/ *n* [U] an expression meaning the practice or principle of having sex with people without being faithful to one person or without being married, used especially in the 1960s and 1970s〔尤指20世紀60年代和70年代的〕自由性愛; 自由性愛主義

free·ly /ˈfrili; ˈfriːli/ *adv* **1** if you can travel, speak, operate etc freely, you can do it as much as you like and in whatever way you like 自由自在地: *In France he could write freely, without fear of arrest.* 在法國他可以自由地寫作, 不用害怕會被捕。**2** without any restrictions on movement 自如地, 順利地: *breathing freely* 自如地呼吸 | *She shook the pen so that the ink flowed more freely.* 她搖了一下鋼筆, 使墨水能更順暢地流出來。**3 freely admit/acknowledge** to agree that something is true, especially when this is difficult 坦率地承認: *I freely admit I made many mistakes.* 我坦率地承認我曾犯許多錯誤。**4** if a piece of writing is translated freely, the translation does not attempt to translate the original words exactly, but gives a general meaning 根據大意地〔翻譯〕 **5 freely available** very easy to obtain 隨手可得到的: *The two research groups are making their findings freely available to each other.* 那兩個研究小組正自由地相互交換研究成果。**6** generously, or in large quantities 慷慨地; 大量地: *Promises were freely given that prices would be low.* 有人作出慷慨的承諾, 說價格會下降。

free·man /ˈfrimən; ˈfriːmən/ *n* [C] someone who is not a slave 自由民, 生來並非奴隸的人

free mar·ket /ˌ· ˈ··/ *n* [C] **1** *technical* a market on the STOCK EXCHANGE in business shares (SHARE[2] (5)) in which the prices are not controlled or fixed【術語】〔證券交易的〕自由市場 **2** a situation in which prices are not controlled or limited in any way〔價格不受控制或限制的〕自由市場

free mar·ket e·con·o·my /ˌ· ˌ·· ·ˈ···/ *n* [C] a system of trade in which prices are allowed to rise and fall without being restricted by the government 自由市場經濟

free mar·ket·eer /ˌ· ··ˈ·/ *n* [C] someone who thinks

F

that prices should be allowed to rise and fall naturally and should not be fixed by the government 支持自由市場經濟的人

Free·ma·son /ˈfriˌmesn̩; ˈfriːˌmeɪsən/ *n* [C] a man who belongs to a secret society, in which each member helps the other members to become successful 共濟會成員

Free·ma·son·ry /ˈfriˌmesn̩rɪ; ˈfriːmeɪsənri/ *n* [U] the system and practices of Freemasons 共濟會制度及活動

free par·don /ˌ· ˈ··/ *n* [C] *law* the official act of forgiving someone for a crime【法律】特赦, 赦免

free pe·ri·od /ˌ· ˈ···/ *n* [C] a period of time in a school day when a student does not have a class〔學校裡的〕自修課, 空課

free·phone /ˈfrifon; ˈfriːfəʊn/ *n* [U] *BrE* an arrangement by which a company or organization pays the cost of telephone calls made to it【英】免費電話, 對方付費電話〔由接電話的公司或組織支付電話費的辦法〕

free port /ˌ· ˈ·/ *n* [C] a port where goods from all countries can be brought in and taken out without being taxed 自由港; 免稅港

free·post /ˈfripost; ˈfriːpəʊst/ *n* [U] *BrE* an arrangement by which a company or organization pays the cost of letters that you send to it by post【英】免費郵遞, 收件方付資郵遞〔由收信的公司或組織付郵資的郵遞辦法〕

free-range /ˌ· ˈ·◂/ *adj* **1** farm animals that are free-range are not kept in small CAGEs but are allowed to move around in a large enclosed area 放養的: *free-range hens* 放養的母雞 **2** food that is free-range comes from these farm animals 由放養的家禽產的: *free-range eggs* 放養雞生的蛋 —compare 比較 BATTERY (2)

free·si·a /ˈfriʒɪə; ˈfriːziə/ *n* [C] a plant with pleasant smelling flowers 小蒼蘭

free·stand·ing /ˈfriˋstændɪŋ; ˌfriːˈstændɪŋ◂/ *adj* standing alone without being fixed to a frame, wall, or other support 獨立式的; 非附屬的; 自力撐持的

free·style /ˈfriˌstaɪl; ˈfriːstaɪl/ *n* [U] a competition in which swimmers use the CRAWL² (2) method of swimming 自由式游泳(比賽): *the 100m freestyle* 100米自由泳比賽

free·think·er /ˌfriˋθɪŋkɚ; ˌfriːˈθɪŋkə/ *n* [C] someone who has their own opinions, ideas, and beliefs, rather than accepting other people's 思想自由的人, 自由思想家 —**freethinking** *adj*

free trade /ˌ· ˈ·◂/ *n* [U] a situation in which the goods coming into or going out of a country are not controlled or taxed 自由貿易

free verse /ˌ· ˈ·/ *n* [U] poetry that does not have a fixed structure〔無固定格律的〕自由詩 —compare 比較 BLANK VERSE

free·way /ˈfriˌwe; ˈfriːweɪ/ *n* [C] *AmE* a very wide road in the US, usually in cities, built for fast travel【美】高速公路: *the Ventura freeway* (通往)文圖拉(市的)高速公路 —compare 比較 MOTORWAY, EXPRESSWAY, HIGHWAY (1)

free·wheel /ˈfriˋhwil; ˌfriːˈwiːl/ *v* [I] to ride a bicycle or drive a vehicle downhill, without using power from your legs or the engine〔騎腳踏車或開汽車下坡時〕靠慣性滑行

free·wheel·ing /ˈfriˋhwilɪŋ; ˌfriːˈwiːlɪŋ◂/ *adj informal* not worried about rules or what will happen in the future【非正式】隨心所欲的; 不考慮規章[後果]的: *A lot of the girls envied me my independent, freewheeling life.* 許多女孩子羨慕我的那種隨心所欲的生活。

free will /ˌ· ˈ·/ *n* [U] **1 do sth of your own free will** to do something because you want to, not because someone else has forced you to 自願做某事: *He went of his own free will.* 他是自願去的。**2** the belief that human effort rather than God or FATE (2) can affect what happens in life 自由意志論

freeze¹ /friz; friːz/ *v past tense* **froze** /froz; frəʊz/ *past participle* **frozen** /ˈfrozn̩; ˈfrəʊzən/

1 ▶LIQUID 液體◀ [I,T] if a liquid freezes, or something freezes it, it becomes hard and solid because the temperature is very cold (使)結冰, 凝固: *The water at the edge of the lake froze last night.* 湖邊的水昨晚結冰了。| **freeze sth** *The cold weather can even freeze petrol in car engines.* 寒冷的天氣甚至能使汽車發動機裡的汽油凝固。—compare 比較 MELT (1), THAW¹ (1)

2 ▶EARTH 土地◀ [I,T] if something such as earth that contains liquid freezes, or something freezes it, it becomes hard because of cold temperatures (使)凍硬; (使)封凍: *The ground was frozen under the thin snow.* 地面在這層薄雪的覆蓋下都凍硬了。

3 ▶MACHINE/ENGINE 機器/發動機◀ also 又作 **freeze up** [I,T] if a machine, engine, pipe etc freezes, or something freezes it, the liquid inside it becomes solid with cold, so that it does not work properly (使)凍住; (使)凍到不能正常運轉: *The water pipes have frozen up.* 水管已經凍住了。

4 ▶FOOD 食品◀ [I,T] to make food extremely cold so that you can preserve it for a long time, or to be able to be preserved in this way 冷藏, 冷凍; 適合冷藏: *I'm going to freeze some of these beans.* 我打算把一些豆冷藏起來。| *Tomatoes don't freeze well.* 番茄不宜冷凍。

5 it's freezing *spoken* used to say that the temperature is extremely cold【口】太冷了: *It's freezing in here – can't we shut a few windows?* 這裡面太冷了, 我們就不能關幾扇窗子嗎? —see 見 COLD¹ (USAGE)

6 ▶FEEL COLD 感到寒冷◀ [I] *spoken* if someone freezes, they feel very cold【口】感到很冷, 凍僵: *You'll freeze if you don't put a coat on.* 如果不穿上大衣, 你會凍僵的。| **freeze to death** *spoken* (=feel extremely cold)【口】冷得要死 *Come inside, you must be freezing to death.* 進來, 你一定冷得要死了吧。

7 ▶WAGES/PRICES 工資/價格◀ [T] if a government or company freezes wages, prices etc, they do not increase them, and keep them at a particular level (使)凍結〔在某種水平上〕: *Student grants were frozen at 1989 levels.* 學生助學金凍結在1989年的水平。

8 ▶MONEY/PROPERTY 錢/財產◀ [T] to legally prevent money in a bank from being spent, property from being sold etc 凍結〔存款、財產〕: *The court froze their assets.* 法庭凍結了他們的資產。

9 ▶STOP MOVING 停止移動◀ [I] to stop moving suddenly and stay completely still and quiet 突然停止; 呆住: *I froze and listened; someone was in my apartment.* 我站住不動地聽着; 有人在我的房間裡。| *"Freeze! Drop your weapons!" shouted Officer Greer.* "不許動! 放下武器!" 格里爾警官高聲喊道。

10 freeze to death to become so cold that you die 冷死, 凍死

freeze sb **out** *phr v* [T] to deliberately prevent someone from being involved in something, by making it difficult for them, being unkind to them etc〔通過刁難或用冷淡的態度等〕不讓〔某人〕參加; 把〔某人〕排除在外: *You've got to stop freezing me out of the decision-making.* 你不可以再繼續不讓我參與決策。

freeze over *phr v* [I] if an area or pool of water freezes over, its surface turns into ice 表面結冰, 封凍: *We'll go skating if the lake has frozen over.* 如果湖面結了冰, 我們就去溜冰。

freeze² *n* **1** [C] a fixing of wages, prices etc at a particular level〔工資、價格等的〕凍結: *pay freezes* 工資凍結 **2** [C] a stopping of some activity〔活動〕停止: **[+on]** *a freeze on production* 停產 **3** *BrE* [singular] a period of extremely cold weather【英】嚴寒期 **4** *AmE* a short period of time, especially at night, when the temperature is extremely low【美】〔尤指夜間的〕短時間的天寒地凍 —see also 另見 DEEP FREEZE

freeze-dry /ˌ· ˈ·◂/ *v* [T] to preserve food or drink by freezing and drying it very quickly 使冷凍乾燥〔以保存食物或飲料〕: *freeze-dried coffee* 冷凍乾燥的咖啡

freeze-frame /ˈ· ˌ·/ *n* [U] the process of stopping the action on a moving film at one particular place〔電影

的〕定格, 停幀: *Press the freeze-frame button on the video.* 按錄像機上的定格按鈕。—**freeze-frame** *v* [T]

freez·er /ˈfrizɚ; ˈfriːzə/ *n* [C] **1** a large machine in which food can be stored at very low temperatures for a long time; DEEP FREEZE 冷藏箱, 冷凍櫃, 冰櫃 —see picture on page A10 參見 A10 頁圖 **2** *AmE* a part of a FRIDGE in which food can be stored at very low temperatures for a long time【美】〔冰箱中的〕冷凍室, 冰凍格 —compare 比較 FRIDGE

freez·ing /ˈfrizɪŋ; ˈfriːzɪŋ/ *n* [U] **above/below freezing** above or below the temperature at which water freezes 在冰點以上/以下: *It was well below freezing when we left.* 我們離開時氣溫已降到冰點以下了。

freezing com·part·ment /ˈ·· ·ˌ··/ *n* [C] a part of a FRIDGE in which food can be stored at very low temperatures for a long time〔冰箱中的〕冷凍室, 冰凍格

freez·ing point /ˈ·· ·/ *n* **1** [U] the temperature at which water turns into ice 冰點 **2** [C usually singular 一般用單數] the temperature at which a particular liquid freezes〔液體的〕結冰點, 凝固點: *Alcohol has a lower freezing point than water.* 酒精的結冰點比水低。—compare 比較 BOILING POINT

freight[1] /fret; freɪt/ *n* **1** [U] goods that are carried by ship, train, or aircraft〔船、火車或飛機運載的〕貨物; 貨運: *freight containers* 集裝箱, 貨櫃 **2** [C] *AmE* a FREIGHT TRAIN【美】貨運列車; 集裝箱列車

freight[2] *v* [T] to send goods by air, sea, or train〔用飛機、輪船或火車〕運送, 託運〔貨物〕

freight·er /ˈfretɚ; ˈfreɪtə/ *n* [C] a ship or aircraft that carries goods 貨船; 運貨飛機

freight·lin·er /ˈfretˌlaɪnɚ; ˈfreɪtˌlaɪnə/ *n* [C] *especially BrE* a train that carries large amounts of goods in special containers【尤英】集裝箱貨運列車

freight train /ˈ· ·/ *n* [C] a train that carries goods 貨運列車; 集裝箱列車

French[1] /frɛntʃ; frentʃ/ *n* **1** the language of France, and some other countries 法語: *How do you ask for directions in French?* 你怎樣用法語問路? **2** the language and literature of France as a subject of study 法國語言文學: *She's studying French at London University.* 她在倫敦大學學習法國語言文學。**3 the French** the people of France 法國人: *The French celebrate 14th July.* 法國人慶祝 7 月 14 日國慶節。

French[2] *adj* **1** belonging to or involved with France or its people 法國的; 法國人的: *an excellent French wine* 一種極好的法國葡萄酒 **2** belonging to or involved with the French language 法語的: *an introduction to French grammar* 法語語法入門 **3 take French leave** to leave your job without permission 未經許可離開工作, 擅離職守, 擅自曠工[缺席, 缺勤] **4 pardon/excuse my French** *spoken* used to say sorry for swearing【口】原諒我的粗話, 請原諒我言辭不恭

French bean /ˌ· ˈ·/ *n* [C] *BrE* a bean with a long green case that is picked when it is young and soft; GREEN BEAN【英】青菜豆

French bread /ˌ· ˈ·/ *n* [U] white bread in the shape of a thick stick 法式長條麵包

French chalk /ˌ· ˈ·/ *n* [U] CHALK[1] (2) used for drawing lines on cloth when making clothes〔做衣服時在布上畫線的〕滑石, 白粉

French doors /ˈ· ˌ·/ *n* [plural] *especially AmE* FRENCH WINDOWS【尤美】落地窗, 落地玻璃門

French dress·ing /ˌ· ˈ··/ *n* [U] a mixture of oil and VINEGAR that is put on raw vegetables〔用油和醋調製成的〕色拉調料

French fry /ˌ· ˈ·/ *n* [C usually plural 一般用複數] *especially AmE* a long thin piece of potato cooked in fat【尤美】炸馬鈴薯條; CHIP[1] (3a) *BrE*【英】

French horn /ˌ· ˈ·/ *n* [C] a HORN[1] (4), that is shaped like a circle, with a wide bell-like opening 法國號

French kiss /ˌ· ˈ·/ *n* [C] a kiss made with your mouths open and with your tongues touching〔將舌頭伸入對方嘴內的〕法式接吻, 濕吻

French let·ter /ˌ· ˈ··/ *n* [C] *informal old-fashioned* a CONDOM【非正式, 過時】避孕套, 陰莖套

French loaf /ˌ· ˈ·/ *n* [C] *BrE* a long thin white LOAF of bread; FRENCH STICK【英】法式長條麵包

French·man /ˈfrɛntʃmən; ˈfrentʃmən/ *n plural* **Frenchmen** /-mən; -mən/ [C] a man born in France or one who has French parents 法國人

French pol·ish /ˌ· ˈ··/ *n* [U] a clear liquid put on wooden furniture to protect it and make it shine 罩光漆

French seam /ˌ· ˈ·/ *n* [C] a double SEAM (1) used when making clothes, which hides the edges that have been cut 法式線縫, 來去線縫

French stick /ˌ· ˈ·/ *n* [C] a long thin white LOAF of bread 法式長條麵包

French toast /ˌ· ˈ·/ *n* [U] pieces of bread put into a mixture of egg and milk and then cooked in hot oil 法式炸麵包片

French win·dows /ˌ· ˈ··/ *n* [plural] a pair of light doors made of glass in a frame, usually opening out on to a garden or BALCONY (1) 落地窗, 落地玻璃門

French·wom·an /ˈfrɛntʃˌwʊmən; ˈfrentʃˌwʊmən/ *n plural* **Frenchwomen** /-ˌwɪmɪn; -ˌwɪmɪn/ [C] a woman born in France or one who has French parents 法國女子

fre·net·ic /frəˈnɛtɪk; frɪˈnetɪk/ *adj* frenetic actions are very fast, uncontrolled and excited 瘋狂的; 狂熱的; 激動的: *a frenetic departure* 發瘋似的離去

fren·zied /ˈfrɛnzɪd; ˈfrenzid/ *adj* frenzied activity is done with a lot of anxiety or excitement and not much organization or control 狂亂的; 瘋狂似的; 異常激動的: *frenzied efforts to find a solution* 發瘋似地努力尋求解決辦法 —**frenziedly** *adv*

fren·zy /ˈfrɛnzɪ; ˈfrenzi/ *n* [C,U] **1** a state of uncontrolled excitement or emotion 瘋狂似的激動; 瘋狂; 狂熱: *religious frenzies* 宗教狂熱 | **in a frenzy** *She pleaded with them in a frenzy to release her son.* 她發瘋似地祈求他們釋放她的兒子。| **a frenzy of passion/remorse etc** *They fell into a frenzy of helpless alarm at the news.* 聽到這個消息, 他們不知所措, 驚恐萬狀。**2 a frenzy of preparation/activity etc** a period of sudden energetic activity 一陣慌亂的準備/一陣活躍等: *The house was in a frenzy of activity as my aunts prepared for the wedding.* 我的姑姑們在籌備這次婚禮時, 家裡出現一片無比熱鬧的景象。

adverbs of frequency 頻率副詞

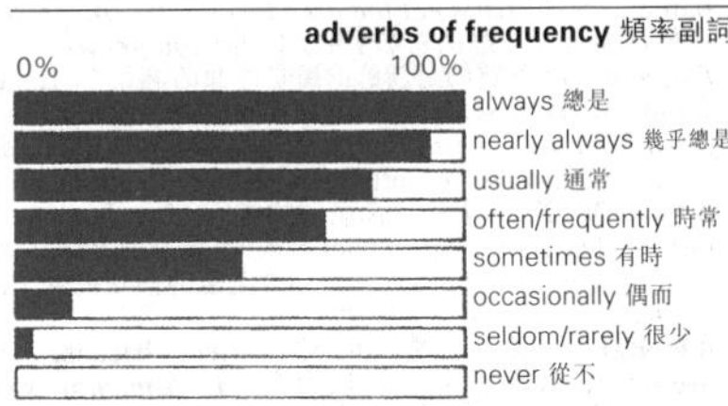

fre·quen·cy /ˈfrikwənsɪ; ˈfriːkwənsi/ *n* **1** [U] the number of times that something happens 發生的次數, 發生率: [+of] *The frequency of mining accidents has steadily decreased over the past 20 years.* 採礦事故發生的頻率在過去的 20 年裡已逐步降低。| **high/low frequency** (=happening very often or not often) 高/低發生率 *The high frequency of cases of diarrhoea is because of poor hygiene.* 腹瀉病例發生頻繁是由於衛生差引起的。| **with increasing frequency** (=more and more often) 越來越頻繁地 **2** [U] the fact that something happens a lot 頻繁: *We are concerned about the frequency of crime in the area.* 我們對該地區頻繁的犯罪活動感到擔心。**3** [C] *technical* the number of radio waves for every second that a radio signal is broadcast【術語】〔無線電廣播每秒鐘的〕頻率, 周率: *This station broadcasts on three different* W3

F

frequencies. 這個電台以三種不同的頻率廣播。**4** [C,U] the rate at which a sound WAVE² (4) moves up and down〔聲波的〕振動頻率: **high/low frequency** (=sounding high or low) 高/低頻率 *The whistle is of such a high frequency the human ear cannot detect it.* 這種哨聲頻率很高，人耳覺察不出來。

3 **fre·quent¹** /ˈfrikwənt; ˈfriːkwənt/ *adj* happening often 經常發生的，頻繁的: *I try to maintain frequent contact with my children.* 我盡可能和我的孩子經常保持聯繫。| *Her headaches are becoming less frequent.* 她不那麼經常頭痛了。| **a frequent visitor/user/correspondent etc** (=someone who often visits, uses something etc) 常客/長期用戶/經常通信的人 *The Governor became a frequent visitor.* 總督成了常客。—opposite 反義詞 INFREQUENT —see picture at 參見 FREQUENCY 圖

fre·quent² /frɪˋkwɛnt; frɪˈkwent/ *v* [T] *formal* to go to a particular place often【正式】常去，常到〔某地方〕: *The bar was frequented by actors from the nearby theatre.* 這家酒吧是附近劇院的演員們經常光顧的地方。

3
2 **frequently** /ˈfrikwəntlɪ; ˈfriːkwəntli/ *adv* very often or many times 經常地，頻繁地: *Sperm whales frequently dive to search for squid.* 抹香鯨經常潛入水中尋找魷魚。

fres·co /ˈfrɛsko; ˈfreskəʊ/ *n* [C] a painting made on a wall by using WATERCOLOUR paint on a surface of wet PLASTER¹ (1)〔用水彩顏料在濕灰漿牆面上畫的〕(濕)壁畫 —compare 比較 MURAL

2
2 **fresh** /frɛʃ; freʃ/ *adj*

1 ►NEW 新的◄ new or recently made, added etc to replace something or add to it 新的; 新做的; 新增的: *I'll just make some fresh coffee.* 我就新煮點咖啡吧。| *There's been no fresh news of the fighting since yesterday.* 自昨天起就沒有關於戰鬥的新消息了。| **a fresh attempt/look/approach etc** (=done again in a new way) 再次努力/重新看/新方法等 *We need to have a fresh look at the problem.* 我們得重新看一看這個問題。| **fresh information/evidence/facts** (=new facts etc that change a situation) 新信息/新證據/新事實等: *This fresh evidence may prove his innocence.* 這項新的證據可能證明他是無辜的。| **a fresh sheet/copy/page/towel etc** (=clean, new, and not used before) 新的牀單/副本/一頁/毛巾等 *You'll have to start again on a fresh sheet of paper.* 你得拿一張白紙重新再畫。

2 ►FOOD/FLOWERS 食品/花◄ **a)** fresh food is good because it was very recently produced, picked, or prepared 新鮮的: *Let's eat the bread while it's still fresh.* 我們趁麵包還新鮮把它吃了吧。| *Did you get fresh or frozen peas?* 你買的是新鮮的還是冷凍的豌豆? | **fresh from the oven/sea/garden etc** *The beans are picked fresh from the garden.* 這些豆是剛從菜園裡摘來的。**b)** fresh flowers have recently been picked〔花〕新摘的

3 ►COOL/CLEAN 涼快的/乾淨的◄ looking, feeling or tasting pleasantly clean or cool 涼爽的，清新的: *the fresh coolness of the air after rain* 雨後空氣的清新涼爽 | *a fresh clean taste* 清新的味道

4 ►NOT TIRED 不疲倦的◄ full of energy because you are not tired 精神飽滿的，精力充沛的: *Somehow she managed to seem fresh and lively even at the end of the day.* 即使是在一天將過去的時候，她還是設法顯得神清氣爽，很有活力。

5 fresh air air that is outside a building or town, and is cleaner〔室外或城外的〕新鮮空氣: *Let's open the windows and have some fresh air in here!* 我們打開窗戶，放點新鮮空氣進來吧!

6 fresh from/fresh out of sth having just finished your education or training, and not having a lot of experience 剛從某處畢業〔經驗不多〕的: *a pleasant young man, fresh from university* 剛從大學畢業、舉止文雅的年輕人

7 ►WEATHER 天氣◄ wind or weather that is fresh is cold〔風、天氣〕涼的: *It's a bit fresh today.* 今天有點涼。

8 ►WATER 水◄ fresh water contains no salt〔水〕淡的

9 be fresh out of sth *AmE spoken* to have just used your last supplies of something【美口】剛用盡某物: *I'm fresh out of cough drops – I'll have to stop at the drug store.* 我剛吃光了止咳糖——我得在藥店停一下。

10 a fresh complexion healthy-looking skin on your face〔臉上的〕好氣色

11 fresh-made/fresh-cut/fresh-grated *especially AmE* having just been made, cut etc【尤美】新做的/新切的/新磨碎的: *fresh-ground coffee* 新磨的咖啡 —see also 另見 FRESHLY

12 fresh as a daisy *informal* not tired and ready to do things【非正式】精神飽滿的

13 fresh in your/their mind recent enough to be remembered clearly〔剛過去不久因而〕記憶猶新的: *She wants to write about her visit while it's still fresh in her mind.* 她想趁記憶猶新的時候把她的這次參觀寫下來。

14 make a fresh start to start something again in a completely new and different way after being unsuccessful 從頭開始，從新開始: *After the accident, they decided to make a fresh start in another town.* 事故之後他們決定在另一個城鎮從新開始。

15 get/be fresh with sb a) to behave or speak rudely or without respect for someone 對某人放肆[無禮]: *Don't you get fresh with me, son!* 別對我無禮，兒子! **b)** to show someone in a rudely confident way that you think they are sexually attractive 對某人說不規矩的話/動手動腳: *He started getting fresh with me.* 他開始對我不規矩。

—**freshness** *n* [U]

fresh·en /ˈfrɛʃən; ˈfreʃən/ *v* **1** [T] also 又作 **freshen up** to make something look clean, new, and attractive, or smell pleasant 使乾淨; 使面目一新; 使吸引人; 使氣味清新: *I think I'll freshen up the paintwork in the bathroom.* 我想我得將浴室裡的油漆刷新一遍。**2** to make something feel cool 使感覺涼快: *Freshen your skin with avocado body lotion.* 用鱷梨潤膚露涼快涼快皮膚吧。**3** [I] if wind or the weather freshens, it gets colder〔風、天氣〕變涼

freshen (sb ↔) **up** *phr v* [I,T] to wash your hands and face in order to feel clean and comfortable 梳洗: *He hurried into the bathroom to freshen up before the meeting.* 他在開會前急忙進浴室梳洗一下。

fresh·er /ˈfrɛʃɚ; ˈfreʃə/ *n* [C] *BrE* a student who has just started at a college or university【英】〔學院或大學的〕一年級新生: *a freshers' party* 一年級新生聚會

fresh-faced /ˌ· ˈ·/ *adj* having a young, healthy-looking face 氣色好的: *a fresh-faced youth* 氣色好的年青人

fresh·ly /ˈfrɛʃlɪ; ˈfreʃli/ *adv* **freshly ground/picked/made etc** recently ground, picked, made etc 新磨的/新摘的/新做的等: *freshly ground pepper* 新磨的胡椒粉

fresh·man /ˈfrɛʃmən; ˈfreʃmən/ *n* [C] *AmE* a student in the first year of HIGH SCHOOL or university【美】〔高中或大學的〕一年級學生

fresh·wa·ter /ˈfrɛʃˌwɔtɚ; ˈfreʃwɔːtə/ *adj* **1** having water that contains no salt 淡水的: *freshwater lakes* 淡水湖 **2** living in water that contains no salt 生活在淡水中的: *freshwater crabs* 淡水蟹 —compare 比較 SALTWATER

fret¹ /frɛt; fret/ *v* **fretted, fretting 1** [I,T] *especially spoken* to feel worried about small or unimportant things, or to make someone feel like this【尤口】(使)煩惱，(使)發愁: *Don't you fret – everything will be all right.* 別煩惱——一切都會好的。| **[+about/over]** *Nicki was always fretting over something or other.* 尼基總是在為這為那發愁。**2** [T] to make something gradually smaller and weaker by rubbing it over a long period of time 磨細; 磨損

fret² *n* **1** [C] one of the raised lines on the NECK (=long straight part) of a VIOLIN, GUITAR etc〔小提琴、結他等定音的〕品，柱，馬 **2 be/get in a fret** *BrE informal* to become worried or anxious about something【英，非正式】焦慮不安: *Aunt Joan always gets in a fret if we're late.* 如果我們遲到，瓊姑姑總是焦慮不安。

fret·ful /ˈfrɛtfəl; ˈfretfəl/ *adj* anxious and complaining, especially about small or unimportant things〔尤指為無足輕重的事〕煩惱的; 發牢騷的: *The child was tired* *and fretful.* 這孩子又疲倦又煩躁不安。—**fretfully** *adv* —**fretfulness** *n* [U]

fret·ted /ˈfrɛtɪd; ˈfretɨd/ *adj* cut or shaped into complicated patterns as decoration 刻成回紋[萬字]圖案的

fret·work /ˈfrɛtˌwɝk; ˈfretwɜːk/ *n* [U] patterns cut into thin wood, or the activity of making these patterns 回紋格子細工, 萬字浮雕細工

Freud·i·an /ˈfrɔɪdɪən; ˈfrɔɪdiən/ *adj* **1** connected with or according to Sigmund Freud's ideas about the way the mind works, and the way it can be studied 弗洛伊德學說的; 根據弗洛伊德學說的 **2** a Freudian remark or action is connected with the ideas about sex that people have in their minds but do not usually talk about〔言語或行動〕與性壓抑有關的

Freudian slip /ˌ··· ˈ·/ *n* [C] something you say that is different from what you intended to say, and shows your true thoughts〔泄露真實想法的〕漏嘴, 口誤, 失言

Fri the written abbreviation of 縮寫= FRIDAY

fri·a·ble /ˈfraɪəbḷ; ˈfraɪəbəl/ *adj technical* friable rocks or soil are easily broken into very small pieces or into powder【術語】脆的; 易碎的

fri·ar /ˈfraɪɚ; ˈfraɪə/ *n* [C] a man who belongs to a Christian group, whose members in the past travelled around teaching about Christianity and asking for money and food〔古時基督教的〕托缽修士; 雲遊傳道修士 —compare 比較 MONK

fric·as·see /ˌfrɪkəˈsi; ˈfrɪkəseɪ/ *n* [C,U] a dish made of small pieces of meat in a thick white SAUCE (1) 原汁煨肉塊

fric·a·tive /ˈfrɪkətɪv; ˈfrɪkətɪv/ *n* [C] a sound, such as /f/ or /z/, made by forcing your breath through a narrow opening between your lips, or between your tongue and your lips or teeth 摩擦音〈如 /f/ 或 /z/〉

fric·tion /ˈfrɪkʃən; ˈfrɪkʃən/ *n* [U] **1** disagreement, angry feelings, or unfriendliness between people〔人們之間的〕不合, 衝突: **cause/create friction** *Restrictions on trade have caused friction between these two nations.* 貿易限制引起兩國之間的衝突。**2** the rubbing of one surface against another 摩擦: *Check your rope frequently, as friction against the rock can wear it down.* 要經常檢查繩索, 因為與岩石摩擦會使它磨損。**3** in science, friction is the natural law that prevents one surface from sliding easily over another surface 摩擦力: *Heat can be produced by chemical reactions or friction.* 熱可由化學反應或摩擦力產生。

Fri·day /ˈfraɪdɪ; ˈfraɪdi/ written abbreviation 縮寫為 **Fri** *n* [C,U] the day between Thursday and Saturday. In Britain, Friday is considered the fifth day of the week, and in the US it is considered the sixth day of the week 星期五〔在英國, 星期五被認為是一週的第五天; 在美國則被認為是第六天〕: *Mom said she mailed the letter last Friday.* 媽媽說她在上星期五把信寄出了。| **on Friday** *The committee meeting is on Friday.* 委員會的會議在星期五舉行。| **on a Friday** *My birthday is on a Friday this year.* 我今年的生日是在星期五。| **Friday morning/evening etc** *Can you meet me Friday morning?* 星期五上午你能來接我嗎? | **on Fridays** (=each Friday) 每星期五 | **the Friday** *BrE* (=the Friday of the week being mentioned)【英】那個星期五, 所說到的那個星期五 *Mr Jones flew in on the Friday and left on the following Wednesday.* 瓊斯先生在星期五乘飛機來, 接着的星期三離開。

2 **fridge** /frɪdʒ; frɪdʒ/ *n* [C] a special cupboard for keeping food cold; REFRIGERATOR 電冰箱, 雪櫃 —see picture on page A10 參見 A10 頁圖

fridge-freez·er /ˌ· ˈ··/ *n* [C] *BrE* a large fridge with a part that keeps food frozen【英】有冷藏室的電冰箱

1 **friend** /frɛnd; frend/ *n* [C]

1 **1 ►PERSON YOU LIKE** 你喜歡的人◄ someone who you like very much and like to spend time with 朋友, 友人: *Jerry, I'd like to introduce you to my friend Lucinda.* 傑里, 我想將你介紹給我的朋友露辛達。| **be friends with sb** *My parents have been friends with the Murkets for twenty years.* 20 年來我的父母和默克特一家是好朋友。| **friend of mine/yours/Billy's etc** *A friend of mine told me this joke yesterday.* 我的一位朋友昨天告訴我這個笑話。| **best friend** (=the friend you like best) 最好的朋友 *One of Tricia's best friends is getting married tomorrow.* 特里西婭的一位最好的朋友於明天結婚。| **good/close friend** (=one of the friends you like most) 好朋友/密友 *One of my good friends just had a baby.* 我的一位好友剛生了小孩。| **old friend** (=one you have known a long time) 老朋友 *Bruce is an old friend of mine.* 布魯斯是我的老朋友。| **friend of a friend** *I met Stephano through a friend of a friend.* 我通過一位朋友的朋友認識了斯特凡諾。

2 make friends to meet people and become friendly with them 交朋友, 建立友好關係: *Jenny has always found it easy to make friends at school.* 珍妮在學校總是很容易交朋友。| **[+with]** *Have you made friends with your neighbors yet?* 你和鄰居建立起友好關係了嗎?

3 be just (good) friends used to say that you are not having a romantic relationship with someone 只是(好)朋友而已: *Ben's not her boyfriend, I think they're just good friends.* 本不是她的男朋友, 我認為他們只是好朋友而已。

4 ►SUPPORTER 贊助者; 支持者◄ someone who supports a theatre, arts organization, CHARITY (2) etc by giving money or help 贊助者; 支持者: *We would like to invite you to become a friend of the orchestra.* 我們想請你當管弦樂隊的贊助人。

5 ►NOT AN ENEMY 不是敵人◄ someone who is not an enemy and will not harm you or cause trouble for you 自己人: *Who goes there? Friend or foe?* 甚麼人?自己人還是敵人? | *Don't worry, you're among friends.* 別擔心, 你是自己人。

6 be no friend of/to to oppose someone or something 反對, 不贊成, 不支持: *I'm no friend of the plan, as you know.* 你知道, 我反對這項計劃。

7 ►AT PUBLIC OCCASION 在公共場合◄ used to address someone or a group of people in a parliament, meeting, or other formal public occasion 朋友〔在議會、會議或其他正式公共場合使用的稱呼語〕: *Friends, we are gathered here today to witness the marriage of Nick and Jo.* 朋友們, 今天我們聚在這裡來見證尼克和喬的婚禮。

8 Friend a member of the Society of Friends; a QUAKER 基督教教友會[公誼會]教友

9 our/your friend used to talk about someone you do not know, who has done something annoying 我們的/你們的那位朋友〔指你不喜歡的不認識的人〕: *Our friend with the loud voice is back.* 我們的那位大嗓門朋友回來了。

10 have friends in high places to know important people who can help you 有重要人物幫忙

11 a friend in need someone who helps you when you need it 患難之交, 真正的朋友

friend·less /ˈfrɛndlɪs; ˈfrendləs/ *adj literary* having no friends and no one to help you【文】無朋友的; 孤獨無助的

-friendly /frɛndlɪ; frendli/ *suffix* [in adjectives 構成形容詞] **1** not difficult for particular people to use〔為某種人所〕容易使用的, 方便…的: *a user-friendly computer* 用戶易操作的電腦, 方便使用的電腦 | *a customer-friendly shopping environment* 方便顧客的購物環境 **2** not harming something 對…無害的: *eco-friendly washing powder* (=not harming the environment) 對環境無害的洗衣粉

friend·ly¹ /ˈfrɛndlɪ; ˈfrendli/ *adj* **1** behaving towards someone in a way that shows you like them and are ready to talk to them or help them 友好的, 友善的: *She's cheerful and friendly the whole time.* 她整段時間都興高采烈, 態度友好。| *a friendly smile* 親切的微笑 | **[+to/towards]** *The local people are always friendly to visitors.* 當地人總是對遊客很友好。**2 be friendly with sb** to be friends with someone 與某人很要好: *Betty's very friendly with* 2 3 *the Jacksons.* 貝蒂同傑克遜一家人非常要好。**3** not at war with your own country, or not opposing you 友好的, 非敵對的: *friendly nations* 友好國家 **4** *BrE* a friendly game is played for pleasure or practice, and not because it is important to win【英】〔比賽〕友誼的: *a friendly match against AC Milan* 與AC米蘭隊的友誼賽 **5 environmentally friendly/ozone friendly etc** not damaging to the environment etc 對環境無害的/不破壞臭氧層的等: *environmentally friendly washing powders* 對環境無害的洗衣粉 **6 friendly fire** bombs, bullets etc that accidentally kill people who are fighting on the same side 誤殺自己人的火力[砲火] —see also 另見 USER FRIENDLY —**friendliness** *n* [U]

friendly² *n* [C] *BrE* a game played for pleasure or practice, and not because it is important to win【英】友誼賽

friendly so·ci·e·ty /ˈ·· ·,···/ *n* [C] an association in Britain that people regularly pay small amounts of money to, which then provides them with money when they become old or ill〔英國〕互濟會, 互助會, 互助儲金會

3 **friend·ship** /ˈfrɛndʃɪp; ˈfrendʃɪp/ *n* **1** [C] a relationship between friends 友誼: *Our friendship developed quickly over the weeks that followed.* 在隨後的幾個星期裡我們的友誼發展很快。| **form a friendship** (=make friends with someone) 建立友誼 *The two boys formed a deep and lasting friendship.* 這兩個男孩子建立了深厚持久的友誼。| **strike up a friendship** (=begin to be friends with someone you have just met)〔見面不久即〕結交 **2** [U] the feelings and behaviour that exist between friends 友情; 友好的行為: *I could always rely on Gary for friendship and support.* 我總能依靠加里的友情和支持。

fri·er /ˈfraɪɚ; ˈfraɪə/ *n* [C] another spelling of FRYER fryer 的另一種拼法

fries /fraɪz; fraɪz/ *n* [plural] *especially AmE* pieces of potato cut into pieces, usually long and thin, and then cooked in hot fat【尤美】炸馬鈴薯條

Frie·si·an /ˈfriʒən; ˈfriːziən/ *n* [C] *especially BrE* a type of cow that is black and white【尤英】霍斯坦種乳牛, 黑白花牛, 荷蘭牛; HOLSTEIN *AmE*【美】

frieze /friz; friːz/ *n* [C] a thin border along the top of the wall of a building or in a room, usually decorated with pictures, patterns etc〔牆壁頂部沿邊的〕橫條裝飾; 雕帶; 飾帶

frig /frɪg; frɪg/ *v*

frig about/around *phr v taboo especially BrE*【諱, 尤英】**1** [I] to waste time doing unnecessary or unimportant things 閒混; 虛度光陰: *Stop frigging about and help!* 不要遊手好閒了, 來幫個忙吧! **2** [T **frig** sb/sth **around/about**] to treat someone badly or unfairly 虐待, 不公平地對待, 欺壓

frig·ate /ˈfrɪgɪt; ˈfrɪgɨt/ *n* [C] a small, fast warship used especially for protecting other ships 護衛艦, 護航艦

frig·ging /ˈfrɪgɪŋ; ˈfrɪgɪŋ/ *adj* [only before noun 僅用於名詞前] *adv taboo spoken* used to emphasize something you are saying when you are angry, annoyed etc【諱, 口】該死的, 他媽的: *I can't open the frigging door!* 我開不了這該死的門!

fright /fraɪt; fraɪt/ *n* **1** [singular] the feeling you have when something frightens you 恐怖; 驚嚇: **give sb a fright** (=do something that makes someone feel afraid) 使某人吃驚, 嚇着某人 *You gave me such a fright creeping up on me like that!* 你偷偷朝我湊過來, 嚇了我一跳! | **get/have a fright** *I got an awful fright when your dog rushed out at me.* 你的狗朝我衝過來, 嚇了我一大跳。| **get/have the fright of your life** (=to feel extremely afraid) 感到極度恐懼 **2** [U] a feeling of fear 驚嚇, 恐懼: *The child was wild with fright and began to scream.* 這孩子嚇壞了, 開始尖叫。**3 take fright** to be very afraid of something, especially so that you run away from it 受驚嚇〔尤指因而逃走〕: *The bird took fright and flew away.* 那隻鳥受驚飛走了。**4 look a fright** *old-fashioned* to look untidy or unattractive【過時】很難看, 怪模怪樣, 醜陋 —see also 另見 STAGE FRIGHT

fright·en /ˈfraɪtn̩; ˈfraɪtn/ *v* [T] **1** to make someone feel afraid 使害怕, 使驚嚇: *Don't stand so near the edge, you're frightening me!* 別那麼靠邊站, 你要把我嚇壞了! | **frighten sb to death/frighten sb out of their wits** (=make someone feel extremely afraid) 使某人嚇得半死/使某人嚇得魂不附體 *She'll be frightened to death when she sees the way you drive.* 看到你那樣開車, 她會嚇得半死的。**2 frighten sb into/out of (doing) sth** to force someone to do something or not to do something by making them afraid 嚇得某人做某事/嚇得某人不敢做某事: *The lawyers frightened the old lady into signing the paper.* 律師們嚇唬那位老太太在文件上簽名。

frighten sb ↔ **away** *phr v* [T] to make a person or animal go away by making them feel afraid 嚇走〔某人〕: *Terrorist activity in the area has frightened most tourists away.* 該地區的恐怖主義活動已經把大多數遊客嚇走。

frighten sb/sth ↔ **off** *phr v* [T] to make a person or animal so nervous or afraid that they go away or do not do something they were going to do 嚇走; 嚇得不做: *The investors were frightened off by the company's low profits that year.* 投資者被該公司那年的低利潤嚇走了。

fright·ened /ˈfraɪtn̩d; ˈfraɪtnd/ *adj* feeling afraid 受驚的, 害怕的: *a frightened animal* 受驚的動物 | [**+of**] *I was frightened of being left by myself in the house.* 我害怕自己一個人被留在屋裡。| **frightened to do sth** *I'll be frightened to look out of the airplane window.* 我從飛機的舷窗往外看會害怕的。| [**+that**] *She's frightened that her ex-husband will find her.* 她怕前夫會找到她。

fright·en·ers /ˈfraɪtn̩ɚz; ˈfraɪtnəz/ *n* [plural] *BrE slang*【英俚】**put the frighteners on sb** to make someone do what you want by threatening them 恐嚇某人〔使其做某事〕

fright·en·ing /ˈfraɪtn̩ɪŋ; ˈfraɪtn-ɪŋ/ *adj* making you feel afraid or nervous 令人害怕的, 嚇人的, 可怕的: *That's a frightening thought.* 那是個可怕的想法。| **it is frightening (to do sth)** *It's frightening to think how easily children can be hurt.* 想到小孩很容易受到傷害, 怪可怕的。—**frighteningly** *adv*

fright·ful /ˈfraɪtfəl; ˈfraɪtfəl/ *adj* **1** *especially BrE* unpleasant or bad【尤英】不愉快的; 可怕的; 壞的: *There's been a frightful accident on the motorway.* 高速公路上發生了一宗可怕的意外事故。**2** *BrE old-fashioned* used to emphasize how bad something is【英, 過時】極度的, 極大的; 很糟的: *a frightful mess* 一團糟, 一塌糊塗的事 —**frightfulness** *n* [U]

fright·ful·ly /ˈfraɪtfəlɪ; ˈfraɪtfəli/ *adv BrE old-fashioned* very【英, 過時】非常, 十分

fri·gid /ˈfrɪdʒɪd; ˈfrɪdʒɨd/ *adj* **1** a woman who is frigid does not like having sex〔女子〕性冷感的 **2** not friendly or kind 冷淡的; 不友好的: *The guard looked at us with a frigid stare.* 守衛冷冰冰地盯着我們。**3** a place that is frigid is very cold 寒冷的, 酷寒的 —**frigidly** *adv* —**frigidity** /frɪˈdʒɪdətɪ; frɪˈdʒɪdɨti/ *n* [U]

frill /frɪl; frɪl/ *n* [C] **1** a decorative edge on a piece of cloth made by another piece of cloth with many small folds in it〔布的〕飾邊, 褶邊: *a frill on the bottom of the skirt* 裙子下擺的飾邊 **2 without frills/with no frills** without attractive but unnecessary details or decorations 不帶花哨裝飾的, 毫無矯飾的: *a no-frills deal* 無額外收費的交易

frill·y /ˈfrɪlɪ; ˈfrɪli/ *adj* having many decorative folds of cloth 有飾邊的, 有褶邊的: *a little girl's frilly dress* 有褶邊的女童連衣裙

fringe¹ /frɪndʒ; frɪndʒ/ *n* [C] **1** *BrE* the part of your hair that hangs over your forehead【英】劉海〔垂在額前的頭髮〕; bangs (BANG¹ (3)) *AmE*【美】—see picture on page A6 參見A6頁圖 **2** a decorative edge of hanging threads on a curtain, piece of clothing etc〔帷幕、衣服等上的〕繸穗, 緣飾, 流蘇 **3 on the fringe of a)** at the part of something that is farthest from the centre 在…的邊緣; 在…的外圍: *It was easier to move around on the fringe of the crowd.* 在人羣的外圍比較容易走動。**b)** not quite belonging to or accepted by a group of people who share the same job, activities etc 屬於…的邊緣的: *a small group on the fringes of the art world* 藝術界邊緣的一小羣人 **4 the right wing/nationalist/radical etc fringe** a group of people within an organization or political party who have extreme ideas that most people do not agree with 右翼/民族主義/激進的極端分子等: *The terrorist fringe condemned the decision.* 恐怖主義的極端分子譴責這個決定。**5 the fringe,** also 又作 **fringe theatre** the performance of plays that are unusual or that try to make people think differently 實驗戲劇(演出); 非傳統的戲劇(演出) —see also 另見 **the lunatic fringe** (LUNATIC (3))

fringe² *adj* [only before noun 僅用於名詞前] different from the most usual or accepted way of thinking or doing things 邊緣的; 非正統的, 非主流的: *The environment is no longer a fringe issue in Europe.* 在歐洲, 環境不再是一個邊緣的問題了。

fringe³ *v* [T] to be around the edge of something; BORDER 在…的邊緣: *A line of trees fringed the pool.* 水池周圍種了一行樹。

fringe ben·e·fit /ˈ· ,···/ *n* [C usually plural 一般用複數] an additional service or advantage given with a job besides wages; PERK¹〔工資外的〕補貼, 附加福利; 附帶的好處; 邊緣福利: *The pay is awful but there are several fringe benefits.* 工資很差, 不過有幾種小額補貼。

fringe thea·tre /,· ˈ···/ *n* [U] *BrE* plays by new writers, often on difficult subjects or written in unusual ways, that are not performed in the main theatres【英】實驗戲劇

frip·pe·ry /ˈfrɪpərɪ; ˈfrɪpəri/ *n* [C] an unnecessary and useless object or decoration 多餘無用的東西; 花哨的裝飾品: *She spends all her money on fripperies.* 她把所有的錢都花在花哨無用的東西上。

fris·bee /ˈfrɪzbɪ; ˈfrɪzbi/ *n* [C,U] *trademark* a piece of plastic shaped like a plate that you throw to someone else to catch as a game【商標】〔遊戲用的〕飛盤, 飛碟

frisk /frɪsk; frɪsk/ *v* **1** [T] also 又作 **frisk down** *AmE*【美】to search someone for hidden weapons, drugs etc by feeling their body with your hands 搜〔某人〕的身: *We were frisked at the airport, can you believe it?* 我們在機場竟被搜身了, 你能相信嗎? —see picture on page A21 參見 A21 頁圖 **2** [I] to run and jump playfully 歡躍, 跳蹦: *The lambs were frisking around the pen.* 羔羊在羊圈裡蹦跳。

frisk·y /ˈfrɪskɪ; ˈfrɪski/ *adj* full of energy, fun, and cheerfulness 活躍的; 活潑的; 歡蹦亂跳的: *a frisky colt* 一匹歡蹦亂跳的馬駒 | *He's still frisky, even at eighty years old!* 他在八十歲的高齡還很活躍! —**friskily** *adv* —**friskiness** *n* [U]

fris·son /friˋsɑn; ˈfriːsɒn/ *n* [C] a sudden feeling of excitement or fear〔突然的〕興奮感; 恐懼; 震顫: *a frisson of alarm* 一陣驚恐的戰慄

frit /frɪt; frɪt/ *adj BrE dialect* frightened【英, 方言】受驚的; 害怕的

frit·ter¹ /ˈfrɪtɚ; ˈfrɪtə/ *n* [C] a thin piece of fruit, vegetable, or meat covered with a mixture of eggs and flour and cooked in hot fat〔有水果、蔬菜或肉餡的〕油炸餡餅: **apple/corn/banana fritter** (=made of apple, corn etc) 油炸蘋果/玉米/香蕉餡餅

fritter²

fritter sth ↔ **away** *phr v* [T] to waste time, money, or effort on something small or unimportant〔在微不足道的事情上〕浪費〔時間、金錢或力氣〕: **[+on]** *They frittered their pocket-money away on sweets.* 他們把零用錢都浪費在買糖果上。

fritz /frɪts; frɪts/ *n* [singular] *AmE informal* **be on the fritz** if something electrical is on the fritz, it is not working properly【美, 非正式】〔電器〕出故障

fri·vol·i·ty /frɪˋvɑlətɪ; frɪˈvɒlɪ̣ti/ *n* **1** [U] lack of serious or sensible thought or behaviour〔思想或行為的〕輕浮, 輕佻: *Your frivolity is out of place on such a solemn occasion.* 你的輕浮舉動在這種嚴肅的場合很不適宜。**2** **frivolities** [plural] **a)** silly or amusing actions or words, especially in a situation where you should be serious or sensible 輕浮的話; 不嚴肅的舉動; 無聊的話[行為] **b)** unimportant or unnecessary things 無關緊要的事: *Student life should be more than parties and other frivolities.* 學生生活應該不僅僅是聚會和其他無關緊要的活動。

friv·o·lous /ˈfrɪvələs; ˈfrɪvələs/ *adj* **1** not serious or sensible, especially in a way that is not suitable for a particular occasion 不嚴肅的, 草率的: *The court discourages frivolous law suits.* 法院不鼓勵草率的訴訟。**2** a frivolous person likes having fun rather than doing serious or sensible things 輕浮的 —**frivolously** *adv*

frizz /frɪz; frɪz/ *v* [T] *informal* to make your hair curl very tightly【非正式】使〔頭髮〕緊緊鬈曲 —**frizz** *n* [U]

friz·zle /ˈfrɪzḷ; ˈfrɪzəl/ *v* [I,T] *informal* also 又作 **frizzle up** to dry or burn something, or to be dried or burnt, especially into a curly shape【非正式】(把…) 燒得捲起來; (使…) 乾得捲起來

frizz·y /ˈfrɪzɪ; ˈfrɪzi/ *adj* frizzy hair is tightly curled〔頭髮〕緊緊鬈曲的

fro /fro; frəʊ/ *adv* —see 見 TO AND FRO

frock /frɑk; frɒk/ *n* [C] **1** *old-fashioned* a woman's or girl's dress【過時】〔婦女或女孩穿的〕長服: *a party frock* 宴會穿的長裙 **2** a long loose piece of clothing worn by some Christian MONKs〔基督教教士穿的〕教士長袍

frock coat /,· ˈ·/ *n* [C] a knee-length coat for men, worn in the 19th century〔19 世紀男子穿的〕長禮服

frog /frɑg; frɒg/ *n* [C] **1** a small green animal that lives near water and has long legs for jumping 蛙 —compare 比較 TOAD **2 have a frog in your throat** *informal* to have difficulty in speaking because of a sore throat【非正式】〔因喉嚨痛〕說話困難, 聲音沙啞 **3 Frog** *informal* an offensive word for a French person【非正式】法國佬〔具冒犯性〕

frog 蛙

frog·man /ˈfrɑgmən; ˈfrɒgmən/ *n* [C] someone who swims under water using special equipment to help them breathe, especially as a job 蛙人; 潛水員

frog·march /ˈfrɑg,mɑrtʃ; ˈfrɒgmɑːtʃ/ *v* [T] *BrE* to force someone to walk somewhere by having two people on either side of them who hold their arms very tightly【英】將〔某人〕反綁雙臂押走

frog·spawn /ˈfrɑgspɔn; ˈfrɒgspɔːn/ *n* [U] frog's eggs 蛙卵

frol·ic¹ /ˈfrɑlɪk; ˈfrɒlɪk/ *v* [I] to play in an active, happy way; FRISK (2) 嬉戲, 歡快地玩耍: **[+around/about/over]** *The kids spent all day frolicking around in the surf.* 孩子們整天在歡快地玩着拍岸的浪花。

frolic² *n* [C often plural 常用複數] a cheerful, enjoyable game or activity 嬉戲, 嬉鬧: *Everyone joined in the Saturday night frolics.* 大家都參加了星期六晚上的歡鬧聚會。

frol·ic·some /ˈfrɑlɪksəm; ˈfrɒlɪksəm/ *adj especially literary* active and liking to play【尤文】活躍的; 愛嬉戲的: *frolicsome kittens* 喜歡嬉戲的小貓

from /frəm; frəm; *strong* 強讀 frɑm; frɒm/ *prep* S1 W1 **1** starting at a particular place, position, or condition 自…, 從…, 由…〔表示起點、開始位置或開始時的狀況〕: *How do you get from here to Colchester?* 從這裡到科爾切斯特怎麼走? | *running from one side of the building to the other* 從大樓的一邊跑向另一邊 | *The hotel is on the main road from Caernarfon.* 旅館位於從卡那封出來的大路上。| *dropped from a height of six feet* 從六英尺的高度落下的 | *translating from French into English* 從法語翻譯成英語 | **go from A to B** (=go from one point or situation to another) 從 A 到 B *People will choose different methods of going from A to B.* 由 A 到 B 人們會選擇不同方法。| **go from bad to worse** (=get worse) 越來越糟糕 *When she arrived, things just went from bad*

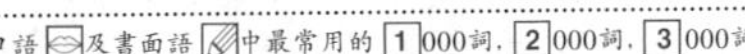

to worse! 她到達後, 情況每況愈下! **2 from house to house/shop to shop/place to place etc a)** calling at every house, shop, etc 挨家挨戶/一家一家商店地/到處等: *She went from house to house asking if anyone had seen him.* 她挨家挨戶問有沒有人看見過他。**b)** in different houses, places etc 在每家每戶/在各家商店/到處等: *From office to office things work differently.* 在每個辦公室, 情況都不一樣。| *It will vary from time to time and from place to place.* 這會因時因地而不同。| *Everything goes wrong from time to time.* (=sometimes) 不管甚麼東西都有出故障的時候。**3** starting at a particular time 從〔某時〕起: *He'll be here tomorrow from about seven o'clock onwards.* 明天從七點鐘左右起他會在這兒。| *in a week from now* 從現在起一週內 | **from morning to night** (=without stopping) 從早到晚, 不停地 *housewives who work from morning to night* 從早到晚幹個不停的家庭主婦 | **from now on** (=from this time onwards) 從現在起 *From now on, I will only be working in the mornings.* 從現在起我只在上午工作。—see 見 SINCE[3] (USAGE) **4** beginning at a particular limit or price 從〔某個限度或價格〕起: *The sizes range from a hundred down to twenty.* 大小從100號至20號不等。| *The yield from this type of investment can be anything from five to ten percent.* 這種投資的收益從百分之五至百分之十不等。**5** if you see, watch, or do something from a place, this is where you are when you see, watch, or do it 從〔某處看或做〕: *From the top of the hill, you can see for miles.* 從山頂你可以看到好幾英里遠。| *There's a man watching us from behind that fence.* 有個人正從籬笆後面看着我們。**6** used to express a distance〔表示距離〕距..., 離...: *We live about five km from Boston.* 我們住在離波士頓大約五公里的地方。| *a large Victorian house only fifty yards from my workplace* 離我的工作場所只有五十碼的一座維多利亞式的大房子 | *It's about an hour and a half from Scarborough.* 離斯卡伯勒大約有一個半小時的路程。**7** if something is moved or taken from a place or person, it is removed, taken away or taken out 從...移走, 從...拿走, 從...拿出: *She pulled her chair away from her desk.* 她把椅子從自己的寫字枱邊拉開。| *I had to take that new toy away from him.* 我只好把新玩具從他那兒拿走。| *Subtract three from 15.* 從15中減去3。| *He took a knife from his pocket.* 他從口袋裡掏出刀子。| *His absence from class has been noted.* 學校已經注意到他缺課。**8** used to say what the origin of something is 來自...; 源自...: *He gets his good looks from his mother.* 他好看的相貌得自於他母親的遺傳。| *I'll show you a short extract from one of our training videos.* 我將給你們看我們的一個訓練錄像的片段。| *Do you know where the information came from?* 你知道信息的來源嗎? | *an infectious disease which he got from another sick dog* 他從另一條病狗染來的傳染病 | *Members are chosen from a list drawn up by the Home Secretary.* 成員是從內政大臣擬定的名單中選出來的。| *I bought it from a shop in the market.* 我從市場上的一家商店買了這東西。| *I got this from Colin.* 我是從科林那兒得到這個東西的。**9** sent or given by someone 從〔某人〕寄來; 從〔某人那裡〕得到: *I've received a bill for nineteen dollars from the hospital.* 我已經收到醫院寄來的一張十九美元的賬單。| *I had a phone call from John.* 我接到了約翰打來的電話。| *You need to get permission from the owner.* 你需要得到主人的許可。| *with lots of love from Elaine and Martin* 帶着伊萊恩和馬丁深深的愛[深深愛你的伊萊恩和馬丁] **10 you can tell him from me...** *spoken* used to ask someone to tell another person something, when you are annoyed or determined【口】你可以替我轉告他...〔不高興時請人傳話時的用語〕: *Well, you can tell him from me that I'll be making an official complaint.* 好吧, 你可以告訴他說我要正式投訴。**11** someone who comes from a particular place lives, works, or belongs there 來自〔某個地方〕: *We invited speakers from all the regions.* 我們邀請了來自各地的演講者。| *Students from all faculties will have access to the machines.* 各院系的學生都將可以使用這些機器。| *Alison from the Job Centre is on the phone.* 我是就業服務中心的阿莉森。〔打電話時用語〕| **I'm from/I come from Devon/New York etc** (=born in Devon, New York etc) 我是德文郡人/我是紐約人等 **12** used to state the cause of something 因為..., 由於...: *mothers who are exhausted from all the sleepless nights* 由於這些不眠之夜而精疲力竭的母親們 | *Death rates from accidents have declined.* 事故的死亡率已經下降。| **suffer from** (=be affected by; have) 患〔病〕; 因...而受苦 *Mum suffers from migraines.* 媽媽患偏頭痛。**13** used to introduce the reason for, or origin of, an opinion or judgement 據...; 憑...: *From what I've read, the company seems to be in difficulties.* 據我在報章上所看到的, 這家公司似乎遇到困難。| *It's obvious from a quick glance that the plan has changed dramatically.* 稍微一瞥就能明顯看到這個計劃已經有了很大變化。| **from my point of view** (=how something affects you) 從我的觀點看 *These changes are ideal from my point of view.* 從我的觀點看, 這些變化很理想。| *From Clarisse's point of view, it's very distressing indeed.* 在克拉麗斯看來, 這確實十分令人苦惱。| **from memory** (=according to what I can remember) 憑我的記憶說, 就我所能回憶的說來 *From memory, the film wasn't as good as the book.* 憑我的記憶說, 這部電影不如書好。**14** used to state the substance that is used to make something 由...〔做的〕: *Bread is made from flour, water, and yeast.* 麵包是由麵粉、水和酵母做的。**15** used after words such as 'protect', 'prevent', or 'keep', to introduce the situation or action that is stopped, avoided, or prevented 免於〔表示阻止、避免、防止〕: *These problems have prevented me from completing the work.* 這些問題使我無法完成工作。| *people who have been disqualified from driving* 已被取消駕駛資格的人 **16** used when you are comparing things, and saying how they are similar or different 與...不同〔用於比較〕: *She's quite different from her sister.* 她和她的姐姐很不同。| *Our two cats are so alike, I can never tell one from the other.* 我們的兩隻貓很相像, 我從來就無法區分出來。

from·age frais /frɔˌmɑʒ ˈfre; ˌfrɒmɑːʒ ˈfreɪ/ *n* [U] *French* a soft white mild cheese you can eat with a spoon【法】稀乳酪, 液體鮮乳酪

frond /frɑnd; frɒnd/ *n* [C] a leaf of a FERN or PALM[1] (2)〔蕨類或棕櫚樹的〕葉

front 前面

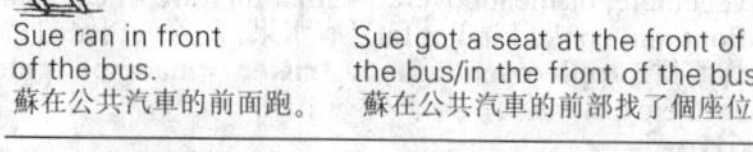

Sue ran in front of the bus.
蘇在公共汽車的前面跑。

Sue got a seat at the front of the bus/in the front of the bus.
蘇在公共汽車的前部找了個座位。

front[1] /frʌnt; frʌnt/ *n*

1 ►GROUP/LINE 一羣/一排◄ **the front** the front of a group or line of people or things is the position that is furthest forward in the direction that they are facing or moving 最前部, 最前面: **[+of]** *She always sits at the front of the class.* 她總坐在教室的最前面。| **in/at the front** *I think I can see them, they're right at the front.* 我想我可以看見他們, 他們就在最前面。| **the front of the line/queue/crowd** *TV reporters shoved their way to the front of the crowd.* 電視記者推擠到人羣的最前面。

2 ►FORWARD SIDE/SURFACE 前部/正面◄ **the front** the side or surface of something that is in the direction

that it faces or moves 前部; 前面: [+of] *Where did that scratch on the front of my car come from?* 我的車子前部的那處刮痕是哪裡來的? —compare 比較 REAR[1] (1)
3 the front the most important side or surface of something, that you look at first 正面, 頭版: **on the front** *Get a postcard with a picture of our hotel on the front of it.* 買一張正面印着我們旅館照片的明信片。| **[+of]** *She's on the front of the Radio Times.* 她出現在《廣播時報》的頭版上。—opposite 反義詞 BACK[2] (2) —compare 比較 REAR[1] (1)
4 ▶BUILDINGS 建築物◀ the front the most important side, where you go in〔最重要的〕一面, 正面
5 ▶BOOK 書籍◀ the front the first pages 扉頁
6 in front of sth a) near the side of something that is in the direction that it faces or moves 在某物前面: *right in front of the car* 在車子的正前面 —opposite 反義詞 BEHIND[1] (1) —see picture on page A1 參見A1頁圖 **b)** near the side of a building where you go in 在〔建築物前門的〕正前面: *She parked in front of the office.* 她在辦公室前面停了車。
7 in front of sb a) ahead of someone, in the direction that they are facing or moving 在某人的前面: *Come out here in front of the class.* 出來站在全班的前面。**b)** if you say or do something in front of someone you do it where they can see or hear you 在某人的面前: *Don't swear in front of the children!* 不要當着小孩的面罵人! **c)** if you have problems or difficulties in front of you, you will soon need to deal with them 某人面臨着〔難題或困難〕
8 in front a) in the most forward or leading position; ahead 在最前面的位置, 在前方: *Mrs Ramsay's horse was well in front.* 拉姆齊夫人的馬遙遙領先。| *He drove straight into the car in front.* 他一下子就撞上了前面的車子。—compare 比較 BEHIND[1] (1) **b)** in the area nearest the most forward part of something, or the entrance to a building 在〔建築物的〕前面[門前]
9 out front also 又作 **out the front/out in front** *BrE*【英】in the area near the entrance to a building 在門外, 在外面: *Hurry up! The taxi is out front.* 快! 計程車就在門外。
10 in/up front also 又作 **in the front** *especially BrE*【尤英】in the part of a car where the driver sits 在〔汽車的〕前座: *"Get in the car, kids." "Can I sit in front, Mom?"* "孩子們, 上車。" "媽媽, 我能坐在前面嗎?"
11 be brought/called/hauled in front of sb to have to see someone in authority about something you have done wrong〔因做錯事〕被帶到/被叫到/被拉到某人面前: *My whole section was called in front of the manager.* 我們全部門的人都被叫到經理面前。
12 sit in front of to spend time using or watching something such as a computer or television〔花時間〕使用〔電腦〕; 觀看〔電視〕: *You've spent all day just sitting in front of the television.* 你整天都在看電視。
13 ▶WEATHER 天氣◀ [C] *technical* the place where two areas of air of different temperatures meet, often shown as a line on weather maps【術語】鋒: **warm/cold front** (=an area of warm or cold air) 暖鋒/冷鋒
14 on the publicity/money/health front etc in a particular area 在宣傳/金錢/健康等方面: *Constant effort is needed on the publicity front.* 宣傳方面需要不斷努力。
15 up front *informal*【非正式】**a)** money that is paid up front is paid before work is done, or goods are supplied 預先, 事先〔付款〕: *We need two hundred pounds up front.* 我們需要預付二百英鎊。**b)** directly and clearly from the start〔一開始就〕明確地: *Jorge wanted to help her, but she'd told him up front she did not need it.* 豪爾赫想要幫她, 可她明確地告訴他她不需要幫助。—see also 另見 UPFRONT
16 ▶SEA 海洋◀ the front *especially BrE* the part of a town next to the sea, between the beach and the shops, hotels etc; SEAFRONT【尤英】海濱城市; 臨海地區
17 ▶BODY 身體◀ your chest, or the part of your body that faces forward 胸前; 前面: *I've spilled some soup down my front.* 我把一些湯濺到胸前了。
18 on all fronts in every area of the activity that you are involved in 在各方面: *We're making rapid progress on all fronts.* 我們在各方面進展都很快。
19 be a front for *informal* to be used for hiding a secret or illegal activity【非正式】成為〔祕密或非法活動〕的掩護者[物], 為…作掩護[當幌子]: *Could his business be a front for drug smuggling?* 他的公司會是掩護毒品走私的商行嗎?
20 put on/show a front to behave in a way that is braver or happier than you feel 裝出〔勇敢或高興〕的樣子: *I know you're scared, but you've got to put on a brave front.* 我知道你害怕, 但你得表現出勇敢的樣子。
21 ▶ORGANIZATION 組織機構◀ [singular] used in the name of a political party or unofficial military organization 陣線〔用於政黨或非正式軍事組織的名稱〕: *the People's Liberation Front* 人民解放陣線
22 ▶WAR 戰爭◀ [C] a line along which fighting takes place during a war; FRONT LINE 前線, 前方: *trucks heading towards the Western Front* 向西部前線駛去的卡車 —see also 另見 HOME FRONT
23 ▶CHURCH 教堂◀ [C] a side of a large, important church building〔大教堂的〕一面: *the west front* 西面, 朝西的一面

USAGE NOTE 用法說明: FRONT
WORD CHOICE 詞語辨析: **in front of, behind, at/in the front of, at/in the back of, face, opposite, before**
In front of (opposite **behind**) is used when one thing is separate from the other. 某個東西不與另一個東西相連時, 用 in front of (反義詞 behind) : *A child ran out in front of the bus* (=in the road outside the bus). 一個小孩跑到了公共汽車的前面。
At/in the front of (opposite **at/in the back of**) is used when one thing is inside or part of the other. 某一個東西位於另一個東西之中或是其一部分時, 用 at/in the front of (反義詞 at/in the back of) : *The child took a seat at/in the front of the bus* (=in the front part of the bus). 這個小孩在公共汽車的前部坐了下來。
If a building is in front of something, it **faces**. it 如果說某建築物在某物前面, 這棟建築物就是面向 (face) 這個物體: *The hotel faced the Mediterranean.* 這家旅館面向地中海。
A person or place that faces another one exactly, with a space between, is **opposite** it. If the bus stop is *opposite the station* it is not *in front of the station* but on the other side of the road. 一個人或地方正面對着另一個人或地方, 但中間有間隔, 那麼這個人或地方是在對面 (opposite)。如果公共汽車站是在車站的對面 (opposite), 它不是在車站的前面 (in front of), 而是在馬路的對面: *I live opposite Greg.* 我住在格雷格家的對面。
One event may happen **before** another. 一件事發生在另一件事之前時用 before: *Let's have a drink before dinner* (NOT 不用 *in front of dinner*). 我們在晚餐前喝點吧。

front² *adj* [only before noun 僅用於名詞前] **1** at, on, or in the front of something (在) 前面的; 前部的: *Your front teeth are going to have to be straightened.* 你的門牙得去弄正一下。| **front door/room/garden** (=at the front of a house) 前門/前廳/前花園 | **front seat/row** *Good news! I got us front row seats!* 好消息! 我給大家弄到了前排的座位! —opposite 反義詞 BACK[3] (1) **2** *informal* a front man or organization acts lawfully in business as a way of hiding a secret or illegal activity【非正式】起掩護作用的, 作幌子的: *a front organization for importing heroin* 一個進口海洛因活動的掩護組織 **3** *technical* a front vowel sound is made by raising your tongue at the front of your mouth【術語】〔元音〕前舌音的 —opposite 反義詞 BACK[3] (7)

F

front³ *v* **1** [I,T] if a building fronts onto the sea, a road etc, the front of the building faces it 面對, 面向: **[+onto]** *Our hotel fronts onto a main road.* 我們的旅館面向一條大路。| **front sth** *houses fronting the lake* 面向湖的房屋 **2 be fronted by/with** to be covered or decorated at the front with something 正面飾有…的: *Victor led us into a large building fronted with marble.* 維克托把我們領進一棟正面牆由大理石砌成的大樓。**3** [T] to lead something such as a group or television programme by being the person that the public see most 領導〔一羣人〕; 主持〔電視節目〕: *She's fronting a weekly current affairs program.* 她在主持一個每週時事節目。

front for sb/sth *phr v* [T] *informal* to act as the person or organization used for hiding the real nature of a secret or illegal activity【非正式】充當…的掩護, 替…作掩護: *Police suspected her of fronting for a gang of forgers.* 警方懷疑她替一幫偽造者作掩護。

front·age /ˋfrʌntɪdʒ; ˈfrʌntɪdʒ/ *n* [U] the part of a building or piece of land that is along a road, river, etc〔建築物的〕正面; 臨路地; 臨河地

front·al /ˋfrʌntl; ˈfrʌntl/ *adj* [only before noun 僅用於名詞前] *formal*【正式】**1** at or connected with the front part of something 前面的, 正面的: *the frontal area of the brain* 大腦的前區 **2** towards the front of something 向前端的, 朝正面的: *From the frontal approach, the house looks grand and imposing.* 這座房屋從正面看上去雄偉壯麗。**3 full frontal** showing people with no clothes on, from the front 正面全裸的: *full frontal nudity* 全身正面赤裸, 一絲不掛 **—frontally** *adv*

frontal sys·tem /ˈ‥ ˌ‥/ *n* [C] *technical* a weather FRONT¹ (13)【術語】鋒系

front-and-center /ˌ‥ ˈ‥◂/ *adj AmE* very important and needing attention【美】重大的, 首要的, 中心的, 需要關注的: *Prayer in schools has become a front-and-center issue for the White House.* 學校禱告已經成為白宮的中心議題。

frontbench /ˌ· ˈ·◂/ *n* [C] the front row of seats on each side of the British parliament, on which the leaders of the political parties sit〔英國議會的〕前(排)座(位)〔為各政黨領導人的席位〕—compare 比較 BACKBENCH

front·bench·er /ˌfrʌntˋbɛntʃɚ; ˌfrʌntˈbentʃə◂/ *n* [C] someone who sits on a front bench in the British parliament〔英國議會中的〕前座議員 —compare 比較 BACKBENCHER

front door /ˌ· ˈ·/ *n* [C usually singular 一般用單數] the main entrance door to a house, at the front〔房屋的〕前門, 正門 —compare 比較 BACK DOOR (1)

fron·tier /frʌnˋtɪr; ˈfrʌntɪə/ *n* **1 the frontier** an area where people have never lived before, that not much is known about, especially in the western US before the 20th century〔尤指 20 世紀前美國西部的〕邊遠地區, 荒野地區; 邊疆: *the settlement of the Oklahoma frontier* 俄克拉何馬州邊遠地區的新拓居地 | *space, the final frontier* 太空, 最後一塊未開拓的疆域 **2** [C] *especially BrE* the border of a country, where people cross from one country to another【尤英】國境, 邊境: **[+between/with]** *Lille is close to the frontier between France and Belgium.* 里爾緊靠法國和比利時的邊境。| **on/at the frontier** *Troops established a road block on the frontier.* 部隊在邊境設立了路障。**3 the frontiers of knowledge/physics etc** the limit of what is known about something 知識/物理的新領域等: **push back the frontiers** (=discover new things) 開拓新領域 **4 roll back the frontiers** to make something such as government power smaller 使〔如政府權力等〕變小, 削減

fron·tiers·man /frʌnˋtɪrzmən; ˈfrʌntɪəzmən/ *n* [C] a man who lived in the American frontier〔美國的〕邊遠地區居民; 邊疆開拓者

fron·tis·piece /ˋfrʌntɪsˌpis; ˈfrʌntɨspiːs/ *n* [C] a picture or photograph at the beginning of a book, usually opposite the page with the title on it〔書籍的〕卷首插圖, 扉畫

front line /ˌ· ˈ·◂/ *n* **1 the front line** the place where fighting happens in a war; FRONT¹ (22)〔戰爭中的〕前線, 前方: *troops in the front line* 前線部隊 **2 in the front line a)** doing something that has not been done before 在…第一線; 在…最前線: *in the front line of the fight against cancer* 在抗癌鬥爭的第一線 **b)** likely to be blamed for an organization's mistakes〔因所屬組織的錯誤〕可能受指責, 可能要承擔過失的責任 **—front-line** *adj* [only before noun 僅用於名詞前]: *front-line conditions* 前線的形勢

front man /ˈ· ·/ *n* [C usually singular 一般用單數] a person who speaks for an organization, for example an illegal one, but is not the leader of it〔某組織的〕出面人; 代表人; 發言人

front mat·ter /ˈ· ˌ‥/ *n* [U] all the pages at the very beginning of a book, including the page with the title on it〔書籍的〕前面各頁

front money /ˈ· ˌ‥/ *n* [singular] money that is paid for something before you get it 預付款

front of·fice /ˌ· ˈ‥/ *n* [singular] *AmE* the managers of a company【美】〔公司的〕管理層; 管理部門

front page /ˌ· ˈ·/ *n* [C] the first page of a newspaper〔報紙的〕頭版

front-page /ˈ· ·/ *adj* [only before noun 僅用於名詞前] *informal* interesting, important, or exciting enough to be printed on the front page of a newspaper【非正式】〔報紙〕頭版的; 重要的; 轟動的: *a front-page story* 頭版報道

front room /ˌ· ˈ·/ *n* [C] the main room in a house where you usually sit; LIVING ROOM 起居室, 客廳; 前廳

front-run·ner /ˌ· ˈ‥/ *n* [C] the person or thing that is most likely to succeed in a competition〔競爭中的〕領先者: *Thomson and Palmer are the front-runners for promotion.* 湯姆森和帕爾默最有希望得到提拔。

frost¹ /frɔst; frɒst/ *n* **1** [U] ice that looks white and powdery and covers things that are outside when the temperature is very cold 霜: *The grass and trees were white with frost.* 草和樹上蓋滿了白霜。**2** [C] very cold weather, when water freezes〔天氣〕嚴寒, 冰凍: **late/early frost** *Even in May we can sometimes get a late frost.* 就算在五月份, 我們有時都會遇到春寒冰凍的天氣。| **hard frost** (=extremely cold weather) 嚴寒, 酷寒 *Our pipes burst in the hard frost.* 我們的管道在嚴寒中爆裂。—see also 另見 FROSTY, FROSTED

frost² *v* [T] *especially AmE* to cover a cake with a mixture of powdery sugar and liquid; ICE²【尤美】在〔糕餅〕上撒糖霜

frost up also 又作 **frost over** *phr v* [I] to become covered in frost 佈滿霜, 結霜: *The car door's all frosted up and I can't get it open.* 車門結滿了霜, 我打不開它。

frost·bite /ˋfrɔstˌbaɪt; ˈfrɒstbaɪt/ *n* [U] a condition caused by extreme cold, that makes your fingers, toes etc swell, become darker and sometimes drop off 霜害, 凍傷 **—frostbitten** /-bɪtn̩; -bɪtn/ *adj*

frost·ed /ˋfrɔstɪd; ˈfrɒstɨd/ *adj* covered with FROST¹ (1), or with something that looks like frost 結霜的; 有霜狀表面的

frosted glass /ˌ‥ ˈ·◂/ *n* [U] glass that is not transparent 磨砂玻璃: *a frosted glass screen* 磨砂玻璃屏風

frost·ing /ˋfrɔstɪŋ; ˈfrɒstɪŋ/ *n* [U] **1** *especially AmE* a sweet substance put on cakes and made from powdery sugar and liquid; ICING【尤美】〔撒在糕餅上的〕糖霜 **2** a rough surface that is not shiny 磨砂面

frost·y /ˋfrɔstɪ; ˈfrɒsti/ *adj* **1 a)** extremely cold 嚴寒的: *frosty air* 冷冽的空氣 **b)** covered with FROST¹ (1) 覆蓋着霜的, 結霜的: *She stumbled, falling heavily on the frosty ground.* 她絆了一下, 重重地摔在結霜的地面上。**2** unfriendly 不友好的; 冷淡的: *"This is a members-only club," said the doorman with frosty politeness.* "這俱樂部只接待本會會員。" 看門人冷淡而禮貌地說道。| **frosty smile/expression/stare** *He gave me a frosty stare.* 他冷冷地瞪了我一眼。**—frostily** *adv*

froth¹ /frɔθ; frɒθ/ *n* **1** [singular, U] small BUBBLES¹ (1) that form on top of a liquid that has air mixed in it 泡沫, 泡: *He carefully wiped the froth from his moustache.* 他小心地抹去小鬍子上的泡沫。**2** [singular, U] small, white BUBBLEs[1] (1) of SALIVA around a person's or animal's mouth〔人或動物嘴裡流出的〕白沫 **3** [U] talk or ideas that are attractive but have no real value or meaning〔動人的〕空談; 空想: *The book has too much froth and not enough fact.* 這本書空話太多, 事實很少。

froth² *v* [I] **1** also 又作 **froth up** if a liquid froths it produces or contains BUBBLEs[1] (1) on top 起泡沫; 含有泡沫: *When you first open the bottle the beer will froth for a few seconds.* 剛打開瓶子時, 啤酒會起幾秒鐘泡沫。**2** if someone's mouth froths, SALIVA comes out as small white BUBBLEs[1] (1) 口吐白沫 **3 froth at the mouth a)** *informal* to be extremely angry【非正式】氣急敗壞, 氣得要命: *By the time I got out of the traffic jam I was frothing at the mouth.* 當我從堵塞的交通中脫身出來時, 我氣得要命。**b)** to have SALIVA coming out of your mouth as small white BUBBLEs[1] (1) 口吐白沫

froth·y /ˋfrɒθɪ; ˈfrɒθi/ *adj* **1** a liquid that is frothy has lots of small BUBBLEs[1] (1) on top 表面起泡沫的: *a cup of hot frothy cappuccino* 一杯熱騰騰、冒着泡的意大利白咖啡 **2** a frothy book, film etc is enjoyable but not serious or important〔書、電影等〕有趣但淺薄的; 不嚴肅的 —**frothily** *adv*

frown¹ /fraun; fraʊn/ *v* [I] to make an angry, unhappy, or confused expression, moving your EYEBROWs together 皺眉: *She saw him frown as he read the letter.* 她看見他在讀信的時候皺眉頭。| [+at] *Mattie frowned at him disapprovingly.* 馬蒂不滿地朝他皺眉頭。

frown on/upon sb/sth *phr v* [T usually passive 一般用被動態] to disapprove of something, especially someone's behaviour 不贊成, 反對〔尤指某人的行為〕: *Even though divorce is legal it is still frowned upon.* 儘管離婚是合法的, 人們仍然不太贊同。

frown² *n* [C usually singular 一般用單數] the expression on your face when you frown 皺眉: **with a frown** *He looked at her with a puzzled frown.* 他困惑不解地皺着眉頭看着她。

frow·zy /ˋfrauzɪ; ˈfraʊzi/ also 又作 **frowsty** /ˋfraustɪ; ˈfraʊsti/ *BrE*【英】—*adj* **1** someone who is frowzy is not very clean or tidy and smells bad 邋遢的; 不整潔的; 骯髒難聞的: *a frowzy old woman who kept cats* 一個養了許多貓的、邋遢的老太太 **2** a house or room that is frowzy has no fresh air in it and smells bad〔房屋或房間〕氣味難聞的; 霉臭的: *The air in the room had become stale and frowzy.* 房間裡的空氣不流通, 氣味難聞。

froze /froz; frəʊz/ the past tense of FREEZE[1]

fro·zen¹ /ˋfrozn̩; ˈfrəʊzən/ the past participle of FREEZE[1]

frozen² *adj* **1** frozen food has been stored at a very low temperature in order to preserve it〔食物〕冷凍的, 冷藏的: *frozen meat* 冷凍肉 **2 be frozen (stiff)** *spoken* to feel very cold【口】凍僵的, 凍壞的: *I'm frozen! Put the fire on.* 我凍僵了! 把爐子打開。**3** earth that is frozen is so cold it has become very hard〔土地〕凍硬的: *The ground was frozen beneath our feet.* 我們腳下的地都凍硬了。**4** a river, lake etc that is frozen has a layer of ice on the surface〔河、湖等〕結冰的 **5 be frozen with fear/terror/fright** to be so afraid, shocked etc that you cannot move 被嚇呆了, 被嚇得無法動彈

fruc·ti·fy /ˋfrʌktə͵faɪ; ˈfrʌktʃfaɪ/ *v* [I,T] *technical* to produce fruit or to make a plant produce fruit【術語】(使)結果實 —**fructification** /͵frʌktəfəˋkeʃən; ͵frʌktʃfɪʃˈkeɪʃən/ *n* [U]

fruc·tose /ˋfrʌktos; ˈfrʌktəʊs/ *n* [U] a kind of natural sugar in fruit juices and HONEY (1)〔果汁或蜂蜜中的〕(天然)果糖

fru·gal /ˋfrugl̩; ˈfruːgəl/ *adj* **1** careful to only buy what is necessary 節儉的, 節約的: *As children we were taught to be frugal and hard-working.* 小時候大人教我們要節儉和勤勞。**2** a frugal meal is a small meal of plain food〔膳食〕少量的; 簡便的, 簡單的: *We sat down to a frugal breakfast.* 我們坐下來吃了一頓簡單的早餐。—**frugally** *adv* —**frugality** /fruˋgælətɪ; fruːˈgælʃti/ *n* [U]

fruit¹ /frut; fruːt/ *n plural* **fruit** or **fruits** **1** [C,U] something such as an apple, BANANA, or STRAWBERRY that grows on a tree or other plant, and tastes sweet 水果: *fresh fruit and vegetables* 新鮮蔬果 | *a bowl of fruit* 一盤水果 —see also 另見 DRIED FRUIT, SOFT FRUIT —see picture on page A8 參見A8頁圖 **2** [C,U] *technical* the part of a plant, bush, or tree that contains the seeds【術語】果實 **3 the fruit/fruits of sth** the good results that you have from something, after you have worked very hard 某事物的成果 **4 bear fruit** if a plan or activity bears fruit, it produces the good results that you intended〔計劃或活動〕取得成果, 有成效 **5 in fruit** *technical* trees, plants etc that are in fruit are producing their fruit【術語】在結果實 **6 the fruits of the earth/nature** all the natural things that the earth produces, such as fruit, vegetables, or minerals 大地/大自然的果實〈如水果、蔬菜或礦物等〉**7** [C] *old-fashioned slang* an insulting way of talking to or about a man who is a HOMOSEXUAL【過時, 俚】男同性戀者〔侮辱性的詞語〕**8 old fruit** *old-fashioned slang BrE* used by men as a way of addressing a man that they know well【過時, 俚, 英】老兄〔對朋友的稱呼〕 S2 W2

fruit² *v* [I] *technical* if a tree or a plant fruits, it produces fruit【術語】〔樹或植物〕結果實

fruit bat /ˋ· ·/ *n* [C] a large BAT[1] (1) that lives in hot countries and eats fruit 狐蝠, 熱帶大蝙蝠

fruit·cake /ˋfrut͵kek; ˈfruːtkeɪk/ *n* **1** [C,U] a cake that has dried fruit in it 水果[果脯, 果子]蛋糕 **2** [C] *informal* someone who seems to be mentally ill or behaves in a strange way【非正式】怪人, 瘋子: *She's a bit of a fruitcake.* 她有點怪。—see also 另見 **nutty as a fruitcake** (NUTTY (3))

fruit·er·er /ˋfrutərə; ˈfruːtərə/ *n* [C] *BrE old-fashioned* someone who sells fruit【英, 過時】水果商

fruit fly /ˋ· ·/ *n* [C] a small fly that eats fruit or decaying plants 果蠅

fruit·ful /ˋfrutfəl; ˈfruːtfəl/ *adj* **1** something you do that is fruitful has good results 富有成效的: *Today's meeting proved more fruitful than last week's.* 今天的會議證明比上星期的有成效。—opposite 反義詞 FRUITLESS **2** *literary* land that is fruitful produces a lot of corn, vegetables, fruit etc【文】〔土地〕多產的, 豐饒的; 果實纍纍的 —**fruitfully** *adv* —**fruitfulness** *n* [U]

fru·i·tion /fruˋɪʃən; fruːˈɪʃən/ *n* [U] *formal* the successful result of a plan, idea etc【正式】〔計劃、想法等〕實現; 完成: **come to fruition/be brought to fruition** *All his plans had come to fruition.* 他所有的計劃都實現了。

fruit·less /ˋfrutlɪs; ˈfruːtləs/ *adj* failing to achieve what was wanted, especially after much effort 無成效的, 無結果的: **fruitless attempt/search/journey** *a fruitless attempt to settle the dispute* 試圖解決爭端的徒勞的努力 | *So far, their search has been fruitless.* 到目前為止, 他們的搜尋工作毫無結果。—opposite 反義詞 FRUITFUL (1) —**fruitlessly** *adv* —**fruitlessness** *n* [U]

fruit ma·chine /ˋ· ·͵·/ *n* [C] *BrE* a machine in which you put a coin, that gives money back if you make three pictures of the same thing appear【英】吃角子老虎機; SLOT MACHINE *AmE*【美】

fruit sal·ad /͵· ˋ··/ *n* [C,U] a dish of many different types of fruit cut into small pieces 水果沙拉[沙律]

fruit·y /ˋfrutɪ; ˈfruːti/ *adj* **1** tasting or smelling strongly of fruit 有水果味的: *a very fruity wine* 帶濃郁果香的葡萄酒 **2** a voice or laugh that is fruity sounds low and pleasant〔聲音〕圓潤的; 洪亮的;〔微笑〕甜美的 **3** *BrE informal* a remark, story etc that is fruity is about sex and slightly shocking or offensive【英, 非正式】〔話語、故事等〕猥褻的; 低級趣味的

frump /frʌmp; frʌmp/ *n* [C] a woman who is frumpy 衣着過時的女子; 老古董, 古板的人

frump·y /ˋfrʌmpɪ; ˈfrʌmpi/ also 又作 **frump·ish** /ˋfrʌmpɪʃ;

F

'frʌmpɪʃ/ *adj* a woman who is frumpy looks unattractive because she dresses in old-fashioned clothes〔女子〕衣着過時的; 古板的

frus·trate /ˈfrʌstret; frʌˈstreɪt/ *v* [T] **1** if something frustrates you it makes you feel annoyed or angry because you are unable to do what you want 使惱怒, 使灰心喪氣: *I think the fact that he's working with amateurs really frustrates him.* 我看他和非專業人員一起幹活的事實在使他感到沮喪。**2** to prevent someone's plans, efforts or attempts from succeeding 挫敗; 阻撓: *Their attempts to speak to him were frustrated by the guards.* 他們想跟他說話, 但被警衛攔住了。—compare 比較 THWART[1]

frus·trat·ed /ˈfrʌstretɪd; frʌˈstreɪtɪ̇d/ *adj* **1** feeling annoyed, upset, and impatient, because you cannot control or change a situation, or achieve something 灰心喪氣的, 泄氣的, 沮喪的: **get frustrated** *He gets frustrated when he can't win.* 他贏不了的時候便垂頭喪氣。| **[+with/at]** *I can't understand this. I just get frustrated with it.* 我無法理解這一點。我只是對此感到沮喪。| **sexually frustrated** (=feeling dissatisfied because you cannot have sex) 性慾上不滿足的 **2 a frustrated poet/actor/dancer etc** someone who wants to develop a particular skill but has not been able to do this 失意的詩人/演員/舞蹈員等

frus·trat·ing /ˈfrʌstretɪŋ; frʌˈstreɪtɪŋ/ *adj* making you feel annoyed, upset, or impatient because you cannot do what you want to do 令人沮喪[泄氣, 不快, 不耐煩]的

frus·tra·tion /frʌsˈtreʃən; frʌˈstreɪʃən/ *n* **1** [C,U] the feeling of being annoyed, upset, or impatient, because you cannot control or change a situation, or achieve something 失意; 失望; 沮喪; 受挫: *It wasn't what he said that made me cry – it was sheer frustration.* 讓我哭的不是他說的話 —— 而是徹底的失望。| **in/with frustration** *Souness watched in frustration as his team lost yet again.* 索內斯失望地看着他的球隊又輸了。**2** [U] the fact of being prevented from achieving what you are trying to achieve 受挫: **[+of]** *The frustration of his ambitions made him a bitter man.* 他的雄心壯志受挫, 使他充滿怨恨。

S3 **fry**[1] /fraɪ; fraɪ/ *v past and past participle* **fried 1** [I,T] to cook something in hot fat or oil, or to be cooked in hot fat or oil 煎, 炸, 炒: *Fry the onions until they are golden.* 把洋蔥炒至金黃色。—see picture on page A10 參見A10頁圖 **2** [I,T] *AmE slang* to kill someone, or to be killed, as a punishment in the ELECTRIC CHAIR【美俚】(被) 以電刑處死, 坐電椅 —see also 另見 DEEP FRY, FRIES, STIR-FRY —**fried** *adj*

fry[2] *n* [plural] **1** very young fish 魚苗, 魚秧; 小魚 —see also 另見 **small fry** (SMALL[1] (12)) **2 fries** [plural] *AmE* long thin pieces of potato that have been cooked in fat【美】油炸馬鈴薯條; chips (CHIP[1] (3a)) *BrE*【英】

fry·er, frier /ˈfraɪɚ; ˈfraɪə/ *n* [C] **1 deep fat fryer/deep fryer** *AmE* a big deep pan for frying food【美】油炸鍋 **2** *AmE* a chicken that has been specially bred to be fried【美】〔適合油炸的〕嫩雞

frying pan /ˈ·· ˌ·/ *n* [C] **1** a round flat pan with a long handle, used for frying food 長柄平底煎鍋; SKILLET *AmE*【美】—see picture at 參見 PAN[1] 圖 **2 out of the frying pan and into the fire** to go from a bad situation to one that is even worse 跳出油鍋又落入火坑〔比喻境況愈來愈糟〕

fry-up /ˈ· ·/ *n* [C] *informal BrE* a meal of fried food such as eggs, BACON, potatoes etc【非正式, 英】簡單油煎菜〈如煎雞蛋、熏肉、馬鈴薯等〉

ft 1 the written abbreviation of 縮寫= FOOT[1] (3) 英尺: *a board 6ft x 4ft* 6英尺×4英尺的木板 **2 Ft** the written abbreviation of 縮寫= FORT, used in names of places 城堡〔用於地名〕: *Ft. Lauderdale* 勞德代爾堡

fuch·sia /ˈfjuʃə; ˈfjuːʃə/ *n* **1** [C,U] a garden bush with hanging bell-shaped flowers in two colours of red, pink, or white 倒掛金鐘〔花卉名〕**2** [U] a bright pink colour 紫紅色

fuck[1] /fʌk; fʌk/ *v taboo spoken*【諱, 口】**1 Fuck off!** an offensive way of telling someone to go away 滾開!〔冒犯用語〕: *Fuck off you stupid bastard!* 滾開, 你這雜種! **2** [I,T] to have sex with someone (與…) 性交 **3 fuck it/you/her/John!** used to emphasize that you are annoyed or angry at someone or something 他媽的! / 滾你媽的蛋! / 滾她媽的蛋! / 約翰這混蛋!〔罵人用語〕: *Oh fuck it! I'm going home early!* 嗬, 他媽的! 我要早回家了!

fuck around also 又作 **fuck about** *BrE*【英】*phr v* [I] *taboo spoken* to waste time or behave in a silly or careless way【諱, 口】閒混; 瞎搞; 幹蠢事

fuck sb **around** also 又作 **fuck** sb **about** *BrE*【英】*phr v* [I] *taboo spoken* to make someone angry or annoyed by wasting their time【諱, 口】粗暴地對待; 瞎弄; 浪費時間: *The telephone company has been fucking me around all week.* 電話公司整個星期都在耍弄我。

fuck sb ↔ **off** *phr v* [T] *taboo spoken* to make someone feel annoyed or angry【諱, 口】使煩厭; 使生氣: *Steve really fucks me off when he doesn't write down my phone messages.* 史蒂夫不記下人家給我的電話留言, 使我確實很生氣。

fuck sb ↔ **over** *phr v* [T] *AmE taboo* to treat someone very badly【美諱】虐待〔某人〕: *Bev had been fucked over so many times she no longer expected life to be fair.* 貝夫已經被虧待許多次了, 她不再指望生活是公平的。

fuck sb ↔ **up** *phr v* [T] *taboo spoken* to make someone very unhappy and confused so that they cannot control their life【諱, 口】搞糟, 弄亂; 毀掉: *Heroin fucks you up.* 海洛因會把你毀了。

fuck up *phr v taboo spoken* [I,T **fuck** sth ↔ **up**] to make a mistake or do something badly【諱, 口】犯錯誤; 把事情搞糟: *You really fucked up this time.* 這次你真把事情搞糟了。

fuck with sb *phr v* [T] *taboo spoken* to annoy someone or make them angry【諱, 口】使某人惱怒, 使某人生氣: *I wouldn't fuck with Alfie if I were you.* 要是我是你, 就不會激怒阿爾菲。

fuck[2] *interjection taboo* used when you are annoyed about something【諱】他媽的, 混賬, 見鬼: *Fuck! I forgot my keys!* 他媽的! 我忘了帶鑰匙!

fuck[3] *n taboo spoken*【諱, 口】**1** [C usually singular 一般用單數] the act of having sex 性交 **2 the fuck** used when you are angry to emphasize what you are saying〔發怒時用於強調〕他媽的; 究竟, 到底: *Get the fuck out of here!* 你他媽的滾出去! | **who/why/what etc the fuck** *What the fuck do you think you're doing?* 你他媽的究竟想做甚麼? **3 not care/give a fuck** to not care at all what happens 毫不在乎

fuck all /ˈ· ·/ *n* [U] *BrE taboo spoken* nothing【英, 諱, 口】甚麼都沒有: *I don't know why they employ him. He does fuck all anyway.* 我不知道他們幹嘛要雇他。反正他甚麼事也不做。

fucked up /ˌ· ˈ·/ *adj taboo* very unhappy and confused, so that you cannot control your life properly【諱】亂糟糟的: *She's pretty fucked up.* 她相當一塌糊塗。

fuck·er /ˈfʌkɚ; ˈfʌkə/ also 又作 **fuck** *BrE*【英】—*n* [C] *taboo spoken* someone who you dislike very much, think is stupid etc【諱, 口】討厭透頂的人, 混蛋; 笨蛋

fuck·head /ˈfʌkˌhɛd; ˈfʌkhed/ *n* [C] *AmE taboo spoken* someone you dislike or think is stupid【美, 諱, 口】討厭的人, 混蛋; 笨蛋: *Get lost, fuckhead.* 走開, 混蛋。

fuck·ing /ˈfʌkɪŋ; ˈfʌkɪŋ/ *adj* [only before noun 僅用於名詞前] *taboo spoken*【諱, 口】**1** used to emphasize that you are angry or annoyed 該死的: *I wish that fucking parrot would shut up!* 我希望那隻該死的鸚鵡會住嘴! **2** used to emphasize your opinion of something 非常〔用於強調〕: *He's a fucking good football player.* 他足球踢得非常好。

fuck·ing A /ˌfʌkɪŋ ˋe; ˌfʌkɪŋ ˈeɪ/ *interjection AmE taboo* used when you are very surprised, shocked etc by something【美諱】他媽的〔表示驚訝、震驚等〕: *Fucking*

A! I never thought L.A. would be this hot. 他媽的！我從來沒想到洛杉磯會這麼熱。

fuck-up /ˈ· ·/ *n* [C] *taboo spoken* a situation that has been dealt with very badly【諱，口】一團糟: *Relations with the staff were bad, so any change in the schedule was seen as 'yet another fuck-up by the management'.* 公司與職員的關係很壞，因此日程表上有任何變化都被看作"管理部門又一次搞糟了"。

fud·dle¹ /ˈfʌdḷ; ˈfʌdl/ *v* [T] *BrE informal* if something, especially alcohol or drugs, fuddles you or your mind, it makes you unable to think clearly【英，非正式】〔尤指酒精或毒品〕使昏醉；使糊塗: *Too much drink fuddles your brain.* 喝酒太多會讓你腦子糊塗。

fuddle² *n* [singular] *informal*【非正式】**in a fuddle** feeling very confused and unable to think clearly 頭腦糊塗的: *Poor old Tom. Since his wife died he's been in a terrible fuddle.* 可憐的老湯姆，自從妻子去世後他就一直糊糊塗塗的。

fud·dled /ˈfʌdḷd; ˈfʌdld/ *adj* unable to think clearly, especially because you are drunk or old〔尤指由於酒醉或年老而〕頭腦糊塗的，思想混亂的

fud·dy-dud·dy /ˈfʌdɪ ˌdʌdɪ; ˈfʌdi ˌdʌdi/ *n* [C] someone who has old-fashioned ideas and attitudes 守舊的人；老古董: *You're such an old fuddy-duddy. Most women wear trousers these days!* 你太頑固保守了，如今多數婦女都穿長褲了！—**fuddy-duddy** *adj*

fudge¹ /fʌdʒ; fʌdʒ/ *n* **1** [U] a soft creamy light brown sweet food 奶油軟糖 **2 a fudge** *especially BrE* an attempt to deal with a situation that does not solve its problems completely, or only makes it seem better【尤英】勉強應付；作表面上的改善；敷衍了事

fudge² *v* **1** [I,T] to avoid giving exact details or a clear answer about something 迴避；敷衍；搪塞: **fudge the issue** (=avoid a particular subject) 迴避問題 *politicians fudging the issue of arms sales* 迴避武器出售問題的政治家 **2** [T] to change important figures or facts to deceive people 捏造: *Sibley has been fudging his data for years now.* 西布利好幾年來一直在捏造數據。

fudge³ *interjection* used when you are angry or annoyed, instead of saying a more offensive word 胡說，瞎說〔用於生氣或煩惱時，代替更具冒犯性的詞語〕: *Oh fudge! I've left my wallet at home!* 哎，媽的！我把皮夾子遺在家裡了！

fudg·y /ˈfʌdʒɪ; ˈfʌdʒi/ *adj AmE* slightly sticky with a strong sweet chocolate taste【美】帶濃烈巧克力甜味而有點黏的

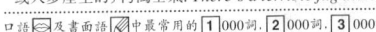

2 2 **fu·el¹** /ˈfjuəl; ˈfjuːəl/ *n* **1** [C,U] a substance such as coal, gas, or oil that can be burned to produce heat or energy 燃料: *Don't leave the engine switched on. It wastes fuel.* 別讓發動機開着。這浪費燃料。| *Coal is one of the cheapest fuels.* 煤是最廉價的燃料之一。**2** [U] something that makes someone's anger, hatred etc worse 火上加油的東西；使〔怒氣、怨恨等〕更激烈的東西: **fuel to sth** *His behaviour was only fuel to her jealousy.* 他的行為只能使她更加妒忌。**3 add fuel to the fire/flames** to make a situation a lot worse than it was already 火上澆油

fuel² *v past tense* **fuelled** *BrE*【英】, **fueled** *AmE*【美】**1** [T] to make a situation worse or make someone's feelings stronger 使惡化；使感情更強烈: *The attempts to stop the strike only fuelled the workers' resentment.* 制止罷工的企圖只能使工人更加不滿。**2** [T] to put oil, petrol etc in a vehicle 給〔車輛〕加油 **3** also 又作 **fuel up** [I] if a vehicle fuels up, fuel is put into it 加油，加燃料: *It's amazing that some planes can fuel up in mid air.* 有些飛機能在空中加油，這真令人吃驚。

fuel in·jec·tion /ˈ·· ·ˌ··/ *n* [U] a method of putting liquid fuel directly into an engine, which allows a car to ACCELERATE more quickly 燃油噴射

fug /fʌg; fʌg/ *n* [singular] *BrE informal* air inside a room that feels heavy and unpleasant because of smoke, heat, or too many people【英，非正式】〔房間內因煙霧、熱氣或人多產生的〕污濁空氣: *There's a terrible fug in here. Let's open a window.* 這裡面空氣污濁得可怕，我們開扇窗子吧。—**fuggy** *adj*

fu·gi·tive¹ /ˈfjudʒətɪv; ˈfjuːdʒə̇tɪv/ *n* [C] someone who is hiding, especially from the police, and is trying to avoid being caught 逃犯；逃亡者: **[+from]** *a fugitive from justice* 在逃的罪犯

fugitive² *adj* [only before noun 僅用於名詞前] **1** trying to escape 企圖逃跑的 **2** *literary* lasting for a very short time【文】短暫的: *rare and fugitive visits* 難得而短暫的訪問

fugue /fjug; fjuːg/ *n* [C,U] a way of writing music using a tune that is repeated regularly in different keys (KEY² (4)) by different voices, instruments etc, or a piece of music written this way 賦格（曲）

-ful¹ /fəl; fəl/ *suffix* [in adjectives 構成形容詞] **1** full of something 充滿…的: *an eventful day* 多事的一天 **2** having the quality of something or causing something 有…性質的；引起…的: *restful colours* 寧神怡目[素淡]的色彩 | *Is it painful?* 痛嗎？—**-fully** /fəlɪ; fəli/ [in adverbs 構成副詞]: *shouting cheerfully* 高興地呼喊

-ful² /fʊl; fʊl/ *suffix* [in nouns 構成名詞] **1** the amount of a substance needed to fill a particular container 充滿…所需的量: *two cupfuls of milk* 滿滿兩杯牛奶 **2** as much as can be carried by or contained in a particular part of the body〔身體部位〕充滿…的: *carrying an armful of flowers* 抱着一抱花

ful·crum /ˈfʌlkrəm; ˈfʊlkrəm/ *n plural* **fulcrums** *or* **fulcra** /-krə; -krə/ [C] the point on which a LEVER (=bar) turns, balances, or is supported in turning or lifting something〔槓桿的〕支點

ful·fil *BrE*【英】, **fulfill** *AmE*【美】/fʊlˈfɪl; fʊlˈfɪl/ *v* [T] 3 3 **1** if a hope, promise, wish etc is fulfilled, the thing that you had hoped, promised, wanted etc happens or is done〔希望、諾言、願望等〕實現；履行: *Visiting Disneyland has fulfilled a boyhood dream.* 到迪士尼樂園參觀實現了童年的夢想。| *Eisenhower finally fulfilled his election pledge to end the war in Korea.* 艾森豪威爾終於履行他的競選諾言，結束了朝鮮戰爭。**2 fulfil a need** to provide something that someone needs 滿足需要 **3 fulfil a requirement/condition** to reach a standard that is necessary, especially one that has been officially decided 符合要求/條件: *Much of the electrical equipment failed to fulfill safety requirements.* 許多電器未能符合安全要求。**4 fulfil a role/function/duty etc** to do the things you are supposed or expected to do because of your job, position in society etc 承擔角色/履行職責/履行義務等: *Does the established Church fulfil any useful function in modern society?* 英國國教在現代社會發揮着甚麼有用的作用嗎？**5** if your work fulfils you, it makes you feel satisfied because you are using all your skills, qualities etc 充分發揮〔才能等〕 **6 fulfil yourself** to feel satisfied because you are using all your skills, qualities etc 充分發揮自己的才能: *She succeeded in fulfilling herself both as an actress and as a mother.* 她作為一個演員和母親，兩者都做得十分出色。**7 fulfil your potential** to be as successful as you possibly could be 充分發揮潛能: *While he is very competent, he is not really fulfilling his potential.* 他固然很能勝任工作，但沒有真正充分發揮出他的潛力。**8 fulfil a prediction/prophecy** to happen in a way someone has said something would happen 應驗預言

ful·filled /fʊlˈfɪld; fʊlˈfɪld/ *adj* satisfied with your life, job etc because you feel that it is interesting, useful, or important, and you are using all your skills 滿意的；滿足的: *I'm sure I'd feel more fulfilled if I had a job that involved working with people, caring for people.* 要是我能得到一份與人打交道、關心人的工作，我肯定會更滿意。

ful·fil·ling /fʊlˈfɪlɪŋ; fʊlˈfɪlɪŋ/ *adj* a job, relationship etc that is fulfilling makes you feel satisfied because it allows you to use all your skills and qualities〔工作、關係等〕使人滿意的；使人滿足的: *A career in nursing still provides one on the most fulfilling of jobs.* 護理職業仍

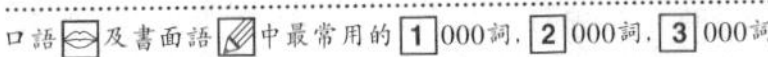

是一種很令人滿足的工作。

ful·fil·ment *BrE*【英】, **fulfillment** *AmE*【美】/fʊl-ˈfɪlmənt; fʊlˈfɪlmənt/ *n* [U] **1** the feeling of being satisfied, especially in your job, because you are using all your skills and qualities〔尤指工作中的〕滿足感: **sense/feeling of fulfilment** *Being responsible for so many people gave her a tremendous sense of fulfilment.* 要向這麼多人負責使她獲得巨大的滿足感。| **seek fulfilment** (=try to find it) 尋找滿足 **2 fulfilment of a wish/need etc** an occasion when something that is wanted, needed etc happens or is given 願望的實現/需要的滿足等 **3 fulfilment of a promise/duty/condition etc** the action of doing what you have promised, your duty, what you have been asked to do etc 履行諾言/職責/滿足條件等: *The offer of this contract is subject to the fulfilment of certain conditions.* 這份合同的要約需要首先滿足某些條件。

full[1] /fʊl; fʊl/ *adj*

1 ▶CONTAINER/ROOM/PLACE ETC 容器/房間/地點等◀ also 又作 **full up** if something such as a container, room, or place is full, no more things or people can go in it 滿的; 裝滿的; 擠滿的: *a full box of cereal* 滿滿的一箱麥片 | *The class is full, but you can register now for next term.* 這個班已經滿了, 不過你現在可以登記下學期的。| **[+of]** *We walked in to find the kitchen full of smoke.* 我們走進去, 發現廚房裡滿是煙。| **full to the brim** (=filled to the top of something) 滿滿的, 滿到邊的 *a cup full to the brim with water* 滿滿一杯水 | **full to bursting** *BrE* (=very full)【英】很滿的 *The room was full to bursting.* 房間擠得水泄不通。

2 ▶COMPLETE/TOTAL 完整的/全部的◀ **a)** including all parts or details 完整的, 詳盡的, 全面的: *Please write your full name and address on the form.* 請在表格上寫下你的全名和詳細地址。| *We have a full range of new cars.* 我們有各種款式的新車。| **the full story** (=everything someone knows about something)〔所知道的〕全部事實 *I still don't think he's telling us the full story.* 我仍然認為他沒有把全部事實都告訴我們。**b)** the highest level or greatest amount of something 最高水平的; 最多的: *Weissman and I are in full agreement on this issue.* 威斯曼和我在這個問題上是完全一致的。

3 be full of a) to feel or express a strong emotion〔表達強烈感情〕充滿…的: *children full of excitement at Christmas* 聖誕節時萬分興奮的孩子們 | *He's full of guilt about the death of his daughter.* 他對女兒的死深感內疚。**b)** to think or talk about one thing all the time 一心想着; 總是談論: *He was full of his plans for travelling around the world.* 他總是想着他那些周遊世界的計劃。| **be full of yourself** (=only think about yourself) 自以為是 *Brad's all right, but he's a little too full of himself.* 布拉德不錯, 可他有點自視過高。**c)** to contain many things of the same kind 有許多…的: *a sky full of stars* 佈滿星星的天空 | *His essay is full of mistakes.* 他的論文錯誤百出。

4 ▶TIME 時間◀ **a)** lasting the whole time 持續整段時間的; 整整的: *My father spent three full hours trying to explain one problem in my math book.* 爸爸花了整整三小時想解釋我的數學書裡的一個問題。**b)** filled with many things to do 忙碌的, 日程排得很滿的: *I've had a full week. I'm looking forward to staying home tonight.* 我已經忙了整個星期。我指望着今晚能留在家裡。

5 ▶FOOD 食品◀ *informal*【非正式】also 又作 **full up** *BrE* having eaten so much food that you cannot eat any more【英】飽的, 吃飽的: *No more, thanks. I'm full.* 不再吃了, 謝謝。我飽了。| **do sth on a full stomach** (=do physical activity just after a meal) 剛吃飽了就做某事

6 at full speed as fast as possible 全速地: *Parker was driving at full speed when he hit the wall.* 帕克在全速開車時撞到了牆壁上。

7 rise to your full height/draw yourself up to your full height to stand up very straight 挺直身子站起來

8 fall/lie full length to fall or lie flat, with your body stretched out 直挺挺地倒下/躺下

9 ▶CLOTHING 衣服◀ a full skirt, pair of trousers etc is made with a lot of material and fits loosely 寬鬆的, 肥大的: *full sleeves* 寬鬆的袖子 | *a dress with a full skirt* 下擺寬鬆的連衣裙

10 full marks *BrE* the highest number of points that you can get for school work【英】〔學校作業等〕滿分

11 ▶BODY 身體◀ **a)** a full face, figure, etc is rounded or large in an attractive way 豐滿的 **b)** used to mean fat when you do not want to offend someone 圓胖的, 豐腴的: *clothes for the fuller figure* 適合比較豐腴身材的衣服

12 in full view of sb so that everybody watching can see everything 使某人能看到全部; 為某人所一覽無餘: *The argument happened on stage in full view of the audience.* 這場爭論發生在台上, 觀眾看得一清二楚。

13 have/lead a full life to do many different and interesting things 過着充實的生活/豐富的人生

14 full flavour *BrE*【英】, **full flavor** *AmE*【美】a pleasantly strong taste 濃味: *This wine has a wonderful full flavour.* 這種葡萄酒的味道醇厚可口。—see also 另見 FULL-BODIED

15 ▶SOUND 聲音◀ a full sound is pleasantly loud or strong 洪亮的: *the full sound of the cello section* 大提琴部分的洪亮聲音 —opposite 反義詞 THIN[1] (7)

16 be full of crap/shit *taboo spoken* used to say that you think what someone is saying is wrong or stupid【諱, 口】一派胡言, 胡扯: *Don't listen to Jerry. He's full of crap.* 別聽傑里的。他一派胡言。

17 in full a) if you pay an amount of money in full, you pay the whole amount〔付款〕全數地, 全部地: *The debt must be paid in full by 31 January 1998.* 這筆債必須在1998年1月31日前全數還清。**b)** if you write or copy something in full, you write it in its complete form 全文地, 完整地; 詳細地

18 to the full in the best or most complete way 充分地; 十足地; 全面地: *To appreciate this opera to the full, you should read the story first.* 你想充分欣賞這齣歌劇, 應當先讀這故事。—see also 另見 FULLY, **come/turn full circle** (CIRCLE[1] (7)), **be full of beans** (BEAN[1] (4)), **(at) full belt** (BELT[1] (6)), **(at) full blast** (BLAST[1] (4)), **in full cry** (CRY[2] (8)), **full member** (MEMBER (1)), **(at) full pelt** (PELT[2] (3)), **be in full swing** (SWING[2] (7)), **at full tilt** (TILT[2] (1)), **have your hands full** (HAND[1] (32))

full[2] *adv* directly 直接地; 正好: **[+on/in]** *The ball struck him full on the chest.* 球正好打在他的胸部。—see also 另見 **know full well** (KNOW[1] (19))

full·back /ˈfʊl,bæk; ˈfʊlbæk/ *n* [C] a player in a football team who plays in a particular position, or the position that they play in〔足球的〕後衛

full beam /ˌ· ˈ·/ *n* [U] *BrE* lights at the front of a car that are on as brightly as possible【英】〔汽車前燈的〕遠光, 強光; HIGH BEAM *AmE*【美】

full-blood·ed /ˌ· ˈ··◂/ *adj* [only before noun 僅用於名詞前] **1** involving very strong feelings or emotions〔感情〕強烈的; 激烈的: **full-blooded argument/fight etc** (=an angry or violent argument etc) 激烈的爭論/爭吵等 *The argument ended up as a full-blooded screaming match.* 這場爭論最後演變成一次激烈的尖叫比賽。**2** having parents, grandparents etc from only one race of people 純血統的: *There are very few full-blooded Cherokee Indians left.* 現在純血統的徹羅基印第安人所餘無幾了。

full blown /ˌ· ˈ·/ *adj* **1** having all of the qualities of something in its most complete or advanced stage 成熟的; 充分發展的: *The border fighting has turned into a full blown war.* 邊境的衝突已經演變成一場全面戰爭。| *full-blown AIDS* 晚期愛滋病 **2** *often literary* a full-blown flower is completely open【常文】〔花〕盛開的

full board /,· '·/ *n* [U] a hotel that offers full board provides people with three meals a day〔旅館提供一日三餐的〕全食宿: *A two night break costs £125 full board.* 兩夜的全食宿需要 125 英鎊。—compare 比較 HALF BOARD

full-bod·ied /,· '··◂/ *adj* tasting strong and rich〔味道〕濃郁的; 醇厚的: *a full-bodied red wine* 味道醇厚的紅葡萄酒

full-court press /,· · '·/ *n* [singular] **1** a method of attacking in the game of BASKETBALL〔籃球賽中的〕全場緊逼 **2** *AmE informal* the use of pressure or influence by one group on another【美, 非正式】〔施加壓力或影響的〕全面出擊, 全面攻勢: *The DEA and the Justice Department put a full court press on the drug baron.* 毒品管理局和司法部向大毒梟發動全面攻勢。

full-cream /,· '·◂/ *adj BrE* full-cream milk has not had the cream removed【英】〔牛乳〕全脂的

full dress /,· '·/ *n* [U] special clothes worn for official occasions and ceremonies 禮服: *officers in full battle dress* 身穿正規戰鬥服的軍官 —**full-dress** *adj* —see also 另見 EVENING DRESS, MORNING DRESS

ful·ler's earth /,fʊləz 'ɜ·θ; ,fʊləz 'ɜːθ/ *n* [U] dried clay made into a powder and used to make oil clearer and cleaner 漂白土, 漂泥

full-face /,· '·◂/ *adj* a full-face photograph or picture of someone shows the whole of their face〔照片或圖片〕正面的 —compare 比較 PROFILE[1] (1)

full-fat /,· '·◂/ *adj BrE* full-fat milk or cheese has not had any of the fat taken out【英】〔乳品〕全脂的

full-fledged /,· '·◂/ *adj especially AmE*【尤美】**1** completely developed, trained, or established 全面發展的; 經過全面訓練的; 成熟的; FULLY-FLEDGED (1) *BrE*【英】: *a full-fledged lawyer* 經過充分訓練的律師 **2** a young bird is full-fledged when it has grown all its feathers and can fly〔鳥〕羽毛豐滿的; FULLY-FLEDGED (2) *BrE*【英】

full-grown /,· '·◂/ *adj AmE* a full-grown animal, plant, or person has developed to their full size and will not grow any bigger【美】〔動物、植物或人〕完全長成的; 成熟的; 發育完全的; FULLY-GROWN *BrE*【英】: *A full-grown male elephant may weigh 2,000 pounds.* 成年的雄性大象體重可達 2000 磅。

full house /,· '·/ *n* [C usually singular 一般用單數] **1** an occasion at a cinema, concert hall, sports field etc when someone is sitting in every seat〔電影院、音樂廳、體育場等〕滿座, 滿席, 客滿: *Speaking to a full house at the auditorium, he outlined his plan.* 他在滿座的禮堂裡對聽眾演說, 概述了他的計劃。**2** three cards of one kind and a pair of another kind in a game of cards〔紙牌戲中的〕滿堂紅, 滿貫〔一組牌中三張點數相同, 另外兩張點數相同〕

full-length[1] /,· '·◂/ *adj* **1 full-length mirror/photograph/portrait** a mirror etc that shows all of a person, from their head to their feet 全身鏡/照片/肖像: *a full-length portrait of the queen* 女王的全身肖像 **2 full-length skirt/dress/coat** a full length skirt etc reaches the ground, or is the longest possible for that particular type of clothing 垂地長裙/垂地連衣裙/長大衣: *a full-length evening dress* 垂地的晚禮服 **3 full-length play/book/film** a play, book etc of the normal length 足本[未刪節]的戲劇/書/電影

full-length[2] *adv* [only after verb 僅用於動詞後] someone who is lying full-length is lying flat with their legs straight out 腳伸直地, 平躺地: *Alison was stretched out full-length on the couch.* 阿莉森舒展手腳, 平躺在長沙發上。

full lock /,· '·◂/ *adv BrE* if you turn a car's STEERING WHEEL full lock, you turn it as far as it can be turned【英】完全鎖定〔即把汽車方向盤轉到頭〕

full moon /,· '·/ *n* [singular] the moon when it looks completely round 滿月, 圓月 —compare 比較 NEW MOON, HALF MOON

full·ness also 又作 **fulness** *BrE*【英】/'fʊlnɪs; 'fʊlnǝs/ *n* [U] **1 in the fullness of time** when the right time comes; EVENTUALLY 在適當的時候, 在時機成熟的時候; 總有一天: *I'm sure he'll tell us what's bothering him in the fullness of time.* 我肯定他會在適當的時候把他的煩惱告訴我們。**2** satisfaction 滿足, 完美: *the human search for fullness in life* 人類對完美生活的尋求 **3** the condition of being full 飽滿; 充滿; 充分

full-page /,· '·◂/ *adj* [only before noun 僅用於名詞前] covering all of one page, especially in a newspaper or magazine〔尤指報紙或雜誌〕全頁的, 整版的: *a full-page advertisement* 整版廣告

full pro·fes·sor /,· ·'··/ *n* [C] *AmE* a teacher at an American university who has reached the highest position and has gained TENURE (=the right to keep the job as long as they want it)【美】正教授, 終身教授 —see also 另見 ASSISTANT PROFESSOR, ASSOCIATE PROFESSOR

full-scale /,· '·◂/ *adj* [only before noun 僅用於名詞前] **1** to the fullest amount or degree possible 最大限度的; 徹底的; 全面的: *a full-scale inquiry into the train crash* 對列車撞毀事故的全面調查 **2** a drawing, model, copy etc of something that is full-scale is the same size as the thing it represents 照原尺寸的, 與實物一樣大小的

full-size /,· '·◂/ *adj* of the largest possible size 全尺寸的; 最大號的: *I need a full-size wrench to loosen this.* 我需要一把最大號的扳手來鬆開這東西。

full stop[1] /,· '·/ *n* **1** [C] *BrE* a point (.) that marks the end of a sentence or the shortened form of a word【英】句號; PERIOD[1] (5) *AmE*【美】—see picture at 參見 PUNCTUATION MARK 圖 **2** *AmE* [singular] the state of being completely stopped, usually in a car【美】完全停止: *The car can accelerate from a full stop to 60 mph in five seconds.* 這輛車能在五秒鐘內從完全停止加速到時速 60 英里。**3 come to a full stop** to stop completely, especially because of a problem or difficulty〔由於問題或困難而〕完全停頓下來: *Production came to a full stop when the generator blew up.* 發電機一爆炸, 生產就完全停頓下來了。

full stop[2] *interjection BrE* used to say that you have definitely decided something, and you will not change your decision; PERIOD[1] (6)【英】就是這樣, 不必多說; 沒有商量: *I don't have a reason. I just don't want to go, full stop.* 我沒有理由。我就是不想去, 不必多說了。

full-term /,· '·◂/ *adj* born after a PREGNANCY of a normal length 足月出生的: *a full-term baby* 足月出生的嬰兒 —compare 比較 PREMATURE (2)

full time /,· '·/ *n* [U] *BrE* the end of the normal period of playing time in a sports game, especially football【英】〔尤指足球的〕比賽時間結束, 終場: *At full time neither team had scored.* 到了比賽時間結束時, 兩隊都沒有得分。—see also 另見 HALF TIME

full-time /,· '·◂/ *adj, adv* **1** working or studying for the number of hours that work is usually done〔工作或學習〕全日制的[地]; 專職的[地]: *She works full-time, and has two kids.* 她全日工作, 而且有兩個孩子。| **full-time staff/student** *They're looking for full-time staff at the library.* 圖書館正招聘專職工作人員。**2 full-time job a)** a job that you do for all the normal working hours in a week 全日制工作, 專職工作 **b)** hard work that you are not being paid for that takes a lot of your time〔全日而不付酬的〕艱苦工作: *Looking after three children all day is a full-time job.* 整天照顧三個小孩是件不得空閒的累活。—compare 比較 PART-TIME S3

ful·ly /'fʊlɪ; 'fʊli/ *adv* **1** completely 完全地; 充分地; 徹底地: *We are fully committed to the idea of political reform.* 我們全心全意堅守並遵行政治改革的思想。**2** used to emphasize how big, far away etc something is 足足; 至少〔強調大、遠等〕: *The nearest big town is fully 300 miles away.* 最近的大城鎮在足足 300 英里之外。 S2 W2

fully-fash·ioned /,·· '··◂/ *BrE adj* clothing that is fully fashioned is made to fit the shape of the body exactly【英】〔衣服〕完全合身的, 完全照體形剪裁的

fully-fledged /,·· '·◂/ *adj especially BrE*【尤英】**1** completely developed, trained, or established 全面發展的; 經過全面訓練的; 成熟的; FULL-FLEDGED (1) *AmE*【美】: *After seven years of training she's now a fully-fledged doctor.* 她經過七年的訓練, 現在已是個完全合格的醫生。**2** a young bird is fully-fledged when it has grown all its feathers and can fly〔鳥〕羽毛豐滿的; FULL-FLEDGED (2) *AmE*【美】

fully-grown /,·· '·◂/ *adj* a fully-grown animal, plant, or person has developed to their full size and will not grow any bigger〔動物、植物或人〕完全長成的; 成熟的; 發育完全的; FULL-GROWN *AmE*【美】

ful·mi·nate /ˈfʌlmə,net; ˈfʊlmɪneɪt/ *v* [I+**against/at**] *formal* to speak angrily against something【正式】怒斥; 嚴厲譴責: *an article fulminating against American Imperialism* 一篇嚴厲譴責美帝國主義的文章 —**fulmination** /,fʌlməˈneʃən; ,fʊlmɪˈneɪʃən/ *n* [C,U]

ful·ness /ˈfulnɪs; ˈfʊlnɪs/ *n* [U] another spelling of FULLNESS fullness 的另一種拼法

ful·some /ˈfulsəm; ˈfʊlsəm/ *adj formal* a fulsome piece of writing, speech etc gives too much praise to be sincere【正式】〔作品或講話等〕過分恭維的; 虛偽的; 令人厭惡的: *His speech was packed with fulsome praise for the managing director.* 他的演說充滿過分恭維總經理的言辭。—**fulsomely** *adv* —**fulsomeness** *n* [U]

fum·ble /ˈfʌmbḷ; ˈfʌmbəl/ *v* **1** [I] to hold or try and move something with your hands carelessly or awkwardly 瞎弄; 笨手笨腳地摸: [+**for/with**] *Steve fumbled drunkenly with the keys, dropping them on the floor.* 史蒂夫醉酒後手忙腳亂地用鑰匙開鎖, 結果鑰匙掉到地板上。**2** [I+**for/with**] if you fumble with your words when you are speaking, you have difficulty saying something 支支吾吾地說話, 笨嘴笨舌地說 **3** [I,T] *AmE* to drop a ball after catching it【美】接 (球) 不穩; 失 (球) —**fumble** *n* [C]

F

fume /fjum; fjuːm/ *v* [I] **1** to be angry, usually without saying anything 生氣〔通常不說話〕: *She sat in the car, fuming about what she had heard.* 她坐在車裡, 對剛才聽到的話感到怒不可遏。| [+**at**] *AmE* (=show you are angry by saying a lot of things to someone)【美】發怒, 怒氣沖沖地說話 **2** to give off smoke or gases 冒煙; 冒氣

3 **fumes** /fjumz; fjuːmz/ *n* [plural] strong-smelling gas or smoke that is unpleasant to breathe in〔氣體、煙霧的〕難聞的氣味: *strong smell of paint fumes* 濃烈的油漆味

fu·mi·gate /ˈfjumə,get; ˈfjuːmɪgeɪt/ *v* [T] to clear disease, BACTERIA, insects etc from somewhere using chemicals, smoke, or gas〔為消毒、殺菌、殺蟲等而用化學品、煙或氣〕熏蒸; 煙熏 —**fumigation** /,fjuməˈgeʃən; ,fjuːmɪˈgeɪʃən/ *n* [U]

2 3 **fun¹** /fʌn; fʌn/ *adj* **1** [only before noun 僅用於名詞前] a fun activity or experience is enjoyable〔活動或經歷〕有趣的, 令人愉快的; 好玩的: *It was a fun night out – we'll have to do it again sometime.* 這次晚上出去很好玩——我們甚麼時候得再去一次。**2** someone who is fun is enjoyable to be with because they are cheerful and amusing〔人〕有趣的, 能給人快樂的: **a fun person/girl/guy etc** *especially AmE*【尤美】*She's a fun person to be around.* 有她在場就很有趣。| **good/great fun** *BrE*【英】*The O'Brian boys were great fun.* 奧布萊恩家的男孩子們很有趣。

2 **fun²** *n* [U] **1** an experience or activity that is very enjoyable and exciting 有趣的經歷[活動]; 令人興奮的經歷[活動]; 嬉戲, 享樂; 樂趣: *It's no fun to be working inside when the weather's nice.* 天氣晴朗的時候在屋裡工作很無趣。| **good/great fun** *BrE*【英】*Why don't you come with us? It'll be great fun.* 你為甚麼不跟我們來呢? 會玩得很痛快的。| **have fun** (=to have an enjoyable time) 玩得[過得]很愉快 *The children were having so much fun, I hated to call them inside.* 孩子們玩得這麼開心, 我捨不得把他們叫進來。| **What fun!** (=that sounds very enjoyable!) 多有趣啊! **2 for fun** also 又作 **for the fun of it** if you do something for fun, you do it because you enjoy it and not for any other reason 鬧着玩地; 為了好玩: *We drove all the way to the beach, just for fun.* 我們從老遠開車到海灘去, 只是為了好玩。**3 full of fun** playful and liking amusement 很喜歡玩的, 很愛玩鬧的: *Jan's always so cheerful and full of fun.* 簡總是這麼高興, 愛玩鬧。**4 fun and games** playful activities 嬉鬧, 歡鬧: *My job isn't all fun and games you know – I work hard as well.* 我的工作不都是玩玩鬧鬧的, 你要知道——我也努力工作的。**5 not be my idea of fun** used to talk about an activity, situation etc that is exciting or interesting to other people but is not for you 對我來說很沒有趣味: *Digging up old bones in a hot desert is not my idea of fun.* 在炎熱的沙漠發掘古老的骨頭不是我心目中好玩的事。**6 in fun** if you make a joke or say something about someone in fun, you do not intend it to be insulting 開玩笑似的[地]; 鬧着玩的[地]: *Don't get upset Chris, she only said it in fun.* 不要苦惱了, 克里斯, 她那句話只是說着玩而已。**7 make fun of sb/sth** to make a joke about someone that is insulting or makes them feel bad 嘲弄某人/某物; 拿某人/某物開玩笑: *The kids at school always made fun of Jill's clothes.* 學校裡的孩子總取笑吉爾穿的衣服。**8 like fun** *AmE spoken* used when you think something will not happen, or when something is not true【美口】當然不, 決不: *"I'm going to Barbara's house." "Like fun you are! Come and finish your chores first."* "我要去巴巴拉的家。" "你不能去呢! 先來幹完你的雜活。" —see also 另見 FUNNY, **figure of fun** (FIGURE¹ (14)), **poke fun at** (POKE¹ (4))

func·tion¹ /ˈfʌŋkʃən; ˈfʌŋkʃən/ *n* **1** [C] the purpose that something is made for, or the job that someone does〔事物的〕功能; 作用;〔人的〕職責: *The function of a cash-machine is to provide people with cash when the bank is shut.* 自動提款機的作用是在銀行關門的時候讓人提取現金。| **perform a function** *In your new job you will be expected to perform many different functions.* 在新工作崗位上, 你可能要履行許多不同的職責。**2** [C] a large party or ceremonial event, especially for an important or official occasion 盛大聚會; 儀式, 典禮: *This room may be hired for weddings and other functions.* 這個房間可以被租來舉行婚禮和其他儀式。**3** [U] the way in which something works or the way in which it is used 用途; 功能: *Bauhaus architects thought that function was more important than form.* 包豪斯學派的建築師認為功能比形式重要。**4 a function of a)** if one thing is a function of another, it is produced by or varies according to the other thing 隨…變化[產生]的因素 **b)** *technical* a mathematical quantity that changes according to how another mathematical quantity changes【術語】函數: *In x=5y, x is a function of y.* 在 x=5y 中, x 是 y 的函數。**5** [C] one of the basic operations performed by a computer〔電腦的〕基本功能

function² *v* [I] **1** if something functions, it works in the way it is supposed to 運轉, 工作: *When the camera is functioning properly the green light comes on.* 照相機運作正常時, 綠燈就亮起來。**2** if something functions in a particular way, it works in that way〔以某種方式〕運作, 運轉: *Can you explain exactly how this new system will function?* 你能解釋一下這個新系統究竟是怎樣運作的嗎? **3 not function** if someone cannot function, they cannot do the activities that people normally do 不能正常活動: *She nurses people in their homes who are too ill to function alone.* 她上門護理生活不能自理的病人。

function as sth *phr v* [T] to be or work as something 起…作用, 作…用: *Athens functioned as a centre of trade in the thirteenth century.* 雅典在13世紀時是貿易中心。

func·tion·al /ˈfʌŋkʃənḷ; ˈfʌŋkʃənəl/ *adj* **1** designed to be useful rather than beautiful or decorative 為實用而設計的, 實用的: *It's not fast – it's just a solid, functional car.* 這輛車速度不快——只是一輛結實、實用的車。**2** working in the way that something is supposed to 正常運轉的: *With a few minor adjustments the filter will be functional again.* 略經調整後, 過濾器將又可以用了。**3** having a useful purpose 有用途的; 有功能的 —**functionally** *adv*

func·tion·al·is·m /ˋfʌŋkʃənl̩ɪzəm; ˈfʌŋkʃənəlɪzəm/ *n* [U] the idea that the most important thing about a building, piece of furniture etc is that it is useful 功能主義, 功能論; 實用主義 —**functionalist** *n* [C] —**functionalist** *adj*

func·tion·a·ry /ˋfʌŋkʃənˏɛrɪ; ˈfʌŋkʃənəri/ *n* [C] someone who has a job doing unimportant or boring official duties〔做繁瑣工作的〕職員, 工作人員; 公務人員

function key /ˈ·· ·/ *n* [C] *technical* a key on the KEYBOARD¹ (1) of a computer that tells the machine to do something【術語】〔電腦的〕功能鍵

function word /ˈ·· ·/ *n* [C] a word such as a PRONOUN or PREPOSITION that is used in place of another word or shows the relationship between two words. For example, in the sentences 'The cat is hungry. It hasn't been fed yet', 'it' is a function word. 功能詞〔如代詞、介詞等, 用於代替一詞或表明兩詞之間的關係。例如句子 The cat is hungry. It hasn't been fed yet 中, it 是個功能詞〕

[3] [1] **fund¹** /fʌnd; fʌnd/ *n* [C] **1** an amount of money that is collected and kept for a particular purpose 基金; 專款; 資金: *The school's funds for sports and music have been seriously depleted.* 這所學校的體育和音樂基金已接近耗盡。| **set up a fund** (=begin to collect money) 設立基金, 開始籌款 *His grandparents set up a fund for his college education.* 他的祖父母為他設立了一個大學教育基金。—see also 另見 FUNDING, TRUST FUND —see 見 MONEY (USAGE) **2** an organization that is responsible for collecting and spending an amount of money 基金會: *We give to the Children's Fund every Christmas.* 我們每年聖誕節向兒童基金會捐款。—compare 比較 CHARITY (2) **3 a fund of** a large supply of something 大量的: *He was a large man with a strong Texan drawl and a fund of stories.* 他身材魁梧, 說話帶着很濃的得克薩斯州腔, 能講許多故事。**4 be short of funds** to have little or no money 缺錢, 手頭拮据; 經費不足: *The Museum is so short of funds it may sell the painting.* 博物館十分缺錢, 可能會把這幅畫賣了。**5 in funds** having enough money to do what is necessary 手頭有錢

[3] [3] **fund²** *v* [T] **1** to provide money for an activity, organization, event etc 為〔活動、組織、事件等〕提供資金; 資助: *The project is jointly funded by several local companies.* 這項目是由當地幾家公司聯合出資的。**2** *technical* to change the arrangements for paying a debt, so that you have more time to pay【術語】將〔短期貸款〕轉為長期有息借款

[2] [2] **fun·da·men·tal¹** /ˏfʌndəˋmɛntl̩; ˌfʌndəˈmentl◂/ *adj* **1** affecting the simplest and most important parts of something 根本的; 基本的; 基礎的: *She's not just in a bad mood, she must have a fundamental psychological problem.* 她不僅僅是心情不好, 肯定有根本的心理問題。| **fundamental change/difference** *a fundamental difference in opinion* 看法的根本區別 | **fundamental mistake/error** *His fundamental mistake was to rely too much on other people.* 他的根本錯誤是過分依賴其他人。**2** very necessary and important as a part of something from which everything else develops 必不可少的; 十分重要的: [+to] *Water is fundamental to survival.* 水對生存是必不可少的。

fundamental² *n* **the fundamentals of** the most important ideas, rules etc that something is based upon 基本原理; 基本規則: *I couldn't even grasp the fundamentals of mechanics.* 我連力學的基本原理都弄不懂。

fun·da·men·tal·is·m /ˏfʌndəˋmɛntl̩ˏɪzəm; ˌfʌndəˈmentəlɪzəm/ *n* [U] **1** the practice of following religious laws very strictly 原教旨主義; 基要主義 **2** a belief that some Christians have that everything in the Bible is completely true〔基督教〕原教旨主義; 基要主義信仰

fun·da·men·tal·ist /ˏfʌndəˋmɛntl̩ɪst; ˌfʌndəˈmentəl̩ɪst/ *n* [C] **1** someone who follows religious laws very strictly 原教旨主義者; 基要主義者: *Muslim fundamentalists* 穆斯林原教旨主義者 **2** a Christian who believes that everything in the Bible is completely true 信奉基要主義的基督信徒 —**fundamentalist** *adj*: *a fundamentalist doctrine* 原教旨主義信條; 基要主義信條

fun·da·men·tal·ly /ˏfʌndəˋmɛntl̩ɪ; ˌfʌndəˈmentəli/ *adv* in every way that is important or basic 根本上; 基本上: *They are good friends even though their views on many things are fundamentally different.* 他們雖然對許多事情的看法根本不同, 但還是好朋友。

fund·ing /ˋfʌndɪŋ; ˈfʌndɪŋ/ *n* [U] an amount of money used for a specific purpose 專款, 撥款: *Funding may be available from the UN.* 聯合國也許會提供撥款。

fund rais·er /ˈ· ˌ··/ *n* [C] a person or event that collects money for a specific purpose 募捐者; 募捐活動

fu·ne·ral /ˋfjunərəl; ˈfjuːnərəl/ *n* [C] **1** a religious ceremony for burying or burning a dead person 葬禮, 喪禮: *The funeral will be held at St. Martin's church.* 葬禮將在聖馬丁教堂舉行。| **funeral procession/car/service etc** *The mayor gave the funeral oration.* 市長致悼詞。**2 it's your funeral** *spoken* used to warn someone that they, and no one else, must deal with the result of their actions【口】你該要操心了, 你該要倒霉了〔警告某人, 需要為其行動的後果負責的只是他自己, 而不是別人〕: *If you show up late again, it's your funeral.* 如果你再次遲到, 那倒霉的是你自己。

funeral di·rec·tor /ˈ··· ·ˌ··/ *n* [C] someone who is paid to organize a funeral 喪葬承辦者, 殯儀業人員; UNDERTAKER *BrE*【英】

funeral home /ˈ··· ˌ·/ also 又作 **funeral par·lour** /ˈ··· ˌ··/ *especially AmE n* [C] the place where a body is kept before a funeral【尤美】殯儀館

fu·ne·ra·ry /ˋfjunəˏrɛrɪ; ˈfjuːnərəri/ *adj* [only before noun 僅用於名詞前] related to a funeral or a grave 葬禮的; 喪葬的: *a funerary urn* 骨灰甕[缸]

fu·ne·re·al /fjuˋnɪrɪəl; fjʊˈnɪəriəl/ *adj* sad, slow, and suitable for a funeral 悲哀的; 沉重的; 適合於葬禮的: *funereal music* 哀樂 —**funereally** *adv*

fun·fair /ˋfʌnˏfɛr; ˈfʌnfeə/ *n* [C] *BrE* a noisy outdoor event where you can ride on machines, play games to win prizes etc; FAIR³ (1)【英】露天遊樂場〔喧鬧的大型戶外活動, 有機動遊戲、攤位遊戲等〕

fun·gal /ˋfʌŋgəl; ˈfʌŋgəl/ also 又作 **fun·gous** /ˋfʌŋgəs; ˈfʌŋgəs/ *adj technical* connected with or caused by a fungus【術語】真菌的; 由真菌引起的: *a fungal infection* 真菌感染

fun·gi·cide /ˋfʌndʒəˏsaɪd; ˈfʌndʒ̍ɪsaɪd/ *n* [C,U] a chemical used for destroying fungus 殺真菌劑

fun·goid /ˋfʌŋgɔɪd; ˈfʌŋgɔɪd/ *adj technical* like a fungus【術語】真菌狀[性]的: *fungoid growths* 真菌植物

fun·gus /ˋfʌŋgəs; ˈfʌŋgəs/ *n plural* **fungi** /-dʒaɪ; -dʒaɪ/ *or* **funguses** **1** [C,U] a simple fast-growing type of plant, such as a MUSHROOM¹ or MOULD¹ (1) 真菌〈如傘菌或黴菌〉**2** [U] this type of plant, especially considered as a disease 真菌類植物 (病)

fun house /ˈ· ·/ *n* [C] *AmE* a building at a FUNFAIR in which there are things that amuse or shock people【美】〔遊樂場中的〕遊樂宮

fu·nic·u·lar /fjuˋnɪkjələ; fjʊˈnɪkjʊlə/ *n* [C] a small railway that goes up a hill or a mountain, pulled by a thick metal rope〔登山〕纜索鐵路

funk¹ /fʌŋk; fʌŋk/ *n* [U] **1** a style of music with a strong RHYTHM that is based on JAZZ and African music〔以爵士樂和非洲音樂的強勁節奏為基礎的〕鄉土爵士樂 **2 in a (blue) funk** *informal* very unhappy, worried, or afraid about something【非正式】沮喪; 焦慮; 驚恐: *She's been in a funk ever since she failed that exam.* 自從她那次考試不及格後, 她就一直很沮喪。**3** *AmE informal* a strong

F

smell that comes from someone's body【美, 非正式】〔身體發出的〕惡臭, 狐臭, 體臭

funk² *v* [T] *BrE old-fashioned* to avoid doing something because it is difficult, or because you are afraid to do it【英, 過時】〔因困難或害怕而〕逃避, 畏縮

funk·y /ˈfʌŋkɪ; ˈfʌŋki/ *adj informal*【非正式】**1** modern, fashionable, and interesting 新款的; 時髦的: *We found some really funky shoes at the market yesterday.* 我們昨天在市場上找到一些非常時髦的鞋子。**2** funky music is simple with a strong RHYTHM that is easy to dance to〔音樂〕樸實而節奏強烈的

fun·nel¹ /ˈfʌnl; ˈfʌnl/ *n* [C] **1** a tube used for pouring liquids or powders into a container with a narrow opening 漏斗: *Use a funnel to pour the oil into the bottle.* 用漏斗把油倒進瓶裡。—see picture at 參見 LABORATORY 圖 **2** *BrE* a metal CHIMNEY for letting smoke out from a steam engine or steam ship【英】〔蒸汽機或輪船的〕〔金屬〕煙囪 —compare 比較 SMOKESTACK

funnel² *v* **funnelled, funnelling** *BrE*【英】, **funneled, funneling** *AmE*【美】[I,T] to pass or be passed through a narrow opening, especially to pass a large amount of something through it (使)流經漏斗; (使)通過小口子: **[+through/into]** *The crowd funnelled through the narrow streets.* 人羣熙熙攘攘地穿過狹小的街道。| **funnel sth into sth** *He funneled the petrol into the can.* 他用漏斗把汽油倒進罐裡。

fun·nies /ˈfʌnɪz; ˈfʌniz/ *n* **the funnies** *AmE informal* a number of different CARTOONS (1) in newspapers or magazines【美, 非正式】〔報紙或雜誌上〕(滑稽)連環漫畫欄

fun·ni·ly /ˈfʌnɪlɪ; ˈfʌnḷli/ *adv* **1** in an odd or unusual way 古怪地; 異常地: *She's been behaving funnily lately.* 她近來行為古怪。**2 funnily enough** *spoken* used to say that something is unexpected or strange【口】奇怪的是; 說來也巧: *Funnily enough, I was just about to call you when you called me.* 說來也巧, 我正要打電話給你, 你就打電話給我了。**3** in an amusing way 滑稽地, 有趣地

1 3 **fun·ny** /ˈfʌnɪ; ˈfʌni/ *adj*

1 ►AMUSING 逗人笑的◄ making you laugh 使人發笑的, 有趣的; 滑稽的: *He was telling funny anecdotes about Hollywood.* 他正在講有關荷里活的趣聞軼事。| **hysterically/hilariously funny** *Everyone except me seemed to find her mistakes hilariously funny.* 除了我, 大家似乎都覺得她的錯誤極其可笑。

2 ►STRANGE 奇怪的◄ unusual and difficult to explain 古怪的; 難以解釋的: *I had a funny feeling that something was going to happen.* 我莫名其妙地感覺到有事要發生了。| *It was a funny sort of day, hot but with huge rain clouds.* 這天有點奇怪, 很熱但又有大片的雨雲。

3 ►DISHONEST 不誠實的◄ seeming to be illegal or dishonest, although you are not exactly sure why 非法的; 不老實的; 耍花招的: *There's something funny going on here.* 這裡正進行一些可疑的活動。| **funny business** (=activities that are illegal or dishonest) 非法活動; 欺騙活動 *When I checked the accounts I realized that there was some funny business going on.* 我檢查賬目時意識到有人做了手腳。

4 go funny *informal* if something goes funny it stops working properly【非正式】出毛病, 出故障: *I just turned it on and the picture went all funny.* 我剛一開機, 畫面就出毛病了。

5 ►ILL 生病的◄ feeling slightly ill 不大舒服的: *I always feel funny after a long ride in the car.* 長時間坐汽車後我總覺得不大舒服。

6 ►CRAZY 發瘋的◄ *BrE* slightly crazy【英】有點發瘋的, 精神有點失常的: *After his wife died he went a bit funny.* 他在妻子去世後變得有點瘋瘋癲癲的。

7 see the funny side of sth to be able to laugh in a difficult or bad situation〔在困境中〕看到某事可笑的一面: *Fortunately, the patient saw the funny side of the mix up and decided not to take us to court.* 幸好, 病人看到這回糟糕事另有可笑的一面, 決定不起訴我們。

Frequencies of the adjective **funny** in spoken and written English. 形容詞 funny 在英語口語和書面語中的使用頻率

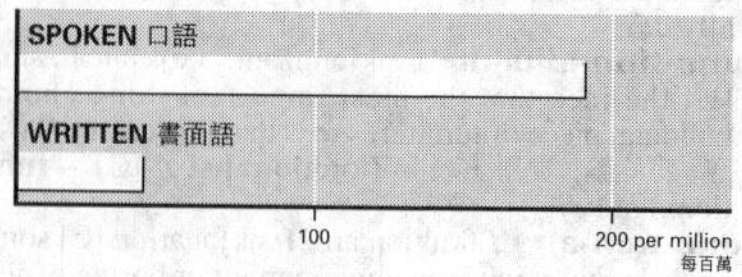

Based on the British National Corpus and the Longman Lancaster Corpus 據英國國家語料庫和朗文蘭卡斯特語料庫

This graph shows that the adjective **funny** is much more common in spoken English than in written English. This is because it is used in a lot of common spoken phrases. 本圖表顯示, 形容詞funny在英語口語中的使用頻率遠遠高於書面語, 因為口語中有很多常用片語是由funny構成的。

funny (*adj*) **SPOKEN PHRASES**
含 funny 的口語片語

8 it's funny used to say that you do not really understand why something happens, but it does and you think it is strange, interesting, worrying etc 真奇怪; 真有趣; 真令人擔心: *It's funny, but I've known her for years and I don't even know her name.* 真奇怪, 我認識她好幾年了, 卻連她的名字也不知道。| **it's funny (that)** *It's funny Jack didn't come. I hope he's ok.* 傑克沒來, 真奇怪, 希望他還好吧。| **it's funny how** *It's funny how you remember the words of songs, even ones you don't really like.* 真有趣, 你能記住許多歌的歌詞, 甚至連你並不真正喜歡的也記得。

9 that's funny used when you are surprised by something that has happened and you can not explain it 真莫名其妙, 真怪: *That's funny! I'm sure I put my wallet down there, and now it's gone.* 真怪了! 我肯定將皮夾子放在那裡的, 現在不見了。

10 the funny thing is used to say what the strangest or most amusing part of a story or situation is 最奇怪的是; 最有趣的是: *But the funny thing is, after they'd argued for ages about where to go, the car wouldn't start.* 不過最有趣的是, 他們爭論了很久去甚麼地方之後, 車子卻發動不了。| *The funny thing is, I sort of knew this would happen.* 最奇怪的是, 我有點知道會發生這事。

11 it's not funny used to tell someone not to laugh at or make jokes about something you think is very serious 這不是好笑的事, 這一點也不可笑: *It's not funny! I'm the one who's going to get blamed for this, you know.* 這不是好笑的事! 你可知道, 因此事而受責怪的人將是我。

12 very funny! used when someone is laughing at you or making a joke and you do not think it is funny 真滑稽!〔反話〕一點也不好笑!: *Oh very funny! Instead of laughing you could try and help.* 哼, 真滑稽! 你可以來幫忙試試, 而不是笑。| *Very funny! Who's hidden my car keys?* 一點也不好笑! 誰藏了我的汽車鑰匙?

13 what's so funny? used when someone is laughing and you want to know why 有甚麼好笑?: *Hey, what's so funny? Did I say something stupid?* 嗨, 甚麼事這樣好笑? 我說了蠢話嗎?

14 funny little used to describe something or someone that is small and unusual 又小又怪的: *I got it in that funny little shop in Market Street.* 我在市場街的那家又小又怪的商店買到這東西的。

15 funny old used to describe something or someone that is strange but that you like or think is interesting 滑稽的: *Yes, he's a funny old man – you never*

know what he's going to say. 是的，他是個很滑稽的傢伙 —— 你永遠也猜不到他會說甚麼。
16 I'm not being funny, but... used when you are going to say something that may seem strange or amusing but is actually serious 我不是想開玩笑，但...: *I'm not being funny, but I quite liked it in hospital.* 我不是開玩笑，但我曾經很喜歡住醫院。
17 funny peculiar or funny ha-ha? *BrE* used when someone has described something as funny and you want to know if they mean that it is strange or amusing 【英】是奇怪還是有趣?: *"You are funny, Albert." "How do you mean? Funny peculiar or funny ha-ha?"* "你很妙，阿爾伯特。" "你指的是甚麼意思? 是奇怪還是有趣?"

funny bone /'.. ./ *n* [singular] the soft part of your elbow that particularly hurts when you hit it hard〔肘部的〕鷹嘴突，尺骨端〔受碰時會有酥麻感的敏感部位〕

funny farm /'.. ./ *n* [C] *informal humorous* an expression meaning a PSYCHIATRIC HOSPITAL that some people consider offensive【非正式，幽默】精神病院〔有些人認為該詞具有冒犯性〕

funny mon·ey /'.. ,../ *n* [U] *informal* money that has been printed illegally【非正式】假紙幣 —see also 另見 COUNTERFEIT[1]

funny pa·pers /'.. ,../ *n* [plural] *AmE informal* another expression meaning FUNNIES【美，非正式】(滑稽) 連環漫畫欄

fun run /'. ,./ *n* [C] an event in which people run a long distance in order to collect money, usually for CHARITY 為(慈善)募捐而舉行的長跑活動

fur[1] /fɝ; fɜː/ *n* **1** [U] the thick soft hair that covers the bodies of some types of animal, for example cats or dogs〔貓、狗等動物的〕軟毛 **2** [C,U] the fur-covered skin of an animal, especially used for making clothes〔尤指用於做衣服的〕毛皮: *Traders exchanged whiskey for furs.* 商人用威士忌酒換毛皮。| *a fur coat* 毛皮大衣 **3** [C] a coat or piece of clothing made of fur 毛皮大衣，毛皮衣物: *She wore a small fur wrapped around her neck.* 她脖子上圍着一條小毛皮圍脖。**4** a hard grey chemical substance that sometimes forms on the inside of water-pipes and containers〔水管和容器內的〕水垢，水鏽; SCALE[1] (11) *AmE*【美】**5 the fur starts/begins to fly** used to say that an angry argument or fight starts 發生激烈的爭論[打鬥]: *The fur really started to fly when she saw the state of the kitchen.* 她看到廚房的樣子時，激烈的爭吵真正開始了。—see also 另見 FURRY

fur[2] *v* [I] also 又作 **fur up** *especially BrE* to become covered with FUR[1] (4)【尤英】生水垢

fur·bish /'fɝbɪʃ; 'fɜːbɪʃ/ *v* [T] also 又作 **furbish up** to improve the appearance of, or decorate something old 改善...的面貌; 翻新; 磨光; 擦亮 —compare 比較 REFURBISH (1)

fu·ri·ous /'fjʊrɪəs; 'fjʊəriəs/ *adj* **1** [not before noun 不用於名詞前] extremely angry 狂怒的，暴怒的: *I've never been so furious in my whole life.* 我這輩子從來沒有這樣大發雷霆過。| [**+with/at/about etc**] *He was furious with himself for not standing up to Gillman.* 他對自己未能勇敢地面對吉爾曼而生自己的氣。**2** [only before noun 僅用於名詞前] done with a lot of energy, effort, or anger 猛烈的，強烈的，激烈的: *There was a sudden furious barking from the backyard.* 後院突然傳來一陣狗的狂吠聲。| **furious debate/argument** *a furious debate in Parliament over the new tax* 議會對新稅項的激烈辯論 —**furiously** *adv*

furl /fɝl; fɜːl/ *v* [T] to roll or fold something such as a flag, umbrella, or sail 捲起，摺起〔旗、傘或帆等〕—**furled** *adj*: *a furled newspaper* 摺起來的報紙

fur·long /'fɝlɔŋ; 'fɜːlɒŋ/ *n* [C] a unit for measuring length, equal to 201 metres and used in horse racing 弗隆〔長度單位，相當於201米，用於賽馬中〕—see table on page C4 參見 C4 頁附錄

fur·lough /'fɝlo; 'fɜːləʊ/ *n* [C,U] a period of time when a soldier or someone working in another country can return to their own country〔軍人或在國外工作的人的〕(回國) 休假: **on furlough** *a young soldier home on furlough* 回國休假的年輕士兵

fur·nace /'fɝnɪs; 'fɜːnɪs/ *n* [C] **1** a large container in which a very hot fire is made, to produce power or heat, or to melt metals〔用於產生動力、熱量或用以熔化金屬的〕火爐; 熔爐 —see also 另見 BLAST FURNACE **2 be like a furnace** *spoken* to be extremely hot【口】熱得像個火爐: *Let's open a window, it's like a furnace in here!* 我們開扇窗吧，這裡熱得像個火爐!

fur·nish /'fɝnɪʃ; 'fɜːnɪʃ/ *v* [T] **1** to put furniture and other things into a house or room 為〔房屋或房間〕配備家具: *The apartment was furnished in Art Deco style.* 這套公寓佈置了裝飾派藝術風格的家具。| **furnish sth with sth** *a room furnished with a desk and swivel chair* 擺放着書桌和轉椅的房間 **2** to supply or provide something 供應，提供: *They were asked to furnish capital for the new enterprise.* 有人要求他們為這家新企業提供資金。| **furnish sb/sth with** *The gardener furnished me with the necessary information.* 那園丁向我提供了必要的信息。—**furnished** *adj*: *a furnished flat* 配備家具的公寓套房

fur·nish·ings /'fɝnɪʃɪŋz; 'fɜːnɪʃɪŋz/ *n* [plural] the furniture and other things in a room, such as curtains, baths etc〔房間裡如桌椅、窗簾、浴缸等的〕家具，室內陳設

fur·ni·ture /'fɝnɪtʃɚ; 'fɜːnɪtʃə/ *n* [U] large movable objects such as chairs, tables, and beds that you use in a room to make it comfortable to live or work in〔大型可移動的〕家具: *The small room was crammed with furniture.* 那間小房間裡塞滿了家具。| *office furniture* 辦公室家具

F

fu·ro·re /'fjʊrɔr; fjʊ'rɔːri/ *BrE*【英】, **fu·ror** /'fjʊrɔr; 'fjʊərɔː/ *AmE*【美】—*n* [singular] a sudden expression of anger or excitement among a large group of people about something that has happened〔一大羣人突然產生的〕騷動; 狂熱: *The security leaks have caused a considerable furore within government circles.* 安全漏洞已在政府中引起極大的騷動。

fur·ri·er /'fɝɪɚ; 'fʌriə/ *n* [C] someone who makes or sells fur clothing 皮衣製造者; 皮貨商

fur·row[1] /'fɝo; 'fʌrəʊ/ *n* [C] **1** a deep line or fold in the skin of someone's face, especially on the forehead〔人臉部，特別是前額的〕皺紋 **2** a long, narrow cut or hollow area in the surface of something〔某物表面的〕溝，壟溝，犁溝: *There were furrows in the tarmac to drain off the rainwater.* 柏油碎石路面上有許多排雨水的溝。**3** a long narrow cut made in the ground with a PLOUGH[1] (1)〔田裡的〕犁溝，壟溝

furrow[2] *v* **1** [I,T] to make the skin on your face form deep lines or folds, especially because you are worried or angry (使)〔臉部〕起皺紋〔尤指煩惱或生氣時〕: *Her husband's brows were furrowed in concentration.* 她丈夫皺着眉頭，顯得聚精會神。**2** [T] to make a deep cut or hollow area in something 犁; 在...開出溝槽 —**furrowed** *adj*: *a furrowed brow* 皺緊的眉頭

fur·ry /'fɝɪ; 'fɜːri/ *adj* covered with fur, or looking or feeling as if covered with fur 覆蓋着毛皮的; 毛茸茸的; 柔軟的: *furry little kittens* 毛茸茸的小貓 | *a large furry towel* 一條軟蓬蓬的大毛巾

fur·ther[1] /'fɝðɚ; 'fɜːðə/ *adv*
1 ▶MORE 更多地◀ if you do something further you do it more, or to a greater degree 進一步地; 在更大程度上; 再; 更: *I will develop this point further next week.* 我將在下星期進一步闡述這一論點。| *Things were further complicated by the fact that she did not speak Spanish.* 由於她不會說西班牙語，事情變得更加複雜。| [**+into/away etc**] *Marcus sank further into debt.* 馬庫斯的債台越築越高。| **delay/detain sth/sb further** (=make you wait) 耽擱某事/讓某人久等 *After we've finished this I won't detain you any further.* 我們完成這件事後，我就不會耽擱你了。

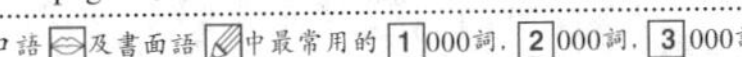
口語 及書面語 中最常用的 1 000詞，2 000詞，3 000詞

2 ▶DISTANCE 距離◀ *especially BrE* used to say that a place is a long way from or more distant than another place; FARTHER【尤英】更遠; 再往前地: *I don't think I can move a step further.* 我看我一步都走不動了。| **[+up/away/along etc]** *A little further up Main Street is an old house that's being restored.* 順着大街往前一點是一座正在修復的老房子。—see 見 FARTHER¹ (USAGE)
3 take sth further to do something at a more serious or higher level, especially by talking about it 進一步地做某事〔尤指討論它〕: *Would you be willing to take this research further?* 你願意進一步從事這項研究嗎? | **take the matter further** (=discuss a subject at a higher level and with more important people) 進一步討論這事 *I'm going to take the matter further and discuss this with your parents.* 我打算把這事進一步和你的父母討論一下。
4 ▶TIME 時間◀ further back/on/ahead etc used to say how much more distant something is in the past or future 再以前/再以後/更遠的未來等: *Five years further on, a cure has still not been found.* 五年過去了, 仍未找到對症療藥。| *The records don't go any further back than 1960.* 這些記錄中沒有早於1960年的。| **further down the road** (=in the future) 將來, 在更遠的未來 *Further down the road we're looking at using up our timber resources.* 在更遠的未來, 我們會看到我們的木材資源耗竭的前景。
5 go (one step) further to do or say more than before 進一步地做; 進一步地說: *Some argued that we should go one step further and get rid of him altogether.* 有人主張我們再大膽一些, 徹底把他打發掉。
6 ▶IN ADDITION 而且◀ [sentence adverb 句子副詞] *formal* used to introduce something additional that you want to talk about; FURTHERMORE【正式】此外; 而且: *He promised not to identify his informant, and further, not to quote him directly.* 他答應不去指明提供信息的人, 而且不直接引述他的話。
7 further to *formal* used in letters or in formal speech to mention a previous subject you want to discuss more【正式】再者; 又及〔某事的更多的討論, 用於信件或正式演說中〕: *Further to your letter of February 5th, we can confirm your order.* 又及, 貴方2月5日來函已悉, 我方可以確認貴方的定單。
8 nothing can be further from the truth used when you want to say that something is totally untrue 這完全不真實
9 sth must not go any further used to say that something you are telling someone is secret or private 某事不可外傳
10 nothing is further from sb's mind *spoken* used to say that you have not been thinking about something, especially when you really have been thinking about it【口】某人的腦子裡根本沒有考慮〔某事〕: *"Did you come here to see Peter?" "No, nothing could be further from my mind!"* "你是來這裡看彼得嗎?" "不是, 我腦子裡根本就沒想到這回事!"

further² *adj* [only before noun 僅用於名詞前] **1** more or additional 更多的; 附加的: *Are there any further questions?* 還有甚麼問題嗎? | **a further 10 miles/5 minutes/£500 etc** *Cook gently for a further ten minutes.* 再用微火多煮十分鐘。**2 until further notice** until you are told that something has changed 直至另行通知: *Lacunza ordered the suspension of the elections until further notice.* 拉昆扎命令暫停選舉, 何時舉行另行通知。

further³ *v* [T] to help something succeed or become successful 促進, 推動: *He dedicated his life to furthering the cause of world peace.* 他一生致力於推動世界和平事業。| **further sb's career** *Alan had been using her to further his career.* 阿倫一直在利用她來幫助自己向上爬。

fur·ther·ance /ˈfɝðərəns; ˈfɜːðərəns/ *n* [U] *formal*【正式】**1 the furtherance of** the development or progress of something ...的發展, ...的進展: *the furtherance of science* 科學的發展 **2 in furtherance of** in order to help something progress or become complete 為了促進...; 為了進一步完善...

further ed·u·ca·tion /ˌ.. ..ˈ../ *n* [U] *BrE* education for adults after leaving school that is not at a university【英】繼續教育, 進修教育, 成人教育 —compare 比較 HIGHER EDUCATION

fur·ther·more /ˈfɝðɚˌmor; ˌfɜːðəˈmɔː/ *adv* [sentence adverb 句子副詞] *formal* in addition to what has already been said【正式】此外; 而且; 不僅如此; 更有甚者: *Furthermore, my aim is to provide the best service possible under these difficult circumstances.* 此外, 我的目標是在這樣困難的條件下盡可能提供最好的服務。

fur·ther·most /ˈfɝðɚˌmost; ˈfɜːðəməʊst/ *adj formal* most distant【正式】最遠的: *In the furthermost corner sat a tall thin man.* 在最遠的角落裡坐着一位瘦高個子的男人。| **[+from]** *in the corner furthermost from the door* 在離門最遠的角落裡

fur·thest /ˈfɝðɪst; ˈfɜːðɪ̩st/ *adj, adv* **1** at the greatest distance from a place or point in time; FARTHEST 最遠的[地]: *There was a huge tapestry on the furthest wall.* 在最遠處的牆上掛着一幅巨大的織花壁毯。| **[+away/from]** *He walked slowly toward the end of the jury box furthest from the judge.* 他慢慢地向陪審團席離法官最遠的那端走去。—see 見 FARTHER¹ (USAGE) **2** to the greatest degree or amount or more than before 最大程度的[地]; 最大限度的[地]: *Maltby's book has probably gone furthest in explaining these events.* 莫爾特比的書可能是把這些事件解釋得最詳細的。

fur·tive /ˈfɝtɪv; ˈfɜːtɪv/ *adj* behaving as if you want to keep something secret 偷偷摸摸的, 鬼鬼祟祟的: *There was something furtive about his appearance.* 他的樣子有點鬼鬼祟祟的。| **furtive glances/looks** *Christine kept stealing furtive glances at me.* 克莉絲廷不斷地偷偷瞥我。—**furtively** *adv* —**furtiveness** *n* [U]

fu·ry /ˈfjʊrɪ; ˈfjʊəri/ *n* **1** [U] extreme, often uncontrolled anger 暴怒, 狂怒: *I was shaking with fury.* 我氣得發抖。**2** [C] a feeling of extreme anger 暴怒, 狂怒; 激動: **in a fury** *"Go on then!" shouted Jamie in a fury. "See if I care!"* "那繼續吧!" 詹米怒不可遏地叫着, "看我在乎不在乎!" | **fly into a fury** (=quickly become very angry) 勃然大怒 *Paul flew into one of his furies.* 保羅又大怒起來。**3 much to sb's fury/to the fury of sb** if something is done much to someone's fury, it makes them very angry 使某人怒不可遏: *The report was leaked to the press, much to the president's fury.* 這個報告泄露給了報界, 這使總統怒不可遏。**4 a fury of** a state of very busy activity or strong feeling〔感情、活動等〕的激烈, 熱烈; 狂熱: *She was listening with such a fury of concentration that she did not notice Arthur had left.* 她正聚精會神地聽着, 沒注意阿瑟已經離開。**5 like fury** *informal* with great effort or energy【非正式】奮力地; 使勁地; 猛烈地: *We went out and played like fury.* 我們到外面拼命地玩了一場。**6 the fury of the wind/sea/waves etc** used to describe bad weather conditions 狂風/怒海/狂浪等: *At last the fury of the storm lessened.* 暴風雨的勢頭終於減弱了。**7** [C] **Fury** one of the three snake-haired goddesses in ancient Greek stories, who punished crime〔古希臘故事裡的〕復仇三女神之一

furze /fɝz; fɜːz/ *n* [U] a wild bush with PRICKLY stems and bright yellow flowers 荊豆

fuse¹ /fjuz; fjuːz/ *n* [C] **1** a short thin piece of wire that is inside electrical equipment and prevents damage by melting and stopping the electricity when there is too much power〔電器中的〕保險絲: *two 13 amp fuses* 兩個13安培的保險絲 | **blow a fuse** (=make it melt by putting too much electricity through it) 熔斷保險絲 **2** also 又作 **fuze** *AmE*【美】a thing that delays a bomb, FIREWORK etc from exploding until you are a safe distance away or makes it explode at a particular time〔炸彈、煙火具等的〕導火索, 導火線; 定時引信: *The fuse was set to go off at 6 p.m.* 引信設定在下午6點起爆。**3 a short**

fuse if someone has a short fuse, they get angry very easily〔人〕易發火, 脾氣急躁 —see also 另見 **blow a fuse** (BLOW¹ (23))

fuse² *v* [I,T] **1** to join together, or to make something join together, to become a single thing 結合; 熔合; 合併: **[+together]** *The egg and sperm fuse together as one cell.* 卵和精子結合成為一個細胞。**2** *BrE* if an electrical system or electrical equipment fuses or you fuse them, it stops working because a fuse has melted【英】(使) 因保險絲熔斷而中斷工作: *The lights have fused again.* 電燈又因保險絲熔斷而熄滅了。**3** if metals, rocks etc fuse or you fuse them, they become joined together by being heated (使)〔金屬、岩石等〕熔化在一起, 熔合 **4** *technical* if a rock or metal fuses or you fuse it, it becomes liquid by being heated【術語】(使)〔岩石或金屬〕熔化: *Lead fuses at quite a low temperature.* 鉛在相當低的溫度下就會熔化。

fuse box /ˈ· ·/ *n* [C] a box that contains the fuses of the electrical system of a house or other building 保險絲盒

fused /fjuzd; fjuːzd/ *adj BrE* if a piece of electrical equipment is fused, it is fitted with a fuse【英】〔電器〕裝有保險絲的

fu·se·lage /ˈfjuzl̩ˌɑʒ; ˈfjuːzəlɑːʒ/ *n* [C] the main part of a plane, in which people sit or goods are carried〔飛機的〕機身 —see picture at 參見 AIRCRAFT 圖

fu·si·lier /ˌfjuzl̩ˈɪr; ˌfjuːzl̩ˈɪə/ *n* [C] a soldier in the past who carried a light gun called a MUSKET〔舊時〕滑膛槍手, 火槍手

fu·sil·lade /ˌfjuzl̩ˈed; ˌfjuːzl̩ˈleɪd/ *n* [singular] **1** a rapid series of loud noises, especially shots from a gun〔尤指槍砲的〕連續齊射 **2** a rapid series of questions or remarks 連珠砲似的問題; 一連串的話

fu·sion /ˈfjuʒən; ˈfjuːʒən/ *n* [U] **1** the combination or joining together of separate things, ideas, or groups 融合; 合成: *Her work is a fusion of several different styles of music.* 她的作品融合了幾種不同風格的音樂。**2** a joining together of separate things by heating them 熔合; 熔化 —compare 比較 FISSION —see also 另見 NUCLEAR FUSION

fusion bomb /ˈ·· ˌ·/ *n* [C] another word for a HYDROGEN BOMB hydrogen bomb 的另一種說法

3 **fuss¹** /fʌs; fʌs/ *n* **1** [singular] nervous or anxious behaviour that is usually about unimportant things〔通常指對小事〕緊張不安; 大驚小怪, 小題大作: **be a fuss** *James said he'd better be getting back or there'd be a fuss.* 詹姆斯說他最好還是回去, 不然有人就會大驚小怪。| **get/be in a fuss** *She gets in such a fuss before people come to dinner.* 她在客人來吃飯之前總是要手忙腳亂一番。**2** [singular,U] attention or excitement that is unnecessary or unwelcome 過於關心; 過於興奮: *They wanted a quiet wedding without any fuss.* 他們想要舉行一個安靜的婚禮, 不想弄得沸沸揚揚。**3 make/kick up a fuss (about)** to complain or become angry about something, especially when this is not necessary〔因…〕大吵大鬧;〔因…〕大驚小怪: *Josie kicked up a fuss because she thought the soup she ordered was too salty.* 喬西大吵大鬧了一番, 因為她認為她點的湯太鹹了。**4 make a fuss of** *BrE*【英】**make a fuss over** *AmE*【美】to pay a lot of attention to someone, to show that you are pleased with them or like them 對…體貼備至; 過分寵愛; 過分關心: *Make a fuss of your dog when he behaves properly.* 狗兒守規矩的時候就要寵寵牠。

fuss² *v* **1** [I] to worry a lot about things that may not be very important 大驚小怪, 小題大作; 過於焦慮; 過於煩惱: *I wish you'd stop fussing – I'll be perfectly all right.* 我希望你不要小題大作了 — 我會很好的。**2** [I] to pay too much attention to small, unimportant details 過於講究細節: **[+with/around/about]** *Paul was fussing with his clothes, trying to get his tie straight.* 保羅在不厭其煩地整理衣服, 試圖把領帶弄直。**3 be not fussed (about)** *BrE spoken* used when you do not think it matters what happens or is done【英口】(對…) 無所謂: *"Where do you want to go?" "I'm not fussed."* "你要去哪兒?" "我無所謂。" **4** [I] *AmE* to behave in an unhappy or angry way【美】吵鬧: *The baby woke up and started to fuss.* 嬰兒醒了, 開始吵鬧。

fuss over sb/sth *phr v* [T] to pay a lot of or too much attention to someone, especially to show that you are pleased with them or like them 過於體貼; 過於關心

fuss·pot /ˈfʌspɑt; ˈfʌs-pɒt/ *BrE*【英】, **fuss·bud·get** /ˈfʌsˌbʌdʒɪt; ˈfʌsˌbʌdʒl̩t/ *AmE*【美】—*n* [C] someone who is very fussy 瞎忙的人; 大驚小怪的人; 愛吹毛求疵的人

fuss·y /ˈfʌsɪ; ˈfʌsi/ *adj* **1** too concerned or worried about small, usually unimportant details, and difficult to please 愛挑剔的; 過於講究的; 難以取悅的: *Leonora was fussy about her looks.* 莉奧諾拉對自己的外表過於講究。| **fussy eater** (=someone who dislikes many types of food) 挑食的人 —compare 比較 FASTIDIOUS **2 not be fussy** *spoken* used when you do not mind what decision is made, where you go etc【口】無所謂, 隨便: *"Do you want to go out or just rent a movie?" "I'm not fussy."* "你要到外面去還是就租部電影看?" "我無所謂。" | **[+who/what/how etc]** *Geese are not fussy whose grass they eat.* 鵝不介意吃的草是誰家的。**3** fussy clothes, objects, buildings etc are too detailed and decorated〔衣服、物體、建築物等〕過分裝飾的: *The furniture looked comfortable, nothing fussy or too elaborate.* 這家具看起來很舒適, 不過分裝飾, 也不太精雕細琢。**4** with small, exact, and careful actions, sometimes showing nervousness〔動作〕過分注意細節的, 緊張的: *She patted her hair with small fussy movements.* 她拍了拍頭髮, 顯得有點緊張。—**fussily** *adv* —**fussiness** *n* [U]

fus·ti·an /ˈfʌstʃən; ˈfʌstiən/ *n* [U] **1** a type of rough heavy cotton cloth, worn especially in the past〔尤指舊時的〕粗斜紋布 **2** *literary* words that sound important but have very little meaning【文】浮誇而無多大意義的話 —**fustian** *adj*

fus·ty /ˈfʌstɪ; ˈfʌsti/ *adj* **1** if rooms, clothes, buildings etc are fusty, they have an unpleasant smell, because they have not been used for a long time〔房間、衣服、建築物等〕發霉味的 **2** *informal* ideas or people that are fusty are old-fashioned【非正式】〔思想或人〕過時的; 守舊的: *These fusty ideas about education should be brought up-to-date.* 這些守舊的教育思想應當予以更新。—**fustiness** *n* [U]

fu·tile /ˈfjutl̩; ˈfjuːtaɪl/ *adj* actions that are futile are useless because they have no chance of being successful 無用的; 徒勞的: *a futile attempt to save the paintings from the flames* 試圖將那些畫從大火中搶救出來的徒勞之舉 | **be futile to do sth** *It was futile to continue the negotiations.* 繼續談判是無濟於事的。—**futility** /fjuˈtɪlətɪ; fjuːˈtɪlˌti/ *n* [U]

fu·ton /ˈfutɑn; ˈfuːtɒn/ *n* [C] a flat soft CUSHION used for sleeping on, especially in Japan〔尤指日本的〕蒲團, 日本牀墊 —see picture at 參見 BED¹ 圖

fu·ture¹ /ˈfjutʃɚ; ˈfjuːtʃə/ *adj* [only before noun 僅用於名詞前] **1** likely to happen, become, or exist at a time after the present 將來的, 未來的: *Careful accounting may help to predict future costs.* 認真的會計工作可能有助於預估將來的費用。| **future wife/husband etc** (=someone who will be your wife, husband etc) 未婚妻/夫; 未來的妻子/丈夫 **2** *technical* in grammar, being the form of a verb used to show a future act or state【術語】〔語法中的〕將來式[時]的: *the future tense* 將來時態 **3 for future reference** something kept for future reference is kept in order to be used or looked at in the future 供日後參考 1 1

future² *n* 1 2

1 the future the time after the present 將來, 未來: *Write an essay of 500 words describing your plans for the future.* 寫一篇500字的文章, 描述一下你對未來的計劃。| *Most science fiction stories are set in the future.* 大部分科幻小說都是以未來為背景的。

2 in future also 又作 **in the future a)** at some time in the future 在將來的某個時候: *In the future we will be using a much more sophisticated computer system.* 將來我們會使用一種更加精密的電腦系統。| **in the near/immediate future** (=soon) 在不久的將來, 不久 *The recession shows no signs of easing in the immediate future.* 這次經濟衰退沒有呈現不久就會緩和的跡象。| **in/for the forseeable future** (=for as long as you can imagine or plan for) 在可預見的將來 *We will not be hiring anyone else in the forseeable future.* 我們在可預見的將來不會再聘人。| **in the distant future** (=a very long time ahead in the future) 在遙遠的將來 *Space travel to other planets may be possible in the distant future.* 到其他行星的太空旅行在遙遠的未來將可能實現。**b)** from now until a much later time 今後: *I'll sleep in her room in future to prevent her sleepwalking.* 我今後要睡在她的房間裡, 以防止她夢遊。

3 ►WHAT WILL HAPPEN TO YOU 前途◄ [C] what someone or something will do or what will happen to them in the future 未來要做的事; 前途; 前景: *The islands should have the right to decide their own future.* 這些島嶼應當有權決定自己的前途。| **sth/sb's future is uncertain** *For young adults in the inner cities, the future is uncertain.* 對市中心貧民區的年輕人來說, 前途是渺茫的。

4 ►POSSIBILITY OF SUCCESS 成功的可能性◄ [singular,U] a chance or possibility of success at a later time 前途, 成功的可能性: *I'd like to discuss my future in the company.* 我想討論一下我在公司裡的前途。| **the future of sth** *Ferguson is optimistic about the future of the business.* 弗格森對公司的前途充滿希望。| **a future in sth** *He felt there was no future in farming these days.* 他覺得如今種田沒有前途。| **have a great/promising/bright future** (=to seem likely to do well in a job, sport etc) 前程遠大/前途無量/前途光明

5 the future *technical* in grammar, the form of a verb that shows that the act or state that has been described will happen or exist at a later time【術語】〔語法中的〕將來式[時]: *In the sentence, 'I will leave tomorrow', the verb 'will' indicates the future.* 在 I will leave tomorrow 一句中, 動詞 will 表示將來。

6 futures [plural] *technical* goods, money, land etc that will be supplied or exchanged in the future at a time and price that has already been agreed【術語】〔貨物、錢幣、土地等〕期貨(交易)

7 look to the future to plan for what will happen or think about what could happen in the future 計劃未來, 考慮未來, 寄希望於將來

future per·fect /ˌ.. ˈ../ *n technical*【術語】**the future perfect** in grammar, the form of a verb that shows that the action described by the verb will be complete before a particular time in the future, formed in English by 'will have' or 'shall have'〔語法中的〕將來完成式 —**future perfect** *adj*

futures mar·ket /ˈ.. ˌ../ *n* [C] *technical* the buying and selling of futures (FUTURE[2] (6)); FORWARD MARKET【術語】期貨市場

fu·tur·is·m /ˈfjutʃəˌrɪzəm; ˈfjuːtʃərɪzəm/ *n* [C] a style of painting, music, and literature in the early 20th century that express the violent, active qualities of modern life, machines, science etc〔20世紀初期繪畫、音樂和文學中的〕未來主義, 未來派 —**futurist** *n* [C]

fu·tur·is·tic /ˌfjutʃəˈrɪstɪk; ˌfjuːtʃəˈrɪstɪk◄/ *adj* **1 futuristic design/building/film etc** a building, film etc that is so unusual and modern in appearance that it looks as if it belongs in the future instead of the present 未來主義設計/建築/電影等: *The futuristic sports stadium is the pride of the city.* 那座未來派風格的體育場是該城的驕傲。**2** futuristic ideas, books etc imagine what may happen in the future, especially through scientific developments〔尤指根據科學發展〕想像的; 幻想的; 未來派的: *Orwell's disturbing futuristic novel, '1984'* 奧威爾的那部令人不安的描寫未來的小說《一九八四》

fu·tu·ri·ty /fjuˈturətɪ; fjʊˈtjʊərʒti/ *n formal*【正式】**1** [U] the time after the present; FUTURE[2] (1) 將來, 未來 **2** [C] an event or possibility that may happen in the future 未來事件; 未來性

futz /fʌts; fʌts/ *v*

futz around *phr v* [I] *AmE informal* to waste time, especially by doing small, unimportant jobs slowly【美, 非正式】閒蕩; 閒混: *I spent the entire day just futzing around.* 我一整天都在閒混。

fuzz[1] /fʌz; fʌz/ *n* [U] **1** thin soft hair or a hairlike substance that covers something〔覆蓋在某物上的〕茸毛; 細毛: *When Jack was born he had a fuzz of black hair on his head.* 傑克出生的時候頭上長着短細的黑毛髮。**2** a small amount of soft material that has come from clothing etc〔衣服上脫落的小撮〕絨毛; LINT (1) *AmE*【美】**3 the fuzz** an insulting way of talking to or about the police, used especially in the 1960s and 1970s 警察〔侮辱性用語, 尤用於20世紀60年代和70年代〕

fuzz[2] *v* [T] to make something fuzzy 使模糊; 使成絨毛狀

fuzz·y /ˈfʌzɪ; ˈfʌzi/ *adj* **1** unclear or confused and lacking details 模糊的, 不明確的: **fuzzy account/description etc** *She gave a rather fuzzy account of what had happened.* 她很模糊地描述了所發生的事。**2** if a sound or picture is fuzzy, it is unclear〔聲音或圖片〕不清楚的: *Some of the photos were so fuzzy it was hard to tell who was who.* 有些照片很模糊, 很難說出誰是誰。**3** having short soft hair, fur etc that stands upright 毛茸茸的: *I stroked the kitten's fuzzy back.* 我撫摸小貓毛茸茸的背。—**fuzzily** *adv* —**fuzziness** *n* [U]

f-word /ˈɛf wɝd; ˈef wɜːd/ *n* [singular] a word used when you are talking about the word FUCK but do not want to say it because it is rude. It is not used instead of the word 'fuck' 粗話〔指 fuck 一詞〕: *Mommy, Billy said the f-word.* 媽媽, 比利說粗話。

fwy *AmE*【美】the written abbreviation for 縮寫= FREEWAY

FX /ˌɛf ˈɛks; ˌef ˈeks/ **1** an abbreviation for 縮寫= FOREIGN EXCHANGE **2** an abbreviation for 縮寫= SPECIAL EFFECTS

FY *AmE*【美】the abbreviation for 縮寫= FISCAL YEAR

-fy /faɪ; faɪ/ *suffix* [in verbs 構成動詞] another form of the suffix -IFY 後綴 -ify 的另一種形式

G,g

G, g /dʒi; dʒiː/ *plural* **G's, g's** the seventh letter of the English alphabet 英語字母表的第七個字母

g the written abbreviation of 縮寫= GRAM

G¹ *n* **1** also 又作 **g** [C,U] the fifth note in the musical SCALE¹ (8) of C MAJOR¹ (4), or the musical KEY based on this note G音〔C大調音階中的第五個音〕; G調 **2** [C] *technical* the amount of force caused by GRAVITY (1) on an object that is lying on the Earth【術語】重力: *Astronauts endure a force of several G's during take-off.* 宇航員在起飛時要承受等於他體重好幾倍的重力。**3** [U] *AmE informal* a GRAND (=$1,000)【美, 非正式】1,000美元

G² *adj AmE* a film that is G has been officially approved as suitable for people of any age【美】〔影片〕經正式批准適合各種年齡的觀眾觀看的; U *BrE*【英】—compare 比較 PG

G & T /ˌdʒi ən ˋti; ˌdʒiː ən 'tiː/ *n* [C,U] gin and tonic; a popular alcoholic drink served with ice and a thin piece of LEMON (1) 加奎寧水的杜松子酒〔飲用時加冰和一薄片檸檬〕

G7 /ˌdʒi ˋsɛvən; ˌdʒiː 'sevən/ *n* **the G7** the Group of Seven; the seven richest industrial nations in the world: Canada, France, Germany, Britain, Italy, Japan, and the US 七國集團〔指世界七大工業發達國家: 加拿大、法國、德國、英國、意大利、日本和美國〕

gab /gæb; gæb/ *v* **gabbed, gabbing** [I+**about**] *informal* to talk continuously, usually about things that are not important【非正式】喋喋不休, 閒聊: *You two were gabbing so much you didn't even see me!* 你們倆閒聊得那麼起勁, 根本沒有看見我。—see also 另見 **the gift of the gab** (GIFT (4)) —**gab** *n* [U] —**gabby** *adj*

gab·ar·dine, gaberdine /ˋgæbɚˌdin; 'gæbədiːn/ *n* **1** [U] a strong material which does not allow water to go through and is often used for making coats 軋別丁, 華達呢〔一種防水布料, 多用於做上衣〕**2** [C] a coat made from gabardine 華達呢大衣

gab·ble¹ /ˋgæbḷ; 'gæbəl/ *v* **gabbled, gabbling** [I,T] to say something so quickly that people cannot hear you or understand you properly 咕嚕, 急促不清地說話: *Just calm down, stop gabbling, and tell me what has happened.* 請冷靜下來, 說話別太急, 告訴我發生了甚麼事。| **gabble away/on** *Gina tends to gabble away when she's excited.* 吉娜一激動, 說話就會急促不清, 絮絮叨叨。

gabble² *n* [singular,U] a lot of talking that is difficult to understand, when several people are talking at the same time〔幾個人同時說話〕混雜的說話聲: *A gabble of voices came from the next room.* 隔壁房間傳來嘈雜不清的說話聲。

gab·er·dine /ˋgæbɚˌdin; 'gæbədiːn/ *n* another spelling of GABARDINE gabardine的另一種拼法

ga·ble /ˋgebḷ; 'geɪbəl/ *n* [C] the upper end of a house wall where it joins with a sloping roof and makes a shape like a TRIANGLE (2) 三角牆: *the gable end of the barn* 穀倉有三角牆的一端

ga·bled /ˋgebḷd; 'geɪbəld/ *adj* having one or more gables 有三角牆的: *a gabled cottage* 有三角牆的小屋

gad /gæd; gæd/ *v* **gadded, gadding**

gad about/around *phr v* [I] *informal* to go out and enjoy yourself, going to many different places, especially when you should be doing something else【非正式】閒蕩, 外出尋樂〔尤指本應做點別的甚麼事〕: *While I'm at home cooking, he's gadding about with his friends.* 我在家做飯, 而他卻在跟他的朋友一起尋樂。

gad·a·bout /ˋgædəˌbaut; 'gædəbaʊt/ *n* [C] *informal* someone who goes out a lot or travels a lot in order to enjoy themselves【非正式】遊蕩的人, 遊手好閒的人

gad·fly /ˋgædˌflaɪ; 'gædflaɪ/ *n* [C] **1** a fly that bites cattle and HORSES 虻, 牛虻 **2** someone who annoys other people by criticizing them〔愛批評別人而〕惹人討厭的人

gad·get /ˋgædʒɪt; 'gædʒɨt/ *n* [C] a small, useful, and cleverly-designed machine or tool 小巧, 設計精巧的機械[裝置]: *a clever gadget for sharpening knives* 精巧的磨刀器具 —see 見 MACHINE¹ (USAGE)

gad·get·ry /ˋgædʒətrɪ; 'gædʒɨtri/ *n* [U] modern gadgets in general 小巧的機械[工具]: *I don't understand how all this electronic gadgetry works.* 所有這些精巧的電子器具是如何工作的, 我不太懂。

Gae·lic¹ /ˋgelɪk; 'geɪlɪk/ *n* [U] one of the Celtic languages, especially spoken in parts of Scotland and in Ireland 蓋爾語〔尤指蘇格蘭部分地區和愛爾蘭講的一種凱爾特語言〕

Gaelic² *adj* speaking Gaelic, or connected with Gaelic 講蓋爾語的; 蓋爾語的

Gaelic foot·ball /ˌ·· ˈ··/ *n* [U] a game played in Ireland between two teams of 15 players, using a round ball that can be kicked or hit with the hands 蓋爾足球〔通行於愛爾蘭的一種足球運動, 兩隊各15人, 使用圓形球, 可足踢亦可手擊〕

gaff /gæf; gæf/ *n* [C] **1** a stick with a hook at the end, used to pull big fish out of the water〔將大魚拖出水面的〕手鉤 **2** *British slang* someone's house【英俚】〔某人的〕房屋 —see also 另見 **blow the gaff** (BLOW¹ (14))

gaffe /gæf; gæf/ *n* [C] an embarrassing mistake made in a social situation or in public; FAUX PAS〔在社交場合或當眾〕出醜, 失禮, 失言: *The consul's comments were a major diplomatic gaffe.* 領事的評論是一次重大的外交失言。

gaf·fer /ˋgæfɚ; 'gæfə/ *n* [C] **1** the person who is in charge of the lighting in making a cinema film〔電影拍攝時負責照明的〕照明電工 **2** *informal humorous* an old man【非正式, 幽默】老頭 **3** *BrE informal* a man who is in charge of people, especially in a factory【英, 非正式】〔尤指工廠裡的〕工頭, 領班

gag¹ /gæg; gæg/ *v* **gagged, gagging 1** [I] to be unable to swallow and seem about to bring up food from your stomach 作嘔: *The foul stench made her gag.* 那種惡臭令她想吐。| [+**on**] *He almost gagged on his first mouthful of food.* 他吃第一口便差點吐了出來。**2** [T] to put a piece of cloth over someone's mouth to stop them making a noise 用布塞進〔某人的嘴, 使其不能出聲〕: *Thugs gagged her and tied her to a chair.* 暴徒用布塞住她的嘴, 把她綁在一把椅子上。| **bound and gagged** (=tied and gagged) 被捆綁着又被塞住嘴 **3** [T] to stop people saying what they want to say and expressing their opinions 壓制〔某人〕言論自由, 限制〔某人〕發言: *an attempt to gag political activists* 壓制政治活動家發言的企圖 | **gagging clause/writ/order** (=a legal agreement or official order that stops you from speaking about something in public) 限制公開言論的條款/法令/命令 **4 gag me with a spoon!** *AmE spoken* used especially by older children to express a strong feeling of dislike【美口】我快吐了!〔尤為較大的孩子用來表示強烈的厭惡感〕

gag² *n* [C] **1** *informal* a joke or funny story【非正式】玩笑, 笑話: *the same old gags* 老一套的笑話 **2** a piece of cloth put over someone's mouth to stop them making a noise 塞口布〔用來蓋住某人的嘴使其不能發聲〕**3 gag order** an order made by the court to prevent any public reporting of a case which is still being considered by a

G

court of law〔法庭禁止公開報道一起正在審理的案件的〕禁聲令

ga·ga /ˋgɑgɑ; ˈgɑːgɑː/ *adj* [not before noun 不用於名詞前] *informal*【非正式】**1** an insulting word used to describe someone who is confused because they are old〔因年老而〕糊塗的〔侮辱性用語〕: *Sid keeps forgetting my name. I think he's going a bit gaga.* 西德老是忘記我的名字。我看他有點老糊塗了。**2** having a strong but often temporary feeling of love for someone; INFATUATED 狂熱的, 着迷的: **[+about/over]** *fans go gaga over the the pretty-baby looks of Sridevi* 對斯利德維漂亮寶貝般的美貌着了迷的仰慕者

gage /gedʒ; geɪdʒ/ *n* an American spelling of GAUGE gauge 的美式拼法

gag·gle /ˋgægl; ˈgægəl/ *n* **1 a gaggle of tourists/children etc** a noisy group of people 喧鬧的遊客/兒童等: *a gaggle of teenage girls* 一羣喧鬧的少女 **2 a gaggle of geese** a number of geese (GOOSE[1] (1)) together 一羣鵝

gai·e·ty /ˋgeətɪ; ˈgeɪəti/ *n old-fashioned*【過時】**1** [U] the fact that someone or something is cheerful and fun 快樂, 歡樂, 高興: *Lars enjoyed the warmth and gaiety of these occasions.* 拉斯享受着這些場合的溫暖和歡樂氣氛。**2 gaieties** enjoyable events or activities 歡娛; 令人歡樂的事件[活動]: *Elaine missed the gaieties of life in Paris.* 伊萊恩懷念巴黎生活時的那些歡娛。—see also 另見 GAY[1]

gai·ly /ˋgelɪ; ˈgeɪli/ *adv* **1** in a happy cheerful way 快樂地, 歡樂地: *He walked past whistling gaily.* 他歡樂地吹着口哨走過去。**2** in a way that shows you do not care about, or do not realize, the effects of your actions 不顧後果地; 冒失地: *They gaily went on talking after the film had started.* 電影開演後他們還毫無顧忌地說話。**3 gaily coloured/painted/decorated etc** having bright cheerful colours 色彩鮮豔/塗上豔麗油漆/裝飾花哨的: *gaily coloured tropical birds* 色彩豔麗的熱帶鳥

2 2 **gain[1]** /gen; geɪn/ *v*

1 ►GET STH 得到某物◄ [T] to obtain or achieve something important or valuable 獲得〔珍貴物品〕; 成就〔重要事情〕: *She gained high grades in English and Math.* 她的英語和數學得了高分。| *After gaining independence in 1957, it was renamed 'Ghana'.* 1957 年獲得獨立後, 它改名為"加納"。| *when radical left parties gained control of local authorites* 當時激進的左派政黨取得了對地方當局的控制權

2 ►GET GRADUALLY 逐漸獲得◄ [I,T] to gradually get more and more of a useful or valuable quality, skill etc 逐漸獲得〔有用或寶貴的品質、技藝等〕: **gain experience/support/a reputation etc** *The Greens are gaining more and more support.* 綠黨正獲得越來越多的支持。| *You'll gain useful experience in working with computers.* 你在使用電腦的過程中會得到有用的經驗。| **gain in popularity/confidence etc** (=become more popular, more confident etc) 變得越來越受歡迎/越來越有信心等 | **gain currency** (=when an idea becomes more popular)〔某種觀點〕流行起來: *These ideas have gained currency in recent years.* 這些想法近幾年已變得很流行。

3 ►GET AN ADVANTAGE 獲益◄ [I,T] to get an advantage from a situation, opportunity, or event (使)〔從某局勢、機會或事件中〕獲益, 獲利: **gain (sth) from** *It was the better-educated women who gained most from this expansion of opportunities.* 受過良好教育的婦女在這次機會的增加中受益最多。| **stand to gain** (=or likely to get an advantage) 可能受益 *Who is it who really stands to gain from these tax cuts?* 誰真正能從這些減稅中受益? | **there's nothing to be gained** (=it will not help you) 無濟於事 *There's nothing to be gained by losing your temper.* 發脾氣是無濟於事的。

4 gain weight/speed/height to increase in weight, speed, or height 增加體重/速度/高度: *Carrie's gained a lot of weight recently.* 卡麗的體重最近增加了很多。

5 gain access (to sth) a) to manage to enter a building 進入〔建築物〕: *New ramps will help the disabled gain better access.* 新修的斜道將使殘疾人進出更方便。**b)** to manage to see someone or use something 得以見到某人[使用某物]: *People should be able to gain easy access to this sort of information.* 人們應當能夠很容易地接觸到這種信息。

6 gain entrance/entry a) to enter a building that is locked 進入〔上了鎖的建築物〕: *Thieves gained entry through the skylight.* 小偷是從天窗進入的。**b)** to join or become part of a system or organization 加入, 成為一部分: *At the age of 48 she gained entrance to the Civil Service.* 她在 48 歲時加入了公務員的行列。

7 gain ground make steady progress and become more popular, more successful etc 穩步發展, 變得更受歡迎[更成功]: *The anti-smoking lobby has steadily gained ground in the last decade.* 向議員遊說的反吸煙團體在過去十年中取得越來越大的成功。

8 gain time to deliberately do something to give yourself more time to think 贏得時間: *Maybe if we said you were sick we could gain some time.* 如果我們說你病了, 也許可以拖延一下時間。—opposite 反義詞 LOSE (12)

9 ►CLOCK 鐘錶◄ [I,T] if a clock or watch gains or gains time, it goes too fast〔鐘錶〕走得太快 —opposite 反義詞 LOSE (15)

10 ►ARRIVE 到達◄ [T] *formal or literary* to reach a place after a lot of effort or difficulty【正式或文】〔經過很大努力或困難之後〕到達: *The swimmer finally gained the river bank.* 那位游泳者終於到達河岸。—see also 另見 **nothing ventured, nothing gained** (VENTURE[1] (4))

gain on/upon sb/sth *phr v* [T] to gradually get closer to a person, car etc that you are chasing 逼近, 趕上: *Quick – they're gaining on us!* 快 —— 他們要趕上我們了!

USAGE NOTE 用法說明: GAIN

WORD CHOICE 詞語辨析: **gain, get, win, earn, make**

You can **gain** something useful or necessary whether or not you deserve it. Though you may **gain** weight, strength, a scholarship, a fortune, etc usually people speak of **gaining**, or less formally **getting**, things that you cannot touch such as experience, knowledge, education, and satisfaction. You especially **gain** (or **get**) things of this sort that other people give you, for example: support, recognition, popularity and respect. gain 用於指獲得有用或需要的東西, 不論你是否應得到。雖然 gain 可以用於指體重、力量、獎學金、財產等的獲得, 但更經常的是用於不可觸及的東西〔此時也可用 get, 但不如 gain 正式〕, 如經驗、知識、教育、滿足等的獲得。gain (或 get) 尤指獲得的這類東西是別人給予你的, 例如: 支持、承認、聲望、尊敬等。

If you **win** something solid like a television or money, you get it partly by chance. win 用於實在有形的東西, 例如一台電視機或錢財, 你在一定程度上是靠運氣得到這些東西的: *Carla won $1,000 in Las Vegas!* 卡拉在拉斯維加斯贏了 1,000 美元!

If you **win** something you cannot touch, such as support, recognition, popularity, favour, or respect, you gain it by your own effort or abilities, usually from someone else. win 用於抽象的東西, 如支持、認可、聲望、寵信或尊敬, 你是靠自己的努力或能力從他人那裡獲得的: *People disliked him at first, but his reliability soon won their approval.* 人們開始時不喜歡他, 但他為人可靠, 很快贏得人們的認可。You can also **win** new friends. win 還可以用來指贏得新朋友。

If you say that someone **wins** *a scholarship/a place at university* etc, it means they did something to get it, and probably that other people tried to get it as well (compare *gained*). *She won a prize* could mean either that she got it by luck (eg in a game), or by her own efforts. 用 win 來指某人贏得獎學金或大學的入學資格等, 意味着此人做了某事才得到它, 其他人可能也曾經設法得到它〔比較 gained〕。She won a prize 可能意味着她可能是靠運氣得獎〔如在某項比賽中〕, 也可能是靠自己的努力。

You **earn** (or less formally **get**) money for work you do. earn 指通過工作掙錢〔或用不那麼正式的 get〕: *He earns/gets £400 a week* (NOT 不用 *gains*). 他每週掙 400 英鎊。You can also **earn** something that you deserve such as support, recognition, popularity, or respect. earn 還可以用於你應該得到的東西, 如支持、認同、聲望或尊敬: *The newspaper quickly earned a reputation for fair, impartial reporting.* 這家報紙很快因其公正、無偏見的報道而贏得了聲譽。| *Take a break, now you've earned it!* 休息一下吧, 你該歇一會了!

You can also **make** money, especially from your own business or in a way that does not involve working. 掙錢可以用 make, 特別是從自己的生意或者以某種不需要工作的方式賺錢: *He made a profit of $50,000 on Wall Street last month.* 他上個月在華爾街獲利 50,000 美元。

3 **gain²** *n* **1** [C,U] an increase in the amount or level of something〔某物數量或水平的〕增加, 提高: *a gain in weekly output* 每週產量的增加 | *weight gain* 重量增加 **2** [C] an advantage or improvement, especially one achieved by planning or effort〔靠計劃或努力得到的〕受益; 改進: *The new machinery has produced big efficiency gains.* 新機器帶來了很大的效益。| *a policy that brought Japan considerable gains in the post-war period* 使日本在戰後大大受益的一項政策 **3** [U] financial profit, when this seems to be the only thing you are interested in〔財務〕收益, 獲利: *companies that care only about short-term gain* 只關心短期收益的公司 | **for gain** *Some of these tribes used to sell their women for gain.* 這些部落中有一部分在過去曾為了獲利而出售他們的女眷。**4 ill-gotten gains** *humorous* money or advantages obtained dishonestly【幽默】不義之財; 以不義的手段獲得的利益 —see also 另見 CAPITAL GAINS

gain·ful /ˋgenfəl; ˈgeɪnfəl/ *adj* **gainful employment/work/activity** *formal* work or activity for which you are paid【正式】有報酬的工作/活動 —**gainfully** *adv*: *gainfully employed* 有職業有收入的

gain·say /genˋse; ˌgeɪnˈseɪ/ *v past tense and past participle* **gainsaid** /-ˋsɛd; -ˈsed/ [T usually in negatives 一般用於否定句] *formal* to say that something is not true, or to disagree with someone【正式】否認, 反對: *It may be very difficult to gainsay the claim.* 反對這種主張可能很難。

gait /get; geɪt/ *n* [singular] the way someone walks 步態, 步伐: *He moved off again with a slow shuffling gait.* 他緩慢地拖着腳又走開了。

gai·ter /ˋgetɚ; ˈgeɪtə/ *n* [C usually plural 一般用複數] a cloth or leather covering worn below the knee by men in past times〔舊時男人穿在膝蓋以下的布質或皮質的〕護腿

gal /gæl; gæl/ *n* [C] **1** *AmE informal* a girl or woman【美, 非正式】女孩, 女子: *She's a great gal.* 她是個了不起的女孩。**2** *BrE old-fashioned* an UPPER-CLASS pronunciation of girl【英, 過時】girl 這個詞的上層社會發音

gal. the written abbreviation of 縮寫= GALLON

ga·la /ˋgelə; ˈgɑːlə/ *n* [C] **1** a public entertainment or performance to celebrate a special occasion 慶典, 演出盛會: **gala night/event etc** *a gala night at the opera* 歌劇院的盛大演出之夜 **2** *BrE* a sports competition, especially in swimming【英】運動會〔尤指游泳比賽〕

ga·lac·tic /gəˋlæktɪk; gəˈlæktɪk/ *adj* related to a galaxy 星系的

gal·ax·y /ˋgæləksɪ; ˈgæləksi/ *n* [C] **1** one of the large groups of stars that make up the universe 星系 **2 the Galaxy** the large group of stars in which our sun and its PLANETs are 銀河, 銀河系 **3** [singular] a large number of things that are similar 一大批〔相似的東西〕: *A whole galaxy of pills and tablets was lined up on the table.* 桌子上擺着各式各樣的藥丸和藥片。

gale /gel; geɪl/ *n* [C] **1** a very strong wind 大風: *The fence was blown down in the gale.* 籬笆在大風中被吹倒了。| **it is blowing a gale** *BrE* (=it is very windy)【英】正在颳大風 —see picture on page A13 參見 A13 頁圖 **2 a gale/gales of laughter** a sudden loud sound of laughter〔突發的〕一陣大笑聲/陣陣大笑聲: *Gales of laughter came from the next room.* 隔壁房間傳來陣陣大笑聲。

gale-force /ˈ· ·/ *adj* a gale-force wind is strong enough to be dangerous or cause damage〔風〕高強度的〔指具有危險性或可能造成災害的大風〕—**gale-force** *adv*: *blowing gale-force* 颳大風

gall¹ /gɔl; gɔːl/ *n* **1 have the gall to do sth** to do something rude and unreasonable that most people would be too embarrassed to do 厚顏無恥地做某事: *Being a Tory politician, he still had the gall to be interviewed on TV and claim all the credit.* 他是個英國保守黨政客, 但仍敢厚着臉皮在電視上接受採訪, 並聲稱一切都歸功於他。**2** [U] *old-fashioned* anger and hate that will not go away【過時】〔難以消除的〕憤恨 **3** [U] *old use* BILE【舊】膽汁 **4** [C] a swelling on a tree or plant caused by damage from insects or infection〔樹或植物上的〕癭, 蟲癭 **5** [C] a painful place on an animal's skin, caused by something rubbing against it〔動物皮膚上的〕擦傷, 擦傷處

gall² *v* [T] to make someone feel upset and angry because of something that is unfair〔因某事不公正而〕使惱怒, 激怒: **it galls sb (that)** *It really galls me they could blame my Vicky for their own screw-up.* 他們自己把事情弄糟, 竟然責怪我們的維基, 這實在使我感到惱火。

gal·lant¹ /ˋgælənt; ˈgəlænt/ *adj old-fashioned* a man who is gallant is kind and polite towards women【過時】〔對女子〕殷勤有禮的

gal·lant² /ˋgælənt; ˈgælənt/ *adj old use* brave【舊】勇敢的, 英勇的: *gallant deeds* 英勇的行為 —**gallantly** *adv*

gal·lant³ /ˋgælənt; ˈgælənt/ *n* [C] *old use* a well-dressed young man who is kind and polite towards women【舊】時髦紳士, 對女子獻殷勤的穿着考究的男子

gal·lan·try /ˋgæləntrɪ; ˈgæləntri/ *n* [U] *formal*【正式】**1** courage, especially in a battle 英勇, 勇敢〔尤指作戰勇敢〕: *a medal for gallantry* 英雄獎章 **2** polite attention given by men to women〔男子對女子所表現的〕殷勤

gall blad·der /ˈ· ˌ··/ *n* [C] the organ in your body in which BILE is stored 膽囊 —see picture at 參見 DIGESTIVE SYSTEM 圖

gal·le·on /ˋgælɪən; ˈgæliən/ *n* [C] a sailing ship used mainly by the Spanish from the 15th to the 17th century〔15 世紀至 17 世紀主要為西班牙人用的〕帆船

gal·le·ry /ˋgælərɪ; ˈgæləri/ *n* [C] **1 a)** a large building where people can see famous pieces of art 美術館: *an exhibition of African art at the Hayward Gallery* 海沃德美術館的非洲藝術展覽 **b)** [C] a small privately owned shop or STUDIO (3) where you can see and buy pieces of art 畫廊, 字畫店〔陳列並出售繪畫等藝術品的小型私人商店或畫室〕**2 a)** [C] an upper floor or BALCONY built out from an inner wall of a hall, theatre, or church, from which people can watch a performance, DEBATE¹ (1, 2) etc〔大廳、劇場或教堂裡的〕樓座, 樓上旁聽席: *the public gallery in Congress* 國會的旁聽席 —see picture at 參見 THEATRE 圖 **b) the gallery** the people sitting in a gallery 樓座觀眾 **3 play to the gallery** to do or say something just because you think it will please people and make you popular 譁眾取寵, 討好觀眾 **4** [C] a level passage under the ground in a mine or CAVE¹〔礦山或山洞裡的〕水平巷道, 坑道 —see also 另見 PRESS GALLERY, SHOOTING GALLERY 3

gal·ley /ˋgælɪ; ˈgæli/ *n* [C] **1** a long low Greek or Roman ship with sails which was rowed by SLAVEs in the past〔古代希臘、羅馬由奴隸划槳的〕低舷大帆船 **2** a kitchen on a ship 船上的廚房: *The fire extinguishers are stored in the galley.* 滅火器存放在船上的廚房裡。**3 a)** a TRAY used by printers which holds TYPE[1] (3) 活字盤 **b)** also 又作 **galley proof** a sheet of paper on which a PRINTER (2) prints a book so that mistakes can be put right before it is divided into pages 長條校樣

Gal·lic /ˋgælɪk; ˈgælɪk/ *adj* typical of France or French people 法國的, 法國人的: *Gallic charm* 法國的魅力

gal·ling /ˋgɔlɪŋ; ˈgɔːlɪŋ/ *adj* making you feel upset and angry because of something that is unfair〔因某事不公平而〕使人惱怒的, 令人生氣的: *The most galling thing is that the guy who got promoted is less qualified than me.* 最令人生氣的是, 那個得到晉升的傢伙, 資格根本比不上我。

gal·li·vant /ˋgæləˌvænt; ˈgælɨvænt/ *v* [I] *informal or humorous* to spend time enjoying yourself and going from place to place for pleasure【非正式或幽默】閒逛, 遊蕩, 尋歡作樂: **gallivant about/around** *She spent six months gallivanting around Europe.* 她花了六個月的時間在歐洲到處遊玩。

gal·lon /ˋgælən; ˈgælən/ *n* [C] **1** *BrE* a unit for measuring liquids, equal to 4.5435 litres【英】加侖〔液量單位, = 4.5435 升〕**2** *AmE* a unit for measuring liquids, equal to 3.785 litres【美】加侖〔= 3.785 升〕—see table on page C3 參見C3 頁附錄

gal·lop[1] /ˋgæləp; ˈgæləp/ *v* **1** [I] if a horse gallops, it moves very fast with all its feet leaving the ground together〔馬〕飛奔, 疾馳: **[+along/across/towards etc]** *wild horses galloping over the sand* 在沙地上飛奔的野馬 **2** [I,T] if you gallop, you ride very fast on a horse or you make it go very fast 騎馬奔馳, 策馬疾馳: **[+along/across/towards etc]** *I watched as Jan galloped away.* 我看着簡策馬奔馳而去。**3** [I always+adv/prep] to move very quickly 快速移動, 飛跑: *Ian came galloping down the stairs.* 伊恩迅速跑下樓梯。

gallop through sth *phr v* [T] *informal* to do a job, some work etc very quickly【非正式】匆匆地做完: *Neil galloped through his homework.* 尼爾匆匆做完作業。

gallop[2] *n* **1 a)** [singular] the movement of a horse at its fastest speed when all four feet leave the ground together〔馬〕飛跑, 疾馳: **break into a gallop** (=begin to go very fast) 飛跑起來 **b)** [C] a ride on a horse when it is galloping 騎馬奔跑 **2 at a gallop a)** at the fastest speed possible when riding a horse〔騎馬〕以最快速度: *Rogers set off at a gallop.* 羅傑斯騎馬奔馳而去。**b)** *informal* very quickly【非正式】急速地, 飛快地

gal·lop·ing /ˋgæləpɪŋ; ˈgæləpɪŋ/ *adj* [only before noun 僅用於名詞前] rapidly increasing or developing 快速增加的, 飛速發展的: **galloping inflation** *galloping inflation of 20 to 30%* 劇烈的通貨膨脹, 通貨膨脹率為 20% 至 30%

gal·lows /ˋgæloz; ˈgæləʊz/ *n plural* **gallows** [C] a structure used for killing criminals by hanging them from a rope 絞刑架

gallows hu·mour *BrE*【英】, **gallows humor** *AmE*【美】/ˈ·· ˌ··/ *n* [U] humour which makes very unpleasant or dangerous things seem funny 絞刑架下的幽默, 大難臨頭的幽默

gall·stone /ˋgɔlˌston; ˈgɔːlstəʊn/ *n* [C] a hard stone which can form in your GALL BLADDER 膽 (結) 石

Gal·lup poll /ˋgæləpˌpol; ˈgæləp pəʊl/ *n* [C] *trademark* a count of people's opinions on a subject, especially to find out how they will vote in an election【商標】蓋洛普民意測驗

ga·loot /gəˋlut; gəˈluːt/ *n* [C] *AmE informal* someone who is not at all graceful and does not dress neatly【美, 非正式】衣冠不整行為粗俗的人: *You clumsy galoot!* 你這笨蛋!

ga·lore /gəˋlɔr; gəˈlɔː/ *adj* [only after noun 僅用於名詞後] in large amounts or numbers 大量的, 許多的: *There are bargains galore in the sales this year.* 今年的大減價期間有許多便宜貨。

ga·losh·es /gəˋlɑʃəz; gəˈlɒʃɨz/ *n* [plural] *old-fashioned* rubber shoes worn over ordinary shoes when it rains or snows【過時】〔下雨或下雪時套在普通鞋外面的〕橡膠套鞋

ga·lumph /gəˋlʌmf; gəˈlʌmf/ *v* [I always+adv/prep] *informal* to move in a noisy, heavy, and awkward way【非正式】腳步嘈雜地行進, 笨拙地行進

gal·van·ic /gælˋvænɪk; gælˈvænɪk/ *adj* **1** *formal* making people react suddenly with strong feelings or actions【正式】使人震驚的: *The bomb warning had a galvanic effect.* 炸彈的警告引起一場恐慌。**2** *technical* connected with the production of electricity by the action of acid on metal【術語】〔由化學作用〕產生電流的

gal·va·nise /ˋgælvəˌnaɪz; ˈgælvənaɪz/ *v* a British spelling of GALVANIZE galvanize 的英式拼法

gal·va·nis·m /ˋgælvəˌnɪzəm; ˈgælvənɪzəm/ *n* [U] *technical* the production of electricity by the use of chemicals, especially as in a BATTERY (1)【術語】用化學藥品產生電〔尤指由原電池產生電〕

gal·va·nize also 又作 **-ise** *BrE*【英】/ˋgælvəˌnaɪz; ˈgælvənaɪz/ *v* [T] to shock or surprise someone so that they do something to solve a problem, improve a situation etc 激勵, 刺激〔某人〕: **galvanize sb into (doing) sth** *The possibility of defeat finally galvanized us into action.* 失敗的可能性最終促使我們採取行動。

gal·va·nized also 又作 **-ise** *BrE*【英】/ˋgælvəˌnaɪzd; ˈgælvənaɪzd/ *adj* **galvanised iron/metal etc** metal with a covering of ZINC made using electricity 鍍鋅鐵/鍍鋅金屬等

gam·bit /ˋgæmbɪt; ˈgæmbɨt/ *n* [C] **1** something that you do or say which is intended to give you an advantage in an argument 精心策劃的一着, 策略: *a clever debating gambit* 巧妙的辯論策略 | **opening gambit** (=the thing you say first) 開場白 **2** a planned series of moves at the beginning of a game of CHESS〔國際象棋中的〕開局時的一系列走棋

gam·ble[1] /ˋgæmbl̩; ˈgæmbəl/ *v* **1** [I] to risk money or possessions on the result of something uncertain, such as a card game, a race or a horse 賭博: *We're forbidden to drink or gamble.* 我們被禁止飲酒和賭博。| **gamble on sth** *Jack loves gambling on the horses.* 傑克喜歡賭馬。| **gamble heavily** (=gamble often, using a lot of money) 豪賭 **2** [I,T] to do something that involves a lot of risk, and that will not succeed unless things happen the way you would like them to 投機, 冒險: **gamble on** *They're gambling on Johnson being fit for Saturday's game.* 他們把賭注押在約翰遜可以應付星期六的比賽。| **gamble sth on sth** *Potter gambled everything on his new play being a hit.* 波特孤注一擲, 指望他的新戲會轟動。| **gamble with** *We can't relax our safety standards – we'd be gambling with people's lives.* 我們不能放鬆我們的安全標準 —— 否則我們就是拿人們的生命來冒險。—**gambler** *n* [C]

gamble sth ↔ **away** *phr v* [T] to lose money by gambling 賭輸掉: *Nielsen gambled his inheritance away.* 尼爾森把繼承的遺產都輸光了。

gamble[2] *n* [singular] an action or plan that involves a risk but that you hope will succeed 冒險, 碰運氣: *We've never used this agency before, so it's a bit of a gamble.* 我們以前從來沒有用過這家代理機構, 所以有點冒險。| **take a gamble** *I think she's taking a gamble setting up her own business like that.* 我認為她那樣創立自己的公司是在冒險。| **a gamble pays off** (=brings success) 賭贏, 取得成功 *Ellen had to admit the gamble had paid off.* 埃倫不得不承認冒險取得了成功。

gam·bling /ˋgæmblɪŋ; ˈgæmblɪŋ/ *n* [U] **1** the practice of risking money or possessions on the result of something uncertain, such as a card game, or a horse race 賭博: *They had always strongly disapproved of gambling.* 他們一向是強烈反對賭博的。**2 gambling den** a place where people go to gamble illegally 賭窟

gam·bol /ˋgæmbl̩; ˈgæmbəl/ *v* [I always+adv/prep] to jump or run around in a lively active way〔活潑地〕跳

G

躍; 嬉戲: *lambs gambolling in a field* 在田野裡跳躍奔跑的羔羊 —**gambol** *n* [C]

game¹ /gem; geɪm/ *n*

1 ▶ACTIVITY OR SPORT 活動或運動◀ [C] **a)** an activity or sport in which people compete with each other according to agreed rules 遊戲; 運動: *What's your favorite game?* 你最喜愛的運動是甚麼? | *Dan's never liked card games.* 丹從來不喜歡打牌。**b)** an occasion when a game is played 比賽: *Did you see the game on TV last night?* 你昨天晚上在電視上看了這場比賽嗎? | *Let's have a game of chess.* 我們來下盤棋吧。**c) your game** how well you play a particular game 球技[運動技巧, 玩遊戲的技巧等]; 比賽技巧: **raise/improve your game** *Liam's taking lessons to improve his game.* 利亞姆正在聽課, 以改進他的比賽技巧。**d) games** a large organized sports event 大型運動會: *the Olympic Games* 奧林匹克運動會 **e)** *BrE* organized sports as a school subject or lesson【英】體育課: *We have games on Thursdays.* 我們星期四上體育課。—compare 比較 MATCH¹ (2) —see also 另見 BALL GAME, BOARD GAME, WAR GAME

2 ▶PART OF A MATCH 比賽的一部分◀ [C] one of the parts into which a single competition is divided, for example in tennis or BRIDGE¹ (4) 一局, 一盤: *Graf leads, two games to one.* 嘉芙以兩局比一局領先。

3 ▶CHILDREN'S GAME 兒童遊戲◀ [C] a children's activity in which they play with toys, pretend to be someone else etc 遊戲: *a game of hide-and-seek* 捉迷藏遊戲 | *Look! Now you've spoilt our game!* 瞧! 你把我們的遊戲搞砸了!

4 ▶BE A GAME 一場遊戲◀ [C] to be something that you do to enjoy yourself rather than for a serious purpose 玩笑: *Some of those kids think life's just a game.* 有些孩子認為生活就是一場遊戲。

5 play games/silly games (with) to behave in a dishonest or unfair way in order to get what you want 欺騙, 耍花招: *Are you sure he's really interested, and not just playing silly games with you?* 你確信他真的感興趣, 不是在跟你耍花招嗎?

6 give the game away to spoil a surprise or secret by doing or saying something that lets someone guess what the secret is 泄露祕密: *Lynn gave the game away by laughing when Kim walked in.* 林恩在基姆走進來的時候笑了出來, 泄露了祕密。

7 ▶ANIMALS/BIRDS 動物/鳥◀ [U] wild animals, birds, and fish that are hunted for food, especially as a sport 獵物, 野味 —see also 另見 BIG GAME

8 beat/play sb at their own game to beat someone or fight back against them by using the same methods that they use 以其人之道還治其人之身: *Jackie decided to play Dean at his own game and left without paying the bill.* 傑基決定用同樣的方法整一整迪恩, 所以沒付賬單就離開了。

9 what's her game/your game etc? *spoken* used to ask what the true reason for someone's behaviour is【口】她/你為甚麼這樣做?〔用來詢問某人的行為的真正原因〕: *Reg is being very nice all of a sudden. What's his game?* 雷格突然變得非常和藹可親。他在耍甚麼花招?

10 advertising/public relations etc game *informal* the profession of advertising etc【非正式】廣告業/公共關係業等

11 a game of chance a game in which you risk money on the result 碰運氣的遊戲, 賭錢的遊戲: *Poker is a game of chance.* 撲克牌是一種碰運氣的遊戲。

12 the game's up *spoken* used to tell someone that something wrong or dishonest that they have done has been discovered【口】事已敗露, 東窗事發: *Come on, Don. The game's up. I know where you've hidden it.* 得了吧, 唐, 你已經敗露了。我知道你把它藏在甚麼地方。

13 be on the game *slang* to be a PROSTITUTE【俚】當妓女, 賣淫

14 make game of *old-fashioned* to make fun of someone【過時】取笑, 同...開玩笑 —see also 另見 FAIR GAME, away game/match (AWAY²), **fun and games** (FUN² (4)), **the name of the game** (NAME¹ (13))

game² *adj* **1** willing to try something dangerous, new, or difficult 願意嘗試〔某些危險、新鮮或困難的事〕的: *If you're game, we can do it now.* 如果你願意嘗試的話, 我們現在就可以做。| **[+for]** *We're game for a change.* 我們願意改變一下。| **game to do sth** *"Who's game to have a try?"* 誰敢試一試? **2 game leg** *old-fashioned* an injured or painful leg【過時】受傷的腿, 疼痛的腿 —**gamely** *adv*

game·keep·er /ˈ· ˌ··/ *n* [C] someone whose job is to look after wild animals and birds that are kept to be hunted on private land〔私人土地上的〕獵場看守人

game park /ˈ· ·/ *n* [C] a GAME RESERVE 野生動物保護區

game plan /ˈ· ·/ *n* [C] a plan for achieving success, especially in business or sports 方案, 策略〔尤指商業或體育比賽方面〕: *The former coach blamed the defeat on no game plan and no inspiration.* 前任教練把這次失敗歸咎於缺少比賽方案和激勵。

game point /ˈ· ·/ *n* [C,U] the situation in a game such as tennis in which one player will win the game if they win the next point 局點〔網球等比賽中再贏一分那局即獲勝的時刻〕—compare 比較 MATCH POINT

game re·serve /ˈ· ·ˌ·/ *n* [C] a large area of land that is designed for wild animals to live in safely 野生動物保護區

game show /ˈ· ·/ *n* [C] a television programme in which people play games or answer questions to win prizes 電視有獎競賽節目

games·man·ship /ˋgemzmənˌʃɪp; ˈgeɪmzmənʃɪp/ *n* [U] the ability to succeed by using the rules of a game to your own advantage〔巧妙運用比賽規則的〕制勝能力

gam·ete /ˋgæmit; ˈgæmiːt/ *n* [C] a type of cell which joins with another cell, starting the development of a baby or other young creature 配子〔一種與另一細胞結合會產生胚胎的細胞〕

game war·den /ˈ· ˌ··/ *n* [C] someone whose job is to look after wild animals in a GAME RESERVE〔野生動物保護區的〕看守人

gam·ey, gamy /ˋgemɪ; ˈgeɪmi/ *adj* having the strong taste of wild animals that are hunted for food 有濃烈的野味味道的

ga·mine /gæˋmin; ˈgeɪmiːn/ *n* [C] a small thin girl or woman who looks like a boy 男孩氣的女孩, 假小子 —**gamine** *adj*: *a gamine hairstyle* 假小子的髮式

gam·ing /ˋgemɪŋ; ˈgeɪmɪŋ/ *n* [U] *old-fashioned* playing cards or other games of chance for money; GAMBLING【過時】賭錢遊戲, 賭博: *gaming tables* 賭桌

gam·ma /ˋgæmə; ˈgæmə/ *n* [C] the third letter of the Greek alphabet 伽瑪〔希臘語字母表的第三個字母, 即 Γ, γ〕

gamma glob·u·lin /ˌgæməˋglɑbjulɪn; ˌgæmə ˈglɒbjʊlɪn/ *n* [U] a natural substance in your body which is a type of ANTIBODY, and gives protection against some diseases 丙種球蛋白〔人體的一種抗體, 能防止某些疾病〕

gamma ray /ˈ·· ·/ *n* [C usually plural 一般用複數] a beam of light with a short WAVELENGTH (2), that can pass through solid objects γ射線, 伽瑪射線

gam·mon /ˋgæmən; ˈgæmən/ *n* [U] *BrE* meat from a pig's leg which has been preserved using salt【英】醃豬腿: *gammon steak* 醃火腿排

gam·my /ˋgæmɪ; ˈgæmi/ *adj BrE old-fashioned* a gammy leg or knee is injured or painful【英, 過時】〔腿或膝〕受傷的, 疼痛的

gam·ut /ˋgæmət; ˈgæmət/ *n* [singular] the complete range of possibilities 全部可能性; 整個範圍: **[+of]** *College life opened up a whole gamut of new experiences.* 大學生活提供了各種全新體驗。| **run the (whole) gamut** (=include or experience all the possibilities between two extremes) 包括各種可能性, 經歷全部的歷程 *Her feelings that day ran the whole gamut of emotions.* 她那天百感交集。

G

gam·y /ˋgemɪ; ˈgeɪmi/ *adj* another spelling of GAMEY gamey 的另一種拼法

-gamy /gəmɪ; gəmi/ *suffix* [in U nouns 構成不可數名詞] marriage to a particular number or kind of people 結婚: *bigamy* (=being married to two people) 重婚 | *monogamy* 一夫一妻制 —**gamous** *suffix* [in adjectives 構成形容詞]

gan·der /ˋgændɚ; ˈgændə/ *n* [C] **1** a male GOOSE[1] (1a) 雄鵝 **2 have/take a gander at** *spoken* to look at something【口】看一看

3 **gang[1]** /gæŋ; gæŋ/ *n* **1** a group of young people who spend time together, and often cause trouble and fight against other groups〔常聚在一起鬧事打鬥的〕一幫年輕人: *a skinhead gang* 一夥光頭仔 | *members of a notorious gang* 聲名狼藉的幫派的成員 | [+**of**] *a gang of kids hanging around the mall* 在購物中心附近閒逛的一幫小夥子 **2** [C] a group of criminals who work together 一羣合夥作案的罪犯: *Several gangs were operating in the area.* 好幾個罪犯團夥在這個地區活動。| [+**of**] *a gang of smugglers* 一個走私幫 **3** *humorous* a group of friends, especially young people【幽默】一羣朋友〔尤指年輕人〕: *The whole gang will be there next weekend.* 朋友們下個週末全部都會到那兒。**4** a group of workers or prisoners doing physical work together〔幹體力活的〕一羣工人, 一羣囚犯 —see also 另見 CHAIN GANG

gang[2] *v*

gang up on sb *phr v* [T] to join together into a group to attack someone or oppose them 合夥打擊[反對]: *I hate school! They all gang up on me!* 我討厭上學! 他們都合起夥來對付我!

gang-bang /ˈ· ˌ·/ *n* [C] **1** *informal* an occasion when several people have sex with each other at the same time【非正式】集體淫亂 **2** a GANG RAPE 輪姦 —**gang-bang** *v* [I,T]

gang·bust·ers /ˋgæŋˌbʌstɚz; ˈgæŋˌbʌstəz/ *n* **come on like gangbusters** *AmE informal* to begin to do something very eagerly and with a lot of energy【美, 非正式】非常熱情, 非常起勁地開始做某事: *You can't come on like gangbusters with women – be more subtle!* 對女人你不能只憑熱情衝動 —— 應該更巧妙細微些!

gang·land /ˋgæŋˌlænd; ˈgæŋlænd/ *adj* **a gangland killing/murder/shooting etc** a killing etc connected with the world of organized and violent crime 黑社會兇殺/黑社會謀殺/黑社會槍殺等: *Sharp may have been the victim of a gangland revenge killing.* 夏普可能已經成了黑社會報復性兇殺的受害者。

gan·gling /ˋgæŋglɪŋ; ˈgæŋglɪŋ/ *adj* unusually tall and thin, and not at all graceful in the way you move 又高又瘦而動作笨拙的: *an awkward gangling teenager* 一位瘦長而笨手笨腳的青少年

gan·gli·on /ˋgæŋglɪən; ˈgæŋgliən/ *n* [C] *technical*【術語】**1** a painful raised area of skin that is full of liquid, often on the back of your wrist 腱鞘囊腫 **2** a mass of nerve cells 神經節

gan·gly /ˋgæŋglɪ; ˈgæŋgli/ *adj* another form of GANGLING gangling 的另一形式

gang·plank /ˋgæŋˌplæŋk; ˈgæŋplæŋk/ *n* [C] a board for walking on between a boat and the shore, or between one boat and another〔船和岸之間或船與船之間的〕跳板, 步橋

gang rape /ˈ· ·/ *n* [C] an occasion when several men attack a woman to force her to have sex with them 輪姦

gan·grene /ˋgæŋgrin; ˈgæŋgriːn/ *n* [U] the decay of the flesh of part of your body because blood has stopped flowing there as a result of illness or injury 壞疽 —**gangrenous** *adj*

gang·ster /ˋgæŋstɚ; ˈgæŋstə/ *n* [C] a member of a violent group of criminals 歹徒, 犯罪團夥成員: *a gangster movie* 描寫盜匪的影片

gang·way /ˋgæŋˌwe; ˈgæŋweɪ/ *n* [C] **1** a space between two rows of seats in a theatre, bus, or train; AISLE (1)〔劇場、公共汽車或火車上座位間的〕過道 **2** a large GANGPLANK 大跳板, 大步橋 **3 gangway!** *spoken* used to tell people in a crowd to let someone go through【口】讓路! 閃開!〔用來請擁擠的人羣給某人讓路〕

gan·ja /ˋgændʒə; ˈgændʒə/ *n* [U] *slang* MARIJUANA【俚】大麻

gan·net /ˋgænɪt; ˈgænɪt/ *n* [C] **1** a large sea bird that lives in large groups on cliffs〔羣居在懸崖上的〕鰹鳥, 塘鵝 **2** *BrE* someone who eats a lot【英】食量大的人

gan·try /ˋgæntrɪ; ˈgæntri/ *n* [C] a large metal frame which is used to support heavy machinery or railway signals〔支承重型機器或鐵路信號燈的〕台架

gaol /dʒel; dʒeɪl/ *n,v* a British spelling of JAIL jail 的英式拼法

gaol·bird /ˋdʒelˌbɝd; ˈdʒeɪlbɜːd/ *n* [C] a British spelling of JAILBIRD jailbird 的英式拼法

gaol·er /ˋdʒelɚ; ˈdʒeɪlə/ *n* [C] a British spelling of JAILER jailer 的英式拼法

gap 缺口

Ken squeezed through a gap in the fence.
肯從籬笆的一個缺口擠了過去。

gap /gæp; gæp/ *n* [C]

1 ▶A SPACE 間隔◀ a space between two objects or two parts of an object because of something that is missing 缺口, 裂縫: [+**in**] *The neighbors' dog got in through a gap in the hedge.* 鄰居的狗從樹籬的缺口鑽進來。| [+**between**] *Lou has big gaps between her front teeth.* 露的門牙間有很大的縫。

2 ▶DIFFERENCE 差別◀ a big difference between two situations, amounts, groups of people etc 差距; 差額; 差別: [+**between**] *the widening gap between the rich and the poor* 貧富之間不斷擴大的差距 | **fill the gap** *Donors will be asked to fill the gap between state funding and actual costs.* 將請捐款人填補國家撥款和實際費用之間的差額。| **bridge the gap** (=reduce the amount or importance of a difference) 填補空缺, 彌補差距 *His films attempt to bridge the gap between tradition and modernity.* 他的影片企圖彌合傳統和現代風格之間的差距。—see also 另見 **the generation gap** (GENERATION)

3 ▶STH MISSING 缺少的東西◀ something that is missing that stops something else from being good or complete 空白, 缺漏: [+**in**] *There are huge gaps in my knowledge of history.* 我的歷史知識很貧乏。| *Frank's death has left a big gap in my life.* 弗蘭克死後, 我的生活變得極度空虛難受。

4 ▶IN A MOUNTAIN 在山裡◀ a low place between two higher parts of a mountain 山峽, 山口

5 ▶IN TIME 在時間上◀ a period of time between two periods of time when nothing is happening 間隙: *an awkward gap in the conversation* 談話中出現的一次令人尷尬的停頓

6 gap in the market an opportunity to develop a particular product and sell it because it has not been developed yet 市場空白〔開發銷售一種尚無人開發的產品的機會〕

gape /gep; geɪp/ *v* [I] **1** to look at something for a long time, especially with your mouth open, because you are very surprised or shocked 瞠目結舌[目不轉睛]地注視: *What are all these people gaping at?* 這些人目不轉睛地都在看甚麼呀? —see 見 GAZE[1] (USAGE) **2** also 又作 **gape open** to come apart or open widely 裂開, 敞開:

Dan stood at the door, his shirt gaping open. 丹敞開襯衫站在門口。—**gape** *n* [C]

gap·ing /ˋgepɪŋ; ˈgeɪpɪŋ/ *adj* [only before noun 僅用於名詞前] a gaping hole, wound, or mouth is very wide and open 裂開的, 敞開的

gap-toothed /ˌ· ˈ·◂/ *adj* having wide spaces between your teeth 牙齒間隙縫很大的

2 **gar·age¹** /gəˋrɑʒ; ˈgærɑːʒ/ *n* [C] **1** a building for keeping a car in, usually next to a house〔通常緊靠房屋的〕車庫, 汽車間 —compare 比較 CARPORT —see picture on page A4 參見 A4 頁圖 **2** a place where motor vehicles are repaired 汽車修理廠[站]: *My car's at the garage.* 我的車子在修理廠。**3** *BrE* a place where you buy petrol; PETROL STATION【英】加油站

garage² *v* [T] to put or keep a vehicle in a garage 將汽車開進[停放]在車庫

garage sale /ˈ·· ˌ·/ *n* [C] *AmE* a sale of used furniture, clothes etc from people's houses, usually held in someone's garage【美】舊物出售〔指將家裡的舊家具、舊衣物等擺在自家的車庫裡出售〕

gar·am ma·sa·la /ˌgarəm məˋsalə; ˌgɑːrəm məˈsɑːlə/ *n* [U] a mixture of SPICES which gives a hot taste to food, used especially in Indian cooking 有辣味的混合香料〔尤用於印度式烹調〕

garb¹ /garb; gɑːb/ *n* [U] *formal or literary* a particular style of clothing, especially clothes that show your type of work or look unusual【正式或文】〔尤指顯示工作類型或樣式特別的〕制服, 服裝, 裝束: *clothed in priestly garb* 穿着牧師服裝的

garb² *v* **be garbed in** *literary* to be dressed in a particular type of clothes【文】穿着…服裝的: *singers garbed in costumes of gold* 穿着金色服裝的歌手

3 **gar·bage** /ˋgarbɪdʒ; ˈgɑːbɪdʒ/ *n* [U] **1** *especially AmE* waste material, such as paper, empty containers, and food thrown away【尤美】垃圾; RUBBISH¹ (1) *BrE*【英】: *Can you take the garbage out when you go?* 你走的時候能把垃圾帶出去嗎? **2** stupid words, ideas etc 蠢話, 廢話, 愚蠢的看法: *You're talking garbage.* 你在說廢話。**3 garbage in, garbage out** used to say that if you put bad information into a computer, you will get bad results〔電腦運算中〕錯進, 錯出〔用來表示若將垃圾信息輸入電腦, 所輸出的也是垃圾〕—see graph at 參見 RUBBISH¹ 圖表

garbage can /ˈ·· ˌ·/ *n* [C] *AmE* a container with a lid for holding waste until it can be taken away【美】垃圾箱, 垃圾桶; DUSTBIN *BrE*【英】—see picture on page A4 參見 A4 頁圖

garbage col·lec·tor /ˈ·· ·ˌ··/ *n* [C] *AmE* someone whose job is to remove waste from garbage cans【美】垃圾清潔工; DUSTMAN *BrE*【英】

garbage dis·po·sal /ˈ·· ·ˌ··/ *n* [C] *AmE* a small machine in the kitchen SINK which breaks vegetable waste into small pieces【美】〔廚房洗滌槽裡將廢棄蔬菜切碎的〕小型垃圾處理機; WASTE DISPOSAL (1) *BrE*【英】

garbage man /ˈ·· ˌ·/ *n* [C] *AmE* a garbage collector【美】垃圾清潔工

garbage truck /ˈ·· ˌ·/ *n* [C] *AmE* a large vehicle which goes from house to house to collect the contents of garbage cans【美】垃圾車; DUST CART *BrE*【英】

gar·ban·zo /garˋbanzo; gɑːˈbænzəʊ/ also 又作 **garbanzo bean** /·ˈ·· ˌ·/ *n* [C] another word for CHICK-PEA, used especially in the western US 鷹嘴豆〔chick-pea 的另一名稱, 尤用於美國西部〕

gar·bled /ˋgarbḷd; ˈgɑːbəld/ *adj* a garbled statement or report is very unclear and confusing〔陳述、報告〕含混不清的, 極其混亂的: *The papers had some garbled version of the story.* 對這件事報紙上有一些含糊不清的報道。| *a garbled phone message* 很不清楚的電話留言

gar·çon /ˌgarˋsɔ̃; ˈgɑːsɒn/ *n* [C] *French* a waiter, especially in a French restaurant【法】〔法國餐館裡的〕男服務員, 男侍

1 1 **gar·den¹** /ˋgardṇ; ˈgɑːdn/ *n* **1** [C] *especially BrE* a piece of land around or next to your house where there is usually lawn (=area of grass) and an area where you grow flowers, plants, or vegetables【尤英】宅旁花園, 菜園; YARD (3) *AmE*【美】: *Grace is out in the garden mowing the lawn.* 格雷斯在外面庭園的草坪上刈草。| **rose garden/herb garden etc** (=where a particular type of plant is grown) 玫瑰園/藥草園等 —see picture on page A4 參見 A4 頁圖 **2** [C] *AmE* the part of a garden that has flowers and plants in it【美】〔庭園裡的〕園圃〔指種有花木的部分〕: *We're thinking of planting a little garden in our yard.* 我們想在院子裡栽種一個小花圃。**3 gardens** [plural] a large area of land where plants and flowers are grown so that the public can go and see them 公園: *the Botanic Gardens at Kew* 基尤的植物園 **4 Gardens** *BrE* used in the name of streets【英】〔用於街道的名稱〕: *number 211 Roland Gardens* 羅蘭德街 211 號 —see also 另見 KITCHEN GARDEN, MARKET GARDEN, **lead sb up the garden path** (LEAD¹ (18))

garden² *v* [I] to work in a garden, keeping it clean, making plants grow etc 從事園藝 —**gardening** *n* [U]: *Since he's retired he's become very interested in gardening.* 他退休後對園藝很感興趣。

garden cen·tre /ˈ·· ˌ··/ *n* [C] *BrE* a place that sells plants, flowers and equipment for gardens; NURSERY (4)【英】〔出售植物、花卉和園藝用具的〕花卉商店

garden cit·y /ˌ·· ˈ··/ *n* [C] *BrE* a town that has been designed to have a lot of trees, areas of grass, and open spaces【英】花園城市 —compare 比較 NEW TOWN

gar·den·er /ˋgardnɚ; ˈgɑːdnə/ *n* [C] **1** someone who enjoys growing flowers and plants 園藝愛好者: *Mom has always been a good gardener.* 母親一直很善於種植花卉。**2** someone whose job is to work in gardens 園藝工人, 園丁, 花匠

garden flat /ˈ·· ˌ·/ *n* [C] *BrE* an apartment on the lowest floor of a house, which has a door leading to the garden【英】花園公寓〔指位於樓房最底層, 有門通向花園的套房〕

gar·de·ni·a /garˋdinɪə; gɑːˈdiːniə/ *n* [C] a large white pleasant-smelling flower that grows on a bush 梔子屬植物

garden par·ty /ˈ·· ˌ··/ *n* [C] *BrE* a formal party for a lot of people which is held in a large garden【英】〔在大花園裡舉行的有許多人參加的正式的〕花園招待會; LAWN PARTY *AmE*【美】

garden-va·ri·e·ty /ˈ·· ·ˌ···/ *adj* [only before noun 僅用於名詞前] *AmE* very ordinary and not very interesting【美】非常一般的, 平淡無奇的: *He's just one of your garden-variety singers.* 他只是一名不起眼的歌手。

gar·gan·tu·an /garˋgæntʃuən; gɑːˈgæntʃuən/ *adj* extremely large; GIGANTIC 巨大的: *What a gargantuan bed!* 多大的一張牀啊!

gar·gle¹ /ˋgargḷ; ˈgɑːgəl/ *v* [I+with] to clean the inside of your mouth and throat by blowing air through water or medicine in the back of your throat 漱口, 漱喉: *Gargling with salt water may help your sore throat.* 用鹽水漱口可能對你的喉嚨痛有好處。

gargle² *n* **1** [C,U] liquid that you gargle with 漱口液 **2** [singular] the act of gargling 漱口

gar·goyle /ˋgargɔɪl; ˈgɑːgɔɪl/ *n* [C] an ugly stone figure of a person or animal that carries rain water from the roof of an old building, especially a church〔教堂等古老建築物屋頂上奇形怪狀的石雕人物或動物形狀的〕排水嘴

gar·ish /ˋgɛrɪʃ; ˈgeərɪʃ/ *adj* very brightly coloured in a way that is unpleasant to look at 花哨的: *Many of the rugs are too garish for my taste.* 這裡許多地毯色彩太花哨, 我不欣賞。—**garishly** *adv* —**garishness** *n* [U]

gar·land¹ /ˋgarlənd; ˈgɑːlənd/ *n* [C] a ring of flowers or leaves that is given to someone to wear around their neck〔送給某人戴於頸部的〕花環

garland² *v* [T] *literary* to decorate someone or something, especially with flowers【文】用花環裝飾

gar·lic /ˋgarlɪk; ˈgɑːlɪk/ *n* [U] a plant like a small onion, 3 used in cooking to give a strong taste 大蒜: *a clove of garlic* (=single section of it) 蒜瓣 | *a garlic press* (=tool used to crush garlic) 搗蒜器 —**garlicky** *adj*: *his garlicky breath* 他帶有大蒜味的呼吸 —see picture on page A9 參見 A9 頁圖

gar·ment /ˈgɑrmənt; ˈgɑːmənt/ *n* [C] *formal or technical* a piece of clothing【正式或術語】〔一件〕衣服 —see picture at 參見 CLOTHES 圖

gar·ner /ˈgɑrnɚ; ˈgɑːnə/ *v* [T] *formal* to take or collect something, especially information【正式】收集〔尤指信息〕

gar·net /ˈgɑrnɪt; ˈgɑːnɪ̈t/ *n* **1** [C] a dark red stone used as a jewel 石榴石 **2** [U] a dark red colour 石榴紅色, 暗紅色

gar·nish¹ /ˈgɑrnɪʃ; ˈgɑːnɪʃ/ *n* [C] something that you add to food to decorate it〔添加在食物上的〕裝飾菜

garnish² *v* [T] **1** to add something to food in order to decorate it 在〔食物〕上加飾菜: **garnish sth with** *Garnish each dish with a slice of lemon.* 在每盤菜上配一片檸檬。**2** also 又作 **garnishee** *technical* to take money from someone's wages because they have not paid their debts【術語】扣發〔債務人的工資〕

gar·ret /ˈgærɪt; ˈgærɪ̈t/ *n* [C] a small uncomfortable room at the top of a house 頂樓, 閣樓 —compare 比較 ATTIC

gar·ri·son¹ /ˈgærəsn; ˈgærɪ̈sən/ *n* [C] a group of soldiers living in a town or FORT and defending it 衛戍部隊, 要塞駐軍: *The garrison was called out when news of the enemy's advance was received.* 收到敵人推進的情報後, 衛戍部隊受命出動。| *a garrison town* 有守備部隊駐防的城鎮

garrison² *v* [T] to send a group of soldiers to defend or guard a place 派兵駐防: *Our regiment will garrison a coastal town.* 我們團將駐防一個沿海城鎮。

gar·rotte /gəˋrot; gəˈrɒt/ *v* [T] to kill someone using a metal collar or wire which is pulled tightly around their neck〔用金屬環或金屬絲〕勒殺 —**garrotte** *n* [C]

gar·ru·lous /ˈgærələs; ˈgærələs/ *adj* always talking a lot 饒舌的, 喋喋不休的: *Ian isn't normally this garrulous!* 伊恩通常不是這樣饒舌的! —**garrulously** *adv* —**garrulousness** *n* [U]

gar·ter /ˈgɑrtɚ; ˈgɑːtə/ *n* [C] **1** a band of ELASTIC (=material that stretches) worn around your leg to keep a sock or STOCKING up 吊襪鬆緊帶 **2** *AmE* one of four pieces of elastic fixed to a woman's underwear and to her stockings to hold them up【美】〔女子內衣和長統襪的〕吊帶; SUSPENDER (1) *BrE*【英】

garter belt /ˈ·· ˌ·/ *n* [C] *AmE* a piece of women's underwear with garters hanging down from it which fasten onto STOCKINGS (1) and hold them up【美】〔女子內衣上的〕吊襪束腰帶; SUSPENDER BELT *BrE*【英】

garter snake /ˈ·· ˌ·/ *n* [C] a harmless American snake with lines of colour along its back 美洲無毒束帶蛇

gas¹ /gæs; gæs/ *n plural* **gases** also 又作 **gasses** **1** [C,U] a substance like air, which is not solid or liquid, and usually cannot be seen 氣, 氣體: *hydrogen gas* 氫氣 | **a gas cylinder** (=for storing gas) 儲氣桶 **2** [U] a substance of this type which is burnt for heating or cooking〔供取暖、烹調用的〕可燃氣: *a gas oven* 煤氣爐 | *Can you light the gas for me?* 你能幫我點燃煤氣爐嗎? **3** [U] a substance of this type used to poison people or to control them 毒氣, 麻醉氣: *Police fired tear gas into the crowd.* 警察朝人羣發射催淚瓦斯。**4** [U] *AmE* GASOLINE【美】汽油 **5 gas mark 4,5,6 etc** *BrE* a measurement of the temperature of a gas OVEN【英】〔測量煤氣烤箱溫度的〕煤氣刻度 4,5,6 等 **6** *AmE slang* the condition of having gas in your stomach【美俚】腹脹, 胃脹; WIND¹ (9) *BrE*【英】**7** [singular] *AmE* something that is fun and makes you laugh a lot【美】有趣的事, 令人發笑的事: *The state fair was a real gas.* 這次的州博覽會真是有趣。

gas² *v* **1** [T] to poison or kill someone with gas 用毒氣殺死 **2** [I] *informal* to talk for a long time about unimportant or boring things【非正式】空談, 閒聊: *They were just standing there gassing away.* 他們站在那兒聊個沒完。

gas sth ↔ **up** *phr v* [I,T] *AmE* to put petrol in a car【美】給〔汽車〕加油: *We'd better gas up before we go.* 我們在走之前最好給汽車加滿油。

gas·bag /ˈgæsˌbæg; ˈgæsbæg/ *n* [C] *informal* someone who talks too much; WINDBAG【非正式】誇誇其談的人, 廢話連篇的人

gas cham·ber /ˈ· ˌ··/ *n* [C] a large room in which people or animals are killed with poisonous gas〔用毒氣殺害人或動物的〕毒氣室

gas·e·ous /ˈgæsɪəs; ˈgæsiəs/ *adj* like gas or in the form of gas 似氣體的, 氣態的

gas-fired /ˌ· ˈ·◂/ *adj especially BrE* using gas as a fuel【尤英】燃氣的: *a gas-fired central heating system* 燃氣中央供暖系統

gas-guz·zler /ˈ· ˌ··/ *n* [C] *AmE informal* a car that uses a lot of petrol【美, 非正式】耗油量大的汽車, 油老虎 —**gas-guzzling** *adj*

gash /gæʃ; gæʃ/ *n* [C] **1** a large deep wound from a cut〔大而深的〕切口, 傷口: *a deep gash on his leg* 他腿上一處很深的傷口 **2** a long deep hole in something 深而長的裂縫: *The trench cut a brown gash through the green lawn.* 壕溝在綠色的草坪上切開一條棕色的大裂縫。—**gash** *v* [T]

gas·hold·er /ˈgæsˌholdɚ; ˈgæsˌhəʊldə/ *n* [C] a very large round metal container or building from which gas is carried in pipes to buildings 大型儲氣罐, 煤氣供應室

gas·i·fy /ˈgæsəˌfaɪ; ˈgæsɪ̈faɪ/ *v* [I,T] to change into a gas, or to make something do this 成為氣體, 氣化 —**gasification** /ˌgæsəfəˋkeʃən; ˌgæsɪ̈fɪ̈ˈkeɪʃən/ *n* [U]

gas·ket /ˈgæskɪt; ˈgæskɪ̈t/ *n* [C] **1** a flat piece of material, often rubber, placed between two surfaces so that steam, oil, gas etc cannot escape 墊圈, 密封墊 **2 blow a gasket a)** if a vehicle blows a gasket, steam or gas escapes from the engine〔發動機〕漏氣 **b)** *informal* to become very angry【非正式】勃然大怒

gas·light /ˈgæsˌlaɪt; ˈgæslaɪt/ *n* **1** [U] the light produced from burning gas 煤氣燈光 **2** [C] also 又作 **gas lamp** a lamp in a house or on the street which gives light from burning gas 煤氣燈

gas·man /ˈgæsˌmæn; ˈgæsmæn/ *n* [C] *BrE* someone who comes to your home to see how much gas you have used or to repair your gas system【英】煤氣抄表員, 煤氣裝置修理員

gas mask /ˈ· ·/ *n* [C] a piece of equipment worn over your face to protect you from poisonous gases 防毒面具 —see picture at 參見 MASK¹ 圖

gas me·ter /ˈ· ˌ··/ *n* [C] a piece of equipment that measures how much gas is used in a building 煤氣表

gas·o·hol /ˈgæsəhɑl; ˈgæsəhɒl/ *n* [U] *AmE* petrol with a small amount of alcohol in it, which can be used in cars and is cheaper than petrol【美】酒精－汽油混合燃料〔即加有少量酒精的汽油, 較汽油便宜, 用於汽車〕

gas·o·line, gasolene /ˈgæsḷˌin; ˈgæsəliːn/ *n* [U] *AmE* a liquid obtained from PETROLEUM, used mainly for producing power in the engines of cars【美】汽油; PETROL *BrE*【英】

gas·om·e·ter /gæsˋɑmətɚ; gæˈsɒmɪ̈tə/ *n* [C] a GASHOLDER 大型儲氣罐, 煤氣供應室

gasp¹ /gæsp; gɑːsp/ *v* [I,T] **1** to breathe in suddenly, quickly, and in a way that can be heard, especially because you are surprised or afraid〔因驚訝或害怕, 出聲地〕喘息; 喘氣: *"My leg! My leg!" he gasped. "I think it's broken!"* "我的腿! 我的腿!" 他喘着氣喊道。"我想是腿斷了!" | **[+with]** *Ollie gasped with pain and slumped forward.* 奧利痛得直吸氣, 向前栽倒。| **[+at]** *The audience gasped at the splendour of the costumes.* 如此華麗的服裝, 觀眾們倒吸一口氣。**2** [I] to breathe quickly and deeply because you are having difficulty breathing〔由於呼吸困難而〕急促地深呼吸: **gasp for air/breath** *Brendan climbed slowly, gasping for breath.* 布倫達上氣不接下氣地慢慢爬着。**3 be gasping** *BrE spok-*

en to be very thirsty【英口】非常口渴的: *Put the kettle on, love, I'm gasping.* 親愛的, 燒壺水吧, 我渴得要命。**4 be gasping for** *BrE spoken* to feel that you urgently need something such as a drink or cigarette【英口】渴望得到〔煙、酒等〕: *I'm gasping for a pint!* 我渴望喝上一杯啤酒。

gasp² *n* [C] **1** an act of taking in your breath suddenly in a way that can be heard, especially because you are surprised or afraid〔尤指因驚訝或害怕〕喘氣, 抽氣: **[+of]** *With a gasp of pure horror, Stormgren jumped up and ran.* 斯托姆格倫嚇得倒抽了一口氣, 跳起來就跑。| **give a gasp** *She gave a little gasp and clutched George's hand.* 她輕輕地抽了一口氣, 抓住了喬治的手。**2** an act of taking in air quickly because you are having difficulty breathing〔因呼吸困難而〕急促呼吸: *Between gasps Michael said that he was allergic to cats.* 邁克爾上氣不接下氣地說他對貓有過敏反應。**3 at your last gasp** about to die 奄奄一息, 即將斷氣: *He rolled his eyes as though at his last gasp.* 他轉動着眼珠, 好像快要斷氣似的。

gas pedal /ˈ· ˌ··/ *n* [C] *AmE* the thing that you press with your foot to make a car go faster; ACCELERATOR (1)【美】〔汽車的〕油門 —see picture on page A2 參見 A2 頁圖

gas per·me·a·ble lens /ˌ· ···· ˈ·/ *n* [C] a kind of CONTACT LENS that allows oxygen to reach your eyes 透氧式隱形眼鏡

gas ring /ˈ· ·/ *BrE n* [C] a metal ring that gets hot when gas passes through it, used for cooking food【英】環形爐頭; BURNER (2) *AmE*【美】

gas sta·tion /ˈ· ˌ··/ *n* [C] *AmE* a place where you can buy petrol and oil for motor vehicles【美】加油站; PETROL STATION *BrE*【英】

gas·sy /ˈgæsɪ; ˈgæsi/ *adj BrE* a gassy drink has too much gas in it【英】〔飲料等〕氣過多的: *This beer is really gassy.* 這種啤酒的氣實在太多。—**gassiness** *n* [U]

gas·tric /ˈgæstrɪk; ˈgæstrɪk/ *adj* [only before noun 僅用於名詞前] *technical*【術語】**1** related to your stomach 胃的: *gastric ulcers* 胃潰瘍 **2 gastric juices** the acids in your stomach that break food into smaller parts 胃液 **3 gastric flu** an illness that makes you VOMIT¹ and gives you DIARRHOEA 胃腸性感冒

gas·tri·tis /gæsˈtraɪtɪs; gæˈstraɪtɪ̥s/ *n* [U] an illness which makes the inside of your stomach become swollen, so that you feel a burning pain 胃炎

gas·tro·en·te·ri·tis /ˌgæstroˌɛntəˈraɪtɪs; ˌgæstrəʊentəˈraɪtɪ̥s/ *n* [U] an illness which makes your stomach and INTESTINE become swollen 胃腸炎

gas·tro·nom·ic /ˌgæstrəˈnɑmɪk; ˌgæstrəˈnɒmɪk◂/ *adj* [only before noun 僅用於名詞前] connected with the art of cooking good food or the pleasure of eating it 烹飪法的, 美食的: *sampling the gastronomic delights of Thailand* 品嘗泰國的美食 —**gastronomically** /-klɪ; -kli/ *adv*

gas·tron·o·my /gæsˈtrɑnəmɪ; gæˈstrɒnəmi/ *n* [U] the art and science of cooking and eating good food 烹飪法, 美食學

gas tur·bine /ˌ· ˈ··/ *n* [C] an engine in which a wheel of special blades is driven round at high speed by hot gases 燃氣輪機

gas·works /ˈgæsˌwɝks; ˈgæswɜːks/ *n plural* **gasworks** [C] a place where gas is made from coal 煤氣廠

2 2 **gate¹** /get; geɪt/ *n* [C] **1** a frame that you can open and close to get through a fence, wall etc at the entrance to a place 大門, 柵欄門: *a garden gate* 花園門 | *In front of him were the wrought-iron gates of the palace.* 他面前是宮殿的鍛鐵門。—compare 比較 DOOR (1) —see picture on page A4 參見 A4 頁圖 **2** the place where you leave an airport building to get on a plane〔機場大樓裡的〕登機門: *Air France flight 76 leaves from gate 6A.* 法航 76 次航班從 6A 號門起飛。**3 Irangate/Watergate/Contragate etc** used with the name of a place or a person to give a name to an event involving dishonest behaviour by a politician or other public official 伊朗門事件/水門事件/孔特拉門事件等 **4** *BrE*【英】**a)** the number of people who go in to see a sports event, especially a football match〔體育比賽, 尤指足球比賽的〕觀眾人數 **b)** the amount of money that these people pay 門票收入

gate² *v* [T] *BrE* to prevent a student from leaving a school as a punishment for behaving badly【英】〔作為對學生行為不端的一種處罰〕禁止離校外出

gâ·teau /gɑˈto; ˈgætəʊ/ *n plural* **gâteaux** /-toz; -təʊz/ [C,U] *BrE* a large sweet cake, often filled and decorated with cream, fruit, chocolate etc【英】奶油(水果)大蛋糕

gate·crash /ˈgetˌkræʃ; ˈgeɪtkræʃ/ *v* [I,T] to go to a party that you have not been invited to 不請自到, 擅自參加〔未受邀請的聚會〕—**gatecrasher** *n* [U]

gated com·mu·ni·ty /ˌ·· ·ˈ···/ *n* [C] *AmE* an area of shops, houses etc with a fence or wall around it and an entrance that is guarded【美】有大門的社區〔指某地區的商店、房屋等有籬笆或牆圍繞, 並有人看守大門〕

gate·house /ˈgetˌhaus; ˈgeɪthaʊs/ *n* [C] a small building next to the gate of a park or at the entrance to the land surrounding a big house 門房

gate·keep·er /ˈgetˌkipɚ; ˈgeɪtˌkiːpə/ *n* [C] someone whose job is to open and close a gate 看門人

gate-leg ta·ble /ˌ·· ˈ··/ *n* [C] a table that can be made larger by moving a leg out to support a folding part 可部分摺疊的桌子

gate·post /ˈgetˌpost; ˈgeɪtpəʊst/ *n* [C] **1** one of two strong upright poles fixed to the ground to support a gate 大門兩邊的門柱 —see picture on page A4 參見 A4 頁圖 **2 between you, me and the gatepost** *BrE spoken* used to say that you are going to tell someone your opinion, but you want it to be a secret【英口】你我私下說說

gate·way /ˈgetˌwe; ˈgeɪt-weɪ/ *n* **1** [C] the opening in a fence, wall etc that can be closed by a gate〔籬笆或圍牆上的〕出入口 **2 the gateway to a)** a place, especially a city, that you can go through in order to reach another much bigger place〔通向更廣闊地區的〕通道, 門戶〔尤指一座城市〕: *St. Louis is the gateway to the West.* 聖路易斯是通往西部的門戶。**b)** a way of achieving something 途徑, 手段: *Hard work is the gateway to success.* 努力工作是獲得成功的手段。**3** [C] a way of connecting two computer networks (NETWORK¹ (4)) that would otherwise not be able to be connected〔連接兩個電腦網絡的〕網關

gath·er¹ /ˈgæðɚ; ˈgæðə/ *v* 2 2

1 ►COME TOGETHER 聚集◄ [I] to come together and form a group 聚集, 集合: *On Fridays the men gather together at the mosque.* 每到星期五這些男人就聚集在清真寺。| *Tens of thousands of people had gathered outside the US embassy.* 數以萬計的人聚集在美國大使館外面。| **gather around/round** *I'd like everyone to gather round so I can demonstrate how the system works.* 我想請大家聚攏過來, 這樣我好演示系統是如何工作的。| **gather together** *Could the bride's family all gather together for a photo?* 請新娘一家人聚在一起拍一個照, 好嗎? | **be gathered** *Dozens of photographers were gathered outside Jagger's villa.* 好幾十名攝影師聚集在賈格爾的別墅外面。

2 ►KNOW/THINK 了解/思考◄ [T not in progressive 不用進行式] to know something or think something is true, because of something that you have heard or seen 推斷, 推測, 知道, 認為: *You two know each other, I gather.* 我想你們兩人是互相認識的。| **gather (that)** *I gather you've had some problems with our sales department.* 我想你和我們的銷售部有過一些爭執。| **from what I can gather/as far as I can gather** (=this is what I believe to be true) 據我所知 *She's his niece, from what I can gather.* 據我所知, 她是他的姪女。

3 ►COLLECT 收集◄ [T] **a)** to search for things of the same type in several different places and collect them together 搜集, 採集: *Thelma went along the lane gath-*

G

ering blackberries. 塞爾瑪沿着鄉間小道採摘黑莓。**b)** to collect information, ideas etc for example in order to write a book or a report 收集〔信息、主意等〕: *Floyd's gathering ideas for his new novel.* 弗洛伊德正為他的新小說收集點子。

4 gather speed/force to move faster or become stronger 加快速度/加大力量: *The cart gathered speed as it coasted down the hill.* 手推車滑行下山時逐漸加快了速度。

5 gather dust if something useful gathers dust, it is not being used 閒置: *You may as well take these books – they're just gathering dust.* 你還不如把這些書拿走吧——它們反正閒置着沒人看。

6 gather momentum a) to gradually move faster, especially because of going down a hill 增加動量[速度] **b)** if a plan or process gathers momentum, it develops quickly and affects more and more people 勢頭日益增強: *A major anti-corruption campaign was gathering momentum.* 當時一場大規模的反腐敗運動的勢頭在日益增強。

7 ▶CLOTH 布◀ [T] **a)** to pull material into small folds 給…打褶襇: *The skirt is gathered at the waist.* 這條裙子的腰部有褶襇。**b)** to pull material or a piece of clothing closer to you 拉近: *Moira gathered her skirts round her and climbed the steps.* 莫伊拉提起她的裙子爬上台階。

8 gather yourself/gather your strength to prepare yourself for something you are going to do, especially something difficult〔為某事, 尤指難事〕做好準備: *I need to rest and gather my strength for the exam.* 我需要休息一下, 為考試做好準備。

9 ▶CLOUDS 雲朵◀ [T] to gradually increase in number 積聚: *Storm clouds were gathering so we hurried home.* 暴風雨雲在空中聚集, 所以我們趕快回家。

10 the gathering darkness/dusk/shadows etc *literary* the time in the evening when it is getting dark【文】黃昏時分: *the evening's gathering shadows* 傍晚漸濃的夜色

11 gather sb to you/gather sb up *old-fashioned* to take someone into your arms and hold them in order to protect them or show them love【過時】擁抱, 抱住

gather sth ↔ **in** *phr v* [T] to collect crops together 收〔莊稼〕: *gathering in the harvest* 在收莊稼

gather sth ↔ **together/up** *phr v* [T] to pick up lots of things from different places 集攏, 拾攏: *Paul gathered up his papers and left the room.* 保羅把他那些文件資料收集起來便離開房間。| *She gathered up some of the children's clothes and stuffed them in a bag.* 她收拾起孩子們的一些衣服, 塞進包裡。

gather² *n* [C] a small fold produced by pulling cloth together 褶襇

gath·er·ing /ˈgæðrɪŋ; ˈgæðərɪŋ/ *n* [C] **1** a meeting of a group of people 集會: *a select gathering of 20 or 30 people* 20或30個特邀人士的集會 **2** a fold or group of folds in cloth 褶襇

gauche /goʃ; gəʊʃ/ *adj* lacking confidence and experience in social situations, so that you often say or do the wrong thing 不善交際的: *a mature, successful businesswoman, not a gauche teenager, flushing with girlish embarrassment* 一個成熟的成功女商人, 而不是一個不善交際的小姑娘, 卻像姑娘般窘得漲紅了臉 **—gauchely** *adv* **—gaucheness** *n* [U]

gau·cho /ˈgaʊtʃo; ˈgaʊtʃəʊ/ *n* [C] a South American COWBOY (1)〔南美洲的〕加烏喬牧人

gau·dy /ˈgɔdɪ; ˈgɔːdi/ *adj* clothes, colours etc that are gaudy are too bright and look cheap〔衣服、顏色等〕俗麗的: *gaudy jewelry* 俗麗的珠寶 **—gaudily** *adv* **—gaudiness** *n* [U]

gauge¹ also 又作 **gage** *AmE*【美】/gedʒ; geɪdʒ/ *n* [C]
1 ▶INSTRUMENT 儀器◀ an instrument for measuring the size or amount of something 測量儀器, 量規: *a rain gauge* 雨量計 | *the fuel gauge in a car* 汽車上的燃料表
2 ▶WIDTH 寬度◀ a) the width of thin metal objects such as wire, or screws〔金屬線、螺釘等的〕直徑; 寬度: *a narrow-gauge screw* 細徑螺絲 **b)** the width of thin material such as metal or plastic sheets〔金屬片或塑料片等的〕厚度: *heavy gauge black polythene* 重而厚的黑色聚乙烯塑料
3 ▶RAILWAY 鐵道◀ the distance between the lines of a railway or between the wheels of a train〔鐵軌的〕軌距,〔火車輪的〕輪距: **broad/narrow gauge** (=with more/less than the standard distance between the rails) 寬軌距/窄軌距
4 ▶GUN 槍砲◀ the width of the BARREL¹ (3) of a gun 槍管口徑: *a 12-gauge shotgun* 12口徑的獵槍
5 ▶MEASURE 量度◀ a standard measure of weight, size etc to which objects can be compared 標準量度, 標準尺寸

gauge² *v* [T] **1** form a correct idea of how people feel about something or what they are likely to do〔對人們的情感和意圖〕正確估計: *The city council failed to gauge the strength of local feeling on this issue.* 市政會未能正確估計當地人關注這個問題的熱切程度。| **[+what/how etc]** *It is difficult to gauge what the other party's next move will be.* 很難判定另一方下一步要做甚麼。**2** to calculate something by using a particular instrument or method〔用量具或方法〕測量: *The thermostat will gauge the temperature and control the heat.* 恆溫器可測量溫度, 控制熱度。

gaunt /gɔnt; gɔːnt/ *adj* **1** very thin and pale, especially because of illness or continued worry〔由於生病或長期煩惱〕瘦削的, 憔悴的: *I looked into her face and it was gaunt with exhaustion.* 我審視她的臉, 發覺她由於精疲力竭而顯得很憔悴。**2** a building, mountain etc that is gaunt looks very plain and unpleasant〔建築物、山等〕平淡無奇的, 難看的: *a gaunt cathedral* 荒涼的大教堂 **—gauntness** *n* [U]

gaunt·let /ˈgɔntlɪt; ˈgɔːntlɪt/ *n* **1** [C] a long GLOVE (1) that covers someone's wrist and protects their hand, for example in a factory 長手套, 防護手套 **2** [C] a GLOVE (1) covered in metal, used for protection by soldiers in past times〔舊時士兵戴的〕鐵護手套 **3 throw down the gauntlet** to invite someone to fight or compete over a disagreement 挑戰〔由於爭執〕**4 pick up/take up the gauntlet** to accept the invitation to fight or compete over a disagreement 接受挑戰 **5 run the gauntlet** to be criticized or attacked by a lot of people 受到眾人的批評[攻擊]: *Once again Clinton had to run the gauntlet of the press.* 克林頓又一次受到新聞界的廣泛攻擊。

gauze /gɔz; gɔːz/ *n* [U] **1** very thin transparent material with very small holes in it, often used for curtains〔常用作窗簾的〕薄紗, 紗羅 **2** also 又作 **gauze bandage** *AmE* thin cotton with very small holes in it that is used for tying around a wound【美】〔包紮傷口的〕紗布 **—gauzy** *adj*

gave /gev; geɪv/ the past tense of GIVE¹

gav·el /ˈgævl; ˈgævəl/ *n* [C] a small hammer that the person in charge of a meeting, law court, AUCTION¹ etc hits on a table in order to get people's attention〔會議主席、法官、拍賣人等用的〕小木槌

ga·votte /gəˈvɑt; gəˈvɒt/ *n* [C] a fast, cheerful French dance, or the music for this dance 加伏特舞〔一種歡快的法國舞蹈〕; 加伏特舞曲

gawd /gɔd; gɔːd/ *interjection* used to represent the word 'god' when it is said in this way as an expression of surprise, fear etc 天哪!〔表示驚訝、恐懼時, 用來代替god這個詞〕

gawk /gɔk; gɔːk/ *v* [I] to look at something for a long time, in a way that looks stupid 呆呆地看: **[+at]** *Don't just stand there gawking at those girls!* 別站在那兒盯着那些女孩傻看!

gaw·ky /ˈgɔkɪ; ˈgɔːki/ *adj* moving in a nervous and awkward way, as if you cannot control your arms and legs 行動舉止笨拙的: *a gawky, long-legged teenager* 一個舉止笨拙的長腿少年 **—gawkiness** *n* [U]

gawp /gɔp; gɔːp/ *v* [I] *BrE* to look at something for a long time, especially with your mouth open because you are surprised【英】〔由於驚訝〕張口凝視: *tourists gawping at Buckingham Palace* 驚異地呆望着白金漢宮的遊客

3 **gay[1]** /ge; geɪ/ *adj* **1** sexually attracted to people of the same sex as yourself; HOMOSEXUAL 同性戀的: **gay rights/community etc** (=the rights etc of gay people) 同性戀者權利/同性戀者社區等 *a gay rights demonstration* 爭取同性戀者權利的示威活動 **2** *old-fashioned* bright or attractive【過時】鮮豔的: *gay colours* 鮮豔的色彩 **3** *old-fashioned* cheerful and excited【過時】快樂的, 興奮的: *She felt excited and quite gay.* 她感到興奮, 非常快樂。**4 with gay abandon** in a careless and thoughtless way 任意地, 縱情地, 放縱地 —see also 另見 GAILY, GAIETY —**gayness** *n* [U]

gay[2] *n* [C] someone who is HOMOSEXUAL, especially a man〔尤指男〕同性戀者

gaze[1] /gez; geɪz/ *v* [I always+adv/prep] to look at someone or something for a long time, giving it all your attention often without realizing you are doing so〔尤指無意識地〕凝視, 盯着看: **[+into/at etc]** *Patrick was gazing into the fire.* 帕特里克凝視着爐火。| *We gazed up at the stars.* 我們抬頭凝望着星星。

USAGE NOTE 用法説明: GAZE

WORD CHOICE 詞語辨析: **look, gaze, stare, gape**

These words all describe **looking** at someone or something for a long time. 這些詞都描寫長時間看着 (look at) 某人或某物。

You may **gaze** at something interesting or beautiful without realizing you are doing it. 你可能會不知不覺地凝視 (gaze at) 有趣或美麗的東西: *He stood gazing at Helen/at the breathtaking landscape.* 他站在那裡凝視着海倫/凝視着令人驚嘆的風景。

If you **stare** at someone or something, you look directly at them for a long time without moving your eyes, for example because you are angry, very interested, or are thinking hard about something. 如果你瞪着眼睛看 (stare at) 某人或某物, 這表示你由於生氣、很感興趣或者努力思考甚麼而目不轉睛地直視着他們: *She stared at the page for several minutes, uncertain what to write.* 她盯着這一頁紙好幾分鐘, 拿不定主意要寫甚麼。| *Why are you staring at me like that?* 你為甚麼那樣盯着我?

You **gape** at something with your mouth open when you are very surprised or shocked. 當你非常驚奇或震驚時, 你張着口呆看 (gape at) 某物: *He just stood and gaped as the building began to crumble.* 他站在那裡, 目瞪口呆看着大樓開始倒塌。

gaze[2] *n* [singular] a long steady look 凝視, 注視: *a curious gaze* 好奇的凝視 | **lower your gaze** *Ellen smiled uncomfortably and lowered her gaze.* 埃倫很不自在地笑一笑, 目光向下移去。| **meet sb's gaze** (=look directly at someone who is looking at you) 與某人凝視的目光相遇 *He didn't dare to meet her gaze.* 他不敢與她凝視的目光相遇。

ga·ze·bo /gəˋzibo; gəˈziːbəʊ/ *n* [C] a small building in a garden, where you can sit and look at the view〔花園內的〕涼亭, 觀景亭

ga·zelle /gəˋzɛl; gəˈzel/ *n* [C] a type of small DEER, which jumps very gracefully and has large beautiful eyes 瞪羚

ga·zette[1] /gəˋzɛt; gəˈzet/ *n* [C] **1** *BrE* an official newspaper, especially one from the government giving important lists of people who have been employed by them etc【英】公報〔尤指政府公報〕**2** *AmE* a newspaper【美】報紙

gazette[2] *v* [T] *BrE*【英】**1 be gazetted** *formal* to be officially given a specific military job【正式】被正式任命〔某軍職〕**2** to give someone an official job, especially in the military forces 正式任命〔某人擔任某公職, 尤指軍職〕

gaz·et·teer /ˌgæzəˋtɪr; ˌgæzəˈtɪə/ *n* [C] a list of names of places, printed as a dictionary or as a list at the end of a book of maps 地名詞典,〔地圖冊後的〕地名索引

gaz·pa·cho /gəzˋpɑtʃo; gæzˈpætʃəʊ/ *n* [U] a cold Spanish soup made from TOMATO, GREEN PEPPER, CUCUMBER, and onion〔用番茄、青椒、黃瓜和洋葱製作的〕西班牙涼菜湯

ga·zump /gəˋzʌmp; gəˈzʌmp/ *v* [T] *BrE informal* to sell a house to another person who offers you more money than someone that you have already agreed to sell it to【英, 非正式】〔房價議定後〕抬價改售他人: *We were gazumped at the last minute.* 原同意賣給我們的房子在最後一刻被以更高的價格賣給另一人。

GB /ˌdʒi ˋbi; ˌdʒiː ˈbiː/ the written abbreviation of 縮寫= Great Britain

Gb the written abbreviation of 縮寫= GIGABYTE

GBH /ˌdʒi bi ˋetʃ; ˌdʒiː biː ˈeɪtʃ/ *n* [U] *BrE* grievous bodily harm; the serious crime of attacking someone and injuring them【英】嚴重的人身傷害

GCE /ˌdʒi si ˋi; ˌdʒiː siː ˈiː◂/ *n* [C] General Certificate of Education; a school examination in one of a range of subjects, taken in England and Wales before 1988 by students aged 15 or over〔英格蘭和威爾斯〕普通教育證書 (考試)

GCSE /ˌdʒi si ɛs ˋi; ˌdʒiː siː es ˈiː/ *n* [C] General Certificate of Secondary Education; a school examination in one of a range of subjects that is taken by students aged 15 or over in Britain〔英國〕普通中等教育證書 (考試)

g'day /gəˋde; gəˈdeɪ/ *interjection AustrE & NZE* an informal way of saying 'hello'【澳和新西蘭】你[你們]好〔説 'hello' 的一種非正式方式〕

GDP /ˌdʒi di ˋpi; ˌdʒiː diː ˈpiː/ gross domestic product; the total value of all goods and services produced in a country, in one year, except for income received from abroad 國內生產總值 —compare 比較 GNP

gear[1] /gɪr; gɪə/ *n* 3

1 ►IN CARS ETC 在汽車裡等◄ [C,U] the machinery in a vehicle that turns power from the engine into movement 排擋: *The new model has five forward gears.* 這種新型號的汽車有五個前進擋。| *driving cautiously along in third gear* 用第三擋小心駕駛前進 | **bottom gear** *BrE*【英】, **low gear** *AmE*【美】(=the gear used for driving slowly) 最低擋〔即用於慢行的排擋〕| **in gear** (=with a gear connecting the engine to the wheels, and therefore ready to move) 掛着排擋 *Don't turn off the engine while you're still in gear.* 還掛着擋時不要關發動機。

2 ►MACHINERY 機器◄ a piece of machinery that performs a particular job〔某種用途的〕機器: *the landing gear of a plane* 飛機的起降架 | *heavy lifting gear* 重型起重機

3 ►EQUIPMENT 設備◄ a set of equipment or tools you need for a particular activity〔某種用途的〕一套設備[工具]: *He's crazy about photography – he's got all the gear.* 他對攝影着迷——所有的器材他都有。| *We'll need camping gear when we go away.* 我們外出時需要帶宿營器具。

4 ►CLOTHES 衣服◄ a set of clothes that you wear for a particular occasion or activity〔為某個場合或活動穿的成套〕服裝: *Bring your rain gear.* 帶上你的雨衣。| *You have to wear protective gear for this.* 為這個你得穿上防護服。

5 change gear *BrE*【英】, **shift gear** *AmE*【美】**a)** to move a vehicle into a different gear 換擋 —see picture on page A3 參見 A3 頁圖 **b)** to start something in a different way, especially in the amount of energy or effort you use 改變方式〔做某事, 尤指精力或力氣的改變〕: *The boss expects us to be able to change gear just like that.* 老闆指望我們能夠不問來由就忽地為他加一把勁。

6 in top gear *BrE*【英】, **in high gear** *AmE*【美】**a)** the gear used at high speeds 掛最高擋 **b)** doing something with the greatest possible effort and energy 全力以赴: *During this period, Japan's export industries were in top*

gear. 在這個時期, 日本的出口工業突飛猛進地發展。| *The Republican's propaganda machine moved into high gear.* 共和黨的宣傳機器開足了馬力。

7 be thrown out of gear if a process is thrown out of gear, something prevents it from happening in the way that was planned 亂了套

8 ▶DRUGS 毒品◀ [U] *slang* a word meaning illegal drugs, used by people who take drugs【俚】毒品

gear² *v* [T] **1 be geared to** to be organized in a way that is suitable for a particular purpose or situation 適應; 使適合於〔某目的〕: *The typical career pattern was geared to men whose wives didn't work.* 典型的職業模式是為那些妻子不工作的男子設計的。| **be geared to do sth** *The course curriculum is geared to span three years.* 這門課程是按三年學完設計的。**2 be geared up** to be well prepared for something you have to do 一切準備就緒: [+for] *The party is all geared up for the election.* 該黨已為選舉作好了準備。| *We need to be geared up to deal with this sort of emergency.* 我們需要為處理這種緊急情況作好準備。

gear·box /ˋgɪr͵bɑks; ˈgɪəbɒks/ *n* [C] a metal box containing the gears of a vehicle〔車輛的〕齒輪箱, 變速箱

gear·ing /ˋgɪrɪŋ; ˈgɪərɪŋ/ *n* [U] *technical* the relationship between the amount of money that a company is worth and the amount that it owes in debts【術語】配稱, 資本搭配〔即資本和負債的關係〕

gear le·ver /ˈ· ͵··/ *n* [C] a metal rod that you move in order to control the gears of a vehicle〔車輛的〕換擋桿, 變速桿 —see picture at 參見 BICYCLE¹ 圖

gear shift /ˈ· ·/ *n* [C] *AmE* a gear lever【美】〔車輛的〕換擋桿, 變速桿 —see picture on page A2 參見 A2 頁圖

gear stick /ˈ· ·/ *n* [C] *BrE* a gear lever【英】〔車輛的〕換擋桿, 變速桿 —see picture on page A2 參見 A2 頁圖

geck·o /ˋgɛko; ˈgekəʊ/ *n* [C] a type of small LIZARD 壁虎

gee¹ /dʒi; dʒiː/ *interjection especially AmE* used to show that you are surprised or annoyed【尤美】哎呀, 哇〔用來表示驚奇或生氣〕: *Aw, gee, Mom, do we have to go?* 呀, 哎呀, 媽媽, 我們非走不可嗎?

gee² *v*

gee up *phr v* **1** [T] *BrE informal* to encourage someone to try harder【英, 非正式】激勵: **gee** sb ↔ **up** *The team needs a captain who can gee them up a bit.* 這個隊需要有個能夠激勵他們加把幹勁的隊長。**2 gee up!** used to tell a horse to go faster 快跑〔用於讓馬快走〕

gee·gaw /ˋdʒigɔ; ˈdʒiːgɔː/ *n* [C] another spelling of GEWGAW gewgaw 的另一種拼法

gee-gee /ˈ· ·/ *n* [C] *BrE* a word meaning a horse, used by or to children, or when talking about HORSE RACING【英】馬〔兒童用語或談論賽馬時的用語〕

geek /gik; giːk/ *n* [C] *slang especially AmE* someone who is boring and wears clothes that are unfashionable【俚, 尤美】討厭鬼〔指令人生厭、穿着不入時的人〕—**geeky** *adj*

geese /gis; giːs/ the plural of GOOSE¹ (1)

gee whiz /͵· ˈ·/ *interjection AmE old-fashioned* used to show that you are surprised or annoyed【美, 過時】哎呀, 哇〔用來表示驚奇或生氣〕

geez /dʒiz; dʒiːz/ *interjection* another spelling of JEEZ jeez 的另一種拼法

gee·zer /ˋgizɚ; ˈgiːzə/ *n* [C] *informal* a man【非正式】男子: *a funny old geezer* 一個滑稽的老人 | *Some stupid geezer had moved my bags.* 有個愚蠢的傢伙移動了我的行李。

Gei·ger count·er /ˋgaɪgɚ ͵kauntɚ; ˈgaɪgə ͵kaʊntə/ *n* [C] an instrument for finding and measuring RADIOACTIVITY 蓋革計數器〔尋找和測量放射性的儀器〕

gei·sha /ˋgeʃə; ˈgeɪʃə/ also 又作 **geisha girl** /ˈ·· ·/ *n* [C] a Japanese woman who is trained in the art of dancing, singing, and providing entertainment, especially for men〔日本〕藝妓

gel¹ /dʒɛl; dʒel/ *n* [C,U] a thick, wet substance that is used in various bath or beauty products〔用於洗浴或美容產品中的〕凝膠, 凍膠: *hair gel* 髮膠

gel² *v* **gelled, gelling** [I] **1** if a liquid gels it becomes firmer or thicker; JELL (2) 形成膠體, 膠化 **2** if an idea or plan gels it becomes clearer or more definite〔想法和計劃〕變得更清楚[更明確]: *My ideas gelled as I talked the problem over.* 在討論這個問題時我的想法變得更明確了。**3** if two or more people gel, they start working well together as a group 開始合作

gel³ /gɛl; gel/ *n* [C] *old-fashioned* used to represent the word 'girl', when it is said in this way【過時】女孩〔用來表示 girl 這個詞〕

gel·a·tine /ˋdʒɛlətin; ˈdʒelətiːn/ also 又作 **gel·a·tin** /-tn̩; -tɪ̮n/ *AmE*【美】*n* **1** [U] a clear substance obtained from boiled animal bones, used for making JELLY 動物膠 **2** [C] a piece of coloured plastic that is put over a light to change its colour〔改變燈光色彩的〕彩色塑料板

ge·lat·i·nous /dʒəˋlætənəs; dʒɪ̮ˈlætɪ̮nəs/ *adj* in a state between solid and liquid, like a JELLY (4) 凝膠的, 凝膠狀的

geld /gɛld; geld/ *v* [T] to remove the TESTICLES of a horse 割去〔馬的〕睾丸

geld·ing /ˋgɛldɪŋ; ˈgeldɪŋ/ *n* [C] a horse that has been gelded 閹過的雄馬, 去勢的馬

gel·ig·nite /ˋdʒɛlɪg͵naɪt; ˈdʒelɪgnaɪt/ *n* [U] a very powerful explosive 葛里炸藥〔一種烈性炸藥〕

gem /dʒɛm; dʒem/ *n* [C] **1** a beautiful stone that has been cut into a special shape; jewel 寶石, 珠寶: *precious gems* 珍貴的寶石 **2** something that is very special or beautiful 精品: *The capital, Tallin, is an architectural gem.* 首都塔林是個建築精品。**3** a very helpful or useful person 難能可貴的人, 非常有用的人: *Ben, you're a real gem!* 本, 你實在是個難能可貴的人!

Gem·i·ni /ˋdʒɛmə͵naɪ; ˈdʒemɪ̮naɪ/ *n* **1** [singular] the third sign of the ZODIAC, represented by TWINS¹ and believed to affect the character and life of people born between May 21 and June 21 雙子宮[座]〔黃道第三宮, 據信該宮影響出生於5月21日至6月21日之間人們的性格和生活〕**2** [C] someone who was born between May 21 and June 21 出生於雙子宮[座]時段〔即5月21日至6月21日〕的人

Gen. a written abbreviation of 縮寫= General

gen¹ /dʒɛn; dʒen/ *n* [U] *BrE informal* information【英, 非正式】信息, 情報: [+on] *She has all the gen on cheap flights.* 她對各廉價航班信息十分靈通。

gen² *v* **genned, genning**

gen up *phr v* [T] *BrE informal* to learn a lot of information about something for a particular purpose【英, 非正式】了解事實; 知道詳情: [+on] *It's a good idea to gen up on the company's product before the interview.* 在面試前先了解該公司產品的詳細情況, 是個好主意。

-ge·nar·i·an /dʒəˋnɛrɪən; dʒəˈneərɪən/ *suffix* [in nouns and adjectives 構成名詞和形容詞] someone who is a particular number of DECADES (=periods of 10 years) old ... 十歲至...十九歲的人: *an octogenarian* (=between 80 and 89 years old) 一位八旬的老人 | *a septuagenarian ex-judge* 一位七十幾歲的前任法官

gen·darme /ˋʒɑndɑrm; ˈʒɒndɑːm/ *n* [C] a French policeman 法國警察

gen·der /ˋdʒɛndɚ; ˈdʒendə/ *n* **1** [C,U] *formal* the fact of being male or female【正式】性別: *Discrimination on grounds of race or gender is forbidden.* 嚴禁種族或性別歧視。**2 a)** [U] the system in some languages of marking words such as nouns, adjectives, and PRONOUNS as being MASCULINE (4), FEMININE (2), or NEUTER¹ (2) 性〔指某些語言中將名詞、形容詞和代詞分為陽性、陰性或中性的一種系統〕**b)** [C] a group such as FEMININE (2) into which words are divided in this system 性〔詞在這種系統中所分成的類, 如陰性〕

gender bend·er /ˈ·· ͵··/ *n* [C] *informal* someone, often a popular singer or entertainer, who behaves or dresses in a way typical of someone of the opposite sex【非正式】男扮女裝或女扮男裝者〔尤指舉止或服裝模仿異性的

G

流行歌手或演員〕

gender-spe·cif·ic /'·· ·,··/ *adj* for males only, or females only 限定性別的: *This law is gender-specific, singling out women.* 這項法律是限定性別的，專門適用於婦女。

S2 W2 **gene** /dʒin; dʒiːn/ *n* [C] a small part of the material inside the NUCLEUS of a cell, that controls the development of the qualities that have been passed on to a living thing from its parents 基因

ge·ne·al·o·gy /,dʒini`ælədʒɪ; ,dʒiːni'ælədʒi/ *n* **1** [U] the study of the history of families 家譜學, 宗譜學 **2** [C] an account of the history of a family, especially when shown in a drawing that shows how each person is related to the others 家譜, 系譜圖 —**genealogist** *n* [C] —**genealogical** /,dʒiniə`lɑdʒɪkḷ; ,dʒiːniə'lɒdʒɪkəl◂/ *adj* —**genealogically** /-kḷɪ; -kli/ *adv*

gene pool /'· ·/ *n* [C] all of the genes available to a particular SPECIES〔某物種的〕基因庫

gen·e·ra /`dʒɛnərə; 'dʒenərə/ the plural of GENUS

S1 W1 **gen·e·ral**[1] /`dʒɛnərəl; 'dʒenərəl/ *adj*

1 ▶NOT DETAILED 不詳細的◀ describing only the main features of something, not the details 大體的, 大致的: *a general introduction to computing* 電腦操作概論 | **general idea** *I've got a general idea of how I want the new room to look.* 新房間應該如何佈置，我有了一個大致的想法。| **in general terms** (=without considering specific details) 大體上, 總的說來 *The minister talked in general terms about the need for fairer taxation.* 部長籠統地談了更公平的稅收的必要性。

2 in general a) usually or in most situations 一般說來, 大體說來: *In general, about 10% of the candidates are eventually offered positions.* 一般說來，大約10%的求職者最終得到了職位。**b)** as a broad subject 總體上: *We're trying to raise awareness about the environment in general and air pollution in particular.* 我們正在努力從總體上增強環境意識，特別提高對空氣污染的意識。

3 ▶AS A WHOLE 總體上◀ considered in terms of a whole situation, group, etc, not of the specific parts that it consists of; OVERALL[1] 總體的, 普遍的: *There are a few intelligent ones, but the general standard isn't very high.* 有幾個很聰明的，但總體水平並不很高。| *We were impressed by the quality of their work and the general air of professionalism.* 他們的工作質量和總體的專業精神給我們留下了深刻印象。| **a general anaesthetic** (=for the whole body, not one part of it) 全身麻醉劑

4 ▶ORDINARY/NOT SPECIFIC 普通的/非特定的◀ of an ordinary kind, not one particular kind 普通的: *I spend about 10 hours a week doing general cooking and cleaning.* 我每星期大約花10小時來進行普通烹調和掃除。| *How widespread is AIDS in the general population?* 愛滋病在總人口中傳播有多廣? | *It's a good general fertilizer.* 它是一種很好的普通肥料。

5 ▶MOST PEOPLE 大多數人◀ shared by or affecting most people, or most of the people in a group 普遍的: *Keynes' view of economics gained general acceptance in the 1930's.* 凱恩斯的經濟學觀點在20世紀30年代被普遍接受。| *How soon can the drug be made available for general use?* 這種藥需要多長時間才能夠普遍使用?

6 the general area/neighbourhood/location not the exact place or direction, but somewhere near 整個地區/街區/場所: *Several bombs landed in the same general area.* 好幾顆炸彈落在大概同一個地區。

7 ▶JOB 職位◀ used in the name of a job to show that the person who does this job has complete responsibility 全面負責的: *the general manager* 總經理 | *the Attorney General* 首席檢察官, 司法部長

8 as a general rule used to say what happens in most cases 在一般情況下, 通常: *He doesn't give interviews as a general rule, but he's prepared to make an exception in this case.* 他通常不接受採訪，但這一次他準備破例。

9 the general public ordinary people, who do not have important positions or belong to specific groups 公眾: *Health education is aimed at the general public as well as at high-risk groups.* 健康教育是針對普通老百姓和高危人羣的。| *The doors opened to the general public last night at the Klondyke Building.* 克朗代克大樓昨晚向公眾開放。

10 in the general interest in a way that helps or brings advantage to most people 對大多數人有好處的, 符合大部分人利益的: *It's in the general interest to invest in public transportation.* 投資公共交通可為大多數人帶來利益。—see also 另見 GENERALLY

general[2] *n* [C] an officer of very high rank in the army or air force〔陸軍和空軍的〕上將 —see table on page C6 參見C6頁附錄

general coun·sel /,··· '··/ *n* [C] **1** the chief legal officer of a US company〔美國公司裡的〕首席法律顧問 **2** a firm of US lawyers that gives general technical advice〔美國的〕綜合性律師事務所

general de·liv·er·y /,··· ·'···/ *n* [U] *AmE* a post office department to which you can send letters for someone who is travelling and which will keep them until they are collected【美】郵件存局候領處; POSTE RESTANTE *BrE*【英】

general e·lec·tion /,··· ·'··/ *n* [C] an election in which all the people voting in a country vote at the same time to choose a government 普選, 大選

general head·quar·ters /,··· ·'··/ *n* [plural] the place from which the actions of an organization, especially a military one, are controlled 總司令部

gen·e·ral·ise /`dʒɛnərəl,aɪz; 'dʒenərəlaɪz/ *v* a British spelling of GENERALIZE generalize 的英式拼法

gen·e·ral·i·ty /,dʒɛnə`rælətɪ; ,dʒenə'ræləti/ *n* **1** [C often plural 常用複數] a very general statement that avoids mentioning details or specific cases 概括, 籠統的話: *Can we stop dealing in generalities and start suggesting practical steps to take?* 我們不要再說空話，開始建議一下採取的實際步驟，好嗎? **2 the generality of** most of; the MAJORITY (1) of 大多數的: *Temporary workers are considerably younger than the generality of workers.* 臨時工比大多數工人年輕多了。**3** [U] *formal* the quality of being true or useful in most situations【正式】普遍性, 共通性

gen·e·ral·i·za·tion also 又作 **-isation** *BrE*【英】/,dʒɛnərələ`zeʃən; ,dʒenərəlaɪ'zeɪʃən/ *n* **1** [C] a general statement or opinion that is only partly true because it is based on only a few cases or incomplete knowledge〔依據不足的〕概括, 泛論: *You're making too many generalizations about an issue that you don't really understand.* 你對一個你並不真正了解的問題作了太多的推論。| **sweeping generalization** (=saying that something is true in every case or situation) 籠統的概括: *Please! No sweeping generalizations like "all women are bad drivers".* 對不起，不要一概而論，說甚麼"所有的女子駕車都不行"。**2** [U] the act of making generalizations 歸納, 概括

gen·e·ral·ize also 又作 **-ise** *BrE*【英】/`dʒɛnərəl,aɪz; 'dʒenərəlaɪz/ *v* **1** [I] to make a general statement about a number of different things or people without mentioning any details 籠統地表達, 概括地論述: *It's difficult to generalize about the typical Republican voter.* 對典型的共和黨選民的特徵進行概括是很難的。**2** [I] to form a general principle or opinion after considering only a small number of facts or examples 概括, 歸納: *It's stupid to generalize and say that all young people are rude.* 泛泛而論說所有的年輕人都很粗魯是愚蠢的。| **[+from]** *We can generalize from the samples and conclude that nitrogen levels have increased.* 我們可以從這些樣品得出一般的結論: 氮的含量已經提高了。**3** [T] *formal* to put a principle, statement, or rule into a more general form so that it covers a larger number of examples【正式】推廣, 擴大〔原則、論述或規律的〕應用範圍: *I will first illustrate it by a simple example and then gen-*

eralize it. 我將先用一個簡單的例子說明, 然後再把它普遍化。

general know·ledge /,… '··/ *n* [U] knowledge of facts about many different subjects 常識, 一般知識: *a general knowledge quiz* 常識測驗

1 1 **gen·er·al·ly** /ˈdʒɛnərəlɪ; ˈdʒenərəli/ *adv* **1** in a general way, considering without details or specific cases 大體上, 大致: *The system has generally been found very easy to use.* 人們大體上覺得這個系統很容易使用。| *She's not really ill, just generally run-down.* 她並不是真正生病了, 只是感到全身疲憊。**2** by or to most people 普遍地, 廣泛地: *The plants are generally regarded as weeds.* 這些植物一般都被認為是雜草。| *So, is the plan generally acceptable?* 那麼, 這項計劃大多數人都可以接受嗎? **3** usually or most of the time 通常地: *Jonathan says he generally gets in to work by 8.00.* 喬納森說他通常不到八點就來到並開始工作。**4 generally speaking** used to introduce a statement that is true in most cases but not always 一般來說: *Generally speaking, the more expensive the stereo, the better it is.* 一般說來, 立體聲音響的價格越貴, 質量就越好。

general prac·tice /,… '··/ *n* **1** [U] the work of a doctor or lawyer who deals with all the ordinary types of illness or legal case, rather than one specific type 普通醫生[普通律師]的工作 **2** [C] a group of lawyers or doctors who do all kinds of work 普通律師事務所; 普通醫生診所

general prac·ti·tion·er /,… ·'···/ *n* [C] a doctor who is trained in general medicine and treats people in a particular area or town; GP〔在某一地區或城市行醫的非專科〕普通醫生, 全科醫生

general-pur·pose /,… '··◂/ *adj* [only before noun 僅用於名詞前] a general-purpose product, vehicle etc is suitable for most situations or jobs that such things are normally used for 多用途的, 多功能的: *general-purpose glue* 多用途膠水

gen·er·al·ship /ˈdʒɛnərəl,ʃɪp; ˈdʒenərəlʃɪp/ *n* [U] the skill of leading an army, developing plans for battle etc〔軍事上的〕指揮才能

general staff /,… '·/ *n* **the general staff** the group of military officers who work for a commanding officer 參謀部〔指某指揮官的全體參謀〕

general store /'… ,·/ *n* [C] *AmE* a shop that sells a wide variety of goods, especially one in a small town【美】〔尤指小鎮上的〕雜貨店

general strike /,… '·/ *n* [C] a time when most of the workers in a country refuse to work in order to protest about working conditions, wages, etc〔全國性的〕總罷工, 大罷工

2 **gen·e·rate** /ˈdʒɛnə,ret; ˈdʒenəreɪt/ *v* [T] **1** to produce or create something 產生, 創造: *a useful technique for generating new ideas* 能產生新創意的有用技術 | *The program would generate a lot of new jobs.* 這個項目將創造許多新職位。| **generate sales/profits/income etc** *What sales volume would be required to generate an income of $96,000?* 需要多大的銷售額才能產生 96,000 美元的收入? **2 generate excitement/interest/ill-feeling** to produce strong feelings among a large number of people〔在一大羣人之中〕引起興奮/興趣/敵意: *News of the Queen's visit is generating a lot of excitement.* 女王訪問的消息使人們興奮不已。**3** to produce heat, electricity, or another form of energy 產生〔熱能、電能或其他能量〕: *The flowing water is used to drive turbines, which generate electricity.* 流水被用來驅動渦輪機, 渦輪機產生電力。

2 2 **gen·e·ra·tion** /,dʒɛnəˈreʃən; ,dʒenəˈreɪʃən/ *n* **1** [C] **a)** all people of about the same age 一代 (人): *My generation never knew an America before Vietnam.* 我這代人不認識越戰之前的美國。| [also+plural verb *BrE* 英] *The younger generation don't know what hard work is.* 年輕一代不知道甚麼叫艱苦的工作。**b)** all the members of a family of about the same age〔家庭中的〕一代 (人): *We're the fourth generation of Carters to live in this house.* 我們是住在這棟房子的第四代卡特家人。| *a second-generation Canadian* (=whose parents are Canadian but whose grandparents were not) 第二代加拿大人〔其父母是加拿大人, 祖父母卻不是〕| **the generation gap** (=the lack of understanding between generations caused by their different attitudes and experiences) 代溝 **2** [C] the average period of time between the birth of a person and the birth of that person's children 一代人的時間〔指一個人的出生與此人的孩子出生之間的平均時間〕: *Within a generation Japan regained the status of a great power.* 日本在一代人的時間裡重新獲得強國的地位。**3** [C] all the members of a group of things which have been developed from a previous group〔某種事物的〕一代: *the latest generation of anti-tank missiles* 最新一代的反坦克導彈 **4** [U] the process of producing something or making something happen 產生, 發生: *the generation of electricity* 發電

gen·e·ra·tive /ˈdʒɛnə,retɪv; ˈdʒenərətɪv/ *adj especially technical* able to produce something【尤術語】有生產力的, 能生成的

generative gram·mar /,… '··/ *n* [C,U] the description of a language using rules that produce all the sentences of the language that are correct according to the rules of grammar 生成語法

gen·e·ra·tor /ˈdʒɛnə,retɚ; ˈdʒenəreɪtə/ *n* [C] a machine that produces electricity 發電機: *a coal-powered generator* 燃煤發電機

ge·ner·ic /dʒəˈnɛrɪk; dʒ$_{\text{ə}}$ˈnerɪk/ *adj* **1 generic name/term/label etc** a word that describes a whole class of things 屬名/通稱等〔用來描述一類事物的詞〕: *Misogyny is the generic term for all hostile feelings and actions towards women.* misogyny 是針對婦女的一切敵對情感和行為的通稱。**2** *technical* belonging to or typical of a GENUS【術語】屬的, 類的 **3** *especially AmE* a generic product does not have a TRADEMARK【尤美】無商標的, 未註冊的 (1) —**generically** /-klɪ; -kli/ *adv*

gen·e·ros·i·ty /,dʒɛnəˈrɑsətɪ; ,dʒenəˈrɒsəti/ *n* **1** [U] willingness to give money, time etc in order to help or please someone 慷慨, 大方: *an act of great generosity* 十分慷慨的行為 **2** [C] an act of being generous 慷慨大方的行為

gen·e·rous /ˈdʒɛnərəs; ˈdʒenərəs/ *adj* **1** willing to give money, spend time etc, in order to help people or give them pleasure 慷慨的, 大方的: **[+to]** *She's always very generous to the kids.* 她對小孩總是很大方。| **it is generous of sb (to do sth)** *What lovely presents – it's very generous of you!* 多麼可愛的禮物 —— 你非常大方啊! | **generous with your help/time/money etc** *I'd like to thank Simon, who's been very generous with his time.* 我想感謝西蒙, 他很慷慨地付出了許多時間。**2** larger than the usual or expected amount〔比通常或預想的〕大量的, 豐富的: *a generous glass of port* 一大杯波爾圖葡萄酒 | *We offer a generous salary and benefits package.* 我們提供一攬子豐厚的薪水和津貼。| *generous welfare payments* 豐厚的福利津貼 **3** sympathetic in the way you deal with people, and tending not to criticize them, get angry, or treat them unkindly 寬宏大量的: *She was generous enough to overlook my little mistake.* 她非常寬宏大量, 不計較我的小錯誤。| *not a very generous attitude* 不很寬厚的態度 —**generously** *adv*: *Please give generously to the refugee fund.* 請為難民基金慷慨解囊。

gen·e·sis /ˈdʒɛnəsɪs; ˈdʒenəsəs/ *n formal* **the genesis of** the beginning or origin of something〔某事物〕的起源: *a discovery that was to be a genesis of modern physics* 成為現代物理學起源的一項發現

gene ther·a·py /'· ,···/ *n* [U] a way of treating certain diseases by adding to the body a GENE that it does not have 基因治療法

ge·net·ic /dʒəˈnɛtɪk; dʒəˈnetɪk/ *adj* connected with GENES or GENETICS 基因的, 遺傳學的: *genetic defects* 遺傳性缺陷 | *These abnormalities may have a genetic basis.* 這

些畸形可能和基因有關。

ge·net·ic·ally /dʒəˋnɛtɪkḷɪ; dʒəˈnetɪkli/ *adv* **1** in a way that is connected with GENETICS 遺傳學上 **2 genetically engineered** a vegetable, VIRUS etc that is genetically engineered has been produced by a method that involves changing the structure of its GENE*s* 基因改造的

genetic code /·,·· ˈ·/ *n* [C] the arrangement of GENE*s* that controls the way a living thing develops 遺傳密碼, 基因密碼

genetic en·gin·eer·ing /·,·· ··ˈ··/ *n* [U] the science of changing the GENETIC structure of an animal, plant, or human in order to affect the way it develops 遺傳[基因]工程學 —**genetic engineer** *n* [C]

genetic fin·ger·print /·,·· ˈ···/ *n* [C] the pattern of GENETIC information which is different for each person or animal 基因指紋

genetic fin·ger·print·ing /·,·· ˈ····/ *n* [U] the process of examining someone's GENETIC structure, especially in order to find out if they are guilty of a crime 基因指紋分析, 基因鑑定〔尤用於司法的犯罪鑑定〕

ge·net·ics /dʒəˋnɛtɪks; dʒəˈnetɪks/ *n* [plural] the study of how the nature and development of living things is affected by their GENE*s* (=the parts of their cells that pass on characteristics from their parents) 遺傳學 —see also 另見 GENE, HEREDITY —**geneticist** /-təsɪst; -tɪsɪst/ *n* [C]

ge·ni·al /ˋdʒinjəl; ˈdʒiːniəl/ *adj* having a cheerful and friendly character or manner 親切的, 和藹的, 友好的 —**genially** *adv* —**geniality** /ˌdʒinɪˋælətɪ; ˌdʒiːniˈælɪti/ *n* [U]

ge·nie /ˋdʒinɪ; ˈdʒiːni/ *n* [C] a magical spirit in old Arabian stories〔古代阿拉伯故事中的〕妖怪, 神靈

gen·i·tal /ˋdʒɛnətḷ; ˈdʒenɪtl/ *adj* connected with or affecting the outer sex organs 外生殖器的: *genital herpes* 生殖器疱疹 | *genital mutilation* 生殖器毀傷 —**genitally** *adv*

gen·i·tals /ˋdʒɛnətḷz; ˈdʒenɪtlz/ also 又作 **gen·i·ta·li·a** /ˌdʒɛnəˋteljə; ˌdʒenɪˈteɪliə/ *technical n* [plural] the outer sex organs【術語】外生殖器, 外陰部

gen·i·tive /ˋdʒɛnətɪv; ˈdʒenɪtɪv/ *n* [C] *technical* a form of the noun in some languages, which shows a relationship of possession or origin between one thing and another【術語】〔某些語言中名詞的〕屬格, 所有格 —**genitive** *adj*

ge·ni·us /ˋdʒinjəs; ˈdʒiːniəs/ *n* **1** [U] a very high level of intelligence, mental skill, or artistic ability, which only a few people have 天才, 天賦: **a writer/work/woman etc of genius** *an imaginative novelist of great genius* 一位想像力豐富的偉大天才小說家 | *The film reveals Fellini's genius.* 這部影片展示了費里尼的天賦。| **a stroke of genius** (=a very clever idea) 天才之舉 **2** [C] someone who has an unusually high level of intelligence, mental skill or artistic ability 有天才的人, 天才: *a musical genius* 一位音樂天才 | *You can't compare him with a true genius like Einstein.* 你不能拿他與愛因斯坦這樣的曠世奇才相比。| **be a genius at sth** *Watch your money – Lou's a genius at cards.* 當心你的錢——露是個玩牌天才。**3 have a genius for (doing) sth** to be especially good at doing something 有(做)某事的天才: *Bernard had a genius for bringing out the best in his students.* 伯納德有讓學生發揮出最佳才能的本事。| *Warhol's genius for publicity* 沃荷的宣傳天才 **4** [U] the special quality of a particular group of people, period of time etc〔某一羣體的人、某個時期等的〕特徵: *the French artistic genius* 法國的藝術特徵

genius lo·ci /ˌdʒinjəs ˋlosaɪ; ˌdʒiːniəs ˈləʊsaɪ/ *n* [singular] *Latin* the typical character of a place and the feelings it produces in people【拉丁】地方的風格[特色]

gen·o·cide /ˋdʒɛnəˌsaɪd; ˈdʒenəsaɪd/ *n* [U] the deliberate murder of a whole group or race of people 大屠殺, 種族滅絕: *the genocide of the Jews during the Holocaust* 大屠殺時期對猶太人的種族滅絕 —**genocidal** /ˌdʒɛnəˋsaɪdḷ; ˌdʒenəˈsaɪdl◂/ *adj*

ge·nome /ˋdʒinom; ˈdʒiːnəʊm/ *n* [C] *technical* the total of all the GENE*s* that are found in one type of living thing【術語】基因組, 染色體組: *the human genome* 人類基因組

gen·re /ˋʒɑnrə; ˈʒɒnrə/ *n* [C] *formal* a particular type of art, writing, music etc, which has certain characteristics that all examples of this type share【正式】〔藝術、寫作、音樂等的〕類型, 體裁: *Science fiction as a genre is relatively new.* 科幻小說作為一種體裁是比較新的。| *Leon's movies are outstanding examples of the genre.* 利昂的影片是這種體裁的傑出榜樣。

gent /dʒɛnt; dʒent/ *n* [C] **1** *informal especially BrE* a GENTLEMAN【非正式, 尤英】紳士: *Quite the gent, he was – in a dress shirt, top hat, and black overcoat.* 他一派紳士風度: 穿着禮服襯衫, 戴着高頂大禮帽, 穿着黑大衣。**2 the gents** [singular] *BrE* a public toilet for men【英】男廁所; MEN'S ROOM *AmE*【美】

gen·teel /dʒɛnˋtil; dʒenˈtiːl/ *adj* **1** behaving and speaking in an unnatural and very polite way, because you want people to think you belong to a high social class〔言談舉止〕假裝上等人的 **2** *old-fashioned* of a high social class【過時】上流社會的: *a genteel neighbourhood* 上流社會街區 —**genteelly** *adv*

gen·tian /ˋdʒɛnʃən; ˈdʒenʃən/ *n* [C] a small plant with blue flowers that grows in mountain areas 龍膽屬植物

gentian vi·o·let /,·· ˈ···/ *n* [U] a purple ANTISEPTIC² (1) liquid that is used to treat burns or stings 龍膽紫, 甲基紫〔一種殺菌劑, 用於治療燒傷、蟲螫傷〕

gen·tile /ˋdʒɛntaɪl; ˈdʒentaɪl/ *n* [C] someone who is not Jewish 非猶太人 —**gentile** *adj*

gen·til·i·ty /dʒɛnˋtɪlətɪ; dʒenˈtɪlɪti/ *n* [U] *formal* the quality of appearing to belong to a high social class【正式】裝出來的彬彬有禮, 假斯文: *her pretensions to gentility* 她自命屬於上流社會的種種裝腔作勢

gen·tle /ˋdʒɛntḷ; ˈdʒentl/ *adj* **1** kind and careful in your character or behaviour and not at all violent or unpleasant 和藹友善的, 温和的, 不粗暴的: *Be gentle when you brush the baby's hair.* 給嬰兒梳頭髮時要輕柔些。| *Lynne was a sweet, gentle girl.* 林恩是個可愛温和的女孩。| *a little gentle mockery* 無傷大雅的小嘲弄 | **[+with]** *He was incredibly gentle with her during her illness.* 在她生病期間, 他對她温柔得難以置信。**2** not strong, loud, forceful, or extreme 輕柔的, 輕聲的, 和緩的: *Take a little gentle exercise.* 做一點輕微的鍛鍊。| *Mother's gentle laughter* 母親輕柔的笑聲 | *the gentle warmth of the evening sun* 夕陽的和煦 **3** a gentle wind or rain is soft and light〔風、雨等〕輕柔的: *a gentle breeze clearing the mist* 吹散薄霧的微風 **4** a gentle hill or slope is not steep or sharp〔山或坡〕不陡的, 平緩的: *the gentle contours of the South Downs* 南部丘陵平緩的輪廓 —see also 另見 GENTLY —**gentleness** *n* [U] (S3 W3)

gen·tle·folk /ˋdʒɛntḷˌfok; ˈdʒentlfəʊk/ *n* [plural] *old use* people belonging to the higher social classes【舊】上流社會的人

gen·tle·man /ˋdʒɛntḷmən; ˈdʒentlmən/ *n* [C] **1** a man who always behaves towards other people in a polite and honourable way and who can be trusted to keep his promises 紳士, 彬彬有禮、言而有信的男士: *a real gentleman* 正人君子 | *Martin – always the perfect gentleman – got to his feet when my mother walked in.* 馬丁始終是十足的紳士派頭, 我母親走進來的時候他便站了起來。**2** a polite word for a man, used especially when talking to or about a man you do not know 先生〔對男士客氣的稱呼, 尤用於你所不認識的人〕: *Could you serve this gentleman please, Ms Bath?* 巴思女士, 請為這位先生服務好嗎? | **ladies and gentlemen** (=used at the beginning of a speech) 女士們, 先生們〔用於講話的開頭〕**3** *old-fashioned* a man from a high social class, especially one whose family owns a lot of property【過時】有身分的人, 紳士〔尤指來自富裕家庭的人〕 (S3 W2)

gentleman farm·er /,··· ˈ··/ *n* [C] *BrE* a man belonging to a high social class who owns and runs a farm for pleasure rather than profit【英】〔經營農場作為消遣的〕鄉紳

gen·tle·man·ly /ˋdʒɛntl̩mənlɪ; ˈdʒentlmənli/ *adj* a man who is gentlemanly is polite, honourable, and always careful to consider other people's feelings 有禮貌的, 寬容周到的, 紳士風度的

gentleman's a·gree·ment /ˏ··· ˑ·ˋ·/ *n* [C] an agreement that is not written down, made between people who trust each other 君子協定

gen·tle·wo·man /ˋdʒɛntl̩ˏwʊmən; ˈdʒentlˌwʊmən/ *n* [C] *old use* a woman who belongs to a high social class【舊】女士; 貴婦; 淑女

3 **gent·ly** /ˋdʒɛntlɪ; ˈdʒentli/ *adv* **1** in a gentle way 輕柔地, 溫柔地: *I patted her gently on the shoulder.* 我輕輕地拍了拍她的肩膀。| *The road curved gently upwards.* 路緩緩向上蜿蜒。**2 gently!** *BrE spoken* used to tell someone to be careful when they are handling something, moving something etc【英口】小心點!〔要某人觸碰或移動某物時當心〕: *Gently, Sammy, you don't want to break it.* 小心點, 薩米, 別把它打破了。| **gently does it** *Careful when you lift that desk – gently does it!* 抬起那張桌子時要小心——輕點兒搬!

gen·tri·fic·ation /ˏdʒɛntrɪfɪˋkeʃən; ˌdʒentrɪ̇fɪ̇ˈkeɪʃən/ *n* [U] the process by which a street that poor people used to live in is changed when people with more money go to live there 地區貴族化〔指較富有的人居住在原來窮人居住的地方的過程〕—**gentrify** /ˋdʒɛntrɪfaɪ; ˈdʒentrɪ̇faɪ/ *v* [T usually passive 一般用被動態]

gen·try /ˋdʒɛntrɪ; ˈdʒentri/ *n* [plural] *old-fashioned* people who belong to a high social class【過時】上流社會人士, 紳士階層: **the landed gentry** (=the gentry who own land) 擁有土地的紳士階層, 地主階級

gen·u·flect /ˋdʒɛnjʊˏflɛkt; ˈdʒenjᵊflekt/ *v* [I] to bend your knee when in church or a holy place as a sign of respect 屈膝; 跪拜〔以示禮拜〕—**genuflection** /ˏdʒɛnjuˋflɛkʃən; ˌdʒenjᵊˈflekʃən/ *n* [C,U]

3 3 **gen·u·ine** /ˋdʒɛnjʊɪn; ˈdʒenjuɪ̇n/ *adj* **1** a genuine feeling, desire etc is one that you really feel, not one you pretend to feel in order to deceive people; sincere〔感情、慾望等〕真誠的: *The reforms are motivated by a genuine concern for the disabled.* 這些改革是出自於對殘疾人的真誠關心。**2** something genuine really is what it seems to be; real〔物品〕真正的: *It's either a genuine diamond or a very good fake.* 它要麼是塊真鑽石, 要麼是一件很好的贗品。**3** someone who is genuine is honest and friendly and you feel you can trust them 真心實意的: *Dan's a real genuine guy.* 丹確實是個誠實可靠的人。**4 the genuine article** *informal* a person, or sometimes a thing, that is a true example of their type【非正式】〔某類型的人或物中〕真正的代表: *If you want to meet a real Southerner, Jake is the genuine article.* 如果你想見到一名真正的南方人, 傑克就是個典型。—**genuinely** *adv*: *He genuinely believes in what he sells.* 他真心相信他賣的東西。—**genuineness** *n* [U]

ge·nus /ˋdʒinəs; ˈdʒiːnəs/ *n plural* **genera** /ˋdʒɛnərə; ˈdʒenərə/ [C] *technical* one of the groups into which scientists divide animals or plants, below a FAMILY (5) and above a SPECIES【術語】〔動植物的〕屬 —see also 另見 GENERIC

ge·o- /dʒio; dʒiːəʊ/ *prefix technical* concerning the Earth or its surface【術語】地球的, 地面的: *geophysics* 地球物理學 | *geopolitical* 地緣政治學的

ge·o·cen·tric /ˏdʒioˋsɛntrɪk; ˌdʒiːəʊˈsentrɪk◂/ *adj* having the Earth as the central point, or measured from the centre of the Earth 以地球為中心的, 地心的: *Ptolemy's geocentric model of the universe* 托勒密的地球中心宇宙模型

ge·o·de·sic dome /ˏdʒiodɛsɪk ˋdom; ˌdʒiːəʊdiːsɪk ˈdəʊm/ *n* [C] *technical* a large building shaped like a ball, made from small flat pieces that are connected together to form POLYGONs【術語】網格球形大型建築

ge·og·ra·phy /dʒiˋɑgrəfɪ; dʒiˈɒgrəfi/ *n* [U] **1** the study of the countries, seas, rivers, towns etc of the world 地理學: *a geography lesson* 地理課 —see also 另見 PHYSICAL GEOGRAPHY, POLITICAL GEOGRAPHY **2 the geography of** the way all the parts of a building, city etc are arranged〔建築物、城市等的〕佈局: *The geography of the old section of Boston is really complicated.* 波士頓舊區的佈局確實很複雜。—**geographer** *n* [C] —**geographical** /ˏdʒiəˋgræfɪkl̩; ˌdʒiːəˈgræfɪkəl◂/ *adj*: *a geographical area* 地理區域 —**geographically** /-kl̩ɪ; -kli/ *adv*

ge·ol·o·gy /dʒiˋɑlədʒɪ; dʒiˈɒlədʒi/ *n* [U] the study of the rocks, soil etc that make up the Earth, and of the way they have changed since the Earth was formed 地質學 —**geologist** *n* [C] —**geological** /ˏdʒiəˋlɑdʒɪkl̩; ˌdʒiːəˈlɒdʒɪkəl◂/ *adj*: *geological periods* 地質時期 —**geologically** /-kl̩ɪ; -kli/ *adv*

ge·o·met·ric /ˏdʒiəˋmɛtrɪk; ˌdʒiːəˈmetrɪk◂/ also 又作 **ge·o·met·ri·cal** /-trɪkl̩; -trɪkəl/ *adj* **1** like the shapes and lines in GEOMETRY, especially in having regular patterns 幾何圖形的: *a geometric design* 幾何圖形的設計 **2** related to GEOMETRY 幾何的, 幾何學的 —**geometrically** /-kl̩ɪ; -kli/ *adv*

geometric pro·gres·sion /ˏ···· ·ˋ··/ *n* [U] a set of numbers in order, in which each is multiplied by a specific number to produce the next number in the series (as in 1, 2, 4, 8, 16,...) 幾何級數, 等比級數〈如1, 2, 4, 8, 16, ...〉—compare 比較 ARITHMETIC PROGRESSION

ge·om·e·try /dʒiˋɑmətrɪ; dʒiˈɒmɪ̇tri/ *n* [U] the study in MATHEMATICS of the angles and shapes formed by the relationships of lines, surfaces, and solid objects in space 幾何學

ge·o·phys·ics /ˏdʒioˋfɪzɪks; ˌdʒiːəʊˈfɪzɪks/ *n* [U] the study of the movements of parts of the Earth, and the forces involved with it, including the weather, the sea beds etc 地球物理學 —**geophysical** *adj* —**geophysicist** *n* [C]

ge·o·pol·i·tics /ˏdʒioˋpɑlətɪks; ˌdʒiːəʊˈpɒlɪ̇tɪks/ *n* [U] the study of the effects of a country's position, population etc on its political character and development 地理政治學, 地緣政治學 —**geopolitical** /ˏdʒiopəˋlɪtɪkl̩; ˌdʒiːəʊpəˈlɪtɪkəl◂/ *adj*

Geor·die /ˋdʒɔrdi; ˈdʒɔːdi/ *n BrE*【英】**1** [C] someone from Tyneside in NE England〔英格蘭東北部的〕泰恩賽德人 **2** [U] a way of speaking typical of people from Tyneside 泰恩賽德人的說話方式 —**Geordie** *adj*

George /dʒɔrdʒ; dʒɔːdʒ/ *n* **by George!** *old-fashioned spoken* used when you are pleasantly surprised【過時, 口】確實, 的確〔用來表示驚喜〕: *By George, I think you're right!* 可不是嗎, 我認為你是對的!

geor·gette /dʒɔrˋdʒɛt; dʒɔːˈdʒet/ *n* [U] a light strong material, used for making clothes 喬其紗〔輕而結實的材料, 用於製作衣服〕

Geor·gian /ˋdʒɔrdʒən; ˈdʒɔːdʒən/ *adj* **1** Georgian buildings, furniture etc come from the 18th century, when Britain was ruled by the Kings George the First, Second, and Third〔英國18世紀建築物、家具等〕喬治一世至三世國王時期風格的: *an elegant Georgian townhouse* 一座典雅的喬治王朝時期風格的城市住宅 **2** connected with the country of Georgia, in the Caucasus 格魯吉亞的

ge·o·sta·tion·ar·y /ˏdʒioˋsteʃənɛrɪ; ˌdʒiːəʊˈsteɪʃənəri◂/ also 又作 **geosynchronous** *adj* a geostationary spacecraft or SATELLITE (1) goes around the Earth at the same speed as the Earth moves, so that it is always above the same place on the Earth〔宇宙飛船、衛星〕與地球旋轉同步的

ge·ra·ni·um /dʒəˋrenɪəm; dʒəˈreɪniəm/ *n* [C] a plant with red, pink, or white flowers and round leaves 天竺葵

ger·bil /ˋdʒɝbl̩; ˈdʒɜːbəl/ *n* [C] a small animal with fur, a tail and long back legs that is often kept as a pet 沙鼠

ge·ri·at·ric /ˌdʒɛrɪˋætrɪk; ˌdʒeriˈætrɪk◂/ *adj* **1** [only before noun 僅用於名詞前] connected with the medical care and treatment of old people 老年醫學的; 老年病學的: *The geriatric ward at the hospital is under threat of closure.* 這家醫院的老年病病房受到關閉的威脅。**2** *informal* too old to work properly or effectively【非正式】老朽的: *geriatric judges* 老朽的法官 | *another of those geriatric 1960s rock bands* 另一支老朽的20世紀60年代的搖滾樂隊

ge·ri·at·rics /ˌdʒɛrɪˋætrɪks; ˌdʒeriˈætrɪks/ *n* [U] the medical treatment and care of old people 老年醫學; 老年病學 —compare 比較 GERONTOLOGY —**geriatrician** /ˌdʒɛrɪəˋtrɪʃən; ˌdʒeriəˈtrɪʃən/ *n* [C]

germ /dʒɝm; dʒɜːm/ *n* [C] **1** *not technical* a bacterium (BACTERIA) that can make you ill【非術語】病菌: *This disinfectant kills all known germs.* 這種消毒劑能殺死所有的已知病菌。**2 the germ of an idea/theory/feeling etc** the early stage of an idea, feeling etc that may develop into something bigger and more important 思想的/理論的/感情等的萌芽: *This doctrine contains the germ of Hegel's later philosophy.* 這一學說包含着黑格爾後期哲學的萌芽。—see also 另見 WHEATGERM, GERM WARFARE

Ger·man /ˋdʒɝmən; ˈdʒɜːmən/ *n* **1** [C] someone who comes from Germany 德國人 **2** [U] the language of Germany, Austria, and parts of Switzerland 德語〔德國、奧地利和瑞士部分地區的語言〕—**German** *adj*

ger·mane /dʒɝˋmen; dʒɜːˈmeɪn/ *adj formal* an idea, remark etc that is germane to something is connected with it in an important and suitable way; RELEVANT【正式】關係密切而恰當的: **[+to]** *It's an interesting idea, but not really germane to the main argument.* 這是一種有趣的想法, 但跟主要論點沒有多大關係。| *economic solutions germane to the present-day environment* 與當今環境息息相關的經濟解決辦法

Ger·man·ic /dʒɝˋmænɪk; dʒɜːˈmænɪk/ *adj* **1** connected with the language family that includes German, Dutch, Swedish and English 日耳曼語系的〔包括德、荷、瑞典、英語諸語種〕**2** typical of Germany or the Germans 德國的, 德國人的

German mea·sles /ˌ·· ˈ··/ *n* [U] an infectious disease that causes red spots on your body, and can damage an unborn child; RUBELLA 風疹, 德國麻疹

German shep·herd /ˌ·· ˈ··/ *n* [C] a large dog rather like a WOLF that is often used by the police, for guarding property etc 德國牧羊犬, 阿爾薩斯狼狗; ALSATIAN *BrE*【英】—see picture at 參見 DOG[1] 圖

ger·mi·cide /ˋdʒɝməˌsaɪd; ˈdʒɜːmɪ̇saɪd/ *n* [C,U] a substance that kills BACTERIA 殺菌劑

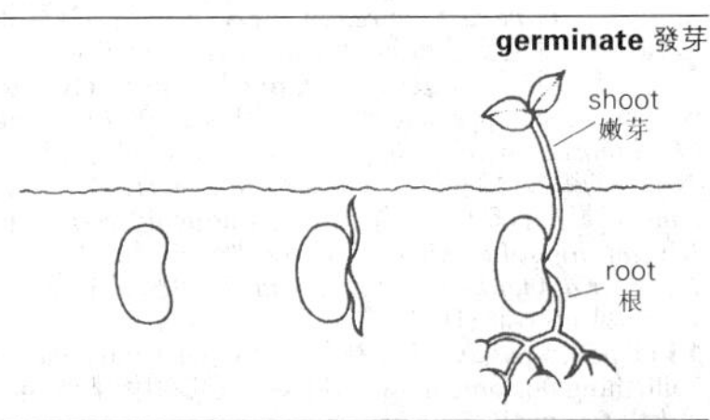

germinate 發芽

ger·mi·nate /ˋdʒɝməˌnet; ˈdʒɜːmɪ̇neɪt/ *v* **1** [I,T] if a seed germinates or if it is germinated, it begins to grow 發芽: *Carnation seeds will germinate at a low temperature.* 康乃馨的種子在低溫下會發芽。**2** [I] if an idea, feeling etc germinates, it begins to develop〔想法、感覺等〕開始形成, 萌芽: *The idea of forming a business partnership began to germinate in his mind.* 建立一種商業夥伴關係的想法開始在他的頭腦中萌發。—**germination** /ˌdʒɝməˋneʃən; ˌdʒɜːmɪ̇ˈneɪʃən/ *n* [U]

germ war·fare /ˌ· ˈ··/ *n* [U] the use of harmful BACTERIA in war to cause illness and death among the enemy 細菌戰

ge·ron·i·mo /dʒɪˋranɪmo; dʒəˈrɒnɪ̇məʊ/ *interjection* a shout used by children when jumping off a high place 傑羅尼莫!〔兒童從高處跳下時的喊聲〕

ger·on·toc·ra·cy /ˌdʒɛrənˋtakrəsɪ; ˌdʒerɒnˈtɒkrəsi/ *n* [C,U] government by old people, or a government that consists of old people 老人統治, 老人政府

ger·on·tol·o·gy /ˌdʒɛrənˋtalədʒɪ; ˌdʒerɒnˈtɒlədʒi/ *n* [U] the scientific study of old age and the changes it causes in the body 老年學 —compare 比較 GERIATRICS —**gerontologist** *n* [C] —**gerontological** /dʒəˌrantəˋladʒɪkl̩; dʒəˌrɒntəˈlɒdʒɪkəl◂/ *adj*

ger·ry·man·der·ing /ˋdʒɛrɪˌmændərɪŋ; ˈdʒerimændərɪŋ/ *n* [U] the practice of changing the size and borders of an area for election purposes, to deliberately give one group or party an unfair advantage over the others 不公正地劃分選區〔以使某團體或政黨在選舉中不公正地獲得有利地位〕

ger·und /ˋdʒɛrənd; ˈdʒerənd/ *n* [C] *technical* a noun in the form of a PRESENT PARTICIPLE, that describes an action or experience, such as 'shopping', in the sentence 'I like shopping'; VERBAL NOUN【術語】動名詞

ge·stalt /gəˋʃtalt; gəˈʃtɑːlt/ *n* [C] *technical* a whole thing that is different from all its parts put together and has qualities that are not present in any of its parts【術語】格式塔, 完形〔整體, 非其各個組成部分的相加, 具有後者所沒有的特性〕: *gestalt psychology* 格式塔心理學

ge·sta·po /gəˋstapo; geˈstɑːpəʊ/ *n* [C] the secret police force used by the state in Germany during the NAZI period 蓋世太保〔納粹時期德國的祕密警察〕

ges·ta·tion /dʒɛsˋteʃən; dʒeˈsteɪʃən/ *n* **1** [U] *technical* the process by which a child or young animal develops inside its mother's body before birth【術語】懷孕, 妊娠 **2** also 又作 **gestation period** [singular] **a)** *technical* the time during which a child or young animal develops inside its mother's body【術語】懷孕期, 妊娠期 **b)** the time it takes to develop an idea, plan etc before it is made known〔想法、計劃等的〕醞釀期

ges·tic·u·late /dʒɛsˋtɪkjəˌlet; dʒeˈstɪkjʊ̈leɪt/ *v* [I] to make movements with your arms and hands, usually while speaking, because you are excited, angry, or cannot think of the right words to use〔講話時〕做手勢: *Jane gesticulated wildly and shouted "Stop! Stop!"* 簡發狂似地做手勢, 喊着"停下! 停下!" —**gesticulation** /ˌdʒɛstɪkjəˋleʃən; dʒeˌstɪkjʊ̈ˈleɪʃən/ *n* [C,U]: *Wild gesticulations of the hands accompanied his speech.* 他講話時手發狂似地比劃着。

ges·ture[1] /ˋdʒɛstʃɚ; ˈdʒestʃə/ *n* **1** [C,U] a movement of 3
part of your body, especially your hands or head, to show what you mean or how you feel 手勢, 姿勢: *Jim raised his hands in a despairing gesture.* 吉姆舉起雙手, 做出絕望的手勢。| *This form of sign language is rich in gesture.* 這種形式的手語的手勢很豐富。**2** [C] something that you say or do, often something small, to show your feelings or intentions 表示, 姿態: *It was a kind gesture to offer to drive me home.* 提出要駕車送我回家是一種善意的表示。| **a gesture of friendship/goodwill/support etc** *The miners went on strike too, as a gesture of solidarity with the railway workers.* 礦工們也舉行罷工, 作為與鐵路工人團結的表示。—**gestural** *adj*

gesture[2] *v* [I always+adv/prep] to use a movement of your hand to tell someone something, or show them what you mean 用手勢示意: **[+to/towards etc]** *"It's somewhere over there." He gestured vaguely at a group of buildings.* "在那邊某個地方。"他含含糊糊地指着一羣樓房。| **gesture for sb to do sth** *The lieutenant gestured for Cook to enter his office.* 中尉用手勢示意庫克到他的辦公室去。

ge·sund·heit /gəˋzʊndhaɪt; gəˈzʊndhaɪt/ *interjection AmE* used to wish someone good health when they have just sneezed (SNEEZE[1] (1))【美】祝你健康〔對打噴嚏者的祝願〕

G

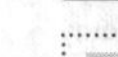

get /gɛt; get/ *v past tense* **got** /gɑt; gɒt/ *past participle* **got** *especially BrE*【尤英】**gotten** /ˈgɑtn̩; ˈgɒtn/ *especially AmE*【尤美】, *present participle* **getting**

① **RECEIVE/OBTAIN 收到/得到**
② **MOVE/GO/TRAVEL 移動/去/旅行**
③ **HAVE/OWN 有/擁有**
④ **BECOME/MAKE STH BECOME 成為/使某物成為**
⑤ **UNDERSTAND 理解**
⑥ **OTHER MEANINGS 其他意思**

① **RECEIVE/OBTAIN 收到/得到**

1 ►RECEIVE 收到◄ [T not in passive 不用被動態] to be given or receive something 收到: *Sharon always seems to get loads of mail.* 莎倫好像總是收到大量的郵件。| *Why do I always get socks for Christmas?* 為甚麼我在聖誕節總是收到襪子? | **get sth from/off sb** *Jordan says he got the drugs off a friend.* 喬丹說他從一個朋友那裡弄到毒品。| **get a shock/surprise/thrill etc** *He'll get a real shock when he sees the bill.* 他見到賬單時會大吃一驚。—see graph at 參見 RECEIVE 圖表

2 ►OBTAIN 獲得◄ [T] to obtain something 獲得, 得到: *Where did you get that painting?* 你是從哪裡弄到那幅畫的? | *There's no place in town you can get a good haircut.* 鎮上找不到一個理髮像樣的地方。| **get sb sth** *He's just popped out to get me some stamps.* 他剛跑出去幫我買些郵票。| **get sth for sb** *Gerrard was sent to get help for his sister.* 傑勒德被派去找人幫助他姐姐。—see 見 OBTAIN (USAGE)

3 ►GET BY BUYING 買到◄ [T] to buy something 買到: *That cat-basket? I got it on Harlow Market.* 那個貓籃? 我在哈洛市場買到的。| **get sth for $20/£100/50p etc** *You can't get a decent CD player for under $500.* 不到500美元無法買到一台不錯的CD播放機。| **get sth free/cheap etc** *Dee gets all her clothes cheap from charity shops.* 迪所有的衣服都是從慈善商店廉價購買的。| **get sb sth** *While you're out, could you get me a newspaper?* 你出去的時候能幫我買份報紙嗎? | **get sth for sb** *She got a ticket for Bobby as well.* 她也為博比買了一張票。—see graph at 參見 BUY 圖表

4 ►GET MONEY BY SELLING 售得◄ [T] to receive a particular amount of money for something when you sell it〔售賣某物〕得到...錢: *How much are you expecting to get for your house?* 你這幢房子打算賣多少錢? | **get £10/50p/$100 etc for** *Ian got $500 for that old car of his.* 伊恩的那輛舊車賣了500美元。

5 ►GET AN ILLNESS 患病◄ [T not in passive 不用被動態] to catch an illness, especially one that is not very serious 得〔病, 尤指不嚴重的疾病〕: *It's fairly unusual for adults to get measles.* 成年人得麻疹是相當不尋常的。| **get sth off/from** *He seems to have got a cold off one of the kids at playgroup.* 他似乎是從幼兒遊戲組的孩子那裡染上感冒的。

6 ►JOB 工作◄ [T] to be given or offered a new job or position, especially because of your own efforts 得到, 找到〔一份新的工作或職位, 尤指通過自己的努力〕: *Why don't you get yourself a job instead of lazing around all day?* 你為甚麼不為自己找份工作, 以免整天無所事事呢? | **get promotion** (=be offered a more important, better paid job than the one you are already doing) 得到提升, 得到晉升 *Some people have been here for years and have never got promotion.* 有些人已經在這裡好幾年了, 但從來沒晉升過。

7 ►EARN MONEY 掙錢◄ [T not in passive 不用被動態] to be earning a particular amount of money 掙得: *How much do you think Stewart gets?* 你認為斯圖爾特掙多少錢? | **get £3,000/£5/$100,000 etc a day/hour/year etc** *Tracey gets five dollars an hour canning fruit.* 特雷西裝水果罐頭每小時掙五美元。

② **MOVE/GO/TRAVEL 移動/去/旅行**

8 ►ARRIVE 到達◄ [I always+adv/prep] to arrive somewhere 到達: *What time will we get there?* 我們甚麼時候到那裡? | **get to/as far as/up to etc** *Next day they got to the camp, tired and hungry.* 第二天他們到達營地, 又累又餓。

9 get the train/bus/ferry etc to travel somewhere on a train, bus etc 搭乘火車/公共汽車/渡船等: *I'm getting the train home tonight.* 我今天晚上乘火車回家。

10 ►MOVE 移動◄ [I always+adv/prep] to move to or go somewhere 移動, 去: [**+out of/over/into etc**] *Get out of my house!* 從我家滾出去! | *Somehow, water had gotten in through the lining.* 不知怎麼地, 水從內襯滲了進來。

11 ►MAKE STH MOVE 使某物移動◄ [T] to make something move to a different place or position, especially with some difficulty〔尤指費力地〕移動: **get sth out/through/off etc** *How on earth are they going to get that piano down the stairs?* 他們究竟打算怎樣把那台鋼琴從樓梯搬下去?

③ **HAVE/OWN 有/擁有**

12 have got *especially BrE* [T] to possess or own something【尤英】擁有: *What kind of car has she got?* 她有甚麼樣的車? | *Darren's got a Master's Degree in Linguistics.* 達倫擁有語言學碩士學位。

13 [T] to have particular features or characteristics 具有〔某種特徵〕: *She's got an awful temper.* 她的脾氣很壞。| *Mr Williams is about 80, and he's got a shiny bald head.* 威廉斯先生大約80歲, 他的頭禿得油光閃亮。

④ **BECOME/MAKE STH BECOME 成為/使某物成為**

14 [linking verb 連繫動詞] to change from one state, feeling etc to another; become〔狀態、感情等的〕變成, 變得: **get angry/cold/upset etc** *When I tried to talk to him about it, he just got really angry.* 我想跟他談一談這件事時, 他便暴跳如雷。| *This is getting silly.* 這變得越來越荒謬了。| **get lost/trapped/ caught etc** (=to become lost, trapped etc) 迷路/被困/被捉等 *Just think of all those people getting killed out there.* 想想在那裡被屠殺的那些人們吧。| *Nick's getting married in September.* 尼克打算9月份結婚。| **get hot/cold/warm etc** *It's getting quite chilly out there.* 外邊已經很冷了。| *Eat your dinner before it gets cold.* 吃飯吧, 免得涼了。—see 見 BECOME (USAGE)

15 [T not in passive 不用被動態] to make someone or something do something 促使[某人或某物]做某事: **get sb/sth to do sth** *Get Chris to wash his jeans occasionally.* 讓克里斯偶爾洗洗牛仔褲。| **get sth doing sth** *I wonder if Frankie could get this video working.* 我不知道弗蘭基能否把這台錄像機修好。

16 get going/moving/cracking etc to make yourself do something or move somewhere more quickly 趕快開始; 趕快去: *What are we all waiting for? Let's get moving!* 我們還在等甚麼? 趕快走吧!

17 get to see/know/understand etc to gradually begin to see, know, understand etc 逐漸明白/知道/理解等: *I'm sure the kids will soon get to like each other.*

我相信這些孩子很快就會互相喜歡的。

18 get to do sth to be able to do something, especially when this is difficult or unusual 能做某事〔尤指困難或不尋常的事〕: *Since the divorce, he hardly ever gets to see Jenny.* 自從離婚之後，他就幾乎見不到詹妮了。

⑤ **UNDERSTAND 理解**

19 [T not in passive or progressive 不用被動態或進行式] *informal* to understand something【非正式】理解: **get the message/hint** (=to finally understand what someone has been trying to tell you, in an indirect way) 終於理解了某信息/某暗示 *I get the message – you just don't want me to come with you.* 我懂你的意思——你不想讓我和你一起去。| **get what/how/who etc** *She still doesn't get what the movie's about.* 她仍然不懂這部影片到底是想説些甚麼。

20 get it *spoken* to understand something, especially after it has been explained to you several times【口】懂得，明白，理解〔尤用於多次解釋之後〕: *Oh, the paper's supposed to go in this way up. I get it.* 啊，紙得這面朝上放進去，我明白了。

21 not get it *spoken* to not understand something, especially a joke【口】不懂，不明白〔尤指笑話〕: *He just didn't get it.* 他就是不明白。

⑥ **OTHER MEANINGS 其他意思**

22 ►BRING 帶來◄ [T] to bring someone or something back from somewhere; FETCH (1) 帶來: *Run upstairs and get a pillow.* 跑上樓去拿個枕頭來。| **get sb/sth from** *She's just gone to get the kids from Mary-Ann's house.* 她剛去瑪麗安家把孩子們帶回來。| **go and get (sb) sb/sth** *Go and get me a cloth, would you?* 去幫我拿塊布來，行嗎？

23 ►REACH A POINT 達到某一點◄ [I always+adv/prep] to reach a particular point or stage of something 到達: **get to/as far as/up to etc** *He's already got up to page 200.* 他已經讀到第200頁了。| *When you get to the end of the test paper, read it through.* 試卷做完後，再通讀一遍。

24 ►CLOTHES 衣服◄ **get sth on/off etc** to put a piece of clothing on or take it off 穿上衣服/脱去衣服等: *You'd better get those wet things off.* 你最好把那些濕衣服脱掉。

25 ►COOK 烹調◄ [T not in passive 不用被動態] to prepare a meal 做飯: *Who's going to get the dinner tonight?* 今天晚上誰做飯？| **get sb dinner/lunch etc** *He expects her to get him his dinner every night.* 他指望她每天晚上給他做飯。

26 you get *spoken* used to say that something happens or exists【口】〔用來表示某事確實發生、某物確實存在〕: *I didn't know you got tigers in Europe.* 我不知道歐洲有老虎。

27 get the door/phone etc *spoken* to answer the door, a telephone etc【口】開門/接電話等: *Can you get the door for me? I'm in the bath!* 請你幫我去開門，好嗎？我在洗澡！

28 you've got me there *spoken* used to say you do not know the answer to something【口】你把我難倒了: *"So how do you spell 'rhythm' then?" "You've got me there."* "那麼 rhythm 是怎麼拼寫的？""你把我難倒了。"

29 ►RADIO/TELEVISION 廣播/電視◄ [T not in passive or progressive 不用被動態或進行式] to be able to receive a particular radio signal, television station etc 收聽到；收看到: *Can you get satellite TV here?* 你這裡可以收看衛星電視嗎？

30 ►PUNISH 懲罰◄ [T not in passive or progressive 不用被動態或進行式] *spoken* to do something to harm or hurt someone who has harmed or hurt you【口】報復: **get sb for sth** *I'm going to get you for that!* 我要為那事找你報復！

31 ►ATTACK 攻擊◄ [T not in passive or progressive 不用被動態或進行式] to attack or harm someone 攻擊，傷害: *Good luck with the diving – and mind the sharks don't get you!* 祝你潛水運氣好——注意別讓鯊魚襲擊你！

32 get sth fixed/done/mended etc to spend time and effort fixing something, finishing a job etc 把某物修理好/把某事做完/把某物補好等: *It's about time we got the kitchen repainted.* 是重新油漆一遍廚房的時候了。

33 it (really) gets me *spoken* used to say that something really annoys you【口】這事（確實）使我氣惱: *It really gets me the way he leaves wet towels on the bathroom floor.* 他老是把濕毛巾扔在浴室的地板上，這確實令我生氣。

34 get you/him/her *spoken humorous* used to say that someone is trying to seem more important, clever etc than they really are【口，幽默】瞧瞧你/他/她〔用來表示某人好像有些自以為了不起〕: *Get you, talking about going on a luxury cruise!* 你別吹牛了，説甚麼乘豪華遊船出遊呢！

get about *BrE*【英】*phr v* [I] **1** to be able to go or travel to different places 四處走動，旅行: *She's eighty now, and doesn't get about much any more.* 她現在八十歲了，不再經常出門走動了。**2** if news or information gets about, it is told to a lot of people〔新聞或消息〕傳開: *I don't mind you knowing, but I don't really want it to get about.* 我不介意你知道，但我確實不想讓它傳開。**3** *informal* if someone gets about, they have sexual relationships with a lot of different people【非正式】與許多人發生性關係

get sth ↔ **across** *phr v* [T not in passive 不用被動態] to succeed in communicating ideas, information etc to someone else 將〔想法、信息〕傳達給某人: **get sth across to sb** *How can I get it across to you people how important this is?* 我怎麼做才能讓你們這些人理解這件事的重要性？

get along *phr v* [I] **1** if two or more people get along, they have a friendly relationship 相處融洽: *If you two are going to share a room, you'd better learn how to get along.* 如果你們兩個人要同住一間房，你們最好要學會如何融洽相處。| [**+with**] *I've always found him a bit difficult to get along with.* 我總是覺得他有點難於相處。**2** to progress in something you are doing 進展: *How's your granddaughter getting along at university?* 你的孫女在大學過得怎麼樣？**3** *spoken* to continue with something that you were doing before【口】繼續幹〔以前做的事〕: *I'd like to stay and chat, but I really must be getting along.* 我想留下來聊天，但我確實必須繼續幹活了。

get around *phr v* **1** [I] to be able to go or travel to different places 可以四處走動，旅行 **2** [I] if news or information gets around or gets round, a lot of people come to hear about it〔新聞或消息〕傳開: *It quickly got around that Joshua was back in town.* 喬舒亞已經回城的消息很快就傳開了。**3** [T **get around** sb] to gently persuade someone to do what you want by being nice to them 哄: *Freddie knows exactly how to get around his mother.* 弗雷迪很善於説服他的母親。**4** [T **get around** sth] to find a way of dealing with a problem, especially by trying to avoid it 應付[迴避]某問題: *Bill's rather stupidly promised her a week in Paris – I don't know how he's going to get around that one.* 比爾很不明智地答應她在巴黎待一週——我不知道他打算如何處理這個問題。

get around to *phr v* [T not in passive 不用被動態] to finally do something that you have been intending to do for some time 終於去做〔一直打算做的事〕: *I don't know when we'll get around to doing any more decorating.* 我不知道我們甚麼時候會進行更多的裝飾。

get at sb/sth *phr v* [T] **1** *informal* to criticize someone repeatedly in an annoying way【非正式】不斷地挖苦，一再批評: *She can't think why Moira's always getting at her.* 她不知道莫伊拉為甚麼老是挖苦她。**2** [not in passive 不用被動態] to seem to be saying something

G

that other people do not completely understand 暗指, 暗示: *What exactly are you getting at, Helen?* 你到底想說甚麼, 海倫? **3** to be able to reach something 及得到, 能夠着: *You have to use a ladder to get at the jars on the top shelves.* 你得用梯子才能夠着架子最高那幾格上的罐子。**4** to use threats to influence the decision of people who are involved in a court case 使用恐嚇來影響審判的結果: *At least eight members of the jury had been got at.* 陪審團至少有八個成員受到恐嚇。**5** to find something out, especially the truth about a situation 查明真相: **get at the truth/facts/information etc** *They're prepared to use any means possible to get at the truth.* 他們準備運用各種可能的手段來查明真相。

get away *phr v* [I] **1** to succeed in leaving a place, especially when this is not easy〔尤指費力地〕走開, 離開, 脱身: *There's a meeting after work, but I should be able to get away by seven.* 下班後要開會, 但我在7點前應該可以離開。**2** to escape from someone who is chasing you or trying to catch you 逃離, 逃避: *The three men got away in a stolen car.* 那三個人乘坐一輛偷來的車子逃掉了。| **[+from]** *Gillie managed to get away from the man and call the police.* 吉利設法逃離了那個人並且報了警。**3** *informal* to take a holiday away from the place you normally live【非正式】外出度假: *Will you manage to get away this summer?* 今年夏天你能夠外出度假嗎? **4 get away!** *BrE spoken* used to say you are very surprised by something or do not believe it【英口】〔用來表示你對某事十分驚訝或不相信某事〕: *"He's been invited to a garden party at Buckingham Palace." "Get away!"* "他被邀請參加白金漢宮的花園招待會。" "我才不信哩!" **5 the one that got away** something good that you nearly had or that nearly happened, but did not 幾乎到手的好東西, 幾乎發生的好事

get away from *phr v* [T not in passive 不用被動態] **1** to begin to talk about other things rather than the subject you are supposed to be discussing 離題: *I think we're getting away from the main issue.* 我想我們偏離了主題。**2 there's no getting away from** *spoken* used to say that a fact must be dealt with or considered【口】不得不面對[考慮]: *There's no getting away from it – we just can't afford to move house at the moment.* 我們眼下沒有錢搬家——這個問題無法迴避。**3 get away from it all** an expression used especially in advertisements meaning to have a relaxing holiday 過個輕鬆的假期〔尤用於廣告中〕: *get away from it all in sunny Barbados.* 在陽光燦爛的巴巴多斯過個輕鬆的假期。

get away with *phr v* [T not in passive 不用被動態] **a)** to not be caught or punished for something you have done wrong〔做錯事而〕不被發覺[不受懲罰]: *I don't know how they manage to get away with paying such low wages.* 我不知道為甚麼他們支付這麼低的工資仍然逍遙法外。| **get away with murder** *informal* (=repeatedly do something wrong, and not get caught or punished)【非正式】不斷做壞事而不被發覺[受懲罰] *Just because he's been working here a long time, he thinks he can get away with murder.* 就因為他已在這裡工作很久, 他認為自己可以做錯事而不受處罰。**b)** *spoken* to be able to do something, even though it is not the best thing to do【口】能做某事〔儘管這樣做並不恰當〕: *I think you could just about get away with wearing navy shoes with that dress.* 我看你穿那件連衣裙又穿一雙深藍色鞋子, 儘管不相配, 但問題不大。

get back *phr v* **1** [I] to return to a place 回到某地: *We'll probably get back at about nine.* 我們可能在9點左右回來。**2** [I+to] to start doing something again or talking about something again 繼續做某事[談某事]: *Let's get back to the main point of the discussion.* 我們還是回到討論的主要問題吧。**3** [T **get** sth ↔ **back**] to have something returned to you 取回, 拿回: *Did you get your books back?* 你把你的書拿回來了嗎? **4** [T **get** sb **back**] *informal* to do something to hurt or harm someone who has hurt or harmed you【非正式】報復: *Don't worry. I'll get her back for this!* 別擔心。我會就這件事向她報復的!

get back at sb *phr v* [T not in passive 不用被動態] to do something to hurt or harm someone who has hurt or harmed you 報復: *He only asked Jean for a date to get back at his ex-girlfriend.* 他只叫吉恩跟他約會, 以此來報復以前的女朋友。

get back to sb *phr v* [T] *especially spoken* used to say that you will try to talk to someone again later, especially on the telephone【尤口】過一會兒再與某人說話〔尤用於打電話〕: *I'm a bit busy at the moment – can I get back to you?* 我現在有點忙——我能過一會兒再給你打電話嗎?

get behind *phr v* [I+with] if you get behind with a job, payments, rent etc, you have not done or paid as much of it as you should have done by now〔工作、付款、房租等〕落後; 拖欠, 脱期: *Try not to get too far behind with your work.* 盡量使你的工作不要落在後面太遠。

get by *phr v* [I] to have enough money to buy the things you need, but no more〔錢〕勉強夠花: *Her old age pension gives her barely enough to get by.* 她的養老金僅僅能供她勉強過活。| **get by on £5/$20/$100 etc** *With four kids to feed, Josie gets by on just $75 a week.* 喬西得供養四個孩子, 僅靠每星期75美元過活。

get down *phr v* **1** [T not in passive 不用被動態 **get** sb **down**] to gradually make someone feel unhappy and tired 漸漸使〔某人〕不高興[疲倦]: *All this waiting and delay is really getting her down.* 這樣的等待和耽擱實在讓她受不了。**2** [T **get** sth ↔ **down**] to write something, especially something that someone is saying 筆錄, 記下〔尤指某人說的話〕: *a group of reporters trying to get down every word he said* 想記下他的一言一語的一羣記者 **3** [T] to succeed in swallowing something 吞下某物 **4** [I] *BrE* an expression used especially by children meaning to leave the table after a meal【英】餐後離開餐桌〔尤為兒童所用〕

get down to sth *phr v* [T] to finally start doing something that needs a lot of time or energy 終於開始做〔需要花費許多時間或精力的事〕: *After Christmas I'm going to get down to some serious job-hunting.* 聖誕節後我打算開始認真地找工作了。| **get down to doing sth** *Isn't it time you got down to marking those papers?* 難道不是你應該評卷的時候了?

get in *phr v* **1** [I] to succeed in entering a place 進入某地: *They arrived at the stadium in good time, but they still couldn't get in.* 他們老早就到了體育場, 但是仍然進不去。**2** [I] if a train, plane etc gets in at a particular time, that is the time it arrives〔火車、飛機等〕到達: *What time does the bus get in?* 公共汽車甚麼時候到? **3** [I] to be elected to a position of political power 當選〔政治性職務〕: *It's unlikely the Liberal Democrats will get in again.* 自由民主黨再次當選是不太可能的。**4** [I] to arrive home 到家: *I'll phone her as soon as I get in.* 我一到家就會給她打電話。**5** [T **get** sth ↔ **in**] to gather together something such as crops and bring them to a sheltered place 收割: *The whole village was involved with getting the harvest in.* 整個村莊都在收割莊稼。**6** [T **get** sb ↔ **in**] to ask someone to come to your home or workplace to do a job, especially to repair something 請…來幫忙[修理]: *We'll have to get the engineer in.* 我們得把工程師請來幫忙。**7** [T **get** sth **in**] to send something to a particular place or give it to a particular person 遞送, 送交: *Please can you get your assignments in by Thursday.* 請你們在星期四以前把作業交上來。| *We have to get an insurance claim in as quickly as possible.* 我們得盡快把保險索賠要求交出去。**8** [I] to succeed in getting a place at a university, college etc 被錄取: *How many of your students got in this year?* 你們今年有多少學生考上大學?

get in on *phr v* [T not in passive 不用被動態] *informal* to become involved in something that other people are doing or planning【非正式】參與〔活動〕: **get in on**

the act (=get involved in something exciting, interesting, important etc) 參加: *Now the Republicans are hoping to get in on the act.* 現在共和黨希望能參與進來。

get in with sb *phr v* [T] *informal* to become friendly with someone, especially someone who could be helpful to you in some way【非正式】與…拉上關係〔尤指對自己有用的人〕: *He spends all his time trying to get in with the boss.* 他把所有的時間都用來巴結老闆。

get into *phr v* **1 what's got into sb** *spoken* used to express surprise that someone is behaving very differently from the way they usually behave【口】(某人) 中了甚麼邪〔用來對某人行為異常表示驚訝〕: *I don't know what's got into Danny – he's suddenly started doing all the cooking and cleaning.* 我不知道丹尼怎麼回事——他突然開始一手包辦做飯和打掃衛生的工作。**2 get (sb) into a temper/state etc** to become angry or make someone angry, become upset or make someone upset etc (使) 發脾氣/緊張不安等: *Don't get into a mood about it.* 別為這發脾氣。**3 get (sb) into trouble/difficulties etc** to do something that causes trouble for yourself or for someone else (使某人) 陷入麻煩/(使某人) 遇到困難等: *That's another fine mess you've got me into.* 你讓我又一次陷入難以擺脱的困境。**4** [T not in passive 不用被動態] to start doing something habitually 染上〔習慣〕, 習慣於: **get into the habit/way/routine etc of** *He had gotten into the habit of walking home through the park.* 他養成了步行穿過公園走回家的習慣。**5** [T not in passive 不用被動態] *informal* to begin to be interested in an activity or subject【非正式】開始對〔某種活動或某個話題〕感興趣: *Lots of my friends are getting into Green politics.* 我的許多朋友開始對環保政治感興趣。**6 cannot get into** *informal* if you cannot get into clothes, they are too small for you【非正式】〔衣服太小〕穿不進去

get off *phr v* **1** [I] to start a journey 開始旅行, 出發: *They're planning to get off by midday.* 他們正打算中午前出發。**2** [T **get** sth **off**] to send a letter, parcel etc by mail 郵寄, 寄出: *I'll have to get this letter off by tonight.* 我得在今晚前把這封信寄出去。**3** [I] if a criminal gets off, they get little or no official punishment for their crime〔罪犯〕逃脱 (應得的) 懲罰: *Financial fraudsters often get off because the details of the case are too complex to be understood by juries.* 金融詐騙者經常能逃脱懲罰, 因為陪審團無法弄懂異常複雜的案情。**4** [T **get** sb **off** sth] to help someone avoid being punished for a crime or something they have done wrong 幫助〔某人〕逃避懲罰: *I'll pay anything you ask if you manage to get her off.* 要是你能讓她免受懲罰, 你要多少錢我就給你多少錢。**5** [I **get** sb **off**] to succeed in making someone, especially a baby, go to sleep 使入睡〔尤指嬰兒〕: *Guy's upstairs trying to get the baby off.* 蓋伊在樓上哄孩子睡覺。| **get sb off to sleep** *Has she got the baby off to sleep yet?* 她把孩子哄睡着了嗎? **6** [I] *AmE informal* to have an ORGASM【美, 非正式】達到性高潮 **7** [I,T] to finish work and leave your workplace at the end of the day 下班: *What time do you get off work?* 你甚麼時候下班? | **[+at]** *Shelley gets off at five-thirty.* 謝利五點半下班。**8 Get off!** *spoken* used to tell someone to stop touching you or to keep away from something【口】滾開!〔用來叫某人不要觸摸你或不要動某物〕**9 tell sb where to get off** *spoken* to tell someone that they are asking you for too much or are behaving in a way you will not accept【口】叫某人規矩些, 教訓某人: *"She expects me to look after her kids all the time." "If I were you I'd tell her where to get off."* "她指望我隨時照看她的孩子。" "要是我, 我就要她別太過分了。"

get off on sth *phr v* [T not in passive 不用被動態] *informal* to become excited by something, especially sexually excited【非正式】因…感到興奮〔尤指性興奮〕

get off to *phr v* [T not in passive 不用被動態] to start to do something in a particular way〔以某種方式〕開始〔做某事〕: **get off to a good/bad start** *As far as school goes, Johnnie has got off to an extremely good start.* 就學業來説, 約翰尼已經有了一個非常好的開端。

get off with *phr v* [T not in passive 不用被動態] *informal* to start a sexual relationship with someone【非正式】與〔某人〕發生性關係: *She spent the whole evening trying to get off with Phil.* 她花了一整個晚上想與菲爾上牀。

get on *phr v*

1 [I] *especially BrE* if two or more people get on, they have a friendly relationship with each other【尤英】友好相處: **[+with]** *How does Gina get on with her colleagues?* 吉娜與她的同事相處得怎麼樣?

2 ►PROGRESS 進展◄ [I] to make progress in something you are doing; GET ALONG (2) 取得進展, 進步: *He's new here, but he seems to be getting on fine.* 他是新來的, 但他好像挺適應的。

3 be getting on a) if time is getting on, it is getting late〔時間〕晚了: *Tell Rea to hurry – it's getting on.* 告訴雷快點——時候不早了。**b)** *informal* if someone is getting on, they are getting old【非正式】〔人〕變老: *We're both getting on now.* 我們倆現在都老了。

4 ►CONTINUE DOING STH 繼續做某事◄ [I] to continue with something you were doing before 繼續做 **[+with]** *Get on with your work!* 繼續幹你的工作吧!

5 ►ABLE TO DO STH 能做某事◄ [I] to be able to do something, in spite of problems or difficulties〔儘管有問題、有困難〕能對付下去: *I don't know how we'll manage to get on without you.* 沒有你我不知道我們怎麼能維持下去。

6 get it on *AmE* to have sex【美】發生性關係, 性交: *Do you think those two have got it on yet?* 你認為那兩個人發生了性關係嗎?

7 Get on with it! *spoken* used to tell someone to hurry【口】快一點!: *Will you lot stop messing around and get on with it!* 你們可否停止瞎胡鬧, 快一點幹呢?

8 let sb get on with it a) *spoken* used to say that you do not care what someone does, even though it might have bad results【口】任憑某人做他的事: *Well, if she wants to go ahead and ruin her career, let her get on with it.* 好吧, 如果她執意這樣幹下去, 把自己的事業毀掉, 那也就隨她吧。**b)** to let someone do something without your help or advice 讓某人自己去做某事: *Why can't my parents ever just let me get on with it?* 為甚麼我的父母不能就讓我自己去做呢?

9 Get on/along with you! *old-fashioned spoken* used to say you do not believe what someone has said【過時, 口】別胡扯!

be getting on for *phr v* [T not in passive 不用被動態] **be getting on for 90/10 o'clock/2,000 etc** to be almost that age, time, number etc 接近 90 歲/10 點鐘/2,000 等: *Mrs McIntyre must be getting on for 90 by now.* 麥金太爾女士現在恐怕接近 90 歲了。| *They paid getting on for $100,000 for it.* 他們為此付了將近 10 萬美元。

get onto *phr v* [T not in passive 不用被動態] **1** to speak or write to someone, especially someone you want to help you 對…講; 寫信給; 與…接觸: *I'm afraid I can't help you – you'd better get onto the Foreign Office.* 恐怕我無法幫助你——你最好同外交部聯繫。**2** to find out about someone who has been doing something wrong 發覺, 識破〔某人進行不良勾當〕: *Why did the police fail to get onto this gang earlier?* 警方為甚麼沒有早些發覺這夥罪犯呢? **3** to be elected as a member of a committee, a political organization etc 當選〔委員會、政治組織等的〕成員: *Very few women ever get onto industry's controlling bodies.* 很少有婦女能被選為工業管理機構的成員。**4** to begin to talk about a subject after you have been discussing something else〔討論其他事情後〕開始談論〔某新話題〕: *After a few minutes they got onto the subject of the election.* 幾分鐘後他們開始談論選舉這個話題。

get out *phr v* **1** [I] to escape from somewhere 逃離,

G

逃走: *How on earth did the dog manage to get out?* 那條狗究竟是怎麼逃走的? | **[+of]** *No-one's ever gotten out of this jail.* 從來沒有人從這所監獄裡逃走過。**2** [T **get** sb **out**] to help someone escape from or leave somewhere 幫〔某人〕逃跑[離開某地]: *Asylum seekers have appealed to the President to help get them out.* 尋求避難的人呼籲總統幫助他們離開。**3** [I] if information gets out, a lot of people know about it though it is meant to be secret〔本應保密的消息〕泄露: *We have to make absolutely certain that none of this gets out.* 我們得絕對保證消息一點也不會泄露出去。| **get out that** *It's bound to get out that he's retiring soon.* 他很快將退休的消息肯定會泄露出去。**4** [T **get** sth ↔ **out**] to succeed in producing or publishing something 生產, 公布, 出版, 發表: *They said they'd try and get the catalog out by the end of the month.* 他們說他們會盡量在月底前把目錄印好。**5** [T **get** sth ↔ **out**] to succeed in saying something, especially when this is very difficult 說出〔尤指難以啟齒之事〕: *I wanted to tell him I loved him, but couldn't get the words out.* 我想告訴他我愛他, 但難以說出口。

get out of *phr v* [T not in passive 不用被動態] **1** to avoid doing something you have promised to do or are supposed to do 逃避, 擺脫〔承諾或應該做的事〕: *See if you can get out of that meeting tomorrow.* 看看你明天是否能不去開那個會。| **get out of doing sth** *Danny's always trying to get out of taking the kids to school.* 丹尼總是想逃避送小孩上學的責任。**2** [**get** sb **out of**] to help someone to avoid doing something they are supposed to do 幫〔某人〕逃避[擺脫]〔本應做的事情〕: *Wendy wants you to try and get her out of classes tomorrow.* 温迪要你想辦法幫她免掉明天的課。| **get sb out of doing sth** *OK, I'll see if I can get you out of having to testify.* 好吧, 我來看看是否能幫你免於作證。**3** [**get** sth **out of** sb] to force or persuade someone to tell you something or give you something 迫使[勸說]〔某人〕說出[拿出] **4** [**get** sth **out of** sth] to gain pleasure or enjoyment from something 從...中得到快樂[享受]: *I don't know what people get out of listening to deafeningly loud music.* 我不知道人們從震耳欲聾的音樂中得到些甚麼樂趣。

get over *phr v* **1 a)** [T not in passive 不用被動態] to get well again after an illness 從〔疾病中〕康復過來: *She's still trying to get over that bout of flu she had.* 她還在努力從那場流感中復元過來。**b)** to begin to feel better after an upsetting emotional experience〔從令人心煩意亂的感情經歷之後〕恢復: *Some people never really get over the early death of a parent.* 有些人永遠無法徹底克服父親或母親早逝所帶來的傷痛。**2** [T **get** sth ↔ **over**] to succeed in communicating ideas, information etc to other people 把...說清楚, 使理解: *There's no point in having brilliant ideas unless you can get them over.* 有了好的想法如果不傳達給別人也就沒有意義了。**3** [T **get** sth **over**] to do and finish something difficult that you have to do 完成〔必須做的某困難事情〕: *Angela says she'll be in touch when she gets her exams over.* 安傑拉說她考試完畢就和你聯繫。| **get sth over with** *I'll speak first if you like – I'd rather get it over with quickly.* 如果你願意, 我想先說 —— 我倒希望能快點結束這件事。**4** [**get over** sth] to successfully deal with problems, difficulties etc 成功地處理問題、困難等: *Once we've got over the first few months, we should be making a reasonable profit.* 我們只要把頭幾個月對付過去, 就會開始獲取相當不錯的利潤。**5 can't/couldn't get over** *spoken* used to say that you are very surprised, shocked, or amused by something【口】對...十分驚訝; 對...感到十分好笑: *Carrie couldn't get over how thin and pale he looked.* 他看上去又瘦又蒼白, 卡里感到十分驚訝。| **I just can't/couldn't get over it** *They suddenly fired all the company directors. I just can't get over it.* 他們突然開除了公司所有的經理。我感到十分驚訝。

get round *phr v BrE*【英】**1** [I] if news or information gets round, it is told to a lot of people〔新聞或消息〕傳開: **get round that** *It wasn't long before it got round that Tracey was going out with James.* 不久消息就傳開了, 說是特雷西已經開始和詹姆斯交往。**2** [T **get round** sth] to find a way of dealing with a problem, especially by trying to avoid it 解決; 避免; 迴避: *There's no way your mother can stay here – we'll just have to get round it somehow.* 你的母親絕對不能待在這裡 —— 我們要想個甚麼辦法解決這個問題。**3** [T **get round** sb] to gently persuade someone to do what you want by being nice to them〔用友善的態度〕說服 (某人): *He's determined he won't give in – see if you can get round him.* 他決定不妥協, 看看你是否能說服他。

get round to *phr v* [T not in passive 不用被動態] *BrE* to finally do something that you have been intending to do for some time, but have not because you were too busy, too lazy etc【英】終於去做〔久想做的事〕: *I haven't even got around to unpacking from my holiday yet!* 我度假回來後連行李都還沒有打開!

get through *phr v* **1** [T not in passive 不用被動態] to come to the end of a difficult or unpleasant experience or period of time 消磨, 度過〔艱難或不愉快的〕一段時間: *It's going to be hard to get through the next couple of days.* 度過未來這幾天時間是很難的。**2** [I,T] to pass a test, examination etc 通過〔考試〕: *I'm afraid your daughter failed to get through her mid-term exams.* 很遺憾你的女兒沒有通過期中考試。**3** [T **get** sb/sth **through** sth] to make sure someone or something passes an examination, test etc 保證〔某人或某事〕通過審查[考試]: *You'll never get that old car through its smog test.* 你永遠也無法保證使那輛舊車能通過煙霧測驗。**4** [T **get** ↔ sth **through**] to succeed in having a plan, new law etc approved by an official group 使〔計劃、新法律等〕獲得批准[通過]: *Once again we failed to get the Bill through Parliament.* 我們又一次未能使該法案在議會通過。**5** [I] to succeed in reaching someone by telephone〔電話〕與某人聯繫上: **[+to]** *At last I managed to get through to one of the managers.* 我終於用電話與一名經理聯繫上。**6** [T **get through** sth] to use a lot of something or spend a lot of money 花費, 耗費: *He gets through at least $500 every weekend.* 他每個週末至少花 500 美元。

get through to *phr v* [I,T **get** sth **through to** sb] to succeed in making someone understand something, especially when this is difficult〔尤指困難地〕使 (某人) 明白: **get it through to sb (that)** *You must try and get it through to them that this is no joke.* 你必須設法使他們明白這不是開玩笑的。

get to sb *phr v* [T] *informal* to make you feel very annoyed or upset【非正式】使...生氣[煩惱]: *I know they're being unfair, but don't let them get to you.* 我知道他們很不公平, 但你不必為他們生氣。—see 見 REACH (USAGE)

get together *phr v* **1** [I] if two or more people get together, they meet each other 聚集, 相聚: *We must get together some time for a drink.* 我們甚麼時候必須聚一聚喝一杯。| **[+with]** *It's ages since I got together with the gang from school.* 我已經很久沒有跟學校那幫人相聚了。**2** [I] if two people get together, they start a romantic or sexual relationship 開始談情說愛, 開始有性關係: *Those two should get together – they have a lot in common.* 那兩個人應該開始談情說愛了 —— 他們多投契。**3 get yourself together** to begin to be in control of your life, your emotions etc 自制; 振作; 集中心思: *She needs a bit of time to get herself together.* 她需要一點時間才能使自己振作起來。**4 get it together** *spoken*【口】**a)** [I] to begin to be in control of your life, your emotions etc 自制; 振作; 集中心思: *If this team doesn't get it together by next month, we'll all be fired.* 如果這個隊到下個月還不振作起來, 我們都將被開除。**b)** if two people get it together, they begin to develop a romantic or sexual relationship with each other 開始談情說愛,

開始有性關係

get up *phr v* **1** [I] to wake up and get out of your bed after sleeping, especially in the morning〔尤指早晨〕起牀: *What time did you get up this morning?* 你今天早晨甚麼時候起牀的? **2** [T **get** sb **up**] to make someone wake up and get out of their bed, especially in the morning 叫…起牀: *Get me up at seven, would you?* 七點叫我起牀, 好嗎? **3** [T] to stand up 起立, 站起來: *No, please don't get up.* 不, 請不要站起來。**4** [I] if a wind or storm gets up, it starts and gets stronger〔風、暴風雨〕開始並增強 **5** [T **get** sth **up**] to organize something 組織: *She's getting a collection up for Sue's birthday.* 她在為蘇的生日組織募捐。**6 get sb up as** *BrE* to dress someone as someone or something else【英】把〔某人〕打扮[裝扮]成: *He arrived at the party got up as Count Dracula.* 他打扮成吸血鬼的模樣來參加聚會。**7 get it up** *informal* to get an ERECTION (1)【非正式】勃起 **8 get up speed/steam** to begin to move or travel faster 加速前進

get up to *phr v* [T] to do something, especially something slightly bad 幹〔尤指輕微的壞事〕: *Go upstairs and see what the kids are getting up to.* 上樓看看孩子們在搗甚麼亂。

get·a·way /ˈgɛtəˌwe; ˈgetəweɪ/ *n* [C] **make a getaway** to escape from somewhere after doing something criminal, or to get away from an unpleasant situation 逃跑: *The thieves made a getaway through a downstairs window.* 盜賊從樓下的一扇窗子逃走了。| **getaway car** (=a car used by criminals to escape after a crime) 罪犯做案後逃逸用的汽車

get-go /ˈ· ·/ *n* **from the get-go** *AmE informal* from the beginning【美, 非正式】從一開始: *From the get-go, I knew these tapes were special.* 一開始我就知道這些磁帶不一般。

get-to·geth·er /ˈ· ·ˌ·· / *n* [C] a friendly informal meeting or party 聚會; 聯歡會: *a family get-together* 家庭聚會

get·up /ˈgɛtˌʌp; ˈgetʌp/ *n* [C] *informal* a set of clothes, especially strange or unusual clothes【非正式】〔尤指奇特或不尋常的〕服裝: *I hardly recognized him in that getup!* 他穿上奇裝異服, 我幾乎認不出來了!

get-up-and-go /ˌ· · · ˈ·/ *n* [U] *informal* energy, and determination to do things【非正式】幹勁, 雄心: *He was the only candidate who had some get-up-and-go.* 他是唯一的一個有幹勁的候選人。

gew·gaw /ˈgjugɔ; ˈgjuːgɔː/ *n* [C] a cheap brightly coloured piece of jewellery or decoration〔便宜花哨的〕珠寶, 裝飾品

gey·ser /ˈgaɪzɚ; ˈgiːzə/ *n* [C] **1** a natural spring of hot water that sometimes rises suddenly into the air 間歇噴泉 **2** a machine fixed to a wall over a bath or SINK and used for heating water in some British houses〔一些英國家庭裡的〕熱水器

ghast·ly /ˈgæstlɪ; ˈgɑːstli/ *adj* **1** a ghastly situation, person, experience etc is one that you do not like or enjoy at all 討厭的, 令人不快的: *What ghastly weather!* 多麼糟糕的天氣! | *I hope they don't bring their ghastly children with them.* 我希望他們不會帶他們那些討厭的的小孩來。| *It was absolutely ghastly.* 絕對的令人厭惡。**2** making you very frightened, upset or shocked 可怕的, 恐怖的: *a ghastly accident* 可怕的事故 **3 look/feel ghastly** to look or feel ill, upset, or unhappy 看上去/感覺有病[煩惱; 不高興]: *Are you alright? You look ghastly!* 你沒事吧? 你臉色很不好! —**ghastliness** *n* [U]

ghat /gɔt; gɔːt/ *n* [C] *IndE & PakE*【印度和巴基斯坦】**1** a set of steps leading down to a river or lake〔通向河邊或湖邊的〕台階 **2** a place where dead bodies are burnt in a ceremony 舉行火葬儀式的地方

ghee /gi; giː/ *n* [U] melted butter made from the milk of a cow or BUFFALO, used in Indian cooking〔乳牛或水牛奶製成用來做菜的〕酥油, 奶油〔用於印度烹調〕

gher·kin /ˈgɝkɪn; ˈgɜːkɨn/ *n* [C] a small type of CUCUMBER that has been preserved in VINEGAR〔醋醃的〕小黃瓜

ghet·to /ˈgɛto; ˈgetəʊ/ *n plural* **ghettos** *or* **ghettoes** [C] **1** a part of a city where people of a particular race or class live separately from the main population, usually in bad conditions〔通常條件很差的〕少數民族聚居區, 貧民區 **2** a part of a city where Jews were forced to live in former times〔以前的〕猶太人居住區: *She was born in a Polish ghetto.* 她出生在一個波蘭的猶太人區。

ghetto blast·er /ˈ·· ˌ··/ *n* [C] *informal* a large radio and TAPE RECORDER that can be carried around, and is often played very loudly in public places【非正式】便攜式大型收錄機, 手提錄音機〔通常在公共場所大聲播放〕; BOOM BOX *AmE*【美】

ghet·to·ize *v* also 又作 **-ise** *BrE*【英】/ˈgɛtoaɪz; ˈgetəʊaɪz/ [T] **1** to force people to live in a ghetto 強迫人們居住在聚居區[貧民區] **2** to make part of a town become a ghetto 使成為聚居區[貧民區]

ghi /gi; giː/ *n* [U] another spelling of GHEE ghee 的另一種拼法

ghost[1] /gost; gəʊst/ *n* [C] **1** the spirit of a dead person that some people think they can feel or see in a place 鬼, 幽靈: *The ghosts of past landlords are said to haunt this pub.* 據說過去店主的幽靈在這家酒吧出沒。| **ghost story** *We used to scare each other by telling ghost stories at night.* 我們過去經常在晚上講鬼故事來相互嚇人。—see also 另見 HOLY GHOST **2 the ghost of a smile/sound etc** a smile etc that is so slight you are not sure it happened 一絲微笑/一點兒聲音等: *He had the ghost of a smile on his lips.* 他嘴角掛着一絲微笑。**3** a GHOST WRITER 代筆人, 捉刀人 **4** a second image that is not clear, especially on a television picture〔尤指電視圖像〕重像, 重影 **5 give up the ghost** *humorous*【幽默】**a)** to die 死 **b)** if a machine gives up the ghost, it does not work any more and cannot be repaired〔機器〕報廢: *My car's finally given up the ghost – I'm selling it for scrap.* 我的車終於報廢了 —— 我正打算把它當廢鐵賣掉。**6 not a ghost of a chance** not even a slight chance of doing something, or of something happening 毫無機會: *There's not a ghost of a chance of finding the missing child now.* 現在要找到那個丟失的小孩完全沒有可能。

ghost[2] *v* [T] to write something as a GHOST WRITER 代人寫

ghost·ly /ˈgostlɪ; ˈgəʊstli/ *adj* slightly frightening and seeming to be connected with ghosts or spirits 幽靈似的, 像鬼似的: *a ghostly stare* 有點嚇人的凝視 —**ghostly** *adv*: *ghostly pale* 臉色蒼白得可怕 —**ghostliness** *n* [U]

ghost town /ˈ· ·/ *n* [C] a town that used to have a lot of people living and working in it, but now has very few 被廢棄的城鎮

ghost train /ˈ· ·/ *n* [C] a small train ride at a British FUNFAIR, that is designed to frighten you by taking you through a dark place full of SKELETON*s* (1) and things that jump out at you〔英國遊樂場裡的〕魔鬼列車, 幽靈列車〔列車載着遊客在黑暗中行駛, 到處都是骷髏和怪物向你撲來〕

ghost writ·er /ˈ· ˌ··/ *n* [C] someone who writes a book or story for another person who then says it is their own work 代筆人, 捉刀人 —**ghost-write** *v* [T]

ghoul /gul; guːl/ *n* [C] **1** an evil spirit in stories that takes bodies from graves and eats them 食屍鬼〔傳說中從墳墓裡挖屍體吃的魔鬼〕**2** someone who gets pleasure from unpleasant things such as accidents that shock other people 從恐怖事件中取樂的人 —**ghoulish** *adj* —**ghoulishness** *n* [U]

GHQ /ˌdʒi etʃ ˋkju; ˌdʒiː eɪtʃ ˈkjuː/ *n* [U] General Headquarters; the place that a large military operation is controlled from 總司令部, 軍事行動指揮所

GI /ˋdʒi ˋaɪ; ˌdʒiː ˈaɪ/ *n* [C] a soldier in the US army, especially during the Second World War〔尤指第二次世界大戰時的〕美國兵

gi·ant[1] /ˋdʒaɪənt; ˈdʒaɪənt/ *adj* [only before noun 僅用於

名詞前] extremely big and much bigger than other things of the same type 巨大的，特大的：*a giant sized box of detergent* 特大盒的洗滌劑 | *a giant supermarket just outside town* 城外的一家特大超市

giant² *n* [C] **1** a very tall, strong man in children's stories who is often bad and cruel〔兒童故事中的〕兇惡巨人 **2** a very large, successful company 興旺的大公司：*the German chemicals giant, BASF* 德國化學產品巨頭巴斯夫公司 **3** a very big man 身材特別高大的人，巨人 **4** someone who is very good at doing something 偉人；卓越人物：*Scorcese is a giant of the American cinema.* 史高西斯是美國電影界的巨擘。

gi·ant·ess /ˈdʒaɪəntɪs; ˈdʒaɪəntes/ *n* [C] an extremely tall strong woman in children's stories who is often bad and cruel〔兒童故事中的〕兇殘女巨人

giant kil·ler /ˈ·· ˌ··/ *n* [C] *BrE* a person, sports team etc that defeats a much stronger opponent【英】能打敗強大對手的人[運動隊]

giant pan·da /ˌ·· ˈ··/ *n* [C] a PANDA (1) 大熊貓

gib·ber /ˈdʒɪbɚ; ˈdʒɪbə/ *v* [I] to speak quickly in a way that no one can understand, especially because you are very frightened or shocked〔尤指由於害怕或受驚而〕說話急促不清：*The little boy was soaking wet and gibbering with agitation.* 這小男孩渾身濕透，激動得語無倫次。

gib·ber·ing /ˈdʒɪbərɪŋ; ˈdʒɪbərɪŋ/ *adj BrE* so frightened, shocked, or excited that you speak quickly in a way that no one can understand【英】〔因害怕、受驚或激動而〕說話急促不清的：**a gibbering wreck** (=someone who is very shocked or frightened) 受驚的人，被嚇壞的人

gib·ber·ish /ˈdʒɪbərɪʃ; ˈdʒɪbərɪʃ/ *n* [U] something you write or say that has no meaning, or is very difficult to understand 胡扯，令人費解的話：*You're talking gibberish!* 你在胡扯！

gib·bet /ˈdʒɪbɪt; ˈdʒɪbɪ̈t/ *n* [C] a wooden frame on which criminals were hanged (HANG¹ (3)) in the past with a rope around their neck 絞刑架

gib·bon /ˈgɪbən; ˈgɪbən/ *n* [C] a small animal like a monkey, with long arms and no tail, that lives in trees in Asia 長臂猿[猴]

gibe /dʒaɪb; dʒaɪb/ *n* [C] another spelling of JIBE jibe 的另一種拼法

gib·lets /ˈdʒɪblɪts; ˈdʒɪblɪ̈ts/ *n* [plural] the inside parts of a bird that can be eaten, and are taken out before the bird is cooked〔可食用的家禽的〕內臟

gid·dy¹ /ˈgɪdi; ˈgɪdi/ *adj* **1** feeling slightly sick and unable to balance, because everything seems to be moving; DIZZY (1) 頭暈的，眩暈的：*Just watching those kids spinning makes me feel giddy.* 僅僅是看那些孩子轉圈就使我頭暈。**2 be giddy with sth** to be very happy because something good has happened 因〔某事而〕開心，高興：*Amanda was giddy with success.* 阿曼達因成功而飄飄然。**3** [only before noun 僅用於名詞前] making you feel as if you may fall 令人頭暈的，令人眩暈的：*a giddy height* 令人眩暈的高度 **4** *old-fashioned* silly and not interested in serious things【過時】輕率的，輕浮的：*Fiona's very pretty but a bit giddy.* 菲奧納很漂亮，但是有點輕浮。—**giddily** *adv* —**giddiness** *n* [U]

giddy² *v*

giddy up [I] used to command a horse to go faster 快走，趕快〔對馬的吆喝〕

gift /gɪft; gɪft/ *n* [C]

1 ►OBJECT 物體◄ something that you give someone on a special occasion or to thank them 禮物：*The earrings were a gift from my aunt.* 這雙耳環是我姑姑送給我的禮物。| **make sb a gift of sth** *Grandma made me a gift of her silver.* 祖母把她的銀餐具作為禮物送給我。| **free gift** *Enjoy a free gift with any purchase of $20 or more.* 購物滿20美元可獲贈禮品一份。

2 ►ABILITY 能力◄ a natural ability; TALENT (1) 天賦，才能：*Donne's poetic gift* 多恩的詩才 | **[+for]** *Dee has a gift for making everyone feel at ease.* 迪有一種能讓大家放鬆的才能。—see also 另見 GIFTED

3 a gift *BrE informal* something that is easier or cheaper than you expected【英，非正式】比預料容易[便宜]的東西：*The exam paper was a gift.* 這次考試比想像的容易。

4 the gift of the gab *informal* an ability to speak confidently and to persuade people to do what you want【非正式】口才，辯才

5 be in someone's gift *BrE informal* to be in someone's power to give a favour to someone they choose【英，非正式】由某人授予[委派]：*The chairmanship of this committee is in the gift of the minister.* 該委員會主席是由部長委派的。

6 never/don't look a gift horse in the mouth *informal* used to tell someone to be grateful for something that has been given to them, instead of asking questions about it or finding something wrong with it【非正式】對禮物不要挑剔 —see also 另見 **God's gift to women/men etc** (GOD (15))

gift cer·tif·i·cate /ˈ· ·ˌ···/ *n* [C] *AmE* a special piece of paper that is worth a particular amount of money when it is exchanged for goods in a shop【美】購物禮券；GIFT TOKEN *BrE*【英】

gift·ed /ˈgɪftɪd; ˈgɪftɪ̈d/ *adj* having a natural ability to do one or more things extremely well 有天賦的，有才華的：*a gifted pianist* 天才橫溢的鋼琴家 | **gifted child** (=one who is extremely intelligent) 天才兒童

gift shop /ˈ· ·/ *n* [C] a shop that sells small things that are suitable for giving as presents 禮品商店

gift to·ken /ˈ· ˌ··/ *n* [C] a special piece of paper that is worth a particular amount of money when it is exchanged for goods in a shop 購物禮券；GIFT CERTIFICATE *AmE*【美】

gift vou·cher /ˈ· ˌ··/ *n* [C] a gift token 購物禮券

gift-wrap /ˈ· ·/ *v* [T] to wrap a present with attractive coloured paper〔用花紙〕包裝〔禮品〕：*Would you like it gift-wrapped?* 你想用花紙把它包起來嗎？

gig¹ /gɪg; gɪg/ *n* [C] **1** a performance by a musician or a group of musicians playing modern popular music or JAZZ¹ (1)〔現代流行音樂或爵士樂〕演奏會 **2** a small carriage with two wheels and pulled by one horse 雙輪小馬車

gig² **gigged, gigging** *v* [I] to give a performance of modern popular music or JAZZ¹ (1) 演奏現代流行音樂[爵士樂]

gig·a·byte /ˈgɪgəbaɪt; ˈgɪgəbaɪt/ *n* [C] *technical* one BILLION BYTES【術語】千兆字節

gi·gan·tic /dʒaɪˈgæntɪk; dʒaɪˈgæntɪk/ *adj* extremely big 巨大的，龐大的：*a gigantic skyscraper* 巨大的摩天樓 —**gigantically** /-klɪ; -kli/ *adv*

gig·gle¹ /ˈgɪgl̩; ˈgɪgəl/ **giggled, giggling** *v* [I] to laugh quietly and often like a child, because something is funny, or because you are nervous or embarrassed 咯咯地笑，傻笑：*If you can't stop giggling you'll have to leave the classroom.* 如果你還咯咯地笑個不停，你就得離開課室。—**giggly** *adj*

giggle² *n* **1** [C] a quiet, repeated laugh 咯咯地笑，傻笑：*She broke into a nervous giggle whenever the manager spoke to her.* 每當經理對她說話，她就緊張得傻笑起來。**2 have (a fit of) the giggles** *informal* to be unable to stop giggling【非正式】咯咯笑個不停 **3 give sb the giggles** *informal* to make someone unable to stop giggling【非正式】讓某人咯咯笑個不停 **4 a giggle** *especially BrE informal* something that you think is fun to do that will not hurt anyone or anything【尤英，非正式】玩笑，逗樂：*We used to hide Mum's keys for a giggle.* 我們過去經常把母親的鑰匙藏起來和她鬧着玩。

gig·o·lo /ˈʒɪgəˌlo; ˈʒɪgələʊ/ *n plural* **gigolos** [C] a man who has sex with women for money 男妓

gild /gɪld; gɪld/ *v* [T] **1** to cover something with a thin layer of gold or with something that looks like gold 給…鍍金，給…塗上金色：*an ornate gilded mirror* 華麗的鍍金鏡子 **2** *literary* to make something look as if it is covered in gold【文】給…染上金色：*The autumn sun gilded the lake.* 秋天的太陽把湖面染成金色。**3 gild the lily**

BrE to spoil something by trying to improve it when it is already good enough【英】畫蛇添足，弄巧成拙

gill[1] /gɪl; gɪl/ *n* [C] **1** one of the organs on the sides of a fish through which it breathes 魚鰓 —see picture at 參見 FISH[1] 圖 **2** one of the thin pale lines on the bottom of a MUSHROOM[1]〔蘑菇的〕菌褶 **3 green/pale about the gills** *informal* looking sick because you are shocked, afraid, or ill【非正式】〔因受驚、害怕或生病〕臉露病容的；面如土色的

gill[2] /dʒɪl; dʒɪl/ *n* [C] a measure of liquid equal to 0.142 litres 吉耳〔液量單位，等於0.142升〕—see table on page C5 參見C5頁附錄

gil·lie /ˈgɪlɪ; ˈgɪli/ *n* [C] a man who acts as a guide to someone who is fishing or shooting for sport in Scotland〔蘇格蘭的〕漁獵嚮導

gilt[1] /gɪlt; gɪlt/ *n* **1** [U] a thin shiny material, such as gold or something similar, used to cover objects for decoration 金色塗層，鍍金材料 **2** [C] a SHARE[2] (5) that is GILT-EDGED 金邊股票 **3** [C] *especially AmE* a young female pig【尤美】小母豬

gilt[2] *adj* [only before noun 僅用於名詞前] covered with gilt 鍍金的: *gilt lettering* 鍍金的字體

gilt-edged /ˌ· ˈ·◂/ *adj technical* gilt-edged stocks (STOCK[1] (3)) or shares (SHARE[2] (5)) do not give you much INTEREST (=additional money) but are considered very safe as they are sold mainly by governments【術語】〔多為政府發行的證券、股票等〕金邊的；保險的；優質的

gim·crack /ˈdʒɪmˌkræk; ˈdʒɪmkræk/ *adj* [only before noun 僅用於名詞前] cheap and badly made 低廉劣質、粗製濫造的

gim·let /ˈgɪmlɪt; ˈgɪmlɪ̵t/ *n* [C] **1** a tool that is used to make small holes in wood so that you can put screws in easily 鏍絲錐；手鑽〔用於在木頭中鑽孔〕 **2 gimlet-eyed/gimlet eyes** if someone is gimlet-eyed, or has gimlet eyes, they look at things very hard and notice every detail 目光敏銳的/敏銳的目光 **3** an alcoholic drink made with GIN (1) or VODKA and LIME[1] (1) 兼烈雞尾酒〔用杜松子酒或伏特加及酸橙汁調製的一種酒〕

gim·me /ˈgɪmɪ; ˈgɪmi/ *spoken* a short form of 'give me' that many people think is incorrect【口】給我〔give me的一種簡略說法，許多人認為這種形式不正確〕: *Gimme that! It's mine!* 把那給我！是我的！

gim·mick /ˈgɪmɪk; ˈgɪmɪk/ *n* [C] *informal*【非正式】**1** a trick or an object that makes you notice a product and want to buy it 推銷花招，噱頭〔指一種伎倆或物品，能使你注意到某商品並願意購買〕: *advertising gimmicks* 廣告花招 **2** something unusual that someone does to make people notice them〔為引人注目而搞的〕奇招 —**gimmicky** *adj* —**gimmickry** *n* [U]

gin /dʒɪn; dʒɪn/ *n* **1** [C,U] a strong alcoholic drink made mainly from grain 杜松子酒〔用糧食釀製的烈性酒〕—see also 另見 PINK GIN, GIN AND TONIC **2** [C] a trap for catching small animals or birds〔捕獵小動物或鳥的〕陷阱，羅網 —see also 另見 COTTON GIN

gin and ton·ic /ˌ· · ˈ··/ *n* [C,U] a popular alcoholic drink served with ice and a thin piece of LEMON (1) or LIME[1] (1) 加奎寧水的杜松子酒〔一種常見的含酒精飲料，飲用時加冰和一片檸檬或酸橙〕

gin·ger[1] /ˈdʒɪndʒə; ˈdʒɪndʒə/ *n* [U] a root with a very strong hot taste that is used in cooking, or the plant that has this root 薑 —see picture on page A9 參見A9頁圖

ginger[2] *adj* **1** *BrE* hair or fur that is ginger is bright orange-brown in colour【英】〔頭髮或毛皮〕薑黃色的，赤黃色的 —see picture on page A6 參見A6頁圖 **2** [only before noun 僅用於名詞前] flavoured with ginger 薑味的

ginger[3] *v BrE*【英】

ginger sth ↔ **up** *phr v* [T] to make something more exciting 使〔某事〕更加令人興奮

ginger ale /ˌ·· ˈ·/ *n* [C,U] a non-alcoholic drink that tastes of ginger and is often mixed with alcohol 薑味汽水〔不含酒精，但常加酒飲用〕

ginger beer /ˌ·· ˈ·/ *n* [C,U] a non-alcoholic drink with a strong taste of ginger 薑啤〔有強烈薑味但不含酒精的飲料〕

gin·ger·bread /ˈdʒɪndʒəˌbrɛd; ˈdʒɪndʒəbred/ *n* **1** [U] a sweet cake or BISCUIT (1) with ginger in it 薑餅 **2 gingerbread man** a piece of gingerbread in the shape of a person 人形薑餅

ginger group /ˈ·· ·/ *n* [C] *BrE* a group of people within a political party or organization that tries to persuade the other members to support their ideas【英】〔政黨或組織內部的〕積極派，激進派 —compare 比較 LOBBY[1] (2)

gin·ger·ly /ˈdʒɪndʒəlɪ; ˈdʒɪndʒəli/ *adv, adj* if you move gingerly or touch something gingerly you do it in a careful way because you are afraid it will be dangerous or painful 小心翼翼地[的]，輕手輕腳地[的]: *He gingerly felt his way along the dark tunnel.* 他在漆黑的隧道裡小心翼翼地摸索着走。

ginger nut /ˈ·· ·/ *BrE*【英】, **ginger snap** *AmE*【美】*n* [C] a hard BISCUIT (1) with ginger in it 薑味餅乾

ging·ham /ˈgɪŋəm; ˈgɪŋəm/ *n* [U] cotton cloth that has a pattern of small squares in white and one dark colour 白色和深色方格相間的棉布: *a red and white gingham tablecloth* 紅白相間的方格桌布 —see picture on page A16 參見A16頁圖

gin·gi·vi·tis /ˌdʒɪndʒəˈvaɪtəs; ˌdʒɪndʒɪ̵ˈvaɪtɪ̵s/ *n* [U] a medical condition in which your GUMs are red, swollen, and painful〔齒〕齦炎

gi·nor·mous /dʒaɪˈnɔrməs; dʒaɪˈnɔːməs/ *adj BrE informal* extremely large【英，非正式】非常大的: *Look Mum! It's ginormous!* 瞧，媽媽！真大啊！—**ginormously** *adv*

gin rum·my /ˌ· ˈ··/ *n* [U] a type of RUMMY (=card game for two people) 金羅美牌戲

gin·seng /ˈdʒɪnsɛŋ; ˈdʒɪnseŋ/ *n* [U] medicine made from the root of a Chinese plant, that some people think keeps you young and healthy 人參；人參製成的藥品

gin sling /ˌ· ˈ·/ *n* [C] a drink made from GIN (1) mixed with water, sugar, and LEMON or LIME juice 甜味杜松子混調酒〔用水、糖和檸檬汁或酸橙汁調製〕

gin trap /ˈ· ·/ *n* [C] a GIN (2)〔捕獵小動物或鳥的〕陷阱，羅網

gip·sy /ˈdʒɪpsɪ; ˈdʒɪpsi/ *n* [C] a British spelling of GYPSY gypsy 的英式拼法

gi·raffe /dʒəˈræf; dʒɪ̵ˈrɑːf/ *n* [C] an extremely tall African animal with a very long neck and legs and pale brown fur with dark spots 長頸鹿

gird /gɝd; gɜːd/ *v past tense and past participle* **girded** or **girt** /gɝt; gɜːt/ [T] *literary*【文】**1 gird (up) your loins** *biblical or humorous* to get ready to do something【聖經或幽默】準備 **2** to fasten something around you 將〔某物〕圍在身上

gir·der /ˈgɝdə; ˈgɜːdə/ *n* [C] a strong beam, made of iron or steel, that supports a floor, roof, or bridge 大梁，桁

gir·dle /ˈgɝdl̩; ˈgɜːdl/ *n* [C] **1** a piece of women's underwear which fits tightly around her stomach, bottom, and HIPS[1] (1) and makes her look thinner〔女子的〕緊身褡 **2** *ScotE* a GRIDDLE【蘇格蘭】平底鍋

girl /gɝl; gɜːl/ *n* [C] S1 W1

1 ►CHILD 孩子◄ a female child 女孩: *Don't do that, you naughty girl!* 別那樣做，你這個調皮的女孩！| **little girl** *spoken*【口】*I used to go there on vacation when I was a little girl.* 我還是個小女孩時，我經常到那兒度假。

2 ►DAUGHTER 女兒◄ a daughter 女兒: *They have two girls and a boy.* 他們有兩個女兒，一個兒子。

3 ►WOMAN 女性◄ a word meaning a woman, which is sometimes considered offensive by women 女人〔有時被婦女視為具有冒犯性〕: *the office girls* 辦公室女郎

4 girls [plural] used by a woman to address a group of other women that she knows well 姐妹們，同伴們〔相熟女子間的友好稱呼〕: *Come on girls!* 來吧，好姐妹！

5 the girls *informal* a woman's female friends【非正式】〔女子的〕女伴們: *a night out with the girls* 跟女伴們外出玩耍一晚

6 old girl a) *informal* an old woman【非正式】老婦人: *Surely the old girl's dead by now?* 那位老婦人現在肯定已經不在了吧? **b)** *old-fashioned* used to address a woman you know well【過時】大姐〔稱呼熟知的某婦女〕: *Listen, old girl, I think you need some rest.* 聽我說, 大姐, 我認為你需要休息一下。—see also 另見 OLD GIRL
7 factory girl/shop girl/office girl *old-fashioned* a young woman who works in a factory, shop, office etc【過時】女工/女店員/女辦事員等
8 my girl *old-fashioned* used by an older person to address a girl or woman who is younger than they are, or when they are annoyed【過時】我的姑娘〔年長的人對年輕女性的稱呼, 或當說話人氣惱時的用語〕: *Just remember who you're talking to, my girl!* 要記住你是在跟誰說話, 我的姑娘!
9 *old-fashioned* a woman who you are having a romantic relationship with【過時】女情人, 情婦
10 ►SERVANT 女僕◄ *old-fashioned* a woman servant【過時】女僕, 女傭

girl Fri·day /,· '··/ *n* [C] a girl or woman worker who does several different jobs in an office 女祕書; 女助理, 女助手

girl·friend /ˋgɝl,frɛnd; 'gɜːlfrend/ *n* [C] **1** a girl or woman that you have a friendly, loving relationship with, usually over a fairly long period of time 女朋友: *Shirley was his first serious girlfriend.* 雪莉是他第一位認真的女朋友。| **ex-girlfriend** (=a former girlfriend) 以前的女朋友 **2** a woman who you are having a romantic relationship with 女情人, 情婦 **3** *especially AmE* a woman's female friend【尤美】女子的女伴: *She's out with one of her girlfriends.* 她跟她的一位女伴出去了。—see also 另見 BOYFRIEND

girl·hood /ˋgɝlhʊd; 'gɜːlhʊd/ *n* [U] the period of her life when a woman is a girl 女性的童年, 少女時期 —see also 另見 BOYHOOD

G

girl·ie[1], girly /ˋgɝlɪ; 'gɜːli/ *adj informal*【非正式】**1 girlie magazine/calendar etc** a magazine etc with pictures of women with no clothes on 登有裸體女人照片的雜誌/日曆等 **2** a woman who is girly behaves in a silly way, for example by pretending to be shy or always thinking about how she looks〔女人〕行為愚蠢的 **3** *spoken* suitable only for girls rather than men or boys【口】只適合女孩子的: *Pink's a girlie color!* 粉紅色是屬於女孩子的顏色!

girlie[2] *n* [C] an offensive word used by men to address a woman who they think is less sensible or intelligent than a man 傻妞〔冒犯語, 男人認為女人不如他們聰明時使用〕

girl·ish /ˋgɝlɪʃ; 'gɜːlɪʃ/ *adj* behaving like a girl, or looking like a girl 女孩似的, 少女似的: *a peal of girlish laughter* 一陣女孩子般的笑聲 —**girlishly** *adv*

girl scout /,· '·/ *n* [C] a SCOUT (=member of the Girl Scouts Association in the US) 女童子軍成員 —see also 另見 BOY SCOUT

girl·y /ˋgɝlɪ; 'gɜːli/ *adj* another spelling of GIRLIE[1] girlie 的另一種拼法

gi·ro /ˋdʒaɪro; 'dʒaɪərəʊ/ *n BrE*【英】**1** [C] a cheque paid by the government to someone who is unemployed〔政府發放的〕失業救濟支票 **2** [U] a system of BANKING in Britain in which a central computer can send money from one BANK ACCOUNT to another electronically〔英國〕銀行直接轉賬電腦系統

girt /gɝt; gɜːt/ the past participle of GIRD

girth /gɝθ; gɜːθ/ *n* **1** [C] the size of something or someone large when they are measured around their middle 圍長;〔人的〕腰圍: *the enormous girth of the tree* 樹的巨大圍長 | *Maxwell heaved his considerable girth into the long, sleek car.* 馬克斯韋爾使勁把自己粗大的腰身挪進那輛線條優美的長轎車裡。**2** [C] a band of leather which is passed tightly around the middle of a horse to keep a SADDLE[1] (1) or load firmly in position〔馬的〕肚帶 —see picture at 參見 HORSE[1] 頁圖

gis·mo /ˋgɪzmo; 'gɪzməʊ/ *n* [C] another spelling of GIZMO gizmo 的另一種拼法

gist /dʒɪst; dʒɪst/ *n* **the gist** the main idea and meaning of what someone has said or written 要旨, 要點: **[+of]** *The gist of his argument is that full employment is impossible.* 他的論點的要旨是全民就業是不可能的。| **get the gist** (=understand the main meaning of something) 理解要點 *Don't worry about all the details – as long as you get the gist of it.* 不要擔心細枝末節, 只要你理解要點就行了。

git /gɪt; gɪt/ *n* [C] *BrE slang* an unpleasant and annoying person, especially a man【英俚】討厭的人〔尤指男人〕: *You miserable git!* 你這可恥的討厭鬼!

gite /ʒit; ʒiːt/ *n* [C] *French or BrE* a holiday house in France【法或英】〔法國的〕度假別墅

S1 W1

give[1] /gɪv; gɪv/ *v past tense* **gave** /gev; geɪv/ *past participle* **given** /ˋgɪvən; 'gɪvən/

① PROVIDE/SUPPLY 提供/供應
② TELL SB STH/PROVIDE INFORMATION 告訴某人某事/提供信息
③ DO STH 做某事
④ PRODUCE A FEELING/ILLNESS/RESULT 產生感情/傳染疾病/得出結果
⑤ ALLOW 允許
⑥ JUDGE 判斷
⑦ TIME 時間
⑧ THINK ABOUT STH 考慮某事
⑨ LIKE STH 喜歡某物
⑩ BEND/BREAK 彎曲/斷裂
⑪ OTHER MEANINGS 其他意思

① **PROVIDE/SUPPLY 提供/供應**

1 [T] to provide or supply someone with something 給予, 供給: **give sb sth** *Researchers were given a £10,000 grant to continue their work.* 研究人員得到10,000英鎊的資助以繼續他們的工作。| *Can you give me a ride to the office on Tuesday?* 星期二你能讓我搭你的車去辦公室嗎? | *He went to Las Vegas. He has a friend there who will give him a job.* 他去了拉斯維加斯。他在那裡有個朋友, 要給他一份工作。| *The doctor gave him something for the pain.* 醫生給了他一些止痛藥。| **give sth to sb** *The firm gives a generous discount to companies that place large orders.* 公司給定貨量大的公司優厚的折扣。

2 [T] to give something to someone by putting it near them or in their hand 交給, 遞給, 拿給: **give sb sth** *A policeman gave me a ticket for speeding.* 警察遞給我一張超速罰單。| **give sth to sb** *Why don't you give those packages to me while you find out about the train?* 你在打聽火車情況時, 何不把那些包裹交給我呢?

3 [T] to provide someone with something as a present〔作為禮物〕贈送: **give sb sth** *Jon always gives her flowers on her birthday.* 喬恩總是在她生日的時候給她送花。

4 [I,T] to give money, food etc in order to help people

who are poor〔向窮人〕捐贈, 捐助: *He gives generously to the church.* 他經常向教會慷慨解囊。| **give sth to sb** *They regularly give 5% of their income to charity.* 他們定期把收入的 5% 捐給慈善機構。

② TELL SB STH/PROVIDE INFORMATION 告訴某人某事/提供信息

5 [T] to tell someone information or details about something 告訴, 提供〔信息〕: *a brochure giving holiday details* 提供度假資訊的小冊子 | *The first chapter gives a broad outline of the topic.* 第一章對這個主題進行了概述。| *You will be asked to give evidence when the case is brought to trial.* 案子開始審理時, 你將被要求出庭作證。| **give sb sth** *When will you be able to give us your answer?* 你甚麼時候能給我們答覆? | **give (sb) information/a description/an example etc** *Dad gave me some information on buying a new car.* 爸爸告訴我一些有關買新車的信息。| **give (sb) advice/instructions/a warning etc** *The instructions the manufacturer gave aren't very clear.* 廠家提供的使用說明不大清楚。| **give (sb) an account/report/message etc** *The newspaper gave a disturbing account of the murder.* 報紙對這次謀殺案做了令人不安的報道。—see 見 SAY[1] (USAGE)

6 give sb your word/promise to promise to do something 答應某人, 允諾某人: *I gave him my word not to repeat anything of what he'd told me.* 我答應他不把他說的話告訴給別人。

7 give sb to understand/believe *formal* to make someone believe that something will happen or is true【正式】使某人理解/相信〔某事確將發生或確有其事〕: *I was given to understand that the contract would be approved by the end of the week.* 我被告知這個合同週末前就會得到批准。

8 give it to me straight *spoken* used when you want someone to tell you something unpleasant directly【口】直接告訴我〔用於要求某人將壞消息直接告訴你〕

③ DO STH 做某事

9 give (sb/sth) a smile/laugh/shout/push etc to smile, laugh, shout etc 對〔某人/某物〕微笑/笑/喊叫/推等: *He gave me a quick smile and a hug.* 他對我微微一笑並把我擁抱了一下。| *Ooh, the baby just gave a kick!* 噢, 嬰兒剛剛踢了一下。

10 give (sb/sth) assistance/help/support etc to do something to help someone or something be successful 給〔某人/某物〕協助/幫助/支持等: *Committee members agreed to give the policy of increasing wheel-chair access their full support.* 委員會成員同意全力支持增加輪椅通道的政策。

11 give (sb) a hand *spoken* to help someone do something, especially something that involves physical work【口】幫助〔某人〕做某事〔尤指體力活〕: *Can you give me a hand? I need to move this box.* 你能幫我一下嗎? 我需要搬動這個箱子。

12 give sb a call/ring *BrE*【英】**/bell** *BrE*【英】**/buzz** to call someone on the telephone 打電話給某人: *I'll give you a call about seven, okay?* 我大約 7 點給你打電話, 好嗎?

13 give a speech/concert/performance etc to talk, play an instrument etc in front of a group of people 發表演講/舉行音樂會/進行演出等: *Seamus Heaney is giving a poetry reading Thursday evening.* 沙默斯·希尼將於星期四晚上舉行詩歌朗誦會。| *She gave a performance of great beauty and sweetness.* 她的表演非常優美, 悅耳動人。

14 give a party/dance etc to be the person who organizes a party etc, especially at your own home〔尤指在自己家裡〕舉辦聚會/舞會等: *Julie is giving a wedding shower for Lori next Saturday.* 朱莉下星期六要為洛麗舉辦結婚送禮會。

15 give sth a try/shot/go *BrE*【英】**/whirl** to be willing to attempt to do something 願意試做某事: *I'm not usually much good at these sorts of games, but I'll give it a go.* 我通常不大擅長這些種類的遊戲, 不過我願意試試。

16 ▶JOB 工作◀ [T] to ask someone to do a job or task 叫〔某人〕做〔某事〕: *My algebra teacher always gives us a lot of homework.* 我的代數老師總是給我們大量的功課。| *Give Mike something to do – he's just sitting there.* 給邁克甚麼事幹吧 —— 他在那兒乾坐。

17 give (sb) trouble/a hard time/problems etc to do something that causes problems or makes a situation difficult for someone 給〔某人〕添麻煩/讓〔某人〕吃苦頭/令〔某人〕傷腦筋等: *This new computer program is giving us a little bit of trouble.* 這個新的電腦程序給我們添了一點麻煩。| *She's always giving her mother a hard time these days.* 這些日子她總是讓她母親不好過。

18 give (sb) a signal/alarm/sign etc to say or do something that tells someone what to do in a particular situation 向〔某人〕發出信號/發出警報/做手勢等: *The man who was controlling the traffic gave me the signal to move forward.* 管理交通的那個人向我發出往前走的信號。

④ PRODUCE A FEELING/ILLNESS/RESULT 產生感情/傳染疾病/得出結果

19 [T] to produce a particular emotional or physical feeling (使) 產生〔情感或感覺〕: **give sb sth** *He gave us quite a shock, appearing suddenly like that.* 他像那樣突然出現, 讓我們大吃一驚。| *The heat gave me a real headache.* 高温讓我頭疼難耐。| *Targets help give workers a sense of achievement.* 指標有助於讓工人們產生成就感。

20 [T] to infect someone with the same illness you have 傳染〔疾病〕: **give sb sth** *Don't come too close – I don't want to give you my cold!* 別靠得太近 —— 我不想把感冒傳給你! | **give sth to sb** *It's very unlikely a doctor could give hepatitis to a patient.* 醫生不太可能會把肝炎傳染給病人。

21 [T] to produce a particular effect, solution, result etc 產生〔效果、解決辦法、結果等〕: *The fields that had not been fertilized gave surprisingly high yields.* 那些未施肥的田地產量高得驚人。| *The camera's focus should be set to give maximum resolution.* 相機的焦距應當調整到能夠產生最高的解像度。

⑤ ALLOW 允許

22 [T] to allow something or someone to do something 允許, 許可: *Women were given the vote in the early 1900's.* 婦女在 20 世紀初被賦予投票權。| *I gave the students the freedom to choose their own topics.* 我允許學生自由選擇自己的話題。| **give (sb) permission/consent** *Her father finally gave his consent to her marriage.* 她父親終於同意了她的婚事。| **give sb a chance/opportunity to do sth** *These meetings give everyone a chance to express their opinions.* 這些會議給大家一個表達自己觀點的機會。

23 give sb authority/responsibility/control etc to allow someone to have power or control over something 賦予某人權力/責任/控制權等: *Schools have recently been given responsibility for their own budgets.* 學校最近被授權進行獨立預算。

24 [I] to be willing to change what you think or do in a situation according to what else happens 願意〔根據情況對想法、做法〕改變; 作出讓步: *If only he'd give a little, we'd have this whole thing settled by now.* 當時他如果稍作讓步, 現在這整件事情我們已經解決了。

⑥ JUDGE 判斷

25 [T] to decide how much time a criminal will have to spend in prison 判處〔犯人若干時間的〕監禁: **give sb sth** *The judge gave her two years.* 法官判決她二年監禁。| *He was given life for murdering three women.* 他因謀殺三名女子而被判處終身監禁。

26 give sth out/offside etc *BrE* to decide that a player or a ball is playing against the rules【英】判定〔球〕出界/〔球員〕越位等: *The linesman gave the ball out.* 巡邊員判球出界。

G

⑦ **TIME 時間**

27 give sb time/a few weeks/all day etc to allow someone or a situation to have enough time to develop, do something etc 給某人時間/幾個星期時間/一整天時間等: *Give him time. It's always hard to adjust to a new place.* 給他一些時間吧。適應一處新地方總是很難的。| **give sb time to do sth** *Flexible working hours could give working parents more time to spend with their children.* 彈性工作時間能給上班的父母更多時間和孩子們在一起。

28 I give it six weeks/a month etc *spoken* used when you think that something is not going to continue successfully for very long【口】我估計不會超過六個星期/一個月等〔某事就會失敗、結束〕: *Steve and Celia are going to get married? I give it six weeks.* 史蒂夫和西莉亞要結婚了嗎? 我估計他們的婚姻不到六個星期就會崩潰。

⑧ **THINK ABOUT STH 考慮某事**

29 give (sth) thought/attention/consideration etc to spend some time thinking about something carefully 思考/注意/考慮〔某事〕等: *Congress has been giving the crime bill serious consideration.* 國會一直在認真考慮這項犯罪法案。| *I'll give the matter some thought and let you know my decision next week.* 這件事我要考慮一下, 下週告訴你我的決定。| **not give sth a second thought/another thought** (=not think or worry about something) 對某事不予考慮[毫不擔心] *Don't give it a second thought. I'll take care of the whole thing.* 你不必擔心, 我會處理這件事。

30 give (sb) the impression/sense/idea etc to make someone think about something in a particular way 給〔某人〕留下印象/感覺/想法等: **give (sb) the impression that** *Paul didn't want to give Mr Bergman the impression that he was avoiding him.* 保羅不想讓伯格曼先生覺得自己在迴避他。

⑨ **LIKE STH 喜歡某物**

31 give me sth (any day/time) *spoken* used to say that you like something much more than something else【口】我更喜歡某物: *I don't like spicy food much. Give me meat and potatoes any day.* 我不大喜歡辛辣的食物, 我比較喜歡肉和馬鈴薯。

32 give anything/a lot/your right arm etc *spoken* used when you want something very much【口】願意付出一切等〔表示十分想要某物〕: *I'd give my right arm for a complexion like that.* 我要是有那樣的膚色該有多好。

⑩ **BEND/BREAK 彎曲/斷裂**

33 [I] if a material gives, it bends or stretches when you put pressure on it 變曲, 伸展: *The leather will give a little after you've worn the shoes a while.* 鞋子穿了一段時間後, 皮革就會略微伸展。

34 [I] if something such as a chair or shelf gives, it breaks suddenly 斷裂: *The branch suddenly gave beneath him.* 樹枝突然在他腳下斷裂。

⑪ **OTHER MEANINGS 其他意思**

35 not give a damn/toss *BrE*【英】**/shit etc** *spoken* used when you do not care at all about something【口】毫不在乎: *I don't give a damn what you think.* 我對你的想法毫不在乎。

36 ►MAKE STH HAVE A PARTICULAR QUALITY 使某物具有某種品質◄ [T not in progressive 不用進行式] to add a quality or characteristic to a person, place, thing etc 為〔某人、某地、某物等〕增添〔品質或特點〕: *The new sponsor gives the theatre some respectability.* 新的贊助者為劇院提高了一些聲望。| **give a smell/taste/look etc** *Rub the salad bowl with a clove of garlic to give a delicate tang.* 用一瓣蒜頭擦拭色拉碗, 讓它帶有一種幽香。| *Her tan gave her a healthy look.* 她那曬黑的皮膚使她看起來很健康。

37 give (sth) coherence/form/shape etc to organize something, especially something such as an idea or situation 使〔某物〕連貫/形成/成形: *The painter takes his emotions and gives them artistic form.* 畫家把自己的感情用藝術形式表現出來。

38 give (sb/sth) credit/respect/priority etc to treat something or someone in a way that shows it is important or has value 對〔某人/某物〕進行讚揚/表示尊敬/給予優先權等: *You have to give him credit for trying to learn the language.* 他努力學習這門語言, 你得表揚他。| *Top priority should be given to finishing on schedule.* 應該最先考慮的是要按時完成。

39 don't give me that *spoken* used when you do not believe someone's excuse or explanation【口】別給我來那一套〔表示不相信某人的借口或解釋〕: *"I'm sorry I'm late. My car broke down." "Oh, don't give me that."* "對不起, 我遲到了。我的車壞了。" "啊, 別來那一套。"

40 give sb what for *informal* to tell someone angrily that you are annoyed with them【非正式】痛罵某人

41 ►PAY 支付◄ [T] to be willing to pay a particular amount of money for something 願意付〔一定數額的錢來購買某物〕: **give sb sth for** *He said he'd give us £700 for our old Ford.* 他說他願意出700英鎊買我們的那輛舊福特車。

42 give as good as you get to fight or argue with someone using the same amount of skill or force that they are using 針鋒相對, 毫不示弱地反擊[反駁]

43 give or take a few minutes/a penny/a mile etc if a number, time, or amount is correct give or take a few minutes etc, it is approximately correct 相差不了幾分鐘/一便士/一英里等: *You can usually predict how tall a child will be as an adult, give or take a couple of inches.* 你通常可以預計一個孩子長大後的身高, 相差不了兩三英寸。

44 I'll give you that *spoken* used when you accept that something is true, even though you do not like it or disagree with other parts of it【口】那點我承認, 那點我接受: *Yes, he's handsome, I'll give you that, but he's really arrogant.* 是的, 他長得帥, 這點我承認, 不過他真的很傲慢。

45 I give you the chairman/prime minister/groom etc *BrE spoken* used at the end of a speech to invite people to cheer or APPLAUD (1) a special guest【英口】我提議為主席/總理/新郎等歡呼[鼓掌]

46 What gives? *spoken* used when you want to ask what is happening【口】發生了甚麼事?

47 ►SEX 性◄ [T] *old-fashioned* if a woman gives herself to a man, she has sex with him【過時】〔女子〕委身於〔男子〕—see also 另見 **give way** (way¹ (31))

give away *phr v* [T] **1** [**give** sth ↔ **away**] to give something to another person because you do not want it any longer or because they need it more than you 送掉, 捐贈, 分送〔將不需要的東西送給別人〕: *I need to give away some of these old baby clothes.* 我需要把這些舊的嬰兒衣服送出去一些。| **give sth away to** *He gave away immense amounts of money to charity.* 他把大筆大筆的錢捐給慈善機構。**2** [**give** sth ↔ **away**] if a company gives away something, they give things to people in order to persuade them to buy that company's products〔公司為爭取顧客而〕贈送, 送發: *They're giving a plastic model skeleton away with a children's book on the body.* 他們向購買一本關於身體構造的兒童書的顧客贈送塑料人體骨架模型。**3** [**give** sth ↔ **away**] to do something that shows what you really think or what is really true 表露, 流露: *Katheryn studied the jurors' faces, but they gave away no clues as to the verdict.* 凱瑟琳打量陪審員的臉, 可是他們沒有透露出判決的線索。**4** [**give** sb **away**] to show that someone is doing something wrong 敗露, 露馬腳: **give yourself away** *Most shoplifters give themselves away by constantly looking around for cameras.* 大多數商店盜竊犯不停地四處尋找攝像機, 因而露出馬腳。**5** [**give** sth ↔ **away**] to tell someone something that you should keep secret 泄露〔祕密〕: *I was afraid the kids would give the whole thing away.* 恐怕孩子會把整件事

說出去。| **give the game away** (=tell someone a secret plan, idea etc) 泄露祕密 **6** **[give** sth ↔ **away]** to lose something by doing something silly or stupid〔由於做了蠢事而〕喪失, 丟失: *The goalkeeper gave away two goals.* 守門員丟了兩分。| *I swear the Democrats are just giving this election away.* 我斷言民主黨正斷送這次選舉。 **7** **[give away** sth] to give someone something such as a prize in a ceremony〔儀式上〕頒發〔獎品等〕: *The university chancellor gave away our diplomas.* 大學校長向我們頒發畢業證書。 **8** **[give** sb ↔ **away]** when a man, especially the BRIDE's father, gives the bride away, he walks with her to the front of the church and formally gives permission for her to marry〔在婚禮上, 尤指新娘的父親〕將〔新娘〕交給新郎: *She asked her eldest brother to give her away.* 她請她的長兄把她交給新郎。

give sth ↔ **back** *phr v* [T] **1** to return something to the person who owned it before 返還, 歸還: **give sth ↔ back to sb** *She read the letter, signed it, and gave it back to Rae.* 她讀了信, 簽上名, 然後還給雷。| **give sb back sth** *I need to give Jack back the money he lent me.* 我得把傑克借我的錢還給他。| **give sb sth back** *Mom! Tell Josh to give me my pens back!* 媽媽! 告訴喬希把我的幾枝筆還給我! **2** if you give someone back a quality, ability, or characteristic, you make them have it again after they had lost it; RESTORE (5) 使〔某人〕恢復〔品質、能力或特點〕: *The operation gave him back his sight.* 這次手術使他恢復了視力。

give in *phr v* **1** [I] to unwillingly agree to someone's demands after they have spent a lot of time arguing with you, trying to persuade you etc 讓步: *They argued back and forth until finally Buzz gave in.* 他們反覆爭論, 直到最後布茲讓步為止。| **[+to]** *O'Neill was giving in to pressure from London to hurry the reforms.* 倫敦施壓, 奧尼爾開始讓步, 加快進行改革。 **2** [I] to stop playing, fighting etc and accept that you will be defeated 屈服, 投降: *They weren't a particularly good team, but they refused to give in and accept defeat.* 他們並不是一支特別好的球隊, 但他們拒絕屈服, 不肯認輸。 **3** **[T give** sth ↔ **in]** *BrE* to give something such as an official paper or piece of work to someone【英】呈交, 交上〔公文或工作〕; **hand in** (HAND²) *AmE*【美】: *Rosa decided to give in her notice.* 羅莎決定遞交辭職通知。| *You were supposed to give this work in four days ago.* 你四天前就應該交上這份作業了。

give in to *phr v* [T] to no longer control a strong emotion or desire 向〔強烈感情或慾望〕屈服: *If you feel the urge for a cigarette, try not to give in to it.* 如果煙癮上來, 盡量要把它控制。

give of sth *phr v* [T] if you give of yourself, your time or money, or your best, you do things for other people without expecting them to do anything for you 獻出〔自身、時間或金錢, 或你最大的力量, 以幫助他人而不指望回報〕: *professionals who give of their free time to help underprivileged youngsters* 把業餘時間用來幫助社會下層青年的專業人士

give off sth *phr v* [T] to produce a smell, light, heat, a sound etc 發出〔氣味、光、熱、聲音等〕: *Chives give off a delicate oniony scent.* 細香蔥發出淡淡的洋蔥味。

give off 發出〔氣味〕

The milk gave off a bad smell.
牛奶發出臭味。

give on/onto sth *phr v* [T not in passive 不用被動態] if a window, door, building etc gives on or onto a particular place, it leads to that place or you can see that place from it〔窗、門、建築物等〕通向, 面朝: *a gate giving on to the main road* 通往大路的入口 | *a small window giving onto fields* 面朝田野的小窗

give out *phr v* **1** **[T give** sth ↔ **out]** to give something to a number of different people, especially to give information to people〔向多人〕分發, 發佈, 公佈〔信息等〕: *Students were giving out leaflets to everyone on the street.* 學生正向街上的每個人分發傳單。| *You had no right to give my telephone number out.* 你無權公佈我的電話號碼。 **2** [I] if a part of your body gives out, it stops working properly〔人體某一部分〕出故障: *I am so frightened that my legs give out, and I reach for the railing.* 我嚇得兩腿發軟, 便伸手去抓欄杆。 **3** [I] if a supply of something gives out, there is none left 耗盡, 用光: *My money began to give out.* 我的錢開始用光了。| *predictions that the world's oil supply would soon give out* 世界石油供應快將耗盡的預測 **4** **[T give out** sth] to produce light, heat, a sound, a gas etc 發出〔光、熱、聲音、氣體等〕: *A palm-oil lamp gave out yellowish light.* 棕櫚油燈發出淡黃色的光。 **5** **[T give** sth ↔ **out]** *BrE formal* to announce something, especially officially【英, 正式】〔尤指官方〕宣佈, 公佈, 發表: *Mr Banks gave out the last verse of the hymn.* 班克斯先生宣讀了那首讚美詩的最後一節。| **give out that** *It was given out that the prime minister was to undergo minor surgery.* 據宣佈, 首相將要接受小手術。 **6** [I] *especially AmE* to end【尤美】結束: *She parked near the spot where the blacktop gave out.* 她把車子停在瀝青路的盡頭處。

give over *phr v* [I,T] *BrE spoken* used to tell someone angrily to stop doing something or to be quiet【英口】住手, 閉嘴〔表示憤怒地要某人停止做某事或住嘴〕: *"We're going to thrash you lot five-nil." "Oh, give over!"* "我們要把你們這幫人打成五比零。" "啊, 別胡說八道!" | **give over doing sth** *Oh, give over complaining, we're nearly there.* 啊, 別抱怨了, 我們就快到了。

give over to *phr v* [T] **1** **be given over to** to be used for a particular purpose 被用於〔某一目的〕: *The best land near the village was given over to vineyards.* 村子附近最好的地被用作葡萄園。| *Two days were given over to the celebrations.* 兩天的時間被用來搞慶祝活動。 **2** **[give** sb/sth ↔ **over to]** to allow yourself or your life to be completely controlled by another person, a feeling, or an activity 受制於〔某人〕; 放任〔感情〕; 致力於〔活動〕: *a life given over to sexual excess* 縱慾過度的一生 | **give yourself over to** *After her husband's death, she gave herself over to her work.* 她丈夫去世之後, 她便完全埋頭於工作。 **3** **[give** sth/sb ↔ **over to]** to give the responsibility for something or someone to someone else 交託給: *His mother gave him over to his uncle's care when he was very small.* 在他很小的時候, 他母親把他交給他舅舅照看。

give up *phr v* **1** **[I,T give** sth ↔ **up]** to stop doing something or having something, especially something that you do regularly 放棄〔擁有某物或做某事, 尤指經常做的事情〕: *Shaun's giving up his karate, he's bored with it.* 肖恩打算放棄空手道, 他已經對它感到厭倦。| *When Ed left, she gave up hope of ever marrying.* 埃德離開時, 她徹底放棄了結婚的希望。| **give up doing sth** *I've given up expecting him to change.* 我已經不指望他會改變。| **give up a job/career/work etc** *Peter had given up a promising career in law to become a teacher.* 彼得放棄了很有前途的律師職業, 當了一名教師。| **give up smoking/drinking/alcohol/cigarettes etc** (=stop doing something that is unhealthy) 戒煙/戒酒/戒酒/戒煙等: *I gave up smoking when I got pregnant.* 我懷孕後便把煙戒了。 **2** **[I,T give** sth ↔ **up]** to stop attempting to do something, especially something difficult, without completing it 放棄, 中止〔尤指難事〕: *They searched for the ball for a while, but eventually gave up and went home.* 他們找了一會兒球, 但最終還是放棄, 回家去了。| **give up doing sth** *I gave up trying to persuade him to get a degree.* 我不再試圖勸說他去拿個學位。| **give it/that up** *"Give it up," Anna advised me. "You'll never get him to agree."* "放棄吧," 安娜勸我說, "你永遠也無法說服他同意的。" |

G

I give up *spoken* (=used when you do not know the answer to a question or joke) 【口】我放棄, 我不懂〔表示不知道問題的答案或聽不懂笑話〕 *"Why did the chicken cross the road?" "I give up. Why?"* "那隻雞為甚麼走過馬路?" "不知道。為甚麼?" **3** [T **give** sb **up**] to allow yourself or someone else to be caught by the police or enemy soldiers 自首, 投案, 投降: **give yourself up** *The police issued a statement urging the fugitive to give himself up.* 警方發表聲明, 敦促逃亡者自首。**4** [T **give up** sth] to agree to do something during the time you would normally spend doing things you enjoy 讓出, 騰出〔時間〕: *The club secretary will need to give up an hour or two a week to do the correspondence.* 俱樂部的祕書每星期需要騰出一兩個小時來處理信函。**5** [T **give** sth/sb ↔ **up**] to give someone else possession of something you have 放棄, 讓出〔所有權〕: *thoughts that Israel might give up some of the occupied territory* 認為以色列可能讓出一些被佔領土的想法 | **give sth ↔ up to sb** *John gave up his seat to an elderly lady on the bus.* 約翰在公共汽車上把座位讓給一位老太太。| **give sb up for adoption** (=allow your child to become legally part of someone else's family) 把孩子交託〔給他人〕撫養 **6** [T **give** sb ↔ **up**] to end a relationship with someone, especially a romantic relationship 斷絕關係〔尤指愛情關係〕: *He's started going out with Emma, but he doesn't want to give up this other girl!* 他已開始和埃瑪交往, 但他又不想斷絕與另一女孩的關係! **7 give sb up for dead/lost etc** to believe that someone is dead and stop looking for them 認為某人已死/失蹤等〔而不再尋找〕: *The ship sank and the crew were given up for dead.* 船沉了, 全體船員被認為已經喪生。—see also 另見 **give up the ghost** (GHOST¹ (5))

give up on sb *phr v* [T] to stop hoping that someone will change, do something etc 對〔某人〕不抱希望: *He'd been in a coma for six months, and doctors had almost given up on him.* 他已經昏迷六個月, 醫生們幾乎已經放棄他能活過來的希望。

give yourself **up to** sth *phr v* [T] to allow yourself to feel some emotion completely, without trying to control it 使〔自己〕陷入〔某種感情而不加控制〕: *He gave himself up to despair.* 他陷入絕望, 不能自拔。

give² *n* [U] the ability to bend or stretch when put under pressure 伸展性, 彈性: *The rope has quite a bit of give in it.* 這繩子相當有伸展性。

give-and-take /ˌ· · ˈ·/ *n* [U] a willingness between two people or groups to understand each other, and to let both of them have some of the things they want 互相忍讓: *In any relationship there always has to be some give-and-take.* 在任何關係中, 互相忍讓是必須的。

give·a·way¹ /ˈgɪvəˌwe; ˈgɪvəweɪ/ *n* **1** [singular] something that makes it easy for you to guess something 使人容易猜中[露出真相]的東西, : **be a clear/dead giveaway** *He'd been smoking dope; his glazed eyes were a dead giveaway.* 他一直在吸毒, 他那目光呆滯的眼睛徹底暴露了這一點。**2** [C] something that a shop gives you when you buy a product 〔商店給顧客的〕贈品

giveaway² *adj* [only before noun 僅用於名詞前] giveaway prices are extremely cheap 〔價格〕極其便宜的

give·back /ˈgɪvbæk; ˈgɪvbæk/ *n* [C] *AmE* an amount of money or goods that you receive from some companies if you buy a product from them 【美】〔一些公司給的〕回扣, 贈品

giv·en¹ /ˈgɪvən; ˈgɪvən/ *adj* [only before noun 僅用於名詞前] **1** a given time, date etc is one that has been previously arranged 〔時間、日期等〕特定的, 預定的: *At a given time we'll all start shouting and cheering.* 在預定時間我們大家都要開始高聲歡呼。**2 at any given time/point etc** at any particular time, point etc 在任何特定的時間/地點等: *The distance from the centre of a circle to the edge is the same at any given point.* 從圓心到圓周上任何一點的距離都是相同的。**3 be given to (doing) sth** to tend to do something, especially something that you should not do 往往會做某事〔尤指不該做的事〕: *She is given to making wild accusations.* 她往往作出荒唐的指控。**4 take sth as given** to base your argument on the belief that something is clearly true 想當然

given² *prep* used to say that something is not surprising when you consider the situation it happened in; CONSIDERING² 如果考慮到: *Given the circumstances, you've coped well.* 考慮到各種情況, 你已經算是處理得很好了。| [+that] *Given that there was so little time, I think they've done a good job.* 考慮到沒有多少時間, 我認為他們算是做得不錯了。

given³ *n* [C] *formal* a basic fact that you accept as being true 【正式】認為正確的基本事實

given⁴ the past participle of GIVE

given name /ˈ· · ·/ *n* [C] *AmE* your FIRST NAME 【美】名字

giz·mo /ˈgɪzmo; ˈgɪzməʊ/ *n* [C] *informal* a word meaning a small piece of equipment, used when you cannot remember or do not know its correct name 【非正式】小玩意兒, 小東西〔忘記或不知道某物的名稱時用語〕

giz·zard /ˈgɪzəd; ˈgɪzəd/ *n* [C] the stomach of a bird 〔鳥的〕砂囊, 胗

gla·cé /glæˈse; ˈglæseɪ/ *adj* [only before noun 僅用於名詞前] glacé fruits, especially cherries (CHERRY), have been covered in sugary liquid 〔水果〕糖漬的, 蜜餞的

glacé i·cing /ˌ·· ˈ··/ *n* [U] *BrE* a type of ICING used to decorate cakes 【英】〔裝飾糕餅的〕糖霜

gla·cial /ˈgleʃəl; ˈgleɪʃəl/ *adj* **1** involving ice and glaciers, or formed by glaciers 冰的, 冰川的, 冰川形成的: *a glacial valley* 冰谷 **2** a glacial look or expression is extremely unfriendly 〔神色、表情〕冷峻的, 冷冰冰的 **3** extremely cold 極冷的: *a glacial wind* 刺骨的寒風 —**glacially** *adv*

gla·ci·a·tion /ˌglesɪˈeʃən; ˌgleɪsiˈeɪʃən/ *n* [U] *technical* the process in which land is covered by glaciers, or the effect this process has 【術語】冰川作用

gla·ci·er /ˈgleʃɚ; ˈglæsiə/ *n* [C] a large mass of ice which moves slowly down a mountain valley 冰川 —see picture on page A12 參見 A12 頁圖

glad /glæd; glæd/ *adj* **gladder, gladdest 1** pleased and happy about something 高興的: *"The doctor says she'll be well again soon." "I'm so glad."* "醫生說她很快就會恢復健康。" "我真高興。" | **[+(that)]** *I'm really glad I don't have to go back there again.* 我真高興我不必再回到那兒去了。| **[+about]** *Deep down he felt glad about the news.* 聽到這個消息他發自內心地感到高興。| **glad to know/see/hear** *We were all glad to hear you passed your exams.* 我們得知你通過了考試都很高興。| **be/feel glad for sb** *When I heard they were getting married I felt genuinely glad for them both.* 我聽到他們要結婚的消息時, 真心為他們倆高興。**2 be glad of sth** to be grateful for something 為某事感激: *Thanks Marge, I'll be glad of the help.* 謝謝瑪吉, 我非常感謝你的幫助。**3 be glad to do sth** to be very willing and eager to do something 很樂於做某事: *"Would you give me a hand?" "I'd be glad to."* "你能幫我一下忙嗎?" "我很樂意。" | **be only too glad to** (=extremely willing) 非常樂意: *I'd be only too glad to let you take the kids today.* 我非常樂意今天由你照看孩子們。**4 I would be glad if** used to say you would be pleased if someone would do something for you 如果〔某人能為你做某事〕, 我將十分高興: *I would be glad if you could arrange it for me.* 如果你能幫我安排一下我將非常高興。**5** making people feel happy 令人高興的: *a glad day for everyone* 每一個人都很開心的一天 **6 glad rags** *informal* your best clothes that you wear for special occasions 【非正式】〔特殊場合穿的〕最好的衣服 **7 glad tidings** *old-fashioned* good news 【過時】好消息 **8 give sb the glad eye** *BrE old-fashioned* to look at someone in a way that shows you are sexually attracted to them 【英, 過時】向某人送秋波 —see also 另見 GLAD-HAND, GLADLY —**gladness** *n* [U]

This graph shows how common the different grammar patterns of the adjective **glad** are. 本圖表所示為形容詞glad構成的不同語法模式的使用頻率。

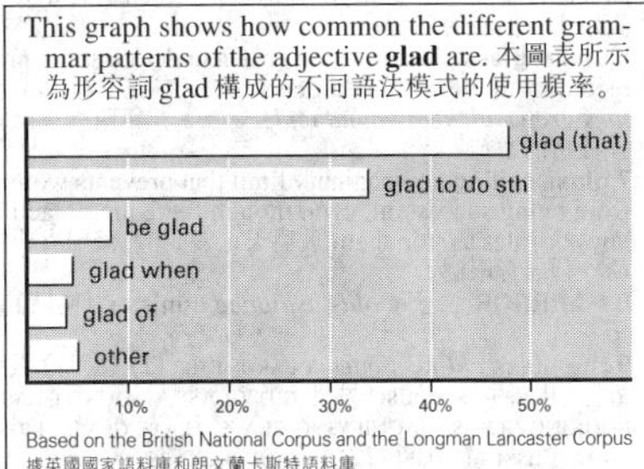

Based on the British National Corpus and the Longman Lancaster Corpus
據英國國家語料庫和朗文蘭卡斯特語料庫

glad·den /ˋglædn̩; ˈglædn/ *v* [T] **gladden sb's heart** *old-fashioned* to make someone feel pleased and happy【過時】使某人高興, 使某人快樂: *It gladdened the old man's heart to see his grandchildren playing in the yard.* 老人看到自己的孫子在院子裡玩, 心裡很高興。

glade /gled; gleɪd/ *n* [C] *literary* an open space in a wood or forest【文】林間空地

glad-hand /ˌ· ˈ·/ *v* [I,T] to give someone a very friendly welcome or be nice to them in order to get what you want〔為得到想要的東西而〕熱烈歡迎, 態度友好: *politicians gladhanding in the crowds* 在人羣中頻頻打招呼的政客

glad·i·a·tor /ˋglædɪˌetɚ; ˈglædieɪtə/ *n* [C] a soldier who fought against other men or wild animals in a public place in Roman times in order to entertain people 角鬥士〔指古羅馬在公共場所互相搏鬥或與野獸搏鬥以供人娛樂的鬥士〕—**gladiatorial** /ˌglædɪəˋtɔrɪəl; ˌglædiəˈtɔːriəl◂/ *adj*

glad·i·o·lus /ˌglædɪˋoləs; ˌglædiˈəʊləs/ *plural* **gladioli** /-laɪ; -laɪ/ *n* [C] a garden plant with long leaves and brightly-coloured flowers 唐菖蒲, 劍蘭

glad·ly /ˋglædlɪ; ˈglædli/ *adv* **1** willingly or eagerly 樂意地, 熱切地: *I would gladly have done it for him.* 我本來會很樂意地為他做這事。**2** happily 高興地, 快樂地: *"Here's Michelle!" he said gladly.* "米歇爾來了!"他高興地説道。

glam·or /ˋglæmɚ; ˈglæmə/ *n* [U] an American spelling of GLAMOUR glamour 的美式拼法

glam·o·rize also 又作 **-ise** *BrE*【英】/ˋglæməraɪz; ˈglæməraɪz/ *v* [T] to make something seem more attractive than it really is 使更吸引人, 使更有魅力, 美化: *a widespread perception that Hollywood movies tend to glamorize war* 普遍認為荷里活電影往往美化戰爭 —**glamorization** /ˌglæmərаɪˋzeʃən; ˌglæməraɪˈzeɪʃən/ *n* [U]

glam·or·ous /ˋglæmərəs; ˈglæmərəs/ *adj* a person, place, or activity that is glamorous seems very attractive and exciting, because it is beautiful or is connected with wealth and success〔人物、地方或活動〕有魅力的, 令人嚮往的, 刺激的: *a glamorous film star* 富有魅力的電影明星 | *glamorous couples in chauffeur-driven limousines* 私人司機駕駛的豪華轎車裡一對對光彩奪目的夫婦 | *Tatiana's glamorous lifestyle* 塔蒂阿娜富於刺激的生活方式 —**glamorously** *adv*

glam·our *usually* 一般作 **glamor** *AmE*【美】/ˋglæmɚ; ˈglæmə/ *n* [U] **1** the attractive and exciting quality that something has because it is connected with wealth and success〔由財富與成功產生的〕魅力, 誘惑力: *Young actors are often dazzled by the glamor of Hollywood.* 年輕演員經常被荷里活的誘惑力弄得眼花繚亂。**2** strong personal attractiveness〔強烈的〕個人魅力 **3 glamour girl** an actress who is beautiful but is not very good at acting 漂亮但演技不佳的女演員

3 **glance¹** /glæns; glɑːns/ *v* [I always+adv/prep] **1** to quickly look at someone or something once 一瞥, 看一眼: [**+at/towards/up etc**] *He glanced nervously at his watch.* 他緊張不安地看一下手錶。| *Nadine glanced round to see if there was anyone that she knew.* 納丁快速環視一下, 看看是否有她認識的人。**2** to read something very quickly 快速閱讀: [**+at/over/etc**] *Can you glance through these figures and tell me what you think of them?* 你能粗略看一下這些數字, 然後把意見告訴我嗎? **3** to flash 閃耀, 閃光: *light glancing on the water* 水面上閃耀着的光

glance off *phr v* [I,T] to hit a surface at an angle and then move away from it in another direction 擦過, 掠過: *The bullet glanced off the side of the car.* 子彈從汽車邊上擦過。

USAGE NOTE 用法説明: GLANCE

WORD CHOICE 詞語辨析: **glance, have/take a quick look, glimpse, catch/get a glimpse of**

If you **glance** at something, you look at it quickly. glance at 意指對某物很快地看一眼: *After the first ten minutes the interviewer started yawning and glancing at his watch.* 頭十分鐘過後, 面試考官開始打呵欠, 看錶。

In spoken English you often use **have/take a (quick) look**, especially to check if something is correct or working properly. 英語口語經常使用 have/take a (quick) look, 特別是檢查某物是否正確, 是否運轉正常時: *Could you just have a quick look at the engine for me?* 你能幫我看一眼發動機嗎?

If you **glimpse** (or more commonly **catch/get a glimpse of**) someone or something, you see them by chance, for a very short time. glimpse〔或更常用的 catch/get a glimpse of〕意指偶然看到某人或某物, 而且時間很短: *I can't describe him well, I only caught a glimpse of him as he drove off.* 我無法準確地把他描述出來, 我只是在他開車離開時碰巧看到他一眼。

glance² *n* [C] **1** a quick look 一瞥, 很快的一看: **give/take/shoot/throw a glance (at)** (=look at someone or something quickly)〔朝…〕一瞥, 看一眼: *He gave her a quick glance as she walked into the room.* 她走進房間時他朝她看了一眼。| **exchange glances** (=look at each other quickly) 交換目光, 互相看一眼 **2 at a glance** if you know something at a glance, you know it as soon as you see it 看一眼便知道: *He'll be able to tell if the diamonds are genuine at a glance.* 他看一眼便能認出這些鑽石的真假。**3 at first glance** when you first look at something 乍一看, 最初看到時: *At first glance the place seemed deserted.* 乍一看, 這地方似乎空無一人。 3

glanc·ing /ˋglænsɪŋ; ˈglɑːnsɪŋ/ *adj* **a glancing blow** a hit that partly misses so that it does not have its full force 擦邊而過的一擊, 斜擊 —**glancingly** *adv*

gland /glænd; glænd/ *n* [C] an organ of the body which produces a substance that the body needs, such as SWEAT² (1) or SALIVA 腺: *Mumps make your glands swell up.* 腮腺炎使你的淋巴腺腫大。| *the pituitary gland* 腦垂體腺

glan·du·lar /ˋglændʒəlɚ; ˈglændjʊlə/ *adj* related to the glands, or produced by the glands 腺的, 由腺產生的

glandular fe·ver /ˌ··· ˈ··/ *n* [U] *BrE* an infectious disease which makes your LYMPH GLANDs swell up and makes you feel weak for a long time afterwards【英】腺熱, 傳染性單核白細胞增多症; MONONUCLEOSIS *AmE*【美】

glare¹ /glɛr; gleə/ *v* [I] **1** to look angrily at someone for a long time 怒目而視: **glare at sb** *She glared at him accusingly.* 她用責備的眼光怒視着他。**2** [always+adv/prep] to shine with a very strong bright light which hurts your eyes 發出刺眼的強光: [**+through/in**] *The sun glared through the car windscreen.* 強烈的陽光透過擋風玻璃照進車裡。

glare² *n* **1** [singular] a bright unpleasant light which hurts your eyes 刺眼的強光: *the harsh glare of the desert sun* 沙漠上刺眼的陽光 **2** [C] a long angry look 怒視: *She gave him an icy glare.* 她以冷冰冰的目光怒視着他。**3**

the glare of publicity the full attention of newspapers, television etc, especially when you do not want it 眾目睽睽

glar·ing /ˈglɛrɪŋ; ˈgleərɪŋ/ *adj* **1** very bad and very noticeable 糟透的; 十分顯眼的: *the glaring absence of any reliable information* 可靠消息的明顯缺乏 | **glaring error/mistake** *The report contained a number of glaring errors.* 報告中有許多很明顯的錯誤。**2** too bright and difficult to look at 耀眼的: *the glaring light of the headlamps* 前燈耀眼的光 —**glaringly** *adv*

glas·nost /ˈglɑsnɑst; ˈglæznɒst/ *n* [U] *Russian* a word meaning the willingness of a country or organization to show what it is doing and discuss its decisions, used especially about the government of the former USSR【俄】公開性, 開放性〔指某國或某組織願意公開表示目前在幹些甚麼並公開討論決策; 此詞尤用於前蘇聯政府〕

glass 玻璃杯

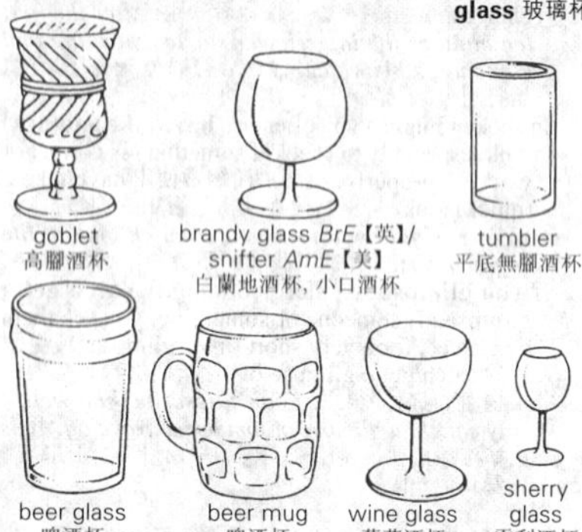

glasses 眼鏡

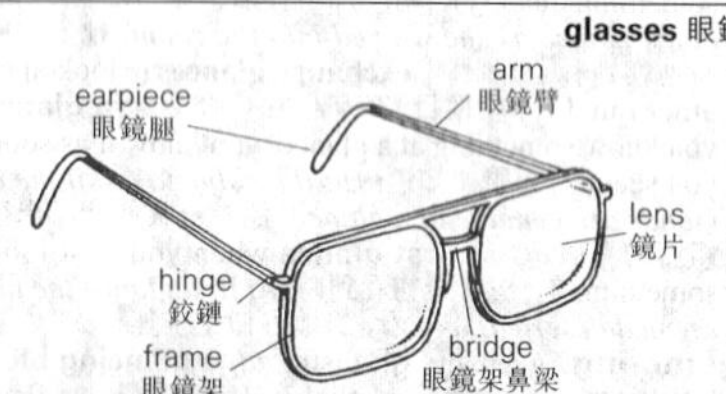

G

glass¹ /glæs; glɑːs/ *n*
1 ►TRANSPARENT 透明的◄ [U] a transparent solid substance, for example used for making windows and bottles 玻璃: *a glass bowl* 玻璃碗 | *Polly cut herself on a piece of broken glass.* 波莉被一片碎玻璃割傷了。
2 ►FOR DRINKING 用於喝東西◄ [C] a container used for drinking made of glass, or the drink in it 玻璃杯; 杯中的東西: *a wine glass* 葡萄酒杯 | **[+of]** *a glass of red wine* 一杯紅葡萄酒
3 ►FOR EYES 用於眼睛◄ **glasses** [plural] a set of two pieces of specially cut glass in a frame, which you wear in order to see more clearly 眼鏡: *I hate wearing glasses.* 我討厭戴眼鏡。| *I need a new pair of glasses.* 我需要一副新眼鏡。—see also 另見 OPERA GLASSES, FIELD GLASSES
4 ►GLASS OBJECTS 玻璃製品◄ [U] objects which are made of glass, especially ones used for drinking and eating; GLASSWARE 玻璃器皿: *a priceless collection of Venetian glass* 一套價值連城的威尼斯玻璃器皿收藏品
5 people in glass houses shouldn't throw stones used to say that you should not criticize someone for having a fault if you have the same fault yourself 玻璃屋裡的人不要扔石頭〔表示你如果有某種毛病, 便不要指責別人有同樣的毛病〕
6 under glass plants that are grown under glass are protected from the cold by a glass cover 在温室裡: *tomatoes grown all year round under glass* 一年四季在温室裡種植的番茄
7 glass ceiling an imaginary limit that prevents women from being successful, even though there are no actual laws or rules to stop them 玻璃天花板〔指妨礙婦女成功的一種無形限制〕
8 ►MIRROR 鏡子◄ *old-fashioned* a mirror【過時】鏡子
9 the glass *old-fashioned* a BAROMETER (1)【過時】氣壓計, 晴雨計 —see also 另見 CUT GLASS, GROUND GLASS, LOOKING GLASS, MAGNIFYING GLASS, PLATE GLASS, **raise your glasses** (RAISE¹ (12)), STAINED GLASS

glass² *v*
glass sth ↔ **in** *phr v* [T] to cover something with glass, or to build a glass structure around something 用玻璃把〔某物〕罩住; 圍繞〔某物〕建起玻璃結構

glass·blow·er /ˈglæsˌbloə; ˈglɑːsˌbləʊə/ *n* [C] someone who shapes hot glass by blowing air through a tube 吹玻璃工

glass fi·bre /ˌ· ˈ··◄/ *n* [U] FIBREGLASS 玻璃纖維

glass·ful /ˈglæsˌful; ˈglɑːsfʊl/ *n* [C] the amount of liquid a glass will hold 一玻璃杯的量

glass·house /ˈglæsˌhaus; ˈglɑːshaʊs/ *n* [C] *BrE*【英】**1** a building which is used for growing plants and is made of glass; GREENHOUSE 玻璃暖房, 温室 **2 the glasshouse** *slang* a military prison【俚】軍事監獄

glass·ware /ˈglæsˌwɛr; ˈglɑːsweə/ *n* [U] glass objects, especially ones used for drinking and eating 玻璃製品〔尤指用於飲食的玻璃器皿〕

glass wool /ˌ· ˈ·/ *n* [U] *BrE* FIBREGLASS【英】玻璃纖維

glass·y /ˈglæsɪ; ˈglɑːsi/ *adj* **1** smooth and shining, like glass〔像玻璃一樣〕光滑的: *the glassy green waters of the Hudson River* 哈得孫河平滑如鏡的綠色河水 **2 glassy eyes/stare** eyes that show no feeling or understanding, and do not move 目光呆滯的眼睛/眼神

glassy-eyed /ˌ·· ˈ·◄/ *adj* having still eyes and an expression that shows no feeling or understanding 目光呆滯的, 眼睛無神的: *They had him doped-up. He was sort of glassy-eyed.* 他們對他施用了麻醉品。他有點目光呆滯。

glau·co·ma /glɔˈkomə; glɔːˈkəʊmə/ *n* [U] an eye disease in which increased pressure inside your eye gradually makes you lose your sight 青光眼

glau·cous /ˈglɔkəs; ˈglɔːkəs/ *adj technical* a glaucous leaf or plant has a fine white powdery surface【術語】〔葉子或植物〕表面起白霜的

glaze¹ /glez; gleɪz/ *v* **1** [I] also 又作 **glaze over** if your eyes glaze over, they show no expression because you are very bored or tired〔因無聊或疲倦〕變得目光呆滯 **2** [T] to cover plates, cups etc made of clay with a thin liquid that gives them a shiny surface 給〔陶瓷碗碟等〕上釉 **3** [T] to cover fruit, cake, or meat with a liquid which gives it an attractive shiny surface 在〔水果、蛋糕或熟肉表面〕澆液漿 **4** [T] to fit glass into window frames in a house, door etc 給…裝玻璃

glaze² *n* **1** [C] a liquid that is used to cover plates, cups etc made of clay and give them a shiny surface 釉 **2** [U] liquid which is put onto fruit, cake, or meat to give it an attractive shiny surface〔澆在水果、蛋糕或熟肉上使之光滑好看的〕液漿 **3** [U] a transparent covering of oil paint spread over a painting 透明色料, 光油

glazed /glezd; gleɪzd/ *adj* **glazed look/eyes/expression etc** if you have a glazed look etc your eyes show no expression because you are very bored or tired〔由於無聊或疲倦而〕目光呆滯的神色/眼睛/表情等

gla·zi·er /ˈgleʒə; ˈgleɪziə/ *n* [C] someone whose job is to fit glass into window frames 裝玻璃工

glaz·ing /ˈglezɪŋ; ˈgleɪzɪŋ/ *n* [U] glass that has been used to fill windows 窗用玻璃 —see also 另見 DOUBLE-GLAZING

gleam¹ /glim; gliːm/ *v* [I] **1** to shine softly 發微光, 閃爍: *The spire of the Golden Temple gleamed in the autumn sun.* 金廟的尖塔在秋日的陽光下閃閃發光。| **[+with]** *the table's surface gleaming with wax polish* 上了蠟的桌面閃閃發亮 **2 gleam with happiness/joy etc** if your eyes or face gleam with a feeling, they show it 〔眼睛或臉部〕露出喜悅的光芒等: *His face gleamed with amusement.* 他滿臉開心的神色。—**gleaming** *adj*: *gleaming glass skyscrapers* 閃閃發亮的玻璃摩天樓

gleam² *n* [C] **1** a small pale light, especially one that shines for a short time 〔尤指短暫的〕微光, 閃光: **[+of]** *They saw the gleam of a lamp ahead.* 他們看到前面一盞燈閃爍的微光。**2** the brightness of something that shines 閃光, 亮光: **[+of]** *the sudden gleam of white teeth* 突然露出光亮雪白的牙齒 **3** a sudden expression that appears for a moment on someone's face or in their eyes 閃現: **[+of]** *A gleam of satisfaction crossed her face.* 她的臉上閃現出滿足的神情。

glean /glin; gliːn/ *v* **1** [T] to find out facts and information slowly and with difficulty 緩慢艱難地搜集〔事實、信息〕: **glean sth from** *I've managed to glean a few details about him from his friends.* 我已經設法從他朋友那兒弄到有關他的幾點情況。**2** [I,T] to collect grain that has been left behind after the crops have been cut 〔收割後〕拾落穗

glean·ings /ˈglinɪŋz; ˈgliːnɪŋz/ *n* [plural] small pieces of information that you have found out with difficulty 好不容易搜集到的零星消息

glebe /glib; gliːb/ *n* [U] **1** *poetic* earth or soil【詩】土地, 大地 **2** *BrE* land given to a priest to provide part of his income【英】給予牧師的土地〔以提供其部分收入〕

glee /gli; gliː/ *n* **1** [U] a feeling of satisfaction and excitement because something good has happened to you or something bad has happened to someone else 〔由於好事發生於自己, 或壞事發生於他人所產生的〕滿足, 興奮: *The kids watched with glee as I tried to catch the hamster.* 在我試圖逮住那隻倉鼠時, 小孩們沾沾自喜地看着。**2** [C] a song for three or four voices together 三部重唱曲, 四部重唱曲

glee club /ˈ· ·/ *n* [C] *AmE* a group of people who sing together for enjoyment【美】合唱組, 合唱團

glee·ful /ˈglifəl; ˈgliːfəl/ *adj* really enjoying the fact that something good has happened to you or that something bad has happened to someone else 〔由於好事發生於自己或壞事發生於他人而〕心滿意足的, 幸災樂禍的 —**gleefully** *adv* —**gleefulness** *n* [U]

glen /glɛn; glen/ *n* [C] a deep narrow valley in Scotland or Ireland 〔蘇格蘭或愛爾蘭的〕峽谷, 幽谷

glib /glɪb; glɪb/ *adj* **1** glib remarks, explanations etc are difficult to believe because they are said easily and without thinking 〔評論、解釋等〕輕率的: *glib generalizations about the problem of racism* 對種族主義問題輕率的概括 **2** someone who is glib says things to persuade people without being certain that they are true 能說會道的, 油腔滑調的: *glib politicians with their easy solutions* 能言善辯的政客和他們所認為能輕而易舉解決問題的辦法 —**glibly** *adv* —**glibness** *n* [U]

glide¹ /glaɪd; glaɪd/ *v* [I always+adv/prep] to move smoothly and quietly, as if no effort was being made 滑行, 滑動: **[+across/over etc]** *a snake gliding across the path* 一條蛇從小道滑行而過 | *The plane glided to a halt just short of the control tower.* 飛機滑行到緊挨控制塔的地方停了下來。

glide² *n* [C] **1** a smooth, quiet movement that seems to take no effort 滑行, 滑動 **2** the act of moving from one musical note to another without a break in sound 滑音, 延音 **3** *technical* a vowel which is made by moving your tongue from one position to another one【術語】滑音 —see also 另見 DIPHTHONG

glid·er /ˈglaɪdɚ; ˈglaɪdə/ *n* [C] a light plane without an engine 滑翔機

glid·ing /ˈglaɪdɪŋ; ˈglaɪdɪŋ/ *n* [U] the sport of flying in a glider 〔乘滑翔機飛行的〕滑翔運動 —see also 另見 HANG GLIDING

glim·mer¹ /ˈglɪmɚ; ˈglɪmə/ *n* [U] **1 a glimmer of hope/doubt/recognition** a small sign of hope, doubt etc 一線希望/一絲懷疑/似曾相識的神情 **2** a light that is not very bright 微光: *the glimmer of a candle* 蠟燭微弱的光線

glimmer² *v* [I] to shine with a light that is not very bright 發出微光: *A light glimmered at the end of the hall.* 一盞電燈在大廳盡頭發出微光。

glim·mer·ing /ˈglɪmərɪŋ; ˈglɪmərɪŋ/ *n* [C often plural 常用複數] a small sign of thought or feeling 模糊的想法, 一點感覺: *glimmerings of interest* 絲毫興趣

glimpse¹ /glɪmps; glɪmps/ *n* [T] **1** to see someone or something for a moment without getting a complete view of them 一瞥, 看一眼: *I glimpsed her face in the crowd, but then she was gone.* 我在人羣中瞥見她的臉, 但隨即她就消失了。—see 見 GLANCE² (USAGE) **2** to begin to understand something for a moment 開始懂得: *He glimpsed the despair that she must have felt.* 他開始體會到她肯定感受過的那種失望。

glimpse² *n* [C] **1** a sight of someone or something that you only have for a short time and that is not complete 一瞥, 一看: **get/catch a glimpse of** *I caught only a glimpse of the president's car.* 我只瞥見總統的汽車。| **fleeting glimpse** (=a very short one) 很快的一瞥 —see 見 GLANCE² (USAGE) **2** a short experience of something that helps you begin to understand it 〔有助於理解某事的〕一次短暫經歷: *a glimpse of what life might be like in the future* 使我領會未來生活可能是甚麼樣子的一次短暫經歷

glint¹ /glɪnt; glɪnt/ *v* [I] **1** if a shiny surface glints, it gives out small flashes of light 閃爍, 閃光: *Her gold bracelet glinted in the morning sunlight.* 她的金手鐲在早晨的陽光裡閃閃發光。**2** if your eyes glint, they shine and show an unfriendly feeling 眼睛發亮〔顯示不友善的感情〕: *Derek's eyes glinted when he saw the money.* 德里克看到錢眼睛就發亮。

glint² *n* [C] **1** a look in someone's eyes which shows an unfriendly feeling 不友好的眼神: *There was an evil glint in her eyes.* 她露出不懷好意的眼神。**2** a flash of light from a shiny surface 〔光滑的表面上發出的〕閃光

glis·ten /ˈglɪsn̩; ˈglɪsən/ *v* [I] to shine and look wet or oily 〔油亮或潮濕物〕閃光: *Her dark hair glistened in the moonlight.* 她的黑髮在月光下閃閃發亮。| **[+with]** *The boy's back was glistening with sweat.* 那個男孩背上的汗水閃閃發亮。

glitch /glɪtʃ; glɪtʃ/ *n* [C] **1** a small fault in the working of something 小故障, 差錯 **2** a false electronic signal caused by a sudden increase in the supply of electric power 〔由於電源突增而產生的〕假電子信號, 脈衝干擾

glit·ter¹ /ˈglɪtɚ; ˈglɪtə/ *v* [I] to shine brightly with flashing points of light 閃爍, 閃光: *The blades of their swords glittered in the sunlight.* 他們的劍刃在陽光下閃閃發亮。

glitter² *n* [U] **1** brightness consisting of many flashing points of light 光亮, 閃光: *the glitter of his gold cigarette case* 他的金煙盒發出的閃光 **2** the attractiveness of a place or a way of living which is connected with rich or famous people; GLAMOUR (1) 〔地方或生活方式的〕魅力, 誘惑力: *Jersey City is a world away from the glitter of Manhattan.* 澤西市遠離曼哈頓的繁華魅力, 是另外一個世界。**3** very small pieces of shiny paper that are used for decoration 〔用於裝飾的〕閃光紙屑 —**glittery** *adj*

glit·te·ra·ti /ˌglɪtəˈrɑtɪ; ˌglɪtəˈrɑːti/ *n* [plural] rich, famous, and fashionable people whose activities are often reported in newspapers and magazines 知名人士, 名流

glit·ter·ing /ˈglɪtərɪŋ; ˈglɪtərɪŋ/ *adj* **1** giving off many small flashes of light 閃光的: *glittering jewels* 閃光的首飾 **2** very successful, and connected with rich and famous people 〔與富人、名人相連的〕輝煌的, 光彩的: *a*

G

glittering career in the diplomatic service 在外交工作生涯的輝煌成就 **—glitteringly** *adv*

glitz /glɪts; glɪts/ *n* [U] the exciting, attractive quality which is connected with rich, famous and fashionable people; GLAMOUR (1)〔與富人、名人、時髦人們有關的〕魅力, 富麗堂皇: *show business glitz* 娛樂行業的魅力 **—glitzy** *adj*

gloam·ing /ˋglomɪŋ; ˈgləʊmɪŋ/ *n* [U] **the gloaming** *poetic* the time in the early evening when it is becoming dark; DUSK【詩】黃昏

gloat /glot; gləʊt/ *v* [I] to show in an unpleasant way that you are happy about your own success or about someone else's failure 幸災樂禍, 洋洋得意: **[+over]** *Dick was still gloating over Scotland's 5-0 defeat.* 迪克還在因為蘇格蘭5比0告負而幸災樂禍。**—gloat** *n* [singular]: *I bet Sam's having a gloat over that one.* 我敢打賭, 薩姆肯定在為那個幸災樂禍。**—gloatingly** *adv*

glob /glɑb; glɒb/ *n* [C] *informal* a small amount of something soft or liquid that has a round shape【非正式】〔柔軟物〕一小團, 〔液體〕一滴: *globs of mud sticking to the cat's fur* 黏在貓身上一團團的泥

3 **glo·bal** /ˋglobḷ; ˈgləʊbəl/ *adj* **1** affecting or including the whole world 全球的, 世界的: *AIDS is a global problem which needs a global response.* 愛滋病是個全球問題, 需要全球合力對付。**2** considering all parts of a problem or a situation together 全面的, 整體的: *The report takes a global view of the company's problems.* 這份報告全面審視了該公司的各種問題。**—globally** *adv*

global warm·ing /ˌ·· ˈ··/ *n* [U] a general increase in world temperatures caused by increased amounts of CARBON DIOXIDE around the Earth 全球氣溫變暖

globe /glob; gləʊb/ *n* [C] **1** a round object with a map of the Earth drawn on it 地球儀 **2 the globe** the world 地球, 世界: *We export our goods all over the globe.* 我們的商品出口到世界各地。**3** an object shaped like a ball; SPHERE (1) 球, 球狀物

globe·trot·ter /ˋglobˌtrɑtɚ; ˈgləʊbtrɒtə/ *n* [C] *informal* someone who travels to many different countries【非正式】〔去許多不同國家的〕環球旅行者 **—globetrotting** *adj*

glob·u·lar /ˋglɑbjəlɚ; ˈglɒbjʊlə/ *adj* in the shape of a globule or a globe 小珠狀的, 球狀的

glob·ule /ˋglɑbjul; ˈglɒbjuːl/ *n* [C] a small drop of a liquid, or of a solid that has been melted〔液體或熔化固體的〕一滴: *tiny globules of mercury* 細小的水銀珠

glock·en·spiel /ˋglɑkənˌspil; ˈglɒkənspiːl/ *n* [C] a musical instrument consisting of many flat metal bars of different lengths, which is played with special hammers〔用小槌敲擊發聲的〕鐘琴

glogg /glɔg; glɒg/ *n* [U] *AmE* a hot drink made with red wine and SPICES[1] (1)【美】格洛格〔一種由紅葡萄酒和香料製成的熱飲〕

glom /glɑm; glɒm/ *v* [I,T] *AmE informal* to take something, especially an idea, opinion etc, and make it your own【美, 非正式】吸收, 接受〔想法、意見等〕: **[+onto]** *Watch how the kids glom onto this new style.* 看看這些孩子怎樣接納這種新款式的。

gloom /glum; gluːm/ *n* [singular,U] **1** *especially literary* almost complete darkness【尤文】朦朧: *A tall figure appeared in the canyon's gloom.* 一個高個子人影出現在峽谷的暗處。**2** a feeling of great sadness and lack of hope 憂鬱, 絕望: *The officers sat sunk in gloom.* 軍官們憂愁滿懷地坐着。

gloom·y /ˋglumɪ; ˈgluːmi/ *adj* **1** sad because you think the situation will not improve 陰鬱的, 沮喪的: *When I saw their gloomy faces, I knew something was wrong.* 我看見他們那憂愁的臉時就知道出事了。**2** making you feel that things will not improve 令人沮喪的, 令人掃興的: *a gloomy economic forecast* 令人沮喪的經濟預測 **3** dark, especially in a way that seems sad 陰暗的, 幽暗的: *Ezra Pound's daughter visited him in his gloomy study in Carlyle Mansions.* 埃茲拉·龐德的女兒在卡萊爾大宅他那陰暗的書房裡看望了他。**—gloomily** *adv* **—gloominess** *n* [U]

glop /glɑp; glɒp/ *n* [U] *AmE informal* a thick soft wet mass, especially of food that looks too unpleasant to eat【美, 非正式】黏稠的糊狀物質〔尤指太難看, 以致難以食用的食品〕**—gloppy** *adj*

glo·ri·fied /ˋglorəˌfaɪd; ˈglɔːrɪ̣faɪd/ *adj* [only before noun 僅用於名詞前] made to seem like something more important 被吹捧的, 被美化的: *The so-called college was no more than a glorified school.* 那個所謂的學院只不過是一所被美化的學校。

glo·ri·fy /ˋglorəˌfaɪ; ˈglɔːrɪ̣faɪ/ *v* [T] **1** to make someone or something seem more important or better than they really are 吹捧, 頌揚: *films which glorify violence* 頌揚暴力的影片 **2 glorify God/the Lord etc** to give praise and thanks to God 讚美上帝/主等 **—glorification** /ˌglorəfəˋkeʃən; ˌglɔːrɪ̣fɪ̣ˈkeɪʃən/ *n*: **[+of]** *the glorification of war* 對戰爭的頌揚

glo·ri·ous /ˋglorɪəs; ˈglɔːriəs/ *adj* **1** having or deserving great fame, praise, and honour 輝煌的, 光榮的, 榮耀的: *It was a glorious political career while it lasted.* 在當時, 那是一段光輝的政治生涯。| *a glorious victory* 光榮的勝利 **2** very beautiful, attractive, or impressive 壯麗的, 吸引人的: *glorious colours* 燦爛的色彩 | *a glorious sight* 壯麗的景色 **3** extremely enjoyable; WONDERFUL 極其愉快的, 極好的: *We spent three glorious weeks in Hawaii.* 我們在夏威夷度過了令人愉快的三週。**4 glorious day/summer/weather** weather etc that is very nice because it is sunny and clear 晴朗的一天/美好的夏季/宜人的天氣 **—gloriously** *adv*

glo·ry¹ /ˋglorɪ; ˈglɔːri/ *n* **1** [U] the importance, honour, and praise that people give someone or something they admire a lot 光榮, 榮譽: *As a child he dreamt of future glory as an Olympic champion.* 他小時候就夢想將來獲得奧林匹克冠軍的榮耀。| **covered in/with glory** *The team finished the season covered with glory.* 該隊滿載榮譽地結束了賽季。**2** [C] something that is especially beautiful, or makes you feel proud 極其漂亮的東西; 榮耀的事, 值得驕傲的事: *the glories of Roman architecture* 羅馬建築的輝煌 | **crowning glory** (=the final completion of something successful) 至高無上的榮譽 *The Oscar was the crowning glory of her career.* 獲得奧斯卡獎是她事業中的最高榮譽。**3** [U] a beautiful and impressive appearance 壯觀; 輝煌: *After years of neglect the palace has been restored to its former glory.* 這座年久失修的宮殿現在又恢復了往日的輝煌。| **in all its/their etc glory** *Wild flowers in all their glory carpeted the meadow.* 野花盛開, 如地毯般把草坪鋪滿了。**4 bask/bathe in sb's reflected glory** to share some of the importance and praise that belongs to someone close to you 分享某人的榮譽, 沾某人的光 **5 Glory (be) to God/Jesus etc** *spoken* used to say that God deserves praise, honour, and thanks【口】榮耀歸於上帝/耶穌等 **6 glory days** a time in the past when someone was admired 輝煌歲月: *his glory days on the high school football team* 他在高中足球隊的威風日子 **7 to the (greater) glory of** *formal* in order to increase the honour that is given to someone or something【正式】為了(增加)...的榮耀: *Bach composed to the greater glory of God.* 巴赫為了增加上帝的榮耀而作曲。**8 go to glory** *old use* to die【舊】作古, 仙逝

glory² *v*

glory in sth *phr v* [T not in passive 不用被動態] to enjoy something very much such as praise or people's attention 因〔受到讚揚、引人注意〕而欣喜

gloss¹ /glɔs; glɒs/ *n* **1** [singular,U] shiny brightness on a surface〔表面的〕光澤, 光亮: *shoes shined to a high gloss* 擦得鋥亮的鞋子 | *The gloss had gone from her dark hair.* 她的黑髮已失去光澤。**2** [singular,U] a pleasant appearance of something, which is better than the truth 假象, 虛假的外表: *The General's image soon lost its gloss.* 將軍的形象只是虛飾, 很快就給揭穿了。**3** [C] an explanation of a piece of writing, especially in a note at the end of a page or book 註釋, 註解 **4 gloss finish/print** a surface or photograph that has been made shiny 光面〔照片等上光的表面〕—compare 比較 MATT

gloss² *v* [T] to provide an explanation of a piece of writing, especially in a note at the end of a page or book 註釋, 註解

gloss over sth *phr v* [T] to deliberately avoid talking about unpleasant facts or say as little as possible about them 故意避免談論〔不愉快的事情〕: *She glossed over the details of her divorce and changed the subject.* 她避免談到她離婚的細節, 改變了話題。

glos·sa·ry /ˈglɑsərɪ; ˈglɒsəri/ *n* [C] a list of explanations of words, especially unusual ones, at the end of a book〔書末的〕詞彙表

gloss paint /ˌ· ˈ·/ *n* [C,U] paint which looks shiny after it dries 有光塗料 —compare 比較 EMULSION (2)

gloss·y¹ /ˈglɔsɪ; ˈglɒsi/ *adj* **1** shiny and smooth 平滑而有光澤的, 光滑的: *the cat's glossy fur* 貓的光滑的毛 **2** *AmE* trying too hard to be attractive or perfect【美】虛飾的: *He may have glossy manners, but Gordon's no gentleman.* 戈登可能圓滑世故, 但他卻不是正人君子。—**glossiness** *n* [U]

glossy² *n* [C] **1** *BrE* also 又作 **glossy magazine** a fashion magazine printed on good quality, shiny paper, usually with lots of colour pictures【英】〔用高級有光紙印刷的〕時尚雜誌 **2** a photograph printed on shiny paper 光面照片〔指用有光紙印刷的彩色照片〕

glot·tal stop /ˌ·· ˈ·/ *n* [C] *technical* a speech sound made by completely closing and then opening your glottis, which in English may take the place of a /t/ between vowel sounds or may be used before a vowel sound【術語】喉塞音, 聲門閉塞音

glot·tis /ˈglɑtɪs; ˈglɒtɪs/ *n* [C] the space between your VOCAL CORDS, which produce the sound of your voice by movements in which this space is opened and closed 聲門 —**glottal** *adj* —see picture at 參見 RESPIRATORY 圖

gloves 手套

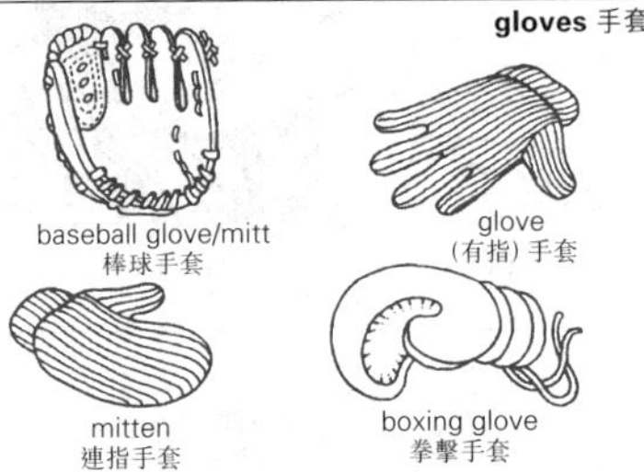

glove /glʌv; glʌv/ *n* [C] **1** a piece of clothing which covers your hand, especially one which has separate parts for each finger〔尤指有指〕手套 —compare 比較 MITTEN **2** a large leather glove used in BOXING 拳擊手套 **3** a large leather glove used to catch the ball in BASEBALL 棒球手套 —see also 另見 **fit (sb) like a glove** (FIT¹ (1))

glove com·part·ment /ˈ· ·ˌ··/ also 又作 **glove box** /ˈ· ·/ *n* [C] a small shelf in a car in front of the passenger seat where small things such as maps can be kept〔汽車前排乘客座位前存放地圖等小物件的〕貯物箱 —see picture on page A2 參見 A2 頁圖

gloved /glʌvd; glʌvd/ *adj* wearing a glove 戴手套的

glove pup·pet /ˈ· ˌ··/ *n* [C] a PUPPET (1) that you put over your hand 手套式木偶, 掌中木偶

glow¹ /glo; gləʊ/ *n* [singular] **1** a soft steady light, especially from something that is burning without flames〔尤指沒有火焰的燃燒物發出的〕光亮, 光輝: *The glow from the dying fire lit his face.* 快要熄滅的火光照亮了他的臉。| *the glow of city lights on the horizon* 城市燈火在地平線上的亮光 **2** brightness of colour, especially colours like red and orange〔尤指紅色和橙色的〕鮮豔: *the glow of copper pans hanging in the kitchen* 掛在廚房裡的黃銅平底鍋的亮光 **3** the bright colour your face or body has after exercise or when you are very pleased and excited〔運動後或興奮時臉部或身體發出的〕紅潤光澤: *a healthy rosy glow in her cheeks* 她臉頰呈現的健康紅潤 **4 a glow of pleasure/satisfaction/happiness etc** a strong feeling of pleasure etc 強烈的愉快/滿足/幸福等

glow² *v* [I] **1** to shine with a soft, steady light 發出柔和穩定的光: *We saw a lamp glowing in the garden.* 我們看見花園裡有盞燈亮着。**2** to produce a red light and heat without flames〔無焰地〕發光生熱: *His cigarette glowed in the dark.* 他的香煙在黑暗中發亮。**3** if your face or body glows, it is red or hot as a result of exercise or strong emotion〔由於運動或強烈情感〕面部[身體]發紅[發熱] **4 glow with pride/pleasure/triumph etc** to look very happy because you feel proud etc 由於自豪/愉快/勝利等容光煥發: *The boys emerged scrubbed and glowing with happiness.* 男孩子們洗得乾乾淨淨, 喜氣洋洋地出現了。

glow·er /ˈglaʊɚ; ˈglaʊə/ *v* [I+at] to look angrily at someone 怒視 —**gloweringly** *adv*

glow·ing /ˈgloɪŋ; ˈgləʊɪŋ/ *adj* **1 glowing report/account/description etc** a report etc full of praise 熱情讚揚的報告/敘述/描寫等: *Her supervisor gave her a glowing reference.* 她的主管上司為她寫了一封充滿讚美的推薦信。**2 in glowing terms** using a lot of praise 以讚揚的詞句: *He speaks of you in glowing terms.* 他總是以十分讚賞的口吻談到你。—**glowingly** *adv*

glow-worm /ˈ· ·/ *n* [C] an insect which gives out light from its body 螢火蟲

glu·cose /ˈglukos; ˈgluːkəʊs/ *n* [U] a natural form of sugar that exists in fruit 葡萄糖

glue¹ /glu; gluː/ *n* [C,U] a sticky substance used for joining things together 膠, 膠水 3

glue² *v present participle* **gluing** *or* **glueing** [T] **1** to join two things together using a special sticky substance 膠合, 黏合, 黏貼: **glue sth together** *I managed to glue the pieces back together.* 我把碎片又黏合起來了。**2 be glued to** *informal* to look at something with all your attention【非正式】盯着眼看, 審視: *Those kids are glued to the TV all day.* 那些孩子整天圍着電視看。**3 glued to the spot** unable to move because you are very surprised, frightened, interested etc〔由於驚恐或極感興趣而〕動彈不得的

glue-snif·fing /ˈ· ˌ··/ *n* [U] the habit of breathing in gases from glues or similar substances in order to produce an artificial state of excitement: SOLVENT ABUSE〔使人產生興奮的〕吸膠毒 —**glue sniffer** *n* [C]

glue·y /ˈgluɪ; ˈgluːi/ *adj* **1** sticky like glue〔像膠一樣〕有黏性的 **2** covered with glue 塗膠的

glum /glʌm; glʌm/ **glummer, glummest** *adj* sad and not talking much; GLOOMY 沉默寡言的; 憂鬱的: *Hey, don't look so glum. Everything will be OK!* 嗨, 別悶悶不樂, 一切都會好的! —**glumly** *adv* —**glumness** *n* [U]

glut¹ /glʌt; glʌt/ *n* [C usually singular 一般用單數] a supply of something that is more than you need 供應過剩: [+of] *a glut of oil on the market* 市場上油的供應過剩

glut² *v* **glutted, glutting** [T] **1 be glutted with** to be supplied with too much of something ...供應過剩, 充斥: *The shops are glutted with oranges.* 商店裡的橙子供應過剩。**2 glut yourself on sth** to eat too much 過度地吃某物

glu·ten /ˈglutn̩; ˈgluːtn/ *n* [U] a sticky PROTEIN substance that is found in flour made of wheat 麵筋, 麩筋

glu·ti·nous /ˈglutənəs; ˈgluːtɪnəs/ *adj* very sticky 很黏的, 黏性很大的

glut·ton /ˈglʌtn̩; ˈglʌtn/ *n* [C] **1** someone who eats too much 貪食者 **2 a glutton for punishment** someone who seems to enjoy working hard or doing something unpleasant 不辭勞苦[任勞任怨]的人 —**gluttonous** *adj* —**gluttonously** *adv*

glut·ton·y /ˈglʌtn̩ɪ; ˈglʌtəni/ *n* [U] *formal* the bad habit of eating and drinking too much【正式】暴食暴飲, 大吃大喝

gly·ce·rine /ˈglɪsərɪn; ˈglɪsərɪn/ *n* [U] a thick sweet transparent liquid made from fats and used in medicines, explosives, and foods 甘油, 丙三醇

gm the written abbreviation of 縮寫= GRAM

GMT /ˌdʒi ɛm ˈti; ˌdʒiː em ˈtiː/ *n* [U] Greenwich Mean Time; the time as measured at Greenwich in London, that is used as an international standard for measuring time 格林尼治標準時間

gnarled /nɑrld; nɑːld/ *adj* **1** a gnarled tree or branch is rough and twisted with hard lumps〔樹或樹枝〕粗糙的; 扭曲的; 多節的 **2** gnarled hands or fingers are twisted, rough, and difficult to move, usually because they are old〔手或手指〕扭曲的; 粗糙的; 行動困難的

gnarl·y /ˈnɑrlɪ; ˈnɑːli/ *adj AmE slang*【美俚】**1** a word meaning very good or excellent, used by young people 很好的, 頂呱呱的〔年輕人用語〕: *"My mom said I can go out tonight!" "Gnarly, man! Let's go."* "我媽媽說今天晚上我可以出去!" "太好了, 夥計! 我們走吧。" **2** a word meaning not good enough, used by young people 不夠好的〔年輕人用語〕

gnash /næʃ; næʃ/ *v* [T] **gnash your teeth** to move your teeth against each other so that they make a noise, especially because you are unhappy or angry〔不高興或生氣時〕咬牙切齒 —**gnash** *n* [C]

gnash·ers /ˈnæʃəz; ˈnæʃəz/ *n* [plural] *BrE informal* teeth【英, 非正式】牙齒

gnat /næt; næt/ *n* [C] a small flying insect that bites〔會飛的〕叮人小蟲

gnaw /nɔ; nɔː/ *v* [I always+adv/prep, T] to keep biting something hard 咬, 啃: **[+away/at/on]** *Val gnawed at her fingernails.* 瓦爾咬自己的手指甲。| **gnaw sth** *a dog gnawing a bone* 啃着骨頭的狗 | **gnaw a hole in sth** *A rat had gnawed a hole in the box.* 老鼠在箱子上咬了一個洞。

gnaw at sb *phr v* [T] to make someone feel worried or frightened 使煩惱, 驚嚇: *Something's gnawing at Celia – she's been very moody.* 有件事在讓西莉亞煩惱——她心情很不好。

gnaw·ing /ˈnɔɪŋ; ˈnɔːɪŋ/ *adj* [only before noun 僅用於名詞前] painful or worrying, especially only slightly but for a long time〔輕微但長時間〕令人痛苦的, 揪心的: *gnawing doubts about her own abilities* 懷疑自己的能力而令她揪心

gnome /nom; nəʊm/ *n* [C] **1** a creature in children's stories like a little old man with a pointed hat who lives under the ground and guards gold, jewels etc〔兒童故事裡地下守護金子、珠寶等的〕土地神 **2** a stone or plastic figure representing one of these creatures 土地神石像[塑像]: *a garden gnome* 花園土地神石像

gno·mic /ˈnomɪk; ˈnəʊmɪk/ *adj* gnomic remarks are short, clever, and difficult to understand〔言論〕簡短慧黠而晦澀的: *gnomic predictions about the future of the economy* 對未來經濟精奧的預測 —**gnomically** /-klɪ; -kli/ *adv*

GNP /ˌdʒi ɛn ˈpi; ˌdʒiː en ˈpiː/ *n* [singular] Gross National Product; the total value of all the goods and services produced in a country, usually in a single year 國民生產總值

gnu /nu; nuː/ *n* [C] a large southern African animal with a tail and curved horns; WILDEBEEST〔南非的〕牛羚

go 去, 走

Nick's gone to Pairs for the weekend.
尼克去巴黎度週末。

Derek's been to Paris three times.
德里克去過巴黎三次。

go¹ /go; gəʊ/ *v past tense* **went** /wɛnt; went/ *past participle* **gone** /gɔn; gɒn/ *3rd person singular present tense* **goes** /goz; gəʊz/

① TO MOVE AWAY FROM THE SPEAKER 離開說話人
② TO BE IN OR PASS INTO A PARTICULAR STATE 處於或進入某種狀態
③ TO START TO DO SOMETHING OR TO DO SOMETHING 開始做某事或做某事
④ POSITION 位置
⑤ SOUND 聲音
⑥ TO FINISH OR STOP 完成或結束
⑦ OTHER MEANINGS 其他意思

① TO MOVE AWAY FROM THE SPEAKER 離開說話人

1 ►LEAVE SOMEWHERE 離開某地◄ [I] to leave a place to go somewhere else; DEPART 離去; 離開: *I wanted to go, but Anna wanted to stay.* 我想走, 但安娜想留下來。| *It's late; I must be going.* 時候不早了, 我該走了。| *What time does the last train go?* 最後一趟火車甚麼時候離開? | *The doctor hasn't gone yet.* 醫生還沒走。

2 go and do sth to go somewhere in order to do something 去做某事: *I'll just go and get my coat.* 我去拿一下我的大衣。| *It's time you went and saw the doctor.* 是你去看醫生的時候了。

3 ►VISIT 去◄ *past participle* 過去分詞 also 又作 **been** [I] to visit a place or go to a place and then leave it 去: *Nancy has gone to Paris.* (=she is in Paris now) 南希去巴黎了。| *Nancy has been to Paris.* (=she has visited

Paris in the past) 南希去過巴黎。| *The doctor hasn't been here yet.* 醫生還沒有來過。—see 見 VISIT (USAGE)

4 ►MOVE/TRAVEL 移動/旅行◄ [I always+adv/prep] to travel or move in a particular way, in a particular direction or a particular distance 行走; 旅行: **[+by/up/to etc]** *We went by bus.* 我們是乘公共汽車去的。| *I want to go home.* 我想回家。| *Where are you going?* 你要去哪兒? | *They all went away and left me alone.* 他們都走了, 留下我一個人。| **be going somewhere** (=intend to go somewhere) 打算去某地 *We're going to my parents' for Christmas.* 我們打算去我父母家過聖誕節。| **go to hospital/prison etc** (=go to hospital in order to get medical treatment, to prison as a punishment etc) 上醫院/坐牢等

5 go for sth to go somewhere in order to take part in a particular activity 去參加某種活動: *Let's go for a swim before lunch.* 我們午餐前去游泳吧。

6 go shopping/swimming/fishing etc to go somewhere in order to visit the shops, swim etc 去購物/游泳/釣魚等: *Dinah's gone skiing in Aspen.* 黛娜到阿斯彭滑雪去了。

7 go flying/laughing etc *spoken* to move in a particular way or to do something as you are moving【口】去飛行/一面走一面笑等: *The plate went crashing to the floor.* 那個盤子"砰"地掉在地板上摔碎了。

8 ►BE SENT 送出, 寄出◄ [I] to be sent or passed on 被寄出, 被傳遞: *Make sure this package goes tonight.* 要保證這包裹今晚就寄出去。| **[+by/through/to etc]** *That letter should go by special delivery.* 那封信應該用特種快遞寄出。| *Complaints must go through the proper channels.* 投訴必須通過適當的渠道。| **go before a board/committee etc** *Your suggestion will go before the committee next week.* 你的建議將於下星期提交委員會。

② TO BE IN OR PASS INTO A PARTICULAR STATE 處於或進入某種狀態

9 ►BECOME 變為◄ [linking verb 連繫動詞] to become something different and often not so good, either naturally or by changing deliberately〔自然或人為地〕變〔壞、糟〕: *The company went bankrupt last year.* 該公司去年破產了。| **go bad/sour etc** *The milk went sour.* 牛奶變酸了。| **go grey/white etc** *Jessica went bright red with shame.* 傑西卡羞得滿臉通紅。| **go mad/deaf/bald etc** *I think you're going crazy.* 我想你發瘋了。| **go wild/mad/white etc with sth** *The crowd was going wild with excitement.* 人羣激動得發狂。—see 見 BECOME (USAGE)

10 ►BE IN A PARTICULAR STATE 處於某種狀態◄ [linking verb 連繫動詞] to be or remain in a particular, usually bad, state 處於〔某種狀態, 通常指不好的狀態〕: *All her complaints went unheard.* 她的一切抱怨都沒人理睬。| *After these attacks he went in fear of his life.* 這些攻擊之後他便為自己的生命安全擔憂。| **go hungry** (=have nothing to eat) 挨餓 *When food is short it's often the mother who goes hungry.* 食物短缺時, 挨餓的常常是母親。

③ TO START TO DO SOMETHING OR TO DO SOMETHING 開始做某事或做某事

11 ►START STH 開始某事◄ [I] to start doing something 開始: *The signal to begin a race is 'Ready, get set, go!'* 賽跑的起跑信號是"各就各位, 預備, 跑!" | *The preparations have been completed and we're ready to go.* 預備工作已經完成, 我們準備開始。| **get going (on sth)** *You'd better get going on this contract if you want to finish on time.* 如果你想按時完成, 最好開始執行合同。

12 ►OPERATE 運轉◄ [I] if a machine goes it works properly 運轉, 運行: *My watch isn't going.* 我的手錶不走了。

13 go to church/school etc to regularly attend church, school etc 去做禮拜/上學等: *Joey's too young to go to Cubs.* 喬伊年紀太小, 不能參加幼年童子軍。| *Iain didn't go to university.* 伊恩沒有上大學。—see graph at 參見 ATTEND 圖表 —see 見 JOIN¹ (USAGE)

14 ►HAPPEN 發生◄ [I always+adv/prep] to happen or develop in a particular way 發生, 進展: **go well/smoothly/swimmingly etc** *The party went well.* 晚會開得很好。| *Everything's going fine at the moment.* 目前一切進展順利。| **how are things going/how's it going/how goes it?** *How are things going at school, Joanna?* 在學校學習情況怎樣, 喬安娜? | **the way things are going** (=used before you give your opinion of what is going to happen next) 看目前的情況〔用在表達自己的意見之前〕*The way things are going, we're going to miss the bus.* 看目前的情況, 我們會搭不上公共汽車。

15 be going to do sth a) to intend to do something 打算做某事: *Wendi's going to ring us from the station.* 溫迪打算從車站給我們打電話。**b)** to be certain or expected to happen in the future 將要[就要; 預期]做某事: *Do you think it's going to rain?* 你認為會下雨嗎? —see also 另見 GONNA

16 ►MAKE A MOVEMENT 做動作◄ [I always +adv/prep] to make a particular movement 做某種動作: **[+like/up/down etc]** *While he was describing her, he went like this with his hands.* 他在描述她時, 用手這樣比劃。

17 don't go doing sth *spoken* used to tell someone not to do something, especially something that is wrong or bad【口】不要做某事〔用來告誡某人不要做某事, 尤指錯事、壞事〕: *It's a secret, so don't go telling everyone.* 這是祕密, 所以不要告訴任何人。

18 have gone and done sth *spoken* used when you are surprised by what someone has done【口】居然做了某事, 真的做了某事〔用來對某人所做的事表示驚訝〕: *Kay's gone and lost the car keys!* 凱真的把車鑰匙丟了! | **have gone and done it** (=have really made a big mistake) 確實犯了大錯誤[做了大錯事] *Tom's really gone and done it this time.* 湯姆這次確實做了大錯事。

19 go it alone to do something, especially start a business, alone 獨自幹, 單幹〔尤指開辦企業〕: *Hamish decided to go it alone and set up his own company.* 哈米什決定單幹, 自己開公司。

20 go one better to do something better than someone else had done it, or get something better than they have 做得比…要好; 得到的比…好: *We went one better and got a colour printer.* 我們更勝一籌, 獲得一台彩色打印機。

21 go far to succeed in whatever you choose to do 大有前途, 事事成功: *Ginny's a smart girl, and I'm sure she'll go far.* 金尼是個聰明的女孩, 我肯定她大有前途。

22 go too far to go beyond the limits of what is reasonable or acceptable 太過分: *I think he went too far when he called you a fat idiot!* 他把你叫成大胖白痴, 我認為他這樣做太過分了。

23 go do sth *spoken* used to tell someone to go away when you are angry【口】滾〔生氣時用來叫某人走開〕: *Go jump in the lake!* 滾開, 去跳湖吧!

24 here goes/here we go *spoken* used just before you do something that is exciting, dangerous etc【口】我這就開始了〔在馬上就開始做刺激或危險的活動前說的話〕: *Well, here goes. Wish me luck!* 好吧, 這就開始。祝我好運吧!

④ POSITION 位置

25 ►BE PLACED 被放置◄ [I always+adv/prep, not in progressive 不用進行式] if something goes somewhere, that is its usual position 放, 擺〔指擺放在通常位置〕: **[+in/under/on etc]** *Where do these plates go?* 這些盤子該放在甚麼地方? | *The sofa can go against the wall.* 這張沙發可靠牆放。

26 ►FIT 適配◄ [I not in progressive 不用進行式] to fit or be contained in something 容納, 裝下: *All that food won't go in this little cupboard.* 這個小食品櫥裝不下所有的食品。

27 ►COLOUR 顏色◄ [I] if two colours go, they look good together 匹配, 相稱, 和諧: *Pink and orange don't go.* 粉紅色和橙黃色不相配。

28 ►DIVIDE 除◄ [I not in progressive 不用進行式] to divide a number, especially so as to get a whole number in the answer 除〔尤指整除〕: *Three into two won't go.* 三除二除不盡。| **go into** *Two goes into ten five times.* 十除以二得五。

⑤ SOUND 聲音

29 ►SONG/STORY 歌曲/故事◄ [I always+adv/prep, T, not in progressive 不用進行式] to be said or sung in a particular way 說; 唱; 據傳: *How does the story go?* 故事是怎麼講的? | *The tune goes something like this.* 曲調大概是這樣的。| **go that** *The story goes that he was poisoned by his wife.* 據說他被妻子毒死了。

30 ►MAKE A SOUND 發出聲音◄ [T] to make a particular sound 發出〔某種聲音〕: *Ducks go 'Quack'.* 鴨子的叫聲是"嘎嘎"。| *The cannon suddenly went boom.* 大砲突然轟隆作響。

31 ►WHISTLE/BELL 鳴笛/響鈴◄ [I] to make a noise as a warning or signal 響, 鳴〔作為警告或信號〕: *A bell goes to mark the end of each class.* 每堂課結束時以鈴響表示。

32 ►SAY 說◄ [T] *spoken* to say something【口】說: *She goes to me: "I hope you've got a licence for that thing!"* 她對我說:"我希望你已給那玩意領了個執照!"

33 here/there sb goes again *spoken* used when someone has annoyed you by continuing to do something they know you do not like【口】某人又來了〔表示某人又在做你所不喜歡的事而讓你生氣〕: *There she goes again – complaining about the way things are run around here.* 她又來了 — 抱怨這裡的管理方式。

⑥ TO FINISH OR STOP 完成或結束

34 ►DISAPPEAR 消失◄ [I] to no longer exist; disappear 消失: *Has your headache gone yet?* 你頭痛好了嗎? | *My pen's gone; who's taken it?* 我的筆不見了。誰把它拿走了?

35 have to/must/can go if someone or something has to go, you have to get rid of them 不得不/必須/可以去掉: *That secretary will have to go; she can't even type.* 那位祕書必須走, 她連打字都不會。

36 ►GET WORSE 每況愈下◄ [I] to get worse or be lost altogether 每況愈下; 完全丟失: *Dad's sight is starting to go.* 爸爸的視力開始每況愈下。

37 ►DIE 死◄ [I] used to mean to die when you do not want to say this directly 沒了, 走了〔指人死, 婉辭說法〕: *Now that his wife's gone, he's all on his own.* 他的妻子沒了, 他一切都要靠自己。| **dead and gone** (=dead) 去世的

38 ►BECOME DAMAGED 損壞◄ [I] to become weak, damaged etc or stop working properly 變得不如從前, 損壞, 停止正常運轉: *My old sweater had started to go at the elbows.* 我的舊運動衫肘部已經開始磨損了。| *The bulb's gone in the bathroom.* 浴室的燈泡壞了。

39 ►BE SPENT 被花掉◄ [I] to be spent or used up 被花掉, 用完: *I don't know where all my money goes!* 我不知道我所有的錢花到哪裡去了! | **[+on]** *Half her salary goes on the rent.* 她工資的一半花在房租上。| **not go far** *$20 doesn't go far these days.* 如今20美元很不經用。

40 ►BE SOLD 被賣掉◄ [I] to be sold 賣掉: **go for sth** *That lovely house went for £30,000.* 那棟漂亮的房子賣了30,000英鎊。| **go to sb** *Each lot will go to the highest bidder.* 每件貨品都將賣給出價最高的人。| **Going, going, gone** (=used to say something has been sold) 要賣了, 要賣了, 成交〔用來宣布某物成交〕 *"Any more bids?" said the auctioneer; "Going ... going ... gone – to the man in the grey hat."* "還有人出價嗎?" 拍賣人說道, "要賣了…要賣了…成交 — 買主是戴灰色帽子的那個人。" | **be going cheap** (=not cost very much) 廉價出售 *I bought some mugs because they were going cheap.* 我買了幾個大杯子, 因為它們都賣得很便宜。

41 ►TIME 時間◄ [I always+adv/prep] to pass〔時間〕消逝: **[+slowly/quickly etc]** *The summer is going fast.* 夏天正飛快地過去。

42 there goes sth *spoken* used to show your disappointment when something stops you doing what you wanted to do【口】…消失了〔用來對不能做到你所想做的事表示失望〕: *Well, there goes my chance of stardom!* 哎, 我成為明星的機會沒了。

⑦ OTHER MEANINGS 其他意思

43 ►REACH 到達◄ [I always+adv/prep, not in progressive 不用進行式] to reach as far as is stated 到達, 通往: **[+to/from/down etc]** *Does this road go to the station?* 這條路通往車站嗎? | *The valley goes from east to west.* 這個山谷呈東西走向。| *This belt won't go around my waist.* 這條皮帶不夠我的腰圍。

44 what sb says goes *informal* someone is in authority and other people must do as they say【非正式】某人的話必須照辦: *You might not like it, but Phil's in charge, and what he says goes.* 你可能不喜歡, 但菲爾管事, 他說了就必須照辦。

45 anything goes used to say that anything someone says or does is acceptable 甚麼都行: *With this season's fashions, anything goes.* 就這個季節的時裝來說, 甚麼式樣都可以。

46 ►HELP 幫助◄ [I] to help to make, prove, or show something 有助於: *Which qualities go to make a good teacher?* 當個好教師要有哪些素質? | **go to show** *It just goes to show, you never know what's going to happen next.* 這只是有助於說明, 你無法知道下一步會發生甚麼事。

47 be going *informal* to be available to be used【非正式】可資利用的, 現成的: *Are there any jobs going in your firm?* 你們公司目前有現成職位嗎? | **be going spare** *I'll have that cupcake if it's going spare.* 那塊紙杯蛋糕要是沒有人吃, 我就把它吃了。

48 to go a) still remaining before something happens 離…還剩下〔若干時間〕: *Only ten days to go to Christmas!* 離聖誕節只剩十天了! **b)** still to be dealt with before you have finished what you are doing〔在完成之前〕還要做: *Laura's sat six exams and has two more to go.* 勞拉已參加了六次考試, 還要參加兩次。**c)** still to travel before you reach the place you are going to〔到達目的地之前〕還要走: *Only another five miles left to go.* 再走五英里就到了。**d)** *AmE* if you buy food from a restaurant to go, you buy it to take away and eat at home or somewhere else【美】帶到餐館外吃的, 外帶的: *Two chicken dinners with corn to go.* 兩份外帶的雞肉餐加玉米。—compare 比較 TAKE-OUT (1)

49 as someone/something goes compared with the average person or thing of that type 就某類人/事情而言: *He's not bad, as politicians go.* 就一般政治家而言, 他不算差了。| **as things go** *£100,000 for a four-bedroomed house isn't bad as things go these days.* 就現在的一般情況來說, 10萬英鎊買一座四間臥室的房子算不錯了。

50 there you go *spoken* used to say that something that has happened cannot be changed or was what you expected【口】事已至此; 事情正如你所料: *Well, there you go, better luck next time.* 嗯, 事情已無法改變, 祝你下次好運。

51 churchgoer/theatregoer etc someone who regularly goes to church, the theatre etc 經常去做禮拜的人/看戲的人等

52 theatregoing/churchgoing etc the act of regularly going to the theatre, to church etc 經常去看戲/做禮拜等

53 go it *BrE old-fashioned*【英, 過時】**a)** to go very fast 快速行進 **b)** to behave very excitedly or carelessly 舉止失措; 輕率 —see also 另見 GOING¹, GOING², GONE², GONE³, **as far as it goes** (FAR¹ (18)), **go as far as to do sth** (FAR¹ (26)), **go halves on (sth)** (HALF² (12))

go about *phr v* **1** [T **go about** sth] also 又作 **set about** to begin working at something; TACKLE[1] (1) 着手〔做某事〕: *I don't know what is the best way to go about it.* 我不知道着手做此事最好的方法是甚麼。| **go about doing sth** *I wouldn't have the faintest idea how to go about writing a novel.* 我一點也不懂怎樣着手寫一本小說。**2** [T **go about** sth] to do something that you usually do 從事〔日常事務〕: *The townspeople were going about their business as usual.* 市民與平時一樣都在忙着各自的事情。**3** [I] *BrE* if a ship goes about, it turns to go in the opposite direction【英】〔船〕調頭行駛 **4 go about with sb** to go around with someone 常與某人結伴外出

go after sth/sb *phr v* [T not in passive 不用被動態] to try to get or catch something or someone 追逐, 追求: *I've decided to go after that job in Ohio.* 我已經決定要把俄亥俄州的那份工作爭取到手。

go against sb/sth *phr v* [T not in passive 不用被動態] **1** if you go against someone's wishes or ideas, you do the opposite of what they want 違背: *She went against her counsel's advice.* 她沒有照律師給她的忠告去做。**2** if a decision, judgment etc goes against you, it is unfavourable to you and you lose 對…不利: *José's lawyer intimated the case might go against him.* 何塞的律師暗示他可能敗訴。| *The vote went against the government.* 政府在這次表決中失利。**3** to not be in agreement with something 與…相反, 與…不符: *Such ideas went against his Calvinist upbringing.* 這樣的想法與他清教主義的教養格格不入。| **go against the grain** (=be hard for someone to do because it does not agree with their beliefs, ideas etc until then) 違反(某人的)信念[思想等] *It just went against the grain for men to salute a woman officer.* 過去男子不願意向女軍官敬禮。

go ahead *phr v* [I] **1** to begin 開始: *Go ahead, we're all listening.* 開始吧, 我們都在聽着。| *"Do you mind if I smoke?" "No, go right ahead."* "我吸煙你介意嗎?" "不, 請吧。" | **go ahead with (doing) sth** *Their solicitor is asking if you want to go ahead with the deal?* 他們的律師問你是否打算把這筆交易進行下去。| **go ahead and do sth** *The newspaper decided to go ahead and publish the story.* 這家報紙決定發表這篇報道。**2** also 又作 **go on ahead** to go somewhere before the other people in your group 先走, 先行: *You go ahead and we'll catch you up later.* 你先走, 我們隨後就趕上來。| **go ahead of sb** *Kemp went ahead of the convoy to take a look.* 肯普比護送車隊先走一步去看看情況。**3** to take place 發生, 舉行: *The sale went ahead as planned.* 大減價按計劃舉行。—see also 另見 GO-AHEAD[1]

go along *phr v* [I] to continue with a plan, activity etc 繼續進行〔某計劃、活動〕: *I'm sure she was making her speech up as she went along.* 我確信她是一面講, 一面編造下面接着講些甚麼。

go along with sb/sth *phr v* [T] **1** to agree with or support someone or something 同意, 贊成, 支持: *They were happy to go along with our suggestions.* 他們樂意支持我們的建議。| **not go along with sth** *informal* (=disapprove of particular behaviour or ideas)【非正式】不同意, 不贊成, 反對 **2 go along with you!** *BrE informal* used to say that you do not believe what someone is saying to you【英, 非正式】我不信!

go around also 又作 **go round** *phr v* **1 go around doing sth** if you go around doing something, especially something people do not approve of, you often do it 經常做某事〔尤指人們不贊同的事〕: *You can't go around accusing people like that.* 你不能老是那樣指責人。**2** [I, T **go around** sth] to usually dress or behave in a particular way 通常穿着; 習慣於: *She often goes around the house naked.* 她常常在屋子裡一絲不掛到處走動。| **go around with your eyes shut** (=not notice what is happening around you) 不注意周圍發生的事 **3** [I,T, usually in progressive 一般用進行式] if an illness, some news etc is going around it is being passed from one person to another〔疾病、消息〕流傳, 傳播: *There's a rumor going around that Eddie's broke.* 傳説埃迪破產了。| **go around the school/office etc** *A new flu bug's going around the office.* 一種新的感冒病菌在辦公室傳播。**4 go around with sb/go around together** also 又作 **go about** to often go out with someone 常與某人外出/常一起外出: *I used to go around with a really bad crowd.* 我過去常與一羣壞人一起在外面鬼混。**5** [I] to be enough for everyone to have some 足夠分配: *Is there enough ice-cream to go around?* 冰淇淋夠大家吃嗎? | *There were never enough textbooks to go around.* 課本總是不夠。**6** [I] to move in a circular way 轉動, 旋轉: *The wheels went around faster and faster.* 輪子轉得越來越快。| **go around and around** (=go round in a circular way many times) 不停旋轉 —see also 另見 **go around in circles** (CIRCLE[1] (6)) **7 what goes around comes around** an expression meaning that your chance will come again if you are patient 只要有耐心, 機會將再來

go at sth/sb *phr v* [T not in passive 不用被動態] *informal*【非正式】**1** to start to do something with a lot of energy; TACKLE[1] (1) 開始賣力幹: *Harry went at the problem like a bull at a barn door.* 哈里幹勁十足地着手解決這個問題。**2** to attack someone or start to fight 攻擊, 打擊: *The two girls went at each other like animals.* 那兩個女孩子像動物一樣拚命厮打起來。| **go at it** *The boxers went at it until officials pulled them apart.* 拳擊運動員拳來拳往, 直到裁判們把他們拉開才停下來。

go away *phr v* [I] **1** to leave a place or a person 離開, 走開: *Go away! Leave me alone!* 走開! 別管我! **2** to spend some time somewhere else, especially on holiday 外出〔度假〕: *Are you going away this year?* 你今年外出度假嗎? **3** if a problem, unpleasant feeling etc goes away, it disappears〔問題、不愉快的感覺等〕消失: *His stutter went away once his mother was home.* 他媽媽一回家他的口吃就消失了。

go back *phr v* [I] **1** to return to a place you have been to before or to something you were doing before 返回, 回復: *I think we ought to go back now.* 我想我們現在應該回去了。| *Once you've made the decision I'm afraid there's no going back.* 你一旦作了決定恐怕就不能反悔。| **go back for sth** (=go back to get something) 回去取某物 *I had to go back for my passport.* 我只好回去拿護照。| **go back to (doing) sth** *Melissa's decided to go back to teaching now Timmy's at school.* 既然蒂米已經開始上學, 梅麗薩決定回去教書。| **go back out/inside/downstairs etc** *It's cold out here – let's go back into the kitchen.* 外面很冷 —— 我們回到廚房裡去吧。**2** [always+adv/prep] to have been made, built, or started at some time in the past 追溯: *The old dairy goes back to Tudor times.* 這座古老的乳品店可追溯到都鐸王朝時代。

go back on sth *phr v* [T] to break or not succeed in keeping to an agreement or promise 違背〔約定, 承諾〕: **go back on your word/promise etc** *You can rely on Sarah; she won't go back on her word.* 你可以信賴莎拉, 她不會食言的。

go by *phr v* **1** [I] to pass〔時間〕過去: *Two years went by.* 兩年過去了。| *Never let a good opportunity go by.* 決不要放過一次好機會。**2** [T not in passive 不用被動態 **go by** sth] to use the information or advice you get from a person, a book, a set of rules etc 依據, 遵循: *Don't go by that old map; it's out of date.* 別使用那張舊地圖, 它已經過時了。| **go by the book** (=obey rules very strictly) 嚴格遵守規則 **3** [T not in passive 不用被動態 **go by** sth] to form an opinion or judgment of someone or something from something else 根據…作判斷: *You can't always go by appearances.* 你不能總是以外表來判斷。

go down *phr v* [I]

1 ►GO DOWNSTAIRS 下樓◄ to go to a lower floor of a building 下樓: *We went down for dinner at nine o'clock.* 我們9點下樓吃晚餐。| *The elevator was going down.* 電梯正在往下走。

G

2 ▶**BECOME LOWER** 變低◀ to not be so expensive, high etc 降低, 下降: *Your temperature seems to be going down.* 你的體温似乎在下降。| *Tomatoes have gone down.* (=they cost less than before) 番茄降價了。
3 ▶**STANDARD** 標準◀ if something goes down, its quality or standard gets worse〔質量、標準〕降低, 下降: *This neighbourhood has really gone down in the last few years.* (=more poor people have moved there) 這個街區最近幾年居民的經濟情況下降了不少。| **go down in sb's opinion/estimation** (=respect someone less) 對某人的評價下降 *Fiona's gone down in my estimation since I found out her political views.* 我知道了菲奧娜的政治觀點後, 對她的評價已經下降。
4 **go down well/badly etc** to get a particular sort of reaction from someone 反應很好/不佳等: *Matt's joke went down like a lead balloon.* 馬特講的笑話人家反應冷淡。
5 ▶**SINK** 下沉◀ to disappear from sight or below a surface 消失, 沉沒: *Ten men died when the ship went down.* 船沉沒時有十人死亡。| *The sun was going down behind the mountains.* 太陽正在落山。
6 ▶**BECOME FLATTER** 變得更平◀ to become less swollen or lose air 消腫; 癟下: *The swelling will go down if you rest your foot.* 如果讓你的腳休息休息, 腫塊就會消退。
7 ▶**FOOD/DRINK** 食品/飲料◀ to pass down your throat 被嚥下, 被吞下: *I couldn't get the pill to go down.* 我無法把藥丸吞下去。| *That meringue went down very nicely.* 那種蛋白酥很順溜就吃下去了。
8 ▶**BE REMEMBERED** 被記住◀ [always+adv/prep] to be recorded or remembered in a particular way 被記錄下來, 被記住: **[+as/in]** *The talks went down as a landmark in the peace process.* 會談作為和平進程的里程碑名垂後世。| **go down in history** (=be remembered for many years) 載入史冊 *Her work will go down in history.* 她的業績將載入史冊。
9 ▶**REACH** 到達◀ [always+adv/prep] to reach as far as a particular place 到達, 延伸到: *Some steps went down to the beach.* 有些台階一直延伸到海灘。
10 ▶**GO SOUTH** 往南去◀ to go further south in a country or go from a city to somewhere less important 往南去; 從城市到小地方: **[+to]** *We're going down to the country for the weekend.* 我們打算去鄉下過週末。
11 ▶**SPORT** 體育運動◀ **a)** to lose a match or competition 輸了〔一場比賽或競賽〕: *Chang went down to Sampras in the third set.* 張德培在第三盤輸給了森柏斯。**b)** to move down to a lower position in an official list of teams or players〔在運動隊或運動員的正式排名中〕降級: **[+to]** *United went down to the second division.* 聯隊降為了乙級隊。
12 ▶**COMPUTER** 電腦◀ to stop working for a short time 暫停運轉, 死機: *Overloading caused all the computers to go down.* 過載使所有的電腦都死機。
13 **go down on your knees** to bend your body so that your knees are on the ground, supporting your weight 下跪: *Nick went down on one knee to ask her to marry him.* 尼克單腿跪下向她求婚。
14 **go down on all fours** to bend your body so that your knees and your hands are on the ground, supporting your weight 匍匐, 趴下
15 ▶**LIGHTS** 燈◀ *literary* if lights go down, they become less bright【文】〔燈光〕暗下來: *The lights went down and the curtain rose on an empty stage.* 燈暗下來, 帷幕開啟, 顯現空蕩的舞台。
16 ▶**FROM UNIVERSITY** 從大學◀ *BrE* to leave a university after doing a degree or at the end of each TERM[1] (9)【英】〔獲得學位後或學期末〕離開大學: **[+from]** *Emily went down from Oxford with a first class degree.* 埃米莉以一等學位從牛津大學畢業。
17 ▶**TO PRISON** 進監獄◀ *slang* to be sent to prison【俚】入獄: *Bert went down for five years.* 伯特被判五年監禁。

go down with sth *phr v* [T not in passive 不用被動態] *informal* to become ill, especially with an infectious disease【非正式】感染上〔傳染病〕: *The children have gone down with mumps.* 孩子們染上了腮腺炎。

go for sb/sth *phr v* [T not in passive 不用被動態] **1** to attack someone physically or with words 攻擊; 抨擊: *Lorna really went for me when I disagreed.* 我表示不同意時洛娜竟動手打我。**2** to try to get or win something 爭取得到, 爭取贏得: *Oona's going for that job in sales.* 烏納正爭取得到那份銷售工作。| *Jackson is going for his second gold medal here.* 傑克遜正在爭取他在這裡的第二塊金牌。| **go for it** *informal* (=do everything you can to get something)【非正式】盡力爭取 *If you really want the job, go for it!* 如果你真的想要那份工作, 就努力爭取吧! —see also 另見 **go for broke** (BROKE[2] (3)) **3** to choose or take something 挑選; 拿: *In a small garden, go for dwarf varieties to maximize space.* 在小花園, 要選擇矮生品種以盡量利用空間。**4** *informal* to like something or find something or someone attractive【非正式】喜歡; 覺得…吸引人: *Annie tends to go for older men.* 安妮喜歡年紀較大的男人。**5** *spoken* to also be true about someone or something else【口】對…也適用: *I told him to work harder, and that goes for you, too.* (=you have to work harder, too) 我告訴他工作努力些, 這句話對你也適用。**6** to be sold for a particular price 賣得〔某價錢〕: *How much did that Alpha Romeo go for?* 那輛阿爾法·羅密歐車賣了多少錢? **7 go for nothing** to be wasted 白費: *All that hard work went for nothing when the project was dropped.* 項目被終止了, 所有的艱苦工作全都白費。—see also 另見 **have a lot going for you/not have much going for you** (GOING[2] (4))

go in *phr v* [I] **1** to enter a building 進入戶內: *Dad wants me to go in before it gets dark.* 父親要我在天黑前進屋。**2** when the sun or the moon goes in, it becomes covered with cloud〔日、月〕被雲遮住 **3** to join someone in order to start a business etc 加入〔共同辦企業〕: **[+with]** *They want me to go in with them on the new venture.* 他們要我和他們一起搞這個新企業。

go in for sth *phr v* [T] **1** to do an exam or take part in a competition 參加〔考試、競賽〕: *Are you going in for the Proficiency exam?* 你打算參加水平考試嗎? **2** to like something or do something often because you enjoy it 喜歡, 愛好: *I don't go in for garden gnomes.* 我不喜歡花園土地神塑像。| **go in for doing sth** *Maggie goes in for improving her mind.* 瑪吉致力於提高自己的智力。**3** to choose something as your job 從事〔某種工作〕: *Have you thought of going in for nursing?* 你考慮過從事護理工作嗎?

go into sth *phr v* [T]
1 ▶**JOB** 工作◀ [not in passive 不用被動態] to enter a particular profession or business 從事〔某職業〕, 進入〔某行業〕: *Sophie wants to go into the army.* 索菲想參軍。| **go into partnership** *Frank's going into partnership with a friend.* 弗蘭克打算與一個朋友合夥。
2 ▶**TIME/MONEY/EFFORT** 時間/錢/力氣◀ [not in passive 不用被動態] to be spent or used to get, make, or do something 用在: *Years of research have gone into this book.* 寫這本書時花了許多年做研究。
3 ▶**EXPLAIN/DESCRIBE** 解釋/描述◀ to explain or describe something in detail 詳細解釋; 詳細描述: *I don't want to go into the matter now.* 我現在不想詳細解釋這件事。| **go into details** *Clare wouldn't go into details about her problems.* 克萊爾不願詳細說明她的問題。
4 ▶**CONSIDER** 考慮◀ to examine something thoroughly 徹底調查, 深究: *My broker is going into the question of long-term cover.* 我的經紀人正深入調查長期保險問題。
5 ▶**HIT** 碰撞◀ [not in passive 不用被動態] if a vehicle goes into a tree, wall, or another vehicle, it hits it〔車等〕撞在…上: *His car went into a lamppost in the high street.* 他的車子撞在大街的一個路燈柱上了。

6►DIVIDE 除◄ [not in passive 不用被動態] *informal* if a number goes into another number, the second number can be divided by the first【非正式】可整除: *12 goes into 60 five times.* 12除60得5。

7►BEGIN A MOVEMENT 開始動作◄ [not in passive 不用被動態] if a vehicle or its driver goes into a particular movement, it starts to do it〔車輛、駕駛員等〕開始做〔某種動作〕: *The plane had gone into a nosedive and crashed.* 飛機開始垂直俯衝, 然後墜毀。

8►SPEECH 演說◄ [not in passive 不用被動態] to begin a long speech, often when it is not necessary 開始〔冗長的演說〕: *Norman went into a long monologue about crime.* 諾曼開始一個人滔滔不絕地談論起犯罪問題來。

go off *phr v*

1►EXPLODE 爆炸◄ [I] to explode 爆炸: *The bomb went off at 6.30 this morning.* 炸彈在上午6時30分爆炸。

2►MAKE A NOISE 發出響聲◄ [I] to make a loud noise 發出巨響: *Our neighbor's car alarm is always going off in the middle of the night.* 我們鄰居汽車的報警器總是在半夜響起來。

3►STOP WORKING 停止工作◄ [I] if a machine goes off, it stops working 停止運轉: *The central heating goes off at 9 o'clock.* 中央供暖系統9點鐘停開。| *Suddenly, all the lights went off.* 突然所有的燈都熄滅了。

4 go off well/badly etc to happen in a particular way 進展很好/很糟糕等: *The party went off swimmingly.* 聚會開得很順利。

5►FOOD 食品◄ [I] *BrE* if food goes off, it goes bad【英】〔食品〕變質, 腐敗: *The milk's gone off.* 牛奶變質了。

6►STOP 停止◄ [I] *BrE* if a pain goes off, you stop feeling it【英】〔疼痛〕消失

7►STOP LIKING SB/STH 不再喜歡某人/某物◄ [T **go off** sb/sth] *BrE informal* to stop liking something or someone【英, 非正式】不再喜歡: *Val went off coffee when she was pregnant.* 瓦爾在懷孕的時候不再喜歡喝咖啡了。| **go off doing sth** *I've gone off cooking lately.* 我最近失去了做飯的興趣。

8►SLEEP 睡◄ [I] *informal* to go to sleep【非正式】入睡: **go off to sleep** *Has the baby gone off to sleep yet?* 寶寶睡着了嗎?

9►GET WORSE 變壞◄ [I] *BrE informal* to get worse【英, 非正式】變壞: *The service in this restaurant has really gone off.* 這家餐館的服務質量確實下降了。

go off with sth/sb *phr v* [T] *informal*【非正式】**1** to leave your husband, wife, partner etc in order to have a relationship with someone else〔拋棄配偶〕移情別戀於...: *She's gone off with her husband's best friend.* 她與她丈夫最好的朋友私奔了。**2** to take something away from a place without having permission 私自拿走: *Who's gone off with my pen?* 誰拿走了我的鋼筆?

go on *phr v*

1►CONTINUE AN ACTION 繼續某動作◄ [I] to continue without stopping or changing 繼續下去: *We can't go on like this; I want a divorce!* 我們不能這樣繼續下去了, 我要離婚! | **go on with sth** *Go on with your work until I come back.* 繼續做你的工作, 等我回來。| **go on doing sth** *You can't go on drinking so much – you're not doing yourself any good.* 你不能再喝這麼多的酒——你是在害自己。| **go on and on** (=continue for a long time) 長時間繼續下去 *The noise seemed to go on and on.* 噪音似乎沒完沒了。

2►DO STH NEXT 接着做某事◄ [I] to do something after you have finished doing something else 進而做某事: **go on to sth** *Let's go on to the next item on the agenda.* 我們轉到議程的下一項吧。| **go on to do sth** *She went on to become a successful surgeon.* 她進而成為一名成功的外科醫生。

3►HAPPEN 發生◄ to take place or happen 發生, 進行: *What's going on in the kitchen?* 廚房裡發生了甚麼事? | *There's something fishy going on here.* 這裡有些事不對勁。—see also 另見 GOINGS-ON

4►USE AS PROOF 用作證據◄ [T not in passive 不用被動態 **go on** sth] to base an opinion or judgment on something 以〔某事〕為根據〔作出判斷〕: *Police haven't much to go on in their hunt for the killer.* 警方在追查殺手時沒有多少線索。

5►BEGIN TO WORK 開始工作◄ [I] if a machine goes on, it begins to operate〔機器〕開始運轉: *The heat goes on automatically at 6 o'clock.* 暖氣在6點鐘自動開始供應。

6►TIME 時間◄ [I] to pass 過去: *As time went on, I grew very fond of him.* 隨着時間的推移, 我變得非常喜歡他了。

7►CONTINUE WITH A STORY/EXPLANATION ETC 繼續講故事/解釋等◄ [I] to continue talking, especially after stopping or changing to a different subject〔尤指停止或改變話題後〕接着講, 繼續說: *Go on, I'm listening.* 說下去吧, 我在聽着。| [**+with**] *After a short pause Maria went on with her story.* 瑪麗亞稍停片刻之後繼續講她的故事。| **go on to do sth** *The councillor went on to explain where the new supermarket would be.* 市議員接着解釋新的超級市場會在甚麼地方。

8►BEHAVE IN THE SAME WAY 以同樣的方式行事◄ [I always+adv/prep] to often behave in a particular way 常以某種方式行事: *The way she's going on she'll have a nervous breakdown.* 她這樣繼續下去會精神崩潰的。

9►COMPLAIN 抱怨◄ [I] *BrE* to continue to complain or ask someone to do something【英】不斷抱怨, 不斷要求〔某人做某事〕: **go on at sb about sth** *I wish you'd stop going on at me about my weight!* 我希望你不要再向我嘮叨我的體重! | **go on at sb to do sth** *Mum kept going on at him to tidy his room.* 媽媽不停地叫他整理他的房間。

10 be going on (for) to be nearly a time, age, number etc 接近〔某時間、年齡、數目等〕: *Nancy must be going on for 60, you know.* 你知道的, 南希肯定快60歲了。| *Jenny's one of those wise teenagers who's 16 going on 70.* (=she seems older than she is, or thinks she is) 詹妮就是那種看上去很老成但實際上只有16歲的聰明少女。

11►MEDICINE 藥◄ [T not in passive 不用被動態 **go on** sth] to begin to take a type of medicine 開始服用〔某種藥物〕: **go on the pill** *Dani's too young to go on the pill.* 丹尼太年輕, 不能服避孕藥。

12►GO IN FRONT OF 在其他人之前走◄ [I] to go somewhere before the other people you are with 先走, 先行: *Bill went on in the car and I followed on foot.* 比爾坐車先走, 我步行跟在後面。

13►TALK TOO MUCH 說太多◄ [I] *informal* to talk too much【非正式】沒完沒了地說, 嘮叨個沒完: *You don't half go on!* 你真是嘮叨個沒完! | **go on and on** *They went on and on about the importance of safety belts.* 他們不停地嘮叨安全帶如何重要。

14►DEVELOP 發展◄ [I] *BrE informal* to develop or make progress【英, 非正式】發展, 進展: *How's the work going on?* 工作進展得怎麼樣?

15 go on a) used to encourage someone to do something 繼續吧〔用來鼓勵某人去做某事〕: *Go on, have another cookie.* 來, 再吃一塊曲奇餅。**b)** also 又作 **go on with you** *BrE spoken* used to tell someone that you do not believe them【英口】我才不信: *I told her she had the most beautiful eyes I'd ever seen. "Oh, go on with you!" she said, blushing with pleasure.* 我告訴她說, 她的眼睛是我見過的最漂亮的眼睛。"唷, 我才不信呢!" 她說道, 高興得漲紅了臉。

16 to be going on with/to go on with *informal, BrE* if you have enough of something to be going on with, you have enough to use at present until the situation improves【非正式, 英】暫時夠用: *Have you got enough money to be going on with?* 你的錢暫時夠用嗎?

17 go on the dole *BrE informal* to begin to claim money from the government because you are not working【英, 非正式】開始領取失業救濟金

go out *phr v* [I]
1 ►FOR ENTERTAINMENT 為了娛樂◄ to leave your house, especially in order to enjoy yourself 出去〔尤指娛樂〕: *Are you going out tonight?* 你今晚要出去嗎? | *Let's go out for a walk.* 我們出去散步吧。| **go out doing sth** *Liam goes out drinking every Friday.* 利亞姆每個星期五都出去喝酒。| **go out to do sth** *Can I go out to play now?* 現在我能出去玩嗎? | **go out and do sth** *You should go out and get some fresh air.* 你應該出去呼吸一些新鮮空氣。
2 ►WITH BOY/GIRL 和男孩/女孩◄ to spend a lot of time with someone and have a romantic relationship with them 交往, 談戀愛: **go out with sb** *Jean used to go out with my brother.* 吉恩與我兄弟談過戀愛。| **go out together** *How long have you been going out together?* 你們已經交往多久了?
3 ►FIRE/LIGHT 火/燈◄ to stop burning or shining 熄滅: *The candle spluttered and went out.* 蠟燭劈啪作響, 然後就滅了。—see 見 FIRE¹ (USAGE)
4 ►ON TV/RADIO 在電視上/廣播裡◄ to be broadcast on television or radio〔在電視或無線電中〕廣播: *The program goes out live at 5 o'clock on Mondays.* 這個節目每週一5點現場直播。
5 ►MOVE ABROAD 到國外◄ to travel to a place far away, often in order to live there 出國〔常指移居〕: *They've gone out to Australia.* 他們已經移居澳大利亞了。
6 ►STRIKE 罷工◄ *BrE* also 又作 **go out on strike** to stop working because of a disagreement【英】罷工
7 go out like a light *informal* to go to sleep very quickly【非正式】很快睡着: *As soon as his head touched the pillow, he went out like a light.* 他的頭一碰枕頭就睡着了。
8 ►NOT BE FASHIONABLE/USED 不再流行/不再使用◄ to stop being fashionable or used 不再流行, 不再用: *Flared trousers are going out again.* 喇叭褲又過時了。—opposite 反義詞 **come in** (COME¹)
9 ►SEA 海洋◄ to go back to its lower level〔潮水〕退去: *The tide's going out.* 潮水正在退去。—opposite 反義詞 **come in** (COME¹)
10 ►MAKE PUBLIC 公開◄ to let everyone know about something 公開, 公佈: *Word went out that the President was dead.* 總統去世的消息公佈了。
11 heart/thoughts go out to sb to have a lot of sympathy for someone 十分同情某人: *Our hearts go out to the victim's family.* 我們非常同情受害者的家庭。
12 ►TIME 時間◄ [always+adv/prep] *literary* to end【文】結束, 終結: *March went out with high winds and rain.* 三月在勁風斜雨中結束。

go over *phr v*
1 ►GO NEAR SB/STH 走近某人/某物◄ [I] to go nearer to someone or something 走近, 走過去: *Blake went over and sat on the bed.* 布萊克走過去坐在牀上。| **[+to]** *Chiara went over to the bar.* 奇阿拉向酒吧走去。| **go over to do sth** *He had gone over to say goodbye.* 他走過去道別去了。
2 ►EXAMINE 檢查◄ [T, **go over** sth] to look at something or think about something carefully 仔細審查, 仔細考慮: *I had gone over and over what happened in my mind.* 我對發生的事進行了反覆思考。
3 ►SEARCH 搜查◄ [T, **go over** sth] to search something very carefully 仔細搜查: *The police have been over the apartment with a fine-tooth comb.* 警方對這套公寓房仔細搜查了一遍。
4 ►VISIT 參觀◄ [T, **go over** sth] to visit a building etc to decide whether to buy or rent it〔買房或租房前〕看〔房子〕: *We'd been over several houses before finding this one.* 我們看了好幾幢房子才找到這一幢。
5 ►REPEAT 重複◄ [T, **go over** sth] to repeat something in order to learn it or understand it 再來一遍, 温習: *Maybe if I went over it all again I would see what she meant.* 也許如果我把它再看一遍, 我就能明白她的意思。
6 go over well/badly etc if a speech, performance etc goes over well, the people listening like it〔演講、表演〕獲得成功/失敗等: **[+with]** *His speech went over well with the Left of the party.* 他的演講受到該黨左派的歡迎。
7 ►CHANGE 改變◄ [I] to change your beliefs, religion, habits etc 改變信仰[宗教、習慣等]: **go over from sth to sth** *Lloyd George went over to Labour in 1951.* 勞埃德·喬治於1951年改入工黨。| **go over to doing sth** *I've gone over to drinking black coffee.* 我已經改喝清咖啡。
8 ►TV/RADIO 電視/無線電廣播◄ [I] to change to a broadcast from another place 轉移地點播放: **[+to]** *We're going over to the White House for an important announcement.* 我們要轉到白宮播放一項重要公告。
9 ►CLEAN 清除◄ [T] to clean something 清除, 打掃: *Liz went over the carpet with the hoover.* 利茲用吸塵器清掃地毯。

go round also 又作 **go around** *phr v* [I]
1 ►BE ENOUGH 足夠◄ to be enough for everyone 足夠分給每個人: *Are there enough chairs to go around?* 有足夠的椅子給大家坐嗎?
2 ►ILLNESS/NEWS ETC 疾病/消息等◄ if an illness, news etc goes around, it is passed from one person to another 流傳, 傳播: *There's a lot of flu going around at the moment.* 眼下流感在大肆傳播。
3 go round in your head if words, sounds etc go round in your head, you continue to hear them for a long time 在腦中縈繞: *That stupid song kept going around in my head.* 那支乏味的歌一直在我的腦中縈繞。
4 ►DRESS/BEHAVE 穿戴/舉止◄ to usually dress or behave in a particular way〔穿着、行為〕習慣於: *These shoplifters go round in pairs.* 這些盜竊商店貨物的小偷總是兩個人一起活動。| **go around doing sth** *You can't go around telling people what to do all the time!* 你不能老是這樣對人家指手劃腳!
5 go around with sb/go round together to often go out with someone 與某人交往/常在一起 —see also 另見 **go round in circles** (CIRCLE¹ (6))

go slow *phr v* [I] *BrE* to put as little effort as possible into your work, as a form of STRIKE² (1)【英】怠工 —see also 另見 GO-SLOW

go through *phr v* **1** [T, **go through** sth] to suffer or experience something bad 經受, 經歷〔壞事、苦事〕: *How does she keep smiling after all she's been through?* 她經歷了這一切後怎麼還能滿臉笑容? **2** [T, **go through** sth] to use something and have none left; **get through** (GET) 用光: *Austria was so expensive – we went through all our money in one week.* 去奧地利一趟十分昂貴——我們在一週內花光了所有的錢。**3** [I,T, **go through** sth] if a law goes through, or goes through Parliament, it is officially accepted〔法律〕被通過: *The Bill went through Parliament without a vote.* 法案未經表決就在議會通過了。**4** [I] if a deal or agreement goes through, it is officially accepted〔交易或協定〕獲正式認可: *Your application for a loan has gone through.* 你的貸款申請已被接受。**5** [T, **go through** sth] *BrE* to slowly make a hole in something【英】磨破, 穿破: *My toe has gone through my sock.* 我的腳趾把襪子磨破了。**6** [T, **go through** sth] to practise something, for example a performance 練習, 排練: *Let's go through the whole thing again, from the beginning.* 我們從頭開始完整地練習一遍。**7** [T, **go through** sth] to look at or for something carefully 仔細檢查, 仔細尋找: *Dave went through his pockets looking for the keys.* 戴夫翻遍了他的衣袋找鑰匙。**8** [I,T, **go through** sth] to read a document from beginning to end 從頭到尾閱讀: *Could you just go through this file and mark anything that's relevant?* 請你通讀一下這份文件, 把相關的地方標出來, 好嗎?

go through with sth *phr v* [T] to do something you had promised or planned to do, even though it causes problems or you are no longer sure you want to do it 做〔承諾或計劃要做的事情〕, 將〔某事〕進行到底: *Jenny* *felt she couldn't go through with the abortion.* 詹妮感到自己不能照她原來說的去做流產。

go to sth *phr v* [T, not in passive 不用被動態] **1 go to great lengths/go to a lot of trouble** to take a lot of trouble to do something〔為做某事〕費了不少氣力/花了不少功夫: *They went to great lengths to make sure I felt at home.* 為了使我住得舒服自在, 他們費了不少力。**2 go to great expense** to spend a lot of money to do something〔為做某事〕花了很多錢 **3** to begin to experience or do something 開始經歷, 開始做: *Shh! Daddy's trying to go to sleep.* 噓!爸爸正在試圖睡覺。| *Britain and Germany went to war in 1939.* 英國和德國於1939年開戰。**4** to be given to someone 被給予, 送給: *All the money raised will go to local charities.* 所有籌到的錢都將捐給當地慈善機構。

go together *phr v* [I] **1** if two things go together, they look, taste etc good together〔外形、味道等〕相配, 協調: *Pork and apple go well together.* 豬肉和蘋果的味道很相配。—see 見 FIT[1] (USAGE) **2** if two people are going together, they are having a romantic relationship 戀愛: *I didn't know Sharon and Les were going together.* 我原來不知道雪倫和萊斯在談戀愛。

go under *phr v* [I] **1** if a business goes under, it has serious problems and fails〔企業〕倒閉, 破產, 垮掉: *Many restaurants go under in the first year.* 許多餐館在第一年就倒閉了。**2** if a ship or something that is floating goes under, it sinks beneath the surface〔船等〕沉沒: *The Titanic finally went under, watched by those survivors who had found a place in the lifeboats.* 那些擠上救生艇的倖存者看着鐵達尼號最終沉沒了。

go up *phr v* [I]

1 ▶INCREASE 增加◀ *spoken* to increase in number or amount【口】增多: *I see cigarettes are going up again.* (=are getting more expensive) 我發現香煙又漲價了。

2 ▶BE BUILT 建立起來◀ *spoken* to be built【口】建立起來: *New houses are going up all around the town.* 城裡到處都在建新房子。

3 ▶EXPLODE/BURN 爆炸/燃燒◀ *spoken* to explode or be destroyed in a fire【口】爆炸; 被燒毀: *The whole building went up in flames.* 整座大樓在大火中燒毀。—see also 另見 **go up in smoke** (SMOKE[1] (5))

4 ▶SHOUT 叫喊◀ if a shout or a CHEER goes up, people start to shout or CHEER 開始呼喊[歡呼]

5 ▶THEATRE 劇場◀ if the curtain goes up at a theatre, it opens for the performance to start〔帷幕〕開啟, 演出開始: *The curtain went up on an empty stage.* 帷幕開啟, 顯現空蕩的舞台。

6 ▶REACH 到達◀ to reach as far as a particular place 到達, 延伸: [+to] *The trees go right up to the beach.* 這些樹一直延伸到海灘。

7 ▶TO UNIVERSITY 上大學◀ *BrE* to go to a university to begin a course of study【英】上大學: [+to] *She went up to Oxford in 1975.* 她1975年上了牛津大學。

8 ▶TO TOWN 進城◀ *BrE* to go to a town or city from a smaller place【英】進城: [+to] *I like to go up to town for Christmas shopping.* 我喜歡進城為聖誕節購物。

go with *phr v* [T not in passive 不用被動態]

1 ▶MATCH/SUIT 匹配/適合◀ if one thing goes with another, they look, taste etc good together 與…匹配, 與…協調: *That shade of blue goes with your eyes.* 那種藍色和你的眼睛很協調。—see 見 FIT[1] (USAGE)

2 ▶BE PART OF STH 成為某物的一部分◀ to be included as part of something 是…的一部分: *The house goes with the job.* 這棟房子屬於這個職位。| **go with doing sth** *Responsibility goes with becoming a father.* 當了父親也就有了責任。

3 ▶EXIST TOGETHER 共存◀ to often exist with something else 伴隨: *Ill health often goes with poverty.* 貧病常相隨。

4 ▶BOY/GIRL 男孩/女孩◀ *informal* to have someone as your boyfriend or girlfriend or to have a sexual relationship with someone【非正式】與某人談戀愛; 與某人發生性關係: *Is Martin still going with Jane?* 馬丁還在跟簡交往嗎?

5 ▶AGREE 同意◀ to accept someone's idea or plan 同意, 接受〔看法, 計劃〕: *Let's go with John's original proposal.* 我們贊成約翰原來的提議吧。

go without *phr v* [I,T] **1** to be able to live without something or without doing something 沒有某物[不做某事]而能過活: *We can't afford a holiday, so we'll just have to go without.* 我們沒錢度假, 所以我們只好不去度假。| **go without sth** *She had gone without food to feed the children.* 她曾經沒有食物餵她的孩子。**2 it goes without saying** used to say that something is so obvious that it does not need to be said 不用說, 不言而喻: *It goes without saying that young doctors should work fewer hours.* 不用說, 年輕醫生的工作時間應該短一些。

[1] **go[2]** *n plural* **goes**

1 ▶TRY 嘗試◀ [C] an attempt to do something 嘗試: **have a go** *"I can't open this jar." "Let me have a go."* "我打不開這個罐子。""讓我試試看。" | **have a go at (doing) sth** *Daisy had six goes at her driving-test before she passed.* 黛西考了六次才通過駕駛考試。| **at one go** *Ruby blew out all her candles at one go.* 露比一口氣吹滅所有的蠟燭。| **give sth a go** (=try to do sth even though you do not think you will succeed) 試做某事 *I don't think I can make him change his mind, but I'll give it a go.* 我並不認為我能使他改變主意, 但我會試試看。

2 ▶IN A GAME 遊戲中◀ [C] someone's turn in a game etc〔遊戲中等〕輪到某人的機會: *Whose go is it?* 輪到誰了? | *If you throw a two you miss a go.* 如果擲到兩點, 你就要錯過一輪。| **have a go on sth** *Can I have a go on your computer?* 我能用一下你的電腦嗎? | **3p/5p/10p a go** *Guess the weight of the cake, 10 pence a go.* 猜一猜這蛋糕的重量, 猜一次10便士。

3 make a go of sth *informal* to make a business, marriage etc succeed【非正式】使〔企業、婚姻等〕成功: **make a go of it** *Do you think they'll make a go of it with this restaurant?* 你認為他們開這家餐館會成功嗎?

4 on the go *informal* very busy or working all the time【非正式】忙個不停: *I'm on the go all day and then collapse into bed at about 10 o'clock.* 我整天忙個不停, 然後大約十點就癱倒在牀上。

5 it's no go *spoken* used to say that something has not happened or that it will not happen【口】〔某事〕未發生; 不會發生: *I went and asked for a rise but it was no go, I'm afraid.* 我去要求提高工資, 但很遺憾, 白跑一趟。—see also 另見 NO-GO AREA (2)

6 all the go *old-fashioned* very fashionable【過時】十分流行的

7 it's all go *BrE spoken* it is very busy【英口】非常忙碌: *It's all go in the toy department in December.* 玩具部在12月非常繁忙。

8 have a go at sb *spoken, especially BrE* to complain【口, 尤英】抱怨: *Mark's bound to have a go at me for spending all this money.* 馬克肯定會埋怨我把這筆錢都花光了。

9 have a go *spoken, especially BrE*【口, 尤英】**a)** to attack someone physically 打, 打架: *A whole gang of yobs were standing around, just waiting to have a go.* 一幫無賴漢四處站着, 只等着打架。**b)** to try to catch someone who you see doing something wrong, rather than waiting for the police〔不等警察到來〕企圖自行抓壞人: *The public should not be encouraged to have a go.* 不應鼓勵公眾自行抓壞人。

10 ▶ENERGY 活力◀ [U] *BrE* liveliness and energy【英】勁頭, 活力: *The children are full of go this morning.* 孩子們今天上午精力充沛。—see also 另見 GET-UP-AND-GO

goad[1] /god; gəʊd/ *v* [T] **1** to make someone do some-

G

thing by annoying them or encouraging them until they do it 驅使, 唆使: **goad sb into (doing) sth** *Kathy goaded him into telling her what he had done.* 凱茜促使他把他所幹的事告訴了她。| **goad sb on** *Duval was goaded on by the need for more money.* 杜瓦爾是受需要更多的錢這一動機的驅使才繼續幹下去的。**2** to push animals ahead of you with a sharp stick〔用尖棒〕驅趕〔牲畜〕

goad² *n* [C] **1** a sharp stick for making cattle move forward〔趕牛的〕尖棒 **2** something that forces someone to do something 驅動人行動的事物

go-a·head¹ /ˈ·.,·/ *n* **give sb the go-ahead/get the go-ahead** to give or be given permission for something to start 給予某人許可/得到准許: *The film was given the go-ahead, and production started in May.* 這部影片得到了拍攝許可, 攝製工作五月份開始。

go-ahead² *adj BrE* using or encouraging new methods or ideas and therefore likely to succeed; PROGRESSIVE¹ (1)【英】開拓進取的: *This go-ahead company introduced profit-sharing.* 這家開拓進取的公司引入分紅制。

S2 W1 **goal** /gol; gəʊl/ *n* [C] **1** something that you hope to achieve in the future; aim 目標, 目的: **achieve a goal** *We've achieved our goal of building a shelter for the homeless.* 我們已經達到了為無家可歸的人建收容所的目標。| **long-term goal/short-term goal** (=that you hope to achieve after a long or short time) 長期目標/短期目標 **2** the action of making the ball go into the scoring (SCORE² (1)) area in games such as football or HOCKEY, or the point won by doing this〔足球、曲棍球等〕得分: **score a goal** *Baggio scored the first goal for Italy.* 巴治奧為意大利進了頭一個球。**3** the area between two posts where the ball must go for a point to be won 球門: **keep goal** (=be the goalkeeper) 當守門員 —see picture on page A23 參見A23頁圖

goal·ie /ˈgolɪ; ˈgəʊli/ *n* [C] *informal* a goalkeeper【非正式】守門員 —see picture on page A23 參見A23頁圖

goal·keep·er /ˈgol,kipɚ; ˈgəʊl,kiːpə/ *n* [C] the player in a sports team who has to try to stop the ball going into his team's goal 守門員 —see picture on page A23 參見A23頁圖

goal·less /ˈgol·lɪs; ˈgəʊl-ləs/ *adj* **a goalless draw** a match where no goals are scored (SCORE² (1)) 無進球[零比零]的比賽

goal line /ˈ· ·/ *n* [C] a line that marks the end of a playing area, where the goal is placed 球門線, 端線

goal·mouth /ˈgol,maʊθ; ˈgəʊlmaʊθ/ *n* [C] the area directly in front of the GOAL (3) 球門區

goal·post /ˈgol,post; ˈgəʊlpəʊst/ *n* [C usually plural 一般用複數] **1** one of the two posts, with a bar along the top or across the middle, that form the GOAL (3) in games like football and HOCKEY〔足球、曲棍球等的〕球門柱 **2 move the goalposts** *BrE informal* to change the rules, limits etc while someone is trying to do something, and make it more difficult for them【英, 非正式】〔在某人做某事時〕改變規則[限制等]〔對其增大難度〕

goal·ten·der /ˈgol,tɛndɚ; ˈgəʊl,tendə/ *n* [C] *AmE* a GOALKEEPER【美】守門員

goat /got; gəʊt/ *n* [C] **1** an animal a little like a sheep that can climb steep hills and rocks 山羊 **2 get sb's goat** *spoken* to make someone extremely annoyed【口】使某人十分惱怒: *I'll tell you another thing that really got my goat.* 我要告訴你另一件着實令我惱怒的事。**3 act/play the goat** *BrE informal* to behave in a silly way【英, 非正式】行為愚蠢 **4 old goat** an unpleasant old man, especially one who annoys women in a sexual way 令人生厭的老頭〔尤指老色鬼〕—see also 另見 BILLY GOAT

goat 山羊

goa·tee /goˈti; gəʊˈtiː/ *n* [C] a small pointed BEARD on the end of a man's chin 山羊鬍子 —see picture on page A6 參見A6頁圖

goat·herd /ˈgot,hɝd; ˈgəʊthɜːd/ *n* [C] someone who looks after a group of goats〔山羊的〕牧羊人

goat·skin /ˈgot,skɪn; ˈgəʊt,skɪn/ *n* **1** [C,U] leather made from the skin of a goat, or a wine container made from this 山羊皮革;〔裝葡萄酒的〕山羊皮囊 **2** [C] the skin of a goat 山羊皮

gob¹ /gɑb; gɒb/ *n* [C] *informal*【非正式】**1** *BrE* an impolite word meaning your mouth【英】嘴〔粗俗用語〕: *Shut your gob!* 住嘴! **2** a mass of something wet and sticky〔黏性物的〕一塊, 一團: [+of] *a gob of spit* 一團痰 **3 gobs** *AmE informal* a large amount of something【美, 非正式】大量: *gobs of money* 大量的錢

gob² *v* [I] *BrE informal* to blow a small amount of liquid out of your mouth; SPIT¹ (1)【英, 非正式】吐〔痰、唾沫〕, 啐

gob·bet /ˈgɑbɛt; ˈgɒbɪ̱t/ *n* [C] a small piece of something, especially food 一小片, 一小塊〔尤指食物〕

gob·ble /ˈgɑbḷ; ˈgɒbəl/ *v informal*【非正式】**1** [I,T] also 又作 **gobble up** to eat something very quickly or in a way people do not consider polite 狼吞虎嚥, 大嚼〔某物〕: *Don't gobble your food!* 別大口大口地吃東西! **2** [T] also 又作 **gobble up** to finish a supply of something quickly 很快消耗掉: *Inflation has gobbled up our wage increases.* 通貨膨脹抵銷了我們工資的增長。**3** [I] to make a sound like a TURKEY (1) 發出像火雞的叫聲 —**gobble** *n* [C]

gob·ble·dy·gook, gobbledegook /ˈgɑbḷdɪ,guk; ˈgɒbəldiguːk/ *n* [U] *informal* complicated language, especially in an official document, that seems to have no meaning【非正式】複雜而看來並無實質意義的語言〔尤指公文用語〕

gob·bler /ˈgɑblɚ; ˈgɒblə/ *n* [C] *AmE informal* a TURKEY (1)【美, 非正式】火雞

go-be·tween /ˈ·.,·/ *n* [C] someone who takes messages from one person or group to another, because the two sides cannot meet or do not wish to meet 中間人: *Martin acted as a go-between in the negotiations.* 馬丁在談判中充當中間人。

gob·let /ˈgɑblɪt; ˈgɒblɪ̱t/ *n* [C] a cup made of glass or metal, with a base and a stem but no handles〔玻璃或金屬製〕無柄高腳杯 —see picture at 參見 GLASS¹ 圖

gob·lin /ˈgɑblɪn; ˈgɒblɪ̱n/ *n* [C] a small, often ugly creature in children's stories that likes to trick people〔童話中的〕小妖精

gob·smacked /ˈgɑb,smækt; ˈgɒbsmækt/ *adj BrE spoken* very surprised, pleased, or disappointed【英口】非常吃驚[高興, 失望]的

gob·stop·per /ˈgɑb,stɑpɚ; ˈgɒb,stɒpə/ *n* [C] *BrE* a large round hard sweet【英】大糖球; JAWBREAKER (1) *AmE*【美】

go-cart /ˈ· ·/ *n* [C] an American spelling of GO-KART go-kart 的美式拼法

God /gɑd; gɒd/ *n* [singular, not with *the* 不與 the 連用] **1** the BEING² (2) who Christians, Jews, and Muslims pray to 上帝, 主; 真主 —see also 另見 **act of God** (ACT¹ (10)) **2 God/oh God/my God/good God** *spoken* used to add force to what you are saying, when you are surprised, annoyed, or amused【口】天啊!〔驚訝、惱怒或開心時用於加強語氣〕: *Oh God, how embarrassing!* 天啊, 多麼令人難堪! **3 I swear/hope/wish etc to God** used to emphasize that you promise, hope or wish that something is true 我對天發誓/衷心希望: *I hope to God nothing goes wrong.* 我衷心希望一切順利。**4 God knows** *spoken*【口】**a)** used to show that you are annoyed because you do not know something, or because you think that something is unreasonable 天曉得〔表示生氣〕: **God knows who/what/how etc** *God knows what she's doing in there.* 天曉得她在那兒幹甚麼。| **God only knows** *It'll cost God only knows how much.* 只有天曉得要花多少錢。**b)** used to add force to what you are saying 上天

為證〔以強調語氣〕: *God knows, it hasn't been easy.* 老天爺為證, 事情辦到現在這個樣子很不容易。**5 what/how/where/who in God's name** *spoken* used to add force to a question when you are angry or surprised【口】究竟甚麼/如何/哪裡/誰〔生氣或驚訝時用於加強語氣〕: *Where in God's name have you been?* 你到底去了甚麼地方? **6 God forbid** *spoken* used to say that you very much hope that something will not happen【口】但願〔某事〕不會發生: **[+(that)]** *God forbid that she should ever hurt you.* 老天爺在上, 但願她不會傷害你。**7 honest to God** *spoken* used to emphasize that you are not lying or joking【口】絕對是真的; 絕對當真: *Honest to God, I didn't tell her!* 對老天爺說實話, 我沒有告訴她! **8 God almighty** *spoken* used to express surprise, shock, annoyance, or anger【口】萬能的上帝〔用來表示驚訝、震驚、惱怒或氣憤〕 **9 God help you/him etc** *spoken* used to warn someone【口】你/他等就有麻煩了〔用於警告某人〕: *God help you if Tom comes home and you're still here!* 要是湯姆回家而你還在這裡的話, 那就只好求上帝幫助你了。**10 God help us** *spoken, usually humorous* used when you think that something bad is going to happen【口, 一般幽默】願上帝保佑我們〔用於認為某壞事將要發生〕: *"Simon's doing the cooking." "God help us!"* "西蒙在做飯。" "上帝保佑!" **11 God bless** *spoken* used to show your affection for someone【口】上帝保佑〔用來向某人表示關愛〕: *Goodnight, Jenny – God bless.* 晚安, 詹妮 —— 上帝保佑。**12 God willing** *spoken* used to say that you hope there will be no problems【口】如上帝許可〔用來表示希望一切順利〕: *We'll be moving next month, God willing.* 如上帝許可, 我們下個月搬家。**13 God-given** received from God 上帝賜予的, 天賦的: *a God-given talent for singing* 天賦的唱歌才華 | **a God-given right** (=the right to do something without asking anyone else's opinion) 上帝給的權利〔指無須徵求任何人意見而做某事的權利〕 **14 God give me strength!** *spoken* used when you are becoming annoyed【口】上帝給我力量!〔用於開始感到惱怒時〕 **15 God's gift to women/men etc** someone who thinks they are perfect or extremely attractive 上帝對女人/男人等的恩賜〔指自以為完美無缺或十分漂亮的人〕: *Paul thinks he's God's gift to the film industry.* 保羅認為他是電影界的天賜之物。**16 God rest his/her soul** also 又作 **God rest him/her** *old-fashioned* used to show respect when speaking about someone who is dead【過時】上帝讓他/她安息〔用於談及死者時表示敬意〕 **17 play God** to behave as though you have the power to do whatever you like 表現得似乎自己可以隨意而為: *scientists who think they can play God with their genetic experiments* 認為在做基因實驗時可以隨心所欲的科學家 **18 by God** *old-fashioned* used to add force when you are expressing determination or surprise【過時】老天作證〔表示決心或驚訝時用來加強語氣〕 —see also 另見 **there but for the grace of God** (GRACE[1] (6)), **in the lap of the gods** (LAP[1] (5)), **thank God/goodness/heavens** (THANK (2))

USAGE NOTE 用法說明: GOD

FORMALITY AND POLITENESS 正式和禮貌

In informal spoken English the following expressions are very common. They are used in a non-religious way, but some people would consider them to be offensive. **Oh (my) God/My God/Good God/God!** are all used to show strong surprise, fear, excitement or annoyance, or to emphasize what is said. 下列詞語在英語口語中十分常見。它們都用於非宗教意義, 但有些人認為這種用法是冒犯。Oh (my) God/My God/Good God/God! 都可用來表示非常吃驚、害怕、激動或惱怒, 或強調所說的話: *Oh God, what's that?* 天啊, 那是甚麼? | *My God, I forgot to lock the door.* 天啊, 我忘了鎖門。| *God he was sexy!* 天啊, 他很性感! | *Good God no!* 啊呀, 不!

For God's sake is used to draw attention strongly to a particular point. for God's sake 用來把注意力吸引到某一點上: *How can she do that, she's only seven for God's sake!* 她怎麼能做那件事呢, 天哪, 她只有七歲! It is also used with orders to make them stronger, or to show annoyance. 也可與命令連用以起強調作用, 或表示惱怒: *For God's sake shut up!* 看在老天爺的份上, 住嘴!

Thank God shows you are happy and pleased about something. thank God 用來表示對某事感到高興和滿意: *Thank God you're here!* 謝天謝地你來了! | *Thank God for that!* 為那事感謝上帝!

God (only) knows is a strong way of saying 'I don't know'. God (only) knows 是 I don't know (我不知道) 的強調說法。

SPELLING 拼法

God is always written with a capital letter in these expressions. 在這些詞語中, God 的第一個字母要大寫。

GRAMMAR 語法

God is not used with *the.* God 不與 the 連用: *I pray to God every night* (NOT 不用 *the God*). 我每天晚上向上帝祈禱。

god /gɑd; gɒd/ *n* [C] **1** a male BEING who is believed to control the world or part of it, or represents a particular quality 神, 男神: *Mars, the god of war* 戰神馬爾斯 **2** [C] someone or something to which you give too much importance or respect 被過分重視或崇拜的人[物]: *material wealth became their god* 物質財富成為他們極度崇拜的東西 **3 the gods a)** *informal* the seats high up and at the back of a theatre【非正式】〔劇院中的〕高層後座 **b)** the force that some people believe controls their lives, bringing them good or bad luck 神, 老天爺: *The gods are against me!* 老天爺在跟我作對!

god·aw·ful /ˌ· ˈ··◂/ *adj* [only before noun 僅用於名詞前] *informal* very bad or unpleasant【非正式】糟透的, 令人憎惡的

god·child /ˈgɑdˌtʃaɪld; ˈgɒdtʃaɪld/ *plural* **godchildren** /-ˌtʃɪldrən; -ˌtʃɪldrən/ *n* [C] the child that a GODPARENT promises to help and to teach Christian values to〔基督教的〕教子, 教女

god·dam·mit /ˈgɑdˋdæmɪt; gɒˈdæmɪ̈t/ *interjection especially AmE* used to express annoyance, anger etc【尤美】該死, 要命

god·damn, goddam /ˈgɑdˋdæm; ˈgɒdæm/ also 又作 **goddamned** /-ˋdæmd; -dæmd/ *adj* [only before noun 僅用於名詞前] *spoken* a word used to express annoyance or give force to an expression【口】該死〔表示惱怒或加強語氣〕: *Where's the goddamn key?* 該死的鑰匙到哪兒去了? **—goddamn, goddam, goddamned** *adv*: *I just did something so goddamned stupid.* 我剛才做了極其愚蠢的事。

god·daugh·ter /ˈgɑdˌdɔtɚ; ˈgɒdˌdɔːtə/ *n* [C] a girl that a GODPARENT promises to help and to teach Christian values to〔基督教的〕教女

god·dess /ˈgɑdɪs; ˈgɒdɪ̈s/ *n* [C] a female BEING[3] (1) who is believed to control the world or part of it, or represents a particular quality 女神: *Aphrodite, goddess of love* 愛情女神阿佛洛狄忒

god·fa·ther /ˈgɑdˌfɑðɚ; ˈgɒdˌfɑːðə/ *n* [C] **1** a man who promises to help a child and to teach him or her Christian values〔基督教的〕教父 **2** *slang* the head of a criminal organization or MAFIA group【俚】〔犯罪組織或黑手黨的〕首領, 教父

god·fear·ing /ˈ· ˌ··/ *adj old-fashioned* leading a good life following the rules of the Christian religion【過時】遵守〔基督教〕教規的; 正直善良的

god·for·sak·en /ˈgɑdfɚˋsekən; ˈgɒdfəseɪkən/ *adj* a godforsaken place is far away from where people live and contains nothing interesting, attractive, or cheerful

G

〔指地方〕被上帝遺棄的, 冷落的, 偏遠的: *Do you really enjoy living in this godforsaken dump?* 你真的喜歡住在這個偏遠的髒地方嗎?

god·head /ˈgɑdhɛd; ˈgɒdhed/ *n* **the Godhead** *formal* a word meaning God, used by Christians to mean the Father, the Son, and the Holy Spirit【正式】上帝

god·less /ˈgɑdlɛs; ˈgɒdləs/ *adj old-fashioned* not showing respect for God or belief in a god【過時】不敬上帝的, 不信神的 —**godlessly** *adv*

god·like /ˈgɑdˌlaɪk; ˈgɒdlaɪk/ *adj* like a god or with a quality suitable for a god 如神的, 具有神之品質的: *surveying the world with godlike calm* 用神般的冷靜審視世界

god·ly /ˈgɑdlɪ; ˈgɒdli/ *adj old-fashioned* obeying God and leading a good life【過時】虔誠的, 敬畏神的 —**godliness** *n* [U]

god·moth·er /ˈgɑdˌmʌðɚ; ˈgɒdˌmʌðə/ *n* [C] a woman who promises to help a child, and to teach him or her Christian values〔基督教的〕教母

god·par·ent /ˈgɑdˌpɛrənt; ˈgɒdˌpeərənt/ *n* [C] someone who promises to help a child, and to teach him or her Christian values〔基督教的〕教父, 教母

god·send /ˈgɑdˌsɛnd; ˈgɒdsend/ *n* [singular] something good that happens to you when you really need it 天賜之物, 及時雨: *That cheque from Sandy was a real godsend.* 桑迪的那張支票真是天賜之物。

god·son /ˈgɑdˌsʌn; ˈgɒdsʌn/ *n* [C] a boy that a godparent promises to help and to teach Christian values to〔基督教的〕教子

god·speed /ˈgɑdˌspid; ˌgɒdˈspiːd/ *n* [U] *old use* used to wish someone good luck especially before a journey【舊】幸運, 順利〔祝某人好運氣, 尤用在出發旅行之前〕

God squad /ˈ· ·/ *n slang* an insulting way of describing Christians who try to persuade other people to become Christians【俚】上帝使團〔侮辱性詞語, 指勸人入教的基督徒〕

go·er /ˈgoɚ; ˈgəʊə/ *n* [C] **1 cinema-/concert-/theatre-goer** someone who regularly goes to theatres etc 常看電影/常聽音樂會/常看戲的人 **2** *BrE spoken* a woman who often has sex with different men【英口】蕩婦: *one of my mum's friends who's a bit of a goer* 我媽媽的一個有些蕩婦行為的朋友

go·fer /ˈgofɚ; ˈgəʊfə/ *n* [C] *informal* someone who carries messages or gets or takes things for their employer【非正式】勤雜工

go-get·ter /ˌ· ˈ··/ *n* [C] someone who is likely to be successful because they are very determined and have a lot of energy 志在必得的人: *She's a real go-getter.* 她確實是個志在必得的人。

gog·gle /ˈgɑgl; ˈgɒgəl/ *v* [I] to look at something with your eyes wide open in surprise or shock〔由於驚訝、震驚〕瞪大眼睛看: **[+at]** *They were goggling at us as if we were freaks.* 他們瞪眼看着我們, 好像我們是怪物似的。

goggle box /ˈ·· ·/ *n* [C usually singular 一般用單數] *BrE informal* a television【英, 非正式】電視機

goggle-eyed /ˌ·· ˈ·◂/ *adj* with your eyes wide open and looking directly at something 瞪大眼睛的: *staring goggle-eyed at the women* 瞪大眼睛看那些女人

gog·gles /ˈgɑglz; ˈgɒgəlz/ *n* [plural] something that protects your eyes, made of two round pieces of glass or plastic with an edge that fits against your skin 護目鏡

go-go danc·er /ˈ· · ,··/ *n* [C] a woman who dances with sexy movements in a bar or NIGHTCLUB〔酒吧或夜總會的〕跳色情舞蹈的舞女 —**go-go dancing** *n* [U]

go·ing[1] /ˈgoɪŋ; ˈgəʊɪŋ/ *n* [U]

1 ►LEAVING 離開◄ the act of leaving a place 離去: *His going will be no great loss to the company.* 他的離去對公司不會造成甚麼大損失。

2 ►SPEED 速度◄ the speed at which you travel or work 行走速度; 工作速度: *We climbed the mountain in three hours, which wasn't bad going.* 我們在三小時內爬上山, 這樣的速度還算不錯。| **hard/rough/slow going** *I'm getting the work done, but it's slow going.* 我正在完成這項工作, 但進展很慢。

3 heavy going if a book, play etc is heavy going, it is boring and difficult to understand〔書、戲劇等〕乏味且難懂的

4 while the going's good *especially BrE* before someone stops you from doing what you want【尤英】趁沒有人阻止前: *Let's get out while the going's good.* 我們趁現在這個機會快走吧。

5 ►GROUND 地面◄ the condition of the ground, especially for a horse race 地面狀況〔特指是否適合賽馬〕— see also 另見 **comings and goings** (COMING[1] (2))

going[2] *adj* **1** [not before noun 不用於名詞前] *informal* available【非正式】可獲得的, 可找到的: *Are there any jobs going where you work?* 你工作的地方有空缺嗎? **2 the biggest/best/nicest ... going** the biggest, best etc of a particular thing 當今最大的/最好的/最美好的: *Jim's the biggest fool going.* 吉姆是當今最大的傻瓜。**3 the going rate** the usual cost of a service or job 通常價格: *£15 per hour is the going rate for tuition.* 每小時15英鎊是現行的學費。**4 have a lot going for you/not have much going for you** to have or not have many advantages and good qualities that will bring success 你有很多/你沒有甚麼有利條件: *Stop being so depressed. You have a lot going for you.* 別這麼沮喪。你有很多有利條件。**5 a going concern** a business which is making a profit and is expected to continue to do so 生意興隆〔且將繼續興隆〕的企業

going-o·ver /ˌ·· ˈ··/ *n* **1** a thorough examination of something to make sure it is all right 全面的檢查: *The car needs a good going-over.* 這輛車需要好好檢查一下。**2 give sb a going-over** *especially BrE* to hit someone and hurt them【尤英】把某人痛打一頓

goings-on /ˌ·· ˈ·/ *n* [plural] activities or events that are strange, especially ones that involve sex or make you think something dishonest may be happening〔怪異的, 尤指色情或不正當的〕活動; 事件: *There are certainly some strange goings-on at that house, I reckon.* 我看那棟房子裡肯定有怪事。

goi·tre *BrE*【英】, **goiter** *AmE*【美】/ˈgɔɪtɚ; ˈgɔɪtə/ *n* [C,U] a disease of the THYROID GLAND that makes your neck very swollen 甲狀腺腫大

go-kart also 又作 **go-cart** *AmE*【美】/ˈgoˌkɑrt; ˈgəʊ kɑːt/ *n* [C] a small vehicle with an engine, made of an open frame on four wheels and used in races 微型賽車 —**go-karting** *n* [U]

gold[1] /gold; gəʊld/ *n* **1** [U] a valuable soft yellow metal that is an ELEMENT (=simple substance) and is used for making coins, jewellery etc 黃金: **strike gold** (=find it in the ground)〔在地下〕發現黃金 **2** [U] coins, jewellery etc made of this metal 金幣, 金首飾等: *Vanessa wore so much gold it's no wonder she was mugged.* 瓦內莎戴了那麼多金首飾, 怪不得遭到搶劫。**3** [C,U] the colour of this metal 金色, 金黃色: *The room was decorated in golds and blues.* 房間是用各種金色和藍色來裝飾的。**4** [C] *informal* a GOLD MEDAL【非正式】金質獎章, 金牌 **5 gold digger** *old-fashioned slang* a woman who tries to attract rich men【過時, 俚】勾引富有男子的女人 —see also 另見 **have a heart of gold** (HEART (13))

gold[2] *adj* **1** made of gold 金質的: *a gold chain* 金鏈 **2** having the colour of gold 金色的, 金黃色的: *gold buttons* 金黃色的鈕扣 | *gold velvet curtains* 金色的絲絨窗簾 —compare 比較 GOLDEN

gold·brick /ˈgoldˌbrɪk; ˈgəʊldbrɪk/ also 又作 **gold·brick·er** /-ˌbrɪkɚ; -brɪkə/ *n* [C] *AmE informal* someone who stays away from their work, especially with the false excuse that they are ill【美, 非正式】裝病逃避工作的人 —**goldbrick** *v* [I]

gold card /ˌ· ˈ·/ *n* [C] a special CREDIT CARD that gives you additional advantages or services, such as a high spending limit〔信用卡〕金卡

gold dust /ˈ· ·/ *n* [U] **1** gold in the form of a fine powder 金粉 **2 be like gold dust** to be very valuable and difficult to find 十分珍貴的, 不可多得的: *Good secretaries are like gold dust.* 好祕書是不可多得的寶貴人才。

3 **gold·en** /ˋgoldn̩; ˈgəʊldən/ *adj* **1** having a bright, rich, yellow colour, like gold 金色的, 金黃色的, 金子般的: *golden sunlight* 金色的陽光 | *golden hair* 金黃色的頭髮 —see picture on page A5 參見 A5 頁圖 **2** made of gold 金質的: *a golden crown* 金王冠 **3 a golden opportunity** a good chance to get something valuable or to be very successful 絕好的機會: *Don't turn the job down – it's a golden opportunity.* 不要拒絕那份工作——這是個絕好的機會。**4 golden boy/girl** someone who is popular and successful 大受歡迎的成功男孩/女孩: *the golden girl of US tennis* 美國網球女明星 **5** [only before noun 僅用於名詞前] a golden period of time is one of great happiness or success〔時期〕非常幸福的, 非常成功的: *the golden summers of childhood* 童年幸福的夏天 **6 golden oldie** a popular song written several years ago that people still enjoy listening to 多年前創作而仍受喜愛的歌曲

golden age /ˈ‥ ˌ·/ *n* [usually singular 一般用單數] an unusually good time of great achievement and happiness, especially in the past〔尤指過去的〕黃金時代: *the golden age of film* 電影的黃金時代

golden an·ni·ver·sa·ry /ˌ‥ ‥ˈ···/ *n* [C] *AmE* a GOLDEN WEDDING【美】結婚50週年紀念日, 金婚紀念日

golden brown /ˌ‥ ˈ·◂/ *adj* a light brown colour 淺棕色的: *Bake the biscuits until golden brown.* 把餅乾烘烤到淺棕色。

golden ea·gle /ˌ‥ ˈ‥/ *n* [C] a large light brown bird that lives in northern parts of the world 金鵰

golden hand·shake /ˌ‥ ˈ‥/ *n* [C] *BrE* a large amount of money given to someone when they leave their job【英】〔離職時的一大筆〕退職金, 遣散費

golden ju·bi·lee /ˌ‥ ˈ···/ *n* [C] *BrE* the date that is exactly 50 years after some important event, especially of becoming king or queen【英】〔某重要事件, 尤指國王、女王加冕〕50週年紀念日 —compare 比較 DIAMOND JUBILEE, SILVER JUBILEE

golden par·a·chute /ˌ‥ ˈ···/ *n* [C] *BrE informal* part of a business person's contract which states that they will be paid a large sum of money when the contract ends【英, 非正式】金降落傘〔指商業人員合約的一部分, 規定合約終止時, 他將獲得一大筆錢〕

golden rai·sin /ˌ‥ ˈ‥/ *n* [C] *AmE* a small pale RAISIN (=dried fruit) used in baking【美】〔烘烤食物使用的〕無核葡萄乾; SULTANA *BrE*【英】

golden re·triev·er /ˌ‥ ·ˈ‥/ *n* [C] a fairly large dog with silky light brown fur 金毛拾獚

golden rule /ˌ‥ ˈ·/ *n* [usually singular 一般用單數] a very important principle, way of behaving etc that should be remembered 重要的原則; 重要的行為準則

golden syr·up /ˌ‥ ˈ‥/ *n* [U] *BrE* a sweet, thick liquid made from sugar that is used in cooking【英】〔用於烹調的〕金黃色糖漿

golden wed·ding /ˌ‥ ˈ‥/ also 又作 **golden wedding an·niver·sa·ry** /ˌ‥ ˈ‥ ‥ˌ···/ *BrE informal n* [C] the date that is exactly 50 years after a wedding【英, 非正式】結婚50週年紀念日, 金婚紀念日; GOLDEN ANNIVERSARY *AmE*【美】—compare 比較 DIAMOND WEDDING, SILVER WEDDING

gold·field /ˋgoldˌfild; ˈgəʊldfiːld/ *n* [C] also 又作 **goldfields** *plural* an area of land where gold can be found 金礦區, 採金地

gold·finch /ˋgoldˌfɪntʃ; ˈgəʊldˌfɪntʃ/ *n* [C] a small singing bird with yellow feathers on its wings 黃雀

gold·fish /ˋgoldˌfɪʃ; ˈgəʊldˌfɪʃ/ *n* [C] a small shiny orange fish often kept as a pet 金魚

goldfish bowl /ˈ‥ ˌ·/ *n* [C] **1** a round glass bowl in which fish are kept as pets 金魚缸 **2 live in a goldfish bowl** to be in a situation in which people can know everything about your life 置身於沒有隱私的境地

gold leaf /ˌ· ˈ·/ *n* [U] gold which has been beaten into extremely thin sheets for use in decoration 金葉, 金箔

gold med·al /ˌ· ˈ‥/ *n* [C] a round, flat piece of gold given to someone for a special achievement, especially for winning a race or competition 金質獎章, 金牌 —see also 另見 BRONZE MEDAL, SILVER MEDAL

gold med·al·list *BrE*【英】, **gold medalist** *AmE*【美】/ˌ· ˈ···/ *n* [C] someone who wins a gold medal 金質獎章獲得者, 金牌獲得者

gold·mine /ˋgoldˌmaɪn; ˈgəʊldmaɪn/ *n* [C] **1** *informal* a business or activity that produces large profits【非正式】〔產生巨額利潤的〕財源, 寶庫: *I bet that shop's a real goldmine.* 我敢說那家商店是個真正的金礦。**2** a deep hole or system of holes underground from which rock containing gold is taken 金礦 **3 be sitting on a goldmine** to own something very valuable, especially without realizing this 擁有非常寶貴的東西〔尤指自己並不知道〕

gold plate /ˌ· ˈ·/ *n* [U] **1** a layer of gold on top of another metal 鍍金層 **2** dishes, spoons etc made of gold 金質餐具 —**gold-plated** *adj*: *Is it solid gold or gold-plated?* 這是純金的還是鍍金的?

gold-rimmed /ˌ· ˈ·◂/ *adj* having a gold edge or border 鑲金邊的: *gold-rimmed glasses* 金邊玻璃杯

gold rush /ˈ· ·/ *n* [C] a situation when a lot of people hurry to a place where gold has just been discovered 淘金熱〔湧向剛剛發現金子的地區〕

gold·smith /ˋgoldˌsmɪθ; ˈgəʊldˌsmɪθ/ *n* [C] someone who makes things out of gold 金匠

gold stan·dard /ˈ· ˌ‥/ *n* **the gold standard** the use of the value of gold as a fixed standard on which to base the value of money〔貨幣的〕金本位

go·lem /ˋgoləm; ˈgəʊləm/ *n* [C] *AmE informal* a stupid person【美, 非正式】傻瓜, 蠢人

golf /gɑlf; gɒlf/ *n* [U] a game in which the players hit a small white ball into holes in the ground with a set of golf clubs using as few hits as possible 高爾夫球運動: **a round of golf** (=a game of golf) 一場高爾夫球 —**golfer** *n* [C] 2 3

golf ball /ˈ· ·/ *n* [C] **1** a small hard white ball used in the game of golf 高爾夫球 **2** a small ball in an electric TYPEWRITER that has the letters of the alphabet on it, and that moves to print them onto paper〔電動打字機的〕球形字頭 **3** an electric TYPEWRITER that operates in this way 有球形字頭的電動打字機 —compare 比較 DAISYWHEEL PRINTER

golf club /ˈ· ·/ *n* [C] **1** an organization of people who play golf, or the land and buildings they use 高爾夫球俱樂部 **2** a long wooden or metal stick used for hitting the ball in the game of golf 高爾夫球杆 —see picture on page A23 參見 A23 頁圖

golf course /ˈ· ·/ *n* [C] an area of land that golf is played on 高爾夫球場

golf·ing /ˋgɑlfɪŋ; ˈgɒlfɪŋ/ *n* [U] the activity of playing golf 打高爾夫球: *Ian goes golfing on Sundays.* 伊恩每星期日去打高爾夫球。

golf links /ˈ· ·/ *plural* **golf links** *n* [C] a golf course, especially by the sea〔尤指海邊的〕高爾夫球場

go·li·ath /gəˋlaɪəθ; gəˈlaɪəθ/ *n* [C] a person or company that is very large, strong, and powerful; GIANT[2] 巨人; 大公司: *How can a small computer company compete with the goliaths of the industry?* 一家小電腦公司怎麼能跟該行業的大公司競爭呢?

gol·li·wog /ˋgɑlɪˌwɑg; ˈgɒliwɒg/ *n* [C] a child's DOLL[1] (1) made of cloth, like a man with a black face, white eyes, and short black hair 黑臉白眼、短頭髮的男布娃娃

gol·ly[1] /ˋgɑlɪ; ˈgɒli/ *interjection old-fashioned* used to express surprise【過時】天啊〔用來表示驚訝〕

golly[2] *n* [C] *informal* a golliwog【非正式】黑臉白眼、短頭髮男布娃娃

-gon /gən; gən *strong* 強讀 gɑn; gɒn/ *suffix* [in nouns 構成名詞] a shape with a particular number of sides and angles ...邊形; ...角形: *a hexagon* (=with six sides) 六邊形 | *a polygon* (=with many sides) 多邊形

go·nad /ˋgɑnæd; ˈgəʊnæd/ *n* [C] *technical* the male or female sex organ in which the SPERM (1) or eggs (EGG[1] (3)) are produced【術語】性腺, 生殖腺; 睾丸; 卵巢

gon·do·la /ˋgɑndələ; ˈgɒndələ/ *n* [C] **1** a long narrow boat with a flat bottom and high points at each end, used on the CANALs in Venice in Italy〔意大利威尼斯運河的〕平底船 **2** the place where passengers sit that hangs beneath an AIRSHIP or BALLOON[1] (2)〔飛船或氣球下的〕吊籃, 吊艙 **3** the enclosed part of a CABLE CAR where the passengers sit〔纜車的〕車廂

gon·do·lier /ˌgɑndəˋlɪr; ˌgɒndəˈlɪə/ *n* [C] a man who rows a gondola in Venice 威尼斯平底船船夫

gone[1] /gɔn; gɒn/ the past participle of go

gone[2] *adj informal*【非正式】**1 be gone** to be showing the effects of taking drugs or drinking alcohol〔因吸毒或飲酒而〕神志不清的: *Look at Michelle – she's totally gone!* 瞧瞧米歇爾——她完全醉了! **2 be gone on sb** to be very fond of someone and think they are very attractive 迷戀上[傾心於]某人: *Our Kate's really gone on that boy next door.* 我們的凱特真的迷戀上隔壁的那個男孩了。**3 be five/six/seven etc months gone** *BrE informal* to have been PREGNANT for a particular length of time【英, 非正式】已經懷孕五個月/六個月/七個月等

gone[3] *prep BrE informal* used like 'past', to mean later than a particular time or older than a particular age【英, 非正式】過了〔與 past 的用法相似, 指過了某個時間或某一年齡〕: *When we got home it was gone midnight.* 我們到家時已經過了半夜。

gon·er /ˋgɑnɚ; ˈgɒnə/ *n informal*【非正式】**be a goner** someone who will soon die, or is in an impossible situation 即將死去[陷入絕境]的人: *If Mark's still inside the plane, he's a goner.* 如果馬克還在飛機裡, 他就完了。

gong /gɔŋ; gɒŋ/ *n* [C] a round piece of metal that hangs in a frame and that you hit with a stick to give a deep ringing sound, used for example to call people somewhere, often to announce that a meal is ready 鑼

gon·na /ˋgɔnə; ˈgɒnə/ a way of saying 'going to', which many people think is incorrect 即將, 打算〔意為 going to, 許多人認為這種用法不正確〕: *This isn't gonna be easy.* 這將很不容易。

gon·or·rhe·a, gonorrhoea /ˌgɑnəˋriə; ˌgɒnəˈriːə/ *n* [U] a disease of the sex organs that is passed on during sex; VD 淋病

gon·zo jour·nal·is·m /ˋgɑnzo ˌdʒɝnl̩ɪzəm; ˈgɒnzəʊ ˌdʒɜːnəlɪzəm/ *n* [U] *AmE informal* reporting in newspapers which is concerned with shocking or exciting the reader and not with giving true information【美, 非正式】尋求轟動效應的新聞報道〔指一種報紙上的報道, 其目的不在於提供信息, 而在於使讀者震驚或激動〕—**gonzo journalist** *n* [C]

goo /gu; guː/ *n* [U] *informal*【非正式】**1** an unpleasantly sticky substance〔令人生厭的〕黏糊糊的東西: *What's all this goo at the bottom of the bag?* 袋底的這些黏糊糊的東西是甚麼? **2** words or feelings that are too emotional or romantic 過分多情的話; 過分多情 —see also 另見 GOOEY

S1 W1 **good[1]** /gʊd; gʊd/ *adj comparative* 比較級 **better** /ˋbɛtɚ; ˈbetə/ *superlative* 最高級 **best** /bɛst; best/

1 ►OF A HIGH STANDARD 高標準的◄ of a high standard 良好的: *a good reputation* 良好的聲譽 | *a good quality cloth* 優質布料 | *a good Muslim* 一名規規矩矩的穆斯林 | *This book is not as good as her last one.* 這本書不如她的上一本好。| *His test scores were good, but hers were even better.* 他的考試分數很好, 可是她的更好。| *We received the best medical treatment.* 我們得到最好的醫療。| **very/extremely/pretty etc good** *Mike's done an extremely good job of painting the windows.* 邁克把窗子油漆得非常好。| **(not) good enough** *Your work's simply not good enough.* 你的工作實在不夠好。| **be too good for sb** *informal*【非正式】*David doesn't deserve to have a girlfriend like Kate – she's much too good for him!* 戴維配不上有像凱特這樣的女朋友, 對戴維來說凱特是太好了! —opposites 反義詞 BAD[1] (2), POOR (3)

2 ►OF THE RIGHT KIND 對頭的◄ having qualities that are worth praising 值得稱讚的, 良好的: *He is a good husband.* 他是個好丈夫。| *$50 is a very good price.* 50美元是個很好的價格。| *That's good news!* 那是好消息! | *They've had a really good idea.* 他們的想法確實很好。| **any good** *"Is your new doctor any good?" – "Yes, she's OK."* "你們那位新醫生行嗎?" "行, 她還不錯。" —opposite 反義詞 BAD[1] (1)

3 no good/not much good/not any good a) not very useful 不太有用: *This radio's not much good, is it?* 這台收音機不怎麼好用, 是嗎? | **it is no good doing sth** *It's no good talking to him – he never listens.* 跟他講沒用——他從來不聽。| **no good for sth** *These glasses are no good for champagne.* 這些玻璃杯不適合用來喝香檳酒。| **no good to sb** *A car's not much good to me, since I can't drive!* 汽車對我沒有多大用處, 因為我不會開車! **b)** bad 不好的, 壞的: *The movie wasn't much good.* 這部電影不怎麼好。

4 ►SKILFUL 熟練的◄ **a)** clever or skilful 聰明的, 熟練的: *She's a good skier.* 她是個滑雪能手。| **good at sth/doing sth** *Alfred is very good at languages.* 阿爾弗雷德很擅長學習語言。| **good with sth/sb** (=skilful at using something or dealing with someone) 擅長使用某物/與某人打交道 *My receptionist is very good with people.* 我的接待員很會與人打交道。—opposites 反義詞 BAD[1] (2), POOR (5)

5 be no good at/not be much good at/not be very good at not to be skilful at something or doing something 不擅長(做)某事: *You're not very good at reading maps, are you?* 你不太擅長看地圖, 是嗎?

6 ►STRONG 強有力的◄ strong; likely to be successful, to persuade people etc 有說服力的, 有分量的: *I want an explanation, and it had better be good!* 我需要有個解釋, 最好是有說服力的解釋! | *That's a good point.* 那是個很有力的論點。| *You have a fairly good chance of winning.* 你獲勝的機會相當大。—opposites 反義詞 POOR (3), WEAK (5)

7 ►ENJOYABLE 令人愉快的◄ enjoyable; pleasant 令人愉快的, 合意的: *It's good to see you again.* 很高興再次見到你。| *That was good fun.* 那非常好玩。| **have a good time/day/weekend etc** *The kids had a very good time at the zoo.* 孩子們在動物園玩得很開心。| **too much of a good thing** (=something which stops being pleasant because you have too much of it or it continues for too long) 過了頭的好事 —see also 另見 **the good old days** (OLD (16))

8 ►SUITABLE 合適的◄ **a) good for sth/good for doing sth** suitable for something 適合某事/適合做某事: *It's a good day for a trip to the mountains.* 今天的天氣很適合到山裡去玩。| *This is the best knife for cutting vegetables.* 這是最適合切菜用的刀子。| *Those cards would be good for the invitations.* 那些卡片做請柬用很合適。**b) good for sb** *especially AmE* convenient for someone【尤美】對某人是方便的: *Ten o'clock is good for me.* 十點鐘對我很合適。| *So we're all meeting at the beach? That's good for me.* 那麼我們大家都在海灘碰頭嗎? 這對我很合適。

9 ►HELPFUL 有幫助的◄ helpful 有幫助的, 有益的: *good advice* 有益的忠告 | *That's a very good example.* 那是個很好的例子。| *She'll be a good influence on him.* 她對他會產生很好的影響。| **be good for sth** (=help it to develop or be produced) 對某物有幫助 *This weather is very good for business.* 這樣的天氣對生意很有幫助。| *It's been a good year for apples.* 今年是蘋果的好年頭。—opposites 反義詞 BAD[1] (2), POOR (3)

10 ►IN A GOOD CONDITION 狀況良好◄ in a satisfactory condition for use; not broken, damaged, decayed, OUT-OF-DATE etc 狀況良好的; 未壞的; 未過期的: *You need*

good shoes for hiking. 徒步旅行需要穿結實的鞋子。| **good for three days/a week etc** (=to be used during that time) 能用三天／一星期等 *This ticket is good for one month.* 這張票一個月有效。| **as good as new** (=in perfect condition, especially after being cleaned or repaired) 〔通過清洗或修理〕像新的一樣 *They've fixed the car, and it's as good as new.* 他們把車修好了, 現在車像新的一樣。—see also 另見 **pay good money for** (MONEY (5))

11 ►HEALTHY 有益健康的◄ healthy 有益健康的: *This water isn't good to drink.* 這水不宜飲用。| **feel good** *I don't feel too good.* 我感到不大舒服。| *He's feeling better today.* 他今天感覺好多了。| **be good for sb** *Milk is good for you.* 喝牛奶對你有好處。| *It isn't good for children to watch too much TV.* 兒童不宜看太多電視。

12 ►SHOWING APPROVAL 表示讚許◄ **Good** *spoken* 【口】**a)** used to show that you are pleased about something 好〔對某事感到滿意〕: *Good, I'm glad you've got it under control.* 好, 我很高興你把它控制住了。| *"Seven minus two is five". "Good".* "七減二等於五。""對。" **b)** used when something has been decided or agreed 行, 好〔用於決定或同意某事時〕: *Good. We'll use the new one, then.* 好, 那麼我們就用新的。

13 ►CHILD 兒童◄ a word meaning well-behaved, used especially about a child 守規矩的, 乖的〔尤指兒童〕: *She's such a good baby.* 她真是一個乖孩子。| *Be a good girl, now.* 做個乖女孩, 聽見了嗎? | **as good as gold** (=extremely well-behaved) 十分有教養的, 非常乖的

14 ►KIND 好心的◄ kind 好心的, 慈善的: **good about** *I had some time off work when my mother was ill, but my boss was very good about it.* 我母親生病的時候我請了幾天假, 老闆對此非常諒解。| **good of sb (to do sth)** *formal* 【正式】*It was good of you to come to the funeral.* 你能來參加葬禮十分感謝。| **good to sb** (=an expression meaning kind to someone, used especially to defend someone) 對某人友善的〔尤用來為某人辯護〕*Mr Hawkins has always been very good to me.* 霍金斯先生一直對我很好。

15 ►LARGE 大的◄ large in amount, area, or range 〔數量、面積或範圍〕相當大的: *They stock a good range of furniture.* 他們備有各式各樣的家具。| *a good crop of mangoes* 芒果的大豐收 | *I've travelled a good distance.* 我走了很長一段路。| **a good while** *informal* (=quite a long time) 【非正式】長時間, 很久 *We'd waited a good while by now.* 我們已經等了很久。—see also 另見 GOODISH

16 ►MORALLY RIGHT 有道德的◄ morally right 有道德的, 高尚的: *a good man* 正派人 | *I still think it was a good thing to do.* 我仍然認為這是件該做的好事。| **my/his etc good deed for the day** *informal* (=something you do that helps someone else, especially something boring or unimportant) 【非正式】我／他等做的善事〔尤指區區小事〕| **the good guys** *informal* (=the people who represent morally right behaviour, especially in films) 【非正式】〔電影裡的〕正派人物 | **be no good** *informal* (=be a morally bad person) 【非正式】品行不端的人 *Stay away from Gerry. He's no good.* 離格里遠點, 他不是好東西。—opposite 反義詞 BAD[1] (3)

17 ►COMPLETE 完整的◄ complete; thorough 完整的, 全面的, 徹底的: *Take a good look at it.* 好好地看它一眼。| *She had a good cry.* 她痛快地哭了一場。| *That needs a good washing.* 那需要好好地洗一洗。| **good and ...** *informal* (=very or completely) 【非正式】非常, 完全 *Don't rush me; I'll do it when I'm good and ready.* 別催我, 我完全準備好了我就會做的。

18 a good deal a lot 大量, 許多: *They went out a good deal.* 他們經常外出。| **a good deal of trouble/time etc** *I went to a good deal of trouble to get this ticket.* 我費了好大勁才弄到這張票。

19 a good deal larger/better etc also 又作 **a good bit larger/better etc** *BrE* much larger, better etc 【英】大得多／好得多等: *Their kitchen is a good deal wider than ours.* 他們的廚房比我們的寬多了。

20 a good friend someone who you know very well and like very much 好朋友

21 hold good if a law, rule, reason etc holds good it is or remains effective or true 〔法律、規則、理由等〕有效, 適用: *theories that hold good for all countries* 適用於各國的理論 | *These words, uttered in 1848, still hold good today.* 這些話雖然是1848年說的, 但在今天仍然適用。

22 the good good people generally; those who do what is right 好人: *Christians believe that the good go to heaven when they die.* 基督徒認為好人死後上天堂。—see also 另見 **the great and the good** (GREAT (21))

23 be too good to be true/to last *informal* to seem to be so good that you think something must be wrong, or expect something bad to happen 【非正式】好得令人難以置信, 好得令人覺得有問題: *She found out he was married – I knew he was too good to be true!* 她發現他是結了婚的 —— 我就知道他不會有這麼好!

24 in good time (for sth/to do sth) if you arrive somewhere in good time to do something, you arrive early enough to do it 早早地〔到某地以便不耽誤做某事〕

25 in her/their etc own good time *informal* someone who does something in their own good time does not do it when other people want them to, but only when they are completely ready to do it 【非正式】在她／他們等認為最適合自己的時間

26 as good a time/place etc as any *usually spoken* used to say that although a time etc is not perfect, there will not be a better one 【一般口】與其他時間／地點等不相上下〔用來表示某一時間等雖不完美, 但不會有更好的〕: *Well, I suppose this is as good a spot as any to set up camp.* 好吧, 我想在這個地方紮營不比任何其他地方壞。

27 good for nothing *informal* someone who is good for nothing is completely useless and worthless 【非正式】〔人〕完全沒用的, 一文不值的 —see also 另見 GOOD-FOR-NOTHING

28 to be good for a meal/a few drinks etc *informal* be likely to give you something 【非正式】可能給一頓飯吃／幾杯酒喝等: *My uncle should be good for a few bucks.* 我叔叔應當會給幾塊錢。

29 good offices [plural] *formal* services provided, especially by someone in a position of power, that help someone out of a difficulty 【正式】〔有權勢的人的〕幫忙, 照顧: *Through the good offices of the ambassador we were given special permission to travel.* 由於大使的幫助, 我們獲得旅行特許。

30 be in sb's good books *informal* if you are in someone's good books, they like you or approve of you more than they usually do 【非正式】為某人所另眼相看: *I'll ask my boss for the day off – I'm in her good books at the moment.* 我要向老闆請一天假 —— 我目前正得到她的好感。

31 the good book *old-fashioned, sometimes humorous* the Bible 【過時, 有時幽默】《聖經》

32 good Samaritan someone who gives help to people in trouble 行善的人: *Mrs Hoare was the good Samaritan who came to our rescue.* 霍爾女士就是那位救援我們的善人。

33 in good faith *formal* sincerely 【正式】真誠地, 誠實地: *I promised you that in good faith, but I can't do it, I'm afraid.* 我當時確是真誠地答應你辦這件事, 不過現在我恐怕做不了。

34 a good three miles/ten years etc at least three miles, ten years etc, and probably more 至少三英里／十年等: *It's a good mile away.* 那裡距離此地至少一英里。| *He's a good ten years younger than her.* 他比她至少小十歲。

35 be good for another three years/hundred miles etc something that is good for a particular length of time is not in good condition but will probably last for that length of time 可再對付用三年／可再走一百英里等: *Nonsense, my bike's good for a few miles yet!* 胡說, 我的自行車還能騎幾英里!

G

36 a good few/many *informal* quite a lot of something【非正式】許多, 大量: *I've done this a good few times now.* 我到現在已經做了許多遍了。| *"How many people were there?" "Oh, a good many."* "那裡有多少人?" "噢, 很多人。"
37 as good as done/finished/yours etc used to say that something is almost done etc, or definitely will be soon 可以說已經做完/完成/就是你的等: *The work is as good as finished.* 這件工作可以說已經完成。
38 as good as dead/ruined/useless etc in a state that is not much better than being dead, ruined etc 差不多死了/毀了/廢了等: *If he finds out, I'm as good as dead!* 如果他發現, 我就沒命了!
39 give as good as you get *BrE informal* to react to someone who attacks or harms you by doing equal damage to them【英, 非正式】以牙還牙
40 have a good thing going to be doing something that is and will continue to be successful 成功地做着某事: *They've got a good thing going with that little business of theirs.* 他們的那個小生意做得很紅火。
41 be as good as your word to keep your promise 守信用, 信守諾言: *He said he'd see what he could do, and he was as good as his word.* 他答應盡力幫忙, 而且他說話算數。
42 a good word for sb/sth a favourable remark about someone or something 為某人/某事說的一句好話: **have a good word (to say) for sb/sth** *I'm afraid no one had a good word to say for her.* 恐怕沒人說她的好話。| **put in a good word for sb** *When you see the CEO, put in a good word for me.* 你見到行政總裁的時候幫我說句好話。
43 be onto a good thing *informal* to have found a way of getting a lot without paying money or working hard【非正式】找到了不必花錢[不必努力工作]便大有所獲的辦法
44 make good also 又作 **make it good** an expression meaning to become successful and rich after being poor, used especially in newspapers 變富; 獲得成功〔尤用於報紙上〕: *a boy from a hick town who made good in New York* 在紐約獲得成功的一位來自偏僻鄉鎮的男孩
45 make good a debt/loss etc an expression meaning to pay someone money that you owe, or provide money instead of what has been lost, used especially in business 償還債務/賠償損失等〔尤用於生意〕: *The loss to the company was made good by contributions from its subsidiaries.* 公司的這一損失由各子公司的捐助彌補了。
46 make good your escape *literary* to succeed in escaping【文】成功逃跑
47 the good life a simple, natural way of living 樸素自然的生活方式 —see also 另見 **so far so good** (FAR¹ (21)), **while the going's good** (GOING¹ (4)), **for good measure** (MEASURE¹ (9)), **bad/good sailor** (SAILOR (2)), **that's/it's all well and good** (WELL³ (5))

Frequencies of the adjective **good** in spoken and written English 形容詞good在英語口語和書面語中的使用頻率

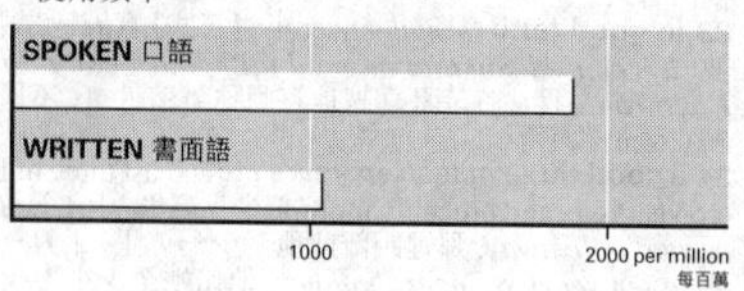

Based on the British National Corpus and the Longman Lancaster Corpus
據英國國家語料庫和朗文蘭卡斯特語料庫

This graph shows that the adjective **good** is much more common in spoken English than in written English. This is because it has some special uses in spoken English and is used in some common spoken phrases. 本圖表顯示, 形容詞good在英語口語中的使用頻率遠遠高於書面語, 因為它在口語中有特殊的用法, 並用在一些常見的口語片語中。

good (*adj*) **SPOKEN PHRASES**
含good的口語片語

48 good used to say that you are pleased that something happens or is done 好〔用來表示對某事發生或辦成很高興〕: *"I could do it tomorrow if you want." "Good."* "如果你需要的話, 我可以明天做。" "好。" used to tell someone that you think their work or what they are doing is good〔用來告訴某人你對他的工作滿意〕: *Good, that's the way, keep going.* 幹得好, 就是這樣, 繼續幹吧。**49 oh good** used to say that you are pleased that something you didn't know about happens or is done 好啊〔用來對原來不知道的事情的發生或完成表示高興〕: *"I've invited Danny and Marilyn to dinner tonight." "Oh good."* "我請了丹尼和瑪麗琳今晚來吃飯。" "好啊。" **50 good morning/afternoon/evening** used to say hello to someone in the morning, afternoon or evening 早上好/下午好/晚上好: *Good afternoon everyone. Sorry I'm late.* 大家下午好。對不起我遲到了。**51 what a good girl/boy/dog etc** used to tell a child or animal that it has behaved well or done something well 多乖的女孩/男孩/狗等: *What a good girl! Mummy's going to give you a nice chocolate.* 多乖的孩子! 媽媽要給你一塊好吃的巧克力。**52 good idea/point/question** used when someone says or suggests something interesting or important that you had not thought of before 好主意/說得對/問題提得好: *"But tomorrow's Sunday, the bank will be closed." "Yes, good point."* "不過明天是星期天, 銀行會關門。" "是的, 說得對。" **53 that's no good** used to say that something is not suitable or convenient 不合適, 不方便: *"I could do it next week." "That's no good. I'll be away."* "我可以下星期做。" "那不行, 下星期我不在家。" **54 that's/it's not good enough** used to say that you are not satisfied with something and you are annoyed about it 那/這不好〔表示對某事不滿意和氣惱〕: *Look, it's just not good enough. I've been waiting an hour!* 你瞧, 這就不怎麼好。我已經等了一個小時了! **55 good luck** used to say that you hope that someone is successful or that something good happens to them 祝你好運: *"When's the exam?" "Next week." "Well, good luck and stay calm."* "考試是在甚麼時候?" "下星期。" "祝你好運, 不要緊張。" **56 good luck to him/them** used to say that you hope someone is successful, although you think it is very unlikely that they will be 祝他/他們好運〔表示儘管認為某人成功的可能性不大仍祝其成功〕: *Good luck to them. You've got to respect them for trying.* 祝他們好運。他們敢於一試, 你得對他們表示敬意。**57 good for you/her** also 又作 **good on you/her** *BrE, AusE* used to say that you approve of or are pleased with what someone has done or decided【英, 澳】幹得好, 好樣的: *"I told him to go away and leave me alone." "Good for you."* "我告訴他走開, 別管我。" "幹得好。" **58 it's a good thing** also 又作 **it's a good job** *BrE* used to say that you are glad something happened, because there would have been problems if it had not happened【英】這是件好事, 幸虧: *It's a good thing you were in. I lost my keys.* 幸虧你在家。我的鑰匙丟了。| **and a good thing/job too** *BrE*【英】*She's gone, and a good thing too.* 她走了, 這倒是好事。**59 good old John/Karen etc** used to praise someone, especially because they have behaved in the way that you would expect them to 好樣的: *Good old Roger! I knew he wouldn't let us down.* 羅傑是好樣的! 我知道他不會讓我們失望的! **60 good grief/god/lord/heavens/gracious!** used to express surprise, anger, or other strong feelings 天啊〔用來表示驚奇、憤怒或其他強烈感情〕: *"It's going to cost us £500 to repair it." "Good grief!"* "修理它我們得花 500 英鎊。""天啊!" **61 be a good laugh** *BrE* to be enjoyable or amusing【英】令人愉快, 令人開心: *You should come to the club with us some time, it's always a good laugh.* 你應該甚麼時候跟我們去俱樂部玩玩, 那裡總是很好玩的。**62 be good for a laugh** to be enjoyable, or amusing to do, although not useful, important etc 可博得一笑: *Let's go watch the guys trying to skate. That should be good for a laugh.* 我們去看看那些人學滑冰。應該會挺滑稽的。**63 that's a good one** used to tell someone that you do not believe something they have said and think it is a joke or a trick 我不信, 開玩笑吧: *You won $50,000? Very funny, that's a good one!* 你贏了 50,000 美元? 真好笑, 我才不信哩! **64 all in good time** used when someone wants you to hurry but you are not going to 不急, 別急: *"When are we going to open our presents, Mom?" "All in good time, Billy, all in good time."* "我們甚麼時候打開禮物呢, 媽媽?" "別急, 比利, 別急。" **65 if you know what's good for you** used to threaten someone that something bad will happen to them if they don't do something 你要是知道好歹: *Do as he says, if you know what's good for you!* 如果你知道好歹的話, 就照他說的做吧! **66 would you be good enough to/be so good as to...?** *formal* used to ask someone very politely to do something【正式】你能否...?〔用來客氣地請人做某事〕: *Would you be good enough to help me with my bags.* 請你幫我搬一下我這些行李, 好嗎? **67 good day** *BrE old-fashioned* used to say 'hello' or 'goodbye'【英, 過時】你好; 再見 **68 very good** *BrE old-fashioned* used to tell someone in a position of authority over you that you will do what they have told you to【英, 過時】好〔用於對有權勢的人說話, 表示將按他吩咐的去做〕: *"Tell the men to come in." "Very good, sir."* "叫那些人進來。" "好的, 先生。" **69 (jolly) good show** *old-fashioned BrE* used to express your satisfaction with something【過時, 英】太好了, 真棒

good² *n*

1 ►ADVANTAGE 好處◄ gain or advantage 利益, 好處: **do sb (a power of/the world of) good** (=to bring someone (a lot of) advantages or improvement) 對某人有 (很大的) 好處 *It'll do you good to have a vacation.* 度假對你會有好處。| *That little talk with the boss certainly did him the world of good!* 與老闆的那次短暫談話確實對他有很大好處! | **for the good of** (=to help something) 為了有助於... *I hate swimming – I only go for the good of my health.* 我不喜歡游泳, 我只是為了健康才去的。| **for your/his/their own good** *Come on, drink up the medicine – it's for your own good!* 好了, 把藥喝下——這是為你自己好! | **do more harm than good** *I don't think you should go – it's bound to do more harm than good.* 我認為你不應該去——這肯定是弊多利少。| **the common/general good** *formal* (=the advantage of everyone in society or in a group)【正式】公益

2 do no good/not do any good to not have any useful effect 沒有用處: *Try and persuade her if you like, but I don't think it'll do any good!* 如果你願意, 想辦法說服她吧, 但我認為這沒有甚麼用!

3 What's the good of...?/What good is...? *informal* used to say that having or doing something brings you no advantage【非正式】...有甚麼用?〔表示不會帶來好處〕: *What's the good of buying a boat if you're too busy to use it?* 如果你忙得沒有時間划船, 買條船有甚麼用? | *What good is money when you haven't any friends?* 如果沒有朋友, 錢有甚麼用?

4 ►GOOD BEHAVIOUR 良好的行為◄ [U] actions or behaviour that are morally right or that follow religious principles 合乎道德的行為, 遵守教規的行為: *She is definitely an influence for good on those boys.* 她給那些男孩子的影響肯定是有益的。| *There's good in him, in spite of his violent behaviour.* 儘管他舉止粗暴, 但他是有善心的。| **good and evil** *the eternal struggle between good and evil* 善惡之間的永恒鬥爭 —see also 另見 DO-GOODER

5 be up to no good *informal* to be doing or planning something wrong or dishonest【非正式】正在做壞事, 打算做壞事: *Anyone waiting around on street corners at night must be up to no good.* 晚上在街角遊蕩的人肯定想幹壞事。

6 for good also 又作 **for good and all** *informal* if someone closes something, leaves, stays etc for good, they close it, leave etc permanently【非正式】永遠: *We've separated from each other before, but I think it's for good this time.* 我們以前分開過, 但我覺得這一次分別是永久的。

7 be £10, $50 etc to the good to have made a profit of £10, $50 etc 淨賺 10 英鎊, 50 美元等

8 [singular] *technical* a particular article that is produced in order to be sold【術語】商品: *a good that could have been obtained more cheaply elsewhere* 本來可從其他地方便宜買到的商品 —see also 另見 GOODS (1)

good³ *adv AmE* a word meaning well, which some people think is incorrect【美】好好地〔與 well 意思相同, 有人認為這種用法不正確〕: *Listen to me good!* 好好聽我說!

good af·ter·noon /· ˌ··ˈ·/ *interjection, n* [C] an expression meaning hello, used when you are greeting someone in the afternoon 下午好

good·bye /gudˋbaɪ; gʊdˈbaɪ/ *interjection, n* [C] used when you are leaving or being left by someone 再見: *"Goodbye, John, see you tomorrow."* "再見, 約翰, 明天見。" | **say goodbye** *I just have to say goodbye to Fred.* 我得跟弗雷德道別。| **say your goodbyes** *We said our goodbyes and left.* 我們告辭後便離開了。

good day /· ˈ·/ *interjection, n* [C] **1** *especially AustrE, NZE* an expression meaning hello, used when you are greeting someone especially in the morning or afternoon【尤澳, 新西蘭】日安, 你好〔意思與 hello 同, 多用於上午或下午打招呼〕 **2** *especially BrE, old fashioned* an expression used to say hello or goodbye【尤英, 過時】你好; 再見

good eve·ning /· ˈ··/ *interjection, n* [C] an expression meaning hello used when you are greeting someone in the evening 晚上好 —compare 比較 GOOD NIGHT

good faith /ˌ· ˈ·/ *n* **in good faith** if an agreement, deal etc is made in good faith, it is made honestly with no intention to deceive anyone 誠實無欺: *a contract drawn up in good faith* 真心誠意草擬的合同

good-for-noth·ing /ˌ· · ˈ··◂/ *n* [C] someone who is lazy or has no skills 飯桶, 無用的人 —**good-for-nothing** *adj* [only before noun 僅用於名詞前]

Good Fri·day /ˌ· ˈ··/ *n* [C,U] the Friday before the Christian holiday of EASTER 受難日〔復活節前的星期五〕

good-heart·ed /ˌ· ˈ··◂/ *adj* kind and generous 好心腸的

good-hu·moured *BrE*【英】, **good-humored** *AmE*【美】/ˌ· ˈ··◂/ *adj* naturally cheerful and friendly 愉快而友好的: *Jo is always remarkably good-humoured whatever happens.* 無論發生了甚麼事, 喬總是非常開朗。—**good-humouredly** *adv*

good·ie /ˋgudɪ; ˈgʊdi/ also 又作 **goody** *n* [C] *informal humorous* someone in a book or film who is good and does things you approve of【非正式, 幽默】〔書或電影中的〕好人

good·ish /ˋgudɪʃ; ˈgʊdɪʃ/ *adj* [only before noun 僅用於名詞前] *BrE informal*【英, 非正式】**1 a goodish distance/number etc** quite a long way, quite a lot etc 相當遠/多等 **2** fairly good but not very good 尚好〔但並非很好的〕

good-look·ing /ˌ· ˈ··◂/ *adj* someone who is good-looking has an attractive face 好看的, 漂亮的 —see 見 BEAUTIFUL (USAGE) —**good-looker** *n* [C]

good looks /ˌ· ˈ·/ *n* [plural] the attractive appearance of someone's face 美貌, 漂亮的容貌: *the young actor's romantic good looks* 年輕演員漂亮而迷人的容貌 | **keep your good looks** (=still be attractive) 保持美貌 *She's certainly kept her good looks.* 她確實保持了她的美貌。

good·ly /ˈgudlɪ; ˈgʊdli/ *adj* [only before noun 僅用於名詞前] **1 a goodly number/sum/amount etc** *old-fashioned* a large amount【過時】大量, 許多: *a goodly number of people* 相當多的人 **2** *old use* pleasant in appearance or good in quality【舊】好看的, 質量好的

good mor·ning /· ˈ··/ *interjection, n* [C] an expression meaning hello, used when you are greeting someone in the morning 早上好

good-na·tured /ˌ· ˈ··◂/ *adj* naturally kind and helpful and not easily made angry 和藹的, 性情溫和的 —**good-naturedly** *adv* —**good-naturedness** *n* [U]

good·ness /ˈgudnɪs; ˈgʊdnɪ̵s/ *n* [U]

1 my goodness!/goodness (gracious) me! *spoken* used when you are surprised or sometimes angry【口】〔用來表示驚訝, 有時表示憤怒〕: *My goodness, you did buy a lot!* 啊呀, 你買了這麼多!

2 have the goodness to do sth *formal* used to show extreme politeness when asking someone to do something【正式】〔用來十分客氣地〕請〔某人〕做某事: *Will you have the goodness to excuse me?* 你願意原諒我嗎?

3 for goodness' sake *spoken* used when you are annoyed or surprised【口】看在老天爺面上〔用來表示煩躁或驚訝〕: *For goodness' sake stop arguing!* 看在老天爺面上, 別吵了!

4 goodness (only) knows *spoken* used to emphasize that you are not sure about something or to make a statement stronger【口】天曉得, 誰也不知道〔用來強調你對某事沒有把握或加強語氣〕: *That bar's been closed for goodness knows how long.* 天曉得那家酒吧已經關了多久。| *Goodness knows, I tried to help him!* 天曉得, 我還想辦法幫過他哩!

5 ►BEING GOOD 好◄ the quality of being good 善良的品質: *Claire has an essential goodness of character.* 克萊爾本性善良。

6 ►BEST PART 精華部分◄ the best part, especially the part of food which is good for your health〔尤指食品的〕精華: *All the goodness of an egg is in the yolk.* 蛋的精華在蛋黃裡。

good night /· ˈ·/ *interjection, n* [C] an expression used when you are leaving or being left by someone at night, especially before going to bed or to sleep 晚安〔晚上分別時尤指就寢前用語〕: *Good night. Sleep well.* 晚安, 睡個好覺。—compare 比較 GOOD EVENING —see also 另見 **kiss sb goodbye/goodnight etc** (KISS[1] (1))

goods /gudz; gʊdz/ *n* [plural] **1** things that are produced in order to be sold 商品: *The demand for goods and services is lower this year.* 今年對商品和服務的需求比較低。| *electrical goods* 電器商品 | **consumer goods** (=televisions, washing machines etc) 消費品 **2 come up with the goods/deliver the goods** to do what other people need or expect 滿足要求, 不負所望, 履行諾言: *Tony makes a lot of promises but rarely comes up with the goods.* 托尼經常作很多承諾, 但很少履行。**3** possessions which can be moved, as opposed to houses, land etc 動產: **sb's worldly goods** (=everything someone owns) 某人的家當 **4 have/get the goods on sb** *especially AmE* to have or find proof that someone is guilty of a crime【尤美】掌握[發現]某人的罪證[把柄]: *Face it, Bukowski, we got the goods on you!* 面對現實吧, 布閣夫斯基, 我們抓住你的把柄了! **5** *BrE* heavy things which can be carried by road, train etc【英】〔用公路或火車運輸的笨重的〕貨物; FREIGHT[1] (2) *especially AmE*【尤美】: *a goods train* 貨運列車 **6 he's/she's/it's the goods** *spoken* used to say that you really like someone or something【口】他/她/它就是我喜歡的: *Emma thinks he's the goods!* 埃瑪認為他是她的意中人! —see also 另見 DRY GOODS

goods and chattels *n* [plural] *law* personal possessions【法律】私人財產

good-tempered *adj* cheerful and not easily made angry 好脾氣的, 隨和的

goodwill *n* [U] **1** kind feelings towards or between people and a willingness to be helpful 好意, 親善 **2** the success of a company, and its good relationship with its customers, calculated as part of its value when it is sold〔出售公司時計算在其價值內的〕商譽: *We paid £60,000 for the store, plus £5,000 for goodwill.* 我們付60,000英鎊買下這家商店, 另外加5,000英鎊買它的商譽。

good·y[1] /ˈgudɪ; ˈgʊdi/ *n plural* **goodies** [C usually plural 一般用複數] *informal*【非正式】**1** something that is nice to eat 好吃的東西: *We brought lots of goodies for the picnic.* 我們為野餐買了許多好吃的東西。**2** something attractive, pleasant, or desirable 吸引人的東西, 好東西: *The CD is given away as an extra goody when you buy the CD player.* 買CD唱機的時候額外贈送這張唱片。**3** a GOODIE 好人

goody[2] *interjection* a word used especially by children to express pleasure 高興〔兒童用語〕

goody-good·y /ˈ·· ˌ··/ also 又作 **goody-two-shoes** /ˌ·· ˈ· ·/ *AmE n* [C] someone who likes to seem very good and helpful in order to please their parents, teachers etc【美】假正經的人, 假裝的乖孩子〔喜歡裝成品行端正、樂於助人以取悦父母、老師的人〕

goo·ey /ˈguɪ; ˈgu:i/ *adj informal*【非正式】**1** sticky, soft and often sweet 黏、鬆軟而甜的: *gooey cakes* 黏性甜餅 **2** expressing your love for someone in a way that other people think is silly; SENTIMENTAL〔以某種可笑的方式〕對〔某人〕表示喜愛的; 多愁善感的: *Babies make her go all gooey.* 只要見到嬰兒, 她就喜歡得不知道怎麼辦好了。

goof[1] /guf; gu:f/ also 又作 **goof up** *v* [I] *especially AmE* to make a silly mistake【尤美】犯愚蠢的錯誤: *The restaurant totally goofed up our reservations.* 餐館把我們預定的座位全部弄錯了。—**goof-off** /ˈ· ·/ *n* [C] —**goof-up** /ˈ· ·/ *n* [C]

goof around *phr v* [I] *AmE informal* to spend time doing silly things【美, 非正式】閒蕩, 瞎混; MESS ABOUT *BrE*【英】

goof off *phr v* [I] *AmE informal* to waste time or avoid doing any work【美, 非正式】混日子, 逃避工作: *Wayne's been goofing off at school and his report card shows it.* 韋恩在學校一直是混日子, 他的成績單說明了這一點。

goof[2] *n* [C] *informal especially AmE*【非正式, 尤美】**1** someone who is silly 傻瓜, 蠢人 **2** a silly mistake 愚蠢的錯誤, 差錯: *a goof on the spelling test* 拼寫測試上犯的錯誤

goof·y /ˈgufɪ; ˈgu:fi/ *adj informal* stupid or silly【非正式】愚蠢的, 傻的: *a goofy grin* 傻笑 —**goofily** *adv* —**goofiness** *n* [U]

goo·gly /ˈguglɪ; ˈgu:gli/ *n* **1** [C] a ball bowled (BOWL[2] (2)) in CRICKET (2) in such a way that it looks as if it will go in one direction but goes in the other〔板球的〕外曲線球, 變向球 **2 bowl sb a googly** *BrE* to ask someone a question that is intended to trick them【英】向某人提出愚弄他的問題

goo-goo eyes /ˌ· · ˈ·/ *n* [plural] *AmE humorous* a silly look that shows you love someone【美, 幽默】含情脈脈的目光: **make goo-goo eyes at sb** *Look at them, making goo-goo eyes at each other.* 瞧他們, 眉來眼去的。—**goo-goo eyed** *adj*

gook /guk; gu:k/ *n* [C] *AmE* a very offensive word for someone from a country in the Far East【美】外國佬〔對遠東國家人的冒犯用語〕

goo·ly, goolie /ˈgulɪ; ˈgu:li/ *n* [C usually plural 一般用複數] *BrE slang* an impolite word meaning a TESTICLE【英俚】睾丸〔粗俗的詞語〕

goon /gun; gu:n/ *n* [C] *informal*【非正式】**1** *especially BrE* a silly or stupid person【尤英】傻瓜, 蠢人 **2** *especially AmE* a violent criminal that is paid to frighten or attack people【尤美】〔受雇傭來恐嚇或襲擊別人的〕暴力罪犯

goop /gup; guːp/ *n* [U] *AmE informal* a thick, slightly sticky substance【美, 非正式】濃而稍黏的物質: *What's that goop you're putting on your hair?* 你往頭髮上塗的黏糊糊的東西是甚麼?

goose¹ /gus; guːs/ *n* **1 a)** [C] *plural* **geese** /gis; giːs/ a bird that is similar to a duck but larger and makes a hissing (HISS (1)) or honking (HONK² (1)) noise 鵝 **b)** a female goose 雌鵝 —compare 比較 GANDER (1) **2** [U] the cooked meat of this bird 鵝肉 **3** *old-fashioned* a silly person【過時】傻瓜, 蠢人 **4 kill the goose that lays the golden egg** to destroy the thing that brings you profit or success 殺鵝取金蛋, 殺雞取卵 —see also 另見 WILD-GOOSE CHASE, **wouldn't say boo to a goose** (BOO² (3)), **cook someone's goose** (COOK¹ (6))

goose² *v* [T] *AmE informal* to touch or press someone on their bottom as a rude joke【美, 非正式】碰或按某人的臀部〔作為一種粗俗的玩笑〕

goose·ber·ry /ˈgusˌbɛrɪ; ˈgʊzbəri/ *n* [C] **1** a small round green fruit with a sour taste that grows on a bush 醋栗 —see picture on page A8 參見 A8 頁圖 **2 play gooseberry** *BrE informal* to be the unwanted third person who is with two people who are having a romantic relationship and want to be alone together【英, 非正式】充當(情侶間的)"電燈泡"

goose·bumps /ˈgusˌbʌmps; ˈguːsbʌmps/ *n* [plural] *AmE* goose pimples【美】雞皮疙瘩

goose·flesh /ˈgusflɛʃ; ˈguːsfleʃ/ *n* [U] *especially BrE* goose pimples【尤英】雞皮疙瘩

goose pim·ples /ˈ· ˌ··/ *n* [plural] a condition in which your skin is raised up in small points because you are cold or frightened〔因冷或害怕而〕起雞皮疙瘩

goose·step /ˈgusˌstɛp; ˈguːs-step/ *n* **the goosestep** a way of marching, used by soldiers in some countries, in which each step is taken without bending your knee〔一些國家部隊使用的〕正步走 **—goosestep** *v* [I]

GOP /ˌdʒi o ˈpi; ˌdʒiː əʊ ˈpiː/ *n* **the GOP** *AmE* Grand Old Party; the Republican Party in US politics【美】老大黨〔美國共和黨的別稱〕

go·pher /ˈgofɚ; ˈgəʊfə/ *n* [C] a North and Central American animal like a large rat that lives in holes in the ground〔生活在北美洲和中美洲的〕地鼠

Gor·di·an knot /ˈgɔrdɪən ˈnɑt; ˌgɔːdiən ˈnɒt/ *n* **cut the Gordian knot** to quickly solve a difficult problem by determined action〔大刀闊斧地〕解決難題, 快刀斬亂麻

gore¹ /gor; gɔː/ *v* [T] if an animal gores someone, it wounds them with its horns or TUSKs〔動物用角或獠牙〕頂傷, 牴傷

gore² *n* **1** [U] *literary* blood that has flowed from a wound and become thicker and darker【文】〔傷口流出的〕已變濃發黑的血 **2** [C] a piece of material that gets wider towards the bottom, used in making a skirt〔縫製裙子的布料〕加寬下襬的襇幅 —see also 另見 GORY

gorge¹ /gɔrdʒ; gɔːdʒ/ *n* [C] **1** a deep narrow valley with steep sides 峽谷 **2 make sb's gorge rise** to make someone feel sick or very angry about something 令某人作嘔; 令某人憤怒: *When they saw the burned-out homes it made their gorge rise.* 他們看見被燒毀的家園時, 感到怒火中燒。

gorge² *v* **1 gorge yourself on/with** to eat until you are too full to eat any more 拚命地吃, 飽塞: *We gorged ourselves on ripe plums.* 我們大嚼成熟的李子。**2 be gorged with** to have eaten so much of something that you are completely full 肚子塞滿, 飽食

3 **gor·geous** /ˈgɔrdʒəs; ˈgɔːdʒəs/ *adj informal*【非正式】**1** extremely beautiful or attractive 極其漂亮的, 極其吸引人的: *a gorgeous blonde* 極其漂亮的金髮女郎 | *gorgeous silks* 極其漂亮的絲綢 **2** extremely pleasant or enjoyable 令人十分愉快[開心]的: *What a gorgeous afternoon!* (=warm and sunny) 天氣多好的下午! **—gorgeously** *adv* **—gorgeousness** *n* [U]

gor·gon /ˈgɔrgən; ˈgɔːgən/ *n* [C] **1** *informal* an ugly frightening woman【非正式】醜陋可怕的女人 **2 Gorgon** one of the three sisters in ancient Greek stories with snakes on their heads that made anyone who looked at them change into stone 戈耳戈, 蛇髮女怪〔古希臘傳說中三個蛇髮姐妹中的一位, 見到她的人會變成石頭〕

go·ril·la /gəˈrɪlə; gəˈrɪlə/ *n* [C] **1** a very large African monkey that is the largest of the APEs¹ (1) 大猩猩 **2** *slang* an ugly, strong man who is employed to protect an important person【俚】〔雇來保護要人的〕彪形大漢

gorm·less /ˈgɔrmlɪs; ˈgɔːmləs/ *adj BrE informal* stupid, especially in appearance【英, 非正式】傻乎乎的: *a gormless grin* 傻笑 **—gormlessly** *adv* **—gormlessness** *n* [U]

gorse /gɔrs; gɔːs/ *n* [U] a PRICKLY bush with bright yellow flowers, which grows in the countryside 荊豆

gor·y /ˈgɔrɪ; ˈgɔːri/ *adj* **1** *informal* clearly describing or showing violence, blood, and killing【非正式】渲染暴力、血腥和殺戮的: *That film was too gory for me.* 我覺得那部影片過多渲染了暴力。**2 all the gory details** *often humorous* all the interesting details about an unpleasant event【常幽默】〔一次不愉快事件的〕所有有趣的細節: *Come on, I want to hear all the gory details.* 給我講講吧, 我想聽聽這件可怕事情所有的細節。**3** *literary* covered in blood【文】血跡斑斑的, 血淋淋的 —see also 另見 GORE² **—gorily** *adv* **—goriness** *n* [U]

gosh /gɑʃ; gɒʃ/ *interjection* used to express surprise〔用來表示驚訝〕: *Gosh, it's cold.* 啊呀, 真冷啊! 2

gos·ling /ˈgɑzlɪŋ; ˈgɒzlɪŋ/ *n* [C] a young GOOSE¹ (1) 小鵝, 幼鵝

go-slow /ˌ· ˈ·◂/ *n* [C] **1** *BrE* a way of protesting against an employer by working as slowly as possible【英】怠工; SLOWDOWN² (2) *AmE*【美】—compare 比較 WORK-TO-RULE **2** *WAfrE* a TRAFFIC JAM【西非】交通堵塞

gos·pel /ˈgɑspl; ˈgɒspəl/ *n* **1 Gospel** [C] one of the four stories of Christ's life in the Bible 福音書〔《聖經》中有關耶穌生平的四福音書之一〕**2** [C usually singular 一般用單數] a particular set of ideas that someone believes in very strongly and tries to persuade other people to accept 信條, 教義: **spread/preach the gospel** *spreading the gospel of monetarism* 散播貨幣主義的信條 **3** also 又作 **gospel truth** /ˌ·· ˈ·/ [U] something that is completely true 真理, 絕對真理: **take sth as gospel** *Don't take everything she says as gospel.* 別把她所說的話都當作真理。**4** also 又作 **gospel mu·sic** /ˈ·· ˌ··/ [U] a style of Christian music usually performed by Black singers in which religious songs are sung strongly and loudly 福音音樂〔通常由黑人歌手有力地大聲演唱的基督教歌曲〕: *a gospel choir* 福音唱詩班

gos·sa·mer /ˈgɑsəmɚ; ˈgɒsəmə/ *n* [U] **1** *literary* a very light thin material【文】薄紗 **2** light silky thread which SPIDERs leave on grass and bushes 蜘蛛絲

gos·sip¹ /ˈgɑsəp; ˈgɒsɪp/ *n* **1** [C,U] conversation or information about other people's behaviour and private lives, often including unkind or untrue remarks 流言蜚語, 街談巷議, 閒話: *What's the latest gossip?* 最近有些甚麼閒話? | **have a gossip** *Phil's in there having a gossip with Maggie.* 菲爾在那裡面跟瑪吉閒聊。| **idle gossip** (=gossip not based on facts) 無中生有的流言蜚語 **2** [C] someone who likes talking about other people's private lives 愛談論別人私生活的人

gossip² *v* [I] to spend time talking to someone about other people's behaviour and private lives or about other things that do not concern you 說閒話, 說長道短: **[+about]** *Julie was gossiping about Jane and Mick's affair.* 朱莉正在聊簡和米克的風流韻事。

gossip col·umn /ˈ·· ˌ··/ *n* [C] a regular article in a newspaper or magazine about the behaviour and private lives of famous people〔報刊雜誌上定期登載的〕關於名人行為和私生活的專欄 **—gossip columnist** *n* [C]

gos·sip·y /ˈgɑsəpɪ; ˈgɒsɪpi/ *adj informal*【非正式】**1** a gossipy person likes to gossip 愛說閒話的, 愛談論別人私生活的 **2** talk or writing that is gossipy, is informal and full of gossip 說人閒話的, 充滿流言蜚語的, 閒聊式

G

的: *a long, gossipy letter* 閒聊式的長信

got /gɑt; gɒt/ the past tense and a participle of GET —see 見 GOTTEN (USAGE)

got·cha /ˈgɑtʃə; ˈgɒtʃə/ *interjection* **1** a word meaning 'I've got you' that is used to surprise someone, or to show them that you have gained a sudden advantage over them 抓到你了〔I've got you 的連音, 用來使某人吃驚或表示你突然間佔了他的上風〕 **2** a word meaning 'I understand' 我明白了: *"Yeah, okay, 5 o'clock, gotcha."* "是的, 好, 五點鐘, 我明白了。"

Goth·ic /ˈgɑθɪk; ˈgɒθɪk/ *adj* **1** the Gothic style of building was common in Western Europe between the 12th and 16th centuries. Its main features were pointed ARCH*es*[1] (1,2), tall PILLAR*s* (1), and tall thin pointed windows. 哥特式的, 哥特風格的〔指 12 至 16 世紀流行於西歐的建築風格。其主要特徵是尖形拱門, 高大廊柱和又高又狹的尖形窗戶〕 **2** a Gothic story, film etc is about frightening things that happen in mysterious old buildings, and lonely places, and was popular in the early 19th century 哥特派的〔發生在神祕古老的建築、偏僻地方的嚇人故事、電影等, 這種風格流行於 19 世紀初〕 **3** Gothic writing, printing etc has thick decorated letters 哥特式〔粗筆畫加裝飾的書寫和印刷字體〕

got·ta /ˈgɑtə; ˈgɒtə/ *spoken* a short form of 縮略式= 'have got to', 'has got to', 'have got a', or 或 'has got a', which most people think is incorrect【口】要, 得; 有〔一個、一件等; 被大多數人視為不正確〕: *We gotta go now.* 我們現在得走了。

got·ten /ˈgɑtn̩; ˈgɒtn/ *AmE*【美】the past participle of GET: *You've gotten us into a lot of trouble.* 你給我們惹了許多麻煩。—see also 另見 ILL-GOTTEN

USAGE NOTE 用法說明: GOTTEN

GRAMMAR 語法

In British English, **got** is the past participle of **get**, but in American English, **gotten** is more commonly used as the past participle. 在英國英語中用 got 是 get 的過去分詞, 但在美國英語中用 gotten 作為過去分詞更為常見: *Kim's gotten engaged!* 基姆已經訂婚了! | *He'd gotten up early that day.* 那天他起牀很早。**Got** is used in British English to mean 'possess'. got 在英國英語中用來表示"擁有": *We've got two cars.* 我們有兩輛車。It may also be used this way in American English, though Americans usually use 'have'.在美國英語中也可以這樣用, 但美國人通常用 have: *We have two cars.* 我們有兩輛車。**Got** is also used in British English to mean 'buy' or 'receive'. got 用在英國英語中也可表示"買"或"收到": *Tim has just got a new bicycle.* 蒂姆剛買了[得到]輛新自行車。In American English, you can say either: *Tim has just gotten a new bicycle.* or *Tim just got a new bicycle.* 在英國英語中, 說以上兩句均可。**Got** is used in both British and American English to mean 'must'. got 在英國英語和美國英語中都可以表示 must (必須): *I've got to talk to him.* 我必須跟他談談。In American English, if you say *I've gotten to talk to him*, you mean you have succeeded in talking to him 在美國英語中, 如果你說 I've gotten to talk to him, 意思是說你已經跟他談過了, but in both British and American English you would usually say 不過在英國英語和美國英語中, 通常說的是: *I got to talk him.* 我跟他談過了。**Gotten** is not used in British English. 英國英語不用 gotten。

gou·ache /guˋɑʃ; gʊˈɑːʃ/ *n* **1** [U] a method of painting using colours that are mixed with water and made thicker with a type of GUM[1] (3) 水粉畫法 **2** [C] a picture produced by this method 水粉畫

Gou·da /ˈgaʊdə; ˈgaʊdə/ *n* [U] a yellow Dutch cheese that does not have a very strong taste 高德乾酪〔味道較淡的黃色荷蘭乾酪〕

gouge[1] /gaʊdʒ; gaʊdʒ/ *v* [T] to make a deep hole or cut in the surface of something 在〔某物表面〕鑿洞, 鑿槽: *The desks were scratched and gouged.* 這些桌子的桌面上有許多劃痕並被鑿了不少洞槽。

gouge sth ↔ **out** *phr v* [T] **1** to make a hole in something such as rock etc by removing material that is on the surface 掘出, 挖出: *Glaciers gouged out narrow valleys during the Ice Age.* 冰川在冰期開出了窄的峽谷。**2 gouge sb's eyes out** to remove someone's eyes with a pointed weapon 挖出某人的眼睛

gouge[2] *n* [C] a hole or cut made in something, usually by a sharp tool or weapon〔利器鑿成的〕孔, 洞, 槽

gou·lash /ˈgulæʃ; ˈguːlæʃ/ *n* [C,U] a dish from Hungary made of meat cooked in liquid with a hot tasting pepper〔匈牙利的〕辣椒燉肉

gourd /gɔrd; gʊəd/ *n* [C] a round fruit whose outer shell can be used as a container 葫蘆〔果實〕 **2** the container made from this fruit 葫蘆〔容器〕

gour·mand /ˈgurmənd; ˈgʊəmənd/ *n* [C] someone who is too interested in eating and drinking 貪吃貪喝的人

gour·met[1] /ˈgurme; ˈgʊəmeɪ/ *adj* [only before noun 僅用於名詞前] producing or connected with very good food and drink 製作[關於]美食佳釀的: *a gourmet cook* 能做出精美菜餚的廚師

gourmet[2] *n* [C] someone who knows a lot about food and wine and who enjoys good food and wine 美食家

gout /gaʊt; gaʊt/ *n* [U] a disease that makes your toes, fingers, and knees swollen and painful 痛風(病) —**gouty** *adj*

gov·ern /ˈgʌvɚn; ˈgʌvən/ *v* **1** [I,T] to officially and legally control a country and make all the decisions about taxes, laws, public services etc 管理, 統治〔國家〕: *The country was governed by a small military élite.* 這個國家被少數軍事頭目統治。**2** [T] if rules, principles etc govern the way a system or situation works, they control how it happens or what happens〔規則、原則等〕規定, 管制, 制約: *rules governing the export of live animals* 管制活牲畜出口的條例 | *the laws that govern the universe* 制約宇宙的規律 **3** [T] to affect the grammar of another word and make it have a particular form〔語法中〕支配〔另一詞, 決定該詞應具有何種形式〕 **4** [T] *old-fashioned* to control a strong or dangerous emotion【過時】抑制, 控制〔強烈或危險的感情〕

gov·ern·ess /ˈgʌvɚnɪs; ˈgʌvənɪs/ *n* [C] a female teacher who lives with a rich family and teaches their children at home〔住在富有家庭中管教孩子的〕家庭女教師

gov·ern·ing /ˈgʌvɚnɪŋ; ˈgʌvənɪŋ/ *adj* **1** [only before noun 僅用於名詞前] having the power to control an organization, country etc 統治的, 執政的, 管理的: **governing body** (=the group of people controlling an institution) 主管機構 *the university's governing body* 大學的主管機構 | **governing party** (=the political party that is governing a country) 執政黨 **2 governing principle** a principle that has the most important influence on something 指導原則: *Freedom of speech for all is one of the governing principles in a democracy.* 所有人均享有言論自由是民主國家的指導原則之一。—see also 另見 SELF-GOVERNING

gov·ern·ment /ˈgʌvɚnmənt; ˈgʌvəmənt/ *n* **1** also 又作 **Government** [C] the group of people who govern a country or state 政府: *The new military government does not have popular support.* 新上台的軍人政府沒有得到廣泛的支持。| [also+plural verb *BrE* 英] *The Government are planning further cuts in public spending.* 政府正計劃進一步削減公共支出。| **government policy/funding/statistics** *Government statistics show an increase in unemployment.* 政府統計數字顯示失業率有所上升。| **form a government** (=become the government after an election in a parliamentary system) 組織政府, 組閣 *Which party will form the next goverment?* 哪一個黨將組織下一屆政府? | **under a government** (=during the period of a government) 在某屆政府執政期間 *changes in policy under the last Labour government* 上

屆工黨政府的政策調整 **2** [U] a form or system of government 政府形式[體制]: *the return to democratic government* 恢復民主政體 | **local government** (=the government of towns, cities etc) 地方政府 | **central government** (=the government of a whole country) 中央政府 **3** [U] the act or process of governing 治理, 管理: *Government has been entrusted to the elected politicians.* 治理的任務已委託給當選的政治家。| **be in government** (=be governing a country) 在執政中 *How long have the Christian Democrats been in government?* 基督教民主黨已經執政多久了? **4** [U] *especially AmE* the degree to which the government controls economic and social activities【尤美】管理經濟與社會活動的程度: *a pledge of less government and greater personal freedom* 減少對經濟與社會活動的干預、增加個人自由的承諾

government health warn·ing /,··· '· ,··/ *n* [C] *BrE* a notice that, by law, must be put on some products, for example cigarettes, to warn people that they are dangerous to their health【英】政府健康警告〔根據法律必須印製在一些諸如香煙等的產品之上, 警告人們該產品有害健康〕

3 **gov·er·nor** /ˋɡʌvənɚ; ˈɡʌvənə/ *n* [C] **1** also 又作 **Governor a)** the person in charge of governing a state in the US〔美國〕州長 **b)** the person in charge of governing a country that is under the political control of another country 總督〔政治上受另一國家控制的國家首腦〕**2** *especially BrE* a member of a committee that controls an organization or institution【尤英】〔指導、監督某組織或機構的〕董事, 理事: *a school governor* 學校董事 **3** *BrE* the person in charge of a prison【英】典獄長; WARDEN (2) *AmE*【美】: *After the riot the prison governor resigned.* 典獄長在暴亂後辭職。**4** a part of a machine that controls how the machine works, especially by limiting it in some way〔機器上的〕調節器 **5** *BrE* a GUVNOR【英】老闆, 先生 —see also 另見 GUBERNATORIAL

Governor-Gen·e·ral /,··· '···/ *n* [C] someone who represents the King or Queen of Britain in other Commonwealth countries which are not REPUBLICS〔英聯邦國家中英國以外非共和制國家的〕總督: *the Governor-General of Australia* 澳大利亞總督

gov·ern·or·ship /ˋɡʌvənɚʃɪp; ˈɡʌvənəʃɪp/ *n* [U] the position of being governor, or the period during which someone is governor〔州長、總督等的〕職位; 任期

govt a written abbreviation of 縮寫= GOVERNMENT

gown /ɡaʊn; ɡaʊn/ *n* [C] **1** a long dress worn by a woman on formal occasions 女禮服: *Arabella wore a blue silk evening gown.* 阿拉貝拉穿着藍色的絲綢晚禮服。**2** a long loose piece of clothing worn for special ceremonies by judges, teachers, lawyers, and members of universities〔法官、教師、律師、大學成員在特殊儀式上穿的〕長袍 **3** a long loose piece of clothing worn in a hospital by someone doing or having an operation 外科手術服 —see also 另見 DRESSING GOWN

GP /ˌdʒi ˋpi; ˌdʒiː ˈpiː/ *n* [C] *especially BrE* general practitioner; a doctor who is trained in general medicine and treats people in a particular area or town【尤英】〔在某特定區域或城鎮行醫的〕全科醫生, 普通醫師

GPA /ˌdʒi pi ˋe; ˌdʒiː piː ˈeɪ/ *n* [C] grade point average; the average of a student's marks over a period of time in the US education system〔美國教育體制中的〕平均分

3 **grab**[1] /ɡræb; ɡræb/ *v* **grabbed, grabbing** [T]
3 **1 ▶WITH YOUR HAND** 用手◀ to take hold of someone or something with a sudden or violent movement 攫取, 抓住: *The policeman grabbed his shoulder.* 警察抓住他的肩膀。| **grab sth from sb** *I managed to grab the gun from Bowen.* 我把槍從鮑文手裡搶了過來。| **grab hold of** *Kay grabbed hold of my arm to stop herself falling.* 凱抓住我的手臂, 以免摔倒。

2 ▶FOOD/SLEEP 食品/睡◀ *informal* to get some food or sleep quickly because you are busy【非正式】〔因忙碌而〕趕緊, 抓緊〔吃或睡〕: *I managed to grab an hour's sleep this afternoon.* 今天下午我抓緊時間睡了一個小時。| **grab a bite to eat** *Let's grab a bite to eat before we go.* 我們走之前趕緊吃點甚麼吧。

3 ▶GET STH FOR YOURSELF 為自己獲取某物◀ to take something for yourself, especially in an unfair way〔尤指通過不公平手段〕霸佔, 擄取, 強奪: *Bob tried to grab the profit for himself.* 鮑伯想把利潤佔為己有。| *Try to get there early and grab a seat.* 想辦法早點到那兒佔個座位。

4 how does sth grab you? *spoken* used to ask someone if they would be interested in doing a particular thing【口】你對某事是否有興趣?: *How does the idea of a trip to Spain grab you?* 你對到西班牙旅行的想法感興趣嗎?

5 grab a chance/opportunity *informal* to take the opportunity to do or have something immediately【非正式】抓住機會: *Grab your chance to travel while you're still young!* 趁你還年輕, 抓住機會去旅遊!

grab at *phr v* [T] **1** to quickly and suddenly put out your hand in order to take hold of something〔迅速伸手〕抓住: *Donny hid behind his mother, grabbing at her skirt.* 多尼藏在母親身後, 拽着她的裙子。**2** to immediately try to take an opportunity that someone offers you 抓住〔機會〕: *Melanie grabs at every invitation that comes her way.* 每次遇到邀請, 梅蘭妮都不放過。

grab[2] *n* **1 make a grab for/at** to suddenly try to take hold of something〔猛然去〕抓: *I made a grab for the revolver.* 我迅速伸手去抓左輪手槍。**2 be up for grabs** *informal* if a job, prize, opportunity etc is up for grabs, it is available for anyone who wants to try to have it【非正式】〔工作、獎金、機會等〕人人都可以爭取得到的, 供爭奪的 **3** [C] a piece of machinery used for taking hold of things 抓具, 抓斗挖土機

grab bag /'· ,·/ *n AmE*【美】**1** [C] a container filled with small presents that you put your hand in to pick one out 摸彩袋; LUCKY DIP (1) *BrE*【英】**2** [singular] *informal* a situation in which things are decided by chance【非正式】碰運氣 **3** [singular] a mixture of different things or styles; RAGBAG〔各種東西或樣式的〕混合: *A grab bag of different kinds of music accompanies the film.* 這部電影的配樂是由各種音樂混雜在一起的。

grace[1] /ɡres; ɡreɪs/ *n*
1 ▶WAY OF MOVING 移動方式◀ [U] a smooth controlled way of moving that is attractive to look at, especially because it seems natural and relaxed 優美, 優雅自然: *Lena had the grace and poise of a model.* 莉娜具有模特兒般的優雅和體態。

2 ▶BEHAVIOUR 行為◀ **a)** [U] polite and pleasant behaviour 彬彬有禮: *Jenny answered their questions with grace and dignity.* 詹妮體面有禮地回答了他們的問題。| **have the (good) grace to do sth** (=be polite enough to do something) 有做某事的氣量 *Meg didn't even have the grace to apologize.* 梅格連道歉的氣量也沒有。**b) graces** [plural] the skills needed to behave in a way that is considered polite and socially acceptable 風度: *social graces* 社交風度

3 ▶MORE TIME 更多的時間◀ [U] more time that is added to the period you are allowed for finishing a piece of work, paying a debt etc 寬限: **a day's/week's etc grace** *I got a day's grace to finish my essay.* 我得到一天的寬限來完成我的論文。

4 with (a) good/bad grace willingly and cheerfully, or in an unwilling and angry way 大方地/勉強地: *Kevin smiled and accepted his defeat with good grace.* 凱文微笑着, 大方地接受自己的失敗。

5 ▶GOD'S KINDNESS 上帝的恩典◀ [U] God's kindness shown to people because he loves them 上帝的恩典: **by/through the grace of God** (=because of God's kindness) 承蒙上帝的恩典 *By the grace of God, Alan wasn't hurt.* 承蒙上帝的恩典, 阿倫沒有受傷。

6 there but for the grace of God (go I) used to say how lucky you feel that you are not in the same bad situation as someone else 要不是上帝的恩典(我也遭殃)〔表示沒有遭到某人那樣的厄運〕

7 ▶**PRAYER** 禱告◀ [C,U] a prayer thanking God, said before a meal〔飯前的〕感恩禱告: **say grace** *Who will say grace?* 誰來做感恩禱告?
8 be in sb's good graces to be liked and approved by someone at a particular time 受到某人的眷顧[青睞]
9 ▶**SOUL** 心靈◀ [U] the state of someone's soul when it has been freed from evil, according to Christian belief 恩典, 恩寵〔基督教教義, 指靈魂無罪時的狀態〕: **be in a state of grace** (=to have been forgiven for what you have done wrong when you die) 在恩典的狀態〔死時生平所做錯事得到寬恕〕
10 Your/His etc Grace used as a title for talking to or about a DUKE, DUCHESS, or ARCHBISHOP〔對公爵、公爵夫人或大主教的尊稱〕閣下
11 the Graces three beautiful Greek goddesses who often appear in art〔希臘〕美慧三女神 —see also 另見 **fall from grace** (FALL¹ (13)), **saving grace** (SAVE¹ (13))
grace² *v* [T] **1 grace sth/sb with your presence** an expression meaning to bring honour to an occasion or group of people by being present, often used jokingly when someone comes late or does not often come to meetings etc 以你的蒞臨來給某事/某人增光〔常用來給遲到或經常缺席的人開玩笑〕: *Ah so you've decided to grace us with your presence!* 啊, 這麼說你已經決定光臨, 給我們增輝添彩! **2** to make a place or an object look more beautiful or attractive 美化, 使優美: *His portrait now graces the wall of the drawing room.* 他的畫像現在給客廳的牆壁添了光彩。
grace·ful /ˋgresfəl; ˈgreɪsfəl/ *adj* **1** moving in a smooth and attractive way, or having an attractive shape〔動作, 線條〕優美的, 雅緻的: *a slim graceful figure* 修長的優美身材 **2** behaving in a polite and pleasant way 優雅得體的, 體面的: *a graceful apology* 得體的道歉 —**gracefully** *adv*: *When I am no longer needed, I shall retire gracefully.* 當不再需要我的時候, 我將體面地退休。—**gracefulness** *n* [U]
grace·less /ˋgreslɪs; ˈgreɪsləs/ *adj* **1** not being polite, especially when someone has been kind to you 無禮貌的, 不知情理的: *She was utterly graceless, showing no gratitude for all we had done.* 她沒有一點禮貌, 對我們所做的一切沒表示任何感激。**2** moving or doing something in a way that seems awkward〔動作、行為等〕笨拙的 **3** something that is graceless is unattractive and unpleasant to look at〔外觀〕難看的, 不優美的: *graceless architecture* 難看的建築 —**gracelessly** *adv* —**gracelessness** *n* [U]
gra·cious /ˋgreʃəs; ˈgreɪʃəs/ *adj* **1** behaving in a polite, kind, and generous way, especially to people of a lower class 有禮貌的; 仁慈的; 和藹的, 親切的〔尤指對較低階層的人們〕: *Thank you for your gracious hospitality.* 感謝你的盛情款待。**2** having the kind of expensive style, comfort, and beauty that only rich people can afford 豪華舒適的, 華美的: *gracious colonial houses* 豪華舒適的殖民時期式樣的房子 | *the gracious ease of the hotel foyer* 旅館門廳的豪華舒適 | **gracious living** (=an easy way of life enjoyed by rich people)〔富人的〕安逸生活 **3** a word meaning kind and forgiving, used to describe God 仁慈的, 寬恕的〔用於形容上帝〕—**graciously** *adv* —**graciousness** *n* [U]
gracious! *interjection old-fashioned* used to express surprise or to emphasize 'yes' or 'no'【過時】〔用來表示驚訝或對"是"與"否"加以強調〕: **good gracious!/gracious me!/goodness gracious!** *Good gracious! What have you done to your hair?* 天哪, 你把頭髮弄成甚麼樣子了? | *"You aren't disappointed, are you?" "Good gracious, no, of course not."* "你沒有失望吧?" "啊呀, 不, 當然不。"
grad /græd; græd/ *n* [C] *AmE informal* a GRADUATE¹【美, 非正式】畢業生
grad·a·ble /ˋgredəbl; ˈgreɪdəbəl/ *adj* an adjective which is gradable can be used in the COMPARATIVE¹ (4) or SUPERLATIVE² (1) forms, or with words such as 'very', 'fairly', and 'almost'〔形容詞〕可分級的〔指可以有比較級或最高級形式或可被 very, fairly, almost 等詞修飾的〕—**gradability** /ˌgredəˋbɪlətɪ; ˌgreɪdəˈbɪlɨti/ *n* [U]
gra·da·tion /greˋdeʃən; grəˈdeɪʃən/ *n* [C] *formal* a small change, or a stage in a set of changes or degrees of development【正式】小變化, 層次, 階段: *There are many gradations of colour between light and dark blue.* 淡藍和深藍之間有許多層次。
grade¹ /gred; greɪd/ *n*
1 ▶**STANDARD** 標準◀ [C,U] a particular standard or level of quality that a product, material etc has〔產品, 材料等的〕等級, 級別: *Grade A eggs* 甲級雞蛋 | *low-grade steel* 低等鋼
2 ▶**COMPANY** 公司◀ [C] the level of importance you have or the level of pay you receive in a company or organization〔職務, 工資〕級別: *Wilma has a lot of responsibility but she's still on a secretarial grade.* 威爾瑪負責很多事情, 但還是在祕書級。
3 make the grade to succeed or reach the necessary standard 成功, 達到標準: *Nina'll never make the grade as a professional tennis player.* 尼娜永遠也達不到職業網球運動員的水平。
4 ▶**SCHOOL YEAR** 學年◀ [C] a particular year of a school course in the American school system〔美國學校的〕年級: *Bobby's in the second grade.* 博比在讀二年級。
5 ▶**MARK IN SCHOOL** 學習成績◀ [C] *especially AmE* a mark given for a particular piece of work in school, or for your work during all or part of a year【尤美】成績, 分數: *You need good grades to go to college.* 你要有好的成績才能上大學。
6 ▶**SLOPE** 斜坡◀ [C] *AmE* degree of slope, especially in a road or railway【美】〔尤指道路或鐵路的〕坡度; GRADIENT *BrE*【英】
grade² *v* [T] **1** to separate things, or arrange them in order according to their quality or rank 給〔物品〕分等級: *potatoes graded according to size* 根據大小分等級的馬鈴薯 **2** *especially AmE* to give a mark to an examination paper or to a piece of school work【尤美】給〔試卷或作業〕評分: *Matt's busy at home grading papers.* 馬特正在家忙着評卷子。**3** to give a particular rank and level of pay to a job 給〔某職位〕評定級別和工資等級
grade cross·ing /ˋ· ˌ··/ *n* [C] *AmE* a place where a road and railway cross each other, usually with gates that shut the road while the train passes【美】公路、鐵路交叉處〔通常有柵欄在火車通過時將道路關閉〕; LEVEL CROSSING *BrE*【英】
grad·ed /ˋgredɪd; ˈgreɪdɨd/ *adj* designed to suit different levels of learning〔學習〕分級的: *graded coursebooks* 分級教科書
grade point av·e·rage /ˋ· · ˌ···/ *n* [C] GPA 平均分
grade school /ˋ· ˌ·/ *n* [C] *AmE* an ELEMENTARY SCHOOL【美】小學
gra·di·ent /ˋgredɪənt; ˈgreɪdiənt/ *n* [C] a degree of slope, especially in a road or railway〔尤指道路或鐵路的〕坡度; GRADE¹ (6) *AmE*【美】: *a steep gradient* 陡坡
grad school /ˋ· ·/ *n* [C] *AmE informal* a GRADUATE SCHOOL【美, 非正式】研究生院
grad·u·al /ˋgrædʒuəl; ˈgrædʒuəl/ *adj* **1** happening, developing, or changing slowly over a long period of time 逐漸的, 逐步的: *Computerization has resulted in the gradual disappearance of many manual jobs.* 電腦化逐步取代了許多手工活。| *I noticed a gradual change in her behaviour.* 我注意到她的舉止逐漸發生了變化。**2** a gradual slope is not steep〔坡〕緩的, 不陡的 —**gradualness** *n* [U]
grad·u·al·ly /ˋgrædʒuəlɪ; ˈgrædʒəli/ *adv* in a way that happens or develops slowly over a long period of time 逐漸地, 逐步地: *The rock gradually wears away due to the action of the water.* 由於水沖刷的作用, 岩石逐漸磨損。
grad·u·ate¹ /ˋgrædʒuɪt; ˈgrædʒuɨt/ *n* [C] **1** someone who has completed a university degree course, especially for a first degree〔尤指完成學士學位課程的〕大學畢業生:

a history graduate 歷史系的大學畢業生 | **[+of]** *a graduate of Birmingham University* 伯明翰大學的畢業生 —compare 比較 UNDERGRADUATE **2** *AmE* someone who has completed a course at a college, school etc【美】畢業生: *a high-school graduate* 中學畢業生

graduate² /ˋgrædʒʊˏɪt; ˈgrædʒueɪt/ *adj* **1** [only before noun 僅用於名詞前] *AmE* a graduate student is studying for a MASTER's or a DOCTORATE degree after receiving their first degree【美】攻讀碩士[博士]研究生的; POSTGRADUATE² (1) *BrE*【英】**2** graduate studies or courses are done after receiving your first degree 研究生〔課程〕

graduate³ *v* **1** [I] to obtain a degree, especially a first degree, from a college or university〔尤指以學士學位〕大學畢業: **[+from]** *Mitch graduated from Stanford with a degree in Law.* 米奇畢業於史丹福大學, 獲法學學位。**2** [I] *AmE* to complete your education at HIGH SCHOOL【美】中學畢業: **[+from]** *Jerry graduated from high school last year.* 傑里去年中學畢業。**3 graduate (from sth) to** to start doing something that is bigger, better or more important〔從某處〕升級到: *Bob played college baseball but never graduated to the Majors.* 鮑勃在大學是棒球隊隊員, 但從來沒有升級加入職業棒球隊。**4** [T] *especially AmE* to give a degree or DIPLOMA to someone who has completed a course【尤美】向〔畢業生〕授予學位[文憑]

grad·u·at·ed /ˋgrædʒʊˏetɪd; ˈgrædʒueɪtɪd/ *adj* **1** divided into different levels or GRADEs¹ (1) 分級的: *graduated rates of taxation* 分級稅率 **2** a tool or container that is graduated has small marks on it showing measurements 標有刻度的

graduate school /ˈ··· ˌ·/ *n* [C] *AmE* a college or university where you can study for a MASTER's or a DOCTORATE degree after receiving your first degree, or the period of time when you study for these degrees【美】研究生院

grad·u·a·tion /ˌgrædʒʊˋeʃən; ˌgrædʒuˈeɪʃən/ *n* **1** [U] the time when you complete a university degree course or your education at an American HIGH SCHOOL〔美國中學或大學的〕畢業: *After graduation Helen went into accountancy.* 海倫畢業後從事會計工作。**2** [U] a ceremony at which you receive a university degree or a DIPLOMA from an American HIGH SCHOOL〔美國大學或中學的〕畢業典禮: *graduation day* 畢業典禮日 **3** [C] a mark showing measurement on an instrument or container for measuring 刻度

Grae·co- /griko; griːkəʊ/ *prefix* another spelling of GRECO greco 的另一種拼法

graf·fi·ti /grəˋfitɪ; grəˈfiːti/ *n* [U] rude, humorous, or political writing and pictures on the walls of buildings, trains etc〔在牆上、火車上等的〕亂塗亂抹, 塗鴉

graft¹ /græft; grɑːft/ *n* **1** [C] a piece of healthy skin or bone taken from someone's body and put in or on another part of their body that has been damaged 移植皮, 移植骨: *Her severe burns were treated with skin grafts.* 她的重度燒傷得到植皮治療。**2** [C] a piece cut from one plant and tied to or put inside a cut in another, so that it grows there〔切取於某植物的〕供嫁接用的接穗 **3** [U] *informal especially BrE* hard work【非正式, 尤英】艱苦的工作: *I was too tired to talk after a hard day's graft.* 一天艱苦的工作之後我累得連說話的力氣都沒有了。**4** [U] *especially AmE* the practice of obtaining money or advantage by the dishonest use of influence, especially political influence【尤美】貪污, 受賄;〔尤指通過政治影響〕以權謀私: *Theo rose to power through graft and corruption.* 西奧靠貪污賄賂上台。

graft² *v* **1** [I,T] to put a piece of skin or bone from one part of someone's body onto another part that has been damaged 移植〔皮膚、骨〕: **graft sth onto** *They grafted skin from his thigh onto his badly burned face.* 他們把他大腿的皮膚移植到他嚴重燒傷的臉上。**2** [I,T+on/onto] to join a part of a flower, plant, or tree onto another flower, plant, or tree〔花、草或樹〕嫁接 **3 graft sth onto** to try to combine an idea, style etc with another idea or style 將〔某想法、風格等〕與〔另一想法、風格〕結合起來: *modern institutions grafted onto medieval traditions* 結合中世紀傳統的現代制度 **4** [I] *informal especially BrE* to work hard【非正式, 尤英】努力地工作

graft off sb ↔ *phr v* [T] *especially AmE* to get money or advantages from someone by the dishonest use of influence, especially political influence【尤美】〔以不正當手段利用權勢〕向〔某人〕索賄, 謀取私利: *politicians who graft off each other* 互相撈取好處的政客

Grail /grel; greɪl/ *n* **the Grail** —see 見 HOLY GRAIL

grain /gren; greɪn/ *n*

1 ►FOOD 食物◄ a) [U] the seeds of crops such as corn, wheat, or rice that are gathered for use as food, or these crops themselves 穀物, 糧食 **b)** [C] a single seed of corn, wheat etc 穀粒

2 ►OF WOOD ETC 木頭等的◄ the grain the natural arrangement of the threads or FIBREs (3) in wood, flesh, rock, and cloth, or the pattern you see as a result of this 紋理: *Cut the wood in the direction of the grain.* 順着木頭的紋理把木頭劈開。—see picture at 參見 KNOT¹ 圖

3 a grain of sympathy/truth/doubt etc a small amount of truth etc 一點點同情/真實性/懷疑等: *They don't have a grain of common sense between them.* 他們兩人沒有一點兒常識。

4 ►SMALL PIECE 顆粒◄ [C] a single, very small piece of a substance such as sand, salt etc〔沙、鹽等的〕顆粒 —see picture on page A7 參見 A7 頁圖

5 go against the grain if something that you have to do goes against the grain, you do not like doing it, because it is not what you would naturally do 違背本人的意願: *It went against the grain for her to be so strict.* 這麼嚴格是她不願意的。

6 ►MEASURE 計量單位◄ [C] the smallest measure of weight, used for medicines, equal to .0648 gram 格令〔最小重量單位, 等於 0.0648 克, 用於稱量藥品〕—see table on page C3 參見 C3 頁附錄 —see also 另見 **take sth with a pinch/grain of salt** (SALT¹ (3))

G

grain·y /ˋgrenɪ; ˈgreɪni/ *adj* a photograph that is grainy has a rough appearance, as if the images are made up of spots 顆粒狀的, 似有顆粒狀的〔指照片看起來很粗糙, 其圖像似由顆粒組成〕

gram, gramme /græm; græm/ written abbreviation 縮寫= **g** or **gm** *n* [C] the basic unit for measuring weight in the METRIC system 克〔公制基本單位〕—see table on page C3 參見 C3 頁附錄 3

-gram /græm; græm/ *suffix* [in nouns 構成名詞] a message delivered as an amusing surprise 給人驚喜的有趣訊息: *On his birthday we sent him a kissagram* (=a girl who was paid to give him a message and kiss him). 他生日的那天我們派一個女孩給他送去賀卡並親吻他一下。

gram·mar /ˋgræmɚ; ˈgræmə/ *n* **1** [U] the rules by which words change their forms and are combined into sentences, or the study or use of these rules 語法 (學): *I find German grammar very difficult.* 我覺得德語語法很難。| *I often have to correct his grammar.* 我經常得糾正他的語法。**2** [C] a particular description of grammar or a book that describes grammar rules 語法書: *Have you seen that new French grammar?* 你見過那本新的法語語法書嗎? 3 3

gram·mar·i·an /grəˋmɛrɪən; grəˈmeəriən/ *n* [C] someone who studies and knows about grammar 語法學家

grammar school /ˈ·· ˌ·/ *n* [C] **1** a school in Britain for children over the age of 11 who have to pass a special examination to go there 文法學校〔英國的一種學校, 為11歲以上的兒童設立, 但必須通過一種特殊考試才能錄取〕—compare 比較 COMPREHENSIVE SCHOOL **2** *AmE old-fashioned* an ELEMENTARY SCHOOL【美, 過時】小學

gram·mat·i·cal /grəˋmætɪkḷ; grəˈmætɪkəl/ *adj* **1** [only before noun 僅用於名詞前] concerning grammar 語法的: *grammatical rules* 語法規則 **2** correct according to the rules of grammar 語法正確的, 符合語法的 —**grammatically** /-kḷɪ; -kli/ *adv*

gramme /græm; græm/ *n* [C] another spelling of GRAM gram 的另一種拼法

gram·o·phone /ˈgræməfon; ˈgræməfəʊn/ *n* [C] *old-fashioned* a RECORD PLAYER【過時】留聲機

gram·pus /ˈgræmpəs; ˈgræmpəs/ *n* [C] a sea animal like a WHALE 逆戟鯨, 虎鯨

gran /græn; græn/ *n* [C] *BrE informal* grandmother【英, 非正式】祖母, 奶奶; 外祖母, 外婆

gra·na·ry¹ /ˈgrænərɪ; ˈgrænəri/ *n* [C] a place where grain, especially wheat, is stored 糧倉〔尤指儲存小麥的倉庫〕

granary² *adj* [only before noun 僅用於名詞前] *BrE* granary bread is bread which contains whole grains of wheat【英】〔麵包〕全麥的

2 3 **grand¹** /grænd; grænd/ *adj* **1** a grand building, occasion etc is very impressive 壯觀的, 盛大的, 隆重的: *We attended a grand ceremony at the Palace.* 我們在王宮參加了一個隆重的典禮。| **on a grand scale** *Preparations for the wedding are taking place on a grand scale.* 婚禮的準備工作正在大規模地進行。**2** a grand plan or idea aims to achieve something very impressive 宏偉的: *As a young minister he was full of grand ideas for social reform.* 作為一位年輕的部長, 他心裡充滿對社會改革的宏偉想法。**3** people who are grand are rich and important but often too proud 有錢有勢而神氣活現的: *A very grand-looking gentleman entered the room.* 一位十分神氣的紳士走進房間。**4** *informal or dialect* very good, pleasant, or enjoyable【非正式或方言】極好的, 非常愉快[令人開心]的: *We had a grand day out at the seaside.* 我們在海邊度過了非常愉快的一天。| *Wasn't it grand to see Ted again?* 再次見到特德真好, 不是嗎? **5 grand total** the final total you get when you add up several numbers or amounts 總計 **6 the Grand Old Man of** a man who has been involved in an activity or a profession for a long time and is highly respected〔某活動、某行業的〕元老、老前輩: *the Grand Old Man of British theatre* 英國戲劇的老前輩 —**grandly** *adv* —**grandness** *n* [U]

grand² *n* [C] **1** *plural* **grand** *informal* a thousand pounds or dollars【非正式】一千英鎊, 一千美元: *That new car of his cost him fifteen grand.* 他那輛新車花了他一萬五千英鎊。**2** *informal* a GRAND PIANO【非正式】大鋼琴

2 **gran·dad** *especially BrE*【尤英】, **granddad** *especially AmE*【尤美】/ˈgræn,dæd; ˈgrændæd/ *n* [C] **1** *informal* grandfather【非正式】爺爺; 外公 **2** *BrE informal* an impolite way of addressing an old man【英, 非正式】老頭〔對老年人的一種不禮貌的稱呼〕: *Hurry up, grandad!* 快點, 老頭!

gran·dad·dy, granddaddy /ˈgræn,dædɪ; ˈgrændædi/ *n* [C] *AmE informal*【美, 非正式】**1** grandfather 爺爺; 外公 **2 the grandaddy of** the first or greatest example of something〔某一行中最傑出的〕老祖宗, 祖師爺: *Louis Armstrong, the grandaddy of all jazz trumpeters* 爵士音樂號手的祖師爺路易·阿姆斯特朗

grandad shirt /ˈ·· ,·/ *n* [C] a shirt without a collar 無領襯衫 —see picture on page A17 參見 A17 頁圖

3 **grand·child** /ˈgrænd,tʃaɪld; ˈgræntʃaɪld/ *plural* **grandchildren** /-,tʃɪldrən; -,tʃɪldrən/ *n* [C] the child of your son or daughter 孫子[女]; 外孫[女] —see picture at 參見 FAMILY 圖

grand·dad /ˈgræn,dæd; ˈgrændæd/ *n* [C] the usual American spelling of GRANDAD grandad 的一般美式拼法

grand·dad·dy /ˈgræn,dædɪ; ˈgrændædi/ *n* [C] another spelling of GRANDADDY grandaddy 的另一種拼法

grand·daugh·ter /ˈgrænd,dɔtɚ; ˈgræn,dɔːtə/ *n* [C] the daughter of your son or daughter 孫女; 外孫女 —see picture at 參見 FAMILY 圖

gran·dee /grænˋdi; grænˈdiː/ *n* [C] **1** a Spanish or Portuguese NOBLEMAN of the highest rank in former times 大公〔從前西班牙或葡萄牙的最高爵位〕**2** a politician of the highest social class who has a lot of influence〔極有影響的〕社會最上層政客

gran·deur /ˈgrændʒɚ; ˈgrændʒə/ *n* [U] impressive beauty, power, or size 壯麗, 雄偉: *the grandeur of the mountains* 山巒的壯麗 —see also 另見 **delusions of grandeur** (DELUSION (2))

grand·fa·ther /ˈgrænd,fɑðɚ; ˈgrænd,fɑːðə/ *n* [C] the father of your father or mother 祖父; 外祖父 —see picture at 參見 FAMILY 圖 3

grandfather clock /ˈ··· ,·/ *n* [C] an old-fashioned tall clock which stands on the floor 老式的落地鐘

grand fi·na·le /,· ·ˈ··/ *n* [C] the last and most impressive or exciting part of a show or performance〔節目或演出的〕終曲, 終場, 壓軸戲

gran·dil·o·quent /grænˋdɪləkwənt; grænˈdɪləkwənt/ *adj formal* using words that are too long and formal in order to sound important; POMPOUS【正式】浮誇的, 華而不實的〔指使用華麗的辭藻以顯得重要〕—**grandiloquence** *n* [U]

gran·di·ose /ˈgrændɪ,os; ˈgrændiəʊs/ *adj* grandiose plans sound very important or impressive, but will never really happen because they are not practical〔計劃〕浮誇的, 不切合實際的: *It's just another of Wheeler's grandiose schemes.* 這只是惠勒的又一個不切實際的計劃。

grand ju·ry /,· ˈ··/ *n* [C] *law* a group of people in the US who decide whether someone charged with a crime should be judged in a court of law【法律】〔美國的〕大陪審團 —**grand juror** *n* [C]

grand lar·ce·ny /,· ˈ···/ *n* [U] *AmE law* the crime of stealing very valuable goods【美, 法律】嚴重盜竊罪〔指盜竊十分珍貴的物品〕

grand·ma /ˈgrændmɑ; ˈgrænmɑː/ *n* [C] *informal* grandmother【非正式】祖母, 奶奶; 外婆

grand mal /,græn ˋmæl; ,grɒn ˈmæl/ *n* [U] *technical* a serious form of EPILEPSY【術語】重度癲癇發作

grand mas·ter /,· ˈ··/ *n* [C] a CHESS player of a very high standard 國際象棋大師

grand·moth·er /ˈgrænd,mʌðɚ; ˈgræn,mʌðə/ *n* [C] the mother of your mother or father 祖母; 外祖母 —see picture at 參見 FAMILY 圖

grand op·e·ra /,· ˈ···/ *n* [C,U] an OPERA with a serious subject in which all the words are sung 大歌劇

grand·pa /ˈgrændpɑ; ˈgrænpɑː/ *n* [C] *informal* grandfather【非正式】爺爺; 外公

grand·par·ent /ˈgrænd,pɛrənt; ˈgræn,peərənt/ *n* [C usually plural 一般用複數] one of the parents of your mother or father 祖父[母]; 外祖父[母]: *My grandparents live in Sussex.* 我的祖父母都住在蘇塞克斯郡。—see picture at 參見 FAMILY 圖

grand pi·an·o /,· ·ˈ··/ *n* [C] the type of large piano often used in concerts〔通常在音樂會上使用的〕大鋼琴 —compare 比較 UPRIGHT PIANO

grand prix /grɑ̃ ˋpri; ,grɒn ˈpriː/ *n* [C] one of a set of international races, especially a car race 國際大獎賽〔尤指賽車〕

grand slam /,· ˈ·/ *n* [C] **1** the winning of all of a set of important sports competitions in the same year〔同年各項重要比賽的〕全勝 **2** a hit in BASEBALL which gets four runs (RUN² (17)) because it is a HOME RUN and there are players on all the bases (BASE² (8))〔棒球中的〕滿壘全壘打 **3** the winning of all of the tricks (TRICK¹ (11)) possible in one game of cards, especially in BRIDGE¹ (4)〔撲克牌, 尤指橋牌中的〕大滿貫

grand·son /ˈgrænd,sʌn; ˈgrænsʌn/ *n* [C] the son of your son or daughter 孫子; 外孫 —see picture at 參見 FAMILY 圖

grand·stand /ˈgrænd,stænd; ˈgrændstænd/ *n* [C] a large structure that has many rows of seats where people sit and watch sports competitions, games, or races〔體育比賽場地的〕大看台

grand·stand·ing /ˈgrænd,stændɪŋ; ˈgrædstændɪŋ/ *n* [U] *AmE* an action that is intended to make people notice and admire you【美】引人注意的動作, 譁眾取寵的行為: *His opening the new school is just a piece of po-*

litical grandstanding. 他主持這所新學校的成立典禮只是一種譁眾取寵的政治舉措。

grand tour /ˌ· ˈ·/ *n* [C] **1** *humorous* an occasion when someone takes you around a building to show it to you 【幽默】參觀: *They took us on a grand tour of their new house.* 他們領我們參觀了他們的新居。**2 the grand tour** a trip round Europe made in former times by young English or American people from rich families as a part of their education 環歐旅行〔指舊時英美富家子弟作為其教育的一部分所作的環歐洲旅行〕

grange /grendʒ; greɪndʒ/ *n* [C] a large country house with farm buildings 鄉間大屋, 莊園

gran·ite /ˈgrænɪt; ˈgrænɪ̈t/ *n* [U] a very hard grey rock, often used in building 花崗岩, 花崗石

3 **gran·ny¹, grannie** /ˈgrænɪ; ˈgræni/ *n* [C] *informal* grandmother【非正式】祖母; 奶奶; 外婆: *Look what granny's bought you!* 瞧奶奶給你帶甚麼來了!

granny², grannie *adj* [only before noun 僅用於名詞前] *BrE* of a style typically used by old women【英】老太太式樣的: *granny shoes* 老奶奶鞋

granny flat /ˈ·· ·/ *n* [C] *BrE* a separate place inside or next to someone's house, that is designed for an old relative to live in 老奶奶住房〔指在住宅內部或隔壁專供年老親戚居住的一套居室〕

granny knot /ˈ·· ˌ·/ *n* [C] a REEF KNOT in which the two pieces of string are crossed in the wrong way〔兩條繩反向打的〕老奶奶結

gra·no·la /grəˋnolə; grəˈnəʊlə/ *n* [U] *AmE* breakfast food made from mixed nuts, grains, and seeds【美】〔用堅果、穀物和種子混合製成的〕早餐食品

1 **grant¹** /grænt; grɑːnt/ *n* [C] an amount of money given
2 to someone, especially by the government for a particular purpose〔政府發給的〕補助金: *We're hoping to get a grant from the local council for the project.* 我們正希望能從本地市政會為這個項目得到一筆撥款。| **student grant** (=a grant to pay for a student's education at university) 助學金

2 **grant²** *v* [T] **1** *formal* to give someone something that
2 they have asked for, especially official permission to do something【正式】給予, 准予〔尤指官方授權〕: **grant sb sth** *The Norton consortium has been granted permission to build a shopping mall.* 諾頓財團已獲准建立一家購物中心。| **grant sb's request** *Your request for housing benefit has been granted.* 你的住房補貼申請已經得到批准。**2** to admit that something is true although it does not make much difference to your opinion 承認〔確有某事, 但不影響自己的看法〕: **I grant you** *Darren's not an intellectual, I grant you, but he does work hard.* 達倫不是一個知識分子, 這不假; 但他確實工作很努力。| **granted** (=used when you admit that what someone has said is true) 不錯; 我承認〔用來表示承認某人所說為事實〕 *Granted, we don't want to scare them, but it's time we applied some pressure.* 不錯, 我們不想把他們嚇住, 但現在是我們施加點壓力的時候了。**3 take it for granted (that)** to believe that something is true without making sure 想當然地認為: *Sorry! I just took it for granted that you'd want to come.* 對不起!我想當然地認為你會願意來。**4 take sb/sth for granted** to expect that someone will always be there when you need them and never show them any special attention or thank them 視某人/某事為當然〔因而對其從不特別關注或感謝〕: *I'm sick and tired of my husband taking me for granted!* 我丈夫覺得我一切理當如此, 真令我感到生氣和厭倦!

grant-main·tained /ˌ· ˈ··◂/ *adj* a grant-maintained school in Britain receives its money directly from the central government rather than from the local government 直接由中央政府資助的〔學校〕

gran·u·lar /ˈgrænjələ; ˈgrænjʊ̈lə/ *adj* consisting of or covered with granules 由顆粒組成的; 佈滿顆粒的

gran·u·lat·ed /ˈgrænjəletɪd; ˈgrænjʊ̈leɪtɪ̈d/ *adj* granulated sugar is in the form of small white grains rather than powder〔白糖〕砂狀的

gran·ule /ˈgrænjul; ˈgrænjuːl/ *n* [C] a small hard piece of something 細粒, 小粒: *coffee granules* 咖啡晶

grape /grep; greɪp/ *n* [C] a small round juicy fruit that grows on a VINE and is often used for making wine 葡萄: *a bunch of grapes* 一串葡萄 —see picture on page A8 參見A8頁圖

grape·fruit /ˈgrepˌfrut; ˈgreɪpfruːt/ *n* [C] a round yellow CITRUS fruit with a thick skin, like a large orange 西柚, 葡萄柚 —see picture on page A8 參見A8頁圖

grape·vine /ˈgrepˌvaɪn; ˈgreɪpvaɪn/ *n* [C] **1 hear sth on the grapevine** to hear about something because the information has been passed from one person to another in conversation 從傳聞聽到某事: *I heard about his resignation on the grapevine.* 我聽說了有關他辭職的傳聞。**2** a climbing plant on which grapes grow; VINE (1) 葡萄〔植物〕

graph /græf; græf/ *n* [C] a drawing that uses a line or lines to show how two or more sets of measurements are related to each other 圖表〔指用線條表示兩組或多組計量之間關係的圖表〕: *Martin showed me a graph of their recent sales.* 馬丁給我看了一張有關他們最近銷售額的圖表。—see picture at 參見 CHART¹ 圖

graph·ic /ˈgræfɪk; ˈgræfɪk/ *adj* **1 a graphic account/description etc** a very clear description of an event that gives a lot of details, especially unpleasant ones 清楚詳細的敘述/描寫等〔尤指包含令人不愉快的細節的〕: *Cookson gives a graphic account of her unhappiness as a child.* 庫克遜詳盡地描述了她童年的不幸。**2** [only before noun 僅用於名詞前] connected with or including drawing, printing, or designing 繪畫的; 印刷的; 平面造型設計的: *a graphic artist* 平面造型藝術家 | *the graphic arts* 平面造型藝術

graph·i·cally /ˈgræfɪklɪ; ˈgræfɪkli/ *adv* **1** if you describe something graphically, you describe it very clearly with a lot of detail 清晰詳細地: *Stella described the scene so graphically that I could almost imagine I was there.* 斯特拉十分詳盡地描述了這一場面, 我幾乎就像身臨其境一樣。**2** *formal* using a graph【正式】用圖表: *statistics represented graphically* 用圖表表示的統計資料

graphic de·sign /ˌ·· ·ˈ·/ *n* [U] the art of combining pictures, words, and decoration in the production of books, magazines etc〔書、雜誌等的〕平面造型設計 —**graphic designer** *n* [C]

graph·ics /ˈgræfɪks; ˈgræfɪks/ *n* [plural] drawings or images that are designed to represent objects or facts, especially in a computer program〔尤指電腦程序中的〕圖, 圖表 —see also 另見 COMPUTER GRAPHICS

graph·ite /ˈgræfaɪt; ˈgræfaɪt/ *n* [U] a soft black substance that is a kind of carbon, used in pencils, paints, and electrical equipment 石墨〔碳的一種形式, 用於鉛筆、油漆和電氣設備中〕

gra·phol·o·gy /græˋfɑlədʒɪ; græˈfɒlədʒi/ *n* [U] the study of HANDWRITING in order to understand people's characters 筆跡學 —**graphologist** *n* [C]

graph pa·per /ˈ· ˌ··/ *n* [U] paper with many squares printed on it, used for drawing GRAPHS〔有格子的〕標繪紙, 坐標紙

-gra·phy /grəfɪ; grəfi/ *suffix* used in nouns to mean the making of a copy or picture of something〔用於名詞, 意為製作或複製圖像的技術〕: *radiography* 射線照相, X光照相 | *photography* 攝影

grap·ple /ˈgræpḷ; ˈgræpəl/ *v* [I] to fight or struggle with someone, holding them tightly 扭打, 揪鬥: **[+with]** *Two men grappled with a guard at the door.* 兩個男人和一個門衛在門口扭打。

grapple with sth *phr v* [T] to try hard to deal with a difficult problem 盡力解決〔某困難問題〕: *The Government is grappling with major areas of social policy.* 政府正努力處理社會政策的主要領域。

grap·pling i·ron /ˈ·· ··/ also 又作 **grappling hook** /ˈ·· ·/

n [C] an iron tool with several hooks that you tie to a rope and use to hold a boat still, look for objects on the bottom of a river etc 抓鉤〔帶若干彎鉤的鐵製工具, 繫於繩上用以固定船隻或在河底尋物〕

grasp¹ /græsp; grɑːsp/ *v* [T] **1** to take and hold something firmly 抓牢, 握緊: *Make sure you grasp the rope with both hands.* 一定要用雙手抓緊繩索。| **grasp hold of sth** *Paula grasped hold of my arm.* 葆拉緊緊抓住我的胳膊。**2** [not in progressive 不用進行式] to completely understand a fact or an idea, especially a complicated one 理解, 領會〔尤指複雜的意思〕: *They failed to grasp the full significance of his remarks.* 他們沒有領會他的話的全部意義。**3 grasp a chance/opportunity** to eagerly and quickly use an opportunity to do something 〔急切地〕抓住機會 **4 grasp the nettle** *BrE* to deal with an unpleasant situation firmly and without delay【英】果斷地處理棘手問題

grasp at sth *phr v* [T] **1** to eagerly try to use an opportunity 急切嘗試利用〔一次機會〕: *He was ready to grasp at any excuse, however flimsy.* 他隨時準備找個藉口, 不管這種藉口是如何牽強。**2** to try to hold on to something 企圖抓住

grasp² *n* [singular] **1** the way you hold something or your ability to hold it 抓, 握: *The book slipped from his grasp and fell to the floor.* 書從他的手裡滑落到地板上。| *Take a firm grasp on the rope.* 抓緊繩子。**2** your ability to understand a complicated idea or situation 〔對複雜概念或棘手狀況的〕理解力: **a good/poor grasp of** *You seem to have a good grasp of the subject.* 看來你對這個題目理解得很透徹。| **beyond sb's grasp** (=too difficult for them to understand) 超乎某人的理解力 **3** your ability to achieve or gain something 力所能及; 把握; 掌握: **within sb's grasp** *Success is now within our grasp.* 現在我們已經成功在握。**4** *especially literary* control or power【尤文】控制, 權力

G

grasp·ing /ˈgræspɪŋ; ˈgrɑːspɪŋ/ *adj* too eager to get money and unwilling to give any of it away or spend it 貪財而吝嗇的: *Hanson was a hard, grasping man.* 漢森是個苛刻貪財又吝嗇的人。

 2
 2

grass¹ /græs; grɑːs/ *n*

1 ▶IN FIELDS 在田野◀ **a)** [U] a very common plant with thin green leaves that grows in fields and is often eaten by animals 草: *a blade of grass* 一根草 | *Please keep off the grass.* 請勿踐踏草地。**b)** [C] a particular kind of grass 〔專指某種草〕: *sea grasses* 大葉藻

2 ▶DRUG 毒品◀ [U] *slang* MARIJUANA【俚】大麻

3 ▶CRIMINAL 罪犯◀ [C] *BrE informal* someone, usually a criminal, who gives information about other criminals to the police; INFORMER【英, 非正式】告密者, 通風報信者〔通常指向警方告發其他罪犯〕; STOOLPIGEON *AmE*【美】—see also 另見 SUPERGRASS

4 not let the grass grow under your feet to not waste time or delay starting something 不浪費時間, 做事不拖沓

5 put sb out to grass *informal* to make someone leave their job because they are too old to do it effectively【非正式】使某人離職〔由於年老而不能有效工作〕: *an old judge being put out to grass* 即將被迫離職的老法官 —see also 另見 GRASS ROOTS, **snake in the grass** (SNAKE¹ (3))

grass² *v* [I] *BrE informal* if a criminal grasses on other criminals, he tells the police about their activities【英, 非正式】〔罪犯〕向警方告發[告密]: **[+on]** *That bastard must have grassed on us!* 那個雜種肯定把我們給告發了! | **grass sb up** *BrE*【英】: *I wonder who grassed us up?* 不知道誰告發了我們?

grass sth ↔ **over** *phr v* [T] to cover land with grass 〔在地上〕覆蓋草皮

grass·hop·per /ˈgræsˌhɑpɚ; ˈgrɑːsˌhɒpə/ *n* [C] an insect that has long back legs for jumping and that makes short loud noises 蚱蜢, 蝗蟲 —see also 另見 **knee-high to a grasshopper** (KNEE-HIGH¹ (2))

grass·land /ˈgræsˌlænd; ˈgrɑːslænd/ also 又作 **grasslands** [plural] *n* [U] a large area of land covered with wild grass 草原

grass roots /ˌ· ˈ·/ *n* **the grass roots** the ordinary people in an organization, rather than the leaders 〔組織中除領袖外的〕普通民眾 —**grass roots** *adj*: *We are hoping for full participation at grass roots level.* 我們希望基層民眾充分參與。

grass snake /ˈ· ·/ *n* [C] a common snake that is not poisonous 遊蛇

gras·sy /ˈgræsɪ; ˈgrɑːsi/ *adj* covered with grass 長滿草的: *sitting on a grassy bank* 坐在長滿草的河岸上

grate¹ /gret; greɪt/ *n* [C] the metal bars and frame that hold the wood, coal etc in a FIREPLACE 〔壁爐的〕金屬爐架

grate² *v* **1** [T] to rub cheese, fruit etc against a rough or sharp surface in order to break them into small pieces 磨碎〔乾酪、水果等〕: *grated carrot* 磨碎的胡蘿蔔 —see picture on page A11 參見 A11 頁圖 **2** [I] to make an unpleasant sound 發出刺耳的摩擦聲: **[+on/against]** *the sound of chalk grating against the blackboard* 粉筆摩擦黑板的刺耳聲 **3** [I] to have an annoying effect on someone's nerves 使某人感到煩躁: **[+on]** *Hardy's constant questions were beginning to grate on me.* 哈代不斷提出問題, 開始使我煩躁。—see also 另見 GRATING²

grate·ful /ˈgretfəl; ˈgreɪtfəl/ *adj* **1** feeling that you want to thank someone because of something kind that they have done 感謝的, 感激的: *Dr Cameron has received hundreds of letters from grateful patients.* 卡梅隆醫生收到數百封向他表示感謝的病人來信。| **[+for]** *I'm so grateful for all your help.* 我非常感謝你的幫助。| **be grateful to sb for sth** *He was extremely grateful to Gladstone for his support.* 他非常感謝格拉德斯通的支持。| **be grateful that** *I'm very grateful that you didn't tell my husband about this.* 我非常感激你沒有告訴我丈夫這件事。| **deeply/eternally grateful** (=extremely grateful) 非常感謝, 感激不盡 **2 be grateful for small mercies** used in a bad situation to say that things could be worse than they are 慶幸〔境況未惡化〕: *Well, be grateful for small mercies – at least you've still got a job!* 好啦, 應感到慶幸了 — 至少你還有個工作! **3 I would be grateful if you could/would ...** *formal* used to make requests in formal situations or letters【正式】如果你能…我將感激不盡〔用於在正式場合或信件中提出請求〕: *We would be most grateful if you could confirm these arrangements immediately.* 如蒙貴方立即確認安排事項, 我方感激不盡。—opposite 反義詞 UNGRATEFUL —**gratefully** *adv*: *We gratefully accepted their offer.* 我們十分感激地接受了他們的提議。—**gratefulness** *n* [U]

grat·er /ˈgretɚ; ˈgreɪtə/ *n* [C] a tool used for grating food 〔食品〕磨碎器, 擦子: *a cheese grater* 乾酪磨碎器

grat·i·fy /ˈgrætəˌfaɪ; ˈgrætɪ̵faɪ/ *v* [T] *formal*【正式】**1 be gratified** to feel pleased and satisfied 感到高興和滿意: *I was very gratified to hear how much they liked my work.* 我非常高興聽到他們說有多喜歡我幹的活兒。**2** to satisfy a desire 滿足〔慾望〕: *Hoping to gratify my curiosity, I opened the door.* 為了滿足我的好奇心, 我打開了門。—**gratification** /ˌgrætəfəˈkeʃən; ˌgrætɪ̵fɪ̵ˈkeɪʃən/ *n* [C,U]

grat·i·fy·ing /ˈgrætəˌfaɪɪŋ; ˈgrætɪ̵faɪ-ɪŋ/ *adj* pleasing and satisfying 令人欣慰的, 使人滿足的: *It's gratifying to know they liked our project.* 得知他們喜歡我們的項目, 真令人欣慰。—**gratifyingly** *adv*

grat·ing¹ /ˈgretɪŋ; ˈgreɪtɪŋ/ *n* [C] a metal frame with bars across it, used to cover a window or hole 〔窗或洞的〕格柵: *Leaves clogged the grating over the drain.* 樹葉把排水管上的格柵堵住了。

grating² *adj* a grating sound is hard and unpleasant 〔聲音〕刺耳的: *a harsh grating laugh* 刺耳難聽的笑聲 —**gratingly** *adv*

grat·is /ˋgretɪs; ˈgrætəs/ *adj, adv* provided without payment; free 免費: *Medical advice was provided gratis.* 醫療諮詢是免費提供的。

grat·i·tude /ˋgrætəˏtjud; ˈgrætətjuːd/ *n* [U] the feeling of being grateful 感激(之情): *Tears of gratitude filled her eyes.* 她的眼裡充滿感激的淚水。| *I couldn't adequately express my gratitude to Francis.* 我對弗朗西斯的感激之情難以言盡。| [+for] *I didn't get a single word of gratitude for all my trouble.* 我沒有聽到一句對我的辛勞表示感謝的話。| **deepest gratitude** (=very great gratitude) 萬分的感激 —opposite 反義詞 INGRATITUDE —see also 另見 **owe a debt of gratitude to sb** (DEBT (4))

gra·tu·i·tous /grəˋtjuətəs; grəˈtjuːətəs/ *adj* **gratuitous violence/insults/cruelty etc** violence etc that is done for no reason and causes unnecessary harm or offence 不必要的暴力/無端的侮辱/無端的殘酷(行為)等 —**gratuitously** *adv* —**gratuitousness** *n* [U]

gra·tu·i·ty /grəˋtjuətɪ; grəˈtjuːəti/ *n* [C] *formal*【正式】**1** a small gift of money given to someone for a service they provided; TIP¹ (2) 小費, 賞錢 **2** *especially BrE* a large gift of money given to someone when they leave their job, especially in the army, navy etc【尤英】〔尤指陸軍、海軍等的〕退職金, 退伍金

grave¹ /grev; greɪv/ *n* [C] **1** the place in the ground where a dead body is buried 墳墓 —compare 比較 TOMB **2 the grave** *especially literary* death【尤文】死亡: *Had his spirit returned from the grave to haunt them?* 是不是他的鬼魂從墳墓裡回來纏上了他們? **3 sb would turn/spin in their grave** used to say that someone who is dead would strongly disapprove of something happening now 某人於九泉之下不得安寧〔表示某人在九泉之下也不會贊成〕: *The way Bill plays that piece would have Mozart turning in his grave.* 比爾那樣演奏那首曲子莫扎特在九泉之下也不會贊成。—see also 另見 **dig your own grave** (DIG¹ (4)), **from the cradle to the grave** (CRADLE¹ (4)), **have one foot in the grave** (FOOT¹ (21)), **silent as the grave** (SILENT (6)), **a watery grave** (WATERY (5))

grave² *adj* **1** very serious and worrying 嚴重的; 令人擔憂的: *This decision may have very grave consequences.* 這一決定可能產生非常嚴重的後果。| *I have grave doubts about his ability.* 我對他的能力十分懷疑。**2** looking or sounding quiet and serious, especially because something important or worrying has happened〔由於發生重大事情, 表情或說話〕嚴肅的: *Turnbull's face was grave as he told them about the accident.* 特恩布爾在告訴他們這次事故時表情十分嚴肅。—**gravely** *adv*: *Adam nodded gravely.* 亞當嚴肅地點點頭。—see also 另見 GRAVITY (2, 3)

grave³ /grɑv; grɑːv/ *adj* a grave ACCENT¹ (4) is a mark put above a letter in some languages such as French to show the pronunciation, for example è 有沉[抑]音符〔法語等語言中加在字母之上表示發音的符號〕的 —compare 比較 ACUTE (7), CIRCUMFLEX

grave·dig·ger /ˋgrevˏdɪgɚ; ˈgreɪvˌdɪgə/ *n* [C] someone whose job is to dig graves 掘墓人

grav·el /ˋgrævḷ; ˈgrævəl/ *n* [U] small stones, used to make a surface for paths, roads etc 礫石, 碎石: *a gravel path* 石子小道 | *a gravel pit* (=a place where gravel is dug out of the ground) 礫石採掘坑

grav·elled /ˋgrævḷd; ˈgrævəld/ *adj* a gravelled path or road has a surface made of gravel〔小道或道路〕用礫石[碎石]鋪成的

grav·el·ly /ˋgrævəlɪ; ˈgrævəli/ *adj* **1** a gravelly voice has a low, rough sound 嗓音低啞的 **2** covered with or mixed with gravel 鋪礫[碎]石的; 含礫[碎]石的: *gravelly soil* 含礫石的土壤

gra·ven /ˋgrevən; ˈgreɪvən/ *adj* **graven image** *literary* an image or figure that has been made out of stone, wood, or metal【文】〔用石、木或金屬製作的〕雕像

grave·side /ˋgrevˏsaɪd; ˈgreɪvsaɪd/ *n* [singular] **at the graveside** beside a grave, especially when someone is being buried there〔尤指某人下葬時〕在墳墓邊上

grave·stone /ˋgrevˏston; ˈgreɪvstəʊn/ *n* [C] a stone above a grave showing details of the person buried there; HEADSTONE 墓碑

grave·yard /ˋgrevˏjɑrd; ˈgreɪvjɑːd/ *n* [C] **1** an area of ground where people are buried, often next to a church〔常挨近教堂的〕墓地 —compare 比較 CEMETERY, CHURCHYARD **2** a place where things that are no longer wanted or useful are left 垃圾場: *a graveyard for old cars* 廢舊汽車堆放場

graveyard shift /ˋ·· ˏ·/ *n* [C] *especially AmE* a regular period of working time at night【尤美】夜班

grav·i·tas /ˋgrævɪtæs; ˈgrævɪtæs/ *n* [U] *formal* a seriousness of manner that people respect【正式】〔令人肅然起敬的〕莊嚴態度

grav·i·tate /ˋgrævəˏtet; ˈgrævəteɪt/ *v* [I always+adv/prep] *formal* to be attracted to something and therefore move towards it or become involved with it【正式】被吸引到: [+to/towards] *Very sporty students tended to gravitate towards others with similar interests.* 酷愛體育的學生往往會因志趣相投而互相吸引。

grav·i·ta·tion /ˏgrævəˋteʃən; ˌgrævəˈteɪʃən/ *n* [U] **1** *technical* the force that causes two objects to move towards each other because of their MASS¹ (5)【術語】引力 **2** the act of gravitating towards something 受吸引

grav·i·ta·tion·al /ˏgrævəˋteʃənəl; ˌgrævəˈteɪʃənəl◂/ *adj* connected with or resulting from the force of gravity 與引力有關的; 產生於引力的: *the planet's gravitational field* 這顆行星的引力場

grav·i·ty /ˋgrævətɪ; ˈgrævəti/ *n* [U] **1** *technical* the force that causes something to fall to the ground or to be attracted to another PLANET【術語】重力, 引力, 地心吸力 **2** *formal* the extreme and worrying seriousness of a situation【正式】〔局勢的〕嚴重性: *Carl did not seem to understand the gravity of this situation.* 卡爾似乎不理解這種情況的嚴重性。**3** an extremely serious way of behaving, speaking etc 嚴肅〔指舉止、言談等的態度〕: *The Consul spoke slowly and with great gravity.* 領事講話緩慢, 而且十分嚴肅。—see also 另見 CENTRE OF GRAVITY

gra·vy /ˋgrevɪ; ˈgreɪvi/ *n* [U] **1** a SAUCE made from the juice that comes from meat as it cooks, mixed with flour〔調味用的〕肉汁〔由烹調肉類時產生的汁水與麵粉混合製成〕**2** *slang, especially AmE* money, profit, or something that you like that is gained when you do not expect it【俚, 尤美】意外之財, 意外所得

gravy boat /ˋ·· ·/ *n* [C] a long JUG (1) that you pour gravy from〔長形有柄帶嘴〕盛肉汁用的器皿

gravy train /ˋ·· ˏ·/ *n* **the gravy train** *informal* an organization, activity, or business from which many people can make money or profit without much effort【非正式】不費甚麼氣力便可從中獲利的組織[活動、買賣], 美差

gray /gre; greɪ/ *adj, n, v* the usual American spelling of GREY grey 的一般美式拼法

graze¹ /grez; greɪz/ *v*

1 ►EAT GRASS 吃草◄ a) [I] if an animal grazes, it eats grass that is growing (動物)吃草: *The sheep continued to graze.* 羊繼續吃草。**b)** [T] to let animals eat grass 放牧: *fields where they used to graze their sheep* 他們過去經常牧羊的田野

2 ►INJURE YOURSELF 傷到自己◄ [T] to break the surface of your skin by rubbing it against something 擦傷: *Oliver grazed his knee when he fell over.* 奧利佛跌倒時擦傷了膝蓋。

3 ►TOUCH STH 碰觸某物◄ [T] to touch something lightly while passing it 擦過, 掠過: *As the plane climbed away, its wing seemed to graze the treetops.* 飛機爬升時, 機翼似乎擦過樹梢。

4 ►EAT 吃◄ [I] to eat small amounts of food all through the day instead of having regular meals 整天少量地吃東西而不定時進食

G

5 ►TELEVISION 電視◄ [I] to keep changing television CHANNELs, watching only a little of each programme 不停切換頻道

graze² *n* [C] a wound caused by rubbing that slightly breaks the surface of your skin〔皮膚的〕擦傷

GRE /ˌdʒi ɑr ˈi; ˌdʒiː ɑːr ˈiː/ *n* [C] Graduate Record Examination; an examination taken by students in the US who have done a first degree and want to go to GRADUATE SCHOOL〔美國〕研究生入學考試

grease¹ /gris; griːs/ *n* [U] **1** animal fat that is soft after being melted〔熔化了的〕動物油脂 **2** any thick oily substance, especially one used to make parts of machines work smoothly 潤滑油

grease² *v* [T] **1** to put grease on something 給…塗油脂: *Grease the pan before you pour the batter in.* 將麵糊倒入鍋裡之前，要在鍋底塗上油脂。**2 grease sb's palm** to give someone money in a secret or dishonest way in order to persuade them to do something〔向某人〕行賄 **3 like greased lightning** *informal* extremely fast【非正式】閃電般，非常快地: *He disappeared like greased lightning when the police arrived.* 警察到達時他閃電般消失了。

grease gun /ˈ· ·/ *n* [C] a tool for forcing grease into machinery 注油槍，油槍

grease mon·key /ˈ· ˌ··/ *n* [C] *slang* someone who repairs car engines or other machinery; MECHANIC【俚】汽車修理工，機器修理工

grease·paint /ˈgrisˌpent; ˈgriːs-peɪnt/ *n* [U] a thick soft kind of paint that actors use on their face or body〔演員塗在臉上或身上的〕油彩

grease·proof pa·per /ˈgrisˌpruf ˈpepɚ; ˌgriːs-pruːf ˈpeɪpə/ *n* [U] *BrE* a kind of paper that GREASE¹ (1) cannot pass through, used in cooking and for wrapping food【英】〔用於烹調、包裝食品的〕防油紙，蠟紙; WAXED PAPER *AmE*【美】

greas·er /ˈgrisɚ; ˈgriːsə/ *n* [C] **1** someone who puts GREASE on machinery to make it run smoothly 潤滑工 **2** *AmE slang* a very offensive word for someone from Latin America, especially Mexico【美俚】拉美佬; 墨西哥佬〔對拉丁美洲人，尤其是墨西哥人的冒犯用語〕

greas·y /ˈgrisɪ; ˈgriːsi/ *adj* **1** covered in grease or oil 多脂的，沾油脂的: *greasy food* 多脂的食品 | *greasy hair* 油膩膩的頭髮 **2** slippery 滑的: *The roads are greasy after the rain.* 雨後道路很滑。**3** too polite and friendly in a way that seems insincere or unpleasant; SMARMY 諂媚的，虛情假意的 —**greasily** *adv* —**greasiness** *n* [U]

greasy spoon /ˌ·· ˈ·/ *n* [C] a small cheap restaurant that mainly serves fried (FRY¹ (1)) food〔主要供應油炸食品的〕廉價小餐館

great /gret; greɪt/ *adj*

① VERY GOOD 很好
② A LOT/VERY MUCH 很多
③ LARGE 大的
④ IMPORTANT 重要的
⑤ FAMILY 家庭
⑥ OTHER MEANINGS 其他意思

G

① VERY GOOD 很好

1 *spoken*【口】**a)** very good; excellent 非常好的，好極的: *We had a great time at the fair.* 我們在遊樂場玩得非常愉快。| *You can come after all? Great!* 你最終還是可以來？太好了！| *It's great to see you again!* 再次見到你太好了。**b)** used when you really think that something is not good, satisfactory or enjoyable at all〔用來表示其實認為某事不好，不令人滿意或不令人愉快〕: *"Daniel's cancelled the party." "Oh great!"* "丹尼爾取消了聚會。""那太好了！"〔此為反話〕

2 ►IN GOOD HEALTH 身體健康◄ feeling well and happy 感到健康快樂的: *I feel great this morning!* 今天早上我感覺棒極了！

3 ►SKILFUL/SUCCESSFUL 熟練的/成功的◄ a) considered to be one of the best in the world and therefore admired by many people 偉大的，卓越的: *a great work of art* 偉大的藝術品 | *one of the greatest boxers of all time* 迄今最偉大的拳擊手之一 **b)** able to do something well 擅長的: [+at] *Joanna's great at chess.* 喬安娜精通國際象棋。

4 the greats the most famous and successful performers, especially in sport or entertainment 大人物，巨擘〔尤指體育或娛樂方面〕: **the all-time greats**: *Charlie Chaplin is one of the all-time cinema greats.* 查理·卓別林是電影史上罕見的偉大演員。

5 be no great shakes to not be very good or skilful 並不好; 並不高明: *Alex thinks he's an ace at tennis, but he's no great shakes.* 亞歷克斯認為自己是網球高手，可是他的水平並不怎麼樣。

6 ►VERY SUITABLE 很合適的◄ *informal* to be very useful or suitable for something【非正式】非常有用的，非常合適的: [+for] *This knife's great for peeling vegetables.* 這把刀非常適合削蔬菜皮。

7 go great guns *informal* to do something very fast and successfully【非正式】順利地快速大幹: *Their campaign began slowly, but now they're going great guns.* 他們的運動開始時很慢，但現在進展很快。

② A LOT/VERY MUCH 很多

8 great care/pleasure/strength etc a lot of care etc 極大的關心/快樂/力氣等: *Take great care with those glasses.* 拿那些玻璃杯時要非常小心。| *It gives me great pleasure to introduce tonight's speaker.* 介紹今晚的演講人，我非常高興。

9 a great deal a lot 許多，大量: *I've travelled a great deal.* 我到過很多地方。| [+of] *I have a great deal of work right now.* 我此刻有許多工作要做。

10 a great number/quantity/extent etc a very large number etc 許多/大量/很大程度等: *Agnes survived the accident and went on to live to a great age* (=she was very old when she died). 阿格尼斯在事故中倖免於難，後來活到很大的年紀。| **the great many** (=very many) 非常多的 | **the great majority** (=almost all) 絕大多數 *a proposal supported by the great majority of members* 得到絕大多數成員支持的提案

11 great friend/admirer etc a very good friend, a very keen admirer etc 很要好的朋友/十分熱烈的愛慕者

12 be a great one for writing/sailing/football etc *BrE* to enjoy writing, sailing, football etc very much【英】酷愛寫作/帆船運動/足球等: *Adam's a great one for football – he never misses a match.* 亞當酷愛足球——他從來不錯過任何一場比賽。

13 a great talker/reader etc someone who enjoys doing a lot of talking, reading etc 愛說話的人/熱衷於讀書的人等

③ LARGE 大的

14 ►VERY LARGE 很大的◄ very large and impressive 巨大的，壯觀的: *The great northern plain is divided by two rivers.* 北部的大平原被兩條河分開。| *a great herd of buffalo* 一大羣水牛 —see 見 BIG (USAGE)

15 great big/stupid/fat etc *spoken* used to emphasize how big, stupid etc something or someone is【口】巨大的/極愚蠢的/極肥胖的等: *They live in a great big house.* 他們住在一棟巨大的房子裡。

16 huge/enormous great *BrE spoken* used to emphasize how big something is【英口】巨大的, 龐大的: *There's a huge great spider in the bath.* 浴缸裡有一隻碩大的蜘蛛。

④ **IMPORTANT** 重要的

17 ►IMPORTANT 重要的◄ [only before noun 僅用於名詞前] especially important or serious 特別重要的; 格外嚴重的: *a great state occasion* 國家的盛典 | *the great political issues of our time* 這時代的重大政治問題

18 the great advantage of/the great thing about the most important advantage of something〔某物〕最主要優點: *The great thing about nylon is that it's extremely tough.* 尼龍的最大優點是極其牢固。

19 ►HAVING INFLUENCE 具有影響◄ having a lot of influence or power as a result of what you have achieved 強大的, 偉大的: *We must strive to make our country great again.* 我們必須努力奮鬥, 使祖國再次強大起來。| *the great man himself* 這位偉人自己

20 the Great used in the name or title of someone or something to show their importance〔用於某人的名字、頭銜或某物的名稱中, 以示其重要性〕: *King Alfred the Great* 阿爾弗雷德大帝

21 the great and the good *formal or humorous* people who are considered important【正式或幽默】大人物

⑤ **FAMILY** 家庭

22 great-grandmother/great-grandfather etc the grandmother etc of one of your parents (外) 曾祖母/(外) 曾祖父等 —see picture at 參見 FAMILY 圖

23 great-granddaughter/great-nephew etc the GRANDDAUGHTER of your child; the GRANDSON of your brother or sister etc (外) 曾孫女/姪[甥] (外) 孫等 —see picture at 參見 FAMILY 圖

⑥ **OTHER MEANINGS** 其他意思

24 Great Scott/Great Heavens! *old-fashioned* used to express surprise【過時】天哪!〔表示驚訝〕

25 Greater used before the name of a city to mean the city and its outer areas〔用於城市名稱前, 指該市及其周邊地區〕: *Greater Manchester* 大曼徹斯特

26 be great with child *biblical* to be PREGNANT【聖經】懷孕 —**greatness** *n* [U]

great·coat /ˋgret͵kot; ˈgreɪtkəʊt/ *n* [C] a long heavy coat 厚大衣

great-grand·child /· ˈ··/ *n* [C] the GRANDCHILD of your child 曾孫(女), 曾外孫(女)

3 **great·ly** /ˋgretlɪ; ˈgreɪtli/ *adv formal* [usually before verb or participle 一般用於動詞或過去分詞前] extremely or very much【正式】非常, 很: *We greatly regret the trouble we have caused.* 我們對所引起的麻煩感到非常抱歉。| *a greatly improved design* 得到極大改善的設計

grebe /grib; griːb/ *n* [C] a bird similar to a duck 鸊鷉

Gre·cian /ˋgriʃən; ˈgriːʃən/ *adj literary* from ancient Greece, or having a style or appearance that is considered typical of ancient Greece【文】古希臘的; 古希臘式的

Gre·co-, Graeco- /ˋgriko; griːkəʊ/ *prefix* **1** of ancient Greece; Greek 古希臘的; 希臘的 **2** ancient Greek and 古希臘和: *Greco-Roman art* 古希臘-羅馬藝術

greed /grid; griːd/ *n* [U] **1** a strong desire for more food or drink than you need 貪食, 貪喝: **pure greed** *It's pure greed but I'd love some more of that cake.* 這完全是貪吃, 不過我很想再吃一點那塊蛋糕。**2** a strong desire for more money, power, possessions etc than you need 貪婪: *a man driven by greed and envy* 受貪婪和妒嫉驅使的人

greed·y /ˋgridɪ; ˈgriːdi/ *adj* **1** wanting more food or drink than you need 貪吃的, 貪喝的: *Don't be greedy – leave some cake for us.* 別貪心 —— 給我們留點蛋糕。| *You greedy pig!* 你這貪吃豬! **2** always wanting more money, possessions etc〔對金錢、財產等〕貪婪的, 渴望的: **greedy for profit/power/fame etc** *The company had become too greedy for profit.* 這家公司對利潤過分貪婪。—**greedily** *adv* —**greediness** *n* [U]

Greek¹ /grik; griːk/ *n* **1** [U] the language of modern or ancient Greece 希臘語; 古希臘語 **2** [C] someone from Greece 希臘人 **3** [C] *AmE* a member of a SORORITY or FRATERNITY (2) at an American college or university【美】〔美國大學裡的〕女生[男生]聯誼會會員 **4 it's all Greek to me** *informal* used to say that you cannot understand something【非正式】我(對此)一竅不通

Greek² *adj* **1** from or connected with Greece 來自希臘的; 希臘的 **2 Greek god** *informal* a very attractive man【非正式】美男子

1 **green¹** /grin; griːn/ *adj*

2 **1 ►COLOUR** 顏色◄ having the colour of grass or leaves 綠色的: *Go on – the traffic lights have turned green!* 走吧 —— 信號燈已經變綠色了! | *green eyes* 綠色的眼睛 —see picture on page A5 參見 A5 頁圖

2 ►GRASSY 長滿草的◄ covered with green grass 鋪滿綠草的, 長滿綠草的: *green fields* 綠油油的農田

3 ►FRUIT/PLANT 水果/植物◄ very young, or not yet ready to be eaten 尚未成熟的: *The bananas are still green.* 香蕉還沒熟。| *new green shoots on the roses* 玫瑰叢上的嫩綠色新芽

4 ►WITHOUT EXPERIENCE 沒有經驗的◄ *informal* young and lacking experience【非正式】年輕而無經驗的: *a new batch of very green recruits* 新招來的一批生手

5 ►ILL 生病的◄ *informal* looking pale and unhealthy because you are ill【非正式】〔臉色〕蒼白的, 不健康的: *George looked a bit green the next morning.* 喬治第二天早上看上去臉色有點蒼白。| **green around/about the gills** (=looking ill or frightened) 臉色蒼白; 面無人色

6 ►ENVIRONMENT 環境◄ connected with the environment 環境的: *green issues* 環境問題

7 ►POLITICS 政治◄ belonging to the Green political party 綠黨的

8 green with envy wishing very much that you had something that someone else has 十分嫉妒的

9 the green-eyed monster *humorous or literary* jealousy【幽默或文】嫉妒

10 have green fingers *BrE*【英】, **have a green thumb** *AmE*【美】to be good at making plants grow 擅長園藝

11 the green stuff *AmE informal* money【美, 非正式】錢

green² *n* **1** [C,U] the colour of grass and leaves 綠色: *a room decorated in pale blues and greens* 以淺藍色和綠色裝飾的房間 **2 greens** [plural] **a)** *informal* vegetables with large green leaves【非正式】綠色闊葉蔬菜; 青菜: *Eat your greens.* 要吃青菜。**b)** *AmE* leaves and branches used for decoration, especially at Christmas【美】〔尤指聖誕節用於裝飾的〕青枝綠葉 —compare 比較 GREENERY **3** [C] a level area of grass, especially in the middle of a village〔村莊中心部位的〕一塊草地: *playing cricket on the green* 在村裡草地上打板球 —see also 另見 BOWLING GREEN, VILLAGE GREEN **4** [C] a smooth flat area of grass around each hole on a GOLF COURSE 球洞區〔高爾夫球場上每個球洞四周的平坦草地〕—see picture on page A23 參見 A23 頁圖 **5 Green** [C] someone who supports the Green political party 綠黨支持者 (spoken) 2 (written) 3

green³ *v* **1** to fill an area with growing plants in order to make it more attractive 綠化: *the challenge of greening the city* 綠化城市的挑戰性任務 **2** to make a person or organization realize the importance of environmental problems 使〔某人、某組織〕意識到環境問題的重要性: *the greening of public opinion* 使輿論認

識到環境問題如何重要

green·back /ˋgrin͵bæk; ˈgriːnbæk/ *n* [C] *AmE informal* an American BANKNOTE【美, 非正式】美鈔

green bean /͵· ˈ·/ *n* [C] a long thin green vegetable which is picked before the beans inside it grow 青菜豆, 嫩菜豆; FRENCH BEAN *BrE*【英】—see picture on page A9 參見 A9 頁圖

green belt /ˈ· ·/ *n* [C,U] an area of land around a city where building is not allowed, in order to protect fields and woods〔城市周圍的〕綠化帶

green card /͵· ˈ·/ *n* [C] **1** a British motor insurance document that you need when you drive abroad〔英國〕綠色保險證〔在國外開車時使用〕**2** a document that a foreigner must have in order to work legally in the US〔美國的〕綠卡

green·e·ry /ˋgrinərɪ; ˈgriːnəri/ *n* [U] green leaves and plants 綠葉和綠色植物

green·field site /ˋgrinfild ͵saɪt; ˈgriːnfiːld ͵saɪt/ *n* [C] a piece of land that has never been built on before〔從未建過房子的〕地皮

green·fly /ˋgrinflaɪ; ˈgriːnflaɪ/ *n plural* **greenflies** [C] a very small green insect that feeds on and damages young plants 蚜蟲

green·gage /ˋgrinˋgedʒ; ˈgriːngeɪdʒ/ *n* [C] a juicy greenish-yellow PLUM[1] (1) 青梅子, 青李子

green·gro·cer /ˋgrin͵grosə; ˈgriːn͵grəʊsə/ *n* [C] *especially BrE*【尤英】**1** someone who owns or works in a shop selling fruit and vegetables 蔬菜水果商; 菜[水果]販 **2 greengrocer's** a greengrocer's shop 蔬菜水果店

green·horn /ˋgrin͵hɔrn; ˈgriːnhɔːn/ *n* [C] *informal* someone who lacks experience and can be easily deceived【非正式】沒有經驗的人, 生手, 新手

green·house /ˋgrin͵haus; ˈgriːnhaʊs/ *n* [C] a glass building used for growing plants that need warmth, light, and protection 溫室, 暖房

greenhouse ef·fect /ˈ·· ·͵·/ *n* [singular] the gradual warming of the air surrounding the Earth as a result of heat being trapped by POLLUTION 溫室效應 —see also 另見 GLOBAL WARMING

greenhouse gas /ˈ·· ͵·/ *n* [C] a gas, especially CARBON DIOXIDE or METHANE, that is thought to trap heat above the Earth and cause the greenhouse effect 溫室氣體〔被認為導致溫室效應的氣體, 尤指二氧化碳或甲烷〕

green·ish /ˋgrinɪʃ; ˈgriːnɪʃ/ *adj* slightly green 略帶綠色的: *a greenish tinge* 一抹綠色

green light /ˈ· ·/ *n* [C] **1** the colour of a TRAFFIC LIGHT that shows cars they can go forward 交通綠燈 **2 give sb the green light** to allow a project, plan etc to begin 給某人開綠燈〔允許某工程、計劃等啟動〕: *The government has given the green light to Sunday trading.* 政府已經給星期日貿易開了綠燈。

green·light /ˋgrin͵laɪt; ˈgriːnlaɪt/ *v* [T] to give official permission for something to be started 正式批准〔某事〕啟動

green on·ion /͵· ˈ··/ *n* [C] *AmE* an onion with a small white round part and a long green stem, usually eaten raw【美】大葱; SPRING ONION *BrE*【英】

green pa·per /͵· ˈ··/ *n* [C] a document produced by the British government containing proposals to be discussed, that may later be used in making laws 綠皮書〔英國政府編製的一種文件, 提出建議以供討論; 日後可能用作立法的依據〕—compare 比較 WHITE PAPER, BILL[1] (2)

green pep·per /͵· ˈ··/ *n* [C] a vegetable with green flesh and white seeds that you can cook or eat raw in SALADS 青椒, 甜椒

green pound /͵· ˈ·/ *n* [C,U] the value of the pound STERLING when exchanged for farm products in the EC 綠色英鎊〔指在歐共體內使用英鎊購買農產品時英鎊的價值〕

green rev·o·lu·tion /͵· ··ˈ··/ *n* [singular] **1** an increase in the amount that is produced by crops, such as wheat, due to improved scientific methods of farming 綠色革命〔指由於改進科學耕作法而產生的諸如小麥等農作物產量的增加〕**2** the new interest in protecting the environment that has developed in many parts of the world 環境革命〔指在世界許多地方出現的對保護環境的新興趣〕

green sal·ad /͵· ˈ··/ *n* [C] a SALAD made with LETTUCE and other raw green vegetables〔萵苣和其他綠色生蔬菜製作的〕綠色色拉

green tea /͵· ˈ·/ *n* [U] light-coloured tea made from leaves that have been heated with steam 綠茶

Green·wich Mean Time /ˋgrɪnɪdʒ ˋmin ͵taɪm; ͵grenɪtʃ ˈmiːn taɪm/ abbreviation 縮寫為 **GMT** *n* [U] the time as measured at Greenwich in London 格林尼治(平均)時間

greet /grit; griːt/ *v* [T] **1** to say hello to someone or welcome them 問候, 迎接, 招呼: *Mr Grimshaw got up from behind his desk to greet me.* 格里姆肖先生從桌後站起來迎接我。| **greet sb with a smile/kiss etc** *Billie greeted us with a cheerful grin.* 比莉燦爛一笑給我們打招呼。**2** [always+adv/prep] to react to something in a particular way 對〔某事〕作出反應: **be greeted with** *The proposal was greeted with bursts of laughter.* 對這項提議的反應是陣陣笑聲。**3** to be the first thing you see or hear when you arrive somewhere 最先映入〔某人的〕眼簾; 傳入〔某人的〕耳中: *As we entered, complete chaos greeted us.* 我們走進去時, 一片混亂景象映入眼簾。

greet·ing /ˋgritɪŋ; ˈgriːtɪŋ/ *n* [C] **1** words you use or something you do when you meet someone 問候, 招呼: *I said good morning to Diane, but she didn't return my greeting.* 我向黛安道早安, 可是她對我的招呼沒有回應。| **exchange greetings** (=greet each other) 互相問候 **2** [usually plural 一般用複數] a message saying that you hope someone will be happy, healthy etc 祝賀, 問候語, 祝願詞: *birthday greetings* 生日賀詞 **3 greetings!** *formal or humorous* used to say hello to someone【正式或幽默】你好! 喂!

greet·ings card /ˈ·· ͵·/ *n* [C] a card that you send to someone on their birthday, at Christmas etc〔生日、聖誕節等的〕賀卡

gre·gar·i·ous /grɪˋgɛrɪəs; grɪˈgeəriəs/ *adj* **1** friendly and preferring to be with others rather than alone; SOCIABLE[1] 愛交際的, 不喜獨處的 **2** *technical* gregarious animals tend to live in a group【術語】〔動物〕傾向於羣居的 —**gregariously** *adv* —**gregariousness** *n* [U]

Gre·go·ri·an cal·en·dar /grɛˋgorɪən ˋkæləndə; grɪ͵gɔːriən ˈkælɪ̣ndə/ *n* [singular] the system of arranging the 365 days of the year in months and giving numbers to the years from the birth of Christ, used in the West since 1582 公曆, 陽曆〔自1582年起在西方使用的曆法〕

Gregorian chant /·͵··· ˈ·/ *n* [C,U] a kind of church music for voices alone 格列高利聖咏〔一種無伴奏的合唱形式的宗教音樂〕

grem·lin /ˋgrɛmlɪn; ˈgremlɪ̣n/ *n* [C] an imaginary evil spirit that is blamed for problems in machinery, especially when no scientific explanation can be found〔傳說中使機器設備產生無法用科學解釋的故障的〕小妖精

gre·nade /grɪˋned; grɪ̣ˈneɪd/ *n* [C] a small bomb that can be thrown by hand or fired from a gun 手榴彈, 槍榴彈: *a hand grenade* 手榴彈

gren·a·dier /͵grɛnəˋdɪr; ͵grenəˈdɪə◂/ *n* [C] a soldier in a famous REGIMENT[1] (1) of the British army 擲彈兵〔英國軍隊某著名兵團的士兵〕

gren·a·dine /͵grɛnəˋdin; ˈgrenədiːn/ *n* [U] a sweet liquid made from POMEGRANATES that is used in drinks〔用於飲料的〕石榴糖漿

grew /gru; gruː/ *v* the past tense of GROW

grey[1] usually 一般作 **gray** *AmE*【美】/gre; greɪ/ *adj*

1 ►COLOUR 顏色◄ having a colour of black mixed with white, like the colour of ash 灰色的: *an old lady with grey hair* 頭髮灰白的老太太 | *a grey sky* 灰色的天空

2 ►HAIR 頭髮◄ having grey hair (有) 灰白頭髮的: **go**

grey *My brother went grey in his forties.* 我哥哥在四十多歲的時候頭髮就白了。—see picture on page A6 參見A6頁圖
3 ▶FACE 臉◀ looking pale because you are tired, frightened, or ill〔人由於疲倦、害怕或生病而〕臉色蒼白的: *Noel's face was gray with fatigue.* 諾埃爾累得臉色蒼白。
4 ▶BORING 乏味的◀ boring and unattractive; GLOOMY 單調乏味的; 暗淡的; 陰鬱的: *the grey anonymous men in government offices* 政府部門裡那些了無生氣的無名小卒
5 ▶OF OLD PEOPLE 老年人的◀ *BrE* connected with old people【英】老年人的: *the grey vote* 老年人的投票
6 grey area an area of law or science that cannot be dealt with in a definite way because it is outside those areas that have clear rules and limits 灰色領域〔指法律或科學中未有明確規則和範圍, 因而難以處理的那些領域〕

grey² usually 一般作 **gray** *AmE*【美】*n* [C,U] the colour of smoke and rain clouds 灰色: *dull greys and browns* 各種暗灰色和棕色 —see picture on page A5 參見A5頁圖

grey³ usually 一般作 **gray** *AmE*【美】*v* [I] if someone greys, their hair becomes grey〔頭髮〕開始變灰白色: *Jim's beginning to gray at the temples.* 吉姆已經開始兩鬢斑白。

grey·hound /ˈgreˌhaund; ˈgreɪhaʊnd/ *n* [C] a type of thin dog that can run very fast and is used in races 靈猩〔一種身體瘦長, 跑得很快的犬, 常用於比賽〕—see picture at 參見 DOG¹ 圖

grey·ish usually 一般作 **grayish** *AmE*【美】/ˈgreɪʃ; ˈgreɪ-ɪʃ/ *adj* slightly grey 略帶灰色的

grey mat·ter /ˈ· ˌ··/ *n* [U] *informal* your intelligence【非正式】智力

grid /grɪd; grɪd/ *n* **1** [C] a metal frame with bars across it 金屬格柵 —see also 另見 CATTLE GRID **2** [C] a pattern of straight lines that cross each other and form squares 方格圖案 **3 the grid** *BrE* the network of electricity supply wires that connects POWER STATIONS【英】電力網, 輸電網: *the national grid* 全國電力網 **4** [C] a system of numbered squares printed on a map so that the exact position of any place can be found〔地圖上的〕坐標方格 **5** [C] a set of starting positions for all the cars in a motor race〔汽車賽中的〕賽車出發點

grid·dle /ˈgrɪdḷ; ˈgrɪdl/ *n* [C] a round iron plate that is used for cooking flat cakes on top of a STOVE¹ (2) or over a fire〔用來烙餅的〕圓形平底鍋

grid·dle·cake /ˈgrɪdḷˌkek; ˈgrɪdlˌkeɪk/ *n* [C] *AmE* a PANCAKE (2)【美】烙餅, 烤餅

grid·i·ron /ˈgrɪdˌaɪɚn; ˈgrɪdaɪən/ *n* [C] **1** an open frame of metal bars for cooking meat or fish over a very hot fire〔用來燒烤肉或魚的〕烤架 **2** *AmE* a field marked in white lines for American football【美】〔畫有白線的〕美式足球場

grid·lock /ˈgrɪdlɑk; ˈgrɪdlɒk/ *n* [U] *especially AmE*【尤美】**1** a situation in which streets in a city are so full of cars that they cannot move〔街道上車輛過多造成的〕交通堵塞 **2** a situation in which nothing can happen, usually because people disagree strongly〔由於強烈的意見分歧而造成的〕僵局: *Clinton is in gridlock with the Congress.* 克林頓與國會陷入僵局。—**gridlocked** *adj*

grief /grif; griːf/ *n* **1** [U] extreme sadness, especially because someone you love has died 極度悲傷〔尤指因所愛之人去世而感受的悲痛〕: **[+over/at]** *The grief she felt over Helen's death was almost unbearable.* 她因海倫的去世而感到悲痛難當。**2** [C] something that makes you feel extremely sad 傷心事, 不幸: *It was a grief to him that he had never had any children.* 他一直沒有小孩, 這是他的傷心事。**3 good grief!** *spoken* used when you are slightly surprised or annoyed【口】哎喲!〔用於略感驚訝或氣惱之時〕: *Good grief! This must have cost you a fortune! Where did you get the money?* 哎呀! 這肯定花了你很多錢! 你從哪裡弄到這錢的? **4 come to grief** to fail, or to be harmed or destroyed in an accident 失敗;〔在事故中〕受損; 被毀: *The expedition shortly came to grief on Vanikoro Reef.* 這次探險不久就在瓦尼科羅因觸礁而失敗。**5 give sb grief** *informal* to criticize someone in an annoying way【非正式】數落[責備]某人: *I'd better go home now – my Mum'll give me grief if I'm not back for dinner.* 我最好是現在回家——如果我不回去吃晚飯, 我媽會罵我。

grief-strick·en /ˈ· ˌ··/ also 又作 **grief-struck** /ˈ· ·/ *adj* feeling very sad because of something that has happened 感到極度悲傷的, 悲痛欲絕的

griev·ance /ˈgrivəns; ˈgriːvəns/ *n* [C,U] something that you complain about because you feel you have been treated unfairly 不平, 委屈, 不滿, 抱怨, 牢騷: **[+against]** *Anyone who has a legitimate grievance against the company can take it to the committee.* 對公司有正當不滿情緒的人可以把意見提交給委員會。| **air your grievances** (=tell other people you feel you have been treated unfairly) 把你的委屈講出來 *The meetings provide employees with an opportunity to air their grievances.* 這些會議使雇員有機會申訴自己的不滿。| **nurse a grievance** (=think about it continuously) 心存不滿 | **sense of grievance** (=a feeling that you have been treated unfairly) 委屈感 *Grant's deep sense of grievance at not being promoted* 格蘭特對沒有得到晉升而感到的極度委屈

grieve /griv; griːv/ *v* **1** [I,T] to feel extremely sad, especially because someone you love has died〔尤指所愛之人去世而〕感到悲痛[傷心]: *People need time to grieve after the death of a loved one.* 人們在所愛之人去世後需要一段哀悼的時間。| **grieve sth** *The family grieved the loss of its only son.* 這家人為他們獨子的去世而傷心。**2** [T] if something grieves you, it makes you feel very unhappy 使傷心: **it grieves sb to think/say/see etc** *It grieves me to think of all the money we've spent on that ungrateful brat.* 想到我們在那個忘恩負義的小壞蛋身上所花的那些錢真讓我傷心。

grieved /grivd; griːvd/ *adj literary* very sad and upset【文】悲傷的, 傷心的: **be grieved (at)** *I am deeply grieved at this sad news.* 我聽到這個悲慘的消息深感悲傷。

griev·ous /ˈgrivəs; ˈgriːvəs/ *adj* **1** *formal* very serious and likely to be very harmful【正式】嚴重的; 可能很有害的: *a grievous error* 嚴重錯誤 | *a grievous shortage of hospital beds* 醫院牀位的嚴重短缺 **2** *especially literary* a grievous wound or pain is severe and hurts a lot【尤文】〔傷痛〕劇烈的 —**grievously** *adv* —**grievousness** *n* [U]

grievous bod·i·ly harm /ˌ·· ˌ··· ˈ·/ *n* [U] *BrE law* serious injury caused by a criminal attack; GBH【英, 法律】〔因罪犯襲擊而造成的〕身體嚴重受傷, 重傷

grif·fin, gryphon /ˈgrɪfɪn; ˈgrɪfən/ *n* [C] an imaginary animal in stories that has a lion's body and an EAGLE's wings and head〔神話中的〕獅身鷹首獸

grif·ter /ˈgrɪftɚ; ˈgrɪftə/ *n* [C] *AmE informal* someone who dishonestly obtains something, especially money【美, 非正式】以不正當方式獲取某物〔尤指錢財〕的人 —**grift** *v* [T]

grill¹ /grɪl; grɪl/ *v* **1** [I,T] if you grill something, or if it grills, you cook it by putting it close to very strong direct heat 燒烤, 烤製: *Grill the burgers for eight minutes each side.* 把這些製作漢堡包的牛肉片每面烤八分鐘。**2** [T] to ask someone a lot of difficult questions in order to make them explain their actions, opinions etc 對〔某人〕嚴加盤問: *I was grilled by customs officers for several hours.* 我被海關官員盤問了好幾個小時。

grill² *n* [C] **1** *BrE* a part of a COOKER (1) in which very strong heat from above cooks food on a metal shelf below【英】〔爐具中熱力自上而下的〕烤架; BROILER (1) *AmE*【美】: *Pop it under the grill for five minutes.* 把它放在烤架下烤上五分鐘。**2** a flat frame with metal bars across it that can be put over a fire, so that food can be cooked quickly on it 柵狀烤架 **3** a place where you can buy and

G

eat grilled food 燒烤店, 燒烤餐館: *Henry J. Bean's Bar and Grill* 亨利·J.比恩酒吧燒烤餐館 —see also 另見 MIXED GRILL **4** a grille〔門窗〕護欄;〔汽車散熱器的〕護柵

grille, grill /grɪl; grɪl/ *n* [C] **1** a frame with metal bars or wire across it that is put in front of a window or door for protection 門窗護欄 **2** the metal bars at the front of a car that protect the RADIATOR (2)〔汽車散熱器的〕護柵

gril·ling /ˈgrɪlɪŋ; ˈgrɪlɪŋ/ *n* **give sb a grilling** to ask someone a lot of difficult questions in order to make them explain their actions or opinions 嚴加盤問某人

grill pan /ˈ· ·/ *n* [C] a square flat pan, used under a GRILL[2] (1)〔用在烤架下的〕平底方盤 —see picture at 參見 PAN[1] 圖

grim /grɪm; grɪm/ *adj* **grimmer, grimmest**

1 ►SITUATION/NEWS 情況/消息◄ making you feel worried and unhappy 令人擔憂發愁的: *There's more grim news from the war zone.* 戰區傳來更多令人擔憂的消息。| **things look grim (for)** *Things look pretty grim for farmers right now.* 對農民來説目前情況相當嚴峻。| **grim prospect** (=something bad that will probably happen) 堪憂的前景

2 ►PLACE/BUILDING ETC 地點/建築物等◄ unpleasant and unattractive 令人不愉快的, 討厭的: *a grim industrial town* 令人生厭的工業城鎮

3 ►PERSON 人◄ looking or sounding very serious because the situation is very bad〔神色或口氣〕嚴肅的, 嚴酷的: *The grim-faced judge sentenced Burke to life-imprisonment.* 面孔鐵板的法官判處伯克終身監禁。| **grim determination** (=serious determination in spite of difficulties or dangers) 堅韌不拔的決心

4 feel grim *informal* to feel ill【非正式】感覺病了: *I felt a bit grim the morning after the party.* 聚會後的第二天早晨我感覺有點不舒服。

5 ►OF BAD QUALITY 劣質的◄ *BrE informal* very bad in quality【英, 非正式】質量很低的: *You should see some of her recent essays – they're pretty grim.* 你應該看看她最近寫的一些文章——質量很差。

6 hold/hang on for grim death *BrE informal* to hold something very tightly because you are afraid【英, 非正式】嚇得緊緊抓住〔某物〕—**grimly** *adv*: *Arnold smiled grimly.* 阿諾德陰冷地笑了笑。—**grimness** *n* [U]

G

gri·mace[1] /grɪˋmes; grɪˈmeɪs/ *v* [I] to twist your face in an ugly way because you do not like something, because you are feeling pain, or because you are trying to be funny〔因感到疼痛或開玩笑而〕扭曲臉部, 做怪相: *Toni muttered and grimaced at each tug of the comb.* 托妮每梳一下頭髮嘴裡便咕噥一聲並裝鬼臉。| **[+with]** *Baggio lay grimacing with pain.* 貝吉奧躺在那裡痛得嘴歪眼斜。

grimace[2] *n* [C] an expression you make by twisting your face because you do not like something or because you are feeling pain 臉部扭曲, 怪相, 鬼臉〔指不喜歡某物或感到疼痛時的面部表情〕: *Bernie gave a grimace of disgust and left the room.* 伯尼做了一個表示厭惡的鬼臉, 離開了房間。

grime /graɪm; graɪm/ *n* [U] dirt that forms a black layer on surfaces〔表面的〕塵垢, 污垢: *black with grime* 因污垢而發黑

grim·y /ˈgraɪmɪ; ˈgraɪmi/ *adj* covered with dirt 滿是污垢的, 蒙上灰塵的: *grimy windows* 蒙着灰塵的窗子

grin[1] /grɪn; grɪn/ *v* [I] **grinned, grinning 1** to smile widely 露着牙齒笑, 咧着嘴笑: *Grinning sheepishly, James admitted he was seeing Sue.* 詹姆斯尷尬地露齒一笑, 承認他正和蘇約會。| **[+at]** *Stop grinning at me, you stupid jackass!* 別朝我咧着嘴笑, 你這傻瓜! | **[+with]** *grinning with delight* 高興得咧着嘴笑 | **grin from ear to ear** (=grin very widely) 笑容滿面 **2 grin and bear it** to accept and bear an unpleasant or difficult situation without complaining, usually because you realize there is nothing you can do to make it better 苦笑着忍受, 逆來順受〔通常因知道無法挽救而接受某一尷尬局面或困境〕

grin[2] *n* [C] a wide smile 露齒笑, 咧嘴笑: *a broad grin* 合不攏嘴的笑 | *Take that cheeky grin off your face!* 別那樣厚着臉皮笑! —see also 另見 **wipe the smile/grin off sb's face** (WIPE[1] (7))

grind[1] /graɪnd; graɪnd/ *v past tense and past participle* **ground** /graʊnd; graʊnd/

1 ►INTO SMALL PIECES 變成碎末◄ [T] **a)** also 又作 **grind up** [T] to break something such as corn or coffee beans into small pieces or powder, either in a machine or between two hard surfaces 把〔玉米、咖啡豆等〕碾碎, 磨成粉末 **b)** *AmE* to cut food, especially raw meat, into very small pieces by putting it through a machine【美】〔用機器將食物, 尤指肉〕絞碎; MINCE[1] (1) *BrE*【英】

2 ►SMOOTH/SHARP 光滑的/鋒利的◄ [T] to make something smooth or sharp by rubbing it on a hard surface or by using a machine 磨光, 磨利: *a stone for grinding knives and scissors* 磨刀剪的石頭 | *The lenses are ground to a high standard of precision.* 鏡片被磨到很高的精確度。

3 ►PRESS STH DOWN 向下擠壓某物◄ [T always+adv/prep] to press something down into a surface and rub it with a strong twisting movement 用力旋轉地擠壓: **grind sth into/in** *He dropped a cigar butt and ground it into the carpet with his heel.* 他扔下雪茄煙頭, 用腳後跟把它踩進地毯裡。

4 grind your teeth to rub your upper and lower teeth together making a noise 把牙齒磨得嘎嘎響

5 grind to a halt a) if a vehicle grinds to a halt, it stops gradually〔車輛〕慢慢停下來: *Traffic ground to a halt as it approached the accident site.* 車輛在靠近事故現場時慢慢停了下來。**b)** if a country, organization, or process grinds to a halt, it gradually stops working〔國家、組織或進程〕逐漸停頓, 慢慢癱瘓: *As more and more workers joined the strike, Britain's economy was grinding to a halt.* 由於越來越多的工人參加罷工, 英國的經濟逐漸趨於停滯。

6 grind the faces of the poor to make poor people work very hard and give them almost nothing in return 壓榨窮人 —see also 另見 **have an axe to grind** (AXE[1] (4))

grind sb ↔ **down** *phr v* [T] to treat someone in a cruel way for such a long time that they lose all courage and hope; OPPRESS 長期欺壓某人〔使其達到絕望地步〕: *Years of dictatorship had ground the people down.* 多年的獨裁統治已使人民處於絕境。

grind on *phr v* [I] to continue for an unpleasantly long time 令人厭煩地長期持續: *Winter grinds on until March.* 冬季一直要持續到三月份。

grind sth ↔ **out** *phr v* [T] to produce information, writing, music etc in such large amounts that it becomes boring 大量撰寫, 大量提供〔信息、文字或音樂作品等〕: *Frank just keeps grinding out detective stories.* 弗蘭克不停地大量撰寫偵探故事。

grind[2] *n* **1** [singular] something that is hard work and physically or mentally tiring 令人疲勞[厭倦]的苦事: *I find the journey to work a real grind.* 我認為每天上班的行程真辛苦。| **the daily grind** (=things that you have to do every day that are boring) 乏味的日常苦差使 **2** [C] *AmE informal* a student who never does anything except study; SWOT[1]【美, 非正式】埋頭學習[死讀書]的學生

grind·er /ˈgraɪndɚ; ˈgraɪndə/ *n* [C] a machine for crushing coffee beans, PEPPERCORNS etc into powder 研磨機, 碾磨機: *a pepper grinder* 辣椒碾磨機

grind·ing /ˈgraɪndɪŋ; ˈgraɪndɪŋ/ *adj* [only before noun 僅用於名詞前] **1 grinding poverty/misery** a situation that makes your life very difficult and unhappy, and never seems to improve 貧困/痛苦不堪 **2** a grinding noise is the continuous unpleasant noise of machinery parts rubbing together〔指機器部件互相摩擦產生的聲音〕持續而刺耳的

grind·stone /ˈgraɪndˌston; ˈgraɪndstəʊn/ *n* [C] a large round stone that is turned like a wheel while tools, knives etc are rubbed against it to make them sharp〔用來磨快刀等工具的〕砂輪 —see also 另見 **keep your nose to**

the grindstone (NOSE[1] (15))

grin·go /ˋgrɪŋgo; ˈgrɪŋgəʊ/ *n plural* **gringos** [C] an offensive word for someone from North America, used by people in Latin American countries 外國佬〔拉丁美洲國家的人對北美洲人的冒犯用語〕

grip[1] /grɪp; grɪp/ *n*

1 ▶FIRM HOLD 緊握◀ [C usually singular 一般用單數] the way you hold something tightly or your ability to do this 緊握; 握緊: *Don't loosen your grip on the rope or you'll fall.* 抓住繩索別鬆手, 不然你會掉下去。

2 ▶POWER 權力◀ [singular] power and control over someone or something〔對某人或某事物的〕控制: **have a grip on sth** *The chancellor doesn't seem to have a very firm grip on the economy.* 這位總理看來沒有牢牢地控制住經濟。

3 come/get to grips with to understand and deal with a difficult problem or situation 了解並應付〔困難問題或局面〕: *I've never really got to grips with this new technology.* 我還從來沒有真正了解這種新技術。

4 lose your grip to become less confident and less able to deal with a situation〔對某局面〕信心不足; 失去控制: *I handled that interview very badly – I must be losing my grip.* 今天的面試我表現很糟糕 —— 我大概是無能為力了。

5 get/keep a grip on yourself to start controlling your emotions when you have been very upset〔在生氣一段時間之後〕開始控制自己的感情: *Stop being hysterical and get a grip on yourself.* 別歇斯底里的, 冷靜下來。

6 be in the grip of to be experiencing a very unpleasant situation that cannot be controlled or stopped 處於〔無法控制的不利局勢〕之中: *a country in the grip of famine* 受饑荒困擾的國家

7 ▶STOP STH SLIPPING 制止某物滑動◀ [C] **a)** a special part of a handle that has a rough surface so that you can hold it firmly without it slipping 有粗糙表面的把手〔可以緊握而不滑動〕: *a racquet with a rubber grip* 帶防滑橡膠手柄的球拍 —see picture on page A23 參見A23頁圖 **b)** the ability of something to stay on a surface without slipping 黏力, 防滑力: *I want some tennis shoes with a good grip.* 我要幾雙防滑力很好的網球鞋。

8 ▶FOR HAIR 用於頭髮◀ [C] *BrE* a HAIRGRIP【英】髮夾

9 ▶CAMERAMAN 攝影師◀ [C] someone whose job is to move the cameras around while a television show or film is being made〔拍電視節目或電影時〕管理攝像[攝影]機的工作人員

10 ▶BAG 袋, 包◀ [C] *old-fashioned* a bag or case used for travelling【過時】旅行袋[箱]

grip[2] *v* **gripped, gripping 1** [I,T] to hold something very tightly 緊握: *I gripped the handrail tightly and tried not to look down.* 我緊緊抓住扶手, 盡量不往下看。**2** [T] to have a strong effect on someone or something 對〔某人或某事物〕具有強烈影響: *a country gripped by economic problems* 受經濟問題嚴重影響的國家 | *Panic suddenly gripped me when it was my turn to speak.* 輪到我說話時, 我突然驚慌起來。**3** [T] to hold someone's attention and interest 吸引〔某人的〕注意[興趣]: *a story that really grips you* 確實能吸引你的故事 **4** [T] if something grips a surface, it stays on it without slipping 緊附於〔某表面而不滑動〕: *Radial tires grip the road well.* 子午線輪胎在路面上防滑能力很好。—see also 另見 GRIPPING

gripe[1] /graɪp; graɪp/ *v* [I] to complain about something continuously and in an annoying way 不停地抱怨, 發牢騷: [+about] *Joe came in griping about how cold it was outside.* 喬走進來, 抱怨外面太冷。

gripe[2] *n informal*【非正式】**1** [C] something unimportant that you complain about 抱怨〔尤指小事情〕: *My main gripe was the price of refreshments.* 我主要抱怨的是點心的價格。**2 the gripes** *old-fashioned* sudden bad stomach pains【過時】胃絞痛

gripe wa·ter /ˈ· ˌ··/ *n* [U] *BrE* a liquid medicine given to babies when they have stomach pains【英】驅風劑〔治療小兒腹痛的藥水〕

grip·ing /ˋgraɪpɪŋ; ˈgraɪpɪŋ/ *adj* a griping pain is a sudden severe pain in the stomach〔胃腸突然〕絞痛的

grip·ping /ˋgrɪpɪŋ; ˈgrɪpɪŋ/ *adj* a gripping film, story etc is very exciting and interesting〔電影、故事等〕扣人心弦的, 引人入勝的 —**grippingly** *adv*

gris·ly /ˋgrɪzlɪ; ˈgrɪzli/ *adj* extremely unpleasant, usually because death, decay, or destruction is involved〔通常因涉及死亡、腐朽、破壞而〕令人極其厭惡的: *the grisly discovery of human remains in the cellar* 地窖中屍體的可怕發現

grist /grɪst; grɪst/ *n* **(all) grist to the mill** something additional that can be used for your advantage in a particular situation 可用來〔為自己〕謀利的事: *Any publicity is good – it's all grist to the mill.* 任何宣傳都是好的 —— 都可以用來謀取利益。

gris·tle /ˋgrɪsl; ˈgrɪsəl/ *n* [U] the part of meat that is not soft enough to eat〔肉食中的〕軟骨 —**gristly** *adj*

grit[1] /grɪt; grɪt/ *n* [U] **1** very small pieces of stone or sand that are scattered on frozen roads to make them less slippery〔撒在結冰的道路上防滑用的〕沙礫, 沙粒 **2** *informal* determination and courage【非正式】堅毅, 勇氣 **3 grits** *AmE* HOMINY grain that is roughly crushed before cooking, often eaten for breakfast【美】粗碾的穀物〔常於早餐食用〕—**gritty** *adj*

grit[2] *v* [T] **gritted, gritting 1** to scatter grit on a frozen road to make it less slippery 在結冰的道路上撒沙礫〔以防滑〕**2 grit your teeth** to use all your determination to continue in spite of difficulties 咬緊牙關, 下定決心: *Just grit your teeth and hang on – it will be over soon.* 咬緊牙關堅持下去吧, 事情很快會過去的。

grit·ter /ˋgrɪtɚ; ˈgrɪtə/ *n* [C] *BrE* a large vehicle that puts salt or sand on the roads in winter to make then less icy【英】〔冬天在道路上撒沙或鹽防滑的〕撒沙車, 撒鹽車; SALT TRUCK *AmE*【美】

griz·zle /ˋgrɪzl̩; ˈgrɪzəl/ *v* [I] *BrE informal*【英, 非正式】**1** if a baby or child grizzles, they cry quietly and continuously〔嬰兒或孩子〕不停地小聲哭泣 **2** to complain continuously in an annoying way 不停地抱怨

griz·zled /ˋgrɪzl̩d; ˈgrɪzəld/ *adj literary* having grey or greyish hair【文】頭髮花白的

griz·zly bear /ˌ·· ˈ·/ also 又作 **grizzly** *n* [C] a very large brownish-grey bear that lives in the Rocky Mountains of North America〔北美落基山脈的〕大灰熊

groan[1] /gron; grəʊn/ *v* [I] **1** to make a long deep sound because you are in pain, upset, or disappointed〔因疼痛、心煩或失望而〕呻吟, 發出低沉的聲音: *The kids all groaned when I switched off the TV.* 我關掉電視時孩子們都發出不滿的哼哼聲。| **moan and groan** (=complain a lot) 不停地抱怨 *I'm tired of him moaning and groaning all the time.* 他一天到晚不停地發牢騷, 我都聽膩了。**2** to make a sound similar to someone groaning 發出低沉的嘎吱聲: *The old tree groaned in the wind.* 老樹在風中嘎吱作響。**3** if a table groans with food there is a very large amount of food on it〔在桌子上〕擺放大量的食品

groan[2] *n* [C] **1** a long deep sound that you make when you are in pain or do not want to do something〔疼痛時的〕呻吟;〔不願做某事時發出的〕哼哼聲: *Casey let out a groan of protest at having to go to bed.* 凱塞不願上牀睡覺, 哼了一聲表示抗議。**2** *literary* a long low sound like someone groaning【文】低沉的聲響: *The door opened with a groan.* 門嘎吱一聲開了。

groat /grot; grəʊt/ *n* **1 groats** [plural] grain, especially OATS with the outer shell removed 去殼穀物〔尤指去殼燕麥〕**2** [C] a former British coin that had a low value 格羅特〔英國從前的低面值硬幣〕

gro·bag, growbag /ˋgrobæg; ˈgrəʊbæg/ *n* [C] *BrE* a large plastic bag containing specially prepared earth for growing vegetables【英】〔裝有種植蔬菜用的特別配製的土壤的〕大塑料袋

gro·cer /ˈgrosɚ; ˈgrəʊsə/ *n* [C] **1** someone who owns or works in a shop that sells food such as flour, sugar, food in cans, and other things used in the home 食品雜貨店主[店員] **2 grocer's** a grocer's shop 食品雜貨店

gro·cer·y /ˈgrosərɪ; ˈgrəʊsəri/ *n* **1 groceries** [plural] goods sold by a grocer or a SUPERMARKET 食品雜貨 **2** also 又作 **grocery store** /ˈ··· ·/ [C] *AmE* a SUPERMARKET【美】超級市場

gro·dy /ˈgrodɪ; ˈgrəʊdi/ *adj AmE slang* a word meaning very unpleasant or offensive, used especially by children【美俚】太討厭, 真噁心〔尤為兒童用語〕

grog /grɑg; grɒg/ *n* [U] **1** a mixture of strong alcoholic drink, especially RUM[1], and water 攙水的烈性酒〔尤指朗姆酒〕 **2** *informal* any alcoholic drink【非正式】烈性酒

grog·gy /ˈgrɑgɪ; ˈgrɒgi/ *adj* weak and unable to walk steadily or think clearly because you are ill or very tired〔因生病或勞累而〕身體虛弱的, 行走不穩的, 頭腦昏沉的: *I felt really groggy after 15 hours on the plane.* 我乘了15個小時飛機之後, 感到昏昏沉沉的。—**groggily** *adv*

groin /grɔɪn; grɔɪn/ *n* [C] **1** the place where the tops of your legs meet the front of your body 腹股溝 —see picture at 參見 BODY 圖 **2** a GROYNE 海岸防波堤

grom·met /ˈgrɑmɪt; ˈgrɒmɪ̣t/ *n* [C] **1** a small metal ring used to make a hole in cloth or leather stronger 金屬扣眼 **2** a small piece of plastic put into a child's ear in order to remove liquid from it 去水塞〔放入兒童耳中以除去耳內液體的塑料製品〕

groom[1] /grum; gruːm/ *v* **1** [T] to take care of animals, especially horses, by cleaning and brushing them 照料〔動物, 尤指刷洗馬匹〕 **2** [I,T] to take care of your own appearance by keeping your hair and clothes clean and tidy 修飾, 打扮: *a well-groomed woman in her twenties* 打扮整潔的二十來歲的女子 **3** [T] to prepare someone for an important job or position in society by training them over a long period 培養, 培訓: **groom sb for sth** *Tim was being groomed for a managerial position.* 蒂姆正在受訓以擔任一個經理職位。| **groom sb to do sth** *Clare's father is grooming her to take his place when he retires.* 克萊爾的父親正在培養她, 以便在自己退休後她能接班。**4** [I,T] if an animal grooms itself or another animal, it cleans its own fur and skin or that of the other animal〔動物為自己或另一動物〕梳理皮毛 —**grooming** *n* [U] —see also 另見 WELL-GROOMED

groom[2] *n* [C] **1** a BRIDEGROOM 新郎 **2** someone whose job is to feed, clean, and take care of horses 馬夫

grooms·man /ˈgrumzmən; ˈgruːmzmən/ *n* [C] *AmE* a friend of a BRIDEGROOM who has special duties at a wedding【美】男儐相; USHER[1] (1) *BrE*【英】

groove[1] /gruv; gruːv/ *n* [C] **1** a thin line cut into a surface, especially to guide the movement of something〔尤指用於引導某物的〕凹槽: *The bolt slid easily into the groove.* 螺栓輕而易舉地滑入槽裡。**2 be in a groove** to be living or working in a situation that has been the same for a long time and that is unlikely to change 墨守成規, 一成不變

groove[2] *v* [T] to make a long narrow track in something 在〔某物〕上開槽 —**grooved** *adj*

groov·y /ˈgruvɪ; ˈgruːvi/ *adj* a word meaning fashionable, modern, and fun, used especially in the 1960s 時髦的, 新潮的, 有趣的〔此詞尤用於 20 世紀 60 年代〕

grope[1] /grop; grəʊp/ *v* **1** [I always+adv/prep] to try to find something that you cannot see by feeling with your hands〔在黑暗中〕摸索: **[+for/through/around etc]** *Ginny groped for her glasses on the bedside table.* 吉尼在牀邊小几上摸找眼鏡。| *groping around in the dark* 在黑暗中四處摸索 **2 grope your way along/across etc** to go somewhere by feeling the way with your hands because you cannot see〔因看不見而用手〕摸索着走/穿過等: *I groped my way along the wall to the door.* 我摸着牆走到門口。**3** [I] to try hard to find the right words to say, or the right solution to a problem but without any real idea of how to do this 努力搜尋〔恰當的言辭或解決辦法〕: **[+for]** *Accusations of misconduct left Keeler groping for a response.* 行為不端的指責使得基勒不得不設法作出反應。**4** [T] *informal* to move your hands over someone's body to get sexual pleasure, especially when they do not want you to do this【非正式】〔為得到性快感〕撫摸某人〔尤指當對方不願意的時候〕

grope[2] *n* [C] *informal* an act of groping (GROPE[1] (4))【非正式】撫摸

gross[1] /gros; grəʊs/ *adj*

1 ►TOTAL 總共的◄ a) a gross amount of money is the total amount before any tax or costs have been taken away〔扣去稅或成本之前〕總的, 毛的: *a gross profit of $15 million* 1500 萬美元的毛利 | *gross receipts* (=the gross amount of money received) 進款總額 —compare 比較 NET[3] (1) **b)** a gross weight is the total weight of something, including its wrapping 毛重的

2 gross negligence/misconduct/injustice etc behaviour that is clearly wrong and unacceptable 明顯的過失/行為不端/不公平等: *a gross exaggeration of the truth* 對真實情況的嚴重誇張

3 ►RUDE 粗魯的◄ behaviour that is gross is extremely rude and completely unacceptable〔行為〕極端粗魯的, 完全不能接受的

4 ►NASTY 令人厭惡的◄ *spoken* very unpleasant to look at or think about【口】看上去[想起來]令人厭惡的: *Ooh, gross! I hate spinach!* 啊, 討厭! 我討厭吃菠菜!

5 ►FAT 胖的◄ extremely fat and unattractive 極胖而難看的 —**grossly** *adv*: *grossly overweight* 嚴重超重 —**grossness** *n* [U]

gross[2] *adv* **earn £20,000/$30,000 etc gross** to earn £20,000 etc before tax has been taken away 稅前收入 20,000 英鎊 / 30,000 美元等: *a junior executive earning more than $30,000 gross* 稅前收入為三萬多美元的初級行政人員

gross[3] *v* [T] to gain an amount as a total profit, or earn it as a total amount, before tax has been taken away 獲得…的總利潤[毛利, 稅前收入]: *This type of store may gross $8 million or more annually.* 這類商店每年可獲得八百萬美元或更多的毛利。

gross sb **out** *phr v* [T] *spoken AmE* to make someone wish they had not seen or been told about something because it is so unpleasant【口, 美】但願某人沒看過[聽過]〔如此惡劣的事情〕

gross[4] *determiner n plural* **gross** [C] a quantity of 144 things 羅〔即 12 打, 144 個〕: *a gross of candles* 一羅蠟燭

gross do·mes·tic prod·uct /ˌ· ··· ˈ··/ *n* [singular] *technical* the GDP; the total value of all the goods and services produced in a country, except for income received from abroad【術語】國內生產總值 —compare 比較 GROSS NATIONAL PRODUCT

gross mar·gin /ˌ· ˈ··/ *n* [C] the financial difference between what something costs to produce and what it is sold for 毛利

gross na·tion·al prod·uct /ˌ· ··· ˈ··/ *n technical* [singular] the GNP; the total value of all the goods and services produced in a country, including income from abroad【術語】國民生產總值 —compare 比較 GROSS DOMESTIC PRODUCT

gross prof·it /ˌ· ˈ··/ *n* [C] GROSS MARGIN 毛利

gro·tesque[1] /groˈtɛsk; grəʊˈtesk/ *adj* **1** strange or unusual in a way that is shocking or offensive 怪誕的, 荒唐的: *The idea of my best friend becoming my stepmother was too grotesque to contemplate.* 我最好的朋友成為我繼母的想法過於荒唐, 無法細想。**2** extremely ugly in a strange or unnatural way 極醜陋的, 怪異的: *a grotesque figure with a huge head* 長着大腦袋的醜陋人形 —**grotesquely** *adv*

grotesque[2] *n* **1** [C] an image of someone who is strangely ugly 某人奇醜的形象 **2 the grotesque** a grotesque style in art〔藝術中的〕怪誕[奇異]風格

grot·to /ˈgrɑto; ˈgrɒtəʊ/ *n* [C] a small natural CAVE[1], or one that someone has made in their garden 天然小洞穴; 花園中挖掘的洞室

grot·ty /ˈgrɒtɪ; ˈgrɒti/ *adj BrE informal* nasty, dirty, or unpleasant【英, 非正式】令人厭惡的; 骯髒的; 令人不快的: *a grotty little bedsit* 一間骯髒的小臥室兼起居室 —**grottily** *adv* —**grottiness** *n* [U]

grouch¹ /graʊtʃ; graʊtʃ/ *n informal*【非正式】**1** [C] someone who is always complaining 總是發牢騷的人: *My grandad is such an old grouch.* 我爺爺牢騷不斷。**2** [C] something unimportant that you complain about 所抱怨的小事: *One of his main grouches is that they never put the top back on the toothpaste.* 他主要的抱怨是, 他們從來不把牙膏蓋蓋回去。

grouch² *v* [I+about] *informal* to complain in an angry way; GRUMBLE¹ (1)【非正式】怒氣沖沖地抱怨

grouch·y /ˈgraʊtʃɪ; ˈgraʊtʃi/ *adj* in a bad temper, especially because you are tired〔尤指因疲倦而〕脾氣壞的 —**grouchiness** *n* [U]

ground¹ /graʊnd; graʊnd/ *n*

① EARTH SURFACE 地面
② AREA 地方
③ SUBJECT 主題
④ OPINION/ATTITUDE 觀點/態度
⑤ REASON 理由
⑥ SUCCESS/ADVANTAGE 成功/優勢
⑦ HIDE/FIND 隱藏/找到
⑧ COLOUR/PAINT 顏色/顏料
⑨ OTHER MEANINGS 其他意思

① EARTH SURFACE 地面

1 [U] the surface of the earth 地面: *The leaf slowly fluttered to the ground.* 葉子慢慢地飄落到地上。| *The air raids were followed by military action on the ground.* 空襲之後是地面軍事行動。| **below/above ground** *miners working 10-hour shifts below ground* 每一班在地下工作十小時的礦工 —compare 比較 FLOOR¹ (1) —see 見 LAND¹ (USAGE)

2 ►SOIL 土壤◄ [U] the soil on and under the surface of the earth 土, 土地: *Dig the ground over in autumn.* 秋天要翻土。| *marshy ground* 沼澤地

3 ►UNDER THE SEA 在海底◄ [U] the bottom of the sea 海底: *Our ship touched ground.* 我們的船擱淺了。

② AREA 地方

4 ►OPEN LAND 空曠之地◄ [U] an area of land without buildings or trees〔無建築物或樹木的〕空地: *a view across open ground* 空曠地帶的景色 | *They're building a car lot on some waste ground across the street.* 他們正在街對面那塊廢棄的空地上建造停車場。

5 grounds [plural] **a)** a large area of land or sea that is used for a particular activity or sport〔用於某項活動或運動的〕一大片場地[海域]: *hunting grounds* 狩獵場 | *fishing grounds* 漁場 **b)** the land or gardens around a large house, hospital etc〔大房子、醫院等周圍的〕庭園, 場地

6 parade/recreation/burial etc ground an area of land that is used for a particular purpose 閱兵場/遊樂場/墓地等 —see also 另見 PLAYGROUND

7 ►SPORTS 體育◄ [C] *BrE* the place where a sport such as football or CRICKET (2) is played; STADIUM【英】〔足球、板球等的〕球場, 體育場: *the team's home ground* (=where they usually play) 該隊的主球場

8 cover a lot of ground to travel a very long distance 走了不少路, 旅行到過很多地方: *You certainly covered a lot of ground on your travels.* 你確實去過不少地方。

③ SUBJECT 主題

9 ►AREA OF KNOWLEDGE 知識領域◄ [U] an area of knowledge, ideas, experience etc 知識[概念, 經驗]領域, 範圍: **go over the same ground** (=talk about the same things again) 又談論同樣的事, 老調重彈 *The article says nothing new – it just goes over the same old ground.* 這篇文章沒有講甚麼新內容 —— 只是老調重彈。| **be on familiar ground/be on your own ground** (=be talking about or dealing with a subject you know a lot about) 談論或處理你所熟知的領域 *Keith's on familiar ground. He's worked with this type of computer before.* 基思駕輕就熟, 他以前用過這種電腦。

10 be on dangerous/safe ground to be expressing ideas that are likely or unlikely to offend or embarrass someone 處於危險/安全境地〔指提出的看法可能或不大可能冒犯某人或使其難堪〕

11 cover a lot of ground to give information about many different parts of a subject 涉及〔某話題的〕諸多方面: *It's absurd to try to cover so much ground in such a short lecture.* 想在如此短的講座中涉及這麼大的範圍是荒謬的。

④ OPINION/ATTITUDE 觀點/態度

12 the middle ground the area of political opinion that most people agree about 中間立場〔為大多數人所贊同的政治觀點〕: *the middle ground between two passionately opposed views* 兩種激烈對立觀點之間的中間立場

13 common ground an area of opinion that two people or groups share〔兩人或兩個團體的〕共同看法: *We hope to find some common ground as a basis for agreement.* 我們希望達成某些共識作為協議的基礎。

14 shift/change your ground to begin to use different reasons or ideas to support your opinions 改變立場

15 hold your ground to continue to support a particular opinion in spite of opposition 堅持立場

16 the moral high ground an opinion that is regarded as morally better than others 高道義立場〔被視為在道義上較其他觀點更為高尚的觀點〕

⑤ REASON 理由

17 ►REASON 理由◄ [C usually plural 一般用複數] a reason, especially one that makes you think that something is true or correct 理由, 根據: **grounds for (doing) sth** *Jim has strong grounds for asking for more money.* 吉姆有充分的理由索要更多的錢。| **on moral/legal etc grounds** *He refused to sign the contract on moral grounds.* 他以道德為由拒絕簽署那份合同。| **on grounds of** *The divorce was granted on grounds of adultery.* 因有通姦情形, 離婚得到批准。| **on the grounds that** *Zoe was awarded compensation on the grounds that the doctor had been negligent.* 佐伊被判給賠償金, 根據是醫生玩忽職守。

⑥ SUCCESS/ADVANTAGE 成功/優勢

18 get off the ground if a plan, a business idea etc gets off the ground, or if you get it off the ground, it starts to be successful〔計劃、經商點子等〕開始獲得成功: *It took a while for the business to get off the ground, but it's making a profit now.* 這家公司經過相當一段時間之後才取得進展, 但現在已經開始贏利了。

19 gain ground a) to get an advantage and become more successful 取得優勢, 變得比較有利: *The Repub-*

licans have been gaining ground in the opinion polls. 共和黨在民意測驗中逐漸取得優勢。**b)** if an idea, belief etc gains ground, it starts to become accepted or believed by more people〔主張、信仰等〕開始被更多的人接受: *a theory gaining ground among academics* 被學術界愈來愈多的人接受的一種理論
20 lose ground to lose an advantage and become less successful 失去優勢, 失利

⑦ HIDE/FIND 隱藏/找到
21 go to ground *BrE* to hide from someone, especially the police【英】躲避〔某人, 尤指警察〕
22 run sb to ground *BrE* to succeed in finding someone after a long search【英】長期搜尋之後找到某人: *I finally ran Luke to ground in the basement store room.* 我終於在地下貯藏室找到了盧克。

⑧ COLOUR/PAINT 顏色/顏料
23 ▶BACKGROUND 背景◀ [C] the colour that is the background for a design 背景: *white flowers on a blue ground* 藍底白花
24 ▶PAINT 顏料◀ [C] the first covering of paint on a painting 底色

⑨ OTHER MEANINGS 其他意思
25 fertile ground/breeding ground a situation in which it is easy for something to develop 沃土/滋生地: *The universities were a fertile ground for left-wing radicalism.* 大學是左翼激進主義的沃土。| *a breeding ground for germs* 細菌的滋生地
26 on the ground in the actual place where something, especially a war, is happening, rather than in another place where it is being discussed 在現場〔尤指戰爭現場, 而非討論的場所〕: *While the politicians talked of peace, the situation on the ground remained tense.* 政治家在談論和平的時候, 現場局勢仍然很緊張。
27 on your own ground/on home ground in the place or situation that is most familiar to you 在你最熟悉的地方/在你最了解的情況下: *I wouldn't dream of meeting my ex-husband again unless I was on home ground.* 除非是在我熟知的地方, 否則我做夢也不想再見到我的前夫。
28 work/drive yourself into the ground to work so hard that you become extremely tired 拚命工作, 使自己極度勞累: *Kay's working herself into the ground trying to meet her deadlines.* 凱拚命地工作, 想在最後期限內完成任務。
29 grounds *plural* the small pieces of something such as coffee which sink to the bottom of a liquid 沉澱物, 渣滓: *coffee grounds* 咖啡渣
30 ▶ELECTRICAL 電氣的◀ [singular] *AmE* a wire that connects a piece of electrical equipment to the ground for safety【美】地線; EARTH[1] (8) *BrE*【英】—see also 另見 **break fresh/new ground** (BREAK[1] (33)), **cut the ground from under sb's feet** (CUT[1] (25)), **have/keep both feet on the ground** (FOOT[1] (16)), **stand your ground** (STAND[1] (8)), **stand your ground** (STAND[1] (17)), **suit sb down to the ground** (SUIT[2] (1)), **be thin on the ground** (THIN[1] (12)), **hit the ground running** (HIT[1] (22))

ground² *v* **1** [T usually passive 一般用被動態] to stop an aircraft or pilot from flying 使〔飛機、飛行員〕停飛: *All planes are grounded until the fog clears.* 所有的飛機都停飛, 直至霧散為止。**2** [I,T] if you ground a boat or if it grounds, it hits the bottom of the sea so that it cannot move〔船舶〕擱淺 **3 be grounded in/on** to be based on something 以…為根據, 建立在…基礎上: *David's values are grounded in a Protestant work ethic.* 大衛的價值觀建立在新教的工作道德基礎之上。**4** [T] *informal* to stop a child going out with their friends as a punishment for behaving badly【非正式】不許〔孩子〕與朋友一起出去玩〔作為表現不好的懲罰〕: *I got home at 2 am and Dad grounded me on the spot.* 我早晨兩點回家, 爸爸當場罰我不准出去。**5** [T] *AmE* to make a piece of electrical equipment safe by connecting it to the ground with a wire【美】把〔電器裝置〕接地〔以確保電器安全〕; EARTH[2] *BrE*【英】—see also 另見 WELL-GROUNDED

ground sb **in** sth *phr v* [T usually passive 一般用被動態] to teach someone the basic things they should know in order to be able to do something 對〔某人〕進行基本訓練: *The recruits were grounded in combat techniques.* 新兵接受作戰技術的基本訓練。

ground³ *adj* [only before noun 僅用於名詞前] ground coffee or nuts have been broken up into powder or very small pieces, using a special machine〔咖啡或堅果用特製機器〕磨成粉末或顆粒的, 磨碎的

ground⁴ the past tense and past participle of GRIND[1]

ground bait /'· ·/ *n* [U] food that you throw onto a river, lake etc when you are fishing in order to attract fish〔捕魚時投入河、湖等中的〕誘餌

ground beef /,· '·/ *n* [U] *AmE* BEEF[1] (1) that has been cut up into very small pieces, often used to make HAMBURGERS【美】〔做漢堡包的〕牛肉末; MINCE[2] *BrE*【英】

ground·break·ing /ˈgraʊnd,brekɪŋ; ˈgraʊnd,breɪkɪŋ/ *adj* groundbreaking work involves making new discoveries, using new methods etc 開闢新天地的

ground cloth /'· ·/ *n* [C] *AmE* a piece of material that water cannot pass through which people sleep on when they are camping【美】〔野營時睡覺用的〕鋪地防潮布; GROUNDSHEET *BrE*【英】

ground con·trol /'· ·,·/ *n* [U] the people on the ground who are responsible for guiding the flight of SPACECRAFT or aircraft〔航天、航空的〕地面控制人員

ground cov·er /'· ,··/ *n* [U] plants that cover the soil 地被植物

ground crew /'· ·/ *n* [C] the group of people who work at an airport looking after the aircraft〔機場的〕地勤人員; GROUND STAFF *BrE*【英】

ground·er /ˈgraʊndɚ; ˈgraʊndə/ *n* [C] a ball hit along the ground in BASEBALL〔棒球中的〕地滾球, 地面球

ground floor /,· '·◂/ *n* **1** [C] *especially BrE* the floor of a building that is at ground level【尤英】〔樓房與地面齊平的〕底層; FIRST FLOOR (2) *AmE*【美】—see 見 FLOOR[1] (USAGE) **2 be/get in on the ground floor** to become involved in a plan, business activity etc from the beginning 從一開始便參加〔某計劃、商務活動等〕

ground for·ces /'· ,··/ *n* [plural] military groups that fight on the ground rather than at sea or in the air 地面部隊

ground glass /,· '·◂/ *n* [U] **1** glass that has been made into a powder 玻璃粉 **2** glass that has been rubbed on the surface so that you cannot see through it, but light passes through it 毛玻璃, 磨砂玻璃

ground·hog /ˈgraʊnd,hɑg; ˈgraʊndhɒg/ *n* [C] a small North American animal that has thick brown fur and lives in holes in the ground; WOODCHUCK 北美土撥鼠, 美洲旱獺

ground·ing /ˈgraʊndɪŋ; ˈgraʊndɪŋ/ *n* **1** [singular] a training in the basic parts of a subject or skill 基礎訓練: [+in] *A thorough grounding in mathematics is essential for the economics course.* 嚴密的數學基礎訓練對經濟學這門課程來説是必不可少的。**2** [C] *AmE* a punishment for a child's bad behaviour in which they are not allowed go out with their friends for a period of time【美】〔因孩子表現不佳〕在一定時間內不許與朋友外出的懲罰

ground·less /ˈgraʊndlɪs; ˈgraʊndləs/ *adj* groundless fears, worries etc are unnecessary because there are no facts to base them on 無根據的: *Fortunately my suspicions proved groundless.* 幸虧我的猜疑後來證明是沒有根據的。

ground lev·el /'· ,··/ *n* [singular] the same level as the surface of the earth, rather than above it or below it 地平面

ground·nut /ˋgraund͵nʌt; ˈgraʊndnʌt/ *n* [C] *BrE technical* a PEANUT or peanut plant【英, 術語】落花生, 花生; 花生植株

ground plan /ˈ· ·/ *n* [C] **1** a drawing of how a building is arranged at ground level, showing the size, position, and shape of walls, rooms etc 樓層平面圖 **2** a plan of how something will happen in the future 大綱, 初步計劃, 草案

ground rent /ˈ· ·/ *n* [C,U] rent paid to the person who owns the land that your house is built on 地租

ground rules /ˈ· ·/ *n* [plural] the basic rules or principles on which future actions or behaviour should be based 基本規則[原則]

ground·sheet /ˋgraund͵ʃit; ˈgraʊndʃiːt/ *n* [C] *BrE* a piece of material that water cannot pass through which people sleep on when they are camping【英】〔野營時睡覺用的〕鋪地防潮布; GROUND CLOTH *AmE*【美】

grounds·man /ˋgraundzmən; ˈgraʊndzmən/ *plural* **groundsmen** /-mən; -mən/ *n* [C] *especially BrE* a man whose job is to take care of large gardens or a sports field【尤英】大花園[運動場]的管理員

ground squir·rel /ˈ· ͵··/ *n* [C] a North American animal that lives in the ground and often damages crops; GOPHER 北美地松鼠, 黃鼠

ground staff /ˈ· ·/ *n* [C] *BrE*【英】**1** the people who take care of the grass and sports equipment at a sports ground〔運動場草坪和運動器材〕管理人員 **2** the group of people who work at an airport looking after the aircraft; GROUND CREW〔機場的〕地勤人員

ground stroke /ˈ· ·/ *n* [C] a way of hitting the ball after it has hit the ground in tennis and similar games〔網球等的〕擊落地球

ground·swell /ˋgraundswɛl; ˈgraʊndswel/ *n* **1** **groundswell of support/opinion etc** a sudden increase in how strongly people feel about something 突然高漲的支持/輿論等 **2** [singular,U] the strong movement of the sea that continues after a storm or strong winds〔暴風雨或大風後的〕海湧, 巨浪

ground·work /ˋgraund͵wɝk; ˈgraʊndwɜːk/ *n* [U] important work that has to take place before another activity, plan etc can be successful 基礎, 根基: *The groundwork for the peace summit was laid during last month's conference.* 和平峯會的基礎是在上月那次會議期間打下的。

1 **group**[1] /grup; gruːp/ *n* [C] **1** several people or things
1 that are all together in the same place〔人或物聚在一處的〕組, 羣, 批: [+of] *a group of tall trees* 一片大樹 | *Get into groups of four.* 分成四個人一組。| [also+plural verb *BrE* 英] *A group of us are going to London for the concert.* 我們中有一羣人要去倫敦聽這場音樂會。**2** several people or things that are connected with each other in some way〔人或物彼此之間有某種聯繫的〕團體; 羣體: [+of] *A group of animal rights activists claimed responsibility for the bomb.* 一個動物權利保護團體聲稱對這一爆炸事件負責。| *the Germanic group of languages* 日耳曼語系 | **income/ethnic etc group** (=people with the same income level, same race etc) 同一收入水平/同一種族等的羣體 **3** several companies that all have the same owner 集團(公司): *a giant textiles group* 龐大的紡織集團 **4** a number of musicians or singers who perform together, usually playing popular music〔通常演奏流行音樂的〕樂團, 樂隊, 組合: *a rock group* 搖滾樂團 —see also 另見 AGE GROUP, BLOOD GROUP, INTEREST GROUP, PLAYGROUP

group[2] *v* **1** [I,T] to come together to make a group or to arrange people or things in a group 聚集成一組; 把人或物分組: [+on/in/together etc] *Can you all group around the piano?* 請大家圍攏在鋼琴周圍好嗎? **2** [T always+adv/prep] to divide people or things into groups or types according to a system〔將人或物〕分類: *The soils can be broadly grouped according to their acidity.* 這些土壤可以按照它們的酸度粗略分類。

group cap·tain /͵· ˈ··◂/ *n* [C] a fairly high rank in the British airforce, or someone who has this rank〔英國的〕空軍上校(軍銜) —see table on page C7 參見C7頁附錄

group·ie /ˋgrupɪ; ˈgruːpi/ *n* [C] someone, especially a young woman, who follows POP muscians to their concerts, hoping to meet them 流行歌星迷〔尤指少女〕

group·ing /ˋgrupɪŋ; ˈgruːpɪŋ/ *n* [C] a set of people, things, or organizations that have the same interests, qualities, or features 興趣、品質或特徵相同的一類人[事物, 組織]: *The unemployed form the largest single grouping of the electorate.* 失業者構成了這個選區最大的一個羣體。

group prac·tice /͵· ˈ··/ *n* [C,U] a group of doctors who work together, in the same building〔幾名醫生在同一棟樓裡一起工作的〕聯合醫療

group ther·a·py /͵· ˈ···/ *n* [U] a method of treating people with emotional or PSYCHOLOGICAL problems by bringing them together in groups to talk about their problems 集體心理治療〔把有情感或心理疾病的患者聚集在一起, 分組讓他們談論自己的問題〕

grouse[1] /graus; graʊs/ *n* **1** [C] *informal* a complaint, especially an unreasonable one【非正式】牢騷〔尤指無理的抱怨〕**2** [C,U] a small fat bird that is hunted and shot for food and sport, or the meat of this bird 松雞; 松雞肉

grouse[2] *v* [I+about] *informal* to complain about something in an angry way: GRUMBLE[1] (1)【非正式】〔生氣地〕發牢騷, 抱怨

grove /grov; grəʊv/ *n* **1** [C] an area of land planted with a particular type of fruit tree 果園, 果樹林: *an orange grove* 柑橘園 —compare 比較 ORCHARD **2** [C] *literary* a small group of trees【文】樹叢, 小樹林 **3 Grove** used in the names of roads …路〔用於路名〕: *Lisson Grove* 利勝路

grov·el /ˋgrɑvḷ; ˈgrɒvəl/ *v* **grovelled, grovelling** *BrE*【英】, **groveled, groveling** *AmE*【美】[I] **1** to behave with too much respect towards someone, because you are asking them to help or forgive you〔因有求於人而〕卑躬屈膝: *There's nothing worse than seeing a man grovel just to keep his job.* 沒有甚麼比看到一個人只是為了保住工作而卑躬屈膝更糟糕的了。**2** to lie or move flat on the ground because you are afraid of someone, or as a way of showing obedience〔因害怕某人或表示順從而〕匍匐在地: *That dog grovels every time you shout.* 每次你一喊, 那條狗就趴在地上。

grow /gro; grəʊ/ *v past tense* **grew** /gru; gruː/ *past participle* **grown** /gron; grəʊn/ 1 1

grow out of 因長大而穿不進〔原來的衣服〕

He's grown out of his clothes.
他長大了, 衣服都不合穿。

1 ▶PERSON/ANIMAL 人/動物◀ [I] to become bigger and develop over a period of time 成長, 長大: *How you've grown since the last time I saw you!* 自上次見到你以來, 你長高了不少啊! | **grow 2 inches/5cm etc** *Stan grew two inches in six months.* 斯坦在六個月中長高了兩英寸。| **growing boy/girl** *Of course he eats a lot – he's a growing boy!* 他當然吃得多—他正在發育!

2 ▶PLANTS/CROPS 植物/作物◀ a) [I] to exist and develop somewhere in a natural way 自然生長: *There's corn growing in that field.* 那塊田裡長着玉米。| *It's too cold for orchids to grow here.* 這裡太冷了, 蘭花無法生長。**b)** [T] to make plants or crops grow by taking care of them 栽, 種植: *We grow all our own*

G

vegetables. 我們吃的蔬菜都是自己種的。—see 見 RAISE[1] (USAGE)

3 ▶HAIR/NAILS 頭髮/指甲◀ **a)** [I] if hair, nails etc grow, they become longer〔頭髮、指甲等〕變長 **b)** [T] if you grow your hair, nails, you do not cut them 留〔長頭髮、長指甲〕

4 ▶INCREASE 增加◀ [I] to increase in amount, size, or degree 增多, 增大, 增強, 增長: *De Niro's reputation continues to grow.* 德·尼羅的聲望在繼續上升。| *Fears are growing for the safety of the crew.* 人們越來越擔心船員們的安全。| **growing concern/interest/disbelief etc** *Scientists view the hole in the ozone layer with growing concern.* 科學家日益關注臭氧層的那個洞。| **a growing number** *A growing number of people are taking part-time jobs.* 越來越多人在從事兼職工作。| **grow in strength/confidence** (=become stronger, more confident) 更加強壯[壯大]/更有信心

5 grow old/hot/worse etc to become old etc over a period of time 逐漸衰老/變熱/惡化等: *She grew impatient with his constant excuses.* 因為他不斷地找藉口, 她越來越不耐煩了。| *I'm scared of growing old.* 我害怕衰老。

6 grow to like/fear/respect etc to gradually start to like etc someone or something 逐漸開始喜歡/害怕/尊敬等: *After a while the kids grew to like Mr Cox.* 不久之後, 孩子開始喜歡上科克斯先生了。

7 ▶IMPROVE 改善◀ [I] to improve in ability or character〔在能力或性格方面〕改善: *She's grown tremendously as a musician since Pallino took her on.* 自從帕利諾雇了她, 她作為樂師的水平大大提高。

8 ▶BUSINESS 生意◀ [T] to make something increase in size or importance 擴大, 增強: *We want to grow the export side of the business.* 我們想要擴大企業的出口業務。

9 it doesn't grow on trees *spoken* used about money, to mean that you should not waste it【口】錢不是從樹上長出來的〔用以表示不可浪費金錢〕

grow apart *phr v* [I] if two people grow apart, their relationship becomes less close〔彼此的關係〕越來越疏遠: *He said the couple had been growing apart for at least a year.* 他說這對夫婦不和至少有一年了。

grow away from sb *phr v* [T not in passive 不用被動態] to begin gradually to have a less close relationship with someone that you loved 與〔所愛之人〕開始逐漸疏遠: *While at university she had grown away from her family.* 她在上大學時就逐漸和家人疏遠起來。

grow into sb/sth *phr v* [T not in passive 不用被動態] **1** to develop over a period of time and become a particular kind of person or thing 成長為: *Susan's grown into a lovely young woman.* 蘇珊已長成為一個可愛的少女。**2** if a child grows into clothes, they become big enough to wear them〔小孩〕長得適合穿〔本來嫌大的衣服〕: *His new jacket's a bit big for him now but he'll soon grow into it.* 他的那件新上衣現在嫌大, 不過很快就會合身了。**3** to gradually learn how to do a job or deal with a situation successfully 逐漸學會[適應]〔工作或情況〕

grow on sb *phr v* [T] if someone or something grows on you, you like them more and more 越來越喜愛: *His music is difficult to listen to, but after a while it grows on you.* 他的音樂很難懂, 但不久會讓你越來越喜歡。

grow out of sth *phr v* [T] **1** if a child grows out of clothes, they become too big to wear them〔小孩〕因長大而穿不進〔原來的衣服〕**2** if a child grows out of a habit, they stop doing it as they get older〔因年齡增長而〕戒除, 改掉〔原有的習慣〕: *She used to bite her nails but seems to have grown out of it.* 她過去經常咬指甲, 但現在似乎已經改掉了。**3** to develop from something small or simple into something bigger or more complicated 由〔小或簡單的事〕發展成〔大或複雜的事〕: *The dispute grew out of an argument between a worker and the foreman.* 這場爭執是從一名工人和工頭的爭論引發的。

grow up *phr v* [I] **1** develop from being a child to being an adult 長大成人: *What do you want to be when you grow up?* 你長大以後想當甚麼? | *I grew up on a farm.* 我是在農場裡長大的。**2 grow up!** *spoken* used to tell someone to behave more like an adult, especially when they have been behaving in a silly way【口】要像個大人樣!〔尤用於某人行為幼稚可笑之時〕**3** to start to exist and become bigger or more important 形成, 興起, 發展: *Trading settlements grew up along the river.* 河的兩岸形成了一些貿易區。

grow·bag /ˈgrobæg; ˈgrəʊbæg/ *n* [C] another spelling of GROBAG grobag 的另一種拼法

grow·er /ˈgroɚ; ˈgrəʊə/ *n* [C] a person or company that grows fruit, vegetables etc in order to sell them〔水果蔬菜等的〕種植者[公司]: *apple growers* 種植蘋果的果農

grow·ing pains /ˈ.. ˌ./ *n* [plural] **1** aches and pains that children can sometimes feel in their arms and legs when they are growing 發育期痛〔兒童發育時的四肢酸痛〕**2** problems and difficulties that are experienced at the beginning of a new activity〔某項新活動所經歷的〕初期困難; 發展時期的困難

growl /graul; graʊl/ *v* **1** [I] if an animal growls it makes a long deep angry sound〔動物〕吼叫: *The dog growled at any stranger who came close.* 有生人走近時, 那條狗就狂吠不已。**2** [I,T] to say something in a low angry voice 怒氣沖沖地低聲說: *"Get out of my way," he growled.* "滾開。"他咆哮道。—**growl** *n* [C]: *The bear gave a sudden growl.* 這隻熊突然發出一聲咆哮。

grown[1] /gron; grəʊn/ *adj* [only before noun 僅用於名詞前] **grown man/woman** an expression meaning an adult man or woman, used especially when you think someone is not behaving as an adult should 成年男子/女子〔尤用於認為某人行為不像一個成年人時〕: *A grown man should know better than to shout and scream.* 成年男子應該明白不應那樣喊叫。—compare 比較 FULL-GROWN, HOMEGROWN

grown[2] the past participle of GROW

grown-up[1] /ˌ. ˈ.◀/ *adj* **1** fully developed as an adult 成年的: *Before you know it, they'll be all grown-up and leaving home.* 轉眼之間, 他們就會長大成人, 離開家庭。**2** behaving like an adult or typical of an adult〔行為〕符合成年人身分的; 具有成年人特點的: *I expect more grown-up behaviour of you now.* 我希望你現在能表現得更像一個成年人。

grown-up[2] /ˈ. ./ *n* [C] a word meaning an adult person, used especially by or to children 成年人, 大人〔尤為兒語〕: *If you're frightened, tell one of the grown-ups.* 如果你害怕, 就跟大人講。

growth /groθ; grəʊθ/ *n*

1 ▶INCREASE IN AMOUNT 數量增加◀ [U] an increase in amount, size, or degree 增多, 增長, 增大, 增強: *efforts to control population growth* 為控制人口增長所作的努力 | **[+in]** *During the 1970's there was rapid growth in oil production and consumption.* 在 20 世紀 70 年代, 石油產量和消費迅速增長。| **growth rate** (=the speed at which something increases or grows) 增長率 *Japan's economic growth rate* 日本的經濟增長率 | **growth area/industry** (=an area of business that is growing very quickly) 迅速增長的〔某企業〕領域/工業

2 ▶PERSON/ANIMAL/PLANT 人/動物/植物◀ [U] the development of the physical size, strength etc of a person, animal or plant over a period of time 成長, 發育, 生長: *Vitamins are essential for healthy growth.* 維生素是健康成長必不可少的。

3 ▶INCREASE IN IMPORTANCE 重要性的增加◀ [singular,U] the gradual development and increase of a particular feeling, idea, or way of living〔某種感覺、想法或生活方式的〕逐漸發展和擴大: **[+of]** *the growth of capitalism* 資本主義的發展 | *Currently there is a growth of interest in African music.* 目前對非洲音樂的興趣有所增長。

4 ▶PERSONAL DEVELOPMENT 個人發展◀ [U] the

G

development of someone's character, intelligence or emotions〔性格、智力或感情的〕發展: **emotional/intellectual/personal etc growth** *A loving home environment is essential for a child's personal growth.* 充滿愛心的家庭環境對小孩的個人發展是必不可少的。
5 ▶SWELLING 腫塊◀ [C] a swelling on your body or under your skin, caused by disease〔由疾病引起, 體內或皮下的〕腫塊, 腫瘤: *a cancerous growth* 癌瘤
6 ▶GROWING THING 生長物◀ [C,U] something which has grown 生長物: *I thought the tree was dead, but there are signs of new growth.* 我原以為這棵樹已經死了, 但它有長出新枝的跡象。

groyne, groin /grɔɪn; grɔɪn/ *n* [C] a low wall built out into the sea to prevent the sea from removing sand and stones from the shore〔海岸的〕防波堤 —see picture on page A12 參見 A12 頁圖

grub[1] /grʌb; grʌb/ *n* **1** [U] *informal* food【非正式】食物: *Let's get some grub.* 我們買點吃的吧。**2** [C] an insect when it is in the form of a small soft white worm 蛆, 蠐螬

grub[2] [I always+adv/prep] *informal* to look for something, especially by moving things, looking under them etc【非正式】尋找〔尤指翻開別的東西, 在下面尋找某物〕: **[+around/about]** *The dog was grubbing around under a bush looking for a bone.* 那條狗在灌木叢下面翻掘, 尋找骨頭。

grub sth ↔ **up/out** *phr v* [T] to dig around something and then pull it out of the ground 將…挖出: *Farmers were encouraged to grub up hedgerows.* 農民被鼓勵挖掉灌木樹籬。

grub·by /ˈgrʌbɪ; ˈgrʌbi/ *adj* **1** fairly dirty 骯髒的: *a grubby handkerchief* 骯髒的手帕 **2** grubby behaviour or activity is morally unpleasant〔行為或活動〕卑鄙的: *the grubby details of Harper's financial dealings* 有關哈珀金融交易的骯髒細節 —**grubbiness** *n* [U]

grub·stake /ˈgrʌbˌstek; ˈgrʌbˌsteɪk/ *n* [U] *AmE informal* money provided to develop a new business in return for a share of the profits【美, 非正式】〔為分紅而投資開發新業務的〕資金, 貸款

grudge[1] /grʌdʒ; grʌdʒ/ *n* [C] **1** a feeling of anger or dislike you have for someone because you cannot forget that they harmed you 懷恨, 怨恨: **[+against]** *He's had a grudge against Bob ever since he was promoted.* 自從鮑伯晉升以來他就對鮑伯懷恨在心。| **bear (sb) a grudge** (=continue to have a grudge)〔對某人〕懷有積怨 **2 grudge fight/match** a fight or competition in sport between two people who dislike each other a lot〔體育中〕冤家對頭的決鬥/比賽

grudge[2] *v* [T] **1** to do or give something very unwillingly; BEGRUDGE 勉強做〔某事〕; 勉強給〔某物〕: **grudge doing sth** *I really grudge paying so much money for such poor service.* 我確實不願意為這麼差勁的服務付這麼多的錢。**2 grudge sb sth** to not want someone to have something 嫉妒: *I don't grudge him his success.* 我並不嫉妒他的成功。

grudg·ing /ˈgrʌdʒɪŋ; ˈgrʌdʒɪŋ/ *adj* done or given very unwillingly 不情願的, 勉強的: *He was looking at Nick with a certain grudging respect.* 他看尼克的目光流露出一種不情願的尊敬。—**grudgingly** *adv*: *He grudgingly admitted that he'd been wrong.* 他勉強承認他錯了。

gru·el /ˈgruəl; ˈgruːəl/ *n* [U] a thin liquid food made of crushed OATS that was eaten in the past by poor or sick people〔過去窮人或病人吃的稀薄的〕燕麥粥, 麥片粥

gru·el·ling *BrE*【英】, **grueling** *AmE*【美】/ˈgruəlɪŋ; ˈgruːəlɪŋ/ *adj* very tiring because you have to use a lot of effort for a long time 非常累人的: *a gruelling 6 hour mountain hike* 非常累人的六小時爬山 —**gruellingly** *adv*

grue·some /ˈgrusəm; ˈgruːsəm/ *adj* very unpleasant and shocking, and usually connected with death or injury; GRISLY〔通常與死亡或傷害相關的〕令人厭惡的, 可怕的: *Spare me all the gruesome details.* 別跟我講那些可怕的細節。—**gruesomely** *adv*

gruff /grʌf; grʌf/ *adj* **1** unfriendly or annoyed, especially in the way you speak〔尤指說話的口氣〕不友好的; 生硬的: *a gruff reply* 生硬的回答 **2** a gruff voice sounds low and rough as if the speaker does not want to talk 低沉而生硬的〔指聲音, 好像說話者不願意講話〕—**gruffly** *adv* —**gruffness** *n* [U]

grum·ble[1] /ˈgrʌmbl; ˈgrʌmbəl/ *v* [I] **1** to keep complaining in an unhappy way 不斷地發牢騷, 抱怨: **[+about/at etc]** *The farmers are always grumbling about the weather.* 農民老是在抱怨天氣。**2** to make a very low sound that gets quieter then louder continuously; RUMBLE[1] (1) 發出時高時低的隆隆聲: *Is that your tummy grumbling?* 那是你的肚子在咕咕叫嗎? **3 mustn't grumble** *BrE spoken* used to say that you are fairly well or that you have no serious problems【英口】還不錯〔用來表示自己的情況沒有甚麼嚴重問題〕: *"How are you today?" "Mustn't grumble."* "你今天好嗎?" "還不錯。" —**grumbler** *n* [C]

grumble[2] *n* [C] **1** something that you feel dissatisfied about and keep complaining about 牢騷, 怨言: *Take your grumbles to the boss – don't bother me with them.* 有怨言去跟老闆說 —— 不要來煩我。**2 have a grumble** to complain about something 發牢騷, 抱怨

grum·bling ap·pen·dix /ˌ·· ·ˈ··/ *n* [singular] *BrE not technical* a condition in which your APPENDIX (1) causes you pain from time to time【英, 非術語】闌尾陣痛

grump·y /ˈgrʌmpɪ; ˈgrʌmpi/ *adj* bad-tempered and tending to complain 脾氣壞又愛發牢騷的 —**grumpily** *adv* **grumpiness** *n* [U]

grunge /grʌndʒ; grʌndʒ/ *n* [U] **1** *AmE informal* dirt; GRIME【美, 非正式】污物, 污垢: *What's all that grunge in the bathtub?* 浴缸裡的那些髒兮兮的東西是甚麼? **2** a style of fashion popular with young people in the early 1990s, in which they wear clothes that look dirty and untidy 邋遢時尚〔20世紀90年代初在年輕人中流行的一種時裝潮流〕**3** a type of loud music played with electric GUITARS popular during this period〔流行於20世紀90年代的〕"頹廢"音樂

grung·y /ˈgrʌndʒɪ; ˈgrʌndʒi/ *adj AmE informal* dirty and sometimes smelling bad in an offensive way【美, 非正式】骯髒的, 骯髒難聞的: *grungy jeans* 骯髒的牛仔褲

grunt[1] /grʌnt; grʌnt/ *v* **1** [I,T] to make short sounds or say a few words in a low rough voice, showing that you do not want to have a conversation〔表示不願意講話時〕發出哼聲; 嘟噥着說: *I tried to cheer him up but he only grunted.* 我想給他打氣, 可他只是嘟噥了一聲。**2** [I] if an animal grunts, especially a pig, it makes short low sounds deep in its throat〔尤指豬等〕發出咕嚕聲

grunt[2] *n* [C] **1** a short low sound made deep in your throat like the sound a pig makes 呼嚕聲, 嘟噥聲, 咕噥聲: *Chris just gave a grunt and went back to sleep.* 克里斯只是哼了一聲, 又睡着了。**2** *AmE slang* an INFANTRY soldier【美俚】步兵

grunt work /ˈ· ·/ *n* [U] *AmE informal* the hard uninteresting part of a piece of work; DONKEYWORK【美, 非正式】〔某項工作中〕困難而單調的部分

Gru·yère /gruˈjɛr; ˈgruːjeə/ *n* [U] a kind of hard cheese with holes in it, from Switzerland 格魯耶爾乾酪〔一種帶孔的瑞士硬乾酪〕

gryph·on /ˈgrɪfən; ˈgrɪfən/ *n* [C] another spelling of GRIFFIN griffin 的另一種拼法

g-spot /ˈdʒi spɑt; ˈdʒiː spɒt/ *n* [C] a centre of sexual feeling in a woman's VAGINA G點

G-string /ˈdʒi strɪŋ; ˈdʒiː ˌstrɪŋ/ *n* [C] a very small piece of cloth, leather etc worn to cover your sexual organs G帶, 遮羞布

GTI /ˌdʒi ti ˈaɪ; ˌdʒiː tiː ˈaɪ/ *adj* a GTI car has a special FUEL system which helps it to go at high speeds 大型旅行車噴射〔大型旅行車噴射型汽車裝有特別燃料系統, 有助於高速行駛〕—compare 比較 FUEL INJECTION

gua·ca·mo·le /ˌgwɑkəˈmolɪ; ˌgwɑːkəˈməʊli/ *n* [U] a Mexican dish made with crushed AVOCADOS 鱷梨色拉〔墨西哥菜餚〕

G

gua·no /ˋgwɑno; ˈgwɑːnəʊ/ *n* [U] solid waste passed from the stomachs of sea birds that is often put on soil to help plants grow 海鳥糞

2 3 **guar·an·tee¹** /ˌgærənˋti; ˌgærənˈtiː/ *v* [T]
1 ►PROMISE STH WILL HAPPEN 許諾某事會發生◄ to promise that something will certainly happen or be done 擔保, 保證: **guarantee (that)** *Take this opportunity, and I guarantee you won't regret it.* 抓住這個機會吧, 我保證你不會後悔的。| **guarantee sth** *The authorities could not guarantee the safety of the UN observers.* 當局無法保證聯合國觀察員的安全。| **guarantee sb sth** *Even if you complete your training I can't guarantee you a job.* 即使你完成了培訓, 我也無法保證你能有工作。
2 ►A PRODUCT 產品◄ to make a formal written promise to repair or replace a product if it has a fault within a specific period of time after you buy it 保修; 包換: **guarantee sth against** *a toaster guaranteed for one year against failure of parts* 零部件保用一年的烤麵包箱
3 ►LEGAL 法律上的◄ to make yourself legally responsible for the payment of money 保證付款
4 ►MAKE STH CERTAIN 確保某事◄ to make it certain that something will happen 保證〔某事必然發生〕: *She soon learned that marriage does not guarantee happiness.* 她很快就發現婚姻不能保證有幸福。
5 ►CERTAIN TO DO STH 肯定做某事◄ **be guaranteed to do sth** to be certain to behave, work, or happen in a particular way 肯定會以某種方式行事[工作, 發生]: *If you yell at him, he's guaranteed to do the opposite of what you want.* 如果你向他大喊大叫, 他肯定會跟你對着幹。
6 ►PROTECT 保護◄ **guarantee sth against** *AmE* to provide complete protection against harm or damage【美】〔為免受傷害或損毀〕提供完全的保護: *Rust-shield guarantees your car against corrosion.* "防鏽盾"保護你的汽車不受腐蝕。

2 **guarantee²** *n* [C]
1 a formal written promise to repair or replace a product without charging, if it has a fault within a specific time after you buy it 保修單; 包換單: *The television comes with a two-year guarantee.* 這台電視有兩年的保修期。| **be under guarantee** (=be protected by a guarantee) 在保用期內 *Your watch will be repaired free if it's still under guarantee.* 你的手錶在保用期內可享受免費修理。**2** a formal and firm promise that something will be done or will happen〔某事必將辦到或發生的〕正式而堅定的承諾: [+of] *Is there a guarantee of work after training?* 培訓結束之後是否保證可以就業? | **give sb a guarantee (that)** *Can you give me a guarantee that the work will be finished on time?* 你能向我保證工作會按時完成嗎? **3 a)** an agreement to be responsible for someone else's promise, especially a promise to pay a debt 擔保〔尤指為保證還債而作的擔保〕 **b)** something valuable given to someone to keep until the owner has kept their a promise, especially to pay a debt〔尤指對債務的〕擔保物; 抵押品 —compare 比較 SECURITY (4), WARRANTY

guar·an·tor /ˋgærəntɚ; ˌgærənˈtɔː/ *n* [C] *law* someone who promises that they will pay for something if the person who should pay for it does not【法律】擔保人

guar·an·ty /ˋgærəntɪ; ˈgærənti/ *n* [C] *AmE law* a formal promise, especially of payment【美, 法律】〔尤指有關付款的〕保證, 保證書 —see also 另見 WARRANTY

3 3 **guard¹** /gɑrd; gɑːd/ *n*
1 ►PERSON 人◄ [C] **a)** someone whose job is to guard a place, person, or object in order to protect them from attack or from thieves 衛兵, 警衛, 門衛: *The guards stopped us at the gate.* 衛兵把我們擋在門口。—see also 另見 SECURITY GUARD **b)** someone whose job is to guard prisoners and prevent them from escaping 獄吏, 監獄看守人
2 be on guard to be responsible for guarding a place or person for a specific period of time 站崗, 執勤: *Who was on guard when the fire broke out?* 火災發生時是誰在執勤?
3 keep/stand/mount guard (over) to guard a person or place 守衛, 看守〔某人或某地〕: *Catherine kept guard over the horses while we looked for water.* 我們找水時凱瑟琳看着馬。
4 ►GROUP 羣◄ [singular] a group of people, especially soldiers, who guard someone or something 一隊守衛〔尤指士兵〕
5 be under (armed) guard to be guarded by a group of people with weapons 在武裝人員的保衛[守衛]下
6 ►THING 事物◄ [C] something that is fitted to a machine or worn on a part of your body to protect you against damage or injury 保護裝置〔指安裝在機器上或戴在身體某部位以防損毀或傷害的裝置〕: *a football player's mouth guard* 橄欖球員的護齒
7 catch/throw/take sb off guard to surprise someone by doing or saying something that they are not ready to deal with〔乘某人不備而做或說某事〕使人驚訝: *Senator O'Hare was caught off guard by the reporter's question.* 記者突然提出的問題讓參議員奧哈爾楞住了。
8 be on your guard to pay careful attention to what is happening so that you avoid being tricked or getting into danger 警惕, 提防: *Be on your guard – they always try to cheat tourists.* 提防點 —— 他們總是想辦法欺騙遊客。| **lower your guard/let your guard down** (=forget to be careful) 放鬆警惕
9 ►ON A TRAIN 火車上◄ [C] *BrE* an official in charge of a train【英】列車長; CONDUCTOR (4) *AmE*【美】
10 ►BOXING 拳擊◄ [singular] the position of your hands in BOXING when you are holding them up to defend yourself〔拳擊中手的〕防禦姿勢
11 the Guards special groups of soldiers in the British army whose original duty was to guard the king or queen 英國的御林軍

guard² *v* [T] **1** to protect a person, place, or valuable object by staying near them and watching them 保衛, 守衛: *The Sergeant told Swift to guard the entrance to the building.* 警官叫斯威夫特守衛大樓的入口處。| **guard sb/sth against** *There is no one to guard these isolated farms against possible attack.* 這幾處孤立的農場門戶大開, 沒有人守衛。**2** to watch a prisoner and prevent them from escaping 看守〔囚犯〕 **3 guard your tongue** *old-fashioned* used to tell someone to be careful of what they say so that they do not tell a secret【過時】管住自己的嘴

guard against sth *phr v* [T] to try to prevent something from happening by being careful〔小心謹慎地〕防止…發生: *Nurses should guard against becoming too emotionally attached to their patients.* 護士應該防止對其看護的病人產生過多的感情依戀。

guard dog /ˋ· ·/ *n* [C] a dog often used by soldiers, police officers etc that is trained to guard a place 軍犬; 警犬

guard·ed /ˋgɑrdɪd; ˈgɑːdɪ̵d/ *adj* a guarded statement, remark etc deliberately does not give much information about your thoughts and feelings〔言辭等〕謹慎的, 有保留的, 提防的: *"What do you want?" Her tone was guarded and hesitant.* "你想要甚麼?" 她的語氣既謹慎又猶豫。—**guardedly** *adv*

guard·house /ˋgɑrdˌhaʊs; ˈgɑːdhaʊs/ *n* [C] a building for soldiers who are guarding the entrance to a military camp〔軍營入口處的〕崗哨樓

guard·i·an /ˋgɑrdɪən; ˈgɑːdiən/ *n* [C] **1** someone who is legally responsible for looking after someone else's child, especially after the child's parents have died 監護人 **2** *formal* someone who guards or protects something, especially an institution or moral principle【正式】〔尤指某種制度或道德準則的〕維護者, 保衛者: [+of] *The US has represented itself as the guardian of democracy.* 美國把自己描繪成民主政治的衛士。

guardian an·gel /ˌ··· ˋ··/ *n* [C] **1** a good spirit who is believed to protect a person or place〔某人或某地的〕守

護天使 **2** someone who helps or protects someone else when they are in trouble 幫助或保護有難者的好人

guard·i·an·ship /ˋgɑrdɪən͵ʃɪp; ˈgɑːdiənʃɪp/ *n* [U] *law* the position of being legally responsible for someone else's child, or the period during which you have this position【法律】監護人的身分[期限]

guard·rail /ˋgɑrd͵rel; ˈgɑːd-reɪl/ *n* [C] **1** a bar or RAIL that is intended to prevent people from falling from a bridge or stairs〔橋或樓梯的〕護欄 **2** *especially AmE* a bar or RAIL[1] (1) intended to prevent drivers from going off the road in a car accident【尤美】〔防止汽車在交通事故中衝出公路的〕護欄

guard·room /ˋgɑrd͵rum; ˈgɑːd-rʊm/ *n* [C] a room, especially in a GUARDHOUSE, for soldiers who are guarding a military camp 衛兵室, 警衛室

guards·man /ˋgɑrdzmən; ˈgɑːdzmən/ *n* [C] **1** a British soldier in the Guards (GUARD[1] (11)) 英國御林軍士兵 **2** a member of the US National Guard 美國國民警衛隊士兵

guard's van /ˋ· ·/ *n* [C] *BrE* the part of a train where the official in charge of it travels, usually at the back【英】〔火車〕列車長車廂〔通常在列車尾〕; CABOOSE *AmE*【美】

gua·va /ˋgwɑvə; ˈgwɑːvə/ *n* [C] a small tropical fruit with pink flesh and many seeds inside 番石榴〔一種小型熱帶水果〕

gu·ber·na·to·ri·al /͵gjubɚnəˋtorɪəl; ͵guːbənəˈtɔːriəl◂/ *adj formal* connected with the position of being a GOVERNOR【正式】州長的

gue·ril·la /gəˋrɪlə; gəˈrɪlə/ *n* [C] another spelling of GUERRILLA guerrilla 的另一種拼法

guern·sey /ˋgɝnzɪ; ˈgɜːnzi/ *n* [C] a SWEATER made of wool with a special pattern of raised stitches across the shoulder〔肩部有用凸針編織的圖案的〕毛衣

guer·ril·la /gəˋrɪlə; gəˈrɪlə/ *n* [C] a member of an unofficial military group, especially one fighting to remove a government from power, that attacks its enemies in small groups unexpectedly 游擊隊員: *guerrilla warfare* 游擊戰 —compare 比較 FREEDOM FIGHTER, TERRORIST

1 3 **guess¹** /gɛs; ges/ *v*

1 ▶WITHOUT BEING SURE 不確信◀ [I,T] to try to answer a question or make a judgment about something without having all the necessary facts, so that you are not sure whether you are correct 猜測: *I'd say he's around 50, but I'm only guessing.* 我想他大約50歲, 不過我只是猜測而已。| **guess what/who/how etc** *Guess how much I had to pay – 3,000 pounds!* 猜一猜我得付多少錢 —— 3,000英鎊! | **guess at** *We can only guess at what caused the crash.* 我們只能猜測這次空難的原因。

2 ▶GUESS CORRECTLY 正確猜出◀ [I,T] to guess something correctly 猜中, 猜對: **[+from]** *"How did you know I won?" "I just guessed from the look on your face."* "你怎麼知道我贏了?" "我只是從你臉上的神色猜出來的。" | **guess that** *I'd never have guessed that you two were brothers.* 我絕對不可能猜出你們倆是兄弟。| **guess sth** *You've guessed my secret.* 你已經猜中了我的祕密。| **have guessed as much** (=have guessed something before someone tells you) 早猜中了 *He told me he was leaving, but I had already guessed as much.* 他告訴我他要走了, 但我事前猜測也是這樣。

3 I guess *spoken especially AmE* used to mean that you suppose something is true or likely【口, 尤美】我想, 我認為〔用來表示你認為某事是真實的或很有可能〕: *I guess I never married because I just didn't find the right girl.* 我想我從來沒結過婚是因為我找不到中意的女孩。| **I guess so/not** *"She wasn't happy?" "I guess not."* "她不高興嗎?" "我想她是不高興。"

4 keep sb guessing to not tell someone what is going to happen next〔不告訴某人下一步將發生甚麼〕讓某人捉摸不定

5 guess what/you'll never guess *spoken* used when you are about to tell someone something that will surprise them【口】猜猜看/你永遠也猜不出: *Guess what! Bradley's resigned.* 你準猜不到, 布拉德利辭職了! | *You'll never guess who I saw today.* 你永遠也猜不出我今天看見誰了。

guess² *n* [C] **1** an attempt to guess something 猜測: *If you're not sure of the answer give us your best guess.* 如果你對答案不確定, 把你最有把握的猜測告訴我們。| *I'll give you three guesses.* 我讓你猜三次。| **make a guess (at)** *I don't know the exact figure but I'll make a guess at it.* 我不知道準確的數字, 不過我要猜測一下。| **rough guess** (=one that is unlikely to be exact) 粗略的猜測 *I'd say she's about 35, but that's only a rough guess.* 我說她大約35歲, 不過那只是粗略的猜測而已。| **wild guess** (=one that is made without much thought) 亂猜 | **have a guess at** *BrE*【英】**/take a guess at** *AmE*【美】(=try to guess something) 猜測 *Take a guess at what's in the third box and you could win a trip to Hawaii.* 猜猜第三個盒子裝的是甚麼, 你可能贏得去夏威夷旅遊的機會。| **at a guess** *spoken* (=used to mean that what you are saying is just a guess)【口】憑猜測〔表示你所說的不過是一種猜測〕 *The girl was twelve years old at a guess.* 我猜這個女孩有十二歲。**2** an opinion formed by guessing 猜想: **my guess is** *My guess is that there won't be many people there today.* 我猜今天那裡不會有許多人。 2
3 be anybody's guess to be something that no one knows 誰也不知道, 誰也拿不準: *What she's going to do with her life now is anybody's guess.* 現在她的日子怎麼過誰也不知道。**4 your guess is as good as mine** *spoken* used to tell someone that you do not know any more than they do about something【口】我跟你一樣不知道

guess·ti·mate /ˋgɛstə͵mət; ˈgestɪ̵mɪ̵t/ *n* [C] *informal* an attempt to judge a quantity by guessing it【非正式】〔對某數量的全憑猜測的〕估計 —**guesstimate** /-tə͵met; -tɪ̵meɪt/ *v* [I,T]

guess·work /ˋgɛs͵wɝk; ˈgeswɜːk/ *n* [U] the method of trying to find the answer to something by guessing 猜測, 推測: *In this study, scientific methods seem to have been replaced by guesswork.* 在這項研究裡, 科學的方法似乎被推測替代了。

guest¹ /gɛst; gest/ *n* [C] 2 2

1 ▶AT YOUR HOUSE 在你家裡◀ someone who is staying in someone else's home because they have been invited 客人, 賓客: *We have guests staying with us.* 有客人住在我們家裡。

2 ▶AT A HOTEL 在旅館◀ someone who is paying to stay in a hotel, GUESTHOUSE etc 旅客, 宿客: *The hotel takes very good care of its guests.* 這家旅館細心照料住宿的客人。

3 ▶AT A RESTAURANT/CLUB 在餐館/俱樂部◀ someone who is invited to a restaurant, theatre, club etc by another person who pays for them〔被邀請去餐館、劇院、俱樂部由另一人請客的〕客人: *I'd like you to be my guest for dinner tonight.* 今天晚上我想請你吃飯。

4 ▶ON A SHOW 演出◀ someone famous who is invited to take part in a show, concert etc, in addition to those who usually take part〔表演、音樂會等的〕特邀名演員[演奏者]: **make a guest appearance** *She is making her first guest appearance on the show.* 她在這場表演中作她的首次特邀演出。

5 be my guest *spoken* used to politely give someone permission to do what they have asked to do【口】請便〔用於禮貌地同意別人的請求〕: *"Do you mind if I look at your notes?" "Of course not. Be my guest."* "我想看一下你的筆記, 你介意嗎?" "當然不介意, 請便。"

6 guest of honour *BrE*【英】**/honor** *AmE*【美】the most important person who has been invited to a special occasion, especially a celebration that is given for them 貴賓

7 guest speaker someone who has been invited to make a speech at a meeting 特邀演講人 —compare 比較 HOST[1] (1)

guest² *v* [I] to take part in a show, concert etc as a guest performer〔以特邀演員身分〕參加演出[音樂會等]

guest book /ˈ· ·/ *n* [C] a book in which everyone who comes to a formal occasion or stays at a hotel writes their name〔正式場合或旅館的〕客人登記簿

guest·house /ˈgɛsthaus; ˈgesthaʊs/ *n* [C] a private house where people can pay to stay and have meals 家庭旅館

guest·room /ˈgɛstˌrum; ˈgest-rʊm/ *n* [C] a room in a private house that is kept for visitors to sleep in 客房〔指私人住宅中供客人使用的臥室〕

guest work·er /ˈ· ˌ··/ *n* [C] a foreign worker, usually from a poor country, working in another country for a limited period 外籍工人〔在另一國家短期工作的人, 通常來自貧窮國家〕

guff /gʌf; gʌf/ *n* [U] *informal* nonsense【非正式】胡說, 廢話: *Don't give me any of that guff.* 別跟我說那些廢話了。

guf·faw /gʌˈfɔ; gəˈfɔː/ *v* [I] to laugh loudly 大笑 —**guffaw** *n* [C]: *A loud guffaw came from the back of the room.* 房間後部傳來一陣大笑。

3 **guid·ance** /ˈgaɪdn̩s; ˈgaɪdəns/ *n* [U] **1** help and advice given to someone about their work, education, personal life etc 指導, 引導: [**+on/about**] *I went to a career counselor for guidance on how to start my job search.* 我到一位就業顧問那裡去討教如何開始找工作。**2** the process of directing a MISSILE (1) in flight〔飛行中導彈的〕制導(過程): *electronic guidance systems* 電子制導系統

guidance coun·sel·or /ˈ·· ˌ···/ *n* [C] *AmE* someone employed in a school to give advice to students about what subjects to study and to help them with personal problems【美】輔導員〔指學校中就如何選課及個人問題向學生提供指導的人員〕—see also 另見 MARRIAGE GUIDANCE

2 **guide**[1] /gaɪd; gaɪd/ *n* [C]
2 **1 ►PERSON 人◄ a)** someone who shows you the way to a place, especially someone whose job is to show a place to tourists 嚮導; 導遊: *a tour guide* 導遊 **b)** someone who advises you and influences the way you live and behave 指導者, 引導者: *The medicine man was the tribe's spiritual guide.* 巫醫是這個部落的精神指導。
2 ►FOR JUDGING STH 用於判斷某事◄ something that provides information on which you can base your judgement, or your method of doing something〔判斷或行事的〕根據: [**+to**] *The opinion polls are not a very reliable guide to how people will vote.* 根據這些民意測驗來判斷人們將如何投票, 並不可靠。
3 ►BOOK 書◄ a) a book that provides information on a particular subject or explains how to do something; HANDBOOK 指南; 手冊: [**+to**] *a guide to North American birds* 北美鳥類指南 **b)** a guidebook 旅行指南
4 ►GIRL 女孩◄ *BrE*【英】**a) the Guides** the Guides Association, which trains girls in practical skills and tries to develop their character 女童子軍 **b)** a member of the Guides Association 女童子軍成員

guide[2] *v* [T] **1** to take someone through or to a place that you know very well, showing them the way 帶領, 引導: [**+along/through/to etc**] *He guided us through the narrow streets to the central mosque.* 他帶領我們穿過狹窄的街道, 來到中央清真寺。**2** to help someone to move in a particular direction 為…引路: *She took her friend's arm to guide her.* 她挽着朋友的胳膊, 為她引路。**3** to strongly influence someone's behaviour, thoughts etc 強烈影響〔行為、思想等〕: *He let himself be guided by his mother's opinion.* 他讓自己為母親的觀點所左右。**4** to show someone the right way to do something, especially something difficult or complicated 指引, 指導〔尤指做困難或複雜的事〕: **guide sb through** *We need a lawyer to guide us through the procedure.* 我們需要一位律師來指導我們完成這一手續。—see also 另見 GUIDING —see 見 LEAD[1] (USAGE)

guide·book /ˈgaɪdˌbʊk; ˈgaɪdbʊk/ *n* [C] a special book about a city, area etc that gives details about the place and its history〔關於城市、地區等的〕旅行指南

guided mis·sile /ˌ·· ˈ··/ *n* [C] a MISSILE (1) that can be controlled electronically while it is flying 導彈

guide dog /ˈ· ·/ *n* [C] *BrE* a dog trained to guide a blind person【英】導盲犬; SEEING EYE DOG *AmE*【美】

guided tour /ˌ·· ˈ·/ *n* [C] a trip around a city, building etc led by someone who tells people about the place 有導遊的遊覽: *a guided tour of the palace* 有導遊引領的對這座宮殿的遊覽

guide·lines /ˈgaɪdˌlaɪnz; ˈgaɪdlaɪnz/ *n* [plural] official instructions about the best way to do something, especially something that could be difficult or dangerous〔尤指可能是困難或危險的事的〕指導方針, 行動準則: [**+for/on**] *Staff have been issued with new guidelines for dealing with infectious patients.* 全體職員都發給了處理感染病人的新規定。

guid·ing /ˈgaɪdɪŋ; ˈgaɪdɪŋ/ *adj* **guiding principle/star/light** a principle, idea, or person that you follow in order to help you decide what you should do in a difficult situation 指導原則/指路星/指路明燈〔在困境中處理問題所遵循的原則、觀念或所遵從的人物〕

guild /gɪld; gɪld/ *n* [C] **1** an organization of people who do the same job, who joined together in the past to help each other improve their businesses 同業公會; 行會 **2** a group of people with the same interest 協會: *the Women's Guild* 婦女協會

guil·der /ˈgɪldɚ; ˈgɪldə/ *n* [C] the former standard unit of money in the Netherlands; GULDEN 盾〔原荷蘭貨幣單位〕

guild·hall /ˈgɪldˋhɔl; ˌgɪldˈhɔːl/ *n* [C] a large building in which members of a guild met in the past 行會[同業公會]會館

guile /gaɪl; gaɪl/ *n* [U] *formal* the use of clever dishonest methods to deceive someone【正式】施詭計, 欺騙 —**guileful** *adj*

guile·less /ˈgaɪllɪs; ˈgaɪl-ləs/ *adj* behaving in an honest way, without trying to hide anything or deceive people 誠實無欺的 —**guilelessly** *adv* —**guilelessness** *n* [U]

guil·le·mot /ˈgɪləˌmɑt; ˈgɪlɪmɒt/ *n* [C] a black and white sea bird with a narrow beak 海鳩

guil·lo·tine[1] /ˈgɪləˌtin; ˈgɪlətiːn/ *n* [C] **1** a piece of equipment used to cut off the heads of criminals, especially in France in the past〔尤指法國以前使用的〕斷頭台 **2** a piece of equipment used to cut large sheets of paper 切紙機, 裁切機 **3** *BrE* the setting of a time limit on the discussion about a proposed law in the British parliament【英】〔英國議會〕對一項法律議案進行討論的時限的規定

guillotine[2] *v* [T] **1** to cut off someone's head using a guillotine 在斷頭台上將…斬首 **2** *BrE* to limit the period of time allowed for the discussion of a proposed law in the British parliament【英】〔英國議會〕限制〔對一項法律議案進行討論的時間〕

guilt /gɪlt; gɪlt/ *n* [U] **1** a strong feeling of shame and sadness because you have done something that you know is wrong 內疚, 自責: [**+about/at**] *Don't you have any feelings of guilt about leaving David?* 你離開大衛難道沒有任何內疚感嗎? | **sense of guilt** *He felt an enormous sense of guilt when he thought about how he'd treated her.* 他想到自己當時那樣對待她, 感到非常內疚。**2** the fact of having broken an official law or moral rule 犯罪: *an admission of guilt* 承認有罪 | *It is up to the prosecution to establish the defendant's guilt.* 控方有責任證實被告有罪。**3** responsibility and blame for something bad that has happened 責任, 罪責: *The teacher said Sonia was impossible to control and that the guilt lay with her parents.* 老師說索尼亞根本不受人管教, 責任可歸咎於她的父母。**4 guilt trip** a feeling of guilt about something 負疚感: **lay/put a guilt trip on sb** *AmE informal* (=make someone feel guilty about something)【美, 非正式】使某人感到內疚

guilt·less /ˋgɪltlɪs; ˈgɪltləs/ *adj* not responsible for a crime or for having done something wrong; INNOCENT[1] (1) 無罪的, 無辜的 —**guiltlessly** *adv*

guilt-rid·den /ˈ· ˌ··/ *adj* feeling so guilty about something that you cannot think about anything else 受內疚感折磨而不能自已的

2 3 **guilt·y** /ˋgɪltɪ; ˈgɪlti/ *adj* **guiltier, guiltiest**

1 ▶ASHAMED 羞愧的◀ feeling very ashamed and sad because you have done something that you know is wrong 羞愧的, 內疚的: [+about] *I feel really guilty about forgetting her birthday again.* 我又忘記了她的生日, 對此我確實感到內疚。| **guilty conscience** *My guilty conscience got the better of me, and I went back to apologize.* 我無法抑制內疚的心情, 便回去道歉。

2 ▶OF A CRIME 關於罪行的◀ having done something that is a crime 犯有罪行的, 有罪的: **guilty of** *The jury found her guilty of murder.* 陪審團裁定她的謀殺罪名成立。| **plead guilty** *law* (=admit in a court of law that you are guilty)【法律】在法庭上認罪 | **not guilty** *law* (=not guilty of the offence you are charged with in a court of law)【法律】無罪的〔指並未犯有在法庭上被指控的罪行〕—opposite 反義詞 INNOCENT[1] (1)

3 responsible for behaviour that is morally or socially unacceptable〔對道德敗壞、社會唾棄的行為〕負有責任的: **guilty of doing sth** *Lately the press has been guilty of reporting scandal in order to sell papers.* 報界近來為了銷售報紙而報道醜聞, 自取其咎。

4 guilty party *formal* the person who has done something illegal or wrong【正式】犯罪的一方, 有過錯的一方 —**guiltily** *adv* —**guiltiness** *n* [U]

This graph shows some of the words most commonly used with the adjective **guilty**. 本圖表所示為含有形容詞 guilty 的一些最常用詞語。

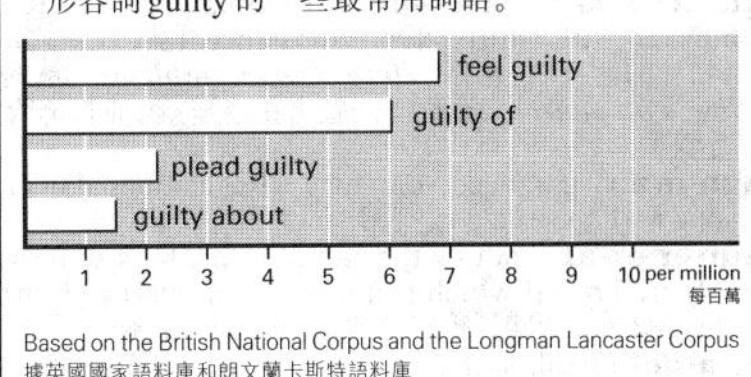

Based on the British National Corpus and the Longman Lancaster Corpus
據英國國家語料庫和朗文蘭卡斯特語料庫

guin·ea /ˋgɪnɪ; ˈgɪni/ *n* [C] a British gold coin or unit of money used in the past, worth £1.05 畿尼〔英國舊時的一種金幣或貨幣單位, 合 1.05 英鎊〕

guinea fowl /ˈ·· ˌ·/ *n* [C] a grey African bird that is often used for food 珍珠雞〔常供食用的一種非洲灰色禽類〕

guinea pig /ˈ·· ˌ·/ *n* [C] **1** a small round animal that has fur, short ears, and no tail, which is kept as a pet 天竺鼠, 豚鼠〔一種小型寵物〕**2** someone who is used in a scientific test to see how successful or safe a new product, system etc is 供科學實驗的人〔為試驗某產品、系統等的效果〕

guise /gaɪz; gaɪz/ *n* [C] *formal* the appearance of something that makes it seem different from how it really is, especially in order to deceive someone【正式】裝扮過的外表, 偽裝: **in/under the guise of** *Advertising material was given to us under the guise of information.* 廣告材料被偽裝成資訊送到我們這裡。| **in a different guise** *It's just the same set of ideas in a different guise.* 這還是老一套的想法, 只是形式不同而已。

3 **gui·tar** /gɪˋtɑr; gɪˈtɑː/ *n* [C] a musical instrument that has six strings and is played by plucking (PLUCK[1] (5)) the strings 結他 —**guitarist** *n* [C]

gu·lag /ˋgulæg; ˈguːlæg/ *n* [C] one of a group of prison camps in the former USSR, where conditions were very bad 古拉格, 前蘇聯勞改營

gulch /gʌltʃ; gʌltʃ/ *n* [C] *AmE* a narrow deep valley formed by flowing water, but usually dry【美】〔由流水沖刷形成, 通常已經乾涸的〕峽谷, 溝壑

gul·den /ˋguldən; ˈgʊldən/ *n* [C] a GUILDER 荷蘭盾

gulf /gʌlf; gʌlf/ *n* [C] **1** a large area of sea partly en- 3
closed by land 海灣: *the Gulf of Mexico* 墨西哥灣 **2** a great difference and lack of understanding between two groups of people, especially in their beliefs, opinions, and way of life 鴻溝, 分歧, 隔閡: [+**between**] *The gulf between management and unions is as wide as ever.* 管理部門和工會之間的分歧依舊嚴重。**3** a deep hollow place in the Earth's surface; CHASM (1)〔地球表面的〕深坑, 深淵

Gulf Stream /ˈ· ·/ *n* [singular] a current of warm water that flows northeastward in the Atlantic Ocean from the Gulf of Mexico towards Europe 墨西哥灣流〔大西洋中從墨西哥灣向東北流向歐洲的暖流〕

gull[1] /gʌl; gʌl/ *n* [C] **1** a large common black and white sea bird that lives near the sea; SEAGULL 海鷗 **2** *literary* someone who is easily deceived【文】易受騙的人

gull[2] *v* [T] *old use* to cheat or deceive someone【舊】欺騙, 詐騙

gul·let /ˋgʌlɪt; ˈgʌlɪ̈t/ *n* [C] the tube through which food goes down your throat 食管

gul·ley /ˋgʌlɪ; ˈgʌli/ *n* [C] another spelling of GULLY gully 的另一種拼法

gul·li·ble /ˋgʌləbḷ; ˈgʌlɪ̈bəl/ *adj* too ready to believe what other people tell you, so that you are easily deceived 輕信的, 易受騙上當的: *Plastic replicas were sold to gullible tourists as ancient relics.* 塑料複製品被當作古代文物賣給了輕信的遊客。—**gullibly** *adv* —**gullibility** /ˌgʌləˋbɪlətɪ; ˌgʌlɪ̈ˈbɪlɪ̈ti/ *n* [U]

gul·ly /ˋgʌlɪ; ˈgʌli/ *n* [C] **1** a small narrow valley, usually formed by a lot of rain flowing down the side of a hill〔山坡上被雨水沖成的〕隘谷, 溝壑 **2** a deep DITCH[1] 深溝

gulp[1] /gʌlp; gʌlp/ *v* **1** [T] also 又作 **gulp** sth ↔ **down** to swallow something quickly 快速吞下: *She gulped down the rest of her coffee and left.* 她匆匆喝掉剩下的咖啡便離開了。**2** [T] also 又作 **gulp** sth ↔ **in** to take in quick large breaths of air 大口吸氣: *We rushed outside and gulped in the sweet fresh air.* 我們跑到外面大口呼吸甘甜的新鮮空氣。**3** [I] to swallow suddenly because you are surprised or nervous〔因驚訝或緊張〕倒吸氣: *I gulped when I saw the bill.* 我看到賬單時倒吸一口氣。

gulp sth ↔ **back** *phr v* [T] to stop yourself from expressing your feelings 抑制, 忍住〔自己的感情〕: *Sandra tried to gulp back her tears.* 桑德拉竭力忍住淚水。

gulp[2] *n* [C] an act of gulping 吞嚥: **take a gulp** *He took a gulp and handed the cup back to Rachel.* 他喝了一大口, 然後把杯子遞還給雷切爾。| **in one gulp/at a gulp** *I've seen him swallow a whole glass of vodka in one gulp.* 我見過他把整杯伏特加酒一飲而盡。

gum[1] /gʌm; gʌm/ *n* **1** [C usually plural 一般用複數] one of the two areas of firm pink flesh at the top and bottom of your mouth, in which your teeth are fixed 齒齦 —see picture at 參見 TEETH 圖 **2** [U] CHEWING GUM 口香糖 **3** [U] a sticky substance found in the stems of some trees 樹膠 **4** [U] *BrE* a special kind of glue used to stick light things such as paper together【英】黏膠 **5** [C] a GUM TREE 桉樹 **6 by gum!** *spoken old-fashioned* used to express surprise【口, 過時】哎喲!〔表示驚訝〕

gum[2] *v* **gummed, gumming** [T always+adv/prep] *BrE* to stick something to something else, using a sticky substance【英】〔用膠〕黏住: **gum sth to/down etc** *A large label had been gummed to the back of the photograph.* 一張大標籤被黏貼在照片的背後。

gum sth ↔ **up** *phr v* [T] *informal* to prevent something from working properly by covering it with a sticky substance【非正式】搞糟; 使出故障〔由於黏性物質覆蓋而不能正常工作〕: *Dirt had got inside the watch and gummed up the works.* 污垢進了手錶裡面, 使機件不能正常工作。

gum·ball /ˋgʌmbɔl; ˈgʌmbɔːl/ *n* [C] *AmE* CHEWING GUM in the form of a small round brightly coloured sweet【美】彩色圓形口香糖

gum·bo /ˋgʌmbo; ˈgʌmbəʊ/ *n* [U] **1** a thick soup made with meat, fish, and OKRA (=a small green vegetable) 秋葵湯〔用肉、魚和秋葵製作的很稠的湯〕 **2** a word used in some parts of the US for OKRA 秋葵〔此詞使用於美國某些地區〕

gum·boil /ˋgʌm͵bɔɪl; ˈgʌmbɔɪl/ *n* [C] a painful swelling on your GUM[1] (1); ABSCESS 齒齦膿腫

gum·boot /ˋgʌm͵but; ˈgʌmbuːt/ *n* [C] *BrE old-fashioned* a tall boot made of rubber worn to keep your feet dry【英, 過時】長統橡膠靴

gum·drop /ˋgʌm͵drɑp; ˈgʌmdrɒp/ *n* [C] a firm transparent sweet that is like JELLY 橡皮糖〔膠凍狀的透明糖食〕

gum·my /ˋgʌmɪ; ˈgʌmi/ *adj* **1** sticky or covered in GUM[1] (3) 黏性的, 塗膠的 **2** a gummy smile shows the gums (GUM[1] (1)) in your mouth 露齒齦的〔微笑〕

gump·tion /ˋgʌmpʃən; ˈgʌmpʃən/ *n* [U] the ability and determination to decide what needs doing and to do it 精明, 魄力, 勇氣: *He probably didn't even have enough gumption to propose to her.* 他可能連向她求婚的勇氣都沒有。

gum·shoe /ˋgʌmˋʃu; ˈgʌm͵ʃuː/ *n* [C] *AmE old-fashioned* a DETECTIVE【美, 過時】偵探

gum tree /ˈ· ·/ *n* [C] **1** a tall tree which produces a strong-smelling oil used in medicine; EUCALYPTUS 桉樹 **2 be up a gum tree** *BrE informal* to be in a very difficult situation【英, 非正式】陷入困境

gun 槍

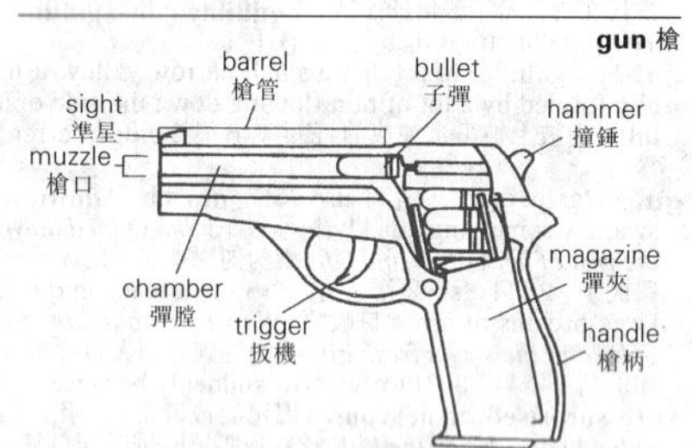

2 2 **gun¹** /gʌn; gʌn/ *n* [C] **1** a weapon from which bullets or SHELLS[1] (3) are fired 槍, 砲 **2** a tool used to send out a liquid, such as paint, GREASE[1] (2), or glue, by pressure 噴射器, 噴射槍〔供噴射諸如油漆、油脂或膠水的工具〕— see also 另見 FLASHGUN, SPRAY GUN **3** *AmE informal* someone who is temporarily put in a position to do a particular job【美, 非正式】被臨時安排做某項工作的人: *He was the sixth gun on the job.* 他是被臨時安排做這份工作的第六個人。**4 hired gun** *AmE informal* someone who is paid to shoot someone else【美, 非正式】〔被雇傭來射殺某人的〕殺手, 刺客, 槍手 —see also 另見 SON OF A GUN, **stick to your guns** (STICK[1]), **jump the gun** (JUMP[1] (11)), **go great guns** (GREAT (7)), **spike sb's guns** (SPIKE[2] (4))

gun² *v* **1** [T] *AmE informal* to make the engine of a car go very fast by pressing the ACCELERATOR (1) very hard【美, 非正式】加速, 猛踩油門: **gun it** (=make a car go fast) 使汽車加速行駛 **2 be gunning for sb** *BrE informal* to be trying to find an opportunity to criticize or harm someone【英, 非正式】伺機批評[加害]: *Ever since I proved he'd made a mistake in the accounts he's been gunning for me.* 自從我證實他的賬目有錯後, 他一直在尋找機會加害於我。

gun sb ↔ **down** *phr v* [T] to shoot someone and badly injure or kill them, especially someone who cannot defend themselves 用槍擊傷; 擊斃〔尤指不能自衛的人〕: *Innocent civilians were gunned down in the street.* 無辜的平民被槍擊倒在街上。

gun·boat /ˋgʌn͵bot; ˈgʌnbəʊt/ *n* [C] **1** a small military ship that is used near a coast〔海岸〕小砲艇 **2 gunboat diplomacy** the practice of threatening to use force against another country to make them agree to your demands 砲艦外交〔指用武力威脅使另一國家屈從的做法〕

gun car·riage /ˈ· ͵· ·/ *n* [C] a frame with wheels on which a heavy gun is moved around 砲架

gun con·trol /ˈ· ·͵·/ *n* [U] laws that restrict the possession and use of guns 槍支管制法

gun dog /ˈ· ·/ *n* [C] a dog trained to find and bring back dead birds shot for sport 獵狗〔指受過訓練能尋找並帶回被射殺禽鳥的犬〕; BIRD DOG *AmE*【美】

gun·fight /ˋgʌn͵faɪt; ˈgʌnfaɪt/ *n* [C] a fight between people using guns 槍戰, 砲戰 —**gunfighter** *n* [C]

gun·fire /ˋgʌn͵faɪr; ˈgʌnfaɪə/ *n* [U] the repeated firing of guns, or the noise made by this 砲火, 砲火聲: *enemy gunfire* 敵人的砲火

gunge¹ /gʌndʒ; gʌndʒ/ *n* [U] *BrE informal* any substance that is dirty, sticky, or unpleasant; GUNK[1]【英, 非正式】污穢、黏性或討厭的東西 —**gungy** *adj*

gunge² *v* **be gunged up with sth** *BrE informal* to be blocked with a dirty sticky substance【英, 非正式】被〔骯髒黏糊的東西〕堵塞

gung-ho /͵gʌŋˋho; ͵gʌŋˈhəʊ/ *adj informal* very eager to do something, especially too eager【非正式】非常急切的, 莽撞的, 操之過急的: *His gung-ho attitude was not appropriate for such delicate negotiations.* 他那急切的態度在這種微妙的談判中是不適宜的。

gunk¹ /gʌŋk; gʌŋk/ *n* [U] *informal* any substance that is dirty, sticky, or unpleasant【非正式】污穢[黏性或討厭]的東西; GUNGE[1] *BrE*【英】: *The milk congealed into a black gunk on the stove.* 牛奶在爐子上凝結成一塊黑色黏糊糊的東西。—**gunky** *adj*

gunk² *v* **be gunked up (with)** *AmE informal* to be blocked with a dirty sticky substance【美, 非正式】被〔黏性的髒東西〕堵塞: *Here's your problem. The fuel line's all gunked up.* 你的問題出在這裡。輸油管全給污垢堵塞了。

gun·man /ˋgʌn͵mæn; ˈgʌnmən/ *n* [C] a criminal or TERRORIST who uses a gun 持槍歹徒; 恐怖分子

gun·met·al /ˋgʌn͵mɛtl̩; ˈgʌn͵metl/ *n* [U] a dull grey coloured metal which is a mixture of COPPER (1), TIN[1] (1), and ZINC 砲銅〔暗灰色的銅、錫、鋅的合金〕

gun·nel /ˋgʌnl̩; ˈgʌnl/ *n* [C] a GUNWALE 舷緣, 舷邊

gun·ner /ˋgʌnɚ; ˈgʌnə/ *n* [C] **1** a soldier, sailor etc whose job is to aim or fire a large gun〔陸軍、海軍的〕砲手 **2** a soldier in the British ARTILLERY (=part of the army which uses heavy guns)〔英國砲兵部隊中的〕砲兵: *Gunner Smith* 砲兵史密斯

gun·ner·y /ˋgʌnərɪ; ˈgʌnəri/ *n* [U] the science and practice of shooting with heavy guns 重砲射擊術, 重砲射擊操作: *a gunnery officer* 重砲射擊軍官

gun·ny·sack /ˋgʌnɪ͵sæk; ˈgʌnisæk/ *n* [C] *AmE* a large bag made from HEMP, in which coal, potatoes etc are stored【美】〔裝貯煤、馬鈴薯等用的〕黃麻袋

gun·point /ˋgʌn͵pɔɪnt; ˈgʌnpɔɪnt/ *n* **at gunpoint** while threatening or being threatened with a gun 用槍威脅, 在槍口威脅下: *The frightened clerk was forced at gunpoint to hand over all the money.* 驚恐的職員在槍口威脅下被迫把所有的錢交出去。

gun·pow·der /ˋgʌn͵paudɚ; ˈgʌn͵paʊdə/ *n* [U] an explosive substance in the form of a powder 火藥

gun·run·ning /ˈ· ͵· ·/ *n* [U] the activity of taking guns into a country secretly and illegally, especially so that they can be used by people who want to fight against their government 私運軍火〔祕密非法帶入某國以供反政府分子使用〕—**gun-runner** *n* [C]

gun·ship /ˋgʌn͵ʃɪp; ˈgʌnʃɪp/ *n* [C] a military HELICOPTER used to protect other helicopters and to destroy enemy guns 武裝直升機

gun·shot /ˋgʌn͵ʃɑt; ˈgʌnʃɒt/ *n* **1** [C] the sound made when a gun is fired 槍砲聲 **2** [U] the bullets fired from a gun〔槍射出的〕子彈: **gunshot wound** (=a wound caused by a bullet) 槍傷 **3 out of/within gunshot** beyond or within the distance that can be reached by a shot fired from a gun 超出槍射程/在槍射程之內

gun-shy /ˈ· ·/ *adj* **1** a GUN DOG that is gun-shy is easily frightened by the noise of a gun〔獵狗〕易被槍聲嚇倒的 **2** *AmE* very careful or frightened about doing something, because of a bad experience in the past【美】〔因過去失敗的經歷而〕非常謹慎的, 提心吊膽的

gun·sling·er /ˈgʌnˌslɪŋɚ; ˈgʌnˌslɪŋə/ *n* [C] *AmE* someone who is very skilful at using guns, especially a criminal【美】熟練的槍手〔尤指罪犯〕

gun·smith /ˈgʌnˌsmɪθ; ˈgʌnˌsmɪθ/ *n* [C] someone who makes and repairs guns 槍砲匠

gun·wale /ˈgʌnl; ˈgʌnl/ *n* [C] *technical* the upper edge of the side of a boat or small ship【術語】舷緣, 舷邊

gup·py /ˈgʌpɪ; ˈgʌpi/ *n plural* **guppies** [C] a small brightly-coloured tropical fish 虹鱂, 孔雀魚〔小型色彩亮麗熱帶魚〕

gur·gle¹ /ˈgɝgl; ˈgɜːgəl/ *v* [I] **1** if something such as a stream gurgles, it makes a low sound, like water flowing through a pipe〔溪水等〕汩汩作響 **2** if a baby gurgles, it makes this kind of sound in its throat〔嬰兒喉中〕發汩汩聲, 發咯咯聲 —**gurgling** *adj*: *a gurgling stream* 汩汩流的小溪

gurgle² *n* [C] the sound of gurgling 汩汩聲, 咯咯聲

gur·ney /ˈgɝnɪ; ˈgɜːni/ *n* [C] *AmE* a long narrow table with wheels used for moving sick people in a hospital【美】〔醫院中移動病人用的〕輪牀

gu·ru /ˈguru; ˈgʊruː/ *n* [C] **1** *informal* someone who knows a lot about a particular subject, and to whom people go for advice【非正式】專家, 權威: *one of the president's foreign policy gurus* 總統的一位外交政策專家 **2** a Hindu religious teacher or leader 古魯〔印度教的宗師或領袖〕

gush¹ /gʌʃ; gʌʃ/ *v* **1** [I always+adv/prep] if a liquid gushes from something, such as a hole or cut, it comes out in large quantities〔液體從某物〕大量湧出, 噴出: **[+out/from/down etc]** *The blood began to gush out, red and frightening.* 血開始湧出, 一片紅色, 十分嚇人。| *oil gushing from the broken pipe* 從破裂的管中噴出來的石油 **2** [T] if something gushes a liquid, large quantities of that liquid come out of it 湧出, 噴出〔大量液體〕: *The wound gushed blood.* 傷口大量出血。**3** [I,T] to express your admiration, pleasure etc too strongly so that people do not think you are sincere 誇張地表達〔愛慕、高興之情〕: *"I simply loved your book," she gushed.* "我實在非常喜歡你的書。" 她裝模作樣地說。**4** [I] if words or emotions gush out, you suddenly express them very strongly〔話語〕迸出;〔感情〕迸發: **[+out]** *All that pent up frustration gushed out in a torrent of abuse.* 被壓抑的挫敗感迸發出來, 他突然破口大罵。

gush² *n* **1** a large quantity of liquid that suddenly flows from somewhere 湧流, 噴出之物: *Gushes of water sprayed out of the pipe.* 水柱從管道噴灑出來。**2 a gush of relief/anxiety etc** a sudden feeling or expression of emotion 一陣寬慰/焦慮等

gush·er /ˈgʌʃɚ; ˈgʌʃə/ *n* [C] an OIL WELL where the natural flow of oil is very strong, so that a pump is not needed 噴油井

gush·ing /ˈgʌʃɪŋ; ˈgʌʃɪŋ/ also 又作 **gush·y** /ˈgʌʃɪ; ˈgʌʃi/ *adj informal* expressing admiration, pleasure etc strongly, so that people may think you are not sincere【非正式】誇大其詞的; 裝腔作勢的 —**gushingly** *adv*

gus·set /ˈgʌsɪt; ˈgʌsɨ̣t/ *n* [C] a small piece of material stitched into a piece of clothing to make it stronger, wider, or more comfortable in a particular place〔衣服的〕襯料

gus·sy /ˈgʌsɪ; ˈgʌsi/ *v*

gussy up *phr v* [I,T] *AmE informal* to make yourself look attractive by wearing your best clothes etc【美, 非正式】(把…) 打扮得漂漂亮亮: **gussy yourself up** *Jolene gussied herself up for the party.* 喬利恩穿得漂漂亮亮地參加聚會。

gust¹ /gʌst; gʌst/ *n*[C] **1** a sudden strong movement of wind 一陣狂風: *A sudden gust of wind blew the door shut.* 一陣狂風把門吹得關上了。**2** a sudden strong feeling of anger, excitement etc 突發的一陣怒氣、興奮等: *A gust of rage swept through him.* 一陣怒火湧上他的心頭。

gust² *v* [I] if the wind gusts, it blows strongly with sudden short movements〔狂風〕一陣陣勁吹: *wind gusting at up to 45 miles per hour* 時速高達 45 英里的狂風

gus·to /ˈgʌsto; ˈgʌstəʊ/ *n* [U] **with gusto** if you do something with gusto, you do it with a lot of eagerness and energy 精力充沛地, 熱忱地: *Brendon always sang hymns with great gusto.* 布倫頓總是精力充沛地唱聖歌。

gust·y /ˈgʌstɪ; ˈgʌsti/ *adj* with wind blowing in strong sudden movements 颳陣風的: *a cold, gusty October night* 寒冷而狂風陣陣的十月夜晚

gut¹ /gʌt; gʌt/ *n*

1 ►COURAGE 勇氣◄ guts [plural] *informal* the courage and determination you need to do something difficult or unpleasant【非正式】〔做困難或不愉快事情所需要的〕勇氣, 魄力, 決心: *Sonia succeeded through sheer guts and determination.* 索尼亞單憑着膽量和決心取得了成功。| **have the guts to do sth** *No one had the guts to tell Paul what a mistake he was making.* 沒有人有膽量告訴保羅他在犯甚麼樣的錯誤。

2 ►BODY PARTS 身體器官◄ a) guts [plural] the organs inside your body 內臟 **b)** the tube through which food passes from your stomach 腸子, 腸道

3 gut reaction/feeling/instinct etc *informal* a reaction or feeling that you are sure is right, although you cannot give a reason for it【非正式】本能的反應/本能的感覺/直覺等: *He had a gut feeling that Sarah was lying.* 他憑直覺感到莎拉在撒謊。

4 hate sb's guts *informal* to hate someone very much【非正式】痛恨某人

5 sweat/slog your guts out *informal* to work very hard【非正式】拚命工作

6 at gut level if you know something at gut level, you feel sure about it, though you could not give a reason 憑直覺, 本能地: *She knew at gut level that he was guilty.* 她本能地知道他有罪。

7 ►STRING 線◄ [U] a type of strong string made from the INTESTINE of an animal 腸線〔用動物腸子製成的十分結實的繩索〕—see also 另見 CATGUT

8 I'll have sb's guts for garters *BrE informal* used to say that you would like to punish someone severely for something they have done【英, 非正式】〔用於表示希望嚴懲某人〕—see also 另見 BEER BELLY, **bust a gut** (BUST¹ (3)), **spill your guts** (SPILL¹ (4))

gut² *v* **gutted, gutting** [T] **1** [usually passive 一般用被動態] to completely destroy the inside of a building, especially by fire 毀壞〔建築物〕內部〔尤指燒毀〕: *The kitchen was completely gutted.* 廚房裡面全被燒毀。**2** to remove the organs from inside a fish or animal in order to prepare it for cooking 取出〔魚或動物內臟, 以備烹調〕 **3** to change something by removing some of the most important or central parts〔通過去除重要的或中心的部分〕改變: *gutting the system from the inside so as to restructure it completely* 去除系統內部以便徹底重建 —see also 另見 GUTTED

gut·less /ˈgʌtləs; ˈgʌtləs/ *adj informal* lacking courage or determination【非正式】缺乏膽量的, 怯懦的 —**gutlessly** *adv* **gutlessness** *n* [U]

guts·y /ˈgʌtsɪ; ˈgʌtsi/ *adj informal* brave and determined【非正式】勇敢的, 堅毅的: *a gutsy young fighter* 一位勇敢的年輕戰士

gut·ted /ˈgʌtɪd; ˈgʌtɨ̣d/ *adj* **1** seriously damaged or completely destroyed 嚴重受損的, 完全毀壞的 **2** *BrE spoken* very shocked or disappointed【英口】十分吃驚的, 非常失望的: *"And how did you feel when Arsenal*

G

scored?" "Totally gutted." "阿仙奴隊得分時你感覺如何?" "徹底震驚。" **3** *BrE spoken* very tired; EXHAUSTED【英口】精疲力竭的: *I was gutted by the end of the week!* 到週末我就精疲力竭!

gut·ter¹ /ˋgʌtɚ; ˈgʌtə/ *n* **1** [C] the edge of a road next to the path, where water collects and flows away〔路邊的〕排水溝 **2** [C] an open pipe or CHANNEL¹ (4), fixed to the edge of a roof to collect and carry away rain water〔屋簷邊的〕雨水槽 —see picture on page A4 參見 A4 頁圖 **3 the gutter** the bad social conditions of the lowest and poorest level of society 社會最底層的惡劣環境: *Men like him usually ended up in jail – or the gutter.* 像他這樣的男人, 下場通常是坐牢或窮困潦倒。**4 the gutter press** *BrE* the newspapers that print shocking stories about people's personal lives【英】〔聳人聽聞地刊登人們私生活新聞的〕低級趣味報紙, 下流報紙 —compare 比較 TABLOID

gutter² *v* [I] *literary* if a CANDLE gutters it burns with an unsteady flame【文】〔燭光〕搖曳不定

gutter out *phr v* [I] *AmE* to become gradually weaker and then stop completely【美】逐漸停止: *What had been a promising film career in the end just guttered out.* 原來很有前途的電影生涯最終灰飛煙滅。

gut·ter·ing /ˋgʌtərɪŋ; ˈgʌtərɪŋ/ *n* [U] the open pipes that are fixed to the edge of the roof of a house to collect and carry away rain water〔屋簷邊的〕雨水槽 —see also 另見 GUTTER¹ (2)

gut·ter·snipe /ˋgʌtɚˌsnaɪp; ˈgʌtəsnaɪp/ *n* [C] *old-fashioned* a dirty, untidy, badly-behaved child from a poor home【過時】又髒又野的窮人家孩子

gut·tur·al /ˋgʌtərəl; ˈgʌtərəl/ *adj* a guttural voice or sound is or seems to be produced deep in the throat〔聲音〕喉中發出的, 像喉中發出的

guv /gʌv; gʌv/ *n BrE spoken* used by men, as a way of addressing a male customer in a shop, taxi etc【英口】先生〔男性用語, 用來稱呼商店、出租車等的男性顧客〕: *Where to, guv?* 上哪兒, 先生?

guv·nor, guv'nor /ˋgʌvnɚ; ˈgʌvnə/ *n BrE spoken*【英口】**1** a man who is in a position of authority over you, usually your employer 老闆, 雇主: *You'll have to speak to the guvnor about that.* 那件事你得跟老闆說。**2** *old-fashioned* used as a way of addressing a man of a higher social class than you【過時】先生〔用來稱呼地位比自己高的男人〕

guy¹ /gaɪ; gaɪ/ *n* [C] **1** *informal* a man【非正式】男人: *Dave's a nice guy when you get to know him.* 戴維是個好人, 你認識他後就知道。**2** a figure of a man burnt every year on Guy Fawkes' Night, in Britain〔在英國每年蓋伊·福克斯之夜焚燒的〕蓋伊·福克斯模擬像 **3** also 又作 **guy rope** a rope that stretches from the top or side of a tent or pole to the ground to keep it in the right position〔帳篷或杆柱的〕固定拉繩, 牽索 **4 guys** [plural] *AmE spoken* used when talking to or about a group of people, male or female【美口】大家, 各位〔用於對同一羣人講話或指一羣人時〕: *Hey you guys! Where are you going?* 嗨, 你們哪! 要上哪兒去? **5 no more Mr Nice Guy!** used to say that you will stop trying to behave honestly and fairly 不再當好好先生了! —see also 另見 **wise guy** (WISE¹ (6))

guy² *v* [T] *old-fashioned* to copy how someone talks or behaves in a way that makes people laugh【過時】模仿〔某人說話或行動以使人發笑〕

Guy Fawkes' Night /ˌgaɪ ˋfɔks naɪt; ˌgaɪ ˈfɔːks naɪt/ *n* [singular] November 5th, when in Britain people light FIREWORKS and burn a GUY¹ (2) on a fire 蓋伊·福克斯之夜〔即11月5日, 在英國屆時人們燃放煙火並焚燒模擬人像〕

guz·zle /ˋgʌzl̩; ˈgʌzəl/ *v* [I,T] *informal* to eat or drink a lot of something, eagerly and quickly【非正式】濫吃, 狂飲: *They've been guzzling beer all evening.* 他們整個晚上都在狂飲啤酒。—see also 另見 GAS-GUZZLER

gym /dʒɪm; dʒɪm/ *n informal*【非正式】**1** [C] a special hall or room that has equipment for doing physical exercise; GYMNASIUM 體育館, 健身房 **2** [U] exercises done indoors for physical development and as a sport, especially as a school subject 體操, 體育: **gym kit/shoes etc** *Do not wear your gym kit outdoors.* 在室外別穿體操服。

gym·kha·na /dʒɪmˋkɑnə; dʒɪmˈkɑːnə/ *n* [C] **1** *BrE* a sporting event at which people on horses compete in races and jumping competitions【英】賽馬大會 **2** *AmE* a car race that involves difficult driving【美】汽車比賽

gym·na·si·um /dʒɪmˋneziəm; dʒɪmˈneɪziəm/ *n* [C] a special hall or room that has equipment for doing physical exercise 體育館, 健身房

gym·nast /ˋdʒɪmnæst; ˈdʒɪmnæst/ *n* [C] someone who is very good at doing physical exercises, especially someone who competes against other people in gymnastic competitions 體操運動員

gym·nas·tics /dʒɪmˋnæstɪks; dʒɪmˈnæstɪks/ *n* [U] **1** a sport involving skilled and controlled physical exercises and movements, often performed in competitions 體操 **2 mental/intellectual/moral gymnastics** very clever thinking 非常聰明的想法 **3 verbal gymnastics** using words in a very clever way 遣詞造句的高超技巧 —**gymnastic** *adj*: *gymnastic skills* 體操技能

gym shoe /ˈ· ·/ *n* [C] a light shoe with a cloth top and a flat rubber bottom used for games and sport, especially at school〔特指在學校裡穿用的〕體操鞋, 運動鞋, 球鞋; PLIMSOLL *BrE*【英】

gym·slip /ˋdʒɪmˌslɪp; ˈdʒɪmˌslɪp/ *n* [C] *BrE*【英】**1** a type of dress without sleeves that girls used to wear over a shirt as a part of their school uniform〔女生穿在襯衫外的〕無袖制服 **2 gymslip mother** a girl who has a baby while she is still at school 懷孕的女中學生

gyn- /dʒaɪn; gaɪn/ *prefix technical* concerning women【術語】與婦女有關的: *gynaecology* (=treatment of women's diseases) 婦科學

gy·nae·col·o·gy *BrE*【英】, **gynecology** *AmE*【美】/ˌdʒaɪnɪˋkɑlədʒɪ; ˌgaɪnl̩ˈkɒlədʒi/ *n* [U] the study and treatment of medical conditions and illnesses affecting only women 婦科(學) —**gynaecologist** *n* [C] —**gynaecological** /ˌdʒaɪnɪkəˋlɑdʒɪkl̩; ˌgaɪnl̩kəˈlɒdʒɪkəl◂/ *adj*

gyp¹ /dʒɪp; dʒɪp/ *n informal*【非正式】**1 give sb gyp** *BrE*【英】**a)** to be painful 疼痛: *My bad leg is really giving me gyp today.* 我受傷的腿今天實在疼痛得不行。**b)** to punish someone or be angry with them because of something they have done 處罰某人; 對某人生氣 **2** [singular] *AmE*【美】**a)** something that you were tricked into buying 被騙買的東西 **b)** a situation in which you feel you have been cheated 欺騙, 詐騙, 騙局: *What a gyp!* 好一個騙局!

gyp² *v* **gypped, gypping** [T] *informal* to cheat someone【非正式】欺騙, 詐騙: *Ten quid? You've been gypped!* 十鎊? 你被騙了!

gyp·sum /ˋdʒɪpsəm; ˈdʒɪpsəm/ *n* [U] a soft white substance that is used to make PLASTER OF PARIS 石膏

gyp·sy also 又作 **gipsy** *BrE*【英】/ˋdʒɪpsɪ; ˈdʒɪpsi/ *n* [C] **1** a member of a dark-haired race that is thought to be of Indian origin, who usually live and travel around in CARAVANS 吉卜賽人 **2** someone who does not like to stay in the same place for a long time; TRAVELLER (2) 不喜歡長時間在同一個地方的人

gy·rate /ˋdʒaɪret; dʒaɪˈreɪt/ *v* [I] *literary* to turn around fast in circles【文】快速旋轉: *The dancers gyrated wildly to the beat of the music.* 舞蹈員隨着音樂的節奏猛烈地旋轉。—**gyration** /dʒaɪˋreʃən; dʒaɪˈreɪʃən/ *n*

gy·ro /ˋdʒaɪro; ˈdʒaɪrəʊ/ *n* [C] *informal* a gyroscope【非正式】陀螺儀, 迴轉儀

gy·ro·scope /ˋdʒaɪrəˌskop; ˈdʒaɪrəskəʊp/ *n* [C] a wheel that spins inside a frame and is used for keeping ships and aircraft steady or as a child's toy 陀螺儀, 迴轉儀 —**gyroscopic** /ˌdʒaɪrəˋskɑpɪk; ˌdʒaɪrəˈskɒpɪk◂/ *adj*

H,h

H, h /etʃ; eɪtʃ/ *plural* **H's, h's** the 8th letter of the English alphabet 英語字母表的第八個字母 —see also 另見 H-BOMB

H_2O /ˌetʃ tu ˋo; ˌeɪtʃ tuː ˈəʊ/ *n* [U] *technical* the chemical sign for water【術語】一氧化二氫〔水的化學符號〕

ha[1] /hɑ; hɑː/ *interjection* used when you are surprised or have discovered something interesting〔表示驚異或發現了某些有趣的事物〕哈!: *Ha! I thought it might be you hiding there!* 哈! 我以為可能是你藏在那兒! —see also 另見 AHA, HA-HA

ha[2] the written abbreviation of 縮寫= HECTARE(S)

ha·be·as cor·pus /ˋhebɪəs ˋkɔrpəs; ˌheɪbiəs ˈkɔːpəs/ *n* [U] *law* the right of someone in prison to come to a court of law so that the court can decide whether they should stay in prison【法律】人身保護狀[令]〔指被拘留的人有權要求及時移交法庭, 以決定其是否應入獄〕

hab·er·dash·er /ˋhæbɚˌdæʃɚ; ˈhæbədæʃə/ *n* [C] *old-fashioned* a shopkeeper who sells haberdashery【過時】男士服飾用品商; 縫紉用品商

hab·er·dash·er·y /ˋhæbɚˌdæʃərɪ; ˈhæbədæʃəri/ *n* **1** [C] *BrE* a shop or part of a large store where things used for making clothes are sold【英】縫紉用品店[部] **2** [C] *AmE old-fashioned* a shop or part of a large store where men's clothes, especially hats, are sold【美, 過時】男士服飾用品〔尤指帽子〕店[部] **3** [U] the goods sold in these shops 男士服飾用品; 縫紉用品

3 **hab·it** /ˋhæbɪt; ˈhæbɪt/ *n*
3 **1 ►STH YOU DO REGULARLY** 慣做的事◄ [C,U] something that you do regularly, often without thinking about it because you have done it so many times before 習慣: *Dalton was a man of regular habits.* 多爾頓是一個遵守習慣的人。| **out of habit/from habit** (=because it is a habit) 出於習慣 *After we moved I kept driving to the old house out of habit.* 我們搬家後, 出於習慣我總是開車回到老房子。| **be in the habit of doing sth** *Jeff was in the habit of taking a walk after dinner.* 傑夫習慣在晚飯後散步。| **get into/get in/out of the habit** (=start/stop doing something regularly) 養成/改掉〔做某事的〕習慣 *Since I stopped taking lessons, I've gotten out of the habit of practising my saxophone.* 自從我沒有上課以後, 我再也沒有練薩克斯管的習慣了。| *She got in the habit of having a drink with us on Fridays.* 她養成了逢星期五和我們一起喝酒的習慣。| **eating/drinking habits** (=how often, how much, and what you eat or drink) 飲食/飲酒習慣 *When she is busy, her eating habits become erratic.* 她一忙飲食習慣就變得毫無規律了。

2 ►ANNOYING BEHAVIOUR 令人討厭的行為◄ [C] something that someone does regularly and that other people find annoying 壞習慣: **have a habit of doing sth** *Glenna has an annoying habit of talking to herself while she's working.* 格倫納有一個壞習慣, 就是一邊工作一邊自言自語。| **a bad/filthy/disgusting habit** *Don't bite your fingernails – it's a disgusting habit.* 別咬指甲, 這是個令人討厭的習慣。

3 ►DRUGS 毒品◄ a strong physical need to keep taking a drug regularly 毒癮: *Many of them get into petty crime to support their habit.* 他們當中有很多人為了滿足毒癮而犯輕罪。| **heroin/cocaine etc habit** *His cocaine habit ruined him physically and financially.* 他的可卡因癮使他的身體和經濟都毀了。| **kick the habit** (=stop taking a drug regularly) 戒除毒癮

4 break the habit to stop doing something that is annoying or bad for your health 擺脱壞習慣: *a new system that's supposed to help you break the smoking habit* 一個幫助你戒煙的新方法

5 don't make a habit of (doing) sth *spoken* used to tell someone who has done something bad or wrong that they should not do it again【口】不要養成做某事的習慣: *You're ten minutes late. I hope you're not going to make a habit of this.* 你遲了十分鐘。我希望你不要養成遲到的習慣。

6 I'm not in the habit of doing sth *spoken* used when you are offended because someone has suggested that you have done something that you have not done【口】我沒有做某事的習慣: *I'm not in the habit of lying to my friends.* 我沒有對朋友撒謊的習慣。

7 old habits die hard used to say that it is difficult to make people change their attitudes or behaviour 舊習難改

8 ►CLOTHES 衣服◄ [C] a long loose piece of clothing worn by people in some religious groups〔某些宗教團體成員穿的〕服裝; 長袍: *a nun's habit* 修女服

9 habit of thought/mind the way someone usually thinks about something, or the attitudes they usually have 已成習慣的思維方式/慣常的態度 —see also 另見 **a creature of habit** (CREATURE (5)), **by/from force of habit** (FORCE[1] (9))

USAGE NOTE 用法説明: HABIT

WORD CHOICE 詞語辨析: **habit, custom, tradition, practice, convention**

A **habit** is usually something someone does again and again, perhaps without them realizing it. habit (習慣) 通常指某人在可能沒有意識到的情況下經常做的事情: *He has an annoying habit of biting his nails.* 他有咬指甲的壞習慣。

A **custom** is usually something which has been done for a long time by a group – for example, a school, company, or society, perhaps every year. custom (習俗) 通常指某一羣人, 如學校、公司或社會, 長久以來可能每年都要做的事情: *the custom of holding exams in June* 六月份舉行考試的習俗 | *a local custom* 當地習俗

A **tradition** is similar to a **custom**, but may be older and passed down from parents to their children. tradition (傳統) 與 custom (習俗) 類似, 但可能更古老, 由父母傳給子女: *the tradition of eating turkey at Thanksgiving* 感恩節吃火雞的傳統 | *a family tradition* 家族傳統

A **practice** is the usual way of doing things in business, law etc. practice (慣例、常規做法) 指商業、法律等領域中的慣常做法: *The normal practice in this company is to send the bill as soon as the job is done.* 本公司的慣例是完成工作後馬上寄出賬單。

The **conventions** of a society are its generally accepted rules of behaviour. 某一社會的 conventions (常規、習俗) 指的是普遍接受的行為準則: *It is a matter of convention for people attending funerals to wear dark clothes.* 人們參加喪禮時穿深色衣服是一種社會習俗。

hab·i·ta·ble /ˋhæbɪtəbl̩; ˈhæbɪtəbəl/ *adj* good enough for people to live in 適宜居住的: *It would cost a fortune to make the place habitable.* 要想讓這個地方變得適宜居住得花一大筆錢。—**habitability** /ˌhæbɪtəˋbɪlətɪ; ˌhæbɪtəˈbɪlɪti/ *n* [U]

hab·i·tat /ˋhæbəˌtæt; ˈhæbɪtæt/ *n* [C] the natural home of a plant or animal〔植物的〕產地;〔動物的〕棲息地:

H

The polar bear's habitat is the icy wastes of the Arctic. 北極熊的棲息地是冰冷的北極荒原。| **natural habitat** *Mountain areas are the natural habitat of the golden eagle.* 山區是金鵰的自然棲息地。

hab·i·ta·tion /ˌhæbəˈteʃən; ˌhæbɪˈteɪʃən/ *n formal*【正式】**1 unfit for human habitation** a building that is unfit for human habitation is not safe or healthy for people to live in 不適合人類居住, 不適宜住人 **2** [U] the act of living in a place 居住: *There was no sign of habitation as far as the eye could see.* 放眼望去, 看不到有人居住的跡象。**3** [C] a house or place to live in 住宅, 住處

habit-form·ing /ˈ·· ˌ··/ *adj* a drug or activity that is habit-forming makes you want to keep taking it, keep doing it etc 使人上癮的; 讓人形成習慣的

ha·bit·u·al /həˈbɪtʃuəl; həˈbɪtʃuəl/ *adj* **1** done as a habit or doing something from habit 已成習慣的: *My father was a habitual gambler.* 我父親賭博成性。| *habitual drinking* 習慣性飲酒 **2** [only before noun 僅用於名詞前] usual or typical of someone 習慣(性)的, 慣常的: *James took his habitual morning walk around the garden.* 詹姆斯如常地繞着花園作晨間散步去了。—**habitually** *adv*: *habitually violent behaviour* 經常性暴力行為

ha·bit·u·ate /həˈbɪtʃuˌet; həˈbɪtʃueɪt/ *v* **be/become habituated to (doing sth)** *formal* to be or gradually become used to something【正式】習慣於(做某事): *Over the centuries, these animals have become habituated to living in such a dry environment.* 經過許多世紀, 這些動物已經習慣於生活在如此乾燥的環境裡。

ha·bit·u·é /həˈbɪtʃuˌe; həˈbɪtʃueɪ/ *n* [C+**of**] *formal* someone who regularly goes to a particular place or event【正式】經常出入某一場所[地方]的人, 常客

ha·ci·en·da /ˌhɑsɪˈɛndə; ˌhæsiˈendə/ *n* [C] a large farm in Spanish-speaking countries〔西班牙語國家的〕大莊園, 大農場

hack¹ /hæk; hæk/ *v* **1** [I always+adv/prep, T always+adv/prep] to cut something into pieces roughly or violently 砍, 劈: **hack away/at etc** *She hacked away at the ice, trying to make a hole.* 她在冰上鑿, 想鑿出一個洞來。| **hack sth into/through etc** *We had to hack a path through the jungle.* 我們只得在叢林中劈出一條路來。**2 can't hack sth** *informal* to feel that you cannot do something that is difficult or boring【非正式】〔由於困難或厭煩〕不願做某事: *I've been doing this job for years, but I just can't hack it anymore.* 這份工作我已經幹了很多年, 再也不想幹了。**3** [I] *AmE* to drive a taxi【美】開計程車 **4** [I,T always+adv/prep] *BrE* to ride a horse along roads or through the country【英】〔在郊外或沿路〕騎馬

hack into *phr v* [T] *informal* to secretly find a way to get into the information on someone else's computer system so that you can use or change it【非正式】侵入〔他人的電腦系統〕

hack² /hæk; hæk/ *n* [C] **1** a writer who does a lot of low quality work, especially writing newspaper articles〔寫報紙文章等的〕蹩腳文人, 雇傭文人: *hack journalism* 雇傭文人寫的報刊文章 —see also 另見 HACKWORK **2** an unimportant politician 二流政客, 政治僕從: *The meeting was attended by the usual old party hacks.* 參加會議的都是那些常見的老黨棍。**3** *AmE informal* a taxi, or a taxi driver【美, 非正式】計程車; 計程車司機 **4** an act of hitting something roughly with a cutting tool 砍, 劈: *Just give it a hack with the axe.* 用斧頭劈一下。**5** an old, tired horse 老馬 **6** a horse you can pay money to ride on 供出租的馬 **7** *BrE* a ride on a horse【英】騎馬

hacked-off /ˌ· ˈ·/ *adj BrE informal* extremely annoyed【英, 非正式】非常生氣的: *I'm really hacked-off; I left my coat on the bus.* 真是氣死我了, 我把外套遺在公共汽車上了。

hack·er /ˈhækə; ˈhækə/ *n* [C] *informal* someone who secretly uses or changes the information in other people's computer systems【非正式】私自存取或篡改(他人)電腦資料的人, 黑客 —**hacking** *n* [U]

hacking cough /ˌ·· ˈ·/ *n* [usually singular 一般用單數] a repeated painful cough with an unpleasant sound 短促頻繁的乾咳

hacking jacket /ˈ·· ˌ··/ *n* [C] *BrE* a woollen JACKET (1) worn when riding a horse【英】騎馬外套, 夾克騎裝

hack·les /ˈhæklz; ˈhækəlz/ *n* [plural] **1 sb's hackles rise** if someone's hackles rise they begin to feel very angry, because someone's behaviour or attitude offends them 被激怒, 勃然大怒: *Laura saw the insolent look on his face, and felt her hackles rising.* 勞拉看到他臉上傲慢的表情時按捺不住心頭的怒火。| **raise sb's hackles** (=make someone angry) 激怒某人 *tactless remarks that were enough to raise anyone's hackles* 足以激怒任何人的不得體的話 **2** the long feathers or hairs on the back of the neck of some animals and birds, which stand up straight when they are in danger〔某些鳥獸遇到危險時會豎起的〕頸背毛, 細長頸羽

hack·ney car·riage /ˈhæknɪ ˌkærɪdʒ; ˈhækni ˌkærɪdʒ/ *n* [C] *BrE*【英】**1** also 又作 **hackney coach** /ˈ·· ·/ *AmE*【美】a carriage pulled by a horse, used in the past like a taxi〔舊時的〕出租馬車 **2** also 又作 **hackney cab** /ˈ·· ·/ *formal* a taxi【正式】出租車, 計程車

hack·neyed /ˈhæknɪd; ˈhæknid/ *adj* a hackneyed phrase, statement etc is boring and does not have much meaning because it has been used so often; TRITE〔言辭等〕陳腐的, 老生常談的

hack·saw /ˈhækˌsɔ; ˈhæksɔː/ *n* [C] a cutting tool with small teeth on its blade, used especially for cutting metal 弓鋸, 鋼鋸 —see picture at 參見 TOOL¹ 圖

hack·work /ˈhækˌwɜk; ˈhækwɜːk/ *n* [U] uninteresting work, especially writing, done to earn money rather than because you enjoy it〔職業性的〕賣文工作;〔雇傭文人的〕平庸作品

had /əd, həd; d, əd, həd; *strong* 強讀 hæd; hæd/ **1** the past tense and past participle of HAVE **2 be had** *informal* to be tricked or be made to look stupid【非正式】上當受騙: *I'm afraid you've been had! This watch is a fake!* 恐怕你是上當了! 這隻錶是假貨!

had·dock /ˈhædək; ˈhædək/ *n plural* **haddock** [C,U] a common fish that lives in northern seas and is often used as food 黑線鱈〔北大西洋產的一種食用魚〕

Ha·des /ˈhediz; ˈheɪdiːz/ *n* [U] the land of the dead in the stories of ancient Greece; HELL¹ (3)〔希臘神話中的〕冥府, 黃泉, 地獄

hadj /hædʒ; hædʒ/ *n* [C] another spelling of HAJ haj 的另一種拼法

hadj·i /ˈhædʒi; ˈhædʒi/ *n* [C] another spelling of HAJJI hajji 的另一種拼法

had·n't /ˈhædnt; ˈhædnt/ short for 縮略式= had not: *If I hadn't seen it myself, I'd never have believed it.* 要不是我親眼看見, 我是怎麼也不會相信的。

hae·ma·tol·o·gy *BrE*【英】, **hematology** *AmE*【美】/ˌhiməˈtɑlədʒɪ; ˌhiːməˈtɒlədʒi/ *n* [U] the scientific study of blood 血液學

haemo- *BrE*【英】, **hemo-** *AmE*【美】/himo, himə; hiːməʊ, hemə/ *prefix technical* concerning the blood【術語】血液的, 與血有關的: *a hemorrhage* (=bleeding) 出血

hae·mo·glo·bin *BrE*【英】, **hemoglobin** *AmE*【美】/ˌhiməˈglobɪn; ˌhiːməˈgləʊbɪn/ *n* [U] a red substance in the blood that contains iron and carries oxygen 血紅蛋白

hae·mo·phil·i·a *BrE*【英】, **hemophilia** *AmE*【美】/ˌhiməˈfɪlɪə; ˌhiːməˈfɪliə/ *n* [U] a serious disease that prevents the blood from becoming thick, so that a person loses a lot of blood easily 血友病

hae·mo·phil·i·ac *BrE*【英】, **hemophiliac** *AmE*【美】/ˌhiməˈfɪlɪˌæk; ˌhiːməˈfɪliæk/ *n* [C] a person who suffers from haemophilia 血友病患者

hae·mor·rhage¹ *BrE*【英】, **hemorrhage** *AmE*【美】/ˈhɛmərɪdʒ; ˈhemərɪdʒ/ *n* [C,U] a serious medical condition in which a person BLEEDs a lot, often inside the body 大量出血〔常指體內〕

haemorrhage² *BrE*【英】, **hemorrhage** *AmE*【美】*v* [I] to have a haemorrhage 大出血; 出血

hae·mor·rhoids *BrE*【英】, **hemorrhoids** *AmE*【美】/ˋhɛmə͵rɔɪdz; ˈheməroɪdz/ *n* [plural] painfully swollen BLOOD VESSELs at the ANUS 痔

haft /hæft; hɑːft/ *n* [C] *technical* a long handle on an AXE¹ (1) or on other weapons【術語】〔斧、刀、槍等的〕柄, 把

hag /hæg; hæg/ *n* [C] an ugly or unpleasant woman, especially one who is old or looks like a WITCH (1) 老醜婆, 母夜叉

hag·gard /ˋhægɚd; ˈhægəd/ *adj* having lines on your face and dark marks around your eyes, especially because you are ill, worried, or have not had enough sleep 〔面容〕憔悴的, 形容枯槁的: *Suddenly, he was looking much older, his face haggard and unshaven.* 他突然看起來老多了, 面容憔悴, 滿面鬍鬚。

hag·gis /ˋhægɪs; ˈhægɪs/ *n* [C,U] a food eaten in Scotland, made from the heart and other organs of a sheep, cut up and boiled in a skin made from the sheep's stomach 肚包羊雜碎〔把羊雜碎放入羊肚中燒的典型蘇格蘭食品〕

hag·gle /ˋhægl̩; ˈhægəl/ *v* [I] to argue, especially when trying to agree about the price of something〔尤指在價格方面〕爭論不休, 討價還價: **haggle with sb over/about** *I had to haggle with the taxi driver over the fare.* 我不得不和計程車司機就車費討價還價。—**haggling** *n* [U]

hag·i·og·ra·phy /͵hægɪˋɑgrəfɪ; ͵hægiˈɒgrəfi/ *n* [C,U] **1** a book about the lives of SAINTs 聖徒傳記 **2** a book about someone that describes them as better than they really are 把主角美化[理想化]的傳記

hag·rid·den /ˋ· ͵··/ *adj literary* always worried by problems in your life【文】受困擾的; 憂心忡忡的

ha-ha¹ /͵· ˋ·/ *interjection* **1** used in writing to represent a shout of laughter 哈哈〔笑聲〕 **2** *spoken* used, sometimes angrily, to show that you do not think something is funny【口】哈哈〔表示某事並不好笑, 有時表示生氣〕: *Oh, very funny, John, ha ha.* 啊, 約翰, 很好笑, 哈哈。

ha-ha² /ˋ· ·/ *n* [C] a wall or fence set in a hole in the ground which divides parts of a park etc without spoiling the view〔不遮住視線的〕界溝中的暗牆; 隱籬

hai·ku /ˋhaɪku; ˈhaɪkuː/ *n* [C] *plural* **haiku** a type of Japanese poem with three lines consisting of five, seven, and five SYLLABLEs 俳句〔一種三行的日本詩體〕

hail¹ /hel; heɪl/ *n* **1** [U] frozen rain drops which fall as hard balls of ice 雹, 冰雹 **2 a hail of bullets/stones** a large number of bullets, stones etc thrown or fired at someone 一陣彈雨/一陣像雹子般襲來的石塊 **3 a hail of criticism/abuse** a lot of criticism etc 連珠砲般的批評/辱罵

hail² *v* [T] to call to someone in order to greet them or try to attract their attention 呼喊; 大聲招呼: *She leaned out of the window and hailed the first passerby.* 她探出窗戶, 高呼她看到的第一個過路人。| **hail a cab/taxi** *The hotel doorman will hail a cab for you.* 旅館門口的侍者會替你叫計程車的。

hail sb/sth **as** sth *phr v* [T often passive 常用被動態] to describe someone or something as being very good, especially in newspapers, magazines etc 把…稱作, 把…譽為: *Lang's first film was immediately hailed as a masterpiece.* 蘭的第一部電影很快被譽為一部傑作。

hail from sth *phr v* [T not in passive 不用被動態] *especially humorous* to have been born in a particular place【尤幽默】出生地是, 來自: *What part of the world do you hail from?* 你來自哪裡?

hail-fel·low-well-met /͵· ··· ˋ·/ *adj old-fashioned* very friendly and cheerful, sometimes in a way that you do not trust【過時】(過分)親熱友好的, 一見如故的: *very cheerful and noisy in a hail-fellow-well-met sort of way* 過分地友好和喧鬧

Hail Ma·ry /͵helˋmɛrɪ; ͵heɪlˈmeəri/ *n* [C] a special Roman Catholic prayer to Mary, the mother of Jesus 萬福馬利亞〔天主教對聖母馬利亞的一種禱辭〕

hail·stone /ˋhel͵ston; ˈheɪlstəʊn/ *n* [C] a small ball of frozen rain 雹塊, 雹子

hail·storm /ˋhel͵stɔrm; ˈheɪlstɔːm/ *n* [C] a storm when a lot of HAIL¹ (1) falls 雹暴

hair /hɛr; heə/ *n* **1** [U] the mass of things like fine threads that grows on your head 頭髮: *She brushed her hair.* 她梳理頭髮。| *I must get my hair cut – it's getting too long.* 我必須去理髮了, 頭髮太長了。| **blond/red/dark hair** *Emma's the one with the red hair.* 那個紅頭髮的是埃瑪。| **short/ long/shoulder-length hair** *Jane has long blond hair.* 簡有一頭長長的金髮。| **straight/curly/ wavy/thick hair** *Her long wavy hair was tied back with a bow.* 她那長長的波浪形頭髮用一個蝴蝶結束在腦後。| **dark-haired/fair-haired/short-haired etc** *He's a tall, fair-haired guy.* 他是一個金髮的高個子。—see picture at 參見 HEAD¹ 圖 **2** [C] one of the long fine things like thread that grows on people's heads and on other parts of their bodies, or similar things that grow on animals〔人、動物的〕毛, 汗毛, 茸毛: *The cat has left white hairs all over the sofa.* 貓在沙發上到處留下白毛。**3 get in sb's hair** *informal* to annoy someone, especially by always being near them【非正式】〔尤指因不斷煩擾而〕惹惱某人 **4 keep your hair on** *spoken* used to tell someone to keep calm and not get annoyed【口】保持冷靜, 別發火 **5 let your hair down** *informal* to enjoy yourself and start to relax, especially after working very hard【非正式】盡情放鬆, 無拘無束〔尤指在緊張的工作過後〕: *The party gave us all a chance to really let our hair down.* 晚會給了我們一個盡情放鬆的機會。**6 make sb's hair stand on end** to make someone very frightened 使某人毛骨悚然 **7 not have a hair out of place** to have a very neat appearance 十分整潔 **8 not turn a hair** to remain completely calm when something bad or surprising suddenly happens 處之泰然, 面不改色, 保持鎮靜 **9 not harm/touch a hair of sb's head** to not harm someone in any way 絲毫無損於某人 **10 the hair of the dog (that bit you)** *humorous* an alcoholic drink that you drink to cure a headache caused by drinking too much alcohol the night before【幽默】用來解宿醉的酒 —see also 另見 **have a good/fine head of hair** (HEAD¹ (4)), **not see hide nor hair of** (HIDE² (4)), **split hairs** (SPLIT¹ (7)), **tear your hair (out)** (TEAR² (11))

hair·breadth /ˋhɛr͵brɛdθ; ˈheəbredθ/ *n* [singular] another spelling of HAIR'S BREADTH hair's breadth 的另一種拼法

hair·brush /ˋhɛr͵brʌʃ; ˈheəbrʌʃ/ *n* [C] a brush you use on your hair to make it smooth 毛刷, 髮刷 —see picture at 參見 BRUSH¹ 圖

hair·cloth /ˋhɛr͵klɔθ; ˈheəklɒθ/ *n* [U] rough material made from animal hair, especially from horses or CAMELs 馬尾襯〔用馬毛、駝毛等動物毛織成的粗面料〕

hair·cut /ˋhɛr͵kʌt; ˈheəkʌt/ *n* [C] **1** the act of having your hair cut by someone 理髮: *I'm going for a haircut.* 我去理髮。**2** the style your hair is cut in 髮型, 髮式: *Do you like my new haircut?* 你喜歡我的新髮型嗎?

hair·do /ˋhɛr͵du; ˈheəduː/ *n plural* **hairdos** [C] *informal* a woman's haircut【非正式】女子髮型

hair·dress·er /ˋhɛr͵drɛsɚ; ˈheə͵dresə/ *n* [C] **1** a person who cuts, washes, and arranges people's hair in particular styles 理髮師, 美髮師 **2 the hairdresser's** the hairdresser's shop 理髮店, 髮廊 —compare 比較 BARBER —**hairdressing** *n* [U]

hair·dry·er, hairdrier /ˋhɛr͵draɪɚ; ˈheə͵draɪə/ *n* [C] a machine that blows out hot air for drying hair〔理髮用的〕吹風器

hair·grip /ˋhɛr͵grɪp; ˈheəgrɪp/ *n* [C] *BrE* a very small thin piece of metal folded in half and used to hold a woman's hair in place【英】髮夾; BOBBY PIN *AmE*【美】—see picture at 參見 PIN¹ 圖

hair·less /ˋhɛrlɪs; ˈheələs/ *adj* with no hair 無頭髮的, 禿頭的

hair·line /ˋhɛr͵laɪn; ˈheəlaɪn/ *n* [C] **1** the line around your

hairstyles 髮型

flattop 平頭

crew cut 板刷頭

bob 短齊髮

dreadlocks"駭人"長髮綹

ponytail
馬尾髮(型)

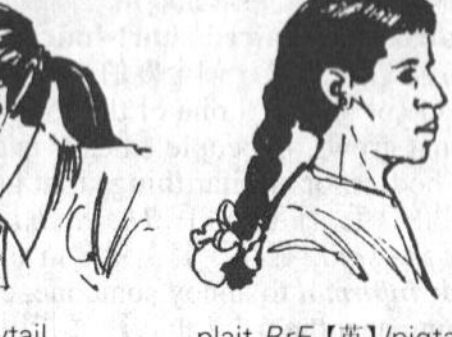
plait *BrE*【英】/pigtail/
braid *AmE*【美】辮子

bun
圓髮髻

plaits *BrE*【英】/pigtails/
braids *AmE*【美】雙辮子

head, especially at the front, where your hair starts growing〔額上的〕髮際線, 頭髮輪廓線: *a receding hairline* 不斷往後退的髮際線〔指頭髮不斷從前額往後禿〕**2 a hairline crack/fracture** a very thin crack 細微的裂縫/骨折: *a hairline fracture in a bone* 骨頭上的細微骨折

hair·net /ˋhɛr,nɛt; ˈheənet/ *n* [C] a very thin net that stretches over your hair to keep it in place 髮網

hair·piece /ˋhɛr,pis; ˈheəpiːs/ *n* [C] a piece of false hair used to make your own hair look thicker〔加在頭髮上使之顯得更濃密的〕小假髮

hair·pin /ˋhɛr,pɪn; ˈheə,pɪn/ *n* [C] a pin made of wire bent into a U-shape to hold long hair in position〔U形〕髮卡; 髮針 —see picture at 參見 PIN[1] 圖

hairpin bend /,·· ˈ·/ *n* [C] a very sharp U-shaped curve in a road, especially on a steep hill〔尤指陡坡處的〕U字形彎路

hair-rais·ing /ˈ· ,··/ *adj* frightening in a way that is exciting 驚險的; 恐怖的: *a hair-raising car chase* 一場驚險的汽車追逐

hair re·stor·er /ˈ· ·,··/ *n* [C,U] a substance or liquid that is supposed to make hair grow again 毛髮再生劑[液]

hair's breadth /ˈ· ·/ *n* [singular] a very small amount or distance 一髮之差, 極細微的距離: *The bullet missed me by a hair's breadth.* 子彈以毫髮之差從我身邊擦過。

hair shirt /,· ˈ·/ *n* [C] a shirt made of rough uncomfortable cloth containing hair, worn in the past by some religious people to punish themselves〔過去有些宗教信徒懲罰自己時穿的〕剛毛襯衣

hair slide /ˈ· ·/ *n* [C] *BrE* a small attractive metal or plastic object used to fasten a woman's hair in place【英】〔金屬或塑料〕小髮夾; BARRETTE *AmE*【美】

hair-split·ting /ˈ· ,··/ *n* [U] the act of paying too much attention to small differences and unimportant details, especially in an argument〔尤指在爭論中的〕吹毛求疵 —see also 另見 **split hairs** (SPLIT[1] (7))

hair spray /ˈ· ·/ *n* [U] a sticky substance that is sprayed (SPRAY[1] (1)) from a container and used to keep hair in place 噴髮膠, 噴髮定型劑

hair·spring /ˋhɛr,sprɪŋ; ˈheəsprɪŋ/ *n* [C] a very small spring inside a watch that helps the watch work correctly〔手錶中的〕游絲, 細彈簧

hair·style /ˋhɛr,staɪl; ˈheəstaɪl/ *n* [C] the style in which someone's hair has been cut or shaped 髮型, 髮式

hair trig·ger /,· ˈ··◂/ *n* [C] **1** a TRIGGER[1] (1) on a gun that needs very little pressure to fire the gun〔槍的〕微力扳機 **2 hair trigger temper** someone who has a hair trigger temper gets very angry easily 火爆的脾氣

hair·y /ˋhɛrɪ; ˈheəri/ *adj* **1** having a lot of body hair〔身體〕多毛的: *He's a skinny guy with hairy legs.* 他是個雙腿多毛的瘦削男子。| *a hairy chest* 多毛的胸脯 **2** *informal* dangerous or frightening, often in a way that is exciting【非正式】驚險的; 令人恐懼的: *We had to climb down the cliff, and that was pretty hairy.* 我們得爬下懸崖, 真驚險啊。—**hairiness** *n* [U]

haj, hadj /hædʒ; hædʒ/ *n* [C] a journey to Mecca for religious reasons, that all Muslims try to make at least once in their life〔伊斯蘭教的〕麥加朝聖

haj·ji, hadji /ˋhædʒi; ˈhædʒi/ *n* [C] used as a title for a Muslim who has made a haj 哈吉〔曾朝覲麥加的伊斯蘭教徒的稱號〕

hake /hek; heɪk/ *n* [C,U] a sea fish, used as food 狗鱈〔一種食用海魚〕

ha·kim /hɑˋkim; hɑːˈkiːm/ *n* [C] a Muslim doctor〔伊斯蘭教的〕醫生

ha·lal, hallal /həˋlɑl; hɑːˈlɑːl/ *adj* halal meat is meat from an animal that has been killed in a way that is approved by Muslim law 哈拉〔哈拉肉指按伊斯蘭教習俗屠宰的牲口的肉〕

hal·berd /ˋhælbɚd; ˈhælbəd/ *n* [C] a weapon with a blade on a long handle, used in past times 戟〔舊時的一種武器〕

hal·cy·on days /ˌhælsɪən ˋdez; ˌhælsiən ˈdeɪz/ *n* [plural] *especially literary* a time when you are very happy【尤文】美好的時光: *She often recalled the halcyon days of her youth.* 她經常回憶起年輕時的美好時光。

hale /hel; heɪl/ *adj* **hale and hearty** someone, especially an old person, who is hale and hearty is very healthy and active〔尤指老人〕精神矍鑠的, 老當益壯的: *still hale and hearty at 74* 74歲高齡仍然精神矍鑠

half[1] /hæf; hɑːf/ *predeterminer, adj* [only before noun 僅用於名詞前] **1** being half of an amount, time, distance, number etc 一半的, 半: *events that happened over half a century ago* 半個多世紀前發生的事情 | *Only half the guests had arrived by seven o'clock.* 七點鐘時只有一半的來賓到達。| *The studio is only half a block away.* 工作室離這兒只有半個街區。| **half a mile/pound/hour etc** (=half of a unit of measurement) 半英里/磅/小時 *half a pound of butter* 半磅黃油 | *It's about half a mile down the road.* 順路走大約半英里遠。| **a half hour/mile etc** *You can't just waltz in a half hour late – we need you here on time.* 你不能晚半小時才大搖大擺地進來, 我們需要你準時來到這裡。**2** if something is half one thing and half something else, it is a combination of those two things 一半...一半...: *A Minotaur is a monster that is half man, half bull.* 彌諾陶洛斯是一個半人半牛的怪

物。**3 half one/two/three etc** *BrE informal* thirty minutes after the hour mentioned【英, 非正式】一點半/兩點半/三點半等: *I rang at about half six.* 我大約在六點半打了電話。**4 half a dozen a)** six 半打, 六個: *half a dozen eggs* 六隻蛋 **b)** several or many 幾個; 多個: *The children seemed to be singing 'Happy Birthday' to half a dozen different tunes.* 孩子們好像用好幾種不同的曲調在唱生日歌。**5 be half the battle** *spoken* used to say that when you have done the most difficult part of an activity, the rest is easy【口】成功了一半: *Getting Jimmy dressed in the mornings is half the battle.* 每天早上只要給吉米穿好衣服, 剩下的事情就好辦了。**6 half the fun/time/trouble etc** the largest part of something 大部分樂趣/時間/麻煩等: *Half the trouble with John is that he never really listens to what you say.* 約翰最麻煩的地方在於他從不真正聽你說話。| *Kids seem to think that climbing up a slide is half the fun.* 孩子們好像認為大部分的樂趣在於爬上滑梯。**7 half a minute/moment/second etc** *spoken* a very short time【口】半分鐘/刻/秒等〔表示時間很短〕: *Hold on, this will only take half a second.* 等一等, 一會兒就行了。**8 have half a mind to do sth** *spoken*【口】**a)** to say that you would like to do something but you probably will not do it, especially when you want to show your disapproval of what someone has done 有點想做某事〔但很可能不做〕: *I have half a mind to tell him what an idiot he is.* 我真想告訴他他有多笨。**b)** used as a not very serious threat to show your disapproval of what someone has done 說不定我會〔表示不太當真的威脅〕: *I have half a mind to tell your mother about this.* 說不定我會把此事告訴你母親。**9 only half the story** an explanation that is not complete, used especially to say that someone is trying to keep something secret 只是〔事件的〕部分真相: *Journalists are convinced that the Congressman was only telling them half the story.* 記者們相信那個眾議員只告訴了他們部分真相。**10 half measures** actions or methods that are not effective in dealing with a difficult problem 不徹底的辦法: *The opposition accused the government of being satisfied with half measures.* 反對黨指責政府滿足於不徹底的辦法。**11 go off at half cock/half cocked** to happen without enough preparation being done, with the result that it is not successful 因準備不足而失敗

1 2 **half²** *n, pron plural* **halves** /hævz; hɑːvz/ [C]

1 ►50%◄ either of the two equal parts into which something is divided or can be divided; $^1/_2$ 一半, 二分之一: *Half of 50 is 25.* 50的一半是25。| *An hour and a half later I was still waiting for him to arrive.* 一個半小時之後, 我還在等着他的到來。| *"How old is Samantha now?" "She's five and a half."* "薩曼莎現在多大了?" "五歲半了。" | *The trade figures improved in the second half of last year.* 貿易數字於去年下半年有所改善。| *Half of the class was working on math problems while the other half divided into reading groups.* 班上的同學有一半在做數學題, 另一半分成了幾個閱讀小組。| *Scott gave her a piece of chocolate and kept the other half for himself.* 司各特給了她一塊巧克力, 另一半留給了自己。| **reduce/cut sth by half** (=make something 50% smaller) 減少/削減一半 *The new policy could cut the world oil production by half.* 這個新政策將使世界石油產量減少一半。| **break/cut sth in half** (=cut something into two equal parts) 分成/切成兩半 *He cut the cake in half.* 他把蛋糕切成兩半。

2 ►NUMBER 數字◄ the number $^1/_2$〔數字〕$^1/_2$, 二分之一: *Three halves make $1^1/_2$.* 三個二分之一相加等於 $1^1/_2$。

3 half past *especially BrE* thirty minutes after the hour mentioned【尤英】〔…點鐘〕以後半小時: **half past one/two/three etc** *Bill came home about half past one.* 比爾大約一點半回到家。| *She said she'd be home by six or half past.* 她說她會在六點或六點半回到家。

4 ►SPORTS EVENT 體育項目◄ either of the two parts into which a sports event is divided 半場: *The Minnesota Vikings pulled ahead to win by seven points in the second half.* 明尼蘇達維京隊在下半場以七分領先而獲勝。

5 ►FOOTBALL ETC 足球等◄ a player who plays in the middle part of the field 中(前)衛

6 ►BEER 啤酒◄ *BrE* a half of a PINT of beer【英】半品脫: *Fancy a quick half down the pub?* 想不想去酒吧呆一小會兒, 喝半品脫啤酒? | *two halves of bitter* 兩份半品脫苦啤酒

7 ►TICKET 票◄ *BrE* a child's ticket, for example on a bus or train, that is cheaper than an adult's ticket【英】兒童半票: *One and a half to Waterloo, please.* 請給我一張去滑鐵盧的大人票和一張兒童半票。

8 and a half *informal* used when you think that something is very unusual or surprising, or very good【非正式】棒極了, 好極了: *That was a meal and a half!* 那頓飯棒極了!

9 your better half/other half *humorous* your husband or wife【幽默】丈夫; 妻子: *Let me introduce you to my better half.* 讓我把你介紹給我的老伴。

10 not do sth by halves to do something very eagerly and using a lot of care and effort 認真地做某事, 不馬虎: *I'm sure it will be a fantastic wedding. Eva never does anything by halves.* 我肯定婚禮一定會辦得非常出色。伊娃辦事從不馬虎。

11 you don't know the half of it *spoken* used to emphasize that a situation is more difficult, complicated, or unpleasant than people realize【口】比你想像的更甚: *"I know it was a dreadful time, just after the war." "You don't know the half of it."* "我知道那時情況很糟糕, 戰爭才剛剛結束。" "比你想像的更糟。"

12 go halves (on sth) to share something, especially the cost of something, equally between two people〔兩人〕平均分攤〔費用〕; 平分, 對半分: *Do you want to go halves on a pizza?* 你要和我合買一個意大利薄餅嗎?

13 how the other half lives how people who are much richer or much poorer than you manage their lives, work, money etc 富人[窮人]是怎樣過日子的: *He's working for a millionaire, so he's getting a taste of how the other half lives.* 他為一個百萬富翁工作, 所以感受到了富人是怎樣生活的。

14 too clever/rich/virtuous etc by half *BrE informal* clever, rich etc in an annoying way【英, 非正式】聰明/富有/高尚等過了頭: *That boy's too arrogant by half.* 那個男孩太傲慢了。

H

half³ *adv* **1** partly, but not completely 部分地, 不完全地: *I was half in love with her by the end of the evening.* 傍晚完結時, 我已經有點愛上她了。| *She was standing there half-dressed, putting on her makeup in front of the mirror.* 她站在鏡子前化妝, 衣服還沒有穿好。| *He seemed to half expect her to come back and apologize.* 他似乎有點期待她回來道歉。| **half-finished/half-empty/half full** *Cups of half-finished tea were on the floor beside the bed.* 牀邊的地板上有幾杯喝了一半的茶。 2
2 used to emphasize something, especially when a situation is extremely bad 極其, 非常〔尤指情況很糟〕: *I had been driven half out of my mind with worry.* 我擔憂得發瘋了。| *The kitten looked half starved.* 小貓看起來餓壞了。**3 half as much/big etc again** larger by an amount that is equal to half the original size 多少/大小等是原來的一倍半: *Roy invested his savings in a new store that was half as big again as the old one.* 羅伊把他的積蓄投資在一家大小是原來一倍半的新店。**4 not half as good/interesting etc (as)** much less good, less interesting etc than someone or something else 遠不如…好/有趣等: *The movie wasn't half as entertaining as the book.* 這部電影遠不如原書好看。| *She can't love you half as much as I do.* 她不可能像我這樣愛你。**5 not half** *BrE spoken* used when you want to emphasize an opinion or statement【英口】極其, 非常: *She doesn't half talk once she gets started.* 她只要一打開話匣子就說個沒完。| *"Did you enjoy it, then?" "Not half!"* "那麼你玩得高興嗎?" "高興極了!" **6 not half bad** an expression

meaning good, used especially when you are rather surprised that something is good〔出乎意料地〕相當好, 很棒: *Actually, the party wasn't half bad.* 實際上, 晚會棒極了。**7 half and half** partly one thing and partly another 各佔一半; 既是…又是…: *"What is she, then, a psychiatrist or a social worker?" "Sort of half and half."* "那麼, 她到底是一位精神科醫生還是社會工作者?" "兩者皆是。"

half-and-half /ˌ· · ˈ·/ *n* [U] *AmE* a mixture that is half milk and half cream, used in coffee or tea【美】〔加入咖啡或茶中的奶油和牛奶摻半的〕稀奶油

half-arsed /ˌhæf ˋɑrst; ˌhɑːf ˈɑːst◂/ *BrE*【英】, **half-assed** /ˌhæf ˋæst; ˌhɑːf ˈæst◂/ *AmE*【美】*adj informal*【非正式】**1** done without enough attention or effort 胡亂的; 敷衍了事的: *He made a half-arsed attempt to clean up after the party.* 晚會結束後, 他敷衍了事地收拾了一下。**2** completely stupid 極愚蠢的: *What a half-assed idea!* 真是個愚蠢的主意!

half·back /ˈhæfˌbæk; ˈhɑːfbæk/ *n* [C] **1** a player in football, RUGBY, HOCKEY etc who plays in the middle part of the field〔足球、橄欖球、曲棍球的〕中(前)衛, 中場球員 **2** a player in American football who, at the start of play, is behind the front line of players and next to the FULLBACK〔美式足球的〕中衛

half-baked /ˌ· ˈ·◂/ *adj* a half-baked idea, suggestion, plan etc has not been properly planned〔想法、建議、計劃等〕不成熟的, 考慮不周全的: *Education has been damaged by the half-baked notions of theorists who've never been in a classroom.* 教育被那些從未進過課室的理論家們草率的觀點所害。

half board /ˌ· ˈ·/ *n* [U] *especially BrE* the price of a room in a hotel that includes breakfast and dinner【尤英】〔包括早餐及晚餐的〕半食宿房價 —compare 比較 FULL BOARD

half-breed /ˈ· ·/ *n* [C] a word which is now considered offensive meaning someone whose parents are of different races, especially one white parent and one Native American parent 混血兒〔父母為不同種族, 尤指一方為白人, 另一方為美洲印第安人。此詞現具冒犯性〕—**half-breed** *adj*

half broth·er /ˈ· ˌ··/ *n* [C] a brother who is the son of only one of your parents 同父異母[同母異父]兄弟

half-caste /ˈ· ·/ *n* [C] a word which is now considered offensive, meaning someone whose parents are of different races 混血兒〔此詞現具冒犯性〕—**half-caste** *adj*

half cock /ˌ· ˈ·/ —see 見 **go off at half cock** (HALF[1] (11))

half-crazed /ˌ· ˈ·◂/ *adj* behaving in a slightly crazy, uncontrolled way 有點發瘋的: *half-crazed with pain* 疼得快發瘋了

half crown /ˌ· ˈ·◂/ *n* [C] a coin used in Britain before 1971. There were eight half crowns in £1 半克朗〔1971年以前的英國銀幣名, 合一英鎊的八分之一〕

half-cup /ˈ· ·/ *n* [C] *AmE* a small container used to measure an amount of food when cooking, or the amount that this holds【美】〔用來量食物的〕小量杯: *Add a half-cup of sugar.* 加上一小杯糖。

half-cut /ˌ· ˈ·/ *adj BrE old-fashioned* drunk【英, 過時】(酒)醉的

half-day /ˈ· ·/ *n* [C] a day when you work or go to school either in the morning or the afternoon, but not all day (上)半天班[學]

half dol·lar /ˌ· ˈ··/ *n* [C] an American or Canadian coin worth 50 cents〔美國或加拿大的〕半元硬幣

half-heart·ed /ˌ· ˈ··◂/ *adj* a half-hearted attempt to do something is done without much effort and without much interest in the result 半心半意的, 敷衍了事的, 不熱心的: *She made a half-hearted attempt to be friendly.* 她敷衍地表示了一下友好。—**half-heartedly** *adv* —**half-heartedness** *n* [U]

half-hol·i·day /ˌ· ˈ···/ *n* [C] *BrE* a morning or afternoon in which you do not have to go to work or school; HALF DAY【英】半日假

half-hour·ly /ˌ· ˈ··◂/ *adj, adv* done or happening every half hour 每半小時的[地]: *the half-hourly chimes of the clock* 半小時一次的鐘鳴

half-length /ˌ· ˈ·◂/ *adj* **1** a half-length coat reaches to just above the knee〔長及膝上的〕半長〔外套〕**2** a half-length painting or picture shows the top half of someone's body 半身〔畫像、照片〕

half-life /ˈ· ·/ *n* [C] the half life of a RADIOACTIVE substance is the length of time it takes to lose half of its RADIOACTIVITY〔放射性物質的〕半衰期

half-light /ˈ· ·/ *n* [U] the dull grey light you see when it is almost dark but not completely dark 半明半暗的光, 灰暗的光線: *Briggs heard the commotion but in the half-light of dawn could not see anyone clearly.* 布里格斯聽到了喧鬧聲, 但在黎明半明半暗的光線中無法看清任何人。

half-mast /ˌ· ˈ·/ *n* **at half-mast a)** a flag that is at half mast has been put at the middle of the pole in order to show respect and sadness for someone important who has died 下半旗〔表示哀悼〕**b)** *BrE humorous* if someone's trousers are at half-mast, they are too short【英, 幽默】〔褲子〕短得半吊着, 短得見踝的

half moon /ˌ· ˈ·/ *n* [C] the shape of the moon when only half of it is showing 半月(形) —compare 比較 FULL MOON, NEW MOON —see picture on page A6 參見A6頁圖

half nel·son /ˌhæf ˋnɛlsn̩; ˌhɑːf ˈnelsən/ *n* [C] a way of holding your opponent's arm behind their back in the sport of WRESTLING〔摔跤姿勢〕側面肩下握頸

half note /ˈ· ·/ *n* [C] *AmE* a musical note which continues for half the length of a WHOLE NOTE【美】〔音樂〕二分音符; MINIM *BrE*【英】—see picture at 參見 MUSIC 圖

half·penny /ˈhepnɪ; ˈheɪpni/ *n* [C] a small coin worth half of one penny, used in Britain in the past〔英國舊時使用的〕半便士小硬幣 —see also 另見 **not have two pennies/halfpennies to rub together** (RUB[1] (11))

half price /ˌ· ˈ·◂/ *adv* at half the usual price 以半價: *Do you like the new carpet? We got it half price in the sale.* 你喜歡那張新地毯嗎? 我們在大減價時以半價買的。—**half-price** *adj*: *half-price sale items* 半價商品

half-sis·ter /ˈ· ˌ··/ *n* [C] a sister who is the daughter of only one of your parents 同父異母[同母異父]姊妹

half step /ˈ· ·/ *n* [C] *AmE* the difference in PITCH[1] (3) between any two notes that are next to each other on a piano【美】半音; SEMITONE *BrE*【英】

half-term /ˌ· ˈ·◂/ *n* [C] *BrE* a short holiday from school in the middle of a TERM[1] (9)【英】〔學校的〕期中假 —compare 比較 MIDTERM[2]

half-tim·bered /ˌ· ˈ··◂/ *adj* a half-timbered house is usually old and shows the wooden structure of the building on the outside walls〔古式房屋建築〕露明木架的

half time /ˌ· ˈ·◂/ *n* [U] a short period of rest between two parts of a game, such as football or BASKETBALL〔足球、籃球比賽等的〕中場休息: *The score at half time was 34-7.* 中場休息時比分為34比7。—see also 另見 FULL TIME

half·tone /ˈhæfˌton; ˌhɑːfˈtəʊn◂/ *n* **1** [U] a method of printing black and white photographs that shows different shades of grey by changing the number of black DOTs in an area of the photograph〔印刷中的〕網目凸版(製版法), 網線凸版 **2** [C] a photograph printed by this method 網版印刷的照片, 網目版圖, 網線凸版畫 **3** [C] *AmE* a HALF STEP【美】半音

half-truth /ˈ· ·/ *n* [C] a statement that is only partly true, especially one that is intended to keep something secret〔為了隱瞞真相的〕半真半假的陳述: *His replies were full of evasions and half-truths.* 他的回答充滿推諉之詞和半真半假的鬼話。

half vol·ley /ˌ· ˈ··/ *n* [C] **1** an action in tennis in which the ball is hit just after it hits the ground〔網球〕一落地跳起即擊的擊球 **2** in CRICKET, a ball that can easily be hit by the BATSMAN just after it hits the ground〔板球〕落

地後跳起時即被擊球手輕易擊中的球, 反彈球

half·way /ˈhæfˈwe; ˌhɑːfˈweɪ◂/ *adj, adv* **1** at a middle point in space or time between two things〔空間、時間的〕中間(的), 半途(的): *We reached the halfway point ten miles into our walk.* 走了十英里後, 我們到達了中間點。| *Grease the muffin tins and fill them halfway with batter.* 將鬆餅烤模塗上牛油, 再把麵糊倒至半滿。| [+up/along etc] *He chased Kevin halfway up the stairs.* 他追凱文一直追到樓梯的中間。| *It was a terrible film – I left halfway through.* 這部電影糟糕得很, 我半途就離場了。| **be halfway there** (=be halfway to achieving something) 完成一半 *If we can just finish this section we'll be halfway there.* 如果我們能幹完這部分, 就算完成一半了。**2 halfway respectable/decent/civil etc** reasonably RESPECTABLE etc 還算正派/體面/文明等: *It's the only halfway decent hotel around here.* 這是附近唯一一家還算體面的旅館。**3 go halfway towards doing sth** to achieve something partly but not completely 完成一部分; 做得不徹底: *These measures only go halfway towards solving the problem.* 這些措施不能徹底地解決這個問題。—see also 另見 **meet sb halfway** (MEET[1] (17))

halfway house /ˌ·· ˈ·/ *n* **1** [singular] something which is a combination of the qualities of two things, but may not be as good as either of those two things by themselves 介乎兩者之間的東西: *His clarinet solos are a kind of halfway house between the styles of Dodds and Russell.* 他的單簧管獨奏既有點多茲的風格, 又有點拉塞爾的風格。**2** [C] a place for former prisoners or people who have had mental illnesses, where they can live until they are ready to live on their own〔為刑滿釋放者或已痊癒的精神病人重返社會而設立的〕過渡教習所[療養所], 重返社會訓練所

half-wit /ˈ· ·/ *n* [C] *informal* a stupid person or someone who has done something stupid【非正式】傻瓜, 笨蛋 —**half-witted** *adj*: *a burly half-witted fellow with one eye* 一個獨眼的壯蠢漢 —**half-wittedly** *adv*

half-year·ly /ˌ· ˈ··/ *adj, adv* done or happening every six months 每隔半年(的), 半年一次(的): *half-yearly meetings in June and December* 於六月和十二月每隔半年開一次的會議

hal·i·but /ˈhæləbət; ˈhælɪ̈bət/ *n* [C] a large flat sea fish used as food 大比目魚〔食用海魚〕

hal·i·to·sis /ˌhæləˈtosɪs; ˌhælɪ̈ˈtəʊsɪ̈s/ *n* [U] a condition in which someone's breath smells very bad 口臭

1 2 **hall** /hɔl; hɔːl/ *n* [C] **1** the area just inside the door of a house or other building that leads to other rooms; HALLWAY (1)〔住宅的〕門廳,〔正門入口處的〕走廊: *We hung our coats on a rack in the entrance hall.* 我們把外套掛在門廳裡的衣架上。**2** a passage in a building or house that leads to many of the rooms; CORRIDOR (1)〔建築物內的〕走廊, 過道: *Each floor of the dorm had ten rooms on both sides of the hall.* 宿舍樓的每一層在走廊的兩邊都有十個房間。**3** a building or large room for public events such as meetings or dances 大廳, 會堂, 禮堂: *Five hundred people filled the lecture hall.* 來了五百人, 把演講廳都擠滿了。| *Carnegie Hall* 卡內基音樂廳 **4 Hall** *especially BrE* part of the name of some large houses in the country【尤英】〔鄉間〕大莊園, 府第: *Haddon Hall* 哈登莊園 **5** *BrE* a place provided by a college or university for students to live in; HALL OF RESIDENCE【英】〔大學的〕學生宿舍 —see also 另見 CITY HALL, MUSIC HALL, TOWN HALL

hal·lal /həˈlɑl; hɑːˈlɑːl/ *adj* another spelling of HALAL halal 的另一種拼法

hal·le·lu·jah /ˌhæləˈlujə; ˌhælɪ̈ˈluːjə◂/ *interjection* **1** used as an expression of thanks, JOY, or praise to God 哈利路亞〔表示感謝、欣喜或讚美上帝〕**2** used when something has finally happened that you think should have happened before 哈利路亞〔表示期望已久的事終於發生〕: *"The bus is here!" "Well, hallelujah."* "公共汽車來了!" "啊, 終於到啦!" —**hallelujah** *n* [C]

hal·liard /ˈhæljəd; ˈhæljəd/ *n* [C] another spelling of HALYARD halyard 的另一種拼法

hall·mark[1] /ˈhɔlˌmɑrk; ˈhɔːlmɑːk/ *n* [C] **1** an idea, method, or quality that is typical of a particular person or thing 特點, 特徵; 標誌: [+of] *Non-violence and simplicity were the hallmarks of Gandhi's philosophy.* 非暴力和簡樸是甘地哲學的特點。| **have all the hallmarks of** *The explosion had all the hallmarks of a terrorist attack.* 這場爆炸事件是一次不折不扣的恐怖襲擊。**2** a mark put on silver, gold, or PLATINUM that shows the quality of the metal, and where and when it was made〔金、銀或白金製品上的〕純度印記

hallmark[2] *v* [T] to put a hallmark on silver, gold, or PLATINUM 在〔金、銀或白金製品〕上打印記

hal·lo /həˈlo; həˈləʊ/ *interjection old-fashioned* a British form of HELLO【過時】hello 的英式拼法

Hall of Fame /ˌ· · ˈ·/ *n* [C] a place in the US where people can go to learn about a particular sport or activity and the famous people connected with it〔美國〕名人紀念館

hall of res·i·dence /ˌ· · ˈ···/ *n* [C] *BrE* a college or university building where students live【英】〔學院或大學的〕學生宿舍樓; DORMITORY[1] (2) *AmE*【美】

hal·lowed /ˈhælod; ˈhæləʊd/ *adj* **1** made holy 神聖的, 奉為神聖的: **hallowed ground** (=land, especially around a church, that has been made holy)〔尤指教堂四周的〕聖地 **2** *sometimes humorous* important and respected【有時幽默】重要而受尊崇的: *a hallowed tradition* 神聖的傳統 | *the hallowed portals* (=doors) *of Broadcasting House* 英國廣播公司中央大樓的神聖入口

Hal·low·een, Hallowe'en /ˌhæloˈin; ˌhæləʊˈiːn◂/ *n* [U] the night of October 31st, when it was believed that the spirits of dead people appeared, and which is now celebrated by children, who dress as WITCH*es*, GHOST*s* etc 萬聖節前夕〔10月31日之夜〕

hal·lu·ci·nate /həˈlusnˌet; həˈluːsɪ̈neɪt/ *v* [I] to see or hear things that are not really there 產生幻覺

hal·lu·ci·na·tion /həˌlusnˈeʃən; həˌluːsɪ̈ˈneɪʃən/ *n* **1** [C, U] the experience of seeing or feeling something that is not really there 幻覺 **2** [C] something which you imagine you can see or hear, but which is not really there 由幻覺產生的形象[聲音]: *drug-induced hallucinations* 由藥物引起的幻覺

hal·lu·ci·na·to·ry /həˈlusnəˌtorɪ; həˈluːsɪ̈nətəri/ *adj formal*【正式】**1** causing hallucinations or resulting from hallucinations (引起)幻覺的; 幻覺導致的: *hallucinatory drugs* 致幻藥物 **2** using strange images, sounds etc like those experienced in a hallucination 似幻覺的, 幻覺般的: *a hallucinatory collage of images* 各種圖像如幻覺般的拼湊

hal·lu·ci·no·gen·ic /həˌlusnəˈdʒɛnɪk; həˌluːsɪ̈nəˈdʒenɪk◂/ *adj* hallucinogenic drugs make people experience hallucinations 引起幻覺的, 致幻的

hall·way /ˈhɔlˌwe; ˈhɔːlweɪ/ *n* [C] **1** the area just inside the door of a house or other building that leads to other rooms; HALL (1)〔住宅的〕門廳,〔正門入口處的〕走廊 **2** a passage in a building or house that leads to many of the rooms; CORRIDOR (1)〔建築物內的〕走廊, 過道

ha·lo /ˈhelo; ˈheɪləʊ/ *n* [C] **1** a bright circle that is often shown above or around the heads of holy people in religious art〔神像頭上的〕光輪 **2** a bright circle of light 暈, 暈圈

hal·o·gen /ˈhælədʒən; ˈhælədʒen/ *n* [U] one of a group of five simple chemical substances that make compounds easily 鹵素

halt[1] /hɔlt; hɔːlt/ *n* [singular] a stop or pause 停止, 停住; 暫停: **bring sth to a halt** (=make something stop moving or continuing) 使…停頓; 使…中止 *Heavy snowfalls brought traffic to a halt on the Brenner Pass.* 大雪使得布倫納山口的交通陷於停頓。| *fuel shortages that have brought the industry to a grinding halt* 使該工業慢慢地停止生產的燃料短缺 | **come/grind/crash etc to a halt**

(=stop moving or continuing) 停下/慢慢停下/猛然停下 *The whole peace process seems to have ground to a halt.* 整個和平進程似乎已慢慢地停頓下來。| *Joe slammed on the brakes and the car skidded to a halt.* 喬猛踩煞車, 汽車便向前滑行着停住了。| **call a halt (to)** (=officially stop an activity from continuing)〔正式〕中止, 停止 *The IRA leadership has called a halt to its campaign of violence.* 愛爾蘭共和軍的領導層已經停止其暴力活動。

halt² *v* **1** [I] to stop moving 停下, 停止: *The parade halted by a busy corner.* 遊行隊伍在一個熱鬧的拐角處停下了。**2 halt!** used as a military command to order someone to stop moving or soldiers to stop marching〔口令〕站住! 立定!: *Company halt!* 全連立定! | *Halt! Who goes there?* 站住! 是誰? **3** [T] to prevent someone or something from continuing with something 阻止: *There were calls to halt the hunting of seals.* 人們呼籲停止捕獵海豹。

hal·ter /ˈhɔltɚ; ˈhɔːltə/ *n* [C] **1** a rope or leather band that fastens around a horse's head, usually used to lead the horse〔馬的〕籠頭, 韁繩 **2** also 又作 **halter top** a type of clothing for women that ties behind the neck and across the back, so that the arms and back are not covered〔女用的在頸及背後繫帶的〕袒肩露背上裝 **3** *literary* a piece of rope used to HANG¹ (3) criminals【文】絞索

hal·ter·neck /ˈhɔltɚˌnɛk; ˈhɔːltənek/ *adj* a halterneck shirt ties around the neck and behind the back, so that the arms and back are not covered〔在頸及背後繫帶〕袒肩露背的〔服裝〕—**halterneck** *n* [C]

halt·ing /ˈhɔltɪŋ; ˈhɔːltɪŋ/ *adj* if your speech or movements are halting, you stop for a moment between words or movements, especially because you are not confident 斷斷續續的; 遲疑不決的: *We carried on a halting conversation in our imperfect German.* 我們用不熟練的德語斷斷續續地進行交談。—**haltingly** *adv*

halve /hæv; hɑːv/ *v* [T] **1** to cut or divide something into two equal pieces 把…分成兩半, 對半分: *Halve the eggplant lengthwise and hollow out the center.* 把茄子縱向地切成兩半, 把中間挖空。**2** to reduce something by a half 將…減半: *The European Union plans to halve production of CFCs by the end of the decade.* 歐盟計劃在本十年末將含氯氟烴的產量減少一半。

halves /hævz; hɑːvz/ the plural of HALF

hal·yard, halliard /ˈhæljɚd; ˈhæljəd/ *n* [C] *technical* a rope used to raise or lower a flag or sail【術語】〔用以升降旗、帆的〕吊索, 升降索

ham¹ /hæm; hæm/ *n* **1** [C,U] the upper part of a pig's leg that has been preserved with salt or smoke, or the meat from this 火腿, 火腿肉: *a ham sandwich* 火腿三明治 | *a seven-pound ham* 七磅重的火腿 **2** [C] *informal* an actor who performs with too much false emotion【非正式】演技做作的演員, 表演過火的演員 **3** [C] someone who receives and sends radio messages for fun rather than as their job 業餘無線電愛好者 **4 hams** [plural] the upper part of a person's or animal's legs 股臀

ham² *v* **ham it up** *informal* to perform with too much false emotion when acting【非正式】做作地表演, 表演過火

ham·burg·er /ˈhæmbɝgɚ; ˈhæmbɜːgə/ *n* **1** [C] very small pieces of BEEF pressed together, cooked, and eaten between two round pieces of bread 漢堡包 **2** [U] *AmE* beef that has been cut into very small pieces【美】牛肉餡, 碎牛肉; MINCE² *BrE*【英】

ham-fist·ed /ˌ· ˈ··◂/ also 又作 **ham-handed** *adj informal*【非正式】**1** not at all skilful with your hands; CLUMSY (1) 笨手笨腳的, 手不靈巧的 **2** not at all skilful or careful in the way that you deal with people〔待人接物〕笨拙的, 不靈巧的: *the government's ham-fisted approach towards the disabled* 政府對待殘疾人士的拙劣手法 —**ham-fistedly, ham-handedly** *adv*

ham·let /ˈhæmlɪt; ˈhæmlɨt/ *n* [C] a very small village 小村莊

ham·mer¹ /ˈhæmɚ; ˈhæmə/ *n* [C]

1 ▶TOOL 工具◀ a) a tool with a heavy metal part on a long handle, used for hitting nails into wood 榔頭, 錘子 —see picture at 參見 TOOL¹ 圖 **b)** a tool like this with a wooden head used to make something flat, make a noise etc 木槌: an *auctioneer's hammer* 拍賣人的木槌

2 come/go under the hammer to be offered for sale at an AUCTION¹ 被拍賣

3 be/go at it hammer and tongs *informal* to fight or argue very loudly【非正式】激烈打鬥[爭吵]

4 ▶PIANO 鋼琴◀ a wooden part of a PIANO that hits the strings inside to make a musical sound 音錘

5 ▶GUN 槍、砲◀ the part of a gun that hits the explosive CHARGE¹ (8) that fires a bullet 擊鐵 —see picture at 參見 GUN¹ 圖

6 ▶SPORT 體育◀ a heavy metal ball on a wire with a handle that is thrown as far as possible, as a sport 鏈球

hammer² *v*

1 ▶HIT STH WITH A HAMMER 用錘擊打某物◀ [I,T] to hit something with a hammer in order to force it into a particular position or shape 錘擊, 錘打; 把…錘進: **hammer sth into/onto** *He hammered the door into its frame.* 他把門錘進門框中。| *The blacksmith then hammers the horseshoe into its final shape.* 鐵匠隨後將馬蹄鐵錘打成形。

2 ▶HIT REPEATEDLY 反覆敲打◀ [I] to hit something many times, especially making a loud noise〔大聲地〕反覆敲打: **[+against/on]** *The rain was hammering against the window.* 雨不停地敲打着窗戶。

3 ▶DEFEAT 擊敗◀ [T] *informal* to defeat someone completely at a sport【非正式】〔在體育比賽中〕徹底擊敗: *Arsenal hammered Manchester United in yesterday's game.* 阿仙奴隊在昨天的比賽中徹底擊敗了曼聯隊。

4 ▶HIT HARD 狠擊◀ [T] *informal* to hit or kick something very hard【非正式】猛擊; 狠踢: *Robinson hammered the ball into the goal.* 羅賓遜猛力將球攻進了球門。

5 hammer away at a) to work hard and continuously at something 接連工作, 不懈地致力於: *I kept hammering away at the essay until it was done.* 我一直在埋頭苦幹, 直到論文寫好為止。**b)** to repeat something continuously until you are sure that people understand or accept what you are saying 重複論及, 反覆說明: *Petersen kept hammering away at his demand for a public inquiry.* 彼得森不斷要求進行一次公開調查。

6 hammer sth home to make sure that people understand what you want to say by speaking in a determined way 明確指出; 強調: *an important point that needs to be hammered home* 需特別強調的一個要點

7 ▶HEART 心◀ [I] if your heart hammers, you feel it beating strongly and quickly〔猛烈快速地〕跳動: *She stood outside the door, her heart hammering.* 她站在門外, 心在怦怦跳動。

hammer ↔ **sth in, hammer sth into sb** *phr v* [T] to repeat something continuously until people completely understand it 不斷重複使某人明白〔某事〕, 反覆灌輸: *The coach hammered his message into the team.* 教練向全隊反覆灌輸他的話。

hammer out sth *phr v* [T] to decide on an agreement, contract etc after a lot of discussion and disagreement〔經詳細的討論及爭議後〕得出〔協議、解決辦法等〕: *The UN is trying to force the warring factions to get together and hammer out a solution.* 聯合國正試圖拉攏各敵對派系一起尋求解決問題的方案。

hammer and sick·le /ˌ·· · ˈ··/ *n* [singular] **1** the sign of a hammer crossing a SICKLE on a red background, used as a sign of COMMUNISM 錘子和鐮刀(圖案)〔共產主義的標誌〕**2** the flag of the former Soviet Union 前蘇聯國旗

ham·mered /ˈhæmɚd; ˈhæməd/ *adj* [only before noun 僅用於名詞前] **1** hammered silver, gold etc has a pattern of small hollow areas on its surface〔金、銀等製品〕鍛造的 **2** *informal* very drunk【非正式】喝得醉醺醺的

ham·mer·ing /ˈhæmərɪŋ; ˈhæmərɪŋ/ *n* [singular] **1 give/take a hammering** to attack or be attacked very severely 發起／受到猛烈攻擊: *Dresden took a real hammering during the war.* 德雷斯頓在戰爭期間受到猛烈攻擊。**2** the sound of someone hitting something with a hammer or with their FISTS (=closed hands) 錘擊聲; 拳擊聲: *There was a hammering at the door.* 有人在使勁敲門。

ham·mock /ˈhæmək; ˈhæmək/ *n* [C] a thing for sleeping in, consisting of a long piece of cloth or a net that is hung between two trees〔帆布或網做的〕吊牀

ham·per¹ /ˈhæmpɚ; ˈhæmpə/ *v* [T] to restrict someone's movements, activities, or achievements by causing difficulties for them 阻礙, 妨礙; 牽制: *Women's progress in the workplace is still hampered by male attitudes.* 婦女在工作上的發展仍受到男性態度的阻擾。

hamper² *n* [C] **1** a basket with a lid, often used for carrying food〔用於攜帶食品的〕有蓋籃子: *a picnic hamper* 野餐籃子 —see picture at 參見 BASKET 圖 **2** *AmE* a large basket that you put dirty clothes in until they can be washed【美】〔放置待洗髒衣物的〕洗衣筐; LAUNDRY BASKET *BrE*【英】

ham·ster /ˈhæmstɚ; ˈhæmstə/ *n* [C] a small animal like a mouse, often kept as a pet 倉鼠〔多作寵物〕

ham·string¹ /ˈhæmˌstrɪŋ; ˈhæmˌstrɪŋ/ *n* [C] a TENDON behind your knee 膕繩肌腱, 膕旁腱, 腿腱

hamstring² *v past tense and past participle* **hamstrung** /-ˌstrʌŋ; -ˌstrʌŋ/ [T often passive 常用被動態] to restrict someone's activities or development so much that they cannot do the job they are supposed to do (受到) 阻礙, (被…) 束縛; 使無能為力: *Police officers claim that they are hamstrung by regulations and paperwork.* 警察聲稱他們被各種規定和文案工作所束縛。

1
1

hand¹ /hænd; hænd/ *n*

① PART OF THE BODY 人體部位
② HELP/WORK 幫助/工作
③ SKILFUL 有某種技能的
④ CONTROL 控制
⑤ DEAL WITH/BE INVOLVED IN 處理/參與
⑥ CLOSE 接近的
⑦ DIRECTLY/NOT DIRECTLY 直接的/非直接的
⑧ OTHER MEANINGS 其他意思

① PART OF THE BODY 人體部位

1 [C] the part at the end of a person's arm, including the fingers and thumb, used to pick up or keep hold of things 手: *He held the pencil in his right hand.* 他用右手握着鉛筆。| *Go wash your hands.* 去洗手。| **hold hands** *They kissed and held hands.* 他們接吻並拉着手。| **take sb by the hand** (=hold sb's hand in order to take them somewhere) 牽着某人的手 *Marika took the child by the hand and led her away.* 馬里卡牽着孩子的手把她帶走了。—see picture at 參見 BODY 圖

2 hand in hand holding each other's hand, especially to show love 手拉手〔尤指表示愛意〕: *They strolled hand in hand through the flower garden.* 他們手拉着手漫步穿過花園。

3 right-handed/left-handed using the right hand for most actions rather than the left, or the left hand rather than the right 慣用右手／左手的: *a left-handed tennis player* 左撇子網球手

4 right/left hander a player who uses mainly the right hand or mainly the left hand 慣用右手／左手的選手[球員]

② HELP/WORK 幫助/工作

5 a hand help with something you are doing, especially something that involves physical work 幫忙, 支援: **give/lend sb a hand** *It's really heavy – can you give me a hand?* 這東西真重 —— 你能幫個忙嗎? | **need a hand** *Tell me if you need a hand.* 需要幫忙就告訴我。—see 見 HELP¹ (USAGE)

6 ►WORKER 工人◄ [C] someone who does physical work on a farm, in a factory etc〔從事體力勞動的〕工人

7 not do a hand's turn *BrE informal* to do no work at all【英, 非正式】一點工作也不做: *He never does a hand's turn to help me.* 他從不幫我。

③ SKILFUL 有某種技能的

8 a dab hand someone who is very good at doing something 能手: *She's a dab hand at making pastry.* 她是做糕點的能手。

9 good with your hands skilful at making things 手巧的, 有一雙靈巧的手

10 turn your hand to to start doing something new or practising a new skill 着手做〔新的事情〕; 開始練習〔新技能〕: *Larry can turn his hand to anything.* 拉里做甚麼工作都行。

11 keep your hand in to keep practising something so you do not lose your skill 繼續練習以保持熟練: *You should work part-time, just to keep your hand in.* 你應該做一份兼職工作, 免得生疏了。

④ CONTROL 控制

12 in the hands of/in sb's hands controlled by someone 在〔某人〕的控制之中, 由〔某人〕支配[掌管]: *The area is already in rebel hands.* 那個地區已經落入叛亂分子的手中。

13 a firm hand strict control of someone 嚴厲管制: *That child is a little monster. She obviously needs a firm hand.* 那個孩子是個小壞蛋, 她顯然需要嚴加管教。

14 get out of hand to become impossible to control 失控: *Deal with the problem before it gets completely out of hand.* 在問題完全失控之前加以處理。

15 take sb/sth in hand to bring someone or something under control 控制, 管制: *It's time these young offenders were taken in hand.* 到了好好管教這些少年犯的時候了。

⑤ DEAL WITH/BE INVOLVED IN 處理/參與

16 in hand being dealt with 在處理之中: *Don't worry – all the arrangements are in hand.* 別擔心, 一切都安排好了。| **have sth in hand** *Give them a call to let them know we have the matter in hand.* 打電話告訴他們我們正在處理這件事。

17 have a hand in to influence or be involved in something 插手, 參與: *I suspect John had a hand in this.* 我懷疑約翰參與了此事。

18 in the hands of/in sb's hands being dealt with by someone 由〔某人〕處理: *The whole affair is now in the hands of the police.* 整件事現在由警方負責處理。

19 in good/safe/capable hands being dealt with or looked after by someone who can be trusted 在可靠的／穩妥的／能幹的人手裡: *We left the project in the capable hands of our deputy manager.* 我們把這個項目交給了能幹的副經理負責。

20 off your hands if something or someone is off your

H

hands, you are not responsible for them any more 不再負責: *We have more free time now the kids are off our hands.* 現在孩子們不用我們看管了, 我們就有更多的自由時間了。

21 have sth/sb on your hands to have a difficult job, problem, or responsibility that you must deal with 手頭有某事待處理〔指困難的事情或問題〕: *They'll have a battle on their hands if they try to build a road here.* 如果他們要在這裡築路, 他們將面臨一場艱難的戰鬥。

⑥ CLOSE 接近的

22 at hand *formal* near in time or space【正式】〔時間或空間上〕接近的, 不遠的: *The great day was almost at hand.* 重要的一天即將到來。| **near/close at hand** *There are shops and buses close at hand.* 附近就有商店和公共汽車。

23 have/keep sth to hand to have or keep something where you can easily reach it 將某物放在手邊

24 on hand close by and ready when needed 在手頭; 在近旁: *The nurse will be on hand if you need her.* 如果你需要護士的話, 她就在附近。

⑦ DIRECTLY/NOT DIRECTLY 直接的/非直接的

25 first hand/at first hand by direct personal experience 第一手的/第一手地; 直接的/直接地: *She stayed there to experience village life at first hand.* 她留在那兒親身體驗鄉村生活。| *first hand eyewitness accounts of the riot* 親身目擊者對暴亂的描述

26 at second/third/fourth hand passed from the first person who actually saw or heard something to a second, third, or fourth person 第二/三/四(道)手: *I may have the story wrong as I heard it at second hand.* 我說的不一定對, 因為我是聽別人說的。—see also 另見 SECOND HAND

27 by hand a) by a person, not a machine 手工的: *Every buttonhole is made by hand.* 所有鈕扣眼都是人手做的。**b)** delivered from one person to another, not sent through the post 親手交的, 非郵遞的

⑧ OTHER MEANINGS 其他意思

28 go hand in hand to be closely connected 密切相關; 同時發生: *High unemployment and high crime often go hand in hand.* 高失業率和高犯罪率常常是密切相關的。

29 get your hands on a) to obtain something 獲取, 得到: *They all want to get their hands on my money.* 他們都想得到我的錢。**b)** to catch someone you are angry with 抓住〔某人〕: *Wait until I get my hands on her, she's borrowed my best skirt.* 等我把她抓住再說, 她借走了我最好的裙子。

30 lay your hands on to find or obtain something 找到; 得到: *I'll bring some tapes if I can lay my hands on them.* 如果找得到的話, 我會帶幾盒錄音帶來。

31 have time on your hands to have a lot of time because you have no work to do 無所事事, 沒事可做

32 have your hands full to be very busy or too busy 非常忙: *I'm sorry I can't help – I have my hands full with problems at home.* 對不起, 我幫不了忙。我自己家裡的問題已經忙不過來了。

33 out of hand if you refuse something out of hand, you refuse immediately and completely 斷然, 即時〔拒絕〕

34 hand in glove closely connected with someone, especially in a bad or illegal activity 與…勾結, 關係密切: *They suspect the politicians are hand in glove with the mafia.* 他們懷疑那些政客與黑手黨互相勾結。

35 right/left hand side the side on your right or left 右邊/左邊: *Keep to the left hand side of the road.* 保持左行。

36 on the one hand ... on the other hand used when comparing different or opposite facts or ideas 一方面…, 另一方面…; 從一方面來說…, 從另一方面來說…: *On the one hand I want to sell the house, but on the other hand I can't bear the thought of moving.* 一方面我想把房子賣掉, 但另一方面我又不願搬家。

37 make/lose/spend hand over fist *informal* to gain, lose, or spend money very quickly and in large amounts【非正式】大量而迅速地賺錢/賠錢/花錢

38 give sb a (big) hand to CLAP[1] (1) loudly in order to show your approval of a performer or speaker 為某人熱烈鼓掌

39 ►CARD GAMES 紙牌遊戲◄ [C] **a)** a set of playing cards held by one person in a game 一手牌: *a winning hand* 一手贏牌 **b)** a game of cards 一局牌: *We played a couple of hands of poker.* 我們打了幾局撲克牌。

40 ►ON A CLOCK 時鐘上◄ [C] a long, thin piece of metal that points at the numbers on a clock 指針: *the hour hand* 時針

41 time/money in hand time or money that is available to be used 手頭現有的時間/金錢: *We still have a couple of weeks in hand before the deadline.* 我們離最後限期還有兩三個星期。

42 at the hands of if you suffer at the hands of someone, they treat you badly 從〔某人〕那裡〔大吃苦頭〕: *They suffered terribly at the hands of the secret police.* 他們吃盡了祕密警察的苦頭。

43 tie/bind sb hand and foot a) to tie someone's hands and feet 捆住〔某人的〕手腳 **b)** to severely restrict someone's freedom to make decisions 束縛: *We're bound hand and foot by all these safety regulations.* 我們被這些安全規則束縛住手腳。

44 sb's hand (in marriage) *old-fashioned* permission or agreement for a man to marry a particular woman【過時】對求婚的應允: *He asked for her hand in marriage.* 他向她求婚。

45 ►WRITING 書寫◄ [singular] the way you write; HANDWRITING 筆跡: *a letter written in a neat hand* 一封筆跡工整的信

46 ►HORSE 馬◄ [C] a unit for measuring the height of a horse, equal to about 10 centimetres 一手之寬〔用於量度馬匹高度的單位, 約 10 厘米〕—see also 另見 FREEHAND, HANDS-ON, HANDS UP, **be an old hand at** (OLD (31)), **bite the hand that feeds you** (BITE[1] (14)), **force sb's hand** (FORCE[2] (6)), **overplay your hand** (OVERPLAY (2)), **shake hands (with)** (SHAKE[1] (5)), **wash your hands of sth** (WASH[1] (5)), **win hands down** (WIN[1] (1))

S2 W2 **hand²** *v* [T] **1** to pass something to someone else 傳, 遞; 交; 給: **hand sb sth** *Can you hand me that book, please?* 請把那本書遞給我, 好嗎? | **hand sth to sb** *She handed her ticket to the ticket collector.* 她把票交給了收票員。**2 you have to hand it to sb** *spoken* used to say that you admire someone【口】你不得不佩服某人: *You have to hand it to her. She's really made a success of that company.* 你不得不佩服她。她的確把那家公司經營得很成功。

hand sth ↔ **around** also 又作 **hand** sth ↔ **round** *BrE*【英】*phr v* [T] to offer something to all the people in a group 分發: *She was busy handing around cups of coffee.* 她在忙着把一杯杯咖啡分給大家。

hand sth ↔ **back** *phr v* [T] **1** to pass something back to someone 交還, 交回: *Kurt examined the document and handed it back to her.* 庫爾特審閱過文件後就交還給她。**2** to give something back to someone it used to belong to 歸還: *The land was handed back to its original owner.* 那幅土地被歸還給原主。

hand sth ↔ **down** *phr v* [T] **1** to give or leave something to people who are younger than you or live after you 傳給〔後代〕: *stories that were handed down from generation to generation* 代代相傳的故事 | *a ring which was handed down from her grandmother* 她祖母傳下來的一隻戒指 —see also 另見 HAND-ME-DOWN **2** to pass something to someone who is below you 遞下來: *The truck driver handed down her rucksack.* 貨車司機把她的背包遞了下來。**3 hand down a decision/ruling/**

sentence etc to officially announce a decision, a punishment etc 公布[宣布]一項決定/裁決/判決等

hand sth ↔ **in** *phr v* [T] to give something to a person in authority 上交; 提交: *Hand your papers in at the end of the exam.* 考試結束後把試卷交上來。

hand sth ↔ **on** *phr v* [T] to give something you have finished dealing with to someone who is waiting for it 交付, 傳遞

hand sth ↔ **out** *phr v* [T] **1** to give something to each member of a group of people; DISTRIBUTE 分發, 散發: *Could you start handing these books out.* 請你把這些書分發出去吧。**2 hand out advice** to give advice, even if people do not want to hear it 出主意 —see also 另見 HANDOUT

hand over *phr v* **1** [T **hand** sb/sth ↔ **over**] to give someone or something to someone else to take care of or to control 把…送交; 交出: *The resistance fighters agreed to hand over the hostages.* 反抗軍的戰士同意交出人質。**2** [I,T **hand** sth ↔ **over**] to give power or responsibility to someone else 移交〔權力、責任等〕: *The captain was unwilling to hand over the command of his ship.* 船長不願把船的指揮權交出來。| *Before handing over to Jim, I'd like to thank you all for your support.* 在把工作移交給吉姆之前, 我要感謝大家對我的支持。

3 **hand·bag** /ˈhænd͵bæg; ˈhændbæg/ *n* [C] a small bag, used by women to carry money and personal things〔女用〕手提包; 手袋; PURSE[1] (3) *AmE*【美】—see picture at 參見 BAG[1] 圖

hand·ball /ˈhænd͵bɔl; ˈhændbɔːl/ *n* **1** [U] a game, played especially in the US, in which you hit a ball against a wall with your hand 手球 (戲)〔用手把球擊向牆壁的美國球戲〕**2** [C] the ball used in this game 手球比賽用的球 **3** [C,U] the offence, in football, of touching the ball with your hands〔足球比賽中的〕手球犯規

hand·bas·ket /ˈhænd͵bæskɪt; ˈhænd͵bɑːskɪt/ *n* —see 見 **go to hell in a handbasket** (HELL[1] (23))

hand·bill /ˈhænd͵bɪl; ˈhænd͵bɪl/ *n* [C] a small printed notice or advertisement 傳單; 廣告單

hand·book /ˈhænd͵bʊk; ˈhændbʊk/ *n* [C] a short book giving information or instructions 手冊, 便覽, 指南

hand·brake /ˈhænd͵brek; ˈhændbreɪk/ *n* [C] *BrE* a piece of equipment in a car that you pull up with your hand to stop the car from moving【英】手煞車; 手閘; EMERGENCY BRAKE *AmE*【美】—see picture on page A2 參見 A2 頁圖

hand·car /ˈhænd͵kɑr; ˈhændkɑː/ *n* [C] *AmE* a small railway vehicle operated by pushing large handles up and down【美】〔鐵路上的〕手泵式四輪小車

hand·cart /ˈhænd͵kɑrt; ˈhændkɑːt/ *n* [C] a small vehicle used for carrying goods, that is pushed or pulled by hand 手推車, 手拉車

hand·craft·ed /ˈhænd͵kræftɪd; ˈhænd͵krɑːftɪd/ *adj* skilfully made by hand, not by machine 用手工做的

hand·cuff /ˈhænd͵kʌf; ˈhændkʌf/ *v* [T] to put handcuffs on someone 給〔某人〕戴上手銬

hand·cuffs /ˈhænd͵kʌfs; ˈhændkʌfs/ *n* [plural] a pair of metal rings joined by a chain for holding a prisoner's wrists together 手銬

hand-eye co·or·di·na·tion /͵· ˈ· ···͵··/ *n* [U] the way in which your hands and eyes work together, especially in sport〔尤指體育運動中的〕手眼協調

hand·ful /ˈhænd͵fʊl; ˈhændfʊl/ *n* **1** [C] an amount that you can hold in your hand 一把: [+of] *a handful of nuts* 一把硬殼果 **2 a handful of** a very small number of people or things 幾個, 少數: *Only a handful of countries have implemented these regulations.* 只有少數國家執行了這些規定。**3 a handful** *informal* someone, especially a child, who is difficult to control【非正式】難管[控制]的人〔尤指孩子〕

hand gre·nade /ˈ· ·͵·/ *n* [C] a small bomb which is thrown by hand 手榴彈

hand·gun /ˈhænd͵gʌn; ˈhændgʌn/ *n* [C] a small gun that you hold in one hand when you fire it 手槍

hand-held /͵· ˈ·◂/ *adj* a hand-held machine or piece of electronic equipment is small enough to hold in your hand when you use it 手持的, 手提的: *a hand-held TV camera* 手提式電視攝像機

hand·i·cap /ˈhændɪ͵kæp; ˈhændikæp/ *n* [C] **1** an inability to use part of your body or mind because it has been damaged〔身體或智力上的〕殘障, 殘疾: *a mental or physical handicap* 一種智力或身體上的殘疾 **2** a condition or situation that makes it difficult for someone to do what they want 缺陷, 不利條件: *Not speaking the language is a real handicap.* 語言不通的確是一個缺陷。**3** a disadvantage given to the stronger competitors in a race or competition, in order to make it fair〔比賽中加給強手的〕不利條件: *She had a handicap of 7 in golf.* 她在高爾夫球比賽中讓了七桿。

hand·i·capped /ˈhændɪ͵kæpt; ˈhændikæpt/ *adj* **1** having serious difficulty using part of your body or mind fully because of injury or damage 殘疾的; 弱智的: **physically/mentally handicapped** *mentally handicapped children* 弱智兒童 | **visually handicapped** (=blind or partly blind) 視障的 **2 the handicapped** people who are physically or mentally handicapped 殘障人士; 弱智人士: *meeting the needs of the handicapped* 滿足殘障人士的需要 **3 be handicapped by** to have difficulties in doing what you want to do, because of a particular problem 受…之阻, 被…妨礙: *Rescue efforts were handicapped by the darkness.* 黑暗使得救援工作受阻。—compare 比較 DISABLED

hand·i·craft /ˈhændɪ͵kræft; ˈhændikrɑːft/ also 又作 **craft** *n* [C usually plural 一般用複數] a skill needing careful use of your hands, such as SEWING, making baskets etc 手工藝; 手藝

handily —see 見 HANDY

hand·i·work /ˈhændɪ͵wɝk; ˈhændiwɜːk/ *n* [U] **1** work that needs skill in using your hands 手工; 手工藝 (品): *When he'd cut the hedge he stood back and admired his handiwork.* 修剪完樹籬後, 他後退幾步欣賞自己的手藝。**2 the handiwork of** something, especially something bad, that has been done by a particular person or group〔尤指壞的〕結果; 所為: *The explosion looks like the handiwork of terrorists.* 這次爆炸看起來像是恐怖分子幹的。

hand job /ˈ· ·/ *n* [C] *taboo slang* the act of exciting a man's sex organs by touching or rubbing them【諱, 俚】手淫

hand·ker·chief /ˈhæŋkɚtʃɪf; ˈhæŋkətʃɪf/ *n* [C] a piece of cloth or thin soft paper for drying your nose or eyes 手帕; 紙巾

han·dle[1] /ˈhændl̩; ˈhændl/ *v* 2 2

1 ▶DEAL WITH STH 處理某事◀ [T] **a)** to deal with a difficult situation or problem 應付〔困難局面〕, 處理〔難題〕: *She couldn't handle the pressures of her new job.* 她無法應付新工作帶來的壓力。**b)** to deal with something by doing what is necessary 處理: *My secretary will handle all the details.* 我的祕書會處理所有的具體問題。

2 ▶DEAL WITH SB 應付某人◀ to deal with people or behave towards them in a particular way, especially to get what you want 對待, 應付〔某人〕: *She's very good at handling difficult customers.* 她很擅長對付挑剔的顧客。| **handle yourself** (=control your behaviour) 控制自己 *advice on how to handle yourself in an interview* 有關在面試中如何表現得體的建議

3 ▶HOLD 拿◀ [T] to pick up, touch, or feel something with your hands 觸; 摸; 碰; 拿: *When the children handle the kittens it makes the mother cat restless.* 孩子們觸摸小貓時, 母貓會覺得不安。

4 ▶CONTROL WITH YOUR HANDS 用手操縱◀ **a)** [T] to control the movement of a vehicle, tool etc 操縱, 操作〔車輛、工具等〕: *The windsurfer handled her board with great skill.* 那個帆板運動員熟練地操縱着她的帆板。**b) handle well/ badly etc** to be easy or difficult to drive or control 容易/不易操縱: *The car handles well, even on wet roads.* 這輛車很好駕駛, 即使是在濕滑的路面上也是如此。

5 ▶IN CHARGE OF 負責◀ [T] to be in charge of 負責: *Ms Brown handles the company's accounts.* 布朗女士負責公司的賬目。

6 ▶MACHINES/SYSTEMS 機器/系統◀ [T] to have the power, equipment, or systems that are necessary to deal with a particular amount of work, number of people etc 處理〔一定數量的工作、人員等〕: *The computers are capable of handling massive amounts of data.* 電腦能處理大量的數據。

7 ▶BUY/SELL 買/賣◀ [T] to buy, sell, or deal with goods or services in business or trade 經銷; 買賣; 處理: *Bennet was charged with handling stolen goods.* 貝內特被控買賣贓物。

3 **handle²** *n* [C] **1** the part of a door, drawer, window etc that you use for opening it 把手 **2** the part of an object that you use for holding it 柄: *a knife with an ivory handle* 一把帶象牙柄的刀 —see pictures at 參見 GUN¹ and 和 TOOL¹ 圖 **3 get a handle on** [T] to start to understand a person, situation etc 開始理解, 了解〔某人、某形勢等〕: *It's difficult to get a handle on exactly how this law will affect us.* 要想確切了解這項法律將會對我們有甚麼影響並不容易。**4** *informal* a name used by someone, especially by a user of CB RADIOS【非正式】民用波段無線電用戶的呼號 —see also 另見 **fly off the handle** (FLY¹ (19))

han·dle·bar mous·tache /ˌhændḷbɑr ˋmʌstæʃ; ˌhændlbɑː məˈstɑːʃ/ *n* [C] a long thick MOUSTACHE which curves upwards at both ends〔兩端上翹的〕翹八字鬍鬚

han·dle·bars /ˈhændḷbɑrz; ˈhændlbɑːz/ *n* [plural] the bar above the front wheel of a bicycle or MOTORCYCLE that you turn to control the direction it goes in〔腳踏車和摩托車等的〕把手 —see picture at 參見 BICYCLE¹ 圖

han·dler /ˈhændlɚ; ˈhændlə/ *n* [C] someone who trains an animal, especially a dog 馴獸師〔尤指馴狗師〕

hand·ling /ˈhændlɪŋ; ˈhændlɪŋ/ *n* [U] **1** the way in which a problem or person is treated or dealt with 處理(方式), 應付(方式): *The President has been much criticized for his handling of health policy.* 總統對醫療衛生政策的處理受到了很多的批評。**2** the act of picking something up, or touching or feeling it with your hands 觸摸; 拿[抱]起: *his gentle handling of the baby* 他溫柔的抱嬰兒動作

handling charge /ˈ·· ˌ·/ *n* [C] the amount charged for dealing with goods or moving them from one place to another 手續費, 搬運費

hand·loom /ˈhændlum; ˈhændluːm/ *n* [C] a small machine for weaving by hand 手織機

hand lug·gage /ˈ· ˌ··/ *n* [U] the small bags that you carry when you are travelling, especially on a plane 手提行李

hand·made /ˈhændˌmed; ˌhændˈmeɪd◂/ *adj* made by hand, not by machine 手工做的: *expensive handmade shoes* 昂貴的手工製作的鞋子

hand·maid·en /ˈhændˌmedṇ; ˈhændˌmeɪdn/ also 又作 **hand·maid** /ˈhændˌmed; ˈhændmeɪd/ *n* [C] **1** *old use* a female servant【舊】女傭, 女僕 **2** *formal* an idea, principle etc that has an important part in supporting or helping another idea etc【正式】輔助, 支持: **[+of]** *Militarism, Ross wrote, is the handmaiden of imperialism.* 羅斯曾寫道, 軍國主義是帝國主義的幫兇。

hand-me-down /ˈ· · ˌ·/ *n* [C usually plural 一般用複數] a piece of clothing which has been used by someone and then given to another person in the family〔年長者穿過傳給年少者的〕舊衣服: *I always had to wear my sister's hand-me-downs.* 我老是得穿姐姐穿過的舊衣服。

hand·out /ˈhændˌaʊt; ˈhændaʊt/ *n* [C] **1** money or goods that are given to someone, for example because they are poor 救濟品; 施捨物: *They only want a helping hand from the government, not a handout.* 他們需要政府的幫助, 而不是施捨。**2** a piece of paper with information given to people who are attending a lesson, meeting etc〔分發給聽眾的〕材料; 講義; 印刷品: *You'll find a full list of references on the last page of the handout.* 你們可以在講義的最後一頁找到一份完整的參考書目。

hand·o·ver /ˈhændˌovɚ; ˈhændəʊvə/ *n* [C] the act of making someone else responsible for something 移交: *Arrangements for the handover of prisoners have been made.* 已經作好了移交戰俘的安排。—see also 另見 **hand over** (HAND²)

hand·picked /ˈhændˋpɪkt; ˌhændˈpɪkt◂/ *adj* someone who is handpicked has been carefully chosen for a special purpose〔人〕精心挑選的: *volunteers handpicked for their ability to speak Spanish* 根據其西班牙語的程度而精心挑選出來的志願者

hand·rail /ˈhændˌrel; ˈhænd-reɪl/ *n* [C] a long bar fixed to the side of a passage or stairs for people to hold while they walk〔通道、樓梯等的〕扶手; 欄杆

hand·saw /ˈhændˌsɔ; ˈhændsɔː/ *n* [C] a small tool for cutting wood etc that has a flat blade and sharp V shaped teeth 手鋸

hands·free /ˈhændzˌfri; ˈhændzfriː/ *adj* [only before noun 僅用於名詞前] a handsfree machine is one that you operate without using your hands 無需用手操縱的

hand·shake /ˈhændˌʃek; ˈhændʃeɪk/ *n* [C] **a)** the act of taking someone's right hand and shaking it, which people do when they meet or leave each other or when they have made an agreement 握手 **b)** the way that someone does this 握手方式: *a nice firm handshake* 堅定有力的握手 —see also 另見 GOLDEN HANDSHAKE

hands off¹ /ˌ· ˈ·/ *interjection* used to warn someone not to touch something 別碰, 別動: *Hands off, that's my candy bar!* 別動, 那是我的糖果條!

hands off² /ˈ· ·/ *adj* [only before noun 僅用於名詞前] letting other people do what they want and make decisions, without telling them what to do 放手的; 不干涉的; 不插手的: *a hands-off style of management* 放手式管理

hand·some /ˈhænsəm; ˈhænsəm/ *adj* **1 a)** a man who is handsome is attractive; GOOD-LOOKING〔男子〕英俊的, 漂亮的 **b)** a woman who is handsome is attractive in a strong healthy way〔女子〕健美的 —see 見 BEAUTIFUL (USAGE) **2** an object, building etc that is handsome is attractive in an impressive way〔建築等〕宏偉的, 雄偉的 **3 a handsome profit/fee/sum etc** a large amount of money 豐厚的利潤/大筆費用/大筆金額等: *He sold the stocks and made a handsome profit for himself.* 他賣掉了股票, 賺了一大筆錢。**4 a handsome gift/offer etc** a generous or valuable gift etc 慷慨的禮物/優惠的報價等: *She received a handsome gift of money from her aunt.* 她從姑媽那兒得到了一大筆錢作為禮物。—**handsomely** *adv*

hands-on /ˈ· ·/ *adj* [only before noun 僅用於名詞前] providing practical experience of something by letting people do it themselves 實際操作的, 親身實踐的: *The computer course includes plenty of hands-on training.* 這個電腦課程包括大量實際操作訓練。

hand·spring /ˈhændˌsprɪŋ; ˈhændsprɪŋ/ *n* [C] a movement in which you turn yourself over completely, first with your hands on the floor and then your feet again 手翻, 前手翻騰越

hand·stand /ˈhændˌstænd; ˈhændstænd/ *n* [C] a movement in which you put your hands on the ground and your legs into the air 手倒立

hands up /ˌ· ˈ·/ *interjection* **1** used to tell people to put one of their hands in the air if they want something or if they know the answer to a question 請舉手: *Hands up everyone who wants a cup of tea.* 想要茶的人請舉手。**2** used when threatening someone with a gun 舉起手來!〔持槍者下的命令〕

hand to hand /ˌ· · ˈ·◂/ *adj, adv* **hand to hand fighting/combat** a way of fighting in a war using hands, knives etc rather than guns 肉搏戰

hand to mouth /ˌ· · ˈ·◀/ *adv* with only just enough money and food to live and nothing for the future 勉強餬口地, 只夠餬口地: *living hand to mouth* 吃了上頓沒下頓 —**hand-to-mouth** *adj*: *a hand-to-mouth existence* 現掙現吃地勉強度日

hand tow·el /ˈ· ˌ··/ *n* [C] a small TOWEL¹ for drying your hands 擦手巾

hand·writ·ing /ˈhændˌraɪtɪŋ; ˈhændˌraɪtɪŋ/ *n* [U] the style of someone's writing 筆跡, 字跡; 書法; 寫字風格: *I recognised her handwriting on the envelope.* 我認出了信封上她的筆跡。

hand·writ·ten /ˈhændˌrɪtn̩; ˌhændˈrɪtn◀/ *adj* written by hand, not printed 手寫的

3 **hand·y** /ˈhændɪ; ˈhændi/ *adj* **1** useful and simple to use 簡便的, 方便的: a *handy little gadget for peeling potatoes* 削馬鈴薯皮的簡便小器具 **2** *informal* near and easy to reach【非正式】手邊的; 附近的: *If there's a pen and paper handy, I'll make a shopping list.* 如果手邊有筆和紙的話, 我要列一份購物清單。| **be handy for** *BrE*【英】*Theo's flat is handy for the shops.* 西奥的住處離商店很近。**3 come in handy** to be useful 遲早有用: *Take a sleeping bag with you – it might come in handy.* 帶一個睡袋去吧, 可能用得着的。**4** good at using something, especially a tool 手巧的, 靈活的: [+with] *He's handy with a screwdriver.* 他善於使用螺絲刀。—**handily** *adv* —**handiness** *n* [U]

hand·y·man /ˈhændɪˌmæn; ˈhændimæn/ *n* [C] someone who is good at doing repairs and practical jobs in the house〔尤指在做家庭小修小補活上〕手巧的人

1 2 **hang¹** /hæŋ; hæŋ/ *v past tense and past participle* **hung** /hʌŋ; hʌŋ/

1 ▶HANG FROM ABOVE 從高處懸下◀ **a)** [T] to fix or put something in a position so that the bottom part is free to move and does not touch the ground 懸掛, 吊起: *Hang your coat on the hook.* 把你的外套掛在鈎上。**b)** [I always+adv/prep] to be fixed in position at the top so that the bottom part is free to move and does not touch the ground 懸掛着, 吊着: [+on/from/out of etc] *A large handbag hung from her shoulder.* 她的肩膀上掛着一個大手袋。| *She sat there with a cigarette hanging out of her mouth.* 她坐在那裡, 嘴裡叼着一根煙。

2 ▶PICTURES ETC 畫、照片等◀ **a)** [I always+adv/prep, T] to fix a picture, photograph etc to a wall, or to be fixed this way 掛: [+on] *A photograph of a handsome soldier hung on the wall.* 牆上掛着一幅一個英俊軍人的照片。**b)** [I always+adv/prep, T] to show a picture publicly or be shown publicly 公開展出: *Her portrait now hangs in the National Gallery.* 她的畫像目前在國家美術館裡展出。**c) be hung with** if the walls of a room are hung with pictures or decorations, the pictures etc are on the walls 掛着, 掛有: *rooms hung with rich tapestries* 掛有華麗壁毯的房間

3 ▶KILL/BE KILLED 殺死/被殺死◀ *past tense and past participle* **hanged** [I,T] to kill someone by dropping them with a rope around their neck, or to die in this way, especially as a punishment for a serious crime (被) 吊死, (被) 絞死: [+for] *They were convicted of genocide and hanged for their crimes.* 他們被判犯了滅絕種族的大屠殺罪而被處以絞刑。| *Corey hanged himself in his prison cell.* 科瑞在囚室裡上吊自殺。

4 hang in the balance to be in a situation in which the end is not certain, and something bad may happen 前景難料; 安危難說: *The future of the airline hangs in the balance.* 該航空公司的前景無法預料。

5 hang by a thread to be in a very dangerous situation 千鈞一髮; 岌岌可危: *For weeks after the accident, her life hung by a thread.* 出事後的幾個星期裡, 她的生命一直岌岌可危。

6 ▶PAPER 紙◀ [T] to fix WALLPAPER¹ on a wall 貼[糊]〔牆紙〕

7 ▶DOOR 門◀ [T] to fix a door in position 安裝〔門〕

8 ▶MIST/SMOKE/SMELL 霧氣/煙/氣味◀ [I+adv/prep] to stay in the air in the same place for a long time 難以散發; 滯留; 懸浮: *The smoke from the bonfires hung in the air.* 空中飄浮着篝火的煙。

9 hang in there also 又作 **hang tough** *informal, especially AmE* to remain brave and determined when you are in a difficult situation【非正式, 尤美】挺下去; 堅持到底: *You're innocent and you'll win, so hang in there!* 你是無辜的, 一定會勝利, 堅持住!

10 hang your head to look ashamed and embarrassed〔羞愧、尷尬地〕垂下頭: *He hung his head and didn't answer her questions.* 他低着頭, 沒有回答她的問題。

11 hang fire to be delayed or prevented from happening or continuing 推遲, 延遲; 停頓: *The whole project is hanging fire until next week's meeting.* 整個項目要等到下週的會議之後再繼續。

12 leave sth hanging in the air to fail to make a definite decision about a question 使某事懸而未決: *important issues left hanging in the air* 懸而未決的重大問題

13 hang a right/left *AmE spoken* used to tell the driver of a car to turn right or left【美口】〔車輛〕往右轉/往左轉

14 hang up your hat *informal* to leave your job, especially at the end of your working life【非正式】不再工作, 退休

15 hang loose *old-fashioned* used to tell someone to stay calm and relaxed【過時】冷靜點; 放鬆些

16 I'll be hanged/I'm hanged if *BrE old-fashioned* used to express annoyance or to say that you will not allow something to happen【英, 過時】豈有此理; 休想: *I'll be hanged if I'll let these people order me around!* 見鬼去吧, 我才不讓這些人支使我!

17 hang it/hang it all *BrE old-fashioned* used to say that you are disappointed or annoyed about something【英, 過時】〔表示失望或厭煩〕見鬼, 該死

18 hang sth *BrE old-fashioned* used to say that you are not going to do something【英, 過時】讓...見鬼去吧, 去它的...〔表示不想做某事〕: *Oh hang the ironing, let's go for a drink.* 熨甚麼鬼衣服, 我們去喝酒吧!

hang about *phr v BrE*【英】**1** [I] *spoken* to move slowly or take too long doing something【口】動作慢吞吞; 拖延: *Don't hang about, we've got a train to catch!* 別慢吞吞的, 我們還要趕火車呢! **2** [I] to spend time somewhere without any real purpose 閒逛, 閒蕩: *There are always kids hanging about down by the shops.* 商店附近總有些孩子在閒逛。**3 hang about with** to spend a lot of time with someone 廝混: *I don't know what he's doing, hanging about with that bunch.* 我不知道他到底在幹甚麼, 整天和那夥人混在一起。**4 hang about!** *spoken* used to ask someone to wait or stop what they are doing【口】等一下, 停一下: *Hang about – I'm nearly ready.* 等等, 我快好了。

hang around *phr v* [I,T] *informal*【非正式】**1** to wait or stay somewhere with no real purpose 閒蕩; 呆等: *I hung around the station for an hour but he never showed up.* 我在車站附近呆等了一小時, 但他始終沒有來。**2 hang around with** to spend a lot of time with someone 廝混: *He hangs around with Luke and Callum.* 他整天和盧克及卡勒姆混在一起。

hang back *phr v* [I] to be unwilling to speak or do something because you are shy 退縮, 躊躇不前: *Don't hang back – go and introduce yourself.* 別猶豫了, 走上前去自我介紹吧。

hang on *phr v* **1** [I] to hold something tightly 緊緊抓住: *We all hung on as the bus swung around a sharp bend.* 公共汽車急轉彎時, 我們趕緊抓住扶手。| [+to] *Hang on to the rail or you'll fall.* 抓緊欄杆, 要不然你會摔倒的。**2 hang on!** *BrE spoken* used to ask or tell someone to wait【英口】等等!: *Hang on! I'll be back in a minute.* 等等! 我一會兒就回來。**3** [I] to continue doing something in spite of difficulties 堅持不懈, 不放棄: *I know you're tired, but try to hang on a bit longer.* 我知

道你累了, 但是再堅持一會兒吧。**4** [T] **hang on** sth to depend on 依賴於, 取決於: *The team's survival in the league hangs on the result of this game.* 該隊能否繼續留在聯賽中將取決於今場比賽。**5 hang on sb's words/every word** to pay close attention to everything someone is saying 傾聽[注意]某人的談話/每一句話

hang on to sth/sb *phr v* [T] to keep something 保留, 保存: *I'd hang on to that letter. You might need it later.* 我會保留着那封信。你以後可能會用得着。

hang out *phr v* **1** [I always+adv/prep] *informal* to spend a lot of time in a particular place or with particular people【非正式】閒蕩; 廝混: *She hangs out with a pretty wild crowd.* 她經常和一羣很不安分的人混在一起。| *That's the corner where all the junkies hang out.* 那是吸毒者經常聚集的一個角落。—see also 另見 HANGOUT **2** [T **hang** sth ↔ **out**] to hang clothes on a piece of string outside in order to dry them 晾曬〔衣服〕: *I've hung out the washing.* 我已經把洗好的衣服晾出去了。**3 let it all hang out** *slang* to relax and do what you like【俚】放縱自己, 做自己想做的事

hang over sth/sb *phr v* [I] if something unpleasant hangs over you, you are worried because it is likely to happen soon〔不愉快的事〕逼近; 威脅着: *The prospect of famine hangs over the whole area.* 整個地區都受到饑荒的威脅。| **be hanging over sb's head** *With the exams hanging over her head she can't sleep at night.* 隨着考試的臨近, 她晚上都睡不着覺。

hang round *phr v* [I,T] = **hang around** (HANG¹)

hang together *phr v* [I] **1** to help each other and work together to achieve an aim 同心協力, 團結一致: *We must hang together if we're going to get out of this mess.* 要想走出困境, 我們就必須同心協力。**2** if a plan, story, set of ideas etc hangs together, it is well-organized and makes sense〔計劃、故事、想法等〕站得住腳; 前後一致; 合情合理: *The case for the defence just doesn't hang together.* 被告方的陳述根本站不住腳。

hang up 掛

Paula is hanging up her suit.
葆拉在掛衣服。

After arguing for ten minutes she hung up.
爭吵了十分鐘後, 她掛斷了電話。

hang up *phr v* **1** [I,T] to finish a phone conversation by putting the telephone down 掛斷電話: *After I hung up I realized I forgot to ask him his telephone number.* 掛了電話後我才想起忘了問他的電話號碼。| **hang up on sb** (=put the phone down before they have finished speaking)〔對方沒有講完即〕掛斷電話 *I was so angry that I hung up on her.* 我一氣之下掛斷了她的電話。**2** [T **hang** sth ↔ **up**] to hang clothes on a hook etc 掛起〔衣服〕**3 be hung up on/about** *informal* to be anxious about something when there is no reason to be【非正式】無端擔心: *She's hung up about people knowing she didn't go to college.* 她老是擔心別人知道她沒有上過大學。—see also 另見 HANG-UP

hang² *n* **get/have the hang of something** *informal* to learn how to do something or use something【非正式】學會: *Using the computer isn't difficult once you get the hang of it.* 一旦你學會後, 使用電腦就一點不難了。

hang·ar /ˈhæŋə; ˈhæŋə/ *n* [C] a very large building where aircraft are kept 飛機庫

hang·dog /ˈhæŋˌdɔg; ˈhæŋdɒg/ *adj* a hangdog expression on your face shows you feel sorry or ashamed about something〔表情〕羞愧的, 慚愧的

hang·er /ˈhæŋə; ˈhæŋə/ *n* [C] a thing for hanging clothes on, consisting of a curved piece of wood or metal with a hook on it 衣架

hanger-on /ˌ·· ˈ·/ *n* [C] someone who spends a lot of time with a person who is important, famous, or rich, because they hope to get some advantage 隨從, 跟班, 依附他人者: *Hollywood celebrities and their hangers-on* 荷里活明星及他們的跟班

hang glid·er /ˈ· ˌ··/ *n* [C] a large frame covered with cloth that you hold on to and fly slowly through the air on, without an engine 懸掛式滑翔機

hang glid·ing /ˈ· ˌ··/ *n* [U] the sport of flying using a hang glider 懸掛式滑翔(運動)

hang·ing /ˈhæŋɪŋ; ˈhæŋɪŋ/ *n* [C,U] **1** the practice or act of punishing someone by putting a rope around their neck and hanging them until they are dead 絞刑: *public hangings* 當眾執行絞刑 | *right-wingers who want to bring back hanging* 想要恢復絞刑的右翼分子 **2 it's/that's no hanging matter** used to say that a problem or mistake is not as bad as someone thinks it is 問題沒那麼嚴重, 不是甚麼大不了的事 **3** a large piece of cloth hung on a wall as a decoration〔掛在牆上作裝飾的〕簾子, 帷幕; 懸掛物: *wall hangings* 掛在牆上的布簾

hang·man /ˈhæŋmən; ˈhæŋmən/ *n* [C] someone whose job is to kill criminals by hanging them 執行絞刑者, 劊子手

hang·nail /ˈhæŋˌnel; ˈhæŋneɪl/ *n* [C] a piece of skin that has become loose near the bottom of the fingernail〔指甲旁的〕倒刺, 甲刺

hang·out /ˈhæŋˌaut; ˈhæŋaʊt/ *n* [C] *informal* a place someone likes to go to often【非正式】常去的地方; 聚集處: *a favourite hangout for artists* 藝術家愛去的地方

hang·o·ver /ˈhæŋˌovə; ˈhæŋəʊvə/ *n* [C] **1** the HEADACHE and sickness that you get the day after you have drunk too much alcohol 宿醉 **2 a hangover from** *BrE* an attitude, habit etc from the past, that is not suitable or practical any more【英】以前遺留下來的態度[習慣]; HOLDOVER *AmE*【美】: *a hangover from her schooldays* 她學生時代遺留下來的習慣

hang-up /ˈ· ·/ *n* [C] *informal* if you have a hang-up about something you feel unreasonably worried or embarrassed about it【非正式】〔無端的〕擔憂, 苦惱, 困擾: *She's got a real hang-up about her nose.* 她老為自己的鼻子感到苦惱。—see also 另見 **hang up** (HANG¹)

hank /hæŋk; hæŋk/ *n* [C] an amount of wool, cotton, or thread that has been wound into a loose ball 線卷, 線球

han·ker /ˈhæŋkə; ˈhæŋkə/ *v*

hanker after/for *phr v* [T] to secretly feel that you want something, over a long period 渴望, 追求: *Lucy had always hankered after a place of her own.* 露茜一直都渴望擁有自己的住處。

han·ker·ing /ˈhæŋkərɪŋ; ˈhæŋkərɪŋ/ *n* [singular] a strong wish to have something 渴望

han·kie, hanky /ˈhæŋkɪ; ˈhæŋki/ *n* [C] *informal* HANDKERCHIEF【非正式】手帕

hank·y-pank·y /ˈhæŋkɪ ˈpæŋkɪ; ˌhæŋki ˈpæŋki/ *n* [U]

humorous sexual activity that is not very serious【幽默】調情, 調戲

Han·sard /ˋhænsɚd; ˈhænsɑːd/ *n* [singular] the official written record of what happens in the British Parliament 英國議會議事錄

han·som /ˋhænsəm; ˈhænsəm/ also 又作 **hansom cab** /ˈ·· ·/ *n* [C] a two-wheeled vehicle pulled by a horse, used in the past as a taxi〔舊時供出租的〕雙輪馬車

Ha·nuk·kah, Chanukah /ˋhɑnɪkə; ˈhɑːnʊkə/ *n* an eight-day Jewish holiday in December〔猶太人的〕獻殿節, 光明節

ha'penny /ˋhepnɪ; ˈheɪpni/ *n* [C] another spelling of HALFPENNY halfpenny 的另一種拼法

hap·haz·ard /ˌhæpˋhæzɚd; ˌhæpˈhæzəd◂/ *adj* happening or done in a way that is not planned or recognized 無計劃的, 沒有條理的, 隨意的: *The training was carried out in a haphazard fashion.* 培訓活動毫無計劃地進行。 —**haphazardly** *adv*

hap·less /ˋhæplɪs; ˈhæpləs/ *adj* [only before noun 僅用於名詞前] *literary* unlucky【文】倒霉的, 不幸的: *Hapless passers-by could be dragged into the argument.* 倒霉的過路人會被拖進這場爭論之中。

hap·ly /ˋhæplɪ; ˈhæpli/ *adv old use* perhaps【舊】可能, 或許

hap'orth /ˋhepɚθ; ˈheɪpəθ/ *n* [singular+**of**] *old-fashioned BrE* an amount that is worth half of one penny【過時, 英】半便士買到的東西

1 **hap·pen** /ˋhæpən; ˈhæpən/ *v* [I] **1** if an event or situa-
1 tion happens, it exists and continues for a period of time, especially without being planned first (偶然) 發生: *The accident happened early on Tuesday morning.* 這場意外在星期二清晨發生。| *No one knew who had fired the gun – it all happened so quickly.* 沒有人知道是誰開槍的, 事情發生得太快了。| *It's impossible to predict what will happen in Cambodia in the next few months.* 無法預料今後幾個月內柬埔寨會發生甚麼事情。| **sth is bound to happen** (=something is certain to happen) 一定會發生 | **sth happens all the time** (=something happens often) 經常發生 *This kind of thing happens all the time.* 這種事經常都會發生。| **whatever happens** *I'll look after you whatever happens.* 不管發生甚麼事, 我都會照顧你的。—see 見 OCCUR[1] (USAGE) —see also 另見 **happen to 2** to be caused as the result of an event or action 發生作用; 產生結果: *She pressed hard on the brake pedal, but nothing happened.* 她使勁地往下踩制動器, 可是車沒有反應。| *What would happen if your parents found out?* 要是你父母發現了, 會怎麼樣呢? **3** to do or have something by chance 碰巧, 湊巧: **happen to do sth** *I happened to meet her on my way home.* 我在回家的路上碰巧遇見了她。| **it happens that** (=by chance, it is true that) 湊巧的是 *It happened that the new person in the office was the woman he had met at Gail's party.* 湊巧的是, 辦公室裡新來的人就是他在蓋爾的晚會上遇到過的那個女人。**4 sb/sth happens to be** used when telling someone something in an angry way, especially because you are annoyed by something they have just said 碰巧, 湊巧〔表示惱怒〕: *That woman you're talking about just happens to be my wife!* 你正在談論的那個女人碰巧是我的妻子! —see also 另見 **accidents will happen** (ACCIDENT (5))

happen by *phr v* [I,T] *AmE* to find a place by chance【美】偶然發現〔某處〕

happen on sb/sth, **happen upon** sb/sth *phr v* [T] to find something or meet someone by chance 偶然碰上; 偶然看到: *They were strolling through the old part of the town when they happened on a tiny Greek restaurant.* 他們在老城區裡遊逛時偶然看見一家希臘小餐館。

happen to sb/sth *phr v* [T] **1** if an event happens to someone or something, they are involved in it and affected by it〔事情〕發生在…身上, 臨到…頭上: *A funny thing happened to me on my way home last night.* 昨晚我在回家的路上發生了一點好笑的事。**2 whatever happened to a)** used when you want to know where someone is and what they are doing, because it is a long time since you saw them〔某人〕最近怎麼樣?: *Whatever happened to Kate Scott?* 凱特·斯科特最近怎麼樣? **b)** used when saying that something such as an idea, quality, or custom seems to have disappeared or been forgotten about〔想法、特點或習俗〕怎麼不見了?: *Whatever happened to the idea of the paperless office?* 怎麼再也不見有人提"無紙辦公室"了?

Frequencies of the verb **happen** in spoken and written English 動詞 happen 在英語口語和書面語中的使用頻率

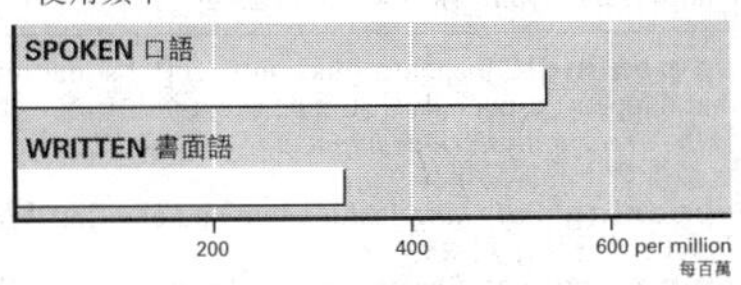

Based on the British National Corpus and the Longman Lancaster Corpus 據英國國家語料庫和朗文蘭卡斯特語料庫

This graph shows that the verb **happen** is much more common in spoken English than in written English. This is because it is used in a lot of common spoken phrases. 本圖表顯示, 動詞 happen 在英語口語中的使用頻率遠遠高於書面語, 因為口語中有很多常用片語是由 happen 構成的。

happen (*v*) **SPOKEN PHRASES**
含 happen 的口語片語

5 what's happening? a) used to ask what people are doing, or what the situation is, especially when you are worried or annoyed about this 發生甚麼事了?: *Hey, what's happening? Why has the light gone out?* 嗨, 發生甚麼事了? 燈為甚麼滅了? | *What's happening here, then? You'd better stop that!* 哎, 你在幹甚麼? 快停下! **b)** *AmE* used when you meet someone you know well, to ask them how they are and what they have been doing【美】近來怎麼樣?: *Hey Carl, what's happening, man?* 嗨, 卡爾, 近來怎麼樣, 老兄? **6 what's going to happen/what happens/what will happen...?** used to ask what the result of something will be 會有甚麼結果?: *What happens if you push this button?* 按下這個按鈕會有甚麼結果? | *What's going to happen when she finds out?* 一旦給她發現了, 會有甚麼結果? **7 whatever happens** used to say that no matter what else happens, one thing will certainly happen 不管發生甚麼事, 無論如何: *Whatever happens in the future, we wish you well.* 不管今後情況如何, 我們都祝你好運。**8 as it happens** used to tell someone something that you think will be useful for them, and is connected with what they have just been talking about 碰巧, 正巧〔用於告訴某人對他有用的事〕: *As it happens I know someone who might be able to give you some advice.* 我正好認識一個人, 可以給你提點意見。**9 it (just) so happens that** used to tell someone about something interesting that is connected with what you have just been talking about 真巧, 碰巧〔用於告訴某人有趣的事, 跟剛提及的事情有關〕: *Now, it just so happens that he had been to the same school as me.* 真巧, 他和我正好上同一所學校。**10 these things happen** used to tell someone not to worry about a mistake they have made, an accident they have caused etc 這算不了甚麼: *These things happen: don't give it another thought.* 這算不了甚麼, 別再想了。**11 anything can happen** used to say that it is impossible to know what will happen 甚麼事也可能發生, 結果無法預料: *Anything can happen in a race like that.* 像這樣的比賽, 結果無法預料。**12 see what happens** used to say that if someone does not know what the result of doing something will be, they should try it and find out〔試一試〕看看會有甚麼結果: *Just turn the switch and see what happens. Is it working?* 試着打開開關, 看看會有甚麼結果。它在轉動嗎? **13 what usually happens is/what tends to happen is** used to say what usually happens in a particular situation〔在某一特定情況下〕通常〔發生的事〕, 往往: *What tends to happen is we meet up for a drink, then go for something to eat.* 我們通常聚在一起喝點酒, 然後去吃點東西。**14 you don't/do you happen to...?** used politely to ask someone if they have or know something 你是否...? 〔婉轉的問法〕: *You don't happen to know his address, do you?* 你知道他的地址嗎?

2 **hap·pen·ing¹** /ˈhæpənɪŋ; ˈhæpənɪŋ/ *n* [C] something that happens, especially a strange event 發生的事〔尤指怪事〕: *recent mysterious happenings on the island* 該島上最近發生的神祕事件

happening² *adj slang* fashionable and exciting【俚】時興的, 流行的; 刺激的

hap·pen·stance /ˈhæpənˌstæns; ˈhæpənstæns/ *n* [U] *AmE* something good that happens by chance【美】巧合: *It was just happenstance that we met.* 我們相遇是個巧合。

hap·pi·ly /ˈhæpɪlɪ; ˈhæpəli/ *adv* **1** in a happy way 高興地, 快樂地: *a happily married couple* 一對幸福的夫婦 **2** [sentence adverb 句子副詞] fortunately 幸運地: *Happily, his injuries were not serious.* 幸好, 他的傷勢並不嚴重。**3** very willingly 很樂意地: *I'd happily go for you.* 我很樂意為你去一趟。

hap·pi·ness /ˈhæpɪnɪs; ˈhæpinəs/ *n* [U] the state of being happy 快樂, 幸福: *She believes she's finally found true happiness.* 她相信自己終於找到了真正的幸福。

1 1 **hap·py** /ˈhæpɪ; ˈhæpi/ *adj* **1** having feelings of pleasure, for example because something good has happened to you 高興的, 快樂的: *Larry looked really happy when we gave him his present.* 我們把禮物送給拉里時, 他看起來高興極了。| *He was a happy child who rarely cried.* 他是一個不愛哭的快樂孩子。| **be happy to be doing sth** *They felt happy to be going home.* 他們為即將回家而感到高興。| **happy that** *I'm happy that everything worked out well in the end.* 我很高興到最後一切都很順利。| **be/feel happy for sb** *I felt really happy for you when I heard you'd passed your exams.* 我聽說你通過了考試, 真為你感到高興。—opposite 反義詞 SAD (1) **2** a happy time, place, occasion etc is one that makes you feel happy〔使人感到〕愉快的; 幸福的: *Some people say that your schooldays are the happiest time of your life.* 有人說學生時代是人一生中最愉快的日子。| **a happy ending** *The story has a happy ending.* 故事的結局很美滿。**3** satisfied or not worried 對...感到滿意[放心]的: **[+about]** *I'm not happy about Dave riding around on that motorbike.* 我對戴夫騎着那輛摩托車到處亂跑很不放心。| **[+with]** *Are you happy with your new car?* 你對新車感到滿意嗎? | **keep sb happy** *I pretended to agree with her, just to keep her happy.* 我假裝贊同她的意見, 只是為了讓她高興。**4 be happy to do sth** to be very willing to do something, especially to help someone 樂意做某事: *I'd be happy to take you in my car.* 我很樂意開車送你去。**5 Happy Birthday/Christmas/Anniversary etc** used when greeting someone on their birthday, at Christmas etc 生日/聖誕節/週年紀念日快樂 **6 the happy event** the time when a baby is born or when two people get married〔嬰兒出生或新人結婚等的〕喜事 **7 a happy medium** a way of doing something that is somewhere between two possible choices and that satisfies everyone 皆大歡喜的折衷辦法 **8 happy as a lark** very happy 非常快樂 **9 not a happy bunny** *BrE*【英】**/not a happy camper** *AmE*【美】*humorous* someone who is not pleased about a situation【幽默】對...感到不滿意 **10** *formal* suitable【正式】恰當的, 得體的: *His choice of words was not a very happy one.* 他用詞不當。

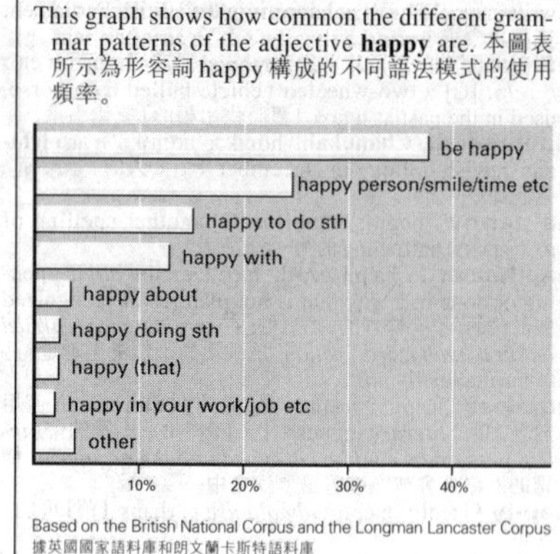

happy-go-luck·y /ˌ.. . ˈ..◂/ *adj* not caring or worrying about what happens 無憂無慮的; 逍遙自在的: *a happy-go-lucky kind of person* 無憂無慮的人

happy hour /ˈ.. ˌ./ *n* [singular] a special time in a bar when alcoholic drinks are sold at lower prices〔酒吧中的〕優惠時間; 快樂時光

har·a·kiri /ˌhɑrəˈkɪrɪ; ˌhærəˈkɪri/ *n* [U] a way of killing yourself by cutting open your stomach, used in former times in Japan to avoid losing your honour〔舊時日本的〕剖腹自殺

ha·rangue¹ /həˈræŋ; həˈræŋ/ *v* [T] to make a loud speech that criticizes or blames someone or tries to persuade people about something 慷慨激昂地演說; 高聲訓斥: *Mr Major was harangued by reporters.* 梅傑先生遭到記者的大聲責問。

harangue² *n* [C] a loud long angry speech that criticizes or blames people, or tries to persuade them 滔滔不絕的高聲訓斥[勸說]: *The principal launched into his usual harangue about standards of behaviour.* 校長開始像往常一樣滔滔不絕地談起了行為準則。

har·ass /ˈhærəs; ˈhærəs/ *v* [T] **1** to treat someone unfairly by threatening them or being continuously unpleasant to them 騷擾: *Black teenagers are being constantly harassed by the police.* 黑人青少年經常遭到警察騷擾。**2** to annoy someone by continually interrupting them 煩擾, 打擾: *Stop harassing me will you! I'm trying to work!* 別煩我了! 我在幹活呢! **3** to continually attack an enemy 不斷攻擊〔敵人〕

har·assed /ˈhærəst; ˈhærəst/ *adj* anxious and tired because you have too many problems or things to do 煩惱的; 疲累的: *The waiter looked harassed so I didn't bother him.* 服務員看起來一臉煩惱的, 所以我沒有叫他。

har·ass·ment /ˈhærəsmənt; ˈhærəsmənt/ *n* [U] **1** unpleasant and often threatening behaviour, or offensive remarks 構成騷擾的言行: **sexual/racial harassment** (=towards someone of a different sex or race) 性/種族騷擾 *sexual harassment in the workplace* 在工作場所的性騷擾 **2** a feeling of anxiety and tiredness because you have too many problems or things to do 煩擾; 疲累

har·bin·ger /ˈhɑrbɪndʒə; ˈhɑːbɪndʒə/ *n* [C+of] *literary* a sign that something is going to happen soon【文】先兆, 預兆

har·bour¹ *BrE*【英】, **harbor** *AmE*【美】/ˈhɑrbə; ˈhɑːbə/ *n* [C] an area of water next to the land where the water is calm, so that ships are safe when they are inside it 港口, 港灣, 海港

harbour² *BrE*【英】, **harbor** *AmE*【美】*v* [T] **1** to protect and hide criminals that the police are searching for 窩藏, 包庇〔罪犯〕**2** to keep bad thoughts, fears, or hopes in your mind for a long time 懷有〔不好的想法、恐懼等〕: **harbour a grudge** *I think he's harbouring some sort of grudge against me.* 我覺得他對我有點懷恨在心。

hard¹ /hɑrd; hɑːd/ *adj*

① FIRM TO TOUCH 堅硬的
② DIFFICULT 困難的
③ INVOLVING WORK AND EFFORT 費力的, 費勁的
④ FULL OF PROBLEMS 棘手的, 艱難的
⑤ UNKIND 無情的
⑥ USING FORCE 用力氣
⑦ UNFORTUNATE 不幸的
⑧ OTHER MEANINGS 其他意思

① FIRM TO TOUCH 堅硬的

1 firm and stiff, and difficult to press down, break, or cut 硬的, 堅固的: *Diamond is the hardest substance known to man.* 鑽石是已知的最堅硬的物質。| *The plums are much too hard to be eaten now.* 李子現在太硬, 不能吃。| *The chairs in the waiting room felt hard and uncomfortable.* 候診室裡的椅子又硬又不舒服。—opposite 反義詞 SOFT (1)

② DIFFICULT 困難的

2 difficult to do or understand 難做的; 難懂的; 困難的, 不易的: *This year's exam was much harder than last year's.* 今年的考試比去年的難得多。| **be hard for sb** *It must be hard for her, bringing up three kids on her own.* 她一個人養育三個孩子一定很不容易。| **be hard to come by** (=be difficult to get or find) 不易得到[找到] *Good jobs are hard to come by these days.* 如今想找份好工作很不容易。| **the hardest thing is** *The hardest thing is going to be telling her parents.* 最難辦的是如何告訴她的父母。—opposite 反義詞 EASY¹ (1)

3 hard to tell/say difficult to know 難以判斷/難說: *It was hard to tell whether Katie really wanted to go.* 很難說凱蒂是否真的想去。

4 find sth hard to believe to think that something is probably not true 認為某事讓人難以置信: *I find it extremely hard to believe that he didn't know.* 他竟然不知道, 這太讓我難以置信了。

5 hard to take difficult to accept or believe 難以接受[相信]: *She found all this sudden concern for her welfare rather hard to take.* 她對所有這些突如其來的對她的幸福的關切感到有點難以置信。

③ INVOLVING WORK AND EFFORT 費力的, 費勁的

6 ►A LOT OF EFFORT 許多努力◄ using or involving a lot of mental or physical effort 費神的; 費力的: *It's been a long hard day.* 今天過得真累啊! | **hard work** *It's not easy running a business – it takes a great deal of hard work.* 要經營一家鋪子真不容易 —— 這需要許多艱苦的努力。

7 hard going a) difficult to do and needing a lot of effort 費勁的, 費力的 **b)** boring 乏味的: *I find most of Sartre pretty hard going.* 我覺得沙特大多數的作品讀起來都很乏味。

8 too much like hard work used to say that you do not want to do something because it will be too much effort 太難了, 太費勁了〔表示不願做某事〕

9 make hard work of to make something you are trying to do seem more difficult than it really is 使〔某事〕看起來更難

10 hard-earned/hard-won achieved after a lot of effort 得來不易的

11 be hard at it *informal* to be very busy doing something【非正式】忙於幹某事: *Sarah was hard at it on her computer.* 莎拉在電腦上忙着。

④ FULL OF PROBLEMS 棘手的, 艱難的

12 a period of time that is hard is one when you do not have enough money and have a lot of problems〔日子〕艱難的, 困苦的, 拮据的: **times are hard** *Times were hard and we were forced to sell our home.* 那時的日子過得很艱難, 我們被迫賣掉了房子。

13 have a hard life to have many problems and not have much money or comfort 生活艱難, 生活拮据: *Miners used to have a very hard life.* 過去礦工們的生活十分艱難。

14 it's hard on/for sb used to say that a situation causes a lot of problems and difficulties for someone〔某人〕過得很不容易: *It's hard on the kids having their father in hospital.* 父親住院了, 孩子們過得很不容易。

⑤ UNKIND 無情的

15 showing no feelings or sympathy 冷酷的, 無情的: *He had a hard face and cold blue eyes.* 他長着一張無情的臉和一雙冷酷的藍眼睛。| *I'm afraid I said some very hard things to her.* 恐怕我對她說了些很刻薄的話。| *You're a hard man, Mr Dawson.* 你是個無情的人, 道森先生。

16 be hard on to treat someone in a way that is unfair, unkind, or too strict〔對某人〕嚴厲的; 無情的; 苛刻的; 不公平的: *You mustn't be too hard on David – he's been under a lot of pressure lately.* 別對戴維太苛刻 —— 他最近一直壓力很大。

17 a hard taskmaster/master someone who makes people work too hard 要求過分嚴格的上司; 對別人過分苛刻的人

18 ►STRONG/NOT AFRAID 勇敢的/不害怕的◄ *informal* strong, ready to fight, and not afraid of anyone or anything【非正式】堅強的, 勇敢的: *I suppose you think you're really hard, don't you!* 我想你以為自己很厲害, 是吧!

19 a hard case *informal* a strong and violent person【非正式】不好惹的人

⑥ USING FORCE 用力氣

20 using force 用力的: *Jane gave the door a good hard push.* 簡使勁地推門。

⑦ UNFORTUNATE 不幸的

21 ►FEEL SORRY FOR SB 為某人感到遺憾的◄ hard luck also 又作 **hard lines** *BrE spoken* used to tell someone that you feel sorry for them【英口】真不幸! 真倒霉! (對別人表示同情)

22 hard cheese *especially BrE spoken* used to tell someone that you do not feel sorry for them【尤英, 口】活該!

23 hard-luck story a story you tell someone to make them feel sorry for you〔為博取別人同情而說的〕不幸的遭遇

⑧ OTHER MEANINGS 其他意思

24 give sb a hard time *informal*【非正式】**a)** to deliberately make someone feel uncomfortable or embarrassed〔故意〕讓某人難堪或難受, 給某人吃苦頭: *Come on guys – stop giving me such a hard time!* 好了, 別再讓我難堪了! **b)** to criticize someone a lot 嚴厲批評某人: *My boss has been giving me a really hard time.* 我的老闆近來動不動就罵我!

25 be hard on sth to have a bad effect on something 對...不利; 把...用壞: *Running 50 miles a week is really hard on the knee joints.* 每週跑50英里真讓膝關節受不了。

26 no hard feelings *spoken* used to tell someone who you have been arguing with that you do not feel anger towards them any more【口】我不生氣, 我不介意〔爭吵後對人說的話〕

27 as hard as nails not feeling any emotions, especially fear or sympathy 無動於衷的, 冷酷無情的

28 learn/do sth the hard way to learn about something by a bad experience or by making mistakes 以吃力的方式學習/做某事

29 hard winter a very cold winter 嚴冬 —opposite 反義詞 MILD¹ (1)

30 ►WATER 水◄ hard water contains a lot of minerals and does not mix easily with soap〔水〕硬的, 含無機鹽的

31 hard facts/information/evidence etc facts, information etc that are definitely true and can be proved 確切[確鑿]的事實/情報/證據等: *Police have several theories, but no hard evidence.* 警方有好幾種說法, 但都缺乏確實的證據。

32 take a (long) hard look at to think about something without being influenced by your feelings 冷靜看待: *We need to take a long hard look at the whole system of welfare payments.* 我們需要認真仔細地審視整套福利支付制度。

33 take a hard line on/over to deal with something in a very strict way 採取強硬態度[立場]: *They've promised to take a hard line on law and order.* 他們承諾在法律與秩序方面採取強硬立場。

34 the hard stuff *informal* strong alcohol or illegal drugs【非正式】烈酒; 烈性毒品

35 a hard left/right a sharp turn to the left or right 猛地向左/向右急轉

36 ►PRONUNCIATION 發音◄ a hard 'c' is pronounced /k/ rather than /s/; a hard 'g' is pronounced /g/ rather than /dʒ/ 發硬音的〈字母c發/k/音而不發/s/音; 字母g發/g/音而不發/dʒ/音〉 —**hardness** *n* [U]: *a material that would combine the flexibility of rubber with the hardness of glass* 能將橡膠的彈性和玻璃的硬度結合起來的一種物料 —see also 另見 **drive a hard bargain** (DRIVE¹ (9))

S1 W2 **hard²** *adv*

1 ►USING ENERGY/EFFORT 用勁/用力◄ using a lot of effort, energy, or attention 費勁地; 費力地: *She had been working hard all morning.* 她整個上午都在努力工作。| *I tried as hard as I could to remember his name.* 我費盡全力想記起他的名字。

2 ►WITH FORCE 用力氣◄ with a lot of force 用力地; 重重地: *Tyson hit him so hard that he fell back on the ropes.* 泰臣給了他一記重拳, 使他倒在欄索上。| *The boys pressed their noses hard against the window.* 男孩們將鼻子緊緊地壓在窗戶上。| *It's raining hard.* 雨下得很大。

3 be hard hit/be hit hard to be badly affected by something that has happened 受到嚴重影響, 受到沉重打擊: *The Italian economy has been particularly hard hit by the world recession.* 意大利的經濟受全球經濟衰退的影響尤為嚴重。

4 be hard put/pressed/pushed (to do sth) *informal* to have difficulty doing something【非正式】難以做到, 做某事有困難: *We'd be hard pushed to get there by 7 o'clock.* 我們很難在7點以前趕到那裡。

5 be hard done by *informal* to be unfairly treated【非正式】受到不公平對待: *The other children felt hard done by because they didn't get any chocolates.* 其餘的孩子都感到自己受到不公平對待, 因為他們沒有得到巧克力。

6 take sth hard *informal* to feel upset about something, especially bad news【非正式】〔尤指因壞消息〕感到不快[難過]: *She's taking it very hard.* 她為此而耿耿於懷。

7 laugh hard/cry hard etc to laugh, cry etc a lot 笑/哭得很厲害: *He laughed so hard he had tears in his eyes.* 他笑得連眼淚都出來了。

8 hard on the heels of happening soon after something 緊接着: *Hard on the heels of the last week's defeat comes news of yet another disaster.* 在上週的失敗後緊接着又傳來不利的消息。

9 be hard on sb's heels to follow close behind or soon after someone 緊跟在某人之後: *They fled in panic with the enemy hard on their heels.* 在敵人的緊追下, 他們恐慌出逃。

10 baked/set hard made firm and stiff by being heated, glued etc 燒硬/黏牢的 —see also 另見 HARD BY, HARD UP, HARD UPON, **play hard to get** (PLAY¹ (10))

hard-and-fast /ˌ· · ˈ·◄/ *adj* **hard and fast rules/regulations** rules that are fixed and that you cannot change 不容改變的規定

hard·back /ˈhɑrdˌbæk; ˈhɑːdbæk/ *n* [C] a book that has a strong stiff cover 硬皮書, 精裝本: *a hardback edition* 精裝本 | **in hardback** *The book sold more than a million copies in hardback.* 這本書的精裝本賣出了一百多萬本。—compare 比較 PAPERBACK

hard·ball /ˈhɑrdˌbɔl; ˈhɑːdbɔːl/ *n* [U] *AmE*【美】**1** the game of BASEBALL rather than SOFTBALL 棒球 **2 play hardball** *informal* to be very determined to get what you want, especially in business or politics【非正式】〔尤指商界或政界中〕採取強硬方式

hard-bit·ten /ˌ· ˈ··◄/ *adj* not easily shocked or upset, because you have had a lot of experience 老練的; 經過磨練的: *a hard-bitten journalist* 一位老練的新聞工作者

hard·board /ˈhɑrdbɔrd; ˈhɑːdbɔːd/ *n* [U] a material made from small pieces of wood pressed together 硬質纖維板; 加壓纖維板

hard-boiled /ˌ· ˈ·◄/ *adj* **1** a hard-boiled egg has been boiled until it becomes solid〔雞蛋〕煮得老[硬]的 —compare 比較 SOFT-BOILED **2** *informal* not showing your emotions and not influenced by your feelings; TOUGH【非正式】不動感情的; 冷酷的

hard·bound /ˈhɑrdˋbaund; ˈhɑːdbaʊnd/ *adj* HARDCOVER 精裝的, 硬皮的

hard by /ˌ· ˈ·/ *adv, prep old use* very near【舊】在近旁, 非常靠近: *in a house hard by the city gate* 城門邊上的一座房子裡

hard can·dy /ˌ· ˈ··/ *n* [C] *AmE* a hard piece of sweet food, which often tastes of fruit【美】(水果) 硬糖; BOILED SWEET *BrE*【英】

hard cash /ˌ· ˈ·/ *n* [U] money that consists of notes and coins, not cheques or CREDIT CARDS 現金, 現鈔

hard ci·der /ˌ· ˈ··/ *n* [U] *AmE* an alcoholic drink made from apples【美】蘋果酒; CIDER (1) *BrE*【英】

hard cop·y /ˈ· ˌ··/ *n* [U] information from a computer that is printed out onto paper 硬拷貝, 硬副本〔指電腦打印出來的信息資料〕—compare 比較 SOFT COPY

hard core /ˌ· ˈ·/ *n BrE*【英】**a) the hard core** the small central group that is most active within a group or organization〔組織中的〕核心力量, 中堅分子, 骨幹: *the hard core of the Communist party* 共產黨的中堅分子 **b)** [singular] a group of people who cannot be persuaded to change their behaviour or beliefs 頑固分子: *a hard core of young offenders* 年青罪犯中的頑固分子

hard-core /ˌ· ˈ·◄/ *adj* **1 hard-core pornography** magazines, films etc that show the details of sexual behaviour, often in an unpleasant way 赤裸裸的色情作品〔書刊、電影等〕**2** [only before noun 僅用於名詞前] having an extremely strong belief or opinion that is unlikely to change 死硬的, 頑固不化的: *hard-core opposition to the government's educational policies* 頑固地反對政府的教育政策

hard court /ˌ· ˈ·/ *n* [C] an area for playing tennis which has a hard surface, not grass 硬地網球場

hard·cov·er /ˈhɑrdˋkʌvə; ˈhɑːdˌkʌvə/ *adj* a hardcover book has a strong stiff cover〔書〕硬皮的, 精裝的

hard cur·ren·cy /ˌ· ˈ···/ *n* [C,U] money that will not lose value because it is from a country that has a strong ECONOMY and can be used in other countries to buy things 硬通貨, 強勢貨幣

hard disk /ˌ· ˈ·/ *n* [C] a part that is fixed inside a computer and is used for permanently storing information〔電腦〕硬磁盤 —compare 比較 FLOPPY DISK

hard-drink·ing /ˈ· ··/ *adj* drinking a lot of alcohol 酗酒的, 喝酒成癮的: *a hard-drinking man* 酒鬼

hard drugs /ˌ· ˈ·/ *n* [plural] very strong illegal drugs such as HEROIN and COCAINE 硬性毒品, 烈性毒品〈如海洛因、可卡因等〉—compare 比較 SOFT DRUG

hard-edged /ˌ· ˈ·◂/ *adj* a hard-edged report, article etc deals with unpleasant subjects or criticizes someone severely in a way that may offend some people 筆鋒犀利的, 批評嚴厲的〔報告、文章等〕

hard·en /ˈhɑrdn̩; ˈhɑːdn/ *v* **1** [I,T] to become firm or stiff, or to make something firm or stiff (使) 變硬; (使) 堅固; (使) 硬化: *Make sure you give the paint enough time to dry and harden.* 你一定要讓油漆有足夠的時間乾透和變硬。**2** [I] to become more strict and determined and less sympathetic 變得更堅定; 變得冷酷無情: *Opposition to the military regime has hardened since the massacres.* 大屠殺後, 反對軍政府的力量更強硬了。| *a hardening of attitudes* 態度變得強硬 | *His face hardened.* 他的臉沉了下來。—compare 比較 SOFTEN (2) **3** [T] if an experience hardens someone, it makes them stronger and more able to deal with difficult or unpleasant situations 使變得堅強, 使更有忍耐力 **4 hardened criminal/police officer etc** a criminal etc who has had a lot of experience of things that are shocking and is therefore less affected by them 死不悔改的罪犯/見怪不怪的警官等 **5 become hardened towards/to** to become used to something shocking because you have seen it many times 對…變得麻木[不在乎] **6 harden your heart** to make yourself not feel pity or sympathy for someone 硬起心腸

hard hat /ˌ· ˈ·/ *n* [C] a protective hat, worn especially by workers in places where buildings are being built〔建築工人的〕安全帽, 防護帽 —see picture at 參見 HAT 圖

hard-head·ed /ˌ· ˈ··◂/ *adj* practical and able to make difficult decisions without letting your emotions affect your judgment 頭腦清醒的, 講究實際的, 不感情用事的: *a hard-headed business tycoon* 精明的商業巨頭 —**hard-headedness** *n* [U]

hard-heart·ed /ˌ· ˈ··◂/ *adj* not caring about other people's feelings 硬心腸的, 沒有同情心的 —**hard-heartedness** *n* [U]

hard-hit·ting /ˌ· ˈ··◂/ *adj* criticizing someone or something in a strong and effective way 激烈批評的: *a hard-hitting report* 措辭尖銳的報告

har·di·ness /ˈhɑrdɪnɪs; ˈhɑːdinɨs/ *n* [U] the ability to bear difficult or severe conditions 堅強; 耐性; 吃苦耐勞的精神

hard la·bour *BrE*【英】, **hard labor** *AmE*【美】/ˌ· ˈ··/ *n* [U] punishment in prison which consists of hard physical work 苦役, 勞役

hard land·ing /ˌ· ˈ··/ *n* [singular] *technical* a sudden fall in economic activity coming after a successful period【術語】硬着陸〔指經濟經過一段時期增長後的突然回落〕

hard left /ˌ· ˈ·◂/ *n* [singular] the part of a political party that believes strongly in SOCIALISM〔堅信社會主義的〕強硬左派

hard-line /ˌ· ˈ·◂/ *adj* having extreme political beliefs, and refusing to change them 立場堅定的, 不妥協的: a *hard-line Marxist* 立場堅定的馬克思主義者 —see also 另見 **take a hard line on/over** (HARD[1] (33))

hard·lin·er /ˌhɑrdˋlaɪnə; ˌhɑːdˈlaɪnə/ *n* [C] a politician who wants political problems to be dealt with in a strong and extreme way 奉行強硬路線者: *Communist hardliners* 共產黨中的強硬派

hard liq·uor /ˌ· ˈ··/ *n* [U] *especially AmE* strong alcohol such as WHISKY【尤美】烈酒〈如威士忌等〉

hard·ly /ˈhɑrdlɪ; ˈhɑːdli/ *adv* **1** almost not 幾乎不; 幾乎沒有: *I hadn't seen him for years but he had hardly changed at all.* 我已多年沒有見到他, 但他幾乎一點都沒變。| **can/could hardly do sth** *The children were so excited they could hardly speak.* 孩子們興奮得幾乎連話都說不出來了。| *I can hardly believe it.* 這簡直讓我難以置信。| **hardly anyone/anything** (=almost no one or almost nothing) 幾乎沒有人/東西 *Hardly anyone writes to me these days.* 現在幾乎沒有人給我寫信了。| **hardly any** (=very few) 幾乎沒有 *There are hardly any cookies left.* 幾乎沒剩下甚麼餅乾了。| **hardly ever** (=almost never) 幾乎從未 *She hardly ever wore a hat.* 她幾乎從未戴過帽子。| **hardly a day/week goes by when/without** (=used to say that something happens almost every day or every week) 幾乎每天/週都… *Hardly a day goes by when I don't think of her.* 我幾乎每天都在想她。—see 見 ALMOST (USAGE) **2** used to say that something had only just happened or someone had only just done something 剛剛: *The day had hardly begun, and he felt exhausted already.* 新的一天才剛剛開始, 他就已經覺得筋疲力盡了。**3** used to say that something is not at all true, possible, correct etc 很難說是…, 一點也不: *It's hardly what I'd call the perfect relationship.* 這絕對不是我所說的完美關係。| **hardly surprising** *It was hardly surprising you didn't pass your exam.* 你考試不及格, 這絲毫不讓人感到意外。| **hardly the time/place/person** (=a very unsuitable time, place, person) 絕不是恰當的時候/地方/人選 *This is hardly the place to talk about our marriage problems.* 這裡絕不是談論我們的婚姻問題的地方。| **you can/could hardly do sth** (=it would not be sensible to do it) 你不應該做某事 *You could hardly blame Jane for being nervous.* 你不該責怪簡過於緊張。| **could hardly be** *The message could hardly be clearer.* 這個意思再清楚不過了。| **hardly a child/beginner etc** *He was fifteen – hardly a kid.* 他已經十五歲了, 絕不是一個小孩子。

USAGE NOTE 用法說明: HARDLY

GRAMMAR 語法

Hardly is a negative word, so it is not used with another negative word. hardly 是一個否定詞, 因此不與另外一個否定詞連用: *hardly any pollution* 幾乎沒有污染 (NOT 不用 *hardly no pollution*) | *We could hardly believe our eyes.* 我們幾乎無法相信自己的眼睛。(NOT 不用 *We couldn't hardly believe our eyes...*)

Hardly usually comes just before the main verb. hardly 往往緊挨着出現在主動詞前: *He could hardly hear her.* 他幾乎聽不見她的話。(NOT 不用 *He hardly could hear her*)

Hardly is used at the beginning of sentences only in very formal or old-fashioned writing. hardly 只有在非常正式或舊式文體中才會用於句首。People would say, and usually write 人們通常會這樣說, 或這樣寫: *The game had hardly begun when it started to rain.* 比賽剛剛開始, 天就開始下起雨來。(compare the formal 比較正式說法: *Hardly had the game begun when it started to rain...*)

Hardly is not the adverb of *hard*. hardly 不是 hard 的副詞形式。You say 應該這樣說: *I tried hard to remember.* 我使勁地回想。| *She works very hard.* 她工作非常努力。(NOT 不用 hardly)

hard-nosed /ˌ· ˈ·◂/ *adj* [usually before noun 一般用於名詞前] not affected by emotions, and determined to get what you want 頑強的, 不屈不撓的, 倔強的: *a hard-nosed approach to business negotiations* 對商業談判所持的一種不屈不撓的態度

hard nut /ˌ· ˈ·/ *n* [C] **1** *informal* someone who is physically or mentally very strong, or thinks that they are strong【非正式】硬漢子 **2 a hard nut to crack** someone or something that is difficult to deal with 難對付的人[事]

hard of hear·ing /ˌ· · ˈ··/ *adj* [not before noun 不用於名詞前] **1** unable to hear very well 聽覺不靈的, 耳背的 **2 the hard of hearing** people who are unable to hear very well 有聽力障礙的人, 失聰者

hard-on /ˈ· ·/ *n* [C] *taboo* an ERECTION (1)【諱】勃起

hard pal·ate /ˌ· ˈ··/ *n* [C] the hard part of the top of your mouth that is at the front behind your teeth 硬顎 —compare 比較 SOFT PALATE

hard porn /ˌ· ˈ·/ *n* [U] *informal* magazines, films etc that show sexual behaviour in an unacceptable, sometimes violent way【非正式】赤裸裸的色情作品〔雜誌、電影等〕: *sales of hard-porn videos* 色情錄像帶的銷售 —compare 比較 SOFT PORN

hard-pressed /ˌ· ˈ·◂/ *adj* **1** having a lot of problems and not enough money or time 處於困境的; 遭受強大壓力的: *Hard-pressed local authorities are finding it difficult to pay for essential services.* 處於困境的地方政府連支付最基本的公共服務費用都有困難。 **2 sb would be hard-pressed to do sth** used to say that it would be difficult for someone to do something 某人難以做到某事: *They'd be hard-pressed to find a better editor.* 他們很難找到一位更好的編輯。

hard right /ˌ· ˈ·◂/ *n* [singular] the part of a political party that believes strongly in RIGHT WING political ideas 強硬右派

hard rock /ˌ· ˈ·/ *n* [U] a type of ROCK MUSIC that has loud electric GUITARs and a strong beat 硬搖滾樂

hard-scrab·ble /ˌ· ˈ··/ *adj AmE* hard-scrabble land is difficult to grow crops on【美】〔土地〕莊稼難以生長的, 貧瘠的

hard sell /ˌ· ˈ·◂/ *n* [singular] a way of selling something in which there is a lot of pressure on you to buy 強行[硬性]推銷(法) —compare 比較 SOFT SELL

hard·ship /ˈhardʃɪp; ˈhɑːdʃɪp/ *n* [C,U] the condition of having very little money so that life is very difficult 艱苦, 貧困: *a time of great economic hardship* 經濟極度困難的時期

hard shoul·der /ˌ· ˈ··/ *n* [singular] *BrE* the area at the side of a big road where you are allowed to stop if you have a problem with your car【英】〔公路旁的〕緊急停車處, 路肩; SHOULDER[1] (9) *AmE*【美】—see picture on page A3 參見 A3 頁圖

hard·top /ˈhardˌtap; ˈhɑːdtɒp/ *n* [C] a car that has a metal roof which cannot be removed 硬頂小客車, 有固定金屬車頂的汽車 —compare 比較 CONVERTIBLE[2]

hard up /ˌ· ˈ·◂/ *adj* not having enough money to buy the things you need, especially for a short period of time〔尤指短期內〕缺錢的, 手頭緊的: *We were too hard up to afford new clothes.* 那時我們手頭緊, 沒有錢買新衣服。

hard up·on /ˈ· ·ˌ·/ also 又作 **hard on** *prep literary*【文】**1** soon after〔時間〕緊接着, 隨即 **2** close behind 緊接…之後

hard·ware /ˈhardˌwɛr; ˈhɑːdweə/ *n* [U] **1** computer machinery and equipment, as opposed to the programmes that make computers work〔電腦〕硬件 —compare 比較 SOFTWARE **2** equipment and tools for your home and garden〔家用或園藝用的〕金屬器件[用具]; 五金製品 **3** the machinery and equipment that is needed to do something 裝備, 設備: *tanks and other military hardware* 坦克和其他軍事裝備

hard-wearing /ˌ· ˈ··◂/ *adj BrE* clothes, materials etc that are hard-wearing will remain in good condition for a long time【英】經穿的, 耐磨的; LONGWEARING *AmE*【美】

hard-wired /ˌ· ˈ·◂/ *adj technical* computer systems that are hard-wired are controlled by HARDWARE rather than SOFTWARE and therefore cannot be easily changed by the user【術語】〔電腦作業〕硬件控制的, 硬連線的

hard·wood /ˈhardˌwʊd; ˈhɑːdwʊd/ *n* **1** [C,U] strong heavy wood from trees such as OAK that take a long time to grow, used for making furniture 硬木〈如橡木〉 **2** [C] a tree that produces this kind of wood 硬木樹; 闊葉樹 —compare 比較 SOFTWOOD

hard-working /ˌ· ˈ··/ *adj* working with a lot of effort 努力工作的, 勤奮的: *a hard-working teacher* 一位努力工作的教師

har·dy /ˈhardɪ; ˈhɑːdi/ *adj* **1** strong and healthy and able to bear difficult living conditions 能吃苦耐勞的; 堅強的; 強壯的: *the hardy fishermen who turned out in these arctic conditions* 在這種極度寒冷的環境中外出的吃苦耐勞的漁民 **2** a hardy plant is able to live through the winter〔植物〕耐寒的

hardy pe·ren·ni·al /ˌ·· ·ˈ···/ *n* [C] **1** a hardy plant that produces flowers for several years 耐寒的多年生植物 —see also 另見 PERENNIAL[2] **2** an idea that is often suggested or discussed 經常提到或談論到的話題

hare[1] /hɛr; heə/ *n plural* **hare** or **hares** [C] **1** an animal like a rabbit but larger, that can run very quickly 野兔 —see picture at 參見 RABBIT[1] 圖 **2 run with the hare and hunt with the hounds** *old-fashioned* to try to support both sides in an argument【過時】兩面討好

hare[2] *v* [I always+adv/prep] *BrE informal* to run or go very fast【英, 非正式】飛跑, 飛奔: [**+off/away**] *He hared off down the road.* 他沿着馬路飛快地跑掉了。

hare·bell /ˈhɛrˌbɛl; ˈheəbel/ *n* [C] a wild plant with bell-shaped blue flowers on a thin stem 圓葉風鈴草, 藍鈴花

hare·brained /ˈhɛrˋbrend; ˈheəbreɪnd/ *adj* a harebrained person, plan etc is very silly and unlikely to succeed〔人、計劃等〕愚蠢的; 輕率的; 不切實際的: *wasting public money on harebrained schemes* 將公帑浪費在一些不切實際的計劃上

hare cours·ing /ˈ· ˌ··/ *n* [U] the sport of chasing a HARE with dogs 用獵犬追蹤野兔的狩獵

hare·lip /ˌhɛrˋlɪp; ˌheəˈlɪp/ *n* [singular,U] the condition of having your top lip divided into two parts because it did not develop properly before birth 兔唇, 唇裂 —**harelipped** *adj*

har·em /ˈhɛrəm; ˈhɑːriːm/ *n* [C] **1** the group of wives or women who lived with a rich or powerful man in some Muslim societies in the past〔舊時有錢或有權的伊斯蘭教徒的〕妻妾, 女眷 **2** part of a Muslim house that is separate from the rest of the house, where only women live〔伊斯蘭教徒的〕女眷居住的內室, 閨房

harem pants /ˈ·· ˌ·/ *n* [plural] loose-fitting women's trousers made from thin cloth 束腰的寬鬆女長褲, 哈倫褲

har·i·cot /ˈhærɪˌko; ˈhærɪkəʊ/ also 又作 **haricot bean** /ˌ··· ˈ·/ *n* [C] a small white bean 菜豆, 扁豆

hark /hark; hɑːk/ *v* **1 hark at him/her!** *BrE spoken* used when you think someone is saying something stupid or unreasonable【英口】暫且聽聽〔某人的蠢話〕: *Hark at him! I bet he couldn't do any better.* 聽他說的! 我敢打賭他也好不到哪裡去! **2 hark!** *old use* used to tell someone to listen【舊】聽着! 留神聽!

hark back *phr v* [I] **1** to remember and talk about things that happened in the past 回想, 談論往事, 追溯過去 **2** to be similar to something in the past 與過去的某事相類似: [**+to**] *music that harks back to the early age of jazz* 類似早期爵士樂的音樂

har·ken /ˈharkən; ˈhɑːkən/ *v* [I] another spelling of HEARKEN hearken 的另一種拼法

har·le·quin /ˈharləkwɪn; ˈhɑːlɪkwɪn/ *n* [C] **1** a character in some traditional plays who wears brightly coloured clothes and plays tricks〔身穿鮮豔服裝的〕滑稽角色, 小丑 **2** a harlequin pattern is made up of DIAMOND shapes in many different colours〔由不同顏色的菱形組成的〕彩色拼塊

har·lot /ˈharlət; ˈhɑːlət/ *n* [C] *old use* a PROSTITUTE【舊】娼妓, 妓女

harm[1] /harm; hɑːm/ *n* [U] **1** damage, injury, or trouble caused by someone's actions or by an event 損害; 危害;

傷害: **do harm to** *Modern farming methods have done considerable harm to the countryside.* 現代農作方式對鄉村造成了很大的損害。| **do more harm than good** (=cause even more problems rather than improving the situation) 壞處多於好處, 弊大於利 *Criticizing people's work often does more harm than good.* 批評別人的工作往往弊多利少。| **where's the harm in that?** *spoken* (=used when you think that something seems a reasonable thing to do)【口】那有甚麼害處呢? | **no harm done** *spoken* (=used to tell someone not to worry about something they have done)【口】沒事兒, 不要緊 **2 come to no harm/not come to any harm** to not be hurt or damaged 沒有受到傷害[損害]: *She was relieved to see the children had come to no harm.* 她看到孩子們沒有受到傷害, 舒了一口氣。**3 mean no harm/not mean any harm** to have no intention of hurting or upsetting anyone 無意傷害別人: *He doesn't mean any harm – he's only joking.* 他沒有惡意, 只是開個玩笑。**4 it does no harm to do sth/there's no harm in doing sth** used to suggest that someone should do something 不妨做某事: *It does no harm to ask.* 不妨問問。| *There's no harm in trying.* 試試也無妨。**5 it wouldn't do sb any harm to do sth** used to suggest that someone should do something that may be helpful or useful 做〔某事〕對〔某人〕並無害處: *It would do you no harm to get some experience first.* 你不妨先積累點經驗。**6 out of harm's way a)** in a safe place 在安全的地方 **b)** if something dangerous is out of harm's way, it is in a place where it is unable to hurt anyone or damage anything 不構成傷害的, 處於不傷害人的地位 —compare 比較 HURT³ —see also 另見 GRIEVOUS BODILY HARM

harm² *v* [T] **1** to damage something 危害, 傷害, 損害〔某事物〕: *Too much direct sunlight will harm the plant.* 陽光直接照射過多會傷害植物。**2 harm sb's image/reputation** to make people have a worse opinion of a person or group 損害某人的形象/名聲 **3** to hurt someone 傷害〔某人〕: *The dogs look fierce, but they wouldn't harm anyone.* 這些狗看起來很兇猛, 但不會傷人。

harm·ful /ˋharmfəl; ˈhɑːmfəl/ *adj* causing or likely to cause harm 有害的; 致傷的: *the harmful effects of smoking* 吸煙的害處 | [**+to**] *chemicals that are harmful to the environment* 對環境有害的化學品 —**harmfully** *adv* —**harmfulness** *n* [U]

harm·less /ˋharmlɪs; ˈhɑːmləs/ *adj* **1** unable or unlikely to hurt anyone or cause damage 無害的; 不致傷的: *The dog seems fierce, but actually he's harmless.* 這條狗看起來很兇, 但實際上不會傷人。**2** not likely to upset or offend anyone 無惡意的: **harmless fun** *It was just a bit of harmless fun.* 這只是個無惡意的玩笑。—**harmlessly** *adv* —**harmlessness** *n* [U]

har·mon·ic /harˋmɑnɪk; hɑˈmɒnɪk/ *adj technical* concerned with the way notes are played or sung together to give a pleasing sound【術語】和聲的: *harmonic scales* 調和音階

har·mon·i·ca /harˋmɑnɪkə; hɑːˈmɒnɪkə/ *n* [C] a small musical instrument that you play by blowing into it and moving it from side to side; MOUTH ORGAN 口琴

har·mo·ni·ous /harˋmonɪəs; hɑːˈməʊniəs/ *adj* **1** harmonious relationships, agreements etc are ones in which people are friendly and helpful to one another〔關係〕和睦的, 融洽的 **2** sounds that are harmonious are very pleasant 音調和諧的, 悅耳的 **3** parts, colours etc that are harmonious look good or work well together〔部分、顏色等〕協調的, 和諧的, 調和的: *The decor is a harmonious blend of traditional and modern.* 這種裝飾風格是傳統和現代的和諧統一。—**harmoniously** *adv* —**harmoniousness** *n* [U]

har·mo·ni·um /harˋmonɪəm; hɑːˈməʊniəm/ *n* [C] a musical instrument like a small piano worked by pumped air 簧風琴

har·mo·nize also 又作 **-ise** *BrE*【英】/ˋharməˌnaɪz; ˈhɑːmənaɪz/ *v* **1** [I] if two or more things harmonize, they work well together or look good together 和諧, 協調: [**+with**] *colours that don't seem to harmonize with each other* 看上去相互不協調的顏色 **2** [T] to make two or more sets of rules, taxes etc the same 使一致, 統一: *harmonizing Europe's widely varying immigration procedures* 統一歐洲各國間相去甚遠的移民程序 **3** [I] to sing or play music in HARMONY 用和聲演唱[演奏]

har·mo·ny /ˋharmənɪ; ˈhɑːməni/ *n* **1** [C usually plural 一般用複數, U] notes of music combined together in a pleasant way〔音樂中的〕和聲: **in harmony** *a choir singing in perfect harmony* 用完美的和聲演唱的唱詩班 **2 be in harmony with** *formal* to agree with another idea, feeling etc, or look good with other things【正式】〔思想、感情等的〕和睦, 一致, 融洽: *Your suggestions are not in harmony with the aims of this project.* 你的建議與本項目的目標不符。**3 live/work in (perfect) harmony** to live or work together without fighting or disagreeing with each other 一起生活/工作得(十分)融洽 **4** [U] the pleasant effect made by different things that form an attractive whole 和諧, 協調: *the harmony of sea and sky* 海天一色 —compare 比較 DISCORD

har·ness¹ /ˋharnɪs; ˈhɑːnɪ̣s/ *n* [C,U] **1** a piece of equipment for controlling a horse, consisting of long pieces of leather held together by metal and worn over the horse's head and shoulders〔馬的〕挽具, 馬具 **2** a piece of equipment used to fasten someone in a place or to stop them from falling 繫帶: *a safety harness* 安全帶 **3 be back in harness** *informal* to have come back to do your usual work【非正式】恢復正常工作 **4 in harness with** working closely with another group 與…密切合作

harness² *v* [T] **1** to control and use the natural force or power of something 利用〔自然界的力量〕: *harnessing the power of the wind to generate electricity* 利用風力發電 **2** to fasten two animals together, or to fasten an animal to something using a harness〔將兩隻動物〕繫拴在一起,〔將動物〕繫到某物上 **3** to put a harness on a horse 給馬套上挽具

harp¹ /harp; hɑːp/ *n* [C] a large musical instrument with strings that are stretched from top to bottom of a frame with three corners 豎琴 —**harpist** *n* [C]

harp² *v*

harp on [I *BrE* 英, T *AmE* 美] *informal* to talk about something continuously, especially in a way that is annoying or boring【非正式】嘮嘮叨叨, 喋喋不休: [**+about**] *My grandfather harps on about the war all the time.* 我的祖父總是喋喋不休地說起戰爭的事。

har·poon /harˋpun; hɑːˈpuːn/ *n* [C] a weapon used for hunting WHALES 捕鯨叉 —**harpoon** *v* [T]

harp·si·chord /ˋharpsɪˌkɔrd; ˈhɑːpsɪkɔːd/ *n* [C] a musical instrument like a PIANO, used in former times 大鍵琴; 古鍵琴〔古時類似鋼琴的一種樂器〕

har·py /ˋharpɪ; ˈhɑːpi/ *n* [C] *literary* a cruel or nasty woman【文】兇惡卑鄙的女人, 潑婦

har·ri·dan /ˋhærədən; ˈhærɪdən/ *n* [C] *old-fashioned* a bad-tempered, unpleasant woman【過時】潑婦, 惡婆, 母夜叉

har·row /ˋhæro; ˈhærəʊ/ *n* [C] a farming machine with sharp metal blades, used to break up the earth before planting crops 耙 —**harrow** *v* [I,T]

har·rowed /ˋhærod; ˈhærəʊd/ *adj* a harrowed look or expression shows that you are very worried or afraid〔樣子或表情〕苦惱的, 憂慮的, 憂傷的; 害怕的

har·row·ing /ˋhærəwɪŋ; ˈhærəʊɪŋ/ *adj* very frightening or shocking and making you feel very upset 折磨人的, 可怕的, 令人痛苦的: *a harrowing experience* 可怕的經歷 | *harrowing video tapes of torture* 令人毛骨悚然的酷刑錄像帶

har·ry /ˋhærɪ; ˈhæri/ *v* **harried, harrying** [T] **1** to keep asking someone for something in a way that is upsetting or annoying 不斷煩擾, 使苦惱 **2** to attack an enemy repeatedly 再三襲擊, 侵擾〔敵人〕

harsh /harʃ; hɑːʃ/ *adj*

1 ►CONDITIONS/WEATHER 條件/天氣◄ difficult to live in and very uncomfortable, cold etc 惡劣的, 艱苦的, 嚴峻的: *The prisoners had to endure harsh living conditions and near starvation.* 犯人們得忍受艱苦的生

H

活條件和極度飢餓。| *the harsh winters of northern China* 中國北方的嚴冬 | **harsh reality** *experiencing the harsh realities of adult life* 體驗成人生活的殘酷現實 **2 ►SOUND/LIGHT/COLOUR** 聲音/光線/顏色◄ unpleasant and too loud or bright 刺耳的; 刺眼的, 耀眼的: *a harsh, croaking voice* 刺耳而沙啞的聲音 | *They stepped out into the harsh sunlight.* 他們走了出去, 外面是刺眼的陽光。**3 ►CRUEL/STRICT** 殘酷的/嚴苛的◄ criticizing, punishing, or treating people in a very cruel or strict way 無情的; 嚴厲的: **harsh criticism** *Brando has had to endure some harsh criticism from the press.* 白蘭度得忍受新聞界對他的嚴厲批評。| *a harsh, authoritarian regime* 無情獨裁的政權 **4 ►LINES/SHAPES ETC** 線條/形狀等◄ ugly and unpleasant to look at 難看的, 醜陋的: *the harsh outline of the factories against the sky* 在天空映襯下醜陋的工廠輪廓 **5 ►CLEANING SUBSTANCE** 清潔用品◄ too strong and likely to damage the thing you are cleaning 太粗糙的; 太強力的 —**harshly** *adv* —**harshness** *n* [U]

hart /hɑrt; hɑːt/ *n* [C] *especially BrE* a male DEER【尤英】公鹿

har·um-scar·um /ˈhɛrəm ˋskɛrəm; ˌheərəm ˈskeərəm/ *adv old-fashioned* in an uncontrolled way and without thinking【過時】冒失地, 魯莽地, 輕率地 —**harum-scarum** *adj*

har·vest¹ /ˈhɑrvɪst; ˈhɑːvɪst/ *n* **1** [C,U] the time when crops are gathered from the fields, or the act of gathering them 收穫期; 收穫, 收割: *harvest time* 收穫時節 **2** [C] the size or quality of the crops that have been gathered 收成; 收穫量: **a poor/bumper harvest** (=a harvest that produces few crops or a lot of crops) 歉收/豐收 **3 reap a harvest** to get good or bad results 獲得成果; 嘗到苦果: *The company is now reaping the harvest of careful planning.* 公司目前嘗到了嚴謹規劃帶來的好處。

harvest² *v* [I,T] to gather crops from the fields 收穫, 收割

har·vest·er /ˈhɑrvɪstə; ˈhɑːvɪstə/ *n* [C] someone who gathers crops 收穫者, 收割者 —see also 另見 **combine harvester** (COMBINE² (1))

harvest fes·ti·val /ˌ.. ˈ.../ *n* [C] *especially BrE* an occasion in the Christian religion when people thank God for the harvest【尤英】收穫感恩節 —compare 比較 THANKSGIVING

harvest moon /ˌ.. ˈ./ *n* [usually singular 一般用單數] the FULL MOON in autumn 秋分前後的滿月

has /əz, həz; z, əz, həz; *strong* 強讀 hæz; hæz/ the third person singular of the present tense of HAVE¹

has-been /ˈ. ./ *n* [C] *informal* someone who was important or popular but who has now been forgotten【非正式】過時的人, 已失去往日風光的人

hash¹ /hæʃ; hæʃ/ *n* **1 make a hash of** *informal* to do something very badly【非正式】把…弄糟: *I made a real hash of my exams.* 我的考試考得一團糟。**2** [U] *informal* HASHISH【非正式】大麻麻醉劑 **3** [C,U] a dish made with cooked meat and potatoes 肉末馬鈴薯泥

hash² *v*

hash sth ↔ up *phr v* [T] *informal* to do something very badly【非正式】把…弄得亂七八糟: *She was so nervous at the interview that she completely hashed it up.* 她面試時太緊張了, 結果表現得極糟。—**hash-up** *n* [C]

hash browns /ˌ. ˈ./ *n* [plural] potatoes that are cut into very small pieces, pressed together, and cooked in oil 煎馬鈴薯餅

hash·ish /ˈhæʃiʃ; ˈhæʃiːʃ/ *n* [U] the strongest form of the drug CANNABIS 大麻麻醉劑

has·n't /ˈhæzn̩t; ˈhæzənt/ the short form of 縮略式= has not: *Hasn't she finished yet?* 她做完了沒有?

hasp /hæsp; hɑːsp/ *n* [C] a flat metal thing used to fasten a door, lid etc 金屬鎖搭, 搭扣

has·sle¹ /ˈhæsl̩; ˈhæsəl/ *n* **1** [C,U] *spoken* something that is annoying, because it causes problems or is difficult to do【口】麻煩: *I don't feel like cooking tonight, it's too much hassle.* 今天晚上我不想做飯, 太麻煩了。| *It's such a hassle not having a washing machine.* 沒有洗衣機真是麻煩。**2** [C] *AmE informal* an argument between two people or groups【美, 非正式】爭論, 爭吵: *hassles with the management* 與管理層的爭論

hassle² *v* **hassled, hassling** *informal*【非正式】**1** [T] to be continuously asking someone to do something in a way that annoys them 煩擾, 不斷打擾: *I wish you'd stop hassling me.* 希望你不要再煩我了。**2** [I+with] to argue with someone 爭論, 爭吵

has·sock /ˈhæsək; ˈhæsək/ *n* [C] **1** a small CUSHION¹ (1) for kneeling on in a church〔教堂裡的〕祈禱跪墊 **2** *AmE* a soft round piece of furniture used as a seat or for resting your feet on【美】坐墊, 腳墊; POUF (1) *BrE*【英】

hast /hæst; hæst/ **thou hast** *old use* a way of saying you have【舊】= you have

haste /hest; heɪst/ *n* [U] **1** great speed in doing something, especially because you do not have enough time 匆忙, 倉促: *I soon regretted my haste.* 我很快就對自己的倉促感到後悔。| **in your haste to do sth** *In his haste to leave he forgot his briefcase.* 他走得很匆忙, 忘了帶公事包。**2 in haste** quickly or in a hurry 匆忙地, 急忙地: *They left in haste, without even saying goodbye.* 他們走得很匆忙, 連再見都沒說。**3 make haste** *old use* to hurry or do something quickly【舊】趕緊, 倉促 **4 more haste less speed** *BrE* used to say that it is useless to do something too quickly【英】欲速則不達

has·ten /ˈhesn̩; ˈheɪsən/ *v* **1** [T] to make something happen faster or sooner 加速, 加緊: *Her death had been hastened by large doses of pain-killing drugs.* 大劑量的止痛藥加速了她的死亡。**2** [I] to do or say something quickly or without delay 搶着, 急忙, 趕快: **hasten to do sth** *I hastened to assure her that there was no danger.* 我趕緊向她保證不會有甚麼危險。**3** [I always+adv/prep] *formal* to go somewhere quickly【正式】趕到某地 **4 I hasten to add** used when you realize that what you have said may not have been understood correctly 我得趕緊補充說: *an exhausting course, which, I hasten to add, was also great fun* 整個課程十分累人, 但我得說, 也十分好玩

hast·y /ˈhestɪ; ˈheɪsti/ *adj* done in a hurry, especially with bad results 倉促完成的; 匆忙的: *He soon regretted his hasty decision.* 他很快就對自己的倉促決定感到後悔。| *a hasty breakfast* 急匆匆的一頓早餐 —**hastily** *adv* —**hastiness** *n* [U]

hats 帽子

hat /hæt; hæt/ *n* [C] **1** a piece of clothing that you wear on your head 帽子: **straw/bowler/woolly etc hat** *She wore an enormous flowery hat.* 她戴着一頂大大的帶花

飾的帽子。**2 keep something under your hat** *informal* to keep something secret【非正式】保守祕密 **3 be wearing your manager's/teacher's etc hat** *informal* to be doing your duty as a manager etc, which is not your only duty【非正式】幹着經理/老師的工作〔指做不只一份工作〕 **4 I take my hat off to** *informal* used to say you admire someone very much because of what they have done【非正式】我欽佩〔某人〕 **5 pass the hat round** *BrE*【英】**/pass the hat (around)** *AmE*【美】to collect money from a group of people, especially in order to buy someone a present〔尤指為了給某人買禮物而〕籌集金錢, 募捐 **6 bowler-hatted/top-hatted etc** wearing a BOWLER hat, etc 戴禮帽/高頂禮帽等的 **7 my hat!** *old-fashioned* used to express great surprise【過時】天哪! 我不信! 胡說! —see also 另見 HARD HAT, **at the drop of a hat** (DROP[2] (5)), **hang up your hat** (HANG[1] (14)), **I'll eat my hat** (EAT (10)), OLD HAT, **be talking through your hat** (TALK[1] (17)), **throw your hat into the ring** (THROW[1] (33))

hat·band /ˈhætˌbænd; ˈhætbænd/ *n* [C] a band of cloth or leather fastened around a hat 帽圈, 帽帶

hat box /ˈ· ·/ *n* [C] a special box used for carrying a hat in 帽盒

hatch[1] /hætʃ; hætʃ/ *v* **1** also 又作 **hatch out** [I,T] if an egg hatches or is hatched, it breaks, letting the young bird, insect etc come out〔蛋〕孵化: *The eggs take three days to hatch.* 這些蛋要三天時間才能孵化。**2** also 又作 **hatch out** [I,T] if a young bird, insect etc hatches or is hatched, it comes out of its egg〔幼禽等〕孵出, 破殼而出: *All the chicks have hatched out.* 小雞都已破殼而出。**3 hatch a plot/plan/deal etc** to form a plan etc secretly 祕密策劃陰謀/計劃/交易等

hatch[2] *n* [C] **1** a hole in a ship or aircraft, used for loading goods, or the door that covers it〔船、飛機上的〕艙口; 艙門 —see picture at 參見 AIRCRAFT 圖 **2** also 又作 **hatchway** a small hole in the wall or floor between two rooms, or the door that covers it〔牆、地板上的〕開口, 活板門: *the hatch between the kitchen and the dining room* 廚房與餐廳之間的小窗口 **3** the act of hatching eggs 孵蛋

hatch·back /ˈhætʃbæk; ˈhætʃbæk/ *n* [C] a car with a door at the back that opens upwards 裝有向上開的後車門的小轎車

hat·check /ˈhætˌtʃɛk; ˈhæt-tʃek/ *n* [C] *AmE old-fashioned* the place in a restaurant, theatre etc where you can leave your coat【美, 過時】〔餐館、劇院等的〕衣帽間

hatch·er·y /ˈhætʃərɪ; ˈhætʃəri/ *n* [C] a place for hatching eggs, especially fish eggs〔尤指魚的〕孵化場

hatch·et /ˈhætʃɪt; ˈhætʃɪ̈t/ *n* [C] a small AXE with a short handle 短柄小斧 —see also 另見 **bury the hatchet** (BURY (8))

hatchet-faced /ˈ·· ˌ·/ *adj* having an unpleasantly thin face with sharp features 尖下巴的, 瘦削臉的

hatchet job /ˈ·· ˌ·/ *n* **do a hatchet job on** *informal* to criticize someone severely and unfairly in a newspaper, on television etc【非正式】〔在報章、電視節目中〕尖刻地攻擊, 詆毀: *Republican columnists did a hatchet job on Dukakis.* 共和黨的專欄作家對杜卡基斯作了尖刻的批評。

hatchet man /ˈ·· ˌ·/ *n* [C] *informal* someone who is employed to make unpopular changes in an organization【非正式】受雇在某機構內進行不受歡迎的改革的人

hatch·ing /ˈhætʃɪŋ; ˈhætʃɪŋ/ *n* [U] fine lines drawn on or cut into a surface〔畫或刻在平面上的〕影線

hatch·way /ˈhætʃˌwe; ˈhætʃweɪ/ *n* [C] a HATCH[2] (2) 開口, 活板門

1 3 **hate[1]** /het; heɪt/ *v* [T not in progressive 不用進行式] **1** to dislike someone very much and feel angry towards them 憎恨, 憎惡, 仇恨: *Jill really hates her stepfather.* 吉爾非常憎恨她的繼父。| **hate sb's guts** *informal* (=hate someone very much)【非正式】恨透某人 **2** *informal* to dislike something very much【非正式】討厭, 不喜歡: *I hate housework.* 我討厭做家務。| *Liz won't eat that, she hates bananas.* 利茲不會吃的, 她不喜歡香蕉。| **hate doing sth** *Paul hates having his photo taken.* 保羅不喜歡別人給他照相。| **hate to do sth** *I hate to see you making a fool of yourself.* 我不喜歡看見你出醜。| **hate sb doing sth** *Jenny's mother hates her staying out late.* 珍妮的母親不喜歡她晚上在外面呆得太晚。| **hate it when** *I hate it when people ask me for money.* 我不喜歡別人向我要錢。**3 I'd hate (sb) to do sth** *spoken* used to emphasize that you really do not want something to happen【口】我不願發生某事: *I'd hate you to go.* 我不希望你走。**4 I hate to think what/how** *spoken* used when you feel sure that something would have a bad result【口】我不敢想…: *I hate to think what would have happened, if you hadn't called the police.* 我不敢想如果你沒有報警會發生甚麼事。**5 I hate to ask/interrupt/disturb etc** *spoken* used to say that you are sorry that you have to ask etc【口】很抱歉, 請問/打斷你/打擾你等: *I hate to ask, but would you be able to give me a lift home tonight?* 很抱歉, 請問你今晚能不能讓我搭你的車回家? **6 I hate to (have to) say this, but...** *spoken* used when saying something that you do not want to say, for example because it is embarrassing【口】我真不好意思告訴你, 但… **—hated** *adj*: *the hated dictator* 令人憎恨的獨裁者 —opposite 反義詞 LOVE

This graph shows how common the different grammar patterns of the verb **hate** are. 本圖表所示為動詞 hate 構成的不同語法模式的使用頻率。

hate sb/sth
hate to do sth
hate doing sth
hate it when
other
10% 20% 30% 40% 50% 60% 70% 80%

Based on the British National Corpus and the Longman Lancaster Corpus
據英國國家語料庫和朗文蘭卡斯特語料庫

hate[2] *n* [U] an angry unpleasant feeling that someone has when they hate someone and want to harm them 憎恨, 仇恨: *Their minds were poisoned with envy and hate.* 他們的心智受到了妒忌和仇恨的毒害。—opposite 反義詞 LOVE[2] (1) —see also 另見 PET HATE

hate·ful /ˈhetfəl; ˈheɪtfəl/ *adj old-fashioned* very bad, unpleasant, or unkind【過時】可恨的, 可惡的, 令人討厭的 **—hatefully** *adv*

hath /hæθ; hæθ/ *old use*【舊】= has

hat·pin /ˈhætˌpɪn; ˈhætˌpɪn/ *n* [C] a long pin that is used to make a woman's hat stay on her head〔女士用於使帽子固定在頭上的〕長飾針 —see picture at 參見 PIN[1] 圖

ha·tred /ˈhetrɪd; ˈheɪtrɪ̈d/ *n* [U] an angry feeling of extreme dislike for someone or something 憎恨, 憎惡, 仇恨: *Her voice was full of hatred and contempt.* 她的聲音裡充滿了仇恨和鄙夷。| **[+of]** *Tom's hatred of authority* 湯姆對權威的憎惡 | **[+for/towards]** *Strangely, the murderer said he never felt hatred for any of his victims.* 奇怪的是, 殺人兇手聲稱自己從未對任何一位受害者懷有仇恨。| **deep hatred** *This experience left him with a deep hatred of politicians.* 這次經歷使他對政客產生了強烈的仇恨。

hat stand /ˈhæt ˌstænd; ˈhæt stænd/ *n* [C] a tall pole with hooks at the top used to hang coats and hats on 衣帽架 —see picture on page A15 參見 A15 頁圖

hat·ter /ˈhætɚ; ˈhætə/ *n* [C] someone who makes or sells hats 製帽匠; 帽商 —see also 另見 **as mad as a hatter** (MAD (14))

hat-trick /ˈ· ·/ *n* [C] a series of three successes, especially in sports such as football when the same person scores (SCORE[2] (1)) three times〔一名運動員在一場比賽

H

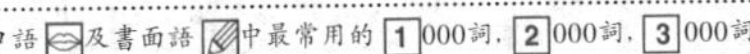
口語及書面語中最常用的 1 000詞, 2 000詞, 3 000詞

中〕連獲三勝〔尤指在足球比賽中連進三球〕: *Saunders scored a hat-trick in the final game of the series.* 桑德斯在聯賽的決賽中連中三元。

haugh·ty /ˋhɔtɪ; ˈhɔːti/ *adj* **haughtier, haughtiest** behaving in a proud unfriendly way 倨傲不遜的, 傲慢的, 目中無人的: *a haughty laugh* 傲然一笑 —**haughtily** *adv* —**haughtiness** *n* [U]

haul¹ /hɔl; hɔːl/ *v* **1** [I always+adv/prep,T] to pull something heavy with a continuous, steady movement 拖, 拉: **haul sth along/in/across etc** *The fishermen were hauling in their nets.* 漁民正在收網。**2 haul sb over the coals** to speak to someone angrily and severely because they have done something wrong 狠狠責備, 訓斥 **3** to carry goods in a vehicle〔用車輛〕運送〔貨物〕**4 haul yourself up/out of etc a)** to succeed in achieving a higher position in society, in a competition etc 提高〔社會地位〕; 取勝: *He hauled himself out of the gutter and became the world heavyweight champion.* 他努力使自己走出社會最低層, 成了世界重量級冠軍。**b)** to pull yourself up, out of etc 起來; 走出: *I see you've managed to haul yourself out of bed.* 你終於起牀了。**5 haul off and hit/punch sb** *AmE informal* to hit someone very hard【美, 非正式】重擊 **6 haul ass** *AmE slang* to hurry【美俚】趕快

haul sb **up** *phr v* [T usually passive 一般用被動態] *informal* to officially bring someone to a court of law to be judged【非正式】傳訊, 把…拉上法庭: *Campbell was hauled up in front of the magistrate.* 坎貝爾被傳訊在地方法院出庭。

haul² *n* [C] **1** a large amount of goods that has been stolen, or found by the police〔一大批〕贓物, 走私物品: *The robbers' haul included a very valuable diamond ring.* 盜賊的贓物中有一枚價值不菲的鑽石戒指。| *Police announced a drugs haul worth two million pounds.* 警方宣布截獲了價值二百萬英鎊的毒品。**2 long/slow haul** something that takes a lot of time and effort 耗時費力的事: **it's been a long haul** *At last we've won our freedom but it's been a long bitter haul.* 我們終於贏得了自由, 但這是通過漫長不懈的努力才得來的。**3** the amount of fish caught when fishing with a net 一網的捕魚量 —see also 另見 LONG-HAUL, SHORT-HAUL

haul·age /ˋhɔlɪdʒ; ˈhɔːlɪdʒ/ *n* [U] **1** the business of carrying goods by road or railway〔公路或鐵路〕貨運業 **2** the charge for this〔公路或鐵路〕貨運費

haul·i·er /ˋhɔljɚ; ˈhɔːliə/ *BrE*【英】, **hau·ler** *AmE*【美】/ˋhɔlɚ; ˈhɔːlə/ *n* [C] someone who owns or manages a haulage business 公路或鐵路貨運業經營者

haunch /hɔntʃ; hɔːntʃ/ *n* **1 haunches** [plural] the part of your body at the back between your waist and legs〔人的〕臀部, 胯部: *They squatted on their haunches playing dice.* 他們蹲坐着玩擲骰子。**2** [C] one of the back legs of a four-legged animal, especially when it is used as meat〔四腿動物的〕一條後腿〔尤指供食用的腰腿肉〕

haunt¹ /hɔnt; hɔːnt/ *v* [T not in progressive 不用進行式] **1** if the spirit of a dead person haunts a place, it appears there often〔鬼魂〕經常出沒於…: *The pub is said to be haunted by the ghost of a former landlord.* 據説這個酒吧裡經常有一位舊房主的鬼魂出沒。**2** to make someone worry or make them sad 纏擾, 煩擾; 縈繞在…心頭: *Clare was haunted by the fear that her husband was having an affair.* 克萊爾總是擔心她丈夫有外遇。**3** to cause problems for someone over a long period of time〔長期〕給〔某人〕帶來麻煩: *an error that would come back to haunt the US Administration for years to come* 一個會在今後幾年給美國政府不斷帶來麻煩的失誤

haunt² *n* [C] a place that someone likes to go to often〔某人〕常去的地方: **a favourite haunt** *The Café Vienna was a favourite haunt of journalists and actors.* 維也納咖啡館是記者和演員最愛光顧的地方。

haunt·ed /ˋhɔntɪd; ˈhɔːntɨd/ *adj* **1** a haunted building is believed to be visited regularly by the spirit of a dead person 鬧鬼的: *a haunted house* 鬧鬼的房子 **2 haunted expression/look** a worried or frightened expression etc 擔驚受怕的表情/樣子

haunt·ing /ˋhɔntɪŋ; ˈhɔːntɪŋ/ *adj* sad but also beautiful and staying in your thoughts for a long time 縈繞於心的, 不易忘懷的: *a haunting melody* 令人難忘的曲調 —**hauntingly** *adv*

haute cou·ture /ˌot kuˋtur; ˌəʊt kuːˈtjʊə/ *n* [U] *French* the business of making and selling very expensive and fashionable clothes for women【法】高級女式時裝業 —**haute couturier** *n* [C]

haute cui·sine /ˌot kwɪˋzin; ˌəʊt kwɪˈziːn/ *n* [U] *French* cooking of a very high standard, especially French cooking【法】(法國式) 高級烹飪

hau·teur /oˋtɝ; əʊˈtɜːʳ/ *n* [U] *formal* a proud, very unfriendly manner【正式】傲慢

Ha·van·a /həˋvænə; həˈvænə/ *n* [C] a type of CIGAR made in Cuba〔古巴產的〕哈瓦那雪茄

have¹ /v, əv, həv; v, əv, həv; *strong* 強讀 hæv; hæv/ *auxiliary verb past tense* **had** /əd, həd; d, əd, həd; *strong* 強讀 hæd; hæd/ *third person singular present tense* **has** /əz, həz; z, əz, həz; *strong* 強讀 hæz; hæz/ *negative short forms* 否定縮略式為 **haven't** /ˋhævn̩t; ˈhævənt/, **hadn't** /ˋhædn̩t; ˈhædnt/, **hasn't** /ˋhæzn̩t; ˈhæzənt/ **1** used with the past participle of another verb to make the perfect tense of that verb 與過去分詞連用構成動詞的完成式: *We have finished the decorating.* 我們已經完成了裝修。| *Have you read that book yet?* 你看過那本書嗎? | *We have been spending too much money.* 我們已經花錢太多了。**2 had better/best** used when telling someone what they should do 最好; 應該: *You'd better phone to say you'll be late.* 你最好打電話去説一聲你要晚到。| *We'd better not tell Jim about our plans just yet.* 我們最好先別把計劃告訴吉姆。**3 have had it** *spoken*【口】**a)** used to say that someone will be in serious trouble for something they have done 完了, 糟了, 遇到麻煩了〔用於表示某人惹來了大禍〕: *Press the wrong button and you've had it!* 你按錯按鈕就完了! **b)** used to say that someone is tired〔用於表示某人〕累壞了: *We'll have to stop for the night – the kids have just about had it.* 我們得停下來過夜了 —— 孩子們已經累壞了。**c)** used to say that something is so old or damaged that it cannot be used any more 已經壞了, 不能用了: *It looks as if your stereo's had it.* 你的立體聲唱機好像壞了。**d) have had it with** used to say you do not want to waste any more time on someone or something that has annoyed you 受夠了, 膩煩了 **4 had sb done sth** if someone had done something 如果〔某人〕做了〔某事〕…: *Had we known about the plans for the factory, we would never have bought the house.* 假如我們知道建工廠的計劃, 我們就不會買這座房子了。

have² *v* [T not usually in passive 一般不用被動態]

1 ►HAVE AN APPEARANCE/QUALITY/FEATURE 具有某種外表/特性/特徵◄ [not in progressive 不用進行式] also 又作 **have got** *especially BrE*【尤英】used when saying what someone or something looks like, what qualities or features they possess etc 具有〔某種外表、特性或特徵〕: *She has dark hair and brown eyes.* 她有一頭深色髮和一雙棕色眼睛。| *I think the idea does have some good points.* 我認為這個主意的確有一些可取之處。| *You need to have a lot of patience to be a teacher.* 當教師必須有很大的耐性。

2 ►INCLUDE/CONTAIN 包括/包含◄ [not in progressive 不用進行式] also 又作 **have got** *especially BrE*【尤英】to include or contain something or a particular number of things or people 包括, 包含, 有: *Japan has a population of over 120 million.* 日本有超過1.2億的人口。| *Our old apartment had a huge kitchen.* 我們過去住的公寓有一個大廚房。| *How many pages has it got?* 它一共有多少頁?

3 ►OWN/BE ABLE TO USE 擁有/具有◄ [not in progressive 不用進行式] also 又作 **have got** *spoken BrE*【英口】**a)** to own something or have been given it to use 有, 擁有: *They used to have a Mercedes Benz.* 他們

曾經擁有一輛平治汽車。| *Has she got a fax machine?* 她有傳真機嗎? | *Have you ever had your own business?* 你自己開過店嗎? **b)** to own a pet or animal 養〔寵物〕: *He's a lovely dog – How long have you had him?* 這隻狗真可愛, 你養了多久了?

4 ▶DO STH 做某事◀ *BrE* a word meaning to do something, used in certain phrases【英】用在某些詞組中表示做某事: **have a look/walk/sleep/talk/think etc** *Do you mind if I have a look at what's on television?* 我看一看電視上播放甚麼節目你不介意吧? | **have a holiday/bath/shower etc** *It's about time she had a holiday.* 她該去度個假了。

5 ▶EAT/DRINK/SMOKE 吃/喝/抽煙◀ to eat, drink, or smoke 吃; 喝; 抽〔煙〕: *She sat down and had another drink.* 她坐下來, 又喝了一杯。| **have lunch/a meal etc** *I usually have breakfast at about 8 o'clock.* 我通常八點左右吃早餐。

6 ▶HAVE AN IDEA/FEELING 有個主意/感覺◀ [not in progressive 不用進行式] also 又作 **have got** *especially BrE*【尤英】to think of an idea or experience a particular feeling 想起〔某個主意〕; 感到: *If you have any good ideas for presents, let me know.* 如果你想到送甚麼禮物的好主意, 就告訴我。| *I have lots of happy memories of my time in Japan.* 在日本的那段日子給我留下了許多美好的回憶。| **have a shock/surprise etc** *When the waiter brought the bill they had a nasty shock.* 服務員拿來賬單時, 他們大吃一驚。

7 ▶HAVE A DISEASE/INJURY/PAIN 生病/受傷/疼痛◀ [not in progressive 不用進行式] also 又作 **have got** *especially BrE*【尤英】to suffer from a disease, injury, or pain 生病; 受傷; 疼痛: *Sarah's got a cold.* 莎拉患了感冒。| *The doctor said he had a broken leg.* 醫生說他的一條腿斷了。

8 ▶EXPERIENCE STH 經歷某事◀ to experience something or be affected by something 經歷, 遇到: **have problems/difficulties/troubles etc** *We've been having a lot of difficulties with our new computer system.* 我們在新電腦系統上遇到了很多困難。| **have an accident/crash** *I'm afraid your son has had a serious accident.* 恐怕你兒子遇到了嚴重的意外事故。| **have a good/terrible etc time** *Thanks for everything – we had a great time.* 謝謝你 —— 我們玩得很開心。

9 have sth stolen/broken/taken etc if you have something stolen, broken etc, someone steals it etc 某物被盜/打破/拿走等: *She had all her jewellery stolen.* 她所有的首飾都被偷了。

10 have your hair cut/your car repaired/your house painted etc to pay a professional person to cut your hair etc for you 請人理髮/修車/粉刷房子等: *Where do you normally have your hair done?* 你通常在哪裡剪髮? | *We'd only just had a new engine put in.* 我們剛請人換了一台新的引擎。

11 have sth ready/done/finished etc to have made something ready to be used, or have finished doing something 準備好/做好/做完某事等: **[+by]** *I should have the car ready by Monday.* 我會在星期一前將車準備好。

12 have sth going/working/on to make a machine operate 使機器運轉/工作/開動: *She always has the TV going at full blast.* 她總是把電視機的聲音開到最大。

13 ▶KEEP/PUT STH IN A PARTICULAR POSITION 使某物保持/將某物放在某個位置◀ [not in progressive 不用進行式] also 又作 **have got** *especially BrE*【尤英】to keep or have put something in a particular position 保持; 放置: **have sth open/closed/out/in/over etc** *I had my eyes half-closed.* 我半閉着眼睛。| *Janice likes to have the window open at night.* 賈尼絲喜歡在晚上開着窗戶。

14 ▶RECEIVE 收到◀ also 又作 **have got** *especially BrE*【尤英】to receive something 收到, 接到: **have a letter/phone call/message** *I had lots of phone calls.* 我接到很多電話。| **have news/information** *Have you had any news yet from Graham?* 你有沒有得到來自格雷厄姆的消息? | **have help/advice etc** *I expect he had some help from his father.* 我估計他得到了父親的幫助。

15 can/could/may I have used when politely asking someone to give you something 能不能把…給我?: *Can I have the bill please?* 請結賬。| *Could we have our ball back?* 能不能把球還給我們?

16 I'll have/we'll have *spoken* used to ask for what you want especially to eat or drink【口】我/我們想要〔尤指食物或飲料〕: *I'll have one vegetable curry and two chapatis please.* 請來一份咖喱蔬菜和兩塊薄煎餅。

17 have a brother/grandmother etc [not in progressive 不用進行式] also 又作 **have got** *especially BrE*【尤英】if you have a brother, grandmother etc, they are part of your family 有個兄弟/祖母等: *She has an uncle who lives in Wisconsin.* 她有一個叔叔住在威斯康辛州。

18 ▶KNOW SB 認識某人◀ [not in progressive 不用進行式] also 又作 **have got** *especially BrE*【尤英】to know someone because you have a relationship with them, work with them etc 認識〔某人〕: *I have a friend who looks like you.* 我有個朋友長得很像你。

19 have a duty/responsibility etc also 又作 **have got** *especially BrE*【尤英】if you have a particular duty, responsibility etc, it is yours and you must do it 有義務/責任等

20 have a job/position/role etc also 又作 **have got** *especially BrE*【尤英】if you have a particular job, position etc, it is yours and you are the one who does it 有一份工作/一個職位/一項職責等

21 ▶EMPLOY/BE IN CHARGE OF 雇用/負責◀ [not in progressive 不用進行式] to employ or be in charge of a group of workers 雇用, 負責管理〔員工〕: *She had more than 20 servants who took care of her every need.* 她有二十多名傭人照顧她各方面的需要。

22 ▶HAVE AN AMOUNT OF TIME 有時間◀ [not in progressive 不用進行式] also 又作 **have got** *especially BrE*【尤英】if you have a particular amount of time, it is available for you to do something 有〔時間〕: *You have 30 seconds to answer the question.* 你有30秒時間回答這個問題。| *I wish I had more time to talk to you.* 真希望能有時間和你多談一會兒。

23 ▶HAVE GOODS/ROOMS AVAILABLE 有現成的商品/房間◀ [not in progressive 不用進行式] also 又作 **have got** *especially BrE*【尤英】if a shop or a hotel has goods or rooms, they are available to you to buy or use〔商店〕供應〔商品〕;〔旅館〕有〔房間〕: *Do you have any single rooms?* 有單人房間嗎? | *They didn't have any sweaters in my size.* 他們沒有我穿的尺碼的毛衣。

24 ▶HAVE BROUGHT STH WITH YOU 帶有某物◀ [not in progressive 不用進行式] also 又作 **have got** *especially BrE*【尤英】to have brought something with you or keep something near you 帶着, 有: *Have you got your pen?* 你帶筆了嗎? | **have sth with you** *I'm afraid I don't have my address book with me.* 我恐怕忘了帶通訊錄了。| **have sth on you** *How much money do you have on you?* 你身上有多少錢?

25 have sb with you also 又作 **have got** *especially BrE*【尤英】if you have someone with you, they are present with you 和某人在一起: *Luckily I had a friend with me who spoke German.* 幸好當時有個會講德語的朋友和我在一起。

26 ▶HOLD SB 捉住某人◀ **have sb by sth** also 又作 **have got** *especially BrE*【尤英】to hold someone violently by a part of their body 捉住, 緊握: *They had him by the throat.* 他們扼住了他的喉嚨。

27 have visitors/guests if you have visitors or guests, they have to come to your home, office etc 來客人, 有客人: *Sorry, I didn't realize you had visitors.* 對不起, 我不知道你家來客人了。

28 have a meeting/party/concert etc to hold an event such as a meeting 舉辦會議/晚會/音樂會等: *We're having a party on Saturday – you're very welcome to come.* 我們會在週六開舞會, 歡迎你來。

29 have an effect/influence/result etc to cause a particular result 產生效果／影響／結果等: *This could have a disastrous effect on the world economy.* 這可能會對世界經濟產生災難性的影響。
30 have the chance/opportunity/honour etc to do sth/of doing sth to be able to do something 能有機會／很榮幸地做某事: *If you have the chance you should go and see it – it's a really good film.* 有機會你應該去看一下，這部電影真的不錯。| *I had the honour of meeting the Duke of Edinburgh.* 我很榮幸地見到了愛丁堡公爵。
31 have a baby/twins etc if a woman has a baby, it is born from her body 生孩子／雙胞胎等: *Anna insisted on having the baby at home.* 安娜堅持要在家裡生孩子。
32 have an operation/treatment etc to be given an operation, treatment etc for a medical problem 做手術／接受治療等
33 ►MAKE SB DO STH 使某人做某事◄ [not in progressive 不用進行式] **a)** make someone start doing something 使〔某人〕做某事: **have sb laughing/crying etc** *Within minutes he had the whole audience laughing and clapping.* 短短幾分鐘內他就使全體觀眾發出陣陣笑聲和掌聲。**b)** to persuade or order someone to do something 勸說[命令]〔某人〕做某事: **have sb doing sth** *She had me doing all kinds of jobs for her.* 她指使我替她做各種各樣的工作。| **have sb do sth** *AmE*【美】*I'll have Hudson show you to your room.* 我會讓赫德森帶你去看你的房間。
34 ►SEX 性◄ [not in progressive 不用進行式] *informal* to have sex with someone【非正式】有〔性關係〕: *I expect she's had lots of men.* 我想她有不少男人。
35 ►NOT ALLOW 不允許◄ **I won't have/we can't have** *spoken* used to say that you do not want or you refuse to allow something to happen【口】我／我們不允許[願意]: *I won't have you walking home on your own – let me call you a taxi.* 我不會讓你自己走回家的 —— 讓我給你叫輛計程車吧！
36 have it coming also 又作 **have got it coming** *spoken* used to say that you are not sorry that something bad has happened to someone, because they deserve it【口】...是應得的; 活該: *I'm not surprised his wife left him – he's had it coming for years.* 他老婆離開他，我絲毫不覺得奇怪 —— 他早就該落到這種下場。
37 I've got it *spoken* used to say you have suddenly thought of the solution to a problem or understand【口】我知道了; 我想出來了
38 you have me there also 又作 **you've got me there** *spoken* used to say that you do not know the answer to a question【口】你把我問住了，我被難倒了
39 I'll have you know *spoken* used to start to tell someone something when you are annoyed with them【口】你給我聽着〔表示不耐煩〕
40 have sb doing sth *especially in questions or negatives* to allow someone to do something or agree that they should do it 允許[同意]某人做某事〔多用於問句或否定式〕: *I wouldn't have you walking home all by yourself.* 我不會讓你獨個兒走回家的。
41 have done with to finish or settle an argument or a difficult situation 結束〔某事〕，了結〔某事〕: *Let's get this sorted out and have done with it.* 我們把這事弄清楚並了結掉吧！
42 have it (that) a) to say that something is true 說，表示: **rumour has it** (=a lot of people are saying) 謠傳 *Rumour has it he's going out with Michele.* 謠傳他和米歇爾在交往。**b)** to be told that something is true 得知，獲悉: **have it on good authority** (=to have been told by someone you can trust) 從可靠渠道得知
43 have it in for *spoken* to want to harm someone【口】圖謀傷害〔某人〕，有意同〔某人〕過不去: *Dean thinks his teachers have it in for him.* 迪安認為他的老師有意和他過不去。
44 have (got) it in you to have a particular quality, skill, or ability 有本事; 有兩下子: *You should have seen the way Dad was dancing – I didn't know he had it in him!* 可惜你沒有看到爸爸的舞姿 —— 我真沒想到他還有這個本事！
45 have (got) something against sb to dislike someone for something they have done 因某事而不喜歡某人: *I don't know what she's got against me.* 我不知道她為甚麼不喜歡我。
46 have (got) nothing against sb *especially spoken* used to say that you do not dislike the person you are talking about【尤口】對某人沒有不好的看法: *I've got nothing against Gary, but I wish he'd show a little more initiative.* 我對加里沒有甚麼看法，但我希望他今後能表現得更主動一些。
47 be not having any (of that) *spoken* to refuse to agree to something, listen to someone etc【口】不同意; 不接受: *I tried to explain to her, but she just wasn't having any.* 我試着向她解釋，但她根本不聽。
48 you've been had *spoken* used to say that someone has been deceived, for example, by being tricked into paying too much money【口】你上當了!: *You paid £200? You've been had!* 你付了 200 英鎊？你上當了！
49 have sth/sb (all) to yourself to be the only person or people in a place, using something, talking to someone else etc 獨自，單獨: *He couldn't wait to have Beth all to himself.* 他巴不得馬上就和貝思單獨在一起。

have sb/sth in also 又作 **have got sb/sth in** *BrE*【英】*phr v* [T] **a)** to have someone in your home in order to do building work etc 雇用某人到家裡幹活: *She won't go to work while she's got the builders in.* 家裡有建築工人在幹活時，她就不去上班。**b)** to have something in your home that you can use, eat etc 家裡有某樣東西

have it off *phr v* [I+with] *BrE slang* to have sex with someone【英俚】與...發生性關係

have on also 又作 **have got on** *especially BrE*【尤英】[T] **1** [**have** sth **on**] to be wearing a piece of clothing or type of clothing 穿着，戴着: *She had on lime-green slacks and a purple nylon shirt.* 她穿着一條酸橙色的便褲和一件紫色的尼龍襯衫。| **have nothing on** (=have no clothes on) 沒穿衣服，光着身子 *Jimmy had nothing on except his socks.* 吉米身上除了襪子外甚麼也沒穿。**2 have the TV/radio/washing machine etc on** to have your television, radio etc switched on and working 開着電視機／收音機／洗衣機等: *Billie has his walkman on all day long.* 比利整天都開着他的隨身聽。**3 be having sb on** *especially BrE* to make someone believe something that is not true, especially as a joke【尤英】〔開玩笑地〕騙人: *He told you he's a Managing Director? He's having you on!* 他告訴你他是個總經理？他在捉弄你呢！**4** [**have** sth **on**] to have arranged to do something, go somewhere etc, especially when this means you cannot do something else〔日程上〕已安排好做某事: *Sorry, I can't do any overtime this weekend – I've got too much on already.* 抱歉，我這個週末不能加班，我已經安排好有很多事要做了。**5** [**have** sth **on** sb] to know about something bad that someone has done 掌握對〔某人〕不利的證據: *What do the police have on him?* 警方掌握了他甚麼證據？**6** [**have nothing on sb/sth**] to not be nearly as good as someone or something else 比不上，不如: *Supermarket vodkas are fine, but they have nothing on brands like Stolichnaya.* 超級市場裡出售的各種伏特加不錯，但都比不上〔俄羅斯的〕斯托利恰耶酒這樣的名牌伏特加。

have sth out *phr v* [T] **1** [**have** sth **out**] **have a tooth/your tonsils etc out** to have a tooth etc removed by a medical operation 拔牙／割除扁桃腺等 **2 have it out with sb** *informal* to settle a disagreement or difficult situation by talking to the person involved, especially when you are angry with them【非正式】與某人把某事說清楚以解決糾紛[困局]〔尤指對他憤怒時〕

have sb up *phr v* [T] *BrE informal* to take someone to court, especially to prove they are guilty of a crime【英，非正式】〔法庭〕傳訊某人; 控告某人: *Last year he was* *had up for drunken driving.* 他去年曾被控酒後駕駛。

[1] **have³** *v* [**have to do sth** also 又作 **have got to do sth** *especially BrE* 尤英] **1** if you have to do something, you must do it because your situation forces you to do it, because you have arranged to do it, or because someone makes you do it 必須, 不得不: *In the end she had to go into a mental hospital.* 最後她不得不進了一家精神病醫院。| *I hate having to get up early in the morning.* 我討厭一早就得起牀。| *We had to do Latin every day.* 我們每天都要學拉丁語。**2** used when saying that it is important that something happens, or that something must happen if something else is to happen 必須, 一定; 只有…才…: *There has to be an end to the violence.* 必須阻止暴力活動。| *You have to believe me!* 你一定要相信我! | *There will have to be a complete ceasefire before the Government will agree to talks.* 只有完全停火後, 政府才會同意談判。**3** used when telling someone how to do something 要, 應該: *First of all you have to mix the flour and the butter.* 首先要將麵粉和黃油拌在一起。**4** used when saying that you are sure that something will happen, or you are sure that something is true 肯定, 必定: *The price of houses has to go up sooner or later.* 房價肯定遲早會上漲。| *None of the others could have done the murder, so it had to be the husband.* 其他人都不可能是殺人犯, 那肯定是她丈夫幹的。**5** *spoken* used when talking about an annoying event which caused you problems【口】不巧〔抱怨某事帶來麻煩〕: *Of course it had to happen on a Sunday, when all the dentists are shut.* 這事偏偏發生在星期天, 所有的牙科診所當時都關門了。**6** *spoken* used when talking about something annoying or surprising that someone does【口】只會, 只能〔對某人所做的事表示不悅或驚奇〕: *She has to go to Marks and Spencers – nowhere else is good enough for her.* 她只會去馬莎百貨買東西, 別處她都看不上。| **do you have to do sth?** (=used to ask someone to stop doing something that annoys you) 你非得要這樣做嗎? *Lieutenant, do you have to keep repeating everything I've just said?* 中尉, 你非得重複我剛剛講過的一切嗎? **7 I have to say/admit/confess** *spoken* used when speaking honestly about something awkward or embarrassing【口】我不得不說/承認/坦白: *I have to say I don't know the first thing about computers.* 老實說, 我對電腦一竅不通。—see also 另見 MUST[1]

ha·ven /ˈhevən; ˈheɪvən/ *n* [C] a place where people go to be safe 安全地; 避難所: *The border region was a natural haven for fugitives.* 邊境地區曾是逃犯們的天然避難所。

have-nots /ˌ· ˈ·/ *n* **the have-nots** the poor people in a country or society 窮人 —see also 另見 HAVES

have·n't /ˈhævn̩t; ˈhævənt/ the short form of 縮略式= have not

hav·er·sack /ˈhævɚˌsæk; ˈhævəsæk/ *n* [C] *BrE old-fashioned* a bag that you carry on your back【英, 過時】背包

haves /hævz; hævz/ *n* **the haves** the rich people in a country or society 有錢人: *the widening gap between the haves and the have-nots* 不斷擴大的貧富差距 —see also 另見 HAVE-NOTS

hav·oc /ˈhævək; ˈhævək/ *n* [U] a situation in which there is a lot of confusion or damage 浩劫, 大破壞: **cause/create havoc** *The Wall Street Crash created havoc and ruin.* 華爾街股市暴跌造成了嚴重的破壞。| **wreak havoc (on)/play havoc with** (=to cause great harm by causing a confusing situation) 對…造成破壞

haw /hɔ; hɔː/ *v* —see 見 **hum and haw** (HUM[1] (4))

hawk¹ /hɔk; hɔːk/ *n* [C] **1** a large bird that hunts and eats small birds and animals 鷹 **2** a politician who believes in using military force 鷹派人物, 主戰派人物: *Meese and other hawks in the Reaganite administration* 列根政府中米斯等主戰派人物 —opposite 反義詞 DOVE[1] (2) **3 watch sb like a hawk** to watch someone very carefully 仔細打量某人, 嚴密監視某人 **4 have eyes like a hawk** to be quick to notice things, especially small details 目光銳利; 具有鷹一般敏銳的眼力

hawk² *v* **1** [T] to try to sell goods by carrying them around〔到處〕叫賣, 兜售 **2** [I] to cough up PHLEGM 咳出〔痰〕

hawk·er /ˈhɔkɚ; ˈhɔːkə/ *n* [C] someone who carries goods from place to place and tries to sell them〔到處〕兜售商品的人, 小販

hawk-eyed /ˈ· ·/ *adj* quick to notice small details 目光敏銳的, 善於觀察的: *hawk-eyed customs officers* 有敏銳觀察力的海關官員

hawk·ish /ˈhɔkɪʃ; ˈhɔːkɪʃ/ *adj* supporting the use of military force 鷹派的, 主戰的 —**hawkishness** *n* [U]

haw·ser /ˈhɔzɚ; ˈhɔːzə/ *n* [C] a thick rope or steel CABLE[1] (2) used on a ship 纜索; 鋼纜

haw·thorn /ˈhɔˌθɔrn; ˈhɔːθɔːn/ *n* [C,U] a small tree that has small white flowers and red berries 山楂 (樹)

hay /he; heɪ/ *n* [U] **1** long grass that has been cut and dried, often used as food for cattle〔作牲畜飼料用的〕乾草, 飼草 **2 hit the hay** *slang* to go to bed【俚】上牀睡覺 **3 make hay while the sun shines** do something while the conditions are favourable 曬草要趁太陽好; 抓緊時機 —see also 另見 **a roll in the hay** (ROLL[2] (10))

hay·cock /ˈhekɑk; ˈheɪkɒk/ *n* [C] a small round pile of hay left in a field to dry〔田地裡的〕小乾草堆

hay fe·ver /ˈ· ˌ··/ *n* [U] a medical condition, like a bad cold (COLD[2] (2)), that is caused by POLLEN (=dust from plants) 枯草熱, 花粉病

hay·loft /ˈheˌlɔft; ˈheɪlɒft/ *n* [C] the top part of a farm building where hay is stored〔穀倉裡〕貯放乾草的頂閣

hay·mak·ing /ˈheˌmekɪŋ; ˈheɪˌmeɪkɪŋ/ *n* [U] the process of cutting and drying hay 製備乾草〔指收割和晾曬〕

hay·rick /ˈherɪk; ˈheɪrɪk/ *n* [C] a haystack 乾草堆

hay·ride /ˈheraɪd; ˈheɪraɪd/ *n* [C] *AmE* an organized ride in a CART filled with hay, usually as part of a social event for young people【美】乘坐裝滿乾草的大車出遊

hay·stack /ˈheˌstæk; ˈheɪstæk/ *n* [C] a large firmly built pile of hay 乾草堆 —see also 另見 **like looking for a needle in a haystack** (NEEDLE[1] (6))

hay·wire /ˈheˌwaɪr; ˈheɪwaɪə/ *adj* **go haywire** *informal* to start working in completely the wrong way【非正式】亂七八糟的, 出差錯的: *The computer went haywire and started printing numbers at random.* 這台電腦出毛病了, 開始胡亂地打印數字。

haz·ard¹ /ˈhæzɚd; ˈhæzəd/ *n* [C] **1** something that may be dangerous, cause accidents etc 危險; 隱患; 會造成危害的事物: *Ice on the road is a major hazard at this time of the year.* 每年的這個時候路上的冰都是個大問題。| **be a hazard to** *Polluted water sources are a hazard to wildlife.* 受污染的水源對野生生物造成危害。| **fire hazard** (=something that may cause a fire) 火災隱患 | **health hazard** (=something that is likely to harm your health) 危害健康的因素 **2** a risk that cannot be avoided〔不可避免的〕風險: **hazard of doing sth** *the economic hazards of running a small farm* 經營小農場的經濟風險 | **occupational hazard** (=a danger that always exists in a job) 職業風險 *Divorce seems to be an occupational hazard for politicians.* 離婚好像是政客們的一種職業風險。

hazard² *v* [T] **1** to say something that is only a suggestion or guess and so might not be correct 斗膽提出; 大膽猜測: **hazard a guess** *Would you like to hazard a guess as to how much he earns?* 你想不想猜猜他掙多少錢? **2** *formal* to risk losing your money, property etc in an attempt to gain something【正式】冒…的風險

hazard light /ˈ·· ·/ *n* [C usually plural 一般用複數] a special light on a vehicle that flashes to warn other drivers of danger〔汽車上的〕危險警告燈

haz·ard·ous /ˈhæzɚdəs; ˈhæzədəs/ *adj* **1 hazardous chemicals/waste/substances etc** *technical* chemicals etc that are dangerous and likely to harm people's health【術語】有害化學物/廢料/材料等 **2 hazardous journey/operation/undertaking etc** a journey etc that involves danger 危險的旅程/手術/任務等

haze¹ /hez; heɪz/ *n* [singular,U] **1** smoke, dust, or MOISTURE in the air which makes it difficult to see through 煙

霧, 靄: [+of] *a haze of cigarette smoke* 香煙的煙霧 | **heat haze** (=a haze that forms in hot weather) 熱氣 **2** the feeling of being very confused and unable to think clearly 懵懂, 迷糊, 迷惑

haze² *v* [T] *AmE* to play tricks on a new college student as part of the ceremony of joining a club【美】戲弄大學新生〔作為入會儀式的一部分〕

haze over *phr v* [I] to become HAZY (1) 起霧: *The sky hazed over.* 天空生起霧靄。

ha·zel¹ /ˈhezḷ; ˈheɪzəl/ *n* [C,U] a small tree that produces nuts 榛樹

hazel² *adj* light brown 淡褐色的: *hazel eyes* 淡褐色的眼睛 —**hazel** *n* [U] —see picture on page A6 參見 A6 頁圖

ha·zel·nut /ˈhezḷˌnʌt; ˈheɪzəlnʌt/ *n* [C] the nut of the HAZEL¹ tree 榛子, 榛實

haz·y /ˈhezɪ; ˈheɪzi/ *adj* **1** not clear because of a slight mist that is caused by heat, smoke etc 霧濛濛的, 朦朧的: *The tower looked dim in the hazy English air.* 塔在英國霧濛濛的空中顯得隱隱約約的。**2** an idea, memory etc that is hazy is not clear or exact〔印象、記憶等〕模糊的, 不清楚的: *My memories of the holiday are rather hazy.* 我對假期的記憶十分模糊。**3 be hazy about** to not know or understand very much about something〔對某事〕不明確, 不了解: *Most people are pretty hazy about Clinton's economic program.* 多數人對克林頓的經濟計劃都不甚了解。—**hazily** *adv* —**haziness** *n* [U]

H-bomb /ˈetʃˌbɑm; ˈeɪtʃ bɒm/ *n* [C] a powerful NUCLEAR bomb 氫彈

HCF /ˌetʃ si ˈɛf; ˌeɪtʃ siː ˈef/ the abbreviation of 縮寫= HIGHEST COMMON FACTOR

H.E. the abbreviation of 縮寫= His Excellency or Her Excellency, used in the title of an AMBASSADOR 閣下〔用於稱呼大使〕

[S1] [W1] **he** /hi; hiː/ *pron* [used as subject of a verb 用作動詞的主詞] **1** used to talk about a male person or animal that has already been mentioned or is already known about 他; 牠〔雄性動物〕: *"Where's Paul?" "He's gone to the cinema."* "保羅在哪兒?" "他去看電影了。" | *Be careful of that dog. He sometimes bites.* 當心那條狗。牠有時咬人。**2** used to talk about anyone, everyone, or an unknown person who may be either male or female 人, 他〔泛指男性或女性〕: *Everyone should do what he considers best.* 每個人做事都應按照自己認為最好的去做。**3 He** used when writing about God〔用於書面語〕上帝

> **USAGE NOTE 用法說明: HE**
> POLITENESS 禮貌程度
> Some people, especially women, do not like the use of **he** to include both men and women in a sentence like 有些人, 特別是女性, 不喜歡使用不分性別的 he 來表示人, 如下句: *Everyone should do what he thinks best.* 每個人都應按照自己認為最好的方法去做事。Instead they use **he or she, she or he,** or **they** 他們常使用 he or she, she or he 或 they 來代替: *Everyone should do what they think best.*
> In writing **he/she** is often used, or simply **s/he**. Often you can write what you want to say in a different way in order to avoid the problem. 在書面表達中經常使用 he/she, 或者是 s/he。人們經常還用其他表達方法來避免出現這個問題。For example say 例如: *People should all do what they think best.* 人們都應該按照自己認為最好的方法去做事。

he- /hi; hiː/ *prefix* a male animal〔動物〕雄(性的): *a he-goat* 一隻雄山羊

-head /hɛd; hed/ *suffix* [in nouns 構成名詞] **1** the top of something 頂部, 上端, 口: *a pithead* (=the top of a coalmine) 礦井口 **2** the place where something begins; SOURCE¹ (1) 源頭; 源泉: *a fountainhead* 泉源

[S1] [W1] **head¹** /hɛd; hed/ *n*

① TOP OF BODY 頭部
② MIND 頭腦, 腦子
③ UNDERSTAND 理解
④ TOP PERSON 首要人物
⑤ TOP/FRONT/MOST IMPORTANT PART 上端/前端/最重要部分
⑥ CALM 冷靜的
⑦ CRAZY 發瘋的
⑧ INTELLIGENT/SENSIBLE 聰明的/明智的
⑨ TOO PROUD 過分自滿
⑩ ALCOHOL/DRUGS 酒/毒品
⑪ FOR EACH PERSON 每人
⑫ OTHER MEANINGS 其他意思

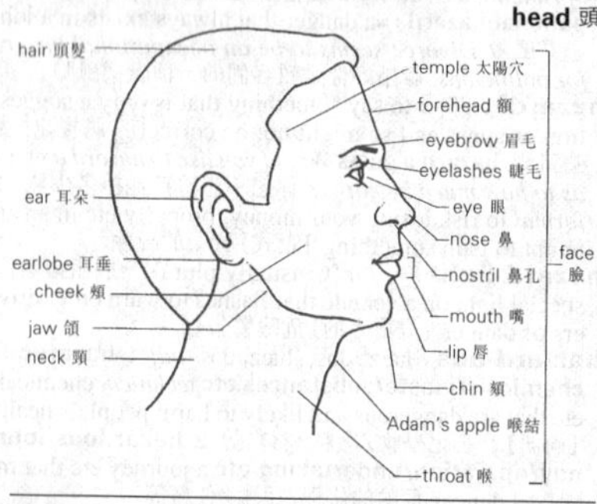

① **TOP OF BODY 頭部**

1 [C] the top part of your body which has your eyes, mouth, brain etc in it 頭, 頭部: *My head aches.* 我頭痛。| *He turned his head and looked at me.* 他轉過頭來看着我。| *severe head injuries* 嚴重的頭部損傷

2 from head to foot/toe over your whole body 從頭到腳, 全身上下: *He was shaking from head to foot.* 他全身上下都在發抖。| *dressed in black from head to toe* 從頭到腳一身黑色衣服

3 a bad/sore head *informal* a pain in your head【非正式】頭痛: *I woke up with a bad head the next morning.* 第二天早上醒來時, 我覺得頭痛。

4 have a good/fine head of hair to have a lot of hair on your head 長有一頭濃密的頭髮

② **MIND 頭腦, 腦子**

5 [C] your mind 頭腦, 腦子: *My head was full of strange thoughts.* 我腦子裡全是些奇怪的想法。| **in/inside sb's head** *All the details are in my head.* 所有的細節都記在我腦子裡。| **do sth in your head** (=calculate something in your mind) 在腦子裡計算 *I can do the figures in my head.* 我可以心算這些數字。

6 sth never entered sb's head used to say that you

never thought of something 從未想過: *"Do you think she's crazy?" "The thought never entered my head!"* "你認為她瘋了嗎?" "我從來沒有這樣的想法。"
7 don't bother/trouble your head about it *spoken* used to tell someone not to worry about something【口】別多想了, 別擔心
8 put sth out of your head *spoken* to stop worrying about something【口】不再為某事擔心
9 can't get something out of your head to be unable to stop thinking about something 禁不住地老想着某事
10 put your heads together *informal* to discuss a difficult problem together【非正式】一起想辦法, 共同商量: *We'll have to put our heads together and see if we can come up with some ideas.* 我們得坐下來一起想想, 看看能不能想出甚麼辦法來。
11 have your head in the clouds to spend too much time thinking about things that you would like to do 想入非非; 耽於空想

③ **UNDERSTAND** 理解
12 get your head round *BrE informal* to understand something difficult【英, 非正式】想通, 理解
13 can't make head nor tail of to be completely unable to understand something 弄不清, 不能理解; 被…弄糊塗: *I can't make head nor tail of this letter – does it mean anything to you?* 我給這封信弄糊塗了, 你看得懂嗎?
14 go over your head to be too difficult for you to understand 太高深而使某人無法理解: *The discussions went completely over my head.* 討論的內容太深奧了, 我根本無法聽懂。
15 get sth into your head *informal* to understand and realize something【非正式】理解, 明白: *I wish he'd get it into his head that I don't want to go out.* 我希望他能明白我不想出去。| **get sth into sb's head** (=make someone understand and realize something) 使某人理解, 使某人明白

④ **TOP PERSON** 首要人物
16 [C] the leader or person in charge of a group or organization 首腦, 首長, 領袖, 主管人: **[+of]** *Eileen is head of the family now.* 艾琳現在成了一家之主了。| *the former head of the FBI, J Edgar Hoover* 前聯邦調查局局長J·埃德加·胡佛
17 head waiter/chef/gardener etc the most senior waiter etc 服務員領班/首席廚師/花匠領班等
18 ►OF A SCHOOL 中小學的◄ [C] *BrE informal* the teacher who is in charge of a school【英, 非正式】校長: **head teacher/the head** *We'll have to ask the head for permission.* 我們必須先徵得校長的同意。

⑤ **TOP/FRONT/MOST IMPORTANT PART** 上端/前端/最重要部分
19 the head of the top or front of something, or the most important part of it 上端, 頂部; 前端; 最重要的部分: **at the head of** *Write your name clearly at the head of each page.* 請將你的名字清楚地寫在每頁紙的上方。| **the head of the table** (=the part where the most important people sit) 首席, 上座 *Frank sat proudly at the head of the table.* 弗蘭克得意地坐在上座。
20 [singular] the large or wide end of a long thin object such as a tool〔工具的〕粗的一端: **[+of]** *the head of a hammer* 錘頭
21 ►PLANT 植物◄ [C] the top of a plant where its leaves and flowers grow 頭狀花序; 葉球

⑥ **CALM** 冷靜的
22 keep your head to remain calm in a difficult or dangerous situation 保持頭腦冷靜: *a leader with a steady nerve and the ability to keep her head in a crisis* 一位處事穩妥、能在危機中保持鎮靜的領袖
23 lose your head to become too anxious to think or behave calmly 慌了神, 失去冷靜, 驚惶失措: *When the engine caught fire, I just lost my head.* 發動機起火時, 我都慌了神了。
24 a clear/cool head the ability to think clearly or calmly in a difficult or dangerous situation 冷靜[清醒]的頭腦: *You need to approach this kind of emergency with a cool head.* 你應該用冷靜的頭腦處理這種緊急情況。

⑦ **CRAZY** 發瘋的
25 be out of your head/off your head *BrE spoken* to be crazy【英口】發瘋的, 精神錯亂的
26 not be right in the head *spoken* to be mentally ill or crazy【口】發瘋的, 精神錯亂的
27 need your head examined *spoken* to be crazy【口】發瘋的, 精神錯亂的, 腦子有問題的: *If you ask me, anyone who believes in UFO's needs their head examined!* 照我看, 相信有不明飛行物的人腦子都有問題。

⑧ **INTELLIGENT/SENSIBLE** 聰明的/明智的
28 have your head screwed on (straight) *informal* to be sensible【非正式】明智的, 理智的, 有頭腦
29 have a good head on your shoulders to be sensible or intelligent 明智的; 聰明的
30 use your head to think about something sensibly 認真思考, 動腦筋

⑨ **TOO PROUD** 過分自滿
31 have a bighead also 又作 **have a swollen head** *BrE informal* to think you are much better, more important, more skilful etc than you are【英, 非正式】自負, 驕傲, 自命不凡
32 go to sb's head *informal* if success goes to someone's head, it makes them feel more important than they really are【非正式】使飄飄然, 沖昏頭腦

⑩ **ALCOHOL/DRUGS** 酒/毒品
33 go to sb's head to make someone quickly feel slightly drunk〔酒〕上頭, 使某人微醉: *The wine went straight to my head.* 我很快就感到酒力了。
34 be out of your head *informal* to not know what you are doing because you have taken illegal drugs or drunk too much alcohol【非正式】〔酗酒或吸毒後〕神智混亂的

⑪ **FOR EACH PERSON** 每人
35 a head/per head for each person 每人, 一個人: **$5/£10 etc a head** *The meal worked out at $50 a head.* 這頓飯算下來每人50美元。

⑫ **OTHER MEANINGS** 其他意思
36 ►COIN 硬幣◄ **heads** the side of a coin which has the king's or queen's head on it 正面, 帶人像的一面 — opposite 反義詞 **tails** (TAIL[1] (5a))
37 keep your head above water to only just manage to continue to live on your income or keep your business working in spite of money problems〔靠自己的收入〕勉強度日; 勉強維持經營
38 keep/get your head down to work steadily and quietly 專心工作, 不分心: *He promised he would get his head down and work for his exams.* 他答應會專心學習, 準備應試。
39 laugh/shout/scream your head off *informal* to laugh, shout etc very loudly【非正式】大笑/高喊/尖叫
40 be banging your head against a brick wall to keep trying to do something which seems impossible 枉費心機, 白費氣力, 試圖幹不可能成功的事: *I feel as if I'm banging my head against a brick wall.* 我覺得自己完全是在白費氣力。
41 take it into your head to do sth to suddenly decide to do something that does not seem sensible 突發

H

奇想, 突然打算做某事〔指不明智的事〕: *They suddenly took it into their heads to go off without telling anyone.* 他們突然心血來潮, 沒有告訴任何人就走了。

42 turn/stand sth on its head to consider a statement or idea in the opposite way from the way in which it was intended 倒過來想

43 give sb their head to give someone the freedom to do what they want to do 放任, 聽任某人自由行動

44 go head to head with *AmE* to deal with someone in a very direct and determined way【美】與某人正面交鋒, 與某人硬碰硬

45 come/bring sth to a head if a problem or difficult situation comes to a head, or if something brings it to a head, it suddenly becomes very bad (使)〔事情〕到了緊要關頭; 突然惡化: *The crisis came to a head when the bank refused to accept our cheques.* 銀行拒絕接受我們的支票, 這使得危機被推至極點。

46 go over sb's head to ask a more important person than the one you would normally ask 越過某人: *My boss was angry because I went over his head to the department manager.* 我的上司很生氣, 因為我越過他去找部門經理。

47 be over your head in debt *AmE* to owe so much money that there is no possibility of paying it all back【美】負債纍纍, 欠了一屁股債

48 have a head for figures/facts/business etc to be good at doing calculations, remembering facts etc 擅長計算/記憶/做生意等

49 have no head for heights to be unable to look down from high places without feeling nervous 有畏高症

50 head and shoulders above the rest/others much better at something than everyone else 遠遠勝過其他人

51 head over heels in love loving someone very much 深深地愛着〔某人〕: *Sam was obviously head over heels in love with his new bride.* 山姆顯然深深地愛着他的新娘。

52 heads will roll *spoken* used to say that some people will be punished severely for something that has happened【口】將要受到嚴厲的懲罰

53 on your own head be it *spoken* used to tell someone that they will be blamed if the thing they are planning to do has bad results【口】責任自負, 落到自己頭上

54 heads up! *AmE spoken* used to warn people that something is falling from above【美口】當心!〔警告別人上面有東西掉下〕

55 do your head in *BrE spoken* to make you feel confused and annoyed【英口】使人煩惱, 使人討厭: *The way he keeps changing his mind about things really does my head in.* 他老是改變主意, 真是煩死我了。

56 ▶BEER 啤酒◀ [C] the layer of small white BUBBLES on the top of a glass of beer〔一杯啤酒上面的〕泡沫

57 ▶RECORDING 錄音◀ [C] the part of a TAPE RECORDER that records sound〔錄音機的〕磁頭

58 head of cattle/sheep etc a particular number of cows, sheep etc 牛/羊等的頭數: *a small farm with 20 head of cattle* 養有20頭牛的小農場

59 head of water/steam pressure that is made when water or steam is kept in an enclosed space 水壓/蒸汽壓力

60 ▶LAND 地方◀ a high area of land that sticks into the sea; HEADLAND 海岬, 陸岬: *Beachy Head* 俾赤岬

61 ▶RIVER/STREAM 河/溪◀ the beginning of a river or stream 源頭

62 ▶INFECTION 感染◀ [C] the white centre of a swollen spot on your skin 膿頭 —see also 另見 **bite sb's head off** (BITE[1] (9)), **bury your head in the sand** (BURY (11)), **hold up your head** (HOLD[1] (38)), **nod your head** (NOD[1] (1)), **off the top of your head** (TOP[1] (16)), **shake your head** (SHAKE[1] (4)), **turn sb's head** (TURN[1] (21)), **do sth standing on your head** (STAND[1] (38))

S2 W2 **head²** *v*

1 ▶GO TOWARDS 朝…行進◀ [I] to go or make something go in a particular direction 朝…前進, 向…去: **[+for/towards/across etc]** *The ship was heading for Cuba.* 船正開往古巴。| *It's about time we were heading home.* 我們該動身回家了。| **head north/south etc** *We headed south towards the capital.* 我們朝南向首都進發。| **be headed (for)** *especially AmE*【尤美】*Where are you guys headed?* 你們要去哪兒?

2 ▶BE IN CHARGE 負責◀ also 又作 **head up** [T] to be in charge of a government, organization, or group of people 主管, 領導: *a delegation headed by former President Jimmy Carter* 一個由前總統吉米·卡特領導的代表團

3 be heading for also 又作 **be headed for** *especially AmE*【尤美】if you are heading for a situation, it is likely to happen to you〔注定〕遭受, 碰到, 面臨: *They're heading for disaster.* 他們正面臨災難。

4 ▶BE AT THE TOP 居於首位◀ [T] **a)** to be at the top of a list or group of people or things 居於首位, 名列第一: *The movie heads the list of Oscar nominations.* 這部影片在奧斯卡提名影片中名列首位。**b) be headed** if a page is headed with a particular word or sentence, it has it on the top 題目是, 標題為: *The page was headed 'Expenses'.* 這一頁的標題為"開支"。

5 ▶BE AT THE FRONT 在前列◀ to be at the front of a line of people 位於隊伍之首; 帶領: *a procession headed by the Reverend Martin Luther King* 由馬丁·路德·金牧師帶領的遊行隊伍

6 ▶FOOTBALL 足球◀ [T] to hit the ball with your head, especially in football 用頭頂〔球〕—see picture on page A23 參見A23頁圖

head off *phr v* **1** [T **head** sth ↔ **off**] to prevent something from happening 阻止, 防止…發生: *They've headed off several crises since they took charge.* 自接手以來, 他們已避免了幾次危機。**2** [T **head** sth ↔ **off**] to stop someone moving in a particular direction by moving in front of them〔在前面〕攔截, 攔擋: *Soldiers headed them off at the border.* 士兵在邊境上將他們攔截住了。**3** [I] to leave to go to another place 離開〔某地〕去〔別處〕: *I'm heading off now.* 我現在要走了。

head·ache /ˈhɛd͵ek; ˈhedeɪk/ *n* [C] **1** a pain in your head 頭痛: **splitting headache** (=a very bad headache) 頭痛欲裂 **2** *informal* an annoying or worrying problem【非正式】使人頭痛的事, 棘手的事, 難題: *Censorship was a constant headache for Soviet newspapers.* 對蘇聯的各家報紙來說, 新聞審查是件讓人頭痛的事。—**headachy** *adj*: *a headachy feeling* 頭痛的感覺

head·band /ˈhɛd͵bænd; ˈhedbænd/ *n* [C] **1** a band that you wear around your head to keep your hair off your face〔紮在額頭上的〕束髮帶 **2** a similar band around a horse's head〔紮在馬頭上的〕繫帶; 頭羈 —see picture at 參見 HORSE[1] 圖

head·bang·er /ˈhɛd͵bæŋɚ; ˈhedbæŋə/ *n* [C] **1** *informal* someone who enjoys HEAVY METAL music and moves their head around violently to the beat of the music【非正式】喜歡聽重金屬音樂的人 **2** someone who behaves in a stupid or crazy way 瘋瘋癲癲的人, 瘋子

head·board /͵hɛdˋbɔrd; ˈhedbɔːd/ *n* [C] the upright wooden board at the end of a bed where your head is 牀頭板

head boy /͵· ˈ·/ *n* [C] the boy who is chosen in a British school each year to represent the school〔英國學校裡每年選出的〕男學生代表

head·butt /ˈhɛd͵bʌt; ˈhedbʌt/ *v* [T] to deliberately hit someone in the stomach with your head 以頭撞某人的肚子

head·case /ˈhɛd͵kes; ˈhedkeɪs/ *n* [C] *slang* a crazy person【俚】瘋子

head·cheese /ˈhɛd͵tʃiz; ˈhedtʃiːz/ *n* [U] *AmE* meat from the head of a pig boiled and pressed【美】〔用豬頭肉煮成的〕碎肉凍; BRAWN (2) *BrE*【英】

head count /ˈ· ·/ *n* **do a head count** to count how many people are present 點人數

head·dress /ˈhɛd͵drɛs; ˈhed-dres/ *n* [C] something that someone wears on their head for decoration on a special occasion 頭飾: *a feathered headdress* 插有羽毛的頭飾

head·ed /ˈhɛdɪd; ˈhedɪ̵d/ *adj* **1 two-headed/three-headed etc** having two heads etc 有兩/三個頭的等 **2 headed notepaper** paper for writing letters that has your name and address printed at the top 印有抬頭的信紙 **3 red-headed/grey-headed etc** having red hair etc 紅頭髮/花白頭髮的等

head·er /ˈhɛdɚ; ˈhedə/ *n* [C] **1** a shot in football made by hitting the ball with your head〔足球的〕頭球 **2** the top of a page, especially on a computer〔尤指電腦屏幕上的〕頁首 **3 take a header** to jump or fall into water with your head going in first 頭朝下跳水[掉進水裡]

head-first /͵· ˈ·◂/ *adv* **1** moving forward with the rest of your body following your head 頭朝前地: **fall/plunge head-first** *I fell head-first down the stairs.* 我一頭栽下樓梯。**2** if you rush into something head-first, you start doing it too quickly without thinking carefully 倉促地, 魯莽地

head·gear /ˈhɛd͵gɪr; ˈhedgɪə/ *n* [U] *informal* hats and other things that you wear on your head【非正式】帽, 頭上戴的東西

head girl /͵· ˈ·/ *n* [C] the girl who is chosen in a British school each year to represent the school〔英國學校裡每年選出的〕女學生代表

head-hunt·er /ˈ· ͵··/ *n* [C] **1** someone who finds people with the right skills and experience to do a particular job, and persuades them to leave their present jobs 物色人才者, 獵頭者 **2** a member of a tribe of people who cut off and keep the heads of their enemies 割取敵人首級作為戰利品的部落成員 —**headhunt** *v* [T]

head·ing /ˈhɛdɪŋ; ˈhedɪŋ/ *n* [C] the title written at the top of a piece of writing 標題, 題目

head·lamp /ˈhɛd͵læmp; ˈhedlæmp/ *n* [C usually plural 一般用複數] a HEADLIGHT〔車輛的〕前燈, 車頭燈

head·land /ˈhɛdlənd; ˈhedlənd/ *n* [C] an area of land that sticks out from the coast into the sea 岬, 海岬 —see picture on page A12 參見 A12 頁圖

head·less /ˈhɛdlɪs; ˈhedləs/ *adj* without a head 無頭的: *a headless corpse* 一具無頭屍體

head·light /ˈhɛd͵laɪt; ˈhedlaɪt/ *n* [C usually plural 一般用複數] one of the large lights at the front of a vehicle〔車輛的〕前燈, 車頭燈 —see picture on page A2 參見 A2 頁圖

S3 **head·line¹** /ˈhɛd͵laɪn; ˈhedlaɪn/ *n* [C usually plural 一般用複數] **1** the title of a newspaper report, which is printed in large letters above the report〔報紙的〕標題, 大字標題: *an eye-catching headline* 醒目的標題 **2 the headlines** the important points of the main news stories that are read at the beginning of a news programme〔廣播或電視的〕新聞提要 **3 hit the headlines/make the headlines** to be reported in newspapers or on radio and television 成了報紙上的新聞; 成為電台或電視報道的新聞: *Computer crime first hit the headlines in 1983.* 電腦罪案在 1983 年首次成為媒體報道的新聞。

headline² *v* [T] **1** [usually passive 一般用被動態] to give a headline to an article or story 給…加標題 **2** *AmE* to appear as the main performer in a show【美】扮演主角, 成為…的主要表演者: *Frank Sinatra headlines this month's production.* 本月推出的影片由法蘭仙納杜拉主演。

head·lock /ˈhɛd͵lɑk; ˈhedlɒk/ *n* [C] a way of holding someone around their neck so that they cannot move〔摔跤中的〕夾頭

head·long /ˈhɛd͵lɔŋ; ˈhedlɒŋ/ *adv* **1** if you rush headlong into something, you start doing it too quickly without thinking carefully 輕率地, 倉促地: **rush headlong into** *Martin just isn't the type to rush headlong into marriage.* 馬丁根本不是會輕率地結婚的人。**2** falling with your head first and the rest of your body following 頭朝下地, 頭在前地 **3** running very quickly without looking where you are going〔奔跑時〕倉皇地, 慌不擇路地: *He fled headlong down a narrow passageway.* 他沿着一條窄路倉皇地逃跑。—**headlong** *adj*: *a headlong dash for the frontier* 向邊境倉皇奔逃

head·man /ˈhɛdmən; ˈhedmən/ *n plural* **headmen** /-mən; -mən/ [C] a chief of a village where a tribe lives 部落的首領, 酋長

head·mas·ter /ˈhɛd͵mæstɚ; ͵hedˈmɑːstə/ *n* [C] *BrE* a male teacher who is in charge of a school【英】〔中小學的〕男校長

head·mis·tress /ˈhɛd͵mɪstrɪs; ͵hedˈmɪstrɪ̵s/ *n* [C] *BrE* a female teacher who is in charge of a school【英】〔中小學的〕女校長

head of·fice /͵· ˈ··/ *n* **1** [C] the main office of a company〔公司的〕總部, 總行 **2** [singular] the managers who work there 總部管理人員

head of state /͵· · ˈ·/ *n* [C] the main representative of a country, such as a queen, king, or president 國家元首

head-on /͵· ˈ·◂/ *adv* **1 meet/crash etc head-on** if two vehicles meet head-on, the front part of one vehicle hits the front part of the other〔車輛〕正面相撞: *Their car collided head-on with a van.* 他們的汽車與一輛小貨車迎頭相撞。**2** if someone deals with a problem head-on, they deal with it in a direct and determined way 面對面地, 毫不迴避地: *It would be best to tackle the situation head-on.* 最好的辦法是正面地解決問題。—**head-on** *adj*: *a head-on collision* 迎面相撞

head·phones /ˈhɛd͵fonz; ˈhedfəʊnz/ *n* [plural] a piece of equipment that you wear over your ears to listen to a radio or recording 耳機, 耳筒

head·piece /ˈhɛd͵pis; ˈhedpiːs/ *n* [C] **1** something you wear on your head for protection 頭盔; 帽子 **2** a decorated title at the top of a page or piece of writing〔頁首或文章開頭的〕花飾圖案

head·quar·tered /ˈhɛd͵kwɔrtɚd; ˈhed͵kwɔːtəd/ *adj* having your headquarters at a particular place 總部設在…的: *Many top companies are headquartered here.* 很多大公司都把總部設在這裡。—**headquarter** *v* [T]

head·quar·ters /ˈhɛd͵kwɔrtɚz; ˈhed͵kwɔːtəz/ *n plural* **headquarters** [C] **1** the main building or offices used by a large organization 總部, 總公司, 總辦事處 **2** *abbreviation* 縮寫為 **HQ** the place from which military operations are controlled〔軍隊的〕司令部, 指揮部, 大本營 W3

head·rest /ˈhɛd͵rɛst; ˈhed-rest/ *n* [C] the top part of a chair or of the front seat in a car that supports the back of your head〔汽車座椅上的〕頭靠, 頭墊 —see picture on page A2 參見 A2 頁圖

head·room /ˈhɛd͵rum; ˈhed-rʊm/ *n* [U] **1** the amount of space above your head, especially when you are in a car〔車輛中乘客頭頂以上的〕頭頂空間 **2** the amount of space above a vehicle when it is under a bridge〔車頂與橋底之間的〕淨空(高度)

head·scarf /ˈhɛdskɑrf; ˈhedskɑːf/ *n* [C] a square piece of cloth that women wear on their heads, tied under their chin (包)頭巾 —see picture at 參見 SCARF¹ 圖

head·set /ˈhɛd͵sɛt; ˈhedset/ *n* [C] a set of HEADPHONES 耳機, 頭戴式受話器

head·ship /ˈhɛdʃɪp; ˈhedʃɪp/ *n* [C] **1** a position of being in charge of an organization 領導地位[職務] **2** *BrE* the job of being in charge of a school【英】〔中小學的〕校長職務

head·shrink·er /ˈhɛd͵ʃrɪŋkɚ; ˈhed͵ʃrɪŋkə/ *n* [C] *informal* a PSYCHIATRIST or PSYCHOANALYST【非正式】精神科醫生; 精神分析專家

head·square /ˈhɛd͵skwɛr; ˈhedskweə/ *n* [C] a HEADSCARF (包)頭巾

head·stand /ˈhɛdstænd; ˈhedstænd/ *n* [C] a position in which you turn your body upside down, with your head and hands on the floor and your legs and feet in the air 倒立

head start /ˈ· ·/ *n* [C] **1** an advantage that helps you to be successful 先起步的優勢; 有利開端; 佔先: *Give your children a head start by sending them to nursery school.* 送你的孩子上幼兒園, 讓他們在學習上有個好的開端。**2** a start in a race in which you begin earlier or further ahead than someone else〔賽跑中〕先起動, 搶先

head·stone /ˈhɛdˌston; ˈhedstəʊn/ *n* [C] a piece of stone on a grave on which the dead person's name is written; GRAVESTONE, TOMBSTONE 墓碑, 墓頭石

head·strong /ˈhɛdˌstrɔŋ; ˈhedstrɒŋ/ *adj* very determined to do what you want, even when other people advise you not to do it 任性的, 固執的: *an impulsive headstrong child* 一個又衝動又固執的孩子

head ta·ble /ˌ· ˈ··/ *n* [C] *AmE* a table at a formal meal where the most important people or those giving speeches sit【美】主桌〔正式宴會上最重要的客人或要發表講話的人所坐的桌子〕; TOP TABLE *BrE*【英】

head teach·er /ˌ· ˈ··/ *n* [C] *BrE* the teacher who is in charge of a school【英】〔中小學的〕校長; PRINCIPAL² (2) *AmE*【美】

head wait·er /ˌ· ˈ··/ *n* [C] the WAITER who is in charge of the other waiters in a restaurant〔餐館的〕服務員領班 —see picture on page A15 參見 A15 頁圖

head·wa·ters /ˈhɛdˌwɔtɚz; ˈhedwɔːtəz/ *n* [plural] the part where a stream starts before it flows into a river 河源, 上游源頭

head·way /ˈhɛdˌwe; ˈhedweɪ/ *n* **make headway a)** to make progress towards achieving something in spite of difficulties 取得進展: **[+towards/in/with etc]** *They had made no headway towards finding a solution.* 他們尚未就解決這個問題取得任何進展。**b)** to move forwards 向前行進

head·wind /ˈhɛdˌwɪnd; ˈhedˌwɪnd/ *n* [C,U] a wind that blows directly towards you when you are moving 逆風, 頂頭風

head·word /ˈhɛdˌwɝd; ˈhedwɜːd/ *n* [C] one of the words whose meaning is explained in a dictionary〔詞典中的〕詞目

head·y /ˈhɛdɪ; ˈhedi/ *adj* [usually before noun 一般用於名詞前] **1** a heady smell, drink etc is pleasantly strong and seems to affect your senses〔氣味、飲料等〕令人陶醉的: *a heady aroma* 醉人的香味 | *a heady combination of wine and brandy* 令人陶醉的葡萄酒和白蘭地混合酒 **2** very exciting in a way that makes you feel as if you can do anything you want to 使人飄飄然的, 使人興奮的: *the heady atmosphere of the early sixties* 六十年代初期的狂熱氣氛

heal /hil; hiːl/ *v* **1** [I] also 又作 **heal up** if a wound or a broken bone heals, the flesh, skin, bone etc grows back together and becomes healthy again〔傷口或折斷的骨〕長好, 癒合: *It took three months for my arm to heal properly.* 我的胳膊過了三個月時間才完全長好。**2** [T] to cure someone who is ill or make a wound heal 醫治; 治癒 **3 heal the wounds/breach/divisions** to make people stop being angry with each other 治癒創傷/彌補裂痕/消除分歧 —see also 另見 FAITH HEALING

heal over *phr v* [I] **1** if a wound or an area of broken skin heals over, new skin grows over it and it becomes healthy again〔傷口或破損的皮膚〕癒合, 痊癒 **2** [I,T] if an argument heals over or is healed over, it is forgotten 忘掉過去的爭吵, 重新和好

heal·er /ˈhilɚ; ˈhiːlə/ *n* [C] someone who is believed to have the natural ability to cure people 醫治者

S1 W1 **health** /hɛlθ; helθ/ *n* [U] **1** your physical condition and how healthy you are 健康 (狀況): *Betty's anxious about her husband's health.* 貝蒂十分擔心她丈夫的健康狀況。| *Smoking can seriously damage your health.* 吸煙會嚴重損害你的健康。| **be in good/excellent/poor health** (=be generally healthy or unhealthy) 身體好/非常好/不好 | **be good/bad for your health** *A low-fat diet is better for your health.* 低脂肪的飲食更有利於你的健康。**2** the state of being healthy (身體) 健康: *Even if you haven't got much money, at least you've got your health.* 即使你沒有太多錢, 但起碼你擁有健康。| **sb is a picture of health** (=used to say that someone looks very healthy) 某人看起來很健康 **3** the work of providing medical services to keep people healthy 醫療保健 (工作): *The government has promised to spend more on health and education.* 政府已經承諾增加醫療保健和教育經費。**4** how successful an economy or organization is〔經濟〕運行狀況;〔機構〕運轉狀況: *The monthly trade figures are seen as an indicator of the health of the economy.* 每月的貿易數字被視為說明經濟情況的指標。**5 drink (to) sb's health** to say that you wish someone will be healthy and happy, and then have a drink of alcohol 為某人的健康乾杯!

health and safe·ty /ˌ· · ˈ··/ *n* [U] an area of government and law concerned with people's health and safety, especially at work 衛生與安全〔指政務和法律範疇, 尤指工作場所的衛生與安全〕

health care /ˈ· ·/ *n* [U] the service of looking after the health of all the people in a country or an area 醫療保健

health cen·ter /ˈ· ˌ··/ *n* [C] *AmE* a building where students go to get medical help or advice【美】〔學生〕醫療中心, 保健中心

health cen·tre /ˈ· ˌ··/ *n* [C] *BrE* a building where several doctors have offices【英】〔包括幾個診所的〕醫療中心, 醫務所

health club /ˈ· ·/ *n* [C] a private club where people can go to exercise in order to become physically stronger and more attractive 健身俱樂部

health farm /ˈ· ·/ *n* [C] a place where people pay to stay so that they can lose weight 健身莊〔人們減肥的一個地方〕

health food /ˈ· ·/ *n* [C,U] food that contains only natural substances 保健食品〔指不含化學物質的天然食品〕

health·ful /ˈhɛlθfəl; ˈhelθfəl/ *adj AmE* likely to make you healthy【美】有利於健康的: *healthful mountain air* 有利於健康的山間空氣

health vis·it·or /ˈ· ˌ···/ *n* [C] a nurse in Britain who visits people in their homes〔英國的〕衛生訪問員〔指上門作健康護理的護士〕

health·y /ˈhɛlθɪ; ˈhelθi/ *adj* S3 W3

1 ►PERSON/ANIMAL 人/動物◄ physically strong and not likely to become ill 健康的, 健壯的: *a healthy baby boy* 健康的男嬰 | *I've always been perfectly healthy until now.* 我的身體一直非常健康。

2 ►MAKING YOU HEALTHY 使人健康◄ likely to make you healthy 有益健康的: *a healthy diet* 健康的飲食

3 ►GOOD FOR YOUR CHARACTER 有利於人的品格◄ [usually in questions or negatives 一般用於疑問句或否定句] good for someone's mind or character 有益於精神[品格]的, 有益於身心的: *I don't think it's healthy for her to spend so much time alone.* 我認為長時間獨處對她的身心健康沒有好處。

4 ►SHOWING GOOD HEALTH 顯示健康◄ showing that you are healthy 顯示健康的: *Her face had a healthy glow.* 她的臉上容光煥發。| *a healthy skin* 健康的皮膚 | **a healthy appetite** (=a desire to eat a lot) 旺盛的食慾

5 ►COMPANY/SOCIETY ETC 公司/社會等◄ a healthy company, society, economic system etc is working effectively and successfully 運作良好的; 興旺發達的: *The economy is looking quite healthy now.* 目前的經濟看起來相當興旺。

6 a healthy respect/contempt/curiosity etc a natural and sensible feeling 自然的尊重/鄙視/好奇心等: *a healthy contempt for silly regulations* 對可笑的規矩自然的鄙視

7 ►AMOUNT 數量◄ large and showing that someone is successful 大量的, 可觀的: *By the end of the year we should make a healthy profit.* 到年底我們應該會有可觀的利潤。—**healthily** *adv* —**healthiness** *n* [U]

heap¹ /hip; hiːp/ *n* [C] **1** a large untidy pile of things〔大而雜亂的〕堆: *a rubbish heap* 垃圾堆 | [+of] *heaps of dead leaves* 落葉堆 | **in heaps** *Dirty clothes lay in heaps on the floor.* 髒衣服成堆地放在地上。**2 heaps of** *informal* a lot of something【非正式】大量, 許多: *Don't worry, we've got heaps of time.* 別擔心, 我們有的是時間。**3** *humorous* an old car that is in bad condition【幽默】破舊的汽車 **4 fall/collapse in a heap** to fall down and lie without moving 癱倒/動彈不了 **5 be struck/knocked all of a heap** *BrE old-fashioned informal* to be suddenly very surprised or confused【英, 過時, 非正式】被突然驚呆, 被弄得慌作一團

heap² *v* [T] **1** also 又作 **heap up** to put a lot of things on top of each other in an untidy way〔雜亂地〕堆積, 堆放: *The ashes from the fire were heaped in a huge pile.* 大火產生的灰燼堆成了一大堆。| **heap sth on/onto** *They had heaped all the rubbish onto the back of the truck.* 他們將所有的垃圾都堆在卡車後面的車斗裡。**2 be heaped with** if a plate is heaped with food, it has a lot on it〔盤子〕堆滿〔食物〕**3 heap praises/insults etc on** to praise, insult etc someone a lot 極力稱讚/百般侮辱等

heaped /hipt; hiːpt/ *adj* **heaped teaspoon/tablespoon etc** an amount of something that is as much as a spoon can hold 滿滿的一茶匙/湯匙: *Add 3 heaped teaspoons of sugar.* 加入滿滿的三茶匙糖。

heaps /hips; hiːps/ *adv* **heaps better/bigger etc** *informal* much better, bigger etc【非正式】好/大得多

hear 聽

Joe can't hear the phone ringing because he's listening to music.
喬聽不見電話鈴聲, 因為他在聽音樂。

S1 W1 **hear** /hɪr; hɪə/ *v past tense and past participle* **heard** /hɝd; hɜːd/

1 ▶HEAR SOUNDS/WORDS ETC 聽到聲音/話語等◀ [I,T not in progressive 不用進行式] to know that a sound is being made, using your ears 聽到, 聽見: *Did you hear that noise?* 你聽見那個聲音嗎? | *I called his name, but he pretended not to hear.* 我叫他的名字, 但他假裝沒聽見。| **hear sb/sth doing sth** *I think I can hear someone knocking.* 我似乎聽到有人在敲門。| **hear sb/sth do sth** *Dixon's going to resign – I heard him say so.* 狄克遜要辭職了——我聽見他是這麼說的。| **hear what** *I'm sorry, I didn't hear what you said.* 對不起, 我沒有聽到你說甚麼。| **be heard to say/ask/remark etc** *One delegate was heard to remark that the conference had been a waste of time.* 有人聽到其中一個代表說這次會議是在浪費時間。

2 ▶LISTEN TO SB/STH 聽◀ [T not usually in progressive 一般不用進行式] to listen to what someone is saying, the music they are playing etc 聽, 聆聽, 傾聽: *Without waiting to hear her answer, he stood up and walked away.* 他沒有聽她的回答, 便站起來走了。| *You can hear that broadcast again on Monday at 9.00.* 你可以在星期一九點再次收聽那個廣播節目。| **hear sb do sth** *Pavarotti is amazing – you should hear him sing 'Nessun dorma'.* 巴伐洛提真棒, 你應該聽聽他唱的《今夜無人能眠》。| **hear what** *Let's hear what he's got to say.* 我們聽聽他怎麼說吧! | **I hear what you're saying** *spoken* (=used to tell someone that you have listened to their opinion)【口】我聽到你的話了, 我明白你的意思 *I hear what you're saying, but we can't ignore the facts.* 我明白你的意思, 但我們也不能不顧事實。

3 ▶BE TOLD STH 被告知某事◀ [I,T not usually in progressive 一般不用進行式] to be told or find out a piece of information 聽說, 被告知, 得知: **hear (that)** *I hear you've been selected to play for the A team.* 聽說你已被選入A隊了。| [+about] *Did you hear about the fire?* 你聽說起火的事了嗎? | **be glad/pleased to hear (that)** *I'm glad to hear your sister's feeling better.* 聽說你姐姐好多了, 我感到很高興。| **so I've heard** *spoken* (=used to say that you already know about something)【口】我已經聽說了 *"Nina's quit her job." "Yes, so I've heard."* "尼娜辭職了。" "哦, 我已經聽說了。" | **hear sth** *We've heard such a lot about you.* 我們已經聽到過很多有關你的事。| **hear what/how/who etc** *When the authorities heard what we were planning, they tried to stop us.* 當局得知我們的計劃後, 便試圖阻止我們。| **hear anything of** (=receive any news about) 聽到有關…的消息 *Have you heard anything of Bob lately?* 你最近收到鮑勃的消息沒有? | **hear sth on the grapevine** (=find out about something in conversation) 從談話中獲悉 | **I've heard it said** *spoken*【口】also 又作 **I've heard tell** *old-fashioned*【過時】(=used when you are repeating something that someone else has told you) 我聽人說 *I've heard it said she's a tough businesswoman.* 我聽人說她是個厲害的女商人。

4 ▶IN COURT 在法庭上◀ hear a case if a court or a committee hears a case, they listen to all the evidence in order to make a decision 審理案件: *The case was heard at Teeside Crown Court on April 10.* 提塞德·克朗法院於4月10日審理了此案。

5 I won't hear of it *spoken* used to say that someone should not do something, especially because you want to help them【口】我不允許; 不要提: *I've offered to pay Simon for fixing my car, but he won't hear of it.* 我提出要酬謝西蒙, 因為他幫我修好了車, 但他拒絕了。

6 I/we haven't heard the last of *spoken* used to say that someone or something will cause more problems for you【口】〔某人或物〕還會給我/我們帶來更多麻煩; 沒完沒了: *I'm sure we haven't heard the last of that woman.* 那個女人肯定還會給我們帶來更多麻煩。

7 I'll/he'll etc never hear the end of it *spoken* used to say that someone will criticize or make jokes about something you have done【口】我/他將會遭到沒完沒了的批評[取笑]: *If my Mum finds out, I'll never hear the end of it.* 如果媽媽知道了, 她會嘮叨個沒完。

8 be hearing things to imagine you can hear a sound when really there is no sound 產生幻聽: **I must be hearing things** *I must be hearing things, I could have sworn you just called my name.* 我一定是聽錯了, 我剛才明明聽見你喊我的名字。

9 (do) you hear me? *spoken* used when you are giving someone an order and want to be certain that they will obey you【口】聽見了嗎? 明白了嗎?: *Now you go straight home. You hear me?* 你馬上回家去, 聽見了嗎?

10 now hear this! *AmE old use* used to introduce an important official announcement【美, 舊】請大家注意聽!〔用於正式通告〕

11 you could hear a pin drop used to say that a place was extremely quiet〔安靜得〕聽得見針落地的聲音: *After she finished telling her story you could have heard a pin drop.* 她講完後, 四周安靜得連一根針掉在地上的聲音都能聽見。

12 I can't hear myself think *spoken* used to say that the place where you are is too noisy【口】這裡太吵了

13 have you heard the one about... used when asking someone if they know a joke 你聽過有關…的笑話嗎?: *Have you heard the one about the turtle and the elephant?* 你聽過有關烏龜和大象的笑話嗎?

14 I've heard that one before *spoken* used when you

do not believe someone's excuse or explanation【口】這藉口我以前已聽過了〔表示不相信某人的解釋〕: *Kept late at the office, were you? I've heard that one before.* 又是在辦公室加班了，是嗎？這個藉口我以前已聽過了。

hear from sb *phr v* [T not in progressive 不用進行式] **1** to receive news from someone, usually by letter〔通常指通過信件〕得到某人的消息: *Have you heard from Sarah lately?* 你最近收到過莎拉的信嗎？| **I look forward to hearing from you** (=used at the end of a letter) 盼儘早賜覆〔信尾套語〕 **2** to listen to someone giving their opinion in a radio or television discussion programme 聽，收聽: *And now we are going to hear from some of the victims of violent crime.* 下面我們將聽到幾位暴力罪行的受害者講講他們的經歷。

hear of sb/sth *phr v* [T] **1 have heard of** to know that someone or something exists because you have been told about them 知道，聽說過: *I've never heard of him!* 我從未聽說過他！**2** [not in progressive 不用進行式] to get news or information about someone or something 得到有關某人[事]的消息: **she/he was last heard of** (=the last time people say they saw someone) 最後一次聽人說見到她/他 *He was last heard of in Lansing, Michigan in 1935.* 人們最後一次聽到他的消息是1935年在密歇根州的蘭辛市。—compare 比較 **hear from** (HEAR) —see also 另見 UNHEARD-OF

hear sb **out** *phr v* [T not in passive 不用被動態] to listen to all of what someone wants to tell you without interrupting them 聽某人說完: *Look, I know you're angry but you could at least hear me out.* 好了，我知道你很生氣，但你起碼聽我把話講完吧。

Hear! Hear! /,· '·/ *interjection especially BrE* used in parliament or in a meeting to say that you agree with the person who is speaking【尤英】好哇！好哇！〔在議會或會議上對某人所說的話表示贊同的呼喊聲〕

hear·er /ˈhɪrɚ; ˈhɪərə/ *n* [C] someone who hears something 聽者

3 2 **hear·ing** /ˈhɪrɪŋ; ˈhɪərɪŋ/ *n* **1** [U] the sense which you use to hear sounds 聽覺: *Speak up, please. My hearing is not too good.* 請大聲一點。我的聽覺不太好。—see also 另見 HARD OF HEARING **2** [C] a meeting of a court or special committee to find out the facts about a case 聽證會；審訊；聆訊 **3 give sb a (fair) hearing** to give someone an opportunity to explain their actions, ideas, or opinions 給某人一個(公平的)解釋機會 **4 in/within sb's hearing** if you say something in someone's hearing, you say it where they can hear you 在某人聽力所及的範圍內: *Don't mention that in John's hearing or he'll go crazy.* 別在約翰聽得見的地方提那件事，否則他會很生氣的。

hearing aid /'·· ·/ *n* [C] a small thing which fits into or behind your ear to make sounds louder, worn by people who cannot hear well 助聽器

hear·ken, harken /ˈhɑrkən; ˈhɑːkən/ *v* [I+to] *literary* to listen【文】傾聽

hear·say /ˈhɪr,se; ˈhɪəseɪ/ *n* [U] something that you have heard about from other people but do not know to be definitely true or correct 傳聞，道聽途說: *I wouldn't take any notice of it, it's just hearsay.* 我不會在意，這只不過是謠言而已。

hearse /hɝs; hɜːs/ *n* [C] a large car used to carry a dead body in a COFFIN at a funeral 靈車

1 1 **heart** /hɑrt; hɑːt/ *n*

1 ▶BODY ORGAN 人體器官◀ [C] the organ in your chest which pumps blood through your body 心(臟): *Eating too many fatty foods is bad for the heart.* 吃太多油膩的食物對心臟不好。| *My heart was beating so fast I thought it would burst.* 我的心跳得很快，好像快要炸開了。| **have heart trouble/have a heart condition** (=have problems with your heart) 患心臟病 | **a weak heart** (=an unhealthy heart) 衰弱的心臟 —see picture at 參見 RESPIRATORY 圖

2 ▶EMOTIONS/LOVE 感情/愛◀ [C] *especially literary* the part of your body that feels strong emotions and feelings【尤文】感情，心情；愛情: *My head said no, but my heart kept saying yes.* 我的理智在說"不行"，但我的感情卻一直在說"行"。| **affairs of the heart** (=matters connected with love) 與愛情相關的事 | **(deep) in your heart** (=used when saying what someone really feels) 在內心(深處) *She still loved him, deep down in her heart.* 在內心深處，她仍愛着他。| **heart and soul** (=completely) 全心全意地，完全地 *You love the boy heart and soul, don't you?* 你是全心全意地愛這個男孩的，是嗎？| **break sb's heart** (=to make someone extremely sad, especially by ending a romantic relationship with them)〔尤指因斷絕戀愛關係〕使某人心碎，使某人傷透了心

3 ▶YOUR CHEST 胸部◀ [C usually singular 一般用單數] the part of your chest near your heart 胸部近心處，心口處: *He put his hand across his heart to show where the pain was.* 他用手按着心口，指出痛楚的地方。

4 ▶SHAPE 形狀◀ [C] a shape used to represent a heart 心形 —see picture at 參見 SHAPE[1] 圖

5 from the heart if you say or mean something from the heart, you really mean it or feel it very strongly 從內心；真心地: *He spoke simply but from the heart.* 他說得很簡單，但卻是出於真心的。| **from the bottom of my heart** *I want to thank you from the bottom of my heart.* 我衷心地感謝你。| **straight from the heart** *What she said came straight from the heart.* 她所說的全是真心話。

6 in your heart of hearts if you know, feel, or believe something in your heart of hearts, you are secretly sure about it although you may not admit it 在心底裡，在內心深處: *Claire knew in her heart of hearts that she would never go back there.* 克萊爾心底裡明白她永遠不會再回到那兒了。

7 ▶IMPORTANT PART OF STH 重要部分◀ the most important part of a problem, question etc 實質；中心，核心；關鍵: **get to the heart of the matter/problem/question etc** *The new book gets to the heart of the controversy over nuclear power.* 這本新書論述了有關核電爭議的中心問題。

8 ▶THE MIDDLE PART OF AN AREA 某地區的中心◀ [C] the middle of an area 中心(地區): **in the heart of** *somewhere deep in the heart of Texas* 深入德克薩斯州腹地的某個地方

9 know/learn something by heart to know or learn something so that you can remember all of it 背誦，熟記: *You have to know all the music by heart.* 你必須把樂曲全部背下來。

10 set your heart on to want something very much 非常想得到，渴望得到: *The coach had set his heart on winning.* 教練一心一意希望能夠獲勝。

11 ▶CARD GAMES 紙牌遊戲◀ **a)** [C] a heart shape printed in red on a playing card 紅心，紅桃 **b) hearts** [plural] the SUIT (=set) of playing cards that have these shapes on them 一套紅桃紙牌: *the ace of hearts* 紅桃A **c)** [C] one of the cards in this set 一張紅桃(紙牌): *Have you got any hearts?* 你有紅桃嗎？

12 kind-hearted/cold-hearted/hard-hearted etc having a kind, unkind, cruel etc character 心腸善良的/冷酷的/狠毒的等

13 have a heart of gold to be very kind 非常仁慈，心地善良

14 have a heart of stone to be very cruel or unsympathetic 鐵石心腸

15 a man/woman after my own heart someone who likes the same things or behaves in the same way that you do 喜好[處事]和我相似的[合我心意的]男人/女人: *Geoff was clear-thinking and decisive – a man after my own heart.* 傑夫是個思路清晰、行動果斷的人，正合我心意。

16 at heart if you are a particular kind of person at heart, that is the kind of person that you really are 本質

上, 心底裡; 實際上: *I've always been a country boy at heart.* 我實質上一直是個鄉村男孩。—see also 另見 **have sb's (best) interests at heart** (INTEREST[1] (5)), **young at heart** (YOUNG[1] (4))

17 close/dear to sb's heart very important to someone 為某人所愛/關注

18 my/his/her heart leapt *literary* used to say that someone suddenly felt happy and full of hope【文】我/他/她的心突然充滿了希望

19 my/his etc heart sank used to say that someone suddenly lost hope and began to feel sad 我/他的心突然往下沉〔指感到失望〕: *Our hearts sank when we heard the results of the voting.* 聽到投票結果後, 我們的心往下一沉。

20 my heart was in my mouth used to say that you suddenly felt very afraid 我突然感到很害怕; 我的心都快跳出來了

21 my heart bleeds (for sb) used to say that you do not really feel any sympathy towards someone 我並不同情某人: *"He's had to sell his Ferrari." "My heart bleeds for him."* "他不得不賣掉了他的法拉利跑車。" "我一點也不同情他。"

22 my/his/her heart goes out to sb used to say that someone feels a lot of sympathy towards another person 我/他/她非常同情某人

23 my/his/her heart isn't in it used to say that someone does not really want to do something 我/他/她的心不在此事上〔指並非真心想做某事〕: *I tried to join in the fun, but somehow my heart wasn't in it.* 我試着和他們一起玩, 但不知怎麼我的心卻不在上面。

24 not have the heart to do something to be unable to do something because it will make someone unhappy 不忍心做某事: *I didn't have the heart to tell my daughter we couldn't keep the puppy.* 我真不忍心告訴女兒我們不能養那隻小狗。

25 be in good heart *formal* to feel cheerful and confident【正式】情緒高昂: *Our troops are in good heart and ready for action.* 我們的部隊士氣高昂, 準備迎接戰鬥。

26 take heart to feel encouraged 鼓起勇氣, 有了信心, 受到鼓舞: *We took heart when we saw the sign, knowing that we were close to home.* 看到路標時我們都振作起來, 因為知道馬上就要到家了。

27 take sth to heart to be very upset by something that someone says or does to you 把某事放在心上, 為某事心煩意亂: *Don't take her criticisms so much to heart.* 別太把她的批評放在心上。

28 do sth to your heart's content to do something as much as you want 痛快地[盡情地]做某事: *After I leave, Joe can sing in the shower to his heart's content.* 我走後, 喬可以在淋浴時盡情地唱歌了。

29 it does your heart good to see/hear used to say that something makes you feel happy 很高興看到/聽到: *It does my heart good to see him running around again.* 看到他又能四處跑來跑去, 我感到很高興。

30 have a heart! *often humorous* used to tell someone not to be too strict or unkind【常幽默】發發善心吧! 做做好事吧!

31 with all your heart with all your strength, energy or emotion 全心全意地, 真心實意地: *Ben hated school with all his heart.* 本打從心裡痛恨上學。

32 have your heart's desire/have everything your heart could desire to get everything that you could possibly want 心想事成, 要甚麼有甚麼

33 know the way to sb's heart *humorous* to know the way to please someone【幽默】知道如何討好某人: *What a great meal! You certainly know the way to a man's heart!* 這頓飯棒極了! 你真懂如何讓我高興!

34 ►VEGETABLE 蔬菜◄ [C] the firm middle part of some vegetables 菜的中心部分: *artichoke hearts* 洋薊心

35 his/her heart is in the right place *informal* used to say that someone is really a kind person, even though they may not appear to be【非正式】他/她的心地還是善良的: *He's a little grouchy sometimes, but his heart's in the right place.* 他有時有點怨天尤人, 但心地還是善良的。—see also 另見 **a broken heart** (BROKEN[2] (10)), **cross my heart** (CROSS[1] (10)), **eat your heart out** (EAT (2)), **change of heart** (CHANGE[2] (1)), **sick at heart** (SICK[1] (9)), **strike at the heart of** (STRIKE[1] (9)), **wear your heart on your sleeve** (WEAR[1] (10)), **win sb's heart** (WIN[1] (3)), **with a heavy heart** (HEAVY[1] (25))

heart·ache /ˈhɑrtˌek; ˈhɑːteɪk/ *n* [U] a strong feeling of great sadness and anxiety 痛心, 傷心

heart at·tack /ˈ· ·ˌ·/ *n* [C] a sudden serious medical condition in which someone's heart stops working, causing them great pain 心臟病發作

heart·beat /ˈhɑrtˌbit; ˈhɑːtbiːt/ *n* [C,U] the action or sound of your heart as it pumps blood through your body 心跳, 心搏: *the amount of blood pumped by each heartbeat* 每次心跳的泵血量

heart·break /ˈhɑrtˌbrek; ˈhɑːtbreɪk/ *n* [U] great sadness or disappointment 心碎, 悲傷; 極度失望

heart·break·ing /ˈhɑrtˌbrekɪŋ; ˈhɑːtˌbreɪkɪŋ/ *adj* making you feel extremely sad or disappointed 使人心碎[悲傷; 極度失望]的: *heartbreaking pictures of starving children* 令人心碎的挨餓兒童的圖片 —**heartbreakingly** *adv*

heart·brok·en /ˈhɑrtˌbrokən; ˈhɑːtˌbrəʊkən/ *adj* extremely sad because of something that has happened 極度傷心的, 心碎的, 悲傷的: *When her parents split up she was heartbroken.* 父母離婚時, 她感到很傷心。

heart·burn /ˈhɑrtˌbɝn; ˈhɑːtbɜːn/ *n* [U] an unpleasant burning feeling in your stomach or chest caused by INDIGESTION〔消化不良引起的〕胃灼熱, 燒心

heart dis·ease /ˈ· ·ˌ·/ *n* [C,U] an illness which prevents someone's heart from working normally 心臟病

heart·en /ˈhɑrtn̩; ˈhɑːtn/ *v* [T usually passive 一般用被動態] to make someone feel happier and more hopeful 使高興; 使振作, 鼓舞: *I was heartened by the news that the operation had been a success.* 手術做得很成功的消息使我感到很高興。—**heartening** *adj* —**hearteningly** *adv* —opposite 反義詞 DISHEARTEN

heart fail·ure /ˈ· ˌ··/ *n* [U] a serious medical condition in which someone's heart stops, often resulting in death 心力衰竭, 心臟停跳

heart·felt /ˈhɑrtˌfɛlt; ˈhɑːtfelt/ *adj* very strongly felt and sincere 衷心的, 誠摯的: *a heartfelt apology* 真誠的道歉

hearth /hɑrθ; hɑːθ/ *n* [C] **1** the area of floor around a FIREPLACE in a house 壁爐前的地板, 壁爐邊 **2 hearth and home** *literary* your home and family【文】温暖的家(庭): *the joys of hearth and home* 温暖快樂的家庭生活

heart·i·ly /ˈhɑrtɪlɪ; ˈhɑːtɪli/ *adv* **1** loudly and cheerfully 開懷地: *He laughed heartily and embraced his brother.* 他開懷大笑着擁抱他的兄弟。**2** completely or very much 完全地; 十分地: **heartily agree/approve of/support etc** *a sentiment with which she heartily agreed* 她完全同意的一種感情 | **heartily fed up with/sick of** *By the end we were heartily fed up with the whole thing.* 到最後我們都給這件事煩死了。**3 eat/drink heartily** to eat or drink a large amount 大吃/大喝

heart·land /ˈhɑrtlænd; ˈhɑːtlænd/ *n* [C] **1 the heartland** the central part of a country or area of land 心臟地帶, 中心區域: *in the Russian heartland* 在俄羅斯的心臟地帶 **2** the most important part of a country or area for a particular activity, or the part where a political group has most support〔國家的〕最重要地區;〔某政黨佔優勢的〕中心地區: *the Democratic heartlands of the Deep South* 民主黨佔優勢的南方腹地

heart·less /ˈhɑrtlɪs; ˈhɑːtləs/ *adj* not feeling any pity 無情的, 冷酷的: *How can you be so heartless?* 你怎麼能如此無情呢? —**heartlessly** *adv* —**heartlessness** *n* [U]

heart-lung ma·chine /ˌ· ˈ· ·ˌ·/ *n* [C] a machine that pumps blood and oxygen around someone's body during a medical operation〔手術時用來維持血液和氧氣供應的〕人工心肺機

heart·rend·ing /ˈhɑrt͵rɛndɪŋ; ˈhɑːt͵rendɪŋ/ *adj* making you feel great pity 使人極度傷心的, 令人悲痛的: *heartrending stories of children being taken from their parents* 關於孩子被人從父母身邊奪走的令人心酸的故事

heart-search·ing /ˈ· ͵··/ *n* [U] the process of examining very carefully your feelings about something or your reasons for doing something 內省, 反省

heart·sick /ˈhɑrt͵sɪk; ˈhɑːt͵sɪk/ *adj* very unhappy or disappointed 悶悶不樂的, 憂傷的, 沮喪的

heart·strings /ˈhɑrt͵strɪŋz; ˈhɑːt͵strɪŋz/ *n* [plural] **tug/tear at sb's heartstrings** to make someone feel strong love or sympathy 牽動某人的心弦〔使人感動或同情〕

heart·throb /ˈhɑrt͵θrɑb; ˈhɑːtθrɒb/ *n* [C] a famous actor, singer etc who is very attractive to women 使〔女性〕着迷的人: *teenage heartthrobs 'Take That'* 讓青少年着迷的 Take That 樂隊

heart-to-heart /͵· · ˈ·◂/ *n* [C] a conversation in which two people say honestly and sincerely what they really feel about something 貼心的談話, 坦率的談心: *Why don't you have a heart-to-heart with him and sort out your problems?* 你為甚麼不和他坦誠地談談, 把問題解決掉呢? —**heart-to-heart** *adj*

heart·warm·ing /ˈhɑrt͵wɔrmɪŋ; ˈhɑːt͵wɔːmɪŋ/ *adj* making you feel happy because you see other people being happy or kind to each other 暖人心房的, 溫馨感人的: *a heartwarming sight* 感人的場面 —**heartwarmingly** *adv*

heart·wood /ˈhɑrt͵wʊd; ˈhɑːtwʊd/ *n* [U] the older harder wood at the centre of a tree〔樹木中心的〕心材

heart·y /ˈhɑrtɪ; ˈhɑːti/ *adj* **1** cheerfully friendly 熱情友好的: *a hearty laugh* 開懷大笑 **2** *old-fashioned* strong and healthy【過時】健壯的 —see also 另見 **hale and hearty** (HALE) **3** a hearty meal is very large〔飯菜〕豐盛的 **4** *especially BrE* with a friendly, noisy and cheerful manner that is not sincere【尤英】假裝開心友好的 —**heartiness** *n* [U] —see also 另見 HEARTILY

S2 W2 **heat¹** /hit; hiːt/ *n*

1 [U] warmth or hotness 熱, 熱量, 熱力: *The heat of the water caused the glass to shatter.* 水的熱度使得玻璃杯子裂開了。| *Black surfaces absorb heat from the sun.* 黑色的表面吸收陽光的熱量。

2 the heat a) very hot weather 酷暑, 炎熱的天氣: *I couldn't stand the heat.* 我無法忍受炎熱的天氣。| **the heat of the day** (=the hottest part of the day) 一天中最熱的時候 **b)** *AmE* the system in a house that keeps it warm in the winter【美】供暖系統, 暖氣設備; HEATING *BrE*【英】

3 [C usually singular 一般用單數] the hot temperature of an OVEN or a heating system〔烤箱或暖氣設備的〕高溫, 溫度: *When the oven reaches the correct heat, the light goes off.* 烤箱達到所需溫度時, 燈就會熄滅。| **turn up/turn down the heat** *She turned up the heat on the cooker.* 她調高了爐子的溫度。

4 in the heat of the moment/argument/battle etc while feeling angry or excited 在最關鍵/辯論最激烈/戰鬥最激烈等的時刻: *In the heat of the argument I said a few things I regret now.* 在爭論最激烈的時刻, 我說了一些令我現在感到後悔不已的話。

5 take the heat out of the situation to make a situation calmer and make people less angry and excited 使局面冷靜[緩和]下來

6 the heat is on/off *spoken* used to say that a situation is very difficult, or that a difficult situation has now ended and you can relax【口】形勢十分嚴峻/已經趨於平穩

7 on heat also 又作 **in heat** *AmE*【美】if a female animal is on heat, her body is ready to have sex with a male〔雌性動物〕發情

8 ►IN A RACE 在比賽中◄ [C] a part of a race or competition whose winners then compete against each other in the next part 分組賽, 預賽 —see also 另見 DEAD HEAT, WHITE HEAT

heat² *v* [I,T] to make something become warm or hot 加熱, 使變熱: *Heat the milk until it boils.* 把牛奶煮開。

heat up *phr v* **1** [I,T] to become warm or hot or to make something become warm or hot (使) 變熱, (把...) 加熱: **heat sth ↔ up** *I heated up the remains of last night's supper.* 我把昨天晚飯剩下的飯菜熱了一下。| **heat up** *The stove takes a while to heat up.* 爐子要過一會兒才能熱起來。**2** [I] if a situation heats up, it becomes dangerous or full of problems〔形勢〕激化, 加劇

heat sth **through** *phr v* [T] to heat food thoroughly 充分加熱〔食物〕

heat·ed /ˈhitɪd; ˈhiːtɪ̈d/ *adj* **1** a heated SWIMMING POOL, room etc is made warm using a heater〔人工〕加熱的; 有暖氣的 **2 heated argument/debate/discussion etc** an argument etc that is full of angry and excited feelings 激烈的爭論/辯論/討論等 —**heatedly** *adv*

heat·er /ˈhitɚ; ˈhiːtə/ *n* [C] a machine for making air or water hotter 加熱器; 暖氣機; 暖爐: *Did you turn the heater off?* 你關掉加熱器了嗎? —see picture on page A2 參見 A2 頁圖

heat ex·haus·tion /ˈ· ·͵··/ *n* [U] weakness and sickness caused by doing too much work, exercise etc when it is hot 中暑 (虛脫)

heath /hiθ; hiːθ/ *n* [C] an area of open land where grass, bushes, and other small plants grow〔雜草和灌木叢生的〕荒野, 荒原

hea·then¹ /ˈhiðən; ˈhiːðən/ *adj old-fashioned* not connected with or belonging to the Christian religion or any of the large established religions【過時】〔不信奉基督教、猶太教或伊斯蘭教等主要宗教的〕異教徒的

heathen² *n old use*【舊】**1 the heathen** *old-fashioned* people who are heathen【過時】異教徒〔總稱〕**2** [C] *old-fashioned* someone who is heathen【過時】異教徒 **3** [singular] *often humorous* someone who refuses to believe in something【常幽默】無信仰的人

heath·er /ˈhɛðɚ; ˈheðə/ *n* [U] a low plant with small purple, pink, or white flowers which grows on hills〔開紫色、粉紅色或白色花的〕石南屬灌木

Heath Rob·in·son /͵hiθ ˈrɑbɪnsn̩; ͵hiːθ ˈrɒbɪ̈nsən/ *adj BrE* a Heath Robinson machine, system etc is very complicated in an amusing way but not at all practical【英】〔機械等〕設計精巧但卻可笑而不實用的; RUBE GOLDBERG *AmE*【美】

heat·ing /ˈhitɪŋ; ˈhiːtɪŋ/ *n* [U] *BrE* a system for making a room or building warm【英】供暖系統, 暖氣設備; the heat *AmE*【美】: *a huge heating bill* 一筆高昂的暖氣費 —see also 另見 CENTRAL HEATING S2

heat light·ning /ˈ· ͵··/ *n* [U] *especially AmE* LIGHTNING¹ (1) without THUNDER or rain【尤美】〔不伴有雷聲或降雨的〕熱閃電

heat·proof /ˈhitpruf; ˈhiːtpruːf/ *adj* heatproof material cannot be damaged by heat 耐熱的, 耐高溫的; 隔熱的

heat pump /ˈ· ·/ *n* [C] part of a machine that takes heat from one place to another 熱泵

heat rash /ˈ· ·/ *n* [C,U] painful or ITCHY red spots on someone's skin caused by heat〔皮膚上的〕痱子

heat-re·sist·ant /ˈ· ·͵··/ *adj* not easily damaged by heat 抗熱的, 耐熱的

heat-seek·ing /ˈ· ͵··/ *adj* a heat-seeking weapon is able to find and move towards the hot gases from an aircraft or ROCKET and destroy it〔武器〕裝有熱跟蹤裝置的, 熱跟蹤的〔指跟蹤飛機、火箭等排出的熱氣〕

heat·stroke /ˈhit͵strok; ˈhiːtstrəʊk/ *n* [U] fever and weakness caused by being outside in the heat of the sun for too long 中暑 —compare 比較 SUNSTROKE

heat wave /ˈ· ·/ *n* [C] a period of unusually hot weather, especially one that continues for a long time 一段非常炎熱的時期, 熱浪期

heave¹ /hiv; hiːv/ *v* **1** [I,T] to pull or lift something very heavy with one great effort〔用很大力氣〕拉; 舉, 抬: **heave sth onto/into/towards etc** *He heaved the pack up onto his back.* 他使勁地將包揹到了背上。| *We heaved* *with all our strength but couldn't shift the old piano.* 我們用盡了全力, 但那架老鋼琴卻紋絲不動。| **heave at/on sth** *He heaved on the rope with all his strength.* 他用盡全力拉動繩子。**2** [T] to throw something heavy using a lot of effort〔用力〕扔, 拋〔重物〕**3 heave a sigh** to breathe out noisily and slowly once, because you are pleased or disappointed 長長地舒[嘆]了一口氣: *She heard him heave a great sigh and then saw that he was crying.* 她聽見他長長地嘆了一口氣, 然後就看見他哭了。| **heave a sigh of relief** *Paolo heaved a great sigh of relief when he heard that she had returned.* 聽說她已經回來了, 保羅寬慰地舒了一口氣。**4** [I] if the sea or someone's chest heaves, it moves up and down with very strong movements 起伏: *Brigg's chest was heaving with exhaustion.* 布里格累得直喘氣, 胸脯不停地上下起伏。**5** [I] *informal* to VOMIT¹【非正式】嘔吐 **6 heave into sight/view** *past tense and past participle* **hove** to appear, especially by getting closer from a distance 逐漸進入視線: *A few moments later a barge hove into view.* 過了一會兒, 一艘大駁船在眼前出現了。—see also 另見 HEAVING

heave to *phr v past tense* **hove to** /ˌhov ˋtu; ˌhəʊv ˈtuː/ [I] *technical* if a ship heaves to, it stops moving【術語】〔船隻〕停止移動

heave² *n* **1** [C] a strong pulling, pushing, or lifting movement〔猛力的〕拉; 推; 舉: *He gave the door a good heave.* 他用力地推了一下門。**2** [U] *literary* a strong rising or falling movement【文】起伏

heave-ho /ˌ· ˈ·/ *interjection* **1** *old-fashioned* used as an encouragement to a person or group of people who are pulling something, especially on ships【過時】用力拉啊〔尤指在船上拉東西時所喊的號子〕**2 give someone the (old) heave-ho** *informal* to end a relationship with someone, or to make someone leave their job【非正式】與某人斷絕關係; 解雇某人

3 **heav·en** /ˋhɛvən; ˈhevən/ *n* **1** also 又作 **Heaven** [singular] the place where God is believed to live and where good people are believed to go when they die 天堂, 天國, 極樂世界 **2** [U] *informal* a very good situation or place【非正式】極好的情況[地方]: **sheer heaven** (=perfect heaven) 絕妙的事 *It was sheer heaven being able to stay in bed all day!* 能整天躺在牀上真是件絕妙的事情。| **heaven on earth** *I had imagined that being married to Max would be heaven on earth.* 我曾經幻想過嫁給馬克斯能讓我過上天堂般美好的日子。**3 for heaven's sake** *spoken*【口】**a)** used to show that you are annoyed or angry〔表示厭煩或生氣〕天哪! 哎呀!: *Oh, for heaven's sake! Do they have to make so much noise?* 啊, 天哪! 他們非得這麼大聲嗎? **b)** used to emphasize a question or request〔強調問題或要求〕看在上帝的份上: *For heaven's sake don't tell Simon about this!* 看在上帝的份上, 不要把這件事告訴西蒙! **4 heaven forbid** *spoken* used to say that you very much hope something will not happen【口】但願不要這樣, 但願不會: *"Will your parents be coming to the party?" "Heaven forbid!"* "你父母會來參加聚會嗎?" "但願不會!" **5 heaven help** *spoken*【口】**a)** used to say that you will be very angry with someone if they do something 饒不了〔某人〕: *Heaven help him if he ever comes back here again!* 要是他回到這裡來, 我一定饒不了他。**b)** used to say that it is dangerous to do something 願上天保佑〔表示做某事很危險〕: *Heaven help anyone who goes in there at night.* 誰要是在夜裡去那兒, 就只能盼老天爺保佑了。**6 heaven (only) knows** *spoken*【口】**a)** used to say that you do not know and cannot imagine what is happening or what will happen 天曉得, 誰知道: *We used to keep in touch, but heaven knows what they're all doing now.* 我們曾經保持聯繫, 但天曉得他們現在在幹些甚麼。**b)** used to emphasize what you are saying〔用以加強語氣〕確實, 的確, 無疑: *I just couldn't get him to stop gambling although heaven knows I tried hard enough.* 我確實力勸過他, 但還是無法使他放棄賭博。**7 what/how/why etc in heaven's name** *spoken* used when asking a surprised and angry question【口】到底[究竟]甚麼/怎麼/為甚麼等: *What in heaven's name did you think you were doing?* 你到底在幹甚麼? **8 the heavens** *literary* the sky【文】天空 **9 the heavens opened** *especially literary* it started to rain very hard【尤文】天下起傾盆大雨來 **10 move heaven and earth** to try very hard to achieve something 竭盡全力, 用盡各種方法 —see also 另見 **be in seventh heaven** (SEVENTH (2)), **thank heavens** (THANK (2))

heav·en·ly /ˋhɛvənlɪ; ˈhevənli/ *adj* **1** *old-fashioned* very beautiful, pleasant, or enjoyable【過時】極好的; 非常美麗的; 令人非常愉快的: *What heavenly weather!* 多好的天氣啊! **2** [only before noun 僅用於名詞前] *biblical* existing in or belonging to heaven【聖經】天堂的, 天國的: *a heavenly choir of angels* 天使聖詩班 | **heavenly Father** (=God) 上帝, 天父 | **the Heavenly Host** (=all the angels)〔所有的〕天使 **3** *literary* existing in or connected with the sky or stars【文】天體的; 天空的

heavenly bod·y /ˌ··· ˈ··/ *n* [C] a star, PLANET or the moon 天體

Heav·ens! /ˋhɛvənz; ˈhevənz/ also 又作 **Good Heavens!, Heavens a·bove!,** /ˌ·· ·ˈ·/ also 又作 **Heavens to Bet·sy!** /ˌhɛvənz tə ˋbɛtsɪ; ˌhevənz tə ˈbetsi/ *AmE*【美】*—interjection* used to express surprise, especially when you are annoyed〔表示惱人的驚訝〕天哪! 我的天!: *Good Heavens what a mess!* 天哪! 多亂呀!

heaven-sent /ˌ·· ˈ·◂/ *adj* happening fortunately at exactly the right time 天賜的; 最合時宜的: *a heaven-sent opportunity* 天賜良機

heav·en·ward /ˋhɛvənwəd; ˈhevənwəd/ also 又作 **heav·en·wards** /-wədz; -wədz/ *adv literary* towards the sky【文】向天上, 朝天空

heav·ily /ˋhɛvɪlɪ; ˈhevəli/ *adv*  3

1 ▶A LOT/IN LARGE AMOUNTS 很多/大量◀ a lot or in large amounts 很多地, 大量地: *It's been raining heavily all day.* 大雨已經下了整整一天了。| **drink/smoke heavily** *Paul was drinking heavily by this time.* 這時保羅已喝了很多酒。

2 ▶VERY 非常◀ very or very much 很大程度上; 非常: **heavily dependent/reliant/influenced** *Japan is heavily dependent on imported oil from the Middle East.* 日本在很大程度上依賴於從中東進口的石油。

3 ▶SLEEP 睡眠◀ if you sleep heavily, you cannot be woken easily 沉沉地: *Joe slept heavily for eight hours.* 喬酣睡了八小時。

4 breathe heavily to breathe slowly and loudly 喘粗氣

5 heavily built having a large broad body that looks strong〔身材〕粗壯的, 強壯的

6 be heavily into *informal* to do something a lot or be very interested in it【非正式】對…非常着迷: *Brenda's heavily into motorbikes.* 布倫達對摩托車着了迷。

7 ▶SLOWLY 緩慢地◀ if you do or say something heavily, you do it slowly, especially because you are sad or bored〔尤因傷心或無聊而〕行動緩慢地: *He was walking heavily, his head down.* 他低着頭, 拖着沉重的步伐緩緩地走。

hea·ving /ˋhivɪŋ; ˈhiːvɪŋ/ *adj BrE informal* very busy or full of people【英, 非正式】熱鬧的; 繁忙的; 擁擠的: [+with] *The place was heaving with showbiz types.* 這個地方到處都是娛樂圈裡的人。

heav·y¹ /ˋhɛvɪ; ˈhevi/ *adj* **heavier, heaviest** 1 1

1 ▶WEIGHT 重量◀ weighing a lot 重的, 沉重的: *I can't lift this case – it's too heavy.* 我提不起這隻箱子, 太重了。| *The baby seemed to be getting heavier and heavier in her arms.* 她手裡抱着的嬰兒好像變得越來越重了。| **how heavy?** (=how much does it weigh) 多重? *How heavy is the parcel?* 這個包裹有多重? —opposite 反義詞 LIGHT² (4)

2 ▶A LOT 許多◀ a lot or in very large amounts 很多的, 大量的: *The traffic was heavier than normal and I was late for work.* 交通異常擁擠, 結果我上班遲到了。| **heavy rain/snow** *flooding caused by heavy rain over*

the weekend 週末大雨引發的洪水 | **heavy use/consumption** *the film's heavy use of special effects* 影片中採用的大量特殊效果
3 heavy smoker/drinker someone who smokes a lot or drinks a lot of alcohol 大量抽煙/喝酒的人
4 ▶SERIOUS/SEVERE 嚴重的/嚴厲的◀ serious or severe 嚴重的, 嚴厲的: *heavy winter storms* 冬天猛烈的暴風雪 | *a heavy burden of responsibility* 沉重的責任 | **heavy fine/penalty** *heavy fines for possession of hard drugs* 對藏有烈性毒品的巨額罰款 | **a heavy cold** (=a very bad cold) 重感冒 *She's in bed with a heavy cold.* 她因重感冒而臥牀不起。| **heavy losses** *Most insurance companies suffered heavy losses last year.* 大多數保險公司去年都遭受嚴重虧損。
5 ▶NEEDING PHYSICAL EFFORT 費力的◀ needing a lot of physical strength and effort 繁重的, 費力的: *heavy manual work* 繁重的體力勞動
6 ▶NEEDING MENTAL EFFORT 費神的◀ not easy or entertaining and needing a lot of mental effort 費神的, 費腦力的: *I want something to read on holiday – nothing too heavy.* 我想找一本假期裡看的書, 要輕鬆點的。
7 heavy going difficult to understand or deal with 難懂的; 難辦的: **find sth heavy going** *I found Balzac's books pretty heavy going.* 我覺得巴爾扎克的書很難懂。
8 be heavy on *informal* to use a lot or too much of something【非正式】大量消耗[使用]: *The car's rather heavy on oil.* 這輛汽車的耗油量很大。
9 heavy schedule/timetable/day etc one in which you have a lot to do in a short time 緊張[工作繁重]的日程/時間表/一天等: *I'd had a heavy day at the office.* 我今天在辦公室過了非常忙碌的一天。
10 heavy sleeper someone who does not wake easily 睡覺時不易醒的人, 睡得很沉的人
11 heavy breathing breathing that is slow and loud 濃重的呼吸, 喘粗氣 —see also 另見 HEAVY BREATHER
12 make heavy weather of sth *BrE* to make something that you are doing seem more difficult or complicated than it really is【英】把某事弄得比實際困難, 對某事小題大做: *All Nick had to do was reorganize the files but he was making heavy weather of it.* 尼克所要做的只是重新整理一下檔案, 但他卻在小題大做。
13 ▶CLOTHES ETC 衣物等◀ clothes, jewellery, or shoes that are heavy are large, thick, and solid〔衣物〕厚重的;〔首飾〕粗大的: *a heavy winter coat* 一件冬天穿的厚大衣

14 ▶BODY/FACE 身材/臉◀ having a large, broad, or thick appearance that is unattractive〔身材〕粗壯的;〔五官〕粗糙的: *a large, heavy-featured woman* 一個高大的、粗眉大眼的女人 | **heavy build** (=a large broad body) 身材粗壯的
15 ▶WITH FORCE 用力◀ hitting something or falling with a lot of force or weight 用力的, 重重的: *the sound of heavy footsteps in the hall* 大廳裡沉重的腳步聲 | *Ali caught him with a heavy blow to the jaw.* 阿里給了他的下巴一記重擊。
16 heavy silence/atmosphere a situation in which people feel sad, anxious, or embarrassed 令人心情沉重的寂靜/沉重的氣氛: *A heavy silence fell upon the room.* 屋子裡頓時陷入沉重的寂靜之中。
17 heavy sky/clouds looking dark and grey as though it will soon rain 陰沉的天空/雲層
18 heavy seas sea with big waves 波浪洶湧的大海: *The ship went down in heavy seas off the coast of Scotland.* 船在蘇格蘭沿海波濤洶湧的大海中沉沒了。
19 ▶FOOD 食物◀ solid and making your stomach feel full and uncomfortable 難消化的: *a heavy meal* 一頓油膩的飯菜 | *heavy fruitcake* 不易消化的水果蛋糕
20 ▶GROUND 地面◀ **a)** soil that is heavy is thick and solid〔土壤〕黏重的 **b)** a sports ground or race track that is heavy is muddy〔運動場地、跑道〕泥濘的: *The going is heavy at Epsom today.* 埃普瑟姆的場地今天很泥濘。
21 ▶SMELL 氣味◀ strong and usually sweet 濃烈的: *a heavy fragrance* 濃濃的香味 | **be heavy with a scent/fragrance/smell** *The garden was heavy with the scent of summer.* 花園裡滿是夏日濃郁的芳香。
22 be heavy with fruit/blossom etc *literary* if trees are heavy with fruit etc they have a lot of fruit etc on them【文】果實纍纍/鮮花滿枝等
23 ▶AIR 空氣◀ unpleasantly warm and not at all fresh because there is no wind 悶熱的: *the damp heavy atmosphere of the rainforest* 雨林中潮濕悶熱的空氣
24 heavy irony/sarcasm remarks that very clearly say the opposite of what you really feel 辛辣的諷刺/嘲笑
25 with a heavy heart *literary* feeling very sad【文】心情沉重地, 悲傷地: *It was with a heavy heart that Kate kissed her children goodbye.* 凱特懷着沉重的心情跟她的孩子們一一吻別。
26 ▶RELATIONSHIP 關係◀ *informal* involving serious or strong emotions【非正式】感情深的, 感情認真的: *She didn't want things to get too heavy at such an early stage in their relationship.* 她不希望在他們交往初期讓感情發展得太深。
27 heavy date *AmE usually humorous* a very important DATE with a BOYFRIEND or GIRLFRIEND【美, 一般幽默】〔男女間的〕重要約會
28 ▶SERIOUS/WORRYING 嚴重的/令人擔憂的◀ *slang* a situation that is heavy makes you feel that people are very angry or have very strong feelings【俚】〔形勢〕危險的, 令人擔憂的, 令人不安的
29 ▶GUNS/WEAPONS 槍砲/武器◀ [only before noun 僅用於名詞前] large and powerful 重型的: *tanks and heavy weaponry* 坦克和重型武器
30 have a heavy foot *AmE informal* to drive too fast【美, 非正式】開快車, 超速駕駛 —**heaviness** *n* [U]

heavy² *adv* **time hangs/lies heavy on your hands** if time hangs or lies heavy on your hands, it seems to pass slowly because you are bored or have nothing to do 時間過得很慢/度日如年

heavy³ *n* [C] **1** [usually plural 一般用複數] *informal* a large strong man who is paid to protect someone or to threaten other people【非正式】打手, 保鏢 **2** a serious male character in a play or film, especially a bad character; VILLAIN (1)〔戲劇或電影中的〕嚴肅的角色〔尤指男性反派人物〕**3 the heavies** *BrE* large, serious newspapers【英】大型的嚴肅報紙

heavy breath·er /,·· '··/ *n* [C] a man who calls a woman on the telephone and does not speak, but breathes loudly, in order to get sexual pleasure 在電話中不說話、對女性喘粗氣進行性騷擾的男子 —**heavy breathing** *n* [U]

heavy cream /,·· '·/ *n* [U] *AmE* thick cream【美】濃稠乳脂; DOUBLE CREAM *BrE*【英】

heavy-du·ty /,·· '··◂/ *adj* **1** heavy duty materials are strong and thick and not easily damaged〔材料〕耐用的, 耐久的: *heavy-duty canvas* 耐久的帆布 **2** heavy-duty machines or equipment are designed to be used for very hard work〔機器〕重型的, 幹重活的 **3** *especially AmE informal* very serious, complicated, or involving strong emotions【尤美, 非正式】〔感情〕深的, 認真的: *a heavy-duty affair* 認真的戀情

heavy goods ve·hi·cle /,·· ',···/ *n* [C] an HGV 大型貨運卡車, 重型卡車

heavy-hand·ed /,·· '··◂/ *adj* done without thinking about other people's feelings 粗暴的; 嚴厲的; 高壓的: *a heavy-handed style of management* 高壓的管理方式 —**heavy-handedly** *adv* —**heavy-handedness** *n* [U]

heavy-heart·ed /,·· '··◂/ *adj literary* very sad【文】心情沉重的

heavy hit·ter /,·· '··/ *n* [C] *AmE*【美】**1** someone who has a lot of power, especially in business or politics〔尤指商界或政界〕舉足輕重的人物, 有權勢的人物, 大亨 **2** a BASEBALL player who hits the ball very hard〔棒球〕強擊手

heavy in·dus·try /,·· '···/ *n* [U] industry that produces large goods such as cars and machines, or materials such as coal, steel, or chemicals 重工業 —compare 比較 LIGHT INDUSTRY

heavy-lad·en /ˌ·· ˈ··◂/ *adj literary*【文】**1** carrying or supporting something very heavy 負載沉重的 **2** having many worries or problems 心情沉重的, 憂心忡忡的

heavy met·al /ˌ·· ˈ··◂/ *n* [U] **1** a type of ROCK[1] (2) music with a strong beat, played very loudly on electric GUITARS 重金屬搖滾樂 **2** *technical* a metal that has a high SPECIFIC GRAVITY, such as gold, MERCURY, and LEAD[3] (1)【術語】重金屬

heavy pet·ting /ˌ·· ˈ··/ *n* [U] sexual activities without actually having sex〔沒有真正性交的〕性愛活動: *teenagers who indulge in heavy petting* 沉溺於性愛遊戲的青少年

heavy-set /ˌ·· ˈ·◂/ *adj* someone who is heavy-set is large or broad and looks strong or fat〔身材〕粗壯的; 矮胖的

heav·y·weight /ˈhɛvɪˌwet; ˈheviweɪt/ *n* [C] **1** someone or something that is very important or has a lot of influence 重量級人物, 有影響力的人物, 要人: *one of the heavyweights of the movie industry* 電影業巨子之一 **2** a BOXER (1) in the heaviest weight group 重量級拳擊手

He·bra·ic /hiˈbre·ɪk; hɪˈbreɪ·ɪk/ *adj* connected with the Hebrew language or people 希伯來語的, 希伯來人的: *Hebraic literature* 希伯來文學

He·brew /ˈhibru; ˈhiːbruː/ *n* **1** [U] the language traditionally used by the Jewish people 希伯來語 **2** [C] a member of the Jewish people, especially in ancient times〔尤指古代的〕希伯來人 —**Hebrew** *adj*

heck /hɛk; hek/ *interjection informal*【非正式】**1** used to show that you are annoyed or to emphasize something you are saying 唉, 見鬼〔用以表示煩惱或加強語氣〕: *Oh heck! I've lost my keys!* 真見鬼! 我的鑰匙丟了! | **a heck of a lot** *a heck of a lot of money* 很多錢 | **where/how/who etc the heck** *Where the heck are we?* 我們到底是在哪兒? **2 what the heck!** *spoken* used to say that you will do something even though you really should not do it【口】管它呢! 不管它!〔用以表示將會做不應做的事〕: *It's rather expensive, but what the heck!* 這個相當貴, 不過管它呢!

heck·le /ˈhɛkl̩; ˈhekəl/ *v* [I,T] to interrupt a speaker at a public meeting〔在公開集會上〕打斷某人的發言, 詰問, 起哄 —**heckler** *n* [C] —**heckling** *n* [U]: *The speaker's voice was drowned by constant heckling.* 發言人的聲音被此起彼落的起哄聲淹沒了。

heck·u·va /ˈhɛkəvə; ˈhekəvə/ *adj spoken* an abbreviation of 縮寫= heck of a; used to emphasize that something is very big, very good etc【口】很大的; 極好的: *That was a heckuva storm last night.* 昨晚的暴風雨真大啊!

hec·tare /ˈhɛktɛr; ˈhektɑː/ *n* [C] a unit for measuring area, equal to 10,000 square metres 公頃〔等於 10,000 平方米〕—see table on page C3 參見 C3 頁附錄

hec·tic /ˈhɛktɪk; ˈhektɪk/ *adj* very busy or full of activity 繁忙的, 忙亂的: *I've had a pretty hectic day at the office.* 我在辦公室裡忙亂了一整天。| *a hectic social life* 繁忙的社交生活 —**hectically** /-klɪ; -kli/ *adv*

hecto- /hɛkto; hektəʊ/ *prefix* 100 times a particular unit 表示"百": *a hectometre* (=100 metres) 一百米 —see table on page C4 參見 C4 頁附錄

hec·tor /ˈhɛktɚ; ˈhektə/ *v* [I,T] to speak to someone in an angry, threatening way 嚇唬, 威脅: *a hectoring, bullying tone of voice* 威嚇欺凌的口氣

he'd /id, hɪd; id, hid; *strong* 強讀 hid; hiːd/ **1** the short form of 縮略式= he had: *By the time I got there he'd gone.* 我趕到那裡時, 他已經走了。**2** the short form for 縮略式= he would: *I'm sure he'd help if he could.* 我相信如果他能做到的話一定會出手幫忙的。

hedge[1] /hɛdʒ; hedʒ/ *n* [C] **1** a row of small bushes or trees growing close together, usually dividing one field or garden from another〔用灌木或矮樹築起的〕樹籬 **2** something that gives you protection in case you lose money〔避免金錢損失的〕防範措施: *Buying a house will be a hedge against inflation.* 買房子是對付通貨膨脹的一種防範手段。

hedge[2] *v* **hedged, hedging 1** [I] to avoid giving a direct answer to a question 避免作正面回答, 規避: *You're hedging again – have you got the money or haven't you?* 你又在閃爍其詞了, 你究竟拿到錢沒有? **2 hedge your bets** to reduce your chances of failure or loss by having several choices available to you 多處下注以減少風險; 腳踏兩隻船: *It's a good idea to hedge your bets by applying to more than one college.* 同時向幾所大學提出申請是個保險的好主意。**3** [T] to make a hedge around an area of land 用樹籬圍起〔地〕

hedge sb/sth **in** *phr v* **be hedged in a)** to be surrounded or enclosed by something 被…包圍: *The building was hedged in with trees.* 大樓四周圍種着樹木。**b)** if you feel hedged in by something, you feel that your freedom is restricted by it 受到…的束縛[限制]

hedge against sth *phr v* [T] to try to protect yourself against possible problems, especially financial loss 採取措施以防招致(財務)損失: *Any well-managed business will hedge against price increases.* 任何一家管理完善的企業都會採取措施防範價格上漲帶來的風險。

hedge·hog /ˈhɛdʒˌhɑg; ˈhedʒhɒg/ *n* [C] a small brown European animal whose body is round and covered with sharp SPINES (=sharp needles) 刺猬

hedgehog 刺猬
spines
刺(毛)

hedge·row /ˈhɛdʒˌro; ˈhedʒrəʊ/ *n* [C] *especially BrE* a line of bushes or small trees growing along the edge of a field or road【尤英】灌木樹籬, 一排樹籬

hedge spar·row /ˈ· ˌ··/ *n* [C] a small common bird that lives in Europe and America〔產於歐洲和美洲的〕籬雀

he·don·ist /ˈhidn̩ˌɪst; ˈhiːdən-ɪst/ *n* [C] someone who believes that pleasure is the most important thing in life 享樂主義者 —**hedonism** *n* [U] —**hedonistic** /ˌhidəˈnɪstɪk; ˌhiːdənˈɪstɪk◂/ *adj*

hee·bie-jee·bies /ˈhibɪ ˈdʒibɪz; ˌhiːbi ˈdʒiːbiz/ *n* **give sb the heebie-jeebies** *informal* to make someone feel nervous【非正式】使某人神經緊張, 使某人坐立不安

heed[1] /hid; hiːd/ *v* [T] *formal* to pay attention to someone's advice or warning【正式】聽從; 注意〔別人的建議或警告〕: *If she had only heeded my warnings, none of this would have happened.* 要是她當初聽從我的警告, 就不會發生這種事了。

heed[2] *n* [U] *formal* **pay/give heed to sth** also 又作 **take heed of sth** to pay attention to something and seriously consider it【正式】注意某事; 慎重考慮某事: **pay no heed to** *Tom paid no heed to her warning.* 湯姆根本沒有理會她的警告。

heed·less /ˈhidlɪs; ˈhiːdləs/ *adj* **heedless of** not paying attention to something 不注意, 不理會, 掉以輕心: *O'Hara rode on, heedless of danger.* 奧哈拉不理會危險, 繼續騎車走去。

hee-haw /ˈhi ˌhɔ; ˈhiː ˌhɔː/ *n* [C] the noise made by a DONKEY 驢叫聲

heel[1] /hil; hiːl/ *n* [C]

1 ►OF YOUR FOOT 腳的◄ the back part of your foot 腳後跟, 踵 —see pictures at 參見 BODY and 和 FOOT[1] 圖

2 ►OF A SHOE 鞋的◄ the raised part of a shoe that is under the back of your foot 後跟, 鞋跟 —see picture at 參見 SHOE[1] 圖

3 high-heeled/low-heeled etc high-heeled or low-heeled shoes have high or low heels〔鞋〕高跟/低跟的

4 ►OF A SOCK 襪子的◄ the part of a sock that covers your heel (襪) 後跟

5 ►OF YOUR HAND 手的◄ the raised part of your hand near your wrist〔近腕處的〕手掌根: *I pressed the paper down firmly with the heel of my hand.* 我用手掌根緊緊地把紙壓下去。

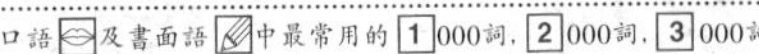

H

6 **heels** [plural] a pair of women's shoes with high heels 〔一雙〕高跟鞋
7 **be on/at sb's heels** to be following closely behind someone, especially in order to catch or attack them 緊跟着某人, 緊隨其後: *The gang were at his heels.* 那幫歹徒緊緊跟在他的身後。
8 **on the heels of** very soon after something 〔時間上〕緊接着, 在...後不久: *Kinnock's resignation came on the heels of the party's fourth defeat.* 該政黨第四次競選失敗後不久, 金諾克就辭職了。
9 **bring sb to heel** to force someone to behave in the way that you want them to 使某人就範, 使某人順從
10 **call sth to heel** if you call a dog to heel, you tell it to come back to you 叫〔狗〕緊隨在主人後面
11 **come to heel a)** if a dog comes to heel, it comes back to its owner when the owner calls it 〔狗〕緊隨在主人後面 **b)** if someone comes to heel they obey you again 〔某人〕服從, 就範
12 **take to your heels** to start running as fast as possible 拔腿逃走: *As soon as he saw me he took to his heels.* 一看到我, 他拔腿就逃。
13 **turn/spin on your heel** to suddenly turn away from someone, especially in an angry or rude way 〔尤指生氣地、無禮地〕突然轉身走掉
14 **under the heel of** completely controlled by a government or group 遭...踐踏; 在...的統治下: *The whole country was under the heel of a tyrannical dictatorship.* 整個國家的人民都活在專制獨裁的統治之下。
15 ►**BAD MAN** 壞人◄ *old-fashioned* a man who behaves badly towards other people【過時】壞蛋, 壞傢伙 —see also 另見 WELL-HEELED, ACHILLES' HEEL, **click your heels** (CLICK (1)), **cool your heels** (COOL² (4)), **dig your heels in** (DIG¹), DOWN-AT-HEEL, **drag your heels** (DRAG¹ (8)), **be hard on sb's heels** (HARD² (9)), **head over heels in love** (HEAD¹ (51)), **be hot on sb's heels** (HOT¹ (15)), **kick your heels** (KICK¹ (11))

heel² *v* **1** [T] to put a heel on a shoe 給〔鞋子〕釘後跟 **2 heel!** *spoken* used when telling a dog to walk next to you【口】跟着我!〔喚狗用語〕**3** [T] to send the ball backwards in RUGBY by hitting it with your heel 〔橄欖球比賽中〕用腳後跟向後傳球

heel over *phr v* [I] if something heels over, it leans to one side as if it is going to fall 傾斜 (要倒): *The ship was heeling over in the wind.* 船在風中向一側傾斜。

hef·ty /ˈhɛftɪ; ˈhefti/ *adj* **1** a hefty person, book etc is big and heavy 高大健壯的; 笨重的: *a hefty volume containing over 1200 pages* 一本一千二百多頁的巨著 **2** a hefty amount of something such as money is very large 大量的, 巨額的: *a hefty fine* 巨額罰款 **3** a hefty blow, kick etc is done using a lot of force 有力的, 重重的: *a hefty punch* 一記重擊 —**heftily** *adv*

he·gem·o·ny /hɪˋdʒɛmənɪ; hɪˈgeməni/ *n* [U] *formal* a situation in which one state or country controls others【正式】〔一國對其他國的〕霸權; 支配權; 領導權

He·gi·ra, Hejira /hiˋdʒaɪrə; ˈhedʒɪrə/ *n* [singular] the journey of Muhammad from Mecca to Medina in AD 622 公元 622 年穆罕默德從麥加到麥地那的逃亡

Hegira cal·en·dar /ˌ··· ˈ···/ *n* [singular] the Muslim system of dividing a year of 354 days into 12 months and starting to count the years from the Hegira 伊斯蘭教曆, 回曆

heif·er /ˈhɛfɚ; ˈhefə/ *n* [C] a young cow that has not yet given birth to a CALF (=baby cow) 〔未生過小牛的〕小母牛 —compare 比較 BULLOCK, OX, STEER

heigh-ho /ˈhe ˋho; ˌheɪ ˈhəʊ/ *interjection old-fashioned* used when you have to accept something that is boring or unpleasant【過時】唉〔表示對沉悶或不愉快的事物無奈地接受〕

S2 W2 **height** /haɪt; haɪt/ *n*
1 ►**TALL** 高◄ **a)** [U] how tall someone is 身高: **sb's height** *State your age, height, and weight.* 說出你的年齡、身高和體重。| **be the same/right etc height** *My daughter's already about the same height as I am.* 我女兒已經幾乎和我一樣高了。**b)** [C,U] the distance between the base and the top of something 高, 高度: *What's the height of the Empire State Building?* 帝國大廈有多高? | **in height** *Some of the pyramids are over 200 feet in height.* 有幾座金字塔的高度超過 200 英尺。—see picture at 參見 LENGTH 圖
2 ►**DISTANCE ABOVE THE GROUND** 離地面的距離◄ [C] a particular distance above the ground 〔離地面的〕高度: *It's a miracle she didn't break her neck falling from that height.* 她從那麼高的地方掉下來居然沒有摔斷脖子, 真是個奇蹟! | *at a height of 10,000 feet* 在離地面 10,000 英尺的高空
3 **gain/lose height** if an aircraft gains height or loses height, it moves higher in the sky or it drops lower in the sky 〔飛機在空中〕上升/下降: *The plane was rapidly losing height.* 飛機正在快速下降。
4 ►**HIGH PLACE** 高處◄ **heights** *plural* **a)** places that are a long way above the ground 高處: *Rachel had always been scared of heights.* 雷切爾過去一直害怕登高。| **have a head for heights** (=not be afraid of heights) 不怕登高, 不畏高 **b)** a particular high place 高地: *the Golan Heights* 戈蘭高地
5 **reach/attain/rise to new heights a)** to reach a very high level of achievement or success 達到新的高度, 取得新的成就: *Her career rose to new heights.* 她的事業取得了新的成就。| **take sth to new heights** *Torville and Dean took ice dancing to new heights.* 托維爾和迪安使冰上舞蹈邁向了新的境界。**b)** to reach a very great level or degree 達到很高的水平[程度]: *War fever had reached new heights.* 戰爭熱又升級了。
6 **the height of** the part of a period of time that is the busiest, hottest etc, or when there is the most activity 最繁忙的時候[季節]; 高潮, 頂點: *the height of the tourist season* 旅遊旺季
7 **be at the height of your success/fame/powers etc** to be at the time when you are most successful, famous etc 處於成功/名聲/權力等的巔峯: *The Beatles were at the height of their fame.* 當時正是披頭四樂隊最出名的時候。
8 **be the height of fashion/stupidity/luxury etc** to be extremely fashionable, stupid etc 是最時髦/愚蠢/奢侈的等: *Flared trousers were considered to be the height of fashion in those days.* 喇叭褲那時被認為是最時髦的服裝。

height·en /ˈhaɪtn̩; ˈhaɪtn/ *v* [I,T] if something heightens a feeling, effect etc, or if a feeling etc heightens, it becomes stronger or increases; INTENSIFY 加強, 增加: *Lemon helps to heighten the flavour.* 檸檬使味道變得更濃。| *Berg uses music to heighten tension in the scene.* 伯格利用配樂來增強該場景的緊張氣氛。| **heighten awareness** (=make people realize something more clearly) 提高意識 *an attempt to heighten their awareness of political issues* 為提高他們的政治意識所作的努力

hei·nous /ˈhenəs; ˈheɪnəs/ *adj formal* very shocking and immoral【正式】極邪惡的, 令人髮指的: *a heinous crime* 滔天罪行 —**heinously** *adv* —**heinousness** *n* [U]

heir /ɛr; eə/ *n* [C] **1** the person who has the legal right to receive the property or title of another person when they die 繼承人: **[+to]** *John was the sole heir to a vast estate.* 約翰是一座大莊園的唯一繼承人。| **the heir to the throne** (=the person who will become king or queen) 王位繼承人 **2** the person who will take over a position or job after you 繼任人, 接班人: *Jonson was his political heir as leader of the Nationalist Party.* 瓊森在政治上接他的班, 成了民族主義政黨的領袖。

heir ap·par·ent /ˌ· ·ˈ··/ *n* [C] an heir whose right to receive the family property, money, or title cannot be taken away 法定繼承人 —compare 比較 HEIR PRESUMPTIVE

heir·ess /ˈɛrɪs; ˈeərɪs/ *n* [C] a woman who will receive a lot of money, property, or a title when an older member of her family dies〔大筆財產或某頭銜的〕女繼承人

heir·loom /ˈɛrˌlum; ˈeəlu:m/ *n* [C] a valuable object that has been owned by a family for many years and that is passed from the older members to the younger members 祖傳寶物, 傳家寶

heir pre·sump·tive /ˌ· ·ˈ··/ *n* [C] an HEIR whose right to receive the family property, money, or title can be taken away if someone else with a better claim is born 假定繼承人〔其繼承權可能因更近的親屬的出生而喪失〕—compare 比較 HEIR APPARENT

heist /haɪst; haɪst/ *n* [C] *AmE informal* an act of robbing something very valuable from a shop, bank etc【美, 非正式】〔貴重物品的〕搶劫: *a jewelry heist* 搶劫首飾 —**heist** *v* [T]

He·ji·ra /hiˋdʒaɪrə; ˈhedʒɪ̈rə/ *n* another spelling of the HEGIRA hegira 的另一種拼法

held /hɛld; held/ past tense and past participle of HOLD¹

hel·i·cop·ter /ˈhɛlɪˌkɑptɚ; ˈhelɪ̈kɒptə/ *n* [C] a type of aircraft with large metal blades on top which turn around very quickly to make it fly 直升(飛)機

helicopter pad /ˈ···· ˌ·/ *n* [C] an area where helicopters can land 直升機停機坪

he·li·o·graph /ˈhilɪəˌgræf; ˈhi:liəgrɑ:f/ *n* [C] an instrument that sends messages by directing flashes of light with a mirror 日光反射信號器

he·li·o·trope /ˈhilɪəˌtrop; ˈhi:liətrəʊp/ *n* **1** [C] a garden plant that has pleasant-smelling pale purple flowers 天芥菜屬植物 **2** [U] the colour of this flower 淺紫紅色〔此種植物花的顏色〕

hel·i·pad /ˈhɛlɪˌpæd; ˈhelipæd/ *n* [C] a HELICOPTER PAD 直升機停機坪

hel·i·port /ˈhɛlɪˌpɔrt; ˈhelipɔ:t/ *n* [C] a small airport for HELICOPTERS 供直升機用的小機場

he·li·um /ˈhilɪəm; ˈhi:liəm/ *n* [U] a gas that is lighter than air, often used in BALLOONS 氦(氣)

he·lix /ˈhilɪks; ˈhi:lɪks/ *n* [C] *technical* a line that curves and rises around a central line; SPIRAL【術語】螺線; 螺旋(形) —see also 另見 DOUBLE HELIX

he'll /ɪl, hɪl; il, hil; *strong* 強讀 hil; hi:l/ **1** the short form of 縮略式= he will **2** the short form of 縮略式= he shall

S1 W3 **hell¹** /hɛl; hel/ *n*

1 ►UNPLEASANT SITUATION 糟糕的情況◄ [singular, U] *informal* a situation, experience, or place that is very unpleasant【非正式】極糟的情況[經歷, 地方]: *Central London was hell the Saturday before Christmas.* 聖誕節前的星期六, 倫敦市中心簡直亂得一團糟。| **sheer hell** (=extremely unpleasant) 糟透了 *"How was your exam?" "Sheer hell!"* "你考得怎麼樣?" "糟透了!" | **hell on earth** *This town is my idea of hell on earth.* 這個小鎮在我眼裡像個人間地獄。

2 ►SUFFERING 痛苦◄ a place or situation in which people suffer very much, either physically or emotionally 令人痛苦的地方[狀態]: *the hell of the battlefield* 戰場這個鬼地方 | **make sb's life hell** *He'll make my life hell if I don't do what he wants.* 如果我不滿足他的要求, 他就不會給我好日子過。| **living hell** *Josh felt trapped in a living hell.* 喬希感覺自己像被困在活地獄裡。

3 ►WHEN YOU DIE 死後◄ also 又作 **Hell** [singular] the place where the souls of bad people are believed to be punished after death, especially in the Christian and Muslim religions〔尤指基督教和伊斯蘭教所說的〕地獄, 陰間

4 how/what/where etc the hell? *spoken* used to show that you are very surprised or angry【口】到底怎麼/甚麼/哪裡等?〔表示驚訝或憤怒〕: *What the hell does he think he's doing?* 他到底認為自己在幹甚麼呢? | *Where the hell have you been?* 你剛才到底上哪兒了?

5 a/one hell of a *spoken* used to emphasize the idea that something is very big, very good, very bad etc【口】〔用以加強語氣〕極, 非常〔大、好、壞等〕: *He's one hell of a good actor.* 他真是個好演員。| *a hell of a lot of money* 一大筆錢 | **have one hell of a time** *We had one hell of a time trying to get here.* 我們費了好大勁才趕到這裡。

6 go to hell! *spoken* used to tell someone that you do not care about them or about what they think【口】見鬼去吧! 管它呢!〔表示不理會某人或其想法〕: *If John doesn't like it, he can go to hell!* 如果約翰不喜歡這樣, 讓他見鬼去吧!

7 feel/look like hell *spoken* to feel or look very ill or tired【口】感覺/看起來不舒服[疲憊]: *I've been feeling like hell all week.* 我整整一星期都感到很不舒服。

8 beat/irritate/scare etc the hell out of sb *informal* to beat, irritate etc someone very much【非正式】把某人打得/激得/嚇得半死

9 (just) for the hell of it *spoken* for no serious reason, or only for fun【口】只是為了好玩, 玩玩而已: *We decided to go for a midnight swim, just for the hell of it.* 我們決定半夜去游泳, 這只是為了好玩。

10 what the hell! *spoken* used to say that you will do something and not worry about any problems it causes【口】管它呢!〔表示不顧後果〕: *What the hell, let's go with them.* 管它呢, 我們和他們一起去吧!

11 to hell with *spoken* used to say that you do not care about something any more【口】讓…見鬼去吧: *To hell with school! I'm going to leave and get a job.* 讓學校見鬼去吧! 我馬上就要離開學校去找工作了。

12 run/work/hurt etc like hell *informal* to run, work etc very quickly or very much【非正式】拚命地跑/拚命地工作/痛得要命等: *We ran like hell and didn't stop until we were safely home.* 我們拚命地跑, 直到安全回到家。

13 like hell/the hell *spoken* used to say that you do not believe what someone has said, or that you disagree with it【口】哪有這種事, 絕不會: *"Like hell you'd pay it back", Wade said wearily.* 韋德有氣無力地說道: "我才不信你會歸還呢。"

14 from hell *informal* the worst you can imagine【非正式】最糟的: *It was disaster after disaster – the holiday from hell!* 倒霉事一件接着一件, 這個假期真是糟透了!

15 mad/weird/ugly etc as hell *especially AmE spoken* very angry, strange etc【尤美, 口】非常生氣的/古怪的/醜陋的等: *I wouldn't ask him now, he's mad as hell.* 我現在不會去問他, 他正暴跳如雷呢!

16 give sb hell *informal* to blame someone angrily【非正式】狠狠地責罵某人: *My dad gave me hell when he found out that I'd borrowed the car.* 父親發現我借了那輛車後, 把我臭罵了一頓。

17 get the hell out (of somewhere) *informal* to leave a place quickly and suddenly【非正式】趕緊離開(某地): *Let's get the hell out of here!* 我們趕緊離開這裡吧!

18 there'll be hell to pay *spoken* used to say that people will be very angry【口】〔某人〕會非常憤怒的: *There'll be hell to pay when the boss finds out.* 要是老闆發現這件事, 那就麻煩了。

19 catch hell *AmE spoken* to be blamed or punished【美口】挨罵, 受責備[懲罰]: *You'll catch hell when your Mom comes home!* 你母親回家後會罵你的!

20 all hell broke loose *informal* used to say that people suddenly become very noisy or angry【非正式】突然喧鬧起來; 一片混亂: *The rival gang arrived and all hell broke loose.* 敵對的一幫人來到後, 這裡就亂成了一片。

21 hell's bells *spoken* also 又作 **hell's teeth** *BrE*【英】used to express great annoyance or surprise【口】見鬼了〔表示極度厭煩或驚訝〕

22 come hell or high water *informal* in spite of any problems or difficulties【非正式】無論有甚麼困難: *I decided I would get the job done by Friday, come hell or high water.* 不管遇到甚麼困難, 我都決心要在星期五之前完成這項工作。

23 go to hell in a handbasket *AmE informal* if a system or organization has gone to hell in a handbasket, it has stopped working properly【美, 非正式】〔系統或機構〕無法正常運作; 出了毛病: *The education system in this state has gone to hell in a handbasket.* 這個國家的教育體系出了很多問題。

24 run/go hell for leather *informal* to run away as fast as possible【非正式】拚命地跑, 狂奔
25 hell on wheels *AmE informal* someone who does exactly what they want and does not care what happens as a result【美, 非正式】我行我素的人; 做事不顧後果的人
26 play (merry) hell with *informal* to make something stop working or happening as it should【非正式】打亂, 攪亂: *The cold weather played hell with the weekend sports schedule.* 寒冷的天氣打亂了週末的體育活動計劃。
27 when hell freezes over *informal* used to say that something will never happen【非正式】永不, 絕不可能 —see also 另見 **not a hope in hell** (HOPE² (5))

hell² *interjection* **1** *especially BrE* used to express anger or annoyance【尤英】見鬼, 該死〔表示憤怒或不耐煩〕: *Oh hell! I've left my purse at home.* 真該死！我把錢包遺在家裡了。**2** *AmE* used to emphasize something you are saying【美】見鬼, 該死〔用來加強語氣〕: *Hell, I don't know!* 見鬼, 我不知道！

hell-bent /ˌ· ˈ·◂/ *adj* [not before noun 不用於名詞前] very determined to do something, especially something that other people do not approve of 堅決的, 不顧一切的: **hell-bent on (doing) sth** *They seemed hell-bent on creating a scandal.* 他們好像一意孤行要製造一個醜聞。

hell·cat /ˈhɛlˌkæt; ˈhelkæt/ *n* [C] *informal* a woman who has a violent temper【非正式】潑婦, 悍婦

Hel·lene /ˈhɛlin; ˈheliːn/ *n* [C] *formal* a Greek, especially an ancient Greek【正式】〔尤指古代的〕希臘人

Hel·len·ic /hɛˈlɛnɪk; heˈlenɪk/ *adj* connected with the history, society, or art of the ancient Greeks 古希臘的

hell-hole /ˈ· ·/ *n* [C] a very unpleasant place 地獄般的地方, 環境極惡劣的地方: *His last apartment was a real hell-hole.* 他上次住的公寓就像地獄一樣。

hell·ish /ˈhɛlɪʃ; ˈhelɪʃ/ *adj informal* extremely unpleasant【非正式】糟透的, 極壞的: *I've had a hellish day at work.* 我今天忙得要命。—**hellishly** *adv*: *a hellishly difficult exam* 極其困難的考試

S1 **hel·lo** /həˈlo; həˈləʊ/ also 又作 **hallo, hullo** *BrE*【英】*interjection* **1** used as a usual greeting〔問候語〕喂, 哈囉, 你好: *Hello, John! How are you?* 喂, 約翰！你好嗎？| **say hello to sb** *She always says hello to me in the street.* 她在街上總是和我打招呼。| **hello there** *Well, hello there! I haven't seen you for ages.* 嗨, 你好！好久不見了。**2** used when answering the telephone or starting a telephone conversation 喂〔打電話用的招呼語〕: *Hello, is Rachel there please?* 喂, 請問雷切爾在嗎？**3** used when calling to get someone's attention 喂〔用以引起別人注意〕: *Hello! Is there anybody home?* 喂！屋裡有人嗎？**4** *BrE* used to show that you are surprised or confused by something【英】嘿〔表示驚訝或不解〕: *Hello! What's happened here?* 嘿！出甚麼事了？

helm /hɛlm; helm/ *n* **1** [C] the wheel or TILLER which guides a ship or boat〔船的〕舵輪 **2 at the helm a)** in charge of something 掌權, 領導: *The company flourished with David Finch at the helm.* 公司在戴維·芬奇的領導下興旺起來。**b)** guiding a ship or boat 掌舵 **3** *old use* a helmet【舊】頭盔

helmets 頭盔

crash helmet 防護頭盔

pith helmet 遮陽帽

see also picture at 另見 **hat** and 和 **cap** 圖

hel·met /ˈhɛlmɪt; ˈhelmɪ̈t/ *n* [C] a strong hard hat worn for protection by soldiers, MOTORCYCLE riders, the police etc 頭盔, 鋼盔, 安全帽 —see also 另見 CRASH HELMET, PITH HELMET

hel·met·ed /ˈhɛlmɪtɪd; ˈhelmɪ̈tɪ̈d/ *adj* wearing a helmet 戴頭盔的

helms·man /ˈhɛlmzmən; ˈhelmzmən/ *n plural* **helmsmen** /-mən; -mən/ [C] someone who guides a ship or boat 舵手

help¹ /hɛlp; help/ *v* S1 W1
1 ►MAKE POSSIBLE OR EASIER 使可能或容易◄ [I,T] to make it possible or easier for someone to do something by doing part of their work or by giving them something they need 幫助, 幫忙: *If there's anything I can do to help, just give me a call.* 如果需要我幫忙, 就給我打個電話。| *She devoted her life to helping the poor and sick.* 她一生致力於幫助窮人和病人。| **help sb (to) do sth** *We all helped him fill out the application form.* 我們大家一起幫他填寫申請表。| *Andy said he would help us to move the furniture.* 安迪說他會幫我們搬家具。| **help sb with sth** *Do you mind helping me with this a minute?* 你能抽點時間幫我一把嗎？| **help (to) do sth** *Part of my job is to help organize conferences.* 我其中一項工作是幫忙籌備會議。| **help sb into/out of/across etc** (=help someone move to a particular place) 扶某人進入/出去/穿過等 *He was so drunk we had to help him into the taxi.* 他醉得很厲害, 我們不得不將他扶進計程車裡。| **help sb on/off with sth** (=help someone put on or take off a piece of clothing) 幫某人穿/脫〔衣服〕*Here, let me help you on with your coat.* 嗨, 我來幫你穿大衣吧！
2 ►BE GOOD FOR 對…有好處◄ [T] to make it easier for something to develop or be improved 有助於, 助長: *The fall in oil prices should help economic development.* 油價下跌將有利於經濟發展。| **help sb (to) do sth** *All this arguing isn't going to help us win the election.* 這樣爭論下去不會幫我們贏得選舉。
3 ►MAKE BETTER 使更好◄ [I,T] to make a situation better, easier, or less painful 使〔形勢〕改善, 好轉; 減輕〔痛苦〕: *Crying won't help.* 哭無助於事。| *It helped a lot to know that someone understood how I felt.* 知道有人理解我的感受, 我感覺好多了。| **help sth** *A couple of aspirin might help your headache.* 吃兩片阿士匹靈可能會減輕你的頭痛。
4 Help! *spoken* used to call people and ask them to help you when you are in danger【口】救命啊！〔求救聲〕
5 can't help it a) to not be responsible for something unpleasant or annoying 沒有辦法; 不是〔某人〕的過錯: *I can't help it if she's late, can I?* 要是她遲到, 我也沒有辦法, 對吧？**b)** to be unable to stop doing something, or change the way that you behave 忍不住, 無法控制自己: *I always get angry with him, I just can't help it.* 我老是對他發火, 我就是控制不了自己。
6 can't/couldn't help doing sth to be unable to stop yourself from doing something 忍不住做某事, 不能停止做某事: *I can't help thinking that we've made a big mistake.* 我不禁感到我們犯了一個大錯誤。| *I couldn't help hearing what you just said.* 我忍不住聽到了你剛剛說的那些話。
7 can't/couldn't help but do sth if you cannot help but do something, it is impossible for you not to do it 不可能不做某事: *I couldn't help but notice the bruise she had under her eye.* 我不能不注意到她眼睛底下的青腫。
8 can't help yourself to be unable to stop yourself from doing something you should not do 忍不住, 無法控制自己: *Sue doesn't always mean to be so rude but sometimes she just can't help herself.* 蘇不是故意要這麼粗暴無禮的, 但有時她就是克制不了自己。
9 help yourself (to sth) a) to take something that you want, such as food, without asking permission 自己取〔食物等〕: *Please help yourself to more; there's plenty of everything.* 請再吃點吧, 還有很多呢！**b)** *informal* to steal something【非正式】偷竊: *Obviously he had been helping himself to the money.* 他顯然一直在偷錢。
10 help sb to sth to serve someone food or drink 為某人取〔食物、飲料〕: *Can I help you to some dessert?* 我

給你拿些甜點好嗎?

11 God help him/them etc *spoken* used to say that something bad may happen to someone【口】他/他們要倒霉了: *If you trust that man with a secret, God help you.* 如果你將祕密告訴那個人, 你就倒霉了!

12 a helping hand help and support 援手, 幫助: **give sb a helping hand** *She's been giving me a helping hand with the children.* 她一直在幫我照顧孩子。

13 it can't be helped *spoken* used to say that there is nothing you can do to change an unpleasant situation【口】無法避免; 沒辦法: *It's going to make a terrible noise, but never mind. It can't be helped.* 這樣會發出可怕的噪音。不過別在意, 這是不可避免的。

14 not if I can help it *spoken* used to say that you are not going to do something【口】不會做某事: *"Are you going to the meeting this afternoon?" "Not if I can help it."* "你今天下午去參加會議嗎?" "能不去就不去。"

15 so help me (God) used when making a serious promise, especially in a court of law 我發誓; 上天作證〔尤在法庭上發誓時用〕

help out *phr v* **1** [I,T] to help someone who is busy by doing some of their work for them 分擔…工作, 幫…一把: *Is there anything I can do to help out?* 我能幫上忙嗎? | **help sb out** *If you haven't got time to finish I'll help you out.* 如果你來不及做完, 我會幫你一把。**2** [T] to give help and support to someone who has problems 幫助〔某人解決難題〕: *He was obviously in some kind of trouble, but I didn't know how I could help him out.* 他顯然遇到了麻煩, 但我不知道應該怎樣幫他。

USAGE NOTE 用法説明: HELP

WORD CHOICE 詞語辨析: **help, assist, give/lend a hand, help out, come to somebody's aid/assistance, aid, give/send aid**

Help and **assist** can both describe people or institutions helping each other do a job. However, **assist** is more formal and often suggests that the person assisting is doing a simple or unimportant part of what has to be done. help 和 assist 都可以用來表示人或機構相互幫助做某事, 但 assist 較正式, 常常暗示提供幫助的一方所做的事比較簡單或佔次要地位: *My company assists businesses in all their office cleaning requirements.* 我的公司協助各企業做辦公室的清潔工作。| *You will assist the administrative officer with day-to-day organization* (Note that **assist** can never mean 'attend' or 'be present at'). 你將協助行政官員做日常的組織工作 (注意 assist 不可用來表示"參加"或"在場")。

In more informal English people often use **give/lend a hand** or **help out**, especially where there is something practical to do and not enough people to do it. 在非正式的英語中, 人們往往用 give/lend a hand 或 help out, 特別是在要做具體工作而又沒有足夠人手的情況下: *Can you give me a hand with the drinks?* 你能幫我端一下飲料嗎? | *I sometimes lend a hand/help out at the old folk's home.* 我有時在老人院裡幫忙。

If someone is in danger or trouble, you may **help** them or more formally **come to their aid/assistance**. 若某人處於危險或困境之中而你施以援手, 可用 help, 或者是語體更正式的 come to their aid/assistance: *My car's broken down, can you help?* 我的車壞了, 你能幫忙嗎? | *If you get into difficulties, the lifeguard will come to your assistance.* 如果你遇到困難, 救生員會來幫你。

If a person, charity, or government helps with money or other necessary things, **aid** (formal) or often **give/send aid** may be used. 若個人、慈善機構或政府通過金錢或其他必需品提供幫助, 可以用 aid (正式) 或常用 give/send aid: *Many projects are aided by Oxfam.* 許多項目都得到樂施會的資助。| *Aid will be sent to the area as soon as possible.* 援助物資將會儘快送往該地區。Informally **help** would be used. 在非正式場合可用 help: *Please help the homeless.* 請幫幫無家可歸的人吧。

GRAMMAR 語法

Help (but not **assist**) is often followed by a verb in the *to* or basic form. help (而不是 assist) 的後面常常跟有某動詞的不定式 (to) 或原形: *He helped me (to) pass my exam* (=I passed NOT 不用 *He helped me passing*...). 他幫助我通過了考試。But note that the expression **can't help...** meaning 'cannot stop yourself...' is only followed by the *-ing* form of a verb. 但應注意, 詞組 can't help... 意為"忍不住...", 後面只能接某一動詞的動名詞形式 (-ing): *I couldn't help laughing.* 我忍不住大笑起來。

You **help/assist/aid** someone, not *to* them. help/assist/aid 直接接幫助的對象, 不加 to。

help² *n* **1** [U] the action of helping someone by doing part of their work or by showing them how to do it 幫助, 幫忙: *If I need any help, I'll call you.* 如果我需要幫助, 我會給你打電話。| **[+with]** *Do you want any help with that?* 那件事你需要幫忙嗎? **2** [U] the fact of being useful or making something easier to do 有幫助的人[物]: *That map isn't much help.* 那張地圖不管用。| **with the help of** *We got it open with the help of a knife.* 我們用刀子把它打開了。| **be of great/little/no help** *I'm sorry I haven't been of much help to you.* 抱歉, 我沒幫上你甚麼忙。**3 be a (big/great/real) help** also 又作 **be a lot of help a)** to be very useful, or give a lot of help (很) 有用; 有 (很大) 幫助: *Thanks. You've been a big help.* 謝謝, 你幫了個大忙。**b)** often used jokingly to say that something is not useful, or someone is not helping you〔開玩笑〕幫倒忙: *A lot of help you've been! Why did you bother to come?* 你真是幫倒忙! 你又何必趕來呢? **4** [U] help which people can give to save someone from danger or difficulty 救助; 援助; 幫助: *She screamed at them to go and get help.* 她高聲叫喊, 讓他們去找救兵。**5** [U] advice, treatment, information, or money which is given to people who need it〔建議、治療、資料或金錢等〕援助, 幫助: *A lot of these children need professional help.* 許多這樣的兒童需要專業人士的幫助。| **[+with]** *You may be able to get help with the rent.* 你可能會獲得租金上的援助。| **beyond help** (=no longer able to be helped or saved) 無可救藥 *I'm afraid the patient is beyond help.* 這個病人恐怕是沒救了。**6 the help** *AmE* someone's servant or servants【美】傭人 S1 W1

help·er /ˈhɛlpɚ; ˈhelpə/ *n* [C] **1** someone who helps another person 幫手; 助手: *She's the cook's helper.* 她是廚師的助手。**2** *AmE* someone who is employed to do some of the work in someone else's home【美】傭人

help·ful /ˈhɛlpfəl; ˈhelpfəl/ *adj* **1** useful in making a situation better or easier 有用的; 有幫助的: **it is helpful (for sb) to do sth** *Sometimes it's helpful to make a list of everything you have to do.* 有時把你要做的事情列成清單是很有用的。| *It'd be helpful for me to know what your plans for the week are.* 了解你這星期的計劃會對我很有幫助。| **helpful in doing sth** *Any information would be helpful in determining what happened.* 任何資料都會幫助我們確定到底發生了甚麼事情。| **helpful suggestions/hints/ideas etc** *Has anybody got any helpful suggestions?* 誰能提出一些有用的建議? **2** always willing to help people 樂於助人的: *She's a helpful child.* 她是個樂於助人的孩子。—**helpfully** *adv* —**helpfulness** *n* [U] S2 W3

help·ing /ˈhɛlpɪŋ; ˈhelpɪŋ/ *n* [C] the amount of food that someone gives you or that you take; SERVING〔食物的〕一份, 一客: *a huge helping of potatoes* 一大份馬鈴薯

help·less /ˈhɛlplɪs; ˈhelpləs/ *adj* **1** unable to look after yourself or to do anything to help yourself 無法照顧自己的; 無助的: *Without proper defences we'd be helpless*

H

against an enemy attack. 如果缺乏適當的防禦手段，我們將無法抵擋敵人的進攻。| *Why is he so helpless?* 他為甚麼會這麼無助呢？**2** unable to control a strong feeling that you have 忍不住的，情不自禁的：[+**with**] *We rolled on the floor, helpless with laughter.* 我們忍不住笑得在地上打滾。| **helpless rage/despair/laughter etc** *fits of helpless laughter* 陣陣開懷大笑 —**helplessly** *adv* —**helplessness** *n* [U]

help·line /ˈhɛlplaɪn; ˈhelplaɪn/ *n* [C] a telephone number that you can ring if you need advice or information 求助熱線

help·mate /ˈhɛlp,met; ˈhelpmeɪt/ also 又作 **help·meet** /-mit; -miːt/ *n* [C] *biblical* a helpful partner, usually a wife【聖經】夥伴，伴侶〔常指妻子〕

hel·ter-skel·ter¹ /ˈhɛltəˋ ˋskɛltəˋ; ˌheltə ˈskeltə/ *adv* quickly and without order or organization 慌慌張張地，手忙腳亂地：*He ran off helter-skelter down the slope.* 他慌慌張張地逃下山坡。

helter-skelter² *n* [C] *BrE* a tall structure in a FAIRGROUND which you sit on at the top and slide round and round to the bottom【英】〔遊樂場內的〕螺旋滑梯

hem¹ /hɛm; hem/ *n* [C] the edge of a piece of cloth that is turned under and stitched down, especially the lower edge of a skirt, trousers etc〔衣服的〕褶邊；〔裙子的〕下襬；〔褲子的〕腳口 —see picture on page A17 參見 A17 頁圖

hem² **hemmed, hemming** *v* **1** [T] to turn under the edge of a piece of material or clothing and stitch it in place 給…縫褶邊 **2** **hem and haw** *AmE* to keep pausing before saying something, and avoid saying it directly【美】〔說話時〕吞吞吐吐，支支吾吾

hem sb **in** *phr v* [T usually passive 一般用被動態] **1** to surround someone closely, in a way that prevents them from moving〔把某人〕圍住：*They were hemmed in by steep mountains on all sides.* 他們四周都是陡峭的高山。**2** to make someone feel that they are not free to do what they want to do 限制住：*She felt hemmed-in by the daily routine.* 她感到自己被一成不變的日常工作所限制。

he-man /ˈ· ·/ *n* [C] *humorous* a strong man with powerful muscles【幽默】肌肉發達的健壯男子

hem·i·sphere /ˈhɛməs,fɪr; ˈhemɪ̣sfɪə/ *n* [C] **1** a half of the earth, especially one of the northern and southern halves above and below the EQUATOR〔地球的〕半球〔尤指赤道以北或以南的北半球或南半球〕**2** one of the two halves of your brain〔大腦的〕半球 **3** half of a SPHERE (=an object which is round like a ball)〔球體的〕一半，半球

hem·line /ˈhɛmlaɪn; ˈhemlaɪn/ *n* [C] the length of a dress, skirt etc〔衣裙下襬的〕底邊；裙子等的長度：*Short hemlines are in this spring.* 今春流行短裙。

hem·lock /ˈhɛmlɑk; ˈhemlɒk/ *n* [C,U] a very poisonous plant, or the poison that is made from it 毒芹；由毒芹提取的毒藥

hemo- /himo, himə; hiːməʊ, hemə/ the American spelling of HAEMO- haemo- 的美式拼法

he·mo·glo·bin /ˌhiməˋglobɪn; ˌhiːməˈgləʊbɪ̣n/ *n* [U] the American spelling of HAEMOGLOBIN haemoglobin 的美式拼法

he·mo·phil·i·a /ˌhiməˋfɪlɪə; ˌhiːməˈfɪliə/ *n* [U] the American spelling of HAEMOPHILIA haemophilia 的美式拼法

he·mo·phil·i·ac /ˌhiməˋfɪlɪæk; ˌhiːməˈfɪliæk/ *n* [C] the American spelling of HAEMOPHILIAC haemophiliac 的美式拼法

hem·or·rhage /ˈhɛmərɪdʒ; ˈhemərɪdʒ/ *n* [C,U] the American spelling of HAEMORRHAGE haemorrhage 的美式拼法

hem·or·rhoids /ˈhɛmərɔɪdz; ˈhemərɔɪdz/ *n* [plural] the American spelling of HAEMORRHOIDS haemorrhoids 的美式拼法

hemp /hɛmp; hemp/ *n* [U] a type of plant that is used to make rope and sometimes to produce the drug CANNABIS 大麻〔用以製繩，有時製成毒品〕

hen /hɛn; hen/ *n* [C] **1** an adult female chicken 母雞 **2** any female bird of which the male is the COCK¹ (5) 雌禽

hence /hɛns; hens/ *adv formal*【正式】**1** [sentence adverb 句子副詞] for this reason 因此，由此，所以：*He's an extremely private person; hence his reluctance to give interviews.* 他是一個極端孤僻的人，因此不願接受採訪。**2** **ten days hence/five months hence etc** ten days from now, five months from now etc 十天/五個月等以後

hence·forth /ˌhɛnsˋfɔrθ; ˌhensˈfɔːθ/ also 又作 **hence·for·ward** /ˌhɛnsˋfɔrwəˋd; ˌhensˈfɔːwəd/ *adv formal* from this time on【正式】從今以後，今後，從現在起：*The company will henceforth be known as "Johnson and Brown."* 公司從今起將稱為"約翰遜－布朗公司"。

hench·man /ˈhɛntʃmən; ˈhentʃmən/ *n plural* **henchmen** /-mən; -mən/ [C] a faithful supporter, especially of a political leader or a criminal〔尤指政治領導人或罪犯的〕忠實支持者，黨羽，嘍囉，狗腿子，心腹

hen house /ˈ· ·/ *n* [C] a small building where chickens are kept 雞舍

hen·na /ˈhɛnə; ˈhenə/ *n* [U] a reddish-brown substance used to change the colour of hair〔紅褐色的〕散沫花染髮劑 —**henna** *v* [T]

hen par·ty /ˈ· ,··/ *n* [C] *informal BrE* a party for women only, that happens just before one of them gets married【非正式，英】〔女性即將結婚前舉行的〕只有女性朋友參加的聚會 —compare 比較 STAG PARTY

hen·pecked /ˈhɛn,pɛkt; ˈhenpekt/ *adj* a man who is henpecked is always being told what to do by his wife, and is afraid to disagree with her〔男人〕怕老婆的，懼內的：*a henpecked husband* 怕老婆的丈夫

hep·a·ti·tis /ˌhɛpəˋtaɪtɪs; ˌhepəˈtaɪtɪ̣s◂/ *n* [U] a disease of the LIVER (1) that causes fever and yellow colour in your skin 肝炎

hepatitis A /ˌ····ˈ·/ *n* [U] a usually less severe form of hepatitis, caused by infected food or water 甲型肝炎

hepatitis B /ˌ····ˈ·/ *n* [U] a severe form of hepatitis passed from one person to another in infected blood 乙型肝炎

hep·ta·gon /ˈhɛptə,gɑn; ˈheptəgən/ *n* [C] a shape with seven sides 七邊形，七角形 —**heptagonal** /hɛpˋtægənl; hepˈtægənəl/ *adj*

her¹ /ɚ, hɚ; ə, hə; *strong* 強讀 hɝ; hɜː/ *determiner* [possessive form of 'she' she 的所有格] **1** belonging to or connected with a woman, girl, or female animal that has been mentioned or is known about〔指女性或雌性動物〕她的：*Maria starts her swimming lessons on Friday.* 瑪麗亞星期五開始上她的游泳課。| *It's her first child.* 這是她的第一個孩子。**2** connected with a country, ship, car etc that has been mentioned〔指國家、船隻、車輛等〕她的：*Her top speed is about 110 miles an hour.* 她的最高時速大約為 110 英里。

her² *pron* [object form of 'she' she 的受[賓]格] **1** a woman, girl, or female animal that has been mentioned or is known about〔指女性或雌性動物〕她：*Janet? I've not seen her for a long time.* 珍妮特？我已經很久沒見過她了。| *Give her the keys.* 把鑰匙給她。| *Is that her over there?* 那邊是她嗎？—see 見 ME (USAGE) **2** a country, ship, car etc that has been mentioned〔指國家、船隻、車輛等〕她：*God bless this ship and all who sail in her.* 願上帝保佑這條船和船上所有的人！

her·ald¹ /ˈhɛrəld; ˈherəld/ *v* [T] **1** to be a sign of something that is going to happen 預示…的發生：*The talks herald a new era in East-West relations.* 會談預示着東西方關係將進入一個新的時代。**2** to say publicly that someone or something will be good or important 公開稱讚：*She has been heralded as one of the country's finest musicians.* 她被譽為是該國最優秀的音樂家之一。

herald² *n* **1** [C] someone who carried messages from a ruler in the past〔古時的〕傳令官 **2** **herald of** a sign that something is soon going to happen …的預兆：

primroses, the first herald of spring 報春花, 春天來臨的首個預兆

he·ral·dic /hɛˋrældɪk; heˈrældɪk/ *adj* connected with heraldry 紋章術的; 紋章學的

her·ald·ry /ˋhɛrəldrɪ; ˈherəldri/ *n* [U] the skill of making or the study of coats of arms (COAT OF ARMS) 紋章術; 紋章學

herb /hɝb; hɜːb/ *n* [C] a small plant that is used to improve the taste of food, or to make medicine〔用於調味或製藥的〕香草; 藥草

her·ba·ceous /hɝˋbeʃəs; həˈbeɪʃəs/ *adj technical* plants that are herbaceous have soft stems rather than wood stems【術語】〔植物〕草本的

herbaceous bor·der /·,·· ˈ··/ *n* [C] part of a garden where plants are grown that live for many years and do not need to be replaced〔花園中種植的多年生的〕綠草帶, 綠緣

herb·al /ˋhɝbḷ; ˈhɜːbəl/ *adj* made of herbs 用草本植物製成的: *herbal tea* 藥草茶 | *herbal remedies* 草藥

herb·al·ist /ˋhɝbḷɪst; ˈhɜːbəl̩st/ *n* [C] someone who grows, sells, or uses HERBS, especially to treat illness 種草藥的人; 草藥商; 草藥醫生

herbal medi·cine /,·· ˈ···/ *n* **1** [U] the practice of treating illness using plants 草藥治療法, 草藥醫學 **2** [C,U] medicine made from plants 草藥

herb gar·den /ˈ· ,··/ *n* [C] a garden in which only HERBS are grown 百草園

herb·i·cide /ˋhɝbɪ,saɪd; ˈhɜːb̩saɪd/ *n* [C,U] *technical* a substance used to kill unwanted plants【術語】除草劑

her·bi·vore /ˋhɝbɪ,vɔr; ˈhɜːb̩vɔː/ *n* [C] an animal that only eats plants 食草動物 —**herbivorous** /hɝˋbɪvərəs; hɜːˈbɪvərəs/ *adj* —compare 比較 CARNIVORE, OMNIVORE

her·cu·le·an /hɝˋkjulɪən; ˌhɜːkjʊˈliːən◂/ *adj* needing great strength or determination 需要花很大力氣[決心]的: *a herculean task* 艱巨的任務

herd¹ /hɝd; hɜːd/ *n* **1** [C] a group of animals of one kind that lives and feeds together〔同一種類並一同棲息的〕獸群: [**+of**] a *herd of cattle* 一群牛 | [also+plural verb in *BrE* 英] *A herd of cows were descending into the valley.* 一群牛正從山上走下來, 進入山谷。—compare 比較 FLOCK¹ (1) **2 the herd** people generally, especially when thought of as being easily influenced〔易受人支配的〕民眾, 老百姓, 芸芸眾生: *She's never been the sort of person to follow the herd.* 她是一個從來不隨大流的人。| **the herd instinct** (=the need to behave in the same way as everyone else) 隨大流的本能

herd² *v* **1** [I always+adv/prep, T] to come together or bring people together in a large group, especially roughly〔尤指粗暴地〕(使) 集合在一起: [**+into/through etc**] *The waiting tourists were herded onto the bus.* 等待着的遊客被趕進大客車裡。**2** [T] to make animals move together in a group 放牧: *herding sheep* 牧羊

herds·man /ˋhɝdzmən; ˈhɜːdzmən/ *n plural* **herdsmen** /-mən; -mən/ [C] a man who looks after a herd of animals 牧人

1 1 **here¹** /hɪr; hɪə/ *adv* **1** in this place 在這裡: *Is George here?* 喬治在這裡嗎? | *Kabul is four hundred miles west of here.* 喀布爾離這裡往西四百英里。| *I knew there would be no one here in this room.* 我早就知道這房間裡沒有人。| *Shall we eat here?* 我們在這裡吃飯好嗎? | **here and now** (=used to emphasize what you are saying) 此時此地〔用來加強語氣〕*I'll tell you here and now that I am not going to resign.* 我現在就告訴你, 我不會辭職。| **on here/out here/down here/over here etc** *It's very cold out here.* 這外面很冷。| *We're over here!* 我們在這兒呢! —compare 比較 THERE² (1) **2** happening now 此時: *I'll be glad when the summer vacation is here.* 暑假來到時, 我會很高興。**3** at this point in a discussion〔討論中〕在這一點上: *There are many reasons for this decline, which we cannot discuss here.* 造成這種下降的原因有很多, 在此我們無法討論。**4 here's/here is/here are/here comes etc** used when introducing something or someone, or showing them to someone〔用以介紹某人或某物〕這就是…: *Here comes Michael now.* 這位就是邁克爾。| *Here's the shop I was telling you about.* 這就是我一直向你提起的那家商店。**5 here/here is/here's/here we are etc** used when you have just found something that you have been looking for 找到了: *Ah, here we are, here's my address book.* 哈, 找到了, 我的地址簿在這裡呢。**6 here's/here/here you are etc** used when you are giving something to someone〔用於把某物給某人時〕給你: *Here's some money for you.* 給你點錢。| *Here are your keys back.* 還你鑰匙。**7 neither here nor there** not important 不重要, 不相干, 無關緊要的: *The hospital needs this machine. The fact that it costs a lot of money is neither here nor there.* 醫院需要這種機器。價格昂貴這一點並不重要。**8 here and there** scattered around in several different places 到處, 各處; 零散地: *Windows were shattered and there was minor damage to buildings here and there.* 窗戶都被打破了, 建築物上到處都是輕微的損傷。**9 here, there, and everywhere** *informal* in many different places【非正式】到處, 各處; 在許多不同的地方: *We've been looking for you here, there, and everywhere.* 我們一直到處在找你。**10 here goes!** used when you are going to try to do something difficult 我這就開始〔做困難的事〕: *I've never ridden a motorbike before, so here goes!* 我以前從未騎過摩托車, 現在就試試看吧! **11 here we go (again)** *informal* used when something unpleasant is beginning to happen again【非正式】〔不愉快的事〕又發生了!: *Janet stormed off in a temper. "Here we go again," Matt thought.* 珍妮特氣沖沖地走了。馬特心想: "又來了!" **12 Here's to** used when you are going to drink something to wish someone good luck, show your respect for them etc〔敬酒時說的祝詞〕為…乾杯, 祝…: *Here's to the happy couple.* 為這幸福的一對乾杯! | *Here's to your new job.* 為你的新工作乾杯! **13 here to stay** if something is here to stay, it has become a part of life and will continue to be so〔某物〕已經成為生活中的一部分

Frequencies of the word **here** in spoken and written English. 單詞 here 在英語口語和書面語中的使用頻率

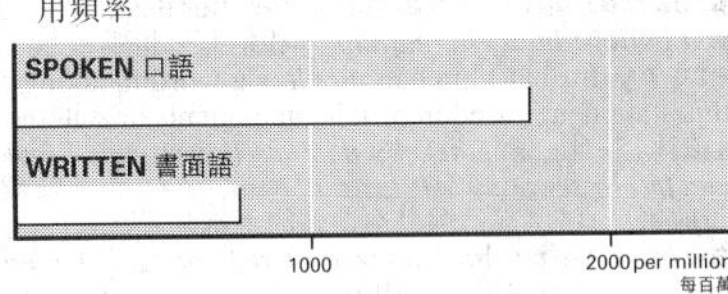

Based on the British National Corpus and the Longman Lancaster Corpus
據英國國家語料庫和朗文蘭卡斯特語料庫

This graph shows that the word **here** is much more common in spoken English than in written English. This is because it has special uses in spoken English and is used in a lot of common spoken phrases. 本圖表顯示, 單詞 here 在英語口語中的使用頻率遠遠高於書面語, 因為它在英語口語中有一些特殊的用法, 而且口語中有很多常用片語是由 here 構成的。

here (*adv*) **SPOKEN PHRASES**
含 here 的口語片語

14 a) used when you are giving or offering something to someone〔把某物給某人時用〕喏: *Here, have my chair. I don't mind standing.* 喏, 坐我的椅子吧。我可以站着。**b)** *BrE* used to get someone's attention or to show that you are annoyed【英】喂〔用來引起別人注意或表示不高興〕: *Here! Just what do you think you're doing?* 喂! 你認為你這是在幹甚麼? **15 here is a)** used when you are giving something to someone〔給別人東西時用〕給你…: *Here's some money. Have a good time.* 給你點錢。好好玩吧! **b)** used to say that someone or something is arriving …來

了: *Ah, look – here's the mailman.* 啊，瞧！郵遞員來了。| **here it is/they are** *Here they are, late as usual.* 他們終於來了，一如以往又遲到了。**c)** used to tell someone that you have found something, or to say where something is …在這兒〔表示發現某物〕: *Oh, here's the knife, it was under these dishes.* 啊，刀子在這兒呢！就在這堆盤子底下。| **here it is/they are** *Here she is, hiding behind the curtains.* 她在這兒呢，藏在簾子後面。**16 here you are/here you go** used when you are giving something to someone〔把東西給某人時用〕給你: *Here you are John, have some cake.* 約翰，給你，吃點蛋糕吧！**17 here we go** used when you are starting to do something or when something is starting to happen（我們）開始了: *Right, here we go, the game's starting.* 好了，開始了，遊戲就要開始了。**18 here goes** used when you are going to try something and you do not know what will happen〔表示準備做某事並對後果不確定〕我要開始了: *O.K. Here goes. Stand back everyone.* 好了，我要開始了。大家往後站。**19 here comes** used when you can see something or someone arriving …來了: *Quick, here comes the bus. Have you got the right money?* 快，公共汽車來了。準備好零錢了嗎？

here² *interjection* **1** used when you are giving or offering something to someone〔用於把某物給某人時〕喏: *Here, have my chair. I don't mind standing.* 喏，坐我的椅子吧。我可以站着。**2** *BrE* used to attract someone's attention or to express annoyance【英】〔用來引起別人注意或表示不高興〕喂！: *Here! Just what do you think you're doing?* 喂！你認為你這是在幹甚麼？

here·a·bouts /ˌhɪrəˋbauts; ˌhɪərəˈbaʊts/ also 又作 **here·about** *AmE*【美】*adv* somewhere near the place where you are（在這）附近，在這一帶: *There must be a public telephone hereabouts.* 這附近肯定有公用電話。

here·af·ter¹ /hɪrˋæftɚ; ˌhɪərˈɑːftə/ *adv* **1** [sentence adverb 句子副詞] *formal* from this time【正式】此後，今後 **2** *formal* after death【正式】死後 **3** *law* in a later part of a legal document【法律】〔法律文件的〕在下文中，此後

hereafter² *n* **the hereafter** a life after death 來世: *Do you believe in the hereafter?* 你相信有來世嗎？

here·by /hɪrˋbaɪ; ˌhɪəˈbaɪ/ *adv law* a word meaning 'by this statement', used in official documents or statements【法律】特此，茲: *I hereby declare that James Lowe is elected to serve as MP for this constituency.* 我特此宣布詹姆斯·洛已經當選為本選區的下議院議員。

he·red·i·ta·ry /həˋrɛdəˌtɛrɪ; hɪ̇ˈredɪ̇təri/ *adj* **1** mental or physical qualities, abilities, or illnesses etc that are hereditary are passed from parent to child in the cells of the body〔品質、體格、能力、疾病等〕遺傳的 **2 a)** *BrE* a position, rank, or title that is hereditary can be passed from an older to a younger person in the same family, usually when the older one dies【英】〔地位、稱號等〕世襲的，承襲的 **b)** having a legal right to receive a position, rank, or title in this way 享有承襲權的: *a hereditary peer* 世襲的貴族

he·red·i·ty /həˋrɛdətɪ; hɪ̇ˈredɪ̇ti/ *n* [U] the process by which mental or physical qualities, abilities, or illnesses pass from parents to children in the cells of the body 遺傳

here·in /hɪrˋɪn; ˌhɪərˈɪn/ *adv formal* in this place, situation, document etc【正式】在此地；在這種情況下；在本文中: *the conditions stated herein* 本文所列條件 —compare 比較 THEREIN

here·in·af·ter /ˌhɪrɪnˋæftɚ; ˌhɪərɪnˈɑːftə/ *adv law* later in this official statement, document etc【法律】〔正式文件〕在下文中: *Messrs Wilson and Cartwright, hereinafter referred to as "the insurers"…* 威爾遜先生和卡特賴特先生，以下稱"承保人"…

here·of /hɪrˋɑv; ˌhɪərˈɒv/ *adv formal or law* connected with or belonging to this【正式或法律】關於這點，在本文中: *every part hereof* 本文中的每個部分 —compare 比較 THEREOF

her·e·sy /ˋhɛrəsɪ; ˈherɪ̇si/ *n* [C,U] **1** a belief that disagrees with the official principles of a particular religion 異教 **2** a belief, statement etc that disagrees with what a group of people believe to be right 異端邪說: *In the 1980s it became economic heresy to challenge monetarist theory.* 20世紀80年代，質疑貨幣主義理論的觀點被看作是經濟學上的異端邪說。

her·e·tic /ˋhɛrətɪk; ˈherɪ̇tɪk/ *n* [C] someone who is guilty of heresy 異教徒；異端分子: *Cranmer was put to death as a heretic.* 克蘭默因信奉異教而被處死。—**heretical** /həˋrɛtɪkḷ; hɪ̇ˈretɪkəl/ *adj*

here·to /hɪrˋtu; ˌhɪəˈtuː/ *adv formal* to this【正式】於此，在此，至此: *my signature hereto appended* 此附上本人簽名

here·to·fore /ˌhɪrtəˋfɔr; ˌhɪətʊˈfɔː/ *adv formal* before this time【正式】此前，在此之前

here·up·on /ˌhɪrəˋpɑn; ˌhɪərəˈpɒn/ *adv formal* at or after this moment【正式】此刻；隨後

here·with /hɪrˋwɪθ; ˌhɪəˈwɪð/ *adv formal* with this letter or document【正式】與此〔信或文件〕一道，隨函附上: *I enclose herewith two copies of the contract.* 隨函附上合同副本兩份。

her·i·ta·ble /ˋhɛrətəbḷ; ˈherɪ̇təbəl/ *adj law* property that is heritable can be passed from the older members of a family to the younger ones; HEREDITARY (2)【法律】〔財產〕可繼承的

her·i·tage /ˋhɛrətɪdʒ; ˈherɪ̇tɪdʒ/ *n* [singular,U] important qualities, customs, and TRADITIONS that have been in a society for a long time 遺產；傳統: *the cultural heritage of Italy* 意大利的文化遺產 —compare 比較 INHERITANCE

her·maph·ro·dite /hɝˋmæfrəˌdaɪt; hɜːˈmæfrədaɪt/ *n* [C] a living thing that has the organs of both male and female 雌雄同體的生物 —**hermaphrodite** *adj* —**hermaphroditic** /hɝˌmæfrəˋdɪtɪk; hɜːˌmæfrəˈdɪtɪk◂/ *adj*

her·met·ic /hɝˋmɛtɪk; hɜːˈmetɪk/ *adj technical* very tightly closed so that air cannot get in or out; AIRTIGHT【術語】密封的，不透氣的 —**hermetically** /-kḷɪ; -kli/ *adv*: *stored in hermetically sealed containers* 保存在密封的容器裡

her·mit /ˋhɝmɪt; ˈhɜːmɪ̇t/ *n* [C] someone who lives alone and has a simple way of life, usually for religious reasons〔一般指出於宗教原因的〕隱士，獨居修道士；遁世者 —compare 比較 RECLUSE

her·mit·age /ˋhɝmɪtɪdʒ; ˈhɜːmɪ̇tɪdʒ/ *n* [C] a place where a hermit lives or has lived 隱居處，隱士住處

hermit crab /ˋ‥ ˌ·/ *n* [C] a kind of CRAB¹ (1) that lives in the empty shells of other sea creatures 寄居蟹

her·ni·a /ˋhɝnɪə; ˈhɜːniə/ *n* [C,U] a medical condition in which an organ pushes through the muscles that are supposed to contain it; RUPTURE¹ (3)〔臟器的〕突出，疝（氣）

he·ro /ˋhɪro; ˈhɪərəʊ/ *n plural* **heroes** [C] **1** a man who is admired for doing something extremely brave 英雄，豪傑，勇士: *He had dared to speak out against injustice, and overnight he became a national hero.* 他敢於站出來抨擊不公正的現象，一夜之間就成了國家英雄。| **war hero** (=a soldier who was very brave in a war) 戰爭英雄 **2** the man or boy who is the main character in a book, film, play etc 男主角，男主人公: *Indiana Jones is the hero of the film.* 印第安那·瓊斯是影片的男主角。**3** someone you admire very much for their intelligence, skill etc 偶像: **sb's hero** *My hero as a boy was the great Di Maggio.* 我兒時的偶像是了不起的〔棒球名將〕迪馬喬。**4** *AmE* a SANDWICH made of a long LOAF of bread filled with meat, cheese etc【美】〔夾有肉、乾酪等的〕長麵包三明治 —see also 另見 HEROINE

he·ro·ic /hɪˋro·ɪk; hɪˈrəʊɪk/ *adj* **1** extremely brave or determined and admired by many people 英雄的，英勇的: *her heroic efforts to save her family* 她為挽救全家人所作的英勇的嘗試 **2** a heroic story, poem etc involves a hero (關於) 英雄的 **3 on a heroic scale/of heroic proportions** very large or great 很大的: *a battle on a heroic scale* 大規模的戰爭 —**heroically** /-klɪ; -kli/ *adv*

heroic coup·let /·,·· ˈ··/ *n* [C] a pair of lines in poetry which end with the same sound and that have five beats in each line〔兩行相互押韻、每行含有五個抑揚音步的〕英雄偶句詩

he·ro·ics /hɪˋro·ɪks; hɪˈrəʊɪks/ *n* [plural] language or behaviour that is too brave for a particular situation〔過分的〕豪言壯語; 逞英雄行為: *America's present need is not heroics, but calm diplomacy.* 美國當前需要的不是逞英雄, 而是冷靜的外交。

her·o·in /ˋhɛro·ɪn; ˈherəʊɪn/ *n* [U] a powerful and illegal drug made from MORPHINE 海洛因, 二乙酰嗎啡: *a heroin addict* 海洛因癮君子

her·o·ine /ˋhɛro·ɪn; ˈherəʊɪn/ *n* [C] **1** the woman or girl who is the main character in a book, film, play etc 女主角, 女主人公: *the tragic heroine of Sophocles' play*〔古希臘劇作家〕索福克勒斯戲劇中悲慘的女主角 **2** a woman who is extremely brave and is admired by many people 女英雄: *a heroine of the French Resistance* 法國抵抗運動的女英雄 **3** a woman you admire very much for her intelligence, skill etc 受崇拜的女人,〔女〕偶像 —see also 另見 HERO

her·o·is·m /ˋhɛro,ɪzəm; ˈherəʊɪzəm/ *n* [U] very great courage 英雄氣概; 大無畏精神, 英勇: *stories of heroism and self-sacrifice* 關於英勇無畏和自我犧牲的故事

her·on /ˋhɛrən; ˈherən/ *n* [C] a large bird with very long legs and a long beak, that lives near water (蒼) 鷺

hero wor·ship /ˈ·· ,··/ *n* [U] great admiration for someone you think is very brave, good, skilful etc 英雄[偶像]崇拜 —**hero-worship** *v* [T]

her·pes /ˋhɝpiz; ˈhɜːpiːz/ *n* [U] a very infectious disease that causes spots on the skin, especially on the face or GENITALS 疱疹

her·ring /ˋhɛrɪŋ; ˈherɪŋ/ *n plural* **herrings** or **herring** [C] a long thin silver sea fish that can be eaten 鯡魚 —see also 另見 RED HERRING

her·ring·bone /ˋhɛrɪŋ,bon; ˈherɪŋbəʊn/ *n* [U] a pattern consisting of a continuous line of V shapes, used in cloth etc〔織物上的〕鯡骨式圖案, 人字形圖案 —see picture on page A16 參見 A16 頁圖

herring gull /ˈ·· ·/ *n* [C] a large white bird that lives near the sea in Britain 銀鷗

3 **hers** /hɝz; hɜːz/ *pron* the possessive form of 'she'; of or belonging to a female person or animal already mentioned〔she 的所有格〕她的 (所有物): *This is my coat. Hers* (=her coat) *is over there.* 這是我的外套。她的 (外套) 在那邊。| *My shoes are brown and hers are red.* 我的鞋子是棕色的, 她的 (鞋子) 是紅色的。| *Paul's a friend of hers.* 保羅是她的朋友。

2 **her·self** /hɚˋsɛlf; əˈself; *strong* 強讀 hɝ-; hɜː-/ *pron* **1**
1 reflexive form of 'she'〔she 的反身代名詞〕她自己: *She hurt herself.* 她 (把自己) 弄傷了。| *She made herself a cup of coffee.* 她給自己煮了杯咖啡。**2** the strong form of 'she' used to emphasize the subject or object of a sentence〔she 的強調形式〕她本人: *It must be true that she's leaving because she told me so herself.* 她的確是要走了, 因為這是她親口對我說的。| *She herself told me.* 她本人告訴我的。**3** *informal* in her usual state of mind or body【非正式】〔身心的〕正常狀態: *She's feeling much more herself today.* 她今天感覺好多了。**4 (all) by herself a)** alone (她) 獨自, 一個人: *She lives by herself.* 她獨自居住。**b)** without help from anyone else 獨力: *The little girl wrote the letter all by herself.* 這個小女孩不用別人幫助, 自己寫了這封信。**5 (all) to herself** for her own use; not having to share (她) 私用的, 獨用的: *She had the house to herself while her parents were gone.* 她父母不在家時, 她一個人住在這座房子裡。

hertz /hɝts; hɜːts/ *n plural* **hertz** [C] a measurement meaning one time each second, used to measure SOUND WAVES〔頻率單位〕赫 (茲), 週/秒, 次/秒

he's /ɪz, hɪz; iz, hiz; *strong* 強讀 hiz; hiːz/ **1** the short form of 縮略式= he is: *He's a writer.* 他是一位作家。| *He's reading.* 他正在看書。**2** the short form of 縮略式= he has: *He's bought a new car.* 他買了一輛新車。

hes·i·tan·cy /ˋhɛzətənsɪ; ˈhezɨtənsi/ also 又作 **hes·i·tance** /-təns; -təns/ *n* [U] the quality of being uncertain or slow in doing or saying something 猶豫, 躊躇, 遲疑 (不決)

hes·i·tant /ˋhɛzətənt; ˈhezɨtənt/ *adj* uncertain about what to do or say because you are nervous or unwilling 猶豫 (不決) 的, 遲疑的, 有疑慮的: *Gail gave me a hesitant little smile.* 蓋爾對我猶豫地微笑了一下。| **hesitant to do sth** *The economist was hesitant to comment on government policy.* 那個經濟學家不大願意對政府政策作出評論。—**hesitantly** *adv*

hes·i·tate /ˋhɛzə,tet; ˈhezɨteɪt/ *v* **1** [I] to pause before saying or doing something because you are not sure or nervous 猶豫, 躊躇, 遲疑 (不決): *Harriet hesitated a moment before replying.* 哈麗雅特猶豫了一會才作出回答。**2 hesitate to do sth** to be unwilling to do something because you are not sure that it is right 不願做某事, 對…有顧慮: *Don't hesitate to contact me if you need any more information.* 如果你需要更多資料, 儘管和我聯繫。—**hesitatingly** *adv*

hes·i·ta·tion /,hɛzəˋteʃən; ,hezɨˈteɪʃən/ *n* [C,U] the action of hesitating 躊躇, 猶豫, 遲疑 (不決): *After some hesitation one of them began to speak.* 猶豫了一會兒之後, 其中一個人開口了。| **have no hesitation in** *I would have no hesitation in declining the post.* 我會毫不猶豫地拒絕這個職位。| **after/without a moment's hesitation** *Without a moment's hesitation she kissed him.* 她毫不猶豫地親吻了他。

hes·si·an /ˋhɛʃən; ˈhesiən/ *n* [U] *BrE* thick rough cloth sometimes used for making sacks (SACK[1] (1))【英】麻袋布, 粗麻布; BURLAP *AmE*【美】

het /hɛt; het/ —see 見 HET UP

hetero- /hɛtəro, -rə; hetərəʊ, -rə/ *prefix formal or technical* other; opposite; different【正式或術語】異的; 雜的; 其他的; 相反的: *heterosexual* (=attracted to the opposite sex) 異性戀的

het·e·ro·dox /ˋhɛtərə,dɑks; ˈhetərədɒks/ *adj formal* heterodox beliefs, practices etc are not approved of by a particular group, especially a religious one【正式】異教的, 異端的, 非正統的 —compare 比較 UNORTHODOX

het·e·ro·ge·ne·ous /,hɛtərəˋdʒinɪəs; ,hetərəʊˈdʒiːniəs/ also 又作 **het·e·ro·ge·nous** /,hɛtəˋrɑdʒənəs; ,hetəˈrɒdʒənəs◂/ *AmE*【美】—*adj formal* consisting of parts or members that are very different from each other【正式】由全然不同的部分[成員]組成的, 混雜的: *a heterogeneous collection of buildings* 風格各異的一組建築 —**heterogeneity** /,hɛtərədʒəˋniətɪ; ,hetərəʊdʒɨˈniːɨti/ *n* [U] —**heterogeneously** *adv*

het·e·ro·sex·u·al /,hɛtərəˋsɛkʃuəl; ,hetərəˈsekʃuəl◂/ *adj* sexually attracted to people of the opposite sex 異性戀的 —compare 比較 BISEXUAL[1] (1), HOMOSEXUAL —**heterosexual** *n* [C] —**heterosexuality** /,hɛtərə,sɛkʃuˋæləti; ,hetərəsekʃuˈælɨti/ *n* [U] —**heterosexually** *adv*

het up /,hɛt ˋʌp; ,het ˈʌp/ *adj* [not before noun 不用於名詞前] *informal* anxious, upset, or slightly angry【非正式】焦慮不安的, 慌張的, 激動的: *Why's Andy so het up?* 安迪為甚麼這樣焦慮不安呢? | **[+about]** *Mike's very het up about his exams.* 麥克對考試感到憂心忡忡。

heu·ris·tic /hjuˋrɪstɪk; hjʊˈrɪstɪk/ *adj formal*【正式】**1** heuristic education is based on discovering and experiencing things for yourself〔教育〕啟發式的 **2** helping you in the process of learning or discovery〔對學習和發現〕有啟發作用的 —**heuristically** /-klɪ; -kli/ *adv*

heu·ris·tics /hjuˋrɪstɪks; hjʊˈrɪstɪks/ *n* [plural,U] the study of how people use their experience to find answers to questions or to improve performance 啟發法, 探索法

hew /hju; hjuː/ *v past tense* **hewed** *past participle* **hewed** or **hewn** /hjun; hjuːn/ *literary*【文】**1** [I,T] to cut something with a cutting tool〔用刀、斧等〕砍, 劈: *hewn stone*

鑿好的石頭 **2 hew a path/channel etc** to cut a path etc through something 開闢道路/渠道等 —see also 另見 ROUGH-HEWN —**hewer** *n* [C]

hewn /hjun; hjuːn/ the past participle of hew

hex¹ /hɛks; heks/ *n* [C] *especially AmE* an evil CURSE² (2) that brings trouble【尤美】〔招致災禍的〕惡毒的詛咒; 不祥之物

hex² *v* [T] *especially AmE* to use magic powers to make bad things happen to someone; CURSE¹ (3)【尤美】施魔法於; 唸惡咒〔使某人遭殃或倒霉〕

hex·a·de·ci·mal /ˌhɛksəˋdɛsəml; ˌheksəˈdesɪməl◂/ also 又作 **hex** *adj technical* hexadecimal numbers are based on the number 16 and are mainly used on computers【術語】十六進制的

hex·a·gon /ˋhɛksəˌgɑn; ˈheksəgən/ *n* [C] a shape with six sides 六邊形, 六角形 —**hexagonal** /hɛkˋsægənəl; hekˈsægənəl/ *adj*

hex·a·gram /ˋhɛksəˌgræm; ˈheksəgræm/ *n* [C] a star shape with six points, made from two TRIANGLES 六角星形

hex·am·e·ter /hɛksˋæmətɚ; hekˈsæmɪtə/ *n* [C] a line of poetry with six main beats 有六韻步的詩行

hey /he; heɪ/ *interjection* a shout used to get someone's attention or to express surprise, interest, or annoyance〔用來引起注意或表示驚訝、興趣或惱怒的喊聲〕嘿, 喂

hey·day /ˋheˌde; ˈheɪdeɪ/ *n* **sb's/sth's heyday** the time when someone or something was most popular, successful, or powerful 某人/某物的全盛時期, 最興盛[最有影響, 最成功]的時期: *a picture of Greta Garbo in her heyday*〔荷里活明星〕格麗泰·嘉寶風華正茂時期的照片

hey pres·to /ˌhe ˋprɛsto; ˌheɪ ˈprestəʊ/ *interjection especially BrE* used to say that something happens so easily that it seems to be magic【尤英】説變就變〔指某事發生得很快, 如同變魔術一般〕

HGV /ˌetʃ dʒi ˋvi; ˌeɪtʃ dʒiː ˈviː/ *n* [C] *BrE* a HEAVY GOODS VEHICLE; a large road vehicle used for moving goods【英】大型貨運卡車, 載重貨車

1 **hi** /haɪ; haɪ/ *interjection informal* hello【非正式】哈囉, 你好, 喂, 嘿: *Hi! How are you?* 嘿! 你好嗎? | **hi there!** *Hi there! I haven't seen you for ages.* 嘿! 好久不見。

hi·a·tus /haɪˋetəs; haɪˈeɪtəs/ *n* [C usually singular 一般用單數] **1** *formal* a break or INTERRUPTION in an activity【正式】停頓, 間斷: *Talks between the two countries have resumed after a six year hiatus.* 兩國間的談判在中斷了六年以後又恢復了。**2** a space where something is missing, especially in a piece of writing〔尤指文稿中的〕脱漏 **3** *technical* a pause between two vowel sounds【術語】元音[母音]分立[分讀]〔指相連兩個元音之間的短暫停頓〕

hi·ber·nate /ˋhaɪbɚˌnet; ˈhaɪbəneɪt/ *v* [I] if an animal hibernates, it sleeps for the whole winter〔動物〕冬眠 —**hibernation** /ˌhaɪbɚˋneʃən; ˌhaɪbəˈneɪʃən/ *n* [U]

hi·bis·cus /haɪˋbɪskəs; haɪˈbɪskəs/ *n* [C,U] a tropical plant with large brightly coloured flowers〔熱帶植物〕木槿

hic·cup¹, hiccough /ˋhɪkʌp; ˈhɪkʌp/ *n* [C] **1** [usually plural 一般用複數] a sudden, quick movement of your DIAPHRAGM (1) that happens repeatedly and uncontrollably for a short time 呃逆, 打嗝(聲): **get/have hiccups** *Don't drink so fast – you'll get hiccups.* 別喝得這麼快, 你會打嗝的。**2** a small problem or delay 小問題; 短暫的耽擱: *Fortunately, the computer problem was only a hiccup.* 幸好電腦的毛病只是一點小問題。

hiccup² *v* **hiccupped, hiccupping** [I] to have hiccups 打嗝

hick /hɪk; hɪk/ *n* [C] *AmE informal* an insulting word for someone who lives in the countryside, and is considered to be less educated than people who live in the city【美, 非正式】鄉巴佬〔此詞具侮辱性〕

hick·ey /ˋhɪkɪ; ˈhɪki/ *n* [C] *AmE* a red mark on someone's skin caused by someone else sucking it as a sexual act【美】〔皮膚上〕用力親吻後留下的紅色痕跡, 吻痕; LOVEBITE *BrE*【英】

hick·o·ry /ˋhɪkərɪ; ˈhɪkəri/ *n* [C,U] a North American tree that produces nuts, or the wood that comes from this tree 山核桃樹; 山核桃木

hid /hɪd; hɪd/ the past tense of HIDE¹

hid·den¹ /ˋhɪdn; ˈhɪdn/ the past participle of HIDE¹

hidden² *adj* **1** difficult to see or find 隱藏的, 隱祕的: *hidden passages and hidden staircases* 隱祕的通道和隱祕的樓梯 **2** not easy to notice or realize 潛在的, 隱含的: *hidden problems* 潛在的問題

hidden a·gen·da /ˌ‥ ‥ˈ‥/ *n* [C] an intended result of a plan or activity that you do not tell other people about 隱祕的動機; 不可告人的目的: *Voters suspected a hidden political agenda.* 選民懷疑背後有暗藏的政治目的。

hide¹ /haɪd; haɪd/ *v past tense* **hid** *past participle* **hidden** /ˋhɪdn; ˈhɪdn/ **1** [T] to deliberately put or keep something in a place where it cannot easily be seen or found 把…藏起來, 隱藏: *My girlfriend keeps hiding my cigarettes.* 我的女友總是把我的香煙藏起來。| **hide sth from sb** *The bushes hid Dave's bike completely from the passers-by.* 灌木叢將戴夫的腳踏車完全擋住了, 路過的人根本無法發現。| **keep sth hidden** *Confidential documents are kept hidden in a secret vault.* 保密文件被藏在一個祕密的保險庫裡。| **hide sth in/under/behind etc** *She hides his letters under her pillow.* 她把他的信都藏在枕頭下面。**2** [I] to go or stay in a place where you hope no one will find you 躲藏, 藏身: *Quick – she's coming – we'd better hide!* 快, 她來了, 我們最好躲起來! | **[+under/behind/in etc]** *Harry hid under the bed until they had gone.* 哈里一直躲在牀下, 直到他們離開。| **hide from** *Kylie tried to hide from the stranger.* 凱里設法躲過那個陌生人。**3** [T] to keep someone in a place where other people will not find them 把〔某人〕藏起來: **hide sb from** *an attempt to hide her children from their violent father* 試圖將她的孩子藏起來, 以躲開他們暴力的父親 **4** [T] to not show your feelings to people 隱藏, 掩蓋〔自己的感情〕: *Paul struggled to hide his disappointment at not getting the job.* 保羅竭力掩藏自己因得不到那份工作而生的失望情緒。**5** [T] to deliberately not tell people facts or information 隱瞞: *He took off his ring to hide the fact that he was married.* 他摘下戒指, 想隱瞞自己已婚的事實。| **hide sth from** *Don't try to hide anything from me.* 別想瞞過我! **6 have nothing to hide** to be willing to tell people about everything you have done, because you have done nothing dishonest, illegal, or immoral 沒甚麼可隱瞞的; 光明磊落: *The company claimed that the deal was legal and that they had nothing to hide.* 公司聲稱這筆交易是合法的, 他們是光明磊落的。**7 hide your light under a bushel** to not tell anyone that you are very good at something〔對自己的特長〕藏而不露

hide² *n* [C] **1** *BrE* a place from which you can watch animals or birds without being seen by them【英】〔可觀察鳥獸行動的〕隱匿處, 埋伏處; BLIND³ (3) *AmE*【美】**2** an animal's skin, especially when it has been removed to be used for leather〔用於製成皮革的〕獸皮: *ox hide gloves* 牛皮手套 **3 have/tan sb's hide** *spoken humorous* to punish someone severely【口, 幽默】剝了某人的皮〔指嚴厲懲罰某人〕**4 not see hide nor hair of** *spoken* to have not seen someone at all recently【口】沒有見到〔某人〕的蹤影: *I haven't seen hide nor hair of him for ages.* 我已經好久沒有見過他的蹤影了。

hide-and-seek /ˌ‥ ‥ ˈ‥/ also 又作 **hide-and-go-seek** /ˌ‥ ‥ ˈ‥/ *AmE*【美】— *n* [U] a children's game in which one player shuts their eyes while the others hide, and then goes to look for them 捉迷藏

hide·a·way /ˋhaɪdəˏwe; ˈhaɪdəweɪ/ *n* [C] a place where you can go when you want to be alone 躲藏處, 藏匿處

hide·bound /ˋhaɪdˏbaund; ˈhaɪdbaʊnd/ *adj* having old-fashioned attitudes and ideas; NARROW-MINDED 古板的, 守舊的, 思想偏狹的: *hidebound reactionaries* 古板的極端保守分子

hid·e·ous /ˋhɪdɪəs; ˈhɪdiəs/ *adj* extremely unpleasant or ugly 極醜的, 極難看的: *a hideous dress* 一條很難看的連衣裙 —**hideously** *adv* —**hideousness** *n* [U]

hide-out /ˋ· ·/ *n* [C] a place where someone goes because they do not want anyone to find them 藏匿處, 躲藏處

hid·ing /ˋhaɪdɪŋ; ˈhaɪdɪŋ/ *n* **1 be/go into hiding** to hide somewhere because you have done something illegal or are in danger〔因犯法或躲避危險〕藏匿, 躲藏: *The gang spent weeks in hiding before they were finally caught.* 那夥罪犯藏匿了幾星期後才被抓獲。**2 give sb/get a good hiding** *spoken informal*【口, 非正式】**a)** used to say that you will physically punish someone 狠揍[痛打]某人/被狠揍[痛打]: *Any more cheek from you and you'll get a good hiding.* 你要是再這麼無禮, 我便狠狠揍你一頓。**b)** to defeat someone or be defeated very seriously, especially in a sports game〔尤指在體育比賽中〕打敗; 大敗 **3 be on a hiding to nothing** *BrE informal* to be completely wasting your time trying to do something【英, 非正式】白白浪費時間, 白費功夫

hiding place /ˋ·· ˏ·/ *n* [C] a place where you can hide or where you can hide something 藏匿處, 躲藏處, 隱藏處

hie /haɪ; haɪ/ *v* [I,T] *old use* to make yourself hurry, or go quickly【舊】(使) 趕緊, (使) 趕忙

hi·er·ar·chy /ˋhaɪəˏrɑrkɪ; ˈhaɪrɑːki/ *n* **1** [C,U] a system within an organization in which people have authority and control over the people in the rank below them, who then have authority over the people below them 等級制度: *a rigid hierarchy* 嚴格的等級制度 **2** [C] the group of people in an organization who have power or control〔組織、團體中的〕統治集團: *All policy decisions were made by the communist hierarchy.* 所有的政策都是由共產黨內的高層成員決定的。—**hierarchical** /ˏhaɪəˋrɑrkɪkḷ; haɪˈrɑːkɪkəl/ *adj* —**hierarchically** /-kḷɪ; -kli/ *adv*

hi·e·ro·glyph·ics /ˏhaɪərəˋglɪfɪks; ˌhaɪrəˈglɪfɪks/ *n* [U] a system of writing that uses pictures to represent words 象形文字 —**hieroglyphic** *adj*: *hieroglyphic script* 象形文字手稿

hi-fi /ˋhaɪ ˋfaɪ; ˈhaɪ faɪ/ *n plural* **hi-fis** **1** [C] a piece of high quality electronic equipment for playing recorded music (高保真度) 音響設備 **2** [U] a way of playing recorded music that is very clear and of very good quality 用高保真度音響設備播放音樂

hig·gle·dy-pig·gle·dy /ˋhɪgḷdɪ ˋpɪgḷdɪ; ˌhɪgəldi ˈpɪgəldi/ *adj* things that are higgledy-piggledy are mixed together in an untidy way 亂七八糟的, 雜亂無章的 —**higgledy-piggledy** *adv*

-high /haɪ; haɪ/ *suffix* [in adjectives 構成形容詞] of a particular height ...高的: *The wall was about chest-high.* (=as high as your chest) 這牆大約有齊胸高。| *a 7000 metre-high mountain* 一座 7000 米高的山

1 1

high¹ /haɪ; haɪ/ *adj*

① MEASUREMENT/DISTANCE 計量/距離
② LARGE AMOUNT/NUMBER 大量/數值大
③ IMPORTANT 重要的
④ SOUND 聲音
⑤ VERY GOOD 很好
⑥ DRUGS/ALCOHOL 毒品/酒精
⑦ HAPPY 高興的
⑧ PROUD 驕傲的
⑨ OTHER MEANINGS 其他意思

high 高的

a high shelf 一個高的架子

a tall building 一幢高樓

① MEASUREMENT/DISTANCE 計量/距離

1 ►FROM BOTTOM TO TOP 從底部到頂部◄ something that is high measures a long distance from its bottom to its top 高的: *the highest mountain in Japan* 日本最高的山 | *a castle surrounded by high walls* 被高牆包圍着的城堡 | **100 feet/30 metres etc high** *a building 20 storeys high* 一幢 20 層高的大樓 | *How high is the Eiffel tower?* 埃菲爾鐵塔有多高? | *a ten-foot high wall* 十英尺高的牆 | **chest/waist/knee etc high** (=as high as your chest etc) 齊胸/腰/膝高 *The grass was knee-high.* 草有齊膝高。

2 ►ABOVE THE GROUND 在地面以上◄ being a long way, or a longer way than usual, above the ground〔離地面〕高的: a *spacious room with a high ceiling* 天花板很高的一個大房間 | *a high shelf* 一個高的架子 | *high in the sky* 在高空 | **high up** *High up among the clouds, we could just see the summit of Everest.* 在高高的雲端中, 我們只能看到珠穆朗瑪峯的頂峯。

3 ►SEA/RIVER ETC 海/河等◄ having risen to a higher level than usual〔水位〕高的: *The river was unusually high.* 這條河的水位異乎尋常地高。| *high tide* 高[滿]潮

② LARGE AMOUNT/NUMBER 大量/數值大

4 a high amount, number, or level is greater than normal〔數值、水平〕高的, 超乎尋常的: *high blood pressure* 高血壓 | *high levels of radiation* 高能級輻射 | *high temperatures* 高温 | **high rent/price/tax etc** *the high cost of insurance* 昂貴的保險費用 | **at high speed** (=very fast) 高速地 *A car was approaching at high speed.* 有一輛車正在高速地駛來。| **high proportion/percentage** (=a very large part of an amount) 高比例/百分比 *A high proportion of married women have part-time jobs.* 很大部分的已婚婦女都在做兼職的工作。

5 ►CONTAINING A LOT 含量高◄ containing a lot of a particular substance or quality〔含量〕高的: *an alloy*

with a high carbon content 高碳含金 | **high in fat/sugar/salt etc** *Beer is high in calories.* 啤酒的熱量很高。

③ IMPORTANT 重要的

6 ►IN SOCIETY/ORGANIZATION 在社會/組織中◄ having an important or powerful position in society or in an organization〔職位或等級〕高的, 高級的; 重要的: *the highest rank in the US Navy* 美國海軍中的最高軍銜 | *the City's highest honour* 該市的最高榮譽 | **high up** (=in a powerful position) 居於高位 *someone high up in the civil service* 在政府文職機構擔任要職的人 | **high office** *With men like Gould in high office, it was easy for the military to influence policy.* 有古爾德這樣的人身居高職, 軍隊就很容易對政策施加影響。| **high society** (=rich people of the highest social class) 上流社會 —see also 另見 HIGH-UP, HIGH-RANKING, **have friends in high places** (FRIEND (10))

7 be high on the list/agenda to be important and need to be dealt with quickly 被列為重要/優先處理事項

④ SOUND 聲音

8 near the top of the range of sounds that humans can hear〔音調〕高的, 尖聲的: *Dogs respond to sounds that are too high for the human ear.* 狗對人耳聽不到的高音有反應。—see also 另見 HIGH-PITCHED

⑤ VERY GOOD 很好

9 high quality/standard/calibre etc very good quality etc 高質量/標準/水準等: *high quality goods* 高質量貨品 | *a high standard of workmanship* 高水平的工藝

10 high opinion/praise/regard etc strong approval, or an expression of strong approval 高度評價/讚揚/尊重等: **have a high opinion of** *I have a high opinion of Miss Boyce's work.* 我對博伊斯小姐的工作評價很高。| **hold sb/sth in high esteem/regard** (=respect them very much) 高度尊重某人/某事 *As an educationalist, he was held in high esteem.* 作為一名教育學家, 他得到人們的高度尊敬。

11 high standards/principles rules of personal behaviour based on the belief that everyone should always be very good and honest 高尚[崇高]的標準/原則: *a man of high moral principles* 具有崇高道德原則的人

12 have high hopes/expectations to hope for or expect very good results or great success 抱有很高的希望/期望: *parents who have such high hopes for their children* 對孩子寄予如此厚望的父母

13 high point/spot the best part of an activity or occasion〔活動的〕高潮/最精彩部分: *Our visit to the Grand Canyon was definitely the high point of our vacation.* 遊覽大峽谷無疑是我們這次度假最精彩的部分。

⑥ DRUGS/ALCOHOL 毒品/酒精

14 [not before noun 不用於名詞前] behaving in an unusually excited way because of taking drugs〔吸食毒品後〕極度興奮的: **[+on]** *They were high on cocaine.* 他們吸食可卡因後顯得極度亢奮。| **get high** (=take a drug to make yourself high) 吸毒以求得飄飄欲仙的感覺 | **high as a kite** (=very high) 飄飄欲仙的

⑦ HAPPY 高興的

15 high spirits feelings of happiness and energy, especially when you are having fun 歡欣, 興高采烈: *I know the kids are a bit noisy but it's just high spirits.* 我知道孩子們有點吵, 但他們只是太高興了。| **in high spirits** *It was a bright sunny day and we set off in high spirits.* 那天陽光明媚, 我們興高采烈地出發了。

16 ►HAPPY/EXCITED 高興的/興奮的◄ happy and excited 高興的; 興奮的: **[+on]** *We were still high on our victory over the champions.* 我們還在為擊敗冠軍隊而興奮不已。

17 have a high old time *old-fashioned* to enjoy an occasion very much【過時】度過愉快的時光, 玩得很痛快

⑧ PROUD 驕傲的

18 be/get on your high horse to behave or talk as if you are better than other people 自高自大, 自以為是

19 high and mighty talking or behaving as if you think you are more important than other people 盛氣凌人的, 不可一世的

⑨ OTHER MEANINGS 其他意思

20 it is high time used to say that something should be done now 到了該做某事的時候: *It's high time you got a job and settled down.* 你該找份工作安頓下來了。

21 ►FOOD 食物◄ cheese, meat etc that is high is not fresh and has a strong smell or taste〔乾酪、肉類等〕不新鮮的; 變質的

22 high wind a strong wind 大風

23 high complexion/colouring a naturally pink or red face 自然紅潤的臉色

24 high drama/adventure events or situations that are very exciting 充滿戲劇性的事件/極刺激的歷險: *a life with moments of high drama* 具有不少刺激經歷的人生

25 ►TIME 時間◄ the middle or the most important part of a particular period of time 趨於頂點的, 全盛的: *high summer* 盛夏 | *the high renaissance* 文藝復興的全盛時期 | **high noon** (=12 o'clock in the middle of the day) 正午 —see also 另見 HIGH SEASON

26 high life/living the enjoyable life that rich people and fashionable people have〔上層社會的〕奢華生活: *the high life of a capital city* 首都的奢華生活

27 high finance the business of dealing with very large sums of money 涉及巨額資金的業務

28 high style/register the style of language used in literature 文學語言風格/語域 —see also 另見 HIGHLY, **in high dudgeon** (DUDGEON), **stink to high heaven** (STINK[1] (1))

USAGE NOTE 用法說明: HIGH

WORD CHOICE 詞語辨析: **high, higher, advanced, tall**

High (opposite **low**) is used of most things, especially when you are thinking only of how far something, or its top, is from the ground. high (反義詞為 low) 可用來描述大多數東西, 尤其是用於描述該物或其頂部離地面的高度: *a high shelf* 高的架子 | *a high mountain* 高山 | *The shelf's too high, I can't reach it.* 架子太高了, 我夠不着。

Many things you cannot touch may also be **high**. 很多人們無法觸摸的東西也可以用 high 來描述: *a high standard* 高標準 | *a high degree of sophistication* 高精密度 | *high technology* 高科技。However, with some words related to education **higher** (or **advanced**) must be used instead. 但在某些與教育有關的詞組中則要用 higher (或 advanced): *higher education* 高等教育 | *advanced teaching/techniques* 高等教歷/高級技術 | *a higher degree/diploma* (but do not confuse this with *High School diploma* etc). 高等學位/高級文憑 (但不要將其與 High School diploma (高中畢業文憑) 等混淆起來)。

Tall (opposite **short**) is used for people and animals. tall (反義詞為 short) 用來描述人或動物: *Your son's*

getting tall, isn't he? 你的兒子越長越高了，不是嗎？
Tall is also used for things that are high and narrow, especially when you are thinking of the complete distance from top to bottom. tall也可用來描述一些高而窄的東西，尤其是在考慮這個東西從頂到底的全距離時: *a tall building like the Sears Tower* 像西爾斯大廈那樣的高樓 | *a tall tree/column/vase/fridge/bottle* 高的樹木/柱子/花瓶/冰箱/瓶子

high[2] *adv*
1 ▶ABOVE THE GROUND 在地面以上◀ at or to a level high above the ground〔離地面〕高高地; 在[向]高處: **[+into/above etc]** *Paula threw the ball high into the air.* 葆拉將球高高地拋向天空。| *flying high in the sky* 在高空飛翔
2 ▶VALUE/COST/AMOUNT 價值/成本/數量◀ at or to a high value, cost, amount etc 高〔價值、成本、數量等〕: *The dollar stayed high after a busy day on the foreign exchanges.* 外匯交易整天頻繁，接近收市時美元價格仍然居高不下。| *He scored higher than anyone else in the class.* 他的分數比班上其他人都要高。
3 ▶SOUND 聲音◀ with a high sound 高音調地: *boy's voices, ringing high above everyone else's* 高過所有人的男孩的嗓音
4 ▶ACHIEVEMENT 成就◀ to a high rank or level of achievement, especially in an organization, business etc 向高的地位[成就]: *Don't set your goals too low. You should always aim high.* 不要將你的目標定得太低。你應該永遠保持着雄心壯志。
5 be left high and dry *informal* to be left without any help or without the things that you need【非正式】孤立無援，陷入困境
6 look/search high and low to try to find someone or something by looking everywhere 到處尋找: *We looked high and low for Sandy but couldn't find her.* 我們到處尋找桑迪，但沒有找到她。
7 hold your head high to behave in a proud confident way, especially in a difficult situation〔尤指在困境中〕充滿自信: *You've kept the family together, I think you can hold your head high.* 你使一家人團結起來，我認為你應該感到自豪。
8 live high on the hog *AmE informal* to enjoy expensive food, clothes etc without worrying about the cost【美，非正式】過奢華的生活: *They've been living high on the hog since Jim got the money from his aunt.* 自從吉姆從他的姑媽那兒得到那筆錢後，他們就一直過着奢華的生活。—see also 另見 **be riding high** (RIDE[1] (7)), **be running high** (RUN[1] (28))

high[3] *n* [C]
1 ▶NUMBER/AMOUNT 數量◀ the highest price, number, temperature etc that has ever been recorded〔價格、數量、溫度等的〕最高點; 最高水平: *The price of oil reached a new high this week.* 本週的石油價格創出了新高。
2 ▶WEATHER 天氣◀ **a)** the highest temperature in a particular day, week, month etc〔某月、週、日的〕最高氣溫: *Highs today were in the mid 20's.* 今天的最高氣溫為二十四、五度。**b)** an area of HIGH PRESSURE[2] that affects the weather 高氣壓(區)
3 ▶DRUGS 毒品◀ a feeling of pleasure or excitement produced by some drugs〔某些毒品帶來的〕極度興奮感，飄飄欲仙的感覺: *The high she got from cocaine never lasted.* 她從可卡因中得到的興奮感總是轉眼即逝。
4 ▶EXCITEMENT 興奮◀ a feeling of happiness or excitement you get from doing something you enjoy 興奮感，歡欣，情緒高漲: **be on a high** *I've been on a high ever since we won the game last week.* 自上週我們比賽獲勝以來，我一直感到興奮不已。
5 ▶SCHOOL 學校◀ a short form of 縮略式= HIGH SCHOOL, used in the name of a school 中學〔用於學校名稱中〕: *She graduated from Reseda High in 1979.* 她於1979年畢業於雷西達中學。
6 on high *biblical* in, to, or from heaven or a high place【聖經】在[從]天堂; 在[從]高處
7 from on high *humorous* from someone in a position of authority【幽默】來自上級的，來自高層的: *an order from on high* 上頭的命令

high·ball /ˈhaɪˌbɔl; ˈhaɪbɔːl/ *n* [C] *especially AmE* an alcoholic drink, especially WHISKY or BRANDY mixed with water or SODA【尤美】高杯酒〔尤指威士忌或白蘭地加水或汽水〕

high beam /ˌ· ˈ·/ *n* [U] *AmE* lights at the front of a car that are on as brightly as possible【美】〔車頭開着的〕遠光燈，高燈 —see also 另見 BRIGHTS

high-born /ˌ· ˈ·◂/ *adj formal* born into the highest social class【正式】出身高貴的

high·boy /ˈhaɪˌbɔɪ; ˈhaɪbɔɪ/ *n* [C] *AmE* a piece of tall wooden furniture with many drawers【美】〔帶有抽屜的〕高腳櫥櫃; TALLBOY *BrE*【英】

high·brow /ˈhaɪˌbraʊ; ˈhaɪbraʊ/ *adj* **1** a highbrow book, film etc is intended for very intelligent people who like serious subjects〔書籍、電影等〕高雅的 **2** someone who is highbrow is interested in serious or complicated ideas and subjects; INTELLECTUAL〔人〕趣味高雅的，文化修養高的 —**highbrow** *n* [C] —compare 比較 LOWBROW

high·chair /ˌhaɪˋtʃɛr; ˌhaɪˈtʃeə/ *n* [C] a special tall chair that a young child sits in to eat〔幼兒吃飯時坐的〕高腳椅 —see picture at 參見 CHAIR[1] 圖

High Church /ˌ· ˈ·◂/ *n* [U] the part of the Church of England that is closest in its beliefs to the Roman Catholic Church〔英國國教的〕高派教會 —compare 比較 LOW CHURCH —**High Church** *adj*

high-class /ˌ· ˈ·◂/ *adj* [usually before noun 一般用於名詞前] of good quality and style, and usually expensive 高級的，上等的: *a high-class restaurant* 高級餐館 —compare 比較 LOW-CLASS

high com·mand /ˌ· ·ˈ·/ *n* [singular] the most important leaders of a country's army, navy etc〔軍隊的〕統帥; 最高指揮部: *the German High Command* 德軍最高指揮部

high com·mis·sion /ˌ· ·ˈ·/ *n* [C] **1** a group of people working for a government or an international organization to deal with a specific problem〔政府或國際組織的〕高級專員公署 **2** a group of people with official duties concerning the relationship of one Commonwealth country with another〔英聯邦國家中負責各英聯邦國家之間關係的〕高級專員公署 —**High Commissioner** *n* [C]

high court /ˌ· ˈ·◂/ *n* [C usually singular 一般用單數] a court of law in Britain that is at a higher level than ordinary courts and that can be asked to change the decisions of a lower court〔英國的〕高等法院

high-def·i·ni·tion /ˌ· ··ˈ··◂/ *adj* [only before noun 僅用於名詞前] a high-definition television or computer shows images very clearly〔電視或電腦〕高清晰度的

higher[1] /ˈhaɪə; ˈhaɪə/ *adj* [the comparative of *high* high 的比較級] **1** [only before noun 僅用於名詞前] more advanced in development or organization〔發展過程或組織結構〕高等的: *the higher forms of mammals, such as the primates and big cats* 高等哺乳類動物，如靈長目動物和大型貓科動物 **2** at a more advanced level of knowledge〔知識〕高等的: *higher mathematics* 高等數學 —see 見 HIGH (USAGE)

high·er[2] *n* [C] the higher level of the Scottish Certificate of Education 蘇格蘭高等教育證書

higher ed·u·ca·tion /ˌ·· ··ˈ··/ *n* [U] college or university education as opposed to school or HIGH SCHOOL 高等教育 —compare 比較 FURTHER EDUCATION

higher-up /ˌ·· ˈ·◂/ *n* [C] *informal* someone who has a high rank in an organization【非正式】〔機構、部門的〕高層人物，要員: *Rumour has it that the higher-ups want to push the schedule forward.* 謠傳高層人物想促使日程提前進行。

highest com·mon fac·tor /ˌ·· ·· ˈ··/ *n* [C] *technical* the largest number that a set of numbers can be divided by exactly【術語】最大公因數: *the highest common factor of 12, 24 and 30 is 6.* 12、24和30的最大公因數是6。

high ex·plo·sive /ˌ· ·ˈ··◂/ *n* [C,U] a substance that explodes with great power and violence 高爆炸藥, 烈性炸藥

high·fa·lu·tin /ˌhaɪfəˈluːtn̩; ˌhaɪfəˈluːtɪ̵n◂/ *adj informal* highfalutin language or behaviour seems silly although it is intended to be impressive【非正式】〔言行〕浮誇的, 做作的

high fi·del·i·ty /ˌ· ·ˈ···◂/ *adj* [usually before noun 一般用於名詞前] high fidelity recording equipment produces sound that is very clear〔音響設備〕高保真度的 —see also 另見 HI-FI

high five /ˌ· ˈ·/ *n* [singular] *especially AmE* the action of hitting someone's open hand with your own above your heads to show that you are pleased about something【尤美】〔兩人〕舉手擊掌〔以示慶賀〕

high-fli·er /ˌ· ˈ··/ *n* [C] someone who is extremely successful in their job or in school〔事業或學業上〕極有成就的人: *a young businessman pegged as a high-flier by the media* 被傳媒稱為成功人士的年輕實業家 —**high-flying** *adj*

high-flown /ˌ· ˈ·◂/ *adj* high-flown language sounds impressive but does not have much real meaning〔言詞〕浮誇的, 空洞的

high-grade /ˌ· ˈ·◂/ *adj* [only before noun 僅用於名詞前] of the best quality 優質的, 高檔的, 上等的: *high-grade beef* 優質牛肉

high-hand·ed /ˌ· ˈ··◂/ *adj* using your authority in an unreasonable way 專橫的, 高壓的, 盛氣凌人的: *high-handed and insensitive management decisions* 專橫而冷漠無情的管理決策 —**high-handedly** *adv* —**high-handedness** *n* [U]

high heels /ˌ· ˈ·/ *n* [plural] women's shoes with high heels 高跟鞋 —**high-heeled** *adj* —see picture on page A17 參見A17頁圖

high jinks also 又作 **hi·jinks** *AmE*【美】/ˈhaɪ ˌdʒɪŋks; ˈhaɪdʒɪŋks/ *n* [U] *old-fashioned* noisy or excited behaviour when people are having fun【過時】嬉鬧, 狂歡作樂: *youthful high jinks* 年輕人的狂歡作樂

high jump /ˈ· ·/ *n* **1 the high jump** a sports event in which someone runs and jumps over a bar that is raised higher each time they jump 跳高〔體育比賽〕 **2 be (in) for the high jump** *BrE informal* if someone is for the high jump, they will be punished for something they have done wrong【英, 非正式】將受到懲罰 —**high jumper** *n* [C]

high·land /ˈhaɪlənd; ˈhaɪlənd/ *adj* [only before noun 僅用於名詞前] **1** coming from or connected to the Scottish Highlands 蘇格蘭高地的: *Highland pipers* 蘇格蘭高地的風笛手 **2** from or about an area with a lot of mountains 高地的, 高原的: *workers in highland Ecuador* 厄瓜多爾高原的工人們

High·land·er /ˈhaɪləndə; ˈhaɪləndə/ *n* [C] someone from the Scottish Highlands 蘇格蘭高地人

Highland fling /ˌ·· ˈ·/ *n* [C] a fast Scottish dance, danced by one person 高地舞〔蘇格蘭的一種單人跳的快舞〕

high·lands /ˈhaɪləndz; ˈhaɪləndz/ *n* [plural] **1 the Highlands** an area in the north of Scotland where there are a lot of mountains 蘇格蘭北部的高地 **2** an area of a country where there are a lot of mountains 高地, 高原: *forested highlands* 森林覆蓋的高地 —compare 比較 LOWLANDS

high-lev·el /ˌ· ˈ··◂/ *adj* [only before noun 僅用於名詞前] **1** done by or involving people who are in powerful positions, for example the government〔政府〕高層的, 由高層人士進行[組成]的: *officials attending a high-level conference on arms control* 參加軍備控制高層會議的官員 **2** at a high level or degree 高度的: *high-level anxiety* 高度憂慮 **3** high-level words or language are very formal or technical〔用詞、語言〕非常正式的; 術語的 **4** a high-level computer language is similar to human language rather than machine language〔電腦語言〕高級的〔接近人類語言〕—compare 比較 LOW-LEVEL

high life /ˈ· ·/ *n* **the high life** a way of life that involves a lot of parties, and expensive food, wine, travel etc〔上層社會的〕奢華生活

high·light[1] /ˈhaɪˌlaɪt; ˈhaɪlaɪt/ *v* [T] **1** to make a problem or subject easy to notice so that people pay attention to it 使…突出, 使注意力集中於: *a test to highlight students' strengths and weaknesses* 能突顯學生優缺點的測試 **2** to mark written words with a special coloured pen, or in a different colour on a computer, so that you can see them easily 在〔書面材料或電腦上〕劃出重點 **3** to make some parts of your hair a lighter colour than the rest 將〔部分頭髮〕染成有光澤的淺色, 挑染 —**highlighting** *n* [U]

highlight[2] *n* **1** [C] the most important, interesting, or enjoyable part of something such as a holiday, performance, or sports competition 最突出[精彩]的部分[場面]: *That weekend in Venice was definitely the highlight of our trip.* 在威尼斯度過的那個週末無疑是我們這次旅行最精彩的部分。**2 highlights** [plural] areas of hair that have been made a lighter colour than the rest〔挑染後〕頭髮上呈淺色的部分 **3** [C] *technical* a light, bright area on a painting or photograph【術語】〔繪畫、照片上的〕強光部分, 最亮部分

high·light·er /ˈhaɪˌlaɪtə; ˈhaɪlaɪtə/ *n* [C] a special light coloured pen used for marking words in a book, article etc〔用來在書上、文章上劃重點的〕淺色彩筆, 螢光筆

high·ly /ˈhaɪlɪ; ˈhaɪli/ *adv* **1** [+adj, adv] very 非常, 極: *highly successful* 非常成功的 | *highly skilled* 十分熟練的 **2** [+adj, adv] to a high level or standard 高度地, 高水平地: *She is a highly educated woman.* 她是個教育水平很高的女人。| *highly paid experts* 薪酬豐厚的專家 **3 highly placed** in an important or powerful position 身居高職的: *a highly placed government official* 身居高職的政府官員 **4 speak/think highly of** to tell other people how good someone is at something or to think they are very good at something 高度稱讚/評價

highly strung /ˌ·· ˈ·◂/ *especially BrE*【尤英】, also 又作 **high-strung** /ˌ· ˈ·◂/ *AmE*【美】— *adj* nervous, and easily upset or excited 容易激動的, 神經質的: *a highly strung child* 神經質的孩子

High Mass /ˌ· ˈ·/ *n* [C,U] a very formal church ceremony in the Roman Catholic Church〔天主教的〕大彌撒

high-mind·ed /ˌ· ˈ··◂/ *adj* having very high moral standards or principles 品德[情操]高尚的, 高潔的: *a high-minded sermon on charity* 以仁愛為題的情操高尚的講道 —**high-mindedly** *adv* —**high-mindedness** *n* [U]

High·ness /ˈhaɪnɪs; ˈhaɪnɪ̵s/ *n* [C] **Your/Her/His Highness** used to speak to or about a king, queen, prince etc 殿下〔用於對國王、王后、王子等的尊稱〕

high-oc·tane /ˌ· ˈ··◂/ *adj* high-octane petrol is of a very high quality〔汽油〕高辛烷值的; 優質的

high-pitched /ˌ· ˈ·◂/ *adj* a high-pitched voice or sound is higher than usual 聲調高的

high-pow·ered /ˌ· ˈ··◂/ *adj* [usually before noun 一般用於名詞前] **1** a high-powered machine, vehicle, or piece of equipment is very powerful 大功率的, 大馬力的, 強有力的: *a high-powered automobile* 大馬力的汽車 **2** having a powerful and important job 幹勁十足的; 積極進取的: *a high-powered publisher* 業務蓬勃的出版商

high-pres·sure[1] /ˌ· ˈ··◂/ *adj* [only before noun 僅用於名詞前] **1** a high-pressure job or situation is one in which you need to work very hard; STRESSFUL 給人很大壓力的, 非常緊張的 **2 high-pressure sales/selling methods etc** very direct and often successful ways of persuading people to buy something 強有力的[強行的]推銷/銷售方法等: *high-pressure sales techniques* 咄咄逼人的推銷手法 **3** containing or using a very high pressure or force of water, gas, air etc〔水、天然氣、大氣等〕高壓的

high-pressure² *n* [U] a condition of the air over a large area that affects the weather 高氣壓

high priest /ˌ· ˈ·/ *n* [C] **1** *informal* someone who is famous for being the best at something such as a type of art or music【非正式】〔藝術、音樂界的〕代表人物: *the high priest of modern jazz* 現代爵士樂的代表人物 **2** a chief PRIEST in some religions 大祭司, 祭司長

high-prin·ci·pled /ˌ· ˈ···◂/ *adj* having high moral standards 品德高尚的, 情操高尚的

high-pro·file /ˌ· ˈ··◂/ *adj* [only before noun 僅用於名詞前] attracting a lot of public attention, usually deliberately〔刻意地〕引人注目的, 高調的: *a high-profile public figure* 一位引人注目的知名人物 —**high profile** *n* [singular]

high-rank·ing /ˌ· ˈ··◂/ *adj* [only before noun 僅用於名詞前] having a high position in a government or other organization〔在政府或其他機構中〕級別[地位]高的

high re·lief /ˌ· ·ˈ·/ *n* [U] **1** a form of art in which figures cut in stone or wood stand out from the surface 高凸浮雕 —compare 比較 BAS-RELIEF **2 throw sth into high relief** to make something very clear and easy to notice 使某物突出

high-rise /ˈ· ·/ *adj* [only before noun 僅用於名詞前] high-rise buildings are tall buildings with many levels〔建築物〕高聳的, 高層的 —compare 比較 LOW-RISE —**high rise** *n* [C]: *They live in a high rise on the East Side.* 他們住在東區的一座高層大廈裡。

high-risk /ˌ· ˈ·◂/ *adj* [only before noun 僅用於名詞前] involving a risk of death, injury, failure etc 高風險的: *high-risk investments* 高風險投資 | *cancer screening for women over 55 and other high-risk groups* 針對55歲以上的婦女及其他高危人士的癌症篩查

high road /ˈ· ·/ *n* [C] *BrE old use* a main road【英舊】大路, 大道, 大街

high rol·ler /ˌ· ˈ··/ *n* [C] *AmE informal* someone who spends a lot of money carelessly or risks a lot of money on games, races etc【美, 非正式】揮金如土的人; 下大賭注賭錢的人

high school /ˈ· ·/ *n* **1** [C,U] a school in the US and Canada for children of 14 or 15 to 18 years old〔美國和加拿大14或15至18歲學生就讀的〕高中 **2** used in the names of some schools in Britain for children from 11 to 18 years old〔英國11至18歲學生就讀的〕中學〔用於校名中〕: *Leytonstone High School for Girls* 雷頓斯通女子中學 —compare 比較 SECONDARY SCHOOL

high seas /ˌ· ˈ·/ *n* **the high seas a)** the areas of ocean around the world that do not belong to any particular country 公海 **b)** *literary* the sea【文】大海, 海洋

high sea·son /ˌ· ˈ··/ *n* [singular,U] *especially BrE* the time of year when businesses make a lot of money and prices are high, especially in the tourist industry; PEAK SEASON【尤英】〔尤指旅遊的〕旺季 —compare 比較 LOW SEASON

high-sound·ing /ˌ· ˈ··◂/ *adj* [only before noun 僅用於名詞前] high-sounding statements, principles etc seem very impressive but are often insincere〔陳述、準則等〕華而不實的, 虛誇的

high-speed /ˌ· ˈ·◂/ *adj* [only before noun 僅用於名詞前] designed to travel or operate very fast 高速的, 快速的: *a high-speed train* 高速列車

high-spir·it·ed /ˌ· ˈ···◂/ *adj* **1** someone who is high-spirited has a lot of energy and enjoys fun and adventure〔人〕生氣勃勃的, 活潑的; 愛冒險的 **2** a horse that is high-spirited is nervous and difficult to control〔馬〕烈性的, 難駕馭的

high street /ˈ· ·/ *n* [C] *BrE* the main street of a town where most of the shops and businesses are【英】〔市鎮商業區的主要街道〕大街: *Camden High Street* 坎登大街 | *peak sales on the high street at Christmas* 聖誕節時大街上的銷售高峯 | **high street banks/shops etc** (=the shops etc that most people use) 大型銀行/商店等 —compare 比較 MAIN STREET (1)

high-strung /ˌ· ˈ·◂/ *adj* an American form of HIGHLY STRUNG highly strung 的美語形式

high ta·ble /ˌ· ˈ··/ *n* [U] *BrE* the table where the most important people at a formal occasion sit【英】貴賓桌

high·tail /ˈhaɪˌtel; ˈhaɪteɪl/ *v* **hightail it** *informal* to leave a place quickly【非正式】快速離開, 急忙逃走: *kids hightailing it down the street on their bikes* 騎腳踏車飛快地駛過街道的孩子們

high tea /ˌ· ˈ·/ *n* [C,U] *BrE* a meal of cold food, cakes etc eaten in the early evening【英】傍晚茶點

high-tech /ˌhaɪˈtɛk; ˌhaɪˈtek◂/ *adj* [usually before noun 一般用於名詞前] **1** using high technology 高科技的: *high-tech industries* 高科技產業 —compare 比較 LOW TECH **2** furniture, designs etc that are high-tech are made in a very modern style〔家具、設計等〕現代風格的, 摩登的 —**high tech** *n* [U]

high tech·nol·o·gy /ˌ· ·ˈ···◂/ *n* [U] the use of the most modern machines and methods in industry, business etc 高科技, 尖端技術

high-ten·sion /ˌ· ˈ··◂/ *adj* **high-tension wires/cables etc** wires etc that have a powerful electric current going through them 高壓電線/電纜等

high tide /ˌ· ˈ·/ *n* **1** [C,U] the point or time at which the sea reaches its highest level 高[滿]潮時 **2** [singular] the time when something is at its best or most successful 成功的頂點, 全盛時期: *The election victory marked the high tide in the party's fortunes.* 大選勝利標誌着該黨時運的頂點。

high-toned /ˌ· ˈ·◂/ *adj* seeming to be concerned with high moral principles 唱高調的, 自命高尚的

high trea·son /ˌ· ˈ··/ *n* [U] the crime of putting your country in great danger, for example by giving military secrets to the enemy 叛國罪, 叛逆罪

high-up /ˈ· ·/ *n* [C] *BrE* someone who has a high rank in an organization; HIGHER-UP【英】〔機構、部門的〕高層人物, 要員

high wa·ter /ˌ· ˈ··/ *n* [U] the period of time during which the water in a river or the sea is at its highest level because of the TIDE¹ (1) 高水位期, 漲潮時 —compare 比較 LOW WATER —see also 另見 **come hell or high water** (HELL¹ (22))

high water mark /ˌ· ˈ·· ·/ *n* [singular] **1** the mark that shows the highest level that the sea or a river reaches 高水位線 **2** the time when someone or something is most successful〔成功的〕頂峯, 頂點, 全盛時期: *the high water mark of Herrera's presidency* 埃雷拉擔任〔委內瑞拉〕總統時最成功的時期

high·way /ˈhaɪˌwe; ˈhaɪweɪ/ *n* [C] **1** *especially AmE* a broad main road that joins one town to another【尤美】公路 —compare 比較 FREEWAY, EXPRESSWAY, MOTORWAY **2** *BrE*【英】**a)** *old-fashioned* any road or street【過時】公路, 大街 **b) the public highway** an expression used in legal documents meaning roads〔用於法律文件中〕公路 **3 highway robbery** *AmE informal* a situation in which something costs you a lot more than it should【美, 非正式】要價太高: *It's highway robbery, charging that much for gas!* 這簡直就是搶錢, 煤氣竟然要這麼多錢! S2

Highway Code /ˌ·· ˈ·/ *n* [singular] the set of official rules and laws about driving and using roads in Britain〔英國的〕公路法規

high·way·man /ˈhaɪˌwemən; ˈhaɪweɪmən/ *n plural* **highwaymen** /-mən; -mən/ [C] someone who stopped people and carriages on the roads and robbed them especially in the 17th and 18th centuries〔尤指17、18世紀的〕攔路搶劫的強盜, 公路響馬

highway pa·trol /ˈ·· ·ˌ·/ *n* [singular] the police who make sure that people obey the rules on main roads in the US〔美國的〕公路巡邏隊

high wire /ˈ· ·/ *n* [C] a tightly stretched rope or wire high above the ground that someone walks along, usually as part of a CIRCUS performance〔走鋼絲表演用的〕繃索, 鋼絲

H

hi·jack[1] /ˈhaɪˌdʒæk; ˈhaɪdʒæk/ *v* [T] **1** to use violence or threats to take control of a plane, vehicle, or ship 騎劫, 劫持〔飛機等〕 **2** to take control of something and use it for your own purposes 控制, 把持: *Some people think the party has been hijacked by right-wing extremists.* 有人認為該黨已經被右翼極端分子所把持。—**hijacker** *n* [C]

hijack[2] *n* [C] *BrE* an act of hijacking a plane, vehicle etc【英】劫持事件

hi·jack·ing /ˈhaɪˌdʒækɪŋ; ˈhaɪdʒækɪŋ/ *n* **1** [C,U] the use of violence or threats to take control of a plane 劫機: *the recent series of airplane hijackings* 最近接二連三的劫機事件 **2** [U] the act of stealing goods from vehicles 盜竊車輛內物品的行為

hi·jinks /ˈhaɪˌdʒɪŋks; ˈhaɪdʒɪŋks/ *n* [plural] an American spelling of HIGH JINKS high jinks的美式拼法

hike[1] /haɪk; haɪk/ *n* [C] **1** a long walk in the mountains or countryside〔在山區或鄉間〕徒步旅行, 遠足: *a hike in the woods* 在林間遠足 **2** *especially AmE informal* a large increase in prices, wages, taxes etc【尤美, 非正式】〔價格、工資、稅率等的〕大幅度上升: *a petition against the proposed tax hikes* 反對擬議中大幅度提高稅率的請願書 **3 take a hike** *AmE spoken* used to tell someone rudely to go away【美口】滾開!

hike[2] *v* **1** [I,T] to walk a long way in the mountains or countryside 徒步旅行, 遠足: **hike sth** *AmE*【美】*He wants to hike the Himalayas.* 他想在喜馬拉雅山區作徒步旅行。| **go hiking** *The kids often go hiking at weekends.* 孩子們經常在週末去遠足。—compare 比較 WALKING[1] (1) **2** also 又作 **hike** sth ↔ **up** [T] *especially AmE* to increase prices, taxes, fees etc, especially by a large amount【尤美】〔大幅度〕提高〔價格、稅款、服務費等〕

hike sth ↔ **up 1** *especially AmE informal* to lift up a piece of your clothing【尤美, 非正式】提起, 拉起〔衣服〕: *She hiked her skirt up to climb the stairs.* 她提起裙子上樓。**2** HIKE[2] (2) 大幅度提高

hik·er /ˈhaɪkɚ; ˈhaɪkə/ *n* [C] someone who walks long distances in the mountains or country for pleasure; WALKER (1) 徒步旅行者, 遠足者

hi·lar·i·ous /həˈlɛrɪəs; hɪˈleərɪəs/ *adj* extremely funny 極好笑的, 極有趣的: *You should have seen that program last night – it was hilarious!* 你真該看看昨晚的節目, 好笑極了!—**hilariously** *adv*

hi·lar·i·ty /həˈlærətɪ; hɪˈlærəti/ *n* [U] laughter, or a feeling of fun 歡笑, 歡鬧: *Gloria's costume caused a good deal of hilarity.* 格洛麗亞的服裝引起了陣陣大笑。

2 2 **hill** /hɪl; hɪl/ *n* [C] **1** an area of land that is higher than the land around it, like a mountain but smaller 小山, 小丘, 山崗 **2** a slope on a road〔路上的〕斜坡: *There's a steep hill ahead – get into low gear.* 前面有個陡坡, 把車子掛到低擋。**3 on the Hill** *AmE* on CAPITOL HILL or in the US government【美】在美國國會[政府]中 **4 over the hill** no longer young, and therefore no longer attractive or good at doing things 不再年輕: *Kathleen thinks she's over the hill, but she's only 32.* 凱瑟琳覺得自己已經老了, 但她只有32歲。**5 it doesn't amount to a hill of beans** *AmE spoken* it is not important【美口】毫無價值, 微不足道

hill·bil·ly /ˈhɪlˌbɪlɪ; ˈhɪlbɪli/ *n* [C] *AmE* an insulting word meaning an uneducated person who lives in the mountains【美】山裡人, 鄉巴佬〔一種帶侮辱性的稱呼〕

hill·ock /ˈhɪlək; ˈhɪlək/ *n* [C] a little hill 小山丘

hill·side /ˈhɪlˌsaɪd; ˈhɪlsaɪd/ *n* [C] the sloping side of a hill〔小山的〕山坡

hill sta·tion /ˈ· ˌ··/ *n* [C] a town in the hills, especially in South Asia, where people go to escape the hot weather〔尤指南亞供避暑用的〕山間小鎮

hill·y /ˈhɪlɪ; ˈhɪli/ *adj* having a lot of hills 多山丘的, 丘陵起伏的: *a hilly region* 多山地區

hilt /hɪlt; hɪlt/ *n* [C] **1** the handle of a sword or knife that is used as a weapon〔刀、劍等武器的〕柄 —see picture at 參見 SWORD 圖 **2 (up) to the hilt** completely, or as much as possible 完全地, 徹底地, 最大限度地: *mortgaged up to the hilt* 已全部抵押的 | *I'd back him to the hilt any day.* 我任何時候都會全力支持他。

him /hɪm; ɪm; *strong* 強讀 hɪm; hɪm/ *pron* object form of 'he'〔he的受[賓]格〕他: *I don't know why he left early, I'll have to ask him about it.* 我不知道他為甚麼提前離開了, 我得問問他。| *It's a great movie, with Sylvester Stallone as we've never seen him before!* 這真是部好電影, 史泰龍有我們從未見過的演出! | *Imagine Ian becoming a pilot, and him so scared of flying too.* 想像一下伊恩成為一名飛行員, 而他是一個如此懼怕飛行的人。—see 見 ME (USAGE)

him·bo /ˈhɪmbo; ˈhɪmbəʊ/ *n* [C] *humorous* a young man who is sexually attractive but is not very intelligent【幽默】徒有其表的年輕男子

him·self /hɪmˋsɛlf; ɪmˈself; *strong* 強讀 hɪmˋsɛlf; hɪmˈself/ *pron* **1** used to emphasize the pronoun 'he', a male name etc 他自己, 他本人〔用於強調he〕: *To her surprise it was the President himself who opened the door.* 出乎她的意料, 是總統本人開的門。| *It must be true, he said so himself.* 這肯定是真的, 是他自己親口說的。| *How can he criticise her work when he has been judged so harshly himself.* 他自己得到的評價如此低, 他還有甚麼資格對她的工作提出批評。**2 not be/feel etc himself** if a man, boy etc is not himself, he does not feel or behave in the way that he usually does because he is nervous or upset 表現/感覺反常: *I think there's something on his mind – he hasn't really seemed himself lately.* 他一定有甚麼心事, 他近來一直表現得不大正常。**3 (all) by himself a)** alone 獨自一人地: *He said he would prefer to spend some time by himself for a while.* 他說他希望獨自一個人呆一段時間。**b)** without help 獨力地, 獨自地: *My son was about 2 years old before he could walk by himself.* 我兒子快兩歲時才會自己走路。**4 (all) to himself** if a man, boy etc has something to himself, he does not have to share it with anyone 獨自享用[擁有]的: *When his brother got married, John finally had a bedroom to himself.* 哥哥結婚後, 約翰終於有了自己一個人用的臥室。**5 a)** the reflexive form of HE〔he的反身代(名)詞〕他自己: *I don't think he hurt himself when he fell.* 我想他摔倒時並沒有傷着自己。| *His name is James but he usually calls himself Jim.* 他的名字叫詹姆斯, 但他通常稱自己為吉姆。| *He spends all day by the fire, talking to himself.* 他整天都呆在火爐邊自言自語。**b)** the reflexive form of HE used after words like EVERYONE, ANYONE, NO ONE etc〔he的反身代(名)詞, 用於everyone, anyone, no one之類的詞語之後〕自己: *Everyone should learn to respect himself.* 人人都應學會尊重自己。—see also 另見 YOURSELF

hind[1] /haɪnd; haɪnd/ *adj* **hind legs/feet** the back legs or feet of an animal with four legs〔四腿動物的〕後腿 —see also 另見 **talk the hind legs off a donkey** (TALK[1] (11))

hind[2] *n* [C] a female DEER 雌鹿

hin·der /ˈhɪndɚ; ˈhɪndə/ *v* [T] to make it difficult for someone to do something or for something to develop 阻礙, 妨礙, 阻止: *High interest rates will hinder economic growth.* 高利率將會阻礙經濟增長。

Hin·di /ˈhɪndɪ; ˈhɪndi/ *n* [U] one of the official languages of India 印地語

hind·most /ˈhaɪndˌmost; ˈhaɪndməʊst/ *adj old use* furthest behind【舊】最後面的 —see also 另見 **devil take the hindmost** (DEVIL (14))

hind·quar·ters /ˈhaɪndˋkwɔrtɚz; ˈhaɪndˌkwɔːtəz/ *n* [plural] the back part of an animal, including the back legs〔動物的〕後臀及後腿 —see picture at 參見 HORSE[1] 圖

hin·drance /ˈhɪndrəns; ˈhɪndrəns/ *n* **1** [C] something or someone that makes it difficult for you to do something successfully 起阻礙作用的人[事]; 障礙物; 阻礙者: **be a hindrance to** *Lack of funding was a serious hindrance to the progress of our research.* 缺少資金嚴重地阻礙了

我們的研究進展。| **be more of a hindrance than a help** (=try to help but cause more problems) 幫倒忙 **2** [U] *formal* the act of making it difficult for someone to do something【正式】阻礙, 妨礙 —see also 另見 **without let or hindrance** (LET² (2))

hind·sight /ˋhaɪnd͵saɪt; ˈhaɪndsaɪt/ *n* [U] the ability to understand facts about a situation only after it has happened 事後聰明, 後見之明: **with the benefit/wisdom of hindsight** (=when hindsight makes it possible to realize what mistakes were made) 通過事後總結/分析 *With the benefit of hindsight it's easy to criticize Lyndon Johnson's fateful decision.* 事後才指責林登·約翰遜的重大失誤當然不難。

Hin·du /ˋhɪndu; ˈhɪnduː/ *n plural* **Hindus** [C] someone who believes in Hinduism 印度教徒 —**Hindu** *adj*: *a Hindu temple* 印度教寺廟

Hin·du·is·m /ˋhɪndu͵ɪzəm; ˈhɪndu-ɪzəm/ *n* [U] the main religion in India, which includes belief in DESTINY and REINCARNATION 印度教〔印度的主要宗教〕

hinge¹ /hɪndʒ; hɪndʒ/ *n* [C] a metal part used to fasten a door to its frame, a lid to a box etc, so that it can swing open and shut〔門、箱等上的〕鉸鏈, 合葉 —see picture at 參見 GLASS¹ 圖

hinge² *v*

hinge on/upon sth *phr v* [T not in progressive 不用進行式] if a result hinges on something happening, it depends on it completely 取決於: *The future prospects of a student hinge on his performance in these examinations.* 一個學生的發展前途取決於他在這些考試中的表現。

hinged /hɪndʒd; hɪndʒd/ *adj* joined by a hinge 用鉸鏈連接的

hint¹ /hɪnt; hɪnt/ *n* [C] **1** something that you say or do in order to tell someone something in an indirect way, so that they can guess what you mean 暗示: **drop a hint (that)** (=give a hint) 作出暗示 *Harry was dropping hints that he wanted to be invited to the party.* 哈里一直在暗示自己希望被邀請參加這次晚會。| **a broad hint** (=one that is deliberately easy to understand) 明顯的暗示 | **take a/the hint** (=understand someone's hint) 領會暗示 *I kept looking at my watch, but Laura wouldn't take the hint – she didn't leave till midnight.* 我不停地看手錶, 但勞拉就是不領會這個提示, 她直到午夜才離開。**2** a very small amount or sign of something〔細微的〕跡象; 少許, 微量: [+of] *There was a hint of anger in his voice.* 他的聲音中帶有一點惱怒。| *a sauce with a hint of garlic* 帶有少許大蒜的調味汁 | **give no hint of/that** *literary*【文】*a blue sky that gave no hint of the storm to come* 沒有一點將要出現暴風雨跡象的藍天 **3** a useful piece of advice about how to do something 有益的建議〔指點〕: [+on] *helpful hints on looking after house plants* 關於種植家居植物的好建議

hint² *v* [I,T] to say something in an indirect way, but so that someone can guess what you mean 暗示, 示意: [+at] *What are you hinting at?* 你在暗示甚麼? | **hint (that)** *I think she was hinting that I might be offered a contract.* 我想她在暗示我可能會獲得一份合同。

hin·ter·land /ˋhɪntə͵lænd; ˈhɪntəlænd/ *n* [singular] an area of land beyond a coast or large river 內地, 腹地

hip¹ /hɪp; hɪp/ *n* [C] **1** one of the two parts on each side of your body between the top of your leg and your waist 臀部 —see picture at 參見 BODY 圖 **2** [usually plural 一般用複數] the red fruit of some kinds of ROSE bushes; ROSE HIP〔紅色的〕薔薇果(實)

hip² *interjection* **hip, hip, hurray!** used as a shout of approval〔表示讚許的喊聲〕加油! 萬歲!

hip³ *adj informal* doing things or done according to the latest fashion【非正式】新潮的, 趕時髦的

hip-bath /ˋhɪp͵bæθ; ˈhɪpbɑːθ/ *n* [C] a bath you can sit but not lie down in 坐浴浴盆

hip flask /ˋ· ·/ *n* [C] a small container for strong alcoholic drinks, made to fit in your pocket〔可放在褲子後袋裡的〕扁平小酒瓶 —see picture at 參見 FLASK 圖

hip hop /ˋ· ·/ *n* [U] a kind of popular dance music with a regular heavy BEAT and spoken words 嘻蹦樂〔節奏強烈、說唱形式的一種流行音樂〕

hip·hug·gers /ˋhɪphʌgəz; ˈhɪphʌgəz/ *n* [plural] *AmE* HIPSTERS【美】褲腰低及臀部的緊身長褲

hip·pie, hippy /ˋhɪpɪ; ˈhɪpi/ *n* [C] someone opposed to the traditional standards of society who wears unusual clothes, has long hair, and takes drugs for pleasure 嬉皮士

hippie 嬉皮士

hip·po /ˋhɪpo; ˈhɪpəʊ/ *n* [C] *informal* a hippopotamus【非正式】河馬

hip pock·et /͵· ˋ··/ *n* [C] a back pocket in a pair of trousers or a skirt〔褲子或裙子的〕後口袋, 後兜

Hip·po·crat·ic oath /͵hɪpəkrætɪk ˋoθ; ͵hɪpəkrætɪk ˈəʊθ/ *n* [singular] the promise made by doctors that they will keep to the principles of the medical profession 希波克拉底誓言〔醫生從業前所立的保證拯救生命和遵守醫德的誓言〕

hip·po·pot·a·mus /͵hɪpəˋpɑtəməs; ͵hɪpəˈpɒtəməs/ *n* [C] a large African animal with a large head, a wide mouth, and thick grey skin, that lives in and near water〔產於非洲的〕河馬

hip·py /ˋhɪpɪ; ˈhɪpi/ *n* [C] another spelling of HIPPIE hippie的另一種拼法

hip·sters /ˋhɪpstəz; ˈhɪpstəz/ *n* [plural] *BrE* trousers that fit tightly over your HIPS and do not cover your waist【英】褲腰低及臀部的緊身長褲; HIPHUGGERS *AmE*【美】

hire¹ /haɪr; haɪə/ *v* [T] **1** *BrE* to pay money to borrow something for a period of hours or days【英】〔短期〕租用; LET¹ (11), RENT¹ (3) *AmE*【美】: *Let's hire a car for the weekend.* 我們這個週末租輛車吧! —see 見 BORROW (USAGE) **2 a)** to employ someone for a short time to do a job for you〔短期〕雇用〔某人〕: *I'm hiring a private detective to trace my ex-husband.* 我雇了一名私家偵探跟蹤我的前夫。**b)** *especially AmE* to employ someone【尤美】雇用, 聘任: **hire and fire** (=employ and dismiss people) 聘用與解雇 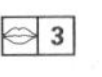

hire sth ↔ **out** *phr v* [T] *BrE*【英】**1** to allow someone to use something for a short time in exchange for money〔短期〕出租; RENT¹ (3) *AmE*【美】: *a little company that hires out boats to tourists* 一家向遊客出租遊船的小公司 **2 hire yourself out** to arrange to work for someone 受雇於某人

USAGE NOTE 用法說明: HIRE

WORD CHOICE 詞語辨析: **hire, hire out, rent, rent out, let out, employ, take on, appoint, charter**

In British English you **hire** things for just a short time and the owner **hires** them **out** to you. 在英國英語中, 短期租用物品用hire, 而物主將物品出租則用hire out: *Let's hire a car for the weekend.* 我們這個週末租輛車吧! | *I'll have to hire a suit for the wedding.* 我得為婚禮租一套禮服。

You **rent** things for a longer period. rent表示租用的時間比較長: *Is that your own fax or do you rent it?* 那台傳真機是你自己的還是租來的? You **rent** a house, room etc and the owner **lets** it **(out)** to you. 租用房屋等用rent, 房主將房屋出租則用let (out)。

In American English, however, you **rent** all of these things, and the owner **rents** them **out**. This is now starting to be used in British English as well. 但在美國英語中, 租用所有物品都用rent, 物主出租所有物品都用rent out。英國英語也在開始採用這種用法。

In American English you **hire** people for any job, but in British English you only **hire** people for a particular purpose for a short time. Otherwise you **employ** them or **take** them **on** (or, more formally, **appoint** them) 在美國英語中, 雇人做任何工作都用 hire, 但在英國英語中, 只有短期雇用某人做某一特定工作才用 hire。如長期雇用則用 employ 或 take on (或者更正式一點, 用 appoint): *We hired a caterer for the wedding reception.* 我們為婚宴雇了一名酒席承辦人。| *Business is good – we'll have to take on more workers.* 生意不錯, 我們得再多雇些工人。

In both American English and British English groups, companies etc may **charter** buses, ships, or planes for a special purpose. 無論在美國或英國英語中, 集團、公司等為某一特定用途包租車輛、船隻或飛機均可用 charter: *UNICEF has chartered a plane to carry supplies to the disaster area.* 聯合國兒童基金會租了一架飛機將物資運往災區。

hire² *n* [U] **1** *BrE* an arrangement by which you borrow something for a short time in exchange for money【英】〔短期〕租用; 出租: *a car hire company* 汽車出租公司 | **for hire** (=available to hire) 可供出租 *boats for hire* 可供出租的小船 | **on hire from** (=being hired) 從...處租用 *The crane is on hire from a construction company.* 吊車是從一家建築公司租來的。**2** *old use* wages【舊】工資, 工錢 —see also 另見 **ply for hire** (PLY¹ (4))

hired hand /ˌ· ˈ·/ *n* [C] *AmE* someone who is employed to help on a farm【美】農場雇工

hire·ling /ˋhaɪrlɪŋ; ˈhaɪəlɪŋ/ *n* [C] someone who will work for anyone who is willing to pay 受雇後聽人使喚者

hire pur·chase /ˌ· ˈ··/ *n* [U] *BrE* a way of buying expensive goods by regularly paying small amounts over a period of time【英】分期付款購買法; INSTALLMENT PLAN *AmE*【美】

hir·sute /ˋhɝsut; ˈhɜːsjuːt/ *adj literary or humorous* having a lot of hair especially on your body and face【文或幽默】〔尤指身體和面部〕多毛的, 毛茸茸的

S1 W1 **his¹** /ɪz; ɪz; *strong* 強讀 hɪz; hɪz/ *determiner* [possessive form of 'he' he 的所有格] **1** used to talk about something that belongs to or is connected with someone who has already been mentioned or who the person you are talking to already knows about (屬於) 他的: *He broke his arm while playing football with his children.* 他與(他的)孩子踢足球時摔斷了胳膊。| *A man of his age shouldn't be running about like that.* 像他這種年紀的人不應該如此東奔西跑。**2** used especially after words like 'everyone', 'anyone', 'no one' etc when you mean 'their' 他的〔尤用於 everyone, anyone, no one 等詞之後〕: *Who cares what everyone else is doing – each to his own, I say.* 誰會在意別人在幹甚麼, 我說呀, 還是各管各的事吧。—compare 比較 THEIR

S1 W2 **his²** *pron* [possessive form of 'he' he 的所有格] **1** used to talk about something that belongs to or is connected with someone who has already been mentioned or who the person you are talking to already knows about (屬於) 他的 (東西); 同他有關的 (人): *That's not Philip's wife – his is a tall blonde woman.* 那不是菲利普的妻子, 他的妻子是個高個子的金髮女人。| **sb/sth of his** *That stupid brother of his ran into my car.* 他那個傻瓜兄弟撞了我的車。**2** used after words like 'everyone', 'anyone', 'no one' etc when you mean 'theirs' 〔用在 everyone, anyone, no one 等詞後〕他的: *Everyone only wants what is his by right.* 每個人都只想得到理應屬於他的東西。—compare 比較 THEIRS

Hi·span·ic /hɪsˋpænɪk; hɪˈspænɪk/ *adj* from or connected with a country where Spanish or Portuguese is spoken 來自說西班牙語[葡萄牙語]國家的; 與說西班牙語[葡萄牙語]國家有關的 —**Hispanic** *n* [C]

hiss /hɪs; hɪs/ *v* **1** [I] to make a noise which sounds like 'ssss' 發出嘶嘶聲: *The snake slowly uncoiled, making a loud hissing noise.* 那條蛇慢慢地伸直了身子, 一邊發出很響的嘶嘶聲。**2** [I,T] to say something in a loud whisper 用噓聲說出: *"Be quiet," she hissed.* "別出聲。" 她噓聲道。**3** [T] to hiss at a performer or speaker that you do not like〔因不滿而對表演者或發言人〕發噓聲 —**hiss** *n* [C] —see picture on page A19 參見 A19 頁圖

hist /hɪst; hɪst/ *interjection old use* a sound used to get someone's attention or to ask someone to be quiet【舊】噓!〔用於引起注意或要求肅靜的聲音〕

his·ta·mine /ˋhɪstəmin; ˈhɪstəmiːn/ *n* [C] a chemical compound that can increase the flow of blood in your body 組胺

his·to·gram /ˋhɪstəˌgræm; ˈhɪstəgræm/ *n* [C] a BAR CHART〔用於統計上的〕條形圖 (表)

his·to·ri·an /hɪsˋtɔrɪən; hɪˈstɔːriən/ *n* [C] someone who studies or writes about history 歷史學家, 史學工作者 

his·tor·ic /hɪsˋtɔrɪk; hɪˈstɒrɪk/ *adj* **1** a historic event or place is important because it is, or will be, remembered as part of history 有重大歷史意義的, 歷史性的: *an historic building* 一座有歷史意義的建築物 | *a historic meeting between two great leaders* 兩位偉大領導人的歷史性會晤 **2** historic times are the periods of time whose history has been recorded 有歷史記載的 —compare 比較 PREHISTORIC

his·tor·i·cal /hɪsˋtɔrɪkḷ; hɪˈstɒrɪkəl/ *adj* **1** connected with the study of history (有關) 歷史的; 歷史學的: *historical research* 史學研究 **2** historical events, facts, people etc happened or existed in the past 歷史上的, 屬於過去的: *Was King Arthur a real historical figure?* 亞瑟王是一位真實的歷史人物嗎? **3** describing or based on events in the past 反映歷史事件的; 基於史實的: a *historical novel* 歷史小說 —**historically** /-kḷɪ; -kli/ *adv* 

historic pres·ent /·ˌ·· ˈ··/ *n* [singular] the present tense, used in some languages to describe events in the past to make them seem more real 歷史現在時〔在一些語言中, 在敘述過去發生的事情時使用現在時式以求生動〕

his·to·ry /ˋhɪstrɪ; ˈhɪstəri/ *n*

1 ▶PAST EVENTS 過去的事件◀ [U] all the things that happened in the past, especially the political, social, or economic development of a nation 歷史: *India has been invaded several times during its history.* 印度在歷史上曾幾次受到侵略。| *Throughout history the achievements of women have been largely ignored.* 在整個歷史過程中婦女的成就在很大程度上都被人忽略了。| **change the course of history** *Those decisions made at the Yalta Conference changed the course of history.* 雅爾塔會議上所作的那些決定改變了歷史的進程。

2 ▶SUBJECT OF STUDY 學科◀ [U] the study of history, especially as a subject in school or university 歷史學: *a degree in European history* 歐洲史學位

3 ▶DEVELOPMENT OF STH 發展過程◀ [singular,U] the development of a subject, activity, institution etc since it started 發展史, 沿革, 發展過程: *the worst disaster in the history of space travel* 太空航行史上最大的災難

4 ▶BOOK 書◀ [C] a book about past events 史書, 史記: *a history of World War II* 第二次世界大戰史記

5 ▶PAST LIFE 過去的生活◀ **a history of** if someone has a history of illness, problems, or criminal activity, these things have happened to them or been done by them in the past 個人經歷, 履歷〈如病史、犯罪記錄等〉: *The defendant had a history of violent assaults against women.* 被告曾有強暴婦女的前科。

6 make history to do something important that will be recorded and remembered 創造歷史, 做出值得載入史冊的重要事情: *Lindbergh made history when he flew across the Atlantic in 1927.* 林白於 1927 年飛越大西洋, 寫下了歷史的新篇章。

7 will go down in history something that will go down in history is important enough to be remembered and recorded 將被載入史冊: *This day will go down in history as the start of a new era in South Africa.* 南非踏入新紀元的這一天將被載入史冊裡。

8 ...and the rest is history used to say that everyone knows the rest of a story you have been telling ...接下來的就是盡人皆知的故事了

9 that's past/ancient history *spoken* used to say that something is not important any more【口】那已是往事了〔表示某事已不再重要〕

10 history repeats itself used to say that things often happen in the same way as they happened before 歷史在不斷重演 —see also 另見 NATURAL HISTORY, CASE HISTORY

his·tri·on·ics /ˌhɪstriˈɑnɪks; ˌhɪstriˈɒnɪks/ *n* [plural] loud, extremely emotional behaviour that is intended to get people's sympathy and attention 矯揉造作, 裝腔作勢 —**histrionic** *adj*

hit¹ /hɪt; hɪt/ *v past tense and past participle* **hit** *present participle* **hitting**

1 ►TOUCH SB/STH HARD 用勁碰某人/物◄ [T] to touch someone or something quickly and usually hard with your hand, a stick etc 打, 擊: **hit sth with** *Billy was hitting a tin can with a spoon.* 比利用匙子敲打着一個罐頭。| **hit sb on the nose/in the stomach/over the head etc** *She hit him playfully over the head with her newspaper.* 她用報紙鬧着玩地打了一下他的頭。| **get hit** *Stand back you lot, or you'll get hit.* 你們全都給我往後站, 否則會被擊中的。—compare 比較 PUNCH¹ (1), SLAP¹ (1)

2 ►HIT/CRASH INTO STH 撞上某物◄ [T] to move into something quickly and hard 撞擊, 碰撞: *The football hit the trash can with a bang.* 足球砰的一聲打在垃圾桶上。| *The driver was drunk and hit three stationary cars.* 司機酒後駕車, 撞上了三輛停着的車。

3 ►ACCIDENTALLY 意外地◄ [T] to move a part of your body quickly and hard against something so that it hurts you〔使身體某部位〕撞[碰]着: **hit sth on/against etc** *I fell and hit my head on the table.* 我摔倒了, 頭撞在桌子上。

4 ►IN SPORT 體育運動中◄ [T] **a)** to make something such as a ball move by hitting it with a bat, stick etc〔用球拍等〕擊打〔球〕: *He hit the shuttlecock gently this time.* 他這次輕擊了一下羽毛球。**b)** to get a point or some points by hitting a ball etc 擊球得分: **hit two goals/a six etc** *The batter hit a home run.* 擊球員打出了一個本壘球。

5 ►WORK A MACHINE ETC 操作機器等◄ [T] to press a part in a machine, car etc to make it work 按, 摁: *Hit the brakes!* 踩煞車!

6 ►HURT SB 傷害某人◄ [T] to deliberately move your hand, a stick etc against someone and hurt them〔用手、棍子等〕打(傷): *Mom, she keeps hitting me!* 媽媽, 她老是打我! | **hit sb with sth** *They used to hit the kids with a leather belt.* 他們過去常用一根皮帶打孩子。| **hit sb over the head/in the stomach etc** *She hit him as hard as she could around his face.* 她用盡力氣在他的臉上亂打一氣。

7 ►BULLETS/BOMBS ETC 子彈/炸彈等◄ [T often passive 常用被動態] to wound someone or damage something with a bullet, bomb etc 擊傷〔某人〕; 擊毀〔某物〕: **hit sb/sth in/on etc** *A second shot hit her in the back.* 第二槍擊中了她的背部。| **be badly hit** *Our ship was badly hit and sank within minutes.* 我們的船受到重擊, 沒過幾分鐘就沉沒了。

8 ►ATTACK 攻擊◄ [I,T usually passive 一般用被動態] to attack someone suddenly〔突然〕攻擊: *The convoy was hit by Afghan government troops.* 車隊遭到阿富汗政府軍的攻擊。

9 ►HURT, BUT NOT PHYSICALLY 造成非肉體上的傷害◄ [T] *informal* to do something that harms someone【非正式】傷害: **hit sb where it hurts** (=in the way you think will be most upsetting for them) 擊中某人的要害, 觸到某人的痛處 *You should hit your husband where it hurts most – in his wallet!* 你應該擊中你丈夫的要害 —— 瞄準他的錢包! | **hit sb when they are down** (=harm someone even though they are already defeated or very weak) 乘人之危打擊某人, 落井下石

10 ►BAD LUCK ETC 惡運等◄ [I,T] if something such as bad luck, illness, bad weather etc hits or hits someone, it suddenly affects them〔惡運、疾病、壞天氣等〕突然襲擊[影響]: *The storm finally hit.* 暴風雨終於來臨了。| *The guilt hit him like a lead weight.* 內疚的感覺像一塊鉛落在他的身上。| **be badly/severely/hard hit** *The company has been badly hit by the drop in prices.* 這家公司因價格下跌而受到重創。| **worst/hardest hit** *the areas of the country hardest hit by the recession* 該國受經濟衰退影響最嚴重的那些地區

11 ►REACH A LEVEL/NUMBER 達到某一水平/數量◄ [T] to reach a particular level or number 達到〔某水平或數量〕: *Youth unemployment has hit the one million mark.* 年輕人的失業人數已達到一百萬。| **hit rock-bottom/hit an all-time low** (=reach an extremely low level) 達到最低點 *World oil prices have hit rock-bottom.* 全球石油價格已跌至最低點。

12 ►PROBLEM/TROUBLE 問題/麻煩◄ [T] to experience trouble, a problem etc 碰到, 遇到〔困難、問題等〕: *I had hit a few snags in my work.* 我在工作上碰到了一些難題。| **hit a bad patch** *spoken* (=have a short period of difficulty)【口】遇到暫時的困難

13 ►REALIZE 意識到◄ [T] if a fact hits you, you suddenly realize its importance and feel surprised or shocked 使〔某人〕突然意識到: *The full meaning of the night's events hit me and I started crying.* 我突然意識到了當晚所發生的事情的全部意義, 然後就開始哭了起來。| **it hits sb** *Suddenly it hit me. He was trying to ask me to marry him.* 我突然明白了。他是在向我求婚。

14 not know what hit you *informal* to be so surprised or shocked by something that you cannot think clearly【非正式】因驚嚇而無法正常思考; 大為驚訝

15 ►ARRIVE 到達◄ [T] *informal* to arrive or go somewhere【非正式】到達〔某地〕: *They hit the main road two kilometres further on.* 他們又前進了兩公里後就到了大路。| **hit town** *especially AmE*【尤美】*I'll look for work as soon as I hit town.* 我一到鎮上就去找工作。

16 hit the road *informal* to start on a journey【非正式】出發, 動身

17 ►TELL SB STH 告訴某人某事◄ [T] *informal* if you hit someone with some information or news, you tell them something surprising or entertaining【非正式】透露〔令人驚訝或有趣的消息〕: *Once you've hit the customer with the price you want to close the deal quickly.* 你一旦將價錢告訴顧客, 就想儘快做成買賣。

18 hit it off (with sb) *informal* if two people hit it off with each other, they like each other as soon as they meet【非正式】〔與某人〕一見如故, 合得來: *I knew you'd hit it off with Mike.* 我早就知道你與邁克會一見如故的。

19 hit the big time *informal* to suddenly become very famous, successful and rich【非正式】突然成名, 突然發跡

20 hit the bottle *informal* to start to drink a lot of alcohol【非正式】開始酗酒, 喝過量的酒

21 hit the dirt/the deck *informal* to fall to the ground because of danger【非正式】〔因遭遇危險而〕突然跌倒在地

22 hit the ground running to start doing something successfully without any delay 立刻着手順利地做某事

23 hit the jackpot a) to win a lot of money 贏得大筆金錢, 中頭彩 **b)** *informal* to have a big success【非正式】大獲成功

24 hit the nail on the head *especially spoken* used to say that what someone has said is exactly right【尤口】正中要害, 一針見血, 說話中肯

25 hit the roof/the ceiling *spoken* to become extremely angry【口】大發雷霆, 暴跳如雷: *Dad hit the roof when*

I got home at 2 am. 我凌晨兩點才回到家裡，爸爸生氣極了。

26 hit the sack *informal* to go to bed【非正式】上牀睡覺

27 hit the spot *informal* if food hits the spot, it stops you being hungry and tastes good【非正式】〔食物〕讓人吃得飽而滿意，切合需要 —see also 另見 **the shit hit the fan** (SHIT¹ (12))

hit back *phr v* [I] to attack or criticize a person or group that has attacked or criticized you 回擊，反擊：**hit back (at sb/sth)** *Stung by Maria's contempt, Philip hit back with a few well-chosen words.* 菲利普因為瑪麗亞蔑視地刺了他幾句，便用兩三句巧妙的話來進行反擊。

hit on *phr v* [T] **1** **[hit on sth]** also 又作 **hit upon** to have a good idea after thinking about a problem for a long time〔經考慮後〕突然想出〔好主意〕：*He hit upon this ingenious method of freezing food.* 他突然靈機一觸，想出了這個巧妙的冷凍食品的辦法。**2** **[hit on sth]** also 又作 **hit upon** to discover something by a lucky chance 偶然發現：*I think you may have hit upon the only error in the whole program.* 我想你可能無意中發現了整個程式中唯一的一處錯誤。**3** **[hit on sb]** *AmE informal* to talk to someone in a way that shows you are sexually attracted to them【美，非正式】用語言挑逗：*Don spent the whole night hitting on anything that moved.* 唐整個晚上都在不擇對象地挑逗別人。

hit out *phr v* [I] **1** to express strong disapproval of someone or something 嚴厲批評，猛烈抨擊：**[+at/against]** *The bishop has hit out at the government's policy on homeless people.* 主教就政府針對無家可歸者的政策進行了猛烈的抨擊。**2** to try to hit someone〔試圖〕打某人：**[+at]** *He hit out at me without thinking.* 他想都沒想就動手打我了。

hit sb **up for** sth *phr v* [T] *AmE spoken* to ask someone for something【美口】要求〔某人〕提供〔某物〕：*Can I hit you up for a loan till Thursday?* 你能否借我點錢，我星期四還給你？

3 **hit²** *n* [C usually singular 一般用單數] **1** a quick, hard touch with your hand or something you are holding〔用手或手持之物的〕打，擊：*That was a hard hit!* 那真是一記重擊！**2** an occasion when something that is aimed at something else touches it, reaches it, or damages it 命中，擊中：*I scored a hit with my first shot.* 我第一槍就命中了目標。| **a direct hit** *Our ship took a direct hit and sank.* 我們的船被擊中下沉了。**3** something such as a piece of music, a film, or a play that is extremely popular 成功並風行一時的事物〈如音樂、電影、戲劇等〉：**a hit single/show etc** *the latest Broadway hit musical, "The Mask"* 轟動全城的百老匯最新音樂劇《面具》| **a big/smash hit** *Chris de Burgh had a smash hit with "Lady in Red".* 克里斯·德伯格的歌曲《紅衣女人》大受歡迎。**4** **be/make a hit with sb** to be liked very much by someone 極受某人喜愛：*Your husband was a big hit with the kids.* 你的丈夫極受孩子們的喜愛。**5** **a hit at sb** a remark that is intended to hurt someone 傷害某人的話 **6** *slang* the action of deliberately breathing in the smoke of an illegal drug【俚】吸毒 **7** *AmE slang* a murder【美俚】謀殺 —see also 另見 HIT MAN

hit-and-miss /ˌ· · ˈ·/ *adj* done in a way that is not planned or organized 碰運氣的，無周詳計劃的

hit-and-run /ˌ· · ˈ·◂/ *adj* [only before noun 僅用於名詞前] **1** a hit-and-run accident is one in which the driver of a car hits a person or another car and then drives away without stopping to help〔交通事故〕撞了人[另一輛車]而逃走的：**hit-and-run driver** (=one who does not stop after an accident) 肇事後逃跑的司機 **2** a hit-and-run military attack is one in which the attackers arrive suddenly and unexpectedly and leave quickly〔軍事行動中〕打了就跑的，攻擊後馬上撤離的

hitch¹ /hɪtʃ; hɪtʃ/ *v* **1** [I,T] *informal* to ask for a free ride from the drivers of passing cars by putting your hand out with your thumb raised; HITCHHIKE【非正式】搭免費便車旅行，搭順風車：**[+across/around/to]** *They hitched all the way across Europe.* 他們搭順風車穿越了整個歐洲。| **hitch a ride with sb** *We hitched a ride with a trucker from New York to Montreal.* 我們搭了一位卡車司機的便車從紐約到了蒙特利爾。**2** **get hitched** *spoken informal* to get married【口，非正式】結婚 **3** [T always+adv/prep] to fasten something such as a TRAILER (1) to the back of a car so that it can be pulled〔將拖車等〕掛上鈎 **4** [T always+adv/prep] to tie a horse to something〔將馬匹〕拴住，套住

hitch sth ↔ **up** *phr v* [T] **1** to pull, especially a piece of clothing, upwards 將〔衣物〕向上拉：*He hitched up his trousers and started to work.* 他把褲子向上拉了拉，開始幹活。**2** **hitch up a horse/wagon/team etc** to tie a horse to something, so that the horse can pull it 把馬/馬車/幾匹馬套在…上：*He hitched up his wagon and headed west.* 他套上馬車向西走了。

hitch² *n* [C] **1** a problem that delays something for a short time〔短暫的〕故障，障礙：*Except for a few technical hitches the show went very well.* 除了一些小小的技術故障外，演出進行得非常順利。| **without a hitch** *The Miss Universe pageant went off without a hitch.* 環球小姐選美大賽進行得非常成功。**2** a short, sudden pull upwards 向上急拉：*He gave his belt a hitch.* 他猛地將腰帶向上提了提。

hitchhike 搭便車旅行

hitch·hike /ˈhɪtʃˌhaɪk; ˈhɪtʃhaɪk/ also 又作 **hitch** *v* [I] to travel by asking drivers of passing cars for free rides 搭免費便車旅行，搭順風車 —**hitchhiker** *n*

hi-tech /ˌhaɪ ˈtɛk; ˌhaɪ ˈtek◂/ another spelling of HIGH-TECH high-tech 的另一種拼法

hith·er /ˈhɪðɚ; ˈhɪðə/ *adj old use* here【舊】這兒，這裡：**hither and thither** (=in many directions) 這兒和那兒，到處 *A little girl was running hither and thither.* 一個小女孩正在四處奔跑。

hith·er·to /ˌhɪðɚˈtu; ˌhɪðəˈtuː◂/ *adv formal* up to this time【正式】到目前為止，迄今，至今：*The printing press made books available to people hitherto unable to afford them.* 印刷機使以前買不起書的人們能買得起書。

hit list /ˈ· ·/ *n* [C] *informal* the names of people, organizations etc who you plan to do bad things to【非正式】〔有計劃地針對某些人或組織的〕打擊名單，襲擊名單：*The company has a hit list of factories it wants to close down.* 公司列出了一份擬關閉的工廠的名單。

hit man /ˈ· ·/ *n* [C] a criminal who is employed to kill someone 職業殺手

hit pa·rade /ˈ· ·ˌ·/ **the hit parade** *n old-fashioned* a list of popular records, usually songs, showing which records have sold the most copies【過時】〔流行歌曲的〕唱片排行榜

HIV /ˌetʃ aɪ ˈvi; ˌeɪtʃ aɪ ˈviː◂/ *n* [U] a kind of VIRUS (=very small living thing that causes disease) that enters the body through blood or sexual activity, and can cause AIDS 人體免疫缺損病毒，愛滋病病毒〔該病毒是透過受感染的血液和性接觸傳播的〕：**be HIV positive** (=have the HIV virus in your body) 愛滋病病毒呈陽性的

hive¹ /haɪv; haɪv/ *n* **1** [C] **a)** also 又作 **beehive** a small box where BEEs are kept 蜂箱 **b)** the group of bees who live together in a hive〔同一蜂箱內的〕蜂羣 **2 a hive of industry/activity etc** *BrE* a place that is full of people who are very busy【英】人羣繁忙的場所, 熙熙攘攘的地方 **3 hives** [U] a skin disease in which a person's skin becomes red and painful 蕁麻疹

hive[2] *v*
hive sth ↔ **off** *phr v* to separate one part of a business from the rest, usually by selling it〔通過出售〕將〔部分業務〕分離出去

hi·ya /ˋhaɪjə; ˈhaɪjə/ *interjection spoken* used to say hello【口】你好!

HM *BrE*【英】the abbreviation for 縮寫= His or Her Majesty

h'm, hmm /həm; m, hm/ *interjection* a sound that you make to express doubt, a pause, or disagreement〔表示懷疑、停頓或不贊同的輕哼聲〕唔, 嗯, 哼, 姆

HMS /ˈ· · ·/ His/Her Majesty's ship; a title for a ship in the British Navy, and for places on the land that are used by the navy 英國皇家海軍艦艇; 英國海軍艦艇陸上基地: *HMS Belfast* 皇家海軍艦艇貝爾法斯特號

hoard[1] /hɔrd; hɔːd/ *n* [C] a collection of things that someone keeps hidden because they like them or consider them to be valuable 藏匿的寶物; 寶庫: [+of] *He kept a little hoard of chocolates in his top drawer.* 他在最上面的抽屜裡藏了一些巧克力糖。

hoard[2] *v* also 又作 **hoard up** [T] to collect and save large amounts of food, money etc 貯藏, 囤積

hoard·er /ˋhɔrdɚ; ˈhɔːdə/ *n* [C] someone who likes to keep things 喜好貯藏東西的人

hoard·ing /ˋhɔrdɪŋ; ˈhɔːdɪŋ/ *n* [C] *BrE*【英】**1** a high fence around a piece of land where something is being built〔建築工地四周的〕圍欄, 圍板 **2** a high fence or board on which large advertisements are stuck 廣告牌[板]; BILLBOARD *AmE*【美】

hoar·frost /ˋhɔrˌfrɔst; ˈhɔːfrɒst/ *n* [U] FROST[1] (1) 白霜

hoarse /hɔrs; hɔːs/ *adj* **1** a hoarse voice sounds rough, as if the speaker has a sore throat〔嗓音〕沙啞的: *His voice was hoarse from laughing.* 他笑得嗓子都沙啞了。**2** a person who is hoarse has a hoarse voice〔人〕嗓音沙啞的 —**hoarsely** *adv* —**hoarseness** *n* [U]

hoar·y /ˋhɔrɪ; ˈhɔːri/ *adj old-fashioned*【過時】**1** very old 非常古老的: *a hoary old joke* 老掉牙的笑話 **2** hoary hair is grey or white〔頭髮〕灰白的, 花白的; 白的 **3** having grey or white hair 頭髮灰白[白]的 —**hoariness** *n* [U]

hoax[1] /hoks; həʊks/ *n* [C] **1** a false warning about something dangerous or bad 惡作劇, 假警告: *a bomb hoax* 虛報有炸彈的惡作劇 | **hoax call** (=a telephone call that gives false information) 惡作劇電話 **2** an attempt to make people believe something that is not true 騙局: *The Hitler Diaries were an elaborate hoax.*《希特拉日記》是一場精心編造的騙局。

hoax[2] *v* [T] to trick someone by means of a hoax 欺騙, 作弄 —**hoaxer** *n* [C]

hob /hɑb; hɒb/ *n* [C] *BrE*【英】**1** the flat top of a COOKER (1) that you cook on〔爐具上的〕爐盤 **2** *old use* a metal shelf next to a fire【舊】〔火堆旁的〕金屬擱架

hob·ble /ˋhɑbḷ; ˈhɒbəl/ *v* **1** [I] to walk with difficulty, especially as a result of an injury to your legs or feet 跛行, 一瘸一拐地走: *an old man hobbling along the street* 在街上一瘸一拐地行走的老頭 **2** [T] to loosely fasten two of an animal's legs together, to stop it from running away〔為防止動物跑掉而鬆鬆地〕捆縛〔動物的腿〕**3** [T] to deliberately make sure that a plan, system etc cannot work successfully 妨礙〔系統等的正常運作〕

hob·ble·de·hoy /ˋhɑbḷdɪˌhɔɪ; ˈhɒbəldihɔɪ/ *n* [C] *old-fashioned* a rude young person【過時】粗魯的年輕人

3 **hob·by** /ˋhɑbɪ; ˈhɒbi/ *n* [C] an activity that you enjoy doing in your free time 業餘愛好, 嗜好: *One of her hobbies is horse-riding.* 她的業餘愛好之一是騎馬。

hob·by·horse /ˋhɑbɪˌhɔrs; ˈhɒbihɔːs/ *n* **1** [C] a child's toy like a horse's head on a stick, which the child pretends to ride on〔兒童放在胯下當馬騎的〕竹馬, 馬頭桿 **2 be on your hobbyhorse** to talk for a long time about a subject you think is very interesting 長時間地談論喜愛的話題

hob·gob·lin /ˋhɑbˌgɑblɪn; hɒbˈgɒblᵻn/ *n* [C] a GOBLIN that plays tricks on people 淘氣的小妖精

hob·nail /ˋhɑbˌnel; ˈhɒbneɪl/ *n* [C] a large nail with a big, flat top, used to make the bottom part of heavy boots and shoes stronger〔釘在笨重鞋子和靴子底部起加固作用的〕平頭釘 —**hobnailed** *adj*

hob·nob /ˋhɑbˌnɑb; ˈhɒbnɒb/ *v* [I] *informal* to spend time talking to people who are in a higher social position than you【非正式】〔與社會地位較高的人〕親近, 親密交談: [+with] *hobnobbing with the bosses at the sports club* 在體育俱樂部裡與上司們親密交談

ho·bo /ˋhobo; ˈhəʊbəʊ/ *n* [C] *plural* **hobos** *AmE* someone, especially in the 1920s, who travelled from place to place because they had no home or job; TRAMP[1] (1)【美】〔尤指20世紀20年代的〕流浪漢, 無業遊民

Hob·son's choice /ˌhɑbsənz ˋtʃɔɪs; ˌhɒbsənz ˈtʃɔɪs/ *n* [U] a situation in which there is only one thing you can do 無選擇餘地〔的局面〕

hock[1] /hɑk; hɒk/ *n* **1** [U] *especially BrE* a German white wine【尤英】霍克酒〔一種德國產的白葡萄酒〕**2** [C] the middle joint of an animal's back leg〔動物後腿上的〕跗關節 —see picture at 參見 HORSE[1] 圖 **3 be in hock** *informal*【非正式】**a)** something that is in hock has been sold temporarily because you need money; pawned (PAWN[2]) 被典當, 被抵押 **b)** to be in debt 負債: *in hock to the big banks* 欠大銀行的債 **4** [C] *especially AmE* a piece of meat from above the foot of an animal, especially a pig【尤美】〔尤指豬的〕腿肉: *pork hocks* 豬腿肉

hock[2] *v* [T] *informal* to sell something temporarily because you are poor and need the money; PAWN[2]【非正式】典當, 抵押

hock·ey /ˋhɑkɪ; ˈhɒki/ *n* [U] **1** *especially BrE* a game played on grass by two teams of 11 players each, with sticks and a ball【尤英】曲棍球; FIELD HOCKEY *AmE*【美】**2** *especially AmE* also 又作 **ice hockey** a team game similar to HOCKEY, but played on ice【尤美】冰球, 冰上曲棍球

ho·cus-po·cus /ˋhokəs ˋpokəs; ˌhəʊkəs ˈpəʊkəs/ *n* [U] a method or belief that you think is based on false ideas 花招, 把戲, 欺騙: *He thinks psychology is a load of hocus-pocus.* 他認為心理學完全是騙人的把戲。

hod /hɑd; hɒd/ *n* [C] a container shaped like a box with a long handle, used for carrying bricks〔運磚用的帶長柄的〕磚斗, 搬運斗

hodge-podge /ˋhɑdʒˌpɑdʒ; ˈhɒdʒ pɒdʒ/ *n* [singular] the American form of the word HOTCHPOTCH hotchpotch 的美式形式

hoe[1] /ho; həʊ/ *n* [C] a garden tool with a long handle used for breaking up the soil 鋤頭, (長柄) 鋤

hoe[2] *v* **hoed, hoeing** [I,T] to break up soil with a hoe 用鋤頭鋤

hog[1] /hɑg; hɒg/ *n* [C] **1** *especially AmE* a pig, especially a fat one for eating【尤美】豬〔尤指供食用的肥豬〕**2** a male pig that is kept for meat〔供食用的〕公豬 —compare 比較 BOAR, SOW[2] **3** *informal* a person who eats too much【非正式】貪吃的人: *You greedy hog!* 你貪吃得像頭豬! **4 go the whole hog** to do something thoroughly 幹到底, 全力以赴: *Why don't we go the whole hog and get wine?* 我們幹嗎不一不做二不休, 索性拿點葡萄酒來呢? **5 go hog wild** *AmE informal* to suddenly do a lot of some activity that you do not usually do【美, 非正式】盡情做某事〔指平常少做的事〕—see also 另見 ROAD HOG —**hoggish** *adj*

hog[2] *v* **hogged, hogging** [T] *informal* to keep or use all of something【非正式】攫取, 把…佔為己有, 獨佔: *Keith's been hogging the bathroom all morning.* 基思整個上午都佔用着浴室。| **hog the road** (=drive badly so that you take up too much space) 佔着馬路當中開車, 霸佔路面

H

Hog·ma·nay /ˌhɑgməˋne; ˈhɒgməneɪ/ *n* [U] New Year's Eve and the parties that take place at that time in Scotland〔蘇格蘭的〕除夕（聚會）

hogs·head /ˋhɑgzˌhɛd; ˈhɒgzhed/ *n* [C] a large container for holding beer, or the amount that it holds 裝啤酒的大桶；一大桶之量

hog·wash /ˋhɑgˌwɑʃ; ˈhɒgwɒʃ/ *n* [U] stupid talk 蠢話，廢話，胡言亂語：*That's a load of hogwash!* 那是一派胡言亂語！

ho ho /ˌho ˋho; ˌhəʊ ˈhəʊ/ *interjection* used to represent the sound of laughter〔表示笑聲〕呵呵

ho-hum /ˌho ˋhʌm; ˌhəʊ ˈhʌm/ *adj informal* boring and ordinary【非正式】沉悶乏味的，無聊的，平平無奇的：*It was a ho-hum sort of day.* 這天過得真乏味。

hoick /hɔɪk; hɔɪk/ *v* [T] also 又作 **hoick up** *BrE informal* to lift or pull something up especially with a sudden movement【英，非正式】〔尤指猛然地〕向上提起：*She hoicked up her skirt and began to dance.* 她向上提了一下裙子，跳起舞來。

hoi pol·loi /ˋhɔɪ pəˋlɔɪ; ˌhɔɪ pəˈlɔɪ/ *n* **the hoi polloi** an insulting word for ordinary people 老百姓，烏合之眾〔此詞具侮辱性〕

hoist¹ /hɔɪst; hɔɪst/ also 又作 **hoist up** *v* [T] **1** to raise, lift, or pull up something, especially using ropes〔尤指用繩子〕吊起，升起，提起：*The sailors hoisted the cargo onto the deck.* 水手們把貨物吊到甲板上。| *hoist the flag* 升旗 **2 be hoist with your own petard** to be harmed or embarassed by something that you planned yourself 搬起石頭砸自己的腳，作繭自縛，害人反害己

hoist² *n* [C] **1** a piece of equipment for lifting heavy objects with ropes 吊升機械，起重機 **2** [usually singular 一般用單數] an upward pull 吊起，提起，升起

hoi·ty-toi·ty /ˋhɔɪtɪ ˋtɔɪtɪ; ˌhɔɪti ˈtɔɪti/ *adj old-fashioned* behaving in a proud way, as if you are important【過時】高傲的，愛擺架子的

ho·key /ˋhokɪ; ˈhəʊki/ *adj AmE* expressing emotions in a way that is too simple, old-fashioned, or silly【美】矯揉造作的；老掉牙的；愚蠢的：*a hokey song* 矯揉造作的歌曲

ho·kum /ˋhokəm; ˈhəʊkəm/ *n* [U] *slang especially AmE* stupid talk, especially talk used to deceive someone or make them admire you【俚，尤美】〔哄騙他人或博取他人稱讚的〕空話，廢話，胡扯；噱頭：*All that talk about improving schools is just a bunch of hokum.* 所有那些關於改善學校條件的話只不過是一堆空話。

hold¹ /hold; həʊld/ *v past tense and past participle* **held** /hɛld; held/

① IN YOUR HANDS/ARMS 在手中/懷抱中
② HAVE/POSSESS 擁有/佔有
③ KEEP/CONTROL 保持/控制
④ SAVE/STORE 保留/保存
⑤ KEEP STH IN A POSITION 使某物保持在某種位置上
⑥ SUPPORT/NOT BREAK 支撐/不斷裂
⑦ NOT CHANGE/CONTINUE 不改變/保持
⑧ RESPONSIBILITY 責任
⑨ OPINION/BELIEF 觀點/信念
⑩ STOP/DELAY STH 停止/拖延〔某事[物]〕
⑪ CONTAIN/INCLUDE 容納/包含
⑫ OTHER MEANINGS 其他意思

① IN YOUR HANDS/ARMS 在手中/懷抱中

1 a) [T] to have something firmly in your hand or arms 握住，抓住；抱住：*He was holding a knife in one hand.* 他一隻手裡握着刀。| *Can you hold the groceries for me while I open the door?* 我開門時你能幫我拿着這些食品雜貨嗎？| *I held the baby in my arms.* 我把嬰兒抱在懷裡。| **hold hands** (=hold each other's hands) 手握着手 *The couple sat, holding hands under a tree.* 那一對夫婦手拉着手坐在樹下。**b)** [T always+adv/prep] to move something that you have in your hands into a particular position 使…處於某種位置：**hold sth out/up/towards etc** *Hold the negative up to the light so we can see.* 把底片對着光拿着，好讓我們看清楚。

2 ►HOLD SB CLOSE 緊抱某人◄ [T] to put your arms around someone in order to comfort them, show you love them etc〔為表示安慰或愛〕緊抱〔某人〕：*She held him tightly, wiping away his tears.* 她緊緊地擁着他，為他擦去眼淚。

② HAVE/POSSESS 擁有/佔有

3 hold a position/rank/job to have a particular job or position, especially an important or powerful one 擔任職務/級別/工作：*Most of the senior positions are held by men.* 大多數高級職位都由男性擔任。

4 ►OWN STH 擁有某物◄ [T] to own or possess something, especially money or land 擁有〔尤指金錢或土地〕：*He holds a half share in the company.* 他擁有該公司一半的股份。

③ KEEP/CONTROL 保持/控制

5 ►ARMY 軍隊◄ [T] if an army holds a place, it either defends it from attack, or controls it by using force 防守，保衛；〔用武力〕佔據：*The French army held the town for three days.* 法軍在這個城鎮守了三天。

6 ►KEEP SB SOMEWHERE 將某人關在某處◄ [T] to keep a person or animal somewhere, and not allow them to leave 關押，扣留：*Police are holding two men in connection with the jewel robbery.* 警方拘留了同搶劫珠寶案有關連的兩名男子。| **hold sb prisoner/hostage/captive** (=to keep someone in a room, prison etc and not allow them to leave) 將某人作為囚犯/人質/俘虜扣押起來

④ SAVE/STORE 保留/保存

7 ►KEEP TO BE USED 保存待用◄ [T] to keep something to be used when it is needed 保存，保留〔以備後用〕：*Our computer holds all the records of births and deaths in Britain since 1950.* 我們的電腦存有 1950 年以來英國所有出生和死亡記錄。

8 hold a place/seat/room etc [T] to save a room, place etc for someone until they want to use it 保留地方/座位/房間等：*They're holding a table for us.* 他們為我們保留了一張桌子。

⑤ KEEP STH IN A POSITION 使某物保持在某種位置上

9 [T always+adv/prep] to make something stay in a particular position 使〔某物〕保持在某種位置上：**hold sth down/up/in place etc** *Ted held the ladder firmly in place.* 特德牢牢地扶住梯子不讓它移動。| *Can you hold the lid down so I can lock the suitcase?* 你能不能把手提箱的蓋子按住，讓我把它鎖上？| *It's only held on with a couple of screws.* 它只用幾個螺釘固定着。| **hold sth open** *Mark held open the door as she came up behind him.* 她跟在馬克後面走過來時，馬克用手扶住門，不讓它關上。

10 ►ARM/LEG/BACK ETC 手臂/腿/背等◄ [T always+adv/prep] to put or keep a part of your body in a particular position 使〔身體某個部位〕保持某種姿勢: **hold sth up/out/straight etc** *Hold out your hand and I'll give you a present!* 伸出手來, 我要送你一件禮物!

⑥ **SUPPORT/NOT BREAK** 支撐/不斷裂

11 ▶BE STRONG ENOUGH 夠堅固◀ **a)** [T] to support the weight of something 承受, 支撐〔重量〕: *Be careful, I don't think that branch will hold you.* 小心, 我覺得那根樹枝承受不了你的重量。**b)** [I] to continue to be able to support the weight of something〔繼續〕支撐住〔重量〕: *I don't think this shelf will hold if we put any more on it.* 我們如果再往擱架上放東西, 我怕它會承受不住。

⑦ **NOT CHANGE/CONTINUE** 不改變/保持

12 ▶AMOUNT/LEVEL 數量/水平◀ [T] to make something continue at a particular rate, level, or number 使保持〔某種速度、水平或數量〕: *hold spending to $10.2 billion* 將支出維持在102億美元 | *Make sure you hold your speed at 30 mph in this area.* 在這個地區一定要將速度保持在每小時30英里。

13 hold sb's interest/attention to make someone continue being interested in something 使某人繼續感興趣, 吸引住…的注意: *Colourful pictures hold the students' interest.* 彩色圖片能使學生保持興趣。

14 ▶WEATHER/LUCK 天氣/運氣◀ also 又作 **hold out** [I] if good weather or good luck holds, it continues unchanged for a long time 保持不變, 持續: *If our luck holds we could reach the final.* 如果我們繼續走運, 我們有望進入決賽。

15 ▶MUSIC 音樂◀ [T] to make a musical note continue for a long time 繼續唱某音符, 保持長音

16 hold a course if an aircraft, ship etc holds a course, it continues to move in a particular direction〔飛機、船隻等〕保持航線: *The ship held a northwesterly course.* 船一直往西北方向行駛。

17 [I] to still be true or continue to have an effect 繼續有效: *What I said yesterday still holds.* 我昨天說的話仍然算數。

18 hold good/hold true to still be true in several different situations 繼續適用[有效]: *This advice will hold good throughout your life.* 這個建議在你一生中都有用。

⑧ **RESPONSIBILITY** 責任

19 hold the fort to be responsible for looking after something while the person usually responsible is not there〔別人不在時〕代為處理事務: *She's holding the fort while the manager's on holiday.* 經理休假時由她負責處理業務。

20 be left holding the baby *BrE*【英】**/the bag** *AmE*【美】to become responsible for something that someone else has started 負責處理別人未辦完的事情; 代人負起全責

21 hold sb responsible/accountable (for sth) to consider someone to be responsible for something, so that they will be blamed if anything bad happens 追究某人的責任, 唯…是問: *I'll hold you personally responsible if anything happens to the boy.* 如果男孩出了甚麼事, 我就唯你是問。

⑨ **OPINION/BELIEF** 觀點/信念

22 [T not in progressive 不用進行式, usually passive 一般用被動態] *formal* to believe something to be true【正式】相信, 認為…是真的: **[+that]** *It is widely held that the council will decide to take military action.* 很多人相信委員會將會決定採取軍事行動。| **hold sb/sth to be sth** *It is held to be his most important novel.* 這被認為是他最重要的一部小說。

23 ▶OPINIONS 觀點◀ **hold an opinion/view/belief etc** to have a particular opinion about something 持有[懷有]觀點/看法/信念: *She holds extreme political views.* 她持有極端的政治觀點。| **commonly held belief** (=something that many people believe to be true) 普遍的看法

24 hold sth dear to think that something is very important 珍視某物: *a threat to everything that I hold dear* 對我所珍視的一切的威脅

25 hold fast to sth *formal* to keep believing in an idea or principles【正式】堅信: *They held fast to their faith in spite of their suffering.* 儘管受苦, 他們仍然堅持自己的信念。

⑩ **STOP/DELAY STH** 停止/拖延〔某事[物]〕

26 hold it! *spoken*【口】**a)** used to interrupt someone〔用來打斷別人說話〕等等!: *Hold it a minute! I've just had a really good idea.* 等等! 我剛剛想到了一個絕妙的好主意。**b)** used to tell someone to wait or to stop what they are doing 停一下! 別動!

27 hold everything! *spoken* used to tell someone to immediately stop what they are doing【口】快停下!: *Hold everything! We have to change it all back again!* 快停下! 我們得全部改回原樣!

28 hold your fire! a military order to tell soldiers to stop shooting〔軍事命令〕停止射擊! 不要開火!

29 hold your horses! *spoken* used to tell someone to stop and think about something【口】停下來想想! 不要倉促行事!

⑪ **CONTAIN/INCLUDE** 容納/包含

30 ▶HAVE SPACE FOR 有空間容納◀ [T not in progressive 不用進行式] to have the space to contain a particular amount of something 能容納: *This pan holds three gallons of water.* 這隻鍋能盛三加侖水。| *The movie theater holds 500 people.* 這家電影院能容納500人。

31 [T] *formal* if the future or a future situation holds something, that may be part of it【正式】〔未來〕包含: *Who knows what the future holds?* 誰知道未來會如何?

⑫ **OTHER MEANINGS** 其他意思

32 hold a meeting/election/party etc [T] to arrange for an event, meeting, election, party etc to happen 舉行會議/選舉/晚會等: *The meeting will be held in the Town Hall.* 會議將在市政廳舉行。

33 [I] also 又作 **hold the line** to wait until the person you have telephoned is ready to answer 不掛斷電話〔等着〕: *Mr Stevenson's busy at the moment – would you like to hold?* 史蒂文森先生現在沒空, 請你不要掛斷等一下好嗎?

34 ▶HAVE A QUALITY 具備某種特質◀ [T] *formal* to have a particular quality【正式】具備某種特質: *Such an emphasis on religion may hold little appeal for modern tastes.* 這種對宗教的注重對現代人來說可能沒有多大吸引力。

35 hold a conversation to have a conversation 談話, 和…交談

36 not hold a candle to *informal* to be much worse than someone or something else【非正式】遠比不上, 無法與…相比

37 hold all the cards to have a strong advantage in a situation 佔絕對上風, 佔極大優勢

38 hold up your head to show pride or confidence in a difficult situation〔在困境中〕決不低頭, 不垂頭喪氣: *I'll never be able to hold up my head in this town again.* 我再也無法在這個城鎮裡抬起頭做人了。

39 hold your own to defend yourself, or to succeed, in a difficult situation〔在困境中〕堅守, 不退讓: *Although he is the youngest competitor, he seems to be holding his own.* 雖然在眾參賽者中他年紀最小, 但他看起來毫不示弱。

40 hold the road if a car holds the road well you can drive it quickly around bends without losing control〔指汽車急轉彎時〕抓地性能良好

41 not hold water if an argument, statement etc does

H

not hold water, it does not seem to be true or reasonable 站不住腳, 不可信: *His explanation of where the money came from just doesn't hold water.* 他對這筆錢的來源的解釋根本站不住腳。

42 hold your drink/liquor/alcohol etc if someone can hold their drink, they are able to drink a lot of alcohol without becoming drunk 酒量很大

43 there's no holding sb *spoken* used when someone is so keen to do something you cannot prevent them from doing it【口】無法阻止某人〔做某事〕: *When he starts talking about football there's no holding him.* 他一談起足球就沒完沒了。—see also 另見 **hold your breath** (BREATH (3)), **hold court** (COURT¹ (5)), **hold your tongue!** (TONGUE (16)), **hold your head high** (HIGH² (7))

hold sth **against** sb *phr v* [T] to allow something bad that someone has done to make you dislike them or want to harm them 對〔某人〕懷恨在心, 對〔某人〕有成見: *It all happened years ago. You can't still hold it against him, surely?* 這都是多年前的事了。你不能還對他懷恨在心, 是吧?

hold back *phr v* **1** [T **hold** sb/sth ↔ **back**] to make someone or something stop moving forward 阻擋, 抑制: *They had erected the barriers to hold back the flood.* 他們築起屏障阻擋洪水。**2** [T **hold back** sth] to stop yourself from feeling or showing a particular emotion 控制〔情感〕: *We struggled to hold back our laughter.* 我們竭力忍住不笑。**3** [T **hold** sb ↔ **back**] to prevent someone from developing or improving 阻礙〔某人的發展〕: *Spending so much time playing sport is holding him back at school.* 他在體育運動上花的時間太多, 影響了學業。**4** [I] to be slow or unwilling to do something especially because you are being careful〔因謹慎而〕猶豫, 躊躇, 退縮: *The tone of his voice made Steven hold back.* 他說話的語氣使史蒂文猶豫起來。**5** [I,T **hold** sth ↔ **back**] to keep something secret 隱瞞: *Tell me about it – don't hold anything back!* 把這事告訴我, 甚麼都別隱瞞!

hold sth/sb ↔ **down** *phr v* [T] **1** to prevent something such as prices from rising 抑制〔價格等的〕上升: *We shall hold down prices until the new year.* 我們會抑制價格上漲, 直至新的一年來臨。| *the best way to hold down inflation* 抑制通貨膨脹的最佳方法 **2** to keep people under control or limit their freedom 限制, 壓制: *held down for centuries by their Ottoman conquerors* 許多個世紀以來受到奧圖曼征服者的壓制 **3 hold down a job** to succeed in keeping a job for a period of time 保住工作[職位]: *He's never held down a job for longer than a few weeks.* 他從未能把一份工作保住幾週以上。

hold forth *phr v* [I] give your opinion on a subject, especially for a long time〔長篇大論地〕發表議論: [+on] *Archer was holding forth on the collapse of society.* 阿切爾正在就社會解體大發議論。

hold off *phr v* **1** [I,T] to delay something 拖延, 推遲: *Buyers have been holding off until the price falls.* 買家們一直按兵不動, 等着價格下跌。| **hold off doing sth** *We will hold off making our decision until Monday.* 我們將推遲到星期一再作決定。**2** [T **hold** sb ↔ **off**] to prevent someone who is attacking you from coming any closer 抵擋, 使同…保持一定距離: *We managed to hold off the gang until the police arrived.* 我們設法擋住了那夥壞蛋, 直到警方趕到。**3** [I] if rain or snow holds off, none of it falls, although you thought it would〔雨、雪等〕延緩, 遲遲不來: *The rain held off until after the game.* 比賽結束後才下起雨來。

hold on *phr v* [I] **1 hold on!** *spoken*【口】**a)** used to tell someone to wait for a short time 等會兒!: *Hold on, I'll just get my coat.* 等一等, 我去拿外衣。**b)** used when you have just noticed something surprising〔表示發現令人驚訝的事〕等等!: *Hold on! Isn't that your brother's car over there?* 等等! 那不是你兄弟的車嗎? **2** to wait for a short period of time〔短時間〕等候: *I'll hold on for another few minutes if you like.* 如果你喜歡的話, 我就再等幾分鐘。| *It's coming soon, just hold on for it.* 它馬上就要來了, 再等一會兒吧。**3** to continue doing something when it is very difficult to do so 堅持下去: *They didn't know if they would be able to hold on until help arrived.* 他們不知道自己是否能夠堅持到援兵到來。

hold on to sb/sth *phr v* [T] **1** to keep your hands or arms tightly around something so that it cannot move or you cannot fall 緊緊抓住[抱住]: *Hold on to the rail or you'll slip!* 抓住欄杆, 否則你會滑倒的! **2** to keep something by not losing it, selling it, or having it taken from you 守住, 保住: *Despite the attacks we held on to the bridge for three more days.* 儘管受到進攻, 我們仍然將大橋守住了三天。| *I think I'll hold on to the records, but you can have the tapes.* 我想我會把唱片留着, 但你可以拿走磁帶。

hold out *phr v* **1** [I] if something such as a supply of something holds out it has not all yet been finished or used〔供給品的〕維持, 持續: *Will the water supply hold out through the summer?* 供水能持續整個夏天嗎? **2** [I] to continue to defend a place that is being attacked 守住: *They'll have to surrender – they can't hold out forever.* 他們遲早得投降, 他們不能永遠守得住。**3 not hold out much hope/prospect of** to not think that something is possible or likely to have a good result 沒有多大希望/前景: *Negotiators are no longer holding out much hope of a peaceful settlement.* 談判人員對和平解決問題不再抱有甚麼希望。

hold out for sth *phr v* [T] to not accept anything less than what you have asked for 堅持要求, 不肯讓步: *The kidnappers are still holding out for the release of all political prisoners.* 綁架者仍堅持要求釋放所有政治犯。

hold out on sb *phr v* [T] *informal* to refuse to give someone information or an answer that they need【非正式】拒絕提供〔資料或答案〕: *Why didn't you tell me straight away instead of holding out on me?* 你為甚麼對我隱瞞消息而不直接告訴我呢?

hold over *phr v* **1** [T **hold** sth **over**] to do or deal with something at a later date 推遲, 使延期: *The game was held over until the following week because of the bad weather.* 由於天氣惡劣, 比賽被推遲到下一週。—see also 另見 HOLDOVER **2** [**hold** sth **over** sb] to use knowledge about someone to threaten them 以…要挾: *He knows I've been in prison and is holding it over me.* 他知道我曾坐過牢, 並以此要挾我。**3 be held over** *AmE* if a play, film, concert etc is held over, it is shown for longer than planned, because it is very good【美】〔戲劇、電影、音樂會等因受歡迎〕公演時間被延長

hold sb **to** sth *phr v* [T] **1** to make someone do what they have promised 使〔某人〕恪守諾言: *"I'll ask him tomorrow." "All right, but I'm going to hold you to that."* "我明天跟他說。""好吧, 不過你要說話算數。" **2** to prevent your opponent in a sports game from getting more than a particular number of points〔在體育比賽中〕不讓對手超過〔某一得分〕: *We held them to 2-2.* 我們把與對方的比分保持在2比2。

hold together *phr v* **1** [I,T **hold** sth **together**] if a group or organization holds together or you hold it together it stays strong and does not break apart (使) 團結, (使) 不分開: *The party was held together by personal loyalty to the leader.* 該黨憑藉對其領袖的忠誠團結在一起。**2** [I] to remain good enough to be used 保持完好: *I hope the washing machine holds together – I can't afford a new one.* 我希望洗衣機能正常運轉, 我沒錢買一台新的。

hold up *phr v* **1** [T **hold** sth ↔ **up**] to support something and prevent it from falling down 支撐: *The roof is held up by pillars.* 屋頂是用柱子支撐着的。**2** [**hold** sb/sth ↔ **up** often passive 常用被動態] to delay someone or something (使) 耽擱, 推遲, 阻延: *The building work has been held up by bad weather.* 由於天氣不好, 建築工程被耽擱下來了。| *Sorry we're late – we were held up at work.* 對不起我們來晚了, 我們在工作中給耽擱了

一會兒。**3 [hold up sth]** to rob or try to rob a place by using violence（試圖）搶劫: *His brother tried to hold up the drugstore and was sent to jail.* 他的兄弟企圖搶劫雜貨店，因此被送進了監獄。—see also 另見 HOLD-UP **4** [I] to remain strong and not become weaker 保持強壯: *His physical condition held up remarkably well.* 他的身體狀況保持得非常好。

hold sb/sth up as *phr v* [T] to use someone or something as an example 將…作為榜樣: *The school is being held up as a model for other inner-city secondary schools.* 這所學校被樹為其他舊城區中學學習的榜樣。

hold with sth *phr v* [T usually in negatives 一般用於否定句] to approve of or agree with something 同意，贊同: *We don't hold with physical violence in this school.* 我們這所學校內不允許有暴力行為。| **hold with doing sth** *I don't hold with letting people smoke in public places.* 我不贊成讓人們在公共場所吸煙。

S2 W3 **hold²** *n*

1 ▶ACTION OF HOLDING STH 拿住某物◀ [singular] the action of holding something tightly; GRIP¹ (1) 握，抓，拿: *She tightened her hold on the rope.* 她抓緊了繩子。| **have/keep hold of** *Make sure you keep hold of my hand when we cross the road.* 過馬路時你一定要拉住我的手。

2 get/take/grab/seize hold of sth to take something and hold it with your hands 抓住，拿住，握住: *Grab hold of the rope and pull yourself up.* 抓住繩子爬上來。| *I took hold of her hand and gently led her away.* 我抓住她的手，小心地帶她離開。

3 get hold of a) to find or borrow something so that you can use it 找來使用: *I need to get hold of a car.* 我得找一輛車。**b)** to find someone for a particular reason〔出於某種原因要〕找到〔某人〕: *I must get hold of Vanessa to see if she can babysit for me.* 我必須找到瓦尼莎，看看她能不能幫我照看一下孩子。

4 on hold waiting to speak or be spoken to on the telephone 等着通電話: **put sb on hold** *Do you mind if I put you on hold?* 你不介意等一會兒吧？

5 put sth on hold to delay doing or starting something 推遲，使延期，擱置

6 take hold to start to have an effect 開始起作用，掌管: *The fever was beginning to take hold.* 發燒開始產生影響了。

7 ▶SPORT 體育◀ [C] a particular position that you hold an opponent in, in a sport such as WRESTLING or JUDO〔摔跤或柔道運動中的〕擒拿技法

8 ▶CLIMBING 攀爬◀ [C] somewhere you can put your hands or feet when you are climbing 供手攀或腳踩之處: *The cliff is steep and it's difficult to find a hold.* 那懸崖很陡，很難找到攀踏的地方。

9 ▶SHIP 船隻◀ [C] the part of a ship below the DECK¹ (1) where goods are stored 底艙，貨艙

10 have a good hold of sth to understand something well 充分理解[掌握]

11 get hold of an idea/impression/story etc to learn or begin to believe something 得到[明白]某個想法/印象/説法等: *Where on earth did you get hold of that idea?* 你到底是從哪兒得來那個想法的？

12 have a hold over/on sb to have power or influence over someone 有左右某人的力量，對某人有影響力: *Ever since he found out about her past, he's had a frightening hold on her.* 自從他發現了她的過去之後，他對她的控制達到令人懼怕的地步。

13 no holds barred no rules or limits 無規則、無限制的，不受約束的: *There are no holds barred when it comes to making a profit.* 賺取贏利是無規則無限制的。

hold·all /ˈhold,ɔl; ˈhəʊld-ɔːl/ *n* [C] *BrE* a large bag for carrying clothes【英】〔裝衣物的〕大旅行袋 —see picture at 參見 BAG 圖

S3 W2 **hold·er** /ˈholdə; ˈhəʊldə/ *n* [C] **1** someone who possesses or has control of a place, land, tickets etc 擁有人，持有人: *Season-ticket holders are furious at the rise in rail fares.* 季票持有人對火車票價上漲極為憤怒。**2 candle/cigarette holder etc** a thing which is used to hold a CANDLE etc 燭台/香煙煙嘴

W3 **hold·ing** /ˈholdɪŋ; ˈhəʊldɪŋ/ *n* [C] something which a person possesses, especially land or shares (SHARE² (5)) in a company 私人擁有的財產〔尤指公司的地產或股份〕—see also 另見 SMALLHOLDING

holding com·pa·ny /ˈ·· ,···/ *n* [C] a company that holds a controlling number of the shares (SHARE² (5)) in other companies 控股公司

holding pat·tern /ˈ·· ,··/ *n* [C] the line of travel that an aircraft follows as it flies over a landing place while it is waiting for permission to land 待降[等待]航線〔指飛機待降時在等待區域的飛行航線〕

hold·o·ver /ˈhold,ovə; ˈhəʊld,əʊvə/ *n* [C] *especially AmE* an action, feeling, or idea that has continued from the past into the present; HANGOVER (2)【尤美】殘餘；遺留物；遺留影響: **[+from]** *Her fear of dogs is a holdover from her childhood.* 她對狗的懼怕是從兒時一直遺留下來的。—see also 另見 **hold over** (HOLD¹)

hold-up 持槍搶劫

hold-up /ˈ· ·/ *n* [C] **1** a situation that stops something from happening for a short time; DELAY¹ (2) 延誤，耽擱: *An unexpected hold-up meant we had fallen 3 weeks behind schedule.* 由於一些意外的延誤，我們已經比原定計劃晚了三週了。**2** a situation in which traffic stops or can only move very slowly 交通阻塞: *There was a hold-up on the highway this morning.* 今天上午公路上堵車了。**3** *informal* an attempt to rob someone by threatening them with a gun【非正式】持槍搶劫 —see also 另見 **hold up** (HOLD¹)

hole¹ /hol; həʊl/ *n* [C] S1 W2

1 ▶SPACE IN STH SOLID 固體物件內的空間◀ an empty space in something solid 洞，孔: **[+in]** *We'll just dig a big hole in the ground and bury the box in it.* 我們只要在地上挖個大洞把盒子埋進去就行了。

2 ▶SPACE STH CAN GO THROUGH 可穿過的空間◀ a space in something that allows things, light etc to get through to the other side; GAP (1)〔可穿過的〕洞，裂口: **[+in]** *The dog got out of the yard through a hole in the fence.* 那條狗從院子籬笆的一個窟窿裡鑽了出去。

3 ▶ANIMAL'S HOME 動物的巢穴◀ the home of a small animal〔小動物的〕窩，洞穴: *a rabbit hole* 兔窩

4 ▶UNPLEASANT PLACE 不舒適的地方◀ *informal* an unpleasant place for living in, working in etc【非正式】令人不舒適的地方: *I've got to get out of this hole.* 我得離開這個破地方。

5 be in a hole to be in a difficult situation 處於困境

6 be full of holes an idea or plan that is full of holes can easily be proved wrong or has many faults〔想法、計劃等〕漏洞[破綻]百出，問題很多

7 ▶GOLF 高爾夫球◀ a) a hole in the ground that you try to get the ball into in the game of GOLF 球洞，球穴 —see picture on page A23 參見 A23 頁圖 **b)** one part of a GOLF COURSE with this kind of hole at one end 球洞區〔遠

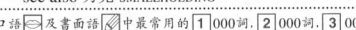

處有一球洞的擊球區〕: *an 18 hole golf course* 有18個洞的高爾夫球場
8 hole in one an act of hitting the ball in GOLF from the starting place into the hole with only one hit〔高爾夫球運動中〕一桿進洞
9 make a hole in sth *informal* to use a large part of an amount of money, food etc【非正式】用去…的大部分, 大量消耗: *The cost of the house repairs made a big hole in my savings.* 修房子花掉了我一大筆積蓄。
10 need something like a hole in the head *spoken* used to say that you definitely do not need or want something【口】絕對不需要…
11 hole-and-corner secret or hidden, especially in a dishonest way 偷偷摸摸的, 鬼鬼祟祟的, 不光明正大的: *hole-and-corner meetings* 偷偷摸摸召開的會議 —see also 另見 BLACK HOLE, WATERING HOLE

hole² *v* [T] **1 be holed** if a ship or boat is holed, it has a hole in it〔船隻〕出現破洞 **2** also 又作 **hole out** [I] to hit the ball into the hole in GOLF〔高爾夫球運動中〕擊球入洞

hole up *phr v* [I always+adv/prep] *informal* to hide somewhere for a period of time【非正式】藏匿: **[+with/in]** *He escaped on his way to prison and holed up with his girlfriend.* 他在去監獄的路上逃走, 和他女朋友一同躲藏起來。

hole in the heart /ˌ· · · ˈ·/ *n* [singular,U] a medical condition, where the two sides of someone's heart are not properly separated 心穴徵, 心膜缺損

hole-in-the-wall /ˌ· · · ˈ·/ *n* [C] **1** *BrE informal* CASH DISPENSER【英, 非正式】自動提款機 **2** *AmE* a small dark store or restaurant【美】狹小黑暗的店鋪或餐館

2 2 **hol·i·day¹** /ˈhɑləˌde; ˈhɒlɪ̈di/ *n* **1** *BrE* also 又作 **holidays** a time of rest from work, school etc【英】〔不用上班、上學的〕假期, 休假日; VACATION¹ (1) *AmE*【美】: *Everyone at work is ready for a holiday.* 每個上班的人都準備休假了。| *The school holidays start on Wednesday.* 學校假期從星期三開始。| **on (your) holiday** *Jackie's been on holiday for the last two weeks.* 傑基前兩週一直在休假。**2** *BrE* also 又作 **holidays** a period of time when you travel to another place for pleasure【英】出外度假時期: *We're going to Spain for our holidays.* 我們將去西班牙度假。| **have a holiday** *I didn't have a proper holiday this year.* 我今年沒有好好度過假。**3** a day fixed by law on which people do not have to go to work or school 法定假日, 公共假日: **public holiday** *Martin Luther King Day is now a public holiday in most states.* 馬丁·路德·金紀念日現在在多數州裡都是一個公共假日。| **national holiday** *The 4th of July is a national holiday in the US.* 7月4日是美國國慶節。| **bank holiday** *BrE*【英】*We're going to Devon for the bank holiday weekend.* 我們將去德文郡度過長週末。

This graph shows how common the nouns **holiday** and **vacation** are in British and American English. 本圖表所示為名詞holiday和vacation在英國英語和美國英語中的使用頻率。

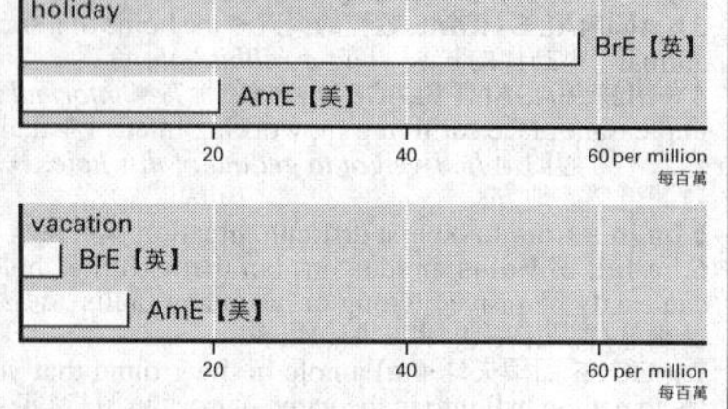

Based on the British National Corpus and the Longman Lancaster Corpus
據英國國家語料庫和朗文蘭卡斯特語料庫

In British English the word **holiday** is used to mean a time of rest from work, school etc, or a period of time when you travel to another place for pleasure. Americans use **vacation** for this meaning. In both American and British English **holiday** is used to mean a day fixed by law on which people do not have to go to work or school. In both American and British English **vacation** is used to mean one of the periods of time each year when universities are closed. 在英國英語中, 單詞holiday是指不用去上班、上學等的休假日或假期, 也指外出度假的時期, 而美國英語則用vacation表示這些意思。holiday在美國英語和英國英語中都用來指人們不用上班、上學的法定假日; vacation在美國英語和英國英語中都用來指大學的假期。

holiday² *v* [I] *BrE* to spend your holiday in a place【英】度假; VACATION² *AmE*【美】: **[+in/at]** *They're holidaying in Majorca.* 他們正在馬霍卡島上度假。

holiday camp /ˈ··· ˌ·/ *n* [C] *BrE* a place where people go for their holidays and where activities are organized for them【英】度假營

holiday home /ˈ··· ˌ·/ *n* [C] *BrE* a house that someone owns where they go during their holidays【英】度假別墅, 度假屋

hol·i·day·mak·er /ˈhɑlədeˌmekɚ; ˈhɒlɪ̈diˌmeɪkə/ *n* [C] *BrE* someone who has travelled to another place for a holiday【英】到外地度假者; VACATIONER *AmE*【美】—**holidaymaking** *n* [U]

hol·i·er-than-thou /ˌ··· ˈ·/ *adj* behaving in a way that shows that you think you are morally better than other people 自以為道德上高人一等的

hol·i·ness /ˈholɪnɪs; ˈhəʊlinɪ̈s/ *n* **1** [U] the quality of being pure and good in a religious way 神聖: *God's holiness* 上帝的神聖 **2 Your/His Holiness** used as a title for addressing or talking about the Pope〔對教皇的尊稱〕陛下, 聖座

ho·lis·tic /hoˈlɪstɪk; həʊˈlɪstɪk/ *adj* **1** based on the principle that a person or thing is more than just their many small parts added together 整體(論)的, 全面的: *a holistic approach to education* 教育的整體論方法 **2 holistic medicine** medical treatment based on the belief that the whole person must be treated, not just the part of their body that has a disease 整體醫學 —**holistically** /-klɪ; -kli/ *adv*

hol·ler /ˈhɑlɚ; ˈhɒlə/ *v* [I,T] *especially AmE informal* to shout loudly【尤美, 非正式】呼喊, 大叫: *The kid just kept hollering until she got her way.* 那孩子一直不停地叫喊, 直到她得到她想要的東西。| **holler at sb** *Stop hollering at me! I'll be there in a second!* 別喊了! 我馬上就來! —**holler** *n* [C]

hol·low¹ /ˈhɑlo; ˈhɒləʊ/ *adj* **1** having an empty space inside 空(心)的, 中空的: *The children hid in the hollow tree.* 孩子們躲在空心的樹裡。**2 hollow face/eyes etc** eyes etc that sink inwards 凹陷的臉頰/雙眼等: *I could feel her appraising me with those hollow, dead eyes.* 我可以感覺到她在用那雙深凹、一動不動的眼睛打量我。**3** a sound that is hollow is low and clear like the sound made when you hit something empty〔聲音〕空洞的, 低沉的 **4** feelings or words that are hollow are not sincere〔感情、語言〕虛假的, 無誠意的: *hollow promises made by corrupt politicians* 腐敗政客的空口諾言 **5 hollow laugh/voice etc** a hollow laugh or voice is one that makes a weak sound and is without emotion 乾巴巴的笑聲/聲音等: *He gave a little hollow laugh and didn't reply.* 他乾笑了一聲, 沒有回答。—**hollowly** *adv* —**hollowness** *n* [U]

hollow 中空的

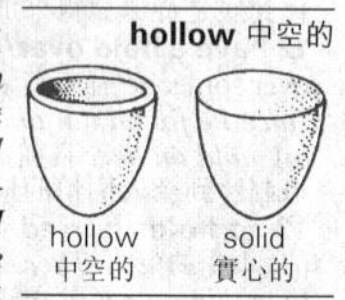

hollow² *n* a place in something that is at a slightly lower level than its surface 淺坑, 凹陷處: *The cat had tried to* *hide in a hollow in the ground.* 那隻貓試圖躲進地面上的一個淺坑裡。

hollow³ *v*

hollow sth ↔ **out** *phr v* [T] to make a hole or empty space by removing the inside part of something 把…挖空[掏空], 使成中空

hol·ly /ˈhalɪ; ˈhɒli/ *n* [U] a small tree with dark green sharp leaves and red berries (BERRY), or the leaves and berries of this tree used as a decoration at Christmas 冬青樹; 〔常用作聖誕節裝飾的〕冬青樹葉及漿果

hol·ly·hock /ˈhalɪˌhak; ˈhɒlihɒk/ *n* [C] a tall thin garden plant with many flowers growing together 蜀葵(花)

Hol·ly·wood /ˈhalɪˌwʊd; ˈhɒliwʊd/ *n* [singular] a city in California where films are made and many famous actors live 荷里活, 好萊塢〔美國著名影城, 位於加利福尼亞州〕

hol·o·caust /ˈhaləˌkɔst; ˈhɒləkɔːst/ *n* [C] **1** a situation in which there is great destruction and a lot of people die 大屠殺: *a nuclear holocaust* 核浩劫 **2 the Holocaust** the killing of millions of Jews by the Nazis in the 1930s and 1940s 〔20世紀30和40年代納粹黨進行的〕對猶太人的大屠殺

hol·o·gram /ˈhaləgræm; ˈhɒləgræm/ *n* [C] a kind of photograph made with a LASER that looks as if it is not flat when you look at it from an angle 〔用雷射光[激光]製作的〕(立體)全息圖

hols /halz; hɒlz/ *n* [plural] *BrE old-fashioned spoken* holidays【英, 過時, 口】假期; 出外度假時期

Hol·stein /ˈholstaɪn; ˈhɒlstən/ *n* [C] *especially AmE* a black and white cow【尤美】霍斯坦種乳牛, 黑白花牛; FRIESIAN *BrE*【英】

hol·ster /ˈholstɚ; ˈhəʊlstə/ *n* [C] a leather object worn on a belt for carrying a small gun 〔繫在腰帶上的〕手槍皮套

3 **ho·ly** /ˈholɪ; ˈhəʊli/ *adj* **1** connected with God and religion; SACRED (有關)上帝[宗教]的, 神聖的: *the holy city of Benares* 貝拿勒斯聖城 | *anointed with holy water* 塗了聖水的 **2** very religious 虔誠的: *a holy man* 虔誠的人 **3 holy cow/cats/shit/mackerel etc** *spoken especially AmE* used to express surprise, admiration, or fear【口, 尤美】天啊! 上帝呀!〔表示驚訝、讚美或恐懼〕 **4 a holy terror** *informal* a child who causes trouble【非正式】搗蛋鬼, 頑皮的小孩 —see also 另見 **take (holy) orders** (ORDER¹ (20))

Holy Bi·ble /ˌ·· ˈ··/ *n* [singular] the BIBLE (1)《聖經》

Holy Com·mu·nion /ˌ·· ·ˈ··/ *n* [U] COMMUNION (2) 聖餐(儀式)

Holy Fam·i·ly /ˌ·· ˈ···/ *n* [singular] Jesus, his mother Mary, and her husband Joseph 聖家庭〔指耶穌、聖母馬利亞以及馬利亞的丈夫約瑟〕

Holy Fa·ther /ˌ·· ˈ··/ *n* [singular] used to address the Pope 羅馬教皇

Holy Ghost /ˌ·· ˈ·/ *n* [singular] the HOLY SPIRIT 聖靈

Holy Grail /ˌ·· ˈ·/ *n* [singular] **1** something that you try very hard to get or achieve but never can 無法實現的夢想 **2** the cup believed to have been used by Christ before his death 〔耶穌死前用過的〕聖杯

Holy Land /ˈ·· ·/ *n* [singular] the parts of the Middle East where most of the events mentioned in the Bible happened 聖地〔指中東的一些地區,《聖經》上記載的大部分事件發生於此〕

holy of ho·lies /ˌ·· · ˈ··/ *n* [singular] **1** *humorous* a room in a building where only important people are allowed to go【幽默】最神聖的地方〔指只許重要人物進入的房間〕 **2** the most holy part of a Jewish temple 猶太教會堂的內殿, 至聖所

Holy See /ˌ·· ˈ·/ *n* [singular] *formal* the office of the Pope【正式】聖座, 宗座〔羅馬教皇的聖職〕

Holy Spir·it /ˌ·· ˈ··/ *n* [singular] God in the form of a spirit according to the Christian religion 聖靈

holy war /ˈ·· ˌ·/ *n* [C] a war that is fought to defend the beliefs of a religion 聖戰〔維護信仰而進行的戰爭〕

Holy Week /ˈ·· ·/ *n* [singular] the week before Easter in the Christian church 〔基督教〕復活節前的一週, 受難週

Holy Writ /ˌ·· ˈ·/ *n* [U] **1** a piece of writing that people treat as if it were completely true in every detail 至高無上的權威著作; 箴言, 真言 **2** *old-fashioned* the Bible【過時】《聖經》

hom·age /ˈhamɪdʒ; ˈhɒmɪdʒ/ *n* [singular] *formal* something you do to show respect and honour for an important person【正式】崇敬, 致敬: **pay homage to sb** (=show respect and honour for someone) 向某人致敬 *The film pays homage to Woody Allen, using some of his best comic lines.* 該影片採用了〔美國著名喜劇演員和導演〕活地·亞倫最精彩的喜劇台詞表達對他的崇敬。

hom·burg /ˈhambɝg; ˈhɒmbɜːg/ *n* [C] a soft hat for men, with a wide edge around it 霍姆堡氈帽〔一種男用的寬邊軟氈帽〕

home¹ /hom; həʊm/ *n* 1 1

1 ▶PLACE WHERE YOU LIVE 居住的地方◀ [C,U] the house, apartment, or place where you live 家, 住家: *They have a comfortable home on the outskirts of the town.* 他們在城郊有一個舒適的家。| **at home** *Her daughter lives at college during the week and at home on the weekends.* 她的女兒平時住在大學校園裡, 週末則住在家裡。| **work from home** *BrE* (=do your work at home instead of at a company)【英】在家辦公 | **make your home somewhere** *A family of swallows had made their home under the roof.* 一窩燕子在屋簷下安了家。

2 ▶WHERE YOU CAME FROM/BELONG 家, 家鄉◀ [C,U] the place where you came from or where you usually live, especially when this is the place where you feel happy and comfortable 〔使人感到親切、愉快的〕家, 家鄉, 故鄉: **make somewhere your home** *She was born in Italy, but she's made Charleston her home.* 她在意大利出生, 但在〔美國〕查爾斯頓安家。| **back home** (=used to talk about the place where your family and friends live) 在家鄉 *Sherri said she misses friends and family back home.* 雪莉說她很想念家鄉的朋友和親人。

3 be/feel at home a) to feel comfortable in a place or with a person 舒適自在, 不拘束: **[+in]** *I'm already feeling at home in the new apartment.* 我在新公寓裡已經感到習慣自如了。| **[+with]** *Penny is very much at home with Roger's family.* 彭尼與羅傑的家人相處時毫不拘束。 **b)** to feel happy or confident about doing or using something 駕輕就熟, 運用自如: **[+with/in]** *I've never felt particularly at home with computers.* 我對電腦一向不太在行。

4 ▶IN YOUR COUNTRY 在本國◀ **at home** in the country where you live, as opposed to foreign countries 在本國, 在國內: *improved sales of trucks both at home and abroad* 提高了國內外市場上的貨車銷量 | *I miss the hot weather we have at home in India.* 我很懷念我的祖國印度那炎熱的天氣。

5 ▶FAMILY 家庭◀ [C,U] the place where a child and his or her family live 家, 家庭: **leave home** *He didn't leave home until he was 21.* 他直到21歲才離開家(自立)。| **come from a broken home** *old-fashioned* (=come from a family in which one parent has left the home)【過時】來自破碎的家庭〔指單親家庭〕

6 ▶PROPERTY 財產◀ [C] a house, apartment etc considered as property which you can buy or sell 〔作為財產的〕住宅, 住房: *Attractive, modern homes for sale.* 有漂亮的現代化住宅出售。

7 ▶FOR TAKING CARE OF SB 用於照料某人◀ [C] a place where people who are very old or sick, or children who have no family are looked after 〔老人或病人的〕療養所; 〔兒童的〕養育院: *an old people's home* 養老院, 老人院 | *They had to put her mother in a home.* 他們不得不把她的母親送進養老院。—see also 另見 REST HOME

8 dogs'/cats' home a place where animals with no owners are looked after 狗/貓的收容所

9 make yourself at home *spoken* used to tell someone who is visiting you that they should relax【口】請隨便,

H

別拘禮〔招呼客人時説〕: *Make yourself at home while I get some coffee.* 隨便坐吧, 我去倒杯咖啡。
10 make sb feel at home to make someone feel relaxed by being friendly towards them 使某人感到賓至如歸: *I'd like to thank everyone again for making me feel so much at home.* 我要再次感謝大家讓我在此感到賓至如歸。
11 find a home for *BrE* to find a place where something can be kept【英】找地方安置〔某物〕: *I'll have to find a home for the new wine glasses.* 我得找個地方放這些新酒杯。
12 the home of a) the place where something was first discovered, made, or developed 發祥地, 發源地: *America is the home of baseball.* 美國是棒球的發源地。 **b)** the place where a plant or animal grows or lives〔動物、植物的〕產地, 生長[棲息]地: *India is the home of elephants and tigers.* 印度是大象和老虎的生息地。
13 ►SPORTS TEAM 運動隊◄ at home if a sports team plays at home, they play at their own sports field〔球隊〕在主場〔作賽〕
14 home from home *BrE*【英】, **home away from home** *AmE*【美】a place that you think is as pleasant and comfortable as your own house 像家一樣舒適自在的地方
15 what's that when it's at home? *BrE spoken humorous* used to ask what someone means when they use a long or unusual word【英口, 幽默】説白了是甚麼意思?〔要求別人不要使用複雜難懂的詞〕
16 home sweet home used to say how pleasant it is to be in your home 家真好啊!
17 ►GAMES 體育比賽◄ [U] a place in some games or sports which a player must try to reach in order to win a point 終點; 目標; 本壘 —see also 另見 HOME PLATE, HOME RUN

home² *adv* **1** to or at the place where you live 到家, 回家; 在家: *Is Sue home from work yet?* 蘇下班回到家了嗎? | *He stayed home for a week to finish writing his book.* 他在家待了一星期, 好把他的書寫完。| **go home** *I'm going home now. See you tomorrow.* 我現在要回家了, 明天見。| **get home** (=arrive at your home) 回到家, 抵家 *By the time we got home the programme had finished.* 等我們回到家時, 節目已經結束了。| **return home** *After three months touring Europe they returned home to Boston.* 他們在歐洲遊覽了三個月後便回去老家波士頓。 **2 take home** to earn a certain amount of money after tax has been taken off 掙得〔稅後收入〕: *The average store worker takes home around $300 a week.* 普通店員每週的稅後淨收入約為 300 美元。 **3 hit/drive/hammer etc sth home a)** to hit or push something firmly into the correct position 敲/推/錘擊進合適的位置 **b)** to make sure that someone understands what you mean by saying it in an extremely direct and determined way 明確闡述〔使人充分理解〕: *a powerful film with imagery that really drives its message home* 一部採用比喻手法將主題思想闡述清楚的具有巨大影響力的電影 **4 bring sth home to sb** to make you realize how serious, difficult or dangerous something is 使某人充分意識到某事〔的嚴重性、難度或危險性〕 **5 be home and dry** *informal especially BrE* to have succeeded in doing something【非正式, 尤英】大功告成, 達到目的 **6 be home free** *AmE informal* to have succeeded in doing the most difficult part of something【美, 非正式】成功完成某事最困難的部分: *Only one more page of the hard stuff and we're home free.* 只要再多看一頁, 我們就能完成最困難的部分了。—see also 另見 **close to home** (CLOSE² (20))

home³ *adj* [only before noun 僅用於名詞前] **1** connected with or belonging to your home or family 家的, 家庭的: **home address** *Make sure to give us your full home address.* 務必把你的詳細住宅地址告訴我們。| **home life** (=relationship with your family) 家庭生活 *The child has had an unhappy home life.* 這孩子在家裡生活得並不愉快。 **2** connected with a particular country, as opposed to foreign countries 本地的, 國內的: **home market** (=the country where something is made) 國內市場 *These cars are made mainly for the home market, not for export.* 這些汽車主要是為國內市場製造的, 不供出口。 **3** done at home or intended for use in a home 在家做的; 家用的: *home cooking* 家常菜 | *a home computer* 家用電腦 **4** played or playing at a team's own sports field, rather than an opponent's field 在主場進行的; 主隊的: *the home team* 主隊 | *home games* 主場賽事 **5 home bird** *BrE* someone who prefers to stay at home rather than going to parties, travelling etc【英】喜歡留在家裡的人 **6 home truths** facts about someone that are unpleasant for them to know but that are true 令人不快的事實: *It's time she was told a few home truths!* 到了該告訴她一些不中聽的實話的時候了!

home⁴ *v*
home in on *phr v* [T] **1** to aim exactly at an object or place and move directly to it 對準〔某事物或地方〕: *The bat can home in on insects using a kind of 'radar'.* 蝙蝠能憑藉某種"雷達"瞄準昆蟲。 **2** to direct your efforts or attention towards a particular fault or problem 將注意力集中於〔某個問題〕: *We homed in on the fault in the system and fixed it quickly.* 我們集中力量找出系統中的故障並迅速把它修好。

home base /ˈ· ·/ *n* [U] [singular] *AmE* HOME PLATE【美】本壘板

home·bod·y /ˈhomˌbɑdɪ; ˈhəʊmˌbɒdi/ *n* [C] *informal* someone who enjoys being at home【非正式】喜歡留在家裡的人

home·boy /ˈhombɔɪ; ˈhəʊmbɔɪ/ *n* [C] *AmE slang* a friend or someone from the same area or GANG¹ (1) as you【美俚】老鄉, 同鄉; 同夥

home brew /ˌ· ˈ·/ *n* [U] beer made at home 家釀啤酒 —**home brewed** *adj*

home·com·ing /ˈhomˌkʌmɪŋ; ˈhəʊmˌkʌmɪŋ/ *n* [C] **1** an occasion when someone comes back to their home after a long absence〔長期在外後〕返鄉, 回家 **2** *AmE* an occasion when former students return to their high school or college【美】校友返校的聚會, 校友日

Home Coun·ties /ˌ· ˈ··/ *n* [plural] the counties (COUNTY¹) around London 倫敦周圍各郡

home e·co·nom·ics /ˌ· ··ˈ··/ *n* [U] the study of cooking, SEWING, and other skills used at home, taught as a subject at school 家政學

home front /ˌ· ˈ·/ *n* [singular] the people who stay and work in their own country while others go abroad to fight in a war〔戰時的〕大後方(人民)

home·grown /ˈhomˋgron; ˌhəʊmˈgrəʊn◂/ *adj* **1** vegetables that are homegrown are grown in your own garden〔蔬菜〕自家園子裡種植的 **2** made or produced in your own country, town etc 本國製造[出產]的; 本地製造[出產]的: *homegrown entertainment* 國產娛樂節目

home help /ˌ· ˈ·/ *n* [C] *BrE* someone who helps ill or old people in their homes with cleaning, cooking etc【英】〔幫助病人或老人的〕家務助理

home·land /ˈhomˌlænd; ˈhəʊmlænd/ *n* [C] **1** the country where someone was born 祖國, 家鄉 **2** a large area of land in South Africa where part of the black population lived, under the APARTHEID system〔南非種族隔離制度下的〕"黑人家園"

home·less /ˈhomləs; ˈhəʊmləs/ *adj* **1** without a home 無家可歸的: *homeless children* 無家可歸的兒童 **2 the homeless** people who have nowhere to live, and who often live on the streets 無家可歸者, 流浪街頭者 —**homelessness** *n* [U]

home·ly /ˈhomlɪ; ˈhəʊmli/ *adj* **1** *BrE* simple and ordinary in a way that makes you feel comfortable【英】樸實無華的; 家常的: *The cottage had a warm, homely feel.* 那間小屋給人一種溫暖而隨和的感覺。 **2** *AmE* people or faces that are homely are unattractive or ugly【美】相貌平庸的; 醜陋的: *I've never seen such a homely dog in* *my life!* 我這輩子從未見過如此難看的狗！

home·made /ˋhomˋmed; ˌhəʊmˈmeɪd◂/ *adj* made at home and not bought from a shop 自製的，家裡做的：*homemade cake* 自製蛋糕

home·mak·er /ˋhomˌmekɚ; ˈhəʊmˌmeɪkə/ *n* [C] *especially AmE* a woman who works at home cleaning and cooking etc and does not have another job; HOUSEWIFE【尤美】家庭主婦

home mov·ie /ˌ· ˈ··/ *n* [C] a film you make, often of a family occasion, that is intended to be shown at home, not in a cinema〔只供在家裡放映的〕自製影片，記錄家庭活動的影片

Home Of·fice /ˈ· ˌ··/ *n* [singular] the British government department which deals with keeping order inside the country, controlling who enters the country etc〔英國的〕內政部

ho·me·o·path /ˋhomɪəˌpæθ; ˈhəʊmiəˌpæθ/ *n* [C] someone who treats diseases using homeopathy 用順勢療法治病的醫師

ho·me·op·a·thy /ˌhomɪˋɑpəθɪ; ˌhəʊmiˈɒpəθi/ *n* [U] a system of medicine in which a disease is treated by giving extremely small amounts of a substance that has the same effect as the disease 順勢療法 —**homeopathic** /ˌhomɪəˋpæθɪk; ˌhəʊmiəˈpæθɪk◂/ *adj* —**homeopathically** /-klɪ; -kli/ *adv*

home·own·er /ˋhomˌonɚ; ˈhəʊmˌəʊnə/ *n* [C] someone who owns their home 房主，自己擁有住房者

home plate /ˈ· ·/ *n* [singular] the place where you stand to hit the ball in BASEBALL and the last place the player who is running must touch in order to get a point〔棒球運動的〕本壘板 —see picture on page A22 參見 A22 頁圖

hom·er /ˋhomɚ; ˈhəʊmə/ *n* [C] *AmE informal* a home run【美，非正式】〔棒球〕本壘打 —**homer** *v* [I]

home room /ˈ· ·/ *n* [C] *AmE* a classroom where students have to go at the beginning of every school day【美】〔學生每天到校後必須去的〕點到室，年級教室

home rule /ˌ· ˈ·/ *n* [U] the right of the people in a country to control their own affairs, after previously being controlled by another country〔某國取得獨立後實行的〕地方自治

home run /ˌ· ˈ·/ *n* [C] a long hit in BASEBALL which allows the player who hits the ball to run around all the bases (BASE[2] (8)) and get a point〔棒球運動的〕本壘打，全壘打

Home Sec·re·ta·ry /ˌ· ˈ····/ *n* [C,U] the British Government minister who is in charge of the HOME OFFICE〔英國的〕內政大臣

home·sick /ˋhomˌsɪk; ˈhəʊmˌsɪk/ *adj* feeling unhappy because you are a long way from your home 想家的，思鄉的 —**homesickness** *n* [U]

home·spun /ˋhomˌspʌn; ˈhəʊmspʌn/ *adj* **1** homespun ideas are simple and ordinary〔想法〕簡單的，樸實的，平凡的：*homespun philosophy* 樸素的哲學 **2** homespun cloth is woven at home〔布料〕家裡紡的

home·stead[1] /ˋhomˌstɛd; ˈhəʊmsted/ *n* [C] **1** a farm and the area of land around it〔包括四周土地的〕農莊，農家 **2** *AmE old use* a piece of land given by the government【美舊】政府分發的土地

homestead[2] *v* [I,T] *AmE old use* to live and work on a homestead【美舊】在農莊工作及生活 —**homesteader** *n* [C]

home stretch /ˌ· ˈ·/ *n* [singular] **1** also 又作 **home straight** *BrE*【英】the last part of a race where there is a straight line to the finish〔賽跑中的〕最後一段直道[路程] **2** the last part of an activity or journey〔活動的〕最後一部分；〔行程的〕最後階段

home time /ˈ· ·/ *n* [U] *BrE* the time at the end of the school day when you can go home【英】〔學校每天的〕放學時間

home town /ˌ· ˈ·/ *n* [C] the place where you were born and spent your childhood 家鄉，故鄉

home·wards /ˋhomwɚdz; ˈhəʊmwədz/ also 又作 **homeward** *especially AmE*【尤美】— *adv* **1** towards home 向家；向家鄉：*The children were heading homewards.* 孩子們正在往家走。**2 homeward bound** *literary* going towards home【文】向家，朝着家 —**homeward** *adj*: *homeward journey* 歸家的旅程 —opposite 反義詞 OUTWARD (2)

home·work /ˋhomˌwɝk; ˈhəʊmwɜːk/ *n* [U] **1** work that a student at school is asked to do at home〔學生的〕家庭作業，功課 —compare 比較 CLASSWORK **2** something you do to prepare for an important activity〔重要活動之前必要的〕準備工作：**sb has done their homework** (=someone has prepared something well) 某人準備工作做得好 *You could tell that she'd really done her homework.* 可以看得出，她的準備工作的確做得很好。 [S] 2

home·work·er /ˋhomˌwɝkɚ; ˈhəʊmˌwɜːkə/ *n* [C] someone who works from their home 在家辦公的人 —**homeworking** *n* [U]

hom·ey[1], homy /ˋhomɪ; ˈhəʊmi/ *adj AmE* pleasant, like home【美】像在家裡一樣的，舒適自在的：*Flora liked the homey atmosphere of Aunt Fran's farm.* 弗洛拉喜歡弗蘭姑媽的農場中那種像家一樣舒適的氣氛。—compare 比較 HOMELY (1)

homey[2], homie *n* [singular] *AmE* a HOMEBOY【美】老鄉，同鄉；同夥

hom·i·cid·al /ˌhɑməˋsaɪdl̩; ˌhɒmɪ̇ˈsaɪdl◂/ *adj* likely to murder someone 嗜殺（成性）的：*a homicidal maniac* 殺人狂

hom·i·cide /ˋhɑməˌsaɪd; ˈhɒmɪ̇saɪd/ *n* **1** [C,U] *especially AmE* murder【尤美】謀殺，殺人 **2** [U] *AmE* the police department that deals with murder【美】警方負責處理謀殺案件的部門

hom·i·ly /ˋhɑmɪlɪ; ˈhɒmɪ̇li/ *n* [C] *formal*【正式】**1** advice about how to behave that is often unwanted〔道德〕說教，陳詞濫調 **2** *literary* a speech given as part of a Christian church ceremony【文】〔基督教的〕講道，佈道

hom·ing /ˋhomɪŋ; ˈhəʊmɪŋ/ *adj* a bird or animal that has a homing instinct has a special ability that helps it find its way home over long distances〔鳥、動物〕有返回原地之能力的

homing de·vice /ˈ·· ·ˌ·/ *n* [C usually singular 一般用單數] a special part of a weapon that helps it to find the place that it is aimed at〔武器上的〕自動導向裝置，尋的裝置

homing pi·geon /ˈ·· ˌ··/ *n* [C] a PIGEON that is able to find its way home over long distances 信鴿

hom·i·ny /ˋhɑmənɪ; ˈhɒmɪ̇ni/ *n* [U] a food made from crushed SWEET CORN 甜玉米片粥

homo- /homo; həʊməʊ/ *prefix formal or technical* same【正式或術語】相同的，同（一）的：*homosexual* (=attracted to the same sex) 同性戀的 | *homographs* (=words spelt the same way) 同形異義詞

ho·moe·o·path /ˋhomɪəˌpæθ; ˈhəʊmiəˌpæθ/ *n* [C] a British spelling of HOMEOPATH homeopath 的英式拼法

ho·moe·op·athy /ˌhomɪˋɑpəθɪ; ˌhəʊmiˈɒpəθi/ *n* [U] a British spelling of HOMEOPATHY homeopathy 的英式拼法

ho·mo·ge·ne·ous /ˌhoməˋdʒinɪəs; ˌhəʊməˈdʒiːniəs◂/ also 又作 **ho·mo·ge·nous** /həˋmɑdʒənəs; həˈmɒdʒɪ̇nəs/ *adj* consisting of people or things that are all of the same kind 由同種族人組成的；由同類組成的：*a homogeneous community* 同種族人組成的社會 —compare 比較 HETEROGENEOUS —**homogeneously** *adv*

ho·mo·ge·nize also 又作 **-ise** *BrE*【英】/həˋmɑdʒəˌnaɪz; həˈmɒdʒənaɪz/ *v* [T] to change something so that its parts become similar or the same 使成均質；使均勻，使純一：*plans to homogenize the various school systems* 統一各類不同學制的計劃

ho·mo·ge·nized /həˋmɑdʒəˌnaɪzd; həˈmɒdʒɪ̇naɪzd/ *adj* homogenized milk has had the cream on top mixed with the milk〔牛奶〕均質的

hom·o·graph /ˋhɑməˌgræf; ˈhɒməgrɑːf/ *n* [C] a word

that is spelt the same as another, but is different in meaning, origin, grammar, or pronunciation 同形異義詞: *The noun 'record' and the verb 'record' are homographs of each other.* 名詞record和動詞record互為同形異義詞。

hom·o·nym /ˈhɑməˌnɪm; ˈhɒmənɪm/ *n* [C] a word that is spelt the same and sounds the same as another, but is different in meaning or origin. The noun 'bear' and the verb 'bear' are homonyms 同音同形異義詞〔名詞bear和動詞bear是同音同形異義詞〕

ho·mo·pho·bia /ˌhoməˈfobɪə; ˌhəʊməˈfəʊbiə/ *n* [U] hatred and fear of HOMOSEXUAL*s* 對同性戀的憎惡和恐懼 —**homophobic** *adj*

hom·o·phone /ˈhɑməˌfon; ˈhɒməfəʊn/ *n* [C] a word that sounds the same as another but is different in spelling, meaning or origin 同音異形異義詞: *'Knew' and 'new' are homophones.* knew和new是同音異形異義詞。

Ho·mo sa·pi·ens /ˌhomo ˈsepɪɛnz; ˌhəʊməʊ ˈsæpienz/ *n* [U] the type of human being that exists now 智人〔現代人的學名〕

ho·mo·sex·u·al /ˌhoməˈsɛkʃuəl; ˌhəʊməˈsekʃuəl◂/ *n* [C] someone, especially a man, who is sexually attracted to people of the same sex〔尤指男性〕同性戀者 —compare 比較 BISEXUAL[1] (1), HETEROSEXUAL —see also 另見 GAY[1] (1) —**homosexual** *adj* —**homosexuality** /ˌhoməˌsɛkʃuˈælətɪ; ˌhəʊməsekʃuˈælɪ̣ti/ *n* [U]

Hon /ɑn; ɒn/ **1** the written abbreviation of 縮寫= HONOURABLE (1), used in the titles of British NOBLE*s* and Members of Parliament 尊敬的〔用於稱呼英國貴族及議會議員〕: *the Hon Arthur Cobbett* 尊敬的阿瑟·科貝特 **2** the written abbreviation of 縮寫= HONORARY (2) used in official job titles 名譽的〔用於官方職位中〕: *Hon Sec* (=honorary secretary) 名譽祕書

hon /hʌn; hʌn/ *pron AmE spoken* an abbreviation of 縮寫= HONEY, used to address someone you love【美口】親愛的, 寶貝〔用於稱呼心愛的人〕: *Come here, hon, let me tie your shoes.* 來, 寶貝, 讓我給你繫上鞋帶。

hon·cho /ˈhɑntʃo; ˈhɒntʃəʊ/ *n* **the head honcho** *informal especially AmE* the person who is in charge【非正式, 尤美】負責人, 頭兒

hone /hon; həʊn/ *v* [T] **1** to improve your skill at doing something, especially when you are already very good at it 磨練, 訓練; 提高…的技藝: *He set about honing his skills as a draughtsman.* 他着手進一步提高自己的製圖技藝。| **finely honed** (=extremely well-developed) 極度發達的 *finely honed intuition* 極度發達的直覺 **2** to make knives, swords etc sharp 把〔刀、劍等〕磨光[鋒利]

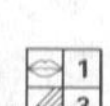

hon·est /ˈɑnɪst; ˈɒnɪ̣st/ *adj*

1 ►CHARACTER 人品◄ someone who is honest does not lie or steal etc 誠實的, 正直的: *It was very honest of him to give them the money back.* 他真是個誠實的人, 把錢還給了他們。| *an old woman with a plain, honest face you could trust* 長着一張平常、誠實可靠的面孔的老婦 | **scrupulously honest** (=always very honest) 極其誠實的 *She is scrupulously honest in all her business dealings.* 她在所有的商業買賣中都極其誠實。

2 ►STATEMENT/ANSWER ETC 講話/回答等◄ not hiding the truth or the facts about something 坦誠的, 直率的, 不隱瞞真相的: *an honest answer* 坦白的回答 | **let's be honest** *Let's be honest – the only reason she married him was for his money.* 說實話, 她嫁給他就是為了他的錢。| **be honest with sb** *I'm not sure if Joe was being completely honest with me when he said he'd never met them before.* 喬說他以前從未見過他們, 我不知道他是不是對我說了實話。| **be honest about sth** *At least he's been honest about it.* 起碼在這件事上他是誠實的。

3 to be honest *spoken* used when you tell someone what you really think【口】說實話, 老實說: *To be honest, I don't like him very much.* 老實說, 我不太喜歡他。

4 honest! *spoken* used to try to make someone believe you【口】真的! 不騙你!: *I didn't mean to hurt him, honest!* 我不是故意傷害他的, 真的!

5 honest to God *spoken* used to emphasize that something you say is really true【口】確實, 千真萬確

6 ►WORK 工作◄ honest work is done without cheating, using your own efforts 用正當手段的, 努力認真的: *I bet he's never done an honest day's work in his life!* 我敢說他這輩子從未認認真真地工作過一天! | **earn an honest living** *young families struggling even to earn an honest living* 要想正正當當謀生都不容易的年青人家庭

7 ►ORDINARY/GOOD PEOPLE 普通的/好人◄ honest people are not famous or special, but behave in a good, socially acceptable way 誠實的; 規矩的: *She came from a good, honest, working-class background.* 她出身於一個良好誠實的工人階級家庭。

8 make an honest woman (out) of *old-fashioned* to marry a woman because she is going to have a baby【過時】因…已懷孕而娶她為妻

hon·est·ly /ˈɑnɪstlɪ; ˈɒnɪ̣stli/ *adv* **1** in an honest way 誠實地, 正直地: *"I don't know," she answered honestly.* 她誠實地回答:"我不知道。" | *Did he come by the money honestly, or was it stolen?* 他的錢是正路來的, 還是偷來的? **2** used to say that you really think that something is true, especially when it seems surprising 真的, 的確: *Does he honestly expect me to believe his story?* 他真的以為我會相信他說的話嗎? **3** *spoken* used when you are shocked or annoyed by something someone has said or done【口】〔用以表示震驚或煩惱〕真是的! 真不像話!: *Honestly! Can't you think of something better to do with your time?* 真不像話! 你難道沒有更好的辦法消磨時間嗎? **4** *spoken* used to try to make someone believe that what you have just said is true【口】真的! 不騙你!: *It wasn't me, honestly!* 那不是我, 真的不是!

honest-to-good·ness /ˌ.. . ˈ../ *adj* [only before noun 僅用於名詞前] simple and good 簡單而美好的, 普通的, 平常的: *plain honest-to-goodness home cooking* 普通家常菜

hon·es·ty /ˈɑnɪstɪ; ˈɒnɪ̣sti/ *n* [U] **1** the quality of being honest 誠實, 正直; 坦誠: *a politician of rare honesty and courage* 具備少見的誠實品德及勇氣的政治家 **2 in all honesty** *spoken* used when telling someone that what you are saying is what you really think【口】說實話: *I must add, in all honesty, that I think the task ahead of us will be difficult.* 我必須補充一句, 說實話, 我認為我們面臨的任務是艱巨的。

hon·ey /ˈhʌnɪ; ˈhʌni/ *n* [U] **1** a sweet sticky substance produced by BEE*s*, used as food 蜂蜜 **2** *especially AmE spoken* used to address someone you love【尤美, 口】親愛的, 寶貝〔用於稱呼心愛的人〕

hon·ey·bee /ˈhʌnɪˌbi; ˈhʌnibiː/ *n* [C] a BEE that makes honey 蜜蜂

hon·ey·comb /ˈhʌnɪˌkom; ˈhʌnikəʊm/ *n* [C] **1** a structure made by BEE*s*, which consists of many six-sided cells in which honey is stored 蜂巢, 蜂窩, 蜂房 **2** something that is arranged or shaped in this pattern 蜂巢[窩]狀物

hon·ey·combed /ˈhʌnɪˌkomd; ˈhʌnikəʊmd/ *adj* [+with] filled with many holes, hollow passages etc 蜂巢[窩]狀的

hon·ey·dew mel·on /ˌhʌnɪdju ˈmɛlən; ˌhʌnidjuː ˈmelən/ *n* [C] a type of MELON 白蘭瓜, 蜜瓜, 甜瓜 —see picture on page A8 參見A8頁圖

hon·eyed /ˈhʌnɪd; ˈhʌnid/ *adj literary* honeyed words or honeyed voices sound soft and pleasant, but are often insincere【文】甜言蜜語的, 阿諛的: *"How kind you are," Brett said in a honeyed voice.* "你真好!"布雷特甜言蜜語道。

hon·ey·moon[1] /ˈhʌnɪˌmun; ˈhʌnimuːn/ *n* [C] **1** a holiday taken by two people who have just got married 蜜月: **on your honeymoon** *We're going to Hawaii on our honeymoon.* 我們要去夏威夷度蜜月。**2** also 又作 **honeymoon period** the period of time when a new government, leader etc has just started and no one criticizes them〔新政府、新領導人上任初期的〕短暫的和諧時期, 蜜月期

honeymoon² *v* [I always+adv/prep] to go somewhere for your honeymoon 外出度蜜月 —**honeymooner** *n* [C]

hon·ey·pot /ˈhʌnɪˌpɑt; ˈhʌnipɒt/ *n* [C] something that is attractive to a lot of people 極有吸引力的事物

hon·ey·suck·le /ˈhʌnɪˌsʌkḷ; ˈhʌniˌsʌkəl/ *n* [C] a climbing plant with pleasant-smelling yellow or pink flowers 忍冬〔一種有香味的攀緣植物〕

honk¹ /hɔŋk; hɒŋk/ *n* **1** a loud noise made by a car horn 汽車喇叭聲 —see picture on page A19 參見A19頁圖 **2** a loud noise made by a GOOSE¹ (1) 雁叫聲

honk² *v* **1** [I,T] if a car horn or a GOOSE¹ (1) honks, it makes a loud noise〔汽車〕鳴(喇叭), 按(喇叭);〔雁〕叫 **2** [I] also 又作 **honk up** *slang* to VOMIT¹【俚】嘔吐

hon·ky, honkie /ˈhɑŋkɪ; ˈhɒŋki/ *n* [C] *AmE slang* an insulting word for a white person【美俚】白鬼子〔對白人的蔑稱〕

hon·ky-tonk¹ /ˈhɑŋkɪ ˌtɑŋk; ˈhɒŋki tɒŋk/ *n* [C] *AmE* a cheap bar where COUNTRY MUSIC is played【美】演奏鄉村音樂的低級酒吧

honky-tonk² *adj* [only before noun 僅用於名詞前] **1** **honky-tonk music/piano** a type of piano music which is played in a cheerful way 歡樂的樂曲/鋼琴曲 **2** *AmE* cheap, brightly-coloured, and not good quality【美】低檔豔俗的

hon·or /ˈɑnɚ; ˈɒnə/ *n* [C,U] the American spelling of HONOUR honour 的美式拼法

hon·or·a·ble /ˈɑnərəbḷ; ˈɒnərəbəl/ *adj* the American spelling of HONOURABLE honourable 的美式拼法

hon·o·rar·i·um /ˌɑnəˈrɛrɪəm; ˌɒnəˈreəriəm/ *n* [C] *formal* a sum of money offered to someone for professional services【正式】〔專業服務〕酬金, 報酬

hon·or·ar·y /ˈɑnəˌrɛrɪ; ˈɒnərəri/ *adj* **1** an honorary title, rank, or university degree is given to someone as an honour〔稱號、官階、學位等〕作為一種榮譽授予的, 榮譽的 **2** an honorary position in an organization is held without receiving any payment〔職位、職務〕名譽的, 名義上的, 無報酬的 **3** an honorary member of a group is treated like a member of that group but does not belong to it〔成員〕名譽的: *They regard her as a kind of honorary man.* 他們將她視作名譽成員。

hon·or·if·ic /ˌɑnəˈrɪfɪk; ˌɒnəˈrɪfɪk◂/ *n* [C] an expression or title that is used to show respect for the person you are speaking to 尊稱, 敬語〔用來表示尊敬的稱號、用語〕

honor roll /ˈ·· ·/ *n* [C] *AmE* a list of the best students in a school or college【美】成績優異者名單; 光榮榜

hon·ors /ˈɑnɚz; ˈɒnəz/ *n* [plural] the American spelling of HONOURS honours 的美式拼法 —see also 另見 **with honours** (HONOUR¹ (12))

honor sys·tem /ˈ·· ˌ··/ *n* [C] *AmE*【美】**1** an agreement between members of a group to obey rules 信用制度〔指自覺遵守規章而不加監督的做法〕: *the school's honor system* 無監考考試制度, 學校的信用制度 **2** a way of recording the fact that a student has achieved a high standard of work 優等生表彰制度

3 **hon·our¹** *BrE*【英】, **honor** *AmE*【美】/ˈɑnɚ; ˈɒnə/ *n*
1 ►RESPECT 尊敬◄ [U] the respect that you, your family, your country etc receive from other people, which makes you feel proud 榮譽; 崇敬, 敬重, 敬意: *For the French team, winning tomorrow's game is a matter of national honour.* 對法國隊來說, 在明天的比賽中獲勝事關國家榮譽。| **sb's honour is at stake** (=someone's honour could be badly affected if they do not succeed) 危及某人的聲譽 *This can't get to the media. The company's honor is at stake here!* 不能讓傳媒知道這件事。此事關係到公司在人們心目中的形象。
2 ►STH THAT MAKES YOU PROUD 讓人引以為榮的事◄ [singular] *formal* something that makes you feel very proud【正式】引以為榮的事, 光榮: **it is an honour to do sth** (=used when saying politely that you are pleased to do something, especially at a formal occasion) 很榮幸做某事 | **have the honour of doing sth** *formal*【正式】*Earlier this year I had the honor of meeting the President and Mrs Bush.* 今年較早時候, 我有幸見到了布殊總統及他的夫人。| **do sb the honour of doing sth** (=make someone proud and happy by doing something for them) 為某人做某事使之感到榮幸, 給面子為某人做某事 | **a rare honour** (=a very special honour) 殊榮
3 in honour of in order to show how much you admire and respect someone 為了表示對…的崇敬: *a memorial in honour of those who died for their country* 為紀念那些為國捐軀者而舉行的儀式
4 ►GIVEN BY A GOVERNMENT 由政府授予的◄ [C] something such as a special title or MEDAL given to someone to show how much people respect them for what they have achieved 榮譽稱號; 榮譽勳章: **highest honour** (=most important honour) 最高榮譽勳章[稱號] *Churchill received many of his country's highest honours.* 丘吉爾曾獲得很多由國家授予的最高榮譽勳章。
5 the place/seat of honour the place which is given to the most important guest 貴賓席, 貴賓座
6 be an honour to to bring admiration and respect to your country, school, family etc because of your behaviour or achievements 為…增光: *a young man who was a great athlete and an honour to his college* 體育出色, 為學院增光的年青人
7 with full military honours if someone is buried with full military honours, there is a military ceremony at their funeral 以隆重的軍葬禮下葬的
8 ►MORAL PRINCIPLES 道德標準◄ [U] strong moral beliefs and standards of behaviour that make people respect and trust you 高尚品德, 氣節: **a matter/point/question of honour** (=something that you feel you must do because of your moral principles) 品德問題 *It is a point of honour with me to repay all my debts promptly.* 儘快地償還所有債務是關係到我的名譽的問題。| **man of honour** *old-fashioned* (=a man who always behaves in a way that is based on high moral standards)【過時】品德高尚的人
9 be/feel honour bound to feel that it is your moral duty to do something 在道義上有責任: *Don't tell Kit either, because she'd feel honour bound to do something about it.* 也別告訴姬特, 因為她會覺得自己有責任為此做點甚麼。
10 on your honour a) if you swear on your honour to do something, you promise very seriously to do it 以名譽擔保 **b)** *old-fashioned* if you are on your honour to do something, you are being trusted to do it【過時】得到信任的
11 do the honours *spoken* to pour the drinks, serve food etc at a social occasion【口】〔在社交場合上〕盡主人之誼〔指倒酒、上菜等〕
12 ►UNIVERSITY 大學◄ *BrE*【英】**a) with honours** if you pass a university degree with honours, you pass it at a level that is higher than the most basic level 以優等成績〔畢業、獲得學位〕**b) First Class/Second Class Honours** the highest or second highest level of degree at a British university〔英國大學中的〕一級/二級榮譽學位[優等成績]
13 Your Honour used when speaking to a judge 法官大人
14 ►SEX 性◄ *old use* if a woman loses her honour, she has sex with a man she is not married to【舊】〔婦女的〕貞操, 貞節 —see also 另見 **guest of honour** (GUEST¹ (6)), MAID OF HONOUR

honour² *BrE*【英】, **honor** *AmE*【美】— *v* [T] **1 be/feel honoured** to feel very proud and pleased 感到榮幸: **be/feel honoured to do sth** *I felt deeply honored to be playing against the former Wimbledon Champion.* 能與溫布頓網球賽的前冠軍球手比賽, 我深感榮幸。**2** to treat someone with special respect 禮待〔某人〕: *our honoured guests this evening* 今晚的貴賓 **3** *formal* to show publicly that someone is respected and admired, especially by praising them or giving them a special title【正式】給…以榮譽, 表彰, 表揚 **4 honour a contract/**

agreement etc to do what you have agreed to do in a contract etc 履行合同/協議 **5 honour a cheque/voucher etc** to accept a cheque etc as payment 接受[承兑]支票/代金券 **6 sb has decided to honour us with their presence** *humorous* used when someone arrives late, or to someone who rarely comes to a meeting, class etc【幽默】某人決定賞光出席了〔用於遲到的或不常參加會議或上課的人〕

Hon·our·a·ble /ˈɑnərəbḷ; ˈɒnərəbəl/ *written abbreviation* 縮寫為 **Hon** *adj* **1** used in Britain in the titles of children whose father is a lord and in the titles of judges and members of parliament 尊敬的〔對英國貴族子女、法官和議員的尊稱〕 **2 Honourable Member** used by British members of parliament when talking to or about each other in the House of Commons 尊敬的議員〔英國下議院議員相互之間的尊稱〕 —compare 比較 RIGHT HONOURABLE

honourable *BrE*【英】, **honorable** *AmE*【美】— *adj* **1** an honourable action or activity deserves respect and admiration〔行為或事件〕光榮的, 值得尊敬的: *My father doesn't think acting is an honorable profession.* 我父親認為當演員不是受人尊敬的行業。**2** behaving in a way that is morally correct and shows you have high moral standards 品行高潔的, 品德高尚的: *a principled and honourable man* 一個講求原則、品德高尚的人 **3** an honourable arrangement or agreement is fair to everyone who is involved in it〔安排或協議〕公平的, 公正的 —**honourably** *adv*

honourable men·tion *BrE*【英】, **honorable mention** *AmE*【美】/ˌ····ˈ··/ *n* [C] a special honour in a competition for work that was of high quality but did not get a prize〔給未獲正式名次但有優異表現者頒發的〕榮譽獎

honours de·gree /ˈ··ˌ·/ *n* [C] a university degree that is above the basic level in one or two particular subjects at a British university〔英國大學的〕榮譽學位, 優等學位: *an honours degree in German* 德語榮譽學位 | **joint honours degree** (=a degree in two main subjects) 雙主修榮譽學位, 聯合榮譽學位

honours list /ˈ·· ˌ·/ *n* [singular] a list of important people in Britain to whom titles are given as a sign of respect〔英國的〕受勳者名冊

hooch, hootch /hutʃ; huːtʃ/ *n* [U] *especially AmE* strong alcoholic drink that has been made illegally【尤美】〔非法製造的〕烈酒

hood /hud; hʊd/ *n* [C] **1** a part of a coat that you can pull up to cover your head〔大衣上的〕風帽, 兜帽: *a fur-lined hood* 有毛皮襯裡的風帽 **2** a cover fitted above a COOKER (1) to remove the smell of cooking〔爐灶上方的〕排風罩, 抽油煙罩 **3** *AmE* the metal covering over the engine on a car【美】汽車引擎蓋: *Check under the hood and see what that noise is.* 打開引擎蓋查查是甚麼聲音。**4** *BrE* a folding cover on a car or PRAM, which gives protection from the rain【英】〔汽車或嬰兒車上用於擋雨的〕摺合式車篷; 篷蓋 **5** a cover that someone puts over their head to prevent them from being recognized〔為了不讓人認出而戴上的〕蒙臉罩 **6** *slang originally AmE* a hoodlum【俚, 原美】惡棍, 暴徒: *gangs of hoods roaming the streets* 聯羣結隊在街上遊蕩的惡棍

-hood /hud; hʊd/ *suffix* [in nouns 構成名詞] the state or time of being something …狀態; …時期: *a happy childhood* 快樂的童年 | *growing to manhood* 長大成人 | *There's not much likelihood.* 那不太可能。

hood·ed /ˈhudɪd; ˈhʊdʒd/ *adj* having or wearing a hood 帶風帽的; 戴着風帽的; 有罩的: *a hooded cape* 帶風帽的斗篷

hood·lum /ˈhudləm; ˈhuːdləm/ *n* [C] *informal* a violent criminal【非正式】惡棍, 暴徒

hoo·doo /ˈhudu; ˈhuːduː/ *n* [U] a type of VOODOO 巫術, 魔法

hood·wink /ˈhudˌwɪŋk; ˈhʊdˌwɪŋk/ *v* [T+into] to trick someone in a clever way so that you can get an advantage for yourself 欺詐, 哄騙

hoo·ey /ˈhuɪ; ˈhuːi/ *n* [U] *AmE* stupid talk; nonsense【美】胡說八道, 瞎話

hoof[1] /huf; huːf/ *n* [C] *plural* **hoofs** *or* **hooves** /huvz; huːvz/ **1** the hard foot of an animal such as a horse, cow etc 蹄 —see picture at 參見 HORSE[1] 圖 **2 on the hoof** *BrE* if you make decisions on the hoof, you make them while you are doing other things, without stopping to think【英】不加思索地〔作決定〕

hoof[2] *v* **hoof it** *slang* to run away quickly【俚】快速逃走

hoof·er /ˈhufɚ; ˈhuːfə/ *n* [C] *AmE slang* a dancer【美俚】舞蹈演員

hoo-ha /ˈhu ˌhɑ; ˈhuː hɑː/ *n* [U] *BrE* noisy talk or excitement about something unimportant【英】吵鬧, 叫嚷; 大驚小怪: *What's all the hoo-ha about?* 幹甚麼這麼吵鬧呀?

hooks 鉤子

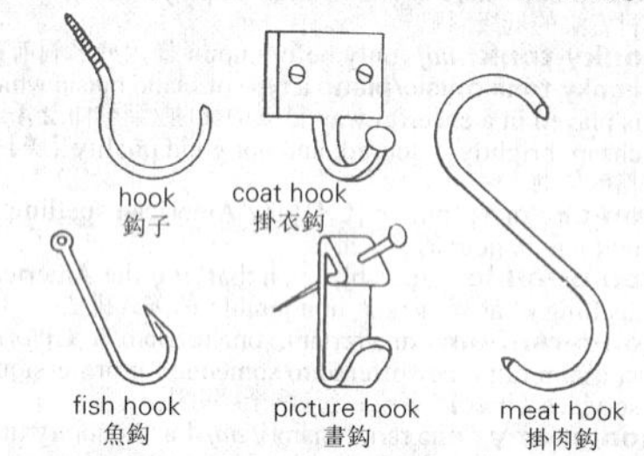

hook[1] /huk; hʊk/ *n* [C]

1 ►FOR HANGING THINGS ON 用來掛東西◄ a curved piece of metal or plastic that you use for hanging things on 掛鉤, 吊鉤: *Put your coat on the hook.* 把你的外套掛在鉤上。

2 ►FOR CATCHING FISH 用來釣魚◄ a curved piece of thin metal with a sharp point for catching fish 魚鉤, 釣鉤: *a fish hook* 魚鉤

3 by hook or by crook if you are going to do something by hook or by crook, you are determined to do it 千方百計地, 下定決心地: *In the old days if you had a deadline, you met it by hook or by crook.* 過去, 如果規定了最後期限, 你就要用盡方法把工作按時完成。

4 let/get sb off the hook to allow someone or help someone to get out of a difficult situation 讓/幫某人脫離困境: *We almost sued the magazine for libel, but in the end we let them off the hook.* 我們差點要控告這家雜誌社誹謗, 但最後我們還是饒了他們。

5 leave/take the phone off the hook to leave or take the telephone RECEIVER (=the part you speak into) off the part where it is usually placed so that no one can call you〔因不想接聽電話而〕摘下電話聽筒

6 ►WAY OF HITTING SB 拳擊方法◄ a way of hitting your opponent in BOXING, in which your elbow is bent〔拳擊中的〕鉤拳

7 hook, line, and sinker if someone believes something hook, line, and sinker, they believe a lie completely 完全地, 無保留地〔相信謊言〕: *She swallowed the whole story hook, line, and sinker.* 她完全地相信了這整件事。

8 ►A TUNE 曲調◄ a part of the tune in a song that makes it very easy to remember 曲調中易記的部分 —see also 另見 BOAT HOOK, **sling your hook** (SLING[1] (4))

hook[2] *v* [T]

1 ►FISH 魚◄ to catch a fish with a hook〔用鉤〕釣魚: *I hooked a 20 pound salmon last week.* 我上週釣了一條20磅重的鮭魚。

2 ►FASTEN 固定◄ [always+adv/prep] to fasten or hang something onto something else 吊, 掛; 把…固定住: **hook sth over/around/onto etc** *He managed to hook his leg* *over the branch.* 他終於設法把一條腿鈎在樹枝上。| **get hooked on/onto** *My jacket got hooked on a rosebush.* 我的上衣被玫瑰叢鈎住了。

3 ►BEND YOUR FINGER/ARM ETC 屈起手指/手臂等◄ [always+adv/prep] to bend your finger, arm, or leg, especially so that you can pull or hold something else 把〔手指、手臂或腿〕屈起〔以拉動或抱住某物〕: **hook sth around/over etc** *Jack hooked his arm around the other man's neck.* 傑克用胳膊摟住另一個人的脖子。

4 ►ATTRACT 吸引◄ *AmE informal* to succeed in attracting someone【美, 非正式】勾引; 吸引

hook sth ↔ up *phr v* [T] *especially AmE* to connect a piece of electronic equipment to another piece of equipment or to an electricity supply【尤美】〔電器〕連接, 接通: *Is the video hooked up to the TV?* 錄像機和電視機連接上了嗎?

hook up with *phr v* [T] *especially AmE*【尤美】**a)** to meet someone and become friendly with them 跟…結交: *I'll give you a few names of people to hook up with out there.* 我會告訴你一些人的名字, 你到那兒後可以和他們結交。**b)** to agree to work together with another organization for a particular purpose 掛鈎〔指與某個組織合作〕

hook·ah /ˈhukə; ˈhʊkə/ *n* [C] a pipe for smoking drugs that consists of a long tube and a container of water 水煙筒

hook and eye /ˌ· · ˈ·/ *n* [U] a small metal hook and ring used for fastening clothes〔衣服上作鈕扣用的〕鈎和環, 鈎眼扣 —see picture at 參見 FASTENER 圖

hook and lad·der /ˌ· · ˈ··/ *n* [C] *AmE* a FIRE ENGINE with long LADDERs fixed to it【美】〔配備有長梯的〕雲梯消防車

hooked /hukt; hʊkt/ *adj* **1** curved outwards or shaped like a hook 鈎狀的: *hooked claws* 鈎爪 | *a hooked nose* 鷹鈎鼻 **2** [not before noun 不用於名詞前] *informal* if you are hooked on a drug, you feel a strong need for it and you cannot stop taking it; ADDICTED (1)【非正式】〔吸毒〕成癮的 **3** [not before noun 不用於名詞前] if you are hooked on something, you enjoy it very much and you want to do it as often as possible 對…上癮的, 對…着迷的: *I got hooked on TV when I was sick.* 我生病期間對電視着了迷。**4** having one or more hooks 有鈎的

hook·er /ˈhukɚ; ˈhʊkə/ *n* [C] *informal* a woman who has sex with men for money; PROSTITUTE【非正式】妓女

hook-nosed /ˈ· ˌ·/ *adj* having a large nose that curves outwards in the middle 長着鷹鈎鼻的

hook-up /ˈ· ·/ *n* [C] a temporary connection between two pieces of equipment such as computers, or between a piece of equipment and an electricity supply〔儀器的〕臨時連接: *a satellite hook-up* 衛星連接[聯播]

hook·y, hookey /ˈhuki; ˈhʊki/ *n* **play hooky** *informal AmE* to stay away from school without permission【非正式, 美】逃學

hoo·li·gan /ˈhulɪgən; ˈhuːlɪ̈gən/ *n* [C] a noisy violent person who causes trouble by fighting etc 流氓, 惡棍: *football hooligans* 足球流氓 —**hooliganism** *n* [U]

hoop /hup; huːp/ *n* [C] **1 jump/go through hoops** to have to do a lot of difficult things as a test of how suitable you are for something 經受考驗[磨練] **2** one of the circular bands of metal or wood around a BARREL¹ (1)〔箍桶用的金屬或木質〕箍 **3** a curved piece of wood or metal that is stuck into the ground and used in the game of CROQUET〔槌球戲中的〕拱門 **4** a large ring that CIRCUS (1) animals are made to jump through or that children used to play with in the past〔馬戲團中供動物鑽過的〕大圈;〔舊時兒童當玩具的〕環 —see also 另見 COCK-A-HOOP, HULA HOOP —**hoop** *v* [T]

hoop-la /ˈhup lɑ; ˈhuːp lɑː/ *n* [U] **1** *especially AmE* excitement about something which attracts a lot of public attention【尤美】喧鬧, 大吹大擂: *all the hoopla that surrounded the trial* 對法庭的審判議論紛紛 **2** *BrE* a game in which prizes can be won by throwing a ring over an object from a distance【英】投環套物遊戲

hoo·ray /hʊˈre; hʊˈreɪ/ *interjection* shouted when you are very glad about something〔表示高興的呼喊聲〕好哇! —see also 另見 **hip hip hooray** (HIP²) —**hooray** *n* [C]

hoose·gow /ˈhusgaʊ; ˈhuːsgaʊ/ *n* [C] *AmE old use* a prison【美舊】監獄

hoot¹ /hut; huːt/ *n* [C] **1** a shout or laugh that shows you think something is funny or stupid〔聽到可笑或愚蠢的事時發出的〕呵喝聲, 噓叫聲; 嘲笑聲: **hoots of laughter/derision** *a speech that was greeted with hoots of derision* 被報以陣陣嘲笑聲的演講 **2** a sound that an OWL makes 貓頭鷹的叫聲 **3** a short clear sound made by a vehicle or ship, as a warning〔汽車喇叭、船的汽笛的〕鳴響聲〔以示警告〕**4 be a hoot** *spoken* to be very funny or amusing【口】很可笑, 很滑稽 **5 don't give a hoot/don't care two hoots** *spoken* used when saying that you do not care about something at all【口】一點也不在乎, 完全不放在心上: *I don't give a hoot for her opinion!* 我根本不在乎她的看法!

hoot² *v* **1** [I,T] if a vehicle or ship hoots, it makes a loud clear noise as a warning〔汽車〕鳴喇叭;〔船〕鳴笛〔以作警告〕: [+at] *The car behind was hooting at me.* 我身後的汽車衝着我鳴喇叭。**2** [I] if an OWL hoots, it makes a long 'oo' sound〔貓頭鷹〕發出鳴叫聲 **3** [I,T] to laugh loudly because you think something is funny or stupid 嘲弄地大笑: [+with] *hooting with laughter* 大聲嘲笑

hoot·er /ˈhutɚ; ˈhuːtə/ *n* [C] **1** *BrE* a piece of equipment that makes a loud noise and is used on cars, ships, or in factories【英】〔汽車的〕喇叭;〔船、工廠的〕汽笛 **2** *BrE slang* your nose【英俚】鼻子 **3 hooters** [plural] *AmE* an offensive word for a woman's breasts【美】一對乳房〔具冒犯性的説法〕

hoo·ver¹ /ˈhuvɚ; ˈhuːvə/ *n* [C] *BrE trademark* VACUUM CLEANER【英, 商標】(胡佛牌) 真空吸塵器

hoover² *v* [I,T] *BrE* to clean a floor, CARPET etc using a VACUUM CLEANER (=a machine that sucks up dirt)【英】用真空吸塵器清潔〔地板、地毯等〕—see picture at 參見 CLEAN² 圖

hooves /huvz; huːvz/ the plural of HOOF

hop¹ /hɑp; hɒp/ *v* **hopped, hopping**

1 ►JUMP 跳躍◄ [I] to move by jumping on one foot〔人〕單足蹦跳: *a child hopping up and down the stairs* 一個在樓梯上來回上下單足蹦跳的孩子

2 [I] if a bird, an insect, or a small animal hops, it moves by making quick short jumps〔鳥、昆蟲、小動物〕(快速小步) 跳躍

3 [I always+adv/prep] *informal* to get into, onto, or out of something, especially a vehicle【非正式】跳上[跳下]〔車輛〕: **[+in/out/on etc]** *Hop in – I'll drive you to the bus stop.* 上車吧, 我送你去公共汽車站。

4 hop a plane/bus/train etc *AmE informal* to get on a plane, bus, train etc, especially after suddenly deciding to do so【美, 非正式】〔尤指突然決定〕乘搭〔飛機、公共汽車、火車等〕: *So we hopped a bus to Phoenix that night.* 因此我們那天晚上便坐上公共汽車到了鳳凰城。

5 hop it! *BrE spoken* used to tell someone to go away【英口】走開! 滾開!

6 hopping mad *informal* very angry【非正式】非常生氣, 暴跳如雷: *Mrs C's going to be hopping mad when she hears!* C 太太聽到這事會非常生氣的!

hop² *n* [C]

1 keep sb on the hop *informal* to make someone very busy【非正式】讓某人十分忙碌: *The children keep me on the hop all day.* 孩子們讓我整天忙個不停。

2 catch sb on the hop to do something when someone is not expecting it and is not ready 使某人措手不及

3 ►JUMP 跳躍◄ a short jump〔小步〕跳躍, 蹦跳

4 ►PLANT 植物◄ [usually plural 一般用複數] part of a flower that is used for making beer, or the tall plant on which it grows 忽布, 啤酒花〔用來釀製啤酒〕

5 ►FLIGHT 飛行◄ a single short journey by plane 短程

飛行: *crossing Australia in a series of hops* 通過一連串短程飛行穿越澳大利亞
6 ►DANCE 跳舞◄ a social event at which people dance 舞會

hop, step, and jump /,· ,· · '·/ *n* [singular] *informal* the TRIPLE JUMP【非正式】三級跳遠

1 1 **hope¹** /hop; həʊp/ *v* [I,T] **1** to want something to happen or be true, and to believe it is possible 希望, 期望, 指望: **hope (that)** *I hope you have a lovely birthday.* 我希望你能過一個快樂的生日。| *I hope I'm not disturbing you.* 希望我沒有打擾你。| *Let's just hope we can find somewhere to park.* 但願我們能找到停車的地方。| **hope to do sth** *Joan's hoping to study Law at Harvard.* 瓊盼望能到哈佛大學唸法律。| **[+for]** *We were hoping for good weather.* 我們在盼望好天氣。| **hope for the best** (=hope that a situation will end well when there is a risk of things going wrong) 抱樂觀的態度, 盡量往好處想 *All we can do is hope for the best and wait.* 我們唯一能做的就是抱着樂觀的態度耐心等待。| **hope against hope** (=continue to hope for something even when it is unlikely to happen) 抱一線希望 *Daniel waited all day, hoping against hope that Annie would change her mind.* 丹尼爾等了一整天, 抱着一絲希望盼安妮會改變主意。

Frequencies of the verb **hope** in spoken and written English 動詞 hope 在英語口語和書面語中的使用頻率

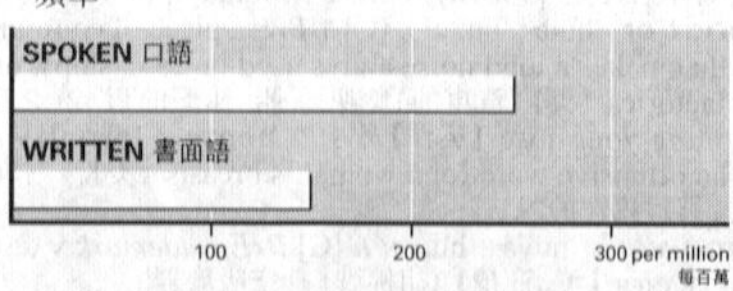

Based on the British National Corpus and the Longman Lancaster Corpus 據英國國家語料庫和朗文蘭卡斯特語料庫

This graph shows that the verb **hope** is much more common in spoken English than in written English. This is because it is used in a lot of common spoken phrases. 本圖表顯示, 動詞 hope 在英語口語中的使用頻率遠遠高於書面語, 因為口語中很多常用片語是由 hope 構成的。

hope (*v*) **SPOKEN PHRASES**
含 hope 的口語片語

2 I hope (that) used to say that you hope something will happen 我希望…: *I hope you're coming to the party.* 我希望你能來參加聚會。| **I do hope (that)** *BrE* (=a polite way of saying that you hope something will happen)【英】我真希望… *It was great to see you and I do hope that we'll meet up again soon.* 很高興能見到你, 我真希望我們不久能再次見面。**3 I hope so** used to say that you hope something that has been mentioned happens or is true 希望如此!: *"Do we get paid this week?" "I certainly hope so!"* "我們這星期能拿到工資嗎?" "希望如此!" **4 I hope not** used to say that you hope something that has been mentioned does not happen or is not true 但願不會!: *I don't think I'm busy that day, at least I hope not anyway.* 我想那天我不會很忙, 至少我是這樣期望的。**5 I am hoping** used to say that you hope something will happen, especially because you are depending on it 我非常希望…: **I am hoping (that)** *I'm hoping he's going to do my car for me because I can't afford to take it to the garage.* 我真的希望他能幫我修修車, 因為我沒錢把車送到修理廠去。| **I'm hoping to do sth** *Oh what a shame! We were hoping to see you today.* 噢, 真可惜! 我們本來以為今天能見到你的。**6 let's hope (that)** used to tell someone that you hope something will happen or will not happen 但願…: *Let's just hope someone finds her bag and hands it in.* 但願有人撿到她的手提包並把它交回來。**7 I should hope so (too)** *BrE* used to say that you feel very strongly that something should happen【英】我(也)希望如此!: *"Well, they should get their money back." "I should hope so too, after being treated like that."* "啊, 他們該把錢要回來。" "我也希望如此, 他們已經吃夠苦頭了。" **8 I hope to God (that)** used to say that you hope very much that something will happen or will not happen, because otherwise there will be serious problems 上帝啊! 但願…〔表示非常希望某事發生或不發生, 否則就會有很大的麻煩〕: *I hope to God I haven't left the car window open.* 上帝啊! 但願我沒有忘了關車窗。

hope² *n* [U] 2
1 ►FEELING 感覺◄ a feeling of wanting something to happen, and a belief that it is likely to happen 希望, 期望, 盼望: **[+for]** *The people are full of hope for the future.* 人們對未來充滿了希望。| **give/offer hope to sb** (=make it possible for people to have hope) 給某人以希望 *This new treatment may offer hope to thousands of cancer patients.* 這種新的治療方法可能會給成千上萬的癌症患者帶來希望。| **lose hope/give up hope** (=stop hoping) 失去/放棄希望 *Michael's parents had almost given up hope of ever seeing him again.* 邁克爾的父母幾乎已經不指望能再見到他了。| **in the hope that** (=because you hope that something will happen) 對…懷有希望 *He showed me a picture of the missing girl in the hope that I might recognize her.* 他給我看了一張失蹤女孩的照片, 希望我能認出她。| **glimmer/ray of hope** (=something that gives you a little hope) 一線希望 *The union's offer to negotiate offered a ray of hope.* 工會提出談判, 這帶來了一線希望。| **live in hope** (=keep hoping for something) 抱有希望 *We haven't had any success yet, but we live in hope.* 我們尚未取得成功, 但我們仍抱着希望。| **not hold out any hope** (=not give someone any reason to hope for something) 不抱希望 *I'm afraid the doctors didn't hold out much hope.* 恐怕醫生們已經不抱多少希望了。
2 ►STH YOU HOPE FOR 希望發生的事◄ [C] something that you hope will happen 希望發生的事: *She told me all her secret hopes and fears.* 她告訴了我她心裡所有的期望和擔憂。| **[+of]** *hopes of fame and fortune* 對名利的期望 | **have hopes of doing sth** (=hope to do it) 希望做某事 *At one time he had hopes of playing at Wimbledon.* 他曾經一度希望自己能參加溫布頓網球賽。| **my one hope is…** *My one hope was that I would see my family again.* 我的一個希望是能再次與家人團聚。| **have high hopes for** (=hope that someone or something will be successful) 對…抱有很高期望 *the high hopes parents have for their children* 父母對子女的厚望 | **hopes are fading** (=people are beginning to lose hope) 希望正在破滅 *The search for survivors continues, but hopes are fading fast.* 尋找生還者的工作仍在繼續, 但希望越來越渺茫。| **pin your hopes on** (=hope that something will happen because all your plans depend on it) 將希望寄託於 *I can't pin my hopes on getting this job.* 我不能指望能獲得這份工作。—see 見 WISH (USAGE)
3 raise/dash sb's hopes to make someone's hopes seem more likely, or make them seem impossible 使某人抱有希望/使某人的希望破滅: *Sally's hopes of meeting someone nice were dashed again.* 莎莉遇上好人的希望又一次破滅了。
4 get/build sb's hopes up to make someone's hopes seem more likely, or to feel that your hopes are more likely to happen 使某人抱有希望: *I don't want to get your hopes up, but I know you're a favorite for the part.* 我不想讓你存有過高的期望, 但我知道你是最有希望擔任這一角色的人選。
5 ►CHANCE 機會◄ [C,U] a chance of succeeding or of something good happening 機會, 可能性: **[+of]** *There*

was no hope of escape. 沒有逃脱的希望了。| **hope that** *There is some hope that we'll find a solution to our problems.* 我們還有一點希望能找到解決問題的方法。| **not a hope!** *spoken* (=used to mean that there is no chance of something happening)【口】沒希望！不可能！*"Do you think they'll refund our money?" "Not a hope!"* "你認為他們會把錢退給我們嗎？" "不可能！" | **not a hope in hell** *spoken* (=not even the smallest chance of success)【口】甚麼希望也沒有！*They don't have a hope in hell of winning this game.* 他們壓根兒沒有希望打贏這場比賽。| **some hope/what a hope!** *BrE spoken humorous* (=used to say that there is no chance that something will happen)【英口, 幽默】沒希望！妄想！*"Your dad might lend you the car." "Some hope!"* "你父親也許會把車借給你。" "不可能！"

6 there's hope for you yet! *spoken* used to say that someone could still be successful, often in a joking way【口】還有希望！

7 be sb's last/only hope to be someone's last or only chance of getting the result they want 是某人最後/唯一的希望: *For many people who couldn't find work, the colonies were the last hope.* 對很多找不到工作的人來説, 去殖民地是他們最後的希望。

8 be beyond hope if a situation is beyond hope it is so bad that there is no chance of any improvement 沒有好轉的希望, 無可救藥: [+of] *Some of these patients are beyond hope of recovery.* 有些病人已經沒有痊癒的希望了。

hope chest /ˈ· ·/ *n* [C] *AmE* things needed for starting a home that young women used to collect before getting married【美】〔女子結婚前準備的〕嫁妝; BOTTOM DRAWER *BrE*【英】

hope·ful¹ /ˈhopfəl; ˈhəʊpfəl/ *adj* **1** believing that what you hope for is likely to happen 抱有希望的, 抱樂觀態度的: [+about] *Everyone's feeling pretty hopeful about the future.* 人人都對未來充滿希望。| **hopeful that** *We're hopeful that the team will be fit for next Saturday's game.* 我們有信心球隊能以良好的狀態參加下星期六的比賽。| **be hopeful of doing sth** *BrE*【英】*The police are hopeful of finding more clues to the murder.* 警方有望找到更多有關這宗謀殺案的線索。**2** *informal* making you feel that what you hope for is likely to happen【非正式】給人以希望的: *Things might get better, but it doesn't look very hopeful right now.* 事情可能會好轉, 但目前看來希望不大。—**hopefulness** *n* [U]

hopeful² *n* [C] someone who is hoping to be successful, especially in acting, music etc〔尤指演藝、音樂界等〕希望獲得成功的人: **young hopefuls** *hundreds of young hopefuls waiting to be auditioned* 幾百個等候試演的希望成名的年輕人

1 **hope·ful·ly** /ˈhopfəlɪ; ˈhəʊpfəli/ *adv* **1** [sentence adverb 句子副詞] used when you are saying what you hope will happen 如果順利的話, 可望…: *Hopefully we can solve the problem.* 如果順利的話, 我們可望解決這個問題。**2** in a way that shows that you are hopeful 懷有希望地, 充滿希望地: *"Will there be any food left over?" he asked hopefully.* 他滿懷希望地問道: "會有剩下的食物嗎？"

3 **hope·less** /ˈhoplɪs; ˈhəʊpləs/ *adj* **1** a hopeless situation is so bad that there is no chance of success or improvement 沒有希望(好轉)的: **be in a hopeless mess/state/condition** *The economy is in a hopeless mess.* 經濟已經無可救藥了。**2** if something that you try to do is hopeless, there is no possibility of it being successful 沒有成功可能的, 無望的: **it is hopeless** *We tried to stop the flames from spreading, but we knew it was hopeless.* 我們試圖阻止火勢蔓延, 但知道這是不可能的。| *a hopeless task* 不可能成功的任務 **3** *informal* very bad at doing something【非正式】糟透的, 不行的, 無能的: *a hopeless cook* 糟糕的廚師 | **be hopeless (at doing sth)** *I've always been hopeless at spelling.* 我的拼寫一向很糟糕。| *Oh, Dan you forgot the potatoes – you're hopeless.* 哎呀, 丹, 你把馬鈴薯忘了。你真糟糕。**4** feeling no hope 絕望的: *hopeless looks on the faces of the refugees* 難民臉上的絕望表情 **5 hopeless case** *often humorous* someone who cannot be helped【常幽默】無藥可救的人: *He had power to cure even hopeless cases.* 他甚至能治癒沒有希望的病人。—**hopelessness** *n* [U]

hope·less·ly /ˈhoplɪslɪ; ˈhəʊpləsli/ *adv* **1** used when emphasizing how bad a situation is, and saying that it will not get better 沒有希望地, 無望地; 完全地: *We found ourselves hopelessly outnumbered by the enemy.* 我們發現敵人的人數已經遠遠超過了我們。**2 be hopelessly in love** to have very strong feelings of love for someone 愛得不可自拔 **3** feeling that you have no hope 絕望地: *staring hopelessly into space* 兩眼絕望地盯着空中

hopped-up /ˌ· ˈ·◂/ *adj AmE slang*【美俚】**1** happy and excited, especially because of the effects of drugs〔尤指因吸毒而〕興奮的, 亢奮的 **2** a hopped-up car, engine etc has been made much more powerful〔汽車、引擎等〕功率增大了的, 馬力更大的: *a hopped-up Mustang* 一輛功率增大了的野馬汽車

hop·per /ˈhɑpɚ; ˈhɒpə/ *n* [C] a large FUNNEL¹ (1) 料斗, 漏斗

hop·scotch /ˈhɑpˌskɑtʃ; ˈhɒpskɒtʃ/ *n* [U] a children's game using squares marked on the ground in which each child has to jump from one square to another 跳房子〔兒童遊戲〕

horde /hɔrd; hɔːd/ *n* [C] a large crowd moving in a noisy uncontrolled way〔吵吵嚷嚷移動着的〕一大羣: **[+of]** *hordes of people milling around the station* 在車站轉來轉去的人羣

ho·ri·zon /həˈraɪzn̩; həˈraɪzən/ *n* **1 the horizon** the line far away where the land or sea seems to meet the sky 地平線: *We could see a ship on the horizon.* 我們能看見一艘船出現在地平線上。**2 horizons** [plural] the limit of your ideas, knowledge, experience〔思想、知識、經驗的〕範圍, 界限; 眼界: *narrow political horizons* 狹隘的政治見解 | **broaden/expand sb's horizons** *a course of study that will broaden your horizons* 一個能開闊眼界的課程 **3 be on the horizon** to seem likely to happen in the future 將要發生: *Business is good now, but there are a few problems on the horizon.* 目前的生意很好, 但有幾個問題已初露端倪了。

hor·i·zon·tal¹ /ˌhɑrəˈzɑntl̩; ˌhɒrɪˈzɒntl◂/ *adj* flat and level 水平的: *a horizontal surface* 水平面 —**horizontally** *adv* —opposite 反義詞 VERTICAL¹ —compare 比較 DIAGONAL —see picture at 參見 VERTICAL¹ 圖

horizontal² *n* **1** [C] a horizontal line or surface 水平線; 水平面 **2 the horizontal** a horizontal position 水平位置

hor·mone /ˈhɔrmon; ˈhɔːməʊn/ *n* [C] a chemical substance produced by your body that influences your body's growth, development and condition 激素, 荷爾蒙 —**hormonal** /hɔrˈmonl̩; hɔːˈməʊnəl/ *adj*

hormone re·place·ment ther·a·py /ˌ· · ˈ· · · ·/ *n* [U] a treatment for women during or after the MENOPAUSE, that adds hormones to the body〔婦女更年期的〕激素[荷爾蒙]補充治療法

horn¹ /hɔrn; hɔːn/ *n*

1 ►OF AN ANIMAL 動物的◄ [C] one of the pair of hard pointed parts that grow on the heads of cows, goats, and other animals〔牛、羊等頭上的〕角

2 ►SUBSTANCE 物質◄ [U] **a)** the substance that animals' horns are made of 角質: *a knife with a horn handle* 一把有角質柄的刀 **b)** [C] a part of an animal's head that stands out like a horn, for example on a SNAIL〔蝸牛等頭上的〕觸角

3 ►ON A CAR 汽車上◄ [C] the thing in a vehicle that is used to make a loud sound as a signal or warning 喇叭: **blow/sound your horn** (=make a noise with your horn) 鳴喇叭, 按喇叭 —see picture on page A2 參見A2頁圖

4 ►MUSICAL INSTRUMENT 樂器◄ [C] **a)** one of several musical instruments that consist of a long metal tube, wide at one end, that you play by blowing〔樂器中的〕號 **b)** a musical instrument made from an animal's horn 號角 —see also 另見 ENGLISH HORN, FRENCH HORN, POST HORN

5 drinking horn/powder horn etc a container in the shape of an animal's horn, used in the past for drinking from, carrying GUNPOWDER etc 角製[形]酒杯／火藥盒

6 draw/pull in your horns to reduce the amount of money you spend 減少開支

7 be on the horns of a dilemma to be in a situation in which you have to choose between two unpleasant or difficult situations 進退維谷, 左右為難 —see also 另見 **blow your own trumpet/horn** (BLOW¹ (21)), **take the bull by the horns** (BULL¹ (3)), **lock horns with sb (over sth)** (LOCK¹ (6))

horn² *v AmE*【美】

horn in *phr v* [I] to interrupt or try to take part in something when you are not wanted 強行參加, 闖入, 侵入: [+on] *He horned in on my date.* 我跟別人約會時他硬插進來。

horn·bill /ˈhɔrnˌbɪl; ˈhɔːnˌbɪl/ *n* [C] a tropical bird with a very large beak 犀鳥

horned /hɔrnd; hɔːnd/ *adj* having horns or something that looks like horns 有角的; 有角狀物的: *horned cattle* 有角的牛

hor·net /ˈhɔrnɪt; ˈhɔːnɪ̈t/ *n* [C] **1** a large black and yellow insect that can sting 大黃蜂 **2 stir up a hornet's nest** to cause a lot of trouble and quarrelling without intending to 捅馬蜂窩, 惹大麻煩

horn of plen·ty /ˌ· · ˈ··/ *n* [C] a CORNUCOPIA (1)〔象徵豐饒的〕角飾, 角狀盛器

horn·pipe /ˈhɔrnˌpaɪp; ˈhɔːnpaɪp/ *n* [C] a traditional dance performed by SAILORS or the music for this dance〔水手跳的〕角笛舞(曲)

horn-rimmed /ˌ· ˈ·◂/ *adj* horn-rimmed SPECTACLES have frames made of plastic that is made to look like horn〔眼鏡〕仿角質框的

horn·y /ˈhɔrnɪ; ˈhɔːni/ *adj* **1** made of a hard substance, such as horn 角製的, 角質的, 硬質的 **2** skin that is horny is hard and rough〔皮膚〕粗硬的 **3** *informal* sexually excited【非正式】性興奮的, 慾火中燒的: *feeling horny* 感到慾火中燒 **4** *informal* sexually attractive【非正式】性感的: *I think he's horny.* 我覺得他很性感。

hor·o·scope /ˈhɔrəˌskop; ˈhɒrəskəʊp/ *n* [C] a description of your character and the things that will happen to you, based on the position of the stars or PLANETS at the time of your birth 根據占星術算命, 星象

hor·ren·dous /hɔˋrɛndəs; hɒˈrendəs/ *adj* **1** frightening and terrible 可怕的, 駭人的: *a horrendous experience* 可怕的經歷 **2** *spoken* extremely unreasonable or unpleasant【口】極不像話的, 極討厭的: *horrendous prices* 嚇人的價格 —**horrendously** *adv*

hor·ri·ble /ˈhɔrəbl; ˈhɒrɪ̈bəl/ *adj* **1** very unpleasant and often frightening or upsetting 可怕的, 嚇人的, 令人恐懼的: *a horrible murder* 恐怖的謀殺案 **2** *spoken* very bad or unpleasant【口】糟糕的, 令人不快的, 極討厭的: *horrible weather* 糟糕的天氣 | *I have a horrible feeling we're going to miss the plane.* 我有一個不祥的預感, 我們會趕不上這班飛機。**3** *spoken* rude and unfriendly【口】粗魯的, 不友好的: *What a horrible man.* 多麼粗魯的男人! —**horribly** *adv*: *Her face was horribly scarred.* 她的臉上有難看的疤。

hor·rid /ˈhɔrɪd; ˈhɒrɪ̈d/ *adj informal especially BrE*【非正式, 尤英】**1** very unpleasant 令人非常不快的, 令人討厭的: *a horrid smell* 極難聞的氣味 **2** behaving in a nasty unkind way 極不友好的: *Don't be so horrid!* 別那麼兇! —**horridly** *adv*

hor·rif·ic /hɔˋrɪfɪk; hɒˈrɪfɪk/ *adj* extremely bad, especially in a way that is frightening or upsetting 令人恐懼的, 可怕的, 恐怖的: *horrific accidents* 可怕的事故 —**horrifically** /-klɪ; -kli/ *adv*

hor·ri·fy /ˈhɔrəˌfaɪ; ˈhɒrɪ̈faɪ/ *v* [T] to make someone feel very shocked and upset or afraid 使震驚, 使害怕, 使毛骨悚然: **horrified to see/hear etc** *We were horrified to see children living in such terrible conditions.* 看到孩子們生活在如此惡劣的環境中, 我們都感到震驚。—**horrifying** *adj*: *horrifying news* 可怕的消息 —**horrifyingly** *adv*

hor·ror /ˈhɔrɚ; ˈhɒrə/ *n* **1** [U] a strong feeling of shock and fear 驚恐; 震驚: *The crowd gasped in horror as Senna's car crashed.* 冼拿的車撞毀時, 人羣嚇得屏住了氣。| **to sb's horror** (=making someone shocked or

horse 馬

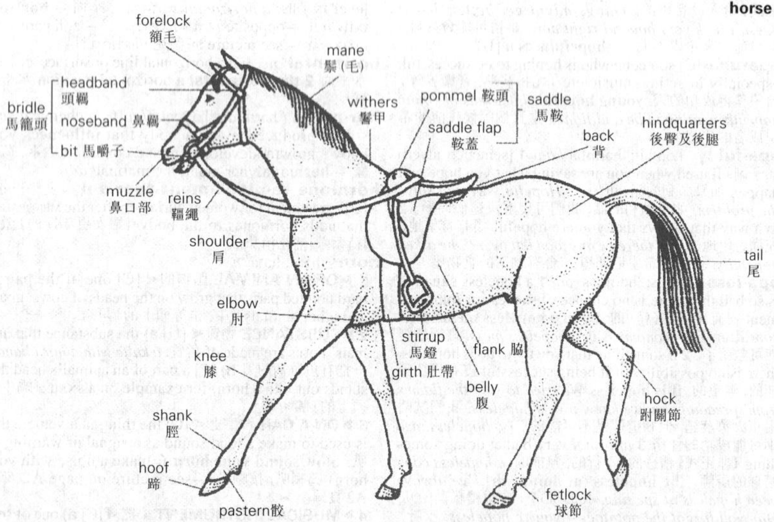

afraid) 使某人震驚地, 使某人恐懼地 *To her horror, Rachel realized her savings account had been cleaned out.* 雷切爾震驚地發現自己的存款已被提空。**2** [C] something that is very terrible, shocking, or frightening 令人驚恐的事: *the horrors of modern warfare* 現代戰爭的恐怖 **3 have a horror of** to be very frightened of something or dislike it very much 非常懼怕; 憎惡, 討厭: *He has a horror of snakes.* 他非常怕蛇。**4 give sb the horrors** to make someone feel unreasonably frightened or nervous 令某人感到非常恐懼[緊張] **5 little horror** *especially BrE* a young child who behaves badly【尤英】淘氣鬼, 討厭鬼〔指小孩子〕**6** [C] something that is extremely ugly 極醜陋的東西

horror film /ˈ‥ ˌ‥/ *BrE*【英】, **horror mov·ie** /ˈ‥ ˌ‥/ *AmE*【美】— *n* [C] a film in which strange and frightening things happen, for example Dracula or Frankenstein 恐怖(影)片

horror sto·ry /ˈ‥ ˌ‥/ *n* [C] **1** *informal* a report about bad experiences, bad conditions etc【非正式】對可怕事件的報道: *horror stories about patients being given the wrong drugs* 有關給病人吃錯藥的可怕報道 **2** a story in which strange and frightening things happen 恐怖故事

horror-struck /ˈ‥ ·/ also 又作 **horror-strick·en** /ˈ‥ ˌ‥/ *adj* suddenly very shocked and frightened 大吃一驚的; 驚恐萬狀的: *He stared horror-struck as the car moved towards the edge of the cliff.* 他眼睜睜看着汽車開向懸崖的邊緣, 嚇得目瞪口呆。

hors de com·bat /ˈɔr də ˈkɑmbɑ; ˌɔː də ˈkɒmbɑː/ *adj French formal* unable to fight because you are wounded【法, 正式】〔因受傷而〕喪失戰鬥能力的

hors d'oeu·vre /ˌɔr ˈdɝv; ˌɔː ˈdɜːv/ *n plural* **hors d'oeuvres** /-ˈdɝvz; -ˈdɜːvz/ [C] food that is served in small amounts before the main part of the meal〔餐前的〕開胃小吃

3 1 **horse¹** /hɔrs; hɔːs/ *n* **1** [C] a large strong animal that people ride on and use for pulling heavy things 馬 **2 the horses** *informal* horse races【非正式】賽馬 **3 straight from the horse's mouth** if you hear something straight from the horse's mouth, you are told it by someone who has direct knowledge of it〔消息〕第一手的, 直接得來的 **4** [C] a piece of sports equipment in a GYMNASIUM used for jumping over; VAULTING HORSE 跳馬, 鞍馬〔體操器械〕**5 horse sense** *old-fashioned* sensible judgement gained from experience; COMMON SENSE【過時】常識 **6** the process of trying to reach an agreement by offering each other things in exchange for other things 討價還價 **7** [U] *old-fashioned slang* HEROIN【過時, 俚】海洛因 —see also 另見 **dark horse** (DARK¹ (9)), **never/don't look a gift horse in the mouth** (GIFT (6)), **be flogging a dead horse** (FLOG (3)), **hold your horses!** (HOLD¹ (29)), **put the cart before the horse** (CART¹ (4)), STALKING HORSE, WHITE HORSES

horse² *v*

horse around/about *phr v* [I] *informal* to play roughly【非正式】胡鬧, 哄鬧: *Stop horsing around, you'll break something!* 別胡鬧了, 你會打破東西的!

horse·back /ˈhɔrsˌbæk; ˈhɔːsbæk/ *n* **on horseback** riding a horse 騎着馬 —**horseback** *adj*

horse·box /ˈhɔrsˌbɑks; ˈhɔːsbɒks/ *n* [C] *BrE* a large vehicle for carrying horses, often pulled by another vehicle【英】運馬拖車, 運馬棚車; HORSE TRAILER *AmE*【美】

horse chest·nut /ˌ· ˈ‥/ *n* [C] **1** a large tree which produces shiney brown nuts and has white and pink flowers 七葉樹 **2** a nut from this tree 七葉樹的堅果

horse-drawn /ˈ· ·/ *adj* [only before noun 僅用於名詞前] pulled by a horse 用馬拉的

horse·fly /ˈhɔrsˌflaɪ; ˈhɔːsflaɪ/ *n* [C] a large fly that bites horses and cattle〔叮咬牛馬的〕虻, 馬蠅

horse·hair /ˈhɔrsˌhɛr; ˈhɔːsheə/ *n* [U] the hair from a horse's MANE and tail, sometimes used to fill the inside of furniture 馬毛〔馬鬃或馬尾的毛〕

horse·man /ˈhɔrsmən; ˈhɔːsmən/ *n plural* **horsemen** /-mən; -mən/ [C] someone who rides horses 騎馬者, 騎手

horse·man·ship /ˈhɔrsmənˌʃɪp; ˈhɔːsmənʃɪp/ *n* [U] the practice or skill of riding horses 騎術, 馬術

horse·play /ˈhɔrsˌple; ˈhɔːspleɪ/ *n* [U] *old-fashioned* rough, noisy behaviour in which older children play by pushing or hitting each other for fun【過時】〔青少年之間的〕嬉戲, 打鬧

horse·pow·er /ˈhɔrsˌpauɚ; ˈhɔːsˌpaʊə/ written abbreviation 縮寫為 **hp** *n* [U] a unit for measuring the power of an engine 馬力〔引擎的功率單位〕

horse rac·ing /ˈ· ˌ‥/ *n* [U] a sport in which horses race against each other 賽馬

horse·rad·ish /ˈhɔrsˌrædɪʃ; ˈhɔːsˌrædɪʃ/ *n* [C,U] a plant whose root has a very strong hot taste and is eaten with meat 辣根

horse-rid·ing /ˈ· ‥/ *n* [U] the activity of riding horses 騎馬 —**horse-riding** *adj*

horse·shit /ˈhɔrsˌʃɪt; ˈhɔːsˌʃɪt/ *AmE taboo* nonsense; BULLSHIT【美諱】屁話, 廢話: *That's total horseshit!* 那完全是廢話!

horse·shoe /ˈhɔrsˌʃu; ˈhɔːʃ-ʃuː/ *n* [C] **1** a curved piece of iron that is nailed on to the bottom of a horse's foot 馬蹄鐵, 馬掌 **2** a sign of good luck in the shape of a horseshoe 馬掌形吉祥物

horse·shoes /ˈhɔrsˌʃuz; ˈhɔːʃ-ʃuːz/ *n* [U] an American outdoor game in which horseshoes are thrown at a post〔美國的〕擲馬蹄鐵套柱遊戲

horse show /ˈ· ·/ *n* [C] a sports event in which people riding horses compete to show their skill in riding 馬術比賽; 馬匹展覽會

horse trail·er /ˈ· ˌ‥/ *n* [C] *AmE* a large vehicle for carrying horses, pulled by another vehicle【美】運馬拖車, 運馬棚車; HORSEBOX *BrE*【英】

horse·whip /ˈhɔrsˌhwɪp; ˈhɔːsˌwɪp/ *v* [T] to beat someone hard with a whip 鞭打〔某人〕

horse·wom·an /ˈhɔrsˌwumən; ˈhɔːsˌwumən/ *n* [C] *plural* **horsewomen** /-ˌwɪmɪn; -ˌwɪmɪn/ a woman who rides horses 女騎手

hors·ey, horsy /ˈhɔrsɪ; ˈhɔːsi/ *adj* **1** very interested in horses and fond of riding horses 愛馬的, 愛騎馬的 **2 horsey face/appearance/smell etc** a face etc that is like a horse's 像馬的臉/外表/氣味等

hor·ti·cul·ture /ˈhɔrtɪˌkʌltʃɚ; ˈhɔːtɪ̇ˌkʌltʃə/ *n* [U] the practice or science of growing flowers, fruit and vegetables 園藝(學) —**horticultural** /ˌhɔrtɪˈkʌltʃərəl; ˌhɔːtɪ̇ˈkʌltʃərəl◂/ *adj* —**horticulturalist** *n* [C] —compare 比較 AGRICULTURE

ho·san·na /hoˈzænə; həʊˈzænə/ *n* [C] *biblical* a shout of praise to God【聖經】和散拿〔讚美上帝用語〕—**hosanna** *interjection*

hose¹ /hoz; həʊz/ *n* [C,U] **1** *BrE* a long rubber or plastic tube which can be moved and bent to put water onto fires, gardens etc【英】軟管, 膠管, 水龍帶; HOSEPIPE *BrE*【英】**2** a word meaning TIGHTS, STOCKINGS (1), or socks, used especially in shops〔尤用於商店〕連褲襪; 長統襪; 短統襪 **3** tight-fitting trousers worn by men in past times〔舊時的〕男式緊身褲

hose² *v* [T] **1** to cover something with water using a hose 用軟管澆水 **2** *AmE slang* to cheat or deceive someone【美俚】欺騙, 哄騙

hose sth/sb ↔ down *phr v* [T] to wash something or someone using a hose 用軟管沖洗: *Would you hose down the car for me?* 你幫我沖洗一下汽車好嗎?

hose·pipe /ˈhozˌpaɪp; ˈhəʊzpaɪp/ *n* [C] *BrE* a long hose【英】長軟管, 長膠管, 水龍帶

ho·sier /ˈhoʒɚ; ˈhəʊzɪə/ *n* [C] *old-fashioned* someone who sells socks and men's underwear【過時】出售襪子和男人內衣褲的零售商

ho·sier·y /ˈhoʒərɪ; ˈhəʊzjəri/ *n* [U] a general word for TIGHTS, STOCKINGS (1), or socks, used in shops and in the clothing industry 襪類〔用於商店及成衣業〕

hos·pice /ˈhɑspɪs; ˈhɒspɪs/ *n* [C] **1** a special hospital where people who are dying are looked after〔晚期病人的〕安養院, 善終醫院 **2** *old use* a house for people who are travelling to stay and rest in【舊】旅客招待所, 旅店

hos·pi·ta·ble /ˈhɑspɪtəbl; ˈhɒspɪtəbəl/ *adj* friendly, welcoming, and generous to visitors 好客的, 殷勤的, 熱情友好的: *The local people were very kind and hospitable.* 當地人十分友善、好客。—**hospitably** *adv*

2 1 **hos·pi·tal** /ˈhɑspɪtl; ˈhɒspɪtl/ *n* [C,U] a large building where sick or injured people are looked after and receive medical treatment 醫院: **in/to/from hospital** *BrE*【英】*He's in hospital, recovering from an operation.* 他手術後正在醫院裡康復。| **in/to/from the hospital** *AmE*【美】*After the accident Jane was rushed to the hospital.* 事故發生後簡被緊急送往醫院。| **be admitted to (the) hospital** (=be brought into a hospital for treatment) 被收進醫院 *A man has been admitted to hospital with gunshot wounds.* 一個受槍傷的男人被收進了醫院。| **hospital bed** (=a place in a hospital for a sick person) 病牀

hos·pi·tal·i·ty /ˌhɑspɪˈtæləti; ˌhɒspɪˈtælɪti/ *n* [U] friendly behaviour towards visitors 好客, 殷勤: *Thanks for your hospitality over the past few weeks.* 感謝你們過去幾星期的熱情款待。—see also 另見 **corporate hospitality** (CORPORATE (4))

hos·pi·tal·ize also 又作 **-ise** *BrE*【英】/ˈhɑspɪtlˌaɪz; ˈhɒspɪtl-aɪz/ *v* [T] **be hospitalized** to be taken into a hospital for treatment 住院, 留醫 —**hospitalization** /ˌhɑspɪtləˈzeʃən; ˌhɒspɪtl-aɪˈzeɪʃən/ *n* [U]

3 **host¹** /host; həʊst/ *n* [C]

1 ►AT A PARTY 在聚會上◄ someone at a party, meal etc who has invited the guests and who provides them with food, drink etc 東道主, 主人: *Our host brought in some more wine.* 主人又拿了一些酒進來。—see also 另見 HOSTESS (1)

2 ►ON TELEVISION 電視中◄ someone who introduces the guests on a television or radio programme; COMPÈRE 節目主持人: *a game show host* 遊戲節目主持人 —see also 另見 HOSTESS (2)

3 ►COUNTRY/GOVERNMENT 國家/政府◄ a country, government or organization that provides the necessary space, equipment etc for a special event 主辦者, 東道國: **host country/government/city etc** *the host city for the next Olympic Games* 下屆奧林匹克運動會的主辦城市 | **play host (to)** (=provide the place, food etc for a special meeting or event) 主辦 *Japan played host to the first World Championship Grand Prix.* 日本主辦了第一屆世界汽車錦標大獎賽。

4 a (whole) host of a large number of 大量, 許多: *a host of possibilities* 許多可能性

5 ►IN CHURCH 在教堂裡◄ **the Host** *technical* the bread that is used in the Christian ceremony of Communion【術語】〔聖餐儀式中的〕聖餅

6 ►ANIMAL/PLANT 動物/植物◄ *technical* an animal or plant on which a smaller animal or plant is living as a PARASITE【術語】寄主, 宿主〔寄生物所寄生的動物或植物〕

7 ►ARMY 軍隊◄ *old use* an army【舊】部隊: *the approaching host* 逐漸逼近的軍隊

8 *old use* a man in charge of a hotel【舊】旅館老闆

host² *v* [T] **1** to provide the place and everything that is needed for an organized event 主辦, 作...的東道主: *Which country is going to host the next World Cup?* 哪個國家將主辦下一屆世界盃? **2** to be the host on a radio or television programme 做〔廣播或電視的〕節目主持人: *a chat show hosted by Oprah Winfrey* 歐普拉·溫弗里主持的清談節目

hos·tage /ˈhɑstɪdʒ; ˈhɒstɪdʒ/ *n* [C] **1** someone who is kept as a prisoner by an enemy so that the other side will do what the enemy demands 人質: **hold sb hostage** (=keep someone as a hostage) 把某人扣作人質 *The group are holding three western tourists hostage.* 這夥人把三名西方遊客挾持作人質。| **take sb hostage** (=seize someone and use them as a hostage) 抓走某人作人質 *the aid-worker who was taken hostage by a rebel militia* 被叛軍抓去當人質的救護人員 **2 give hostages to fortune** to take a risk that may bring trouble in the future, especially by making promises〔尤指因作出許諾而〕承擔風險

hos·tel /ˈhɑstl; ˈhɒstl/ *n* [C] **1** somewhere where people, especially people living away from home, can stay and eat fairly cheaply〔為外地人提供廉價食宿的〕旅舍, 招待所 **2** a YOUTH HOSTEL 青年旅舍 **3** a place where people who have no homes can stay 無家可歸者收容所

hos·tel·ler also 又作 **hosteler** *AmE*【美】/ˈhɑstlə; ˈhɒstələ/ *n* [C] someone travelling from one YOUTH HOSTEL to another 投宿青年旅舍的旅行者

hos·tel·ry /ˈhɑstlrɪ; ˈhɒstəlri/ *n* [C] **1** *old use* a hotel【舊】旅館, 旅店 **2** *BrE humorous* a PUB【英, 幽默】酒館, 酒吧

host·ess /ˈhostɪs; ˈhəʊstɪs/ *n* [C] **1** a woman at a party, meal etc who has invited all the guests and provides them with food, drink etc〔聚會的〕女主人 **2** a woman who introduces the guests on a television or radio show〔廣播或電視節目的〕女主持人 **3** a woman who shows people to seats in a restaurant in the US〔美國飯館裡的〕女領座員; 女侍應

hos·tile /ˈhɑstl; ˈhɒstaɪl/ *adj* **1** angry and deliberately unfriendly towards someone and ready to argue with them 懷有敵意的, 敵對的, 不友善的: *The President was given a hostile reception by a crowd of angry farmers.* 總統受到一羣憤怒的農民很不友好的接待。**2** opposing a plan or idea very strongly 強烈反對的: **[+to/towards]** *Senator Lydon was openly hostile to our proposals.* 萊登參議員公開反對我們的建議。**3** belonging to an enemy 敵人的, 敵方的: *hostile territory* 敵方領土 **4 hostile environment** conditions that are difficult to live in or exist in 逆境, 艱苦的條件

hos·til·i·ty /hɑsˈtɪlətɪ; hɒˈstɪlɪti/ *n* **1** [U] a feeling or attitude that is extremely unfriendly 敵意, 敵對態度: **[+towards/between]** *hostility towards foreigners* 對外國人的敵意 | **open hostility** (=hostility that is clearly shown) 公開的敵意 **2** [U] strong or angry opposition to a plan or idea 強烈的反對: *The reform program was greeted with hostility by conservatives.* 改革方案遭到保守派人士的強烈反對。**3 hostilities** [plural] *formal* acts of fighting【正式】戰鬥, 戰爭: *a cessation of hostilities* 休戰

hos·tler /ˈhɑslə; ˈɒslə/ *n* [C] the usual American spelling of OSTLER ostler的一般美式拼法

1 2 **hot¹** /hɑt; hɒt/ *adj* **hotter, hottest**

① HIGH TEMPERATURE 高溫	⑤ POPULAR 受歡迎的
② HOT TASTE 辣味	⑥ FOLLOWING CLOSELY 緊隨
③ DIFFICULT TO DEAL WITH 棘手的	⑦ OTHER SENSES 其他意思
④ ANGRY 憤怒的	

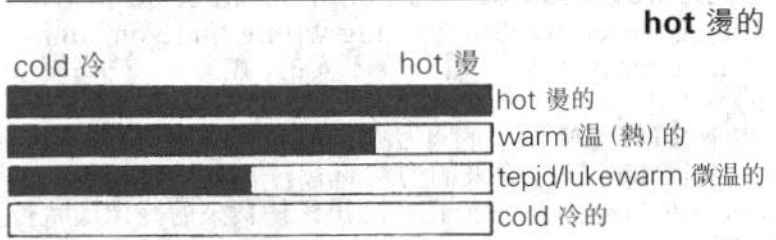

① **HIGH TEMPERATURE** 高温

1 ►WEATHER/FOOD/LIQUID ETC 天氣/食物/液體等◄ having a high temperature 熱的, 燙的; 炎熱的: *It's too hot in here – shall I open a window?* 這裡太熱了, 要開窗嗎? | *a nice hot bath* 舒服的熱水浴 | *How hot is the water?* 水有多熱? | *the hottest summer I can remember* 我記憶中最炎熱的一個夏天 | *hot countries* 熱帶國家 | **red hot** (=used to describe an object or surface that is very hot) 〔物體或表面〕熾熱的, 赤熱的 | **white hot** (=used to describe metal that is extremely hot) 〔金屬〕白熱的 | **boiling/broiling/scorching/baking/roasting hot** (=used to describe weather that is extremely hot) 〔天氣〕炙熱的, 火熱的 *a scorching hot day in August* 八月裡炙熱的一天 | **boiling/scalding hot** (=used to describe liquid that is extremely hot) 〔液體〕滾燙的 | **piping hot** (=used to describe food or water that is nice and hot) 〔食物、水〕熱騰騰的; 滾燙的 *Pour the sauce over the pasta and serve piping hot.* 將醬汁澆在意大利粉上, 趁熱上桌。| **burning hot** (=used to describe the sun or a surface when it is extremely hot) 〔太陽或表面〕炙熱的, 灼熱的 *the burning hot sands of the desert* 沙漠中炙熱的沙子 | **stifling/sweltering hot** *informal* (=used to describe weather or places that are uncomfortably hot) 【非正式】〔天氣或地方〕悶熱的, 熱得令人發昏的 | **be hot as hell** *informal* (=used to describe a place that is extremely hot) 【非正式】〔地方〕熱死人的

2 ►FEELING HOT 感覺熱◄ [not before noun 不用於名詞前] feeling hot in a way that is uncomfortable 〔感覺〕熱的, 熱乎乎的: *I was hot and tired at the end of the day.* 一天結束時我覺得又熱又累。—see 見 COLD (USAGE)

② **HOT TASTE** 辣味

3 food that tastes hot contains pepper etc and has a burning taste 〔食物〕辣的, 辛辣的

③ **DIFFICULT TO DEAL WITH** 棘手的

4 hot issue/topic etc a subject that people disagree strongly about 有爭議的熱門話題: *Abortion is a hot issue on both sides of the Atlantic.* 人工流產在大西洋兩岸都是一個具爭議性的熱門話題。

5 be too hot to handle if a problem or situation is too hot to handle it is impossible to deal with because it is causing too much trouble and anger 〔問題〕太棘手: *The Watergate investigation eventually became too hot to handle.* 對水門事件的調查最終變得不可收拾。

6 be a hot potato *informal* if a subject or problem is a hot potato, it is difficult to deal with 【非正式】是棘手的問題

7 ►DIFFICULT/UNPLEASANT SITUATION 困境◄ [not before noun 不用於名詞前] *informal* if a situation or place becomes too hot for someone, it is because other people are angry with them 【非正式】棘手的, 難辦的: *When things got too hot for him he sold up and left town.* 當問題變得十分難辦時, 他便賣掉全部家當離開了鎮。| **make it hot for** (=cause a lot of trouble for someone) 使〔某人〕難以應付, 讓〔某人〕日子不好過

8 get into hot water to get into a difficult situation by doing something wrong 〔因做錯事而〕陷入困境

④ **ANGRY** 憤怒的

9 hot temper someone who has a hot temper becomes angry very easily 火暴脾氣, 急脾氣 —see also 另見 HOT-TEMPERED

10 get hot under the collar *spoken* to become angry and ready to quarrel 【口】惱怒的, 氣沖沖的

⑤ **POPULAR** 受歡迎的

11 *informal* popular at a particular point in time 【非正式】受歡迎的, 紅極一時的: *Bros was a really hot group a few years ago.* 布洛斯樂隊幾年前紅極一時。| **hot property** (=an actor, singer etc that many theatre or film companies want) 當紅明星 *Michael Jackson soon became the hottest property in show business.* 米高積遜很快便成了演藝界最搶手的明星。

12 be a hot ticket *AmE* to be a very popular and fashionable person whom everyone wants to see 【美】成為紅人: *Jodie Foster seems to be this year's hot ticket.* 茱迪·科士打看來是今年當紅的影星。

⑥ **FOLLOWING CLOSELY** 緊隨

13 in hot pursuit following someone quickly, and closely because you want to catch them 〔因想抓住某人而〕緊追其後, 窮追不捨: *The car sped away with the police in hot pursuit.* 汽車飛馳而去, 警察則在後面緊追不捨。

14 be hot on sb's trail/track to be close to and likely to catch someone you have been chasing 緊緊追蹤某人, 快要逮住某人

15 be hot on sb's heels to be very close behind someone 緊隨某人之後: *Jake came sprinting towards me with Mrs Bass's dog hot on his heels.* 傑克向我衝過來, 後面緊跟着巴斯太太的狗。

16 come hot on the heels of to happen very soon after another event 緊接…之後發生

⑦ **OTHER SENSES** 其他意思

17 ►GOOD AT STH 擅長於◄ *informal* very good at doing something 【非正式】十分擅長於某事: *a hot new guitar player* 優秀的新結他手

18 be hot stuff *spoken* 【口】**a)** to be very good at a particular activity 是個能手: *You should see him on the tennis court – he's really hot stuff.* 你真該看看他在網球場上的表現, 他可真是名好手。**b)** to be sexually attractive 性感

19 not so hot *spoken* not very good 【口】並不怎麼樣, 不很好的: *"How are you feeling?" "Not so hot; I'm really tired."* "你感覺怎麼樣?" "不太好, 我覺得很累。"

20 be in the hot seat to have the job of making difficult and sometimes unpleasant decisions 處於須解決難題、作出棘手決策的職位上

21 be hot on sth *informal* 【非正式】**a)** to know a lot about something 通曉[熟知]某事: *I'm not very hot on European history.* 我對歐洲歷史不大熟悉。**b)** to be very strict about something 對某事要求很嚴格: *They're really hot on punctuality here.* 他們這裡對守時要求十分嚴格。

22 be hot on sb to be sexually attracted to someone 對某人表示出性慾, 迷戀某人

23 be hot at sth *informal* to be very good at doing something 【非正式】做某事拿手, 擅長於某事: *I'm not too hot at basketball.* 我打籃球不太在行。

24 ►COMPETITION 比賽◄ competition that is hot is between people or companies that are trying very hard to win or succeed 激烈的, 緊張的: *Competition for the best jobs is getting hotter all the time.* 對好工作的競爭正日趨激烈。

25 ►NEWS 消息◄ hot news is about very recent events and therefore interesting or exciting 最近的, 炙手可熱的: *a hot news item* 一條最新消息

26 be hot off the press if a newspaper, report etc is hot off the press, it has only just been printed 剛印好; 剛見報

27 hot favourite *BrE* 【英】, **hot favorite** *AmE* 【美】 a competitor that most people expect to win a race or competition 最被看好的選手, 最熱門的參賽者

28 hot tip a very good piece of advice about which horse is likely to win a race 〔有關賭賽馬的〕好建議

29 hot air if someone talks hot air, they make statements which sound impressive, but are really meaningless 大話, 空話: *It's all just hot air – he hasn't the money to pay for it.* 那全是空話, 他花不起這筆錢。
30 hot spot a) a place where there is likely to be trouble, fighting etc 可能發生動亂或戰事的地區, 多事地區 **b)** an area that is popular for a particular activity or type of entertainment〔因某項活動而〕受到人們歡迎的地區, 熱點
31 go hot and cold a) to suddenly feel very worried or frightened by something〔由於擔憂或害怕而〕感到渾身一陣熱一陣冷: *When I saw a police car outside, I went hot and cold all over.* 看到外邊的警車, 我嚇得渾身一陣熱一陣冷。**b)** to experience sudden changes in the temperature of your body because you are ill〔因生病而〕感到渾身一陣熱一陣冷 —see also 另見 **blow hot and cold** (BLOW[1] (15))
32 be hot and bothered *informal* to be so worried and confused by things going wrong that you cannot think clearly【非正式】煩躁不安的, 焦急的; 被搞糊塗的
33 ►STOLEN 偷來的◄ *slang* goods that are hot have been stolen【俚】偷來的: *He was caught trying to sell hot video recorders.* 他在企圖出售偷竊來的錄像機時被拘捕。
34 hot money money that is frequently moved from one country to another in order to make a quick profit〔在各國間頻繁流動以獲利的〕游資, 尋求短期回報的流動資金, 熱錢
35 ►MUSIC 音樂◄ having a strong exciting RHYTHM 節奏強勁的
36 ►SEXUALLY EXCITING 激起性慾的◄ a film, book etc that is hot is sexually exciting〔電影、書籍等〕色情的 —see also 另見 RED-HOT, HOTLY, HOTS

hot² *v* **hotted, hotting**
hot up *phr v* [I] *informal especially BrE* to become more exciting or dangerous with a lot more activity; INTENSIFY【非正式, 尤英】加劇, 變得激烈: *The election campaign is hotting up.* 競選活動正在熱烈起來。

hot-air bal·loon /ˈ·ˈ· ·ˌ·/ *n* [C] a large BALLOON filled with hot air used for carrying people up into the sky 熱氣球

hot·bed /ˈhɑtˌbɛd; ˈhɒtbed/ *n* **be a hotbed of** a place where a lot of a particular kind of activity, especially bad or violent activity, happens 是…的溫牀, 有利於〔壞事〕滋長的地方: *Bavaria was a hotbed of extremist politics in the 1920s and 1930s.* 巴伐利亞在二十世紀二、三十年代曾是極端主義政治的溫牀。

hot-blood·ed /ˌ· ˈ··◄/ *adj* having very strong emotions such as anger or love, that are difficult to control; PASSIONATE 熱血沸騰的, 情感強烈的, 激昂的

hot cake /ˌ· ˈ·/ *n* [C] **be selling/going like hot cakes** *spoken* to be sold very quickly and in large amounts【口】非常搶手, 非常暢銷

hot choco·late /ˌ· ˈ··/ *n* [C,U] a hot drink made with chocolate powder and milk or water 熱巧克力奶

H

hotch·potch /ˈhɑtʃˌpɑtʃ; ˈhɒtʃpɒtʃ/ *especially BrE*【尤英】, usually 一般作 **hodgepodge** *AmE*【美】— *n* [singular] *informal* a number of things mixed up without any sensible order or arrangement; MISHMASH【非正式】雜亂的一大堆東西, 大雜燴

hot-cross bun /ˌ· · ˈ·/ *n* [C] a small round sweet cake, with a cross-shaped mark on top, that is eaten just before Easter〔受難節時吃的〕十字甜麵包

hot dish /ˌ· ˈ·/ *n* [C,U] *AmE* hot food cooked and served in a deep covered dish【美】砂鍋菜餚

hot dog¹ /ˌ· ˈ·/ *n* [C] a cooked SAUSAGE in a long round piece of bread 熱狗〔用長麵包夾住熟香腸〕

hot dog² /ˌ· ˈ·/ *interjection AmE* used to express pleasure or surprise【美】〔用以表示高興或驚訝〕太棒了, 好極了

hot dog³ /ˈ· ·/ *v* [I] *AmE informal* to do a fast and exciting sport, especially skiing (SKI²), in a way that will attract a lot of attention and admiration【美, 非正式】〔尤指在滑雪運動中〕賣弄技巧: *skiers hot dogging down the slopes* 在斜坡上賣弄技巧的滑雪者

S2 W1 **ho·tel** /hoˈtɛl; həʊˈtel/ *n* [C] a building where people pay to stay and eat meals〔供住宿及用膳的〕飯店, 旅館, 旅社, 酒店

ho·tel·i·er /ˌhotəˈlɪr; həʊˈteliei/ *n* [C] someone who owns or manages a hotel 旅館老闆; 旅館經理

hot flush /ˌ· ˈ·/ *especially BrE*【尤英】, usually 一般作 **hot flash** *AmE*【美】— *n* [C] a sudden hot feeling, which women have during their MENOPAUSE〔婦女更年期時的〕潮熱, 陣發性發熱感, (熱) 潮紅

hot·foot¹ /ˈhɑtˌfut; ˌhɒtˈfʊt◄/ *adv informal* moving fast and eagerly【非正式】火速地, 急匆匆地: *We ran hotfoot to the scene of the accident.* 我們火速趕往事故現場。

hotfoot² *v* **hotfoot it** *informal* to walk or run quickly【非正式】急行, 快跑

hot·head /ˈhɑtˌhɛd; ˈhɒthed/ *n* [C] someone who does things too quickly without thinking 性急的人 —**hotheaded** /ˈhɑtˈhɛdɪd; ˌhɒtˈhedɪ̣d◄/ *adj* —**hotheadedly** *adv*

hot·house /ˈhɑtˌhaus; ˈhɒthaʊs/ *n* [C] **1** a heated building, usually made of glass, where flowers and delicate plants can grow 溫室, 暖房 —compare 比較 GREENHOUSE **2** a place or situation where a lot of people are interested in particular ideas or activities 有利於…的地方[環境]; 溫牀: *Vienna was a hothouse of artistic activity.* 維也納是藝術活動的溫牀。**3 hothouse atmosphere/environment etc** conditions in which strong attitudes and emotions develop among a group of people who are separated from ordinary people〔一羣人的〕偏激氣氛/環境等: *the hothouse atmosphere of a girls boarding school* 女子寄宿學校中的偏激氣氛

hot line /ˈ· ·/ *n* [C] **1** a direct telephone line between government leaders in different countries, which is only used in serious situations〔政府首腦之間的〕直通電話, 熱線: *the hot line between Washington and Moscow* 華盛頓和莫斯科之間的熱線 **2** a special telephone line for people to find out about or talk about something〔用於諮詢服務或討論的〕專線電話, 熱線: *Call our crime hot line today.* 今天就撥打我們的舉報罪案熱線電話。

hot·ly /ˈhɑtlɪ; ˈhɒtli/ *adv* **1 hotly debated/disputed/denied etc** discussed etc very angrily or with very strong feelings 受到激烈爭論的/有激烈爭議的/遭到強烈否認的: *The rumor has been hotly denied.* 這個流言遭到強烈的否認。**2 hotly pursued** chased closely by someone 被緊緊追蹤的: *The man ran out of the store hotly pursued by two security guards.* 那個人跑出商店, 後面有兩名保安人員緊追不放。

hot pants /ˈ· ·/ *n* [plural] very short tight women's shorts (SHORT³ (2a)) 女式緊身超短褲, 熱褲

hot·plate /ˈhɑtˌplet; ˈhɒtpleɪt/ *n* [C] a metal surface, usually on a COOKER, that can be heated so that you can cook a pan of food on it〔電爐灶上的〕烤盤, 加熱板

hot·pot /ˈhɑtˌpɑt; ˈhɒtpɒt/ *n* [C,U] *BrE* a mixture of meat, potatoes and onions, cooked slowly together【英】罐燜 (馬鈴薯) 羊肉〔或其他肉類〕; 火鍋

hot rod /ˈ· ·/ *n* [C] *informal especially AmE* an old car that has been fitted with a more powerful engine to make it go very fast【非正式, 尤美】由舊車改裝成的高速汽車

hots /hɑts; hɒts/ *n* **have/get the hots for sb** *informal* to be sexually attracted to someone【非正式】對…具有強烈的情慾

hot·shot /ˈhɑtˌʃɑt; ˈhɒtʃɒt/ *n* [C] *informal* someone who is very successful and confident【非正式】藝高而自負的人; 高手 —**hotshot** *adj*: *a hotshot lawyer* 一位自信十足的律師

hot spring /ˌ· ˈ·/ *n* [C] a place where hot water comes up naturally from the ground 溫泉

hot-tem·pered /ˌ· ˈ··◄/ *adj* having a tendency to become angry easily 性情暴躁的, 火暴脾氣的

hot tub /,· '·/ *n* [C] a heated bath that several people can sit in〔供多人共浴的〕熱水澡缸 —compare 比較 JACUZZI

hot-water bot·tle /,· '·· ,··/ *n* [C] a rubber container full of hot water used to make a bed warm 熱水袋 —see picture at 參見 BOTTLE[1] 圖

hot-wire /'· ·/ *v* [T] *slang* to start the engine of a vehicle, by using the wires of the IGNITION system【俚】用點火裝置電線短路的方法發動〔汽車〕

hou·mous, houmus /'huməs; 'huːməs/ *n* [U] other spellings of HUMMUS hummus 的另一種拼法

hound[1] /haund; haʊnd/ *n* [C] **1** a dog used for hunting 獵狗: **ride to hounds** *BrE old-fashioned* (=go FOXHUNTING)【英, 過時】去獵狐 **2** *informal* a dog【非正式】狗

hound[2] *v* [T] **1** to keep following someone and asking them questions in an annoying or threatening way; HARASS (1) (不斷) 騷擾, 煩擾: *After the court case Lee was hounded relentlessly by the Press.* 案件庭審後, 李不斷受到新聞界的無情騷擾。**2 hound sb out (of)** to make things so unpleasant for someone that they are forced to leave 不斷騷擾某人使之退出, 逼使某人離開…

[1] **hour** /aur; aʊə/ *n* [C]

[1] **1 ►60 MINUTES** 60 分鐘◄ a period of 60 minutes. There are 24 hours in a day 小時: *The flight to Moscow takes just over three hours.* 飛往莫斯科要花三小時多一點的時間。| *Karen is paid $10 an hour.* 卡倫的報酬是每小時 10 美元。| **in an hour/in an hour's time** (=an hour from now) 一小時內 *I'll be back in an hour.* 我一小時內回來。| **an hour's work/wait etc** *The system crashed and I lost three hours' work.* 系統突然癱瘓, 我白幹了三個小時。| **pay/charge by the hour** (=pay or charge someone according to the number of hours it takes to do something) 按小時付費/收費

2 ►DISTANCE 距離◄ the distance you can travel in an hour 一小時行程: **be an hour from** *We're only an hour by car from New York.* 我們離紐約開車只需一小時。| **an hour's drive/walk etc** (=a distance that takes an hour to drive, walk etc) 開車/步行等一小時的路程 *It's only about an hour's drive from here, isn't it?* 從這兒開車只有一小時的路程, 對嗎?

3 ►TIMES FOR BUSINESS/WORK ETC 營業/工作時間◄ **hours** [plural] a fixed period of time in the day when a particular activity, business etc happens〔某一活動、業務的〕(固定) 時間: *hours of business 9.00–5.00* 營業時間: 9 點－5 點 | **office/opening hours** (=when an office or shop is working or open) 辦公/營業時間 | **visiting hours** (=when you can visit someone in hospital)〔醫院的〕探病時間 | **out of hours** *BrE* (=before or after the usual working or business hours)【英】在正常工作或營業時間之外 | **after hours** (=after the time when a business, especially a bar, is supposed to close) 辦公[營業]時間之後;〔尤指酒吧〕關門後 | **lunch/dinner hour** (=the period in the middle of the day when people stop work for a meal) 午餐/晚餐時間 —see also 另見 RUSH HOUR, HAPPY HOUR

4 work long/regular etc hours if you work long, regular etc hours, the period that you work is longer than usual, always the same etc 工作時間長/固定: *the long hours worked by hospital doctors* 醫院醫生很長的工作時間 | **work unsocial hours** (=work in the evenings so that you cannot spend time with family or friends) 在晚間工作〔因而妨礙家庭或社交活動〕| **work all the hours that God sends** (=work all the time that you can) 利用一切可能的時間工作

5 ►TIME OF DAY 一天裡的時間◄ *often plural* a particular period or point of time during the day or night〔一天裡的某個〕時刻, 時間段: **the small hours** (=the period between midnight and two or three o'clock in the morning) 凌晨時分 *The celebrations went on into the small hours.* 慶祝活動一直持續到凌晨時分。| **the hours of darkness/daylight** *literary*【文】*Few people dared to venture out during the hours of darkness.* 很少有人敢在黑夜裡冒險外出。| **at this hour** *spoken* (=used when you are surprised or annoyed by something happening too late at night or too early in the morning)【口】〔因某事發生在凌晨或深夜而表示驚訝或生氣〕這種時候 *Who can be calling at this late hour?* 誰會這麼晚打電話來呢? | **unearthly/ungodly hour** *spoken* (=used when you are complaining about how early or late something is)【口】〔抱怨太早或太晚〕鬼時間/該死的時間, 不適當的時間 *We had to get up at some ungodly hour to catch a plane.* 我們得一大早就起牀去趕飛機。| **at all hours (of the day or night)** *spoken* (=at any time)【口】在任何時間, 隨時 *Our neighbours play loud music at all hours.* 我們的鄰居一天到晚不停地在高聲放音樂。| **till all hours** *spoken* (=until an unreasonably late time at night)【口】直至深夜 *She's up till all hours studying.* 她溫習一直到深夜才睡。| **keep late/regular etc hours** (=go to bed and get up at late, regular etc times) 晚睡晚起/定時作息 —see also 另見 **waking hours/life/day etc** (WAKING)

6 ►LONG TIME 長時間◄ **a) hours** [plural] *informal* a long time or a time that seems long【非正式】長時間: *We had to spend hours filling in forms.* 我們花了很長時間填表。| *I've been waiting here for hours.* 我已經在這兒等了大半天了。| **hours and hours** (=a very long time) 很長時間 *a really boring lecture – and it just went on for hours and hours* 十分枯燥, 沒完沒了的講課 **b) hour after hour** continuously for many hours 連續許多個小時地

7 within hours of only a few hours after doing something or after something happening〔某事發生〕幾小時後: *Within hours of landing, troops had started to advance inland.* 部隊登陸幾小時後, 就開始向內陸挺進。

8 ►O'CLOCK 鐘點◄ the time of the day when a new hour starts, for example one o'clock, two o'clock etc … 點鐘; 鐘點: **strike the hour** (=if a clock strikes the hour, it rings, to show that it is one o'clock, seven o'clock etc)〔時鐘〕在正點報時 | **(every hour) on the hour** (=every hour at six o'clock, seven o'clock etc) (每小時的) 正點 *There are flights to Boston every hour on the hour.* 每小時正點都有航班飛往波士頓。

9 1300/1530/1805 hours used to give the time in official or military reports and orders〔官方或軍隊使用的 24 小時計時制〕13 時/15 時 30 分/18 時 05 分

10 by the hour/from hour to hour if a situation is changing by the hour or from hour to hour, it is changing very quickly and very often〔變化〕快速不斷地, 每小時都有變化: *This financial crisis is growing more serious by the hour.* 這場金融危機正在快速加劇。

11 ►POINT IN HISTORY OR SB'S LIFE 歷史或人一生中的時刻◄ an important moment or period in history or in your life 重要時刻[時期]: **finest hour** *This was our country's finest hour.* 這是我國最光輝的時刻。| **sb's hour of need/glory etc** (=a time when someone needs help, is very successful etc) 某人需要幫助的時刻/光榮時刻 *Don't desert me in my hour of need.* 別在我需要幫助的時候拋下我。

12 of the hour of a particular time, especially the present time 某一刻〔尤指目前〕: *one of the burning questions of the hour* 目前急需解決的問題之一 | **the hero/man of the hour** (=someone who does something very brave, is very successful etc at a particular time) 當時的英雄/成功人士 —see also 另見 **the eleventh hour** (ELEVENTH (2)), HOURLY, ZERO HOUR

hour·glass /'aur,glæs; 'aʊəglɑːs/ *n* [C] **1** a glass container for measuring time in which sand moves slowly from the top half to the bottom in exactly one hour〔計時用的〕沙漏 **2 hourglass figure** a woman who has an hourglass figure has a narrow waist in comparison with her chest and HIPS〔女性的〕蜂腰體型

hour hand /'· ,·/ *n* [C] the shorter of the two pieces on a clock or watch that show you what time it is〔鐘錶上的〕時針

H

hour·ly /ˋaurlı; ˈaʊəli/ *adj* **1** happening or done every hour 每一小時的; 每小時一次的: *hourly news broadcasts* 每小時一次的新聞廣播 **2 hourly pay/earnings/fees etc** the amount you earn or charge for every hour you work 按小時計的工資/收入/費用等 —**hourly** *adv*: *The database is updated hourly.* 數據庫每一小時更新一次。

1 1 **house¹** /haus; haʊs/ *plural* **houses** /ˋhauzız; ˈhaʊzɪ̵z/ *n* [C]

1 ▶WHERE YOU LIVE 住處◀ **a)** a building that you live in, especially one that has more than one level and is intended to be used by one family 房屋, 房子; 住宅: *a four bedroom house* 一幢有四個臥室的房子 | *Why don't you all come over to our house for coffee?* 你們全都上我家去喝杯咖啡如何? | **set up house** (=start to live in a house, especially with another person) 〔尤指和另外一個人一起〕開始有自己的家 | **move house** *BrE* (=leave your house and go to live in another one) 【英】搬家, 遷居 —see picture on page A4 參見 A4 頁圖 **b)** all the people who live in a house 〔住在一幢房子裡的〕一家人: *He gets up at six and disturbs the whole house.* 他六點鐘起牀, 吵醒全家人。

2 keep house to do all the cooking, cleaning etc in a house 做家務, 料理家務

3 ▶LARGE BUILDING 大樓, 大廈◀ **a) opera house/court house etc** a large public building used for a particular purpose 歌劇院/法院等 **b) House** used in the names of office buildings 〔地名中〕大樓, 大廈: *Longman House, Harlow, Essex* 埃塞克斯郡哈洛市朗文大廈

4 hen house/coach house/storehouse etc a building used for keeping animals, goods, equipment etc in 雞舍/客車車庫/倉庫等

5 ▶COMPANY 公司◀ a company, especially one that produces books, lends money, or designs clothes 〔尤指出版社、銀行、服裝公司等〕公司, 商號, 商行: *America's oldest publishing house* 美國歷史最悠久的出版社 | *the House of Dior* 〔巴黎〕迪奧時裝公司

6 in house if you work in house, you work at the offices of a company or organization, not at home 在辦公室裡〔工作〕

7 put/set your own house in order if someone should put or set their own house in order, they should improve the way they behave before criticizing other people 〔在批評別人之前〕把自己的事管好

8 get on like a house on fire *informal* to quickly have a very friendly relationship with someone 【非正式】〔和某人〕很快成為好朋友, 一見如故

9 ▶PARLIAMENT 議會◀ a group of people who make the laws of a country 議院(成員): *The President will address both houses of Congress.* 總統將向國會兩院發表講話。| **the house** (=the house of Commons or Lords in Britain, or the house of representatives in the US) 英國上、下議院; 美國眾議院 —see also 另見 LOWER HOUSE, UPPER HOUSE

10 this house *formal* used to mean the people who are voting in a formal DEBATE when you are stating the proposal that is being discussed 【正式】(辯論後) 參加投票的議員

11 ▶IN A SCHOOL 學校裡◀ a group of children of different ages at the same school which competes against other groups in the school, for example in sports competitions 〔學校裡為進行體育比賽等而分的〕組

12 ▶THEATRE 劇院◀ **a)** the part of a theatre, cinema etc where people sit 觀眾席: **full/packed/empty house** (=a large or small AUDIENCE) 滿座/空場 *The show has been playing to packed houses since it opened.* 該演出自開演以來場場爆滿。—see also 另見 HOUSE LIGHTS **b)** the people who have come to watch a performance; AUDIENCE 觀眾 **c)** a performance that is one of a series during the day 演出場次

13 be on the house if drinks or meals are on the house you do not have to pay for them because they are provided free by the owner of the bar, restaurant etc 由店家出錢, 免費招待

14 house wine ordinary wine that is provided by a restaurant to be drunk with meals 〔餐館裡供應的〕佐餐用葡萄酒: *A glass of house red, please.* 請來一杯貴店供佐餐用的紅葡萄酒。

15 go all round the houses *BrE* to go through an unnecessarily complicated process in order to do something or answer something 【英】兜圈子, 繞彎子

16 ▶ROYAL FAMILY 王室◀ an important family, especially a royal family 〔尤指〕王室, 王朝, 皇族: *the House of Windsor* 温莎王室 —see also 另見 COUNCIL HOUSE, **eat sb out of house and home** (EAT (4)), OPEN HOUSE, PUBLIC HOUSE, **(as) safe as houses** (SAFE¹ (5))

17 bring the house down to make a lot of people laugh, especially when you are acting in a theatre 〔尤指戲劇表演〕博得滿堂喝采

house² /hauz; haʊz/ *v* [T] **1** to provide someone with a place to live 讓…居住, 給…提供住房: *The refugees are being housed in temporary accommodation.* 難民被安置在臨時住房裡。**2** if a building houses something, it is kept there 收藏; 存放: *The library is currently housed in the British Museum.* 該圖書館現設在大英博物館中。

house ar·rest /ˈ·· ,·/ *n* **be under house arrest** to be told that you must stay inside your house by the government 軟禁

house·boat /ˋhaus͵bot; ˈhaʊsbəʊt/ *n* [C] a boat that you can live in 船屋

house·bound /ˋhaus͵baund; ˈhaʊsbaʊnd/ *adj* unable to leave your house, especially because you are ill or old 〔尤指因病或年老而〕出不了門的, 閉門不出的

house·boy /ˋhaus͵bɔı; ˈhaʊsbɔɪ/ *n* [C] *old use* a word which is now considered offensive, meaning a man who is employed to do general work at someone's house 【舊】〔現被視為貶義〕男僕, 家僮

house·break·er /ˋhaus͵brekɚ; ˈhaʊs͵breɪkə/ *n* [C] a thief who enters someone else's house by breaking locks, windows etc; BURGLAR 〔破門入室的〕竊賊 —**house-breaking** *n* [U]

house·bro·ken /ˋhaus͵brokən; ˈhaʊs͵brəʊkən/ *adj AmE* an animal that is housebroken has been trained not to make the house dirty with its URINE and FAECES 【美】〔家養小動物〕訓練後不在室內隨地便溺的; HOUSE-TRAINED *BrE*【英】

house·coat /ˋhaus͵kot; ˈhaʊs-kəʊt/ *n* [C] a long, loose coat worn at home to protect clothes while cleaning etc 家居便服, 〔在家穿的〕寬鬆長袍

house·craft /ˋhaus͵kræft; ˈhaʊs-krɑːft/ *n* [U] *BrE old-fashioned* DOMESTIC SCIENCE 【英, 過時】家政學

house·fly /ˋhaus͵flaı; ˈhaʊsflaɪ/ *n plural* **houseflies** [C] a common type of fly that lives in houses 家蠅, 蒼蠅

house·ful /ˋhausful; ˈhaʊsfʊl/ *n* **a houseful of** a large number of people or things in your house 一屋子, 滿屋〔人或東西〕: *We had a houseful of guests last weekend.* 上週末我們家來了一屋子的客人。

house guest /ˈ· ,·/ *n* [C] a friend or relative who is staying in your house for a short time 暫住客人

house·hold¹ /ˋhaus͵hold; ˈhaʊshəʊld/ *n* [C] *BrE* all the people who live together in one house 【英】一家人; 同住一幢房子的人

household² *adj* [only before noun 僅用於名詞前] **1** connected with looking after a house and the people in it; DOMESTIC 家庭的, 家用的, 家務的: **household goods/products/items** *washing powder and other household products* 洗衣粉及其他家用產品 | *household chores* 家務雜活 **2 be a household name/word** to be very well known 家喻戶曉, 十分出名: *Coca Cola is a household name around the world.* 可口可樂是全世界都家喻戶曉的品牌。

house·hold·er /ˋhaus͵holdɚ; ˈhaʊs͵həʊldə/ *n* [C] *formal* someone who owns or is in charge of a house 【正式】房主; 戶主; 家長

house hus·band /'· ,··/ *n* [C] a husband who stays at home and does the cooking, cleaning etc 操持家務的丈夫

house·keep·er /'haus,kipɚ; 'haʊs,kiːpə/ *n* [C] someone who is employed to manage the cleaning, cooking etc in a house or hotel 管家; 旅館勤雜工人

house·keep·ing /'haus,kipɪŋ; 'haʊs,kiːpɪŋ/ *n* [U] **1** the work and organization of things that need to be done in a house, for example cooking and buying food 家務管理, 料理家務 **2** also 又作 **housekeeping money** an amount of money that is kept and used to pay for food and other things needed in the home 家務開支, 家用錢 **3** jobs that need to be done to keep a system working properly〔維持某個系統正常運轉的〕內務工作

house lights /'· ·/ *n* [plural] the lights in the part of a cinema or theatre where people sit〔影劇院中〕觀眾席照明燈

house·maid /'haus,med; 'haʊsmeɪd/ *n* [C] *old-fashioned* a female servant who cleans someone's house【過時】女傭, 女僕

house·man /'haus,mən; 'haʊsmən/ *n plural* **housemen** /-mən; -mən/ *BrE* [C] someone who has nearly finished training as a doctor and is working in a hospital【英】駐院實習醫生; INTERN *AmE*【美】

house mar·tin /'· ,··/ *n* [C] a small black and white European bird of the SWALLOW² (1) family 毛腳燕〔歐洲的一種鳥〕

house·mas·ter /'haus,mæstɚ; 'haʊs,mɑːstə/ *n* [C] *especially BrE* a male teacher who is in charge of one of the houses (HOUSE¹ (11)) in a school【尤英】〔學校裡負責體育比賽某一分組的〕男督導

house·mis·tress /'haus,mɪstrɪs; 'haʊs,mɪstrɨs/ *n* [C] *especially BrE* a female teacher who is in charge of one of the houses (HOUSE¹ (11)) in a school【尤英】〔學校裡負責體育比賽某一分組的〕女督導

house mu·sic /'· ,··/ *n* [U] a type of popular music 豪斯音樂〔電子樂器演奏的一種流行音樂〕

house of cards /,· · '·/ *n* [singular] **1** a plan that is so badly arranged that is likely to fail 籌劃不周而可能失敗的計劃, 不可靠的計劃 **2** an arrangement of PLAYING CARDS built carefully but easily knocked over 用紙牌搭房子的遊戲

House of Com·mons /,· · '··/ *n* [singular] the part of the British or Canadian parliament whose members are elected by the people〔英國或加拿大議會中的〕下議院

house of God /,· · '·/ *n* [singular] *literary* a church【文】教堂, 禮拜堂

House of Lords /,· · '·/ *n* [singular] the part of the British parliament whose members are not elected but have positions because of their rank or title〔英國議會中的〕上議院, 貴族院

House of Rep·re·sen·ta·tives /,· · ··'···/ *n* [singular] the larger of the two parts of the US Congress or of the parliament of Australia or New Zealand〔美國、澳大利亞、新西蘭國會中的〕眾議院 —compare 比較 SENATE (1)

house of wor·ship /,· · '··/ *n* [C] *especially AmE* a church【尤美】教堂

house·par·ent /'haus,pɛrənt; 'haʊs,peərənt/ *n* [C] someone who looks after a group of children who live together in a special home because they have no families or need special care〔孤兒院等中的〕管理員, 舍監

house par·ty /'· ,··/ *n* [C] a group of people who stay as guests in a large country house 在鄉間別墅裡留宿的客人

house·phone /'haus,fon; 'haʊsfəʊn/ *n* [C] a telephone that can only be used to make calls within a building, especially a hotel〔尤指旅館裡的〕內線電話

house·plant /'haus,plænt; 'haʊsplɑːnt/ *n* [C] a plant that you grow indoors for decoration 室內盆栽植物

house-proud /'haus,praud; 'haʊspraʊd/ *adj* spending a lot of time on keeping your house clean and tidy 注重保持家居整潔的, 熱衷於美化家庭環境的

house·room /'haus,rum; 'haʊsruːm/ *n* [U] *especially BrE*【尤英】**1 not give sth houseroom** to not like something and not want it 不要某物, 不留存某物 **2** space in a house for a person or thing〔房子中住人或擺放東西的〕房間

house-sit /'· ·/ *v* [I] to look after someone's house while they are away〔房主外出時〕代為看管房屋

Houses of Par·lia·ment /,·· · '···/ *n* [singular] the buildings where the British parliament meets, or the parliament itself〔英國的〕議會大廈; 議會

house-to-house /,· · '·◂/ *adj* **house-to-house inquiries/survey/search etc** inquiries etc that are made by visiting each house in a particular area 挨家挨戶的詢問/調查/搜查等: *The abduction sparked a house-to-house search in the Willenhall area.* 劫持案導致威倫霍爾地區進行了一次挨家挨戶的大搜查。

house·tops /'haus,tɑps; 'haʊs-tɒps/ *n* **shout/broadcast/proclaim sth from the housetops** to say something publicly so that everyone will hear or know about it 公開喊叫/播出/聲稱

house-trained /'· ·/ *adj BrE* a pet that is house-trained has been trained not to make the house dirty with its URINE and FAECES【英】〔家養小動物〕訓練後不在室內隨地便溺的; HOUSEBROKEN *AmE*【美】—**housetrain** *v* [T]

house·wares /'haus,wɛrz; 'haʊsweəz/ *n* [plural] *AmE* small things used in the home, for example plates, lamps etc, or the department of a large shop that sells these things【美】家用器皿;〔百貨公司的〕家居用品部

house-warm·ing /'· ,··/ *n* [C] a party that you give to celebrate moving into a new house〔遷入新居後舉行的〕慶祝喬遷聚會: *Are you coming to Jo's housewarming on Friday?* 週五你去參加喬的喬遷慶祝聚會嗎?

house·wife /'haus,waɪf; 'haʊs-waɪf/ *n plural* **housewives** /-waɪvz; -waɪvz/ [C] a married woman who works at home doing the cooking, cleaning etc, but does not have a job outside the house; HOMEMAKER〔不在外工作的〕家庭婦女, 家庭主婦 —**housewifely** *adj*

house·work /'haus,wɝk; 'haʊswɜːk/ *n* [U] work that you do to take care of a house such as washing, cleaning etc 家務(勞動): *I spent all morning doing the housework.* 我整個上午都在做家務。

hous·ing /'hauzɪŋ; 'haʊzɪŋ/ *n* **1** [U] the houses or conditions that people live in 住房; 住房條件; 居住環境: *health problems caused by bad housing* 住房條件差引起的健康問題 **2** [U] the work of providing houses for people to live in 供給住房: *government housing policy* 政府的住房政策 **3** [C] a protective cover for a machine〔機器的〕外罩, 外殼, 護蓋: *the engine housing* 發動機機殼 W2

housing as·so·ci·a·tion /'·· ···,··/ *n* [C] an association in Britain, formed by a group of people so that they can build homes for themselves, or can buy homes of their own〔英國的一種以建房或購房為目的的〕住房互助協會, 房屋協會

housing es·tate /'·· ·,·/ *BrE*【英】, **housing de·vel·op·ment** /'·· ·,···/ *AmE*【美】— *n* [C] a large number of houses that have been built together in a planned way〔經規劃建造的〕住宅區

housing pro·ject /'·· ,··/ *n* [C] *especially AmE* a group of houses or apartments, usually built with government money, for poor families【尤美】〔政府出資建造供低收入家庭居住的〕住房項目, 住宅區

hove /hov; həʊv/ *v* [I] the past tense and past participle of HEAVE¹

hov·el /'hʌvl; 'hɒvəl/ *n* [C] a small dirty place where someone lives, especially a very poor person〔尤指窮人居住的〕簡陋骯髒的住處

hov·er /'hʌvɚ; 'hɒvə/ *v* [I] **1** if a bird, insect, or HELICOPTER hovers, it stays in one place in the air〔鳥、昆蟲〕盤旋;〔直升機〕懸停 **2** to stay nervously in the same place especially because you are waiting for something or are uncertain what to do〔等待或拿不定主意時〕徘徊; 走來

走去: **[+around/about]** *I noticed several reporters hovering around outside the courtroom.* 我注意到幾名記者在法庭外徘徊。**3** [always+adv/prep] to be in an uncertain state 不確定, 搖擺不定: **[+around/between etc]** *The dollar has been hovering around the 110 yen level.* 美元一直在110日圓水平上下擺動。

hov·er·craft /ˈhʌvɚˌkræft; ˈhɒvəkrɑːft/ *n plural* **hovercraft** or **hovercrafts** [C] a vehicle that travels just above the surface of land or water by means of a strong current of air forced out beneath it 氣墊船 —compare 比較 HYDROFOIL

hover mow·er /ˈ·· ˌ··/ *n* [C] a machine for cutting grass that moves just above the ground 氣墊割草機

how¹ /haʊ; haʊ/ *adv*

1 ►QUESTIONS 疑問◄ **a)** used to ask about what way or what method you should use to do something, find out about something, go somewhere etc 怎樣, 如何: *How do you spell foyer?* "foyer"這個詞怎麼拼? | *How should I dress for this job interview?* 我該如何打扮去參加這次招聘面試? | *How on earth do you manage to afford so many holidays?* 你到底有甚麼辦法負擔得起這麼多次度假呢? | *I want to know how you say 'good luck' in Japanese.* 我想知道日語怎樣說"祝你好運"。**b)** used to ask about the amount, size, degree etc of something〔數量、大小、程度〕多少: *How big is the state of Louisiana compared to England?* 與英格蘭相比, 路易斯安那州有多大? | *How many kids do they have now?* 他們現在有幾個孩子? | *How long did you live in Manchester for?* 你在曼徹斯特住了多久? | **how much?** (=used to ask the price of something)〔詢問價格〕多少錢? *How much is that sweater, the blue one?* 那件毛衣多少錢, 那件藍色的? **c)** used to ask about someone's health or about their feelings〔身心感覺〕怎麼樣, 如何: *How's your ankle this morning? Has the swelling gone down?* 你的腳踝今天上午感覺怎麼樣? 腫消下去了嗎? **d)** used to ask about someone's opinion of something or about their experience of something〔看法、經歷〕怎麼樣: *How did your exams go?* 你考試考得怎麼樣? | *How was the play?* 那齣話劇怎麼樣? **e)** used to ask about the way something looks, behaves, or is expressed〔外表、行為、表達〕怎麼樣, 如何: *How does that speech of Macbeth's end, the one about 'a tale told by an idiot'?* 麥克白的那段話是怎麼結尾的, 就是關於"傻瓜講的故事"的那段話? | *How does that song go, anyway?* 好了, 那首歌是怎麼唱的?

2 ►EMPHASIZE 強調◄ used before an adjective or adverb to emphasize the quality you are mentioning〔加強語氣〕多麼, 何等: *He was impressed at how well she could read.* 他對她有這麼高的閱讀水準感到很欽佩。| *"John's been in an accident." "Oh, how awful!"* "約翰出事了。""哦, 太糟了!" | *It depends on how busy they are whether they'll be able to go or not.* 他們能不能去要看他們有多忙。

Frequencies of the word **how** in spoken and written English 單詞how在英語口語和書面語中的使用頻率

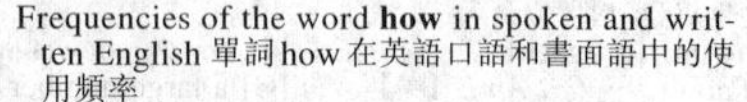

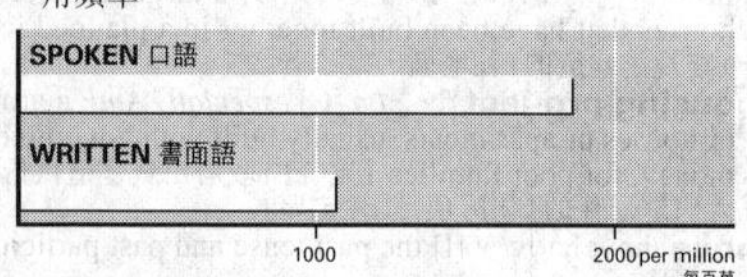

Based on the British National Corpus and the Longman Lancaster Corpus 據英國國家語料庫和朗文蘭卡斯特語料庫

This graph shows that the word **how** is much more common in spoken English than in written English. This is because it is used a lot to ask questions, is used to emphasize what you are saying, and is used in a lot of common spoken phrases. 本圖表顯示, 單詞how在英語口語中的使用頻率遠遠高於書面語, 因為該詞經常用來提問, 或用於強調説話的語氣, 而且口語中很多常用片語是由how構成的。

how (*adv*) **SPOKEN PHRASES**
含how的口語片語

3 how are you? used when you meet someone, to ask if they are well〔見面問候語〕你好嗎?: *"Hi Francie, how are you?" "Fine, thanks, how are you?"* "嗨, 弗蘭西, 你好嗎?""很好, 謝謝, 你呢?"

4 how's it going?/how are you doing? a) used when you meet someone, to ask if they are well, happy etc 你最近好嗎?/你過得好嗎?: *"Hey, how's it going?" "OK."* "嗨, 你最近好嗎?""還好。" **b)** used to ask if someone is happy with what they are doing〔詢問事情進行得是否順利〕怎麼樣: *So how's it going at work these days? Still enjoying it?* 那麼這幾天工作怎麼樣? 仍然很開心嗎?

5 how about...? a) used to make a suggestion about what to do〔徵求意見〕...好嗎? ...行嗎?: *No, I'm busy on Monday. How about Tuesday at seven?* 不行, 我星期一沒空。星期二七點行嗎? | **how about doing sth** *How about putting the sofa closer to the window?* 把沙發挪得離窗戶近一些好嗎? | **how's about** *informal especially AmE*【非正式, 尤美】*How's about going to the beach this afternoon?* 今天下午去海灘好嗎? **b)** used to introduce a new idea, fact etc that has not yet been discussed〔提及新的話題〕...又怎麼樣呢?: *"Mary and Ken are still away." "And how about Billy?"* "瑪麗和肯還沒回來。""那比利呢?"

6 how about you? used to ask someone what they want or what their opinion is, after you have said what you want or what your opinion is〔詢問某人的需求或看法〕你呢?: *I can't stand opera, how about you?* "我受不了歌劇, 你呢?"

7 how do you mean? used to ask someone to explain something they have just said〔要求進一步解釋〕你是甚麼意思?: *"What's your family situation?" "How do you mean?" "Are you married?"* "你的家庭狀況如何?""你是甚麼意思?""你結婚了嗎?"

8 how's that? used to ask someone whether something is satisfactory〔詢問是否滿意〕怎麼樣?: *How's that? Can you see now?* 怎麼樣? 你現在看見了嗎?

9 how come? used to ask why something has happened or been said, especially when you are surprised by it 怎麼會呢?〔尤表示驚訝〕: *How come Dave's home? Isn't he feeling well?* 戴夫怎麼會在家呢? 他不舒服嗎?

10 how do you do? a polite expression used when you meet someone for the first time 您好!〔初次見面時的問候語〕

11 how are things? used when you meet someone, to ask if they are well, happy etc 你好嗎? 最近好嗎?: *"Hello Peter, how are things?" "Oh, not too bad."* "你好, 彼得, 最近好嗎?""哦, 還不錯。"

12 how do you know? used to ask how someone found out about something or why they are sure about something 你怎麼知道?: *"Better bring an umbrella. It's going to rain later." "How do you know?"* "最好帶上一把雨傘, 一會兒要下雨。""你怎麼知道?"

13 how can you/how could you...? used when you are very surprised by or disapprove strongly of something 你怎麼能...?〔表示震驚或強烈反對〕: *William! How could you say such a thing!* 威廉! 你怎麼能説這種話呢?

14 how about that!/how do you like that! used to ask what someone thinks of something that you think is surprising, rude, very good etc〔徵求別人的意見〕你信嗎?: *He lost 15 pounds in a month! How about that!* 他一個月內體重減了15磅! 你説神奇不神奇?

15 how so? used to ask someone to explain an opinion they have given〔要求解釋原因〕為甚麼? 怎麼會這樣?: *"Rick's parents are a little strange, I think." "How so?"* "我覺得里克的父母有些怪。" "為甚麼?" **16 and how!** *AmE old-fashioned* an expression meaning 'yes, very much,' used to strongly emphasize your reply to a question【美, 過時】那還用說! 當然啦!: *"Was Matt drunk?" "And how!"* "馬特醉了嗎?" "那還用說!"

how² *conjunction* **1** used at the beginning of a CLAUSE (2) in which you explain the method of doing something 怎樣…, 如何…: *He has to understand that this is how we do things in this household, even if his mother does them differently.* 他必須明白, 儘管他母親有不同的做法, 但在我們家就是這麼做的。| **how to do sth** *The class teaches students how to plan a budget.* 這堂課教學生怎樣做預算。**2** used at the beginning of a CLAUSE (2) in which you introduce a fact or statement 關於…的事: *We were both traveling across Europe, and that's how we first met.* 我們倆都在環遊歐洲, 我們就是那樣認識的。| *Okay, do you remember how we discussed yesterday the Roman rule of Britain?* 好, 你還記得我們昨天談到的有關古羅馬人統治不列顛的事嗎? **3** *spoken* in whatever way【口】無論用甚麼方法: *In your own house you can act how you want.* 在你自己家裡你可以為所欲為。

how·dah /ˋhaudə; ˈhaʊdə/ *n* [C] a covered seat used for riding an elephant 象轎〔一種架在象背上供人乘坐的有蓋座位〕

how·dy /ˋhaudɪ; ˈhaʊdi/ *interjection AmE* used to say hello in an informal, usually humorous way【美】你好!〔一般為幽默用法的非正式招呼語〕

2 1 **how·ev·er¹** /hauˋɛvɚ; haʊˈevə/ *adv* **1** used when you are adding a fact or piece of information that seems surprising, or seems to disagree with what you have just said 然而, 不過, 但是: *People like this are usually harmless. They can, however, be a nuisance.* 這類人通常是無惡意的。不過他們會討人厭。| *This method has been widely adopted. However, it is not yet clear that it is the best method.* 這種方法一直被廣泛使用, 但還不能肯定這就是最好的方法。—see 見 BUT¹ (USAGE) **2 however hard/serious/long/carefully etc** it makes no difference how hard, serious, long, carefully etc 無論多難/嚴重/長/小心等: *You should report any incident, however serious or minor it is.* 有任何事你都應該報告, 不管事情是大是小。| *We'll have to finish the job, however long it takes.* 無論要花多長時間, 我們都得把這件工作做完。| **however much/many** (=it makes no difference, how much or how many) 無論多少 *I really want the car, however much it costs.* 不管那輛車多貴, 我真的很想要。**3** used to mean how, when you want to show that you find something very surprising (到底) 如何?〔表示驚訝〕: *However did he get that job?* 他到底是怎樣得到那份工作的呢?

however² *conjunction* in whatever way 不管怎樣, 無論如何: *You can do it however you like.* 你可以按自己的意思去做。| *If we win the match we'll be delighted however it happens.* 如果我們能贏這個比賽, 不管怎麼贏的我們都會高興。

how·it·zer /ˋhauɪtsɚ; ˈhaʊɪtsə/ *n* [C] a heavy gun which fires shells (SHELL¹ (2)) high into the air so that they travel a short distance 榴彈砲〔一種能以大仰角射擊近距離目標的重砲〕

howl¹ /haul; haʊl/ *v* **1** [I] if a dog, WOLF, or other animal howls, it makes a long loud sound〔狼、狗等〕嗥叫, 長嚎: *The dogs howled all night.* 那幾隻狗整夜嗥叫。**2** [I] to make a long loud cry because you are unhappy, in pain, or angry〔因悲傷、痛苦、憤怒〕不停地嚎哭; 咆哮: *the constant howling from the baby upstairs* 樓上的嬰兒不斷的哭叫聲 **3** [I,T] to shout or demand something angrily 怒吼, 大聲要求: [+for] *Right wing Republicans have been howling for military intervention.* 右翼共和黨人一直在憤怒地要求進行軍事干預。**4** [I] if the wind howls, it makes a loud high sound as it blows〔風〕怒號: *wind howling in the trees* 在林中怒號的風 **5 howl with laughter** to laugh very loudly 狂笑 **6 be a howling success** to be extremely successful 極其成功

howl sb/sth ↔ **down** *phr v* [T] to prevent someone or something from being heard by shouting loudly and angrily 大聲怒叫以蓋過…的聲音

howl² *n* [C] **1** a long loud sound made by a dog, WOLF or other animal〔狗、狼等的〕嗥叫聲, 長嚎 **2** a loud cry of pain or anger〔痛苦、憤怒的〕嚎叫, 咆哮 **3 howl of laughter** a very loud laugh 狂笑

howl·er /ˋhaulɚ; ˈhaʊlə/ *n* [C] *BrE informal* a stupid mistake that makes people laugh【英, 非正式】可笑的錯誤

how·so·ev·er /ˌhausoˋɛvɚ; ˌhaʊsəʊˈevə/ *adv literary* HOWEVER【文】不管怎樣, 無論如何

how·zat /ˌhauˋzæt; ˌhaʊˈzæt/ *interjection* used in CRICKET when claiming that a player is OUT¹ (37)〔板球比賽中宣布球員〕出局

HP /ˌ· ˈ·/ **1** an abbreviation of 縮寫= HORSEPOWER **2** *BrE*【英】an abbreviation of 縮寫= HIRE PURCHASE: **on HP** *We bought it on HP.* 我們分期付款買下了它。

HQ /ˌetʃ ˋkju; ˌeɪtʃ ˈkjuː/ an abbreviation of 縮寫= HEADQUARTERS

hr *plural* **hrs** a written abbreviation of 縮寫= HOUR

HRH an abbreviation of 縮寫= His or Her Royal Highness

HRT /ˌetʃ ar ˋti; ˌeɪtʃ ɑː ˈtiː/ *n* [U] an abbreviation of 縮寫 = HORMONE REPLACEMENT THERAPY

ht the written abbreviation of 縮寫= HEIGHT

hub /hʌb; hʌb/ *n* [C] **1** the central and most important part of an area, system etc, which all the other parts are connected to〔地域、系統的〕中心, 樞紐: [+of] *York used to be the hub of a vast rail network.* 約克曾經是一個巨大鐵路網的樞紐。**2** the central part of a wheel to which the AXLE is joined (輪) 轂 —see picture at 參見 BICYCLE¹ 圖

hub·bub /ˋhʌbʌb; ˈhʌbʌb/ *n* [singular,U] a mixture of loud noises, especially the noise of a lot of people talking at the same time〔人羣〕喧鬧聲, 嘈雜聲

hub·by /ˋhʌbɪ; ˈhʌbi/ *n* [C] *informal* husband【非正式】老公, 丈夫

hub·cap /ˋhʌbˌkæp; ˈhʌbkæp/ *n* [C] a metal cover for the centre of a wheel on a vehicle〔汽車的〕轂蓋 —see picture on page A2 參見 A2 頁圖

hu·bris /ˋhjubrɪs; ˈhjuːbrɨs/ *n* [U] *literary* great and unreasonable pride【文】傲慢, 自大, 目中無人

huck·le·ber·ry /ˋhʌklˌbɛrɪ; ˈhʌkəlbəri/ *n* [C] a small dark-blue North American fruit that grows on a bush〔產於北美的〕黑果

huck·ster /ˋhʌkstɚ; ˈhʌkstə/ *n* [C] **1** *AmE* someone who uses very strong, direct selling methods, sometimes dishonestly【美】〔有時用欺騙手段的〕強行推銷者 **2** *old-fashioned* someone who sells small things in the street or to people in their houses【過時】〔沿街叫賣或上門兜售的〕小販; 推銷員

hud·dle¹ /ˋhʌdl; ˈhʌdl/ *v* **huddled, huddling 1** [I,T] also 又作 **huddle together/up** if a group of people huddle together, they gather closely together in a group, especially because they are cold or frightened〔尤因寒冷或恐懼而〕擠作一團, 聚成一堆: *A few diehard football fans huddled together in the rain waiting for tickets.* 幾個死硬的足球迷在雨中擠作一團等買票。**2** [I always+adv/prep] to lie or sit with your arms and legs close to your body because you are cold or frightened 蜷縮着身體: *I jumped in bed and huddled under the blankets.* 我跳上牀, 在毯子下蜷着身體。

huddle² *n* [C] **1** a group of people standing or sitting close together, or a group of things placed together in a confused way 緊緊聚在一起的一羣人; 雜亂的一堆東西: [+of] *a huddle of straw huts* 雜亂的一堆茅草屋 **2** a group of players in American football who gather around one player who tells them the plan for the next part of the

H

game〔美式足球運動續賽前〕聚在一起聽取指示的一羣隊員 **3 get/go into a huddle** to form a small group away from other people in order to discuss something 私下集中商量, 進行祕密商談

hue /hju; hjuː/ *n* [C] *especially literary*【尤文】**1** a colour or kind of colour 顏色; 色調; 色度: *Her hair turned a deep golden hue in the light of the sun.* 她的頭髮在陽光下變成了一種深金黃色。**2** a type of opinion, belief etc 一種〔觀點、看法等〕: **of every hue** (=of many kinds) 各種各樣的, 形形色色的 *Political opinions of every hue were represented at the conference.* 形形色色的政治見解在大會上提了出來。

hue and cry /ˌ· · ˈ·/ *n* [singular] angry protests about something 憤怒的抗議

huff¹ /hʌf; hʌf/ *v* [I] *informal*【非正式】**1 huff and puff** to breathe out noisily, especially because you are tired〔尤因疲倦而〕氣喘吁吁: *By the time he got to the top he was huffing and puffing.* 他爬到頂時已經是氣喘吁吁了。**2 huffing and puffing** behaviour that shows that someone disagrees strongly with something such as an official plan〔某人對某事物的〕強烈反對

huff² *n* **in a huff** feeling angry or bad-tempered, especially because someone has offended you〔尤指因受到冒犯而〕生氣, 氣惱: **go off/walk off/leave in a huff** *I told her she was always late and now she's gone off in a huff.* 我説她老是遲到, 她就大發脾氣地走了。

huff·y /ˈhʌfɪ; ˈhʌfi/ *adj informal* in a bad temper【非正式】怒氣沖沖的, 氣鼓鼓的: *It's no use getting all huffy about it.* 生這麼大的氣是沒有用的。—**huffily** *adv*

hug¹ /hʌg; hʌg/ *v* **hugged, hugging** [T] **1** to put your arms around someone and hold them tightly to show love or friendship 熱烈地擁抱〔某人〕: *Jane threw her arms around him and hugged him tight.* 簡張開雙臂緊緊地擁抱他。—see picture on page A21 參見 A21 頁圖 **2** to hold something in your arms close to your chest 抱住〔某物〕: *He was hugging a big pile of books.* 他抱着一大堆書。**3** to move along the side, edge, top etc of something, staying very close to it 靠近[緊挨]…走: *The boat hugged the coast.* 小船貼近海岸航行。**4 hug yourself with joy/delight etc** to feel very pleased with yourself 沾沾自喜

H

hug² *n* [C] the action of putting your arms around someone and holding them tightly to show love or friendship 擁抱, 緊抱: **give sb a hug** *Paul gave me a big hug and smiled.* 保羅熱情地擁抱了我, 臉上充滿微笑。—see also 另見 BEAR HUG

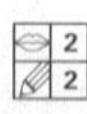

huge /hjudʒ; hjuːdʒ/ *adj* **1** extremely large 巨大的, 龐大的: *huge sums of money* 大筆的錢 | *Your room's positively huge compared to mine.* 你的房間跟我的比確實很大。**2** to a very great degree 程度很大的: **a huge success/disappointment etc** *The play was a huge success.* 這部劇獲得巨大的成功。—**hugely** *adv*: *hugely successful* 極其成功的 —**hugeness** *n* [U]

huh /hʌ; hʌh/ *interjection spoken*【口】**1** *especially AmE* used at the end of a question, often to ask for agreement【尤美】〔用於問句末尾常用作徵求對方認同〕嗯, 啊: *Not a bad little place, huh?* 這個小地方不錯, 嗯? **2** used to show that you have not heard or understood a question〔表示沒聽到或沒聽懂問題〕嗯: *"Carly, are you listening to me?" "Huh?"* "卡利, 你在聽我説話嗎?" "嗯?" **3** used to show disagreement or surprise, or to show that you do not find something impressive〔表示異議、驚訝或對某事印象平平〕嗯, 哼: *"She looks nice." "Huh! Too much make-up, if you ask me."* "她看起來挺漂亮。" "哼! 我倒覺得妝化得太濃了。"

hu·la /ˈhulə; ˈhuːlə/ *n* [singular] a Polynesian dance done by women using gentle movements of the HIPS〔波利尼西亞女子跳的〕呼拉舞, 草裙舞 —**hula** *adj*: *hula skirts* 呼拉舞裙, 草裙

hula hoop /ˈ·· ·/ *n* [C] a large ring which you make swing around your waist by moving your HIPS 呼拉圈

hulk /hʌlk; hʌlk/ *n* [C] **1** a large heavy person or thing 身材龐大的人; 龐然大物; 笨重的人[東西]: *a hulk of a man* 大漢, 壯漢 **2** the main part of an old ship that is not used any more 廢棄的舊船體

hulk·ing /ˈhʌlkɪŋ; ˈhʌlkɪŋ/ *adj* [only before noun 僅用於名詞前] very big and often awkward 大而笨拙的: *a hulking great figure of a man* 男人笨重的身體

hull¹ /hʌl; hʌl/ *n* [C] the main part of a ship 船體, 船身: **wooden-hulled/steel-hulled etc** (=having a wood, steel etc hull) 木質/鋼質等船體 —see picture at 參見 YACHT 圖

hull² *v* [T] to take off the outer part of vegetables, rice, grain etc 除去…外皮[莢、殼等]

hul·la·ba·loo /ˈhʌləbəˌlu; ˌhʌləbəˈluː/ *n* [C usually singular 一般用單數] **1** excited talk, newspaper stories etc, especially when something surprising or shocking is happening; UPROAR〔尤指對使人震驚的事件的〕激烈評論, 集中報道: *the huge hullabaloo over the film in the press* 新聞界對該影片的大肆報道 **2** a lot of noise, especially made by people shouting 吵鬧聲, 喧囂聲

hul·lo /həˋlo; hʌˈləʊ/ *interjection* [C] *especially BrE spoken*【尤英, 口】another spelling of HELLO hello 的另一種拼法

hum¹ /hʌm; hʌm/ *v* **hummed, humming 1** [I,T] to sing a tune by making a continuous sound with your lips closed 哼(曲子): *Carol hummed quietly to herself as she worked.* 卡羅爾一邊工作一邊輕聲地哼着曲子。**2** [I] to make a low, continuous sound 發出嗡嗡聲: *insects humming in the hot summer air* 炎熱的夏日空中嗡嗡飛着的昆蟲 **3** [I] to be very busy and full of activity 忙碌, 活躍: [+with] *Wall Street was humming with rumours.* 華爾街謠言滿天飛。**4 hum and haw** *BrE* to take a long time to say something etc because you are not sure what to say【英】支吾其詞, 吞吞吐吐 —see also 另見 **hem and haw** (HEM² (2))

hum² *n* [singular] a low continuous sound 嗡嗡聲; 低而持續的嘈雜聲: *the hum of bees* 蜜蜂的嗡嗡聲 | *the distant hum of traffic* 遠處嘈雜的車流聲

hu·man¹ /ˋhjumən; ˈhjuːmən/ *adj* **1** belonging to or concerning people, especially as opposed to animals or machines 人的; 人類的: *theories of human behaviour* 人類行為理論 | *The cat's eyes looked almost human.* 那隻貓的雙眼看起來幾乎像人的一樣。**2** human weaknesses, emotions etc are typical of ordinary people 普通人(特有)的: *common human failings such as greed and envy* 貪婪和忌妒等普通人的常見弱點 **3 sb is only human** used to say that someone should not be blamed for what they have done 某人只是個普通人而已〔表示不應苛求〕**4** someone who seems human shows that they have the same feelings and emotions as ordinary people 有人情味的, 有人性的: *He's really not so bad. When you get to know him he seems quite human.* 他實際上沒那麼壞。一旦你對他有所了解, 就會發現他是頗有人情味的。—opposite 反義詞 INHUMAN **5 the human touch** someone, especially someone in authority, who has the human touch deals with people in a kind, friendly way 人情味, 人性: *Senior managers have been accused of lacking the human touch.* 高層管理人員被指責缺乏人情味。**6** mistakes made by a person, rather than by a machine〔錯誤〕人為的 **7** a quality that makes a story interesting because it is about people's feelings, relationships etc〔故事〕有關人的感情的, 有關人與人之間關係的 —see 見 MAN¹ (USAGE)

human² also 又作 **human be·ing** /ˌ·· ˈ··/ *n* [C] a man, woman, or child 人〔男人、女人或小孩〕—see also 另見 MAN¹ (3)

hu·mane /hjuˋmen; hjuːˈmeɪn/ *adj* treating people or animals in a way that is not cruel and causes them as little pain or suffering as possible 人道的, 仁慈的: *Farmers will be asked to consider more humane ways of transporting livestock.* 農民會被要求考慮用更人道的方法來運送家畜。—**humanely** *adv* —opposite 反義詞 INHUMANE

hu·man·is·m /ˈhjumən,ɪzəm; ˈhjuːmənɪzəm/ *n* [U] **1** a system of beliefs concerned with the needs of people and not with religious ideas 人道主義; 人本主義 **2** the study in the Renaissance of the ideas of the ancient Greeks and Romans〔文藝復興時期〕對古希臘、古羅馬思想的研究; 人文主義 —**humanist** *n* [C] —**humanistic** /,hjumənˈɪstɪk; ,hjuːməˈnɪstɪk◂/ *adj*

hu·man·i·tar·i·an /hju,mænəˈtɛrɪən; hjuː,mænɪˈteəriən/ *adj* concerned with improving bad living conditions and preventing unfair treatment of people 博愛的; 人道主義的: *humanitarian aid to the refugees* 向難民提供的人道主義援助 —**humanitarian** *n* [C] —**humanitarianism** *n* [U]

hu·man·i·ties /hjuˈmænətɪz; hjuːˈmænɪtiz/ *n* **the humanities** subjects of study such as literature, history, PHILOSOPHY etc 人文學科〈如文學、歷史、哲學等〉

hu·man·i·ty /hjuˈmænətɪ; hjuːˈmænɪti/ *n* [U] **1** people in general 人, 人類: *30% of humanity lives in conditions of terrible poverty.* 30% 的人生活在極度貧困的條件下。**2** the state of being human and having qualities and rights that all people have 人性, 普通人具有的特性: *We must never forget our common humanity.* 我們永遠不要忘記我們共有的人性。**3** kindness, respect, and sympathy towards other people 仁慈, 博愛, 同情心

hu·man·ize also 又作 **-ise** *BrE* /ˈhjumə,naɪz; ˈhjuːmənaɪz/ *v* [T] to make a system more pleasant or more suitable for people【英】使人性化; 使仁慈: *an attempt to humanize the huge governmental bureaucracy* 使龐大的政府官僚體系人性化的努力

hu·man·kind /ˈhjumən,kaɪnd; ,hjuːmənˈkaɪnd/ *n* [U] people in general 人類

hu·man·ly /ˈhjumənlɪ; ˈhjuːmənli/ *adv* **be humanly possible a)** to do as much as anyone could possibly do 盡最大努力: *Doctors did everything humanly possible to save the child's life.* 醫生們盡了最大努力去挽救那孩子的生命。**b)** if something is humanly possible, it can be done using a great deal of effort 在人力所及範圍內, 人可以做到的: *I'm not sure it will be humanly possible to prevent the disease from spreading.* 我無法肯定人力是否可以阻止該疾病的擴散。

human na·ture /,·· ˈ··/ *n* [U] **1** the qualities or ways of behaving that are natural and common to most people 人性 **2 it's (only) human nature** used to say that a particular feeling or way of behaving is normal and natural〔感情或行為〕是正常的, 是人之常情

hu·man·oid /ˈhjumənɔɪd; ˈhjuːmənɔɪd/ *adj* something, especially a machine, that is humanoid has a human shape and qualities〔尤指機器〕具人的形狀[特性]的, 類人的: *a humanoid robot* 人形的機器人 —**humanoid** *n* [C]

human race /,·· ˈ·/ *n* **the human race** all people, considered together as a single group 人類〔總稱〕—see also 另見 MAN[1] (3)

human re·sourc·es /,·· ·ˈ··/ *n* **1** [plural] the abilities and skills of people 人力資源 **2** the department in a company that deals with employing, training, and helping people; PERSONNEL (2)〔公司的〕人力資源部, 人事部

human rights /,·· ˈ·/ *n* [plural] the basic rights which every person has to be treated in a fair, equal way without cruelty, especially by their government 人權: *flagrant human rights violations* 對人權明目張膽的侵犯

hum·ble[1] /ˈhʌmbl̩; ˈhʌmbəl/ *adj* **1** having a low social class or position〔地位〕卑微的, 低下的: **humble background/origins etc** *Iacocca rose from humble beginnings to become boss of Ford.* 亞科卡出身卑微, 後來成了福特公司的總裁。| *a humble country parson* 地位低下的鄉村牧師 **2** not considering yourself or your ideas to be as important as other people's 謙虛的, 謙卑的: *He thanked us again with a humble smile.* 他帶着謙卑的微笑再次向我們表示感謝。—opposite 反義詞 PROUD (2) **3 my humble apologies** *spoken* used to say you are sorry, but not in a very serious way【口】是我錯〔一種不太認真的口氣〕**4 in my humble opinion** *spoken* used to give your opinion about something in a slightly humorous way【口】敝人以為, 依我愚見〔略帶幽默的說法〕**5** simple and not advanced, but useful or effective 簡單而實用的: **the humble** *high-priced successor to the humble pocket calculator* 取代簡單而實用的袖珍計算器的昂貴的下一代產品 **6 eat humble pie** to admit that you were wrong about something〔低聲下氣地〕承認錯誤; 賠禮道歉 **7 your humble servant** a formal way of ending a letter, used in the past 您卑微的僕人; 卑職; 愚〔舊時信末的自謙詞〕—**humbly** *adv* —see also 另見 HUMILITY

humble[2] *v* **humbled, humbling 1 be humbled** if you are humbled, you realize that you are not as important, good, kind etc as you thought you were 使謙卑, 使感到自慚: *He felt humbled by their offer.* 他們的出價令他自慚形穢。**2** [T] to easily defeat someone who is much stronger than you are〔輕易〕擊敗〔強敵〕: *The mighty US army was humbled by a small South East Asian country.* 強大的美軍竟被一個小小的東南亞國家輕易擊敗。**3 humble yourself** to show that you are not too proud to ask for something, admit you are wrong etc 作出謙恭的姿態; 不恥下問; 勇於認錯 —**humbling** *adj*: *a humbling experience* 自尊心受挫的經歷

hum·bug /ˈhʌm,bʌg; ˈhʌmbʌg/ *n* **1** [U] insincere words or behaviour, especially pretending to feel shocked or disapprove of something 詭計, 花招; 假道學 **2** [U] *old-fashioned* someone who pretends to be someone they are not, or to have qualities or opinions they do not have【過時】騙子, 假冒者 **3** [C] *BrE* a sweet made of hard boiled sugar, usually tasting of mint (MINT[1] (2))【英】薄荷硬糖

hum·ding·er /,hʌmˈdɪŋə; hʌmˈdɪŋə/ *n* [singular] *informal* a very exciting or impressive game, performance, or event【非正式】精彩的比賽[節目, 事件]: **a real humdinger** *Foreman's next match promises to be a real humdinger.* 福爾曼的下一場比賽肯定精彩絕倫。

hum·drum /ˈhʌm,drʌm; ˈhʌmdrʌm/ *adj* boring and ordinary, and having very little variety or interest 單調的, 過於平凡的, 乏味的: **a humdrum existence/job** *a humdrum office job* 單調乏味的辦公室工作

humerus /ˈhjumərəs; ˈhjuːmərəs/ [C] *n technical* the bone between your shoulder and elbow【術語】肱骨

hu·mid /ˈhjumɪd; ˈhjuːmɪd/ *adj* weather that is humid makes you feel uncomfortable because the air feels very hot and wet〔天氣〕潮濕的: *Tokyo is extremely humid in mid-summer.* 仲夏的東京十分悶熱潮濕。—compare 比較 DRY[1] (2)

hu·mid·i·fi·er /hjuˈmɪdə,faɪə; hjuːˈmɪdɪfaɪə/ *n* [C] a machine that makes the air in a room, container etc less dry 加濕器, 增濕器

hu·mid·i·fy /hjuˈmɪdə,faɪ; hjuːˈmɪdɪfaɪ/ *v* [T] to add very small drops of water to the air in a room etc because the air is too dry 使濕潤

hu·mid·i·ty /hjuˈmɪdətɪ; hjuːˈmɪdɪti/ *n* [U] **1** the amount of water contained in the air 濕度; 濕氣: *90% humidity* 90% 濕度 **2** air or weather that is uncomfortably warm and wet 悶熱潮濕的空氣[天氣]

hu·mil·i·ate /hjuˈmɪlɪ,et; hjuːˈmɪlieɪt/ *v* [T] to make someone feel ashamed and upset, especially by making them seem stupid or weak 使蒙羞, 羞辱: *Her boss humiliated her in front of all her colleagues.* 她的老闆在所有同事面前羞辱了她。—**humiliated** *adj*: *I've never felt so humiliated in all my life!* 我這輩子從未感到過如此丟人!

hu·mil·i·at·ing /hju,mɪlɪˈetɪŋ; hjuːˈmɪlieɪtɪŋ/ *adj* making you feel ashamed, embarrassed, and angry because you have been made to look weak or stupid 使蒙受恥辱的, 丟臉的, 不光彩的: *a humiliating defeat* 丟臉的失敗

hu·mil·i·a·tion /hju,mɪlɪˈeʃən; hjuː,mɪliˈeɪʃən/ *n* **1** [U] a feeling of shame and great embarrassment, because you have been made to look stupid or weak 羞辱, 丟臉, 蒙恥: *She would do anything rather than suffer the hu-*

H

miliation of asking her parents for money. 她無論如何都不願厚着臉皮去跟父母要錢。**2** [C usually singular 一般用單數] a situation that makes you feel humiliated 使人蒙羞的情形

hu·mil·i·ty /hju`mɪlətɪ; hjuːˈmɪlɪ̣ti/ *n* [U] the quality of not being too proud about yourself 謙遜, 謙恭 —see also 另見 HUMBLE[1]

humming bird /ˈ·· ·/ *n* [C] a very small brightly-coloured tropical bird whose wings move very quickly 蜂鳥

hum·mock /ˋhʌmək; ˈhʌmək/ *n* [C] a very small hill; HILLOCK 小山丘, 岡

hum·mus, humus /ˋhuməs; ˈhuːməs/ *n* [U] a type of Greek food made from a soft mixture of CHICK PEAs, oil and GARLIC 鷹嘴豆泥〔用鷹嘴豆搗碎後加油、大蒜等製成的希臘食品〕

hu·mor·ist /ˋhjumərɪst; ˈhjuːmərɪ̣st/ *n* [C] someone, especially a writer, who tells funny stories (談吐) 詼諧的人, 〔尤指〕幽默作家

hu·mor·ous /ˋhjumərəs; ˈhjuːmərəs/ *adj* deliberately funny and entertaining, especially in a clever way 幽默的, 詼諧的: *a humorous account of her travels in South America* 對她南美之行的幽默描述 —**humorously** *adv*

hu·mour[1] *BrE*【英】, **humor** *AmE*【美】/ˋhjumɚ; ˈhjuːmə/ *n* **1** [U] the quality in something that makes it funny 幽默, 風趣: *Mr Thorne failed to see the humour in the situation.* 索恩先生看不到這種情景的幽默之處。**2** [U] the way that a particular person or group find certain things amusing〔某人或人羣的〕幽默方式: *English humour* 英國式幽默 | **sense of humour** *Ackroyd's often bizarre sense of humor* 阿克洛伊德常有的奇特幽默感 **3** [U] the ability to understand and enjoy amusing situations or to laugh at things 幽默感, 感受幽默的能力: *Paul radiated humour and charm.* 保羅全身散發着幽默感和魅力。| **sense of humour** *It's vital to have a sense of humor in this job.* 做這份工作必須具備幽默感。**4 good humour** the ability to remain cheerful, especially in situations that would make some people upset or angry〔尤指在不利形勢中的〕良好情緒: *Danny reacted to these criticisms with his usual good humour.* 丹尼以他慣常的好情緒對待這些批評。**5 in a good humour/in a bad humour etc** in a good or bad temper 心情好/壞 —see also 另見 GOOD-HUMOURED **6** [C] one of the four liquids that in the past were thought to be present in the body and to influence someone's character〔舊時認為存在於體內並會影響性格的〕四種體液之一 **7 out of humour** *old-fashioned* in a bad temper【過時】心情不好

humour[2] *BrE*【英】, **humor** *AmE*【美】*v* [T] to agree with someone even though you know they are wrong 遷就, 迎合: *I decided I'd better try and humour him, as I couldn't face another argument.* 我決定最好還是試着迎合他, 因為我不想再和他爭辯了。

hu·mour·less /ˋhjumɚlɪs; ˈhjuːmələs/ *adj* too serious and not able to laugh at things that other people think are amusing 缺乏幽默感的, 一本正經的 —**humourlessly** *adv* —**humourlessness** *n* [U]

hump[1] /hʌmp; hʌmp/ *n* **1** [C] a large round shape that rises above the surface of the ground or a surface 巨大鼓包, 圓形隆起物: *I could just make out the hump of a hill in the distance.* 我只能依稀辨認出遠處隆起的山丘。**2** [C] one of the two raised parts on the back of a CAMEL 駝峯 **3** [C] a raised part on someone's back that is caused by an unusually curved SPINE (1)〔人的〕駝背 **4 be over the hump** to have succeeded in doing the most difficult part of something 完成最困難的部分, 度過最困難的階段 **5 give sb the hump/get the hump** *BrE spoken* to make someone feel angry or upset, or to feel angry or upset【英口】使…生氣[煩惱]/生氣: *He'll get the right hump when he finds out you've drunk all his Scotch.* 一旦他發現你喝光了他的蘇格蘭威士忌, 他一定會發火的。

hump[2] *v* **1** [T always+adv/prep] *BrE informal* to carry something heavy somewhere, especially with difficulty【英, 非正式】揹, 扛, 搬運: **hump sth down/along/across etc** *I just about managed to hump the suitcases upstairs.* 我勉強將那些箱子搬上了樓。**2** [I,T] *slang* to have sex with someone【俚】與…性交

hump·back /ˋhʌmpˌbæk; ˈhʌmpbæk/ *n* [C] another form of HUNCHBACK hunchback 的另一種形式

hump-backed bridge /ˌ· · ˈ·/ also 又作 **hump-back bridge** *n* [C] *especially BrE* a short steep bridge【尤英】弓形橋, 駝峯橋

humpback whale /ˌ·· ˈ·/ *n* [C] a large WHALE 座頭鯨

humph /hʌmf; hʌmf/ *interjection* used to show that you do not believe something or do not approve of something 哼〔表示懷疑、異議〕

hu·mus /ˋhjuməs; ˈhjuːməs/ *n* [U] soil made of decayed plants, leaves etc which is good for growing plants 腐殖質, 腐質土 (壤)

Hun /hʌn; hʌn/ *n* **the Hun** *slang* an insulting word for German people, used especially during the First and Second World Wars【俚】〔第一、二次世界大戰中對德國人的蔑稱〕德國佬

hunch[1] /hʌntʃ; hʌntʃ/ *n* [C] a feeling that something is true or that something is happening, even though you have very little information about it 基於直覺的想法, 預感: *"How did you know that Campbell was a murderer?" "Oh, it was just a hunch."* "你怎麼知道坎貝爾是殺人兇手?" "噢, 那只是直覺。" | **have a hunch (that)** *I had a hunch that something like this would happen.* 我早就預感到這種事會發生。

hunch[2] *v* **1** [I always+adv/prep] to bend down and forwards so that your back forms a curve 弓起背: **[+over]** *She hunched nervously over her drink.* 她弓着背緊張地喝着飲料。**2 hunch your shoulders** to raise your shoulders into a rounded shape, especially because you are cold, anxious etc〔尤因寒冷、緊張等〕聳起雙肩 —**hunched** *adj*

hunch·back /ˋhʌntʃˌbæk; ˈhʌntʃbæk/ *n* [C] an offensive word for someone whose back has a large raised part on it because their SPINE (1) curves in an unusual way 駝背 (的人), 駝子〔冒犯用語〕

hun·dred /ˋhʌndrəd; ˈhʌndrɪ̣d/ *number* **1** 100 百: *a hundred years* 一百年 | *two hundred miles* 兩百英里 **2 a hundred times** many times 許多次: *I've told you a hundred times not to do that!* 我已經無數次警告過你不要那樣幹了! **3 a hundred per cent** *spoken*【口】**a)** completely 百分之百, 完全: *I agree with you a hundred per cent.* 我完全同意你的看法。**b)** well 健康的, 完全復原的: *I'm still not really feeling a hundred per cent.* 我覺得自己仍然沒有完全康復。

USAGE NOTE 用法說明: HUNDRED

GRAMMAR 語法

Singular and plural forms of the number words **dozen, hundred, thousand, million** and **billion** are all used in the same ways. 數詞 dozen、hundred、thousand、million 和 billion 的單、複數形式用法均相同。

When one of these words follows a word showing number or amount, it is not put in the plural and does not have *of* after it. 如出現在具體數字之後, 不必用複數形式, 後面也不加 of: *a/three/several hundred years* 一/三/幾百年 (NOT 不用 *three hundreds of years*) | *ten million people* 一千萬人 | *a few dozen eggs* 幾十隻蛋 | *about fifty thousand miles* 約五萬英里

Where there is no other word showing a number or amount, the plural is used. 如不與具體數字相連, 則用複數形式: *He has hundreds of books* (NOT 不用 *He has hundred of books.*) *It will cost thousands of dollars* (=I do not know how many thousand exactly). 他有幾百冊書。這要花費幾千美元。

hundreds and thou·sands /ˌ.. · ˈ../ *BrE n* [plural] small thin pieces of coloured sugar used to decorate cakes【英】〔蛋糕上作裝飾用的〕彩色珠子糖

hun·dredth /ˈhʌndrədθ; ˈhʌndrɪdθ/ *n* [C] **1** one of the hundred equal parts of something 百分之一 **2** 100th 第一百(個)

hun·dred·weight /ˈhʌndrədˌwet; ˈhʌndrɪdweɪt/ written abbreviation 縮寫為 **cwt** *n* [C] a unit for measuring weight equal to 112 pounds or 50.8 kilograms 英擔〔相當於 112 磅或 50.8 公斤〕—see table on page C4 參見 C4 頁附錄

hung /hʌŋ; hʌŋ/ past tense and past participle of HANG

Hun·gar·ian¹ /hʌŋˈgɛrɪən; hʌŋˈgeəriən/ *n* **1** [U] the language of Hungary 匈牙利語 **2** [C] someone from Hungary 匈牙利人

Hungarian² *adj* from or connected with Hungary 匈牙利的

hun·ger¹ /ˈhʌŋgɚ; ˈhʌŋgə/ *n* **1** [U] lack of food, especially for a long period of time, that can cause illness or death; STARVATION〔尤指長期的〕飢餓; 饑荒: *Thousands of people are dying from hunger every day.* 每天都有成千上萬人因飢餓而死亡。**2** [U] the feeling that you need to eat 飢餓感: *Babies often cry from hunger.* 嬰兒常常因飢餓而哭叫。| **hunger pangs** (=sudden feelings of being hungry) 突如其來的飢餓感 **3 hunger for** a strong need or desire for something 對…的渴求[渴望]: *the West's hunger for material wealth* 西方人對物質財富的渴求

hunger² *v* [I] *literary* to want something very much【文】渴望, 渴求: **[+for/after]** *a nation hungering for change* 渴望變革的國家

hunger strike /ˈ.. ˌ./ *n* [C] a situation in which someone refuses to eat for a long time in order to protest about something 絕食抗議 —**hunger striker** *n* [C]

hung ju·ry /ˌ. ˈ../ *n* [singular] a JURY (1) that cannot agree about whether someone is guilty of a crime〔因意見不一致而〕未能作出裁定的陪審團

hung·o·ver /hʌŋˈovɚ; hʌŋˈəʊvə/ *adj* feeling ill because you have drunk too much alcohol the previous evening 因宿醉而感到難受的, 宿醉的 —see also 另見 HANGOVER

hung par·lia·ment /ˌ. ˈ.../ *n* [C] *BrE* a parliament in which no one political party has more elected representatives than the others added together【英】各黨派勢均力敵的議會

hun·gri·ly /ˈhʌŋgrɪlɪ; ˈhʌŋgrɪli/ *adv* **1** in a way that shows you want to eat something very much 飢餓地: *J. D. ate hungrily, covering the french fries with layers of catsup.* J.D. 狼吞虎嚥, 一邊在炸薯條上澆上厚厚的番茄醬。**2** in a way that shows you very much want something 充滿渴望地: *Her gaze fell hungrily on my diamond ring.* 她的目光充滿渴求地落在我的鑽石戒指上。

3 **hun·gry** /ˈhʌŋgrɪ; ˈhʌŋgri/ *adj* **1** wanting to eat something 飢餓的: *There's tons of food – I hope you're all hungry!* 那兒有好多食物, 希望你們都已經餓了! | **get hungry** *If you get hungry between meals, have a piece of fruit.* 你如果在兩頓飯之間感到餓, 就吃一塊水果。**2** ill or weak as a result of not having enough to eat for a long time 挨餓的: *We can't justify wasting food when half the world is hungry.* 世界上有一半人在挨餓, 我們沒有理由浪費食物。**3 the hungry** people who do not have enough food to eat 挨餓的人 **4 go hungry** to not have enough to eat 吃不飽, 挨餓: *Thousands of families go hungry every day in this country.* 這個國家裡每天都有數以千計的家庭吃不飽肚子。**5 be hungry for** to want or need something very much 渴望得到…: *young people hungry for excitement and adventure* 渴望刺激和冒險的年青人 **6 power-hungry/news-hungry etc** wanting power, news etc very much 渴求權力/消息的

hung-up /ˌ. ˈ./ *adj informal* very anxious and unhappy about a situation【非正式】焦慮的, 擔心的: **[+about]** *She's really hung-up about her parents.* 她十分擔心她的父母。

hunk /hʌŋk; hʌŋk/ *n* [C] **1** a thick piece of something, especially food, that has been cut or torn from a bigger piece〔切下或撕下的〕一大塊, 一大片〔尤指食物〕: **[+of]** *a hunk of bread* 一大塊麵包 —see picture on page A7 參見 A7 頁圖 **2** [C] *informal* a man who is attractive because he is big and strong【非正式】高大健壯的男子

hun·ker /ˈhʌŋkɚ; ˈhʌŋkə/ *v* [I] *AmE* to sit on your heels with your knees bent up in front of you; SQUAT【美】蹲坐, 蹲: **[+down]** *They hunkered down by the fire.* 他們蹲坐在火邊。

hunker down *phr v* [I,T often passive 常用被動態] *AmE* to work hard to completely prepare yourself for a difficult situation【美】認真準備〔以應付艱難的情況〕

hun·kers /ˈhʌŋkɚz; ˈhʌŋkəz/ *n* **on your hunkers** sitting on your heels with your knees bent up in front of you 蹲坐, 蹲: *The little boy was squatting on his hunkers, completely absorbed in his game.* 小男孩蹲着, 完全投入於遊戲之中。

hunk·y /ˈhʌŋkɪ; ˈhʌŋki/ *adj* a man who is hunky is attractive and strong-looking〔男性〕高大健壯的

hun·ky-dor·y /ˌhʌŋkɪ ˈdɔrɪ; ˌhʌŋki ˈdɔːri/ *adj* [not before noun 不用於名詞前] *informal* a situation that is hunky-dory is one in which everyone feels happy and there are no problems【非正式】〔情況〕令人十分滿意的, 一切如意的

hunt¹ /hʌnt; hʌnt/ *v* **1** [I,T] to chase animals and birds in order to catch and kill them 追獵, 獵殺〔鳥獸〕: *At one time man had to hunt to survive.* 從前人類要以打獵為生。| **hunt sth** *hunting big game in Kenya* 在肯尼亞捕獵大型動物 **2** [I] to look hard for something you have lost 搜尋, 尋找: *We've been hunting for the car keys for the last half-hour.* 過去的半小時裡, 我們一直在找汽車鑰匙。**3** [I,T] *BrE* to hunt foxes (FOX¹ (1)) as a sport, riding on horses and using dogs【英】〔騎馬用獵犬〕獵狐 **4** [T] to search for and try to catch someone, especially a criminal 搜捕, 追捕〔罪犯〕: *Police are hunting the killer.* 警方正在追捕殺人兇手。

hunt sb/sth ↔ **down** *phr v* [T] to catch someone in order to kill, hurt, or punish them, after chasing them or trying very hard to catch them〔幾經艱苦下〕追捕到, 捉住

hunt sb/sth ↔ **out** *phr v* [T] **1** to search for someone in order to catch or get rid of them 搜捕, 追捕〔某人〕: *Military Police were ordered to hunt out subversives.* 憲兵隊奉命搜捕顛覆分子。**2** to look for something that you have not used or seen for a long time 搜尋, 尋找〔某物〕: *I must try and hunt out that old tennis racket.* 我必須盡力找到那隻舊網球拍。

hunt² *n* **1** [C] an occasion when people chase animals in order to catch and kill them 打獵, 狩獵: *a tiger hunt* 獵虎 **2** [singular] a search for someone or something that is difficult to find 搜索, 搜尋: **the hunt for** *the hunt for the remains of the Titanic* 對"鐵達尼[泰坦尼克]號"殘骸的搜索工作 | **the hunt is on** (=used to say that people have started looking for someone or something) 開始搜尋 | **have a hunt around for** *informal* (=look for something)【非正式】搜尋, 尋找 *I'll have a hunt around for it in my desk.* 我會在書桌裡找找它。**3** [C] an organized sporting event in Britain in which people riding on horses hunt foxes (FOX¹ (1)) using dogs〔英國的一種體育項目〕騎馬〔用獵犬〕獵狐 **4** [C] *BrE* a group of people who regularly hunt foxes (FOX¹ (1)) together【英】經常在一起獵狐的人

hunt·er /ˈhʌntɚ; ˈhʌntə/ *n* **1** [C] a person or animal that hunts wild animals 獵人, 捕獵野獸的人;〔獵食其他動物的〕獵獸 **2 souvenir/autograph/bargain etc hunter** someone who looks for or collects a particular type of thing 搜集紀念品/簽名/便宜貨的人 **3** [C] a strong horse used in Britain for hunting foxes (FOX¹ (1))〔英國獵狐用的〕狩獵用馬 —see also 另見 BOUNTY HUNTER, FORTUNE HUNTER

hunt·ing /ˈhʌntɪŋ; ˈhʌntɪŋ/ *n* [U] **1** the act of chasing and killing animals for food or for sport〔為獵食或作為運動的〕打獵, 狩獵 **2** the sport of hunting foxes (FOX[1] (1)) in Britain〔英國的〕獵狐運動 **3 job-hunting/househunting etc** the activity of looking for a job, house etc 找工作/房子 **4 go hunting** to hunt for animals, especially as a sport〔尤作為運動〕去打獵 —**hunting** *adj*: *a hunting rifle* 獵槍

hunting ground /ˈ···/ *n* **1** [C] a place where animals are hunted 狩獵場 **2 a happy/good hunting ground for** a place where people who are interested in a particular thing can easily find what they want 能讓人輕易找到自己感興趣東西的地方, ...愛好者的天堂

hunt·ress /ˈhʌntrɛs; ˈhʌntrɨs/ *n* [C] *literary* a female hunter【文】女獵人, 女狩獵者

hunt sab·o·teur /,· ··ˈ·/ *n* [C] *BrE* member of a group that tries to stop people from hunting foxes (FOX[1] (1))【英】阻止獵狐者, 反狩獵活動者

hunts·man /ˈhʌntsmən; ˈhʌntsmən/ *n* [C] *especially BrE*【尤英】**1** a man who hunts animals (男) 獵人, 狩獵者 **2** the person in charge of the dogs in FOXHUNTING〔獵狐時的〕獵犬管理員

hur·dle[1] /ˈhɝdl; ˈhɜːdl/ *n* **1** [C] a frame that a person or horse has to jump over during a race〔跨欄賽跑或馬術表演中用的〕欄架: **clear a hurdle** (=successfully jump over a hurdle) 跨越欄架 **2** [C] a problem or difficulty that you must deal with before you can achieve something〔必須克服的〕障礙, 困難: *Finding enough money was the first hurdle.* 首先需要克服的困難是籌措足夠的資金。| **clear a hurdle** (=deal successfully with a problem) 克服困難 **3 the 100 metres/400 metres hurdles** a race in which the runners have to jump over hurdles 100米/400米跨欄賽跑 **4** [C] a moveable part of a temporary fence around animals or land〔用以圍起動物或土地的〕臨時活動圍欄

hurdle[2] *v* **1** [T] to jump over something while you are running〔跑步過程中〕跨越: *Barrett hurdled the fence and ran off down the street.* 巴雷特跨過護欄沿着街逃走了。**2** [I] to run in hurdle races 進行跨欄賽跑 —**hurdler** *n* [C] —**hurdling** *n* [U]

hur·dy-gur·dy /ˈhɝdɪ,gɝdɪ; ˈhɜːdi ˌgɜːdi/ *n* [C] a small musical instrument that you operate by turning a handle 手搖風琴

hurl /hɝl; hɜːl/ *v* **1** [T always+adv/prep] to throw something violently and with a lot of force, especially because you are angry 猛投, (用力) 投擲〔尤因生氣〕: **hurl sth through/across/over etc** *Demonstrators were hurling bricks through the windows.* 示威者在向窗裡擲磚頭。**2 hurl abuse/insults/accusations etc at sb** to shout at someone in a loud and angry way 漫罵/辱罵/責罵某人等 **3 hurl yourself at/against** to throw yourself at someone or something with a lot of force 向...猛撲過去

hurl·ing /ˈhɝlɪŋ; ˈhɜːlɪŋ/ *n* [U] an Irish ball game played between two teams of 15 players 愛爾蘭式曲棍球

hur·ly-bur·ly /ˈhɝlɪ,bɝlɪ; ˈhɜːli ˌbɜːli/ *n* [U] a lot of busy, noisy activity 騷動, 喧嘩鬧騰: *the hurly-burly of city life* 城市生活的喧囂

hur·ray /həˈre; hʊˈreɪ/ also 又作 **hur·rah** /həˈrɑ; hʊˈrɑː/ *interjection old-fashioned* a shout that shows you are pleased【過時】〔表示高興的呼喊聲〕好哇! 加油! 萬歲! —see also 另見 **hip, hip, hurray!** (HIP[2])

hur·ri·cane /ˈhɝɪ,ken; ˈhʌrɨkən/ *n* [C] a violent storm, especially in the western Atlantic ocean〔尤指大西洋西部的〕颶風 —compare 比較 CYCLONE, TYPHOON, TORNADO —see picture on page A13 參見 A13 頁圖

hurricane lamp /ˈ··· ·/ *n* [C] a lamp that has a strong cover to protect the flame inside from the wind 防風燈

hur·ried /ˈhɝɪd; ˈhʌrid/ *adj* [usually before noun 一般用於名詞前] done very quickly, often too quickly, because you are in a hurry; RUSHED 匆忙完成的, 趕出來的: *We just caught the plane after several hurried phone calls from the airport.* 我們從機場匆忙打了幾個電話後, 剛剛好趕上了飛機。—**hurriedly** *adv*

hur·ry[1] /ˈhɝɪ; ˈhʌri/ *v* **1** [I,T] to do something or go somewhere more quickly than usual, especially because there is not much time 趕緊, 匆忙: *The movie begins as six – we'll have to hurry.* 電影六點開始, 我們得趕快點。| **hurry through/along/down etc** *She hurried down the corridor as fast as she could.* 她以最快速度沿着走廊急匆匆地走了。| **hurry after sb** *John went hurrying off after his girlfriend.* 約翰急着去追他的女朋友了。| **hurry to do sth** *They were hurrying to catch their train.* 他們匆匆忙忙去趕火車。| **hurry sth** *I don't want to have to hurry my meal.* 我不想匆匆忙忙吃飯。**2** [T] to make someone do something more quickly 催促, 使匆忙: *Don't hurry me; I'm working as fast as I can.* 別催我, 我正在儘快幹呢! **3 hurry up!** *spoken* used to tell someone to do something more quickly【口】快點!: *Hurry up, we're late!* 快點, 我們遲到了! | **hurry up with** *Hurry up with the accounts – the boss is waiting for them.* 快把賬做好, 老闆等着要呢! **4** [T always+adv/prep] to take someone or something quickly to a place 急送: **hurry sth to/through/across etc** *Emergency supplies have been hurried to the areas worst hit by the famine.* 應急物資已經被緊急運往饑荒最嚴重的地區。

hurry sb/sth **up** *phr v* [T] to make someone do something more quickly or to make something happen more quickly 催促, 使加快

hurry[2] *n* **1 be in a hurry** to do something, go somewhere, need something etc more quickly than usual, often too quickly 匆匆忙忙, 倉促, 趕時間: *Sorry, I can't stop, I'm in a hurry.* 對不起, 我不能停下, 我有急事。| *You'll make mistakes if you do things in too much of a hurry.* 辦事太匆促會出錯的。| **be in a hurry to do sth** *Why are you in such a hurry to leave?* 你幹嘛這麼急着要走? **2 will not be doing sth (again) in a hurry** *spoken* used to say that you do not want to do something again【口】再也不願幹某事: *We won't be going back there again in a hurry, I can tell you.* 我可以告訴你, 我們再也不願回到那裡去了。**3 in your hurry to do sth** while you are trying to do something too quickly 在匆忙做某事的時候: *In his hurry to leave the room he tripped over a chair.* 他在匆匆忙忙離開房間時, 被椅子絆了一下。**4 be in no hurry/not be in any hurry** to be able to wait because you have plenty of time in which to do something 不急於, 不着急: *I'll wait till you've closed up – I'm not in any hurry.* 我等到你關門, 我不着急。**5 be in no hurry to do sth/not be in any hurry to do sth** to be unwilling to do something or not want to do it soon 不急着做某事: *I'm in no particular hurry to leave.* 我不特別急着要走。**6 (there's) no hurry** *spoken* used to tell someone that they do not have to do something soon【口】不用着急!: *You can give me the money back next month. There's no great hurry.* 你可以下個月還錢給我, 不用急。**7 what's (all) the hurry?/why (all) the hurry?** *spoken* used to say that someone is doing something too quickly【口】急甚麼?: *We've got plenty of time – what's all the hurry?* 我們有的是時間, 急甚麼?

hurt[1] /hɝt; hɜːt/ *v past tense and past participle* **hurt 1** [I,T] if a part of your body hurts, you feel pain in it〔身體〕感到疼痛: *My back hurts.* 我的背痛。| **it hurts** *Where does it hurt?* 哪兒痛? | **hurt sb** *My shoulder's really hurting me.* 我的肩膀使我痛得很。| **hurt like hell** (=hurt very much) 痛死了 **2** [T] if you hurt part of your body you injure it or make it feel painful, especially in an accident〔尤指在意外中〕弄傷, 弄痛〔身體某部位〕: *Several people were seriously hurt in the accident.* 好幾個人在事故中受了重傷。| **hurt your arm/leg/nose etc** *I hurt my finger in the door.* 我的手指讓門夾傷了。| **hurt yourself** (=injure yourself) 弄傷自己 *Careful you don't hurt yourself – it's very sharp.* 小心別傷了你自己, 它很鋒利。**3** [I,T] if something hurts part of your body, it makes it feel painful〔某物〕使〔身體某個部位〕感到疼痛: *The sun's hurting my eyes.* 太陽光刺痛我的雙眼。**4** [T] to cause physical pain to someone 弄痛〔某人〕: *Put* *that thing down – you might hurt someone with it.* 快放下它，你會傷着別人的。**5** [I,T] to make someone feel very upset, unhappy, sad etc 傷害〔感情〕，使傷心：**hurt sb's feelings** *I'm really sorry, I didn't mean to hurt your feelings.* 真對不起，我不是故意傷害你的感情的。| **what hurts is that** *What really hurts is that he never even said goodbye.* 真正令人傷心的是，他甚至沒有和我道別。| **hurt sb** *The last thing I want to do is to hurt you.* 我最不願傷害你。**6 be hurting yourself** to be making yourself feel even more unhappy, upset, sad etc 加重自己的痛苦 **7** [T] to have a bad effect on someone or something, especially by making them less successful or powerful 造成損害，產生不良影響：*Foreign competition has definitely hurt the firm's position in the market.* 來自國外的競爭的確已經對公司的市場地位造成損害。**8 be hurting a)** *AmE informal* to feel very upset, unhappy, sad etc【美，非正式】感到十分痛苦 **b)** if a group, organization etc is hurting, they do not have something important that they need, for example money〔團體、組織等〕急需；缺乏：[+**for**] *Our division in Salem is hurting for competent staff right now.* 我們的塞勒姆分部目前急需精兵強將。**9 it won't/doesn't hurt (sb) to do sth** *spoken* used to say that there is no reason why someone cannot or should not do something【口】做某事不會有壞處：*It won't hurt Julia to get up early for once.* 偶爾早起一次不會對朱莉婭造成甚麼不便。**10 one more won't hurt** *spoken* used to encourage someone to have another drink, piece of chocolate etc【口】〔用於勸人喝酒或吃東西〕再來一杯[塊]不會有問題的！—compare 比較 HARM[2]

hurt[2] *adj* **1** [not usually before noun 一般不用於名詞前] physically injured〔肉體〕受傷的：**badly/seriously hurt** *This man needs a doctor – he's badly hurt.* 這個人需要醫生治療，他傷得很重。**2** very upset or unhappy because someone has said or done something unkind, dishonest, or unfair〔感情上〕受傷害的，痛苦的：*a hurt expression* 痛苦的表情 | **deeply hurt** *I was feeling deeply hurt by what she had just said.* 她剛才說的話深深地傷害了我。

hurt[3] *n* [C,U] a feeling of great unhappiness because someone, especially someone you trust, has treated you unkindly or unfairly〔對感情造成的〕傷害，痛苦：*the hurt caused by the breakup of his marriage* 婚姻破裂對他造成的傷害 —compare 比較 HARM[1]

hurt·ful /ˈhɜːtfəl; ˈhɜːtfəl/ *adj* making you feel very upset or offended〔感情上〕傷害人的，使人痛苦的：*a hurtful remark* 刻薄的話 —**hurtfully** *adv* —**hurtfulness** *n* [U]

hur·tle /ˈhɜːtl̩; ˈhɜːtl/ *v* [I always+adv/prep] if something, especially something big or heavy, hurtles somewhere, it moves or falls very fast〔巨大物體〕飛速移動；快速落下，猛衝：**hurtle down/through/along etc** *Huge pieces of rock went hurtling down the mountainside.* 巨大的岩石塊沿着山坡飛滾而下。

1 1 **hus·band[1]** /ˈhʌzbənd; ˈhʌzbənd/ *n* **1** [C] the man that a woman is married to 丈夫：*Have you met her husband?* 你見過她的丈夫嗎？| **ex-husband** (=a man that a woman used to be married to) 前夫 —see picture at 參見 FAMILY 圖 **2 husband and wife** a man and woman who are married 夫妻，夫婦

husband[2] *v* [T] *formal* to be very careful in the way you use your money, supplies etc and not waste any【正式】節約地使用：*carefully husbanded resources* 謹慎節約使用的資源

hus·band·man /ˈhʌzbəndmən; ˈhʌzbəndmən/ *n* [C] *old use* a farmer【舊】農夫，農民

hus·band·ry /ˈhʌzbəndrɪ; ˈhʌzbəndri/ *n* **1** [U] *technical* farming【術語】農業；飼養業；農牧業：*animal husbandry* 畜牧業 **2** [U] *old-fashioned* careful management of money and supplies【過時】〔對資金、物資的〕節約；管理

hush[1] /hʌʃ; hʌʃ/ *v* **1 hush!** *spoken* used to tell people to be quiet or to comfort a child who is crying or upset【口】噓！〔叫人別出聲〕：*Hush, now. Try to get to sleep.* 噓，別哭了。睡吧。**2** [T] to make someone stop shouting, talking, crying etc 使安靜（下來）**3** [I] to stop shouting, talking, crying etc 安靜（下來）

hush sth ↔ **up** *phr v* [T] to prevent the public from knowing about something dishonest or immoral 隱瞞，遮掩：*The whole affair has been hushed up by school officials.* 校方官員隱瞞了整個事件。

hush[2] *n* **1** [singular] a period of silence that comes after there has been a lot of noise, shouting etc, especially because people are expecting something to happen〔吵鬧過後的〕寂靜，安靜：**a hush falls/descends** (=everyone becomes quiet) 一片寂靜 *A sudden hush descended on the crowd.* 人羣突然變得鴉雀無聲。**2 can we have/let's have a bit of hush** *BrE spoken* used to ask people, especially noisy children, to be quiet【英口】讓我們安靜一點

hushed /hʌʃt; hʌʃt/ *adj* [usually before noun 一般用於名詞前] quiet because people are listening, waiting to hear something, or talking quietly 安靜的，寂靜的：*A hushed courtroom awaited the verdict.* 法庭上一片寂靜，人們在等待裁決。| **hushed tones/voice/whispers etc** (=quiet speech) 輕聲/低聲/小聲耳語

hush-hush /ˌ· ˈ·◂/ *adj informal* an official operation etc that is hush-hush is very secret【非正式】祕密的

hush mon·ey /ˈ· ˌ··/ *n* [U] money that is paid to someone not to tell other people about something embarrassing〔不讓醜事張揚出去的〕封嘴錢

hush pup·py /ˈ· ˌ··/ *n* [C] a small fried cake made of MAIZE flour eaten in the southern states of the US〔美國南部常吃的〕油炸玉米圓子

husk[1] /hʌsk; hʌsk/ *n* [C,U] the dry outer part of grains, seeds etc and some types of nut〔穀粒、種子、某幾類堅果的〕外皮；殼；莢

husk[2] *v* [T] to remove the husks from grains, seeds etc 去除外皮，剝殼

hus·ky[1] /ˈhʌskɪ; ˈhʌski/ *adj* **1** a husky voice is deep, quiet, and rough-sounding, often in an attractive way〔聲音〕沙啞的，嘶啞的：*"Come quickly" she said in a husky whisper.* "快來！"她用沙啞的聲音小聲說。**2** *especially AmE* a man who is husky is big and strong【尤美】〔男子〕高大健壯的 —**huskily** *adv* —**huskiness** *n* [U]

husky[2] *n* [C] a dog with thick hair used in Canada and Alaska to pull SLEDGES over the snow 愛斯基摩犬

hus·sar /hʊˋzɑr; hʊˈzɑː/ *n* [C] a British CAVALRY (2) soldier〔英國軍隊中的〕輕騎兵

hus·sy /ˈhʌsɪ; ˈhʌsi/ *n* [C] *old-fashioned* a woman who is sexually immoral【過時】蕩婦，淫婦：*The shameless hussy!* 這個不要臉的蕩婦！

hus·tings /ˈhʌstɪŋz; ˈhʌstɪŋz/ *n* **the hustings** *BrE* the process of trying to persuade people to vote for you by making speeches etc【英】競選活動〈如拉票、演說等〉：**be at/on the hustings** *All the candidates are out on the hustings.* 所有候選人都在外出進行競選拉票活動。

hus·tle[1] /ˈhʌsl̩; ˈhʌsəl/ *v* **hustled, hustling 1** [T] to make someone move quickly, especially by pushing them roughly 推搡，硬擠；催促：**hustle sb out/into/through etc** *I was hustled out of the building by a couple of security men.* 我被幾個保安人員推出了大樓。| **hustle sb off somewhere** *She hustled the kids off to school.* 她催促孩子們去上學。**2** [I,T] *AmE* to sell or obtain things, especially unofficially or illegally【美】非法買賣：*small time thieves hustling stolen goods on the street* 在街上非法兜售贓物的小偷 **3** [I] *AmE* to do something with a lot of energy and determination【美】拚命幹，努力幹：*C'mon kids, let's hustle!* 來吧，孩子們，我們加把勁！**4** [I] *AmE slang* to work as a PROSTITUTE【美俚】當妓女，賣淫

hustle[2] *n* [U] **1** busy and noisy activity 忙碌；喧鬧：**hustle and bustle** *the hustle and bustle of the market place* 市場上的熙熙攘攘 **2** *AmE* dishonest and illegal ways of getting money【美】非法獲利；欺詐行為

H

hus·tler /ˋhʌslɚ; ˈhʌslə/ *n* **1** [C] *especially AmE* someone who tries to trick people into giving them money【尤美】騙子 **2** [C] *AmE* a PROSTITUTE【美】妓女

hut /hʌt; hʌt/ *n* [C] a small, simple building with only one or two rooms (簡陋的) 小屋, 棚屋, 茅舍: *a wooden hut* 小木屋

hutch /hʌtʃ; hʌtʃ/ *n* [C] **1** a small wooden CAGE used for keeping small animals in, especially rabbits〔尤指關兔子等小動物用的〕小籠子, 小木箱 **2** [C] *AmE* a piece of furniture used for storing and showing dishes【美】碗碟櫃, 餐具櫃; WELSH DRESSER *BrE*【英】

hy·a·cinth /ˋhaɪəˌsɪnθ; ˈhaɪəsɪ̵nθ/ *n* [C] a garden plant with blue, pink, or white bell-shaped flowers and a sweet smell〔植物〕風信子

hy·ae·na /haɪˋinə; haɪˈiːnə/ another spelling of HYENA hyena 的另一種拼法

hy·brid /ˋhaɪbrɪd; ˈhaɪbrɪ̵d/ *n* **1** [C] an animal or plant produced from parents of different breeds or types 雜種動物; 雜交植物; 雜交生成的生物體: *Most modern roses are hybrids.* 現代的玫瑰多數是雜交品種。**2** [C] something that consists of or comes from a mixture of two or more other things〔兩種或兩種以上不同物質組成的〕混合體

hy·dra /ˋhaɪdrə; ˈhaɪdrə/ *n plural* **hydrae** /-drɪ; -dri/ [C] **1** a snake in ancient Greek stories with many heads that grow again when they are cut off〔古希臘神話中頭被斬去後會立即復生的〕多頭蛇 **2** something that is evil and very difficult to get rid of 難於根除的禍患

hy·drant /ˋhaɪdrənt; ˈhaɪdrənt/ *n* [C] a water pipe in a street where you can get water to put on fires that are burning 消防栓; 消防龍頭

hy·drate /ˋhaɪdret; ˈhaɪdreɪt/ *n* [C] *technical* a chemical substance that contains water【術語】水合物, 水化物

hy·draul·ic /haɪˋdrɔlɪk; haɪˈdrɒlɪk/ *adj* [usually before noun 一般用於名詞前] moved or operated by the pressure of water or other liquid 水[液]力的, 水[液]壓的: *a hydraulic pump* 水壓泵, 液壓泵 | *hydraulic brakes* 液壓制動器 —**hydraulically** /-klɪ; -kli/ *adv*

hy·draul·ics /haɪˋdrɔlɪks; haɪˈdrɒlɪks/ *n* [plural] the scientific study of the use of moving liquids 水力學

H

hydro- /haɪdro; haɪdrəʊ/ *prefix* **1** concerning or using water 水的: *hydroelectricity* (=produced by water power) 水力發電; 水電 | *hydrotherapy* (=treatment of disease using water) 水療法 **2** concerning or containing HYDROGEN 含氫的, 氫化的: *hydrocarbons* 烴, 碳氫化合物

hy·dro·car·bon /ˌhaɪdroˋkɑrbən; ˌhaɪdrəˈkɑːbən/ *n* [C] *technical* a chemical compound that consists of HYDROGEN and CARBON (1), such as coal or gas【術語】烴, 碳氫化合物

hy·dro·chlor·ic ac·id /ˌhaɪdrəˋklɔrɪk ˋæsɪd; ˌhaɪdrəklɒrɪk ˈæsɪ̵d/ *n* [U] a strong acid used especially in industry 氫氯酸, 鹽酸

hy·dro·e·lec·tric /ˌhaɪdro·ɪˋlɛktrɪk; ˌhaɪdrəʊ-ɪˈlektrɪk◂/ *adj* using water power to produce electricity 水力發電的: *a hydroelectric power station* 水(力發)電站 —**hydroelectrically** /-klɪ; -kli/ *adv* —**hydroelectricity** /ˌhaɪdroɪlɛkˋtrɪsətɪ; ˌhaɪdrəʊɪlekˈtrɪsɪ̵ti/ *n* [U]

hy·dro·foil /ˋhaɪdrəˌfɔɪl; ˈhaɪdrəfɔɪl/ *n* [C] a large boat that raises itself above the surface of the water when it travels at high speeds 水翼船 —compare 比較 HOVERCRAFT

hy·dro·gen /ˋhaɪdrədʒən; ˈhaɪdrədʒən/ *n* [U] a simple chemical substance that is found in water, and also exists as a gas which is lighter than air 氫

hydrogen bomb /ˈ···ˌ·/ *n* [C] a very powerful NUCLEAR bomb 氫彈

hydrogen per·ox·ide /ˌ··· ·ˈ··/ *n* [U] a chemical liquid used for killing BACTERIA and making hair lighter; PEROXIDE 過氧化氫, 雙氧水

hy·dro·pho·bi·a /ˌhaɪdrəˋfobɪə; ˌhaɪdrəˈfəʊbiə/ *n* **1** [U] *technical* RABIES【術語】狂犬病 **2** fear of water 恐水, 畏水

hy·dro·plane[1] /ˋhaɪdrəˌplen; ˈhaɪdrəpleɪn/ *n* **1** [C] a HYDROFOIL 水翼船 **2** [C] *AmE* a plane that can take off from and land on water; SEAPLANE【美】水上飛機

hydroplane[2] *v* [I] **1** *AmE* if a car hydroplanes, it slides uncontrollably on a wet road【美】〔汽車〕濕路打滑; AQUAPLANE[2] (2) *BrE*【英】**2** if a boat hydroplanes, it travels very quickly just touching the surface of the water〔船〕水上滑行, 掠過水面

hy·e·na, hyaena /haɪˋinə; haɪˈiːnə/ *n* [C] a wild animal like a dog that feeds on the meat of dead animals 鬣狗〔形似狗, 食動物屍體〕

hy·giene /ˋhaɪdʒin; ˈhaɪdʒiːn/ *n* **1** [U] the study and practice of preventing illness or stopping it from spreading by keeping things clean 衛生(學); 保健(學): *public hygiene* 公共衛生 **2** [U] the practice of keeping your body clean 個人衛生

hy·gien·ic /ˌhaɪdʒɪˋɛnɪk; haɪˈdʒiːnɪk/ *adj* clean and likely to prevent bacteria, infections, or disease from spreading 衛生的; 清潔的: *food processed in hygienic conditions* 在衛生的條件下加工的食品 | *That's not very hygienic.* 那不太衛生。—**hygienically** /-klɪ; -kli/ *adv*

hy·gien·ist /ˋhaɪdʒɪənɪst; ˈhaɪdʒiːnɪ̵st/ *n* [C] *BrE* someone who helps a DENTIST by cleaning patients' teeth and giving advice about keeping teeth healthy【英】牙醫助手; DENTAL HYGIENIST *AmE*【美】

hy·men /ˋhaɪmən; ˈhaɪmən/ *n* [C] a piece of skin that partly covers the entrance to the VAGINA of some girls or women who have not had sex 處女膜

hymn /hɪm; hɪm/ *n* [C] a song of praise to God 聖歌, 讚美詩: *a hymn book* 聖歌集

hymn book /ˈ· ·/ also 又作 **hym·nal** /ˋhɪmnl; ˈhɪmnəl/ *technical n* [C] a book containing Christian songs of praise to God【術語】〔基督教〕聖歌集, 讚美詩集

hype[1] /haɪp; haɪp/ *n* [U] attempts to make the public interested in a product, film etc by saying how good it is on television, radio etc〔傳媒的〕大肆宣傳: **media hype** *Despite all the media hype, I found the film very disappointing.* 儘管傳媒大肆宣傳, 我發覺這部影片十分讓人失望。

hype[2] *v* [T] to try to get a lot of public attention for something by saying how good it is on television, radio etc〔通過傳媒〕大肆宣傳

hype sth ↔ **up** *phr v* [T] to make an event, thing, or person seem better or more important than it is 誇大地宣傳, 鼓吹

hyped up /ˌ· ˈ·/ *adj* [not before noun 不用於名詞前] *informal* excited or nervous about something that is going to happen【非正式】〔對即將發生的事感到〕興奮的, 激動的; 緊張的: **[+about]** *Jerry is really hyped up about his exams.* 傑里確實對考試感到很緊張。

hy·per /ˋhaɪpɚ; ˈhaɪpə/ *adj informal* extremely excited or nervous about something【非正式】非常興奮的; 非常緊張的

hyper- /haɪpɚ; haɪpə/ *prefix* more than usual; especially too much 過分(的), 過度(的): *hypersensitive* (=too sensitive) 過度敏感的 | *hyperinflation* 極度通貨膨脹

hy·per·ac·tive /ˌhaɪpɚˋæktɪv; ˌhaɪpərˈæktɪv◂/ *adj technical* a hyperactive child is too active and can only keep still or quiet for very short periods of time【術語】〔兒童〕過分活躍的, 多動的 —**hyperactivity** /ˌhaɪpəækˋtɪvətɪ; ˌhaɪpərækˈtɪvɪ̵ti/ *n* [U]

hy·per·bo·le /haɪˋpɝbəˌlɪ; haɪˈpɜːbəli/ *n* [U] a way of describing something by saying it is much bigger, smaller, worse etc than it actually is 誇張(法)〔一種修辭法〕: *To say 'This chair weighs a ton' is an example of hyperbole.* "這張椅子有一噸重"是一種誇張的說法。—see also 另見 EXAGGERATE —**hyperbolic** /ˌhaɪpɚˋbɑlɪk; ˌhaɪpəˈbɒlɪk◂/ *adj*

hy·per·crit·i·cal /ˌhaɪpɚˋkrɪtɪkl; ˌhaɪpəˈkrɪtɪkəl◂/ *adj* too eager to criticize other people and things, especially about small details 吹毛求疵的, 過分挑剔的, 苛求的 —**hypercritically** /-klɪ; -kli/ *adv*

hy·per·in·fla·tion /ˌhaɪpɚɪnˋfleʃən; ˌhaɪpərɪnˈfleɪʃən/ *n* [U] a rapid rise in prices that seriously damages a country's economy 極度通貨膨脹, 超通貨膨脹

hy·per·mar·ket /ˋhaɪpɚˌmɑrkɪt; ˈhaɪpəˌmɑːkɪ̣t/ *n* [C] *BrE* a very large SUPERMARKET, usually built outside a town【英】巨型超級市場

hy·per·sen·si·tive /ˌhaɪpɚˋsɛnsətɪv; ˌhaɪpəˈsensɪ̣tɪv◂/ *adj* **1** [+to] extremely sensitive to any change in conditions, to pain, to certain chemicals, drugs etc 過敏的 **2** too easily hurt or upset by unimportant things 感情脆弱的: [+to/about] *She's hypersensitive to any form of criticism.* 她經不起任何批評。—**hypersensitivity** /ˌhaɪpɚˌsɛnsəˋtɪvətɪ; ˌhaɪpəsensɪ̣ˈtɪvɪ̣ti/ *n* [U]

hy·per·ten·sion /ˌhaɪpɚˋtɛnʃən; ˌhaɪpəˈtenʃən/ *n* [U] *technical* a medical condition in which your BLOOD PRESSURE is too high【術語】高血壓

hy·phen /ˋhaɪfən; ˈhaɪfən/ *n* [C] a short written or printed line (-) that joins words or SYLLABLES 連字符, 連（字）號: *'Co-operate' can be written with or without a hyphen.* "co-operate"這個詞書寫中連字符可有可無。—compare 比較 DASH² (1)

hy·phen·ate /ˋhaɪfənˌet; ˈhaɪfəneɪt/ *v* [T] to join words or SYLLABLES with a HYPHEN 用連字符[號]連接 —**hyphenation** /ˌhaɪfəˋneʃən; ˌhaɪfəˈneɪʃən/ *n* [U]

hy·phen·a·ted /ˋhaɪfənˌetɪd; ˈhaɪfəneɪtɪ̣d/ *adj* containing a hyphen 帶有連字符[號]的

hyp·no·sis /hɪpˋnosɪs; hɪpˈnəʊsɪ̣s/ *n* **1** [U] a sleep-like state of the brain in which someone's thoughts and actions can be influenced by the person who caused this state（受）催眠狀態: **under hypnosis** (=in a state of hypnosis) 處於被催眠狀態中 *describing details of your early childhood while under hypnosis* 在受催眠狀態下描述你童年時代的細節 **2** [U] the act of hypnotizing (HYPNOTIZE) someone 催眠（術）

hyp·no·ther·a·py /ˌhɪpnoˋθɛrəpɪ; ˌhɪpnəʊˈθerəpi/ *n* [U] the use of hypnosis to treat emotional or physical problems 催眠療法 —**hypnotherapist** *n* [C]

hyp·not·ic¹ /hɪpˋnɑtɪk; hɪpˈnɒtɪk/ *adj* **1** making you feel tired or unable to think clearly, especially because of a regularly repeated sound or movement 催人入眠的, 使人昏昏欲睡的: *The steady ticking of the clock had a hypnotic effect.* 時鐘發出的有規律的滴答聲使人昏昏欲睡。**2** [only before noun 僅用於名詞前] connected with HYPNOSIS 催眠（術）的: *a hypnotic trance* 催眠後的恍惚狀態 —**hypnotically** /-klɪ; -kli/ *adv*

hypnotic² *n* [C] *technical* a drug that helps you to sleep; SLEEPING PILL【術語】安眠藥

hyp·no·tise /ˋhɪpnəˌtaɪz; ˈhɪpnətaɪz/ *v* [T] the British spelling of HYPNOTIZE hypnotize 的英式拼法

hyp·no·tis·m /ˋhɪpnəˌtɪzəm; ˈhɪpnətɪzəm/ *n* [U] the practice of hypnotizing people 催眠（術）

hyp·no·tist /ˋhɪpnətɪst; ˈhɪpnətɪ̣st/ *n* [C] someone who hypnotizes people, especially in public for entertainment〔尤在公共場所以娛樂他人為目的的〕施行催眠術的人, 催眠師

hyp·no·tize also 又作 **-ise** *BrE*【英】/ˋhɪpnəˌtaɪz; ˈhɪpnətaɪz/ *v* [T] **1** to make someone be in a sleep-like state in which their thoughts and actions can be influenced by your suggestions 對…施行催眠術 **2 be hypnotized** to be so interested or excited when seeing or listening to something that you cannot think of anything else 沉醉於, 為…所陶醉: *We were completely hypnotized by Bylsma's performance of the Haydn.* 我們完全陶醉在比爾斯馬所演奏的海頓作品之中。

hy·po /ˋhaɪpo; ˈhaɪpəʊ/ *n* [C] *informal* a HYPODERMIC【非正式】皮下注射器

hypo- /haɪpo; haɪpəʊ/ *prefix technical* less than usual, especially too little【術語】過少（的）; 低於正常（的）: *dying of hypothermia* (=too low body temperature) 死於體溫過低

hy·po·chon·dri·a /ˌhaɪpəˋkɑndrɪə; ˌhaɪpəˈkɒndriə/ *n* [U] a state in which you continuously worry that there is something wrong with your health, even when you are not ill 疑病症, 憂鬱症

hy·po·chon·dri·ac /ˌhaɪpəˋkɑndrɪˌæk; ˌhaɪpəˈkɒndriæk/ *n* [C] someone who always worries about their health, even when they are not ill 疑病症患者, 憂鬱症患者 —**hypochondriac** *adj*

hy·poc·ri·sy /hɪˋpɑkrəsɪ; hɪˈpɒkrɪ̣si/ *n* [U] a way of behaving in which you pretend to have better moral principles than you actually do 偽善, 虛偽: **sheer hypocrisy** *It's sheer hypocrisy for politicians to preach about family values when so many of them are having affairs.* 政客們口口聲聲宣揚家庭的各種重要性是純屬虛偽, 他們中有很多人卻有婚外戀情。

hyp·o·crite /ˋhɪpəˌkrɪt; ˈhɪpəkrɪt/ *n* [C] someone who pretends to be morally good 偽君子, 偽善的人

hyp·o·crit·i·cal /ˌhɪpəˋkrɪtɪkḷ; ˌhɪpəˈkrɪtɪkəl◂/ *adj* behaving in a way that is intended to make people believe that you are morally better than you really are 偽善的, 虛偽的, 假惺惺的: *hypocritical concern for the less privileged members of society* 對社會中處於弱勢地位者假惺惺的關心

hy·po·der·mic¹ /ˌhaɪpəˋdɝmɪk; ˌhaɪpəˈdɜːmɪk◂/ *n* [C] an instrument with a very thin hollow needle used for putting drugs directly into the body through the skin; a SYRINGE 皮下注射器

hypodermic² *adj* used in an INJECTION (1) beneath the skin 用於皮下注射的: *a hypodermic needle* 皮下注射器針頭 —**hypodermically** /-klɪ; -kli/ *adv*

hy·pot·e·nuse /haɪˋpɑtṇˌjus; haɪˈpɒtɪ̣njuːz/ *n* [C] *technical* the longest side of a TRIANGLE that has a RIGHT ANGLE【術語】〔直角三角形的〕斜邊, 弦 —see picture at 參見 SHAPE¹ 圖

hy·po·ther·mi·a /ˌhaɪpəˋθɝmɪə; ˌhaɪpəʊˈθɜːmiə/ *n* [U] a serious medical condition caused by extreme cold 體溫過低

hy·poth·e·sis /haɪˋpɑθəsɪs; haɪˈpɒθɪ̣sɪ̣s/ *n plural* **hypotheses** /-ˌsiz; -siːz/ **1** [C] an idea that is suggested as a possible way of explaining a situation, proving an idea etc, which has not yet been shown to be true 假設, 假說: **put forward a hypothesis** (=suggest a hypothesis) 提出假設 *A number of hypotheses have been put forward concerning the possible origins of mankind.* 人們已經提出了一些關於人類起源的假設。**2** [U] ideas or guesses rather than facts 猜想: *All this is mere hypothesis.* 這一切純屬猜想。

hy·po·thet·i·cal /ˌhaɪpəˋθɛtɪkḷ; ˌhaɪpəˈθetɪkəl◂/ *adj* based only on an idea or suggestion about what might happen or might be true and not on a real situation（基於）假設的, 假定的: *Let's consider a hypothetical case.* 讓我們考慮一個假設的情況吧！| **purely hypothetical** (=completely hypothetical) 純粹假設的 *The question is purely hypothetical.* 這個問題純屬假設。—compare 比較 IMAGINARY —**hypothetically** /-klɪ; -kli/ *adv*

hys·ter·ec·to·my /ˌhɪstəˋrɛktəmɪ; ˌhɪstəˈrektəmi/ *n* [C, U] a medical operation to remove a woman's WOMB 子宮切除（術）

hys·te·ri·a /hɪsˋtɪrɪə; hɪˈstɪəriə/ *n* **1** [U] extreme excitement that makes people cry, laugh, shout etc uncontrollably 歇斯底里: *an outbreak of hysteria among the group's fans* 該組合的熱心追隨者中爆發的一陣歇斯底里 **2** [U] a situation in which a lot of people are affected by the same extreme emotion such as fear or anger which often makes them behave in an unreasonable way〔眾人的〕狂熱情緒的爆發: *anti-communist hysteria* 反共狂熱情緒 | **mass hysteria** *Since the General's death, the population has been gripped by mass hysteria.* 自將軍死後, 全國人民已陷入羣眾性激動情緒的狀態。**3** *technical* a medical condition which upsets someone's emotions and makes them suddenly feel very nervous, excited, anxious etc【術語】癔病 —**hysteric** /hɪsˋtɛrɪk; hɪˈsterɪk/ *adj*

hys·ter·i·cal /hɪsˋtɛrɪkḷ; hɪˈsterɪkəl/ *adj* **1** behaving in a

H

wild, uncontrollable way, especially by shouting or crying because you are extremely excited 歇斯底里的; 狂熱的: *Hysterical fans tried to stop Madonna's car at the airport.* 狂熱的歌迷企圖在機場攔截麥當娜的汽車。**2** *spoken* extremely funny【口】極可笑的, 滑稽的 —**hysterically** /-klɪ; -kli/ *adv*

hys·ter·ics /hɪsˋtɛrɪks; hɪˈsterɪks/ *n spoken*【口】**1 have hysterics** to be extremely upset or angry 暴跳如雷的; 極度心煩的: *Mum'd have hysterics if she knew what you'd done.* 媽媽如果知道你幹的好事, 肯定會暴跳如雷的。**2 be in hysterics/have sb in hysterics** to be laughing uncontrollably or to make someone laugh uncontrollably 狂笑不止/使某人狂笑不止

Hz *n* [C] the written abbreviation for 縮寫= HERTZ

I,i

I, i¹ /aɪ; aɪ/ **1** *plural* **I's, i's** *n* [C] the ninth letter of the English alphabet 英語字母表的第九個字母 **2** the ROMAN NUMERAL representing the number one 羅馬數字 I

1 1 **I²** /aɪ; aɪ/ *pron* used as the subject of a verb when you are the person speaking 我〔用作主語〕: *I've just seen a strange man in your garden.* 我剛才看見你家園子裡有個陌生男人。| *I'm not late again, am I?* 我不是又遲到了吧? —see 見 ME (USAGE)

I³ *AmE* the abbreviation of 縮寫= INTERSTATE (=an important road between states in the US)【美】州際公路: *the point where I95 meets I40* 95號與40號州際公路交會處

-i /-ɪ; -i/ *plural* **-is** *suffix* **1** [in nouns 構成名詞] a person or the language of a particular place or country, especially in Asia〔尤指亞洲〕某地[某國]的人[語言]: *two Pakistanis* 兩個巴基斯坦人 | *speakers of Nepali* 說尼泊爾語的人 **2** [in adjectives 構成形容詞] of a particular place or country 某地的; 某國的: *Bengali food* 孟加拉食品 | *the Israeli army* 以色列軍隊

-ial /əl; iəl/ *suffix* another form of the suffix -AL 後綴 -al 的另一種形式: *a managerial job* (=with the duties of a manager) 管理工作

i·amb /ˈaɪæmb; ˈaɪæm/ also 又作 **i·am·bus** /aɪˋæmbəs; aɪˈæmbəs/ *n* [C] *technical* a unit of RHYTHM (1) in poetry, that has one short or weak beat followed by a long or strong beat, as in the word 'alive'【術語】抑揚格〔詩歌的音步單位, 即一個短或弱音節之後跟着一個長或強音節, 如 alive〕—**iambic** /aɪˋæmbɪk; aɪˈæmbɪk/ *adj*

iambic pen·tam·e·ter /·,·· ·ˈ···/ *n* [C,U] a common pattern of beats in English poetry, in which each line consists of five iambs 抑揚格五音步〔一種常見的英詩節拍模式, 每行有五個抑揚格〕

-ian /ɪən; iən/ *suffix* [in adjectives and nouns 構成形容詞和名詞] another form of the suffix -AN 後綴 -an 的另一種形式: *Dickensian characters* (=like those in Dickens' books) 與狄更斯作品中的人物相似者 | *a librarian* (=someone who works in a library) 圖書館館員

-iana /iˋɑnə; iɑːnə/ *suffix* also 又作 **-ana** [in nouns 構成名詞] a collection of objects, papers, etc, connected with someone or something 一批與某人[某物]有關的物件[資料]: *Churchilliana* 丘吉爾文物總匯 | *Shakespeariana* 莎士比亞研究資料匯編

I·be·ri·an /aɪˋbɪrɪən; aɪˈbɪəriən/ *adj* connected with Spain or Portugal 伊比利亞的, 與西班牙[葡萄牙]有關的: *the Iberian peninsula* 伊比利亞半島

i·bex /ˈaɪbɛks; ˈaɪbeks/ *plural* **ibexes** or **ibex** *n* [C] a wild goat that lives in the mountains of Europe, Asia, and North Africa 北山羊〔一種生活在歐洲、亞洲和北非等地山區的野山羊〕

ib·id /ˈɪbɪd; ˈɪbɪd/ also 又作 **ib·i·dem** /ɪˋbaɪdɛm; ˈɪbɪdem/ *adv Latin* from the same book, writer, or article as the one that has just been mentioned【拉丁】出處同前〔來自剛提過的同一本書、作者或文章〕

-ibility /əbɪlətɪ; ə̩bɪlə̩ti/ *suffix* [in nouns 構成名詞] another form of the suffix -ABILITY 後綴 -ability 的另一種形式: *invincibility* 不可戰勝

-ible /əbl̩; ə̩bəl/ *suffix* [in adjectives 構成形容詞] another form of the suffix -ABLE 後綴 -able 的另一種形式: *irresistible* 不可抗拒的

IBM-com·pat·i·ble /ˌaɪ bi ɛm kəmˋpætəbl̩; ˌaɪ biː em kəmˈpætə̩bəl/ *adj* an IBM-compatible computer is designed to work in the same way as a type of computer made by the IBM company, and can use the same computer PROGRAMS¹ (1) 與 IBM 兼容的〔指電腦與 IBM 公司生產的電腦有相同的操作模式, 並可使用相同的電腦程式〕—**IBM-compatible** *n* [C]

-ic /ɪk; ɪk/ *suffix* [in adjectives 構成形容詞] **1** of, like, or connected with a particular thing …的, 像…的, 與…相關的: *photographic* (=of photography) 攝影的 | *an alcoholic drink* (=containing alcohol) 含酒精的飲料 | *polysyllabic* (=containing several SYLLABLES) 多音節的 | *pelvic* (=of the PELVIS) 骨盆的 | *Byronic* (=like or connected with the poet Byron) 拜倫(式)的 **2** [in nouns 構成名詞] someone who is affected by a particular unusual condition, a mental illness for example 受〔某種異常狀態, 如精神疾病〕困擾的人: *an alcoholic* (=someone who cannot stop drinking alcohol) 酗酒者 —**-ically** /ɪkl̩ɪ; ɪkli/ [in adverbs 構成副詞] *photographically*〔像照片那樣〕逼真地

-ical /ɪkl̩; ɪkəl/ *suffix* [in adjectives 構成形容詞] another form of the suffix -ic (1) 前綴 -ic (1) 的另一種形式: *historical* (=of history) (有關)歷史的 | *satirical* 諷刺的 —**-ically** /ɪkl̩ɪ; ɪkli/ [in adverbs 構成副詞]: *historically* 歷史地

ICBM /ˌaɪ si bi ˋɛm; ˌaɪ siː biː ˈem/ *n* [C] Intercontinental Ballistic Missile; a MISSILE (1) that can travel very long distances 洲際彈道導彈

ice¹ /aɪs; aɪs/ *n* **1** [U] water that has frozen into a solid state 冰: *Would you like some ice in your drink?* 您的飲料中要放點兒冰嗎? | *The wind blew the snow across the ice on the lake.* 風把雪花吹過結了冰的湖面。| *Her hands were as cold as ice.* 她雙手冷冰冰的。**2 keep/put something on ice** to do nothing about a plan or suggestion for a period of time〔將計劃、建議〕擱置, 凍結: *Opposition to Irish home rule was put on ice for the duration of the war.* 反對愛爾蘭自治的建議因戰爭持續而被擱置起來。**3 be (skating) on thin ice** to be in a situation in which you are likely to upset someone or cause trouble 如履薄冰〔處於會惹人不高興或招麻煩的情況〕: *Don't question him too closely about where he got the money – you'd be on very thin ice.* 不要追問他在哪兒弄到了錢, 這樣做只會自找麻煩。**4** [C] **a)** a cold sweet food like ICE CREAM, made with fruit juice instead of milk or cream; SORBET〔像冰淇淋, 但不含牛奶或奶油, 用果汁製成的〕冰凍甜食; 冰糕, 雪芭 **b)** *old-fashioned, especially BrE* an ICE CREAM【過時, 尤英】冰淇淋 **5** [U] *AmE old-fashioned* diamonds【美, 過時】鑽石 —see also 另見 ICY, BLACK ICE, DRY ICE, **break the ice** (BREAK¹ (30)), **cut no ice** (CUT¹ (35)) 2 3

ice² *v* [T] *especially BrE* to cover a cake with ICING (=a mixture made of liquid and powdery sugar)【尤英】〔在糕餅上〕覆蓋糖衣 —compare 比較 FROST²

ice sth ↔ **down** *phr v* [T] *AmE* to cover an injury in ice to stop it from swelling【美】冰敷〔受傷處, 阻止腫脹〕: *Make sure you ice that ankle down as soon as you get inside.* 你進屋後一定要立即把腳踝用冰敷上。

ice over/up also 又作 **be iced over/up** *phr v* [I] to become covered with ice 被冰覆蓋, 結冰: *The lake was iced over by morning.* 到了早晨, 湖面已結了冰。| *The plane's engines had iced up.* 飛機的引擎被凍住了。

Ice Age /ˈ· ·/ *n* [C] one of the long periods of time, thousands of years ago, when ice covered many northern countries 冰川期, 冰河時代

ice axe also 又作 **ice ax** *AmE*【美】/ˈ· ·/ *n* [C] a metal tool, used by mountain climbers to cut into ice〔登山者

I

使用的〕冰鎬; 碎冰斧 —see also 另見 ICE PICK

ice·berg /ˈaɪs͵bɝg; ˈaɪsbɜːg/ *n* [C] a very large mass of ice floating in the sea, most of which is under the surface of the water 冰山 —see also 另見 **the tip of the iceberg** (TIP[1] (7))

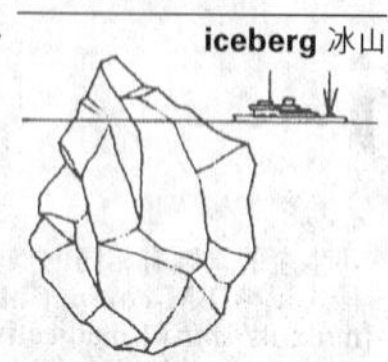

iceberg let·tuce /͵.. ˈ../ *n* [C,U] a firm round, pale green LETTUCE 卷心[球葉]萵苣

ice·bound /ˈaɪs͵baʊnd; ˈaɪsbaʊnd/ *adj* surrounded by ice, especially so that it is impossible to move 冰封的, 被冰封住的: *The Russian Fleet was icebound.* 那支俄羅斯艦隊遭遇了冰封。

ice·box /ˈaɪs͵bɑks; ˈaɪsbɒks/ *n* [C] **1** *AmE old-fashioned* a REFRIGERATOR【美, 過時】電冰箱 **2** a box where food is kept cold with blocks of ice〔裡面放冰塊以冷藏食物的〕冰箱

ice·break·er /ˈaɪs͵brekɚ; ˈaɪs͵breɪkə/ *n* [C] **1** a ship that cuts a passage through floating ice 破冰船 **2** something that you say or do to make people less nervous when they first meet〔第一次見面時〕消除拘謹的話語[舉動]: *This game is an effective icebreaker at the beginning of a semester.* 這場比賽可以有效地消除開學初期的拘謹氣氛。—see also 另見 **break the ice** (BREAK[1] (30))

ice buck·et /ˈ. ͵../ *n* [C] **1** a container filled with ice to keep bottles of wine cold 冰桶〔用於冰鎮葡萄酒〕 **2** a container in which pieces of ice are kept for putting in drinks 冰桶〔用於盛放加入飲料中的小冰塊〕

ice cap /ˈ. ./ *n* [C] an area of ice that permanently covers land or sea, such as that on the North or South Poles 冰蓋, 冰冠〔常年被冰覆蓋的陸地或海洋, 諸如南北極地區〕

ice-cold /͵. ˈ.◂/ *adj* extremely cold 極冷的, 冰冷的: *ice-cold drinks* 冰冷的飲料 | *Her hands were ice-cold.* 她兩手冰涼的。

S2 **ice cream** /͵. ˈ.◂/ *n* **1** [U] a frozen sweet food made of milk or cream, sugar etc, with an added taste of fruit, nuts, chocolate etc 冰淇淋, 雪糕: *vanilla ice cream* 香草冰淇淋 **2** [C] *BrE* a small amount of this food for one person【英】一人份的冰淇淋: *"Mummy, can I have an ice cream?"* "媽, 我能要一份冰淇淋嗎?"

ice-cream so·da /͵. . ˈ../ *n* [C] a mixture of ice cream, sweet SYRUP, and SODA WATER, served in a tall glass〔由冰淇淋、糖漿、蘇打水混合製成的〕冰淇淋蘇打水, 雪糕梳打

ice cube /ˈ. ./ *n* [C] a small block of ice used to make drinks cold〔加入飲料中的〕小方冰塊

iced cof·fee /͵. ˈ../ *n* [C,U] cold coffee with ice and milk, or a glass of this drink〔放了冰塊和牛奶的〕冰咖啡; 一杯冰咖啡

iced tea /͵. ˈ./ *n* [C,U] cold tea with ice, lemon, and sugar, or a glass of this drink 冰茶; 一杯冰茶

ice floe /ˈ. ./ *n* [C] an area of ice floating in the sea, that has broken off from a larger mass〔海洋上的〕浮冰, 冰盤

ice hock·ey /ˈ. ͵../ *n* [U] a sport played on ice, in which players try to hit a hard flat round object into the other team's GOAL (3) with special sticks 冰球運動

Ice·land·er /ˈaɪsləndɚ; ˈaɪsləndə/ *n* [C] someone from Iceland 冰島人

Ice·lan·dic /aɪsˈlændɪk; aɪsˈlændɪk/ *adj* connected with Iceland, its people, or their language 冰島的; 冰島人的; 冰島語的

ice lol·ly /ˈ. ͵../ *plural* **ice lollies** *n* [C] *BrE* a piece of sweet tasting ice on a stick, that you suck【英】冰棍, 冰棒, 雪糕; POPSICLE *AmE*【美】

ice·man /ˈaɪs͵mæn; ˈaɪs-mæn/ *n plural* **icemen** /-͵mɛn; -men/ [C] *AmE* a man who delivered ice to people's houses in the past, so that they could keep food cold【美】送冰人〔過去送冰上門供人們貯藏食物的人〕

ice pack /ˈ. ./ *n* [C] **1** a bag containing ice, used to keep injured or painful parts of your body cold 冰袋〔用以冷敷受傷或疼痛處〕 **2** a large area of crushed ice floating in the sea〔海上〕浮冰羣, 大片浮冰 —compare 比較 PACK ICE

ice pick /ˈ. ./ *n* [C] a sharp tool used for cutting or breaking ice 碎冰錐

ice rink /ˈ. ./ *n* [C] a specially prepared surface of ice where you can ICE-SKATE 溜冰場

ice sheet /ˈ. ./ *n* [C] an ICE CAP 冰蓋, 冰冠

ice-skate /ˈ. ./ *v* [I] to slide on ice wearing ice skates 溜冰, 滑冰 —**ice-skater** *n* [C] —**ice-skating** *n* [U]

ice skate /ˈ. ./ *n* [C usually plural 一般用複數] a special boot with thin metal blades on the bottom, that allows you to move quickly on ice 冰鞋, 溜冰鞋 —compare 比較 ROLLER SKATE

ice wa·ter /ˈ. ͵../ *n* [C,U] very cold water with pieces of ice in it, or a glass of this 冰水; 一杯冰水

ich·neu·mon fly /ɪkˋnjumən flaɪ; ɪkˈnjuːmən flaɪ/ *n* [C] an insect that lays eggs on or inside the LARVA of another insect 姬蜂〔一種將卵產於其他昆蟲幼體表面或體內的昆蟲〕

-ician /ɪʃən; ɪʃən/ *suffix* [in nouns 構成名詞] a skilled worker who deals with a particular thing …能手, …(專)家: *a beautician* (=someone who gives beauty treatments) 美容師 | *a technician* 技術員

i·ci·cle /ˈaɪsɪkl̩; ˈaɪsɪkəl/ *n* [C] a long thin pointed piece of ice hanging from a roof or other surface 冰柱, 垂冰〔自屋頂或其他表面垂下來的冰〕

-icide /ɪsaɪd; ɪsaɪd/ *suffix* also 又作 **-cide** [in nouns 構成名詞] killer; killing 殺害者; 殺: *insecticide* (=chemical substance for killing insects) 殺蟲劑 | *suicide* (=act of killing oneself) 自殺 —**-icidal** /ɪsaɪdl̩; ɪsaɪdl/ [in adjectives 構成形容詞] —**-icidally** /ɪsaɪdl̩ɪ; ɪsaɪdl-i/ [in adverbs 構成副詞]

i·ci·ly /ˈaɪsɪlɪ; ˈaɪsl̩li/ *adv* if you say something icily or look at someone icily you do it in an angry or very unfriendly way 生氣地, 冷淡地, 不友好地: *She started talking, but he glared at her icily.* 她開始說話, 他卻對她怒目而視。

ic·ing /ˈaɪsɪŋ; ˈaɪsɪŋ/ *n* [U] **1** a mixture made from powdery sugar and liquid, used to cover cakes〔覆在糕餅上的〕糖衣, 酥皮; FROSTING (1) *AmE*【美】 **2 the icing on the cake** something that makes a very good experience perfect 錦上添花, 好上加好: *It was a great evening but meeting you here was just the icing on the cake!* 那是一個美好的夜晚, 而在這兒遇到你更是美妙至極!

icing sug·ar /ˈ.. ͵../ *n* [U] *BrE* powdery sugar that is mixed with liquid to make icing【英】〔製糖衣用的〕糖粉; CONFECTIONER'S SUGAR *AmE*【美】

ick·y /ˈɪkɪ; ˈɪki/ *adj informal* very unpleasant, especially to look at, taste, or feel【非正式】〔尤指在視覺、味覺、觸覺上〕非常令人討厭的: *Those dumplings look really icky!* 那些餃子看上去令人噁心!

i·con /ˈaɪkɑn; ˈaɪkɒn/ *n* [C] **1** a small sign or picture on a computer SCREEN[1] (1) that is used to start a particular operation〔電腦屏幕上標示某一操作系統的〕圖標: *To open a new file, click on the icon at the top of the screen.* 要打開新文件, 就點擊屏幕上方的那個圖標。**2** someone famous who is admired by many people and is thought to represent an important idea 偶像, 崇拜對象: *Anita Roddick has been feted as some kind of environmentally conscious feminist icon.* 安妮塔·羅迪克被讚譽為具有環保意識的女權主義偶像。**3** also 又作 **ikon** a picture or figure of a holy person that is used in worship in the Greek or Russian Orthodox Church〔希臘或俄羅斯東正教的〕聖像 —**iconic** /aɪˋkɑnɪk; aɪˈkɒnɪk/ *adj*

i·con·o·clast /aɪˋkɑnə͵klæst; aɪˈkɒnəklæst/ *n* [C] someone who attacks established ideas and customs 攻擊傳統觀念和習俗的人

i·con·o·clas·tic /aɪ͵kɑnəˋklæstɪk; aɪ͵kɒnəˈklæstɪk◂/ *adj* iconoclastic ideas, opinions, writings etc attack established beliefs and customs〔思想、意見、著作等〕反對傳統觀念和習俗的: *Wolfe's theories were revolutionary and iconoclastic.* 沃爾夫的理論是革命性和反傳統的。

i·co·nog·ra·phy /ˌaɪkəˋnɑɡrəfɪ; ˌaɪkəˈnɒɡrəfi/ *n* [U] the way that a particular people, religious or political group etc represent ideas in pictures or images〔特定民族、宗教或政治派別用來表達思想的〕圖示法, 象徵手法: *Crocodiles and hippopotami are both symbols of evil in the iconography of ancient Egypt.* 在古埃及的圖示法中, 鱷魚和河馬都代表邪惡。

-ics /ɪks; ɪks/ *suffix* [in nouns 構成名詞] **1** the scientific study or use of something ...學, ...研究: *linguistics* (=the study of language) 語言學 | *electronics* (=the study or making of electronic apparatus) 電子學 | *acoustics* 聲學 **2** the actions typically done by a particular type of people〔由特定的人做的〕活動: *athletics* (=running, jumping, throwing, etc) 田徑運動 | *acrobatics* 雜技 **3** qualities or events connected with something〔與某物有關的〕性質, 現象: *the acoustics* (=sound qualities) *of the hall* 大廳的音響效果

ic·y /ˋaɪsɪ; ˈaɪsi/ *adj* **1** extremely cold 極冷的: *An icy wind blew from the north.* 刺骨的寒風從北方吹來。| *The bath water was icy cold.* 洗澡水是冰冷的。**2** covered in ice 被冰覆蓋的: *The roads will be icy tonight.* 道路今夜將結冰。**3** an icy comment, look etc shows that you feel annoyed with or unfriendly towards someone〔評語、目光等〕冷冷的, 不友好的: *Jo fixed the other woman with an icy stare.* 喬冷冷地盯着另一個女人。—see also 另見 ICILY —**iciness** *n* [U]

I'd /aɪd; aɪd/ **1** the short form of 縮略式= 'I had' : *I wish I'd been there.* 真希望我當時在那裡。**2** the short form of 縮略式= 'I would' : *I'd leave now if I were you.* 我要是你的話, 現在就走。

ID /ˌaɪ ˋdi; ˌaɪ ˈdiː/ *n* [C,U] a document that shows your name and date of birth, usually with a photograph 身分證明(文件): *Do you have any ID, sir?* 先生, 您有身分證明嗎?

id /ɪd; ɪd/ *n* [U] *technical* according to Freudian PSYCHOLOGY (1), the part of your mind that is completely unconscious but has hidden needs and desires【術語】伊德, 本我〔據弗洛伊德心理學, 這是潛意識的最深一層, 隱藏了需要和慾望〕—compare 比較 EGO (3), SUPEREGO

ID card /ˌaɪ ˋdi kɑrd; ˌaɪ ˈdiː kɑːd/ *n* [C] an IDENTITY CARD 身分證

-ide /aɪd; aɪd/ *suffix* [in nouns 構成名詞] *technical* a chemical compound【術語】...化(合)物: *cyanide* 氰化物 | *sulphide* 硫化物

1 1 **i·dea** /aɪˋdiə; aɪˈdɪə/ *n*

1 ►PLAN/SUGGESTION 計劃/建議◄ [C] a plan or suggestion for a possible course of action, especially one that you think of suddenly〔尤指突然想到的〕計劃, 建議, 想法, 主意: **[+for]** *What gave you the idea for the book?* 是甚麼使你產生寫這本書的想法? | **[+of]** *What do you think about John's idea of recruiting two new people?* 你認為約翰招收兩個新人的主意怎麼樣? | **idea that** *What do you think of this idea that we should all wear uniforms?* 你認為大家都穿制服這個想法怎麼樣? | **it is sb's idea to do sth** *It was Mary's idea to hold the party outside.* 在室外舉行聚會是瑪麗的主意。| **good/great idea** *What a good idea!* 真是好主意! | **have an idea** (=think of an idea) 想到一個主意 *George has had a brilliant idea – let's hire the church hall.* 喬治想出一個絕妙的主意 —— 租用教堂大廳。| **hit on/come up with an idea** (=to think of an idea) 想到一個主意 | **new idea** *These meetings are intended to pool knowledge and inspire new ideas.* 這些會議的目的是集思廣益, 啟發新想法。| **toy with the idea of doing sth** (=think about a plan or suggestion, but not very seriously)〔不很認真地〕考慮〔計劃、建議等〕*We toyed with the idea of going to Paris.* 我們隨便地考慮過是否去巴黎。| **entertain an idea** (=consider it as a possibility) *formal*【正式】考慮一個想法〔認為有可能〕: *There is evidence to show that she entertained the idea of suicide long before this.* 有證據顯示她在此很久之前就考慮過自殺。| **bright idea** (=a very clever idea, often used jokingly to mean a very stupid idea or action) 好主意, 餿主意〔常用於開玩笑, 指非常愚蠢的想法或行為〕*Whose bright idea was it to turn the fridge off, then?* 那麼把冰箱的電源關掉是誰的餿主意?

2 ►KNOWLEDGE 知道◄ [C,U] **a)** a general understanding of something, based on knowing something about it 概括的了解: *Before I undertake this work, I need an idea of the problems involved.* 在着手這項工作前, 我需要大致了解一下有關的問題。| **some idea** (=at least a little knowledge about something)〔對某事的〕一些了解 *You must have some idea of where they went.* 對他們的行蹤你肯定略知一二。| **general/rough idea** (=a not very exact idea) 大致的想法 *Can you give me a rough idea of how much the repairs will cost?* 你能否告訴我修理費用大約是多少? **b)** to not know at all 根本不知道, 一無所知: **have no idea** *I've no idea where she's gone.* 我一點兒也不知道她去哪裡了。| *"When are they arriving?" "No idea."* "他們甚麼時間到?" "不知道。" | **not have the faintest/slightest/foggiest idea** *spoken*【口】*I don't have the foggiest idea how much he earns.* 我一點兒也不知道他掙多少錢。

3 ►AIM/INTENTION 目的/意圖◄ [C,U] the aim, intention, or purpose of doing something〔做某事的〕目的, 意圖: *The idea was to buy a new dress, but we only got as far as the supermarket!* 我們原打算買一件新的連衣裙, 卻只走到了超級市場! | **[+of]** *The idea of the game is get the ball past your opponent.* 這項運動的目的是不讓對手把球攔截掉。| **big ideas** (=plans to become important, successful etc) 遠大的抱負 *He was a man with big ideas – he even dreamed of becoming president.* 他抱負遠大, 甚至夢想做總統。| **have other ideas** (=have different plans from the ones that someone else has for you) 另有打算 *They wanted Mike to go to law school, but he had other ideas.* 他們想讓邁克上法學院, 但他另有打算。

4 ►IMAGE 印象◄ [C,U] an image in your mind of what something is like or should be like 概念, 想法: **[+of]** *Chefs differ in their idea of what makes a good dessert.* 好的餐後甜點應該是甚麼樣子, 廚師們觀點各異。| **not my idea of fun/a good time etc** *Walking up a mountain in the pouring rain isn't my idea of fun.* 在滂沱大雨中爬山, 在我看來毫無樂趣。

5 ►BELIEF 信念◄ [C usually plural 一般用複數] an opinion or belief 意見, 信念: *Jack has some pretty strange ideas.* 傑克有一些相當奇怪的想法。| **[+about]** *traditional ideas about women* 有關婦女的傳統觀念

6 have an idea (that) to be fairly sure that something is true, without being completely sure 猜想, 估計〔認為確有某事, 但無絕對把握〕: *I'm not certain where she is, but I've a pretty good idea.* 我不知道她在哪兒, 但大體上能猜出來。| *Benson? Yes, I have an idea he works in the library.* 本森? 對啦, 我想他在圖書館工作。

7 ►PRINCIPLE 原則◄ [C] a principle or belief about how something is or should be 原則, 信念: **[+of]** *The whole idea of democracy was something strange and new to most people.* 對於當時大部分人來說, 民主這個概念又奇怪又新鮮。| **idea that** *It's based on the idea that all people are created equal.* 它是基於人人生而平等這個信念的。

8 it is a (good) idea to do sth *spoken* used to give someone advice about what to do【口】做某事是個不錯的主意〔用於提供建議〕: *It'd be a good idea to call and let them know you're coming.* 最好打電話讓他們知道你要來。

9 get the idea *informal* to begin to understand something or be able to do something【非正式】開始明白或能做〔某事〕: *Just read through the instructions – you'll get the idea.* 把說明書讀一遍 —— 你會明白的。

10 get the wrong idea to think that something is true when it is not 誤解: *Don't get the wrong idea about Dan and Helen – they're just friends.* 不要誤解丹和海倫, 他倆不過是朋友而已。
11 have the right idea to be using the right kind of method or general principle in something that you are trying to do〔做某事〕方法正確, 方向對頭: *He still makes a few mistakes but I reckon he's got the right idea.* 他還犯一些錯誤, 但我認為他已經找到了竅門。
12 where did you get that idea? *spoken* used to say that what someone thinks is in fact completely wrong【口】你這想法是哪兒來的?〔指對方的想法完全錯誤〕: *No, I'm not seeing Jane. Where did you get that idea?* 不, 我不是去見簡。你這想法是從哪兒來的?
13 put ideas into sb's head to make someone think of doing something that they had not thought of before, especially something stupid or impossible 使某人產生某種念頭〔尤指愚蠢或不切實際的想法〕: *Nick tells me he wants a motorbike. Have you been putting ideas into his head?* 尼克對我說想要一輛摩托車。這個想法是不是你引起的?
14 that's an idea! *spoken* used to say that you like what someone has just suggested【口】好主意!〔用來表示贊同別人的建議〕: *"We could hire a car when we get there." "That's an idea!"* "到那兒之後我們可以租一輛車。" "好主意!"
15 that's the idea *spoken* used to tell someone who is learning to do something that they are doing it the right way, in order to encourage them【口】對了, 就是這樣〔用來鼓勵正在學着做某事的人〕
16 sb's idea of a joke *informal* something that is intended to be a joke but makes you angry【非正式】某人意在開玩笑的做法〔結果卻把人惹生氣了〕: *I suppose hiding the car keys was his idea of a joke!* 我看他把車鑰匙藏起來本是想開個玩笑!
17 you have no idea *spoken* used when you are telling someone that something is extremely good, bad etc【口】你簡直想不到〔用於告訴某人某事好或壞到極端地步〕: *You have no idea how worried I was.* 你簡直想不到我當時多麼着急。
18 the idea! *old-fashioned* used to express surprise or disapproval when someone has said something stupid or strange【過時】甚麼話!〔用於對方說了愚蠢或奇怪的話時, 表示驚訝或不贊成〕—see also 另見 **buck your ideas up** (BUCK²)

I

This graph shows some of the words most commonly used with the noun **idea**. 本圖表所示為含有名詞 idea 的一些最常用詞組。

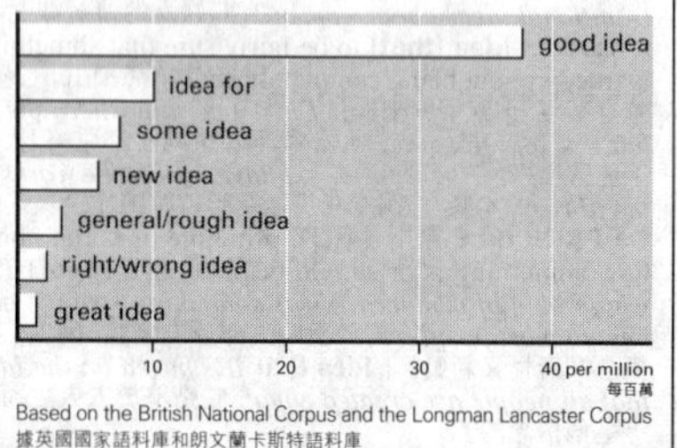

Based on the British National Corpus and the Longman Lancaster Corpus
據英國國家語料庫和朗文蘭卡斯特語料庫

S2 W2 **i·deal¹** /ˌaɪˋdɪəl; ˌaɪˈdɪəl◂/ *adj* **1** the best that something could possibly be 理想的, 最好的: *advice on how to reach your ideal weight* 如何達到理想體重的建議 | *an ideal place for a picnic* 理想的野餐地點 **2** [only before noun 僅用於名詞前] an ideal world, job, system etc is one that you imagine to be perfect, but that is not likely to really exist 想像的; 理想中的〔世界、職業、制度等〕: *In an ideal world there would be no need for a police force.* 在理想的世界中不需要警察。

ideal² *n* [C] **1** a principle or perfect standard that you hope to achieve〔希望實現的〕理想: *Social justice and equality, like many ideals, are difficult to realise.* 社會正義和平等, 如許多理想那樣, 是難以實現的。**2** an idea of what something would be like if it had no faults or problems 完美典型〔想像中完美的事物〕: **[+of]** *the democratic ideal of government* 民主政體的完美典型

i·deal·ise /aɪˋdɪəlˌaɪz; aɪˈdɪəlaɪz/ *v* [T] a British spelling of IDEALIZE idealize 的英式拼法

i·deal·is·m /aɪˋdɪəlˌɪzəm; aɪˈdɪəlɪzəm/ *n* [U] **1** strong belief in principles or perfect standards, even when they are very difficult to achieve in real life 理想主義: *youthful idealism* 青年人的理想主義 | *The movement appealed to their idealism.* 這場運動投合他們的理想主義觀點。**2** *technical* a way of using art to show the world as a perfect place, even though it is not【術語】理想主義〔指通過藝術來表現完美的世界, 儘管事實上世界並不完美〕—compare 比較 REALISM (2), NATURALISM

i·deal·ist /aɪˋdɪəlɪst; aɪˈdɪəlɪst/ *n* [C] someone who tries to live according to principles or perfect standards, especially in a way that is not practical or possible 理想主義者; 空想家

i·deal·is·tic /aɪˌdɪəlˋɪstɪk; aɪˌdɪəˈlɪstɪk◂/ *adj* believing in principles or perfect standards that cannot really be achieved 理想主義(者)的; 空想的: *We were young and idealistic and anything seemed possible.* 當時我們年輕, 充滿幻想, 似乎甚麼事都有可能。—**idealistically** /-klɪ; -kli/ *adv*

i·deal·ize also 又作 **-ise** *BrE*【英】/aɪˋdɪəlˌaɪz; aɪˈdɪəlaɪz/ *v* [T] to imagine or represent something or someone as being perfect or better than they really are 把〔某人、某物〕理想化; 對〔某人、某物〕作理想化的描述: *Boys often idealize their fathers.* 男孩子常常把自己的父親理想化。—**idealization** /aɪˌdɪələˋzeʃən; aɪˌdɪəlaɪˈzeɪʃən/ *n* [U]

i·deal·ly /aɪˋdɪəlɪ; aɪˈdɪəli/ *adv* **1** [sentence adverb 句子副詞] used to describe the way you would like things to be, even though this may not be possible 理想地: *How many orders are you hoping for, ideally?* 在最理想的情況下, 你希望拿到多少訂單? | *Ideally I'd like a job where I can work from home.* 最理想的是我能找到一份能在家裡辦公的工作。**2 ideally suited/placed/qualified etc** having very suitable qualities etc for a particular situation 非常適合/位置理想/條件合適: *He was ideally suited for the job.* 他做這個工作非常合適。

id·em /ˋaɪdɛm; ˈɪdem/ *Latin* from the same book, author etc as the one that has just been mentioned【拉丁】同前, 同上〔指來自剛提過的同一本書、作者等〕

i·den·ti·cal /aɪˋdɛntɪkḷ; aɪˈdentɪkəl/ *adj* exactly the same 完全相同的: *four identical houses* 四幢一模一樣的房子 | **[+to]** *This system is identical to the one used in France.* 這個系統與法國所用的那個完全相同。—**identically** /-klɪ; -kli/ *adv*

identical twin /·,··· ˈ·/ *n* [C usually plural 一般用複數] one of a pair of brothers or sisters born at the same time, who look almost exactly alike 長相酷似的雙胞胎之一, 同[單]卵雙胞胎之一

i·den·ti·fi·a·ble /aɪˋdɛntəˌfaɪəbḷ; aɪˈdentəfaɪəbəl/ *adj* someone or something that is identifiable can be recognized 可識別的, 可辨認出來的: *Only three people in the photograph are identifiable.* 照片上只有三個人可以辨認出來。

i·den·ti·fi·ca·tion /aɪˌdɛntəfəˋkeʃən; aɪˌdentəfəˈkeɪʃən/ *n* [U] **1** official papers or cards, such as your PASSPORT, that prove who you are 身分證明(文件)〈如護照〉: *Do you have any identification?* 你有甚麼身分證明文件嗎? | **means of identification** *My only means of identification was my driver's licence.* 我唯一的身分證明是駕駛執照。—see also 另見 ID **2** your ability to say who someone is because you have seen them before 辨認〔某人的能力〕, 認出: *procedures for the identification of suspects* 辨認嫌疑犯的程序 **3** the act or process of recognizing something 確定〔某物〕: *Correct identification of needs is vital.* 正確判定需求十分關鍵。**4** a strong feeling of sympathy with someone that makes you able to share their feelings 情感相通, 認同: *identification with the heroine of the play* 對劇中女主角的認同

identification pa·rade /ˌ·ˌ···ˈ·· ·ˌ·/ *n* [C] *BrE* a process in which a WITNESS to a crime looks at a group of people to see if they can recognize the criminal【英】列隊辨認〔指目擊者在一羣人中辨認嫌疑犯的過程〕; LINE-UP (4) *AmE*【美】

1 **i·den·ti·fy** /aɪˋdɛntəˌfaɪ; aɪˈdentɪfaɪ/ *v* [T] **1** to recognize and correctly name someone or something 認出〔某人或某物〕, 識別: *I agreed to try and identify the body.* 我同意去辨認那具屍體。| **identify sb/sth** *The aircraft were identified as American.* 那些飛機被認出是美國的。**2** to recognize something or discover exactly what it is, what its nature or origin is, etc 確定; 發現: *The first task is to identify local crime problems.* 首要任務是搞清楚地方犯罪問題。| *Scientists have identified the gene that causes abnormal growth.* 科學家已發現了造成畸形發育的基因。**3** to make it clear to other people who someone is 表明[顯示]身分: **identify sb as sb** *His accent identified him as a Frenchman.* 他的口音表明他是法國人。

identify with *phr v* [T] **1** [**identify with** sb] to feel able to share or understand the feelings of another person 與〔某人〕在感情上認同, 與〔某人〕有同感: *I didn't enjoy the movie because I couldn't identify with any of the characters.* 我不喜歡那部電影, 因為我對裡面的任何人物都不能認同。**2 be identified with** to be closely connected or involved with something such as a political group 與〔政治派別等〕關係緊密: *She has always been identified with the radical left.* 她與激進的左翼派別一直聯繫密切。**3** [**identify** sth **with** sb/sth] to think that something is the same as, or closely connected with, something else 將〔某物〕等同於〔某物〕: *It is a mistake to identify art with life.* 將藝術等同於生活是錯誤的。

i·den·ti·kit /aɪˋdɛntɪˌkɪt; aɪˈdentɪˌkɪt/ *n* [C] *BrE*【英】**1** a method used by the police for producing a picture of a possible criminal from descriptions given by a WITNESS or witnesses 容貌拼具〔指警方根據證人的描述拼出嫌疑犯的頭像的方法〕; COMPOSITE² (2) *AmE*【美】: *an identikit portrait* 容貌拼具拼出的肖像 **2 identikit houses/popstars etc** all exactly the same, and with no interesting or unusual features 千篇一律[毫無個性]的房屋/流行歌手等

2 **i·den·ti·ty** /aɪˋdɛntətɪ; aɪˈdentɪti/ *n* **1** [C,U] **sb's identity** who someone is; someone's name 某人的身分; 某人的姓名: *The identity of the killer is still unknown.* 兇手的身分仍未查明。| **mistaken identity** (=when someone is mistaken for someone else) 誤認〔以為是另一個人〕 *He was chased and shot by the police in a case of mistaken identity.* 他因被誤認而遭警察開槍追捕。**2** [U] the qualities and attitudes you have that make you feel you have your own character and are different from other people 個性; 個人特性: **sense of identity** *He has no sense of his own identity.* 他缺乏自我意識。| **cultural/ethnic/social identity** (=a strong feeling of belonging to a particular group, race etc) 文化/民族/社會認同 | **identity crisis** (=a feeling of uncertainty about who you really are and what your purpose in life is) 身分危機〔指對自己的身分和人生目標感到迷茫〕 **3** [U] *formal* exact SIMILARITY between two things【正式】〔兩件事物〕相同, 一致

identity card /·ˈ··· ·/ *n* [C] a card with your name, date of birth, photograph, and SIGNATURE on it, that proves who you are; ID CARD 身分證

id·e·o·gram /ˋɪdɪəˌgræm; ˈɪdiəgræm/ also 又作 **id·e·o·graph** /-græf; -grɑːf/ *n* [C] a written sign, for example in Chinese, that represents an idea rather than the sound of a word 表意文字〈如漢字〉, 表意符號

i·de·o·lo·gic·al /ˌaɪdɪəˋlɑdʒɪkḷ; ˌaɪdiəˈlɒdʒɪkəl◂/ *adj* based on strong beliefs or ideas, especially political or economic ideas, that may not be practical in real life 意識形態的, 觀念的; 不現實的: *an ideological commitment to privatization* 意識形態上對私有化的堅持 —**ideologically** /-klɪ; -kli/ *adv*

i·de·ol·o·gy /ˌaɪdɪˋɑlədʒɪ; ˌaɪdiˈɒlədʒi/ *n* [C,U] **1** a set of ideas on which a political or economic system is based 〔政治或經濟的〕思想體系, 意識形態: *the ideologies of fascism and capitalism* 法西斯主義和資本主義的意識形態 **2** a set of ideas and attitudes that strongly influence the way people behave 〔強烈影響人的行為的〕思想; 觀念: *an ideology that views women as 'the weaker sex'* 認為婦女是"弱勢性別"的思想 3

ides /aɪdz; aɪdz/ *n* [plural] a date or period of time around the middle of the month in the ancient Roman calendar 古羅馬曆法每月中間的一天[月中的一段時間/中旬]

id·i·o·cy /ˋɪdɪəsɪ; ˈɪdiəsi/ *n* **1** [U] extreme stupidity or silliness 極度愚蠢: *the idiocy of our rulers* 統治者的極度愚蠢 **2** [C] a very stupid remark or action 極愚蠢的言論[行為]

id·i·o·lect /ˋɪdɪəˌlɛkt; ˈɪdiəlekt/ *n* [C,U] *technical* the way in which a particular person uses language【術語】個人言語方式, 個人語型 —compare 比較 DIALECT

id·i·om /ˋɪdɪəm; ˈɪdiəm/ *n* **1** [C] a group of words with a meaning of its own that is different from the meanings of each separate word put together 習語, 成語: *'Under the weather' is an idiom meaning 'ill'.* 習語 under the weather 意為"生病"。**2** [C,U] *literary* a style of expression in writing, speech, or music, that is typical of a particular group of people【文】〔某團體在寫作、言語、音樂方面典型的〕風格, 特色

id·i·o·mat·ic /ˌɪdɪəˋmætɪk; ˌɪdiəˈmætɪk◂/ *adj* **1 idiomatic phrase/expression** an idiom 習慣用語/慣用表達法: *an idiomatic phrase* 習慣短語 **2** typical of the natural way in which someone using their own language speaks or writes 〔說話或書寫〕符合某一語言習慣的, 地道的: *After a year in Madrid, her Spanish was fluent and idiomatic.* 在馬德里住了一年後, 她的西班牙語已很流利地道了。—**idiomatically** /-klɪ; -kli/ *adv*

id·i·o·syn·cra·sy /ˌɪdɪəˋsɪnkrəsɪ; ˌɪdiəˈsɪŋkrəsi/ *n* [C] **1** an unusual habit or way of behaving that someone has 〔個人特有的〕習性, 癖好: *Her idiosyncrasies included talking to her plants.* 她的怪癖之一是對自己種植的草木說話。**2** an unusual or unexpected feature that something has 〔某物的〕異質; 特點: *one of the many idiosyncrasies of English spelling* 英語拼寫眾多特點之一 —**idiosyncratic** /ˌɪdɪosɪnˋkrætɪk; ˌɪdiəsɪnˈkrætɪk◂/ *adj*

id·i·ot /ˋɪdɪət; ˈɪdiət/ *n* [C] **1** a stupid person or someone who has done something stupid 笨蛋, 蠢才: *Some idiot drove into the back of my car.* 有個笨蛋開車撞上了我汽車的尾部。**2** *old use* someone who is mentally ill or has a very low level of intelligence【舊】白痴 —**idiotic** /ˌɪdɪˋɑtɪk; ˌɪdiˈɒtɪk◂/ *adj* —**idiotically** /-klɪ; -kli/ *adv*

idle¹ /ˋaɪdḷ; ˈaɪdl/ *adj* **1** not working or producing anything 不工作的; 空閒的: **lie/stand idle** *We can't leave this expensive machinery lying idle.* 我們不能讓這套昂貴的機械閒置着。| *The whole team stood idle, waiting for the mechanic.* 整隊人乾站着等技工來。**2** lazy 懶惰的: *a crowd of idle students* 一羣懶散的學生 | *Come on, you idle lot!* 快點, 你們這羣懶蟲! **3** not serious, or not done with any definite intention 不認真的; 漫無目的的: *The doctor hated wasting time on idle chatter.* 這個醫生討厭把時間浪費在閒聊上。| *If you say 'no', mean it. Never make idle threats.* 說"不"就是"不", 別作無謂的威脅。**4 the idle rich** rich people who do not have to work 不用工作的富人

idle² *v* **idled, idling 1** [I always+adv/prep] to spend time doing nothing 虛度時間, 閒混, 無所事事: *Tom was idling at the corner when a well-dressed businessman came up to him.* 湯姆正在街角閒逛, 突然一位衣冠楚楚的商人朝他走來。**2** [I,T] if an engine idles or if you idle it, it runs slowly while it is not connected to the system that makes parts move (使)〔發動機低速地〕空轉 **3** [T] to

I

stop using a factory or stop providing work for your workers, especially temporarily〔尤指暫時〕使〔工廠〕閒置; 使〔工人〕閒着

idle sth ↔ **away** *phr v* [T] to spend time in a relaxed way, doing nothing 虛度〔光陰〕, 消磨〔時間〕: *We were just idling away the time by the river.* 我們當時只是在河邊閒逛。

id·ler /ˋaɪdlɚ; ˈaɪdlə/ *n* [C] *old-fashioned* someone who is lazy and does not work【過時】懶漢, 遊手好閒者

i·dol /ˋaɪdḷ; ˈaɪdl/ *n* [C] **1** someone or something that you love or admire very much 偶像: **be the idol of** *a football player who was the idol of the younger boys* 成為小男孩們偶像的足球員 | **TV/pop idol** (=a famous actor or performer that many people admire) 電視/流行樂偶像 *the chance to meet your favorite TV idol* 與你最喜愛的電視偶像見面的機會 **2** a picture or STATUE that is worshipped as a god 神像

i·dol·a·ter /aɪˋdɑlətɚ; aɪˈdɒlətə/ *n* [C] *formal* someone who worships a picture or STATUE of a god【正式】〔神像的〕崇拜者

i·dol·a·tress /aɪˋdɑlətrɪs; aɪˈdɒlətr¦ɪs/ *n* [C] *formal* a woman who worships a picture or STATUE as a god【正式】〔神像的〕女崇拜者

i·dol·a·try /aɪˋdɑlətrɪ; aɪˈdɒlətri/ *n* [U] **1** the practice of worshipping IDOLS 偶像崇拜 **2** too much admiration for someone or something〔對某人或某物的〕過分崇拜: *idolatry of power* 對權力的極度崇拜 —**idolatrous** *adj*

i·dol·ize also 又作 **-ise** *BrE*【英】/ˋaɪdḷˌaɪz; ˈaɪdəl-aɪz/ *v* [T] to admire and love someone so much that you think they are perfect 極度欽佩〔某人〕, 喜愛: *They had one child, a girl whom they idolized.* 他們有一個女兒, 他們對她寵愛備至。

id·yll /ˋaɪdḷ; ˈɪdəl/ *n* [singular] *literary* a place or experience in which everything is peaceful and everyone is perfectly happy【文】平靜快樂的地方; 安寧愉快的經歷: *the rural idyll of peace and plenty* 恬靜富庶的鄉村生活

i·dyl·lic /aɪˋdɪlɪk; ɪˈdɪlɪk/ *adj* very happy and peaceful, with no problems or dangers 快樂祥和的: *an idyllic setting on the shores of a lake* 湖畔恬靜宜人的環境 —**idyllically** /-klɪ; -kli/ *adv*: *idyllically happy* 悠然歡暢

i.e. /ˌaɪ ˋi; ˌaɪ ˈiː/ *Latin* used to explain the exact meaning of something that you have just said【拉丁】即; 也就是〔用於對剛才所說作確切的說明〕: *The film is only open to adults, i.e. people over 18.* 該影片只限成年人觀看, 即18歲以上者。

-ie /ɪ; i/ *suffix* [in nouns 構成名詞] *informal* another form of the suffix -y² (1)【非正式】後綴 -y² (1) 的另一種形式: *dearie* 親愛的

1 1 **if¹** /ɪf; ɪf/ *conjunction* **1** used to talk about something that might happen 假若, 倘若, 如果: *What can you do if your child behaves badly in a public place?* 如果你的孩子在公共場所胡鬧, 你能怎麼辦? | *If you don't leave now I'm calling the police.* 你現在若不離開, 我就報警。| *We can always get a taxi if there's a problem with the car.* 如果車子出了毛病, 我們總可以叫一輛計程車。| **if by any chance** *If by any chance Peter should phone, can you tell him I'll talk to him later?* 萬一彼得來電話, 告訴他我待會兒跟他談, 好嗎? | **if not** *I think there's a train at midday. If not you'll have to wait till 12.30.* 我想正午會有一班火車。要是沒有, 你只好等到12時30分了。**2** used when you are talking about something that always happens in a particular situation 無論何時; 只要: *If I go to bed late I feel dreadful in the morning.* 我如果睡得晚, 第二天早上就感到很不舒服。| *Plastic will melt if it gets too hot.* 塑料過熱就會融化。**3 even if** although something is true or something happens 即使; 雖然: *Even if I did lose a stone, I still wouldn't look skinny.* 即使我的體重減輕一英石, 看上去也不會皮包骨頭。**4** used to mean 'though', when you are describing someone or something that you like 雖然〔用於描述所喜愛的人或物〕: *He's a pleasant child, if a little spoiled.* 他是個很討人喜愛的孩子, 只是有點兒給寵壞了。**5** used like 'whether' when asking or deciding whether something is true or will happen 是否〔詢問或判斷對錯或事情是否會發生時, 與 whether 的用法相似〕: *I rang them to see if I could cancel the appointment.* 我給他們打電話, 看能不能取消約會。| *Ask him if he'll lend me some money.* 問問他能否借我一些錢。| *I wonder if John's home yet.* 我不知道約翰是否到家了。**6** used when saying that you are surprised, upset, angry etc that something has happened or is true〔用於表示由於某事發生或某種情況驚訝、心煩、氣惱等〕: *I'm sorry if you took it that way.* 你要是那樣理解我很遺憾。| *I don't care if he is my brother. He's still an idiot.* 我不在乎他是不是我兄弟, 他就是個笨蛋。**7 if I were you** used when giving advice and telling someone what you think they should do 我要是你的話〔用於給人忠告〕: *If I were you I'd jump at the chance of a job like that.* 我要是你, 就會立即抓住那樣好的工作機會。**8 it isn't as if.../it's not as if...** used when saying that you do not understand why someone is doing something 似乎並不〔用於對某人的做法表示不理解〕: *I can't think why they're being so mean. It's not as if they're short of money.* 我不明白他們怎麼變得這麼吝嗇, 他們似乎並不缺錢啊。

if² *n* **1 ifs and buts** *BrE*【英】**/ifs, ands, or buts** *AmE*【美】if you do not want any ifs and buts, you want someone to do something quickly without arguing〔為故意拖延而作的〕藉口, 託詞: *No ifs and buts – just make sure the job is done by tomorrow!* 別找任何藉口, 一定要保證在明天把工作完成! **2 and it's a big if** used to say that something is not likely to happen 這是一大疑問〔用於表示某事不大可能發生〕: *We can do it if, and it's a big if, we get the money.* 這事我們有錢就能做, 但能否找到錢是一大疑問。

if·fy /ˋɪfɪ; ˈɪfi/ *adj informal* full of uncertainty【非正式】不確定的, 充滿不確定性的: *The whole plan is beginning to look pretty iffy.* 整個計劃開始讓人覺得撲朔迷離。| *I'm a bit iffy about having a party here.* 是否在這裡舉行聚會, 我還沒有拿定主意。

-iform /ɪfɔrm; ¦ɪfɔːm/ *suffix* [in adjectives 構成形容詞] *technical* like or in the shape of something【術語】…樣的, 具有…形狀的: *cruciform* (=cross-shaped) 十字形的

-ify /ɪfaɪ; ¦ɪfaɪ/ *suffix* [in verbs 構成動詞] also 又作 **-fy** **1** to affect something in a particular way, or become something (使) 成為…, (使) …化: *to purify* (=make or become pure) 淨化 | *to clarify the situation* (=make it clear) 澄清情況 **2** to fill someone with a particular feeling 使〔某人〕充滿〔某種感情〕: *They terrify me.* (=fill me with terror) 他們使我充滿恐懼。**3 a)** *informal* to do something in a silly or annoying way【非正式】愚蠢地[令人討厭地]做某事: *to speechify* (=make speeches, use important sounding words) 高談闊論; 誇誇其談 **b)** to make something or someone be like or typical of a person or group 使類似於〔某人或團體〕: *Frenchified* (=like the French) 法國化的

ig·loo /ˋɪglu; ˈɪgluː/ *n* [C] a house made from blocks of hard snow or ice〔用堅硬的雪或冰塊築成的〕小屋

ig·ne·ous /ˋɪgnɪəs; ˈɪgniəs/ *adj technical* igneous rocks are formed from LAVA (=hot liquid rock under the ground)【術語】〔岩石〕火成的

ig·nite /ɪgˋnaɪt; ɪgˈnaɪt/ *v* **1** [I,T] *formal* to start burning or to make something start burning【正式】點燃; 使燃燒: *The fuel is ignited by a high voltage spark.* 這種燃料由高壓火花點燃。**2 ignite controversy/resentment etc** to make people suddenly feel very angry or upset about something 激起爭論/憤怒等

ig·ni·tion /ɪgˋnɪʃən; ɪgˈnɪʃən/ *n* **1** [singular] the electrical part of a vehicle's engine that makes it start working〔汽車引擎的〕點火裝置, 點火開關 —see picture on page A2 參見 A2 頁圖 **2** [U] *formal* the act of starting to burn, or making something do this【正式】着火, 起火燃燒; 點火

ig·no·ble /ɪgˋnobḷ; ɪgˈnəʊbəl/ *adj formal* ignoble thoughts, feelings, or actions are ones that you should feel ashamed or embarrassed about【正式】卑鄙的, 可恥的, 不光彩的 —**ignobly** *adv*

ig·no·min·i·ous /ˌɪgnəˋmɪnɪəs; ˌɪgnəˈmɪniəs/ *adj formal* making you feel ashamed, especially because you seem stupid, unimportant, or dishonest【正式】〔因顯得愚蠢、渺小或奸詐而感到〕丟臉的, 不光彩的: *an ignominious departure* 不光彩的離任 | *another ignominious failure* 又一次令人丟臉的失敗 —**ignominiously** *adv*

ig·no·mi·ny /ˋɪgnəˌmɪnɪ; ˈɪgnəmɪni/ *n formal*【正式】**1** [C] an event or situation that makes you feel ashamed 難堪; 恥辱〔指事件或處境〕: *He came last, an ignominy he could hardly bear.* 他得了最後一名, 這是他難以忍受的恥辱。**2** [U] shame and public dishonour 恥辱; 不名譽: *the ignominy of defeat* 失敗的恥辱

ig·no·ra·mus /ˌɪgnəˋreməs; ˌɪgnəˈreɪməs/ *n* [C] *plural* **ignoramuses** someone who does not know about things that most people know about 無知的人, 愚人

ig·no·rance /ˋɪgnərəns; ˈɪgnərəns/ *n* [U] **1** lack of knowledge or information about something 無知, 愚昧: *My mistake was caused by ignorance, not malice.* 我的錯誤是無知所致, 並非出於惡意。| **keep sb in ignorance** (=not tell someone about something that they should know about) 不讓某人知道〔他應知道的事〕*Adopted children shouldn't be kept in ignorance about their true origins.* 不應該瞞着領養的孩子他們的親生父母是誰。**2 ignorance is bliss** used to say that if you do not know about a problem, you cannot worry about it 無知是福

ig·no·rant /ˋɪgnərənt; ˈɪgnərənt/ *adj* **1** not knowing facts or information that you ought to know 無知的, 沒有學識的, 愚昧的: *an ignorant and uneducated man* 不學無術的人 | [**+of**] *They were ignorant of any events outside their own town.* 他們對鎮外的事情一無所知。| [**+about**] *I'm very ignorant about politics.* 我對政治一竅不通。—see 見 IGNORE (USAGE) **2** caused by a lack of knowledge and understanding 因無知而產生的: *What an ignorant thing to say!* 這話太無知了! | *ignorant opinions* 愚蠢的看法 **3** *BrE spoken* rude or impolite; ILL-MANNERED【英口】粗魯的, 不禮貌的

2 2 **ig·nore** /ɪgˋnor; ɪgˈnɔː/ *v* [T] **1** to behave as if you had not heard or seen someone or something 不管; 忽視; 不理: *Either she didn't see me wave or she deliberately ignored me.* 要麼她沒看見我招手, 要麼就是故意不理我。| *Sam rudely ignored the question.* 山姆粗魯地對這個問題不予理睬。**2** to deliberately pay no attention to something that you have been told or that you know about〔故意對知道的事〕置之不理: *As far as homelessness goes, the vast majority of people just sit back and ignore it.* 對於無家可歸這個問題, 大多數人都袖手旁觀, 熟視無睹。

> **USAGE NOTE 用法說明: IGNORE**
> WORD CHOICE 詞語辨析: **ignore, be ignorant of**
> If you **ignore** something, you know about it or have seen or heard it, but choose not to take notice of it. ignore 是指視而不見、聽而不聞或故意不予理睬: *Some drivers simply ignore speed limits.* 有些司機就是對速度限制視而不見。
> If you are **ignorant of** something, you do not know about it. ignorant of 指對某事不知道, 不了解: *No driver can pretend to be ignorant of speed limits.* 沒有哪個司機能夠佯裝不知道速度限制。

i·gua·na /ɪˋgwanə; ɪˈgwɑːnə/ *n* [C] a large tropical American LIZARD 鬣蜥〔一種大型熱帶美洲蜥蜴〕

i·kon /ˋaɪkan; ˈaɪkɒn/ *n* [C] another spelling of ICON (3) icon (3) 的另一種拼法

il- /ɪl; ɪl/ *prefix* the form used for IN- before l 前綴 in- 用於 l 前的形式: *illogical* (=not logical) 不合邏輯的

i·lex /ˋaɪlɛks; ˈaɪleks/ *n* [C,U] **1** a type of OAK tree with leaves that are always green 聖櫟〔一種常綠橡樹〕**2** *technical* one of a family of trees and bushes including HOLLY【術語】冬青屬植物

ilk /ɪlk; ɪlk/ *n* **of that/his/their ilk** of that type, his type etc 與那個/他/他們同類的: *Irving Berlin and composers of his ilk* 歐文·柏林及其同類作曲家

I'll /aɪl; aɪl/ the short form of 縮略式= 'I will' or 'I shall'

ill¹ /ɪl; ɪl/ *adj* **1** [not usually before noun 一般不用於名詞 3 3
前] *especially BrE* suffering from a disease or not feeling well; sick【尤英】有病的; 不適的: *Bridget can't come – she's ill.* 布麗奇特不能來了, 她生病了。| **feel ill** *I was feeling ill that day, and decided to stay at home.* 我那天不太舒服, 決定待在家裡。| **be taken ill/fall ill** (=become ill) 患病; 病倒 *She was suddenly taken ill at school.* 她突然病倒在學校裡。| **seriously ill** (=very ill) 病重 *seriously ill in hospital* 在醫院裡病得很重 | **mentally ill** (=with a disease of the mind) 患精神病的 | **terminally ill** (=with an illness that you will die from) 病入膏肓的 *a hospice for the terminally ill* 晚期病人的安養院 | **ill health** *He had to resign due to ill health.* 他由於身體欠佳只好辭職。—see also 另見 ILLNESS —see 見 SICK¹ (USAGE) **2** [not before noun 不用於名詞前] *BrE* suffering from the effects of an injury【英】傷的, 受傷的: *The two policemen are still seriously ill with gunshot wounds.* 這兩名警察的槍傷仍然十分嚴重。**3** [only before noun 僅用於名詞前] bad or harmful 壞的, 有害的: *She seemed to have suffered no ill effects from her ordeal.* 她似乎未因這次苦難而受到不良影響。| *accusations of ill treatment by the police* 對警察虐待的指控 **4 ill at ease** nervous, uncomfortable, or embarrassed 緊張, 不自在, 窘迫: *He always felt shy and ill at ease at parties.* 他每次參加聚會都感到害羞和不自在。**5 it's an ill wind (that blows nobody any good)** *spoken* used to say that every problem brings an advantage for someone【口】只有惡風才會對一切人都不利〔即指任何麻煩總會使某些人獲益〕—see also 另見 ILL FEELING, ILL WILL

> This graph shows how common the adjectives **ill** and **sick** are in British and American English. 本圖表所示形容詞 ill 和 sick 在英國英語和美國英語中的使用頻率。
>
> 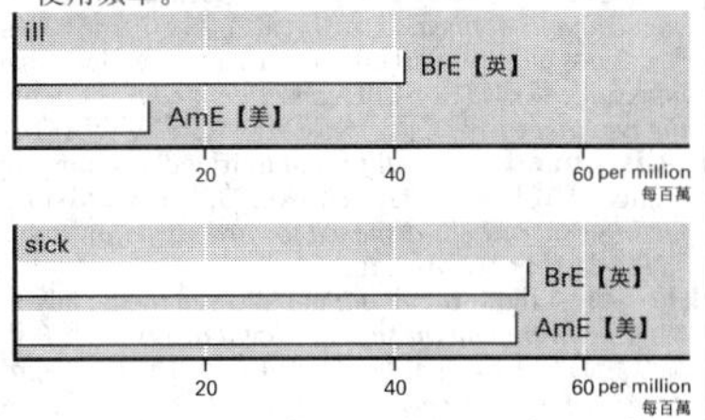
>
>
> Based on the British National Corpus and the Longman Lancaster Corpus
> 據英國國家語料庫和朗文蘭卡斯特語料庫
>
> In British English the word **ill** means not healthy. Americans usually use **sick** for this meaning. In British English **sick** can be used in this way, but is more commonly used in expressions such as **be sick** or **feel sick** meaning to VOMIT or feel that you are going to VOMIT. 英國英語用 ill 表示身體不健康, 而美國英語一般用 sick 表示這個意思。在英國英語裡 sick 也可以這樣用, 但更常見的是用在 be sick 或 feel sick 這樣的片語中, 表示"嘔吐"或"噁心"的意思。

ill² *adv* **1 be ill treated/ill used etc** to be treated badly, unpleasantly, or cruelly 受虐待: *Most of our clients have been ill-treated as children.* 我們的多數委託人在孩提時代都受過虐待。**2** not well or not enough; badly 不好, 不夠; 惡劣地: *She was ill prepared for the ordeal ahead.* 她對未來的嚴峻考驗準備不足。| *"I see one third of a nation ill-housed, ill-clad, ill-nourished." (F.D. Roosevelt)* "我看見一個國家有三分之一的人民屋不遮雨, 衣不蔽體, 食不果腹。" (F.D. 羅斯福) **3 can ill afford (to do) sth** to be unable to do something without making the situation you are in very difficult 難以承擔做某事的後果: *I was wasting time I could ill afford to lose.* 我當時是在浪費我浪費不起的時間。**4 think/speak ill of** *formal* to think or say unpleasant things about someone【正式】對〔某人〕抱有惡感; 說〔某人〕壞話: *She really believes you should never speak ill of the dead.* 她的確認為你不應該講死者的壞話。

ill³ *n* **1** [plural] problems and difficulties 問題; 困難: *Free-market economics was seen as the cure for all our ills.* 自由市場經濟曾被看作是醫治我們一切弊病的良藥。**2** [U] *formal* harm, evil, or bad luck【正式】傷害; 邪惡; 厄運: *She did not like Matthew but she would never wish him ill.* 她雖不喜歡馬修, 但也不會希望他倒霉。

ill-ad·vised /ˌ· ·ˈ·◂/ *adj* not sensible or not wise and likely to cause problems in the future 不理智的〔日後可能惹麻煩〕; 不明智的: *an ill-advised response to the crisis* 對危機作出的不明智反應 | **you would be ill-advised to do sth** (=used to advise someone not to do something stupid) 你要是做某事就太不明智了〔用於忠告別人不要做蠢事〕 *You would be ill-advised to lend him any money.* 你要是借錢給他就太不明智了。—**ill-advisedly** *adv*: *Scott ill-advisedly took matters into his own hands.* 司各特攬下這些事情, 太不明智了。

ill-as·sort·ed /ˌ· ·ˈ··◂/ *adj* an ill-assorted group of people or things do not seem to belong together in a group〔一組人或事物〕不相配的; 拉雜的

ill-bred /ˌ· ˈ·◂/ *adj* rude or behaving badly, especially because your parents did not teach you to behave well 粗魯的〔尤指沒有家教〕; 無教養的: *an ill-bred upstart criticizing everyone else* 對所有人都橫加指責的缺乏教養的暴發戶

ill-con·sid·ered /ˌ· ·ˈ··◂/ *adj* decisions, actions, ideas etc that are ill-considered have not been carefully thought about 考慮不周的: *The program is ill-considered and a waste of everyone's time.* 該方案考慮欠周全, 浪費了大家的時間。

ill-de·fined /ˌ· ·ˈ·◂/ *adj* **1** not described clearly enough 不清楚的, 不明確的: *The party's policies were often vague and ill-defined.* 該黨的政策常常模糊不清, 界定不明。**2** not clearly marked, or not having a clear shape; INDISTINCT 輪廓模糊不清的: *an ill-defined track between the two lakes* 兩湖之間一條時寬時窄、若隱若現的小徑

ill-dis·posed /ˌ· ·ˈ·/ *adj formal* unfriendly or unsympathetic【正式】不友好的; 漠不關心的: **[+towards]** *I was feeling generally ill-disposed toward my fellow man.* 我當時對同伴一般都不友善。

il·le·gal¹ /ɪˋligl; ɪˈliːgəl/ *adj* not allowed by the law 違法的: *They were caught selling illegal drugs.* 他們在販賣違禁藥品時被捕。| **it is illegal to do sth** *It's illegal to drive without a licence.* 無照駕駛是違法的。—opposite 反義詞 LEGAL (1) —**illegally** *adv*

illegal² *n* [C] *AmE spoken* an illegal immigrant【美口】非法移民: *We don't want illegals coming for welfare dollars!* 我們不想收容那些為福利金而來的非法移民!

illegal im·mi·grant /ˌ·ˌ·· ˈ···/ also 又作 **illegal a·li·en** *AmE*【美】/ˌ·ˌ·· ˈ···/ *n* [C] someone who comes to live in a country from abroad, without official permission〔來自國外的〕非法居留者, 非法移民

il·le·gal·i·ty /ˌɪlɪˋgælətɪ; ˌɪlɪˈgæləti/ *n* **1** [U] the state of being illegal 違法, 非法 **2** [C] an action that is illegal 違法行為

il·le·gi·ble /ɪˋlɛdʒəbl; ɪˈledʒəbəl/ *adj* difficult or impossible to read〔字跡〕難以[不能]辨認的: *I'm not sure what this note says – Dad's writing is almost illegible!* 我搞不清這張便條上寫了甚麼 —— 爸爸的字幾乎無法辨認! —opposite 反義詞 LEGIBLE —**illegibly** *adv* —**illegibility** /ɪˌlɛdʒəˋbɪlətɪ; ɪˌledʒəˈbɪləti/ *n* [U]

il·le·git·i·mate /ˌɪlɪˋdʒɪtəmɪt; ˌɪləˈdʒɪtəmət◂/ *adj* **1** born to parents who are not married 私生的 **2** not allowed or acceptable according to established rules or agreements 不合規則[約定]的: *illegitimate use of public funds* 濫用公款 —**illegitimately** *adv* —**illegitimacy** *n* [U]

ill-e·quipped /ˌ· ·ˈ·◂/ *adj* not having the necessary equipment or skills for a particular situation or activity 裝備不足的; 能力欠缺的: *They were ill-equipped for the journey.* 他們這次旅行的裝備不夠充足。| **ill-equipped to do sth** *an inexperienced teacher who was ill-equipped to deal with such children* 一位既缺乏經驗又沒有能力對付這樣的孩子的教師

ill-fat·ed /ˌ· ˈ··◂/ *adj literary* unlucky and leading to serious problems or death【文】不幸的, 倒霉的〔導致嚴重問題甚至死亡的〕: *One of the group was killed on the ill-fated expedition.* 隊伍中有一人死於這場倒霉的遠征。

ill-fa·voured *BrE*【英】, **ill-favored** *AmE*【美】/ˌ· ˈ··◂/ *adj literary or old-fashioned* having an unattractive face; ugly【文或過時】長相醜陋的, 其貌不揚的

ill feel·ing /ˌ· ˈ··/ *n* [U] angry feelings towards someone 敵意, 反感: *Whatever ill feeling there had been between them had vanished by now.* 他們之間以往的恩恩怨怨現在已煙消雲散了。

ill-found·ed /ˌ· ˈ··/ *adj formal* not based on true facts【正式】缺乏根據的, 憑空的: *Unfortunately her faith in British justice proved ill-founded.* 不幸的是, 她對英國司法的信任原來毫無根據。

ill-got·ten /ˌ· ˈ··◂/ *adj* **ill-gotten gains/wealth etc** *especially humorous* money that was obtained in an unfair or dishonest way【尤幽默】來路不正的錢財: *They rushed home to gloat over their ill-gotten gains.* 他們趕緊回家, 對着不義之財沾沾自喜。

il·lib·e·ral /ɪˋlɪbərəl; ɪˈlɪbərəl/ *adj formal*【正式】**1** not supporting freedom of expression or of personal behaviour 不開明的, 狹隘的, 不容異說的: *illiberal and undemocratic policies* 專制、不民主的政策 **2** not generous 吝嗇的, 小氣的 —**illiberally** *adv* —**illiberality** /ɪˌlɪbəˋrælətɪ; ɪˌlɪbəˈræləti/ *n* [U]

il·li·cit /ɪˋlɪsɪt; ɪˈlɪsət/ *adj* not allowed by laws or rules, or strongly disapproved of by society 非法的, 違禁的, 社會不容許的: *an illicit love affair* 有違世俗的愛情 | *illicit diamond trading* 非法鑽石交易 —**illicitly** *adv*

il·lit·e·rate /ɪˋlɪtərɪt; ɪˈlɪtərət/ *adj* **1** someone who is illiterate has not learned to read or write 不識字的, 文盲的 **2** badly written, in an uneducated way〔因未受教育而〕滿紙別字的, 病句連篇的: *It was an illiterate letter, full of mistakes.* 這封信文筆很差, 錯誤連篇。**3 politically/scientifically etc illiterate** knowing very little about politics, science etc 對政治/科學知識等一竅不通 —**illiteracy** *n* [U]

ill-judged /ˌ· ˈ·◂/ *adj formal* an action that is ill-judged has not been thought about carefully enough【正式】判斷不當的, 輕率的: *an ill-judged decision* 輕率的決定

ill-man·nered /ˌ· ˈ··◂/ *adj formal* not polite; behaving badly in social situations【正式】粗魯的;〔在社交場合〕不禮貌的 —opposite 反義詞 WELL-MANNERED

ill-na·tured /ˌ· ˈ··◂/ *adj formal* unpleasant or unkind【正式】令人討厭的, 不友善的: *ill-natured gossip* 流言蜚語

ill·ness /ˋɪlnɪs; ˈɪlnəs/ *n* [C,U] a disease of the body or mind 病, 疾病: *She had all the normal childhood illnesses.* 兒童的常見病她小時候都患過。| *mental illness* 精神疾病 | **serious illness** *an insurance policy that guarantees an income in the event of serious illness* 保證身患重病時仍有收入的保險單 | **minor illness** (=one that is not very serious) 小病, 微恙 *people who go to the doctor even for the most minor illnesses* 那些稍有不適就去找醫生的人 —see also 另見 DISEASE

il·lo·gi·cal /ɪˋlɑdʒɪkl; ɪˈlɒdʒɪkəl/ *adj* **1** not sensible or reasonable 不合理的, 悖理的: *erratic and illogical behaviour* 古怪、乖戾的行為 —opposite 反義詞 LOGICAL (1) **2** not based on the principles of LOGIC 不合邏輯的: *an illogical conclusion* 荒謬的結論 —**illogically** /-klɪ; -kli/ *adv* —**illogicality** /ɪˌlɑdʒɪˋkælətɪ; ɪˌlɒdʒəˈkæləti/ *n* [U]

ill-o·mened /ˌ· ˈ··◂/ *adj literary* likely to bring a lot of problems or suffering in the future【文】不祥的, 很可能導致問題[苦難]的: *an ill-omened business venture* 有不祥之兆的投資

ill-starred /ˌ· ˈ·◂/ *adj literary* unlucky and likely to cause or experience a lot of problems or unhappiness【文】倒霉的, 不吉利的: *an ill-starred love affair* 苦命的愛情

ill-tem·pered /ˌ· ˈ··◂/ *adj formal*【正式】**1** easily made angry or impatient 易怒的, 脾氣暴躁的 **2** an ill-tempered meeting, argument etc is one in which people are angry and often rude to each other〔會議、爭論等〕怒氣沖沖的, 粗魯無禮的: *ill-tempered exchanges in the presidential debate* 總統競選辯論中火藥味十足的唇槍舌劍

ill-timed /ˌ· ˈ·◂/ *adj* happening, done, or said at the wrong time 不合時宜的: *His remarks are ill-timed and inappropriate.* 他那番話說得不是時候, 內容也有失妥當。

ill-treat /ˌ· ˈ·/ *v* [T] to be cruel to someone, especially to a child or animal 虐待〔尤指對孩子或動物〕—**ill-treatment** *n* [U]

il·lu·mi·nate /ɪˈluməˌnet; ɪˈluːmɪ̀neɪt/ *v* [T] **1** to make a light shine on something, or fill a place with light 照射, 照亮, 照明: *The room was illuminated by the glow of the fire.* 房間被爐火照得通明。**2** *formal* to make something much clearer and easier to understand【正式】闡明〔某物〕, 解釋; 使易懂: *His lecture illuminated and explained many scientific phenomena.* 他的講演闡明並解釋了許多科學現象。**3** to decorate buildings, streets, etc with lights for a special occasion〔節日時〕用燈裝飾〔建築物、街道等〕**4** *literary* to make someone look happy or excited【文】使〔某人〕面露喜色, 容光煥發: *A sudden smile illuminated her face.* 突然她的臉上露出了笑容。

il·lu·mi·nat·ed /ɪˈluməˌnetɪd; ɪˈluːmɪ̀neɪtɪ̀d/ *adj* **1** lit up by lights〔用燈〕照亮的, 發光的: *a big illuminated sign over the entrance* 入口處上方的大型燈標 **2 an illuminated book/bible/manuscript etc** a book of a type produced by hand in the Middle Ages, whose pages are decorated with gold paint and other bright colours 綴以顏色的書籍/聖經/手稿等〔指在中世紀以手工製作的一種書籍, 頁面上有金漆及其他亮麗色彩的裝飾〕

il·lu·mi·nat·ing /ɪˈluməˌnetɪŋ; ɪˈluːmɪ̀neɪtɪŋ/ *adj* making things much clearer and easier to understand 使清楚的, 容易理解的: *I didn't find his reply very illuminating.* 我覺得他的答覆意思不太明確。

il·lu·mi·na·tion /ɪˌluməˈneʃən; ɪˌluːmɪ̀ˈneɪʃən/ *n* **1** [U] lighting provided by a lamp, light etc 光亮, 照明: *An electric light bulb provided the only illumination.* 一隻電燈泡提供唯一的照明。| *The illumination is too weak to show the detail of the painting.* 照明太差, 顯示不出這幅畫的細節。**2** [C usually plural 一般用複數] a picture or pattern painted on a page of a book, especially in former times〔尤指舊時書籍中頁面上的〕彩飾, 圖案裝飾: *valuable manuscripts with many illuminations* 帶有許多彩飾的珍貴手稿 **3 illuminations** *especially BrE* a show of coloured lights used to make a town bright and colourful【尤英】〔裝飾城市的〕燈彩, 燈飾: *the famous Blackpool illuminations* 著名的黑池市燈飾 **4** [U] *formal* clear explanation of a particular subject【正式】闡明〔某主題〕: *illumination of a previously unexplored topic* 對以前從未涉及的話題的闡釋

ill-use /ˌɪl ˈjuz; ˌɪl ˈjuːz/ *v* [T usually passive 一般用被動態] *formal* to treat someone badly or unfairly【正式】虐待〔某人〕; 不公正對待〔某人〕: *She's been ill-used by her colleagues.* 她一直受到同事的苛待。—**ill-usage** /-ˈjusɪdʒ; -ˈjuːsɪdʒ/ *n* [U]

il·lu·sion /ɪˈluʒən; ɪˈluːʒən/ *n* [C] **1** an idea or opinion that is wrong, especially about yourself〔尤指對自己的〕幻覺, 幻想: **illusion that** *He cherished the illusion that she loved him.* 他幻想她愛他。| **be/labour under an illusion** (=believe something that is not true) 誤以為, 有錯覺 | **have no illusions about** (=realize the unpleasant truth about something) 對…不存幻想〔意識到使人不愉快的真相〕*He has no illusions about the harsh realities of the economic climate.* 他對經濟局勢的嚴峻現實不抱幻想。**2** something that seems to be different from the way it really is 假象, 錯覺: *The mirrors in the room gave an illusion of greater space.* 鏡子給人一種房間變大了的錯覺。—see also 另見 OPTICAL ILLUSION

il·lu·sion·ist /ɪˈluʒənɪst; ɪˈluːʒənɪ̀st/ *n* [C] someone who does surprising tricks that make things seem to appear or happen〔運用幻術使人感到某物突然出現或某事突然發生的〕魔術師

il·lu·so·ry /ɪˈlusərɪ; ɪˈluːsəri/ also 又作 **il·lu·sive** /ɪˈlusɪv; ɪˈluːsɪv/ *adj formal* false but seeming to be real or true【正式】虛假的, 貌似真實的: *the apparent but illusory successes of the last 15 years* 近15年來虛幻的成功表象

il·lus·trate /ˈɪləstret; ˈɪləstreɪt/ *v* [T] **1** to make the meaning of something clearer by giving examples 舉例說明〔某事物〕: *To illustrate the point, Dr Fisher told a story.* 費舍博士講了個故事來說明這一點。**2** to be an example which shows that something is true or that a fact exists 作為例證說明〔事實〕: *Nixon's downfall illustrates the immense power of the media.* 尼克遜的倒台顯示出媒體的巨大威力。**3** [usually passive 一般用被動態] to put pictures in a book, article etc〔給書籍、文章等〕作插圖: *a beautifully illustrated book* 插圖精美的書 W2

il·lus·tra·tion /ˌɪləsˈtreʃən; ˌɪləˈstreɪʃən/ *n* **1** [C] a picture in a book, article etc, especially one that helps you to understand it〔書籍、文章中的〕插圖; 圖解: *Children like books with lots of illustrations.* 兒童喜歡看有大量插圖的書。**2** [C,U] a story, event, action etc that shows the truth or existence of something very clearly 實例, 例證: [+of] a *striking illustration of 19th century attitudes to women* 19世紀對待婦女的態度的明顯例證 | **by way of illustration** (=as an example) 作為例子 *By way of illustration, I should like to mention a recent case.* 作為一個例子, 我想提一件最近發生的事。**3** [U] the act or process of illustrating something 說明; 圖解, 圖示

il·lus·tra·tive /ɪˈlʌstrətɪv; ˈɪləstreɪtɪv/ *adj* helping to explain the meaning of something 起輔助說明作用的: *an illustrative example* 起輔助說明作用的例子 —see also 另見 ILLUSTRATE (2)

il·lus·tra·tor /ˈɪləsˌtretə; ˈɪləstreɪtə/ *n* [C] someone who draws pictures, especially for books〔尤指圖書的〕插圖畫家

il·lus·tri·ous /ɪˈlʌstrɪəs; ɪˈlʌstriəs/ *adj formal* famous and admired because of what you have achieved in the past【正式】著名的, 傑出的, 卓越的: *I would like to introduce our illustrious guest, Professor Brookes.* 我向大家介紹這位聲譽卓著的嘉賓 —— 布魯克斯教授。

ill will /ˌ· ˈ·/ *n* [U] strong dislike; HOSTILITY 厭惡; 敵意: *At first there was a lot of suspicion and ill will among the team.* 起初, 隊員互相猜忌, 充滿敵意。| **bear sb no ill will** (=feel no dislike or anger towards someone) 對某人不懷敵意

I'm /aɪm; aɪm/ the short form of 縮略式= 'I am' : *I'm a student.* 我是個學生。

im- /ɪm; ɪm/ *prefix* the form used for IN- before b, m, or p 用在b, m或p前, 代替in-: *immobilize* 使固定 | *impossible* 不可能的

im·age /ˈɪmɪdʒ; ˈɪmɪdʒ/ *n* [C] S3 W1

1 ▶PUBLIC OPINION 公眾輿論◀ the general opinion that most people have of a person, organization, product etc〔某人、組織、產品等的〕形象: *The party is seeking to improve its image with women voters.* 該黨正力圖改善它在女性選民心目中的形象。| **project an image** (=make an image) 樹立形象 *The princess aimed to project an image of herself as serious and hard-working.* 公主想為自己塑造一個認真勤奮的形象。

2 ▶IDEA IN MIND 腦海中的想法◀ a picture that you have in your mind, especially about what someone or something is like or the way they look〔腦海中對某人或某物的〕印象, 形象: *She had a clear image of how she would look in twenty years' time.* 二十年後她將是甚麼模樣, 她心中有一個清楚的形象。| *He didn't really conform to the hard-drinking, hard-living image of the political journalist.* 他不太符合政治記者那種飲酒無度、生活艱苦的形象。

3 ▶PICTURE/WHAT YOU SEE 圖像/所見的東西◀ **a)** a picture of an object in a mirror or in the LENS (2) of a camera〔鏡子或照相機鏡頭中的〕映像: *She gazed at her image in the glass.* 她凝視着鏡子中自己的映像。**b)** a picture on the SCREEN[1] (1,2) of a television, cinema, or computer〔電視機、電腦屏幕上或銀幕上的〕圖像: *The image on a computer screen is made up of thousands of pixels.* 電腦屏幕上的圖像是由千萬個像素組成的。**c)** a copy of the shape of a person or thing, especially cut in wood, stone etc〔尤指用木頭或石頭雕刻成的人或物的形狀〕塑像, 雕像: *carved images in the rocks* 刻於岩石上的圖像 **4 ▶DESCRIPTION** 描繪◀ a phrase or word that describes something in a poetic way〔修辭中的〕比喻: *the image of man as a prisoner of the gods* 將人比喻為眾神之囚 **5 be the (very/living/spitting) image of** to look exactly like someone or something else 酷似〔某人或某物〕: *He's the very image of his father.* 他長相酷似他的父親。**6 in the image of** *literary* in the same form or shape as someone or something else【文】與…同形: *According to the Bible, man was made in the image of God.* 據《聖經》說, 人是按照上帝的模樣創造出來的。—see also 另見 MIRROR IMAGE

im·ag·e·ry /ˈɪmɪdʒərɪ; ˈɪmɪdʒəri/ *n* [U] **1** the use of poetic phrases and images to describe something in literature〔文學中的〕意象, 形象化描述; 比喻: *the symbolic imagery of Dylan Thomas* 迪倫·托馬斯的象徵性比喻 **2** the representation of ideas in paintings, films etc〔繪畫、電影等中表達思想的〕意象, 形象化描述: *the romantic imagery of the Pre-Raphaelite painters* 拉斐爾前派畫家創造的浪漫意象

i·ma·gi·na·ble /ɪˈmædʒɪnəbḷ; ɪˈmædʒɨnəbəl/ *adj* **the best/worst/kindest etc imaginable** used to emphasize that something is the best, worst etc example of something that it is possible to imagine 可想像到的最好/壞/善良等的〔用於強調〕: *He was defeated in the most humiliating circumstances imaginable.* 他在人們能夠想像到的最屈辱的情況下被打敗了。| **every imaginable** *Posters were plastered on every imaginable surface.* 只要是能想到的空白的表面都給張貼了海報。

i·ma·gi·na·ry /ɪˈmædʒəˌnɛrɪ; ɪˈmædʒɨnəri/ *adj* not real, but produced from pictures or ideas in your mind 想像的, 虛構的: *All the characters in this book are imaginary.* 本書人物純屬虛構。—compare 比較 IMAGINATIVE

i·ma·gi·na·tion /ɪˌmædʒəˈneʃən; ɪˌmædʒɨˈneɪʃən/ *n* **1** [C,U] the ability to form pictures or ideas in your mind 想像力: *Children often have very vivid imaginations.* 兒童常有生動的想像力。| *With a little imagination, he could visualize the old house as a luxury hotel.* 他稍加幻想, 便可以把這幢舊房子想像成豪華飯店。**2** [U] something that is caused only by your mind, and does not really exist or did not really happen 幻覺, 幻像; 空想: *Did you hear that noise, or was it my imagination?* 你聽到那個聲音了嗎? 還是我的幻覺? **3 in your imagination** only existing or happening in your mind, not in real life 只存在於[發生於]腦海中的, 幻想的: *The difficulties are all in your imagination.* 這些困難全是你想像出來的。**4 capture/catch sb's imagination** to make people feel very interested and excited 使某人出神, 使某人入迷: *His music captured the imagination of a whole generation of young people.* 他的音樂吸引了整整一代年輕人。**5 leave sth to sb's imagination** to deliberately not describe something because you think someone can guess or imagine it 留給某人自己去想像〔因認為人們能夠猜測或想像到, 故意不描述某事〕: *I'll leave the details of the affair to your imagination.* 事情的細節留給你去想像吧。**6 use your imagination!** *spoken* used to tell someone that they can easily guess the answer to a question, so you should not need to tell them【口】動動腦筋!〔用於告訴某人他能輕易猜到答案〕—see also 另見 **not by any stretch of the imagination** (STRETCH[2] (5))

i·ma·gi·na·tive /ɪˈmædʒəˌnetɪv; ɪˈmædʒɨnətɪv/ *adj* **1** someone who is imaginative is good at thinking of new, interesting ideas, and at forming pictures in their mind〔人〕想像力豐富的: *an imaginative child* 想像力豐富的孩子 **2** something that is imaginative contains new and interesting ideas used in a clever way〔某物〕富有想像力的: *imaginative writing* 富有想像力的文章 | *an imaginative solution to the problem* 富有想像力的解決方法 —compare 比較 IMAGINARY —**imaginatively** *adv*

i·ma·gine /ɪˈmædʒɪn; ɪˈmædʒɨn/ *v* [T] **1 ▶MENTAL PICTURE** 心中的圖像◀ [not usually in progressive 一般不用進行式] to form a picture or idea in your mind about what something could be like 想像: **imagine (that)** *Try to imagine that you are a tourist arriving in London for the first time.* 試想像自己是第一次來倫敦的遊客。| *Close your eyes and imagine a tropical island.* 閉上眼睛, 想像一個熱帶島嶼。| **imagine what/how/why etc** *I can just imagine what the place is going to look like in a few years' time.* 我能想像出這個地方幾年之後會變成甚麼樣子。| **imagine sb doing sth** *I can just imagine Sarah running her own business.* 我能想像出莎拉自己開公司的情景。| **imagine doing sth** *It's hard to imagine working in a place like that.* 在那種地方工作, 真是難以想像。| **imagine sb/sth as** *I never knew my grandmother but I always imagine her as a kind, gentle person.* 我從未見過祖母, 但我總把她想像成一個心地善良、和藹可親的人。| **imagine sb in/with/without etc** *Somehow I can't imagine him without a beard.* 不知為甚麼, 我就是想像不出他沒有鬍子的樣子。**2 ▶WRONG IDEA** 錯誤的想法◀ to have a false or wrong idea about something 幻想, 誤以為: *She doesn't love him, he's just imagining it.* 她不愛他, 他不過是在幻想。| *imagined dangers* 憑空臆想出來的危險 | **imagine (that)** *He imagines that people don't like him but they do.* 他誤以為人們不喜歡他, 但事實並非如此。| **imagine sb/sth to be sth** *I was surprised when I saw the farm. I had imagined it to be much bigger.* 看見農場時我大為驚訝——我原來想像它會大得多。**3 ▶THINK STH** 猜想某事◀ [not in progressive 不用進行式] to think that something is true, but without being sure or having proof〔不肯定或沒有根據地〕猜想, 猜測: *You must miss him, I imagine.* 我猜想你一定很想念他。| **imagine (that)** *I imagine she's home by now if you want to phone her.* 如果你要給她打電話, 我想她現在已經到家了。**4 you can't imagine** *BrE spoken* used to emphasize how good, bad etc something is【英口】你想像不到〔用於強調某物好、壞等的程度〕: *You can't imagine what a terrible week we had.* 你簡直想像不出我們經歷了多麼可怕的一個星期。**5 ▶SURPRISED** 感到驚訝◀ **(just) imagine!** *spoken old-fashioned* used to show surprise, shock, or disapproval【口, 過時】真想不到!〔表示驚訝、震驚或反對〕: *He dyed his hair bright yellow! Just imagine!* 真沒想到, 他竟然把頭髮染成了鮮豔的黃色! | **imagine doing sth** *Imagine going all that way for nothing!* 真想不到走了那麼遠卻毫無所獲!

This graph shows how common the different grammar patterns of the verb **imagine** are. 本圖表所示為動詞 imagine 構成的不同語法模式的使用頻率。

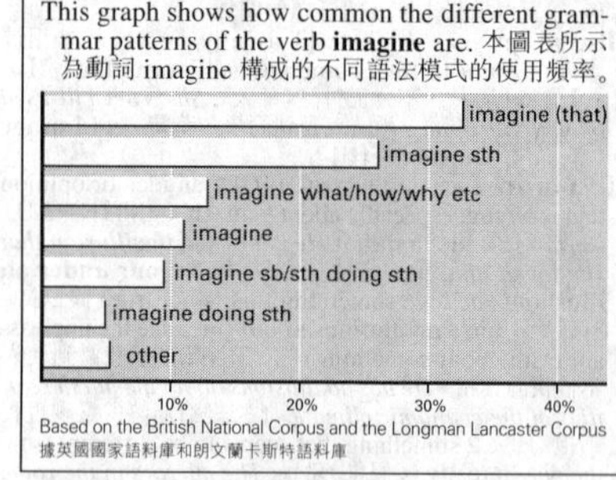

Based on the British National Corpus and the Longman Lancaster Corpus
據英國國家語料庫和朗文蘭卡斯特語料庫

i·ma·gin·ings /ɪˋmædʒɪnɪŋz; ɪ'mædʒɪ̮nɪŋz/ *n* [plural] *literary* situations or ideas that you imagine, but which are not real or true【文】想像的情形[概念]〔實際上是虛妄的〕

im·am /ɪˋmɑm; 'ɪmɑːm/ *n* [C] a Muslim religious leader or priest 伊瑪目〔伊斯蘭教的宗教領袖或祭司〕

im·bal·ance /ɪmˋbæləns; ɪm'bæləns/ *n* [C,U] a lack of a fair or correct balance between two things, which results in problems or unfairness 不平衡; 失調: *a hormonal imbalance* 激素失衡 | **redress an imbalance** (=put it right) 恢復平衡 *an attempt to redress the imbalance between rich and poor* 平均財富的努力

im·be·cile /ˋɪmbəsl; 'ɪmbəsiːl/ *n* [C] **1** someone who is very stupid or behaves very stupidly 蠢人, 笨蛋: *He looked at me as if I was a complete imbecile.* 他看着我, 好像我是個大笨蛋。**2** *old-fashioned* a word meaning someone who is mentally ill, now considered offensive【過時】低能兒〔現代用法中為冒犯用詞〕—**imbecilic** /ˌɪmbəˋsɪlɪk; ˌɪmbɪ̮'sɪlɪk◂/ *adj*

im·be·cil·i·ty /ˌɪmbəˋsɪlətɪ; ˌɪmbɪ̮'sɪlɪ̮ti/ *n* **1** [C,U] very stupid behaviour or an action that is very stupid 愚蠢的行為 **2** [U] the condition of being an imbecile 愚蠢; 低能, 弱智

im·bed /ɪmˋbɛd; ɪm'bed/ *v* **imbedded, imbedding** [T] another spelling of EMBED embed 的另一種拼法

im·bibe /ɪmˋbaɪb; ɪm'baɪb/ *v* [I,T] *formal or humorous*【正式或幽默】**1** to drink something, especially alcohol 喝〔尤指酒〕, 飲: *Having imbibed rather too freely, he fell forward against the table.* 由於酒喝得太多, 他一頭栽在桌子上。**2** to accept and be influenced by qualities, ideas, values etc 接受〔品質、觀點、價值等〕並受到影響: *imbibing radical political ideas* 受激進的政治主張的影響

im·bro·gli·o /ɪmˋbroljo; ɪm'brəʊliəʊ/ *n plural* **imbroglios** [C] a difficult, embarrassing, or confusing situation, especially in politics or public life〔尤指政治或公務中出現的〕錯綜複雜的局面: *He found himself in the greatest imbroglio of his tenure at the UN.* 他發現自己陷入了在聯合國任職期間最大的困境。

im·bue /ɪmˋbju; ɪm'bjuː/ *v*

imbue sb **with** sth *phr v* [T usually passive 一般用被動態] to make someone feel an emotion very strongly 使〔某人〕充滿〔強烈情感〕: *a people deeply imbued with national pride* 內心充滿自豪感的民族

IMF /ˌaɪ ɛm ˋɛf; ˌaɪ em 'ef/ *n* **the IMF** the International Monetary Fund; an international organization that tries to encourage trade between countries and to help poorer countries develop economically 國際貨幣基金組織〔促進國際貿易, 並協助貧窮國家發展經濟的國際組織〕

im·i·tate /ˋɪməˌtet; 'ɪmɪ̮teɪt/ *v* [T] **1** to copy something because you think it is good〔認為是好的而〕仿效〔某物〕: *Do kids really imitate the violence they see on TV?* 孩子真會模仿在電視上看到的暴力嗎? | *Our methods have been imitated all over the world.* 全世界都在效仿我們的辦法。**2** to copy the way someone behaves, speaks, moves etc, especially in order to make people laugh 模仿〔某人的行為、說話、動作等, 尤指引人發笑的模仿〕: *"Give that back!" she screeched, imitating Jess's high-pitched squeal.* "還給我!" 她模仿着傑斯的尖嗓音高聲喊道。—**imitator** *n* [C]

im·i·ta·tion /ˌɪməˋteʃən; ˌɪmɪ̮'teɪʃən◂/ *n* **1** [C,U] an attempt to imitate someone or something, or the act of doing this 模仿, 仿效: *Bill can do a passable imitation of an American accent.* 比爾對美國腔調的模仿還真挺像。| *Children learn a lot by imitation.* 孩子通過模仿學到很多東西。| **a pale imitation** (=something that is much less good than the thing it imitates) 拙劣的仿製品 *The remake of 'Casablanca' was a pale imitation of the original movie.* 重拍的《北非諜影》與原版相比大為遜色。**2** [C] a copy of something 仿製品, 贗品: *The table is a genuine antique not a cheap imitation.* 這張桌子是真品古董, 不是便宜的仿製品。| **imitation leather/wood/ivory etc** (=something that looks like an expensive material but is a copy of it) 人造皮革/木材/象牙等

im·i·ta·tive /ˋɪməˌtetɪv; 'ɪmɪ̮tətɪv/ *adj formal* copying someone or something, especially in a way that shows you do not have any ideas of your own【正式】模仿的〔尤指缺乏個人的思想〕, 仿效的 —**imitatively** *adv* —**imitativeness** *n* [U]

im·mac·u·late /ɪˋmækjəlɪt; ɪ'mækjɪ̮lɪ̮t/ *adj* **1** very clean and tidy 非常潔淨整齊的: *Richard looked immaculate in a white silk dinner jacket.* 理查德穿着白色絲綢禮服上裝, 看上去乾淨利落。**2** exactly correct or perfect in every detail 精確的; 完美的: *Your timing is immaculate!* 你時間把握得分秒不差! —**immaculately** *adv*

Immaculate Con·cep·tion /·,··· ·'··/ *n* the Christian belief that Christ's mother Mary was a VIRGIN (=someone who has never had sex) when Christ was born 無玷成胎(說)〔此說認為聖母馬利亞童貞懷孕生下耶穌〕

im·ma·nent /ˋɪmənənt; 'ɪmənənt/ *adj formal*【正式】**1** a quality that is immanent seems to be naturally present〔指特質〕內在的; 天生的: *Hope seems immanent in human nature.* 抱有希望似乎是人類與生俱來的本性。**2** God or another spiritual power that is immanent is present everywhere〔上帝或另一種精神力量〕無所不在的 —compare 比較 EMINENT, IMMINENT —**immanence, immanency** *n* [U]

im·ma·te·ri·al /ˌɪməˋtɪrɪəl; ˌɪmə'tɪəriəl◂/ *adj* **1** not important in a particular situation; IRRELEVANT 無關緊要的; 不相關的: *The causes of the problem are immaterial now – we need solutions.* 問題的原因現在已無關緊要, 我們需要的是解決方法。**2** *formal* not having a real physical form【正式】非實體的, 無形的

im·ma·ture /ˌɪməˋtjur; ˌɪmə'tʃʊə/ *adj* **1** someone who is immature behaves or thinks in a way that is typical of someone much younger〔行為、思想〕不成熟的: *I married much too young – I was very immature.* 我結婚時太年輕, 當時還很不成熟。**2** not fully formed or developed 發育未全的: *The immature plants are susceptible to frost.* 幼小的植物易受霜凍侵襲。—**immaturity** *n* [U]

im·mea·su·ra·ble /ɪˋmɛʒərəbl; ɪ'meʒərəbəl/ *adj* too big or too extreme to be measured 無法計量的: *This latest scandal has done immeasurable damage to his reputation.* 最近的醜聞給他的名譽造成了難以估計的傷害。—**immeasurably** *adv*: *The company's position has improved immeasurably since last year.* 去年以來, 公司的地位得到極大提高。

im·me·di·a·cy /ɪˋmidɪəsɪ; ɪ'miːdiəsi/ *n* [U] the quality of seeming to happen right now that makes something seem more important or urgent to you 即時; 緊迫; 刻不容緩: *Television brings a new immediacy to world events.* 電視使世界大事更迅捷地呈現在觀眾眼前。

im·me·di·ate /ɪˋmidɪɪt; ɪ'miːdiət/ *adj* S2 W2

1 ►NO DELAY 立即, 不延誤◄ happening or done at once and without delay 立刻的, 即時的: *The police response to the situation was forceful and immediate.* 警方對局面作出迅速有力的反應。| *seek immediate medical attention* 尋求即時醫療護理

2 ►NOW 目前◄ [only before noun 僅用於名詞前] existing now, and needing to be dealt with quickly 目前的〔要迅速處理的〕, 當下的: *Our immediate concern was to stop the fire from spreading.* 我們的當務之急是阻止火勢蔓延。| *I have no immediate plans to leave.* 我目前沒有離開的打算。

3 ►AFTER/BEFORE 之後/之前◄ [only before noun 僅用於名詞前] happening just before or just after someone or something else 最接近的, 緊接的: *My immediate predecessor went to work for a rival firm.* 我最近離開的前任去了一家與我們競爭的公司工作。| *the immediate future* 最近的將來

4 ►NEAR 附近的◄ [only before noun 僅用於名詞前] next to, or very near to, a particular place〔地方〕鄰近的; 緊鄰的: *The immediate area was sealed off after the*

bombing. 轟炸之後, 緊鄰地區被封鎖起來。
5 immediate family/kin people who are very closely related to you, such as your parents, children, brothers, and sisters 直系親屬〈如父母、兒女、兄弟姐妹等〉

im·me·di·ate·ly¹ /ɪˋmidɪɪtlɪ; ɪˈmiːdiətli/ *adv* **1** without delay 即刻, 馬上: *Cook the mixture for ten minutes and serve immediately.* 將混合物烹調十分鐘後即刻上桌。| *As soon as I got their fax, I wrote back immediately.* 我一收到他們的傳真, 就立刻寫了回信。**2** [+adj/adv] very soon before or after something〔某事之前或之後〕立即: *The baby was given up for adoption immediately after birth.* 那個嬰兒剛出生就交給別人領養了。**3** [+adj/adv] very near to something 貼近地: *Charles lives in the apartment immediately above ours.* 查爾斯就住在緊靠我們家樓上的那個公寓套間。**4 immediately involved/concerned/affected etc** very closely involved etc in a particular situation〔與某事〕有直接牽連/關係; 直接〔受某事〕影響: *All those immediately involved will be informed of the decision.* 這個決定將通知所有直接相關人員。

immediately² *conjunction BrE formal* as soon as【英, 正式】一…就…: *Make sure the property you are buying is insured immediately you exchange contracts.* 合同互換之後, 應立刻給所購房產買保險。

im·me·mo·ri·al /ˌɪməˋmɔrɪəl; ˌɪməˈmɔːriəl◂/ *adj* **1 since/from time immemorial** for longer than people can remember 自古以來: *The tribe had inhabited the area since time immemorial.* 自遠古以來, 該部落就在這個地區居住。**2** *formal* starting longer ago than people can remember, or than written history shows【正式】年代久遠沒人記得的; 史前的: *an immemorial custom* 源遠流長的風俗

im·mense /ɪˋmɛns; ɪˈmens/ *adj* extremely large 巨大的: *An immense amount of money and time has been put into finding a cure.* 為尋找治療方法, 已投入了大量金錢和時間。

im·mense·ly /ɪˋmɛnslɪ; ɪˈmensli/ *adv* very much; extremely 非常; 極大地: *We enjoyed the play immensely.* 我們極為欣賞該劇。| *immensely popular* 非常流行的; 非常受歡迎的; 非常有聲望的

im·men·si·ty /ɪˋmɛnsətɪ; ɪˈmensəti/ *n* [U] **1** the great size and seriousness of something such as a problem you have to deal with or a job you have to do〔指規模或困難程度的〕巨大: *the immensity of the task before us* 我們所面臨的極為浩繁的任務 **2** also 又作 **immensities** [plural] the great size of something, especially something that cannot be measured 浩瀚無際: *the immensities of outer space* 浩瀚無際的外太空

im·merse /ɪˋmɝs; ɪˈmɜːs/ *v* [T] **1** *especially technical* to put someone or something deep into a liquid so that it is completely covered【尤術語】使浸沒〔於液體中〕: **immerse sb/sth in** *Immerse your foot in ice cold water to reduce the swelling.* 把你的腳泡在冰涼的水中可以消腫。**2 immerse yourself in** to become completely involved in an activity 潛心於, 專心於: *Jane was determined to immerse herself in the African way of life.* 簡決心潛心研究非洲人的生活方式。—**immersed** *adj*: *completely immersed in his job* 完全投入工作

im·mer·sion /ɪˋmɝʃən; ɪˈmɜːʃən/ *n* [U] **1** the fact of being completely involved in something you are doing 專心〔做某事〕, 投入: *He was well respected, despite his immersion in the murkier side of politics.* 他雖然與政治的黑暗面有很深的牽連, 但仍然很受尊敬。**2 a)** the action of immersing something in liquid, or the state of being immersed 沉浸, 浸沒 **b)** BAPTISM (=a ceremony to introduce someone into a church) in which someone's whole body is put into water〔全身入水的〕洗禮, 浸禮 **3** the language teaching method in which people are put in situations where they have to use the new language〔將學生置於必須使用外語的環境的〕沉浸式語言教學法 **4** *BrE informal* an immersion heater【英, 非正式】浸入式熱水器

immersion heat·er /ˌ···ˌ··/ *n* [C] *BrE* an electric water heater that provides hot water for a house【英】浸入式熱水器〔一種家用電熱水器〕

im·mi·grant /ˋɪməgrənt; ˈɪməgrənt/ *n* [C] someone who comes from abroad to live permanently in another country〔外來〕移民 —compare 比較 EMIGRANT

im·mi·grate /ˋɪməˌgret; ˈɪməgreɪt/ *v* [I] to come into a country in order to live there permanently〔為定居而從外國〕移入 —see also 另見 EMIGRATE

im·mi·gra·tion /ˌɪməˋgreʃən; ˌɪməˈgreɪʃən/ *n* [U] **1** the process of entering another country in order to live there 移民入境: *normal immigration procedures* 正常的移民入境程序 **2** the total number of people who do this 移民人數: *Immigration fell in the 1980s.* 20 世紀 80 年代移民人數下降。**3** also 又作 **immigration control** the place at an airport, sea port etc where officials check the documents of everyone entering the country〔機場、港口等的〕入境檢查處

im·mi·nent /ˋɪmənənt; ˈɪmənənt/ *adj* an event that is imminent will happen very soon 即將發生的; 逼近的: *A declaration of war now seemed imminent.* 現在宣戰似乎已是箭在弦上。| *The company is now in imminent danger of collapse.* 該公司現在瀕臨倒閉。—compare 比較 IMMANENT —**imminence** *n* [U] —**imminently** *adv*

im·mo·bile /ɪˋmobḷ; ɪˈməʊbaɪl/ *adj* **1** not moving at all 不活動的, 固定的: *A few soldiers were lounging around on two immobile tanks.* 幾個士兵懶洋洋地倚在兩輛停駛的坦克上。**2** unable to move or walk normally 不能正常走動的: *Kim's illness had rendered her completely immobile.* 金的病使她完全喪失了活動能力。—**immobility** /ˌɪmoˋbɪlətɪ; ˌɪməˈbɪləti/ *n* [U]

im·mo·bi·lize also 又作 **-ise** *BrE*【英】/ɪˋmoblˌaɪz; ɪˈməʊbəlaɪz/ *v* [T] **1** to prevent someone or something from moving 使〔人或物〕不能動, 使固定: *The broken limb must be immobilized immediately.* 斷肢必須立即加以固定。**2** to stop something from working 使〔某物〕停止運轉: *The car's security device will immobilize the ignition system.* 這輛汽車的安全裝置能使點火系統停止工作。—**immobilization** /ɪˌmoblaɪˋzeʃən; ɪˌməʊbəlaɪˈzeɪʃən/ *n* [U]

im·mod·e·rate /ɪˋmɑdərɪt; ɪˈmɒdərət/ *adj formal* not within reasonable and sensible limits; EXCESSIVE【正式】無節制的; 過度的: *immoderate wage demands* 無理的工資要求 | *immoderate drinking* 酗酒, 暴飲 —**immoderately** *adv*

im·mod·est /ɪˋmɑdɪst; ɪˈmɒdəst/ *adj* **1** having a very high opinion of yourself and your abilities, and not embarrassed about telling people how clever you are etc 驕傲的, 不謙虛的 —opposite 反義詞 MODEST (1) **2** *old-fashioned* behaviour or clothes that are immodest may embarrass or offend people because they do not follow the usual social rules concerning sexual behaviour【過時】〔行為或衣着〕不端莊的, 不正派的, 下流的, 有傷風化的 —**immodestly** *adv* —**immodesty** *n* [U]

im·mo·late /ˋɪməˌlet; ˈɪməleɪt/ *v* [T] *formal* to kill someone or something by burning them【正式】燒死 —**immolation** /ˌɪməˋleʃən; ˌɪməˈleɪʃən/ *n* [U]

im·mor·al /ɪˋmɔrəl; ɪˈmɒrəl/ *adj* **1** morally wrong 不道德的, 道德敗壞的: *They condemned slavery as immoral.* 他們譴責奴隸制是不道德的。**2** not following accepted standards of sexual behaviour 放蕩的, 淫蕩的; 傷風敗俗的 —compare 比較 AMORAL —**immorally** *adv*

im·mo·ral·i·ty /ˌɪməˋrælətɪ; ˌɪməˈræləti/ *n* [U] behaviour that is morally wrong 缺德, 道德敗壞; 傷風敗俗: *the immorality of bombing civilians* 轟炸平民的不道德行為

im·mor·tal /ɪˋmɔrtḷ; ɪˈmɔːtl/ *adj* **1** living or continuing forever 不死的; 永存的: *Plato believed that the soul is immortal.* 柏拉圖認為靈魂不滅。**2** an immortal line, play, song etc is so famous that it will never be forgotten〔詩句、戲劇、歌曲等〕不朽的, 流傳百世的: *Shakespeare's immortal lines* 莎士比亞的不朽詩句 —**immortal** *n* [C]

im·mor·tal·i·ty /ˌɪmɔrˋtælətɪ; ˌɪmɔːˈtæləti/ *n* [U] the condition of living forever or being remembered forever 永生, 長存, 永恆, 永垂不朽

im·mor·tal·ize also 又作 **-ise** *BrE*【英】/ɪˋmɔrtḷ͵aɪz; ɪˈmɔːtəlaɪz/ *v* [T] to make someone or something famous for a long time, especially by writing about them, painting a picture of them etc〔通過著書、畫像等〕使不朽; 使名垂千古: *Dickens' father was immortalized as Mr Micawber in 'David Copperfield'.* 狄更斯的父親作為米考伯先生的原型出現在《塊肉餘生記》中, 從而名留千古。

im·mo·va·ble /ɪˋmuvəbḷ; ɪˈmuːvəbəl/ **1** impossible to move 不可移動的, 固定的: *Lock your bike to something immovable like a railing or lamp-post.* 把自行車鎖到一個固定的地方, 如欄杆或路燈柱上。**2** impossible to change or persuade 堅定不移的, 不為所動的: *The president is immovable on this issue.* 在這個問題上, 總統的立場堅定不移。—**immovably** *adv*

im·mune /ɪˋmjun; ɪˈmjuːn/ *adj* **1** someone who is immune to a particular disease cannot catch it〔對疾病〕有免疫力的 **2** not affected by something such as criticism, bad treatment etc 不受〔批評、虐待等〕影響的: **[+to]** *They're always so rude that I've almost become immune to it.* 他們總是如此粗暴無禮, 我都幾乎習以為常了。**3** specially protected from something unpleasant 豁免的; 可免…的: **[+from]** *Peterson was told he would be immune from prosecution if he co-operated with the police.* 彼得森被告知, 如果他與警方合作, 就可免受起訴。

immune sys·tem /·ˈ· ͵··/ *n* [C] the system by which your body protects itself against disease〔身體的〕免疫系統

im·mu·nise /ˋɪmjə͵naɪz; ˈɪmjʊnaɪz/ *v* a British spelling of IMMUNIZE immunize 的英式拼法

im·mu·ni·ty /ɪˋmjunətɪ; ɪˈmjuːnʒti/ *n* [U] the fact of not being affected by a disease or harmed by something unpleasant 免疫; 免除; 豁免: **[+to]** *immunity to infection* 對傳染病的免疫力 | **[+from]** *They were granted immunity from prosecution.* 他們獲准免受起訴。

im·mu·nize also 又作 **-ise** *BrE*【英】/ˋɪmjə͵naɪz; ˈɪmjʊnaɪz/ *v* [T] to protect someone from a particular illness, especially by putting a substance into their body by INJECTION (1)〔尤指通過注射而〕使〔人〕免疫: **immunize sb against sth** *All girls are routinely immunized against German measles.* 所有女孩都按常規接種德國麻疹疫苗。—compare 比較 VACCINATE —**immunization** /͵ɪmjunəˋzeʃən; ͵ɪmjʊnaɪˈzeɪʃən/ *n* [C,U]

im·mu·no·de·fi·cien·cy /͵ɪmjunodɪˋfɪʃənsɪ; ͵ɪmjʊnəʊdɪˈfɪʃənsi/ *n* [C,U] a medical condition in which your body is unable to fight infection in the usual way 免疫缺陷〔病〕—**immunodeficient** *adj*

im·mu·nol·o·gy /͵ɪmjuˋnɑlədʒɪ; ͵ɪmjʊˈnɒlədʒi/ *n* [U] the scientific study of the prevention of disease and how the body reacts to disease 免疫學

im·mure /ɪˋmjʊr; ɪˈmjʊə/ *v* [T] *formal or literary* to shut someone in somewhere so that they cannot get out【正式或文】監禁, 禁閉

im·mu·ta·ble /ɪˋmjutəbḷ; ɪˈmjuːtəbəl/ *adj formal* never changing or impossible to change【正式】永恆的; 不能改變的: *the immutable principles of liberty and justice* 永恆的自由與公正原則 —**immutably** *adv* —**immutability** /ɪ͵mjutəˋbɪlətɪ; ɪ͵mjuːtəˈbɪlʒti/ *n* [U]

imp /ɪmp; ɪmp/ *n* [C] **1** a small creature in stories who has magic powers and behaves very badly〔故事中有魔法愛作弄人的〕小魔鬼, 小妖精 **2** a child who behaves badly, but in a way that amuses people rather than annoying them 頑童, 小淘氣 —see also 另見 IMPISH

2 **im·pact¹** /ˋɪmpækt; ˈɪmpækt/ *n* [C] **1** the effect or influence that an event, situation etc has on someone or something 影響; 作用: *the environmental impact of increased road traffic* 道路交通增加對環境的影響 | **have an impact (on)** *Warnings about the dangers of smoking seem to have little impact on this age group.* 吸煙有害的警告對這個年齡段的人似乎沒有多大作用。**2** the force of one object hitting another 衝擊力, 撞擊力: *The impact pushed the engine backwards and crushed my legs.* 衝擊力把發動機向後推, 壓傷了我的雙腿。**3 on impact** at the moment when one thing hits another〔與另一物體〕碰撞時: *a missile which explodes on impact* 一枚在撞擊時爆炸的導彈

im·pact² /ɪmˋpækt; ɪmˈpækt/ *v* **[I+on,T]** *especially AmE* to have an important or noticeable effect on someone or something【尤美】產生〔重要或明顯的〕影響: *How will this program impact on the local community?* 這項計劃對當地社區會產生甚麼樣的影響?

im·pact·ed /ɪmˋpæktɪd; ɪmˈpæktʒd/ *adj* a tooth that is impacted is growing under another tooth so that it cannot develop properly 阻生的〔牙齒〕

im·pair /ɪmˋpɛr; ɪmˈpeə/ *v* [T] to make something less good than it usually is or less good than it should be 削弱, 損害, 損傷〔某物〕: *Do not boil the sauce as this can impair the flavor.* 調味汁不要煮沸, 否則影響味道。—**impairment** *n* [U]

im·paired /ɪmˋpɛrd; ɪmˈpeəd/ *adj* not as good as before or not as good as it should be 受損的; 變差的: *a special device for viewers with impaired hearing.* 為患有聽力障礙的觀眾而設的特殊裝置 | *TV reception may be impaired in some areas.* 某些地區電視的接收效果可能會受到影響。

im·pa·la /ɪmˋpɑlə; ɪmˈpɑːlə/ *n* [C] a large brown graceful African animal; ANTELOPE〔非洲的〕黑斑羚

im·pale /ɪmˋpel; ɪmˈpeɪl/ *v* [T often passive 常用被動態] to push a sharp pointed object through something or someone〔以尖物〕刺穿, 插進: *Gregson fell to a horrible death, impaled on the railings below.* 格雷格森跌下去, 身體被下面的柵欄刺穿, 死得很慘。—**impalement** *n* [U]

im·pal·pa·ble /ɪmˋpælpəbḷ; ɪmˈpælpəbəl/ *adj formal*【正式】**1** impossible to touch or feel physically 觸摸不着的, 感覺不到的 —opposite 反義詞 PALPABLE (2) **2** very difficult to understand 難懂的

im·pan·el /ɪmˋpænḷ; ɪmˈpænl/ *v* [T] another spelling of EMPANEL empanel 的另一種拼法

im·part /ɪmˋpɑrt; ɪmˈpɑːt/ *v* [T] *formal*【正式】**1** to give information, knowledge, wisdom etc to someone〔向某人〕傳授〔知識、智慧〕, 透露〔信息〕; 告知 **2** to give a particular quality to something 賦予〔某種品質〕, 給予: *Oregano imparts a delicious flavour to the stew.* 牛至給燉菜一種鮮美的味道。

im·par·tial /ɪmˋpɑrʃəl; ɪmˈpɑːʃəl/ *adj* not giving special favour or support to any one person or group; fair 不偏不倚的; 公正的: *We offer impartial advice on pensions and investments.* 我們對養老金和投資問題提供公正的建議。| *an impartial observer* 不帶偏見的觀察家 —**impartially** *adv* —**impartiality** /͵ɪmpɑrʃɪˋælətɪ; ɪm͵pɑːʃiˈælʒti/ *n* [U]

im·pass·a·ble /ɪmˋpæsəbḷ; ɪmˈpɑːsəbəl/ *adj* a road, path, or area that is impassable is impossible to travel along or through 不能通行的, 無法通過的: *The road is impassable due to snow.* 道路因積雪而無法通行。

im·passe /ˋɪmpæs; æmˈpɑːs/ *n* [singular] a situation in which it is impossible to continue with a discussion or plan because the people involved cannot agree 僵局: **reach an impasse** *Negotiations seemed to have reached an impasse.* 談判似乎陷入了僵局。

im·pas·sioned /ɪmˋpæʃənd; ɪmˈpæʃənd/ *adj* an impassioned speech, request, argument etc is full of strong feeling and emotion〔演說、要求、爭辯等〕充滿激情的, 激昂的: *She appeared on television to make an impassioned appeal to the kidnappers.* 她在電視上向綁架者發出激昂的呼籲。

im·pas·sive /ɪmˋpæsɪv; ɪmˈpæsɪv/ *adj* not showing any emotion or feeling 神情冷漠的; 木然的: *Oscar's face remained impassive throughout the trial.* 在整個審訊中, 奧斯卡都面無表情。—**impassively** *adv* —**impassivity** /͵ɪmpæˋsɪvətɪ; ͵ɪmpæˈsɪvʒti/ *n* [U]

im·pa·tience /ɪmˋpeʃəns; ɪmˈpeɪʃəns/ *n* [U] **1** annoy-

I

ance at having to accept delays, other people's weaknesses etc 不耐煩, 無耐心: *Fiona's impatience with her slower students was beginning to show.* 菲奧娜對遲鈍的學生的不耐煩開始顯露出來。**2** great eagerness for something to happen, especially something that is going to happen soon〔尤指對即將發生的事〕渴望, 企盼

im·pa·tient /ɪm`peʃənt; ɪm'peɪʃənt/ *adj* **1** annoyed because of a situation you cannot control, especially when you have to wait for something 不耐煩的, 無耐心的; 急躁的: *After an hour's delay, passengers were becoming impatient.* 延誤一小時後, 旅客開始焦躁起來。| *I'm coming – don't be so impatient!* 我這就來 —— 耐心點! **2** very eager for something to happen and not wanting to wait 焦急的, 切盼的: **[+for]** *The woman stood there, impatient for me to be gone.* 那女人站在那兒, 焦急地等我離開。| **impatient to do sth** *Glen was clearly impatient to be off.* 葛蘭顯然急着要走。—**impatiently** *adv*

im·peach /ɪm`pitʃ; ɪm'piːtʃ/ *v* [T] *law*【法律】**1** to charge a public official with a serious crime, especially in the US〔尤指在美國〕彈劾〔政府官員〕: *The House Judiciary Committee voted that President Nixon should be impeached.* 眾議院司法委員會投票贊成彈劾尼克遜總統。**2** to say that someone is guilty of a serious crime, especially a crime against the state 指控〔某人犯有嚴重罪行, 尤指危害國家罪〕, 檢舉 —**impeachment** *n* [U]

im·pec·ca·ble /ɪm`pɛkəbl̩; ɪm'pekəbəl/ *adj* completely perfect and without any mistakes 完美的; 無任何錯誤的: *Eliza had impeccable manners.* 伊莉莎的舉止無懈可擊。| *an impeccable performance* 完美的表演 —**impeccably** *adv*: *impeccably dressed* 穿着非常得體

im·pe·cu·ni·ous /ˌɪmpɪ`kjunɪəs; ˌɪmpɪ'kjuːniəs◂/ *adj formal or humorous* having very little money, especially over a long period【正式或幽默】〔尤指長期〕沒錢的: *a gifted but impecunious painter* 一貧如洗的天才畫家 —**impecuniously** *adv* —**impecuniousness** *n* [U]

im·ped·ance /ɪm`pidn̩s; ɪm'piːdəns/ *n* [singular, U] *technical* a measure of the power of a piece of electrical equipment to stop the flow of an ALTERNATING CURRENT【術語】阻抗; 全電阻

im·pede /ɪm`pid; ɪm'piːd/ *v* [T] to prevent something from happening in the normal way, or make it happen more slowly 妨礙, 阻礙; 防止, 延緩: *Storms at sea impeded our progress.* 海上風暴阻礙了我們的航程。

im·ped·i·ment /ɪm`pɛdəmənt; ɪm'pedɪ̯mənt/ *n* [C] *formal*【正式】**1** a physical or nervous problem that makes it difficult for someone to speak or move normally〔生理或神經疾病所致的〕言語[行動]不能自如: *a speech impediment* 口吃, 結巴 **2** a situation or event that makes it difficult or impossible for someone or something to succeed or make progress 阻礙, 障礙(物); 絆腳石: **[+to]** *The main impediment to development is the country's huge foreign debt.* 巨額外債是該國發展的主要障礙。

im·ped·i·men·ta /ˌɪmpɛdə`mɛntə; ɪmˌpedɪ̯'mentə/ *n* [plural] *often humorous* bags, animals, supplies etc that you take with you on a journey, and that may slow you down【常幽默】〔旅行中〕妨礙行進的重負〈如行李、動物、補給等〉

im·pel /ɪm`pɛl; ɪm'pel/ *v* [T] an idea, emotion etc that impels you to do something makes you feel very strongly that you must do it〔想法、情感等〕促使, 驅使: **impel sb to do sth** *Donnelly felt impelled to write and complain.* 唐納利覺得非寫信投訴不可。—compare 比較 COMPEL

im·pend·ing /ɪm`pɛndɪŋ; ɪm'pendɪŋ/ *adj* an impending event or situation, especially an unpleasant one, is going to happen very soon〔尤指不愉快的事情〕逼近的, 即將發生的: *I had a sense of impending doom.* 我有一種厄運即將降臨的預感。| *an impending ecological crisis* 即將發生的生態危機

im·pen·e·tra·ble /ɪm`pɛnətrəbl̩; ɪm'penɪ̯trəbəl/ *adj* **1** impossible to get through, see through, or get into 不能通過的, 不能看透的, 無法進入的: *an impenetrable barrier of thorn bushes* 無法穿過的荊棘灌木叢 | *impenetrable darkness* 漆黑 **2** very difficult or impossible to understand 難以理解的, 費解的: *The document was written in impenetrable lawyer's jargon.* 文件是用晦澀的律師行話寫成的。—**impenetrably** *adv* —**impenetrability** /ɪmˌpɛnətrə`bɪlətɪ; ɪmˌpenɪ̯trə'bɪlɪ̯ti/ *n* [U]

im·pen·i·tent /ɪm`pɛnətənt; ɪm'penɪ̯tənt/ *adj formal* not feeling sorry for something bad or wrong that you have done【正式】不知悔悟的, 沒有悔意的 —**impenitently** *adv* —**impenitence** *n* [U]

im·per·a·tive¹ /ɪm`pɛrətɪv; ɪm'perətɪv/ *adj* **1** extremely important and needing to be done or dealt with immediately 緊急的, 極為重要而必須立即處理的: **it is imperative (that)** *It is absolutely imperative that these safety measures are implemented immediately.* 這些安全措施必須立刻執行。| **it is imperative to do sth** *By now, it had become imperative to evacuate the area.* 撤離該地區已刻不容緩。**2** a voice, manner etc that is imperative is very firm and has a feeling of authority〔嗓音、態度等〕堅定的, 顯示權威的 **3** *technical* an imperative verb is one that expresses a command【術語】祈使的〔動詞〕—**imperatively** *adv*

imperative² *n* [C] **1** something that must be done urgently 緊急的事: *Reducing unemployment has become an imperative for the government.* 減少失業已成為政府的當務之急。**2** *technical* the form of a verb that expresses a command【術語】祈使語氣的動詞形式: *In 'Come here!' the verb 'come' is in the imperative.* 在 Come here! (過來!) 中, come 是祈使語氣。**3** *formal* an idea, belief, or emotion that strongly influences people to behave in a particular way【正式】強烈的慾望; 衝動: *the sexual imperative* 性慾

im·per·cep·ti·ble /ˌɪmpə`sɛptəbl̩; ˌɪmpə'septɪ̯bəl/ *adj* an imperceptible change, movement etc is difficult to see or notice because it is very small〔變化、動作等由於極微小而〕難以察覺的: *an almost imperceptible change of speed* 難以察覺的變速 —**imperceptibly** *adv*: *The daylight faded almost imperceptibly into night.* 天色不知不覺地暗了下來。—**imperceptibility** /ˌɪmpə-ˌsɛptə`bɪlətɪ; ˌɪmpəseptɪ̯'bɪlɪ̯ti/ *n* [U]

im·per·fect¹ /ɪm`pɝfɪkt; ɪm'pɜːfɪkt/ *adj* not completely correct or perfect 有缺點的, 不完美的: *an imperfect knowledge of German* 粗通德語 | *I got it cheap because it's slightly imperfect.* 這東西因為有點小毛病, 所以我很便宜就買到了。—**imperfectly** *adv* —**imperfection** /ˌɪmpə`fɛkʃən; ˌɪmpə'fekʃən/ *n* [C,U]

imperfect² also 又作 **imperfect tense** *n* [singular] *technical* the form of a verb that shows an incomplete action in the past【術語】〔動詞的〕未完成過去式

im·pe·ri·al /ɪm`pɪrɪəl; ɪm'pɪəriəl/ *adj* **1** connected with an EMPIRE or with the person who rules it 帝國的; 皇帝的: *Britain's imperial expansion in the 19th century* 19世紀英帝國的擴張 | *a major imperial power* 一個主要的帝國 **2** [only before noun 僅用於名詞前] connected with the system of weights and measurements based on INCH*es*, miles etc〔以英寸、英里等為基本度量衡單位的制度〕英制的 —compare 比較 METRIC

im·pe·ri·al·is·m /ɪm`pɪrɪəlˌɪzəm; ɪm'pɪəriəlɪzəm/ *n* [U] **1** a political system in which one country rules a lot of other countries, and tries to find more that it can defeat and govern 帝國主義 **2** methods by which a rich or powerful country can get political or trade advantages over poorer countries 富國或強國對貧窮國家在政治或貿易上掠取利益的手段 —compare 比較 COLONIALISM —**imperialist** *n* —**imperialist, imperialistic** /ɪmˌpɪrɪəl`ɪstɪk; ɪmˌpɪəriə'lɪstɪk◂/ *adj*

im·per·il /ɪm`pɛrəl; ɪm'perɪ̯l/ *v formal*【正式】**imperilled** *BrE*【英】, **imperiled** *AmE*【美】[T] to put something in danger 危及: *The whole project was imperilled by a lack of funds.* 資金缺乏危及整個工程。

im·pe·ri·ous /ɪm`pɪrɪəs; ɪm'pɪəriəs/ *adj* giving orders and expecting to be obeyed, in a way that seems too proud 專橫的; 飛揚跋扈的; 傲慢的: *She had an imperious domineering manner which Tim did not like.* 她那飛揚跋扈、作威作福的樣子讓蒂姆很反感。| *an imperious voice* 傲慢的口氣 —**imperiously** *adv* —**imperiousness** *n* [U]

im·per·ish·a·ble /ɪm`pɛrɪʃəbl̩; ɪm'perɪʃəbəl/ *adj formal* formed or made in a way that will exist for a long time or for ever【正式】堅固的; 永存的: *The manufacturers claim that the material is imperishable.* 製造商聲稱這種材料永不磨損。| *imperishable memories* 永不磨滅的記憶 —opposite 反義詞 PERISHABLE

im·per·ma·nent /ɪm`pɝmənənt; ɪm'pɜːmənənt/ *adj formal* not staying the same forever; TEMPORARY【正式】非永久的, 臨時的: *A row of precarious and impermanent wooden huts clung to the hillside.* 一排臨時小木屋緊靠着山坡。—**impermanence** *n* [U]: *The impermanence of the situation worried him.* 局勢動蕩令他憂慮。

im·per·me·a·ble /ɪm`pɝmɪəbl; ɪm'pɜːmiəbəl/ *adj technical* not allowing liquids or gases to pass through【術語】不容〔液體或氣體〕透過的, 不可滲透的: *an impermeable shell membrane* 不透水的蛋殼膜

im·per·mis·si·ble /ˌɪmpɝ`mɪsəbl̩; ˌɪmpɜː'mɪsɪ̵bəl/ *adj formal* something that is impermissible cannot be allowed【正式】不許可的, 不允許的: *an impermissible infringement of the rules* 違反規章, 不能容許

im·per·son·al /ɪm`pɝsn̩l; ɪm'pɜːsənəl/ *adj* **1** not showing any feelings of sympathy, friendliness etc 不表示同情[友善等]的; 冷漠的: *She left a short impersonal note, saying that she was leaving.* 她留下一張措詞冰冷的便條, 說她要走了。**2** a place or situation that is impersonal does not make people feel that they are important or valued〔地方或情況〕沒有人情味的; 冷淡的: *a large impersonal city* 一座人情淡薄的大城市 | *Health care has become increasingly bureaucratic and impersonal.* 衞生保健(制度)越來越繁瑣拖拉, 人情味越來越淡薄。**3** *technical* in grammar, an impersonal sentence or verb is one where the subject is represented by a word such as 'it', as in the sentence 'It rained all day'【術語】〔語法中〕非人稱的, 無人稱的〔指句子或動詞的主語是 it 等詞, 如 It rained all day〕—compare 比較 PERSONAL¹ —**impersonally** *adv*

im·per·so·nate /ɪm`pɝsn̩ˌet; ɪm'pɜːsəneɪt/ *v* [T] **1** to pretend to be someone else by copying their appearance, voice, and behaviour, especially in order to deceive people〔尤指為行騙而〕假扮〔他人〕, 假冒: *He gained access to the building by impersonating a police officer.* 他假扮警察而得以進入大樓。**2** to copy someone's voice and behaviour, especially in order to make people laugh〔尤指為逗人發笑而〕模仿〔某人的說話、動作〕: *Eddie was standing on the table, trying to impersonate John Wayne.* 愛迪站在桌子上, 模仿尊榮的模樣。—**impersonation** /ˌɪmpɝsn̩`eʃən; ɪmˌpɜːsə'neɪʃən/ *n* [C,U]: *On the club circuit, he's renowned for his Elvis impersonations.* 在夜總會的巡迴演出中, 他以模仿皮禮士利而見稱。

im·per·so·nat·or /ɪm`pɝsn̩ˌetɚ; ɪm'pɜːsəneɪtə/ *n* [C] someone who copies the way that other people look, speak, and behave, as part of a performance〔在表演中模仿他人的〕模仿者

im·per·ti·nent /ɪm`pɝtn̩ənt; ɪm'pɜːtɪ̵nənt/ *adj* rude and not respectful, especially to someone who is older or more important〔尤指對尊長〕不禮貌的; 莽撞無禮的: *The question about her age was very impertinent.* 詢問她的年齡太失禮了。—**impertinently** *adv* —**impertinence** *n* [U]

im·per·tur·ba·ble /ˌɪmpɚ`tɝbəbl̩; ˌɪmpə'tɜːbəbəl/ *adj* remaining calm and unworried in spite of problems or difficulties 從容鎮定的, 沉着的, 冷靜的: *His steady, imperturbable nature reassured me.* 他沉着鎮定的性格讓我感到放心。—**imperturbably** *adv* —**imperturbability** /ˌɪmpɚˌtɝbə`bɪlətɪ; ˌɪmpətɜːbə'bɪlɪ̵ti/ *n* [U]

im·per·vi·ous /ɪm`pɝvɪəs; ɪm'pɜːviəs/ *adj* **1** not affected or influenced by something and seeming not to notice it 不受影響的; 無動於衷的: **[+to]** *Janet carried on reading, impervious to the row going on around her.* 珍妮特不受周圍的嘈雜聲影響, 繼續看書。| *He seems to be impervious to criticism.* 他好像對批評毫不在乎。**2** not allowing anything to enter or pass through〔任何東西都〕不能進入的; 不能穿過的: *impervious volcanic rock* 不透水不透氣的火山岩

im·pe·ti·go /ˌɪmpɪ`taɪgo; ˌɪmpɪ̵'taɪgəʊ/ *n* [U] an infectious skin disease 膿疱病〔傳染性皮膚病〕

im·pet·u·ous /ɪm`pɛtʃʊəs; ɪm'petʃʊəs/ *adj* tending to do things very quickly, without thinking carefully first〔做事〕過快的, 魯莽的: *It was an impetuous decision which she soon regretted.* 她作了倉促的決定, 不久就感到後悔。—**impetuously** *adv* —**impetuousness** *n* [U] —**impetuosity** /ˌɪmpɛtʃʊ`ɑsətɪ; ɪmˌpetʃu'ɒsɪ̵ti/ *n* [U]

im·pe·tus /`ɪmpətəs; 'ɪmpɪ̵təs/ *n* [U] **1** feeling an influence that makes people or helps something to develop or continue doing something 刺激; 推動(力); 促進: **gain/lose impetus** *The campaign is already gaining impetus.* 這場運動的氣勢正在增加。| *As a result of this failure, a lot of the initial impetus was lost.* 由於這次失敗, 大大減弱了當初的衝勁。| **[+for]** *Einstein's work provided the impetus for a major shift in the study of physics.* 愛因斯坦的研究成果促使物理學研究發生了重大轉變。**2** *technical* the force that makes an object start moving, or keeps it moving once it has started【術語】〔使物體移動的〕動量, 衝力

im·pi·e·ty /ɪm`paɪətɪ; ɪm'paɪɪ̵ti/ *n formal*【正式】**1** [U] lack of respect for religion or God〔對宗教或上帝〕不虔誠, 褻瀆 **2** [C usually plural 一般用複數] an action that shows a lack of respect for religion or God〔對宗教或上帝的〕不敬的行為 —see also 另見 IMPIOUS

im·pinge /ɪm`pɪndʒ; ɪm'pɪndʒ/ *v*

impinge on/upon *phr v* [T] *formal* to have an effect on someone or something; influence【正式】對...起作用; 影響: *The change of government scarcely impinged on ordinary people's lives.* 政府的更迭對平民百姓的生活幾乎沒有影響。| *We were discussing the way welfare policies impinge on women.* 我們在討論福利政策對婦女的影響。—**impingement** *n* [U]

im·pi·ous /`ɪmpɪəs; 'ɪmpiəs/ *adj formal* lacking respect for religion or God【正式】〔對宗教或上帝〕不恭敬的, 不虔誠的 —**impiously** *adv* —**impiousness** *n* [U] —see also 另見 IMPIETY

imp·ish /`ɪmpɪʃ; 'ɪmpɪʃ/ *adj* behaving badly and causing trouble, but in a way that is amusing rather than serious or annoying; MISCHEIVOUS 調皮搗蛋的, 淘氣的 —**impishly** *adv: Tony grinned impishly at her.* 托尼向她調皮地咧嘴一笑。—**impishness** *n* [U]

im·plac·a·ble /ɪm`plækəbl̩; ɪm'plækəbəl/ *adj* very determined to continue opposing someone or something 決意〔與...〕作對的,〔對...〕毫不寬容的: *an implacable enemy* 死敵 | *The tabloid newspapers remained implacable in their opposition.* 那些小報執意堅持對立觀點。—**implacably** *adv*: *A few organizations remain implacably opposed to Sunday trading.* 一些組織執意反對週日交易。—**implacability** /ɪmˌplækə`bɪlətɪ; ɪmˌplækə'bɪlɪ̵ti/ *n* [U]

im·plant¹ /ɪm`plænt; ɪm'plɑːnt/ *v* **1** to strongly fix an idea, feeling, or way of behaving in someone's mind, so that it becomes part of their character 灌輸〔思想、感情或行為方式〕: *a deep sense of patriotism that had been implanted in him by his father* 他父親向他灌輸了強烈的愛國主義情感 | *The phrase implanted itself in my memory.* 這句話深深地印在我的腦海裡。**2** [T] to put something into someone's body by doing a medical operation 把〔某物〕植入〔體內〕; 移植: *Surgeons successfully implanted an artificial kneejoint.* 外科醫生成功植入一個人造膝關節。—**implantation** /ˌɪmplæn`teʃən; ˌɪmplɑːn'teɪʃən/ *n* [U]

im·plant² /`ɪmplænt; 'ɪmplɑːnt/ *n* [C] something that has been implanted in someone's body in a medical operation〔通過手術被移植人體的〕植入物: *silicone implants*

I

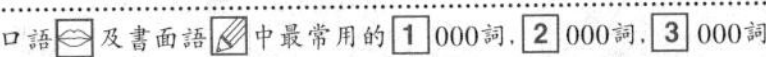

硅酮植入片 —compare 比較 TRANSPLANT[2]

im·plau·si·ble /ɪm`plɔzəbl; ɪm'plɔːzəbəl/ *adj* difficult to believe and therefore unlikely to be true 難以置信的; 不大可能真實的: *an implausible explanation* 讓人難以相信的解釋 | *His excuses were totally implausible.* 他的藉口根本不合情理。—**implausibly** *adv* —**implausibility** /ɪm,plɔzə`bɪlətɪ; ɪm,plɔːzə'bɪləti/ *n* [U]

3 **im·ple·ment**[1] /`ɪmplə,mɛnt; 'ɪmpləment/ *v* [T] **implement a plan/policy/proposal etc** to take action or make changes that you have officially decided should happen〔正式地〕執行計劃/政策/建議等: *We have decided to implement the committee's suggestions in full.* 我們已決定全面實施委員會提出的建議。

im·ple·ment[2] /`ɪmpləmənt; 'ɪmplәmәnt/ *n* [C] a tool or instrument, especially a fairly large one with no motor〔尤指相當大、非馬達驅動的〕工具, 用具, 器具: *ploughs, hoes, and other farming implements* 犁、鋤和其他農具

im·ple·men·ta·tion /,ɪmpləmɛn`teʃən; ,ɪmpləmen'teɪʃən/ *n* [U] the act of implementing a plan, policy etc 實施, 貫徹, 執行: *implementation of the peace plan* 實施和平計劃

im·pli·cate /`ɪmplɪ,ket; 'ɪmplәkeɪt/ *v* [T] **1** to show or seem to show that someone is involved in something wrong or criminal（彷彿）表明〔某人〕與〔錯誤或罪行〕有牽連: **implicate sb in sth** *The letter seemed to implicate Mitchell in the robbery.* 這封信似乎表明米切爾與這件搶劫案有牽連。**2** to show or seem to show that something is the cause of something bad or harmful（彷彿）表明〔某物〕導致〔不好或有害的事〕: *Tobacco has already been implicated as one of the causes of the disease.* 煙草已被認為是導致這種疾病的原因之一。

2 **im·pli·ca·tion** /,ɪmplɪ`keʃən; ,ɪmplә'keɪʃən/ *n* **1** [C usually plural 一般用複數] a possible future effect or result of a plan, action, or event, which must be considered or discussed〔計劃、行為或事件需要考慮或討論的〕可能的影響, 可能的後果: **[+of]** *What are the implications of these proposals?* 這些提議會有甚麼後果? | **have implications for** *This could have serious implications for the company's future.* 這對公司的未來可能會產生嚴重影響。| *You can't just close reactors down – there are all sorts of safety implications.* 反應堆不是説關閉就能關閉的, 有各種各樣的安全問題需要考慮。**2** [C,U] something that you do not say directly but that you seem to want people to believe 含意, 暗示: **[+that]** *I resent the implication that I would have lied to you.* 有人暗示我會對你説謊, 對此我感到很生氣。| **by implication** *The law bans organized protests and, by implication, any form of opposition.* 這條法律禁止有組織的抗議, 言外之意是不許進行任何形式的反對。—see also 另見 IMPLY (1) **3** [U] a situation in which someone is shown to be involved in something wrong or criminal〔某人〕牽涉〔錯誤或罪行〕, 捲入: **[+of]** *the implication of the former Chief of Staff in a major scandal* 前任參謀長捲入一宗重大的醜聞 **4** something that you believe to be shown by a particular situation, action etc〔特定的情況、行動等〕顯示[表明]的內容: **[+in]** *The implication in this case is that he's innocent.* 這個情況表明他是清白無辜的。—see also 另見 IMPLICATE

im·pli·cit /ɪm`plɪsɪt; ɪm'plɪsәt/ *adj* **1 implicit criticism/threat/approval** criticism etc that is suggested or understood without being stated directly 含蓄的批評/隱含的恫嚇/默許: *Her words contained an implicit threat.* 她話裡帶着威脅。| *implicit criticism* 含蓄的批評 —compare 比較 EXPLICIT **2 be implicit in** *formal* to form a central part of something, but without being openly stated【正式】隱含其中的; 不明言的: *Confidentiality is implicit in your relationship with a counsellor.* 在你與律師的關係中, 他會為你保守祕密是不言而喻的。**3 implicit trust/faith** trust etc that is complete and contains no doubts 絕對的信任/信心: *They had an implicit faith in his powers.* 他們絕對相信他的才能。—**implicitly** *adv*: *We trusted Lopez implicitly.* 我們絕對信任洛佩斯。

im·plode /ɪm`plod; ɪm'plәʊd/ *v* [I] to explode inwards 向心聚爆; 內爆 —compare 比較 EXPLODE (1) —**implosion** /ɪm`ploʒən; ɪm'plәʊʒәn/ *n* [C,U]

im·plore /ɪm`plɔr; ɪm'plɔː/ *v* [T] *formal* to ask for something in an emotional way; PLEAD (1)【正式】懇求; 乞求; 哀求: *John, I implore you, stop now before it's too late.* 約翰, 我求你快停下, 不然就來不及了。| **implore sb to do sth** *She implored the soldiers to save her child.* 她乞求那些士兵救她的孩子。

im·ply /ɪm`plaɪ; ɪm'plaɪ/ *v* [T] **1** to suggest that something is true without saying this directly 暗示, 暗指: **imply (that)** *She managed to imply she'd contributed the money without actually saying so.* 她設法暗示了錢是她捐的, 而沒有直接説出來。| *an implied threat* 隱含的威脅 —see 見 INFER (USAGE) **2** if a fact, event etc implies something, it shows that it is likely to be true 意味着〔某事可能是真的〕: *The high level of radiation in the rocks implies that they are volcanic in origin.* 岩石內的高輻射意味着它是火山作用形成的。**3** if a principle, action, idea etc implies something, it makes other actions or conditions necessary〔原則、行動、思想等〕必然包含…: *Democracy implies a respect for individual liberties.* 民主必然包含對個人自由的尊重。

im·po·lite /,ɪmpə`laɪt; ,ɪmpә'laɪt◂/ *adj* not polite; rude 無禮的; 粗魯的: *It was very impolite not to write and thank them.* 不寫信向他們致謝是很不禮貌的。—**impolitely** *adv* —**impoliteness** *n* [C,U]

im·pol·i·tic /ɪm`pɑlətɪk; ɪm'pɒlәtɪk/ *adj formal* not sensible or not behaving in a way that is likely to bring you advantage【正式】不明智的; 失策的: *It was considered impolitic for him to spend too much time with the radicals in the party.* 他花太多時間與黨內的激進分子在一起被認為是不明智的。

im·pon·de·ra·ble[1] /ɪm`pɑndərəbl; ɪm'pɒndәrәbәl/ *adj formal* something that is imponderable cannot be exactly measured, judged, or calculated【正式】無法精確估量的, 難以判斷的

imponderable[2] *n* [C usually plural 一般用複數] *formal* something that cannot be exactly measured, judged, or calculated【正式】無法準確估量的事物: *There are so many imponderables that it is impossible to make an accurate prediction.* 不可估量的情況太多, 所以難以作出準確預測。

im·port[1] /`ɪmpɔrt; 'ɪmpɔːt/ *n* **1** [C] something that is brought into one country from another in order to be sold 進口商品: *cheap imports of grain* 廉價進口的穀物 **2** [U] the process or business of bringing goods into one country from another〔商品的〕進口, 輸入: *The government eventually banned the import of all electrical goods.* 政府最後禁止所有電氣產品的進口。—opposite 反義詞 EXPORT[1] **3** [U] *formal* importance or meaning【正式】重要性; 含意: *a matter of no great import* 一件小事

im·port[2] /ɪm`pɔrt; ɪm'pɔːt/ *v* [T] **1** to bring something into a country from abroad in order to sell it 進口〔商品〕, 輸入: *imported oil* 進口的石油 **2** *technical* to move information from one computer into another【術語】〔從一台電腦到另一台電腦〕輸入〔信息〕—opposite 反義詞 EXPORT[2]

im·por·tance /ɪm`pɔrtn̩s; ɪm'pɔːtәns/ *n* [U] **1** the quality of being important 重要(性): *The doctor stressed the importance of regular exercise.* 醫生強調了經常鍛鍊的重要性。| **attach importance to** (=treat something as if it is important) 給予重視 *Much greater importance is now attached to environmental concerns.* 環境問題越來越受到重視。| **of great/vital/crucial importance** (=very important) 極為重要 *This is an issue of great importance to all disabled people.* 這個問題對於殘疾人士至關重要。**2** the reason why something is important 重要的原因: *The real importance of this law is the protection it gives to female workers.* 這項法律的真正重要意義在於它對女工所提供的保護。

im·por·tant /ɪm`pɔrtn̩t; ɪm'pɔːtәnt/ *adj* **1** an important event, decision, problem etc has a big effect or influence on people's lives or on events in the future 重要的, 重大的: *a very important meeting* 一次極為重要的會議 | *Listen everyone, I've got some important news!* 大家注意, 我有重要消息宣布。| **it is important to do sth** *It is important to explain to the patient what is happening.* 對病人說明病情是很重要的。| **it is important that** *It's vitally important that you understand the danger.* 了解危險所在是極為重要的。| **be important to sb/sth** *Money was the only thing that was important to Carson.* 對卡爾遜來說, 錢是唯一重要的東西。**2** people who are important have a lot of power or influence〔人〕有勢力的; 有影響的: *a very important customer* 一位大客戶 | *an important client* 一位有影響的委託人

im·por·tant·ly /ɪmˋpɔrtn̩tlɪ; ɪmˈpɔːtəntli/ *adv* **1 more/equally/less importantly** [sentence adverb 句子副詞] used to show that the next statement or question is more, equally etc important than what you said before it 更/同等/不太重要的是: *Most importantly, you must keep a record of everything you do.* 更重要的是, 你必須把你所做的事一一記錄下來。**2** in a way that shows you think that what you are saying or doing is important 煞有介事地; 自以為了不起地: *"I've got to look after his books," the youngest boy said importantly.* "我得照管他這些書。"最小的男孩一本正經地說道。| *striding importantly into the room* 神氣十足地大步走進房間

im·por·ta·tion /ˌɪmpɔrˋteʃən; ˌɪmpɔːˈteɪʃən/ *n* **1** [U] the business of buying goods from another country and having them sent to your country to be sold there 進口, 輸入 **2 a)** [U] the act of bringing into a country something new or different such as a new plant, custom, or idea〔將新鮮事物〕引進〔某國家〕 **b)** [C] something that is brought into a country in this way 舶來品, 從外國引進的事物 —compare 比較 IMPORT[1]

import du·ty /ˈ·· ˌ··/ *n* [C,U] a tax on goods that are brought into one country from another country 進口關稅

im·port·er /ɪmˋpɔrtɚ; ɪmˈpɔːtə/ *n* [C] a person, company, or country that buys goods from another country, to be sold or used in their own country 進口者; 進口商; 進口國, 輸入國: *Japan is one of the world's largest importers of tropical timber.* 日本是全球熱帶木材進口大國之一。—opposite 反義詞 EXPORTER

import li·cence /ˈ·· ˌ··/ *n* [C] a document that gives permission for goods to be brought into one country from another 進口許可證

im·por·tu·nate /ɪmˋpɔrtʃənɪt; ɪmˈpɔːtʃʊn̩ət/ *adj formal* always asking for things in an annoying or unreasonable way【正式】糾纏不休的, 無理的: *importunate demands* 蠻橫無理的要求 —**importunately** *adv* —**importunity** /ˌɪmpəˋtjunətɪ; ˌɪmpəˈtjuːn̩əti/ *n* [U]

im·por·tune /ˌɪmpəˋtjun; ˌɪmpəˈtjuːn/ *v* [T] *formal* to ask someone for something repeatedly, especially in an annoying or unreasonable way; beg【正式】〔向某人〕再三要求〔尤指糾纏不休或不合理地〕; 乞求: **[+for]** *importuning passers-by for money* 纏着過路人討錢

2 **im·pose** /ɪmˋpoz; ɪmˈpəʊz/ *v* **1 impose a ban/tax/fine etc (on)** to officially order that something should be forbidden, restricted, taxed etc, or that someone should be punished〔正式〕實施禁令/徵收稅款/懲收罰款等: *The government imposed a ban on the sale of ivory.* 政府禁止買賣象牙。| *We have decided to impose sanctions on countries that break the agreement.* 我們決定對違約國加以制裁。**2 impose a burden/strain etc (on/upon)** to have a bad effect on something or someone by causing them problems 增加負擔/壓力等: *The President's health care proposals would not impose any great burden on the state's finances.* 總統提出的醫療保健計劃不會給國家財政帶來任何巨大的負擔。**3** [T] to force someone to have the same ideas or beliefs as you〔將想法、信仰〕強加於〔某人〕: **impose sth on sb** *parents who impose their own moral values on their children* 把自己的道德價值觀強加於孩子們的父母 **4** [I] to unreasonably expect or ask someone to do something for you when this is inconvenient for them 麻煩〔別人〕: **[+on/upon]** *We could ask them to let us stay the night, but I don't want to impose on them.* 我們可以請求他們讓我們在這裡過夜, 但我不想麻煩他們。

im·pos·ing /ɪmˋpozɪŋ; ɪmˈpəʊzɪŋ/ *adj* large, important-looking, and impressive 壯觀的, 宏偉的; 氣勢雄偉的: *an imposing building* 氣勢宏偉的建築

im·po·si·tion /ˌɪmpəˋzɪʃən; ˌɪmpəˈzɪʃən/ *n* **1** [C usually singular 一般用單數] something that someone unreasonably expects or asks you to do for them, which is inconvenient 無理要求: *I regarded his request for a loan as something of an imposition.* 我認為他的貸款要求有點強人所難。**2** [U] the introduction of something such as a rule, tax, or restriction〔規章、稅種、限制等的〕實施; 徵收: *the imposition of martial law* 實施軍事管制

im·pos·si·ble /ɪmˋpɑsəbl̩; ɪmˈpɒsəbəl/ *adj* S2 W2

1 ►CAN'T BE DONE 不能完成◄ something that is impossible cannot happen or be done 不可能發生的; 辦不到的: *Further research is impossible without more money.* 沒有更多的資金, 進一步研究就不可能。| *This crossword's absolutely impossible!* 這個縱橫填字謎遊戲根本不可能做出來! | *Impossible! It can't be true.* 不可能! 不會是真的! | **find it impossible to do sth** *Members with young children often found it impossible to attend evening meetings.* 有小孩的會員經常無法參加晚間的會議。| **ask the impossible** (=ask for something that cannot be done) 要求不可能做到的事 *Expecting the project to be completed by October was really asking the impossible.* 指望十月前完成這項工程是要人家做辦不到的事。| **do the impossible** (=succeed in doing something that seems impossible) 實現不可能的事 *Somehow, Jen had done the impossible and got us all tickets.* 珍妮不知用甚麼方法, 辦成了不可能做到的事, 給大家都買到了票。| **impossible demands/requests etc** (=demands etc for something that is impossible) 辦不到的要求/請求等

2 ►SITUATION 情形◄ a situation that is impossible is extremely difficult to deal with 極難對付的: *Helen's refusal to cooperate has put me in an impossible position.* 海倫拒絕合作, 使我進退兩難。| *His bad temper is making life impossible for the rest of the family.* 他的壞脾氣讓全家人度日如年。

3 ►PERSON 人◄ someone who is impossible behaves in a very unreasonable and annoying way〔行為〕不講道理的, 令人討厭的: *You're impossible! Yesterday you said you didn't like carrots, and today you won't eat potatoes!* 真拿你沒辦法! 昨天你說不喜歡胡蘿蔔, 今天又不吃馬鈴薯! —**impossibly** *adv*: *impossibly difficult* 極為困難的 | *They were asking an impossibly high price.* 他們要價高得難以接受。—**impossibility** /ɪmˌpɑsəˋbɪlətɪ; ɪmˌpɒsəˈbɪləti/ *n* [C,U] *To walk there would have been a virtual impossibility.* 步行去那裡實際上是不可能的。

im·pos·tor also 又作 **imposter** *AmE*【美】/ɪmˋpɑstɚ; ɪmˈpɒstə/ *n* [C] someone who pretends to be someone else in order to trick people 冒充他人的騙子

im·pos·ture /ɪmˋpɑstʃɚ; ɪmˈpɒstʃə/ *n* [U] *formal* a situation in which someone tricks people by pretending to be someone else【正式】冒名行騙; 招搖撞騙

im·po·tent /ˈɪmpətənt; ˈɪmpətənt/ *adj* **1** unable to take effective action because you do not have enough power, strength, or control 不能採取有效行動的, 無能為力的: *Emergency services seem almost impotent in the face of such a disaster.* 面對這種災難, 急救服務似乎無能為力。| *impotent rage* 無奈的狂怒 **2** a man who is impotent is unable to have sex because he cannot get an ERECTION (1)〔指男子〕無性交能力的, 陽痿的 —**impotently** *adv* —**impotence** *n* [U]

im·pound /ɪmˋpaund; ɪmˈpaʊnd/ *v* [T] *law* if the police or law courts impound your possessions they take them and keep them until you claim them【法律】扣押〔某物

I

直到物主認領): *Last time I went to Rome my car was impounded.* 我上次去羅馬, 汽車被扣了。

im·pov·e·rish /ɪm`pɑvərɪʃ; ɪm'pɒvərɪʃ/ *v* [T] **1** [often passive 常用被動態] to make someone very poor 使貧困, 使赤貧: *Many peasants were impoverished by the land tax.* 土地稅使許多農民一貧如洗。**2** to make something worse in quality 使品質降低: *Crop rotation has not impoverished the soil.* 農作物輪作沒有使土壤貧瘠。—**impoverishment** *n* [U]

im·pov·e·rished /ɪm`pɑvərɪʃt; ɪm'pɒvərɪʃt/ *adj* **a)** very poor 赤貧的: *an impoverished student* 貧困的學生 **b)** worse in quality 質量下降的: *Our lives would be impoverished without music.* 沒有音樂, 我們的生活就會變得更貧乏。

im·prac·ti·ca·ble /ɪm`præktɪkəbl̩; ɪm'præktɪkəbəl/ *adj* something that is impracticable cannot be done even though it seems a good idea 不現實的, 行不通的: *It was an appealing plan but quite impracticable.* 這個計劃有吸引力, 但完全行不通。—**impracticably** *adv* —**impracticability** /ɪm,præktɪkə`bɪlətɪ; ɪm,præktɪkə'bɪlətì/ *n* [U]

im·prac·ti·cal /ɪm`præktɪkl̩; ɪm'præktɪkəl/ *adj* **1** an idea, suggestion, or action that is impractical is not sensible because it would be too difficult, too expensive etc 〔念頭、建議、活動〕不切實際的; 不現實的; 過於昂貴的: *A 24-hour service would be impractical for a small organization like this.* 這樣小的機構提供24小時服務是不切實際的。**2** someone who is impractical is not good at dealing with ordinary practical matters, such as making or repairing things 〔人〕無實踐能力的〈如維修物件〉; 動手能力差的: *a hopelessly impractical man, who couldn't even boil an egg* 一個連雞蛋都不會煮的笨手笨腳的人 —**impractically** /-kl̩ɪ; -kli/ *adv* —**impracticality** /ɪm,præktɪ`kælətɪ; ɪm,præktɪ'kælətì/ *n* [U]: *the sheer impracticality of such a large scale screening program* 如此大規模的甄別計劃絕對不切實際

im·pre·ca·tion /,ɪmprɪ`keʃən; ,ɪmprɪ'keɪʃən/ *n* [C] *formal* an offensive word or phrase that you say when you are very angry; a CURSE² (2) 【正式】罵人的話; 咒罵, 詛咒

im·pre·cise /,ɪmprɪ`saɪs; ,ɪmprɪ'saɪs◂/ *adj* not exact; INACCURATE 不精確的, 不確切的: *a very imprecise method of measurement* 很不精確的測量方法 | *an imprecise term* 不確切的說法 —**imprecisely** *adv* —**imprecision** /-`sɪʒən; -'sɪʒən/ *n* [U]

im·preg·na·ble /ɪm`prɛgnəbl̩; ɪm'pregnəbəl/ *adj* **1** a building that is impregnable is so strong that no one can get into it by force 〔建築物〕攻不破的, 固若金湯的: *an impregnable fortress* 堅不可摧的堡壘 **2** *formal* attitudes, opinions etc that are impregnable cannot be changed or influenced 【正式】〔態度、意見等〕無法改變的, 無法動搖的: *her impregnable obstinacy* 她那頑固不化的倔強 —**impregnably** *adv* —**impregnability** /ɪm,prɛgnə`bɪlətɪ; ɪm,pregnə'bɪlətì/ *n* [U]

im·preg·nate /`ɪmprɛgnet; 'ɪmpregneɪt/ *v* [T] **1** to make a substance spread completely through something, or to spread completely through something 浸透, 浸漬; 使飽和: **[+with]** *The material has been impregnated with disinfectant.* 這種材料已用消毒劑浸漬過。**2** to make a woman or female animal PREGNANT 使懷孕, 使受精

im·pre·sa·ri·o /,ɪmprɪ`sɑrɪ,o; ,ɪmprɪ'sɑːriəʊ/ *n* [C] someone who organizes performances in theatres, concert halls etc 〔劇院、音樂廳的〕演出主辦人; 演出經理

3 **im·press¹** /ɪm`prɛs; ɪm'pres/ *v* [T] **1** [not in progressive 不用進行式] if something or someone impresses you, you admire them because you notice how good, clever, successful etc they are 令人稱羨, 使留下深刻印象: *What impressed us most about the book was its vivid language.* 這本書給我們印象最深的是它生動的語言。| *Steve borrowed his dad's sports car to impress his girlfriend.* 史蒂夫借來他爸爸的跑車以便對女友炫耀。| **be impressed with/by** *We're very impressed with the standard of the children's work.* 這些兒童作品水準之高, 給我們留下了深刻印象。| **be favourably impressed** *I think the boss was favourably impressed by your presentation.* 我認為老闆對你的報告相當滿意。| **be suitably impressed** (=be impressed as you should be) 恰如其分地感到印象深刻 **2** to make the importance of something clear to someone 使〔某人〕了解〔某事的〕重要性: **impress sth on sb** *Father impressed on me the value of hard work.* 父親向我強調努力工作的重要意義。**3** to press something into a soft surface so as to make a mark or pattern as a result of this pressure 把〔某物〕壓入〔柔軟的平面〕; 壓印; 蓋〔印〕於: **be impressed in/on** *patterns impressed in the clay* 壓印在黏土上的圖案

im·press² /`ɪmprɛs; 'ɪmpres/ *n* [C] *formal or literary* a mark or pattern made by pressing something into a surface 【正式或文】印記; 壓痕

impression 壓痕

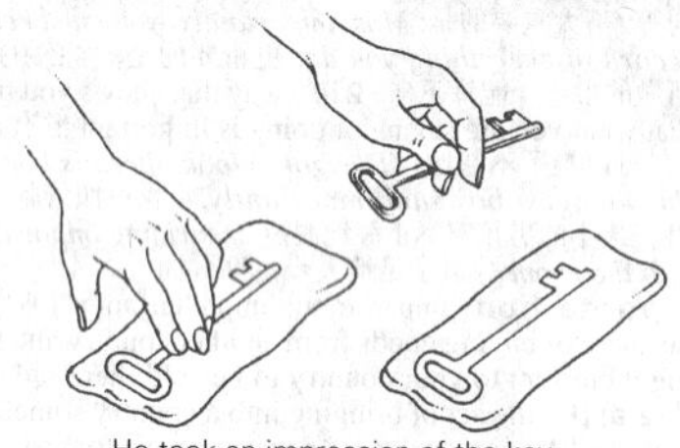

He took an impression of the key.
他壓取了鑰匙的模子。

im·pres·sion /ɪm`prɛʃən; ɪm'preʃən/ *n*

1 ►OPINION 想法◄ [C] the opinion or feeling you have about someone or something because of the way they seem 〔對人、事的〕印象; 感想: **[+of]** *What's your impression of Frank as a boss?* 你對身為老闆的弗蘭克印象如何? | *Now I have a very different impression of England.* 如今我對英格蘭的印象大不相同了。| **first impression** *First impressions can be deceptive.* 第一印象可能是靠不住的。| **create a good/bad impression** *Arriving late won't create a very favourable impression.* 遲到不會給人留下好印象。| **make an impression (on)** (=make someone admire you) 留下好印象 *It was their first meeting, and Richard was determined to make an impression.* 這是他們第一次見面, 理查德決心給人留下好印象。| **have/get the impression (that)** (=think that something is a fact because of the way the situation seems) 覺得 *I get the distinct impression that we're not wanted here.* 我明顯感到我們在這裡是不受歡迎的。| **be under the impression (that)** (=wrongly believe that something is a fact because of the way the situation seems) 原以為, 誤以為 *I'm sorry, I was under the impression that you were the manager.* 對不起, 我誤以為你是經理呢。

2 ►COPYING SB 模仿某人◄ [C] the act of copying the speech or behaviour of a famous person in order to make people laugh 〔對名人言行的〕滑稽模仿: **do an impression (of)** *Jean does a great impression of Tina Turner.* 吉恩模仿天娜·端納真是維妙維肖!

3 ►MARK 印痕◄ [C] a mark left by pressing something into a soft surface 印記; 壓痕: *An impression of a heel was left in the mud.* 泥地上留下了一個腳後跟的印記。

4 ►BOOK 書籍◄ [C] all the copies of a book printed at one time 印次〔一次印刷成的圖書總數量〕—compare 比較 EDITION

im·pres·sion·a·ble /ɪm`prɛʃənəbl̩; ɪm'preʃənəbəl/ *adj* easy to influence, especially because you are young 〔尤因年輕而〕易受影響的: **at an impressionable age** *It's damaging to criticize kids when they're at an impressionable age.* 指責年幼無知的孩子, 有害無益。—**impression-**

ability /ɪm͵prɛʃənə`bɪlətɪ; ɪm͵preʃənəˈbɪlɪ̈ti/ *n* [U]

im·pres·sion·is·m /ɪm`prɛʃən͵ɪzəm; ɪmˈpreʃənɪzəm/ *n* [U] **1** a style of painting used especially in France in the 19th century which uses colour instead of details of form to produce effects of light or feeling 印象主義, 印象派〔不拘泥於細節, 而以色彩來表達光線或感覺的繪畫風格, 盛行於 19 世紀的法國〕**2** a style of music from the late 19th and early 20th centuries that produces feelings and images by the quality of sounds rather than by a pattern of notes 印象主義, 印象派〔以音色而不是旋律來產生效果的音樂風格, 盛行於 19 世紀末 20 世紀初〕—**impressionist** *adj*: *impressionist painters* 印象派畫家

im·pres·sion·ist /ɪm`prɛʃənɪst; ɪmˈpreʃənɪ̈st/ *n* [C] **1** someone who uses impressionism in the paintings or music that they produce 印象派畫家; 印象派作曲家 **2** someone who copies the speech or behaviour of famous people in order to entertain other people 模仿名人的滑稽演員

im·pres·sion·is·tic /ɪm͵prɛʃən`ɪstɪk; ɪm͵preʃəˈnɪstɪk◂/ *adj* based on a general feeling of what something is like, rather than on specific facts or details 僅憑一般印象的; 主觀的: *an impressionistic account of what happened* 對所發生事情單憑印象的描述 —**impressionistically** /-klɪ; -kli/ *adv*

3 **im·pres·sive** /ɪm`prɛsɪv; ɪmˈpresɪv/ *adj* something that is impressive seems very good, large, important etc so that you admire it 給人深刻印象的: *Among the guests was an impressive array of authors and critics.* 來賓中以作家和評論家為之觸目。| *the remains of an impressive Roman villa* 一座令人讚嘆的古羅馬別墅遺跡 —**impressively** *adv* —**impressiveness** *n* [U]

im·pri·ma·tur /͵ɪmprɪ`metɚ; ͵ɪmprɪ̈ˈmeɪtə/ *n* [singular] **1** *usually humorous* approval of something, especially from an important person【一般幽默】〔尤指來自重要人物的〕批准, 認可, 同意 **2** official permission to print a book, especially when this is given by the Roman Catholic Church〔尤指羅馬天主教對書刊的〕印刷出版許可

im·print¹ /`ɪmprɪnt; ˈɪmprɪnt/ *n* [C] **1** the mark left by an object being pressed into or onto something 印記; 壓痕: **[+of]** *the imprint of her hand on the soft sand* 她留在細沙上的手印 **2** *technical* the name of a PUBLISHER as it appears on a book【術語】〔印在書籍上的〕出版者名稱: *This dictionary is published under the Longman imprint.* 這本辭典的出版者是朗文。

im·print² /ɪm`prɪnt; ɪmˈprɪnt/ *v* **1 be imprinted on your mind/ memory** if something is imprinted on your mind or memory, you can never forget it 銘記在心/在腦海中: *The sight of her waving from the window was forever imprinted on my mind.* 她站在窗口揮手的情景永遠留在我的腦海中。**2** [T] to print or press the mark of an object on something 在…上壓印[蓋印]: **be imprinted with** *notepaper imprinted with the Duke's monogram* 印有公爵姓名首字母圖案的信箋

im·pris·on /ɪm`prɪzn̩; ɪmˈprɪzən/ *v* [T] **1** to put someone in prison or to keep them somewhere and prevent them from leaving 監禁; 禁錮: *The government imprisoned or exiled all opposition leaders.* 政府不是把反對派領導人監禁就是流放。**2** if a situation or feeling imprisons people it restricts what they can do〔行為受到〕束縛, 限制: *Many elderly people felt imprisoned in their own homes.* 許多老年人感到自己有如被監禁在家裡似的。

im·pris·on·ment /ɪm`prɪzn̩mənt; ɪmˈprɪzənmənt/ *n* [U] the state of being in prison, or the time someone spends there 囚禁; 服刑: *sentenced to a long term of imprisonment* 被判處長期監禁 | **life imprisonment** (=imprisonment for the rest of your life, or for a long time) 終身監禁, 無期徒刑 *life imprisonment for murder* 因殺人而被判處無期徒刑

im·prob·a·ble /ɪm`prɑbəbl̩; ɪmˈprɒbəbəl/ *adj* **1** not likely to happen or to be true 不大可能發生的; 未必確實的: **it is improbable that** *It seems improbable that he could have driven home in less than an hour.* 他開車一小時之內就到了家, 這似乎不大可能。| **highly improbable** *a highly improbable explanation* 極不可信的解釋 **2** surprising and slightly strange 不可思議的: *Theirs was an improbable partnership.* 他們的合夥關係讓人不可思議。—**improbably** *adv* —**improbability** /ɪm͵prɑbə`bɪlətɪ; ɪm͵prɒbəˈbɪlɪ̈ti/ *n* [C,U]

im·promp·tu /ɪm`prɑmptu; ɪmˈprɒmptjuː/ *adj* done or said without any preparation or planning 無準備的; 即興的; 即席的: *an impromptu party* 即興聚會 —**impromptu** *adv*: *He insists he was speaking impromptu.* 他堅稱自己剛才的是即席講話。

im·prop·er /ɪm`prɑpɚ; ɪmˈprɒpə/ *adj* **1** unacceptable according to the normal standards of moral, social, or professional behaviour 不適當的, 不合適的, 不妥當的: *It is quite improper for you to have an affair with one of your students.* 與自己的學生發生曖昧關係是很不合適的。| **an improper suggestion** (=about sex) 猥褻的話 **2** illegal or dishonest 不合法的; 不誠實的: *allegations of improper banking practices* 對銀行違規經營的指控 **3** not correct according to a set of rules 不正確的; 不合乎規則的: *the improper use of a singular verb with a plural subject* 單數動詞與複數主語的不正確搭配 —**improperly** *adv*: *If you are improperly dressed, you will not be admitted.* 你若衣着不當, 就會被拒入內。

improper frac·tion /·͵·· ˈ··/ *n* [C] *technical* a FRACTION (2) such as 107/8 in which the top number is larger than the bottom number【術語】假分數〔分子大於分母的分數, 如 107/8〕—compare 比較 PROPER FRACTION

im·pro·pri·e·ty /͵ɪmprə`praɪətɪ; ͵ɪmprəˈpraɪɪ̈ti/ *n formal* [C] behaviour or a particular action that is unacceptable according to moral, social, or professional standards【正式】不正當的行為[行動]; 不得體的舉止: *Accusations of impropriety were made against the company's directors.* 對公司董事不正當的行為提出了指控。

im·prove /ɪm`pruv; ɪmˈpruːv/ *v* **1** [T] to make something better 改善, 改進: *a course for students wishing to improve their English* 為想提高英語水平的學生開的一門課 | *Many dishes are greatly improved by adding fresh herbs.* 許多道菜的味道都因加入了新鮮香草而大有改善。**2** [I] become better 變得更好: *Let's hope the weather improves before Saturday.* 但願星期六以前天氣轉好。| *Some wines improve with age.* 有些葡萄酒歷久彌香。—see 見 RAISE¹ (USAGE) 2 1

improve on/upon sth *phr v* [T] to do something better than before or make it better than before 改進, 做得比…更好, 超過: *Bertorelli has scored 165 points, and I don't think anyone will improve on that.* 博托雷利得了 165 分, 我看沒人能超出這個分數。

im·proved /ɪm`pruvd; ɪmˈpruːvd/ *adj* better than before 已改善的: *improved performance throughout the company* 公司上下已改善的工作表現 | *New improved formula!* 新改進的配方!

im·prove·ment /ɪm`pruvmənt; ɪmˈpruːvmənt/ *n* **1** [C, U] an act of improving or a state of being improved 改善, 改進; 提高: **[+in]** *There's certainly been an improvement in the children's behaviour.* 孩子們的行為舉止確實有進步。| **[+to]** *We need to carry out some improvements to the computer system.* 我們需要對電腦系統進行一些改進。| **show an improvement** *This month's trading figures show some improvement.* 本月的貿易統計數字表明情況有所改善。| **room for improvement** (=the possibility of improving even more) 改進餘地 *Your English is much better but there's still room for improvement.* 你的英語比以前好多了, 但還可以再提高。**2** [C] a change or addition that improves something 改進之處: *Power steering is just one of the improvements to be found in the new 160cc model.* 動力轉向裝置只是新 160 立方厘米型號的其中一項改良。**3 be an improvement on** to be better than something similar that existed before 好於〔舊有的同類東西〕, 強於: *The new electronic controls are a big improvement on the old system.* 新型 2

電子操縱裝置是對舊系統的一項很大的改進。

im·prov·i·dent /ɪm`prɑvədənt; ɪm'prɒvɨdənt/ *adj formal* too careless to save any money or to plan for the future【正式】揮霍的; 無遠見的: *the generous but improvident welfare provision of the 1960s* 20世紀60年代慷慨但無遠見的福利供應 —**improvidence** *n* [U] —**improvidently** *adv*

im·pro·vise /`ɪmprə,vaɪz; 'ɪmprəvaɪz/ *v* **1** [I] to do something without any preparation, because you are forced to do this by unexpected events〔事先無準備, 但因出乎意料的事而被迫〕臨時做; 即興作出: *I forgot to bring the notes for my speech, so I just had to improvise.* 我忘了帶發言稿, 只好即席演講。**2** [T] to make something by using whatever you can find because you do not have the equipment or materials that you need〔因缺乏所需用具或材料而〕臨時拼湊: *We improvised a crude shelter using branches.* 我們用樹枝臨時搭了個簡陋的蔽身之所。**3** [I] to perform music, DRAMA or COMEDY that comes straight from your imagination and has never been performed before 即興演奏; 即興表演: *You can't be a good jazz musician if you can't improvise.* 不會即興演奏, 就不能成為一名優秀的爵士樂手。—**improvisation** /,ɪmprəvaɪ`zeʃən; ,ɪmprəvaɪ'zeɪʃən/ *n* [C,U]

im·pru·dent /ɪm`prudn̩t; ɪm'pru:dənt/ *adj formal* not sensible or wise【正式】不明智的, 輕率的, 魯莽的: *It would be rather imprudent to invest in an arms company at the moment.* 目前投資兵器公司是很不明智的。—**imprudently** *adv* —**imprudence** *n* [C,U]

im·pugn /ɪm`pjun; ɪm'pju:n/ *v* [T] *formal* to express doubts about someone's honesty, courage, ability etc【正式】對〔某人的誠實、勇氣、能力等〕表示懷疑: *The honour of our country has been grossly impugned!* 我們國家的榮譽受到了巨大挑戰!

im·pulse /`ɪmpʌls; 'ɪmpʌls/ *n* **1** [C,U] a sudden strong desire to do something before thinking whether it is a sensible thing to do 衝動; 突然的慾望: **impulse to do sth** *Gerry couldn't resist the impulse to skip work and go down to the beach.* 格里抵制不了放下工作去海邊的衝動。| **on impulse** (=because of an impulse) 因一時衝動 *She had invited Joseph on a sudden impulse but was now regretting it.* 她當初一時衝動邀請了約瑟夫, 現在卻後悔了。| **impulse buying** (=buying things without planning or choosing carefully) 未經計劃或細心選擇而購買 **2** [C] an aim or reason that causes a particular kind of activity or behaviour 推動; 動力: *The prime impulse of capitalism is the making of money.* 資本主義的首要推動力是賺錢。**3** [C] *technical* a single push or force moving for a short time in one direction along a nerve or electric wire【術語】神經衝動; (電) 脈衝

im·pul·sion /ɪm`pʌlʃən; ɪm'pʌlʃən/ *n* [U] a sudden strong desire to do something 衝動, 強烈的慾望

im·pul·sive /ɪm`pʌlsɪv; ɪm'pʌlsɪv/ *adj* tending to do things as soon as you think of them, without considering the possible dangers or problems 衝動的; 草率的, 莽撞的: *Arthur Morel was a quick, careless, impulsive boy.* 亞瑟·莫雷爾是個性情急躁、粗心大意、容易衝動的男孩。| *In a burst of impulsive generosity I offered to pay.* 由於一時衝動, 我慷慨地提出付款。—**impulsively** *adv* —**impulsiveness** *n* [U]

im·pu·ni·ty /ɪm`pjunətɪ; ɪm'pju:nɨti/ *n* **do sth with impunity** if you do something wrong or immoral with impunity, there is no risk that you will be punished for it 做錯事而免受懲處: *Men used to be able to violently abuse their wives with almost total impunity.* 過去男人粗暴地虐待妻子幾乎完全不受懲罰。

im·pure /ɪm`pjur; ɪm'pjʊə/ *adj* **1** an impure substance has something else mixed with it, especially something of a lower quality 不純淨的; 攙雜的〔尤指攙有劣質的東西〕: *An added danger was that the group was using impure sodium chlorate in their bombs.* 還有一個危險是這夥人在他們的炸彈中使用了不純的氯酸鈉。—opposite 反義詞 PURE (1) **2** *old-fashioned or humorous* impure thoughts, feelings etc are morally bad, especially because they are about sex【過時或幽默】不道德的, 淫穢的, 下流的: *He tried, without success, to rid his mind of any impure thoughts about Julia.* 他盡力想排除腦海中對朱莉婭的種種邪念, 可是做不到。—opposite 反義詞 PURE (4)

im·pu·ri·ty /ɪm`pjʊrətɪ; ɪm'pjʊərɨti/ *n* **1** [C usually plural 一般用複數] part of an almost pure substance that is of a lower quality 雜質: *All natural minerals contain impurities.* 一切天然礦物都含有雜質。**2** [U] the state of being impure 不純; 攙雜

im·pu·ta·tion /,ɪmpjʊ`teʃən; ,ɪmpjʊ'teɪʃən/ *n formal*【正式】**1** [C] a statement that someone is guilty of a crime or of doing something bad 罪名; 責難的話: *It was the first time she had confronted him with such direct imputations.* 她是第一次以如此直接的指責與他對質。**2** [U] [+of] the act of imputing something 歸罪, 歸咎

im·pute /ɪm`pjut; ɪm'pju:t/ *v*

impute sth **to** sb/sth *phr v* [T] *formal* to say, often unfairly, that someone or something is responsible for something that has happened【正式】〔通常不公平地〕把〔某事〕歸因於〔某人或某物〕: *The police were not guilty of the violence imputed to them.* 警方把歸咎於他們的暴力罪行洗脫了。—**imputable** *adj* —**imputation** /,ɪmpjʊ`teʃən; ,ɪmpjʊ'teɪʃən/ *n* [C,U]

in- /ɪn; ɪn/ *prefix* in some adjectives and nouns, shows a negative, an opposite, or a lack; not 不, 非, 無〔用在某些形容詞和名詞裡表示否定、相反或缺乏之意〕: *insensitive* (=not sensitive) 不敏感的 | *inattention* (=lack of attention) 漫不經心 —compare 比較 UN-

-in /ɪn; ɪn/ *suffix* [in nouns 構成名詞] an activity in which a group of people do something together for a purpose〔一羣人為達到某目的而一起進行的〕活動: *a sit-in* (=where people sit in a place to prevent its usual activity) 靜坐示威 | *a teach-in*〔大學師生共同參加的時事〕專題討論會

in¹ /ɪn; ɪn/ *prep* **1** used with the name of a container, place, or area to say where someone or something is 在〔容器、地點或地區〕裡, 在…內: *There's some sugar in the cupboard.* 碗櫥裡有一些糖。| *My mother was in the kitchen.* 母親在廚房裡。| *He spends a lot of time driving round in his car.* 他花費很多時間駕車到處轉悠。| *She spent the day in bed.* 她在牀上度過了那一天。| *He spent fifteen years in prison.* 他在獄中度過了十五年。**2** used with the names of countries and towns to say where someone or something is 在某國家[某城鎮]: *Mr Fisher is in Boston this week.* 費舍爾先生本週在波士頓。| *The taxi man got lost in Manchester.* 計程車司機在曼徹斯特迷了路。| *My parents live in New Zealand now.* 我父母現住在新西蘭。**3** used with the names of months, years, seasons etc to say when something happens 在某月[某年、某季節等]: *He first visited Russia in 1937.* 他於1937年初訪問俄國。| *These changes first started in the 1840s.* 這些變化最初發生在19世紀40年代。| *He retired in October.* 他已於十月份退休。**4** during a period of time 在…期間: *It was amazing how much we managed to do in a day.* 真想不到我們在一天之內做了這麼多事情。**5** at the end of a period of time 在一段時間之後: *I'll be with you in a minute.* 我馬上就到你那兒。| *I think he'll be a millionaire in a year or two.* 我看他一兩年後就會成為百萬富翁。**6** if you have not done something in several weeks, years etc you have not done it for that period of time 在…期間〔沒做某事〕: *I haven't enjoyed myself so much in years.* 我已多年沒有玩得這麼開心了。**7** included as part of something 包含在…之內: *She said all this in her speech.* 所有這些她在演講中都說了。| *You shouldn't believe everything you read in the newspapers.* 報紙上看到的東西不可全信。**8** working at a particular kind of job 從事某種工作: *She used to be a teacher, but she's in marketing now.* 她以前是教師, 現在從事市場營銷。| *He's been in politics for fifteen years.* 他從政已有十五年了。**9** wearing something 穿着; 穿戴: *He looked* *very handsome in his uniform.* 他穿着制服，看上去很英俊。| *She was dressed in a blue linen suit.* 她身穿藍色亞麻布套裝。**10** using a particular way of talking or writing 以某種方式說[寫]: *Her parents always talk to her in German.* 她的父母和她說話總是用德語。| *She shouted my name in a harsh voice.* 她高聲厲喝我的名字。| *The children are only allowed to write in pencil.* 孩子們只許用鉛筆寫字。**11** arranged so as to form a particular shape or group 排列成某種形狀[羣體]: *The soldiers stood in a line and waited for orders.* 士兵們站成一列，等候命令。| *People were sitting in small groups chatting.* 人們三五成羣地坐着閒聊。| *Arrange the words in alphabetical order.* 將單詞按字母順序排列。**12** used with numbers or amounts to show a proportion 每〔與數字或數量連用，表示比例〕: *One in every 10 children now suffers from asthma.* 現在每十個兒童中有一個患有哮喘。**13** used to show a connection between two things 用來表示兩件事物之間的聯繫: *We need a further increase in investment.* 我們需要進一步增加投資。| *Milk is very rich in calcium.* 牛奶中含有豐富的鈣質。| *She never showed any interest in music.* 她對音樂從未表現出甚麼興趣。| *an expert in human biology* 人體生物學專家 **14** used to show the feelings you have when you do something 處於…中〔用來表示做某事時的感情〕: *She looked at me in horror.* 她驚恐地看着我。| *It was all done purely in fun.* 做這些事純粹是為了好玩兒。**15** used to say how one person should consider another〔用來表示一個人應如何看待另一人〕: *You've got a very good friend in Pat.* 你有個好朋友帕特。| *We have a very good candidate in Peter Dobrowski.* 彼德·朵勃羅夫斯基是我們一個很好的候選人。**16 in that** because 由於: *The situation is rather complicated in that we have two managing directors.* 由於我們有兩位總經理，所以情況很複雜。**17 in all** used when giving a total amount 總共: *There were about 800 people in all.* 總共有 800 人左右。**18 in doing sth** when or by doing something 在做某事時；藉着做某事: *In raising money to support her work, Baker made contact with many organisations that were sympathetic to her ideas.* 貝克在籌款以支持她的工作時，接觸過許多贊同她的想法的機構。

1 1 **in²** *adv* **1** so as to be contained inside something or surrounded by it 在…內，在裡面: *She opened the cupboard and put the tins in.* 她打開碗櫥，把幾個罐頭放進去。| *He picked up a glass and poured some water in.* 他拿起一個玻璃杯，向裡面倒了一些水。**2** inside a building, especially the building where you live or work 在建築物裡〔尤指居住或工作的地方〕: *I'm afraid Mr Stewart won't be in until tomorrow morning.* 恐怕斯圖爾特先生明天上午才能回來。| *She's never in when I call.* 我每次打電話，她都不在。| *We're staying in this evening.* 我們今晚不外出。**3** if a train, boat, or plane is in, it has arrived at a station, airport etc〔車、船、飛機等〕已經到達: *Our train's not in yet.* 我們的火車還沒到站。| *When's her flight due in?* 她乘坐的航班甚麼時候到？**4** if you send something in, you send it to an organization, where it will be dealt with 送至〔某機構〕，遞交: *All entries must be in by next week.* 所有參賽作品必須在下週之前提交。| *Letters have been pouring in from all over the country.* 信件從全國各地紛至沓來。**5** if you write, paint, or draw something in, you add it 填上；着色；加畫: *Fill in your name and address on the form provided.* 在所提供的表格上填上姓名和地址。| *The information is typed in by trained keyboarders.* 信息由專業錄入人員輸入電腦。**6** if clothes, colours etc are in, they are fashionable〔衣服、色彩等〕流行的，時髦的: *Stripes are definitely in this summer.* 條紋時裝在今夏確實流行起來。**7** if a person or team is in, they are batting (BAT² (1)) in a game such as CRICKET (2)〔板球等的〕擊球: *Surrey have chosen to go in first.* 薩里選擇先擊球。**8** if a ball is in during a game, it is inside the area where the game is being played〔球類比賽中，球〕在界內: *Her second serve was just in.* 她第二次發球正好落在界內。**9 be in for sth** if someone is in for something unpleasant, it is going to happen to them 將要遭遇〔不愉快的事〕: *I'm afraid he's in for a bit of a disappointment.* 恐怕他要失望了。**10 be in for it** *informal* if someone is in for it, they are going to be punished【非正式】將受到懲罰: *We're really in for it now.* 現在我們真要受到懲罰了。**11 be/get in on sth** to be involved in something that is happening 參與某事: *I think you ought to be in on this discussion, Ted.* 我看你應加入這場討論，泰德。**12 have (got) it in for sb** *informal* if someone has got it in for you, they do not like you and want to cause problems or difficulties for you【非正式】刁難；伺機報復: *I think the teacher's really got it in for me.* 我看這是老師有意刁難我。**13** if something falls or turns in, it falls or turns towards the centre 朝裡，向中心: *The map had started to curl in at the edges.* 這張地圖的邊緣已開始向內彎曲了。**14** if a boat or the TIDE¹ (1) comes in, it comes towards the shore〔船〕向岸邊移動；〔潮水〕上漲: *The tide was coming in.* 潮水正在上漲。| *The boat drifted in to the shore.* 小船向岸邊漂去。**15 be in with sb** *informal* to be friendly with someone【非正式】與某人友好相處: *She's in with the theatrical crowd.* 她與戲劇界的關係不錯。**16 be in at sth** to be present when something happens 當時在場: *I was lucky enough to be in at the start of the research project.* 我很幸運在研究計劃開始時便已參與。

in³ *adj* **1** *informal* clothes or colours that are in are fashionable【非正式】〔服裝、色彩等〕流行的: *Red is definitely the in colour this year.* 紅色無疑是今年流行的顏色。| *Long skirts are in at the moment.* 時下流行穿長裙。**2** [only before a noun 僅用於名詞前] an in joke is a private joke that is understood by only a small group of people 只為少數人聽得懂的〔笑話〕，只限於小圈子的〔笑話〕

in·a·bil·i·ty /ˌɪnəˋbɪlətɪ; ˌɪnəˈbɪlɪ̣ti/ *n* [singular, U] the fact of being unable to do something 沒辦法，沒能力: *the government's inability to control inflation* 政府無力控制通貨膨脹

in·ac·ces·si·ble /ˌɪnəkˋsɛsəbl̩; ˌɪnəkˈsesɪ̣bəl◂/ *adj* **1** difficult or impossible to reach 難到達的；不可及的: *These mountain villages are completely inaccessible in winter.* 這些山村到冬天就完全無法進入。**2** difficult or impossible to understand or afford 難懂的；得不到的: *an inaccessible subject such as theoretical nuclear physics* 像理論核物理學這樣難懂的學科 —**inaccessibly** *adv* —**inaccessibility** /ˌɪnəkˌsɛsəˋbɪlətɪ; ˌɪnəksesɪ̣ˈbɪlɪ̣ti/ *n* [U]

in·ac·cu·ra·cy /ɪnˋækjərəsɪ; ɪnˈækjʊ̈rəsi/ *n* **1** [C] a statement that is not completely correct 不準確的說法；錯誤，差錯: *I think your report contained various inaccuracies and half-truths.* 我認為你的報告裡有各種各樣的錯誤和半真半假的說法。**2** [U] a lack of correctness 不準確: *As a journalist you simply cannot tolerate inaccuracy.* 作為記者，決不能容忍報道失實。

in·ac·cu·rate /ɪnˋækjərɪt; ɪnˈækjʊ̈rɪ̣t/ *adj* not completely correct 不完全準確的: *an inaccurate translation of the French* 一份不完全正確的法語譯文 —**inaccurately** *adv*

in·ac·tion /ɪnˋækʃən; ɪnˈækʃən/ *n* [U] the fact that someone is not doing anything〔人〕無行動；沒反應: *Several newspapers have criticized the President for his inaction.* 好幾家報紙批評總統無所作為。

in·ac·tive /ɪnˋæktɪv; ɪnˈæktɪv/ *adj* not doing anything or not working 不活動的，不工作的；懶散的 —**inactivity** /ˌɪnækˋtɪvətɪ; ˌɪnækˈtɪvɪ̣ti/ *n* [U]

in·ad·e·qua·cy /ɪnˋædəkwəsɪ; ɪnˈædɪ̣kwɪ̣si/ *n* [U] **1** a feeling that you are unable to deal with situations because you are not as good as other people〔指人〕不夠好，不勝任: *Unemployment can often cause feelings of inadequacy and low self-esteem.* 失業往往使人感到不夠格和自卑。**2** [U] the fact of not being good enough in quality, ability, size etc for a particular purpose〔質量、能力、大小等〕不足，欠缺: [+of] *the inadequacy of local* *health care* 當地醫療保健制度的不健全 **3** [C] a fault or weakness in your character〔性格上的〕缺點, 不足之處: *I'm quite aware of my own inadequacies.* 我很清楚自身的不足之處。

in·ad·e·quate /ɪn`ædəkwɪt; ɪn'ædɪ̈kwɪ̈t/ *adj* **1** not good enough, big enough, skilled enough etc for a particular purpose〔對某一特定目的而言〕不夠好的, 不足的, 不強的: *An inadequate supply of vitamin A can lead to blindness.* 維生素A不足會導致失明。| **[+for]** *The parking facilities are inadequate for such a busy shopping centre.* 停車設施不足以應付這樣熱鬧的購物中心。**2** someone who feels inadequate feels unable to deal with situations because they think they are not as good as other people〔人自以為〕不勝任的; 不夠好的; 能力不足的: *The teacher made us feel inadequate and stupid if we made mistakes.* 我們出錯時, 老師總是讓我們覺得自己能力差, 腦子笨。—**inadequately** *adv*

in·ad·mis·si·ble /ˌɪnəd`mɪsəbḷ; ˌɪnəd'mɪsɪ̈bəl◂/ *adj formal*【正式】**inadmissible evidence** information that is not allowed to be used in a court of law〔在法庭上〕不可接受的證據 —**inadmissibly** *adj* —**inadmissibility** /ˌɪnədmɪsə`bɪlətɪ; ˌɪnədmɪsɪ̈'bɪlɪ̈ti/ *n* [U]

in·ad·vert·ent·ly /ˌɪnəd`vɝtṇtlɪ; ˌɪnəd'vɜːtəntli/ *adv* without realizing what you are doing 粗心大意地; 非故意地: *I inadvertently stepped on his toe.* 我不留神踩了他的腳趾。—**inadvertent** *adj*: *the inadvertent disclosure of sensitive information* 無意中泄露敏感信息 —**inadvertence** *n* [C,U]

in·ad·vis·a·ble /ˌɪnəd`vaɪzəbḷ; ˌɪnəd'vaɪzəbəl◂/ *adj* an action that is inadvisable is not sensible; unwise〔行動〕不可取的, 不明智的, 失策的: *It is inadvisable to climb in these mountains on your own.* 獨自一人爬這幾座山是很不明智的。

in·a·li·en·a·ble /ɪn`eljənəbḷ; ɪn'eɪliənəbəl/ *adj formal* an inalienable right cannot be taken away from you【正式】〔權利〕不可剝奪的

i·nam·o·ra·ta /ɪnˌæmə`rɑtə; ɪˌnæmə'rɑːtə/ *n* [C] *literary or humorous* the woman that a man loves【文或幽默】情婦

i·nane /ɪn`en; ɪ'neɪn/ *adj* extremely stupid or without much meaning 愚蠢至極的; 無意義的, 空洞的: *inane remarks* 空話 | *an inane conversation* 無聊的談話 —**inanely** *adv* —**inanity** /ɪn`ænətɪ; ɪ'nænɪ̈ti/ *n* [C,U]

in·an·i·mate /ɪn`ænəmɪt; ɪn'ænɪ̈mɪ̈t/ *adj* not living 無生命的: *A rock is an inanimate object.* 岩石是沒有生命的物體。

in·ap·pli·ca·ble /ɪn`æplɪkəbḷ; ˌɪnə'plɪkəbəl/ *adj* a description, question, or rule that is inapplicable to a particular subject cannot sensibly be used about it〔描述、問題或規則對特定主題〕不適用的: **[+to]** *These new regulations are inapplicable to us.* 這些新規定對我們不適用。—**inapplicability** /ɪnˌæplɪkə`bɪlətɪ; ˌɪnəplɪkə'bɪlɪ̈ti/ *n* [U]

in·ap·pro·pri·ate /ˌɪnə`proprɪɪt; ˌɪnə'prəʊpri-ɪ̈t/ *adj* **1** not suitable for a particular purpose or situation〔對特定目的或情況〕不合適的; 不恰當的: *I thought his comments were wholly inappropriate on such a solemn occasion.* 我認為他在如此莊嚴的場合說這樣的話極不恰當。| **[+for]** *an inappropriate gift for a child* 不適合送給孩子的禮物 **2** not correct according to generally accepted rules of social, moral, or professional behaviour〔根據普遍接受的社會、道德或專業行為規則〕不適宜的, 不恰當的: *It would be inappropriate for me to discuss her case at this meeting.* 讓我在這個會上討論她的事情是不恰當的。—**inappropriately** *adv*: *inappropriately dressed* 穿着不得體 —**inappropriateness** also 又作 **inappropriacy** *n* [U]

in·apt /ɪn`æpt; ɪn'æpt/ *adj formal* an inapt phrase, statement etc is not right for a particular situation【正式】〔措詞、陳述〕不恰當的, 不適宜的: *a very inapt comment* 很不恰當的評論 —compare 比較 INEPT —**inaptly** *adv* —**inaptness** *n* [U]

in·ar·tic·u·late /ˌɪnar`tɪkjəlɪt; ˌɪnɑː'tɪkjɪ̈lɪ̈t◂/ *adj* **1** not able to express yourself clearly when you speak〔說話時〕詞不達意的, 口齒不清的 **2** speech that is inarticulate is not clearly expressed or pronounced〔話語〕表達不清楚的; 發音不清的: *inarticulate mutterings* 含糊不清的咕噥 —**inarticulately** *adv* —**inarticulateness** also 又作 **inarticulacy** *n* [C,U]

in·as·much /ˌɪnəz`mʌtʃ; ˌɪnəz'mʌtʃ/ *adv formal*【正式】**inasmuch as** used to introduce an additional phrase that explains the rest of your sentence or says in what limited way it is true 鑑於, 由於〔用於開端以說明接下來的說話〕: *Anne is also guilty, inasmuch as she knew what the others were planning.* 安妮知道他們的謀劃, 所以也是有罪的。

in·at·ten·tion /ˌɪnə`tɛnʃən; ˌɪnə'tenʃən/ *n* [U] lack of attention 不注意; 疏忽, 漫不經心: **[+to]** *inattention to detail* 對細節的疏忽

in·at·ten·tive /ˌɪnə`tɛntɪv; ˌɪnə'tentɪv◂/ *adj* not giving enough attention to someone or something 不夠注意的; 漫不經心的: *an inattentive student* 注意力不集中的學生 —**inattentively** *adv* —**inattentiveness** *n* [U]

in·au·di·ble /ɪn`ɔdəbḷ; ɪn'ɔːdɪ̈bəl/ *adj* too quiet to be heard〔聲音小得〕聽不見的: *inaudible muttering* 聽不清的小聲低語 —**inaudibly** *adv* —**inaudibility** /ˌɪnɔdə`bɪlətɪ; ɪnˌɔːdɪ̈'bɪlɪ̈ti/ *n* [U]

in·au·gu·ral /ɪn`ɔgjərəl; ɪ'nɔːgjɪ̈rəl/ *adj* [only before noun 僅用於名詞前] **1 inaugural speech/lecture** the first speech given by someone starting an important job, such as a president or a university PROFESSOR〔總統等的〕就職演說;〔大學教授的〕首次講課 **2 inaugural meeting/concert etc** the first in a series of meetings, concerts etc 會議的開幕式; 音樂會的首場演出

in·au·gu·rate /ɪn`ɔgjəˌret; ɪ'nɔːgjɪ̈reɪt/ *v* [T] **1** if an event inaugurates an important change or period of time, it comes at the beginning of it 開始〔一個重要變化〕; 開創...時代: *The International Trade Agreement inaugurated a period of high economic growth.*《世界貿易協定》開創了一個經濟高速發展的階段。**2** to introduce a new person into an important job such as that of president, by holding a special ceremony 為〔新總統等〕舉行就職典禮 **3** to open a building or service for the first time or to start a public event with a ceremony 舉行〔新建築物〕落成典禮; 為〔公共活動〕舉行開幕式 —**inauguration** /ɪnˌɔgjə`reʃən; ɪˌnɔːgjɪ̈'reɪʃən/ *n* [C,U] *Eight months after Hoover's inauguration came the Wall Street Crash.* 胡佛就任總統八個月後, 就發生了華爾街股市暴跌。

in·aus·pi·cious /ˌɪnɔ`spɪʃəs; ˌɪnɔː'spɪʃəs◂/ *adj formal* seeming to show that future success is unlikely【正式】不祥的, 不吉利的, 凶兆的: *an inauspicious start to the journey* 這次旅行不祥的開始 —**inauspiciously** *adv*

in-be·tween /ˌ· ·`·◂/ *adj informal* in the middle between two points, sizes, periods of time etc【非正式】介於兩者之間的: *Neither the 12 nor the 14 fits properly – I must be an in-between size.* 12碼和14碼都不合適, 我的尺碼肯定在兩者之間。

in·board /`ɪnˌbord; 'ɪnbɔːd/ *n* [C] a motor inside a boat 船內側發動機 — compare 比較 OUTBOARD MOTOR

in·born /ɪn`born; ˌɪn'bɔːn◂/ *adj* an inborn quality or ability is one that you have had naturally since birth 天生的, 與生俱來: *Lincoln had an inborn sense of the truth.* 林肯天生誠實正直。

in·bound /`ɪn`baund; 'ɪnbaʊnd/ *adj AmE* an inbound flight or train is coming towards the place where you are【美】〔班機或火車〕返航的, 回程的

in-bounds /ˌ· `·◂/ *adj AmE* if the ball is in-bounds in a sport, it is in the playing area【美】〔球賽中球〕在界內的

in·bred /ɪn`brɛd; ˌɪn'bred◂/ *adj* **1** having developed as a natural part of your character 天生的: *an inbred responsiveness to music* 對音樂天生的敏感 **2** produced by INBREEDING 近親繁殖的

in·breed·ing /`ɪnˌbridɪŋ; 'ɪnbriːdɪŋ/ *n* [U] the producing of children, animals, or new plants from closely related members of the same family 近親交配; 近親繁殖

in·built /ˋɪnˋbɪlt; ˈɪnbɪlt/ *adj especially BrE* an inbuilt quality, feature etc is part of the character of someone or something and cannot be removed【尤英】內在的; 固有的: *an organization with an inbuilt tendency to expand* 一個有內在擴展趨勢的組織

Inc /ɪŋk; ɪŋk/ the written abbreviation of 縮寫= INCORPORATED; used in the US after the name of a company to show that it has become a CORPORATION (1) 股份有限的〔在美國用於公司名稱後, 表示已成為法人組織〕: *General Motors Inc* 通用汽車股份有限公司 —compare 比較 LTD, PLC

in·cal·cu·la·ble /ɪnˋkælkjələbl̩; ɪnˈkælkjʊləbəl/ *adj* too many or too great to be calculated 數不清的; 不可估量的: *A scandal of this nature would do the school incalculable harm.* 這類醜聞將給學校造成不可估量的損害。—**incalculably** *adv*

in·can·des·cent /ˌɪnkənˋdɛsn̩t; ˌɪnkænˈdesənt◂/ *adj* **1** giving a bright light when heated 熾熱的, 白熾的 **2 incandescent with rage** *BrE* extremely angry【英】怒不可遏的 —**incandescence** *n* [U]

in·can·ta·tion /ˌɪnkænˋteʃən; ˌɪnkænˈteɪʃən/ *n* [C,U] the set of special words that someone uses in magic, or the act of saying these words 咒語; 唸咒語

in·ca·pa·ble /ɪnˋkepəbl̩; ɪnˈkeɪpəbəl/ *adj* **1** [not before noun 不用於名詞前] unable to do something or to feel a particular emotion 無能力〔做某事〕的; 不能〔有某種感情〕的: **[+of]** *incapable of understanding even the simplest instructions* 甚至連最簡單的説明都不懂 | *incapable of pity* 不會有憐憫之心 **2** weak and unable to care for yourself 體弱而不能照顧自己的 —**incapably** *adv* —**incapability** /ˌɪnkepəˋbɪlətɪ; ɪnˌkeɪpəˈbɪlɪti/ *n* [U]

in·ca·pa·ci·tate /ˌɪnkəˋpæsəˌtet; ˌɪnkəˈpæsɪteɪt/ *v* [T often passive 常用被動態] if something such as an illness or accident incapacitates you, it makes you too ill or weak to live and work normally〔疾病或意外事故等〕使無能力〔正常生活和工作〕: *He was permanently incapacitated after the accident.* 這次事故使他終身殘疾, 不能正常生活和工作。—**incapacitation** /ˌɪnkəpæsəˋteʃən; ˌɪnkəpæsɪˈteɪʃən/ *n* [U]

in·ca·pa·ci·ty /ˌɪnkəˋpæsətɪ; ˌɪnkəˈpæsɪti/ *n* [singular, U] **1** the condition of being too ill or weak to live and work normally 無正常生活和工作的能力: *temporary incapacity through illness* 由於疾病而暫時不能正常生活和工作 **2** the inability to do something 無能力〔做某事〕: *the author's incapacity to convey his ideas* 作者無法表達自己的思想

in·car·ce·rate /ɪnˋkɑrsəˌret; ɪnˈkɑːsəreɪt/ *v* [T usually passive 一般用被動態] *formal* to keep someone in a place, especially a prison【正式】監禁, 禁閉 —**incarceration** /ɪnˌkɑrsəˋreʃən; ɪnˌkɑːsəˈreɪʃən/ *n* [U]

in·car·nate¹ /ɪnˋkɑrnɪt; ɪnˈkɑːnɪt/ *adj* [only after noun 僅用於名詞後] **evil/wisdom/the devil etc incarnate** someone who is considered to be the human form of evil, wisdom etc 邪惡/智慧/魔鬼等的化身

in·car·nate² /ɪnˋkɑrnet; ˈɪnkɑːneɪt/ *v* [T] *formal*【正式】**1** to be the human form of a particular quality 成為…的化身 **2** to make something appear in a human form 使〔某物〕具有人形

in·car·na·tion /ˌɪnkɑrˋneʃən; ˌɪnkɑːˈneɪʃən/ *n* **1** [C] the period of time, according to some religions, during which someone is alive in the form of a particular person or animal〔某些宗教中的〕前世, 上輩子: *She believed that in a previous incarnation she had been an Egyptian queen.* 她認為自己前世是一位埃及王后。**2 be the incarnation of goodness/evil/sweetness** to perfectly represent goodness etc in human form 是善良/邪惡/仁慈的化身: *She was the incarnation of perfect wisdom.* 她是完美智慧的化身。**3 the Incarnation** the act of God coming to Earth in the human form of Jesus Christ, according to the Christian religion〔基督教的〕道成肉身〔指上帝化身成基督來到人間〕

in·cau·tious /ɪnˋkɔʃəs; ɪnˈkɔːʃəs/ *adj* done or said without thinking about the possible effects, and therefore causing problems 輕率的; 不謹慎的: *incautious remarks* 輕率的言論 —**incautiously** *adv*

in·cen·di·a·ry¹ /ɪnˋsɛndɪˌɛrɪ; ɪnˈsendiəri/ *adj* [only before noun 僅用於名詞前] **1 incendiary bomb/device/attack etc** designed to cause a fire 燃燒彈/燃燒裝置/火攻等 **2** an incendiary speech or piece of writing is intended to make people angry and is likely to cause trouble〔演講、文章〕煽動性的

incendiary² *n* [C] a bomb designed to cause a fire 燃燒彈

in·cense¹ /ˋɪnsɛns; ˈɪnsens/ *n* [U] a substance which has a pleasant smell when you burn it, and which is used in religious ceremonies〔祭祀時焚燒用的〕香

in·cense² /ɪnˋsɛns; ɪnˈsens/ *v* [T] to make someone extremely angry 使〔某人〕十分憤怒: *Spectators, incensed by the referee's decision, ran onto the field.* 觀眾對裁判的判罰極為憤怒, 衝進了球場。

in·censed /ɪnˋsɛnst; ɪnˈsenst/ *adj* extremely angry 極為憤怒的: *When I reported the matter to Stalin, he became incensed.* 我把此事向史太林匯報時, 他勃然大怒。

in·cen·tive /ɪnˋsɛntɪv; ɪnˈsentɪv/ *n* [C,U] something which encourages you to work harder, start new activities etc 刺激; 動力; 鼓勵: *With prices so low there is little incentive for the farmers.* 價格太低, 因此農民並不積極。| **incentive to do sth** *The chance of a higher salary gives young people the incentive to work harder.* 由於有加薪的機會, 年輕人工作更賣力了。| **tax incentives** (=offers of reduced taxes) 減税優惠 3

in·cep·tion /ɪnˋsɛpʃən; ɪnˈsepʃən/ *n* [singular] *formal* the start of an organization or institution【正式】〔組織、機構的〕開創; 開端: *a history of the Labour Party from its inception to the present day* 工黨建黨至今的歷史

in·ces·sant /ɪnˋsɛsn̩t; ɪnˈsesənt/ *adj* an incessant activity, noise etc continues without stopping, in an annoying way〔令人感到厭煩的活動、噪音等〕持續不斷的, 沒完沒了的: *The child's incessant talking started to irritate her.* 孩子喋喋不休, 使她煩躁起來。—**incessantly** *adv*

in·cest /ˋɪnsɛst; ˈɪnsest/ *n* [U] illegal sex between people who are closely related, for example between a brother and sister, or father and daughter 亂倫

in·ces·tu·ous /ɪnˋsɛstʃuəs; ɪnˈsestʃuəs/ *adj* **1** an incestuous relationship is a sexual relationship between people who are closely related in a family 亂倫的 **2** an incestuous relationship is one in which a small group of people or organizations only help each other, in a way that is unfair to other people〔羣體或組織〕排外的; 小圈子內的: *the incestuous relationship between sport and television* 體育界與電視媒體間的小集團關係 —**incestuously** *adv* —**incestuousness** *n* [U]

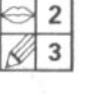

inch¹ /ɪntʃ; ɪntʃ/ *n* [C] **1** a unit for measuring length, equal to 2.54 centimetres 英寸〔長度單位, 等於2.54厘米〕—see table on page C3 參見C3頁附錄 **2** a very small distance 很小的距離: *A bullet thudded into the wall only inches from where I was standing.* 一顆子彈砰的一聲射進離我站的地方只有幾英寸的牆內。| *The bus missed our car by inches.* (=almost hit it) 公共汽車差一點就撞着我們的車。**3** enough rain or snow to cover an area an inch deep 一英寸的積水[積雪]: *Over five inches of rain has fallen in the last week.* 上週降雨量超過了五英寸。**4 every inch a)** completely or in every way 完全地; 不折不扣地: *He looked every inch a gentleman.* 他看上去像個地地道道的紳士。**b)** the whole of an area〔某地區的〕全部: **[+of]** *They're determined to defend every inch of their territory.* 他們決心保衛每一寸領土。**5 give sb an inch and they'll take a yard/mile** used to say that if you allow someone a little freedom or power, they'll try to take a lot more 得寸進尺 **6 inch by inch** moving very gradually and slowly〔移動〕一點一點地, 緩慢地: *Inch by inch the soldiers were driven back.* 這些士兵被逐漸

擊退了。**7 not give/budge an inch** to refuse to change your opinion even slightly about something in spite of attempts to persuade you 寸步不讓: *Neither side is prepared to give an inch in the negotiations.* 談判中雙方都無意作絲毫讓步。**8 beat/thrash sb within an inch of their life** to hit someone so hard and so many times that you almost kill them 幾乎把某人打死

inch² *v* [I always+adv/prep, T always+adv/prep] to move very slowly in a particular direction, or make something do this (使) 緩慢移動: **[+along/towards/around etc]** *I started inching forward along the ledge towards the open window.* 我沿着窗台緩慢地挪向開着的窗子。| **inch sth along/towards etc** *He slowly inched the box forward, unable to lift it.* 由於無法把那隻箱子提起來, 他一點一點地向前挪動它。

in·cho·ate /ɪnˋko·ɪt; ɪnˈkəʊɨt/ *adj formal* inchoate ideas, plans, attitudes etc are only just starting to develop【正式】〔想法、計劃、態度等〕剛開始形成的

in·ci·dence /ˋɪnsədəns; ˈɪnsɨdəns/ *n* [singular] *formal* the number of times something bad happens, for example how many people have a particular illness or how many crimes there are【正式】〔疾病、罪行等壞事的〕發生率: *a survey to determine the incidence of heart defects among premature babies* 確定早產兒心臟發育不全比率的調查 | *the high incidence of alcoholism among the unemployed* 失業者中高比率的酗酒現象

2 **in·ci·dent** /ˋɪnsədənt; ˈɪnsɨdənt/ *n* [C] **1** something that happens, especially something that is unusual〔尤指不平常的〕事件: *After the children had been punished, nobody mentioned the incident again.* 孩子受到懲罰後, 再沒人提起這件事了。| **without incident** (=without anything unusual or unpleasant happening) 沒有發生不尋常[不愉快]的事; 平安無事 *Despite my fears the meal passed without incident.* 儘管我有些擔心, 但吃飯時並未發生甚麼事。**2** a serious or violent event that causes disagreement〔導致爭論的〕嚴重[暴力]事件: *a major diplomatic incident* 重大外交事件

in·ci·den·tal¹ /ˌɪnsəˋdɛntl; ˌɪnsɨˈdentl◂/ *adj* **1** happening or existing in connection with something else that is more important 附帶的; 伴隨的; 次要的: *minor incidental details* 附帶的次要細節 | **incidental expenses** (=small expenses connected with a particular activity)〔與某特定活動相關的〕雜費: *Keep a record of any incidental expenses on your trip.* 把旅途中的雜費都記錄下來。**2** [not before noun 不用於名詞前] happening as a result of something in a way that can be expected〔意料之內〕由…引發的; 免不了的: **[+to]** *Drinking too much is almost incidental to bartending.* 當酒吧侍者幾乎免不了飲酒過度。

incidental² *n* [C usually plural 一般用複數] something that you have to do, buy etc which you had not planned to do or buy 原來沒打算要做的事[要買的東西]: *It's useful to carry extra cash for taxis, tips and other incidentals.* 有必要額外帶些現金用來坐計程車、付小費和其他臨時開支。

3 **in·ci·den·tal·ly** /ˌɪnsəˋdɛntlɪ; ˌɪnsɨˈdentəli/ *adv* **1** [sentence adverb 句子副詞] used when adding more information to what was said before, or when you want to talk about something else you have just thought of 順便提一下〔用來補充說過的事情, 或提及剛想到的事〕: *a beautiful town which, incidentally, is where they filmed 'The French Lieutenant's Woman'* 真是個美麗的小鎮, 順便說一句, 電影《法國中尉的女人》就是在那兒拍攝的 | *Incidentally, this wine goes particularly well with cheese.* 順便提一下, 這種葡萄酒配乾酪特別好。**2** happening in a way that was not planned, but as a result of something else〔情況的發生〕偶然地: *Quite incidentally, I found out some very useful information at the party.* 我在聚會上非常偶然地發現了一些十分有用的信息。

incidental mu·sic /ˌ···· ˈ··/ *n* [U] music played during a play, film etc in order to give the right feeling〔戲劇、電影的〕配樂

in·cin·e·rate /ɪnˋsɪnəˌret; ɪnˈsɪnəreɪt/ *v* [T usually passive 一般用被動態] to burn something completely in order to destroy it 將…燒成灰燼; 燒毀: *All the infected clothing was incinerated.* 所有沾染病菌的衣服都被焚毀了。—**incineration** /ɪnˌsɪnəˋreʃən; ɪnˌsɪnəˈreɪʃən/ *n* [U]

in·cin·e·ra·tor /ɪnˋsɪnəˌretɚ; ɪnˈsɪnəreɪtə/ *n* [C] a machine designed to burn things at a very high temperature in order to destroy them〔廢物〕焚化爐

in·cip·i·ent /ɪnˋsɪpɪənt; ɪnˈsɪpiənt/ *adj* [only before noun 僅用於名詞前] *formal* starting to happen or exist【正式】剛開始的, 早期的: *those tiny yawns that are sure signs of incipient boredom* 那些輕微的哈欠肯定是開始感到厭倦的信號 —**incipiently** *adv*

in·cise /ɪnˋsaɪz; ɪnˈsaɪz/ *v technical*【術語】**1** [T+in/into] to cut a pattern or mark into a surface〔在表面〕雕〔圖案或記號〕, 刻 **2** [T] to cut carefully into something with a sharp knife〔用鋒利的刀〕小心切入

in·ci·sion /ɪnˋsɪʒən; ɪnˈsɪʒən/ *n* [C,U] a cut into something, especially into someone's body using a special knife during a medical operation, or the act of making this kind of cut〔手術〕切口, 切痕; 切開, 切入: *The incision was carefully stitched and bandaged.* 切口被小心翼翼地縫合包紮起來。

in·ci·sive /ɪnˋsaɪsɪv; ɪnˈsaɪsɪv/ *adj* words, remarks etc that are incisive are very clear and direct and deal immediately with the most important part of a subject〔言語〕直截了當的, 切中要害的: *Her questions were well-formulated and incisive.* 她的問題提得很好, 個個切中要害。—**incisively** *adv* —**incisiveness** *n* [U]

in·ci·sor /ɪnˋsaɪzɚ; ɪnˈsaɪzə/ *n* [C] one of the teeth at the front of your mouth which have a sharp edge 門齒, 切牙 —compare 比較 CANINE TOOTH, MOLAR —see picture at 參見 TEETH 圖

in·cite /ɪnˋsaɪt; ɪnˈsaɪt/ *v* [T] to deliberately encourage people to cause trouble, fight, argue etc 煽動, 鼓動, 激起: **incite sb to do sth** *He was charged with inciting the students to riot.* 他被指控煽動學生暴亂。| **incite sb to sth** *inflammatory articles that incited people to violence and hatred* 激起暴力和仇恨的煽動性文章 —**incitement** *n* [U]

in·ci·vil·i·ty /ˌɪnsəˋvɪlətɪ; ˌɪnsɨˈvɪlɨti/ *n* [U] *formal* impolite behaviour【正式】不文明行為, 無禮舉動

in·clem·ent /ɪnˋklɛmənt; ɪnˈklemənt/ *adj formal* inclement weather is unpleasant because it is cold, rainy etc【正式】〔天氣〕惡劣的, 寒冷的, 多雨的 —**inclemency** *n* [U]

in·cli·na·tion /ˌɪnkləˋneʃən; ˌɪnklɨˈneɪʃən/ *n*

1 ►DESIRE 慾望◄ [C,U] a feeling that makes you want to do something 意向; 傾向: *You always follow your own inclinations instead of considering other people's feelings.* 你總是隨心所欲, 不考慮別人的感受。| **inclination to do sth** *I have not the slightest inclination to take unnecessary risks.* 我絲毫不想冒不必要的風險。

2 ►TENDENCY 趨勢◄ [C,U] tendency to think or behave in a particular way〔思想或行為的〕傾向: **inclination to do sth** *an inclination to see everything in political terms* 從政治角度看待一切事物的傾向

3 inclination of the head the movement of bending your neck so that your head is lowered 點頭: *With a slight inclination of the head she showed her approval.* 她微微點了一下頭表示認可。

4 ►SLOPE 斜面◄ [C,U] *formal* a slope or the angle at which something slopes【正式】斜坡; 斜度

in·cline¹ /ɪnˋklaɪn; ɪnˈklaɪn/ *v* [not in progressive 不用進行式] *formal*【正式】

1 ►TEND TO DO STH 傾向於做某事◄ a) to think that a particular belief or opinion is most likely to be right 傾向於〔某個信念或意見〕: **[+to/ towards]** *He has always inclined to the belief that all men are capable of great evil.* 他一直傾向於認為人性本惡。| **incline to do sth** *I incline to accept the official version of events.* 我傾向於接受官方對這些事件的說法。**b)** to tend to behave in a particular way or to show a particular quality 趨向於〔以某種特定方式行事〕; 易於〔顯示出某種習性[品

格〕: **[+to/towards]** *The child has always inclined towards laziness.* 這孩子一直表現得懶散。

2 ▶INFLUENCE 影響◀ [T] if a situation, fact etc inclines you to do or think something, it influences you towards a particular action or opinion 使去做〔某事〕, 使傾向於〔某觀點〕: **incline sb to do sth** *I know that you acted hastily, but that does not incline me to forgive you.* 我知道你做得匆忙, 但我不能因此就原諒你。

3 incline your head to bend your neck so that your head is lowered 點頭

4 ▶TO SLOPE 傾斜◀ [I,T] to be sloping at a particular angle or to make something do this (使) 有斜度, (使) 傾斜

in·cline² /ˋɪnklaɪn; ˈɪnklaɪn/ *n* [C] a slope 斜坡; 斜度: *a steep incline* 陡坡

3 **in·clined** /ɪnˋklaɪnd; ɪnˈklaɪnd/ *adj*

1 ▶TENDING TO DO STH 傾向於做某事◀ [not before noun 不用於名詞前] tending to behave in a particular way 有…意向的; 傾向於…的: **be inclined to do sth** *She's inclined to tell lies.* 她愛說謊。

2 be inclined to agree/think/believe etc to have a particular opinion but not to hold it very strongly 傾向於贊同/認為/相信等: *Arthur has some strange ideas, but on this occasion I'm inclined to agree with him.* 亞瑟有一些奇怪的想法, 但這次我倒是傾向於同意他的觀點。

3 ▶WISHING TO DO SOMETHING 希望做某事◀ [not before noun 不用於名詞前] wanting to do something 想要做…的: **inclined to do sth** *You can even swim in the lake – if you feel inclined to.* 你甚至可以在湖裡游泳——如果你想的話。

4 mathematically/linguistically/musically inclined naturally interested in or good at something such as mathematics or languages 有數學/語言/音樂天賦的: *We sent her to the Arts school because she's very musically inclined.* 我們送她去上藝術學校, 因為她很有音樂天賦。

5 ▶SLOPING 傾斜的◀ sloping or leaning in a particular direction 傾斜的; 有坡度的

in·close /ɪnˋkloz; ɪnˈkləʊz/ *v* [T] another spelling of ENCLOSE enclose 的另一種拼法

in·clos·ure /ɪnˋkloʒɚ; ɪnˈkləʊʒə/ *n* [C,U] another spelling of ENCLOSURE enclosure 的另一種拼法

2 1 **in·clude** /ɪnˋklud; ɪnˈkluːd/ *v* [T] **1** [not in progressive 不用進行式] if a group or a set includes something or someone, it has that thing or person as one of its parts 包括; 含有: *Our tour party included several retired couples.* 我們這個旅遊團有幾對退休夫婦。| *The price includes postage charges.* 這價錢包括郵費。—see 見 COMPRISE (USAGE) **2** to make someone or something part of a larger group or set 使〔某物〕成為整體的一部分; 把〔某人〕算入: *The team is looking strong, especially now they have included Roscoe.* 球隊看上去很強大, 特別是現在有羅斯科加入進來。| **include sth in/on etc** *Teachers must include attendance figures in their monthly reports.* 教師在每月的匯報中必須把出勤率包括進去。| *Is service included in the bill?* 賬單裡包括服務費嗎? **3 include me out** *spoken* a humorous way of saying you do not want to be included in a group【口】把我包括在外〔一種幽默說法〕—opposite 反義詞 EXCLUDE

in·clud·ed /ɪnˋkludɪd; ɪnˈkluːdʒd/ *adj* [only after noun 僅用於名詞後] **myself/John etc included** including myself, John etc 包括我自己/約翰等在內: *Everyone has to go to the dentist's, you included.* 每個人都得去看牙醫, 包括你在內。

2 1 **in·clud·ing** /ɪnˋkludɪŋ; ɪnˈkluːdɪŋ/ *prep* used to introduce something or someone that is included in the larger group or amount you have just mentioned 包括〔用於表示某物或某人是剛才談及的整體的一部分〕: *There were twelve of us, including me and Tom.* 共有十二人, 包括我和湯姆。| *£25.50 including postage and packing* 一共二十五鎊半, 包括郵寄費和包裝費 —opposite 反義詞 EXCLUDING

in·clu·sion /ɪnˋkluʒən; ɪnˈkluːʒən/ *n* **1** [U] the act of including someone or something in a larger group or set, or the fact of being included in one 包含, 包括: *His inclusion in the team has caused a lot of controversy.* 他的入隊, 引起了很多爭議。**2** [C] someone or something that has been included in a larger group or set 包括在整體中的某人[某物]: *With the recent inclusions there will be 28 delegates in all.* 連同新近加入的, 總共有28位代表。

in·clu·sive /ɪnˋklusɪv; ɪnˈkluːsɪv/ *adj* **1** an inclusive price or cost includes everything〔價錢或費用〕包括一切的: *an all-inclusive charge* 包括一切費用在內的價格 | **[+of]** *The rent is £50 a week, inclusive of heating and lighting.* 房租每星期50英鎊, 包括暖氣費和照明費。**2 April to June inclusive/15 to 20 inclusive, etc** including April, June and all the months between them, 15 and 20 and all the numbers between them etc 從四月到六月 (包括四月和六月); 從15到20 (包括15和20)

> **USAGE NOTE 用法說明: INCLUSIVE**
> AmE-BrE DIFFERENCE 美-英用法差異
> Where British English speakers might use **inclusive** in this way 英國英語會這樣用 inclusive: *Monday to Friday inclusive* 週一到週五; American speakers may use **through** 美國英語則會用 through: *Monday through Friday* 週一到週五

in·cog·ni·to /ɪnˋkɑgnɪ,to; ˌɪnkɒgˈniːtəʊ/ *adv* if a famous person travels incognito, they travel without letting people know who they are 隱瞞身分地, 微服地〔諸如名人出遊〕

in·co·her·ent /ˌɪnkoˋhɪrənt; ˌɪnkəʊˈhɪərənt◂/ *adj* **1** thoughts, ideas etc that are incoherent are very badly expressed or badly arranged and are difficult to understand〔思想、觀點等〕條理不清的; 紊亂的: *At times the narrative is completely incoherent.* 有時候敘述完全是前言不搭後語。**2** speaking unclearly 言語不清的: *As the child's temperature soared she became incoherent.* 隨着體溫急劇升高, 女孩開始語無倫次。—**incoherently** *adv* —**incoherence** *n* [U]

in·come /ˋɪn,kʌm; ˈɪŋkʌm/ *n* [C,U] the money that you earn from your work or that you receive from INVESTMENTS〔工作的〕收入;〔投資的〕收益: *Most of my income goes on my rent.* 我的大部分收入都用來支付房租。| **be on a high/low income** *It's only reasonable that people on a high income should pay more tax.* 高收入的人多納稅是合情合理的。| **live within your income** (=to not spend more than you earn) 量入為出 | **unearned income** (=income from property, INVESTMENTS etc) 非勞動收入, 非工資收入〔指來自財產、投資等的收入〕—compare 比較 EXPENDITURE (1) —see 見 PAY¹ (USAGE) 2 1

income tax /ˈ‥ ˌ/ *n* [U] tax paid on the money that you earn (個人) 所得稅

in·com·ing /ˋɪn,kʌmɪŋ; ˈɪnkʌmɪŋ/ *adj* [only before noun 僅用於名詞前] **1** arriving or coming in 正到達的; 進入的: *incoming flights* 正到達的航班 | *the incoming tide* 漲潮 **2** an incoming president, government etc has just been elected or chosen〔總統、政府等〕新當選的: *It is hoped that the incoming administration will inject some life into Capitol Hill.* 希望新一屆政府能給國會注入一些活力。

in·com·mode /ˌɪnkəˋmod; ˌɪnkəˈməʊd/ *v* [T] *formal* to make a situation difficult for someone【正式】使〔某人〕不便; 妨礙

in·com·mo·di·ous /ˌɪnkəˋmodɪəs; ˌɪnkəˈməʊdiəs◂/ *adj formal* inconvenient, difficult, or uncomfortable【正式】不便的, 困難的, 不舒服的

in·com·mu·ni·ca·do /ˌɪnkə,mjunɪˋkɑdo; ˌɪnkəmjuːnɪˈkɑːdəʊ/ *adv* if you are kept incommunicado, you are kept in a place where you cannot see or talk to anyone else 不得與他人接觸地: *The men were arrested and held incommunicado in prison camps.* 這些人被逮捕, 並被監

禁在集中營，不得與外界接觸。

in·com·pa·ra·ble /ɪnˋkɑmpərəbl̩; ɪnˈkɒmpərəbəl/ *adj* so good, beautiful etc that nothing else can even be compared to it 無可比擬的，舉世無雙的：*a writer of incomparable prose* 舉世無雙的散文家 | *the incomparable view of San Marco* 聖馬科美妙絕倫的景色 —**incomparably** *adv*

in·com·pat·i·ble /ˌɪnkəmˋpætəbl̩; ˌɪnkəmˈpætɪ̈bəl◂/ *adj* **1** two people who are incompatible have completely different characters so that it is difficult for them to have a good relationship〔兩個人〕不能和睦相處的，合不來的：*God knows why they ever got married. They're totally incompatible!* 天知道他們為甚麼結為夫妻——他們根本合不來！**2** two beliefs, statements, actions etc that are incompatible cannot exist or be accepted together because they are completely different〔觀點、言論、行為等完全相左而〕不相容的，不能共存的：**[+with]** *His business interests are incompatible with his presidential responsibilities.* 他的商業利益與他的總統職責是不相容的。**3** two things that are incompatible are of different types so that they cannot be used together 不相配的，相互排斥的：*Their blood groups were incompatible.* 他們的血型不相配。—**incompatibly** *adv* —**incompatibility** /ˌɪnkəmˌpætəˋbɪlətɪ; ˌɪnkəmpætɪ̈ˈbɪlɪ̈ti/ *n* [U]

in·com·pe·tence /ɪnˋkɑmpətəns; ɪnˈkɒmpɪ̈təns/ *n* [U] lack of the ability or skill to do your job properly 不勝任，不稱職：*The manager in charge was fired for incompetence.* 主管經理因不稱職而被解雇。

in·com·pe·tent /ɪnˋkɑmpətənt; ɪnˈkɒmpɪ̈tənt/ *adj* not having the ability or skill to do your job properly 不稱職的，不勝任的：*an incompetent teacher* 不稱職的教師 —**incompetent** *n* [C] —**incompetently** *adv*

in·com·plete /ˌɪnkəmˋplit; ˌɪnkəmˈpliːt◂/ *adj* **1** not having all its parts 不完全的，不完整的：*Unfortunately I do not have the information because our records are incomplete.* 很遺憾，由於我們的記錄不完整，我無法提供有關資料。**2** not completely finished 未完成的，未結束的：*an incomplete process* 未完成的程序 —**incompletely** *adv* —**incompleteness** *n* [U]

in·com·pre·hen·si·ble /ˌɪnkɑmprɪˋhɛnsəbl̩; ɪnˌkɒmprɪˈhensɪ̈bəl/ *adj* difficult or impossible to understand 難懂的，不可理解的：*Legal documents are full of incomprehensible jargon.* 法律文書充滿難懂的行話。| *I find your whole attitude quite incomprehensible.* 我覺得你的整個態度很難理解。—**incomprehensibly** *adv* —**incomprehensibility** /ˌɪnkɑmprɪˌhɛnsəˋbɪlətɪ; ɪnˌkɒmprɪhensɪ̈ˈbɪlɪ̈ti/ *n* [U]

in·com·pre·hen·sion /ˌɪnkɑmprɪˋhɛnʃən; ɪnˌkɒmprɪˈhenʃən/ *n* [U] the state of not being able to understand something 不理解，不懂：*"Are you leaving me?" she cried, her face full of incomprehension and rage.* "你要離開我嗎？"她喊道，一臉的迷惑和憤怒。

in·con·cei·va·ble /ˌɪnkənˋsivəbl̩; ˌɪnkənˈsiːvəbəl/ *adj* too strange or unusual to be thought real or possible 難以置信的，不可思議的：*A few years ago a car fuelled by solar energy would have been inconceivable.* 幾年前汽車用太陽能做動力是不可思議的。| **it is inconceivable that** *It seemed inconceivable that a man in such a powerful position could be so stupid.* 似乎難以想像一個身居要職的人竟會如此愚蠢。—**inconceivably** *adv* —**inconceivability** /ˌɪnkənˌsivəˋbɪlətɪ; ˌɪnkənsiːvəˈbɪlɪ̈ti/ *n* [U]

in·con·clu·sive /ˌɪnkənˋklusɪv; ˌɪnkənˈkluːsɪv◂/ *adj* not leading to a clear decision or result 非結論性的，無確定結果的：*The evidence against the two men was inconclusive.* 針對兩個人的不利證據並不令人信服。| *The talks were inconclusive and both parties agreed to further meetings.* 會談沒有取得結果，雙方同意繼續會晤。—**inconclusively** *adv* —**inconclusiveness** *n* [U]

in·con·gru·i·ty /ˌɪnkɑŋˋgruətɪ; ˌɪnkənˈgruːɪ̈ti/ *n* **1** [U] strangeness, especially in being unsuitable, unusual, or unexpected in relation to the things around〔與環境〕不協調，不合適，不相稱：*He was suddenly struck by the incongruity of drinking champagne out of plastic glasses.* 他突然感到用塑料杯喝香檳酒很不協調。**2** [C] an act or event which seems strange or unsuitable because it seems very different from what is happening around it〔與環境〕不相稱，不協調的行為[事件]

in·con·gru·ous /ɪnˋkɑŋgruəs; ɪnˈkɒŋgruəs/ *adj* something that is incongruous seems strange and unsuitable because it is so unexpected in a particular situation and so different from everything around it 不協調的，不相稱的：*The modern building looked incongruous in such a quaint old village.* 這座現代化建築與這個古老雅致的村莊顯得格格不入。—**incongruously** *adv* —**incongruousness** *n* [U]

in·con·se·quen·tial /ˌɪnkɑnsəˋkwɛnʃəl; ɪnˌkɒnsɪ̈ˈkwenʃəl◂/ *adj* not important; INSIGNIFICANT 不重要的；微不足道的：*He made a few inconsequential remarks before moving on to the next guests.* 他寒暄了幾句後便去招呼下一批客人。—**inconsequentially** *adv*

in·con·sid·e·ra·ble /ˌɪnkənˋsɪdərəbl̩; ˌɪnkənˈsɪdərəbəl◂/ *adj* **not inconsiderable** *formal* fairly large or important【正式】相當大規模的；相當重要的：*He has built up a not inconsiderable business empire.* 他已建立起一個規模非同小可的商業帝國。

in·con·sid·er·ate /ˌɪnkənˋsɪdərɪt; ˌɪnkənˈsɪdərɪ̈t◂/ *adj* not caring about the feelings, needs or comfort of other people 不考慮他人的，不為別人着想的：*It was inconsiderate of him to keep us waiting like that.* 讓我們等這麼久，他太不體諒人了。—**inconsiderately** *adv*

in·con·sis·ten·cy /ˌɪnkənˋsɪstənsɪ; ˌɪnkənˈsɪstənsi◂/ *n* **1** [U] changes in someone's behaviour or reactions that make their ideas, wishes etc unclear〔行為或反應的〕反覆無常，出爾反爾：*Inconsistency in management creates unnecessary anxieties among the workforce.* 管理層的出爾反爾在員工中造成了不必要的憂慮。**2** [C usually plural 一般用複數] two statements that cannot both be true because they each state the facts differently〔兩個說法〕不協調，不一致，前後矛盾：*There were several inconsistencies in his report.* 他的報告中有幾處前後矛盾。

in·con·sis·tent /ˌɪnkənˋsɪstənt; ˌɪnkənˈsɪstənt◂/ *adj* **1** ideas or statements that are inconsistent cannot be accepted or believed together because they each state the facts differently〔指主意、說法〕不一致的，前後矛盾的：*The accounts of the witnesses are inconsistent.* 幾位目擊者的說法並不一致。| **[+with]** *What the Government says now is inconsistent with its election promises.* 政府現在的說法與競選時的許諾互相矛盾。**2 be inconsistent with** behaviour that is inconsistent with a particular set of principles or standards is not right according to those principles etc〔行為〕與〔原則、標準〕相悖的，不相稱的：**[+with]** *conduct inconsistent with what is expected of a congressman* 與人們對議員的期望不相稱的行為 **3** inconsistent behaviour, work etc changes too often from good to bad or from situation to situation〔行為、工作等〕時好時壞的，變化無常的：*The team's performance has been highly inconsistent this season.* 該隊在本賽季的發揮極不穩定。| *an inconsistent approach to discipline* 前後不一的處罰手段

in·con·so·la·ble /ˌɪnkənˋsoləbl̩; ˌɪnkənˈsəʊləbəl◂/ *adj* so sad that it is impossible for anyone to comfort you〔悲痛至極而〕無法安慰的，傷心欲絕的：*The boy was inconsolable after the death of his dog.* 小狗死後，那個男孩傷心不已。—**inconsolably** *adv*: *weeping inconsolably* 哭個不停

in·con·spic·u·ous /ˌɪnkənˋspɪkjuəs; ˌɪnkənˈspɪkjuəs◂/ *adj* not easily seen or noticed 不顯眼的，不引人注意的：*She put on an inconspicuous grey dress, hoping she wouldn't be seen in the crowd.* 她穿了一條不顯眼的灰色連衣裙，希望在人羣中不會被發現。—**inconspicuously** *adv* —**inconspicuousness** *n* [U]

in·con·stant /ɪnˋkɑnstənt; ɪnˈkɒnstənt/ *adj formal* unfaithful in love or friendship【正式】〔對友誼或愛情〕不忠實的：*She was charming, but an inconstant and unre-*

liable friend. 她很可愛, 但她不是一個忠實可靠的朋友。—**inconstancy** *n* [U]

in·con·tes·ta·ble /ˌɪnkənˋtɛstəbl̩; ˌɪnkənˈtestəbəl◂/ *adj* clearly true and impossible to disagree with; INDISPUTABLE 無可否認的; 不可爭辯的: *incontestable evidence of her innocence* 她無罪的鐵證 —**incontestably** *adv* —**incontestability** /ˌɪnkənˌtɛstəˋbɪlətɪ; ˌɪnkəntestəˈbɪlɪ̣ti/ *n* [U]

in·con·ti·nent /ɪnˋkɑntənənt; ɪnˈkɒntɪ̣nənt/ *adj* **1** unable to control the passing of food waste from your body 〔大小便〕失禁的 **2** *old use* unable to control your sexual urges【舊】〔性衝動〕不能控制的; 荒淫的 —**incontinence** *n* [U]

in·con·tro·ver·ti·ble /ˌɪnkɑntrəˋvɝtəbl̩; ɪnˌkɒntrəˈvɜːtɪ̣bəl/ *adj* a fact that is incontrovertible is definitely true and no one can prove it to be false; INDISPUTABLE 不容置疑的; 無可辯駁的: *The photograph provides incontrovertible evidence that Martin was at the scene of the crime.* 這張照片提供了馬丁案發時在場的確鑿證據。—**incontrovertibly** *adv* —**incontrovertability** /ɪnˌkɑntrəvɝtəˋbɪlətɪ; ɪnˌkɒntrəvɜːtəˈbɪlɪ̣ti/ *n* [U]

in·con·ve·ni·ence¹ /ˌɪnkənˋvinjəns; ˌɪnkənˈviːniəns/ *n* **1** [C] something that causes you problems or difficulty 不便之處, 麻煩事: *Compared to the trouble we've had in the past, this is only a minor inconvenience.* 與我們過去遇到的困難相比, 這不過是個小麻煩。**2** [U] the state of having problems or difficulty 麻煩, 不便: *We hope the delay has not caused any inconvenience to our customers.* 希望這次延誤沒有給我們的顧客帶來任何不便。

inconvenience² *v* [T] to cause someone problems or difficulty 給〔某人〕帶來不便; 添麻煩; 打擾: *I hope it won't inconvenience you to drive me to the station.* 我希望你開車送我去車站不會給你添麻煩。

in·con·ve·ni·ent /ˌɪnkənˋvinjənt; ˌɪnkənˈviːnjənt◂/ *adj* causing problems or difficulty, often in a way that is annoying; not CONVENIENT 帶來麻煩的; 不方便的: *It's a bit inconvenient for me to get to the centre of town. Can we meet somewhere else?* 我去市中心有點不方便, 我們能否換個地方會面? | *an inconvenient time* 不方便的時間 —**inconveniently** *adv*

3 **in·cor·po·rate** /ɪnˋkɔrpəˌret; ɪnˈkɔːpəreɪt/ *v* [T] to include something as part of a group, system, plan etc 把〔某物〕併入, 包含; 吸收: **incorporate sth into/in** *We've incorporated many environmentally-friendly features into the design of the building.* 我們在這座建築的設計中加進了許多環保特點。| *Our original proposals were not incorporated in the new legislation.* 新立法沒有包括我們當初的提議。—**incorporation** /ɪnˌkɔrpəˋreʃən; ɪnˌkɔːpəˈreɪʃən/ *n* [U]

in·cor·po·rat·ed /ɪnˋkɔrpəˌretɪd; ɪnˈkɔːpəreɪtɪ̣d/ written abbreviation 縮寫為 **Inc** *adj* used after the name of a company in the US to show that it has become a CORPORATION (1) 股份有限的〔在美國用於公司名稱後, 表示成為法人組織〕

in·cor·po·re·al /ˌɪnkɔrˋporɪəl; ˌɪnkɔːˈpɔːriəl/ *adj formal* not existing in any physical form but only as a spirit【正式】無形體的; 非實體的, 精神的 —**incorporeally** *adv*

in·cor·rect /ˌɪnkəˋrɛkt; ˌɪnkəˈrekt◂/ *adj* **1** not correct or true 不正確的; 不真實的: *incorrect spelling* 錯誤的拼寫 **2** not following the rules of polite behaviour 〔行為〕不恰當的; 不合禮節的 —**incorrectly** *adv* —**incorrectness** *n* [U]

in·cor·ri·gi·ble /ɪnˋkɔrɪdʒəbl̩; ɪnˈkɒrɪ̣dʒɪ̣bəl/ *adj often humorous* someone who is incorrigible is bad in a way that cannot be changed or improved【常幽默】〔人〕屢教不改的, 無可救藥的: **an incorrigible liar/gambler/rogue etc** *Peter, you are an incorrigible flirt!* 彼得, 你總喜歡跟女人調情, 真是無可救藥! —**incorrigibly** *adv*

in·cor·rup·ti·ble /ˌɪnkəˋrʌptəbl̩; ˌɪnkəˈrʌptɪ̣bəl◂/ *adj* **1** too honest to be influenced by anything that is illegal or morally wrong 誠實正直的, 剛正不阿的, 廉潔的: *A good judge must be incorruptible.* 好法官必須廉潔。**2** *formal* material that is incorruptible will never decay and cannot be destroyed【正式】〔物質〕不腐蝕的, 不會毀壞的: *Gold was precious because it was incorruptible.* 黃金不會腐蝕, 所以珍貴。—**incorruptibly** *adv*: *incorruptibly honest* 廉潔正直的 —**incorruptibility** /ˌɪnkəˌrʌptəˋbɪlətɪ; ˌɪnkərʌptɪ̣ˈbɪlɪ̣ti/ *n* [U] —see also 另見 CORRUPT¹

in·crease¹ /ɪnˋkris; ɪnˈkriːs/ *v* **1** [I] to become larger in amount, number, or degree 增加, 增大, 增強: *The population of London increased dramatically in the first half of the 20th century.* 20 世紀上半葉, 倫敦的人口大幅度地增長。| *The pain increased steadily until I could think of nothing else.* 疼痛越來越劇烈, 弄得我只覺得痛, 別的甚麼事情都想不了! | **increase in value/price/importance etc** *Investments are certain to increase in value.* 投資一定會增值。| **[+by]** *Food prices increased by 10% in less than a year.* 不到一年, 食品價格就上漲了10%。—see 見 RAISE¹ (USAGE) **2** [T] to make something larger in amount, number, or degree 使增加; 使增大, 使增強: *Now they want to increase our rents!* 如今他們要提高我們的房租! | *political tensions that might increase the likelihood of a nuclear war* 可能引發核戰爭的緊張政局 —**increasing** *adj*: *There is increasing difficulty in finding trained staff.* 越來越難找到訓練有素的職員了。—opposite 反義詞 DECREASE¹ —compare 比較 REDUCE 2 1

in·crease² /ˋɪnkris; ˈɪnkriːs/ *n* [C,U] a rise in amount, number, or degree 增加, 增強, 增大: **[+in]** *an increase in the crime rate* 犯罪率的上升 | **pay/price/tax increase** *Recent tax increases have affected the poor more than the rich.* 新近提高的稅收對窮人的影響比富人大。| **be on the increase** (=be increasing) 正在增加 *Diseases like TB and pneumonia are on the increase.* 像肺結核、肺炎這樣的疾病正在增加。 3 1

in·creased /ɪnˋkrist; ɪnˈkriːst/ *adj* larger than before 增強的, 增大的: *an increased awareness of the risks involved* 對相關風險已有所提高的警惕 3 2

in·creas·ing·ly /ɪnˋkrisɪŋlɪ; ɪnˈkriːsɪŋli/ *adv* more and more all the time [+adj/adv] 不斷增加地, 越來越多地: *The classes at the college have become increasingly full over the past five years.* 在過去的五年中, 這所學院的各班級越來越滿。| [sentence adverb 句子副詞] *Increasingly, it is the industrial power of Japan and South East Asia that dominates world markets.* 主宰世界市場的是日本和東南亞的工業實力 —— 這一情況日益明顯。 2

in·cred·i·ble /ɪnˋkrɛdəbl̩; ɪnˈkredɪ̣bəl/ *adj* **1** too strange to be believed or very difficult to believe 不可相信的, 難以置信的: *She told us the incredible story of her 134 days lost in the desert.* 她向我們講述了在沙漠迷途了134天的驚人經歷。| *It's incredible how much Tom has changed since he met Sally.* 湯姆自認識莎莉後, 他的變化之大讓人難以置信。**2** extremely good or extremely large 極好的; 極大的: *Tony has an incredible singing voice.* 托尼唱歌嗓音好極了。| *They stock an incredible range of goods.* 他們進貨的範圍簡直無所不包。—**incredibility** /ˌɪnkrɛdəˋbɪlətɪ; ɪnˌkredɪ̣ˈbɪlɪ̣ti/ *n* [U]

in·cred·i·bly /ɪnˋkrɛdəblɪ; ɪnˈkredɪ̣bli/ *adv* **1** [+adj/adv] extremely 極端地, 非常地: *I'm sorry I haven't phoned. I've been incredibly busy this week.* 很對不起沒有打電話, 我這週簡直忙得焦頭爛額。**2** [sentence adverb 句子副詞] in a way that is hard to believe 難以置信地: *Incredibly, even though the car was a write-off, he wasn't hurt at all.* 車都報廢了, 他卻毫髮未損, 真不可思議。 3

in·cre·du·li·ty /ˌɪnkrəˋdjulətɪ; ˌɪnkrɪ̣ˈdjuːlɪ̣ti/ *n* [U] a feeling that you cannot believe something; DISBELIEF 不相信; 懷疑: *Matt's comment brought a look of complete incredulity to Jill's face.* 馬特的話使得吉爾滿臉狐疑。

in·cred·u·lous /ɪnˋkrɛdʒələs; ɪnˈkredjʊ̣ləs/ *adj* unable or unwilling to believe something 不能相信的; 不願相信的: *He raised his eyebrows and gave me an incredulous look.* 他眉毛一揚, 用懷疑的神色看了我一眼。—**incredulously** *adv*

in·cre·ment /ˋɪŋkrəmənt; ˈɪŋkrɨmənt/ *n* [C] **1** an amount that is regularly added to the amount that someone is paid each year〔每年薪金的定期〕增加, 增額: *The starting salary is £10,000, but with increments it can rise to £16,500.* 起薪1萬英鎊, 通過年度加薪, 可增加到1.65萬英鎊。**2** the amount by which a number, value, or amount increases〔數字、價值、數量的〕增加額 —**incremental** *adj*

in·crim·i·nate /ɪnˋkrɪmə,net; ɪnˈkrɪmɨneɪt/ *v* [T] to make someone seem guilty of a crime 使〔某人〕顯得有罪; 連累, 牽連: *He refused to speak because he was worried that he would incriminate himself.* 他因擔心自己受到牽連而拒絕講話。| *incriminating evidence* 可顯示有罪的證據 —**incrimination** /ɪn,krɪməˋneʃən; ɪn,krɪmɨˈneɪʃən/ *n* [U]

in·crim·i·na·to·ry /ɪnˋkrɪmənə,torɪ; ɪnˈkrɪmɨnətəri/ *adj* making someone seem to be guilty 使〔某人〕顯得有罪的

in-crowd /ˋ· ·/ *n* **the in-crowd** a small group of people who are admired by other people, for example because they are very fashionable, and who do not let many other people join them〔因時髦等受到羨慕但排外的〕小集團; 小圈子: *I was never one of the in-crowd at school.* 我在學校從來沒有參加過小圈子。

in·crus·ta·tion /,ɪnkrʌsˋteʃən; ,ɪnkrʌsˈteɪʃən/ *n* [C] an amount of dirt, salt etc which forms a hard layer on a surface〔在表面形成的一層硬的〕凝結物; 積垢, 沉積物: **[+of]** *an incrustation of salt on the bottom of the boat* 船底部的鹽垢

in·cu·bate /ˋɪŋkjə,bet; ˈɪŋkjɨbeɪt/ *v* [I,T] **1** if a bird incubates its eggs or if they incubate, they are kept warm by the bird until the young birds come out 孵〔蛋〕;〔蛋〕被孵化 **2** [I,T] *technical* if a disease incubates, or if you incubate it, it develops in your body until you show physical signs of it【術語】〔疾病〕潛伏在體內

in·cu·ba·tion /,ɪnkjəˋbeʃən; ,ɪŋkjɨˈbeɪʃən/ *n* [U] the period between becoming infected with a disease and showing the first physical signs of it〔疾病的〕潛伏期

incubator 恆溫箱

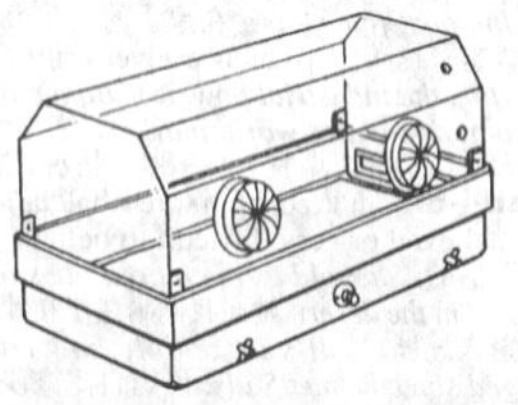

in·cu·ba·tor /ˋɪŋkjə,betə; ˈɪŋkjɨbeɪtə/ *n* [C] **1** a heated container for keeping eggs warm until the young birds etc come out 孵化器, 孵化箱 **2** a piece of hospital equipment used for keeping very small or weak babies alive〔用於放置很小或體弱初生嬰兒的〕恆溫箱

in·cu·bus /ˋɪŋkjəbəs; ˈɪŋkjɨbəs/ *n* [C] **1** someone or something that causes a lot of worries 造成嚴重憂慮的人[事] **2** a male DEVIL that is supposed to have sex with a sleeping woman 夢淫妖〔傳說與睡夢中的女人交合的妖怪〕—compare 比較 SUCCUBUS **3** *literary* a bad dream; NIGHTMARE (1)【文】噩夢, 夢魘

in·cul·cate /ɪnˋkʌlket; ˈɪŋkʌlkeɪt/ *v* [T] *formal* to fix ideas, principles etc in someone's mind【正式】灌輸〔觀念、原則等〕, 教誨: **inculcate sth in/into** *She tries very hard to inculcate traditional values into her students.* 她想方設法給學生灌輸傳統的價值觀。| **inculcate sb with sth** *Schools inculcate children with patriotic ideas from an early age.* 學校從孩子年幼開始就向他們灌輸愛國思想。—**inculcation** /,ɪnkʌlˋkeʃən; ,ɪŋkʌlˈkeɪʃən/ *n* [U]

in·cul·pate /ɪnˋkʌlpet; ˈɪŋkʌlpeɪt/ *v* [T] *formal* to show that someone is guilty of a crime【正式】顯示〔某人〕有罪

in·cum·ben·cy /ɪnˋkʌmbənsɪ; ɪnˈkʌmbənsi/ *n* [C] *formal* the period of time during which someone is an incumbent【正式】〔特指政治職位的〕任期

in·cum·bent[1] /ɪnˋkʌmbənt; ɪnˈkʌmbənt/ *n* [C] *formal*【正式】**1** someone in an official position, especially a political one 任職者, 現任者〔尤指政治職位〕: *Castillo was to be the new incumbent at the City Controller's office.* 卡斯蒂略當時即將就任城市審計辦公室的新主管。**2** a priest who is in charge of a church〔掌管教堂的〕牧師

incumbent[2] *adj formal*【正式】**1 it is incumbent upon sb to do sth** if it is incumbent upon you to do something, it is your duty or responsibility to do it 做某事是某人的職務[責任]: *It is incumbent upon the teacher to maintain discipline.* 教師有責任維護紀律。**2 the incumbent president/priest/Senator etc** the president etc at the present time 現任的總統/牧師/參議員等

in·cur /ɪnˋkɝ; ɪnˈkɜː/ *v* **incurred, incurring** [T] **1** to put yourself in an unpleasant situation by your own actions, so that you lose something, get punished etc〔因自己的舉動而〕招致〔不愉快的事〕, 招惹, 遭受: **incur losses/debts etc** *Milton incurred debts of over $300,000.* 密爾頓負債三十多萬美元。| **incur sb's anger/disapproval etc** *We incurred her displeasure.* 我們把她惹得很不高興。**2 incur expenses** to have to spend money on something 招致花費

in·cur·a·ble /ɪnˋkjʊrəbl; ɪnˈkjʊərəbəl/ *adj* **1** impossible to cure 無法治癒的, 不可救藥的: *an incurable disease* 不治之症 **2** impossible to change 不可改變的: *My mother is an incurable optimist.* 我母親是個不可動搖的樂天派。—**incurably** *adv*: *incurably romantic* 無可救藥地浪漫 —**incurable** *n* [C]

in·cu·ri·ous /ɪnˋkjʊrɪəs; ɪnˈkjʊəriəs/ *adj formal* not naturally interested in finding out about the things around you【正式】〔對周圍〕沒有好奇心的, 不感興趣的: *The child watched with an incurious gaze.* 那個小孩用漠然的眼神看着。

in·cur·sion /ɪnˋkɝʒən; ɪnˈkɜːʃən/ *n* [C] *formal*【正式】**1** a sudden attack into an area that belongs to other people 突襲; 侵入, 侵犯: *a British and French incursion into China in 1857* 1857年英法聯軍侵入中國 **2** the unwanted arrival of something in a place where it does not belong〔不受歡迎的〕進入〔其他地方〕; 來到: *the incursion of tabloid-style reporting into such a famous newspaper* 小報式的報道對如此著名的一家報紙的入侵

in·debt·ed /ɪnˋdɛtɪd; ɪnˈdetɨd/ *adj* **be indebted to** to be very grateful to someone for the help they have given you 對〔某人給予幫助而〕感激的: **greatly/deeply indebted** *I am indebted to my husband for helping me edit the book.* 我很感激我丈夫幫助我編輯這本書。—**indebtedness** *n* [U]

in·de·cen·cy /ɪnˋdisn̩sɪ; ɪnˈdiːsənsi/ *n* [U] *law* behaviour that is sexually offensive, especially INDECENT EXPOSURE【法律】猥褻; 下流〔尤指猥褻的裸露〕: *gross indecency* 低級下流

in·de·cent /ɪnˋdisn̩t; ɪnˈdiːsənt/ *adj* **1** indecent behaviour, movements, clothes etc are likely to shock or offend people, because they involve sex or because they show parts of the body that are usually covered〔行為、動作、衣着等〕下流的, 猥褻的: *You can't go to a dinner party in that dress – it's positively indecent!* 你不能穿那種衣服參加宴會——太不雅觀了! **2** not acceptable 不合適的, 不適當的: *The funeral formalities were performed with almost indecent haste.* 葬禮幾乎是草率了事。—**indecently** *adv*: *indecently dressed* 穿着不體面的

indecent as·sault /·,·· ·ˈ·/ *n* [C,U] *law* an attack on a person which includes sexual violence【法律】強暴猥褻行為

indecent ex·po·sure /·,·· ·ˈ··/ *n* [U] *law* the criminal offence of deliberately showing your sex organs in a place where this is likely to offend people【法律】猥褻暴露, 露陰〔指故意裸露性器官〕—see also 另見 FLASHER

in·de·ci·pher·a·ble /ˌɪndɪˋsaɪfərəbḷ; ˌɪndɪˈsaɪfərəbəl◂/ *adj* impossible to read or understand 難以辨認的, 難以讀懂的: *an indecipherable signature* 難以辨認的簽名

in·de·ci·sion /ˌɪndɪˋsɪʒən; ˌɪndɪˈsɪʒən/ *n* [U] the state of being unable to decide what to do 猶豫不決; 無決斷能力; 優柔寡斷: *tortured by doubt and indecision* 飽受疑惑和優柔寡斷的折磨

in·de·ci·sive /ˌɪndɪˋsaɪsɪv; ˌɪndɪˈsaɪsɪv◂/ *adj* **1** unable to make clear decisions or choices 不果斷的, 猶豫不決的: *an indecisive leader* 優柔寡斷的領導人 **2** having an unclear result; INCONCLUSIVE 結果不明確的; 非結論性的: *a confused indecisive battle* 不分勝負的一場混戰 —**indecisively** *adv* —**indecisiveness** *n* [U]

in·dec·o·rous /ɪnˋdɛkərəs; ɪnˈdekərəs/ *adj formal* behaving in a way that is not polite or socially acceptable【正式】不禮貌的; 不得體的, 不雅的 —**indecorously** *adv*

3 1 **in·deed** /ɪnˋdid; ɪnˈdiːd/ *adv* **1** [sentence adverb 句子副詞] used to emphasize a statement or answer 當然, 確實〔用於強調陳述或答案〕: *"Would it help if you had an assistant?" "It would, indeed."* "你要是有個助手, 會有幫助嗎?" "那是肯定的。" | *There are few, if indeed any, authors with such a gift for dialogue.* 寫對話有如此天賦的作家, 即使真的有, 也十分少。**2** *formal* used to introduce additional information that emphasizes what you have just said【正式】甚至; 其實〔用來補充內容, 強調剛說過的話〕: *I didn't mind at all. Indeed, I was pleased.* 我一點也不介意, 事實上我非常高興。**3** *especially BrE* used to emphasize the word 'very' in expressions such as 'very good indeed' and 'very much indeed'【尤英】確實, 實在〔在 very good indeed 和 very much indeed 這類的片語中用來強調 very〕: *I am very sorry indeed for my foolish behaviour.* 我對自己的愚蠢行為深感抱歉。| *Thank you very much indeed.* 萬分感謝。**4** *especially BrE spoken* used to express disbelief, surprise, or annoyance at something you have been told【尤英, 口】真的, 真是〔表示對所聽到消息的懷疑、驚訝、惱火等〕: *"He's taken a three hour lunch break." "Has he, indeed?"* "他午間休息了三個小時。" "他真的這樣做?" | *"Why would anyone say such a horrible thing?" "Why, indeed?"* "怎麼會有人說這樣惡劣的話?" "是呀, 怎麼會呢?"

in·de·fat·i·ga·ble /ˌɪndɪˋfætɪgəbḷ; ˌɪndɪˈfætɪgəbəl/ *adj formal* determined and never becoming tired【正式】堅定的, 堅持不懈的: *an indefatigable campaigner for human rights* 不屈不撓的人權運動者 —**indefatigably** *adv*

in·de·fen·si·ble /ˌɪndɪˋfɛnsəbḷ; ˌɪndɪˈfensəbəl◂/ *adj* **1** too bad to be excused or defended 不可原諒的; 無法辯解的: *indefensible behaviour* 不可原諒的行為 **2** impossible or very difficult to defend from military attack〔對武裝攻擊〕無法防禦的, 無法保衛的 —**indefensibly** *adv*

in·de·fin·a·ble /ˌɪndɪˋfaɪnəbḷ; ˌɪndɪˈfaɪnəbəl◂/ *adj* an indefinable feeling, quality etc is difficult to describe or explain〔情感、品質等〕難以描述的, 難以解釋的: *She felt a sudden indefinable sadness.* 她突然感到一種難以名狀的悲傷。—**indefinably** *adv*

in·def·i·nite /ɪnˋdɛfənɪt; ɪnˈdefənət/ *adj* **1** an indefinite action or period of time has no definite end arranged for it〔行動或時間〕無限期的: *an indefinite ban on imports of gold* 無限期禁止黃金進口的禁令 **2** not clear or definite; VAGUE 不清楚的, 不明確的; 模糊的: *indefinite opinions* 模糊不清的意見 —**indefiniteness** *n* [U]

indefinite ar·ti·cle /ˌ·ˌ··· ˈ···/ *n* [C] the word 'a' or 'an' in the English language or a word in another language that is used like 'a' or 'an' 不定冠詞〔如英語中的 a 或 an, 以及其他語言中與 a 或 an 功能相似的詞語〕—compare 比較 DEFINITE ARTICLE —see also 另見 ARTICLE[1] (4)

in·def·i·nite·ly /ɪnˋdɛfənɪtlɪ; ɪnˈdefənətli/ *adv* **1** for a period of time for which no definite end has been arranged 無限期地: *Negotiations have been suspended indefinitely.* 談判已無限期中止。**2** without giving clear or exact details〔細節〕不清楚地; 模糊粗略地

in·del·i·ble /ɪnˋdɛləbḷ; ɪnˈdeləbəl/ *adj* **1** impossible to remove or forget; permanent 難以去掉的, 難以忘記的; 永恒的: *The teacher's words left an indelible impression on me for years to come.* 在後來的歲月裡, 老師的話讓我難以忘懷。**2 indelible ink/pencil/marker etc** ink etc that makes a permanent mark which cannot be removed 不褪色墨水/鉛筆/記號筆等 —**indelibly** *adv*: *a moment indelibly imprinted on my mind* 刻骨銘心的一刻

in·del·i·cate /ɪnˋdɛləkət; ɪnˈdeləkət/ *adj* likely to embarrass or shock people 令人窘迫的; 令人震驚的: *He made an indelicate remark at the dinner table.* 他在飯桌上說了一些很粗鄙的話。—**indelicately** *adv* —**indelicacy** *n* [U]

in·dem·ni·fi·ca·tion /ɪnˌdɛmnəfəˋkeʃən; ɪnˌdemnəfəˈkeɪʃən/ *n law*【法律】**1** [U+for/against] the act of paying, or promising to pay, someone for loss, injury, or damage〔對所受損失、損傷或損壞的〕賠償, 賠償承諾 **2** [C,U+for] a payment made to someone for loss, injury or damage 賠償金, 賠款

in·dem·ni·fy /ɪnˋdɛmnəˌfaɪ; ɪnˈdemnəfaɪ/ *v* **indemnified, indemnifying** [T] *law*【法律】**1** [+against/for] to promise to pay someone if something they possess is damaged or lost 保證〔遇損壞或損失時〕賠償 **2** [+for] to pay someone money because of loss, injury, or damage that they have suffered 賠償〔損失、傷害、損毀等〕, 補償

in·dem·ni·ty /ɪnˋdɛmnətɪ; ɪnˈdemnəti/ *n law*【法律】**1** [U] protection against loss or damage, especially in the form of a promise to pay for any losses or damage〔尤指以保證賠償形式的〕保障, 保護 **2** [C] a payment for the loss of money, goods etc 賠償金

in·dent[1] /ɪnˋdɛnt; ɪnˈdent/ *v* **1** [T] to start a line of writing further towards the middle of the page than other lines〔在書寫的一行中〕縮格 **2** [I+for] *especially BrE* to order goods by writing on an official form【尤英】〔填寫訂單〕訂購

in·dent[2] /ˋɪndɛnt; ˈɪndent/ *n* [C+for] *especially BrE*【尤英】**1** an order for goods to be sent abroad, or for supplies for an army 出口訂貨; 軍需訂貨 **2** an official written order for goods 正式書面訂貨單

in·den·ta·tion /ˌɪndɛnˋteʃən; ˌɪndenˈteɪʃən/ *n* [C] **1** a cut into the surface or edge of something 凹口, 凹陷, 缺口: *The bite left deep indentations.* 這一咬留下了深深的齒痕。**2** a space at the beginning of a line of writing〔書寫時的〕行首空格 **3** [C,U] the act of indenting 縮格, 縮排

in·dent·ed /ɪnˋdɛntɪd; ɪnˈdentəd/ *adj* an indented edge or surface has cuts or marks in it〔邊緣或表面呈〕鋸齒狀的; 有凹痕的: a *deeply indented coastline* 蜿蜒曲折的海岸線

in·den·ture /ɪnˋdɛntʃɚ; ɪnˈdentʃə/ also 又作 **indentures** *plural* — *n* [C] a formal contract, especially in former times, between an APPRENTICE[1] and his master〔舊時的〕正式師徒契約

in·de·pen·dence /ˌɪndɪˋpɛndəns; ˌɪndəˈpendəns/ *n* [U] 2
1 political freedom from control by the government of another country 政治獨立: [+from] *Nigeria gained independence from Britain in 1960.* 尼日利亞於 1960 年脫離英國獨立。| *minority groups striving for political independence* 追求政治獨立的少數民族 **2** the time when a country becomes politically independent 國家獲得獨立的時期: *The country has made great advances since independence.* 該國自獨立以來發展迅速。**3** the freedom and ability to make your own decisions in life, without having to ask other people for permission, help, or money〔個人生活的〕獨立, 自主: *financial independence* 經濟獨立 | *I was enjoying a new feeling of independence.* 我沉浸在一種獨立自主的嶄新感覺之中。

Independence Day /··ˈ·· ˌ·/ *n* [singular] the FOURTH OF JULY 美國獨立紀念日〔7月4日〕

in·de·pen·dent /ˌɪndɪˋpɛndənt; ˌɪndəˈpendənt◂/ *adj* 2

1 ►COUNTRY/ORGANIZATION 國家/機構◄ [no comparative 無比較級] not governed or controlled by another country or organization 獨立的, 自主的: *India became independent in 1947.* 印度於 1947 年獨立。| *The independent role of the Police Commission must never be compromised.* 警務委員會的獨立身分絕對不能受到損害。| **independent school/broadcasting etc** *especially BrE* (=not owned or paid for by the government) 【尤英】民辦[私立]學校/獨立廣播等
2 ►PERSON 人◄ a) confident and able to do things by yourself in your own way, without wanting help or advice from other people 獨立的, 不需要別人幫助的; 有主見的: *I quite like living alone, it's made me more independent.* 我很喜歡獨居, 這樣我能更加獨立。| **[+of]** *study material that helps the student to be independent of the teacher* 有助於學生自學的學習材料 **b)** [no comparative 無比較級] having enough money to live so that you do not have to depend on other people 經濟自立的, 自力謀生的: *financially independent* 經濟自立的 | **[+of]** *Robert aimed to be independent of his parents by the time he was twenty.* 羅伯特的目標是在二十歲時脱離父母自立。
3 of independent means having your own income from property, INVESTMENTS etc 靠財產、投資等獲取個人收入的: *a woman of independent means* 自立謀生有自己收入的女人
4 independent inquiry/opinion/advice etc something that is done or given by people who are not involved in a particular situation and who can therefore be trusted to be fair in judging it 獨立的調查/觀點/建議等: *There have been demands for an independent inquiry into allegations of police misconduct.* 有人要求對警方涉嫌濫用職權的指控進行獨立調查。
5 ►SEPARATE 分離的◄ existing separately and not connected with or influenced by any others 獨立的; 不受別人影響的: *Three independent studies in three different countries all arrived at the same conclusion.* 在三個不同國家獨立進行的三項研究得出了相同的結論。| **[+of]** *reports from two separate sources entirely independent of one another* 根據兩個完全獨立的信息來源所作的報道 —**independently** *adv*: *two systems that operate independently of each other* 兩套獨立運行的系統

Independent *n* [C] a politician who does not belong to a political party 無黨派政治家

independent clause /ˌ···· ˈ·/ *n* [C] *technical* a CLAUSE (2) which can make a sentence by itself, for example 'she went home' in the sentence 'She went home because she was tired.'; MAIN CLAUSE【術語】獨立子句〔即能獨立成句的子句, 如 She went home because she was tired. 中的 she went home 也稱主句〕

in-depth /ˈ· ·/ *adj* [only before noun 僅用於名詞前] **in-depth study/ investigation/report etc** an examination or description of something that is thorough and complete so that all the details are considered 深入的研究/調查/報道等: *scientists doing an in-depth study of the causes of lung cancer* 正在對肺癌病因作深入研究的科學家

in·de·scri·ba·ble /ˌɪndɪˋskraɪbəbl; ˌɪndɪsˈkraɪbəbəl◄/ *adj* something that is indescribable is so terrible, so good, so strange etc that you cannot describe it, or it is too difficult to describe 難以名狀的; 無法形容的: *a feeling of indescribable joy* 難以形容的喜悦 | *There was an indescribable tension in the room.* 房間內有一種難以名狀的緊張氣氛。—**indescribably** *adv*: *indescribably squalid conditions* 難以形容的骯髒環境

in·de·struc·ti·ble /ˌɪndɪˋstrʌktəbl; ˌɪndɪˈstrʌktəbəl◄/ *adj* too strong to be destroyed 不可摧毀的; 堅不可摧的: *indestructible optimism* 堅定不移的樂觀精神 | *These toys are great because they're practically indestructible.* 這些玩具真不錯, 幾乎怎麼玩都不壞。—**indestructibly** *adv* —**indestructibility** /ˌɪndɪˌstrʌktəˋbɪlətɪ; ˌɪndɪstrʌktəˈbɪləti/ *n* [U]

in·de·ter·mi·na·ble /ˌɪndɪˋtɝmɪnəbl; ˌɪndɪˈtɜːmənəbəl◄/ *adj* impossible to find out or calculate exactly 難以查明的; 無法準確計算的: *water of indeterminable depth* 深不可測的水域 —**indeterminably** *adv*

in·de·ter·mi·nate /ˌɪndɪˋtɝmənɪt; ˌɪndɪˈtɜːmənət◄/ *adj* impossible to know about definitely or exactly 難以肯定的, 無法確定的: *a girl of indeterminate age* 年齡難以確定的女孩 —**indeterminately** *adv* —**indeterminacy** *n* [U]

in·dex¹ /ˋɪndɛks; ˈɪndeks/ *n plural* **indices** /-dəˌsiz; -dəsiːz/ or **indexes** [C] **1** an alphabetical list of names, subjects etc at the back of a book, with the numbers of the pages where they can be found〔書後人名、題目等的〕索引 **2** a set of cards, each with a name or piece of information on it, arranged in alphabetical order, as used in a library; CARD INDEX〔用於圖書館等處的〕卡片索引 **3** a sign by which the level of something can be judged or measured〔用於判斷或量度水平的〕標誌: *This may be taken as an index of economic growth.* 這可以視為經濟增長的指標。**4** *technical* a system by which prices, costs etc can be compared to those of a previous date【術語】〔用於比較今昔價格、費用等的〕指數

index² *v* [T] **1** to make an index for something 為〔某物〕編索引 **2 [+to]** to arrange for the level of wages, PENSIONs etc to increase or decrease according to the level of prices 使〔工資、養老金等〕與物價指數掛鉤 —**indexation** *n* [C]

index card /ˈ·· ·/ *n* [C] one of the cards in an index 索引卡片

index fin·ger /ˈ·· ˌ··/ *n* [C] the finger next to your thumb; FOREFINGER 食指

index-linked /ˌ·· ˈ·◄/ *adj technical BrE* index-linked wages, PENSIONs etc, increase or decrease according to the rise or fall of prices【術語, 英】〔工資、養老金等〕與物價升降掛鉤的

In·di·a ink /ˋɪndɪə ˌɪŋk; ˈɪndiə ˌɪŋk/ *n* [U] black ink used especially for Chinese or Japanese writing with a brush〔中國或日本寫毛筆字用的〕墨, 墨汁

In·di·an¹ /ˋɪndɪən; ˈɪndiən/ *n* **1** [C] someone from India 印度人 **2** [C] someone from one of the races that lived in North, South, and Central America before Europeans arrived〔美洲的〕印第安人

Indian² *adj* **1** from or connected with India 印度的 **2** connected with Indians 印度人的; 印第安人的

Indian corn /ˌ··· ˈ·/ *n* [U] *old-fashioned, especially AmE* MAIZE【過時, 尤美】玉米

Indian file /ˈ··· ·/ *n* [U] if people walk in Indian file, they walk one behind another; SINGLE FILE 單列縱隊

Indian giv·er /ˌ··· ˈ··/ *n* [C] *AmE informal* an expression that is now considered offensive meaning someone who gives you something and then takes it back【美, 非正式】送禮物後又索回的人〔今認為具冒犯意思〕—**Indian giving** *n* [U]

Indian ink /ˌ··· ˈ·/ *n* [U] *BrE* black ink used especially for Chinese or Japanese writing with a brush【英】〔中國或日本寫毛筆字用的〕墨, 墨汁

Indian sum·mer /ˌ··· ˈ··/ *n* [C] **1** a period of warm weather in the autumn 秋季的和暖天氣; 小陽春 **2** a happy or successful time, especially near the end of your life or CAREER¹ (1) 幸福[成功]的時期〔尤指晚年或事業晚期〕

Indian wrest·ling /ˌ··· ˈ··/ *n* [U] *AmE* a game in which you stand facing someone with your foot touching theirs, and try to push them over by pushing their hand【美】推比賽〔兩人相向而立, 以一足相抵, 一掌互推, 身體失去平衡者為負〕

india rub·ber /ˌ··· ˈ··◄/ *n old-fashioned*【過時】**1** [U] rubber used for making toys, removing pencil marks etc〔製玩具或擦鉛筆字跡用的〕橡皮: *an india rubber ball* 橡皮球 **2** [C] *BrE* a piece of rubber used for removing pencil marks; ERASER【英】〔擦鉛筆字跡用的〕橡皮

in·di·cate /ˋɪndəˌket; ˈɪndəkeɪt/ *v*

1 ►FACTS 事實◄ [T] to show that a particular situation exists or that something is likely to be true 表明; 表示: *The survey results seem to indicate a connection between poor housing conditions and bad health.* 調查結果表明, 居住條件差與健康不佳之間似乎存在着關係。| **indicate that** *This indicates that rape is more widespread than people believe.* 這表明, 強姦案比人們認為的要普遍。

2 ►POINT AT 指向◄ [T] to direct someone's attention to something, for example by pointing 指, 指着〔以引起注意〕: *"She's the one I was telling you about," whispered Toby, indicating a girl in a cheap cotton dress.* "她就是我跟你說過的那個人,"托比指着一位身穿廉價棉布衣服的女孩小聲地說道。

3 ►YOUR WISHES/INTENTIONS 希望/意願◄ [T] to say or do something to make your wishes, intentions etc clear〔說或做某事〕表明〔意向等〕: *The Russians have already indicated their willingness to cooperate.* 俄國人已經表明了樂意合作的意向。| **indicate that** *Ralph patted the sofa to indicate that she should join him.* 拉爾夫拍拍沙發, 示意讓她坐過來。

4 ►A SIGN FOR 為…的標誌◄ [T] to be a sign for something; REPRESENT 標誌着; 代表: *The symbols indicate different groups of sounds.* 這些符號表示不同的音羣。

5 ►IN A CAR 在汽車裡◄ [I,T] *BrE* to show the direction in which you intend to turn in a vehicle, using lights or your hands; signal【英】〔用指示車燈或手勢〕指示〔轉彎方向〕: *Don't forget to indicate before you pull out.* 駛離所在車道前別忘發信號。—see picture on page A3 參見A3頁圖

6 ►TREATMENT 治療◄ be indicated *formal* if a particular kind of treatment is indicated, the need for it is shown【正式】顯示有…的需要

Frequencies of **indicate** and **show** in spoken and written English 動詞 indicate 和 show 在英語口語和書面語中的使用頻率

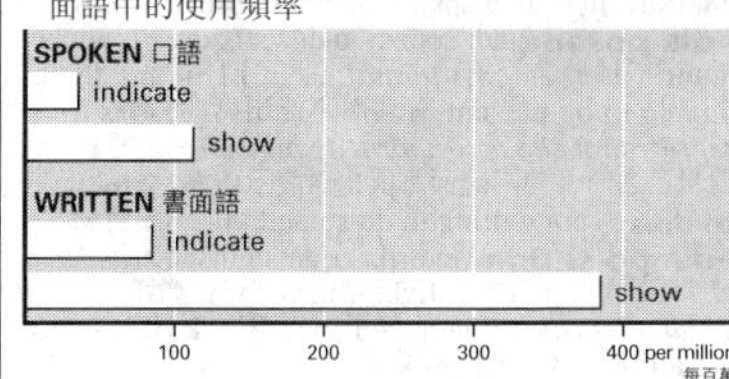

Based on the British National Corpus and the Longman Lancaster Corpus 據英國國家語料庫和朗文蘭卡斯特語料庫

This graph shows that **show** is much more common than **indicate** in both spoken and written English. This is because **show** is much more general in meaning and is more commonly used in informal English than **indicate**. 本圖表顯示, show 在英語口語和書面語中的使用頻率都遠遠高於 indicate。這是因為 show 的語義比較廣泛, 在非正式場合中比 indicate 更常用。

3 **in·di·ca·tion** /ˌɪndəˋkeʃən; ˌɪndʒˈkeɪʃən/ *n* [C,U] a sign that something is probably happening or that something is probably true 跡象: **[+of]** *He gave no indication of his own feelings at all.* 他一點兒也沒有顯露自己的感情。| **[+that]** *a clear indication that they were in financial difficulty* 他們遭遇財政困難的明顯跡象 | **every indication** (=very clear signs) 種種跡象 *The two leaders greeted each other with every indication of good feeling.* 兩位領導人十分友好地互致問候。

in·dic·a·tive¹ /ɪnˋdɪkətɪv; ɪnˈdɪkətɪv/ *adj* **1 be indicative of** to be a clear sign that a particular situation exists or that something is likely to be true 顯示出; 指明; 表明; 象徵: *This behaviour is indicative of her whole attitude, I'm afraid.* 恐怕這種行為表明了她的整個態度。**2** *technical* an indicative verb form is used for making statements【術語】〔動詞〕陳述語氣的

indicative² *n* [C,U] *technical* the form of a verb that is used to make statements. For example, in the sentences 'Penny passed her test', and 'Michael likes cake', the verbs 'passed' and 'likes' are in the indicative.【術語】〔動詞的〕陳述語氣〈如 Penny passed her test. 和 Michael likes cake. 中的 passed 和 likes〉

in·di·ca·tor /ˋɪndəˌketə; ˈɪndʒkeɪtə/ *n* [C] **1** something that can be regarded as a sign which shows you in what way a situation is changing 指示者; 指示物: *All the main economic indicators suggest that trade is improving.* 所有的主要經濟指標都表明貿易正在改善。**2** *BrE* one of the lights on a car that flash to show which way the car is turning【英】〔汽車上的〕轉向指示燈; TURN SIGNAL *AmE*【美】**3** a POINTER (1) on a machine that shows the temperature, pressure, speed etc〔機器設備中表示溫度、壓力、速度等的〕指針 —see picture on page A2 參見A2頁圖

in·di·ces /ˋɪndəˌsiz; ˈɪndʒsiːz/ the plural of INDEX

in·dict /ɪnˋdaɪt; ɪnˈdaɪt/ *v* [I,T] *law especially AmE* to officially charge someone with a criminal offence【法律, 尤美】控告; 起訴〔某人〕: **indict sb for sth** *He was indicted for fraud before a grand jury.* 他在大陪審團前被指控犯有欺詐罪。—**indictment** *n* [C,U]

in·dict·a·ble /ɪnˋdaɪtəbḷ; ɪnˈdaɪtəbəl/ *adj law especially AmE* an indictable offence is one for which you can be indicted【法律, 尤美】〔罪行〕可被控告的

in·dict·ment /ɪnˋdaɪtmənt; ɪnˈdaɪtmənt/ *n* **1 be an indictment of** to be a very clear sign that a system, method etc is very bad or very wrong〔制度不善、方法錯誤等的〕明顯象徵: *The fact that these children cannot read is a damning indictment of our education system.* 這些孩子不能閱讀, 分明顯示出我們的教育制度有問題。**2** [C] *law especially AmE* an official written statement charging someone with a criminal offence【法律, 尤美】起訴書, 訴狀 **3** [U] *law especially AmE* the act of officially charging someone with a criminal offence【法律, 尤美】起訴, 指控, 控告

in·die /ˋɪndɪ; ˈindi/ *n* [C] a small independent company, especially one that produces records of popular music or television programmes〔製作流行樂唱片或電視節目的〕小型獨立公司

indie mu·sic /ˈ·· ˌ··/ *n* [U] records of popular music produced by a small independent company〔由小型獨立公司出品的〕獨立音樂唱片

in·dif·fer·ence /ɪnˋdɪfərəns; ɪnˈdɪfərəns/ *n* [U] lack of interest or concern 缺乏興趣; 漠不關心: *He always treats Jane with complete indifference.* 他對簡總是極其冷淡。| **be a matter of indifference to** (=be something that someone does not care about)〔對某人〕完全無所謂 *Whether you stay or leave is a matter of total indifference to me.* 你是留是走對我根本無所謂。

in·dif·fer·ent /ɪnˋdɪfərənt; ɪnˈdɪfərənt/ *adj* **1** not caring about what is happening, especially about other people's problems or feelings〔尤指對別人的困難或感情〕不關心, 不在乎: **[+to]** *Customs officials were indifferent to their plight.* 海關官員對他們的困境無動於衷。**2** not particularly good; MEDIOCRE 不太好的; 一般的; 平庸的: *an indifferent cook* 手藝平平的廚師 —**indifferently** *adv*

in·di·ge·nous /ɪnˋdɪdʒənəs; ɪnˈdɪdʒənəs/ *adj* indigenous animals, plants etc have always lived or grown naturally in the place where they are, as opposed to others that were brought there〔動、植物等〕土生土長的; 本地的: **[+to]** *There were no snakes indigenous to the islands.* 這些島嶼過去不產蛇。—**indigenously** *adv*

in·di·gent /ˋɪndədʒənt; ˈɪndɪdʒənt/ *adj formal* not having much money or many possessions; POOR (1)【正式】貧困的, 貧窮的 —**indigence** *n* [U] —**indigent** *n* [C]

in·di·ges·ti·ble /ˌɪndɪˋdʒɛstəbḷ; ˌɪndɪˈdʒestʒbəl◄/ *adj* **1** food that is indigestible cannot easily be broken down in the stomach into substances that the body can use〔食

I

物〕難消化的 —opposite 反義詞 DIGESTIBLE **2** facts that are indigestible are not easy to understand〔事實〕難懂的, 不好理解的: *indigestible statistics* 看不懂的統計數字 —**indigestibly** *adv*

in·di·ges·tion /ˌɪndəˋdʒɛstʃən; ˌɪndɪˈdʒestʃən◂/ *n* [U] pain that you get when your stomach cannot deal with food that you have eaten 消化不良(症): *You'll get indigestion eating that fast!* 你吃得那麼快會消化不良的!

in·dig·nant /ɪnˋdɪgnənt; ɪnˈdɪgnənt/ *adj* expressing anger and surprise, because you feel insulted or unfairly treated〔由於受辱或受不公平待遇而表示〕氣憤的, 憤慨的, 憤憤不平的: *Harriet was indignant at the suggestion that she might need help.* 哈麗特對有人暗示她可能需要幫助十分惱火。| *anger expressed by an indignant snort* 以氣憤的哼聲來表示的憤怒 —**indignantly** *adv*: *"Of course I didn't tell her!" Sasha said indignantly.* "我當然沒有告訴她!"薩莎氣憤地說。

in·dig·na·tion /ˌɪndɪgˋneʃən; ˌɪndɪgˈneɪʃən/ *n* [U] feelings of anger and surprise because you feel insulted or unfairly treated〔因受辱或受到不公平待遇而感到〕憤慨, 義憤, 憤怒: *Chamberlain found, to his great indignation, that he was not to be included in the team.* 張伯倫發現他將被排斥在小組之外, 因此感到十分氣憤。| *anger fuelled by righteous indignation* 由於義憤而燒得更旺的怒火 | **[+at]** *Her indignation at such rough treatment was understandable.* 遭受如此粗暴的待遇, 她大為光火是可以理解的。

in·dig·ni·ty /ɪnˋdɪgnətɪ; ɪnˈdɪgnəti/ *n* [C,U] a situation that makes you feel very ashamed, unimportant, and not respected 侮辱; 輕蔑: *She suffered many such indignities during her years with their family.* 她與他們一家相處的幾年裡蒙受了許多屈辱。| **the indignity of** *At least the general was spared the indignity of a public trial.* 這位將軍至少得以免受公審之辱。

in·di·go /ˋɪndɪˌgo; ˈɪndɪgəʊ/ *n* [U] a dark purplish blue colour 靛藍色 —**indigo** *adj*

in·di·rect /ˌɪndəˋrɛkt; ˌɪndəˈrekt◂/ *adj* **1** not by the fastest, easiest, or straightest way 遲緩的; 費力的; 迂迴的: *They took an indirect route, avoiding the town centre.* 他們繞道而行, 避開了市中心。**2** not said in a clear direct way〔說話〕間接的, 不直截了當的: *It was an indirect way of asking me to leave.* 那是轉彎抹角地要我離開的方法。**3** the indirect result of an action is not caused directly by it, but by something else which that action caused 間接引致的: *The accident was an indirect result of the bus being late.* 這次事故是公共汽車晚點間接造成的。—opposite 反義詞 DIRECT[1] —**indirectly** *adv*: *Perhaps I was indirectly to blame for the misunderstanding.* 也許我應為這個誤解承擔間接責任。

indirect dis·course /ˌ... ˈ../ *n* [U] *AmE technical* INDIRECT SPEECH【美, 術語】間接引語

indirect ob·ject /ˌ... ˈ../ *n* [C] *technical* the second OBJECT[1] (6) of a verb in a sentence, which is the person or thing that the DIRECT OBJECT is given to, said to, made for etc. For example, in the sentence 'I asked him a question', the indirect object is 'him'.【術語】間接受詞, 間接賓語〈如 I asked him a question. 中的 him〉

indirect speech /ˌ... ˈ./ *BrE*【英】**indirect discourse** *AmE*【美】*n* [U] *technical* the style used to report what someone said without repeating their actual words. For example, in the sentence 'Julia said that she didn't want to go', the clause 'that she didn't want to go' is indirect speech. Her actual words were 'I don't want to go'.【術語】間接引述, 間接引語〔即不引用實際話語〕〈如 Julia said that she didn't want to go. 中 that she didn't want to go 為間接引語。Julia 實際上說是 I don't want to go.〉

indirect tax·a·tion /ˌ... ..ˈ../ *n* [U] a system of collecting taxes by adding an amount to the price of goods and services that people buy 間接課稅〔附加於商品或服務的稅〕

in·dis·cer·ni·ble /ˌɪndɪˋsɝnəbl; ˌɪndɪˈsɜːnəbəl◂/ *adj* very difficult to see, hear, or notice 難以看到的; 難以聽見的; 難以察覺的: *The path was almost indiscernible in the mist.* 小路在濃霧之中幾乎無法看清楚。

in·dis·ci·pline /ɪnˋdɪsəplɪn; ɪnˈdɪsəplən/ *n* [U] a lack of control with the result that people behave badly 缺乏約束, 無紀律: *Indiscipline among the troops eventually led to a riot.* 軍紀不嚴最終導致騷亂。—see also 另見 DISCIPLINE[1] (1)

in·dis·creet /ˌɪndɪˋskrit; ˌɪndɪˈskriːt◂/ *adj* careless about what you say or do, especially by talking about things which should be kept secret 言行失檢的; 輕率的, 不慎重的〔尤指泄露機密〕: *It was very indiscreet of Colin to tell them about our plan.* 科林跟他們談論我們的計劃, 太不謹慎了。—**indiscreetly** *adv*

in·dis·cre·tion /ˌɪndɪˋskrɛʃən; ˌɪndɪˈskreʃən/ *n* **1** [U] a lack of careful thought or good judgment in the things that you say or do〔說話或行為〕輕率, 不謹慎: *the startling indiscretion of her statement to the press* 她向媒體發表談話時令人吃驚的輕率 **2** [C] an action or remark that shows a lack of careful thought or good judgment 魯莽的言行, 輕率的言行 **3** [C] something you do that is morally or socially unacceptable 有失檢點的行為: *The indiscretions of his youth were not entirely forgotten.* 他年輕時行為不檢還沒有被完全遺忘。

in·dis·crim·i·nate /ˌɪndɪˋskrɪmənɪt; ˌɪndɪˈskrɪmənət◂/ *adj* **1** indiscriminate killing, violence, damage etc is done without any thought about who is harmed or what is damaged〔殺戮、暴力、破壞等〕不加區別的, 盲目隨意的, 不分青紅皂白的: *the indiscriminate slaughter of innocent civilians* 濫殺無辜平民 **2** not thinking carefully before you make a choice〔選擇〕任意的, 不假思索的 —**indiscriminately** *adv*

in·di·spen·sa·ble /ˌɪndɪˋspɛnsəbl; ˌɪndɪˈspensəbəl◂/ *adj* someone or something that is indispensable is so important or useful that it is impossible to manage without them 必需的, 不可或缺的: *a piece of equipment that modern divers regard as indispensable* 被現代潛水員視作不可或缺的一件裝備 —**indispensably** *adv* —**indispensability** /ˌɪndɪˌspɛnsəˋbɪlətɪ; ˌɪndɪspensəˈbɪləti/ *n* [U]

in·dis·posed /ˌɪndɪˋspozd; ˌɪndɪˈspəʊzd/ *adj* [not before noun 不用於名詞前] *formal*【正式】**1** ill and therefore unable to be present 有病而不能出席的: *Mrs Rawlins regrets that she is temporarily indisposed.* 羅林斯太太對自己臨時身體不適而不能出席表示遺憾。**2 indisposed to do sth** not willing to do something 不願意做某事

in·dis·po·si·tion /ˌɪndɪspəˋzɪʃən; ɪnˌdɪspəˈzɪʃən/ *n formal*【正式】**1** [C,U] a slight illness 小病, 微恙: *his wife's sudden indisposition* 他妻子突感不適 **2** [U] an unwilling attitude 不情願, 不樂意

in·dis·pu·ta·ble /ˌɪndɪˋspjutəbl; ˌɪndɪˈspjuːtəbəl/ *adj* an indisputable fact is so certain that it must be true 無可爭辯的, 不容置疑的: *The evidence was indisputable.* 這個證據不容置疑。—**indisputably** *adv*: *He was indisputably in the wrong.* 毫無疑問是他的錯。

in·dis·so·lu·ble /ˌɪndɪˋsɑljəbl; ˌɪndɪˈsɒljəbəl◂/ *adj formal* an indissoluble relationship cannot be destroyed【正式】〔關係〕牢不可破的: *an indissoluble union* 牢不可破的聯盟 —**indissolubly** *adv* —**indissolubility** /ˌɪndɪˌsɑljəˋbɪlətɪ; ˌɪndɪsɒljəˈbɪləti/ *n* [U]

in·dis·tinct /ˌɪndɪˋstɪŋkt; ˌɪndɪˈstɪŋkt◂/ *adj* an indistinct sound, image, or memory cannot be seen, heard, or remembered clearly〔聲音、影像〕不清楚的,〔記憶〕模糊的: *She muttered something indistinct.* 她含含糊糊地嘟噥了甚麼。—**indistinctly** *adv* —**indistinctness** *n* [U]

in·dis·tin·guish·a·ble /ˌɪndɪsˋtɪŋgwɪʃəbl; ˌɪndɪˈstɪŋgwɪʃəbəl/ *adj* things that are indistinguishable are so similar that you cannot see any difference between them 難以分辨的, 難以區分的: **[+from]** *an artificial material that is almost indistinguishable from real silk* 與真絲幾乎無法區分的人造材料 —**indistinguishably** *adv*

in·di·vid·u·al[1] /ˌɪndəˋvɪdʒuəl; ˌɪndəˈvɪdʒuəl◂/ *adj* **1** [only before noun 僅用於名詞前] considered separately from other people or things in the same group 單獨的, 個別

的: *Each individual leaf on the tree is different.* 樹上每片葉子都不相同。| *the needs of the individual customer* 每位顧客的需求 **2** [only before noun 僅用於名詞前] belonging to or intended for one person rather than a group 個人的, 供一個人的: *Everyone has their own individual opinions.* 每人都有各自的觀點。| *The children get far more individual attention in these small classes.* 在這些小班裡面, 孩子得到多得多的個別關注。| *individual portions of butter* 一人份的黃油 **3** an individual style, way of doing things etc is different from anyone else's; DISTINCTIVE〔風格、做事方式等〕獨特的, 與眾不同的: *a tennis player with a very individual style* 風格卓異的網球手 | *a very individual way of dressing* 非常個性化的衣着方式

1 **individual²** *n* [C] **1** one person, considered separately from the rest of the group or society that they live in 個人, 個體: *the rights of the individual* 個人權利 | *It is important to know the HIV test can vary from individual to individual.* 對人體免疫缺損病毒的檢測可能因人而異, 了解這一點很重要。**2** a person with thoughts, feelings, and ideas of their own 有自己的思想、感情和觀念的人: *With adequate support, any child will grow into a fully developed individual.* 有了適當的支持, 每個孩子都會充分成長為性格獨立的人。**3** *informal* a person of a particular kind, especially one who is unusual in some way【非正式】有某種特點的人〔尤指在某些方面與眾不同的人〕: *a strange-looking individual in a green jacket* 身穿綠色上衣、長相怪異的人

in·di·vid·u·al·is·m /ˌɪndəˋvɪdʒuəlˌɪzəm; ˌɪndɪˈvɪdʒuəlɪzəm/ *n* [U] **1** the belief that the rights and freedom of individual people are the most important rights in a society 個人主義〔視個人權利和自由至上的信仰〕: *capitalism, which encouraged competition and individualism* 鼓勵競爭、提倡個人主義的資本主義 **2** the behaviour or attitude of someone who does things in their own way without being influenced by other people 我行我素〔的行為或態度〕—**individualist** *adj*

in·di·vid·u·al·ist /ˌɪndəˋvɪdʒuəlɪst; ˌɪndɪˈvɪdʒuəlɪst/ *n* [C] someone who does things in their own way and has different opinions from most other people 按自身意願做事的人, 有自己獨特性的人: *a rebel and an individualist* 叛逆、我行我素的人 —**individualistic** /ˌɪndəˌvɪdʒuəlˋɪstɪk; ˌɪndɪvɪdʒuəˈlɪstɪk◂/ *adj* —**individualistically** /-klɪ; -kli/ *adv*

in·di·vid·u·al·i·ty /ˌɪndəˌvɪdʒuˋælətɪ; ˌɪndɪvɪdʒuˈælɪti/ *n* [U] the quality that makes someone or something different from all other things or people 個性; 特性: *a strict regime, that left little room for individuality* 幾乎不給個性留下任何空間的嚴厲政權

in·di·vid·u·al·ize also 又作 -ise *BrE*【英】/ˌɪndəˋvɪdʒuəlˌaɪz; ˌɪndɪˈvɪdʒuəlaɪz/ *v* [T] to make something different so that it fits the special needs of a particular person or place 使有個性, 使有特色〔以適應特定的人或地方的特殊需要〕: *an individualized learner program* 個性化的學習課程

in·di·vid·u·al·ly /ˌɪndəˋvɪdʒuəlɪ; ˌɪndɪˈvɪdʒuəli/ *adv* separately, not together in a group 分別地, 各自地: *The bridegroom thanked them all individually.* 新郎向大家一一道謝。| [sentence adverb 句子副詞] *Individually, they're nice kids, but in a group they can be a nightmare!* 這些孩子個個都很乖, 但要是聚在一起, 他們就可能成為混世魔王。

in·di·vid·u·ate /ˌɪndəˋvɪdʒuˌet; ˌɪndɪˈvɪdʒueɪt/ *v* **1** [T] to make someone or something clearly different from others of the same kind 使有區別, 使區別開來: *The characters are beautifully individuated in the play.* 劇中人物各具個性, 處理得極為得體。**2** [I] *AmE* to have an idea of yourself as an independent person, separate from other people【美】自覺是獨立的人, 個體化

in·di·vis·i·ble /ˌɪndəˋvɪzəbl̩; ˌɪndɪˈvɪzɪbəl◂/ *adj* something that is indivisible cannot be separated or divided into parts 分不開的, 不可分割的 —**indivisibly** *adv* —**indivisibility** /ˌɪndəˌvɪzəˋbɪlətɪ; ˌɪndɪvɪzɪˈbɪlɪti/ *n* [U]

Indo- /ɪndo; ɪndəʊ/ *prefix* **1** of India; Indian 印度的; 印度人的 **2** Indian and 印度和…的: *the Indo-Pakistani border* 印巴邊界

in·doc·tri·nate /ɪnˋdɑktrɪnˌet; ɪnˈdɒktrɪneɪt/ *v* [T] to train someone to accept a particular set of political or religious beliefs and not consider any others 向〔某人〕灌輸〔政治或宗教思想, 使其排斥其他思想〕: *People were indoctrinated not to question their leaders.* 人們被灌輸對領導人不得置疑的觀念。—**indoctrination** /ɪnˌdɑktrɪˋneʃən; ɪnˌdɒktrɪˈneɪʃən/ *n* [U]: *objective discussion, free from propaganda and indoctrination* 不受任何宣傳和思想灌輸影響的客觀討論

Indo-Eu·ro·pe·an /ˌ·· ··ˋ··◂/ *adj* the Indo-European group of languages includes English, French, Hindi, Russian, and most of the languages of Europe and N India 印歐語系的〔印歐語系包括英語、法語、印地語、俄語和多數歐洲和印度北部的語言〕

in·do·lent /ˋɪndələnt; ˈɪndələnt/ *adj formal* lazy【正式】懶惰的 —**indolently** *adv* —**indolence** *n* [U] *a life of luxury and indolence* 奢侈懶散的生活

in·dom·i·ta·ble /ɪnˋdɑmətəbl; ɪnˈdɒmɪtəbəl/ *adj* **indomitable spirit/courage etc** determination or courage that can never be defeated 不屈不撓的精神/勇氣等: *a woman of indomitable strength* 意志堅強的女人 —**indomitably** *adv*

in·door /ˋɪnˌdor; ˈɪndɔː/ *adj* [only before noun 僅用於名詞前] used or happening inside a building 在室內使用的, 戶內的: *an indoor swimming pool* 室內游泳池 | *indoor shoes* 室內穿的鞋 —opposite 反義詞 OUTDOOR

in·doors /ˋɪnˋdorz; ˌɪnˈdɔːz◂/ *adv* into or inside a building 在室內; 往室內: *Let's go indoors and have something to eat.* 我們進屋吃點東西。| *It rained all afternoon, so we had to stay indoors.* 雨整整下了一個下午, 我們只好呆在屋裡。—opposite 反義詞 OUTDOORS

in·dorse /ɪnˋdɔrs; ɪnˈdɔːs/ *v* another spelling of ENDORSE endorse 的另一種拼法

in·du·bi·ta·ble /ɪnˋdjubɪtəbl; ɪnˈdjuːbɪtəbəl/ *adj formal* definitely true without any possible doubt【正式】不容置疑的, 明確無誤的 —**indubitably** *adv*: *"Are you sure we can rely on you?" "Indubitably."* "你肯定我們能依賴你嗎?" "儘管放心好啦。"

in·duce /ɪnˋdjus; ɪnˈdjuːs/ *v* [T] **1** to make someone decide to do something, especially something that seems unwise 勸誘〔某人做某事, 尤指不好的事〕, 誘導: **induce sb to do sth** *Nothing would induce me to vote for him again.* 沒有甚麼能誘使我再投他的票了。| *What could have induced you to do such a ridiculous thing?* 到底是甚麼誘使你做出這麼荒謬可笑的事來? **2** to make a woman give birth to her baby, by giving her a special drug〔用藥物〕為〔產婦〕引產: *She had to be induced because the baby was four weeks late.* 她的孩子晚了四星期仍未出生, 因此要給她引產。**3** *formal* to cause a particular physical condition【正式】誘發〔某種身體反應〕: *This drug may induce drowsiness.* 這種藥可能會引起睡意。

in·duce·ment /ɪnˋdjusmənt; ɪnˈdjuːsmənt/ *n* [C,U] something such as money or a gift that you are offered to persuade you to do something 引誘物〔使某人做某事而贈送的金錢或禮物〕: **inducement to do sth** *They offered her a share in the business as an inducement to stay.* 他們把公司的股份送給她, 誘使她留下來。

in·duct /ɪnˋdʌkt; ɪnˈdʌkt/ *v* [T often passive 常用被動態] *formal*【正式】**1** [+into] to officially place someone, especially a priest, in their new job, rank, position etc in a special ceremony〔舉行儀式〕使〔牧師、神父等〕正式就職 **2** *AmE* to officially introduce someone into a group or organization, especially the army【美】正式吸收…為成員〔尤指入伍〕

in·duc·tee /ˌɪndʌkˋti; ˌɪndʌkˈtiː/ *n* [C] *AmE* someone who is being or has just been introduced into the army【美】剛應召入伍者

in·duc·tion /ɪnˋdʌkʃən; ɪnˈdʌkʃən/ *n* **1** [C,U] the introduction of someone into a new job, company, official position etc〔新工作、公司、官方職位等的〕入門: *an induction course* 入門課程 **2** [C] a ceremony in which someone is officially introduced into an official position or an organization 就職儀式; 入會儀式 **3** [C,U] the process of making a woman give birth to her baby by giving her a special drug〔藥物〕引產（術）**4** [U] *technical* the production of electricity in one object by another that already has electrical or MAGNETIC power【術語】電磁感應 **5** [U] *technical* a process of thought that uses known facts to produce general rules or principles【術語】歸納（法）—compare 比較 DEDUCTION (1)

induction coil /·ˈ·· ·/ *n* [C] *technical* a piece of electrical equipment that changes a low VOLTAGE to a higher one【術語】感應線圈〔用於增加電壓〕

in·duc·tive /ɪnˋdʌktɪv; ɪnˈdʌktɪv/ *adj technical*【術語】**1** using known facts to produce general principles 歸納的, 歸納法的 **2** connected with electrical or MAGNETIC induction 電感的; 磁感的

in·due /ɪnˋdju; ɪnˈdjuː/ *v* [T] another spelling of ENDUE endue 的另一種拼法

in·dulge /ɪnˋdʌldʒ; ɪnˈdʌldʒ/ *v* **1** [I,T] to let yourself do or have something that you enjoy, especially something that is considered bad for you（使）〔自己〕沉溺於, 沉湎於: **[+in]** *Most of us were too busy to indulge in heavy lunchtime drinking.* 我們大多數人都忙得不能在午飯時盡情飲酒。| *Eva had never been one to indulge in self pity.* 伊娃從不是那種沉湎於自憐自哀的人。| **indulge yourself** *I haven't had strawberries and cream for a long time, so I'm really going to indulge myself* (=eat a lot). 我好久沒吃奶油草莓了, 真要大吃一頓。| **indulge sth** *Ray has enough money to indulge his taste for expensive wines.* 雷有足夠的錢來盡情享受昂貴的葡萄酒。**2** [T] to let someone have or do whatever they want, even if it is bad for them 放縱, 縱容, 遷就: **indulge sb's every whim** *His mother pampered and spoiled him, indulging his every whim.* 他母親對他縱容嬌慣, 千依百順。

in·dul·gence /ɪnˋdʌldʒəns; ɪnˈdʌldʒəns/ *n* **1** [U] the habit of eating too much, drinking too much etc 放縱飲食 —see also 另見 SELF-INDULGENCE **2** [C] something that you do or have for pleasure, not because you need it 嗜好, 愛好: *An occasional glass of sherry was his only indulgence.* 偶爾喝一杯雪利酒是他唯一的嗜好。**3** [C,U] freedom from punishment by God, or a promise of this, which was sold by priests in the Middle Ages〔歐洲中世紀由神父出售的〕免罪, 赦免 **4** [U] *old use* permission【舊】允許, 許可

in·dul·gent /ɪnˋdʌldʒənt; ɪnˈdʌldʒənt/ *adj* willing to allow someone, especially a child, to do what they want, even if this is not good for them〔尤指對孩子〕溺愛的, 縱容的, 放縱的: *a camping trip paid for by their indulgent grandparents* 由溺愛孫輩的祖父母出資的野營旅行 —**indulgently** *adv*

1 **in·dus·tri·al** /ɪnˋdʌstrɪəl; ɪnˈdʌstriəl/ *adj* **1** connected with industry or the people working in it 工業的; 產業工人的: *industrial pollution* 工業污染 | *industrial output* 工業產量 | **industrial accident/injury** (=happening at work) 工業事故/工傷 **2** having many industries, or industries that are well developed 有很多工業的, 工業發達的: *an industrial nation* 工業國 **3** of the type used in industry 工業用的: *industrial detergents* 工業用洗滌劑 —compare 比較 INDUSTRIOUS —**industrially** *adv*

industrial ac·tion /·,··· ˈ··/ *n* [U] *BrE* a protest such as a STRIKE (=stopping work) used by workers in a disagreement with their employer【英】工業行動〈如罷工〉

industrial ar·chae·ol·o·gy /·,··· ··ˈ···/ *n* [U] the study of the history of old factories, machines etc 工業考古學〔研究早期工廠、機器的歷史等〕

industrial art /·,··· ˈ·/ *AmE n* [U] a subject taught in school about how to use tools, machinery etc【美】〔學校中教授怎樣使用工具、機器等的〕工藝課

industrial dis·pute /·,··· ·ˈ·/ *n* [C] a disagreement between a group of workers and their employer 勞資糾紛

industrial es·pi·o·nage /·,··· ˈ····/ *n* [U] attempts to steal secret information from another company in order to help your own company 企業諜報活動

industrial es·tate /·,··· ·ˈ·/ *BrE* a piece of land on the edge of a town planned as a place for factories and small businesses【英】〔圈劃在城市邊緣供建立工廠和小型企業用的〕工業區

in·dus·tri·al·is·m /ɪnˋdʌstrɪəl,ɪzəm; ɪnˈdʌstriəlɪzəm/ *n* [U] the system by which a society gets its wealth through industries and machinery 工業主義, 產業主義〔指主要依靠工業和機械獲得財富的體制〕

in·dus·tri·al·ist /ɪnˋdʌstrɪəlɪst; ɪnˈdʌstriəlɪst/ *n* [C] the owner or manager of a factory, industrial company etc 工業家, 實業家

in·dus·tri·al·ize also 又作 **-ise** *BrE*【英】/ɪnˋdʌstrɪəl,aɪz; ɪnˈdʌstriəlaɪz/ *v* [I, T] if a country or place is industrialized or if it industrializes, it develops a lot of industry（使）工業化

in·dus·tri·a·lized /ɪnˋdʌstrɪə,laɪzd; ɪnˈdʌstriəlaɪzd/ *adj* having a lot of factories, mines, industrial companies etc（已實現）工業化的: *the industrialized nations of the West* 西方工業化國家

industrial re·la·tions /·,··· ·ˈ··/ *n* [plural] the relationship between workers and employers 勞資關係

industrial rev·o·lu·tion /·,··· ··ˈ··/ *n* [singular] the period, especially in the 18th and 19th centuries in Europe, when machines were invented and the first factories were established〔尤指歐洲在 18、19 世紀發明機器、建立第一批工廠的〕工業革命, 產業革命

industrial tri·bu·nal /·,··· ·ˈ··/ *n* [C] a type of court in Britain to which individual workers can make complaints against their employers〔英國的〕勞資關係審裁處, 行業糾紛審理委員會

in·dus·tri·ous /ɪnˋdʌstrɪəs; ɪnˈdʌstriəs/ *adj* tending to work hard 勤勞的, 勤奮的 —**industriously** *adv* —**industriousness** *n* [U] —compare 比較 INDUSTRIAL

in·dus·try /ˋɪndəstrɪ; ˈɪndəstri/ *n* **1** [U] the production of goods, especially in factories 工業; 製造業: *a decline in manufacturing industry* 製造業的衰退 | **heavy industry** (=the production of large goods such as aircraft, cars etc)〔生產飛機、汽車等大型產品的〕重工業 | **light industry** (=the production of small goods)〔生產小型產品的〕輕工業 **2** [singular] the people and organizations that work in industry〔工業的〕從業人員; 產業組織: *an agreement that will be welcomed by both sides of industry* (=employers and workers) 將受到勞資雙方歡迎的協定 **3** [C] a particular type of industry, trade, or service〔某一工業、貿易或服務的〕行業: *the coal industry* 煤炭工業 | *Italy's thriving tourist industry* 蓬勃發展的意大利旅遊業 | **service industries** (=businesses that provide services, such as hotels and banks) 服務業 **4** [singular] an area of work which is not really an industry but which has grown too large 行業〔比喻為工業, 指其規模過大〕: *another book from the Shakespeare industry* 莎士比亞研究的又一本專著

-ine /aɪn; aɪn/ *suffix formal or technical*【正式或術語】**1** of or concerning something 具有…屬性的: *equine* (=of horses) 馬的, 馬科的 **2** made of or like something 由…製成的, …狀的: *crystalline* 結晶狀的

i·ne·bri·ate /ɪnˋibrɪɪt; ɪˈniːbriɪt/ *n* [C] *old-fashioned* someone who is often drunk【過時】酒鬼, 酗酒者 —**inebriate** *adj*

i·ne·bri·a·ted /ɪnˋibrɪ,etɪd; ɪˈniːbrieɪtɪd/ *adj formal*【正式】drunk 喝醉的 —**inebriation** /ɪn,ibrɪˋeʃən; ɪ,niːbriˈeɪʃən/ *n* [U]

in·ed·i·ble /ɪnˋɛdəbl; ɪnˈedəbəl/ *adj* not suitable for eating 不宜食用的: *The food was so burnt as to be inedible.* 食物焦得太厲害, 不能吃了。

in·ed·u·ca·ble /ɪnˋɛdʒəkəbl; ɪnˈedjʊkəbəl/ *adj formal* impossible or very difficult to educate【正式】難以教育

的, 不可教育的

in·ef·fa·ble /ɪnˋɛfəbḷ; ɪn'efəbəl/ *adj formal* too great or beautiful to be described in words【正式】〔好或美得〕難以名狀的, 不可言喻的: *ineffable joy* 難以形容的喜悦 —**ineffably** *adv* —**ineffability** /ɪn͵ɛfəˋbɪlətɪ; ɪn͵efə'bɪlɨti/ *n* [U]

in·ef·fec·tive /͵ɪnəˋfɛktɪv; ͵ɪnɨ'fektɪv◂/ *adj* something that is ineffective does not achieve what it is intended to achieve 無效果的, 不起作用的, 不奏效的: *The various treatments for AIDS have so far proved ineffective.* 愛滋病的種種療法迄今都不見效果。—**ineffectively** *adv* —**ineffectiveness** *n* [U]

in·ef·fec·tu·al /͵ɪnəˋfɛktʃuəl; ͵ɪnɨ'fektʃuəl◂/ *adj* not having the ability, confidence, or personal authority to get things done 無能力的, 無信心的, 無威望的: *an ineffectual leader* 無能的領導人 | *an ineffectual attempt* 無效的嘗試 —**ineffectually** *adv*

in·ef·fi·cient /͵ɪnəˋfɪʃənt; ͵ɪnɨ'fɪʃənt◂/ *adj* a worker, organization, or system that is inefficient does not work well and wastes time, money, or energy 效率差的; 不稱職的: *an inefficient heating* system 效果差的供暖系統 | *Local government was inefficient and corrupt.* 地方政府效率低下, 腐敗成風。—**inefficiently** *adv* —**inefficiency** *n* [C,U] *the inefficiency of the postal service* 郵政服務的低效率

in·el·e·gant /ɪnˋɛləgənt; ɪn'elɪgənt/ *adj* not graceful 不雅的, 不精緻的: *an inelegant belly-flop into the water* 〔指跳水時〕胸腹着水而入的不雅動作 —**inelegantly** *adv* —**inelegance** *n* [U]

in·el·i·gi·ble /ɪnˋɛlɪdʒəbḷ; ɪn'elɨdʒɨbəl/ *adj* not being able to have or do something 無資格〔擁有或做某事〕的, 不合格的: [+for] *Temporary workers are ineligible for the staff discount scheme.* 臨時工沒有資格參加員工折扣計劃。| **ineligible to do sth** *ineligible to vote in the election* 無資格參加選舉投票 —**ineligibility** /͵ɪnɛlɪdʒəˋbɪlətɪ; ɪn͵elɨdʒɨ'bɪlɨti/ *n* [U]

in·e·luc·ta·ble /͵ɪnɪˋlʌktəbḷ; ͵ɪnɪ'lʌktəbəl◂/ *adj literary* impossible to escape from; unavoidable【文】難以逃脱的, 不可避免的 —**ineluctably** *adv*

in·ept /ɪnˋɛpt; ɪ'nept/ *adj* having no skill 沒有技能的: *an inept driver* 技術拙劣的司機 | *Blake was intellectually able but politically inept.* 布萊克很聰慧, 但對政治卻一竅不通。| *He made some inept sexist comment.* 他說了一些不恰當的、帶有性別歧視的話。—**ineptly** *adv* —**ineptitude, ineptness** *n* [U] —compare 比較 INAPT

in·e·qual·i·ty /͵ɪnɪˋkwɑlətɪ; ͵ɪnɪ'kwɒlɨti/ *n plural* **inequalities** [C,U] an unfair situation, in which some groups in society have less money, influence, or opportunity than others〔社會上的〕不平等: *the inequalities still suffered by disabled people* 殘疾人仍然遭受的不平等待遇

in·eq·ui·ta·ble /ɪnˋɛkwɪtəbḷ; ɪn'ekwɨtəbəl/ *adj formal* not equally fair to everyone; UNJUST【正式】不公平的, 不平等的: *an inequitable financial settlement after the divorce* 離婚後不公正的財產處理 —**inequitably** *adv*

in·eq·ui·ty /ɪnˋɛkwɪtɪ; ɪn'ekwɨti/ *n plural* **inequities** [C, U] *formal* unfairness, or something that is unfair【正式】不公正, 偏私; 不平之事: *gross inequities of income and wealth* 收入與財富的嚴重不公平

in·e·rad·i·ca·ble /͵ɪnɪˋrædɪkəbḷ; ͵ɪnɪ'rædɪkəbəl◂/ *adj formal* an attitude or quality of character that is ineradicable can never be completely removed【正式】〔觀點、性格等〕難以根除的, 根深蒂固的 —**ineradicably** *adv*

in·ert /ɪnˋɝt; ɪ'nɜːt/ *adj* **1** not having the strength or power to move 無力活動的: *an inert form lying on the bed* 躺在牀上一動不動的人形 **2** very slow and unwilling to take any action 呆滯的, 遲緩的: *Congress remained inert and skeptical about the proposal.* 國會對這項提案仍然沒有動作並持懷疑態度。**3** *technical* not producing a chemical reaction when combined with other substances【術語】惰性的, 不活潑的: *inert gases* 惰性氣體 —**inertly** *adv* —**inertness** *n* [U]

in·er·tia /ɪˋnɝʃə; ɪ'nɜːʃə/ *n* [U] **1** a tendency for a situation to stay unchanged for a long time〔長期〕維持現狀: *The government's wish to avoid conflict resulted in political inertia.* 政府意欲避免衝突, 結果導致政治上的遲鈍。**2** lack of energy and a feeling that you do not want to do anything 懶惰, 惰性 **3** *technical* the force that keeps an object in the same position or state of movement until it is moved or stopped by another force【術語】慣性 —**inertial** *adj*

inertia reel seat·belt /·͵·· · ˈ··/ *n* [C] a type of SEAT BELT that will unwind if it is pulled normally but not if it is pulled suddenly〔汽車的〕慣性捲筒式安全帶〔突然受力時會自動繃緊〕

inertia sel·ling /·͵·· ˈ··/ *n* [U] *especially BrE* the practice of sending goods to people who have not asked for them, and then demanding payment if the goods are not returned【尤英】慣性銷售〔指將商品送給沒有要求購買的人。若商品沒有退還, 即要求付款〕

in·es·ca·pa·ble /͵ɪnəˋskepəbḷ; ͵ɪnɪ'skeɪpəbəl◂/ *adj* impossible to avoid 不可避免的: *The inescapable conclusion is that Pamela stole the money.* 不可避免的結論是帕米拉偷了錢。—**inescapably** *adv*

in·es·sen·tial /͵ɪnəˋsɛnʃəl; ͵ɪnɨ'senʃəl◂/ *adj formal* not needed; unnecessary【正式】不需要的, 非必需的: *He lived very simply with few inessential items in his apartment.* 他生活非常儉樸, 家裡幾乎沒有不必要的東西。—**inessentials** *n* [plural]

in·es·ti·ma·ble /ɪnˋɛstəməbḷ; ɪn'estɨməbəl/ *adj formal* too much or too great to be calculated【正式】〔由於太多或太大而〕難以計算的, 無法估計的: *The legal case has done inestimable damage to his reputation.* 這樁案子給他的名譽造成了難以估量的損害。—**inestimably** *adv*

in·ev·i·ta·ble /ɪnˋɛvətəbḷ; ɪ'nevɨtəbəl/ *adj* **1** certain to happen and impossible to avoid 必然發生的, 難以避免的: *A further escalation of the crisis now seems inevitable.* 危機的進一步升級現在看來已不可避免。**2** **the inevitable** a situation that is certain to happen 不可避免的事情: *One day the inevitable happened and I was caught sneaking in late.* 有一天, 不可避免的事情發生了: 我遲到了, 想偷偷溜進去時被人發現了。**3** [only before noun 僅用於名詞前] happening so regularly that you know it will happen again 照例必有的: *the inevitable bouts of travel sickness on school trips* 學校旅行中必然出現的旅途噁心嘔吐 —**inevitability** /ɪ͵nɛvətəˋbɪlətɪ; ɪ͵nevɨtə'bɪlɨti/ *n* [U] W3

in·ev·i·ta·bly /ɪnˋɛvətəblɪ; ɪn'evɨtəbli/ *adv* as was certain to happen and could not be prevented 必然地, 不可避免地: *Inevitably, we had overlooked a few points.* 不可避免地, 我們忽略了一些方面。W3

in·ex·act /͵ɪnɪgˋzækt; ͵ɪnɪg'zækt◂/ *adj* not exact 不精確的, 不準確的: *Sociology is an inexact science.* 社會學不是一門精確的科學。—**inexactness** *n* [U]

in·ex·cu·sa·ble /͵ɪnɪkˋskjuzəbḷ; ͵ɪnɪk'skjuːzəbəl◂/ *adj* inexcusable behaviour is too bad to be excused 不可原諒的, 不可寬恕的: *Such rudeness is inexcusable!* 如此莽撞無禮是不可原諒的! —**inexcusably** *adv*

in·ex·haus·ti·ble /͵ɪnɪgˋzɔstəbḷ; ͵ɪnɪg'zɔːstɨbəl◂/ *adj* existing in such large amounts that it can never be finished or used up 無窮無盡的, 用不完的: *a man of inexhaustible energy* 精力旺盛的人 | *an inexhaustible supply of firewood* 用之不竭的柴火 —**inexhaustibly** *adv*

in·ex·o·ra·ble /ɪnˋɛksərəbḷ; ɪn'eksərəbəl/ *adj formal* an inexorable process cannot be stopped【正式】不可阻擋的, 不可更改的: *the inexorable decline of Britain's manufacturing industry* 英國製造業無可挽回的衰敗 —**inexorably** *adv*: *The story moves inexorably towards its tragic conclusion.* 這個故事勢所必然地向悲劇結局發展。—**inexorability** /ɪn͵ɛksərəˋbɪlətɪ; ɪn͵eksərə'bɪlɨti/ *n* [U]

in·ex·pe·di·ent /͵ɪnɪkˋspidɪənt; ͵ɪnɪk'spiːdiənt◂/ *adj formal* a plan or action that is inexpedient is not useful because it is not likely to achieve the result you want【正式】〔計劃或行動〕不明智的〔因為不大可能奏效〕, 沒用的 —**inexpedience, inexpediency** *n* [U]

in·ex·pen·sive /ˌɪnɪkˋspɛnsɪv; ˌɪnɪk'spensɪv◂/ *adj* cheap and of good quality for the price you pay 價錢公道的, 廉價的: *clean and inexpensive accommodation in the centre of town* 市中心整潔價廉的住房 —**inexpensively** *adv* —**inexpensiveness** *n* [U]

in·ex·pe·ri·ence /ˌɪnɪkˋspɪrɪəns; ˌɪnɪk'spɪəriəns/ *n* [U] lack of experience 缺乏經驗: *youthful inexperience* 少不更事

in·ex·pe·ri·enced /ˌɪnɪkˋspɪrɪənst; ˌɪnɪk'spɪəriənst◂/ *adj* not having had much experience 經驗不足的, 不熟練的: *Lyn is still too young and inexperienced to go abroad on her own.* 琳少不更事, 不能一個人去國外。

in·ex·pert /ˌɪnɪksˋpɜt; ɪn'ekspɜːt/ *adj* not good at doing something〔對某事〕不熟練的, 不內行的 —**inexpertly** *adv* —**inexpertness** *n* [U]

in·ex·plic·a·ble /ˌɪnˋɛksplɪkəbl̩; ˌɪnɪk'splɪkəbəl◂/ *adj* too unusual or strange to be explained or understood〔由於不尋常或太奇怪而〕無法解釋的; 費解的: *the inexplicable disappearance of a young woman* 一名年輕女子的離奇失蹤 —**inexplicably** *adv* —**inexplicability** /ɪnˌɛksplɪkəˋbɪlətɪ; ˌɪnɪksplɪkə'bɪləti/ *n* [U]

in·ex·pres·si·ble /ˌɪnɪkˋsprɛsəbl̩; ˌɪnɪk'spresəbəl◂/ *adj* **inexpressible joy/sorrow/relief etc** a feeling or condition that is too strong to be described in words 難以言傳的喜悅/悲傷/欣慰等 —**inexpressibly** *adv*: *He looked inexpressibly sad.* 他看來有說不出的悲傷。

in·ex·press·ive /ˌɪnɪkˋsprɛsɪv; ˌɪnɪk'spresɪv◂/ *adj* a face that is inexpressive shows no emotion at all 無表情的

in·ex·tin·guish·a·ble /ˌɪnɪkˋstɪŋgwɪʃəbl̩; ˌɪnɪk'stɪŋgwɪʃəbəl◂/ *adj literary*【文】**inextinguishable hope/love/spirit etc** hope etc that is so strong that it cannot be destroyed 不可遏制的希望/愛情/精神等 —**inextinguishably** *adv*

in ex·tre·mis /ˌɪn ɪkˋstrimɪs; ˌɪn ɪk'striːmɪs/ *adv Latin formal*【拉丁, 正式】**1** in a very difficult and urgent situation when very strong action is needed 在危急關頭〔需要採取強烈行動〕**2** at the moment of death 在彌留之際

in·ex·tric·a·ble /ˌɪnˋɛkstrɪkəbl̩; ˌɪnɪk'strɪkəbəl◂/ *adj formal* two or more things that are inextricable cannot be separated from each other【正式】分不開的, 解不開的: *Character development is an inextricable part of the novel.* 人物性格發展是這部小說不可分割的一部分。

in·ex·tric·a·bly /ˌɪnˋɛkstrɪkəblɪ; ˌɪnɪk'strɪkəbli/ *adv* **be inextricably linked/connected/mixed etc** if two or more things are inextricably linked etc, they are very closely connected and cannot be separated 緊密相連地, 密不可分地: *Poor health and bad housing conditions are inextricably linked.* 健康不佳與住房條件惡劣有密切關係。

in·fal·li·ble /ɪnˋfæləbl̩; ɪn'fæləbəl/ *adj* **1** always right and never making mistakes 永遠正確的, 從不犯錯誤的: *I'm only human, I'm not infallible.* 我只是平常人, 不可能不犯錯誤。| *an infallible memory* 絕對可靠的記憶 **2** something that is infallible always works or has the intended effect〔事物〕絕對有效的: *He had an infallible cure for a hangover.* 他有對付宿醉絕對靈驗的良方。—**infallibly** *adv* —**infallibility** /ɪnˌfæləˋbɪlətɪ; ɪnˌfælə'bɪləti/ *n* [U]

in·fa·mous /ˋɪnfəməs; 'ɪnfəməs/ *adj* **1** well known for being bad or morally evil 聲名狼藉的, 臭名昭著的: *an infamous traitor* 臭名昭著的叛徒 | *plans to deal with Los Angeles' infamous smog* 治理惡名遠播的洛杉磯煙霧的計劃 —see 見 FAMOUS (USAGE) **2** *literary* evil【文】邪惡的: *infamous behaviour* 無恥的行為 —**infamously** *adv*

in·fa·my /ˋɪnfəmɪ; 'ɪnfəmi/ *n* **1** [U] the state of being evil or well known for evil things 惡名昭彰, 聲名狼藉, 醜惡 **2** [C usually plural 一般用複數] an evil action 醜行, 惡行

in·fan·cy /ˋɪnfənsɪ; 'ɪnfənsi/ *n* [singular, U] **1** the period of a child's life before it can walk or talk 嬰兒期: *She had five children, but four of them died in infancy.* 她生了五個孩子, 但四個死於襁褓之中。**2 in its infancy** something that is in its infancy is just starting to be developed 在初期, 在早期: *Agricultural research is still in its infancy in parts of the Third World.* 農業研究在第三世界的一些地區才剛剛起步。

in·fant¹ /ˋɪnfənt; 'ɪnfənt/ *n* [C] **1** *literary or technical* a very young child or baby【文或術語】幼兒, 嬰兒: *The infant, cradled in Miriam's arms, began to cry.* 米麗亞姆抱在懷中的嬰兒開始哭叫。—see picture at 參見 CHILD 圖 **2 infants** [plural] children in school in Britain between the ages of four and eight〔英國學校裡四至八歲的〕學童 **3 infant school/teacher/class etc** a school etc for children aged between four and eight in Britain〔英國為四至八歲兒童設立的〕兒童學校/教師/班級等

infant² *adj* [only before noun 僅用於名詞前] an infant company, organization etc has just started to exist or be developed〔公司、組織等〕剛成立的, 初創的: *The plan was designed to protect infant industries in Mexico.* 這個計劃是為保護墨西哥的幼稚產業而設計的。

in·fan·ti·cide /ɪnˋfæntəˌsaɪd; ɪn'fæntəsaɪd/ *n* [U] *technical* the crime of killing a child【術語】殺嬰罪

in·fan·tile /ˋɪnfənˌtaɪl; 'ɪnfəntaɪl/ *adj* **1** infantile behaviour seems silly in an adult because it is typical of a child 幼稚的, 孩子氣的: *I was sick of his infantile jokes.* 我很討厭他那些幼稚的笑話。**2** *technical* affecting very young children【術語】嬰幼兒患的: *infantile colic* 嬰兒腸絞痛

infantile pa·ral·y·sis /ˌ··· ·'···/ *n* [U] *old-fashioned* POLIO【過時】脊髓灰質炎, 小兒麻痺症

infant mor·tal·i·ty rate /ˌ·· ·'··· ·/ written abbreviation 縮寫為 **IMR** *n* [C] the number of deaths of babies under one year old, expressed as the number out of each 1,000 babies born alive in a year〔每年每 1,000 名一歲以下嬰兒的〕嬰兒死亡率

infant prod·i·gy /ˌ·· '···/ *n* [C] a child with an extremely high level of ability in music, art, mathematics etc〔極富音樂、藝術、數學等天賦的〕神童: *Mozart, the most famous infant prodigy of all* 名冠天下的神童莫扎特

in·fan·try /ˋɪnfəntrɪ; 'ɪnfəntri/ *n* [U] soldiers who fight on foot 步兵(部隊) —compare 比較 CAVALRY

in·fan·try·man /ˋɪnfəntrɪmən; 'ɪnfəntrimən/ *n plural* **infantrymen** /-mən; -mən/ [C] a soldier who fights on foot 步兵

in·fat·u·at·ed /ɪnˋfætʃʊˌetɪd; ɪn'fætʃueɪtəd/ *adj* having unreasonably strong feelings of love, but only for a short time and especially for someone that you do not know very well〔尤指短時間, 對不十分了解的人〕迷戀的, 痴心的: **[+with]** *John had become infatuated with the French teacher.* 約翰迷戀上了法語老師。

in·fat·u·a·tion /ɪnˌfætʃʊˋeʃən; ɪnˌfætʃu'eɪʃən/ *n* [C,U] unreasonably strong feelings of love that you only have for a short time, especially for someone that you do not know very well 迷戀, 痴心〔尤指短時間, 對不十分了解的人〕: *As I thought, it was another passing infatuation.* 正如我所料想的, 那不過是另一次轉瞬即逝的迷戀。

in·fect /ɪnˋfɛkt; ɪn'fekt/ *v* [T] **1** to give someone a disease 傳染〔疾病給人〕: *People with the virus may feel perfectly well, but they can still infect others.* 帶有這種病毒的人可能毫無病徵, 卻仍可能傳染他人。**2** to put something that spreads disease into food, water, the air etc〔以病菌等〕污染〔食物、水、空氣等〕**3** if your excitement, eagerness etc infects other people, it makes them begin to feel the same way〔情緒等〕感染〔別人〕, 使〔人〕受影響: *Lucy's enthusiasm soon infected the rest of the class.* 露西的熱情很快就感染了班裡的其他人。

in·fect·ed /ɪnˋfɛktɪd; ɪn'fektəd/ *adj* **1** a part of your body or a wound that is infected, has harmful BACTERIA in it which prevent it from healing (HEAL (1))〔身體或傷口〕受到〔細菌〕感染的: *It was only a small cut, but it be-*

came infected. 傷口雖然很小，但還是感染了。**2** food, water etc that is infected contains BACTERIA that spread disease〔食品、水等〕受到細菌污染的

3 **in·fec·tion** /ɪn`fɛkʃən; ɪn'fekʃən/ *n* [C,U] **1** a disease caused by BACTERIA or a VIRUS (1) that affects a particular part of your body〔由細菌或病毒造成對身體某部位的〕感染: *You ought to get some antibiotics for that ear infection.* 你的耳朵感染應該用些抗生素。**2** the act or result of infecting someone 傳染; 傳染病: *Always sterilize the needle to prevent infection.* 注射用針每次都要消毒，以防傳染。

in·fec·tious /ɪn`fɛkʃəs; ɪn'fekʃəs/ *adj* **1** an infectious illness can be passed from one person to another, especially through the air you breathe〔指疾病〕傳染的〔尤指通過空氣〕, 傳染性的: **highly infectious** *There seems to be a highly infectious type of flu going around.* 似乎有一種傳染性極強的流感在流行。**2** someone who is infectious has an illness and could pass it to other people〔人〕患有傳染病並能傳染他人的 **3** infectious feelings or laughter spread quickly from person to another〔情感、笑聲等〕極富感染力的: *Her giggles were infectious and soon we were all laughing.* 她咯咯的笑聲極富感染力，我們很快都笑了起來。—**infectiously** *adv* —**infectiousness** *n* [U]

in·fer /ɪn`fɝ; ɪn'fɜː/ *v* **inferred, inferring** [T] to form an opinion that something is probably true because of other information that you already know〔根據其他資料〕推斷, 推定: **infer sth from** *facts that can be inferred from archaeological data* 可根據考古資料推斷的事實 | **infer that** *It would be wrong to infer that people who are overweight are just greedy.* 根據身體肥胖就斷定別人貪吃是錯誤的。

USAGE NOTE 用法說明: INFER

WORD CHOICE 詞語辨析: **infer, imply**

In formal English the speaker or writer **implies** something, and the listener or reader **infers** it. 在正式英語中，講話者或作者暗示某物用imply，而聽話人或讀者進行推斷則是infer: *His report implied* (=suggested indirectly) *that the building was unsafe.* 他在報告中暗示這幢大樓不安全。*I inferred from his report that the building was unsafe* means that this is what I thought the report meant. 我從他的報告中推斷出這幢大樓不安全，這表示我認為這就是他報告的本意。

Infer is now often used to mean **imply** but some people think that this is not correct. 現在infer常被用來表達imply的意思，但有人認為這種用法不正確: *Are you inferring I'm drunk?* (=are you trying to tell me I'm drunk?) 你是說我喝醉了？

in·fer·ence /`ɪnfərəns; 'ɪnfərəns/ *n* **1** [C] something that you think is true, based on information that you already know 推論, 推斷的結果: **draw inferences** *What inferences have you drawn from this evidence?* 你從這個證據中得出了甚麼推論？**2** [U] the act of inferring something 推理, 推斷: **by inference** *measures directed against the enemies of National Socialism, including by inference all radicals and communists* 針對國家社會主義的敵人——包括類推的一切激進分子和共產黨人——的措施 —**inferential** /ˌɪnfə`rɛnʃəl; ˌɪnfə'renʃəl◂/ *adj*: *inferential evidence* 推論性證據 —**inferentially** *adv*

in·fe·ri·or¹ /ɪn`fɪrɪɚ; ɪn'fɪəriə/ *adj* **1** not good, or less good in quality, value, or skill than someone or something else〔質量、價值、技能等〕差的, 次的: *I felt very inferior among all those academics.* 與那些大學教師在一起，我自慚形穢。| *Pay less, and you get an inferior product.* 便宜沒好貨。| [+to] *This machine is technically inferior to Western models.* 這台機器在技術上不如西方國家的型號。**2** *formal* lower in rank【正式】低級別的, 下級的: *an inferior court of law* 初級法院; 下級法院 —compare 比較 SUPERIOR¹ —**inferiority** /ɪnˌfɪrɪ`ɑrətɪ; ɪnˌfɪəri'ɒrɪ̈ti/ *n* [U]

inferior² *n* [C] someone who has a lower position or rank than you in an organization 下級, 下屬, 部下 —compare 比較 SUPERIOR²

inferiority com·plex /···'·· ˌ··/ *n* [C] a continuous worrying feeling that you are much less important, clever etc than other people 自卑情結; 自卑感

in·fer·nal /ɪn`fɝnl; ɪn'fɜːnl/ *adj* **1** [only before noun 僅用於名詞前] *old-fashioned* used to express anger or annoyance about something【過時】〔用於表示憤怒或煩惱〕可惡的, 惱人的: *I wish the children would stop that infernal noise.* 我真希望孩子們別再瞎聒噪。**2** *literary* connected with HELL【文】陰間的; 地獄的: *the infernal powers of darkness* 地獄中的魔鬼 —**infernally** *adv*

in·fer·no /ɪn`fɝno; ɪn'fɜːnəʊ/ *n* [C] *literary* an extremely large and dangerous fire【文】熊熊烈火, 火海: **raging inferno** (=an extremely violent fire) 極端猛烈的大火 *Within minutes the oilrig had become a raging inferno.* 只幾分鐘工夫，石油鑽塔便成了一片火海。

in·fer·tile /ɪn`fɝtḷ; ɪn'fɜːtaɪl/ *adj* **1** infertile land or soil is not good enough to grow plants in〔土地〕不肥沃的, 貧瘠的, 不毛的 **2** an infertile person or animal cannot have babies 不能生育的, 無生育能力的 —**infertility** /ˌɪnfɚ`tɪlətɪ; ˌɪnfə'tɪlɪ̈ti/ *n* [U]

in·fest /ɪn`fɛst; ɪn'fest/ *v* [T] if insects, rats etc infest a place, they appear in large numbers and usually cause damage〔昆蟲、老鼠等〕成羣侵擾〔一般造成破壞〕, 橫行: [+with] *hair infested with lice* 頭髮裡生滿虱子 | *shark-infested waters* 大批鯊魚出沒的水域 —**infestation** /ˌɪnfɛs`teʃən; ˌɪnfe'steɪʃən/ *n* [C,U] *an infestation of cockroaches* 蟑螂橫行

in·fi·del /`ɪnfədḷ; 'ɪnfɪ̈dəl/ *n* [C] *old use* an insulting word for someone who does not believe what you consider to be the true religion【舊】異教徒, 不信奉正統宗教者〔冒犯用詞〕

in·fi·del·i·ty /ˌɪnfə`dɛlətɪ; ˌɪnfɪ̈'delɪ̈ti/ *n* [C,U] an act of being unfaithful to your wife, husband etc by having sex with someone else〔對丈夫或妻子的〕不貞行為: *Paul sometimes suspected her of infidelity.* 保羅有時懷疑她不貞。

in·field /`ɪnˌfild; 'ɪnfiːld/ *n* [singular] **1** the part of a CRICKET (2) field nearest to the player who hits the ball〔板球場的〕內場 **2** the part of a BASEBALL field inside the four bases〔棒球場的〕內場, 內野 —see picture on page A22 參見A22頁圖 **3** the group of players in the CRICKET (2) or BASEBALL infield〔板球的〕全體內場員,〔棒球的〕全體內野手 —compare 比較 OUTFIELD —**infielder** *n* [C]

in·fight·ing /`ɪnˌfaɪtɪŋ; 'ɪnfaɪtɪŋ/ *n* [U] unfriendly competition and disagreement between members of the same group or organization 內部爭鬥, 內訌: *political infighting* 政治內訌

in·fil·trate /ɪn`fɪltret; 'ɪnfɪltreɪt/ *v* **1** [I always+adv/prep, T] to secretly join an organization or enter a place in order to find out information about them or harm them〔祕密地〕加入〔某組織〕, 進入〔某地方, 以刺探情報或進行破壞〕: *Police attempts to infiltrate neo-Nazi groups were largely unsuccessful.* 警方滲透入新納粹集團的企圖基本上不成功。| [+into] *Enemy forces have been infiltrating into our territory.* 敵軍一直在偷偷向我國境內滲透。**2** [+into] to secretly introduce someone or something into an organization or place〔祕密地〕派人進入〔某組織或地方〕, 使滲透: *plans to infiltrate sabotage agents into the UK* 派破壞分子滲入英國的計劃 —**infiltrator** *n* [C] —**infiltration** /ˌɪnfɪl`treʃən; ˌɪnfɪl'treɪʃən/ *n* [U]

in·fi·nite /`ɪnfənɪt; 'ɪnfɪ̈nɪ̈t/ *adj* **1** very great 極大的: *Hilary takes infinite care over her work.* 希拉里對待工作極為謹慎。**2** without limits in space or time〔空間或時間〕無限的, 無窮無盡的: *The universe is infinite.* 宇宙是無窮無盡的。—compare 比較 INFINITE (1), NONFINITE (2)

I

in·fi·nite·ly /ˈɪnfənɪtlɪ; ˈɪnfɪ̣nɪ̣tli/ *adv* [+adj/adv] very much 極多地: *Living in the country is infinitely preferable to living in London.* 住在鄉下比住在倫敦要好千百倍。

in·fin·i·tes·i·mal /ˌɪnfɪnəˋtɛsəml̩; ˌɪnfɪnɪ̣ˈtesɪ̣məl◂/ *adj* extremely small 極微小的: *infinitesimal changes in temperature* 氣温極微小的變化 —**infinitesimally** *adv*

in·fin·i·tive /ɪnˋfɪnətɪv; ɪnˈfɪnɪ̣tɪv/ *n* [C] *technical* the basic form of a verb, such as 'be', 'make' or 'go', usually used with 'to' in the form 'to be', 'to make', 'to go' etc【術語】〔動詞〕原形, 不定式〈如 be, make 或 go, 一般帶 to, 成為 to be, to make, to go 等〉—see also 另見 SPLIT INFINITIVE

in·fin·i·tude /ɪnˋfɪnəˌtjud; ɪnˈfɪnɪ̣tjuːd/ *n* [singular, U] *formal* a number or amount without limit; INFINITY【正式】〔數目或數量〕無限, 無窮; 無限大: *the vast infinitude of space* 廣闊無垠的太空

in·fin·i·ty /ɪnˋfɪnətɪ; ɪnˈfɪnɪ̣ti/ *n* **1** [U] a space or distance without limits or an end 無垠的空間, 無窮的距離: *The universe stretches away into infinity.* 宇宙無邊無際。**2** [singular] a number that is too large to be calculated 無窮大: **an infinity of** *An infinity of interpretations have been put on the novel.* 對這部小說進行了無窮無盡的解釋。

in·firm /ɪnˋfɝm; ɪnˈfɜːm/ *adj* **1** weak or ill, especially because you are old〔尤指由於年邁而〕體弱多病的: *Her grandmother is now old and infirm.* 她的祖母如今年邁體弱。**2 the infirm** all the people who are weak or ill 體弱多病者

in·fir·ma·ry /ɪnˋfɝmərɪ; ɪnˈfɜːməri/ *n* [C] **1** a hospital 醫院 **2** a room in a school or other institution where people can go if they are ill〔學校等的〕醫務室

in·fir·mi·ty /ɪnˋfɝmətɪ; ɪnˈfɜːmɪ̣ti/ *n* [C,U] bad health or a particular illness 體弱, 身體不佳; 疾病: *She blamed her infirmity on the damp climate.* 她把身體不佳歸咎於潮濕的氣候。

in fla·gran·te de·lic·to /ɪn fləˌgrænte dɪˋlɪkto; ɪn fləˌgrænteɪ dɪˈlɪktəʊ/ *adv Latin, technical or humorous* in the act of having sex, especially with someone else's husband or wife【拉丁, 術語或幽默】〔尤指與別人的丈夫或妻子〕做愛時

in·flame /ɪnˋflem; ɪnˈfleɪm/ *v* [T] *literary* to make someone's feelings of anger, excitement etc much stronger【文】加劇〔憤怒或興奮等情感〕, 使火上澆油: *Seeing her again inflamed all his old desire.* 再次見到她, 激起他所有往日的慾望。

in·flamed /ɪnˋflemd; ɪnˈfleɪmd/ *adj* a part of your body that is inflamed is red and swollen, because it is hurt or infected〔身體部位〕紅腫的, 發炎的

in·flam·ma·ble /ɪnˋflæməbl̩; ɪnˈflæməbəl/ *adj* **1** *BrE* inflammable materials or substances will start to burn very easily【英】易燃的: *Petrol is highly inflammable.* 汽油高度易燃。—opposite 反義詞 NONFLAMMABLE **2** an inflammable temper easily becomes angry or violent 易怒的, 性情暴躁的

in·flam·ma·tion /ˌɪnfləˋmeʃən; ˌɪnfləˈmeɪʃən/ *n* [C,U] swelling and soreness on or in part of your body, which is often red and hot to touch 發炎, 炎症: *an inflammation of the eye* 眼睛發炎

in·flam·ma·to·ry /ɪnˋflæməˌtorɪ; ɪnˈflæmətəri/ *adj* **1** an inflammatory speech, piece of writing etc is likely to make people feel angry〔講話、文字等〕使人激憤的, 煽動性的: *His inflammatory remarks about the homeless were seized on by the press.* 他有關無家可歸者的煽動性講話立刻被媒體利用。**2** *technical* an inflammatory disease, condition etc causes inflammation【術語】〔疾病、環境等〕引發炎症的

in·fla·ta·ble¹ /ɪnˋfletəbl̩; ɪnˈfleɪtəbəl/ *adj* an inflatable object has to be filled with air before you can use it (需)充氣的: *an inflatable mattress* 充氣牀墊

inflatable² *n* [C] a rubber boat filled with air 充氣橡皮艇

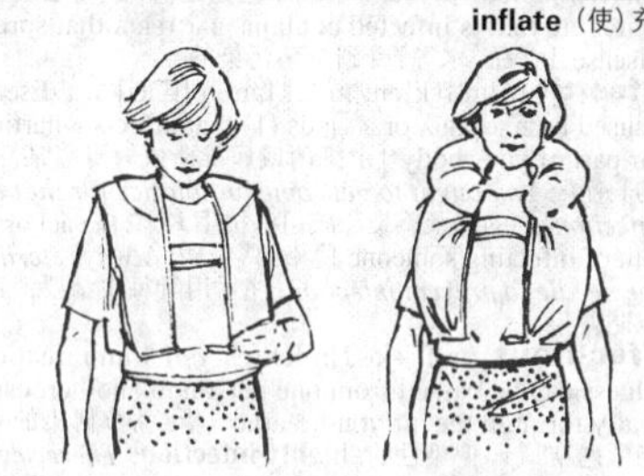
inflate (使)充氣

in·flate /ɪnˋflet; ɪnˈfleɪt/ *v* **1** [I,T] if you inflate something, or if it inflates, it fills with air or gas so that it becomes larger (使)充氣: *It took us half an hour to inflate the dinghy.* 我們用了半小時給橡皮筏充氣。| *Her life jacket failed to inflate.* 她的救生衣充不進氣。**2** [T] to make something seem more important or impressive than it is 吹捧〔某物〕: *Our egos were already inflated by success.* 成功使我們自命不凡。**3** [T] *technical* to make prices increase【術語】使〔價格〕上漲: *The sudden influx of Westerners has inflated house prices out of all proportion.* 西方人突然湧入, 把房價抬得離了譜。

in·flat·ed /ɪnˋfletɪd; ɪnˈfleɪtɪ̣d/ *adj* **1** inflated prices, sums etc are unreasonably high〔價格、數目等〕過高的: *These company directors are paid grossly inflated salaries.* 這些公司董事領取過高的薪水。**2** inflated ideas, opinions etc about something make it seem more important than it really is〔想法、意見〕誇張的, 言過其實的: *people with an inflated idea of their own importance* 自高自大的人 **3** filled with air or gas 充氣的

in·fla·tion /ɪnˋfleʃən; ɪnˈfleɪʃən/ *n* [U] **1** a continuing increase in prices or the rate at which prices increase 物價上漲(率), 通貨膨脹(率): *Inflation is now running at over 16%.* 通貨膨脹率現已超過16%。**2** the process of filling something with air 充氣 —compare 比較 DEFLATION

in·fla·tion·a·ry /ɪnˋfleʃənˌɛrɪ; ɪnˈfleɪʃənəri/ *adj* relating to or causing price increases 價格上漲的, 〔引起〕通貨膨脹的: *inflationary wage increases* 通貨膨脹引起的工資增長 | **inflationary spiral** (=the continuing rise in wages and prices because an increase in one causes an increase in the other) 螺旋形通貨膨脹〔指工資和物價交互影響而持續上漲〕

inflation-proof /·ˋ·· ·/ *adj* protected against price increases 不受通貨膨脹影響的: *inflation-proof pensions* 不受通貨膨脹影響的養老金

in·flect /ɪnˋflɛkt; ɪnˈflekt/ *v* **1** [I] if a word inflects, its form changes according to its meaning or use〔詞形〕屈折變化 **2** [I,T] if your voice inflects or if you inflect it, the sound of it becomes higher or lower as you are speaking〔說話時〕變(音), 轉(調)

in·flect·ed /ɪnˋflɛktɪd; ɪnˈflektɪ̣d/ *adj* an inflected language contains many words which change their form according to their meaning or use〔語言〕屈折變化的: *German is an inflected language.* 德語是屈折變化的語言。

in·flec·tion, inflexion /ɪnˋflɛkʃən; ɪnˈflekʃən/ *n* **1** [U] the way in which a word changes its form to show difference in its meaning or use〔單詞的〕屈折變化 **2** [C] one of the forms of a word that changes in this way, or one of the parts that is added to it 屈折形式, 屈折成分 **3** [C,U] the way the sound of your voice goes up and down when you are speaking〔說話時聲調的〕抑揚頓挫 —**inflectional** *adj*

in·flex·i·ble /ɪnˋflɛksəbl̩; ɪnˈfleksɪ̣bəl/ *adj* **1** inflexible rules, arrangements etc are impossible to change〔規則、協議等〕不可改變的, 不容變更的 **2** unwilling to make even the slightest change in your attitudes or plans etc〔態度、計劃等〕頑固的, 僵化的: *an arrogant man with an inflexible will* 傲慢無禮、剛愎自用的人 **3** inflexible material is stiff and will not bend〔材料〕堅硬的, 不能彎曲的 —**inflexibly** *adv* —**inflexibility** /ɪn͵flɛksə`bɪlətɪ; ɪn͵fleksə̦ˈbɪlə̦ti/ *n* [U]

in·fle·xion /ɪn`flɛkʃən; ɪnˈflekʃən/ *n* [C,U] another spelling of INFLECTION inflection 的另一種拼法

in·flict /ɪn`flɪkt; ɪnˈflɪkt/ *v* **1** [T] to make someone suffer something unpleasant 使〔某人〕遭受〔不愉快的事〕, 使承受: *The judge inflicted the severest possible penalty.* 法官判處了最嚴厲的懲罰。| **inflict sth on/upon sb** *He inflicted a great deal of suffering on his wife and children.* 他讓妻子和幾個孩子吃了很多苦頭。—see graph at 參見 PAIN[1] 圖表 **2 inflict yourself on** *humorous* to visit or be with someone when they do not want you【幽默】不請自來: *Frank's in-laws are inflicting themselves on us for the weekend.* 弗蘭克的姻親不請自來, 要在我們家度週末。—**infliction** /ɪn`flɪkʃən; ɪnˈflɪkʃən/ *n* [U]

in-flight /ˈ· ·/ *adj* [only before a noun 僅用於名詞前] provided during a plane journey 飛行途中提供的: *in-flight entertainment* 飛行旅程中提供的娛樂

in·flow /`ɪn͵flo; ˈɪnfləʊ/ *n* **1** [C] the movement of people, money, goods etc into a place〔人、錢、商品等的〕流入, 湧入: *the inflow of migrants* 移民的湧入 **2** [singular, U] the flow of water into a place〔水〕流入 —opposite 反義詞 OUTFLOW

2 **in·flu·ence**[1] /`ɪnfluəns; ˈɪnfluəns/ *n* **1** [C,U] power to
1 have an effect on the way someone or something develops, behaves, or thinks without using direct force or commands 影響: **[+with]** *She used her influence with the chairman to get me the job.* 她利用對主席的影響力使我得到了這份工作。| **have an influence on** *Claude's work had a major influence on generations of musicians.* 克勞德的作品對幾代音樂家都產生過重要影響。| **under the influence of** (=controlled by the influence of) 在…的影響下 *They had come under the influence of a strange religious sect.* 他們受到一個奇特教派的影響。**2** [C] someone or something that has an influence on other people or things 有影響的人[物]: **be a bad/good influence (on)** *Gaye's mother said I was a bad influence on her daughter.* 蓋伊的母親說我對她女兒產生了很壞的影響。| **outside influences** (=influences from beyond your own group) 外來的影響 *The tribe remains untouched by outside influences.* 這個部落仍然不受外界的影響。**3 under the influence** *informal* drunk【非正式】喝醉了

2 **influence**[2] *v* [T] to have an effect on the way someone
2 or something develops, behaves, thinks etc without directly forcing or commanding them 影響, 起作用: *Bruckner was much influenced by Wagner's orchestral music.* 布魯克納深受華格納管弦樂作品的影響。| *Don't let me influence your decision.* 別讓我影響你的決定。| **influence sb to do sth** *What influenced you to take the job?* 是甚麼影響你接受了這份工作?

in·flu·en·tial /͵ɪnflu`ɛnʃəl; ͵ɪnfluˈenʃəl◂/ *adj* having a lot of influence and therefore changing the way people think and behave 有影響力的: *an influential politician* 一位有影響力的政治家 | **influential in doing sth** *Dewey was influential in shaping economic policy.* 杜威對制定經濟政策頗有影響。| **highly influential** *a highly influential art magazine* 一本極有影響的藝術雜誌

in·flu·en·za /͵ɪnflu`ɛnzə; ͵ɪnfluˈenzə/ *n* [U] *technical* an infectious disease that is like a very bad cold; usually shortened to FLU【術語】流行性感冒〔一般簡寫為 flu〕

in·flux /`ɪn͵flʌks; ˈɪnflʌks/ *n* [C] the arrival of large numbers of people or large amounts of money, goods etc especially suddenly〔人、錢、貨物等突然〕大量湧入: **[+of]** *Tourism has brought a huge influx of wealth into the region.* 旅遊業使財富大量湧入該地區。

in·fo /`ɪnfo; ˈɪnfəʊ/ *n* [U] *informal* information【非正式】信息, 情報

in·fo·mer·cial /ˈɪnfomɝʃəl; ˈɪnfəʊmɜːʃəl/ *n* [C] *AmE* a long television advertisement that provides a lot of information and seems like a normal programme【美】商品信息[電視片, 專題廣告片]〔這類廣告提供大量信息, 看似普通的電視節目〕

in·form /ɪn`fɔrm; ɪnˈfɔːm/ *v* [T] **1** to formally or officially 2
tell someone about something or give them information 2
〔正式〕通知〔某人〕, 告知: *They thought it better to inform the police.* 他們認為最好告知警方。| **inform sb about/of** *Please inform us of any change of address as soon as possible.* 地址如有變更, 請盡早通知我們。| **inform sb (that)** *We regret to inform you that your application has been rejected.* 我們很遺憾地通知你, 你的申請不獲接受。| **inform sb who/why/how etc** *Could you please inform us what books you have in stock?* 能否告知你們庫存中有哪些書籍? **2** *formal* to influence someone's attitude or opinion【正式】影響: *Her experience as a refugee informs the content of her latest novel.* 她的難民經歷對她最新推出的小說的內容有影響。

inform against/on sb *phr v* [T] to tell the police or an enemy information about someone that will harm them 告發, 檢舉: *Treachery intervened when German sympathisers informed on them.* 出了叛徒, 親德分子告發了他們。

in·for·mal /ɪn`fɔrml̩; ɪnˈfɔːməl/ *adj* **1** relaxed and 3
friendly without being restricted by rules of correct behaviour 輕鬆的, 友好的, 不拘禮節的: *The atmosphere at work is fairly informal.* 工作氣氛相當輕鬆。| *The two groups met for informal talks.* 兩個小組會面舉行非正式會談。**2** an informal style of writing or speaking is suitable for ordinary conversations or letters to friends〔言談或書信〕非正式的, 日常使用的, 適於朋友間的 **3** informal clothes are suitable for wearing at home or in ordinary situations〔衣服〕在家穿的, 日常穿的: *Students and teachers shared a taste for informal dress.* 學生和老師都喜歡穿便服。—**informally** *adv* —**informality** /͵ɪnfɔr`mælətɪ; ͵ɪnfɔːˈmælə̦ti/ *n* [U]

in·for·mant /ɪn`fɔrmənt; ɪnˈfɔːmənt/ *n* [C] **1** someone who gives secret information about someone else, especially to the police〔尤指向警方〕提供〔某人的〕祕密消息者, 線人, 告密者: *The FBI were warned about the spy ring by a paid informant.* 一名受雇的線人曾向聯邦調查局報告過該間諜網的情況。—compare 比較 INFORMER **2** *technical* someone who gives information about their language, social customs etc to someone who is studying them【術語】〔為研究者提供語言、風俗等資料的〕資料提供人

in·for·ma·tion /͵ɪnfɚ`meʃən; ͵ɪnfəˈmeɪʃən/ *n* **1** [U] facts 1
or details that tell you something about a situation, 1
person, event etc 情報, 資料, 消息: *For further information phone the number below.* 查詢詳情, 請撥打下面的電話號碼。| **information that** *We have received information that Grant may have left the country.* 我們得到消息, 格蘭特可能已經離開了這個國家。| **[+about/on]** *The book contains information about a wide variety of subjects.* 這本書內容廣泛。| **provide information** *The guide will provide you with information about the area.* 導遊將給你提供該地區的資料。| **additional/ further information** *For further information, please ask at Reception.* 詳細情況請向服務台查詢。| **gather/collect information** *The survey didn't collect any information about temporary workers.* 這次調查沒有收集臨時工的資料。| **relevant/necessary/useful information** *There is a severe lack of relevant information and research about this disease.* 這種疾病的相關資料和研究都極度缺乏。| **detailed information** *Readers requiring more detailed information should consult Herman and McCure.* 想得到更詳細資料的讀者可查閱赫爾曼和麥克丘爾的著作。| **piece of information** *I've one or two useful pieces of information to pass on to you.* 我有一兩條有用的消息告訴你。| **my/our information is** (=used when officially stating what you know about a situation) 我/我們

得到的消息是〔用於發表正式談話〕*Our information is that troops have already invaded the city.* 我們得到的消息是軍隊已侵入這座城市。**2 for your information** *spoken* used when you are telling someone that they are wrong about a particular fact【口】不妨告訴你一下〔用來糾正別人的錯誤〕: *For your information, I've worked as a journalist for six years.* 不妨告訴你一下, 我做記者已有六年了。**3 for information only** written on copies of letters and documents that are sent to someone who needs to know about them but does not have to deal with them 僅供參考〔寫在信件和文件的副本上, 發給需要知道的人, 但對方不用處理〕—see also 另見 **inside information** (INSIDE[4] (2)) **4** [U] *AmE* the telephone service which provides telephone numbers to people who ask for them【美】電話號碼查詢服務; DIRECTORY ENQUIRIES *BrE*【英】—**informational** *adj*

This graph shows some of the words most commonly used with the noun **information**. 本圖表所示為含有名詞 information 的一些最常用詞組。

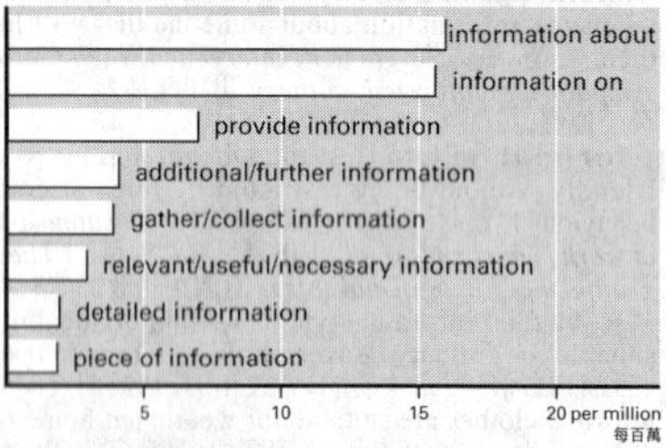

information about
information on
provide information
additional/further information
gather/collect information
relevant/useful/necessary information
detailed information
piece of information

5 10 15 20 per million 每百萬

Based on the British National Corpus and the Longman Lancaster Corpus
據英國國家語料庫和朗文蘭卡斯特語料庫

information cen·tre /ˈ‥ˈ‥ ˌ‥/ *n* [C] a place where you can get information about an area, event etc 信息[資訊]中心

information re·triev·al /‥ˈ‥ ·ˌ‥/ *n* [U] the process of finding stored information, especially on a computer 信息檢索〔尤指從電腦存儲的資料中查找〕; 資訊檢索

information sci·ence /ˌ‥‥ ˈ‥/ *n* [U] the science of collecting, arranging, storing, and sending out information 信息 (科) 學〔收集、整理、儲存和發送資訊的科學〕; 情報 (科) 學

information su·per·high·way /ˌɪnfɚmeʃən ˌsupɚˈhaɪwe; ˌɪnfəmeɪʃən ˌsuːpəˈhaɪweɪ/ *n* [singular] the various systems that can be used to send or obtain information, pictures, films etc by electronic means, for example from a computer in one place to a computer in a different place 信息高速公路〔指用電子方法發送或取得信息、圖畫、影片等的各種系統, 如通過電腦之間的互相傳輸〕

information tech·nol·o·gy /ˈ‥ˈ‥ ·ˌ‥/ *n* [U] the study or use of electronic processes for storing information and making it available; IT 信息技術〔以電子方法儲存和使用信息的科學及其應用〕

information the·o·ry /ˈ‥ˈ‥ ˌ‥/ *n* [U] *technical* the mathematical principles related to sending and storing information【術語】信息論

in·for·ma·tive /ɪnˈfɔrmətɪv; ɪnˈfɔːmətɪv/ *adj* providing many useful facts or ideas 資料豐富的; 增進知識的: *She gave an informative talk on various aspects of child care.* 她就撫育孩子的各方面作了一次內容豐富的講話。—**informatively** *adv* —**informativeness** *n* [U]

in·formed /ɪnˈfɔrmd; ɪnˈfɔːmd/ *adj* **1** having a lot of knowledge or information about a particular subject or situation 了解情況的, 見多識廣的: *Informed sources have denied that the President was involved at all.* 消息靈通人士否認總統與此事有任何關係。**2 well-informed/ill-informed/badly-informed** knowing a lot or not knowing much about what is happening in the world 見多識廣[消息靈通]的/信息閉塞的/信息不準確的: *She seemed to be fairly well-informed about the underlying economic issues.* 她對基礎的經濟問題似乎頗有了解。**3 informed guess/estimate/judgment etc** a guess etc that is based on knowledge of a subject or situation 有根據的猜測/估計/判斷等 **4 keep sb informed** to give someone the latest news and details about a situation 不斷給某人提供〔關於某事的〕最新消息: *Please keep me fully informed of any developments.* 事態如有發展, 請向我提供詳情。

in·form·er /ɪnˈfɔrmɚ; ɪnˈfɔːmə/ *n* [C] someone who is involved in an organization, especially a criminal organization, but who secretly tells the police, the army etc about its activities in return for money 告密者〔向警方、軍方等告密, 並收取金錢作回報的人, 尤指犯罪團夥的成員〕—compare 比較 INFORMANT (1)

in·fo·tain·ment /ˈɪnfoˌtenmənt; ˈɪnfəʊˌteɪnmənt/ *n* [U] *AmE* television programmes that deal with important subjects in a way that people can enjoy【美】〔在電視中用輕鬆方式處理重要問題的〕信息娛樂節目

infra- /ɪnfrə; ɪnfrə/ *prefix technical* below something in a range; beyond【術語】在…之下, 在…之外: *the infra-red end of the spectrum* 光譜的紅外線區 —compare 比較 ULTRA- (1)

in·frac·tion /ɪnˈfrækʃən; ɪnˈfrækʃən/ *n* [C,U+of] *formal* an act of breaking a rule or law【正式】違規行為, 違法行為

infra dig /ˌɪnfrə ˈdɪg; ˌɪnfrə ˈdɪg/ *adj* [not before noun 不用於名詞前] *informal BrE* below the standard of social behaviour that is suitable for a person of your class or rank【非正式, 英】有失身分的: *It's a bit infra dig for her to wear jeans on such a formal occasion.* 她在如此正式的場合穿牛仔褲有點兒失身分。

infra-red /ˌɪnfrə ˈrɛd; ˌɪnfrə ˈred◂/ *adj* infra-red light gives out heat but cannot be seen 紅外線的 —compare 比較 ULTRAVIOLET

in·fra·struc·ture /ˈɪnfrəˌstrʌktʃɚ; ˈɪnfrəˌstrʌktʃə/ *n* [C] the basic systems and structures that a country or organization needs in order to work properly, for example transport, communications, and banking systems 基礎設施〈如運輸、通訊、銀行制度等〉; 基礎結構: *the country's economic infrastructure* 國家的經濟基礎設施 —**infrastructural** *adj*

in·fre·quent /ɪnˈfrikwənt; ɪnˈfriːkwənt/ *adj* not happening often; rare 不經常發生的; 罕見的: *They would make infrequent visits to the house.* 他們偶爾去看一看那所房子。—**infrequently** *adv*: *We see them only very infrequently.* 我們只是偶然看到他們。—**infrequency** *n* [U] —see 見 RARE (USAGE)

in·fringe /ɪnˈfrɪndʒ; ɪnˈfrɪndʒ/ *v* [T] to do something that is against a law or someone's legal rights 違反〔法律〕, 侵犯〔他人權利〕: *Increasing care must be taken not to infringe copyright.* 必須不斷加強注意不要侵犯版權。—**infringement** *n* [C,U] *a minor infringement of the rules* 對規則的輕微違反

infringe on/upon sth *phr v* [T] to limit someone's freedom in some way〔在某方面〕限制〔某人的自由〕: *He found that all the media attention was infringing upon his private life.* 他認為所有的媒體關注都侵犯他的私生活。

in·fu·ri·ate /ɪnˈfjʊrɪˌet; ɪnˈfjʊərieɪt/ *v* [T] to make someone extremely angry 使〔某人〕大怒: *It infuriates me to think of all the money we've wasted.* 一想到我們浪費了那麼多錢, 我就怒火中燒。

in·fu·ri·a·ting /ɪnˈfjʊrɪˌetɪŋ; ɪnˈfjʊərieɪtɪŋ/ *adj* very annoying 非常令人惱火的: *It was infuriating to be so close and yet unable to contact them.* 和他們近在咫尺卻無法聯繫, 真叫人惱火。—**infuriatingly** *adv*

in·fuse /ɪnˈfjuz; ɪnˈfjuːz/ *v* **1** *formal* [T] to fill something or someone with a particular feeling or quality【正式】使充滿〔某種感覺〕; 將〔某品質〕注入〔某物〕: **infuse sth/sb with** *She managed to infuse the situation with humour.*

她設法為緊張氣氛注入一些幽默感。| **infuse sth into** *Hannah wanted desperately to infuse some vitality into their dull marriage.* 漢娜迫切地希望給他們平淡乏味的婚姻注入一些活力。**2** [I,T] if you infuse tea or HERBS or if they infuse, you leave them in very hot water while their taste passes into the water〔用熱水〕泡〔茶或香草〕

in·fu·sion /ɪnˋfjuʒən; ɪnˈfjuːʒən/ *n* **1** [C,U] the act of putting a new feeling or quality into something〔新感覺或品質的〕注入, 灌輸: *What the department needs is an infusion of new ideas.* 這個部門需要注入新思路。**2** [C] a drink made with HERBS in hot water that is usually taken as a medicine 草藥泡劑; 用香草泡的茶

-ing /ɪŋ; ɪŋ/ *suffix* **1** forms the present participle of verbs 構成動詞的現在分詞形式: *They're dancing.* 他們在跳舞。| *to go dancing* 去跳舞 | *a dancing bear* 一頭搖搖晃晃行走的熊 **2** [in U nouns 構成不可數名詞] the action or process of doing something 動作, 過程: *She hates swimming.* 她不喜歡游泳。| *No parking.* (=do not park here) 禁止停車。**3** [in U nouns 構成不可數名詞] **a)** a case or example of doing something 做某事的實例: *to hold a meeting* 舉行一次會議 **b)** a product or result of doing something〔動作的〕產物[結果]: *a beautiful painting* 一幅美麗的繪畫 **4** [in nouns 構成名詞] something used to do something or used for making something 做某事或製作某物的材料: *a silk lining* 絲質襯裡 | *ten metres of shirting* (=cloth for shirts) 十米襯衫布

in·ge·ni·ous /ɪnˋdʒinjəs; ɪnˈdʒiːniəs/ *adj* **1** an ingenious plan, idea, INVENTION etc is the result of clever thinking and new ideas, and works well〔計劃、主意、發明等〕巧妙的, 精妙的: *an ingenious way of making money* 賺錢的妙法 | *an ingenious gadget* 巧妙的小玩意 **2** someone who is ingenious is very good at inventing things or thinking of new ideas〔人〕善於創造發明的, 足智多謀的 —**ingeniously** *adv*

in·gé·nue /ˋændʒə,nu; ˈænʒeɪnjuː/ *n* [C] *French* a young inexperienced girl, especially in a film or play【法】〔尤指電影或戲劇中〕涉世不深的少女

in·ge·nu·i·ty /,ɪndʒəˋnuətɪ; ,ɪndʒəˈnjuːɪ̇ti/ *n* [U] cleverness of inventing things and thinking of new ideas 心靈手巧, 善於創造發明; 足智多謀

in·gen·u·ous /ɪnˋdʒɛnjuəs; ɪnˈdʒenjuəs/ *adj* inexperienced, simple, trusting, and honest 閱歷淺的, 純樸的, 坦誠率直的 —**ingenuously** *adv* —**ingenuousness** *n* [U] —opposite 反義詞 DISINGENUOUS

in·gest /ɪnˋdʒɛst; ɪnˈdʒest/ *v* [T] *technical* to take food into your body【術語】攝取〔食物〕; 咽下 —compare 比較 DIGEST[1] —**ingestion** /ɪnˋdʒɛstʃən; ɪnˈdʒestʃən/ *n* [U]

in·gle·nook /ˋɪŋgl,nuk; ˈɪŋgəlnʊk/ *n* [C] *especially BrE* a seat by the side of a large open fireplace, or the space that it is in【尤英】壁爐邊的座位; 爐邊

in·glo·ri·ous /ɪnˋglorɪəs; ɪnˈglɔːriəs/ *adj literary* causing shame and dishonour【文】不光彩的, 可恥的, 不名譽的: *an inglorious defeat* 可恥的失敗 —**ingloriously** *adv*

in·got /ˋɪŋgət; ˈɪŋgət/ *n* [C] a lump of pure metal in a regular shape, usually shaped like a brick〔純金屬的〕錠

in·grained /ɪnˋgrend; ɪnˈgreɪnd/ *adj* **1** ingrained attitudes or behaviour are firmly established and therefore difficult to change〔態度或行為〕根深蒂固的, 難以改變的: *an ingrained prejudice against all foreigners* 對一切外國人根深蒂固的偏見 **2** ingrained dirt is under the surface of something and very difficult to remove〔污物〕難以除掉的

in·grate /ˋɪngret; ɪnˈgreɪt/ *n* [C] *formal* an ungrateful person【正式】忘恩負義者

in·gra·ti·ate /ɪnˋgreʃɪ,et; ɪnˈgreɪʃieɪt/ *v* **ingratiate yourself (with)** to try hard to get someone's approval, by doing things to please them, expressing admiration etc 使得到〔某人〕的歡心, 討好〔某人〕: *The child glared so fiercely that I tried to ingratiate myself with her by offering candy.* 那個小女孩對我怒目而視, 我只好給她糖果來討好她。

in·gra·ti·at·ing /ɪnˋgreʃɪ,etɪŋ; ɪnˈgreɪʃieɪtɪŋ/ *adj* trying too hard to get someone's approval 極力討好奉承的: *I can't stand that ingratiating manner of his.* 我受不了他那種諂媚的樣子。—**ingratiatingly** *adv*

in·grat·i·tude /ɪnˋgrætə,tjud; ɪnˈgrætɪ̇tjuːd/ *n* [U] ungratefulness 忘恩負義: *I've never seen such ingratitude in all my life!* 我一生中從未見過這樣的忘恩負義!

in·gre·di·ent /ɪnˋgridɪənt; ɪnˈgriːdiənt/ *n* [C] **1** one of the types of food you use to make a particular dish〔烹調用的〕原料, 材料, 成分: *Have we got all the ingredients for a casserole?* 做砂鍋菜的原料都備齊了嗎? **2** a quality you need to achieve something〔完成某事的〕要素, 因素: *Imagination and hard work are the ingredients of success.* 想像力與勤奮工作是成功的要素。

in·gress /ˋɪngrɛs; ˈɪngres/ *n* [U] *literary* the right to enter a place or the act of entering it【文】進入權; 進入

in-group /ˋ· ·/ *n* [C] a small group of people in an organization or activity who like the same things and are friendly with each other, but do not want other people to join them; CLIQUE〔排他性的〕小集團, 小圈子 —**in-group** *adj*

in·growing /,ɪnˋgroɪŋ; ,ɪnˈgrəʊɪŋ◂/ *BrE*【英】, **in·grown** /,ɪnˋgron; ,ɪnˈgrəʊn◂/ *AmE*【美】—*adj* [no comparative 無比較級] an ingrowing TOENAIL grows inwards, cutting into the surrounding skin〔腳趾甲〕向內生長的, 長到肉裡去的

in·hab·it /ɪnˋhæbɪt; ɪnˈhæbɪ̇t/ *v* [T] if animals or people inhabit an area or place, they live there〔動物或人〕居住於〔某地〕: *The island is mainly inhabited by sheep.* 這個島嶼主要棲居着綿羊。—**inhabitable** *adj*

in·hab·i·tant /ɪnˋhæbətənt; ɪnˈhæbɪ̇tənt/ *n* [C] one of the people who live in a particular place 居民: *a city of six million inhabitants* 有六百萬居民的城市

in·ha·lant /ɪnˋhelənt; ɪnˈheɪlənt/ *n* [C,U] a medicine or drug that you breathe in, for example when you have a cold 吸入藥, 吸入劑

in·hale /ɪnˋhel; ɪnˈheɪl/ *v* [I, T] *especially technical* to breathe in air, smoke, or gas【尤術語】吸入〔空氣、煙霧或氣體〕: *It is dangerous to inhale ammonia fumes.* 吸入氨氣是很危險的。| **inhale deeply** (=inhale a lot of air or smoke) 深深吸入 *Myra lit another cigarette and inhaled deeply.* 邁拉又點了一支煙, 深吸了一口。—opposite 反義詞 EXHALE —**inhalation** /,ɪnhəˋleʃən; ,ɪnhəˈleɪʃən/ *n* [C,U]

in·hal·er /ɪnˋhelɚ; ɪnˈheɪlə/ *n* [C] a small plastic tube containing medicine that you breathe in in order to make breathing easier〔內含藥品、用於使呼吸變得較順暢的〕吸入器

in·here /ɪnˋhɪr; ɪnˈhɪə/ *v*

inhere in sth *phr v* [T] *technical* to be a natural part of something【術語】為〔某物〕固有的一部分

in·her·ent /ɪnˋhɪrənt; ɪnˈhɪərənt/ *adj* a quality that is inherent in something is a natural part of it and cannot be separated from it 內在的, 固有的: **[+in]** *I'm afraid the problems you mention are inherent in the system.* 你提及的這些問題恐怕本來就存在於這個體制中。—**inherently** *adv*: *Nuclear power is inherently dangerous and wasteful.* 核動力在本質上既危險又浪費。

in·her·it /ɪnˋhɛrɪt; ɪnˈherɪ̇t/ *v* **1** [I,T] to receive money, property etc from someone after they have died 繼承〔遺產〕: **inherit sth from** *She inherited the land from her grandfather.* 她從祖父那裡繼承了這塊土地。**2** [T] to have a problem caused by mistakes that other people have made in the past 承擔〔他人過去錯誤造成的問題〕: **inherit sth from** *The government claims to have inherited all of its problems from the previous administration.* 政府聲稱所有問題都是前任政府遺留下來的。**3** [T] to have the same character or appearance as your parents 遺傳得到〔父母的性格、外貌〕: **inherit sth from** *Gordon's inherited his father's bad temper.* 戈登的壞脾氣得自父親的遺傳。**4** [T] *informal* to get something that someone else does not want any more【非正式】接

收〔別人不再需要的東西〕: **inherit sth from** *We inherited the furniture from the previous tenants.* 我們從剛搬走的房客那裡接收了這些家具。—see also 另見 DISINHERIT

in·her·i·tance /ɪnˋhɛrətəns; ɪnˈherɪ̇təns/ *n* **1** [C,U] money, property etc that you receive from someone who has died 繼承的遺產: *She had squandered and gambled away her inheritance within a year.* 不出一年, 她就把她所繼承的遺產揮霍賭博掉了。**2** [U] *formal* ideas, beliefs, skills, literature, music etc from the past that influence people in the present【正式】〔仍對人們有影響的思想、信念、技藝、文學、音樂等〕遺產: *our literary inheritance* 我們的文學遺產

inheritance tax /ˈ·˙·· ˌ·/ *n* [U] a tax on the money or property that you give to someone else after you die 遺產稅, 繼承稅

in·her·i·tor /ɪnˋhɛrɪtɚ; ɪnˈherɪ̇tə/ *n* [C] someone who receives money, property etc from someone who has just died 遺產繼承人

in·hib·it /ɪnˋhɪbɪt; ɪnˈhɪbɪ̇t/ *v* [T] **1** to prevent something from growing or developing as much as it might have done otherwise 抑制, 約束: *Failure to set up a good transport network inhibited the expansion of trade.* 未能建立良好的運輸網絡限制了貿易的發展。**2** to make someone feel embarrassed or less confident so that they cannot do or say what they want to 使羞於, 使怯於: **inhibit sb from doing sth** *Being too critical may inhibit a child from asking you things he needs to know.* 過分挑剔會使孩子不敢問你他想知道的事情。| *an inhibiting influence* 有約束作用的影響

in·hib·it·ed /ɪnˋhɪbɪtɪd; ɪnˈhɪbɪ̇tɪ̇d/ *adj* not confident or relaxed enough to do or say what you want to 拘謹的, 束手束腳的: **feel inhibited** *When discussing sexual matters many people feel very inhibited.* 談到性的問題, 許多人都很不自在。—**inhibitedly** *adv*

in·hi·bi·tion /ˌɪnhɪˋbɪʃən; ˌɪnhɪ̇ˈbɪʃən/ *n* [C,U] a feeling of worry or embarrassment that stops you doing or saying what you really want to〔憂慮、窘迫等造成的〕抑制, 顧忌, 拘謹: **lose your inhibitions** (=stop feeling worried etc) 無所顧忌 *That night she finally lost her inhibitions and told him how she felt.* 那天夜裡, 她終於打消所有顧慮, 把自己的心思都告訴他。

in·hos·pi·ta·ble /ˌɪnˋhɑspɪtəbḷ; ˌɪnhɒˈspɪtəbəl/ *adj* **1** an inhospitable place is difficult to live or stay in because of severe weather conditions or lack of shelter〔地方〕荒涼的; 不適宜居住的〔由於天氣惡劣或缺乏遮蔽處〕: *inhospitable desert regions* 荒涼的沙漠地區 **2** unfriendly to a visitor, especially by not welcoming them, offering them food etc 慢待〔尤指不歡迎, 不招待〕客人的, 不好客的

in-house /ˌ· ˈ·◂/ *adj, adv* within a company or organization rather than outside it 公司[組織]內部的; 在機構內部: *We have an in-house training unit.* 我們公司設有一個內部培訓部。| *The keyboarding is done in-house.* 資料輸入在公司內部完成。

in·hu·man /ɪnˋhjumən; ɪnˈhjuːmən/ **1** very cruel without any normal feelings of pity 殘暴的, 無同情心的: *an inhuman tyrant* 野蠻的暴君 | *The slaves were subjected to inhuman discipline.* 奴隸受到殘酷的管束。**2** lacking any human qualities in a way that seems strange or frightening 無人性的, 看似怪異[令人驚恐]的: *a fear of modern technology as something inhuman and threatening* 對現代科技的恐懼, 認為它缺乏人性、構成威脅 | *The interviewer had a cold, almost inhuman, manner.* 面試官態度冷峻, 幾乎沒甚麼人情味。—**inhumanly** *adv*

in·hu·mane /ˌɪnhjuˋmen; ˌɪnhjuːˈmeɪn/ *adj* causing too much suffering and therefore considered cruel and unacceptable 殘忍的, 不人道的: **inhumane treatment/conditions/laws etc** *the inhumane treatment of political prisoners* 對政治犯的虐待 —**inhumanely** *adv*

in·hu·man·i·ty /ˌɪnhjuˋmænətɪ; ˌɪnhjuːˈmænɪ̇ti/ *n* [C usually plural 一般用複數, U] cruel behaviour or acts 殘酷無情的行為[舉止, 行動]: *The book focuses on the inhumanity of the labour camps.* 這本書着重描述勞改營的殘酷情況。

in·im·i·cal /ɪnˋɪmɪkḷ; ɪˈnɪmɪkəl/ *adj formal* very unfavourable for something【正式】極為不利的: *a cold, inimical climate* 寒冷嚴酷的氣候 | **[+to]** *conditions inimical to economic development* 對經濟發展極為不利的條件 —**inimically** /-kḷɪ; -kli/ *adv*

in·im·i·ta·ble /ɪnˋɪmətəbḷ; ɪˈnɪmɪ̇təbəl/ *adj* too good or skilful for anyone else to copy with the same high standard〔高超得〕難以模仿的, 無與倫比的: *the inimitable Billie Holliday* 蓋世無雙的比利·霍力戴 | *singing in his own inimitable style* 以其無與倫比的風格演唱 —**inimitably** *adv* —compare 比較 IMITATE

in·iq·ui·tous /ɪˋnɪkwətəs; ɪˈnɪkwɪ̇təs/ *adj formal* very unfair and morally wrong【正式】極不公正的, 邪惡的: *an iniquitous system of taxes that victimizes the poor* 損害窮人的極不公平的稅收體制 —**iniquitously** *adv*

in·iq·ui·ty /ɪˋnɪkwətɪ; ɪˈnɪkwɪ̇ti/ *n* [C, U] *formal*【正式】**1** the quality of being very unfair or evil, or something that is very unfair 極不公正, 邪惡; 不公正的事 **2 den of iniquity** *humorous* a place where there is a lot of immoral behaviour【幽默】罪惡的淵藪: *Our mother regarded the pub as a den of iniquity.* 我們的母親認為那家酒吧是邪惡的場所。

i·ni·tial[1] /ɪˋnɪʃəl; ɪˈnɪʃəl/ *adj* [only before noun 僅用於名詞前] happening at the beginning; first 開始的, 最初的: *She overcame her initial shyness and really enjoyed the evening.* 她克服了開始時的羞怯, 晚上玩得很高興。| *an initial investment of £5000* 最初投資5000英鎊

initial[2] *n* [C] **1** the first letter of someone's first name 名字的首字母: *"Can I have your initial, Mr Davies?!" "It's G, Mr G Davies."* "戴維斯先生, 您名字的首字母是甚麼?" "是 G, G·戴維斯。" **2 initials** [plural] the first letters of all your names in order 姓名的首字母: *His initials are DPH: they stand for David Perry Hallworth.* 他的姓名的首字母是DPH, 代表大衞·佩里·霍爾沃斯。

initial[3] *v* **initialled, initialling** *BrE*【英】, **initialed, initialing** *AmE*【美】[T] to write your initials on a document to make it official or to show that you agree with something 在〔文件〕上簽上姓名的首字母〔使其正式或表示同意〕: *You have to initial any corrections on a cheque.* 支票上任何更改之處都要簽上你姓名的首字母。

i·ni·tial·ly /ɪˋnɪʃəlɪ; ɪˈnɪʃəli/ *adv* at the beginning 起初: *The president initially appeared to endorse the idea.* 總統起初好像贊同這個想法。

i·ni·ti·ate[1] /ɪˋnɪʃɪˌet; ɪˈnɪʃieɪt/ *v* [T] **1** *formal* to arrange for something important to start, such as an official process or a new plan【正式】開始實施〔重要的事, 如官方程序或新計劃〕; 發起: *The plaintiffs initiated court proceedings in order to recover their debts.* 原告們開始法律訴訟以討回債款。**2** to introduce someone to special knowlege or skills that they did not know about before 向〔某人〕傳授專門知識[技巧]: *During that summer he was initiated into the mysteries of sex.* 那年夏天, 他對性的奧祕獲得了初步了解。**3** to introduce someone into an organization, club, group etc, usually with a special ceremony〔通過特殊儀式〕使〔某人〕加入〔組織、俱樂部、社團等〕: *In August Ivan was initiated into the Oakland chapter of the Hell's Angels.* 八月, 伊凡被邀加入"地獄天使"俱樂部的奧克蘭分部。

initiate[2] *n* [C] someone who has been allowed to join a particular group and has been taught its secrets 被吸納加入某組織並授以訣竅的人

i·ni·ti·a·tion /ɪˌnɪʃɪˋeʃən; ɪˌnɪʃiˈeɪʃən/ *n* [C,U] **1** the process of officially introducing someone into a club or group, or of introducing a young person to adult life, often with a special ceremony〔加入俱樂部或社團的〕正式儀式;〔青年男女的〕成年儀式: *The initiation ceremony involves elaborate dances.* 成年儀式包括各種複雜的舞蹈。**2** the act of starting something such as an official process, a new plan etc〔計劃、方案等的〕發起, 實施

2 **i·ni·tia·tive** /ɪˋnɪʃɪˌetɪv; ɪˈnɪʃətɪv/ *n*
1 ►YOUR OWN DECISIONS 個人的決定◄ [U] the ability to make decisions and take action without waiting for someone to tell you what to do 自主決斷行事的能力; 主動能力: *I wish my son would show a bit more initiative.* 我希望我的兒子能表現得再主動一些。| **use your (own) initiative** *Don't keep asking me for advice. Use your initiative.* 別總是要我給你出主意, 發揮你自己的決斷能力吧。| **on your own initiative** (=without being told what to do) 主動地, 自主地: *Lieutenant Carlos was not obeying orders. He acted on his own initiative.* 卡洛斯中尉沒有服從命令, 而是自己作主。
2 ►PLAN 計劃◄ [C] an important new plan or process that has been started in order to achieve a particular aim or to solve a particular problem 計劃, 措施: *a government initiative to help exporters* 扶助出口商的政府計劃
3 ►ADVANTAGE 優勢◄ **the initiative** the power to gain an advantage by taking actions that will influence events〔能夠影響事情發展的〕主動權: **seize/hold/lose the initiative** *Zhukov was quick to seize the initiative and launched a massive counter attack.* 朱可夫迅速掌握主動, 發動大規模反攻。
4 take the initiative to be the first one to take action to improve a situation or relationship, especially when other people are waiting for someone else to do something 帶頭, 率先〔改善情況或關係, 尤指其他人都在等待某人先行動時〕: *Why don't you take the initiative and arrange a meeting?* 你為甚麼不帶個頭, 安排一個會議呢?
5 ►TO CHANGE A LAW 修改法律◄ [C] *law* a process by which ordinary citizens can propose a change in the law by signing a PETITION[1] (1)【法律】公民〔簽名提出修改法律的〕提案程序

in·ject /ɪnˋdʒɛkt; ɪnˈdʒekt/ *v* [T] **1** to put liquid, especially a drug, into someone's body by using a special needle〔向體內〕注射〔液體, 尤指藥液〕: **inject sth into** *The drug is injected directly into the base of the spine.* 藥物被直接注射入脊椎底部。| **inject sb with** *The patient had been injected with a narcotic drug.* 病人已被注射了麻醉劑。**2** to improve something by adding excitement, interest etc to it 增加〔氣氛、興趣等〕: *They hoped that the adoption of a child would inject new life into their marriage.* 他們希望收養一個孩子能給他們的婚姻生活增添生氣。**3 [+into]** to provide more money, equipment etc for something 投入〔更多的資金、設備等〕

3 **in·jec·tion** /ɪnˋdʒɛkʃən; ɪnˈdʒekʃən/ *n* **1** [C,U] an act of giving a drug by using a special needle 注射: **give sb an injection** *The nurse gave me a tetanus injection.* 護士給我注射了一劑破傷風預防針。**2** [C,U] the act of forcing a liquid into something〔將液體〕注入〔某物〕: *a fuel injection system* 燃油注入系統 **3** [C] an addition of money to something in order to improve it 資金注入〔為了改進某事〕: **[+of]** *a massive injection of public funds* 大量注入公共基金

in-joke /ˈ· ·/ *n* [C] a joke that is only understood by a particular group of people〔只有某圈子裡的人才能聽懂的〕內部笑話

in·ju·di·cious /ˌɪndʒuˋdɪʃəs; ˌɪndʒuːˈdɪʃəs/ *adj formal* an injudicious action, remark etc is not sensible and is likely to have bad results【正式】〔行為、言論等〕不明智的〔可能產生不良後果〕, 不謹慎的: *I thought his choice of words injudicious, to say the least.* 我認為他至少是措辭不當。—**injudiciously** *adv* —**injudiciousness** *n* [U]

In·jun /ˋɪndʒən; ˈɪndʒən/ *n* **honest Injun** *spoken especially AmE* used especially by children to make someone believe they are telling the truth【口, 尤美】是真的, 一點不假〔尤為兒語, 用於使人相信他們說的是真話〕

in·junc·tion /ɪnˋdʒʌŋkʃən; ɪnˈdʒʌŋkʃən/ *n* [C] **1** *law* an order given by a court which forbids someone to do something【法律】〔由法院發出的〕禁(制)令: **[+against]** *The company is seeking an injunction against the strike.* 這家公司正要求法院下令禁止罷工。| **take out an injunction against** (=get an injunction from a court) 取得法院的禁令 *Johnson took out an injunction to prevent the publication going ahead.* 約翰遜取得禁令, 阻止這項出版繼續進行。**2** *formal* a piece of advice or a command from someone in authority【正式】訓諭, 忠告, 指令

in·jure /ˋɪndʒɚ; ˈɪndʒə/ *v* [T] **1** to cause physical harm to someone or to yourself, for example in an accident or an attack 受傷; 傷害: *One of the players injured his knee and had to be carried off.* 一個隊員膝蓋受傷被抬至場外。| **be badly/seriously/critically injured** *Two people have been critically injured in a road accident.* 在一次交通事故中, 有兩人嚴重受傷。**2 injure sb's pride/self-esteem etc** to upset someone by damaging their confidence 傷害某人的自尊心等 —compare 比較 WOUND[3]

in·jured /ˋɪndʒɚd; ˈɪndʒəd/ *adj* **1** having an injury 受傷的: *He isn't injured – just shocked.* 他沒有受傷, 只是受了驚嚇。**2 the injured** injured people 傷者: *Firefighters had to cut open the wreckage in order to get the injured out.* 消防員必須割開殘骸才能救出受傷者。**3 an injured look/expression etc** a look that shows you feel you have been treated unfairly 委屈的樣子/表情等 **4 injured pride/feelings etc** a feeling of being upset or offended because you think you have been unfairly treated 受到傷害的自尊/情感等〔由於覺得受委屈〕 **5 the injured party** *formal* the person who has been unfairly treated in a particular situation【正式】受到不公正待遇的一方

in·ju·ri·ous /ɪnˋdʒurɪəs; ɪnˈdʒʊəriəs/ *adj formal* causing injury, harm, or damage【正式】有害的, 致傷的: *Smoking is injurious to health.* 吸煙危害健康。

in·ju·ry /ˋɪndʒərɪ; ˈɪndʒəri/ *n* **1** [C] a wound or damage to part of your body caused by an accident or attack〔對身體的〕傷害, 損害: **sustain injuries** *formal* (=be injured)【正式】受到傷害 *The driver of the lorry sustained only minor injuries to legs and arms.* 卡車司機只是四肢受了點輕傷。| **internal injuries** (=injuries inside your body) 內傷 **2** [U] physical harm that is caused by an accident or attack〔因事故或攻擊造成的〕人身傷害: *insurance against injury at work* 工傷保險 **3 do yourself an injury** *BrE humorous* to accidentally hurt yourself【英, 幽默】〔意外地〕自我傷害: *Don't lift that tool-box – you'll do yourself an injury!* 別搬那隻工具箱, 會砸着你自己的! —see also 另見 **add insult to injury** (ADD (8)) 2

injury time /ˈ··· ˌ·/ *n* [U] *BrE* playing time added on to a game such as football because of time lost when players are injured【英】〔足球賽中因球員受傷耽誤而延長比賽時間的〕補時

in·jus·tice /ɪnˋdʒʌstɪs; ɪnˈdʒʌstɪs/ *n* **1** [C,U] a situation in which people are treated very unfairly and not given their rights 不公正, 非正義: *the injustice of slavery* 奴隸制的非正義 | *innumerable injustices against the black population* 對黑人難以計數的不公正行為 **2 do sb an injustice** to judge someone's character unfairly 冤枉某人: *It would be doing Brett an injustice to say that he didn't care about other people.* 說布萊特不關心他人是冤枉他了。

ink[1] /ɪŋk; ɪŋk/ n **1** [C,U] coloured liquid used for writing, printing or drawing 墨水 **2** [U] the black liquid in sea creatures such as OCTOPUS and SQUID〔章魚、烏賊等海洋生物分泌出的〕墨汁

ink[2] *v* [T] **1** to put ink on something 塗墨水於〔某物〕 **2** *AmE* to write something in ink, especially your SIGNATURE on a contract etc【美】用墨水書寫〔尤指在合同上用墨水筆簽名〕: *Just ink your name on the bottom line.* 請在底線上簽名。
ink sth ↔ **in** *phr v* [T] to complete something done in pencil by drawing over it in ink 在〔鉛筆底稿上〕用墨水加描

ink·jet print·er /ˋɪŋkdʒɛt ˌprɪntɚ; ˈɪŋkdʒet ˌprɪntə/ *n* [C] an electronic printer, usually connected to a small computer 噴墨打印機 —see picture on page A14 參見A14頁圖

ink·ling /ˋɪŋklɪŋ; ˈɪŋklɪŋ/ *n* **have an inkling** to have a slight idea about something 略知; 模糊的印象: *We had no inkling that he was leaving.* 我們根本不知道他要走。| *No one gave me the slightest inkling of what they were planning.* 他們在盤算甚麼, 沒人給我透露半點消息。

ink pad /ˋ· ·/ *n* [C] a small box containing ink on a thick piece of cloth, used for putting ink onto a stamp (STAMP[1] (2)) that is pressed onto paper (打) 印台

ink·stand /ˋɪŋk͵stænd; ˈɪŋkstænd/ *n* [C] a container for pens and pots of ink, kept on a desk 墨水台

ink·well /ˋɪŋk͵wɛl; ˈɪŋk-wel/ *n* [C] a container for ink which fits into a hole in a desk〔嵌在桌上的〕墨水池

ink·y /ˋɪŋkɪ; ˈɪŋki/ *adj* **1** marked with ink 沾有墨水的: *inky fingers* 沾有墨水的手指 **2** *poetic* very dark【詩】漆黑的: *I stared out into the inky blackness of the night.* 我凝視着外面漆黑的夜色。—**inkiness** *n* [U]

in·laid /͵ɪnˋled; ͵ɪnˈleɪd◂/ *adj* **1** an inlaid box, table, floor etc has a thin layer of another material set into its surface for decoration〔箱子、桌子、地板等〕鑲嵌着…的: **[+with]** *a wooden jewellery box inlaid with ivory* 嵌有象牙的木製珠寶盒 **2 [+in/into]** metal, stone etc that is inlaid into the surface of another material is set into its surface as decoration 鑲入的, 嵌入的

in·land¹ /ˋɪnlənd; ˈɪnlənd/ *adj* [only before noun 僅用於名詞前] an inland area, city etc is not near the coast 內陸的, 內地的

in·land² /ˋɪn͵lænd; ɪnˈlænd/ *adv* in a direction away from the coast and towards the centre of a country 向內陸, 在內地: *The mountains are five miles inland.* 這些山位於內陸五英里處。

Inland Rev·e·nue /͵·· ˋ···/ *n* [singular] the government department which collects national taxes in Britain〔英國的〕政府稅收機關, 稅務局

in-laws /ˋ· ·/ *n* [plural] *informal* your relatives by marriage, especially the father and mother of your husband or wife【非正式】姻親〔尤指岳父母或公婆〕: *We have to spend Christmas with the in-laws.* 我們得和姻親們一起過聖誕節。

in·lay /ˋɪn͵le; ˈɪnleɪ/ *n* **1** [C,U] a material which has been set into the surface of furniture, floors etc for decoration, or the pattern made by this 鑲嵌物; 鑲嵌圖案: *a cedarwood casket with gold inlay* 鑲金的雪松木小盒 **2** [C] a substance used by a DENTIST to fill a hole in a decayed tooth 補牙用的充填物

in·let /ˋɪn͵lɛt; ˈɪnlet/ *n* [C] **1** a narrow area of water reaching from the sea or a lake into the land or between islands 水灣〔海邊、湖邊或島嶼之間的狹長水域〕; 小港: *bays and sheltered inlets along the coast* 沿岸的海灣和可避風浪的小港 **2** the part of a machine through which liquid or gas flows in〔機器上液體或氣體的〕入口, 進口: *a fuel inlet* 燃油注入口

in lo·co pa·ren·tis /ɪn ˋloko pəˋrɛntɪs; ɪn ͵ləʊkəʊ pəˈrentɪs/ *adv Latin, formal or law* having the responsibilities of a parent for someone else's child【拉丁, 正式或法律】〔對別人的孩子〕代盡父母的責任: *As a teacher, you should regard yourself as being in loco parentis.* 作為教師, 你應視自己有代盡父母的責任。

in·mate /ˋɪnmet; ˈɪnmeɪt/ *n* [C] someone who is kept in a prison or MENTAL HOSPITAL〔監獄中的〕囚犯;〔精神病院的〕病人: *One of the inmates has escaped.* 有一名病人[犯人]逃跑了。

in me·mo·ri·am /ɪn məˋmorɪ͵æm; ɪn mɪ̆ˈmɔːriəm/ *prep Latin* an expression meaning 'in memory of', used especially on the stone above a grave【拉丁】〔用在墓碑上表示〕為了紀念〔某人〕

in·most /ˋɪn͵most; ˈɪnməʊst/ *adj* [only before noun 僅用於名詞前] **1** your inmost feelings, desires etc are the ones you feel most strongly and keep private〔感情、慾望等〕內心深處的, 內心隱祕處的 **2** *formal* furthest inside【正式】最深處的: *She consigned the letter to the inmost recesses of her desk.* 她把那封信藏到書桌裡面最隱祕的地方。—opposite 反義詞 OUTERMOST

inn /ɪn; ɪn/ *n* [C] **1** *especially BrE* a small PUB or hotel, especially one in the countryside, built in an old-fashioned style【尤英】〔樣式古老的〕小酒館; 小旅館 **2** a word used in the names of some PUBs and hotels …酒店〔用於某些酒館、旅店的名稱〕: *We're staying at the Holiday Inn.* 我們住在假日酒店。

in·nards /ˋɪnədz; ˈɪnədz/ *n* [plural] **1** *informal* the parts inside your body, especially your stomach【非正式】內臟〔尤指胃部〕 **2** the parts inside a machine 機器的內部

in·nate /͵ɪˋnet; ɪˈneɪt◂/ *adj* an innate quality has been part of your character since you were born〔素質〕天生的, 固有的: *Donna had an innate ability to sense when someone was unhappy.* 唐娜有一種天生的本領, 能覺察出誰心情不好。—**innately** *adv*: *the army's innately conservative values* 軍隊固有的保守價值觀

in·ner /ˋɪnɚ; ˈɪnə/ *adj* [only before noun 僅用於名詞前] **1** on the inside or close to the centre of something 內部的, 靠近中心的: *an inner room* 內室 | *Dial 0171 for inner London.* 往倫敦中心區打電話要撥 0171。| *the inner ear* 內耳 —opposite 反義詞 OUTER **2** connected with your soul or deepest feelings 心靈的, 內心的: *I really enjoy yoga – it gives me a sense of inner calm.* 我很喜歡瑜伽, 它使我感到內心平靜。**3 inner meanings/thoughts etc** meanings or thoughts that are secret and not expressed 含蓄隱晦的意思/思想等: *Sarah suspected that his comment had an inner meaning.* 莎拉懷疑他的評論含有言外之意。**4 inner circle** the few people in an organization, political party etc who control it or share power with its leader〔組織、政黨等的〕核心集團: *The invasion plans were only divulged to the President's inner circle.* 入侵計劃只透露給總統的核心集團。**5 the inner man/woman a)** the soul 靈魂 **b)** *humorous* the desire for food; APPETITE (1)【幽默】食慾, 胃口

inner cit·y /͵·· ˋ··◂/ *n* [C] the part near the middle of a city where the buildings are in a bad condition and the people are poor 市中心貧民區: *the problem of deprivation in our inner cities* 舊城區的貧困問題 —**inner city** *adj*: *squalor in inner-city areas* 貧民區的骯髒窮困

in·ner·most /ˋɪnɚ͵most; ˈɪnəməʊst/ *adj* [only before noun 僅用於名詞前] **1** your innermost feelings, desires etc are the ones you feel most strongly about and do not talk about〔情感、慾望等〕隱祕的, 內心深處的 **2** *formal* furthest inside【正式】最裡面的: *the innermost depths of the cave* 山洞的最深處

inner tube /ˋ·· ·/ *n* [C] **1** the air-filled rubber tube inside a tyre〔輪胎的〕內胎 **2 go inner-tubing** *AmE* to ride on an inner tube either on water or down a snow-covered hill【美】用內胎衝浪[滑雪]

in·ning /ˋɪnɪŋ; ˈɪnɪŋ/ *n* [C] one of the nine playing periods in a game of BASEBALL or SOFTBALL〔棒球或壘球九局比賽的一〕局

in·nings /ˋɪnɪŋz; ˈɪnɪŋz/ *n plural* **innings 1** [C] the period of time when a cricket team or player bats (BAT² (1))〔板球球隊或球員可以擊球的〕局 **2 he/ she had a good innings** *BrE informal* used about someone who has died to say that they had a long life【英, 非正式】他/她享高壽〔指已逝世的人〕: *It's sad. Still, she was 89 – she had a good innings.* 真叫人傷心。不過, 她活了 89 歲, 很長壽了。

inn·keep·er /ˋɪn͵kipɚ; ˈɪn͵kiːpə/ *n* [C] *old use* someone who owns or manages an INN【舊】小旅館老闆; 客棧掌櫃

in·no·cence /ˋɪnəsn̩s; ˈɪnəsəns/ *n* [U] **1** the fact of being not guilty of a crime 清白無罪: *Can you prove your innocence?* 你能證明自己無罪嗎? | **protest your innocence** (=say repeatedly that you are not guilty) 再三申明無罪 *The prisoners continued to protest their innocence.* 犯人們一再申明他們無罪。**2** the state of not having much experience of life or knowledge about evil in the world, especially so that you are easily deceived

閱世不深, 天真, 單純: *In our innocence we believed everything we were told.* 我們太幼稚, 他們所說的我們都信以為真。| *the innocence of childhood* 童年的天真單純 **3 in all innocence** if you do or say something in all innocence, you have no intention of doing harm or of offending anyone 完全沒有惡意

in·no·cent¹ /ˈɪnəsn̩t; ˈɪnəsənt/ *adj* **1** not guilty of a crime 無罪的: *Nobody would believe that I was innocent.* 沒人肯相信我是無罪的。| **[+of]** *He's innocent of murder.* 他沒犯殺人罪。**2 innocent victims/bystanders/people etc** people who get hurt or killed in a war or as a result of a crime though they are not involved in it〔戰爭或犯罪行為〕無辜的受害者/旁觀者/人們等: *innocent victims of ruthless terrorism* 殘忍恐怖主義的無辜受害者 **3** done or said without intending to harm or offend anyone 不帶惡意的: *He was startled by their angry reaction to his innocent remark.* 他們對他那並無惡意的話如此憤怒, 使他大為驚訝。**4** not having much experience of life, so that you are easily deceived; NAIVE 天真無邪的, 閱世不深的: *I was thirteen years old and very innocent.* 我那時十三歲, 年幼無知。—**innocently** *adv*

innocent² *n* [C] someone who does not have much experience of life or knowledge about evil in the world 涉世不深的人

in·noc·u·ous /ɪˋnɑkjʊəs; ɪˈnɒkjuəs/ *adj* not offensive, dangerous, or harmful 無意冒犯的, 不危險的, 無害的: *an innocuous remark* 無惡意的話語 | *Those innocuous-looking cases contain enough explosive to destroy this building.* 那些貌似無害的箱子裡面裝的炸藥足以摧毀這幢大樓。—**innocuously** *adv* —**innocuousness** *n* [U]

in·no·vate /ˋɪnə͵vet; ˈɪnəveɪt/ *v* [I] to start to use new ideas, methods, or inventions 革新, 創新, 改革

3 **in·no·va·tion** /͵ɪnəˋveʃən; ͵ɪnəˈveɪʃən/ *n* **1** [C] a new idea, method, or invention 新觀念, 新方法, 新發明: *recent technological innovations* 最近的技術發明 **2** [U] the introduction of new ideas or methods 革新; 創新: *We must encourage innovation if the company is to remain competitive.* 公司要想保持競爭力, 就必須鼓勵革新。

in·nov·at·ive /ˋɪnə͵vetɪv; ˈɪnə͵veɪtɪv/ *adj* **1** an innovative process, method, plan etc is new, different, and better than those that existed before〔程序、方法、計劃等〕新穎的, 有創新精神的 **2** using clever new ideas and methods 運用新觀念和新方法的: *a young innovative company* 一家富有新意的新公司

in·no·vat·or /ˋɪnə͵vetɚ; ˈɪnəveɪtə/ *n* [C] someone who introduces changes and new ideas 革新者, 創新者

in·nu·en·do /͵ɪnjʊˋɛndo; ͵ɪnjuˈendəʊ/ *n plural* **innuendoes** or **innuendos** **1** [C] an indirect remark about sex or about something bad that someone has done 影射〔性或某人所做的壞事〕的話, 暗諷的話: *lies and innuendoes* 謊言與暗諷 **2** [U] the act of making such unpleasant remarks 含沙射影; 暗諷: *a despicable smear campaign based on rumour, innuendo, and gossip* 以造謠、暗諷和流言蜚語為內容, 為人所不齒的有組織的誹謗行動

In·nu·it /ˋɪnjʊɪt; ˈɪnjuɪt/ *n* [U] *adj* another spelling of INUIT Inuit 的另一種拼法

in·nu·me·ra·ble /ɪˋnjumərəbl̩; ɪˈnjuːmərəbəl/ *adj* very many, or too many to be counted 不可勝數的: *They received innumerable letters of complaint about the programme.* 他們收到了大量對該計劃的投訴信。

in·nu·mer·ate /ɪˋnjumərɪt; ɪˈnjuːmərɪt/ *adj* unable to do calculations or understand basic mathematics 不會計算的, 不會基礎數學的 —**innumeracy** *n* [U]

i·noc·u·late /ɪnˋɑkjə͵let; ɪˈnɒkjəleɪt/ *v* [T] to protect someone against a disease, usually by injecting (INJECT (1)) them with a weak form of it 給〔某人〕接種, 給〔某人〕作預防注射: **[+against]** *All the children had been inoculated against hepatitis.* 所有孩子都注射了肝炎預防針。—compare 比較 IMMUNIZE, VACCINATE —**inoculation** /ɪ͵nɑkjəˋleʃən; ɪ͵nɒkjəˈleɪʃən/ *n* [C,U]

in·of·fen·sive /͵ɪnəˋfɛnsɪv; ͵ɪnəˈfensɪv◂/ *adj* unlikely to offend anyone 不觸犯人的, 不會得罪人的: *Her husband was a small, inoffensive-looking man.* 她丈夫個子不高, 看上去很隨和。—**inoffensively** *adv* —**inoffensiveness** *n* [U]

in·op·e·ra·ble /ɪnˋɑpərəbl̩; ɪnˈɒpərəbəl/ *adj* **1** an inoperable illness or TUMOUR (=lump) cannot be treated or removed by a medical operation〔疾病、腫瘤〕無法用手術治療的: *an inoperable spinal tumour* 不能用手術治療的脊柱腫瘤 **2** an inoperable system or method is not practical and therefore cannot be used〔系統、方法〕不實際的, 行不通的

in·op·e·ra·tive /ɪnˋɑpə͵retɪv; ɪnˈɒpərətɪv/ *adj formal* 【正式】**1** a machine that is inoperative is not working, or is not in working condition〔機器〕不運轉的; 不在工作狀態的 **2** a system or a law that is inoperative is not working or cannot be made to work〔系統、法律〕不能實施的, 無效的

in·op·por·tune /͵ɪnɑpɚˋtjun; ɪnˈɒpətjuːn/ *adj formal* 【正式】**1** an inopportune moment or time is not suitable or good for something〔時間等〕不合適的, 不適宜的: *I'm afraid you've called at rather an inopportune moment.* 我恐怕你的電話打得有些不是時候。**2** happening at an unsuitable or bad time〔時間〕不湊巧的, 不合時宜的: *an inopportune visit* 不合時宜的探訪 —**inopportunely** *adv* —**inopportuneness** *n* [U]

in·or·di·nate /ɪnˋɔrdn̩ɪt; ɪˈnɔːdənɪt/ *adj* far more than you would reasonably or normally expect 超出合理限度的, 過分的: *Testing is taking up an inordinate amount of teachers' time.* 測試工作佔去了教師們太多的時間。—**inordinately** *adv*: *She's inordinately fond of her parrot.* 她溺愛她那隻鸚鵡。

in·or·gan·ic /͵ɪnɔrˋgænɪk; ͵ɪnɔːˈgænɪk◂/ *adj* **1** not consisting of anything that is living 無機的, 無生命的: *inorganic matter* 無機物質 **2** not produced or allowed to develop in a natural way 非自然長成[發展]的 —opposite 反義詞 ORGANIC (1,5) —**inorganically** /-klɪ; -kli/ *adv*

inorganic chem·is·try /͵.... ˈ.../ *n* [U] *technical* the part of chemistry concerning the study of substances that do not contain CARBON【術語】無機化學 —compare 比較 ORGANIC CHEMISTRY

in·pa·tient /ˋɪn͵peʃənt; ˈɪnpeɪʃənt/ *n* [C] someone who stays in a hospital for treatment, rather than coming in for treatment from outside 住院病人 —compare 比較 OUTPATIENT

in·put¹ /ˋɪn͵pʊt; ˈɪnpʊt/ *n* [singular, U] **1** ideas, advice, money, or effort that you put into a job, meeting etc in order to help it succeed 投入(物)〔指向工作、會議等提供的意見、建議、資金、努力等〕: *The conference would not have been such a success without your valuable input.* 沒有您的寶貴投入, 會議不會開得如此成功。**2** *technical*【術語】**a)** electrical power that is put into a machine for it to use〔輸入機器供其使用的〕電力 **b)** information that is put into a computer〔輸入電腦的〕信息 —compare 比較 OUTPUT¹ 3

input² *v past tense and participle* **inputted** or **input** [T] to put information into a computer〔向電腦〕輸入〔信息〕

in·quest /ˋɪnkwɛst; ˈɪŋkwest/ *n* [C] **1** a legal process to find out the cause of someone's death〔調查死因的〕訊問, 審理: **hold an inquest (into)** *An inquest will be held into the death of the actor, Tom Barnard.* 對於演員湯姆·巴納德的死因將進行審訊。**2** an unofficial discussion about the reasons for someone's defeat or failure to do something〔對某人的失敗進行的非正式的〕討論

in·qui·e·tude /ɪnˋkwaɪə͵tjud; ɪnˈkwaɪətjuːd/ *n* [U] *literary* anxiety【文】焦慮; 不安

in·quire, enquire /ɪnˋkwaɪr; ɪnˈkwaɪə/ *v* [I,T] **1** to ask someone for information 詢問, 打聽: *"Are you getting married?" the television interviewer inquired.* "你準備結婚了嗎?" 電視採訪記者問道。| **[+about]** *I am writing to inquire about your advertisement in The Times.* 您在《泰晤士報》刊登廣告, 特此致函詢問詳情。| **in-**

quire whether/why/how etc *The waiter inquired whether we would like to sit near the window.* 侍者問我們是否想靠窗坐着。—see 見 ASK (USAGE) **2 inquire within** used on notices, especially in shop windows, to mean that you can find out more about something inside 詳情請入內查詢〔用於商店櫥窗內的告示, 意思是你若進入店內, 可得知更多情況〕: *Vacancies – inquire within.* 招聘 —— 有意者入內查詢。—**inquirer** *n* [C]

inquire after sb/sth *phr v* [T] to ask someone about someone else, about how they are and what they are doing 問候, 問好: *He called me aside to inquire after my daughter.* 他把我叫到一旁, 打聽我女兒的情況。

inquire into sth *phr v* [T] to ask questions in order to get more information about something 查問, 查究, 調查: *The investigation will inquire into the exact circumstances of the sale.* 這次調查將查問這項銷售的具體情況。

inquire sth **of** sb *phr v* [T] *formal* to ask someone a question about something【正式】向〔某人〕詢問: *He nervously inquired of his host whether he could light a cigarette.* 他不好意思地問主人是否可以吸煙。

in·quir·ing, enquiring /ɪn`kwaɪrɪŋ; ɪn'kwaɪərɪŋ/ *adj* [only before noun 僅用於名詞前] **1** an inquiring look or expression shows that you want to ask about something 〔神色〕有疑問的 **2 an inquiring mind** someone who has an inquiring mind is very interested in finding out more about everything 好探索的精神: *As a child he had a lively inquiring mind.* 他小時候凡事都想問個明白。—**inquiringly** *adv*: *Victor raised an eyebrow inquiringly.* 維克多眉毛一揚, 露出探詢的神色。

3 **in·quir·y, enquiry** /ɪn`kwaɪrɪ; ɪn'kwaɪəri/ *n* **1** [C] a question you ask in order to get information 詢問, 打聽: **[+about]** *We're getting a lot of inquiries from travel companies about our new London-Rio service.* 許多旅行社詢問我們新開設的倫敦－里約熱內盧旅行線路的情況。| **make inquiries** *I don't know who sent the gift, but I'll make discreet inquiries.* 我不知道禮物是誰送的, 但我會小心地打聽一下。| **be helping the police with their inquiries** *BrE* (=be answering questions about a crime)【英】協助警方調查〔罪案〕**2** [U] the act of asking questions in order to get information 查問: *On further inquiry, it emerged that Malcolm had not been involved in the campaign.* 進一步調查表明, 馬爾科姆與該運動無關。| **line of inquiry** (=method of inquiry) 查詢方法 *No definite information yet – but we're following up a most promising line of inquiry.* 現在還沒有確切情報, 但我們正在循着一個可望成功的辦法進行調查。**3 enquiries** the name of a service or office from which you can get information 詢問處; 諮詢處 **4** [C] an official process, in the form of a series of meetings, intended to find out why something happened 〔以一系列會議形式開展的〕官方調查程序: **[+into]** *Local residents are calling for a public inquiry into the accident.* 當地居民要求對這次事故進行公開調查。| **hold/conduct an inquiry** *complaints that the inquiry is being conducted behind closed doors* 對於非公開祕密調查的不滿 **5 scientific inquiry** a process of trying to discover facts by scientific methods 用科學方法調查

inquiry a·gent /·'·· ·,··/ *n* [C] *BrE old-fashioned* a PRIVATE DETECTIVE【英, 過時】私人偵探

in·qui·si·tion /,ɪnkwə`zɪʃən; ,ɪŋkwǀ'zɪʃən/ *n* **1 the Inquisition** the Roman Catholic organization in former times whose aim was to find and punish people who had unacceptable religious beliefs 〔昔日羅馬天主教懲罰異教徒的〕宗教法庭, 異端裁判所 **2** [singular] a series of questions that someone asks you in a threatening or unpleasant way 〔帶威脅、令人不快的〕盤問, 查問: *When I got home I had to face a two-hour inquisition from my parents about where I'd been.* 我回家後遭受父母長達兩小時的盤問, 問我去了哪兒。

in·quis·i·tive /ɪn`kwɪzətɪv; ɪn'kwɪzǀtɪv/ *adj* **1** asking too many questions and trying to find out too many details about something or someone 過分好奇的, 過分好問的, 好追根究底的: *Don't be so inquisitive – it makes people uncomfortable.* 不要打聽個沒完, 弄得人很不舒服。**2** interested in a lot of different things and wanting to find out more about them 好奇的, 愛鑽研的: *a cheerful, inquisitive little boy* 一個快樂、好奇的小男孩 —**inquisitively** *adv*: *He peeped inquisitively into the drawer.* 他好奇地往抽屜裡窺視。—**inquisitiveness** *n* [U]

in·quis·i·tor /ɪn`kwɪzətɚ; ɪn'kwɪzǀtə/ *n* [C] **1** someone who is asking you a lot of difficult questions and making you feel very uncomfortable 〔提出很多難題, 令人不舒服的〕盤問者, 詢問者 **2** an official of the INQUISITION 宗教法庭審判官 —**inquisitorial** /ɪn,kwɪzə`torɪəl; ɪn,kwɪzǀ'tɔːriəl◂/ *adj* —**inquisitorially** *adv*

in·quo·rate /ɪn`kwɔrɪt; ɪn'kwɔːrǀt/ *adj formal* an inquorate meeting does not have enough people to make decisions or vote【正式】〔會議〕未達到法定出席人數的

in re /ɪn `ri; ɪn 'riː/ *prep* an expression used especially in business letters that means 'concerning' 關於〔尤用於商務信函〕

in·roads /`ɪn,rodz; 'ɪnrəʊdz/ also 又作 **inroad** *n* **make inroads into/on a)** to become more and more successful, powerful, or popular and so take away power, trade, votes etc from a competitor or enemy 〔在力量、貿易、選票等方面〕進攻〔競爭者或敵方的領域〕, 侵佔: *Video is making huge inroads into attendance figures at movie theaters.* 錄像帶正在大量奪走電影院的觀眾。**b)** to use more and more of something such as space, time, money, or energy so that there is less available 〔空間、時間、金錢、精力等不斷的〕消耗: *The administrative workload is making massive inroads into our working day.* 行政事務佔去了我們大量的工作時間。

in·sa·lu·bri·ous /,ɪnsə`lubrɪəs; ,ɪnsə'luːbriəs◂/ *adj formal* insalubrious conditions or places are unpleasant and bad for your health【正式】〔條件或地方〕不衛生的, 不利於健康的

ins and outs /,· · '·/ *n* [plural] all the exact details of a complicated situation, problem, system etc 〔複雜的局面、難題等的〕詳情, 細節: *I don't really know all the ins and outs of the matter.* 我並不知道這件事的所有細節。

in·sane /ɪn`sen; ɪn'seɪn/ *adj* **1** *informal* completely stupid or crazy, often in a way that is dangerous【非正式】愚蠢的, 瘋狂的: *I don't know what made Sarah marry him – she must have been totally insane.* 我不明白莎拉為甚麼要嫁給他, 她肯定是發瘋了。| *The whole idea sounds absolutely insane to me.* 整個主意在我看來愚蠢至極。**2** *especially law* someone who is insane is permanently and seriously mentally ill so that they cannot live in normal society【尤法律】(患) 精神病的, 精神失常的, 瘋癲的: *The killer was declared criminally insane.* 這名殺人犯被定為精神失常犯罪。**3 drive sb insane** *informal* to make someone feel more and more annoyed or angry, usually over a long period of time【非正式】逼得某人發瘋〔一般指經過長時間〕: *I had to give up teaching – it was driving me insane.* 我當時不得不放棄教書, 它都要把我逼瘋了。—**insanely** *adv*: *insanely jealous* 發瘋似地妒忌

in·san·i·ta·ry /ɪn`sænə,tɛrɪ; ɪn'sænǀtəri/ *adj* insanitary conditions or places are very dirty and likely to cause disease 骯髒的, 不衛生的, 對健康不利的; UNSANITARY *especially AmE*【尤美】

in·san·i·ty /ɪn`sænətɪ; ɪn'sænǀti/ *n* [U] **1** very stupid actions that may cause you serious harm 極端愚蠢的行為: *It was sheer insanity to drive across the mountains in the dark.* 黑夜駕車翻山越嶺, 簡直荒唐透頂。**2** *especially law* the state of being seriously mentally ill, so that you cannot live normally in society【尤法律】精神錯亂: *The court acquitted Campbell on the grounds of temporary insanity.* 法庭以坎貝爾一時精神錯亂為由而將他無罪釋放。

in·sa·tia·ble /ɪn`seʃəbḷ; ɪn'seɪʃəbəl/ *adj* always wanting more and more of something 貪得無厭的, 不能滿足

的: **insatiable appetite/desire/demand etc** *an insatiable demand for Western consumer goods* 對西方消費品越來越多的需求 —**insatiably** *adv*

in·scribe /ɪnˋskraɪb; ɪnˈskraɪb/ *v* [T] to carefully cut, print, or write words on something, especially on the surface of a stone or coin〔尤指在石頭或硬幣表面細緻地〕雕刻, 印製, 題寫: **inscribe sth in/on etc** *Inside the cover someone had inscribed the words 'To Thomas, with love'.* 在書的內封面上, 題寫了"托馬斯惠存"幾個字。| **inscribe sth with** *The tomb was inscribed with a short epitaph.* 墓碑上刻有簡短的墓誌銘。

in·scrip·tion /ɪnˋskrɪpʃən; ɪnˈskrɪpʃən/ *n* [C] a piece of writing inscribed on a stone, in the front of a book etc 碑文, 題詞

in·scru·ta·ble /ɪnˋskrutəbḷ; ɪnˈskruːtəbəl/ *adj* someone who is inscrutable shows no emotion or reaction in the expression on their face so that it is impossible to know what they are feeling or thinking〔因不露聲色而〕難以理解的, 高深莫測的: *an inscrutable smile* 詭祕的微笑 —**inscrutably** *adv* —**inscrutability** /ɪn͵skrutəˋbɪlətɪ; ɪn͵skruːtəˈbɪlɪ̈ti/ *n* [U]

in·sect /ˋɪnsɛkt; ˈɪnsekt/ *n* [C] a small creature such as a fly or ANT, that has six legs, and sometimes wings 昆蟲: *an insect bite* 昆蟲叮咬的傷口 | *mosquitoes and other flying insects* 蚊子和其他飛蟲

in·sec·ti·cide /ɪnˋsɛktə͵saɪd; ɪnˈsektɪ̈saɪd/ *n* [U] a chemical substance used for killing insects 殺蟲劑, 殺蟲藥 —compare 比較 PESTICIDE —**insecticidal** /ɪn͵sɛktəˋsaɪdḷ; ɪn͵sektɪ̈ˈsaɪdl◂/ *adj*

in·sec·ti·vore /ɪnˋsɛktə͵vɔr; ɪnˈsektɪ̈vɔː/ *n* [C] a creature that eats insects for food 食蟲動物[植物] —**insectivorous** *adj*

in·se·cure /͵ɪnsɪˋkjʊr; ͵ɪnsɪˈkjʊə◂/ *adj* **1** not feeling at all confident about yourself, your abilities, your relationships etc 無自信的, 沒有把握的: *I'd only just started at university and I still felt very shy and insecure.* 當時我剛開始上大學, 還很靦腆而且不自信。**2** a job, INVESTMENT etc that is insecure does not give you a feeling of safety, because it is likely to be taken away or lost at any time〔工作、投資等〕無保障的, 無安全感的: *Running a small business is a very insecure occupation.* 做小買賣是一個沒有甚麼保障的職業。**3** a building or structure that is insecure is not safe, because it is likely to fall down〔建築、結構等〕不牢固的, 可能垮掉的 —**insecurity** *n* [U] *Student teachers often suffer from a great sense of insecurity.* 實習教師常為自信心不足而苦惱。—**insecurely** *adv*

in·sem·i·nate /ɪnˋsɛmə͵net; ɪnˈsemɪ̈neɪt/ *v* [T] to put SPERM into a female animal in order to make her have a baby 使懷孕, 使受精 —**insemination** /ɪn͵sɛməˋneʃən; ɪn͵semɪ̈ˈneɪʃən/ *n* [U] —see also 另見 ARTIFICIAL INSEMINATION

in·sen·sate /ɪnˋsɛnset; ɪnˈsenseɪt/ *adj formal*【正式】**1** not able to feel things; INANIMATE 沒感覺的, 無生命的 **2** unreasonable and crazy 無理智的, 瘋狂的: *insensate rage* 失去理智的狂怒

in·sen·si·bil·i·ty /͵ɪnsɛnsəˋbɪlətɪ; ɪn͵sensɪ̈ˈbɪlɪ̈ti/ *n* [U] **1** *formal* the state of being unconscious【正式】無知覺 **2** *old use* inability to experience feelings such as love, sympathy, anger etc【舊】冷淡, 無感情

in·sen·si·ble /ɪnˋsɛnsəbḷ; ɪnˈsensɪ̈bəl/ *adj formal*【正式】**1** not knowing about something that could happen to you; UNAWARE 沒意識到的, 沒覺察到的: **[+of]** *She remained insensible of the dangers that lay ahead.* 她對即將出現的危險毫無察覺。**2** unable to feel something or be affected by it 無感覺的: **[+to/of]** *insensible to the cold* 感覺不到寒冷 **3** *old use* not conscious【舊】失去知覺的: *He fell to the ground, insensible.* 他跌倒在地, 失去了知覺。—**insensibly** *adv*

in·sen·si·tive /ɪnˋsɛnsətɪv; ɪnˈsensɪ̈tɪv/ *adj* **1** not noticing other people's feelings, and not realizing when they are upset or when something that you do will upset them 麻木不仁的, 缺乏同情心的: *One insensitive official insisted on seeing her husband's death certificate.* 一位不近人情的官員非要看看她丈夫的死亡證明不可。| **[+to]** *She's totally insensitive to Jack's feelings.* 她根本不理會傑克的感情。**2** not paying attention to what is happening or to what people are saying, and therefore not changing your behaviour because of it〔對發生的事或別人的話〕置之不理的, 不作反應的: **[+to]** *Companies that are insensitive to global changes will lose sales.* 對全球變化無動於衷的公司, 其銷售額必會下降。| *Outwardly he seems insensitive to criticism.* 從表面上看, 他似乎對批評漠然處之。**3** not affected by physical effects or changes 身體無感覺的, 麻木的: **[+to]** *insensitive to pain* 無疼痛感 | *insensitive to light* 無光感 —**insensitively** *adv* —**insensitivity** /ɪn͵sɛnsəˋtɪvətɪ; ɪn͵sensɪ̈ˈtɪvɪ̈ti/ *n* [U]

in·sep·a·ra·ble /ɪnˋsɛpərəbḷ; ɪnˈsepərəbəl/ *adj* **1** people who are inseparable are always together and are very friendly with each other〔人〕常在一起的, 親密無間的: *Jane and Sarah soon became inseparable companions.* 簡與莎拉很快就形影不離了。**2** things that are inseparable cannot be separated or cannot be considered separately〔東西〕分不開的, 不可分離的: **[+from]** *In poetry meaning is inseparable from form.* 在詩歌中, 意義與形式不可分離。—**inseparably** *adv* —**inseparability** /͵ɪnsɛpərəˋbɪlətɪ; ɪn͵sepərəˈbɪlɪ̈ti/ *n* [U]

in·sert¹ /ɪnˋsɝt; ɪnˈsɜːt/ *v* [T] **1** to put something inside or into something else 插入, 放進: **insert sth in/into/between** *He inserted a sheet of paper into the printer.* 他把一張紙放入打印機。| *Insert one 20p coin.* 投入一枚 20 便士的硬幣。**2** to add something to the middle of a document or piece of writing〔在文件或文稿中〕加入, 加進: *The manager wanted to insert a clause giving him 30% of any future earnings.* 經理想加入一項條款, 規定他在未來的贏利中可以獲得 30% 的分紅。

insert 插入

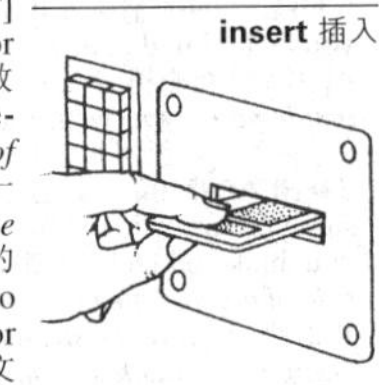

in·sert² /ˋɪnsɝt; ˈɪnsɜːt/ *n* [C] **1** printed pages that are put inside a newspaper or magazine in order to advertise something〔夾在報刊中的〕插頁廣告: *a six-page insert on computer software* 關於電腦軟件的六張插頁廣告 **2** something that is designed to be put inside something else 插入物: *He wore special inserts in his shoes to make him look taller.* 他在鞋裡墊了一些東西, 以使他顯得個子高一點兒。

in·ser·tion /ɪnˋsɝʃən; ɪnˈsɜːʃən/ *n* **1** [U] the act of putting something inside something else 放入, 插入 **2** [C] something that is added to the middle of a document or piece of writing〔文件或文稿中的〕插入物

in-ser·vice /͵· ˋ··◂/ *adj* **in-service training/courses etc** training etc that you do while you are working in a job 在職培訓/課程等

in·set¹ /ˋɪnsɛt; ˈɪnset/ *n* [C] a small picture, map etc in the corner of a page or larger picture etc, which shows more detail or information 嵌入物, 附加物〔尤指附加在大圖片、大地圖角位上, 以顯示細部或提供更詳盡資料的小圖片或小地圖〕: *See inset for a comparison of world grain exporters.* 要對全球糧食出口國比較, 請看附圖。

in·set² /ɪnˋsɛt; ɪnˈset/ *v past tense and past participle* **inset** *or* **insetted** [T] **1** to put something in as an inset on a printed page〔在一頁印刷品中〕嵌入, 加入 **2 be inset with** if something is inset with decorations, jewels etc, it has them set in its surface 被嵌入〔飾品、珠寶等〕

in·shore /͵ɪnˋʃor; ͵ɪnˈʃɔː◂/ *adv* near, towards, or to the shore 靠近海岸, 向海岸: *The fishing boats usually stay close inshore.* 漁船通常逗留在近海海域。—**inshore** *adj*: *an inshore lifeboat* 海岸救生艇

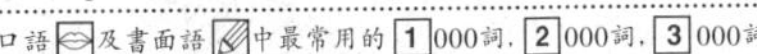

in·side¹ /ɪnˋsaɪd; ɪnˈsaɪd/ *prep*
1 ►CONTAINER 容器◄ in a container or other closed space so that it is completely covered or surrounded 在〔容器或其他封閉的空間〕裡面: *I'll leave the keys inside an envelope.* 我會把鑰匙放在一個信封裡。| *The jewels were locked away inside the safe.* 珠寶都鎖入了保險箱。
2 ►BUILDING/ROOM 建築物/房間◄ in a room or building, especially when you are looking at it from the outside 在房間內, 在樓內〔尤指從外面看〕: *Mail was piled up just inside the doorway.* 在入口處上堆滿了郵件。
3 ►COUNTRY 國家◄ a word meaning in a country or area, used when you want to emphasize that something is happening there and not outside it 在某國家[地區]內部〔強調某事只在那裡發生〕: *Very little is known of events inside Albania.* 幾乎沒有人知道阿爾巴尼亞國內發生的事情。| *The guerrillas were said to be operating from bases inside the war zone.* 據說游擊隊員是從戰區內部的基地出發進行活動的。
4 ►ORGANIZATION 組織◄ a word meaning in an organization or company, used when you want to emphasize that something is happening or known about there, but not outside it 在〔組織或公司的〕內部〔強調某事只在那裡發生〕: *women's influence inside the Party* 婦女在黨內的影響力 | *There have been rumours of bitter disputes inside the company.* 一直有謠傳說公司內部常有激烈的爭執。
5 ►FEELING 情感◄ if you have a feeling inside you, you feel it but do not express it or tell other people about it〔感情〕在心裡: *It's no good bottling all the anger up inside you – you've got to let it out.* 把怒氣憋在心裡不好, 你應當發泄出來。
6 ►HEAD/MIND 頭腦/心靈◄ if something happens inside you, or inside your head or mind, it is part of what you think and feel 在…腦海中, 在…心裡: *Something inside of me told me not to trust him.* 我的直覺告訴我不能相信他。| *Steve's a strange guy – you never know what's going on inside his head.* 斯蒂夫是個怪人, 誰也不知道他腦子裡在想甚麼。
7 ►BODY 身體◄ in your body 在…體內: *She could feel the baby kicking inside her.* 她感到胎兒在腹內踢蹬。| *You'll feel better once you've got a good meal inside you* (=after you have eaten something). 好好吃一頓, 你就會感覺好些的。
8 ►TIME 時間◄ *especially spoken* if you do something inside a particular amount of time, it takes you slightly less than that amount of time to do it【尤口】〔時間〕在…內, 少於…: *Jonson's time of 9.3 seconds was just inside the world record.* 約翰遜用了 9.3 秒, 剛好破了世界紀錄。| **inside (of) two hours/inside (of) fifteen minutes etc** *We did the return trip to Birmingham in just inside three hours.* 我們返回伯明翰用了不到三個小時。

in·side² /ɪnˋsaɪd; ɪnˈsaɪd/ *adv* **1** in something 在〔某物〕裡面: *The car was locked and the keys were inside.* 車已鎖上, 鑰匙卻在車裡。| *The purse had £50 inside.* 錢包裡有 50 英鎊。**2** in a house or other building 在〔房子或其他建築物〕內: *It's raining. We'll have to go inside.* 下雨了, 我們進屋去吧。| *She could hear voices inside, but no-one came to the door.* 她聽到裡面有說話聲, 但沒有人來開門。**3** if you have a feeling inside, you have the feeling but do not show it to other people〔感覺〕在心裡: *You just don't understand how I feel inside!* 你根本不懂我心裡在想甚麼! **4** *informal* in prison【非正式】在監獄裡, 坐牢: *My boyfriend's been inside for a year.* 我的男友在獄裡已一年了。**5 inside of a)** within a particular period of time 在〔一定時間〕之內: *We should get it finished inside of a month.* 我們必須一個月內完成。**b)** *AmE* on the inside of something【美】在〔某物〕內: *There were now about a thousand people inside of the stadium.* 體育館裡約有一千人。

in·side³ /ɪnˋsaɪd; ɪnˈsaɪd/ *n* **1 the inside a)** the inner part of something, which is surrounded or hidden by the outer part 裡面, 內部: *The apple's rotten on the inside.* 這個蘋果裡面爛了。| *The door had been locked from the inside.* 門已從裡面上鎖。—opposite 反義詞 OUTSIDE⁴ (1) **b)** the part of a road that is nearest to the edge on the side where you are driving〔道路的〕內側: *He tried to overtake me on the inside.* 他試圖從內側超過我。**2 inside out** with the usual outside parts on the inside 裡面朝外地: *You've got that jumper inside out.* 你把套頭毛衣穿反了。| *Turn cushion covers inside out to wash them.* 把坐墊套子裡外翻過來洗洗。**3 on the inside** someone who is on the inside is a member of a group or an organization〔團體或組織的〕內部人員: *Someone on the inside must have helped with the robbery.* 這樁搶劫案肯定有內應協助。**4 sb's inside/insides** *informal* someone's stomach【非正式】腸胃; 肚子: *My insides are beginning to complain about the lack of food.* 我開始感到肚子餓。**5 turn sth inside out** to search a place very thoroughly by moving everything that is in it 對某處進行徹底搜尋: *The drug squad turned the apartment inside out.* 緝毒組把公寓搜了個遍。**6 know sth inside out** to know something in great detail 知道得一清二楚: *She knows her subject inside out.* 她對她的課題了解得很透徹。

in·side⁴ /ˈɪnsaɪd; ˈɪnsaɪd/ *adj* **1** on or facing the inside of something 裡面的, 內部的; 朝裡的: *the inside pages of the newspaper* 報紙的裡頁 **2 inside information/the inside story etc** information that is available only to people who are part of a particular group or organization 內部消息; 內幕: *Police believe the robbers may have had inside information.* 警方認為搶劫犯可能得到了內部消息。

inside lane /ˌ·· ˈ·/ *n* [C] **1** the part of a road that is closest to the edge, usually used by slow vehicles〔靠近路邊較多慢速車輛行駛的〕內車道 —see picture on page A3 參見 A3 頁圖 **2** the part of a circular track for racing that is nearest to the centre of the circle and is therefore shorter〔比賽跑道的〕內圈

in·sid·er /ɪnˋsaɪdə; ɪnˈsaɪdə/ *n* [C] someone who has a special knowledge of a particular organization because they are part of it〔團體〕內部的人, 圈內人, 業內人士: *an insider's view of the way that a Japanese company works* 業內人士對日本公司運作方式的看法 —compare 比較 OUTSIDER (3)

insider trad·ing /ˌ·· ˈ··/ also 又作 **insider dealing** *n* [U] illegal buying and selling of a company's shares (SHARE² (5)) involving the use of secret information known only by people connected with the company〔股票的〕內幕交易, 內線交易〔指利用祕密的內幕消息而非法買賣一家公司的股票〕

inside track /ˌ·· ˈ·/ *n* [C] **1** the part of a circular track for racing that is nearest to the centre of the circle and is therefore shorter〔比賽的〕內圈跑道〔最接近圓心, 因此較短〕**2** *AmE* a position that gives someone an advantage over the people they are competing against【美】〔競爭中的〕有利地位, 有利形勢: *the inside track to success in business* 企業成功的有利形勢

in·sid·i·ous /ɪnˋsɪdɪəs; ɪnˈsɪdiəs/ *adj* an insidious danger or problem spreads gradually without being noticed, and causes serious harm〔危險或問題〕暗中為害的,〔禍害〕潛伏的: *an insidious trend towards censorship of the press* 實行新聞審查的逆流 —**insidiously** *adv* —**insidiousness** *n* [U]

in·sight /ˋɪnˌsaɪt; ˈɪnsaɪt/ *n* **1** [U] the ability to understand and realize what people or situations are really like 洞察力, 眼光: *a woman of great insight* 一位極有眼光的婦女 **2** [C] a sudden clear understanding of something, especially something complicated〔尤指對複雜事情的〕頓悟, 猛省: [+into] *The article gives us a real insight into the causes of the present economic crisis.* 這篇文章分析目前經濟危機的原因, 發人深省。

in·sig·ni·a /ɪnˋsɪgnɪə; ɪnˈsɪgniə/ *n plural* **insignia** [C] a BADGE (1) or sign that shows what official or military rank someone has, or which group or organization they belong to〔表示官銜、軍階的〕徽章,〔隸屬某個組織或機構的〕標誌: *the royal insignia* 王權的徽章 | *military insignia* 軍階標誌

in·sig·nif·i·cant /ˌɪnsɪgˋnɪfəkənt; ˌɪnsɪgˈnɪfɪkənt◂/ *adj* too small or unimportant to consider or worry about 不重要的, 價值不大的, 無意義的: *Looking at the Earth from space makes you realize how small and insignificant we all are.* 從太空看地球, 會使你發現我們都是多麼渺小。| *an insignificant difference* 微小的區別 —**insignificantly** *adv* —**insignificance** *n* [U]

in·sin·cere /ˌɪnsɪnˋsɪr; ˌɪnsɪnˈsɪə◂/ *adj* pretending to be pleased, sympathetic etc, especially by saying nice things, but not really meaning what you say 不誠懇的, 虛偽的: *insincere praise* 虛情假意的讚揚, 吹噓 | *an insincere smile* 虛偽的微笑; 諂笑 —**insincerely** *adv* —**insincerity** /ˌɪnsɪnˋsɛrətɪ; ˌɪnsɪnˈserɪ̈ti/ *n* [U]

in·sin·u·ate /ɪnˋsɪnjuˌet; ɪnˈsɪnjueɪt/ *v* [T] **1** to say something which seems to mean something unpleasant without saying it directly, for example saying indirectly that someone is being dishonest 暗示〔令人不快的內容〕; 含沙射影地說: **insinuate that** *Are you insinuating that the money was stolen?* 你是在暗示錢被偷了嗎? **2 insinuate yourself into** to gradually gain someone's love, trust etc by pretending to be friendly and sincere〔假裝友善和誠實〕使自己取得〔某人的喜愛、信任等〕: *He managed to insinuate his way into her affections.* 他終於設法贏得了她的好感。

in·sin·u·a·tion /ɪnˌsɪnjuˋeʃən; ɪnˌsɪnjuˈeɪʃən/ *n* **1** [C] something that someone insinuates 影射, 暗示: *the insinuation that they did not know how to run their own business* 關於他們經營無方的暗示 **2** [U] the act of insinuating something 暗示, 暗指

in·sip·id /ɪnˋsɪpɪd; ɪnˈsɪpɪ̈d/ *adj* **1** food or drink that is insipid does not have much taste〔飲食〕淡而無味的: *an insipid pasta dish* 一盤沒有味道的麵點 **2** not interesting, exciting, or attractive 枯燥無味的, 不吸引人的: *an insipid young man* 木訥的年輕人 —**insipidly** *adv* —**insipidness, insipidity** /ˌɪnsɪˋpɪdətɪ; ˌɪnsɪ̈ˈpɪdɪ̈ti/ *n* [U]

3 2 **in·sist** /ɪnˋsɪst; ɪnˈsɪst/ *v* [I] **1** to say firmly and repeatedly that something is true, especially when other people think it may not be true 堅持宣稱, 堅決認為: **insist that** *Mike insisted that he was right.* 邁克堅決認為自己是對的。| **[+on]** *She kept insisting on her innocence.* 她再三堅持自己無罪。**2** to demand that something should happen and refuse to let anyone say no 堅持主張, 堅決要求, 一定要: **[+on]** *Her parents insisted on speaking to the headmistress.* 她父母堅持要和女校長談話。| *Stay for supper – I insist!* 你一定要留下來吃晚飯! | **insist that** *They insisted that everyone should come to the party.* 他們堅決要求每個人都要來參加晚會。**3 if you insist** *spoken* used when agreeing to do something that you do not really want to do【口】如果你一定要這樣〔用來對你並不真正想做的事表示同意〕: *"Why don't you call them up today?" "Oh, if you insist!"* "你何不今天就給他們打電話?" "好吧, 如果你一定要我這樣辦的話。"

insist on sth *phr v* [T] **1** to think that something is very important, and demand that you have it 認為〔某事〕非常重要〔並堅持得到它〕: *We insist on the highest standards of cleanliness in the hotel.* 我們堅持要酒店的衛生水平達到最高標準。**2** to keep doing something, especially something that is inconvenient or annoying 堅持做〔尤指麻煩或令人討厭的事〕: *She will insist on washing her hair just when I want to have a bath.* 正當我要洗澡的時候, 她偏要去洗頭髮。

in·sis·tence /ɪnˋsɪstəns; ɪnˈsɪstəns/ *n* [U] an act of demanding that something should happen and refusing to let anyone say no 堅決要求, 堅持: **insistence that** *his insistence that they discuss the problem* 他堅持要他們討論這個問題 | **[+on]** *an insistence on punctuality* 堅決主張守時 | **at sb's insistence** (=because someone insisted) 由於某人的堅持 *At her father's insistence, she joined them for a drink.* 由於父親的堅持, 她和他們一起喝了一杯酒。

in·sis·tent /ɪnˋsɪstənt; ɪnˈsɪstənt/ *adj* **1** demanding firmly and repeatedly that something should happen 堅持的, 堅決要求的: **insistent that** *She was insistent that they should all meet for dinner.* 她堅持要大家聚在一起吃晚飯。| **[+on]** *insistent on good manners* 堅持彬彬有禮 **2** making a continuous loud sound that is difficult to ignore〔響聲〕持續不斷的: *the insistent pounding of drums* 持續不斷的擊鼓聲 —**insistently** *adv*

in si·tu /ɪn ˋsaɪtju; ɪn ˈsɪtjuː/ *adv Latin* if something remains in situ, it remains in its usual place【拉丁】在原地, 在原來位置

in·so·far /ˌɪnsoˋfɑr; ˌɪnsəˈfɑː/ *adv* —see 見 **in so far as/in as far as/insofar as** (FAR[1] (30))

in·sole /ˋɪnˌsol; ˈɪnsəʊl/ *n* [C] a foot-shaped piece of cloth, leather etc that you put inside your shoe 鞋墊

in·so·lent /ˋɪnsələnt; ˈɪnsələnt/ *adj* rude and not showing any respect 粗魯無禮的, 傲慢的: *an insolent tone of voice* 傲慢的語氣 | *You insolent child!* 你這個沒禮貌的孩子! —**insolently** *adv* —**insolence** *n* [U]

in·sol·u·ble /ɪnˋsɑljəbḷ; ɪnˈsɒljɪ̈bəl/ *adj* **1** an insoluble problem is or seems impossible to solve〔問題〕(似乎)不能解決的: *insoluble conflicts within the department* 部門內難以調和的衝突 **2** an insoluble substance does not become a liquid when you put it into a liquid〔物質〕不能溶解的 —compare 比較 DISSOLVE (1)

in·sol·va·ble /ɪnˋsɑlvəbḷ; ɪnˈsɒlvəbəl/ *adj especially AmE* an insolvable problem is or seems impossible to solve; INSOLUBLE (1)【尤美】〔問題〕(似乎)不能解決的 —**insolvably** *adv*

in·sol·vent /ɪnˋsɑlvənt; ɪnˈsɒlvənt/ *adj* not having enough money to pay what you owe; BANKRUPT 無償債能力的, 破產的: *insolvent private companies* 無償債能力的私人公司 —**insolvency** *n* [U]

in·som·ni·a /ɪnˋsɑmnɪə; ɪnˈsɒmniə/ *n* [U] the condition of not being able to sleep 失眠

in·som·ni·ac /ɪnˋsɑmnɪæk; ɪnˈsɒmniæk/ *n* [C] someone who cannot sleep easily 失眠症患者 —**insomniac** *adj*

in·so·much /ˌɪnsəˋmʌtʃ; ˌɪnsəʊˈmʌtʃ/ *adv formal*【正式】**1 insomuch that** *especially AmE* to such a degree that【尤美】到…的程度(因此…) **2** another form of the word INASMUCH inasmuch 的另一種形式

in·sou·ci·ance /ɪnˋsusɪəns; ɪnˈsuːsiəns/ *n* [U] *formal* a cheerful feeling of not caring or worrying about anything【正式】無憂無慮: *He strolled through the house with an air of insouciance.* 他在這座房子裡踱來踱去, 一副逍遙自在的樣子。—**insouciant** *adj* —**insouciantly** *adv*

in·spect /ɪnˋspɛkt; ɪnˈspekt/ *v* [T] **1** to examine something carefully in order to find out more about it or that it is not satisfactory 仔細檢查; 檢驗: *I got out of the car to inspect the damage.* 我下車檢查損壞情況。| **inspect sth for cracks/faults etc** (=in order to check that there are no cracks etc) 檢查某物有無裂縫/毛病等 *He carefully inspected the china for cracks.* 他仔細檢查瓷器看有無裂紋。—see graph at 參見 EXAMINE 圖表 **2** to make an official visit to a building, organization etc to check that everything is satisfactory and that rules are being obeyed 視察; 檢閱: *The building is regularly inspected by the fire-safety officer.* 消防安全官定期視察這座大樓。| *General Allenby arrived to inspect the troops.* 艾倫比將軍來此檢閱部隊。

in·spec·tion /ɪnˋspɛkʃən; ɪnˈspekʃən/ *n* [C,U] **1** an official visit to a building or organization to check that everything is satisfactory and that rules are being obeyed 視察; 檢閱: **[+of]** *regular inspections of the prison* 定期視察監獄 | **carry out an inspection** *An inspection was carried out at the school.* 有人來學校視察了一遍。| **tour of inspection** (=an official journey or visit to inspect 3 something) 巡察 **2** a careful examination of something to find out more about it 仔細檢查: **on closer inspection** (=when looked at more closely) 再仔細一看 *On closer inspection, the scrap of paper turned out to be a £20 note.* 再仔細一看, 這張小紙片原來是一張面值20英鎊的鈔票。

in·spec·tor /ɪn`spɛktɚ; ɪn'spektə/ *n* [C] **1** an official whose job is to check that something is satisfactory and that rules are being obeyed 檢查員; 督察員: *ticket inspectors* 查票員 | *a Health and Safety inspector* 健康安全視察員 **2** a police officer of middle rank 督察, 巡官〔中級警官〕: *Inspector Blake* 布萊克巡官 —see also 另見 CHIEF INSPECTOR **3** *BrE* someone whose job is to visit schools and judge the quality of the teaching【英】督學

in·spec·tor·ate /ɪn`spɛktərɪt; ɪn'spektərɨt/ *n* [C] the group of INSPECTORs who officially inspect schools, factories etc〔學校、工廠等的〕檢查團, 督察隊

inspector of tax·es /·,·· · '··/ *n* [C] *BrE* a government official who calculates what tax each person should pay【英】稅務稽查員

in·spi·ra·tion /ˌɪnspə`reʃən; ˌɪnspɨ'reɪʃən/ *n* [C,U] **1** a sudden good idea about what you should do or say 靈感: *I haven't started writing the article yet – I'm still waiting for inspiration.* 我還沒有開始寫那篇文章, 我還在等待靈感。**2** the state of being given encouragement or good ideas about what you should do 鼓舞, 啟示: **divine inspiration** (=inspiration from God or gods) 神的啟示, 神靈感應 **3** a person, experience, place, etc that you get inspiration from 給人以靈感的人物[經歷、地點等]: *The seascapes of Cape Cod were her inspiration.* 科德角的海景給她靈感。**4 be an inspiration to sb** to make someone feel encouraged to be as good, successful etc as possible 給某人以鼓舞: *Maya, who bears her illness with such patience, is an inspiration to us all.* 瑪雅堅忍地對待疾病, 給我們很大的鼓舞。

in·spi·ra·tion·al /ˌɪnspə`reʃənḷ; ˌɪnspɨ'reɪʃənəl◂/ *adj* providing inspiration 鼓舞人心的; 給予靈感的: *Jones proved an inspirational figure in Welsh rugby.* 事實證明, 瓊斯是威爾斯橄欖球運動中能鼓舞人心的人物。

in·spire /ɪn`spaɪr; ɪn'spaɪə/ *v* [T] **1** to encourage someone by making them feel confident and eager to achieve something great 鼓舞, 激勵: *We need a new captain – someone who can inspire the team.* 我們需要一位能振奮士氣的新隊長。| **inspire sb to sth** *I hope this success will inspire you to greater efforts.* 希望這次成功能激勵你更加努力。**2** to make someone have a particular feeling or react in a particular way 使〔某人〕產生〔某種感情或反應〕, 激起, 喚起: *Gandhi's quiet dignity inspired respect even among his enemies.* 甘地不怒自威, 連他的敵人都肅然起敬。| **not inspire confidence** (=make people feel anxious because they do not trust your ability) 難以讓人信任: *His driving hardly inspires confidence.* 他的開車技術難以讓人放心。**3** to give someone the idea for a story, painting, poem etc 給〔某人〕創作靈感: *The story was inspired by a chance meeting with an old Russian duke.* 這個故事的創作靈感來自與一位俄國老公爵的不期而遇。**4** *technical* to breathe in【術語】吸氣

in·spired /ɪn`spaɪrd; ɪn'spaɪəd/ *adj* **1** having very exciting special qualities that are better than anyone or anything else 卓越的, 激動人心的: *an inspired leader* 卓越的領導人 | *Wordsworth's most inspired poems* 華茲華斯極富靈感的詩 **2 inspired guess** a correct guess that is based on feelings rather than facts 憑靈感[直覺]的正確猜測 **3 politically inspired** started for political reasons 基於政治原因: *We suspect that the violence was politically inspired.* 我們認為這次暴力衝突由政治原因導致。

in·spir·ing /ɪn`spaɪrɪŋ; ɪn'spaɪərɪŋ/ *adj* giving people energy, a feeling of excitement, and a desire to do something great 鼓舞人心的; 啟發靈感的: *inspiring music* 激勵人心的音樂 | *King, 27 years old, was a great orator and an inspiring leader.* 27 歲的金是偉大的演說家和鼓舞人心的領袖。

inst /ɪnst; ɪnst/ *adj BrE formal old-fashioned* used after a date in business letters to mean 'of the present month'【英, 正式, 過時】本月〔用於商務信件中的日期後〕: *Thank you for your letter of the 21st inst.* 感謝你本月 21 日的來信。

in·sta·bil·i·ty /ˌɪnstə`bɪlətɪ; ˌɪnstə'bɪlɨti/ *n* [U] **1** uncertainty in a situation that is caused by the possibility of sudden change〔形勢的〕不穩定: *the instability of the market* 市場的變化無常 | *political instability* 政治上的動蕩 **2** mental problems that are likely to cause sudden changes of behaviour〔可能導致行為突然失常的〕精神疾病: *nervous instability* 神經錯亂

in·stall, instal /ɪn`stɔl; ɪn'stɔːl/ *v* [T] **1** to put a piece of equipment somewhere and connect it so that it is ready to be used 安裝〔設備〕, 設置: *They've installed the new network at last.* 他們終於安裝了新網絡。**2** to put someone in an important job or position, especially with a ceremony〔尤指通過特別儀式〕正式任命, 使正式就職: *Churchill was installed as Chancellor of the university.* 丘吉爾被任命為那所大學的校長。**3 install yourself in/at etc** to settle somewhere as if you are going to stay for a long time 把自己安頓在〔某地逗留很長一段時間〕, 安置

in·stal·la·tion /ˌɪnstə`leʃən; ˌɪnstə'leɪʃən/ *n* **1** [C] a piece of equipment that has been fitted in its place 裝置, 設備: *The whole computer installation was nearly new.* 整套電腦設備幾乎是全新的。**2** [U] the act of fitting a piece of equipment somewhere 安裝: *the installation of a new washing machine* 安裝一台新洗衣機 **3** [C] a place where industrial or military equipment, machinery etc has been put〔工業或軍事〕設施, 基地: *nuclear installations* 核設施 **4** [U] *formal* the ceremony of putting someone in an important job or position【正式】就職儀式: *the installation of the new bishop* 新主教的就職儀式

installment plan /·'·· ·/ *n* [singular, U] *AmE* a system of paying for goods by a series of small regular payments【美】分期付款購物法; HIRE PURCHASE *BrE*【英】

in·stal·ment also 又作 **installment** *AmE*【美】/ɪn`stɔlmənt; ɪn'stɔːlmənt/ *n* [C] **1** one of a series of regular payments, that you make until you have paid all the money you owe〔分期付款中的〕每期付款額: *the second instalment of a loan* 一項貸款的第二期還款 | **pay by instalments** *They're letting me pay for the washing machine by instalments.* 他們允許我以分期付款方式買這台洗衣機。**2** one of the parts of a story that appears as a series of parts in a magazine, newspaper etc; EPISODE (2)〔在報刊上分期連載故事的〕一期

in·stance¹ /`ɪnstəns; 'ɪnstəns/ *n* **1 for instance** for example 例如: *You can't rely on her. For instance, she arrived an hour late for an important meeting yesterday.* 她這個人靠不住, 比如說, 昨天有個重要會議, 她晚來了一小時。**2** [C] an example of a particular kind of situation〔特定情況的〕例子, 實例: **[+of]** *instances of injustice* 種種不公的事例 | **in this instance** *Hilary is right about most things, but in this instance I think she was mistaken.* 多數情況下希拉里都是對的, 但這件事上我認為她弄錯了。**3 at sb's instance** *formal* because of someone's wish or request【正式】應某人的請求 **4 in the first instance** at the beginning of a series of actions〔一連串行動的〕第一步, 首先: *Anyone wishing to join the society should apply in the first instance to the secretary.* 任何人加入協會都得先向祕書提出申請。

instance² *v* [T] *formal* to give something as an example【正式】舉…為例: *She instanced the first chapter as proof of his skill in constructing scenes.* 她以第一章為例證明他構思情節的技巧。

in·stant¹ /`ɪnstənt; 'ɪnstənt/ *adj* **1** happening or produced immediately 立刻的, 馬上的: *The women took an instant dislike to one another.* 那些女人立即相互厭惡起來。| *a system that provides instant hot water* 即時熱水供應系統 **2** [only before noun 僅用於名詞前] instant food, coffee etc is in the form of powder and prepared by adding hot water〔食物、咖啡〕速溶的, 調製方便的: *instant coffee* 速溶咖啡

instant² *n* **1** [C usually singular 一般用單數] a moment 片刻, 頃刻: *She caught his eye for an instant.* 她在一瞬間與他的目光相遇。| **in an instant** (=immediately) *When the rain started, the crowd vanished in an instant.* 下雨了, 人羣立刻散盡。**2 the instant (that)** as soon as something happens 一…(就…): *The instant I saw him, I knew he was the man the police were looking for.* 我一看到他就認出他正是警方在尋找的那個人。**3 this instant** *spoken* used when telling someone, especially a child, to do something immediately【口】立即, 此刻〔尤用於催促小孩〕: *Come here this instant!* 趕緊過來!

in·stan·ta·ne·ous /ˌɪnstənˋtenɪəs; ˌɪnstənˈteɪniəs◂/ *adj* happening immediately 即刻的: *The computer gives an instantaneous response.* 電腦瞬間作出反應。—**instantaneously** *adv* —**instantaneousness** *n* [U]

in·stant·ly /ˋɪnstəntlɪ; ˈɪnstəntli/ *adv* immediately 立即, 馬上: *They recognised him instantly.* 他們立刻認出了他。| *All four victims died instantly.* 四名受害人都當即死去。

instant re·play /ˌ.. ˈ../ *n* [C] *AmE* an important moment in a sports game on television that is shown again immediately after it happens【美】〔電視體育比賽節目中重要鏡頭的〕即時重放; ACTION REPLAY *BrE*【英】

1 1 **in·stead** /ɪnˋstɛd; ɪnˈsted/ *adv* **1 instead of** in place of something or someone 代替; 而不是: *We should do something instead of just talking about it.* 我們不能只是談論, 應當做點甚麼。| *You must have picked up my keys instead of yours.* 你肯定拿走了我的鑰匙, 而不是你自己的。| *Could I have tuna instead of ham?* 我可否要金槍魚來代替火腿? **2** in place of something that has just been mentioned 作為替代: *If Joe can't attend the meeting, I could go instead.* 如果喬不能去開會, 我可以代他去。| *We didn't have enough money for a movie, so we went to the park instead.* 我們的錢不夠看電影, 於是去了公園。| [sentence adverb 句子副詞] *Cardew did not join the navy. Instead, he decided to become an actor.* 卡杜沒有參加海軍, 而是決定當演員。

in·step /ˋɪnˌstɛp; ˈɪnstep/ *n* [C] **1** the raised part of your foot between your toes and your ANKLE 腳背 —see picture at 參見 FOOT¹ 圖 **2** the part of a shoe or sock that covers this part 鞋面; 襪背 —see picture at 參見 SHOE¹ 圖

in·sti·gate /ˋɪnstəˌget; ˈɪnstɪgeɪt/ *v* [T] **1** to start something such as a legal process or an official inquiry 開始〔法律程序、正式調查等〕; 發起: *Without evidence it would be impossible to instigate an official investigation.* 沒有證據就不能進行正式調查。**2** to start trouble by persuading someone to do something bad 唆使; 煽動: *A foreign government was accused of having instigated the bloodshed.* 某外國政府被指控煽動了這次流血事件。—**instigator** *n* [C]

in·sti·ga·tion /ˌɪnstəˋgeʃən; ˌɪnstɪˈgeɪʃən/ *n* **1 at sb's instigation** *formal* because of someone's suggestion, request or demand【正式】在某人的建議[請求, 要求]下: *At Canham's instigation, a clerk brought in an electric fan.* 在坎納姆的建議下, 辦事員拿進一台電風扇。**2** [U] the act of starting something 發動; 發起

in·stil *BrE*【英】, **instill** *AmE*【美】/ɪnˋstɪl; ɪnˈstɪl/ *v* [T] to teach someone a way of thinking or behaving over a long period of time 逐漸灌輸〔思想或行為方式〕: **instil sth in/into sb** *They instilled good manners into their children at an early age.* 他們從小就教育孩子要有禮貌。—**instillation** /ˌɪnstɪˋleʃən; ˌɪnstɪˈleɪʃən/ *n* [U]

in·stinct /ˋɪnstɪŋkt; ˈɪnstɪŋkt/ *n* [C,U] a natural tendency or ability to behave or react in a particular way without having to learn it or think about it 本能; 直覺; 天性: **[+for]** *an instinct for self-preservation* 自我保存的本能 | **instinct to do sth** *a lion's instinct to hunt* 獅子的獵食本能 | *My instinct would be to wait and see.* 我的本能反應會是等着瞧。—compare 比較 INTUITION

in·stinc·tive /ɪnˋstɪŋktɪv; ɪnˈstɪŋktɪv/ *adj* based on instinct〔出於〕本能的;〔出於〕天性的;〔出於〕直覺的: *instinctive behaviour* 本能行為 | *an instinctive sympathy with the younger boys* 對小男孩的天生惻隱之心 —**instinctively** *adv*: *Instinctively, we dived for cover.* 我們本能地迅速躲藏起來。

in·sti·tute¹ /ˋɪnstəˌtjut; ˈɪnstɪtjuːt/ *n* [C] an organization that has a particular purpose such as scientific or educational work, or the building where this organization is based 學院; 研究院, 研究所: *The Institute for Contemporary Arts* 當代藝術學院 | *research institutes* 研究所 2

institute² *v* [T] *formal* to introduce or start a system, rule, legal process etc【正式】制定〔制度、規則等〕; 提起〔訴訟〕: *institute divorce proceedings* 提出離婚訴訟

in·sti·tu·tion /ˌɪnstəˋtjuʃən; ˌɪnstɪˈtjuːʃən/ *n* [C] 1

1 ▶FOR SCIENCE/BUSINESS 關於科學/企業◀ a large establishment or organization that has a particular kind of work or purpose 機構, 團體: *the most advanced medical institution in the world* 全球最先進的醫療機構 | *a financial institution* 金融機構

2 ▶HOSPITAL ETC 醫院等◀ a) a large building where old people or ORPHANS live and are looked after by an official organization 慈善機構; 養老院; 孤兒院: *The atmosphere of the institution was rather impersonal.* 這家養老院缺乏人情味。**b)** a word meaning a mental hospital, used when you want to avoid saying this directly 精神病院〔委婉語〕

3 ▶CUSTOM 習俗◀ an established system or custom in society 習俗, 慣例, 制度: *the institution of marriage* 婚姻習俗

4 ▶STARTING STH 開始某事◀ the act of starting or introducing a system, rule etc 開創; 制定: **[+of]** *They approved the institution of a new law.* 他們同意制定一部新法律。

5 ▶PERSON 人物◀ be an institution *humorous* to be so well known in a place that you seem to be a permanent part of it【幽默】在某地為人所熟知的人: *Bill Tucker has been the postman in our village for 40 years. He's become something of an institution.* 比爾·塔克在我們村裡做郵遞員已有40年, 他已經成為我們村的知名人物。—**institutional** *adj*

in·sti·tu·tion·al·ize also 又作 **-ise** *BrE*【英】/ˌɪnstəˋtjuʃənlˌaɪz; ˌɪnstɪˈtjuːʃənəlaɪz/ *v* [T] *old-fashioned* to put someone in a mental hospital or institution for old people etc【過時】把〔某人〕送到精神病院[養老院]

in·sti·tu·tion·al·ized also 又作 **-ised** *BrE*【英】/ˌɪnstəˋtjuʃənlˌaɪzd; ˌɪnstɪˈtjuːʃənəlaɪzd/ *adj* **1 institutionalized violence/racism/corruption** violence etc that has happened for so long in an organization or society that it has become accepted as normal 習以為常的暴力行為/種族歧視/腐敗 **2** *formal* someone who has become institutionalized has lived for a long time in a prison, mental hospital etc and now cannot easily live outside one【正式】長期坐牢[住精神病院]〔已不適應外界生活〕的

in-store /ˌ. ˈ.◂/ *adj* happening within a large shop or DEPARTMENT STORE 發生在大商店[百貨公司]內的: *in-store sales demonstrations* 商店內的銷售展示

in·struct /ɪnˋstrʌkt; ɪnˈstrʌkt/ *v* [T] **1** to officially tell someone what to do 命令; 指示: **instruct sb to do sth** *Our staff have been instructed to offer you every assistance.* 我方工作人員已奉命為您提供一切幫助。| **as instructed** (=in the way that you have been instructed) 依照指示 *We returned the questionnaire as instructed.* 我們依照指示交回調查表。**2** to teach or show someone how to do something 教授, 指導: **instruct sb in sth** *Mr. Andersen was instructing them in the art of screen printing.* 安德遜先生在教他們絲網印刷法。—see 見 TEACH (USAGE) **3** [usually passive 一般用被動態] *formal* to officially inform someone about something【正式】通知: **instruct sb that** *We were instructed that the assembly would not vote until noon.* 我們得到通知, 大會中午才投票。**4** *law* to employ a lawyer to deal with your case in court【法律】聘請〔律師〕出庭: *Once you have decided to proceed with a case, you should instruct a good solicitor.* 一旦你決定打官司, 就應當聘請一位好律師。

3 2 **in·struc·tion** /ɪn`strʌkʃən; ɪnˈstrʌkʃən/ *n* **1 instructions** [plural] the printed information that tells you how to use a piece of equipment etc 操作指南; 使用說明: *We forgot to read the instructions.* 我們忘了看使用說明書。| **follow the instructions** *Follow the instructions on the back of the box.* 按照盒子背面印的說明去做。**2** [C, usually plural 一般用複數] a statement telling someone what they must do 命令, 指示: **instructions to do sth** *He had explicit instructions to check everyone's identity card at the door.* 他接到明確指示, 在入口處檢驗每個人的身分證。| **instructions that** *Mrs Edwards left strict instructions that she was not to be disturbed.* 愛德華茲夫人留下嚴格指示, 不許任何人打擾她。| **on sb's instructions** (=because you have been officially told to do it) 按照某人的吩咐 *On his instructions, the luggage had been sent on.* 按照他的吩咐, 行李已先行送走。| **my instructions are** (=used to tell someone what you have been officially told to do) 我得到的命令是 *My instructions are to give the package to him personally.* 我得到的命令是把包裹當面交給他。**3** [U] *formal* teaching that you are given in a particular skill or subject【正式】講授, 教學; 指導: *religious instruction* 宗教指導 | *driving instruction* 駕駛技術指導 | **[+in]** *You will receive basic instruction in navigation.* 你將接受有關航行的基礎指導。| **under (sb's) instruction** (=while being taught by someone) 在某人的教授下 *Under Stewart's instruction, I slowly mastered the art of glass blowing.* 在斯圖亞特的教導下, 我逐漸學會了玻璃吹製技術。

in·struc·tion·al /ɪn`strʌkʃənḷ; ɪnˈstrʌkʃənəl/ *adj formal* providing instruction【正式】提供指導的; 教學用的: *instructional materials* 教材

instruction ma·nu·al /·ˈ·· ˌ···/ *n* [C] a book that gives you instructions on how to use or look after a machine〔機器的〕使用[維修]手冊

in·struc·tive /ɪn`strʌktɪv; ɪnˈstrʌktɪv/ *adj* providing a lot of useful information, explanations, and knowledge about something 有教育意義的; 有啟發性的; 增長知識的: *an instructive book on photography* 增進攝影知識的書 | *a very instructive experience* 極富教育意義的經歷 —**instructively** *adv*

in·struc·tor /ɪn`strʌktɚ; ɪnˈstrʌktə/ *n* [C] **1** someone who teaches a sport or practical skill〔運動或技藝的〕指導員; 教練; 教員: *a driving instructor* 駕駛教練 | *ski instructors* 滑雪教練 **2** *AmE* someone who teaches in an American college or university before they have finished being trained【美】大學講師: *a social studies instructor* 社會科學講師

2 **in·stru·ment** /`ɪnstrəmənt; ˈɪnstrʊmənt/ *n* [C]

1 ►TOOL 工具◄ a small tool used in work such as science or medicine where very careful movements are necessary〔指用來進行細緻工作的〕器械, 器具: *surgical instruments* 外科 (手術) 器械

2 ►MUSIC 音樂◄ an object such as a piano, horn, VIOLIN etc, used for producing musical sounds; MUSICAL INSTRUMENT 樂器: *stringed instruments* 弦樂器

3 ►FOR MEASURING 測量◄ a piece of equipment for measuring and showing distance, speed, temperature etc 儀器, 儀表: *The pilot studied his instruments anxiously.* 飛行員焦慮地查看各種儀表。| **instrument flying/landing** (=flying or bringing down an aircraft using only instruments) 儀表飛行/着陸

4 ►METHOD 方法◄ [usually singular 一般用單數] a system, method, or law that is used by people in power to get a particular result 制度; 方法; 法律: *Sometimes military force can become an instrument of government policy.* 軍事力量有時會成為政府政策的工具。

5 ►DOCUMENT 文件◄ *formal* a legal document【正式】法律文件

6 *literary*【文】**instrument of fate/God** someone or something that is used by an unseen power which is beyond our control 受命運/上帝擺佈的人[物]

7 instrument of torture a piece of equipment used to make people suffer pain 刑具

in·stru·men·tal[1] /ˌɪnstrə`mɛntḷ; ˌɪnstrʊˈmentl◄/ *adj* **1 be instrumental** *informal* to be important in making something possible【正式】對...重要的, 有幫助的: *Wilson was instrumental in introducing new methods of production.* 在引進新的生產方法上, 威爾遜起了很大作用。**2** instrumental music is for instruments, not for voices 器樂的; 用樂器演奏的 —**instrumentally** *adv* —**instrumentality** /ˌɪnstrəmɛn`tælətɪ; ˌɪnstrʊmenˈtælɪti/ *n* [U]

instrumental[2] *n* [C] a piece of music or a part of a piece of music where no voices are used, only instruments 器樂曲; 樂曲中無人聲只有器樂演奏的部分

in·stru·men·tal·ist /ˌɪnstrə`mɛntḷɪst; ˌɪnstrʊˈmentəlɪst/ *n* [C] someone who plays a musical instrument 樂器演奏者 —compare 比較 VOCALIST

in·stru·men·ta·tion /ˌɪnstrəmɛn`teʃən; ˌɪnstrʊmenˈteɪʃən/ *n* [U] **1** the way in which a piece of music is arranged to be played by several different instruments 器樂曲的譜寫 **2** the set of instruments (INSTRUMENT (3)) used to help in controlling a machine〔用於控制某機器的全部〕儀表: *the complex instrumentation in an aircraft's cockpit* 飛機駕駛艙內複雜的儀表

instrument pan·el /ˈ··· ˌ··/ *n* [C] the board in front of the pilot of an aircraft, where all the instruments (INSTRUMENT (3)) are〔飛機駕駛艙中的〕儀表板

in·sub·or·di·nate /ˌɪnsə`bɔrdṇɪt; ˌɪnsəˈbɔːdənɪt◄/ *adj* refusing to obey someone who has a higher rank than you in the army, navy etc〔軍隊中〕下級不服從的, 違抗命令的 —**insubordination** /ˌɪnsəˌbɔrdṇ`eʃən; ˌɪnsəbɔːdɪˈneɪʃən/ *n* [U]: *Howell was dismissed for gross insubordination.* 豪威爾因為嚴重違抗命令而被開除。

in·sub·stan·tial /ˌɪnsəb`stænʃəl; ˌɪnsəbˈstænʃəl◄/ *adj* **1** *formal* something that is insubstantial is much too small or weak and does not look solid enough【正式】不堅固的; 脆弱的: *a slender rope bridge, terrifyingly insubstantial* 細長的索橋, 不牢固的樣子令人害怕 **2** *literary* not existing as a real object or person【文】非實體的; 虛幻的: *Pale figures, like insubstantial ghosts, moved through the mist.* 影影綽綽的人影, 就像虛幻的幽靈, 在霧中穿行。—**insubstantiality** /ˌɪnsəbstænʃɪ`ælətɪ; ˌɪnsəbstænʃiˈælɪti/ *n* [U]

in·suf·fe·ra·ble /ɪn`sʌfrəbḷ; ɪnˈsʌfərəbəl/ *adj* extremely annoying or unpleasant 令人極厭惡[不快]的: *the insufferable heat* 熾熱難耐 | *Lou can be pretty insufferable at times.* 羅有時很令人討厭。—**insufferably** *adv*: *insufferably arrogant* 傲慢得不能忍受

in·suf·fi·cient /ˌɪnsə`fɪʃənt; ˌɪnsəˈfɪʃənt◄/ *adj* not enough 不足的, 不夠的: *insufficient supplies* 供應不足 | **[+for]** *There were insufficient funds for a research project.* 資金不足以進行一個研究項目。| **insufficient to do sth** *The evidence is quite insufficient to convict him.* 證據不足以給他定罪。—**insufficiently** *adv* —**insufficiency** *n* [singular, U] *an insufficiency of capital* 資本不充足

in·su·lar /`ɪnsəlɚ; ˈɪnsjʊlə/ *adj* **1** not interested in anything except your own group, country, way of life etc 思想狹隘的; 保守的: *In today's small world, we must guard against an insular outlook.* 如今世界已變小, 我們必須防止眼光狹隘。**2** *formal* like or connected with an island【正式】島嶼般的; 島嶼的 —**insularity** /ˌɪnsə`lærətɪ; ˌɪnsjʊˈlærɪti/ *n* [U] *the insularity of the British* 英國人的島民特性

in·su·late /`ɪnsəˌlet; ˈɪnsjʊleɪt/ *v* [T] **1** to cover or protect something so that electricity, sound, heat etc cannot get in or out 使絕緣; 使隔熱; 使隔音: *insulated cables* 絕緣電纜 | **insulate sth from/against** *A bird fluffs up its feathers to insulate itself against the cold.* 鳥抖鬆羽毛以禦寒。**2** to protect someone from unpleasant experiences or unwanted influences 把〔某人〕隔離, 使隔絕〔以免遭受不愉快的經歷或不良影響〕: **insulate sb from sth** *students insulated from the experiences of real life* 受到隔絕而不懂世情的學生

insulating tape /ˈ···· ,·/ *n* [U] narrow material used for wrapping around electric wires to insulate them 絕緣膠帶

in·su·la·tion /ˌɪnsəˋleʃən; ˌɪnsjʊˈleɪʃən/ *n* [U] **1** material used to insulate something, especially a building〔尤指建築物的〕絕緣材料 **2** the act of insulating something or the state of being insulated 隔絕: *Good insulation can save you lots of money on heating bills.* 好的隔熱效果能節省很多取暖費。

in·su·la·tor /ˈɪnsəˌletɚ; ˈɪnsjʊleɪtə/ *n* [C] an object or material that insulates, especially one which does not allow electricity to pass through it〔尤指不導電的〕絕緣體; 隔音材料

in·su·lin /ˈɪnsəlɪn; ˈɪnsjʊlɪn/ *n* [U] a substance produced naturally by your body which allows sugar to be used for energy 胰島素 —see also 另見 DIABETES

in·sult[1] /ɪnˋsʌlt; ɪnˈsʌlt/ *v* [T] to say or do something that is rude and offensive to someone 侮辱; 冒犯: *Nobody insults my family and gets away with it!* 誰也別想侮辱了我的家庭之後就不了了之! | *I hope Andy won't feel insulted if I turn down his invitation.* 要是我拒絕安迪的邀請, 希望他不要介意。| **insult sb by doing sth** *Please don't insult me by offering me money.* 請不要用給我錢的辦法來侮辱我。

in·sult[2] /ˈɪnsʌlt; ˈɪnsʌlt/ *n* [C] **1** a rude or offensive remark or action 辱罵, 凌辱; 侮辱性的言行: *She was shouting insults at her boy friend.* 她正在對她的男朋友破口大罵。| *$200 for all that work? It's an insult.* 幹那麼多工作才給 200 美元? 簡直是對我的侮辱。| **take sth as an insult** *Carol will take it as an insult if you don't come to the party.* 你要是不來參加聚會, 卡羅會認為是對她的不敬。**2 be an insult to sb's intelligence** if something such as a book, lesson, or television programme is an insult to your intelligence, it offends you by being too simple or stupid 對某人智力的侮辱〔指書、課程或電視節目等過於幼稚、愚蠢〕—see also 另見 **add insult to injury** (ADD (8))

in·sult·ing /ɪnˋsʌltɪŋ; ɪnˈsʌltɪŋ/ *adj* very rude and offensive to someone〔對某人〕侮辱的, 無禮的: *insulting remarks* 侮辱性的言論

in·su·pe·ra·ble /ɪnˋsupərəbḷ; ɪnˈsjuːpərəbəl◂/ *adj formal* an insuperable difficulty or problem is impossible to deal with【正式】〔困難或問題〕不能克服的, 無法解決的: *Getting an agreement between the two leaders proved to be an insuperable obstacle.* 要想使兩位領導人達成協議, 簡直不太可能。—**insuperably** *adv*

in·sup·por·ta·ble /ˌɪnsəˋportəbḷ; ˌɪnsəˈpɔːtəbəl◂/ *adj formal* too unpleasant for you to bear【正式】〔極討厭而〕難以忍受的, 不能容忍的: *insupportable behaviour* 難以容忍的行為 | *insupportable pain* 不堪忍受的痛苦

3 2 **in·sur·ance** /ɪnˋʃurəns; ɪnˈʃʊərəns/ *n* **1** [U] an arrangement with a company in which you pay them money each year and they pay the costs if anything bad happens to you, such as an illness or an accident 保險: *health insurance* 健康保險 | *life insurance* (=so that your family receive money if you die) 人壽保險 | **[+against]** *insurance against permanent disability* 終身殘疾保險 | **[+on]** *Do you have insurance on your household contents?* 你買家庭財產保險了嗎? | **claim for sth on your insurance** (=get an insurance company to pay for something)〔就某物〕提出保險索賠 *We can probably claim for the damage on the insurance.* 我們可以讓保險公司賠償損失。| **take out insurance** (=start paying for insurance protection) 買保險 **2** [U] the money that you pay regularly to an insurance company; INSURANCE PREMIUM 保險費: **[+on]** *Insurance on my house is very high.* 我家房子的保險費很高。**3** [U] the business of providing insurance 保險業: *He works in insurance.* 他從事保險業。**4** [singular, U] protection against something bad happening 保障; 預防措施: **[+against]** *I put an extra lock on the door as an added insurance against burglars.* 為了防盜, 我在門上又加了一把鎖。—see also 另見 ASSURANCE (3), NATIONAL INSURANCE

insurance ad·just·er /ˈ·ˈ·· ·,··/ *n* [C] *AmE* someone who is employed by an insurance company to decide how much to pay people who have had an accident, had something stolen etc【美】〔保險公司雇請的〕險損估價人, 保險理算師; LOSS ADJUSTER *BrE*【英】

insurance bro·ker /ˈ·ˈ·· ,··/ also 又作 **insurance agent** *n* [C] someone who arranges and sells insurance as their job 保險經紀人, 保險代理人

insurance pol·i·cy /ˈ·ˈ·· ,···/ *n* [C] a written agreement with an insurance company 保險合同; 保險單

insurance pre·mi·um /ˈ·ˈ·· ,···/ *n* [C] the money that you pay regularly to an insurance company〔定期交納的〕保險費

in·sure /ɪnˋʃur; ɪnˈʃʊə/ *v* **1** [I,T] to buy insurance to protect yourself against something bad happening to you, your family, your possessions etc 給…保險, 為…投保: *Have you insured the contents of your home?* 你給家裡的財產投保了嗎? | **insure (sth/sb) against sth** *It would be wise to insure your property against storm damage.* 為防風暴損毀而給財產保險是明智之舉。| **insure sth for £1000/$2000 etc** *I would advise you to insure the painting for at least £100,000.* 我建議你給這幅油畫至少投保 100,000 英鎊。**2** [T] to provide insurance for something or someone 為〔某物或某人〕提供保險: *Many companies won't insure young drivers.* 許多公司都不願意為年輕的司機提供保險。**3** an American spelling of ENSURE ensure 的美式拼法

insure against sth *phr v* [T] to protect yourself against the risk of something bad happening by planning or preparing 對…採取預防措施: *No matter what precautions you may take, you cannot insure against every eventuality.* 不管你採取甚麼樣的預防措施, 都不能確保萬無一失。

USAGE NOTE 用法說明: INSURE

WORD CHOICE 詞語辨析: **assure, reassure, insure, ensure, make sure**

If you **assure** someone of something, you tell them that it is really true or will happen. assure 是向某人保證某事是真實的或將要發生: *The receptionist assured me that I would not have to wait long.* 接待人員向我保證說不會久等。| *Christianity assures us there is life after death.* 基督教使我們相信人死後可得永生。

You **reassure** someone who is worried by telling them that there is nothing to worry about. reassure 用來向發愁的人表示安慰, 請他們不必擔心: *The doctor reassured me that there would be no pain.* 醫生要我放心, 說不會疼痛的。

You may **insure** something against something bad happening to it by paying money to an insurance company. insure 意思是為防不測而向保險公司投保: *Is the house insured against fire?* 這所房子是否保了火險? | *Julia Roberts' legs are insured for a large amount of money.* 朱麗亞·羅拔絲為她的雙腿投了大額保險。It is also possible to **insure** your life against death, though where something is certain to happen one day the technical British English word is **assure**. insure 也有為死亡而向保險公司投保的用法。然而, 英國英語中關於總有一天會發生的事情的術語是 assure。

If you **ensure** (usually **insure** in American English) that something happens, that means you make certain or **make sure** (more informal) it does happen. ensure〔美國英語中多用 insure〕意思是"確保某事發生", 意同 make sure〔較為不正式〕:

Please ensure that the lights are switched off before leaving the building. 請確保離開大樓前關掉所有電燈。In some situation **assure** can be used in this meaning too where the object is reflexive or what is ensured is something such as success, safety, comfort etc. 如果受詞是反身代詞, 或確保的對象為成功、安全、舒適等, 也可用 assure: *I assured myself of a seat at the front* (=I made sure I got one). 我確保自己在前排有個座位。| *The band's latest release has assured their success in the rock world* (=ensured that they will be successful). 這支樂隊的最新唱片確保了它在搖滾樂壇的成功。

in·sured /ɪn`ʃʊrd; ɪn'ʃʊəd/ *adj* **1** having insurance 已保險的: *Mike's bike was stolen and it wasn't insured.* 邁克的自行車被偷了, 且車子沒受險。| **insured to do sth** *You wouldn't be insured to drive Anne's car.* 你開安妮的車不享受保險。| **[+against]** *Is your house insured against fire?* 你的房子保火險了嗎? **2 the insured** *law* the person or people who are insured【法律】被保險人, 保戶, 受保人

in·sur·er /ɪn`ʃʊrɚ; ɪn'ʃʊərə/ *n* [C] a person or company that provides insurance 承保人; 保險公司: *The insurer will pay the full cost of storm damage.* 保險公司將全額償付風暴造成的損失。

in·sur·gent /ɪn`sɝdʒənt; ɪn'sɜːdʒənt/ *n* [C often plural 常用複數] one of a group of people fighting against the government of their own country 起義者, 暴動者, 叛亂者 —**insurgency** n [U] —**insurgent** *adj*: *the insurgent forces* 叛軍 —see also 另見 COUNTERINSURGENCY

in·sur·moun·ta·ble /ˌɪnsɚ`mauntəbḷ; ˌɪnsə'maʊntəbəl◂/ *adj* a difficulty or problem that is insurmountable is too large or too difficult to deal with〔困難或問題〕不可逾越的; 難以克服的; 難以處理的: *The language barrier proved an insurmountable barrier to their relationship.* 語言障礙是他們關係中難以克服的障礙。

in·sur·rec·tion /ˌɪnsə`rɛkʃən; ˌɪnsə'rekʃən/ *n* [C,U] an attempt by a large group of people within a country to take control using force and violence 起義; 暴動; 造反; 叛亂: *an armed insurrection against the party in power* 反對執政黨的武裝暴亂 —**insurrectionist** *n*

in·tact /ɪn`tækt; ɪn'tækt/ *adj* [not before noun 不用於名詞前] not broken, damaged, or spoiled, usually after something bad has happened 完好無損的; 未受損傷的: *The fireplace was the only thing that remained intact after the tornado.* 龍捲風過後, 只有壁爐完好無損。| *Somehow his reputation survived the scandal intact.* 這場醜聞過後, 不知為甚麼他的名聲竟然絲毫未受影響。

in·ta·gli·o /ɪn`tæljo; ɪn'tɑːliəʊ/ *n* [C,U] the art of cutting patterns into a hard substance or the pattern that you get by doing this 凹雕藝術; 凹雕圖案

in·take /`ɪnˌtek; 'ɪnteɪk/ *n* **1** [singular] the amount of food, drink etc that you take into your body〔食物、飲品等的〕納入量: *Lower your intake of fat and alcohol to improve your health.* 為了增進健康, 減少脂肪和酒精的攝入量。**2** the number of people allowed to enter a school, profession etc〔學校、行業等的人員〕收納數量: *an increase in the intake of foreign students* 收納留學生人數的增加 **3** [C] a tube, pipe, etc through which air, gas, or liquid is taken in〔空氣、可燃氣體或液體注入的〕管道: *air intakes on a jet engine* 噴氣式發動機的進氣口 **4 an intake of breath** a sudden act of breathing in, showing that you are shocked etc 倒吸一口氣〔表示吃驚〕

in·tan·gi·ble /ɪn`tændʒəbḷ; ɪn'tændʒɨbəl/ *adj* an intangible quality or feeling cannot be clearly felt or described, although you know it exists; INDEFINABLE〔性質或感受〕難以捉摸的; 無法形容的; 難以確認的: *The island of Iona has an intangible quality of holiness.* 艾奥納島有一種說不出的神聖感。| *Customer goodwill is an important and intangible asset of a business.* 商譽是企業重要的無形資產。—**intangibly** *adv* —**intangibility** /ɪnˌtændʒə`bɪlətɪ; ɪnˌtændʒɨ'bɪlɨti/ *n* [U]

in·te·ger /`ɪntədʒɚ; 'ɪntɨdʒə/ *n* [C] *technical* a whole number【術語】整數: *6 is an integer, but 6.4 is not.* 6是整數, 而6.4不是。

in·te·gral /`ɪntəgrəl; 'ɪntɨgrəl/ *adj* forming a necessary part of something 構成整體所必需的, 不可缺少的: *Effective communication is an integral part of being a teacher.* 有效的溝通技巧是一名教師不可缺少的部分。| **[+to]** *Her talents are integral to the team's good performance.* 她的才華對於全隊的良好表現是不可或缺的。—**integrally** *adv*

integral cal·cu·lus /ˌ··· '···/ *n* [U] *technical* a method of measuring the distance a moving object has moved at a particular moment, by using your knowledge of its speed until then【術語】積分(學)

in·te·grate /`ɪntəˌgret; 'ɪntɨgreɪt/ *v* **1** [I,T] to join in the life and customs of the group or society that you live in so that you are accepted by them, or to help someone do this (使)融入〔某羣體或社會〕; (使)成為一體: **[+into/with]** *The child was only adopted a year ago, but she has completely integrated into the family's life.* 這個孩子雖然才領養一年, 但她已完全融入了這個家庭的生活中。| *Attempts to integrate the new immigrants have failed.* 同化新移民的努力已告失敗。**2** [T] to combine things that work well together in order to make an effective system 使合併〔成為有效的系統〕, 使結合: *Train and bus services have been fully integrated.* 火車和公共汽車兩種系統已完全結合了起來。| **integrate sth with sth** *The school integrates maths lessons with computer studies.* 學校把數學課與電腦課結合起來。**3** [I,T] to end the separation of races in a place or institution, usually by making separation illegal; DESEGREGATE (使)取消種族隔離: *Laws were passed in the US in order to integrate all schools.* 美國已通過法律, 在所有學校中取消種族隔離。—compare 比較 SEGREGATE

in·te·grat·ed /`ɪntəˌgretɪd; 'ɪntɨgreɪtɨd/ *adj* an integrated system, institution etc combines many different groups, ideas, or parts in a way that works well〔各組成部分〕相互協調的; 綜合的: *an integrated public transport system* 綜合公共交通體系 | *a fully integrated school with children from many races and classes* 兼收不同種族及不同社會階層兒童的學校 —compare 比較 SEGREGATED

integrated cir·cuit /ˌ···· '··/ *n* [C] *technical* a very small set of electronic connections printed on a single piece of SEMICONDUCTOR material instead of being made from separate parts【術語】集成電路

in·te·gra·tion /ˌɪntə`greʃən; ˌɪntɨ'greɪʃən/ *n* [U] **1** the combining of two or more things so that they work together effectively 結合; 綜合; 集成; 整合: *the closer integration of the countries' economies* 各國經濟更密切的聯合 **2** the acceptance of people in a group or society 同化; 融入: *complete integration of racial groups* 不同種族羣體的完全融合 **3** the ending of laws that make people of different races live, work etc separately 種族隔離法規的廢除

in·teg·ri·ty /ɪn`tɛgrətɪ; ɪn'tegrɨti/ *n* [U] **1** the quality of being honest and of always having high moral principles 正直; 誠實: *a man of absolute integrity, with the highest moral standards* 剛正不阿、道德高尚的人 **2** *formal* the state of being united as one complete thing【正式】完整, 完全: *Removing the chapter destroys the integrity of the book.* 去掉這一章會破壞全書的完整。

in·teg·u·ment /ɪn`tɛgjəmənt; ɪn'tegjʊmənt/ *n* [C] *technical* something such as a shell which covers something else【術語】覆蓋物; 外皮〈如甲殼〉

in·tel·lect /`ɪntḷˌɛkt; 'ɪntɨlekt/ *n* **1** [C,U] the ability to understand things and to think intelligently 智力; 理解能力; 思維能力: *new scientific ideas that are a challenge to the human intellect* 對人類智慧構成挑戰的新科學觀點 | *a woman of superior intellect* 聰穎過人的女子 **2** [C] someone who is very intelligent 才智出眾者: *some* *of the greatest intellects in the world of science* 科學界中幾位最偉大的智者

3 **in·tel·lec·tual**[1] /ˌɪntḷˋɛktʃuəl; ˌɪntḷˈlektʃuəl◂/ *adj* **1** an intellectual activity, quality etc involves intelligent thinking in order to understand or enjoy something 智力的; 需用腦力的: *an intellectual film* 寓意深奧的影片 | *The student showed enormous intellectual ability.* 這個學生表現出極高的智力。**2** an intellectual person is well-educated and interested in serious ideas and subjects such as science, literature etc 有知識的, 受過良好教育的: *an intellectual family* 有知識的家庭 —**intellectually** *adv*: *intellectually stimulating* 給人以知識啟迪的 —**intellectualize** *v* [I,T]

intellectual[2] *n* [C] an intelligent, well-educated person who spends a lot of their time thinking about complicated ideas and discussing them 知識分子: *He likes to think of himself as an intellectual.* 他喜歡把自己看成知識分子。—see 見 INTELLIGENT (USAGE)

intellectual prop·er·ty /ˌ····· ˈ···/ *n* [U] *law* something which someone has invented or has the right to make or sell, especially something protected by a PATENT[1] (1), TRADEMARK, or COPYRIGHT【法律】知識產權

3
3 **in·tel·li·gence** /ɪnˋtɛlədʒəns; ɪnˈteḷdʒəns/ *n* [U] **1 a)** the ability to learn, understand, and think about things 智力; 理解力: *a child of low intelligence* 智力低下的孩子 | *Don't act like such an idiot – use your intelligence!* 別幹這種傻事, 動動腦筋! **b)** a high level of this ability 聰穎; 聰明: *a woman of beauty, charm, and intelligence* 美麗、迷人、聰慧的女子 **2 a)** information about the secret activities of foreign governments, the military plans of an enemy etc 情報, 諜報: *intelligence gathering* 情報收集 **b)** a group of people or an organization that gathers this information for their government 情報機構; 諜報人員: *He works for British Intelligence.* 他為英國情報局工作。| *reports from Military Intelligence* 來自軍事情報處的報告

intelligence quo·tient /ˌ·ˈ··· ˌ··/ *n* [C] IQ 智商

3 **in·tel·li·gent** /ɪnˋtɛlədʒənt; ɪnˈteḷdʒənt/ *adj* **1** having a high level of mental ability so that you are good at understanding ideas and thinking quickly and clearly 有智慧的; 聰明的; 悟性強的: *If you're reasonably intelligent the maths involved should present no problems.* 你如果智力還過得去, 這裡所涉及的數學根本不成問題。**2** an intelligent animal is able to think and understand〔動物〕有智能的: *Are there intelligent forms of life on other planets?* 在其他星球上是否有智能生命形式存在? —**intelligently** *adv*

> **USAGE NOTE 用法說明: INTELLIGENT**
> WORD CHOICE 詞語辨析: **intelligent, intellectual**
> An **intelligent** person is someone with a quick and clever mind, but an **intellectual** person is someone who is well-educated and interested in subjects that need long periods of study. A small child, or even a dog, can be **intelligent** but cannot be called **intellectual**. intelligent 指人頭腦敏捷, 智力聰穎; intellectual 則指人受過良好教育, 對需要長期研究的學科感興趣。可以用 intelligent 來形容一個小孩, 甚至一頭狗, 但不能用 intellectual。
> **Intelligent** and **intellectual** are both adjectives, but **intellectual** can also be a noun. intelligent 和 intellectual 都是形容詞, 但 intellectual 還可作名詞: *There are too many intellectuals in the government.* 政府中知識分子太多。

in·tel·li·gent·si·a /ɪnˌtɛləˋdʒɛntsɪə; ɪnˌteḷˈdʒentsiə/ *n* **the intelligentsia** the people in a society who are most highly educated and who are most interested in new ideas and developments, especially in art, literature, or politics〔尤指藝術、文學和政界的〕知識分子; 知識階層

in·tel·li·gi·ble /ɪnˋtɛlɪdʒəbḷ; ɪnˈteḷdʒḷbəl/ *adj* intelligible speech, writing, or ideas can be easily understood〔言語、文章、觀點〕明白易懂的: *He was so drunk that his speech was barely intelligible.* 他醉得說話幾乎讓人聽不懂。| **[+to]** *Newspapers must be intelligible to all levels of readers.* 報紙必須讓各種水平的讀者都看得懂。—**intelligibly** *adv* —**intelligibility** /ɪnˌtɛlɪdʒəˋbɪlətɪ; ɪnˌteḷdʒḷˈbɪḷti/ *n* [U] —opposite 反義詞 UNINTELLIGIBLE

in·tem·per·ate /ɪnˋtɛmpərɪt; ɪnˈtempərḷt/ *adj formal*【正式】**1** not having enough control over your feelings so that you behave in a way that is unacceptable to other people〔行為〕無節制的; 過度的; 放縱的: *an intemperate outburst* 過度的感情發泄 **2** regularly drinking too much alcohol 縱酒的, 酗酒的 —**intemperately** *adv* —**intemperance** *n* [U]

in·tend /ɪnˋtɛnd; ɪnˈtend/ *v* [T] **1** to have something in 3
your mind as a plan or purpose 計劃, 打算, 想要: 1
intend to do sth *I intend to get there as soon after 5 as I can.* 我打算在五點後盡快趕到那裡。| **intend sb/sth to do sth** *I didn't intend her to see the painting until it was finished.* 我原本不想在畫還沒有完成時就讓她看。| *He was insulted by my remark, but I hadn't intended it to be offensive.* 他感到我的話侮辱了他, 但我根本沒有這個意思。| **it is intended that** *It is intended that all new employees will receive appropriate training.* 按計劃所有新員工都要接受適當的培訓。| **fully intend** (=definitely intend) 明確打算 *Kate had fully intended returning home on Sunday but she couldn't get a flight.* 凱特原來打定主意星期日回家, 可是她沒有買到飛機票。—see 見 PROPOSE (USAGE) **2 be intended for sb/sth** to be provided or designed for a particular purpose or person 是為…而準備的; 專供…使用的: *a book intended for young children* 專供幼兒閱讀的書 **3 intended target/victim/destination etc** the person, thing, result etc that an action is intended to affect or reach 預期的目標/被害人/目的地等: *It seems likely that General Rocha was the intended victim.* 羅卡將軍很可能是襲擊的目標。

in·tend·ed /ɪnˋtɛndɪd; ɪnˈtendḷd/ *n* **sb's intended** *old-fashioned or humorous* the person that you are going to marry【過時或幽默】未婚夫; 未婚妻: *Meet my intended, Miss Robinson.* 這是我的未婚妻魯賓遜小姐。

in·tense /ɪnˋtɛns; ɪnˈtens/ *adj* **1** having a very strong ef- 3
fect or felt very strongly 強烈的, 劇烈的: *intense pain* 劇痛 | *The heat was intense.* 天氣酷熱。**2** there is intense activity, effort etc when people are working, trying, or thinking extremely hard 緊張的; 認真的: *a period of intense concentration and study* 全神貫注、力學不倦的時期 **3** having feelings or opinions that are extremely strong, serious etc〔感情或意見〕極為強烈的, 極為嚴肅的: *She can be so intense, it makes me exhausted.* 她有時會過於嚴肅, 讓我感到精疲力竭。| *an intense young man* 十分嚴肅認真的年輕人 —**intensely** *adv*: *intensely exciting* 極度興奮 —**intensity** *n* [U]

in·ten·si·fi·er /ɪnˋtɛnsəˌfaɪr; ɪnˈtensḷfaɪə/ *n* [C] *technical* a word, usually an adverb, that is used to emphasize an adjective, adverb, or verb, for example the word 'absolutely' in the phrase 'that's absolutely wonderful'【術語】〔一般是副詞, 用以加強形容詞、副詞或動詞詞意的〕強調成分; 強調語〈如 that's absolutely wonderful 中的 absolutely〉

in·ten·si·fy /ɪnˋtɛnsəˌfaɪ; ɪnˈtensḷfaɪ/ *v* [I,T] if an activity, effort, feeling etc intensifies, or if you intensify it, it increases in degree or strength 加強, 增強: *Police have now intensified the search for the lost child.* 警方已加緊尋找那個失蹤的孩子。—**intensification** /ɪnˌtɛnsəfəˋkeʃən; ɪnˌtensḷfḷˈkeɪʃən/ *n* [U] *the intensification of the conflict in Bosnia* 波斯尼亞衝突的加劇

in·ten·sive /ɪnˋtɛnsɪv; ɪnˈtensɪv/ *adj* **1** involving a lot of activity, effort, or careful attention in a short period of time 加強的; 集中的: *a one-week intensive course in English* 為期一週的英語強化課程 | *a period of intensive fighting* 戰鬥激烈的時期 **2 intensive farming/agriculture** farming which produces a lot of food from a small area of land 精耕細作; 集約式農業: *Most of low-*

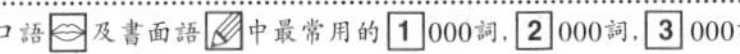

land Britain is intensively cultivated. 大多數的英國低地都進行精耕細作。—**intensively** *adv* —see also 另見 LABOUR-INTENSIVE

intensive care /ˌ·ˌ·· ˈ·/ *n* [U] a department in a hospital that gives special attention and treatment to people who are very seriously ill or badly injured 危重病人監護部, 深切治療部

in·tent¹ /ɪnˋtɛnt; ɪnˈtent/ *n* [U] **1 to all intents (and purposes)** *especially spoken* almost completely【尤口】實際上; 幾乎在一切方面: *To all intents and purposes, their marriage is over.* 他們的婚姻實際上已結束。**2** *formal* what you intend to do; intention【正式】目的; 意圖: *She behaved foolishly but with good intent.* 她雖然幹了蠢事, 但意圖是好的。**3** *law* the intention to do something illegal【法律】(犯罪) 意圖: *arrested for loitering with intent* 因四處遊蕩伺機作案而被捕 | **intent to do sth** *Jefferson was charged with intent to damage property.* 傑斐遜被指控企圖破壞財產。

intent² *adj* **1** giving careful attention to something so that you think about nothing else 專注的, 專心致志的: *watching the game with an intent stare* 目不轉睛地觀看比賽 | [+**on/upon**] *Intent upon her work, she ignored the cold.* 她專心於工作, 不顧寒冷。**2 be intent on (doing) sth** to be determined to do something or achieve something, especially something that may cause damage 執意 (某事)〔尤指會造成破壞的事〕: *Pete seems intent on stirring up trouble.* 皮特好像故意要惹出亂子。—**intently** *adv*: *I noticed her gazing intently at one of the photographs.* 我發覺她全神貫注地看着其中一張照片。—**intentness** *n* [U]

2 **in·ten·tion** /ɪnˋtɛnʃən; ɪnˈtenʃən/ *n* [C,U] something that you intend to do 意圖, 目的; 打算: **have no intention of doing sth** *I have no intention of helping him after what he said to me.* 聽了他對我說的話, 我再也不想幫他了。| **with the intention of doing sth** *They went into town with the intention of visiting the library.* 他們進城的目的是去圖書館。| **intention to do sth** *It is our intention to be the number one distributor of health products.* 我們的目標是成為保健產品第一大批發商。| **good intentions/the best intentions** (=intentions to do something good or kind especially when you do not succeed in doing) 一片好心/一片好意〔尤用於事情沒做成時〕: *So much for all our good intentions!* 我們的一片好心到此為止吧! —see also 另見 WELL-INTENTIONED

in·ten·tion·al /ɪnˋtɛnʃənḷ; ɪnˈtenʃənəl/ *adj* done deliberately and usually intended to cause harm 故意的; 蓄意的: *I did trip him, but it wasn't intentional.* 我是把他絆倒了, 但不是故意的。—**intentionally** *adv*: *intentionally vague promises* 故意含糊其辭的允諾 —opposite 反義詞 UNINTENTIONAL

in·ter /ɪnˋtɝ; ɪnˈtɜː/ *v* **interred, interring** [T] *formal* to bury a dead person【正式】埋葬〔死者〕—opposite 反義詞 DISINTER

inter- /ɪntə; ɪntə/ *prefix* between; among a group 在…之間: *intermarry* (=marry someone of another race, religion, etc)〔不同種族、宗教之間的〕通婚

in·ter·act /ˌɪntəˋækt; ˌɪntərˈækt/ *v* [I] **1** if people interact with each other, they talk to each other and understand each other 交流; 交往; 互相理解: [+**with**] *Vanessa interacts well with other children in the class.* 瓦內莎和班裡的其他孩子相處得很好。**2** if two or more things interact, they have an effect on each other and work together 相互作用, 相互影響: *social and economic factors interacting to produce a recession* 社會因素與經濟因素相互作用造成經濟衰退 | *hormones interacting in the body* 荷爾蒙在體內相互影響

3 **in·ter·ac·tion** /ˌɪntəˋækʃən; ˌɪntərˈækʃən/ *n* [C,U] **1** a process by which two or more things have an effect on each other and work together 相互作用, 相互影響: [+**of**] *the interaction of the tones of demand and supply* 供求消長趨勢的相互作用 | [+**with/between**] *complex interaction between mind and body* 身心之間複雜的相互影響 **2** the activity of talking to other people and understanding them 交流: [+**with/between**] *the degree of interaction between teacher and student* 師生之間交流的程度

in·ter·act·ive /ˌɪntəˋæktɪv; ˌɪntərˈæktɪv◂/ *adj* **1** interactive teaching methods, processes etc involve people working together and discussing what they do 互動的; 相互影響的; 相互配合的 **2 interactive programs** computing programs etc involving communication between a computer and the person using it〔人和電腦〕交互式[互動]程序: *interactive educational software* 交互式[互動]教育軟件 —**interactively** *adv* —**interactivity** /ˌɪntərækˋtɪvɪtɪ; ˌɪntərækˈtɪvə̇ti/ *n* [U]

in·ter a·li·a /ˌɪntəˋelɪə; ˌɪntər ˈeɪliə/ *adv Latin formal* among other things【拉丁, 正式】除了別的事情之外: *The paper discussed, inter alia, political, economic, and judicial issues.* 除了其他方面之外, 這篇論文還討論了政治、經濟和司法問題。

in·ter·breed /ˌɪntəˋbrid; ˌɪntəˈbriːd/ *v past tense and past participle* **interbred** /-ˋbrɛd; -ˈbred/ [I+**with**, T] to produce young animals from parents of different breeds or groups (使) 雜交繁殖 —compare 比較 CROSSBREED¹, INBREEDING

in·ter·cede /ˌɪntəˋsid; ˌɪntəˈsiːd/ *v* [I] to speak in support of someone, especially in order to try to prevent them from being punished 代為請求, 說情: [+**with**] *My good friend, Senator Bowie, interceded with the authorities on my behalf.* 我的好友鮑伊參議員為我向當局求情。—see also 另見 INTERCESSION

intercept 攔截

in·ter·cept /ˌɪntəˋsɛpt; ˌɪntəˈsept/ *v* [T] to stop or catch something or someone that is going from one place to another 攔截, 截住, 阻截: *We rely on the coastguard to intercept boats running drugs from the island.* 我們靠海岸警衛隊攔截從那個小島來的毒品走私船。| *Harker's phone calls had been intercepted.* 哈克的電話被人竊聽了。—**interception** /-ˋsɛpʃən; -ˈsepʃən/ *n* [C,U]

in·ter·cep·tor /ˌɪntəˋsɛptə; ˌɪntəˈseptə/ *n* [C] a light fast military aircraft 截擊機

in·ter·ces·sion /ˌɪntəˋsɛʃən; ˌɪntəˈseʃən/ *n* **1** [U+**with**] an act of interceding 求情, 說情 **2** [C,U] a prayer asking for someone to be helped or cured〔請求救助某人的〕祈禱; 代禱

in·ter·change¹ /ˋɪntəˌtʃendʒ; ˈɪntətʃeɪndʒ/ *n* **1** [singular, U] an exchange, especially of ideas or thoughts〔觀點、思想的〕交流: *the interchange of ideas between students and staff* 學生與教職工的意見交流 **2** [C] a point where a MOTORWAY and a main road join and are connected by several smaller roads〔高速公路的〕立體交叉道

in·ter·change² /ˌɪntəˋtʃendʒ; ˌɪntəˈtʃeɪndʒ/ *v* [I,T] to put each of two things in the place of the other or to be exchanged in this way (使)〔兩者〕交換位置; 互換

in·ter·chan·gea·ble /ˌɪntəˋtʃendʒəbḷ; ˌɪntəˈtʃeɪndʒəbəl/ *adj* things that are interchangeable can be used instead of each other 可以互換的: *interchangeable parts* 可互換的部件 | *These two words are almost interchangeable.* 這兩個單詞幾乎可以互換。—**interchangeably** *adv* —

interchangeability /ˌɪntɚtʃendʒəˋbɪlətɪ; ˌɪntətʃeɪndʒəˈbɪlǝ̍ti/ *n* [U]

in·ter·cit·y /ˌɪntɚˋsɪtɪ; ˌɪntəˈsɪti◂/ *adj* [only before noun 僅用於名詞前] happening between two or more cities, or going from one city to another 城市之間的; 往來於城市之間的: *an intercity train service* 城際列車服務 | *intercity rivalry* 城市之間的競爭

in·ter·col·le·giate /ˌɪntɚkəˋlidʒɪɪt; ˌɪntəkəˈliːdʒǝ̍t/ *adj* intercollegiate competitions are between members of different colleges 學院之間的: *an intercollegiate football game* 校際足球賽

in·ter·com /ˋɪntɚˌkɑm; ˈɪntəkɒm/ *n* [C] a communication system by which people in different parts of a building, aircraft etc speak to each other〔樓房、飛機等〕內部通話系統: *The pilot spoke to the passengers over the intercom.* 飛行員用內部通話設備向乘客講話。

in·ter·com·mu·ni·cate /ˌɪntɚkəˋmjunəˌket; ˌɪntəkəˈmjuːnǝ̍keɪt/ *v* [I+with] **1** *formal* to communicate with each other and exchange information【正式】互相聯繫; 互相通訊; 互通消息 **2** if two rooms intercommunicate, there is a door leading from one to the other〔兩房之間〕相通 —**intercommunication** /ˌɪntɚkəˌmjunəˋkeʃən; ˌɪntəkəmjuːnǝ̍ˈkeɪʃən/ *n* [U]

in·ter·con·nect /ˌɪntɚkəˋnɛkt; ˌɪntəkəˈnekt/ *v* [I+with] if two systems interconnect, they are connected to each other〔兩個系統〕相連: *a set of interconnecting pipes* 一套相連的管道 —**interconnected** *adj*

in·ter·con·ti·nen·tal /ˌɪntɚˌkɑntəˋnɛntəl; ˌɪntəkɒntǝ̍ˈnentl◂/ *adj* happening between two CONTINENTS (=for example Africa and Asia) or going from one continent to another 跨洲的〈例如非洲和亞洲〉; 洲際的: *intercontinental trade* 洲際貿易 | *an intercontinental flight* 洲際飛行

in·ter·course /ˋɪntɚˌkɔrs; ˈɪntəkɔːs/ *n* [U] *formal*【正式】**1** the act of having sex; SEXUAL INTERCOURSE 性交; 性行為 **2** an exchange of ideas, feelings etc which make people or groups understand each other better 交流; 溝通: *social intercourse* 社交

in·ter·de·nom·i·na·tio·nal /ˌɪntɚdɪˌnɑməˋneʃənḷ; ˌɪntədǝ̍nɒmǝ̍ˈneɪʃənəl/ *adj* between or involving Christians from different groups〔基督教〕教派之間的; 涉及不同教派的

in·ter·de·part·men·tal /ˌɪntɚdɪˌpɑrtˋmɛntḷ; ˌɪntəˌdiːpɑːtˈmentl/ *adj* between or involving different departments of a company, government etc〔公司、政府等〕部門之間的; 牽涉不同部門的: *intense interdepartmental rivalry* 部門之間的激烈競爭

in·ter·de·pen·dence /ˌɪntɚdɪˋpɛndəns; ˌɪntədɪˈpendəns/ *n* [U] a situation in which people or things depend on each other 互相依賴

in·ter·de·pen·dent /ˌɪntɚdɪˋpɛndənt; ˌɪntədɪˈpendənt◂/ *adj* depending on or necessary to each other 互相依賴的, 互相需要的: *countries with interdependent economies* 經濟上相互依賴的國家 —**interdependently** *adv*

in·ter·dict /ˋɪntɚˌdɪkt; ˈɪntədɪkt/ *n* [C] **1** *law* an official order from a court telling someone not to do something【法律】〔法庭作出的〕禁令 **2** *technical* a punishment in the Roman Catholic Church, by which someone is not allowed to take part in church ceremonies【術語】〔羅馬天主教禁止某人參加宗教儀式的〕禁令 —**interdict** /ˌɪntɚˋdɪkt; ˌɪntəˈdɪkt/ *v* [T]

in·ter·dis·ci·plin·ary /ˌɪntɚˋdɪsəplɪnɛrɪ; ˌɪntəˌdɪsǝ̍ˈplɪnəri/ *adj* an interdisciplinary course of study includes two or more subjects 跨學科的: *an interdisciplinary course* 跨學科的課程

2 **in·terest**[1] /ˋɪntərɪst; ˈɪntrǝ̍st/ *n*
1 **1 ▶FEELING 情感◀** [singular, U] a feeling that makes you want to pay attention to something or to find out more about it 興趣: *Ruth listened with evident interest.* 露思明顯感興趣地聽着。| [+in] *They share an interest in poetry.* 他們都愛好詩歌。| **lose interest** (=stop being interested) 失去興趣 *The older ones soon lost interest in the game.* 年紀大一些的人很快就失去對那個遊戲的興趣了。| **take an interest (in)** (=be interested in something) (對…) 產生興趣: *Babies soon begin to take an interest in the world around them.* 嬰兒很快就開始對周圍的事物產生興趣。| **show/express interest** (=say you are interested in something or want to buy it) 表現出/表達出興趣 *Ben has shown an interest in learning French.* 本表示想學法語。| *Several football clubs have expressed an interest in Giggs.* 好幾家足球俱樂部都已表示對傑斯感興趣。

2 ▶QUALITY 性質◀ [U] a quality or feature of something that attracts your attention or makes you want to know more about it 引起關注或好奇心的性質; 趣味: *Add interest to your decor with a patterned border.* 用帶圖案的花邊給你的裝飾增加趣味。| **of interest** (=interesting) 有趣的; 能引起興趣的 *Tourist information will give you a list of local places of interest.* 旅遊信息中心將給你一份地方名勝目錄。| **of general interest** (=that everyone wants to know about) 廣為感興趣的 *a subject of general interest* 普遍感興趣的話題 | **of special/particular interest** *This book will be of particular interest to those studying British Politics since 1900.* 那些研究 1900 年以來英國政治的人會特別對這本書感興趣。| **be of no interest (to)** (=not be interesting to someone) 絲毫不感興趣 *Your private problems are of no interest to me.* 對你的私人問題我毫無興趣。

3 ▶ACTIVITY 活動◀ [C] something that you enjoy doing or a subject that you enjoy studying when you are not working 興趣; 愛好: *Her main interest in life is tennis.* 她生活中的主要愛好是網球。| *List your leisure time interests on the back of the form.* 在表格背面列出你的業餘愛好。

4 ▶MONEY 錢◀ [U] **a)** a charge made for borrowing money〔借貸的〕利息: *competitive rates of interest* 有競爭力的利率 | **[+on]** *The interest on the loan is 16.5% per year.* 貸款年利率為 16.5%。**b)** money paid to you by a bank or financial institution when you keep money in an account there 存款利息 —see also 另見 COMPOUND INTEREST, SIMPLE INTEREST

5 ▶ADVANTAGE 優勢◀ [C,U] the things that bring advantages to someone or something 利益, 好處: **be in your (best) interest(s)** (=be helpful for you) 對你 (最) 有利 *It would be in your interests to do as he says.* 按他說的去做, 對你有好處。| **look after/protect/safeguard your interests** *The company is endeavouring to protect its own interests.* 這家公司正竭力維護自身利益。| *the national interest* 國家利益 | **have sb's (best) interests at heart** (=care about someone and want to improve their situation) (極為) 關心某人的利益 *Private employment agencies may not have your best interests at heart.* 私人職業介紹所可能並不關心你的利益。

6 be in the public/national interest be good or necessary for the safety or success of a country and its people 出於公眾/國家利益: *The documents were kept secret 'in the public interest'.* 這些文件"出於公眾利益"而被保密。

7 in the interest(s) of justice/efficiency etc in order to make a situation or system fair, efficient etc 出於公正/效率等的考慮: *In the interest of justice, I must speak the truth.* 為了維護正義, 我必須說實話。

8 (just) out of interest/as a matter of interest *spoken* used to say that you are asking a question only because you are interested and not because you need to know【口】(只是) 出於興趣〔提問時用〕: *Just out of interest, how much did they offer you?* 只是出於感興趣問一下, 他們打算給你多少錢? | *As a matter of interest, where did you meet him?* 我只是感興趣問一下, 你是在哪裡遇見他的?

9 have no interest in doing sth not to want to do something 不想做某事: *I have no interest in continuing this conversation.* 我不想繼續談下去。

10 declare an interest (in sth) to state that you are connected with something or someone, and so cannot be completely fair and independent when making a decision involving them 宣布〔與某事〕有利害關係: *I must declare an interest here, the second candidate is a friend of mine.* 我必須在此宣布有關利害關係, 第二位候選人是我的朋友。

11 human interest/love interest the part of a story or film which is interesting because it is about people's lives or romantic relationships〔小說或影片中的〕人們的生活/風流韻事情節

12 pay sb back with interest *informal* to harm or offend someone in an even worse way than they have harmed you【非正式】向某人加倍報復

13 ►SHARE IN COMPANY 公司股份◄ [C] *technical* a share in a company, business etc【術語】權益; 股份: *She's sold all her interests in the company.* 她把她在這家公司的股份全部賣掉了。| **controlling interest** (=enough shares to control what decisions are taken) 控股權益 *Müller has a controlling interest in the factory.* 米勒有這家工廠的控股權。

14 ►POWERFUL GROUP 權力集團◄ [C] *technical* a group of people in the same business who share aims or ideas【術語】利益集團; 利益相關者: *landed interests* 地產業主 | *shipping interests* 運輸業主 —see also 另見 SELF-INTEREST, VESTED INTEREST

This graph shows some of the words most commonly used with the noun **interest**. 本圖表所示為含有名詞 interest 最常用的一些詞組。

interest in	
of interest	
public/national interest	
lose interest	
special interest	
particular interest	
best interests	
general interest	

10 20 30 40 per million 每百萬

Based on the British National Corpus and the Longman Lancaster Corpus 據英國國家語料庫和朗文蘭卡斯特語料庫

interest² *v* [T] **1** to make someone feel interested 使〔某人〕感興趣: *Here's an article which might interest you.* 這裡有一篇文章, 也許你會感興趣。| *What interests me is all the history of these places.* 使我感興趣的是這些地方的歷史。| **it may interest you to know** *spoken* (=used to introduce a fact which you think may surprise someone)【口】你聽了可能會感興趣 *It may interest you to know that she is now head of a major company.* 你聽了可能會感興趣: 她現在是一家大公司的老闆。**2 could I interest you in a drink/a meal etc?** *spoken* used as a polite way of offering someone something【口】可否賞臉跟我喝一杯/吃頓飯等?

S1 W2 **in·terest·ed** /ˈɪntərɪstɪd; ˈɪntrɨstɨd/ *adj* **1** giving a lot of attention to something because you want to find out more about it 很感興趣的, 關心的: **[+in]** *I'm not really interested in politics.* 我對政治不太感興趣。| *Carrie's fourteen now, and all she's interested in is clothes.* 嘉莉十四歲了, 只對穿戴感興趣。| **be interested to hear/know/see etc** *I'd be very interested to hear your opinion.* 我非常想聽聽你的意見。—opposite 反義詞 UNINTERESTED **2** *informal* eager to do or have something【非正式】熱切的: *I offered to help but they weren't interested.* 我主動幫忙, 他們卻不着急。| **to be interested in doing sth** *Sheila's interested in starting her own business.* 希拉很想自己開一家公司。| **[+in]** *Would you be interested in a secondhand Volvo?* 您想不想買一輛二手的富豪汽車? **3 interested party/group** a person or group that is directly or personally concerned with a situation and is likely to be affected by its results 當事人/團體: *All interested parties should write to the chairman of the inquiry.* 所有當事人都應給調查委員會主席寫信。—**interestedly** *adv* —see also 另見 DISINTERESTED

interest-free /ˌ·· ˈ·◂/ *adj* an interest-free LOAN¹ (1) has no interest charged on it〔貸款〕無息的: *interest-free credit* 免息信貸

interest group /ˈ·· ˌ·/ *n* [C] a group of people who join together to try to influence the government in order to protect their own particular rights, advantages etc〔試圖左右政府決策以保護自身利益的〕利益集團

in·terest·ing /ˈɪntərɪstɪŋ; ˈɪntrɨstɪŋ/ *adj* unusual or exciting in a way that keeps your attention 有趣的, 令人關注的: *an interesting film* 有趣的影片 | *I found his talk very interesting.* 我覺得他的講話很引人入勝。| **it is interesting to see/know etc** *It would be interesting to see figures supporting this argument.* 看看支持這個論點的一些數字會很有意思。| **it is interesting that** *It's interesting that no one remembers seeing the car.* 竟沒人記得見過這輛車, 真是有趣。—see 見 BORING (USAGE) S1 W2

in·terest·ing·ly /ˈɪntərɪstɪŋlɪ; ˈɪntrɨstɪŋli/ *adv* **1** [sentence adverb 句子副詞] used to introduce a fact that you think is interesting 有趣的是: *Interestingly enough, Pearson made no attempt to deny the rumour.* 說來真有意思, 皮爾森沒有試圖否認謠傳。**2** in an interesting way 有趣地

interest rate /ˈ·· ˌ·/ *n* [C] the PERCENTAGE amount charged by a bank etc when you borrow money or paid to you by a bank when you keep money in an account there〔銀行貸款或存款的〕利率: *The government intends to keep interest rates low.* 政府打算保持低利率。

in·ter·face¹ /ˈɪntɚˌfes; ˈɪntəfeɪs/ *n* [C] **1** *technical* the part of a computer system through which two different machines are connected【術語】接口 **2** the way in which two subjects, events etc affect each other 相互作用, 相互影響 **3** *technical* the surface where two things touch each other【術語】〔兩個物體接觸的〕界面

interface² *v* [I, T+with] *technical* if you interface two parts of a computer system, or if they interface, you connect them【術語】(使) 聯繫, (使) 接合

in·ter·fere /ˌɪntɚˈfɪr; ˌɪntəˈfɪə/ *v* [I] to deliberately get involved in a situation that does not concern you, and try to influence what happens in a way that annoys people 介入; 干涉; 干預: *I wish you'd stop interfering – you've caused enough problems already.* 我希望你別再插手, 你惹的麻煩已經夠多了。| *the interfering old busybody* 多管閒事的老傢伙 | **[+in]** *Some people believe it's not the church's job to interfere in politics.* 有人認為干預政治不是教會應做的事。

interfere with sth/sb *phr v* [T] **1** to prevent something from succeeding or from happening in the way that was planned 妨礙, 阻止: *Anxiety can interfere with children's performance at school.* 憂慮緊張會影響孩子在學校的表現。**2** if something interferes with a radio or television broadcast, it spoils the sound or picture that you receive 干擾〔廣播或電視播送〕**3** to touch a child sexually 對〔兒童〕性侵犯: *He was arrested for interfering with young boys.* 他因猥褻男童而被捕。

in·ter·fer·ence /ˌɪntɚˈfɪrəns; ˌɪntəˈfɪərəns/ *n* [U] **1** an act of interfering 干涉; 干預; 妨礙; 擾亂: *I resent his interference in my work.* 我討厭他干預我的工作。| *Industrial relations should be free from state interference.* 勞資關係應不受政府干預。**2** unwanted noise on radio or television or on the telephone, or faults in the television picture〔收音機、電視機、電話等受到的〕干擾: *The bad weather's causing a lot of television interference.* 惡劣的天氣給電視接收造成很大干擾。**3** *especially AmE* the act of blocking another player in ICE HOCKEY, American football etc by standing in front of them【尤美】〔冰上曲棍球、美式橄欖球等中的〕掩護阻擋; OBSTRUCTION (4) *BrE*【英】**4 run interference** *AmE*【美】**a)** the act of protecting a player who has the ball in American football by blocking players from the opposing team〔美式

足球比賽中為保護本方持球隊員而〕掩護阻擋 **b)** the act of helping someone to achieve something by dealing with people or problems that might cause trouble〔為幫助某人成就某事而〕對付可能製造麻煩的人[事]

in·ter·fer·on /ˌɪntɚˈfɪran; ˌɪntəˈfɪərɒn/ *n* [U] a chemical substance that is produced by your body to fight against VIRUS*es* that cause disease〔體內產生的抗病毒的〕干擾素

in·ter·ga·lac·tic /ˌɪntɚgəˈlæktɪk; ˌɪntəgəˈlæktɪk◂/ *adj* between the large groups of stars in space 星系之間的: *intergalactic travel* 星系間旅行

in·ter·im¹ /ˈɪntərɪm; ˈɪntərɪm/ *adj* [only before noun 僅用於名詞前] an interim arrangement, report, payment etc is used or accepted temporarily, until a final or complete one is made; PROVISIONAL 過渡期間的; 臨時的: *an interim report* 中期報告 | *He received an interim payment of £10,000.* 他收到暫時支付的 10,000 英鎊。

interim² *n* **in the interim** in the period of time between two events; MEANWHILE 在此期間; 與此同時: *The child will be adopted but a relative is looking after him in the interim.* 孩子將由人領養, 但現在這段時間暫由一名親屬照管。

in·te·ri·or¹ /ɪnˈtɪrɪɚ; ɪnˈtɪəriə/ *n* **1** [C usually singular 一般用單數] the inner part or inside of something 內部: *His new Porsche has red bodywork with a black leather interior.* 他新買的保時捷車身是紅色的, 內飾是黑色皮革。—opposite 反義詞 EXTERIOR¹ (1) **2 the interior** the part of a country that is farthest away from the coast 內地, 腹地: *The interior of the country is mainly desert.* 這個國家的內陸地帶主要是沙漠。**3 Minister/Department of the Interior** the minister or department that deals with matters within a country rather than abroad 內政部長/內政部

interior² *adj* [only before noun 僅用於名詞前] inside or indoors 內部的, 裡面的; 室內的: *The interior walls are all painted white.* 室內牆壁都漆成了白色。—opposite 反義詞 EXTERIOR² (1)

interior de·co·ra·tor /·ˌ··· ˈ····/ also 又作 **interior de·sign·er** /·ˌ··· ·ˈ··/ *n* [C] someone whose job is to plan and choose the colours, materials, furniture etc for the inside of people's houses 室內設計師

in·ter·ject /ˌɪntɚˈdʒɛkt; ˌɪntəˈdʒekt/ *v* [I,T] to interrupt what someone else is saying with a sudden remark 突然插入(話): *"That's absolute rubbish!" he interjected.* "全是廢話!" 他突然插語道。

in·ter·jec·tion /ˌɪntɚˈdʒɛkʃən; ˌɪntəˈdʒekʃən/ *n* **1** [C] a word or phrase used to express a strong feeling such as shock, pain, or pleasure; EXCLAMATION 感嘆語, 感嘆詞 **2** [C,U] an INTERRUPTION or the act of interrupting 打斷〔別人的話〕; 插嘴

in·ter·lace /ˌɪntɚˈles; ˌɪntəˈleɪs/ *v* [I, T] to join things together by weaving and twisting them over and under each other, or to be joined in this way (使) 交織; (使) 交錯: *The threads were interlaced with strands of gold.* 這些線是夾雜着金絲編成的。

in·ter·lard /ˌɪntɚˈlard; ˌɪntəˈlɑːd/ *v* [T+with] *literary* to add things that are not necessary to a speech or piece of writing, such as foreign phrases【文】〔在講話或文章中〕夾雜〔不必要的內容〕〈如外來詞語等〉

in·ter·link /ˌɪntɚˈlɪŋk; ˌɪntəˈlɪŋk/ *v* [I, T] to connect or be connected with something else (使) 連結: *a chain of interlinking loops* 連結成鏈的套環

in·ter·lock¹ /ˌɪntɚˈlak; ˌɪntəˈlɒk/ *v* [I, T] if two or more things interlock or are interlocked, they fit firmly together (使) 連鎖; (使) 相互扣住; (使) 連結: *a puzzle with 500 fully interlocking pieces* 由 500 個緊密相連的圖塊組成的拼圖

in·ter·lock² /ˈɪntɚlak; ˈɪntəlɒk/ *n* [C] *technical* a special part of a computer that prevents particular operations happening unless other operations have already happened【術語】聯鎖裝置

in·ter·loc·u·tor /ˌɪntɚˈlakjətɚ; ˌɪntəˈlɒkjʊ̈tə/ *n* [C] *formal* the person who is speaking to you【正式】對話者, 參加談話的人

in·ter·lop·er /ˌɪntɚˈlopɚ; ˈɪntələʊpə/ *n* [C] someone who enters a place or group where they should not be 擅自進入者, 闖入者: *The village women stared at the interloper with curiosity.* 村裡的女人們好奇地盯着這位不速之客。

in·ter·lude /ˈɪntɚˌlud; ˈɪntəluːd/ *n* [C] **1** a period of time or an event that is different from what happens before and afterwards 間歇: *a brief interlude of peace before a return to the battlefield* 重返戰場之前的短暫平靜 **2** a short period of time between the parts of a play, concert etc〔戲劇、音樂會等的〕幕間休息 **3** a short piece of music, talk etc used to fill such a period〔幕間休息時的〕幕間音樂[講話等]

in·ter·mar·riage /ˌɪntɚˈmærɪdʒ; ˌɪntəˈmærɪdʒ/ *n* [U] **1** marriage between members of different races, families, or social groups〔不同種族、家族、門第間的〕通婚: *intermarriage between black and white* 黑人與白人通婚 **2** marriage within your own family or within a small group of relatives 近親結婚: *intermarriage between cousins* 堂[表]兄弟姐妹間的通婚

in·ter·mar·ry /ˌɪntɚˈmærɪ; ˌɪntəˈmæri/ *v* [I+**with**] **1** if two groups or races intermarry, people from each group marry people from the other 不同家族[種族]之間通婚 **2** to marry someone within your own group or family 近親結婚: *It is not unusual for royal cousins to intermarry.* 皇室成員近親結婚並不少見。

in·ter·me·di·a·ry /ˌɪntɚˈmidɪˌɛrɪ; ˌɪntəˈmiːdiəri/ *n* [C] a person or organization that tries to help two other people or groups to agree with each other 調解人; 中間人: *Jackson acted as an intermediary between the two parties.* 傑克遜在雙方之間充當調解人。—**intermediary** *adj*: *an intermediary role in the negotiations* 談判中調解人的角色

in·ter·me·di·ate /ˌɪntɚˈmidɪɪt; ˌɪntəˈmiːdiət◂/ *adj* **1** an intermediate stage in a process of development is between two other stages 中間的, 居中的: *an intermediate stage during which the disease is dormant* 疾病處於潛伏狀態的中期 **2** an intermediate class, course etc is at a level between the first level and advanced level 中級程度的, 中等水平的

intermediate school /··ˈ··· ˌ·/ *n* [C] *AmE* a JUNIOR HIGH SCHOOL or MIDDLE SCHOOL【美】初級中學

intermediate tech·no·lo·gy /ˌ····· ·ˈ···/ *n* [C,U] a practical science which is suitable for use in developing countries because it is cheap and simple 中間技術〔適用於發展中國家的廉價而簡單的實用科學技術〕

in·ter·ment /ɪnˈtɝmənt; ɪnˈtɜːmənt/ *n* [C, U] *formal* the act of burying a dead body【正式】安葬; 埋葬

in·ter·mez·zo /ˌɪntɚˈmɛtso; ˌɪntəˈmetsəʊ/ *n* [C] a short piece of music, especially one that is played between the main parts of a concert, OPERA etc〔音樂會、歌劇等的〕間奏曲

in·ter·mi·na·ble /ɪnˈtɝmɪnəbl; ɪnˈtɜːmɪ̈nəbəl/ *adj* very long and boring 冗長乏味的: *interminable delays* 無休止的拖延 —**interminably** *adv*: *an interminably long speech* 喋喋不休的沉悶講話

in·ter·min·gle /ˌɪntɚˈmɪŋgl; ˌɪntəˈmɪŋgəl/ *v* [I, T usually passive 一般用被動態] to mix together or mix something with something else (使) 混合; (使)〔...與...〕混在一起: [+**with**] *reds and oranges intermingled with pink* 與粉紅色混在一起的各種紅色和橙色

in·ter·mis·sion /ˌɪntɚˈmɪʃən; ˌɪntəˈmɪʃən/ *n* [C] *especially AmE* a short period of time between the parts of a play, concert etc【尤美】幕間休息; INTERVAL (5) *BrE*【英】

in·ter·mit·tent /ˌɪntɚˈmɪtnt; ˌɪntəˈmɪtənt◂/ *adj* happening repeatedly for short periods, but not regularly or continuously 間歇的; 斷斷續續的: *The weather forecast is for sun, with intermittent showers.* 天氣預報為天晴, 有間歇陣雨。—**intermittently** *adv*

in·ter·mix /ˌɪntɚˈmɪks; ˌɪntəˈmɪks/ *v* [I,T] to mix

together, or mix things together（使）混合；（使）混雜

in·tern[1] /ɪn`tɝn; ɪnˈtɜːn/ *v* [T] to put someone in prison or limit their movements for political reasons or during a war, without charging them with a crime〔指戰時或出於政治原因〕拘留，扣押：*Seven hundred men were interned in the camps.* 七百人被關押於集中營。

in·tern[2] /`ɪntɝn; ˈɪntɜːn/ *AmE* someone who has nearly finished training as a doctor and is working in a hospital【美】實習醫師；HOUSEMAN *BrE*【英】

2 **in·ter·nal** /ɪn`tɝnḷ; ɪnˈtɜːnl/ *adj* **1** [only before noun 僅用於名詞前] inside something rather than outside 內部的，裡面的：*They've knocked down a couple of internal walls.* 他們已拆掉了幾面內牆。| *the internal measurements of the car* 汽車的內部空間大小 **2** inside your body 體內的：*The X-rays showed there were no internal injuries.* X 光片顯示沒有內傷。| *an internal examination* 內科檢查 **3** within an organization, place etc rather than outside it〔機構、地方等〕內部的：*There's to be an internal inquiry into the whole affair.* 對整個事件將進行內部調查。| *the internal mail* 內部郵件 **4** within a particular country 國內的：*internal trade* 國內貿易 | *Internal security became a priority after the bomb attack.* 炸彈襲擊後，國內安全成為一項必須首先解決的問題。**5** existing in your mind 內心的：*internal doubts* 心裡的疑慮 —**internally** *adv*: *The matter will be dealt with internally.* 這件事將在內部解決。| *This medicine must not be taken internally.* 此藥不得內服。—opposite 反義詞 EXTERNAL

internal com·bus·tion en·gine /ˌ··· ˈ·· ˌ··/ *n* [C] an engine that produces power by burning petrol 內燃機

in·ter·nal·ize also 又作 **-ise** *BrE*【英】/ɪn`tɝnḷˌaɪz; ɪnˈtɜːnəlaɪz/ *v* [T] if you internalize a particular belief, attitude, pattern of behaviour etc it becomes part of your character 使〔信仰、態度、行為模式等〕內在化〔成為性格的一部分〕—**internalization** /ɪnˌtɝnḷə`zeʃən; ɪnˌtɜːnəlaɪˈzeɪʃən/ *n* [U]

internal med·i·cine /ˌ·· ˈ···/ *n* [U] *AmE* a type of medical work in which doctors say what is wrong with a person and treat illnesses but do not do operations【美】內科（學）

Internal Rev·e·nue Ser·vice /ˌ·· ˈ··· ˌ··/ also 又作 **Internal Revenue** *n* [singular] the department that collects national taxes in the US〔美國〕國內稅務局 —compare 比較 INLAND REVENUE

3 1 **in·ter·na·tion·al**[1] /ˌɪntɚ`næʃənḷ; ˌɪntəˈnæʃənəl◂/ *adj* connected with or involving more than one nation 國際的：*an international peace-keeping force* 國際維持和平部隊 | *an international conference* 國際會議

international[2] *n* [C] **1** an international sports game 國際體育比賽 **2** *BrE* someone who plays for one of their country's sports teams【英】國際體育比賽選手

international date line /ˌ····· ˈ· ·/ *n* [singular] an imaginary line that goes from the NORTH POLE to the SOUTH POLE, to the east of which the date is one day later than it is to the west 國際日期變更線，日界線

In·ter·na·tion·ale /ˌɪntɚnæʃə`nɑl; ˌɪntənæʃəˈnæl/ *n* **the Internationale** the international SOCIALIST[1] (1) song 國際歌

in·ter·na·tion·al·is·m /ˌɪntɚ`næʃənḷˌɪzəm; ˌɪntəˈnæʃənəlɪzəm/ *n* [U] the belief that nations should work together and help each other 國際主義 —**internationalist** *n*

in·ter·na·tion·al·ize also 又作 **-ise** *BrE*【英】/ˌɪntɚ`næʃənḷˌaɪz; ˌɪntəˈnæʃənəlaɪz/ *v* [T] to make something international or bring it under international control 使國際化；把…置入國際共管之下 —**internationalization** /ˌɪntɚˌnæʃənḷə`zeʃən; ˌɪntənæʃənəlaɪˈzeɪʃən/ *n*

in·ter·na·tion·al·ly /ˌɪntɚ`næʃənḷɪ; ˌɪntəˈnæʃənəli/ *adv* in many different parts of the world 世界地，國際性地：*A recent investment boom should help firms to compete internationally.* 最近的投資景氣應有助於各企業進行國際競爭。| **internationally famous/recognized/celebrated etc** *Callas quickly became internationally famous.* 卡拉斯很快就聞名世界。

International Mon·e·ta·ry Fund /ˌ····· ˈ···· ·/ *n* the IMF 國際貨幣基金組織

in·ter·ne·cine /ˌɪntɚ`nisɪn; ˌɪntəˈniːsaɪn◂/ *adj formal* internecine fighting, disputes etc happen between members of the same group or nation【正式】內部鬥爭的；自相殘殺的；內訌的：*bitter internecine strife* 激烈的內部衝突

in·tern·ee /ˌɪntɝ`ni; ˌɪntɜːˈniː/ *n* [C] someone who is put into prison during a war or for political reasons, usually without a TRIAL[1] (1)〔戰時或由於政治原因〕被拘留者，拘留犯：*a call for the release of all internees* 要求釋放所有被拘留者的呼籲

In·ter·net /`ɪntɚˌnɛt; ˈɪntənet/ *n* **the Internet** a computer system that allows millions of computer users around the world to exchange information 互聯網

in·tern·ist /`ɪntɝnɪst; ˈɪntɜːnɪst/ *n* [C] *AmE* a doctor who has a general knowledge about all illnesses and medical conditions but who does not do operations【美】內科醫師

in·tern·ment /ɪn`tɝnmənt; ɪnˈtɜːnmənt/ *n* **1** [U] the act of keeping people in prison or in special camps for political reasons, without charging them with a crime 拘留〔指由於政治原因關押於監獄或集中營〕**2** [C] the period of time during which someone is kept in this way 拘留期

in·ter·pen·e·trate /ˌɪntɚ`pɛnəˌtret; ˌɪntəˈpenɪtreɪt/ *v* [I, T] *formal* to spread through something or spread through each other【正式】貫穿；滲透；相互貫穿；相互滲透 —**interpenetration** /ˌɪntɚˌpɛnə`treʃən; ˌɪntəpenɪˈtreɪʃən/ *n* [C, U]

in·ter·per·son·al /ˌɪntɚ`pɝsənḷ; ˌɪntəˈpɜːsənəl◂/ *adj* involving relations between people 人與人之間的；人際關係的：*interpersonal skills* 人際交往技巧

in·ter·plan·e·ta·ry /ˌɪntɚ`plænəˌtɛrɪ; ˌɪntəˈplænɪtəri◂/ *adj* [only before noun 僅用於名詞前] between the PLANETS 行星間的：*interplanetary travel* 星際旅行

in·ter·play /`ɪntɚˌple; ˈɪntəpleɪ/ *n* [U] the way in which two people or things react with one another or affect each other 相互作用；相互影響

In·ter·pol /`ɪntɚˌpol; ˈɪntəpɒl/ *n* [singular] an international police organization that helps national police forces to catch criminals 國際刑（事）警（察）組織

in·ter·po·late /ɪn`tɝpəˌlet; ɪnˈtɜːpəleɪt/ *v* [T] *formal*【正式】**1** to put additional words into a piece of text 在文本中插入〔字句〕**2** to interrupt someone by saying something 插〔話〕—**interpolation** /ɪnˌtɝpə`leʃən; ɪnˌtɜːpəˈleɪʃən/ *n* [C,U]

in·ter·pose /ˌɪntɚ`poz; ˌɪntəˈpəʊz/ *v* [T] *formal*【正式】**1** to put yourself or something else between two other things 使介入〔兩者之間〕；使插入：*Local activists interposed between party leaders and the people.* 地方政治活動分子插入了黨派領袖和羣眾之間。**2** to introduce something between the parts of a conversation or argument 插〔話〕：*"That might be difficult," interposed Regina.* "那可能有困難。"雷吉娜插嘴說。

in·ter·pret /ɪn`tɝprɪt; ɪnˈtɜːprɪt/ *v* **1** [T] to believe that 3
someone's actions or behaviour or an event as having a particular meaning 把〔某人的行為或某一事件〕理解為；解釋為：**interpret sth as** *The EC's refusal to intervene in Bosnia should not be interpreted as a sign of weakness.* 不可把歐共體拒絕干涉波斯尼亞的局勢視為軟弱的表現。**2** [I,T] to change words spoken in one language into another 口譯：*They spoke good Spanish, and promised to interpret for me.* 他們西班牙語說得很好，而且答應為我作口譯。—see also 另見 TRANSLATE (1) **3** [T] to explain the meaning of something 解釋，闡釋：*Freud's attempts to interpret the meaning of dreams* 弗洛伊德解釋夢的含義的嘗試 **4** [T] to perform a part in a play, a piece of music etc in a way that shows your feelings

about it or what you think it means〔表演者根據自己對戲劇、音樂等的感受或理解來〕表演, 演繹; 體現

2 **in·ter·pre·ta·tion** /ɪnˌtɝprɪˋteʃən; ɪnˌtɜːprɨ̵ˈteɪʃən/ *n* [C, U] **1** an attempt to explain the reason for an event, a result, someone's actions etc 解釋, 說明, 闡明: *One possible interpretation is that they want you to resign.* 一種可能的解釋是, 他們想要你辭職。| **put an interpretation on** (=explain something in a particular way) 對…作某種解釋 *It's difficult to put an accurate interpretation on the survey results.* 對調查結果難以做出精確的解釋。**2** the way in which someone performs a play, a piece of music etc and shows what they think and feel about it〔體現表演者對戲劇、音樂等的觀點或感受的〕表演, 演繹: *Laurence Olivier's brilliant interpretation of Henry V* 勞倫斯·奧利弗扮演亨利五世的精彩演出

in·ter·pre·ta·tive /ɪnˋtɝprɪˌtetɪv; ɪnˈtɜːprɨ̵tətɪv/ *adj* concerned with explaining the reasons for something or with the way someone performs a play, piece of music etc〔對某事原委〕解釋的, 闡釋的;〔對表演或音樂〕藝術處理的: *an interpretative framework* 起解釋作用的框架 | *interpretative skills* 藝術處理技巧

in·ter·pret·er /ɪnˋtɝprɪtɚ; ɪnˈtɜːprɨ̵tə/ *n* [C] **1** someone who changes spoken words from one language into another, especially as their job 口譯者, 傳譯員 —see also 另見 TRANSLATOR **2** a computer PROGRAM[1] (1) that changes an instruction into a form that can be understood directly by the computer〔電腦的〕解釋程序

in·ter·pre·tive /ɪnˋtɝprɪtɪv; ɪnˈtɜːprɨ̵tɪv/ *adj* INTERPRETATIVE 解釋的; 藝術處理的

interpretive cen·ter /ˈ·ˋ··· ˌ··/ *n* [C] *AmE* a room or building where visitors and tourists can receive historical information about the place they are visiting【美】講解中心〔給遊客提供旅遊點歷史的詢問處〕

in·ter·ra·cial /ˌɪntɚˋreʃəl; ˌɪntəˈreɪʃəl◂/ *adj* between different races of people 不同種族間的: *interracial harmony* 種族間的和睦 —**interracially** *adv*

in·ter·reg·num /ˌɪntɚˋrɛgnəm; ˌɪntəˈregnəm/ *n plural* **interregnums** or **interregna** /-nə; -nə/ [C] **1** a period of time when a country has no king or queen, because the new ruler has not yet started to rule〔新王即位前的〕空位期 **2** a period of time when a company, organization etc has no leader, because the new leader has not started their job 空位過渡期〔由於新領導人尚未接任而使公司、機構等沒有領導的一段時期〕

in·ter·re·late /ˌɪntɚrɪˋlet; ˌɪntərɪˈleɪt/ *v* [I,T] if two things interrelate or you interrelate them, they are connected and have an effect on each other (使) 相互關聯; (使) 相互影響: *a model interrelating population, capital, and natural resources* 聯繫人口、資本與自然資源的模型

in·ter·re·lat·ed /ˌɪntɚrɪˋletɪd; ˌɪntərɪˈleɪtɨ̵d◂/ *adj* things that are interrelated are connected and have an effect on each other 相互關聯的; 相互影響的: *Unemployment and inflation are interrelated.* 失業與通貨膨脹是相互聯繫的。| *Many interrelated factors are at work here.* 這裡許多相互關聯的因素在起作用。

in·ter·re·la·tion·ship /ˌɪntɚrɪˋleʃənʃɪp; ˌɪntərɪˈleɪʃənʃɪp/ also 又作 **interrelation** /-rɪˋleʃən; -rɪˈleɪʃən/ *n* [C,U] a connection between two things that makes them affect each other 相互聯繫, 相互關係

in·ter·ro·gate /ɪnˋtɛrəˌget; ɪnˈterəgeɪt/ *v* [T] **1** to ask someone a lot of questions for a long time in order to get information, sometimes using threats〔長時間地〕訊問; 審問; 盤問: *The police interrogated the suspect for several hours.* 警察盤問了這名嫌疑犯好幾個小時。**2** *technical* to try to get information directly from a part of a computer【術語】〔在電腦上〕查詢〔資料〕: *We're having trouble in interrogating the database.* 我們在查詢電腦數據庫時遇到了麻煩。—**interrogator** *n* [C]: *He refused to tell his interrogators anything.* 他拒絕向訊問者提供任何資料。—**interrogation** *n* [C,U]

in·ter·ro·ga·tion mark /·ˌ··ˋ·· ˌ·/ *n* [C] *formal* a QUESTION MARK【正式】問號

in·ter·rog·a·tive[1] /ˌɪntəˋrɑgətɪv; ˌɪntəˈrɒgətɪv◂/ *adj technical* an interrogative sentence, PRONOUN etc, asks a question or has the form of a question【術語】〔句子、代詞等〕疑問的: *'Who' and 'what' are interrogative pronouns.* who 和 what 都是疑問代名詞。—**interrogatively** *adv*

interrogative[2] *n technical*【術語】**1 the interrogative** the form of a sentence or verb that is used for asking questions〔句子或動詞的〕疑問形式: *Put this statement into the interrogative.* 把這個陳述句改為疑問句。**2** [C] a word such as 'who', or 'what' that is used in asking questions 疑問詞〈如 who, what〉

in·ter·rupt /ˌɪntəˋrʌpt; ˌɪntəˈrʌpt/ *v* **1** [I,T] to stop someone from continuing what they are saying or doing by suddenly speaking to them, making a noise etc 打斷〔某人的〕講話; 中斷〔某人的〕行動; 打擾: *Don't interrupt – I haven't finished yet.* 別插嘴, 我還沒說完呢。| **interrupt sb** *She began to explain but I interrupted her.* 她開始解釋, 但我打斷了她。**2** [T] to make a process or activity stop temporarily 使〔過程、活動〕暫時停止: *My studies were interrupted by the war.* 我的學業由於戰爭而暫時中止。**3** [T] *literary* if something interrupts a line, surface, view etc it stops it from being continuous【文】中斷〔直線、平面、風景等的連續性〕—**interruption** /-ˋrʌpʃən; -ˈrʌpʃən/ *n* [C,U]: *Let's go somewhere where we can talk without interruption.* 我們去找個說話不受打擾的地方吧。

in·ter·sect /ˌɪntɚˋsɛkt; ˌɪntəˈsekt/ *v* **1** [I,T] if two lines or roads intersect, they meet or go across each other (和…) 相交, (和…) 交叉 **2** [T usually passive 一般用被動態] to divide an area with several lines, roads etc〔用線或路把一個區域〕分隔: *The plain is intersected by a network of canals.* 平原上運河網絡縱橫交錯。

in·ter·sec·tion /ˌɪntɚˋsɛkʃən; ˌɪntəˈsekʃən/ *n* [C] **1** a place where roads, lines etc cross each other, especially where two roads meet〔尤指兩條道路的〕交叉口, 十字路口;〔線的〕交點 **2** [U] the act of intersecting something 橫斷; 交叉

in·ter·sperse /ˌɪntɚˋspɝs; ˌɪntəˈspɜːs/ *v* [T usually passive 一般用被動態] **1 be interspersed with** if something is interspersed with a particular kind of thing, it has a lot of them in it〔大量〕點綴着, 散佈着: *sunny periods interspersed with occasional showers* 間或有陣雨的晴朗天氣 **2 intersperse sth with** to put something in between pieces of speech or writing, parts of a film etc 在某物中夾雜

in·ter·state[1] /ˌɪntɚˋstet; ˌɪntəˈsteɪt◂/ *n* [C] *AmE* a very wide road for long distance travel【美】州際公路

interstate[2] *adj* [only before noun 僅用於名詞前] involving different states, especially in the US〔尤指美國〕州際的: *interstate commerce* 州際貿易 —**interstate** *adv*: *travelling interstate on company business* 為公司業務從一個州去另一個州

in·ter·stel·lar /ˌɪntɚˋstɛlɚ; ˌɪntəˈstelə◂/ *adj* [only before noun 僅用於名詞前] happening or existing between the stars 星際的; 恒星之間的

in·ter·stice /ɪnˋtɝstɪs; ɪnˈtɜːstɨ̵s/ *n* [C usually plural 一般用複數] *formal* a small space or crack between things placed close together【正式】裂縫; 空隙; 間隙: *small plants in the interstices of the rock* 岩石裂縫中長出的小草

in·ter·twine /ˌɪntɚˋtwaɪn; ˌɪntəˈtwaɪn/ *v* [I,T] **1** if two things intertwine or are intertwined, they are twisted together (使) 纏繞; (使) 交織在一起: *intertwining stems* 枝幹盤結 **2 be (closely) intertwined** if two situations, ideas etc are intertwined, they are closely connected with each other〔局勢、觀點等〕緊密相關: *The problems of crime and unemployment are closely intertwined.* 犯罪問題與失業問題密切相關。

in·ter·val /ˋɪntɚvl; ˈɪntəvəl/ *n* [C] **1** the period of time between two events, activities etc〔兩件事情、兩種活動等之間的〕間隔, 間歇: *He left the room, returning after* 

a short interval with a message. 他離開房間，隔了一會兒就回來報告一條消息。| **[+between]** *The interval between arrest and trial can be up to six months.* 從逮捕到審判之間的間隔可達六個月。**2 sunny/bright intervals** short periods of fine weather between cloudy, rainy weather etc〔陰雨天中的〕短暫晴朗 **3 at weekly/20 minute etc intervals** every week, 20 minutes etc 每週/每20分鐘等: *The bell rang at half-hourly intervals.* 每半小時響鈴一次。**4 at regular intervals a)** something that happens at regular intervals happens often 每隔一定時間: *The phone rang at regular intervals all afternoon.* 整個下午每隔一定時間電話鈴就響一次。**b)** objects that are placed at regular intervals have all been placed at the same distance from each other〔物件〕按相同間距〔擺放〕: *Trees had been planted at regular intervals.* 樹已按相同間距栽種。**5** *BrE* a short period of time between the parts of a play, concert etc【英】〔戲劇、音樂會等〕幕間休息; INTERMISSION *especially AmE*【尤美】: *We can get some drinks in the interval.* 我們可以在幕間休息時喝點甚麼。**6** *technical* the amount of difference in PITCH[1] (6) between two musical notes【術語】音程

in·ter·vene /ˌɪntɚˋvin; ˌɪntəˈviːn/ *v* [I] **1** to do something to try and stop a quarrel, or a war, or to deal with a problem, especially one that you are not directly involved in〔尤指本身不直接牽涉在內，但為了停止爭吵、戰爭或解決問題而〕干涉，干預: **[+in]** *The police don't usually like to intervene in disputes between husbands and wives.* 警方通常不願意干預夫妻之間的爭吵。| *The Federal Reserve Bank had to intervene to protect the value of the dollar.* 聯邦儲備銀行不得不干預以保護美元的幣值。**2** if an event intervenes it happens in a way that prevents or interrupts something else〔某事發生對另一事件形成〕阻礙，使中斷: *He was just establishing his career when the war intervened.* 他剛剛開始創建自己的事業，戰爭便爆發了。**3** if a period of time intervenes, it comes between two events〔時間〕介於兩件事情之間

in·ter·ven·ing /ˌɪntɚˋvinɪŋ; ˌɪntəˈviːnɪŋ◂/ *adj* **the intervening years/months/decades etc** the amount of time between two events 兩件事情之間的那些年/那些月/幾十年等: *I hadn't seen him since 1980, and he had aged a lot in the intervening years.* 我自1980年以來就沒見過他，這期間他老了不少。

3 **in·ter·ven·tion** /ˌɪntɚˋvɛnʃən; ˌɪntəˈvenʃən/ *n* [C,U] the act of intervening in something such as an argument or activity to influence what happens 干涉，干預；介入: *government intervention to regulate prices* 政府干預調整物價

in·ter·ven·tion·is·m /ˌɪntɚˋvɛnʃənˌɪzəm; ˌɪntəˈvenʃənɪzəm/ *n* [U] **1** the belief that a government should try to influence trade by spending government money 干預主義〔認為應由政府出資干涉貿易的主張〕**2** the belief that a government should try to influence what happens in foreign countries 干涉主義〔主張干預其他國家的事務〕—**interventionist** *adj*

3 2 **in·ter·view**[1] /ˈɪntɚˌvju; ˈɪntəvjuː/ *n* **1** [C,U] a formal meeting at which someone is asked questions in order to find out whether they are suitable for a job, course of study etc〔求職、入學等的〕面試、面談: **[+for]** *He has an interview next Thursday for a job on the Los Angeles Times.* 他下週四參加《洛杉磯時報》的求職面試。**2** [C] an occasion when a famous person is asked questions about their life, experiences, or ideas for a newspaper, magazine, TV programme etc〔報紙、雜誌、電視的〕採訪；訪談: **[+with]** *an interview with the President* 對總統的採訪 | **give an interview** *Mellor gave an off-the-cuff interview to reporters outside his home.* 梅勒在屋外接受記者們的即席採訪。**3** [C] an official meeting with someone who asks you questions〔與提問者的〕正式晤談，接見，會見: *a police interview* 警察問訊

2 **interview**[2] *v* [T] **1** to ask someone questions, in order to find out if they are good enough for a job, course of study etc 對〔求職者、學校考生等〕進行面試: *We're interviewing six candidates this afternoon.* 我們今天下午要對六位候選人進行面試。**2** to ask a famous person questions about their life or ideas 採訪〔名人〕**3** to ask someone questions officially 向〔某人〕正式提問

in·ter·view·ee /ˌɪntɚvjuˋi; ˌɪntəvjuːˈiː/ *n* [C] the person who answers the questions in an interview 接受面試者；被採訪者

in·ter·view·er /ˈɪntɚˌvjuɚ; ˈɪntəvjuːə/ *n* [C] the person who asks the questions in an interview 採訪者；〔對候選人〕進行面試的人

in·ter·war /ˌɪntɚˋwɔr; ˌɪntəˈwɔː◂/ *adj* happening or connected to the period between the First and the Second World Wars 在第一次與第二次世界大戰之間的: *the interwar years* 兩次世界大戰之間的歲月

in·ter·weave /ˌɪntɚˋwiv; ˌɪntəˈwiːv/ *v past tense* **interwove** /-ˋwov; -ˈwəʊv/ *past participle* **interwoven** /-ˋwovən; -ˈwəʊvən/ **1 be interwoven** if two lives, problems etc are interwoven they are closely connected in a complicated way〔兩個生命、問題等〕交織在一起: *The histories of our two families are closely interwoven.* 我們兩個家族的歷史緊密地連結在一起。**2** [T] to weave two or more things together 使交錯編織: *silk interwoven with gold and silver threads* 金線和銀線交錯編織而成的絲製品 **3** [T] to mix together different styles or methods 使〔不同的風格、方法〕混合

in·tes·tate /ɪnˋtɛstet; ɪnˈtesteɪt/ *adj law*【法律】**die intestate** to die without having made a WILL (=an official statement about who you want to have your property after you die) 去世時沒有立遺囑

in·tes·tine /ɪnˋtɛstɪn; ɪnˈtestɪn/ *n* [C] the long tube that takes food from your stomach out of your body 腸 —**intestinal** *adj*: *intestinal bacteria* 腸道細菌 —see also 另見 LARGE INTESTINE, SMALL INTESTINE

in-thing /ˌ· ˈ·/ *n* **be the in-thing** *informal* to be very fashionable at the moment【非正式】目前極時髦的

in·ti·ma·cy /ˈɪntəməsɪ; ˈɪntɪməsi/ *n* **1** [U] a state of having a close personal relationship with someone 親密，親近: *the intimacy and friendliness of family life* 家庭生活的親密友好 | **[+between]** *a surprising lack of intimacy between parents and children* 父母與子女之間令人吃驚的疏遠 **2 intimacies** *plural* remarks or actions of a type that happen only between people who know each other very well 親昵的言語[行為]: *The women often met to exchange initimacies about their social life.* 婦女們常常見面，親密地談起她們的社交生活。**3** [U] a word meaning sex, used especially by lawyers and police when they want to avoid using the word 'sex' 性行為〔尤指律師和警方的委婉用語〕: *Intimacy took place on several occasions.* 曾發生過數次性行為。

in·ti·mate[1] /ˈɪntəmɪt; ˈɪntɪmɪt/ *adj*

1 ►FRIENDS 朋友◄ having an extremely close relationship 親密的: *intimate friends* 親密的朋友 | **be on intimate terms with** *She's on intimate terms with important people in the government.* 她與政府要員關係密切。

2 ►PRIVATE 私人的◄ connected with very private or personal matters 隱私的，個人的: *Valerie always tells me about the most intimate details of their relationship.* 瓦萊麗總是把他們之間的隱私細節告訴我。

3 an intimate knowledge of sth very detailed knowledge of something as a result of careful study or a lot of experience〔因細心研究或經驗豐富而〕精通某事

4 ►RESTAURANT/MEAL/PLACE 飯店/餐飲/地方◄ private and friendly so that you feel comfortable 幽靜親切的〔因此使人感覺舒服的〕: *The Wisteria café has a pleasant intimate atmosphere.* 紫藤咖啡館的氣氛親切宜人。| *an intimate meal for two* 親密幽靜的兩人用餐〔環境〕

5 ►CONNECTION 關聯◄ **intimate link/connection etc** a very close connection between two things〔兩者間的〕密切聯繫

6 ►SEXUAL 性的◄ **a)** connected with sex 與性有關的: **intimate relations/contact** *The virus can only be trans-*

mitted through intimate contact. 這種病毒只能通過性接觸來傳播。**b) be intimate with** *formal* to have sex with someone【正式】與…發生性關係 —**intimately** *adv*

in·ti·mate² /ˋɪntəˌmet; ˈɪntɪ̣meɪt/ *v* [T] *formal* to make people understand what you mean without saying it directly【正式】暗示; 提示: **intimate that** *He intimated, politely but firmly, that we were not welcome.* 他有禮貌但很堅決地暗示我們是不受歡迎的。

in·ti·mate³ /ˋɪntəmɪt; ˈɪntɪ̣mɪ̣t/ *n* [C] a close personal friend 知己, 密友, 至交

in·ti·ma·tion /ˌɪntəˋmeʃən; ˌɪntɪ̣ˈmeɪʃən/ *n* [C,U] *formal* an indirect or unclear sign that something may happen【正式】先兆; 預兆: *the first intimations of the approaching conflict* 衝突即將發生的最初預兆

in·tim·i·date /ɪnˋtɪməˌdet; ɪnˈtɪmɪ̣deɪt/ *v* [T] to frighten someone by behaving in a threatening way, especially in order to make them do what you want 恐嚇, 恫嚇, 威脅〔尤指強迫某人做某事〕: *Buildings were bombed in an attempt to intimidate the opposition.* 幾幢大樓被炸, 目的是威脅反對派。—**intimidation** *n* [U] *allegations of police intimidation* 對警察使用恐嚇手段的指控

in·tim·i·dat·ed /ɪnˋtɪməˌdetɪd; ɪnˈtɪmɪ̣deɪtɪ̣d/ *adj* [not before noun 不用於名詞前] feeling worried and less confident, for example because you are in a difficult situation or other people seem better than you〔因陷於困境或自卑而〕膽怯的; 畏縮的: *I was shy, and felt intimidated by the older students.* 我很靦腆, 看見年紀比我大的學生就膽怯。

in·tim·i·dat·ing /ɪnˋtɪməˌdetɪŋ; ɪnˈtɪmɪ̣deɪtɪŋ/ *adj* making you feel worried and less confident 令人緊張不安的: *Some people find interview situations very intimidating.* 有些人認為面試的環境令人緊張不安。

1 1 **in·to** /ˋɪntə; ˈɪntə; *before vowels* 在元音前 ˋɪntu; ˈɪntʊ; *strong* 強讀 ˋɪntu; ˈɪntuː/ *prep*

1 ▶INSIDE CONTAINER, PLACE, AREA 在容器、地點、區域之內◀ in order to be inside something or to be in a place or area 進入; 到…裡面: *I saw Jim this morning; he was going into the paper shop.* 我今天上午看見吉姆, 當時他正走進一家報刊零售店。| *Sue got back into bed and pulled the quilt over her head.* 蘇回到牀上, 拉過被子蒙住頭。| *I've got to go into town this morning and do some shopping.* 我今天上午得進城去買些東西。| *They decided to put £1000 into an investment account.* 他們決定將1000英鎊存入投資賬戶。

2 ▶INVOLVED IN STH 捲入某事◀ becoming involved in a situation or activity 從事; 捲入: *At the age of 16, I went into the printing trade as an apprentice.* 我16歲時加入印刷業當學徒。| *Sorry, I haven't time to go into all these details now.* 對不起, 我目前沒有時間說明全部細節。| *She puts a lot of time and effort into her work.* 她把大量時間和精力投入到工作中。| *You'll get into trouble if you're not careful.* 你如果不細心就會遇到麻煩。

3 ▶DIFFERENT APPEARANCE, SITUATION 不同的外貌、情況◀ in a different situation or a different physical form 處於不同情況, 具有不同外形: *They're going to move Ian into a different class.* 他們打算把伊恩轉入另一個班。| *You'll have to eat your vegetables if you want to grow into a big strong boy.* 你如果想長成一個高大強壯的孩子, 就得吃蔬菜。| *Put the car into reverse.* 掛上倒擋倒車。| *Cut the cake into pieces.* 把蛋糕切成小塊。

4 ▶HIT, TOUCH, MEET 碰撞, 接觸, 遇見◀ coming near, or hitting someone or something in a sudden or violent way 靠近; 〔突然或劇烈地〕撞擊: *Fred bumped into her knocking her over.* 弗雷德和她撞個滿懷, 把她撞倒了。| *He lost control of the car and it crashed into the wall.* 他對汽車失去控制, 車子撞在牆上。| *I ran into Brad* (=met him) *at the Bluebird last night.* 我昨晚在"藍鳥"遇見了布萊德。

5 be into sth *spoken* to like and be interested in something【口】對〔某物〕感興趣; 喜歡: *I've really got into French films lately.* 我近來對法國電影很着迷。

6 *spoken* used when you are dividing one number by another【口】除〔用一個數目除另一數目〕: *Eight into twenty four is three.* 8除24等於3。

7 ▶TIME 時間◀ at or until a certain time 在[直到]〔某個時間〕: *Andy and I talked well into the night.* 安迪和我一直談到深夜。| *John was well into his forties before he got married.* 約翰結婚時已經四十多歲了。

8 ▶DIRECTION 方向◀ in a particular direction 朝…方向: *Sue stared straight into the camera.* 蘇盯着照相機的鏡頭。| *Make sure you're speaking directly into the microphone.* 說話時一定要對準話筒。

in·tol·e·ra·ble /ɪnˋtɑlərəbl̩; ɪnˈtɒlərəbəl/ *adj* too difficult, unpleasant, annoying etc for you to bear〔太困難、太討厭、太煩人而〕難以忍受的: *The arms race was placing an intolerable strain on the Russian economy.* 軍備競賽給俄羅斯的經濟帶來難以承受的壓力。—**intolerably** *adv*

in·tol·e·rant /ɪnˋtɑlərənt; ɪnˈtɒlərənt/ *adj* not willing to accept ways of thinking and behaving that are different from your own 不能包容的; 不容異己的; 心胸狹窄的: **[+of]** *intolerant of other people's political beliefs* 不能容忍他人的政治信仰 —**intolerantly** *adv* —**intolerance** *n* [U] *nationalistic rivalry and racial intolerance* 民族間的對抗和種族間的互不相容

in·to·na·tion /ˌɪntoˋneʃən; ˌɪntəˈneɪʃən/ *n* [C,U] **1** the way in which the level of your voice changes in order to add meaning to what you are saying, for example by going up at the end of a question 語調〈如疑問句的結尾是升調〉; 音調 **2** [U] the act of intoning something 吟誦

in·tone /ɪnˋton; ɪnˈtəʊn/ *v* [T] say something slowly and clearly without making your voice rise and fall much as you speak〔以平直的音調緩慢清晰地〕吟誦: *The priest intoned the blessing.* 神父吟誦賜福詞。

in to·to /ɪn ˋtoto; ˌɪn ˈtəʊtəʊ/ *adv Latin* as a whole; totally【拉丁】全然; 完全, 全部: *They accepted the plan in toto.* 他們完全接受這個計劃。

in·tox·i·cant /ɪnˋtɑksəkənt; ɪnˈtɒksɪ̣kənt/ *n* [C] *technical* something that makes you drunk, especially an alcoholic drink【術語】致醉物〔尤指酒精飲料〕

in·tox·i·cat·ed /ɪnˋtɑksəˌketɪd; ɪnˈtɒksɪ̣keɪtɪ̣d/ *adj* **1** drunk 喝醉的: *The driver was clearly intoxicated.* 司機顯然喝醉了。**2** happy, excited, and unable to think clearly, especially as a result of love, success, power etc〔因愛情、成功、權力等而〕極為興奮的; 陶醉的: *intoxicated with the experience of freedom* 陶醉於自由的經歷 —**intoxicate** *v* [T]

in·tox·i·cat·ing /ɪnˋtɑksəˌketɪŋ; ɪnˈtɒksɪ̣keɪtɪŋ/ *adj* **1** intoxicating drinks can make you drunk〔飲料〕致醉的 **2** making you feel happy, excited, and unable to think clearly 令人極興奮的; 令人陶醉的: *the intoxicating combination of her beauty, wit and charm* 讓人陶醉的美貌、智慧與魅力在她身上的結合

in·tox·i·ca·tion /ɪnˌtɑksəˋkeʃən; ɪnˌtɒksɪ̣ˈkeɪʃən/ *n* [U] the state of being drunk 醉酒

in·tra- /ɪntrə; ɪntrə/ *prefix formal or technical*【正式或術語】**1** inside; within 在…之內(的): *intra-departmental* (=within a department) 部門內部的 | *intracranial pressure* (=inside the head) 顱內壓力 **2** into 進入: *an intravenous injection* (=into a VEIN) 靜脈注射

in·trac·ta·ble /ɪnˋtræktəbl̩; ɪnˈtræktəbəl/ *adj formal*【正式】**1** an intractable problem is very difficult to deal with or find an answer to 難解決的; 難對付的: *the seemingly intractable problem of human greed* 人類的貪婪這個似乎難以解決的問題 **2** having a strong will and difficult to control 倔強的, 難以管束的: *They found the islanders intractable, resisting their offers of gifts.* 他們發現島民性格執拗, 不願接受他們贈送的禮物。—**intractably** *adv* —**intractability** /ɪnˌtræktəˋbɪlətɪ; ɪnˌtræktɪ̣ˈbɪlɪ̣ti/ *n* [U]

in·tra·mu·ral /ˌɪntrəˋmjurəl; ˌɪntrəˈmjʊərəl◂/ *adj especially AmE* intramural courses, competitions etc happen within a school or college and are intended for the students of the school or college【尤美】〔課程、比賽等〕校內的 —opposite 反義詞 EXTRAMURAL

in·tran·si·gent /ɪnˋtrænsɪdʒənt; ɪnˈtrænsɪ̣dʒənt/ *adj formal* unwilling to change your ideas or behaviour in a way that seems unreasonable【正式】〔執拗地〕不妥協的; 不讓步的: *an intransigent attitude* 不妥協的態度 —**intransigence** *n* [U] —**intransigently** *adv*

in·tran·si·tive /ɪnˋtrænsətɪv; ɪnˈtrænsɪ̣tɪv/ *adj technical* an intransitive verb has a subject but no object. For example, in the sentence 'my cup broke', 'break' is intransitive. Intransitive verbs are marked [I] in this dictionary.【術語】〔動詞〕不及物的〔即有主語而無賓語的動詞, 如 my cup broke 中的 break。在本辭典中, 不及物動詞以 [I] 標明〕—**intransitive** *n* [C] —**intransitively** *adv* —opposite 反義詞 TRANSITIVE

in·tra·state /ˌɪntrəˋstet; ˌɪntrəˈsteɪt◂/ *adj AmE* within one state, especially in the US【美】〔美國〕州內的: *intrastate commerce* 州內貿易 —compare 比較 INTERSTATE²

in·tra·ve·nous /ˌɪntrəˋvinəs; ˌɪntrəˈviːnəs◂/ *adj* **1 intravenous injection** an INJECTION that is done into a VEIN (=tube in the body taking blood back to the heart) 靜脈注射 **2 intravenous drugs/fluids etc** drugs etc that are put directly into a vein 靜脈注射用的藥物/液體等 —**intravenously** *adv*

in tray /ˈ· ·/ *n* [C] a container on your desk in which you keep work and letters that need to be dealt with〔存放待處理文件或信件的〕公文格 —compare 比較 OUT TRAY —see picture at 參見 TRAY 圖

in·trench /ɪnˋtrɛntʃ; ɪnˈtrentʃ/ *v* [T] another spelling of ENTRENCH entrench 的另一種拼法

in·trep·id /ɪnˋtrɛpɪd; ɪnˈtrepɪ̣d/ *adj especially literary* willing to do dangerous things or go to dangerous places【尤文】無畏的, 勇敢的: *intrepid explorers* 勇敢的探險家

in·tri·ca·cy /ˋɪntrəkəsɪ; ˈɪntrɪkəsi/ *n* **1** [C usually plural 一般用複數] one of the small parts or details that together form a pattern, system, method etc〔構成一幅圖案、一個系統或一種方法的〕細節: **the intricacies of** *I still haven't mastered the intricacies of the filing system.* 我還是沒有掌握文件歸檔系統錯綜複雜的細節。**2** [U] the state of containing a large number of parts or details 錯綜複雜; 盤根錯節: *designs of amazing intricacy and sophistication* 極為複雜精妙的設計

in·tri·cate /ˋɪntrəkɪt; ˈɪntrɪkɪ̣t/ *adj* containing many small parts or details that all work or fit together 錯綜複雜的: *intricate patterns* 花紋精緻的圖案

in·trigue¹ /ɪnˋtrig; ɪnˈtriːg/ *v* **1** [T] if something intrigues you, you are very interested by it, especially because it seems strange or mysterious〔尤指因某事奇特或神祕而〕激起興趣; 引起好奇心; 迷住: *I was intrigued by his request.* 他的請求引起了我的好奇。**2** [I] *literary* to make secret plans to harm someone or make them lose their position of power【文】密謀; 施詭計〔傷害某人或奪去其權勢〕: *While King Richard was abroad, the barons had been intriguing against him.* 理查德國王在國外時, 貴族們一直在密謀反對他。

in·trigue² /ˋɪntrig; ˈɪntriːg/ *n* **1** [U] the act or practice of secretly planning to harm someone or make them lose their position of power 陰謀; 密謀; 詭計: *It's an exciting story of political intrigue and murder.* 那是一個關於政治陰謀和謀殺的扣人心弦的故事。| *a web of intrigue* 一套陰謀詭計 **2** [C] a secret plan to harm someone or make them lose their position of power〔傷害某人或奪去其權勢的〕陰謀

in·tri·guing /ɪnˋtrigɪŋ; ɪnˈtriːgɪŋ/ *adj* something that is intriguing is very interesting because it is strange, mysterious, or unexpected〔由於奇特、神祕或出人意料而〕引起好奇心的; 令人感興趣的: *an intriguing discovery* 令人感興趣的發現 —**intriguingly** *adv*: *The book is intriguingly titled "The Revenge of The Goldfish"!* 這本書有一個引人入勝的書名, 叫做《金魚的復仇》!

in·trin·sic /ɪnˋtrɪnsɪk; ɪnˈtrɪnsɪk/ *adj* being part of the nature or character of someone or something 本質的, 內在的, 固有的: *The job is of little intrinsic interest.* 這份工作本身沒甚麼樂趣。| *intrinsic goodness* 天生的善良 | **[+to]** *problems that are intrinsic to the situation* 這種局勢必然帶來的困難 —**intrinsically** /-klɪ; -kli/ *adv*

in·tro /ˋɪntro; ˈɪntrəʊ/ *n* [C] *informal* the introduction to a song, piece of writing etc【非正式】〔歌曲、文章等的〕引子

in·tro- /ɪntrə; ɪntrə/ *prefix* into, especially into the inside 向內: *introspection* (=examining your own feelings) 內省, 反省

in·tro·duce /ˌɪntrəˋdjus; ˌɪntrəˈdjuːs/ *v* [T]

1 ▶WHEN PEOPLE MEET 人們相遇時◀ if you introduce someone to another person, you formally tell them each other's names, for example at a party or meeting 介紹, 引見; 使相互認識: *"Have you two been introduced? Tom, this is Greg."* "有人給你們介紹了嗎? 湯姆, 這位是格雷格。" | **introduce sb to sb** *I was introduced to Mrs Myers.* 我被引見給邁爾斯太太。| **introduce yourself** (=formally tell someone who you are)〔正式的〕自我介紹 *Let me introduce myself; my name is Melody Johnson.* 讓我自我介紹一下, 我叫梅洛迪·約翰遜。

2 ▶MAKE STH HAPPEN/EXIST 使某事物發生/存在◀ to make a change, plan, system etc happen or exist for the first time 引進〔變革、計劃、制度等〕, 實施; 推行: *plans to introduce a new system of welfare payments* 實施新的福利費支付系統的計劃 | *The teachers' association wanted to introduce a new kind of test.* 教師協會想引進一種新型的測試方法。

3 ▶BRING TO A PLACE 帶到某地◀ to take or bring something to a place for the first time from somewhere else 首次引入〔某物〕, 使傳入: **introduce sth to/into** *The grey squirrel was introduced into Britain from North America.* 灰松鼠是由北美傳入英國的。

4 ▶NEW EXPERIENCE 新經歷◀ **introduce sb to sth** to show someone something or tell them about it for the first time 使某人初次嘗試某物: *Malcolm introduced me to the joys of wine-tasting.* 馬爾科姆讓我初次嘗到品酒的樂趣。

5 ▶TELEVISION/RADIO 電視/廣播◀ to speak at the beginning of a TV or radio programme and say what is going to happen〔在電視或廣播節目開始時為節目〕作開場白: *Tonight's programme will be introduced by James Adams.* 今晚的節目將由詹姆斯·亞當斯作開場白。

6 ▶BE THE START OF 為…的開始◀ if an event introduces a particular period or change, it is the beginning of it〔某事的發生〕作為[標誌着]〔一個時期或變化的〕開始: *The death of Pericles in 429 BC introduced a darker period in Athenian history.* 公元前 429 年伯里克利之死標誌着雅典歷史上一段黑暗時期的開始。

7 ▶LAW 法律◀ to formally present a new law to be discussed and voted on, especially in the British parliament〔尤指在英國議會, 將一項新法律〕提交討論

8 ▶PUT STH INTO 把某物放入◀ *technical* to put something carefully into something else【術語】小心地把〔某物〕放入〔另一物裡〕: *Fuel was introduced into the jet pipe.* 燃油注入噴管。

in·tro·duc·tion /ˌɪntrəˋdʌkʃən; ˌɪntrəˈdʌkʃən/ *n*

1 ▶START TO USE 開始使用◀ [U] the act of making something start to be used or exist for the first time〔初次〕採用: **[+of]** *the introduction of new working methods* 採用新的工作方法 | *Since their introduction, compact discs have taken over from records.* 激光唱片面世後, 已經取代了〔傳統〕唱片。

2 ▶BRING STH TO A PLACE 把某物帶到一個地方◀ **a)** [U] the act of bringing something to a place for the first time from somewhere else 初次引入, 帶到: **[+of]** *the introduction of Buddhism to China nearly 2000 years ago* 約 2000 年前佛教傳入中國 **b)** [C] something that is brought into a place for the first time from somewhere else 初次傳入的東西: *The potato was a sixteenth century introduction.* 馬鈴薯是十六世紀傳進來的。

3 ▶**WHEN MEETING SB** 見面時◀ [C often plural 常用複數] the act of formally telling two people each other's names when they first meet 介紹, 引見: *There isn't time for formal introductions.* 沒時間作正式引見。
4 ▶**BOOK/SPEECH** 書/演講◀ [C] a written or spoken explanation at the beginning of a book or speech 引言, 序言, 導言; 開場白: *In the introduction there's a brief account of Lawrence's life.* 序言裡對勞倫斯的生平有一個簡要的說明。
5 ▶**EXPLANATION** 解釋◀ [C] something that provides a way of learning about something for the first time〔提供初學者學習途徑的〕入門指導: **[+to]** *This little book is a very good introduction to geometry.* 這本小書是一本很好的幾何學入門讀物。
6 ▶**LETTER** 信◀ [C] an official letter that explains who you are, given to someone you have not met before 介紹信
7 ▶**PUT STH INTO STH** 把某物放入某物◀ [U] *technical* the act of putting something into something else【術語】放入: **[+of]** *the introduction of air into the heating system* 將空氣注入暖氣系統中

in·tro·duc·to·ry /ˌɪntrəˋdʌktərɪ; ˌɪntrəˈdʌktəri◂/ *adj* **1 introductory remarks/paragraph etc** things that someone says or writes at the beginning of a book, speech etc in order to explain what it is about〔書、講話等的〕開場白/導言段落等 **2 introductory course/ lesson etc** a course, lesson etc that is intended for people who have never done a particular activity before 基礎教程/入門課等 **3 introductory offer** a special low price to encourage people to buy a new product〔推銷新產品的〕特惠價格, 特價優惠: *Don't miss our introductory offer!* 不要錯過我們的新產品特價優惠!

in·tro·spec·tion /ˌɪntrəˋspɛkʃən; ˌɪntrəˈspekʃən/ *n* [U] the process of thinking deeply about your own thoughts and feelings to find out their real meaning 內省, 反省: *He stopped his introspection to listen.* 他停止內省, 開始傾聽。

in·tro·spec·tive /ˌɪntrəˋspɛktɪv; ˌɪntrəˈspektɪv/ *adj* tending to think deeply about your own thoughts, feelings etc (好) 內省的; (好) 反省的: *a shy and introspective person* 一個靦腆內向的人 —**introspectively** *adv*

in·tro·vert /ˋɪntrəˌvɝt; ˈɪntrəvɜːt/ *n* [C] someone who thinks mainly about their own thoughts and personal life and does not enjoy spending time with other people 性格內向的人 —opposite 反義詞 EXTROVERT

in·tro·vert·ed /ˋɪntrəˋvɝtɪd; ˈɪntrəvɜːtɪ̆d/ *adj* someone who is introverted spends a lot of time thinking about their own problems and interests and finds it difficult to talk to other people 性格內向的; 不善交際的: *The young girl had become nervous and introverted.* 那個女孩變得神經質並不愛與人交往。—opposite 反義詞 EXTROVERTED —**introversion** /ˌɪntrəˋvɝʃən; ˌɪntrəˈvɜːʃən/ *n* [U]

in·trude /ɪnˋtrud; ɪnˈtruːd/ *v* **1** [I] to interrupt someone or become involved in their private affairs in an annoying and unwanted way, especially with the result that you upset or offend them 打擾〔別人的私事, 尤指令對方不快或感到受冒犯〕; 干涉; 侵擾: *Would I be intruding if I came with you?* 我要是和你一起去, 會不會打擾你? | **[+into/on/upon]** *It would be very insensitive to intrude on their private grief.* 干涉人家不願公開的傷心事, 太不明事理了。**2** **[I+on]** to have an unwanted effect on a situation〔不受歡迎地〕強加於

in·trud·er /ɪnˋtrudɚ; ɪnˈtruːdə/ *n* [C] **1** someone who illegally enters a building or area, usually in order to steal something 非法闖入者〔常指小偷〕: *The police think the intruder got in through an unlocked window.* 警察認為闖入者是由未鎖的窗子進來的。**2** someone who is in a place where they are not wanted 不請自來者: *They had always regarded me as an unwelcome intruder.* 他們一直把我看作不受歡迎的不速之客。

in·tru·sion /ɪnˋtruʒən; ɪnˈtruːʒən/ *n* [C,U] **1** an unwanted event or person in a situation that is private〔討厭的事或人的〕干擾, 侵擾: *She considered Pam's presence in the kitchen an intrusion.* 她認為帕姆待在廚房是一種干擾。| **[+into/on/upon]** *I resented this intrusion into my domestic affairs.* 我討厭這種對我家事的干涉。**2** something that has an unwanted effect on a situation, on people's lives etc〔對某種情況、別人生活等的〕侵襲; 打擾: *the intrusion of Western values on a culture that has existed for centuries* 西方價值觀對一種已存在幾百年的文化的侵襲

in·tru·sive /ɪnˋtrusɪv; ɪnˈtruːsɪv/ *adj* affecting someone's private life or interrupting them in an unwanted and annoying way 干涉的; 打擾的: *They found the television cameras too intrusive.* 他們認為電視攝像機太討厭了。

in·trust /ɪnˋtrʌst; ɪnˈtrʌst/ *v* another spelling of ENTRUST entrust 的另一種拼法

in·tu·it /ɪnˋtjuɪt; ɪnˈtjuːɪ̆t/ *v* [I,T] *formal* to understand that something is true through your feelings rather than your thoughts【正式】憑直覺知道

in·tu·i·tion /ˌɪntjuˋɪʃən; ˌɪntjuˈɪʃən/ *n* **1** [U] the ability to understand or know something by using your feelings rather than by carefully considering the facts 直覺力: *women's intuition* 女人的直覺 | *Imagination and intuition are vital to good science.* 想像力和直覺對於成功的科學研究是至關重要的。**2** [C] an idea about what is true in a particular situation based on strong feelings rather than facts 直覺感知, 直覺知識: *He had an intuition there was trouble brewing.* 他憑直覺感到麻煩就要發生。

in·tu·i·tive /ɪnˋtjuɪtɪv; ɪnˈtjuːɪ̆tɪv/ *adj* **1** an intuitive idea is based on feelings rather than on knowledge or facts〔想法〕憑直覺獲知的: *He seemed to have an intuitive awareness of how I felt.* 他好像憑直覺就知道我的感受。**2** someone who is intuitive is able to understand situations using their feelings without being told or having any proof〔人〕有直覺的 —**intuitively** *adv* —**intuitiveness** *n* [U]

In·u·it /ˋɪnjuɪt; ˈɪnjuɪ̆t/ *n* [C] a member of a race of people living in the very cold northern areas of North America 伊努伊特人〔居住在北美北部嚴寒地區〕—compare 比較 ESKIMO —**Inuit** *adj*

in·un·date /ˋɪnʌnˌdet; ˈɪnʌndeɪt/ *v* [T] **be inundated a)** to receive so much of something that you cannot easily deal with it all 收到太多而應接不暇: *After the broadcast, we were inundated with requests for more information.* 節目播出之後, 不斷收到提供詳情的請求, 使我們無法應付。**b)** *formal* to be covered with water【正式】被水淹沒 —**inundation** /ˌɪnənˋdeʃən; ˌɪnənˈdeɪʃən/ *n* [C,U]

in·ure /ɪnˋjur; ɪˈnjʊə/ *v*
inure sb **to** sth *phr v* [T usually passive 一般用被動態] to make someone become used to something unpleasant, so that they are no longer upset by it 使習慣[適應]〔令人不愉快的事物〕: *Nurses soon became inured to the sight of suffering.* 護士們很快就習慣了那些病痛的場面。

in·vade /ɪnˋved; ɪnˈveɪd/ *v* **1** [I,T] to enter a country, town, or area using military force, in order to take control of it 武力入侵, 侵略, 侵佔: *Hitler invaded Poland in 1939.* 希特勒在 1939 年入侵波蘭。**2** [T] to go into a place in large numbers, especially when you are not wanted〔尤指不受歡迎地〕湧入; 蜂擁而入: *Every summer the town is invaded by tourists.* 每年夏天, 大量遊客湧入小鎮。| *Fans invaded the pitch at half-time.* 球迷在中場休息時湧入球場。**3** [T] to affect someone in an unwanted and annoying way 侵擾〔某人〕: *Her image invaded his mind with immense power.* 她的形象勢不可擋地佔據了他的頭腦。| **invade sb's privacy** *Does that give you an excuse to invade my privacy?* 這就給你藉口來干涉我的私事嗎? | **invade sb's territory** (=start to deal with things that they think they should deal with)〔認為該做的事就去做〕越權去做 —see also 另見 INVASION

in·vad·er /ɪnˋvedɚ; ɪnˈveɪdə/ *n* [C] someone in an army that enters a country or town by force in order to take control of it 侵略者: *Invaders from the south ransacked the town.* 來自南面的侵略軍把小鎮洗劫一空。

in·val·id[1] /ɪnˋvælɪd; ɪnˈvælɪ̈d/ *adj* **1** a contract, ticket, claim etc that is invalid is not legally or officially acceptable〔合約、票、要求等〕無效的; 作廢的: *Without the right date stamped on it, your ticket will be invalid.* 票上若沒有加蓋正確的日期就是廢票。**2** reasons, opinions etc that are invalid are not based on clear thoughts or accurate facts〔觀點、理由等〕站不住腳的: *Their argument was manifestly invalid.* 他們的論點顯然站不住腳。—opposite 反義詞 VALID (1)

in·va·lid[2] /ˋɪnvəlɪd; ˈɪnvəliːd/ *n* [C] someone who cannot look after themselves because of illness, old age, or injury 病人; 病弱者; 年邁者; 傷殘者; 殘疾者: *I resented being treated as an invalid.* 我討厭別人把我當病人看待。—**invalid** *adj*

in·va·lid[3] *v*

invalid sb **out** *phr v* **be invalided out** to have to leave the army, navy etc because you are ill or injured〔軍人因病或傷而〕退役

in·val·i·date /ɪnˋvæləˌdet; ɪnˈvælɪ̈deɪt/ *v* [T] **1** to show that something such as a belief or explanation is wrong 證明〔信念或解釋〕是錯誤的: *The theory was invalidated by later findings.* 這個理論被後來的發現推翻了。**2** to make a document, ticket, claim etc no longer legally or officially acceptable 使〔文件、票券、所有權等〕無效

invalid chair /ˈ··· ˌ·/ *n* [C] *BrE old-fashioned* a WHEELCHAIR【英, 過時】輪椅

in·va·lid·it·y /ˌɪnvəˋlɪdətɪ; ˌɪnvəˈlɪdɪ̈ti/ *n* [U] **1** the state of being too ill, old, or injured to work 傷殘; 年邁; 病殘: *invalidity benefit* 病殘救濟金 **2** the state of being not legally or officially acceptable〔法律或官方上〕無效: *How is the invalidity of an agreement to be decided?* 一項協議無效是如何決定的?

in·val·u·a·ble /ɪnˋvæljəbḷ; ɪnˈvæljuəbəl/ *adj* extremely useful 極有價值的: *Your advice has been invaluable to us.* 你的建議對我們非常寶貴。

in·var·i·a·ble /ɪnˋvɛrɪəbḷ; ɪnˈveəriəbəl/ *adj* **1** always happening in the same way, at the same time etc 恆定的, 不變的; 始終如一的: *His invariable answer was "Wait and see."* 他的回答總是那句話: "等着瞧吧。" **2** *technical* never changing【術語】不變的; 常數的: *Mass, unlike weight, is invariable.* 與重量不同, 質量是不變的。

in·var·i·a·bly /ɪnˋvɛrɪəblɪ; ɪnˈveəriəbli/ *adv* if something invariably happens or is invariably true, it almost always happens or is true, so that you expect it 始終不變地; 永遠如此地; 可預測地: *It invariably rains when I go there.* 我每次去那兒都肯定下雨。| *The security guards were invariably ex-servicemen.* 保安人員毫無例外地都是退伍軍人。

in·va·sion /ɪnˋveʒən; ɪnˈveɪʒən/ *n* **1** [C,U] an occasion when one country's army enters another country by force, in order to take control of it 侵犯, 入侵, 侵略: *the invasion of Normandy* 對諾曼底的入侵 **2** [C] the arrival in a place of a lot of people or things, often where they are not wanted〔不受歡迎的人或物〕湧入; 蜂擁而來: *the annual invasion of teenagers and hippies for the Glastonbury Pop Festival* 每年一度吸引大批青少年和嬉皮士的格拉斯頓伯里流行音樂節 **3 invasion of privacy** a situation in which someone tries to find out personal details about another person's private affairs in a way that is upsetting and often illegal 對隱私的侵犯

in·va·sive /ɪnˋvesɪv; ɪnˈveɪsɪv/ *adj* invasive medical treatment involves cutting into someone's body〔治療〕需手術的: *invasive surgery* 侵入性外科手術

in·vec·tive /ɪnˋvɛktɪv; ɪnˈvektɪv/ *n* [U] *formal* rude and insulting words that someone says when they are very angry【正式】咒罵: *a stream of invective* 一連串咒罵

in·veigh /ɪnˋve; ɪnˈveɪ/ *v*

inveigh against sb/sth *phr v* [T] *formal* to criticize someone or something strongly【正式】猛烈抨擊

in·vei·gle /ɪnˋvegḷ; ɪnˈveɪgəl/ *v*

inveigle sb **into** sth *phr v* [T] *formal* to persuade someone to do what you want, especially in a dishonest way【正式】誘騙〔某人〕做〔某事〕: *She had inveigled me into taking messages to her lover.* 她誘騙我給她的情人送信。

in·vent /ɪnˋvɛnt; ɪnˈvent/ *v* [T] **1** to make, design, or produce something new for the first time 發明; 創造: *Alexander Bell invented the telephone in 1876.* 亞歷山大·貝爾於 1876 年發明了電話。**2** to think of an idea, story etc that is not true, usually in order to deceive people 捏造, 編造〔觀點、故事等〕; 虛構: *They invented a very convincing alibi.* 他們編造了很有説服力的不在犯罪現場的證據。

> **USAGE NOTE 用法説明: INVENT**
> WORD CHOICE 詞語辨析: **invent, discover**
> You **invent** something that did not exist before, such as a machine or a method. invent 表示發明過去不存在的事物, 如機器或方法: *Who invented the computer?* 誰發明了電腦?
> You **discover** something that existed before but was not known, such as a place, thing, or fact. discover 表示發現過去就存在但不為人知的事物, 如地點、物體或事實等: *In the sixties, oil was discovered under the North Sea.* 20 世紀 60 年代, 在北海海底發現了石油。

in·ven·tion /ɪnˋvɛnʃən; ɪnˈvenʃən/ *n* **1** [C] a useful machine, tool, instrument etc that has been invented 發明物〈如機器、工具、儀器等〉: *The dishwasher is a wonderful invention.* 洗碗機是一項奇妙的發明。**2** [U] the act of inventing something 發明: *The invention of the computer has revolutionized the business world.* 電腦的發明使商界徹底發生了變革。**3** [C,U] a story, explanation etc that is not true 虛構的故事; 編造的解釋; 假話: *They subsequently admitted that the story was pure invention.* 他們後來承認他們的説法純屬虛構。**4** [U] the ability to think of new and clever ideas 發明才能; 創造力: *They accused the painter of a total lack of invention.* 他們指責這位畫家毫無創造力。

in·ven·tive /ɪnˋvɛntɪv; ɪnˈventɪv/ *adj* able to think of new, different, or interesting ideas 善於發明創造的; 有創造力的: *one of the most talented and inventive drummers in modern music* 現代音樂界最有才華、最有創造力的鼓手之一 —**inventively** *adv* —**inventiveness** *n* [U] *mechanical inventiveness* 機械發明能力

in·ven·tor /ɪnˋvɛntɚ; ɪnˈventə/ *n* [C] someone who has invented something, or whose job is to invent things 發明者; 發明家: *the inventor of the vacuum cleaner* 真空吸塵器的發明者

in·ven·tory /ˋɪnvənˌtorɪ; ˈɪnvəntri/ *n* **1** [C] a list of all the things in a place〔一個地方所有東西的〕詳細目錄; 清單: *We made a complete inventory of everything in the apartment.* 我們把這公寓套間裡的所有東西開列了一份詳細清單。**2** [U] *AmE* all the goods in a shop; STOCK[1] (2)【美】存貨; 庫存

in·verse[1] /ɪnˋvɝs; ˌɪnˈvɜːs◂/ *adj* [only before noun 僅用於名詞前] **1 in inverse proportion/relation to** getting bigger at the same rate as something else gets smaller, or getting smaller at the same rate as something else gets bigger 與…成反比: *Clearly, the amount of money people save increases in inverse proportion to the amount they spend.* 顯然, 人們的儲蓄與他們的花費成反比。**2** *technical* exactly opposite, especially in order or position【術語】〔尤指次序或位置〕相反的; 逆向的: *an inverse correlation* 逆向關聯 —**inversely** *adv*

inverse[2] *n* [C] *technical* the complete opposite of something【術語】相反; 顛倒

in·ver·sion /ɪnˋvɝʃən; ɪnˈvɜːʃən/ *n* [C,U] **1** *formal* the changing of something so that it is the opposite of what it was before, or of turning something upside down【正

式】反向; 倒置; 顛倒 **2** *technical* a kind of weather condition in which the air nearest the ground is cooler than the air above it【術語】逆温〔指越接近地面氣温越低〕

in·vert /ɪn`vɝt; ɪn'vɜːt/ *v* [T] *formal* to put something in the opposite position to the one it was in before, especially by turning it upside down【正式】使反向; 使顛倒; 使倒置

in·ver·te·brate /ɪn`vɝtəbrɪt; ɪn'vɜːtɪ̈brɪ̈t/ *n* [C] a living creature that does not have a BACKBONE (1) 無脊椎動物 —compare 比較 VERTEBRATE —**invertebrate** *adj*

inverted com·ma /ˌ·ˌ·· '··/ *n* [C usually plural 一般用複數] *BrE*【英】**1** one of a pair of marks (" ") or (' ') that are put at the beginning and end of a written word, sentence etc to show that someone said it or wrote it, or when writing the title of a book, song etc; QUOTATION MARK 引號 —see picture at 參見 PUNCTUATION MARK 圖 **2 in inverted commas** *spoken* used to show that a word you are using to describe something is only what it is usually called, and not what you think it really is【口】所謂的〔表示用來描述某物的詞只是它通常的名稱, 而不是你所認為的意思〕: *Her friends, in inverted commas, all disappeared when she was in trouble.* 當陷入困境時, 她那些所謂的"朋友"全都消失了。

inverted snob·ber·y /ˌ··· '···/ *n* [U] *BrE* the idea that everything that is typical of the upper classes must be bad【英】倒轉的勢利觀點〔認為屬於上層社會的一切事物都必然是壞的觀點〕

3 **in·vest** /ɪn`vɛst; ɪn'vest/ *v* **1** [I,T] to give money to a company, business, or bank, in order to get a profit 投資; 入股: **invest (sth) in sth** *Jones invested $7 million in an ultra-modern video studio.* 瓊斯把700萬美元投資於一個超現代的電視演播室。| **invest heavily** (=invest a lot of money) 投入巨資 *Maxwell had invested heavily in the bond market.* 馬克斯維爾已在債券市場上投入巨資。**2** [T] to use a lot of time, effort etc in order to make something succeed 投入〔大量時間、精力等以成就某事〕: **invest sth in sth** *I've invested a lot of time and effort in this project, and I don't want it to fail.* 我在這個項目上投入了大量時間和精力, 我不想它失敗。

invest in sth *phr v* [T] **1** to buy something in order to sell it again when the value increases and so make a profit 買進〔以便高價賣出賺錢〕: *Oliver made a fortune by investing in antique furniture.* 奧利弗買賣古董家具發了財。**2** to buy something because it will be useful for you 買〔對自己有用的東西〕: *It's about time you invested in a new shirt!* 你該買件新襯衫了!

invest sb/sth **with** sth *phr v* [T often passive 常用被動態] *formal*【正式】**1** to officially give someone power to do something 授權給: *invested with the authority to enforce his recommendations* 被授權執行他的建議 **2** to make someone or something seem to have a particular quality or character 使似乎具有〔某種特性或品質〕: *Richard's heavy-rimmed glasses invested him with an air of dignity.* 理查德的厚邊眼鏡使他顯得很威嚴。

2 **in·ves·ti·gate** /ɪn`vɛstəˌget; ɪn'vestɪ̈geɪt/ *v* **1** [I,T] to try to find out the truth about something such as a crime, accident, or scientific problem 查明〔犯罪、事故或科學問題等的真相〕; 調查; 審查: *The allegations were investigated, and found to be untrue.* 經過調查發現所有指控都不符合事實。| *I heard a noise and went downstairs to investigate.* 我聽見響聲, 就下樓去看個究竟。**2** [T] to try to find out more about someone's character, actions etc, because you think they may have been involved in a crime〔由於可能牽涉犯罪而〕調查〔某人〕: *Penney was already being investigated by the police on suspicion of murder.* 彭尼因有殺人嫌疑而已經被警方調查過了。

2 **in·ves·ti·ga·tion** /ɪnˌvɛstə`geʃən; ɪnˌvestɪ'geɪʃən/ *n* **1** [C] an official attempt to find out the reasons for something such as a crime, accident, or scientific problem〔針對犯罪、事故或科學問題而進行的正式〕調查, 探究: *a criminal investigation* 犯罪調查 | **[+into]** *The authorities are planning to launch a full-scale investigation into the crash which claimed over 200 lives.* 當局計劃對這樁造成二百餘人死亡的墜機事件展開全面調查。**2** [U] the act of investigating something 調查: *the investigation of computer fraud* 對利用電腦詐騙的調查 | **under investigation** (=being investigated) 正在調查中 *The whole issue is still under investigation.* 整個事件仍在調查之中。

in·ves·ti·ga·tive /ɪn`vɛstəˌgetɪv; ɪn'vestɪ̈gətɪv/ *adj* **investigative journalism/report/work** work or activities that involve investigating something 調查性新聞報道/報告/工作

in·ves·ti·gat·or /ɪn`vɛstəgetɚ; ɪn'vestɪ̈geɪtə/ *n* [C] someone who investigates things, especially crimes〔尤指針對犯罪的〕調查員, 偵察員: *Government investigators are going through the financial records.* 政府調查人員正在審查賬目。

in·ves·ti·ga·to·ry /ɪn`vɛstəgəˌtorɪ; ɪn'vestɪ̈gətəri/ *adj* connected with investigating something 與調查有關的

in·ves·ti·ture /ɪn`vɛstətʃɚ; ɪn'vestɪ̈tʃə/ *n* [C] *formal* a ceremony at which someone is given an official title【正式】授銜儀式: *the investiture of the Prince of Wales* 冊封威爾斯親王的儀式

in·vest·ment /ɪn`vɛstmənt; ɪn'vestmənt/ *n* **1** [C,U] the money that people or organizations have put into a company, business, or bank in order to get a profit, or to make a business activity successful 投資〔的款項〕: **[+in]** *Wellings made a number of high-risk investments in the property market during the late 80s.* 20世紀80年代後期韋林斯在房地產市場進行了許多項高風險投資。| *new measures aimed at attracting foreign investment into South Africa* 旨在吸引外國投資到南非的新措施 **2** something that you buy or do because it will be useful for later 投資: **a good/sound investment** *The lessons cost me over $500, but I consider them a good investment.* 這些課程花了我五百多美元, 但我認為這是很好的投資。**3** [C,U] a large amount of time, energy, emotion etc that you spend on something〔大量時間、精力、情感等的〕花費: *a huge investment of time and effort* 時間和精力的大量投入 1

in·vest·or /ɪn`vɛstɚ; ɪn'vestə/ *n* [C] someone who gives money to a company, business, or bank in order to get a profit 投資者 3

in·vet·e·rate /ɪn`vɛtərɪt; ɪn'vetərɪ̈t/ *adj* [only before noun 僅用於名詞前] **1 inveterate liar/smoker/womanizer etc** someone who smokes a lot, lies a lot etc and cannot stop 慣於説謊的人/煙癮很大的人/沉迷女色等的人: *a voracious reader and inveterate talker* 一個看起書來如飢似渴、説起話來喋喋不休的人 **2 inveterate fondness/distrust/hatred etc** an attitude or feeling that you have had for a long time and cannot change 根深蒂固的喜愛/懷疑/仇恨等 —**inveterately** *adv*

in·vid·i·ous /ɪn`vɪdɪəs; ɪn'vɪdiəs/ *adj* unpleasant, especially because it is likely to offend people or make you unpopular 令人不快的; 惹人反感的: *an invidious task* 招人不滿的任務 —**invidiously** *adv* —**invidiousness** *n* [U]

in·vi·gi·late /ɪn`vɪdʒəˌlet; ɪn'vɪdʒɪ̈leɪt/ *BrE v* [I,T] to watch the people who are taking an examination and make sure that they do not cheat【英】〔考試〕監考; PROCTOR[2] *AmE*【美】—**invigilator** *n* [C] —**invigilation** /ɪnˌvɪdʒə`leʃən; ɪnˌvɪdʒɪ̈'leɪʃən/ *n* [U]

in·vig·o·rat·ed /ɪn`vɪgəˌretɪd; ɪn'vɪgəreɪtɪ̈d/ *adj* feeling healthier, stronger, and having more energy than you did before 感到〔比原來〕更健康[強壯, 精力充沛]: *He felt invigorated after his day in the country.* 在鄉下住了一天, 他感到精神充沛多了。—**invigorate** *v* [T]

in·vig·o·ra·ting /ɪn`vɪgəˌretɪŋ; ɪn'vɪgəreɪtɪŋ/ *adj* making you feel more active, and healthy 使精力充沛的; 使健康強壯的: *an invigorating swim before breakfast* 早餐前的健身游泳 —**invigoratingly** *adv*

in·vin·ci·ble /ɪn`vɪnsəbl; ɪn'vɪnsɪ̈bəl/ *adj* **1** an invincible team, army etc is too strong to be destroyed or defeated〔隊伍、軍隊等〕不可消滅的; 無敵的: *the once invincible East German athletics team* 曾經戰無不勝的東德田徑隊 **2** an invincible belief, attitude etc is extremely strong and cannot be changed〔信念、態度等〕不屈不撓的; 堅定不移的: *her invincible determination* 她那堅定不移的決心 —**invincibly** *adv* —**invincibility** /ɪnˌvɪnsəˋbɪlətɪ; ɪnˌvɪnsəˈbɪləti/ *n* [U]

in·vi·o·la·ble /ɪnˋvaɪələbl̩; ɪnˈvaɪələbəl/ *adj formal* an inviolable right, law, principle etc is extremely important and should not be got rid of【正式】〔權利、法律、原則等〕不可違背的; 不可侵犯的 —**inviolably** *adv* —**inviolability** /ɪnˌvaɪələˋbɪlətɪ; ɪnˌvaɪələˈbɪləti/ *n* [U]

in·vi·o·late /ɪnˋvaɪəlɪt; ɪnˈvaɪələt/ *adj formal* something that is inviolate cannot be attacked, changed, or destroyed【正式】不受打擊[改變, 損毀]的

in·vis·i·ble /ɪnˋvɪzəbl̩; ɪnˈvɪzəbəl/ *adj* **1** something that is invisible cannot be seen 看不見的; 無形的: *The house was surrounded by trees and invisible from the road.* 這所房子樹木環繞, 從路上是看不見的。| **[+to]** *germs that are invisible to all but the most powerful microscopes* 只有用最大倍數的顯微鏡才可看見的細菌 **2 invisible earnings/exports/trade etc** earnings etc that are connected with services rather than products 無形收益/輸出/貿易等: *Insurance is one of Britain's largest invisible exports.* 保險業是英國最大的無形輸出之一。—**invisibly** *adv* —**invisibility** /ɪnˌvɪzəˋbɪlətɪ; ɪnˌvɪzəˈbɪləti/ *n* [U]

invisible ink /ˌ···ˈ·/ *n* [U] secret ink that cannot be seen on paper until it is heated〔遇熱才能看見的〕隱形墨水

in·vi·ta·tion /ˌɪnvəˋteʃən; ˌɪnvəˈteɪʃən/ *n* **1** [C] a written or spoken request to someone, inviting them to go somewhere or do something〔書面或口頭〕邀請: **[+to]** *Did you get an invitation to the party?* 你收到參加聚會的請柬了嗎?| **invitation to do sth** *Shortly afterwards, Dawson received an invitation to speak at a scientific conference.* 不久之後, 道森應邀在一次科學會議中發言。| **accept an invitation** *President Yeltsin has accepted an invitation to visit the White House in June.* 葉利欽總統已接受了六月份訪問白宮的邀請。| **decline an invitation** *formal* (=to not accept an invitation)【正式】謝絕邀請 | **by invitation only** (=only those people who have been invited can attend) 憑請柬參加〔即只讓受到邀請的人參加〕**2** [C] a card inviting someone to attend a party, wedding etc 請柬: *Have you sent out all the wedding invitations yet?* 婚禮請柬都發出了嗎? **3 without invitation** without having been invited 並未受到邀請: *They were always dropping by to visit, usually without invitation.* 他們常常來串門, 通常不請自來。**4** [singular, U] encouragement to do something 鼓動[激勵]〔做某事〕: **take sth as an invitation to do sth** *He seemed to take my silence as an invitation to talk.* 他似乎把我的沉默理解為鼓勵他講話。**5 at sb's invitation** also 又作 **at the invitation of sb** if you go somewhere or do something at someone's invitation, you go there or do it because they have invited you to 應某人的邀請 **6 open/standing invitation** an invitation to do something, especially to visit someone, at any time you like 不受限制/長期有效的邀請〔尤指可隨時探望某人〕: *My cousin Diana is living in China, and I have an open invitation to visit her.* 我的堂[表]姐[妹]戴安娜現住在中國, 她邀請我隨時去看她。**7 be an open invitation for/to sb** to make it very easy for someone to rob you or harm you 公開讓人〔來搶劫或傷害〕: *Leaving the car unlocked like that is just an open invitation to thieves.* 離開汽車而不上鎖等於擺明了讓竊賊來偷。

2 2 **in·vite¹** /ɪnˋvaɪt; ɪnˈvaɪt/ *v* [T] **1** to ask someone to come to a party, wedding, meal etc 邀請: **invite sb to sth** *Who should we invite to the party?* 我們應請誰來參加聚會? | **invite sb to do sth** *I'm thinking of inviting them to spend the summer with me in Italy.* 我正考慮邀請他們和我一起在意大利過夏天。| **invite sb for a drink/meal etc** *Why don't you invite her for a drink at the club one evening?* 你何不找一天晚上請她在俱樂部喝酒? | **be invited** *I'm afraid I wasn't invited.* 恐怕我沒有被邀請。**2** *formal* to politely ask someone to do something【正式】〔禮貌地〕請求〔某人做某事〕: **invite sb to do sth** *The interviewer invited Senator Axelmann to comment on recent events.* 採訪記者請艾克舍爾曼參議員評論近來的事件。**3** to encourage something bad such as trouble or criticism to happen to you, especially without intending to〔尤指無意地〕招致〔麻煩或批評等不好的事〕; 引誘: *Any government that sells arms to these dictators is inviting trouble.* 任何賣武器給這些獨裁者的政府都是自找麻煩。

invite sb **along** *phr v* [T] to ask someone if they would like to come with you when you are going somewhere〔去某地時〕邀請〔某人〕同往: *We were going to the beach and I decided to invite her along.* 我們正要去海灘, 我決定請她同去。

invite sb **back** *phr v* [T] to ask someone to come to your home, hotel etc after you have been out somewhere together〔在與某人一同外出之後〕再邀請他到自己的住處: *Richard often used to invite me back for coffee after the show.* 理查德常常在看完演出後請我到他家裡喝咖啡。

invite sb **in** *phr v* [T] to ask someone to come into your home 邀請〔某人〕進屋: *Mr Vosset came to the door but didn't invite me in.* 弗塞特先生來到門口, 但並未請我進去。

invite sb **over** *phr v* [T] to ask someone to come to your home, usually for a drink or a meal 邀請〔某人〕來家裡〔通常是請他喝酒或吃飯〕: *Max has invited me over for dinner.* 馬克斯已經邀請了我去他家吃飯。

in·vite² /ˋɪnvaɪt; ˈɪnvaɪt/ *n* [C] *informal* an invitation to a party, meal etc【非正式】〔聚會、吃飯等的〕邀請

in·vit·ing /ɪnˋvaɪtɪŋ; ɪnˈvaɪtɪŋ/ *adj* an inviting sight, smell, offer etc is very attractive and makes you want to go somewhere or do something〔景象、氣味、建議等〕誘人的; 吸引人的: *The log fire looked warm and inviting.* 篝火看上去温暖誘人。—**invitingly** *adv*: *She smiled invitingly.* 她很迷人地笑了笑。

in vi·tro fer·ti·li·za·tion /ɪn ˌvaɪtro fɝtələˋzeʃən; ɪn ˌviːtrəʊ fɜːtəlaɪˈzeɪʃən/ *n* [U] *technical* a process in which a human egg is fertilized (FERTILIZE) outside a woman's body; IVF【術語】體外受精

in·vo·ca·tion /ˌɪnvəˋkeʃən; ˌɪnvəˈkeɪʃən/ *n literary* [C, U] a request for help, especially from a god【文】〔尤指祈求神靈的〕救助: **[+to]** *an invocation to Zeus* 向宙斯的求助

in·voice¹ /ˋɪnvɔɪs; ˈɪnvɔɪs/ *n* [C] a list of goods that have been supplied or work that has been done, showing how much you owe for them 發票; 發貨清單; 已完成工作的清單〔單上注明應支付的款項〕

invoice² *v* [T] **1** to send someone an invoice 寄送發票〔給某人〕**2** to prepare an invoice for goods that have been supplied or work that has been done 開發票[發貨清單]

in·voke /ɪnˋvok; ɪnˈvəʊk/ *v* [T] *formal*【正式】**1** to use a law, principle, or THEORY to support your views 援引〔法律、原則或理論以支持自己的論點〕: *Such legislation has frequently been invoked to silence political opposition.* 這類法規常常被援引以壓制政治反對派的言論。**2** to make a particular idea, image or feeling appear in people's minds〔在腦海中〕喚起〔某個想法、形象或感受〕; 引起, 產生: *His earlier novels invoke a romanticized picture of life in the countryside.* 他早期的小說使人腦海中浮現一幅鄉村生活的浪漫圖畫。**3** to ask for help from someone more powerful than you, especially a god 祈求〔有權力者, 尤指神靈〕幫助: *Isagoras invoked the aid of King Cleomenes.* 伊薩哥拉斯向克萊奧梅尼國王求助。**4** to make spirits appear by using magic〔用魔法〕使〔靈魂〕顯現: *invoking the spirits of their dead ancestors* 為死去的先人招魂

in·vol·un·ta·ry /ɪnˋvɑlənˌtɛrɪ; ɪnˈvɒləntəri/ *adj* an involuntary movement, sound, reaction etc is one that you make suddenly and without intending to because you cannot control yourself〔動作、聲音、反應等〕無意識做出的; 非故意的: *an involuntary cry of shock* 不由自主的驚叫 —**involuntarily** *adv* —**involuntariness** *n* [U]

2 1 **in·volve** /ɪn`vɑlv; ɪn'vɒlv/ *v* [T] **1** to include something as a necessary part or result 包含〔必要的部分或結果〕, 包括, 需要: *What will the job involve?* 這份工作包括甚麼? | *I didn't realize putting on a play involved so much work.* 我沒有想到演出一場戲需要做這麼多的工作。| **involve doing sth** *Every day each of us makes decisions that involve taking a chance.* 每天我們每個人做出的決定都包含碰運氣的成分。**2** to include or affect someone or something 涉及; 影響: *These changes will involve everyone on the staff.* 這些變化將涉及每一位職員。| *an accident involving a coach and two cars* 涉及一輛長途汽車和兩輛汽車的事故 | *charges involving accusations of widespread corruption* 涉及大規模貪污的控訴 **3** to ask or allow someone to take part in something〔邀請或允許某人〕參與: **involve sb in sth** *Try to involve as many children as possible in the game.* 盡量讓多些孩子參與遊戲。| *We want to involve the workforce at all stages of the decision-making process.* 我們希望在決策過程中的各個階段都有職工參與。**4 involve yourself** to take part actively in a particular activity 積極參與: [+in] *The US has so far been extremely unwilling to involve itself in the crisis in Bosnia.* 直到現在, 美國仍然極不願意捲入波斯尼亞的危機中去。

2 3 **in·volved** /ɪn`vɑlvd; ɪn'vɒlvd/ *adj* **1 be involved** to take part in an activity or event, or be connected with it in some way 參與某活動[某事件]的; 與某活動[某事件]有關聯的: [+in] *More than 30 software firms were involved in the project.* 三十多家軟件公司參與了這項工程。| **deeply/heavily involved** (=be involved a lot) 大量參與 *At law school Hilary became heavily involved in student politics.* 在法學院, 希拉里積極參與學生政治活動。| **get involved in an argument/discussion/fight etc** *I don't want to get involved in some lengthy argument about who is to blame.* 我不想捲入誰該承擔責任的冗長爭論。| *The Mafia could well be involved.* 黑手黨很可能與此事有牽連。**2 be involved in an accident/fight/crash etc** to be one of the people in an accident, crash etc 牽涉進一次事故/打鬥/墜機等: *I'm afraid your son's been involved in an accident.* 恐怕你兒子牽涉在一次事故之中。**3 work/effort etc involved in doing sth** [not before noun 不用於名詞前] the work, money, effort, risk etc that is involved in doing something is the amount that is needed in order to succeed in doing it 為成就某事必須做的工作/付出的努力等: *Most people don't realize the amount of effort that is involved in writing a novel.* 大多數人都不明白寫一本小說要花多少心血。| *I would never go climbing on my own – there's too much risk involved.* 我絕不會一個人去爬山, 那樣太冒險了。**4 be involved with sb** to be having a sexual relationship with someone, especially someone you should not have a relationship with 與〔某人〕有不正當的性關係: *Matt's involved with a married woman at work.* 馬特與同事中一名有夫之婦有染。**5** having so many different parts that it is difficult to understand; complicated 複雜難懂的: *The plot was so involved that very few people knew what was going on.* 情節太複雜, 幾乎沒人知道是怎麼回事。

3 **in·volve·ment** /ɪn`vɑlvmənt; ɪn'vɒlvmənt/ *n* [U] **1** the act of taking part in an activity or event, or the way in which you take part in it 捲入; 牽連: [+in] *President Clinton defended US involvement in Haiti's domestic affairs.* 克林頓總統為美國干預海地內政進行辯護。| *What exactly was his involvement in the murder?* 他與這件謀殺案到底有甚麼牽連? **2** the feeling of excitement and satisfaction that you get from an activity 滿足; 興奮: *a student's emotional involvement in the learning experience* 學生在學習過程中的情感滿足

in·vul·ne·ra·ble /ɪn`vʌlnərəbl̩; ɪn'vʌlnərəbəl/ *adj* someone or something that is invulnerable cannot be harmed or damaged if you attack or criticize them〔人或物〕無法傷害的; 攻不破的; 無懈可擊的: *Gerry's confidence seemed to make him invulnerable.* 格里的自信使他似乎無懈可擊。| [+to] *The castle was invulnerable to attack.* 這座城堡固若金湯。—**invulnerably** *adv* —**invulnerability** /ˌɪnvʌlnərə`bɪlətɪ; ɪnˌvʌlnərə'bɪlɨti/ *n* [U] —compare 比較 VULNERABLE

in·ward /`ɪnwəd; 'ɪnwəd/ *adj* **1** [only before noun 僅用於名詞前] felt or experienced in your own mind but not expressed to other people 內心的; 精神的: *a feeling of inward satisfaction* 內心的滿足感 | *inward panic* 潛藏於心的惶恐 **2** moving towards the inside or centre of something 向內的; 朝向中心的 —**inwardly** *adv*: *I managed to smile, but inwardly I was furious.* 我勉強裝出笑容, 心裡卻氣得很。—opposite 反義詞 OUTWARD

inward-look·ing /'·· ˌ··/ *adj* an inward-looking person or group is more interested in themselves than in other people〔人或團體〕只關注自身的: *an inward-looking and isolated country community* 一個閉關自守、與世隔絕的鄉間社區

in·wards /`ɪnwədz; 'ɪnwədz/ *especially BrE*【尤英】, **inward** *especially AmE*【尤美】—*adv* towards the inside of something 向內: *A breeze blew the curtains inward for a moment.* 微風把窗簾向屋裡吹了一會兒。—opposite 反義詞 OUTWARDS

i·o·dine /`aɪəˌdaɪn; 'aɪədiːn/ *n* [U] a dark blue chemical substance used on wounds to prevent infection 碘

i·on /`aɪən; 'aɪən/ *n* [C] *technical* an atom which has been given a positive or negative force by adding or taking away an ELECTRON【術語】離子

-ion /ən; ən/ *suffix* [in nouns 構成名詞] the act, state, or result of doing something 行為, 狀態; 〔行動的〕結果: *the completion* (=completing) *of the task* 任務完成 | *his election* (=he was elected) *to the post* 他在該職位上的當選 | *several volcanic eruptions* 數次火山爆發

I·on·ic /aɪ`ɑnɪk; aɪ'ɒnɪk/ *adj* made in the simply decorated style of ancient Greek building〔古希臘〕愛奧尼亞建築風格的〔風格簡單〕: *an Ionic column* 愛奧尼亞式柱子

i·on·ize also 又作 **-ise** *BrE*【英】/`aɪənˌaɪz; 'aɪənaɪz/ *v* [I,T] to form ions or make them form (使) 形成離子 —**ionization** /ˌaɪənə`zeʃən; ˌaɪənaɪ'zeɪʃən/ *n* [U]

i·on·i·zer also 又作 **-iser** *BrE*【英】/`aɪənaɪzə; 'aɪənaɪzə/ *n* [C] a machine used to make the air in a room more healthy by producing negative IONS 負離子發生器〔用於使室內空氣清新〕

i·on·o·sphere /aɪ`ɑnəˌsfɪr; aɪ'ɒnəsfɪə/ *n* **the ionosphere** the part of the ATMOSPHERE (1) which is used to help send radio waves around the Earth 電離層

i·o·ta /aɪ`otə; aɪ'əʊtə/ *n* [singular] **1 not one iota** not even a small amount 一點也不: *It's no use talking to him – it won't make an iota of difference.* 跟他說沒用——一點作用也沒有。**2** the Greek letter 'I' 希臘字母 I

IOU /ˌaɪ o `ju; ˌaɪ əʊ 'juː/ *n* [C] *informal* a note that you sign to say that you owe someone some money【非正式】借條, 借據

IPA /ˌaɪ pi `e; ˌaɪ piː 'eɪ◂/ *n* [singular] the International Phonetic Alphabet; a system of special signs, used to represent the sounds made in speech 國際音標

ip·so fac·to /`ɪpso `fækto; ˌɪpsəʊ 'fæktəʊ/ *adv Latin formal* used to show that something is known from or proved by the facts【拉丁, 正式】根據事實本身〔用來表示某事是根據事實得知或有事實依據〕

IQ /ˌaɪ `kju; ˌaɪ 'kjuː/ *n* [C] intelligence quotient; your level of intelligence, measured by a special test, with 100 being the average result 智力商數〔智力的水平, 用特殊測驗測試, 以 100 為平均數〕: *an IQ of 130* 智商為 130

ir- /ɪ; ɪ/ *prefix* the form used for IN- before r; not 不; 否, 沒有〔在 r 之前用來代替 in-〕: *irregular* (=not regular) 不規則的

IRA /ˌaɪ ɑr `e; ˌaɪ ɑːr 'eɪ/ *n* the Irish Republican Army; an illegal organization that wants to unite Northern Ireland

I

and the Republic of Ireland 愛爾蘭共和軍 —see also 另見 SINN FEIN

i·ras·ci·ble /ɪˋræsəbḷ; ɪˈræsɨbəl/ *adj formal* easily becoming angry【正式】易怒的: *He was an irascible, energetic little man.* 他是個脾氣暴躁、精力充沛的小個子男人。—**irascibly** *adv* —**irascibility** /ɪˌræsɪˋbɪlətɪ; ɪˌræsɨˈbɪlɨti/ *n* [U]

i·rate /aɪˋret; ˌaɪˈreɪt◂/ *adj* extremely angry, especially because you think you have been treated unfairly 極憤怒的〔尤指認為受到不公平待遇時〕: *The company received several complaints from irate customers.* 公司收到幾名怒氣沖沖的顧客投訴。—**irately** *adv*

ire /aɪr; aɪə/ *n* [U] *literary* anger【文】憤怒: *the ire of angry enemies* 憤怒的敵人的怒火

ir·i·des·cent /ˌɪrəˋdɛsṇt; ˌɪrɨˈdesənt◂/ *adj* showing colours that seem to change in different lights〔因光線不同而〕變色的: *The painting has a shimmering iridescent quality.* 這幅油畫閃爍着微光, 色彩隨光線的變化而變化。—**iridescence** *n* [U]

i·rid·i·um /ɪˋrɪdɪəm; ɪˈrɪdiəm/ *n* [U] a rare metal used in medicine 銥

i·ris /ˋaɪrɪs; ˈaɪərɨs/ *n* [C] **1** a tall plant with long, thin leaves and large purple, yellow, or white flowers 鳶尾屬植物 **2** the round coloured part of your eye, that surrounds the black PUPIL (2)〔瞳孔周圍的〕虹膜 —see picture at 參見 EYE[1] 圖

I·rish[1] /ˋaɪrɪʃ; ˈaɪərɪʃ/ *n* **the Irish** people from Ireland 愛爾蘭人

Irish[2] *adj* from or connected with Ireland 愛爾蘭的

Irish cof·fee /ˌ·· ˈ··/ *n* [C,U] coffee with cream and WHISKY added 愛爾蘭咖啡〔加奶油和威士忌酒的咖啡〕

I·rish·man /ˋaɪrɪʃmən; ˈaɪərɪʃmən/ *n* [C] a man from Ireland 愛爾蘭男人

Irish Set·ter /ˌ·· ˈ··/ *n* [C] a type of large dog with long hair 愛爾蘭諜犬〔一種長毛大狗〕

Irish stew /ˌ·· ˈ·/ *n* [C,U] a dish of meat, potatoes, and onions boiled together 馬鈴薯洋蔥燉肉

I·rish·wom·an /ˋaɪrɪʃˌwʊmən; ˈaɪərɪʃˌwʊmən/ *n* [C] a woman from Ireland 愛爾蘭女人

irk /ɝk; ɜːk/ *v* [T] if something irks you, it makes you feel annoyed, especially because you feel you cannot change the situation 使惱怒; 使氣憤〔尤指因對局勢無能為力時〕: *Luna never told me what irked her that Sunday morning.* 盧娜從沒告訴我那個星期日早上是甚麼把她惹惱了。

irk·some /ˋɝksəm; ˈɜːksəm/ *adj formal* annoying【正式】惱人的: *an irksome journey* 一次惱人的旅行

S3 W2 **i·ron[1]** /ˋaɪən; ˈaɪən/ *n*

1 ►METAL 金屬◄ [U] a common hard metal that is used to make steel, is MAGNETIC and is found in very small quantities in food and blood 鐵: *There were huge iron gates in front of the mansion.* 這宅第前面有兩扇巨大的鐵門。| *iron ore* 鐵礦石 | *Spinach is full of iron.* 菠菜含豐富鐵質。

2 ►FOR CLOTHES 用於衣物◄ [C] a thing that you use for making clothes smooth, which has a heated flat metal base 熨斗

3 have several irons in the fire to be involved in several different activities or have several plans 同時從事數種不同活動; 同時有數項計劃

4 ►SPORT 運動◄ [C] a GOLF CLUB (2) made of metal rather than wood〔高爾夫球〕鐵頭球棒 —see picture on page A23 參見 A23 頁圖

5 ►CHAINS 鎖鏈◄ irons [plural] *especially literary* a chain used to prevent a prisoner from moving【尤文】鐐銬: **clap sb in irons** *old use* (=put chains on them)【舊】給某人戴上鐐銬

6 have a will of iron/an iron will to have an extremely strong and determined character 具有堅強的意志 —see also 另見 **pump iron** (PUMP[2] (8)), **rule sb/sth with a rod of iron** (RULE[2] (6)), **strike while the iron is hot** (STRIKE[1] (24))

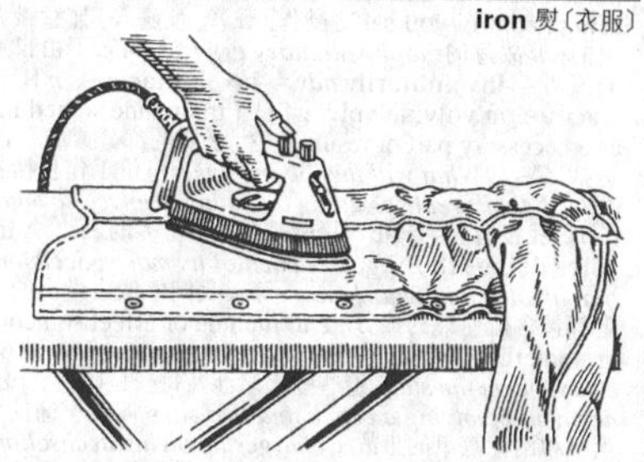

iron 熨〔衣服〕

iron[2] *v* [T] to make clothes smooth using an iron〔用熨斗〕熨平: *Have you ironed my shirt?* 你把我的襯衫熨過了嗎? —see also 另見 IRONING

iron sth **out** *phr v* [T] **1** to solve or get rid of problems or difficulties, especially small ones 消除, 解決〔尤指小問題或困難〕: *We need to iron out a few operating problems first.* 我們需要先解決幾個操作上的問題。| **iron out the kinks** *AmE* (=deal with small problems so that you can succeed)【美】處理小問題 *You'll need to iron out the kinks in your routine before you go on stage.* 你在登台表演之前, 有必要處理那套動作中的一些小毛病。**2** to remove folds from your clothes by ironing them 用熨斗熨平〔衣褶〕

iron[3] *adj* [only before noun 僅用於名詞前] very firm and strong or determined 極堅強的; 極堅定的: *iron discipline* 鐵的紀律

Iron Age /ˈ·· ·/ **the Iron Age** the period of time about 3,000 years ago when iron was first used for making tools, weapons etc〔約 3,000 年前的〕鐵器時代 —compare 比較 BRONZE AGE, STONE AGE

Iron Cur·tain /ˌ·· ˈ··/ **the Iron Curtain** the name that was used for the border between the Communist countries of Eastern Europe and the rest of Europe 鐵幕〔原指東歐共產黨國家與其他歐洲國家的邊界〕

iron-grey *BrE*【英】, **iron-gray** *AmE*【美】/ˌ·· ˈ·◂/ *adj* iron-grey hair is a dark grey colour 鐵灰色的

i·ron·ic /aɪˋrɑnɪk; aɪˈrɒnɪk/ also 又作 **i·ron·i·cal** /-ɪkḷ; -ɪkəl/ *adj* **1** using words that are the opposite of what you really mean, especially in a joking way, or to show that you are annoyed 具有諷刺意味的〔尤指出於開玩笑或表示不快〕, 諷刺的: *As the rain lashed down, my mother's one ironic comment was: "An ideal day for a wedding."* 大雨傾盆而下時, 媽媽說了一句帶諷刺意味的話: "真是結婚的理想日子。" —compare 比較 SARCASTIC **2** an ironic situation is one in which something strange and unexpected happens, especially in a way that seems amusing〔情況〕有諷刺意味的; 出乎意料的; 令人啼笑皆非的: *Your car was stolen at the police station! How ironic!* 你的車在警察局被偷, 真讓人哭笑不得!

i·ron·i·cal·ly /aɪˋrɑnɪklɪ; aɪˈrɒnɪkli/ *adv* **1** [sentence adverb 句子副詞] used when talking about a situation that seems strange, unexpected, and often amusing 具有諷刺意味的是; 出乎意料的是; 讓人哭笑不得的是: *Ironically, his cold got better on the last day of his holiday.* 具有諷刺意味的是, 他的感冒竟在假期的最後一天好了。**2** in an ironic way 用諷刺的方式: *"Oh, no problem!" said Terry, ironically.* "啊, 沒問題!" 特里說道, 很有挖苦的味道。

i·ron·ing /ˋaɪənɪŋ; ˈaɪənɪŋ/ *n* [U] **1** the activity of making clothes smooth with an iron 熨衣服: **do the ironing** *I hate doing the ironing.* 我討厭熨衣服。**2** clothes that are waiting to be ironed or have just been ironed 待熨[剛熨好]的衣物

ironing board /ˈ··· ·/ *n* [C] a small narrow table used for making clothes smooth with an iron 熨衣板

iron lung /ˌ·· ˈ·/ *n* [C] a large machine with a metal case that fits round your body and helps you to breathe 鐵肺; 人工呼吸器

i·ron·mon·ger's /ˋaɪɚnˌmʌŋgɚz; ˈaɪənˌmʌŋgəz/ *n* [singular] *BrE old-fashioned* a shop that sells equipment and tools for your home and garden【英, 過時】五金商店 —**ironmongery** *n* [U]

iron-on /ˈ·· ·/ *adj* labels that you can stick to your clothes using a hot iron〔標籤〕可用熨燙法黏附於衣服上的

iron ra·tions /ˌ·· ˈ··/ *n* [plural] small amounts of high energy food, carried by soldiers, climbers etc〔士兵、登山運動員等隨身攜帶的〕應急口糧〔即量小但能量高的食品〕

i·ron·stone /ˋaɪɚnˌston; ˈaɪənstəʊn/ *n* [U] a type of rock that contains a lot of iron 含鐵礦石

i·ron·ware /ˋaɪɚnˌwɛr; ˈaɪənweə/ *n* [U] articles made of iron 鐵器

i·ron·work /ˋaɪɚnˌwɝk; ˈaɪənwɜːk/ *n* [U] fences, gates and other parts of buildings made of iron bent into attractive shapes〔房屋的〕鐵製構件〈如柵欄、大門等〉

i·ron·y /ˋaɪrənɪ; ˈaɪərəni/ *n* [U] **1** the use of words that are the opposite of what you really mean, in order to be amusing or to show that you are annoyed 反語: **heavy irony** (=a lot of irony) 強烈的反語 *"Of course Michael won't be late: you know how punctual he always is," she said with heavy irony.* "當然, 邁克爾不會遲到, 你知道他一貫守時。"她用強烈的諷刺口吻說道。—compare 比較 SARCASM **2** a situation that seems strange and unexpected or amusing, or the reason it is like this 具有諷刺意味[出乎意料, 令人啼笑皆非]的情況[原因]: *The tragic irony is that the drug was supposed to save lives.* 可悲的諷刺在於這藥本來應該是用來挽救生命的。—see also 另見 DRAMATIC IRONY

ir·ra·di·ate /ɪˋredɪˌet; ɪˈreɪdieɪt/ *v* [T] **1** *technical* to treat someone or something with X-RAYS or similar beams【術語】用 X 射線或類似的射線來治療[處理]: *The tomatoes are irradiated to make them stay fresh longer.* 番茄經 X 線照射後可延長保鮮期。**2** *literary* to make something look bright by shining light onto it【文】照耀; 使發光 —**irradiation** /ɪˌredɪˋeʃən; ɪˌreɪdiˈeɪʃən/ *n* [U]

ir·ra·tion·al /ɪˋræʃənḷ; ɪˈræʃənəl/ *adj* **1** irrational behaviour, feelings etc seem strange because they are not based on clear thought or reasons〔行為、感受等〕不合理的; 荒謬的: *My sister keeps telling me that my fear of flying is irrational.* 我妹妹不斷對我講害怕坐飛機是沒道理的。**2** someone who is irrational tends to behave or do things without thinking clearly or without good reasons 無理性的; 失去理智的: *He's becoming increasingly irrational.* 他越來越沒理智了。—**irrationally** *adv* —**irrationality** /ɪˌræʃəˋnælətɪ; ɪˌræʃəˈnæləti/ *n* [U]

ir·rec·on·ci·la·ble /ɪˋrɛkənˌsaɪləbḷ; ɪˌrekənˈsaɪləbəl◂/ *adj* irreconcilable opinions, positions etc are so strongly opposed to each other that it is not possible for them to reach an agreement〔觀點、立場等〕不能一致的; 勢不兩立的; 不可調和的: *The differences between the Israelis and the Palestinians seemed completely irreconcilable.* 以色列人和巴勒斯坦人之間的分歧似乎完全不可調和。| **[+with]** *This belief was irreconcilable with the Church's doctrine of salvation.* 這種信仰與教會的救贖教義是不相容的。—**irreconcilably** *adv*

ir·re·cov·er·a·ble /ˌɪrɪˋkʌvərəbḷ; ˌɪrɪˈkʌvərəbəl◂/ *adj* something that is irrecoverable is lost or has gone and you cannot get it back 不能挽回的, 無法補救的: *irrecoverable costs* 無法挽回的損失 —**irrecoverably** *adv*

ir·re·deem·a·ble /ˌɪrɪˋdiməbḷ; ˌɪrɪˈdiːməbəl◂/ *adj* **1** *especially literary* too bad to be corrected or repaired【尤文】〔因太壞、太糟而〕無法補救的; 不可救藥的 **2** *technical* irredeemable STOCK[1] (3) cannot be exchanged for money【術語】〔證券〕不能償還的; 不可贖回的 —**irredeemably** *adv*: *irredeemably wicked* 邪惡透頂

ir·re·du·ci·ble /ˌɪrɪˋdjusəbḷ; ˌɪrɪˈdjuːsəbəl◂/ *adj* an irreducible sum, level etc cannot be made smaller or simpler〔金額、水平等〕不能縮減的; 不能簡化的 —**irreducibly** *adv*

ir·re·fu·ta·ble /ˌɪrɪˋfjutəbḷ; ˌɪrɪˈfjuːtəbəl◂/ *adj* an irrefutable statement, argument etc cannot be disproved and must be accepted〔聲明、論點等〕無可辯駁的; 必須接受的: *irrefutable evidence* 駁不倒的證據 —**irrefutably** *adv*

ir·re·gard·less /ˌɪrɪˋgardlɪs; ˌɪrɪˈgɑːdləs/ *adv* **irregardless of** *AmE non-standard* a word meaning REGARDLESS, that many people consider to be incorrect【美, 不規範】不管怎樣〔許多人認為這個詞是不正確的〕

ir·reg·u·lar[1] /ɪˋrɛgjəlɚ; ɪˈregjələ/ *adj* **1** having a shape, surface, pattern etc that is not even, smooth, or balanced〔形狀、外表、圖案等〕不規則的〔即不平整、不光滑或不對稱的〕: *a face with irregular features* 五官不勻稱的面孔 | *irregular handwriting* 歪歪扭扭的字跡 **2** not happening at points in time that are at an equal distance from each other 無規律的〔即不是按同樣的時間間隔發生的〕,〔時間〕間隔不一致的: *His heartbeat sounded irregular.* 他的心跳聽起來不規則。**3** not doing something at the expected time every day, week etc when you should do it or when something normally happens〔做事〕不按時的, 不定期的: *Jason's attendance at school has been somewhat irregular.* 賈森一直是不定期地上學。| *irregular meals* 吃飯不定時 **4** *formal* not obeying the usually accepted legal or moral rules【正式】不合法的; 不合道德規範的: **highly irregular** (=extremely irregular) 極不合常規的; 極不道德的 *It would be highly irregular for a minister to accept payments of this kind.* 身為部長接受這類報酬是極不合法的。**5 irregular word/verb/plural etc** a word etc that does not follow the usual pattern of grammar〔語法中〕不規則的詞/動詞/複數形式等: *'Go' is an irregular verb.* go 是不規則動詞。**6** *AmE* a word meaning CONSTIPATED (=unable to pass food waste from your body) used when you want to avoid saying this directly【美】便祕的〔委婉的用法〕—**irregularly** *adv* —**irregularity** /ˌɪrɛgjəˋlærətɪ; ɪˌregjəˈlærəti/ *n* [C,U]: *He lived a life of complete irregularity.* 他的生活一點規律都沒有。

irregular[2] *n* [C] a soldier who is not an official member of a country's army 非正規軍人

ir·rel·e·vance /ɪˋrɛləvəns; ɪˈreləvəns/ also 又作 **ir·rel·e·van·cy** /-vənsɪ; -vənsi/ *n* **1** [U] a lack of importance in a particular situation 不相干; 無關緊要: *The irrelevance of his remark irritated her.* 他那些不相干的話讓她很惱火。**2** [C] someone or something that is not important in a particular situation 無關緊要的人[物]

ir·rel·e·vant /ɪˋrɛləvənt; ɪˈreləvənt/ *adj* **1** something that is irrelevant is not important because it is not connected with the situation or subject that you are dealing with, or it has no effect or influence on a situation 不重要的; 不相干的: *Age is irrelevant if he can do the job.* 如果他能做好這個工作, 年齡是無關緊要的。| **[+to]** *Her comments seemed irrelevant to the real issue.* 她的評論似乎與問題的實質沒有關聯。**2** having no real or useful purpose 沒用的, 沒意義的: *Students viewed Latin as boring and irrelevant.* 學生們認為拉丁語枯燥無用。—**irrelevantly** *adv*

ir·re·li·gious /ˌɪrɪˋlɪdʒəs; ˌɪrɪˈlɪdʒəs◂/ *adj formal* opposed to religion or not having any religious feeling【正式】反宗教的; 無宗教信仰的

ir·re·me·di·a·ble /ˌɪrɪˋmidɪəbḷ; ˌɪrɪˈmiːdiəbəl◂/ *adj formal* so bad that it is impossible to make it better【正式】不可救藥的; 無法糾正的 —**irremediably** *adv*

ir·rep·a·ra·ble /ɪˋrɛpərəbḷ; ɪˈrepərəbəl/ *adj* irreparable damage, harm etc is so bad that it can never be repaired or made better〔破壞、傷害等〕不能修復的; 無法彌補的: *irreparable damage to his heart* 對他的心臟造成永久的傷害 —**irreparably** *adv*

ir·re·place·a·ble /ˌɪrɪˋplesəbḷ; ˌɪrɪˈpleɪsəbəl◂/ *adj* too special, valuable, or unusual to be replaced by anything

I

else〔因特別或貴重而〕獨一無二的; 不可代替的: *the loss of several great works of art, many of them irreplaceable* 幾件偉大藝術品的丟失, 其中不少是舉世無雙的

ir·re·pres·si·ble /ˌɪrɪˋprɛsəbḷ; ˌɪrɪˈpresɨbəl◂/ *adj* full of energy, confidence, and happiness so that you never seem unhappy〔精力、信心、快樂〕壓抑不住的; 控制不了的: *an irrepressible optimist* 精力充沛的樂觀主義者 —**irrepressibly** *adv*

ir·re·proach·a·ble /ˌɪrɪˋprotʃəbḷ; ˌɪrɪˈprəʊtʃəbəl◂/ *adj formal* something such as someone's behaviour that is irreproachable is so good that you cannot criticize it【正式】〔行為等〕無可指責的; 無可挑剔的 —**irreproachably** *adv*

ir·re·sis·ti·ble /ˌɪrɪˋzɪstəbḷ; ˌɪrɪˈzɪstɨbəl◂/ *adj* **1** so attractive, desirable etc that you cannot prevent yourself from wanting it 無法抗拒的; 富有誘惑力的: *Chocolate is irresistible for a lot of people.* 巧克力的誘惑力對於許多人來說是無法抗拒的。| **find sb/sth irresistible** *Men find Natalie irresistible.* 男人們覺得無法抗拒納塔莉的魅力。**2** too strong or powerful to be stopped or prevented〔力量太大而〕不可抗拒的; 不可避免的: *I had an irresistible urge to kiss him!* 我有一種抑制不住的慾望要親吻他! —**irresistibly** *adv*

ir·res·o·lute /ɪˋrɛzəˌlut; ɪˈrezəluːt/ *adj formal* unable to decide what to do; uncertain【正式】沒有決斷力的; 猶豫不決的 —**irresolutely** *adv* —**irresolution** /ɪˌrɛzəˋluʃən; ɪˌrezəˈluːʃən/ *n* [U]

ir·re·spec·tive /ˌɪrɪˋspɛktɪv; ˌɪrɪˈspektɪv/ *adv* **irrespective of** used when saying that a particular fact such as someone's age or race, something's size etc has no effect on a situation and is not important 不顧...; 不考慮...; 不問...〔用來表示某事實, 如年齡、種族、某物的大小等, 對某事沒有影響, 不重要〕: *The course is open to anyone irrespective of age.* 這門課沒有年齡限制。

ir·re·spon·si·ble /ˌɪrɪˋspɑnsəbḷ; ˌɪrɪˈspɒnsɨbəl◂/ *adj* doing careless things without thinking or worrying about the possible bad results 不負責任的: **be (highly) irresponsible of sb to do sth** *It was highly irresponsible of him to leave the children on their own in the pool.* 他把孩子單獨留在游泳池裡, 真是太不負責任了。—**irresponsibly** *adv* —**irresponsibility** /ˌɪrɪˌspɑnsəˋbɪlətɪ; ˌɪrɪspɒnsɨˈbɪlɨti/ *n* [U]

ir·re·trie·va·ble /ˌɪrɪˋtrivəbḷ; ˌɪrɪˈtriːvəbəl◂/ *adj formal*【正式】**1** an irretrievable situation cannot be made right again 不能挽回的; 無法復原的: *the irretrievable breakdown of their marriage* 他們的婚姻已無法挽救 **2 irretrievable loss** the loss of something that you can never get back 不可彌補的損失 —**irretrievably** *adv*: *irretrievably lost* 永遠失去

ir·rev·e·rent /ɪˋrɛvərənt; ɪˈrevərənt/ *adj* having a lack of respect for organizations, customs, beliefs etc〔對組織、習俗、信仰等〕不尊敬的; 不恭的: *an irreverent laugh* 無禮的一笑 —**irreverently** *adv* —**irreverence** *n* [U]

ir·re·ver·si·ble /ˌɪrɪˋvɝsəbḷ; ˌɪrɪˈvɜːsɨbəl◂/ *adj* **irreversible damage/change/decline etc** damage, change etc that is so serious or so great that you cannot change something back to how it was before 不可挽回的損失/不可逆轉的變化/不可逆轉的衰退等 —**irreversibly** *adv*

ir·rev·o·ca·ble /ɪˋrɛvəkəbḷ; ɪˈrevəkəbəl/ *adj* an irrevocable decision, action etc cannot be changed or stopped〔決定、行動等〕不可更改的, 不可取消的; 不可撤回的 —**irrevocably** *adv*: *machines that irrevocably changed the pattern of rural life* 使農村生活模式發生不可逆轉的變化的機器

ir·ri·gate /ˋɪrɪˌget; ˈɪrɨgeɪt/ *v* [T] **1** to supply land or crops with water 灌溉〔土地[莊稼]〕**2** *technical* to wash a wound with a flow of liquid【術語】沖洗〔傷口〕—**irrigation** /ˌɪrəˋgeʃən; ˌɪrɨˈgeɪʃən/ *n* [U]

ir·ri·ta·ble /ˋɪrətəbḷ; ˈɪrɨtəbəl/ *adj* **1** getting annoyed quickly or easily 易怒的: *Jo was tired, irritable, and depressed.* 喬疲憊、急躁而且情緒低落。**2** *technical* very sensitive and sore【術語】過敏的; 紅腫的; 疼痛的: *irritable skin* 過敏的皮膚 —**irritably** *adv* —**irritability** /ˌɪrətəˋbɪlətɪ; ˌɪrɨtəˈbɪlɨti/ *n* [U]

ir·ri·tant /ˋɪrətənt; ˈɪrɨtənt/ *n* [C] **1** something that makes you feel annoyed over a period of time 使人〔在某段時間內〕煩躁的事物: *Low flying aircraft are a constant irritant in this area.* 低空飛行的飛機使這個地區終日不得安寧。**2** a substance that can make a part of your body painful and sore〔使身體某部分腫痛的〕刺激物

ir·ri·tate /ˋɪrəˌtet; ˈɪrɨteɪt/ *v* [T] **1** to make someone feel annoyed or impatient over a long period, especially by repeatedly doing something〔尤指不斷重複做某事而〕使〔人長期〕煩躁; 激怒 **2** to make a part of your body painful and sore 使〔身體的一部分〕疼痛: *This cream may irritate sensitive skin.* 這種潤膚霜對過敏性皮膚可能有刺激。

ir·ri·tat·ed /ˋɪrəˌtetɪd; ˈɪrɨteɪtɨd/ *adj* **1** feeling annoyed and impatient about something 惱火的; 急躁的: **[+about/at/with/by]** *John was irritated by the necessity for polite conversation.* 約翰對於必須彬彬有禮地談話很不耐煩。**2** painful and sore 疼痛的; 發炎的

ir·ri·tat·ing /ˋɪrəˌtetɪŋ; ˈɪrɨteɪtɪŋ/ *adj* an irritating habit, situation etc is annoying〔習慣、情況等〕煩人的; 使人不快的: *She has an irritating habit of interrupting everything you say.* 她有一個很煩人的習慣: 你說甚麼她都打斷你。—**irritatingly** *adv*

ir·ri·ta·tion /ˌɪrəˋteʃən; ˌɪrɨˈteɪʃən/ *n* **1** [U] the feeling of being annoyed about something, especially something annoying that happens repeatedly or for a long time 煩惱〔尤指反覆發生或持續很長一段時間的事〕, 不快: *Newspaper reports of yet more scandals are a constant source of irritation for the government.* 報紙上登載的醜聞接二連三, 使政府的煩惱連續不斷。**2** [C] something that makes you annoyed 令人氣惱的事物: *The children are just an irritation for him when he's trying to work.* 他剛要工作, 孩子就來搗亂。**3** [U] a painful, sore feeling on a part of your body〔身體某部位的〕疼痛: *irritation of the skin* 皮膚疼痛

ir·rup·tion /ɪˋrʌpʃən; ɪˈrʌpʃən/ *n* [C] *formal* a sudden rush of people into a place【正式】〔人〕突然湧入: *an irruption of the audience onto the stage* 觀眾突然湧到台上

is /s, z; s, z *strong* 強讀 ɪz; ɪz/ the third person singular of the present tense of BE 動詞 be 的第三人稱單數現在式

-i·sa·tion /əzeʃən; aɪzeɪʃən/ *suffix* a British spelling of -IZATION -ization 的英式拼法

ISBN /ˌaɪ ɛs bi ˋɛn; ˌaɪ es biː ˈen/ *n* a number that is given to every book 國際標準圖書編號

-ise /aɪz; aɪz/ *suffix* [in verbs 構成動詞] a British spelling of -IZE -ize 的英式拼法

-ish /ɪʃ; ɪʃ/ *suffix* **1** [in nouns 構成名詞] the people or language of a particular country or place〔某國或某地的〕人[語言]: *Are the British unfriendly?* 英國人不友善嗎? | *learning to speak Turkish* 學說土耳其語 | *She's Swedish.* 她是瑞典人。**2** [in adjectives 構成形容詞] of a particular place 某地方的: *Spanish food* (=from Spain) 西班牙食品 **3** [in adjectives 構成形容詞] typical of or like a particular type of person 屬於[類似]某種類型的人的: *foolish behaviour* (=typical of a fool) 愚蠢的行為 | *Don't be so childish!* (=Don't behave like a child) 別這麼孩子氣! | *snobbish* 勢利的 **4** [in adjectives 構成形容詞] the ending of some adjectives that show disapproval〔作為一些形容詞的後綴表示貶義〕: *selfish* 自私的 | *raffish* 粗俗的 **5** [in adjectives 構成形容詞] rather; quite 相當: *youngish* (=not very young, but not old either) 還算年輕 | *tallish* 個子略高的 | *reddish hair* 淺紅色的頭髮 **6** [in adjectives 構成形容詞] *spoken* about; **approximately** (APPROXIMATE[1])【口】大約, 大致: *We'll expect you eightish.* (=at about 8 o'clock) 我們希望你八點左右來。| *He's fortyish.* (=about 40 years old) 他大約四十歲。

Is·lam /ˋɪsləm; ˈɪslɑːm/ *n* [U] **1** the Muslim religion, which was started by Muhammad and whose holy book is the Koran 伊斯蘭教〔由穆罕默德創立，經典是《可蘭經》〕 **2** the people and countries that follow this religion 伊斯蘭教徒；伊斯蘭國家 —**Islamist** *n* [C] —**Islamic** /ɪzˋlæmɪk; ɪzˈlæmɪk/ *adj*

2 **is·land** /ˋaɪlənd; ˈaɪlənd/ *n* [C] **1** a piece of land completely surrounded by water 島嶼：*a small island in the middle of the lake* 湖中央的小島 | *the Hawaiian Islands* 夏威夷羣島 —see also 另見 DESERT ISLAND **2** a place that is different in some way from the area that surrounds it〔與周圍地區不盡相同的〕地方，處所：**an island of peace/calm etc** *The park is an island of peace in the noisy city.* 在這座喧囂的城市中，這個公園是一塊寧靜的地方。

is·land·er /ˋaɪləndɚ; ˈaɪləndə/ *n* [C] someone who lives on an island 島民，島上居民

isle /aɪl; aɪl/ *n* [C] a word for an island, used in poetry or in names of islands 島〔用於詩歌或島名〕：*the Scilly Isles* 錫利羣島

is·let /ˋaɪlɪt; ˈaɪlɨt/ *n* [C] a very small island 小島

is·m /ˋɪzəm; ˈɪzəm/ *n* [C] *informal* used to describe a set of ideas or beliefs whose name ends in 'ism', especially when you think that they are not sensible or practical【非正式】主義，學説〔用來稱呼名稱以ism結尾的思想或信仰；尤指你認為這種理論不合理或不實際〕

-ism /ɪzəm; ɪzəm/ *suffix* [in nouns 構成名詞] **1** a political belief or religion based on a particular principle or the teachings of a particular person 政治信仰；宗教：*socialism* 社會主義 | *Buddhism* 佛教 **2** the action or process of doing something〔做某事的〕行為[過程]：*his criticism of my work* (=he CRITICIZES it) 他對我工作的批評 **3** an action or remark that has a particular quality 具有某種特徵的行為[評論]：*her witticisms* (=funny or WITTY remarks) 她詼諧[俏皮]的評論 **4** the state of being like something or someone, or having a particular quality 像某物[某人]；具有某種特徵：*heroism* (=being a HERO; bravery) 英雄氣概 | *magnetism* (=being MAGNETIC) 磁性 **5** illness caused by too much of something 由於某物過多而引起的疾病：*alcoholism* 酗酒 **6** the practice of treating people unfairly because of something 歧視：*sexism* (=making unfair differences between men and women) 性別歧視 | *racism* 種族歧視 | *heightism* (=against people who are very tall or short) 身高歧視

is·n't /ˋɪznt; ˈɪzənt/ the short form of 縮略式= 'is not'

iso- /aɪso; aɪsəʊ/ *prefix technical* the same all through or in every part; equal【術語】同；等：*an isotherm* (=line joining places of equal temperature) 等溫線

i·so·bar /ˋaɪsəˌbɑr; ˈaɪsəbɑː/ *n technical* a line on a weather map joining places where the air pressure is the same【術語】〔氣象圖上的〕等壓線

i·so·late /ˋaɪslˌet; ˈaɪsəleɪt/ *v* [T] **1** to prevent a country, political group etc from getting support from other countries or groups etc, so that it becomes weaker 孤立〔國家或政治團體等〕：*The US has sought to isolate Cuba both economically and politically.* 美國一直想在經濟和政治上孤立古巴。**2** *technical* to separate a substance, disease etc from other substances so that it can be studied【術語】分離〔物質、疾病等以作研究〕：[+from] *The hepatitis B virus has been isolated from breast milk.* 乙型肝炎病毒已從母乳中分離出來。**3** to separate an idea, word, problem etc so that it can be examined or dealt with by itself 分離〔觀點、單詞、問題等〕：**isolate sth from** *It is impossible to isolate political responsibility from moral responsibility.* 不可能把政治責任與道德責任分離開來。**4** to make someone feel separate from other people in a society or group, and make them feel lonely or unhappy〔在社會、團體中〕使〔某人〕孤立：**isolate sb from** *Presley's phenomenal early success isolated him from his friends.* 皮禮士利年紀輕輕便成就超羣，這使他在朋友們中陷於孤立。**5** to make a place separate from other places so that people cannot enter it 使某地與其他地方隔離：*villages which have been isolated by recent flooding* 由於不久前的洪水而與外界隔絕的一些村莊 **6** to keep someone separate from other people, especially because they have a disease 把〔某人，尤指病人〕與其他人隔離：**isolate sb from** *New-born babies must be isolated from possible contamination.* 新生兒必須隔離，以免受感染。

i·so·lat·ed /ˋaɪslˌetɪd; ˈaɪsəleɪtɨd/ *adj* **1** an isolated building, village etc is far away from any others〔建築物、村莊等〕孤零零的；偏僻的：*Not many people visit this isolated spot.* 沒有多少人來這個偏僻的地方。**2** feeling alone and unable to meet or speak to other people〔人〕孤單的：*Young mothers often feel isolated and cut off from the rest of the world.* 年輕的媽媽常常感到孤獨，好像與外界失去了聯繫。**3** an isolated action, event, example etc happens only once, and is not likely to happen again〔行動、事件、例子等〕孤立的；個別的：**an isolated incident/episode** *Police say that last week's protest was an isolated incident.* 警方說上週的抗議是個別的事件。 3

i·so·la·tion /ˌaɪslˋeʃən; ˌaɪsəˈleɪʃən/ *n* [U] **1** the state of being completely separate from any other place, group etc 隔離；孤立；分離：*Because of its geographical isolation, the area developed its own unique culture.* 由於地理位置的隔絕，該地區發展了自己獨特的文化。**2** a feeling of being lonely and unable to meet or speak to other people 孤獨；孤單：*Retirement can often cause feelings of isolation.* 退休生活常讓人感到孤獨。**3 in isolation** if something exists or is considered in isolation, it exists or is considered separately from other things that are connected with it 孤立地：*Taken in isolation, these events have no particular significance, but there is, in fact, an underlying pattern.* 孤立地看，這些事件毫無特殊意義，但事實上卻有一個潛在的模式。**4** the act of deliberately separating one group, person, or thing from others〔故意把一個團體、人或物體〕隔離；孤立：*isolation of political prisoners* 對政治犯的隔離

i·so·la·tion·is·m /ˌaɪslˋeʃənɪzəm; ˌaɪsəˈleɪʃənɪzəm/ *n* [U] a disapproving word for beliefs or actions that are based on the political principle that your country should not be involved in the affairs of other countries 孤立主義〔用於指信仰或行為的貶義詞，指一個國家不應捲入其他國家的事務〕—**isolationist** *n* [C] —**isolationist** *adj*

isolation pe·ri·od /··ˈ·· ˌ···/ *n* [C] the period of time that someone with an infectious illness needs to be kept apart from other people〔傳染病患者的〕隔離期

i·so·met·rics /ˌaɪsəˋmɛtrɪks; ˌaɪsəˈmetrɪks/ *n* [plural] exercises that make your muscles stronger by pushing against each other 等長運動〔一種以互推動作來增強肌肉的運動〕

i·sos·ce·les tri·an·gle /aɪˋsɑslˌiz ˋtraɪæŋgl; aɪˌsɒsəliːz ˈtraɪæŋgəl/ *n* [C] a three-sided shape in which two of the sides are the same length 等腰三角形 —compare 比較 EQUILATERAL TRIANGLE, SCALENE TRIANGLE —see picture at 參見 SHAPE[1] 圖

i·so·therm /ˋaɪsəˌθɝm; ˈaɪsəθɜːm/ *n* [C] *technical* a line on a weather map joining places where the temperature is the same【術語】〔氣象圖上的〕等溫線，恆溫線

i·so·tope /ˋaɪsəˌtop; ˈaɪsətəʊp/ *n* [C] *technical* one of the possible different forms of an atom of a particular ELEMENT (=simple chemical substance)【術語】同位素

Is·rae·li /ɪzˋrelɪ; ɪzˈreɪli/ *n* [C] someone from Israel 以色列人

Is·rael·ite /ˋɪzrɪəlˌaɪt; ˈɪzrəlaɪt/ *n, adj* (in the Bible) (a person) of the ancient kingdom of Israel 古以色列人；〔《聖經》中〕古以色列王國的

is·sue[1] /ˋɪʃu; ˈɪʃuː/ *n*

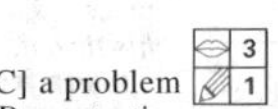

1 ►**SUBJECT/PROBLEM** 話題/問題◄ [C] a problem or subject that people discuss 問題；議題：*Drugs testing of employees is a sensitive issue.* 對雇員進行毒品檢查是個敏感問題。| *the immigration issue* 移民問題 | **raise**

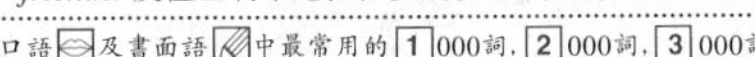

the issue (=say that a problem should be discussed) 提出問題〔表示該問題需要討論〕*We should raise the issue of discrimination with the council.* 我們應向委員會提出討論歧視問題。| **sth is not the issue** *spoken* (=used to say that something is not the important part of what you are discussing) 【口】某事不是談論的主要問題 *Unemployment is not the issue – the real problem is the decline in public morality.* 失業不是主要問題，真正的問題是公眾道德水準的下降。| **not be an issue** (=not be a problem) 不是問題 *I just got a raise, so money's no longer an issue.* 我剛加了薪，所以錢不再是問題了。| **avoid/dodge/duck/evade the issue** (=avoid discussing a problem or subject) 逃避討論某問題[某話題] *When asked about the bill, the senator tried to duck the issue.* 當問及這項議案時，參議員試圖迴避這個問題。| **confuse/cloud the issue** (=make a problem or subject more difficult by talking about things that are not directly connected with it) 把問題搞亂，把問題搞得模糊不清: *clouding the issue with uninformed judgements* 以缺乏根據的判斷把問題弄得模糊不清 | **what's the big issue?** *spoken* (=used when you do not think that something is a problem and you cannot understand why people are worried or arguing) 【口】有甚麼大不了的〔用於表示你認為某事不是問題，不明白為甚麼其他人擔心或爭論〕

2 ►MAGAZINE 雜誌◄ [C] a magazine or newspaper printed for a particular day, week, or month〔雜誌、報紙的〕期; 號: *the latest issue of Vogue* 最新一期的《時尚》

3 at issue the problem or subject at issue is the most important part of what you are discussing or considering 問題的焦點: *What is at issue is the extent to which exam results reflect a student's ability.* 問題的關鍵是，考試成績在多大程度上反映學生的能力。

4 take issue with to disagree or argue with someone about something〔向某人對某事〕提出異議: *It is difficult to take issue with his analysis.* 對他的分析很難有不同看法。

5 make an issue (out) of sth to argue about something, especially in a way that annoys other people because they do not think it is important 挑起爭端〔尤指對方認為是小題大作〕: *I was upset by Eleanor's remarks, but decided not to make an issue of it.* 我對埃莉諾的話很惱火，但還是決定不去理會她。

6 ►SET OF THINGS FOR SALE 待售之物◄ [C] a new set of something such as shares (SHARE² (5)) or stamps, made available for people to buy〔新股票或郵票的〕發行: *a new issue of bonds* 新發行的債券

7 ►ACT OF GIVING STH 給予某物◄ [singular] the act of officially giving people something to use〔正式〕發給; 分配: *the issue of identity cards to all non-residents* 發身分證給無定居身分的居民

8 die without issue *old use and law* to die without having any children【舊和法律】死後無嗣

2 **issue²** *v* [T] **1** to officially make a statement, give an order, warning etc 發表〔聲明〕; 頒布; 發出〔命令、警告等〕: *Silva issued a statement denying all knowledge of the affair.* 西爾瓦發表聲明，宣稱對此事一無所知。| *a warning issued by the Surgeon General*〔美國〕衛生局局長發出的警告 **2** to provide something for each member of a group 分給〔團體中每個成員〕; 配發: **issue sb with** *All the workers were issued with protective clothing.* 所有工人都配發了防護服。**3** to officially produce something such as new stamps, coins, or shares (SHARE² (5)) and make them available for people to buy 正式發行〔新郵票、硬幣、股票等〕

issue forth *phr v* [I] *literary* to go or come out of a place【文】〔從某處〕發出: *A low grunt issued forth from his throat.* 他喉嚨裡發出一陣低沉的咕噥聲。

issue from *phr v* [T] *formal* if something, especially a sound or liquid, issues from somewhere, it comes out of it【正式】〔尤指聲音或液體〕來自，產生於: *Smoke issued from the factory chimneys.* 煙從工廠煙囪中冒出。

-ist /ɪst; ɪ̈st/ *suffix* **1** [in nouns 構成名詞] someone who believes in a particular religion or set of principles or ideas〔某宗教、主義的〕信仰者: *a Buddhist* 佛教徒 | *a Scottish Nationalist* 蘇格蘭民族黨黨員 **2** [in adjectives 構成形容詞] connected with or showing a particular political or religious belief 與某政治[宗教]信仰有關的; 顯示某政治[宗教]信仰的: *her socialist views* 她的社會主義觀點 | *He's very rightist.* (=supports the political RIGHT³ (4b)) 他是個極右派。**3** [in nouns 構成名詞] someone who studies a particular subject, plays a particular instrument or does a particular type of work〔某學科的〕研究者;〔某樂器的〕演奏者;〔某工作的〕從事者: *a linguist* (=someone who studies or learns languages) 語言學家 | *a novelist* (=someone who writes NOVELs) 小說家 | *a guitarist* (=someone who plays the GUITAR) 結他手 | *a machinist* (=someone who operates a machine) 機械師 — see also 另見 -OLOGIST **4** [in adjectives 構成形容詞] treating people unfairly because of something 歧視的: *a very sexist remark* (=making unfair differences between men and women) 嚴重的性別歧視言論 **5** [in nouns 構成名詞] someone who treats people unfairly because of something 歧視分子: *They're a bunch of racists.* 他們是一羣種族歧視分子。

isth·mus /ˋɪsməs; ˈɪsməs/ *n* [C] a narrow piece of land with water on both sides, that connects two larger areas of land 地峽: *the Isthmus of Panama* 巴拿馬地峽

IT /ˌaɪ ˋti; ˌaɪ ˈtiː/ *n* [U] the study or use of electronic processes for storing information and making it available; INFORMATION TECHNOLOGY 信息技術

it /ɪt; ɪt/ *pron* [used as subject or object 用作主詞或受詞] **1** used to talk about the thing, situation, idea etc that has already been mentioned or that the person you are talking to already knows about 它，這，那〔指已經提及或已為對方所知曉的事物、情況、想法等〕: *"What should I do with the key?" "Oh just leave it on the table."* "這把鑰匙我怎麼辦?" "噢，把它放在桌子上就可以了。" | *There were people crying, buildings on fire. It was terrible!* 有人在哭喊，樓房在燃燒。這簡直太可怕了! | *She complained about the food so much that I was sorry I mentioned it in the end.* 她對食物如此不滿，因此我對自己最後提到食物感到十分抱歉。**2** the situation that someone is in now〔指某人目前所處的境況〕: *I can't stand it any longer. I'm resigning.* 我再也忍受不了了，我要辭職。| *How's it going Bob? I haven't seen you for ages.* 鮑勃，近況如何?我們好久不見了。| *And the worst of it is the car isn't even paid for yet.* 最糟糕的是這輛車子還沒有付錢。**3** used as the subject or object of a verb when the real subject or object is later in the sentence〔用作動詞的主詞或受詞，而真正的主詞或受詞置於句子的後部〕: *It makes me sick the way she thinks everyone's in love with her.* 她以為人人都喜歡她，這真讓我噁心。| *What's it like being a sailor?* 當水手是甚麼滋味? | *Apparently it's cheaper to fly than go by train.* 顯然，乘飛機比坐火車便宜。| *It's a pity you couldn't come.* 你來不了，真遺憾。**4** used with the verb 'be' to make statements about the weather, the time, distances etc〔與動詞 be 連用來構成句子，表明天氣、時間、距離等〕: *It's over 200 miles from London to Manchester.* 從倫敦到曼徹斯特有二百多英里。| *It was 4 o'clock and the mail still hadn't come.* 四點鐘了，郵件還沒到。| *It had obviously been snowing but none of it stuck to the ground.* 顯然曾經下過雪，但地上並沒有積雪。| *Can you believe she's forgotten it's my birthday today?* 你相信她忘了今天是我的生日嗎? **5** used to emphasize that one piece of information in a sentence is more important than the rest〔用來強調句子裡的某條信息比其他部分重要〕: *It was Jane who paid for the meal yesterday.* (=it was Jane and not another person) 昨天是簡付飯錢的。| *It was the meal that Jane paid for yesterday.* (=it was a meal and not something else) 簡昨天付的是飯錢。| *It was yesterday that Jane paid for the meal.* (=it was yesterday and not at another time) 簡是昨天付飯錢的。**6** used as the subject of 'seem', 'appear', 'look' and 'happen'〔用作 seem, appear, look 和 happen 的主詞〕: *It seems that no one really knows where he's gone.* 似乎沒有人真正知道他去了哪裡。| *Since it happened to be such a nice day they thought they'd go to the beach.* 既然碰巧趕上一個好天氣, 他們覺得應當去海邊。**7** used to talk about a child or an animal when you do not know what sex they are〔用來指性別不明的孩子或動物〕: *What will you call it if it's a boy?* 要是男孩的話, 你想給他取個甚麼名字? **8 a) it's me/John/a car etc** used to give the name of a person or thing when it is not already known 是我/約翰/一輛汽車等〔用來表明某人或某物的名字[名稱]〕: *"Who was that at the door?" "It was a man selling house insurance."* "門口那個人是誰?" "是一個賣房屋保險的人。" | *"I can't quite make out what it's a photograph of." "Oh, it's our new boat."* "我看不出這張照片上的是甚麼。" "啊, 是我們新買的一條船。" **b) it's me/John etc** used to say who is speaking on a telephone 是我/我是約翰等〔用來説明打電話的是誰〕: *Hello, it's Carmel here. Is Polly there, please?* 喂, 我是卡梅爾, 請問波莉在嗎? **9 if it weren't for/ if it hadn't been for** if something had not happened 要不是; 要是沒有: *We would have arrived much earlier if it hadn't been for the snow.* 要不是下雪, 我們早就到了。**10 a)** *informal* a particular ability or quality【非正式】〔表示某種能力或品質〕: *In a job like advertising, you've either got it or you haven't!* 像廣告這種職業, 你要麼有這份才能, 要麼沒有! **b)** *slang* SEXUAL INTERCOURSE【俚】性交: *Have you done it with him yet?* 你已經和他發生性關係了嗎? **11 this is it!** *spoken* used to say that something you expected to happen is actually going to happen【口】就是它!〔表示你預計發生的事真要發生了〕**12 That's it!** *spoken*【口】**a)** used to say that a particular situation has finished 完了! 沒有了!〔表示某個情況已結束〕*You can have one more cookie and then that's it!* 你可以再吃一塊小甜餅, 吃完就沒了! **b)** used to praise someone because they have done something correctly 做得對! 就是這樣!〔用來稱讚某人做對事情〕**13 think you're it** *informal* to think you are more important than you are【非正式】自以為了不起: *Just because he got a higher mark he really thinks he's it.* 他因為分數比別人高就自以為了不起。

I·tal·i·an[1] /ɪˈtæljən; ɪˈtæliən/ *n* [U] **1** the language of Italy 意大利語 **2** someone from Italy 意大利人

Italian[2] *adj* from or connected with Italy 意大利的

I·tal·i·a·nate /ɪˈtæljəˌnet; ɪˈtæliəneɪt/ *adj literary* with an Italian style or appearance【文】意大利風格的; 意大利特色的

i·tal·i·cize also 又作 **-ise** *BrE*【英】/ɪˈtæləˌsaɪz; ɪˈtælɪ̈saɪz/ *v* [T] to put or print something in italics 把…排成斜體; 用斜體字印刷〔某物〕—**italicized** *adj*

i·tal·ics /ɪˈtælɪks; ɪˈtælɪks/ *n* [plural] a type of printed letters that lean to the right, often used to emphasize particular words 斜體字〔常用來表示強調〕: **in italics** *This example is written in italics.* 這個例句是用斜體排印的。—compare 比較 ROMAN —**italic** *adj*: *italic script* 斜體書法

Italo- /ɪtælo; ɪtæləʊ/ *prefix* Italian 意大利(人)的: *the Italo-Austrian border* 意(大利)奧(地利)邊界

itch[1] /ɪtʃ; ɪtʃ/ *v* **1** [I,T] if part of your body or your clothes itch, you have an unpleasant feeling on your skin that makes you want to rub it with your nails (使) 發癢: *My feet were itching terribly.* 我的腳癢得厲害。| **itch sb** *AmE*【美】: *The label on this shirt itches me.* 這件襯衫上的商標刺得我發癢。**2 be itching to do sth** *informal* to want to do something very much as soon as possible【非正式】急切地想做某事: *You could tell they were itching to leave.* 你能看出他們急着要離開。

itch[2] *n* [singular] **1** an uncomfortable feeling on your skin that makes you want to rub it with your nails 癢 **2** *informal* a strong desire to do or have something【非正式】〔想做某事、要某物的〕強烈願望: **[+for]** *an itch for adventure* 進行探險的強烈願望

itch·y /ˈɪtʃɪ; ˈɪtʃi/ *adj* **1** part of your body that is itchy has an unpleasant feeling that makes you want to rub it with your nails 發癢的: *My eyes sometimes get red and itchy in the summer.* 夏天我的眼睛有時會紅腫發癢。**2** clothes that are itchy make you have this feeling on your skin〔衣服〕令人發癢的: *These tights are all itchy.* 這些緊身衣讓人渾身發癢。**3** wanting to go somewhere new or do something different 渴望〔去新的地方、做不同的事情〕: *He's had that job now for about eight years, and he's starting to get itchy.* 他做那份工作約八年了, 現在開始不安心了。**4 have itchy feet** *especially BrE informal* to want to travel or go somewhere new【尤英, 非正式】腳癢〔想旅行或去新的地方〕: *I've only been back home for a few months and I've already got itchy feet.* 我回家不過才幾個月, 就又想出門了。**5 itchy fingers** *informal* someone with itchy fingers is likely to steal things【非正式】手癢〔想偷東西〕: *I tucked the bills deep into my pocket, away from itchy fingers.* 我把鈔票藏在口袋深處, 以防扒手偷走。**6 itchy palm** *informal* an official who has an itchy palm is willing to dishonestly accept money 手心癢〔指官員想接受賄賂〕—**itchiness** *n* [U]

it'd /ˈɪtəd; ˈɪtəd/ *usually spoken*【一般口】the short form of 縮略式= 'it would' or 'it had': *I'd do it if I thought it'd help.* 如果我認為這樣做有用, 我就會去做的。

-ite /aɪt; aɪt/ *suffix* **1** [in nouns 構成名詞] a follower or supporter of a particular idea or person〔某個思想或人的〕支持者, 追隨者: *a group of Trotskyites* (=followers of Trotsky's political ideas) 一羣托洛茨基分子 | *the Pre-Raphaelites* 拉斐爾前派藝術家 **2** [in adjectives 構成形容詞] connected with a particular set of religious or political ideas, or with the ideas of a particular person 具有〔某宗教、政治或某人〕觀點的: *his Reaganite opinions* 他的列根主義觀點 **3** someone who lives in a particular place or belongs to a particular group 住在…的人; 屬於…組織的人: *a Brooklynite* (=someone from Brooklyn) 布魯克林區的人 | *the Israelites* (=in the Bible)〔《聖經》中的〕古以色列人

i·tem /ˈaɪtəm; ˈaɪtəm/ *n* **1** [C] a single thing, especially part of a list, group, or set〔尤指清單上、一羣或一組事物中的〕一項; 一件; 一條: *The professor wanted to see item 15, the Egyptian pot.* 教授想看第 15 件, 那個埃及壺。| **[+of]** *an item of furniture* 一件家具 **2** [C] a single, usually short, piece of news in a newspaper or magazine, or on TV〔報紙、雜誌、電視上的〕一條 (短) 消息: *He sat at the kitchen table with the paper reading each item aloud.* 他坐在廚房餐桌前, 拿着報紙大聲朗讀每條新聞。**3 be an item** *informal* if two people are an item, they have a sexual relationship【非正式】有性關係: *They're not an item any more.* 他們不再有性關係了。 W1

i·tem·ize also 又作 **-ise** *BrE*【英】/ˈaɪtəmˌaɪz; ˈaɪtəmaɪz/ *v* [T] to make a list and give details about each thing on the list 分條列舉; 詳細列舉 —**itemized** *adj*: *an itemized bill* 逐項開列的賬單

i·tin·e·rant /aɪˈtɪnərənt; aɪˈtɪnərənt/ *adj* [only before noun 僅用於名詞前] *formal* travelling from place to place, especially to work【正式】〔尤指工作上〕巡迴的; 流動的: *itinerant labourers* 流動勞工

i·tin·e·ra·ry /aɪˈtɪnəˌrɛrɪ; aɪˈtɪnərəri/ *n* [C] a plan or list of the places you will visit on a journey 旅行計劃; 預定行程: *His itinerary would take him from Bordeaux to Budapest.* 他的旅行計劃是從波爾多到布達佩斯。

-itis /aɪtɪs; aɪtɪ̈s/ *suffix* [in U nouns 構成不可數名詞] **1** an illness or infection that affects a particular part of your body〔身體某部分的〕炎症: *tonsillitis* (=infection of the TONSILS) 扁桃體炎 **2** *humorous* the condition of having too much of something or liking something too much【幽默】…迷; …癖: *televisionitis* (=watching too much television) 電視癖

it'll /ˈɪtl; ˈɪtl/ *usually spoken*【一般口】the short form of 縮略式= 'it will': *It'll be dark before they get back.* 他

們回來之前天就會黑了。

it's /ɪts; ɪts/ **1** the short form of 縮略式= 'it is': *It's raining.* 正在下雨。**2** a short form of 縮略式= 'it has': *It's been cloudy all day.* 已經陰了一整天。

its /ɪts; ɪts/ *determiner* the possessive form of IT〔it 的所有格形式〕: *The baby had fallen out of its crib.* 嬰兒從嬰兒牀上跌落下來。| *I must admit the plan does have its merits.* 我必須承認這項計劃確有它的優點。

it·self /ɪt`sɛlf; ɪt'self/ *pron* **1** the reflexive form of IT〔it 的反身形式〕: *The cat lay on the sofa, washing itself.* 貓躺在沙發上給自己舔乾淨。| *It is generally felt that the government has made an idiot of itself.* 人們普遍認為政府自己做了一件大蠢事。**2** used to emphasize the pronoun 'it'〔用來強調代詞 it〕: *We've checked the wiring and the aerial so the problem maybe the television itself.* 線路和天線我們都檢查過了，所以問題也許在電視機本身。**3 in itself** considered without other related ideas or situation 就其本身而言: *There is a little infection in the lung which in itself is not important.* 肺部有些感染，但就其本身而言並沒甚麼關係。**4 (all) by itself a)** alone 獨自: *Will the dog be safe left in the car by itself?* 把狗獨自留在車裡安全嗎? **b)** without help 無需外力地: *The door seemed to open all by itself.* 那扇門好像是自己打開的。**5 (all) to itself** if something has something else to itself, it does not have to share that thing with others 全部為自己所有; 非共用: *This idea deserves a chapter to itself.* 這個觀點值得單獨寫一章。

it·sy-bit·sy /ˌɪtsɪ `bɪtsɪ; ˌɪtsi 'bɪtsi◂/ also 又作 **it·ty-bit·ty** /ˌɪtɪ `bɪtɪ; ˌɪti 'bɪti◂/ *adj* [only before noun 僅用於名詞前] *spoken humorous* very small【口, 幽默】極小的

-i·tude /ətjud; ᵻtjuːd/ also 又作 **-tude** [in nouns 構成名詞] *suffix formal* the state of having a particular quality【正式】有...特性: *certitude* (=being certain) 必然(性) | *exactitude* 精確(性)

ITV /ˌaɪ ti `vi; ˌaɪ tiː 'viː/ *n* [U] Independent Television; a group of British television companies that are paid for by advertising〔英國〕獨立電視公司〔由幾家電視公司組成, 靠廣告收入維持〕

-ity /ətɪ; ᵻti/ also 又作 **-ty** *suffix* [in nouns 構成名詞] the state of having a particular quality, or something that has that quality 具有某種特性的狀態; 具有某種特性的事物: *with great regularity* (=regularly) 很有規律地 | *such stupidities* (=stupid actions or remarks) 如此荒謬的言行

IUD /ˌaɪ ju `di; ˌaɪ juː 'diː/ *n* [C] a small plastic or metal object used inside a woman's UTERUS (=place where a baby develops) to prevent a baby being born; COIL[2] (4)〔婦女用〕子宮內避孕器

IV /ˌaɪ `vi; ˌaɪ 'viː/ *n* [C] *AmE* medical equipment that is used to put liquid directly into your blood【美】〔靜脈〕滴注器; DRIP[2] (3) *BrE*【英】

I've /aɪv; aɪv/ *usually spoken*【一般口】the short form of 縮略式= 'I have': *I've never been here before.* 我以前從未來過這兒。

-ive /ɪv; ɪv/ *suffix* [in nouns and adjectives 構成名詞和形容詞] someone or something that does something or can do something (能)做某事的人[物]: *an explosive* (=substance that can explode) 炸藥 | *a detective* (=someone who tries to discover facts about crimes) 偵探 | *the adoptive parents* (=who ADOPT a child) 養父養母

IVF /ˌaɪ vi `ɛf; ˌaɪ viː 'ef/ *technical* a process in which a human egg is fertilized (FERTILIZE (1)) outside the woman's body; IN VITRO FERTILIZATION【術語】體外受精

i·vied /`aɪvɪd; 'aɪvid/ *adj literary* covered with ivy【文】常春藤覆蓋的

i·vo·ry /`aɪvərɪ; 'aɪvəri/ *n* **1** [U] the hard smooth yellowish-white substance from the TUSKs (=long teeth) of an ELEPHANT 象牙(質): *an ivory chess set* 一副象牙國際象棋 **2** [U] a yellowish white colour 象牙色; 乳白色 **3** [C often plural 常用複數] something made of ivory, especially a small figure of a person or animal 象牙製品〔尤指小型人像或動物像〕: *a collection of Chinese ivories* 中國象牙製品藏品 **4 the ivories** [plural] *informal* the KEYS (=parts you press down) of a piano【非正式】鋼琴鍵 —see also 另見 **tickle the ivories** (TICKLE[1] (5)) **5** *AmE humorous* someone's teeth【美, 幽默】〔某人的〕牙齒 **6 ivory tower** a place or situation where you are separated from the difficulties of ordinary life and so are unable to understand them 象牙塔〔脫離現實生活中困境的小天地〕: *ivory tower linguists* 象牙塔中的語言學家

i·vy /`aɪvɪ; 'aɪvi/ *n* [C, U] a climbing plant with dark green shiny leaves 常春藤 —see also 另見 POISON IVY

Ivy League /ˌ·· `·◂/*adj* connected with a group of old and respected universities in the eastern US 常春藤名牌大學的〔與美國東部歷史悠久、聲譽卓著的一批大學有關的〕: *an Ivy League college* 一所常春藤名牌大學

-ization /əzeʃən; aɪzeɪʃən/ *suffix* makes nouns from verbs ending in -IZE 加在以 -ize 結尾動詞之後使之成為名詞: *civilization* 文明 | *crystallization* 結晶

-ize also 又作 **-ise** *BrE*【英】/aɪz; aɪz/ *suffix* [in verbs 構成動詞] **1** to make something have more of a particular quality 使某物更大程度地具有某種特點: *We need to modernize our procedures.* (=make them more modern) 我們要使我們的程序現代化。| *Americanized spelling* (=spelling made more American) 美式拼寫 | *privatized transport systems* (=put back into private ownership) 私有化的運輸系統 **2** to change something to something else, or be changed to something else 轉變; 變成: *The liquid crystallized.* (=turned into CRYSTALS) 液體結晶了。**3** to speak in a particular way 以某種方式講話: *to soliloquize* (=speak a SOLILOQUY, to yourself) 自言自語 | *I sat and listened to him sermonizing.* (=speaking solemnly, as if in a SERMON) 我坐着聽他那布道式的講話。**4** to put into a particular place 置於某處: *She was hospitalized after the accident.* 她在事故發生後被送往醫院。

iz·zat·so /ɪ,zæt`so; ɪˌzæt'səʊ/ *interjection AmE* used to show that you do not believe something that someone has just said【美】真的嗎?〔用來表示不相信某人剛剛說的話〕

J,j

J, j /dʒe; dʒeɪ/ *plural* **J's, j's** *n* [C] the tenth letter of the English alphabet 英語字母表的第十個字母

J the written abbreviation of 縮寫= JOULE

jab¹ /dʒæb; dʒæb/ *v* **jabbed, jabbing** [I,T] to push something into or towards something else with short quick movements 戳, 刺, 捅; 猛擊: **jab sb with sth** *Stop jabbing me with your elbow!* 別用胳膊肘捅我! | [+at] *She jabbed at the elevator buttons.* 她迅速按了一下電梯按鈕。

jab² *n* [C] **1** a sudden hard push, especially with a pointed object or your FIST (=closed hand) 〔用尖物或拳頭〕擊, 推, 戳: **right/left jab** (=with your right or left hand) 用右手/左手擊打 **2** *BrE informal* an INJECTION (1) given to prevent you from catching a disease; SHOT¹ (15)【英, 非正式】預防針: *a typhoid jab* 傷寒預防針

jab·ber /ˋdʒæbɚ; ˈdʒæbə/ *v* [I,T] to talk quickly, excitedly, and not very clearly 急促、激動而含糊不清地說話 —**jabber** *n* [singular,U]

jack¹ /dʒæk; dʒæk/ *n* [C]

1 ▶TOOL FOR LIFTING 起重工具◀ a piece of equipment used to lift a heavy weight off the ground, such as a car, and support it while it is in the air 起重器, 千斤頂: *a hydraulic jack* 液壓千斤頂

2 ▶CARD GAMES 紙牌遊戲◀ a card used in card games that has a man's picture on it and is worth less than a queen and more than a ten 〔紙牌中介於王后和十之間的〕"J" 牌, 傑克: *a pair of jacks* 一對傑克

3 ▶ELECTRICAL 電的◀ an electronic connection for a telephone or other electric machine 插座, 插孔

4 ▶CHILDREN'S GAME 兒童遊戲◀ **a) jacks** [plural] a children's game in which the players try to pick up small objects while bouncing (BOUNCE) and catching a ball 拋接子遊戲〔一面拍球一面設法拾起小物件〕 **b)** a small metal or plastic object that has six points, used in this game 〔拋接子遊戲中用的〕帶有六個尖端的金屬[塑料]小物件

5 ▶BALL 球◀ a small white ball at which players aim larger balls in the game of bowls (BOWL¹ (3a)) 〔滾木球戲中用作靶子的〕小白球

6 I'm all right, Jack *BrE usually spoken* someone with an I'm all right Jack attitude is happy with their life and does not care about other people【英, 一般口】反正我過得挺好〔指自己生活得很快活, 對別人卻漠不關心〕

7 ▶PERSON 人◀ **every man jack** *BrE old-fashioned* every single person; everyone【英, 過時】每個人: *Every man jack of them is without a job.* 他們誰都沒有工作。

8 jack shit/diddly *AmE spoken* an impolite expression meaning nothing at all【美口】一點都不〔不禮貌說法〕: *He knows jack shit about cars.* 他對汽車一竅不通。—see also 另見 JUMPING JACK, UNION JACK

jack² *v*

jack sb **around** *phr v* [T] *AmE slang* to waste someone's time by deliberately making things difficult for them【美俚】故意刁難〔某人〕以浪費其時間: *Stop jacking me around and make up your mind!* 別浪費我的時間了, 立定主意吧!

jack sth ↔ **in** *phr v* [T] *BrE informal* to stop doing something【英, 非正式】停止做: *I'd love to jack in my job and go live in the Bahamas.* 我會樂於辭去工作, 去巴哈馬居住。

jack off *phr v* [I,T] *AmE taboo* to MASTURBATE【美諱】手淫

jack sb/sth ↔ **up** *phr v* [T] **1** to lift something heavy off the ground using a jack 〔用起重器〕頂[托]起〔重物〕: *Jack the car up higher – I can't get the tire off.* 把車再托高些, 不然車胎拿不下來。**2** *informal* to increase prices, sales etc by a large amount【非正式】大幅度提高〔價格、銷量等〕: *jacking up their profit margins* 大幅度提高他們的盈利率 **3 be jacked up** *AmE informal* to be excited and nervous【美, 非正式】又興奮又緊張

jack·al /ˋdʒækəl; ˈdʒækɔːl/ *n* [C] a wild animal like a dog that lives in Asia and Africa and eats the remaining parts of dead animals 〔亞洲和非洲的〕豺, 胡狼

jack·ass /ˋdʒækˌæs; ˈdʒæk-æs/ *n* [C] **1** *BrE old-fashioned or AmE informal* an annoying stupid person【英, 過時或美, 非正式】傻瓜, 蠢貨 **2** a male ASS (=animal similar to a horse) 公驢

jack·boot /ˋdʒækˌbut; ˈdʒækbuːt/ *n* [C] a boot worn by soldiers that covers their leg up to the knee 長筒軍靴 —**jackbooted** *adj*

jack·daw /ˋdʒækˌdɔ; ˈdʒækdɔː/ *n* [C] a black bird like a CROW¹ (1) that sometimes steals small, bright objects 寒鴉

jack·et /ˋdʒækɪt; ˈdʒækɪ̣t/ *n* [C] **1** a short, light coat 夾克, 外套: *a denim jacket* 牛仔布夾克 | *Gene has to wear a jacket and tie to work.* 吉恩必須穿着外套打着領帶去上班。—see also 另見 DINNER JACKET, LIFE JACKET —see picture on page A17 參見 A17 頁圖 **2** a stiff piece of folded paper that fits over the cover of a book to protect it; DUST JACKET 〔書籍的〕護封; 書套 **3** *AmE* a stiff paper cover that protects a record【美】唱片封套; SLEEVE (4) *BrE*【英】 **4** a cover that surrounds and protects some types of machines 〔機器的〕外罩, 保護罩 2 3

jacket po·ta·to /ˈ·· ·ˌ·/ *n* [C] *BrE* a potato baked with its skin on【英】帶皮烤的馬鈴薯

Jack Frost /ˌ· ˈ·/ *n* [singular] a way of describing FROST¹ (1) as a person, used especially when talking to children 〔擬人化的〕霜〔常用於與兒童說話時〕

jack·ham·mer /ˋdʒækˌhæmɚ; ˈdʒækˌhæmə/ *n* [C] *AmE* a large powerful tool used to break hard materials such as the surface of a road【美】風鑽; 鑿岩機; PNEUMATIC DRILL *BrE*【英】

jack-in-the-box /ˈ· · · ˌ·/ *n* [C] a children's toy shaped like a box with a figure inside that springs out when the box is opened 玩偶匣〔內裝小人, 盒蓋開啟, 小人即跳出〕

jack-knife¹ /ˈ· ·/ *n plural* **jack-knives** /-ˌnaɪvz; -naɪvz/ [C] **1** a knife with a blade that folds into its handle 摺刀 **2** a DIVE² (1) in which you bend at the waist when you are in the air 屈體跳水

jack-knife² *v* **jack-knifing, jack-knifed** [I] if a large vehicle with two parts jack-knifes, the back part swings towards the front part 〔前後鉸接的車輛〕發生彎折: *The truck skidded and jack-knifed.* 那輛鉸接卡車打滑後發生了彎折。

jack-of-all-trades /ˌ· · ˈ· ·/ *n* [singular] someone who can do many different types of work, but who often is not very skilled at any of them 博而不精的人

jack-o'-lan·tern /ˌdʒæk ə ˋlæntɚn; ˌdʒæk ə ˈlæntən/ *n* [C] a PUMPKIN (1) that has a face cut into it and a CANDLE put inside to shine through the holes 南瓜燈籠〔在南瓜上挖出人面形窟窿, 內點蠟燭〕

jack·pot /ˋdʒækˌpɑt; ˈdʒækpɒt/ *n* [C] a large amount of money that you can win in a game that is decided by chance 〔在靠運氣的遊戲中可贏得的〕巨額獎金 —see also 另見 **hit the jackpot** (HIT¹ (23))

jack·rab·bit /ˋdʒækˌræbɪt; ˈdʒækˌræbɪ̣t/ *n* [C] a large North American HARE (=animal like a large rabbit) with very long ears 〔北美洲的〕長耳大野兔

J

Jack Rob·in·son /ˌdʒæk ˋrɑbɪnsn̩; ˌdʒæk ˈrɒbɪnsən/ *n* **before you can say Jack Robinson** *old-fashioned* very quickly or suddenly【過時】迅速地; 突然地

Jack the Lad /ˌ· · ˋ·/ *n* [singular] *BrE spoken* a young man who enjoys drinking beer and going out with his male friends, and who thinks he is sexually attractive【英口】〔愛喝啤酒、常與男性夥伴外出、自以為很有性魅力的〕青年男子

Jac·o·be·an /ˌdʒækəˋbiən; ˌdʒækəˈbiːən◂/ *adj* belonging to or typical of the period between 1603 and 1625 in Britain, when James I was king of England 英王詹姆斯一世時期 (1603–1625) 的: *Jacobean drama* 詹姆斯一世時代的戲劇

Jac·o·bite /ˋdʒækəˌbaɪt; ˈdʒækəbaɪt/ *n* [C] someone in the 17th or 18th centuries who supported King James II of England and wanted one of his DESCENDANTS to rule England〔17或18世紀〕擁護詹姆斯二世並主張由他的後裔來統治英國的人 —**Jacobite** *adj*

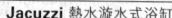

Jacuzzi 熱水漩水式浴缸

Ja·cuz·zi /dʒəˋkuzi; dʒəˈkuːzi/ *n* [C] *trademark* a large indoor bath that makes hot water move in strong currents around your body【商標】〔室內〕熱水漩水式浴缸 —compare 比較 HOT TUB, SPA (2)

jade /dʒed; dʒeɪd/ *n* **1** [U] a hard, usually green stone often used to make jewellery 碧玉, 翡翠 **2** [U] the light green colour of this stone 綠玉色, 翡翠綠 —see picture on page A5 參見A5頁圖 **3** [C] *old use* a woman, especially a rude or immoral woman【舊】〔尤指粗魯或淫蕩的〕婦女; 蕩婦

ja·ded /ˋdʒedɪd; ˈdʒeɪdɪ̇d/ *adj* someone who is jaded is no longer interested in or excited by life, especially because they have experienced too many things〔尤因飽經世故而〕對世事冷漠: *magnificent meals to tempt the most jaded appetites* 可挑起最厭食之人胃口的美饌佳餚

Jaf·fa /ˋdʒæfə; ˈdʒæfə/ *n* [C] *BrE* a large orange, especially one that comes from Israel【英】〔尤指產於以色列的〕雅法橙

J

jag /dʒæg; dʒæg/ *n* [C] *informal*【非正式】**crying/shopping/talking etc jag** a short period of time when you suddenly cry etc without controlling how much you do it〔不加控制的〕一陣大哭/狂買/喋喋不休等

jag·ged /ˋdʒægɪd; ˈdʒægɪ̇d/ *adj* having a rough, uneven edge or surface, often with sharp points on it 鋸齒狀的; 凹凸不平的: *the jagged rocks of St. Saviour's Point* 聖基督角的鋸齒狀岩石 —**jaggedly** *adv*

jag·u·ar /ˋdʒægwɑr; ˈdʒægjuə/ *n* [C] a large South American wild cat with brown and yellow fur with black spots〔產於南美的〕美洲豹

jai a·lai /ˋhaɪ əˌlaɪ; ˌhaɪ əˈlaɪ/ *n* [U] a game played by two, four, or six people in which they use an object like a basket on a stick to throw a ball 回力球〔一種用一頭有籃筐的棒拋球, 由二、四或六人參加的遊戲〕

jail¹ also 又作 **gaol** *BrE*【英】/dʒel; dʒeɪl/ *n* [C,U] a place where criminals are kept as part of their punishment, or where people who have been charged with a crime are kept before they are judged in a law court; PRISON (1) 監獄

jail² also 又作 **gaol** *BrE*【英】—*v* [T] to put someone in jail 監禁; 拘留: *They ought to jail him for life.* 他們應把他終身監禁。

jail·bird also 又作 **gaolbird** *BrE*【英】/ˋdʒelˌbɝd; ˈdʒeɪlbɜːd/ *n* [C] *informal* someone who has spent a lot of time in prison【非正式】長期坐牢的人

jail·break also 又作 **gaolbreak** *BrE*【英】/ˋdʒelˌbrek; ˈdʒeɪlbreɪk/ *n* [C] an escape or an attempt to escape from prison, especially by several people〔尤指多人的〕越獄

jail·er also 又作 **gaoler** *BrE*【英】/ˋdʒelɚ; ˈdʒeɪlə/ *n* [C] *old-fashioned* someone who is in charge of guarding a prison or prisoners【過時】監獄看守, 獄卒

Jain /dʒaɪn; dʒaɪn/ *n* [C] someone whose religion is Jainism 耆那教教徒 —**Jain** *adj*

Jain·is·m /ˋdʒaɪnɪzəm; ˈdʒaɪnɪzəm/ *n* [C] a religion of India that is against violence towards any living things 耆那教〔印度的一種宗教, 反對暴力和殺生〕

jal·a·pe·ño /ˌhɑləˋpenjo; ˌhæləˈpeɪnjəʊ/ *n* [C] a small, very hot green PEPPER used especially in Mexican food 墨西哥青辣椒〔極辣, 尤用於墨西哥食物〕

ja·lop·y /dʒəˋlɑpɪ; dʒəˈlɒpi/ *n* [C] *old-fashioned* a very old car in bad condition【過時】破舊的汽車 —see also 另見 BANGER (2)

jam¹ /dʒæm; dʒæm/ *n* **1** [C,U] a very thick sweet substance made from boiled fruit and sugar and eaten especially on bread; CONSERVE 果醬: *strawberry jam* 草莓醬 **2** [C] a situation in which it is difficult or impossible to move because there are so many people, things, cars etc close together 擁擠; 堵塞: **traffic jam** *Sorry we're late. We got stuck in a traffic jam.* 對不起, 我們來晚了, 因為路上堵車。**3 be in a jam** *informal* to be in a difficult or uncomfortable situation【非正式】處於困境 **4 jams** [plural] *AmE* brightly coloured trousers that stop above your knee【美】〔長及膝蓋以上的〕彩色短褲 **5 jam tomorrow** *BrE informal* good things that you are promised if you are patient enough to wait for them【英, 非正式】許而不與的好東西〔指對耐心的人來說美好的事物總會到來〕—see also 另見 JAM SESSION

jam² *v*

1 ►PUSH HARD 用力推◄ [T] to push something somewhere using a lot of force, or to push too many things into a small place 用力推擠, 塞進〔將許多物件塞進一個小處所〕: **jam sth into/under/on** *I'll never jam all my clothes into one suitcase.* 我不會把我的衣服都塞進一個箱子裡。| **be jammed (up) against sth** (=pushed tightly against something) 與某物緊緊塞在一起

2 ►MACHINE 機器◄ also 又作 **jam up** [I,T] if a lock or a moving part of a machine jams, or if you jam it, it no longer works properly because something is preventing it from moving (使) 卡住; (使) 發生故障: *The front roller has jammed on the photocopier.* 複印機的前滾筒卡住了。

3 ►BLOCK 堵塞◄ also 又作 **jam up** [T] if a lot of people or vehicles jam a place, they block it so that it is difficult to move〔人、車〕堵塞〔某地〕: *Crowds jammed the entrance to the stadium.* 體育場入口處堵滿了人。—see also 另見 JAMMED (2)

4 ►MUSIC 音樂◄ [I] to play music informally with others without practising first 未經練習的非正式演奏, 即興演奏 —see also 另見 JAM SESSION

5 jam on the brakes to slow down a car suddenly by putting your foot down hard on the BRAKE¹ (1) 猛踩煞車

6 jam the switchboard if telephone calls jam the switchboard, so many people are telephoning the same organization that its telephone system cannot work properly 使電話線路堵塞

7 ►RADIO 無線電◄ [T] to deliberately prevent broadcasts or other electronic signals from being received by sending out noise on the same WAVELENGTH 干擾〔無線電廣播或其他電子信號〕

8 sb is jamming *AmE spoken* used to say that someone is doing something well【美口】某人幹得好

jamb /dʒæm; dʒæm/ *n* [C] a side post of a door or window〔門、窗的〕側柱

jam·ba·la·ya /ˌdʒæmbəˋlaɪə; ˌdʒæmbəˈlaɪə/ *n* [U] a dish from the southern US containing rice, and SEAFOOD 什錦飯〔美國南部食品, 由米飯和海鮮烹調而成〕

jam·bo·ree /ˌdʒæmbəˋri; ˌdʒæmbəˈriː/ *n* [C] **1** a big noisy party or celebration, usually outdoors 喧鬧的大型聚會[慶祝]〔通常在露天舉行〕**2** a large meeting of scouts (SCOUT¹ (1)) or guides (GUIDE¹ (4)) 童子軍大會

jammed /dʒæmd; dʒæmd/ *adj* **1** [not before noun 不用於名詞前] impossible to move because of being stuck between two or more surfaces 夾住不能動的: *The child had got his finger jammed in the door.* 那孩子的一個手指被門夾住了。**2** *AmE* full of people or things; jam-packed【美】擠滿人[物]的: *The place is jammed. We'll never get in.* 那地方太擁擠了, 我們絕對進不去。

jam·mies /ˋdʒæmɪz; ˈdʒæmiz/ *n* [plural] *informal* PYJAMAS【非正式】睡衣褲

jam·my /ˋdʒæmɪ; ˈdʒæmi/ *adj BrE slang*【英俚】**1** **jammy bastard/cow/bugger etc** an impolite expression meaning someone who has been very lucky 走運的傢伙〔粗俗詞語〕**2** very easy 非常容易的

jam-packed /ˌ· ˈ·◂/ *adj informal* full of people or things that are very close together【非正式】擠滿人[物]的: [+with] *The square was jam-packed with revelers celebrating the New Year.* 廣場上擠滿了慶祝新年的狂歡者。

jam ses·sion /ˈ· ˌ··/ *n* [C] an occasion when JAZZ¹ (1) or ROCK¹ (2) musicians play music together informally 爵士樂[搖滾樂]非正式演奏會, 即興演奏會

Jan /dʒæn; dʒæn/ the written abbreviation of 縮寫= January

Jane Doe /ˌdʒen ˋdo; ˌdʒeɪn ˈdəʊ/ *n* [singular] *AmE* a woman whose name is not known, especially one who is involved in a law case【美】某甲, 某女〔指不知姓名的婦女, 尤指訴訟案件中的女當事人〕—compare 比較 JOHN DOE

jan·gle /ˋdʒæŋgḷ; ˈdʒæŋgəl/ *v* **1** [I,T] if metal objects or bells jangle or if you jangle them, they make a sharp sound when they hit each other (使)〔金屬物件或鈴鐺〕發出尖銳的聲音: *jangling bracelets* 叮噹作響的手鐲 **2** also 又作 **jangle on** [T usually passive 一般用被動態] to make someone feel nervous or upset 使焦躁不安: *jangled nerves* 緊張不安的神經 —**jangle** *n* [singular]

jan·i·tor /ˋdʒænətɚ; ˈdʒænɪ̥tə/ *n* [C] *AmE or ScotE* someone who looks after a school or other large building【美或蘇格蘭】〔學校或大樓的〕看門人, 門房; CARETAKER (1) *BrE*【英】

Jan·u·a·ry /ˋdʒænjuˌɛrɪ; ˈdʒænjuəri/ written abbreviation 縮寫為 **Jan** *n* [C,U] the first month of the year, between December and February 一月: **in January** *Our new office is opening in January 2000.* 我們的新辦事處定於2000年1月開始辦公。| **last/next January** *I haven't heard from him since last January.* 從去年一月到現在, 我沒有收到過他的信。| **on January 29th** (also 又作 **on 29th January** *BrE* 英) *Rosie's party was on January 29th.* 羅齊的聚會是在1月29日。(spoken as 讀作: *on January the twenty-ninth* or 或 *on the twenty-ninth of January* or 或 (*AmE* 美) *on January twenty-ninth*)

Jap·a·nese¹ /ˌdʒæpəˋniz; ˌdʒæpəˈniːz◂/ *n* **1** [U] the language of Japan 日語 **2** **the Japanese** people from Japan 日本人

Japanese² *adj* from or connected with Japan 來自日本的, 與日本有關的

Japanese lan·tern /ˌ··· ˈ··/ *n* [C] a paper decoration, usually with a light inside〔裝飾用〕紙燈籠

jape /dʒep; dʒeɪp/ *n* [C] *old-fashioned* a trick or joke【過時】把戲; 玩笑

jar¹ /dʒɑr; dʒɑː/ *n* [C] **1** a round glass container with a wide lid, used for storing food such as JAM¹ (1) and HONEY (1)〔用來盛果醬、蜂蜜等的玻璃〕廣口瓶 **2** the amount of food, drink, etc contained in a jar 一廣口瓶所裝之量: *half a jar of peanut butter* 半瓶花生醬 **3** [singular] the shock of two things hitting each other, or a sudden pain from something hitting you〔兩物碰撞引起的〕震動; 突然的痛楚: *It must have been the jar of the impact that broke her ankle.* 肯定是由於碰撞的震動把她的腳踝折斷了。**4** a round container made of clay, stone etc used especially in the past for keeping food or drink in〔過去用來盛食物或飲料、用黏土或石頭等製成的〕壜, 罐 **5** *BrE informal* a glass of beer【英, 非正式】一杯啤酒: *We'd had a few jars down the pub.* 我們已在小酒館喝了幾杯啤酒。

jar² *v* **jarred, jarring 1** [T] to slightly hurt a part of your body by hitting it against something 撞傷〔身體的一部分〕: *Alice landed badly, jarring her ankle.* 艾麗斯落地姿勢不好, 扭傷了腳踝。**2** [I,T] if you jar something or if two things jar, they are suddenly shaken or hit (使)〔某物〕震動; 相撞: *Oops, sorry, did I jar your elbow?* 哎喲, 對不起, 我撞着你的手肘了嗎? **3** [I,T] also 又作 **jar on** to make someone feel slightly annoyed or uncomfortable 令〔人〕略感不快[不舒服]: **jar on sb's nerves** *The baby's screaming was starting to jar on my nerves.* 那個嬰兒的尖叫聲開始使我心煩。**4** [I] to be different in style or appearance from something else and therefore look strange 不和諧, 不相配: [+with] *a modernistic lamp that jarred with the rest of the room* 與房間其他地方不相稱的一盞非常時髦的燈 —**jarring** *adj*

jar·gon /ˋdʒɑrgən; ˈdʒɑːgən/ *n* [U] technical words and expressions that are used mainly by people who belong to the same professional group and are difficult to understand〔難懂的〕行話, 術語: *documents full of legal jargon* 全是法律術語的文件

jas·mine /ˋdʒæzmən; ˈdʒæzmɪ̥n/ *n* [C,U] a climbing plant with sweet-smelling small white or yellow flowers 茉莉, 素馨

jas·per /ˋdʒæspɚ; ˈdʒæspə/ *n* [U] a red, yellow, or brown stone that is not very valuable〔呈紅、黃、棕等顏色不大值錢的〕碧玉

jaun·dice /ˋdʒɔndɪs; ˈdʒɔːndɪ̥s/ *n* [U] a medical condition in which your skin and the white part of your eyes become yellow 黃疸(病)

jaun·diced /ˋdʒɔndɪst; ˈdʒɔːndɪ̥st/ *adj* **1** tending to judge people and things unfavourably, often because you have had disappointing experiences yourself〔由於受過挫折而對世事〕有偏見的: *a jaundiced view of life* 有偏見的人生觀 | **with a jaundiced eye** (=thinking of people and situations in a jaundiced way) 帶着偏見的眼光 **2** suffering from jaundice 患黃疸病的

jaunt /dʒɔnt; dʒɔːnt/ *n* [C] a short journey for pleasure 短途旅遊 —**jaunt** *v* [I]

jaun·ty /ˋdʒɔntɪ; ˈdʒɔːnti/ *adj* jaunty actions, clothes etc show that you are confident and cheerful〔動作、衣着等〕滿懷信心的, 愉快的: **at a jaunty angle** *His hat was tilted at a jaunty angle.* 他歪戴着帽子, 顯得輕鬆愉快。—**jauntily** *adv* —**jauntiness** *n* [U]

jav·e·lin /ˋdʒævlɪn; ˈdʒævəlɪ̥n/ *n* [C] **1** a light SPEAR for throwing, now used mostly in sport〔現多用於體育運動的〕標槍 **2** **the javelin** a sporting event in which competitors throw a javelin 擲標槍〔比賽項目〕

jaw¹ /dʒɔ; dʒɔː/ *n* **1** [C] the lower part of your face that moves when you eat 頷, 下顎: *Tyson punched his opponent on the jaw.* 泰臣一拳狠狠打在對手的下顎上。—see picture at 參見 HEAD¹ 圖 **2** **sb's jaw dropped** used to say that someone looked surprised or shocked〔用來形容某人驚訝或震驚得〕張口結舌: *Her jaw dropped when I told her Jean had left her husband.* 我告訴她吉恩已與丈夫分手, 她驚訝得說不出話來。**3** **jaws** [plural] **a)** the mouth of a person or animal, especially a dangerous animal〔尤指猛獸的〕嘴: *a crocodile snapping its jaws* 鱷魚的嘴開合時劈啪作響 **b)** the two parts of a machine or tool that move together to hold something tightly〔工具或機器的〕夾住東西的部分, 鉗口 **4** [C usually singular 一般用單數] the shape of someone's jaw, especially when it shows something about their character〔某人的〕下顎形狀〔尤指顯示其性格〕: *She's got a very determined jaw.* 她個性堅毅。**5 the jaws of death/defeat/despair** *literary* a situation in which you almost die, are almost defeated etc【文】生死關頭/勝負關頭/絕望邊緣 **6 the jaws of a cave/tunnel etc** the entrance to a place which is dark and dangerous 黑暗而危險處的入口 **7 have a jaw** *old-fashioned* to have a conversation【過時】聊天

jaw² *v* [I] *informal* to talk【非正式】閒談

jaw·bone /ˋdʒɔˋbon; ˈdʒɔːbəʊn/ *n* [C] one of the two big bones of the jaw, especially the lower jaw 頜骨〔尤指下頜骨〕; 顎骨 —see picture at 參見 SKELETON 圖

jaw·break·er /ˋdʒɔˏbrekɚ; ˈdʒɔːˌbreɪkə/ *n* [C] *AmE* a round hard sweet【美】圓形硬糖; GOBSTOPPER *BrE*【英】

jay /dʒe; dʒeɪ/ *n* [C] a noisy brightly-coloured European bird of the CROW[1] (1) family 樫鳥〔一種產於歐洲、羽毛豔麗的鴉屬鳥〕—see also 另見 BLUEJAY

jay·walk·ing /ˋdʒeˏwɔkɪŋ; ˈdʒeɪˌwɔːkɪŋ/ *n* [U] the act of crossing streets with traffic in a careless and dangerous way 不遵守交通規則胡亂穿越馬路 —**jaywalker** *n* [C]

jazz¹ /dʒæz; dʒæz/ *n* [U] **1** music originally played by black Americans with a strong beat and parts in which performers can play alone 爵士樂: *a jazz band* 爵士樂樂隊 **2 and all that jazz** *spoken* and things like that【口】諸如此類的東西: *I'm fed up with rules, responsibilities and all that jazz.* 我對規則、責任等諸如此類的東西感到厭煩。

jazz² *v*

jazz sth ↔ **up** *phr v* [T] *informal* to make something more attractive or exciting【非正式】使更活潑; 使更誘人: *Jazz up your everyday meals with our new range of seasonings.* 用我們新系列的調味品使你的一日三餐更有味道。—**jazzed-up** *adj*

jazz·y /ˋdʒæzɪ; ˈdʒæzi/ *adj informal*【非正式】**1** bright, colourful or very modern in appearance〔外表〕炫麗的; 花哨的: *jazzy writing paper* 色彩鮮豔的信紙 **2** in the style of jazz music 爵士樂風格的

jct the written abbreviation of 縮寫= JUNCTION

jeal·ous /ˋdʒɛləs; ˈdʒeləs/ *adj* **1** feeling angry and unhappy because someone has something that you would like; ENVIOUS 嫉妒的, 妒忌的: [+**of**] *Why are you so jealous of his success?* 你為甚麼這麼嫉妒他的成功? | **make sb jealous** *It makes me jealous, seeing all these women with babies.* 看見這些女人都有孩子, 真讓我嫉妒。**2** feeling angry and unhappy because someone you like or love is showing interest in another person, or another person is showing interest in them 吃醋的: *She gets jealous if I even look at another woman.* 我即使只看別的女人一眼, 她也會醋意大發。| **jealous husband/wife/lover** *You're acting like a jealous husband.* 你的表現就像一個愛吃醋的丈夫。**3 jealous of** wanting to keep or protect something that you have because you are proud of it〔因對某物引以自豪而〕珍惜的; 小心守護的: *a country jealous of its heritage* 珍惜其文化遺產的國家 —**jealously** *adv*: *a jealously guarded secret* 小心守着的祕密

jeal·ous·y /ˋdʒɛləsɪ; ˈdʒeləsi/ *n* [C,U] a feeling of being jealous 妒忌; 嫉妒 (之情)

jeans /dʒinz; dʒiːnz/ *n* [plural] trousers made of DENIM (=a strong, usually blue cotton cloth) 粗斜紋藍布褲, 牛仔褲

jeep, Jeep *trademark*【商標】/dʒip; dʒiːp/ *n* [C] a type of car made for travelling over rough ground 吉普車

jeer /dʒɪr; dʒɪə/ *v* [I,T] to laugh unkindly at someone to show that you strongly disapprove of them 嘲笑; 嘲弄: [+**at**] *Of course they jeered at you – you lost the game, right?* 他們當然嘲笑你——你輸了比賽, 對吧? —**jeer** *n* [C]: *hurtful jeers* 刻薄的嘲笑

jeer·ing /ˋdʒɪrɪŋ; ˈdʒɪərɪŋ/ *adj* a jeering remark or sound is unkind and shows disapproval〔說話、聲音〕不友好的; 有惡意的: *jeering laughter* 嘲笑聲 —**jeering** *n* [U] —**jeeringly** *adv*

jeez /dʒiz; dʒiːz/ *interjection AmE* used to strongly express feelings such as surprise, anger, etc【美】哎呀〔用來強烈地表示驚訝、氣憤等〕

Je·ho·vah /dʒɪˋhovə; dʒɪˈhəʊvə/ *n* a name given to God in the OLD TESTAMENT (=first part of the Bible) 耶和華〔《聖經·舊約》中對上帝的稱呼〕

Jehovah's Wit·ness /·,·· ˈ··/ *n* [C] a member of a religious organization that believes the end of the world will happen soon and sends its members to people's houses to try to make them join 耶和華見證人〔一個宗教教派的成員。該教派認為世界末日即將來臨, 並派信徒上門傳教, 試圖勸人們加入〕

je·june /dʒɪˋdʒun; dʒɪˈdʒuːn/ *adj formal*【正式】**1** ideas that are jejune are too simple〔觀點〕幼稚的: *jejune political opinions* 幼稚的政治觀點 **2** writing or speech that is jejune is boring〔文章、講話〕枯燥乏味的

Jek·yll and Hyde /ˏdʒɛkɪl ənd ˋhaɪd; ˌdʒekḷ ənd ˈhaɪd/ *n* [C] someone who is sometimes nice but at other times is unpleasant 具有善惡兩重性格的人

jell /dʒɛl; dʒel/ *v* [I] **1** also 又作 **gel** *BrE*【英】if a thought, plan etc jells, it becomes clearer or more definite〔思想、計劃等〕定形, 成形; 具體化: *Things were confused before, but they are really starting to jell now.* 情況曾經很混亂, 但現在確實開始清楚明朗了。**2** also 又作 **gel** if a liquid jells it becomes firmer, or thicker〔液體〕凝成膠狀

jel·lied /ˋdʒɛlɪd; ˈdʒelid/ *adj* [only before noun 僅用於名詞前] *especially BrE* cooked or served in jelly【尤英】煮成膠凍狀的: *jellied eels* 鱔魚凍

Jell-o, jello /ˋdʒɛlo; ˈdʒeləʊ/ *n* [U] *AmE trademark* JELLY (1)【美, 商標】果凍

jel·ly /ˋdʒɛlɪ; ˈdʒeli/ *n* **1** [C,U] *BrE* a soft solid substance made with sweetened fruit juice and GELATINE【英】果凍(甜食); JELLO *AmE*【美】: *raspberry jelly* 山莓果凍 **2** [U] *AmE* a very thick sweet substance made from boiled fruit and sugar with no pieces of fruit in it; clear JAM[1] (1)【美】〔不含水果碎粒的〕果醬; 清果醬: *a peanut butter and jelly sandwich* 花生醬果醬三明治 **3** [U] *especially BrE* a soft solid substance made from meat juices and GELATINE; ASPIC【尤英】肉凍 **4** [U] substance that is solid but very soft, and moves easily when you touch it 膠凍, 膠凍狀物: *frogs' eggs floating in a protective jelly* 在有保護作用的膠凍狀物內漂浮的青蛙卵 **5 feel like/turn to jelly** if your legs, knees etc feel like jelly, they start to shake because you are frightened or nervous〔腿、膝蓋等由於恐懼或緊張而〕開始顫抖

jelly ba·by /ˈ·· ,··/ *n* [C] *BrE trademark* a small soft sweet made in the shape of a baby in a variety of colours【英, 商標】膠糖娃娃〔一種做成娃娃形狀、有各種顏色的軟糖〕

jelly bean /ˈ·· ·/ *n* [C] a small soft sweet with different tastes and colours that is shaped like a bean 軟心豆粒糖〔有不同顏色和味道〕

jel·ly·fish /ˋdʒɛlɪˏfɪʃ; ˈdʒelifɪʃ/ *n* [C] a round transparent sea animal that sometimes stings people 水母; 海蜇

jelly roll /ˈ·· ,·/ *n* [C] *AmE* a long thin cake that is rolled up with JAM[1] (1) or cream inside【美】〔夾有果醬或奶油的〕蛋糕卷, 瑞士卷; SWISS ROLL *BrE*【英】

jem·my /ˋdʒɛmɪ; ˈdʒemi/ *BrE*【英】, **jimmy** *AmE*【美】*n* [C] a metal bar used especially by thieves to break open locked doors, windows etc〔竊賊用來撬開門窗等的〕金屬撬棍 —**jemmy** *v* [T+**open**]

je ne sais quoi /ʒɛ nə ˏse ˋkwɑ; ʒə nə seɪ ˈkwɑː/ *n French, often humorous*【法, 常幽默】**a certain je ne sais quoi** a good quality that you cannot easily describe 難以形容的好品質: *The place looks pretty old and crumbly, but it does have a certain je ne sais quoi.* 這地方看上去相當破舊, 但確實有一種難以形容的美。

jen·ny /ˋdʒɛnɪ; ˈdʒeni/ *n* [C] a SPINNING JENNY 詹尼多軸紡紗機

jeop·ar·dize also 又作 **-ise** *BrE*【英】/ˋdʒɛpɚdˏaɪz; ˈdʒepədaɪz/ *v* [T] to risk losing or spoiling something important or valuable 使〔重要或珍貴事物〕處於危險之中; 危害

jeop·ar·dy /ˈdʒɛpɚdɪ; ˈdʒepədi/ *n* **in jeopardy** in danger of being lost or harmed 在危險中〔會失去或受到危害〕: **put/place sth in jeopardy** *The killings could put the whole peace process in jeopardy.* 這些殺人事件會危及整個和平進程。

jerk[1] /dʒɝk; dʒɜːk/ *v* **1** [I,T] to pull something suddenly and roughly 急拉; 猛拉: **[+at/on]** *Don't keep jerking at the drawer, it won't open.* 不要不停地猛拉那個抽屜, 打不開的。**2** [I,T] to move or make something move in short, sudden movements (使) 顛簸行進: **jerk to a stop/halt** *Suddenly the train jerked to a halt.* 火車猛然煞車, 停了下來。

jerk sb **around** *phr v* [T] *AmE informal* to waste someone's time or deliberately make things difficult for them【美, 非正式】浪費〔某人〕時間; 故意刁難〔某人〕

jerk off *phr v* [I,T] *taboo especially AmE* to MASTURBATE【諱, 尤美】手淫

jerk out *phr v* [I,T] to say something quickly and nervously 快速而緊張地說: *I jerked out some stupid remark.* 我情急之下說了一些蠢話。

jerk[2] *n* **1** [C] a sudden quick movement 猛的一動: **with a jerk** *The train moved off with a jerk.* 火車猛地一顛開動了。| **give sth a jerk** (=pull something suddenly) 猛地一拉某物 —see also 另見 PHYSICAL JERKS **2** [C] *informal* a stupid man who does not care about the effects of his actions【非正式】〔不顧行為後果的〕蠢人; 笨蛋: *Tim's such a jerk! He always says the wrong thing.* 蒂姆是個笨蛋! 他總是說錯話。

jer·kin /ˈdʒɝkɪn; ˈdʒɜːkɪn/ *n* [C] a short jacket that covers your body but not your arms 無袖外套

jerk·wa·ter /ˈdʒɝkˌwɔtɚ; ˈdʒɜːkwɔːtə/ *adj* [only before noun 僅用於名詞前] *AmE spoken* a jerkwater place, organization etc is small and uninteresting【美口】〔地方、組織等〕無足輕重的; 小而乏味的

jerk·y[1] /ˈdʒɝkɪ; ˈdʒɜːki/ *adj* movements that are jerky are rough, with many starts and stops〔在行進中〕不平穩的; 顛簸的: *The bus came to a jerky halt.* 公共汽車顛簸着停下來。—**jerkily** *adv* —**jerkiness** *n* [U]

jerky[2] *n* [U] *AmE* meat that has been cut into thin pieces and dried in the sun or with smoke【美】〔切成薄片, 曬過或熏過的〕肉乾

jer·o·bo·am /ˌdʒɛrəˈboəm; ˌdʒerəˈbəʊəm/ *n* [C] a very large wine bottle 大酒瓶

Jer·ry /ˈdʒɛrɪ; ˈdʒeri/ *n plural* **Jerries** [C] *especially BrE* an insulting word meaning a German【尤英】德國佬〔侮辱的稱呼〕

jer·ry-built /ˈdʒɛrɪˌbɪlt; ˈdʒeribɪlt/ *adj* built cheaply, quickly, and badly 匆促草率建成的, 偷工減料蓋成的

Jer·sey /ˈdʒɝzɪ; ˈdʒɜːzi/ *n* [C] a light brown cow 澤西種乳牛

jer·sey /ˈdʒɝzɪ; ˈdʒɜːzi/ *n* **1** [C] a shirt made of soft material worn by players of sports such as football and RUGBY〔足球員、橄欖球員等穿的〕緊身運動套衫 **2** [C] a piece of clothing made of wool that covers the upper part of your body and your arms; SWEATER 毛衣, 套頭毛衣 **3** [U] a soft material made of cotton or wool 棉[毛]質的柔軟衣料

Je·ru·sa·lem ar·ti·choke /dʒəˌrusələm ˈɑrtɪtʃok; dʒəˌruːsələm ˈɑːtɪtʃəʊk/ *n* [C] an ARTICHOKE (2) 菊芋 —see picture on page A9 參見 A9 頁圖

jest[1] /dʒɛst; dʒest/ *n* **1 in jest** something you say in jest is intended to be funny, not serious〔說話〕開玩笑地 **2** [C] *old-fashioned* something that you say or do to amuse people; joke【過時】笑話; 玩笑

jest[2] *v* [I+about] *old use* to say things that you do not really mean in order to amuse people【舊】說笑話; 開玩笑: **I jest!** *spoken* (=used to say that you are joking)【口】我是說着玩的! —**jestingly** *adv*

jest·er /ˈdʒɛstɚ; ˈdʒestə/ *n* [C] a man employed in the past by a king or ruler to entertain people with jokes, stories etc〔昔時為國王或統治者說笑逗樂的〕弄臣

Je·su·it /ˈdʒɛʒuɪt; ˈdʒezjuɪt/ *n* [C] a man who is a member of the Roman Catholic religious Society of Jesus 天主教耶穌會會士

Je·sus[1] /ˈdʒizəs; ˈdʒiːzəs/ also 又作 **Jesus Christ** /ˌ·· ˈ·/ *n* the person who Christians believe was the son of God, and whose life and teachings Christianity is based on 耶穌〔基督徒認為他是上帝的兒子, 他的生平和傳教活動是基督教信仰的基礎〕

Jesus[2] *interjection slang* used to express anger or surprise【俚】天啊〔用來表示憤怒或驚訝〕: *Oh Jesus! What are we going to do?* 哦, 天啊! 我們該怎麼辦?

USAGE NOTE 用法說明: JESUS

FORMALITY AND POLITENESS 正式程度與禮貌程度

Jesus!, **Christ!** and **Jesus Christ!** are all used in a non-religious way in very informal spoken English. They have the same uses as **God!**, but are even stronger. Jesus!, Christ! 和 Jesus Christ! 都以非宗教意義用於非正式的口語中, 用法與 God! 相同, 但語氣更強: *Jesus, that hurts.* 哎呀, 太痛了。| *Jesus! What are you going to live on?* 天啊! 你打算靠甚麼生活?

Some people, especially those who believe in the Christian religion, are offended by these uses of these words. 有些人, 特別是信仰基督教的人, 對這些詞用作感嘆詞感到反感。

jet[1] /dʒɛt; dʒet/ *n* **1** [C] an aircraft with a jet engine 噴氣式飛機: **jet fighter/aircraft** *British jet fighters have joined the UN forces.* 英國的噴氣式戰鬥機已加入聯合國部隊。**2** [C] a narrow stream of liquid or gas that comes quickly out of a small hole, or the hole itself〔液體、氣體的〕噴射流: *a water jet* 水柱 **3** [U] a hard black stone that is used for making jewellery 煤玉, 黑玉

jet[2] *v* **jetted, jetting** [I always+adv/prep] **1** *informal* to travel by plane, especially when you go to many different places【非正式】坐飛機旅行〔尤指去很多不同的地方〕: *business executives jetting around the world* 坐飛機周遊世界的企業行政人員 **2** if a liquid or gas jets out from somewhere, it comes quickly out of a small hole〔液體、氣體〕噴射, 噴出

jet-black /ˌ· ˈ·◂/ *adj* very dark black 烏黑的: *jet-black hair* 烏黑的頭髮

jet en·gine /ˌ· ˈ··/ *n* [C] an engine that pushes out a stream of hot air and gases behind it, used in aircraft 噴氣發動機 —see picture at 參見 AIRCRAFT 圖

jet foil /ˈ· ·/ *n* [C] a boat that rises out of the water on structures that look like legs when it is travelling fast 噴流水翼船

jet lag /ˈ· ·/ *n* [U] the tired and confused feeling that you can get after flying a very long distance 飛行時差綜合症 —**jet-lagged** *adj*

jet-pro·pelled /ˌ· ·ˈ·◂/ *adj* using a jet engine for power 噴氣發動機推進的

jet pro·pul·sion /ˌ· ·ˈ··/ *n* [U] the use of a JET ENGINE for power 噴氣推進

jet·sam /ˈdʒɛtsəm; ˈdʒetsəm/ *n* [U] things that are thrown from a ship and float on the sea towards the shore〔漂浮至岸邊的〕從船上投進海裡的物品 —see also 另見 **flotsam and jetsam** (FLOTSAM (2))

jet set /ˈ· ·/ *n* **the jet set** *old-fashioned* rich and fashionable people who travel a lot【過時】常乘飛機旅行又時髦的有錢階層 —**jet-setter** *n* [C]

jet-ski /ˈ· ·/ *n* [C] a small fast boat that one or two people can ride on for fun〔供一人或兩人乘坐遊玩的〕噴氣式滑水橇

jet stream /ˈ· ·/ *n* [singular,U] a current of very strong winds high above the Earth's surface〔地球高空上的〕急流

jet·ti·son /ˈdʒɛtəsn̩; ˈdʒetɪsən/ *v* [T] **1** to get rid of methods, ideas, or ways of doing things 除掉, 擺脫〔做

事的方法、想法或方式〕: *The new President quickly jettisoned most of the previous economic policies.* 新上任的總統很快便廢除了大部分舊有的經濟政策。**2** to throw things away, especially from a moving plane or ship〔尤指從正在行進中的飛機或船上〕拋出〔物品〕, 丟棄

jet·ty /ˈdʒɛtɪ; ˈdʒeti/ *n* [C] a wide wall or flat area built out into the water, used for getting on and off ships 突堤; 碼頭 —compare 比較 PIER (1) —see picture on page A12 參見A12頁圖

Jew /dʒu; dʒuː/ *n* [C] a member of the group of people whose religion is Judaism, who lived in ancient times in the land of Israel, some of whom now live in the modern state of Israel and others in various countries throughout the world 猶太人; 猶太教徒〔古時猶太人居住在以色列地, 現在他們中有的住在現代的以色列國, 還有許多人散居在世界各地〕—**Jewish** *adj*: *the Jewish religion* 猶太教 | *My husband is Jewish.* 我丈夫是猶太人。

jew·el /ˈdʒuəl; ˈdʒuːəl/ *n* [C] **1** a small valuable stone, such as a diamond 寶石 **2 jewels** [plural] jewellery or decorative objects made with valuable stones 寶石飾物; 首飾 **3** a very small stone used in the machinery of a watch〔鐘錶內的〕寶石軸承; 鑽 **4** *informal* someone who is very important to you, or the best things in a group of things【非正式】寶貴的人[物品]; 珍寶: *The Matisse was the jewel of her art collection.* 馬蒂斯的畫是她的藝術品收藏中的珍品。**5 the jewel in the crown** the best or most valuable part of something 皇冠上的珠寶〔指某物最好或最有價值的部分〕—see also 另見 CROWN JEWELS

jew·elled *BrE*【英】, **jeweled** *AmE*【美】/ˈdʒuəld; ˈdʒuːəld/ *adj* decorated with jewels 鑲有寶石的: *the famous jewelled eggs of Fabergé* 著名的鑲有寶石的法貝熱復活節彩蛋

jew·el·ler *BrE*【英】, **jeweler** *AmE*【美】/ˈdʒuələ˞; ˈdʒuːələ/ *n* [C] **1** someone who owns or works in a shop that sells jewellery 珠寶商; 寶石商 **2** someone who makes or repairs jewellery 寶石匠

jewellery 珠寶, 首飾

earrings 耳環

sleeper 耳環圈

stud 耳釘

clip-on 夾式耳環

necklace 項鏈

bracelet 手鐲

ring 戒指

3 **jew·el·lery** *BrE*【英】, **jewelry** *AmE*【美】/ˈdʒuəlrɪ; ˈdʒuːəlri/ *n* [U] small things that you wear for decoration, such as rings or NECKLACES 珠寶, 首飾: *a piece of jewellery* 一件首飾 —see also 另見 COSTUME JEWELLERY

Jew·ess /ˈdʒuɪs; ˈdʒuːɪs/ *n* [C] *old-fashioned* a word meaning a Jewish woman, now usually considered offensive【過時】猶太女人〔此詞現在一般視為具有冒犯性〕

Jew·ry /ˈdʒurɪ; ˈdʒuːri/ *n* [U] *old use* the Jewish people【舊】猶太人

Jez·e·bel /ˈdʒɛzəbl̩; ˈdʒezəbəl/ *n* [C] *old use* a sexually immoral woman【舊】蕩婦

jib[1] /dʒɪb; dʒɪb/ *n* [C] **1** a small sail 艏三角帆, 小帆 —compare 比較 MAINSAIL —see picture at 參見 YACHT 圖 **2** the long part of a CRANE[1] (1)〔起重機的〕懸臂

jib[2] *v* **jibbed, jibbing** [I] if a horse jibs, it stops suddenly and will not move〔馬〕突然停步, 不肯走動

jib at sth *phr v* [T] *especially BrE informal* to become suddenly unwilling to do or accept something【尤英, 非正式】突然不肯做[接受]〔某事〕: *If he jibbed at five hundred pounds, he'll hardly pay four thousand!* 他如果連五百英鎊都不肯付, 就更別說四千英鎊了!

jibe[1], **gibe** /dʒaɪb; dʒaɪb/ *n* [C] an unkind remark intended to make someone seem silly 嘲諷的話: *She was tired of his constant jibes.* 她受夠了他沒完沒了的挖苦。

jibe[2] *v* [I+with] *AmE* if two statements, reports etc jibe, the information in them matches【美】〔兩個陳述、報告等〕相一致, 符合

jibe at sb/sth *phr v* [T] to say something that is intended to make someone seem silly 嘲諷, 挖苦

jif·fy /ˈdʒɪfɪ; ˈdʒɪfi/ also 又作 **jiff** /dʒɪf; dʒɪf/ *n* [singular] *spoken*【口】**in a jiffy** very soon 很快; 一會兒: *I'll be with you in a jiffy.* 我很快就來你這兒。

Jiffy bag /ˈ·· ·/ *n* [C] *BrE trademark* a thick soft envelope, used for posting things that might break【英, 商標】〔供郵寄易碎物品用的〕有襯墊的大封套

jig[1] /dʒɪg; dʒɪg/ *n* [C] a type of quick dance, or a piece of music for this dance 吉格舞(曲)〔一種輕快的舞蹈或為這種舞蹈伴奏的樂曲〕

jig[2] *v* **jigged, jigging 1** [I] to dance a jig 跳吉格舞 **2** [I always+adv/prep] to move up and down with quick short movements 上下急動; 蹦跳

jig·ger /ˈdʒɪgə˞; ˈdʒɪgə/ *n* [C] a small amount of alcoholic drink, or the cup this is measured with 少量的酒; 量酒的小杯

jig·gered /ˈdʒɪgə˞d; ˈdʒɪgəd/ *adj* [not before noun 不用於名詞前] *BrE old-fashioned*【英, 過時】**I'll be jiggered!** used when you are very surprised 我感到吃驚!〔表示非常驚奇〕

jig·ger·y-po·ker·y /ˌdʒɪgərɪ ˈpokərɪ; ˌdʒɪgəri ˈpəʊkəri/ *n* [U] *BrE informal* secret dishonest activity to make something seem what it is not【英, 非正式】詐騙; 騙局: *social jiggery-pokery behind the scenes* 幕後的卑鄙社交勾當

jig·gle /ˈdʒɪgl̩; ˈdʒɪgəl/ *v* **jiggled, jiggling** [I,T] to move or make something move from side to side with short quick movements (使)急速地左右擺動

jigsaw 拼圖玩具

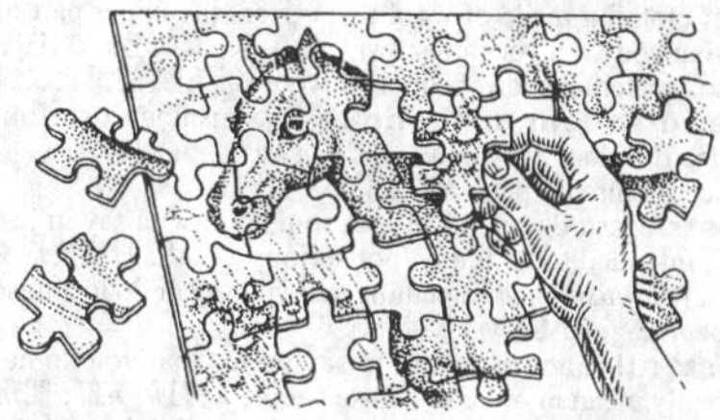

jig·saw /ˈdʒɪgˌsɔ; ˈdʒɪgsɔː/ *n* [C] **1** also 又作 **jigsaw puz·zle** /ˈ·· ˌ··/ a picture cut up into many pieces that you try to fit together 拼圖玩具 **2** a special SAW (=cutting tool) for cutting out shapes in thin pieces of wood 線

鋸, 鏤花鋸 —see picture at 參見 TOOL[1] 圖

ji·had /dʒɪˋhɑd; dʒɪˈhɑːd/ *n* [C] a holy war fought by Muslims〔伊斯蘭教的〕聖戰

jilt /dʒɪlt; dʒɪlt/ *v* [T] to end a relationship with someone 拋棄〔情人〕, 和…分手

Jim Crow /ˌdʒɪm ˋkro; ˌdʒɪm ˈkrəʊ/ *n AmE* a system of laws and practices in the US that separated black and white people【美】〔美國的〕歧視黑人的法律[做法]

jim·my /ˋdʒɪmɪ; ˈdʒɪmi/ *n* [C] the American form of the word JEMMY jemmy 的美式拼寫 —**jimmy** *v* [T]

jin·gle[1] /ˋdʒɪŋgl; ˈdʒɪŋgəl/ *v* **jingled, jingling** [I,T] to shake metal things together so that they make a sound like small bells 使〔金屬物件〕發出叮噹聲: *Stop jingling those coins in your pocket.* 別把口袋裡的硬幣弄得叮噹作響。

jingle[2] *n* **1** [C] a short song used in advertisements〔廣告中的〕短歌 **2** [singular] the sound of small metal objects being shaken together〔小金屬物件撞擊發出的〕叮噹聲 —see picture on page A19 參見 A19 頁圖

jin·go·is·m /ˋdʒɪŋgoɪzəm; ˈdʒɪŋgəʊɪzəm/ *n* [U] a strong belief that your own country is better than others 沙文主義; 極端愛國主義: *a mood of warlike jingoism* 好戰的沙文主義情緒 —**jingoistic** /ˌdʒɪŋgoˋɪstɪk; ˌdʒɪŋgəʊˈɪstɪk◂/ *adj*

jinks /dʒɪŋks; dʒɪŋks/ *n* —see 見 HIGH JINKS

jinn /dʒɪn; dʒɪn/ *n* [C] a GENIE 妖魔, 精靈

jinx /dʒɪŋks; dʒɪŋks/ *n* [singular] a strange power that brings bad luck 不祥之物: **[+on]** *So many things have gone wrong, we're beginning to think there's a jinx on the whole wedding.* 那麼多事情不對頭, 我們開始認為整個婚禮交了噩運。

jinxed /dʒɪŋkst; dʒɪŋkst/ *adj* often having bad luck, or making people have bad luck 倒霉的; 帶來噩運的

jit·ter·bug /ˋdʒɪtɚˌbʌg; ˈdʒɪtəbʌg/ *n* [singular] a popular fast JAZZ dance in the 1940s 吉特巴舞〔一種20世紀40年代流行的快節奏爵士舞〕

jit·ters /ˋdʒɪtɚz; ˈdʒɪtəz/ *n* **get the jitters** *informal* to feel anxious, especially before an important event or before something difficult【非正式】〔尤指在重大或困難事件發生之前〕感到緊張[恐慌]: *It's my driving test next week, and I've got the jitters already.* 下週我要參加駕駛考試, 我現在已經感到很緊張了。

jit·ter·y /ˋdʒɪtərɪ; ˈdʒɪtəri/ *adj informal* anxious or nervous【非正式】焦慮的; 緊張的

jive[1] /dʒaɪv; dʒaɪv/ *n* [C] **1** a very fast dance, popular especially in the 1930s and 40s, performed to SWING[2] (5) music〔尤其流行於20世紀30和40年代, 伴隨搖擺樂跳的快節奏〕搖擺舞 **2** [U] *AmE informal* statements that you do not believe are true【美, 非正式】假話; 花言巧語: *Don't give me any of that jive!* 別對我花言巧語!

jive[2] *v* **1** [I] to dance a jive 跳搖擺舞 **2** [T] *AmE informal* to try to make someone believe something that is not true, as a joke【美, 非正式】胡扯; 開玩笑, 愚弄

Jnr *adj BrE*【英】the written abbreviation of 縮寫= JUNIOR

Job /dʒob; dʒəʊb/ *n* **1 Job's comforter** someone who tries to make you feel more cheerful, but actually makes you feel worse 反讓人更難過的安慰者 **2 have the patience of Job** to be extremely patient 極有耐心

1 1

job /dʒɑb; dʒɒb/ *n*

① WORK 工作
② STH YOU MUST DO 責任, 義務
③ DO STH WELL/BADLY 幹得好/幹得差
④ COMPUTERS 電腦
⑤ CRIME 罪行
⑥ OTHER MEANINGS 其他意思

① WORK 工作

1 [C] the regular paid work that you do for an employer 工作; 職位; 職業: **get/find a job (as sth)** *Eventually, Mary got a job as a waitress.* 瑪麗終於找到了一份服務員的工作。| **take a job** (=accept a job that is offered to you) 接受一份工作 *I was so desperate that I took the first job that came along.* 我求職心切, 第一份出現的工作就接受了。| **lose a job** *At least there's no danger of you losing your job.* 你至少沒有失業的危險。| **temporary/permanent job** *It's a temporary job, but I'm hoping it'll be made permanent.* 那是份臨時工作, 但我希望能成為固定的。| **offer (sb) a job** *Well, Ms Taylor, we'd like to offer you the job.* 嗯, 泰勒女士, 我們想聘請你。| **part-time/full-time job** (=a job you do for only part of the day or week, or all of the day or week) 兼職/全職工作 | **apply for a job** (=try to get a job) 申請工作 *I've applied for a job at the university.* 我申請了一份在大學裡的工作。| **job satisfaction** (=the enjoyment that you get from doing your job) 工作滿足感 | **leave/quit a job** *Oh Rick, you didn't quit your job, did you?* 里克, 你沒把工作辭掉吧? | **change jobs** (=get a different job) 轉換工作 | **hold down a job** (=keep a job) 保住工作 | **job security** (=how permanent your job is likely to be) 就業保障〔指職位的固定性如何〕| **Saturday/summer/holiday job** (=a job that you only do on Saturdays etc) 在星期六/暑期/假日做的工作 | **steady job** (=a job that is likely to continue) 穩定的工作 | **be out of a job** (=not have a job) 失業 *If the project fails we'll all be out of a job.* 如果計劃失敗, 我們都將失業。| **know your job** (=be very experienced at the work you do) 對自己的工作很內行 | **job losses** *Four hundred more job losses were announced this week.* 本週宣布再有四百人失業。—see also 另見 JOB DESCRIPTION

2 on the job a) as part of a particular job 作為工作的一部分: *Most clerical training is done on the job.* 大部分文書培訓都是在職進行的。**b)** doing a particular job 從事某種工作: *We'll put our best people on the job.* 我們會安排最優秀的人做這項工作。**c)** *BrE spoken* having sex【英口】在性交時

3 I'm only doing my job *spoken* used to say that it is not your fault if you have to do something in your work that other people do not like【口】我只是在做我的工作〔用來表示你所做的事情雖然有人不喜歡, 但那屬於你的職責範圍, 並非你的過錯〕

4 it's more than my job's worth *BrE spoken* used to tell someone that you cannot do what they want because it is against your company's rules【英口】我的職位會保不住〔用於告訴某人你不能按照他們的意願做事, 因為那違反了公司的規章〕

5 jobs for the boys *BrE* work that someone in power has given to their friends, especially work that is not necessary【英】〔當權者〕給自己人安排的職位〔尤指沒有必要的職位〕

② STH YOU MUST DO 責任, 義務

6 [C] something that you have to do which involves working or making an effort 費勁的事: *Fixing the roof is going to be the biggest job.* 修繕屋頂將是一件最大的工作。| **odd jobs** (=small things that need to be done, especially in the house or garden)〔尤指房子或花園裡的〕雜活 | **get on with a job** (=continue doing a job) 繼續工作 | **the job in hand** (=the work that you are doing now) 手頭的工作

7 ▶DUTY 責任◀ [singular] if it is your job to do some-

J

thing, it is your duty to do it 職責; 責任: *Leave the dishes – that's my job.* 盤碟留給我, 那是我的工作。| **it is sb's job (to do sth)** *It's my job to make sure that the work's finished on time.* 確保工作按時完成是我的責任。

8 fall down on the job to fail to do something you were supposed to do 未能完成該做的事

9 a job of work *BrE old-fashioned* something that you have to do, whether you enjoy it or not【英, 過時】〔無論是否喜歡〕非做不可的事

③ DO STH WELL/BADLY 幹得好/幹得差

10 do a good/great/marvellous job (with) to do something very well 幹得很好: *You've done a great job raising your kids.* 你在培養孩子方面幹得十分出色。

11 make a good/bad job of sth *BrE* to do something well or badly【英】把某事做好/做壞: *Sarah made a really good job of that presentation.* 莎拉的那個報告真是精彩。

12 do the job *informal* if something does the job, it is effective in doing what you want it to do【非正式】〔某物〕管用: *That little screwdriver should do the job.* 那把小螺絲刀應該管用。

13 Good job! *AmE spoken* used to tell someone they have done something well【美口】幹得好!〔稱讚某人做事出色〕

④ COMPUTERS 電腦

14 [C] an action done by a computer (一件) 工作, 作業

⑤ CRIME 罪行

15 [C] *informal* a crime in which money is stolen from a bank, company etc【非正式】〔從銀行、公司等〕盜竊: *a bank job* 搶劫銀行 | **an inside job** (=one done by a member of the organization in which it happens) 內賊作案; 監守自盜

⑥ OTHER MEANINGS 其他意思

16 it's a good job *BrE spoken* used to say that it is lucky that something happened【英口】真幸運〔用來表示幸虧做了某事〕: *It's a good job you had your safety belt on.* 幸好你繫了安全帶。

17 have a job doing/to do sth *BrE spoken* to have difficulty doing something【英口】做某事很困難: *I had an awful job getting that stain out.* 我費了好大勁才把那污漬去掉。

18 make the best of a bad job *especially BrE* to do the best that you can in a situation that you do not like but cannot change【尤英】〔在不喜歡但無法改變的情況下〕盡力而為

19 give sth up as a bad job *BrE* to accept that something is not going to succeed and stop trying to do it【英】因感到無望而放棄做某事

20 just the job *BrE spoken* exactly what is needed for a particular situation【英口】正是需要的東西: *That table you gave us was just the job!* 你給我們的那張桌子正合我們需要!

21 ►KIND OF THING 某種東西◄ *spoken* used to say that something is of a particular type【口】〔用來說明某物屬於某類型〕: *Jack's got a new car – a red two-seater job.* 傑克買了一輛新車, 是紅色兩個座位的那種。

22 a job lot *BrE* a mixed group of things that are sold together【英】混合出售的一批物品: *a job lot of furniture* 混雜出售的一批家具 —see also 另見 BLOW JOB, HAND JOB, NOSE JOB

USAGE NOTE 用法說明: JOB

WORD CHOICE 詞語辨析: **job, work, post, position, line of work/business, do, occupation, trade, profession, vocation, career**

What you do to earn your living is your **job** [C], especially if you work for someone else. job〔可數名詞〕指謀生的工作, 尤指為他人所雇: *I need a part-time job.* 我需要一份兼職工作。| *a boring job delivering pizzas* 外送意大利薄餅的乏味工作

Work [U] is something you are paid for doing, especially regularly. work〔不可數名詞〕指有報酬的工作, 尤指固定工作: *She wants to return to work after having the baby.* 她想生完孩子後繼續工作。But it can also be used where there is no payment or you are not working for someone else. 但也可指無報酬的工作, 或不為他人雇用: *voluntary work* 志願工作 | *housework* 家務 | *her work as a self-employed trainer* 她當自雇教練

Post and **position** are more formal words for a particular job in a company etc. post 和 position 是較為正式的用語, 指在公司等機構裡某個專門的職位: *He was appointed to the post/position of professor of English at Stanford University.* 他被聘任為史丹福大學的英語教授。

In spoken English, the kind of work or job someone does may be called their **line of work/business**, or the verb **do** is often used, especially in questions. 口語中, 某人從事的行業可稱為 line of work/business. 動詞 do 也很常用, 尤其用於問句: *What do you do?* 你是做甚麼工作的? | *I'd like to get into that line of work!* 我想從事那種職業!

More formally, your kind of work or job is your **occupation** [C]. occupation〔可數名詞〕表示所從事的職業, 是更正式的用語。On a form you might see 在申請表中可能看到: *Please state your name and occupation.* 請填寫你的姓名和職業。

A **trade** is a skilled kind of work in which you make or do things with your hands. trade 指有專門技術的手工行業: *She's an electrician by trade.* 她的職業是電工。

A **profession** is a kind of work such as that of a doctor or lawyer, for which you need special training and a good education. Some **professions**, such as teaching and nursing, are also called **vocations**, which suggests that people do them in order to help others rather than to earn a lot of money. profession 指需要受過特殊訓練和良好教育的工作, 如醫生和律師。一些旨在幫助他人, 而不是為了掙錢的職業, 如教書和護理, 也可稱作 vocation。

A **career** is a type of work that you do or hope to do for most of your life. career 指終生從事的事業: *Her political career began 20 years ago.* 她的政治生涯始於 20 年前。

This graph shows some of the words most commonly used with the noun **job**. 本圖表所示為含有名詞 job 的一些最常用詞組。

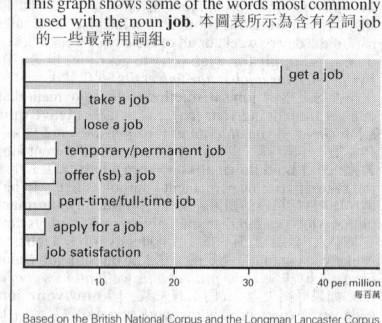

Based on the British National Corpus and the Longman Lancaster Corpus
據英國國家語料庫和朗文蘭卡斯特語料庫

job·ber /ˋdʒɑbɚ; ˈdʒɒbə/ *n* [C] *especially BrE* someone whose job is buying and selling stocks (STOCK[1] (3)) and shares (SHARE[2] (5))【尤英】證券[股票]經紀人

job·bing /ˋdʒɑbɪŋ; ˈdʒɒbɪŋ/ *adj BrE*【英】**jobbing gardener/painter etc** someone who does small pieces of work for different people 打零工的園丁/漆匠等

job cen·tre /ˈ· ˌ··/ *n* [C] a British government service where jobs are advertised and training courses are provided for people who are looking for work〔英國政府的〕就業服務中心

job de·scrip·tion /ˈ· ·ˌ··/ *n* [C] an official list of the work and responsibilities that you have in your job〔正式的〕工作職責說明

job·less /ˋdʒɑblɪs; ˈdʒɒbləs/ *adj* without a job; UNEMPLOYED[1] 無業的; 失業的

job-shar·ing /ˈ· ˌ··/ *n* [U] an arrangement by which two people both work PART-TIME doing the same job 職位共享〔兩人分擔一份全職工作〕—**job-share** *n* [C]

jobs·worth /ˋdʒɑbzwɝθ; ˈdʒɒbzwɜːθ/ *n* [C] *BrE informal* someone who follows the rules of their job too exactly without using any imagination【英, 非正式】工作中墨守成規的人, 工作死板的人

jock /dʒɑk; dʒɒk/ *n* [C] **1** *BrE informal* an insulting word for someone from Scotland【英, 非正式】蘇格蘭佬〔侮辱的稱呼〕**2** *AmE informal* an insulting word for someone who does a lot of sport【美, 非正式】運動員〔對酷愛運動的人的侮辱性稱呼〕

jock·ey[1] /ˋdʒɑkɪ; ˈdʒɒki/ *n* [C] someone who rides horses in races 賽馬騎師

jockey[2] *v* **1 jockey for position** to try to get into the best position or situation 爭取最有利的位置: *businessmen jockeying for position at the bar* 搶佔酒吧最好位置的商人 **2** [T] to gradually persuade someone to do something 逐漸說服〔某人做某事〕; 誘使: **jockey sb into doing sth** *Do you think you can jockey them into accepting our offer?* 你覺得你能說服他們接受我們的提議嗎?

jockey shorts /ˈ·· ·/ *n* [plural] *trademark* a type of men's cotton underwear that fits very tightly【商標】喬基褲〔一種男式棉質緊身內褲〕

jock·strap /ˋdʒɑkˌstræp; ˈdʒɒkstræp/ *n* [C] a piece of men's underwear that supports their sex organs during sport〔男人運動時用的〕下體護身帶

jo·cose /dʒoˋkos; dʒəˈkəʊs/ *adj literary* joking【文】開玩笑的 —**jocosely** *adv* —**jocoseness, jocosity** /dʒoˋkɑsətɪ; dʒəˈkɒsɪ̣ti/ *n* [U]

joc·u·lar /ˋdʒɑkjələ; ˈdʒɒkjʊ̈lə/ *adj formal* joking or humorous【正式】開玩笑的; 幽默的: *jocular remarks* 詼諧幽默的話 —**jocularly** *adv* —**jocularity** /ˌdʒɑkjəˋlærətɪ; ˌdʒɒkjʊ̈ˈlærɪ̣ti/ *n* [U]

joc·und /ˋdʒɑkənd; ˈdʒɒkənd/ *adj literary* cheerful and happy【文】愉快的; 歡樂的 —**jocundly** *adv* —**jocundity** /dʒoˋkʌndətɪ; dʒəʊˈkʌndɪ̣ti/ *n* [U]

jodh·purs /ˋdʒɑdpɚz; ˈdʒɒdpəz/ *n* [plural] a special type of trousers that you wear when riding horses 馬褲

Joe Bloggs /ˌdʒo ˋblɑgz; ˌdʒəʊ ˈblɒgz/ *BrE*【英】, **Joe Blow/Schmo** /-ˋblo, -ˋʃmo; -ˈbləʊ, -ˈʃməʊ/ *AmE*【美】*n* [singular] *spoken* the ordinary average person【口】普通人, 常人

jog[1] /dʒɑg; dʒɒg/ *v* **jogged, jogging 1** [I] to run slowly and steadily, especially as a way of exercising〔尤指為鍛鍊身體而〕慢跑: *two figures jogging along the beach* 沿海灘慢跑的兩個人 **2** [T] to knock or push something lightly by mistake〔非故意〕輕碰, 輕推: *You jogged my elbow.* 你輕輕碰了一下我的肘部。**3 jog sb's memory** to make someone remember something 使某人記起某事: *Perhaps this photo will help to jog your memory.* 也許這張照片能幫助你回憶。

jog along *phr v* [I] *informal* to continue in the same way as usual【非正式】如常進行, 照舊繼續

jog[2] *n* [singular] **1** a slow steady run, especially done as a way of exercising〔尤指為鍛鍊身體而進行的〕慢跑: **go for a jog** *Mike goes for a two-mile jog every morning.* 邁克每天早上慢跑兩英里。**2** a light knock or push done by accident〔意外地〕輕碰, 輕推

jog·ger /ˋdʒɑgɚ; ˈdʒɒgə/ *n* [C] someone who runs slowly and steadily as a way of exercising〔健身鍛鍊的〕慢跑者

jog·ging /ˋdʒɑgɪŋ; ˈdʒɒgɪŋ/ *n* [U] the activity of running slowly and steadily as a way of exercising〔作為健身鍛鍊的〕慢跑

jogging suit /ˈ·· ·/ *n* [C] loose thick cotton clothes that you wear when you are running for exercise〔寬鬆厚身的棉質〕慢跑運動服

jog·gle /ˋdʒɑgl; ˈdʒɒgəl/ *v* [I,T] *informal* to shake or move up and down slightly【非正式】〔上下〕輕微搖晃

jog trot /ˈ· ·/ *n* [singular] a slow steady run 小跑; 慢跑 —**jog-trot** *v* [I]

john /dʒɑn; dʒɒn/ *n* [C] *AmE*【美】**1** *informal* a toilet【非正式】衛生間, 廁所 **2** *slang* the customer of a PROSTITUTE【俚】嫖客

John Bull /ˌ· ˈ·/ *n old-fashioned*【過時】**1** [U] England or the English people 英國; 英國人 **2** [C] an insulting word for an Englishman, especially one who does not like foreigners〔尤指不喜歡外國人的〕英國佬〔侮辱性稱呼〕

John Doe /ˌ· ˈ·/ *n* [singular] *AmE* a man whose name is not known, especially one who is involved in a law case【美】某甲, 某男〔尤指訴訟程序中對不知真實姓名的男當事人的稱呼〕—compare 比較 JANE DOE

John Han·cock /ˌdʒɑn ˋhænkɑk; ˌdʒɒn ˈhænkɒk/ *n* [C] *AmE informal* your signature【美, 非正式】親筆簽名

john·ny /ˋdʒɑnɪ; ˈdʒɒni/ *n* [C] **1** *BrE slang* a CONDOM【英俚】避孕套 **2** *old-fashioned* a man【過時】男人 **3** *AmE slang* a PENIS【美俚】陰莖

Johnny-on-the-spot /ˌ·· · · ˈ·/ *n* [singular] *AmE informal* someone who immediately offers to help, takes an opportunity etc【美, 非正式】隨時提供幫忙的人; 隨時利用機會的人

johns /dʒɑnz; dʒɒnz/ *n* [plural] —see 見 LONG JOHNS

john thom·as /ˌdʒɑn ˋtɑməs; ˌdʒɒn ˈtɒməs/ *n* [C] *slang* a PENIS【俚】陰莖

joie de viv·re /ˌʒwɑ də ˋvivr; ˌʒwɑː də ˈviːvrə/ *n* [U] *French* a feeling of pleasure and excitement because you are alive【法】〔由於活着而產生的〕快樂興奮

join[1] /dʒɔɪn; dʒɔɪn/ *v* S1 W1

1 ►CONNECT 連接◄ **a)** [T] to connect or fasten things together 連接, 接合; 連結: *Join the two pieces of wood with strong glue.* 用強力膠水把兩塊木頭黏合起來。| *The hip bone is joined to the thigh bone.* 髖骨和股骨相連。**b)** [I,T] to come together and become connected 匯合, 聚合: *Where does the river join the sea?* 這條河在甚麼地方入海?

2 ►GROUP/ORGANIZATION 羣體/組織◄ [T] to become a member of an organization, society, or group 成為…的一員, 加入, 加盟: *When did you join the Labour party?* 你何時加入工黨的? | *Woods joined the Daily Dispatch as a reporter in 1960.* 伍茲於 1960 年進入《每日快報》當記者。

3 ►ACTIVITY 活動◄ [T] to begin to take part in an activity that other people are involved in 參加〔活動〕: **join a course/class/scheme etc** *I joined the class halfway through the second term.* 我在第二個學期中途插入這個班。| *Church leaders have joined the campaign to end foxhunting.* 教會領袖參加了禁止捕獵狐狸的運動。

4 join a queue/line/row etc to go and stand at the end of a line of people 排隊: *Meanwhile, Carl joined the queue for tickets.* 同時, 卡爾排隊買票。

5 join sb (for sth) to meet someone in order to do something together 與某人作伴(做某事): *I'm going to the theatre tonight. Would you care to join me?* 我今晚去劇院, 你願意一起去嗎?

6 join sb in doing sth to do or say something together

with someone else 與某人一起説[做]某事: *I'm sure you'll all join me in thanking today's speaker.* 我相信你們都會和我一起感謝今天的演講者。
7 join hands if people join hands, they hold each other's hands 攜手
8 join the club! *spoken* used to say that you and a lot of other people are in the same situation【口】大家都一樣!〔指你和其他許多人的境況一樣〕: *"I can't find a job at all." "Yeah? Join the club!"* "我根本找不到工作。" "是嗎? 我們都一樣!"
9 join battle *formal* to begin fighting【正式】開始交戰
10 be joined in marriage/holy matrimony *formal* to be married【正式】結婚, 結成夫婦 —see also 另見 **join/combine forces** (FORCE[1] (7)), **if you can't beat 'em, join 'em** (BEAT[1] (20))

join in *phr v* [I,T] to take part in an activity as one of a group of people 參加〔活動〕; 加入進來: *Come on, Ian, join in! You can sing!* 伊恩, 你也來! 你會唱歌! | **join in the fun/party** *We couldn't wait to join in the fun.* 我們迫不及待地參加進去一起玩。

join up *phr v* [I] to become a member of the army, navy, or airforce 從軍

join up with sb/sth *phr v* [T] *informal* to combine with other people in order to do something【非正式】與〔某人〕結夥〔幹某事〕: *We joined up with a couple from Derbyshire to make a quiz team.* 我們和德比郡的一對夫婦組成一個問答比賽小組。

join with sb *phr v* [T] *formal* to do or say something together, as a group【正式】與…一同做[説]: **join with sb in doing sth** *Please join with me in praying for Sarah's recovery.* 請和我一起祈禱莎拉早日康復。

USAGE NOTE 用法説明: JOIN
WORD CHOICE 詞語辨析: **join, enrol(l) in/at, enlist in, go to, come to, attend, join in, participate in**

If you go to be with someone, you **join** them. join 指和某人在一起: *He was looking forward to joining his wife/family in Detroit* (NOT 不用 *joining with them*). 他盼望着在底特律與妻子/家人團聚。

You may also **join** (=become a member of) many kinds of groups of people, such as a club, a team, a political party, a tour group, a company, a church, or a congregation (NOT 不用 *join in*). A country may **join** the EU, the UN, or another international organization. join 還可指加入各種各樣的團體, 如俱樂部、隊伍、政黨、旅遊團、公司、教會、教堂會眾等。一個國家可以加入歐盟、聯合國或其他國際組織。

You may **join** the army, navy etc or more formally **enlist in** it. You **go to** war (NOT 不用 *join* it). 可以用 join 指參加軍隊〔陸軍、海軍等〕, 更正式的説法是 enlist in。"參軍打仗" 是 go to war。

You may **join** a class, course, or university at the beginning, but the more official word is **enrol in/at** (*AmE* **enroll**). join 可表示在開學時加入一個班、修讀一個課程或入讀大學, 但更正式的用語是 enrol in/at〔美 enroll〕: *I want to enrol in/join the linguistics class* (NOT 不用 *join to*). 我想上語言學的課。| *Diane has enrolled at the University of Essex.* 黛安入讀了埃塞克斯大學。When you **go** regularly **to** a class, school etc, you formally **attend** it (NOT 不用 *attend to* it). 經常地聽課或上學等, 是 attend (出席)。

You usually **go/come to** or more formally **attend** an event such as a meeting, football game, wedding, church service or official dinner (NOT 不用 *join*). 參加一項活動, 如會議、足球比賽、婚禮、教堂禮拜或正式宴會, 通常用 go/come to, 較正式的用語是 attend: *Are you coming to my birthday party?* 你打算來參加我的生日聚會嗎?

If you actively take part in something that a group is doing, you **join in** or more formally **participate in** what it does. join in 或更正式的用語 participate in 是指積極參加一羣人正在做的某事: *I hope you will participate in all our club activities.* 我希望你能參加我們俱樂部的所有活動。| *Chris joined in the class discussion enthusiastically.* 克里斯積極地參與課堂討論。

You **go to**, **attend**, or more actively **participate in** a conference. "參加會議" 可用 go to 或 attend, 而 participate in 表示更積極地參加。

join² *n* [C] a place where two parts of an object are connected or fastened together〔兩個物體的〕連接處: **you can hardly see the join** *It's been glued back together so well, you can hardly see the join.* 這東西黏得很好, 你幾乎看不出其中的接口。

join·er /ˈdʒɔɪnə; ˈdʒɔɪnə/ *n* [C] someone who makes wooden doors, window frames etc〔製造木門、窗框等的〕細木工人 —compare 比較 CARPENTER

join·er·y /ˈdʒɔɪnərɪ; ˈdʒɔɪnəri/ *n* [U] the trade and work of a joiner 細木工行業[手藝] —compare 比較 CARPENTRY

joint¹ /dʒɔɪnt; dʒɔɪnt/ *adj* [only before noun 僅用於名詞前] **1** shared, owned by, or involving two or more people or groups 共享的; 共有的; 共同的: *a joint bank account* 共有的銀行賬戶 | *joint first prize* 共同獲得的頭獎 | *joint army and airforce operations* 陸軍與空軍的聯合行動 **2 joint effort** a situation in which two or more people work together 共同努力: *"Who cooked the meal?" "Well it was a joint effort really."* "這頓飯是誰做的?" "這是我們共同努力的成果。" **3 joint venture** a business activity begun by two or more people or companies working together 合資經營項目; 合資企業 **4 joint resolution** *law* a decision or law agreed by both houses of the US Congress and signed by the President【法律】〔由美國國會眾議院和參議院兩院同意並經總統簽署的〕共同決議 —**jointly** *adv*: *tenants who are jointly responsible for their rent* 共同分擔房租的房客

joint² *n* [C] **1** a part of your body where two bones meet 骨關節: *knee joint* 膝關節 **2** *BrE* a large piece of meat for cooking, usually containing a bone【英】〔供烹調的〕一大塊肉〔一般帶有骨頭〕: *a joint of beef* 一大塊牛肉 **3** a place where two things or parts of an object are joined together〔兩個物體或部分的〕接合處; 匯合處: *Rain penetrates the joints between the concrete panels.* 雨水滲過水泥板的接合處。**4 out of joint a)** if a bone in your body is out of joint, it has been pushed out of its correct position〔骨〕脱臼, 脱節 **b)** if a system, group etc is out of joint, it is not working properly〔系統、組織〕混亂, 不協調: *Something is out of joint in our society.* 我們的組織出了毛病。—see also 另見 **put sb's nose out of joint** (NOSE[1] (18)) **5** *informal* a cheap bar, club, or restaurant【非正式】廉價酒館[俱樂部、餐廳]: *a hamburger joint* 廉價漢堡包店 —see also 另見 CLIP JOINT **6** *slang* a cigarette containing CANNABIS【俚】〔含有大麻的〕香煙 —see also 另見 **case the joint** (CASE[2] (2))

joint³ *v* [T] to cut meat into joints (JOINT[2] (2)) 把〔肉〕切成大塊

joint·ed /ˈdʒɔɪntɪd; ˈdʒɔɪntɨd/ *adj* having joints and able to move and bend 有活動關節的: *a jointed puppet* 關節能活動的木偶

joint hon·ours /ˌ· ˈ··/ *n* [U] a university degree course in Britain in which two main subjects are studied〔英國大學的〕聯合學位課程〔即攻讀兩門主要學科〕—compare 比較 SINGLE HONOURS

joint-stock com·pa·ny /ˌ· ˈ· ˌ···/ *n* [C] *AmE technical* a company that is owned by all the people with shares (SHARE[2] (5)) in it【美, 術語】股份公司

joist /dʒɔɪst; dʒɔɪst/ *n* [C] one of the beams that support a floor or ceiling〔支撐地板或天花板的〕托梁

2 3 **joke¹** /dʒok; dʒəʊk/ *n* [C]
1 ►STH FUNNY 有趣的事◄ something that you say or do to make people laugh, especially a funny story or trick 笑話, 玩笑: *Do you know any good jokes?* 你知道甚麼好玩的笑話嗎? | *Don't get mad – it was only a joke!* 別發火, 那不過是個玩笑! | **crack/make a joke** (=say something funny) 開玩笑 | **tell a joke** (=tell a short funny story) 講一個笑話 | **get the joke** *informal* (=understand why a joke is funny) 【非正式】明白笑話〔為甚麼好笑〕| **play a joke on sb** (=trick them) 戲弄某人 | **dirty joke** (=about sex) 猥褻的笑話 | **sick joke** (=about something unpleasant) 令人不悅的笑話 | **have a joke** (=not mean something seriously) 開個玩笑〔表示不嚴肅〕*I was only having a joke!* 我不過是開個玩笑!
2 ►STH ANNOYING 討厭的事◄ *informal* a situation which is so silly or unreasonable that it makes you angry【非正式】荒唐可笑的事: *The whole meeting was a complete joke.* 整個會議完全是一場鬧劇。
3 go/get beyond a joke a situation that gets beyond a joke has become serious and worrying〔情況〕不是鬧着玩的; 嚴肅的: *I haven't heard from them for three weeks now – it's gone beyond a joke.* 我至今已有三週沒有收到他們的信, 這不是鬧着玩的事了。
4 be no joke used to emphasize that a situation is serious or that someone really means what they say 並非開玩笑〔用來強調情況嚴重或某人的說話是認真的〕: *These rail strikes every week are no joke.* 鐵路罷工每週都有, 絕不是開玩笑的事。| **it's no joke** *It's no joke, I think she really means to kill herself.* 我認為她的確想自殺, 絕不是鬧着玩的。
5 take a joke to be able to laugh at a joke about yourself 經得起開玩笑: *Your problem is you just can't take a joke!* 你的問題是你經不起開玩笑!
6 make a joke of to treat something serious as if it was intended to be funny 拿〔嚴肅的事〕開玩笑: *Sure, he made a joke of it but he was clearly hurt.* 不錯, 他確實拿它開玩笑, 但他明顯地受到傷害。
7 not get the joke to not understand why someone thinks a situation is funny 不明白有甚麼好笑: *"Is that a proposition?" I asked, but she didn't get the joke.* "你是想勾引我嗎?" 我問道, 但她卻不明白其中有甚麼好笑。
8 sb's idea of a joke *spoken* a situation that someone else thinks is funny but you do not【口】某人的鬼主意, 某人開玩笑的方式: *I suppose hiding the car key was his idea of a joke.* 他大概認為把別人的車鑰匙藏起來很好玩。
9 the joke's on you/her etc used to say that the person who was trying to make other people seem silly now seems silly themselves〔想開別人的玩笑反而〕把玩笑開到自己身上了; 被戲弄的反而是自己 —see also 另見 IN-JOKE, PRACTICAL JOKE, **standing joke** (STANDING¹ (4))

3 **joke²** *v* [I] **1** to say things that are intended to be funny 開玩笑, 說笑話: **[+about/with]** *It's serious, Donny, don't joke about it!* 事情很嚴重, 唐尼, 別開玩笑了! **2 you're joking!/you must be joking!** *spoken* used to tell someone that what they are suggesting is so strange or silly that you cannot believe that they are serious【口】你(一定)是在開玩笑吧!〔用來表示某人說的話很奇怪或愚蠢, 你無法相信他們是認真的〕: *What! Buy a house on my salary? You must be joking!* 甚麼? 用我的薪水買房子? 你一定是在開玩笑吧? **3 only joking** *BrE spoken* used to say that you did not really mean what you just said【英口】只是說着玩的, 開個玩笑而已〔用來表示剛才所說並不是認真的〕: *Only joking, darling – I love you really!* 親愛的, 只不過開個玩笑, 我真的很愛你! **4 joking apart/aside** *BrE* used before you say something serious after you have been joking【英】說正經的〔用來表示停止開玩笑, 開始說嚴肅的事〕: *Joking apart, she is a very talented painter.* 說正經的, 她真是一位很有才華的畫家。—**jokingly** *adv*

jok·er /ˈdʒokɚ; ˈdʒəʊkə/ *n* [C] **1** *informal* someone who behaves in a way you think is stupid【非正式】傻瓜, 蠢人: *Some joker had nailed it to the floor.* 不知哪個笨蛋把它釘在地板上了。**2** a PLAYING CARD that has no fixed value and is only used in some card games〔某些紙牌遊戲中可充作任何點數的〕百搭牌 **3** someone who makes a lot of jokes 愛開玩笑的人 **4 the joker in the pack** something or someone whose effect on future events cannot be known 難以預料的事; 難以捉摸的人

jok·ey, joky /ˈdʒokɪ; ˈdʒəʊki/ *adj BrE* not serious and tending to make people laugh【英】滑稽的, 令人發笑的: *Her jokey manner put us at ease.* 她詼諧的態度讓我們放鬆下來。—**jokily** *adv* —**jokiness** *n* [U]

jol·li·fi·ca·tion /ˌdʒɑləfəˈkeʃən; ˌdʒɒlɪ̠fɪ̠ˈkeɪʃən/ *n* [C, U] *old-fashioned* fun and enjoyment【過時】歡樂, 歡鬧

jol·ly¹ /ˈdʒɑlɪ; ˈdʒɒli/ *adj* **jollier, jolliest** *especially BrE*【尤英】**1** happy and cheerful 快樂的, 愉快的: *Everybody was in a very relaxed and jolly mood.* 大家的心情都很輕鬆愉快。**2** *old-fashioned* very pleasant and enjoyable【過時】令人愉快的: *a very jolly occasion* 令人非常愉快的時刻

jolly² *adv BrE old-fashioned*【英, 過時】**1** very 很, 非常: *Sounds like a jolly good idea to me.* 在我聽起來, 這個主意很好。**2 jolly well** used to emphasize that you are annoyed 真是〔用於強調自己很不耐煩〕: *I wish he'd jolly well hurry up.* 但願他真能快一些。**3 jolly good!** *spoken* used to say that you are pleased by what someone has just said【口】說得好!〔用來表示你對某人剛剛所說的話感到滿意〕

jolly³ *v* [T] **jolly sb into doing sth** *BrE informal* to gently persuade someone to do something【英, 非正式】哄某人做某事
jolly sb **along** *phr v* [T] *BrE* to try to make someone do something faster by encouraging them【英】鼓勵〔某人加快行動〕: *You'll have to jolly people along if you want to get this work finished.* 如果你想把這件事完成, 就要鼓勵一下人們。
jolly sth ↔ **up** *v* [T] *BrE* to make a place brighter and more cheerful【英】使〔某地方〕更明亮宜人

jolly⁴ *n* [C] **1 get your jollies** *AmE spoken* to get pleasure from a particular experience or activity【美口】〔從某經歷或活動中〕得到快樂 **2** *BrE old-fashioned* an informal event at which people have fun and enjoy themselves【英, 過時】尋歡作樂的活動

Jolly Ro·ger /ˌ·· ˈ··/ *n* a black flag with a picture of bones on it, used in former times by PIRATES; SKULL AND CROSSBONES (1)〔昔日海盜使用的〕骷髏旗

jolt¹ /dʒolt; dʒəʊlt/ *v* **1** [I,T] to move suddenly and roughly, or to make someone or something move in this way (使)突然移動[顛簸]: *The car jolted and Rachel was thrown backwards.* 汽車猛地搖晃, 使蕾切爾向後摔去。**2** [T] to give someone a sudden shock 使〔某人〕震驚

jolt² *n* [C] **1** a sudden rough shaking movement〔突然的〕震動, 搖晃: *I felt every jolt of the bus.* 我感到公共汽車每一次的搖晃。**2** a sudden shock 震驚: **with a jolt** *I realized with a jolt that they must have gone without me.* 我驚訝地意識到他們一定是扔下我走了。

Jo·nah /ˈdʒonə; ˈdʒəʊnə/ *n* [C] someone who seems to bring bad luck 帶來噩運的人

Jones·es /ˈdʒonzɪz; ˈdʒəʊnzɪ̠z/ *n* —see 見 **keep up with the Joneses** (KEEP¹)

josh /dʒɑʃ; dʒɒʃ/ *v AmE old-fashioned*【美, 過時】**1** [I+with] to talk to someone in a joking way〔用開玩笑的口吻〕與〔某人〕說話 **2** [T] to laugh at someone in a friendly way〔無惡意地〕嘲弄: *The guys josh him and call him an egghead.* 那些人逗他, 叫他書呆子。

joss stick /ˈdʒɑs ˌstɪk; ˈdʒɒs ˌstɪk/ *n* [C] a stick of INCENSE¹〔祭供時用的〕線香

jos·tle /ˈdʒɑsl̩; ˈdʒɒsəl/ *v* [I,T] to push or knock against someone in a crowd, especially so that you can get somewhere or do something before other people〔在人羣中〕推, 撞〔尤指讓自己前往某處或比其他人早做某事〕: *The couple were shoved and jostled by reporters as they left the courtroom.* 這對夫婦離開法庭時受到記者們的推撞。

jot¹ /dʒɑt; dʒɒt/ *v* **jotted, jotting**
jot sth ↔ **down** *phr v* [T] to write something quickly 匆匆記下: *Let me jot down your number and I'll call you tomorrow.* 讓我記下你的號碼, 明天給你回電話。

jot² *n* **not a jot** *BrE old-fashioned* not at all or none at all【英, 過時】一點也不; 一點也沒有: *It doesn't make a jot of difference.* 一點兒影響都沒有。

jot·ter /ˈdʒɑtɚ; ˈdʒɒtə/ *n* [C] *BrE* a small book for writing notes in【英】便條本, 便箋簿

jot·tings /ˈdʒɑtɪŋz; ˈdʒɒtɪŋz/ *n* [plural] *informal* short notes, usually written to remind yourself about something【非正式】〔為提醒自己而寫的〕簡短記事

joule /dʒul; dʒuːl/ *n* [C] *technical* a measure of energy or work【術語】焦耳〔能或功的單位〕

jour·nal /ˈdʒɝnl̩; ˈdʒɜːnl/ *n* [C] **1** a serious magazine produced for professional people or those with a particular interest〔供專業人士或具有某種興趣的人讀的〕期刊, 雜誌: *the British Medical Journal*《英國醫學雜誌》 **2** *literary* a written record that you make of the things that happen to you each day; DIARY (1)【文】日記; 日誌

jour·nal·ese /ˌdʒɝnl̩ˈiz; ˌdʒɜːnəlˈiːz/ *n* [U] language that is typical of newspapers 新聞用語

jour·nal·is·m /ˈdʒɝnl̩ˌɪzəm; ˈdʒɜːnəl-ɪzəm/ *n* [U] the job or activity of writing news reports for newspapers, magazines, television or radio 新聞業; 新聞工作

3 **jour·nal·ist** /ˈdʒɝnl̩ɪst; ˈdʒɜːnəl-ɪ̥st/ *n* [C] someone who writes news reports for newspapers, magazines, television, or radio 新聞工作者; 新聞記者 —compare 比較 REPORTER

3 2 **jour·ney¹** /ˈdʒɝni; ˈdʒɜːni/ *n* [C] **1** *especially BrE* a trip from one place to another, especially over a long distance【尤英】〔尤指長途的〕旅行, 旅程: *a train journey across Europe* 橫跨歐洲的長途火車旅行 | *I have a 25-minute journey to work.* 我上班路上要用 25 分鐘。| **break your journey** (=stop somewhere for a time to rest) 中途停留休息 **2** *literary* the process by which something gradually changes and develops【文】歷程, 過程: *our journey through life* 我們的人生歷程 —see 見 TRAVEL (USAGE)

journey² *v* [I always+adv/prep] *literary* to travel【文】旅行

jour·ney·man /ˈdʒɝnɪmən; ˈdʒɜːnimən/ *n* [C] *old-fashioned*【過時】**1** a trained worker who works for someone else〔為他人雇用的〕熟練工人 **2** an experienced worker whose work is reasonable but not excellent〔技術合格但並不出色的〕熟手

jour·no /ˈdʒɝno; ˈdʒɜːnəʊ/ *n* [C] *informal* a JOURNALIST【非正式】新聞工作者; 新聞記者

joust /dʒaust; dʒaʊst/ *v* [I] to fight with LANCE*s* (=long sticks) while riding a horse 騎着馬用長矛比武 —**joust** *n* [C]

J

Jove /dʒov; dʒəʊv/ *n* **by Jove!** *BrE old-fashioned* used to express surprise or to emphasize something【英, 過時】哎呀!〔用來表示驚訝或強調某事〕: *By Jove, you're right!* 哎呀, 你說得對!

jo·vi·al /ˈdʒovɪəl; ˈdʒəʊviəl/ *adj* friendly and cheerful 友好的; 高興的: *a jovial smile* 友善的微笑 —**jovially** *adv* —**joviality** /ˌdʒovɪˈælətɪ; ˌdʒəʊviˈælɪ̥ti/ *n* [U]

jowl /dʒaul; dʒaʊl/ *n* [C] **1** [usually plural 一般用複數] the skin that covers your lower jaw on either side of your face 下頜垂肉 **2 heavy-jowled** having large jowls that hang down slightly 有下頜垂肉的, 雙下巴的 —see also 另見 **cheek by jowl** (CHEEK¹ (4))

3 **joy¹** /dʒɔɪ; dʒɔɪ/ *n* **1** [U] great happiness and pleasure 歡欣, 愉快, 喜悅: **to sb's joy** *To Beth's surprise and joy, she was awarded first prize.* 貝思得了頭獎, 使她又驚又喜。| **jump for joy** (=be very pleased) 高興得跳起來 **2** [C] something or someone that gives you happiness and pleasure 使人高興的事物[人]: *the joys and sorrows of bringing up a family* 養育子女的苦與樂 | **be a joy to use/drive etc** (=be very pleasant to use/drive etc) 使用〔某物〕/駕駛〔某車〕是件樂事 *The new Merc's a joy to drive.* 駕駛這輛新的平治汽車真是件樂事。**3** [U only in questions or negatives 僅用於疑問句或否定句] *BrE spoken* success in doing what you are trying to do【英口】成功: *You could ask the library to trace the book, but I doubt you'll get any joy.* 你可以請圖書館查找這本書, 但我看不會有甚麼結果。

joy² *v*
joy in sth *phr v* [T] *literary* to be happy because of something【文】由於...而高興

joy·ful /ˈdʒɔɪfəl; ˈdʒɔɪfəl/ *adj* very happy, or likely to make people very happy 歡樂的; 令人高興的: *the joyful news* 令人高興的消息 —**joyfully** *adv* —**joyfulness** *n* [U]

joy·less /ˈdʒɔɪlɪs; ˈdʒɔɪləs/ *adj* without any happiness at all 不高興的, 不快樂的: *a joyless marriage* 毫不快樂的婚姻 —**joylessly** *adv* —**joylessness** *n* [U]

joy·ous /ˈdʒɔɪəs; ˈdʒɔɪəs/ *adj literary* very happy, or likely to make people very happy【文】歡樂的; 令人愉快的: *a joyous occasion* 歡樂的場合 —**joyously** *adv* —**joyousness** *n* [U]

joy·rid·ing /ˈdʒɔɪˌraɪdɪŋ; ˈdʒɔɪˌraɪdɪŋ/ *n* [U] the crime of stealing a car and driving it in a fast and dangerous way for fun 偷盜汽車並開快車兜風 —**joyride** *v* [I] —**joyrider** *n* [C]

joy·stick /ˈdʒɔɪˌstɪk; ˈdʒɔɪˌstɪk/ *n* [C] an upright handle that you use to change the direction in which something such as a plane moves〔飛機等的〕操縱桿

JP /ˌdʒe ˈpi; ˌdʒeɪ ˈpiː/ *n* [C] a JUSTICE OF THE PEACE; a MAGISTRATE in Britain〔英國〕治安法官; 地方官

Jr *AmE* the written abbreviation of 縮寫= JUNIOR; used after the name of a man who has the same name as his father【美】小〔置於與父親同名的男子姓名後〕: *Alan Parks, Jr.* 小阿倫·帕克斯

jub·i·lant /ˈdʒubl̩ənt; ˈdʒuːbɪ̥lənt/ *adj* extremely happy and pleased because you have been successful, or full of people who feel this way〔因成功而〕歡騰的; 興高采烈的: *jubilant celebrations* 歡騰的慶祝活動 —**jubilantly** *adv*

ju·bi·la·tion /ˌdʒubl̩ˈeʃən; ˌdʒuːbɪ̥ˈleɪʃən/ *n* [U] *formal* happiness and pleasure because you have been successful【正式】〔因成功而〕歡欣, 愉快: *shouts of jubilation from the crowd* 人羣發出的歡呼聲

ju·bi·lee /ˈdʒubl̩ˌi; ˈdʒuːbɪ̥liː/ *n* [C] a date that is celebrated because it is exactly 25 years, 50 years etc after an important event〔重要事件25年、50年等的〕週年紀念 —see also 另見 DIAMOND JUBILEE, GOLDEN JUBILEE, SILVER JUBILEE

Ju·da·is·m /ˈdʒudɪˌɪzəm; ˈdʒuːdeɪ-ɪzəm/ *n* [U] the Jewish religion based on the Old Testament of the Bible, the Talmud, and the later teachings of the RABBI*s* 猶太教 —**Judaic** /dʒuˈde·ɪk; dʒuːˈdeɪ-ɪk/ *adj*

Ju·das /ˈdʒudəs; ˈdʒuːdəs/ *n* [C] someone who is disloyal to a friend; TRAITOR 出賣朋友的人; 叛徒

jud·der /ˈdʒʌdɚ; ˈdʒʌdə/ *v* [I] if a vehicle or machine judders, it shakes violently〔車輛或機器〕劇烈震動: *The engine juddered to life.* 引擎劇烈震動着發動起來。—**judder** *n* [C]

judge¹ /dʒʌdʒ; dʒʌdʒ/ *n* [C] **1** the official in control of a court who decides how criminals should be punished 法官; 審判官: **federal judge/high court judge** (=a judge in a particular court) 聯邦法官/高等法院法官 **2** someone who decides on the result of a competition〔比賽的〕裁判員, 評判: *The panel of judges included several well-known writers.* 評判小組中包括幾位著名作家。**3 be no judge** *informal* to not have enough skill or knowledge to be able to give an opinion on a particular subject【非正式】...並非鑑定人〔指沒有足夠的技能或知識來評價某事〕: *I don't like this wine – not that I'm any judge of these things.* 我不喜歡這種酒, 但我不是這玩意兒的鑑賞家。**4 a good/bad judge of** someone whose opinion on something is usually right or wrong 對...判斷力很好/很差的人: *Sandra's a very good judge of character.* 桑德拉很善於鑑別人的性格。**5 let me be the judge of that** *spoken* used to tell someone angrily that you do not need their advice【口】由我來決定〔憤怒地向某人表示你不需要他的勸告〕—see also 另見 **as sober as a judge** (SOBER[1] (1))

2 3 **judge²** *v* **judged, judging**

1 ►OPINION 看法◄ [I,T] to form or give an opinion about someone or something after thinking carefully about all the information you know about them〔認真考慮後〕認為; 判斷; 斷定; 評價: *It seems a good idea, but without all the facts it's hard to judge.* 這看來是個好主意, 但在所有細節都不清楚的情況下, 難以作出決斷。| **judge sb/sth by sth** *Teachers tend to be judged by their students' exam grades.* 人們常以學生的考試成績來判斷教師的優劣。| **judge sb/sth on sth** *Why can't they judge me on my brains, not my looks?* 他們為甚麼不能憑我的智力而不是我的相貌來評價我呢? | **judge that** *I judged that Williams was a spy.* 據我判斷, 威廉斯是個間諜。| **judge sb/sth (to be) sth** *Their reunion was judged to be a great success.* 他們的重新統一被認為是極成功的。| **judge who/what/how etc** *Well, Sam, can you judge where they might go next?* 好吧, 山姆, 你能斷定他們下一步可能去哪兒嗎? | **judge sth/sb (to be) good/bad/fair etc** *The headmaster was judged incompetent by school inspectors.* 校長被督學評定為不稱職。| **judge it unwise/expedient/ inappropriate etc to do sth** *At that point we judged it wise to leave them alone.* 在那種情況下, 我們認為不去打擾他們是明智的。

2 ►GUESS 猜測◄ [I,T] to guess an amount, distance, height, weight etc; ESTIMATE 猜測, 估計: *"How long will it take?" "It's impossible to judge."* "要花多長時間?" "無法估計。" | **judge sb/sth to be sth** *Trevor judged the distance to be about 30 yards.* 特雷弗估計距離大約為30碼。| **judge how far/long/wide etc sth is** *In this fog, we can't judge how far it is to the other side of the river.* 在這樣的大霧天氣, 我們很難估計離河對岸有多遠。

3 judging by/from used to say that you are making a guess based on what you have just seen, heard or learned 依據〔所見、所聞、所聽〕來判斷: *Judging by the look on Adam's face, the news must have been terrible.* 從亞當的表情來看, 那肯定是可怕的消息。

4 ►COMPETITION 競賽◄ [I,T] to decide on the result of a competition 裁判, 評判: *Who's judging the talent contest?* 這次才能比賽誰是評判? | **judge sb on sth** *Competitors will be judged on speed and accuracy.* 根據速度和準確性來評判參賽者。

5 ►CRITICIZE 批評◄ [I,T] to form an opinion about someone, especially in an unfair or criticizing way〔尤指不公正或批判地〕(對…) 作出評價: *What right have you to judge the way they live?* 你有甚麼權利對他們的生活方式說三道四?

6 ►LAW 法律◄ [T] to decide whether someone is guilty of a crime in court〔在法庭上〕審判, 審理

7 It's not for me to judge *spoken* used to say that you do not think you have the right to give your opinion about something【口】輪不到我來判斷〔指你認為自己沒有權利對某事發表意見〕

8 as far as I can judge used to say that you think what you are saying is true, but you are not sure 據我判斷〔用來說明你相信自己說的話沒錯, 但沒有十足把握〕

9 don't judge a book by its cover used to say that you should not form an opinion based only on the way something looks 不要以封面來評定一本書; 不要以貌取人〔指不可憑事物的外表作出判斷〕

2 **judg·ment** also 又作 **judgement** *BrE*【英】/ˈdʒʌdʒmənt; ˈdʒʌdʒmənt/ *n*

1 ►OPINION 看法◄ [C,U] an opinion that you form after thinking carefully about something〔認真思考後的〕意見; 看法; 評價: **in sb's judgment** *In my judgment, we should accept his offer.* 依我看, 我們應接受他的建議。| **pass judgment** (=give your opinion or criticism) 作出評論[批評] | **reserve judgment** (=refuse to decide before you have all the facts)〔在掌握全部事實之前〕拒絕作出判斷

2 ►ABILITY TO DECIDE 決斷力◄ [U] the ability to make decisions about situations or people 判斷力: *The minister's remarks show a lack of political judgement.* 部長的談話顯示他缺乏政治判斷力。| **sound judgment** (=good judgment) 良好的判斷力 *sound editorial judgment* 良好的編輯判斷力

3 ►LAW 法律◄ [C,U] an official decision given by a judge or a court of law〔法官或法庭的〕審判, 判決: *a judgment delivered by the European court* 歐洲法庭作出的判決

4 against your better judgment if you do something against your better judgment, you do it even though you do not think it is the right thing to do〔做某事〕違心的; 明知是不對的: *In the end I agreed to lend her the money, but it was against my better judgment.* 我終於還是同意把錢借給她, 但這樣做違背我的心願。

5 a judgment something unpleasant that happens which seems like a punishment for the things you have done wrong 報應; 天譴

6 sit in judgment over sb to criticize someone's behaviour, especially unfairly 對某人的行為進行批評〔尤指不公正的批評〕

7 judgment call *AmE* a decision you have to make yourself because there are no fixed rules in a situation【美】裁判員的判決〔指由於沒有固定的規章可循而必須自行作出的決定〕—see also 另見 LAST JUDGMENT, VALUE JUDGMENT

judg·ment·al also 又作 **judgemental** *BrE*【英】/dʒʌdʒˈmɛntl; dʒʌdʒˈmentl/ *adj* too quick and willing to criticize people 輕率批評人的

judgment day /ˈ·· ·/ also 又作 **day of judgment** *n* [singular, not with *the* 不與 the 連用] the time after death when everyone is judged by God for what they have done in life, according to Christianity and some other religions〔基督教等的〕最後審判日〔指人死後, 上帝按各人所行的進行審判〕

ju·di·ca·ture /ˈdʒudɪkətʃɚ; ˈdʒuːdɪkətʃə/ *n* **the judicature** *formal* judges and the organization, power etc of the law【正式】司法系統; 司法權

ju·di·cial /dʒuˈdɪʃəl; dʒuːˈdɪʃəl/ *adj* **1** connected with a court of law, judges, or their decisions 法庭的; 法官的; 裁決的: *the judicial system* 司法系統 —compare 比較 EXECUTIVE² (1), LEGISLATIVE (2) **2** behaviour that is judicial is sensible and shows good judgment〔行為〕明智的, 有判斷力的 —**judicially** *adv*

ju·di·cia·ry /dʒuˈdɪʃɪˌɛrɪ; dʒuːˈdɪʃəri/ *n* **the judiciary** *formal* all the judges in a country who, as a group, form part of the system of government【正式】司法部; 司法系統[部門]

ju·di·cious /dʒuˈdɪʃəs; dʒuːˈdɪʃəs/ *adj formal* done in a sensible and careful way【正式】明智的; 審慎的: *a judicious choice* 明智的選擇 —**judiciously** *adv* —**judiciousness** *n* [U]

ju·do /ˈdʒudo; ˈdʒuːdəʊ/ *n* [U] a sport from the Far East, in which you try to throw your opponent onto the ground 柔道

jug /dʒʌg; dʒʌg/ *n* [C] **1** *BrE* a container for liquids with

jugs 罐, 壺

measuring jug *BrE*【英】/measuring cup *AmE*【美】量杯

jug *AmE*【美】細口瓶

jug *BrE*【英】/ pitcher *AmE*【美】〔有柄帶嘴的〕壺, 罐

J

a handle and a SPOUT (=for pouring)【英】〔有柄帶嘴的〕壺, 罐; PITCHER (1) *AmE*【美】**2** also 又作 **jug·ful** /ˈdʒʌgful; ˈdʒʌgfʊl/ the amount of liquid that a jug will hold 一壺的容量: *a jug of milk* 一壺牛奶 **3 in (the) jug** *BrE old-fashioned* in prison【英, 過時】坐牢

jug-eared /ˈdʒʌg ˌɪrd; ˈdʒʌg ˌɪəd/ *adj* having large ears that stick out 長着一對招風耳的

jugged hare /ˌ· ˈ·/ *n* [U] *BrE* a dish made of HARE that has been cooked in liquid【英】清燉野兔肉, 罐燜野兔

jug·ger·naut /ˈdʒʌgɚˌnɔt; ˈdʒʌgənɔːt/ *n* [C] **1** *BrE* a very large vehicle, that carries goods over long distances【英】〔長途運輸用的〕重型貨車; SEMI (3) *AmE*【美】**2** something large and powerful that destroys everything it meets 有強大毀滅力量的物體; 強大的摧毀力

jug·gle /ˈdʒʌgl; ˈdʒʌgəl/ *v* **1** [I,T] to keep three or more objects moving through the air by throwing and catching them very quickly (用…) 玩雜耍〔同時拋接數件物品〕: **[+with]** *juggling with plates* 拋耍盤子 **2** [I,T] if you juggle two or more jobs, activities etc, you try to fit all of them into your life 試圖應付〔兩個或更多的職務、活動等〕: *juggling the needs of your family with the demands of the job* 嘗試應付家庭的需要與工作的要求 **3** [T] to arrange numbers, information etc in the way that you want 篡改〔數字、資料等〕: *No amount of financial juggling could hide the fraud.* 假賬造得再多也掩蓋不了這欺詐行為。—**juggler** *n* [C] —see also 另見 **juggling act** (ACT[1] (12))

jug·u·lar /ˈdʒʌgjəlɚ; ˈdʒʌgjələ/ *n* [C] **1** a jugular vein 頸靜脈 **2 go for the jugular** *informal* to criticize or attack someone very strongly, especially in order to harm them【非正式】強烈批評[攻擊]〔某人, 尤指為了要傷害對方〕

jugular vein /ˌ··· ˈ·/ *n* [C usually singular 一般用單數] the large VEIN (=tube) in your neck that takes blood from your head back to your heart 頸靜脈

juice[1] /dʒus; dʒuːs/ *n* **1** [C,U] the liquid that comes from fruit and vegetables, or a drink that is made from this〔水果、蔬菜的〕汁; 水果[蔬菜]汁飲料: *a carton of orange juice* 一紙盒橙汁 **2** [U] the liquid that comes out of meat when it is cooked 肉汁 **3 gastric/digestive juice(s)** the liquid inside your stomach that helps you to DIGEST[1] (1) food 胃液/消化液 **4** [U] *informal* something that produces power, such as petrol or electricity【非正式】能源〈如汽油或電力〉—see also 另見 **stew in your own juice** (STEW[2] (2))

juice[2] *v* [T] to get the juice out of fruit or vegetables; SQUEEZE[1] (2) 榨〔水果或蔬菜的〕汁

juice sth ↔ **up** *phr v* [T] *AmE informal* to make something more interesting or exciting【美, 非正式】使有生氣, 使活躍

juiced /dʒust; dʒuːst/ *adj AmE old-fashioned* drunk【美, 過時】喝醉了的

juic·er /ˈdʒusɚ; ˈdʒuːsə/ *n* [C] **a)** *AmE* a small kitchen tool used for getting juice out of fruit【美】〔廚房用的小型〕榨果汁器; LEMON SQUEEZER *BrE*【英】**b)** an electric machine for doing this 電動榨果汁機

juic·y /ˈdʒusɪ; ˈdʒuːsi/ *adj* **1** containing a lot of juice 多汁的, 多液的: *a juicy steak* 多汁的牛排 **2 juicy stories/gossip/details** *informal* stories etc that contain interesting or shocking information, especially about people's sexual behaviour【非正式】有趣[繪聲繪色]的故事/流言/細節〔尤與人們的性行為有關〕**3** *informal* involving a lot of money【非正式】大筆錢款的: *a big fat juicy cheque* 一張很大額的支票 **4** *informal* giving you work to do that will lead to a feeling of satisfaction【非正式】〔工作〕給人以滿足感的: *a juicy part in 'Moby Dick'*《白鯨記》中一個可有充分發揮的角色 —**juiciness** *n* [U]

ju·jit·su /dʒuˈdʒɪtsu; ˌdʒuːˈdʒɪtsuː/ *n* [U] a type of fighting from Japan, in which you hold, throw, and hit your opponent 柔術, 柔道

ju·ju /ˈdʒudʒu; ˈdʒuːdʒuː/ *n* [C,U] a type of West African magic involving objects with special powers, or one of these objects〔使用帶有魔力的物件的〕非洲西部巫術

juke-box /ˈdʒuk ˌbɑks; ˈdʒuːk bɒks/ *n* [C] a machine in public bars that plays music when you put money in〔酒吧內的〕投幣式自動唱機

ju·lep /ˈdʒulɪp; ˈdʒuːlɪ̣p/ *n* —see 見 MINT JULEP

Ju·ly /dʒuˈlaɪ; dʒʊˈlaɪ/ written abbreviation 縮寫為 **Jul** *n* [C,U] the seventh month of the year, between June and August 七月: **in July** *a society founded in July 1890* 成立於 1890 年 7 月的學會 | **last/next July** *Anne's starting work next July.* 安妮將於明年七月開始工作。| **on July 12th** (also 又作 **on 12th July** *BrE* 英) *"When's the concert?" "On 12th July."* "音樂會甚麼時候舉行?" "7 月 12 日。" (spoken as 讀作: *on the twelfth of July* or 或 *on July the twelfth* or 或 *(AmE 美) on July twelfth)*

jum·ble[1] /ˈdʒʌmbl; ˈdʒʌmbəl/ *n* **1** [singular] an untidy mixture of things〔東西〕混亂, 雜亂的一堆: **[+of]** *a jumble of thoughts and feelings* 雜亂的想法與情感 **2** [U] *BrE* things to be sold at a jumble sale【英】供義賣的舊雜貨; RUMMAGE[2] (2) *AmE*【美】

jumble[2] also 又作 **jumble up** *v* [T often passive 常用被動態] to mix things together so that they are not in a neat order 使混亂, 使雜亂: *In his excitement Ben's words became jumbled.* 本興奮得語無倫次。

jumble sale /ˈ·· ·/ *n* [C] *BrE* a sale of used clothes, books etc in order to get money to help a local church, school etc; RUMMAGE SALE【英】舊雜貨的義賣〔以捐助本地教會、學校等〕

jum·bo /ˈdʒʌmbo; ˈdʒʌmbəʊ/ *adj* [only before noun 僅用於名詞前] *informal* larger than other things of the same type【非正式】〔同類中〕特大的, 巨大的: *jumbo-sized hot dogs* 巨無霸熱狗

jumbo jet /ˈ·· ·/ also 又作 **jumbo** *n* [C] a very large aircraft for carrying passengers 巨型噴氣式客機, 珍寶客機

jump[1] /dʒʌmp; dʒʌmp/ *v*

1 ►UPWARDS 向上地◄ **a)** [I] to push yourself suddenly up in the air using your legs 跳, 躍: **[+over/across/onto etc]** *He jumped over the wall and ran off.* 他跳牆而逃。| **jump up and down** *The kids love jumping up and down on their beds.* 孩子喜歡在他們的牀上跳上跳下。| **jump clear** (=jump out of danger) 跳離危險 *We managed to jump clear of the car before it hit the wall.* 在汽車撞到牆前, 我們及時跳了出來。**b)** [T] to go over or across something by jumping 跳過〔某物〕, 躍過: *They jumped the barriers to avoid paying for tickets.* 他們為了逃票而跳過柵欄。

2 ►DOWNWARDS 向下地◄ [I] to let yourself drop from a place that is above the ground 跳下, 躍下: **[+out/down etc]** *Three people saved themselves by jumping from the window.* 三人從窗戶跳下得以撿回性命。

3 ►MOVE FAST 快速移動◄ [I always+adv/prep] to move quickly or suddenly in a particular direction〔朝某方向〕快速[突然]移動: **[+out/away/up etc]** *Matt jumped up to fetch the TV guide.* 馬特突然起身去取電視節目指南。

4 ►IN FEAR/SURPRISE 由於恐懼/驚訝◄ [I] to make a quick sudden movement because you are surprised or frightened〔因驚訝或受驚而〕突然一跳: *Sorry, I didn't mean to make you jump.* 對不起, 我不是有意嚇你一跳的。| **jump out of your skin** (=move suddenly because you are very surprised) 嚇了一大跳

5 ►MACHINE 機器◄ [I] if a machine jumps, it makes a wrong movement 錯誤地跳動: *The typewriter jumps every time you press 'a'.* 每次按 a, 打字機都跳鍵。

6 ►KEEP CHANGING 不斷變化◄ [I] to change quickly from one place, position, idea etc to another, often missing something that comes in between〔地方、位置、思想等, 常漏掉中間部分而〕突然轉換: **jump from sth to sth** *Cathy's conversation jumped wildly from one topic to another.* 卡西談話時胡亂地從一個話題突然轉到另一個話題。| **jump ahead** *I can't resist jumping ahead when I read crime novels.* 我看偵探小說時, 總是忍不住跳過一些章節。

7 ▶INCREASE 增加◀[I] to increase suddenly and by a large amount〔數量〕突然上升, 暴漲: [**+to**] *ICA's profits jumped to £20 million last year.* 國際合作署的利潤去年猛增到二千萬英鎊。
8 ▶ATTACK 攻擊◀[T] *informal* to attack someone suddenly【非正式】突然襲擊〔某人〕: *Somebody jumped him in the park last night.* 他昨天晚上在公園裡遭人襲擊。
9 jump down sb's throat *informal* to suddenly speak angrily to someone【非正式】突然訓斥某人: *You don't have to jump down my throat! I was only asking how you were.* 你用不着對我這麼生氣! 我只是問候你而已。
10 jump to conclusions to form an opinion about something before you have all the facts〔在掌握全部事實之前〕倉促作出結論: *Don't jump to conclusions – he may just want to be friends.* 別急着下結論, 他也許只想和我們交朋友。
11 jump the gun to start doing something too soon, especially without thinking about it properly〔沒有認真考慮而〕過早地做某事
12 jump for joy to be extremely happy and pleased 高興至極: *You don't have to jump for joy, but at least smile!* 你不必高興得跳起來, 但至少笑一笑!
13 (go) jump in a lake! *spoken* used to tell someone rudely to go away【口】滾開!〔粗魯地叫別人離開〕
14 jump to it! *spoken* used to order someone to do something immediately【口】趕快!〔命令某人立即做某事〕
15 jump bail to leave a town, city, or country where a court of law has ordered you to stay until your TRIAL[1] (1) 棄保潛逃
16 jump rope *AmE* to jump over a rope as you pass it over your head and under your feet as a game【美】跳繩; SKIP *BrE*【英】—see also 另見 JUMP ROPE
17 jump the queue *BrE*【英】, **jump in line** *AmE*【美】to join a line of people in front of others who were already waiting 不按次序排隊, 插隊; cut in line (CUT[1] (17)) *AmE*【美】—see also 另見 QUEUE-JUMP
18 jump a light to drive past red TRAFFIC LIGHTS 闖紅燈
19 jump a claim *AmE old-fashioned* to claim someone else's land as your own【美, 過時】強佔他人的土地
20 jump a train *especially AmE* to travel on a train, especially a goods train, without paying【尤美】不買票乘火車〔尤指運貨火車〕
21 jump ship to leave a ship on which you are working as a sailor, without permission〔水手〕擅自離船
22 ▶SEX 性◀[I,T] *AmE taboo* to have sex with someone【美諱】(與…)性交
23 ▶CAR 汽車◀ [T] *AmE* to start a car in which the BATTERY[1] (1) has lost power by connecting it to the BATTERY of another car; JUMP-START (1)【美】用跨接法起動〔汽車〕

jump at sth *phr v* [T] to eagerly accept the chance to do something 馬上接受〔機會〕: *Yvonne jumped at the chance of a trip to Asia.* 伊芳欣然接受了這次到亞洲旅行的機會。

jump in *phr v* [I] to interrupt someone or suddenly join a conversation 打斷某人的話; 突然插話

jump on sb *phr v* [T] *informal* to criticize or punish someone, especially unfairly【非正式】〔尤指不公正地〕批評; 懲罰: [**+for**] *Ryder used to jump on me for every little mistake.* 賴德以前常常對我犯的每一個小錯誤都嚴加斥責。

jump out at sb *phr v* [T] if something jumps out at you, it is extremely easy to notice〔某物〕很明顯, 明擺着

jump² *n* [C]
1 ▶UP 向上◀ an act of pushing yourself suddenly up into the air using your legs 跳, 躍: *That was his best jump of the competition.* 那是他在比賽中最好的一跳。
2 ▶DOWN 向下◀ an act of letting yourself drop from a place that is above the ground 跳下: *a parachute jump* 跳傘
3 ▶STH YOU JUMP OVER 跳過的物體◀ a fence, gate, or wall for jumping over in a race or competition 比賽中需要跳過的障礙物〈如柵欄或牆〉: *Her horse cleared all the jumps in the first round.* 她的馬在第一輪比賽中躍過了所有的障礙物。
4 ▶INCREASE 增加◀ a sudden large increase in an amount or value〔數量或價值的〕激增: [**+in**] *a jump in inflation rates* 通貨膨脹率的劇增
5 ▶PROGRESS 進展◀ a large or sudden change, especially when it improves things 巨大[突然]的變化〔尤指改善〕: *a great jump forward for human rights* 人權的極大改善
6 stay one jump ahead of sb *informal* to keep your advantage over the people you are competing with by always being the first to do something new or better【非正式】保持領先優勢〔常常率先改善或創新〕
7 have the jump on sb *informal especially AmE* to have an advantage because you started doing what was necessary before your competitor【非正式, 尤美】〔由於比競爭對手先開始做必須做的事而〕佔有優勢, 搶在某人之前 —see also 另見 HIGH JUMP, LONG JUMP, RUNNING JUMP

jump ball /ˈ· ·/ *n* [C] the act of throwing the ball up in a game of BASKETBALL, so that one player from each team can try to gain control of it〔籃球比賽中的〕跳球, 爭球 —see picture on page A22 參見 A22 頁圖

jumped-up /ˌ· ˈ·◂/ *adj* [only before noun 僅用於名詞前] *BrE* believing that you are more important than you really are, because you have improved your social position【英】〔剛發跡而〕自命不凡的: *some jumped-up little bureaucrat* 某個暴發的小官僚

jump·er /ˈdʒʌmpɚ; ˈdʒʌmpə/ *n* [C] **1** *BrE* a piece of clothing made of wool that covers the upper part of your body and arms; SWEATER【英】套頭毛衣 **2** *AmE* a dress without SLEEVES usually worn over a shirt【美】〔通常穿在襯衣外面的〕無袖連衣裙; PINAFORE *BrE*【英】**3** a person or animal that jumps 跳躍的人[動物] S3

jump·er ca·bles /ˈ·· ˌ··/ *n* [plural] *AmE* JUMP LEADS【美】跳線, 跨接線

jump·ing jack /ˌ·· ˈ·/ *n* [C] a jump that is done from a standing position with your arms and legs pointing out to the side; STAR JUMP 跳躍運動〔兩腿分開、兩臂舉起原地跳躍〕

jumping-off point /ˌ·· ˈ· ˌ·/ *n* [C] a place to start from, especially at the beginning of a journey〔旅程的〕起點, 出發地點

jump jet /ˈ· ·/ *n* [C] *especially BrE* an aircraft that can take off and land by going straight up and down【尤英】垂直起降式噴氣機

jump-leads /ˈdʒʌmp lidz; ˈdʒʌmp liːdz/ *n* [plural] *BrE* thick wires used to connect the batteries (BATTERY[1] (1)) of two cars in order to start one that has lost power【英】〔用以連接兩輛汽車的電瓶以發動其中一輛的〕跳線, 跨接線

jump rope /ˈ· ·/ *n* [C] *AmE* a long piece of rope that children use for jumping over【美】〔跳繩遊戲用的〕繩子, 跳繩; SKIPPING ROPE *BrE*【英】

jump shot /ˈ· ·/ *n* [C] the action in BASKETBALL in which you throw the ball towards the basket as you jump in the air〔籃球的〕跳起投籃 —see picture on page A22 參見 A22 頁圖

jump-start /ˌ· ˈ·/ *v* [T] **1** to start a car whose BATTERY[1] (1) has lost power by connecting it to the battery of another car 用跨接法起動〔汽車〕 **2** to help a process or activity start or become more successful 推動〔過程或活動〕, 促進: *lowering taxes to jump-start the economy* 降低稅收以推動經濟發展 —**jump start** *n* [C]

jump·suit /ˈdʒʌmpsut; ˈdʒʌmpsuːt/ *n* [C] a piece of clothing like a shirt and a pair of trousers joined together, worn by women 女式連衫褲

jump·y /ˈdʒʌmpɪ; ˈdʒʌmpi/ *adj* worried or excited especially because you are expecting something bad to happen〔尤指因預計將發生不祥之事而〕心驚肉跳的 —**jumpily** *adv* —**jumpiness** *n* [U]

3 **junc·tion** /ˈdʒʌŋkʃən; ˈdʒʌŋkʃən/ *n* [C] a place where one road, track etc joins another〔公路、鐵軌等的〕聯接點, 匯合處, 交叉口: *the junction of Abbot's Road and Church Street* 阿伯特路與教堂街的交叉口

junc·ture /ˈdʒʌŋktʃə; ˈdʒʌŋktʃə/ *n* **at this juncture** *spoken formal* at this point in an activity or period of time【口, 正式】值此之際: *At this juncture I'd like to suggest we take a short break.* 在這個時刻, 我建議大家休息一下。

June /dʒun; dʒuːn/ written abbreviation 縮寫為 **Jun** *n* [C,U] the sixth month of the year, between May and July 六月: **in June** *My birthday is in June.* 我的生日在六月。| **last/next June** *I finished school last June.* 我去年六月完成了學業。| **on June 1st** (also 又作 **on 1st June** *BrE* 英) *We met on June 1st.* 我們在 6 月 1 日見過面。(spoken as 讀作: *on June the first* or 或 *on the first of June* or 或 *(AmE* 美*) on June first*)

jun·gle /ˈdʒʌŋgl; ˈdʒʌŋgəl/ *n* **1** [C,U] a thick tropical forest with many large plants growing very close together 熱帶叢林 **2** [singular] a place that is very untidy and where a lot of things have been placed close together〔堆滿東西的〕雜亂的地方: *This place is turning into a jungle already.* 這個地方已變得一片凌亂。**3** [singular] a situation in which it is difficult to become successful or get what you want, especially because a lot of people are competing with each other〔尤因競爭者眾多〕難以成功的局面: *You've got to be tough – it's a jungle out there.* 你必須堅強一些, 那個地方競爭激烈。—see also 另見 CONCRETE JUNGLE, **law of the jungle** (LAW (10))

jungle gym /ˈ·· ˌ·/ *n* [C] *AmE* a large frame made of metal bars for children to climb on【美】〔兒童玩的〕攀登架; CLIMBING FRAME *BrE*【英】

3 **Ju·ni·or** /ˈdʒunjə; ˈdʒuːniə/ written abbreviation 縮寫為 **Jr** *AmE*【美】, **Jnr** *BrE*【英】[only after noun 僅用於名詞後] used after the name of a man who has the same name as his father 小〔置於與父親同名的男子姓名之後〕: *John J. Wallace, Jr.* 小約翰·J·華萊士

junior[1] *adj* **1** [only before noun 僅用於名詞前] having a low rank in an organization or profession〔在組織或行業中〕級別[職位]低的: *a junior doctor* 初級醫生 —opposite 反義詞 SENIOR[1] **2 be junior to sb** to have a lower rank than someone〔級別〕低於某人 —see also 另見 SENIOR[1]

junior[2] *n* **1 be two/five/ten etc years sb's junior** to be two, five, ten etc years younger than someone 比某人小兩歲/五歲/十歲等: *She married a man seven years her junior.* 她嫁給一個比她小七歲的男人。**2** [C] *especially BrE* someone who has a low rank in an organization or profession【尤英】低級職位的人: *an office junior* 初級職員 **3** [C] *BrE* a pupil in a JUNIOR SCHOOL【英】小學生 **4** [C] *AmE* a student in the year before the final year of HIGH SCHOOL or university【美】〔四年制大學或高中的〕三年級學生 —compare 比較 FRESHMAN; SENIOR[2] (2); SOPHOMORE **5** [singular] *AmE especially humorous* a way of speaking to or about your son【美, 尤幽默】〔指自己的〕兒子: *What are we going to do about junior if we go out tonight?* 我們今晚如果外出, 兒子怎麼辦? —see also 另見 SENIOR[2]

junior col·lege /ˌ··· ˈ··/ *n* [C,U] a college in the US or Canada where students take a course of study that continues for two years; COMMUNITY COLLEGE〔美國或加拿大的〕兩年制專科學院

junior high school /ˌ··· ˈ· ·/ also 又作 **junior high** *n* [C,U] a school in the US and other countries for children aged 12 to 13 or 14 初級中學〔美國等國家 12 至 13 或 14 歲的孩子上的學校〕—compare 比較 MIDDLE SCHOOL, SENIOR HIGH SCHOOL

junior school /ˈ··· ˌ·/ *n* [C,U] a school in Britain for children aged 7 to 11 小學〔英國 7 至 11 歲的孩子上的學校〕

junior var·si·ty /ˌ··· ˈ···/ *n* [C,U] *AmE* a team of younger or less experienced sports players who represent a school or college【美】〔學校或學院的〕體育代表隊二隊, 乙級隊〔年齡較小或經驗較淺的〕—compare 比較 VARSITY (1)

ju·ni·per /ˈdʒunəpə; ˈdʒuːnɪ̥pə/ *n* [C,U] a small bush that produces berries (BERRY) and has leaves that are green all year 檜, 刺柏

junk[1] /dʒʌŋk; dʒʌŋk/ *n* **1** [U] old or unwanted objects that have no use or value 廢舊雜物: *I must get rid of all this junk.* 我必須把這些廢舊雜物都丟掉。**2** [C] a Chinese sailing boat 中國平底帆船 **3** [U] *slang* a dangerous drug, especially HEROIN【俚】毒品〔尤指海洛因〕**4** *spoken* JUNK FOOD【口】〔多熱量、少營養的〕劣質[垃圾]食物

junk[2] *v* [T] to get rid of something because it is old or useless 丟掉〔廢舊物品〕

junk bond /ˈ· ·/ *n* [C] a BOND[1] (1) which has a high risk and is often sold to pay for a TAKEOVER 低檔債券, 風險債券, 垃圾債券

jun·ket /ˈdʒʌŋkɪt; ˈdʒʌŋkɪ̥t/ *n* **1** [U] a sweet dish made from thickened milk 乳凍甜食 **2** [C] *informal especially AmE* a free trip that is paid for by government money【非正式, 尤美】公帑旅行, 公費旅遊

junk food /ˈ· ·/ *n* [U] *informal* food that is not healthy because it contains a lot of fat, sugar, or CARBOHYDRATE【非正式】〔高脂肪、高糖分、高碳水化合物的〕不利健康的劣質食品, 垃圾食品

junk·ie, junky /ˈdʒʌŋkɪ; ˈdʒʌŋki/ *n* [C] *slang*【俚】**1** someone who takes dangerous drugs and is dependent on them 有毒癮者 **2 television/soap opera etc junkie** *humorous* someone who likes something so much that they seem to be dependent on it【幽默】看電視/肥皂劇等上癮的人, 電視/肥皂劇迷: *a television junkie* 電視迷

junk mail /ˈ· ·/ *n* [U] letters that advertisers send to people 垃圾郵件〔指商家寄給消費者的廣告信件〕

junk shop /ˈ· ·/ *n* [C] a shop that buys and sells old things〔收售舊貨的〕舊貨商店

junk·y /ˈdʒʌŋkɪ; ˈdʒʌŋki/ *n* [C] another spelling of JUNKIE junkie 的另一種拼法

junk yard /ˈ· ·/ *n* [C] *AmE* a place where old or unwanted things can be left, bought, and sold【美】廢品舊貨棧 —compare 比較 DUMP[2] (1), TIP[1] (4)

jun·ta /ˈdʒʌntə; ˈdʒʌntə/ *n* [C] a military government that has gained power by using force〔靠武力取得政權的〕軍政府

Ju·pi·ter /ˈdʒupətə; ˈdʒuːpɪ̥tə/ *n* [singular] a large PLANET that moves around the sun 木星 —see picture at 參見 SOLAR SYSTEM 圖

ju·rid·i·cal /dʒʊˈrɪdɪkḷ; dʒʊˈrɪdɪkəl/ *adj formal* connected with judges or the law【正式】司法上的, 法律上的

jur·is·dic·tion /ˌdʒurɪsˈdɪkʃən; ˌdʒʊərɪ̥sˈdɪkʃən/ *n* [U] the right to use an official power to make legal decisions 司法權; 審判權; 管轄權: *That area is not within the State Police's jurisdiction.* 那個地區不在州警察局的管轄範圍之內。

ju·ris·pru·dence /ˌdʒurɪsˈprudṇs; ˌdʒʊərɪ̥sˈpruːdəns/ *n* [U] *formal* the science or study of law【正式】法學, 法律學

ju·rist /ˈdʒurɪst; ˈdʒʊərɪ̥st/ *n* [C] *formal* someone who has a very detailed knowledge of law【正式】法學家, 法律學者

ju·ror /ˈdʒurə; ˈdʒʊərə/ *n* [C] a member of a JURY 陪審員; 評判員

ju·ry /ˈdʒurɪ; ˈdʒʊəri/ *n* [C] **1** a group of 12 ordinary people who listen to details of a case in court and decide whether someone is guilty or not〔由 12 位公民組成的〕陪審團: *The jury finds the defendant not guilty.* 陪審團認為被告無罪。| **sit on a jury** (=be part of a jury) 擔任陪審員 **2** a group of people chosen to judge a competition〔競賽的〕評判委員會 **3 the jury is out on sth** used to say that something is still not yet certain 陪審團仍在商議中〔指某事仍然沒有定論〕: *The jury is still out as to the overall impact of the programme.* 關於該計劃的整體影響, 評委會仍在進行商議。—see also 另見 GRAND JURY

jury box /'·· ·/ *n* [C usually singular 一般用單數] the place where the jury sits in a court 陪審團席

jury du·ty /'·· ,··/ *n* [U] *AmE* a period of time during which you must be part of a jury【美】〔一段時間內〕擔任陪審員的義務; JURY SERVICE *BrE*【英】

ju·ry·man /ˈdʒʊrɪmən; ˈdʒʊərimən/ *n* [C] a male member of a jury 男陪審員

jury serv·ice /'·· ,··/ *n* [U] *BrE* a period of time during which you must be part of a jury【英】擔任陪審員的義務; JURY DUTY *AmE*【美】

jur·y·wom·an /ˈdʒʊrɪˌwʊmən; ˈdʒʊəriˌwʊmən/ *n* [C] a female member of a jury 女陪審員

1 **just¹** /dʒəst; dʒəst; *strong* 強讀 dʒʌst; dʒʌst/ *adv* **1** ex-
1 actly 正好, 恰好: *Thank you. That's just what I need.* 謝謝, 那正是我需要的。| *The house was large and roomy; just right for us.* 那幢房子大而寬敞, 正適合我們。| *She looks just like her mother.* 她看上去就像她媽媽。**2** only 僅僅, 只是: *He's not a thief, just a little boy who likes biscuits.* 他不是賊, 只是個愛吃餅乾的小男孩。| *It'll just take a few minutes.* 只需花幾分鐘。**3** if something has just happened, it happened only a short time ago 剛剛〔發生〕, 方才: *John's just told me that he's getting married.* 約翰剛剛告訴我他要結婚了。| *I've just been out shopping.* 我剛才出去買東西了。**4** if you are just doing something, or just about to do something you are starting to do it or going to do it soon 剛要〔做某事〕, 正準備: *He was just leaving when the phone rang.* 他正準備離開時, 電話鈴響了。| *I'll just change my clothes, if you don't mind waiting a minute.* 如果你不介意等一下, 我就去換衣服。**5** used to emphasize something you are saying〔用於加強語氣〕: *I needed some fresh air, so work would just have to wait.* 我需要一點新鮮空氣, 工作就只好等一等。| *He just got in his car and drove off.* 他徑直鑽進汽車, 開車走了。**6 just before/after/over etc** only a short time before, after etc 稍前/稍後/剛剛超過等: *We moved here just after our son was born.* 兒子出生不久我們就搬到這兒來了。| *I saw her just before she died.* 就在她去世前不久, 我見過她。| *It's just under three centimeters long.* 差一點兒才夠三厘米長。**7 (only) just** if something just happens or is just possible, it does happen or is possible, but it almost did not happen or was not possible 勉強地, 不太可能地: *He just managed to get home before dark.* 他趕及在天黑前到家。| *Those pants only just fit you now.* 那幾條褲子你現在穿勉強合身。**8 just about** almost 幾乎, 差不多: *The plums are just about ripe now.* 李子差不多都熟了。| *Just about everybody will be affected by the tax increases.* 幾乎每個人都將受到加稅的影響。**9 just as** equally as 和…一樣: *Brad is just as good as the others.* 布拉德和其他人完全一樣。**10 just then** at exactly that moment 正在那時: *Just then there was a sound in the hall.* 正在那時, 大廳裡傳來響聲。**11 just the thing** *informal* exactly the right thing【非正式】正合適的東西: *This soup is just the thing for a cold winter's day.* 寒冷的冬天裡喝這種湯正合適。**12** *informal* completely【非正式】完全地: *She was just horrified at my choice of husband.* 她對於我選擇的丈夫大感吃驚。—see also 另見 **just my luck** (LUCK¹ (7))

Frequencies of the adverb **just** in spoken and written English 副詞 just 在英語口語和書面語中的使用頻率

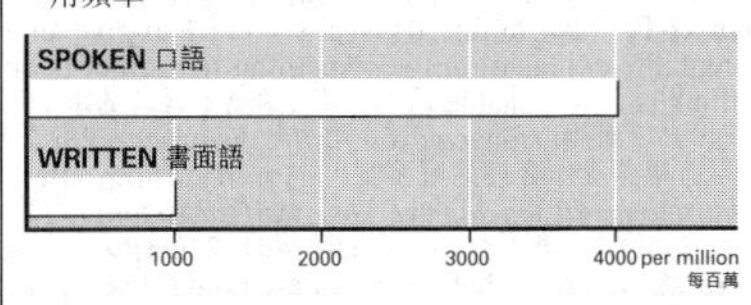

Based on the British National Corpus and the Longman Lancaster Corpus 據英國國家語料庫和朗文蘭卡斯特語料庫

This graph shows that the adverb **just** is much more common in spoken English than in written English. This is because it is very commonly used in spoken English to mean 'exactly' or to mean 'a short time before or after'. It also has special uses in spoken English and is used in a lot of common spoken phrases. 本圖表顯示, 副詞just在英語口語中的使用頻率遠遠高於書面語, 因為它在口語中常常用來表示"正好"或"稍前/稍後"的意思。它在口語中還有許多特殊用法, 而且口語中有很多常用片語都是由just構成的。

just (*adv*) **SPOKEN USES AND PHRASES**
含 just 的口語用法及片語

13 just a) used to pause while you think what to say next or think how to describe something〔用於短暫停頓, 以便思考接着說甚麼或如何描述某事等〕: *When I told him the news he just ... he just sat there and didn't say a word.* 我告訴他這個消息時, 他嗯…坐在那兒一言不發。| *It wasn't an argument, it was just, it was more like a discussion.* 那不是爭論, 那是嗯…倒更像是討論。**b)** used when politely asking something or telling someone to do something〔用於禮貌地要求某事或請某人做某事〕: *Could I just say a few words before we start?* 我們開始前, 能否讓我先說幾句話? **c)** used when firmly telling someone to do something〔用於嚴厲地命令某人做某事〕: *Look, just shut up for a minute!* 喂, 把你的嘴閉一會兒! **14 just a minute/second/moment a)** used to ask someone to wait for a short time while you do something 請稍等一下〔當你做某事時請別人等一等〕: *Just a minute, I'll see if I can find it for you.* 稍等一下, 我看看能否給你找到它。**b)** used to interrupt someone in order to ask them something, disagree with them etc 請等一下〔用於打斷別人的話, 以詢問某事或表示不同意等〕: *Just a minute, I'm not sure I agree with your last point.* 請等一下, 我不同意你說的最後一點。**15 just now a)** a moment ago or a very short time ago 剛才: *Where have my glasses gone? I had them just now.* 我的眼鏡哪裡去了? 我剛才還戴着呢。**b)** *especially BrE* at the moment【尤英】現在, 眼下: *We're busy just now, can you come back later?* 我們現在很忙, 你過一會再來好嗎? **16 would just as soon** if you would just as soon do something, you would prefer to do it 寧願, 寧可: *I'd just as soon not be here when she comes.* 她來的時候, 我寧可不在這裡。**17 may just/might just** might possibly 也許, 有可能: *You could try Renee; she might just know where they live now.* 你不妨問問蕾妮, 她也許知道他們現在住在哪兒。**18 not just yet** not quite yet 還不能: *I can't leave just yet. I've still got a couple of letters to write.* 我現在還不能離開, 還有幾封信要寫。**19 it's just that** used when explaining the reason for something, especially when someone thinks there is a different reason 只是〔用來說明原因, 尤其在有人認為另有原因時使用〕: *No, I do like Chinese food, it's just that I'm not hungry.* 不, 我的確喜歡中國菜, 只是我現在不餓。**20 just think/look/listen** used to tell someone to imagine, look at or listen to the same thing that you are imagining, looking at, or listening to 且想想/看看/聽聽〔自己想像、看見或聽見的事物〕: *Just think – in a week we'll be lying on a beach in the sun!* 你想想——一星期後我們將躺在沙灘上曬太陽! **21 be just looking** to be looking at things in a shop without intending to buy anything〔在商店裡〕隨便逛逛〔不準備購物〕: *"Can I help you?" "No thanks, I'm just looking."* "你要甚麼?" "不, 謝謝。我只是隨便看看。" **22 just because ... doesn't mean** used to say that although one thing is true, another thing is not necessarily true 儘管…但不表示…: *Just because you're older than me doesn't mean you can tell me what to do.* 儘管你年紀比我大, 但不表示你有權命令我。**23 it's/that's just as well** used to say that it is lucky that something hap-

J

pens because otherwise there would be problems 幸虧, 幸而: *It's just as well Kathy didn't come to the film. She'd have hated it.* 幸虧凱西沒來看這部電影, 她會討厭這電影的。**24 might just as well** if you might just as well do something, it would be sensible, or a good idea to do it 還不如…〔用來表示做某事是明智或恰當的〕: *There's no point in waiting here. We might just as well go home.* 在這兒等沒有意義, 我們還不如回家。**25 just the same** used to say that your opinion is the same about something, although someone has said something to try to change your opinion 儘管那樣〔表示不管別人怎樣說, 你對某物的看法仍然一樣〕: *"The new model is a lot better." "Just the same, I'd rather have the old one I'm used to."* "新型號好得多。" "儘管如此, 我仍然喜歡我熟悉的舊型號。" **26 isn't she just/aren't they just** *old-fashioned* used to strongly agree with something someone has said about a person or thing【過時】沒錯, 的確〔對某人的話表示強烈贊同〕: *"He's a selfish, rude, ignorant man!" "Isn't he just!"* "他是個自私、粗魯又無知的傢伙!" "可不是嘛!" **27 just testing a)** used to tell someone that you only asked them something to check if they knew the answer 只是問問/考考你〔用來表示之所以發問是想看某人是否知道答案〕: *"What's the capital of France?" "Paris, of course!" "Just testing."* "法國的首都是哪裡?" "當然是巴黎!" "只是想考考你。" **b)** used when you have made a mistake, to pretend that you only did it to see if someone would notice 只是試驗〔做錯事時, 用來假裝你做此事只是為了試驗別人有沒有注意到〕: *"That isn't how you spell 'receive'!" "I know, just testing!"* "receive這個詞不是這樣拼的!" "我知道, 只是試試你能不能看出來!" **28 just on** *BrE* almost exactly【英】差不多, 將近: *It's just on three o'clock.* 快到三點整。**29 just so a)** with everything arranged neatly and tidily 井然有序, 有條不紊: *Her house always has to be just so.* 她的房子總是收拾得井井有條。**b)** *old-fashioned* used to say yes or agree with something【過時】對; 是這樣; 正是如此

USAGE NOTE 用法說明: JUST

AmE-BrE DIFFERENCE 美國英語與英國英語的區別

Time adverbs **just, already**, and **yet** are often used with the simple past tense in American English. 美國英語中, 時間副詞 just, already 和 yet 常與一般過去式連用: *The bell just rang* (=it rang a short time ago). 鈴剛響過。| *I already saw him.* 我已經見過他。| *Did you eat yet?* 你吃過飯了嗎?

This use is also fairly common now in British English, but it is still considered more correct to say 這種用法現在在英國英語中也相當普遍, 但人們仍然認為更準確的說法是: *The bell has just rung.* 鈴剛響過。| *I've already seen him.* 我已經見過他。| *Have you eaten yet?* 你吃過飯了嗎?

S3 W3 **just²** /dʒʌst; dʒʌst/ *adj* **1** morally right and fair 正義的, 公正的, 公平的: *A medal of honour was his just reward.* 一枚榮譽獎章是對他最公正的獎賞。| *I think this is a just punishment bearing in mind the seriousness of the crime.* 考慮到罪行的嚴重性, 我認為這是很公正的懲罰。**2 get your just deserts** to be punished or suffer in a way that other people think you deserve 得到應有的懲罰, 罪有應得: *I hope that he's caught and gets his just deserts.* 我希望他被抓住並得到應有的懲罰。—**justly** *adv*: *These men are criminals, but they must be dealt with justly.* 這些人雖然是罪犯, 但也應公正對待。

W2 **jus·tice** /ˈdʒʌstɪs; ˈdʒʌstɨ̣s/ *n* **1** [U] fairness in the way people are treated 正義; 公正; 合理: *Sometimes I wonder if there's any justice in this world.* 我有時候懷疑世上還有沒有公義。—opposite 反義詞 INJUSTICE —see also 另見 POETIC JUSTICE **2** [U] the system by which people are judged in courts of law and criminals are punished 司法制度; 審判; 法律制裁: *This has restored my faith in British justice.* 這件事使我恢復了對英國司法制度的信心。| **escape justice** (=avoid being punished for a crime) 〔犯罪後〕逃避法律制裁 **3 bring sb to justice** to catch someone who you think is guilty of a crime and arrange for them to go to court 將犯人緝拿歸案: *We will not rest until her killer is brought to justice.* 不把殺害她的兇手繩之於法, 我們決不罷休。**4 justice has been done/served** used to say that someone has been treated fairly or has been given a punishment they deserve 正義得以伸張 **5 do justice to sb/sth** also 又作 **do sb/sth justice** to treat or represent someone or something in a way that is fair and shows their best qualities 公平對待某人/某物; 充分展現某人/某物的最佳素質: *The photo doesn't do her justice – she was really beautiful.* 這張照片沒有把她拍好——她其實很美。| *It's impossible to do justice to Mahler's music without a full orchestra.* 沒有完整的管弦樂隊, 馬勒的音樂就不可能得到充分展現。**6 do yourself justice** to do something such as a test well enough to show your real ability 〔在考試等中〕充分發揮自己的能力: *Sara panicked in the exam and didn't do herself justice.* 莎拉在考試中由於緊張未能充分發揮自己的水準。**7** also 又作 **Justice a)** [C] *AmE* a judge in a law court【美】法官 **b)** [C] *BrE* the title of a judge in the High Court【英】〔高等法院的〕法官的頭銜 **8** [U] the quality of being right and deserving fair treatment 正確; 公正: *No one doubts the justice of our cause.* 沒有人懷疑我們的動機的合理性。—see also 另見 **rough justice** (ROUGH[1] (14))

Justice of the Peace /ˌ··· ·ˈ·/ abbreviation 縮寫為 **JP** *n* [C] someone who judges less serious cases in small law courts and, in the US, can perform marriage ceremonies 地方官; 治安法官〔在美國還有證婚權〕

jus·ti·fi·a·ble /ˈdʒʌstəˌfaɪəbl; ˈdʒʌstɨ̣faɪəbəl/ *adj* actions, reactions, decisions etc that are justifiable are done for good reasons 〔行為、反應、決定等〕有道理的: *justifiable anger* 情有可原的憤怒 —**justifiably** *adv*

justifiable hom·i·cide /ˌ····ˈ···/ *n* [U] *law* a situation in which you are not punished for killing someone, usually because you did it to defend yourself【法律】正當殺人〔一般指因自衛而殺人, 因此不受懲罰〕

jus·ti·fi·ca·tion /ˌdʒʌstəfəˈkeʃən; ˌdʒʌstɨ̣fɨ̣ˈkeɪʃən/ *n* [C,U] **1** a good and acceptable reason for doing something 正當的理由, 可接受的理由: *The committee could see no justification for a pay rise.* 委員會找不出提高工資的恰當理由。**2 in justification (of)** to explain why an idea or action is right 為…辯解〔解釋為何某想法或行動是正確的〕

jus·ti·fied /ˈdʒʌstəˌfaɪd; ˈdʒʌstɨ̣faɪd/ *adj* **1** having an acceptable explanation or reason 有正當理由的, 有合理解釋的: *I think your conclusions were fully justified.* 我認為你的結論完全合理。| **be justified in doing sth** *Under the circumstances, the principal was justified in expelling this student.* 在這種情況下, 校長完全有理由開除這名學生。**2 right/left justified** *technical* printed material that is right or left justified has a straight edge where all the words line up on the left or right of a page【術語】〔印刷品中的文字在頁面〕右側/左側對齊的

jus·ti·fy /ˈdʒʌstəˌfaɪ; ˈdʒʌstɨ̣faɪ/ *v* [T] **1** to give an acceptable explanation for something that other people think is unreasonable 證明〔別人認為不合理的事〕有道理; 為…辯護: *How can you justify the expense?* 你怎樣對這筆開支作合理的解釋呢? | **justify doing sth** *It's hard to justify making everyone wait for so long.* 對讓大家等這麼久是很難作出合理的解釋的。**2 justify yourself (to sb)** to prove that what you are doing is reasonable (向某人) 為自己辯護: *I'm in charge here; I don't have to justify myself to you.* 這裡由我負責, 我沒有必要為我的行為向你解釋。**3** to be a good and acceptable reason for something 是…的正當理由: *Nothing justifies murdering another human being.* 沒有任何正當的理由可以為殺人這種罪行辯解。

jut /dʒʌt; dʒʌt/ *v* **jutted, jutting** [I always+adv/prep] also 又作 **jut out** something that juts up or out sticks up or out further than the other things around it 突出, 伸出: *Tall jagged rocks jutted out over the beach.* 高聳嶙峋的岩石在海灘上延伸出來。

jute /dʒut; dʒuːt/ *n* [U] a natural substance that is used for making rope and rough cloth〔用於製繩子和粗布的〕黃麻纖維

ju·ve·nile /ˈdʒuvənl; ˈdʒuːvənaɪl/ *adj* **1** [only before noun 僅用於名詞前] *especially law* connected with young people who are not yet adults【尤法律】少年的: *juvenile crime* 少年罪行 **2** silly and typical of a child rather than an adult 幼稚的, 年幼無知的: *a very juvenile sense of humour* 很幼稚的幽默感 —**juvenile** *n* [C]

juvenile de·lin·quent /,··· ·ˈ··/ *n* [C] a child or young person who behaves in a criminal way 少年罪犯 —**juvenile delinquency** *n* [U]

jux·ta·pose /ˌdʒʌkstəˋpoz; ˌdʒʌkstəˈpəʊz/ *v* [T] *formal* to put things together, especially things that are not normally together, in order to compare them or to make something new【正式】把…並列[並置]〔以作比較或製作新東西〕—**juxtaposition** /ˌdʒʌkstəpəˋzɪʃən; ˌdʒʌkstəpəˈzɪʃən/ *n* [C,U]

K,k

K, k /ke; keɪ/ *plural* **K's, k's** *n* [C] the eleventh letter of the English alphabet 英語字母表的第十一個字母

K, k 1 *informal*【非正式】an abbreviation of 縮寫= one thousand 一千: *salary of £30k a year* 年薪三萬英鎊 **2** an abbreviation of 縮寫= KILOBYTE (=a measurement of computer information) 千字節〔電腦的信息單位〕

ka·bob /kəˋbɑb; kəˈbɑːb/ *n* [C] an American spelling of KEBAB kebab 的美式拼法

kaf·fee·klatch /ˋkæfeˌklætʃ; ˈkæfeɪklætʃ/ *n* [C] *AmE* an informal social situation when people drink coffee and talk【美】咖啡敘談會

kaf·fir /ˋkæfɚ; ˈkæfə/ *n* [C] *SAfrE taboo* an offensive word for a black African, used only by white people【南非, 諱】非洲黑鬼〔白人對非洲黑人的冒犯用語〕

kaf·tan /ˋkæftən; ˈkæftæn/ *n* [C] another spelling of CAFTAN caftan 的另一種拼法

Ka·lash·ni·kov /kəˋlæʃnɪkɑf; kəˈlæʃnɪkɒf/ *n* [C] a type of RIFLE (=long gun) that can fire very quickly 卡拉什尼科夫步槍, AK47 步槍

kale /kel; keɪl/ *n* [C,U] a dark green CABBAGE (=type of vegetable) 羽衣甘藍

ka·lei·do·scope /kəˋlaɪdəˌskop; kəˈlaɪdəskəʊp/ *n* [C] **1** a pattern, situation, or scene that is always changing and has many details or bright colours 千變萬化的圖案[情況; 景致]: **[+of]** *the kaleidoscope of American ethnic groups* 五光十色的美國各民族 **2** a tube with mirrors and pieces of coloured glass at one end, that shows coloured patterns when you turn it 萬花筒

ka·lei·do·scop·ic /kəˋlaɪdəˌskɑpɪk; kəˌlaɪdəˈskɒpɪk◂/ *adj* kaleidoscopic scenes, colours, or patterns change often and quickly〔景致、色彩或圖案〕千變萬化的 —**kaleidoscopically** /-klɪ; -kli/ *adv*

kam·i·ka·ze /ˌkæmɪˋkɑzɪ; ˌkæmɪˈkɑːzi◂/ *adj* **1 kamikaze pilot** a pilot who deliberately crashes his plane on enemy camps, ships, etc knowing he will be killed 神風隊飛行員 **2 kamikaze attitude/behaviour** willingness to take risks, without caring about your safety 敢於冒險不計自身安危的態度/行為: *kamikaze lorry drivers* 不顧生命危險的卡車司機

kan·ga /ˋkæŋgə; ˈkæŋgə/ *n* [C] a woman's dress from Africa, consisting of a long piece of cloth wound around the body 肯加衣裙〔源於非洲婦女的衣着, 用一條長布包纏身軀而成〕

kan·ga·roo /ˌkæŋgəˋru; ˌkæŋgəˈruː◂/ *n* [C] an Australian animal that moves by jumping and carries its babies in a POUCH (=a special pocket of skin) 袋鼠

kangaroo court /ˌ··· ˈ·/ *n* [C] an unofficial court that punishes people unfairly "袋鼠法庭"〔私設的判案不公的法庭〕

ka·o·lin /ˋkeəlɪn; ˈkeɪəlɪn/ *n* [U] a type of white clay used for making cups, plates etc, and also in medicine 高嶺土, 瓷土

ka·pok /ˋkepɑk; ˈkeɪpɒk/ *n* [U] a very light material like cotton used for filling soft things like cushions (CUSHION[1] (1)) 木棉

ka·put /kəˋpʊt; kəˈpʊt/ *adj* [not before noun 不用於名詞前] *spoken* broken【口】壞了的; 不能使用的: **go kaput** (=become broken) 壞了; 不能用了

kar·a·o·ke /ˌkɑrəˋokɪ; ˌkæriˈəʊki/ *n* **1** [U] the activity of singing to recorded music for entertainment 卡拉 OK〔以錄好的音樂作伴奏跟着唱〕**2** [C] a machine that plays recorded music which people can sing to 卡拉 OK 伴唱機

kar·at /ˋkærət; ˈkærət/ *n* [C] an American spelling of CARAT carat 的美式拼法

ka·ra·te /kɑˋrɑtɪ; kəˈrɑːti/ *n* [U] a style of fighting from the Far East, in which you kick and hit with your hands 空手道〔源自遠東的一種徒手搏擊術〕

kar·ma /ˋkɑrmə; ˈkɑːmə/ *n* [U] **1** the force that is produced by the things you do in your life and that will influence you in the future, according to the Hindu and Buddhist religions〔印度教、佛教中的〕羯磨; 業〔指現世活動將影響來世報應〕**2** *informal* luck resulting from your actions; FATE【非正式】命運; 因果報應 —**karmic** *adj*

ka·ty·did /ˋketɪˌdɪd; ˈkeɪtidɪd/ *n* [C] *AmE* a type of large GRASSHOPPER that makes a noise like the sound of the words 'katy did'【美】螽斯〔一種大型蚱蜢〕

kay·ak /ˋkaɪæk; ˈkaɪæk/ *n* [C] a type of light CANOE[1] 小皮艇, 輕型獨木舟

ka·zoo /kəˋzu; kəˈzuː/ *n* [C] a simple musical instrument that you play by holding it to your lips and making sounds into it 卡祖笛

Kb an abbreviation of 縮寫= KILOBYTE

KC /ˌke ˋsi; ˌkeɪ ˈsiː/ *n BrE* King's Counsel; the highest level of BARRISTER (=lawyer who speaks in court) when the ruler is a king【英】王室法律顧問; 大律師 —compare 比較 QC

ke·bab /kɪˋbæb; kəˈbæb/ also 又作 **kabob** *AmE*【美】*n* [C] small pieces of meat and vegetables cooked on a stick 烤肉串

kedg·e·ree /ˋkɛdʒəˌri; ˈkedʒəriː/ *n* [U] a cooked dish of fish, rice, and eggs mixed together 魚蛋燴飯

keel[1] /kil; kiːl/ *n* **1** a bar along the bottom of a boat that keeps it steady in the water〔船的〕龍骨 —see picture at 參見 YACHT 圖 **2 on an even keel** steady without any sudden changes 平穩的; 穩定的: *Now that the crisis is over, we must try to get things back on an even keel.* 既然危機已結束, 我們就應設法使情況恢復穩定。

keel[2] *v*

keel over *phr v* [I] to fall over sideways 翻倒, 傾覆: *Several soldiers keeled over in the hot sun.* 幾名士兵在烈日下暈倒了。

keel·haul /ˋkilˌhɔl; ˈkiːlhɔːl/ *v* [T] **1** *usually humorous* to punish someone severely【一般幽默】嚴懲〔某人〕**2** to pull someone under the keel of a ship with a rope as a punishment 把〔某人〕縛於船底施以拖刑

keen[1] /kin; kiːn/ *adj*

1 ►INTERESTED/EAGER 感興趣的/渴望的◄ *especially BrE* someone who is keen is very interested in something or is eager to do it【尤英】熱衷的, 渴望的, 熱切的: *a keen photographer* 熱衷於攝影的人 | **[+on]** *Daniel's very keen on tennis.* 丹尼爾非常喜愛打網球。| **keen to do something** *She's out of hospital and keen to get back to work.* 她已經出院, 並急於重返工作崗位。

2 ►ATTRACTED 着迷的◄ *especially BrE*【尤英】**be keen on sb** to be very attracted to someone 對某人十分着迷: *He must be pretty keen on her – they've been dancing all night.* 他肯定迷上她了 — 他倆整夜都在跳舞。

3 ►CLEVER 聰明的◄ someone with a keen mind is quick to understand things 頭腦敏捷的

4 ►COMPETITION 競爭◄ **keen competition** a situation in which people compete strongly 激烈的競爭: *We won the contest in the face of keen competition.* 在激烈的競爭中我們贏得了比賽。

5 ►SIGHT/SMELL/HEARING 視覺/嗅覺/聽覺◄ a keen sense of smell or keen sight or hearing is an extremely

good ability to smell etc 靈敏的, 敏銳的: *Dogs have a very keen sense of smell.* 狗有十分靈敏的嗅覺。
6 ▶SHARP 鋒利的◀ *literary* a keen knife or blade is extremely sharp【文】〔刀、刃〕鋒利的
7 ▶WIND 風◀ *old-fashioned* a keen wind is cold and strong【過時】〔風〕刺骨的
8 keen as mustard *BrE informal*【英, 非正式】**a)** extremely eager 極其渴望的 **b)** very quick to understand things 非常聰穎的 —**keenly** *adj* —**keenness** *n* [U]

keen² *v* [I] *old use* to sing a loud, sad song for someone who has died【舊】〔為死者〕哀號, 哀歌, 唱輓歌

1 1 **keep¹** /kip; ki:p/ *v past tense and past participle* **kept** /kɛpt; kept/
1 ▶NOT GIVE BACK 不歸還◀ [T] to have something and not need to give it back 保留; 保存; 留下: *You can keep it. I don't need it.* 你留着吧, 我不需要了。| *Try it for a week and we guarantee you'll want to keep it.* 試用一週, 我們保證你會想把它留下的。
2 ▶NOT LOSE 不丟失◀ [T] to continue to have something and not lose it or get rid of it 保管, 保藏: *No, we're going to keep the house in Vermont and rent it out.* 不, 我們打算留下佛蒙特州的房子, 把它租出去。| *It's not getting a job that's the problem – it's keeping it!* 找個工作不是難事, 問題是怎樣保住它!
3 ▶NOT CHANGE/MOVE 不變/不動◀ [I, linking verb 連繫動詞] to continue to be in a particular state, condition, or place and not change or move 保持〔某種狀態〕; 保持不動[不變]: *I'm trying to cut his hair but he won't keep still.* 我在為他剪頭髮, 但他動個不停。| **keep warm/safe/dry etc** *With this wind it's so difficult to keep warm!* 風這麼大, 很難保暖呢! | **keep left/right** (=stay to the left or right of a path or road as you move) 靠左側/右側〔行走〕
4 ▶MAKE SB/STH NOT CHANGE/MOVE 使某人/某物不變/不動◀ [T] **a)** to make someone stay in a place 使〔某人〕停留於某處: *How long are they going to keep her in the hospital?* 他們想讓她在醫院裡住多久? **b)** to make someone or something continue being in a particular state or situation 使〔某人或某物〕保持〔某種狀態〕: **keep sb warm/safe etc** *Take my overcoat. It'll keep you warm.* 拿上我的大衣, 可以給你保暖。| *some toys to keep the kids busy* 能讓孩子們忙碌一陣子的玩具 | **keep sth clean/open etc** *We try to keep the major roads open right through winter.* 我們設法使主要道路整個冬天暢通無阻。| **keep sb/sth doing sth** *I'll try not to keep you waiting.* 我會盡量不讓你久等。| *Keep the engine running.* 別讓發動機熄火。| **keep sb in suspense** (=keep someone waiting anxiously to know a result) 使某人焦急等待〔結果〕 *How much longer are you going to keep us in suspense?* 你還想再讓我們等多久才告訴我們結果? | **keep on the right side of sb** (=not do anything to annoy them) 盡量別惹惱某人 *Keep on the right side of Mrs Salazar, she's very strict.* 別去惹惱薩拉查夫人, 她可是很嚴厲的。
5 ▶DO STH REPEATEDLY 反覆做某事◀ [I,T] to continue doing an activity or repeat the same action several times 繼續[重複]做: **keep (on) doing sth** *I keep forgetting to mail this letter.* 我老是忘記把這封信寄出。| *Daddy! Melanie keeps on hitting me!* 爸爸, 梅勒妮老是打我!
6 ▶DELAY SB 使某人耽擱◀ [T] to delay someone 阻止; 拖延: *He should be here by now. What's keeping him?* 他現在本該到這兒了, 甚麼事把他耽擱了?
7 ▶STORE STH 存放某物◀ [T always+adv/prep] to leave something in one particular place so that you can find it easily 存放: **keep sth in/on/under etc** *I always keep a first aid box in the car, in case we have an accident.* 我總是在車裡放一個急救箱, 以便出事時用。
8 keep a record/account/diary etc to regularly record written information somewhere 定期記錄/記賬/寫日記等
9 keep your promise/word etc to do what you have promised to do 履行諾言: *How do I know you'll keep your word?* 我怎麼知道你會履行諾言?
10 keep a secret to not tell anyone about a secret that you know 保守祕密: *Can I trust all of you to keep a secret?* 我能相信你們所有人都會保守祕密嗎?
11 keep to yourself also 又作 **keep yourself to yourself** *BrE* to live a very quiet private life and not do many things that involve other people【英】深居簡出, 不與人交往; 不理會別人的事
12 keep guard/watch to guard a place or watch around you all the time 守衛; 防守; 看守
13 ▶FOOD 食物◀ [I] if food keeps, it stays fresh enough to still be eaten 保鮮: *Eat the salmon because it won't keep till tomorrow.* 把這條鮭魚吃了吧, 明天就不新鮮了。
14 keep your head to stay calm in a difficult situation or an EMERGENCY〔在困境或緊急情況中〕保持冷靜: *Just keep your head and try to steer in the direction of the skid.* 保持冷靜, 朝打滑的方向打方向盤。
15 ▶ANIMALS 動物◀ [T] to own and look after animals 飼養: *We keep chickens and a couple of pigs.* 我們養了一些雞和幾頭豬。
16 ▶SHOP 商店◀ [T] *BrE old-fashioned* to own a small business and work in it【英, 過時】經營〔小店鋪〕: *Frank used to keep a butcher's on Park Road.* 弗蘭克曾在帕克路開過一家肉鋪。
17 ▶LOOK AFTER 照料◀ [T] to take care of someone, providing them with money, food etc 照顧; 供養: **keep sb in sth** *There's enough money there to keep you in silk stockings for a year!* 那裡有足夠的錢供你豐衣足食一年之久!
18 ▶PROTECT 保護◀ [T] *formal* to guard or protect someone【正式】保護, 保衛: **keep sb (from harm)** *The Lord bless you and keep you.* 上帝賜福於你並保佑你。
19 ▶CELEBRATE STH 慶祝某事◀ [T] *old-fashioned* to do the things that are traditionally done to celebrate something such as Christmas【過時】慶祝〔節日〕: *People don't keep Christmas the way they used to do.* 人們如今過聖誕節的方式與過去不同。—see also 另見 **keep in touch** (TOUCH² (6)), **home/keep your eye on sb** (EYE¹ (3)), **keep house** (HOUSE¹ (2)), **keep pace with** (PACE¹ (5)), **keep sb company** (COMPANY (2)), **keep the peace** (PEACE (5)), **keep time** (TIME¹), **keep your hand in** (HAND¹ (11)), **keep/lose track of** (TRACK¹ (8))

Frequencies of the verb **keep** in spoken and written English 動詞 keep 在英語口語和書面語中的使用頻率

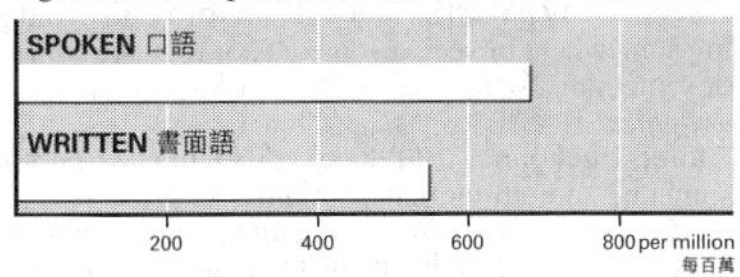

Based on the British National Corpus and the Longman Lancaster Corpus 據英國國家語料庫和朗文蘭卡斯特語料庫

This graph shows that the verb **keep** is more common in spoken English than in written English. This is because the expression **keep doing sth** is very commonly used in spoken English to mean 'continue to do something' or 'do something repeatedly'. **Keep** is also used in a lot of common spoken phrases. 本圖表顯示動詞 keep 在英語口語中的使用頻率高於書面語, 因為 keep doing sth 在英語口語中使用十分普遍, 表示"持續做某事"或"重複做某事"。keep 還用於許多常見的口語片語中。

keep (*v*) **SPOKEN PHRASES**
含 keep 的口語片語

20 keep going used to encourage someone who is doing something and to tell them to continue 繼續做下去〔用於鼓勵〕: *"Well done, that's it, keep going!"*

"幹得不錯, 就是那樣, 繼續做下去!"

21 keep it used to tell someone that they can keep something you have given them or lent them 你留着吧: *Keep it. I've got plenty more at home.* 你留着吧, 我家裡還有很多呢。

22 keep quiet used to tell someone not to say anything or make any noise 安靜點, 小點聲: *Keep quiet! I'm trying to watch the game.* 安靜一點! 我要看比賽!

23 keep away/back! used to tell someone not to go near something or to move away from something 離遠一點! 不要靠近!: *Keep back everyone – this is dangerous!* 大家離遠一點, 這裡危險!

24 keep down! used to tell someone to keep near the ground so they cannot be seen, shot etc 趴下!

25 keep it down used to tell someone to be quieter 安靜一點: *Keep it down, will you. We're trying to sleep.* 請小點聲, 我們要睡覺了。

26 how are you keeping? used to ask if someone is well 你身體好嗎?: *"Hi, Mark! How are you keeping?" "Oh, not so bad."* "你好, 馬克, 近來身體怎麼樣?" "還可以。"

27 keep the change used when paying someone, to tell them they can keep the extra money you have given them 不用找錢: *"That's $18." "Here's $20. Keep the change."* "這要 18 美元。" "這是 20 美元, 不用找零了。"

28 keep your hair/shirt on! used to tell someone to be more calm, patient etc 保持冷靜!; 耐心點!: *Keep your hair on! We've got plenty of time.* 耐心點! 我們有的是時間。

29 it'll keep used to say that you can tell someone something or do something later 以後告訴你; 以後再做: *"I'd love to hear about it but I've got to go." "Don't worry, it'll keep."* "我很想聽聽, 但現在就得走。" "別擔心, 我以後再告訴你。"

30 that'll keep you going used to tell someone that what you are giving them will last for some time 夠你用一段時間: *Here's £50 – that'll keep you going for a while.* 這是 50 英鎊, 夠你用一陣子的。

keep at *phr v* [T] **1** [**keep** sb **at** sth] to force someone to continue to work hard 逼迫〔某人〕繼續苦幹: *She kept us at it until eight o'clock!* 她竟要我們一直幹到八點! **2** [**keep at** sth] to continue working hard at something 堅持苦幹: *Let's just keep at it until we're finished.* 讓我們堅持下去, 直到幹完為止。

keep away *phr v* [I,T **keep** sb/sth **away**] to avoid going somewhere or seeing someone, or to make someone or something do this (使) 遠離: *You keep away from my daughter!* 你離我女兒遠點兒!

keep back *phr v* **1** [T **keep** sth ↔ **back**] to not tell someone something that you know 隱瞞〔某事〕: *I got the feeling he was keeping something back.* 我感到他有甚麼事隱瞞着。**2** [T **keep** sth ↔ **back**] *especially BrE* to not give or pay something that you were going to give 【尤英】留下, 扣除: *They kept back some of his wages to pay for the damage.* 他們扣下他的一部分工資以賠償損失。

keep sb/sth ↔ **down** *phr v* [T] **1** to control something and prevent it from increasing 控制, 抑制〔某物以防止其增長〕: *You can use herbicides to keep down the weeds.* 你可以用除草劑控制雜草的生長。**2** to be able to not VOMIT something (=pass it back up from your stomach) after you have eaten or drunk it 〔在吃喝之後〕阻止…嘔[吐]出: *I could hardly keep anything down for about three days.* 這三天我幾乎甚麼都咽不下去。

keep from *phr v* [T] **1** [**keep** sth **from** sb] to not tell someone something that you know 隱瞞, 不把…告訴〔某人〕: *You won't be able to keep the truth from her father.* 事實真相你是瞞不了她父親的。**2** [**keep** sb/sth **from** sth] to prevent someone from doing something or prevent something happening 阻止; 避免: **keep sb from doing sth** *Mulligan was the only person who kept us from running amok completely.* 馬利根是唯一阻止我們的人, 使我們沒有完全任性胡為。| **keep (yourself) from doing sth** *I could hardly keep from laughing, it was so funny.* 太滑稽了, 我簡直忍不住笑起來。| **keep sth from doing sth** *You put the potatoes in salted water to keep them from turning black.* 把馬鈴薯放到鹽水裡以防變黑。

keep sb **in** *phr v* [T] *BrE* to force someone to stay inside, especially as a punishment in school 【英】使〔某人〕留在裡面; 罰…課後留校〔尤作為學校中的一種懲罰〕

keep in with sb *phr v* [T] *BrE* to try to stay friendly with someone, especially because this helps you 【英】與〔某人〕友好相處〔尤因這樣做對自己有利〕; 獲得…的歡心: *You should try to keep in with Benson – he has a lot of influence around here.* 你應想辦法討好本森, 他在這一帶很有影響力。

keep off *phr v* **1** [T **keep** sth ↔ **off**] to prevent something affecting something else 防止; 避開; 使免受〔某物〕的影響: *They have these transparent covers to keep the dust off.* 他們用這些透明蓋子來遮擋灰塵。**2** [I] if rain keeps off, it does not fall 〔雨〕不下

keep on *phr v* **1 keep on doing sth** to continue doing something 繼續做某事: *I've told him to stop but he keeps on scratching it!* 我叫他停下來, 他還是刮個不停! **2** [T **keep** sb **on**] to continue to employ someone 繼續雇用: *If you're good they might keep you on after Christmas.* 你如果表現不錯, 聖誕節後他們或許會繼續用你。**3** [I] *informal* to talk continuously in an annoying way 【非正式】喋喋不休地說: [**+at/about**] *Do you have to keep on about your medical problems the whole time?* 你有必要沒完沒了地談你那些醫學問題嗎?

keep out *phr v* **1 keep out!** used on signs to tell people to stay away from a place or not enter it 切勿接近! 閒人免進! (用於警示牌) **2** [T **keep** sth ↔ **out**] to prevent someone or something getting into a place 阻止〔某人或某物〕進入: *Take this. It should at least keep the rain out.* 拿上這個, 至少可以擋擋雨。

keep out of sth *phr v* [T] to try not to become involved in something 不捲入; 避開: *We've always tried to keep out of local politics.* 我們總是盡可能不捲入地方政治中。

keep to *phr v* [T] **1** [**keep to** sth] to stay on a particular road, course, piece of ground etc 不離開〔某一道路、方向、地方等〕: *It's best to keep to the paved roads.* 最好不要偏離鋪過的道路。**2** [**keep to** sth] to do what you have promised or agreed to do 履行, 實施: *Keep strictly to the terms of the contract.* 嚴格執行合同條款。**3 keep sth to yourself** to keep something secret 保守祕密: *It's official. We're leaving, but do me a favour and keep it to yourself will you.* 這是公事。我們即將啟程, 但請幫忙保密, 你自己知道就行了。**4 keep to the point/subject etc** to talk or write only about the subject you are supposed to be talking about 緊扣要點/主題等 **5** [**keep** sth **to** sth] to prevent an amount, degree, or level from going higher than it should 防止〔數量、程度或水平〕高於應有的限度: *Can you please keep costs to a minimum?* 請你把成本保持在最低水平行嗎? **6 keep to your room/bed** to stay in your room or bed because you are ill or upset 〔因有病或心煩而〕不出門/不下牀

keep up *phr v* **1** [T **keep** sth ↔ **up**] to prevent something from falling or going to a lower level 使不掉下來; 使不下降: *The shortage of supplies is keeping the price up.* 供應不足使價格保持堅挺。**2** [I,T **keep** sth ↔ **up**] to continue doing something, or to make something continue (使) 繼續: *Keep up the good work!* 繼續好好幹! | *I don't think I can keep this up any longer.* 我認為這事我再也堅持不下去了。**3** [I] to manage to go or learn as fast as someone 〔進展、學習等〕跟上〔某人〕, 不落後: *Slow down, Davey can't keep up.* 放慢速度, 戴維跟不上了。| [**+with**] *I'm having trouble keeping up with the rest of the class.* 跟上全班的學習我有困難。**4** [I] to continue to read and learn about a particular subject 跟上〔某學科〕: [+with] *It's hard to keep up with the changes in computer technology.* 要跟上電腦技術的變化是很難的。**5 keep your spirits/strength/morale etc up** to try to stay happy, strong, confident etc 保持愉快心境/體力/士氣等: *We sang as we marched, to keep our spirits up.* 我們一面行進一面唱歌, 以保持高昂的情緒。**6** [T **keep** sb **up**] *informal* to prevent someone from going to bed【非正式】不讓〔某人〕上牀睡覺: *I hope I'm not keeping you up.* 我希望我沒有耽誤你上牀休息。**7 keep up appearances** to pretend that everything in your life is normal and happy even though you are in trouble, especially financial trouble 裝面子; 擺闊氣〔儘管遇到錢財方面的麻煩〕**8 keep up with the Joneses** to try to have all the possessions that your friends have because you want people to think that you are as good as them 與朋友比闊氣

keep² *n* **1** [U] all the things such as food, clothing etc that you need to keep you alive, or the cost of providing this 生活必需品〈如食物、衣服等〉; 生活費: **earn your keep** (=do things in return for the things that are provided for you) 自謀生活 *It's time you got a job and started earning your keep.* 是你找工作養活自己的時候了。**2 for keeps** *informal* for ever【非正式】永遠; 永久: *I'm going to settle this argument for keeps!* 我要一勞永逸地解決這場爭論! | *Marriage ought to be for keeps.* 婚姻應當是永久性的。**3** [C] a large strong tower, usually in the centre of a castle〔城堡的〕主樓

keep·a·way /ˈ· ··/ *n* [U] *AmE* a children's game in which you try to catch a ball that is being thrown between two other people【美】〔兒童的〕傳球遊戲〔截住另外兩人之間拋接的球〕; **piggy in the middle** (PIGGY¹ (2)) *BrE*【英】

keep·er /ˈkipɚ; ˈkiːpə/ *n* [C] **1** someone whose job is to look after a particular place 看守人, 管理員: *a lighthouse keeper* 燈塔管理員 | **shopkeeper/storekeeper** (=who owns and works in a shop) 店主 **2** someone who cares for or protects animals 動物園管理員; 獵場管理員: **zookeeper/gamekeeper** *The zoo keeper ordered the public away from the lion house.* 動物園管理員囑咐公眾遠離獅舍。—see also 另見 GAMEKEEPER **3** also 又作 **goalkeeper** someone who guards the GOAL (3) in a sport〔體育運動的〕守門員

keep fit /ˌ· ˈ·◂/ *n* [U] *BrE* a class in which you do exercises to keep yourself healthy【英】健身〈課〉—**keep-fit** *adj*

keep·ing /ˈkipɪŋ; ˈkiːpɪŋ/ *n* [U] **1 in sb's keeping** being looked after or guarded by someone 由某人照顧[保管] **2 in safe keeping** being carefully guarded somewhere 被安全保管 **3 in keeping/out of keeping (with sth)** suitable or not suitable for a particular occasion or purpose〈與某物〉協調[一致]/不協調[不一致]: *Please ensure your remarks are in keeping with the seriousness of the occasion.* 你要確保自己的言談與該場合的嚴肅性相協調。

keep·sake /ˈkipˌsek; ˈkiːpseɪk/ *n* [C] a small object that reminds you of someone 小紀念品

keg /kɛg; keg/ *n* [C] a round wooden container with a flat top and bottom, used especially for storing beer; BARREL¹ (1)〔尤指盛啤酒用的〕圓木桶: **keg beer/bitter** (=beer etc served from a keg) 桶裝啤酒/苦啤酒

keg·ger /ˈkɛgɚ; ˈkegə/ *n* [C] *AmE slang* a big party, usually outside, where beer is served from KEGS【美俚】大型露天啤酒會

keis·ter /ˈkistɚ; ˈkaɪstə/ *n* [C] *AmE old-fashioned* BUTTOCKS (=part of your body that you sit on)【美, 過時】臀部

kelp /kɛlp; kelp/ *n* [U] a type of large brown SEAWEED 巨藻, 大型褐藻

kel·vin /ˈkɛlvɪn; kelvɪn/ *n* [C] a unit for measuring temperature 開〔開爾文溫標的計量單位〕

ken¹ /kɛn; ken/ *n* **beyond your ken** outside your knowledge or understanding 超出…的知識範圍[理解程度]

ken² *v* [I,T] *ScotE* to know【蘇格蘭】知道; 認識: *D'ye ken John Peel?* 你認識約翰·皮爾嗎?

ken·nel /ˈkɛnl; ˈkenl/ *n* [C] **1** a small HUT where a dog sleeps 狗舍, 狗窩 **2** also 又作 **kennels** *BrE* a place where dogs are bred (BREED¹ (1,2)) or can stay while their owners are away【英】養狗場; 狗房; 狗繁殖場

kept the past tense and past participle of KEEP¹

kept wom·an /ˌ· ˈ··/ *n* [C] *old-fashioned* a woman who is given a place to live, money and clothes by a man who visits her regularly for sex【過時】〔受供養的〕情婦, 姘婦

kerb *BrE*【英】, **curb** *AmE*【美】/kɝb; kɜːb/ *n* [C] the edge of the PAVEMENT (=raised path) at the side of a street〔街道的〕路緣 —see picture on page A4 參見 A4 頁圖

kerb craw·ler *BrE*【英】, **curb crawler** *AmE*【美】/ˈ· ˌ··/ *n* [C] a man who drives his car slowly along the road looking for a PROSTITUTE (=woman who has sex for money) 駕車沿路緩慢行駛尋找娼妓的人 —**kerb crawling** *n* [U]

ker·chief /ˈkɝtʃɪf; ˈkɜːtʃɪf/ *n* [C] **1** a square piece of cloth, worn especially by women in former times around their head or neck〔舊時婦女用的〕方頭巾; 圍巾, 披肩 **2** *old-fashioned* a handkerchief【過時】手帕

ker·fuf·fle /kəˈfʌfl; kəˈfʌfəl/ *n* [C,U] *BrE informal* unnecessary noise and activity; FUSS¹ (2)【英, 非正式】吵鬧, 喧嘩; 混亂

ker·nel /ˈkɝnl; ˈkɜːnl/ *n* [C] **1** the centre part of a nut or seed, usually the part you can eat〔堅果或種子的〕核, 仁 **2** something that forms the most important part of a statement, idea, plan etc 核心, 要點, 要素: *There may be a kernel of truth in what he says.* 他說的話也可能有真實的成分。

ker·o·sene, kerosine /ˈkɛrəˌsin; ˈkerəsiːn/ *n* [U] *AmE, AustrE, NzE* an oil that is burnt for heat and used in lamps for lighting【美, 澳, 新西蘭】〔供取暖和照明用的〕煤油; PARAFFIN (1) *BrE*【英】

kes·trel /ˈkɛstrəl; ˈkestrəl/ *n* [C] a type of small FALCON 茶隼, 紅隼

ketch /kɛtʃ; ketʃ/ *n* [C] a small sailing ship with two masts (MAST (1)) 雙桅小帆船

ketch·up /ˈkɛtʃəp; ˈketʃəp/ also 又作 **catsup** *especially AmE*【尤美】*n* [U] a thick red liquid made from tomatoes (TOMATO) that you eat with food 番茄醬

ket·tle /ˈkɛtl; ˈketl/ *n* [C] **1** a metal or plastic container with a lid, a handle, and a SPOUT (=for pouring), used to boil water〔煮開水用的〕水壺 —see picture on page A10 參見 A10 頁圖 **2 put the kettle on** to boil water in a kettle 用水壺煮水: *I'll put the kettle on for tea.* 我要煮水沏茶。**3 another/a different kettle of fish** *informal* used to say that a situation that is very different from one that you have just mentioned【非正式】完全不同的兩回事: *She enjoys public speaking but being on TV is a different kettle of fish.* 她喜歡當眾演講, 但上電視就完全是另一回事了。**4 a fine/pretty kettle of fish** a situation that will cause you problems 困境; 尷尬的局面

ket·tle·drum /ˈkɛtlˌdrʌm; ˈketldrʌm/ *n* [C] a large metal drum with a round bottom, used in an ORCHESTRA 定音鼓, 銅鼓 —see also 另見 TIMPANI

kew·pie doll /ˈkjupɪ ˌdɑl; ˈkjuːpi dɒl/ also 又作 **kewpie** *n* [C] a type of American plastic DOLL¹ (1) with a fat body and a curl of hair on its head 丘比特娃娃〔身體肥胖、頭有鬈髮的塑料娃娃〕

K

key¹ /ki; kiː/ *adj* very important and necessary for success or to understand something 極為重要的, 關鍵的: *Put your most experienced players in the key positions.* 把最有經驗的選手放在關鍵位置上。| **key points/questions/issues etc** (=most important) 關鍵要點/問題等 *You can summarize the key points of his speech in a few lines.* 你可以用幾句話來總結他的講話要點。| **key mover/player** (=most important person in achieving a result, change etc) 關鍵人物

key² *n* [C] S2 W3
1 ►LOCK 鎖◄ a small specially shaped piece of metal

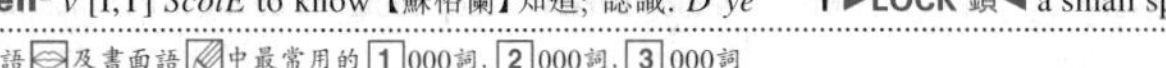

which you put into a lock and turn in order to lock or unlock a door, start a car etc 鑰匙
2 ►IMPORTANT PART 重要部分◄ **the key** the part of a plan, action, etc, that everything else depends on〔計劃、行動等的〕關鍵（部分）: **[+to]** *Concentration is the key to effective study.* 集中精力是有效學習的關鍵。
3 ►MACHINE/MUSICAL INSTRUMENT 機器/樂器◄ the part of a machine, computer, or musical instrument that you press with your fingers to make it work 鍵: *Press the ESCAPE key to exit.* 按ESCAPE鍵退出。| *She ran her fingers over the piano keys.* 她用手指在鋼琴鍵上掃過。
4 ►MUSICAL NOTES 音調◄ a set of musical notes with a particular base note, and the quality of sound that they have〔音樂的〕調, 主音: *a tune played in the key of C* 用C調演奏的曲子
5 ►MAP/DRAWING 地圖/圖紙◄ the part of a map, technical drawing etc that explains the signs etc on it 圖例, 符號說明
6 ►ISLAND 島◄ a small flat island, especially one near the coast of Florida〔尤指靠近佛羅里達海岸的〕低島, 小島; 礁: *the Florida Keys* 佛羅里達羣島
7 ►TEST ANSWERS 測試答案◄ the printed answers to a test or to the questions in a TEXTBOOK[1] that are used to check your work〔教科書中附有的測驗或問題的〕答案, 題解 —see also 另見 LOW-KEY

key³ *v* [T] *especially BrE* to prepare a surface so that a covering such as paint will stick to it【尤英】〔為塗油漆等〕處理好〔表面〕
key sth ↔ **in** *phr v* [T] to put information into a computer by using a KEYBOARD[1] (1)〔用鍵盤〕把〔信息〕輸入電腦 —see also 另見 KEYED UP
key sth **to** sth *phr v* [T usually passive 一般用被動態] *especially AmE* to slightly change a system, plan etc so that it works well with something else【尤美】〔對體系、計劃等略加改動〕使適合於〔另一事物〕: **be keyed to the needs of** (=match the needs of) 適於…的需要 *The daycare hours are keyed to the needs of working parents.* 日間託兒服務的時間是根據在職家長的需要制定的。

 **key·board¹** /ˈkiˌbɔrd; ˈkiːbɔːd/ *n* [C] **1** a row or several rows of keys (KEY² (3)) on a musical instrument like a piano or a machine like a computer〔樂器或機器上的〕鍵盤: *a computer keyboard* 電腦鍵盤 —see picture on page A14 參見A14頁圖 **2** also 又作 **keyboards** [plural] a musical instrument with a keyboard that can sound like a piano, drums etc 鍵盤樂器

keyboard² *v* **1** [I] to use the KEYBOARD[1] (1) of a computer, printing machine etc 操作〔電腦、打印機等的〕鍵盤 **2** [T] to put information into a computer by using a KEYBOARD[1] (1) 用鍵盤將〔資料〕輸入電腦 —**keyboarder** *n* [C]

key card /ˈ· ·/ *n* [C] a special plastic card that you put in an electronic lock to open a door etc〔電子門鎖的〕鑰匙卡

keyed up /ˌ· ˈ·/ *adj* [not before noun 不用於名詞前] worried or excited 緊張的; 興奮的: **[+about]** *Don't get all keyed up about the exam.* 對這次考試不要過於緊張。

key·hole /ˈkiˌhol; ˈkiːhəʊl/ *n* [C] the hole containing a lock that you use a key in 鎖眼, 鑰匙孔

keyhole sur·ge·ry /ˌ·· ˈ···/ *n* [U] a medical operation that is done through a very small hole in the body 微創外科手術, 栓孔手術〔只在身體上切一小口進行的手術〕

key·note /ˈkiˌnot; ˈkiːnəʊt/ *n* [C] **1** the main point in a piece of writing, system of beliefs, activity etc, that influences everything else; THEME (1) 主旨, 要旨; 基調: **[+of]** *Stability was the keynote of the reign of Queen Mary I.* 穩定是女王瑪麗一世統治時期的基調。**2 keynote address/speech** a speech that introduces a formal meeting〔正式會議的〕基調演說/主題發言 **3** the note on which a musical key is based〔音樂的〕基調; 主音

key·pad /ˈkiˌpæd; ˈkiːpæd/ *n* [C] **1** a small KEYBOARD[1] (1) which you hold in your hand, such as the REMOTE CONTROL for a television〔電視遙控器等能拿在手上操作的〕小型鍵盤 **2** the part of a computer KEYBOARD[1] (1) that has the number and command keys on it〔電腦鍵盤的〕擴充鍵盤, 輔助鍵盤〔數字鍵和命令鍵部分〕

key ring /ˈ· ·/ *n* [C] a metal ring that you keep keys on 鑰匙圈

key sig·na·ture /ˈ· ˌ···/ *n* [C] a set of marks at the beginning of a line of written music to show which KEY² (4) it is in〔樂譜上的〕調號

key·stone /ˈkiˌston; ˈkiːstəʊn/ *n* [C usually singular 一般用單數] **1** the large central stone in an ARCH[1] (1) that keeps the other stones in position 拱頂石 —see picture at 參見 ARCH[1] 圖 **2** the most important part of an idea, belief etc 主旨, 基礎; 基本原則: **[+of]** *Social justice is the keystone of our policies.* 社會正義是我們政策的基石。

key·stroke /ˈkiˌstrok; ˈkiːstrəʊk/ *n* [C] the action of pressing a key on a TYPEWRITER or computer KEYBOARD[1] (1)〔對打字機或電腦鍵盤的〕按鍵, 擊鍵

kg the written abbreviation of 縮寫= KILOGRAM or KILOGRAMS

KGB /ˌke dʒi ˈbi; ˌkeɪ dʒiː ˈbiː/ *n* **the KGB** the secret police of the former USSR 克格勃, (前蘇聯) 國家安全委員會〔前蘇聯的祕密警察機關〕

kha·ki /ˈkɑkɪ; ˈkɑːki/ *n* [U] **1** a dull green-brown or yellow-brown colour 土黃色, 卡其黃, 黃褐色 —see picture on page A5 參見A5頁圖 **2** cloth of this colour, especially when worn by soldiers 卡其布〔尤指士兵穿的軍服用料〕—**khaki** *adj*

kha·kis /ˈkɑkɪz; ˈkɑːkiz/ *n* [plural] *AmE* trousers made of KHAKI (2) cloth【美】卡其褲

kha·lif /ˈkelɪf; ˈkeɪlɪ̣f/ *n* [C] another spelling of CALIPH caliph的另一種拼法

kha·li·fate /ˈkeləˌfet; ˈkeɪlɪ̣feɪt/ *n* [C] another spelling of CALIPHATE caliphate的另一種拼法

khan /kɑn; kɑːn/ *n* [C] a ruler or official in Asia, or their title 可汗, 汗〔亞洲一些國家統治者或官員的尊稱〕

kHz the written abbreviation of 縮寫= KILOHERTZ

kib·ble¹ /ˈkɪbḷ; ˈkɪbəl/ *n* [U] *especially AmE* small round pieces of dry dog food【尤美】〔圓形小塊〕乾狗食

kibble² *v* [T] *especially BrE* to crush grain into small pieces【尤英】把〔穀物〕磨成粗粒

kib·butz /kɪˈbuts; kɪˈbʊts/ *n* [C] a type of farm in Israel where many people live and work together〔以色列的〕合作農莊, 居民點, 基布茲

kib·itz /ˈkɪbɪts; ˈkɪbɪts/ *v* [I] *AmE* to make unhelpful comments while someone is doing something【美】〔在某人正在做某事時〕妄加評論 —**kibitzer** *n* [C]

ki·bosh /ˈkaɪbɑʃ; ˈkaɪbɒʃ/ *n* **put the kibosh on sth** *old-fashioned informal* to stop a plan, idea etc from developing; RUIN²【過時, 非正式】阻止〔某計劃、想法等〕; 使…破滅

kick¹ /kɪk; kɪk/ *v*
1 ►HIT WITH YOUR FOOT 用腳碰撞◄ [I,T] to hit something with your foot 踢: *She kicked me under the table.* 她在桌子下踢了我一下。| *Joe, stop kicking!* 喬, 別踢了! | **kick sth down/over etc** *The police kicked the door down.* 警察把門踢倒了。| **kick sth around/towards etc** *Billy was kicking a ball around the yard.* 比利繞着院子踢球。| **kick sb in the head/face/stomach etc** *I got kicked in the face playing rugby.* 我打橄欖球時臉被踢了一下。
2 ►MOVE YOUR LEGS 移動雙腿◄ [I,T] to move your legs as if you were kicking something 蹬, 踩: *The cow may kick a bit when you milk her.* 擠奶時, 奶牛可能會有一點踢蹬。| **kick your legs** *They danced and sang and kicked their legs high in the air.* 他們邊跳邊唱, 把腿踢得很高。
3 ►KICK A GOAL 踢進球門◄ [T] to SCORE² (1) by kicking 踢入〔球門〕得分: **kick a goal** *He kicked two penalty goals in the last ten minutes.* 在最後十分鐘, 他踢進了兩個罰球。
4 kick a habit to stop doing something that is a harmful

habit 戒除惡習: *Some smokers find it surprisingly easy to kick the habit.* 有些吸煙者發現戒除這一惡習原來出奇地容易。
5 be kicking yourself/will kick yourself/could have kicked yourself *spoken* used to say that someone is annoyed with themselves because they realize that they have made a mistake or missed a chance【口】懊悔, 自責: *I could have kicked myself for getting her name wrong.* 我弄錯了她的名字, 真該自責。| *You'll kick yourself when I tell you the answer.* 我把答案告訴你時, 你會懊悔的。| *I bet they are kicking themselves now.* 我敢說他們正後悔不已。
6 kick sb when they are down to criticize or attack someone who is already in a weak position or having difficulties 落井下石: *The newspapers cannot resist kicking a man when he is down.* 報紙總忍不住要幹落井下石的事。
7 kick sb in the teeth *informal* to disappoint or DISCOURAGE someone very much, especially when they need support or hope【非正式】使某人大失所望[大為泄氣]〔尤指在其需要幫助或鼓勵之時〕: *Why is it that whenever I ask you for help you kick me in the teeth?* 為甚麼我每次求你幫忙你都讓我失望?
8 kick (sb's) ass *AmE slang*【美俚】**a)** to punish or defeat someone 懲罰; 打敗: *We really kicked their ass today, didn't we?* 我們今天好好教訓了他們一頓, 對吧? **b)** to have fun in a noisy violent way 熱鬧一下: *Come on, let's kick some ass!* 來啊, 我們一起熱鬧一下!
9 kick over the traces *BrE* to free yourself from control and start to behave as if there are no moral restrictions【英】擺脫約束; 放任, 放縱: *Haven't you ever felt you must go out and kick over the traces?* 你是否曾經覺得必須到外面去放縱一下自己?
10 kick sb upstairs to move someone to a job that seems to be more important than their present one but actually means that they have less influence 使明升暗降
11 kick your heels to waste time waiting for something 無聊地等: *We were sitting around kicking our heels for half the day.* 我們坐在那兒無聊地等了半天。
12 kick the bucket *humorous informal* to die【幽默, 非正式】死, 蹬腿兒

kick about/around *phr v* **1 be kicking about/around (sth) a)** to be lying somewhere untidily, especially when forgotten 被隨意放着: *You should find a copy of the report kicking around somewhere.* 你應該能在甚麼地方找到那份報告的副本, 它只是被隨意擱在某處罷了。| *Goodness knows how many bottles he has kicking about his flat.* 天知道有多少瓶子被他隨意丟在公寓裡。**b)** to be travelling around a place with no fixed plan 漫無目的地到處旅行: *He's been kicking around Australia for eight months.* 他在澳大利亞各地周遊了八個月。**2** [T] **kick sth ↔ about/around** to discuss an idea with a group of people in order to decide whether it is good or not 商量, 討論, 談論: *Perhaps we could kick one or two of these ideas around for a while.* 也許我們可以在這些觀點中挑一兩個來花點時間討論一下。**3** [T] **kick sb about/around** to treat someone badly and unfairly 虐待, 欺淩: *She was tired of being kicked around by her boss.* 她膩透了老闆對她的欺淩。

kick (out) against *phr v* [T] to react strongly against something 反對; 反抗: *She has kicked out against authority all her life.* 她一生都在反抗權威。

kick in *phr v* **1** [I] *informal* to begin to have an effect or come into operation【非正式】開始產生效果; 開始運作: *I could feel the painkillers kick in.* 我能感到止痛藥開始起效了。| *Other benefits kick in at a certain level of income.* 在收入處於某一水平時享有其他津貼。**2** [I, T] *AmE* to join with others in giving money or help; CONTRIBUTE【美】湊份子捐助: *He doesn't really want to kick in and help.* 他並不真正願意捐助。| *We're going to buy Bob a present – do you want to kick in something?* 我們打算給鮑勃買份禮物, 你也算一份嗎? **3 kick sb's face/sb's head in** to severely wound someone by kicking them 嚴重踢傷某人的臉/頭: *He threatened to kick my head in.* 他威脅說要踢死我。**4** [T] to kick a door so hard that it breaks open 把〔門〕踢開, 踢壞: *We had to get the police to kick the door in.* 我們只好讓警察把門踹開。

kick off *phr v* **1** [I] when a game of football kicks off, it starts〔足球比賽〕開球: *The match kicks off at 3 o'clock.* 比賽三點開始。**2** [I,T] if you kick off a meeting, event etc, or if it kicks off, it starts〔會議、事情等〕開始: *The meeting kicked off at 11.00.* 會議於 11 點開始。| *Right, who would like to kick off?* 好吧, 誰先發言? | **kick sth ↔ off (with)** *I'm going to kick off today's proceedings with a few remarks about next year's budget.* 我先講幾句下一年的預算, 以此來開始今天的議程。**3** [T] **kick your shoes ↔ off** to remove your shoes by shaking them off your feet 抖落掉腳上穿的鞋: *I slumped into the armchair and kicked off my shoes.* 我一屁股坐到沙發上, 抖落掉腳上的鞋子。

kick sb **↔ out** *phr v* [T] to make someone leave or dismiss them 攆走; 開除〔某人〕: *Bernard's wife had kicked him out.* 伯納德的太太把他攆了出去。| **[+of]** *He's been kicked out of the golf club.* 他被開除出高爾夫俱樂部。

kick up sth **↔** *phr v* [T] **1 kick up a fuss/row** to loudly complain and show you are annoyed about something〔因不滿而〕大吵大鬧: *He was kicking up an awful fuss about his cold meal.* 他因他那份冷餐而大吵大鬧。**2** to make something, especially dust, go up into the air while you are walking〔走路時〕揚起塵土: *As they marched, the soldiers kicked up clouds of dust.* 士兵行進時, 揚起一團團塵土。

kick² *n* **1** [C] an act of hitting something with your foot 踢; 蹬: *Brazil scored with the last kick of the match.* 巴西隊在比賽中最後一腳射門得分。| **give sb/sth a good kick** (=to kick them hard) 用力踢某人/某物 *If the outer door won't open just give it a good kick.* 外門如果打不開, 就使勁踢開它。**2** [C] an opportunity, allowed by the referee, for one team in a game of football or RUGBY to kick the ball without being stopped by the other team〔足球或橄欖球中的〕任意球: *a free kick* 任意球 | **take a kick** *Pearce came forward to take the kick.* 皮爾斯跑到前面踢任意球。**3 a kick up the arse/backside etc** *informal* severe criticism or punishment for something you have done wrong【非正式】嚴厲批評; 嚴懲: *Phil needs a good kick up the arse.* 得好好教訓一下菲爾。**4 be a kick in the teeth** *informal* to be very disappointing or discouraging, especially when you need support or hope【非正式】令人大失所望, 令人大為泄氣〔尤指在需要幫助或鼓勵時〕: *Her refusal to see me was a real kick in the teeth.* 她拒絕見我, 讓我大為失望。**5 get a kick out of sth/get a kick from sth** to really enjoy doing something 從做某事中得到樂趣: *Alan gets a real kick out of his job.* 阿倫從他的工作中得到真正的樂趣。**6 give sb a kick** to give someone a strong feeling of pleasure 給某人以極大樂趣: *It gives her a kick to get you into trouble.* 給你製造麻煩使她得到極大的樂趣。**7 do sth for kicks/get your kicks from sth** *informal* to do something, especially something dangerous or harmful, in order to get a feeling of excitment【非正式】為尋求刺激而幹某事〔尤指危險或有害的事〕: *Apparently she steals from supermarkets just for kicks.* 顯然, 她在超級市場偷東西只是為了尋找刺激。**8 have a kick (to it)** *informal* to have a strong effect or taste, especially alcohol【非正式】〔尤指烈性酒〕有勁; 有濃烈的味道 **9 be on a health/decorating/Italian food etc kick** *informal* to have a strong new interest【非正式】熱衷於保健/裝飾/意大利式食物等: *I'm on a health kick at the moment.* 目前我正熱衷於保健。

kick-ass /'· ·/ *adj AmE slang* strong, powerful, and sometimes violent【美俚】強壯的; 粗暴的: *a kick-ass attitude that will get him into trouble* 會給他招惹麻煩的蠻橫態度

kick·back /ˈkɪkˌbæk; ˈkɪkbæk/ *n* [C,U] *slang* money that you pay secretly or dishonestly for someone's help; BRIBE【俚】酬金, 回扣; 賄賂

kick·ball /ˈkɪkˌbɔl; ˈkɪkbɔːl/ *n* [U] an American children's game, similar to BASEBALL, in which you kick the ball rather than hit it〔按棒球規則進行的美國〕兒童足球遊戲

kick·box·ing /ˈkɪkˌbɑksɪŋ; ˈkɪkˌbɒksɪŋ/ *n* [U] a form of BOXING in which you kick as well as PUNCH (=hit) 跆拳道

kick·off /ˈkɪkˌɔf; ˈkɪk-ɒf/ *n* [C usually singular 一般用單數] **1** the time when a game of football starts, or the first kick〔足球比賽的〕開球; 比賽開始: *Kickoff is at 3.00.* 足球比賽三點開始。**2** *informal* the beginning of a new activity【非正式】〔新活動的〕開始, 序幕

kick·stand /ˈkɪkˌstænd; ˈkɪkstænd/ *n* [C] a thing that supports a bicycle or MOTORCYCLE when it is not moving, and keeps it in an upright position〔腳踏車或摩托車的〕撐腳架

kick-start[1] /ˈ· ·/ *v* [T] **1** to do something to help a process or activity start or develop more quickly 啟動; 促進: *lowering interest rates to kick-start the economy* 通過降低利率來促進經濟 **2** to start a MOTORCYCLE using your foot 用腳發動〔摩托車〕

kick-start[2] also 又作 **kick-start·er** /ˈ· ,··/ *n* [C] the part of a MOTORCYCLE that you press with your foot to start it〔摩托車的〕腳踏起動器

1 2 **kid**[1] /kɪd; kɪd/ *n* **1** [C] *informal* a child【非正式】小孩, 兒童: **the kids** (=children that you are responsible for)〔由某人負責照管的〕孩子們 *I'm taking the kids to the zoo today.* 我今天要帶孩子們去動物園。—see 見 CHILD (USAGE) **2** [C] *informal* a young person【非正式】年輕人: *college kids* 大學生 **3** [C] *informal* a son or daughter【非正式】孩子; 兒子; 女兒 **4 kid's stuff** *BrE*【英】**/kid stuff** *AmE*【美】something that is very easy or boring 非常容易[乏味]的事情 **5** [C,U] a young goat, or the leather made from its skin 小山羊; 小山羊皮革 **6 treat/handle someone with kid gloves** to treat someone very carefully because they easily become upset 小心謹慎地對待某人〔尤指易生氣的人〕

kid[2] *v* **kidded, kidding** *informal*【非正式】**1** [I,T] to say something that is not true, especially as a joke〔尤指作為玩笑〕戲弄; 嘲笑; 欺騙: **just/only kidding** *spoken*【口】*Don't get mad, I was only kidding.* 別生氣, 我剛才不過是開個玩笑。| **you're kidding (me)** *spoken*【口】*You won $5,000? You're kidding!* 你贏了五千美元? 騙人! **2** [T] to make yourself believe something untrue or unlikely 欺騙, 哄騙〔自己〕: **not kid yourself (that)** *Don't kid yourself he'll ever change.* 別欺騙自己以為他會改的。**3 no kidding a)** *spoken* used when you do not completely believe someone, or are surprised by what they say【口】不是開玩笑吧: *Carlotta's 39? No kidding?* 卡洛塔 39 歲了? 不是開玩笑吧? **b)** used to warn someone that you mean what you say 說真的; 不騙你 **4 I kid you not** *spoken* used to emphasize that you are telling the truth【口】跟你說正經的, 騙你不是人 —**kidder** *n* [C] *AmE*【美】

kid around *phr v* [I] to behave in a silly way 胡鬧: *Stop kidding around and listen to me.* 別胡鬧了, 聽我說。—**kidding** *n* [U]

kid[3] *adj informal especially AmE*【非正式, 尤美】**kid sister/brother** your kid sister or brother is younger than you are 小妹妹/弟弟

kid·die, kiddy /ˈkɪdɪ; ˈkɪdi/ *n* [C] *especially BrE informal* a young child【尤英, 非正式】小孩 —**kiddie** *adj*: *a kiddie seat* 兒童座位

kid·do /ˈkɪdo; ˈkɪdəʊ/ *n* [C usually singular 一般用單數] *especially AmE spoken* a way of addressing someone you know, usually a young person【尤美口】年輕人, 小伙子〔對認識的人, 一般對年輕人的一種稱呼〕: *Come on kiddo, let's go.* 喂, 小伙子, 我們走吧。

kid·nap /ˈkɪdnæp; ˈkɪdnæp/ *v* **kidnapped, kidnapping** also 又作 **kidnaped, kidnaping** *AmE*【美】[T] to take someone away illegally, usually by force, in order to get money for returning them 綁架; 誘拐; 劫持 —**kidnapper** *n* [C]

kid·nap·ping /ˈkɪdnæpɪŋ; ˈkɪdnæpɪŋ/ also 又作 **kidnap** *especially BrE*【尤英】—*n* [C,U] the crime of kidnapping someone 綁架; 誘拐; 劫持: *the recent series of kidnappings* 近來發生的一連串綁架事件 | *a kidnap attempt* 綁架企圖

kid·ney /ˈkɪdnɪ; ˈkɪdni/ *n* **1** [C] one of the two organs in your lower back that separate waste liquid from your blood and make URINE 腎, 腎臟 **2** [C,U] one or more of these organs from an animal, used as food 腰子〔指供食用的動物腎臟〕: *steak and kidney pie* 牛排和腰子餡餅

kidney bean /ˈ·· ·/ *n* [C] a dark red bean that is shaped like a KIDNEY 菜豆, 四季豆 —see picture on page A9 參見 A9 頁圖

kill[1] /kɪl; kɪl/ *v*

1 ►MAKE SB/STH DIE 使某人/某物死亡◄ [I,T] to make a living thing die 弄死; 殺死: *His parents were killed in a plane crash.* 他的父母死於飛機失事。| *What's the best way to kill weeds?* 甚麼是除草的最好辦法? | *Drug abuse can kill.* 濫用藥物可以致命。| **kill yourself** *You're going to kill yourself on that motorcycle.* 你騎那輛摩托車會送命的。| *The jury returned a verdict that he killed himself with an overdose.* 陪審團作出裁決, 認定他因過量服藥而喪命。

2 ►MAKE STH STOP/FAIL 使某物停止/失敗◄ [T] to make something stop or fail, or turn off the power to something 使停止; 使失敗; 使關閉: *Nothing that the doctor gives me kills the pain.* 醫生給我的藥都不止痛。| *Quick! Kill the lights.* 快! 關燈! | *You've got to kill that story before it gets printed* (=prevent it being printed). 你得在刊印之前刪掉這篇報道。| **kill the conversation** (=stop people talking) 使談話中止 | **kill a beer/bottle of wine etc** *AmE spoken* (=finish drinking)【美口】喝光一杯啤酒/一瓶葡萄酒等 *Let's kill these beers and go.* 我們把這幾杯啤酒喝光再走吧。| **kill the ball** (=completely stop a fast moving ball) 截球, 停球 | **kill your speed** (=drive slowly) 減速行駛

3 ►BE ANGRY WITH SB 對某人生氣◄ [T] *informal* to be very angry with someone【非正式】對〔某人〕大發雷霆: *Maria will kill me if I'm late again.* 如果我再遲到, 瑪麗亞一定會對我大發雷霆。

4 ►MAKE SB TIRED/SAD 令某人疲倦/難過◄ [T] to make someone feel extremely tired, unhappy etc 使極度疲倦[難過等]: **it kills me/her/them** *It kills me to see him working so hard for nothing.* 看見他工作如此艱辛而沒有任何回報, 真讓我難過。

5 the suspense is killing me *spoken* used to say you are impatient to know the result of something【口】這樣懸而不決真讓我受不了

6 my head is/feet are etc killing me *spoken* used to say that a part of your body is hurting a lot【口】我的頭/腳等痛得要命: *I've walked miles and my feet are killing me.* 我步行了好幾英里路, 腳痛得要命。

7 ►MAKE SB LAUGH 令某人大笑◄ [T] to make someone laugh a lot at something 使發笑: *You really killed them tonight, Frenchie!* 弗蘭奇, 你今晚可真讓他們笑死了! | **kill yourself laughing** (=laugh a lot) 讓自己笑個半死

8 it won't kill sb (to do something) *spoken* used when saying that someone could easily do something, and ought to do it【口】(做某事) 對某人來說十分容易〔因此應該去做〕: *It wouldn't kill you to give me a bit of help.* 幫我一點小忙不會要你的命的。

9 kill time to do something that is not very useful or interesting while you are waiting for something to happen 消磨時光, 打發時間

10 kill two birds with one stone to achieve two things with one action 一石二鳥, 一舉兩得, 一箭雙雕

11 kill someone with kindness to be too kind to someone 對待某人好得過分, 寵壞某人
12 ►SPOIL STH'S APPEARANCE 破壞某物的外表◄ [T] if something kills the way something else looks, the two things look wrong together 破壞; 搞糟: *That hat kills her whole outfit.* 那頂帽子令她全身的衣着打扮失色不少。
13 it will kill or cure used to say that what you plan to do will either work very well or fail completely 不是一舉成功, 就是一敗塗地
14 kill the fatted calf to welcome someone home with a big meal etc after they have been away for a long time 盛宴款待〔長期離家歸來的人〕—see also 另見 **dressed to kill** (DRESSED (4)), **kill the goose that lays the golden egg** (GOOSE[1] (4))
kill sth ↔ **off** *phr v* [T] to cause the death of a lot of living things 使〔生物〕大量死亡; 使滅絕: *Pollution is rapidly killing off plant life.* 污染使大量植物迅速死亡。

USAGE NOTE 用法説明: KILL
WORD CHOICE 詞語辨析: **kill, murder, execute, put to death, kill oneself, commit suicide, slaughter, assassinate, massacre**
Kill is the general word meaning to make someone or something die. kill是表示“使人或物死亡”的普通用詞: *My uncle was killed in a plane crash.* 我叔叔死於飛機失事。| *A sharp frost can kill young plants.* 一場急降的霜凍能凍死幼苗。
Murder means to kill someone deliberately and illegally. murder指蓄意、非法地殺害某人: *Davies is accused of murdering his wife and their three young children.* 戴維斯被指控謀殺他的妻子和他們三個年幼的孩子。
If someone is killed legally as a punishment for a crime, they are **executed** or **put to death**. 如果某人因犯罪而被依法處決, 他就是被 executed 或 put to death: *Should serial killers be executed?* 連環殺手應當被處死嗎? | *Thousands of revolutionaries were put to death after the coup.* 成千上萬的革命者在政變後被處死。
If someone **kills himself or herself**, they **commit suicide**. kill himself or herself意為“自殺”(commit suicide)。
Slaughter is the technical word for killing animals for food, leather etc but it is also used to describe the violent and unnecessary killing of a large number of people. slaughter是屠宰動物〔供食用或製革〕的術語, 但也指使用暴力殺害大批無辜者: *Thousands of people are slaughtered every year in road accidents.* 每年都有成千上萬的人死於交通事故。
To **assassinate** someone means to murder an important, famous, and usually powerful person for political reasons. assassinate指為了政治原因刺殺一名重要而著名的, 而且通常是有權勢的人物: *Who really assassinated President Kennedy?* 到底是誰刺殺了甘迺迪總統?
To **massacre** means to kill large numbers of ordinary people, especially people who cannot defend themselves. massacre指大量屠殺平民, 尤其是沒有自衛能力的人: *Hundreds of men, women, and children were massacred in the attack.* 在這次襲擊中, 有數百個男女和兒童遭到屠殺。

kill² *n* **1** the act of killing a hunted animal 捕殺: *The hawk's talons grip tight as it makes its kill.* 老鷹捕殺獵物時雙爪緊緊收攏。**2 move in/close in for the kill** to come nearer to something and prepare to kill, defeat, or destroy 逐漸靠近以伺機殺死[擊敗, 摧毀]: *Enemy submarines were moving in for the kill.* 敵人的潛艇正靠近目標準備攻擊。| **be in at the kill** (=watch something being killed, someone being defeated etc) 目擊某物被毀[某人被擊敗等] **3** [singular] an animal killed by another animal, especially for food〔尤指作食物而被殺死的〕獵獲物

kill·er /ˋkɪlɚ; ˈkɪlə/ *n* [C] **1** a person, animal, or thing that kills 殺手; 殺生的人[動物; 事物]: *Heart disease is America's number one killer.* 心臟病是美國的頭號殺手。—see also 另見 SERIAL KILLER **2** *AmE slang* something or someone that is very attractive or very good【美俚】極有吸引力的人[物]; 極好的人[物]: *a killer movie* 一部絕好的電影 —see also 另見 LADY-KILLER **3 a/the killer instinct** a desire to succeed that is so strong that you are willing to harm other people 嗜殺的本性 —**killer** *adj*: *a killer disease* 致命的疾病

killer whale /ˈ·· ·/ *n* [C] a black and white WHALE that eats meat 逆戟鯨, 虎鯨, 殺人鯨

kill·ing¹ /ˋkɪlɪŋ; ˈkɪlɪŋ/ *n* [C] **1** a murder 謀殺: *a series of gangland killings* 一系列的黑社會謀殺案 **2 make a killing** *informal* to make a lot of money in a short time【非正式】發橫財

killing² *adj informal*【非正式】**1** extremely tiring 令人精疲力竭的: *a killing workload* 令人疲憊不堪的工作負擔 **2** *old-fashioned* very funny【過時】滑稽的, 好笑的 —**killingly** *adv*

kill·joy /ˋkɪlˌdʒɔɪ; ˈkɪldʒɔɪ/ *n* [C] someone who spoils other people's pleasure 令人掃興的人

kiln /kɪln; kɪln/ *n* [C] a special OVEN for baking clay pots, bricks etc〔燒製陶器、磚頭等的〕窰

ki·lo /ˋkɪlo; ˈkiːləʊ/ *n plural* **kilos** [C] an informal word for KILOGRAM kilogram的非正式用詞: *The box weighs 6 kilos.* 這個箱子重六公斤。

kilo- /kɪlə; kɪlə/ *prefix* 1,000 times a particular unit 千; 一千倍: *a kilogram* (=1,000 grams) 一千克 —see table on page C4 參見C4頁附錄

kil·o·byte /ˋkɪləˌbaɪt; ˈkɪləbaɪt/ also 又作 **K** *n* [C] a unit for measuring computer information equal to 1,024 BYTES〔電腦信息單位〕千字節〔相等於1,024個字節〕

kil·o·gram /ˋkɪləˌgræm; ˈkɪləgræm/ *n* [C] a unit for measuring weight equal to 1,000 grams 千克, 公斤 —see table on page C3 參見C3頁附錄

kil·o·hertz /ˋkɪləˌhɝts; ˈkɪləhɜːts/ written abbreviation 縮寫為 **kHz** *n* [C] a unit for measuring wave lengths, especially of radio signals, equal to 1,000 HERTZ 千赫(兹)

kil·o·me·tre *BrE*【英】, **kilometer** *AmE*【美】/ˋkɪləˌmitɚ; ˈkɪləˌmiːtə/ *n* [C] a unit for measuring length, equal to 1,000 metres 千米, 公里 —see table on page C3 參見C3頁附錄 

kil·o·watt /ˋkɪləˌwɑt; ˈkɪləwɒt/ *n* [C] a unit for measuring electrical power equal to 1,000 WATTS 千瓦

kilowatt hour /ˌ··· ˈ·/ *n* [C] the amount of ENERGY produced by a KILOWATT in one hour 千瓦時

kilt /kɪlt; kɪlt/ *n* [C] a type of thick skirt, traditionally worn by Scottish men 褶襉短裙〔蘇格蘭男子的傳統服飾〕—**kilted** *adj*

kil·ter /ˋkɪltɚ; ˈkɪltə/ *n* **out of kilter** not working as well as usual 失常, 失調: *Things in my life seem all out of kilter lately.* 近來我的生活中似乎一切都不正常。

ki·mo·no /kəˋmonə; kɪˈməʊnəʊ/ *n* [C] **1** a traditional piece of Japanese clothing like a long coat, that is worn at special ceremonies〔日本的〕和服 **2** *especially AmE* a long, loose piece of clothing worn informally indoors, especially by women【尤美】〔尤指婦女在家中穿的〕寬鬆晨衣

kin /kɪn; kɪn/ *n* [plural] **1** *informal* also 又作 **kinfolk** your family【非正式】家人, 家屬; 親屬 **2 next of kin** *formal* your most closely related family【正式】最近的親屬: *We'll have to notify the next of kin of his death.* 我們將把他去世的消息告知他最近的親屬。—compare 比較 KINDRED¹ (1) —see also 另見 KITH AND KIN

-kin /kɪn; kɪn/ also 又作 **-kins** /kɪnz; kɪnz/ *suffix* [in nouns 構成名詞] a word meaning something small, used espe-

K

cially to children 小…〔尤用於對兒童說話時〕: *a lambkin* 小羔羊

kind¹ /kaɪnd; kaɪnd/ *n* **1** [C] a type or sort or person or thing 種; 類: [+of] *What kind of fish is this?* 這是哪一種魚? | *Are you in some kind of trouble?* 你遇到某種麻煩了嗎? | *victimization of the worst kind* 最惡劣的一種迫害 | **all kinds of** *They sell all kinds of different things.* 他們出售各種各樣的東西。| **of this kind** *Operations of this kind always carry risks.* 這種手術總是有風險的。| **of its kind** *the best wine of its kind* 同類酒中最好的 **2 kind of** also 又作 **kinda** *AmE spoken*【美口】**a)** slightly or in some ways 有點; 有幾分: *I'm kind of glad I didn't win.* 我倒是有點高興我沒有贏。**b)** used when you are explaining something and want to avoid giving the details 大致是這樣: *I kind of made it look like the post office had lost his letter.* 總之, 我把它弄得看起來好像是郵局把他的信丟了。**3 a kind of (a)** *especially spoken* used to say that your description of something is not exact【尤口】稍稍, 幾分: *a kind of a reddish-brown* 略呈紅的棕色 **4 something of the/that kind** *spoken* something similar to what has been mentioned【口】類似所提及的某事物: *"Are you sure he was wearing jeans?" "Well, something of the kind."* "你肯定他穿的是牛仔褲嗎?" "唔, 類似那種褲子。" **5 nothing/anything of the kind** used to emphasize what you are saying when you disagree with someone 完全不是那樣: *I never said anything of the kind!* 我從來沒說過那種話! **6** [U] people or things that are similar in some way or belong to the same group 相似的人[事物]; 同一類的人[事物]: **sb's (own) kind** *Grace only made friends among her own kind.* 格雷絲只與跟自己同一類的人交朋友。**7 be the kind** to be a person of a particular type 屬於某種類型的人: *She may not be the marrying kind.* 她可能不是那種想結婚的人。| **be the kind to do sth** *He's not the kind to get excited about money.* 他不是那種見錢就心動的人。**8 two/three etc of a kind** two or three people or things that are of the same type 屬於同一類的兩/三個人[事物]等: *You and your brother are two of a kind.* 你和你弟弟兩人屬於同一類型。**9 one of a kind** the only one of a particular type of something; UNIQUE 唯一的, 獨一無二的: *Each plate is handpainted and one of a kind.* 每隻盤子都是手工繪製, 因此也是獨一無二的。**10 of a kind** used to say that something is not as good as it should be 名不符實的: *Elections of a kind are held, but there is only one party to vote for.* 有些所謂的選舉進行了, 但只有一個黨派參加競選。**11 payment in kind** a method of paying someone with goods or services instead of money 以實物[服務]〔而非錢款〕支付, 以貨代款 **12 respond/retaliate etc in kind** to react by doing the same thing as someone else has just done 以同樣方式回應/反擊等: *If other papers cut their prices, we'll have to respond in kind.* 如果其他報紙降價, 我們也只好用降價回應。

USAGE NOTE 用法說明: KIND

FORMALITY 正式程度

Remember that **would you be kind enough to/would you be so kind as to...?** are formally polite. When you are speaking or writing informally they may sound unfriendly and it would be better to say, for example 要記住 would you be kind enough to/would you be so kind as to...? 是正式場合下的禮貌說法, 而在非正式的口語或書面語中, 這種說法則可能聽起來並不友善, 因此用其他說法會更好, 例如: **Please could you.../Could you possibly...?**

On the other hand, **kind of** and **sort of** meaning that something is uncertain or partly true (mainly before adjectives and verbs) are used only in informal contexts. 但是, 表示某事不確定或只是部分真實的 kind of 和 sort of〔主要用於形容詞和副詞前〕只用於非正式場合中: *I kinda like that color.* 我有點喜歡那種顏色。| *"Did he help you?" "Well, kind of."* (=not as much as I hoped) "他幫你忙了嗎?" "嗯, 可以說幫了一點。"〔意指不如我希望的那樣〕

In very informal speech you sometimes use **kind of** and **sort of** to make a serious statement sound weaker or amusing. 在很不正式的口語中, 有時用 kind of 和 sort of 來減弱話語的嚴肅性或使其滑稽有趣: *He sort of came up to me and pushed me. So I kind of hit him in the face.* 他湊到我面前推我, 於是我就那麼給了他一記耳光。Some people do not consider this to be good English. 有些人認為這種用法不是規範的英語。

GRAMMAR 語法

Kind(s) of or **sort(s) of** is regularly used in the singular or plural before singular and uncountable nouns. 在單數名詞和不可數名詞前可用單數的 kind of 或 sort of, 也可以用複數的 kinds of 或 sorts of: *one kind of flower/person/bread* 一種花/人/麵包 | *many kinds of car/person/cheese/attraction* 許多種類的車/人/乳酪/吸引力 | *several sorts of paint* 幾種油漆

The plural **kinds of/sorts of** is also used before plural nouns in more informal English. 在較為非正式的英語裡, 複數名詞前也用 kinds of/sorts of: *these/many kinds of flowers/programs/people* 這些/許多種類的花/程序/人 (but NOT 但不用 *this kind/sort of programs*, though you can more formally say 不過可用更正式的說法 *programs of this kind/sort*)。

Remember that whether **kind** or **sort** itself is singular or plural also relates to the word used just before. 要記住 kind 或 sort 用單數還是複數取決於用在其前面的詞語: *this/one/each/every kind of...* 這/一/每一/各種… | *another sort of cheese* 另一種乳酪 but you say 但說 *these/ten/many/all/a few kinds of...* 這些/十個/許多/所有/少數種類的… | *in other kinds of school* 在其他類別的學校 | *shops of all sorts* 各種各樣的商店。In informal spoken English people do say things like 在非正式的口語中, 人們確實也用如下的說法: *Those kind/sort of questions are very difficult* 那種題目非常難, but some people think this is incorrect. 但有些人認為這種用法不正確。

kind² *adj* **1** saying or doing things that show that you care about other people and want to help them or make them happy 體貼的; 親切的; 和藹的: *It's really kind of you to let us use your pool.* 感謝你讓我們使用你的游泳池。| *Ms Jarvis is unable to accept your kind invitation.* 賈維斯女士不能接受你的友好邀請。| [+to] *He's been very kind to me.* 他對我一直很友善。—see 見 KINDLY² (USAGE) **2** not causing harm or suffering 關照的, 厚待的: *Life has been very kind to me.* 我的生活一向不錯。| *I need a soap that's kinder to my skin.* 我需要一種對皮膚較為柔和的肥皂。**3 would you be kind enough to do sth/be so kind as to do sth** *formal* used to make a polite request【正式】勞駕, 請您…好嗎: *Would you be kind enough to close the door, please?* 勞駕, 請您關上門好嗎? —opposite 反義詞 UNKIND —see also 另見 KINDLY², KINDNESS

kin·der·gar·ten /ˈkɪndəˌgartn; ˈkɪndəgɑːtn/ *n* [C,U] **1** *AmE* a school or class for young children, usually aged five, that prepares them for normal school【美】〔通常為五歲兒童開設的〕幼兒園, 學前班 **2** *BrE* a school for children aged two to five【英】〔為二歲至五歲兒童開辦的〕幼兒園 —compare 比較 NURSERY

kind-heart·ed /ˌ· ˈ··◂/ *adj* kind and generous 好心的; 仁慈的; 慷慨的 —**kind-heartedly** *adv* —**kind-heartedness** *n* [U]

kin·dle /ˈkɪndl; ˈkɪndl/ *v* [I,T] **1** to start burning, or to make something start burning 點燃; (使) 燃燒起來: **kindle a fire** (=make a fire using small pieces of wood etc) 點火; 生火 **2 kindle excitement/interest etc** to make someone interested, excited etc 引起興奮/興趣等: *The love of poetry was kindled in him by her teaching.* 她的教學引發了他對詩歌的興趣。

kin·dling /ˋkɪndlɪŋ; ˈkɪndlɪŋ/ *n* [U] small pieces of dry wood, leaves etc that you use for starting a fire 引火物〈如乾的木柴、樹葉等〉

kind·ly¹ /ˋkaɪndlɪ; ˈkaɪndli/ *adv* **1** in a kind way; generously 友善地; 親切地: *Mr Nunn has kindly agreed to let us use his barn for the dance.* 納恩先生很友好地同意我們用他的穀倉舉行舞會。**2** *spoken formal* a word meaning 'please', which is often used when you are annoyed【口, 正式】請〔常用來表示不快〕: *Will you kindly put that book back?* 請你把那本書放回去好嗎? **3 not take kindly to** to be unwilling to accept a situation because it annoys you 不願意接受: *Eddie would not take kindly to her working.* 埃迪不會接受她去工作。**4 look kindly on** to approve of someone or something 贊成, 同意: *He hoped the committee would look kindly on his request.* 他希望委員會會同意他的請求。**5 think kindly of** to have fond thoughts about someone 懷念, 想念: *Think kindly of me when I'm gone.* 我走後希望還能記着我。

kindly² *adj* kind and caring for other people 友善的; 親切的; 和藹的; 體貼的: *Mrs Gardiner was a kindly old soul.* 加德納夫人是個和藹可親的老人。—**kindliness** *n* [C]

USAGE NOTE 用法說明: KINDLY

FORMALITY 正式程度

A request like **would you kindly...?** or **kindly shut the door!** is formally polite. In informal contexts it sounds as though you are annoyed and **could you possibly...?** would be more usual. 像 Would you kindly...? 或 Kindly shut the door! 這樣的請求是正式而客氣的。但在非正式場合下, 這種說法顯得說話人好像不耐煩, 比較常用的說法是 Could you possibly...?

WORD CHOICE 詞語辨析: **kindly, kind**

Kindly is either the adverb of **kind**. kindly 既是 kind 的副詞形式: *He kindly opened the door for me* 他體貼地為我開門, or an adjective with a slightly different meaning from **kind** which is much less common 同時又是形容詞, 但意思與 kind 略有不同, 而且也不很常見: *She is a kindly person.* 她是個和藹可親的人。

The adjective **kindly** describes a person's general character. **Kind** may also do this, but often describes someone's behaviour at one particular moment. 形容詞 kindly 用於描寫一個人的總體性格。kind 也有這個用法, 但常描寫某人在某特定時刻的行為: *It was kind of you to help me.* 謝謝你友好的幫忙。| *She's often kind to me* (NOT 不用 *kindly*). 她常友善待我。

kind·ness /ˋkaɪndnɪs; ˈkaɪndnɨs/ *n* **1** [U] kind behaviour towards someone 仁慈; 和藹; 好意; 體貼: *I can't thank you enough for your kindness.* 我對你的好意感激不盡。**2** [C] a kind action 友好的行為: **do sb a kindness** *It would be doing him a kindness to tell him the truth.* 把實情告訴他對他是件好事。—see also 另見 **kill someone with kindness** (KILL¹ (11))

kin·dred¹ /ˋkɪndrɪd; ˈkɪndrɨd/ *n* [U] **1** *old use* your family【舊】家人; 親屬 —compare 比較 KIN **2** [+with] *formal* a family relationship; KINSHIP【正式】親屬關係, 血緣關係

kindred² *adj* [only before noun 僅用於名詞前] **1 a kindred spirit** someone who thinks and feels the way you do 志趣相投的人 **2** *formal* belonging to the same group or family【正式】同宗的; 同類的; 同源的

ki·net·ic /kɪˋnɛtɪk; kɪˈnetɪk/ *adj technical* connected with movement【術語】運動的; 動力的

kinetic art /ˌ·ˌ·· ˈ·/ *n* [U] art, such as SCULPTURE, that has moving parts 動態藝術〈如動態雕塑〉

kinetic en·er·gy /ˌ·ˌ·· ˈ···/ *n* [U] *technical* the power of something moving, such as running water【術語】動能〈如流水的能量〉

ki·net·ics /kɪˋnɛtɪks; kɪˈnetɪks/ *n* [U] *technical* the science that studies the action or force of movement【術語】動力學

kin·folk /ˋkɪnˌfok; ˈkɪnfəʊk/ *n* [plural] an American form of KINSFOLK kinsfolk 的美語形式

king /kɪŋ; kɪŋ/ *n* [C] 1

1 ▶RULER 統治者◀ a man who is ruler of a country because he is from a royal family 國王: *He became king on the death of his father.* 他在父親死後成為國王。| [+of] *Henry VIII, King of England* 英格蘭國王亨利八世

2 ▶THE BEST 最好者◀ **a)** someone that you think does a particular thing the best 最優秀的人: [+of] *the King of Rock 'n' Roll* 搖滾樂之王 **b)** something that is the best of its type〔同類事物中的〕最優秀者: [+of] *the king of Swiss cheeses* 瑞士乳酪中的極品

3 ▶CHESS 國際象棋◀ the most important piece in a game of CHESS 王〔國際象棋中最重要的棋子〕

4 ▶CARDS 紙牌◀ a playing card with a picture of a king on it 老 K〔繪有國王圖像的紙牌〕

5 ▶IMPORTANT 重要的◀ **be king** if something is king at a particular time, it has a big influence on people 極具影響: *back in the days when jazz was king* 在往昔爵士樂極為盛行的年代

6 king of the jungle/of beasts the most important male animal 叢林之王/百獸之王: *The lion is king of the jungle.* 獅子是叢林之王。

7 a king's ransom an extremely large amount of money 一筆巨款

8 live like a king to have a very good quality of life 養尊處優 —see also 另見 QUEEN¹

king·dom /ˋkɪŋdəm; ˈkɪŋdəm/ *n* [C] **1** a country governed by a king or queen 王國: *the kingdom of Thailand* 泰王國 **2 the kingdom of** an imaginary place where a particular thing or quality has the greatest influence〔以某物或某品質為主宰的〕領域: *the kingdom of love* 愛情王國 **3 the animal/plant/mineral kingdom** one of the three parts into which the natural world is divided 動物界/植物界/礦物界〔大自然三界〕**4 the kingdom of heaven/God** heaven 天國 **5 blow sb/sth to kingdom come** *informal* to completely destroy someone or something【非正式】把〔某人〕送上西天; 徹底摧毀〔某物〕**6 wait till kingdom come** to wait for ever 永遠等待 3

king·fish·er /ˋkɪŋˌfɪʃɚ; ˈkɪŋˌfɪʃə/ *n* [C] a small brightly-coloured bird with a blue body that eats fish in rivers 翠鳥〔一種食河魚的鳥〕

king·ly /ˋkɪŋlɪ; ˈkɪŋli/ *adj* good enough for a king, or typical of a king 國王的; 配得上國王身分的; 有皇家氣派的: *a kingly feast* 豪華盛宴

king·mak·er /ˋkɪŋˌmekɚ; ˈkɪŋˌmeɪkə/ *n* [C] someone who influences the choice of people for important jobs 對任命要職人員有影響力的人

king·pin /ˋkɪŋˌpɪn; ˈkɪŋˌpɪn/ *n* [C usually singular 一般用單數] **1** the most important person or thing in a group〔在某羣體中〕最重要的人[事物]; 領袖 **2** *technical* a thin strong piece of metal used in hinges (HINGE¹)【術語】〔鉸鏈的〕中心軸, 轉向立軸

King's Coun·sel /ˌ· ˈ··/ *n* a KC 王室法律顧問

King's Eng·lish /ˌ· ˈ··/ *n* **the King's English** *old-fashioned* correct English, as it is spoken in Britain【過時】標準[規範]英語 —see also 另見 QUEEN'S ENGLISH

king's ev·i·dence /ˌ· ˈ···/ *n* **turn King's evidence** *BrE* to give information about other criminals in order to get a less severe punishment【英】〔罪犯為減刑〕提供對同案犯不利的證據, 〔罪犯〕作為污點證人指控同黨; STATE'S EVIDENCE *AmE*【美】—see also 另見 QUEEN'S EVIDENCE

king·ship /ˋkɪŋʃɪp; ˈkɪŋʃɪp/ *n* [U] the official position

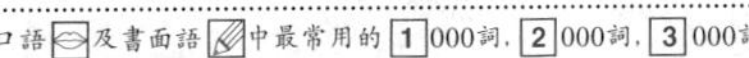

K

or condition of being a king 王權; 王位: *the responsibilities of kingship* 王權的責任

king-size /ˈ· ·/ also 又作 **king-sized** *adj* **1** very large, and usually the largest size of something 大號的; 特大號的: *a king-size bed* 特大的牀 **2** *informal* very big or strong【非正式】極大的; 極強烈的: *a king-size thirst* 極強的渴望

kink¹ /kɪŋk; kɪŋk/ *n* [C] **1** a twist in something that is normally straight 扭結; 絞纏: [+in] *The water hose had a kink in it.* 水龍軟管有一處扭結。**2** something strange or dangerous in your character〔某人性格中〕奇特[危險]的成分; 怪癖

kink² *v* [I,T] to get or give something a kink (使) 扭結; (使) 絞纏

kink·y /ˈkɪŋkɪ; ˈkɪŋki/ *adj* **1** *informal* someone who is kinky, or does kinky things, has strange ways of getting sexual excitement【非正式】〔性行為〕變態的 **2** kinky hair has a lot of small curves〔頭髮〕鬈曲的 —**kinkiness** *n* [U] —**kinkily** *adv*

kins·folk /ˈkɪnzˌfok; ˈkɪnzfəʊk/ also 又作 **kinfolk** *AmE*【美】*n* [plural] *old-fashioned* your family【過時】家人; 親屬

kin·ship /ˈkɪnʃɪp; ˈkɪnʃɪp/ *n* **1** [U+with] *literary* a family relationship【文】親屬關係: *the ties of kinship* 親屬關係 **2** [singular,U] a strong connection between people 緊密聯繫: [+with/between] *Poe shows his kinship with his literary ancestors.*〔美國小說家〕愛倫·坡顯示出他和他的文學先輩之間的密切聯繫。

kins·man /ˈkɪnzmən; ˈkɪnzmən/ *n* [C] *old use* a male relative【舊】男性親戚

kin·swom·an /ˈkɪnzˌwʊmən; ˈkɪnzˌwʊmən/ *n* [C] *old use* a female relative【舊】女性親戚

ki·osk /kɪˋɑsk; ˈkiːɒsk/ *n* [C] **1** a small building in the street where newspapers, sweets etc are sold〔街上出售報紙、糖果等的〕小亭 **2** *BrE old-fashioned* a public telephone box【英, 過時】公用電話亭

kip¹ /kɪp; kɪp/ *n* [singular,U] *BrE informal* a period of sleep【英, 非正式】一段睡眠時間: **have a kip** (=sleep for a short time) 睡一覺 | **get some kip** *I'm going to lie down and try to get some kip.* 我想躺下睡一會兒。

kip² *v* **kipped, kipping** [I] *BrE informal*【英, 非正式】**1** to sleep 睡覺 **2** to lie down in order to sleep 躺下睡覺: [+down] *kipping down for the night* 晚間上牀睡覺

kip·per /ˈkɪpɚ; ˈkɪpə/ *n* [C] a type of fish that has been preserved using smoke and salt 醃後熏製的鯡魚 —**kippered** *adj*: *kippered herring* 熏鯡魚

kirk /kɝk; kɜːk/ *n ScotE*【蘇格蘭】**1** [C] a church 教堂 **2** **the Kirk** the Church of Scotland 蘇格蘭教會

kirsch /kɪrʃ; kɪəʃ/ *n* [U] a strong alcoholic drink made from CHERRY (1) juice 櫻桃酒〔一種烈性酒〕

kis·met /ˈkɪzmɛt; ˈkɪzmet/ *n* [U] *literary* the things that will happen to you in your life; FATE (1)【文】命運, 天命

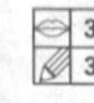
3
3

kiss¹ /kɪs; kɪs/ *v* **1** [I,T] to touch someone with your lips as a greeting or to show them love 吻: *They kissed again, passionately.* 他們再一次熱烈地親吻。| **kiss sb on** *Did he kiss you on the cheek or on the mouth?* 他吻了你的臉還是嘴? | **kiss sb goodbye/goodnight etc** *Kiss Daddy goodnight.* 親親爸爸說晚安。**2** [T] to touch something with your lips as a sign of respect 用唇接觸〔以示敬意〕: *She raised the Crucifix to her lips and kissed it.* 她把十字架舉到嘴邊親吻了一下。**3 sb can kiss goodbye to sth/kiss sth goodbye** *informal* used when you think it is certain that someone will lose their chance of getting or doing something【非正式】〔某人〕肯定會失去…的機會: *If you don't work harder you can kiss goodbye to your chances of going to university.* 如果你不加把勁學習, 你上大學的機會肯定十分渺茫。**4 kiss sth away/better** *spoken* an expression meaning to take away the pain of something by kissing someone, used especially with children【口】親親就不痛了; 吻掉〔尤用於對孩子說話〕: *Here, let Mommy kiss it better.* 來, 讓媽媽親親就不那麼痛了。**5 kiss my ass** *AmE taboo slang* an insulting expression used to show that you do not respect someone【美, 諱, 俚】去你的〔侮辱性用語〕**6 kiss (sb's) ass** *AmE taboo slang* to be too nice to someone who can give you something you want【美, 諱, 俚】拍馬屁, 巴結〔某人〕—compare 比較 KISS-ASS **7** [T] *literary* if the wind, sun etc kisses something, it gently moves or touches it【文】〔風、陽光等〕輕拂; 輕觸

kiss up to sb *phr v* [T] *AmE informal* to try to please someone in order to get them to do something for you【美, 非正式】〔為了讓某人做某事而〕奉承: *That guy got his promotion by kissing up to the boss.* 那傢伙對老闆阿諛奉承才得到了提升。

kiss² *n* [C] **1** an act of kissing 吻, 接吻: *Do you remember your first kiss?* 你記得你的初吻嗎? | **give sb a kiss** *Come and give your old Grandma a kiss.* 過來吻一下奶奶。**2 the kiss of death** *informal* something that spoils or ruins a plan, activity etc【非正式】損害[破壞]計劃[活動等]的事 —see also 另見 FRENCH KISS, KISS OF LIFE, **blow sb a kiss** (BLOW¹ (16))

kiss·a·gram *n* [C] another spelling of KISSOGRAM kissogram 的另一種拼法

kiss-ass /ˈ· ·/ *adj* [only before noun 僅用於名詞前] *AmE slang* a very impolite word used to describe the behaviour of someone who tries too hard to please other people【美俚】拍馬屁的〔粗俗用語〕

kiss·ing cous·in /ˌ·· ˈ··/ *n* [C] *AmE old-fashioned* someone you are not closely related to, but whom you know well【美, 過時】關係不太親密但很熟悉的人

kiss of life /ˌ· · ˈ·/ *n* **1 give sb the kiss of life** *especially BrE* to make someone start breathing again by blowing air into their lungs when they have almost DROWNED etc【尤英】對某人進行人工呼吸 **2** something that helps you continue an activity that you thought would fail 使…起死回生的事物: *a grant that was a kiss of life to the project* 使這項工程起死回生的撥款

kiss·o·gram, kissagram /ˈkɪsəˌgræm; ˈkɪsəgræm/ *n* [C] a humorous greeting for your BIRTHDAY etc that is delivered by someone in a special COSTUME, or the person who delivers it and kisses you 親吻電報〔一種幽默的祝賀生日等的方式, 由穿着特殊服裝的人轉達祝辭並親吻被祝賀者〕; 送親吻電報的人

kit¹ /kɪt; kɪt/ *n* **1 shaving/sewing/repair kit** [C] a set of tools, equipment etc that you use for a particular purpose or activity 剃鬚/縫紉/修理等用的成套工具 **2** [C] something such as furniture that you buy in parts and put together yourself 成套的組合部件〈如家具〉: *He made the model from a kit.* 他用一套元件組裝成模型。**3** *BrE* [U] a set of clothes and equipment that you use when playing a sport【英】〔運動用的〕成套服裝和用品: *football kit* 成套足球用品 **4** [U] a set of clothes and equipment used by soldiers, SAILORS etc〔士兵、水手等的〕成套服裝和設備: *survival kit* 一套救生用品 **5 the whole kit and caboodle** *old-fashioned* everything【過時】全部, 一切 —see also 另見 FIRST AID KIT, TOOL KIT

kit² *v* **kitting, kitted** *especially BrE*【尤英】

kit sb **out** *phr v* [T] **1** to provide someone with the clothes and equipment they need for an activity 向〔某人〕提供〔進行某種活動〕所必需的服裝和設備 **2 be kitted out/up** to have the correct clothes and equipment to do a particular activity 配備必需的裝備: *all kitted out in waterproof clothes* 配齊了防水服裝

kit bag, kitbag /ˈkɪt bæg; ˈkɪt bæg/ *n* [C] *especially BrE* a long narrow bag used by soldiers, SAILORS etc, for carrying their clothes and other possessions【尤英】〔士兵、水手等使用的長而窄的〕背包; 行李袋

kitch·en /ˈkɪtʃɪn; ˈkɪtʃɪn/ *n* [C] **1** the room where you prepare and cook food 廚房: *Can you help me carry these dishes into the kitchen?* 你能幫我把這些碟子拿到廚房去嗎? | *the kitchen table* 廚房用桌 **2 everything but the kitchen sink** *humorous* used when someone has brought too many things with them【幽默】能帶來的都帶了〔用於表示某人帶來過多的東西〕

kitchen cab·i·net /ˌ·· ˈ···/ *n* [C] an informal group of people who advise the leader of the government〔政府首腦的〕私人顧問團, 智囊團, "廚房內閣"

kitchen gar·den /ˌ·· ˈ··/ *n* [C] a part of a garden where you grow your own fruit and vegetables 家庭菜園

kitchen roll /ˈ·· ·/ *BrE*【英】also 又作 **kitchen tow·el** /ˈ·· ˌ··/ *n* [U] thick paper used for cleaning up small amounts of liquid, food etc 廚房潔紙

kitchen sink dra·ma /ˌ·· ˈ· ˌ··/ *n* [C] *BrE* a serious play or film about problems that families have at home【英】廚房水槽劇〔描寫家庭問題的嚴肅劇或電影〕

kite¹ /kaɪt; kaɪt/ *n* [C] **1** a light frame covered in coloured paper or plastic that you let fly in the air on the end of one or two long strings 風箏 **2** a type of HAWK (=bird that eats small animals) 鳶〔鷹的一種, 以小動物為食〕 **3** *AmE informal* an illegal cheque【美, 非正式】空頭支票; 假支票 **4 fly a kite** to make a suggestion to see what people will think of it 試探輿論 —see also 另見 **go fly a kite** (FLY¹ (21)), **high as a kite** (HIGH¹ (14))

kite² *v* **kited, kiting** [I,T] *AmE informal*【美, 非正式】**1** also 又作 **kite up** to raise the cost of something 提高(費用): *Soaring medical costs keep kiting up insurance premiums.* 迅速增加的醫療費用使得保險費猛升。**2** to obtain money using an illegal cheque 開〔空頭支票〕; 使用假支票騙錢

kite-fly·ing /ˈ· ˌ··/ *n* [U] **1** the game or sport of flying a kite 放風箏 **2** the act of telling people about an idea, plan etc in order to get their opinion 試探風聲[反應]

kith and kin /ˌkɪθ ən ˈkɪn; ˌkɪθ ən ˈkɪn/ *n* [plural] *old-fashioned* family and friends【過時】家人和朋友, 親友

kitsch /kɪtʃ; kɪtʃ/ *n* [U] kitsch decorations, films etc that are made without much serious thought and are SENTIMENTAL and often amuse people because of this 俗氣的裝飾; 庸俗的文藝作品 —**kitsch** *adj*

kit·ten /ˈkɪtn̩; ˈkɪtn/ *n* [C] **1** a young cat 小貓 **2 have kittens** *informal* to be very anxious or upset about something【非正式】焦慮; 煩躁

kit·ten·ish /ˈkɪtn̩ɪʃ; ˈkɪtn-ɪʃ/ *adj old-fashioned* a kittenish woman behaves in a silly way in order to attract men【過時】〔女人〕賣弄風情的, 搔首弄姿的

kit·ty /ˈkɪtɪ; ˈkɪti/ *n* **1** [C usually singular 一般用單數] the money that people have collected for a particular purpose〔為某目的〕湊集起來的錢款: *How much money is there left in the kitty?* 公共儲金還剩下多少錢? **2** [C usually singular 一般用單數] the money that the winner of a game of cards receives〔紙牌戲中的〕全部賭注 **3** [C] a word for a cat, used especially by children 小貓, 貓咪〔尤為兒語〕

kitty-cor·ner /ˌ·· ˈ··/ *adv AmE informal* on the opposite corner of a street from a particular place【美, 非正式】在街道斜對面; 成對角線地: **[+from/to]** *The drugstore is kitty-corner from the bank.* 藥店在銀行的斜對面。

ki·wi /ˈkiwɪ; ˈkiːwiː/ *n* [C] **1** a New Zealand bird that has very short wings and cannot fly 鷸鴕, 幾維〔新西蘭的一種短翅不會飛翔的鳥〕 **2** *informal* someone from New Zealand【非正式】新西蘭人

kiwi fruit /ˈ·· ·/ *n* [C] a small sweet fruit with a brown skin, which is green inside 奇異果, 獼猴桃 —see picture on page A8 參見 A8 頁圖

KKK /ˌke ke ˈke; ˌkeɪ keɪ ˈkeɪ/ *n* the abbreviation of 縮寫 = Ku Klux Klan

klans·man /ˈklænzmən; ˈklænzmən/ *n* [C] *AmE* a member of the Ku Klux Klan【美】三 K 黨成員

klax·on /ˈklæksən; ˈklæksən/ *n* [C] a loud horn that was fixed onto police cars and other official vehicles in the past〔舊時安裝在警車及其他官方車輛上的〕高音喇叭, 警報器

Kleen·ex /ˈklinɛks; ˈkliːneks/ *n* [C,U] *trademark* a TISSUE (1)【商標】健力氏[可麗舒]紙巾; 紙巾

klep·to·ma·ni·a /ˌklɛptəˈmenɪə; ˌkleptəˈmeɪniə/ *n* [U] a mental illness in which you have a desire to steal things 盜竊癖, 偷竊狂

klep·to·ma·ni·ac /ˌklɛptəˈmenɪæk; ˌkleptəˈmeɪniæk/ also 又作 **klep·to** /ˈklɛpto; ˈkleptəʊ/ *informal*【非正式】*n* [C] someone suffering from kleptomania 有盜竊癖的人, 偷竊狂者

klutz, clutz /klʌts; klʌts/ *n* [C] *AmE* someone who drops things and falls easily【美】笨手笨腳的人 —**klutzy** *adj*

km *n* the written abbreviation of 縮寫 = KILOMETRE

knack /næk; næk/ *n informal*【非正式】**1** [singular] a special skill or ability that you usually gain by practice 竅門, 技能, 本領: *There's a knack to starting our lawn mower.* 發動我們那台刈草機有個竅門。**2 have a knack of doing sth** to have a tendency to do something 有做某事的習慣: *He has a knack of saying the wrong thing.* 他總愛說一些不合時宜的話。

knack·er /ˈnækɚ; ˈnækə/ also 又作 **knacker out** *v* [T] *BrE spoken*【英口】**1** to become extremely tired 使精疲力竭: **knacker yourself out** *Slow down – you'll knacker yourself out!* 放慢點兒, 你這樣會累壞的! **2 knacker your elbow/hand etc** to hurt your elbow etc so that you cannot use it 使胳膊肘/手等嚴重受傷致殘

knack·ered /ˈnækɚd; ˈnækəd/ *adj BrE spoken*【英口】**1** extremely tired 極累的, 精疲力竭的 **2** too old or broken to use 舊[破]得不能用的: *a knackered old bike* 舊得不能騎的腳踏車

knackers' yard /ˈ·· ˌ·/ also 又作 **knacker's** *n* [C] *BrE*【英】**1** a place where horses are killed 宰馬場 **2 ready for the knacker's yard** too old to be useful or work properly 舊得不能用

knap·sack /ˈnæpˌsæk; ˈnæpsæk/ *n* [C] a bag that you carry on your shoulders 背包

knave /nev; neɪv/ *n* [C] **1** *BrE* the playing card with a value between the ten and queen; JACK¹ (2)【英】傑克〔jack, 紙牌中介於十點與王后之間的一張牌〕—see also 另見 **cards** (CARD¹ (7)) **2** *old-fashioned* a dishonest boy or man【過時】狡詐的男孩[男人] —**knavish** *adj* —**knavishly** *adv*

knav·e·ry /ˈnevərɪ; ˈneɪvəri/ *n* [C,U] *old use* dishonest behaviour【舊】無賴行為, 不誠實的行為

knead /nid; niːd/ *v* [T] **1** to press a mixture of flour and water many times with your hands 揉, 捏〔濕麵粉〕: *Knead the dough for three minutes.* 將麵團揉三分鐘。—see picture on page A11 參見 A11 頁圖 **2** to press someone's muscles many times in order to help cure pain 按摩, 推揉

knee¹ /ni; niː/ *n* [C] **1** the joint that bends in the middle of your leg 膝, 膝蓋: *Lift using your knees, not your back.* 用膝蓋頂起來, 別用背部。—see picture at 參見 BODY 圖 **2** the part of your clothes that covers your knee〔褲子的〕膝部: *holes in both knees* 褲子膝部的破口子 **3 on sb's knee** on the top part of your legs when you are sitting down 在某人膝上: *Daddy, can I sit on your knee?* 爸爸, 我能坐你的腿上嗎? **4 with your knees knocking (together)** feeling very afraid or very cold 怕[冷]得雙膝顫抖 **5 on your knees** in a way that shows you have no power or are very sorry 跪下〔表示沒有能力或悲傷〕: *He begged me, on his knees, to forgive him.* 他雙膝跪下乞求我原諒他。**6 bring sb/sth to their knees a)** to defeat a country or group of people in a war〔在戰爭中〕打敗〔某一國家或一隊人馬〕 **b)** to have such a bad effect on an organization, activity etc that it cannot continue 使〔組織、活動等〕難以繼續: *The recession has brought many companies to their knees.* 經濟衰退使許多公司難以維持。**7 put sb over your knee** *old-fashioned* to punish a child by hitting them【過時】打孩子〔以示懲罰〕 **8 on bended knee(s)** *old-fashioned* in a way that shows great respect for someone【過時】跪着〔表示對某人極大的敬意〕: *worshipping on bended knee* 跪拜 —see also 另見 **knee/elbow pad** (PAD¹ (1)), **learn/be taught sth at your mother's knee** (MOTHER¹ (5)), **the bee's knees** (BEE (4)), **weak at the knees** (WEAK (11))

knee² *v* [T+in] to hit someone with your knee 用膝蓋碰撞: *I kneed him in the groin.* 我用膝蓋撞擊他的陰部。

K

knee breech·es /'· ,··/ *n* [plural] tight trousers that end at your knee, worn especially in the past〔尤指舊時人們穿的〕齊膝緊身短褲

knee cap /'· ·/ *n* [C] the bone at the front of your knee 髕骨, 膝蓋骨 —see picture at 參見 SKELETON 圖

knee·cap /ˈniˌkæp; ˈniːkæp/ *v* **kneecapped, kneecapping** [T] to shoot someone's kneecaps as an unofficial punishment 槍擊〔某人〕的膝蓋骨〔作為一種非法的報復手段〕

knee-deep /,· '·◂/ *adj* **1** deep enough to reach your knees 齊膝深的: [+in] *knee deep in mud* 陷入齊膝深的爛泥 **2** *informal* having a lot of something【非正式】非常多的: [+in] *knee deep in work* 工作繁多

knee-high¹ /,· '·◂/ *adj* **1** tall enough to reach your knees 齊膝高的, 沒膝的: *knee-high grass* 齊膝高的草 **2 knee-high to a grasshopper** *old-fashioned* used when talking about the past to say that someone was a very small child then【過時】〔某人〕還是很小的孩子時

knee-high² *n* [C] a sock that ends just below your knee〔高及膝蓋下的〕長統襪

knee-jerk /'· ·/ *adj* a knee-jerk reaction, opinion etc is what you feel or say about a situation from habit, without thinking about it 本能[自動]反應的

kneel 跪

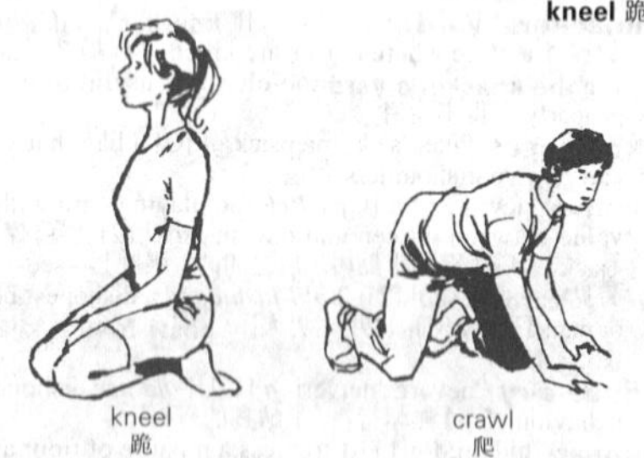

kneel 跪　crawl 爬

kneel /nil; niːl/ also 又作 **kneel down** *v past tense and past participle* **knelt** /nɛlt; nelt/ also 又作 **kneeled** *AmE*【美】[I] to be in or move into a position where your body is resting on your knees 跪着, 跪下: *a statue of a kneeling figure* 一尊下跪者的塑像 | [+on] *We knelt on the floor to have a good look at the map.* 我們跪在地板上仔細查看地圖。

knee-length /'· ·/ *adj* long or tall enough to reach your knees 長[高]及膝部的: *a knee-length skirt* 長及膝部的裙子

knees-up /'· ·/ *n* [C] *BrE informal* a noisy party【英, 非正式】喧鬧的集會: *After the wedding there was a bit of a knees-up.* 婚禮之後是一小陣子喧鬧的慶祝活動。

knell /nɛl; nel/ *n* [C] *literary* the sound of a bell being rung slowly because someone has died【文】喪鐘 —see also 另見 DEATH KNELL

knew /nju; njuː/ *v* the past tense of KNOW¹

knick·er·bock·ers /ˈnɪkɚˌbɑkɚz; ˈnɪkəˌbɒkəz/ *n* [plural] short loose trousers that fit tightly at your knees, worn especially in the past〔尤指舊時穿的膝部紮緊的〕燈籠褲

knick·ers /ˈnɪkɚz; ˈnɪkəz/ *n* [plural] *BrE informal*【英, 非正式】**1** a piece of women's underwear worn between your waist and the top of your legs; PANTIES 女用短襯褲: *a pair of frilly knickers* 一條鑲褶邊的女用短襯褲 —see picture at 參見 UNDERWEAR 圖 **2** *AmE* KNICKERBOCKERS【美】〔膝部紮緊的〕燈籠褲 **3 get your knickers in a twist** *BrE spoken* to get upset【英口】感到不快, 惱火

knick-knack /ˈnɪk ˌnæk; ˈnɪk næk/ *n* [C] a small object used as a decoration 小裝飾品, 小擺設: *They had various knick-knacks on the top of the bookcase.* 他們的書櫃頂上放有各種小擺設。

knives 刀

table knife 餐刀
vegetable knife 切菜刀
fish knife 魚刀
penknife/pocket knife 小摺刀
scalpel 手術刀
bread knife 切麵包刀
carving knife 切肉刀
dagger 短劍; 匕首

knife¹ /naɪf; naɪf/ *n plural* **knives** /naɪvz; naɪvz/ [C] **1** a metal blade fixed into a handle, used for cutting or as a weapon〔有柄的〕刀: *knife and fork* 刀叉 | *He had been stabbed with a knife.* 他被刀扎傷了。| **kitchen/bread/vegetable etc knife** (=knife used in the kitchen, for cutting bread etc) 廚房用刀/麵包刀/菜刀等 —see picture on page A11 參見 A11 頁圖 **2 the knives are out** *informal* used to say that people are being extremely unfriendly to each other【非正式】劍拔弩張 **3 have/get your knife into someone** *informal* to dislike someone and be very unfriendly towards them【非正式】討厭[敵視]某人 **4 twist/turn the knife** to say something that makes someone more upset about a subject they are already unhappy about 火上澆油 **5 under the knife** *humorous* having a medical operation【幽默】在手術刀下, 做手術 **6 you could cut the atmosphere/air with a knife** used to say that you felt the people in a room were angry with each other〔屋內人之間的緊張氣氛〕使人透不過氣 —see also 另見 PAPER KNIFE

knife² *v* [T+in] to put a knife into someone's body; STAB¹ (1) 用刀扎〔某人〕

knife-edge /'· ·/ *n* **1 be on a knife-edge a)** to be in a situation in which the result is extremely uncertain 對結果毫無把握: *Success or failure is balanced on a knife-edge.* 是成功還是失敗仍是未知數。**b)** very anxious about the future result of something 急於知道結果, 對結果焦慮不安: *She is on a knife-edge about her promotion.* 她急於想知道自己晉升的情況。**2** [singular] something that is narrow or sharp 窄長[鋒利]的東西: *The cliff narrowed down to a knife-edge.* 懸崖逐漸變窄, 形似刀刃。

knight¹ /naɪt; naɪt/ *n* [C] **1** a man with a high rank in former times who was trained to fight while riding a horse 騎士, 武士: *knights in armour* 披盔戴甲的騎士 —see also 另見 WHITE KNIGHT **2** a man who has received a knighthood and has the title 'SIR' (4) before his name 爵士〔受封為爵士的人, 其名前冠有 Sir 這一頭銜〕**3** the CHESS piece with a horse's head on it〔國際象棋中的〕馬 **4 a knight in shining armour** a brave man who saves someone from a dangerous situation 救人於危難之中的勇士

knight² *v* [T] to give someone the rank of knight 封〔某人〕為爵士

knight-er·rant /,· '··/ *n* [C] a knight in former times who travelled looking for adventure〔舊時的〕遊俠騎士

knight·hood /ˈnaɪthʊd; ˈnaɪthʊd/ *n* [C,U] a special rank or title that is given to someone by the King or Queen in Britain〔由英國國王或女王授予的〕爵士封號[頭銜]

knight·ly /ˈnaɪtlɪ; ˈnaɪtli/ *adj literary* connected with being a knight or typical of a knight, especially by behaving with courage and honour【文】騎士的; 俠義的; 勇敢

而高尚的: *knightly deeds of chivalry* 騎士般的俠義行為

knit /nɪt; nɪt/ *v past tense and past participle* **knitted** *or* **knitting** [I,T] **1** also 又作 **knit up** to make clothing out of wool using two KNITTING NEEDLES〔用毛線和兩根編織針〕編織, 針織: **knit sb sth** *She's knitting me a sweater.* 她在給我織毛衣。—compare 比較 CROCHET **2** *technical* to use a PLAIN (=basic) knitting stitch【術語】織平針: *Knit one, purl one.* 平織一針, 反織一針。**3** to join people, things or ideas more closely, or to be closely connected 使〔人、物或想法〕緊密結合: **[+together]** *Wherever they live, the Jewish people are knit together by a common faith.* 猶太人無論住在哪裡, 共同的信仰都把他們緊緊連在一起。| **well/closely/tightly etc knit** (=with all the parts joined closely) 緊密結合的 *a closely knit community* 緊密團結的社區 **4 [+together]** a bone that knits after being broken grows into one piece again〔折骨〕癒合 **5 knit your brows** to show you are worried, thinking hard etc by moving your EYEBROWS together 緊皺眉頭〔表示憂慮、思索等〕—**knitter** *n* [C] —see also 另見 CLOSE-KNIT

knit·ting /ˈnɪtɪŋ; ˈnɪtɪŋ/ *n* [U] something that is being knitted 編織物

knitting nee·dle /ˈ·· ˌ··/ *n* [C] one of the two long sticks with round ends that you use to knit something 編織針 —see picture at 參見 NEEDLE¹ 圖

knit·wear /ˈnɪtˌwɛr; ˈnɪt-weə/ *n* [U] knitted (KNIT (1)) clothing 針織品, 編織的衣物: *a knitwear shop* 針織品商店

knives /naɪvz; naɪvz/ *n* the plural of KNIFE¹

knob /nɑb; nɒb/ *n* [C] **1** a round handle or thing that you turn to open a door, turn on a radio etc 球形把手; 旋鈕 **2 a knob of** a small piece of something 一小塊: *Melt a knob of butter in the pan.* 用平底鍋融化一小塊黃油。**3** *BrE taboo slang* a PENIS【英, 諱, 俚】陰莖 **4 with (brass) knobs on** *BrE old-fashioned* used especially by children to reply to an insult【英, 過時】〔尤為小孩反唇相譏時用語〕更是那樣: *"Idiot!" "Same to you, with knobs on!"* "你是白痴!" "你才是呢, 你是個大白痴!"

knob·bly /ˈnɑblɪ; ˈnɒbli/ also 又作 **knob·by** /ˈnɑbɪ; ˈnɒbi/ *AmE*【美】*adj* with hard parts that stick out from under the surface of something 帶有似球形突出物的; 多結節的: *knobbly knees* 突出的膝蓋骨

1 3 **knock¹** /nɑk; nɒk/ *v*

1 ▶DOOR/WINDOW 門/窗◀ [I] to hit a door or window with your closed hand to attract the attention of the people inside 敲門[窗]: *Why don't you knock before you come in?* 你進來前為甚麼不敲門? | **[+at/on]** *I turned to see Jane knocking frantically on the taxi window.* 我轉過身看見簡發瘋似地敲着計程車的車窗。

2 ▶HIT/MAKE STH MOVE 碰撞/使某物移動◀ [I always+adv/prep, T] to hit someone or something with a short quick action, so that it moves, falls down etc 碰撞; 碰倒, 撞倒: *Don't knock the camera, the picture will be blurry.* 別碰相機, 不然照片就模糊了。| **knock sth ↔ down/off/over etc** *The dog managed to knock over a table.* 那條狗竟然弄翻了桌子。| **knock sth ↔ against/into/in** *I need a hammer to knock these tent pegs in.* 我需要一把錘子把這些固定帳篷的樁子敲進去。| **knock sb/sth flying** *BrE informal* (=hit something or someone so that they move a long distance)【英, 非正式】把某人/某物撞得很遠 *Holly ran through the crowd, knocking people flying.* 霍莉衝過人羣, 把周圍的人撞得四散。| **knock a hole in** (=make a hole in something) 在…上撞出一個洞

3 ▶HIT SB HARD 用力撞擊某人◀ **a) knock sb flat/knock sb to the ground** to hit someone so hard that they fall down 撞倒某人: *His assailant knocked him to the ground and ran off with his briefcase.* 襲擊者把他撞倒在地上, 搶了他的皮包跑了。**b) knock sb unconscious/senseless** to hit someone so hard that they fall unconscious 擊昏某人: *The blast from the explosion knocked him unconscious.* 他被爆炸的衝擊波擊昏了。**c) knock the living daylights out of/hell out of** *informal* to hit someone many times or very hard【非正式】多次猛擊某人

4 I'll knock your block off *spoken* used when threatening to hit someone very hard【口】我會把你痛打一頓: *If you touch her, I'll knock your block off!* 你要是碰她一下, 我就會狠狠揍你一頓!

5 knock it off *spoken* used to tell someone to stop doing something, because it is annoying you【口】〔因受干擾而叫某人〕停下來: *"Hey, knock it off!" Jesse shouted furiously.* "喂, 給我停下來!" 傑西憤怒地吼道。

6 ▶CRITICIZE 批評◀ [T] to criticize someone or their work, especially in an unfair or annoying way 指責, 責難; 批評: *Some movie reviewers seem to knock every picture they see.* 有些電影評論家似乎對他們所觀看的每一部影片都加以批評。| **don't knock it** *spoken* (=used to tell someone not to criticize something)【口】別指責 *"Bungee jumping! You must be crazy!" "Don't knock it till you've tried it."* "綁緊跳? 你瘋了吧?" "你沒試過就先別瞎說。"

7 knock sb/sth into shape *informal* to make changes to something in order to make it good enough【非正式】使人/事物更完善: *We've only got until Thursday to knock this play into shape.* 我們必須在星期四之前把劇本修改好。

8 ▶MAKE A NOISE 發出噪音◀ [I] if an engine or pipes etc knock, they make a noise like something hard being hit, usually because something is wrong with them〔發動機、管道等因出毛病而〕發出爆震[碰撞]聲

9 ▶BALL 球◀ [T always+adv/prep] to kick or hit a ball somewhere 踢〔球〕; 擊〔球〕: **knock sth about/past/back etc** *We were just knocking a ball about in the yard.* 我們只是在院子裡踢球。

10 knock the stuffing out of *informal* to make someone lose their confidence【非正式】使某人氣餒: *Getting such low grades this semester seems to have knocked the stuffing out of him.* 這學期得這麼低的分數, 似乎使他信心全無了。

11 knock sb's socks off also 又作 **knock 'em dead** *spoken* to surprise and please someone by being very impressive【口】令某人又驚又喜: *Go out there and knock 'em dead, kid.* 孩子, 走出去給他們一個驚喜。

12 knock some sense into sb/into sb's head *informal* to make someone learn to behave in a more sensible way【非正式】讓某人得個教訓/懂事一些: *Who knows. Maybe getting arrested will knock some sense into him.* 誰知道, 也許被抓起來能讓他以後懂事一些。

13 knock spots off *BrE spoken* to be much better than someone or something【英口】比〔某人或某物〕強得多; 遠遠勝過: *Our new computer system knocks spots off the old one.* 我們的新電腦系統比舊的強多了。

14 knock sth on the head *BrE informal* to prevent you from doing something you have planned【英, 非正式】阻止某人做某事; 破壞〔計劃〕: *I wanted to go for a picnic, but the rain's knocked that on the head.* 我本想去野餐, 可這場雨使計劃泡了湯。

15 knock (sb's) heads together *informal* to talk angrily to people who are quarrelling or behaving stupidly【非正式】強制令某人停止〔爭吵或胡鬧〕: *If you kids don't settle down I'm going to come up and knock your heads together!* 如果你們這幫孩子再不安靜下來, 我就要來教訓你們了!

16 you could have knocked me down with a feather *old-fashioned* used to emphasize how surprised you were by something【過時】令某人驚訝不已: *When I heard I'd won, you could have knocked me down with a feather.* 聽說我贏了, 這使我大為驚訝。

17 knock the bottom out of *informal* to make something, such as a price much lower or weaker【非正式】使〔價格等〕大跌[疲軟]: *A rise in interest rates would completely knock the bottom out of the property market.* 提升利率可能使房地產市場價格大跌。—see also 另見 **with your knees knocking (together)** (KNEE¹ (4))

knock around also 又作 **knock about** *BrE*【英】*phr v informal*【非正式】
1 ▶HIT SB 打某人◀ [T **knock** sb **about/around**] to hit someone several times 多次打〔某人〕: *My father used to knock me and my brother around a lot.* 父親以前常打我和弟弟。
2 ▶RELAX 放鬆◀ [I,T] to spend time in a relaxing way, without doing anything very important 悠閒地度過: **knock around town/the house etc** *We spent the weekend just knocking around the house.* 我們就在家裡悠閒地度過了週末。
3 ▶TRAVEL 旅行◀ [I,T **knock around** sth] to travel to different places 到各處旅行; 漫遊; 流浪: *I've knocked around a few places in my life.* 我這輩子去過一些地方。
4 ▶IDEAS 主意◀ [T **knock** sth ↔ **around**] to discuss and think about an idea, plan etc with other people 討論, 商討: *We've been knocking around a few ideas.* 我們一直在討論一些想法。
5 ▶BALL 球◀ [T **knock** sth **about**] *BrE* to play a game with a ball, but not in a serious way【英】玩〔球〕, 打〔球〕
6 ▶BE SOMEWHERE 在某處◀ [I] *BrE* if something or someone is knocking around a place, it is somewhere in that place but you are not sure exactly where【英】在甚麼地方, 在某處: *Is there a screwdriver knocking about anywhere?* 能在甚麼地方找到一把螺絲刀嗎?

knock back *phr v* [T] *informal*【非正式】**1** [**knock** sth ↔ **back**] to quickly drink large quantities of an alcoholic drink 狂飲, 豪飲: **knock it/them back** *spoken*【口】*Steve can really knock it back – he's drunk five pints already.* 史蒂夫真能喝, 已經喝了五品脫啤酒了。**2** [**knock** sb **back** sth] to cost you a lot of money 使花費〔大筆錢〕: *Our summer holiday knocked us back £600 this year.* 我們今年度暑假花費了600英鎊。**3** [**knock** sb **back**] *BrE* to surprise or shock someone【英】使吃驚; 使震驚: *The news of her death really knocked him back.* 她去世的消息着實使他大吃一驚。

knock down *phr v* [T]
1 ▶DRIVING A CAR 駕車◀ [**knock** sb **down**] to hit someone with a car while you are driving, so that they are hurt or killed〔駕車〕把〔某人〕撞倒: *He was knocked down by a drunk driver.* 他被一名醉漢開車撞倒。| **get knocked down** *Someone said a kid got knocked down by a truck.* 有人說一個小孩被卡車撞倒了。
2 ▶DESTROY 摧毀◀ [**knock** sth ↔ **down**] to destroy a building or part of a building 摧毀, 拆毀〔建築物或其部分〕: *We knocked down one of the walls to make a bigger kitchen.* 我們拆掉了一面牆使廚房變大。
3 ▶REDUCE PRICE 減價◀ [**knock** sth ↔ **down**] *informal* to reduce the price of something by a large amount【非正式】使大幅降價: *The new stove we bought was knocked down from $800 to $550.* 我們新買的爐子的價錢從800美元降到了550美元。—see also 另見 KNOCKDOWN
4 ▶ASK SB TO REDUCE PRICE 討價還價◀ [**knock** sb **down to**] *informal* to persuade someone to reduce the price of something they are selling you【非正式】使降價, 殺〔某人的〕價: *I tried to knock him down to £50.* 我試圖把他的要價壓到50英鎊。
5 ▶DRINK 飲酒◀ [**knock** sth ↔ **down**] *AmE informal* to quickly drink large quantities of an alcoholic drink【美, 非正式】狂飲, 豪飲
6 ▶PROVE STH WRONG 證明某事錯誤◀ [**knock** sth ↔ **down**] *BrE informal* to prove that an idea, plan etc is not good or right【英, 非正式】證明〔某主意、計劃等〕不妥[不對]: *They knocked the proposal down on the grounds that it was impractical.* 他們以不切實際為由否定了這個建議。

knock sth **into** sth *phr v* [T] to make two rooms into one room by taking away the wall that divides them 拆掉…的隔牆〔把兩間房變為一間房〕: *We knocked the sitting room and the dining room into one.* 我們拆掉了客廳與飯廳之間的隔牆, 使兩室合二為一。

knock off *phr v informal*【非正式】
1 ▶STOP WORK 停止工作◀ [I] to stop working at the end of the day, before lunch etc 停止工作; 下班: *What time do you knock off for lunch?* 你們甚麼時候歇工吃午飯? | **knock off early** *Is it okay if I knock off a little early today?* 我今天早點下班行不行? | **knock off work** *Alex usually knocks off work about 5:30.* 亞歷克斯通常約五點半下班。| **knock off for the day** *We knocked off for the day at eight.* 我們八點鐘收工。
2 ▶REDUCE A PRICE 減價◀ [T **knock** sth ↔ **off**] to reduce the price of something by a particular amount 從價錢中減去: *He said he'd knock off a couple of pounds if I bought two.* 他說我如果買兩個就可以少收幾英鎊。
3 ▶REDUCE AMOUNT 減量◀ [T **knock** sth ↔ **off**] to take a particular amount away from a total〔從總量中〕去掉: *We're knocking off one mark for each mistake.* 每出一個錯我們就減掉一分。
4 ▶PRODUCE 製造◀ [T **knock** sth ↔ **off**] to produce something quickly and easily〔快速輕鬆地〕做出; 做完: *Roland makes huge amounts of money knocking off copies of famous paintings.* 羅倫靠快速仿製名畫, 賺取大筆大筆的錢。
5 ▶MURDER 謀殺◀ [T **knock** sb **off**] to murder someone 殺害〔某人〕
6 ▶STEAL 偷◀ [T **knock** sth ↔ **off**] *BrE* to steal something, especially easily【英】〔尤指不費力地〕偷竊
7 ▶SEX 性◀ [T **knock** sb **off**] *BrE slang* to have sex with someone【英俚】與…性交

knock out *phr v* [T]
1 ▶UNCONSCIOUS 無知覺的◀ [**knock** sb/sth **out**] to make someone become unconscious 使失去知覺, 把…擊昏: *Tyson knocked out his opponent in Round 5.* 泰森在第五回合將對手擊昏。| *The shock from an electric eel is powerful enough to knock a man out.* 一條電鰻的電擊足以把一個人擊昏。—see also 另見 KNOCKOUT[1] (2)
2 ▶DEFEAT 擊敗◀ [**knock** sb/sth **out**] to defeat a person or team in a competition so that they can no longer take part 擊敗, 淘汰: **knock sb out of** *Indiana knocked Purdue out of the semifinals.* 印第安納隊將珀杜隊淘汰出半決賽。—see also 另見 KNOCKOUT[1] (4)
3 ▶ADMIRE 欽佩◀ [**knock** sb **out**] *informal* to make you feel surprised and full of admiration【非正式】令人驚嘆; 使極其欽佩: *The music was just brilliant – it really knocked me out.* 這音樂太美妙了, 真讓我着迷。
4 ▶SHOCK 震驚◀ [**knock** sb **out**] *informal* to shock someone so much that they do not know what to say or do【非正式】使驚得目瞪口呆: *When she told me the real truth it just totally knocked me out.* 她把真相告訴我後, 我簡直驚呆了。
5 ▶PRODUCE WITH DIFFICULTY 費力地做出◀ [**knock** sth ↔ **out**] *BrE informal* to produce something, especially when you find this difficult【英, 非正式】〔尤指吃力地〕做成: *It took him several years to knock out a book on the subject.* 他花了好幾年才就這個主題寫出了一本書。| **knock sth ↔ out of** *Let's see if we can knock a decent sound out of this old piano.* 我們來試試看能不能讓這架舊鋼琴發出像樣的聲音吧。
6 ▶PRODUCE EASILY 輕易地做出◀ [**knock** sth ↔ **out**] *AmE informal* to produce something easily and quickly, especially so that it is not of very good quality【美, 非正式】草草弄成, 匆匆弄出;〔輕易地〕完成: *We can knock out about 50 dresses in a day.* 我們一天能做出大約50件連衣裙。
7 knock yourself out *informal* to work very hard in order to do something well【非正式】〔為做好某事而〕苦幹: *The Nelsons really knocked themselves out to give Amy a nice wedding.* 為了把艾美的婚禮辦得圓滿, 納爾遜一家人真是竭盡全力。

knock over *phr v* [T] **1** [**knock** sb **over**] to hit someone with a car while you are driving, so that they are hurt or killed〔開車〕撞傷; 撞死: *Beth was knocked over by a motorcyclist when she was crossing the street.* 貝思橫過馬路時被摩托車撞傷。**2** [**knock** sth ↔ **over**] *AmE* *informal* to rob a place such as a shop or bank and threaten or attack the people who work there【美, 非正式】搶劫〔商店、銀行等〕

knock sth ↔ **together** *phr v* [T] *informal* to make something quickly, using whatever you have available【非正式】〔以現有材料〕迅速拼湊: *We should be able to knock something together with what's in the fridge.* 就冰箱裡現有的東西, 我們應該能拼湊出一點甚麼。

knock up *phr v* [T] **1** [**knock** sth ↔ **up**] *informal* to make something quickly and without using much effort【非正式】倉促製成; 趕做: *A local carpenter knocked up some kitchen units for us out of old pine.* 一位本地木匠用舊松木給我們趕製了幾件廚房用具。**2** [**knock** sb ↔ **up**] *BrE informal* to wake someone up by knocking on their door【英, 非正式】敲門把〔某人〕喚醒: *What time do you want me to knock you up in the morning?* 你想我早上幾點敲門把你叫醒? **3** [**knock sb up**] *informal* to make a woman PREGNANT【非正式】使〔女子〕懷孕

knock² *n* **1** [C] the sound of something hard hitting a hard surface 敲擊聲: *a loud knock at the door* 很響的敲門聲 | *a knock in the engine* 發動機的爆震聲 **2** [C] the action of something hard hitting your body 撞擊: *He got a knock on the head when he fell.* 他跌倒時頭被撞了一下。**3 take a knock** *informal* to have some bad luck or trouble【非正式】倒霉, 遇到麻煩: *Clive's taken quite a few hard knocks lately.* 克萊夫近來受到不少挫折。

knock·a·bout /ˈnɑkəˌbaʊt; ˈnɒkəbaʊt/ *adj BrE* knockabout entertainers make people laugh with their silly behaviour, for example by falling over things and pushing each other around【英】〔演員〕以喧鬧笨拙的表演引人發笑的

knock·down /ˈnɑkˌdaʊn; ˈnɒkdaʊn/ *adj* [only before noun 僅用於名詞前] a knockdown price is very cheap 〔價格〕很低的 —see also 另見 **knock down** (KNOCK¹)

knock-down-drag-out /ˈ· · ˌ· ·/ *adj AmE* using the most extreme methods to win【美】激烈的; 不惜一切手段的: *a knock-down-drag-out political campaign* 激烈的政治運動

knock·er /ˈnɑkɚ; ˈnɒkə/ *n* **1** [C] a piece of metal on an outside door that you use to knock loudly〔門上供敲門用的〕門環 **2 knockers** [plural] *slang* an offensive word meaning a woman's breasts【俚】〔女人的〕乳房〔冒犯用語〕 **3** [C] someone who is always criticizing 愛挑剔的人

knock-kneed /ˌ· ˈ·◂/ *adj* having knees that point inwards slightly 膝外翻的

knock·off /ˈnɑkˌɔf; ˈnɒkɒf/ *n* [C] *AmE informal* a cheap copy of something expensive【美, 非正式】〔貴重物品的〕廉價仿製品

knock-on /ˈ· ·/ *adj* **have a knock-on effect** to start a process in which each part is directly influenced by the one before it 引起連鎖反應: *These price rises will have a knock-on effect throughout the economy.* 這些價格的上漲將給整個經濟帶來連鎖反應。

knock·out¹ /ˈnɑkˌaʊt; ˈnɒk-aʊt/ *n* [C] **1** an act of knocking your opponent down in BOXING so that he cannot get up again〔拳擊中〕擊倒對手: *The fight ended in a knockout.* 這場比賽以一方被擊倒而結束。**2 knockout punch/blow a)** a hard hit that knocks someone down so that they cannot get up again 把對手打倒的一擊 —see also 另見 **knock out** (KNOCK¹) **b)** an action or event that causes defeat or failure 導致失敗的行為[事件]: *High interest rates have been a knockout blow to the business.* 高利率一直是對企業的致命打擊。**3** *informal* someone or something that is very attractive or successful【非正式】極有魅力的人[物]; 非常成功的人[物]: *Baby, you're a knockout.* 寶貝, 你太迷人了。**4** *BrE* a competition in which winning players or teams continue playing until there is only one winner【英】淘汰賽

knockout² *adj informal* making someone unconscious【非正式】使人昏迷的: *knockout pills* 麻醉藥, 蒙汗藥 | *the knockout punch* 把對手擊昏的一拳

knock-up /ˈ· ·/ *n* [C] *BrE* a short time before a game when the players practise, especially in tennis【英】〔尤指網球的〕賽前練習

knoll /nol; nəʊl/ *n* [C] a small round hill 土墩, 小圓丘

knot 結; 節疤

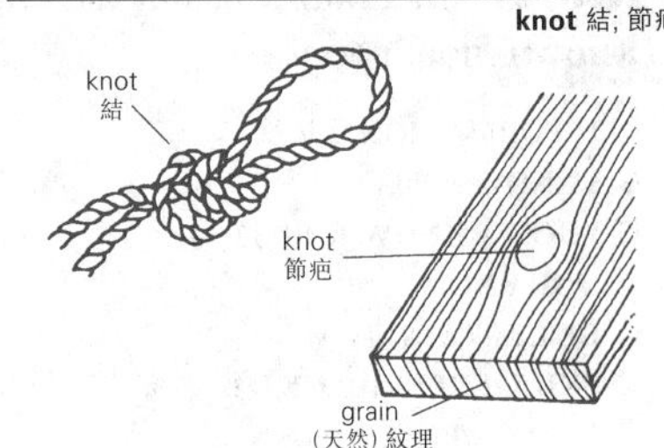

knot¹ /nɑt; nɒt/ *n* [C]

1 ►TIED STRING 綁好的繩◄ a join made by tying together two ends of rope, cloth, string etc〔繩索、布條、線等兩端打成的〕結: *Here, let me fix the knot in your tie.* 來, 我替你把領帶上的結整理一下。| *Can you help me undo this knot?* 你能幫我解開這個結嗎?

2 ►HAIR 毛髮◄ **a)** a mass of hairs, threads etc accidentally twisted together 絞成一團的頭髮[線等]: *I can't get the knots out of my hair.* 我分不開纏結在一起的頭髮。**b)** a way of arranging your hair into a tight round shape at the back of your head 髮髻, 圓髻

3 ►SHIP'S SPEED 船速◄ written abbreviation 縮寫為 KT, a measure of speed used for ships and aircraft that is about 1,853 metres per hour 節〔即 1,853 米 / 小時, 船和飛機的速度單位〕

4 ►PEOPLE 人◄ a small group of people standing close together〔站在一起的〕一小羣人

5 ►HARD MASS 硬結◄ a hard mass that is formed by a lot of things that are close together 硬結, 隆起(物): *a knot of muscles* 肌肉塊

6 ►WOOD 木頭◄ a hard round place in a piece of wood where a branch once joined the tree〔木材上枝與幹分離處的〕節, 節疤

7 a knot in your stomach/throat etc a hard uncomfortable feeling in your stomach etc caused by a strong emotion such as fear or anger〔恐懼或生氣等強烈情緒導致的〕心窩揪緊/喉嚨哽住等 —see also 另見 GORDIAN KNOT, **at a rate of knots** (RATE¹ (7)), **tie the knot** (TIE¹ (4)), **tie yourself (up) in knots** (TIE¹ (5))

knot² *v* **knotted, knotting 1** [T] to tie together two ends of rope, cloth, string etc 使打結, 使纏結 **2** [I,T] **a)** if hair or threads knot they become twisted together (使)〔頭髮、線〕絞纏 **b) knot your hair** to arrange and fasten your hair into a tight round shape at the back of your head 把頭髮梳理成一個圓髻 **3** [I,T] if a muscle or other part of your body knots, or is knotted it feels hard and uncomfortable (使)〔肌肉〕暴突, (使)〔身體某部分〕緊揪: *Fear and anxiety knotted her stomach.* 恐懼和焦慮使她胃部緊揪。

knot·ted /ˈnɑtɪd; ˈnɒtɪ̣d/ *adj*

1 ►FULL OF KNOTS 多結的◄ [only before noun 僅用於名詞前] containing a lot of knots 多結的: *pieces of knotted string* 幾根打有許多結的繩子

2 ►MUSCLE 肌肉◄ if a muscle or other part of your body is knotted, it feels hard and uncomfortable 暴突的, 揪緊的: *knotted shoulder muscles* 肩膀暴突的肌肉

3 Get knotted! *BrE spoken* used to tell someone rudely to go away or that you do not agree with them【英口】滾開! 見鬼去!

4 ►HANDS 手◄ knotted hands or fingers are twisted because of old age or too much work〔手或手指因年老或過度勞累形成的〕骨節突出彎曲的

knot·ty /ˈnɑtɪ; ˈnɒti/ *adj* **1** difficult to solve 難以解決的: *a knotty problem* 棘手的問題 **2** knotty wood contains a lot of KNOTs (=hard round places)〔木材〕多節(疤)的

know¹ /no; nəʊ/ *v past tense* **knew** /nju; njuː/ *past participle* **known** /non; nəʊn/

① INFORMATION 信息
② I KNOW 我知道
③ I DON'T KNOW 我不知道
④ YOU KNOW 你知道
⑤ BE CERTAIN 有把握
⑥ SKILL/EXPERIENCE 技術/經驗
⑦ PERSON/PLACE 人/地點
⑧ LANGUAGE/MUSIC ETC 語言/音樂等
⑨ REALIZE 意識到
⑩ RECOGNIZE 認出
⑪ EXPERIENCE 體驗
⑫ SPOKEN PHRASES 口語片語
⑬ OTHER MEANINGS 其他意思

① INFORMATION 信息

1 [I,T not in progressive 不用進行式] to have information about something 知道; 了解: *Who knows the answer?* 誰知道答案? | *Do you happen to know the time?* 你知道現在幾點鐘嗎? | *When are they arriving? Maybe Mrs. Mott knows.* 他們甚麼時候到達? 也許莫特太太知道。| *instructions telling you everything you need to know* 寫明所有須知事項的説明書 | *Marriage cancels a will, didn't you know that?* 婚姻使遺囑無效, 這一點你竟然不知道? | *I had spoken without knowing all the facts.* 我當時是在並不了解全部事實的情況下説的。| **know what/where/when etc** *Do you know what I'm supposed to be doing?* 你知道我現在該做甚麼嗎? | *I don't know where to go.* 我不知道應該到哪裡去。| **know about** *The council has known about the leak for six months.* 委員會獲悉消息泄露的情況已六個月了。| **know all about** *spoken*【口】*We know all about David and what he's been up to!* 我們對於戴維以及他一直在搞些甚麼都十分了解! | **know (that)** *She knew that her father was sick, but not how serious it was.* 她知道父親病了, 但不知病情嚴重到甚麼程度。| **knowing that** (=because you know) 了解到 *I went to bed early knowing that I had to get up at six a.m.* 我知道早晨六點就得起牀, 所以早早就睡了。| **want to know** (=want to be told) 想知道 *I want to know what happened.* 我想知道發生了甚麼事。| *I thought you'd want to know immediately.* 我以為你立刻就想知道呢。| *"When do I start?" Carlos wanted to know.* "我甚麼時候開始?" 卡洛斯問道。| **I'm dying to know** *spoken* (=I am very eager to find out)【口】我急切地想知道 *I'm dying to know who won!* 我極想知道誰贏了! | **without sb knowing** (=secretly, privately, or without someone being told) 祕密地, 私下地 *You can't do anything without the whole town knowing.* 你幹任何事都不可能瞞得了全鎮的人。| **know to do sth** (=know that you should do it) 知道該做甚麼 *She knows not to tell anyone about it.* 她知道不可以把這件事告訴任何人。| **know sth/sb to be sth** (=know that something is true about them) 知道某物/某人確是某種情況 *a story which he knew to be true* 他知道確有其事的一個故事 | *I know him to be a good worker.* 我知道他做起事來確實很賣力。| **how do you know?** *spoken* (=how did you find out or what makes you think that?)【口】你是怎麼知道的? 你為甚麼這樣認為? *How did he know our names?* 他是怎麼知道我們的名字的? | *"Jason won't want to be involved." "How do you know?"* "賈森不想參與這件事。" "你為甚麼這樣認為?" | **as you/we know** *spoken*【口】*As you know, there's been a tremendous revival of interest in the project.* 你知道, 人們對這個計劃重新又有了極大的興趣。| **as/so far as I know** (=I believe that it is true, but I am not certain) 據我所知 *No other athlete, so far as I know, has won so many medals.* 據我所知, 還沒有其他運動員得過這麼多獎牌。| **know for certain/sure** *I think she's going but I don't know for sure.* 我認為她要去, 但我不敢肯定。| **know from experience** *I know from experience that he's got a foul temper.* 根據我的經驗判斷, 他是個脾氣暴躁的人。| **I wouldn't know** *spoken* (=I do not know, and I am not the person you should ask)【口】我不知道〔你不應該問我〕*"When is he coming back?" "I wouldn't know."* "他甚麼時候回來?" "我不知道。" | **know the way** (=know how to get to a place) 知道路 *Does he know the way to your house?* 他知道去你家的路嗎?

2 let sb know to tell someone about something 讓某人知道, 將某事告訴某人: *When it stops, let me know.* 它停下來的時候, 告訴我一聲。| *Give him this medicine, and let us know if he's not better in two days.* 給他服這種藥, 兩天後要是他沒有好轉, 請告訴我們。| *Thank you for your application; we'll let you know.* (=we will tell you soon whether you have been successful) 謝謝你的申請, 我們會把結果通知你。| **let it be known (that)** (=let other people know what your opinions or intentions are) 讓人知道〔自己的意見或意圖〕*The Prince has let it be known that he does not approve of his son's behaviour.* 親王已讓大家知道他不認同兒子的行為。

3 know sth inside out also 又作 **know sth backwards** to know something extremely well 熟知某事: *We expect you to know these codes inside out, men.* 我們指望你們能對這些密碼倒背如流, 夥計們。

② I KNOW 我知道

4 I know *spoken*【口】**a)** used to say that you have suddenly had an idea, thought of a solution to a problem, etc 我知道了〔表示靈機一觸〕: *"What should we do?" "I know, we could ask Anne to help."* "我們該怎麼辦?" "我知道, 可以請安妮幫忙。" **b)** used to agree with someone or to say that you feel the same way 我知道〔表示贊同或有同感〕: *"I'm so worn out!" "Yeah, I know."* "我累壞了。" "嗯, 我知道。" **c)** used to prevent someone from objecting to what you say by saying the objection first 我知道〔用來搶先提出反對意見, 以阻止某人反對你的説法〕: *It sounds silly, I know, but try it anyway.* 我知道這聽起來很愚蠢, 但無論如何試一試吧。| *I know, I know, I should have had the car checked out before now.* 我知道, 我知道, 我早應該把車開去檢查一下的。

③ I DON'T KNOW 我不知道

5 I don't know *spoken*【口】**a)** used to say that you do not have the answer to a question 我不知道〔表示不知道某問題的答案〕: *"When did they arrive?" "I don't know."* "他們甚麼時候到的?" "不知道。" | *"Why did you do that?" "I don't know."* "你為甚麼那樣做?" "我不知道。" **b)** used to show that you disagree slightly with what has just been said 我不清楚〔表示略有異議〕: *"I* *couldn't live there." "Oh, I don't know. It might not be so bad."* "我不能住那兒。" "是嗎? 我不大了解, 也許沒那麼糟吧。" **c)** used when you are not sure about something 我拿不準〔表示沒有把握〕: *Oh, I don't know, sixty, seventy?* 我也說不準, 六十, 七十? | **[+if/whether/that]** *I don't know if I would want to teach.* 我拿不準是否想去教書。**d)** used to show that you are slightly annoyed 我不知道〔表示有點不耐煩〕: *Oh, I don't know! You're hopeless!* 噢, 我不知道! 你真令人失望!

6 I don't know how/why etc used to criticize someone 我不明白怎麼會/為甚麼等〔用於批評某人〕: *I don't know how people could treat a child like that.* 我真不明白人們怎麼會那樣對待一個孩子。

7 I don't know whether you want to...? *spoken* used to ask someone politely to do something【口】能否請你…?〔用於有禮貌地請人做某事〕: *I don't know whether you want to respond to that?* 能否請你對此作出回應?

8 I don't know about you but... *spoken* used to give an opinion, suggestion, or decision of your own which might be different from that of the person listening【口】我不知道你怎麼想, 但…; 我不敢苟同〔表示異議〕: *I don't know about you, but I'm going home.* 你怎麼想我不知道, 但我可要回家了。

9 I don't know how to thank you/repay you *spoken formal* used to thank someone【口, 正式】真不知該怎樣感謝你/報答你〔用於表示感謝〕

④ YOU KNOW 你知道

10 you know *spoken*【口】**a)** used to emphasize a statement 你知道〔用於強調〕: *There'll be trouble, you know.* 你知道會有麻煩的。| *I don't like to brag but, you know, I did do pretty well.* 我不喜歡自吹自擂, 不過你知道, 我的確幹得很出色。**b)** used when you need to keep someone's attention, but cannot think of what to say next 你知道〔用於要保持對方的注意力但又想不出下面說甚麼時〕: *I was just, you know, looking through my slides before you came.* 剛才, 你知道, 你來之前我是在看我的這些幻燈片呢。**c)** used when you are explaining or describing something and want to give more information 你知道的〔用於在解釋或描述某事時希望提供更多的信息〕: *That padding that you put on the car, you know, that stuff on the doors.* 你安裝在車裡的那種襯墊, 你知道, 就是車門上的那種材料。

11 you know/do you know *spoken* used to start talking about something, or make someone listen【口】你知道/你知道嗎〔用於開始談及某事或使人注意聽你講話〕: *You know your cousin? You'll never guess what she did!* 你知道你表妹嗎? 你絕對猜不到她幹了些甚麼! | *You know, it's a sad thing about this guy.* 你知道, 這個人真是夠慘的。| *Do you know, when I went out this morning that man was still there.* 你知道嗎? 我今天早晨出去時, 那個人還在那裡。| **(do) you know what/something?** *But do you know what? He got fired.* 你知道嗎? 他被解雇了。

⑤ BE CERTAIN 有把握

12 [I,T not in progressive 不用進行式] to be sure about something〔對某事〕確信: *I just know I won't get the job.* 我就知道我不會得到這份工作。| *I knew you'd say that.* 我早知道你會這麼說。| *The boy stared at him uncertainly, not knowing whether to believe him.* 那個男孩疑惑地盯着他, 不知道該不該相信他的話。| **how do you know?** (=what makes you feel certain?) 你怎麼知道? *How do you know he won't do it again?* 你怎麼知道他不會再做這樣的事?

⑥ SKILL/EXPERIENCE 技術/經驗

13 [T not in progressive 不用進行式] to have learned a lot about something or be skilful and experienced at doing something 精通, 熟悉; 懂得: *I don't know enough history to make a comparison.* 我對歷史了解不多, 不能加以比較。| *I taught him everything he knows.* 他現在通曉的東西都是我教給他的。| **know how to** *Do you know how to change a fuse?* 你知道怎麼換保險絲嗎? | **know about** *I have a friend who knows about antiques.* 我有一個朋友對古董很在行。| **know all about** *Politicians know all about the power of language.* 政治家們十分了解語言的力量。| **know what you are doing** (=have enough skill and experience to deal with something properly) 有足夠的技術和經驗做好某事 | **know what you are talking about** *You listen to Aunt Kate, she knows what she's talking about.* 你聽聽凱特姨姨的話, 她在這方面很在行。| **know your job/subject** also 又作 **know your stuff** (=be good at and know all you should know about a job or subject) 對某項工作/話題非常了解[很在行]

14 think you know everything/think you know all the answers to behave in a way that is too confident, always trying to give people advice 過於自信, 自以為甚麼都知道

15 know a thing or two *informal* to have a lot of useful information gained from experience【非正式】富有經驗, 見多識廣; 明白事理

⑦ PERSON/PLACE 人/地點

16 [T] to be familiar with a person, place, etc 熟悉〔某人、某地等〕: *I've known her for twenty years.* 我認識她有二十年了。| *Are you really thinking of leaving Kevin for a guy you barely know?* 你真打算為一個你剛剛認識的人而離開凱文? | *Anyone who knows his work and who knows Wales will see the connection.* 任何熟悉他的作品又熟悉威爾斯的人, 都會看出两者之間的聯繫。| *Do you know the Boy's Club in Claremont?* 你熟悉克萊爾蒙特的男孩俱樂部嗎? | **know sb well** *We did not know each other well enough to talk freely.* 我們之間當時還沒有熟悉到可以隨意交談的地步。| **get to know** *I'm getting to know the neighbors.* 我開始跟鄰居混熟了。| *You need time to get to know a new instrument.* 你需要一段時間才能熟悉一件新工具。| **as we know it** (=in the form that we are familiar with) 我們所熟知的 *That will mean an end to the Tory Party as we know it.* 那將意味着我們所熟知的英國保守黨的終結。| **know sb/sth inside out** (=be very familiar with them) 對某人/某事物十分熟悉 *We need someone who knows the area inside out.* 我們需要一個對此地十分熟悉的人。| *That's the thing about Mom, she knows me inside out.* 媽媽的問題就在這裡, 她對我太了解了。| **know sb by sight** (=often see them, but not know them well) 與某人面熟 *I know her by sight, but I don't think I've ever spoken to her.* 我只是和她面熟, 但我想我從來沒有和她說過話。| **knowing him/if I know him** (=I know what he is like and expect him to do a particular thing) 我了解他 *Knowing Sumi, my note's probably still in her pocket.* 我了解蘇米, 我的字條可能還在她的衣袋裡呢。| *He'll be chatting up the women, if I know Ron!* 我了解羅恩這個人, 他可能還在和那些女人聊得起勁哩!

⑧ LANGUAGE/MUSIC ETC 語言/音樂等

17 know a language to be able to speak, read, and understand a foreign language 懂一門語言: *I know some French.* 我懂一點兒法語。

18 know a song/a tune/a poem etc to be able to sing a song, play a tune, say a poem etc because you have learned it 能唱某首歌/演奏某支曲子/朗誦某首詩等: *Do you know all the words to 'As Time Goes By'?* 你知道《當時光流逝》的全部歌詞嗎? | **know sth (off) by heart** (=to have learned it and be able to repeat it from memory) 能把…背誦出來

⑨ REALIZE 意識到

19 [I,T] to realize, find out about, or understand something 意識到; 發現; 了解: *Miss Brown knew as soon as she came in that something was wrong.* 布朗小姐一進來就發覺有點不對頭。| *Hardly knowing what he was*

doing, Nick pulled out a cigarette. 尼克下意識地拿出一支煙。| *I know I have been avoiding the issue.* 我知道自己一直在迴避這個問題。| **(do/if) you know what I mean?** *spoken* (=used to ask if someone has understood you)【口】你明白我的意思嗎? *It's nice to have a change sometimes. Know what I mean?* 間或改變一下是件好事。明白我的意思嗎? | **I/she etc should have known** *spoken* (=used to say that someone ought to have realized something)【口】我/她等本該意識到 *I should have known it would take this long.* 我早就應該知道需要這麼長的時間。| **I might have known** *BrE spoken* (=I should not be surprised that something has happened, but I am annoyed)【英口】我就知道 *I might have known you'd be mixed up in this mess!* 我就知道你會牽涉到這種亂七八糟的事情裡去! | **know exactly/precisely** *I know exactly how you feel.* 我完全清楚你目前是甚麼心情。| **know perfectly well/full well/only too well** *You know perfectly well what I mean.* 你完全明白我的意思。| **sb will never know/no one will ever know** (=no one will realize that something has happened) 誰也不會知道 *Just take it, no one will ever know.* 你拿着吧, 不會有人知道的。| **and you know it** *spoken*【口】*This has nothing to do with gratitude and you know it.* 這與感激不感激沒關係, 這你知道。| **if I had known/if I'd have known** *If I had known they were in trouble, I'd have gone to help.* 我當時要是知道他們有麻煩, 我是會去幫忙的。| **little did she know** *literary*【文】*As she closed the door, she little knew that this was the last time she would leave this house.* 她關上門的時候, 一點也不知道這是她最後一次離開這所房子。

⑩ RECOGNIZE 認出

20 [T] to be able to recognize someone or something 認出: *Honestly, it had been so long, I hardly knew her.* 說實話, 隔了這麼長時間, 我幾乎認不出她了。| **[+by]** *He looked very different, but I knew him by his voice.* 他外表變化很大, 但我憑他的嗓音認出了他。

21 know sth from sth to understand the difference between one thing and another 分辨, 區分出來: *Lloyd doesn't even know his right from his left.* 勞埃德甚至分不出自己的左邊和右邊。| *She knows right from wrong; she can't claim she was insane.* 她分得清好歹, 她不能聲稱自己曾經有過精神錯亂。

22 not know sb from Adam *informal* to not know who someone is at all【非正式】完全不認識某人

⑪ EXPERIENCE 體驗

23 [T] to live through an experience 經歷; 體驗: **[+about]** *I know all about being poor, so don't think I don't.* 我知道貧窮是甚麼滋味, 所以別以為我不明白。

24 I've never known used to say that you have never heard of or experienced something as surprising as the thing you are describing 我從不知道: *This weather is amazing. I've never known anything like it!* 這種天氣真令人吃驚, 我從未經歷過這樣的天氣!

25 I've never known sb to do sth used to say that someone never does something 從來不知道某人會做某事: *I've never known him to iron anything.* 我從來沒有見到過他熨衣服。

26 sb/sth is not known to be sth also 又作 **sb/sth has never been known to do sth** used to say that there is no information that says that a person or animal behaves in a particular way 據知某人/某事物不是某種情況[不會做某事]: *This species is not known to be vicious.* 據知這個物種並不兇猛。

27 I've known sb to do sth also 又作 **sb has been known to do sth** used to say that someone does something sometimes, even if it is unusual 我聽說過某人做某事: *Watch it. He's been known to eat a whole pizza himself!* 注意看。據說他可以吃下一整塊意大利薄餅!

⑫ SPOKEN PHRASES 口語片語

28 you never know used to say that it is possible that something good may happen 也許; 很難說: *I might be able to catch the earlier train, you never know.* 我也許能趕上早一點的那班火車, 這很難說。

29 how should I know?/how am I to know?/how do I know? used to say that it is not reasonable to expect that you should know something 我怎麼會知道?: *"What's it like?" "I haven't seen it, so how should I know?"* "它是甚麼樣子的?" "我沒見過, 怎麼會知道?"

30 how was I to know?/how did I know? used as an excuse or to say that you are sorry (當時)我怎麼會知道?: *It's not my fault – how was I to know it would rain!* 這不能怪我, 我怎麼知道會下雨?

31 I ought to know used to emphasize that you know about something because you made it, experienced it etc 我應該知道: *"Are you sure there's no sugar in it?" "Of course. I ought to know, I made it!"* "你肯定這裡面沒放糖嗎?" "當然。我應當知道, 因為是我親手做的!"

32 not that I know of used when answering a question to say that you believe that the answer is 'no', but there may be facts that you do not know about 據我所知沒有: *"Andrew didn't phone today, did he?" "Not that I know of."* "安德魯今天沒有來電話, 是嗎?" "據我所知沒有。"

33 if you must know used when you are annoyed at having to give information to someone 如果你一定要知道〔表示不耐煩〕: *"Where is it?" "In an envelope, if you must know," said James impatiently.* "它在哪兒?" "在一個信封裡, 如果你一定要知道的話。" 詹姆斯不耐煩地說。

34 for all I know used to say that you do not know about something and it does not really matter because you are not involved or affected 說不定: *It cost millions. It could be billions for all I know.* 它花費了數百萬, 可能花了幾十億也說不定呢。

35 there's no knowing it is impossible to know 不可能知道: *There is no knowing what she will do next.* 沒法知道她下一步要幹甚麼。

36 (I'm/I'll be) damned if I know! used to emphasize that you do not know something, and are annoyed or think something is hopeless 鬼才知道!: *"Whatever are we going to do?" "Damned if I know."* "我們到底要幹甚麼?" "鬼才知道。"

37 Heaven/God/who/goodness knows! a) used to say that you do not have any idea what an answer might be, and do not expect to know 天知道!〔表示對某事一無所知, 也不想知道〕: *"Where do you think he's disappeared to this time?" "God knows!"* "你認為他這次又跑到哪裡去了?" "天知道!" **b)** used to emphasize a statement 天曉得!〔用於加強語氣〕: *I haven't seen her for goodness knows how long.* 天曉得我有多長時間沒有見到她了。| *It might make us more efficient, which heaven knows we need.* 它也許能讓我們更有效率, 老天爺知道這是我們需要的。

38 not want to know *informal* to refuse to listen to a complaint or a problem【非正式】不想知道; 不想聽: *We phoned the council about the damage, but they just didn't want to know.* 我們打電話向委員會報告損毀情況, 但他們根本不想聽。

39 knowing my luck used to say that you expect something bad will happen because you are usually unlucky 知道不走運〔表示自己可能要倒霉, 因為運氣通常不佳〕: *Knowing his luck, he'll get hit with a golf ball or something.* 他知道自己運氣不好, 也許會被高爾夫球打中或出點別的甚麼毛病。

40 (well,) what do you know! used to express surprise 真想不到!: *Well, what do you know – look who's arrived!* 啊, 真想不到, 你看誰來了?

41 the next thing you know used to say that something happens suddenly and unexpectedly 突然又: *One minute everybody's laughing and the next thing you know, they're all arguing!* 他們一會兒哈哈大笑, 一會

兒又突然爭吵起來!

42 I will (want to) know the reason why an expression meaning you will want an explanation, used in a threatening way 我倒想知道原因何在〔有威脅之意〕: *It had better be right this time, or I'll know the reason why.* 這回最好不要出錯, 否則我就要你作出解釋。

43 if you know what's good for you used to tell someone that they should do something, or you will harm them in some way 如果你知道好歹: *You'll just keep your mouth shut about this if you know what's good for you!* 如果你不想吃苦頭的話, 對這件事你就閉上嘴吧!

44 you know who/what used to talk about someone or something without mentioning their name 你知道的那人[物]〔用來談論某人或某物而不必指名道姓〕: *I saw you know who yesterday.* 我昨天看見了你知道的那個人。

⑬ **OTHER MEANINGS** 其他意思

45 be known as to also be called something 被稱為: *Chicago is known as 'the windy city'.* 芝加哥被稱為'風城'。

46 know better a) to be wise or experienced enough to avoid making mistakes 有頭腦, 明事理(而不至於): **know better than to...** *She ought to know better than to expect any help from Roger.* 她應該明白不能指望羅傑幫忙。**b)** to know or think you know more than someone else (自認為) 知道得比某人多: *They said it was gold, but Sharon knew better.* 他們說那是金子, 但莎倫知道並非如此。

47 know best used to say that someone should be obeyed or that their way of doing things should be accepted because they are experienced〔表示由於某人經驗豐富而〕最具權威: *I think I know best how to deal with my own staff!* 我認為如何對待我手下的職員, 我最清楚。| **Mother/Father etc knows best** *Don't argue. Daddy knows best!* 不要爭辯了, 爸爸比你懂!

48 know your own mind to be confident and have firm ideas about what you want and like 有自信心; 有自己的想法

49 you will be delighted/pleased to know that *formal* used before you give someone information that they will be pleased to hear【正式】你會很高興/樂意知道: *You will be pleased to know that we have accepted your offer.* 你一定樂意知道, 我們已接受了你的提議。— see also 另見 **know no bounds** (BOUND[4] (6)), **know the ropes** (ROPE[1] (2)), **know the score** (SCORE[1] (5)), **know your place** (PLACE[1] (30)), **not know what hit you** (HIT[1] (14))

know of sb/sth *phr v* [T] to have been told or to have read that something exists, but not know much about it 聽說〔但所知不多〕, 知道有…: *I know of one company that makes these things.* 我聽說有一家公司生產這類物品。

USAGE NOTE 用法說明: KNOW

WORD CHOICE 詞語辨析: **know, find out, hear/read about, get to know, learn, study**

If you **know** a fact, person, or place, or how to speak a language, drive a car etc, you have information about it in your mind, or the skills to do it. 知道 (know) 某一事實、某個人或某個地方, 或者能講某種語言、會開車等等, 就意味着擁有相關的信息或相關的技術。

Often you **know** something only after you have **heard or read about** it, or if you have **found it out** (especially deliberately) or **got to know** about it (especially by chance). 知道 (know) 某事常常是在聽說到 (hear about) 或從書裡讀到 (read about) 這件事之後, 或者是由於有意識地發現 (find out) 或偶然得知 (get to know) 這件事: *When he heard about the affair he became extremely angry.* 他聽說這件事後極為憤怒。| *I use my dictionary to find out the correct pronunciation* (NOT 不用 *know*). 我用詞典查找正確的讀音。| *During the visit we got to know something about the American way of life.* 訪問期間我們了解到某些美國的生活方式。You also **get to know** a person. get to know 也指結識一個人。

If you **learn** something, that may mean that you **find it out**, but this is a formal use of the word. learn 可以指發現某事 (find it out), 但這是該詞的正式用法: *He learnt the news/that he had won a prize.* 他已得知這個消息/他得了獎。Usually to **learn** means to make an effort to remember something you have found out or been taught, or to practise a skill, so that you then **know** it. 通常 learn 指努力記住所發現或別人所教的某種東西, 或努力練習一種技能, 這樣才會懂得 (know): *I'm trying to learn the names of all the students in my class* (NOT 不用 *know*). 我正在努力記住我班上所有學生的名字。| *She is learning English/learning to drive.* 她在學習英語/學習開車。

If you spend time learning about something, especially in a school, university etc you **study** it. study 指花時間學習 (learn about) 某物, 尤指在學校、大學等地方學習: *Gina is studying engineering at London University.* 吉娜正在倫敦大學攻讀工程學。

know² *n* **in the know** *informal* having more information about something than most people【非正式】知情, 熟知內情: *People in the know say that interest rates will have to rise again soon.* 知道內情的人說, 利率將很快再次上升。

know-all /'· ·/ *n* [C] *BrE informal* someone who behaves as if they know everything【英, 非正式】自以為無所不知的人; KNOW-IT-ALL *AmE*【美】

know-how /'· ·/ *n* [U] *informal* practical ability or skill【非正式】實用本領; 技能; 知識; 竅門: *Jeff needs more technical know-how to do his new job.* 要做好這項新的工作, 傑夫需要更多的技能。

Frequencies of the verb **know** in spoken and written English 英語口語和書面語中動詞 know 的使用頻率

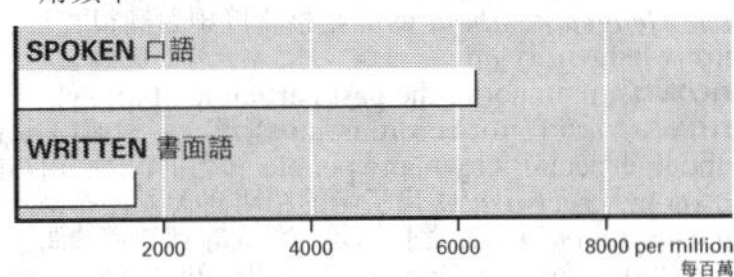

Based on the British National Corpus and the Longman Lancaster Corpus
據英國國家語料庫和朗文蘭卡斯特語料庫

This graph shows that the verb **know** is much more common in spoken English than in written English. This is because it is used in a lot of common spoken phrases. These are marked *spoken* in the entry. 本圖表顯示動詞 know 在英語口語中的使用頻率遠遠高於書面語, 因為該詞用於許多常用的口語片語中。在詞條中這些片語都有 *spoken*【口】標記。

know·ing /ˈnoɪŋ; ˈnəʊɪŋ/ *adj* showing that you know all about something 會意的, 心照不宣的: *He said nothing but gave us a knowing look.* 他一言不發, 只是會意地看了我們一眼。

know·ing·ly /ˈnoɪŋlɪ; ˈnəʊɪŋli/ *adv* **1** in a way that shows you know about something secret or embarrassing 會意地: *She smiled knowingly at us.* 她會意地對我們一笑。**2** deliberately 故意地, 有意地: *He would never knowingly upset people.* 他從來不故意讓別人生氣。

know-it-all /'· · ·/ *n* [C] *informal especially AmE* someone who behaves as if they know everything【非正式, 尤美】自以為無所不知的人; KNOW-ALL *BrE*【英】

K

2 1 **knowl·edge** /ˋnɑlɪdʒ; ˈnɒlɪdʒ/ *n* [U] **1** the facts, skills, and understanding that you have gained through learning or experience 知識; 學問; 認識: *You need specialist knowledge to do this job.* 做這項工作要有專門知識。| [+of] *His knowledge of ancient civilizations is unrivalled.* 他在古代文明方面的學問無人能比。| [+about] *We now have greater knowledge about the risks of using these chemicals.* 我們現在對於使用這些化學品的危險性已有了更多的認識。**2 in the knowledge that** knowing that something has happened or is true 已知道, 了解到: *Kay smiled, secure in the knowledge that she was right.* 凱笑了, 她很有把握知道自己是對的。**3 not to your knowledge** *spoken* used to say that something is not true, based on what you know【口】據...所知某事並不確實: *"Is it true that she's leaving the company?" "Not to my knowledge."* "她要離開這家公司, 這是真的嗎?" "據我所知不是這樣。" **4** information that you have about a particular situation, event etc 消息, 信息: **in full knowledge of** (=knowing all the details of a situation) 充分了解... *He acted in full knowledge of the possible consequences.* 他這麼做時完全明白所有可能的後果。| **deny all knowledge of sth** (=say that you do not know anything about it) 否認知道某事 *Evans denied all knowledge of the robbery.* 伊文斯說對這樁搶劫案一概不知。| **come to sb's knowledge** *formal* (=become known about)【正式】被某人獲悉[知道] *The incident first came to our knowledge about a fortnight ago.* 我們是大約兩週前第一次聽說這次事故的。| **bring sth to sb's knowledge** *formal* (=give someone information they did not know)【正式】將某事告訴某人 **5 to the best of your knowledge** used to say that you think something is true, although you may not have all the facts 就某人所知: *To the best of my knowledge the new project will be starting in June.* 據我所知, 新項目將於六月開始進行。**6 without your knowledge** without knowing what is happening 在某人不知情的情況下: *He was annoyed to find the contract had been signed without his knowledge.* 他發現合同已在他不知情的情況下簽署, 這使他很惱火。—see also 另見 GENERAL KNOWLEDGE, **common knowledge** (COMMON[1] (3)), **working knowledge** (WORKING[1] (5))

knowl·edge·a·ble /ˋnɑlɪdʒəbḷ; ˈnɒlɪdʒəbəl/ *adj* knowing a lot 有知識的; 博學的: [+about] *Graham's very knowledgeable about wines.* 格雷厄姆對酒很在行。—**knowledgeably** *adv*

known[1] /non; nəʊn/ the past participle of KNOW[1]

3 **known[2]** *adj* [only before noun 僅用於名詞前] known about, especially by many people 知名的, 眾所周知的: *a known crack dealer* 出了名的精明商人 | *Yes, yes, it's a known problem.* 對, 對, 這是一個大家都知道的問題。| **be known for** (=be famous for) 以...知名 *The Saumur region is known for its sparkling wines.* 梭繆地區以出產香檳酒而聞名。—see also 另見 **little-known, well-known**

knuck·le[1] /ˋnʌkḷ; ˈnʌkəl/ *n* **1** [C] the joints in your fingers including the ones where your fingers join your hands 指節; 掌指關節 **2** [C] a piece of meat around the lowest leg joint 膝關節部分的肉, 肘子: *a knuckle of pork* 豬肘子 **3 near the knuckle** *BrE informal* rude, or likely to give offence【英, 非正式】粗魯的; 近乎下流的: *Some of his jokes are a bit near the knuckle.* 他的一些笑話近乎下流。—see also 另見 **a rap on/over the knuckles** (RAP[2] (5))

knuckle[2] *v*

knuckle down *phr v* [I] *informal* to suddenly start working or studying hard【非正式】(突然)開始努力工作[學習]: *If he doesn't knuckle down soon, he'll never get through those exams.* 他如果不立即開始用功, 就決不會通過那些考試。

knuckle under *phr v* [I] *informal* to accept someone's authority or orders without wanting to【非正式】屈服; 認輸

knuckle-dust·er /ˈ·· ˌ··/ *n* [C] a metal covering for the backs of the fingers, used as a weapon 指節銅套〔一種武器〕

knuck·le·head /ˋnʌkḷˌhɛd; ˈnʌkəlhed/ *n* [C] *AmE spoken* used to address someone who you like who has done something stupid【美口】小傻瓜〔用來稱呼自己喜愛但又做了蠢事的人〕: *You knucklehead, you can't go around saying things like that!* 你這個小傻瓜, 不可以到處去講那種話!

ko·a·la /koˋɑlə; kəʊˈɑːlə/ also 又作 **koala bear** /·ˌ·· ˈ·/ *n* [C] an Australian animal like a small bear with no tail that climbs trees 樹袋熊, 樹熊, 無尾熊, 考拉〔產於澳大利亞似熊的一種無尾樹棲動物〕

kohl /kol; kəʊl/ *n* [U] a black pencil used around women's eyes to make them more attractive 眼線筆〔女性化妝用品〕

kook /kuk; kuːk/ *n* [C] *AmE informal* someone who is silly or crazy【美, 非正式】傻瓜; 狂人 —**kooky** *adj*

kook·a·bur·ra /ˋkʊkəˌbʌrə; ˈkʊkəbʌrə/ *n* [C] an Australian bird whose song sounds like laughter 笑翠鳥〔產於澳大利亞、叫聲似笑聲的一種鳥〕

Ko·ran, Qur'an /kəˋræn; kɔːˈrɑːn/ *n* **the Koran** the holy book of the Muslims《古蘭經》,《可蘭經》〔伊斯蘭教的經典〕—**Koranic** *adj*

kor·ma /ˋkɔrmə; ˈkɔːmə/ *n* [U] an Indian dish made with meat and cream 考莫〔一種用肉和奶油做成的印度菜餚〕: *chicken korma* 雞肉考莫

ko·sher /ˋkoʃɚ; ˈkəʊʃə/ *adj* **1 a)** kosher food is prepared according to Jewish law〔食品〕按猶太教規製成的 **b)** kosher restaurants or shops sell food prepared in this way〔餐館或商店〕供應符合猶太教規食物的 **2** *informal* honest or lawful; actually being what is claimed【非正式】誠實可靠的; 合法的; 真正的: *Are you sure this offer is kosher?* 你確實認為這個建議可靠嗎?

kow·tow /kaʊˋtaʊ; ˌkaʊˈtaʊ/ *v* [I+to] *informal* to be too eager to obey or be polite to someone in authority【非正式】順從, 巴結, 唯命是從

KP /ˌke ˋpi; ˌkeɪ ˈpiː/ *n* [U] *AmE* work that soldiers or children at a camp have to do in a kitchen【美】炊事值勤, 幫廚

kph the written abbreviation of 縮寫= kilometres per hour 千米[公里]/小時

kraal /krɑl; krɑːl/ *n* [C] **1** a village in South Africa with a fence around it〔用柵欄圍起來的〕(南非) 柵欄村莊 **2** *SAfrE* an enclosed piece of ground in which cows, sheep, etc are kept at night【南非】牲畜欄

kraut /kraʊt; kraʊt/ *n* [C] *slang* an insulting word for someone from Germany【俚】德國佬〔侮辱性用語〕

Krem·lin /ˋkrɛmlɪn; ˈkremlɪ̣n/ *n* **the Kremlin a)** the government of Russia and the former USSR 俄羅斯政府; 前蘇聯政府 **b)** the government buildings of Russia and the former USSR in Moscow 克里姆林宮〔位於莫斯科的俄羅斯和前蘇聯政府大樓〕

krill /krɪl; krɪl/ *n* [U] small SHELLFISH 磷蝦(羣)

Kriss Krin·gle /ˌkrɪs ˋkrɪŋgḷ; ˌkrɪs ˈkrɪŋgəl/ *n* [singular] *AmE* another name for SANTA CLAUS【美】聖誕老人〔Santa Claus 的另一叫法〕

kro·na /ˋkronə; ˈkrəʊnə/ *n plural* **kronor** /-nɔr; -nɔː/ or **kronur** /-nɚ; -nə/ the standard unit of money in Sweden and Iceland 克朗〔瑞典和冰島的標準貨幣單位〕

kro·ne /ˋkronɛ; ˈkrəʊnə/ *n plural* **kroner** /-nɛr; -nə/ [C] the standard unit of money in Denmark and Norway 克朗〔丹麥和挪威的貨幣單位〕

Kru·ger·rand /ˋkrugəˌrænd; ˈkruːgəˌrænd/ *n* [C] a South African gold coin〔南非的〕克魯格[富格林]金幣

kryp·ton /ˋkrɪptɑn; ˈkrɪptɒn/ *n* [U] a gas that is an ELEMENT (=basic substance), found in the air 氪(氣)

Kt the written abbreviation of 縮寫= KNIGHT

kt the written abbreviation of 縮寫= KNOT[1] (3)

ku·dos /ˋkjudɑs; ˈkjuːdɒs/ *n* [U] admiration and respect that you get for being important or doing something important 榮譽, 光榮; 名聲; 威信

Ku Klux Klan /ˌku klʌks ˋklæn; ˌkuː klʌks ˈklæn/ *n* **the**

Ku Klux Klan a secret American political organization of Protestant white men who oppose people of other races or religions 三 K 黨〔反對其他種族或宗教的美國白種男性新教徒的祕密政治組織〕

kum·quat /ˈkʌmkwɑt; ˈkʌmkwɒt/ *n* [C] the American spelling of CUMQUAT cumquat 的美式拼法

kung fu /ˌkʌŋ ˈfu; ˌkʌŋ ˈfuː/ *n* [U] an ancient Chinese fighting art in which you attack people with your hands and feet 中國功夫[拳術]

Kurd /kɝd; kɜːd/ *n* [C] a member of a people living in countries such as Iran, Iraq, and Turkey 庫爾德人〔居住在伊朗、伊拉克和土耳其等國〕

kvetch /kvɛtʃ; kvetʃ/ *v* [I] *AmE informal* to continually complain about something【美, 非正式】〔對某事〕不斷抱怨 —**kvetch** *n* [C]

kw the written abbreviation of 縮寫= KILOWATT

kwe·la /ˈkwelə; ˈkweɪlə/ *n* [U] a kind of dance music popular among black South African people 奎拉舞曲〔南非黑人喜愛的一種舞曲〕

kwh the written abbreviation of 縮寫= KILOWATT HOUR

L, l

L, l /ɛl; el/ *plural* **L's, l's** *n* [C] **1** the 12th letter of the English alphabet 英語字母表的第十二個字母 **2** the number 50 in the system of ROMAN NUMERALS 羅馬數字 50

l **1** the written abbreviation of 縮寫= LITRE **2** the written abbreviation of 縮寫= line **3** also 又作 **L** the written abbreviation of 縮寫= lake

la /lɑ; lɑː/ *n* [singular] the sixth note in a musical SCALE[1] (8), according to the SOL-FA system 全音階第六音

Lab the written abbreviation of 縮寫= LABOUR PARTY

lab /læb; læb/ *n* [C] *informal* a LABORATORY【非正式】實驗室

3 **la·bel[1]** /ˋlebḷ; ˈleɪbəl/ *n* [C] **1** a piece of paper or other material that is stuck onto something and gives information about it 標籤, 標記: *a luggage label* 行李標籤 **2** the name of a record company 唱片公司名: *their new release on the Ace Sounds label* 由 Ace Sounds 唱片公司給他們灌製的新唱片 **3** a word or phrase which is used to describe a person, group, or thing, but which is unfair or not correct〔用以描述人、組織或事物的〕稱號, 外號, 綽號;〔以不公平或不正確的稱號將人扣上的〕帽子: *Men tend to accept these arrangements in order to avoid attracting the 'sexist' label.* 男人往往願意接受這些安排, 以免被扣上"性歧視"的大帽子。

label[2] *v* **labelled, labelling** *BrE*【英】, **labeled, labeling** *AmE*【美】[T] **1** to fix a label onto something or write information on something 貼標籤於; 用標籤標明: *Label the diagram as shown.* 按所示在圖表上標明。| **label sth poison/secret etc** *The file was labelled 'Top Secret'.* 該文件被標為"絕密"。**2** to use a word or phrase to describe someone or something, but often unfairly or incorrectly〔用稱號、外號、綽號〕描述〔某人或某物〕; 給…扣帽子: **label sb/sth (as) sth** *The newspapers had unjustly labelled him a troublemaker.* 報界都不公正地給他扣上鬧事者的帽子。

la·bi·a /ˋlebɪə; ˈleɪbiə/ *n* [plural] the outer folds of the female sex organ 陰唇

la·bi·al /ˋlebɪəl; ˈleɪbiəl/ *n* [C] *technical* a speech sound made using one or both lips【術語】唇音 —**labial** *adj* —see also 另見 BILABIAL

la·bor /ˋlebɚ; ˈleɪbə/ *n* [U] the American spelling of LABOUR labour 的美式拼法

la·bor·a·tory /ˋlæbrəˌtorɪ; ləˈbɒrətri/ *n* [C] a special room or building in which a scientist tests and prepares substances 實驗室: *a research laboratory* 研究實驗室 | **laboratory experiments/animals etc** *tests on laboratory animals* 在實驗室動物身上做的試驗 —see also 另見 LANGUAGE LABORATORY 3

Labor Day /ˋ·· ·/ *n AmE* a public holiday in the US on the first Monday in September【美】勞工節〔九月的第一個星期一, 為美國的公眾假日〕

la·bored /ˋlebɚd; ˈleɪbəd/ *adj* the American spelling of LABOURED laboured 的美式拼法

la·bor·er /ˋlebərɚ; ˈleɪbərə/ *n* [C] the American spelling of LABOURER labourer 的美式拼法

labor-in·ten·sive /ˌ·· ·ˈ··◂/ *adj* the American spelling of LABOUR-INTENSIVE labour-intensive 的美式拼法

laboratory 實驗室

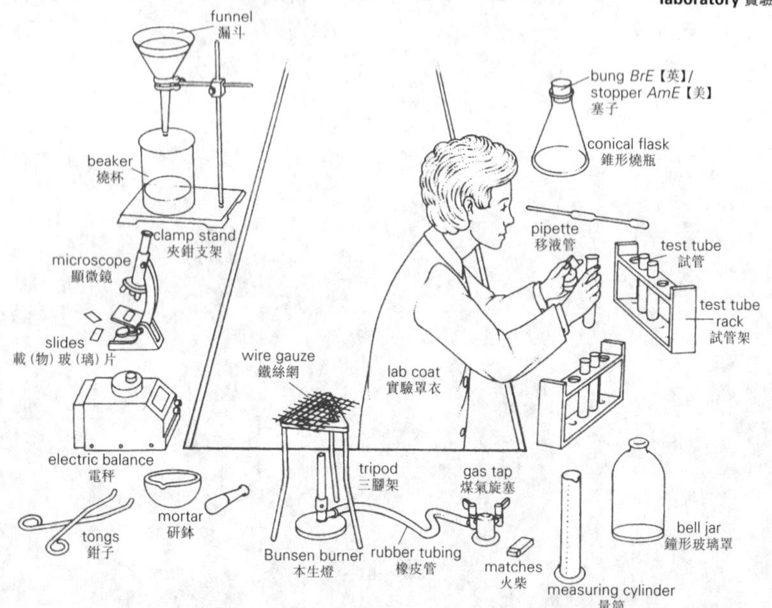

la·bo·ri·ous /ləˋbɔrɪəs; ləˈbɔːriəs/ *adj* **1 laborious task/process/method etc** a job or piece of work that is difficult and needs a lot of effort 費勁的工作/過程/方法等: *the laborious task of collating all the evidence* 核對所有證據的艱苦工作 **2** seeming to be done slowly and with difficulty 緩慢而吃力的: *laborious progress through the work* 工作的進展緩慢而吃力 —**laboriously** *adv*: *Selina was laboriously copying out her homework.* 塞琳娜當時在吃力地抄寫作業。—**laboriousness** *n* [U]

labor-sav·ing /ˈ·· ˌ··/ *adj* the American spelling of LABOUR-SAVING labour-saving 的美式拼法

labor u·nion /ˈ·· ˌ··/ *n* [C] *AmE* an organization that represents the ordinary workers in a particular trade or profession, especially in meetings with employers【美】〔尤指在某一行業中代表普通工人與雇主交涉的〕工會; TRADE UNION *BrE*【英】

3 1 **la·bour¹** *BrE*【英】, **labor** *AmE*【美】/ˋlebɚ; ˈleɪbə/ *n*
1 ►WORK 工作◄ [U] effort or work, especially physical work 努力, 工作〔尤指體力勞動〕: *The garage charges £30 an hour for labour.* 汽車修理廠每小時收取 30 英鎊的工錢。| **manual labour** (=work with tools you hold in your hands) 體力勞動 *Building still involves a lot of manual labour.* 建築仍然包含許多體力勞動。| **withdraw your labour** (=protest by stopping work) 停工〔抗議〕 *Workers withdrew their labour for twenty-four hours.* 工人停工二十四小時。—see also 另見 HARD LABOUR
2 ►WORKERS 勞動者◄ [U] all the people who work for a company or in a country 員工, 工人: *Organized labour banded together to fight the anti-union laws.* 有組織的工人聯合起來反對反工會法。| **skilled/unskilled labour** *a shortage of skilled labour* 缺乏熟練工人 | **cheap labour** (=people who are paid very low wages) 廉價勞工 | **labour costs/shortages etc** *Immigrants may help to solve labour shortages.* 移民可以有助於解決勞動力短缺的問題。—see also 另見 LABOUR FORCE
3 ►BABY 嬰兒◄ [singular,U] the process in which a baby is born by being pushed from its mother's body, or the period of time during which this happens 分娩; 產程: **be in labour** *Meg was in labour for 6 hours.* 梅格分娩了6個小時。| **go into labour** *Diane went into labour at 2 o'clock.* 黛安娜2點鐘開始分娩。| **labour pains/ward/room** *No men were allowed in the labour room.* 產房內禁止男士進入。
4 a labour of love something that is hard work but that you do because you want to 心甘情願所做的苦工
5 my/your labours *formal* a period of hard work【正式】我/你的一段時間的辛勤工作: *We sat down to rest after our labours.* 苦幹了一陣子後, 我們坐下來休息。

labour² *BrE*【英】, **labor** *AmE*【美】*v* **1** [I,T] to try very hard to do something; struggle 努力做〔某事〕; 奮爭: **[+over]** *I've been labouring over this report all morning.* 整個早上我都忙於做這份報告。| **labour to do sth** *Ray had little talent but laboured to acquire the skills of a writer.* 雷伊沒有甚麼才能, 但努力學習寫作技巧。**2** [I] to work hard 辛勤工作: *Marina had laboured late into the night to finish her essay.* 為完成文章, 瑪麗娜工作到深夜。**3 labour under a delusion/misconception/misapprehension etc** to believe something that is not true 錯覺, 誤解 **4 labour the point** to describe or explain something in too much detail or when people have already understood it 過於詳細地講述某事 **5** [I] if an engine labours it turns too slowly and with difficulty 〔引擎〕緩慢而困難地運轉

Labour³ *n* [U,not with *the* 不與 the 連用] the British LABOUR PARTY〔英國〕工黨: *We all vote Labour in this house.* 在本院中我們都投工黨的票。

Labour⁴ *adj* supporting or connected with the British LABOUR PARTY 支持工黨的; 與工黨有關的: *a Labour MP* 工黨下議院議員 | *Labour policies* 工黨的方針政策

labour camp *BrE*【英】, **labor camp** *AmE*【美】/ˈ·· ·/ *n* [C] a prison camp where prisoners have to do hard physical work 勞動營, 勞改營

la·boured *BrE*【英】, **labored** *AmE*【美】/ˋlebɚd; ˈleɪbəd/ *adj* showing signs of effort and difficulty 吃力的, 費勁的: *laboured breathing* 費力的呼吸

la·bour·er *BrE*【英】, **laborer** *AmE*【美】/ˋlebərɚ; ˈleɪbərə/ *n* [C] someone whose work needs strength rather than skill, especially someone who works outdoors 體力勞動者, 工人〔尤指戶外勞動者〕: *a farm labourer* 農場工人

labour ex·change /ˈ·· ·ˌ·/ *n* [C] a former British government office where people went to find jobs 職業介紹所〔舊時英國的政府機構〕—compare 比較 JOB CENTRE

labour force *BrE*【英】, **labor force** *AmE*【美】/ˈ·· ·/ *n* **the labour force** all the people who work for a company or in a country 勞動力

labour-in·ten·sive *BrE*【英】, **labor-intensive** *AmE*【美】/ˌ·· ·ˈ··◂/ *adj* an industry or type of work that is labour-intensive needs a lot of workers 勞動密集型的: *labour-intensive farming methods* 勞動密集型的耕作法 —see also 另見 CAPITAL INTENSIVE

labour mar·ket *BrE*【英】, **labor market** *AmE*【美】/ˈ·· ˌ··/ *n* **the labour market** the combination of workers available and jobs available in one place at one time 勞工市場, 勞動力市場: *married women re-entering the labour market* 重新進入勞動力市場的已婚婦女

labour move·ment *BrE*【英】, **labor movement** *AmE*【美】/ˈ·· ˌ··/ *n* **the labour movement** the political parties representing working people, and all other organizations which have the same beliefs and aims 工人運動

Labour Par·ty /ˈ·· ˌ··/ *n* **the Labour Party** a political party in Britain and some other countries that aims to improve social conditions for ordinary working people and poorer people〔英國和其他一些國家的〕工黨, 勞工黨

labour re·la·tions *BrE*【英】, **labor relations** *AmE*【美】/ˈ·· ·ˌ··/ *n* [plural] the relationship between employers and workers 勞資關係: *a company with good labour relations* 勞資關係和諧的公司

labour-sav·ing *BrE*【英】, **labor-saving** *AmE*【美】/ˈ·· ˌ··/ *adj* [only before noun 僅用於名詞前] **labour-saving device/gadget/equipment etc** something that makes it easier for you to do a particular job 節省勞力的裝置/器具/設備等

Lab·ra·dor /ˋlæbrəˌdɔr; ˈlæbrədɔː/ *n* [C] a large dog with fairly short black or yellow hair 拉布拉多獵犬, 紐芬蘭拾獚 —see picture at 參見 DOG¹ 圖

la·bur·num /ləˋbɝnəm; ləˈbɜːnəm/ *n* [C,U] a small tree with long hanging stems of yellow flowers and poisonous seeds 金鏈花; 金鏈花屬植物

lab·y·rinth /ˋlæbəˌrɪnθ; ˈlæbərɪnθ/ *n* [C] **1** a large network of paths or passages which cross each other, making it very difficult to find your way; MAZE (3) 迷宮; 曲徑: **[+of]** *a labyrinth of long corridors* 迷宮似的長廊 **2** something that is very complicated and difficult to understand 複雜難懂的事物: **[+of]** *a labyrinth of EC directives* 錯綜複雜的歐共體的指示 —**labyrinthine** /ˌlæbəˋrɪnθɪn; ˌlæbəˈrɪnθaɪn◂/ *adj*: *the labyrinthine complexity of bureaucracy* 官僚主義的繁文縟節

lace¹ /les; leɪs/ *n* **1** [U] a fine cloth made with patterns of many very small holes 網眼織物, 花邊: *a handkerchief trimmed with lace* 飾有花邊的手絹 | *lace curtains* 網眼紗簾 —see also 另見 LACY —see picture on page A16 參見 A16 頁圖 **2** [C] a string that is pulled through special holes in shoes or clothing to pull the edges together and fasten them 鞋帶; 繫帶 —see picture at 參見 SHOE¹ 圖

lace² *v* [T] **1** also 又作 **lace up** to pull something together or fasten something by tying a LACE¹ (2) 繫〔(鞋)帶〕, 用帶子將…繫緊: *Lace up your shoes or you'll trip over.* 把鞋帶繫好, 否則你會絆倒。| **lace sth to** *The canvas was laced to a steel frame.* 油畫布被固定在鋼製的畫框內。**2** to pass a string or LACE¹(2) through holes in something such as a pair of shoes 將線[繩, 帶]穿過〔鞋子等〕的孔眼 **3** to add a small amount of alcohol or a drug to a drink 給〔飲料〕攙酒[藥物]: **lace sth with** *coffee laced with Irish whiskey* 攙有愛爾蘭威士忌的咖啡 **4 be laced with** if a book, lesson, speech etc is laced with something, it has a lot of a particular quality all through it〔書、課文、演講等中〕攙有…: *The novel is laced with sexual imagery.* 這本小説攙雜着大量的性描述。**5** *literary* to weave or twist something together【文】把〔某物〕交織在一起: *Hannah laced her fingers together.* 漢娜把手指扣在一起。

la·ce·rate /ˈlæsəˌret; ˈlæsəreɪt/ *v* [T] to tear skin or flesh with something sharp〔用鋭器〕撕裂, 劃破, 割傷〔皮膚或肉體〕: *badly lacerated by bomb fragments* 被炸彈碎片嚴重割傷

la·ce·ra·tion /ˌlæsəˈreʃən; ˌlæsəˈreɪʃən/ *n* [C,U] *technical* serious cuts in your skin or flesh【術語】〔皮膚或肉體的〕嚴重劃破, 撕裂, 割傷: **[+to]** *multiple lacerations to the upper arms* 上臂的多處割傷

lace-up /ˈ· ·/ *n* [C usually plural 一般用複數] *especially BrE* shoes fastened with laces (LACE[1] (2))【尤英】繫帶的鞋 —**lace-up** *adj: shiny black lace-up shoes* 光亮的黑色繫帶鞋

lach·ry·mal /ˈlækrəml; ˈlækrɪməl/ *adj technical* connected with tears【術語】眼淚的: *lachrymal glands* 淚腺

lach·ry·mose /ˈlækrəˌmos; ˈlækrɪməʊs/ *adj formal*【正式】**1** often crying; TEARFUL 愛哭的; 淚汪汪的: *Avril was feeling tired and lachrymose.* 阿夫里爾累得想哭。**2** making you feel sad 使人傷感的: *lachrymose drama* 催人淚下的戲劇

3 2 **lack**[1] /læk; læk/ *n* [singular, U] the state of not having something, or of not having enough of it 沒有; 不足; 缺乏: **[+of]** *Lack of vitamin B can produce a variety of symptoms.* 缺少維生素B會引發多種症狀。| **a complete/distinct/marked/total lack of** *Rosie was showing a marked lack of interest in her school work.* 羅茜明顯表露出對學業缺乏興趣。| **for/through lack of** (=because there is a lack of) 因缺乏… *new mums, exhausted through lack of sleep* 由於缺乏睡眠而疲憊不堪的新媽媽們 | **no lack of** (=used when there is a lot of something) 不缺 *There was no lack of willing helpers.* 不乏自願幫助者。

3 **lack**[2] *v* **1** [T] to not have something that you need, or not have enough of it 沒有; 缺乏: *Alex's real problem is that he lacks confidence.* 亞歷士的真正問題是缺乏信心。**2 lack for nothing** *formal* to have everything that you need【正式】應有盡有: *Russell's parents made sure that he lacked for nothing.* 拉塞爾的父母設法確保他甚麼都不缺。

lack·a·dai·si·cal /ˌlækəˈdezɪkl; ˌlækəˈdeɪzɪkəl◂/ *adj* not showing enough interest in something or not putting enough effort into it 無精打采的; 懶散的: *David has a rather lackadaisical approach to his work.* 大衛對工作的態度相當懶散。—**lackadaisically** /-klɪ; -kli/ *adv*

lack·ey /ˈlækɪ; ˈlæki/ *n* [C] someone who behaves like a servant by always doing what someone else tells them to 走卒, 唯命是從者

lack·ing /ˈlækɪŋ; ˈlækɪŋ/ *adj* [not before noun 不用於名詞前] **1 be lacking in** to not have enough of something such as a quality or skill 缺乏〔某種品質或技能〕: *She seems to be sadly lacking in tact.* 她似乎太不夠老練了。**2** if something that you need is lacking, you do not have it 缺少的, 沒有的: *Financial backing for the project is still lacking.* 這個項目仍然缺少財政支持。**3** *old-fashioned* not very intelligent【過時】智力欠缺的: *The poor lad's a bit lacking.* 這個可憐的小伙子智力有點欠缺。

lack·lus·tre *BrE*【英】, **lackluster** *AmE*【美】/ˈlækˌlʌstɚ; ˈlækˌlʌstə/ *adj* not very exciting, impressive etc; dull 毫無生氣的; 無光澤的; 乏味的: *a lacklustre performance* 不精彩的演出 | *lacklustre hair* 乾枯的頭髮

la·con·ic /ləˈkɑnɪk; ləˈkɒnɪk/ *adj* using only a few words to say something〔語言〕簡短的 —**laconically** /-klɪ; -kli/ *adv*

lac·quer[1] /ˈlækɚ; ˈlækə/ *n* [U] **1** a liquid painted onto metal or wood to form a hard shiny surface〔塗在金屬、木材上的〕漆 **2** *old-fashioned* a transparent liquid that you put on your hair so that it keeps its shape【過時】〔用於固定髮型的〕噴髮膠

lacquer[2] *v* [T] **1** to cover something with LACQUER[1] (1) 用漆塗蓋: *a black lacquered box* 塗了黑漆的箱子 **2** to use LACQUER[1] (2) on your hair 給〔頭髮〕噴定型髮膠

la·crosse /ləˈkrɔs; ləˈkrɒs/ *n* [U] a game played on a field by two teams of ten players, in which each player has a long stick with a net on the end of it and uses this to throw, catch and carry a small ball 兜網球, 長曲棍球〔用帶網的曲棍來擲球、捕球、持球的隊際運動〕

lac·tate /ˈlækˌtet; lækˈteɪt/ *v* [I] *technical* to produce milk in your breasts【術語】泌乳

lac·ta·tion /lækˈteʃən; lækˈteɪʃən/ *n* [U] *technical* the production of milk in a mother's breasts for her baby, or the period during which this milk is produced【術語】泌乳; 泌乳期

lac·tic /ˈlæktɪk; ˈlæktɪk/ *adj technical* connected with milk【術語】乳汁的

lactic a·cid /ˌ·· ˈ··/ *n* [U] an acid found in sour milk and used to help keep food fresh 乳酸

lac·tose /ˈlæktos; ˈlæktəʊs/ *n* [U] a type of sugar found in milk, sometimes used as a food for babies and sick people 乳糖

la·cu·na /ləˈkjunə; ləˈkjuːnə/ *n plural* **lacunae** /-ni; -niː/ or **lacunas** [C] *formal* an empty space in a piece of writing, where something is missing【正式】〔文章中的〕脱漏

lac·y /ˈlesɪ; ˈleɪsi/ *adj* made of LACE[1] (1) or looking like lace 網眼織物的; 網眼狀的; 有花邊的; (似)帶子的: *lacy underwear* 網眼織物做的內衣 | *a plant with delicate, lacy leaves* 長着精巧網狀葉子的植物

lad /læd; læd/ *n* [C] *old-fashioned or literary*【過時或文】**1** a boy or young man 男孩; 少年, 男青年, 小伙子: *Things were different when I was a lad.* 我年輕的時候, 情況不大相同。**2 the lads** *BrE spoken* a group of men you know and work with or spend your free time with【英口】夥伴: *a night out with the lads* 和夥伴們外出的一個通宵 | **one of the lads** (=a member of your group of friends) 夥伴之一 **3** a boy or man who works with horses; STABLE BOY 馬倌, 馬夫 **4 a bit of a lad** *BrE spoken* a man that people like even though he behaves rather badly【英口】放蕩不羈的人: *That Charlie's a bit of a lad, isn't he?* 那個查理是個放蕩鬼, 對不對? —compare 比較 LASS —see also 另見 JACK THE LAD

lad·der[1] /ˈlædɚ; ˈlædə/ *n* [C] **1** a piece of equipment for climbing a wall, the side of a building etc, consisting of two long pieces of wood, metal, or rope, joined to each other by RUNGS (=steps) 梯子 —see also 另見 ROPE LADDER, STEPLADDER **2** a series of jobs by which you gradually become more important within an organization〔在機構內逐漸晉升的〕階梯, 途徑: *clerical workers on the bottom rung of the ladder* 在晉升階梯底層的辦事員 **3** *BrE* a long thin hole in knitted (KNIT (1)) clothing, STOCKINGS or TIGHTS where stitches have broken【英】〔織物的〕抽絲, 脱針, 脱線; RUN[2] (19) *AmE*【美】**4** a list of players of a game such as SQUASH or tennis who play each other regularly in order to decide who is the best〔壁球或網球等運動中的〕名次排列表 —see also 另見 SNAKES AND LADDERS

ladder[2] *v* [I,T] *BrE* if a STOCKING (1) or a pair of TIGHTS ladders or is laddered, a long thin hole is made in them【英】(使)〔褲襪等〕發生抽絲現象; RUN[2](19) *AmE*【美】

lad·die, laddy /ˈlædɪ; ˈlædi/ *n* [C] *informal especially BrE* a boy【非正式, 尤英】男孩, 少年, 小伙子

la·den /ˈledn; ˈleɪdn/ *adj literary*【文】**1** heavily loaded with something 裝滿的, 滿載的: **[+with]** *a Christmas tree laden with presents* 掛滿了禮物的聖誕樹 | **fully/**

heavily laden *The lorry was fully laden.* 這貨車滿載了。 **2 laden with troubles/problems etc** full of troubles etc 充滿憂慮/問題等: *Antonia was laden with doubts about the affair.* 關於此事安東尼亞滿腹疑慮。

ladies' man /ˈ‥ ·/ *n* [C] a man who likes to spend time with women and thinks they enjoy being with him 喜歡與女人廝混的男人

ladies' room /ˈ‥ ·/ *n* [C] *AmE* a women's toilet【美】女廁所, 女洗手間; the ladies *BrE*【英】

la·ding /ˈledɪŋ; ˈleɪdɪŋ/ *n* [C,U] —see 見 BILL OF LADING

la·dle¹ /ˈledl̩; ˈleɪdl/ *n* [C] a large deep spoon with a long handle, used for lifting liquid out of a container 長柄勺: *a soup ladle* 湯勺 —see picture at 參見 SPOON¹ 圖

ladle² *v* [T] to serve soup or other food onto plates or bowls, especially using a ladle〔尤指用長柄勺〕舀, 盛

ladle sth ↔ **out** *phr v* [T] to give someone too much of something such as advice or praise, without thinking carefully about it〔不假思索地〕大量給予〔建議或稱讚〕; 隨便濫給: *ladling out compliments* 大肆恭維

2 2 **la·dy** /ˈledɪ; ˈleɪdi/ *n plural* **ladies** [C]

1 ►WOMAN 婦女◄ **a)** a word meaning woman, used because people think it is a more polite word 女士; 夫人; 小姐〔禮貌用語〕: *Give your coat to the lady over there.* 把你的外衣交給那位女士。| *The young lady at reception sent me up here.* 接待處的小姐讓我來這裡的。| *the ladies' darts team* 女子擲鏢隊 | **tea lady/cleaning lady etc** (=a woman who does a particular job) 端茶小姐/清潔女工等 | **lady doctor/councillor etc** (=a polite word, which many women find offensive, for a woman doctor, councillor, etc) 女醫生/女議員〔禮貌用語, 很多婦女認為這類詞具冒犯性〕—see also 另見 DINNER LADY **b)** *approving especially AmE* a woman, especially one with a strong character【褒, 尤美】女士, 夫人; 小姐〔尤指個性很強的女性〕: *She's a real smart lady.* 她是位很時髦的女性。

2 ►POLITE WOMAN 文雅的女性◄ a woman who is always polite and behaves very well 舉止文雅的女人, 淑女: *Sheila always tries to be a lady.* 希拉總是盡力做個淑女。

3 ►WOMAN OF HIGH CLASS 貴婦◄ a woman born into a high social class in Britain〔英國的〕貴婦人, 貴族小姐: *a lady of noble birth* 貴族出身的小姐

4 ►WIFE/GIRL FRIEND 妻子/女友◄ *old-fashioned or literary* a man's wife or female friend【過時或文】妻子; 女友: *the captain and his lady* 船長和他的妻子

5 ►WHEN SPEAKING TO A WOMAN 稱呼婦女時◄ *AmE* a way of addressing a woman, which many women consider to be offensive【美】太太, 女士, 小姐〔稱呼婦女的一種方式, 很多女性認為具冒犯性〕: *Hey, lady, watch where you're going!* 嘿, 女士, 瞧你走到哪兒去了!

6 the ladies *BrE* a women's toilet【英】女廁所, 女洗手間; LADIES ROOM *AmE*【美】—compare 比較 **the gents** (GENT (2))

7 Lady a) used as the title of the wife or daughter of a British NOBLEMAN or the wife of a KNIGHT¹ (2) 太太, 夫人, 小姐〔用作對英國貴族女眷或爵士妻子的稱呼〕: *Lady Diana* 黛安娜小姐 **b)** *BrE* used in the title of women with a high official position【英】職位高的女人〔用在其稱呼之前〕: *Lady President* 女總統

8 the lady of the house *old-fashioned* the most important woman in a house, usually the mother of a family【過時】女主人

9 lady of leisure *often humorous* a woman who does not work and has a lot of free time【常幽默】休閒夫人: *So you're a lady of leisure now that the kids are at school?* 孩子們都上學去了, 你當起休閒夫人啦?

10 lady friend *often humorous* a man's female friend; GIRLFRIEND【常幽默】女性朋友; 女友: *I saw him with his new lady friend.* 我看見他與新的女友在一起。—see also 另見 BAG LADY, FIRST LADY, OLD LADY, OUR LADY

la·dy·bird /ˈledɪˌbɝd; ˈleɪdibɜːd/ *BrE*【英】, **la·dy·bug** /ˈledɪˌbʌg; ˈleɪdibʌg/ *n* [C] *AmE* a small round BEETLE (=a type of insect) that is usually red with black spots【美】瓢蟲

la·dy·fin·ger /ˈledɪˌfɪŋgɚ; ˈleɪdiˌfɪŋgə/ *n* [C] *AmE* a small cake shaped like a finger, used to make DESSERTs【美】手指餅乾〔用於製作甜品〕

lady-in-wait·ing /ˌ‥ ·ˈ‥/ *n* [C] a woman who looks after and serves a queen or PRINCESS〔女王或公主的〕女侍臣, 女官, 宮廷女侍

lady-kill·er /ˈ‥ ˌ‥/ *n* [C] *informal* a man who is very attractive to women but treats them badly【非正式】使女人傾心的男人: *Matt thinks he's such a lady-killer.* 馬特自認為是一位使女人傾倒的男人。

la·dy·like /ˈledɪˌlaɪk; ˈleɪdilaɪk/ *adj old-fashioned* behaving in the polite, quiet way that was once supposed to be typical of or suitable for women【過時】貴婦人似的, 舉止似大家閨秀的: *scratching herself in a way that was certainly not ladylike* 她搔癢的樣子肯定有失大家閨秀的風度

Lady Muck /ˌ‥ ˈ·/ *n* [C] *humorous* a woman who has a very high opinion of her own importance【幽默】自命不凡的女人: *Look at Lady Muck over there with her parasol.* 瞧那邊那個打着太陽傘的神氣女人。

la·dy's fin·gers /ˈ‥ ˌ‥/ *n* [plural] OKRA 秋葵

la·dy·ship /ˈledɪˌʃɪp; ˈleɪdiʃɪp/ *n* **1 your ladyship/her ladyship** used as a way of speaking to or talking about a woman with the title of Lady 夫人, 小姐〔對有 Lady 頭銜女子的尊稱〕: *Her ladyship is waiting for you in the drawing-room.* 夫人正在客廳等你。**2** *BrE spoken* a humorous way of talking about a woman who thinks she is very important【英口】貴夫人, 嬌小姐〔對自負女人的幽默稱謂〕: *Do you think her ladyship will be joining us?* 你認為夫人她會加入我們嗎?

lag¹ /læg; læg/ **lagged, lagging** *v* **1** [I] to move or develop more slowly than others 落後, 拖後: *Britain was still lagging in the space race.* 在太空競賽方面英國仍落在後面。| **[+behind]** *Jessica always lags behind, looking in shop windows.* 傑西卡總是落在後面看各種商店櫥窗。**2** [T] *BrE* to cover water pipes etc with a special material to prevent heat from being lost【英】給〔水管等〕加上外罩保暖: *We've had the hot-water tank lagged.* 我們已給熱水箱加上了保暖外罩。

lag² *n* [C] a delay or period of waiting between one event and a second event; TIME LAG〔兩起事件之間的〕延遲, 間歇; 時差 —see also 另見 JET LAG, OLD LAG

la·ger /ˈlɑgɚ; ˈlɑːgə/ *n BrE*【英】**1** [C,U] a light-coloured 3
beer or a glass of that beer (一杯) 淡啤酒: *Two halves of lager, please.* 請來兩杯半品脫淡啤酒。**2 lager lout** a young man who drinks too much and then behaves violently or rudely〔酒醉後有暴力行為或舉止粗魯的〕年輕酒徒

lag·gard /ˈlægɚd; ˈlægəd/ *n* [C] *old-fashioned* someone or something that is very slow or late【過時】遲緩[落後]的人[物] —**laggardly** *adj*

lag·ging /ˈlægɪŋ; ˈlægɪŋ/ *n* [U] the material used to protect a water pipe or container from heat or cold〔覆蓋水管或容器的〕隔熱[保温]材料

la·goon /ləˈgun; ləˈguːn/ *n* [C] **1** a lake of sea water partly or completely separated from the sea by sand, rock etc 瀉湖, 鹹水湖, 環礁湖: *a tropical lagoon* 熱帶瀉湖 —see picture on page A12 參見 A12 頁圖 **2** *AmE* a small lake which is not very deep, near a larger lake or river【美】〔大湖或江河附近的〕小而淺的淡水湖

lah-di-dah /ˌlɑ dɪ ˈdɑ; ˌlɑː diː ˈdɑː/ *adj spoken* talking and behaving as if you think you are better or from a higher class than you really are【口】裝腔作勢的, 故作斯文的

laid /led; leɪd/ past tense and past participle of LAY²

laid-back /ˌ· ˈ·◄/ *adj* relaxed and seeming not to be worried about anything 自在的, 不在乎的: *I don't know how you can be so laid-back about your exams.* 我弄不懂你對考試怎麼會如此不在乎。

lain /len; leɪn/ the past participle of LIE¹

lair /lɛr; leə/ *n* [C] **1** the place where a wild animal hides and sleeps 獸穴[窟]; 野獸躲藏處 **2** a place where you go to hide or to be alone 藏身處; 獨處的地方: *The police*

L

tracked the rapist to his lair. 警察跟蹤找到了強姦犯的藏身處。

laird /lɛrd; leəd/ *n* [C] a Scottish landowner 蘇格蘭地主 —compare 比較 SQUIRE(1)

lais·sez-faire, laisser-faire /ˌlɛse ˋfɛr; ˌleseɪ ˈfeə/ *n* [U] *French* the principle of allowing private businesses to develop without any state control【法】〔國家不限制私營企業發展的〕自由放任主義: *laissez-faire policies* 自由放任政策

la·i·ty /ˋleətɪ; ˈleɪəti/ *n* **the laity** all the members of a religious group apart from the priests 一般信徒, 俗人

3 3 **lake** /lek; leɪk/ *n* **1** [C] a large area of water surrounded by land 湖: *boating on the lake* 在湖上划船 | *Lake Michigan* 密歇根[密執安]湖 **2 wine lake/milk lake etc** a very large amount of wine, milk etc that is not needed or used 酒池/奶池等〔指生產過量的葡萄酒/牛奶等〕—see also 另見 MOUNTAIN (3)

lake·side /ˋlekˌsaɪd; ˈleɪksaɪd/ *adj* beside a lake 湖邊的, 湖濱的: *a lakeside restaurant* 湖濱飯店 —**lakeside** *n* [singular]

lakh /læk; læk/ *number IndE & PakE* a hundred thousand【印和巴】十萬〔盧比〕

lam¹ /læm; læm/ *v*

lam into sb *phr v* [T] *BrE informal* to hit someone or speak angrily to them【英, 非正式】狠擊; 怒斥

lam² *n* **on the lam** *AmE informal* escaping from someone, especially the police【美, 非正式】在潛逃中: *Sykes was recaptured after three weeks on the lam.* 賽克斯潛逃三個星期後又被抓獲了。

la·ma /ˋlɑmə; ˈlɑːmə/ *n* [C] a Buddhist priest in Tibet of China, Mongolia etc 喇嘛〔西藏、蒙古等地的佛教僧侶〕

La·ma·is·m /ˋlɑməɪzəm; ˈlɑːmə-ɪzəm/ *n* [U] a form of the Buddhist religion common in Tibet of China, Mongolia etc 喇嘛教

lamb¹ /læm; læm/ *n* **1** [C] a young sheep 羔羊, 小羊 **2** [U] the meat of a young sheep 羔羊肉: *roast lamb with mint sauce* 薄荷汁烤羊肉 **3** [C] *spoken* someone gentle and loveable, especially a child【口】溫柔可愛的人〔尤指小孩〕: *Benny's asleep now, the little lamb.* 班尼正在睡覺, 像可愛的小羔羊。**4 like a lamb** quietly and without any argument 似羔羊般順從地: *Suzie went off to school like a lamb today.* 蘇齊今天乖乖地去上學了。**5 like a lamb to the slaughter** used when someone is going to do something dangerous but do not realize it 像送去屠宰的羔羊〔指將做危險之事而未覺察者〕

lamb² *v* [I] *technical* to give birth to lambs【術語】生產羊羔: *The ewes are lambing this week.* 本週母羊將要產羊羔。

lam·ba·da /læmˋbɑdə; læmˈbɑːdə/ *n* [singular, U] a sexy DISCO dance from Brazil 朗巴達舞〔巴西的一種色情迪斯科舞〕

lam·baste /læmˋbest; læmˈbeɪst/ also 又作 **lam·bast** /-ˋbæst; -ˈbæst/ *v* [T] to attack or criticize someone very strongly 猛烈攻擊; 抨擊: *Her new play was really lambasted by the critics.* 她的新劇本遭到了評論家的猛烈抨擊。

lam·bent /ˋlæmbənt; ˈlæmbənt/ *adj literary*【文】**1** clever in a gentle and amusing way 伶俐的, 巧妙的, 詼諧的: *lambent wit* 雋智 **2** a lambent light or flame shines softly and pleasantly〔光或火焰〕閃爍的, 柔和的

lamb·skin /ˋlæmˌskɪn; ˈlæmˌskɪn/ *n* **1** [C,U] the skin of a lamb, with the wool still on it〔帶羊毛的〕羔羊皮: *lambskin gloves* 羔羊皮手套 **2** [U] leather made from the skin of lambs 羔羊皮, 羔皮革

la·mé /lɑˋme; ˈlɑːmeɪ/ *n* [U] cloth containing gold or silver threads 有金銀線的織物, 金銀錦緞: *a gold lamé evening skirt* 有金銀線的晚裝女裙

lame¹ /lem; leɪm/ *adj* **1** unable to walk properly because your leg or foot is injured or weak 瘸的, 跛的: **go lame** (=become lame) 變成瘸子 **2** a lame explanation or excuse does not sound very believable〔解釋或藉口〕無說服力的, 站不住腳的: *Nancy came out with some lame excuse about missing the bus again.* 南茜又一次搬出未趕上公共汽車這種牽強的藉口。—see also 另見 LAMELY **3 lame duck** a person, business etc that is experiencing difficulties and needs to be helped 跛足鴨〔遭遇困難需要幫助的人或企業等〕**4 lame duck president/administration etc** *especially AmE informal* a president, government etc whose period in office will soon end【尤美, 非正式】任期即將結束的總統/政府等 —**lameness** *n* [U]

lame² *v* [T usually passive 一般用被動態] to make a person or animal unable to walk properly 使〔人或動物〕跛[瘸]; 使殘廢

lame·brain /ˋlembren; ˈleɪmbreɪn/ *n* [C] *AmE informal* a stupid person【美, 非正式】笨蛋, 蠢貨: *Don't do it that way, lamebrain; you'll break it.* 別那樣弄, 笨蛋; 你會把它弄壞的。

lame·ly /ˋlemlɪ; ˈleɪmli/ *adv* if you say something lamely, you do not sound confident and other people find it difficult to believe you〔說話〕不自信地, 令人難以相信地: *"But I still love you," he added rather lamely.* "但我還是愛你的。"他很不自信地補充道。

la·ment¹ /ləˋmɛnt; ləˈment/ *v* **1** [I,T] to express feelings of great sadness about something 為…悲痛, 哀悼; 痛惜; 悲嘆: *The nation lamented the death of its great war leader.* 全國為戰時的偉大領袖之死而悲痛。| [+over] *lamenting over her luck in love* 為她戀愛的不幸而悲嘆 **2** [T] to express annoyance or disappointment about something you think is unsatisfactory or unfair 抱怨: *another article lamenting the decline of popular television* 又一篇抱怨大眾化電視走下坡路的文章

lament² *n* [C] a song, piece of music, or something that you say, that expresses a feeling of sadness 輓歌, 哀樂, 悼詞: *A lone piper played a lament.* 孤單的風笛手吹奏了一首哀樂。

lam·en·ta·ble /ˋlæməntəbḷ; ˈlæməntəbəl/ *adj formal* very unsatisfactory or disappointing【正式】可嘆的, 令人惋惜的; 讓人失望的: *Riley showed a lamentable lack of tact.* 賴利顯得束手無策, 令人失望。—**lamentably** *adv*

lam·en·ta·tion /ˌlæmənˋteʃən; ˌlæmənˈteɪʃən/ *n* [C, U] *formal* deep sadness or something that expresses it【正式】悲痛, 悲慟, 哀悼: *There was lamentation throughout the land at the news of the defeat.* 聽到戰敗的消息, 舉國為之悲慟。

lam·i·nar flow /ˌlæmɪnɚ ˋflo; ˌlæmɪ̣nə ˈfləʊ/ *n* [U] *technical* a smooth flow of liquid or gas over a solid surface【術語】層流

lam·i·nate /ˋlæməˌnɪt; ˈlæmɪ̣nɪ̣t/ *n* [C,U] laminated material 層壓板材

lam·i·nated /ˋlæməˌnetɪd; ˈlæmɪ̣neɪtɪd/ *adj* **1** laminated material has several thin sheets joined on top of each other 由薄片疊成的; 層壓的: *laminated glass* 層壓玻璃 **2** covered with a layer of thin plastic or metal 由塑料[金屬]薄片覆蓋的: *wood laminated with plastic* 由塑料薄層覆蓋的木製品 —**laminate** *v* [T]

lamp /læmp; læmp/ *n* [C] **1** an object that produces light by using electricity, oil, or gas 燈: *a table lamp* 枱燈 —see also 另見 HEADLAMP, STANDARD LAMP, STREETLAMP, SAFETY LAMP —see picture at 參見 LIGHT¹ 圖 **2** a piece of electrical equipment used to provide a special kind of heat, especially as medical treatment〔尤指治療用的〕發熱燈;〔發出熱射線等的〕照射器: *an infrared lamp* 紅外線燈 —see also 另見 SUNLAMP, BLOWLAMP

lamp·black /ˋ· ·/ *n* [U] a fine black colouring material made from SOOT (=the black powder produced by smoke) 燈黑〔由燈上煤炱製成的黑色顏料〕

lamp·light /ˋlæmpˌlaɪt; ˈlæmp-laɪt/ *n* [U] the soft light produced by a lamp 燈光: *Her eyes shone in the lamplight.* 她的眼睛在燈光下閃閃發亮。

lamp·light·er /ˋlæmpˌlaɪtɚ; ˈlæmpˌlaɪtə/ *n* [C] someone whose job was to light lamps in the street in the past 燈夫〔舊時點街燈者〕

lam·poon /læmˋpun; læmˈpuːn/ *v* [T] to write about

someone, especially a politician, in a way that makes them seem stupid 用文章諷刺[挖苦]〔政客等〕—**lampoon** *n* [C]

lamp-post /'· ·/ *n* [C] **1** *especially BrE* a tall pole supporting a lamp that lights a street or public area【尤英】路燈柱, 燈桿 —see picture on page A4 參見A4頁圖 **2** *AmE* a pole supporting an old-fashioned type of lamp【美】〔舊式燈的〕燈桿

lamp·shade /ˈlæmpˌʃed; ˈlæmpʃeɪd/ *n* [C] a decorative cover fixed over a lamp to reduce or direct its light 燈罩 —see picture at 參見 LIGHT¹ 圖

LAN /læn; læn/ *n* [C] *technical* local area network; a system for communicating by computer in a large place such as an office building【術語】局部(地區)網(絡)〈如辦公樓內的電腦通訊系統〉

lance¹ /læns; lɑːns/ *n* [C] a long thin pointed weapon that was used in the past by soldiers on horses〔昔日騎兵用的〕長矛

lance² *v* [T] to cut a small hole in someone's flesh with a sharp instrument to let out PUS (=yellow liquid produced by infection)〔用鋒利的刀子〕切開: *to lance a boil* 切開癤子

lance cor·po·ral /ˌ· ˈ···/ *n* [C] a low level rank in the Marines or the British army, or someone who has this rank〔美國海軍陸戰隊或英國陸軍中的〕一等兵 —see table on page C6 參見C6頁附錄

lanc·er /ˈlænsɚ; ˈlɑːnsə/ *n* [C] a soldier belonging to a REGIMENT (=part of the army) that used to be armed with lances 長矛輕騎兵, 槍騎兵

lan·cet /ˈlænsɪt; ˈlɑːnsɪ̣t/ *n* [C] **1** a small very sharp pointed knife with two cutting edges, used by doctors to cut flesh〔醫療用的〕手術刀, 柳葉刀 **2 lancet arch/window** *technical* a tall narrow ARCH¹ (1) or window that is pointed at the top【術語】尖拱/尖窗

1 1 **land¹** /lænd; lænd/ *n*

1 ►NOT SEA 非海洋◄ [U] the solid dry part of the Earth's surface 陸地: *After 21 days at sea we sighted land.* 經過21天的海上航行, 我們見到了陸地。| **by land** *It's quicker by land than sea.* 走陸路要比走海路快捷。| **on land** *The crocodile lays its eggs on land.* 鱷魚在陸地上產卵。

2 ►GROUND 土地◄ [U] ground, especially when used for farming or building on 土地〔尤指耕作或建築用地〕: *the use and management of land* 土地的使用和管理 | *fertile land* 肥沃的土地 | *high land prices* 昂貴的地價

3 ►COUNTRY 國土◄ [C] *especially literary* a country【尤文】國土, 國家: *people of many lands* 很多國家的人們 | **native land** (=the land where you were born) 祖國 *She returned at last to her native land.* 最終她回到了自己的祖國。

4 ►NOT CITY 非城市◄ **the land** the countryside thought of as a place that is quiet and peaceful, or as a place where people grow food 鄉村, 農村; 田地: *We want to leave London and get back to the land.* 我們要離開倫敦回到鄉村。| **live off the land** (=grow or catch all the food you need) 靠土地生活

5 ►PROPERTY 財產◄ [U] also 又作 **lands** *plural* the area of land that someone owns 地產, 田產: *Get off my land!* 從我的土地上滾開! | *The Duke's lands lay south of the mountains.* 公爵的地產在山南。

6 see/find out how the land lies to try to discover what the situation really is before you make a decision〔作出決定前〕了解情況, 摸清現狀[形勢]

7 in the land of the living *spoken humorous* awake【口, 幽默】醒着: *Now you're back in the land of the living you can put the kettle on.* 既然你醒了, 你可以把水壺放上去了。

8 land of milk and honey an imaginary place where life is easy and pleasant〔虛構中的〕乳蜜之鄉, 富饒之地

9 the land of nod *old-fashioned* an expression meaning sleep, used especially when talking to children【過時】睡夢之鄉〔尤用於和孩子說話時〕—see also 另見 **be/live in cloud-cuckoo-land** (CLOUD¹ (6)), DRY LAND, **the lie of the land** (LIE³ (3))

USAGE NOTE 用法說明: LAND

WORD CHOICE 詞語辨析: **world, earth, land, ground, floor, soil, country**

When you are talking about **the world** as a whole, compared with other planets, you often call it **the Earth** (or **the earth**). 與其他行星相比較, the world 作為整體提及時常叫作 the Earth (或 the earth): *From space, the earth looks like a shining blue ball.* 從太空中看, 地球像是一個發光的藍球。But in some phrases *the* is not usually used. 但在某些短語中通常不用 the: *Billions of people live on earth* (NOT usually 一般不用 *on the earth* and definitely NOT 一定不用 *in the earth*). 地球上住着數十億的人。

The hard surface of the world, when it is compared with the area covered by sea, is called **land** [U], but when you are comparing it with the air you say **the ground** or, on a larger scale, **(the) earth**. 當與海域相比較時, 地球的硬表層叫作 land〔不可數〕, 但當與太空相比較時, 則叫作 the ground, 規模更大的叫作 (the) earth: *After a week adrift at sea, we spotted land.* 經過一星期的海上漂浮, 我們見到了陸地。| *The horse fell to the ground.* 馬倒在地上。| *I won't relax until we're safely back on the ground.* 要到我們安全返回地面時我才會鬆口氣。| *Once a meteor from outer space fell to earth here.* 曾經有一顆流星從外太空掉落到了這裡的地面上。| *The earth shook and huge cracks appeared.* 大地震動, 巨大的裂縫出現了。

Inside a building the surface you walk on is usually called the **floor** (but it is called **the ground** outside). 室內供行走的地面稱為 the floor〔而室外則稱作 the ground〕: *The dishes crashed to the kitchen floor.* 盤子掉到廚房的地板上碎了。| *The ground's too wet for camping.* 地面太濕了, 不能紮營。

An area thought of as property is a piece of **land** [U]. land〔不可數〕指當作財產的一塊地: *the high price of land in Tokyo* 東京昂貴的地價 | *He owns a lot of land in New Mexico* (NOT 不用 **earth** or 或 **ground** or 或 **big land**). 他在新墨西哥州擁有很多地產。Also when you are talking about large areas, especially when it is used for a particular purpose, you say **land**. 當談論到大片面積的地, 特別是用於特定的用途, 其也稱作 land: *The land isn't much good for raising corn.* 這塊地不大適合種植玉米。| *Much of the land here is used for industry.* 這裡的大部分土地用於工業。

A smaller area is likely to be called a piece of **ground** [U]. 小塊地可稱作 a piece of ground [U]: *a small piece of ground where I could plant potatoes* 一小塊我可以種馬鈴薯的地 | *a patch of waste ground behind the house* 屋後的一塊荒地

The substance that plants grow in is **soil** [U] or **earth** [U] or (*AmE*) **dirt** [U]. 生長植物的土為 soil〔不可數〕或 earth〔不可數〕或 dirt〔美, 不可數〕: *The soil/earth is pretty good here.* 這裡的土壤很好。| *The kids were playing on a mound of dirt in the yard.* 小孩在院內的土堆上玩耍。But when you are talking about its quality, type, or condition, you usually use **soil**. 但當談論土質、土壤類型或狀況的時候, 通常用 soil 一詞: *soil erosion* 土壤的侵蝕 | *To improve clay soil, dig in as much sand as you can.* 要改良黏土, 盡量多攙入點沙。

Land that is not covered in buildings is **the country**, often compared with the town or city. 通常, 與城鎮相比較而言, 沒有樓羣覆蓋的地方為 the country: *Why don't we take a trip to the country and get*

L

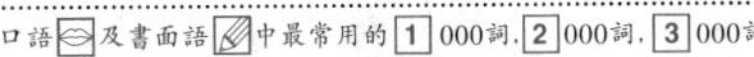

some fresh air? (NOT 不用 *land*). 我們為何不到郊外旅行呼吸點新鮮空氣？

You call a country a **land** [C] only if you want to communicate a particular meaning. 只有在傳達特殊的意義時，才可稱國土為 land〔可數〕。In a story, perhaps, or to show your feelings about a country you might say 或許，在一個故事中或要表達對一個國家的感情時，可以說：*My homeland/native land is India* (=that is the country I feel I belong to). 我的祖國是印度〔=我認為我屬於那個國度〕。| *He visited many foreign lands* (=strange and mysterious countries). 他去過了很多充滿異域風情的國度〔=陌生和神祕的國家〕。Compare this with the following which is a report of simple facts. 將這和下面的例句相比較，下面的例句是簡單事實的記述：*I come from India.* 我來自印度。| *He visited many foreign countries.* 他去過了許多國家。

S2 W3 **land²** *v*

1 ►PLANE 飛機◄ [I,T] if an aircraft lands or if a pilot lands it, it moves down onto the ground（使）着陸，（使）降落：*We are due to land at Heathrow at 12:50.* 我們〔的航班〕定於 12 點 50 分在希思羅機場降落。

2 ►ARRIVE BY BOAT/PLANE 乘船/乘飛機抵達◄ [I] to arrive somewhere in an aircraft, boat etc〔乘飛機、船等〕到達〔某地〕：*1969, when the first men landed on the moon* 1969 年，當人類首次登上月球

3 ►GOODS/PEOPLE 貨物/乘客◄ [T] to put something or someone on land from an aircraft or boat〔從飛機或船上〕卸下〔貨物〕；使〔乘客〕下飛機[船]：*Troops were landed by helicopter.* 軍隊乘直升機降落。| *Trawlers were landing their catch at the harbour.* 拖網漁船正在港口卸魚獲。

4 ►FALL/COME DOWN 掉下/落下◄ [I always+adv/prep] to come down through the air onto something 從空中落到〔某物上〕：**[+in/on/under etc]** *Louis fell out of the tree and landed in a holly bush.* 路易斯從樹上掉下來落到冬青樹叢中。| *I felt a few drops of rain landing on my head.* 我覺得頭上落了幾滴雨。

5 ►PROBLEMS 問題◄ [I always+adv/prep] to be given to someone unexpectedly, and cause problems that they will have to deal with〔出乎意料地〕送達〔某人，引發需要解決的問題〕：**[+in/on/under etc]** *Just when I thought my problems were over, this letter landed on my desk.* 正當我認為所有問題都解決了時，這封信送到了我的桌上。

6 ►JOB/CONTRACT ETC 工作/合同等◄ [T] *informal* to succeed in getting a job, contract etc that was difficult to get【非正式】謀取〔一份難得的工作、合同等〕：*Fay landed a plum job with the BBC.* 費伊從英國廣播公司謀得一份好差事。| **land yourself sth** *Bill's just landed himself a part in a Broadway show.* 比爾剛在百老匯演出中謀到了一個角色。

7 ►FISH 魚◄ [T] to catch a large fish 捕到〔大魚〕

8 land a punch/blow to succeed in hitting someone 擊中〔某人〕—see also 另見 **fall/land on your feet** (FOOT¹ (18))

land sb **in** sth *phr v* [T] **1 land sb in trouble/hospital/court etc** to cause serious problems for someone 使某人陷入困境/得病住院/捲入訴訟之中：*We all knew his drinking would land him in court one day.* 我們都認為他的酗酒總有一天會使他給送上法庭。**2 land sb in it** *spoken* to get someone into trouble by saying that they did something wrong【口】使某人陷入困擾之中：*Micky landed me in it by saying I was the last one to use the photocopier.* 米基說我是最後一個使用影印機的人，這使我陷入了麻煩中。

land on sb *phr v* [T] *AmE informal* to speak angrily to someone【美，非正式】痛斥〔某人〕：*Dale landed on him for forgetting the documents.* 戴爾因他忘了文件而痛斥了他一頓。

land up *phr v* [I always+adv/prep] *informal* to finally get into a particular place, situation, or position after a lot of things have happened to you【非正式】〔歷經許多事後〕最終落到〔某一處境〕：**land up in/on etc** *We landed up in a bar at 3 am.* 凌晨 3 點鐘我們終於到達了一家酒吧。| *Be careful that you don't land up in serious debt.* 當心，切勿債台高築。

land sb **with** sth *phr v* [T usually passive 一般用被動態] *informal* to give someone something unpleasant to do, because no one else wants to do it【非正式】讓人做〔無人願做的〕事：*Maria's been landed with all the tidying up as usual.* 像往常一樣，所有的收拾工作都留給了瑪麗亞。

land a·gent /ˈ· ,··/ *n* [C] someone who looks after land, cattle, farms etc that belong to someone else〔包括看管農田、牲畜等在內的〕地產管理人

lan·dau /ˈlændɔ; ˈlændɔː/ *n* [C] a four-wheeled carriage that is pulled by horses and has two seats and a top that folds back in two parts 活頂雙座四輪馬車

land·ed /ˈlændɪd; ˈlændɨd/ *adj* [only before noun 僅用於名詞前] **1 landed gentry/family/nobility** a family or group that has owned a lot of land for a long time 擁有大量土地的鄉紳/家族/貴族 **2** including a lot of land 包括大量土地的：*landed estates*〔包含大量土地的〕地產

land·fall /ˈlænd,fɔl; ˈlændfɔːl/ *n* [C usually singular 一般用單數] the first land that you see or arrive at after a long journey by sea or air〔長時間飛行或航行後的〕初見陸地；首次登上陸地：*We made our landfall just south of Stornoway.* 我們恰好在斯托諾韋的南面首次登陸。

land·fill /ˈlænd,fɪl; ˈlændfɪl/ *n* **1** [U] the practice of burying waste under the soil, or the waste buried in this way 廢棄物的埋填；埋填的廢棄物 **2** [C] a place where this waste is buried 廢棄物埋填場

land·ing /ˈlændɪŋ; ˈlændɪŋ/ *n* [C] **1** the floor at the top of a set of stairs or between two sets of stairs 樓梯〔過渡〕平台，樓梯過道 —see picture on page A4 參見 A4 頁圖 **2** an act of arriving on land or of bringing something onto land from the sea or air 登陸，着陸；降落：*troop landings in Normandy in 1944* 1944 年盟軍在諾曼第的登陸 | **crash landing/emergency landing** (=an aircraft's sudden landing because of trouble with the engine etc) 強行〔摔機〕着陸/緊急着陸

landing charge /ˈ·· ,·/ *n* [C] *technical* money that you have to pay when goods are unloaded at a port【術語】卸貨費，上岸費，着陸費

landing craft /ˈ·· ,·/ *n* [C] a flat-bottomed boat that opens at one end to allow soldiers and equipment to land directly onto a shore 登陸艇

landing field /ˈ·· ·/ *n* [C] a LANDING STRIP 小型飛機場；飛機起落場；機場跑道

landing gear /ˈ·· ·/ *n* [U] an aircraft's wheels and wheel supports〔飛機等的〕起落架，起落裝置 —see picture at 參見 AIRCRAFT 圖

landing net /ˈ·· ·/ *n* [C] a net on a long handle used for lifting a fish out of the water after you have caught it 抄網〔用以撈取上了鉤的較大的魚〕

landing stage /ˈ·· ·/ *n* [C] a wooden structure onto which passengers and goods are landed from boats 浮碼頭，囤船

landing strip /ˈ·· ·/ *n* [C] a level piece of ground that has been prepared for aircraft to use; AIRSTRIP〔機場的〕簡易跑道

land·la·dy /ˈlænd,ledɪ; ˈlænd,leɪdi/ *n* [C] **1** the woman that you rent a room, building, or piece of land from 女房東，女地主 **2** a woman who owns or is in charge of a PUB〔酒店、酒館等的〕女店主

land·less /ˈlændlɪs; ˈlændləs/ *adj* owning no land 不擁有土地的，沒有土地的

land·locked /ˈlænd,lɑkt; ˈlændlɒkt/ *adj* a landlocked country is surrounded by other countries and has no coast 陸圍的，被內陸包圍的

land·lord /ˈlænd,lɔrd; ˈlændlɔːd/ *n* [C] **1** the man that W3 you rent a room, building, or piece of land from 房東, 地主 **2** a man who owns or is in charge of a PUB〔酒店、酒館等的〕店主

land·lub·ber /ˈlændˌlʌbɚ; ˈlændˌlʌbə/ *n* [C] *old-fashioned* someone who does not have much experience of the sea or ships【過時】旱鴨子〔不諳航海的人或蹩腳水手〕

land·mark /ˈlændˌmɑrk; ˈlændmɑːk/ *n* [C] **1** an event, idea, or discovery that marks an important part of someone's life, of the development of knowledge etc〔個人生活或知識發展中的〕里程碑; 重大轉折: *The discovery of penicillin was a landmark in the history of medicine.* 青黴素的發現是醫藥史上的里程碑。| **landmark discovery/decision etc** *the landmark decision to join NATO* 加入北約組織的重大決定 **2** something that is easy to recognize, such as a tall tree or building, and will help you know where you are 地標, 陸標

land·mass /ˈlændˌmæs; ˈlændmæs/ *n* [C] *technical* a large area of land【術語】地塊, 大陸〔塊〕

land·mine /ˈlændmaɪn; ˈlændmaɪn/ *n* [C] a kind of bomb hidden in the ground that explodes when someone walks or drives over it 地雷

land of·fice /ˈ· ˌ··/ *n* [C] a government office in the US that records the sales of all public land〔美國〕土地管理局

land·own·er /ˈlændˌonɚ; ˈlændˌəʊnə/ *n* [C] someone who owns a large amount of land 土地擁有者, 地主 —**landowning** *adj*: *the landowning aristocracy* 擁有大批土地的貴族 —**landownership** *n* [U]

land re·form /ˈ· ·ˌ·/ *n* [C,U] the political principle of sharing farm land so that more people own some of it 土地改革

land re·gis·try /ˈ· ˌ···/ *n* [C] a government office in Britain that keeps records about the sales and ownership of land〔英〕土地管理局, 土地登記處

Land Rov·er /ˈ· ˌ··/ *n* [C] *BrE trademark* a type of strong car made for travelling over rough ground【英, 商標】越野車

3 **land·scape¹** /ˈlændskep; ˈlændskeɪp/ *n* **1** [C] an area of countryside or land, considered in terms of how attractive it is to look at〔陸上的〕風景, 景致, 景色: *the beauty of the New England landscape in autumn* 美麗的新英格蘭秋色 | *a desolate urban landscape* 城市荒涼的景色 **2** [C] a picture showing an area of countryside or land 風景照, 風景畫: *Cézanne's landscapes* 塞尚的風景畫 **3** [U] the painting or drawing of landscapes in art 風景繪畫, 山水繪畫 **4 the political/intellectual etc landscape** the general situation in which a particular activity takes place 政治/知識界的概貌: *She dominated the intellectual landscape of Paris.* 她掌控着巴黎知識界的整體情況。**5** [U] *technical* LANDSCAPE MODE【術語】橫向格式 —see also 另見 **a blot on the landscape** (BLOT² (2))

landscape² *v* [T often passive 常用被動態] to make a park, garden etc look attractive and interesting by planting trees and bushes, making different levels etc 用園藝美化〔公園、花園等〕

landscape ar·chi·tec·ture /ˌ·· ˈ····/ *n* [U] the profession or art of planning the way an area of land looks, including roads, buildings, and planted areas 園林建築業, 園林建築術 —**landscape architect** *n* [C]

landscape gar·den·ing /ˌ·· ˈ···/ *n* [U] the profession or art of arranging gardens and parks so that they look attractive and interesting 園藝業, 園藝學 —**landscape gardener** *n* [C]

landscape mode /ˈ·· ˌ·/ *n* [C] *technical* a piece of paper, picture, etc that has its longer edge at the top and bottom【術語】橫向格式 —opposite 反義詞 PORTRAIT MODE

land·scap·er /ˈlændskepɚ; ˈlændskeɪpə/ *n* [C] *AmE* someone whose job is to arrange plants, paths etc in gardens and parks【美】園藝師

land·slide /ˈlændˌslaɪd; ˈlændslaɪd/ *n* [C] **1** a sudden fall of a lot of earth or rocks down a hill, cliff etc 山崩, 滑坡, 塌方 **2** a victory in an election in which one person or party gets a lot more votes than all the others 一面倒的勝利,〔競選中〕一方選票佔壓倒性多數: **by a landslide** *The SNP candidate won by a landslide.* 蘇格蘭國民黨候選人以壓倒性多數獲勝。| *a landslide victory* 一面倒的勝利

land·slip /ˈlændˌslɪp; ˈlændslɪp/ *n* [C] a small landslide〔小規模的〕山崩; 滑坡; 塌方; 山泥傾瀉

land·ward /ˈlændwɚd; ˈlændwəd/ *adj* facing towards the land and away from the sea 朝岸的, 向陸地的: *the landward side of the hill* 朝向陸地的山坡 —**land·wards** /ˈlændwɚdz; ˈlændwədz/ *adv*

lane /len; leɪn/ *n* [C] **1** a narrow road between fields or houses, especially in the countryside〔尤指鄉間〕小道; 小巷; 胡同; 里弄: *a dusty lane leading to some cottages* 通向幾座鄉間村舍的小土路 **2** the two or three parallel areas on a main road which are divided by painted lines to keep fast and slow traffic apart 車道, 行車線: **the inside/outside lane** *Use the outside lane for overtaking only.* 只能使用外車道超車。| **the fast lane** (=the lane for going past other vehicles) 快車道 **3** used in the names of roads …巷〔用於路名〕: *a hotel in Park Lane* 園林巷內的酒店 **4** one of the narrow parallel areas marked for each competitor in a running or swimming race 跑道; 泳道: *The champion is running in lane five.* 上屆冠軍正在第五跑道上跑。**5** a line or course along which ships or aircraft regularly travel between ports or airports〔船舶或飛機的〕航線, 航道: *busy shipping lanes* 繁忙的海運航道 —see also 另見 **life in the fast lane** (FAST LANE (2)) 3 3

lan·guage /ˈlæŋgwɪdʒ; ˈlæŋgwɪdʒ/ *n* 2 1

1 ▶ENGLISH/FRENCH/ARABIC ETC 英語/法語/阿拉伯語等◀ [C,U] a system of communication by written or spoken words, which is used by the people of a particular country or area〔某國家或地區的書面或口頭的〕語言〔文字〕: *the Japanese language* 日語 | *How many languages do you speak?* 你能説幾種語言? | **native language** (=the first language you learned) 母語 *Andrea's native language is German.* 安德烈的母語是德語。| **modern language** (=a language that is still spoken today) 當代語言 | **dead language** (=a language that is no longer spoken) 過時語言 | **the language barrier** (=the difficulty of communicating with people who speak a different language) 語言上的障礙

2 ▶COMMUNICATION 溝通◀ [U] the use of written or spoken words to communicate〔書面或口頭的〕語言〔文字〕: *the origins of language* 語言的起源

3 ▶COMPUTERS 電腦◀ [C,U] *technical* a system of instructions and commands for operating a computer【術語】電腦語言: *a programming language such as BASIC or Pascal* 程式[序]語言, 如BASIC語言〔初學者通用符號指令碼〕或帕斯卡語言

4 ▶STYLE/TYPE OF WORDS 詞語的風格/類型◀ [U] the kind of words and style used in one kind of writing or by people in a particular job or activity 行語, 專門用語, 術語: *medical language* 醫學用語 | *poetic language* 詩詞用語

5 ▶SOUNDS/SIGNS/ACTIONS 聲音/手勢/動作◀ [U] a way of expressing meaning or giving information through sounds, signs, movements etc〔使用聲音、手勢、動作等的〕表達方式: *the language of music* 音樂語彙

6 ▶SWEARING 謾罵◀ [U] *informal* words that most people think are offensive【非正式】粗話, 罵人話: *You never heard such language! It was disgusting.* 你從未聽過如此粗魯的語言!真噁心! | **mind/watch your language** (=stop swearing) 注意你的語言, 別咒罵了

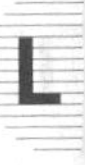

7 strong language a) angry words used to tell people exactly what you mean 措辭強硬的話, 激烈的言辭 **b)** words that most people think are offensive; swearing 粗話, 罵人話

8 speak the same language if two people speak the same language, they have similar attitudes and opinions

有共同語言〔表示兩個人看法和觀點一致〕—see also 另見 BODY LANGUAGE, SIGN LANGUAGE

language la·bor·a·tory /'·· ·,···/ *n* [C] a room in a school or college where you can learn to speak a foreign language by listening to TAPEs and recording your own voice 語言實驗室

lan·guid /ˋlæŋgwɪd; 'læŋgwɪd/ *adj* **1** moving slowly and making very little effort, but in an attractive way 悠然的, 慵懶的, 緩緩的: *Sebastian left with a languid wave of the hand.* 塞巴斯蒂安緩緩地揮了揮手就離開了。**2** lazily slow and peaceful 懶洋洋的, 悠閒的: *a languid afternoon by the river* 在河邊懶洋洋度過的下午 —**languidly** *adv*

lan·guish /ˋlæŋgwɪʃ; 'læŋgwɪʃ/ *v* [I] **1** to be forced to stay somewhere where you are unhappy 受煎熬: *Shaw languished in a Mexican jail for fifteen years.* 肖在墨西哥監牢裡受了十五年的煎熬。**2** to become weaker or less successful 變得(越來越)衰弱: *Local food production languished through lack of government support.* 得不到政府的支持, 地方的食品生產漸漸失去了活力。| *The conversation was languishing.* 談話軟弱無力, 沒有效果。**3** [+for] to become ill and unhappy because you want someone or something very much〔因渴望得到某人或某物而〕變得憔悴, 悶悶不樂

lan·guor /ˋlæŋgɚ; 'læŋgə/ *n especially literary*【尤文】**1** [C,U] a pleasant feeling of tiredness or lack of strength 倦怠 **2** [U] pleasant or heavy stillness of the air 平靜, 沉悶: *the languor of a hot afternoon* 炎熱午後的沉悶 **3** [C] a feeling of sadness because you want someone or something very much 愁悶 —**languorous** *adj* —**languorously** *adv*

lank /læŋk; læŋk/ *adj* lank hair is thin, straight and unattractive〔頭髮〕稀疏的, 平直而難看的 —**lankly** *adv* —**lankness** *n* [U] —see picture on page A6 參見 A6 頁圖

lank·y /ˋlæŋkɪ; 'læŋki/ *adj* unattractively tall and thin 瘦高難看的: *long lanky legs* 又瘦又長的細腿 —**lankiness** *n* [U]

lan·o·lin /ˋlænəlɪn; 'lænəl-ɪ̵n/ *n* [U] an oil that is in sheep's wool and is used in skin creams 羊毛脂

lan·tern /ˋlæntɚn; 'læntən/ *n* [C] **1** a lamp that you can carry consisting of a metal or glass container surrounding a flame or light 燈籠, 提燈—see picture at 參見 LIGHT[1] 圖 **2** *technical* a structure at the top of a tower or LIGHTHOUSE, that has windows on all sides【術語】〔燈塔上的〕燈室 —see also 另見 CHINESE LANTERN, MAGIC LANTERN

lantern-jawed /,·· '·◂/ *adj* having a long narrow jaw and cheeks that sink inwards 下巴突出且雙頰深陷的

lan·yard /ˋlænjɚd; 'lænjəd/ *n* [C] **1** a short piece of rope, used on a ship to tie things〔船上繫物的〕短繩 **2** a thick string with a knife or whistle on it, that sailors wear around their necks〔水手用以繫小刀或哨子等的〕頸帶, 項帶

lap[1] /læp; læp/ *n*

1 ►LEGS 腿◄ [C] the upper part of your legs when you are sitting down〔人坐着時〕腰以下到膝為止的大腿部: *Come and sit on my lap, Ginny.* 吉尼, 過來坐在我的膝上。

2 ►RACE 賽跑◄ [C] one journey around or along a running track, race course etc〔跑道等的〕一圈; 一次往返: *Hill finished a lap ahead of his team-mate.* 希爾比他的隊友先跑完一圈。| **do/run/swim a lap** *Come on, let's do a few laps in the pool.* 快來, 讓我們在游泳池內游幾個來回。| **lap of honour** *BrE*【英】, **victory lap** *AmE*【美】(=a lap that you do after winning)〔優勝者的〕繞場一周

3 ►PART OF JOURNEY 部分旅程◄ [singular] a part of a long journey 長途旅行中的一段: *The last lap of their journey was by ship.* 他們最後的一段旅程是坐船。

4 in the lap of luxury having an easy, comfortable life with plenty of money, possessions etc 處在優裕、舒適的生活環境中

5 in the lap of the gods if the result of something is in the lap of the gods, you do not know what will happen 在神的掌控之中(的), 未來之事難以預料(的)

6 drop/dump sth in sb's lap *spoken* to make someone responsible for dealing with something difficult【口】把難事推給某人去做: *Ben just dumped all this work in my lap and told me to get on with it.* 班恩就把這工作全部往我身上一推, 讓我來完成它。

lap[2] *v*

1 ►SEA/LAKE/RIVER 海/湖/河◄ [I,T] if water laps something or laps against something such as the shore or a boat, it moves against it or hits it in small waves〔波浪〕輕輕拍打, 沖刷: **[+against]** *The water of the lake lapped gently against the rocks.* 湖水輕輕地拍打岩石。

2 ►DRINK 飲, 喝◄ [I, T] if an animal laps something, it drinks it by making small tongue movements〔動物〕舔飲

3 ►IN A RACE 在比賽中◄ **a)** [T] to pass a competitor in a race after having completed a whole lap more than they have 領先〔另一競賽者〕一圈: *Casey gave up after being lapped twice.* 凱西在被人超過了兩圈之後放棄了比賽。**b)** [I] to make a single journey around a track, race course etc in a particular time〔在特定時間內〕跑完一圈

4 ►PARTLY COVER 部分重疊◄ [I,T] *technical* if one thing laps another, a part of one covers part of the other; OVERLAP[1]【術語】(使) 部分重疊; 疊蓋

5 ►FOLD/WRAP 摺疊/包住◄ [T always+adv/prep] *literary* to fold or wrap something around something else【文】包住; 包圍; 裹住 —**lapping** *n* [U]

lap ↔ sth **up** *phr v* [T] **1** to get a lot of pleasure and enjoyment from something, without worrying about whether it is good, true etc〔不分良莠地〕欣然接受: *She seems to be lapping up all the attention she's getting.* 她似乎為自己得到的注意而高興。| *They sat listening to his story, spellbound, lapping it up.* 他們坐下來聽他的故事, 全都入了迷, 被吸引住了。**2** to drink all of something eagerly 暢飲

lap·a·ra·scope /ˋlæpɚəskop; 'læpərəskəʊp/ *n* [C] *technical* a piece of equipment with a lighted tube that a doctor uses to look inside someone's body【術語】腹腔鏡

lap·a·ros·cop·y /,læpəˋrɑskəpɪ; ,læpə'rɒskəpi/ *n* [C, U] *technical* an examination or medical operation on the inside of someone's body, using a laparoscope【術語】腹腔鏡檢查[手術]

lap belt /'· ·/ *n* [C] a type of safety belt that fits across your waist when you are sitting in the back of a car〔汽車上的〕安全帶

lap·dog /ˋlæp,dɔg; 'læpdɒg/ *n* [C] **1** a small pet dog 小寵物狗, 叭兒狗 **2** someone who is completely under the control of someone else and will do anything they say 趨炎附勢[仰人鼻息]的人

la·pel /ləˋpɛl; lə'pel/ *n* [C] the part of the front of a coat or JACKET (1) that is joined to the collar and folded back on each side〔西服上衣或夾克的〕翻領

lap·i·da·ry[1] /ˋlæpə,dɛrɪ; 'læpɪ̵dəri/ *adj* [only before noun 僅用於名詞前] *technical* connected with the cutting or polishing of valuable stones or jewels【術語】寶石雕刻[加工]的

lapidary[2] *n* [C] someone who is skilled in cutting and polishing jewels and valuable stones 玉石匠, 寶石匠

lap·is laz·u·li /ˋlæpɪs ˋlæzjəlɪ; ,læpɪ̵s 'læzjʊli/ *n* **1** [C, U] a valuable bright blue stone 天青石, 青金石 **2** [U] a bright blue colour 天青石色, 青金石色

lap robe /'· ·/ *n* [C] *AmE* a small thick BLANKET[1] (1) used to cover your legs when your are travelling【美】〔用來蓋腿的〕毛毯, 膝毯

lapse[1] /læps; læps/ *n* [C] **1** a short time when someone is careless or forgetful〔短暫的〕疏忽; 健忘: **[+in]** *There haven't been any lapses in security recently.* 近來在保安方面沒有出現過疏忽大意。| **[+of]** *A single lapse of* concentration cost Becker the game. 一時的失誤使得貝克爾輸掉了比賽。| **a memory lapse** (=when you cannot remember something for a short time) 一時記錯 **2** [C] a failure to do something you should do, especially to behave correctly〔尤指舉止〕疏忽, 過失, 過錯: *He didn't offer Darren a drink and Marie did not appear to notice the lapse.* 他沒有給達倫飲料, 瑪麗看來也沒有發現這一疏忽。**3** [C usually singular 一般用單數] a period of time between two events〔兩事件中的〕時間間隔: *The usual time lapse between request and delivery is two days.* 從要求訂購到交貨一般要兩天。| **[+of]** *a lapse of about ten seconds* 約十秒鐘的間隔

lapse² *v* [I] **1** to gradually come to an end or to stop for a period of time 慢慢地結束; 中止: *I let the conversation lapse and Kelly finally spoke up.* 我讓談話慢慢中止, 凱莉最終發言了。**2** if a contract, agreement, legal right etc lapses, it comes to an end, for example because an agreed time limit has passed〔合同、協議、合法權利等如因期限已過而〕終止, 失效

lapse into sth *phr v* [T] **1 lapse into silence/sleep/a daydream etc** to go into a quiet or less active state 陷入沉默／進入睡眠／做起白日夢等: *The girl lapsed into a sulky silence.* 女孩生起了悶氣。| *He lapsed into a coma and died two days later.* 他陷入了昏迷, 兩天後就死了。**2** to start behaving or speaking in a different and usually less good or acceptable way 陷入, 進入〔一般指背離正道〕: *Following his death, the Empire lapsed into chaos.* 他死後, 帝國就陷入了混亂之中。| *She would sometimes deliberately lapse into another dialect.* 她有時會故意用另一種方言說話。

lapsed /læpst; læpst/ *adj* [only before noun 僅用於名詞前] **1** no longer having the beliefs you had, especially religious beliefs 背棄的, 背教的: *a lapsed Catholic* 離經叛道的天主教徒 **2** *law* not used any more【法律】不再使用的, 過時的, 失效的

lap·top /ˈ· ·/ *n* [C] a small computer that you can carry with you 膝上型電腦; 手提電腦: *executives with their laptops* 配備有手提電腦的行政主管 —**lap·top** *adj*

lap·wing /ˈlæpˌwɪŋ; ˈlæpˌwɪŋ/ *n* [C] a small black and white European bird with raised feathers on its head; PEEWIT 田鳧(鳥); 麥雞

lar·board /ˈlarbɚd; ˈlɑːbəd/ *n* [U] *old-fashioned* the left side of a ship; PORT (4)【過時】左舷

lar·ce·nist /ˈlarsn̩ɪst; ˈlɑːsənɪst/ *n* [C] *law* a thief【法律】竊賊

lar·ce·ny /ˈlarsn̩ɪ; ˈlɑːsəni/ *n* [C, U] *law* the act or crime of stealing【法律】偷竊罪 —see also 另見 PETTY LARCENY

larch /lartʃ; lɑːtʃ/ *n* [C,U] a tree that looks like a PINE tree but drops its leaves in winter 落葉松

lard¹ /lard; lɑːd/ *n* [U] white fat from pigs that is used in cooking 豬油

lard² *v* [T] **1 be larded with sth** if a speech, piece of writing etc is larded with particular types of words or phrases, there are a lot of them in it〔講話和文章等〕大量使用[穿插]某類詞語: *a speech larded with Biblical quotations* 穿插很多聖經引文的講話 **2** to put small pieces of BACON onto meat before cooking it〔烹調前〕把小塊醃肉片鋪在〔其他〕肉上

lard-ass /ˈ· ·/ *n* [C] *AmE spoken* an insulting word for someone who is fat【美口】肥豬〔侮辱性詞語〕

lar·der /ˈlardɚ; ˈlɑːdə/ *n* [C] a small room or large cupboard for storing food in a house〔家中的〕食品貯藏室; 食品貯藏櫃

S1 W1 **large** /lardʒ; lɑːdʒ/ *adj*

1 ►BIG 大的◄ bigger or more than usual in number, amount, or size 大量的; 巨大的: *Los Angeles is the second largest city in the US.* 洛杉磯是美國第二大城市。| *The T-shirt comes in Small, Medium and Large.* 這種T恤有小號、中號和大號的貨。| *This could create a large number of new jobs.* 這可以創造一大批新的就業機會。| *The town has a large population of elderly people.* 該鎮的老年人口眾多。—see 見 WIDE (USAGE), BIG (USAGE)

2 ►PERSON 人◄ a large person is very tall and wide 身材高大的: *A large man with a shotgun blocked our path.* 一個身材高大、手持獵槍的人擋住了我們的去路。—see 見 FAT¹ (USAGE)

3 be at large if a dangerous person or animal is at large, they have escaped from somewhere and may cause harm or damage〔危險人物或動物〕在逃的; 不受控制的: *Two of the escaped prisoners are still at large.* 兩名逃犯仍逍遙法外。

4 the world/country/public at large people in general 全世界／全國／全體民眾: *The organization provides information on health issues to the public at large.* 這個組織向全體民眾提供關於健康問題的資料。

5 ►MORE GENERAL 更加普遍的◄ **the larger issues/view/picture** the important general facts and questions about a situation, problem etc 更重大的問題／更主要的觀點／更大的局面: *a useful book about the conflict, which helps to explain the larger picture* 一本關於這場衝突的有用書籍, 有助於解釋更廣泛的局勢

6 (as) large as life *spoken* used when someone has appeared or is present in a place where you did not expect to see them【口】確確實實(就在眼前)〔用於表示沒有料到某人的出現〕: *I turned a corner and there was Joe, as large as life.* 我在拐角處轉了個彎, 那不是喬嗎, 確確實實是他。

7 larger than life someone who is larger than life attracts a lot of attention because they are more amusing, attractive, or exciting than most people〔比多數人〕更有趣更具吸引力的, 與眾不同的, 極不平常的

8 in large part/measure *formal* mostly【正式】大部分, 基本上 —see also 另見 **by and large** (BY² (5)), **loom large** (LOOM² (3)), **writ large** (WRIT²) —**largeness** *n* [U]

large in·tes·tine /ˌ· ·ˈ··/ *n* [C] the lower part of your BOWELS, where food is changed into solid waste matter 大腸 —compare 比較 SMALL INTESTINE

large·ly /ˈlardʒlɪ; ˈlɑːdʒli/ *adv* mostly or mainly 大半地, 主要地: *The state of Nevada is largely desert.* 內華達州大部分是沙漠。| *Kevin's success is largely due to sheer hard work.* 凱文的成功主要靠踏踏實實的苦幹。 S3 W2

large-scale /ˌ· ˈ·◄/ *adj* [only before noun 僅用於名詞前] **1** using or involving a lot of effort, people, supplies etc 大規模的: *a large-scale rescue operation* 大規模的營救行動 **2** a large-scale map, model etc is drawn or made bigger than usual, so that more details can be shown〔地圖、模型等〕大型的, 用大比例尺製作的

lar·gesse, largess /larˈdʒɪs; lɑːˈʒes/ *n* [U] *formal* the quality or act of being generous and giving money or gifts to people who have less than you, or the money or gifts that you give【正式】慷慨的贈與; 賞金; 贈送之物

larg·ish /ˈlardʒɪʃ; ˈlɑːdʒɪʃ/ *adj informal* fairly big【非正式】相當大的

lar·go¹ /ˈlargo; ˈlɑːgəʊ/ *adj, adv technical* played or sung slowly and seriously【術語】演奏[唱]緩慢的[地], 莊嚴的[地]

largo² *n* [C] *technical* a piece of music played or sung slowly and seriously【術語】緩慢而莊嚴的樂章, 廣板

lar·i·at /ˈlærɪət; ˈlæriət/ *n* [C] *AmE* a LASSO¹【美】套索

lark¹ /lark; lɑːk/ *n* [C] **1** a small brown singing bird with long pointed wings; SKYLARK 百靈科鳥; 雲雀 **2** *informal* something that you do to amuse yourself or as a joke, especially something bad【非正式】玩笑, 玩樂〔尤指惡作劇〕: **do sth for a lark** *They hid her passport for a lark.* 他們把她的護照藏起來, 以此取樂。**3 blow/sod etc that for a lark** *BrE spoken* used when you stop doing something or refuse to do something because it needs too much effort【英口】開玩笑〔某事太費精力而不想幹時的用語〕: *Paint the whole room? Sod that for a lark!* 油漆整個房間? 簡直是開玩笑! **4 this dieting/exercise/gardening lark** *BrE spoken* used to describe an activity that you think is silly or unpleasant【英口】節食／鍛鍊／栽培花木這種無聊的事〔用於自認為愚蠢或使人不快的

活動〕: *Salad again? How long are you going to keep up this healthy eating lark?* 又是沙拉? 這種所謂的健康食物你還要吃多久? **5 be up with the lark** to get up very early 很早起牀 —see also 另見 **happy as a lark** (HAPPY (8))

lark² *v*

lark about/around *phr v* [I] *BrE informal* to have fun by behaving in a silly way【英, 非正式】胡鬧, 鬧着玩: *A group of kids was larking about near the shops.* 一羣小孩正在商店附近嬉鬧。

lar·va /ˋlɑrvə; ˈlɑːvə/ *n plural* **larvae** /-vi; -viː/ [C] a creature like a fat WORM that is a young insect which has left the egg and has not yet changed into an insect with wings〔昆蟲的〕幼蟲, 幼體 —**larval** *adj*

lar·yn·gi·tis /ˌlærɪnˋdʒaɪtɪs; ˌlærən̩ˈdʒaɪtəs/ *n* [U] an illness which makes talking difficult because your larynx and throat are swollen 喉炎

lar·ynx /ˋlærɪŋks; ˈlærɪŋks/ *n plural* **larynges** /ləˋrɪndʒiz; ləˈrɪndʒiːz/ or **larynxes** [C] *technical* the hollow box-like part in your throat where you make voice sounds【術語】喉 —see picture at 參見 RESPIRATORY 圖

la·sa·gne *BrE*【英】, **lasagna** *AmE*【美】/ləˋzɑnjə; ləˈsænjə/ *n* [C,U] a type of Italian food made with flat pieces of PASTA, meat or vegetables, cheese and a SAUCE made with milk〔一種意大利〕鹵汁寬麵條

las·civ·i·ous /ləˋsɪvɪəs; ləˈsɪviəs/ *adj* showing strong sexual desire 好色的, 淫蕩的; 猥褻的: *Mandy gave him a lascivious wink.* 曼迪挑逗地瞟了他一眼。—**lasciviously** *adv* —**lasciviousness** *n* [U]

la·ser /ˋlezɚ; ˈleɪzə/ *n* [C] a piece of equipment that produces a powerful narrow beam of light that can be used in medical operations, to cut metals, or to make patterns of light for entertainment 激光(器), 雷射(裝置): *laser surgery* 激光(外科)手術

laser disk /ˈ·· ˌ·/ *n* [C] a computer DISK that can be read by laser light 激光磁碟[盤], 雷射光碟[盤]

laser print·er /ˈ·· ˌ··/ *n* [C] a machine connected to a computer system that prints by using laser light 激光[雷射]打印機 —see picture on page A14 參見 A14 頁圖

lash¹ /læʃ; læʃ/ *v*

1 ▶TIE 捆紮◀ [T always+adv/prep] to tie something tightly to something else with a rope, or tie two things together〔用繩〕把…與…捆在一起, 把…捆在一起: **lash sth to/onto etc** *The oars were lashed to the sides of the boat.* 槳拴在船的兩側。

2 ▶WIND/RAIN ETC 風/雨等◀ [I always+adv/prep, T] to hit against something with violent force 猛擊: *The rain lashed her face.* 雨點擊打着她的臉。| *waves lashing the shore* 波浪猛烈地拍擊岸邊 | **[+against/down/across]** *The wind lashed violently against the door.* 風猛烈地撞擊着大門。

3 ▶HIT 擊打◀ [I,T] to hit someone very hard with a whip, stick etc 鞭打, 抽打: *The guards would lash any of the prisoners who fell behind.* 衛兵總會鞭打落在後面的犯人。

4 ▶TAIL 尾巴◀ [I,T] if an animal lashes its tail or its tail lashes, it moves it from side to side quickly and strongly, especially because it is angry〔尤指動物生氣時〕擺動尾巴, 用尾巴抽動

5 ▶CRITICIZE 批評◀ [T] a word meaning to criticize someone angrily, used especially in newspapers 抨擊: *Judge lashes drug-dealers.* 法官猛烈抨擊毒品販子。

6 lash sb into a fury/rage/frenzy etc to deliberately make a group of people have strong violent feelings 煽動〔羣眾〕: *The crowd was being lashed into a frenzy by the speaker.* 人羣的憤怒情緒正被演講者煽動起來。

lash out *phr v* [I] **1** to suddenly speak angrily to someone 猛烈抨擊, 痛斥: **[+at]** *I used to lash out at my children for no reason.* 過去我經常無緣無故地訓斥我的孩子。**2** to try to hit someone, with a series of violent, uncontrolled movements 瘋狂地攻擊: *In its panic, the bear started to lash out.* 熊在驚慌之中開始猛擊。

lash² *n* [C] **1** a hit with a whip, especially as a punishment 鞭打: *They were each given fifty lashes.* 他們每人挨了五十鞭。**2** [usually plural 一般用複數] one of the hairs that grow around the edge of your eyes; EYELASH 睫毛 **3** a sudden or violent movement like that of a whip 突然猛烈的一甩: *With a lash of its tail, the lion sprang at its prey.* 獅子猛地甩了一下尾巴就向牠的獵物撲了過去。**4** the thin piece of leather at the end of a whip 鞭梢

lash·ing /ˋlæʃɪŋ; ˈlæʃɪŋ/ *n* [C] **1 lashings of** *BrE old-fashioned* a large amount of food or drink【英, 過時】大量的〔食品或飲料〕: *apple pie with lashings of cream* 塗有大量奶油的蘋果餡餅 **2** a punishment of hitting someone with a whip 鞭笞 **3** a rope that fastens something tightly to something else 捆綁用的繩索, 繫索

lash-up /ˈ· ·/ *n* [C] *BrE informal* an arrangement of things, for example electrical equipment or wires, put together quickly to be used for only a short time【英, 非正式】應急辦法, 應急之物, 臨時湊合的東西

lass /læs; læs/ also 又作 **las·sie** /ˋlæsɪ; ˈlæsi/ *n* [C] *ScotE & NEngE*【蘇格蘭和英格蘭北部】**1** a girl or young woman 女孩, 少女 **2** a girlfriend 女友 —compare 比較 LAD

las·si·tude /ˋlæsəˌtjud; ˈlæsətjuːd/ *n* [U] *formal*【正式】**1** tiredness and lack of energy 疲倦, 疲乏 **2** laziness or lack of interest 懶惰, 厭倦: *Cheam was accused of moral lassitude.* 奇姆被指責為不仁不義。

las·so¹ /læˋsu; ləˈsuː/ *n* [C] a rope with one end tied in a circle, used to catch cattle and horses, especially in the western US〔尤指美國西部套捕牛、馬等用的〕套索

lasso² *v* [T] to catch an animal using a lasso〔用套索〕套捕

last 最近的

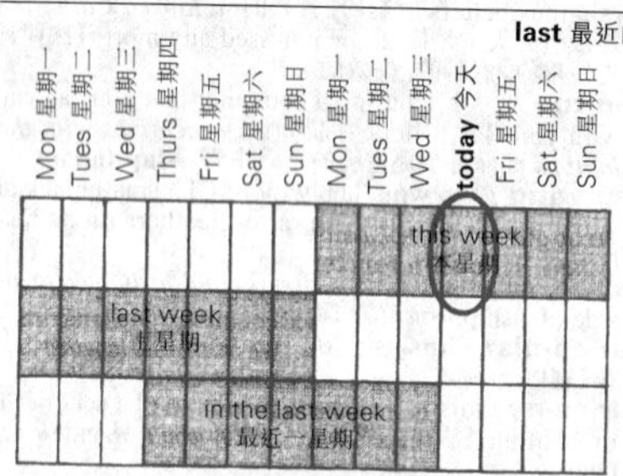

last¹ /læst; lɑːst/ *determiner* **1** most recent; the nearest one to the present time 最近的, 最近一段時間的, 最近一次的: *I haven't seen you since the last meeting.* 自從上次會面後, 我再沒有見到你。| **last night/week/year etc** *Did you watch the game on TV last night?* 昨晚你在電視上看比賽了沒有? | *Fashion has changed in the last twenty years.* 在過去的二十年中時裝潮流發生了變化。| **(the) last time** (=the most recent occasion) 上一次 | *The last time I spoke to Bob he seemed happy enough.* 上次我跟鮑勃說話的時候, 他顯得夠高興的。—compare 比較 NEXT¹ (2) **2** happening or existing at the end, with no others after 最後的: *I didn't read the last chapter of the book.* 我還沒有讀這本書的最後一章。| *Anna was the last person to see him alive.* 安娜是最後一個見到他活着的人。**3** remaining after all others have gone, been used etc 最後剩下的: *Is this your last cigarette?* 這是你最後一支煙嗎? | *These are the last four birds of their kind still in existence.* 這些鳥是這類鳥中僅存的四隻。**4 the last person/thing a)** one that you did not expect at all 最未料到的人[事]: *She's the last person I'd expect to meet in a disco.* 我怎麼也想不到會在迪斯科舞廳中見到她。**b)** one that you do not want at all, that is most unsuitable etc 最不想要的人[事]; 最不合適的人[事]: *The* *last thing we wanted was for the newspapers to find out what was going on.* 我們最不希望報界發現所發生的事。**5 last thing (at night)** at the very end of the day 在一天的末了: *Take a couple of these pills last thing at night to help you get to sleep.* 晚上睡前吃兩顆藥丸以幫助入睡。**6 on your last legs** *informal*【非正式】**a)** very tired 很疲倦的: *Sarah looks as if she's on her last legs.* 莎拉看上去似乎很疲憊。**b)** very ill and likely to die soon 病危的 **7 on its last legs** *informal* old or in bad condition, and likely to stop working soon【非正式】老化的, 糟透的: *We'll have to get a new lawn mower this year – the old one is really on its last legs.* 今年我們得買一台新的割草機 —— 原來那台真的不好用了。**8 have the last word a)** to make the last statement in an argument, which gives you an advantage〔在爭論中〕作最後的陳述〔具有一定優勢〕**b)** to be the person who makes the final decision on something 作最終的裁定, 為最後的決定者: *The finance committee always has the last word on expenditure.* 在開支上財政委員會總是最後的決定者。**9 be the last word in** to be the best, most modern, or most comfortable example of something 在…方面是最好[現代; 舒適]的: *It's the last word in luxury holidays.* 這是最舒服的豪華假期。

1 1 **last²** *adv* **1** most recently before now 最近, 上次: *When I last saw her, she was working in New York.* 我上次見到她時, 她正在紐約工作。**2** after everything or everyone else 最後: *They told me I'd be interviewed last.* 他們告訴我, 我最後一個接受面試。| *Mix together flour, butter, and sugar, and add the eggs last.* 把麵粉、牛油和砂糖混在一起, 最後加上雞蛋。| **last of all** (=used when giving a final point or piece of information) 最後(一點[一條]) *Last of all, I'd like to thank the catering staff for a splendid meal.* 最後我要感謝提供美餐的員工們。**3 last but not least** used when mentioning the last person or thing in a list, to emphasize that they are still important 最後但並非最不重要的(一點): *Last but not least, let me introduce Jane, our new secretary.* 最後但同樣重要的是, 讓我來介紹簡, 我們新來的祕書。

1 1 **last³** *n, pron* **1 the last** the person or thing that comes after all the others 最後的人[事物]: *He was the first to arrive and the last to leave.* 他是最早到又最晚走的一個人。| *I think this box is the last.* 我想這個盒子是最後一個。**2 at (long) last** if something happens at last, it happens after you have waited a long time 最終, 終於: *I'm so pleased that Jane's managed to get a job at last.* 簡終於找到工作了, 我真為此感到高興。—see 見 LASTLY (USAGE) **3 the day/week/year etc before last** the day, week etc before the one that has just finished 前天/上上週/前年等: *I sent the letter off the week before last.* 上上週我把信寄出了。**4 the last of** the remaining parts of something 最後剩下的…: *Joan took the last of the meat from the dish and passed it to her mother.* 瓊拿起了盤中最後剩下的肉遞給她母親。**5 haven't heard the last of** if you have not heard the last of a problem, it has not yet finished and it may cause problems for you in the future …還未了結: *I have a nasty feeling we haven't heard the last of this.* 我有一種不好的感覺, 這件事還沒有了結。**6 the last I heard** *spoken* used to tell someone the most recent news that you know about a person or situation【口】最近聽到的消息〔告訴別人知道的最新消息時的用語〕: *The last I heard, she was going back to college to study law.* 最近聽說, 她正打算回校去學習法律。**7 to the last** *formal* until the end of an event or the end of someone's life【正式】直到終了; 至死: *He died in 1987, insisting to the last he was innocent.* 他死於 1987 年, 至死仍堅稱自己是清白的。

1 2 **last⁴** *v* **1** [I always+adv/prep, linking verb 連繫動詞] to continue for a particular length of time 持續: [+for/until/through etc] *The hot weather lasted for the whole month of June.* 炎熱的天氣在六月份持續整整一個月。| **last an hour/ten minutes etc** *Each lesson lasts an hour.* 每堂課持續一小時。| *The ceasefire didn't last long.* 停火時間不長。**2** [I] to continue to exist or remain in good condition for a long time 繼續存在, 保持良好狀態: *This good weather won't last.* 這種好天氣不會持續很久。| *We wondered whether all this concern about the environment would really last.* 我們對於所有這種對環境的關心是否會真的保持下去感到懷疑。**3** [I+adv/prep] to manage to remain in the same situation, even when this is difficult 盡力維持原狀: *They won't be able to last much longer without fresh supplies.* 沒有新的供應, 他們就不能維持多久了。| *The new manager is very inexperienced – I doubt if he'll last long.* 新經理很沒有經驗 —— 我懷疑他是否能繼續待下去。**4** [linking verb 連繫動詞] to be enough for someone to use 足夠〔某人〕使用 **last (sb) two days/three weeks etc** 讓〔某人〕夠用兩天/三週等: *The water supply should last another 48 hours.* 供水可以再用 48 小時。| *We only had $50 to last us the rest of the month.* 我們只有 50 美元來度過這個月餘下的日子。

last⁵ *n* [C] a piece of wood or metal shaped like a human foot, used by a shoemaker 鞋楦

last call /ˌ· ˈ·/ *n* [C] *AmE* the words used by the person who is in charge of a bar when it is going to close and people can order just one more drink【美】最後一杯〔酒吧負責人在酒吧快打烊時的用語〕; LAST ORDERS *BrE*【英】

last-ditch /ˌ· ˈ·◂/ *adj* **a last-ditch attempt/effort etc** a final attempt to achieve something before it is too late 最後的圖謀/努力等: *The negotiators made a last-ditch effort to reach an agreement.* 談判者為達成協議盡了最後的努力。

last hur·rah /ˌ· ·ˈ·/ *n* [C usually singular 一般用單數] *AmE* a final effort, event etc at the end of a long period of work etc【美】最後的努力[一搏]

last·ing /ˈlæstɪŋ; ˈlɑːstɪŋ/ *adj* strong enough, well enough planned etc to last for a very long time 持久的, 耐久的: *The reforms will bring lasting benefits.* 改革將帶來長遠的利益。| *a lasting peace settlement* 持久的和平協議 | **leave a lasting impression** *Our first meeting left a lasting impression on me.* 我們的第一次見面給我留下了不可磨滅的印象。

last judg·ment /ˌ· ˈ··/ *n* **the last judgment** the time after death when everyone is judged by God for what they have done in life, according to Christianity and some other religions; JUDGMENT DAY〔基督教及其他一些宗教所稱的上帝對人類的〕末日審判; 最終審判(日)

last·ly /ˈlæstlɪ; ˈlɑːstli/ *adv* [sentence adverb 句子副詞] used when you want to say one more thing at the end of a list 最後(一點): *Lastly, could I ask all of you to keep this information secret.* 最後, 我請求各位對這一消息嚴守祕密。

USAGE NOTE 用法說明: LASTLY

WORD CHOICE 詞語辨析: **lastly, last of all, finally, in the end, at last**

Lastly, last of all and **finally** are often used to end a set of points where time is not involved. lastly、last of all 和 finally 都常用以結束不考慮時間因素的一系列要點: *There are three reasons why I hate him: first(ly) he's rude, second(ly) he's a liar, and lastly/last of all/finally he owes me money* (NOT 不用 *at last*). 我討厭他有三個原因: 第一, 他很粗魯; 第二, 他是個騙子; 最後一點是他欠我錢。

Last (of all) and **finally** also end a set of actions, often at points of time. last (of all) 和 finally 亦用來結束一系列動作, 經常按照時間的順序排列: *First I get dressed, next I bring in the paper, then I feed the cat, and last/finally I fix my breakfast* (NOT 不用 *at last*). 首先我穿好衣服, 然後把報紙拿進來, 接着餵貓, 最後準備早餐。

Finally is also used, like **in the end**, just to mark something as happening after a long period of time.

L

finally 和 in the end 一樣, 僅用來表示很長時間後發生的事: *I tried hard and finally/in the end I managed it.* 我盡了很大努力, 最終我成功了。| *He fell ill and finally died/in the end he died.* 他病倒了, 最終撒手人寰。

At last has a similar use, but only when something good happens after a period of time. at last 用法相仿, 區別在於經過一段時間後所發生的是好事: *I tried and at last I managed it.* 我盡了努力, 終於完成了。| *At last I have a good dictionary!* (=I have waited a long time to find one). 我終於有了一本好詞典〔=我等了好長時間才找到它〕。

last-minu·te /ˌ· ˈ··◂/ *adj* [only before noun 僅用於名詞前] happening or done as late as possible within a process, event, or activity 最後一分鐘的, 緊要關頭的: *last-minute changes to the script* 手稿最後一刻的改動

last name /ˌ· ˈ·/ *n* [C] *especially AmE* a SURNAME【尤美】姓

last or·ders /ˌ· ˈ··/ *n* [plural] *BrE* the words used by the person who is in charge of a bar or PUB when it is going to close and people can order just one more drink【英】最後一杯〔酒吧負責人在酒吧快打烊時的用語〕; LAST CALL *AmE*【美】

last post /ˌ· ˈ·/ *n* **the last post** the tune played on a BUGLE at British military funerals, or to call soldiers back to camp for the night〔英國〕軍人葬禮號;〔軍人的〕夜間回營號

last rites /ˌ· ˈ·/ *n* [plural] the ceremony performed in some religions, especially the Catholic religion, for people who are dying〔尤指天主教〕為臨終者舉行的聖禮

lat the written abbreviation of 縮寫 = LATITUDE

latch[1] /lætʃ; lætʃ/ *n* [C] **1** a small metal bar that drops into a U-shaped object to keep doors, gates, windows etc closed〔門或窗的〕閂: *Gwen lifted the latch and opened the gate.* 格溫提起門閂開門。**2** *especially BrE* a kind of lock for a door that you can open from the inside by turning a handle but that you need a key to open from the outside【尤英】碰鎖, 碰簧鎖: **on the latch** (=shut but not locked) 閂上〔關上但沒有鎖上〕 *Ray went out, leaving the door on the latch.* 雷伊走出去, 把門閂上了。

latch[2] *v* [T] to fasten a door, window etc with a latch 用碰(簧)鎖鎖上〔門窗等〕

latch on *phr v* [I] *BrE informal* to understand【英, 非正式】理解: *He's so thick it took him ages to latch on.* 他這麼笨, 花了很長時間才能理解。

latch onto sb/sth *phr v* [T] *informal*【非正式】**1** to follow someone and keep trying to talk to them, get their attention etc, especially when they would prefer to be left alone 纏住…不放: *He latched onto Sandy at the party and wouldn't go away.* 在派對上他纏住桑迪不放。**2** get very interested in something so that you spend a lot of time thinking about it or discussing it 對〔某事〕深感興趣: *It's the kind of issue that the media really latch onto.* 這確實是媒體深感興趣的問題。

latch·key /ˈlætʃˌki; ˈlætʃkiː/ *n* [C] **1** a key that opens a lock on an outside door of a house or apartment〔住所大門的〕碰(簧)鎖的鑰匙; 公寓門上的鑰匙 **2 latchkey kid** *old-fashioned* a child whose parents both work and who spends time alone in the house after school【過時】掛鑰匙的兒童〔父母都外出上班的孩子, 放學後獨自待在家中〕

S1 W1 **late**[1] /let; leɪt/ *adj*

1 ▶AFTER EXPECTED TIME 晚於預期時間◀ arriving, happening, or done after the time that was expected, agreed, or arranged 晚的, 遲的; 遲到的: *Sorry I'm late – I overslept.* 對不起, 來晚了——我睡過頭了。| *The train was late.* 火車晚點了。| *We apologize for the late departure of flight AZ709.* 我們為 AZ709 航班的延誤起飛表示道歉。| *Are we too late to get tickets?* 我們是不是太晚了而拿不到門票了? | [+for] *Cheryl overslept and was late for school.* 徹麗爾睡過了頭, 上學遲到了。

2 ▶AFTER USUAL TIME 晚於通常時間◀ happening or done after the usual or normal time 晚的: *a late breakfast* 晚早餐 | *The harvest was rather late this year.* 今年的收穫季節來得相當晚。

3 ▶NEAR THE END 將近末尾◀ [only before noun 僅用於名詞前] near to the end of a period of time 晚期的, 後期的: *the late eighteenth century* 十八世紀末期 | *Paul's in his late forties.* 保羅快五十歲了。

4 as late as used to express surprise that something considered old-fashioned was still happening so recently〔過時的東西〕到…如此晚的時候仍然在發生〔表示驚訝〕: *Capital punishment was still used in Britain as late as the 1950s.* 直到 20 世紀 50 年代英國還在沿用死刑。

5 ▶PAYMENTS ETC 支付等◀ **a)** paid, given back etc after the agreed date 遲付的, 遲還回的: *There are strict penalties if repayments on the loan are late.* 若不能按時支付貸款會有嚴格的處罰。**b) be late with** to pay something, bring something back etc after the agreed date 遲交款的, 遲還回的: *We try never to be late with the rent.* 我們盡量不拖欠租金。

6 ▶EVENING 晚上◀ [only before noun 僅用於名詞前] near the end of the day 臨近一天之末的: *the late movie* 夜場電影 | *We stopped by for a late drink.* 我們夜裡順便拜訪來喝一杯。

7 her late husband/the late president etc used to talk about someone who has died 她的先夫/已故總統等

8 a late developer a child whose physical size or character develops slowly 發育晚的孩子

9 it's (a little) late in the day used to show disapproval because someone has done something too late for it to be effective 已(有點)晚了〔抱怨做事太晚而失去效用〕: *It's a little late in the day to say you're sorry!* 說對不起已有點晚了!

10 late of *formal* having lived in a place until fairly recently【正式】不久前住在〔某地〕的: *Billy Hicks, late of this parish* 不久前住在這一教區的比利·希克斯

late[2] *adv* **1** after or later than the usual time 晚於〔通常時間〕: *The stores are open late on Thursdays.* 這些商店星期四開門晚。| *Ellen has to work late tonight.* 艾倫今晚得工作到很晚。**2** after the arranged or expected time 遲, 晚; 遲於安排[預期]的時間: *The bus came ten minutes late.* 公共汽車晚到了十分鐘。**3** near to the end of a period of time or an event〔時期或事件〕臨近末尾: **late in August/the evening/1995** *The wedding took place late in May.* 婚禮在五月底舉行。**4 of late** *formal* recently【正式】最近: *Maureen hasn't been feeling too well of late.* 莫琳最近一直感到不太舒服。**5 late in life** if you do something late in life, you do it at an older age than most people do it 比一般人年歲大一點〔幹某事〕 **6 better late than never** used to say that you are glad someone has done something, or that they should do something, although they are late 遲做總比不做好 — see also 另見 **be running late** (RUN[1] (48)) 

late-break·ing /ˈ· ˌ··/ *adj* late-breaking news concerns events that happen just before a news broadcast or just before a newspaper is printed〔消息〕剛得到的;〔事件〕剛發生的

late·com·er /ˈletˌkʌmɚ; ˈleɪtˌkʌmə/ *n* [C] someone who arrives late 遲到者, 後來者; 新進者

late·ly /ˈletlɪ; ˈleɪtli/ *adv* recently 近來, 最近: *I've been feeling ill just lately.* 最近我感到不適。

late-night /ˈ· ·/ *adj* [only before noun 僅用於名詞前] happening late at night 深夜的, (後)半夜的: *late-night television* 午夜的電視節目 | *late-night shopping* 晚間購物

la·tent /ˈletn̩t; ˈleɪtənt/ *adj* something that is latent is present but hidden, and may develop or become more noticeable in the future 潛在的, 潛伏的: *The virus remains latent in the body for many years.* 該病毒在體

內潛伏了許多年。| *latent aggression* 潛在的侵略 — **latency** *n* [U]

latent heat /ˌ·· ˈ·/ *n* [U] *technical* the additional heat necessary to change a solid into a liquid, or a liquid into a gas【術語】潛熱

1 1 **lat·er¹** /ˈletə; ˈleɪtə/ *adv* **1** after the time you are talking about or after the present time 後來, 此時以後: *I'm going out for a bit – I'll see you later.* 我出去一會兒 —— 回頭見。| **two years later/three weeks later etc** *He became Senator two years later.* 兩年後他成了參議員。| **later that day/ morning/week** *The baby died later that night.* 嬰兒在那晚的後半夜夭折。| **later in the day/week/year** *The dentist could fit you in later in the week.* 牙醫可以在後半週給你補牙。—see 見 LASTLY (USAGE) **2 later on** at some time later or in the future 過後, 以後, 將來: *I can't eat all of this – I'll finish it later on.* 我吃不下所有的東西 —— 我過後才吃完它。**3 not later than** used when saying that something must be done by a particular time in the future 不得晚於, 須早於: *Completed entry forms should arrive not later than 31st July.* 填寫好的參加表格不得晚於 7 月 31 日遞交。

later² *adj* [only before noun 僅用於名詞前] **1** coming in the future or after something else 較晚時候的, 以後的: *The role of marketing is dealt with in a later chapter.* 市場銷售的作用會在稍後的一章中述及。| *The launch was postponed to a later date.* 發射延期了。**2** more recent 更新近的: *The engine has been greatly improved in later models.* 在新近的型號中引擎作了很大的改進。**3 in later years/life** when someone is older 在晚年: *Using a sunscreen when you are young helps you to have healthy skin in later years.* 年輕的時候使用防曬油會使你在年老時擁有健康的皮膚。

lat·e·ral¹ /ˈlætərəl; ˈlætərəl/ *adj technical* connected with the sides of something, or movement to the side【術語】側面的; 橫 (向) 的: *The wall is weak and requires lateral support.* 牆體不堅固, 需要側面的支撐。—**laterally** *adv*

lateral² *n* [C] *technical* something that is at the side or comes from the side【術語】在側面的東西; 橫向伸出的東西

lateral think·ing /ˌ··· ˈ··/ *n* [U] a way of thinking in which you use your imagination to make connections between things that are not normally thought of together 橫向思考 (法)

lat·est¹ /ˈletɪst; ˈleɪtɪ̈st/ *adj* [only before noun 僅用於名詞前] the most recent or the newest 最近的; 最新的: *all the latest gossip* 最近所有的流言蜚語 | *Metallica's latest album* 金屬製品樂隊的最新專輯

latest² *n* **1 the latest** *informal* the most recent news, fashion, or technical improvement【非正式】最新消息 [款式; 技術改進]: *the latest in computer software* 最新的電腦軟件 **2 at the latest** no later than the time mentioned 最遲, 最晚: *I should be back by 11 o'clock at the latest.* 我最遲 11 點會回來。

la·tex /ˈletɛks; ˈleɪteks/ *n* [U] **1** a thick whitish liquid produced by some plants, especially the rubber tree 膠乳; (尤指橡膠樹的) 橡漿 **2** an artificial substance similar to this, used in making paint, glue etc (人工的) 膠乳

lath /læθ; lɑːθ/ *n* [C] /læθs; lɑːðz/ a long flat narrow piece of wood used in building to support PLASTER (=material used to cover walls) (木) 板條

lathe /leð; leɪð/ *n* [C] a machine that shapes wood or metal, by turning it round and round against a sharp tool 車牀

la·ther¹ /ˈlæðə; ˈlɑːðə/ *n* [singular, U] **1** a white mass of BUBBLEs produced by mixing soap in water (肥皂水等的) 泡沫 **2** a white mass that forms on a horse's skin when it has been sweating (SWEAT¹ (1)) (馬的) 汗沫 **3 in a lather** *BrE informal* very anxious, especially because you do not have enough time【英, 非正式】(尤指因時間不足而) 緊張不安, 着急, 焦躁 —**lathery** *adj*

lather² *v* **1** [I] to produce a lather 起泡沫: *This soap lathers really well.* 這種肥皂真的易起泡沫。**2** [T] to cover something with lather (用泡沫) 覆蓋 (某物) **3** [T] *informal* to hit someone violently【非正式】狠擊 (某人)

Lat·in¹ /ˈlætn; ˈlætɪn/ *n* **1** [U] the language of the ancient Romans 拉丁語; 拉丁系語言 **2** [C] someone who comes from Southern Europe 拉丁人 (指歐洲南部的人)

Latin² *adj* **1** written in Latin 用拉丁語寫成的: *a Latin text* 拉丁文版本 **2** connected with a nation that speaks a language such as Italian, Spanish, or Portuguese that developed from Latin 拉丁語系各民族的 (如意大利人、西班牙人, 或葡萄牙人)

Latin A·mer·i·can /ˌ·· ·ˈ···◂/ *adj* connected with South or Central America 拉丁美洲的

La·ti·no /læˈtino; læˈtiːnəʊ/ *n* [C] *AmE* someone living in the US whose family came from a Central or South American country【美】(居住在美國的) 拉丁美洲人 — **Latino** *adj*: *Latino culture* 拉丁美洲文化

lat·i·tude /ˈlætəˌtjud; ˈlætɪ̈tjuːd/ *n* **1** [C,U] *technical* the distance north or south of the EQUATOR (=the imaginary line around the middle of the world) measured in degrees【術語】緯度 —compare 比較 LONGITUDE —see picture at 參見 EARTH¹ 圖 **2 latitudes** [plural] an area at a particular latitude 特指的緯度區域: *At these latitudes you often get strong winds.* 在這些緯度地區經常有大風。**3** [U] *formal* freedom to choose what you do or say【正式】自由度, 選擇的餘地: *Pupils enjoy considerable latitude in deciding what they want to study.* 小學生們想學甚麼有相當大的選擇餘地。—**latitudinal** /ˌlætəˈtjudənḷ; ˌlætɪ̈ˈtjuːdɪ̈nəl/ *adj*

lat·i·tu·di·na·ri·an /ˌlætəˌtudṇˈɛrɪən; ˌlætɪ̈tjuːdɪ̈ˈneəriən/ *n* [C] *formal* someone who is willing to accept other people's beliefs and behaviour【正式】樂於接納他人信仰和行為的人 —**latitudinarian** *adj*

lat·ke /ˈlɑtkə; ˈlɑːtkə/ *n* [C] a Jewish food like a round flat PANCAKE made from raw potato 馬鈴薯烙餅 (猶太食品)

la·trine /ləˈtrin; ləˈtriːn/ *n* [C] a toilet that is outdoors in a camp or military area (營地或軍營的) 戶外廁所

lat·ter¹ /ˈlætə; ˈlætə/ *n* **the latter** *formal* the second of two people or things just mentioned【正式】(剛提及的兩個人或物中的) 後者: *The system brings both financial and environmental benefits, the latter being especially welcome.* 該制度對財政和環境都有益處, 後者特別受歡迎。—opposite 反義詞 FORMER² (1) 2

latter² *adj* [only before noun 僅用於名詞前] *formal*【正式】**1** being the second of two people or things, or the last in a list just mentioned (兩者之中的) 後者 (的); (剛提到的列單之中的) 最後者 (的): *In the latter case, buyers pay a 15% commission.* 在後一種的情況下, 購買者付 15% 的佣金。**2** the latter part of a period of time is nearest to the end of it 末期的, 後期的: *Celebrations are planned for the latter part of November.* 慶祝計劃在十一月下旬舉行。

latter-day /ˈ·· ·/ *adj* [only before noun 僅用於名詞前] **a latter-day Versailles/Tsar/Robin Hood etc** something or someone that exists now but is like a famous thing or person that existed in the past 當今的凡爾賽/沙皇/羅賓漢等: *ruling his business empire like a latter-day Tsar* 像當代的沙皇一樣統治着他的商業帝國

Latter-Day Saints /ˌ·· ·ˈ·/ *n* [plural] the MORMONs 末世聖徒, 摩門教教徒

lat·ter·ly /ˈlætəlɪ; ˈlætəli/ *adv formal*【正式】**1** recently 近來, 最近: *Jim's behaviour has been a little strange latterly.* 吉姆的舉止近來一直有點古怪。**2** towards the end of a period of time (一段時間的) 末期: *O'Rourke retired after a 15-year career with Bisons, latterly as chief executive.* 奧羅克在比森斯公司工作了 15 年, 後來以總裁身分退休。—compare 比較 FORMERLY

lat·tice /ˈlætɪs; ˈlætɪ̈s/ *n* [C] **1** also 又作 **lat·tice·work** /ˈlætɪsˌwɝk; ˈlætɪ̈swɜːk/ a pattern or structure made of long flat narrow pieces of wood, plastic etc that are arranged so that they cross each other and the spaces between them are shaped like diamonds (DIAMOND (2)) 格

L

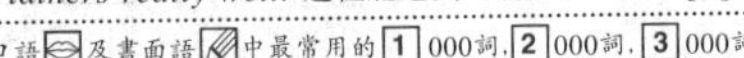

子圖案[結構] **2 lattice window** a type of window made of a pattern of many small pieces of glass shaped like diamonds (DIAMOND (2)) 格子窗 **3** *technical* a regular arrangement of objects over an area or in space【術語】晶格; 格構

laud /lɔd; lɔːd/ *v* [T] *formal* to praise someone or something【正式】稱讚, 讚美

lau·da·ble /ˈlɔdəbḷ; ˈlɔːdəbəl/ *adj formal* deserving praise or admiration, even if not completely successful【正式】值得稱讚[讚美]的: *a laudable attempt* 值得稱讚的嘗試 —**laudably** *adv*

lau·da·num /ˈlɔdənəm; ˈlɔːdənəm/ *n* [U] a substance containing the drug OPIUM, used in the past to control pain and help people to sleep 鴉片酊[酒]

lau·da·to·ry /ˈlɔdəˌtɔri; ˈlɔːdətəri/ *adj formal* expressing praise or admiration【正式】表達稱頌[讚美]的: *a laudatory biography* 頌揚性的傳記

2 2 **laugh¹** /læf; lɑːf/ *v*

1 ►MAKE SOUND 發出聲音◄ [I] to make the sounds and movements of the face that people make when they think something is funny 發出笑聲, 笑: *Jonathan kept pulling funny faces at me, and I couldn't stop laughing.* 喬納森一直朝我扮鬼臉, 我禁不住大笑。| [+at/about] *I couldn't understand why they were all laughing at me.* 我不明白他們為甚麼都在笑我。| **burst out laughing** (=suddenly start laughing) 突然放聲大笑 *When we saw what had happened to the cake we burst out laughing.* 當我們見到蛋糕變成的模樣時, 我們爆發出一陣大笑。| **laugh your head off** (=laugh loudly and a lot) 大笑不止 | **laugh out loud** (=suddenly laugh loudly) 突然放聲大笑

2 ►SPEAK 說話◄ [T] to say something in a voice that shows you are amused 笑着說: *"You look ridiculous!" Nick laughed.* "你看起來很可笑!"尼克笑着說。

3 be laughing *spoken* to be happy or in a good situation, for example because something has had a successful result for you【口】正高興; 處於佳境中: *Well they paid me, didn't they, so I'm laughing.* 喏, 他們付錢給我了, 是不是, 所以我正高興呢。

4 don't make me laugh *spoken* used when someone has just told you something that is completely untrue, asked for something impossible etc【口】別跟我說笑話了: *"Do you think we'll finish this today?" "Don't make me laugh."* "你認為我們今天會完成這個嗎?" "別跟我說笑話了。"

5 no laughing matter *informal* something serious that should not be joked about【非正式】嚴肅的事, 不是鬧着玩的事: *Losing your job is no laughing matter.* 把工作丟了, 這可不是鬧着玩的事。

6 be laughing all the way to the bank *informal* to be in a good situation because you have made a lot of money without making much effort【非正式】一路笑着去銀行〔因賺錢容易而開心愉快〕

7 be laughed out of court *especially BrE* if a person or idea is laughed out of court, the idea is not accepted because people think it is completely stupid【尤英】對…一笑了之; 不予考慮: *We can't propose that! We'd be laughed out of court!* 我們不能提那建議!我們會被瞧不起的!

8 sb will be laughing on the other side of their face *spoken* used unkindly to mean that although someone is happy or confident now, they will be in trouble or in difficulty later【口】〔某人將〕轉笑為哭, 轉喜為憂

9 laughing stock someone who has done something so stupid that everyone laughs at them 笑柄, 笑料: *He was the laughing stock of the school!* 他是全校的笑料!

10 not know whether to laugh or cry to feel upset or annoyed by something bad or unlucky that has happened 哭笑不得: *And when I couldn't find the passports – honestly, I didn't know whether to laugh or cry!* 而當我找不到護照的時候 —— 說真的, 我不知道該哭還是笑!

11 you have to laugh *spoken* used to say that, even though a situation is annoying or disappointing, you can also see that there is something funny about it【口】〔儘管情況令人心煩或失望, 但還是覺得滑稽而〕不由得好笑

12 laugh in sb's face to behave towards someone in a way that shows that you do not respect them or care about what they think 當面嘲笑[取笑]: *I asked them not to park in front of my garage, but they just laughed in my face.* 我請他們別在我的車庫前停車, 他們卻當面嘲笑我。

13 laugh up your sleeve to be secretly happy, especially because you have played a trick on someone or criticized them without them knowing 暗笑, 竊笑, 偷笑

laugh at sb/sth *phr v* [T] **1** to treat someone or something as if they are stupid, by laughing or making funny and unkind remarks about them 嘲笑, 取笑: *I can't go to school wearing that – everyone'll laugh at me.* 我不能穿着它去上學 —— 大家會取笑我的。**2** to seem not to care about something that most people would worry about 不在乎, 不當一回事: *Young offenders just laugh at this sort of sentence.* 年輕的冒失鬼們對這種判決根本不在乎。

laugh sth ↔ **off** *phr v* [T] to pretend that something is less serious than it really is by laughing or joking about it 用笑擺脫; 用笑話來排除; 對…一笑了之: *I tried to tell him he was drinking too much but he just laughed it off.* 我告訴他, 他喝得太多了, 可是他只是一笑了之。

laugh² *n* [C] **1** the sound you make when you laugh 笑聲: *a nervous laugh* 神經質的一笑 | **give a laugh** *She gave a little laugh and squeezed my arm.* 她輕輕的大笑一聲, 並捏我的手臂。**2 have a (good) laugh** *BrE*【英】**a)** *informal* to have fun and enjoy yourself【非正式】盡情地笑; 玩得很痛快: *We always have a good laugh when Kevin comes to stay.* 每當凱文來的時候, 我們總是玩得很痛快。**b)** to laugh about something in a happy way with other people 把…當笑話: *It was a nightmare at the time, but afterwards we all had a good laugh about it.* 那時候這事極可怕, 但是後來我們都把它當成笑話。**3 be a (good) laugh** *BrE informal*【英, 非正式】**a)** to be amusing and fun to be with 和…一起很愉快: *I hope Sarah comes – she's a real laugh.* 我希望莎拉會來 —— 她真是個有趣的人。**b)** if an occasion, activity etc is a good laugh, you enjoy yourself and have fun 是件開心痛快的事: *We all went to the beach last night – it was a really good laugh.* 昨晚我們都去沙灘了 —— 那真是件開心痛快的事。**4 do sth for a laugh** *BrE informal* to do something because you think it will be fun, not for a serious reason【英, 非正式】做某事只是為了取樂 **5 have the last laugh** to be successful, win an argument etc in the end, after other people have criticized you, defeated you etc earlier〔經歷非議、失敗等〕最終獲勝[成功] **6 be a laugh a minute** *informal* to be very funny, cheerful, and amusing; sometimes used humorously to mean the opposite【非正式】有趣, 快樂, 令人好笑;〔有時幽默地指〕無趣, 不快 3

laugh·a·ble /ˈlæfəbḷ; ˈlɑːfəbəl/ *adj* so bad, silly, or unbelievable that it makes you want to laugh 可笑的, 荒唐的: *The profit figures are laughable!* 這些利潤數字是荒唐的! —**laughably** *adv*

laugh·ing gas /ˈ·· ·/ *n* [U] *informal* a gas that is sometimes used to stop you feeling pain during an operation【非正式】〔手術中止痛的〕笑氣, 一氧化二氮

laughing jack·ass /ˌ·· ˈ··/ *n* [C] *informal* a KOOKABURRA【非正式】笑翠鳥

laugh·ing·ly /ˈlæfɪŋli; ˈlɑːfɪŋli/ *adv* **1** if something is laughingly called something or described in a particular way, you think it is so bad that the name or description seems stupid 開玩笑地: *This room is laughingly referred to as the 'Quality Control Centre'.* 這個房間被戲稱為"質量控制中心"。**2** if you do something laughingly, you are laughing while you do it 帶笑地(做)

laugh lines /ˈ· ·/ *n* [plural] the American form of LAUGHTER LINES laughter lines 的美語形式

laugh·ter /ˈlæftɚ; ˈlɑːftə/ *n* [U] the act of laughing or sound of people laughing 笑; 笑聲: *We could hear riotous laughter from next door.* 我們能夠聽到隔壁房間狂歡的笑聲。| **roar/howl/shriek with laughter** (=laugh very loudly) 發出哄笑／狂笑／尖笑聲 | **dissolve into laughter** (=start to laugh when you have been trying not to) 情不自禁地大笑

laughter lines /'· ·/ *n* [plural] *BrE* lines on your skin around your eyes which can be seen when you laugh 【英】〔眼睛周圍的〕笑紋; LAUGH LINES *AmE* 【美】

2 **launch**[1] /lɔntʃ; lɔːntʃ/ *v* [T]

1 ▶START STH 開始做某事◀ to start something, especially an official, public, or military activity that has been carefully planned 發動, 發起, 開始進行: **launch a campaign/appeal/inquiry** *Police have launched a murder enquiry following the discovery of a woman's body.* 發現女屍後, 警方開始進行謀殺案的調查。| **launch an attack/assault/offensive** *The press launched a vicious attack on the President.* 新聞界對總統發起了惡意的攻擊。

2 ▶PRODUCT 產品◀ to make a new product, book etc available for sale for the first time 把〔新產品、新書等〕投放市場, 出版, 發行: *It was a party to launch her new novel.* 就發行她的新小説而舉行了招待會。

3 ▶BOAT 船◀ to put a boat or ship into the water 將〔船或艦〕下水

4 ▶SKY/SPACE 天空/太空◀ to send a weapon or SPACECRAFT into the sky or into space 發射〔武器或太空船〕: *A test satellite was launched from Cape Canaveral.* 實驗人造衛星從卡納維拉爾角發射升空。

5 launch yourself forwards/up/from etc to jump up and forwards into the air with a lot of energy 〔用力〕撲向前／躍起／從…撲過去等

launch into sth *phr v* [T] to suddenly start a description or story, or suddenly start criticizing something 突然開始〔描述、敍述、抨擊〕: *The preacher launched into an attack on adultery.* 傳教士突然開始抨擊通姦。

launch out *phr v* [I always+adv/prep] to start something new, especially something that involves risk 開始, 着手〔新事情, 尤指有風險的事〕: **[+into]** *Dickson left his father's firm and launched out into business on his own.* 狄克森離開了他父親的公司, 開創自己的事業。

launch[2] *n* [C] **1** an occasion at which a new product, book etc is made available or made known 〔新產品的〕投放市場, 〔新書的〕發行: *the launch of our new hatchback* 有倉門式後背的新款小汽車的推出 **2** a large boat with a motor 遊艇, 汽艇

launch·er /'lɔntʃɚ; 'lɔːntʃə/ *n* [C] a structure from which a weapon, ROCKET, or SPACECRAFT is sent into the sky 發射架, 發射裝置

launch pad /'· ·/ also 又作 **launching pad** /'·· ·/ *n* [C] a base from which a ROCKET or MISSILE is sent up into the sky 〔火箭、導彈的〕發射台, 發射坪

laun·der /'lɔndɚ; 'lɔːndə/ *v* [T] **1** to put money which has been obtained illegally into legal businesses and bank accounts, so that you can hide it or use it 洗〔黑錢〕〔即把非法得來的錢注入合法的生意中或存入銀行, 以便隱藏或使用〕 **2** *formal* to wash and IRON[2] clothes, sheets etc 【正式】洗熨〔衣服等〕—**laundered** *adj*

laun·der·ette /ˌlɔndə'rɛt; ˌlɔːndə'ret/ also 又作 **laundrette** /lɔn'drɛt; lɔːn'dret/ *BrE n* [C] a place where you can go to wash your clothes in machines that work when you put coins in them 【英】〔裝有投幣洗衣機的〕自助洗衣店

laun·dry /'lɔndrɪ; 'lɔːndri/ *n* **1** [C] a place or business where clothes etc are washed and ironed (IRON[2]) 洗熨衣服的地方, 洗衣房; 洗衣店 **2** [U] clothes, sheets etc that need to be washed or have just been washed 待洗[洗過]的衣物

laundry bas·ket /'·· ˌ··/ *n* [C] **1** *BrE* a large basket that you put dirty clothes in until you wash them 【英】〔放置待洗髒衣服的〕洗衣筐; HAMPER[2] (2) *AmE* 【美】—see picture at 參見 BASKET 圖 **2** a basket used for carrying wet clothes that have been washed 〔裝已洗濕衣的〕籃子

laundry list /'·· ·/ *n* [C] *AmE* a list you write to remind you of things you have to do or buy 【美】〔提醒〕要做之事[購物]的清單

laur·e·ate /'lɔrɪɪt; 'lɔːriət/ *n* [C] someone who has won an important prize, especially the NOBEL PRIZE 重要獎項〔尤指諾貝爾獎〕獲得者: *Nigeria's Nobel laureate, Wole Soyinka* 尼日利亞的諾貝爾獎獲得者, 沃雷·索因卡 —see also 另見 POET LAUREATE

laur·el /'lɔrəl; 'lɒrəl/ *n* **1** [C,U] a small tree with smooth shiny dark green leaves that do not fall in winter 月桂樹 **2 rest/sit on your laurels** to be satisfied with what you have achieved and therefore stop trying to achieve anything new 滿足於已有成績, 不求上進 **3 look to your laurels** to work hard in order not to lose the success that you have achieved 盡力保住已獲得的成功

lav /læv; læv/ *n* [C] *BrE spoken* a lavatory 【英口】廁所, 洗手間

la·va /'lɑvə; 'lɑːvə/ *n* [U] **1** hot liquid rock that flows from a VOLCANO 〔火山噴出的〕岩漿, 熔岩 **2** this rock when it has become cold and solid 火山岩

lav·a·to·ri·al /ˌlævə'torɪəl; ˌlævə'tɔːriəl◂/ *adj* lavatorial humour or jokes are about going to the toilet or about sex 〔有關上廁所或性方面的幽默或笑話〕低級粗俗的

lav·a·to·ry /'lævəˌtorɪ; 'lævətəri/ *n* [C] *formal* a toilet or the room a toilet is in 【正式】廁所, 洗手間

lav·en·der /'lævəndɚ; 'lævəndə/ *n* **1** [C,U] a plant that has purple flowers with a strong pleasant smell 薰衣草 **2** [U] the dried flowers of this plant, often used to make things smell nice 晾乾的薰衣草花 **3** [U] a pale purple colour 淺紫色

lavender bag /'··· ˌ·/ *n* [C] a small bag containing dried lavender that you put in a drawer to make your clothes smell nice 存放乾薰衣草花的袋子

lavender wa·ter /'··· ˌ··/ *n* [U] a PERFUME[1] (1) made from lavender oil and alcohol 薰衣草香水

la·ver /'lɑvɚ; 'lɑːvə/ *n* [U] a type of sea plant that you can eat 紫菜

laver bread /'·· ·/ *n* [U] a dish made from laver that is boiled and then cooked in butter 紫菜麵包〔由紫菜和黃油製的食品〕

lav·ish[1] /'lævɪʃ; 'lævɪʃ/ *adj* **1** lavish gifts, meals etc are large and generous, and look as if they have cost a lot of money 過分多的, 過分鋪張的, 過分豐盛的: *They would organize lavish dinners for potential customers.* 他們會設下鋪張的宴會招待潛在客戶。| *a lavish production of 'Tosca', with fine costumes and elaborate stage sets* 採用華麗服裝和精美舞台布景巨資打造的〔歌劇電影〕《托斯卡》 **2 be lavish with** to give something very generously 過分慷慨地給與, 過於大方地出手: *He's never very lavish with his praises.* 他從不隨便誇獎。—**lavishly** *adv*: *lavishly decorated with fruit and flowers* 裝點着大量水果和花朵 —**lavishness** *n* [U]

lavish[2] *v*

lavish sth **on/upon** sb *phr v* [T] to give someone a lot of something such as expensive presents, love, or praise 〔過分〕慷慨地給予〔某人〕〈如貴重禮物、愛或誇獎〉: *Roberta lavished attention on the children.* 羅波塔對孩子們關懷備至。

law /lɔ; lɔː/ *n*

1 ▶SYSTEM OF RULES 規則體系◀ [singular, U] the whole system of rules that citizens of a country or place must obey 法律（體系）, 法規: **against the law** (=illegal) 違法的 *Sex discrimination is against the law.* 性別歧視是違法的。| **break the law** (=do something illegal) 犯法 *There were easy profits for businessmen who were prepared to break the law.* 對於有心以身試法的商人而言盈利是容易的。| **against the law (for sb) to do sth** *It is against the law for children to work before they are fifteen.* 兒童在十五歲以前工作是違法的。| **become law** (=be officially made a law) 立法, 成為法律 *The Criminal Justice Bill became law amidst much controversy.*

《刑事審判法案》在許多爭議中成為了法律。| **by law** (=according to the law) 依照法律 *Seatbelts must, by law, be worn by all passengers.* 依照法律, 乘客必須繫上安全帶。| **keep/stay/remain/operate within the law** (=make sure that what you do is legal) 在法律許可範圍之內進行 *They make tough business deals, but are always careful to operate within the law.* 他們做一些棘手的買賣, 但總會小心翼翼地在法律許可的範圍內進行。| **tax law/divorce law/libel law etc** (=all the laws relating to tax etc) 稅法/離婚法/誹謗法等 *a specialist in company law* 公司法專家 | *She's a partner in a major New York law firm.* 她是紐約一家大律師事務所的合夥人。—see also 另見 CRIMINAL LAW, LAW FIRM

2 ►A RULE 規則◄ [C] a rule that people in a particular country, city or local area must obey 法則, 法令: *Under the new law, any gathering of over 10 people is considered a crime.* 按照新的法律, 任何超過十人的集會均被視為犯罪。| **[+on]** *European laws on equal opportunities* 歐洲的均等機會法 | **[+against]** *There ought to be a law against cutting down trees.* 應該制定一項禁止伐樹的法律。

3 there's no law against (it) *spoken* used to tell someone who is criticizing you that you are not doing anything wrong【口】沒有法律規定說不可以 (這樣)

4 ►POLICE 警察◄ the law the police 警方, 警察: *I think she may be in trouble with the law.* 我想她會和警察惹上麻煩。| **I'll have the law on you** *spoken* (=used to threaten someone that you will call the police)【口】我要叫警察了 *Get away from my car or I'll have the law on you!* 離開我的車, 否則我要叫警察了!

5 law and order a situation in which people respect the law, and crime is controlled by the police, the prison system etc 法律和秩序, 法治: *The soldiers were brought in to restore law and order after the riots.* 騷亂發生後士兵被派來維持治安。

6 have the law on your side to be legally right in what you are doing〔做事〕合法

7 ►SPORT 體育運動◄ [C] one of the rules that say how a sport should be played 運動規則: *the laws of football* 足球規則

8 ►BUSINESS/ART 商業/藝術◄ [C] a way in which things happen in an activity such as business or art, which is thought of as a rule because it seems impossible to change 規則: *the law of supply and demand* 供需規律 | *the law of perspective* 透視法

9 ►NATURAL LAW 自然規律◄ [C] a statement that describes and explains how nature works 法則, 定律: *the laws of nature* 自然法則 | *the Second Law of Thermodynamics* 熱力學第二定律 | *the law of gravity* 萬有引力定律

10 the law of the jungle a) the idea that people should only look after themselves and not care about other people, if they want to succeed 想要成就, 莫顧他人 **b)** the principle that only the strongest creatures will stay alive 叢林法則; 弱肉強食法則; 強者生存原則

11 the law of averages the PROBABILITY that one result will happen as often as another if you try something often enough 平均律, 均值定理, 概率: *By the law of averages you'll have to throw a six eventually.* 根據概率你最後必須擲出六點。

12 be a law unto himself/herself etc to behave in an independent way and not worry about the usual rules of behaviour or what other people do or think 我行我素, 獨斷專行

13 take the law into your own hands to do something illegal in order to put right something that you think is unjust, for example by violently punishing someone instead of informing the police 不通過法律擅自處理; 用私刑處罰: *vigilantes who take the law into their own hands* 擅自執法的治安會成員

14 go to law to go to court in order to settle a problem 提起訴訟, 打官司 —see also 另見 CIVIL LAW, COMMON LAW, **lay down the law** (LAY²), POOR LAW, ROMAN LAW, SOD'S LAW, **unwritten law** (UNWRITTEN)

law-a·bid·ing /ˈ· ·,··/ *adj* **law-abiding citizens/people/neighbours etc** people who respect and obey the law 守法的公民/人民/鄰居等

law·break·er /ˈ· ,··/ *n* [C] someone who does something illegal 犯法的人, 違法的人 —**law-breaking** *n* [U]

law·court /ˈlɔ,kɔrt; ˈlɔːkɔːt/ *n* [C] a room or building where legal cases are judged 法庭, 法院

law en·force·ment /ˈ· ·,··/ *n* [U] the job of making sure that the law is obeyed 執法

law enforcement a·gent /ˈ· ··,··/ *n* [C] *AmE* a policeman or policewoman【美】警察

law firm /ˈ· ·/ *n* [C] *especially AmE* a company that provides legal services and employs many lawyers【尤美】律師事務所

law·ful /ˈlɔfəl; ˈlɔːfəl/ *adj formal or law*【正式或法律】**1** considered by the government or law courts to be legal and correct 合法的; 依法的; 法定的: *a lawful marriage* 合法婚姻 **2** allowed by law 法律許可的: *doubts as to whether these dealings were lawful* 對這些交易是否合法的懷疑 | *lawful forms of protest* 法律許可的抗議形式 —**lawfully** *adv* —**lawfulness** *n* [U]

law·less /ˈlɔlɪs; ˈlɔːləs/ *adj* not obeying the law, or not controlled by the law 不守法的; 不受法律控制的: *lawless terrorists* 無法無天的恐怖分子 | *a lawless frontier town* 不受法律控制的邊境城鎮 —**lawlessly** *adv* —**lawlessness** *n* [U]

Law Lords /ˈ· ·/ *n* **the Law Lords** the members of the British House of Lords holding high positions in the legal profession, and who form the highest court in the British legal system 英國上議院中擁有高級司法職位的議員; 最高法庭的法官

law·mak·er /ˈlɔ,mekɚ; ˈlɔːmeɪkə/ *n* [C] *especially AmE* any elected official responsible for making laws【尤美】立法者, 立法官員

law·man /ˈlɔmæn; ˈlɔːmæn/ *n plural* **lawmen** /-mɛn; -men/ [C] *AmE* any professional officer who is responsible for making sure that the law is obeyed【美】執法者, 執法官員

lawn /lɔn; lɔːn/ *n* **1** [C] an area of ground in a garden or park that is covered with short grass〔草修剪得很短的〕草坪, 草地: **mow the lawn** (=cut the grass) 修剪草坪 **2** [U] a fine cloth made from cotton or LINEN 上等細棉布; 上等細麻布

lawn bowl·ing /ˈ· ,··/ *n* [U] *AmE* a game played on grass in which you try to roll a big ball as near as possible to a smaller ball called the JACK¹ (5)【美】草坪滾木球遊戲; BOWLS *BrE*【英】

lawn chair /ˈ· ·/ *n* [C] *AmE* a light chair like a folding bed, that you can sit or lie on outside when the sun is shining【美】草地躺椅; SUN LOUNGER *BrE*【英】—see picture at 參見 CHAIR¹ 圖

lawn mow·er /ˈ· ,··/ *n* [C] a machine that you use to cut grass 刈草機, 割草機

lawn par·ty /ˈ· ,··/ *n* [C] *AmE* a formal party held outside in the afternoon, especially in a large garden【美】〔尤指在大花園裡舉行的正式〕草坪招待會; GARDEN PARTY *BrE*【英】

lawn sign /ˈ· ·/ *n* [C] *AmE* a sign that you put in front of your house before an election to say which person or political party you support【美】〔選舉前貼在屋前的〕草坪告示〔寫上所支持的人或政黨〕

lawn ten·nis /,· ˈ··/ *n* [U] *formal* TENNIS【正式】網球, 草地網球

law school /ˈ· ·/ *n* [C,U] a school in the US where you study to become a lawyer after your BACHELOR'S DEGREE〔美國已獲學士學位的學生為取得律師資格就讀的〕法學院

law·suit /ˈlɔ,sut; ˈlɔːsuːt/ *n* [C] a charge, claim, or complaint against someone that is made in a court of law by a private person or company, not by the police or state;

SUIT¹ (4) 訴訟〔非刑事案件〕: **file a lawsuit** *Local people filed a private lawsuit against the oil company over water contamination.* 當地百姓對石油公司造成水污染提起了私人訴訟。

3 2 **law·yer** /ˈlɔjɚ; ˈlɔːjə/ *n* [C] someone whose job is to advise people about laws, write formal agreements, or represent people in court 律師 —see also 另見 ADVOCATE², ATTORNEY, BARRISTER, SOLICITOR

USAGE NOTE 用法说明: LAWYER
WORD CHOICE 詞語辨析: **lawyer, counsellor/counselor, attorney, barrister, solicitor**
In American English a **lawyer** is often called a **counsellor** (also spelt 又拼作 **counselor**) or, especially if he or she speaks in court, an **attorney**. 在美國英語中, lawyer 常被稱做 counsellor, 若在法庭上辯護尤稱 attorney。
In British English a **lawyer** who speaks in court is called a **barrister**, while a **solicitor** works mainly from an office, but may also appear in the less formal and important courts. 在英國英語中, 在法庭上作辯護的 lawyer 被稱作 barrister, 而 solicitor 主要從事事務性的工作, 但也可在不太正式和次重要的法庭上出庭。

lax /læks; læks/ *adj* **1** not strict or careful enough about standards of behaviour, work, safety etc; SLACK¹ (1) 不嚴格的, 疏忽的; 鬆散的: *lax security* 不嚴格的保安措施 **2** muscles or arms or legs that are lax are not firm or strong and therefore tend to hang loosely〔肌肉、臂或腿〕鬆弛的 —**laxly** *adv* —**laxity** *n* [U] —**laxness** *n* [U]

lax·a·tive /ˈlæksətɪv; ˈlæksətɪv/ *n* [C] a medicine or something that you eat which makes your BOWEL*s* empty easily 通便藥, 輕瀉劑 —**laxative** *adj*

1 2 **lay¹** /le; leɪ/ *v* the past tense of LIE¹

lay 平放

laying a dress on the bed 把裙子平放在牀上

lying on the bed 平躺在牀上

lay² *v past tense and past participle* **laid** /led; leɪd/
1 ►PUT SB/STH DOWN 把某人/某物放下◄ [T always+adv/prep] to put someone or something down carefully into a flat position 把〔某人/某物〕平放: **lay sth in/on/under etc** *Laying my coat carefully on the bed, I crept towards the door.* 我把外套小心地放在牀上, 然後悄悄地向門走去。| *The bodies were laid under the trees to await burial.* 屍體被放在樹下準備埋葬。| *Sharon laid her hand on my arm.* 雪倫把手放在我胳膊上。
2 lay bricks/carpet/concrete/cables etc to put or fix bricks, a carpet etc in the correct place, especially on the ground or floor 砌磚/鋪地毯/鋪水泥/鋪設電纜等: *The man's coming to lay the carpet on Saturday.* 星期六有人會來鋪地毯。| *laying an oil pipeline across the desert* 鋪設一條橫貫沙漠的輸油管道
3 ►EGGS 蛋◄ [I,T] if a bird, insect etc lays eggs, it produces them from its body 下〔蛋〕; 產〔卵〕: *The flies lay their eggs on decaying meat.* 蒼蠅在變腐的肉上產卵。
4 ►RISK MONEY 賭錢◄ [T] to risk an amount of money on the result of a race, sports game etc; BET² (1) 押〔賭注〕; 用…打賭: **lay £5/$10 etc on** *She laid £5 on the favourite, Golden Boy.* 她把五英鎊押在最喜歡的賽馬"金童"身上。
5 lay the blame on to blame someone for something that has happened 責怪, 責備: *Then both sides start trying to lay the blame on each other!* 然後雙方開始設法互相指責!
6 lay a charge/proposal etc *formal* to make a statement, suggestion etc in an official or public way【正式】〔正式或公開地〕提出控告/建議等: *Your employer has laid a serious charge against you.* 你的雇主已對你提出了嚴重指控。| *Several proposals have been laid before the committee.* 幾項建議已提交給委員會。
7 lay sth open/bare to remove what covers, hides, or shelters something 使某物暴露
8 lay sth ↔ waste to destroy or damage everything in a place, especially in a war〔尤指戰爭中〕把某物徹底摧毀; 夷為平地
9 lay stress/emphasis on to emphasize something because you regard it as very important 強調: *a political philosophy that lays great stress on individual responsibility* 着重強調個人責任的政治哲學
10 lay plans/a trap etc to carefully prepare something, especially something that will harm someone else 制定計劃/設圈套等
11 lay the table to put the cloth, plates, knives, forks etc on a table, ready for a meal 擺好餐桌〔準備用飯〕
12 ►HAVE SEX 發生性行為◄ [T] *slang* to have sex with someone【俚】與…性交: **get laid** (=find someone to have sex with) 尋找機會發生性關係
13 lay sb/sth flat to hit someone or something and knock them down 擊倒某人/某物: *Laid him flat with a single punch!* 只一拳就將他擊倒在地!
14 lay yourself open to blame/criticism/ridicule etc to do something that makes it possible that you will be blamed, criticized etc 使自己受到責備/批評/奚落等: *I don't want to lay myself open to charges of nepotism.* 我不想別人指責我任人唯親。
15 lay sth on the line a) to state something, especially a threat, demand, or criticism, in a very clear way 表明某事〔尤指威脅、要求或批評〕**b)** to risk losing your life, your job etc, especially in order to help someone〔尤指為了幫助別人而〕冒〔犧牲、失業等〕危險
16 lay sb low a) [usually passive 一般用被動態] if an illness lays someone low, they are unable to do their normal activities for a period of time 使某人病倒: *She's been laid low with flu for a week.* 她因患流感病(倒)了一星期。**b)** *literary* to knock someone down or injure them seriously【文】把某人擊倒; 使某人重傷
17 lay the ghost (of) to finally get rid of something from your past that has been worrying you 擺脱某事 —see also 另見 **lay your hands on** (HAND¹ (30)), **lay/provide the foundation(s) for** (FOUNDATION (5)), **not lay a finger on** (FINGER¹ (5)), **put/lay your cards on the table** (CARD¹ (12))

lay about sb *phr v* [T] *literary or old-fashioned* to attack someone violently【文或過時】猛烈攻擊〔某人〕: *He laid about his attackers with his stick.* 他用棍子狠揍攻擊他的人。

lay sth **↔ aside** *phr v* [T] **1** to store something to use in the future 儲存〔某物〕待用[備用]: *She'd managed to lay aside a few pounds each week from her wages.* 她設法每週從薪水中存上幾個英鎊。**2** to stop using, doing, or preparing something, for a short time 暫時把〔某事〕擱在一邊: *The building plans may have to be laid aside till things improve.* 在情況得到改善前, 建築規劃可能只得擱置起來。

lay sth **↔ down** *phr v*
1 ►TOOLS/WEAPONS 工具/武器◄ [T]to put down your tools, weapons etc as a sign that you will stop using them 放下: *Lay down your weapons and walk slowly towards the door!* 放下武器, 慢慢走到門邊去!
2 ►OFFICIALLY STATE 正式闡述◄ [usually passive 一般用被動態] to officially state rules that must be

L

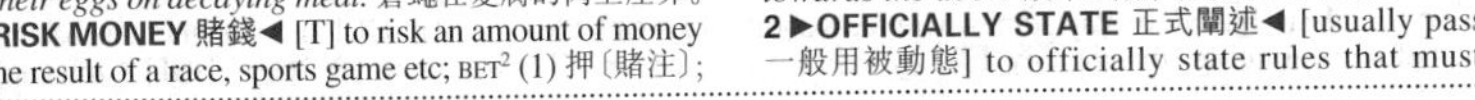

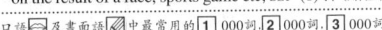

obeyed, systems that must be used etc or state something officially or firmly〔正式或堅決地〕闡述, 聲明: *The regulations lay down a rigid procedure for checking safety equipment.* 規則明定了檢驗安全設備的嚴格程序。| **lay down that** *It is laid down in the regulations that all members must carry their membership cards at all times.* 根據規定, 所有成員必須隨身攜帶會員證。
3 lay down your life *formal* to lose your life, for example in a war, in order to help other people【正式】犧牲生命: *prepared to lay down his life for his comrades* 他準備為同志們犧牲自己的生命
4 lay down the law to tell other people what to do, how they should think etc, in an unpleasant or rude way〔用嚴厲或粗魯的方式〕發號施令
5 ►START 開始◄ to start building or making something by doing the first part of the work 開始建造; 開始做: *Crick and Watson laid down the foundations of modern genetic research.* 克里克和沃森為現代遺傳學研究奠定了基礎。
6 ►WINE ETC 酒等◄ to store something, especially wine, to use in the future 儲存〔尤指酒〕
lay sth ↔ **in** *phr v* [T] to obtain and store a large supply of something to use in the future 儲存〔某物〕
lay into sb *phr v* [T] to attack someone physically or with words 痛打; 抨擊: *You should have heard her laying into Tommy!* 你一定聽到了她痛斥湯米!
lay off *phr v* **1** [T **lay** sb ↔ **off**] to stop employing a worker, especially for a period in which there is not much work to do〔尤指在生意蕭條期臨時性地〕解雇〔雇員〕: *Harry was laid off for six months during the recession.* 在營業衰退時期, 哈里被停雇了六個月。**2** [I,T **lay off** sth] *informal* to stop doing, having, or using something【非正式】停止, 中止: *I think you'd better lay off alcohol for a while.* 我想你最好一段時間內不要飲酒。| **lay off doing sth** *Just lay off hassling me, would you!* 你就別和我爭了, 行不行!
lay on *phr v* [T] **1** [**lay** sth ↔ **on**] to provide food, entertainment etc in a very generous way〔慷慨〕提供〔食物等〕; 款待; 安排: *The organizers have laid on a huge meal for us.* 組織者款待了我們一頓豐盛的飯菜。| *It's great! – transportation, hotel, food, it's all laid on.* 太好了! —— 交通、旅館、食物, 一切都安排妥當了。**2** [**lay** sth **on** sb] to give someone something such as a responsibility or problem that is hard to deal with 把〔責任或困難等〕推給〔某人〕: *Sorry to lay this on you, but we need someone to go to Italy next week.* 很抱歉把此事交給你, 但是我們下週需要有人去意大利。**3 lay it on (a bit thick)** *informal*【非正式】**a)** to praise or admire someone or something too much, especially in order to please someone 拍馬奉承〔尤指刻意取悅某人〕**b)** to state or describe something in a way that goes beyond the truth; EXAGGERATE 過分吹噓[渲染]
lay sb/sth **out** *phr v* [T]
1 ►SPREAD 鋪展◄ to spread something out 鋪開, 展開: *Lay out the map on the table and let's have a look.* 把地圖鋪在桌上, 讓我們看一下。
2 ►ARRANGE 佈置◄ to arrange or plan a building, town, garden etc 佈置, 設計〔建築、城鎮、花園等〕: *The garden is laid out in a formal pattern.* 這花園是按正規式樣設計的。
3 ►SPEND 花費◄ *informal* to spend money, especially a lot of money【非正式】花費〔尤指大筆錢〕: **lay out sth on** *We've just laid out £500 on car repairs.* 我們剛花了500英鎊修車。—see also 另見 OUTLAY
4 ►HIT 擊打◄ to knock someone down, especially hard enough to make them unconscious 擊倒, 打昏〔某人〕: *One of the guards had been laid out and the other was missing.* 一個衛兵被打昏, 另一個衛兵則不知去向。
5 ►BODY 屍體◄ to prepare a dead body so that it can be buried 給…作殯葬準備
lay over *phr v* [I] *AmE* to stay somewhere for a short time before continuing your journey【美】途中停留
lay to *phr v* [I,T **lay** sth **to**] *technical* if a ship lays to or if you lay it to, it stops moving【術語】(使)〔船〕停駛
lay sb/sth ↔ **up** *phr v* [T] **1 be laid up (with)** to have to stay in bed because you are ill or injured〔因患病或受傷〕臥牀不起: *laid up for a week with flu* 因流感臥牀一週 **2 lay up problems/difficulties etc** to do something that will cause problems in the future〔做某事〕自找麻煩: *I tell you, she's just laying up trouble for herself, she really is.* 我說, 她就是自討苦吃, 她就是這樣。**3** *old-fashioned* to collect and store something to use in the future【過時】儲存〔某物〕備用: *laying up firewood for the winter* 為冬季儲存木柴

USAGE NOTE 用法說明: LAY
GRAMMAR 語法
You **lay** [T] something somewhere, but you **lie** [I] somewhere. 把某物放在某處用 lay〔及物動詞〕, 但是躺在某處用 lie〔不及物動詞〕: *He laid his things on the bed* 他把東西放在牀上 but 但用 *He lay on the bed* (NOT 不用 *lied*) 他躺在牀上. In spoken British English you will also sometimes hear things like 在英國口語中有時也會聽到: *I want to lay down* (instead of 而不是 *I want to lie down*) 我想躺下 but some people consider this to be incorrect. 但是有人認為這種用法不正確。
A third verb **lie** [I] **(lying, lied, lied)** means 'to tell a lie'. **Lied** should not be confused with **lived.** 第三個動詞 lie〔不及物動詞〕的意思是"說謊"。切勿將 lied 與 lived 相混淆: *She lied when she said she lived in Beverley Hills.* 她說自己住在比華利山是說謊。

lay³ *n* [C] **1 the lay of the land** *especially AmE*【尤美】**a)** the situation that exists at a particular time〔特定時候的〕形勢, 情況: *I'll go in and get the lay of the land – see if Pam's in a better mood.* 我進去了解情況, 看看帕姆的心情好點沒有。**b)** the appearance of an area of land, the way it slopes etc 地形, 地貌 **2 be a great/good lay** *slang* to be good to have sex with【俚】是夠騷的娘們[騷貨, 性交對象] **3** *literary* a poem or song【文】詩; 歌
lay⁴ *adj* [only before noun 僅用於名詞前] **a)** not trained or knowing much about a particular profession or subject 非專業的; 外行的: *To the lay observer, these technical terms are incomprehensible.* 對於外行人來說, 這些專業術語不易理解。**b)** not in an official position in the church 非神職的: *a lay preacher* 非神職傳教士
lay·a·bout /ˋleə͵baut; ˈleɪəbaʊt/ *n* [C] *BrE informal* a lazy person who avoids work, responsibility etc【英, 非正式】遊手好閒之徒; 躲避工作[責任]的人; 不務正業的人
lay·a·way /ˋleə͵we; ˈleɪəweɪ/ *n* [U] *AmE* a method of buying goods in which the goods are kept by the seller for a small amount of money until the full price is paid【美】分期累積預付購貨法〔指預付定金留貨, 付足貨款後再交貨的方式〕: *I've put the dress on layaway.* 我已付定金預購了服裝。—**layaway** *adj*: *a layaway plan* 預購計劃
lay-by /ˈ· ·/ *n* [C] *BrE* a space next to a road where vehicles can stop【英】路側停車帶

layer〔覆蓋〕層

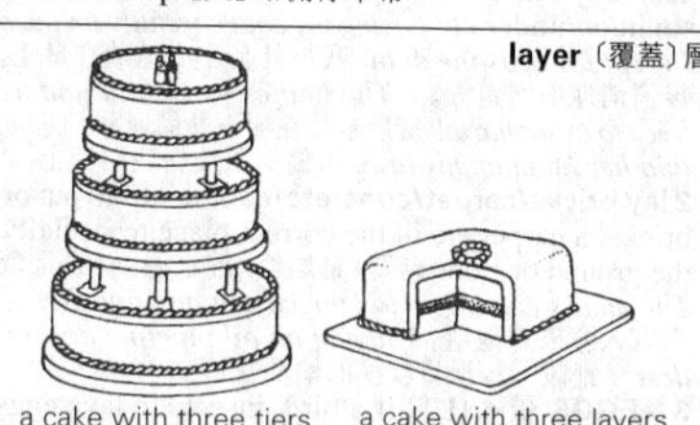

a cake with three tiers 一個三層蛋糕
a cake with three layers 一塊三層蛋糕

lay·er¹ /ˋleə; ˈleɪə/ *n* [C] **1** an amount of a substance that covers all of a surface〔覆蓋〕層: **[+of]** *A thick layer of* 3 3 *dust lay on the furniture.* 家具上蒙了一層厚厚的灰塵。 **2** one of several levels of substances lying one on top of another〔物質〕層: **[+of]** *a thin layer of coal between two layers of rock* 兩層岩石間薄薄的一層煤 | *He pulled off layer upon layer of clothing.* 他把衣服一件件地脱掉。—see also 另見 OZONE LAYER **3** one of several different levels in a complicated organization, system, set of ideas etc〔組織、系統、思想等的〕層次: **[+of]** *There are many layers of meaning to be discovered in the poem.* 在這首詩中有許多層含義有待解讀。| *major changes that have eliminated two layers of management* 消除雙層管理的重大變動 **4 multi-layered/single-layered etc** having a lot of layers, one layer etc 多/單層等的

layer[2] *v* [T] **1** to make a layer of something or put something down in layers 鋪一層…; 把…堆成層: *potatoes layered with cheese* 夾有幾層乳酪的馬鈴薯 **2** to cut someone's hair in layers rather than all to the same length 把〔頭髮〕分層剪短

lay·ette /le`ɛt; leɪ'et/ *n* [C] a complete set of clothing and other things a new baby needs 全套新生兒用品

lay fig·ure /'· ,··/ *n* [C] a model of the human body used in painting or drawing〔供繪畫用的〕人體模型

lay·man /'lemən; 'leɪmən/ *n plural* **laymen** /-mən; -mən/ [C] **1** someone who is not trained in a particular subject or type of work, especially when they are being compared with someone who is 門外漢, 外行人: **the layman** (=laymen in general)〔泛指〕外行人 *technical terms not easily understood by the layman* 門外漢不易理解的專業術語 | **in layman's terms** (=used when explaining something in simple language) 用外行的話說 *the GNP or, in layman's terms, the amount of goods produced by a country* 國民生產總值, 或是用外行的話說, 一個國家所生產貨物的總量 **2** someone who is not a priest but is a member of a church 非神職教徒, 平信徒, 普通信徒

lay-off /'· ·/ *n* [C] the act of stopping a worker's employment because there is not enough work〔因工作清淡而導致的〕臨時解雇: *more lay-offs in the car industry* 在汽車製造業較多暫遭解雇的工人 —see also 另見 **lay off** (LAY[2])

lay·out /'le,aut; 'leɪaʊt/ *n* [C] **1** the way in which something such as a town, garden, or building is arranged〔城鎮、花園或建築物等的〕佈局, 設計 **2** the way in which writing and pictures are arranged on a page〔文章和畫的〕版面編排, 版面設計 —see also 另見 **lay sb/sth out** (LAY[2])

lay·o·ver /'le,ovɚ; 'leɪəʊvə/ *n* [C] *AmE* a short stay between parts of a journey, especially a long plane journey【美】〔尤指長途飛行的〕中途停留; STOPOVER *BrE*【英】

lay·per·son /'le,pɝsn; 'leɪ,pɜːsən/ *n plural* **laypersons** [C] a word for a LAYMAN used when the person could be a woman or a man 外行, 門外漢; 普通信徒

lay read·er /,· '··/ *n* [C] someone in Christian churches who is not a priest but who has been given authority to lead a religious service and PREACH (1)〔基督教堂裡被授權在儀式中領讀經文的〕平信徒讀經員

lay-up /'· ·/ *n* [C] a throw in BASKETBALL made from very close to the basket or from under it〔籃球的〕打板進籃; 籃下單手跳投

lay·wom·an /'le,wumən; 'leɪ,wʊmən/ *n plural* **laywomen** /-,wɪmɪn; -,wɪmɪn/ [C] **1** a woman not trained in a particular subject or type of work, especially when she is being compared with someone who is〔女性〕外行人 **2** a woman who is not a priest but is a member of a church〔女性〕非神職教徒, 平信徒, 普通信徒

laze /lez; leɪz/ *v* [I always+adv/prep] to relax and enjoy yourself in a lazy way 懶散度日, 混日子: *Warren spent the afternoon lazing in the sun.* 沃倫懶懶地曬太陽消磨了整個下午。| **laze about/around** *lazing around when they should have been working* 他們該工作的時候卻吊兒郎當 —**laze** *n* [singular]

la·zy /'lezɪ; 'leɪzi/ *adj* **1** disliking work and physical activity, and never making any effort 懶惰的, 不努力的: *the laziest boy in the class* 班上最懶的男孩 | *I was feeling lazy so I called a taxi.* 我懶得走, 所以叫了計程車。 **2** a lazy period of time is spent doing nothing except relaxing〔時段〕懶洋洋度過的: *a lazy Sunday* 懶洋洋的星期日 **3** moving slowly 慢吞吞的; 緩慢的: *a lazy river* 水流緩慢的河 —**lazily** *adv* —**laziness** *n* [U]

la·zy·bones /'lezɪ,bonz; 'leɪzibəʊnz/ *n* [C] *informal* a word for a lazy person, often used in a friendly way to someone you like【非正式】懶鬼, 懶骨頭〔通常表示友好〕: *Come on, lazybones! Get out of bed.* 快起來, 懶鬼! 該起牀了。

lb *plural* **lbs** the written abbreviation of 縮寫= pound, a unit of weight equal to 0.454 kilograms 磅〔重量單位, 等於 0.454 千克〕: *a 3lb bag of flour* 一袋三磅重的麵粉

lbw /,ɛl bi `dʌblju; ,el biː 'dʌbəljuː/ *adv* leg before wicket; a way in which your INNINGS can end in CRICKET (2), when the ball hits your leg that is in front of your WICKET〔板球中的〕(擊球員) 腿碰球 (犯規) 出局

LCD /,ɛl si `di; ,el siː 'diː/ *n* [C] **1** liquid crystal display; the part of a watch, CALCULATOR, or small computer where numbers and letters are shown by means of an electric current that is passed through a special liquid 液晶顯示 —see picture on page A14 參見 A14 頁圖 **2** the written abbreviation of 縮寫= LOWEST COMMON DENOMINATOR

LCM the written abbreviation of 縮寫= LOWEST COMMON MULTIPLE

lea /li; liː/ *n* [C] *poetical* an area of land with grass【詩】草地, 草原

leach /litʃ; liːtʃ/ also 又作 **leach out** *v* [I,T] *technical* if a substance leaches or is leached from a larger mass such as the soil, it is removed from it by water passing through the larger mass【術語】(使) 濾掉, (使) 流失: *Nitrates from agricultural fertilizers leached into the rivers.* 農業肥料中的硝酸鹽流失到河中。

lead[1] /lid; liːd/ *v past tense and past participle* **led** /lɛd; led/

① GO SOMEWHERE 去某地
② CONTROL 控制
③ WIN 贏
④ CAUSE STH 引發某事
⑤ LIVE 過生活
⑥ BE BEST/FIRST 最好/領先
⑦ OTHER MEANINGS 其他意思

① GO SOMEWHERE 去某地

1 ▶GO IN FRONT 走在前面◀ [I,T] to go in front of a group of people or vehicles〔走在前面〕給…帶頭; 為…開路: *You lead and we'll follow.* 你帶路, 我們跟着。| *A truck with a jazz band on it was leading the parade.* 一輛載着爵士樂隊的卡車在遊行隊伍前開道。| *a procession led by a man on a horse* 由一名騎士帶領的隊伍 | **lead the way** (=go in front and show the way) 領路, 引路

2 ▶GUIDE SB 引導某人◀ **a)** [T always+adv/prep] to take someone to a place by going with them 為〔某人〕帶[引]路: **lead sb through/to/along etc** *An official led me along the corridor to a large office.* 一位官員領我沿着走廊走到一間大的辦公室。 **b)** [T] to take a person or animal somewhere while holding the person's arm or pulling a rope tied to the animal 引導〔人〕; 牽引〔動物〕: **lead sb up/down/through etc sth** *The hostages were blindfolded and led to a waiting car.* 人質被蒙上眼睛, 帶到一輛正在等候的汽車上。| *A groom was leading a racehorse out of the stable.* 馬夫牽着一匹賽馬走出馬廄。

3 ▶ROAD/WIRE 道路/電線◀ [I] if something such as a path, pipe, or wire leads somewhere or leads in a particular direction, it goes there or goes in that direction 通到; 通往, 通向: **[+down/into/towards etc]** *a flight of steps leading down to the beach* 一段通往下面沙灘的台階 | *animal tracks that led into the woods* 通向森林的野獸腳印 | *The thieves cut the wires leading to the surveillance cameras.* 小偷切斷了連接監視攝影機的電線。| *Where does this road lead?* 這條路通到哪裡?

4 ▶DOOR 門◀ [I] if a door or passage leads to a particular room or place, you can get there by going through it 進入: **[+to/into]** *a door leading to the conference room* 進入會議室的門

② CONTROL 控制

5 ▶BE IN CHARGE 負責◀ [T] to be in charge of something such as an important activity, a group of people, or an organization, especially a political party 領導, 率領, 帶領: *a communist-led striker* 共產黨領導的罷工 | *Major will lead the Conservative Party at the next election.* 在下屆選舉中梅傑將領導保守黨。| *Inspector Roberts is leading the investigation into Susan Carr's murder.* 羅伯茨警官在負責蘇珊·卡爾謀殺案的調查。

6 lead sb astray to encourage someone to do bad or immoral things that they would not normally do 把某人引入歧途: *We think Harry was led astray by some of the older boys.* 我們認為哈里是被一些大孩子引入歧途的。

7 ▶CONVERSATION 談話◀ [I,T] to direct a conversation or discussion, especially so that it develops in the way you want 引導〔談話或討論〕: *Mary led the conversation around to the topic of salaries.* 瑪麗引導談話圍繞着薪資話題進行。

8 lead sb by the nose *informal* to make someone do anything you want them to【非正式】牽着某人的鼻子走, 使某人完全聽命於自己

③ WIN 贏

9 [I,T] to be winning a game or competition〔遊戲或競賽中〕勝過, 領先: **lead by ten points/two sets/four frames etc** *Agassi was leading by two sets when rain stopped play.* 當下雨中止比賽時, 阿加西領先兩盤。| **lead sb/sth** *Brazil led Germany 1-0.* 巴西以 1:0 領先德國。| *Schumacher led the race from start to finish.* 舒馬赫自始至終領先。| *With two minutes to play the Lakers are still leading.* 還有最後兩分鐘, 湖人隊仍然領先。

④ CAUSE STH 引發某事

10 [T] to be the thing that makes someone decide to do something 使得, 引導〔某人做某事〕: **lead sb to do sth** *What led you to take up acting as a career?* 甚麼讓你開始從事演藝事業的? | *Ian's death led me to rethink what I wanted out of life.* 伊恩的死讓我重新思考生活中自己追求甚麼。

11 lead sb to believe/expect/understand *formal* to make someone think something is true, especially when it is not【正式】使某人相信/期望/理解〔尤指不真實的情況〕: *We were led to believe that all the money from the concert was going to charity.* 我們誤以為所有音樂會所得的錢都要捐給慈善事業。

⑤ LIVE 過生活

12 lead a normal/exciting/dull etc life to have a particular kind of life 過正常/刺激/枯燥乏味等的生活: *We lead a very quiet life since Ralph retired.* 自從拉爾夫退休後, 我們過着非常平靜的生活。

⑥ BE BEST/FIRST 最好/領先

13 [I,T] to be more successful than other people, companies, or countries in a particular activity or area of business or study〔在某項活動或領域中〕領先: *US companies lead the world in biotechnology.* 美國公司在生物科技領域上領先於世界。| *Asian-American students under 12 lead in literacy and numeracy.* 12歲以下的亞裔美國學生在識字認數上佔優。| **lead the field** (=be the most successful person etc in a particular area of business or study) 在某領域中領先 *a company that leads the field in software applications* 在應用軟件領域領先於世界的公司

14 lead the way to be the first to do something, especially something good or successful, which is likely to encourage others to do the same thing 帶頭, 先行: *The Japanese led the way in using industrial robots.* 日本在工業機器人應用方面處於領先地位。

⑦ OTHER MEANINGS 其他意思

15 market-led/demand-led/service-led etc in which the market, demand etc is the most important influence on the way something happens 由市場/需求/服務等推動的: *a demand-led recovery* 由需求推動的經濟復蘇

16 this leads me to... *spoken* used in a speech or discussion to introduce a new subject and connect it with what you have just said【口】這使我聯想到…: *This leads me to our sales targets for next year.* 這使我聯想到明年的銷售目標。

17 lead sb a dance *informal* to make someone feel worried and confused, especially because they do not know what you are going to do next【非正式】使人感到憂慮[不知所措]: *Once they were married, Gwen led her poor husband a hell of a dance.* 他們結婚後, 格溫讓她可憐的丈夫感覺非常迷茫。

18 lead sb up the garden path *informal* to deceive someone【非正式】欺瞞某人

19 [I+with,T] to play a particular card as your first card in one part of a game of cards 率先出(牌): *He led with the eight of hearts.* 他先出了一張紅桃八。

20 lead with your left/right to hit someone mainly with your left or right hand in BOXING〔拳擊中主要〕用左拳/右拳出擊

lead into sth *phr v* [T not in passive 不用被動態] if one subject, discussion etc leads into another, the second one follows naturally from the first because there is a clear connection between them 引發, 引起: *Fox mentioned the Korean deal, which led into a general discussion on our prospects in Asia.* 福克斯提到了韓國的政策, 從而引發了關於我們在亞洲發展前景的廣泛討論。

lead off *phr v* **1** [I,T] to start something such as a meeting, discussion, or performance by saying or doing something〔以說或做某事〕作為開頭: *I'd like to lead off by thanking Rick Jones for finding the time to be with us today.* 我首先要感謝里克·瓊斯今日到來。| **lead off with** *John, would you lead off with your views on the merger?* 約翰, 請你先談談對合併的看法好嗎? | **lead sth ↔ off** *Hal led off the evening with some folk songs.* 哈爾唱了幾首民歌來作為晚會的開始。**2** [I,T] if a road, room etc leads off a place, it connects directly with that place〔路、房間等〕(與…) 相連接, 通向: **lead off from sth** *Go on for about 100 yards and you'll see a path leading off from the main road.* 再走大約 100 碼, 你就能見到一條通向主道的路。| **lead off sth** *a dining room leading off the hall corridor* 與大廳走廊相連接的飯廳 **3** [I] *AmE* to be the first player to try to hit the ball in an INNING (=period of play) in a game of BASEBALL【美】〔棒球比賽在一局中〕率先擊球

lead to sth *phr v* [T not in passive 不用被動態] to make something happen or exist as a result 導致…: *an* *investment program that will lead to the creation of hundreds of new jobs* 會創造上百個新職位的投資規劃 | *The bank has offered a reward for any information leading to the arrest of the men.* 銀行對能使這些人被繩之以法的任何情報提供了獎賞。

lead up to sth *phr v* [T not in passive 不用被動態] **1** if events lead up to something important that happens, they come before it, and often cause it 作為…的先導, 引起: *The book describes the trial and the events leading up to it.* 本書敘述該次審判以及導致其發生的一系列事件。**2** to gradually introduce a subject into a conversation, especially a subject that may be embarrassing or upsetting for you or the person you are talking to 漸漸引入〔話題, 尤指可能使說者或聽者尷尬或不舒服的話題〕: *I suppose all this talk about "business opportunities" is leading up to a request for money?* 我想這關於"商業機會"的所有談話是不是開口要錢的頭一步?

USAGE NOTE 用法說明: LEAD

WORD CHOICE 詞語辨析: **lead, show the way, take, bring, guide, see, direct, tell the way**

To **lead** is to **show the way** by going first. to lead 指在前面領路 (show the way): *You lead and we'll follow.* 你帶路, 我們跟着。| *She led them down the mountain.* 她把他們領下山。

More usually to show someone the way you just **take or bring** them somewhere. 給人帶路更通常的用法是把某人 take 或 bring 到某處: *Please pick him up and take him to the hotel/bring him to my house* (NOT usually 一般不用 *lead*). 請接他去旅館/把他帶到我家裡。

Roads, tunnels, corridors etc. may **lead** to places, but cars, planes etc usually **take** you there. 道路、隧道和走廊等通向某地可用 lead, 但是汽車、飛機等載人去某地通常用 take: *This road leads to/takes you to Chicago* 這條路通往芝加哥 but 但是 *The train took me to Grand Central Station* 火車把我送到大中央車站 (NOT 不用 *led*, unless you were following behind the train! 除非你跟在火車後面!)

If someone needs a lot of help you **guide** them somewhere in order to show them the way and explain things. 某人若需要很多幫助, 用 guide 表示給他帶路並沿途講解: *We'll need someone to guide us through the hills.* 我們需要有人帶我們參觀這山區。| *He guides tourists around the castle.* 他帶領遊客參觀城堡。

See someone somewhere may be used especially if you go with someone to a place because there may be some danger rather than because they do not know the way. 如果和某人去某地不是因為對方不認識路, 而是怕有危險, 可用 see someone somewhere: *It's very late – Do you want me to see you home?* 很晚了──你要我送你回家嗎?

To **direct** (slightly formal) is to explain to someone how to get to a place, but not to go with them. To direct〔稍正式的用法〕指告訴某人如何去某地, 但並沒有一同去: *Could you direct me to the station, please?* 可以告訴我去車站的路嗎? Less formally you **tell** someone **the way**. 給某人指路略為不正式的說法是 tell someone the way: *Can you tell me the way to the station, please?* 能不能告訴我去車站的路?

GRAMMAR 語法

Remember the past tense and past participle of **lead** are both **led**. 記住 lead 的過去式和過去分詞都是 led: *She's led an interesting life* (NOT 不用 *lead*). 她過着有趣的生活。

lead 領先 (地位)

Number 4 is in the lead. 4 號隊員領先。

[2] [2] **lead²** *n*

1 ►RACES ETC 比賽等◄ the lead the position in front of everyone else in a race or competition 領先的地位: **be in the lead** *Le Mond was in the lead after the third lap.* 利·蒙德在第三圈後處於領先的地位。

2 take the lead a) to go ahead of the other competitors in a race or competition 居領先地位: *South Korea has taken the lead in ship-building.* 韓國在造船業中已居領先地位。**b)** to take the responsibility for organizing something 負責〔組織某事〕: *It's up to the older members to take the lead and explain things to the newcomers.* 該由老會員負責給新會員作講解。**c)** to be the first to do something, hoping that others will copy you 帶頭: *The Americans have taken the lead in banning nuclear tests.* 美國人已帶頭禁止核試。

3 ►WINNING AMOUNT 贏的數量◄ [singular] the distance, number of points etc by which one competitor is ahead of another〔距離、得分等的〕超前量; 領先程度: [**+over**] *The Bulls had a 17 point lead over the Celtics by halftime.* 公牛隊上半場結束時領先凱爾特人隊 17 分。| [**+of**] *The latest polls give the Republicans a lead of 32%.* 最近的選舉中共和黨獲 32% 的優勢。

4 ►EXAMPLE 榜樣◄ [C] a suggestion or example for people to copy 引導; 典範, 榜樣: **give (sb) a lead** *It's up to you to give a moral lead.* 你得樹立一個道德的榜樣。| **follow sb's lead** *You say what you think is best. I'll follow your lead.* 你說你的想法最好, 我會聽你的。

5 ►INFORMATION 消息◄ [C] a piece of information that may help you to make a discovery or help find the answer to a problem; CLUE[1] (1) 線索: *The police have several leads as to the location of the stolen goods.* 警察掌握了幾條被偷物資位置的線索。

6 ►PERFORMER 表演者◄ a) [C] the main acting part in a play, film etc 主角: *playing the lead in an amateur production of 'Hamlet'* 在業餘愛好者製作的《哈姆雷特》一劇中扮演主角 **b) lead singer/guitarist etc** the main singer, GUITAR player etc in a musical group 主唱/首席結他手等

7 ►FOR DOG 狗用的◄ [C] *BrE* a piece of rope, leather etc fastened to a dog's collar in order to control it; LEASH[1] (1)【英】〔牽狗的〕繩子; 皮帶

8 ►ELECTRIC WIRE 電線◄ [C] *BrE* an electric wire used to connect a piece of electrical equipment to the power supply【英】導線, 引線, 連接線; CORD[1](3) *AmE*【美】

9 be your lead if it is your lead in a game of cards, you have the right to play your card first〔某人〕先出牌

lead³ /lɛd; led/ *n* **1** [U] a soft heavy easily melted greyish-blue metal, used for water pipes, covering roofs etc 鉛: *lead piping* 鉛管 **2** [C,U] the central part of a pencil 鉛筆芯 **3 go down like a lead balloon** if a suggestion or joke goes down like a lead balloon, people do not like it at all〔建議或笑話〕無人感興趣 **4** [U] *AmE old-fashioned* bullets【美, 過時】子彈: *They filled him full of lead.* 他們朝他狂射子彈。**5 leads** [plural] **a)** sheets of lead used for covering a roof〔蓋屋頂用的〕鉛片 **b)** narrow pieces of lead used for holding small pieces of glass together

L

to form a window〔固定窗玻璃的〕鉛框 —see also 另見 BLACK LEAD, WHITE LEAD

lead·ed gas /ˌlɛdɪd ˋgæs; ˌledɪ̣d ˈgæs/ *n* also 又作 **leaded gasoline** /ˌ.. ˈ.../ [U] *AmE* petrol containing lead【美】含鉛汽油; LEADED PETROL *BrE*【英】

leaded lights /ˌlɛdɪd ˋlaɪts; ˌledɪ̣d ˈlaɪts/ *n* [plural] *BrE* windows with thin narrow pieces of lead (LEAD³ (1)) separating small pieces of glass shaped like squares or diamonds (DIAMOND (2))【英】鉛框玻璃窗

leaded pet·rol /ˌlɛdɪd ˋpɛtrəl; ˌledɪ̣d ˈpetrəl/ *n* [U] *BrE* petrol containing lead (LEAD³ (1))【英】含鉛汽油; LEADED GAS *AmE*【美】

leaded win·dows /ˌlɛdɪd ˋwɪndoz; ˌledɪ̣d ˈwɪndəʊz/ *n* [plural] LEADED LIGHTS 鉛框玻璃窗

lead·en /ˋlɛdn̩; ˈledn/ *adj* **1** *literary* dark grey【文】深灰色的: *a leaden sky* 灰暗的天空 **2** without happiness, excitement, or energy 陰鬱的; 死氣沉沉的, 沉悶的: *a leaden performance* 沉悶的演出

3 1 **lead·er** /ˋlidɚ; ˈliːdə/ *n* [C]

1 ▶IN CONTROL 控制着◀ the person who directs or controls a team, organization, country etc 領導者, 領袖, 首領, 首長: *The prize was awarded to President de Klerk and the ANC leader Nelson Mandela.* 這個獎授給了德克拉克總統和非洲國民大會領導人納爾遜·曼德拉。| *a born leader* 天生的領袖 | **[+of]** *the leader of the local black community* 當地黑人社區的領袖

2 ▶RACE 比賽◀ the person, organization etc that is in front of all the others in a race or competition 領先者: *Schumacher was now catching up and challenging the leaders.* 舒馬赫正追上來, 直逼領先者。| **[+in]** *leaders in the field of information technology* 資訊科技領域的領先者 —see also 另見 MARKET LEADER

3 ▶NEWSPAPER 報紙◀ *BrE* a piece of writing in a newspaper giving the paper's opinion on a subject; EDITORIAL【英】社論

4 ▶MUSICIAN 音樂家◀ *BrE* the main VIOLIN player in an ORCHESTRA【英】首席小提琴手; CONCERTMASTER *AmE*【美】

5 ▶MUSICAL DIRECTOR 音樂指揮◀ *AmE* someone who directs the playing of a musical group; CONDUCTOR (1)【美】樂團指揮

6 ▶TAPE 磁帶◀ *technical* the part at the beginning of a film or recording tape which has nothing on it【術語】〔膠卷、磁帶等前端的〕空白段

7 ▶BRANCH 枝條◀ *technical* a long thin branch that grows from the stem of a bush or tree beyond other branches【術語】〔樹幹或枝上的〕頂枝

8 ▶FISHING 釣魚◀ *technical* a short piece of a special string used to tie the hook onto the end of a fishing line (LINE¹ (16))【術語】接鈎繩

3 2 **lead·er·ship** /ˋlidɚʃɪp; ˈliːdəʃɪp/ *n* **1** [U] the position of being the leader of a team, organization etc 領導地位, 領導權: *Burns took over the leadership of the party.* 伯恩斯奪取了政黨領導權。| **under sb's leadership** (=while a particular person is leader) 在某人的領導下 **2** [U] the quality of being good at leading a team, organization, country etc 領導才能, 領導素質: *someone with vision and leadership* 既有洞察力又有領導才能的人 **3** [C] all the people who lead a group, organization etc [also+plural verb *BrE* 英] 領導人員, 領導層: *The party leadership are in agreement on this matter.* 黨的全體領導層在此問題上取得一致。**4** [U] the position of being in front of others in a competition 領先地位: *the company's leadership in robot technology* 公司在機器人技術上的領先地位

lead-free /ˌlɛd ˋfri; ˌled ˈfriː◂/ *adj* lead-free petrol contains no LEAD³ (1); UNLEADED〔汽油〕無鉛的

lead-in /ˋlid ˌɪn; ˈliːd ɪn/ *n* [C] remarks made by someone to introduce a radio or television show〔介紹廣播或電視節目的〕開場白; 介紹

2 **lead·ing¹** /ˋlidɪŋ; ˈliːdɪŋ/ *adj* [only before noun 僅用於名詞前]

1 ▶MOST IMPORTANT/BEST 最重要的/最佳的◀ best, most important, or most successful 最好的; 最重要的; 最成功的: *the leading software provider in the domestic PC markets* 國內個人電腦市場的最佳軟件供應商 | *a leading heart specialist* 最好的心臟病專家

2 leading edge a) *technical* the front edge of something【術語】〔物體的〕前緣 **b)** the area of an activity where the most modern and advanced equipment and methods are used 前沿領域: *working at the leading edge of genetic engineering* 工作在遺傳工程學的前沿 —see also 另見 LEADING-EDGE

3 leading light a respected person who leads a group or organization, or is important in a particular area of knowledge or activity 受人尊敬的領導人物; 有影響的重要人物

4 leading question a question that deliberately tricks someone into giving the answer you want 誘導性問題

5 leading lady/man the woman or man who acts the most important female or male part in a film, play etc 扮女/男主角的演員 —see also 另見 LEADING ARTICLE

lead·ing² /ˋlɛdɪŋ; ˈledɪŋ/ *n* [U] *technical*【術語】**1** lead (LEAD³ (1)) used for covering roofs, for window frames etc〔蓋屋頂用的〕鉛片;〔固定窗玻璃的〕鉛框 **2** the space left between lines of print on a page〔印刷品的〕行間隔

leading ar·ti·cle /ˌlidɪŋ ˋɑrtɪkl̩; ˌliːdɪŋ ˈɑːtɪkəl/ *n* [C] *BrE* a piece of writing in a newspaper giving the paper's opinion on a subject; EDITORIAL【英】報紙的評論文章, 社論

leading-edge /ˌlidɪŋ ˋɛdʒ; ˌliːdɪŋ ˈedʒ/ *adj* [only before noun 僅用於名詞前] leading-edge machines, systems etc are the most modern and advanced ones that exist〔機器、系統等〕最現代的, 最先進的: *It uses leading-edge voice-recognition software.* 它運用最先進的語音識別軟件。

lead-off /ˋlid ɔf; ˈliːd ɒf/ *adj AmE* happening or going first or before others【美】最先發生的, 開頭的

2 2 **leaf¹** /lif; liːf/ *n plural* **leaves** /livz; liːvz/

1 ▶PLANT 植物◀ [C] one of the flat green parts of a plant that are joined to its stem or branches 樹葉, 葉子: *a flowering bush with large shiny leaves* 長着光亮大葉子的開花灌木 | **be in leaf/come into leaf** *The forest was just coming into leaf.* 森林裡的樹剛開始長葉。

2 take a leaf out of sb's book to copy the way someone else behaves because you admire them 學某人的樣, 以某人為榜樣

3 turn over a new leaf to decide you will change the way you behave and become a better person 翻開新的一頁; 改過自新; 重新做人

4 ▶PAPER 紙◀ [C] *technical* a thin sheet of paper, especially a page in a book【術語】紙頁,〔尤指書的〕一頁 —see also 另見 LOOSE-LEAF, OVERLEAF

5 ▶OF TABLE 桌子的◀ [C] a part of the top of a table that can be taken out to make the table smaller 活動桌面板

6 ▶METAL 金屬◀ [U] metal, especially gold or silver, in a very thin sheet; GOLD LEAF 金屬箔〔尤指金、銀箔〕—see also 另見 **shake like a leaf** (SHAKE¹ (1))

leaf² *v*

leaf through sth *phr v* [T] to turn the pages of a book quickly, without reading it properly 匆匆翻閱: *I was leafing through an old school magazine when I came across your photo.* 當我匆匆翻閱一本學校的舊雜誌時, 我發現了你的相片。

leaf·age /ˋlifɪdʒ; ˈliːfɪdʒ/ *n* [U] the leaves on a tree or plant; FOLIAGE 葉子〔總稱〕

leaf·let¹ /ˋliflɪt; ˈliːflɪ̣t/ *n* [C] a small piece of printed paper giving information or advertising 散頁印刷品; 傳單; 廣告單張: *a leaflet on skin cancer* 有關皮膚癌的傳單

leaflet² *v* [I,T] to give out leaflets in a particular area (向…) 散發傳單: *He's leafleting the neighborhood.* 他正在居民區散發傳單。

leaf mould *BrE*【英】, **leaf mold** *AmE*【美】/ˈ· ·/ *n* [U] dead decaying leaves that form a rich surface on soil 腐葉土

leaf·y /ˈlifi; ˈliːfi/ *adj* **1** having a lot of leaves 多葉的: *leafy green vegetables such as spinach* 菠菜之類的多葉綠色蔬菜 **2** having a lot of trees and plants 多樹木的, 茂密的: *a leafy suburb* 樹木茂密的郊外

2 **league¹** /lig; liːg/ *n* [C] **1** a group of sports teams or players who play games against each other to see who is best 體育運動聯合會: *Spurs finished fourth in the league this season.* 本賽季熱刺隊在聯賽中獲第四名。—compare 比較 CONFERENCE (3) **2 be in a different league from/not be in the same league as** to be much better, or much worse, than someone or something else 和…在不同的檔次上/不在同一等級上: *They're not in the same league as the French at making wine.* 他們釀葡萄酒的水準比不上法國人。**3 be in league** to be working together secretly, especially for a bad purpose 暗中合謀, 私下勾結: **[+with]** *Union leaders were accused of being in league with the Mafia.* 工會領袖被指控與黑手黨勾結。**4** a group of people or countries who have joined together because they have similar aims, political beliefs etc 聯盟, 同盟: *the Young Communist League* 共青團 **5** an old unit for measuring, equal to about five kilometres 里格〔舊時長度單位, 約五公里〕

league² *v* [I, T] *formal* to join together with other people, especially in order to fight for or against something【正式】(與…) 聯合, (與…) 結成同盟

league ta·ble /ˈ· ˌ··/ *n* [C] *especially BrE* a list that shows the positions of people, teams, or organizations that are competing against each other【尤英】比賽名次表

3 **leak¹** /lik; liːk/ *v* **1** [I,T] if a container, pipe, roof etc leaks, or if it leaks gas, liquid etc, there is a small hole or crack in it that lets the gas or liquid flow out or flow through (使) 漏; (使) 滲: *The roof always leaks when it rains.* 一下雨, 屋頂總是漏水。| **leak sth** *My car seems to be leaking oil.* 我的汽車好像正在漏油。**2** [I] if a gas or liquid leaks, it gets in or through a hole in something 〔氣體、液體〕漏出: **[+into/through/out of etc]** *Gas was leaking out of the pipes.* 煤氣從管子裡漏出來了。**3** [T] to deliberately give secret information to a newspaper, television company etc 泄露〔祕密給報紙、電視台等〕: **leak sth to** *Details of his business dealings were leaked to the press.* 他的商務來往的詳情已被泄露給新聞界了。**4 leak like a sieve** to leak very badly 漏得很厲害

leak out *phr v* [I] if secret information leaks out, a lot of people find out about it 泄露: *News of his dismissal soon leaked out.* 他被免去職務的消息不久便泄露出去。

leak² *n* [C] **1** a small hole that lets liquid or gas flow into or out of something 漏洞, 裂縫: *There's a leak in the car radiator.* 汽車的散熱器上有條裂縫。**2 a gas/oil/water leak** an escape of gas or liquid through a hole in something 煤氣/油/水的泄漏 **3** a situation in which secret information is deliberately given to a newspaper, television company etc 〔向報紙、電視台等〕透露祕密: *a leak suggesting that the hospital is to be closed* 透露醫院要關閉的消息 **4 take/have a leak** *slang* to pass water from your body; URINATE【俚】小便, 撒尿 —see also 另見 **spring a leak** (SPRING² (9))

leak·age /ˈlikɪdʒ; ˈliːkɪdʒ/ *n* [C,U] **1** an example of gas, water etc leaking, or the amount of gas or liquid that has leaked 漏出; 滲出; 漏出量 **2** the deliberate spreading of information that should be kept secret 〔祕密的〕泄露, 透露

leak·y /ˈlikɪ; ˈliːki/ *adj* having a hole or other fault so that liquid or gas passes through a container, roof, pipe etc 漏的; 有漏洞的; 有裂縫的: *the constant dripping of a leaky tap* 水龍頭漏水不止 —**leakiness** *n* [U] —see picture on page A18 參見 A18 頁圖

3 **lean¹** /lin; liːn/ *v past tense and past participle* **leaned** or **leant** /lɛnt; lent/ *especially BrE*【尤英】**1** [I always+adv/prep] to move or bend your body in a particular direction 屈身: **[+forward/back etc]** *Robert was leaning forward, talking to the people in front.* 羅拔正向前彎着身和前面的人說話。| *They were leaning over her, trying to wake her up.* 他們彎下身去想把她弄醒。**2** [I] to slope or bend from an upright position 傾斜, 彎曲: *trees leaning in the wind* 在風中傾斜的樹木 **3** [I always+adv/prep] to support yourself or be supported in a sloping position against a wall or other surface 倚, 靠: **[+on/against]** *He was leaning on the bar with a drink in his hand.* 他手上拿着一杯飲料, 正靠在酒吧的櫃台上。| *There was a ladder leaning against the wall.* 牆上斜靠着一部梯子。**4** [T always+adv/prep] to put something in a sloping position where it is supported 〔把某物〕斜靠着放: **lean sth on/against sth** *Gail leant her head on his shoulder.* 嘉兒把頭靠在他的肩上。

lean on sb/sth *phr v* [T] **1** to depend on someone or something for support and encouragement, especially at a difficult time 依靠, 倚賴〔尤指在困難時刻〕: *It's good to know you've got friends to lean on.* 很高興知道你已找到可以信賴的朋友。**2** *informal* to try to influence someone, especially by threatening them【非正式】〔對某人〕施加壓力〔尤指通過恐嚇〕: **lean on sb to do sth** *Lean on them to pay up.* 威脅他們把錢付清。

lean towards sth *phr v* [T] to tend to support, or begin to support, a particular set of opinions, beliefs etc 傾向於支持, 開始支持: *My wife is voting Democrat but I'm leaning towards the Republicans.* 我妻子準備投民主黨的票, 但是我傾向支持共和黨。

lean² *adj* **1** thin in a healthy and attractive way 苗條的, 健美的: *lean and athletic looking* 外表健美的 —see 見 THIN (USAGE) **2** lean meat does not have much fat on it 〔肉〕瘦的, 脂肪少的 **3** a lean organization, company etc uses only as much money and as many people as it needs, so that nothing is wasted 〔組織、公司等〕節儉的; 精簡的 **4** a lean period is a very difficult time because there is not enough money, business etc 不景氣的: *a lean year for business* 生意不景氣的一年 —**leanness** *n* [U]

lean³ *n* [U] the fleshy part of meat and not the bone or fat 瘦肉

lean·ing /ˈlinɪŋ; ˈliːnɪŋ/ *n* [C] a tendency to prefer or agree with a particular set of beliefs, opinions etc; INCLINATION (2) 傾向, 偏愛: *Fran has Conservative leanings.* 弗蘭有親保守黨的傾向。| **[+towards]** *a leaning towards the Right* 右翼傾向

leant /lɛnt; lent/ the past tense and past participle of LEAN¹

lean-to /ˈ· ·/ *n* [C] a small roughly made building that rests against the side of a larger building 靠着大屋所建的單坡屋頂小屋, 披屋

leap¹ /lip; liːp/ *v past tense and past participle* **leapt** /lɛpt; lept/ *especially BrE*【尤英】, **leaped** *especially AmE*【尤美】

1 ►JUMP 跳◄ **a)** [I always+adv/prep] to jump high into the air or to jump in order to land in a different place 跳, 跳躍: *Jen leapt across the stream.* 詹恩跳過了小溪。**b)** [T] *literary* to jump over something【文】跳過, 躍過〔某物〕: *Brenda leaped the gate and ran across the field.* 布倫黛躍出了大門跑過田野。

2 ►MOVE FAST 快速移動◄ [I always+adv/prep] to move very quickly and with a lot of energy 敏捷地移動; 迅速地反應: **[+up/out/into etc]** *I leapt up the stairs three at a time.* 我一步三級地躍上樓梯。| **leap to your feet** *Morgan leapt to his feet and started shouting.* 摩根立刻跳起來開始大叫大嚷。| **leap to sb's assistance/defence etc** *Wendi leaped to his assistance.* 温蒂趕緊去援助他。

3 ►INCREASE 增加◄ [I] to increase quickly and by a large amount 迅速大幅增加: *The price of gas leapt 15% overnight.* 煤氣價格一夜之間就上漲了 15%。

4 leap at the chance/opportunity/offer to accept a chance, opportunity, or offer very eagerly 抓住機會; 急忙接受: *They were offering a free holiday in the Algarve, so naturally I leapt at the chance.* 他們正在提供去阿爾加維的免費度假, 我自然趕緊抓住這個機會。

5 leap out at you if something you are looking at leaps out at you, it is very easy for you to notice because it is unusual or unexpected 特別引人注目, 很容易注意到〔非同尋常或意料之外的事〕
6 ►HEART 心臟◄ [I] *especially literary* if your heart leaps, you feel a sudden surprise, happiness, or excitement【尤文】突然感到驚奇[幸福; 激動]: *My heart leaped when I saw Paul at the airport.* 當我在機場看到保羅的時候, 我感到驚喜萬分。—see also 另見 **look before you leap** (LOOK¹ (10))

leap² *n* [C] **1** a big jump 跨躍: *Bill cleared the ditch with a single leap.* 比爾一躍就跳過了水溝。**2 by/in leaps and bounds** if someone or something increases, develops, grows etc by leaps and bounds, they increase etc very quickly 迅速地, 突飛猛進地: *Andrew's German is improving by leaps and bounds.* 安德魯的德語進步得很快。**3** a sudden large increase in the number or amount of something 數量的激增: **[+in]** *a leap in prices* 物價猛漲 **4** a mental process that is needed to understand something difficult or see the connection between two very different ideas 思維的發揮: **a leap of imagination** *It takes a great leap of imagination to see John as a teacher.* 要發揮豐富的想像力才能看得出約翰是一位老師。**5 a leap in the dark** something you do, or a risk that you take, without knowing what will happen as a result 冒險舉動, 輕舉妄動; 瞎闖

leap·frog¹ /ˈlipˌfrɑg; ˈliːpfrɒg/ *n* [U] a children's game in which someone bends over and someone else jumps over them 跳背遊戲

leapfrog 跳背遊戲

leapfrog² *v* [I,T] to achieve something more quickly than usual by missing some of the usual stages 越過, 超越, 越級: *Nigel leapfrogged two ranks and was made a colonel.* 奈傑爾越了兩級升為上校。

leapt /lɛpt; lept/ the past tense and past participle of LEAP¹

leap year /ˈ· ·/ *n* [C] a year, which happens every fourth year, when February has 29 days instead of 28 閏年〔每四年一次, 二月份有29天而不是28天〕

1 1 **learn** /lɝn; lɜːn/ *v past tense and past participle* **learned** or **learnt** /lɝnt; lɜːnt/ *especially BrE*【尤英】
1 ►SUBJECT/SKILL 科目/技藝◄ [I,T] to gain knowledge of a subject, or skill in an activity, by experience, by studying it, or by being taught 學習; 學到; 學會: *What's the best way to learn a language?* 學習語言的最佳方法是甚麼? | *Children are usually very quick at learning.* 小孩通常學得很快。| **[+about]** *I am very keen to learn about the town's history.* 我很想了解該城鎮的歷史。| **learn (how) to do sth** *I learnt to drive when I was 17.* 我17歲那年學會了開車。| **learn how/what/who etc** *In the first lesson we'll learn how to format a text file.* 第一課我們將學習如何安排文本文件的版式。—compare 比較 TEACH, see 見 KNOW¹ (USAGE)
2 ►FIND OUT 發現◄ [I,T] *formal* to find out information, news etc by hearing it from someone else【正式】獲悉, 得知, 聽到: **[+of/about]** *We were all saddened to learn of her death.* 得知她的死訊, 我們都很難過。| **learn sth** *Where did you learn the news?* 你在哪裡聽到這個消息的? | **learn (that)** *May was pleased to learn that he had arrived safely.* 知道他安全抵達, 梅很高興。| **learn who/what/whether etc** *We have yet to learn who will be the new manager.* 我們還未聽說誰將是新的經理。
3 ►REMEMBER 記住◄ [T] to get to know something so well that you can easily remember it; MEMORIZE 背誦, 記住: *The actor was busy learning his lines.* 那名男演員正在忙於背台詞。
4 ►CHANGE YOUR BEHAVIOUR 改變行為◄ [T] to gradually understand a situation and start behaving in the way that people expect you to behave〔漸漸〕懂得, 〔慢慢〕領悟: **learn (that)** *They have to learn that they can't just do whatever they like.* 他們得明白他們不能隨心所欲地做事。| **learn to do sth** *gamblers who had learned to modify their behaviour* 學會改正行為的賭徒
5 learn from your mistakes to improve the way you do things because of mistakes you have made 從錯誤中學習
6 learn (sth) the hard way to understand a situation or develop a skill by learning from your mistakes and bad experiences〔從錯誤和教訓中〕學會 (某事)
7 learn your lesson to suffer so much because you did something wrong or stupid, that you will not do it again 得到教訓: *I really learned my lesson when I got sunburned last year on vacation.* 當我去年度假曬傷了皮膚時, 我真的得到了教訓。—see also 另見 **live and learn** (LIVE¹ (27))

This graph shows how common the different grammar patterns of the verb **learn** are. 本圖所示為動詞 learn 構成的不同語法模式的使用頻率。

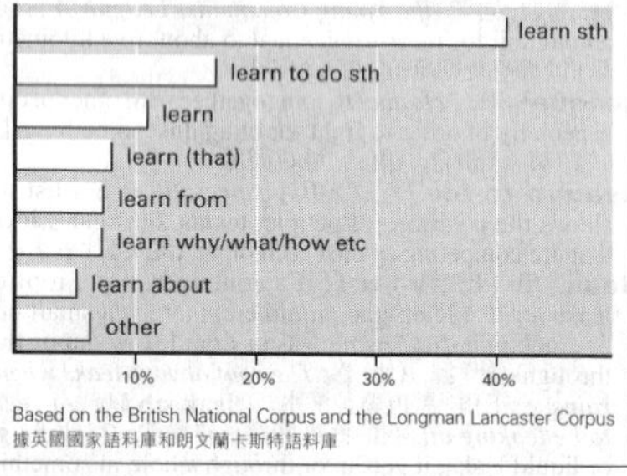

Based on the British National Corpus and the Longman Lancaster Corpus
據英國國家語料庫和朗文蘭卡斯特語料庫

learn·ed /ˈlɝnɪd; ˈlɜːnɪ̇d/ *adj formal*【正式】**1** having a lot of knowledge because you have read and studied a lot 有學問的; 博學的 **2 learned books/works etc** books etc to be used by advanced students 學術性書籍/著作等 —**learnedly** *adv*

learn·er /ˈlɝnə; ˈlɜːnə/ *n* [C] **1** someone who is learning to do something 學習者; 初學者: *Jill's a very quick learner.* 吉爾是一位善於學習的人。| **[+of]** *a grammar book for learners of English* 英語初學者的語法書 **2** also 又作 **learner driver** *BrE* someone who is learning to drive a car【英】實習司機, 見習司機

learner's per·mit /ˈ·· ˌ·/ *n* [C] *AmE* an official document that gives you permission to learn to drive【美】駕駛學習證; PROVISIONAL LICENCE *BrE*【英】

learn·ing /ˈlɝnɪŋ; ˈlɜːnɪŋ/ *n* [U] knowledge gained through reading and study 知識, 學問: *a man of great learning* 學問淵博的人

learning curve /ˈ·· ·/ *n* [C] the rate at which you learn a new skill 學習曲線

learning dis·a·bil·i·ty /ˈ·· ··ˌ···/ *n* [C] a mental problem that affects a child's ability to learn things 學習障礙, 學習能力缺陷

learnt /lɝnt; lɜːnt/ the past tense and past participle of LEARN

lease¹ /lis; liːs/ *n* [C] **1** a legal agreement which allows you to use a car, building etc for a period of time, in return for rent 租約, 租契: **take out a lease** (=sign a lease so that you can rent something) 簽租約 *We've taken out a lease on an office building.* 我們已經簽了一幢辦公樓的租約。**2 a new lease of life** *especially BrE*【尤英】, **a new lease on life** *AmE*【美】**a)** if someone has a new lease of life, they become healthy, active, or happy again after being weak, ill, or tired 重新恢復生氣: *The vacation has given me a new lease of life.* 假期使我重新恢復

了精力。**b)** if something has a new lease of life, improvements are made that mean it will last longer 延長使用壽命: *Give dirty rugs a new lease of life with our super steam cleaner!* 使用我們的高效能蒸汽除垢器能延長髒地毯的使用壽命!

lease² *v* [T] **1** also 又作 **lease out** to use or let someone use buildings, property etc on a lease 出租: **lease sb sth/lease sth to sb** *They decided to lease the building to another company.* 他們決定把樓租給另外一家公司。**2** to pay to use expensive machinery or equipment for a long period, instead of buying it 長期租用〔某物〕: *We lease all our computers.* 我們長期租用所有的電腦。

lease·back /ˈlisˌbæk; ˈliːsbæk/ *n* [C,U] *technical* an arrangement in which you sell or give something to someone, but continue to use it by paying them rent【術語】售後回租〔租用已出售的財產〕

lease·hold /ˈlisˌhold; ˈliːshəʊld/ *adj especially BrE* leasehold property is owned only for as long as is stated in a lease【尤英】根據地契年期而擁有的, 租賃的 —compare 比較 FREEHOLD —**leasehold** *adv*: *Buying leasehold is cheaper.* 按地契年期購買便宜些。

lease·hold·er /ˈlisˌholdɚ; ˈliːshəʊldə/ *n* [C] someone who lives in a leasehold house, apartment etc〔房屋等〕承租人

leash¹ /liʃ; liːʃ/ *n* [C] *especially AmE*【尤美】**1** a piece of rope, leather etc fastened to a dog's collar in order to control it〔牽狗的〕繩子; 皮帶; LEAD² (7) *BrE*【英】: **be on leash** *All dogs must be on a leash by order of the Parks Department.* 園林部門規定所有的狗都必須用帶子牽着。**2 have sb on a leash** *humorous* to be able to control someone【幽默】能控制某人: *Jerry's wife has him on a tight leash.* 傑里的老婆牢牢地控制着他。

leash² *v* [T] *AmE* to put a leash on a dog【美】〔用牽狗繩〕繫住〔狗〕

1 1 **least¹** /list; liːst/ *determiner, pron* **1 at least a)** not less than a particular number or amount 至少, 起碼〔就數量而言〕: *It will take you at least 20 minutes to get there.* 到那裡至少要花掉你 20 分鐘。| *He had been dead for at least a fortnight.* 他死了至少有兩星期。| **at the very least** (=not less than and probably much more than) 最起碼 *It would cost $1 million at the very least.* 最起碼要付一百萬美元。**b)** even if nothing else is true, or even if nothing else happens 不管怎樣, 無論如何: *I think you should at least consider his offer.* 我認為你至少應考慮他的建議。| *Well, at least I don't spend all my money on drink like some people.* 好了, 不管怎樣, 我不會像有些人那樣把所有的錢都花在喝酒上。**c)** used when you are mentioning an advantage that makes certain problems or disadvantages seem less serious 至少, 起碼〔用於指出某些問題或不利條件的優點〕: *At least he was safe now.* 至少他現在是安全的。| *The film wasn't very interesting, but at least it filled the time.* 電影沒有多少意思, 但起碼打發了時間。**d)** used when you are correcting or changing something that you have just said 至少, 起碼〔用於糾正剛說過的話〕: *Mary was depressed all evening. Or at least it seemed that way.* 瑪麗整夜情緒都很低落。至少看起來如此。| *She has no plans to return to England yet, at least as far as I know.* 她還沒有回英國的計劃, 至少據我所知是這樣。**2** the smallest in number, amount, or importance〔數量、重要性〕最小; 最少: *It's not always wise to buy the one that costs the least.* 買最便宜的貨並非總是明智之舉。| *Those with the least money pay the least in taxes.* 收入最少的人納稅也最少。**3 not the least/not in the least/not the least bit** none at all, or not at all 一點也不: *It doesn't matter in the least if you're a bit late.* 如果你遲來些, 一點也沒有關係。| *She didn't seem the least bit worried.* 她似乎一點也不擔憂。| *He came up without the least hesitation and asked me what I was doing there.* 他毫不猶豫地走過來問我在那兒幹甚麼。**4 the least sb could do** used when saying what you think someone should or could do to help someone else 起碼能〔為別人〕做的事: *The least he could do is give them some money towards the rent.* 他起碼能給他們一些錢付房租。**5 to say the least** used to show that something is worse or more serious than you are actually saying 退一步講, 至少可以說: *He was rather offended, to say the least.* 說得輕點, 他相當惱火。**6 the least of your worries** something you are not worried about because there are other more important problems 最不擔心的事: *Deciding what to wear for the trial is the least of my worries.* 穿甚麼衣服參加選拔賽是我最不擔心的。

least² *adv* **1** less than anything or anyone else 最少, 最小: *It happened when we least expected it.* 此事在我們最沒有料想到的時候發生了。| *He was the least experienced of the teachers.* 他是教師中經驗最少的。| *The tax hits those who can least afford it.* 稅收使那些最交不起稅的人受到打擊。**2 least of all** especially not a particular person〔在多者中〕最不的: *No one knew where he was, least of all his family.* 沒有人知道他在哪裡, 更不用說他的家人了。**3 not least** *formal* especially【正式】尤其, 特別: *The president's speeches were alarming, not least to the country's allies.* 總統的演講令人恐慌, 對那些盟國尤其如此。

least com·mon mul·ti·ple /ˌ· ·· ˈ···/ LOWEST COMMON MULTIPLE 最小公倍數

least·wise /ˈlistˌwaɪz; ˈliːstwaɪz/ also 又作 **least·ways** /-wez; -weɪz/ *adv AmE informal* at least; anyway【美, 非正式】至少; 無論如何: *He was there a minute ago, leastwise that's what Sue said.* 剛才他還在那兒, 至少蘇是那麼說的。

leath·er¹ /ˈlɛðɚ; ˈleðə/ *n* [U] **1** animal skin that has been treated to preserve it, and is used for making shoes, bags etc〔動物的〕皮, 皮革: *a book bound in leather* 皮面裝幀的書 —see picture on page A16 參見 A16 頁圖 **2 leathers** [plural] special leather clothes worn for protection by someone riding a MOTORCYCLE〔騎摩托車穿的〕皮革防護衣 —see also 另見 **run/go hell for leather** (HELL¹ (24)) 3

leather² *adj* made of leather 皮製的: *a leather jacket* 皮夾克

leath·er·ette /ˌlɛðəˈrɛt; ˌleðəˈret/ *n* [U] a cheap material made to look like leather 人造革, 人造皮; NAUGAHYDE *AmE*【美】

leath·er·y /ˈlɛðərɪ; ˈleðəri/ *adj* hard and stiff like leather rather than soft or smooth 似皮革的; 堅韌的: *leathery skin* 粗糙的皮膚

1 1 **leave¹** /liv; liːv/ *v past tense and past participle* **left** /lɛft; left/

① LEAVE A PLACE, VEHICLE 離開某地、某交通工具	④ REMAIN 剩下
② LEAVE YOUR JOB, HOME, WIFE ETC 離職, 離開家/妻子等	⑤ NOT DO STH 不做某事
③ LEAVE STH SOMEWHERE 留某物於某處	⑥ STATE/POSITION 狀態/形勢
	⑦ DECIDE/CHOOSE 決定/選擇
	⑧ DEATH 死亡
	⑨ OTHER MEANINGS 其他意思

① LEAVE A PLACE, VEHICLE 離開某地、某交通工具

1 ►LEAVE 離開◄ [I,T] to go away from a place or a person 離開; 前往, 出發: *What time did you leave the office?* 你甚麼時候離開辦公室的? | *They were so noisy that the manager asked them to leave.* 他們吵鬧得以致於經理請他們離開。| **[+for]** *They're leaving for Rome in the morning.* 他們打算早晨動身去羅馬。| **leave to do sth** *Franca left early to meet her mother.* 弗蘭卡很早出門去接她母親。| **leave sb doing sth** *Ann left Keith dozing in the chair.* 安由着基思在椅子上打瞌睡。

2 ►TRAIN/SHIP ETC 火車/船等◄ [T] to get off a train, ship etc 下〔火車、船等〕: *Make sure to check the overhead luggage compartments before you leave the plane.* 下飛機前別忘了檢查頭頂上的行李箱。

3 leave sb to sth to go away and let someone continue what they are doing 離開後讓某人繼續做某事: *I'll leave you to your work.* 我走了, 你接着幹吧。

4 leave him to himself/leave her to herself etc to go away from someone so that they are alone 讓他/她獨自待着

② LEAVE YOUR JOB, HOME, WIFE ETC 離職, 離開家/妻子等

5 ►HOME/SCHOOL ETC 家/學校等◄ [I,T] to stop living at your parents' home, stop going to school etc 離〔家〕; 離〔校〕: *Zoe wants to be a hairdresser when she leaves school.* 佐伊離校後想當一位美髮師。| *Tom wants to leave home.* 湯姆想離開家。

6 ►HUSBAND/WIFE ETC 丈夫/妻子等◄ [I,T] to stop living with someone you had a close relationship with 離開〔親密的人〕: **leave sb for sb** (=leave in order to live with someone else) 離開某人與另一人同居 *Jan's husband's left her for another woman.* 簡的丈夫離開她要和另一個女人同居。

7 ►COUNTRY/PLACE 國家/地方◄ [I,T] to stop living in a country, town etc and go somewhere else 遷離: *They're leaving Minneapolis to live in Santa Fe.* 他們即將離開明尼阿波利斯去聖菲居住。

8 ►JOB/COMPANY 工作/公司◄ [I,T] to stop working for a particular organization or being a member of a group 離職; 脫離〔某團體〕: *Bill's leaving the company after 25 years' service.* 比爾在工作了25年後要離開公司了。| *We are concerned about the number of young people leaving the church.* 我們關心年輕人離教的人數。| **a leaving present** (=for someone who is leaving) 臨別禮品

9 leave sb alone to stop annoying or upsetting someone 不去打擾某人, 讓某人獨自待着: *Why can't you just leave her alone?* 你為甚麼不能讓她一個人待會兒?

10 leave sth alone to stop touching something 別碰某物: *Will you leave that piano alone?* 你別碰那架鋼琴好嗎? | **leave it/this alone** *Leave it alone or you'll break it!* 別碰它, 否則你會把它弄壞的!

11 leave go of/leave hold of *BrE* to stop holding something【英】放開, 鬆手; 放掉: *Leave go of me!* 放開我!

12 leave it at that used to say that you have said or done enough about something 就到此為止; 別再爭論下去了: *Let's leave it at that for today.* 我們今天就到此為止。

③ LEAVE STH SOMEWHERE 留某物於某處

13 ►LET STH REMAIN 使某物仍處於某種狀態◄ [T always+adv/prep] to let something or someone stay where they are when you go away 把〔某物或某人〕留在原處: **leave sth in/on etc** *Someone's left their car in the middle of the driveway.* 有人把車留在車道中間。| *If you leave that on the floor, it'll get trodden on and broken.* 如果你把這留在地板上, 它會被踩碎的。| *I've left the kids with Sandra.* 我把孩子們留給仙杜拉照顧了。

14 ►FORGET STH 忘記某物◄ [T always+adv/prep] to forget to take something with you when you leave a place 丟下, 遺忘: **leave sth behind/in/on etc** *Oh no! I've left the paperwork in my office.* 哎呀不好! 我把要做的文書工作忘在辦公室了。

15 ►FOR SB TO FIND 讓某人找到◄ [T] to put something in a place where someone else can find it 留, 留下〔把某物放在某人找得到的地方〕: *Miriam always leaves a spare key under the plant.* 米里亞姆總是把一把備用的鑰匙留在那棵樹下。| *I'll leave you some milk in the fridge.* 我會在冰箱裡給你留些牛奶。

16 ►LETTER/MESSAGE 信件/口信◄ [T] to leave a letter, package, message etc somewhere for someone〔給某人〕留下〔信件、包裹、口信等〕: *If you'd care to leave your name and number, he'll call you right back.* 如果你願意留下姓名和電話號碼的話, 他一回來就會給你打電話。| **leave sth for sb/leave sb sth** *Lucy left a note for you.* 露茜給你留了一張便條。| *Who left me this message?* 誰給我留了這個口信?| **leave word with sb** (=leave a message with someone) 給某人留下口信 *Could you leave word with my secretary if you can't make it?* 如果你辦不成的話, 能否給我的祕書留一個口信?

④ REMAIN 剩下

17 ►BE LEFT 被剩下◄ [T] to remain after everything else has been taken away or used 剩下, 剩餘; 留下來: *I'll have another brandy if there's any left.* 如果還有剩餘的話, 我就再喝一杯白蘭地。| *By 5 o'clock there was hardly anyone left in the office.* 到5點的時候, 辦公室裡幾乎走得沒有人了。| **have sth left** *How much time do we have left to finish this?* 我們還剩多少時間完成這個? | **be left over** (=remain after you have used or spent all the rest) 餘下, 用後剩下 *If there's any money left over, you can keep it for yourself.* 如果錢還有剩餘, 就歸你了。

⑤ NOT DO STH 不做某事

18 ►DELAY 推遲◄ [T] to not do something until later 留待, 留到: *Let's leave the dishes for tomorrow.* 我們把盤子留到明天洗吧。| *Leave it another week, then tell him he'll have to decide.* 把此事再往後放一週, 到時告訴他必須作出決定。| *Leave the batter to stand for 15 minutes.* 讓麵糊擱置15分鐘。| **leave sth for now** *Leave the filing for now. You can do it later.* 文檔整理現在暫時擱一下, 你可以稍後再做。

19 ►NOT DO STH 不做某事◄ [T] to not do something that you ought to do 留下, 不去做〔該做的事〕: *I couldn't face the ironing so I just left it.* 我怕熨燙衣服, 所以我就沒有去做。

20 ►NOT EAT/DRINK 不吃/喝◄ [T] if you leave food or drink, you do not eat it because you do not like it or you have had enough〔因不喜歡或已吃飽而把食物或飲料〕留下來不吃[不喝]: *If you don't like the stew, just leave it.* 如果你不喜歡燉菜, 就把它留下來吧。

21 leave sb/sth be to not disturb or annoy someone, or not touch or move something 不要去打擾, 不去管〔某人〕; 別動〔某物〕: *Just leave Jenny be and she'll sort things out for herself.* 別打擾珍妮, 她自己會把事情處理好的。

22 leave well (enough) alone to not try to change a situation in case you make it worse than it was before 不要弄巧成拙; 不如維持現狀為好: *If I were you I would leave well alone.* 我要是你, 我會維持原狀, 免得弄巧成拙。

23 leave sb to their own devices to not tell someone what to do or offer them help, but let them do what they decide to do 聽某人自便; 不要支配[幫助]某人

⑥ STATE/POSITION 狀態/形勢

24 [T] **a)** to make something stay, or let something stay in a particular state or position 使〔某物〕留下[處於]〔某種狀態或位置〕: *How did you leave things after the*

meeting? 會議後你把事情處理得怎樣? | **leave sth open/empty/untidy etc** *I wish you'd stop leaving the door open.* 我希望你別老開着門。| *The trial left a lot of questions unanswered.* 試驗留下了許多沒有得到解答的問題。| **leave sth on/off/out etc** *Leave the television on, will you?* 開着電視, 好嗎? | **leave sth doing sth** *I'll just leave the engine running while I pop in.* 我順便去一下那兒的時候, 會讓引擎繼續開着。**b)** if something leaves you in a particular condition, you are in that condition as a result of it 使〔某人〕落到某種地步: *Paying for the repairs left Jim without a cent.* 付了修理費後吉姆已身無分文。| *Frankly, their rudeness left me speechless.* 坦率地講, 他們的粗魯使我無話可說。| **leave sb doing sth** *Carla's narrow escape left her shaking with terror.* 卡拉死裡逃生, 嚇得渾身發抖。

⑦ **DECIDE/CHOOSE 決定/選擇**

25 ►LET SB DECIDE/TAKE RESPONSIBILITY 讓某人決定/負責◄ [T] to let someone decide something or take responsibility for something 把…留交〔某人決定或負責〕; 委託; 交由: **leave sth with sb** *Leave it with me and I'll fix it for you.* 把它留給我, 我會幫你修好的。| **leave sth to sb** (=let someone choose or decide) 把某事交由某人〔選擇或決定〕 *I've always left financial decisions to my wife.* 我總是把財務大權交給妻子負責。| **leave doing sth to sb** *I'll leave buying the tickets to you.* 我把買票的事交給你去辦。| **leave sb to do sth** *BrE*【英】*I'll leave you to choose which film we see.* 我讓你來選擇我們看哪部電影。| **leave it to me** (=I'll take responsibility for it) 我來負責 *Leave it to me. I'll make sure it gets posted.* 把它交給我吧, 我保證把它寄出去。| **leave it (up) to sb to do sth** *We left it to Dad to get the packing done.* 我們把打包的事交給爸爸負責。| *I'll leave it up to you to decide.* 我把這件事交給你決定。| **leave sth to chance** (=take no action and just wait and see what happens) 聽天由命; 順其自然

26 leave sb with no choice/option to force someone to do something because there is nothing else they can do 讓某人別無選擇: *You leave me with no option but to resign.* 你讓我別無選擇, 只有辭職。

⑧ **DEATH 死亡**

27 ►WHEN YOU DIE 臨死時◄ [T] **a)** to give something to someone after you die 遺贈; 遺留: *The old lady left $5 million.* 老婦人遺留下了五百萬美元。| **leave sth to sb/sth** *He had left all his money to charity.* 他把所有的錢都遺贈給了慈善事業。| **leave sb sth** *Hugo left me his mother's ring.* 雨果把他母親的戒指遺贈給了我。**b)** to have members of your family still alive when you die〔去世後〕遺下: *Collins leaves a wife and three children.* 柯林斯遺下了妻子和三個孩子。

⑨ **OTHER MEANINGS 其他意思**

28 leave a space/gap etc to deliberately make a space etc when you are doing something 留有餘地[空間等]: *Leave a 10 centimetre gap between the young plants.* 秧苗之間留下 10 厘米的空間。| **leave room** *Drivers should always leave plenty of room for cyclists.* 司機總是應該給騎車人留出足夠的空間。

29 leave a mark/stain/scar etc to make a mark etc that remains afterwards 留下記號/污跡/疤痕等: *The cut was deep and left a terrible scar.* 刀口很深, 留下了可怕的傷疤。| *William had left a trail of muddy footprints across the floor.* 威廉在地板上留下了一串泥腳印。

30 leave sb cold to not interest or excite someone at all 絲毫引不起某人的興趣: *Modern Jazz leaves me cold, I'm afraid.* 現代爵士樂恐怕引不起我一點兒興趣。

31 leave sb/sth standing *informal* to be much better, quicker etc than someone or something else【非正式】遠遠勝過某人/某物: *Anna leaves all her classmates standing.* 安娜遠遠超過了她所有的同班同學。

32 leave a lot to be desired to be very unsatisfactory 令人極不滿意, 有很大的改進餘地: *Your conduct this term has left a lot to be desired.* 這學期你的品行有很多地方仍有待改進。

33 leave a bad taste in your mouth if an experience leaves a bad taste in your mouth, remembering it upsets you or makes you feel uncomfortable 留下了壞的感覺[印象]: *The things she said really left a nasty taste in my mouth.* 她說的事情確實給我留下了惡劣的印象。

34 leave no stone unturned to do everything that you can in order to find something or solve a problem 千方百計, 竭盡全力: *Jarvis left no stone unturned in his search for the manuscript.* 賈維斯竭盡全力尋找手稿。

35 leave sth aside/leave sth to one side to not think about or consider something for a time, so that you can think about something else〔暫時〕把某事擱置起來: **leaving aside** (=used to say that you do not want to consider something for a time) 暫不考慮 *Leaving aside the question of expense, what's your opinion?* 暫不考慮費用問題, 你的意見如何? —see also 另見 **take it or leave it** (TAKE[1] (18a))

leave sb/sth **behind** *phr v* [T] **1** to forget to take something with you when you leave a place 忘了帶, 遺忘: *I think I left my credit card behind at the restaurant.* 我想我把信用卡遺忘在餐廳裡了。**2** to move far ahead of someone who cannot run, walk, or drive as fast as you can 將〔某人〕拋在後面: **leave sb far behind** *BrE*【英】/ **leave sb way behind** *especially AmE*【尤美】*I was soon left far behind.* 很快我就被遠遠地拋在了後面。**3** to let something or someone stay in a place when you go away, especially permanently〔尤指永久地〕離開〔某物或某人〕: *Sooner or later we have to leave our parents behind.* 遲早我們都得離開父母。**4 be/get left behind** to not work as well or as quickly as someone else, so that you make less progress than they do 落後: *You'll have to put in some extra work at night if you don't want to get left behind.* 如果你不希望落後的話, 就得開夜車。

leave off *phr v* [I,T] *informal* to stop doing something【非正式】停止: *I wish the rain would leave off for five minutes.* 我希望雨能停五分鐘。| *Let's start again from where we left off.* 讓我們從中斷處重新開始。| **leave off (doing) sth** *BrE*【英】: *Leave off shouting! I can't hear myself think in here.* 別喊了! 我在這兒沒法思考了。

leave sb/sth **out** *phr v* [T] **1** to not include someone or something in a group, list, activity etc 遺漏, 漏掉: *You've left out a zero in this phone number.* 你在這電話號碼中漏掉了一個零。| **leave sb/sth out of sth** *Kidd has been left out of the team.* 基德被球隊除了名。**2 be/feel left out** to feel as if you are not accepted or welcome in a social group 被忽視[冷落]/覺得被忽視[冷落]: *All the others seemed to know each other and I began to feel left out.* 其他所有人似乎都彼此互相認識, 我開始感到被冷落了。**3 leave it out!** *BrE spoken* used to tell someone to stop lying, pretending, or being annoying【英口】〔用於告知某人〕別撒謊[裝蒜, 煩人]了!

3 2 **leave²** *n*

1 ►HOLIDAY 假期◄ [U] time that you are allowed to spend away from your work, especially in the armed forces 假期, 假日; 〔尤指軍人的〕休假: *I've applied for three days' leave.* 我已經請了三天假。| **be on leave** *I'm in command while Farringdon is on leave.* 法林頓休假期間我負責指揮。

2 sick/maternity/compassionate leave time that you are allowed to spend away from work because you are ill, because you have had a baby, or because of a personal problem such as the death of a relative 病假/產假/私事假

3 leave of absence a period of time that you are allowed to spend away from work for a particular purpose

准假: *She's been given leave of absence to attend a computer course.* 她獲准休假參加電腦課程培訓。

4 take leave of your senses to become crazy and behave in a strange way 發瘋: *You want to marry him? Have you taken leave of your senses?* 你要嫁給他? 你是不是瘋了?

5 ►PERMISSION 許可◄ [U] *formal* permission to do something, especially something you would not normally be allowed to do【正式】許可, 准許: *All this was done entirely without my leave.* 所有這些都是在根本沒有得到我許可的情況下進行的。| **leave to do sth** *Julia had special leave to do her exams at home.* 茱麗亞獲得特許在家完成考試。| **ask leave** *He asked leave to speak to her in private.* 他請求允許私下和她談話。

6 without so much as a by your leave *old-fashioned* without asking permission, in a way that seems very rude【過時】未經許可, 擅自: *How dare you come marching into my office without so much as a by your leave?* 你怎敢未經許可擅自闖入我的辦公室?

7 take leave of sb/take your leave *formal* to say goodbye to someone【正式】向某人告別/離開

8 by your leave *old use* used when asking permission to do something【舊】請允許我〔用於徵求許可做某事〕; 對不起; 請原諒 —see also 另見 **take French leave** (FRENCH² (3))

leav·en¹ /ˈlɛvən; ˈlevən/ also 又作 **leav·en·ing** /ˈlɛvənɪŋ; ˈlevənɪŋ/ *n* **1** [U] a substance, especially YEAST, that is added to a mixture of flour and water so that it will swell and can be baked into bread 酵母, 麵肥 **2** [C,U] *literary* a small amount of a quality that makes an event or situation less boring and more interesting or cheerful【文】使事件[情景]變得有趣[生動]的東西

leaven² *v* [T] **1** *formal* to make something less boring and more interesting or cheerful【正式】使〔某物〕變得有趣[生動, 高興] **2** *old-fashioned* to add leaven to a mixture of flour and water【過時】加發酵劑[酵母]於〔麵粉和水的混合物〕; 使發酵; 使發鬆 —see also 另見 UNLEAVENED

leaves /livz; liːvz/ the plural of LEAF

leave-tak·ing /ˈ· ··/ *n* [C] *literary* an act of saying goodbye when you go away【文】告別, 辭別

leav·ings /ˈlivɪŋz; ˈliːvɪŋz/ *n* [plural] *old-fashioned* things that are left because they are not wanted, especially food【過時】〔尤指食物的〕剩餘物, 殘餘 —compare 比較 **leftovers** (LEFTOVER² (1))

lech¹, letch /lɛtʃ; letʃ/ *n* [C] *BrE informal* a lecher【英, 非正式】淫蕩的人, 好色之徒

lech², letch *v*

lech after/over sb *phr v* [T] *BrE informal* to show sexual desire for a woman in a way that is unpleasant or annoying【英, 非正式】對〔某女人〕抱有性慾: *a middle-aged man leching after young girls* 對年輕女子抱有性慾的中年男子

lech·er /ˈlɛtʃə; ˈletʃə/ *n* [C] an insulting word for a man who is always thinking about sex or trying to get sexual pleasure 淫蕩的人, 好色之徒〔侮辱性詞語〕

lech·er·ous /ˈlɛtʃərəs; ˈletʃərəs/ *adj* a lecherous man is always thinking about sex or trying to get sexual pleasure〔男人〕縱慾的; 淫蕩的, 好色的 —**lecherously** *adv*

lech·er·y /ˈlɛtʃərɪ; ˈletʃəri/ *n* [U] too much interest in or desire for sex 好色, 色慾, 淫蕩

lec·tern /ˈlɛktən; ˈlektən/ *n* [C] a high, sloping surface for putting an open book or notes on while you are giving a lecture, SERMON etc〔桌面傾斜的〕書桌; 讀經台

3 3 **lec·ture¹** /ˈlɛktʃə; ˈlektʃə/ *n* [C] **1** a long talk given to a group of people on a particular subject, especially as a method of teaching in universities〔尤指大學中的〕講座; 講課; 演講: **[+on/about]** *a lecture on medieval art* 關於中世紀藝術的講座 | **give a lecture** *She's giving a series of lectures on molecular biology.* 她正在作分子生物學的系列講座。**2** an act of criticizing someone or warning them about something in a long, serious talk, in a way that they think is unfair or unnecessary〔冗長、嚴肅、但其對象認為不公平或不必要的〕教訓, 告誡; 訓斥: **[+on/about]** *My aunt gave me a long lecture about the dangers of drink.* 姨媽長篇大論地告誡我酗酒的種種危害。

lecture² *v* **1** [T] to talk angrily or seriously to someone in order to criticize or warn them, in a way that they think is unfair or unnecessary 教訓, 告誡; 訓斥: *I wish you'd stop lecturing me!* 我希望你不要再教訓我! | **lecture sb about/on** *Mrs Reed was continually lecturing her children about their behaviour.* 里德太太不斷批評自己孩子的行為。**2** [I] to talk to a group of people on a particular subject, especially as a method of teaching at a university 講授, 講課, 作講座; 演講

lec·tur·er /ˈlɛktʃərə; ˈlektʃərə/ *n* [C] **1** someone who gives a lecture (LECTURE¹ (1)) 講課者, 講授者; 演講者: *a brilliant lecturer* 才華橫溢的演講者 **2** someone who has the lowest teaching rank at a British university or college〔英國大學或學院中的〕講師 —see 見 PROFESSOR (USAGE) **3** *AmE* someone who makes speeches in different places on a subject they know well【美】〔就自己熟知的某一主題在不同地方演講的〕演講者

lec·ture·ship /ˈlɛktʃəˌʃɪp; ˈlektʃəʃɪp/ *n* [C] the lowest teaching rank at a British university or college 講師職位〔英國大學或學院中最低的教學級別〕: **[+in]** *a lectureship in mathematics* 數學講師職位

LED /ˌɛl i ˈdi; ˌel iː ˈdiː/ *n* [C] *technical* light emitting diode; a small piece of equipment on a watch, computer screen etc that produces light when electricity passes through it【術語】發光二極管

led /lɛd; led/ the past tense and past participle of LEAD¹

-led /lɛd; led/ *suffix* [in adjectives 構成形容詞] having a particular thing as the most important or effective cause, influence etc 以…為先導的, 以…為重點的: *an export-led economic recovery* 以出口為先導的經濟復蘇

ledge /lɛdʒ; ledʒ/ *n* [C] **1** a narrow flat surface of rock that is parallel to the ground 岩架; 岩礁 **2** a narrow flat shelf or surface, fixed to a wall〔固定於牆上的〕窄平的架子[表面]; 壁架: **window ledge** (=narrow shelf below a window) 窗台

led·ger /ˈlɛdʒə; ˈledʒə/ *n* [C] **1** a book recording the money received and spent by a business, bank etc 總賬, 分類賬 **2** a ledger line〔五線譜的〕加線

ledger line /ˈ·· ·/ *n* [C] a line on which you write musical notes that are too high or low to be recorded on a STAVE¹ (1)〔五線譜的〕加線

lee /li; liː/ *n* [singular] **1 the lee of a wall/hedge etc** the part of a wall etc that provides shelter from the wind 牆/籬等的背風[避風]處 **2** the side of something, especially a ship, that is away from the wind〔尤指船的〕背風面, 下風面 **3 the lees** the thick substance that collects at the bottom of a bottle of wine; SEDIMENT〔酒瓶中的〕沉澱物, 沉渣 —compare 比較 DREGS —see also 另見 LEE SHORE

leech /litʃ; liːtʃ/ *n* [C] **1** a small soft creature that fixes itself to the skin of animals in order to drink their blood 螞蟥, 水蛭 **2** someone who takes advantage of other people, usually by taking their money, food etc 吸血鬼, 佔他人便宜者〔通常榨取錢財、食物等〕**3** *old use* a doctor【舊】醫生

leek /lik; liːk/ *n* [C] a vegetable with a long white stem and long flat green leaves, which tastes a little like an onion 韭蔥 —see picture on page A9 參見 A9 頁圖

leer /lɪr; lɪə/ *v* [I] to look at someone in an unpleasant way that shows that you find them sexually attractive〔色迷迷地〕斜眼瞅[瞟, 瞥]: **[+at]** *Stop leering at those girls!* 別色迷迷地瞅那些女孩子! —**leer** *n* [C]: *a disgusting leer* 令人厭惡的色迷迷的眼神

leer·y /ˈlɪrɪ; ˈlɪəri/ *adj informal* careful in the way that you deal with something or someone because you do not trust them; WARY【非正式】懷有戒心的, 不信任的: **[+of]** *I was very leery of him after I found out he had lied* to *Jennifer.* 我發現他對珍妮弗說謊後, 我對他很留神。

lee shore /ˌ· ˈ·/ *n* [singular] *technical* a shore which the wind from the sea is blowing onto【術語】背風岸, 下風岸

lee·ward /ˈliwɚd; ˈliːwəd/ *adj technical*【術語】**1** the leeward side of something is the side that is sheltered from the wind 背風的, 下風的 **2** a leeward direction is the same direction as the wind is blowing 向下風方向的, 順風的: **to leeward** *The ship cruised slowly to leeward.* 船順風緩慢航行。—**leeward** *adv* —opposite 反義詞 WINDWARD[1]

lee·way /ˈliˌwe; ˈliːweɪ/ *n* [U] **1** freedom to do things in the way you want to〔按個人意願做事的〕餘地; 靈活性: *Our reporters have a lot of leeway in what they write.* 我們的記者寫報道有很大的靈活性。**2** *BrE* time that you have lost that means you are at a disadvantage【英】時間的損失; 落後: *Janet's got a lot of leeway to make up in her studies after her illness.* 珍妮特病好以後有許多落後的學業要補上。**3** *technical* the sideways movement of a ship caused by strong wind【術語】〔航船因強風而引起的〕偏航

1 1 **left¹** /lɛft; left/ *adj* [only before noun 僅用於名詞前] **1** on the side of your body that contains your heart〔身體〕左側的: *She held out her left hand.* 她伸出左手。—opposite 反義詞 RIGHT[1] (4a) **2** on, by, or in the direction of your left side 左邊的, 左面的, 左方的: *Hank had scribbled notes in the left margin.* 漢克在左邊的空白處草草地作了筆記。| *Take a left turn at the crossroads.* 在十字路口向左拐。**3 have two left feet** *informal* to be very awkward in the way you move; be CLUMSY (1)【非正式】行動非常笨拙 **4 the left hand doesn't know what the right hand is doing** used to say that one part of a group or organization does not know what the other parts are doing〔指某一集團或組織的一部分不知道其他部分在做甚麼〕互不溝通 —opposite 反義詞 RIGHT[1] —see also 另見 LEFT-OF-CENTRE, LEFT WING[1]

left² *adv* towards the left side 向左地, 朝左地: *Turn left after the gas station.* 過了加油站向左轉。—opposite 反義詞 RIGHT[2] (4)

left³ *n* **1** [singular] the left side or direction 左側, 左方, 左面: *Take the next road on the left.* 下一條路左轉。| *On your left you can see the Houses of Parliament.* 在左邊你可以看到議會大廈。| *Our house is just to the left of the school.* 我家就在學校的左邊。**2 the left/the Left** political parties or groups, such as Socialists and Communists, that want money and property to be divided equally, and generally support workers rather than employers 左派政黨[組織] **3** [C] a hit made with your left hand 左手的一擊, 左手拳: *I caught him on the chin with a straight left.* 我用一記左直拳擊中他的下巴。

left⁴ the past tense and past participle of LEAVE[1]

left field /ˈ· ·/ *n* [singular] **1** a position in BASEBALL in the left side of the OUTFIELD〔棒球運動中的〕左外場 **2 (way) out in left field** *AmE informal* strange or unusual【美, 非正式】奇怪的, 怪誕的, 不常見的: *Some of his ideas are way out in left field.* 他的有些想法很古怪。**3 come from out in left field** *AmE informal* to be very surprising or unexpected【美, 非正式】令人驚訝, 出乎意料: *His comment about Kia's hair came from out in left field.* 他對基亞頭髮的評價非常令人驚訝。

left field·er /ˈ· ˌ··/ *n* [C] someone who plays on the left side of a BASEBALL field〔棒球運動中的〕左外場球員, 左外野手

left-hand /ˌ· ˈ·◂/ *adj* [only before noun 僅用於名詞前] **1** on the left side of something 左手的, 左邊的: *We live about halfway down the street on the left-hand side.* 我們住在這條街的左邊, 大約往下走半條街。**2** curving to the left 向左轉彎的: *a left-hand bend* 左彎處 **3** always using your left hand to do a particular thing 慣用左手的, 左撇子的: *David was a left-hand bowler.* 大衛是左手投球手。—opposite 反義詞 RIGHT-HAND

left-hand drive /ˌ· · ˈ·/ *adj* a left-hand drive vehicle has the STEERING WHEEL on the left side〔方向盤在左邊的〕左座駕駛的, 左御的 —**left-hand drive** *n* [singular]

left-handed (慣)用左手的

Dad is left-handed. 爸爸是左撇子。 She caught the ball left-handed. 她用左手接球。

left-hand·ed /ˌ· ˈ··◂/ *adj* **1** someone who is left-handed uses their left hand for most things, especially writing〔尤指寫字〕慣用左手的, 左撇子的 **2** done with the left hand 用左手做的, 左手操作的: *a left-handed shot* 左手射擊 **3** made to be used by left-handed people 為慣用左手的人做的: *left-handed scissors* 左手用的剪刀 **4 left-handed compliment** *AmE* a statement that seems to express admiration or praise, but at the same time is insulting【美】〔含有侮辱意味的〕虛情假意的恭維 —**left-handed** *adv* —**left-handedness** *n* [U] —opposite 反義詞 RIGHT-HANDED

left-hand·er /ˌ· ˈ··/ *n* [C] **1** someone who uses their left hand, especially for throwing a ball 左撇子, 慣用左手的人〔尤指左撇子投手〕**2** a hit made with your left hand 左手的一擊, 左手拳 —opposite 反義詞 RIGHT-HANDER

left·ie /ˈlɛftɪ; ˈlefti/ another spelling of LEFTY lefty 的另一種拼法

left·ist /ˈlɛftɪst; ˈleftɪst/ *adj* supporting LEFT-WING politics, groups, or ideas 左派的, 左翼的: *leftist views* 左翼觀點 | *a prominent leftist student group* 著名的左派學生團體 —**leftism** *n* [U] —**leftist** *n* [C]

left lug·gage of·fice /ˌ· ˈ·· ˌ··/ *n* [C] *BrE* a place in a station, airport etc where you can pay to leave your bags and get them later【英】〔車站、機場等的〕行李寄存處

left-of-cen·tre *BrE*【英】, **left-of-center** *AmE*【美】/ˌ· · ˈ··◂/ *adj* having ideas or opinions that agree more with the LEFT[3] (2) in politics than with the RIGHT[3] (4b) 傾向於左派的, 中間偏左的

left·o·ver¹ /ˈlɛftˌovɚ; ˈleftəʊvə/ *adj* [only before noun 僅用於名詞前] remaining after all the rest has been used, eaten etc 剩餘的, 未用完的; 未吃完的: *Any leftover vegetables can be used to make a soup.* 任何剩下的蔬菜都可以用來做湯。

leftover² *n* **1 leftovers** [plural] food that has not been eaten at the end of a meal 剩飯菜: *Give the leftovers to the dog.* 把吃剩的飯菜餵狗。**2** [singular] an object, habit, method etc that remains from an earlier time, even though you would expect it to have gone 遺留物〔過去留下的東西、習慣、方法等〕: *They still slept with the lights on, a leftover from more dangerous times.* 他們還是亮着燈睡覺, 這是從前危險時期養成的習慣。

left·ward /ˈlɛftwɚd; ˈleftwəd/ *adj* on or towards the left 在左邊的, 向左邊的: *a leftward bend* 向左的轉彎處 —opposite 反義詞 RIGHTWARD —**leftward/leftwards** *adv*

left-wing¹ /ˌ· ˈ·◂/ *adj* supporting the political aims of groups such as Socialists and Communists, such as the idea that money and property should be divided more fairly 左翼的, 激進(派)的: *She's very left-wing.* 她很激進。| *a left-wing newspaper* 左翼報紙 —opposite 反義詞 RIGHT-WING —**left-winger** *n* [C]

left wing² /ˌ· ˈ·/ *n* [singular] the group of people, within a larger political group, whose ideas are more left-wing than those of other members of the group 左翼, 左派(人士): *He's on the left wing of the Conservative Party.*

他是保守黨中的左派。| *The party has a small but powerful left wing.* 黨內有一小股強有力的左翼勢力。

left·y, leftie /ˈlɛftɪ; ˈlefti/ *n* [C] **1** *informal especially BrE* a humorous or slightly insulting way of talking about someone who has left-wing political ideas【非正式, 尤英】左派分子〔幽默或損人〕**2** *informal especially AmE* someone who uses their left hand to write, throw etc【非正式, 尤美】左撇子 —**lefty** *adj*: *My lefty friends keep telling me I'm a fascist.* 我的左派朋友們老說我是個法西斯分子。

leg[1] /lɛg; leg/ *n*
1 ▶BODY PART 身體部位◀ [C] either of the two long parts of your body that your feet are joined to, or a similar part on an animal or insect 腿: *Angie broke her leg skiing.* 安吉滑雪時摔斷了腿。| *A spider has 8 legs.* 蜘蛛有八條腿。| *She's got long skinny legs.* 她的腿又瘦又長。—see picture at 參見 BODY 圖
2 ▶FOOD 食物◀ [C,U] the leg of an animal when eaten as food 腿肉: *roast leg of lamb* 烤羊腿
3 ▶FURNITURE 家具◀ [C] one of the upright parts that supports a piece of furniture 腿腳, 支架: *a chair leg* 椅子腿
4 ▶CLOTHING 衣服◀ [C] the part of your trousers that covers your leg 褲腿: *The legs of my jeans were covered in mud.* 我的牛仔褲褲腿上沾滿了泥。
5 ▶JOURNEY/RACE 旅程/比賽◀ [C] a part of a long journey, race, process etc that is done one part at a time〔旅程、賽程、過程等的〕一段: *the final leg of the Tour de France* 環法單車賽賽程的最後一段
6 four-legged/two-legged etc having four legs, two legs etc 四條腿的/兩條腿的等: *four-legged animals* 四條腿的動物 —see also 另見 CROSS-LEGGED, BOW-LEGGED
7 leg room space in which to put your legs comfortably when you are sitting in a car, theatre etc〔汽車、戲院等座位前的〕供伸腿的空間, 腿部活動空間
8 not have a leg to stand on *informal* to be in a situation where you cannot prove or legally support what you say【非正式】〔論點等〕沒有根據, 站不住腳: *If you didn't sign a contract, you won't have a leg to stand on.* 如果你不簽合同, 你就沒有法律上的支撐。
9 pull sb's leg *informal* to make a joke by telling someone something that is not actually true【非正式】愚弄某人, 開某人的玩笑
10 be on its last legs *informal* to be in very bad condition and about to stop working【非正式】糟糕(的); 即將停止運作(的): *The Chevy really is on its last legs now.* 現在這輛雪佛萊汽車快要不行了。
11 get your leg over *BrE slang* to have sex with someone【英俚】與〔某人〕性交
12 ▶SPORT 運動◀ [C] *BrE* one of the parts of a special football competition that is played in two parts【英】〔足球賽的〕半場
13 have legs *informal especially AmE* if a piece of news has legs, people continue to be interested in it and talk about it【非正式, 尤美】〔新聞〕不脛而走, 談論熱烈: *These allegations don't have legs – they'll be forgotten by next week.* 這些說法沒人會感興趣——到下週就會被忘得一乾二淨了。—see also 另見 **break a leg** (BREAK[1] (46)), LEG-PULL, LEG-UP, PEG LEG, SEA LEGS, **shake a leg** (SHAKE[1] (11)), **show a leg** (SHOW[1] (22)), SQUARE LEG, **stretch your legs** (STRETCH[1] (12))

leg[2] *v* **leg it** *BrE informal* to run in order to escape from someone or something【英, 非正式】跑; 逃脫: *We saw him coming, and legged it out of the house.* 我們見他來了, 就從屋裡逃了出來。

leg·a·cy /ˈlɛgəsɪ; ˈlegəsi/ *n* [C] **1** a situation that exists as a result of things that happened at an earlier time 遺留之物〔遺留下來的狀況〕: **[+of]** *The civil wars in the region are largely a legacy of apartheid.* 這個地區的內戰在很大程度上是種族隔離的後遺症。**2** money or property that you receive from someone after they die 遺產, 遺贈物: *a legacy from her aunt* 她姨媽留下的一份遺產

le·gal /ˈligl; ˈliːgəl/ *adj* **1** allowed, ordered, or approved by law 法律允許的, 合法的, 法定的: *He had twice the legal limit of alcohol in his bloodstream.* 他血液中的酒精含量是法定限度的兩倍。| *plans to make the carrying of identity cards a legal requirement* 使攜帶身分證成為法定要求的計劃 | **the legal age for** *the legal age for voting* 選舉的法定年齡 **2** [only before noun 僅用於名詞前] concerned with or connected with the law (有關)法律的: *free legal advice* 免費法律諮詢 | *a costly legal dispute* 代價高昂的法律糾紛 **3 take legal action/proceedings** to use the legal system to settle an argument, put right an unfair situation etc 採取法律行動/提起法律訴訟: *Unless the money is paid immediately we shall be forced to take legal action.* 如不立刻付款, 我們將被迫採取法律行動。—opposite 反義詞 ILLEGAL[1] —see also 另見 LEGALLY

le·gal·ese /ˌliglˈiz; ˌliːgəlˈiːz/ *n* [U] *informal* language used by lawyers that is difficult for most people to understand【非正式】法律行話〔大多數人難以理解的律師用語〕

le·gal·ise /ˈliglˌaɪz; ˈliːgəlaɪz/ *v* [T] a British spelling of LEGALIZE legalize 的英式拼法

le·gal·ist·ic /ˌliglˈɪstɪk; ˌliːgəˈlɪstɪk◀/ *adj* too concerned about small legal details, and not concerned enough about what is really important 拘泥於法規[條文]的 —**legalistically** /-klɪ; -kli/ *adv* —**legalism** /ˈliglɪzəm; ˈliːgəlɪzəm/ *n* [U]

le·gal·i·ty /lɪˈgælətɪ; lɪˈgæləti/ *n* [U] the fact of being allowed by law 合法性, 法律性: *Some people questioned the legality of the US's attack on Baghdad.* 有人對美國攻擊巴格達的合法性提出了質疑。

le·gal·ize also 又作 **-ise** *BrE*【英】/ˈliglˌaɪz; ˈliːgəlaɪz/ *v* [T] to make a law that allows people to do something that was not allowed before 使合法化, 使得到法律認可: *the campaign to legalize cannabis* 使大麻合法化的運動 —**legalization** /ˌliglə̩ˈzeʃən; ˌliːgəlaɪˈzeɪʃən/ *n* [U]

le·gal·ly /ˈliglɪ; ˈliːgəli/ *adv* **1** according to the law 依據法律, 法律上: *Legally he's still my husband.* 法律上他還是我的丈夫。| *The ship was legally authorized to carry 200 passengers.* 這艘船依照法律規定可載200名乘客。| *Which of them is legally responsible for the accident?* 他們之中誰負這次事故的法律責任? **2 legally binding** an agreement or document that is legally binding must be obeyed by law〔協議或文件〕具有法律約束力的

legal pad /ˈ‥ ˌ/ *n* [C] a PAD[1] (2) of yellow writing paper with lines, of a type sold in the US 標準拍紙簿

legal pro·fes·sion /ˈ‥ ‥ˌ‥/ *n* **the legal profession** lawyers, judges, and other people who work in courts of law or advise people about legal problems 法律界〔律師、法官、法庭工作人員、法律顧問等〕

legal-size /ˈ‥ ˌ/ *adj AmE* legal-size paper is 14 inches (INCH[1] (1)) long and 8 inches wide【美】〔紙張〕大小適合於法律文件的〔14英寸長8英寸寬〕; 法定尺寸的

legal sys·tem /ˈ‥ ˌ‥/ *n* [C] the laws and the way they work in a particular country 法律體制, 法制

legal ten·der /ˌ‥ ˈ‥/ *n* [U] coins or bank notes that are officially allowed to be used as money 法定貨幣

leg·ate /ˈlɛgɪt; ˈlegə̩t/ *n* [C] an important official representative 使節

leg·a·tee /ˌlɛgəˈti; ˌlegəˈtiː/ *n* [C] *law* someone who is given money or property after another person dies【法律】遺產承受人, 受遺贈人

le·ga·tion /lɪˈgeʃən; lɪˈgeɪʃən/ *n* [C] **1** an office that represents a government in a foreign country but is lower in rank than an EMBASSY 公使館: *the Cuban legation* 古巴公使館 **2** the people who work in this office 公使館全體人員

le·ga·to /lɪˈgɑto; lɪˈgɑːtəʊ/ *adj, adv technical* played or sung so that each note connects to the next one without pauses between them【術語】〔音樂中〕連奏的[地]

le·gend /ˈlɛdʒənd; ˈledʒənd/ *n* **1** [C] an old, well-known story, often about brave people, adventures, or magical events 傳說, 傳奇(故事): *the legend of Rip Van Winkle who slept for 100 years* 瑞普·凡·温克爾昏睡百年的傳説 **2** [U] all stories of this kind 民間傳說: *Celtic legend* 凱爾特人的民間傳説 **3** [C] someone who is famous and admired for being extremely good at doing something〔某領域中的〕傳奇式人物: *Pelè, Maradona, and other footballing legends* 貝利、馬拉多納以及其他足球傳奇人物 —see also 另見 LIVING LEGEND **4** [C usually singular 一般用單數] **a)** *literary* words that have been written somewhere, for example on a sign【文】〔牌匾等上的〕鐫刻文字, 銘文: *A sign above the door bore the legend 'patience is a virtue'.* 門上方的匾上題寫着"忍耐即美德"。**b)** *old-fashioned* the words that explain a picture, map etc【過時】〔圖片、地圖等的〕文字説明, 圖例

le·gen·da·ry /ˈlɛdʒəndˌɛrɪ; ˈledʒəndəri/ *adj* **1** famous and admired 非常有名的, 大名鼎鼎的, 傳奇式的: *the legendary Babe Ruth, one of the greatest baseball players of all time* 傳奇式人物貝布·魯思, 歷史上最偉大的棒球運動員之一 **2** talked or read about in legends 傳説(中)的: *legendary sea monsters* 傳説中的海怪

le·ger·de·main /ˌlɛdʒə·dɪˈmen; ˌledʒədəˈmeɪn/ *n* [U] *old-fashioned* skilful use of your hands when performing tricks【過時】魔術, 戲法

-legged /lɛgɪd; legɪ̵d/ *suffix* [in adjectives 構成形容詞] having legs of a particular type or number 有…腿的: *four-legged animals* 四條腿的動物 | *a long-legged runner* 長腿賽跑運動員

leg·gings /ˈlɛgɪŋz; ˈlegɪŋz/ *n* [plural] **1** women's tight trousers without a ZIP[1] (1), which stretch to fit the shape of your body 女式緊身褲 **2** trousers worn to protect your legs 綁腿, 裹腿; 護腿

leg·gy /ˈlɛgɪ; ˈlegi/ *adj* a woman or child who is leggy has long legs〔女人或小孩〕腿細長的: *a leggy blonde* 雙腿修長的金髮美女 —**legginess** *n* [U]

le·gi·ble /ˈlɛdʒəbl̩; ˈledʒɪ̵bəl/ *adj* written or printed clearly enough for you to read〔字跡〕可以辨認的, 易讀的: *Her handwriting was so tiny it was barely legible.* 她的字寫得這麼小, 簡直都看不清楚。—**legibly** *adv* —**legibility** /ˌlɛdʒəˈbɪlətɪ; ˌledʒɪ̵ˈbɪlɪ̵ti/ *n* [U] —opposite 反義詞 ILLEGIBLE

le·gion[1] /ˈlidʒən; ˈliːdʒən/ *n* [C] **1** a large group of soldiers, especially in ancient Rome〔尤指古羅馬的〕軍團 **2** *literary* a large number of people【文】〔人的〕眾多, 大批, 無數

legion[2] *adj* [not before noun 不用於名詞前] *literary* very many; NUMEROUS【文】眾多的, 大批的: *The stories of her adventures were legion.* 她的歷險故事多極了。

le·gion·a·ry /ˈlidʒənˌɛrɪ; ˈliːdʒənəri/ *n* [C] a member of a legion (古羅馬)軍團士兵

le·gion·naire /ˌlidʒənˈɛr; ˌliːdʒəˈneə/ *n* [C] a member of a legion, especially the French Foreign Legion〔尤指法國外籍軍團的〕士兵

legionnaire's dis·ease /ˌ··ˈ· ·ˌ·/ *n* [U] a serious lung disease 軍團病, 退伍軍人協會會員病〔一種嚴重的肺部疾病〕

leg i·rons /ˈ· ˌ··/ *n* [plural] metal circles or chains that are put around a prisoner's legs 腳鐐

le·gis·late /ˈlɛdʒɪsˌlet; ˈledʒɪ̵sleɪt/ *v* [I] to make a law about something 制定法律, 立法: **[+against/for/on]** *There are plans to legislate against computer-related crime.* 已經有打擊電腦犯罪的立法計劃了。

2 **le·gis·la·tion** /ˌlɛdʒɪsˈleʃən; ˌledʒɪ̵ˈsleɪʃən/ *n* [U] **1** a law or set of laws 法規, 法律: *an important piece of human rights legislation* 人權法規中的重要部分 | *legislation governing minimum wage rates* 規定最低工資率的法規 **2** the act of making laws 制定法律, 立法

le·gis·la·tive /ˈlɛdʒɪsˌletɪv; ˈledʒɪ̵slətɪv/ *adj* **1** a legislative institution has the power to make laws 有立法權的: *a legislative assembly* 立法議會 **2** concerned with laws or with making laws 法律的, 立法的: *new legislative measures to stem the flow of drugs into the US* 阻止毒品流入美國的新法律措施 —compare 比較 EXECUTIVE[2] (1), JUDICIAL (1)

le·gis·la·tor /ˈlɛdʒɪsˌletə; ˈledʒɪ̵sleɪtə/ *n* [C] someone who has the power to make laws or belongs to an institution that makes laws 立法者, 立法機關成員

le·gis·la·ture /ˈlɛdʒɪsˌletʃə; ˈledʒɪ̵sleɪtʃə/ *n* [C] an institution that has the power to make or change laws 立法機關: *the Iowa state legislature* 艾奧瓦[衣阿華]州立法機關 —compare 比較 EXECUTIVE[1] (2), JUDICIARY

le·git /ləˈdʒɪt; lɪ̵ˈdʒɪt/ *adj* [not before noun 不用於名詞前] *spoken*【口】**1** legal or following official rules; LEGITIMATE[1] (1) 合法的, 守規則的: *Don't worry, the deal's strictly legit.* 不用擔憂, 這項交易是完全合法的。**2** honest and not trying to deceive people 誠實不欺人的: *Are you sure he's legit?* 你敢肯定他沒有騙人?

le·git·i·mate[1] /lɪˈdʒɪtəmɪt; lɪˈdʒɪtɪ̵mɪ̵t/ *adj* **1** correct, allowable, or operating according to the law 合法的, 法律許可的, 依法的: *The Mafia uses legitimate business operations as a front.* 黑手黨利用合法經營作掩護。**2** fair, correct, or reasonable according to accepted standards of behaviour 公正的, 正當的, 合理的: *Is this a legitimate use of taxpayers' money?* 這是正當使用納稅人的錢嗎? | *I think that's a perfectly legitimate question.* 我認為那是一個完全正當的問題。**3** legitimate children are born to parents who are legally married to each other 合法婚姻所生的, 婚生的 —**legitimately** *adv* —**legitimacy** *n* [U]

le·git·i·mate[2] /lɪˈdʒɪtəˌmet; lɪˈdʒɪtɪ̵meɪt/ *v* [T] the usual American form of LEGITIMIZE legitimize 的一般美語形式

le·git·i·mize also 又作 **-ise** *BrE*【英】/lɪˈdʒɪtəˌmaɪz; lɪˈdʒɪtɪ̵maɪz/ *v* [T] **1** to make something that is unfair or morally wrong seem acceptable and right 使〔某種不公平或不正當的事〕被接受, 使顯得正當: *Mussolini's use of symbols from ancient Rome to try to legitimize Fascist policies* 墨索里尼使用古羅馬的象徵符號企圖使法西斯政策正當化 **2** to make something official or legal that had not been before 使〔某事〕得到公開承認, 使〔某事〕合法化 **3** to make a child LEGITIMATE[1] (3) 使〔某小孩〕認定為婚生子

leg·less /ˈlɛglɪs; ˈlegləs/ *adj BrE informal* drunk【英, 非正式】爛醉如泥的

leg·o /ˈlɛgo; ˈlegəʊ/ *n* [U] *trademark* a toy consisting of plastic pieces of various sizes that can be fitted together to build things【商標】樂高玩具〔由各種大小的塑料模塊組成〕

leg-pull /ˈ· ·/ *n* [C usually singular 一般用單數] *BrE* a joke in which you make someone believe something that is not true【英】愚弄人 —see also 另見 **pull sb's leg** (LEG[1] (9))

leg room /ˈ· ·/ *n* [U] space for your legs in front of the seats in a car, theatre etc〔汽車、戲院等的座下〕供伸腿的空間, 腿的活動餘地

leg·ume /ˈlɛgjum; ˈlegjuːm/ *n* [C] **1** a plant of the bean family that has seeds in a POD (=a long thin case) 豆科植物 **2** *especially AmE* a bean, PEA, LENTIL etc, used as food【尤美】食用豆類 —**leguminous** /lɪˈgjumənəs; lɪˈgjuːmɪ̵nəs/ *adj*

leg-up /ˈ· ·/ *n* **give sb a leg-up** *informal*【非正式】**a)** to help someone to get up to a high place by joining your hands together so they can use them as a step〔雙手交叉〕讓〔某人〕踩着登高 **b)** *especially BrE* to help someone to succeed in their job【尤英】助〔某人〕一臂之力

leg·warm·er /ˈ· ˌ··/ *n* [C] a piece of clothing made from wool, which covers the lower part of your leg 暖腿套

leg·work /ˈlɛgˌwɝk; ˈlegwɜːk/ *n* [U] *informal* the hard boring work that has to be done in order to achieve something【非正式】跑腿活, 跑外工作

lei /le; leɪ/ *n* [C] a circle made of flowers you put around someone's neck as a greeting, especially in Hawaii〔尤指在夏威夷迎客時套在客人頸上的〕花環

3 **lei·sure** /ˈliʒɚ; ˈleʒə/ *n* [U] **1** time when you are not working or studying and can relax and do things you enjoy 空閒, 閒暇, 業餘時間: *gardening, sailing, and other leisure pursuits* 園藝、帆船運動和其他業餘愛好 | **leisure time** *In her leisure time she visits museums and galleries.* 在空閒的時候, 她去參觀博物館和美術館。| **the leisure industry** (=the business of providing leisure activities) 休閒娛樂行業, 提供業餘活動的行業 **2 at your leisure** as slowly as you want and when you want 有空時; 方便時: *Take the leaflets home and read them at your leisure.* 把這些傳單拿回家, 閒暇時閱讀。**3 gentleman/lady of leisure** *humorous* someone who does not have to work【幽默】〔不須工作的〕有閒先生/女士

leisure cen·tre /ˈ·· ˌ··/ *n* [C] *BrE* a place where you can do many different sports activities, exercise classes etc【英】休閒中心, 娛樂中心; 健身中心

lei·sured /ˈliʒɚd; ˈleʒəd/ *adj* **1** having no regular work and a lot of leisure time, especially because you are rich〔尤因富有而〕有空閒的, 悠閒自在的 **2** leisurely 從容的, 不慌不忙的

lei·sure·ly /ˈliʒɚli; ˈleʒəli/ *adj* moving or done in a relaxed way, without hurrying 從容的, 不慌不忙的: *a leisurely stroll* 悠閒的散步 | *working at a leisurely pace* 不慌不忙地幹活 —**leisurely** *adv*: *The great ship sailed leisurely across the bay.* 這艘巨輪緩緩地橫渡海灣。—**leisureliness** *n* [U]

leisure suit /ˈ·· ·/ *n* [C] *AmE* an informal suit popular during the 1970s, consisting of a shirt-like JACKET and trousers made of the same material【美】〔20 世紀 70 年代流行的〕休閒套裝

lei·sure·wear /ˈliʒɚˌwɛr; ˈleʒəweə/ *n* [U] a word meaning clothes that are made to be worn when relaxing or playing sport, used especially by shops or by the companies that make these clothes 休閒服, 運動服, 便服

leit·mo·tif, leitmotiv /ˈlaɪtmoˌtif; ˈlaɪtməʊˌtiːf/ *n* [C] **1** a musical phrase that is played at various times during an OPERA or similar musical work to represent a particular character or idea〔音樂用語〕主導主題; 主旋律 —compare 比較 MOTIF (3) **2** a feature that appears often in something such as a book, a speech, or an artist's work〔書、演說、藝術作品等中的〕主題, 主旨

lem·ming /ˈlɛmɪŋ; ˈlemɪŋ/ *n* [C] **1** a small rat-like animal that is known for killing itself by following other lemmings and jumping into the sea in large numbers 旅鼠 **2** someone who copies other people's actions and ideas without thinking about it 盲目仿效者

lem·on /ˈlɛmən; ˈlemən/ *n* **1** [C, U] a fruit with a hard yellow skin and sour juice 檸檬: *fish served with slices of lemon* 配上檸檬片的魚 —see picture on page A8 參見 A8 頁圖 **2** [U] *BrE* a drink made from this fruit【英】檸檬汁 **3** [U] a pale yellow colour 淡黃色 —see picture on page A5 參見 A5 頁圖 **4** [C] *AmE informal* something that is useless because it fails to work or work properly【美, 非正式】無用之物, 易出故障之物: *He has an old Dodge that's a real lemon.* 他有一輛舊道奇車, 那真是輛爛車。**5** [C] *BrE informal* a silly person【英, 非正式】傻瓜, 笨蛋: *I felt such a lemon when I realized I'd gone on the wrong day.* 當我意識到去錯了日子, 我感到自己真是個傻瓜。

3 **lem·on·ade** /ˌlɛmənˈed; ˌleməˈneɪd◀/ *n* [U] **1** a drink made from lemons, sugar, and water 檸檬水 **2** *BrE* a sweet colourless FIZZY drink【英】檸檬汽水

lemon curd /ˌ·· ˈ·/ *n* [U] *BrE* a sweet food made of eggs, butter, and lemon juice, eaten on bread【英】檸檬酪〔由蛋、黃油、檸檬汁製成〕

lemon sole /ˌ·· ˈ·/ *n* [C] a flat fish used as food 檬鰈〔可食用的一種扁魚〕

lemon squeez·er /ˈ·· ˌ··/ *n* [C] a small kitchen tool for getting the juice out of a lemon 檸檬榨汁器〔廚房用具〕

lend 借出, 借給

I borrowed $20. 我借了 20 美元。 My friend lent me $20. 我的朋友借給我 20 美元。

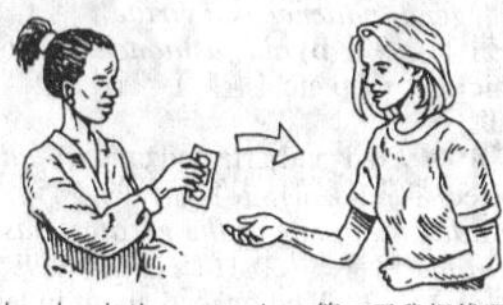

I paid her back the next day. 第二天我把錢還給了她。

lend /lɛnd; lend/ *v past tense and past participle* **lent** /lɛnt; lent/

1 ▶MONEY/CAR/BOOK ETC 錢/汽車/書籍等◀ a) [T] to let someone borrow money from you or use something that you own, which they will give you back later 借給〔某人錢或東西〕, 借出: **lend sb sth** *I wish I'd never lent him my car.* 但願我從未把汽車借過給他。| *Can you lend me $20 till Friday?* 你能不能借我 20 美元, 到星期五還給你? | **lend sth to sb** *Reluctantly, I agreed to lend it to her.* 我勉強同意把它借給她。**b)** [I,T] if a bank or financial institution lends money, it lets someone borrow it on condition that they pay it back, often gradually, with an additional amount as interest 貸出; 貸〔款〕: *We aim to lend money at reasonable rates of interest.* 我們力求以合理的利率貸出款項。| **lend sth to sb** *US banks lent billions of dollars to Third World countries in the 1970s.* 20 世紀 70 年代美國的銀行貸給第三世界數十億美元的款項。—see 見 BORROW (USAGE)

2 lend (sb) a hand to help someone do something, especially something that needs physical effort 幫助〔某人〕做事〔尤指需要體力的事〕

3 lend an ear to listen to someone, especially in a sympathetic way 聽, 〔尤指同情地〕傾聽

4 lend itself to to be suitable for being used in a particular way 適用於: *None of her books really lends itself to being made into a film.* 她的書沒有一本真正適合於拍成電影。

5 ▶GIVE A QUALITY 增添某種特性◀ [T] *formal* to give a situation, event etc a particular quality【正式】給予, 增添〔某種特性〕: *The Duke's presence lent the occasion a certain air of dignity.* 公爵的光臨使場面增添了幾分莊嚴感。| **lend sth to sth** *His soft accent lends a kind of warmth to his words.* 他柔和的聲調給他的話注入了一點温情。

6 lend support/assistance to support or help someone 提供支持/幫助

7 lend weight to to make an opinion, belief etc seem more likely to be correct 使〔意見、看法等〕更可信: *The new evidence lends weight to the theory that the killer was a man.* 新證據使得兇手是一名男性的推測變得更可信。

8 lend your name/voice to to announce publicly that you support something someone is trying to do 公開支持, 聲援 —**lender** *n* [C]

lend·ing li·bra·ry /ˈ·· ˌ···/ *n* [C] a library that lends books, records etc for people to use at home〔可外借書籍、唱片等的〕圖書館 —compare 比較 REFERENCE LIBRARY

lending rate /ˈ·· ·/ *n* [C] the rate of INTEREST[1] (4) that you have to pay to a bank or other financial institution when you borrow money from them; INTEREST RATE 借貸利率, 貸款利率

2 2 **length** /lɛŋθ; leŋθ/ *n*

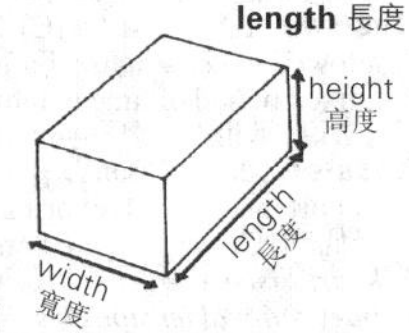

1 ►SIZE 尺寸◄ [C,U] the measurement of something from one end to the other 長, 長度: **[+of]** *The fish can grow to a length of four feet.* 這種魚可長到四英尺長。| **2 feet in length/10 metres in length etc** *Vehicles of over 3 metres in length pay an additional toll.* 汽車超過三米長要付額外的通行費。| *pieces of string of different lengths* 不同長度的繩子 —compare 比較 BREADTH, WIDTH

2 ►TIME 時間◄ [C,U] the amount of time that you spend doing something or that something continues for 時間長度: *reducing the average length of stay in hospital* 降低平均住院時間 | **not for any length of time** (=not for very long) 一刻也不 *I didn't want to be left alone with him for any length of time.* 我一刻也不願和他單獨在一起了。

3 ►BOOKS/FILMS ETC 書/電影等◄ [C, U] the amount of writing in a book, or the amount of time that a film, play etc continues for〔書的〕字數[頁數];〔電影、戲劇等的〕長度: *We had to cut the length of the book by two-thirds.* 我們得削減此書三分之二的長度。| *Films of this length are pretty unusual.* 這樣長度的電影很少見。

4 go to any lengths/great lengths to do sth to be willing to use any methods to achieve something that you are very determined to achieve 千方百計/竭盡全力做某事: *Gerald is prepared to go to any lengths to get his daughter back.* 傑拉爾德準備竭盡全力去把他的女兒要回來。

5 at length a) if you talk at length about something, you talk about it for a long time 長時間地: *We've already discussed the subject at great length in previous meetings.* 在以前的會議中, 我們已經用了很長時間討論了這一題目。**b)** *literary* after a long time【文】長時間後, 最後, 最終: *"How have you been?" she said at length.* "你怎麼樣了?" 她最終問了一句。

6 the length and breadth of in or through every part of a large area 各處, 四面八方

7 walk/travel/drive the length of walk, travel etc the whole distance along something 沿着〔某物〕走/開完全程: *They walked the length of the pier.* 他們沿着長堤走到頭。

8 ►PIECE 根◄ [C] a piece of something long and thin 細長的物件: **[+of]** *a length of steel tubing* 一根鋼管

9 ►IN RACES 在比賽中◄ [C] the measurement from one end of a horse, boat etc to the other, used when saying how far one is ahead of another 一馬位, 一艇位〔比賽中超出的長度〕: *The horse won by three lengths.* 這匹馬以領先三個馬位而獲勝。

10 ►SWIMMING 游泳◄ [C] the distance from one end of a swimming pool to the other 游泳池的長度: *I was really bad at swimming – I could barely do a length.* 我真的游不好 —— 游泳池的一個長度我幾乎都游不了。—see also 另見 **at arm's length** (ARM[1] (10)), FULL-LENGTH, **measure your length** (MEASURE[2] (5)), SHOULDER-LENGTH

length·en /ˈlɛŋθən; ˈleŋθən/ *v* [I,T] to make something longer or to become longer (使) 延長, (使) 加長: *Can you lengthen this skirt for me?* 你能不能為我加長這條裙子? | *The days lengthened as summer approached.* 隨着夏天臨近, 白天延長了。—opposite 反義詞 SHORTEN

length·ways /ˈlɛŋθˌwez; ˈleŋθweɪz/ also 又作 **length·wise** /-waɪz; -waɪz/ *adv* in the direction or position of the longest side 縱長地; 縱向地; LONGWAYS *AmE*【美】: *Lay the bricks lengthways.* 縱向地砌磚。

length·y /ˈlɛŋθɪ; ˈleŋθi/ *adj* **1** continuing for a long time, often too long 長時間的, 過長的: *a lengthy court trial* 漫長的庭審 **2** a speech, piece of writing etc that is lengthy is long and often contains too many details〔講話、文章等〕冗長的, 過於詳盡的 —**lengthiness** *n* [U] —**lengthily** *adv*

le·ni·ent /ˈlinɪənt; ˈliːniənt/ *adj* not strict in the way you punish someone or control their behaviour 寬大的, 仁慈的: *Judges have been accused of being far too lenient in rape cases.* 法官被指責在審理強姦案件中過分寬容。| *a very lenient sentence* 極為寬大的判決 —**leniently** *adv* —**leniency** also 又作 **lenience** *n* [U]

lens /lɛnz; lenz/ *n* [C] **1** a piece of curved glass or plastic which makes things look bigger or smaller, for example in a pair of GLASSes or in a TELESCOPE[1] 凸透鏡; 凹透鏡; 透鏡; 鏡片: *Jan wears glasses with thick lenses.* 簡戴着鏡片很厚的眼鏡。—see picture at 參見 GLASS[1] 圖 **2** the part of a camera through which the light travels before it hits the film〔照相機、攝影機的〕鏡頭: *a standard 50mm lens* 50 毫米標準鏡頭 —see picture at 參見 CAMERA 圖 **3** the clear part inside your eye that focuses (FOCUS[1] (3)) so you can see things clearly〔眼球的〕晶狀體 —see picture at 參見 EYE[1] 圖 **4** one of a pair of small curved pieces of plastic that fit closely to your eyes to help you see better; CONTACT LENS 隱形眼鏡

Lent /lɛnt; lent/ *n* [U] the period before Easter during which Christians traditionally eat less food or stop doing something that they enjoy〔基督教的〕大齋期 —**Lenten** *adj*

lent the past tense and past participle of LEND

len·til /ˈlɛntl̩; ˈlentl/ *n* [C] a small round seed like a bean, dried and used for food 小扁豆

len·to /ˈlɛnto; ˈlentəʊ/ *adj, adv technical* music that is played lento is played slowly【術語】〔音樂〕緩慢的[地]

Le·o /ˈlio; ˈliːəʊ/ *n* **1** [singular] the sign of the ZODIAC represented by a lion and believed to affect the character and life of people born between 23 July and 22 August 獅子宮[座] **2** [C] someone who was born between 23 July and 22 August 獅子宮[座]時段 (7 月 23 日至 8 月 22 日) 出生的人

le·o·nine /ˈliəˌnaɪn; ˈliːənaɪn/ *adj* connected with lions, or like a lion in character or appearance 獅子的; 獅子般勇猛的, 獅子般雄壯的

leop·ard /ˈlɛpɚd; ˈlepəd/ *n* [C] **1** a large animal of the cat family, with yellow fur and black spots, which lives in Africa and South Asia 豹 **2 a leopard can't change its spots** used to say that people cannot change their character 本性難移

le·o·tard /ˈliətɑrd; ˈliːətɑːd/ *n* [C] a tight-fitting piece of women's clothing that covers your whole body from your neck to the top of your legs and is worn for exercise or dancing〔運動或跳舞穿的〕女式緊身連衣褲 —see picture at 參見 UNDERWEAR 圖

lep·er /ˈlɛpɚ; ˈlepə/ *n* [C] **1** someone who suffers from the disease of leprosy 麻瘋病人 **2** someone that people avoid because they have done something that people disapprove of〔因做了不為人讚許的事〕別人避之唯恐不及的人: *They treated me as if I was some kind of leper.* 他們把我當作某種讓人避之唯恐不及的人。

lep·re·chaun /ˈlɛprəˌkɔn; ˈleprɪ̣kɔːn/ *n* [C] an imaginary creature in the form of a little old man, in old Irish stories〔愛爾蘭古代民間傳說中的〕矮妖精

lep·ro·sy /ˈlɛprəsɪ; ˈleprəsi/ *n* [U] a very serious infectious disease in which the flesh and nerves are gradually destroyed 麻瘋病 —**leprous** *adj*

ler·gy /ˈlɝgɪ; ˈlɜːgi/ *n* [C] another spelling of LURGY lurgy 的另一種拼法

les·bi·an /ˈlɛzbɪən; ˈlezbiən/ *n* [C] a woman who is sexually attracted to other women 女同性戀者 —**lesbian** *adj*: *lesbian writers* 女同性戀作家 —**lesbianism** *n* [U]

lese-ma·jes·ty /ˈliz ˈmædʒɪstɪ; ˌliːz ˈmædʒɪ̣sti/ *n* [U] **1** *humorous* behaviour that shows a lack of respect towards an important person【幽默】犯上行為 **2** *law* a crime against a king or government【法律】冒犯君主罪，叛逆罪

le·sion /ˈliʒən; ˈliːʒən/ *n* [C] *technical*【術語】**1** a wound 傷口，損傷: *multiple lesions to the skin* 皮膚上的多處傷口 **2** a dangerous change in part of someone's body such as their lungs or brain, caused by injury or illness〔因傷、病而致的〕損傷，損害；病變: *cerebral lesions* 大腦損傷

-less /lɪs; ləs/ *suffix* [in adjectives 構成形容詞] **1** without something 無…的: *a childless couple* (=who have no children) 無子女的夫婦 | *It's quite harmless.* (=will not harm you) 它的確無害。| *He was hatless.* (=wore no hat) 他沒戴帽子。| *endless complaints* (=that never end) 沒完沒了的抱怨 **2** never doing something 永不…的: *a tireless helper* (=who never gets tired) 永不知疲倦的助人為樂者 **3** unable to be treated in a particular way 不能…的: *on countless occasions* (=too many to be counted) 在無數場合中

S1 W1 **less**[1] /lɛs; les/ *adv* **1** not so much; to a smaller degree 不那麼多；更[較]少地；至更[較]小程度: *I found the second half of the play less interesting than the first.* 我發現劇本的第二部分沒有第一部分般有趣。| *We go to Paris less frequently now.* 現在我們較不常去巴黎了。| *You ought to smoke less.* 你應該少吸點煙了。—opposite 反義詞 MORE[1] (1) **2 less and less** gradually becoming smaller in amount or degree 越來越少[小]: *Our trips became less and less frequent.* 我們外出的次數越來越少了。**3 much/still less** *formal* certainly not【正式】更不用說，更何況: *They did not intend even to tell the authorities about the experiments, still less seek their approval.* 他們甚至不想告訴當局有關試驗的事，更不用說尋求當局的批准了。

S1 W1 **less**[2] *determiner, pron* **1 a)** not as much 不那麼多，更[較]少: *You ought to eat less salt.* 你應該少吃點鹽。| *Most of the workers were paid £5 per day, but some received even less.* 大多數工人每天得五英鎊工資，但有些工人得到的甚至更少。| *Give him less of the medicine if it seems to upset him.* 如果用藥看來使他不舒服的話，就給他少一點。| *a distance of less than 100 metres* 不足100米的距離 **b)** used to mean fewer or not as many, but often considered incorrect in this meaning 為數更少，為數不那麼多〔此用法常被認為不正確〕: *There were less people there than we expected.* 那裡的人比我們預料的為少。**2 no less than** used when you are giving a number, to emphasize that it is surprisingly large 不少於，多達: *The book has been translated into no less than 40 languages.* 此書已翻譯成多達40種語言。**3 less than helpful/perfect etc** not at all helpful, perfect etc 一點也沒有幫助/不完善等: *Doctors have been less than successful in treating this condition.* 在治療這種病上，醫生一直沒有獲得成功。**4 in less than no time** very quickly or very soon 很快地，很迅速地: *The debts increased alarmingly, and in less than no time they found that they owed over $10,000.* 負債增長驚人，很快他們發現已經欠了一萬多美元。**5 nothing less than** used to emphasize how important or serious something really is 簡直是: *His appearance in the show was nothing less than a sensation.* 他在演出中的亮相簡直是轟動一時的事件。**6 no less** used to emphasize that the person or thing you are talking about is very important 正是〔強調談及的人、物很重要〕: *The building was opened by no less a person than the Prince of Wales.* 為大樓主持揭幕典禮的正是威爾士王子。| *His case is supported by the Police Complaints Committee no less.* 他的案子正是由警察投訴委員會支持的。**7 less of** *spoken* used to tell someone, usually a child, to stop doing something【口】不要做…〔通常對小孩說的話〕: *Less of that noise, please!* 請不要吵！**8 not ... any the less** just as much 不減少，仍然不變，還是那麼多: *I know he's done a dreadful thing, but I don't love him any the less.* 我知道他做了件很不好的事，但我仍然一樣愛他。

less[3] *prep* taking away or not counting a particular amount 減去，不計: *What is 121 less 36?* 121減去36是多少？| *He gave us our money back less the $2 service charge.* 他把錢還給我們，但扣除了兩美元服務費。

les·see /lɛˋsi; leˈsiː/ *n* [C] *law* someone who is legally allowed to use a house, building, land etc agreement for a fixed period of time in return for payment to the owner【法律】承租人，租戶 —compare 比較 LESSOR

less·en /ˈlɛsn̩; ˈlesən/ *v* [I,T] to become smaller in size, importance, or value, or make something do this（使）降低，（使）減少: *Garlic is supposed to lessen the risk of heart disease.* 大蒜被認為可以降低心臟病的發病率。| *International tensions lessened after the end of the Cold War.* 冷戰結束後國際緊張局勢緩和了。

less·er /ˈlɛsɚ; ˈlesə/ *adj* [only before noun 僅用於名詞前] **1** *formal* not as large, as important, or as much as something else【正式】更小的，次要的，更少的: *They originally asked for $5 million, but finally settled for a lesser sum.* 他們原先要求五百萬美元，但最後同意較少的金額。| **to a lesser extent/degree** *the growing influence of Tokyo, and to a lesser extent Frankfurt, as financial centers* 作為金融中心，東京的影響正在提高，其次是法蘭克福 —see also 另見 **lesser mortals** (MORTAL[2] (1)) **2 the lesser of two evils** the less unpleasant or harmful of two unpleasant choices 兩害之較輕者 **3 lesser known** not well known or not as well known as others 比較鮮為人知的，知名度較小的: *a lesser known French poet* 比較鮮為人知的法國詩人 **4** used in the names of some types of animal, bird, or plant that are slightly smaller than the main type〔用於鳥獸、植物的名字中，表示比主要品種〕略小的

les·son /ˈlɛsn̩; ˈlesən/ *n* [C] 

1 ▶LEARNING A SKILL 學習技能◀ a period of time in which someone is taught a particular skill, for example how to play a musical instrument or drive a car 課；課程: *piano lessons* 鋼琴課 | **take lessons** *She's started taking driving lessons.* 她已開始上駕駛課。| **[+on/in]** *lessons in social etiquette* 社交禮儀課

2 ▶IN SCHOOL 在學校◀ *BrE* a period of time in which students in a school are taught a particular subject【英】一堂課；CLASS[1] (3)) *AmE*【美】: *What did you do last lesson?* 上一堂課你們幹甚麼了？| *boring Maths lessons* 乏味的數學課 | **[+in/on]** *lessons on eight different subjects every week* 每週上八個科目的課

3 ▶WARNING 警告◀ an experience, especially an unpleasant one, that makes you more careful in the future 經驗，〔尤指〕教訓: *Pearl Harbor was a painful lesson for the US.* 珍珠港事件對美國是一場慘痛的教訓。

4 let that be a lesson to you *spoken* used to warn someone that they must be more careful in order to avoid the same bad experience happening to them again【口】引以為誡

5 ▶BOOK 書◀ a part of a book that is used for learning a particular subject, especially in school〔課本中的〕課: *Turn to lesson 25.* 翻到第25課。

6 ▶CHURCH 禮拜◀ a short piece that is read from the Bible during a religious ceremony〔宗教儀式中〕選讀的《聖經》經文 —see also 另見 **learn your lesson** (LEARN (7)), **teach sb a lesson** (TEACH (6))

les·sor /lɛˋsɔr; leˈsɔː/ *n* [C] *law* someone who allows someone else to use their house, building, land etc for a period of time for payment【法律】出租人 —compare 比較 LESSEE

lest /lɛst; lest/ *conjunction formal*【正式】**1** in order to make sure that something will not happen 免得，以免，唯恐: *She pulled away from the window lest anyone see them.* 她從窗口躲開了，免得有人見到她們。**2** used to show that someone is afraid or worried that a particular thing might happen〔與表示害怕或擔心的詞連用〕: *The child watched them, nervous lest they hurt themselves.* 小孩看着牠們，怕牠們自己傷了自己。| *He paused, afraid lest he say too much.* 他停頓下來，唯恐說得太多。

-let /lɪt; lɪ̣t/ *suffix* [in nouns 構成名詞] **1** a small kind of something 小: a *booklet* (=small paper-covered book) 小冊子 | *a piglet* (=young pig) 小豬 **2** a band worn on a particular part of your body 佩帶的環形物: *an anklet* (=worn on the ankle) 腳鐲

1 1 **let¹** /lɛt; let/ *v past tense and past participle* **let** *present participle* **letting**

1 ▶ALLOW 允許◀ [T not in passive 不用被動態] **a)** to allow someone to do something 讓, 允許: *I wanted to go out but my Dad wouldn't let me.* 我要出去, 但爸爸不允許。| **let sb do sth** *She won't let her children play by the river.* 她不許她的孩子在河邊玩。| *Don't let your boss hear you say that.* 別讓你的老闆聽到你那麼說。| **let sb have sth** (=give something to someone) 給某人某物 *I can let you have a copy of the report.* 我可以給你一份這篇報告的副本。—see graph at 參見 PERMIT¹ 圖表 —see graph at 參見 FORBID 圖表 **b)** to allow something to happen 使〔某事發生〕: **let sth do sth** *Max let the door swing open.* 馬克斯使門旋轉而開。| *She didn't let her anger show.* 她壓住怒火。| *It'll drive you crazy if you let it.* 如果你放任它, 它會把你逼瘋。—see 見 CAN (USAGE) —see graph at 參見 PERMIT¹ 圖表

2 let go to stop holding something 放手, 鬆開: *Let go! You're hurting me.* 鬆開手!你把我弄痛了。| **let go of** *She wouldn't let go of the rope.* 她不會鬆開繩子的。

3 let sb go a) to allow a person or animal to leave a place where they have been kept 放掉某人, 放走某人: *They said they wouldn't let her go until her family paid the ransom.* 他們說她家付贖金後才會放她走。**b)** a phrase meaning to dismiss someone from their job, used to avoid saying this directly 解雇某人〔委婉說法〕: *I'm afraid we're going to have to let you go.* 恐怕我們得讓你走人了。

4 let yourself go a) to allow yourself to relax completely in a social situation, and not worry about what other people think 放鬆自己, 放縱自己 **b)** to take less care of your appearance than usual 不修邊幅, 不注意外表: *She's really let herself go since her husband died.* 自從她丈夫死後, 她就很不注意打扮了。

5 let sth go for £2/$150 etc *informal* to sell something for a low price【非正式】以 2 英鎊/150 美元等賤賣

6 let sb know to tell someone something 讓某人知道, 告訴某人: *I'd appreciate it if you'd let me know as soon as possible.* 如蒙盡快賜告, 本人不勝感激。| **let sb know if/whether** *Let us know if you need any more information.* 如果你需要更多的信息, 請告訴我們。

7 let alone used to say that because one thing does not happen or is not true etc, another thing cannot possibly happen or be true 更不用說, 更談不上: *The baby can't even crawl yet, let alone walk!* 這孩子連爬都不會, 更不用說走了!

8 ▶WISH 願望◀ *literary* used to express a wish that something will happen or will not happen【文】〔用來表達願望〕讓: **(not) let sb/sth do sth** *Don't let him be the one who died, she prayed.* 但願死的不是他, 她祈求說。| **let there be** *Let there be roses and sparkling champagne.* 要是有玫瑰和泛泡沫的香檳酒該多好。

9 let yourself be bullied/imposed on etc to allow other people to treat you badly 容忍被別人欺負/強加於〔某事〕等: *Don't let yourself be pushed around.* 別讓人擺佈你。

10 never let a day/week go by without... to do something every day or every week 每天/每週都〔做某事〕: *I never let a day go by without phoning my mother.* 我沒有一天不給媽媽打電話。

11 ▶ROOM/BUILDING 房間/大樓◀ [T] to allow someone to use a room or building in return for money every week or month; LEASE² (1) 出租: *Interhome has over 20,000 houses to let across Europe.* 英特霍姆地產公司在全歐洲有兩萬多幢房屋出租。| **let sth to sb** *I've let my spare room to a Japanese student.* 我把空餘的房間租給了一個日本學生。| **To Let** *BrE*【英】**/For Let** *AmE*【美】(=words on a sign outside a building to show that it is empty and can be rented)〔空屋〕出[招]租 —compare 比較 HIRE¹ (1), RENT¹ (3)

12 ▶IMAGINE 想像◀ *formal*【正式】**a) let us suppose/say/ imagine** used to ask a reader or listener to imagine that something is true, as a way of helping them understand what you are talking about 假設/假如說/設想: *Let us suppose that interest rates go up again. What effect will this have on the property market?* 假設利率再次上升, 這對房地產市場會有甚麼影響? **b) let sth be/ equal/represent** used in mathematics or science to mean that one thing can be imagined as representing another 假設某物為/等於/代表: *Let angle A be 45°.* 設角 A 為 45°。

13 let sb alone also 又作 **let sb be** to stop annoying someone, or asking them things 不打擾某人: *Your mother's tired – let her alone!* 你媽媽累了 —— 別打擾她!

14 let sth drop/rest to stop discussing something or trying to deal with something that has been annoying you or worrying you 停止談論某事, 別去管某事: *He's apologized, so I think you should let it drop now.* 他已道歉, 所以我想你現在應該不要再提這件事情。

15 let sth go/pass to decide not to react to something bad or annoying that someone has done or said 對某事不計較: *I know you didn't mean to offend her, so we'll let it pass this time.* 我知道你不是有意傷害她, 所以這次我們對此事就不計較了。

16 let sth ride a) if you let a situation ride, you let it continue for a time before deciding whether to take any action〔作決定前〕放任某情況持續一段時間 **b)** if you let a remark that has annoyed you ride, you do not say anything about it 對惱人的話不理睬

17 let drop/fall to say a piece of information as though by accident, although really you want someone to know about it 似不經意脫口而出: *She decided that she would casually let drop the news about having the baby.* 她決定似不經意地把懷了孩子的事說出去。

18 let slip to accidentally say a piece of information that you did not want someone to know 走漏〔祕密〕

19 let yourself in for *informal* to do something that will cause you a lot of trouble【非正式】給自己招來〔麻煩〕: *I don't think Carol realizes what she's letting herself in for.* 我不認為嘉露認識到她在給自己招來甚麼麻煩。

20 let sb have it *informal*【非正式】**a)** to shout at someone because you are angry with them 大聲訓斥某人: *Mrs Bates really let him have it for leaving the classroom early.* 由於他早了離開教室, 貝茨女士大聲訓斥他。**b)** to hit or shoot someone 打擊某人; 向某人射擊 —see also 另見 **let fly** (FLY¹ (20)), **let your hair down** (HAIR (5)), **let it all hang out** (HANG¹), **live and let live** (LIVE¹ (28)), **let sth rip** (RIP¹ (5))

Frequencies of the verb **let** in spoken and written English 動詞 let 在英語口語和書面語中的使用頻率

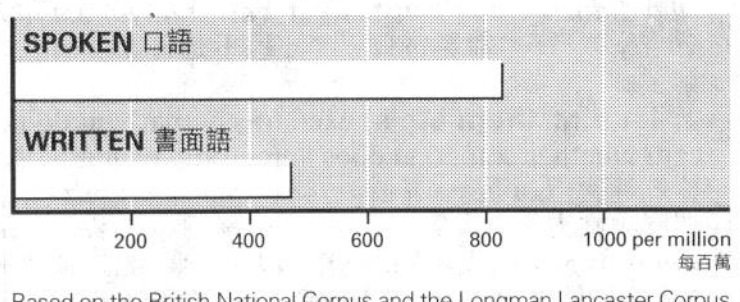

Based on the British National Corpus and the Longman Lancaster Corpus 據英國國家語料庫和朗文蘭卡斯特語料庫

This graph shows that the verb **let** is much more common in spoken English than in written English. This is because it is more commonly used in spoken English than **allow**, which is more formal and is more common in written English. **Let** is also used in a lot of common spoken phrases. 本圖表顯示, 動詞 let 在英語

口語中的使用頻率遠遠高於書面語, 因為它在英語口語中比allow使用得更加普遍, 而allow較為正式, 在書面語中使用得較普遍。let也用於許多常用口語片語中。

let (*v*) SPOKEN PHRASES
含let的口語片語

21 let's used to suggest to someone that you and they should do something together 讓我們〔一起〕: *Come on, let's dance!* 來吧, 讓我們一起跳舞! | *Right, let's get these plates washed.* 對, 讓我們把這些盤子洗了吧。| *Let's move on to the report itself: any comments?* 讓我們繼續來看報告本身: 有意見嗎? | **let's not** *Let's not talk about work now.* 我們大家現在別談工作。| **don't let's** *BrE*【英】*Don't let's quarrel.* 我們大家不要吵! —see 見 PROPOSE (USAGE)
22 let's see a) used to say that you are going to try to do something 讓我們試試看: **let's see if/whether** *Let's see if I can get the car to start.* 讓我試試看我能否把車起動。**b)** used when pausing to remember something or find a piece of information 讓我們想一下, 讓我們找一找: *Now, let's see...here it is: "Video recorder, good condition, £75".* 好吧, 讓我們找找看…在這裡: "錄影機, 性能良好, 75英鎊。" | *Let's see, oh, I wanted to ask what you are doing next Wednesday.* 讓我想一下, 哦, 我想問下星期三你打算幹甚麼。**c)** used to ask someone to show you something 讓我們看一下: *"Come on, let's see." "No, it's a secret!"* "過來, 讓我們看一下。" "不, 這是祕密!" | *Let's see your new dress.* 讓我們看一下你的新衣服。| *Right, let's see what you can do with that guitar!* 對, 讓我們瞧瞧你能用那結他演奏些甚麼曲子!
23 let me see/think used when pausing to think of some information or think what to do next 讓我想一想: *You sent it to, um, let me see, ... Mike Toghill.* 你把它寄給, 嗯, 讓我想一想, …邁克·托格希爾。
24 let me do sth a) used to politely offer to do something for someone 讓我〔為你〕做某事: *Here, let me help you with those bags.* 喂, 讓我幫你拿那些袋子。**b)** used to tell someone what you are going to do next 讓我做某事, 我要做某事: *Let me just take your blood pressure.* 我要量一下你的血壓。| *Let me finish this typing then I'll make us some coffee.* 讓我打完這些字, 然後給大家煮些咖啡。
25 let's say used to ask someone to imagine something in order to discuss it or understand it better 譬如說: *OK, you buy an object – let's say a bicycle – for $100. How much interest would you have to pay?* 好吧, 你買一樣東西 —— 譬如說是一輛腳踏車 —— 要100美元。你需要付多少利息? | **let's say (that)** *Let's say you did fail your exams, you could retake them, couldn't you?* 假如說你的確沒有通過考試, 你可以再考一次, 不是嗎?
26 let's just say used to say that you are not going to tell someone all the details about something 知道…就夠了〔用於不打算告訴某人所有細節時〕: *"So who did it?" "Let's just say it wasn't anyone in this family."* "那是誰幹的呢?" "知道不是這家裡的人就夠了。"
27 let him/them etc a) used to say that you do not care whether someone does something or not 隨他/他們等去: *Let her tell everyone, then – I don't care.* 那麼讓她去告訴大家好了 —— 我不在乎。| *Well, if he wants to go and kill himself, let him!* 哦, 如果他要去自殺, 那就讓他去好了! **b)** used to say that someone else should do something instead of you 讓他/他們等去〔做某事〕: *Let them clear up the mess, it's their fault.* 讓他們去打掃這堆髒東西, 這是他們的過失。
28 let's hope used to say that you hope something will happen, so that there will not be problems 我們希望〔某事會發生〕: *Let's just hope he got your letter in time.* 我們只希望他及時收到你的信。
29 let's face it/let's be honest used to say that you must accept an unpleasant fact 我們認了吧: *Let's face it, Ben, no one's going to lend us any more money.* 我們認了吧, 班恩, 沒有人再會借錢給我們了。
30 let well (enough) alone to not try to change a situation, because you may make it worse 維持現狀, 不畫蛇添足: *He's happier now – I'd let well enough alone if I were you.* 他現在比過去開心 —— 我要是你, 我不會去改變目前的狀況。
31 let me tell you! used to emphasize that a feeling you had was very strong 告訴你吧!: *I was pretty surprised, let me tell you!* 我感到很吃驚, 告訴你吧!
32 I'll/we'll let it go at that used to tell someone that you will not punish or criticize them any more for something bad they have done 我/我們不再懲罰[批評]〔某人〕: *Well you've missed your favorite program so we'll let it go at that.* 算了, 你已經錯失了你所喜愛的節目, 所以我們就不再批評你了。

let sb/sth ↔ **down** *phr v* [T] **1** to make someone feel disappointed because you have not behaved well or not done what you said you would do 讓〔某人〕失望, 失信於〔某人〕: *I'm counting on you to support me – don't let me down!* 我指望你支持我呢 —— 別讓我失望! | **let sb down badly** *She felt badly let down by her friends.* 她覺得她的朋友們對她大大失信了。**2 a)** to give something to someone who is in a lower place than you are 把〔某物〕放下來: *Let down a rope so that I can climb up.* 把繩子放下來我好爬上去。**b)** to move something that is on a string, rope etc downwards 把〔繫在繩子等上的某物〕向下放: *Let the basket down gently.* 把籃子小心地往下放。**3 let your hair down** *informal* to relax and enjoy yourself, especially after working hard【非正式】〔尤指辛勞後〕使某人放鬆: *The Christmas party gives everyone a chance to let their hair down.* 聖誕晚會給了大家輕鬆一下的機會。**4** *BrE* to allow the air to escape from something so that it loses its shape and firmness【英】使某物中的氣跑掉: *Someone's let my tyres down!* 有人把我輪胎的氣放掉了! **5 let the side down** *BrE informal* to cause embarrassment or disappointment to your friends, family, team etc, for example by not behaving as they expect you to behave【英, 非正式】讓〔親友、團隊等〕丟臉, 辜負了〔親友、團隊等〕 **6 let sb down lightly** to give someone bad news in a way that will not upset them too much 委婉地把壞消息告知某人 **7** to make a piece of clothing longer 加長〔衣服〕: *I'm going to let down this old dress for my daughter.* 我打算加長這件舊衣服給女兒穿。

let sb/sth ↔ **in** *phr v* [T] **1** to open the door of a room, building etc so that someone can come in 讓〔某人〕進來: *I unlocked the door and let him in.* 我開門讓他進來。| *My mother let herself in.* 我媽自己進來了。**2** to allow light, water, air etc to enter a place 讓〔光線、水、空氣等〕進入: *The windows don't let in much light.* 這些窗戶採光不足。**3 let sb in on** to tell someone about a secret plan, idea etc, and trust them not to tell other people 讓某人知道並讓其嚴守〔祕密、計劃等〕

let sb/sth **into** sth *phr v* [T] **1** to allow someone to come into a room or building 讓〔某人〕進入: *Who let you into my office?* 誰讓你進我的辦公室? **2 let sb into a secret** to tell someone something secret or private 告訴某人祕密 **3 be let into** *technical* if something such as a window or a decoration is let into a wall, brick etc, it is placed so that it is level with the surface it is in【術語】鑲入, 嵌入

let sb/sth **off** *phr v* [T] **1** to not make someone do a piece of work which they should be doing 免除〔某人應做之事〕: *Since you practiced the piano yesterday, I'll let you off today.* 由於你昨天練習了鋼琴, 今天我就讓你免了。| **let sb off sth** *She let her son off his chores.* 她免了她兒子的家務。**2** to not punish someone 免處罰〔某人〕: *I'll let you off this time, but don't do it again.* 這次

我就饒了你，但是不要再這麼做了。| **let sb off with sth** *The judge let two of the three prisoners off with only a reprimand.* 法官對三名犯人中的兩名只訓斥了一頓，免於處罰。| **let sb off lightly** (=give someone a less serious punishment than they deserve) 輕罰某人 **3 a)** to fire a gun 開〔槍〕**b)** to make a bomb or FIREWORK explode 扔[引爆]〔炸彈〕，放〔煙火〕—see also 另見 **let sb off the hook** (HOOK[1] (4)), **let off steam** (STEAM[1] (4))

let on *phr v* [I,T] *informal* to tell someone something that was meant to be a secret【非正式】泄露〔祕密〕，透露：*I think he knows more about it than he's letting on.* 我認為關於此事，他知道的比他透露給我們的要多。| **let on (that)** *Don't let on that I told you.* 不要告訴別人是我對你說的。| **let on who/why/how etc** *You mustn't let on who gave it to us.* 你千萬別說出去誰把它給我們的。

let out *phr v* **1** [T **let** sb ↔ **out**] to allow someone to leave a room, building etc 放…出去；釋放：*Let the dog out, will you?* 讓狗出去，行嗎？| *He was in a high-security jail and would probably never be let out.* 他關在戒備森嚴的監獄裡；可能永遠也不會被釋放出來。| **let sb out of sth** *Quietly, I let myself out of her apartment.* 我悄悄走出了她的公寓。**2** [T **let** sth ↔ **out**] to allow light, water, air etc to leave a place 讓〔光線、水、空氣等〕跑掉：*Close the door, you're letting all the heat out.* 關上門，你把暖氣都放跑了。**3 let out a scream/cry/roar etc** to make a sound, especially a loud sound 發出尖叫聲/叫喊聲/吼叫聲等：*She let out a sudden scream.* 她突然尖叫起來。**4** [T **let** sth ↔ **out**] to make a piece of clothing wider or looser, especially because the person it belongs to has become fatter 加寬，加大〔衣服〕**5** [T **let** sth ↔ **out**] *especially BrE* to allow someone to use a room, building etc in exchange for money【尤英】出租〔房間、大樓等〕—see 見 HIRE[1] (USAGE) **6** [I] *AmE* if a school, film etc lets out, it ends, so that the people attending it can leave【美】放學，散場：*What time does the play let out?* 戲甚麼時候散場？—see also 另見 **let the cat out of the bag** (CAT (2))

let up *phr v* [I] **1** if something, such as bad weather or an unpleasant situation, lets up, it stops or becomes less serious 停止，結束；緩和：*When do you think this rain will let up?* 你認為這場雨甚麼時候會停？**2 not let up** if someone does something without letting up, they do it continuously, especially in an annoying way〔尤指惱人地〕不停〔做某事〕：*I wish you'd stop nagging! You just never let up, do you?* 我希望你停止嘮叨！你就是沒完沒了，是不是？

let² *n* **1** [C] *BrE*【英】**a)** a period during which a house or flat is rented to someone; RENT[1] (1)〔房屋或公寓的〕出租期：*a long let* 長期出租 **b)** a house or flat that can be rented 出租的房屋[公寓] **2 without let or hindrance** *law* happening freely without being prevented in any way【法律】毫無障礙地

letch /lɛtʃ; letʃ/ another spelling of LECH lech 的另一種拼法

let·down /ˈlɛtˌdaun; ˈletdaʊn/ *n* [singular] *informal* an event, performance etc that is not as good as you expected it to be; disappointment【非正式】失望；令人失望的事：*The ending of the book was a real letdown.* 這本書的結尾確實是敗筆。—see also 另見 **let down** (LET[1])

le·thal /ˈliθəl; ˈliːθəl/ *adj* **1** causing death, or having the power to cause death 致命的，致死的，具殺傷力的：*a lethal dose of a drug* 藥品的致死劑量 **2** *often humorous* likely to be dangerous or dangerously effective【常幽默】危險的，危害的：*That cocktail looks pretty lethal.* 那雞尾酒看起來相當濃烈。**3 a lethal combination** a very bad or dangerous combination of two or more things 惡劣[危險]的組合：*Alcohol and tranquillizers are a lethal combination.* 烈酒和鎮靜劑搭配在一起極為危險。

le·thar·gic /lɪˈθɑrdʒɪk; lɪ̆ˈθɑːdʒɪk/ *adj* feeling as if you have no energy and no interest in doing anything 無精打采的，懶洋洋的：*The hot weather was making us all lethargic.* 炎熱的天氣使我們昏昏欲睡。—**lethargically** /-klɪ; -kli/ *adv*

leth·ar·gy /ˈlɛθədʒɪ; ˈleθədʒi/ *n* [U] the feeling of being lethargic 無精打采，懶洋洋：*New mothers often complain of tiredness, lethargy and mild depression.* 剛當上媽媽的人經常訴說疲倦、乏力和輕微的抑鬱。

let's /lɛts; lets/ the short form of 縮略式＝'let us'：*C'mon, let's go!* 來吧，我們一起走吧！—see 見 PROPOSE (USAGE)

let·ter¹ /ˈlɛtə; ˈletə/ *n* [C] S1 W1 **1** a written or printed message that is usually put in an envelope and sent by mail 書信：*Bart's writing a letter to his parents.* 巴特正在給他父母寫信。| *I got a long letter from Melanie today.* 今天我收到梅拉妮的一封長信。| **mail a letter** *AmE*【美】*Can you mail this letter for me on your way out?* 你在出去時能順道替我寄這封信嗎？| **post a letter** *BrE*【英】*I'm just going to post a letter.* 我正要去寄信。**2** any of the signs in writing or printing that represent a speech sound 字母：*'B' is a capital letter, 'b' is a small letter.* B 是大寫字母，b 是小寫字母。**3 do sth to the letter** to pay exact attention to the details of an agreement, rule, set of instructions etc 嚴格按照字面做某事；不折不扣做某事：*He kept his promise to the letter.* 他不折不扣地遵守諾言。| *I followed all the instructions to the letter, but it still wouldn't work.* 我嚴格地執行所有指示，但仍行不通。**4 the letter of the law** the exact words of a law or agreement rather than the intended or general meaning〔法律或協議的〕字面含義：*various methods of avoiding taxes while adhering to the letter of the law* 既按法律字面含義遵守法規、又可避免納稅的各種辦法 **5** *AmE* a large cloth letter to put on to clothes, given as a reward for playing in a school or college sports team【美】校隊隊衣上的大寫字母〔作為對優秀運動員的獎勵〕：*She got her letter in track.* 在賽跑中她獲得了校隊字母的獎勵。**6 English/American/German letters** [plural] *formal* the study of the literature of a particular country or language【正式】英國/美國/德國文學[語言]：*a major figure in English letters at the turn of the century* 世紀交替時期的一位英國文學大師 —see also 另見 CHAIN LETTER, DEAD LETTER, DEAR JOHN LETTER, LETTER OF CREDIT, MAN OF LETTERS, OPEN LETTER

letter² *v* [I] *AmE* to earn a LETTER[1] (5) in a sport【美】贏得運動項目的校隊字母獎勵：**[+in]** *He lettered in basketball at Brandeis.* 他在布蘭迪斯舉行的籃球賽中獲得校名首字母獎勵榮譽。

letter³ *adj AmE* LETTER-SIZE【美】信紙尺寸的

letter bomb /ˈ·· ˌ·/ *n* [C] a small bomb hidden in a package and sent to someone in order to kill or harm them 郵件炸彈

let·ter·box /ˈlɛtəˌbɑks; ˈletəbɒks/ *n* [C] **1** a narrow hole in a door, or a special box where letters, packages etc are delivered〔收方設的〕信箱 **2** *BrE* a box in a post office or street, in which letters can be posted【英】〔郵局設的〕郵箱，郵筒；MAILBOX *AmE*【美】

let·tered /ˈlɛtəd; ˈletəd/ *adj formal*【正式】**1** well educated 有學問的 **2 badly lettered/carefully lettered** with badly drawn, beautifully drawn etc letters or words 字寫得差的/字寫得工整的：*a brightly lettered sign on the boy's door* 男孩門上寫有亮閃閃字跡的牌子

let·ter·head /ˈlɛtəˌhɛd; ˈletəhed/ *n* [C] the name and address printed at the top of a sheet of writing paper 信箋抬頭，箋頭〔印於信箋上端的名稱和地址〕

let·ter·ing /ˈlɛtərɪŋ; ˈletərɪŋ/ *n* [U] **1** written or drawn letters, especially of a particular type, size, colour etc 字體：*a yellow board with black lettering* 上有黑字的黃色牌子 **2** the art of writing or drawing letters or words 字母圖案繪製術，印字，刻字，燙印

letter of cred·it /ˌ·· ˈ··/ *n* [C] an official letter from a bank allowing a particular person to take money from another bank〔銀行開出的〕信用證，信用狀

letter-per·fect /ˌ·· ˈ··◂/ *adj AmE* correct in every detail【美】正確無誤的，一字不差的：*The District Attorney's* *case was letter-perfect.* 該名地方檢察官的案情陳述完全正確。

letter-qual·i·ty /ˈ·· ˌ···/ *adj* a letter-quality PRINTER (1) produces print that is good enough to be used for business letters, reports etc 打印質量佳的

letter-size /ˈ·· ·/ also 又作 **letter** *adj AmE* paper that is letter-size is 8½ inches (INCH[1] (1)) wide and 11 inches long【美】信紙大小的〔寬 8½ 英寸, 長 11 英寸〕

let·ting /ˈlɛtɪŋ; ˈletɪŋ/ *n* [C] *BrE* a house or apartment that can be rented【英】可租用的房屋[公寓]: *a holiday letting* 假日出租公寓

let·tuce /ˈlɛtɪs; ˈletʒs/ *n* [C,U] a round vegetable with thin green leaves used in SALADS 生菜, 萵苣 —see picture on page A9 參見 A9 頁圖

let·up /ˈlɛtˌʌp; ˈletʌp/ *n* [singular, U] a pause or a reduction in a difficult, dangerous, or tiring activity 中止, 暫息, 減弱: *There is no sign of a letup in the fighting.* 戰鬥無停息的跡象。| *We were working seven days a week with no letup.* 我們一星期連續不停地工作了七天。—see also 另見 **let up** (LET[1])

leu·co·cyte /ˈljukəˌsaɪt; ˈluːkəsaɪt/ *n* [C] *technical* another spelling of LEUKOCYTE【術語】leukocyte 的另一種拼法

leu·cot·o·my /luˈkɑtəmɪ; luːˈkɒtəmi/ *n* [C] *BrE* a LOBOTOMY【英】葉切斷(術), 腦白質切斷(術)

leu·ke·mi·a also 又作 **leukaemia** *BrE*【英】/ljuˈkimɪə; luːˈkiːmiə/ *n* [U] a type of CANCER in which the blood contains too many WHITE BLOOD CELLs, causing weakness and sometimes death 白血病

leu·ko·cyte /ˈljukəˌsaɪt; ˈluːkəsaɪt/ *n* [C] *technical* one of the cells in your blood which fights against infection; WHITE BLOOD CELL【術語】白血球, 白細胞

lev·ee[1] /ˈlɛvɪ; ˈlevi/ *n* [C] a special wall built to stop a river flooding (防洪) 堤, 堤岸

lev·ee[2] /ˈlɛvɪ; ˈlevi/ *n* [C] *old use* a meeting in which a king receives visits from important people【舊】〔國王的〕召見, 接見

S1 W1 **lev·el[1]** /ˈlɛvl; ˈlevəl/ *n* [C]

1 ►AMOUNT 數量◄ a) the measured amount of something that exists at a particular time or in a particular place〔測得的〕數量, 數值: *Inflation had dropped to its lowest level in 30 years.* 通貨膨脹降到了 30 年來的最低值。| **[+of]** *concern about the level of carbon monoxide in the air* 對空氣中一氧化碳的含量的關注 | **high/low levels** *High levels of radiation were found in the sea.* 在海洋中探測到高能級輻射。**b)** the amount of a quality that someone has or that exists in a situation 水平, 水準, 程度: *a very high level of commitment among the workforce* 工人們的極度投入 | *These simple exercises can dramatically reduce stress levels.* 這些簡單的運動能迅速減輕緊張的程度。

2 ►HEIGHT 高度◄ the height of something in relation to the ground or to another object 水平高度; 相對高度: *Hold out your arm at the same level as your shoulder.* 伸出你的手臂與肩同高。| **at eye level** (=at the same height as your eyes) 與眼睛相同高度

3 ►LIQUID 液體◄ the height of the surface of a liquid from the ground or from the bottom of a container 液體的高度: *Check the water level in the car radiator.* 檢查一下汽車散熱器內水的高度。—see also 另見 SEA LEVEL, WATER LEVEL

4 ►STANDARD 標準◄ a particular standard of skill or ability, for example in education or sport 標準, 水平, 水準, 級別: *Students at this level tend to have a lot of problems with grammar.* 這一水平的學生在語法上會有很多問題。| *By 21, she was regularly playing at international level.* 她 21 歲就經常在國際級的比賽中演奏。| *an advanced level coursebook* 高級程度課本

5 ►FLOOR/GROUND 地板/地面◄ a floor or piece of ground, especially when considered in relation to another floor or piece of ground that is higher or lower 高低不同的地面[層面]: *The town is built on different levels.* 這個城鎮建在高低不同的地面上。| *The medical center should be on one level for the convenience of patients.* 為了方便病人, 醫療中心應該設在同一層樓上。

6 ►RANK OF JOB 工作的級別◄ all the people or jobs within an organization, industry etc that have similar amounts of importance and responsibility 等級, 級別: *Training was offered at each level in the department.* 部門內各級人員都要進行培訓。| *Decisions like this can only be made at board level.* 這種決定只能由董事會作出。

7 at local level/at national level happening within a small area or the whole area of a country 地區級的/國家級的: *Decisions are made at local and not national level.* 決定是由地區而不是由國家作出的。

8 on/at one level ... on/at another level used when you are considering something in one way and then in another way 一方面…另一方面: *At one level I really enjoy the work, but at another level I feel I should be doing something more challenging.* 一方面我確實喜歡這工作, 但是另一方面我感到應該做些更具挑戰性的事。

9 on a practical level/on a personal level etc used to talk about something, considering it in a practical, personal etc way 從實際的角度/從個人的角度等: *On a more practical level, we should consider how we are going to find the money.* 從比較實際的角度, 我們應該考慮怎樣找到這筆錢。

10 be on the level *informal* to be honest【非正式】老實的, 誠實的, 真誠的: *I'd like to buy that bloke's car, but I'm not sure he's on the level.* 我想買那個傢伙的車子, 但我不知道他是否老實。

11 ►TOOL 工具◄ *especially AmE* a tool used for checking that a surface is flat; SPIRIT-LEVEL【尤美】水準儀, 水準器

level[2] *adj* **1** a surface, piece of land etc that is level is flat and does not slope in any direction 平的, 平坦的, 水平的: *Make sure the ground is completely level before you lay the turf.* 鋪草皮前要確定地面完全平整。**2 be level a)** two things that are level are at the same height as each other 同等高度: **[+with]** *The top of the tree was level with the roof of the house.* 樹頂和屋頂一樣高。**b)** *BrE* two sports teams, competitors etc that are level have the same number of points【英】同等比分: **draw level** (=get enough points to be level) 拉平比分 *Faldo has drawn level with Ballesteros on twelve under par.* 佛度拉平了與巴列斯特羅斯的比分, 都負十二桿。| **finish level** *The two teams finished level, with 10 points each.* 兩隊終局比分拉平, 各得 10 分。—see also 另見 LEVEL-PEGGING **3 do your level best** to try as hard as possible to do something 盡力〔去做某事〕: *I'll do my level best to help you.* 我會盡力幫助你。**4 a level voice/look/gaze** a steady voice, look etc, that shows you are calm or determined 平靜[堅定]的聲音/神色/目光 **5 level spoon(ful)/cup** an amount of a substance, that is just enough to fill a spoon or cup, used as a measure in cooking 平杓/平杯

level[3] *v* **levelled, levelling** *BrE*【英】, **leveled, leveling** *AmE*【美】[T] **1** to make something flat and even 推倒, 平坦, 把…弄平, 整平: *Pat levelled the wet concrete with a piece of wood.* 帕特用一片木頭抹平濕混凝土。**2** to knock down or destroy a building or area completely 推倒, 夷平: *The bombing raid levelled a large part of the town.* 空襲把這城鎮的一大部分地區夷為了平地。**3 level the score** *BrE* to make the score in a game or competition equal【英】使比分拉平, 使比分相同

level sth **at** *phr v* [T] **1** to aim something such as a weapon at someone or something 用〔某物〕瞄準, 對準 **2 level a charge/accusation/criticism at** to publicly criticize someone or say they are responsible for a crime, mistake etc 針對〔某人〕的指控/指責/批評: *Outrageous accusations were levelled against some of Hollywood's most famous stars.* 粗暴的指責是針對好萊塢某些著名的影星。

level off/out *phr v* **1** [I] to stop climbing or falling, and continue at a fixed height 作水平飛行, 平飛: *After climbing steeply through woodland the path levelled off.* 小路穿過陡峭的林地後變得平坦。| *The plane levelled out at 30,000 feet.* 飛機在三萬英尺的高空作水平飛行。 **2** [I] to become steady in development or growth 變得平穩: *Inflation has begun to level off.* 通脹開始趨於平穩。**3** [T **level** sth ↔ **off/out**] to make something flat and smooth 使〔某物〕平坦[平整]

level with sb *phr v* [T] *informal* to speak honestly to someone, not hiding any unpleasant facts from them【非正式】直言相告: *He asked Ron to level with him about what people were saying about him.* 他要求羅恩直言不諱地告訴他人們對他的議論。—see also 另見 **be on the level** (LEVEL[1] (10))

level cross·ing /ˌ‥ ˈ‥/ *n* [C] *BrE* a place where a road and railway cross each other, usually protected by gates【英】〔公路與鐵路的〕平面交叉點, 平交道口

level-head·ed /ˌ‥ ˈ‥◂/ *adj* calm and sensible in making judgments or decisions 穩健的, 頭腦清醒的

lev·el·ler *BrE*【英】, **leveler** *AmE*【美】/ˋlɛvl̩ɚ; ˈlevələ/ *n* [C] something, especially death or illness, that makes people of all classes and ranks seem equal 使人平等的事物〔尤指死亡或疾病〕

level-peg·ging /ˌ‥ ˈ‥/ *n* **be level-pegging** *BrE* if competitors in a race, election etc are level-pegging, they are equal and it is difficult to know who will win【英】勢均力敵, 不分高低

level play·ing-field /ˌ‥ ˈ‥ˌ·/ *n* [singular] a situation in which different companies, countries etc can all compete fairly with each other because no one has special advantages 公平的競爭基礎: *It's not really a level playing-field when one country is subsidizing its car industry with massive government grants.* 當一國給予其汽車工業大量的政府補貼, 這就不是一個真正的公平競爭。

le·ver[1] /ˋlɛvɚ; ˈliːvə/ *n* [C] **1** a long thin piece of metal that you use to lift something heavy by putting one end under the object and pushing the other end down 槓桿 **2** a stick or handle fixed to a machine, that you move to make the machine work〔機器的〕控制桿[柄] —see also 另見 GEAR LEVER **3** something you use to influence a situation to get the result that you want〔影響局勢的〕方法, 手段

lever[2] *v* [T] **1** to move something with a lever〔用槓桿〕撬動: **lever sth off/up/out etc** *Marc grunted as he levered the stone into place.* 馬克一邊嘟囔一邊用槓桿把石頭撬正。**2** to make someone leave a particular job, situation etc 擠走〔某人〕: **[+out]** *They're trying to lever him out of his job as CEO.* 他們正試圖把他從行政總裁的職位上擠走。

le·ver·age[1] /ˋlɛvərɪdʒ; ˈliːvərɪdʒ/ *n* [U] **1** influence that you can use to make people do what you want 影響: *Diplomatic leverage by the US persuaded several governments to cooperate.* 美國施加外交影響說服一些國家進行合作。**2** the action, power, or use of a lever 槓桿作用, 槓桿力量

leverage[2] *v* [T] *AmE technical* to make money available, using a particular method【美, 術語】舉債經營, 借貸經營: *using public funds to leverage private investment* 借用公共基金經營私人投資

lev·e·ret /ˋlɛvərɪt; ˈlevərɪ̵t/ *n* [C] a young HARE[1] (1) 小野兔

le·vi·a·than /lɪˋvaɪəθən; lɪˈvaɪəθən/ *n* [C] **1** something very large and strong 龐然大物: *a leviathan of a ship* 龐大的巨輪 **2** a very large and frightening sea animal 海中巨獸

lev·i·tate /ˋlɛvəˌtet; ˈlevɪ̵teɪt/ *v* [I] to rise and float in the air by magic〔靠魔力〕浮在空中, 飄浮 —**levitation** /ˌlɛvəˋteʃən; ˌlevɪ̵ˈteɪʃən/ *n* [U]

lev·i·ty /ˋlɛvətɪ; ˈlevɪ̵ti/ *n* [U] *formal* lack of respect or seriousness when you are dealing with something serious【正式】輕浮, 輕率

lev·y[1] /ˋlɛvɪ; ˈlevi/ *v* [T] **levy a tax/charge etc** to officially make someone pay a tax etc 徵稅/徵費等: **[+on]** *A new tax has just been levied on all electrical goods.* 對所有電器商品剛開始徵收新稅。

levy[2] *n* [C] an additional sum of money, usually paid as a tax 稅款, 稅額

lewd /lud; luːd/ *adj* using rude words or movements that make you think of sex 好色的, 下流的, 淫蕩的: *lewd comments* 下流的評論 —**lewdly** *adv* —**lewdness** *n* [U]

lex·i·cal /ˋlɛksɪkl̩; ˈleksɪkəl/ *adj technical* dealing with words, or related to words【術語】詞彙的

lex·i·cog·ra·phy /ˌlɛksəˋkɑgrəfɪ; ˌleksɪˈkɒgrəfi/ *n* [U] the skill, practice, or profession of writing dictionaries 詞典編纂學; 詞典編纂; 詞典編纂業 —**lexicographer** *n* [C] —**lexicographical** /ˌlɛksəkoˋgræfɪkl̩; ˌleksɪkəˈgræfɪkəl/ *adj*

lex·i·col·o·gy /ˌlɛksɪˋkɑlədʒɪ; ˌleksɪˈkɒlədʒi/ *n* [U] *technical* the study of the meaning and uses of words【術語】詞彙學

lex·i·con /ˋlɛksɪkɑn; ˈleksɪkən/ *n* **1 the lexicon** *technical* all the words and phrases used in a language or that a particular person knows【術語】〔某種語言或某人知曉的〕全部詞彙 **2** [C] a book containing an alphabetical list of words with their meanings 詞典

lex·is /ˋlɛksəs; ˈleksɪ̵s/ *n* [U] *technical* all the words in a language【術語】〔某種語言的〕全部詞彙

ley line /ˋle ˌlaɪn; ˈleɪ laɪn/ *n* [C] an imaginary line connecting old buildings, places etc that is believed to follow an ancient track that has special power 史前地貌的假想線

li·a·bil·i·ty /ˌlaɪəˋbɪlətɪ; ˌlaɪəˈbɪlɪ̵ti/ *n* **1** [U] legal responsibility for something, especially for paying money that is owed, or for damage or injury 責任, 義務: **[+for]** *Tenants have legal liability for any damage they cause.* 承租人對於他們造成的任何損壞負有法律責任。**2 liabilities** *technical* the amount of debt that must be paid【術語】負債, 債務 **3** [singular] someone or something that is likely to cause problems for someone 妨礙的人[物]: *A kid like Tom would be a liability in any classroom.* 像湯姆這樣的孩子放到任何班上都是個累贅。**4 liability to sth** the amount that something is likely to be affected by a particular kind of problem, illness etc 易有〔某種〕傾向: *The patient may suffer greater liability to bacterial diseases.* 這病人可能更易患細菌性疾病。—see also 另見 LIMITED LIABILITY ✍ 2

li·a·ble /ˋlaɪəbl̩; ˈlaɪəbəl/ *adj* **1 be liable to do sth** to be likely to do or say something or to behave in a particular way, especially because of a fault or natural tendency 易於〔做某事〕, 傾向於…的: *The car is liable to overheat on long trips.* 這輛汽車跑長途容易過熱。**2** [not before noun 不用於名詞前] legally responsible for the cost of something 有賠償責任的: **[+for]** *Manufacturers are liable for any defects in the equipment.* 製造商對設備的任何缺陷都負有賠償責任。**3** likely to be affected by a particular kind of problem, illness etc 易出問題的, 易得病的: **[+to]** *You're more liable to injury when you don't get regular exercise.* 要是你不經常鍛鍊, 會更易受傷。**4** *law* likely to be legally punished or forced to do something by law【法律】可能受處罰的, 可能承擔有法律義務的: **[+to]** *Anyone found trespassing is liable to a maximum fine of $100.* 任何人擅自闖入, 一經發現, 最高可被罰款 100 美元。| **[+for]** *All males between 18 and 60 are liable for military service.* 所有 18 歲到 60 歲的男性公民都有服兵役的義務。

li·aise /lɪˋez; liˈeɪz/ *v* **[I+with]** to exchange information with someone who works in another organization or department so that you can both be more effective 聯絡, 聯繫: *Part of Anne's job as a librarian is to liaise with local schools.* 作為圖書館管理員, 安妮的部分工作是聯絡當地的學校。

li·ai·son /lɪəˌzɑn; liˈeɪzən/ *n* **1** [singular, U] the regular exchange of information between groups of people, es-

L

pecially at work, so that each group knows what the other is doing 聯絡, 聯繫: **[+between]** *close liaison between army and police* 軍方和警方的密切聯繫 | **in liaison with** *The project has been set up in liaison with the art department.* 該項目已經與藝術部門建立了聯繫。 **2** [C] a word meaning a sexual relationship between a man and a woman who are not married to each other, used to avoid saying this directly〔男女間的〕私通〔委婉語〕

liaison of·fi·cer /·ˈ·· ˌ···/ *n* [C] someone whose job is to talk to different departments or groups and to tell each of them about what the others are doing 聯絡官

li·ar /ˋlaɪɚ; ˈlaɪə/ *n* [C] someone who tells lies 說謊者

Lib *BrE*【英】the written abbreviation of 縮寫= LIBERAL[3] —**Lib** *adj*

lib /lɪb; lɪb/ *n* —see 見 AD LIB, WOMEN'S LIB

li·ba·tion /laɪˋbeʃən; laɪˈbeɪʃən/ *n* [C] a gift of wine to a god 祭酒, 奠酒

lib·ber /ˋlɪbɚ; ˈlɪbə/ *n* **women's libber** —see 見 WOMEN'S LIB

Lib Dem /ˌlɪb ˋdɛm; ˌlɪb ˈdem◂/ *n* [C] *BrE* LIBERAL DEMOCRAT【英】自由民主黨〔中間黨派〕—**Lib Dem** *adj*

li·bel¹ /ˋlaɪbḷ; ˈlaɪbəl/ *n* [C,U] an act of writing or printing untrue statements about someone so that other people are likely to have a bad opinion of them 誹謗, 誹謗性文字: *Holt sued the newspaper for libel.* 霍爾特控告該報社誹謗。| *a libel action* (=a court case against someone for libel) 誹謗訴訟案 —compare 比較 SLANDER¹ (2)

libel² *v* **libelled, libelling** *BrE*【英】, **libeled, libeling** *AmE*【美】[T] to write or print a libel against someone 誹謗〔某人〕

li·bel·lous *BrE*【英】, **libelous** *AmE*【美】/ˋlaɪbələs; ˈlaɪbələs/ *adj* containing untrue written statements about someone which could make other people have a bad opinion of them 誹謗的, 中傷的: *libellous gossip* 誹謗性的流言

2 **lib·e·ral¹** /ˋlɪbərəl; ˈlɪbərəl/ *adj* **1** willing to understand and respect other people's ideas, opinions, and feelings 心胸寬闊的, 尊重別人想法[意見; 感情]的: *Young people nowadays take a more liberal attitude towards sexuality.* 當今的年輕人對性行為採取更加開明的態度。**2** supporting or allowing gradual political and social changes〔思想〕開放的, 支持[主張]變革的: *a more liberal policy on issues of crime and punishment* 對待犯罪及量刑的更加開明的政策 **3** given in large amounts 豐富的, 充足的: *a liberal supply of drinks* 飲料的充足供應 **4** generous with your money 慷慨大方的 **5** not exact 不拘一格的, 不拘泥字面的: *a liberal interpretation of the original play* 對原劇的自由詮釋 **6 liberal education** a kind of education which encourages you to develop a large range of interests and knowledge and respect for other people's opinions 通才教育

liberal² *n* [C] someone with liberal opinions or principles 開明人士: *a society dominated by white bourgeois liberals* 白人資產階級開明人士主導的社會

Liberal³ *n* [C] someone who supports or belongs to the former LIBERAL PARTY or the LIBERAL DEMOCRATS in Britain〔英國前〕自由黨支持者[黨員], 自由民主黨支持者[黨員] —**Liberal** *adj*

liberal arts /ˌ··· ˈ·/ *n* [plural] the areas of learning which develop someone's ability to think and increase their general knowledge, rather than developing technical skills 文科

Liberal Dem·o·crats /ˌ··· ˈ···/ *n* [plural] a British political party of the centre〔英國的〕自由民主黨 —**Liberal Democrat** *adj*

lib·e·ral·is·m /ˋlɪbərəlˌɪzəm; ˈlɪbərəlɪzəm/ *n* [U] liberal opinions and principles, especially on social and political subjects 自由主義

lib·e·ral·i·ty /ˌlɪbəˋræləti; ˌlɪbəˈræləti/ *n* [U] *formal*【正式】**1** understanding of, and respect for, other people's opinions 寬容, 開明: *a spirit of liberality and fairness* 開明公平的精神 **2** the quality of being generous 慷慨大方

lib·e·ral·ize also 又作 **-ise** *BrE*【英】/ˋlɪbərəlˌaɪz; ˈlɪbərəlaɪz/ *v* [T] to make a system, laws, or moral attitudes less strict 使自由化; 放鬆對...的限制 —**liberalization** /ˌlɪbərələˋzeʃən; ˌlɪbərəlaɪˈzeɪʃən/ *n* [U]

Liberal Par·ty /ˈ··· ˌ··/ *n* [singular] a former British political party of the centre〔舊時英國的〕自由黨

liberal stud·ies /ˌ··· ˈ··/ *n* [plural] *especially BrE* subjects that are taught in order to increase student's general knowledge and their ability to write, speak, and study more effectively【尤英】文科科目 —compare 比較 LIBERAL ARTS

lib·e·rate /ˋlɪbəˌret; ˈlɪbəreɪt/ *v* [T] **1** to free someone from feelings or conditions that make their life unhappy or difficult 使解脫, 使解放: **[+from]** *liberated from shame* 從羞愧中解脫出來 | *the liberating power of education* 教育的解放力量 **2** to free prisoners, a city, a country etc from someone's control 釋放, 解放〔囚犯、城市、國家等〕—**liberator** *n* [C] —**liberation** /ˌlɪbəˋreʃən; ˌlɪbəˈreɪʃən/ *n* [U]

lib·e·rat·ed /ˋlɪbəˌretɪd; ˈlɪbəreɪtɪd/ *adj* free to behave in the way you want, and not restricted by old rules of social and sexual behaviour〔在社交和男女關係上〕不受約束的, 思想解放的: *the magazine for the liberated woman* 面向思想解放的婦女的雜誌

lib·er·tar·i·an /ˌlɪbɚˋtɛrɪən; ˌlɪbəˈteəriən/ *n* [C] someone who believes strongly that people should be free to do and think what they want to 自由論者 —**libertarian** *adj*

lib·er·tine /ˋlɪbɚˌtin; ˈlɪbətiːn/ *n* [C] someone who leads an immoral life and always looks for pleasure, especially sexual pleasure 放蕩不羈的人, 淫蕩的人 —**libertine** *adj*

lib·er·ty /ˋlɪbɚtɪ; ˈlɪbəti/ *n*

1 ►FREEDOM 自由◄ [U] the freedom and the right to do whatever you want without asking permission or being afraid of authority 自由, 自由權: *People will resent these restrictions on their liberty.* 人們會憎恨這些對他們自由的限制措施。

2 ►LEGAL RIGHT 合法權利◄ [C usually plural 一般用複數] a particular legal right〔某種〕合法權利: *liberties such as freedom of speech that we take for granted* 合法權利, 諸如我們認為理所當然的言論自由

3 ►WITHOUT PERMISSION 未經許可◄ [singular] something you do without asking permission, which may offend or upset someone else 擅自的行為, 冒犯的舉動, 放肆的行為: *What a diabolical liberty!* 多麼放肆的舉動! | **take the liberty of doing sth** *I took the liberty of cancelling the reservation for you.* 我擅自取消了你的預訂。

4 be at liberty to do sth *formal* to have the right or permission to do something【正式】有權做某事, 獲許可做某事: *I'm afraid that I am not at liberty to discuss these matters.* 恐怕我無權討論這些問題。

5 take liberties with sb/sth a) to make unreasonable changes in something such as a piece of writing 隨便地改動某物: *The film-makers took too many liberties with the original novel.* 製片人對原著改動太多了。**b)** *old-fashioned* to treat someone without respect by being too friendly too quickly, especially in a sexual way【過時】與某人相處時太放肆, 太隨便對待某人〔尤指性行為上〕: *He's been taking liberties with our female staff.* 他對待我們的女職員太隨便了。

6 at liberty if a prisoner or an animal is at liberty, they are no longer in prison or enclosed in a small place〔犯人或動物〕不受拘禁的, 獲得自由的

li·bi·do /lɪˋbido; lɪˈbiːdəʊ/ *n* [C,U] *technical* someone's desire to have sex【術語】性慾 —**libidinous** /lɪˋbɪdṇəs; lɪˈbɪdɪnəs/ *adj*

Li·bra /ˋlibrə; ˈliːbrə/ *n* **1** [singular] the seventh sign of the ZODIAC, represented by a pair of SCALES, and believed to affect the character and life of people born between September 23rd and October 23rd 天秤宮[座] **2** [C] someone who was born between September 23rd and October 23rd 天秤宮[座]時段〔9月23日至10月23日〕出生的人

li·brar·i·an /laɪˋbrɛrɪən; laɪˈbreəriən/ *n* [C] someone who works in a library 圖書館管理員 —**librarianship** *n* [U]

2 1 **li·bra·ry** /ˋlaɪˌbrɛrɪ; ˈlaɪbrəri/ *n* [C] **1** a room or building containing books that can be looked at or borrowed 圖書館, 圖書室: *a public library* 公共圖書館 | *the college library* 大學[學院]圖書館 | *a library book* 圖書館的書 —compare 比較 BOOKSHOP **2** a group of books, records etc, collected by one person 私人收藏的書籍[唱片等] **3** a set of books, records etc that are produced by the same company and have the same general appearance〔同一公司出版、外觀相同的〕叢書[唱片集等]: *a library of modern classics* 現代古典文庫

library pic·tures /ˈ··· ˌ··/ *n* [plural] *BrE* pictures shown in a television programme that were made at a previous time【英】〔電視節目中放映的〕資料圖片

li·bret·tist /lɪˋbrɛtɪst; lɪˈbretəst/ *n* [C] someone who writes librettos〔歌劇的〕歌詞作者

li·bret·to /lɪˋbrɛto; lɪˈbretəʊ/ *plural* **librettos** *n* [C] the words of an OPERA or musical play〔歌劇、音樂劇的〕歌詞〔腳本〕

lice /laɪs; laɪs/ *n* the plural of LOUSE¹ (1)

3 2 **li·cence** *BrE*【英】, **license** *AmE*【美】/ˋlaɪsn̩s; ˈlaɪsəns/ *n*

1 ►DOCUMENT 文件◄ [C] an official document giving you permission to own or do something for a period of time 許可證, 執照, 證書: *a firearms license* 槍支許可證 | *How much is the licence fee?* 許可證的費用是多少? | **lose your licence** (=have your driving licence taken by the police as punishment) 被扣留駕駛執照

2 ►FREEDOM 自由◄ [U] **a)** freedom to do or say what you think is best〔行動、言論的〕自由, 不受拘束: *Headteachers should be allowed greater licence in the exercise of their power.* 應允許校長在行使權利中有更大的自由。**b)** freedom to behave in a way that is sexually immoral 放縱, 淫蕩

3 artistic/poetic licence the way in which a writer or painter changes the facts of the real world to make their story, description, or picture of events more interesting or more beautiful 藝術/詩的破格[奔放], 打破常規

4 ►RIGHT TO DO STH 做某事的權利◄ [C] official permission to do something, which seems to give someone the right to do something that is wrong 許可, 特許: **[+for]** *Church groups see the new laws as a licence for promiscuity.* 各教派視新的法律為對男女濫交的認同。| **licence to print money** (=an officially approved plan in which there is no control over how much money is spent) 允許濫印鈔票〔意指正式批准但對開銷不加以控制的計劃〕

5 under licence if something is sold, made etc under licence it is sold etc with the permission of a company or organization 獲許可〔出售、生產等〕

li·cense also 又作 **licence** *BrE*【英】/ˋlaɪsn̩s; ˈlaɪsəns/ *v* [T usually passive 一般用被動態] to give official permission for someone to do something or for an activity to take place 批准, 許可: **be licensed to do sth** *The restaurant is now licensed to sell alcohol.* 這間餐廳現在獲准售酒。

li·censed also 又作 **licenced** /ˋlaɪsn̩st; ˈlaɪsənst/ *adj* **1** *BrE* having a licence to sell alcoholic drinks【英】獲准售酒的, 許可售酒的: *a licensed restaurant* 許可售酒的餐館 **2** a car, gun etc that is licensed is one that someone has official permission to own or use 領有執照的, 正式許可擁有[使用]的 **3** having been given official permission to do a particular job 獲准執業的: *a licensed private investigator* 獲准執業的私人偵探

licensed vict·ual·ler /ˌ·· ˈ···/ *n* [C] *BrE technical* an owner of a shop or PUB who is allowed to sell alcoholic drink【英, 術語】特許出售酒類店鋪[酒吧]的老闆

li·cen·see /ˌlaɪsn̩ˋsi; ˌlaɪsənˈsiː/ *n* [C] someone who has official permission to do something 執照持有人, 許可證持有人

license plate /ˈ·· ·/ *n* [C] *AmE* one of the signs with numbers on it at the front and back of a car【美】〔汽車的〕牌照, 車牌; NUMBER PLATE *BrE*【英】—see picture on page A2 參見A2頁圖

licens·ing hours /ˈ··· ˌ··/ *n* [plural] the hours during which it is legal to sell alcohol in Britain〔英國的〕合法售酒時間, 許可售酒時間

licensing laws /ˈ··· ˌ·/ *n* [plural] *BrE* the laws that say when and where you can sell alcohol【英】售酒法〔規定酒類的銷售時間和地點〕

li·cen·ti·ate /laɪˋsɛnʃɪɪt; laɪˈsenʃiət/ *n* [C] someone who has been given official permission to practise a particular art or profession 有從事某種專業資格的人, 持有專業證書者: *a licentiate of the Royal College of Music* 皇家音樂學院證書持有者

li·cen·tious /laɪˋsɛnʃəs; laɪˈsenʃəs/ *adj formal* behaving in a sexually immoral or uncontrolled way【正式】淫蕩的; 放蕩的 —**licentiously** *adv* —**licentiousness** *n* [U]

li·chee /ˋlaɪtʃi; ˈlaɪtʃiː/ *n* [C] another spelling of LYCHEE lychee 的另一種拼法

li·chen /ˋlaɪkən; ˈlaɪkən/ *n* [U] a grey, green, or yellow plant that spreads over the surface of stones and trees 地衣 —compare 比較 MOSS

lick¹ /lɪk; lɪk/ *v* 3

lick 舔

1 ►TONGUE 舌頭◄ [T] to move your tongue across the surface of something in order to eat it, clean it etc 舔, 舔吃: *The dog jumped up and licked her face.* 狗跳起來舔她的臉。

2 ►SPORT 體育運動◄ [T] *informal* to defeat an opponent【非正式】擊敗〔對手〕: *I reckon we could lick the best teams in Georgia.* 我估計我們能擊敗喬治亞州最強的隊。

3 ►FLAMES/WAVES 火焰/波浪◄ [I,T] *literary* if flames or waves lick something, they touch it again and again with quick movements【文】〔火焰〕吞捲; 〔波浪〕拍擊: **[+at/against]** *Soon the flames were licking at the curtains.* 很快火焰便吞捲着窗簾。

4 have (got) sth licked *informal* to have succeeded in dealing with a difficult problem【非正式】使〔難題〕得到解決

5 lick your lips to feel eager and excited because you are expecting to get something good 舔唇嚮往, 熱切期盼

6 lick your wounds to quietly think about the defeat or disappointment you have just suffered〔舔癒傷口〕重整旗鼓

7 lick sb's boots to obey someone completely because you fear them or want to please them 巴結[奉承]某人 —see also 另見 BOOT-LICKING, **knock/lick sb into shape** (SHAPE¹ (7))

lick sth ↔ **up** *phr v* [T] to drink or eat something by licking it 舔飲, 舔吃

lick² *n* **1** [C usually singular 一般用單數] an act of licking something with your tongue 舔: *Can I have a lick of your ice cream?* 我可以舔一下你的冰淇淋嗎? **2 a lick of paint/colour etc** a small amount of paint etc put onto the surface of something to improve its appearance 少量油漆/顏料等 **3 give sth a lick and a promise a)** *BrE* to wash or clean something quickly and carelessly【英】馬虎地清洗[清掃]某物 **b)** *AmE* to do a job quickly and carelessly【美】草率地做某事 **4 at a great lick/at a hell of a lick** *informal especially BrE* very fast【非正式, 尤英】迅速地 **5** [C] *informal* an act of hitting someone【非正式】一擊

lick·e·ty-split /ˌlɪkətɪ ˋsplɪt; ˌlɪkə̬ti ˈsplɪt/ *adv AmE old-fashioned* very quickly【美, 過時】快速地, 迅速地

lick·ing /ˋlɪkɪŋ; ˈlɪkɪŋ/ *n* [singular] *informal*【非正式】**1** a defeat in a sports competition or match〔體育競賽或比賽的〕失敗, 挫折: *We got a real licking in the final.* 在決賽中我們被打得慘敗。**2** a severe beating as a punishment 狠揍, 痛打〔作為懲罰〕

lic·o·rice /ˋlɪkərɪs; ˈlɪkərɪs/ *n* [U] the American spelling of LIQUORICE liquorice 的美式拼法

lid /lɪd; lɪd/ *n*

1 ►COVER 蓋子◄ [C] a cover for the open part of a pot, box, or other container〔容器的〕蓋子: *Can you get the lid off this jar for me?* 你能幫我打開這個罐子的蓋嗎? | *a dustbin lid* 垃圾桶蓋

2 keep the lid on to control a situation so that it does not become worse 控制…的局勢: *keeping the lid on inflation* 控制通貨膨脹 | *She was trying to keep the lid on her simmering anger.* 她盡力按捺住難以控制的怒火。

3 ►EYE 眼睛◄ [C] an EYELID 眼瞼

4 put the lid on *informal* to do something that finally ruins or ends someone's plans or hopes【非正式】毀滅〔希望〕; 結束〔計劃〕

5 take the lid off sth/lift the lid on sth to let people know the true facts about a bad or shocking situation 揭露〔真相〕, 披露〔醜聞〕: *Their latest documentary takes the lid off the world of organized crime.* 他們最近的文件揭開了集團犯罪的真相。

lid·ded /ˋlɪdɪd; ˈlɪdə̬d/ *adj* **1 heavy-lidded eyes** eyes with large EYELIDs 眼皮重垂的眼睛 **2** a lidded container, pot etc has a lid〔容器〕帶蓋子的

li·do /ˋlido; ˈliːdəʊ/ *n* [C] *especially BrE* an outdoor public area, often at a beach, lake etc, for swimming and lying in the sun【尤英】海[湖]濱浴場, 露天游泳池

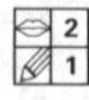
lie¹ /laɪ; laɪ/ *v present participle* **lying** *past tense* **lay** /le; leɪ/ past *participle* **lain** /len; leɪn/

1 ►FLAT POSITION 放平的位置◄ a) [I always+adv/prep] to be in a position in which your body is flat on the floor, on a bed etc 躺, 平臥: **[+on/in/there etc]** *He was lying on the bed smoking a cigarette.* 他正躺在牀上抽煙。| *Don't lie in the sun for too long.* 不要在日光下躺得時間太長。| **lie still/awake/dead etc** *She would lie awake at nights worrying.* 她擔憂得每夜都躺着無法入睡。**b)** also 又作 **lie down** [I always+adv/prep] to put yourself in a position in which your body is flat on the floor or on a bed 躺下: **[+on/in/there etc]** *Lie on the floor and stretch your legs upwards.* 平躺在地板上, 雙腿向上伸展。**c)** [I always+adv/prep] to be in a flat position on a surface 被平放: **[+on/in/there etc]** *The papers were lying neatly on his desk, waiting to be signed.* 文件正整齊地擺放在他的桌上, 等待簽署。

2 ►EXIST 存在◄ [I always+adv/prep] if an idea or a quality lies in a particular action, person etc, it exists or is expressed in that action, person, etc 存在, 在於: **[+in/with/outside etc]** *The answer must lie in finding alternative sources of power.* 答案必定在於找到替代的能源。| **the future lies in** (=something will be very important in the future) …在未來至關重要 *The future lies in multimedia.* 多媒體在未來處在很重要的地位。

3 ►BE IN A PLACE 在某個地方◄ [I always+adv/prep] if a town, village, etc lies in a particular place, it is in that place 位於: **[+in/on/below]** *The town lies in a small wooded valley.* 該城鎮坐落於一個林木茂盛的山谷中。

4 lie ahead/lie before you/lie in store if something lies ahead of you etc, it is going to happen to you in the future 將要發生: *How will we cope with the difficulties that lie ahead?* 我們將如何處理以後出現的困難呢? | *I was wondering what lay in store for us.* 我正想知道我們以後會遇到甚麼事情。

5 lie open/empty/undisturbed etc to be open etc 處於打開/空/未擾亂的狀態等: *The book lay open on the table.* 書本在桌子上翻開着。| *The town now lay in ruins.* 該城鎮現已成為一片廢墟。

6 lie in wait (for) a) to remain hidden in a place and wait for someone so that you can attack them 埋伏着等待: **[+for]** *a giant crocodile lying in wait for its prey* 埋伏着等待獵物的巨鱷 **b)** if something unpleasant lies in wait for you, it is going to happen to you〔不快的事〕將會發生

7 lie low to remain hidden because someone is trying to find you or catch you 躲藏: *We'll have to lie low until tonight.* 我們得躲藏至今晚。

8 lie at the heart of *formal* to be the most important part of something【正式】處在…中最重要的地位: *the issue that lies at the heart of the present conflict* 在目前衝突中至關重要的那個問題

9 lie heavy on *formal* if something lies heavy on you, it makes you feel unhappy【正式】使…感到不安, 沉重地壓在: *The feelings of guilt lay heavy on him.* 犯罪感使他感到不安。

10 lie second/third/fourth etc *BrE* to be in second, third etc position in a competition【英】〔在競賽中〕名列第二/第三/第四等: *Liverpool are lying third in the football championship.* 利物浦隊在足球錦標賽中名列第三。

11 ►DEAD PERSON 死者◄ [I always+adv/prep] if someone lies in a particular place, they are buried there 被埋葬: **here lies …** (=written on a gravestone) …被埋葬於此〔寫於墓碑上〕*Here lies Percival Smythe.* 珀西瓦爾·史密瑟長眠於此。

12 lie in state if an important person who has died lies in state, their body is put in a public place so that people can go and show their respect for them〔遺體〕停放於某處供瞻仰

13 ►STAY 停留◄ [I always+adv/prep] *old use* to spend the night somewhere【舊】〔在某處〕過夜: *He was to lie that night at a neighbour's.* 他那晚要在鄰居家過夜。— see also 另見 **let sleeping dogs lie** (SLEEP¹ (6))

lie about/around *phr v* **1** [I,T] if something is lying around, it has been left somewhere untidily, rather than being in its proper place 零亂地擺放着: *If you leave your shoes lying around like that, you'll trip over them.* 如果你把鞋子這樣到處亂放, 你會被它們絆倒的。| **lie around/about sth** *Papers and books lay around the room in complete chaos.* 房間內到處放着報紙和書, 簡直亂七八糟。**2** [I] if you lie around, you spend time lying down and not doing anything 無所事事地閒躺着混日子: *I felt so lazy just lying around on the beach all day.* 我整天只是在海濱躺着, 感到太懶散了。

lie behind sth *phr v* [T] if something lies behind an action, it is the real reason for the action even though it may be hidden 是〔某行為〕的原因: *I knew that something else lay behind his sudden interest in football.* 我知道他突然對足球感興趣是另有原因的。

lie down *phr v* **1** [I] to put yourself in a position in which your body is flat on the floor or on a bed 躺下: *You must lie down and rest.* 你必須躺下休息。**2 take sth lying down** *informal* to accept bad treatment without complaining【非正式】屈從, 逆來順受: *I'm not going to take this lying down! You'll be hearing from my lawyer.* 我不會就此屈服! 你等着我的律師找你。

lie in *phr v BrE* [I] to remain in bed in the morning for longer than usual【英】遲起, 睡懶覺: *I can't wait to be able to lie in this weekend!* 要到本週末才能睡個懶覺, 我可等不了!

lie with sb *phr v* [T] **1** if a power, duty etc lies with someone, they have that power etc 是某人的〔權力、職責等〕, 決定於某人: *The responsibility for this problem lies firmly within the government.* 這個問題的責任完全在於政府。**2** *old use* to have sex with someone【舊】和〔某人〕性交

lie² *v past tense* **lied** *present participle* **lying 1** [I] to deliberately tell someone something that is not true 說謊: *I could tell from her face that she was lying.* 我可以從她的表情上看出她在說謊。| **lie to sb** *I would never lie to you.* 我再也不會向你說謊了。| **lie through your teeth** (=say something that is completely untrue) 撒彌天大謊

2 [I] if a picture, account etc lies, it does not show the true facts or the true situation 造成假象, 欺騙: *Statistics can often lie.* 統計資料往往會給人假象。| *The camera never lies.* 照相機從不騙人。

lie³ *n* **1** [C] something that you say or write that you know is untrue 謊言, 假話: *There's no truth in her story. It's all lies!* 她的話沒有一句是真的, 全是謊言! | **tell a lie** *I always know when he's telling lies.* 我總是知道甚麼時候他在說謊。| **tell sb a lie** *Of course it's true. I wouldn't tell you a lie.* 當然這是真的, 我不會對你說謊的。| **pack of lies** (=a story or set of statements that is completely untrue) 一派胡言, 一堆謊話 *Their whole account of the event was a pack of lies.* 他們對事件的描述全是一派胡言。| **barefaced lie** (=a shocking lie) 無恥的謊言 | **white lie** (=a lie that is not serious, or one that is told to avoid upsetting someone) 無關緊要的謊言, 善意的謊言 **2 give the lie to** *formal* to show that something is untrue【正式】揭穿...的謊言: *This report gives the lie to the company's claim that there has been no pollution.* 這份報告揭穿了公司聲稱沒有污染的謊言。**3 the lie of the land/the way the land lies** the way that a situation is developing at a particular time〔某一時期〕形勢的發展, 情況的變化: *I want to see how the land lies before I decide whether or not to take the job.* 在決定是否接受這份工作以前, 我先要觀察一下形勢的發展。**4 (I) tell a lie** *BrE spoken* used when you realize that something you have just said is not correct【英口】說錯了〔用於意識到自己剛說的話不對時〕: *It was £25, no, tell a lie, £35.* 是 25 英鎊, 不, 說錯了, 是 35 英鎊。

lie de·tec·tor /ˈ· ·,··/ *n* [C] a piece of equipment used especially by the police to check whether someone is lying, by measuring sudden changes in their heart rate 測謊器

lie down /ˈlaɪˌdaʊn; ˈlaɪdaʊn/ *n* [singular] *BrE* a short rest, usually on a bed【英】〔一般躺在牀上的〕小睡, 小憩: *I'm going upstairs to have a lie down.* 我要上樓去躺着休息一下。

lief /lif; liːf/ *adv old use* willingly or gladly【舊】樂意地, 高興地

liege /lidʒ; liːdʒ/ *n* [C] **1** also 又作 **liege lord** a lord who was served and obeyed in the Middle Ages〔中世紀的〕君主, 王侯 **2** also 又作 **leigeman** someone who had to serve and obey a lord in the Middle Ages〔中世紀的〕臣民

lie-in /ˈ··/ *n* [singular] *BrE* an occasion when you stay in bed longer than usual in the morning【英】睡懶覺

li·en /ˈliən; ˈliːən/ *n* [C+on] *law* the legal right to keep something that belongs to someone who owes you money, until the debt has been paid【法律】扣押權, 留置權

lieu /lu; ljuː/ *n* **in lieu (of)** instead of 代替: *extra time off in lieu of payment* 用額外的休假來代替付款

Lieut the written abbreviation of 縮寫= LIEUTENANT

lieu·ten·ant /luˈtɛnənt; lefˈtenənt/ *n* **1 a)** [C] a fairly low rank of an officer in the army, navy, or air force, or a fairly high rank in the US police 陸軍中尉; 海軍上尉; 空軍上尉;〔美警察部隊的〕中尉, 少尉 **b)** an officer who has this rank 擁有上尉[中尉, 少尉]頭銜的官員 **2 lieutenant colonel/general/Governor etc** an officer or official with the rank below COLONEL, GENERAL², GOVERNOR etc 中校/中將/副州長等 **3** [C] someone who does work for, or in place of, someone in a higher position; DEPUTY (1) 代理官員; 副職官員 —see table on page C6 參見 C6 頁附錄

1 1

life /laɪf; laɪf/ *n plural* lives /laɪvz; laɪvz/

① PERIOD OF LIVING 一生
② HUMAN EXPERIENCES 人的經歷
③ LIFE AND DEATH 生和死
④ LIVING THINGS 生物
⑤ REAL/TRUE 真的/真實的
⑥ HOW LONG STH CONTINUES 某事物的持續時間
⑦ ACTIVITY/EXCITEMENT 活動/興奮
⑧ OTHER MEANINGS 其他意思

① PERIOD OF LIVING 一生

1 [C,U] the period between a person's birth and death during which they are alive 一生, 壽命: *Learning goes on throughout life.* 學習是一生的事。| *You have your whole life ahead of you.* 你前面還有漫長的一生呢。| **in your life** *I'd never seen the woman before in my life.* 我以前從未見過這個女人。| **spend your life** *She spent her life moving from one town to another.* 她的一生在從一個城鎮搬到另一個城鎮的顛簸之中度過。| **all your life** (=for the whole of your life) 整個一生 *I've lived in Mayo all my life.* 我一生都住在梅奧。| **early life** (=the part of your life when you were young) 早年, 年青時期的生活 *We don't know much about the poet's early life.* 我們對這位詩人的早年生活知道得不多。| **in later life** (=in the later part of your life) 在晚年〔生活中〕*My grandfather was troubled with illness in later life.* 我祖父晚年時受到疾病的折磨。| **late in life** (=when you are older than the usual age) 晚於一般年齡 *She had her children late in life.* 她晚年得子。| **for life** (=not changing for the rest of your life) 終生(不變) *As far as I'm concerned, when you get married it's for life.* 對我而言, 一旦你結了婚, 那是終生的事。| **working life** (=the part of your life when you are working) 工作生活, 工作生涯 *Norman had started his working life in the shipyards.* 諾曼在船廠開始了他的工作生涯。

② HUMAN EXPERIENCES 人的經歷

2 ►A PERSON'S EXPERIENCES 個人經歷◄ [C usually singular 一般用單數] the kind of experience that someone has during their life 經歷, 生活: *a life spent at sea* 海上的經歷 | **lead a happy/exciting/normal etc life** *Maria led a full and happy life.* 瑪莉亞過着充實而幸福的生活。| **a hard life** (=a life full of difficulty and trouble) 艱難的生活 **live a life of crime/sacrifice etc** *Marc dreamed of getting rich and living a life of luxury.* 馬克夢想致富並過着豪華的生活。—see also 另見 LIFE STORY

3 ►TYPICAL EXPERIENCES 獨特的經歷◄ [C,U] all the experiences and activities that are typical of a particular way of living〔特定的〕生活(方式);〔某種〕生活經歷: **army/city/country etc life** *Isobel was bored with country life and longed for London.* 伊索貝爾厭倦了鄉村生活, 渴望去倫敦。| **the life of a soldier/film star etc** *According to his book, the life of a rock star is not a happy one.* 據他的書所稱, 搖滾樂明星的生活並不幸福。| **married life** *after 25 years of married life* 25 年的婚姻生活之後

4 private/social/sex etc life activities in your life that are private, done with friends, concerned with sex etc 私/社交/性生活: *She enjoys a very active social life.* 她喜歡活躍的社交生活。

5 ►ALL HUMAN EXPERIENCE 所有的人生經驗◄ [U] all human existence considered as a variety of activities and experiences 世事, 處事經驗: *My Aunt Julia had very little experience of life.* 我姨媽茱麗亞的生活經驗很少。|

L

life's rich pattern 人生經歷的豐富模式 | *Life was hard in the mining communities.* 採礦社區的生活很艱辛。

6 way of life the way someone chooses to live their life 生活方式: *a traditional way of life* 傳統的生活方式 | *the American way of life* 美國的生活方式

7 quality of life the level of health, comfort, and pleasure in someone's life 生活質素

8 be sb's (whole) life to be the most important thing or person in someone's life 是某人的(全部)生活; 是某人的生活寄託: *Music is Laura's whole life.* 音樂是羅拉全部生活的寄託。

9 start/make a new life to completely change your life, for example by moving to another place 開始新生活〈如去異地謀生〉: *They emigrated to Australia to start a new life there.* 他們移民到澳洲, 在那裡開始新生活。

③ LIFE AND DEATH 生和死

10 ►ALIVE NOT DEAD 活着的◄ [C,U] the state of being alive 生, 生存: *Miss Byatt thinks her life is in danger.* 拜厄特小姐認為她的生命有危險。| *Smoke detectors protect life and property.* 煙霧警報器使生命和財產得到保障。| **save sb's life** *A seatbelt could save your life.* 座椅安全帶可以救命。| **risk your life** *Two fire fighters risked their lives to rescue the children.* 兩名消防員冒着生命危險營救孩子們。| **risk life and limb** (=do something that is very dangerous) 出生入死 | **lose your life** (=die) 喪生 *Thousands lost their lives in the earthquake.* 成千上萬的人在地震中罹難。| **take your own life** (=deliberately kill yourself) 自殺 | **give your life/lay down your life** (=die in order to save other people or because of a strong belief) 捐軀 | **take sb's life** (=kill someone) 殺死某人 | **take your life in your (own) hands** (=put yourself in danger of death) 冒生命危險 *Every time you cross these busy roads you take your life in your hands.* 人們每次穿過這幾條繁忙的道路都冒着生命危險。

11 a matter of life and death a serious situation in which someone might die 生死攸關的事

④ LIVING THINGS 生物

12 [U] **a)** the quality that animals and plants have and that rocks, machines, and dead bodies do not have 生命, 性命: *the seeds of life* 生命的萌芽 | **bring sth to life** (=make something live) 賦予〔某物〕以生命 *In the story the artist brings the statue to life.* 在小說中, 藝術家賦予塑像以生命。**b)** living things, such as people, animals, or plants 生物, 有生命之物〈如人、動物、植物等〉: *Is there life on other planets?* 其他行星上有生物嗎? | **animal/plant/bird life** *The island is rich in bird life.* 該島鳥類繁多。

⑤ REAL/TRUE 真的/真實的

13 real life what really happens as opposed to what happens in people's imaginations or in stories 真實生活: *a real life drama* 取自真實生活的戲劇 | **in real life** *In real life crimes are never solved by amateur detectives.* 在現實生活中犯罪案件從未被業餘偵探偵破過。

14 paint/draw from life to paint or draw something real, not from another picture 寫生

15 be true to life to represent life as it really is 真實反映生活的: *I prefer stories that are true to life.* 我喜歡真實反映生活的故事。

⑥ HOW LONG STH CONTINUES 某事物的持續時間

16 [singular] **a)** the period of time during which something takes place or exists〔某事物的〕存在期: **[+of]** *during the life of the present parliament* 本屆國會的任期期間 **b)** the period of time during which something is still good enough to use or fresh enough to eat 使用期; 有效期; 保鮮期: **[+of]** *What's the average life of a passenger aircraft?* 客機的平均服役期是多久? — see also 另見 SHELF LIFE

⑦ ACTIVITY/EXCITEMENT 活動/興奮

17 [U] activity or movement 活動; 動靜: **sign of life** *The door was open but there was no sign of life.* 門開着卻沒有動靜。

18 come to life to start to become exciting or interesting 變得令人興奮[有趣]: *The game really came to life in the second half.* 下半場, 比賽變得很刺激。

19 bring sth to life to make something more exciting or interesting 使〔某事物〕更令人振奮[有趣]: *Her songs bring our history to life again.* 她的歌曲又一次使我們的歷史活現了。

20 full of life very cheerful and active 充滿活力: *Katie seemed young and full of life.* 凱蒂看上去很年輕, 充滿了活力。

21 come to life/roar into life/splutter into life etc to suddenly start working 突然開始運作[工作]: *Finally the car spluttered into life.* 最後小轎車突然噼啪幾聲發動起來了。

22 be the life and soul of the party to be the person who brings fun and excitement to a social group or occasion〔在社會團體或社交場合中〕最活躍的人

⑧ OTHER MEANINGS 其他意思

23 get a life! *spoken* used to tell someone you think they are boring【口】別無聊!

24 that's life *spoken* used when you are disappointed or upset that something has happened but realize that you must accept it【口】生活就是這樣〔表示無奈地接受令人失望或生氣之事〕: *Oh well, that's life!* 算了, 生活就是這樣!

25 have the time of your life to have a very enjoyable time 玩得很高興: *The kids had the time of their lives at the waterslide.* 這些孩子玩水上滑梯玩得很高興。

26 make life difficult/easier etc to make it difficult, easier etc to do something 使〔做某事〕變得困難/較容易等: *This constant complaining isn't going to make life any easier!* 這種不停的埋怨於事無補!

27 for dear life with the greatest possible effort and strength, especially in order to avoid harm 拚命地, 竭盡全力地〔尤指為避免傷害〕: *Vera was clinging onto the branch for dear life.* 薇拉拚命抱住那根樹枝。

28 cannot for the life of me *spoken* used to say that you cannot remember or understand something even when you try hard【口】無論如何不能, 無法: *I cannot for the life of me see why you are so annoyed.* 我怎麼也無法理解你為甚麼如此煩惱。

29 not on your life *spoken* used to say that you definitely will not do something【口】決不〔做某事〕

30 ►PRISON 監獄◄ [U] also 又作 **life imprisonment** the punishment of being put in prison for the rest of your life 終身監禁: *He was sentenced to life imprisonment for the murder.* 他因謀殺罪被判終身監禁。—see also 另見 LIFE SENTENCE

31 the race/game/fright etc of your life the best race you have ever run, the best game you have ever played 生平最出色的賽跑/最佳的比賽/最大的驚嚇等

32 be the life and soul of the party to make people feel happy by talking a lot, telling jokes etc 成為聚會上的活寶

33 ►BOOK/FILM 書/電影◄ [U] the story of someone's life; BIOGRAPHY 人物故事, 傳記: *Boswell's Life of Johnson* 鮑斯韋爾所著的《約翰遜傳記》

34 the next life/the life to come a continued existence that is expected after death 下一世/來生

35 the woman/man in your life the woman or man with whom you have a sexual or romantic relationship 生命中的女人/男人〔指性生活的對象或情人〕—see also 另見 HIGH LIFE, LOW LIFE, CHANGE OF LIFE, **as large as life** (LARGE (6)), **lease of life** (LEASE[1] (2))

USAGE NOTE 用法說明: LIFE

WORD CHOICE 詞語辨析: **life, living**

In general, the word **life** relates to the whole experience of living while the word **living** is more about the physical needs of living, for example, how much money you need, etc. 一般來說，life 一詞與整個人生經歷有關，而 living 一詞則較多關於生活上的物質需要，例如：你需要多少錢，等等：*He had a good life*（他生活得很好）means that he had a lot of good experiences and enjoyed it but 這句話的意思是他有許多美好的生活經歷並且感到快樂，但 *They have a pretty good living*（他們日子過得很好）means they have enough food, money etc. 這句話的意思是他們有足夠的食物和錢等。

If you **make or earn a living** doing something, the work you do means you can provide yourself with the things that are necessary for life. 如果以做某事來 make or earn a living，指所幹的工作能供給生活所需的物品：*Joanne earns a living as a dancer in a nightclub.* 喬安妮在夜總會當舞女，以此謀生。

If you **make a life** for yourself somewhere, you go there and find work, establish a home etc. 去異地 make a life 指去那裡找到了工作並且建立家庭等：*thousands of refugees, making a new life across the border* 成千上萬的難民，越過邊境去尋求新的生活。

The way in which someone or a group of people generally lives is their **way of life**, or less often their **way of living**. 某人或一羣人平常的生活方式即是說他們的 way of life，或較少使用的 way of living。

If you are thinking more of the sort of rooms people live in, whether they have things like water, heating etc, you talk about their **living** conditions (NOT 不用 *life conditions*). 如果考慮較多人們居住空間之類的事，像他們是否有水、暖氣等，那麼談論的是他們的 living conditions（生活條件）：*the appalling living conditions of millions of old people* 無數老人惡劣的生活條件

If you are thinking of the level of comfort of someone's life, and how much money they have to spend on things that are not necessary, you talk about their **standard of living**. 如果考慮某人的生活舒適度，在非必需品上得花多少錢，那麼談論的是他們的 standard of living（生活水平）：*Most Americans have a higher standard of living than Europeans.* 大多數美國人的生活水平比歐洲人高。

The **cost of living** is how much people need to spend in order to buy necessary things. cost of living 指基本的生活費用：*The cost of living keeps rising, but my salary stays the same* (NOT 不用 *the cost of life*). 基本的生活費用不斷上漲，而我的工資卻原封未動。

If you are thinking more of the type of food that someone enjoys eating, the exercise they take, and what they do when they are not working, you talk about their **lifestyle**. 如果考慮多一點某人愛吃的食物種類、運動的類型及工作之餘做甚麼，那麼談論的是他們的 lifestyle（生活方式）：*The typical lifestyle of a 60s rock star included lots of alcohol, sex and drugs.* 20世紀60年代搖滾樂明星的典型生活方式包括了大量的酒精、性生活和毒品。

If you are talking about how enjoyable someone's life is, you call it their **quality of life**. 如果談論的是某人的生活如何愉快，那麼指的是他們的 quality of life（生活質量）：*Having a decent washing machine would improve the quality of my life no end!* 有一台好的洗衣機會大大改善我的生活質量！

GRAMMAR 語法

When talking about **life** [U] in general, you never use *the*. 泛指生活時不用冠詞 the: *Life is hard* (NOT 不用 *The life...*) 生活很艱難。| *She loves life in the city.* 她熱愛城市生活。

life as·sur·ance /ˈ· ·ˌ··/ *n* [U] *BrE* LIFE INSURANCE【英】人壽保險

life belt /ˈ· ·/ *n* [C] **1** *BrE* a LIFE BUOY【英】救生圈 **2** *AmE* a special belt you wear in the water to prevent you from sinking【美】救生帶

life·blood /ˈ· ·/ *n* [U] **1** the most important thing needed by an organization, relationship etc to continue to exist or develop successfully 生命線，命脈：*Communication is the life-blood of a good marriage.* 溝通是良好婚姻的命脈。**2** *literary* your blood【文】人的血液

life·boat /ˈlaɪfˌbot; ˈlaɪfbəʊt/ *n* [C] **1** a boat that is sent out to help people who are in danger at sea（海上）救生艇[船] **2** a small boat carried by ships in order to save people if the ship sinks〔船上備用的〕救生艇

life buoy /ˈ· ·/ *n* [C] a large ring made out of material that floats, which you throw to someone who has fallen in the water, to prevent them from drowning 救生圈

life cy·cle /ˈ· ˌ··/ *n* [C] all the different levels of development that an animal or plant goes through during its life〔生物的〕生活周期；生命環

life ex·pec·tan·cy /ˌ· ·ˈ···/ *n* [C] **1** the length of time that a person or animal is expected to live〔人或動物的〕預期壽命，平均（期望）壽命 **2** the length of time that something is expected to continue to work, be useful etc〔某物的〕平均有效期，預期使用壽命

life form /ˈ· ·/ *n* [C] a living thing such as a plant or animal 生物：*life forms on other planets* 其他行星上的生物

life guard /ˈ· ·/ *n* [C] someone who works at a beach or swimming pool to help swimmers who are in danger〔海濱或游泳池的〕救生員

life his·to·ry /ˌ· ˈ···/ *n* [C] all the events and changes that happen during the life of a living thing 生活史

life in·sur·ance /ˈ· ·ˌ··/ *n* [U] a type of insurance that someone makes regular payments into so that when they die their family will receive money 人壽保險

life jack·et /ˈ· ˌ··/ *n* [C] a piece of clothing that can be filled with air and worn around your upper body to stop you from sinking in the water 救生衣

life·less /ˈlaɪflɪs; ˈlaɪfləs/ *adj* **1** *especially literary* dead or appearing to be dead【尤文】死的；看似無生命的 **2** lacking the positive qualities that make something or someone interesting, exciting, or active 單調的，無生氣的，無活力的：*The actors' performances were lifeless.* 演員們的表演單調乏味。**3** not living, or not having living things on it 無生機的，沒有生物的：*The surface of the moon is arid and lifeless.* 月球表面乾旱沒有生命。—**lifelessly** *adv* —**lifelessness** *n* [U]

life·like /ˈlaɪfˌlaɪk; ˈlaɪflaɪk/ *adj* a lifelike picture, model etc looks exactly like a real person or thing〔圖畫、模型等〕生動的，逼真的：*a very lifelike statue* 栩栩如生的塑像

life·line /ˈlaɪflaɪn; ˈlaɪflaɪn/ *n* [C] **1** something which someone depends on completely 生命線，命脈：*The telephone is her lifeline to the rest of the world.* 電話是她與外界聯繫的命脈。**2** a rope used for saving people in danger, especially at sea〔尤指用於海上的〕救生索

life·long /ˈlaɪfˈlɔŋ; ˈlaɪflɒŋ/ *adj* [only before noun 僅用於名詞前] continuing or existing all through your life 終身的，畢生的：*a lifelong friend* 終身的朋友

life peer /ˌ· ˈ·/ *n* [C] someone who has the rank of a British PEER[1] (2) but who cannot pass it on to their children〔不可世襲的〕終身貴族

life peer·ess /ˌ· ˈ··/ *n* [C] a woman who has the rank of a British PEER but cannot pass it on to her children〔不可世襲的〕終身女貴族

life pre·serv·er /ˈ· ·ˌ··/ *n* [C] *AmE* something such as a LIFE BELT or LIFE JACKET that can be worn in the water to prevent you from sinking【美】救生用品；救生帶；救生衣

lif·er /ˈlaɪfɚ; ˈlaɪfə/ *n* [C] *informal* someone who has been sent to prison for life【非正式】無期徒刑犯人

life raft /ˈ· ·/ *n* [C] a small rubber boat that can be filled

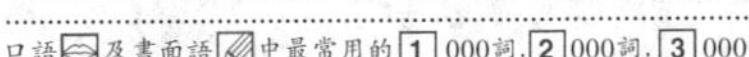

with air and used by passengers on a sinking ship 救生筏

life·sav·er /ˈlaɪfˌsevɚ; ˈlaɪfseɪvə/ *n* [C] **1** someone or something that helps you avoid a difficult or unpleasant situation 幫助解決困難的人[物], 救星: *Thanks for all your help, Carrie, you've been a real lifesaver!* 謝謝你的幫助, 卡麗, 你真是位救星! **2** a LIFE GUARD 救生員

life·sav·ing /ˈlaɪfˌsevɪŋ; ˈlaɪfseɪvɪŋ/ *n* [U] the skills necessary to save a person from drowning〔救溺水者的〕救生術: *She has a bronze medal in lifesaving.* 她有一枚救生銅章。

life sci·en·ces /ˌ· ˈ···/ *n* [plural] subjects such as BIOLOGY that are concerned with the study of humans, plants and animals 生命科學〈如生物學〉

life sen·tence /ˌ· ˈ··/ *n* [C] the punishment of sending someone to prison for life 無期徒刑

life-size /ˈ· ·/ also 又作 **life-sized** *adj* a picture or model of something or someone that is life-size is the same size as they are in real life 與實物[真人]大小一樣的: *a life-sized statue of the president* 與真人大小一樣的總統雕像

3 **life·span** /ˈlaɪfspæn; ˈlaɪfspæn/ *n* [C] the average length of time that someone will live or that something will continue to work〔人的〕平均壽命;〔物的〕使用期: *Men have a shorter lifespan than women.* 男人的平均壽命比女人短。—compare 比較 LIFETIME

life story /ˈ· ˌ··/ *n* [C] the story of someone's whole life 傳記, 生平故事: *For some reason, she insisted on telling me her whole life story.* 因某種原因, 她堅持要給我講述她一生的經歷。

life·style /ˈlaɪfˌstaɪl; ˈlaɪfstaɪl/ *n* [C] the way someone lives, including the place they live in, the things they own, the kind of job they do, and the activities they enjoy 生活方式: *a luxurious lifestyle* 奢侈的生活方式

life sup·port sys·tem /ˈ· ·· ˌ··/ *n* [C] **1** a piece of equipment that keeps someone alive when they are extremely ill〔病重時使用的〕生命維持系統 **2** a piece of equipment that keeps people alive in conditions where they would not normally be able to live, such as in space〔宇航員的〕生命保障系統 **3** a natural system that is necessary for life to continue, for example the process that produces oxygen for people to breathe〔維持生命所必需的〕自然的維生系統

life·time /ˈlaɪfˌtaɪm; ˈlaɪftaɪm/ *n* [C usually singular 一般用單數] **1** the period of time during which someone is alive or something exists 一生, 終生; 生存期: *During her lifetime she had witnessed two world wars.* 她一生經歷了兩次世界大戰。**2 the chance/experience etc of a lifetime** the best opportunity, experience etc that you will ever have 千載難逢的機遇/經歷等 —compare 比較 LIFESPAN

life vest /ˈ· ·/ *n* [C] *AmE* a LIFE JACKET【美】救生衣

2 2 **lift¹** /lɪft; lɪft/ *v*

1 ►MOVE STH WITH YOUR HANDS 用手搬某物◄ [T] to take something in your hands and raise it, move it, or carry it somewhere 舉起, 抬起, 抱起: *He tried to lift the sleeping girl, but she was too heavy.* 他試圖抱起正在睡覺的女孩, 但是她太重了。| **lift sth onto/out of/off etc** *I lifted down my suitcase and opened it.* 我放下手提箱, 把它打開。—see 見 RAISE¹ (USAGE)

2 ►RAISE 升起◄ also 又作 **lift up** [I,T] to move something upwards, into the air, or to move upwards into the air 抬起〔某物〕; 向上升: *He lifted both hands in a gesture of despair.* 他舉起雙手, 一副絕望的樣子。| *At high speeds the front of the boat would lift out of the water.* 在高速行駛中, 船的頭部會抬離水面。

3 ►HEAD/EYES 頭/眼睛◄ [T] to move your head or eyes upwards so that you can look at someone or something 抬〔頭或眼看事物〕: *Brig lifted his head as the others came into the room.* 當其他人進來的時候, 布里格抬起頭來。| *She lifted her gaze from her book for a minute.* 她把目光從書本上抬起來停了一會兒。

4 ►CONTROLS/LAWS 控制措施/法律◄ [T] to remove a rule or a law that says that something is not allowed 解除, 撤銷〔限制〕: *the lifting of sanctions* 撤銷制裁

5 ►CLOUDS/MIST 雲/霧◄ [I] if cloud or mist lifts, it disappears〔雲或霧〕消散

6 ►BY PLANE 用飛機◄ [T] to take people or things to or from a place by aircraft 空運〔人或物〕: *More troops are being lifted into the area as the fighting spreads.* 隨着戰爭的擴散, 更多的軍隊正被空運到這個地區。

7 not lift a finger *informal* to do nothing to help【非正式】一點都不幫忙

8 lift sb's spirits to make someone feel more cheerful and hopeful 使某人心情較開朗

9 ►SAD FEELINGS 悲傷的情緒◄ [I] if feelings of sadness lift, they disappear〔悲傷〕消失: *Jan's depression seemed to be lifting at last.* 簡的沮喪情緒看來終於逐漸消失了。

10 ►USE SB'S IDEAS/WORDS 使用某人的觀點/話語◄ [T] to copy words, ideas, music etc that someone else has written 剽竊, 抄襲: *The words were lifted from an article in a medical journal.* 這段文字是從某醫學雜誌上的一篇文章中抄來的。

11 ►STEAL 偷◄ [T] *informal* to steal something【非正式】偷〔某物〕

12 ►VOICE 嗓音◄ also 又作 **lift up** [T] *literary* if you lift your voice, you speak, shout, or sing more loudly【文】提高〔嗓音〕

13 ►INCREASE 增加◄ [T] to increase the amount or level of something 增加〔某物〕的量, 提高〔某物〕的水平: *This policy lifted Canadian exports of wheat and flour.* 這個政策增加了加拿大小麥和麵粉的出口量。

14 ►VEGETABLES 蔬菜◄ [T] to dig up vegetables that grow under the ground 掘出〔長在地下的蔬菜〕: *lifting potatoes* 挖馬鈴薯

lift off *phr v* [T] if an aircraft or space vehicle lifts off, it leaves the ground and rises into the air〔飛機〕起飛;〔太空船〕升空

lift² *n* 

1 ►IN A BUILDING 在建築物內◄ [C] *BrE* a machine that you can ride in, that moves up and down between the floors in a tall building【英】電梯; 升降機; ELEVATOR (1) *AmE*【美】: *She pressed the button to call the lift.* 她按鍵叫電梯。| **take the lift** *They took the lift down to the bar.* 他們乘電梯去樓下的酒吧。

2 ►IN A CAR 在車上◄ [C] *BrE* if you give someone a lift, you take them somewhere in your car【英】〔讓某人〕搭便車; RIDE² (1) *AmE*【美】: *Do you want a lift into town?* 你要搭便車進城嗎? | **give sb a lift** *I'll give you a lift back to London.* 我讓你搭便車回倫敦。

3 ►MAKE SB HAPPIER 使某人較高興◄ **give sb a lift** to make someone feel more cheerful and more hopeful 使某人精神振奮

4 ►LIFTING MOVEMENT 提升的運動◄ a movement in which something is lifted or raised up 被抬起[被舉起]的運動: *the gentle lift and sway of the dinghy* 小艇輕微的起伏搖晃

5 ►WIND/AIRCRAFT 風/飛機◄ [U] the pressure of air that keeps something up in the air or lifts it higher 升力, 浮力 —see also 另見 CHAIRLIFT, SKI LIFT

lift-off /ˈ· ·/ *n* [C,U] the moment when a vehicle that is about to travel in space leaves the ground〔太空船的〕發射: *Ten seconds to lift-off!* 離發射還有十秒! —compare 比較 TAKE-OFF (1)

lig·a·ment /ˈlɪgəmənt; ˈlɪgəmənt/ *n* [C] a band of strong material in your body, similar to muscle, that joins bones or holds an organ in its place 韌帶

lig·a·ture /ˈlɪgətʃɚ; ˈlɪgətʃə/ *n* [C] *technical* something such as a thread used for tying a BLOOD VESSEL to stop someone bleeding【術語】〔綁着血管、止血用的〕結紮線, 縛線

L

lights 燈

lampshade 燈罩
light 燈
bulb 燈泡
lamp 燈
fluorescent light/strip light *BrE*【英】熒光燈
spotlight 聚光燈
oil lamp 油燈
standard lamp *BrE*【英】/ floor lamp *AmE*【美】落地燈
desk lamp/angle-poise lamp *BrE*【英】活動(枱)燈
lantern 燈籠

1 1 **light¹** /laɪt; laɪt/ *n*

1 ▶NATURAL/ARTIFICIAL LIGHT 自然光/人造光◀ **a)** [U] the energy from the sun, a flame, a lamp etc that allows you to see things 光, 光線: *the morning light streaming in through the windows* 穿過窗戶照進來的晨光 | *We could see a tiny glimmer of light in the distance.* 我們可以看到遠處有一點微微閃爍的光。| **good/strong/bright light** *The light isn't good enough to take a photograph.* 光線亮度不夠, 沒法拍照。| **poor/dim/fading light** *In the fading light she could just make out the shape of a tractor.* 光線漸漸暗下來, 她只能看清拖拉機的輪廓。| **by/in the light of** (=using the light produced by something) 利用…的光 *She was trying to read by the light of a flickering candle.* 她正嘗試利用搖曳的燭光看書。| **in/into the light** (=out of the shadows where there is light) 在亮處/走進亮處 *Come into the light where I can see you.* 走到亮的地方去, 好讓我可以看到你。| **soft/warm light** *The valley was bathed in the soft light of dawn.* 山谷沐浴在黎明的柔光中。| **cold/harsh light** *the cold blue light of the Arctic* 北極的藍色冷光 | **blinding/dazzling light** (=extremely bright light) 耀眼的光 *a sudden flash of blinding light* 耀眼的光突然一閃 | **a beam/ray of light** (=a thin line of light) 光柱/光束 *the beam of light from her flashlight* 從她的手電筒射出的光柱 **b)** [C] a particular type of light, with its own particular colour, level of brightness etc〔有某種光色、亮度的〕光: *Monet painted a series of river views in different lights.* 莫奈用不同的光色畫了一系列的河上風景。—see also 另見 NORTHERN LIGHTS, **a trick of the light** (TRICK¹ (10))

2 the light the light produced by the sun during the day 日光: *We worked for as long as the light lasted.* 我們一直幹到天黑。

3 first light *literary* the first light that appears in the morning sky; DAWN¹ (1)【文】曙光, 黎明: **at first light** *The search continued at first light next morning.* 第二天黎明搜查繼續進行。

4 ▶LAMP/ELECTRIC LIGHT ETC 燈/電燈等◀ [C] **a)** an electric light 電燈: *the neon lights of the city* 城市的霓虹燈 | *lights from the hotel shining on the wet sidewalk* 旅館的燈光照在潮濕的人行道上 | **turn/switch/put on ↔ the light** *Please turn the light on.* 請開燈。| **turn/switch/put off ↔ the light** also 又作 **turn etc the light out** *Alan switched the overhead light off.* 艾倫關掉了頭頂上的燈。| **the light is/comes/goes/on** *The street lights are coming on now.* 現在街燈亮了。| **the light goes off/out** *Suddenly all the lights in the house went out.* 忽然屋內所有的燈都熄滅了。| **turn the lights down/dim the lights** (=make lights less bright) 把燈光調暗 *Sarah turned the lights down low to add a touch of romance.* 莎拉把燈光調暗來增加一點浪漫的氛圍。| **the house lights** (=the lights in a cinema, theatre etc) 影院[劇場等]的燈光 —see also 另見 **the bright lights** (BRIGHT (13)) **b)** something such as a lamp or a TORCH¹ (1) 燈; 手電筒: *Shine a light over here, will you?* 請把燈往這邊照, 可以嗎?

5 ▶TRAFFIC CONTROL 交通控制◀ [C usually plural 一般用複數] one of a set of red, green and yellow lights used for controlling traffic; TRAFFIC LIGHTS 交通信號燈: *We waited for the lights to change.* 我們等待交通信號燈轉換。| *The driver had failed to stop at a red light.* 紅燈亮起時司機沒有停車。—see also 另見 GREEN LIGHT, RED LIGHT DISTRICT, **jump a light** (JUMP¹ (18))

6 ▶ON A VEHICLE 在車上◀ [C, usually plural 一般用複數] one of the lights on a car, bicycle etc, especially a HEADLIGHT〔汽車、腳踏車等的〕車燈〔尤指前燈〕: *You've left your lights on.* 你忘了關車燈。—see also 另見 BRAKE LIGHT, PARKING LIGHT

7 be/stand in sb's light to prevent someone from getting all the light they need to see or do something 擋住某人的光線: *Could you move to the left a little – you're standing in my light.* 你能靠左一點嗎 —— 你擋住了我的光線。

8 ▶FOR A CIGARETTE 用於香煙◀ **a light** a match or CIGARETTE LIGHTER to light a cigarette 火柴; 打火機: **have you got a light?** *BrE*【英】**/do you have a light?** *AmE*【美】你有火嗎?

9 set light to to make something start burning 給〔某物〕點火: *The candle fell over and set light to the barn.* 蠟燭倒了, 把穀倉點着。

10 in a new/different/bad etc light if someone or something is seen or shown in a new, different etc light, you begin to understand them in a particular way or make someone else do this 從新的/不同的/壞的角度看: *There was Brian, pushing the pram, and I suddenly saw him in a new light.* 布賴恩就在那裡, 推着嬰兒車, 我突然對他有新的看法。| *an incident that presented the company in the worst possible light* 使公司形象嚴重受損的事件

11 in the light of *BrE*【英】**/in light of** *AmE*【美】if you do or decide something in the light of something else, you do it after considering that thing 考慮到〔某事物〕, 根據, 鑑於: *In light of the tragic news about our chairman, we have cancelled the 4th of July celebrations.* 鑑於主席遭受慘變, 我們已經取消了 7 月 4 日的慶祝活動。| **in (the) light of experience** (=as a result of your experience of something) 根據經驗

12 come to light/be brought to light if new information comes to light, it becomes known〔新消息〕為人所知/被披露出來

13 throw/shed/cast light on to provide new information that makes a difficult subject or problem easier to understand〔提供新資料〕使〔難題〕更容易理解: *These discoveries may throw some new light on the origins of the universe.* 這些發現可能會使人進一步了解宇宙的起源。

14 see the light a) to suddenly understand something 忽然理解, 頓悟 **b)** to begin to believe in a religion very strongly 開始虔誠地信仰某宗教

15 see the light (of day) a) if an object sees the light of day, it is taken from the place where it has been hidden, and becomes publicly known 公開, 問世, 發表: *Some of the Pentagon papers will never see the light of day.* 有些五角大樓的文件永遠也不會公開。**b)** if a law, decision etc sees the light of day, it comes into existence for the first time〔法律、決定等〕出台, 頒布
16 ►IN YOUR EYES 在某人眼中◄ [singular, U] *literary* an expression in your eyes that shows an emotion or intention【文】眼神: *There was a murderous light in his eyes.* 在他的眼中有一股殺氣。
17 light and shade brightness and darkness in a painting〔畫中的〕亮部與暗部
18 light at the end of the tunnel something that gives you hope for the future after a long and difficult period 經歷長期磨難後終於看到希望: *It's been a hard few months, but we're finally beginning to see the light at the end of the tunnel.* 這幾個月很艱難, 但是我們終於開始見到曙光。
19 have your name in lights *informal* to be successful and famous in theatre or films【非正式】在舞台上[電影中]成名, 在演藝界中成名
20 go/be out like a light *informal* to go to sleep very quickly because you are very tired【非正式】〔因很疲倦而〕很快入睡
21 a leading light in/of *informal* someone who is important in a particular group【非正式】〔某組織中的〕權威人士, 重要人物: *She's one of the leading lights of the local dramatic society.* 她是當地戲劇界的權威人士。
22 according to your own lights *formal* according to your own personal opinions or ideas of right and wrong【正式】根據個人的是非[道德]觀
23 ►WINDOW 窗◄ [C] *technical* a window or other opening in a roof or wall that allows light into a room【術語】窗; 天窗; 採光口
24 ►FOOD 食品◄ lights [plural] *old-fashioned* the lungs of sheep, pigs etc used as food【過時】〔供食用的羊、豬等的〕肺 —see also 另見 **in the cold light of day** (COLD[1] (14)), **hide your light under a bushel** (HIDE[1] (7)), **be all sweetness and light** (SWEETNESS (2))

1 1

light² *adj*

① NOT DARK 淺色的
② NOT HEAVY 不重的
③ WITHOUT MUCH FORCE 不強烈的
④ NOT DIFFICULT/SEVERE 不難的/不嚴厲的
⑤ SMALL AMOUNT 少量
⑥ FOOD AND DRINK 食品和飲料
⑦ NOT VERY SERIOUS 不很嚴肅的
⑧ OTHER MEANINGS 其他意思

① NOT DARK 淺色的

1 ►COLOUR 顏色◄ a light colour or light skin is pale and not dark〔顏色或皮膚〕淡色的, 淺色的: *the lightest shade of blue* 最淺的藍色色調 | **light orange/grey etc** *light green curtains* 淡綠色的窗簾 —compare 比較 DARK[1] (2); DEEP[1] (7)
2 ►DAYLIGHT 白晝◄ it is light if it is light, there is the natural light of day 天亮, 天明: **it gets light** (=it becomes light) 天亮, 天明 *It gets light at about 4:00 in the summer.* 夏天大約4點鐘天就亮了。
3 ►ROOM 房間◄ a room that is light has plenty of light in it, especially from the sun 明亮的〔尤指陽光充足〕: *The studio was light and spacious.* 這間工作室明亮寬敞。—opposite 反義詞 DARK[1] (1)

② NOT HEAVY 不重的

4 not weighing very much, or weighing less than you expect 輕的, 比預計輕的: *You can carry this bag – it's fairly light.* 你可以拿這個袋子 —— 它相當輕。| **as light as air/as light as a feather** (=extremely light) 分量極輕/輕如羽毛 —opposite 反義詞 HEAVY[1] (1) —see also 另見 LIGHTEN, LIGHTWEIGHT
5 be a kilo/pound etc (too) light if something is a kilo etc light, it weighs that amount less than it should weigh 少了一公斤/磅等〔指較應有的重量輕〕
6 light clothes are thin and not very warm〔衣服〕薄的, 不溫暖的: *She took a light sweater in case the evening was cool.* 她帶了一件薄毛衣, 以防晚上天氣涼。—opposite 反義詞 THICK[1] (1)

③ WITHOUT MUCH FORCE 不強烈的

7 ►WIND 風◄ blowing without much force 微弱的: *a light breeze* 微風 —opposite 反義詞 STRONG (17)
8 ►SOUND 聲音◄ very quiet 很輕的: *There was a light tap at the door.* 有輕輕的敲門聲。—opposite 反義詞 LOUD[1] (1)
9 ►TOUCH 接觸◄ very gentle and soft 輕柔的: *She gave him a light kiss on the cheek.* 她在他的臉頰上輕柔地吻了一下。—see also 另見 LIGHTLY (1)

④ NOT DIFFICULT/SEVERE 不難的/不嚴厲的

10 ►WORK/EXERCISE 工作/鍛鍊◄ not very tiring 不累的, 輕鬆的: *She only has a few light duties around the house.* 她只負責房子裡這兒那兒的一些輕鬆工作。
11 ►PUNISHMENT 懲罰◄ not very severe 不嚴厲的: *I thought the sentence was too light.* 我認為這判決太輕。—opposite 反義詞 HARSH (3)
12 make light work of to finish a job quickly and easily 輕易地完成〔某事〕

⑤ SMALL AMOUNT 少量

13 small in amount, or less than you expected 少量的, 較預計少的: *The traffic seems very light today.* 今天的交通似乎並不擁擠。| **a light meal/lunch etc** (=a meal in which you only eat a small amount) 吃得不多的一頓飯/午餐等
14 a light smoker/drinker/eater etc someone who does not smoke etc very much 抽煙/飲酒/吃飯少的人

⑥ FOOD AND DRINK 食品和飲料

15 a) food or alcoholic drink that is light either does not have a strong flavour or is easy to DIGEST[1] (1) 清淡的; 濃度低的; 易消化的: *a light white wine* 淡白葡萄酒 | *a light dessert* 清淡的甜食 —compare 比較 FULL-BODIED, HEAVY[1] (19) **b)** not containing much fat 低脂肪的: *a new light cheese spread with only half the fat* 只含一半脂肪的新低脂肪乾酪醬

⑦ NOT VERY SERIOUS 不很嚴肅的

16 not serious in meaning, style, or manner, and only intended for entertainment〔意義、風格或方式〕不嚴肅的; 供消遣的: *an evening of light music* 輕音樂晚會 | **light reading** *Christie bought a woman's magazine for a little light reading.* 克里斯蒂買了一本女性雜誌作消遣性讀物。| **a light touch** (=a relaxed and pleasant style)

輕鬆愉快的風格 *Your writing style is very formal; you should aim for a lighter touch.* 你的寫作風格很拘謹; 你應該追求較輕快的風格。| **on a lighter note/in a lighter vein** (=used when you are introducing a joke, funny story etc after you have been speaking about something serious) 說點輕鬆的話題〔用於在嚴肅話題結束後引入笑話等〕—see also 另見 LIGHTLY (4)

17 light relief something that is pleasant and amusing after something sad or serious〔悲傷或嚴肅的事情後的〕調劑: *I'm glad you've arrived – we could all do with a little light relief!* 我很高興你已經到了 —— 我們都需要略微輕鬆輕鬆。

18 make light of to joke about something or treat it as not being very serious, especially when it is important〔尤指〕拿〔重要的事〕開玩笑, 不把…當一回事, 輕視: *He makes light of getting fired, but I know how angry he is.* 他把被解雇不當一回事, 但我知道他是多麼生氣。

⑧ **OTHER MEANINGS** 其他意思

19 be light on your feet to be able to move quickly and gracefully 步履輕盈

20 light sleep sleep from which you wake up easily 睡得不沉

21 a light sleeper someone who wakes up easily if there is any noise etc 睡覺易醒的人

22 ►SOIL 土壤◄ easy to break into small pieces 鬆軟的 —opposite 反義詞 HEAVY[1] (20a)

23 light head someone who has a light head feels unsteady, for example because they are ill or have drunk too much alcohol〔因生病、醉酒而〕頭腦眩暈 —see also 另見 LIGHT-HEADED

24 ►HEART 心情◄ *literary* someone who has a light heart feels happy and not worried【文】愉快的, 無憂無慮的 —see also 另見 LIGHT-HEARTED —**lightness** *n* [U]: *a lightness of touch* 輕鬆的手法

3 3 **light**[3] *v past tense and past participle* **lit** /lɪt; lɪt/ or **lighted** **1** [T] to deliberately make something start to burn〔使某物〕燃燒, 點燃: *I lit another cigarette.* 我又點了一枝香煙。| **put a lighted match/candle to sth** *Martin put a lighted match to the papers.* 馬丁用一根點燃的火柴點燃文件。—see also 另見 FIRE (USAGE) **2** [I] to start to burn 開始燃燒: *The fire won't light.* 火點不着。**3** [T usually passive 一般用被動態] to give light to something 照亮〔某物〕: *His bedroom was lit by a bare electric bulb.* 他的臥室用沒有燈罩的電燈泡照明。| **well/poorly etc lit** also 又作 **well/poorly etc lighted** *The room was brightly lit.* 這房間燈火通明。—see also 另見 LIGHTEN **4 light sb into/along etc** also 又作 **light sb's way** *old-fashioned* to provide light for someone while they are going somewhere【過時】用燈給某人照路; 拿燈引路

light on/upon sth *phr v* [T] *literary*【文】**1** to fly to something and sit on it; ALIGHT 飛落〔某物上〕**2** to find something pleasant by accident 偶然發現〔美好的東西〕: *His eye lit on a ruby ring.* 他偶然看到一枚紅寶石戒指。

light out *phr v* [I] *AmE informal* to run away because you are afraid【美, 非正式】〔因驚慌而〕逃走, 溜掉

light up *phr v* **1** [T **light** sth ↔ **up**] to give light to a place or to shine light on something 照亮〔某處〕; 把光照在〔某物〕上: *A flare lit up th night sky.* 火焰照亮了夜空。—see also 另見 LIGHTING UP TIME **2 a)** [I] if someone's face or eyes light up, they show pleasure, excitement etc〔臉上或眼中〕流露出喜悅[興奮]: **light up with joy/pride etc** *His face lit up with glee.* 他一臉高興。**b)** [T **light** sth ↔ **up**] to make someone's face or eyes show pleasure or excitement 使〔某人的臉或眼〕流露出喜悅[興奮]: *Suddenly a smile lit up her face.* 忽然她臉上綻放出笑容。**3** [I] to become bright with light or colour 變得明亮: *As the screen lit up, he typed in a code.* 當螢光屏變亮時, 他輸入密碼。**4** [I] *informal* to light a cigarette【非正式】點香煙

light[4] *adv* **travel light** to travel without much luggage 輕裝地旅行

light air·craft /ˌ· ˈ··/ *n* [C] a small plane 輕型飛機

light ale /ˌ· ˈ·/ *n* [U] a type of fairly weak pale beer 淡啤酒

light bulb /ˈ· ·/ *n* [C] the glass object inside a lamp that produces light and has to be replaced regularly 燈泡

light·en /ˈlaɪtn̩; ˈlaɪtn/ *v* **1** [T] to reduce the amount of work, worry, debt etc that someone has 使〔工作、擔憂、負債等〕減輕, 減少, 緩和: *Maybe we should hire another secretary to lighten Barbara's workload.* 或許我們應該再雇一位祕書以減輕芭芭拉的工作負擔。**2** [I] if someone's face or expression lightens, they begin to look more cheerful〔臉或表情〕變得高興: *His whole face would lighten when anyone mentioned Nancy.* 當別人一提起南茜, 他就滿臉喜悅。**3** [I,T] to become brighter or less dark, or to make something brighter etc (使) 變亮, (使) 明亮: *As the sky lightened we were able to see where we were.* 天亮了, 我們能看清自己在甚麼地方。—compare 比較 DARKEN **4** [I,T] to reduce the weight of something or become less heavy (使) 變輕 **5 lighten up!** *AmE spoken* used to tell someone not to be so serious about something【美口】別認真! 別當真!: *It was a joke, Kath – lighten up!* 這是一個玩笑, 凱瑟 —— 別當真!

light·er /ˈlaɪtɚ; ˈlaɪtə/ *n* [C] **1** a small object that produces a flame for lighting cigarettes etc 打火機; 點火器 **2** a large, open, low boat used for loading and unloading ships〔用於裝卸貨物的〕駁船

light·er·age /ˈlaɪtərɪdʒ; ˈlaɪtərɪdʒ/ *n* [U] the service of moving goods on a lighter, or the charge made for this service 駁運; 駁運費

light-fin·gered /ˌ· ˈ··◂/ *adj* **1** likely to steal things 慣於偷竊的 **2** able to move your fingers easily and quickly, especially when you play a musical instrument〔尤指演奏樂器〕手指靈巧的

light-foot·ed /ˌ· ˈ··◂/ *adj* able to move quickly and gracefully 步履輕盈的

light-head·ed /ˌ· ˈ··◂/ *adj* unable to think clearly or move steadily, for example during a fever or after drinking alcohol; DIZZY (1)〔發熱或飲酒後〕神志不清的; 腳步不穩的; 眩暈的: *The sun and the wine had made him a little light-headed.* 陽光和酒使他有些頭暈。—**light-headedness** *n* [U]

light-heart·ed /ˌ· ˈ··◂/ *adj* **1** not intended to be serious 非嚴肅的, 輕鬆的: *a light-hearted comedy* 輕鬆的喜劇 **2** cheerful and not worried about anything 輕鬆愉快的, 無憂無慮的: *I found her in a light-hearted mood.* 我覺得她心情輕鬆愉快。—**light-heartedly** *adv* —**light-heartedness** *n* [U]

light heav·y·weight /ˌ· ˈ···/ *n* [C] a BOXER (1) who weighs between 72.5 and 79.5 kilograms〔體重在 72.5 到 79.5 公斤之間的〕輕[次]重量級拳擊手 —**light heavyweight** *adj*

light·house /ˈlaɪtˌhaʊs; ˈlaɪthaʊs/ *n* [C] a tower with a powerful flashing light that guides ships away from danger 燈塔

light in·dus·try /ˌ· ˈ···/ *n* [U] the part of industry which produces small goods, such as things used in the house 輕工業

light·ing /ˈlaɪtɪŋ; ˈlaɪtɪŋ/ *n* [U] the lights that light a room, building, or street, or the quality of the light produced〔照明的〕光線; 照明設備: *Better street lighting might help to reduce crime.* 改善街道的照明可能有助於減少犯罪。 ⊜3

lighting up time /ˌ·· ˈ· ˌ·/ *n* [U] *BrE* the time of the evening when the street lights come on and you must put your car lights on【英】〔車輛的〕規定開燈時間

light·ly /ˈlaɪtli; ˈlaɪtli/ *adv* **1** with only a small amount of weight or force; gently 輕輕地, 輕微地: *Martin kissed his bride lightly on the cheek.* 馬丁輕輕地吻了吻他新娘的臉頰。**2** using or having only a small amount of something 少許, 少量: *Rub a casserole lightly with*

olive oil. 用少許橄欖油擦砂鍋。| *lightly armed soldiers* 輕武裝士兵 **3** without worrying, or without appearing to be worried 輕鬆地; 無憂無慮地: *Ma chuckled lightly and went back upstairs.* 媽媽輕鬆地笑了笑, 轉身上了樓。**4** done without serious thought 輕率地, 不慎重地: **take sth lightly** *Divorce is not a matter you can afford to take lightly.* 離婚不是一樁能草率對待的事。**5 escape/get off lightly** to be punished in a way that is less severe than you deserve 逃脱重罰

light me·ter /ˈ· ˌ··/ *n* [C] an instrument used by a photographer to measure how much light there is〔攝影用的〕曝光表

light·ning¹ /ˈlaɪtnɪŋ; ˈlaɪtnɪŋ/ *n* [U] **1** a powerful flash of light in the sky caused by electricity and usually followed by thunder 閃電: **be struck by lightning** (=be hit by lightning) 被閃電擊中[雷擊] —see picture on page A13 參見 A13 頁圖 **2 like lightning** extremely quickly 迅如閃電: *The horse streaked like lightning down the track.* 馬在跑道上閃電般飛奔。

lightning² *adj* very fast, and often without warning 很快的〔往往沒有任何預兆〕: *a lightning attack* 突擊 | **at/with lightning speed** (=extremely quickly) 以閃電般的速度

lightning bug /ˈ·· ·/ *n* [C] *AmE* an insect with a tail that shines in the dark; FIREFLY【美】螢火蟲

lightning con·duc·tor /ˈ·· ·ˌ··/ *BrE*【英】, **lightning rod** /ˈ·· ·/ *AmE*【美】—*n* [C] a metal wire or bar connecting the highest point of a building to the ground to protect the building from lightning 避雷器, 避雷針

lightning strike /ˌ·· ˈ·/ *n* [C] *BrE* a STRIKE (=act of stopping work) without any warning【英】〔事先沒有警告的〕閃電式罷工

light pen /ˈ· ·/ *n* [C] a piece of equipment like a pen used to draw lines on a computer screen〔用於在電腦螢光屏上畫線的〕光筆

light rail·way /ˌ· ˈ··/ *BrE*【英】, **light rail** /ˌ· ˈ·/ *AmE*【美】— *n* [C] an electric railway system that uses light trains and usually carries only passengers, not goods〔載客用的〕輕便鐵路, 輕軌

light·ship /ˈlaɪtˌʃɪp; ˈlaɪtˌʃɪp/ *n* [C] a small ship that stays near a dangerous place at sea and guides other ships using a powerful flashing light〔導航用的〕燈船

light show /ˈ· ·/ *n* [C] a series of moving coloured lights, especially at a POP concert〔尤指流行音樂會上的〕燈光表演

lights-out /ˌ·ˈ·/ *n* [U] the time at night when a group of people who are in a school, the army etc must put the lights out and go to sleep〔學校、軍隊等〕熄燈(就寢)時間

light·weight¹ /ˈlaɪtˌwet; ˈlaɪt-weɪt/ *n* [C] **1** someone who has no importance or influence, or who does not have the ability to think deeply 微不足道的人, 無足輕重的人; 思想淺薄的人: *an intellectual lightweight* 智力平庸的人 **2** a BOXER (1) who weighs between 59 and 61 kilograms〔體重為 59 至 61 公斤的〕輕量級拳擊手 **3** someone or something of less than average weight 重量低於平均的人[物]

lightweight² *adj* **1** weighing less than average 較平均重量輕的: *special lightweight fabric* 特別輕的織物 **2** showing a lack of serious thought 思想浮淺的, 淺薄的: *She's written nothing but lightweight novels.* 她只寫了一些淺薄的小説。

light year /ˈ· ·/ *n* [C] **1** the distance that light travels in one year, about 9,500,000,000,000 kilometres, used for measuring distances between stars 光年 **2** also 又作 **light years** *plural informal* a very long time【非正式】很長的時間: *It all seems light years ago now.* 這一切現在看來都是很久以前的事了。

lig·ne·ous /ˈlɪgnɪəs; ˈlɪgniəs/ *adj technical* like wood【術語】木的, 木質的; 木頭似的

lig·nite /ˈlɪgnaɪt; ˈlɪgnaɪt/ *n* [U] a soft substance like coal, used as FUEL¹ (1) 褐煤

lik·a·ble, likeable /ˈlaɪkəbḷ; ˈlaɪkəbəl/ *adj* likable people are nice and easy to like〔人〕可愛的, 討人喜歡的: *a friendly likeable little boy* 友善可愛的小男孩

like¹ /laɪk; laɪk/ *prep* **1** similar in some way to something else 像, 相似: *My mother has a car like yours.* 我媽媽有一輛車與你的相似。| *He crawled out of the hut on his belly, like a snake.* 他像蛇一樣匍匐着爬出了小屋。| **very like** *He's very like his brother.* 他很像他的哥哥。| **look/sound/feel/taste/seem like** *The building looked like a church.* 這座建築物看來像教堂。| *At last he felt like a real soldier.* 他終於感到像一名真正的士兵。| **just like** (=exactly like) 完全像 *She was just like all the other girls.* 她跟所有其他女孩完全一樣。| **like new** (=in perfect condition) 像新的 *The carpet just needs a good clean and it'll be like new.* 地毯只需好好地清洗一下, 就會像新的一樣。**2 nothing like/anything like** used to say that something is not at all similar to something else, or to ask whether it is similar 一點也不像/是否像〔用於指某物不像另一物或詢問是否相似〕: *The course was nothing like what I'd expected.* 這門課程一點也不像我期望的那樣。| *Was the film anything like the book?* 這部電影拍得是否和原著相似? **3 like this/like so** *spoken* used when you are showing someone how to do something【口】就像這樣〔用於教人做事時〕: *You have to fold the corners back, like so.* 你得把角往回摺疊, 就像這樣。**4** typical of a particular person 符合〔某人〕的特點: *It's not like Steven to be late.* 史提芬一向不遲到的。**5 what is sb/sth like?** used when asking someone to describe or give their opinion of a person or thing 某人/某物怎樣, 如何〔用於叫某人形容某人[物]或發表意見〕: *Have you met the new boss? What's he like?* 你見到新老闆沒有? 他這個人怎樣? **6** for example 例如, 像: *far-off countries like Australia and China* 遙遠的國家, 如澳大利亞和中國 | *nutritious foods like eggs and fish* 營養食品, 如雞蛋和魚 **7 something like** not much more or less than a particular amount; about 大概, 大約: *The machinery alone will cost something like thirty thousand pounds.* 單是機器就要花費大約三萬英鎊。**8 more like** used when giving an amount or number that you think is more accurate than one that has been mentioned 更可能像(是)〔提供較之前提及的更準確的數量或數字〕: *The builders say they'll be finished in three months, but I think it'll be more like six.* 建築商説他們會在三個月內完工, 但是我認為更可能會是六個月。**9 there's nothing like** *spoken* used to say that a particular thing is the best【口】沒有甚麼比得上〔用於指某事物是最好的〕: *There's nothing like a nice cup of tea!* 喝杯好茶最令人暢快! **10 that's more like it** *spoken* used to tell someone that what they are doing or suggesting is more satisfactory than what they did or suggested before【口】那比較像樣〔用於告訴某人他現在的行動或建議比以前好〕

like² *v* [T not usually in progressive 一般不用進行式] **1** to enjoy something or think that it is nice 喜歡, 喜愛, 愛好: *I like your new dress.* 我喜歡你的新裙子。| *Bill doesn't like Chinese food.* 比爾不喜歡中國菜。| **like sth best** (=prefer it) 最喜歡某物 *Which of these colours do you like best?* 這幾種顏色你最喜愛哪種? | **like doing sth** *I like swimming, playing tennis, and things like that.* 我愛好游泳、打網球及諸如此類的運動。| **like to do sth** *I like to see the children enjoying themselves.* 我喜歡看到孩子玩得開心。| **like sth about sth/sb** *What I like about this job is the flexibility.* 這工作我喜歡的是它的靈活性。| **like it** *I don't like it when you look at me like that!* 我不喜歡你那樣看着我! | *It was a great place for a vacation. You'd have liked it there.* 那是度假的好地方, 要是你到那裡會喜歡它的。| **like the idea/thought of (doing) sth** *Sandra didn't like the idea of being so far from home.* 仙杜拉不想離家那麼遠。| **like the look/sound of** *I don't like the look of that black cloud over there. We'd better go in.* 我看那邊的那塊烏雲不太妙, 我們最好進屋裡去。| **get to like sth** *informal* (=begin to like it)【非正式】開始喜歡某物 *I don't think I'll ever* *get to like modern art.* 我不認為我還會喜歡現代藝術。**2** to think that someone is nice or enjoy being with them 喜歡〔某人〕: *I don't think he likes me – he never talks to me.* 我不認為他喜歡我——他從來沒有跟我說過話。**3** to prefer that something is done in one particular way or at one particular time rather than another 要〔某事以特定的方式或在某時間做〕, 想; 希望: **like sth** *"How do you like your coffee?" "Black, please."* "你喜歡喝甚麼樣的咖啡?" "不加牛奶的, 謝謝。" | *I like films with action in them. None of this boring romantic stuff.* 我喜歡動作片, 不喜歡這種乏味的言情片。**4** to think that it is good to do something, so that you do it regularly or want other people to do it regularly 喜好〔認為做某事有益, 於是定期做或想其他人也定期做〕: **like to do sth** *I always like to get up early in the summer.* 夏天我總是喜歡早起。| **like sb to do sth** *We like our students to take a full part in college social and sports activities.* 我們希望學生全面參與學院的社交和體育活動。**5 not like to do sth/not like doing sth** *especially BrE* to not want to do something because you do not feel it is polite, fair, nice etc【尤英】不願意做某事〔因認為是無禮、不公平、不友善等〕: *I don't like bothering him when he's busy.* 他忙的時候, 我不願意打擾他。**6** to approve of something or have a good opinion of it 贊成, 同意〔某事〕: *I really didn't like the way he avoided giving us direct answers.* 我確實不贊成他迴避正面答覆我們的做法。| **like sb doing sth** *Claus doesn't like anyone arguing with him.* 克勞斯討厭任何人和他爭論。| **like sb to do sth** *I'd like you to be honest with me.* 我要你對我誠實。

Frequencies of the verb **like** in spoken and written English 動詞 like 在英語口語和書面語中的使用頻率

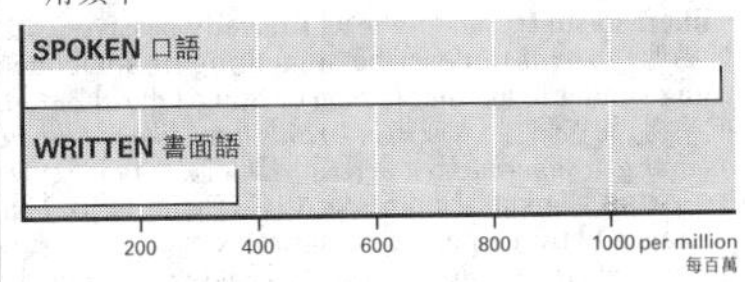

Based on the British National Corpus and the Longman Lancaster Corpus
據英國國家語料庫和朗文蘭卡斯特語料庫

This graph shows that the verb **like** is much more common in spoken English than in written English. This is because it is used in a lot of common spoken phrases.
本圖表顯示, 動詞 like 在英語口語中的使用頻率遠遠高於書面語, 因為口語中很多常用片語是由 like 構成的。

like (*v*) **SPOKEN PHRASES**
含 like 的口語片語

7 I'd like used to say what you want 我想要: **I'd like sth** *I'd like a cheeseburger.* 我想要乾酪漢堡包。| **I'd like you/John etc to do sth** *I'd like her to be at tomorrow's meeting.* 我想要她出席明天的會議。**8 would you like ...? a)** used to ask someone if they want something 你想要…嗎?〔用於問某人是否要某物〕: **would you like sth** *Would you like some more cake?* 你還想要些蛋糕嗎? | **would you like to do sth?** *Well, would you like to come shopping with me?* 那麼, 你願意和我一起去購物嗎? | **would you like me/her etc to do sth?** *Would you like me to pick you up in the morning?* 你要我早晨來接你嗎? **b)** also 又作 **How would you like ...?** used to offer someone something that someone does not expect, but that you know they will like 你覺得…如何?〔用於徵求某人對某建議的意見, 對方沒料想有此一問, 但估計會同意〕: **(How) would you like to do sth?** *How would you like to go to the camp in the mountains this summer?* 今年夏天去山上的營地你覺得怎麼樣? **9 would like** used to express politely what you want to happen or do 想要〔用於禮貌地表達願望〕: *We'd really like a holiday in Italy, but it's so expensive.* 我們真想去意大利度假, 但是太貴了。| **would like to do** *I'd just like to comment on a few things that were said.* 我想就說過的一些事發表一下意見。| **would like sb to do** *We'd like you to come in for a second interview on Monday, if possible.* 若可能的話, 請你星期一來作第二次面試。| **would like (to have) sth done** *I'd like to have the report finished by tomorrow.* 我想明天完成這份報告。**10 if you like** *especially BrE*【尤英】**a)** used to suggest or offer something 如果你願意〔用於提出建議〕: *If you like, I could go with you to the doctor's.* 如果你願意, 我可以陪你去看醫生。**b)** used to agree to something, even if it is not what you want yourself 要是你喜歡〔用於表示贊同, 即使並非自己所願〕: *"Can we have spaghetti tonight?" "If you like."* "今晚我們吃意大利麵條好嗎?" "你喜歡就行。" **c)** used to suggest one possible way of describing something or someone 可以說是〔用於提出形容某物或人的可行方法〕: *This experience was, if you like, a door that opened up a whole new world.* 這次經歷, 可以說, 是開啟整個新天地的門戶。**11 whatever/anything etc you like** *especially BrE* whatever you want【尤英】你想要怎樣就怎樣: *"Which play shall we go to see?" "Oh, whichever you like."* "我們去看哪部話劇?" "哦, 你想看哪部就看哪部吧。" | *Come and stay with us for as long as you like.* 來我家住, 你願待多久就待多久。**12 I like that! a)** used to say that you like what someone has said, shown you etc 我喜歡!〔用於表示贊同他人所言、所示等〕: *"That's a great story!" he said, roaring with laughter, "I really like that!"* "這故事太棒了!" 他大聲地笑着說, "我真的喜歡極了!" **b)** *especially BrE* used to say that what someone has said or done is rude and unfair【尤英】虧你說得出口[幹得出來]!〔用於表示對粗魯和不公正言行的反感〕: *"I thought you were older than her." "Well, I like that!"* "我以為你的年紀比她大。" "嘿, 虧你說得出口!" **13 how would you like...? a)** used to ask someone if they want something, especially when you already know they want it 你想要…嗎?〔用於問某人是否要某物, 尤用於已知道他想要時〕: **how would you like sth?** *How would you like a cup of coffee?* 給你來杯咖啡好嗎? | **how would you like to do sth?** *Say, how would you like to go to Italy next summer?* 你說, 明年夏天去意大利怎麼樣? **b)** used to ask someone to imagine how they would feel if something bad happened to them instead of to you or someone else 你會怎麼想〔用於叫某人想像自己遇到壞事時, 會有甚麼感覺〕: **how would you like it if?** *How would you like it if you got home to find you'd been burgled?* 如果你回到家發現被盜, 你會怎麼想? | **How would you like sb doing sth?** *How would you like your boss calling you an idiot?* 老闆叫你白痴, 你會感覺如何? **14 how do you like? a)** used to ask someone for their opinion of something 你覺得怎樣?〔用於徵詢意見〕: *How do you like my new jacket?* 你覺得我的新短上衣怎樣? **b) how do you like that?** used to ask someone what they think after you have done something or told them something surprising, unpleasant etc 你對這事有何想法?〔做了某事, 或告訴了對方令人驚訝、討厭的事情後, 問他們的想法〕**15 (whether you) like it or not** used to emphasize that something unpleasant is true or will happen and cannot be changed 不管[無論]你喜不喜歡〔強調令人討厭的事是真的或即將發生, 並且無法改變〕: *You're coming to your grandparents' today whether you like it or not!* 不管你喜不喜歡, 今天你都要去祖父母家! **16 I'd like to see you/him do sth** used to say that you do not believe someone can do something 我倒要看看你/他做某事〔表示不相信某人能做某事〕: *I'd like to see you run as fast as that!* 我倒要看看你跑那麼快! **17 I'd like to think/believe**

L

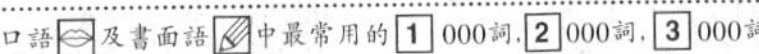

(that) a) used to say that you wish or hope something is true, when you are not sure that it is 我但願[希望]…〔用於表示希望某事是真的, 但不肯定〕: *I'd like to believe that one day he'll be well enough to lead a normal life.* 我但願他有一天會康復到能過正常人的生活。**b)** used to say that you think you do something well, especially when you do not want to make yourself seem better than other people 我倒認為…〔表示認為自己做得好, 尤用於不想自誇時〕: *I'd like to think that my work is as good as anybody's here.* 我倒認為我的工作和這裡任何一個人的都一樣好。

like[3] *n* **1 sb's likes and dislikes** all the things you like and do not like 某人的好惡[愛憎]: *All the children have their likes and dislikes when it comes to food.* 在吃的方面, 所有孩子都有他們的好惡。**2 and the like** and similar things 諸如此類, 等等: *He was interested in natural disasters, such as volcanoes, earthquakes and the like.* 他對自然災害很感興趣, 如火山、地震等等。**3 the like of sb/sth** also 又作 **sb's/sth's like** something similar to someone or a particular person or thing, or of equal importance or value 像某人[物]一樣〔重要或有價值〕的〔人/物〕: *He gave a superb performance, the like of which has never been seen since.* 他的表演精彩絕倫, 後無來者。| *The man was a genius. We shall not see his like again.* 他是位天才, 我們不會再見到這樣的人物。**4 the likes of** *spoken*【口】**a)** used to talk about someone you do not like 類似…的人〔用於談論不喜歡的人〕: *I'd never vote for the likes of him!* 我決不會投他那種人的票! **b)** used to talk about people of a particular type or social class …的一類人〔用以談論某種人〕: *Those expensive restaurants with fancy food aren't for the likes of us.* 那些飯菜講究、收費昂貴的餐廳不是為我們這種人開的。

like[4] *adj* [only before noun 僅用於名詞前] *formal*【正式】**1** similar in some way 相似的, 相像的: *They understand each other because they are of like mind.* 他們彼此理解, 因為他們志趣相投。**2 be like to do sth** *old use* to be likely to do something【舊】有可能做某事

like[5] *conjunction especially spoken*【尤口】**1** in the same way as 像…一樣的方式: *Don't talk to me like you talk to a child.* 不要像跟孩子說話一樣跟我說話。**2 like I say/said** used when you are repeating something that you have already said 正如我說的/說過的那樣: *Like I said, I don't mind helping out on the day.* 正如我說過的, 那天去幫忙我沒意見。**3** as if 好像, 似乎: *I acted like I couldn't see them.* 我裝得好像看不見他們一樣。

like[6] *adv spoken*【口】**1** used in speech to fill a pause while you are thinking what to say next〔用在說話中墊補思考下文時出現的停頓〕嗯: *This bloke will look at it for me, like, and he'll tell me what it needs.* 這傢伙會替我查看它, 嗯, 他會告訴我它需要甚麼。**2 as like as not/like enough** probably 很可能: *The car will be written off as like as not.* 這輛汽車很可能報廢。

-like *n* /laɪk; laɪk/ *suffix* [in adjectives 構成形容詞] typical of, or suitable to something 像…似的, 有…特徵的; 適於…的: *a jelly-like substance* 膠凍狀的物質 | *child-like simplicity* 孩子般的單純 | *ladylike behaviour* 貴婦人似的舉止

like·a·ble /ˈlaɪkəbḷ; ˈlaɪkəbəl/ *adj* another spelling of LIKABLE likable的另一種拼法

like·li·hood /ˈlaɪklɪˌhʊd; ˈlaɪklihʊd/ *n* [singular, U] **1** the degree to which something can reasonably be expected to happen; PROBABILITY 可能(性): [+of] *taking steps to reduce the likelihood of disease* 採取措施減少染病的可能 | [+(that)] *a greater likelihood that you will make a profit* 獲利的更大可能性 **2 in all likelihood** almost certainly 幾乎肯定地, 極可能地: *If I refused, it would in all likelihood mean I'd lose my job.* 如果我拒絕, 那就極可能意味着我會丟掉工作。

like·ly[1] /ˈlaɪklɪ; ˈlaɪkli/ *adj* **likelier, likeliest 1** something that is likely will probably happen or is probably true 可能的; 可能發生的; 可能是真的: *Snow showers are likely in the next 24 hours.* 未來的 24 小時內可能有陣雪。| *the likely cost of the operation* 手術可能的費用 | *the likeliest outcome of the talks* 會談最有可能的結果 | **likely to do sth** *remarks that are likely to offend some war veterans* 可能會冒犯某些退伍軍人的話語 | **more than likely (that)** (=almost certain) 幾乎肯定的, 極可能的 *Ian had been sick too, so it's more than likely you caught it from him.* 伊恩也生過病, 所以幾乎可以肯定你是從他那兒傳染的。**2** [only before noun 僅用於名詞前] as suitable or almost certain to produce good results 很合適的; 很可能成功的: *a likely candidate* 可能當選的候選人 | *Search all the most likely places first – maybe he's hiding in the cellar.* 首先搜索所有最有可能躲藏的地方 —— 可能他正躲在地窖中。| **likely-looking** (=seeming likely to produce results) 可能產生結果的 **3 a likely story** *spoken* used to tell someone you do not believe what they have just said【口】說得像真的似的〔告訴某人你不相信他剛說過的話〕

likely[2] *adv* **1** probably 大概, 很可能: *I'd very likely have done the same thing in your situation.* 在你那種情況下, 我很可能做同樣的事。| **likely as not** *spoken* (=probably)【口】很可能 *Likely as not, we'll never be told what really happened.* 很可能, 我們永遠也不會被告知到底發生了甚麼事。**2 not likely!** *spoken especially BrE* used to disagree strongly, or to say that something will not happen【口, 尤英】才不呢! 決不可能!〔表示強烈反對或某事不會發生〕: *"He said you'd be giving them a lift." "Not likely!"* "他說你會讓他們搭便車。" "決不可能!"

like-mind·ed /ˌ· ˈ··◂/ *adj* having similar interests and opinions 趣味相投的, 想法一致的 —**like-mindedness** *n* [U]

lik·en /ˈlaɪkən; ˈlaɪkən/ *v*

liken sb/sth **to** sb/sth *phr v* [T usually passive 一般用被動態] *formal* to describe something or someone as being similar to another person or thing【正式】將〔某人或某物〕比作〔另一人或物〕: *Critics have likened the new theater to a supermarket.* 評論家將新劇院比作超級市場。

like·ness /ˈlaɪknɪs; ˈlaɪknəs/ *n* **1** [C,U] similarity in appearance between people; RESEMBLANCE〔人的外表〕相似, 相像: [+to] *Hugh's uncanny likeness to his father* 休和他父親出奇的相像 **2** [C] a painting or photograph of a person, especially one that looks very like the person; PORTRAIT[1] (1)〔尤指酷似本人的〕畫像, 肖像; 相片: *That's a remarkable likeness of Julia.* 那是朱莉亞一張非常出眾的肖像。

like·wise /ˈlaɪkˌwaɪz; ˈlaɪk-waɪz/ *adv* **1** *formal* in the same way; similarly【正式】同樣地; 相似地: *I was up at dawn, and my host likewise.* 我天一亮就起牀, 主人也是這個時候起牀。| **do likewise** *Nanny put on a shawl and told the girls to do likewise.* 南妮披上披肩, 並且告訴女孩們也這樣做。| [sentence adverb 句子副詞] *There has been an upsurge of interest in chamber music. Likewise opera is receiving a boost from increased record sales.* 人們對室內樂的興趣大增, 同樣地, 歌劇因唱片銷量的增長而受到了推動。**2 likewise** *spoken* used to return someone's greeting or polite comment【口】〔用於回答問候或客氣的評論〕也, 同樣: *"You're always welcome at our house." "Likewise."* "歡迎你隨時來我家作客。" "彼此彼此。"

lik·ing /ˈlaɪkɪŋ; ˈlaɪkɪŋ/ *n* **1 have a liking for sth** *formal* to like something【正式】喜歡某物: *a liking for chocolate* 喜歡吃巧克力 **2 take a liking to sb** to like someone you have just met〔剛見面便〕喜歡上某人 **3 to your liking** *formal* being just what you wanted【正式】對你的胃口, 合你的心意: *I hope everything in the suite was to your liking, Sir.* 先生, 我希望套房內的一切都合你的心意。

li·lac /ˈlaɪlək; ˈlaɪlək/ *n* **1** [C] a small tree with pale purple or white flowers 丁香 **2** [U] a pale purple colour 淡紫色 —**lilac** *adj*: *a lilac dress* 淡紫色的連衣裙 —see picture on page A5 參見 A5 頁圖

lil·li·pu·tian /ˌlɪləˋpjuʃən; ˌlɪlɪ̵ˈpjuːʃən◂/ *adj* extremely small compared to the normal size of things〔同正常物體比較〕極小的

Li·lo /ˋlaɪlo; ˈlaɪləʊ/ *n* [C] *BrE trademark* a rubber MATTRESS filled with air and used as a bed or for floating on water【英, 商標】充氣墊〔用作牀或於水上漂浮〕

lilt /lɪlt; lɪlt/ *n* [singular] a pleasant pattern of rising and falling sound in someone's voice or in music 抑揚頓挫的聲音; 優美的旋律 —**lilting** *adj*: *a lilting melody* 優美的曲調

lil·y /ˋlɪlɪ; ˈlɪli/ *n* [C] one of several types of plant with large bell-shaped flowers of various colours, especially white 百合(花) —see also 另見 **gild the lily** (GILD (3)), WATER LILY

lily-liv·ered /ˌ·· ˈ··◂/ *adj old-fashioned* lacking courage【過時】膽小的, 懦弱的

lily of the val·ley /ˌ·· · ˈ··/ *n* [C] a plant with several small white bell-shaped flowers 鈴蘭

lily pad /ˈ·· ·/ *n* [C] the leaf of the WATER LILY that floats on the surface of the water 睡蓮的漂浮葉

lily-white /ˌ·· ˈ·◂/ *adj* **1** *literary* pure white【文】純白的: *lily-white skin* 白皙的皮膚 **2** *informal* morally perfect【非正式】道德高尚的: *You're not so lily-white yourself!* 你本人也並非如此品格端正!

li·ma bean /ˋlaɪmə bin; ˈliːmə biːn/ *n* [C] a flat bean that grows in tropical America, or the plant that produces it 利馬豆

limb /lɪm; lɪm/ *n* [C] **1 out on a limb** alone and without help or support 孤立無援: *All the other EU governments have signed the agreement, leaving Britain out on a limb.* 所有其他歐盟國家的政府都簽署了協議, 這使英國孤立無援。| **go out on a limb** (=take a risk) 冒險 **2** an arm or leg 肢; 手臂; 腿 **3** a large branch of a tree 大樹枝 **4 strong-limbed/long-limbed etc** having strong, long etc arms and legs 四肢強壯的/四肢長的等 —see also 另見 **tear sb limb from limb** (TEAR² (10))

lim·ber¹ /ˋlɪmbɚ; ˈlɪmbə/ *v*

limber up *phr v* [I] to do gentle exercises in order to make your muscles stretch and move easily, especially when preparing for a race, competition etc〔尤指在賽跑、比賽等前〕做熱身運動

limber² *adj* able to move and bend easily; SUPPLE 易彎曲的; 柔軟靈活的

lim·bo /ˋlɪmbo; ˈlɪmbəʊ/ *n* **1 be in limbo** to be in an uncertain situation in which it is difficult to know what to do 處於不確定的狀態: *I'm in limbo now until I know whether I've got the job.* 我現在心中沒有着落, 要一直到我知道是否得到那份工作。**2 the limbo** a West Indian dance in which the dancer leans backwards and goes under a stick that is lowered gradually〔西印度羣島的〕林波舞〔舞者向後彎腰通過逐步降低的橫杆〕

lime¹ /laɪm; laɪm/ *n* **1** [C] a small juicy green fruit with a sour taste, or the tree this grows on 酸橙(樹) —see picture on page A8 參見A8頁圖 **2** [C] a tree with pleasant-smelling yellow flowers; LINDEN 椴樹 **3** [U] a white substance obtained by burning LIMESTONE, used for making cement, marking sports fields etc; QUICKLIME 石灰; 生石灰 —see also 另見 BIRDLIME

lime² *v* [T] *technical* to add lime to soil to control acid【術語】撒石灰於〔土壤中以控制酸性〕

lime·ade /ˌlaɪmˋed; ˌlaɪmˈeɪd/ *n* [U] a drink made from the juice of limes 酸橙飲料

lime green /ˌ· ˈ·◂/ *n* [U] a light yellowish green colour 淺黃綠色, 酸橙綠色 —**lime-green** *adj* —see picture on page A5 參見A5頁圖

lime·light /ˋlaɪmˌlaɪt; ˈlaɪmlaɪt/ *n* [singular] a situation in which someone receives a lot of attention, especially from newspapers, television etc 公眾關注的中心: **be in the limelight** *Tad loves being in the limelight.* 塔德喜歡成為公眾關注的焦點。| **steal the limelight** *She's afraid this new actor will steal the limelight from her.* 她害怕這位新演員會搶去她的風頭。

lim·e·rick /ˋlɪmərɪk; ˈlɪmərɪk/ *n* [C] a humorous short poem, with three long lines and two short ones 五行打油詩〔三句長, 兩句短〕

lime·scale /ˋlaɪmˌskel; ˈlaɪmskeɪl/ *n* [U] a hard white or grey substance that forms on the inside of pipes, TAPS and water containers 水鹼

lime·stone /ˋlaɪmˌston; ˈlaɪmstəʊn/ *n* [U] a type of rock that contains CALCIUM 石灰岩

li·mey /ˋlaɪmɪ; ˈlaɪmi/ *n* [C] *AmE old-fashioned* a slightly insulting word for a British person【美, 過時】英國佬〔略帶冒犯〕

lim·it¹ /ˋlɪmɪt; ˈlɪmɪ̵t/ *n* S2 W2

1 ▶GREATEST AMOUNT ALLOWED 最大的限量◀ [C] the greatest amount, number, speed etc that is allowed 限度, 極限: *a 55 mph speed limit* 55英里的時速限制 | **[+to/on]** *Is there any limit to the amount of time we have?* 我們的時間有沒有限制? | **set a limit (on)** *attempts to set limits on consumer waste* 試圖設定生活垃圾的限量 | **lower/upper limit** (=lowest or highest point something is allowed to reach) 最低/最高限度 *an upper limit for pollution levels* 污染水平的最高限度

2 ▶GREATEST AMOUNT POSSIBLE 可能的最大量◀ also 又作 **limits** [C] the greatest possible amount of something that can exist or be obtained〔現有的或可獲取的〕最大量[限度]: **[+of]** *the limits of human knowledge* 人類知識的限度 | **to the limit** *Our finances are already stretched to the limit.* 我們的財力已經用到了極限。| **there is no limit (to)** *There's no limit to what you can do if you try.* 如果你努力, 成就無可限量。

3 ▶PLACE 地方◀ [C] the furthest point or edge of a place, that must not be passed〔不可以通過的〕界限, 邊界: *The public is not allowed within a 2-mile limit of the missile site.* 公眾禁止進入導彈發射場兩英里以內的範圍。

4 within limits within the time, level, amount etc considered acceptable 在合理限度內: *You can come and go when you want – within limits.* 你可以自由來去——但要有分寸。

5 know your limits *informal* to know what you are good at doing and what you are not good at【非正式】知道長處和短處: *I know my limits. I'm not an administrator.* 我有自知之明。我不是搞行政管理的料。

6 have your limits *informal* to have a set of ideas about what is reasonable to do, and to not accept behaviour that does not follow those ideas【非正式】有〔行為的〕準則: *You cannot smoke pot in this house. Even I have my limits!* 你不可以在這屋內抽大麻。甚至連我都有原則!

7 there are limits! *spoken* used to express shock or disapproval of someone's behaviour【口】要有個分寸〔對某人的行為表示震驚或不贊成〕—see also 另見 **the sky's the limit** (SKY (3))

8 be the limit *spoken* to be so annoying that you upset someone【口】令人無法容忍, 太過分: *Have you lost your glasses again? You really are the limit!* 你又把眼鏡弄丟了? 你真是太過分了!

9 be over the limit to have drunk more alcohol than is legal or safe for driving〔駕駛〕飲酒過量

10 off limits *especially AmE* beyond the area where someone is allowed to go【尤美】禁止入內: *That area of beach was off limits to us 'city kids'.* 我們"城市孩子"禁止進入沙灘的那個範圍。

limit² *v* **1** [T] to stop an amount or number from increasing beyond a particular point〔在量或數上〕限制, 限定: *a decision to limit imports of foreign cars* 限制外國汽車進口的決定 | **limit sth to** *Seating is limited to 500.* 限定500個座位。**2** [T] to stop someone from using as much of something as they want or from behaving in the way they want〔使用或行為上〕限制: *Obviously I'm limited by my pension situation.* 顯然, 我受到養老金狀況的限制。| **limit yourself to sth** *We must limit ourselves to one gallon of water per day.* 我們必須限定自己每天最多使用一加侖水。**3 be limited to** to exist or happen

only in a particular place, group, or area of activity 局限於〔某地方、團體或範圍〕: *Her traveling has been limited to a few French resorts.* 她的旅行局限於一些法國旅遊勝地。

3 **lim·i·ta·tion** /ˌlɪmə`teʃən; ˌlɪmɪ'teɪʃən/ *n* **1** [U] the act of limiting something 限制: **[+of]** *the limitation of armaments* 軍備限制 —see also 另見 **damage limitation** (DAMAGE[1] (7)) **2** [C usually plural 一般用複數] a limit on how good someone or something can be, what they are able to do etc〔某人或物的〕局限, 不足之處: **have your limitations** *It's a good little car, but it has its limitations.* 這是一輛很好的小汽車, 但是有它的不足之處。

2 **lim·it·ed** /`lɪmɪtɪd; 'lɪmɪtɪd/ *adj* **1** not very great in amount, number, ability etc, and impossible to improve or increase 有限的〔不可能改善或增加〕: *My time is more limited now that I have a baby.* 由於我有了孩子, 我的時間就更有限了。| *families on limited incomes* 收入低的家庭 | *a student of limited intelligence* 智力平平的學生 **2 Limited** written abbreviation 縮寫為 **Ltd** used after the name of British business companies that have LIMITED LIABILITY 負有限責任的〔置於英國有限公司名稱之後〕—compare 比較 INCORPORATED

limited com·pa·ny /ˌ… '…/ *n* [C] a company whose owners only have to pay a limited amount if the company gets into debt (股份) 有限公司 —compare 比較 PUBLIC LIMITED COMPANY

limited e·di·tion /ˌ… ·'··/ *n* [C] a fixed number of copies of a book, picture etc produced at one time〔書畫等〕特定版, 限量版, 限數本

limited li·a·bil·i·ty /ˌ… ··'···/ *n* [U] *technical* the legal position of being responsible for paying only a limited amount of debt if something bad happens to yourself or your company【術語】有限責任

limited liability com·pa·ny /ˌ… ··'… ˌ…/ *n* [C] *technical* a LIMITED COMPANY【術語】(股份) 有限 (責任) 公司

lim·it·ing /`lɪmətɪŋ; 'lɪmɪtɪŋ/ *adj* **1** preventing any improvement or increase in something 限制性的: **limiting factor** *A limiting factor in health care is the way resources are distributed.* 資源的分配方式是醫療保健的一個限制性因素。**2** *informal* preventing someone from developing and doing what they are interested in【非正式】有局限的〔阻止某人發展或做有興趣的事〕: *The job's OK, but it's sort of limiting.* 這工作不錯, 但有點束縛。

lim·it·less /`lɪmɪtlɪs; 'lɪmɪtləs/ *adj* without a limit or end 無限的: *limitless possibilities* 無限的可能 —**limitlessly** *adv* —**limitlessness** *n* [U]

lim·o /`lɪmo; 'lɪməʊ/ *n* [C] *informal* a limousine【非正式】大型豪華轎車; 中型客車

lim·ou·sine /`lɪməˌzin; 'lɪməziːn/ *n* [C] **1** a big expensive comfortable car 大型豪華轎車 **2** a small comfortable bus that people take to and from airports in the US〔美國往返機場的〕中型客車

limp[1] /lɪmp; lɪmp/ *adj* not firm or strong 軟的; 不強壯的: *a limp handshake* 無力的握手 | *His limp body collapsed forward.* 他軟弱的身體向前癱倒了。—**limply** *adv* —**limpness** *n* [U]

limp[2] *v* [I] **1** to walk slowly and with difficulty because one leg is hurt or injured〔因受傷而〕跛行, 一瘸一拐地走 —see picture on page A24 參見 A24 頁圖 **2** if a ship or aircraft limps somewhere, it goes there slowly, because it has been damaged〔船或飛機因損壞而〕緩慢地前進

limp[3] *n* [C] the way someone walks when they are limping 跛行: *Young walked with a slight limp.* 楊格走路有一點跛。

lim·pet /`lɪmpɪt; 'lɪmpɪt/ *n* [C] a small sea animal with a shell, which holds tightly onto the rock where it lives 蝛, 帽貝 —see picture at 參見 SHELL[1] 圖

lim·pid /`lɪmpɪd; 'lɪmpɪd/ *adj literary* clear or transparent【文】清澈的, 透明的: *limpid blue eyes* 清澈的藍眼睛 —**limpidly** *adv* —**limpidness** *n* [U] —**limpidity** /lɪm`pɪdətɪ; lɪm'pɪdɪti/ *n* [U]

limp-wrist·ed /ˌ· '··◂/ *adj* a man who is limp-wristed is considered to lack strong, traditionally male qualities〔男子〕缺乏陽剛氣的

lim·y /`laɪmɪ; 'laɪmi/ *adj* containing or covered in LIME[1] (3) 含有石灰的, 石灰質的: *limy particles* 石灰微粒

linch·pin, lynchpin /`lɪntʃˌpɪn; 'lɪntʃˌpɪn/ *n* **the linchpin of** the person or thing in a group, system etc that is most important, because everything depends on them〔團體、制度等的〕關鍵人物[部分]

linc·tus /`lɪŋktəs; 'lɪŋktəs/ *n* [U] *BrE* a liquid medicine used for curing coughs【英】止咳糖漿

lin·dane /`lɪnden; 'lɪndeɪn/ *n* [U] a chemical for killing insects, that is dangerous to people 林丹〔殺蟲劑, 對人體有害〕

lin·den /`lɪndən; 'lɪndən/ *n* [C] *AmE or poetic* a LIME[1] (2) tree【美或詩】椴樹

1 1 **line[1]** /laɪn; laɪn/ *n*

① LONG THIN MARK 線條
② SHAPE/EDGE 輪廓/邊緣
③ OPINION/ATTITUDE 看法/態度
④ WAY/METHOD 方式/方法
⑤ TELEPHONE LINE 電話線
⑥ STRING 繩子
⑦ WRITING/WORDS 寫作/詞句
⑧ ROW OF PEOPLE/THINGS 人/物的排
⑨ LIES/EXCUSES 謊言/藉口
⑩ RAILWAY LINE 鐵路線
⑪ DIRECTION 方向
⑫ WORK/INTEREST 工作/興趣
⑬ OBEY 服從
⑭ WAR 戰爭
⑮ DO THE SAME 做同樣的事
⑯ OTHER MEANINGS 其他意思

① **LONG THIN MARK 線條**

1 [C] a long thin, usually continuous mark on a surface 線, 線條: *A wiggly line showed where the river was.* 一條彎彎曲曲的線標示着河的位置。| **straight line** *Can you draw a straight line?* 你能畫一條直線嗎? | **dotted line** (=a broken straight line drawn or printed on paper) 虛線 *Sign your name on the dotted line.* 在虛線處簽上你的名字。

2 [C] a long thin mark used to show a limit or border 界線; 邊界線: *a broken white line in the middle of the road* 道路中間的白色虛線 | *If the ball goes over the line, it's out of play.* 如果球出了界, 就成了死球。

3 [C] an imaginary line, for example one that shows the limits of an area of land 設想的線, 想像的線〈如邊界線〉: *the line that divides northern and southern Ireland* 北愛爾蘭和南愛爾蘭的邊界線 | *lines of longitude* 經線

4 county line/state line *AmE* a border between two counties, states etc【美】縣界/州界

5 ►ON SB'S FACE 在某人的臉上◄ [C] a line on the

skin of someone's face or skin; WRINKLE[1] (1)〔皮膚上的〕紋路; 皺紋: *a forehead etched with deep lines* 刻着深深皺紋的前額

6 the line *technical* the EQUATOR【術語】赤道

② **SHAPE/EDGE** 輪廓/邊緣

7 [C usually plural 一般用複數] the outer shape of something long or tall〔長或高的物件的〕輪廓, 外形: *a dress that follows the lines of the body* 合身的連衣裙 | *I admired the ship's clean elegant lines.* 我欣賞這艘船簡潔優雅的輪廓。

③ **OPINION/ATTITUDE** 看法/態度

8 [C usually singular 一般用單數] an attitude or belief, especially one that is stated publicly〔尤指公開發表的〕態度, 看法: **[+on]** *What's the candidate's line on abortion?* 候選人對人工流產是甚麼態度? | **the party line** (=the official opinion of a political party) 政黨的路線[方針] *By supporting Robertson, she's going directly against the party line.* 她支持羅伯遜, 直接反對黨的方針。

9 take a firm/hard/strict etc line on to have a very strict attitude towards something〔對某事〕採取堅定的/強硬的/嚴格的態度等: *a judge notorious for taking a tough line on drug users* 以對吸毒者採取嚴厲態度而著稱的法官

④ **WAY/METHOD** 方式/方法

10 line of action/thought/reasoning etc a way or method of doing something or thinking about something 行為/思維/推理的方式[方法]等: **line of inquiry** (=a way of trying to find out about something) 詢問[查問, 調查]方式 *Police are following several lines of inquiry.* 警察正在使用幾種方式進行調查。| **line of argument** (=a way of persuading someone about something) 游説方法 *Which line of argument is Clarke likely to take?* 克拉克會採用哪種游説方法?

11 along those/similar/different etc lines done or doing something in that way, a similar way etc 用那些/相似的/不同的等方法: *We've both been thinking along the same lines.* 我們兩人一直都以同樣的方法在思考。| **something along those lines** (=something like that) 諸如此類的事 *They're organizing a trip to the beach or something along those lines.* 他們正在組織去海濱的旅遊或諸如此類的事。| **along the lines of** (=in a particular way) 以某種方式 *We'll probably end up doing something along the lines of what you're suggesting.* 我們很可能最終會按照你所建議的方式做點甚麼。

12 on the right lines done or doing something in the right kind of way 正確的, 對的: *These new proposals are certainly on the right lines.* 這些新建議肯定是正確的。

⑤ **TELEPHONE LINE** 電話線

13 [C usually singular 一般用單數] a telephone wire or connection 電話線(路): *We rent the line from British Telecom.* 我們租用英國電話公司的電話線。| **on the line** *There's a fault on the line.* 電話線路出現故障。| **bad line** (=a line that is not working properly so that you cannot easily hear the other person talking) 線路不良〔聽不清楚對方説話〕

14 hold the line *spoken* used to politely ask the person who is on the telephone to wait for a short time【口】請別掛斷電話: *Hold the line, please. I'll put you through to Mr Bork.* 請不要掛斷電話。我給你接通博克先生。

⑥ **STRING** 繩子

15 ►DRYING CLOTHES 晾衣服◄ [C] a piece of string or rope that you hang wet clothes etc on in order to dry them; CLOTHESLINE, WASHING LINE 晾衣繩: **the line** *You'd better get your washing off the line – it's raining.* 你最好把晾在繩子上的衣服收下來 — 下雨了。

16 ►FISHING 釣魚◄ [C] a strong thin string with a hook on the end, used for catching fish 釣魚線

⑦ **WRITING/WORDS** 寫作/詞句

17 [C] a line of words on a page, for example in a poem or a report〔詩或報告中的〕一行字: *a few lines from Shakespeare* 選自莎士比亞作品的幾行詩

18 ►ACTOR'S SPEECH 演員的台詞◄ [plural] the words of a play or performance that an actor learns 台詞: *After 30 years on the stage, I still forget my lines.* 當了30年演員, 我仍記不住台詞。

19 ►PUNISHMENT 處罰◄ **lines** [plural] *BrE* a punishment given to school children that consists of writing the same thing a lot of times【英】罰寫〔對小學生的處罰〕: *Take a hundred lines!* 罰寫一百遍!

20 drop sb a line *informal* to write a short letter to someone【非正式】給某人寫短信[便條]: *Drop me a line and let me know how you're getting on.* 給我寫一封短信, 告訴我你過得怎麼樣。

⑧ **ROW OF PEOPLE/THINGS** 人/物的排

21 [C] a row of people or things next to each other 排, 列, 行: **[+of]** *a line of poplar trees beside the road* 路旁的一排楊樹 | **in a line** *four little boys standing in a line* 站成一行的四個小男孩

22 [C] *AmE* a row of people standing one behind the other while waiting for something【美】〔人在等候時排的〕隊; QUEUE[1] (1) *BrE*【英】: *I was talking with Karen in the lunch line.* 排隊等候午餐時我和卡倫聊天。—see picture at 參見 PUSH[1] 圖

⑨ **LIES/EXCUSES** 謊言/藉口

23 shoot a line/spin (sb) a line to tell someone things that are not true in order to persuade them or to make them admire you 吹牛/编造謊言〔以說服某人或博取歡心〕

24 don't give me that line *spoken* used to tell someone that you do not believe their excuse【口】別跟我來那一套〔表示不相信對方的藉口〕: *"We just haven't had enough time to..." "Oh, don't give me that line."* "我們實在沒有足夠的時間..." "哦, 別跟我來那一套。"

⑩ **RAILWAY LINE** 鐵路線

25 a track that a train travels along 鐵路(線); 路軌: **the line** *A train had broken down further along the line.* 一列火車在前面的鐵路線上拋錨了。| **railway line** *a bridge over the railway line* 架在路軌上空的橋 | **the Brighton/ Manchester/Cambridge etc line** (=a line that goes to Brighton etc) 布賴頓/曼徹斯特/劍橋等鐵路線 | **Piccadilly/Victoria/Central etc line** (=a line on London's UNDERGROUND system)〔倫敦的〕皮卡迪利/維多利亞/中央等地鐵線

⑪ **DIRECTION** 方向

26 [C usually singular 一般用單數] the direction or imaginary line along which something travels between two points in space〔某物行進的〕方向: **in a straight line** *Light travels in a straight line.* 光沿直線傳播。| **line of fire/attack/movement etc** (=the direction in which someone shoots, attacks, moves etc) 射擊/進攻/運動等的方向 *I was directly in the animal's line of attack.* 野獸撲過來, 我首當其衝。| **line of vision** (=the direction in which you are looking) 視線的方向

⑫ **WORK/INTEREST** 工作/興趣

27 ►JOB 工作◄ [C usually singular 一般用單數] the kind of work someone does 專業, 行業: **line of business** *What line of business is he in?* 他是幹哪一行的? | **be in the building/retail etc line** 從事建築業/零售業等 —see 見 JOB (USAGE)

28 in the line of duty if you do something in the line of duty, you do it as part of your job〔做某事是〕應盡的

職責: *Don't thank me, madam – it's all in the line of duty.* 不用謝, 夫人, 這都是我的份內事。
29 be in sb's line to be the type of thing that someone is interested in or good at 是某人感興趣的事; 是某人的專長: *I'm afraid cookery isn't really in my line.* 恐怕烹飪不是我真正的專長。

⑬ **OBEY 服從**
30 fall into line *informal* to start to do something in the way that a company, organization etc wants you to【非正式】〔做事與公司、組織等〕取得一致: *Don't worry, I'm sure he'll soon fall into line and sign with the rest of us.* 不用擔心, 我肯定他很快會同意並和我們其餘的人簽訂合同。
31 bring sb into line *informal* to make someone behave the way you want them to【非正式】使某人行動一致: *The right wing of the party has got to be brought into line.* 必須使這個政黨的右翼採取一致的行動。
32 be out of line *AmE* if someone's behaviour is out of line, it is unacceptable【美】〔行為〕不可接受, 出格

⑭ **WAR 戰爭**
33 ▶WAR 戰爭◀ [C often plural 常用複數] a row of military defences in front of the area that an army controls during a war 防線: **behind the line(s)** (=in the area where your enemy is) 在敵區 *Parachutists dropped behind the lines.* 傘兵降落在敵區。| **enemy lines** *The base was stationed 100 miles inside enemy lines.* 基地駐紮在敵軍防線內 100 英里處。
34 [C] the line of positions that an army has when it is fighting a battle 前線: *the line of battle* 戰線

⑮ **DO THE SAME 做同樣的事**
35 in line with if something changes in line with something else, it changes in the same way and at the same rate 與…一致, 符合〔某物〕: *Pensions will be increased in line with inflation.* 退休金將隨着通貨膨脹而相應提高。
36 bring sth into line with to make something work or happen according to a particular system or set of rules 使某物與〔制度或規則〕一致: *British law will have to be changed to bring it into line with the latest European ruling.* 英國的法律將要修改, 以使它符合歐洲最新的規定。
37 along religious/party/ethnic lines if people divide along religious, party etc lines they divide according to which religion, political party, or other group they belong to 按照宗教/政黨/民族路線〔劃分〕

⑯ **OTHER MEANINGS 其他意思**
38 a thin/fine line between only a slight difference between two things, one of which is something bad〔兩事〕之間的細小差別〔其中之一是壞事〕: *There's a very fine line between tax evasion and fraud.* 避稅和詐騙之間只有一線之差。
39 be in line for sth to be very likely to get or be given something 很有可能獲得某物: *Ted's in line for the chairmanship.* 特德很有可能當主席。| **first/second etc in line for** *She's about second in line for the management job.* 她大概是第二個有望爭取到管理工作的人選。
40 be on the line *informal* if your job, position etc is on the line, there is a possibility you might lose it【非正式】〔工作、職位等〕有失去的可能: *From now on, all our jobs are on the line.* 從現在起, 我們都有失業的危險。
41 somewhere along the line *informal* during the time that you are involved in an activity or process【非正式】在活動[過程]中的某段時間: *Somewhere along the line, Errol seemed to have lost interest in their marriage.* 有段時間, 埃羅爾似乎對他倆的婚姻失去了興趣。
42 ▶PRODUCT 產品◀ [C] a type of goods for sale in a shop〔貨物的〕種類, 類型: *this season's new lines from Paris* 來自巴黎的本季度的新款式 | **discontinue a line** (=stop selling a type of goods) 停止銷售某種商品
43 on line communicating with or by means of a computer 與〔電腦〕聯接着: **[+to]** *The system is on line to the bank's mainframe computer.* 這系統與銀行的電腦主機聯接着。| *We need to bring the network back on line.* 我們需要使網絡恢復聯接狀態。—see also 另見 ONLINE
44 ▶COMPANY 公司◀ [C usually singular 一般用單數] a company that provides a system for moving goods by sea, air, road etc 運輸公司: *a shipping line* 海運公司 | *the Cunard line* 丘納德輪船公司
45 be in the firing line/in the line of fire a) to be one of the people who could be criticized or blamed for something 成為批評[指責]的對象: *As one of the President's chief advisers, he's bound to be in the firing line.* 作為總統的主要顧問之一, 他勢必成為批評的對象。**b)** to be in a place where a bullet etc might hit you 可能遭到槍擊
46 ▶SPORT 運動◀ [C] a row of players in a game such as American football or RUGBY that is formed when they move into position before play starts again〔美式足球或橄欖球等的〕進攻線; 防守線
47 get a line on *informal* to get information about someone or something【非正式】獲得〔某人或事〕的消息: *Have we got any kind of line on that guy Marston?* 有沒有得到任何關於馬斯頓那傢伙的消息?
48 ▶DRUG 毒品◀ [C] *informal* an amount of an illegal drug in powder form, arranged in a line before it is taken【非正式】〔粉末狀毒品在吸食前排成的〕一行: **[+of]** *a line of coke* 一行可卡因
49 ▶FAMILY 家族◀ [singular] the people that came or existed before you in your family〔家庭中的〕長輩, 先輩: *She comes from a long line of actors.* 她出身演員世家。| **be of sb's line** (=be their GRANDCHILD, GREAT-GRANDCHILD etc) 某人的孫輩[曾孫輩等] *There was no-one directly of James's line to succeed to the throne.* 詹姆斯家族沒有直系孫輩繼承王位。—see also 另見 **draw the line** (DRAW[1] (35)), **hard lines** (HARD[1] (21)), **hook, line and sinker** (HOOK[1] (7)), **lay sth on the line** (LAY[2] (15)), **picket line** (PICKET[1] (1)), **the poverty line/level** (POVERTY (2)), **read between the lines** (READ[1] (11)), **spin a story/yarn/line** (SPIN[1] (6))

line² *v* [T] **1** to cover the inside of a piece of material with another material 給〔某物〕加襯裡: *Are those curtains lined?* 那些窗簾加襯裡了嗎? | **line sth with** *a coat lined with silk* 有絲綢襯裡的外衣 **2** to form a layer over the inner surface of something 形成內襯: *the mucus that lines the stomach* 胃內壁的黏液 | **line sth with** *The bird lined its nest with feathers.* 鳥在窩內墊上羽毛。**3** [usually passive 一般用被動態] to form rows along something 沿〔某物〕排列成行: *tree-lined avenues* 林蔭道 | *Crowds lined the route to the palace.* 人羣在通往皇宮的路上夾道排列。**4 line your own pockets** to make yourself richer, especially by doing something dishonest 撈一把; 中飽私囊

line up *phr v* **1** [I,T] to form a row or arrange people or things in a row (使) 排成行: *Line up, everybody!* 大家排好隊! | **line sb/sth ↔ up** *The men were being lined up for an inspection.* 男人們正在排隊接受檢查。**2** [T] to make arrangements so that something will happen or that someone will be available for an event 安排〔某事〕; 安排〔某人〕出席: **line sb/sth up** *Sue's lined up some excellent speakers for tonight.* 蘇為今晚邀請了幾位出色的演講者。—see also 另見 LINE-UP

lin·e·age /ˈlɪnɪɪdʒ; ˈlɪni-ɪdʒ/ *n* [C,U] *formal* the way in which members of a family are descended (DESCEND) from other members【正式】血統, 世系, 家系: *a family of ancient lineage* 古老世家

lin·e·al /ˈlɪnɪəl; ˈlɪniəl/ *adj* **1** *formal* related directly to someone who lived a long time before you【正式】直系

的, 嫡系的: *lineal descendants* 直系後代 **2** another form of LINEAR linear的另一種拼法 —**lineally** *adv*

lin·e·a·ment /ˋlɪnɪəmənt; ˈlɪniəmənt/ *n* [C usually plural 一般用複數] *formal*【正式】**1** a feature of your face 容貌; 面部輪廓 **2** a typical quality 特徵

lin·e·ar /ˋlɪnɪɚ; ˈlɪniə/ *adj* **1** consisting of lines, or in the form of a straight line 線的; 直線的: *a linear diagram* 線條圖 **2** [only before noun 僅用於名詞前] concerning length 長度的: *linear measurements* 長度測量 **3** involving a series of directly connected events, ideas etc 涉及一連串直接相關的事物的; 線性的: *linear thinking* 線性思維 —compare 比較 LATERAL THINKING —**linearly** *adv* —**linearity** /ˌlɪnɪˋærətɪ; ˌlɪniˈærəti/ *n* [U]

linear ac·cel·e·ra·tor /ˌ··· ˈ····/ *n* [C] *technical* a piece of equipment that makes PARTICLES (=small pieces of atoms) travel in a straight line at increasing speed【術語】直線加速器〔使粒子沿着直線加速運動的裝置〕

linear per·spec·tive /ˌ··· ·ˈ··/ *n* [U] a way of drawing and painting that gives the appearance of distance or depth 直線透視法〔表現距離或深度的畫法〕

line·back·er /ˋlaɪnˌbækɚ; ˈlaɪnˌbækə/ *n* [C] a player in American football who tries to TACKLE[1] (3) members of the other team〔美式足球的〕中後衛, 線後衛

lined /laɪnd; laɪnd/ *adj* **1** a coat, skirt etc that is lined has a piece of thin material covering the inside〔外衣、裙子等〕有襯裡的: *a fleece-lined jacket* 有羊毛襯裡的夾克 **2** paper that is lined has straight lines printed or drawn across it〔紙〕印[畫]有直線的 **3** skin that is lined has WRINKLES on it〔皮膚〕有皺紋的

line draw·ing /ˈ· ˌ··/ *n* [C] a DRAWING consisting only of lines 線條畫

line drive /ˈ· ·/ *n* [C] a BASEBALL hit with great force in a straight line fairly near the ground〔棒球中擊出的〕平直球

line·man /ˋlaɪnmən; ˈlaɪnmən/ *n plural* **linemen** /-mən; -mən/ [C] **1** *especially AmE* someone whose job is to take care of railway lines or telephone wires【尤美】〔鐵路的〕養路工人;〔電話線的〕線務員; LINESMAN (2) *especially BrE*【尤英】**2** *AmE* a player in the front line of a sports team【美】進攻線衛; 防守線衛

line man·age·ment /ˈ· ˌ···/ *n* [U] **1** the system of passing information and instructions in an organization by which each person tells the one immediately higher or lower than them in rank 直線管理〔指組織內部直屬上下級之間傳送信息〕**2** the group of managers in a company who are responsible for its main activities, such as production and sales 公司負責生產、推銷等主要活動的管理層

line man·a·ger /ˈ· ˌ···/ *n* [C] **1** a manager in a company who is responsible for the main activities of production, sales etc 公司負責生產、推銷等主要活動的經理 **2 sb's line manager** someone who is one level higher in rank than you in a company and is in charge of your work 某人的頂頭上司

lin·en /ˋlɪnɪn; ˈlɪnɪn/ *n* [U] **1** sheets, TABLECLOTHS etc 家庭日用織品: *bed linen* 牀單 | *table linen* 桌布 **2** cloth made from the FLAX plant, used to make high quality clothes, home decorations etc 亞麻布〔用於製作優質衣服、家庭裝飾等〕: *a linen jacket* 亞麻布製的短外衣 **3** *old use* underwear【舊】內衣褲

linen bas·ket /ˈ·· ˌ··/ *n* [C] a LAUNDRY BASKET 待洗衣物筐 —see picture at 參見 BASKET 圖

linen cup·board /ˈ·· ˌ··/ *n* [C] a special cupboard in which sheets, TOWELS etc are kept〔牀單、毛巾等〕家庭日用織品儲存櫃

line of scrim·mage /ˌ· · ˈ··/ *n* [C] a line in American football where the ball is placed at the beginning of a particular PLAY[2] (3)〔美式足球的〕爭球線

line-out /ˈ· ·/ *n* [C] the way of starting play again in a RUGBY UNION game, when the ball has gone off the field 界外球〔英式聯合會橄欖球出界後繼續比賽的方式〕

line print·er /ˈ· ˌ··/ *n* [C] a machine that prints information from a computer at a very high speed〔電腦的〕行式打印機 —**line printing** *n* [U]

lin·er /ˋlaɪnɚ; ˈlaɪnə/ *n* **1** [C] a piece of material used inside something in order to protect it〔起保護作用的〕襯裡, 襯墊: *a trash can liner* 垃圾筒的襯墊 | *nappy liners* 尿布襯墊 **2** [C] a large passenger ship, especially one of several owned by a company〔輪船公司的〕郵輪, 大客輪: *an ocean liner* 遠洋郵輪 —see also 另見 AIRLINER, CRUISE LINER **3** [C,U] *informal* EYELINER【非正式】眼線筆

liner notes /ˈ·· ·/ *n* [plural] *AmE* printed information about a record that appears on its cover【美】〔唱片封套上的〕說明文字

lines·man /ˋlaɪnzmən; ˈlaɪnzmən/ *n plural* **linesmen** /-mən; -mən/ [C] **1** an official in a sport who decides when a ball has gone out of the playing area〔球類運動中〕邊線裁判; 巡邊員; 司線員 —see picture on page A23 參見 A23 頁圖 **2** *especially BrE* someone whose job is to take care of railway lines and telephone wires【尤英】〔鐵路的〕養路工人;〔電話線的〕線務員; LINEMAN (1) *especially AmE*【尤美】

line-up /ˈ· ·/ *n* [C usually singular 一般用單數] **1** a group of people, especially performers, who have agreed to be involved in an event 全體參與人員〔尤指演員〕: *Tonight's line-up includes Suzanne Vega.* 今晚的演出陣容包括蘇珊妮·維加。**2** the players in a sports team who play in a particular game〔出賽的〕運動員陣容: **starting line-up** (=the first ones to play in a game) 開場陣容 **3** a set of events or programmes arranged to follow each other 一系列項目[節目]: *the best line-up of radio entertainment in the world* 世界上最佳的廣播娛樂節目系列 **4** *especially AmE* a row of people examined by a WITNESS to a crime in order to try to recognize a criminal【尤美】〔待目擊者辨認的〕一排嫌疑犯; IDENTIFICATION PARADE *BrE*【英】

ling /lɪŋ; lɪŋ/ *n* [U] a plant very like HEATHER 石南〔一種植物〕

-ling /lɪŋ; lɪŋ/ *suffix* [in nouns 構成名詞] a small, young, or unimportant kind of something 小, 幼; 不重要: *a duckling* (=young duck) 小鴨 | *minor Prussian princelings* (=unimportant princes) 次要的普魯士小王公

lin·ger /ˋlɪŋgɚ; ˈlɪŋgə/ *v* [I] **1** to stay somewhere a little longer, especially because you do not want to leave〔尤指因不願意離開而〕逗留, 徘徊: **[+over/on etc]** *They lingered over coffee and missed the last bus.* 他們慢吞吞地喝咖啡, 沒有趕上末班車。**2** [always+adv/prep] to continue looking at or dealing with something for longer than is usual 盯着〔某物〕; 拖延〔某事〕: **[+on/over etc]** *Mike couldn't help letting his eyes linger on her face.* 米克的雙眼不由自主地盯着她的臉。**3** also 又作 **linger on** to be slow to disappear 緩慢消失: *The taste lingers in your mouth.* 這味道在你嘴裡很久不會消失。**4** also 又作 **linger on** to be dying slowly so that you stay alive for a long time although you are extremely weak 苟延殘喘: *Horribly wounded he lingered on to die two years later.* 他傷勢嚴重, 但是拖了兩年才死。—**lingerer** *n* [C]

lin·ge·rie /ˌlɑnʒəˋre; ˈlænʒəri/ *n* [U] women's underwear 女式內衣褲

lin·ger·ing /ˋlɪŋgərɪŋ; ˈlɪŋgərɪŋ/ *adj* slow to finish or disappear 拖延的, 久纏不去的: *lingering doubts about the need for reform* 對於是否需要改革持續不斷的疑問 | **a lingering death** (=slow and often painful) 漫長(痛苦)的死亡 —**lingeringly** *adv*

lin·go /ˋlɪŋgo; ˈlɪŋgəʊ/ *n* [C usually singular 一般用單數] *informal*【非正式】**1** a language, especially a foreign one 語言〔尤指外語〕: *I'd like to go to Greece, but I don't speak the lingo.* 我想去希臘, 可是不會說希臘語。**2** words used only by a group of people who do a particular job or activity 行話, 術語: *the estate agent's baffling lingo* 難懂的房地產經紀人行話

lin·gua fran·ca /ˌlɪŋgwə ˋfræŋkə; ˌlɪŋgwə ˈfræŋkə/ *n* [C] a language used between people whose main lan-

L

guages are different〔母語不同的人之間使用的〕通用語: *English serves as a lingua franca in many countries.* 英語是很多國家的通用語。

lin·gual /ˋlɪŋgwəl; ˈlɪŋgwəl/ *adj* **1** related to the tongue 舌的 **2** a lingual sound is made by the movement of the tongue 舌音的 —see also 另見 BILINGUAL

lin·gui·ni /lɪŋˋgwinɪ; lɪŋˈgwiːni/ *n* [plural] long thin flat pieces of PASTA〔意大利〕扁麵條

lin·guist /ˋlɪŋgwɪst; ˈlɪŋgwɪ̈st/ *n* [C] **1** someone who studies and is good at foreign languages 研究並通曉幾種外語的人 **2** someone who studies or teaches linguistics 語言學家

3 **lin·guis·tic** /lɪŋˋgwɪstɪk; lɪŋˈgwɪstɪk/ *adj* related to language, words, or linguistics 語言的; 語言學的: *a child's linguistic development* 兒童的語言發展 —**linguistically** /-klɪ; -kli/ *adv*

lin·guis·ti·cian /ˌlɪŋgwɪsˋtɪʃən; ˌlɪŋgwɪ̈ˈstɪʃən/ *n* [C] a LINGUIST (2) 語言學家

lin·guis·tics /lɪŋˋgwɪstɪks; lɪŋˈgwɪstɪks/ *n* [U] the study of language in general and of particular languages, their structure, grammar, and history 語言學 —compare 比較 PHILOLOGY

lin·i·ment /ˋlɪnəmənt; ˈlɪnɪ̈mənt/ *n* [U] a liquid containing oil that you rub on your skin to cure soreness and stiffness 皮膚擦劑〔用以消除疼痛和僵硬〕

lin·ing /ˋlaɪnɪŋ; ˈlaɪnɪŋ/ *n* [C,U] a piece of material covering the inside of a box, piece of clothing etc〔盒子、衣服等的〕襯裡, 裡子: *The coat has a silk lining.* 這件外衣有絲綢襯裡。| *brake linings* 制動裝置襯面 —see picture at 參見 SHOE[1] 圖

2 **link[1]** /lɪŋk; lɪŋk/ *v* **1 be linked** if people or events are linked, they are connected in some way 有聯繫, 有關聯: *Police think the murders are linked.* 警方認為這些謀殺案有關連。| **[+with/to]** *They believe that this illness is linked to the use of chemical pesticides.* 他們相信這種病和使用化學殺蟲劑有關係。**2** [T] to connect computers, broadcast systems etc, so that electronic messages can be sent between them 聯繫〔電腦、廣播系統等, 使電子信息能在它們之間傳遞〕, 連接: **link sth to** *You can link your TV to your stereo for better sound.* 你可以把電視機連接到立體聲設備上, 以獲得更好的音響效果。| **link sth with** *We'll link your PC with our network via modem.* 我們將通過調制解調器把你的個人電腦和我們的網絡連接。**3** [T] to connect two or more things together 把〔兩個或以上的事物〕聯繫在一起: *These traditional stories link the past and the present.* 這些傳統故事把過去和現在聯繫在一起。**4** [T] to believe that one fact or situation is connected with or caused by another〔某事或情況〕和…有聯繫; 由…引起: **link sth to/with** *There are compelling reasons for linking crimes like burglary and car theft with poverty.* 有令人信服的理由認為入屋行竊和偷車等罪行是由貧窮引起的。**5** [T] to join one place to another 連接〔另一處〕: *the coastal highway linking Saigon and Hanoi* 連接西貢和河內的海濱高速公路 **6 link arms** to bend your arm and put it through someone else's bent arm 挽着手臂

link up *phr v* [I] to make a connection with something 連接; 聯繫: **[+with]** *The train links up with the ferry at Holyhead.* 這趟列車連接霍利黑德渡口。| *My work links up with previous research.* 我的工作和以前的研究相聯繫。—see also 另見 LINKUP

link 鏈, 環

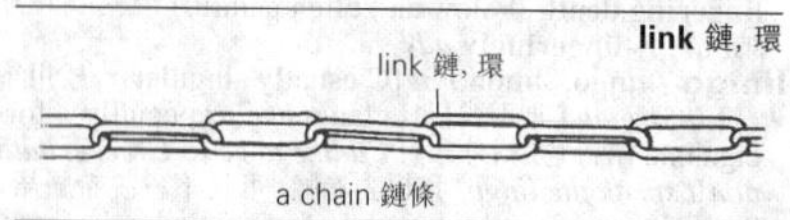

3
2 **link[2]** *n* [C] **1** a relationship between two things or ideas, in which one is caused or affected by the other〔兩種事物或思想的因果〕關聯: **[+between]** *the link between smoking and cancer* 抽煙和癌症之間的關連 **2** a relationship between two or more people, countries, organizations etc〔人、國家、組織等之間的〕聯繫, 關係: **[+with/between]** *They have severed all political links with the Left.* 他們已經同左翼斷絕了所有政治上的聯繫。**3** one of the rings in a chain〔鏈的〕一環 **4 rail/road/telephone link** something that joins two places and allows you to travel or communicate between them 鐵路/公路/電話線連接: *a transatlantic conference via satellite link* 通過衛星連接的橫越大西洋的會議 **5 link in the chain** one of the steps involved in a process 過程中的一環 **6 weak link** the weakest part of a plan or the weakest member of a team〔計劃中的〕薄弱環節;〔一隊中〕最弱的隊員 —see also 另見 CUFF LINK, LINKS, MISSING LINK

link·age /ˋlɪŋkɪdʒ; ˈlɪŋkɪdʒ/ *n* **1** [singular, U] a condition in a political or business agreement, by which one country or company agrees to do something, only if the other promises to do something in return 關聯原則〔政治或商業協議中, 一方同意做某事, 以換取對方做某事的條件〕**2** [singular,U] a LINK[2] (1) 因果關聯 **3** [C] a system of links or connections 連接, 接合

link·man /ˋlɪŋkmən; ˈlɪŋkmæn/ *n* [C] a man whose job is to introduce all the separate parts of a radio or television broadcast〔廣播或電視節目的〕男主持人

links /lɪŋks; lɪŋks/ *plural* **links** *n* a piece of ground near the sea on which GOLF is played〔海濱的〕高爾夫球場

link·up /ˋlɪŋkˌʌp; ˈlɪŋk-ʌp/ *n* [C] a connection between computers, broadcasting systems etc that sends electronic messages between them〔電腦、廣播系統等的〕連接

link·wom·an /ˋlɪŋkˌwʊmən; ˈlɪŋkˌwʊmən/ *n* [C] a woman whose job is to introduce all the separate parts of a radio or television broadcast〔廣播或電視節目的〕女主持人

lin·net /ˋlɪnɪt; ˈlɪnɪ̈t/ *n* [C] a small brown singing bird 朱頂雀

li·no /ˋlaɪno; ˈlaɪnəʊ/ *n* [U] *BrE informal* linoleum【英, 非正式】油氈

li·no·cut /ˋlaɪnoˌkʌt; ˈlaɪnəʊkʌt/ *n* **1** [U] the art of cutting a pattern on a block of linoleum 油氈浮雕藝術 **2** [C] a picture printed from such a block 油氈浮雕版畫

li·no·le·um /lɪˋnolɪəm; lɪ̈ˈnəʊliəm/ *n* [U] smooth shiny material in flat sheets used to cover a floor〔鋪地用的〕油氈

Li·no·type /ˋlaɪnoˌtaɪp; ˈlaɪnəʊtaɪp/ *n* [U] *trademark* a system for arranging TYPE[1] (3) in the form of solid metal lines【商標】萊諾鑄排機〔用於印刷的排字系統〕

lin·seed /ˋlɪnˌsid; ˈlɪnsiːd/ *n* [U] the seed of the FLAX (1) plant 亞麻籽

linseed oil /ˌ‥ ˈ‥/ *n* [U] the oil from linseed used in some paints, inks etc 亞麻籽油〔用於某些油漆、墨水中〕

lint /lɪnt; lɪnt/ *n* [U] **1** *especially AmE* soft light pieces of thread or wool that come off cotton, wool, or other material【尤美】絨屑, 飛花; FLUFF *BrE*【英】**2** *BrE* soft material used for protecting wounds【英】〔裹傷口的〕軟敷料

lin·tel /ˋlɪntl̩; ˈlɪntl/ *n* [C] a piece of stone or wood across the top of a window or door, forming part of the frame〔門、窗上的〕過梁

li·on /ˋlaɪən; ˈlaɪən/ *n* [C] **1** a large yellowish-brown animal of the cat family that eats meat, and lives in Africa and parts of Southern Asia 獅子: *the lion's roar* 獅子的吼聲 —see also 另見 LIONESS **2** *especially literary* someone who is very important, powerful, or famous【尤文】要人; 名人 **3 the lion's share (of)** the largest part of something〔某物〕最大的一份: *The Department of Defense will take the lion's share of the federal budget.* 國防部將佔去聯邦預算的最大份額。**4 in the lion's den** among people who are your enemies 身處敵穴 **5 be thrown/ tossed to the lions** to be put in a dangerous or unpleasant situation 被送到危險[難堪]的境地

li·on·ess /ˋlaɪənɪs; ˈlaɪənes/ *n* [C] a female lion 母獅

lion-heart·ed /ˌ‥ ˈ‥◂/ *adj literary* very brave【文】非常勇敢的

li·on·ize also 又作 **-ise** *BrE*【英】/ˋlaɪən͵aɪz; ˈlaɪənaɪz/ *v* [T] to treat someone as being important or famous 視〔某人〕為要人[名人] —**lionization** /͵laɪənəˋzeʃən; ˌlaɪənaɪˈzeɪʃən/ *n* [U]

2 **lip** /lɪp; lɪp/ *n* **1** [C] one of the two edges of your mouth where your skin is redder or darker 嘴唇: *Marty kissed me right on the lips!* 馬蒂就吻在我的嘴唇上! —see picture at 參見 HEAD[1] 圖 **2** [U] *informal* a word meaning rude, angry talk, used especially by adults to children【非正式】無禮[唐突]的話〔此詞尤在成年人對兒童的話中使用〕: **give sb lip** *Don't give me any of your lip!* 不許對我無禮! **3 thin-lipped/full-lipped etc** with lips that are thin, round etc 薄嘴唇的/厚嘴唇等的 **4** [C usually singular 一般用單數] the edge of something you use to pour liquid from〔容器的〕嘴, 開口: *There's a crack in the lip of that jug.* 那個水壺的壺嘴上有一條裂縫。**5** [C] the edge of a hollow or deep place in the land, usually one made out of rock〔通常由岩石形成的洞或深凹地勢的〕邊緣: *the lip of the canyon* 峽谷的邊緣 **6 my lips are sealed** *spoken* used to say that you will keep a secret【口】我會保密 **7 sth will not pass my lips** used to say that you will not talk about something that is secret 我不會說出某事〔指祕密的事〕: *Don't worry, not a word of this shall pass my lips!* 放心, 關於此事一個字也不會從我嘴裡說出去! **8 on everyone's lips** being talked about by everyone 大家正在談論的: *a name that will soon be on everyone's lips* 很快就會成為大家談論的名字 **9** [C] *BrE spoken* an angry expression【英口】怒容: *Look at the lip on her!* 瞧她那氣憤的樣子! —see also 另見 **lick your lips** (LICK[1] (5)), **read sb's lips** (READ[1] (15)), **keep a stiff upper lip** (STIFF[1] (9))

lip balm /ˈ· ·/ *n* [C,U] *AmE* a substance used to protect dry lips【美】〔防乾燥的〕潤唇膏

lip gloss /ˈ· ·/ *n* [C,U] a substance used to make lips look very shiny 亮唇膏, 唇彩

lip·id /ˋlaɪpɪd; ˈlɪpɪ̈d/ *n* [C] *technical* one of several types of FATTY substances in living things, such as fat, oil, or WAX[1] (1)【術語】脂質〈如脂肪、油或蠟〉

lip·o·suc·tion /ˋlɪpo͵sʌkʃən; ˈlɪpəʊˌsʌkʃən/ *n* [U] a way of removing fat from someone's body using SUCTION 抽脂肪, 脂肪抽吸法

lip·py /ˋlɪpɪ; ˈlɪpi/ *adj BrE informal* not showing respect in the way that you speak to someone【英, 非正式】〔與某人說話時〕出言不遜的

lip-read /ˋlɪp ͵rid; ˈlɪp riːd/ *v* [I,T] to understand what someone is saying by watching the way their lips move, especially because you cannot hear〔尤因失聰而〕唇讀, 觀察唇形以理解〔語義〕—**lip-reading** *n* [U]

lip salve /ˈ· ·/ *n* [C,U] *especially BrE* a substance used to make sore lips feel better【尤英】〔舒緩疼痛的〕護唇油膏

lip ser·vice /ˈ· ˌ··/ *n* **pay lip service to** to say that you support or agree with something without doing anything to prove your support 空口答應, 口惠而實不至: *They're only paying lip service to women's rights.* 他們只是口頭上支持婦女的權利。

lip·stick /ˋlɪp͵stɪk; ˈlɪpˌstɪk/ *n* [C,U] a piece of a substance shaped like a small stick, used for adding colour to your lips 唇膏, 口紅 —see picture at 參見 MAKE-UP 圖

lip synch /ˋlɪp sɪŋk; ˈlɪp sɪŋk/ *n* [U] the action of moving your lips at the same time as a recording is being played, to give the appearance that you are singing〔放錄音時〕對口型假唱 —**lip-synch** *v* [I]

liq·ue·fac·tion /͵lɪkwɪˋfækʃən; ˌlɪkwɪ̈ˈfækʃən/ *n* [U] *technical* the act of making something a liquid or of becoming a liquid【術語】液化(作用)

liq·ue·fy /ˋlɪkwə͵faɪ; ˈlɪkwɪ̈faɪ/ *v* [I,T] *formal* to become liquid, or make something become liquid【正式】(使)液化: *Some gases liquefy at cold temperatures.* 有些氣體在寒冷的溫度下會成為液體。

li·ques·cent /lɪˋkwɛsn̩t; lɪˈkwesənt/ *adj technical* becoming or tending to become liquid【術語】液化性的; 易融化的

li·queur /lɪˋkɝ; lɪˈkjʊə/ *n* [C,U] a sweet and very strong alcoholic drink, drunk in small quantities after a meal〔飯後淺酌的〕利口酒, 甜酒 —compare 比較 LIQUOR

liq·uid[1] /ˋlɪkwɪd; ˈlɪkwɪ̈d/ *n* **1** [C,U] a substance that is not a solid or a gas, which flows, is wet, and has no fixed shape 液體, 液態物: *Water is a liquid.* 水是液體。**2** [C] *technical* either of the CONSONANT sounds /l/ and /r/【術語】流音〔指/l/和/r/〕—see also 另見 WASHING-UP LIQUID

liquid[2] *adj* **1 liquid oxygen/soap etc** oxygen etc in the form of a liquid, instead of its usual gas or solid form 液態氧/肥皂液等 **2** clear and shiny, like water 清澈的, 明亮的: *liquid green eyes* 清澈明亮的綠眼睛 **3** *literary* liquid sounds are clear and pure【文】〔聲音〕清脆的 **4** easily exchanged or sold to pay debts 易變為現金的: *liquid funds* 流動資金 —see also 另見 LIQUID ASSETS **5 liquid refreshment** *humorous* drink, especially alcoholic drink【幽默】飲料〔尤指酒類〕

liquid as·sets /ˌ·· ˈ··/ *n* [plural] *technical* the money that a company or person has, and the property they can easily exchange for money【術語】〔公司或個人擁有的〕流動資產

liq·ui·date /ˋlɪkwɪ͵det; ˈlɪkwɪ̈deɪt/ *v* **1** [I,T] to close a business or company in order to pay its debts 停業清盤〔公司以償還債務〕, 清算 **2** [T] *technical* to pay a debt【術語】償還〔債務〕, 清償: *The stock will be sold to liquidate the loan.* 將出售股票以償還貸款。**3** [T] *informal* to kill someone【非正式】殺死〔某人〕

liq·ui·da·tion /͵lɪkwɪˋdeʃən; ˌlɪkwɪ̈ˈdeɪʃən/ *n* [C,U] **1** the act of closing down a company in order to pay its debts by selling its assets (ASSET (1)) 停業清盤〔指公司停業, 出售資產以還債〕, 清算: **go into liquidation** *land being sold off because the builder has gone into liquidation* 由於建築商已經停業清盤而正在削價變賣的土地 **2** the act of paying a debt〔債務的〕清償

liq·ui·da·tor /ˋlɪkwɪ͵detɚ; ˈlɪkwɪ̈deɪtə/ *n* [C] an official who ends the trade of a company, so that its debts can be paid 公司資產清算[盤]人

liquid gas /ˌ·· ˈ·/ *n* [U] gas changed to liquid by extreme cold〔氣體遇上極冷而凝結成的〕液態氣體

li·quid·i·ty /lɪˋkwɪdətɪ; lɪˈkwɪdɪ̈ti/ *n* [U] *technical*【術語】**1** a situation in which you have money or goods that can be sold to pay debts 擁有流動資產 **2** the state of being LIQUID[1] (1) 液態

liq·uid·ize also 又作 **-ise** *BrE*【英】/ˋlɪkwə͵daɪz; ˈlɪkwɪ̈daɪz/ *v* [T] to crush fruit or vegetables into a thick liquid 把〔水果或蔬菜〕榨出濃汁

liq·uid·iz·er also 又作 **-iser** *BrE*【英】/ˋlɪkwə͵daɪzɚ; ˈlɪkwɪ̈daɪzə/ *n* [C] *BrE* a small electric machine that makes solid foods into liquids; BLENDER【英】榨汁機

liquid lunch /ˌ·· ˈ·/ *n* [C] *humorous* a LUNCH in which you mainly have alcoholic drinks rather than eating food【幽默】〔以酒為主的〕液態午餐

liq·uor /ˋlɪkɚ; ˈlɪkə/ *n* [U] **1** *AmE* a strong alcoholic drink, such as WHISKY【美】烈酒〈如威士忌〉—compare 比較 LIQUEUR **2** *BrE technical* alcoholic drink【英, 術語】酒精類飲料

liq·uo·rice *BrE*【英】, **licorice** *especially AmE*【尤美】/ˋlɪkərɪs; ˈlɪkərɪs/ *n* **1** [U] a black substance produced from the root of a plant, used in medicine and sweets〔藥用、製糖果的〕甘草根浸出物 **2** [C,U] a sweet or sweets made from this substance 甘草糖

liquorice all·sorts /͵lɪkərɪs ˋɔlsɔrts; ˌlɪkərɪs ˈɔːlsɔːts/ *n* [plural] *BrE* a mixture of differently shaped brightly coloured sweets containing liquorice【英】什錦甘草糖果

liquor store /ˈ·· ·/ *n* [C] *AmE* a shop where alcohol is sold【美】賣酒的商店; OFF-LICENCE *BrE*【英】

lir·a /ˋlɪrə; ˈlɪərə/ *n plural* **lire** /-re; -reɪ/ *or* **liras** [C] the standard unit of money in Malta and Turkey, and used in Italy before the euro 里拉〔馬爾他和土耳其的標準貨幣單位, 也是意大利在使用歐元前的貨幣單位〕

lisle /laɪl; laɪl/ *n* [U] cotton material, used in the past for GLOVEs and STOCKINGs 萊爾線〔舊時用來織手套和長襪〕

L

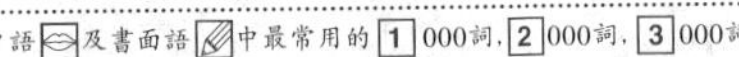
口語及書面語中最常用的 1 000詞, 2 000詞, 3 000詞

lisp¹ /lɪsp; lɪsp/ *v* [I,T] to speak, pronouncing 's' sounds as 'th' 咬舌(說話); 口齒不清地說話〔把 s 發成 th 音〕

lisp² *n* [singular] if someone has a lisp, they lisp when they speak 說話時咬舌[口齒不清]: *She speaks with a slight lisp.* 她說話有點口齒不清。

lis·som, lissome /ˈlɪsəm; ˈlɪsəm/ *adj literary* a body that is lissom is thin and graceful【文】〔身材〕清瘦優雅的: *her slender lissom figure* 她修長優美的身材

S1 W1 **list¹** /lɪst; lɪst/ *n* [C] **1** a set of words, numbers etc written one below the other, for example so that you can remember them 名單, 清單, 目錄: *a shopping list* 購物清單 | *an alphabetical list* 按字母順序列出的名單 | **[+of]** *Make a list of the things you have to do.* 把必須做的事情列成清單。| **at the top/bottom of the list** (=regarded as most or least important) 最緊要的/最不緊要的 **2 enter the lists** *BrE* to become involved in an argument, competition, etc【英】捲入〔爭論、競爭等中〕—see also 另見 CIVIL LIST, **be on the danger list** (DANGER (4)), HIT LIST, MAILING LIST, SHORT LIST, WAITING LIST

S2 W3 **list²** *v* **1** [T] to write a list, or mention things one after the other 列出清單; 列舉: *The guidebook lists 1,000 hotels and restaurants.* 這本導遊書列出了1,000家旅館和餐廳。**2** [I] if a ship lists, it leans to one side〔船〕傾斜 **3** [I] *old use* to listen【舊】聽, 聞

list·ed build·ing /ˌ·· ˈ··/ *n* [C] a building of historical interest in Britain, that is protected by a government order〔英國登錄入冊的〕文物保護建築物

S1 W1 **lis·ten¹** /ˈlɪsn̩; ˈlɪsən/ *v* [I] **1** to pay attention to what someone is saying or to a sound that you can hear〔注意地〕聽: *listening to music* 聽音樂 | *Listen! There's a strange noise in the engine.* 聽! 引擎內有一種奇怪的雜音。| **[+to]** *I like listening to the radio.* 我喜歡聽收音機。| **listen hard** (=try to hear something that is very quiet) 盡力去聽〔很輕的聲音〕| **listen intently** (=very carefully and with interest) 留意聽, 留神聽 **2** *spoken* used to tell someone to pay attention to what you are about to say【口】聽着, 聽好〔用於告訴某人留意你要說的話〕: *Listen, I'm sure we can work this out, if everybody calms down.* 聽着! 如果大家冷靜下來, 我肯定我們能解決這件事。**3** to consider carefully what someone says to you 聽從, 聽信: *I told him not to go, but he just wouldn't listen.* 我告訴他不要去, 可是他就是不聽。| **[+to]** *I wish I'd listened to your advice.* 我要是當初聽你的勸告就好了。

listen for sth/sb *phr v* [T] to pay attention so that you are sure you will hear a sound 留心聽: *Listen for the moment when the music changes.* 留心聽音樂變化的那一瞬間。

listen in *phr v* [I] **1** to listen to a broadcast on the radio 收聽電台廣播: **[+to]** *I must remember to listen in to the news at noon.* 我一定要記住聽午間新聞。—see also 另見 **tune in** (TUNE²) **2** to listen to someone's conversation without them knowing it 偷聽, 竊聽: **[+on]** *It sounded like someone was listening in on the extension.* 聽起來好像有人在分機上偷聽。

listen out *phr v* [I] *BrE informal* to listen carefully, especially for an unexpected sound【英, 非正式】注意聽, 留心聽〔尤指突如其來的聲音〕: **listen out for** *Listen out for the baby in case she wakes up.* 注意聽寶寶有沒有醒來。

listen up *phr v* [I] *especially AmE spoken* used to get people's attention so they can hear what you are going to say【尤美, 口】注意, 聽着〔用於吸引別人的注意, 使他們能聽見你將要說的話〕: *Hey everybody, listen up!* 喂, 各位, 注意!

USAGE NOTE 用法說明: LISTEN

Grammar 語法

Remember you can only **listen to** (or sometimes **for**) something. 別忘記, 聽某事只能用 listen to〔有時用 for〕: *He's listening to music* (NOT 不用 *He's listening music*). 他正在聽音樂。

listen² *n* [singular] *BrE informal* an act of listening【英, 非正式】聽: *Have a listen to this new album!* 聽一聽這張新唱片!

lis·ten·a·ble /ˈlɪsn̩əbl̩; ˈlɪsənəbəl/ *adj informal* pleasant to hear【非正式】悅耳動聽的

lis·ten·er /ˈlɪsn̩ɚ; ˈlɪsənə/ *n* [C] **1** someone who listens, especially to the radio〔尤指電台廣播的〕收聽者, 聽眾: *Some of our regular listeners have complained about the new program schedule.* 有些長期聽眾對我們的新節目表有不滿。—compare 比較 VIEWER (1) **2 a good listener** someone who listens patiently and sympathetically to other people 耐心聽別人說話的人

lis·ten·ing de·vice /ˈ··· ·ˌ·/ *n* [C] a piece of equipment that allows you to listen secretly to other people's conversations; a BUG¹ (5) 竊聽器 —compare 比較 HEARING AID

lis·te·ri·a /lɪˈstɪriə; lɪˈstɪəriə/ *n* [U] a type of BACTERIA that makes you sick 李斯特菌

list·ing /ˈlɪstɪŋ; ˈlɪstɪŋ/ *n* **1** [C] something that is on a list〔清單中的〕列項 **2 listings** [plural] lists of films, plays, and other events with the times and places at which they will happen〔電影、戲劇等的〕節目表

list·less /ˈlɪstlɪs; ˈlɪstləs/ *adj* feeling tired and not interested in things 倦怠的, 無精打采的, 懶洋洋的: *The heat was making me listless.* 炎熱的天氣使我懶洋洋的。—**listlessly** *adv* —**listlessness** *n* [U]

list price /ˈ· ·/ *n* [C] a price that is suggested for a product by the people who make it〔廠商的〕定價

lit¹ /lɪt; lɪt/ the past tense and past participle of LIGHT²

lit² an abbreviation of 縮寫= LITERATURE or LITERARY

lit·a·ny /ˈlɪtn̩ɪ; ˈlɪtəni/ *n* [C] **1** a long prayer in the Christian church in which the priest says a sentence and the people reply 連禱, 應答祈禱 **2** something that takes a long time to say that repeats phrases, or sounds like a list 冗長乏味的陳述; 反覆的贅述: *a long litany of complaints* 絮絮叨叨的抱怨

li·tchi /ˈlitʃi; ˈlaɪtʃiː/ *n* [C] another spelling of LYCHEE lychee 的另一種拼法

lite beer /ˌlaɪt ˈbɪr; ˌlaɪt ˈbɪə/ *n* [U] *AmE* beer that has fewer CALORIEs than normal beer【美】萊特啤酒〔熱量比一般的啤酒低〕

li·ter /ˈlitɚ; ˈliːtə/ *n* [C] the American spelling of LITRE litre 的美式拼法

lit·er·a·cy /ˈlɪtərəsɪ; ˈlɪtərəsi/ *n* [U] **1** the state of being able to read and write 有讀寫能力, 有文化: *a new adult literacy campaign* 新的成年人識字運動 **2 computer literacy** the ability to understand and use computers 使用電腦的能力

lit·e·ral¹ /ˈlɪtərəl; ˈlɪtərəl/ *adj* **1** the literal meaning of a word or expression is its basic or original meaning〔詞的〕本義的, 原義的, 字面意思的: **literal meaning/sense/interpretation etc** *A trade war is not a war in the literal sense.* 貿易戰不是字面意義上的戰爭。—compare 比較 FIGURATIVE (1) **2 literal translation** a translation that gives a single word for each original word instead of giving the meaning of the whole sentence in a natural way 直譯, 逐字翻譯 **3 literal-minded** not showing much imagination; PROSAIC 缺乏想像力的, 乏味的 —**literalness** *n* [U]

literal² *n* [C] *BrE technical* a printing mistake, especially in the spelling of a word; TYPO【英, 術語】印刷錯誤〔尤指拼寫錯誤〕

lit·e·ral·ly /ˈlɪtərəlɪ; ˈlɪtərəli/ *adv* **1** according to the most basic or original meaning of a word or expression 按照原義, 根據字面意思: *'Inspire' literally meant 'to breathe into'.* inspire 的原義是"吸入"。| **mean sth literally** (=mean exactly what you say) 意思和字面所說的一樣 *I know I said I felt like quitting, but I didn't mean it literally!* 我知道我說過想退出, 可是這說來有點誇張。**2 take sb/sth literally** to only understand the most basic meaning of words, phrases etc, often with the result that you do not understand what someone really means 僅僅

從字面上理解某人/某事物: *Christians who take the Bible literally* 只從字面上理解《聖經》的基督徒 **3** used to emphasize that something is actually true 的確〔用於加強語氣〕, 確實: *The Olympic Games were watched by literally billions of people.* 奧林匹克運動會確實有幾十億人觀看。**4** *spoken* used to emphasize something you say that is already expressed strongly【口】簡直〔用於加強本已強烈的語氣〕: *Dad was literally blazing with anger.* 爸爸簡直是火冒三丈。

2 **lit·e·ra·ry** /ˈlɪtəˌrɛrɪ; ˈlɪtərəri/ *adj* **1** connected with LITERATURE 文學的: *a literary prize* 文學獎 | *literary criticism* 文學評論 **2** typical of the style of writing used in literature rather than in ordinary writing and talking〔文風〕常見於文學〔有別於一般書面語和口語〕; 典雅的: *a very literary style of writing* 非常典雅的文體 **3** liking literature very much, and studying or producing it 愛好文學的, 從事文學研究[創作]的: *a literary woman* 女文人 —**literariness** *n* [U]

lit·e·rate /ˈlɪtərɪt; ˈlɪtərɪ̈t/ *adj* **1** able to read and write 能讀會寫的, 識字的 —compare 比較 NUMERATE **2 computer literate/musically literate etc** having enough knowledge to use a computer, play a musical instrument etc 會使用電腦的/會演奏樂器的等 **3** well educated 受過良好教育的 —opposite 反義詞 ILLITERATE (1) —see also 另見 LITERACY —**literately** *adv* —**literateness** *n* [U]

lit·e·ra·ti /ˌlɪtəˈretaɪ; ˌlɪtəˈrɑːti/ *n* **the literati** *formal* a small group of people in a society who know a lot about literature【正式】文學家, 文人學士

2 **lit·e·ra·ture** /ˈlɪtərəˌtʃʊr; ˈlɪtərətʃə/ *n* [U] **1** books, plays, poems etc that people think have value 文學(作品): *one of the great works of English literature* 英國文學巨著之一 **2** works such as these that are studied as a subject〔作為學科研究的〕文學: *a course in modern African literature* 非洲現代文學課程 **3** all the books, articles, etc on a particular subject〔某一學科的〕著述, 文獻資料: *literature on the history of science* 科學史的文獻資料 **4** printed information produced by organizations that want to sell something or tell people about something〔促銷商品或提供信息的〕印刷品; 宣傳品: *Do you have any sales literature available?* 你們有沒有推銷商品的印刷品?

lithe /laɪð; laɪð/ *adj* having a body that moves easily and gracefully〔動作〕靈活優美的: *the dancer's lithe long-limbed body* 舞蹈表演者優美修長的身材 —**lithely** *adv*

lith·i·um /ˈlɪθɪəm; ˈlɪθiəm/ *n* [U] a soft silvery ELEMENT (=simple substance) that is the lightest known metal 鋰〔已知的最輕的金屬〕

lith·o·graph¹ /ˈlɪθəˌgræf; ˈlɪθəgrɑːf/ *n* [C] a printed picture made by lithography 平版印刷畫, 石版畫

lithograph² *v* [T] to print a picture by lithography 用平版印刷術印刷

li·thog·ra·phy /lɪˈθɑgrəfɪ; lɪˈθɒgrəfi/ *n* [U] a process for printing patterns, pictures, etc from something that has been cut into a piece of stone or metal〔石板、金屬板的〕平版印刷術 —**lithographic** /ˌlɪθəˈgræfɪk; ˌlɪθəˈgræfɪk◂/ *adj*

lit·i·gant /ˈlɪtəgənt; ˈlɪtɪ̈gənt/ *n* [C] *law* someone who is making a claim against someone or defending themselves against a claim in a court of law【法律】訴訟當事人

lit·i·gate /ˈlɪtəˌget; ˈlɪtɪ̈geɪt/ *v* [I,T] *law* to take a claim or complaint against someone to a court of law【法律】提出訴訟; 起訴〔某人〕

lit·i·ga·tion /ˌlɪtəˈgeʃən; ˌlɪtɪ̈ˈgeɪʃən/ *n* [U] *law* the process of taking claims to a court of law, in a non-criminal case【法律】〔民事案件的〕訴訟, 訟爭

li·ti·gious /lɪˈtɪdʒɪəs; lɪˈtɪdʒəs/ *adj formal* too willing to take any disagreements to a court of law【正式】好訟爭的, 好打官司的 —**litigiousness** *n* [U]

lit·mus /ˈlɪtməs; ˈlɪtməs/ *n* [U] a chemical that turns red when touched by acid, and blue when touched by an ALKALI 石蕊〔遇酸變紅, 遇鹼變藍〕

litmus pa·per /ˈ·· ˌ··/ *n* [U] paper containing litmus used to test whether a chemical is an acid or an ALKALI 石蕊試紙

litmus test /ˈ·· ˌ·/ *n* [singular] **1** something that makes it clear what someone's attitude, intentions etc are〔某人的態度、意圖等的〕檢驗辦法, 試金石: *The election will be an interesting litmus test on the 'greening' of politics.* 選舉將是檢驗"環保"政治的有趣的試金石。**2** a test using litmus paper 石蕊試驗

li·to·tes /ˈlaɪtoˌtiz; ˈlaɪtətiːz/ *n* [U] *technical* a way of expressing your meaning by using a word that has the opposite meaning with a negative word such as 'not', for example by saying 'not bad' when you mean 'good'【術語】曲言法, 反敍法〈如以"不壞"表示"好"〉

li·tre *BrE*【英】, **liter** *AmE*【美】/ˈlitə; ˈliːtə/ *n* [C] **1** the basic unit for measuring an amount of liquid, in the METRIC system 升〔公制容量單位〕—see table on page C3 參見C3頁附錄 **2 1.3/2.4 etc litre engine** a measurement that shows the size and power of a vehicle's engine 1.3/2.4升等的引擎〔汽車引擎的大小和功率的測量〕

lit·ter¹ /ˈlɪtə; ˈlɪtə/ *n* **1** [U] bits of waste paper, containers etc that people have thrown away and left on the ground in a public place〔扔在公共場所的〕垃圾, 廢棄物: *Please take your litter away with you.* 請把垃圾隨身帶走。—compare 比較 GARBAGE, RUBBISH, TRASH **2** [C] a group of baby animals such as dogs or cats which one mother gives birth to at the same time 一窩〔小狗、小貓等〕**3 cat/kitty litter** [U] small grains of a special substance that you put in a container where your cat gets rid of its solid and liquid waste 貓沙〔特殊物質的顆粒, 放在容器中供貓便溺用〕: *a litter tray* 貓沙盤 **4** [U] STRAW (1) that a farm animal sleeps on〔家畜睡覺用的〕褥草 **5 a litter of** a group of things arranged in a very untidy way 雜亂的一堆: *a litter of notes, papers and textbooks* 亂糟糟的一堆筆記、紙張和課本 **6** [C] a very low bed for carrying important people on, used in former times〔舊時載重要人物的〕轎

litter² *v* **1** also 又作 **litter up** [T] if things litter an area there are a lot of them in that place, scattered in an untidy way〔在某處〕亂丟東西; 把〔某處〕弄亂: *Clothes littered the floor.* 地板上到處都是亂丟的衣服。| **be littered with** *The road was littered with debris.* 路上遍地瓦礫。**2 be littered with** if something is littered with things, there are a lot of those things in it 充滿〔某物〕: *History is littered with examples of failed colonialism.* 歷史上有許多殖民主義失敗的例子。**3** [I,T] to leave bits of waste paper etc on the ground in a public place〔在公共場所〕亂扔〔廢棄物〕**4** [I] *technical* if an animal such as a dog or cat litters, it gives birth to babies【術語】〔狗、貓等動物〕產仔

lit·te·ra·teur /ˌlɪtərəˈtɜ; ˌlɪtərəˈtɜː/ *n* [C] someone who is interested in literature, especially a writer whose work is not considered to be very good 文人〔尤指作品一般的作家〕

litter bin /ˈ·· ·/ also 又作 **litter bas·ket** /ˈ·· ˌ··/ *BrE*【英】*n* [C] a container in a public place for people to put things in that they are throwing away, such as papers or cans〔公共場所的〕垃圾箱

lit·ter·bug /ˈlɪtəˌbʌg; ˈlɪtəbʌg/ also 又作 **litter lout** *BrE*【英】*n* [C] someone who leaves waste on the ground in public places〔在公共場所〕亂扔廢物者, 垃圾蟲

lit·tle¹ /ˈlɪtl̩; ˈlɪtl/ *adj* 1 1

1 ▶SIZE 尺寸◀ small in size 小的: *a little house* 小屋 | *their little group of supporters* 他們為數不多的支持者 | **a little bit of** *especially BrE* (=a small piece of something)【尤英】一小片[塊, 段等]的 *little bits of paper all over the floor* 地板上到處都是小紙片 | **little tiny** *spoken* (=extremely small)【口】極小的 *a little tiny puppy* 極小的狗 | **a little something** *informal* (=a small present)【非正式】小禮物 *I promised the kids a little something if they ate all their dinner.* 我答應孩子, 如果他們把晚餐全部吃完的話, 我會送給他們小禮品。

2 used about something or someone that is small to show

that you like or dislike them, or that you feel sorry for them 小的〔用於小的人或物，表示喜歡、厭惡或同情〕: **nice little/clever little etc** *a nice little house* 漂亮的小屋 | *a clever little gadget* 靈巧的小裝置 | *It wasn't a bad little car.* 那是一輛不錯的小汽車。| **nasty little/silly little etc** *another of her silly little jokes* 她的另一個愚蠢的玩笑 | *a boring little man* 無聊的小個子男人 | **poor little/pathetic little** (=used when you feel sympathetic) 可憐的小…〔表示同情〕 *her sad little face looking up at me* 她痛苦的小臉仰起來看着我 | *a poor little bird with a broken wing* 斷了一隻翅膀的可憐的小鳥

3 done in a way that is not very strong or noticeable; slight 微弱的; 不明顯的; 輕微的: *a wry little smile* 微微的苦笑

4 ►TIME/DISTANCE 時間/距離◄ short in time or distance 短的: *I can have a nice little nap in the car.* 在汽車內我可以舒服地小睡片刻。| *You'll find it a little way along this path.* 沿着這條小路走不遠你就會找到它。| **a little while** (=a short period of time) 一會兒 *He arrived a little while ago.* 他剛到一會兒。| *We sat there for a little while longer.* 我們在那裡多坐了一會兒。

5 ►YOUNG 年輕的◄ young and small 年輕的, 幼小的: *a cute little puppy* 可愛的小狗 | *We didn't have toys like this when I was little.* 在我小時候, 我們沒有這樣的玩具。| **a little boy/girl** *two little boys playing in the street* 兩個在街上玩的小男孩 | **your little girl/boy** (=your son or daughter who is still a child) 你的小女兒/兒子〔意指仍然是兒童〕 *Mum, I'm 17 – I'm not your little girl any longer.* 媽, 我 17 歲了 — 我不再是你的小女兒了。| **little brother/sister** (=a younger brother or sister who is still a child) 小弟弟/小妹妹

6 ►UNIMPORTANT 不重要的◄ a) not important 不重要的: *I'm too busy to worry about little things like broken windows.* 我無暇顧及窗戶破了之類的小事。**b)** used jokingly when you really think that something is important 微不足道的〔用於開玩笑, 實指某事很重要〕: *There's just that little matter of the £5,000 you owe me.* 就是你欠我 5,000 英鎊這件小事情。

7 a little bird told me *humorous spoken* used to say that someone who you are not going to name has told you something about another person【幽默, 口】有人告訴我〔某人的事, 不願意透露消息來源時使用〕: *A little bird told me you're getting married soon.* 有人告訴我你快要結婚了。

8 the little woman *spoken* an expression meaning someone's wife, often considered offensive especially by women【口】老婆, 婆娘〔指某人的妻子, 常被認為是冒犯用語, 尤其是婦女〕

Frequencies of **a little** and **a bit** in spoken and written English a little 和 a bit 在英語口語和書面語中的使用頻率

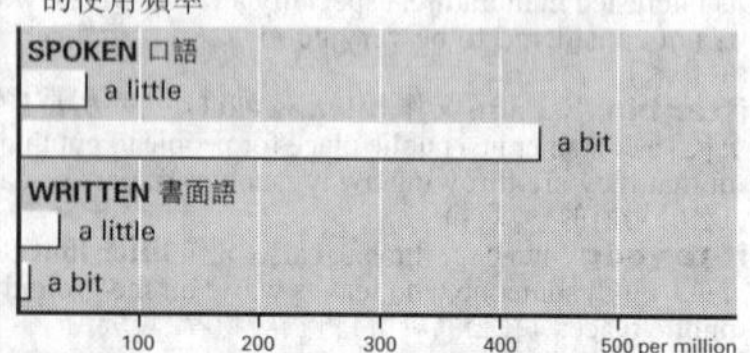

Based on the British National Corpus and the Longman Lancaster Corpus
據英國國家語料庫和朗文蘭卡斯特語料庫

This graph shows that **a bit** is much more common in spoken English than **a little**. This is because **a bit** is informal and is therefore more commonly used in ordinary conversation. However, in written English **a little** is more common than **a bit**. 本圖表顯示, a bit 在英語口語中的使用頻率遠遠高於 a little, 因為 a bit 是非正式用語, 所以在日常對話中用得較為普遍。但 a little 在書面語中的使用頻率遠遠高於 a bit。

USAGE NOTE 用法說明: LITTLE

Word choice 詞語辨析: **little, small**

Little often suggests that you are talking about someone or something small that you are fond of or feel sympathetic towards. little 通常表示談到的人或東西既小又令你喜歡或同情: *What a sweet little dog!* 多麼可愛的小狗！| *A little old lady lived in the house opposite.* 一個矮小的老太太住在對面的房子裡。

Small simply describes the size of something. small 只描述某物的大小: *My daughter's room is smaller than mine.* 我女兒的房間比我的小。| *He packed his things into a small bag.* 他把自己的東西裝進一個小包內。You also use **small** when you are giving information and facts. 當提供信息和事實時也可以用 small: *There has been a small increase in production.* 產量稍有增長。

Little can also suggest that someone or something is unimportant. little 也可以表示人或物是不重要的: *What a silly little man!* 多麼無足輕重的蠢傢伙！When you are speaking it often sounds more friendly or polite to say something is **little** rather than **small**. 說話時談到某物, 用 little 比 small 友善或有禮貌: *I have a little problem, can you help me?* 我有個小問題, 你能幫我嗎? makes the problem sound less serious or urgent than 使問題的嚴重或緊急程度小於: *I have a small problem* and 而 *We're going to have a little test* 我們要做一個小測試 sounds a little less frightening than 則不及以下這句駭人: *We're going to have a small test.*

little² *quantifier*

1 only a small amount or hardly any of something 一點兒; 少得幾乎沒有: *Little is known about these areas of the moon.* 月球上這些地區鮮為人知。| *There's little to be gained from an official complaint.* 從正式投訴中得不到甚麼。| *I paid little attention to what the others were saying.* 我不大注意別人在說甚麼。| **very little** *During that period I ate very little and slept even less.* 那段期間我吃得不多, 睡得更少。| *There's very little money left.* 沒剩下多少錢了。| *There seems very little point in continuing this discussion.* 看來繼續進行這場討論已沒有多少意義。| **little or no** *peasants who have little or no land* 少地或無地的農民 | **little of** *Little of their wealth now remains.* 現在他們的財富已所剩無幾。| **do little to help/benefit etc** *The new filing system has done little to improve efficiency.* 新的歸檔系統沒有提高多少效率。| **as little as possible** (=the smallest amount that you can have or do) 盡可能少的 *He always writes as little as possible.* 他總是盡可能少寫。| **little real effect/importance etc** (=used to emphasize that there is hardly any effect etc)〔用於強調〕很少實際效果/極不重要等 *The laboratory tests are of little real value.* 這些化驗沒有多少真正的價值。| **precious little** (=very little) 很少 *There's precious little good news.* 現在好消息少得可憐。—see 見 FEW (USAGE)

2 a little also 又作 **a little bit** a small amount 少量的: *I told him a little bit about it.* 關於此事我告訴了他一點點情況。| *Fortunately I had a little time to spare.* 很幸運, 我有一點空閒時間。| *She speaks a little French.* 她會說一些法語。| *A little over half the class can swim.* 班上有一半多一點的人會游泳。| **a little more/less** *He poured me out a little more wine.* 他又給我倒了一點酒。| *"Would you like some more coffee?" "Just a little, thanks."* "你還要點咖啡嗎?" "一點點就夠了, 謝謝。" | **a little of** *The city is regaining a little of its former splendour.* 這座城市正在回復一些昔日的輝煌。

3 ►TIME/DISTANCE 時間/距離◄ a short time or distance 短時間; 短距離: *a little over 60 years ago* 六十幾年前 | *We walked on a little and then turned back.* 我們走了一會兒, 然後就折返。

4 what little the small amount that there is, that is possible etc 僅有的一點; 盡可能的一點: *We did what little we could to help.* 我們盡了僅有的一點力量。| *The firemen recovered what little remained of the bodies.* 消防員發現了屍體僅剩的一點殘骸。

1 1 **little³** *adv* **1 a little** also 又作 **a little bit** to a small degree 稍許, 一點兒: *She trembled a little as she spoke.* 她說話時有些顫抖。| *I was a little bit disappointed with my test results.* 我的測驗成績令我有點沮喪。| **a little more/better/ further etc** *We shall have to wait a little longer to see what happens.* 我們得再等一會兒才能看到會發生甚麼事情。**2** not much or only slightly 很少, 略微: *The pattern of life here has changed little since I was a boy.* 從我小時候至今這裡的生活模式幾無改變。| **little known/understood etc** (=not known etc by many people) 鮮為人知 *a little known corner of the world* 世上鮮為人知的角落 | **little more/better etc (than)** *His voice was little more than a whisper.* 他的聲音和耳語差不了多少。| **very little** *The situation has improved very little, in spite of all our efforts.* 雖然我們花了氣力, 但情況仍無多大改觀。| **as little as possible** *I try to disturb her as little as possible when she's working.* 在她工作的時候, 我盡可能不去打擾她。**3 little did sb think/realize** also 又作 **sb little thought/realized** used to mean that someone did not think or realize that something was true 某人沒有想到/認識到〔某事是真的〕: *Little did he realize that we were watching his every move.* 他沒有意識到我們正在觀察他的一舉一動。**4 little by little** gradually 逐漸地: *Little by little things returned to normal.* 情況逐漸回復正常。**5 more than a little/not a little** *formal* extremely【正式】極度地, 極端地: *Graham was more than a little frightened by what he had seen.* 格雷厄姆被自己所看到的事嚇了一大跳。**6 (just) that little bit extra/harder/better etc** more, harder etc by a small amount that will have an important effect 更多一點的/更努力一點的/更好一點的等〔會有重要的影響〕: *people who work just that little bit harder than anyone else* 工作比別人更盡力一點的人

Little Bear /ˌ·· ˈ·/ *especially BrE*【尤英】, **Little Dip·per** /ˌ·· ˈ··/ *especially AmE*【尤美】— *n* **the Little Bear** a group of stars 小熊星座

little fin·ger /ˌ·· ˈ··/ *n* [C] the smallest finger on your hand 小指

Little League /ˈ·· ˌ·/ *n* a BASEBALL LEAGUE for children in the US〔美國〕少年棒球聯合會

little peo·ple /ˈ·· ˌ··/ *n* [plural] **1** all the people in a country or organization who have no power 老百姓, 平民: *It's the little people who bear the brunt of taxation.* 承擔稅收的主力是平民百姓。**2 the little people** fairies (FAIRY (1)), especially Irish LEPRECHAUNS 小仙子;〔尤指愛爾蘭傳說中的〕矮妖精

lit·to·ral /ˈlɪtərəl; ˈlɪtərəl/ *n* [C] *technical* an area of land near the coast【術語】沿海地區, 海岸地區 —**littoral** *adj*

li·tur·gi·cal /lɪˈtɝdʒɪkḷ; lɪˈtɜːdʒɪkəl/ *adj* [only before noun 僅用於名詞前] related to church services and ceremonies 教堂儀式的, 禮拜儀式的 —**liturgically** /-kḷɪ; -kli/ *adv*

lit·ur·gy /ˈlɪtɚdʒɪ; ˈlɪtədʒi/ *n* **1** [C,U] a way of praying in a religious service using a fixed order of words, prayers etc 禮拜儀式 **2 the Liturgy** the written form of these services 禮拜公禱文, 祈禱書

liv·a·ble, liveable /ˈlɪvəbḷ; ˈlɪvəbəl/ *adj* **1** also 又作 **livable in** *BrE* a place that is livable in is suitable to live in; HABITABLE【英】適宜居住的 **2** if your life is livable, you can bear it; ENDURABLE〔生活〕能忍受的

1 1 **live¹** /lɪv; lɪv/ *v*

① IN A PLACE/TIME 在某處/某時
② LIVE IN A PARTICULAR WAY 以某種方式生活
③ BE ALIVE 活着
④ SEXUAL RELATIONSHIP 性關係
⑤ LIVE FOR A REASON 為某種理由而活
⑥ IN YOUR MIND 在心中
⑦ OTHER MEANINGS 其他意思

① IN A PLACE/TIME 在某處/某時

1 ►IN A PLACE/HOME 在某處/某家◄ [I always+adv/prep] to have your home in a particular place〔在某處〕居住: **live in/at/with/near etc** *Where do you live?* 你住在哪裡? | *We used to live in Bakersfield.* 我們過去住在貝克斯菲爾德。| *They have one daughter who still lives with them.* 他們有一個女兒還和他們住在一起。| **live at home** (=live with your parents) 住在家裡〔和父母住在一塊〕| **look for a place to live** (=look for a house to live in) 找住處 | **live rough** *BrE* (=have no home and sleep outdoors)【英】無家可歸, 風餐露宿

2 ►PLANT/ANIMAL 植物/動物◄ [I always+adv/prep] a plant or animal that lives in a particular place grows there or has its home there〔在某處〕生長[棲息]: **live in/on/near etc** *The birds live only on this island.* 這種鳥只棲息在這個島上。

3 ►AT A PARTICULAR TIME 在某時◄ [I always+adv/prep] to be alive at a particular time or when particular events happen〔在某時或某事發生時〕生存, 活着: **[+before/in/at]** *Pythagoras lived a century before Socrates.*〔古希臘數學家〕畢達哥拉斯生活在蘇格拉底之前一個世紀。| *He lived during the time of the plague.* 在瘟疫流行期間他還活着。

4 ►TO BE KEPT SOMEWHERE 被置於某處◄ [I always+adv/ prep] *informal especially BrE* to be kept in a particular place【非正式, 尤英】被放置在某處: **live in/on etc** *Where does this dish live?* 這盤子放在哪裡?

② LIVE IN A PARTICULAR WAY 以某種方式生活

5 [I always+adv/prep,T] to have a particular type of life, or live in a particular way 過…生活; 以〔某種方式〕生活: **live in/under/like etc** *These people are living in appalling conditions.* 這些人生活在極其惡劣的環境之中。| *He lived like a king.* 他過着國王一樣的生活。| **live well** (=have plenty of money, food etc) 生活過得很富裕 | **live a quiet/active/healthy life** *Ben has to live a quiet life.* 本得過平靜的生活。| **live the life of** *She lived the life of an aristocrat.* 她過着貴族的生活。| **live a life of crime/luxury** *a movie star living a life of luxury* 過着奢華生活的電影明星 | **live in fear (of)** *Colin lives in fear of having a heart attack.* 科林生活在恐懼中, 怕心臟病發作。| **live from day to day** (=deal with each day as it comes without making plans) 日復一日地得過且過 | **be living on the breadline** (=be very poor) 生活貧困 | **live out of a suitcase** (=travel a lot, especially as part of your work) 經常奔走旅行〔尤指是工作的一部分〕

6 ►LIVE BY DOING STH 靠做某事生活◄ [I] to keep yourself alive by working, eating etc 靠〔工作, 吃某食物等〕為生: *They earn barely enough to live.* 他們賺的錢剛夠餬口。| **live by doing sth** *They live by hunting and killing deer.* 他們靠捕殺鹿為生。| **live on beans/potatoes/grass etc** (=eat only a particular type of food)〔只是〕以豆/馬鈴薯/草等維持生命 *living on a diet of bread and cheese* 靠吃麵包和乾酪維持生命 | **live out of tins/cans** (=eat mainly food from cans, not fresh food) 主要吃罐頭食品 | **live on benefit/welfare/£40 a week**

L

etc (=have only a small amount of money with which to buy food, pay bills etc) 靠撫恤金/福利救濟/每週40英鎊等來過活 *I challenge anyone to try to live on the state pension.* 我要出道難題，看誰能靠政府養老金生活。
7 live it up *informal* to do things that you enjoy and spend a lot of money【非正式】享樂，過花天酒地的生活：*living it up at the Hotel California* 在加利福尼亞酒店享樂一番
8 ►LIVE BY A PRINCIPLE/RULE ETC 按照某種原則/規律等生活◄ [I] to always behave according to a particular set of rules or ideas 總是按…的規定[觀念]行事：*people who live by the Bible* 以《聖經》為行事準則的人
9 live by your wits to get money by being clever or dishonest, and not by doing an ordinary job 靠要小聰明[不誠實手段]賺錢
10 live a lie to pretend all the time that you feel or believe something when actually you do not 過虛偽的生活：*I had to divorce him, I couldn't go on living a lie.* 我得和他離婚，我不能繼續過着虛偽的生活。
11 ►EXCITING LIFE 令人興奮的生活◄ [I] to have an exciting life 過有樂趣[意義]的生活：*We're beginning to live at last!* 我們終於開始好好地生活了！

③ BE ALIVE 活着

12 ►BE/STAY ALIVE 活着，生存◄ [I] to be alive or be able to stay alive 活着；生存：*Without light, plants couldn't live.* 沒有陽光，植物就無法生存。| *He is extremely ill and not expected to live.* 他病得很重，看來活不成了。| *The baby only lived a few hours.* 嬰兒只活了幾個小時。| *Females live longer on average than males.* 女人一般來説比男人壽命長。| **give sb six months/a year etc to live** (=expect someone who is ill to only live for six months etc) 預期某病人只能活六個月/一年等 | **live to see/witness sth** (=live long enough to see it) 活着見到某事 *I'm glad she did not live to witness the break-up of her daughter's marriage.* 我很欣慰，她活着時沒有看到女兒婚姻破裂。
13 the best/greatest/worst... that ever lived someone who was better, greater etc at doing something than anyone else in the past or present 迄今為止最好的/最偉大的/最差的〔做某事的人〕：*I think Jimi Hendrix was definitely the greatest guitarist that ever lived.* 我認為吉米·亨德里克斯肯定是迄今為止最偉大的結他演奏家。
14 be living on borrowed time to be still alive after the time that you were expected to die 比預期活得更久

④ SEXUAL RELATIONSHIP 性關係

15 live with/together [I] if two people live together, they live with each other in a sexual relationship without getting married 和…(未婚)同居：*We wanted to live together and have a child.* 我們想同居並生個小孩。| *the man she's been living with for the last four years* 最近四年和她同居的男人
16 live in sin *old-fashioned* to live together and have a sexual relationship without being married【過時】同居；姘居

⑤ LIVE FOR A REASON 為某種理由而活

17 live for sb/sth if you live for someone or something, they are so important to you that they seem to be your main reason for living 為某人/某事物而活：*He lived for his art.* 他為自己的藝術而活着。| *All through the football season, I lived for Saturdays.* 在整個足球賽季，我為星期六而活着。
18 live and breathe sth to enjoy doing something so much that you spend most of your time on it 投身於某事：*Politics is the stuff I live and breathe.* 我投身於政治活動，如魚得水。
19 live for the day when to want something to happen very much 盼望有一天〔某事發生〕：*She lives for the day when she can have an apartment of her own.* 她盼望有一天能有自己的公寓。

⑥ IN YOUR MIND 在心中

20 live in a world of your own/live in a dream world to have strange ideas about life that are not like those of other people 活在自己想像的世界裡/活在夢幻的世界裡
21 live in the past to have old-fashioned ideas and attitudes 生活在過去之中〔觀點和態度過時〕：*You can't go on living in the past.* 你不能繼續生活在過去之中。
22 live in sb's memory/live with sb to continue to exist in someone's memory 活在某人的記憶中：*The expression of terror on my son's face lived with me for years.* 兒子臉上的驚恐表情在我的記憶中留存了好多年。
23 ►IMAGINE STH 想像某事物◄ [I always+adv/prep] to imagine that you are experiencing something 想像正在經歷某事：**[+in/through etc]** *an old actress living in her past glory* 沉醉在昔日光輝中的年邁女演員

⑦ OTHER MEANINGS 其他意思

24 ►STILL HAVE INFLUENCE 仍有影響◄[I] if someone's idea or work lives, it continues to influence people〔某人的觀念和作品〕繼續影響〔人們〕：*Shakespeare's words live with us still.* 莎士比亞的話仍然影響着我們。
25 as long as I live used to emphasize that you will always do or feel something 只要我還活着〔用於強調〕：*I'll never forget it as long as I live.* 只要我還活着，我永遠也不會忘記它。
26 not live sth down if you cannot live down something bad that you have done, people do not forget about it 無法使人忘記〔自己做過的壞事〕：*I was tempted to admit defeat, but I would never have lived it down.* 我很想承認失敗，但是我永遠無法讓人忘記它。
27 you live and learn used to say that you have just heard or learnt something surprising 真是活到老學到老〔用於表示剛得知令人驚訝的事〕
28 live and let live used to say that you should accept other people's behaviour, even if it seems strange 自己活也得讓別人活〔表示對他人奇怪行為的寬容〕
29 you haven't lived used to say that someone's life will be boring if they do not have a particular experience 你白活了〔用於表示某人的生活因未有某種經歷而枯燥乏味〕：*You haven't lived until you've tasted champagne.* 沒有嚐過香檳酒的話，你就算白活了。
30 sb will live to regret it used to say that someone will wish that they had not done something 某人將會對所做的事感到懊悔：*If you marry him, you'll live to regret it.* 如果你和他結婚，你早晚會後悔的。
31 if I live to be 100/1,000 etc used to say that you will never understand something 即使我活到100歲/1,000歲等〔用於表示永遠也不能理解某事〕：*If I live to be a thousand years old, I'll never see why she does these things!* 即使我活到一千歲，我也無法明白她為甚麼做這些事！
32 live to fight/see another day to continue to live or work after a failure or after you have dealt with a difficult situation〔經歷失敗或困難處境後〕繼續生存[工作]下去：*A lot of stores like ours have closed down, but we'll live to see another day.* 像我們這樣的商店很多都倒閉了，但我們繼續經營下去。
33 long live the King/Queen! etc *spoken* used as an expression of loyal support【口】國王/女王萬歲！
34 long live democracy/America/the people etc used to show support for an idea, principle, or nation 民主/美國/人民等萬歲〔對某思想、原則或國家表示支持〕

live in *phr v* [I] if someone who does paid work in a place lives in, they live at that place 住宿在工作場所 — see also 另見 LIVE-IN

live off sth/sb *phr v* [T] to get your income or food from a supply of money or from another person 靠〔某經濟來源或某人〕過活：*Mom used to live off the interest from her savings.* 媽媽過去靠存款的利息過日子。| *Rick disapproves of people who are living off the welfare.* 里

克不贊同靠福利救濟過日子的人。| **live off the land** (=get food from growing vegetables, hunting etc) 靠土地〔種植蔬菜、打獵等〕生存

live on *phr v* [I] to continue to exist 繼續存在着: *Alice's memory will live on.* 大家會懷念愛麗思的。—see also 另見 LIVE[1] (24)

live out *phr v* **1** [I] when someone who does paid work in a place lives out, they do not live in that place 不住在工作場所 **2** [T] **live out sth** to experience or do something that you have planned or hoped for 實現某事〔已計劃或想做的事〕: *The money enabled them to live out their dreams.* 這筆錢可以使他們實現自己的夢想。**3 live out your life in/on/along etc** to continue to live in a particular way or place until you die 以〔某種方式〕/在〔某地方〕終老: *He lived out his life in solitude.* 他在孤獨中度過餘生。

live through sth *phr v* [T] to experience difficult or dangerous conditions 經歷〔艱難或險境〕: *It was hard to describe the nightmare she had lived through.* 她所經歷的恐懼難以描述。

live up to sth *phr v* [T] if something or someone lives up to a standard, reputation, or promise, they do as well as they were expected to, do what they promised etc 符合〔標準〕; 不負〔盛名〕; 履行〔諾言〕: *The bank is insolvent and will be unable to live up to its obligations.* 銀行已經破產, 將無力履行其義務。| **live up to your expectations** *The book certainly lived up to his expectations.* 這本書無疑符合他的期望。

live with sth *phr v* [T] to accept a difficult situation that is likely to continue for a long time 忍受, 容忍〔可能為時長久的困難局面〕: *You have to learn to live with stress.* 你得學會承受壓力。

S3 W3 **live²** /laɪv; laɪv/ *adj*

1 ▶LIVING 活的◀ [only before noun 僅用於名詞前] not dead or artificial; living 活的〔非死的或人造的〕; 有生命的: *They are campaigning against experiments on live animals.* 他們正在開展反對用活的動物做實驗的運動。—compare 比較 DEAD[1] (1)

2 live broadcast/programme etc a programme that is seen or heard on television or radio at the same time as it is being made 〔電視或廣播的〕現場直播[實況轉播]/現場直播的節目等

3 live performance/act/music etc a performance in which the entertainer performs for people who are watching rather than for a film, record etc 〔為觀眾所作的〕現場表演/節目/音樂(會): *Did the introduction of CDs affect the interest in live music?* 雷射唱片流行以後, 有沒有影響大眾對現場音樂表演的興趣? | *Madonna live in concert* 麥當娜現場演唱會 | **live recording** (=a recording made of a live performance) 實況錄製 | **live audience** (=the people who watch a live performance) 現場觀眾 *It's always different singing in front of a live audience.* 在現場觀眾面前演唱總是不一樣的。

4 ▶ELECTRIC 帶電的◀ a wire or equipment that is live has electricity flowing through it 〔電線、設備〕通電的, 帶電的 —see also 另見 LIVE WIRE (2)

5 ▶BULLETS/BOMBS 子彈/炸彈◀ a live bullet, bomb etc still has the power to explode because it has not been used 會爆炸的: *live ammunition* 會爆炸的彈藥

6 live match a match that has not yet been used to produce a flame 未用過的火柴

7 live coals pieces of coal that are burning 正在燃燒的煤

8 live issue/concern an issue that still interests or worries people 當前大家關注的問題

9 ▶COMPUTER 電腦◀ when a computer system is put into live use, it is used in a real situation by ordinary people instead of just being tested by the people who designed it 〔電腦系統〕已投入使用的

10 live yoghurt yoghurt containing BACTERIA that are still alive 含活菌的酸乳酪

11 a real live ... *spoken* an expression used to emphasize that something surprising has been seen or exists, used especially to or by children【口】活生生的..., 真的〔用於強調, 指看到或存在的事物令人驚訝, 尤為兒語〕: *We saw a real live elephant!* 我們看到一頭真的大象!

live³ *adv* **1 broadcast a programme/show/speech etc live** to broadcast something at the same time as it actually happens 現場直播節目/演出/講話等: *We will be broadcasting the program live from Austin.* 我們將從奧斯丁現場直播這個節目。**2 perform live** to perform in front of people who have come to watch, rather than for a film, record etc 〔在觀眾面前〕現場演出[表演]

live·a·ble /ˈlɪvəbl; ˈlɪvəbəl/ *adj* another spelling of LIVABLE livable的另一種拼法

-lived /lɪvd; lɪvd/ *suffix* [in adjectives 構成形容詞] lasting or living for a particular length of time 壽命...的, 生活...的: *Her enthusiasm was short-lived.* (=did not last long) 她的熱情很短暫。| *to come from a long-lived family* 出生於一個長壽的家族

lived-in /ˈ· ·/ *adj* a place that looks lived-in has been used often by people so that it does not seem too new 〔地方看上去像〕有人住過的: **have a lived-in look** *often humorous*【常幽默】*Jared's apartment has that lived-in look.* 賈里德的房子看上去不像簇新的。

live-in /ˈlɪv ɪn; ˈlɪv ɪn/ *adj* [only before noun 僅用於名詞前] **1 live-in maid/nanny etc** a worker who lives in the house where they work 住在雇主家的女傭/保姆等 **2 live-in lover/boyfriend etc** a phrase meaning someone who lives with their sexual partner without being married to them, used especially by people who do not approve of this (未婚)同居的情人/男朋友等〔尤為不贊成同居的人使用〕

live·li·hood /ˈlaɪvlɪˌhud; ˈlaɪvlihʊd/ *n* [C,U] the way you earn money in order to live 生計: *New fishing regulations will threaten our livelihood.* 新的捕魚條例將威脅到我們的生計。

live·long /ˈlɪvˌlɔŋ; ˈlɪvlɒŋ/ *adj AmE old-fashioned*【美, 過時】**all the livelong day** a phrase meaning all day, used when this seems like a long time to you 整整一天〔用於似乎時間很漫長時〕

live·ly /ˈlaɪvlɪ; ˈlaɪvli/ *adj* S3

1 ▶FULL OF ENERGY 充滿活力的◀ someone who is lively has a lot of energy and is very active 充滿活力的, 精力充沛的, 活潑的: *He'd always been a bright and lively child.* 他向來是個聰明活潑的孩子。

2 ▶FULL OF INTEREST 充滿興趣的◀ something that is lively is exciting and involves quick, intelligent thinking 〔某事〕激烈的〔包含敏銳的思考〕, 熱烈的: *That was a pretty lively debate!* 那是一場相當熱烈的辯論。| **a lively interest** (=strong interest) 濃厚的興趣 *Eric has a lively interest in Eastern cuisine.* 艾里克對東方烹飪有着濃厚的興趣。

3 ▶EXCITING 讓人激動的◀ a place or situation that is lively is exciting because a lot of things are happening 〔地方或情況〕激動人心的〔因發生了很多事情〕: *Not exactly a lively vacation, was it?* 假期不很刺激, 是嗎?

4 ▶COLOUR 顏色◀ very bright 鮮豔的: *a dress of lively reds and yellows* 鮮豔的紅黃色連衣裙

5 lively imagination someone with a lively imagination tends to invent stories, descriptions etc that are not true 生動的想像力

6 make things lively (for sb) to make a situation more exciting or more difficult for someone 使〔某人〕感到更激動[困難]: *Our trainer was threatening to make life lively for us if we didn't improve.* 教練威脅我們, 如果我們沒有改進就有我們好受的。

7 Look/step lively! *spoken* used to tell someone to hurry【口】趕快! 走快點! —**liveliness** *n* [U]

liv·en /ˈlaɪvən; ˈlaɪvən/ *v*

liven up *phr v* **1** [I,T] to become more exciting, or to make an event become more exciting (使)活躍起來: *The* *party really livened up when Mattie arrived.* 馬蒂來到後，聚會真的熱鬧了起來。| **liven sth ↔ up** *Why don't we play some games? That'll liven things up!* 我們為甚麼不玩些遊戲？那樣會使氣氛活躍起來！**2** [T] to make something look, taste etc more interesting or colourful 使〔某物〕更好看[更有趣味]: **liven sth ↔ up** *Why not liven up the room with some flowers?* 為甚麼不用一些花把房間點綴得更漂亮呢？**3** [I,T] to become more interested or excited, or to make someone feel like this (使) 變得更有興趣[興奮]: *I'm sure she'll liven up when she sees Malcolm.* 我確信她見到馬爾科姆後會高興的。

liv·er /ˋlɪvɚ; ˈlɪvə/ *n* **1** [C] a large organ in your body which produces BILE (1) and cleans your blood〔人體的〕肝臟 —see picture at 參見 DIGESTIVE SYSTEM 圖 **2** [U] the livers of animals used as food〔供食用的〕動物肝臟 **3 a clean/fast etc liver** someone who lives their life in a morally good, exciting etc way 潔身自好/生活放蕩等的人

live rail /ˌlaɪv ˋrel; ˌlaɪv ˈreɪl/ *n* [C] a thick metal bar along a railway track that supplies electricity to trains〔鐵道上向火車供電的〕電軌

liv·e·ried /ˋlɪvərɪd; ˈlɪvərid/ *adj* wearing LIVERY (1) 穿制服的: *a liveried servant* 穿制服的僕人

liv·er·ish /ˋlɪvərɪʃ; ˈlɪvərɪʃ/ *adj BrE informal* slightly ill, especially after eating or drinking too much【英，非正式】患病的〔尤指暴飲暴食之後〕

liver saus·age /ˈ·· ˌ··/ *n* [U] *BrE* a type of cooked soft SAUSAGE made mainly of LIVER (2)【英】肝泥香腸; liverwurst *AmE*【美】

liv·er·wort /ˋlɪvɚˌwɝt; ˈlɪvəwɜːt/ *n* [C,U] a small flat green plant without flowers that grows in wet places 葉苔

liv·er·wurst /ˋlɪvɚˌwɝst; ˈlɪvəwɜːst/ *n* [U] *AmE* a type of cooked soft SAUSAGE made mainly of LIVER (2)【美】肝泥香腸; liver sausage *BrE*【英】

liv·e·ry /ˋlɪvərɪ; ˈlɪvəri/ *n* **1** [C,U] a type of old-fashioned, expensive-looking uniform for servants〔樣子昂貴的舊式〕僕人制服 **2** [U] *poetic* natural bright colours that cover something【詩】〔覆蓋物體的〕鮮豔的自然色彩 **3** [C,U] *BrE* a set of colours and designs used by a company on its property and vehicles【英】〔公司財產或汽車上的〕標誌性的色調[圖案] —see also 另見 LIVERIED

livery com·pa·ny /ˈ··· ˌ···/ *n* [C] one of the GUILDs (=ancient trade associations) of London〔倫敦的〕同業公會

liv·e·ry·man /ˋlɪvərɪmən; ˈlɪvərimən/ *n plural* **livery·men** /-mən; -mən/ [C] someone who works in a LIVERY COMPANY〔倫敦的〕同業公會會員

livery sta·ble /ˈ··· ˌ··/ *n* [C] a place where people pay to have their horses kept, fed etc or where horses can be hired〔付錢寄養馬匹的〕代養馬房; 馬匹出租處

lives /laɪvz; laɪvz/ the plural of LIFE

live·stock /ˋlaɪvˌstɑk; ˈlaɪvstɒk/ *n* [plural, U] the animals that are kept on a farm 牲畜，家畜

live wire /ˌlaɪv ˋwaɪr; ˌlaɪv ˈwaɪə/ *n* [C] **1** *informal* someone who is very active and has a lot of energy【非正式】活躍分子，精力充沛的人 **2** a wire that has electricity passing through it 載電線，火線

liv·id /ˋlɪvɪd; ˈlɪvɪ̀d/ *adj* **1** extremely angry; FURIOUS 非常憤怒，暴怒的: *Mom will be livid if she finds out.* 媽媽要是發現了，會非常生氣的。**2** a mark on your skin that is livid is dark blue and grey〔皮膚傷痕呈現〕烏青色的: *livid bruises* 烏青色的傷痕 **3** *literary* a face that is livid is very pale【文】〔臉色〕蒼白的 —**lividly** *adv*

L

liv·ing¹ /ˋlɪvɪŋ; ˈlɪvɪŋ/ *adj* **1** alive now 活(着)的: *one of the greatest living composers* 當今最偉大的作曲家之一 **2 living proof** if someone is living proof of a particular fact, they are a good example of how true it is 活證據: *I'm living proof that you don't need a college degree to be successful.* 沒有大學學位也能獲得成功，我就是活證據。**3 in living memory** for as long as anyone can remember 在人們的記憶裡: *the worst storm in living memory* 人們的記憶中最厲害的風暴 **4 in/within living memory** a long time ago but within the lives of people who are still alive〔很久以前，但仍然〕在今人的記憶中: *the worst recession in living memory* 人們的記憶中最嚴重的經濟衰退 **5 living things** anything that lives, such as plants, animals or people 生物 **6 living language** a language that is still spoken today 現在仍使用的語言，活語言

living² *n* **1** [C usually singular 一般用單數] the way that you earn money or the money that you earn 生計; 收入: *It's not a great job, but it's a living.* 這不是一份了不起的工作，卻是生計。| **do sth for a living** (=as your job) 做某事以維持生計 *So what do you do for a living?* 你是幹哪行的？| **earn/make a living** *It's hard to make a decent living as a musician.* 當音樂家想生活過得好是很難的。| **scrape/scratch a living** (=get just enough to eat or live) 勉強為生 —see 見 LIFE (USAGE) **2 the living** all the people who are alive as opposed to dead people 活着的人 **3** [U] the way in which someone lives their life 生活方式: *the stresses of city living* 城市生活的壓力 **4** [C] the position or income of a PARISH priest; BENEFICE 教區牧師的聖職[聖俸] —see also 另見 **cost of living** (COST¹ (1)), **in the land of the living** (LAND¹ (7)), STANDARD OF LIVING 

living death /ˌ·· ˈ·/ *n* [singular] a life that is so unpleasant, it would seem better to be dead 生不如死的生活

living fos·sil /ˌ·· ˈ··/ *n* [C] *technical* an animal or plant of a very ancient type, that has not changed and still exists【術語】活化石

living hell /ˌ·· ˈ·/ *n* [singular] a situation that causes you a lot of suffering for a long time 活地獄〔使人長期受苦的情況〕: *Walter made my life a living hell.* 沃爾特使我受盡了折磨。

living le·gend /ˌ·· ˈ··/ *n* [C] someone who is famous for being extremely good at something〔某方面極為擅長的〕活着的傳奇人物: *John Lee Hooker isn't just a great blues player – he's a living legend.*〔美國歌手、結他手兼作詞家〕約翰·李·胡克不只是偉大的勃魯斯音樂演奏家——他是活着的傳奇人物。

living quar·ters /ˈ·· ˌ··/ *n* [plural] the part of an army or industrial camp etc where the soldiers or workers live and sleep〔軍營或工業區內的〕生活區

living room /ˈ·· ·/ *n* [C] the main room in a house where people relax, watch television etc 起居室，客廳 —compare 比較 DRAWING ROOM, FRONT ROOM, LOUNGE¹ (3), PARLOUR (2)

living stan·dard /ˈ·· ˌ··/ *n* [C usually plural 一般用複數] the level of comfort and wealth that people have; STANDARD OF LIVING 生活水平[水準]: *a decline in the country's living standards* 該國生活水平的下降

living wage /ˌ·· ˈ·/ *n* [singular] wages high enough to allow you to buy the things that you need to live 基本生活工資

living will /ˌ·· ˈ·/ *n* [C] *AmE* a document explaining what medical or legal decisions should be made if you become so ill that you cannot make those decisions yourself【美】活遺囑，生前囑咐〔一種文件，說明當事人病危無法作決定時，應採取哪種醫療或法律決定〕

liz·ard /ˋlɪzɚd; ˈlɪzəd/ *n* [C] a type of REPTILE that has four legs, and a long tail 蜥蜴

lizard 蜥蜴

ll the written abbreviation of 縮寫= 'lines', used in books〔書中的〕行

lla·ma /ˋlɑmə; ˈlɑːmə/ *n* [C] a South American animal with thick woolly hair, rather like a camel without a hump 亞美利加駝，美洲駝

LLB *n* [C] Bachelor of Laws; a first university degree in law 法學士

LLD *n* [C] Doctor of Laws; a DOCTORATE in law 法學博士

LLM *n* [C] Master of Laws; a MASTER's degree in law 法學碩士

lo /lo; ləʊ/ *interjection old use* look; used to tell someone to pay attention to something that is surprising【舊】看哪, 瞧〔用於叫人注意出乎意料的事〕—see also 另見 LO AND BEHOLD

2 3 **load¹** /lod; ləʊd/ *n* [C]

1 ►AMOUNT OF STH 某物的量◄ a large quantity of something that is carried by a vehicle, person etc〔車輛、人等的〕負載物: *Take this load of wood over to the barn.* 把這批木頭搬到倉庫裡去。—see also 另見 **shed its load** (SHED² (8))

2 a load/loads (of sth) *informal especially BrE* a lot of something【非正式, 尤英】很多, 大量 —see graph at 參見 MANY 圖表: *We got a load of complaints about the loud music.* 我們收到對吵鬧的音樂聲的很多投訴。| *Don't worry, there's loads of time.* 不用擔心, 時間很充裕。| **loads to do/see/eat etc** *There was loads to eat at the party.* 聚會上有很多吃的。—see graph at 參見 MANY 圖表

3 truckload/carload etc the biggest amount or number of something that a vehicle can carry 滿滿一卡車/一輛汽車等: *a busload of tourists* 滿滿一輛公共汽車的遊客

4 a load of crap/rubbish/bull etc *spoken especially BrE* used to say that something is complete nonsense or stupid【口, 尤英】十足的廢話[蠢話]: *I never heard such a load of crap in all my life!* 我一生中從未聽到過這種十足的胡言亂語!

5 ►WORK 工作◄ the amount of work that a person or machine has to do〔一個人或一台機器的〕工作量, 負荷: *The computer couldn't handle the load and crashed.* 電腦應付不了負荷而死機。| **a light/heavy load** (=not much work, or a lot of work) 輕鬆的/繁重的工作 *Hans has a heavy teaching load this semester.* 這學期漢斯的教學負擔很重。| **work load** *My work load has doubled since Mandy left.* 自從曼蒂走後, 我的工作量加倍了。

6 a heavy/difficult load to bear a responsibility or worry that is difficult to deal with 沉重的/難以承受的負擔: *Coping with her mother's long illness was a heavy load to bear.* 應付她母親的長期疾病是個難以承受的重擔。—see also 另見 **be a load/weight off your mind** (MIND¹ (15))

7 ►WASHING 洗滌◄ a quantity of clothes etc that are washed together in a washing machine〔洗衣機的一次〕洗衣量: *Do all the whites in one load.* 把所有白色的衣物用洗衣機一起洗。

8 get a load of *spoken* used to tell someone to look at or listen to something surprising or funny【口】看, 聽〔令人驚奇或可笑的事, 用於叫人注意〕: *Get a load of that weird hairdo!* 瞧那稀奇古怪的髮型!

9 ►WEIGHT 重量◄ the amount of weight that the frame of a building or structure can support〔建築物或結構的〕承重量: *a load-bearing wall* 承重牆

10 ►ELECTRICITY 電◄ an amount of electrical power 電荷

load² *v* **1** also 又作 **load up** [I,T] to put a load of something on or into a vehicle 把…裝上[裝進]〔運輸工具〕: *Have you finished loading up?* 你裝完貨了嗎? | **[+with]** *The boat called at Lerwick to load up with fresh vegetables.* 船停靠在勒威克裝新鮮蔬菜。| **load sth** *It took an hour to load the van.* 把貨物裝進運貨車花了一小時。| **load sth into/onto** *Be careful loading that piano into the truck!* 把鋼琴裝上貨車要小心! **2** [T] to put bullets into a gun, a film into a camera etc 給〔槍〕上子彈; 給〔相機〕裝入膠卷: **load sth with** *Did you load it with 200 or 400 film?* 你裝了 200 還是 400 的膠卷? | **load sth into** *Can you load the CD into the player, please?* 請你把雷射唱片放入唱機中好嗎? **3** [T] to put a PROGRAM¹ (1) into a computer 把程式輸入電腦: **load sth into/from** *You have to load it from the A drive.* 你得把程式從A驅動器中輸到電腦裡去。**4 load sb with** to give someone a lot of things to carry 讓某人拿[搬運]〔很多東西〕: *Em always loaded the kids with groceries to carry.* 埃姆總是讓孩子們提着許多雜貨。

load sb/sth down *phr v* [T usually passive 一般用被動態] **1** to give someone more responsibility, work etc than they can deal with 給〔某人〕過重的負擔: *Jane felt loaded down with money worries.* 簡被金錢的煩惱壓得透不過氣來。**2** to make someone carry too many things 使〔某人〕攜帶太多東西: *She staggered home loaded down with shopping bags.* 她拿着大包小包的購物袋, 搖搖晃晃地往家走。

load·ed /ˈlodɪd; ˈləʊdɪd/ *adj*

1 ►VEHICLE 運載工具◄ carrying a load of something 有負載的, 裝着貨的: *a loaded truck* 裝了貨的貨車

2 ►GUN/CAMERA 槍/相機◄ containing bullets, film etc 裝了子彈的; 裝上膠卷的: *a loaded pistol* 上了子彈的手槍

3 ►RICH 富有的◄ [not before noun 不用於名詞前] *informal* very rich【非正式】富有的, 很有錢的: *Giles can afford it – he's loaded.* 賈爾斯花得起這筆錢 — 他有的是錢。

4 ►FULL 充滿的◄ **be loaded with** *informal* to be full of a particular quality, attitude etc, or contain a lot of something, especially something bad【非正式】充斥着〔某素質、態度等〕; 充滿…〔尤指不好的東西〕: *Your paper's loaded with spelling mistakes.* 你的試卷全是拼寫錯誤。| *a voice loaded with menace* 充滿威脅的嗓音

5 ►WORD/STATEMENT 詞/陳述◄ a loaded word, statement etc has more meaning, especially a negative meaning, than you first think〔單詞、陳述等〕有暗含意義的〔尤指負面意思〕: *He 'deserved' it? That's a loaded word.* 這是他"應得"的嗎? 那是話中有話的詞。

6 loaded question a question that is unfair because it makes you answer in a particular way 不公正的問題, 有偏袒的問題〔誘導人以某種方式去回答〕—compare 比較 **leading question** (LEADING¹ (4))

7 ►DRUNK (酒)醉的◄ *informal* very drunk【非正式】酩酊大醉

8 the dice/odds are loaded against sb/sth used to say that someone or something is not likely to succeed or win 敗局已定〔用於表示某人/某事不會成功〕

9 loaded dice DICE¹ (1) that have weights in them so that they always fall with the same side on top 灌鉛骰子, 做了手腳的骰子〔總是擲出某一面〕

load·ing /ˈlodɪŋ; ˈləʊdɪŋ/ *n* [U] an amount added to the cost of an insurance agreement because of special risks, profits etc〔保險協議的〕附加費

load·sa /ˈlodzə; ˈləʊdzə/ *adj spoken* a lot of【口】很多的, 許多的: *He gets to shoot loadsa bad guys and snog the girlies.* 他槍殺許許多多壞蛋, 並贏得妞兒們歡心。

load·star /ˈlodˌstɑr; ˈləʊdstɑː/ *n* [C] another spelling of LODESTAR lodestar 的另一種拼法

load·stone /ˈlodˌston; ˈləʊdstəʊn/ *n* [C] another spelling of LODESTONE lodestone 的另一種拼法

loaf¹ /lof; ləʊf/ *n plural* **loaves** /lovz; ləʊvz/ [C] **1** bread that is shaped and baked in one piece and can be cut into SLICES〔麵包的〕一條: *a loaf of bread* 一條麵包 **2 meat/nut loaf** meat or nuts that have been cut very finely, pressed together, and baked〔切得很細、壓在一起, 然後焙烤的〕肉/果仁糕 **3 use your loaf** *BrE old-fashioned* used to tell someone to be more sensible or think harder【英, 過時】〔告訴某人〕機靈點, 動動腦筋

loaf² *v* [I] *informal* to waste time in a lazy way when you should be working【非正式】虛度光陰; 閒蕩: **loaf around/about** *They spend all day loafing around on street corners.* 他們整天在街角閒蕩。

loaf·er /ˈlofɚ; ˈləʊfə/ *n* [C] **1** a flat leather shoe that does not need to be fastened onto your foot 平跟船鞋; 懶漢鞋 —see picture at 參見 SHOE¹ 圖 **2** someone who loafs around 遊手好閒者

loam /lom; ləʊm/ *n* [U] good quality soil consisting of sand, clay, and decayed plants 沃土, 壤土 —**loamy** *adj*

L

loan¹ /lon; ləʊn/ *n* **1** [C] an amount of money that your borrow from a bank etc〔銀行等的〕借款: **take out a loan** (=borrow money) 借款 | **repay a loan** *We're repaying the loan over a three-year period.* 我們以三年期償還貸款。| **bank loan** (=money lent by a bank) 銀行貸款 | **student loan** (=money lent to students) 學生貸款 **2** [singular] the act of lending something 借出: **[+of]** *Thanks for the loan of your camera.* 謝謝你借相機給我。| **give sb the loan of sth** (=lend someone something) 借某物給某人 **3 on loan** if something such as a painting or book is on loan, someone is borrowing it〔畫或書等〕暫借(的): *The book I wanted was out on loan.* 我要的書借出去了。| *pictures on loan from the Louvre* 從羅浮宮借來的畫

loan² *v* [T] **1** *especially AmE* to lend someone something, especially money【尤美】借給〔某人某物〕〔尤指錢〕: **loan sb sth/loan sth to sb** *Can you loan me $5?* 你能借我5美元嗎? **2** *BrE* to lend something valuable, such as a painting, to an organization【英】把〔貴重物品〕出借〔某機構〕: *The family loaned their collection of paintings for the exhibition.* 這家族把收藏的畫借給了展覽會。—see 見 BORROW (USAGE)

loan cap·i·tal /ˈ· ˌ···/ *n* [U] the part of a company's money that was borrowed to help start it〔幫助公司成立的〕借入資本

lo and be·hold /ˌ· · ·ˈ·/ *interjection humorous* used to make someone pay attention when you are going to mention something surprising that has happened【幽默】瞧, 真怪呀〔用於使人注意將提及的令人驚訝的事〕

loan shark /ˈ· ·/ *n* [C] someone who lends money at very high rates of INTEREST¹ (4) and will often use threats or violence to get the money back 放高利貸者

loan·word /ˈlonˌwɝd; ˈləʊnwɜːd/ *n* [C] a word taken into one language from another 外來語, 借詞 —see also 另見 BORROWING (1)

loath /loθ; ləʊθ/ *adj* **be loath to do sth** *formal* to be unwilling to do something【正式】不願意做某事: *Sarah was loath to tell her mother all that had happened.* 莎拉不願意告訴媽媽所發生的一切。

loathe /loð; ləʊð/ *v* [T not in progressive 不用進行式] to hate someone or something very much 厭惡, 憎恨: *Lucinda loathes spiders.* 露辛達討厭蜘蛛。| **loathe doing sth** *I absolutely loathe travelling.* 我絕對憎惡外出旅行。

loath·ing /ˈloðɪŋ; ˈləʊðɪŋ/ *n* [singular, U] a very strong feeling of hatred 強烈的厭惡[憎恨]: **[+for]** *The more he called me 'Sugar', the more my loathing for him increased.* 他越叫我"寶貝", 我越討厭他。

loath·some /ˈloðsəm; ˈləʊðsəm/ *adj* very unpleasant or cruel; DISGUSTING 令人厭惡[憎恨]的: *How I detest you, you loathsome creature!* 我實在討厭你, 你這可恨的傢伙! —**loathsomeness** *n* [U]

loaves /lovz; ləʊvz/ the plural of LOAF

lob /lɑb; lɒb/ *v* **lobbed, lobbing** [T] **1** *informal* to throw something somewhere, especially over a wall, fence etc【非正式】扔〔尤指越過牆、籬笆等〕: **lob sth into/at/over etc** *The kids were lobbing pine cones into the neighbor's yard.* 孩子們把松果扔進鄰居的院子中。**2** to throw or hit a ball in a slow high curve, especially in a game of tennis or CRICKET (2)〔打網球或板球時〕將〔球〕挑高: *Martinez lobbed the ball high over Graf's head.* 馬天妮絲將球挑過嘉芙的頭頂。—**lob** *n* [C] —see picture on page A22 參見A22頁圖

L

lob·by¹ /ˈlɑbɪ; ˈlɒbi/ *n* [C] **1** a wide passage or large hall just inside the entrance to a public building〔公共場所入口處的〕門廊, 大廳: *a hotel lobby* 旅館大堂 —compare 比較 FOYER (1) **2** a group of people who try to persuade a government that a particular law or situation should be changed〔游說政府更改某項法律或改變某種局面的〕羣眾團體: *The tobacco lobby is trying to change the no smoking laws.* 煙草游說團正企圖更改禁煙法。—see also 另見 LOBBY² **3** an attempt to persuade a government to change a law, make a new law etc〔試圖說服政府更改法律、制定新法律的〕游說: **[+of]** *a mass lobby of Parliament by women's organizations* 婦女團體對議會的大量游說 —see also 另見 LOBBY² **4 a)** a hall in the British Parliament where members of parliament and the public meet〔英國議院中的〕民眾接待廳 **b)** one of the two passages in the British Parliament where members go to vote for or against a BILL¹ (2)〔英國議院中的〕投票走廊〔其一供投贊成票, 另一供投反對票〕

lobby² *v* [I,T] to try to persuade the government or someone with political power that a law or situation should be changed 游說〔政府或政治上的掌權者更改法律或改變局面〕: **[+for/against]** *The group is lobbying for a reduction in defense spending.* 該團體正在游說, 以期削減國防開支。| **lobby sb to do sth** *We've been lobbying our State Representative to support the new health plan.* 我們一直在勸說我們的州議員支持新的保健計劃。—**lobbyist** *n* [C]

lobby sth **through** *phr v* [T] to get a law officially approved by the government by lobbying〔通過游說使政府〕通過〔某法律〕: *After months of debate the bill was finally lobbied through Parliament.* 經過數月的辯論, 議會最終通過了這項法案。

lobe /lob; ləʊb/ *n* [C] **1** the soft piece of flesh at the bottom of your ear; EARLOBE 耳垂 **2** *technical* a round part of an organ in your body, especially in your brain or lungs【術語】〔尤指腦、肺等的〕葉 —**lobed** *adj*

lo·bot·o·my /loˈbɑtəmɪ; ləʊˈbɒtəmi/ *n* [C] a medical operation to remove part of someone's brain in order to make them less violent, rarely done now 葉切斷(術), 腦白質切斷(術)〔過去用來減少暴力行為的手術, 現已罕用〕; LEUCOTOMY *BrE*【英】—**lobotomize** also 又作 **-ise** *BrE*【英】*v* [T]

lob·ster /ˈlɑbstɚ; ˈlɒbstə/ *n* **1** [C] a sea animal with eight legs, a shell, and two large CLAWS 龍蝦 **2** [U] the meat of this animal used for food 龍蝦肉

lobster 龍蝦

claw/pincer 螯, 鉗

lob·ster·pot /ˈlɑbstɚpɑt; ˈlɒbstəpɒt/ *n* [C] a trap shaped like a basket in which lobsters are caught〔誘捕〕龍蝦籠

lo·cal¹ /ˈlokḷ; ˈləʊkəl/ *adj* **1** connected with a particular place or area, especially the place you live in 地方性的, 當[本]地的〔尤指居住地的〕: *the local hospital* 當地醫院 | *members of the local community* 本地社區的成員 **2** *technical* affecting or limited to one part of your body【術語】〔身體上〕局部的: *a local infection* 局部感染 | **local anaesthetic** *The tooth was removed under local anaesthetic.* 在局部麻醉下把牙拔掉。

local² *n* [C] **1** [often plural 常用複數] someone who lives in the place where you are or the place that you are talking about 本地人, 當地居民: *We asked one of the locals to recommend a hotel.* 我們請一位當地人介紹一家旅館。**2** *BrE* a pub near where you live, especially one where you often drink【英】〔尤指經常光顧的〕住處附近的小酒館: *I usually have a pint or two at my local on Friday nights.* 星期五晚上我通常在鄰近的小酒館裡喝上一兩品脫。**3** *AmE* a bus, train etc that stops at all regular stopping places【美】〔每站都停的〕普通公共汽車[列車]〔與快車相對〕**4** *AmE* a branch of a TRADE UNION【美】〔工會的〕地方分會

lo·cal /ˌloˈkæl; ˌləʊˈkæl◂/ *adj* another spelling of LOW-CAL low-cal 的另一種拼法

local ar·e·a net·work /ˌ·· ˌ··· ˈ··/ *n* [C] *technical* LAN【術語】〔電腦〕局部(地區)網絡

local au·thor·i·ty /ˌ·· ·ˈ···/ *n* [C] *BrE* the group of people elected or paid to be the government of a particular area, town, or city in Britain【英】〔英國市、鎮等的〕地方當局: *The local authority are considering his grant application.* 地方當局正在考慮他的補助金申請。

local call /ˈ·· ˌ·/ *n* [C] a telephone call to a place near you that does not cost much money 市內通話

local col·our *BrE*【英】, **local color** *AmE*【美】/ˌ·· ˈ··/ *n* [U] additional details in a story or picture that give you a better idea of what a place is really like〔小說或圖畫中使場面逼真的〕地方色彩, 鄉土氣息: *His description of the smells from the market added a touch of local colour.* 他對菜市場的種種氣味的描述, 使作品添加了一點地方色彩。

local coun·cil /ˌ·· ˈ··/ *n* [C] the group of people responsible for providing houses, schools, parks etc in a small area such as a town or DISTRICT〔負責鎮或行政區的住房、學校、公園等的〕地方議會

lo·cale /loˋkæl; ləʊˈkɑːl/ *n* [C] the place where something happens or where the action takes place in a book or a film〔書或電影中某事發生的〕地點, 現場: *We need a tropical locale for this scene.* 我們需要一個熱帶地方作為這個場景。

local gov·ern·ment /ˌ·· ˈ···/ *n* [C,U] the government of cities, towns etc by elected representatives of the people living in them〔市、鎮等經選舉產生的〕地方政府

local his·to·ry /ˌ·· ˈ···/ *n* [U] the history of a particular area 地方史, 地方誌 —**local historian** /ˌ·· ·ˈ···/ *n* [C]

lo·cal·i·ty /loˋkælətɪ; ləʊˈkæləti/ *n* [C] a small area of a country, city etc 地區: **in the locality** (=near to the place you are talking about) 在這個地區, 在附近 *What kind of leisure facilities are there in the locality?* 附近有哪些休閒設施?

lo·cal·ize also 又作 **-ise** *BrE*【英】/ˋloklˌaɪz; ˈləʊkəlaɪz/ *v* [T] *formal*【正式】**1** to find out exactly where something is 找出…的確切位置: *A mechanic is trying to localize the fault.* 技師正在尋找故障所在。**2** to limit the effect that something has, or the size of area it covers 使〔某物的影響〕限於局部, 限制…的範圍 —**localization** /ˌlokləˋzeʃən; ˌləʊkəlaɪˈzeɪʃən/ *n* [U]

lo·cal·ized also 又作 **-ised** *BrE*【英】/ˋloklˌaɪzd; ˈləʊkəlaɪzd/ *adj formal* a word meaning within one small area, used especially to talk about something unpleasant or unwanted【正式】局部的, 小範圍的〔尤指令人不快或討厭的事物〕: *localized flooding* 局部的洪水泛濫 | *a localized infection* 局部感染

S2 **lo·cal·ly** /ˋloklɪ; ˈləʊkəli/ *adv* **1** near the area where you are or the area you are talking about 在本地, 在當地: *I live locally, so it's easy to get to the office.* 我住在本地, 所以上班很方便。**2** in particular small areas 局部地: *Most of the country will be dry, but there will be some rain locally.* 全國大部分地區天氣乾燥, 但局部地區有雨。

local pa·per /ˌ·· ˈ··/ *n* [C] **1** a newspaper that gives mainly local news〔以刊載當地新聞為主的〕地方報紙 **2** *AmE* a newspaper printed in a town which contains local, national, and international news【美】〔在某城市發行的〕地方報紙〔包括本地、國家和國際新聞〕

local ra·di·o /ˌ·· ˈ···/ *n* [U] a radio service that broadcasts programmes for a particular area of the country 地方廣播電台, 地區廣播

local rag /ˌ·· ˈ·/ *n* [C] *BrE informal* a local newspaper【英, 非正式】地方報紙

local time /ˈ·· ·/ *n* [U] the time of day in a particular part of the world 當地時間: *We'll arrive in Boston at 4:00 local time.* 我們將於當地時間四點到達波士頓。

S3 W3 **lo·cate** /ˋloket; ləʊˈkeɪt/ *v* **1** [T] to find the exact position of something 找出〔某物〕的準確位置: *We couldn't locate the source of the radio signal.* 我們無法確定無線電信號的來源。**2 be located in/by/near etc** to be in a particular position 位於[坐落在]…/…邊上/…附近等: *The business is located right in the center of town.* 商店正好位於市中心。**3** [I always+adv/prep] *AmE* to come to a place and start a business, company etc there【美】將〔公司等〕設立〔在某處〕: **[+in/at etc]** *We are offering incentives for companies to locate in our city.* 我們正在鼓勵企業來本市設立公司。

lo·ca·tion /loˋkeʃən; ləʊˈkeɪʃən/ *n* **1** [C] a particular place or position, especially in relation to other areas, buildings etc〔尤指與其他地區、建築物等有關的〕地點, 位置: *Could you give me your precise location?* 你能給我你的精確位置嗎? —see 見 POSITION¹ (USAGE) **2** [C, U] a place outside or away from a film STUDIO where scenes are filmed〔電影的〕外景拍攝地: *It was hard to find a suitable location for the desert scenes.* 要找到拍攝沙漠鏡頭的合適外景地很困難。| **on location** *Most of the movie was shot on location in Africa.* 這部影片大部分是在非洲的外景地拍攝的。**3** [U] the act of finding the position of something〔某物的〕定位: *The main problem for engineers was the location of underground rivers in the area.* 工程師的主要問題是定位這地區的地下河流。 S3 W2

Frequencies of the nouns **location, place** and **spot** in spoken and written English 名詞 location, place 和 spot 在英語口語和書面語中的使用頻率

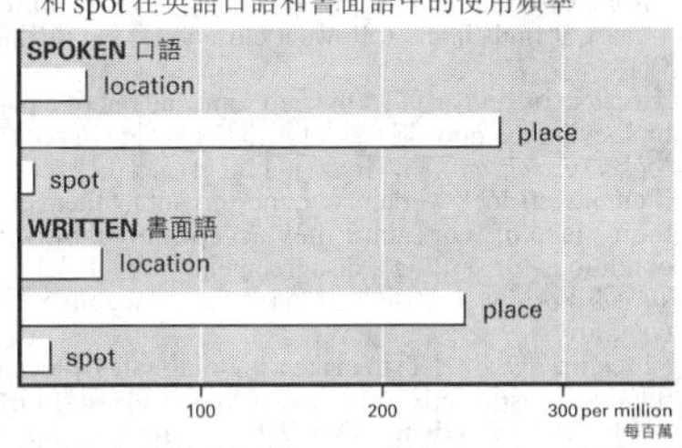

Based on the British National Corpus and the Longman Lancaster Corpus
據英國國家語料庫和朗文蘭卡斯特語料庫

This graph shows that **place** is much more common than **location** or **spot** in both spoken and written English. This is because **place** is the most general of the three words. **Location** is used to mean a particular place or position, especially in relation to other buildings, areas etc. **Spot** is used to mean a pleasant place or area where you spend time or do something.
本圖表顯示, 在英語口語和書面語中 place 的使用頻率遠遠高於 location 或 spot, 因為 place 在這三個詞中是最普通的。location 用於表示某一特定地點或位置, 尤其是和其他建築物和地區等有關。spot 用於表示某人愉快地度日或做事的地方或地區。

loch /lɑk; lɒx/ *n* [C] *ScotE* a lake or a part of the sea partly enclosed by land【蘇格蘭】湖;〔部分伸入陸地的〕海灣: *Loch Ness* 尼斯湖

lo·ci /ˋlosaɪ; ˈləʊsaɪ/ the plural of LOCUS

lock¹ /lɑk; lɒk/ *v* S2 W3

1 ►FASTEN SOMETHING 拴住某物◄ [I,T] to fasten something with a lock or be fastened with a lock 鎖住〔某物〕: *Did you lock the car?* 你把車鎖好了嗎? | *I can't get the door to lock.* 我沒法把門鎖上。

2 ►PUT STH IN A SAFE PLACE 把某物放在安全的地方◄ [T always+adv/ prep] to put something in a safe place and lock the door, lid etc 把〔某物〕鎖藏起來: **lock sth up/away/in etc** *Joe locked the money in the safe.* 喬把錢鎖藏在保險箱內。

3 be locked together/in an embrace if two people are locked together or locked in an embrace, they are holding each other very tightly〔兩個人〕緊緊摟[抱]住: *The fighters were locked together.* 拳擊手揪扭在一起。| *lovers locked in a deep embrace* 緊緊擁抱在一起的情人

4 lock arms to join your arms tightly together with someone else 臂挽着臂: *The police locked arms to form a barrier against the protesters.* 警察們臂挽着臂組成一道阻擋抗議者的壁壘。

5 be locked in battle/combat/dispute etc to be involved in a serious argument, fight etc with someone 捲

L

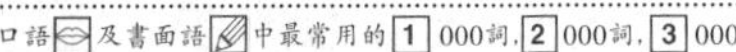

入門爭/戰鬥/爭論之中: *We found ourselves locked in a costly legal battle.* 我們發現捲進了一場代價高昂的訴訟之中。

6 lock horns with sb (over sth) to argue or fight with someone (為某事)與某人爭吵[打架]

7 ►WHEEL/PART OF A MACHINE 輪子/機器的部件◄ [I] to become fixed in one position and impossible to move 卡住〔不能運轉〕: *The wheels suddenly locked.* 輪子突然卡住不動了。—**lockable** *adj*

lock sb/sth **away** *phr v* [T] **1** to put something in a safe place and lock the door, lid etc 把…鎖藏起來: *We locked all our valuables away before we went on vacation.* 我們外出度假之前把所有貴重物品都鎖藏起來了。**2** to put someone in prison 把〔某人〕關進監獄

lock sb **in** *phr v* [T] to prevent someone from leaving a room or building by locking the door 把〔某人〕鎖在〔房間或建築物〕裡面: *Help me, somebody – I'm locked in.* 來人哪, 救救我 — 我被鎖在裡面了。

lock onto sth *phr v* [T] if a MISSILE locks onto a TARGET, it finds it and follows it closely 〔導彈〕鎖定〔目標〕

lock sb **out** *phr v* [T] **1** to keep someone out of a place by locking the door 把〔某人〕鎖[關]在門外: *Oh no, I've locked myself out!* 啊, 不好了, 我把自己關在門外啦! **2** if employers lock workers out, they do not let them enter their place of work until they accept the employers' conditions for settling a disagreement 不讓〔工人〕進廠〔直到爭執按雇主的條件解決時為止〕—see also 另見 LOCKOUT

lock up *phr v* **1** [I,T] to make a building safe by locking the doors, especially at night 〔尤指在夜間〕鎖好〔建築物的〕門: **lock sth up** *Don't forget to lock up the warehouse.* 別忘了鎖倉庫。**2** [T **lock** sth **up**] to put something in a safe place and lock its door, lid etc 把〔某物〕鎖藏起來 **3** [T **lock** sb **up**] *informal* 【非正式】 **a)** to put someone in prison 把〔某人〕關進監獄: *Rapists should be locked up.* 應把強姦犯關進監獄。**b)** *often humorous* to put someone in a hospital for people who are mentally ill 【常幽默】把〔某人〕關進精神病院 **4 be locked up (in sth)** if your money is locked up, you have put it into a business, INVESTMENT etc and cannot easily move it or change it into CASH¹ 把〔錢〕擱死〔在不易兌成現金的地方〕

2 **lock²** *n*

1 ►ON A DOOR 在門上◄ [C] a thing for fastening a door, drawer etc, that you can only open with a key 鎖: *The rear doors are fitted with childproof locks.* 後門都裝上了兒童安全鎖。| **pick a lock** (=use something like a pin to open a lock, especially for an illegal purpose) 捅開鎖〔尤指用於非法目的〕

2 under lock and key a) kept safely in a box, cupboard etc that is locked 安全地鎖藏着: *Dad keeps all his liquor under lock and key.* 爸爸把他所有的酒都鎖藏起來了。**b)** kept in a place such as a prison 被關押着

3 lock, stock, and barrel including every part of something 全部, 完全: *He moved the whole company, lock, stock, and barrel, to Mexico.* 他把整家公司都搬到了墨西哥。

4 ►HAIR 頭髮◄ a) [C] a small BUNCH of the hair on your head 一綹頭髮: *a stray lock of hair* 一綹散亂的頭髮 **b) locks** [plural] *poetic* your hair 【詩】頭髮: *long flowing locks* 飄逸的長髮

5 ►ON A RIVER ETC 在河上等◄ [C] a part of a CANAL (1) or river that is closed off by gates so that the water level can be raised or lowered to move boats up or down a slope 〔運河、河流的〕水閘, 船閘

6 ►IN A FIGHT 在搏鬥中◄ [C] a HOLD² (7) which WRESTLERS use to prevent their opponent from moving 〔摔跤中的〕抱, 夾: *a head lock* 夾頭

7 ►VEHICLE 運載工具◄ [C, U] *especially BrE* the degree to which a vehicle's STEERING WHEEL can be turned in order to turn the vehicle 【尤英】〔汽車方向盤的〕轉動程度: **on full lock** (=turned as far as possible) 最大的轉動程度

8 ►MACHINE 機器◄ [U] the state of a machine when it is stopped in such a way that it cannot be operated 鎖定狀態: *in the lock position* 處在鎖定位置

lock·er /ˈlɑkɚ; ˈlɒkə/ *n* [C] **1** a small cupboard where you leave your outdoor clothes, bags etc while you work or play sports 〔工作或運動時供存放衣物等的〕鎖櫃, 寄物櫃 **2** *AmE* a very cold room used for storing food in a restaurant or factory 【美】〔餐館或工廠用於儲存食物的〕冷藏室: *a meat locker* 肉類冷藏室

locker room /ˈ·· ·/ *n* [C] a room in a sports building, school etc where people change their clothes and leave them in lockers 〔體育館、學校等的〕衣物間; 更衣室

lock·et /ˈlɑkɪt; ˈlɒkɪ̈t/ *n* [C] a piece of jewellery that you wear around your neck on a chain, with a small metal case in which you can put a picture, a piece of hair etc 紀念品飾盒〔懸在項鏈上, 可以存放照片、頭髮等的金屬小盒〕

lock·jaw /ˈlɑkˌdʒɔ; ˈlɒkdʒɔː/ *n* [U] *non technical* TETANUS 【非術語】破傷風

lock keep·er /ˈ· ˌ··/ *n* [C] someone whose job is to open and close the gates of a LOCK² (5) or a CANAL (1) 水閘[閘門]管理員

lock·out /ˈlɑkˌaut; ˈlɒk-aʊt/ *n* [C] a period of time when a company does not allow workers to go back to work, especially in a factory, until they accept its working conditions 閉廠〔公司在工人接受工作條件前不讓其返回工作場所的一段時間〕—see also 另見 **lock out** (LOCK¹), compare 比較 STRIKE² (1)

lock·smith /ˈlɑkˌsmɪθ; ˈlɒkˌsmɪθ/ *n* [C] someone who makes and repairs locks 鎖匠

lock·step /ˈlɑkˌstɛp; ˈlɒkstep/ *n* **in lockstep** *especially AmE* following rules and accepted ideas without thinking 【尤美】因循守舊

lock·up /ˈlɑkˌʌp; ˈlɒk-ʌp/ *n* [C] a small prison where a criminal can be kept for a short time, often in a village or small town 〔尤指鄉鎮上的〕臨時拘留所, 監牢

lock-up gar·age /ˌ· · ˈ··/ *n* [C] *BrE* a garage that you can rent to keep cars, goods etc in 【英】可租用的車庫

lo·co /ˈloko; ˈləʊkəʊ/ *adj AmE informal* crazy 【美, 非正式】發瘋的: **go loco** *That guy's going loco!* 那傢伙在發瘋! —see also 另見 IN LOCO PARENTIS

lo·co·mo·tion /ˌlokəˈmoʃən; ˌləʊkəˈməʊʃən/ *n* [U] *formal or technical* movement or the ability to move 【正式或術語】運動(能力); 移動(能力)

lo·co·mo·tive¹ /ˌlokəˈmotɪv; ˌləʊkəˈməʊtɪv/ *n* [C] *technical or AmE* a railway engine 【術語或美】機車; 火車頭

locomotive² *adj technical* connected with movement 【術語】與運動有關的

lo·co·weed /ˈlokoˌwid; ˈləʊkəʊwiːd/ *n* [C] a plant that grows in America and makes animals ill if they eat it 瘋草〔生長於美洲, 動物食後會得病〕

lo·cum /ˈlokəm; ˈləʊkəm/ *n* [C] *BrE* a doctor or priest who does another doctor's or priest's work while they are on holiday, ill etc 【英】〔醫生或牧師的〕臨時代理人

lo·cus /ˈlokəs; ˈləʊkəs/ *n plural* **loci** /ˈlosaɪ; ˈləʊsaɪ/ [C] **1 locus of** *formal* a place or position where something is particularly known to exist or happen 【正式】〔某事存在或發生的〕地點, 場所: *areas identified as the locus of poverty and deprivation* 被認為是貧窮和匱乏的地區 **2** *technical* the set of all points given by a particular rule in mathematics 【術語】〔數學上的〕軌跡

lo·cust /ˈlokəst; ˈləʊkəst/ *n* [C] an insect that lives mainly in Asia and Africa and flies in a very large group, eating and destroying crops 蝗蟲: *a swarm of locusts* 一大羣蝗蟲

lo·cu·tion /loˈkjuʃən; ləʊˈkjuːʃən/ *n technical* 【術語】 **1** [U] a style of speaking 講話的風格 **2** [C] a phrase, especially one used in a particular area or by a particular group of people 〔某地區或階層使用的〕慣用語; 行話

lode /lod; ləʊd/ *n* [C usually singular 一般用單數] an amount of ORE (=metal in its natural form) 礦藏 —see also 另見 MOTHER LODE

lode·star, loadstar /ˈlodˌstɑr; ˈləʊdstɑː/ *n especially literary* 【尤文】**1** [singular] a principle or fact that guides someone 準則, 指導原則: *the economic lodestar for achieving low interest rates* 實現低利率的經濟準則 **2** the POLE STAR, used as a guide by sailors 北極星

lode·stone, loadstone /ˈlodˌston; ˈləʊdstəʊn/ *n* [C,U] *old use* iron, or a piece of iron that acts as a MAGNET (1) 【舊】天然磁石

lodge[1] /lɑdʒ; lɒdʒ/ *v*

1 ▶STAY SOMEWHERE 暫住在某處◀ [I always+adv/prep] to pay someone rent so you can live in a room in their house 租住, 寄宿, 寄住: **[+at/with etc]** *Paul lodged with a family in Bristol when he first started work.* 保羅剛開始工作時寄住在布里斯托爾的一戶人家裡。

2 lodge a complaint/protest/appeal etc *BrE* to make a formal or official complaint, protest etc 【英】提出控告/抗議/上訴等: *They lodged a complaint against the doctor for negligence.* 他們控告醫生疏忽。

3 ▶BE STUCK 卡住◀ [I always+adv/prep,T usually passive 一般用被動態] to become firmly stuck somewhere, or make something become stuck (使)卡住, (使)固定在…裡: **[+in/down etc]** *The fishbone lodged in her throat.* 魚刺卡在她的喉嚨內。| **be lodged in/down etc** *The bullet was lodged in his spine.* 那顆子彈嵌在他的脊椎骨裡。

4 ▶PUT SB SOMEWHERE 安排某人住在某處◀ [T] to give or find someone a place to stay for a short time, usually for payment 供…寄住; 給…找寄住處〔通常要付錢〕: *a building used to lodge prisoners of war* 一座關押戰俘的建築物 | **lodge sb in/at etc** *The refugees were lodged in old army barracks.* 難民被安置在舊兵營中。

5 ▶IN A SAFE PLACE 在安全的地方◀ [T] *formal* to put something in an official place so that it is safe 【正式】把〔某物〕存放〔在正規的地方〕: **lodge sth with sb** *Be sure to lodge a copy of the contract with your solicitor.* 一定要在你的律師那兒留一份合同副本。

lodge[2] *n* [C] **1** a small house built on the land of a large country house 〔鄉村大宅院中的〕小屋, 側屋 **2** a room for someone whose job is to see who enters a building or around a building 〔建築物的〕門房, 管理員室: *the porter's lodge* 傳達室 **3** a small house in country or mountain areas, used by hunters, skiers (SKI[2]) etc 〔鄉村或山間供獵人、滑雪者等使用的〕小屋, 小舍 **4 a)** an organisation of FREEMASONS 共濟會的分會: *a Masonic lodge* 共濟會的分會 **b)** the building where this group meets 共濟會分會集會處 **5** a BEAVER's home 〔河狸的〕洞穴 **6** *AmE* a hotel in the mountains 【美】山區旅館 **7** *AmE* a WIGWAM 【美】〔印第安人居住的〕棚屋

lodg·er /ˈlɑdʒɚ; ˈlɒdʒə/ *n* [C] *especially BrE* someone who pays rent to live in a house with its owner 【尤英】房客; ROOMER *AmE* 【美】: **take in a lodger** (=start having a paying guest in your home) 收房客

lodg·ing /ˈlɑdʒɪŋ; ˈlɒdʒɪŋ/ *n* [singular, U] **1** a place to stay 寄宿處: **board and lodging** *BrE* 【英】: *It's £70 a week for board and lodging.* 食宿費每週70英鎊。—compare 比較 BOARD[1] (9), ROOM AND BOARD **2 lodgings** *plural* a house where you pay rent to the owner so you can live in one of their rooms 〔出租房間的〕公寓

lodging house /ˈ·· ·/ *n* [C] *BrE* a building where rooms can be rented for a few days or weeks 【英】〔按日或星期出租房間的〕公寓; ROOMING HOUSE *AmE* 【美】

loft[1] /lɔft; lɒft/ *n*

1 ▶ON A FARM 在農場裡◀ [C] a raised area in a BARN used for keeping HAY (1) or other crops 〔穀倉內貯放乾草或其他作物的〕廐樓: *a hayloft* 貯放乾草的廐樓

2 ▶UNDER A ROOF 在屋頂下面◀ [C] *BrE* a room or space under the roof of a building; ATTIC 【英】頂樓; 閣樓

3 ▶TYPE OF ROOM/BUILDING 房間/建築物的樣式◀ [C] *especially AmE* 【尤美】**a)** a room that is on a raised level within another room 〔房間裡的〕閣樓房間 **b)** a building that has this feature 有閣樓的建築物: *a loft apartment* 閣樓式公寓

4 ▶FOR BIRDS 供鳥用的◀ [C] a set of CAGEs used to keep PIGEONs in 鴿舍

5 ▶IN A CHURCH 在教堂裡◀ the place where a church ORGAN (2) is 〔教堂的〕風琴樓: *the organ loft* 風琴樓

loft[2] *v* [T] to hit a ball very high in GOLF or CRICKET 〔高爾夫球或板球中將球〕擊高[吊高]

loft·y /ˈlɔfti; ˈlɒfti/ *adj* **1** seeming to think you are better than other people 高傲的, 傲慢的: *a lofty manner* 傲慢的舉止 **2** lofty ideas, beliefs, attitudes etc are of an unusually high moral quality 〔理想、信仰、態度等〕高尚的, 崇高的: *lofty ideals of equality and social justice* 平等和社會正義的崇高理想 **3** *literary* lofty mountains, buildings etc are very high 【文】〔山、建築物等〕巍峨的, 高聳的 —**loftily** *adv* — **loftiness** *n* [U]

log[1] /lɔg; lɒg/ *n* [C] **1** a thick piece of wood cut from a tree 〔樹上砍下的〕大木頭; 原木, 圓材 **2** an official recorded or written record of something, especially a journey in a ship or plane 航海日誌; 飛行日誌; 航行紀錄 **3** a LOGARITHM 對數 —see also 另見 **it's as easy as falling off a log** (FALL[1] (29)), **sleep like a log/top** (SLEEP[1] (1)) 

log[2] *v* **logged, logging 1** [T] to make an official record of events, facts etc 正式記錄〔事件、事實等〕**2** [T] to travel a particular distance or for a particular length of time, especially in a plane or ship 飛行[航行]〔若干距離或小時〕: *The pilot has logged 1,200 flying hours.* 飛行員已經飛行了1,200小時。**3** [I,T] to cut down trees 砍伐(樹木)

log in/on *phr v* [I] to do the necessary actions on a computer system that will allow you to begin using it 進入電腦系統

log off/out *phr v* [I] to do the actions that are necessary when you finish using a computer system 退出電腦系統

lo·gan·ber·ry /ˈlogənˌbɛrɪ; ˈləʊgənbəri/ *n* [C] a soft dark red fruit similar to a RASPBERRY 羅甘莓〔似懸鉤子的深紅色果子〕—see picture on page A8 參見A8頁圖

log·a·rith·m /ˈlɔgəˌrɪðəm; ˈlɒgərɪðəm/ *n* [C] *technical* a number representing another number in a mathematical system so that complicated multiplying may be done as simple addition; LOG[1] (3) 【術語】〔數學中的〕對數

log book /ˈ· ·/ *n* [C] **1** *BrE* an official document containing details about a vehicle and the name of its owner 【英】車輛登記證 **2** a LOG[1] (2) 航海[飛行]日誌

log cab·in /ˌ· ˈ··/ *n* [C] a small house made of logs (LOG[1] (1)) (原木)小木屋

loge /loʒ; ləʊʒ/ *n* [C] *AmE* a set of seats at the side of the lower BALCONY in a theatre or concert hall 【美】〔劇院或音樂廳的〕樓上前座

log·ger /ˈlɔgɚ; ˈlɒgə/ *n* [C] someone whose job is to cut down trees; LUMBERJACK 伐木工人

log·ger·heads /ˈlɔgɚˌhɛdz; ˈlɒgəhedz/ *n* **be at loggerheads (with sb)** if two people or groups are at loggerheads, they disagree very strongly (與某人)不和, 爭吵: *Clare's at loggerheads with her boss over the new working hours.* 克萊爾在新定的工作時間上和老闆爭吵起來。

log·ging /ˈlɔgɪŋ; ˈlɒgɪŋ/ *n* [U] the work of cutting down trees in a forest 伐木: *the logging industry* 伐木業

lo·gic /ˈlɑdʒɪk; ˈlɒdʒɪk/ *n* **1** [U] the science or study of careful reasoning using formal methods 邏輯學 **2** [U] a set of reasons someone uses in order to reach an opinion 推理方法: *I couldn't follow Pete's logic.* 我不能理解皮特的邏輯。**3** [singular, U] sensible reasons or reasonable thinking 合乎邏輯的道理; 合理的想法: **there is a (certain) logic in/to** *There is a certain logic in bringing Simon with us because he does know the area.* 我們帶西門來是有道理的, 因為他確實熟悉這地方。| **logic behind an idea/statement etc** *I fail to see the logic behind that idea.* 我不理解這想法背後的道理。**4** [U] *tech-*

nical a set of choices that a computer uses to solve a problem【術語】〔電腦的〕邏輯

3 **lo·gic·al** /ˈlɑdʒɪkḷ; ˈlɒdʒɪkəl/ *adj* **1** seeming reasonable and sensible 合情合理的: *It's a logical site for a new supermarket, with the housing development nearby.* 隨着附近住房的發展, 這裡開設新超級市場是合情合理的。| *a logical conclusion* 合理的結論 —opposite 反義詞 ILLOGICAL (1) **2** based on a series of facts, reasons, and ideas that are connected in a correct and intelligent way 合乎邏輯的: *The detective has to discover the murderer by logical deduction.* 偵探必須通過邏輯推理來找出兇手。—**logically** /-kḷɪ; -kli/ *adv* —**logicality** /ˌlɑdʒɪˈkælətɪ; ˌlɒdʒɪˈkælə̇ti/ *n* [U]

lo·gi·cian /loˈdʒɪʃən; ləˈdʒɪʃən/ *n* [C] someone who studies or is skilled in logic 邏輯學家

-logist /lədʒɪst; lədʒə̇st/ *suffix* [in nouns 構成名詞] another form of the suffix -OLOGIST 後綴 -ologist 的另一種拼法

lo·gis·tics /loˈdʒɪstɪks; ləˈdʒɪstɪks/ *n* **1 the logistics of** the practical arrangements that are needed in order to make a plan or activity successful〔使計劃或活動成功的〕統籌安排, 後勤 (工作): *the complex logistics of supplying food to the famine areas* 給饑荒地區提供食物的複雜的後勤工作 **2** [U] the study or skill of moving soldiers, supplying them with food etc 後勤學; 物流學;〔軍隊和食物供給等的〕調度技巧 —**logistic** also 又作 **logistical** *adj* —**logistically** /-kḷɪ; -kli/ *adv*

log·jam /ˈlɔgˌdʒæm; ˈlɒgdʒæm/ *n* [C] **1** a problem or difficult situation that must be dealt with〔必須處理的〕僵局, 困難局面: *There's a logjam of bills before Congress.* 國會面臨處理議案的僵局。**2** a tightly packed mass of floating LOGS on a river〔河道中輸送木材時的〕木材堵塞

LOGO /ˈlogo; ˈləʊgəʊ/ *n* [U] an easy computer language that is often used in schools〔電腦的〕Logo 語言〔常用於學校〕

lo·go /ˈlogo; ˈləʊgəʊ/ *n plural* **logos** [C] a small design that is the official sign of a company or organization〔公司或組織的〕標識, 標誌

log·roll·ing /ˈlɔgˌrolɪŋ; ˈlɒgˌrəʊlɪŋ/ *n* [U] **1** *AmE informal* the practice in the US Congress of helping a member to pass a bill, so that they will do the same for you later【美, 非正式】〔美國國會議員的〕互相贊成票〔以通過彼此支持的法案〕**2** *AmE* the practice of praising or helping someone, so that they will do the same for you later【美】相互吹捧[幫忙] **3** a sport in which two people stand on and roll a log floating on water, each person trying to make the other fall off 水上踩滾木遊戲〔兩人同站在一根漂浮在水面的圓木上, 設法使對手落水〕

-logue also 又作 **-log** *AmE*【美】/lɔg; lɒg/ *suffix* [in nouns 構成名詞] something spoken; talk 言語; 談話: *a monologue* (=speech by one person) 獨白

-logy /lədʒɪ; lədʒi/ *suffix* [in nouns 構成名詞] another form of the suffix -OLOGY 後綴 -ology 的另一種拼法: *genealogy* 系譜 (學)

loin /lɔɪn; lɔɪn/ *n* **1** [C,U] a piece of meat from the lower part of an animal's back〔動物的一塊〕腰肉 **2 loins** [plural] *especially literary*【尤文】**a)** the part of your body below your waist and above your legs 腰部 **b)** the area directly around your sexual organs 下身, 下部 **3 the fruit of your loins** *biblical or humorous* your children【聖經或幽默】兒女 —see also 另見 **gird (up) your loins** (GIRD (1))

loin·cloth /ˈlɔɪnˌklɔθ; ˈlɔɪnklɒθ/ *n* [C] a piece of cloth that men in some hot countries wear around their loins〔熱帶國家男人用以蔽體的〕(纏) 腰布

loi·ter /ˈlɔɪtə; ˈlɔɪtə/ *v* [I] **1** to stand or wait somewhere, especially in a public place, without any clear reason〔尤指在公共場所〕閒逛; 遊蕩: *Watch out for any strangers loitering in residential streets.* 要當心任何在住宅區街上徘徊的陌生人。**2** to move or travel slowly, or to keep stopping when you should keep moving 磨蹭; 走走停停: *Don't loiter on the way home, there's heavy snow forecast.* 別在回家的路上磨蹭, 天氣預報有大雪。—**loiterer** *n* [C]

loi·ter·ing /ˈlɔɪtərɪŋ; ˈlɔɪtərɪŋ/ *AmE*【美】, **loitering with in·tent** /ˌ···· ·ˈ·/ *BrE*【英】*n* [U] *law* the offence of staying in a place for a long time without having any reason to be there, so that it seems as if you are going to do something illegal【法律】伺機作案

loll /lɑl; lɒl/ *v* **1** [I always+adv/prep] to sit or lie in a very lazy and relaxed way 懶洋洋地坐[躺]: **[+around/about/beside etc]** *We spent our vacation lolling around beside the pool.* 我們懶洋洋地在游泳池邊上度假。**2** [I,T] if your head or tongue lolls or if you loll your head, you allow it to hang in a relaxed uncontrolled way (使)〔頭或舌〕垂下

lol·li·pop also 又作 **lollypop** *AmE*【美】/ˈlɑlɪˌpɑp; ˈlɒlipɒp/ *n* [C] **1** *BrE* frozen juice or ICE CREAM on a stick【英】冰棍, 冰棒; POPSICLE *AmE*【美】**2** a hard sweet made of boiled sugar on a stick 棒棒糖

lollipop la·dy /ˈ··· ˌ··/ *n* [C] *BrE* a woman whose job is to help school children cross a road safely【英】〔幫助學生安全地過馬路的〕女交通糾察

lollipop man /ˈ··· ˌ·/ *n* [C] *BrE* a man whose job is to help school children cross a road safely【英】〔幫助學生安全地過馬路的〕男交通糾察

lol·lop /ˈlɑləp; ˈlɒləp/ *v* **[I+around/across/about]** *informal* to run with long awkward steps【非正式】笨拙地大步跑: *Simon's dog came lolloping up the beach.* 西門的狗笨拙地沿着海灘跑。

lol·ly /ˈlɑlɪ; ˈlɒli/ *n BrE informal*【英, 非正式】**1** [C] **a)** frozen juice or ICE CREAM on a stick; LOLLIPOP (1) 冰棍 **b)** a hard sweet made of boiled sugar on a stick; LOLLIPOP (2) 棒棒糖 **2** [U] *old-fashioned* money【過時】錢

lol·ly·pop /ˈlɑlɪˌpɑp; ˈlɒlipɒp/ *n* [C] an American spelling of LOLLIPOP lollipop 的美式拼法

lone /lon; ləʊn/ *adj* [only before noun 僅用於名詞前] *especially literary*【尤文】**1** completely alone, and sometimes seeming sad 孤獨的, 孤單的; 孤寂的: *a lone figure standing at the bus stop* 站在巴士站的孤單身影 —see 見 ALONE (USAGE) **2 lone mother/father/parent** someone who is looking after their children on their own 單身母親/單身父親/單親

lone·ly /ˈlonlɪ; ˈləʊnli/ *adj* **1** unhappy because you are alone and feel that you do not have anyone to talk to 孤單的, 寂寞的: *Don't you get lonely being on your own all day?* 你整天獨自一人不感到寂寞嗎? **2** *especially literary* a place that is lonely is a long way from where people live and very few people go there【尤文】荒涼的, 荒無人煙的: *a lonely beach* 荒涼的海灘 —see also 另見 LONESOME, ALONE (USAGE) —**loneliness** *n* [U] 3

lonely hearts /ˌ·· ˈ·/ *n* **lonely hearts club/page/column** a club or an advertisement page of a newspaper that is used by people who want to meet a friend or a lover 微友[愛侶]俱樂部/專版/專欄

lon·er /ˈlonə; ˈləʊnə/ *n* [C] someone who prefers to be alone or someone who has no friends 喜歡獨處的人; 孤獨的人: *Ken's always been a bit of a loner, even at school.* 肯恩總是有點孤僻, 甚至上學時也是那樣。

lone·some /ˈlonsəm; ˈləʊnsəm/ *adj especially AmE*【尤美】**1** feeling very unhappy because you are alone or have no friends 孤寂的, 孤單的, 孤獨的: *Beth is lonesome without the children.* 孩子們不在身邊, 貝思感到寂寞。**2** a lonesome place is one that is a long way from where people live and very few people go there 荒僻的, 荒無人煙的: *a lonesome spot near the canyon* 靠近峽谷人煙稀少的地方 **3 on/by your lonesome (self)** *informal* alone【非正式】單獨, 獨自: *What are you doing sitting there all on your lonesome?* 你獨自一個坐在那裡幹甚麼?

lone wolf /ˌ· ˈ·/ *n* [C] a loner 喜歡獨處的人; 孤獨的人

long[1] /lɔŋ; lɒŋ/ *adj*

1 ►OBJECT/LINE 物體/線◄ measuring a great length

or a greater length than usual from one end to the other 長的: *Cher used to have really long hair.* 謝爾以前有非常長的頭髮。| *The line to get into the movie was so long we gave up.* 看電影的隊伍排得那麼長, 我們放棄不看了。| *The Aleutian Islands form the longest archipelago in the world.* 阿留申羣島形成了世界上最長的羣島。—opposite 反義詞 SHORT¹ (1) —see picture on page A6 參見A6頁圖

2 ►TIME 時間◄ continuing for a large amount of time 長時間的, 長久的: *I thought the play was a little too long.* 我以為這個劇有點兒太長了。| *recovering from a long illness* 久病復康 | *People who exercise regularly generally live longer, healthier lives.* 經常運動的人一般更長壽, 更健康。| **a long time** *They've been married a long time.* 他們已經結婚很長時間了。| **get longer** *The days are beginning to get longer.* 白天開始變長。| **for the longest time** *AmE spoken* (=for a very long time)【美口】在很長的時間裡 *I thought for the longest time that his name was Don, but it's really Ron.* 長久以來, 我都以為他的名字叫多恩, 但實際上是叫羅恩。—opposite 反義詞 SHORT¹ (4)

3 ►DISTANCE 距離◄ continuing or travelling a great distance from one place to another 長距離的: *a long distance runner* 長跑運動員 | **long walk/flight/drive** *It's a long walk to the shops from here.* 從這裡去商店要走很遠。| **a long way** *We're still a long way from Aberdeen.* 我們到阿伯丁還有很長一段路。—opposite 反義詞 SHORT¹ (4)

4 ►HOW LONG 多長; 多久◄ [usually after noun 一般用於名詞後] having a particular length or continuing for a particular amount of time〔距離或時間〕長的; 長久的: *How long is the concert going to be?* 音樂會要開多久? | **an hour/two metres/three pages etc long** *The room is about 10 metres long and 5 metres wide.* 這房間大約10米長, 5米寬。| *The article should be about 1,500 words long.* 這篇文章應該在1,500字左右。

5 ►BOOKS/NAMES/LISTS ETC 書/名字/清單等◄ books, lists etc that are long contain a lot of pages, details etc 頁數多的; 詳細的: *War and Peace is one of the longest novels I've ever read.*《戰爭與和平》是我看過的最長的小說之一。| *He has a long, unpronounceable last name.* 他的姓很長, 很難唸。—opposite 反義詞 SHORT¹ (16)

6 ►CLOTHING 衣服◄ long dresses, trousers, sleeves etc cover your body to the ANKLEs or wrists〔衣服、褲子、袖子等〕長的: *a long ballgown* 長禮服

7 all day/year/summer etc long during all of the day etc 整個一天/一年/夏天等

8 ►SEEMING TOO LONG 似乎過長的◄ *spoken* seeming to continue for a longer time or distance than is usual, especially because you are bored, tired etc【口】〔因不耐煩、疲倦等而覺得時間或距離〕顯得過長的: *It's been a long week and all I want to do is go home.* 過了漫長的一個星期, 我想做的事就是回家。

9 ►WORK 工作◄ if you work long hours or a long day, you work for more time than is usual 工作時間特別長的: *Doctors often work long hours.* 醫生經常長時間工作。

10 go a long way/have come a long way to be likely to be successful and achieve things, or to have been successful and achieved things 可望成功/大有進展: *Genetic research has come a long way in the last few years.* 基因的研究在最近幾年裡大有進展。

11 go a long way towards doing sth to help greatly in achieving something 對做某事大有幫助: *Your contributions will go a long way towards helping children in need.* 你的捐助對有困難的孩子們大有幫助。

12 a little of sth goes a long way *spoken* used to say you do not need much of something【口】有一些就夠了: *A little ketchup goes a long way.* 有一點番茄醬就美味極了。

13 at long last after a long period of time; finally〔長時間以後〕最終; 終於: *The house sold, at long last, in September.* 那房子終於在九月份賣掉了。

14 long time no see *spoken* used to say hello when you have not seen someone for a long time【口】很久不見〔用於打招呼〕

15 the long and the short of it *spoken* used when you are trying to tell someone something complicated in only a few words【口】長話短說, 總而言之: *Well, the long and the short of it is that we missed the train.* 好吧, 總而言之, 我們錯過了火車。

16 not by a long chalk/shot *informal* not at all or not nearly【非正式】絕對沒有, 遠遠沒有: *Oh, I've not finished yet – no, not by a long chalk.* 哦, 我還沒有完成——不, 還差得很遠。

17 how long is a piece of string? *BrE spoken* used when you think there is no certain answer to a question【英口】很難說: *"How long will it take to finish?" "How long is a piece of string?"* "要花多長時間才能完成?" "很難說。"

18 a long memory an ability to remember things that happened a long time ago 好記性: *Those of you with long memories may recall Cooper's fight with Muhammad Ali.* 你們之中記性好的人可能還記得庫珀和穆罕默德·阿里的拳賽。

19 ►VOWEL 元音◄ a long vowel in a word is pronounced for a longer time than a short vowel with the same sound〔元音〕長的

20 long odds if there are long odds against something happening, it is very unlikely that it will happen 可能性不大

21 long drink a) a large cold drink, containing little or no alcohol, served in a tall glass〔用深口杯盛, 無酒精或低酒精的〕大杯冷飲 **b)** if you take a long drink, you drink a large amount of liquid at one time 痛飲

22 long in the tooth *informal* too old【非正式】太舊了: *Some of our vehicles are getting a bit long in the tooth.* 我們有些汽車有點破舊了。—see also 另見 **as long as your arm** (ARM¹ (11)), **a long face** (FACE¹ (2)), **long/slow haul** (HAUL² (2)), **in the long run** (RUN² (4)), **a long shot** (SHOT¹ (12)), **it's a long story** (STORY (8)), **cut a long story short** (STORY (11)), **in the long/short/medium term** (TERM¹ (10)), **take the long view (of)** (VIEW¹ (10))

long² *adv* 1 1 **1** for a long time 長久地, 長期地: *Have you been waiting long?* 你是否等了很長時間? | *It took me longer than I thought it would to paint the kitchen.* 油漆廚房所花的時間比我所想的要長。| *How long have you lived in New Jersey?* 你在新澤西州住了多久? **2** at a time that is a long time before or after a particular time 很久以前; 很久以後: **long before/after** *This all happened long before you were born.* 這事都發生在你出生前很久的時候。| **long ago/since** *If they'd stayed out of the war it would have been over long ago.* 如果他們不插手的話, 這場戰爭早就結束了。| **sth won't be long** *especially spoken* (=used when something is going to happen soon)【尤口】某事很快會發生 *Dinner won't be long – only five minutes.* 晚餐很快就好了——只需五分鐘。| **sb won't be long** *spoken* (=used to say that someone will be ready, back etc soon)【口】某人馬上就準備好[回來等] *Wait here, I won't be long.* 在這裡等, 我馬上就回來。| **it wasn't long before** (=used when something happens very soon after a particular event) 很快[不久]就... *It wasn't long before we realized Dan had left.* 我們不久便意識到丹恩走了。**3 no longer/not any longer** used when something used to happen in the past but does not happen now 不再: *The extra workers won't be needed any longer.* 不再需要額外的工人。**4 for long** [usually in questions and negatives 一般用於疑問句和否定句] for a long time 長久地, 長期地: *I haven't known them for very long.* 我已經很久沒有聽到他們的消息了。**5 before long** soon 很快, 不久: *It looks like it's going to rain before long.* 看來馬上就要下雨了。**6 as/so long as** used

to say that one thing can happen or be true only if another thing happens or is true 只要, 假如: *You can go out to play as long as you stay in the back yard.* 只要不出後院, 你可以出去玩。**7 so long** *spoken especially AmE* goodbye【口, 尤美】再見

long³ *v* [I] to want something very much, especially when it seems unlikely to happen soon 渴望, 盼望: **long to do/have sth** *I long to see her again.* 我盼望再見到她。| **long for sth** *Patsy longed for some excitement, something new.* 帕齊渴望一些刺激, 一些新東西。| **long for sb to do sth** *I was longing for him to go.* 我渴望他走。| **longed-for** *the birth of a longed-for daughter* 盼望已久的女兒的出生 —see also 另見 LONGING

long⁴ the written abbreviation of 縮寫= LONGITUDE

long-a·wait·ed /ˌ·ˈ··◂/ *adj* [only before noun 僅用於名詞前] a long-awaited event, moment etc is one that you have been expecting for a long time 期待的: *We finally got our long-awaited pay rise.* 我們終於得到了久久盼望的加薪。

long·boat /ˈlɔŋˌbot; ˈlɒŋbəʊt/ *n* [C] a type of big rowing boat used especially for travelling on the sea〔尤用於航海的〕大划艇

long·bow /ˈlɔŋˌbo; ˈlɒŋbəʊ/ *n* [C] a large BOW³ (1) made from a long thin curved piece of wood, used in former times for hunting or fighting〔舊時用於打獵或打仗的〕長弓, 大弓

long-dis·tance /ˌ· ˈ··◂/ *adj* [only before noun 僅用於名詞前] **1 long-distance runner/driver etc** someone who runs, travels etc a long distance 長跑運動員/長途司機等 **2 long-distance call** a telephone call to a place that is far away 長途電話 —**long-distance** *adv*

long di·vi·sion /ˌ· ·ˈ··/ *n* [C,U] a method of dividing one large number by another〔算術的〕長除法

long-drawn-out /ˌ· · ˈ·◂/ *adj* continuing for a longer time than necessary〔時間〕拖長了的, 冗長的: *The official enquiry was a long-drawn-out process.* 官方調查冗長緩慢。

lon·gev·i·ty /lɑnˈdʒɛvətɪ; lɒnˈdʒevə̇ti/ *n* [U] **1** *formal* long life【正式】長壽: *The inhabitants enjoy good health and longevity.* 此地的居民健康長壽。**2** *technical* the length of a person or animal's life【術語】〔人或動物的〕壽命

long·hand /ˈlɔŋˌhænd; ˈlɒŋhænd/ *n* [U] ordinary writing by hand, as opposed to SHORTHAND, TYPING etc 普通書寫〔與速記、打字等相對〕

long-haul /ˈ· ·/ *adj* a long-haul aircraft or flight goes a very long distance without stopping〔飛機〕長途運輸的; 長途飛行的 —compare 比較 SHORT-HAUL —see also 另見 **long/slow haul** (HAUL² (2))

long·horn /ˈlɔŋhɔrn; ˈlɒŋhɔːn/ *n* [C] a cow with long horns, kept for meat〔供食用的〕長角牛

long·house /ˈlɔŋhaus; ˈlɒŋhaʊs/ *n* [C] a kind of house, about a hundred feet long, that was used by some NATIVE AMERICAN tribes 長屋〔一些印第安部落的房子, 約一百英尺長〕

long·ing¹ /ˈlɔŋɪŋ; ˈlɒŋɪŋ/ *n* [singular,U] a strong feeling of wanting something or someone; YEARNING 渴望, 盼望: *an expression of heartfelt longing* 殷切期待的表情 | **[+for]** *a longing for peace* 對和平的渴望

longing² *adj* [only before noun 僅用於名詞前] wanting something very much 渴望的, 盼望的: *a longing glance* 渴望的一瞥 —**longingly** *adv*: *Inez was gazing longingly at him.* 伊內茲以渴望的目光凝視着他。

L

long·ish /ˈlɔŋɪʃ; ˈlɒŋɪʃ/ *adj informal* fairly long【非正式】略長的; 相當長的

lon·gi·tude /ˈlɑndʒəˌtud; ˈlɒndʒə̇tjuːd/ *n* [C,U] a position on the Earth that is measured in degrees east or west of a MERIDIAN (=an imaginary line drawn from the top point of the Earth to the bottom)〔地球的〕經度: *The town is at longitude 21° east.* 這個鎮位於東經21度。—compare 比較 LATITUDE (1) —see picture at 參見 EARTH¹ 圖

lon·gi·tu·di·nal /ˌlɑndʒəˈtudn̩l; lɒndʒə̇ˈtjuːdə̇nəl◂/ *adj* **1** going from top to bottom, not across 縱長的, 縱向的: *longitudinal muscles* 縱向肌 **2** *formal* related to the development of something over a period of time【正式】歷時性的: *longitudinal research on populations* 對人口的縱觀研究 **3** *technical* measured according to longitude【術語】經度的 —**longitudinally** *adv*

long johns /ˈlɔŋ dʒɑnz; ˈlɒŋ dʒɒnz/ *n* [plural] warm underwear with long legs 長內褲

long jump /ˈ· ·/ *n* **the long jump** a sport in which each competitor tries to jump further than anyone else 跳遠 —**long jumper** *n* [C]

long-last·ing /ˌ· ˈ··◂/ *adj* continuing for a long time 持久的: *long-lasting effects* 持久的效果

long-life /ˌ· ˈ·◂/ *adj BrE* long-life milk, batteries etc are treated so that they stay fresh or continue working for a long time【英】〔經過處理的牛奶、電池等〕保鮮期[使用期]長的, 經久耐用的

long-lived /ˌlɔŋ ˈlaɪvd; ˌlɒŋ ˈlɪvd◂/ *adj* living or existing a long time 長壽的; 長期存在的: *He comes from a long-lived family.* 他生在長壽家庭。| *long-lived discontent* 長期存在的不滿 —compare 比較 SHORT-LIVED

long-lost /ˌ· ˈ·◂/ *adj* [only before noun 僅用於名詞前] lost or not seen for a long time 丟失很久的; 長久未見的: *long-lost treasures* 丟失很久的珍寶 | **long-lost relative/uncle/friend etc** *a long-lost cousin* 久未見面的表弟

long-play·ing rec·ord /ˌ· ·· ˈ··/ also 又作 **long-play·er** /ˌ· ˈ··/ *n* [C] an LP 密紋[慢轉]唱片

long-range /ˌ· ˈ·◂/ *adj* [only before noun 僅用於名詞前] **1** a long-range decision, plan etc is about a period far in the future〔決定、計劃等〕長遠的, 長期的: *long-range weather forecast* 遠期天氣預報 **2** a long-range missile, bomb etc is able to hit something that is a long way away〔導彈、炸彈等〕遠程的, 遠距離的

long-run·ning /ˌ· ˈ··◂/ *adj* [only before noun 僅用於名詞前] a long-running battle, show etc has been happening for a long time〔戰鬥、表演等〕持續長時間的: *the long-running dispute over farm subsidies* 對農業津貼曠日持久的爭論

long·ship /ˈlɔŋʃɪp; ˈlɒŋˌʃɪp/ *n* [C] a long narrow open ship used by the Vikings〔北歐海盜使用的〕狹長無蓋戰船

long·shore·man /ˈlɔŋˌʃɔrmən; ˈlɒŋʃɔːmən/ *n* [C] someone whose job is to load and unload ships at a DOCK¹ (1) 碼頭工人; DOCKER *BrE*【英】

long·sight·ed /ˌlɔŋˈsaɪtɪd; ˌlɒŋˈsaɪtə̇d◂/ *adj especially BrE* able to see objects or read things clearly only when they are far from your eyes【尤英】遠視的; FAR-SIGHTED (2) *AmE*【美】—opposite 反義詞 SHORT-SIGHTED (1)

long-stand·ing /ˌ· ˈ··◂/ *adj* having continued or existed for a long time 持續長久的; 長期存在的: **long-standing argument/debate etc** *a long-standing feud between the two families* 兩家的世仇 | **long-standing arrangement/offer/relationship etc** *We have a long-standing tradition of hunting every fall.* 我們有一個長期沿襲的傳統, 每年秋季都去打獵。

long-suf·fer·ing /ˌlɔŋˈsʌfərɪŋ; ˌlɒŋˈsʌfərɪŋ◂/ *adj* patient in spite of problems and other people's annoying behaviour〔長期〕耐心忍受的: *Tom goes out drinking every night, leaving his longsuffering wife to look after the children.* 湯姆每晚都出去喝酒, 讓含辛茹苦的妻子照顧孩子。

long-term /ˌ· ˈ·◂/ *adj* continuing for a long period of time into the future, or connected with what will happen in the distant future 長期的; 有長期打算的: *long-term loans* 長期貸款 | *the long-term implications of the crisis* 這場危機造成的長期影響 —see also 另見 **in the long/short/ medium term** (TERM¹ (10))

long-time /ˌ· ˈ·◂/ *adj* [only before noun 僅用於名詞前] having existed or continued to be a particular thing for a long time 長時間的: *a long-time supporter of civil rights* 始終不渝的民權支持者

long ton /ˌ· ˈ·/ *n technical* a British unit of weight equal to 2,240 pounds【術語】噸, 長噸〔英制重量單位, 等於 2,240 磅〕

lon·gueur /lɔŋˋgɝ; lɒŋˈgɜː◂/ *n* [C usually plural 一般用複數] *literary* a very boring part of a book or period of time【文】〔書〕乏味的部分; 乏味的時期

long va·ca·tion /ˌ· ·ˈ··/ also 又作 **long vac** /ˌ· ˈ·/ *informal*【非正式】—*n* [C] *BrE* the period of three months in the summer when university students have holidays【英】〔大學的〕暑假〔三個月〕; SUMMER VACATION *AmE*【美】

long wave /ˌ· ˈ·◂/ written abbreviation 縮寫為 **LW** *n* [U] radio broadcasting or receiving on waves of 1,000 metres or more in length 長波 —compare 比較 MEDIUM WAVE, SHORT WAVE

long·ways /ˈlɔŋˌwez; ˈlɒŋweɪz/ also 又作 **long·wise** /-waɪz; -waɪz/ *AmE*【美】*adv* in the direction of the longest side; LENGTHWAYS 縱向[長]地

long-wear·ing /ˌlɔŋˈwɛrɪŋ; ˌlɒŋˈweərɪŋ◂/ *adj AmE* long-wearing clothes, shoes etc remain in good condition for a long time even when they are used a lot【美】〔衣服、鞋子等〕耐用的, 耐穿的; HARD-WEARING *BrE*【英】

long-wind·ed /ˈlɔŋˋwɪndɪd; ˌlɒŋˈwɪndɪd◂/ *adj* continuing for too long or using too many words in a way that is boring 冗長乏味的, 絮絮叨叨的: *Bray's explanation was unnecessarily long-winded.* 布雷的解釋不必那麼絮叨。—**longwindedly** *adv* —**longwindedness** *n* [U]

long·wise /ˈlɔŋˌwaɪz; ˈlɒŋwaɪz/ *adv* the usual American form of LONGWAYS; LENGTHWAYS 縱向[長]地〔longways 的一般美式拼法〕

loo /lu; luː/ *n plural* **loos** [C] *BrE informal* a toilet【英, 非正式】衛生間, 洗手間, 廁所

loo·fah, loofa /ˈlufɑ; ˈluːfə/ *n* [C] a rough kind of SPONGE[1] (1), made from the dried inner part of a tropical fruit 絲瓜絡

look up 查找, 查閱

He looked up the word in his dictionary. 他翻詞典查這個詞。

1 1 **look[1]** /luk; lʊk/ *v*

1 ►SEE 看◄ [I] to turn your eyes towards something, so that you can see it 看, 瞧, 望: *Sorry, I didn't see – I wasn't looking.* 對不起, 我沒有看見 — 我沒在看。| *If you look carefully you can see that the painting represents a naked man.* 如果你仔細看, 你會看出這幅畫畫的是一個裸體男子。| **[+at]** *"It's time we left," Ian said, looking at his watch.* "我們該走了。"伊恩看了看錶說。| *Look at me when I'm talking to you!* 我和你說話時, 要看着我! | **[+away/over/down etc]** *Dad looked up from his paper and smiled.* 爸爸從報紙上抬起頭來笑了笑。| *I saw you, I was looking through the window.* 我看到你了, 我正望向窗外呢。—see 見 GAZE[1] (USAGE)

2 ►SEARCH 尋找◄ [I] to try and find something using your eyes〔用眼睛〕尋找: *We looked everywhere but we couldn't find it.* 我們到處都找遍了, 但沒有找到。| **look in/under/between etc** *Try looking under the bed.* 試着在牀底下找一找。

3 ►SEEM 看似◄ [linking verb 連繫動詞] to seem to be something, especially by having a particular appearance 看上去, 看起來: *How do I look in this dress?* 我穿這件連衣裙看起來怎樣? | **look like** *The intruder was holding what looked like a shotgun.* 闖入者手裡握着看似獵槍一樣的東西。| **look as if** *You look as if you haven't slept all night.* 你看上去似乎整夜沒有睡覺。| **it looks as if** (=seems likely) 好像是 *The cause of death seems clear – it looks as if he was poisoned.* 死因似乎很清楚 — 他好像是中毒。| **look good/impressive etc** *The plan looks good at the moment, but none of the details have been thought of.* 計劃此刻看來很好, 但細節問題都沒有考慮過。| **look happy/pale/tired etc** *I thought Reg was looking very tired.* 我覺得雷格看上去很疲憊。

4 be looking to do sth *informal* to be planning or expecting to do something【非正式】正打算[期待]做某事: *We're looking to buy a new car early next year.* 我們正打算明年初買一輛新轎車。

5 look daggers at *informal* to look at someone with a very angry expression on your face【非正式】怒視〔某人〕

6 look sb up and down to look at someone examining them carefully from their head to their feet, as if you are judging their appearance 上下打量某人

7 look sb in the eye/face to look directly at someone when you are speaking to them, especially to show that you are not afraid of them or that you are telling the truth 正眼看某人〔尤表示無畏或真誠〕: *Owen was burning with humiliation. He dared not look his father in the eye.* 歐文羞愧得無地自容, 不敢正眼看父親。

8 look down your nose at *informal* to behave as if you think that someone or something is not good enough for you【非正式】看不起, 輕視, 對…不屑一顧: *He looks down his nose at anyone or anything foreign.* 他看不起外國人或洋東西。

9 ►FACE A DIRECTION 朝着某方向◄ if a building looks in a particular direction, it faces that direction〔建築物〕面向, 朝向: *The cabin looks east, so we get the sun first thing in the morning.* 小屋朝東, 所以我們早上第一眼看到的是太陽。

10 look before you leap used to say that it is wise to think about possible dangers or difficulties before doing something 三思而後行

Frequencies of the verb **look** in spoken and written English 動詞 look 在英語口語和書面語中的使用頻率

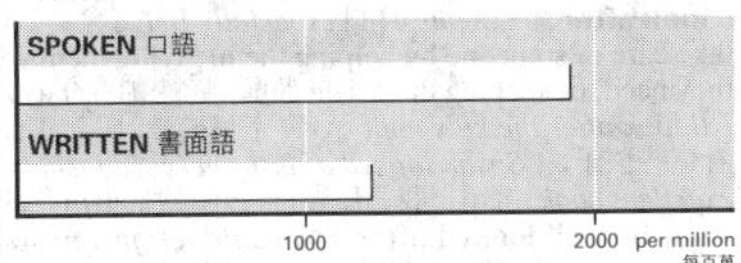

Based on the British National Corpus and the Longman Lancaster Corpus 據英國國家語料庫和朗文蘭卡斯特語料庫

This graph shows that the verb **look** is much more common in spoken English than in written English. This is because it has special uses in spoken English and is used in a lot of common spoken phrases. 本圖表顯示, 動詞 look 在英語口語中的使用頻率遠遠高於書面語, 因為它在口語中有特殊的用法並用於許多常見的口語片語中。

look (*v*) **SPOKEN USES AND PHRASES**
含 look 的口語用法和片語

11 look a) used to tell someone to look at something that you think is interesting, surprising etc 瞧, 當心, 注意, 留神〔用於讓某人注意有趣、驚訝的事等〕: *Look! There's a fox!* 瞧, 有一隻狐狸! **b)** used to get someone's attention so that you can tell them something 瞧, 注意〔用於讓人注意接着要說的事〕: *Look. Why don't you think about it and give me your*

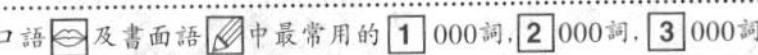

answer tomorrow? 瞧, 你為甚麼不考慮一下此事, 明天給我答覆呢? | *Look, I've had enough of this. I'm going home.* 瞧, 這我已經受夠了, 我要回家了。**12 it looks like/it looks as if** used to say that something seems to be likely or true 看起來好像: *There are no buses so it looks like we'll be walking home.* 沒有公共汽車了, 看來我們要走路回家了。**13 look out!** used to warn someone that they are in danger 注意! 當心!: *Look out! There's a car coming.* 當心! 一輛汽車開過來了。**14 Look at that!** used to tell someone to look at something that you think is interesting, bad etc 瞧瞧那!: *Look at that! What a horrible mess!* 瞧瞧那! 簡直是一團糟! **15 Look who's here!** used when someone arrives unexpectedly 看誰來了!: *Well, look who's here! It's Jill and Paul!* 哎, 看誰來了! 是吉爾和保羅! **16 don't look now** used when you see someone you want to avoid 別看他: *Oh no! Don't look now but here comes Tony.* 哦不! 真是冤家路窄, 東尼來了。**17 look what you're doing/look where you're going etc** used to tell someone to be careful 瞧你在幹甚麼/瞧你往哪兒走〔用於告訴某人要小心〕: *Look where you're putting your feet, there's mud all over the carpet.* 瞧你腳踩過的地方, 地毯上到處都是泥巴。**18 not be looking yourself** to appear tired, unhappy, ill etc, when you are not usually 看上去不是某人平時的狀態〔顯得疲倦、不快、滿面病容等〕: *She should take a break – she hasn't been looking herself lately.* 她應該休息一下 —— 最近她看上去不像平時那樣健康。**19 look what you've done!** used to angrily tell someone to look at the result of a mistake they have made or something bad they have done 瞧你幹了些甚麼!: *Look what you've done – my jacket's ruined!* 瞧你幹的事 —— 我的短上衣給毀了! **20 look here** *old-fashioned* used to get someone's attention in order to tell them something, especially when you are annoyed with them【過時】聽着〔尤用於生某人氣時, 讓人注意要説的話〕: *Look here, you can't say things like that to me!* 聽着, 你不能這樣跟我説話! **21 (I'm) just looking** used when you are in a shop, to say that you are only looking at things, but do not intend to buy anything now (我) 只是看看〔不打算現在就買〕: *"Can I help you?" "No, thank you. I'm just looking."* "你要買甚麼嗎?" "不, 謝謝。我只是看看。"

look after sb/sth *phr v* [T] *especially BrE*【尤英】**1** to take care of someone by helping them, giving them what they need, or keeping them safe 照顧, 照料: *Don't worry, I'll look after the kids tomorrow.* 不用擔心, 明天我會照看這些孩子。| *Susan looked after us very well, she's an excellent cook.* 蘇珊把我們照顧得很好, 她是很出色的廚師。| **be well looked after** *You could tell just by looking at the horse that it had been well looked after.* 你只要看一下這匹馬就會知道牠被照料得很好。**2** to be responsible for dealing with something 負責處理: *I'm leaving you here to look after the business until I get back.* 在我回來之前, 我讓你料理生意。**3 look after yourself** *spoken especially BrE* used when you are saying goodbye to someone in a friendly way【口, 尤英】好好照顧自己〔友好的離別用語〕**4 be able to look after yourself** to not need anyone else to take care of you 能照顧好自己: *Don't worry about Maisie – she can look after herself.* 不用擔心梅西 —— 她能照顧好自己。

look ahead *phr v* [I] to plan future situations, events etc, or to think about the future 向前看, 作未來的打算, 考慮將來: *Looking ahead, we must expect radical changes to be made in our system of government.* 展望未來, 我們確信政體將作徹底改革。

look around/round *BrE*【英】*phr v* **1** [I] to search 尋找: **[+for]** *Jason's going to start looking around for a new job.* 賈森正打算開始找新的工作。**2** [I,T] to look at what is in a place such as a building, shop, town etc, especially when you are walking 參觀, 邊走邊看: *Do we have to pay to look around the castle?* 我們參觀城堡要付錢嗎? | *Let's look round the shops.* 我們一道去逛逛商店吧。

look at sb/sth *phr v* [T] **1** to turn your eyes towards something, so that you can see it 看〔某物或某人〕: *The twins looked at each other and smiled.* 這對雙胞胎相視而笑。**2** to read something quickly, but not thoroughly, in order to form an opinion of it 泛泛地閱讀: *I really can't comment on the report – you see, I've not had time to look at it yet.* 我真的無法評論這報告 —— 你瞧, 我還沒有時間看一下呢。**3** if someone with a special skill, such as a doctor, looks at something that is damaged or broken, they examine it and try to find out what is wrong with it〔醫生等〕檢查, 察看: *You should get the doctor to look at that cut.* 你應該找醫生檢查一下那傷口。| *Can you look at my car? There's a strange noise coming from the front wheel.* 你能檢查一下我的汽車嗎? 前輪發出怪怪的噪音。**4** to study and consider something, especially in order to decide what to do 仔細地研究[考慮]〔尤指要決定做甚麼〕: *We need to look very carefully at ways of improving our efficiency.* 我們需要仔細研究提升效率的方法。**5 look at ...!** *spoken* used when you are talking about something as an example of a situation【口】看看...!〔用於指視某物為榜樣或引以為戒〕: *Look at Mrs Godfrey, smoking killed her!* 瞧瞧戈弗雷夫人, 抽煙把她的命都送掉了! **6** to think about something in a particular way〔以某種方法〕思考: *I'd like to be friends again, but Richard doesn't look at it that way.* 我願意重新成為朋友, 可是理查德不這麼想。**7 not much to look at** *informal* if someone is not much to look at, they are not attractive【非正式】相貌不好看[不吸引人]

look back *phr v* [I] **1** to think about something that happened in the past 回憶起, 回顧: **[+on/to]** *When I look back on those days I realize I was desperately unhappy.* 當我回想起那些日子, 我認為我痛苦透了。| **looking back on it** *informal*【非正式】*Looking back on it, I still can't figure out what went wrong.* 回顧過去的事, 我仍找不到甚麼地方出錯了。**2 never look back** to become more and more successful, especially after a particular event〔尤指在某事之後〕越來越成功: *After winning the scholarship he never looked back.* 贏得獎學金以後, 他便一帆風順。

look down on sb/sth *phr v* [T] to think that you are better than someone else, for example because you are more successful, or of a higher social class than they are 輕視, 瞧不起: *Mr Garcia looks down on anyone who hasn't had a college education.* 加西亞先生看不起任何未受過大學教育的人。

look for sb/sth *phr v* [T] **1** to try to find something that you have lost, or someone who is not where they should be 尋找: *I'm looking for Steve – have you seen him?* 我在找史提夫 —— 你見過他嗎? | *Detectives are still looking for the prisoner who escaped three days ago.* 偵探們仍在找三天前越獄的犯人。—see graph at 參見 SEARCH² 圖表 **2 be looking for** to be trying to find a particular kind of thing or person that you need or want 正設法尋找〔所需的某物或某人〕: *I'm sorry, we're really looking for someone with no family commitments.* 對不起, 我們其實在尋找沒有家累的人。| **be what/who you are looking for** *Salubrious! That's just the word I was looking for.* 有益健康的! 那正是我在找的字眼。**3 be looking for trouble** *informal* to be behaving in a way that makes it likely that problems will happen【非正式】在自找麻煩: *You're looking for trouble if you say things like that to me!* 你要是那樣對我説話, 你是在自找麻煩!

look forward to *phr v* [T] to be excited and pleased about something that is going to happen〔興奮地〕期待, 盼望: *I'm really looking forward to our vacation.* 我熱切期待着我們假期的到來。| **look forward to doing sth** *My mother says she's looking forward to meeting you.*

我母親說她盼望着與你見面。—see 見 WAIT (USAGE)

look in *phr v* [I] *informal* to make a short visit to someone, while you are going somewhere else, especially if they are ill or need help【非正式】探望, 作短暫訪問〔尤在某人生病或需要幫忙時〕: **[+on]** *I promised to look in on Dad and see if he's feeling any better.* 我答應去探望爸爸, 看他是否好一點了。

look into sth *phr v* [T] to try to find out the truth about a problem, crime etc in order to solve it 調查〔問題、罪行等〕: *Police are looking into the disappearance of two children.* 警察正在調查兩個孩子失蹤的事。

look on *phr v* **1** [I] to watch something happening, without being involved in it or trying to stop it 旁觀: *Only one man tried to help us, the rest just looked on in silence.* 只有一個人設法幫助我們, 其餘的人都只是袖手旁觀。**2** also 又作 **look upon** [T **look on** sb/sth] to consider something in a particular way, or as a particular thing 看作, 視為: **[+as]** *I look on him as a good friend.* 我視他為好朋友。| **[+with]** *I look upon all my nephews and nieces with equal affection.* 我對我的姪兒姪女都一樣疼愛。

look sth ↔ **out** *phr v* [T] to search for and find a particular thing amongst your possessions〔從自己的東西中〕找出: *I'll look out some of my old books for you to read.* 我將從我的舊書中找幾本給你看。

look out for sth *phr v* [T] **1** to pay attention to what is happening around you, so that you will notice a particular person or thing if you see them 注意察看〔周圍情況, 以便找到〕: **[+for]** *Look out for your Aunt while you're at the station.* 你在車站的時候, 留神尋找你的姨媽。| *He's looking out for a nice apartment downtown.* 他正在留意尋找一套位於市中心的舒適公寓。**2 look out for yourself/for number one** to think only about what will bring you an advantage, and not think about other people 只從個人利益考慮〔不管他人〕

look sth/sb ↔ **over** *phr v* [T] to examine something quickly, without paying much attention to detail 迅速地檢查, 瀏覽: *Do you have a few minutes to look these samples over?* 你有沒有幾分鐘的時間很快地看看這些樣品? —see also 另見 OVERLOOK

look round *phr v* [I,T] *especially BrE* to LOOK AROUND【尤英】到處看看

look through sb/sth *phr v* [T] **1** to look for something among a pile of papers, in a drawer, in someone's pockets etc 翻閱, 翻找: *I've looked through all my papers but I still can't find the contract.* 我翻閱了所有文件, 但依然沒有找到那份合同。**2** to not notice or pretend not to notice someone you know, even though you see them (假裝) 沒有注意到: **look straight/right through sb** *I saw Fiona in the street yesterday and she looked straight through me.* 昨天我在街上看到菲安娜, 而她裝着沒有看到我。

look to sb/sth *phr v* [T] **1** to depend on someone to provide help, advice etc 指望, 依靠: **[+for]** *We look to you for support.* 我們指望得到你的支持。| **look to sb to do sth** *They're looking to the new manager to make the company profitable.* 他們指望新經理使公司贏利。**2** to pay attention to something, especially in order to improve it 注意〔改進等〕: *We must look to ways of encouraging new ideas.* 我們必須想方設法鼓勵新思維。

look up *phr v* **1** [I] if a situation is looking up, it is improving〔形勢〕好轉, 改善: **things are looking up** *Now the summer's here things are looking up!* 夏天到了, 情況正在好轉! **2** [T **look** sth ↔ **up**] if you look up information in a book, on a computer etc, you try to find a particular bit of information there〔在書、電腦中〕查找, 查閱: *Look up the word in the dictionary.* 翻翻辭典查一下這個詞。| *I'll just look up the train times.* 我將查一下火車時刻表。**3** [T **look** sb ↔ **up**] to visit someone you know, especially when you are in the place where they live for a different reason 看望, 拜訪: *Don't forget to look me up when you come to Atlanta.* 你來亞特蘭大時, 別忘了來看看我。

look up to sb *phr v* [T] **1** to admire or respect someone 仰慕; 尊敬〔某人〕: *I've always looked up to Bill for his courage and determination.* 我一直很敬重比爾, 他既勇敢又果斷。

look² *n* S1 W1

1 ►LOOKING AT STH 看某物◄ [C usually singular 一般用單數] an act of looking at something 看, 瞧: **have/take a look at** *Let me have a look at that – I think it's mine.* 讓我看一下那個東西 —— 我想它是我的。| **have a good/close look** (=look carefully) 仔細地看, 細心看 *If you have a good look you can just see the lighthouse.* 如果你仔細看, 剛好能看得見燈塔。| **take one look** *I took one look at the coat and then decided it wasn't worth £50.* 我看了看那件外套後, 確定它不值50英鎊。—see 見 GLANCE¹ (USAGE) | **have/take a look around** also 又作 **have/take a look round** *BrE* (=look at all the things in a particular place)【英】〔在某處〕四下察看 *I have a special interest in old houses. Do you mind if I take a look around?* 我對老房子特別感興趣, 我四下看看你介意嗎?

2 ►EXPRESSION 表情◄ [C] an expression that you make with your eyes or face, especially to show someone that you are angry, or that you do not like them 眼色; 神色, 面部表情〔尤指向某人表示憤怒或厭惡〕: **give sb a look** *Mike gave him such a severe look he didn't dare argue.* 邁克以他如此嚴厲的眼光看他, 他不敢爭論了。| **dirty look** (=unfriendly look) 不友好的表情 *Why has Jake been giving me dirty looks all morning?* 為甚麼傑克整個早上都沒有給我好臉色看?

3 ►APPEARANCE 外表◄ [C usually singular 一般用單數] the appearance of something or someone 外觀, 外表: *The whole area has a very seedy look to it.* 整個地區看上去很破舊。| *Mr Flynn had a tired, ill look in his eyes.* 弗林先生的眼中顯出倦意和病態。| **by the look(s) of it/him** (=it seems that) 從外表看, 看樣子 *The doctor's back from holiday by the looks of it.* 看樣子醫生是度假回來。| **not like the look of** (=think that something bad has happened or will happen because of something's appearance) 看來已[會]出問題 *We should turn back now, it's getting dark and I don't like the look of those rain clouds.* 我們現在應該回去, 天越來越黑, 雨雲密佈, 看來要下雨。

4 ►SB'S BEAUTY 某人的美貌◄ looks [plural] someone's physical attractiveness 吸引人的外貌: *Fiona's got everything – looks, money and youth.* 菲安娜甚麼都有了 —— 美貌、金錢和青春。| **lose your looks** (=become less attractive) 容顏衰老 *When she lost her looks she found it difficult to get an acting part.* 當她容顏衰老後, 她覺得很難找到演戲的角色。| **good looks** (=attractive appearance) 美貌 *You get your good looks from your mother.* 你的美貌是你媽媽遺傳給你的。

5 ►FASHION 時尚◄ [singular] a fashionable style in clothes, hair, furniture etc〔服裝、頭髮、家具等的〕時髦樣式[款式, 風格]: *The hippy look is back again.* 嬉皮士風格復甦了。

look·a·like /ˈlʊkəˌlaɪk; ˈlʊkəlaɪk/ *n* [C] *informal* someone who looks very similar to someone who is famous【非正式】長相極像名人的人: *a Marilyn Monroe lookalike* 一個長得酷似瑪麗蓮·夢露的人

look·er /ˈlʊkə; ˈlʊkə/ *n* [singular] *informal* someone who is attractive, usually a woman【非正式】美貌迷人者〔通常指女人〕: *She's a real looker!* 她真是個美人!

looker-on /ˌ·· ˈ·/ *n plural* **lookers-on** [C] someone who watches something happening without taking part in it; ONLOOKER 旁觀者

look-in /ˈ· ·/ *n* [singular] *informal*【非正式】**1 get/have a look-in** to have a chance to take part in or succeed in something 有參與[成功]的機會: *Their team was so good that we barely got a look-in.* 他們的隊這麼棒, 我們簡直毫無希望。**2** a short visit 短暫的探訪 —see also 另見 **look in** (LOOK¹)

look·ing glass /'·· ·/ *n* [C] *old-fashioned* a MIRROR[1] (1)【過時】鏡子

look·out /'lʊk,aut; 'lʊk-aʊt/ *n*

1 be on the lookout for to watch a place or situation continuously in order to find something you want or to be ready for problems or opportunities 監視, 留神觀察: *Police were on the lookout for anyone behaving suspiciously.* 警察隨時注意可疑的人。| *We're always on the lookout for new business opportunities.* 我們隨時留意新的商機。

2 keep a lookout to keep watching carefully for something or someone, especially for danger 密切注視〔尤指危險〕: **keep a sharp/special lookout** *When you're driving keep a sharp lookout for cyclists.* 駕駛時要特別注意騎腳踏車的人。

3 ►PERSON 人◄ [C] someone whose duty is to watch carefully for something, especially danger 監視者, 守望者: *A lookout reported an enemy plane approaching.* 監視哨報告説一架敵機正在飛近。

4 ►PLACE 地方◄ [C] a place for a lookout to watch from 哨所, 瞭望台: *a coastguard lookout on the clifftop* 海邊懸崖頂上的哨所

5 it's your/their own lookout *BrE spoken* used to say that what someone has chosen to do is their own problem or risk, and no one else's【英口】那是你們/他們自己的事〔與別人不相干〕: *If he wants to ruin his health with all these drugs, that's his own lookout.* 如果他要用所有這些毒品毀掉自己的健康, 那是他自己的事。

6 be a poor/bad lookout for sb *BrE spoken* used to say that something bad or unsatisfactory is likely to happen【英口】對某人不是件好事, 事情不妙: *It'll be a poor lookout for James if she finds that letter.* 如果她發現那封信, 詹姆斯就慘了。

look-see /'· ·/ *n* [C] *AmE informal* a quick look at something【美, 非正式】一瞥: **have a look-see** *Can you wait a minute? I just want to have a look-see.* 你能否等一下? 我只想去看一眼。

loom[1] /lum; lu:m/ *n* [C] a frame or machine on which thread is woven into cloth 織布機

loom[2] *v* [I] **1** [always+adv/prep] to appear as a large, unclear shape, especially in a threatening way〔尤指陰森森地〕隱約出現[聳現]: **[+up/out/ahead etc]** *A tall figure loomed up out of the mist.* 一個高大的人影從霧中隱隱出現。**2** if a problem or difficulty looms, it is likely to happen very soon〔問題或困難〕逼近, 臨近: *I must start revising – final exams are looming.* 我必須開始溫習功課了 —— 期末考試正逐漸逼近。**3 loom large** to seem important, worrying, and difficult to avoid 顯得重要[令人擔憂, 無法迴避]: *Fear of failure loomed large in his mind.* 失敗的恐懼沉重地壓在他的心頭。

loon /lun; lu:n/ *n* [C] **1** a large North American bird that eats fish and that makes a long wild sound〔北美〕潛鳥 **2** a silly or strange person 傻子; 怪人 —see also 另見 **crazy as a loon** (CRAZY[1] (7))

loon·y /'lunɪ; 'lu:ni/ *n* [C] *informal* someone who is crazy or strange【非正式】瘋子; 怪人: *Her brother's a complete loony.* 她的弟弟是個十足的瘋子。—**loony** *adj*: *loony ideas* 瘋狂的念頭

loony bin /'·· ·/ *n* [C] *humorous* a hospital for people who are mentally ill【幽默】瘋人院, 精神病院

loony tune /'·· ·/ *n* [C] *AmE* a loony【美】瘋子; 怪人

loop[1] /lup; lu:p/ *n* [C]

1 ►SHAPE OR LINE 形狀或線條◄ a shape like a curve or a circle made by a line curving back towards itself 圈, 環: *The road formed a loop around the peninsula.* 道路繞着半島形成一個圓環。

2 ►TO FASTEN STH 扣住某物◄ something that has this curved shape, especially when used as a handle or to hold something in place 拎環, 襻〔尤用作把手或扣住某物〕: *a belt loop* 皮帶環 | *The best bicycle locks are made of a loop of solid metal.* 最好的腳踏車鎖是用堅固的金屬做成的環形鎖。

3 ►IN WOMAN'S BODY 在婦女體內◄ a curved metal or plastic object that is put inside a woman's UTERUS (=place where a baby develops) to prevent her from becoming PREGNANT〔一種置入子宮內的〕避孕環

4 ►COMPUTER 電腦◄ a set of commands in a computer PROGRAM[1] (1) that are intended to be followed repeatedly〔電腦程式中的〕循環, 回路

5 ►PLANE 飛機◄ a pattern like a circle made by a plane flying upwards, backwards, and then downwards〔飛機〕翻跟斗; 翻圈飛行

6 ►FILM/TAPE 膠片/磁帶◄ a film or TAPE[1] (1a) loop contains images or sounds that are repeated again and again 環形膠片; 環形磁帶〔可循環播放〕

7 ►RAILWAY 鐵路◄ a railway line that leaves the main track and then joins it again further on〔鐵路的〕會車線

8 in the loop/out of the loop *AmE informal* part of a group of people who make decisions about important subjects, or not part of this group【美, 非正式】在〔決策〕圈內/圈外: *White House officials insist the Secretary of State is still in the loop.* 白宮官員堅持説國務卿仍然是在決策圈內。

9 knock/throw sb for a loop *AmE informal* to surprise and upset someone【美, 非正式】使某人驚慌[煩惱]: *Yeah, the news really knocked me for a loop.* 是, 這消息確實令我驚慌失措。

loop[2] *v* **1** [T always+adv/prep] to fasten or join something with a loop〔用環〕扣[套]住: **loop sth over/around/together etc** *Loop the wire over the gate to keep it shut.* 用鐵絲繞在門上把它關住。**2** [I,T] to make a loop or make something into a loop 使成圈[環]; 把…繞成圈: *a rug with looped threads* 用繩圈做成的小地毯 **3** [I] to move in a circular direction that forms the shape of a loop 繞轉成圈: *little streams that loop through the valley* 環繞山谷的小溪 **4 loop the loop** to fly a plane in a loop 翻跟斗飛行

loop·hole /'lup,hol; 'lu:phəʊl/ *n* [C] a small mistake in a law that makes it possible to avoid doing something that the law is supposed to make you do〔法律中的〕漏洞, 空子: *tax loopholes* 稅收上的漏洞

loop·y /'lupɪ; 'lu:pi/ *adj informal*【非正式】**1** crazy or strange 發瘋的, 瘋狂的; 奇怪的 **2 go loopy** *spoken*【口】**a)** *BrE* to become extremely angry【英】變得狂怒 **b)** to become mentally ill 變得精神失常

loose[1] /lus; lu:s/ *adj*

1 ►NOT FIXED 未固定的◄ not firmly fixed in place 鬆的, 鬆動的: *One of my buttons is loose.* 我的一顆鈕扣鬆了。| *a loose floorboard* 鬆動的地板 | **come/work loose** (=become loose) 變得鬆動 *A piece of stair carpet had come loose.* 樓梯上的一塊地毯鬆了。

2 ►ROPE/CHAIN ETC 繩/鏈等◄ a rope, chain etc that is loose is not fastened as firmly or pulled as tight as it should be 鬆開的, 未繫牢的

3 ►CLOTHES 衣服◄ clothes that are loose are big and do not fit your body tightly 寬大的, 不合身的: *a loose sweatshirt* 寬鬆的運動衫

4 ►FREE 自由的◄ an animal or person that is loose is free to move around and not tied to anything or shut in anywhere.〔動物或人〕自由的, 無束縛的, 沒有擊[關]住: **break/get loose** (=get free) 掙脱束縛 *Somehow the horses had broken loose during the night.* 不知怎的馬在夜間掙脱了束縛。| **turn/let sth loose** (=let something go free) 讓某物自由 *Don't let your dog loose if there are any sheep around.* 如果周圍有羊, 不要放開你的狗。

5 ►NOT TOGETHER 不在一起◄ not tied together, fastened to anything else, or put together in one package 未繫[未包]在一起的; 散裝的: *Do they sell these olives loose?* 這些橄欖零賣嗎? | *Do you like loose tea, or teabags?* 你要茶葉還是茶包? | *Her hair fell loose around her shoulders.* 她的頭髮鬆散地披在肩上。

6 ►CLOTH/A KNOT ETC 布/繩結等◄ tied or woven in a way that is not tight 疏鬆的, 沒繫牢的: *a loose knot* 沒繫牢的結 | *a loose weave* 鬆織法

7 ▶NOT EXACT 不嚴謹的◀ [usually before noun 一般用於名詞前] not exact or thoroughly done 不嚴謹的; 不精確的: **loose translation/interpretation etc** *This is only a loose translation of the original paper.* 這只是原文的一篇不精確的譯文。

8 ▶NOT CONTROLLED 沒有控制的◀ not strictly controlled or organized 控制[組織]不嚴的: *a loose, informal trading system* 組織不嚴的、非正規的貿易制度

9 ▶IMMORAL 道德敗壞的◀ *old-fashioned* behaving in a way that is considered to be sexually immoral【過時】放蕩的, 淫蕩的: *a loose woman* 蕩婦

10 ▶TALK 談話◀ *old-fashioned* not careful about what you say or who is listening【過時】說話隨便[輕率]的: *There's been a bit of loose talk about it.* 對這件事有些不負責任的話。

11 ▶BODY WASTE 身體排泄物◀ *not technical* having a problem in which the waste from your BOWELs has too much liquid in it【非術語】稀薄的: *loose motions* 稀濕的大便 | *He's a bit loose in the mornings.* 他早上都有點腹瀉。

12 cut loose a) to free yourself from the influence of someone or something 去掉[擺脫]影響: *Anna had finally managed to cut loose from her father's domineering influence.* 安娜終於擺脫了父親的專橫對她的影響。**b)** *AmE informal* to start enjoying yourself in a happy, noisy way after a period of controlled behaviour【美, 非正式】〔壓抑過後的〕放任, 發泄: *After the exams we'll really have a chance to cut loose.* 考試過後, 我們真的有機會輕鬆輕鬆了。

13 let sb loose on sth to allow someone to deal with something in the way they want to 讓某人隨意做某事: *Whatever you do, don't let Derek loose on the garden!* 不管你做甚麼, 千萬別讓德里克在花園裡任意胡為!

14 be at a loose end also 又作 **be at loose ends** *AmE*【美】to have nothing to do 無所事事, 閒着: *I was at a loose end so I decided to go see an old movie.* 我閒着沒事, 所以決定去看一部老電影。

15 loose ends parts of something that have not been completed or properly done 未完成[做好]的部分: **tie up the loose ends** (=complete something, or deal with any remaining problems) 完成某事; 收拾殘局 *It's a good report but there are still a few loose ends to be tied up.* 這是一份很好的報告, 但仍有少量沒有說清楚的部分有待完善。

16 loose change coins that you have in your bag or pocket 零錢: *I've got twenty quid and a bit of loose change as well.* 我有二十英鎊和一些零錢。

17 hang/stay loose *AmE spoken* used to tell someone to stay calm, or not to worry about something【美口】保持鎮靜, 別緊張 —**loosely** *adv*: *Just tie it loosely.* 只要大致捆一捆就行。| *Loosely translated it means 'watch out'.* 大致上可把它譯成"當心"。—**looseness** *n* [U]

loose² *v* [T] **1** to untie someone or something, especially an animal 放開〔尤指動物〕; 釋放 **2** *literary* to fire an ARROW (1), a shot from a gun etc【文】射〔箭〕; 放〔槍〕**3** to make something unpleasant begin 使不愉快的事情出現: *The recent court case has loosed a spate of racist attacks.* 最近法院處理的案件使種族攻擊大量爆發。

loose sth **on/upon** *phr v* [T] to allow something dangerous or destructive to begin to affect a situation or other people 使〔有危險或有害的事〕開始影響[侵襲]〔某局面或其他人〕: *A potentially lethal drug has been loosed upon unsuspecting kids looking for a quick high.* 一種可能致命的毒品已經開始侵擾毫無戒備之心又急於追求快感的年輕人。

loose³ *adv* loosely 很鬆地; 不嚴密地, 不嚴謹地 —see also 另見 **play fast and loose with** (FAST² (10))

loose⁴ *n* **be on the loose** if a criminal or dangerous animal is on the loose, they have escaped from prison or from their cage〔罪犯或危險動物〕在逃

loose-fit·ting /,· '··◂/ *adj* loose-fitting clothes are loose on your body, so that they are comfortable〔衣服〕寬鬆的: *wearing jeans and a loose-fitting jacket* 身着牛仔褲和寬鬆的短上衣

loose-leaf /,· '·◂/ *adj* having pages that can be put in and removed easily 活頁的: *a loose-leaf binder* 活頁夾

loos·en /ˈlusn; ˈluːsən/ *v* **1** [I,T] to make something less tight or less firmly fixed, or to become less tight or less firmly fixed (使) 變鬆; 鬆開: *You'll need a spanner to loosen that bolt.* 你需要扳子來擰鬆這個螺栓。| *Check the plug – there may be a loosened connection.* 檢查一下插頭 —— 可能鬆掉了。**2** [T] to unfasten something, especially something you are wearing 解開〔尤指穿着的衣物〕: *Harry loosened his tie.* 哈利解開他的領帶。**3** [T] to make laws, rules etc less strict 使〔法律、規定等〕放寬: *It was time to loosen economic constraints.* 該是放寬經濟限制的時候了。**4 loosen your grip/hold a)** to reduce the control or power you have over someone or something 放鬆對...的控制[操縱]: *as communism began to loosen its hold on eastern Europe* 正當共產主義開始放鬆對東歐的控制 **b)** to start holding someone less tightly than you were before 放鬆[鬆開]抓着〔某人〕的手: **[+on]** *The policeman loosened his grip on my arm.* 警察放鬆了抓着我手臂的手。**5 loosen sb's tongue** to make someone talk more freely than usual, for example by making them drunk 使某人說話不那麼拘束〈如將其灌醉等〉

loosen up *phr v* **1** [I, T **loosen** sth ↔ **up**] to exercise your muscles and joints to make them work more easily, especially before playing a sport or running; WARM-UP (1)〔尤指運動或跑步前〕活動肌肉和關節; 熱身 **2** [I] to stop worrying and become more relaxed 無拘無束, 放鬆: *Try and loosen up a bit!* 盡量放鬆一點!

loot¹ /lut; luːt/ *n* [U] **1** *informal old-fashioned* goods or money that have been stolen【非正式, 過時】〔偷來的〕贓物 **2** goods taken by soldiers from a place where they have won a battle 戰利品, 掠奪物 **3** *AmE informal humorous* things that you have bought or been given in large amounts【美, 非正式, 幽默】大量購買[贈送]之物: *Jodie came home from the mall with sacks of loot.* 喬迪從購物中心滿載而歸。

loot² *v* [I, T] to steal things, especially from shops or homes that have been damaged in a war or RIOT²〔尤指在戰爭或暴亂中〕搶劫, 洗劫, 掠奪: *Shops were looted and burned down.* 商店遭搶劫並被燒毀。—**looting** *n* [U] —**looter** *n* [C]

lop /lɑp; lɒp/ *v* **lopped, lopping** [T] to cut branches from a tree, especially with a single strong movement 砍掉〔樹枝, 尤指猛地一下砍掉〕

lop sth **off** *phr v* [T] **1** to cut a part of something off, especially a branch of a tree 砍掉〔某物的部分, 尤指樹枝〕**2** to remove a particular amount from a price or charge〔從價錢中〕削減: *They lopped $15 off the price.* 他們削價 15 美元。

lope /lop; ləʊp/ *v* [I always+adv/prep] to run easily with long steps 輕鬆地跑: **[+along/across/up etc]** *Brad loped across the field towards home.* 布拉德蹦跳着穿過田地跑回家。—**lope** *n* [singular]

lop-eared /,· '·◂/ *adj* a lop-eared animal such as a rabbit has long ears that hang down〔兔子等動物〕耳朵長而垂下的

lop·sid·ed /,· '··◂/ *adj* **1** having one side that is lower or heavier than the other 歪斜的: *a lopsided grin* 咧着歪斜的嘴笑 **2** unequal or uneven in a way that seems unfair 不平等[平衡, 公正]的: *a lopsided ratio of men to women* 男女的比例失衡

lo·qua·cious /loˈkweʃəs; ləʊˈkweɪʃəs/ *adj formal* liking to talk a lot, sometimes too much【正式】話多的; 饒舌的 —**loquaciously** *adv* —**loquacity** /loˈkwæsətɪ; ləʊˈkwæsəti/ *n* [U]

lo·quat /ˈlokwɑt; ˈləʊkwɒt/ *n* [C] the small yellowish fruit of a tree that grows mostly in China and Japan 枇杷

Lord /lɔrd; lɔːd/ *n* [singular] **1** also 又作 **the Lord** a title of God or Jesus Christ 上帝; 耶穌: *Thank you, Lord, for your blessings.* 感謝上帝的恩賜。**2 the Lords a)** the members of the British House of Lords considered as a group 英國上議院全體議員 **b)** the House of Lords 上議院 **3 Lord (only) knows** *spoken* used when you do not know the answer to something【口】(只有) 天知道〔用於不知道答案時〕: *Lord knows where I left that bag.* 天曉得我把那袋子留在哪裡了。**4 (good) Lord!/Oh Lord!** *spoken* used when you are suddenly surprised, annoyed or worried about something【口】天哪! 主啊!〔表示驚訝、惱怒或憂慮〕: *Good Lord! Is that the time?* 天哪! 時候到了嗎? **5 Lord willing** *spoken* used to say that you hope nothing will prevent something from happening【口】按上帝的旨意, 按上帝的安排: *We'll finally be able to take that trip this year, Lord willing.* 我們終於今年能夠安排去那裡旅行, 但願這是上帝的旨意。**6 the Lord's Day** Sunday, considered as the holy day of the Christian religion 星期天〔基督教的禮拜日〕 **7** *BrE* the title of someone who has a particular type of official job【英】大人, 閣下〔對某些官員的尊稱〕: *Lord Mayor of London* 倫敦市長大人

3 2 **lord¹** *n* **1** [C] a man who has rank in the ARISTOCRACY, especially in Britain, or his title〔尤指英國的〕貴族 (頭銜): *Lord Hailsham* 黑爾什姆勳爵 —compare 比較 LADY (7) **2** [C] a man in medieval Europe who was very powerful and owned a lot of land〔中世紀歐洲的〕領主; 莊園主: *the feudal lords* 封建領主 **3 my lord** used to address a judge or BISHOP (1) in Britain, and in the past to address a lord 大人, 閣下〔對英國的法官、主教的尊稱, 舊時也用來稱呼貴族〕 **4 your lord and master** *humorous* someone who must be obeyed because they have power over you【幽默】主人; 上司〔指要服從的人〕

lord² *v* **lord it over sb** to behave in a way that shows you think you are better or more powerful than someone else 對某人作威作福, 在某人面前擺架子: *the outer office where Carol lorded it over her assistants* 嘉露對她的助手發號施令的外面辦公室

lord·ly /ˈlɔrdlɪ; ˈlɔːdli/ *adj* **1** behaving in a way that shows you think you are better or more important than other people 傲慢的, 高傲的: *Sebastian has a lordly disdain for such everyday affairs.* 塞巴斯蒂安對這類日常事務擺出高傲輕蔑的樣子。**2** very grand or impressive 富麗堂皇的; 貴族氣派的: *a lordly feast* 盛大的筵席 —**lordliness** *n* [U]

lord·ship /ˈlɔrdʃɪp; ˈlɔːdʃɪp/ *n* [C] **1 your/his lordship** used when talking to or talking about a LORD¹ (1), or when addressing a British judge or BISHOP (1) 爵爺; 大人; 閣下〔用於稱呼或提及貴族或尊稱英國的法官或主教時〕 **2 his lordship** *BrE spoken* a humorous way of talking about a man who thinks he is very important【英口】大人, 老爺〔談論自命不凡者的幽默方式〕: *So when will his lordship be back?* 那麼, 老爺甚麼時候回來? **3** [U+**over**] the power of a lord or the period of time when he rules〔貴族的〕權力; 統治時期 —compare 比較 LADYSHIP (1)

Lord's Prayer /ˌ· ˈ·/ *n* **the Lord's Prayer** the most important prayer of the Christian religion〔基督教的〕主禱文, 天主經

lore /lɔr; lɔː/ *n* [U] knowledge or information about a subject, for example nature or magic, that is not written down but is passed from person to person〔口頭流傳的關於某一主題的〕知識; 傳說: *This story has become part of the county lore of Ayrshire.* 這個故事已經成為艾爾郡傳說的一部分。

lor·gnette /lɔrnˋjɛt; lɔːˈnjet/ *n* [C] a pair of GLASSES with a long handle at the side that you hold in front of your eyes 長柄眼鏡

lorn /lɔrn; lɔːn/ *adj poetical* sad and lonely; FORLORN【詩】淒涼的, 孤苦伶仃的 —see also 另見 LOVELORN

3 **lor·ry** /ˈlɔrɪ; ˈlɒri/ *n* [C] *BrE*【英】**1** a large vehicle for carrying heavy goods; TRUCK¹(1) 大卡車, 運貨汽車 **2 it fell off the back of a lorry** *spoken humorous* used to say that something was probably stolen【口, 幽默】多半是偷來之物

lose /luz; luːz/ *v past tense and past participle* **lost** /lɔst; lɒst/ 1 1

1 ►NOT HAVE ANY MORE 不再擁有◄ [T] to stop having something that is important to you or that you need 喪失, 失去〔重要或需要的東西〕: *I can't afford to lose my job, I have a family to support.* 我可不能失去工作, 我要養家餬口。| *I lost a lot of money on that deal.* 我在那樁交易上賠了很多錢。| *We're going to lose five teachers when the schools are merged.* 學校合併時, 我們會失去五位教師。| **lose everything** *If they're lucky they'll make a fortune, if they're unlucky they stand to lose everything.* 如果運氣好, 他們會發大財; 如果運氣不好, 他們就會一無所有。

2 ►NOT WIN 未贏◄ [I,T] to not win a game, argument, war etc 輸掉〔比賽、辯論、戰爭等〕: *I'm not playing tennis with her any more – I always lose.* 我再也不和她打網球了 — 我總是輸。| **lose to/against** *Cuba lost to Canada in the world volleyball championships.* 古巴在世界排球錦標賽中輸給了加拿大。| **lose a game/fight/election etc** *Are they in danger of losing this battle?* 他們是不是有輸掉這場戰爭的危險? | **lose by 1 goal/10 votes/20 points etc** *Smithson lost by 7,008 votes.* 史密森輸了7,008票。| **lose sb sth** (=be the reason why someone does not win something) 是某人失敗的原因 *Allegations of corruption lost him the election.* 貪污的傳言使他在這次選舉中落敗。—opposite 反義詞 WIN¹ (1)

3 ►CANNOT FIND 找不着◄ [T] to be unable to find someone or something 丟失, 找不到: *Whatever you do, don't lose those keys.* 無論你做甚麼事, 千萬別丟失這些鑰匙。| *Make sure you don't lose each other in the crowd.* 你們務必注意別在人羣中走散了。

4 lose your memory/sight/voice etc to stop having a particular ability or sense 失去記憶/視力/嗓音等: *She lost her sight in a car accident.* 她在一次車禍中失明了。| **lose your voice** (=temporarily not be able to speak) 失去嗓音〔暫時不能說話〕 *A few days before our first concert I got a cold and lost my voice.* 我們第一次開音樂會的前幾天, 我得了感冒, 嗓子啞了。

5 lose an arm/leg etc to have an arm, leg etc cut off after injury in an accident or in war〔因受傷而〕失掉手臂/腿等: *He lost his right arm in a motorbike accident.* 他在摩托車事故中失去了右臂。

6 lose your temper/head/nerve/rag etc to become angry, nervous etc 發怒/失去理智/感到膽怯等: *It is vital that you do not lose your head* (=that you manage to stay calm) *even in the most serious crisis.* 關鍵是你不要失去理智, 即使在最緊要的危急關頭。| *I really wanted to do the jump, but lost my nerve* (=stopped feeling brave and confident) *at the last minute.* 我真想跳過去, 但在最後卻膽怯了。

7 lose your way/bearings to not know where you are or which direction you should go 迷路/迷失方向: *It's very easy to lose your way in the forest.* 在森林中很容易迷路。

8 lose your balance/footing to become unsteady or fall 失去平衡/失足: *Sam lost his footing on the snowy bank.* 山姆在積雪的堤岸上失足摔倒。

9 lose interest/hope/heart etc to stop being interested in something, having hope etc 失去興趣/希望/勇氣等: *Don't lose heart – there are plenty of other jobs you could apply for.* 不要灰心 — 有很多別的工作你可以申請。

10 lose your mother/father/wife etc used to say that someone's mother etc has died 喪母/父/妻等: *Paul's been very depressed since losing his mother.* 自從母親去世後, 保羅的情緒一直很低落。| **lose the baby** (=used when a woman's baby dies before it is born) 流產

11 lose weight to become thinner 體重減輕: *Kay's lost a lot of weight.* 凱伊體重輕了不少。| **lose 20lbs/3st/5kg**

I'd like to lose at least 7 pounds before I go on vacation. 我希望在度假前至少能減去7磅。

12 lose your mind to become crazy or to stop behaving sensibly 發瘋; 失去理智: *Have you lost your mind? It's really dangerous to go climbing there without a guide.* 你是不是瘋了? 沒有嚮導到那裡去爬山真的很危險。

13 lose your life to die 喪命: *His grandfather lost his life in a mining accident.* 他的祖父在一次採礦事故中喪生。

14 ▶TIME 時間◀ [T] to waste time because of delays, INTERRUPTIONs etc〔因耽擱、打擾等〕浪費, 失去〔時間〕: **lose time/2days/3hours etc** *We lost a lot of valuable time waiting for the others to arrive.* 為了等其他人到來, 我們失去了許多寶貴的時間。| **there's no time to lose** (=it is neccessary to hurry) 抓緊時間 *Hurry, there's no time to lose.* 趕快, 沒有時間磨蹭了。| **lose no time in doing sth** (=do something immediately) 馬上做某事 *George could see how serious it was and lost no time in calling the doctor.* 喬治看到情況十分嚴重, 立刻就叫醫生。—opposite 反義詞 GAIN[1] (8)

15 ▶CLOCK/WATCH 鐘/錶◀ [T] if a clock or watch loses time, it works too slowly 走慢: **lose time/5 minutes/1 hour** *This old watch loses about 2 minutes in every hour.* 這隻舊錶每小時大約慢兩分鐘。—opposite 反義詞 GAIN[1] (9)

16 ▶CONFUSE 混淆◀ to confuse someone when you are trying to explain something to them〔試圖解釋時〕把〔某人〕搞糊塗: *I'm sorry, you've lost me now – could you start again?* 抱歉, 你已經把我搞糊塗了—可不可以重新來一遍?

17 ▶ESCAPE FROM 擺脱◀ to escape from someone who is chasing or following you 甩掉〔追趕着的人〕: *His car was much faster but I eventually managed to lose him.* 他的汽車比我的快多了, 但最後我還是甩掉了他。

18 lose yourself in sth to be so involved in something that you do not notice anything else 全神貫注於某事: *It's easy to lose yourself in the magic of this film.* 你很容易被這部電影的魅力所吸引。

19 have nothing to lose to be in a situation in which you should attempt to do something, because you may be successful, and it will not make things worse if you are not〔應該嘗試做某事, 因為有可能成功, 即使不成功也〕不會損失甚麼: *You might as well apply for the job – you've got nothing to lose.* 你不妨申請這份工作—你不會損失甚麼的。

20 have a lot to lose/have too much to lose to be in a situation in which you will suffer very much if you do not succeed in doing something〔如果不成功〕損失會很大

21 lose sight of a) to stop being able to see someone or something 看不見…: *Soon we had lost sight of the boat as it sailed off downstream.* 船向下游駛去, 我們很快就看不見它了。**b)** to forget to consider something important 忘記考慮〔重要事情〕: *She was enjoying herself so much, she'd almost lost sight of the purpose of her visit.* 她正玩得這麼高興, 幾乎忘了她此行的目的。

22 lose touch (with) a) to not speak to, write to, or see someone for a long time, so that you do not know where they are (和…)失去聯繫: *I've lost touch with all my old school friends.* 我已經和所有老校友失去了聯繫。**b)** to not know the most recent information about something and therefore be unable to understand it properly〔不知某事的近況而〕(對…)不明白: *When you're living abroad it's so easy to lose touch with what's happening back home.* 當你在國外生活時, 很容易對國內發生的事不了解。

23 lose it *spoken*【口】**a)** to become crazy 發瘋: *I reckon Jack's losing it – he was walking the dog in his pyjamas.* 我想傑克發瘋了—他穿着睡衣在遛狗。**b)** be unable to stop yourself laughing, crying, shouting etc 情不自禁地笑[哭, 喊等]: *Then she started doing this funny little dance and I just lost it completely.* 然後她開始跳這個滑稽的小舞蹈, 我就情不自禁地笑個不停。

24 lose face to do something that makes people not trust or respect you any more, especially in a public situation 丟面子, 出醜〔尤指在公共場合〕

25 lose height if an aircraft loses height it falls to a lower height in the sky〔飛機〕降低高度

lose out *phr v* [I] to not get something such as a job, business contract, or profit because someone else gets it instead 失利, 輸掉: *On this occasion both the dealer and the client lost out.* 在這件事上買賣雙方都輸了。| **lose out to sb** *We lost out to a French company as they could do the job more cheaply.* 我們輸給了一家法國公司, 因為他們能以更低的價格做這工作。| **lose out on sth** *Why is it that women always seem to lose out on career opportunities?* 為甚麼在就業機會上婦女似乎總是輸家?

los·er /ˈluːzə; ˈluːzɚ/ *n* [C] **1** someone who has lost a competition or game〔競爭或比賽中的〕失敗者, 輸家: *The losers walked dejectedly off the field.* 輸掉比賽的運動員沮喪地離開運動場。| **good/bad loser** (=someone who behaves well or badly after losing) 輸得起/輸不起的人 **2** someone who is in a worse situation than they were, because of something that has happened 不幸者, 倒霉的人: *The real losers if Bailey died would be his kids.* 如果貝利死了, 真正不幸的人會是他的孩子。**3** someone who is never successful in life, work, or relationships〔在生活、工作或關係方面〕總是輸的人, 老是失敗的人: **a born loser** *I swear Joe's a born loser.* 我肯定喬是個天生的失敗者。

loss /lɒs; lɔs/ *n* 

1 ▶NO LONGER HAVING STH 不再擁有某物◀ [C, U] the fact of no longer having something you used to have 失去, 喪失: *Job losses were common in the 1980s.* 在20世紀80年代, 失業是很普遍的。| **[+of]** *a temporary loss of memory* 暫時失去記憶 | **weight/blood etc loss** *rapid hair loss* 迅速掉髮

2 ▶MONEY 錢◀ [C,U] money that has been lost by a business, person, government etc 虧損, 損失: *losses amounting to £12,000* 總共達12,000英鎊的虧損 | *profit and loss* 盈虧 | **make a loss** *The company made a loss of $250,000 in its first year.* 公司在第一年虧損了25萬美元。| **sell/operate sth at a loss** (=sell something or do something with the result that you have less money than you had in the beginning) 虧本銷售/經營某物

3 ▶LIFE 生命◀ [C,U] the death of someone 死亡: *My sympathy for your loss.* (=of someone you love) 我為你親人的去世致哀。| **suffer heavy losses** *The US forces withdrew after suffering heavy losses.* 美軍在遭到重大傷亡後撤退了。| **loss of life** *formal*【正式】*The blaze was overcome without loss of life.* 大火被撲滅了, 沒有造成人命損傷。

4 be at a loss to be confused and uncertain about what to do or say 困惑, 不知所措: *I was at a complete loss as to how to find the money in time.* 我完全不知道怎樣能及時弄到這筆錢。| **be at a loss for words** (=be unable to think what to say) 不知説甚麼才好

5 ▶FEELING 感受◀ [U] a feeling of being sad or lonely because someone or something is not there any more 傷感, 孤獨感: **sense of loss** *I still feel an aching sense of loss, even though Allen died four years ago.* 儘管艾倫已經去世四年, 我仍然有一種痛楚的失落感。

6 ▶PROBLEM 問題◀ [singular] a disadvantage caused by someone or something leaving or being removed〔因某人或某物的離去或挪移而造成的〕損失: **a great loss** *We see your going as a great loss to the company.* 我們把你的離去視為公司的重大損失。

7 that's your/their loss *spoken* used to say that something will affect someone in a much worse way than it will affect you【口】那是你的/他們的損失: *Well, if he doesn't want to come it's his loss.* 好吧, 如果他不願意來, 那是他的損失。

8 ▶GAME 比賽◀ [C] an occasion on which a competi-

L

tion or game is lost; DEFEAT[1] 輸, 失敗: [+to] *The loss to the Lions meant we were out of the playoffs.* 比賽輸給雄獅隊意味着我們不能進入決勝加賽。—see also 另見 **cut your losses** (CUT[1] (31)), **be a dead loss** (DEAD[1] (13))

loss ad·just·er /'· ·,··/ *n* [C] *BrE* someone who is employed by an insurance company to decide how much should be paid to people who make CLAIM*s* on their insurance【英】〔保險公司雇用的〕險損估價人; INSURANCE ADJUSTER *AmE*【美】

loss lead·er /'· ,··/ *n* [C] something that is sold at a very low price to make people go into a shop 虧本促銷商品

lost[1] /lɔst; lɒst/ *adj*

1 ►CANNOT BE FOUND 找不到◄ something that is lost is something you had but cannot now find; MISSING 找不到的, 遺失的: *The lost file eventually turned up among Branson's papers.* 丟失的檔案結果在布蘭森的文件堆中出現。

2 ►CANNOT FIND YOUR WAY 迷路◄ unable to find your way or not knowing where you are 迷路的: *Police are generally happy to give directions to lost tourists.* 警察一般都樂於為迷路的遊客指路。| **get lost** (=become lost) 迷路 *I got thoroughly lost on the way here.* 我在來這裡的路上完全迷了路。

3 ►WASTED 浪費的◄ [only before noun 僅用於名詞前] not used properly; wasted 用得不恰當的; 浪費的, 錯過的: *It'll be impossible to make up the lost time.* 不可能把浪費的時間補回來。| **lost opportunities/chances etc** *lost market opportunities* 錯過的市場機遇

4 feel/be lost (in the crowd) to not feel confident about what to do or how to behave, especially among people you do not know 感到陌生〔尤指在陌生人中膽怯〕: *Will your child feel lost at a nursery?* 你的孩子在託兒所怕生嗎?

5 Get lost! *spoken* used to tell someone rudely to go away【口】〔粗魯地叫別人〕走開!, 滾開!

6 ►IN THOUGHT ETC 在思考中等◄ [not before noun 不用於名詞前] thinking so hard about something or being so interested in something that you do not notice what is happening around you 想得出神; 沉浸於: [+in] *I was lost in the beauty of the scenery.* 我被這美麗的景色迷住了。| **lost in thought** *Poirot remained lost in thought.* 波伊羅特仍然想得出神。| **lost to the world** *Alex sat reading, lost to the world.* 亞歷士坐着看書, 沉醉在書中的世界裡。

7 get lost (in sth) to be forgotten or not noticed in a complicated process or busy time〔在複雜的過程或繁忙時間中〕被遺忘[忽略]: *It's easy for your main points to get lost in a long speech.* 在長篇演講中你的主要觀點很容易被忽略。

8 ►NOT UNDERSTAND 不理解◄ be lost to be completely confused by a complicated explanation〔被複雜的解釋〕弄糊塗: *"Did you understand the instructions?" "No, I'm totally lost."* "你看得懂這些使用說明嗎?" "不, 我被徹底弄糊塗了。"

9 be lost on sb if something is lost on someone, they do not understand or want to accept it 為某人所不理解[接受]: *All my warnings were completely lost on Beth.* 我所有的警告貝思根本聽不進去。

10 be lost for words to be unable to say anything because you are very surprised, upset etc〔因非常驚訝、煩惱等而〕說不上話來: *It's not often Glenda's lost for words.* 格倫達說不上話來不是常有的事。

11 ►NOT EXISTING 不存在的◄ not existing or owned any more 不復存在的, 不再擁有的: *the lost dreams of her youth* 她那些逝去的青春夢想

12 ►DESTROYED/KILLED 毀壞的/被殺的◄ destroyed, ruined, or killed 毀滅的; 遭難的; 被殺死的: **lost at sea/lost in battle etc** *The whole crew was lost at sea.* 全體船員葬身大海。

13 a lost cause something that has no chance of succeeding 注定失敗的事: *Trying to interest my son in classical music is a lost cause.* 我試圖讓兒子對古典音樂感興趣是注定無法成功的。

14 lost soul *often humorous* someone who does not seem to know where they are or what to do【常幽默】失魂落魄者; 茫然若失的人 —see also 另見 **give sb up for dead/lost etc** (GIVE[1]), **make up for lost time** (MAKE[1]), **there is no love lost between** (LOVE[2] (11))

lost[2] the past tense and past participle of LOSE

lost-and-found /,· · '·/ *n* **the lost-and-found** a place where things that are lost are kept until someone comes to claim them 失物招領處; LOST PROPERTY *BrE*【英】

lost prop·er·ty /,· '···/ *n BrE*【英】**1** [U] things that have been found in public places because people have lost or forgotten them 待領失物 **2** [C] also 又作 **lost property office** *BrE* a place where these things are kept until someone comes to claim them; LOST-AND-FOUND【英】失物招領處

lot /lɑt; lɒt/ *n*

1 ►LARGE AMOUNT 大量◄ a lot also 又作 **lots** *informal*【非正式】a large quantity or number 大量, 許多: *The stereo cost a lot, but it was worth it.* 這台立體聲音響很貴, 但物有所值。| *"How much ice cream do you want?" "Lots, please."* "你要多少冰淇淋?" "要很多, 謝謝。" | [+of] *There were lots of people at the party.* 聚會上來了很多人。| **a lot to do/see/eat etc** *There's a lot to do before the wedding.* 婚禮前有許多事情要做。| **an awful lot** (=a very large amount) 很多, 極多

2 ►MUCH 許多◄ [+comparative] if something is a lot or lots better, easier etc, it is much better, easier etc ...得多〔用於比較〕: *Benny can run lots faster than me.* 班尼能跑得比我快得多。| *Andrea always had a lot more money than I had.* 安德烈亞的錢總是比我多得多。

3 have a lot on *BrE*【英】**/have a lot going on** *AmE*【美】to be very busy, with a lot of things to do in a short time 很忙, 要趕做很多事情

4 have a lot on your mind to have a lot of problems that you are worried about 有很多操心的問題, 心事重重

5 thanks a lot *spoken*【口】**a)** thank you very much 非常感謝 **b)** used when you are annoyed about something and do not really mean thank you at all 謝謝〔反語, 用於生氣時〕: *"I forgot to bring your money." "Well, thanks a lot!"* "我忘記把你的錢帶來。" "哦, 還得謝謝你!"

6 ►TO BE SOLD 待售◄ [C] something that is sold, especially at an AUCTION[1]〔尤指拍賣的〕物品, 拍賣品: *Lot fifteen was a box of old books.* 第十五號拍賣品是一箱舊書。

7 have a lot to answer for to be responsible for a bad situation〔壞情況〕要對負責: *Jerry's got a lot to answer for. If it weren't for him, Ann would never have left Denver.* 傑里得負責任。若不是他的緣故, 安決不會離開丹佛。

8 the lot *especially BrE* the whole quantity or number【尤英】全部[全數]: *I can't believe you ate the whole lot!* 我無法相信你竟然全吃下去了!

9 ►FILM 電影◄ [C] a building and the land surrounding it where films are made; a film STUDIO (2) 電影攝製場: *the Universal Studios lot* 環球影片公司的攝製場

10 ►SB'S LOT 某人的命運◄ *sometimes humorous* the work, responsibilities, social position etc that you have, especially when they could be better【有時幽默】〔尤指不好的〕命運, 運氣: *She seems happy enough with her lot in life.* 她似乎對自己的命運感到滿意。

11 ►PEOPLE 人們◄ [singular] *BrE informal* a group of people, especially one you do not completely approve of【英, 非正式】〔尤指某人不完全贊同的〕一羣人, 一批人: *Come on you lot, hurry up!* 加油, 你們這幫傢伙, 趕快! | **the lot of you/them etc** (=all of you, them etc) 你們/他們等所有的人 *Outside, the lot of you!* 出去, 你們所有的人!

12 ►GROUP OF THINGS 一批東西◄ *BrE informal* a

group of things【英, 非正式】一批[組]東西: *Let's drop this lot off and go home.* 讓我們送走這批東西, 然後回家。

13 ▶OF LAND 土地的◀ [C] *especially AmE* an area of land used for building on or for another particular purpose【尤美】一塊地〔用於建屋或其他用途〕: *We could turn that vacant lot into a playground.* 我們可以把那塊空地改成遊戲場。| *a used-car lot* 舊車場 —see also 另見 PARKING LOT

14 have a lot on your plate *informal especially BrE* to have a lot of difficult problems to deal with【非正式, 尤英】有很多難題要處理: *Leave Mum alone – she's got a lot on her plate at the moment.* 別打擾媽媽 — 此刻她有許多難事要處理。

15 draw lots to decide on someone or something by choosing one piece of paper, object etc from among many〔用以作決定的〕抽籤, 抓鬮: *They drew lots to see who would go first.* 他們抽籤看誰先走。

16 throw in/cast your lot with sb to join or support someone, so that what happens to you depends on what happens to them 與某人共命運〔加入或支持對方〕: *They threw their lot in with the allies.* 他們與盟友共命運。

17 by lot by drawing lots 用抽籤[抓鬮]的方法: *In Athens at that time, judges were chosen by lot.* 在那時候的雅典, 法官是通過抽籤來選定的。—see also 另見 **bad egg/lot/sort/type** (BAD[1] (16)), **fall to sb's lot** (FALL[1]), **a fat lot of good/use** (FAT[1] (5))

loth /loθ; ləʊθ/ *adj* [not before noun 不用於名詞前] another spelling of LOATH loath的另一種拼法

lo·tion /ˈloʃən; ˈləʊʃən/ *n* [C,U] a liquid mixture that you put on your skin or hair to clean or protect it〔抹在皮膚或頭髮上起清理或保護作用的〕洗液, 洗劑; 護膚液: *suntan lotion* 防曬液

lot·sa /ˈlɑtsə; ˈlɒtsə/ *quantifier spoken*【口】a short form of 縮略式= lots of

3 **lot·te·ry** /ˈlɑtərɪ; ˈlɒtəri/ *n* **1** [C] a system of raising money for the state or a CHARITY (2), in which people buy numbered tickets and some people win prizes 抽彩票給獎法: *a lottery ticket* 彩票 —compare 比較 RAFFLE[1], DRAW[2] (2) **2** [singular] an uncertain or risky situation 碰運氣[冒險]的事: *The legal system is nothing but a lottery these days.* 法律制度如今全是碰運氣。

lo·tus /ˈlotəs; ˈləʊtəs/ *n* [C] **1** a white or pink flower that grows on the surface of lakes in Asia 蓮花, 荷花: *lotus blossom* 蓮花叢 **2** the shape of this flower used in decorative patterns, especially in ancient Egyptian art〔尤指古埃及藝術中的〕蓮[荷]花裝飾圖案 **3** a fruit that gives you a pleasant dreamy feeling after you eat it, according to Ancient Greek stories 落拓棗, 忘憂果〔據古希臘傳說, 食後會有一種愉快的、如夢如幻的感覺〕

lotus-eat·er /ˈ·· ˌ··/ *n* [C] someone who has a lazy, pleasant life and is not interested in other things 生活懶散、圖安逸不問世事的人

loud¹ /laʊd; laʊd/ *adj* **1** making a lot of noise 大聲的, 喧鬧的: *a loud bang* 響亮的撞擊聲 | *That music's too loud.* 那音樂聲太吵了。**2** someone who is loud talks too loudly and confidently〔人〕說話過於大聲自信的: *The more Tom drank, the louder he became.* 湯姆喝得越多, 說話聲音越大。**3** loud clothes are unpleasantly bright〔衣服〕花哨的, 刺眼的: *Butch was wearing a loud checked suit.* 巴奇穿着紮眼的格子套裝。**4 be loud in your praise/opposition etc** to express your approval or disapproval very strongly 竭力贊同/反對等 —**loudly** *adv* —**loudness** *n* [U]

loud² *adv* **1** loudly 響亮地, 大聲地: *Could you speak a little louder?* 你能不能說得大聲點? | *You've got the telly on too loud.* 你把電視機開得太響了。**2 loud and clear** in a way that is very easily understood 容易理解: *Sally got her message across loud and clear.* 莎莉把她的信息表達得很清楚, 容易理解。**3 out loud** in such a way that people can hear you; ALOUD 大聲地: *Read it out loud, so we can all hear.* 把它大聲地唸出來, 這樣我們都能聽到。| *If you've got anything to say, say it out loud.* 如果你有話要說, 就大聲地說出來。| **laugh out loud** *Leo laughed out loud at her suggestion.* 利奧大聲地嘲笑她的建議。—see also 另見 **actions speak louder than words** (ACTION (15)), **for crying out loud** (CRY[1] (8))

loud·hail·er /ˌlaʊdˈhelə; ˌlaʊdˈheɪlə/ *n* [C] *especially BrE* a thing shaped like a tube that is wide at one end, that you speak through to make your voice louder; MEGAPHONE【尤英】喇叭筒, 擴音器

loud·mouth /ˈlaʊdˌmaʊθ; ˈlaʊdmaʊθ/ *n* [C] someone who talks too much and says offensive or stupid things 多嘴饒舌的人; 總說不中聽的話的人 —**loudmouthed** /ˈlaʊdˌmaʊðd; ˈlaʊdmaʊðd/ *adj*

loud·speak·er /ˈlaʊdˈspikə; ˌlaʊdˈspiːkə/ *n* [C] **1** a SPEAKER (3) 揚聲器 **2** a piece of equipment used to make sounds louder 擴音器, 喇叭: *Music blared from a loudspeaker.* 響亮的音樂從擴音器中傳出。

lough /lɑk; lɒk/ *n* [C] *IrE* a lake or a part of the sea almost surrounded by land【愛爾蘭】湖;〔幾乎為陸地所環繞的〕海灣: *Lough Neagh* 內伊湖

lounge¹ /laʊndʒ; laʊndʒ/ *n* [C] **1** a small comfortable public room in a hotel or other building used by many people〔旅館等中的〕休息室: *the television lounge* 電視室 **2** a WAITING ROOM at an airport〔機場的〕等候室: *the departure lounge* 候機室 **3** *especially BrE* a comfortable room where you relax in your home【尤英】〔住所中的〕起居室 **4** *BrE* a lounge bar【英】酒吧雅座 —see also 另見 COCKTAIL LOUNGE, SUN LOUNGE

lounge² *v* [I] **1** [always+adv/prep] to stand or sit in a lazy way 懶洋洋地站[坐]着: **[+in/on etc]** *young lads lounging in doorways* 懶洋洋地站在門口的小伙子 **2 lounge around/about** *BrE* to spend time doing nothing【英】閒逛, 百無聊賴地消磨[打發]時間: *He was just lounging around all day.* 他只是整天無所事事。

lounge bar /ˈ· ·/ *n* [C] *BrE* a room with comfortable furniture in a PUB; SALOON BAR【英】〔小酒館中的〕雅座酒吧

loung·er /ˈlaʊndʒə; ˈlaʊndʒə/ *n* [C] **1** someone who is lazy and does no work 遊手好閒的人 **2** a piece of garden furniture like a light narrow bed, used for lying in the sun〔花園中曬太陽用的〕躺椅; SUN LOUNGER *AmE*【美】

lounge suit /ˈ· ·/ *n* [C] *BrE old-fashioned* a suit that a man wears during the day, especially to work in an office【英, 過時】〔尤指日常在辦公室上班時穿的〕西裝; BUSINESS SUIT *AmE*【美】

lour /laʊr; ˈlaʊə/ *v* [I] a British spelling of LOWER³ lower³的英式拼法

louse¹ /laʊs; laʊs/ *n* [C] **1** *plural* **lice** a small wingless insect that lives on people's or animals' skin and hair 蝨子 **2** *plural* **louses** *informal* someone who is nasty and unpleasant【非正式】卑鄙小人: *"You louse!" she yelled.* "你這個卑鄙小人!" 她叫罵道。

louse² *v*

louse up *phr v AmE informal*【美, 非正式】**1** [T **louse sth up**] to make something worse rather than better, or to spoil something 把…弄亂[搞糟, 搞壞]: *I don't want to louse up your life.* 我不想破壞你的生活。**2** [I] to do something badly〔做事〕差, 不好: **[+on]** *Chris really loused up on his exams.* 基斯考試真的考得很糟。

lou·sy /ˈlaʊzɪ; ˈlaʊzi/ *adj* **lousier, lousiest 1** *especially spoken* very bad, unpleasant etc【尤口】非常糟糕的; 令人作嘔的: *What lousy weather!* 多麼糟糕的天氣! | *I feel lousy.* 我感覺很難受。**2** *spoken* small, useless, or unimportant【口】不起眼的; 不起作用的; 微不足道的: *Harry wouldn't lend me ten lousy quid!* 哈里連區區十英鎊都不借給我! **3 lousy with sth** *AmE spoken*【美口】**a)** a place that is lousy with people of a particular kind is too full of them〔某處〕滿是〔某種人〕: *The town was lousy with tourists.* 鎮上擠滿了遊客。**b)** someone who is lousy with money has a lot more of it than they need〔某人〕有大量的錢 **4** covered with lice (LOUSE¹ (1)) 佈滿蝨子的

lout /laut; laʊt/ *n* [C] a rude, violent man 舉止粗野的人: *Get up, you lazy lout!* 起來, 你這又懶惰又粗魯的傢伙! —see also 另見 **lager lout** (LAGER (2)) —**loutish** *adj* —**loutishly** *adv* —**loutishness** *n* [U]

lou·vre *BrE*【英】, **louver** *AmE*【美】/ˈluvɚ; ˈluːvə/ *n* [C] **1** a narrow piece of wood, glass etc, in a door or window, sloping outwards to let some light in and keep rain or strong sun out〔窗或門上的〕葉板〔用來擋雨或強光〕**2 louvre window/door** a door or window made of these pieces of wood, glass etc 百葉窗/門 —**louvred** *adj*: *louvred shutters* 百葉窗

lov·a·ble, loveable /ˈlʌvəbl; ˈlʌvəbəl/ *adj* friendly and attractive 友善可愛的, 討人喜歡的: *a lovable kitten* 可愛的小貓 | *not a very lovable child* 不十分討人喜歡的孩子

love¹ /lʌv; lʌv/ *v*

1 ►ROMANTIC ATTRACTION 愛情的吸引力◄ [T not in progressive 不用進行式] to have a strong feeling of caring for and liking someone, combined with sexual attraction 愛情, 戀愛, 性愛: *I love you, really. Do you love me?* 我真的愛你。你愛我嗎? | *He was the only man she had ever loved.* 他是她唯一愛過的男人。

2 ►CARE ABOUT 關心◄ [T not in progressive 不用進行式] to care very much about someone, especially a member of your family or a close friend〔尤指對家庭成員、親密朋友的〕關心, 鍾愛: *Children need to feel loved.* 孩子需要感到有人關心他們。| **much-loved/greatly-loved/well-loved** *one of America's best-loved TV personalities* 美國觀眾最喜愛的電視名人之一 | **loved ones** (=people you love) 鍾愛的人 *women caring for loved ones who had been injured in the war* 照料在戰爭中受傷的親友的婦女

3 ►LIKE/ENJOY 喜歡/喜愛◄ [T not in passive 不用被動態] to like something very much or enjoy doing something very much 喜歡〔某物〕; 喜愛〔做某事〕: **love doing sth** *Max found that he really loved teaching.* 馬克斯發現他很喜歡教書。| **love sth** *I love carrots.* 我喜歡吃胡蘿蔔。| *She loves anything to do with figures.* 她喜歡一切和數字有關的事。| **love to do sth** *We all love to talk about ourselves.* 我們都喜歡談論自己。| *I love the way she sings that.* 我喜歡她那種唱歌方式。| **I'd love to** *spoken* (=used to say you would really like to do something)【口】我確實願意〔做某事〕*"Would you like to come swimming with us?" "I'd love to."* "你願意和我們一起去游泳嗎?" "我很願意。" | *I'd have loved to have stayed till the end.* 我很想一直逗留到結束。| *I'd love to know just why they did that.* 我真想知道他們到底為甚麼那樣做。

4 I must love you and leave you *spoken* used to tell someone that you have to go, especially when you wish you could stay longer【口】我得走了〔尤用於希望逗留的時間能長些〕

5 ►LOYALTY 忠誠◄ [T not in progressive 不用進行式] to have a strong feeling of loyalty to your country, an institution etc 熱愛〔國家、組織等〕: *He really loved the police force.* 他非常熱愛警隊。

6 I love it! *spoken* used when you are amused by something, especially by someone else's mistake or bad luck【口】好玩! 太有趣了!〔尤用於被他人的差錯或壞運逗樂的時候〕: *"Henry was telling the prof all about relativity." "I love it! I love it!"* "亨利告訴教授所有關於相對論的東西。" "太有趣了! 太有趣了!"

7 she's going to love you/he's going to love this etc *spoken*【口】**a)** used to say that someone will enjoy something 某人會喜歡你[某事等]: *Listen guys, you're going to love this.* 大家聽着, 你們會喜歡聽的。**b)** used jokingly to say that someone will not be pleased about something〔用於開玩笑地表示〕某人不會喜歡某事: *I'm going to love telling him we've changed our minds again.* 我不會高興地告訴他我們又改變主意了。—see also 另見 LOVER

love² *n*

1 ►FOR FAMILY/FRIENDS 對家人/朋友◄ [U] a strong feeling of caring about someone, especially a member of your family or a close friend〔尤指對家人、親密朋友的〕愛, 關心, 關愛: *What these kids need is love and support.* 這些孩子需要的是關心和支持。| **[+for]** *a mother's love for her child* 母親對孩子的愛 —opposite 反義詞 HATE², HATRED

2 ►ROMANTIC 浪漫的◄ [U] a strong feeling of liking and caring about someone, especially combined with sexual attraction 戀愛, 愛情, 性愛: *She's seen him every day this week – it must be love!* 這個星期她每天都見他 —— 那肯定是戀愛! | *a love song* 情歌 | **be/fall in love (with)** *I think I'm falling in love with your brother.* 我想我愛上了你的哥哥。| **madly in love/very much in love/head over heels in love** *It was obvious that they were very much in love.* 很明顯他們在熱戀之中。| **love at first sight** (=when you love someone the first time you see them) 一見鍾情 | **true love** (=strong romantic love that remains for ever) 不變的真愛

3 ►PERSON YOU LOVE 鍾愛的人◄ [C] someone that you feel a strong romantic and sexual attraction to 所愛的人: *He was her first love.* 他是她第一個愛上的人。| **the love of your life** (=the person that you have loved most of your life) 一生中最心愛的人

4 ►PLEASURE/ENJOYMENT 快樂/樂趣◄ a) [singular,U] a strong feeling of pleasure and enjoyment that something gives you 熱愛: **love of/for** *a love of nature* 對大自然的熱愛 **b)** [C] something that gives you a lot of pleasure and enjoyment 愛好, 喜愛: *Sailing was her great love.* 帆船運動是她最大的愛好。

5 make love a) to have sex with someone that you love 做愛, 性交: **make love to/with** *"I want to make love with you," she breathed.* "我想和你做愛。" 她小聲地說。**b)** *old use* to say loving things to someone, to kiss them etc【舊】〔向某人〕示愛

6 send your love (to) to ask someone to give your loving greetings to someone else when they see them, write to them etc 向某人致意[問候]: *Aunt Mary sends her love to you.* 瑪麗姑媽向你問好。

7 give my love to *spoken* used to ask someone to give your loving greetings to someone else【口】轉達我對〔某人〕的問候: *"Bye! Give my love to Jackie."* "再見! 請轉達我對傑基的問候。"

8 love (from)/lots of love/all my love expressions used at the end of a letter to a friend, a member of your family, or someone you love 愛你的…/深愛你的/全心愛你的〔用於寫給朋友、家人或所愛之人的信的末尾〕: *See you soon. Lots of love, Clare.* 希望很快能見到你。深愛你的, 克萊爾。

9 (my) love *spoken*【口】**a)** *especially BrE* a word used when you are talking to someone you love【尤英】親愛的〔用於對所愛的人說話時〕: *Hurry up, love!* 趕快, 親愛的! **b)** *BrE* a friendly way of talking to someone who you do not know, especially to a woman【英】親愛的〔對陌生人說話的友好方式, 尤其是對婦女〕: *Are you OK, love?* 你沒事吧, 親愛的?

10 be a love and.../... there's a love *spoken, especially BrE* expressions used when you are asking someone to do something, used especially to children and members of your family【口, 尤英】乖乖的〔用於要孩子和家人做某事〕: *Say hello to your auntie, there's a love.* 乖乖的, 向阿姨問好。

11 there is no love lost between if there is no love lost between two people, they dislike each other〔兩人之間〕沒有好感, 互相厭惡: *There's never been any love lost between Paul and Geoff.* 保羅和傑夫兩個人彼此憎恨。

12 ►TENNIS 網球◄ [U] an expression meaning no points, used in the game of tennis〔網球比賽中的〕零分

13 not for love or/nor money *informal* if you cannot get something or do something for love or money, it is impossible to obtain or to do【非正式】無論怎樣也不,

决不: *I can't get hold of that book for love nor money.* 我無論如何也找不到那本書。

14 for the love of God/Mike etc *old-fashioned spoken* used to show that you are extremely angry, disappointed etc【過時, 口】看在上帝的份上〔用於表示怒不可遏、沮喪等〕

15 love nest *humorous* a place where two people who are having a romantic relationship live or meet each other【幽默】愛巢〔情人同居或幽會的地方〕—see also 另見 **a labour of love** (LABOUR[1] (4))

love af·fair /ˈ· ·,·/ *n* [C] **1** a romantic sexual relationship, usually between two people who are not married to each other〔尤指非夫妻間的〕性關係; 風流韻事: *a passionate love affair* 火熱的性關係 —see also 另見 AFFAIR (3) **2** a strong enjoyment of something〔對某物的〕強烈興趣, 熱愛, 酷愛: *the great American love affair with the automobile* 美國人對汽車的酷愛

love·bird /ˈlʌv,bɝd; ˈlʌvbɜːd/ *n* [C] **1** a small brightly coloured PARROT[1] (1) 情侶鸚鵡 **2 lovebirds** *humorous* two people who show by their behaviour that they love each other very much【幽默】一對情侶

love bite /ˈ· ·/ *n* [C] *especially BrE* a red mark on someone's skin caused by someone else sucking it as a sexual act【尤英】愛的吮痕〔做愛時被對方在皮膚上吮出的紅印痕〕; HICKEY *AmE*【美】

love·child /ˈlʌvtʃaɪld; ˈlʌvtʃaɪld/ *n* [C] a word used especially in newspapers meaning a child whose parents are not married 私生子〔報紙用語〕

love·less /ˈlʌvlɪs; ˈlʌvləs/ *adj* without love 沒有愛的: *a loveless marriage* 沒有愛情的婚姻

love let·ter /ˈ· ,··/ *n* [C] a letter that someone writes to tell someone else how much they love them 情書

love life /ˈ· ·/ *n* [C,U] the part of your life that involves your love relationships, especially sexual ones 愛情生活〔尤指性生活〕

love·lorn /ˈlʌv,lɔrn; ˈlʌvlɔːn/ *adj literary* sad because the person you love does not love you【文】失戀的, 因失戀而憔悴的

2 3 **love·ly¹** /ˈlʌvlɪ; ˈlʌvli/ *comparative* 比較級 **lovelier** *superlative* 最高級 **loveliest** *adj* **1** *especially BrE* beautiful or attractive【尤英】美麗的; 可愛的: *What a lovely baby!* 多麼可愛的嬰兒! | *Her hair's a lovely shade of red.* 她的頭髮是漂亮的紅色。| **look lovely** *You look lovely in blue.* 你穿藍衣服看上去很漂亮。**2** *informal especially BrE* friendly and pleasant【非正式, 尤英】親切的, 令人愉快的: *Richard's a lovely person.* 理察是一個討人喜歡的人。**3** *BrE spoken* used to say that something is not at all enjoyable, or good【英口】令人敗興的; 糟透了的: *"The cat threw up all over the carpet!" "Lovely!"* "貓吐得整張地毯都是!" "太糟糕了!" | *You've made a lovely mess in here.* 你把這裡弄得亂糟糟的。**4** *spoken especially BrE* very pleasant, enjoyable, or good【口, 尤英】令人愉快[高興]的; 美好的: *That was a lovely cup of tea.* 這是一杯上好的茶。| *Thank you for a lovely evening.* 謝謝你讓我們度過了一個美好的夜晚。**5 lovely and warm/cold etc** *BrE spoken* used to emphasize how good something is【英口】非常暖和/寒冷等〔用於強調〕: *This bread's lovely and fresh.* 這麵包新鮮極了。**6** *BrE spoken* used to show that you are pleased with something【英口】好極了〔用於表示對某事滿意〕: *Push it right across. That's it, lovely.* 把它直接推過去。對, 棒極了。—**loveliness** *n* [U]

lovely² *n* [C] *old-fashioned* an attractive woman【過時】美人, 美女: *Samantha, a nineteen year old Liverpool lovely* 薩曼莎, 十九歲的利物浦美女

love·mak·ing /ˈlʌv,mekɪŋ; ˈlʌv,meɪkɪŋ/ *n* [U] sexual activity, especially the act of having sex 做愛, 性交 —see also 另見 **make love** (LOVE[2] (5))

3 **lov·er** /ˈlʌvɚ; ˈlʌvə/ *n* [C] **1** a sexual partner 性夥伴[伴侶]: *a jealous lover* 愛吃醋的性伴侶 **2** someone who has a sexual relationship for a long time with someone they are not married to〔長期保持性關係的〕情人: *Arabella had had many lovers.* 阿拉貝拉有過很多情人。—compare 比較 MISTRESS (1) **3** someone who enjoys doing a particular thing very much or is very interested in it〔…的〕愛好者: *music lovers* 音樂愛好者

love·seat /ˈlʌv,sit; ˈlʌvsiːt/ *n* [C] **1** a seat in the shape of an S for two people, designed so that they can face each other 情人座〔面對面的S形雙人座〕**2** *AmE* a small SOFA for two people【美】雙人小沙發

love·sick /ˈlʌv,sɪk; ˈlʌv,sɪk/ *adj* spending all your time thinking about someone you love, especially someone who does not love you 單戀, 害相思病的: *You're acting like a lovesick teenager!* 你像一個害相思病的少年!

lov·ey /ˈlʌvɪ; ˈlʌvi/ *n* [C] *BrE spoken* a word used to address a woman or child, that many women think is offensive【英口】親愛的, 寶貝〔對女人或孩子的稱呼, 很多婦女認為是冒犯語〕—see also 另見 LUVVIE

lovey-dov·ey /,lʌvɪ ˈdʌvɪ; ,lʌvi ˈdʌvi◂/ *adj informal* behaviour that is lovey-dovey is too romantic; SENTIMENTAL【非正式】情意綿綿的; 過分多情的: *Josh went all lovey-dovey when I said I was pregnant.* 當我説我懷孕了, 喬希就變得温柔多情起來。

lov·ing /ˈlʌvɪŋ; ˈlʌvɪŋ/ *adj* **1** [only before noun 僅用於名詞前] behaving in a way that shows you love someone 鍾愛的, 表示愛意的: *in memory of my loving wife* 悼念我的愛妻 | *What that child needs is plenty of loving care and attention.* 那孩子所需要的是很多充滿愛的關心和照顧。**2 peace-loving/home-loving etc** thinking that peace, your home etc is very important 熱愛和平的/愛家的: *a peace-loving nation* 熱愛和平的國家 | *Molly's a real home-loving type.* 莫莉是一個非常愛家型的人。—**lovingly** *adv*: *Anna stroked the baby's cheek lovingly.* 安娜慈愛地撫摸嬰孩的臉頰。

loving cup /ˈ·· ·/ *n* [C] a very large cup with two handles that was passed around at formal meals in former times 愛杯〔舊時正式宴會上供賓客傳飲的雙柄大酒杯〕

loving kind·ness /,·· ˈ··/ *n* [U] *especially literary* gentle and sincere friendship or love【尤文】慈愛, 仁愛; 温厚誠摯的友誼

low 低矮的

a low wall 低矮的牆

shallow water 淺水區

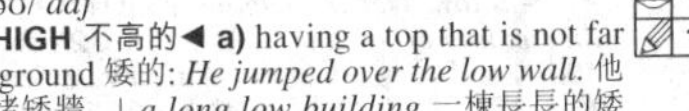

low¹ /lo; ləʊ/ *adj* 1 1

1 ►NOT HIGH 不高的◄ **a)** having a top that is not far above the ground 矮的: *He jumped over the low wall.* 他跳過了那堵矮牆。| *a long low building* 一棟長長的矮房子 **b)** at a point that is not far above the ground 低的,

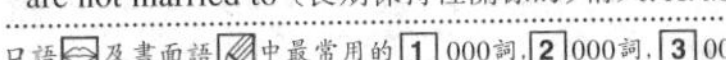

口語 及書面語 中最常用的 1 000詞, 2 000詞, 3 000詞

下面的: *low clouds* 低垂的雲 | *Put the books on the lowest shelf.* 把書放在最下面的書架上。**c)** below the usual height 低於一般高度的: *a low bridge* 矮橋 | *The river is low for this time of year.* 每年的這個時候, 河水比較低。

2 ►SMALL AMOUNT 少量◄ a) small, or smaller than usual, in amount, value etc〔數量、價值等〕少的: *The price of oil is at its lowest for 10 years.* 石油的價格是10年來最低的。| *families existing on very low incomes* 低收入家庭 | **low-cost/low-budget etc** *There's a desperate need for good low-cost housing.* 對價廉物美的住屋有着急迫的需求。**b) low in** having less than the usual amount of a substance or chemical〔某種物質或化學品等〕含量低的: *food that is low in calories* 低熱量食品 | **low-fat/low-salt etc** *I only smoke low-tar cigarettes.* 我只抽焦油含量低的香煙。| *low-alcohol beer* 低酒精度啤酒 **c) in the low 20s/50s etc** a number, temperature etc in the low 20s etc is around 21, 22, or 23, but no higher〔數字、溫度等〕在20多一點〔21–23〕/50多一點〔51–53〕等: *Daytime temperature will be in the low 30s.* 白天溫度將在31度至33度之間。

3 ►BELOW USUAL LEVEL 低於一般水平◄ small, or smaller than usual, in level or degree〔水平或程度〕低的; 小於平常的: *In this sort of investment, the risks are fairly low.* 在這種投資中, 風險相當小。| *Morale has been low since the latest round of job-cuts.* 自最近一輪裁員以來, 士氣一直很低落。| **low-risk/low-priority etc** *a low-security prison* 警戒不嚴的監獄, 低度設防監獄

4 ►STANDARDS/QUALITY 標準/質量◄ below an acceptable or usual level or quality〔水平或質量〕低於可接受[平常]程度的: *Their safety standards seem to be pretty low.* 他們的安全標準似乎相當低。| *Cost-cutting has led to a lower quality of service.* 削減成本導致了服務質量的降低。

5 ►SUPPLY 供應◄ a) a supply of something that is low is nearly finished 短缺的, 將耗盡的: **be/get/run low (on)** *We're running low on coffee.* 我們的咖啡不多了。| *Stocks are getting low.* 庫存快耗盡了。

6 ►SOUND 聲音◄ a low voice, sound etc is quiet or deep 低聲的, 輕聲的: *I heard a low moaning noise.* 我聽到低沉的呻吟聲。| *The volume is too low – turn it up.* 音量太低了 — 開響一點。| *a low whisper* 低聲耳語

7 ►LIGHT 光線◄ a light that is low is not bright 暗淡的: *low romantic lighting in a restaurant* 餐館裡具有浪漫色彩的暗淡燈光

8 ►HEAT 熱度◄ if you cook something on a low heat or in a low OVEN, you cook it using only a small amount of heat〔烹調時〕低溫的, 低熱度的

9 ►BATTERY 電池◄ a BATTERY that is low does not have much power left in it〔電力〕不足的

10 ►CLOTHES 衣服◄ a low dress, BLOUSE etc does not cover your neck and the top of your chest〔衣服〕領口低的, 低胸的

11 ►UNHAPPY 不高興的◄ [not before noun 不用於名詞前] unhappy and without much hope for the future 不高興的, 情緒低落的: *She's still feeling pretty low about failing that exam.* 她考試不及格, 情緒仍很低落。| **in low spirits** *Terry seems to be in rather low spirits today.* 泰里今天似乎情緒相當低落。

12 ►DISHONEST 不誠實的◄ *old-fashioned or humorous* behaviour that is low is not fair or honest【過時或幽默】卑鄙的, 卑劣的: *a low trick* 卑鄙的詭計

13 of low birth/breeding *old-fashioned* not from a high social class【過時】出身低微的 —see also 另見 **be at a low ebb** (EBB¹ (2)), **—lowness** *n* [U]

low² *adv* **1** in or to a low position or level 低; 低水平地: *He bent low over the engine.* 他俯身察看引擎。| *Turn the heating down low.* 把暖氣關小。**2** near the ground 高出地面不多地, 不高地: *Watch out for low-flying aircraft.* 當心低空飛行的飛機。**3** if you play or sing musical notes low, you play or sing them with quiet deep notes〔彈奏或唱歌時〕用低音調, 低沉地: *Sing those bars an octave lower.* 這幾小節用低八度唱。**4 search/look high and low** *informal* to look everywhere in order to find something【非正式】到處尋找 **5 lie low a)** to hide from people who are trying to catch you 躲藏, 隱匿 **b)** to wait and try not to be noticed by anyone 避免引人注目, 等候機會: *Just lie low for a while.* 別出頭露面, 等一會兒。**6 lay sb low** to knock someone down onto the ground or to make someone feel very weak 擊倒某人; 使某人身體虛弱: *laid low by flu* 因流感而病倒 **7 be brought low** *old-fashioned* to become much less rich or important【過時】變得遠不如原來富有[重要] —see also 另見 LOWLY

low³ *n* **1** [C] a low price or level 低價; 低水平: **fall to a new low/hit a new low** (=be worth less than ever before) 降到新低點/達到新低點 *The pound has fallen to a new low against the dollar.* 英鎊對美元的匯價降到了新低。| **all-time low** (=much lower or worse than ever before) 前所未有的低[差] *Profits hit an all-time low this month.* 這個月的利潤降到了歷史上最低點。**2** [C] a bad situation in someone's personal life〔某人生活中的〕低潮: **all-time low** (=a worse situation than ever before) 最差的境況 *1963 marked an all-time low in his family life.* 1963 年是他家庭生活最糟的一年。| **highs and lows** (=good times and bad times) 好與差的時期 *the highs and lows in their marriage* 他們婚姻生活中的高潮和低潮 **3** [C usually singular 一般用單數] **a)** an area of low pressure in the air 低氣壓區: *a low moving in over the Pacific* 從太平洋上空移入的低氣壓區 **b)** a low temperature 低温: *The overnight low will be 8°C.* 晚間低温為攝氏8度。**4 the lowest of the low a)** *informal* someone you think is completely unfair, cruel, immoral etc【非正式】最不公正[殘忍, 不道德等]的人: *Property barons are among the lowest of the low.* 房地產巨頭是最卑劣之徒。**b)** *often humorous* someone from a low social class【常幽默】社會地位低微的人

low⁴ *v* [I] *especially literary* if cattle low, they make a deep sound【尤文】〔牛〕哞哞叫

low beam /ˌ· ˈ·/ *n* **be on low beam** if the lights at the front of a car are on low beam, they light only a short distance of the road ahead and are not very bright〔汽車前燈的〕近距離光

low·born /ˌloˈbɔrn; ˌləʊˈbɔːn◄/ *adj old-fashioned* coming from a low social class【過時】出身低微的

low·brow /ˈloˌbrau; ˈləʊbraʊ/ *adj* not interested in or connected with literature, art etc 對文學、藝術等不感興趣的; 與文學、藝術等無關的, 庸俗的: *lowbrow television shows* 庸俗的電視節目 —compare 比較 HIGHBROW

low-cal, lo-cal /ˌloˈkæl; ˌləʊˈkæl◄/ *adj informal* low-cal food or drink does not contain many CALORIES【非正式】〔食物或飲料〕低熱量的

Low Church /ˌ· ˈ·◄/ *n* [U] the part of the Church of England that believes in the importance of faith and studying the BIBLE rather than in religious ceremonies〔英國〕低教會派〔認為信仰及對《聖經》的研習比宗教儀式重要〕—compare 比較 HIGH CHURCH

low-class /ˌ· ˈ·◄/ *adj* **1** *old-fashioned* WORKING CLASS【過時】工人階級, 勞工階級: *a low-class bar* 工人酒吧 **2** not good quality 質量低劣的

low-cut /ˌ· ˈ·◄/ *adj* a low-cut dress is shaped so that it shows your neck and the top of your chest〔連衣裙〕低胸的

low·down /ˈloˌdaun; ˈləʊdaʊn/ *n* **the lowdown (on)** *informal* the most important facts about something or someone【非正式】〔關於某事物或某人的〕最重要情況: *Give me all the lowdown on what happened at the meeting.* 告訴我會議的所有重點。

low-down /ˈ· ·/ *adj* [only before noun 僅用於名詞前] *informal* dishonest and unkind【非正式】卑劣的, 卑鄙的: *What a low-down, dirty trick.* 多麼卑劣骯髒的勾當!

low·er¹ /ˈloə; ˈləʊə/ *adj* **1** [only before noun 僅用於名詞前] below something else, especially beneath some- 

thing of the same type〔尤指在同類中處於〕較下的; 下層的: *Nina chewed her lower lip anxiously.* 尼娜焦慮不安地咬着下唇。| *the lower limbs* (=legs) 下肢 **2** [only before noun 僅用於名詞前] at or near the bottom of something 在底部的; 接近底部的: *the lower slopes of the mountain* 山腳 **3** smaller in number or amount〔數字或數量〕較小的: *Temperatures will be lower over the weekend.* 週末氣温會下降。**4** [only before noun 僅用於名詞前] less important than something else of the same type〔同類中〕次重要的, 較低級的: *the lower levels of management* 較低級的管理層

lower² *v*

1 ▶REDUCE 減少◀ [I,T] to reduce something in amount, degree, strength etc, or to become less 減少, 降低: *After 20 minutes lower the temperature to 325°.* 20分鐘後, 將温度降到325度。| *drugs to lower blood pressure* 降血壓的藥 | **lower your voice** (=make it quieter) 壓低嗓音 *Helen lowered her voice as they approached.* 當他們走近時, 海倫壓低了嗓音。

2 ▶MOVE DOWN 降下◀ [T] to move something down from higher up 把〔某物〕移低, 降下: *The flags were lowered to half-mast.* 下了半旗。| **lower sth down/into/between etc** *They lowered the coffin into the grave.* 他們把棺材放到墓穴中。

3 lower yourself [usually in negatives 一般用於否定句] to behave in a way that makes people respect you less 降低〔自己的〕身分: *I wouldn't lower myself to speak to her after what she's done.* 她做了那樣的事以後, 我不會自降身分和她說話。

4 lower the tone *often humorous* to make a conversation, a social situation etc less polite, for example by telling rude jokes【常幽默】敗壞〔談話、社交場合等〕的格調: *They thought an influx of students would lower the tone of the neighborhood.* 他們認為學生的湧入會使這一帶的風氣變差。

5 lower your eyes to look down 向下看: *Katrina lowered her eyes demurely.* 卡特里娜含羞地垂下眼睛。—**lowered** *adj*: *Zoe watched through lowered eyelashes.* 佐伊透過垂下的眼睫毛向外觀察。

low·er³ also 又作 **lour** *BrE*【英】/ˈlauə; ˈlaʊə/ *v* [I] **1** when the sky or the weather lowers, it becomes dark because there is going to be a storm〔暴風雨前的天〕變昏暗;〔天氣〕變險惡: *lowering clouds* 陰沉沉的雲 **2** *literary* to look threatening or annoyed; FROWN¹【文】露慍色; 皺眉: *lowering at us across the table* 隔着桌子生氣地看着我們

lower case /ˌ.. ˈ.◂/ *n* [U] letters in their small forms, such as a, b, c etc 小寫字體〈如a, b, c等〉—compare 比較 CAPITAL¹ (3) —opposite 反義詞 UPPER CASE —**lower case** *adj*: *lower case letters* 小寫字母

lower class /ˌ.. ˈ.◂/ also 又作 **lower classes** *n* [C] *old-fashioned* the social class that has less money, power, or education than anyone else【過時】下層階級, 勞工階級 —see also 另見 WORKING CLASS —**lower-class** *adj*

Lower House /ˌ.. ˈ./ also 又作 **Lower Cham·ber** /ˌ.. ˈ../ *n* [singular] a group of elected representatives who make laws in a country, for example the HOUSE OF COMMONS in Britain or the HOUSE OF REPRESENTATIVES in the US〔某國議會的〕下院〈如英國的下議院、美國的眾議院〉

lower or·ders /ˌ.. ˈ../ *n old-fashioned* **the lower orders** an expression meaning people of a low social class, used especially by people who consider themselves to be better and more important【過時】下層社會〔尤為自視為上層社會的人所用〕

lowest com·mon de·nom·i·na·tor /ˌ.. ˌ.. ˈ..../ *n* [U] **1** *technical* the smallest number that the bottom numbers of a group of fractions (FRACTION (2)) can be divided into exactly【術語】最小公分母 **2** the biggest possible number of people, including people who are very easily influenced or are willing to accept low standards〔容易受影響或願意接受低水準的〕社會大眾: *Television quiz shows often seem to target the lowest common denominator.* 電視問答競賽節目經常似乎以迎合大眾的趣味為目標。

lowest com·mon mul·ti·ple /ˌ.. ˌ.. ˈ.../ *n* [C] *technical* the smallest number that two or more numbers divide into exactly【術語】最小公倍數: *12 is the lowest common multiple of 4 and 6.* 12是4和6的最小公倍數。

low-fat /ˌ. ˈ.◂/ *adj* containing or using only a small amount of fat 含脂肪少的; 低脂肪的: *a low-fat, high-fibre diet* 低脂肪高纖維膳食

low-fly·ing /. ˈ..◂/ *adj* flying close to the ground 低空飛行的

low gear /ˌ. ˈ./ *n* [C,U] one of a vehicle's GEARs that you use when you are driving at a slow speed〔車輛的〕低速擋, 低速齒輪傳動裝置

low-key /ˌ. ˈ.◂/ *adj* not intended to attract a lot of attention to an event, subject, or thing 低調的: *The reception was a low-key affair.* 那個招待會是一次低調的活動。| *a low-key approach to establishing women's rights* 確立婦女權利的低調處理方法

low·lands /ˈloləndz; ˈləʊləndz/ *n* [plural] an area of land that is lower than the land around it 低地: *the Scottish lowlands* 蘇格蘭低地 —**lowland** *adj* [only before noun 僅用於名詞前]: *lowland farming* 低地耕作 —**lowlander** *n* [C] —compare 比較 HIGHLANDS

low-lev·el /ˌ. ˈ..◂/ *adj* a low-level computer language is used to give instructions to a computer and is similar to the language that the computer operates in〔電腦語言〕低階的, 低級的〔類似於電腦作業指令的〕—compare 比較 HIGH-LEVEL (4)

low life /ˈ. ./ *n* **1** [U] the life and behaviour of people from a low social class, especially those who are involved in criminal activities 下層社會的生活〔尤指犯罪活動〕: *a novel about low life in Chicago in the 1930s* 描寫20世紀30年代芝加哥下層社會生活的小說 **2** also 又作 **lowlife** [C] *AmE informal* someone who is involved in crime or who is bad【美, 非正式】罪犯; 惡棍: *Pete turned out to be a real lowlife.* 彼得原來是個十足的惡棍。—**low-life** *adj AmE informal*【美, 非正式】: *some low-life hooker Joe's taken up with* 某個和喬相好的低級妓女

low·lights /ˈloˌlaɪts; ˈləʊlaɪts/ *n* [plural] a dark colour that can be added to change the natural colour of some of your hair 深色染髮劑 —compare 比較 **highlights** (HIGHLIGHT² (2))

low·ly /ˈlolɪ; ˈləʊli/ *adj sometimes humorous* low in rank, importance, or social class; HUMBLE¹ (1)【有時幽默】〔等級、重要性或社會地位等〕低下的, 低級的; 卑微的: *He had left his lowly origins far behind.* 他已經徹底擺脫了低微的出身。| *Don't ask me, I'm just a lowly cleaner.* 別問我, 我只不過是一個普通的清潔工人。—**lowliness** *n* [U]

low-ly·ing /ˌ. ˈ..◂/ *adj* **1** low-lying land is not far above the level of the sea〔土地〕高出海面不多的 **2** below the usual level 低於一般水平的: *low-lying mist* 低層的霧

low-paid /ˌ. ˈ.◂/ *adj* providing or earning only a small amount of money 薪水低的: *low-paid jobs in catering* 飲食行業中的低薪工作

low-pitched /ˌ. ˈ.◂/ *adj* **1** a low-pitched musical note or sound is deep〔音符〕低音的;〔聲音〕低沉的: *the low-pitched hum of the generator* 發電機低沉的嗡嗡聲 **2** a low-pitched roof is not steep〔屋頂〕不陡的, 緩坡的

low point /ˈ. ./ *n* [C usually singular 一般用單數] the worst moment of a situation or activity〔情況或活動〕最糟的時刻: *For him, the low point came with a phone call from the police.* 對他來說, 最糟糕的時刻是警察打來電話那一刻。

low-pressure /ˌ. ˈ../ *n* [U] a condition of the air over a large area that affects the weather 低氣壓

low pro·file /ˌ. ˈ../ *n* **keep a low profile** to be careful not to attract attention to yourself or your actions 保持低姿態: *We'd better keep a low profile until the whole thing blows over.* 我們最好保持低調直到整件事情過去。

—**low-profile** *adj*: *a low-profile campaign* 低姿態的〔競選〕活動

low·rid·er /ˈloraɪdɚ; ˈləʊraɪdə/ *n* [C] *AmE* a big car that has its bottom very close to the ground, or a young man who drives this type of car【美】低底盤轎車; 年輕的低底盤轎車駕駛者

low-rise /ˈ· ·/ *adj* [only before noun 僅用於名詞前] a low-rise building does not have many STOREYS〔建築物〕層數少的 —compare 比較 HIGH-RISE

low-risk /ˌ· ˈ·◂/ *adj* [only before noun 僅用於名詞前] likely to be safe or without difficulties 低風險的: *a low-risk investment* 低風險投資

low sea·son /ˈ· ˌ··/ *n BrE* the time of year when there is the least business for hotels, shops etc; OFF-SEASON【英】〔旅館、商店等的營業〕淡季 —compare 比較 HIGH SEASON

low-spir·it·ed /ˌ· ˈ···◂/ *adj* unhappy; DEPRESSED (1) 悶悶不樂的, 沒精打采的, 情緒消沉的: *He was a dull, low-spirited companion.* 他是一個乏味的、情緒消沉的夥伴。

low-tech /ˌ· ˈ·◂/ *adj* not using the most modern machines or methods in business or industry〔商業或工業〕低技術的, 技術簡單的 —opposite 反義詞 HIGH-TECH

low tide /ˌ· ˈ·/ *n* [C,U] the time when sea water is at its lowest level〔海水的〕低潮 (時間): *You can walk across to the island at low tide.* 在低潮時你可以徒步走到對面的島上。—opposite 反義詞 HIGH TIDE (1)

low wa·ter /ˌ· ˈ··/ *n* [U] the time when the water in a river or the sea is at its lowest level because of the TIDE[1] (1)〔河、海的〕低水位, 低潮

low water mark /ˌ· ˈ·· ˌ·/ *n* [C] **1** a mark showing the lowest level reached by a river or other area of water 低潮線, 低水位線 **2** the worst time in someone's life, job etc〔某人生活或工作等中〕最不順利的時期, 最低點: *Our fortunes had reached their low water mark.* 我們的時運到了最倒霉的時候。

lox /lɑks; lɒks/ *n* [U] *especially AmE* SALMON that has been treated with smoke in order to preserve it【尤美】熏鮭魚, 熏大麻哈魚

loy·al /ˈlɔɪəl; ˈlɔɪəl/ *adj* always supporting your friends, principles, country etc〔對…〕忠貞的, 忠實的, 忠誠的: **[+to]** *Dennis will always be loyal to this government, whatever it does.* 無論這屆政府做甚麼, 丹尼斯對它忠貞不渝。| *a loyal supporter of the team* 球隊的忠實支持者 —**loyally** *adv*

loy·al·ist /ˈlɔɪəlɪst; ˈlɔɪəlɪ̈st/ *n* [C] someone who continues to support a government or country, when a lot of people want to change it〔支持某政府或國家的〕忠誠分子 —**loyalist** *adj*

loy·al·ty /ˈlɔɪəltɪ; ˈlɔɪəlti/ *n* **1** [U] the quality of remaining faithful to your friends, principles, country etc 忠誠, 忠貞: **[+to/towards]** *These people feel a lot of loyalty to the company.* 這些人都對公司忠心耿耿。**2** [C usually plural 一般用複數] a feeling of support for someone or something 忠心, 忠於…的感情: *Don't let political loyalties affect your judgment.* 不要讓政治傾向影響你的判斷。| **divided loyalties** (=two strong feelings of loyalty that you must choose between) 相互抵觸的忠誠 *the agony of divided loyalties for the children in a divorce* 離婚中孩子左右為難的痛苦

loz·enge /ˈlɑzɪndʒ; ˈlɒzɪ̈ndʒ/ *n* [C] **1** a small flat sweet, especially one that contains medicine〔含有藥物的〕小塊扁糖, 糖錠, 藥糖: *a cough lozenge* 止咳糖 **2** a shape similar to a square, with two angles of less than 90° opposite each other and two angles of more than 90° opposite each other 菱形

LP /ˌɛl ˈpi; ˌel ˈpiː/ *n* [C] long playing record; a record that turns 33 times per minute, and usually plays for between 20 and 25 minutes on each side 慢轉[密紋]唱片

L-plate /ˈɛl plet; ˈel pleɪt/ *n* [C] a flat white square with a red letter L on it, that must be fixed to the back and front of a car being driven by a learner in Britain L字車牌, 學車牌〔在英國掛在學習駕駛者車輛的前後〕

LRV /ˌɛl ɑr ˈvi; ˌel ɑː ˈviː/ *n* [C] Light Rail Vehicle; a type of train whose tracks run in or between streets, used especially in cities in the US〔尤指在美國城市中行走的〕輕軌火車

LSD /ˌɛl ɛs ˈdi; ˌel es ˈdiː/ *n* [U] an illegal drug that makes you see things as more beautiful, strange, frightening etc than usual, or see things that do not exist; ACID[1] (2) 麥角酰二乙胺〔一種迷幻藥〕

Lsd, £sd /ˌɛl ɛs ˈdi; ˌel es ˈdiː/ *n* [U] *BrE old-fashioned*【英, 過時】**1** the abbreviation of 縮寫=pounds, SHILLINGS, and pence, the system of money used in Britain before 1971 英鎊, 先令和便士〔1971年前英國使用的貨幣體係〕 **2** money 錢

Lt. the written abbreviation of 縮寫= LIEUTENANT

Ltd the written abbreviation of 縮寫= LIMITED (2), used in the names of companies or businesses 有限(責任)公司〔用於公司或企業名稱〕: *M. Dixon & Son Ltd* 狄克遜父子有限公司 —compare 比較 INC, PLC

lu·bri·cant /ˈlubrɪkənt; ˈluːbrɪkənt/ *n* [C,U] a substance such as oil that you put on surfaces that rub together, especially parts of a machine, in order to make them move smoothly and easily 潤滑劑[油]

lu·bri·cate /ˈlubrɪˌket; ˈluːbrɪkeɪt/ *v* [T] to put a lubricant on something in order to make it move more smoothly 使潤滑, 給…加潤滑劑[油]: *Lubricate all moving parts with grease.* 給所有活動部件加潤滑油。—**lubrication** /ˌlubrɪˈkeʃən; ˌluːbrɪˈkeɪʃən/ *n* [U]

lu·bri·cious /luˈbrɪʃəs; luːˈbrɪʃəs/ *adj formal* too interested in sex, in a way that seems unpleasant or unacceptable【正式】淫蕩的, 猥褻的 —**lubriciously** *adv*

lu·cid /ˈlusɪd; ˈluːsɪ̈d/ *adj* **1** expressed in a way that is clear and easy to understand 表達清楚的, 易於理解的: *a lucid and accurate account of the day's events* 對當日事件清楚而精確的描述 **2** a word meaning able to understand and think clearly, used especially about someone who is not always able to do this〔尤指總是迷迷糊糊的人〕神志還清醒的, 頭腦還清楚的: *In her more lucid moments the old lady would talk about her past.* 在頭腦較清醒的時候, 老太太會談起她過去的事。—**lucidly** *adv* —**lucidity** /luˈsɪdətɪ; luːˈsɪdɪ̈ti/ *n* [U]

Lu·ci·fer /ˈlusəfɚ; ˈluːsɪ̈fə/ *n* the devil 魔王

luck[1] /lʌk; lʌk/ *n* [U]

1 ►GOOD FORTUNE 好運◄ something good that happens by chance 好運, 幸運: **have luck (with sth)** *Did you have any luck with the job application?* 你申請這份工作有甚麼進展嗎? | *You're not having much luck today, are you?* 你今天運氣欠佳, 是不是? | **Good luck!/Best of luck!** *Good luck tomorrow in the exam!* 祝明天考試好運! | **wish sb luck** *Tom wished me luck in the race and left.* 湯姆祝我在比賽中好運, 然後離開了。

2 ►CHANCE 機會◄ the way in which good or bad things happen to people by chance 運氣: *There's no skill in roulette, it's all a matter of luck.* 輪盤賭博沒有甚麼技巧, 完全是碰運氣的事。| **good/bad luck** *We seem to have had a lot of bad luck lately.* 我們近來似乎惡運連連。| **sheer/pure luck** *It was sheer luck you were there to help.* 全靠運氣, 你在那裡幫忙。

3 any luck? *spoken* used to ask someone if they have succeeded in doing something【口】做好了嗎? 成功了嗎?: *"I phoned them about the car." "Any luck?" "Yes, it'll be ready on Tuesday."* "我給他們打電話講汽車的事。""能弄好嗎?""對, 星期二就能弄好了。"

4 do sth for luck to do something because you think it might bring you good luck 為帶來好運而做某事: *John always carried a rabbit's foot for luck.* 約翰總是帶着一隻兔腳, 認為會帶來好運。

5 be in luck to be able to do or get something, especially when you did not expect to〔出乎意料的〕走運: *We're in luck – the train hasn't gone yet.* 我們運氣好——火車還沒有開走。

6 be out of luck to be prevented from getting or doing something by bad luck 不走運: *I'm sorry, you're out of* *luck! I sold the last one this morning.* 對不起, 你運氣不好! 最後一個我今天早上賣掉了。

7 just my luck! *spoken* used to say that you are not surprised something bad has happened to you, because you are usually unlucky【口】我總是運氣不好! 我總是不走運!: *He's married, is he? Just my luck!* 他已經結婚了, 是不是? 我總是不走運!

8 no such luck! *spoken* used to say you are disappointed, because something good that could have happened did not happen【口】沒這樣的運氣〔表示失望〕: *"Did you get a rise then?" "No such luck!"* "那麼你得到加薪了嗎?" "沒這樣的運氣!"

9 with (any) luck/with a bit of luck *spoken* if things happen in the way that you want; HOPEFULLY【口】要是走運的話; 但願: *With any luck, there'll be some food left.* 運氣好的話, 會有些食物剩下來。

10 better luck next time! used to say that you hope someone will be more successful the next time they try to do something〔祝某人〕下次好運些!

11 good luck to sb *spoken* used to say that you do not mind what someone does, because it does not affect you and may help them【口】祝某人好運〔用於表示不介意某人做的事, 因不會受到影響, 但對他有幫助〕: *Well if she wants to go on her own, good luck to her, but I'm staying here.* 好吧, 如果她自己要去, 祝她好運, 但我會留在這裡。

12 luck is on sb's side if luck is on someone's side, things go well for them 某人走運[交好運]: *Luck was on my side; all the traffic lights were green.* 我很走運, 一路全是綠燈。

13 as luck would have it used to say that something happened by chance 碰巧: *As luck would have it, the bar was shut when we got there.* 真不巧, 我們到那酒吧的時候, 它已經關門了。

14 be down on your luck to have no money because you have had a lot of bad luck over a period of time〔因不走運而〕窮困潦倒: *You really find out who your friends are when you're down on your luck!* 在你窮困潦倒的時候, 你才能發現誰是你的朋友!

15 the luck of the draw the result of chance rather than something you can control 碰運氣的事: *You can't be sure of getting a ticket – it's all in the luck of the draw.* 你不可能保證買到票——這都是碰運氣的事。

16 stroke of luck something very fortunate, happening by chance 真巧, 真幸運: *What a stroke of luck, bumping into David in the street like that!* 真巧, 在街上就那樣碰到了大衛!

17 some people have all the luck! *spoken* used when someone else has got something that you would like【口】有些人就是運氣好!〔用於別人得到你所喜愛的東西時〕: *Rich parents as well? Some people have all the luck!* 還有富有的父母? 有些人真是運氣好!

18 a run of bad luck a period of time when a lot of bad things happen to you 一段倒霉的日子

19 try/chance your luck to do something because you hope you will be successful, even though you know you may not be 碰碰運氣: *The Hotel Europa was full, so we decided to try our luck elsewhere.* 歐羅巴酒店已經客滿, 所以我們決定到別處去碰碰運氣。

20 bad/hard/tough luck! *spoken especially BrE* used to express sympathy when something unpleasant has happened to someone【口, 尤英】真不幸!〔用於表示同情〕: *Oh bad luck! I'm sure you'll pass next time.* 哦, 真不幸! 我相信下次你會及格的。—compare 比較 **tough luck** (TOUGH¹ (7))

21 worse luck! *BrE spoken* unfortunately【英口】真倒霉!: *I've got to work this Saturday, worse luck!* 這個星期六我得工作, 真倒霉!

22 (one) for luck *spoken* used when you take or add something for no particular reason【口】(取或加一個)祈求好運〔用於無緣無故拿去或添加某物時〕

23 trust to luck to hope that things will happen in the way that you want, even though you cannot control them 靠運氣〔希望得償所願〕: *I decided to just apply for the job and trust to luck for the rest.* 我決定就去申請一下這份工作, 剩下的事情就全靠運氣了。—see also 另見 **hard-luck story** (HARD¹ (23)), **push your luck** (PUSH¹ (10))

luck² *v*

luck out *phr v* [I] *AmE informal* to be lucky【美, 非正式】走運: *Yeah, we really lucked out, got a parking space right in front.* 是, 我們真走運, 正好在前面有一個停車位。

luck·i·ly /ˈlʌkɪlɪ; ˈlʌkɪli/ *adv* as a result of good luck 幸運地: *Luckily she can take a joke.* 她幸而經得起開玩笑。| **luckily for sb** *Luckily for us, the rain held off all day.* 我們真幸運, 一整天沒有下雨。 S3

luck·less /ˈlʌklɪs; ˈlʌkləs/ *adj literary* having no luck in something you are trying to do【文】〔做某事而〕運氣不好的, 不幸的: *He died in the desert like so many other luckless explorers.* 他像許多不幸的探險者一樣死在沙漠中。

luck·y /ˈlʌkɪ; ˈlʌki/ *adj* **1** having good luck; fortunate 運氣好的; 幸運的: **be lucky (enough) to do/be** *You were lucky to catch him in.* 你真幸運能在他家裡碰見他。| *John was lucky enough to be selected for the team.* 約翰真幸運, 能被選入球隊。| **lucky (that)** *He's lucky he didn't break his neck.* 他幸好脖子沒有斷。| **[+with]** *We've been very lucky with the weather.* 我們很幸運, 天氣一直很好。| **think/count yourself lucky** *You can count yourself lucky he didn't hear you.* 算你幸運, 他沒有聽到你説甚麼。**2** resulting from good luck 由好運產生的: *I didn't really know your name – it was just a lucky guess.* 我真的不知道你的名字——只是碰運氣猜中的。| *a lucky escape* 僥倖的逃脱 **3** bringing good luck 帶來好運的, 吉祥的: *a lucky charm* 吉祥飾物 **4 I/you should be so lucky!** *spoken* used to say that someone wants something that is unreasonable and not likely to happen【口】我/你沒有那種福氣!〔用於表示某人的要求不合理及不大可能實現〕: *You want a transfer to the London office? You should be so lucky!* 你想調到倫敦的辦事處去工作? 你沒這運氣! **5 lucky you/me etc!** *spoken* used to say that someone is fortunate to be able to do something【口】我/你真幸運!〔指某人有幸能做某事〕: *"I'm going out tonight." "Lucky you."* "今晚我會外出!" "你真幸運。" —see also 另見 **thank your lucky stars** (THANK (6)), **third time lucky** (THIRD¹) S2 W3

lucky dip /ˌ·· ˈ·/ *n BrE*【英】**1** [C] a game in which you put your hand into a container filled with small objects, and choose one without looking 摸彩袋, 運氣袋; GRAB BAG (1) *AmE*【美】**2** [singular] a situation in which what happens depends on chance 由運氣[機遇]來決定的事

lu·cra·tive /ˈlukrətɪv; ˈluːkrətɪv/ *adj* a job or activity that is lucrative lets you earn a lot of money; PROFITABLE〔職業或活動〕可賺大錢的; 盈利的: *Flynn had a lucrative contract at Warners.* 弗林在華納公司有一份很賺錢的合同。

lu·cre /ˈlukɚ; ˈluːkə/ *n* **filthy lucre** money or wealth, used to show disapproval 骯髒錢, 不義之財

Lud·dite /ˈlʌdaɪt; ˈlʌdaɪt/ *n* [C] someone who is strongly opposed to using modern machines and methods 堅決反對使用現代機器、現代方法的人

lu·di·crous /ˈludɪkrəs; ˈluːdʒkrəs/ *adj* completely unreasonable, stupid, or unsuitable; RIDICULOUS 荒唐的, 愚蠢荒謬的, 可笑的: *She turned up wearing a ludicrous flowery hat.* 她戴着一頂可笑的花帽到來。—**ludicrously** *adv*: *The test was ludicrously easy.* 這次測驗是意想不到的容易。—**ludicrousness** *n* [U]

lu·do /ˈludo; ˈluːdəʊ/ *n* [U] *BrE trademark* a game played with COUNTERS (=small flat round objects) on a board【英, 商標】魯多〔一種用小的籌碼在紙板上玩的遊戲〕; PARCHEESI *AmE*【美】

lug¹ /lʌg; lʌg/ **lugged, lugging** *v* [T] to pull or carry something heavy with difficulty 吃力地拖[拉]〔重物〕: **lug sth**

up/down/around etc *I lugged my suitcase up the stairs and rang the bell.* 我費勁地提着箱子上樓梯, 按門鈴。

lug² *n* [C] **1** a part of something that sticks out and can be used as a handle or a support〔用作柄、把手等的〕耳狀物 **2** *BrE humorous* an ear; LUGHOLE【英, 幽默】耳朵 **3** a LUGWORM 沙蠋 **4** *AmE old-fashioned* a rough, stupid, or awkward person【美, 過時】笨拙的粗人: *You big lug!* 你這個大笨蛋!

luge /luʒ; luːʒ/ *n* [C] a vehicle with blades instead of wheels on which you slide down a track made of ice 仰臥滑行用的小雪橇

lug·gage /ˋlʌgɪdʒ; ˈlʌgɪdʒ/ *n* [U] the cases, bags etc carried by someone who is travelling 行李 —see also 另見 HAND LUGGAGE

luggage rack /ˈ‥ ˌ‥/ *n* [C] a shelf in a train, bus etc for putting luggage on〔火車、公共汽車等內的〕行李架 —see picture at 參見 RACK¹ 圖

luggage van /ˈ‥ ˌ‥/ *n* [C] *BrE* the part of a train that boxes, cases etc are carried in【英】〔火車的〕行李車

lug·ger /ˋlʌgɚ; ˈlʌgə/ *n* [C] a small boat with one or more lugsails 有斜桁四角帆的小船

lug·hole /ˋlʌghol; ˈlʌghəʊl/ *n* [C] *BrE humorous* an ear【英, 幽默】耳朵

lug·sail /ˋlʌgˌsel; ˈlʌgseɪl/ *n* [C] a four-sided sail that hangs down from a pole attached to the MAST (1) 斜桁四角帆

lu·gu·bri·ous /luˋgjubrɪəs; lʊˈguːbriəs/ *adj literary or humorous* very sad and serious【文或幽默】悲傷的, 憂鬱的: *a lugubrious voice* 悲哀的噪音 —**lugubriously** *adv* —**lugubriousness** *n* [U]

lug·worm /ˋlʌgˌwɝm; ˈlʌgwɜːm/ *n* [C] a small WORM that lives in sand by the sea, often used to catch fish〔常用作釣餌的〕沙蠋

luke·warm /ˌlukˋwɔrm; ˌluːkˈwɔːm◂/ *adj* **1** food, liquid etc that is lukewarm is slightly warm and often not as hot or cold as it should be; TEPID〔食物、液體等〕微温的; 温熱的: *Why do British people like lukewarm beer?* 為甚麼英國人喜歡温熱的啤酒? —see picture at 參見 HOT¹ 圖 **2** not showing much interest or excitement 不熱心的, 冷淡的: *His plan got only a lukewarm response from the committee.* 他的計劃只得到委員會冷淡的反應。

lull¹ /lʌl; lʌl/ *v* [T] **1** to make someone feel calm or sleepy 使平靜下來; 使昏昏欲睡: *The movement of the train gradually lulled me to sleep.* 火車的晃動漸漸使我昏昏欲睡。**2** to make someone feel safe and confident so that they are completely surprised when you attack or cheat them 哄騙, 使放鬆警惕: **lull sb into (doing) sth** *Felix's charm lulled me into believing he loved me.* 費利克斯的魅力騙得我相信他是愛我的。| **lull sb into a false sense of security** (=make someone think they are safe when they are not) 騙某人產生一種虛假的安全感

lull² *n* [C] **1** a short period of time when there is less activity or less noise than usual〔活動或吵聲的〕暫停期, 暫時平靜期: **[+in]** *a brief lull in the conversation* 談話短暫的停止 | *a lull in the fighting* 戰鬥的間歇期 **2 the lull before the storm** a short period of time when things are calm that is followed by a lot of activity, noise, or trouble 暴風雨到來前短暫的平靜

lul·la·by /ˋlʌləˌbaɪ; ˈlʌləbaɪ/ *n* [C] a slow, quiet song sung to children to make them go to sleep 催眠曲, 搖籃曲

lu·lu /ˋlulu; ˈluːluː/ *n* [C] *AmE informal*【美, 非正式】**1** something very good or exciting 出眾之物, 令人興奮的事: *The roller coaster at Magic Mountain is a real lulu.* 魔山的過山車真是妙極了。**2** something extremely silly, bad, embarrassing etc 極傻[糟糕, 尷尬]的事: *She's said some stupid things in her life, but that one was a real lulu!* 她一生中說了一些傻話, 而那一回真是傻透了!

lum·ba·go /lʌmˋbego; lʌmˈbeɪgəʊ/ *n* [U] pain in the lower part of the back 腰痛

lum·bar /ˋlʌmbɚ; ˈlʌmbə/ *adj technical* related to the lower part of the back【術語】腰部的: *pain in the lumbar region* 腰部疼痛

lum·ber¹ /ˋlʌmbɚ; ˈlʌmbə/ *v* **1** [I always+adv/prep] to move in a slow, awkward way 慢而笨拙地移動: **[+after/into/along etc]** *Mrs Moffat lumbered over to us, complaining about her arthritis.* 莫法特太太艱難地走過來, 跟我們訴說她得關節炎的痛苦。**2** [T] *informal* to give someone a job or responsibility that they do not want【非正式】讓〔某人〕做不願意做的事[接受不願要的責任]: **get/be lumbered with** *As usual, Joe got lumbered with the babysitting.* 照例, 喬被迫接受照料小孩的工作。**3** [I] *AmE* to cut down trees to make TIMBER (1)【美】伐木製材

lumber² *n* [U] **1** *BrE informal* large objects that are no longer useful or wanted【英, 非正式】廢舊的笨重物品 **2** trees that have been cut down to be used as wood; TIMBER (1) 木材, 木料

lum·ber·jack /ˋlʌmbɚˌdʒæk; ˈlʌmbədʒæk/ *n* [C] someone whose job is cutting down trees for wood 伐木工人

lumber jack·et /ˈ‥ ˌ‥/ *n* [C] a thick wool jacket, often with a CHECK² (5) pattern〔常有方格圖案的〕厚毛短上衣

lum·ber·man /ˋlʌmbɚmən; ˈlʌmbəmən/ *n* [C] someone whose job is cutting down trees or selling wood 伐木工人; 木材商

lum·ber·mill /ˋlʌmbɚmɪl; ˈlʌmbəmɪl/ *n* [C] *AmE* a building where trees are cut up to make wood【美】木材廠, 鋸木廠; SAWMILL *BrE*【英】

lumber room /ˈ‥ ˌ‥/ *n* [C] *BrE* a room where old furniture, broken machines etc are kept【英】廢舊物品堆藏室

lum·ber·yard /ˋlʌmbɚˌjɑrd; ˈlʌmbəjɑːd/ *n* [C] *AmE* a place where wood is kept before it is sold【美】〔售前堆放木料的〕木材場

lu·mi·na·ry /ˋluməˌnɛrɪ; ˈluːmɪnəri/ *n* [C] someone who is very famous or highly respected for their skill at, or knowledge of, a particular subject 名人, 傑出人物: *luminaries of the women's movement* 婦女運動的傑出人物

lu·mi·nous /ˋlumənəs; ˈluːmɪnəs/ *adj* **1** made of a substance or material that shines in the dark 發光的; 夜明的: *luminous paint* 發光塗料 | *luminous road signs* 發光路標 **2** very brightly coloured, especially in green, pink, or yellow 色彩鮮豔的〔尤指綠色、粉紅色或黃色〕: *luminous socks* 色彩鮮豔的短襪 —**luminously** *adv* —**luminosity** /ˌluməˋnɑsətɪ; ˌluːmɪˈnɒsɪti/ *n* [U]

lum·me /ˋlʌmɪ; ˈlʌmi/ *interjection BrE old-fashioned* used to express surprise【英, 過時】哎呀, 啊〔表示驚訝〕

lump¹ /lʌmp; lʌmp/ *n* [C] **1** a small piece of something solid, without a particular shape〔不定形的〕塊: *There were lumps in the sauce.* 醬汁中有粒狀的東西。| **[+of]** *a lump of coal* 一塊煤 —see picture on page A7 參見 A7 頁圖 **2** something small that sticks out from someone's skin or grows in their body, usually because of an illness〔一般因患病而在皮膚上凸起或在身體內長出的〕腫塊: *Check monthly for lumps on your breasts.* 每月檢查你乳房有沒有腫塊。**3** a small square block of sugar 小方塊糖: *One lump or two?* 要一塊還是兩塊方糖? **4 bring a lump to sb's throat** to make someone feel as if they want to cry 使某人哽結欲泣: *The scene where Laddie dies brought a lump to my throat.* 拉迪死亡的場面使我哽結欲泣。**5 take your lumps** *AmE informal* to accept the bad things that happen to you and not let them affect you【美, 非正式】認倒霉: *Forget about it, Rob, you have to take your lumps and go on.* 忘了它吧, 羅布, 你只有認倒霉並繼續幹。**6** *BrE spoken* someone who is stupid, or CLUMSY (1)【英口】愚蠢的人, 笨拙的人: *You stupid great lump!* 你這個大笨蛋!

lump² *v* **lump it** *informal* to accept a situation or decision you do not like because you cannot change it【非正式】無奈地接受, 勉強同意: **like it or lump it** *I'm going to that party! Like it or lump it!* 我打算去參加那個聚會! 不管喜歡還是不喜歡!

lump sth **together** *phr v* [T] to consider two or more

L

different things as a single type or group, rather than individually or separately 把…合在一起考慮: *Pacifists, atheists and journalists were all lumped together as 'troublemakers'.* 和平主義者、無神論者和記者都被歸為"惹事生非者"。

lump·ec·to·my /lʌmpˋɛktəmɪ; lʌmpˈektəmi/ *n* [C] an operation in which a TUMOUR is removed from someone's body, especially from a woman's breast〔尤指乳房〕腫瘤切除術

lump·ish /ˈlʌmpɪʃ; ˈlʌmpɪʃ/ *adj* awkward or stupid 笨拙的; 愚鈍的

lump sum /ˌ· ˈ·/ *n* [C] an amount of money given in a single payment 一次付款總額: *When you retire you'll get a lump sum of £80,000.* 當你退休時, 你將得到一次總付 80,000 英鎊。

lump·y /ˈlʌmpɪ; ˈlʌmpi/ *adj* covered with or containing small solid pieces 佈滿團塊的; 有團塊的: *a lumpy mattress* 不平整的牀墊

lu·na·cy /ˈlunəsɪ; ˈluːnəsi/ *n* [U] **1** a situation or behaviour that is completely crazy 瘋狂的狀態[行為]: **complete/sheer/pure lunacy** *It would be sheer lunacy to turn down an offer like that.* 拒絕那樣的提議簡直是發瘋。**2** *old-fashioned* mental illness【過時】精神病, 精神失常: *the cause of Hamlet's lunacy* 哈姆雷特精神失常的原因 —see also 另見 LUNATIC

lu·nar /ˈlunɚ; ˈluːnə/ *adj* connected with the moon or with travel to the moon 月球的; 與前往月球有關的: *a lunar eclipse* 月蝕

lunar month /ˌ·· ˈ·/ *n* [C] a period of 28 or 29 days between one NEW MOON and the next 太陰月; 陰曆一個月

lu·na·tic /ˈlunəˌtɪk; ˈluːnətɪk/ *n* [C] **1** someone who behaves in a crazy or very stupid way 瘋狂的人; 愚笨的人: *You lunatic – you nearly drove straight into me!* 你這個蠢貨——你差點(用車)撞我個正着! **2** *old-fashioned* someone who is mentally ill【過時】精神錯亂的人, 瘋子: *a dangerous lunatic* 可能傷害他人的精神病人 **3 the lunatic fringe** *BrE* the people in a political group or organization who have the most extreme opinions or ideas【英】〔政治團體或組織中的〕極端分子 —**lunatic** *adj*: *lunatic behaviour* 瘋狂的行為

lunatic a·sy·lum /ˈ···· ˌ·ˌ··/ *n* [C] *old-fashioned* a hospital where people who are mentally ill are cared for【過時】精神病院

1 2 **lunch**[1] /lʌntʃ; lʌntʃ/ *n* [C,U] **1** a meal eaten in the middle of the day 午餐: **at lunch** *Anna said something at lunch about leaving.* 安娜吃午餐時說了她要走的事。| **have lunch** *When do you usually have lunch?* 你通常甚麼時候吃午飯? | **have some lunch** *I'm starved. Let's have some lunch.* 我餓極了, 我們吃點午餐吧。| **have sth for lunch** *All I had for lunch was a salad sandwich.* 我午餐吃的只是一份沙拉三明治。| **take sb out to lunch** *He decided to take her out to lunch.* 他決定請她吃午飯。| **go to lunch** (=go somewhere to eat lunch) 去吃午餐 *Rory went to lunch in a small Italian restaurant.* 羅里到一家意大利小飯館去吃午餐。| **a working lunch** (=when you discuss business and eat) 工作午餐 | **packed lunch** *BrE*【英】**/bag lunch** *AmE*【美】(=food, usually SANDWICHes, that you take with you to work, school etc)〔上班、上學等帶的〕盒裝午餐〔通常是三明治〕**2 out to lunch** *informal* behaving in a strange and confused way【非正式】舉止有點失常

lunch[2] *v formal*【正式】**1** [I] to eat lunch 吃午飯, 用午餐 **2** [T] to buy someone lunch 給…買午餐

lunch·box /ˈlʌntʃˌbɑks; ˈlʌntʃbɒks/ *n* [C] a box in which food is carried to school, work etc〔帶上學、上班等的〕午餐盒, 便當

lunch break /ˈ· ·/ *n* [C] LUNCH HOUR 午餐時間

lunch·eon /ˈlʌntʃən; ˈlʌntʃən/ *n* [C,U] *formal* lunch【正式】午餐, 午宴

luncheon meat /ˈ·· ·/ *n* [U] meat that has been cooked, then pressed down, and is often sold in a can 午餐肉

luncheon vou·cher /ˈ·· ˌ··/ *n* [C] a special ticket sometimes given to people in Britain by their employers, that can be used to buy meals or food 餐券, 膳食券〔英國一些雇主有時發給員工的特殊餐券, 可用於用餐或購買食物〕

lunch hour /ˈ· ·/ *n* [C] the period of time in the middle of the day when people stop working in order to eat 午餐時間

lunch·room /ˈlʌntʃrum; ˈlʌntʃruːm/ *n* [C] *AmE* a large room in a school or office where people can eat【美】〔學校或辦公室的〕餐廳, 食堂 —compare 比較 CAFETERIA

lunch·time /ˈlʌntʃˌtaɪm; ˈlʌntʃtaɪm/ *n* [C,U] the time in the middle of the day when people usually eat their LUNCH 午餐時間: *a lunchtime drink* 午餐飲料 3

lung /lʌŋ; lʌŋ/ *n* [C] one of the two organs in your body that you breathe with 肺: *Smoking can cause lung cancer.* 吸煙會引起肺癌。—see also 另見 IRON LUNG —see picture at 參見 RESPIRATORY 圖

lunge /lʌndʒ; lʌndʒ/ *v* [I] to make a sudden strong movement towards someone or something, especially using your arm and to attack them 突然向前衝[撲等]〔尤指襲擊某人或某物〕: [**+forwards/at/towards**] *They both lunged forwards to catch the ball.* 他們倆都衝去抓球。—**lunge** *n* [C]: *Brad made a lunge towards his opponent, but missed.* 布拉德撲向對手, 但沒有打着。

lunk·head /ˈlʌŋkˌhɛd; ˈlʌŋkhed/ *n* [C] *AmE informal* someone who is very stupid【美, 非正式】笨蛋, 傻瓜

lu·pin *BrE*【英】, **lupine** *AmE*【美】/ˈlupɪn; ˈluːpɪ̈n/ *n* [C] a plant with a tall stem and many small flowers 羽扇豆

lurch[1] /lɝtʃ; lɜːtʃ/ *v* [I] **1** to move suddenly forwards or sideways, usually because you cannot control your movements 蹒跚而行, 東倒西歪地走: [**+across/into/along etc**] *Frank lurched back to his seat.* 法蘭克踉踉蹌蹌地走回自己的座位。| *The car lurched forward across the grass.* 汽車東歪西扭地穿過了草地。**2 your heart/stomach lurches** used to say that your heart or stomach seems to move as you suddenly feel shocked, frightened etc〔因震驚、驚恐等而〕感到心跳/胃裡翻騰 **3 lurch from one crisis to the next/lurch from one extreme to the other etc** to seem to have no plan and no control over what you are doing 感到束手無策, 無法控制局面

lurch[2] *n* [C] **1** a sudden movement forwards or sideways, usually made because you cannot control your body or a machine〔身體或機器〕突然的晃動: *The train gave a violent lurch.* 火車突然劇烈地晃了一下。**2 leave sb in the lurch** to leave someone at a time when you should stay and help them; DESERT[2] (1) 臨危捨棄某人, 置某人於困難之中(而不顧)

lure[1] /lur; lʊə/ *v* [T] to persuade someone to do something, especially something wrong, by promising them something they want; TEMPT 引誘, 誘惑: **lure sb into/to/away etc** *I think he's trying to lure you away from Jerry.* 我認為他在試圖誘騙你離開傑里。| *prospectors lured to Alaska by the promise of gold* 被黃金引誘到阿拉斯加的淘金者

lure[2] *n* **1** [C usually singular 一般用單數] something that you think is attractive, or the power that something has to attract you 誘惑力, 吸引力: [**+of**] *Settlers were drawn to the West by the lure of free land.* 移民在自由土地的吸引下來到西部。**2** [C] a piece of equipment, such as a plastic bird or fish, used to attract animals or fish so that they can be caught; DECOY (2) 誘捕動物或魚用的假鳥[假魚]; 誘餌

Lu·rex /ˈlurɛks; ˈljʊəreks/ *n* [U] *trademark* a type of thread that looks like metal, usually gold or silver, used in material for making clothes【商標】盧勒克斯(金銀紗)〔用於做衣服〕: *a gold Lurex top* 金紗織成的上裝

lur·gy /ˈlɝgɪ; ˈlɜːgi/ *n* [singular] *BrE humorous* an illness, especially one that is infectious but not serious【英, 幽

默】疾病〔尤指不嚴重的傳染病〕: *Anne's got the dreaded lurgy.* 安妮得了那種可怕的疾病。

lu·rid /ˈlurɪd; ˈlʊərɪ̣d/ *adj* **1** a description, story etc that is lurid is deliberately shocking and involves sex or violence 聳人聽聞的, 可怕的〔指描述、故事等內容包括性或暴力〕: *lurid headlines* 駭人聽聞的標題 | *He told me in lurid detail what would happen to me.* 他把將要發生在我身上的事告訴了我, 細節之處聳人聽聞。**2** too brightly coloured; GAUDY 色彩耀眼的, 俗氣的: *a lurid orange dress* 一件俗氣的橘黃色連衣裙 —**luridly** *adv* —**luridness** *n* [U]

lurk /lɝk; lɜːk/ *v* [I always+adv/prep] **1** to wait somewhere quietly and secretly, usually because you are going to do something wrong 潛伏, 埋伏: [**+around/in/beneath etc**] *A man was lurking around outside the shop.* 一個男人潛伏在商店外面。**2** to exist almost without being seen or known about 暗藏, 潛藏: *childish fears that lurk in all our hearts* 藏在我們所有人心中的幼稚的恐懼

lus·cious /ˈlʌʃəs; ˈlʌʃəs/ *adj* **1** extremely good to eat 甘甜的, 美味的: *a luscious peach* 甘甜的桃子 **2** *informal* a word meaning very sexually attractive, used especially by men【非正式】十分性感的〔尤為男士用語〕: *a luscious young starlet* 性感的年輕小女明星

lush¹ /lʌʃ; lʌʃ/ *adj* **1** plants that are lush grow many leaves and look healthy and strong〔植物〕茂盛的, 繁茂的, 鬱鬱蔥蔥的: *lush tropical vegetation* 茂盛的熱帶草木 **2** very beautiful, comfortable, and expensive 華麗的, 舒適的, 昂貴的: *lush carpets* 華麗的地毯

lush² *n* [C] *AmE informal* an ALCOHOLIC【美, 非正式】酒鬼, 醉漢

lust¹ /lʌst; lʌst/ *n* **1** [C,U] very strong sexual desire, especially when it does not include liking or love 強烈的性慾; 淫慾: *What Len felt for her was pure lust.* 萊恩對她只有肉慾而已。**2** [U+**for**] a very strong desire to have something, usually power or money 強烈的慾望〔通常指對權力或金錢的慾望〕: *hard-faced men driven by a lust for gain* 利慾熏心、麻木不仁的人

lust² *v*

lust after sb/sth *phr v* [T] *often humorous*【常幽默】**1** to be strongly sexually attracted to someone, and think about having sex with them 對〔某人〕有強烈的性慾: *He thinks I'm only lusting after his body!* 他以為我僅僅渴望與他發生肉體關係! **2** to want something very much, especially something that you do not really need 對〔某物〕有強烈慾望, 貪戀〔尤指並不真正需要的東西〕: *This is the shop for those of you lusting after designer clothes.* 這家店是為那些追求名家設計服裝的人而開的。

lus·ter /ˈlʌstɚ; ˈlʌstə/ *n* [singular, U] the American spelling of LUSTRE lustre 的美式拼法

lust·ful /ˈlʌstfəl; ˈlʌstfəl/ *adj* feeling or showing strong sexual desire 色慾的, 好色的: *a jealous, lustful man* 妒忌心強的好色男子 —**lustfully** *adv*: *Max stared at her lustfully.* 馬克斯色迷迷地盯着她看。

lus·tre *BrE*【英】, **luster** *AmE*【美】/ˈlʌstɚ; ˈlʌstə/ *n* [singular, U] **1** an attractive shiny appearance 光澤, 光亮: **add/give lustre to** *A little conditioner will give lustre to your hair.* 用一點護髮素會給你的頭髮帶來光澤。**2** the quality that makes something interesting or exciting 出色, 光彩: **add/give luster to** *Arnold's singing will add lustre to the affair.* 阿諾德的歌唱將會給這個活動增添光彩。

lus·trous /ˈlʌstrəs; ˈlʌstrəs/ *adj* shining in a soft, gentle way 有光澤的, 光亮的: *lustrous black hair* 光亮的黑髮

lust·y /ˈlʌstɪ; ˈlʌsti/ *adj* strong and healthy; powerful 健壯的; 強有力的: *The baby gave a lusty cry.* 嬰兒發出洪亮的哭聲。| *lusty young men* 強壯的小伙子 —**lustily** *adv*: *cheering lustily* 縱情歡呼 —**lustiness** *n* [U]

lute /lut; luːt/ *n* **1** [C] a musical instrument similar to a GUITAR with a round body, played especially in former times 魯特琴〔舊時的一種類似結他的圓形撥弦樂器, 琴身圓形〕**2** [U] *technical* a type of clay or CEMENT used to fill holes or cracks【術語】封泥〔封堵洞穴或裂縫的黏土或水泥〕

Lu·ther·an /ˈluθərən; ˈluːθərən/ *n* [C] a member of the church that follows the teachings and ideas of Martin Luther 路德會教徒 —**Lutheran** *adj*

luv /lʌv; lʌv/ *n BrE informal* an informal way of spelling LOVE when it is used to address someone【英, 非正式】〔love 的非正式拼法, 用於稱呼某人〕: *Come on, luv, don't cry.* 得啦, 親愛的, 別哭了。

luv·vie /ˈlʌvɪ; ˈlʌvi/ *n BrE*【英】**1** another spelling of LOVEY lovey 的另一種拼法 **2** [C] *informal* an actor or actress who behaves to other people in a very friendly way that is not sincere【非正式】〔假裝友善的〕演員

lux·u·ri·ant /lʌgˋʒurɪənt; lʌgˈzjʊəriənt/ *adj* **1** growing strongly and thickly 茂盛的, 濃密的: *a luxuriant black beard* 濃密的黑鬍子 | *luxuriant vegetation* 茂盛的草木 **2** giving a rich effect 華麗的: *luxuriant prose* 詞藻華麗的散文 —**luxuriantly** *adv* —**luxuriance** *n* [U]

lux·u·ri·ate /lʌgˋʒurɪˌet; lʌgˈzjʊərieɪt/ *v*

luxuriate in sth *phr v* [T] to relax and consciously enjoy something 盡情享受: *Melanie was luxuriating in the sunshine when they arrived.* 當他們來到的時候, 梅拉尼正在盡情享受陽光。

lux·u·ri·ous /lʌgˋʒurɪəs; lʌgˈzjʊəriəs/ *adj* very expensive, beautiful, and comfortable 奢華的, 華麗的, 舒適的: *The bathroom was luxurious, with gold taps and a thick carpet.* 浴室很奢華, 配有金水龍頭和厚地毯。—**luxuriously** *adv* —**luxuriousness** *n* [C]

lux·u·ry /ˈlʌkʃərɪ; ˈlʌkʃəri/ *n* **1** [U] very great comfort and pleasure, such as you get from expensive food, beautiful houses, cars etc 奢華, 奢侈: *Caviar for breakfast! I was not used to such luxury.* 早餐吃魚子醬! 我不習慣這種奢侈! | **a life of luxury** *They led a life of luxury, in a huge house in the countryside.* 他們在鄉村的大宅子裡過着奢華的生活。| **luxury apartment/flat/car etc** (=expensive and large) 豪華的房間/套房/汽車等 **2** [C] something expensive that you do not need, but you buy for pleasure and enjoyment 奢侈品: *We can't afford luxuries like piano lessons any more.* 我們再也負擔不起像上鋼琴課這樣奢侈的事。—see also 另見 **in the lap of luxury** (LAP¹ (4)) —compare 比較 NECESSITY (1)

LW the written abbreviation of 縮寫= LONG WAVE

-ly /lɪ; li/ *suffix* **1** [in adverbs 構成副詞] in a particular way 以某種方式: *He did it very cleverly.* (=in a clever way) 這件事他做得很聰明。| *walking slowly* 緩慢地走 **2** [in adverbs 構成副詞] considered in a particular way 從某方面來考慮的: *Politically speaking it was a rather unwise remark.* 從政治上來講, 這是相當愚蠢的評論。| *a financially sound proposal* 財務上可行的建議 **3** [in adjectives and adverbs 構成形容詞和副詞] happening at regular periods of time 定期發生的: *an hourly check* (=done every hour) 每小時一次的檢查 | *They visit monthly.* (=once a month) 他們每個月探望一次。**4** [in adjectives 構成形容詞] like a particular thing in manner, nature, or appearance 舉止像…的; 有…態度[外貌]的: *with queenly grace* 有女王般的優雅風度 | *a motherly woman* (=showing the love, kindness etc of a mother) 慈母般的婦女

ly·ce·um /laɪˋsiəm; laɪˈsiːəm/ *n* [C] *AmE old-fashioned* a building used for public meetings, concerts, speeches etc【美, 過時】〔舉行公眾會議、音樂會或演講等的〕演講廳, 音樂廳, 會堂

ly·chee, litchi /ˈlitʃi; ˈlaɪtʃiː/ *n* [C] a small round fruit with a rough pink-brown shell outside and sweet white flesh inside 荔枝 —see picture on page A8 參見 A8 頁圖

lych·gate, lichgate /ˈlɪtʃˌget; ˈlɪtʃgeɪt/ *n* [C] a gate with a roof leading into the area surrounding a church 通向教堂周圍庭院的有上蓋的門道

Ly·cra /ˈlaɪkrə; ˈlaɪkrə/ *n* [U] *trademark* a material that stretches, used especially for making tight-fitting sports clothes【商標】萊卡〔彈性織物, 尤用於製造緊身運動服〕

ly·ing /ˋlaɪɪŋ; ˈlaɪ-ɪŋ/ the present participle of LIE[1]

lying-in /ˌ·· ˈ·/ *n* [singular] *old-fashioned* the period of time during which a woman stays in bed before and after the birth of a child; CONFINEMENT (2)【過時】產褥期, 產期

lying in state /ˌ·· · ˈ·/ *n* [singular] the period of time when people can come and see the body of someone such as a president or king who has died, to show their respect〔總統或國王等死後的〕遺容瞻仰期

Lyme dis·ease /ˋlaɪm dɪˌziz; ˈlaɪm dɪˌziːz/ *n* [U] a serious illness that is caused by a bite from a TICK[1] (2) 萊姆病〔由蜱叮咬引起的一種嚴重疾病〕

lymph /lɪmf; lɪmf/ *n* [U] a clear liquid that is formed in your body and passes into your blood system 淋巴 —**lymphatic** /lɪmˋfætɪk; lɪmˈfætɪk/ *adj*

lymph gland /ˈ· ·/ *n* [C] a lymph node 淋巴結, 淋巴腺

lymph node /ˈ· ·/ *n* [C] a small rounded SWELLING in your body through which lymph passes to be made pure before entering your blood system 淋巴結

lynch /lɪntʃ; lɪntʃ/ *v* [T] if a crowd of people lynches someone, they HANG[1] (3) them as a punishment, without using the usual legal process〔一夥人〕用私刑絞死〔某人作為懲罰〕: *At that time you could be lynched for being black.* 那時候你可能會因為是黑人而被私刑絞死。—**lynching** *n* [C]

lynch mob /ˈ· ·/ *n* [singular] a group of people that kills someone by hanging (HANG[1] (3)) them, without a legal TRIAL[1] (1) 實施私刑的暴民

lynchpin /ˋlɪntʃˌpɪn; ˈlɪntʃpɪn/ *n* [C] another spelling of LINCHPIN linchpin 的另一種拼法

lynx /lɪŋks; lɪŋks/ *n* [C] a large wild cat that has no tail and lives in forests 猞猁; BOBCAT *AmE*【美】

lyre /laɪr; laɪə/ *n* [C] a musical instrument with strings across a U-shaped frame, used especially in ancient Greece 里拉琴〔古希臘的一種弦樂器, 琴身為U形〕

lyre·bird /ˋlaɪrˌbɝd; ˈlaɪəbɜːd/ *n* [C] a bird with a long U-shaped tail, that lives in Australia 琴鳥〔產於澳大利亞, 有U形長尾〕

lyr·ic[1] /ˋlɪrɪk; ˈlɪrɪk/ *adj* [only before noun 僅用於名詞前] expressing strong personal emotions such as love, in a way that is similar to music in its sounds and RHYTHM (1) 抒情的: *Wordsworth was one of the greatest lyric poets of his time.* 華茲華斯是他那個時代最偉大的抒情詩人之一。

lyric[2] *n* **1 lyrics** [plural] the words of a song, especially a modern popular song〔尤指現代流行歌曲的〕歌詞: *music and lyrics by the Gershwin brothers* 格什溫兄弟創作的歌曲和歌詞 **2** [C] *technical* a poem, usually a short one, written in a lyric style【術語】抒情詩〔通常為短詩〕

lyr·i·cal /ˋlɪrɪkḷ; ˈlɪrɪkəl/ *adj* **1** beautifully expressed in words, poetry, or music 像詩歌[音樂]般抒情的: *Lawrence's lyrical descriptions of the natural world* 勞倫斯對自然界抒情詩般的描寫 **2 wax lyrical** to talk about and praise something in a very eager way 熱情地談論[讚美]: *Simon waxed lyrical on the joys of hill-walking.* 西門興高采烈地談論爬山的樂趣。—**lyrically** /-klɪ; -kli/ *adv*

lyr·i·cis·m /ˋlɪrəˌsɪzəm; ˈlɪrɨsɪzəm/ *n* [U] the romantic or song-like expression of something in writing or music〔寫作或音樂的〕抒情風格, 抒情性

lyr·i·cist /ˋlɪrəsɪst; ˈlɪrɨsɨst/ *n* [C] someone who writes the words for songs, especially modern popular songs〔尤指現代流行歌曲的〕歌詞作者

L

M,m

M, m /ɛm; em/ *plural* **M's, m's** *n* [C] **1** the 13th letter of the English alphabet 英語字母表的第十三個字母 **2** the number 1000 in the system of ROMAN NUMERALs〔羅馬數字系統中的〕1000

M *BrE*【英】the abbreviation of 縮寫= MOTORWAY: *M25* 25號高速公路 | *M1* 1號高速公路

m the written abbreviation of 縮寫= **a)** metre **b)** mile **c)** million **d)** male **e)** married **f)** medium

MA /ˌɛm ˋe; ˌem ˈeɪ/ *n* [C] Master of Arts; a university degree in an arts subject (ART[1] (5)) that you get after studying for a year or two longer after your first degree 文學碩士: *an MA in English literature* 英國文學碩士 | *Vanessa Clark, MA* 瓦内莎·克拉克, 文學碩士 —compare 比較 MSC

Ma, ma /mɑ; mɑː/ *n* [C] *informal*【非正式】**1** mother 媽, 媽媽: *What's for dinner, Ma?* 媽, 午餐吃甚麼? **2** a word meaning 'Mrs', used in some country areas of the US 夫人, 太太〔用於美國一些鄉村地區〕: *old Ma Harris* 老哈里斯夫人

ma'am /mæm; mæm/ *n* **1** *AmE spoken* a polite way of addressing a woman【美口】夫人〔對婦女的禮貌稱呼〕: *May I help you, ma'am?* 夫人, 要我幫忙嗎? **2** *BrE spoken* a way of addressing the Queen, some women in authority, and, especially in the past, women of high social class【英口】夫人; 女士〔對女王、某些有權勢的婦女的尊稱, 尤其過去用於稱呼上流社會的婦女〕

mac /mæk; mæk/ *n* [C] *BrE* a coat worn to keep out the rain; MACKINTOSH【英】雨衣

Mac *n AmE informal* used to address a man whose name you do not know【美, 非正式】老兄, 老弟〔用以稱呼你不知其姓名的男子〕

ma·ca·bre /məˋkɑbrə; məˈkɑːbrə/ *adj* very strange and unpleasant and connected with death, serious accidents etc 恐怖的, 可怕的, 駭人的; 與死亡[嚴重事故等]有關的: *a macabre tale* 令人毛骨悚然的故事 | *a macabre sense of humour* 使人悚然的幽默感

ma·cad·am /məˋkædəm; məˈkædəm/ *n* [U] a road surface made of a mixture of broken stones and TAR[1] (1) or ASPHALT 柏油碎石路面; TARMAC[1] (1) *BrE*【英】

mac·a·ro·ni /ˌmækəˋronɪ; ˌmækəˈrəʊni◂/ *n* [U] a type of PASTA in the shape of small tubes, which is cooked in boiling water 通心粉, 通心麵: *a plate of macaroni* 一盤通心粉 | **macaroni cheese** (=macaroni with a cheese sauce) 乾酪通心麵 —see picture at 參見 PASTA 圖

mac·a·roon /ˌmækəˋrun; ˌmækəˈruːn/ *n* [C] a small round cake made of sugar, eggs, and crushed ALMONDs or COCONUT 蛋白杏仁餅; 蛋白椰子餅

ma·caw /məˋkɔ; məˈkɔː/ *n* [C] a large brightly coloured bird like a PARROT[1] (1), with a long tail 鸚鵡, 金剛鸚鵡

mace /mes; meɪs/ *n* **1** [U] powder made from the dried shell of a NUTMEG, used to give food a special taste〔調味用的〕肉豆蔻乾皮(粉) **2** [C] a heavy ball with sharp points on a short metal stick, used in the past as a weapon〔舊時用作武器的〕狼牙棒, 釘頭錘 **3** [C] a decorated stick that is carried by an official in some ceremonies as a sign of power〔作為權力象徵的〕權杖 **4 Mace** [U] *trademark* a chemical which makes your eyes and skin sting painfully, which some women carry to defend themselves【商標】〔婦女自衛用的〕梅斯催淚毒氣

M

ma·cer·ate /ˋmæsəˌret; ˈmæsəreɪt/ *v* [I,T] *technical* to make something soft by leaving it in water, or to become soft in this way【術語】泡軟, (把…)浸軟 —**maceration** /ˌmæsəˋreʃən; ˌmæsəˈreɪʃən/ *n* [U]

ma·chet·e /məˋʃɛtɪ; məˈʃeti/ *n* [C] a large knife with a broad heavy blade, used as a weapon or a tool〔作武器或工具用的〕寬刃刀, 大砍刀

Mach·i·a·vel·li·an /ˌmækɪəˋvɛlɪən; ˌmækiəˈveliən◂/ *adj* using clever but immoral methods to get what you want 詭計多端的, 狡詐的; 為達到目的而不擇手段的

mach·i·na·tions /ˌmækəˋneʃənz; ˌmækɨˈneɪʃənz/ *n* [plural] secret and clever plans 密謀, 詭計

ma·chine[1] /məˋʃin; məˈʃiːn/ *n* [C] **1** a piece of equipment that uses power such as electricity to do a particular job 機器: *a machine that fills the bottles* 裝瓶機 | *Could you get me a Coke from the machine?* 給我從自動售賣機裡買一罐可樂好嗎? | **sewing/washing machine etc** (=a machine that can sew, wash clothes etc) 縫紉機/洗衣機等 | **by machine** *The letters are sorted by machine.* 信件都是由機器分揀的。**2** a computer 電腦: *a powerful machine that is ideal for software development* 一台對於軟件開發來說很理想的功能強大的電腦 **3** a group of people that controls an organization, especially a political party〔控制某組織, 尤指政黨的〕核心人物; 領導核心: *the party machine* 政黨的核心人物 | *the government's propaganda machine* 政府的宣傳機器 **4 like a well-oiled machine** working very smoothly and effectively 像上足了油的機器一樣;〔工作〕非常順利有效: *The office runs like a well-oiled machine.* 那個辦公室像上足了潤滑油的機器一樣運轉順利。**5** *informal* a vehicle【非正式】汽車: *That's an impressive-looking machine you've got there.* 你那輛車看上去真神氣。**6** someone who works without stopping, or who seems to have no feelings or independent thoughts 機器〔指無休止工作或似乎沒有感覺或獨立思維的人〕: *He was a running machine, born to do nothing but win medals.* 他是一台賽跑機器, 生來就是為了贏得獎牌。—see also 另見 CASH MACHINE, FRUIT MACHINE, TIME MACHINE

USAGE NOTE 用法說明: MACHINE

WORD CHOICE 詞語辨析: **machine, device, thing, appliance, gadget**

You do not usually work a **machine** directly by hand, and it may be large. Often the word is used with another word before it that describes its purpose. machine 通常不是直接用手操縱的機器, 而且它可能很龐大。這個詞常與位於它前面、描述其用途的另外一個詞連用: *The coffee machine has broken down.* 那台咖啡機已經壞了。

Device is more formal. A device may be worked by hand, or be electrical. device 這個詞更正式一些, 它可以是手動的也可以是電動的: *a device for opening bottles* 開瓶器。In spoken English people say **thing**. 在英語口語中人們用 thing 這個詞: *a thing to open bottles with* 一個用來開瓶子的器具。**Device** is used especially for something that is used to measure or protect something else. device 特別用來指測量或保護其他物件的裝置: *a device to find faults in plastic* 檢測塑料瑕疵的儀器 | *a contraceptive device* 避孕用具

An **appliance** is a machine used for a particular purpose in the home, and is called this especially by the people who produce and sell them. appliance 是用於某一具體用途的家用機器, 這種叫法尤為生產和銷售這類機器的人所使用: *a household appliance such as a dishwasher* 家用電器如洗碗機 | *domestic appliances* 家用電器

A **gadget** is a cleverly designed small machine, often one that does a complicated action, and is usually modern. gadget指設計巧妙、常用來做複雜的工作的小機器, 而且通常是現代化的: *My latest gadget is a breadmaker.* 我最近購得的一台小機器是麵包機。

SPOKEN-WRITTEN 口語－書面語

When the word before it describes what the machine is for, people sometimes leave out the word **machine**. 當machine前面的詞描述其用途時, 人們有時會省去machine這個詞: *Can I use your fax (machine)?* 我可以用一下你的傳真機嗎?

When the word before **machine** ends in *-ing*, you can sometimes use the same word ending in *-er* on its own. 當machine前面是一個以-ing結尾的詞, 有時可單獨使用該詞以-er結尾的形式: *Lianne is in charge of the photocopier.* (formal 正式 **photocopying machine**) 利安負責管理那台影印機。

Often you do not use the word **machine** at all to talk about a particular machine. For example, you say **dishwasher**, not **dishwashing machine** and **tumble-drier** not **tumble-drying machine**. 人們通常不用machine這個詞來談論一台具體的機器, 如人們說dishwasher而不說dishwashing machine, 說 tumble-drier 而不說tumble-drying machine。

machine[2] *v* [T] **1** to fasten pieces of cloth together using a SEWING MACHINE 用縫紉機縫 **2** to make or shape something using a machine 用機器製造[加工]

machine code /ˈ·ˌ·/ *n* [C,U] *technical* instructions in the form of numbers which are understood by a computer【術語】機器(代)碼

machine gun /ˈ·ˌ·/ *n* [C] a gun that fires a lot of bullets very quickly 機關槍 —**machinegun** *v* [T]

machine lan·guage /ˈ·ˌ·ˌ··/ *n* [C,U] instructions in a form such as numbers that can be used by a computer 機器語言

machine-made /ˈ·ˌ·/ *adj* made using a machine 機器製造的 —compare 比較 HANDMADE

machine-read·a·ble /·ˌ· ˈ···◂/ *adj* in a form that can be understood and used by a computer 機器可讀的, 電腦可讀的: *information stored in machine-readable form* 以機讀形式儲存的資訊

3 **ma·chin·e·ry** /məˈʃinərɪ; məˈʃiːnəri/ *n* [U] **1** machines, especially large ones 機器, 機械〔尤指大型機械〕: *agricultural machinery* 農業機械 | *an expensive piece of machinery* 一台昂貴的機器 **2** the parts inside a machine that make it work〔使機器運轉的〕部件: *Jack keeps tinkering with the machinery, but the car still won't go.* 傑克一直在擺弄機器, 但汽車還是開不動。**3** system or set of processes for doing something 體系; 機構: *the machinery of government* 政府機構

machine tool /ˈ·ˌ·/ *n* [C] a tool used for cutting and shaping metal, wood etc, usually run by electricity 機牀

machine trans·la·tion /ˈ·ˌ·ˌ··/ *n* [U] translation done by a computer 機器翻譯, 電腦翻譯

ma·chin·ist /məˈʃinɪst; məˈʃiːnəst/ *n* [C] someone who operates a machine, especially in a factory 機工, 機械師

ma·chis·mo /mɑˈtʃizmo; məˈtʃɪzməʊ/ *n* [U] traditional male behaviour that emphasizes how brave, strong, and sexually attractive a man is 大男子氣概

mach·o /ˈmɑtʃo; ˈmætʃəʊ/ *adj informal* macho behaviour emphasizes a man's physical strength, lack of sensitive feelings, and other qualities considered to be typical of men【非正式】富有男子漢氣概的: *Jim likes to pretend he's macho but he's actually quite a vulnerable guy.* 吉姆喜歡裝出一副男子漢氣概, 但他實際上是一個極為脆弱的傢伙。| *He's so concerned with his macho image.* 他非常在意自己的男子漢形象。

macho man /ˈ·· ·/ *n* [C] a man who is always trying to show that he is strong, brave etc 經常着意顯示自己陽剛氣概的人

mack /mæk; mæk/ *n* [C] *BrE*【英】another spelling of MAC mac的另一種拼法

mack·e·rel /ˈmækərəl; ˈmækərəl/ *n plural* **mackerel** [C] a sea fish that has oily flesh and a strong taste 鯖魚〔一種海魚〕

mack·in·tosh /ˈmækɪnˌtɑʃ; ˈmækəntɒʃ/ *n* [C] *old-fashioned especially BrE* a coat worn to keep out the rain; MAC【過時, 尤英】雨衣

ma·cra·mé /ˈmækrəˌme; məˈkrɑːmi/ *n* [U] the art of knotting string together in patterns for decoration 流蘇花邊編結法, 裝飾結編結技藝, 花帶結藝術

mac·ro /ˈmækro; ˈmækrəʊ/ *n plural* **macros** [C] a set of instructions for a computer, stored and used as a unit〔電腦〕宏指令

macro- /ˈmækro; ˈmækrəʊ/ *prefix technical* large, especially concerning a whole system rather than particular parts of it【術語】大的; 巨型的; 宏觀的: *macroeconomics* 宏觀經濟學 | *macromolecular structures* 高分子結構 —compare 比較 MICRO-

mac·ro·bi·ot·ic /ˌmækrobaɪˈɑtɪk; ˌmækrəʊbaɪˈɒtɪk/ *adj* macrobiotic food consists mainly of grains and vegetables, with no added chemicals 攝生飲食的〔指食物主要由穀物和蔬菜構成, 無化學添加劑〕

mac·ro·cos·m /ˈmækrəˌkɑzəm; ˈmækrəʊkɒzəm/ *n* [C] a large, complicated system such as the whole universe or a society, considered as a single unit〔視為單一體系的〕大而複雜的系統; 整個宇宙; 宏觀世界 —compare 比較 MICROCOSM

mac·ro·ec·o·nom·ics /ˌmækroikəˈnɒmɪks; ˌmækrəʊekəˈnɒmɪks/ *n* [U] the study of large economic systems such as those of a whole country or area of the world 宏觀經濟學 —**macroeconomic** *adj*

mad /mæd; mæd/ *adj* **madder, maddest** 2 3

1 ►ANGRY 生氣的◄ [not before noun 不用於名詞前] *informal especially AmE* angry【非正式, 尤美】生氣的: *You make me so mad!* 你真把我氣壞了! | *Stay clear of Tucker – he's mad as hell and looking for a fight.* 離塔克遠一點 —— 他在氣頭上, 正想找人打架呢。| **mad at sb** *AmE*【美】*Don't get mad at me, I'm just telling you what Ray said.* 別對我發火, 我只是在告訴你雷所說的話。| **mad with sb** *BrE*【英】*Mum's really mad with Peter since he borrowed her car.* 媽媽確實很生彼得的氣, 因為他借走了她的汽車。| **go mad** *BrE informal* (=become extremely angry)【英, 非正式】變得極為憤怒, 變得狂怒 *Joe will go mad when he finds out how much I paid for that dress.* 喬要是知道了我買那件衣服花了多少錢, 他會氣得火冒三丈。| **hopping mad** (=very angry) 怒不可遏; 氣得暴跳如雷 | **as mad as a wet hen** *AmE* (=very angry)【美】非常生氣

2 ►CRAZY 瘋狂的◄ *BrE* very silly or unwise; crazy【英】極愚蠢[不明智]的; 瘋狂的: *Surely no one would be mad enough to fly in this weather?* 肯定沒有人會傻到這種地步, 在這樣的天氣中乘飛機旅行吧? | *You've agreed to marry him! Are you mad?* 你已經同意跟他結婚了! 你瘋了嗎? | **stark raving mad** (=completely crazy) 完全瘋了的; 傻透頂的 *My friends all think I'm stark raving mad.* 我的朋友都認為我傻透了。| **barking mad** (=completely crazy, with very strange ideas) 完全瘋了的; 想法古怪的

3 ►MENTALLY ILL 瘋癲的, 患精神病的◄ *old-fashioned, not technical* mentally ill; INSANE (1)【過時, 非術語】瘋癲的; 患精神病的; 精神錯亂的: *Mr Rochester's mad wife* 羅切斯特先生的瘋妻子 | *There was a mad gleam in his bloodshot eyes.* 他充血的雙眼中有一絲瘋癲的神色。

4 ►WILD/UNCONTROLLED 狂暴的/失控的◄ *especially BrE* behaving in a wild, uncontrolled way, without thinking about what you are doing【尤英】舉止狂暴的; 失控的: **a mad dash/rush etc** *We all made a mad dash for the door.* 我們所有人都發瘋似地向門口衝去。|

be mad with rage/grief etc *She was mad with grief when she heard about her son's death.* 當她聽到兒子的死訊時，悲傷得幾乎發瘋了。

5 go mad a) *not technical* to become mentally ill【非術語】變得精神失常，患精神病，發瘋 **b)** *especially BrE* to start behaving in an excited or uncontrolled way【尤英】變得極度激動；變得失去控制：*When Italy scored, the crowd went mad.* 意大利隊得分後人羣變得失去了控制。| *We went a bit mad and ordered a bottle of champagne.* 我們有些激動起來，因此要了一瓶香檳酒。**c)** *BrE* to start feeling crazy because you are very bored, annoyed, or anxious【英】〔因十分無聊、煩躁或憂慮而感到要〕發瘋：*Sometimes I thought I'd go mad with loneliness.* 有時我想我會因孤獨而發瘋。| *I'll go mad if I have to spend another day in that place.* 要是必須在那個地方再待上一天的話，我會發瘋的。**d)** *BrE informal* to become very angry【英，非正式】大怒，極為生氣：*Mum will go mad when she finds out what I paid for this dress.* 要是媽媽知道我買這件衣服花了多少錢，她會氣瘋的。

6 don't go mad *BrE spoken* used to tell someone not to work too hard or to get too excited【英口】別不要命地幹；別太激動：*I know you've got a lot to do before tomorrow morning but don't go mad.* 我知道你明天上午之前有許多事情要做，但也別不要命地幹。

7 you/she etc must be mad (to do sth) *BrE spoken* used when you think someone is very silly or stupid to do something【英口】某人（做某事）太愚蠢：*You've given up your job? You must be mad!* 你辭職了？你真是傻到家啦！

8 be mad about/on sb *BrE informal* to love someone in a strong, uncontrolled way【英，非正式】對某人愛得如醉如痴：*I was totally mad about him.* 我瘋狂地愛上了他。

9 be mad about/on sth *informal BrE* to be very interested in an activity and spend a lot of time on it【非正式，英】痴迷於某事：*He's completely mad about computer games.* 他對電腦遊戲完全着了迷。

10 be mad keen on *BrE informal* to be very interested in something or like it very much【英，非正式】對...極感興趣；非常喜歡：*Giles was mad keen on planes from an early age.* 賈爾斯從早年起就對飛機極感興趣。

11 run/work etc like mad *BrE informal* to run, work etc as quickly as you can【英，非正式】拚命地奔跑/工作等：*She ran like mad to catch the bus.* 她拚命地跑去趕公共汽車。| *We've been working like mad to get the job finished.* 我們一直在拚命地幹以完成這項工作。

12 drive sb mad *BrE* to make someone so bored, annoyed, or anxious that they feel as if they are going crazy【英】逼得某人發瘋：*I wish you'd stop making that noise, it's driving me mad!* 我希望你別再發出那種聲音了，都快把我吵瘋了。

13 power-mad/money-mad/sex-mad etc only interested in power, money etc 只對權/錢/性等感興趣的：*a power-mad dictator* 權迷心竅的獨裁者

14 as mad as a hatter *informal* behaving in a way that is very silly or strange, but unlikely to do any harm【非正式】〔舉止〕瘋狂怪誕的

mad·am /ˋmædəm; ˈmædəm/ *n* **1** a polite way of addressing a woman, especially a customer in a shop 女士〔對婦女，尤其對商店女顧客的禮貌稱呼〕：*Are you being served, Madam?* 女士，有人接待您嗎？**2 Dear Madam** used at the beginning of a business letter to a woman 親愛的女士〔用於寫給婦女的商業信函開頭〕**3 Madam President/Ambassador etc** a way of addressing a woman who has an important official position 總統/大使閣下〔對身居要職的婦女的稱呼〕**4** [C] a woman who is in charge of a BROTHEL (=place where women are paid to have sex with men) 鴇母 **5 a (proper) little madam** *BrE informal* a young girl who expects other people to do what she wants【英，非正式】指望他人聽其使喚的小女孩

Mad·ame /ˋmædəm; ˈmædəm/ *n plural* **Mesdames** /meˋdɑm; meɪˈdæm/ a title used to address a French-speaking woman, especially a married one; MRS 夫人，太太；女士〔對講法語，特別是已婚婦女的稱呼〕：*Madame Lefevre* 勒菲弗夫人

mad·cap /ˋmæd͵kæp; ˈmædkæp/ *adj* a madcap idea seems crazy and unlikely to succeed〔想法〕瘋狂的；魯莽的

mad cow dis·ease /͵· ˈ· ·͵·/ *n* [U] *not technical* BSE【非術語】牛海綿狀腦病，瘋牛病

mad·den /ˋmædn̩; ˈmædn/ *v* [T usually passive 一般用被動態] to make someone extremely angry or annoyed 使狂怒；使極為惱火

mad·den·ing /ˋmædnɪŋ; ˈmædənɪŋ/ *adj* extremely annoying 使人極其惱火的：*maddening delays* 令人十分氣惱的拖延 —**maddeningly** *adv*

made /med; meɪd/ **1** the past tense and past participle of MAKE[1] **2 be made for each other** *informal* to be completely suitable for each other, especially as husband and wife【非正式】〔尤指作為夫妻〕十分合適，完全般配：*Jacinta and Dermot were made for each other.* 賈欣塔和德莫特真是天生的一對。**3 have (got) it made** *informal* to have everything that you need for a happy life【非正式】具備幸福生活所需的一切：*Nice house, good job, lovely family – you've got it made!* 漂亮的房子，稱心的工作，美滿的家庭 —— 你可是一應俱全啦！**4 see what sb is (really) made of** *informal* to find out how strong, brave etc someone is【非正式】認識某人的真才實學[真本領] **5 I'm not made of money** *spoken* used to say that you cannot afford something【口】買不起〔某物〕：*I can't buy you shoes as well – I'm not made of money!* 我不能也給你買鞋 —— 我可不是錢堆的！**6 be made (for life)** *informal* to be so rich that you will never have to work again【非正式】富有得一輩子用不着再幹活：*If the deal is successful I'll be made for life.* 如果這筆交易能成功的話，我就可受用一輩子了。**7 I wasn't made for** *BrE spoken* used to say that you are not enjoying a job or activity【英口】我不喜歡〔某工作或某活動〕：*I wasn't made for housework.* 我不喜歡做家務。

Ma·dei·ra /məˋdɪrə; məˈdɪərə/ *n* [U] a strong sweet wine 馬德拉葡萄酒〔一種烈性甜酒〕

Madeira cake /·ˈ·· ·/ *n* [U] a kind of plain yellow cake 馬德拉蛋糕

Mad·e·moi·selle /͵mædəmwəˋzɛl; ͵mædəmwəˈzel/ *n plural* **Mesdemoiselles** /͵medəmwəˋzɛl; ͵meɪdəmwəˈzel/ a title used to address a young unmarried French-speaking woman; MISS[2] (1) 小姐〔對講法語的年輕未婚婦女的稱呼〕：*Mademoiselle Dubois* 迪布瓦小姐

made-to-mea·sure /͵· · ˈ··◂/ *adj* made-to-measure clothes are specially made to fit you〔衣服〕量體定做的

made-to-or·der /͵· · ˈ··◂/ *adj AmE* made-to-order clothing, furniture etc is made for one particular customer【美】〔服裝、家具等〕定製的

made-up /͵· ˈ·◂/ *adj* **1** a story that is made-up is not true〔故事〕虛構的，不真實的：*This tale of hers is totally made-up.* 她講的這個故事完全是虛構的。—see also 另見 **make up** (MAKE[1]) **2** wearing MAKE-UP (1) on your face 化了妝的：*She was heavily made-up.* 她濃妝豔抹。

mad·house /ˋmæd͵haus; ˈmædhaʊs/ *n* [C] **1** a place with a lot of people, noise, and activity 人多嘈雜而混亂的場所：*This office is like a madhouse.* 這個辦公室吵吵鬧鬧，亂糟糟的。**2** *old use* a MENTAL HOSPITAL【舊】瘋人院，精神病院

mad·ly /ˋmædlɪ; ˈmædli/ *adv* **1** in a wild, uncontrolled way 瘋狂地，發瘋似地：*She was beating madly on the door with her fists.* 她發瘋似地用雙拳捶打着門。**2 madly in love** very much in love 瘋狂地愛着

mad·man /ˋmædmən; ˈmædmən/ *n plural* **madmen** /-mən; -mən/ [C] **1 like a madman** in a wild, uncontrolled way 瘋子似地：*He went racing off like a madman!* 他瘋子般飛快地跑掉了。**2** *not technical* a man who is mentally ill【非術語】瘋子，神經錯亂的人

mad·ness /ˋmædnɪs; ˈmædnəs/ *n* [U] **1** *especially BrE* very stupid behaviour that could be dangerous【尤英】非常愚蠢並可能有危險的行為: **it is/would be madness to do sth** *It would be sheer madness to try to cross the desert on your own.* 你試圖獨自穿越沙漠, 簡直是瘋了。**2** *not technical* serious mental illness【非術語】嚴重精神錯亂 —see also 另見 **there's method in sb's madness** (METHOD (3))

Ma·don·na /məˋdɑnə; məˈdɒnə/ *n* **1 the Madonna** Mary, the mother of Jesus, in the Christian religion 聖母馬利亞〔基督教中耶穌的母親〕**2** [C] a picture or figure of Mary 聖母畫像[雕像]

ma·dras /məˋdrɑs; məˈdrɑːs/ *n* **1** [C,U] a kind of CURRY (=hot-tasting Indian dish) usually made with meat 馬德拉斯〔一種印度辣味咖喱菜餚, 通常加肉烹調〕**2** [U] a kind of cotton cloth with stripes 馬德拉斯條紋棉布

mad·ri·gal /ˋmædrɪgl; ˈmædrɪgəl/ *n* [C] a song for several singers without musical instruments, popular in the 16th and 17th centuries 無伴奏合唱曲〔流行於16與17世紀〕

mad·wom·an /ˋmædˌwʊmən; ˈmædwʊmən/ *n plural* **madwomen** /-ˌwɪmɪn; -wɪmɪn/ [C] *not technical* a woman who is mentally ill【非術語】女瘋子, 瘋女人

mael·strom /ˋmelstrəm; ˈmeɪlstrəm/ *n* [C] **1** a situation full of uncontrollable events or strong emotions that make people feel weak or frightened 極度混亂狀態; 失控狀態: *a maelstrom of conflicting emotions* 矛盾情感的漩渦 **2** a violent storm 暴風雨

maes·tro /ˋmaɪstro; ˈmaɪstrəʊ/ *n* [C] someone who can do something very well, especially a musician 大師〔尤指音樂大師〕

maf·i·a /ˋmɑfɪˌɑ; ˈmɑːfiə/ *n* [singular] **1 the Mafia** a large organised group of criminals who control many illegal activities especially in Italy and the US〔尤指意大利和美國的〕黑手黨 **2** a powerful group of people within an organization or profession who support and protect each other〔某組織或行業內部相互支持並相互保護的〕勢力集團: *the medical mafia* 醫務界的勢力集團

maf·i·o·so /ˌmæfɪˋoso; ˌmɑːfiˈəʊsəʊ/ *n plural* **mafiosi** /-si; -siː/ [C] a member of the Mafia 黑手黨成員

mag /mæg; mæg/ *n* [C] *informal* a magazine【非正式】雜誌

2 **mag·a·zine** /ˌmægəˋzin; ˌmægəˈziːn/ *n* [C] **1** a large thin
2 book with a paper cover that contains news stories, articles, photographs etc, and is sold weekly or monthly 雜誌, 期刊: *a glossy fashion magazine* 用有光紙印刷的時裝雜誌 | *a literary magazine* 文學雜誌 **2** the part of a gun that holds the bullets〔槍的〕子彈夾, 彈匣, 彈倉 —see picture at 參見 GUN[1] 圖 **3** the container that holds the film in a camera or PROJECTOR〔照相機或電影放映機的〕膠卷盒, 底片盒 **4** a room or building for storing weapons, explosives etc 彈藥室; 軍火庫

ma·gen·ta /məˋdʒɛntə; məˈdʒentə/ *n* [U] a bright pink colour 品紅色, 洋紅色 —**magenta** *adj* —see picture on page A5 參見A5頁圖

mag·got /ˋmægət; ˈmægət/ *n* [C] a small creature like a WORM that is the young form of a FLY and lives in decaying food, flesh etc 蛆

Ma·gi /ˋmedʒaɪ; ˈmeɪdʒaɪ/ *n* [plural] **the Magi** the three wise men who brought gifts to the baby Jesus, according to the Christian religion〔根據基督教的說法, 送禮物給剛剛降生的耶穌的〕三博士, 東方三賢

ma·gic¹ /ˋmædʒɪk; ˈmædʒɪk/ *n* [U] **1** a secret power used to control events or do impossible things, by saying special words or performing special actions 魔法, 法術; 巫術: *Do you believe in magic?* 你相信魔法嗎? | **work/do magic** *tales of wizards who could work magic* 關於會施法術的男巫的故事 —see also 另見 BLACK MAGIC, WHITE MAGIC **2** a special, attractive or exciting quality 魅力, 魔力: *These old stories still retain their magic.* 這些老故事仍然保持着吸引力。**3** the skill of doing tricks that look like magic, used by a MAGICIAN, or the tricks a magician does 魔術, 戲法; 巫術 **4 like magic/as if by magic** in a surprising way that seems impossible to explain 像變魔術似地: *The bottle had disappeared as if by magic.* 瓶子像變魔術似地突然消失了。| **work like magic** (=be very effective) 非常有效

magic² *adj* **1** [only before noun 僅用於名詞前] having special powers that are not normal or natural, so that you can do impossible things 有魔力的; 神奇的: *There is no magic formula for instant success.* 沒有立即成功的神方妙法。| **magic spell/charm etc** *a magic hat that makes her invisible* 使她隱身的魔法帽子 | **magic trick** (=a trick in which something happens in a way that seems impossible to explain) 魔術戲法 *His best magic trick is sawing a lady in half.* 他最拿手的魔術戲法是把一位女士鋸成兩半。**2 magic number/word** a number or word that is very important or that has a powerful effect on people 神祕數字/詞彙〔指非常重要或對人們有強烈影響的數字或詞彙〕**3 have a magic touch** to have a special ability to make things work well or to make people happy 有使事情運行良好[使人高興]的特殊才能: *The baby's always quiet for Gary – he has a magic touch.* 這個嬰兒只要和加里在一起就不哭不鬧 —— 加里有一種魔力。**4** [not before noun 不用於名詞前] *BrE spoken* very good or very enjoyable【英口】非常好的; 令人十分愉快的: *"Did you have a good time?" "Yeah, it was magic!"* "玩得痛快嗎?" "是的, 痛快極了!" **5 magic bullet** *informal* a quick, painless cure for illness, or something that solves a difficult problem in an easy way【非正式】魔彈〔指快速而無痛苦的疾病療法或能輕鬆解決難題之物〕

magic³ *v* **magicked, magicking** *BrE*【英】

magic sth/sb **away** *phr v* [T] to make someone or something disappear by using magic 用魔法使…消失: *I wish I could magic us away to a warm beach.* 我希望我能夠施展魔法把我們大家送到一處溫暖的海灘上去。

magic sth ↔ **up** *phr v* [T] to make something appear suddenly and unexpectedly 使…突然[出人意料]地出現

ma·gic·al /ˋmædʒɪkl; ˈmædʒɪkəl/ *adj* **1** very enjoyable, exciting or romantic, in a strange or special way 奇異的, 瑰麗的; 迷人的: *that magical evening we spent together* 我們一起度過的那個迷人的夜晚 **2** containing magic, or done using magic 有魔力的; 用魔法做成的: *magical powers* 神奇的力量 —**magically** /-klɪ; -kli/ *adv*

magic car·pet /ˌ‥ ˈ‥/ *n* [C] a CARPET[1] (1) that people use to travel through the air in children's stories〔童話故事中人們用以在空中飛行的〕魔毯

magic eye /ˌ‥ ˈ·/ *n* [C] *informal* a PHOTOELECTRIC CELL【非正式】電眼〔光電管的俗名〕

ma·gi·cian /məˋdʒɪʃən; məˈdʒɪʃən/ *n* [C] **1** someone in stories who can use magic; WIZARD (1)〔故事中的〕巫師, 術士 **2** an entertainer who performs magic tricks; CONJURER 魔術師, 變戲法的人

magic lan·tern /ˌ‥ ˈ‥/ *n* [C] a piece of equipment used in the past to make pictures shine onto a white wall or surface〔舊時的〕幻燈

magic mush·room /ˌ‥ ˈ‥/ *n* [C] a type of MUSHROOM that has an effect like some drugs, and makes you see things that are not really there 神奇蘑菇, 致幻蘑菇〔一種食用後像某些藥物一樣使人產生幻覺的蘑菇〕

magic wand /ˌ‥ ˈ·/ *n* [C] **1** a small stick used by a MAGICIAN 魔杖 **2 wave a magic wand** *humorous* to solve problems or difficulties immediately【幽默】揮舞魔杖〔立刻解決問題或困難〕: *I can't just wave my magic wand and make your problems disappear!* 我不可能只靠揮舞魔杖便使你的問題消失!

ma·gis·te·ri·al /ˌmædʒɪsˋtɪrɪəl; ˌmædʒəˈstɪəriəl◂/ *adj* **1** a magisterial way of behaving or speaking shows that you think you have authority〔行為或說話方式〕自以為權威的: *his magisterial voice* 他那盛氣凌人的語調 **2** a magisterial book is written by someone who has very great knowledge about a subject 具有學術權威性的: *his*

magisterial study of the First World War 他對第一次世界大戰的權威性研究 **3** connected with or done by a magistrate 與地方法官有關的; 由地方法官經辦的: *magisterial district* 地方法官的管轄區 —**magisterially** *adv*

ma·gis·tra·cy /ˋmædʒɪstrəsɪ; ˈmædʒɨstrəsi/ *n* [U] **1** the official position of a magistrate, or the time during which someone has this position 地方法官的職位[任期]; 治安法官的職位[任期] **2 the magistracy** magistrates considered together as a group〔總稱〕地方法官; 治安法官

ma·gis·trate /ˋmædʒɪsˌtret; ˈmædʒɨstreɪt/ *n* [C] someone who judges less serious crimes in a court of law 地方法官; 治安法官

Magistrates' Court /ˈ··· ˌ·/ *n* [C] the lowest court of law in England and Wales, which deals with less serious crimes〔英格蘭和威爾斯審理輕罪案件的〕地方法庭

mag·ma /ˋmægmə; ˈmægmə/ *n* [U] *technical* hot melted rock below the surface of the Earth【術語】岩漿

mag·na cum lau·de /ˌmægnə kum ˋlɔdɪ; ˌmægnə kʌm ˈlɔːdi/ *adj, adv Latin* at the second of the three highest levels of achievement that American students can reach when they finish their college studies【拉丁】優等成績的; 以優等成績〔美國大學生畢業時取得的三個最高等級成績中的第二等〕—compare 比較 CUM LAUDE, SUMMA CUM LAUDE

mag·nan·i·mous /mægˋnænəməs; mægˈnænɨməs/ *adj* kind and generous, especially to someone that you have defeated in some way 寬宏大量的, 慷慨的〔尤指對被自己擊敗的人〕: *a magnanimous gesture* 寬宏大量的姿態 —**magnanimously** *adv* —**magnanimity** /ˌmægnəˋnɪmətɪ; ˌmægnəˈnɪmɨti/ *n* [U]

mag·nate /ˋmægnet; ˈmægneɪt/ *n* [C] **steel/oil/shipping magnate** a rich and powerful person in a particular industry 鋼鐵/石油/船運業大亨

mag·ne·sia /mægˋniʃə; mægˈniːʃə/ *n* [U] a light, white powder used in medicine and in industry 鎂氧; 氧化鎂 —see also 另見 MILK OF MAGNESIA

mag·ne·si·um /mægˋniʃɪəm; mægˈniːziəm/ *n* [U] a common silver-white metal that burns with a bright yellow light 鎂

mag·net /ˋmægnɪt; ˈmægnɨt/ *n* [C] **1** a piece of iron or steel that can make other metal objects move towards it 磁鐵; 磁石, 吸鐵石 **2** a person or place that attracts many other people or things 有吸引力的人[地方]: *The region has become a magnet for small businesses.* 那裡已變成一個吸引小企業的地區。

mag·net·ic /mægˋnɛtɪk; mægˈnetɪk/ *adj* **1** connected with or produced by MAGNETISM 磁的; 磁性的: *magnetic forces* 磁力 | *a magnetic disk* 磁盤 **2 magnetic personality/charm etc** a personality etc that makes other people feel strongly attracted towards you 具有吸引力的個性/特點等 **3** having the power of a magnet 有磁力[磁性]的: *a magnetic bulletin board* 磁性公告板 —**magnetically** /-klɪ; -kli/ *adv*

magnetic field /·ˌ·· ˈ·/ *n* [U] an area around an object that has magnetic power 磁場

magnetic head /·ˌ·· ˈ·/ *n* [C] **1** the part of a TAPE RECORDER that records sound〔錄音機的錄音〕磁頭 **2** the part of a computer that reads and writes DATA〔電腦讀寫數據的〕磁頭

magnetic me·di·a /·ˌ·· ˈ···/ *n* [plural,U] magnetic methods of storing information for computers, for example FLOPPY DISKS or MAGNETIC TAPE 磁介質〔為電腦儲存信息的介質, 如軟盤或磁帶〕

magnetic north /·ˌ·· ˈ·/ *n* [U] the northern direction shown by the needle on a COMPASS (1) 磁北 —compare 比較 TRUE NORTH

magnetic pole /·ˌ·· ˈ·/ *n* [C] **1** one of the two points that are not firmly fixed but are near the North and South Poles of the Earth, towards which the needle on a COMPASS (1) points〔地球的〕磁極 **2** a POLE[1] (5a)〔磁鐵的〕磁極

magnetic tape /·ˌ·· ˈ·/ *n* [U] TAPE[1] (1a) on which sound, pictures, or computer information can be recorded using magnetism〔錄音、錄像或電腦儲存信息用的〕磁帶; 錄音帶; 錄像帶

mag·net·is·m /ˋmægnəˌtɪzəm; ˈmægnɨtɪzəm/ *n* [U] **1** the physical force by which a MAGNET (1) attracts metal, or which is produced when an electric current is passed through iron or steel 磁力; 磁性 **2** a quality that makes other people feel attracted to you 魅力, 吸引力: *his extraordinary personal magnetism* 他那非凡的個人魅力

mag·net·ize also 又作 **-ise** *BrE*【英】/ˋmægnəˌtaɪz; ˈmægnɨtaɪz/ *v* [T] **1** to make iron or steel able to attract other pieces of metal 使有磁性; 使磁化 **2** to have a powerful effect on people so that they feel strongly attracted to you 強烈吸引, 迷住: *His dark flashing eyes magnetized those around him.* 他那雙炯炯有神的黑眼睛吸引住了周圍的人。

mag·ne·to /mægˋnito; mægˈniːtəʊ/ *n* [C] a piece of equipment containing one or more magnets that is used for producing electricity, especially in the engine of a car〔尤指用於汽車引擎的〕磁電機, 永磁發電機

magnet school /ˈ·· ˌ·/ *n* [C] *AmE* a school that has more classes in a particular subject than usual, and so attracts students from a wide area【美】磁鐵學校, 特別才藝學校〔這種學校在某一學科上開設的課時比一般學校多, 所以學生來源的地域範圍廣〕

mag·ni·fi·ca·tion /ˌmægnəfəˋkeʃən; ˌmægnɨfɨˈkeɪʃən/ *n* **1** [U] the act of magnifying 放大: *The fingerprints showed up clearly under magnification.* 放大後指紋清晰地顯示了出來。**2** [C] the degree to which something is able to magnify things 放大率, 放大倍數: *binoculars with a magnification of ×12* 放大倍數為12倍的雙筒望遠鏡

mag·nif·i·cent /mægˋnɪfəsn̩t; mægˈnɪfɨsənt/ *adj* extremely impressive because of being very big, beautiful etc 宏偉的, 壯麗的; 華麗的, 富麗堂皇的: *The view from the summit was magnificent.* 從山頂望去, 景色壯觀動人。| *a magnificent collection of Mexican art* 一批精美的墨西哥藝術收藏品 | *her magnificent mane of red hair* 她漂亮的長而密的紅髮 —**magnificently** *adv* —**magnificence** *n* [U]

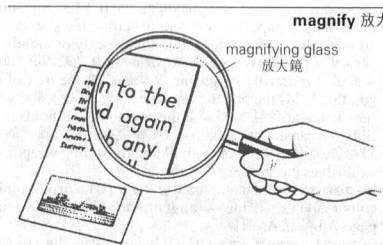

magnify 放大

magnifying glass 放大鏡

mag·ni·fy /ˋmægnəˌfaɪ; ˈmægnɨfaɪ/ *v* [T] **1** to make something look bigger than it is 放大: *The photo shows a human embryo, magnified 150 times.* 這張照片上是一個放大了150倍的人類胚胎。**2** to make something seem more important than it really is 誇張, 誇大: *This report tends to magnify the risks involved.* 這個報告有誇大所涉風險的傾向。**3** *formal* to make a problem much worst or more serious【正式】使〔問題〕加重: *The results of economic mismanagement were magnified by a series of natural disasters.* 經濟管理不善造成的後果因一連串自然災害而變得更加嚴重。**4** *biblical* to praise God【聖經】讚美〔上帝〕—**magnifier** *n* [C]

magnifying glass /ˈ···· ˌ·/ *n* [C] a round piece of glass with a handle, used to make objects or print look bigger

放大鏡 —see picture at 參見 MAGNIFY 圖

mag·ni·tude /ˋmægnə͵tjud; ˈmægnɪtjuːd/ *n* **1** [U] greatness of size or importance 巨大, 龐大; 重要性: *They didn't seem to appreciate the magnitude of the problem.* 他們似乎沒有意識到這個問題的重要性。**2** [C] *technical* the degree of brightness of a star【術語】〔恒星的〕光度, 星等 —see also 另見 ORDER OF MAGNITUDE

mag·no·li·a /mægˋnolɪə; mægˈnəʊliə/ *n* **1** [C] a tree with large white, pink, yellow, or purple flowers that smell sweet 木蘭 **2** [U] a very pale pinkish-white colour 淡桃紅色

mag·num /ˋmægnəm; ˈmægnəm/ *n* [C] **1** a large bottle containing about 1.5 litres of wine, CHAMPAGNE etc〔約裝1.5公升葡萄酒或香檳酒等的〕大酒瓶 **2** a type of large PISTOL 大口徑手槍: *a 44 magnum* 口徑0.44英寸的大口徑手槍

magnum o·pus /͵·· ˋ··/ *n* [singular] *Latin* the most important piece of work by a writer or artist【拉丁】〔作家或藝術家的〕最重要的作品, 代表作

mag·pie /ˋmæg͵paɪ; ˈmægpaɪ/ *n* [C] **1** a bird with black and white feathers and a long tail 喜鵲 **2** *informal* someone who likes collecting things【非正式】愛收集東西的人

mag tape /͵· ˋ·/ *n* [U] *BrE informal* MAGNETIC TAPE【英, 非正式】磁帶

ma·ha·ra·jah, maharaja /͵mɑhəˋrɑdʒə; ͵mɑːhəˈrɑːdʒə/ *n* [C] an Indian prince or king〔印度的〕王子; 國王; 王公; 土邦主

ma·ha·ra·ni, maharanee /mɑhəˋrɑni; ͵mɑːhəˈrɑːniː/ *n* [C] an Indian PRINCESS or queen〔印度的〕公主; 王妃; 土邦主之妻

ma·ha·rish·i /məˋhɑrəʃi; ͵mɑːhəˈriːʃi/ *n* [C] a HINDU holy teacher〔印度教的〕宗教教師

ma·hat·ma /məˋhætmə; məˈhætmə/ *n* a title used for a wise and holy man in India 聖雄, 聖人〔印度對智者、聖賢的稱呼〕

mahjong, mahjongg /mɑˋdʒɑŋ; ͵mɑː ˈdʒɒŋ/ *n* [U] a Chinese game played with small pieces of wood or bone 麻將〔中國的一種牌戲〕

ma·hog·a·ny /məˋhɑgənɪ; məˈhɒgəni/ *n* **1** [C,U] a type of hard reddish brown wood used for making furniture, or the tree that produces this wood〔製家具用的〕桃花心木, 紅木; 桃花心木科的樹 **2** [U] a dark, reddish brown colour 深赤褐色 —**mahogany** *adj*

ma·hout /məˋhaut; mɑːˈhuːt/ *n* [C] *IndE* someone who rides and trains elephants【印】象夫, 御象者, 趕象人, 管象人

maid /med; meɪd/ *n* [C] **1** a female servant, especially in a large house〔尤指大戶人家的〕女僕: *a kitchen maid* 廚房女傭人 **2** *old use* a woman or girl who is not married【舊】未婚女子; 姑娘, 少女 —see also 另見 OLD MAID

maid·en¹ /ˋmedn; ˈmeɪdn/ *n* [C] *literary* a girl who is not married【文】少女; 姑娘

maiden² *adj* **1 maiden flight/voyage** the first journey that a plane or ship makes〔飛機或船的〕首次飛行/航行 **2 maiden speech** *BrE* the first speech that someone makes in parliament【英】〔在議會中的〕首次演説

maiden aunt /͵·· ˋ·/ *n* [C] an AUNT who has never married〔從未結婚的〕姑; 姨

mai·den·hair /ˋmedn͵hɛr; ˈmeɪdnheə/ *n* [U] a kind of FERN 掌葉鐵線蕨, 孔雀草

maid·en·head /ˋmedn͵hɛd; ˈmeɪdnhed/ *n old use*【舊】**1** [U] the state of being a female VIRGIN 童貞; 處女時期 **2** [C] a HYMEN 處女膜

maid·en·ly /ˋmednlɪ; ˈmeɪdnli/ *adj old use* typical of a girl or young woman【舊】少女[年輕女子]所特有的: *maidenly modesty* 少女特有的謙遜

maiden name /ˋ·· ·/ *n* [C] the family name that a woman had before she got married 婦女的娘家姓

maid of hon·our /͵· · ˋ··/ *n* [C] **1** the chief BRIDESMAID at a wedding 首席女儐相, 主要伴娘 **2** an unmarried lady who serves a queen or a PRINCESS 女王[王后, 公主]的未婚侍女 **3** *BrE* a type of small cake【英】牛奶蛋糊[杏仁]小餡餅

maid·ser·vant /ˋmed͵sɝvənt; ˈmeɪd͵sɜːvənt/ *n* [C] *old use* a female servant【舊】女傭人, 女僕 —compare 比較 MANSERVANT

mail¹ /mel; meɪl/ *n* **1 the mail** *especially AmE* the system of collecting and delivering letters, packages etc; POST¹ (1)【尤美】郵政, 郵遞系統: *The mail here's really slow and unreliable.* 這裡的郵遞系統確實是既慢又不可靠。| **in the mail** *Your photos are in the mail.* 你的照片在郵寄途中。| *I'll put the check in the mail.* 我將把支票郵寄過去。| **by mail** *Did you send it by mail?* 你是把它郵寄的嗎? —see also 另見 ELECTRONIC MAIL, SNAIL MAIL **2** [U] the letters, packages etc that are delivered to a particular person or at a particular time 郵件; 郵包: *Did we get any mail this morning?* 我們上午收到甚麼郵件嗎? | **in the mail** *Anything interesting in the mail?* 郵件中有甚麼有趣的東西嗎? —see also 另見 JUNK MAIL **3** [U] armour made of metal worn in the Middle Ages〔中世紀穿的〕鎧甲, 鎖子甲 S3 W3

mail² *v* [T] *especially AmE* to send a letter, package etc to someone【尤美】郵寄〔信件、包裹等〕; POST² (1) *BrE*【英】: **mail sth to sb** *I'll mail it to you tomorrow.* 我明天把它寄給你。 S3

mail·bag /ˋmel͵bæg; ˈmeɪlbæg/ *n* [C] **1** a large, strong bag used for carrying mail on trains etc〔火車等運送郵件的〕郵件袋 **2** *AmE* a bag used to deliver letters to people's houses【美】〔郵遞員向住戶遞送郵件的〕郵袋; POSTBAG *BrE*【英】

mail·box /ˋmel͵bɑks; ˈmeɪlbɒks/ *n* [C] *AmE*【美】**1** a box, usually outside a house, where someone's letters are delivered or collected〔通常置於住宅外的〕信箱 —compare 比較 LETTERBOX **2** a container where you post letters 郵箱, 郵筒; POSTBOX *BrE*【英】

mail car·ri·er /ˋ· ͵···/ *n* [C] *AmE old-fashioned* someone who delivers mail to people's houses【美, 過時】郵遞員

mail drop /ˋ· ·/ *n* [C] *AmE*【美】**1** an address where someone's mail is delivered, which is not where they live 通信地址〔非收件人居住地址〕**2** a box in a post office where your mail can be left〔設在郵局內的〕郵箱

mail·er /ˋmelɚ; ˈmeɪlə/ *n* [C] *especially AmE* a container or envelope used for sending something small by mail【尤美】包裝小郵件用的容器[信封]

mailing list /ˋ·· ·/ *n* [C] a list of names and addresses kept by an organization, so that it can send information or advertising material by mail〔供寄送資料或廣告材料用的〕郵寄名單

mail·man /ˋmel͵mæn; ˈmeɪlmæn/ *n plural* **mailmen** /-͵mɛn; -men/ [C] *AmE* a man who delivers mail to people's houses【美】郵遞員; POSTMAN *BrE*【英】

mail or·der /͵· ˋ··◂/ *n* [U] a method of buying and selling in which the buyer chooses goods at home and orders them from a company which sends them by mail 郵購

mail·shot /ˋmelʃɑt; ˈmeɪlʃɒt/ *n* [C] advertisements or information sent to many people at one time by mail〔大量發送的〕郵寄資料, 郵寄廣告

mail train /ˋ· ·/ *n* [C] a train that carries mail 郵政列車

maim /mem; meɪm/ *v* [T] to wound or injure someone very seriously and often permanently 使受重傷, 使殘疾: *landmines that kill or maim people in the rural areas* 鄉村地區炸死或炸傷人的地雷 | **maimed for life** *Rod was maimed for life in a car smash.* 羅德在一次撞車事故中受重傷, 因而終身殘疾。

main¹ /men; meɪn/ *adj* [only before noun 僅用於名詞前] **1** bigger or more important than all other things, ideas, influences etc of the same kind〔同類中〕主要的, 最重要的; 最大的: *I noted down the main points of her speech.* 我把她講話的要點記了下來。| *The main bed-* S1 W1 *room is at the back of the house.* 主臥室在房子的後部。| *Lack of confidence was the main reason behind the team's defeat.* 缺乏信心是球隊失敗的主要原因。| *Our main concern is that the children are safe.* 我們最關心的是孩子們的安全。| *the main female character in the movie* 電影中的女主人公 **2 the main thing** *spoken* used to say what is the most important thing in a situation【口】最重要的事: *As long as you're not hurt, that's the main thing.* 只要你不受到傷害 —— 這才是最重要的。| *The main thing is not to panic.* 最重要的是不要驚慌。—see also 另見 **with an eye to the main chance** (EYE[1] (36)), **the main drag** (DRAG[2] (7))

main² *n* **1** [C] a large pipe or wire carrying the public supply of water, electricity or gas〔供水、供電、供煤氣的〕總管道; 幹線電纜: *a burst water main in the street* 街上爆裂的自來水總管道 **2 the mains** *BrE*【英】**a)** the place on a wall you can connect something to a supply of electricity 電源插座: *You can run it off batteries or plug it into the mains.* 你可以用電池或者把它插到電源插座上使用。| **at the mains** *Make sure that the television is turned off at the mains.* 一定要把電視機的電源關上。**b) mains gas/electricity/water** the public supply of gas etc through large pipes or wires 由總管道[幹線]輸送的煤氣/電/水: *The heater will run off mains gas or bottled gas.* 加熱器用管道煤氣或罐裝煤氣均可。**3 in the main** mostly 大體上, 基本上: *Her fellow students were in the main from wealthy backgrounds.* 她的同學大都來自富有的家庭。—see also 另見 **with might and main** (MIGHT[2] (1))

main clause /,· '·/ *n* [C] *technical* a CLAUSE that can form a sentence on its own【術語】主句〔能獨立構成句子的分句〕

main course /'· ·/ *n* [C] the main part of a meal 主菜

main drag /,· '·/ *n* **the main drag** *AmE informal* the main street in a town or city where big shops and businesses are【美, 非正式】〔城鎮的〕主要街道, 大街: *cruising along the main drag in Las Vegas* 沿着拉斯維加斯的主要大街慢駛

main·frame /ˋmen,frem; 'meɪnfreɪm/ *n* [C] a large computer that can work very fast and that a lot of people can use at the same time 大型電腦

main·land /ˋmen,lænd; 'meɪnlənd/ *n* **the mainland** the main area of land that forms a country, as compared to islands near it that are also part of that country 大陸, 本土〔與和它一起構成一個國家領土的鄰近島嶼相對而言〕: *a ferry service between the islands and the mainland* 往返各島嶼與大陸之間的輪渡服務 **—mainland** *adj*: *mainland Britain* 英國本土

main line /,· '·◂/ *n* [C] an important railway that connects two cities〔連接兩座城市的〕鐵路幹線: *the main line to Moscow* 通往莫斯科的鐵路幹線 **—mainline** *adj*: *a mainline station* 鐵路幹線車站

main·line /ˋmen,laɪn; 'meɪnlaɪn/ *v* [I,T] *slang* to INJECT illegal drugs into your blood【俚】向自己的血液中注射〔毒品〕: *By that time he was mainlining heroin.* 當時他正在注射海洛因。

main·ly /ˋmenlɪ; 'meɪnli/ *adv* as the largest or most important reason, thing, part of something etc 主要地; 大部分地: *Her illness was caused mainly by worry and stress.* 她的病主要是由焦慮和精神壓力引起的。| *The workforce is mainly made up of women.* 勞動力主要是由婦女構成的。| *the mainly Zulu Inkatha Freedom Party* 主要由祖魯人組成的英卡塔自由黨 | [sentence adverb 句子副詞] *"What did you do all evening?" "Well, we just talked mainly."* "你們整個晚上幹甚麼了?" "噢, 我們主要是聊天而已。" | **mainly because** *I don't go out much, mainly because I have to look after the kids.* 我不大出去, 主要是因為我必須照看孩子們。| **mainly due to** (=caused to a great degree by) 主要由…引起 *Increased sales during the summer were mainly due to tourism.* 夏季銷售額增加主要是由旅遊業帶動的。| **mainly why/what/how** *spoken*【口】*Boredom was mainly why I decided to quit.* 覺得工作枯燥乏味是我決定辭職的主要原因。

main·mast /ˋmen,mæst; 'meɪnmɑːst/ *n* [C] the largest or most important of the MASTS that hold up the sails on a ship〔船的〕主桅, 大桅

main road /,· '·/ *n* [C] a large and important road 大路

main·sail /ˋmen,sl; 'meɪnsəl; *not tech* 非術語 -sel; -seɪl/ *n* [C] the largest and most important sail on a ship〔船的〕主帆 —see picture at 參見 YACHT 圖

main·spring /ˋmen,sprɪŋ; 'meɪnsprɪŋ/ *n* [C] **1 the mainspring of/for** the most important reason or influence that makes something happen …的主要原因: *Romantic love had been the mainspring of Augustini's poetry.* 浪漫的愛情造就了奧古斯丁尼的詩歌。**2** the most important spring in a watch or clock〔鐘錶的〕主發條

main·stay /ˋmen,ste; 'meɪnsteɪ/ *n* **the mainstay of a)** an important part of something that makes it possible for it to work properly or continue to exist …的主要依靠[支柱]: *Agriculture is still the mainstay of the country's economy.* 農業仍然是這個國家經濟的主要支柱。**b)** someone who does most of the important work for a group or organization …的挑大梁的人物[台柱子, 骨幹]: *She was the mainstay of the team.* 她是這個小組的骨幹。

main·stream¹ /ˋmen,strim; 'meɪnstriːm/ *n* **1 the mainstream of** the most usual way of thinking about something or doing something〔思想或行為〕的主流: *Environmental ideas have been absorbed into the mainstream of European politics.* 環境意識已被納入歐洲政治的主流。**2 the mainstream** the people whose ideas about a subject are shared by most people and regarded as normal 主流派人物: *Genet started as a rebel, but soon became part of the literary mainstream.* 吉尼特開始是一位叛逆者, 但不久就成為文學主流派中的一員。**—mainstream** *adj*: *mainstream economic theory* 主流經濟理論

mainstream² *v* [T] *AmE* to include a child with physical or mental problems in an ordinary class【美】把〔生理或心理上有問題的兒童〕安排到普通班級中

Main Street /'· ·/ *n* **1** [C] the most important street, with many shops and businesses on it, in many small towns in the US〔美國許多小城鎮的〕大街, 主街 —compare 比較 HIGH STREET **2** [U] *AmE* ordinary people who believe in traditional American values【美】〔信仰美國傳統價值觀的〕普羅大眾, 老百姓: *The President's new tax hikes won't go down too well on Main Street.* 總統再次提高稅收, 這不會受到普通老百姓的歡迎。

main·tain /menˋten; meɪn'teɪn/ *v* [T] 

1 ▶MAKE STH CONTINUE 使某事繼續◀ to make something continue in the same way or at the same high standard as before 保持; 維持: *Britain wants to maintain its position as a world power.* 英國想保持其世界強國的地位。| *our commitment to maintaining a high-quality service* 我們保持高質量服務的承諾

2 ▶LEVEL/RATE 水平/速度◀ to make a level or rate of activity, movement etc stay the same 保持〔水平或速度〕: *It is important to maintain a constant temperature inside the greenhouse.* 使溫室內的溫度保持恒定是很重要的。

3 ▶MACHINE/BUILDING 機器/建築物◀ to keep a machine, building etc in good condition by looking after it 維修; 保養〔機器、建築物等〕: *The report found that safety equipment had been very poorly maintained.* 報告說安全設備保養得很糟糕。

4 maintain your silence/opposition etc to continue to be silent, to oppose something etc 保持沉默/堅持反對意見等: *Evans has always maintained his allegiance to the trade union movement.* 埃文斯一貫擁護工會運動。

5 ▶SAY 說◀ to strongly express your belief that something is true 斷言〔某事〕屬實; 堅持說…: **maintain (that)** *Critics maintain that these reforms will lead to a decline in educational standards.* 批評者堅稱這些改革會導致教育水平下降。| **maintain your innocence** (=continue to say that you are not guilty of something)

堅稱自己無罪
6 ►MONEY/FOOD 金錢/食物◄ to provide someone with the things they need, such as money or food 供養; 贍養: *How can you maintain a family on $900 a month?* 你每月900美元怎麼能維持一家人的生活呢?
7 maintain life to provide animals, plants etc with the things they need in order to exist 維持〔動植物等的〕生命

2 3 **main·te·nance** /ˈmentənəns; ˈmeɪntənəns/ *n* [U] **1** the repairs, painting etc that are necessary to keep something in good condition 維修; 養護, 保養: **[+of]** *The caretaker is responsible for the maintenance of the school buildings.* 管理員負責保養維修學校的各棟樓房。| **car/building etc maintenance** *evening classes in car maintenance* 汽車維修夜校課程 | **maintenance man** (=a man who looks after buildings and equipment for a school or company)〔為學校或公司看樓或看管設備的〕管理員 **2** *BrE* money paid by someone who is DIVORCED to their former wife or husband【英】〔付給前妻或前夫的〕贍養費; CHILD SUPPORT *AmE*【美】**3** the act of making a state or situation continue 保持; 維持: *the maintenance of good relations between the two countries* 兩國間友好關係的保持

mai·son·ette /ˌmezəˋnɛt; ˌmeɪzəˈnet/ *n* [C] *BrE* an apartment, usually on two floors, that is part of a larger house【英】〔通常佔有兩層樓的〕公寓套房

mai·tre d' /ˌmetrə ˋdi; ˌmetrə ˈdiː/ also 又作 **maître d'hôtel** /ˌmɛtrə doˋtɛl; ˌmetrə dəʊˈtel/ *n* [C] *French* someone who is in charge of a restaurant, and who welcomes guests, gives orders to the waiters etc【法】餐館經理; 餐館服務員領班 —see picture on page A15 參見 A15 頁圖

maize /mez; meɪz/ *n* [U] *BrE* a type of tall plant with large yellow seeds which are used for food【英】玉蜀黍, 玉米; CORN (2a) *AmE*【美】

Maj. the written abbreviation of 縮寫= MAJOR² (1)

ma·jes·tic /məˋdʒɛstɪk; məˈdʒestɪk/ *adj* very big and impressive 雄偉壯麗的; 威嚴的: *the majestic temples of Bangkok* 曼谷雄偉的寺廟 —**majestically** /-klɪ; -kli/ *adv*

ma·jes·ty /ˋmædʒɪstɪ; ˈmædʒɨsti/ *n* [U] **1 Your/Her/His Majesty** used when talking to or about a king or queen 陛下〔對國王或女王的稱呼〕: *The Prime Minister is here to see you, Your Majesty.* 首相前來拜謁, 陛下。| *His Majesty the King* 國王陛下 **2** the quality of being impressive and powerful that something big has 雄偉, 壯麗; 莊嚴; 崇高: *the awesome majesty of the snowcapped Rocky Mountains* 白雪覆頂的落基山脈令人驚嘆的壯麗

3 2 **ma·jor¹** /ˋmedʒɚ; ˈmeɪdʒə/ *adj* **1** [usually before noun 一般用於名詞前] very large or important, when compared to other things or people of a similar kind 較大的; 較重要的; 主要的: *There are two major political parties in the US.* 美國有兩大政黨。| *Mahler's music was a major influence on the young composer.* 馬勒的音樂極大地影響了那位年輕的作曲家。| *one of the major causes of cancer* 癌症的主要病因之一 —opposite 反義詞 MINOR¹ (1) **2** [usually before noun 一般用於名詞前] having very serious or worrying results 後果十分嚴重的; 後果非常令人擔憂的: *The loss of Cantona through injury was a major setback for the team.* 簡東拿因傷缺陣使該隊遭受了嚴重的損失。| **major problem** *This could create major traffic problems.* 這會產生嚴重的交通問題。**3** [not before noun 不用於名詞前] *AmE spoken* very important【美口】非常重要的: *This is major? You got me out of bed for this?* 這就叫做重要? 你把我從牀上弄起來就是為了這個? **4** a major key (KEY² (4)) is based on a musical SCALE in which there are SEMITONES between the third and fourth and the seventh and eighth notes〔音樂〕大音階的, 大調的: *a symphony in D major* D大調交響樂 —compare 比較 MINOR¹ (2)

major² *n* [C] **1** an officer of middle rank in the British or US army or MARINES, or in the US airforce〔英國〕陸軍[海軍陸戰隊]少校;〔美國〕陸軍[空軍、海軍陸戰隊]少校 —see table on page C6 參見 C6 頁附錄 —see also 另見 DRUM MAJOR **2** *especially AmE* the main subject that a student studies at college or university【尤美】〔大學的〕主修科目, 專業: *Her major is history.* 她的主修科目是歷史。—compare 比較 MINOR² (2) **3** *AmE* someone studying a particular subject as their main subject at college or university【美】〔大學中〕主修某科目的學生, 某專業的學生: *She's a history major.* 她是歷史專業的學生。**4 the majors** [plural] the MAJOR LEAGUES〔美〕職業棒球大聯盟, 職業棒球聯合總會 —compare 比較 MINOR LEAGUE

major³ *v*
major in sth *phr v* [T] *especially AmE* to study something as your main subject at college or university【尤美】〔在大學〕主修: *He's majoring in Political Science.* 他主修政治學。

ma·jor·do·mo /ˌmedʒɚˋdomo; ˌmeɪdʒəˈdəʊməʊ/ *n* [C] *old-fashioned* someone in charge of the servants in a large house【過時】大管家, 總管

ma·jor·ette /ˌmedʒəˋrɛt; ˌmeɪdʒəˈret/ *n* [C] a girl who spins a BATON while marching with a band〔樂隊行進時手中轉動着指揮棒的〕女指揮, 女領隊

major gen·e·ral /ˌ·· ˈ···◄/ *n* [C] an officer of high rank in the British or US army or the US airforce〔英〕陸軍少將;〔美〕陸軍[空軍]少將 —see table on page C6 參見 C6 頁附錄

ma·jor·i·ty /məˋdʒɔrətɪ; məˈdʒɒrɨti/ *n* **1** [singular] most of the people or things in a particular group 多數, 大多數〔人或物〕: **[+of]** *The majority of lone parents are divorced or separated women.* 單身父母中大多數是離婚或分居的婦女。| [also+plural verb *BrE* 英] *Among trade union leaders, a majority still believe in public ownership.* 工會領導人中多數仍然相信公有制。| **the great/vast majority** (=almost all of a group) 絕大多數, 幾乎全體 *In the vast majority of cases the disease proves fatal.* 在絕大多數的病例中, 這種疾病結果都是致命的。| **a majority decision** (=a decision made by more people voting for it than against it) 多數人投票贊成的決定 **2 be in the majority** to form the largest part of a group 構成多數, 佔多數: *Young people were in the majority at the meeting.* 這次會議年輕人佔了多數。**3** [C] the difference between the number of votes gained by the winning party or person in an election and the number of votes gained by other parties or people 超過的票數〔選舉中獲勝黨或個人所得票數與其他政黨或候選人所得票數之間的差額〕: *Their majority in the House was reduced by 20.* 他們在議會中的多數議席減少了20席。| **overall majority** (=a situation in which one party wins more votes in an election than all the other parties)〔選舉中一政黨所獲票數超過所有其他政黨所獲票數之和的〕總和多數票 | **by/with a majority** *He won by a majority of 500.* 他以500票的多數獲勝。**4** [U] *law* the age when someone legally becomes a responsible adult【法律】成年; 法定年齡 —opposite 反義詞 MINORITY 3 2

majority lead·er /·ˈ··· ˌ··/ *n* [C] the person who organizes the members of the political party that has the most people elected, in either the House of Representatives or the US Senate〔美國參議院或眾議院中〕多數黨領袖 —compare 比較 MINORITY LEADER

major-league /ˌ·· ˈ·/ *adj* [usually before noun 一般用於名詞前] **1** connected with the Major Leagues〔美國〕職業棒球聯合會的: *playing major-league baseball* 打聯合會職業棒球賽 **2** *especially AmE* important or influential【尤美】重要的; 有影響的: *a major-league player in California politics* 在加州政壇上有影響力的人物

Major Leagues /ˌ·· ˈ·/ *n* [plural] the group of teams that make up American professional baseball〔美國〕職業棒球大聯盟, 職業棒球聯合總會

M

make¹ /mek; meɪk/ *v past tense and past participle* made /med; meɪd/

① PRODUCE STH 製作某物
② DO STH 做某事
③ CAUSE A STATE/SITUATION 導致某種情況
④ FORCE SB TO DO STH 迫使某人做某事
⑤ MONEY 金錢
⑥ BE ADDED TOGETHER 加起來
⑦ BE SUITABLE 適合於
⑧ PRETEND 假裝
⑨ MAKE IT 做成某事
⑩ CALCULATE 計算
⑪ MANAGE 勉強應付
⑫ MAKE WAY 讓路
⑬ ARRIVE 到達
⑭ BE GOOD/IMPORTANT 好/重要
⑮ OTHER MEANINGS 其他意思

① PRODUCE STH 製作某物

1 [T] to produce something by working 做, 製作, 製造; 建造: *I'm going to make a cake for Sam's birthday.* 我打算為薩姆的生日做一個蛋糕。| *Did you make that dress yourself?* 那件衣服是你自己做的嗎? | *a car made in Japan* 一輛日本製造的汽車 | *They're making a documentary about the Civil War.* 他們正在拍一部有關南北戰爭的記錄片。| **make sth out of** *You could make some cushion covers out of those old curtains.* 你可以用那些舊窗簾做一些坐墊罩。| **make sth from** *We made a shelter from leaves and branches.* 我們用樹葉和樹枝搭了一個棚子。| **make sb sth** *Shall I make you a cup of coffee?* 我為你沖杯咖啡好嗎? | **made (out) of** *a blouse made of silk* 絲綢做的女式襯衫

2 to produce something by doing something, often by accident〔常指意外地〕使出現; 使形成: **make a hole/dent etc** *Make a hole in the paper.* 在紙上戳一個洞。| **make a mark/scratch etc** *Who made those marks on the wall?* 牆上那些污跡是誰留下的?

② DO STH 做某事

3 [T] **a)** used with some nouns to mean that someone performs the action of the noun 進行; 作出〔與某些名詞連用, 表示某人完成一個由該名詞表達的行為〕: **make a decision/mistake etc** *It's time to make a decision.* (=to decide) 該是作決定的時候了。| *Come on, you guys – make an effort!* 來吧, 哥們 —— 努力幹吧! | *The company was about to make a major purchase.* 公司當時正打算進行一項大宗的購貨。**b)** used with some nouns of speaking, to mean that someone says something 作出〔與某些與説話有關的名詞連用, 表示某人説某事〕: **make a suggestion/comment/observation etc** *May I make a suggestion?* 我可以提個建議嗎? | *Jackson made a short statement to the press, denying all the charges.* 傑克遜向新聞界作了一個簡短的聲明, 否認所有的指控。

4 make an appointment/arrangement/date etc to arrange to do something, meet someone etc 進行預約/作出安排/進行約會等

5 make a contribution/donation/charge etc to give or ask for money for a particular purpose 捐獻/捐款/收費等: *We have to make a small charge for use of the facilities.* 我們不得不收取少量設施使用費。

6 make an appearance/entrance etc to suddenly appear somewhere or enter a room 突然在某處出現/進入房間等

7 make a start to begin doing something 開始做〔某事〕: **[+on/with]** *I'd better make a start on the ironing.* 我最好開始熨衣服。

③ CAUSE A STATE/SITUATION 導致某種情況

8 [T] to cause a particular state or situation, or make something happen 引起, 導致; 使某事發生: **make sb/sth do sth** *That tune makes me want to dance.* 那支曲子使我想跳舞。| *This lever here makes the heating come on.* 這裡的這根控制桿控制暖氣開啟。| *I like him because he makes me laugh.* 我喜歡他因為他逗我笑。| **make sb/sth** *You could make this a really nice room if you got a new carpet.* 如果你買一塊新地毯, 你就能把這個房間變得十分漂亮。| *the movie that made him a star* 那部使他成為明星的電影 | **make sb ill/happy/popular etc** *The decision made her very unpopular with the staff.* 這一決定使她很不受員工們的歡迎。| *It makes me so angry to see children being treated like that.* 看到孩子們受到那樣的對待我非常氣憤。| **make sb feel good/guilty/sick etc** *Jo's reassuring comments made me feel better.* 喬所説的那些安慰話使我感覺好多了。| **make sb look old/thin etc** *This photo makes her look much older than she really is.* 這張照片使她看起來比實際年齡大得多。| *I like the dress Jan, it makes you look really slim.* 簡, 我喜歡那件連衣裙, 它讓你看起來很苗條。| **make yourself heard/understood etc** *I had to shout to make myself heard above the music.* 我不得不大聲喊叫以使人們在音樂聲中聽到我的話。| **make it clear (that)** *I want to make it clear that I don't agree with this policy.* 我想講清楚, 我不同意這個政策。| **make it known (that)** *He made it known that he would not be running for reelection.* 他公開宣布他不打算競選連任。

9 make trouble/a noise/a mess etc to do something that causes trouble, noise etc 製造麻煩/發出響聲/弄髒[弄亂]等: *The kids had made a terrible mess.* 孩子們把到處搞得又髒又亂。| *Do you have to make such a row?* 難道你們必須這樣大吵大鬧嗎?

10 make sb captain/leader etc to give someone a new job or position in a group, organization etc 任命某人為船長/隊長等: *She's now been made a full partner.* 她現在已成為一名正式股東。

11 make sth the best/worst/most expensive etc to result in something being the best, worst etc of a particular type 使某事成為最好/最差/最昂貴等: *These findings make Britain the country with the worst record on pollution.* 這些調查結果使英國成為污染記錄最糟糕的國家。

④ FORCE SB TO DO STH 迫使某人做某事

12 [T] to force someone to do something, or force something to happen 強迫〔某人做某事〕; 迫使〔某事發生〕: **make sb do sth** *They made us write it out again ten times.* 他們強迫我們再把它寫十遍。| *Marcia made the poor girl cry.* 馬西婭把那個可憐的小姑娘弄哭了。| **be made to do sth** *I was made to wait two hours for an appointment.* 我為了一個約會而被迫等了兩個小時。

⑤ MONEY 金錢

13 [T] to earn or get money 掙得; 獲得〔金錢〕: *She makes about £25,000 a year.* 她每年大約掙25,000英鎊。| *We made $10,000 out of selling the house.* 我們賣

掉那座房子賺了10,000美元。| **make money** *Dunson's one aim in life was to make money.* 鄧森生活中的唯一目的就是賺錢。

14 make a living (doing sth) to earn the money that you need (做某事)謀生: *He makes a living repairing secondhand cars.* 他靠修理二手汽車謀生。

15 make a profit/loss to get or lose money in a trade or business 獲利/賠錢: *The company has made a big loss this year.* 那家公司今年賠了不少錢。—see 見 GAIN¹ (USAGE)

⑥ BE ADDED TOGETHER 加起來

16 [linking verb 連繫動詞] to be a particular number or amount when added together 合計為, 總計: *Two and two make four.* 二加二等於四。| *So if Jan comes that makes four of us.* 這樣, 如果簡來的話我們就有四個人了。

⑦ BE SUITABLE 適合於

17 [linking verb 連繫動詞] to have the qualities, character etc necessary for a particular job, use, or purpose 宜用作; 具備...的素質: *I'm sure Penny will make a very good teacher.* 我相信彭尼會成為一名很好的教師。| *The hall would make an excellent theatre.* 這座大廳可以改裝成一家一流的劇院。| *An old cardboard box makes a comfortable bed for a kitten.* 舊紙箱給小貓當牀是很舒服的。

⑧ PRETEND 假裝

18 make believe to pretend that something is true, especially as a game 假裝〔尤指作為遊戲〕; 假扮: *We made believe we were on a secret island.* 我們假裝在一個人跡罕至的海島上。—see also 另見 MAKE-BELIEVE

19 make like *AmE spoken* to behave in a way that you hope will give people a particular opinion of you【美口】假裝; 裝扮作: *He makes like he's got it all figured out.* 他裝出一副甚麼都明白了的樣子。

20 make as if to do sth to move in a way that makes it seem that you are going to do something 比劃着好像要做某事: *Fred, still grinning, made as if to hit me.* 弗雷德仍然咧嘴笑着, 卻比劃着好像要打我。

⑨MAKE IT 做成某事

21 make it *informal*【非正式】**a)** to arrive somewhere in time for something 及時到達, 趕上: *If we run, we should make it.* 如果跑着去的話, 我們應該還能趕得上。| **[+to]** *I just made it to the bathroom before throwing up.* 我忍住嘔吐, 及時衝進了衛生間。**b)** to be successful in a particular activity or profession 取得成功: *I never thought Clare would make it as an actress.* 我從來沒想到克萊爾會成為一名成功的女演員。| **make it big** *AmE* (=be very successful)【美】取得極大成功 *They've made it big in show business.* 他們在演藝界取得極大成功。**c)** *spoken* to be able to go to an event, meeting etc that has been arranged【口】能參加, 能出席〔已安排好的活動、會議等〕: *I'm really sorry, but I won't be able to make it on Sunday after all.* 非常抱歉, 我星期天還是不能出席。| *We didn't make it to the party in the end.* 我們最終還是沒能參加那個聚會。**d)** to live through an illness or after an accident, or manage to deal with a very difficult experience〔在生病或事故之後〕活下來;〔在一次困難的經歷中〕挺了過來: *Frank was very ill, and the doctors didn't think he'd make it.* 弗蘭克當時病得很厲害, 醫生們認為他挺不過來了。| **[+through]** *I don't know how I'm going to make it through the day.* 我不知道我將如何熬過這一天。

22 make it up *BrE* to become friendly with someone again after you have had an argument【英】和解, 和好: *Have you made it up with your sister yet?* 你與你姐姐已經和好了嗎?

23 make it up to to do something good for someone because you feel responsible for something bad that happened to them 彌補, 補償: *I'll make it up to you one day, I promise.* 我總有一天會給你補償的, 我保證做到。

24 make it quick/snappy *spoken* used to tell someone to do something as quickly as possible【口】趕快: *Two coffees please, and make it snappy.* 請來兩杯咖啡, 越快越好。

25 make it 6 o'clock/4.30 etc *BrE spoken* to think that it is a particular time, according to your watch【英口】〔按自己的錶〕時間為六點/四點半等: *"What time do you make it?" "I make it half past two."* "你的錶現在幾點鐘了?""我的錶兩點半了。"

26 make it with *AmE* to have sex with someone【美】與〔某人〕做愛

⑩ CALCULATE 計算

27 [T] to decide that something is a particular amount or total by calculating 計算為, 算出: *I make that $150 altogether.* 我算出總共為150美元。

⑪ MANAGE 勉強應付

28 make do (with/without) to manage with or without something, even though this is not completely satisfactory (在目前有/沒有某物的情況下)勉強應付: *New clothes are expensive, so you'll just have to make do with what you've got.* 新衣服很貴, 所以你就只能有甚麼穿甚麼了。

⑫ MAKE WAY 讓路

29 make way a) to move to one side so that someone or something can pass〔給某人或某物〕讓路: **[+for]** *The crowd stepped aside, making way for the riders.* 人羣走到一旁, 給騎手們讓路。**b)** to be removed so that something newer or better can be used or made instead 騰出地方: **[+for]** *Several houses were demolished to make way for an office development.* 好幾棟房子被拆除以騰出地方來建一座辦公樓。

30 make your way a) to move towards something, especially slowly or with difficulty〔尤指緩慢或艱難地〕前進: *We made our way down the hill towards the town.* 我們下了小山, 朝鎮上走去。**b)** to slowly become successful in a particular job, activity, or profession 緩慢獲得成功: *Gradually, Henderson began to make his way in politics.* 慢慢地, 亨德森開始在政壇上嶄露頭角。

⑬ ARRIVE 到達

31 [T] *informal* to arrive at or get to a particular place【非正式】到達: *I don't think we're going to make the town before nightfall.* 我認為黃昏之前我們到不了那個城鎮。| *We didn't make the 6:30 train.* 我們沒有趕上六點半的火車。

32 make the meeting/the party/Tuesday etc *spoken* to be able to go to something that has been arranged for a particular date or time【口】能夠參加會議/晚會/星期二的活動等: *I'm sorry, I can't make Friday after all.* 對不起, 星期五我還是來不了。| *Will you be able to make the next meeting?* 你能來參加下一次會議嗎?

33 make a deadline/target/rate to succeed in doing something by a particular time, producing a particular amount etc 在限期內完成/實現目標/達到級別

⑭ BE GOOD/IMPORTANT 好/重要

34 make the papers/headlines/front page etc to be interesting or important enough to be printed in the papers etc 登上報紙/成為頭條新聞/成為頭版新聞等: *News of their divorce made the headlines.* 他們離婚的消息成了頭條新聞。

35 make the team/squad etc to be good enough to be chosen to play in a sports team 被選進運動隊等: *He'll never make the football team.* 他永遠也進不了足球隊。

⑮ OTHER MEANINGS 其他意思

36 make a difference to cause a change, especially an

improvement, in a situation 引起變化〔尤指促進改進〕: *Their help has made a big difference to the team's success.* 他們的幫助對運動隊的成功起了重要的作用。| *I tried to reason with him, but it made no difference.* 我設法勸導他, 但不起作用。| **make all the difference** *That one extra day off made all the difference.* 那額外的一天假起了關鍵作用。**37 make a (phone) call** to speak to someone using a telephone 打電話: *I have to make a few calls.* 我有幾個電話得打。**38 make time** to find enough time to do something, even though you are busy 抽出時間: *Somehow, she always makes enough time to take the kids out.* 不知怎的, 她總是能騰出時間帶孩子們出去。**39 make the bed** to pull the sheets and covers over a bed so that it is tidy after someone has slept in it 整理牀鋪, 鋪牀 **40 make or break** to cause either great success or complete failure 使大為成功或徹底失敗, 或成之或毀之: *Critics can make or break a young performer.* 評論家既能夠捧紅也能夠毀掉一名年輕的演員。**41 it makes a change** *spoken especially BrE* used to say that something is pleasantly different from normal【口, 尤英】有所變化〔用以表示某事與平常不同而令人愉快〕: *It makes a change to get something other than bills in the post!* 從郵件中收到賬單以外的東西, 會使人分外高興! **42 that makes two of us** *spoken* used to agree with someone's opinion or to say that something that happened to them has also happened to you【口】對我來說也是如此, 對我同樣適用: *"I think I've had enough of this party." "That makes two of us."* "我想我對這個聚會已經感到厭煩了。" "我也有同感。" **43 make to do sth** *old use* to seem to be starting to do something【舊】似乎正要做某事: *Greg made to speak, but I stopped him.* 格雷格好像要講話, 但我阻止了他。**44 ►MAKE STH PERFECT** 使某物完美◄ [T] *informal* to provide the qualities that make something complete or successful【非正式】使完美: *The hat really makes the outfit.* 這頂帽子確實給整套服裝錦上添花。—see also 另見 MADE, **make sb's day** (DAY[1] (35)), **make friends** (FRIEND (2)), **make good** (GOOD[1] (44)), **make sense** (SENSE[1] (9))

make away with sb/sth *phr v* [T] **1** *informal* to steal something【非正式】偷竊〔某物〕: *Thieves made away with thousands of dollars worth of jewelry.* 竊賊偷走了價值數千美元的珠寶。**2** *old-fashioned* to kill someone【過時】殺死〔某人〕

make for sth *phr v* [T] **1** to move towards something, or move in a particular direction 朝…走去; 朝…前進: *We made for St. Louis as fast as possible.* 我們以最快的速度向聖路易斯趕去。**2** to be likely to have a particular result or make something possible 有利於; 傾向於; 使可能: *The larger print makes for easier reading.* 大號字體會更方便閱讀。| *Such statements don't exactly make for racial harmony.* 這樣的聲明不利於種族和睦。—see also 另見 **be made for each other** (MADE (2))

make sb/sth **into** sth *phr v* [T] **1** to change something so that it has a different form or purpose 將…製成[變成]: *We can make your room into a study.* 我們可以把你的房間改成一個書房。**2** [T] to change someone's character, job, or position in society 使轉變為〔指改變某人的性格、工作或社會地位〕: *a film which made her into a star overnight* 使她一夜之間成為明星的一部電影

make sth **of** sb/sth *phr v* [T] **1** to understand something in a particular way, or have a particular opinion about something 了解, 理解; 看待: *I don't know what to make of Kristin's recent behaviour at all.* 我一點也不知道該如何解釋克里斯丁最近的行為。| *What do you make of this latest idea?* 你對這個最新的主意有何看法? **2** to use the chances, opportunities etc you have in a way that achieves a particular result〔利用機遇〕有所成就; 塑造: *Your college career is whatever you make of it.* 你的大學生活, 你把它弄成甚麼樣, 它就是甚麼樣。| *I want to make something of my life.* 我想這輩子有所成就。| **make the most of** (=use an opportunity as successfully or usefully as possible) 充分利用 *We only have one day in Paris, so we'd better make the most of it.* 我們在巴黎只待一天, 因此我們最好充分利用這一天時間。**3 make a go of sth** *BrE informal* to make something as successful as possible by trying hard or working hard【英, 非正式】盡力以使某事成功: *She's determined to make a go of the business this time.* 她下決心這次要把生意做得十分成功。**4 make too much of** to treat something as if it is more important than it really is 過分重視: *The press made too much of what was only meant as a joke.* 媒體對那個只是作為兒戲的事情重視過頭了。**5 make a day/night/evening of it** *informal* to decide to spend a whole day, night etc doing something【非正式】花整天/整夜/整個晚上的時間做某事: *Why don't we go for a meal after the movie and really make an evening of it.* 看完電影後我們何不去吃頓飯, 玩它整整一個晚上呢。**6 do you want to make sth (out) of it?** *spoken* used to say that you are willing to have a fight or argument with someone【口】你想弄個明白嗎?〔用來表示願意跟某人打鬥或爭論〕—see also 另見 **see what sb is (really) made of** (MADE (4))

make off *phr v* [I] to leave quickly, especially in order to escape〔尤指為了逃跑〕匆忙離開; 溜掉

make off with sth *phr v* [T] *informal* to take something that does not belong to you【非正式】拿走〔他人之物〕; 搶走: *Two young men attacked him and made off with his wallet.* 兩個年輕男子襲擊了他並搶走了他的錢包。

make out *phr v* **1** [T **make** sth ↔ **out**] to be only just able to hear, see, or understand something〔勉強〕聽出; 看出, 辨認出: *I can scarcely make out his writing.* 我難以看清他的字跡。| **make out who/how/when etc** *We couldn't make out what they were talking about.* 我們聽不清楚他們正在談論甚麼。**2** [T **make** sb ↔ **out**] *informal* to understand someone's character, or what they think, feel, want etc【非正式】了解〔某人的性格或想法、感覺、需要等〕: *Stuart's a strange guy – I can't make him out at all.* 斯圖爾特是個怪人 —— 我一點都搞不懂他。**3 make out a cheque/bill etc** to write a cheque, bill etc 開支票/賬單等: *Make the cheque out to 'Spencer Cross Ltd'.* 把支票開給"斯潘塞·克羅斯有限公司"。**4** [T] *informal* to claim or pretend that something is true when it is not【非正式】假稱; 聲稱; 假裝; 把…說成: **make out (that)** *She always makes out she's the only one who does any work.* 她總是聲稱她是唯一幹了點活的人。| **make sb out to be sth** *Oh, Sean's not as bad as he's made out to be.* 哎呀, 肖恩並沒有人們說的那麼壞。**5 make out a case (for)** to find good enough reasons to prove something or explain why you need something 找到充分理由證明[解釋]〔某事〕: *I'm sure we can make out a case for hiring another assistant.* 我確信我們可以找到充分理由再雇用一位助手。**6** [I] *especially AmE* to succeed or progress in a particular way【尤美】〔在某方面〕取得成功; 取得進展: *How did you make out at the interview?* 你面試情況怎樣? **7** [I] *informal, especially AmE* to kiss and touch someone in a sexual way【非正式, 尤美】親吻愛撫: *making out in the back seats of cars* 在汽車後座親吻撫摸 **8 make out like a bandit** *AmE informal* to get a lot of money or gifts, win a lot etc【美, 非正式】獲得大量金錢[禮物]; 贏得大量錢財: *Those kids make out like bandits every Christmas.* 那些孩子每年聖誕節都會得到不少的禮物。

make sth ↔ **over** *phr v* [T] **1** to officially and legally give money or property to someone else〔正式依法〕轉讓〔錢財〕: *He made over the whole estate to his son.* 他把全部財產轉讓給自己的兒子。**2** *AmE* to change something so that it looks different or has a different use【美】

改造: *I've made that old blue dress over into a skirt.* 我把那件舊的藍色連衣裙改成了一條裙子。—see also 另見 MAKEOVER

make towards sth *phr v* [T] to start moving towards something 朝〔某物〕移動, 移向…: *She made towards the door.* 她朝門走去。

make up *phr v*

1 ▶EXCUSE/EXPLANATION 藉口/解釋◀ [T **make** sth ↔ **up**] to invent a story, explanation etc in order to deceive someone 編造〔說法、解釋等〕: *I think they're making the whole thing up.* 我認為整件事情都是他們編造出來的。—see also 另見 MADE-UP

2 ▶SONG/POEM 歌/詩◀ [T **make** sth ↔ **up**] to invent the words or music for a new song, story, poem etc 編〔歌詞、曲子、故事、詩歌等〕: *We even made up a rude song about it.* 我們甚至寫了一首關於此事的粗俗的歌曲。

3 ▶SB'S FACE 某人的臉◀ [I,T **make** sb ↔ **up**] to put special paint, colour etc on someone's face in order to change the way they look 給〔某人〕化妝[化裝]: *They made him up as an old man for the last act of the play.* 在這齣戲的最後一幕, 他們把他化裝成一個老頭子。—see also 另見 MADE-UP, MAKE-UP

4 ▶PREPARE/ARRANGE 準備/佈置◀ [T **make** sth ↔ **up**] to prepare or arrange something by putting things together 準備; 佈置: *I could make up a bed for you on the couch.* 我可以給你在長沙發上準備鋪蓋。| *Get the chemist to make up this prescription for you.* 讓藥劑師給你配好這個處方。

5 ▶FORM/BE 形成/成為◀ [T **make up** sth] to combine together to form a particular system, group, result etc; CONSTITUTE 形成, 組成, 構成: *Women make up only 30% of the workforce.* 婦女僅佔勞動力的30%。| **be made up of** *The committee is made up of representatives from every state.* 該委員會由來自每個州的代表組成。—see 見 COMPRISE (USAGE)

6 ▶NUMBER/AMOUNT 數目/金額◀ [T **make up** sth] *especially BrE* to complete an amount or number to the level that is needed【尤英】湊足, 補齊: *I saved as much as I could, and my mum made up the rest of the money.* 我盡我所能地攢了一些錢, 不足之數由我媽媽湊齊。| *Do you want to make up a four for tennis?* 你們想湊足四個人打網球嗎?

7 ▶TIME/WORK 時間/工作◀ [T **make** sth ↔ **up**] to work at times when you do not usually work, so that you do all the work that you should have done 補上, 補回: *I'm trying to make up the time I lost while I was sick.* 我正在設法補回我生病期間耽誤的時間。| *Is it OK if I make the work up next week?* 我下星期再補做這些工作可以嗎?

8 ▶FROM CLOTH 用布料◀ [T **make** sth ↔ **up**] to produce something from cloth by cutting and sewing 裁製; 縫製: **[+into]** *I plan on making that material up into a dress.* 我計劃把那塊衣料做成一件連衣裙。

9 ▶FRIENDS 朋友◀ [I] *informal* to become friendly with someone again after you have had an argument【非正式】和好, 和解: **[+with]** *Have you made up with Patty yet?* 你與帕蒂和好了嗎? | **kiss and make up** *When are you two going to kiss and make up?* 你們兩個甚麼時候和好如初呀? —see also 另見 **make up your mind** (MIND[1] (4))

make up for sth *phr v* [T] **1** to make a bad or unpleasant situation seem better, by providing something pleasant 補償: *That one weekend made up for all the disappointments I'd had.* 那一個週末補償了我曾有過的一切失望。**2** to have so much of one quality that it does not matter that you do not have enough of something else 彌補: **make up for sth in/with** *What Jay lacked in experience, he made up for in enthusiasm.* 經驗方面的不足, 傑伊用熱情彌補上了。**3 make up for lost time a)** to work more quickly, or at times when you do not usually work, because something has prevented you from working before 補償失去的時間: *We rehearsed all day Saturday, to make up for lost time.* 我們星期六排練了一整天, 以補回失去的排練時間。**b)** to become involved in an activity very eagerly, because you wish you could have done it earlier in your life 補償早年應做而未做的事: *After all those years apart, we're making up for lost time getting to know each other!* 在分離了那麼多年之後, 我倆正在相互了解, 以補償失去的時間。

make up to sb *phr v* [T] to try to get someone's attention or approval by being friendly or praising them, especially in order to get an advantage for yourself 討好, 奉承, 巴結〔尤指為了本人的利益〕—see also 另見 **make it up to** (MAKE[1] (23))

USAGE NOTE 用法説明: MAKE

COLLOCATION 搭配

There is no simple rule for when to use **make** or **do**. Generally you **make** something that did not exist before. 沒有簡單的規則規定何時用 make, 何時用 do。通常, make 表示製造出以前不存在的東西: you *make lunch/trouble/peace/a noise/a plan/a joke/a mistake/ a speech/a promise* 做午飯/製造麻煩/講和/發出聲音/制定計劃/開玩笑/犯錯誤/發表演講/作出許諾 But other verbs are used in phrases like these 但是在下列短語中應當用其他動詞: *I asked a question.* 我問了一個問題。| *He gave an answer.* 他給予了答覆。| *We nearly had an accident.* 我們差點出了場事故。

Make is also used when someone or something is changed in some way. make 也用於表示某人或某物在某些方面發生了變化: *She made him comfortable.* 她使他覺得很舒服。| *He made a success of it.* 他把它做成了。| *They made friends.* 他們交上了朋友。| *How much money did Shane make?* 沙恩賺了多少錢? But 但說 *They did a lot of harm/damage.* 他們造成了很大的傷害/破壞。

When travel is involved, it is safer to use **go**. 當涉及旅行的時候, 用 go 更穩妥: *They went shopping/for a picnic/on vacation/on a trip.* 他們外出購物/野餐/度假/旅行去了。But you can also say 但也可以說: *They did the shopping* (他們去買了東西), and 及 *They made a trip to Boston.* (他們去了一趟波士頓)。

You **do** other actions. do 用來表示其他的活動: *They did some exercises/some research/a test/the TOEFL exam.* 他們做了一些練習/做了一些研究/參加了一次測驗/參加了托福考試。| *Would you do me a favour?* 你能幫我一個忙嗎? But you 但說 *make fun of someone* (取笑某人), *make use of something* (使用某物), and 及 *make an effort/attempt/start.* (作一次努力/作一次嘗試/開始)。Sometimes you would use **take** instead. 有時會用 take 代替: *take a class/take a look at something/take a ride on something* 上課/看某物一眼/乘坐某交通工具

Do is especially frequent with words that describe work and activities, often ending in *-ing*. do 特別常與表示工作和活動的詞連用, 這類詞常以 -ing 結尾: *Her husband does all the shopping and cooking.* 購物和做飯全由她丈夫做。

GRAMMAR 語法

Apart from in certain fixed phrases, you do not use an adjective immediately after **make**. 除了在某些固定短語中之外, make 後面不直接接形容詞: *She always makes her classes interesting* (NOT 不用 *She always makes interesting her classes*). 她總是使自己的課生動有趣。

You **make** someone do something. 用 make 表示讓某人做某事: *The police officer made them empty*

their pockets (NOT 不用 *The police officer made them to empty their pockets*). 那個警察要他們把口袋掏空。

However, you do use **to** for the second verb when you are writing or speaking in the passive tense. 然而，當用被動語態寫或說時，第二個動詞前一定要用to: *They were made to empty their pockets.* 他們被要求掏空口袋。

make² *n* **1** a particular type of product, made by one company〔由一家公司生產的〕產品樣式；品牌：*What make is your car?* 你的車是甚麼牌子的？| **[+of]** *a different make of computer* 不同品牌的電腦 **2 be on the make** *informal*【非正式】**a)** to be always trying to get an advantage for yourself 總是設法為自己謀求利益 **b)** to be trying to have a sexual relationship with someone 試圖與某人發生性關係

make-be·lieve /ˈ· ·,·/ *n* [U] a state of imagining or pretending that something is real 假想；假裝：*She told me her parents are millionaires, but it's all just make-believe.* 她告訴我她父母是百萬富翁，但這一切都純屬子虛烏有。

make·o·ver /ˋmekovɚ; ˈmeɪkəʊvə/ *n* [C] a process of improving your own or someone else's appearance with new clothes, a new haircut, MAKE-UP (1) etc〔以新衣服、新髮型、化妝品等〕裝扮

mak·er /ˋmekɚ; ˈmeɪkə/ *n* [C] **1 mapmaker/watchmaker etc** someone who makes or produces maps etc 地圖繪製員[生產商]/鐘錶製造商等 **2 decision maker/peacemaker etc** someone who is good at or responsible for making decisions, stopping arguments etc 決策者/調解人等：*She was the peacemaker in a family that was always quarreling.* 在一個爭吵不休的家庭裡她是個和事老。—see also 另見 TROUBLEMAKER **3** also 又作 **makers** [plural] *especially BrE*【尤英】—a firm that makes or produces something 製造商；製造廠：*There's something wrong with my camera; I'm sending it back to the makers.* 我的照相機出毛病了；我要把它送回生產廠家。**4 meet your maker** *humorous* to die【幽默】去見上帝，死

make·shift /ˋmek,ʃɪft; ˈmeɪkʃɪft/ *adj* made for temporary use when you need something and there is nothing better available 權宜的；臨時(代用)的：*a makeshift sofa of crates and cushions* 用木箱和坐墊拼成的臨時沙發

make-up 化妝品

make-up /ˈ· ·/ *n* **1** [U] substances such as powder, creams, and LIPSTICK that some women and also actors put on their faces to improve or change their appearance 化妝品；化裝用品：*eye make-up* 眼部化妝品 —see also 另見 **make up** (MAKE¹) **2** [singular] a particular combination of people or things that form a group or whole〔人或物的〕組成，構成：*The make-up of the team should include both young and experienced players.* 這支隊伍應包括年輕隊員又應包括經驗豐富的隊員。**3 sb's make-up** the qualities, attitudes etc in someone's character 某人的性格：*It's in Bill's make-up to keep on fighting till the end.* 堅持戰鬥到底，這是比爾的性格。**4** [C] *AmE* a test taken in school because you were not able to take a previous test【美】補考

make-weight /ˈ· ·/ *n* [C] someone or something that is added only to make a necessary number or quantity 用來湊足數目的人[物]，充數的人[物]

make-work /ˈ· ·/ *n* [U] *AmE* work that is not important but is given to people to keep them busy【美】〔為使人們有事幹而提供的〕不重要的工作

mak·ing /ˋmekɪŋ; ˈmeɪkɪŋ/ *n* **1** [U] the process or business of making or producing something 製造，製作，生產：**the making of** *an interesting programme about the making of 'Jurassic Park'* 一個關於電影《侏羅紀公園》製作過程的有趣節目 | *involved in the making of policy* 參與政策的制定 | **dress making/decision making etc** *a region famous for cheese making* 一個以製作乾酪而聞名的地區 **2 be the making of sb** to make someone a much better or more successful person 使某人更優秀[更加成功]：*It's a tough course, but I'm sure it will be the making of him.* 這是個艱難的過程，但我敢肯定這會使他更加成功。**3 have the makings of** to have the qualities or skills needed to become a certain kind of person or thing 具有成為〔某種人或物的〕素質[技能]：*Giggs has the makings of a world-class footballer.* 傑斯具有成為一名世界級足球運動員的素質。**4 in the making** in the process of being made or produced 在製造[製作]中：*His book was 20 years in the making.* 他的書寫了20年的時間。**5 of your own making** problems or difficulties that are of your own making have been caused by you and no-one else〔問題或困難〕由自己造成的

mal- /mæl; mæl/ *prefix* bad or badly 壞，不良：*a malformed limb* (=wrongly shaped) 畸形的肢體 | *She maltreats her children.* (=treats them cruelly) 她虐待自己的孩子們。

mal·ad·just·ed /,mæləˋdʒʌstɪd; ,mæləˈdʒʌstɪd◂/ *adj* unable to form good relationships with people because of problems in your character and attitudes 不適應生活環境的；心理失調的 —**maladjustment** *n* [U]

mal·ad·min·i·stra·tion /,mæləd,mɪnəˋstreʃən; ,mælədmɪnɪˈstreɪʃən/ *n* [U] *formal* careless or dishonest management【正式】管理不善；弊政

mal·a·droit /,mæləˋdrɔɪt; ,mæləˈdrɔɪt◂/ *adj formal* not good at dealing with people or problems【正式】不善於與人打交道的，不圓滑的；不老練的 —**maladroitly** *adv* —**maladroitness** *n* [U]

mal·a·dy /ˋmælədɪ; ˈmælədi/ *n* [C] **1** *formal* something that is wrong with a system or organization【正式】〔制度或機構的〕弊病，弊端：*Public education suffers from the same malady as many other government programs.* 公共教育與其他許多政府項目一樣受困於同一弊病。**2** *old use* an illness【舊】疾病

ma·laise /mæˋlez; məˈleɪz/ *n* [singular,U] **1** a feeling of anxiety, dissatisfaction, and lack of confidence within a group of people that is not clearly expressed or understood〔一羣人中潛在的〕焦躁[不滿，缺乏信心的]情緒：*We detected a certain malaise among the staff.* 我們覺察到工作人員中有種莫名的不滿情緒。**2** a feeling of being slightly ill that usually does not last very long〔短期的〕不適，不舒服

mal·a·prop·is·m /ˋmæləprɑp,ɪzəm; ˈmæləprɒpɪzəm/ *n* [C] an amusing mistake made by using a word that sounds similar to the word you intended to say but means something completely different 令人發笑的詞語誤用〔指誤用發音近似而意義完全不同的詞語〕

ma·lar·i·a /məˋlɛrɪə; məˈleəriə/ *n* [U] a disease common in hot countries that is caused when an infected MOSQUITO bites you 瘧疾 —**malarial** *adj*: *malarial fever* 瘧疾

ma·lar·key /mə`lɑrkɪ; mə'lɑːki/ *n* [U] *informal* talk that is meant to impress or deceive you but does not mean anything; NONSENSE【非正式】胡言亂語; 廢話; 蠢話: *All that stuff was a load of malarky!* 那些都是一派胡言!

Ma·lay¹ /mə`le; mə'leɪ/ *n* **1** [C] someone from the largest population group in Malaysia 馬來人 **2** [U] the language of these people 馬來語

Malay² *adj* from or connected with Malaysia 馬來西亞的

mal·con·tent /`mælkən,tɛnt; 'mælkəntent/ *n* [C] *formal* someone who is likely to cause trouble because they are dissatisfied【正式】不滿者, 反叛者

3 2 **male¹** /mel; meɪl/ *adj* **1** belonging to the sex that cannot have babies 男的, 雄的, 公的: *a male lion* 雄獅 | *Women teachers often earn less than their male colleagues.* 女教師掙的錢常常比她們的男同事要少。**2** typical of or connected with this sex 男性特有的; 男性的, 男子的: *male aggression* 男人特有的攻擊性 | *traditional male values* 傳統的男性價值觀 | *differences between male and female longevity* 男女兩性壽命的差異 **3 male plant/flower etc** a plant etc that cannot produce fruit 雄性植物/花朵等 **4** *technical* a male PLUG¹ (1) fits into a hole or SOCKET (1)【術語】〔插頭等〕陽的, 凸形的 **5 male bonding** the forming of strong friendships between men 男子間的牢固友誼之形成 —opposite 反義詞 FEMALE¹ —**maleness** *n* [U]

3 **male²** *n* [C] **1** a male animal 雄性動物: *The male is usually bigger and more brightly coloured than the female.* 雄性動物通常比雌性動物體型大, 顏色也更鮮豔。**2** a man, especially a typical man 男人, 男子: *She wouldn't appeal to your average male.* 她對普通男人不會有甚麼吸引力。| *Police described her attacker as a white male aged about 25.* 警察把襲擊她的人描述為一個大約25歲的白人男子。

male chau·vin·ist /,· '···◂/ *n* [C] a man who believes that men are better than women and who has fixed, traditional ideas about the way men and women should behave 大男人主義者: *Bill was very much the male chauvinist, and wouldn't let his wife go out to work.* 比爾是個十足的大男人主義者, 不願讓妻子出去工作。| **male chauvinist pig** (=an insulting name for a male chauvinist) 奉行大男人主義的蠢豬

mal·e·dic·tion /,mælə`dɪkʃən; ,mælɨ'dɪkʃən/ *n* [C] *formal* a wish or prayer that something bad should happen to someone; CURSE² (2)【正式】詛咒, 咒罵

mal·e·fac·tor /`mælə,fæktɚ; 'mælɨfæktə/ *n* [C] *formal* someone who does evil things【正式】作惡的人, 壞人

ma·lef·i·cent /mə`lɛfəsn̩t; mə'lefɨsənt/ *adj formal* doing or able to do evil things【正式】作惡的, 犯罪的, 有害的 —**maleficence** *n* [U]

male men·o·pause /,· '···/ *n* [singular] *humorous* a period in the middle of a man's life when he feels anxious and unhappy【幽默】男性更年期

male-voice choir /,· · '·/ *n* [C] a large group of male singers 男聲合唱團

ma·lev·o·lent /mə`lɛvələnt; mə'levələnt/ *adj* showing a desire to harm other people 有惡意的; 惡毒的 —**malevolence** *n* [U] —**malevolently** *adv*

mal·feas·ance /,mæl`fizn̩s; mæl'fiːzəns/ *n* [U] *law* illegal activity, especially by a government official【法律】〔尤指政府官員的〕違法行為; 瀆職

mal·for·ma·tion /,mælfɔr`meʃən; ,mælfɔː'meɪʃən/ *n* **1** [C] a part of the body that is badly formed〔身體的〕畸形: *congenital malformations in young children* 幼兒先天的身體畸形 **2** [U] the state of being badly formed 畸形: *bone malformation* 骨骼畸形

mal·formed /mæl`fɔrmd; ,mæl'fɔːmd◂/ *adj* badly formed 畸形的, 變形的

mal·func·tion /mæl`fʌŋkʃən; mæl'fʌŋkʃən/ *n* [C] a fault in the way a machine or computer operates〔機器或電腦的〕故障, 失靈 —**malfunction** *v* [I]

mal·ice /`mælɪs; 'mælɨs/ *n* [U] **1** the desire or intention to deliberately harm someone 惡意, 害人之心: *There was no need for Jane to tell them – she did it out of sheer malice.* 簡沒有必要告訴他們 —— 她這麼做純粹出於惡意。| **bear sb no malice** (=not want to harm someone although they have behaved badly to you) 對某人無懷恨之心 **2 with malice aforethought** *law* a criminal act that is done with malice aforethought is done in a carefully planned and deliberate way【法律】精心策劃的預謀犯罪

ma·li·cious /mə`lɪʃəs; mə'lɪʃəs/ *adj* showing a desire to harm or hurt someone 惡意的, 惡毒的: *malicious gossip* 惡意的閒話 —**maliciously** *adv* —**maliciousness** *n* [U]

ma·lign¹ /mə`laɪn; mə'laɪn/ *v* [T usually passive 一般用被動態] to say or write unpleasant things about someone that are untrue 誹謗, 誣衊, 中傷: *She had seen herself repeatedly maligned in the newspapers.* 她已遭受報紙的多次誹謗。| **much maligned** (=criticized by a lot of people, often unfairly)〔常指不公正地〕受到眾人猛烈批評的 *a much-maligned and controversial film* 一部受到猛烈抨擊的有爭議的電影

malign² *adj formal* harmful【正式】有害的: *a malign influence* 有害的影響 —**malignly** *adv* —**malignity** /mə`lɪgnətɪ; mə'lɪgnɨti/ *n* [U]

ma·lig·nan·cy /mə`lɪgnənsɪ; mə'lɪgnənsi/ *n* **1** [C] *technical* a TUMOUR【術語】惡性腫瘤 **2** [U] *formal* feelings of great hatred【正式】極度憎恨(的情緒)

ma·lig·nant /mə`lɪgnənt; mə'lɪgnənt/ *adj* **1** *technical* a malignant TUMOUR, disease etc is one that develops uncontrollably and is likely to cause death【術語】〔腫瘤、疾病等〕惡性的; 致命的 —compare 比較 BENIGN (2) **2** *formal* showing hatred and a strong desire to harm someone【正式】惡毒的, 惡意的; 立意害人的: *He advanced towards them with a malignant look.* 他朝他們走去, 滿臉兇相。—**malignantly** *adv*

ma·lin·ger /mə`lɪŋgɚ; mə'lɪŋgə/ *v* [I] to avoid work by pretending to be ill 裝病以逃避工作 —**malingerer** *n* [C]

mall /mɔl; mɔːl/ *n* [C] *especially AmE* a large area where there are a lot of shops, usually a covered area where cars are not allowed【尤美】購物中心, 商場

mal·lard /`mælɚd; 'mælɑːd/ *n* [C] a kind of wild duck 綠頭鴨〔一種野鴨〕

mal·le·a·ble /`mælɪəbl̩; 'mæliəbəl/ *adj* **1** something that is malleable is easy to press or pull into a new shape 有展延性的; 可鍛[壓, 拉]的: *malleable steel* 展性鋼 **2** someone who is malleable is easily influenced, changed, or trained〔人〕易受影響的; 易改變的; 易訓練的 —**malleability** /,mælɪə`bɪlətɪ; ,mæliə'bɪlɨti/ *n* [U]

mal·let /`mælɪt; 'mælɨt/ *n* [C] **1** a wooden hammer with a large end 木槌 —see picture at 參見 TOOL¹ 圖 **2** a wooden hammer with a long handle used when playing CROQUET and POLO〔打槌球、馬球用的〕長柄球棍

mal·low /`mælo; 'mæləʊ/ *n* [C,U] a plant with pink or purple flowers and long stems 錦葵 —see also 另見 MARSHMALLOW (2)

mal·nour·ished /mæl`nɝɪʃt; ,mæl'nʌrɪʃt◂/ *adj* ill or weak because of not having enough food to eat, or because of not eating good food 營養不良的

mal·nu·tri·tion /,mælnju`trɪʃən; ,mælnjʊ'trɪʃən/ *n* [U] illness or weakness caused by not having enough food to eat, or by not eating good food 營養不良

mal·o·dor·ous /mæl`odərəs; ,mæl'əʊdərəs/ *adj literary* smelling unpleasant【文】難聞的, 惡臭的

mal·prac·tice /mæl`præktɪs; ,mæl'præktɨs/ *n* [C,U] the act of failing to do a professional duty properly, or of making a mistake while doing it 玩忽職守, 瀆職: *She sued her doctor for malpractice.* 她以醫療失當罪起訴她的醫生。

malt¹ /mɔlt; mɔːlt/ *n* **1** [U] grain, usually BARLEY, that has been kept in water for a time and then dried, used for making beer, WHISKY etc 麥芽 **2** [C] *AmE* a drink made from milk treated with malt, with ICE CREAM and something else such as chocolate added【美】麥乳精, 麥乳精飲料: *Two strawberry malts, please.* 請來兩杯草莓麥乳精飲料。**3** [C,U] also 又作 **malt whisky** —a type of high quality WHISKY from Scotland 麥芽威士忌〔一種蘇格蘭產的優質威士忌〕

malt² *v* [T] to make grain into malt 把…製成麥芽

malt·ed /ˋmɔltɪd; ˈmɔːltɪ̣d/ *n* [C] *AmE* a MALT¹ (2)【美】麥乳精, 麥乳精飲料

Mal·tese /mɔlˋtiz; ˌmɔːlˈtiːz◂/ *adj* from or connected with Malta 馬爾他人的; 馬爾他語的; 馬爾他的

Mal·tese Cross /ˌ·· ˈ·/ *n* [C] a cross with four pieces that become wider as they go out from the centre 馬爾他十字〔十字四部分從中心向外漸寬〕

malt liq·uor /ˌ· ˈ··/ *n* [U] *AmE* a type of beer【美】麥芽啤酒

mal·treat /mælˋtrit; mælˈtriːt/ *v* [T] to treat a person or animal cruelly 虐待, 殘暴地對待 —**maltreatment** *n* [U]

mam /mæm; mæm/ *n* [C] *informal ScotE & NEngE* a mother【非正式, 蘇格蘭及英格蘭北部】母親

ma·ma¹, mamma /ˋmɑmə; ˈmɑːmə/ also 又作 **momma** *n* [C] *AmE informal* a word meaning mother, used by or to children【美, 非正式】媽媽〔兒語〕

ma·ma² /ˋmɑmə; məˈmɑː/ *n* [C] *BrE old-fashioned* a mother【英, 過時】媽媽

mama's boy /ˋmɑməz ˌbɔɪ; ˈmɑːməz ˌbɔɪ/ *n* [C] *AmE* a boy or man who lets his mother look after him and protect him too much, so that people think he is weak【美】嬌生慣養的男孩, 過分依戀母親的男孩; 缺乏男子氣的男人; MUMMY'S BOY *BrE*【英】

mam·ba /ˋmɑmbə; ˈmæmbə/ *n* [C] a poisonous African snake that is black or green 曼巴〔非洲的一種黑色或綠色毒蛇〕

mam·ma /ˋmɑmə; ˈmɑːmə/ *n* [C] another spelling of MAMA¹ mama¹的另一種拼法

mam·mal /ˋmæml; ˈmæməl/ *n* [C] one of the class of animals that drinks milk from its mother's body when it is young 哺乳動物 —**mammalian** /mæˋmelɪən; mæˈmeɪliən/ *adj*

mam·ma·ry /ˋmæmərɪ; ˈmæməri/ *adj technical* [only before noun 僅用於名詞前] connected with or relating to the breasts【術語】乳房的

mammary gland /ˈ··· ˌ·/ *n* [C] *technical* the part of a woman's breast that produces milk, or a similar part of a female animal【術語】乳腺

mam·mo·gra·phy /mæˋmɑgrəfɪ; mæˈmɒgrəfi/ *n* [U] examination of the breasts using X-RAYS to check for signs of CANCER 乳房X線照相術; 乳房造影術

mam·mon /ˋmæmən; ˈmæmən/ *n* [U] money, wealth, and profit, regarded as something that people want or think about too much〔人們過分想要或過分考慮的〕金錢, 財富, 利潤

mam·moth¹ /ˋmæməθ; ˈmæməθ/ *adj* [only before noun 僅用於名詞前] extremely large 巨大的, 龐大的: *a mammoth task* 巨大的任務 | *a mammoth corporation* 龐大的公司

mammoth² *n* [C] a large hairy ELEPHANT that lived on Earth thousands of years ago〔數千年前生活於地球上的〕猛獁, 毛象

mam·my /ˋmæmɪ; ˈmæmi/ *n* [C] *especially IrE* a mother【尤愛爾蘭】母親

man¹ /mæn; mæn/ *n plural* **men** /mɛn; men/ [C]

1 ►MALE PERSON 男人◄ [C] an adult male human 成年男子: *There were two men and a woman in the car.* 車上有兩男一女。| *He's a very kind man.* 他是個非常和藹的人。| *a man's watch* 男式手錶 | *Don't keep him waiting – he's a busy man.* 別讓他老等着 —— 他可是個大忙人。

2 ►STRONG/BRAVE MAN 強壯/勇敢的男子◄ [C usually singular 一般用單數] a man who has the qualities that people think a man should have, such as being brave, strong etc 男子漢, 大丈夫: **be a man** *Go on, be a man. Tell him he has to pay you more.* 堅持下去, 拿出點男子漢的氣概來。告訴他必須給你加錢。| **be man enough to do sth** (=be strong or brave enough) 有足夠的力量[勇氣]去做某事 | **make a man (out) of** (=make a boy or young man start behaving in a confident way) 使一個男孩[年輕男人]樹立信心 *Running his own business has really made a man out of Terry.* 經營他自己的企業使特里真正樹立了信心。

3 ►HUMAN BEING 人◄ **a)** [C] *old-fashioned* a person, either male or female【過時】人: *All men are equal in the eyes of the law.* 法律面前人人平等。**b)** [U] people as a group 人類: *This is one of the worst diseases known to man.* 這是人類已知的最厲害的疾病之一。| *the evolution of man* 人類的進化 | **prehistoric/stone-age man** (=the types of people who lived in the early stages of human development) 史前/石器時期的人類

4 ►WORKER 工人◄ [C] **a)** [usually plural 一般用複數] a man who works for an employer 男雇員: *Bad conditions and low wages were making the men restless.* 惡劣的條件和很低的工資使工人們焦躁不安。**b)** a man who comes to your house to do a job for you, especially to repair something〔上門服務的〕修理工: *Has the man been to fix the TV?* 那個工人來修過電視嗎? | **the gas man/rent man etc** *I waited in all day for the man to come and connect the heater.* 我一整天都在等那個工人來接通暖氣。

5 ►PARTICULAR KIND OF MAN 特定類別的人◄ **a ... man a)** a man who belongs to a particular organization, comes from a particular place, does a particular type of work etc〔屬於某個組織、來自某個地方、從事某種工作等的〕人: *Bernard was a typical Foreign Office Man.* 伯納德是個典型的外交部官員。| *I got it from the vegetable man in the market.* 我從市場上賣菜的那裡買到的。| *I think she married a Belfast man.* 我想她與一位貝爾法斯特男子結了婚。| **an Oxford/Yale/Cambridge man** (=one who has been to a particular university) 牛津/耶魯/劍橋大學畢業生 **b)** a man who likes, or likes doing, a particular thing 喜歡某物[做某事]的人: *I'm more of a jazz man myself.* 我本人更喜歡爵士樂。| *Are you a betting man?* 你喜歡打賭嗎?

6 Man! *spoken*【口】**a)** used for addressing an adult male, especially when you are excited, angry etc 老兄! 老弟!〔用於稱呼成年男子, 尤其當說話人興奮、生氣時〕: *Stop talking nonsense, man!* 別胡說八道了, 老兄! **b)** *especially AmE, CarE* used for addressing someone, especially an adult male【尤美, 加勒比】老兄! 老弟!〔尤用於稱呼成年男子〕: *This party's really great, man!* 這個聚會真是棒極了, 老兄!

7 ►SOLDIER 士兵, 戰士◄ [C usually plural 一般用複數] a soldier or SAILOR who is under the authority of an officer 士兵; 水兵: *The Captain ordered his men to fire.* 上校命令水兵們開火。

8 ►HUSBAND 丈夫◄ [C] *informal* a woman's husband or sexual partner【非正式】丈夫; 情人: *She spent five years waiting for her man to come out of prison.* 她花了五年的時間等她的丈夫出獄。

9 the man *spoken*【口】**a)** used to talk about a man you dislike, a man who has done something stupid etc 傢伙, 小子〔用於談論你不喜歡或做了蠢事的某男子〕: *I don't know why she married him – I can't stand the man myself.* 我不懂她為甚麼與他結婚 —— 我可受不了這個傢伙。| *Don't listen to him the man's a complete idiot.* 別聽他的, 那傢伙是個十足的白痴。**b)** *AmE* someone who has authority over you, especially a white man or police officer【美】頭兒, 上司〔用來指有權管你的某人, 特別是白種人或警官〕

10 a man *old-fashioned spoken* used by a man to mean himself【過時, 口】我〔男子用以指自己〕: *Can't a man*

read his paper in peace? 難道就不能讓我安靜地讀讀報紙嗎?

11 he's your/our man *spoken* used to say that a man is the best person for a particular job, situation etc【口】他是最合適的人: *If you need repairs done in the house, Brian's your man.* 如果你家裡有甚麼需要修理的話, 讓布賴恩來幹最合適。

12 a man of his word a man you can trust, who will do what he has promised to do 守信用的人, 靠得住的人

13 a man of few words a man who does not talk very much 沉默寡言的人

14 be your own man to behave and think independently without worrying about what other people think 獨立自主

15 it's every man for himself *spoken* used to say that people will not help each other【口】自顧自, 不願互相幫忙: *In journalism it's every man for himself.* 在新聞界大家都是自顧自。

16 the man in the street the average man or the average person 老百姓; 普通人, 常人: *This kind of music doesn't appeal to the man on the street.* 這種音樂不會引起一般人的興趣。

17 a man of the people a man who understands and expresses the views and opinions of ordinary people 了解民意的人; 為民眾代言的人

18 a man's man a man who enjoys being with other men and doing male activities, and is popular with men rather than women〔喜歡與其他男人在一起, 從事男人喜歡幹的事的〕男人歡迎的男人

19 ladies' man a man who is popular with women and who likes to go out with a lot of different women〔喜歡在女人中間廝混的〕女人歡迎的男人

20 man and boy if a man has done something man and boy, he has done it all his life 一輩子, 從小到大: *I've worked on that farm man and boy.* 我在那個農場工作了一輩子。

21 be man and wife to be married 結為夫婦

22 live as man and wife to behave as though you are married, although you may not be 像夫妻般生活

23 as one man *especially literary* if a group of people do something as one man, they do it together【尤文】全體一致地: *The audience rose as one man to applaud the singers.* 觀眾全體起立為歌手們鼓掌。

24 to a man/to the last man *especially literary* used to say that all the men in a group do something or have a particular quality【尤文】所有人; 無一例外地: *a disreputable crew, robbers and cutthroats to a man* 一個臭名昭著的團夥, 全部都是些強盜和殺手

25 man-about-town a rich man who spends a lot of time at parties, clubs, theatres etc〔經常出沒於遊樂場所的〕紈袴子弟; 花花公子

26 man of God a religious man, especially a priest 神職人員;〔尤指〕牧師, 神父

27 my (good) man *BrE old-fashioned spoken* used when talking to someone of a lower social class【英, 過時, 口】老兄, 老弟〔對社會階層較低的人說話時的用語〕

28 my man *spoken* used by some black British and American men to greet a friend【口】朋友〔某些英美黑人男子向朋友打招呼的用語〕

29 your man *IrE spoken* used to mean a particular man【愛爾蘭口】那個人〔指某一特定的人〕: *I think your man over there's organizing the music.* 我想那邊那個人正在安排音樂。

30 ▶SERVANT 僕人◀ [C] *old-fashioned* a male servant【過時】男僕: *My man will drive you to the station.* 我的僕人將開車送你去車站。

31 ▶GAME 遊戲◀ [C] one of the pieces you use in a game such as CHESS 棋子

32 every man jack *old-fashioned* each person in a group【過時】〔某一羣體中的〕每一個人

33 kick/hit a man when he's down to treat someone badly when you know that they already have problems 落井下石

34 man's best friend a dog 人類最好的朋友〔指狗〕

35 the man on the Clapham omnibus *BrE* someone who is supposed to represent the attitudes of ordinary people【英】普通人 —see also 另見 BEST MAN, MAN-TO-MAN, NEW MAN, OLD MAN, **be a man/woman of the world** (WORLD[1] (26))

USAGE NOTE 用法說明: MAN

POLITENESS 禮貌程度

Many people no longer use **man** to mean 'men and women in general' because it gives the impression that women are not included. They prefer to use **humans** or **human beings**. 許多人不再用 man 來統稱"男人和女人", 因為這種用法給人的印象是婦女未被包括在內。他們更喜歡用 humans 或 human beings: *abilities found in humans* (rather than 而不用 *in man*) 人類的各種能力。Also you might see 此外還會看到: *every disease known to human kind* (人類已知的各種疾病) rather than 而不是 *every disease known to man/mankind.*

Generally you use the word **person** when it is not important to say whether you are talking about a man or a woman. 一般情況下, 當沒有必要說明是在談論一個男人或女人時, 可用person一詞: *Sandy's a really nice person.* 桑迪真是個好人。| *unemployed people* 失業的人們。

It is also advisable not to use words that contain **man** in the names of jobs, because this seems to mean that only men do that job or that the person is a man. So say that someone is a **chairperson**, rather than a **chairman**, especially when it is a woman. Similarly it is better to say **spokesperson, businesspeople**, or **salesperson**. 在職務名稱中如果含有man, 最好也不要使用, 因為這種名稱似乎意味着只有男人才能擔任這種職務, 或者擔任該職務的是一個男人。所以要說某人是個 chairperson (主席), 而不用 chairman 這個詞, 當這個人是位女性時更應如此。同樣, 最好說 spokesperson (發言人), businesspeople (商人), 或 salesperson (推銷員)。

Sometimes you do not need to use **-man**, **-woman**, or **-person** in the names of jobs at all. For example, people are more likely to say **firefighter** than **fireman, police officer** rather than **policeman**, and in British English, **headteacher** or **head** instead of **headmaster** or **headmistress**. 有時職務名稱中沒有必要使用 -man, -woman 或 -person。例如, 人們更常用的是 firefighter (消防員) 而不是 fireman, police officer (警察) 而不是 policeman; 而在英國英語中人們則會用 headteacher (校長) 或 head 來代替 headmaster 或 headmistress。

man[2] *v* **manned, manning** [T] to work at, use, or operate a system, piece of equipment etc 在〔某系統、設備等上〕工作; 使用, 操縱〔某系統、設備等〕: *The information desk is manned 24 hours a day.* 問訊處每天24小時有人值班。| *the first manned spacecraft* 第一艘載人宇宙飛船

man[3] *interjection especially AmE* used to emphasize what you are saying【尤美】喂; 嘿; 啊呀〔用於強調正在說的話〕: *Man, that was a lucky escape!* 哎呀, 那真是死裡逃生啊!

man·a·cle /ˈmænəkl; ˈmænəkəl/ *n* [C usually plural 一般用複數] an iron ring on a chain that is put around the hands or feet of prisoners 鐐銬, 手銬, 腳鐐 —**manacled** *adj*

man·age /ˈmænɪdʒ; ˈmænɪdʒ/ *v* 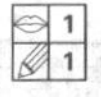

1 ▶DO STH DIFFICULT 做困難之事◀ [I,T] to succeed in doing something difficult, especially after trying very hard 設法做成〔困難的事〕; 努力完成: **manage to do sth** *Jenny managed to pass her driving test on the fifth* *attempt.* 珍妮考了五次才最終通過了駕駛考試。| *How do you manage to stay so slim?* 你是如何把身材保持得這麼苗條的? | *We eventually managed to track down the elusive Ms Lewis.* 我們終於找到了那位難找的劉易斯女士。| **manage sth** *He tried to walk, but managed only a few shaky steps.* 他試圖行走, 但只是顫巍巍地走了幾步。| **manage it** *I said we'd be there by seven, do you think we'll manage it?* 我説我們將在七點鐘之前去到那兒, 你認為我們能做到嗎?

2 ▶DEAL WITH PROBLEMS 處理問題◀ [I] *especially spoken* to succeed in dealing with problems, living in a difficult situation etc【尤口】成功應付難題, 〔在困境等中〕得以對付過去: *Frankly, I don't know how single parents manage.* 坦率地説, 我不知道單身父母日子是怎麼過的。| **[+without]** *How on earth do you manage without a washing machine?* 沒有洗衣機你究竟是怎麼生活的? | **manage with** (=use something even though it is not the best or most suitable thing) 湊合, 將就 *I can't afford to get you a new coat – you'll have to manage with the one you've got.* 我沒有錢給你買新外套 —— 你只能湊合着穿你現有的那一件。

3 ▶LIVE WITHOUT MUCH MONEY 靠不多的錢生活◀ [I] to succeed in buying the things you need to live even though you do not have very much money 〔靠不多的錢〕生活下去, 勉強維持: *I honestly don't know how we'll manage now Keith's lost his job.* 基思失業了, 我確實不知道我們將如何生活下去。| **[+on]** *People like Jim have to manage on as little as $75 a week.* 像吉姆那樣的人們不得不靠每週75美元的微薄收入來勉強過日子。

4 ▶NOT NEED HELP 無需幫忙◀ [I,T] *especially spoken* to be able to do something or carry something without help【尤口】〔無需幫忙〕能幹〔某事〕; 能搬〔某物〕: *"Do you want a hand with those bags?" "No, it's OK, I can manage."* "要我幫忙搬那些行李嗎?" "不用, 沒問題, 我應付得來。" | **manage sth** *You'll never manage that heavy suitcase; let me take it.* 那隻笨重的箱子你是提不動的, 讓我來吧。

5 ▶CAUSE PROBLEMS 引起問題◀ [T] *especially spoken* used jokingly to mean to do something that causes problems【尤口】竟搞得, 竟做出〔用於開玩笑地表示做出成問題的事情〕: **manage to do sth** *The kids had managed to spill paint all over the carpet.* 孩子們竟然把顏料灑了整整一地毯。| *I don't know how I managed to arrive so late.* 我不知道自己怎麼竟然會到得這麼遲。

6 ▶BUSINESS 生意◀ [T] to direct or control a business and the people who work in it; to be the manager of 經營, 管理; 當〔某企業〕的經理: *Managing four restaurants is extremely hard work.* 經營四家飯店是極其艱難的工作。| *He used to manage a famous rock band.* 他過去曾當過一支著名搖滾樂隊的經理。| *The company had been very badly managed.* 那家公司當時一直經營管理不善。

7 ▶TIME/MONEY 時間/金錢◀ [T] to use your time or money effectively, without wasting them 有效使用〔時間或金錢〕: *Helena's never been very good at managing her money.* 海倫娜從來就不太善於理財。

8 ▶KEEP TIDY 保持整潔◀ [T] to succeed in keeping something neat and tidy 把〔某物〕保持得井井有條: *He'll never manage such a big garden on his own.* 他單靠自己是無法料理這麼大的一個花園。| *Silkesse conditioner makes hair easier to manage.* 西爾克西護髮素能使頭髮更易於梳理。

9 ▶CONTROL 控制◀ [T] to control the behaviour of a person or animal, so that they do what you want 駕馭, 控制〔人或動物的行為〕: *Audrey has the knack for managing difficult children.* 奧德麗有本事管住調皮的孩子。

10 ▶BE STRONG ENOUGH 足夠強壯◀ [T] to be able to do something because you are strong enough or healthy enough 強壯[健康]得能做〔某事〕: *Grandad can't manage the stairs any more.* 爺爺再也爬不動樓梯了。| *I can only manage three sit-ups.* 我只能做三個仰臥起坐。

11 ▶EAT/DRINK 吃/喝◀ [T] to be able to eat or drink something 能吃[喝]〔某物〕: *I think I could manage another glass of wine.* 我想我能再喝一杯酒。

12 manage a smile/a few words etc to make yourself say or do something when you do not really want to 勉強笑一笑/説幾句等: *Tina managed a reluctant smile for the camera.* 蒂娜對着鏡頭勉強笑了笑。

13 ▶HAVE TIME FOR 有時間做◀ **manage Wednesday/7:30/lunch etc** to agree to meet someone or do something with them, even though you are busy 安排星期三/7點30分等〔見某人或做某事〕; 安排〔與某人〕吃午飯: *We should meet soon, can you manage Wednesday evening?* 我們應該早點會面, 你星期三晚上行嗎?

man·age·a·ble /ˈmænɪdʒəbl̩; ˈmænɪdʒəbəl/ *adj* easy to control or deal with 易控制的; 易管理的; 易處理的: *My hair's more manageable since I had it cut.* 我的頭髮剪短後變得好梳理多了。—opposite 反義詞 UNMANAGEABLE —**manageability** /ˌmænɪdʒəˈbɪləti; ˌmænɪdʒəˈbɪlə̩ti/ *n* [U]

man·age·ment /ˈmænɪdʒmənt; ˈmænɪdʒmənt/ *n* **1** [U] the act or skill of directing and organizing the work of a company or organization 經營; 管理: *He left the management of the firm to his son.* 他把公司的經營事宜交給了他的兒子。| *They sent me on one of those management training courses.* 他們派我去學那些管理培訓課程中的一門。| **good/bad management** *The company's failure was mainly due to bad management.* 這家公司破產主要是由於經營不善。**2** [singular, U] the people who are in charge of a company or organization 〔公司或組織的〕管理層: *Targets were agreed in consultation between management and staff.* 指標是由管理層和員工協商達成的。| [also+plural verb *BrE* 英] *The management are blaming the workers for the dispute.* 管理層將糾紛歸咎於工人。| *a management decision* 管理層的決定 | **senior/junior management** *talks with senior management* 與高層管理人員的談判 | **middle management** (=in charge of small groups within an organization) 中層管理人員 **3** [U] the act or skill of dealing with a situation that needs to be controlled in some way 管理; 管理技巧: *traffic management* 交通管理 | *better management of the Earth's natural resources* 對地球自然資源更有效的管理

management buy·out /ˌ··· ˈ··/ *n* [C] the buying of shares (SHARE² (5)) of a company by the management so that they control the company 管理層收購

management con·sult·ant /ˈ···ˌ··/ *n* [C] someone who is paid to advise the management of a company how to improve their organization and working methods 管理顧問, 業務顧問

man·ag·er /ˈmænɪdʒə; ˈmænɪdʒə/ *n* [C] **1** someone whose job is to manage part or all of a company or other organization 〔公司或其他機構的〕經理: *a bank manager* 銀行經理 | *the General Manager of Chevrolet* 雪佛萊公司總經理 | *one of our regional managers* 我們的一位地區經理 | *Can I speak to the manager?* 我能跟經理談談嗎? **2** someone who is in charge of the business affairs of a singer, an actor etc 〔歌手、演員等的〕經紀人 **3** someone who is in charge of training and organizing a sports team 〔運動隊的〕管理人, 經理: *Jack Charlton, the Ireland manager* 愛爾蘭隊的領隊傑克·查爾頓 —see also 另見 LINE MANAGER

man·ag·er·ess /ˈmænɪdʒərɪs; ˌmænɪdʒəˈres/ *n* [C] *old-fashioned* a woman who is in charge of a business, especially a shop or restaurant【過時】〔尤指商店或飯店的〕女經理, 女管理人

man·a·ge·ri·al /ˌmænəˈdʒɪrɪəl; ˌmænə̩ˈdʒɪəriəl/ *adj* connected with the job of a manager 經理的; 管理的; 經營的: *a managerial post* 經理職位

managing di·rec·tor /ˌ··· ·ˈ··/ *n* [C] *BrE* someone who is in charge of a large company or organization【英】〔大公司或機構的〕總經理, 總裁

ma·ña·na /mənˈjɑnə; mænˈjɑːnə/ *adv, adj, n Spanish* a

word meaning tomorrow, used when talking about someone who seems too relaxed and always delays doing things【西】明天〔用於談論某個過於散漫、做事拖拉的人〕: *a mañana attitude* 一種明日復明日的態度

man-at-arms /ˌ· · ˈ·/ *n* [C] *old use* a soldier【舊】士兵

Man·cu·ni·an /mænˋkjunɪən; mænˈkjuːniən/ *n* [C] someone who lives in or comes from Manchester 曼徹斯特人 —**Mancunian** *adj*

man·da·la /ˋmændələ; ˈmændələ/ *n* [C] a picture of a circle around a square, that represents the universe in Hindu and Buddhist religions 曼荼羅〔印度教和佛教中象徵宇宙的內方外圓圖案〕

Man·da·rin /ˋmændərɪn; ˈmændərɪn/ *n* [U] the official language of China, spoken by most educated Chinese people〔中國〕官話, 國語, 普通話

mandarin *n* [C] **1** a kind of small orange with skin that is easy to remove 橘子, 柑橘 **2** *BrE* an important official in the Civil Service, especially one who is regarded as having too much influence【英】內務要員, 達官貴人: *the mandarins of Whitehall* 白廳的高官們 **3** an important government official in the former Chinese EMPIRE (1)〔舊時中國帝制時代的〕高級官吏

mandarin or·ange /ˌ··· ˈ··/ *n* [C] a MANDARIN (1) 橘子, 柑橘

man·date¹ /ˋmændet; ˈmændeɪt/ *n* **1** [C] the right and power to carry out certain policies, which is given to a government or elected official by the people who voted for them〔選民對政府或選出的官員執行某些政策的〕授權: **mandate to do sth** *The President was elected with a clear mandate to tackle violent crime.* 總統當選時獲得了解決暴力犯罪問題的明確授權。| **seek a mandate** *They are seeking a mandate for tax reforms.* 他們正在尋求授權以進行稅制改革。**2** [C] an official command given to a person or organization to do something〔對某人或某機構的〕命令; 訓令: *an envoy carrying out the Archbishop's mandate* 執行大主教命令的使節 **3** [C,U] the power given to one country to govern another country 委任統治權, 託管權

man·date² /ˋmændet; mænˈdeɪt/ *v* [T] **1** *especially AmE* to give an official command that something must be done【尤美】命令, 指示: *Austerity measures were mandated by the International Monetary Fund.* 國際貨幣基金組織指示採取緊縮措施。**2** [often passive 常用被動態] to give someone the right or power to do something 授權於〔某人〕, 委任

man·dat·ed /ˋmændetɪd; mænˈdeɪtɨd/ *adj* a mandated country has been placed under the control of another country〔國家〕被託管的: *mandated territories* 託管地

man·da·to·ry /ˋmændəˌtorɪ; ˈmændətəri/ *adj* something that is mandatory must be done because the law says it must be done; COMPULSORY, OBLIGATORY 依法必須做的; 強制性的; 義務的: *Inspection of imported meat is mandatory.* 對進口肉類的檢查是強制性的。| *Drug smuggling carried a mandatory death penalty.* 毒品走私必然會被判死刑。

man·di·ble /ˋmændəbl̩; ˈmændɨbəl/ *n* [C] *technical*【術語】**1** the jaw of an animal or fish, especially the lower jaw〔動物或魚的〕頜〔尤指下頜〕**2** the upper or lower part of a bird's beak 鳥喙的上[下]部 **3** a part like a jaw at the front of an insect's mouth 昆蟲的大顎, 上顎

man·do·lin /ˋmændl̩ɪn; ˌmændəˈlɪn/ *n* [C] a musical instrument with eight metal strings and a round back 曼陀林〔一種八根金屬弦、圓形琴身的樂器〕

man·drake /ˋmændrek; ˈmændreɪk/ *n* [C] a plant from which drugs can be made which help people to sleep, and which was once thought to have magic powers 曼德拉草, 曼陀羅草〔一種可製安眠藥的植物, 舊時被認為有魔力〕

man·drill /ˋmændrɪl; ˈmændrɪl/ *n* [C] a large monkey like a BABOON with a brightly coloured face 山魈〔與狒狒相似, 臉上有鮮明色彩〕

mane /men; meɪn/ *n* [C] **1** the long hair on the back of a horse's neck, or around the face and neck of a lion〔馬、獅頸上的〕鬃毛 —see picture at 參見 HORSE¹ 圖 **2** *informal* a person's long thick hair【非正式】又長又密的頭髮

man-eat·er /ˋ· ˌ··/ *n* [C] **1** an animal that eats human flesh 食人獸 **2** *humorous* a woman who has many sexual partners【幽默】放蕩的女人 —**man-eating** *adj*: *a man-eating tiger* 食人虎

ma·neu·ver /məˋnuvɚ; məˈnuːvə/ *n, v* the American spelling of MANOEUVRE manoeuvre 的美式拼法

ma·neu·ve·ra·ble /məˋnuvərəbl̩; məˈnuːvərəbəl/ *adj* the American spelling of MANOEUVRABLE manoeuvrable 的美式拼法

ma·neu·ve·ring /məˋnuvərɪŋ; məˈnuːvərɪŋ/ *n* [C,U] the American spelling of MANOEUVRING manoeuvring 的美式拼法

man·ful·ly /ˋmænfəlɪ; ˈmænfəli/ *adv* in a brave, determined way 勇敢地; 果斷地: *They struggled manfully on through the wind and rain.* 他們冒着風雨勇敢而艱難地前進。—**manful** *adj*

man·ga·nese /ˋmæŋgəˌniz; ˈmæŋgəniːz/ *n* [U] a greyish-white metal used for making glass, steel etc 錳

mange /mendʒ; meɪndʒ/ *n* [U] a skin disease of animals that makes them lose small areas of fur 獸疥癬, 家畜疥

man·ger /ˋmendʒɚ; ˈmeɪndʒə/ *n* [C] a long open container that horses, cattle etc eat from〔馬、牛等的〕食槽 —see also 另見 **dog in the manger** (DOG¹ (10))

mange·tout /ˌmɑnʒˋtu; ˌmɒnʒˈtuː/ *n* [C] *BrE* a kind of flat PEA whose outer part is eaten as well as the seeds【英】糖莢豌豆〔一種莢和豆均可吃的豌豆〕; SNOW PEA *AmE*【美】

man·gle¹ /ˋmæŋgl̩; ˈmæŋgəl/ *v* [T] **1** [often passive 常用被動態] to damage or injure something badly by crushing or twisting it 壓壞; 扭傷: *The trap closed round her leg, badly mangling her ankle.* 夾子夾住了她的腿, 重傷了她的腳踝。**2** to put clothes through a mangle 用軋液機軋壓〔衣服〕

mangle² *n* [C] a machine with two rollers (ROLLER (1)), used to remove water from washed clothes 軋液機〔用於壓去已洗淨衣服的水分〕

man·go /ˋmæŋgo; ˈmæŋgəʊ/ *n* [C] a tropical fruit with a thin skin and sweet yellow flesh 芒果 —see picture on page A8 參見 A8 頁圖

man·grove /ˋmæŋgrov; ˈmæŋgrəʊv/ *n* [C] a tropical tree that grows in or near water and grows new roots from its branches 紅樹〔一種熱帶樹木, 生於水中或水邊, 並從樹枝上長出新根〕: *a mangrove swamp* 生長紅樹的沼澤地

mang·y /ˋmendʒɪ; ˈmeɪndʒi/ *adj* **1** suffering from MANGE〔獸、畜〕患疥癬的: *emaciated mangy dogs* 瘦骨嶙峋的癩皮狗 **2** *informal* dirty and in bad condition【非正式】髒而破的, 破舊的: *a mangy-looking rug* 看起來又髒又破的舊地毯

man·han·dle /ˋmænˌhændl̩; ˈmænhændl/ *v* [T] **1** to push or handle someone roughly 粗暴地推搡: **manhandle sb into/through etc** *The police manhandled him into the car.* 警察粗暴地把他推進汽車。**2** to move a heavy object using force 用力搬動〔重物〕: **manhandle sth up/into etc** *We managed to manhandle the piano up the stairs.* 我們費力地將鋼琴搬上樓梯。

man·hole /ˋmænˌhol; ˈmænhəʊl/ *n* [C] a hole on the surface of a road covered by a lid, used to examine pipes, wires etc 人孔, 檢修孔〔路面上的有蓋洞口, 用於檢修管道、電線等〕

man·hood /ˋmænhud; ˈmænhʊd/ *n* **1** [U] qualities such as strength, courage, and especially sexual power, that people think a man should have; VIRILITY 男子氣概[氣質]〈如力量、勇氣, 尤指性能力〉: *He took this remark as an insult to his manhood.* 他把這句話看成是對他的男子氣概的污辱。**2** [U] the state of being a man and no longer a boy〔男子的〕成年, 成人: *He had barely reached manhood when he married.* 他剛剛成年便結了婚。**3** [singular]

M

especially literary a word meaning PENIS, used in order to avoid saying this directly【尤文】陽物, 陰莖〔委婉語〕 **4** [U] *literary* all the men of a particular nation【文】〔一個國家的〕全體男子: *America's manhood* 美國全國的男子 —compare 比較 WOMANHOOD

man-hour /ˈ· ˌ·/ *n* [C] the amount of work done by one person in one hour 人時, 工時〔一人一小時完成的工作量〕

man·hunt /ˈmænˌhʌnt; ˈmænhʌnt/ *n* [C] an organized search, especially for a criminal or a prisoner who has escaped〔尤指對罪犯或逃犯的〕搜捕, 追捕

ma·ni·a /ˈmenɪə; ˈmeɪniə/ *n* [C,U] **1** a very strong desire for something or interest in something, especially one that affects a lot of people at the same time 狂熱, 熱衷; 癖好: **[+for]** *A mania for a game called Nibs ran through the school.* 一種名叫尼布斯的遊戲所掀起的狂熱風潮席捲了全校。| **religious/football/disco etc mania** *The whole country is in the grip of football mania.* 整個國家都沉浸在對足球的狂熱中。**2** *technical* a serious mental illness【術語】躁狂症

ma·ni·ac /ˈmenɪˌæk; ˈmeɪniæk/ *n* [C] **1** *informal* someone who behaves in a stupid or dangerous way【非正式】舉止愚蠢[危險]的人, 瘋子: *Some maniac overtook us on a bend.* 一個瘋子在拐彎處超過了我們。**2 a religious maniac/sex maniac etc** *informal* someone who thinks about religion, sex etc all the time【非正式】宗教迷/性慾狂等: *The woman's a sex maniac if you ask me.* 在我看來, 那個女人是個性慾狂。**3** *old-fashioned* someone who is mentally ill【過時】躁狂者; 瘋子, 精神病患者

ma·ni·a·cal /məˈnaɪəkḷ; məˈnaɪəkəl/ *adj* behaving as if you are crazy 瘋狂的; 狂躁的: *maniacal laughter* 瘋狂的笑聲 —**maniacally** /-kḷɪ; -kli/ *adv*

man·ic /ˈmænɪk; ˈmænɪk/ *adj* **1** *informal* behaving in a very anxious or excited way【非正式】急切的, 激動的: *She seemed slightly manic.* 她好像有點激動。**2** *technical* connected with a feeling of great happiness and excitement that is part of a mental illness【術語】躁狂的

manic de·pres·sion /ˌ·· ·ˈ··/ *n* [U] a mental illness that makes people sometimes feel extremely happy and excited and sometimes extremely sad and hopeless 躁狂抑鬱症

manic de·pres·sive /ˌ·· ·ˈ··/ *n* [C] someone who suffers from manic depression 躁狂抑鬱症患者 —**manic-depressive** *adj*

man·i·cure /ˈmænɪˌkjur; ˈmænɨkjʊə/ *n* [C,U] a treatment for the hands and nails that includes cutting and polishing the nails 修指甲 —**manicure** *v* [T]

man·i·cured /ˈmænɪˌkjurd; ˈmænɨkjʊəd/ *adj* **1** manicured hands have nails that are neatly cut and polished〔指甲〕修剪整潔的 **2** manicured gardens or LAWN*s* are very neat and tidy〔花園或草坪〕修剪整齊的 —**manicurist** *n*

man·i·fest¹ /ˈmænəˌfɛst; ˈmænɨfest/ *v* [T] *formal*【正式】**1** to show a feeling, attitude etc 顯示, 表明, 表露〔感情、態度等〕: *They have so far manifested a total indifference to our concerns.* 到目前為止, 他們對我們所關注的事情一直擺出一副漠不關心的態度。**2 manifest itself** to appear or to become easy to see 顯現, 顯露: *Food allergies manifest themselves in a variety of ways.* 食物過敏症狀會以多種方式表現出來。

manifest² *adj formal* plain and easy to see; OBVIOUS【正式】顯而易見的, 明顯的: *a manifest error of judgment* 明顯的判斷錯誤 | **be made manifest** (=be clearly shown) 顯示, 顯露 *Their devotion to God is made manifest in ritual prayer.* 他們對上帝的虔誠在宗教儀式的禱告中明白地顯示出來。—**manifestly** *adv*: *manifestly untrue* 顯然不真實

man·i·fes·ta·tion /ˌmænəfɛsˈteʃən; ˌmænɨfeˈsteɪʃən/ *n formal*【正式】**1** [C] a very clear sign that a particular situation or feeling exists 明顯跡象; 表現: **[+of]** *These latest riots are a clear manifestation of growing discontent.* 這些最近發生的騷亂是不滿情緒日益增長的明顯跡象。**2** [U] the act of appearing or becoming clear 顯現; 顯示, 表明: *Manifestation of the disease often doesn't occur until middleage.* 這種疾病的症狀通常到中年才表現出來。**3** [C] the appearance of a GHOST or a sign of its presence〔鬼魂的〕顯靈

man·i·fes·to /ˌmænəˈfɛsto; ˌmænɨˈfestəʊ/ *n* [C] a written statement by an organized group, especially a political party, saying what they believe in and what they intend to do 宣言

man·i·fold¹ /ˈmænəˌfold; ˈmænɨfəʊld/ *adj formal* many and of different kinds【正式】繁多的, 多種多樣的; 多方面的: *manifold cultural differences* 多方面的文化差異

manifold² *n* [C] *technical* an arrangement of pipes through which gases enter or leave a car engine【術語】〔汽車發動機的〕歧管: *an exhaust manifold* 排氣歧管 —see picture at 參見 ENGINE 圖

man·i·kin, mannikin /ˈmænəkɪn; ˈmænɪkɨn/ *n* [C] **1** a model of the human body, used in art classes or for teaching medical students〔藝術或醫學課用的〕人體模型 **2** *old use* a little man; DWARF¹【舊】矮子, 侏儒

ma·nil·a, manilla /məˈnɪlə; məˈnɪlə/ *n* [U] *old use* strong brown paper used for making envelopes【舊】〔做信封用的〕馬尼拉紙

ma·nip·u·late /məˈnɪpjəˌlet; məˈnɪpjɨleɪt/ *v* [T] **1** to make someone think and behave exactly as you want them to, by skilfully deceiving them or influencing them〔通過巧妙地欺騙或影響而〕操縱, 控制: *I don't like the way she manipulates people.* 我不喜歡她擺佈別人的做法。| *It was a shameless attempt to manipulate public opinion.* 那是一種無恥的圖謀, 企圖操縱輿論。**2** to work skilfully with information, systems etc to achieve the result that you want〔熟練地〕操作, 使用〔信息、系統等〕: *Researchers can manipulate the data in a variety of ways.* 研究員們能以多種方式使用這些數據。**3** *technical* to skilfully move and press a joint or bone into the correct position【術語】推拿正〔骨〕**4** to use skill in moving or handling something 巧妙地移動〔某物〕; 巧妙地處理〔某事〕—**manipulation** /məˌnɪpjuˈleʃən; məˌnɪpjɨˈleɪʃən/ *n* [U]

ma·nip·u·la·tive /məˈnɪpjəˌletɪv; məˈnɪpjɨlətɪv/ *adj* **1** clever at controlling or deceiving people to get what you want 善於控制[欺騙]他人的: *She has a very manipulative side to her character.* 她性格中有愛擺佈人的一面。**2** *technical* connected with the skill of moving bones and joints into the correct position【術語】推拿正骨法的: *manipulative treatment* 推拿法治療 **3** *technical* connected with the ability to handle objects in a skilful way【術語】操作的: *manipulative techniques* 操作技術

ma·nip·u·la·tor /məˈnɪpjuˌletɚ; məˈnɪpjɨleɪtə/ *n* [C] someone who is good at getting what they want by cleverly controlling or deceiving other people 善於擺佈[欺騙]他人者, 操控者

man·kind /mænˈkaɪnd; ˌmænˈkaɪnd/ *n* [U] all humans considered as a group 人類: *a great step forward for mankind* 人類邁進的一大步 —compare 比較 WOMANKIND —see 見 MAN¹ (USAGE)

man·ky /ˈmæŋkɪ; ˈmæŋki/ *adj BrE informal* looking dirty and unattractive【英, 非正式】骯髒難看的: *a manky old sweater* 又髒又舊的毛衣

man·ly /ˈmænlɪ; ˈmænli/ *adj* having qualities that people expect and admire in a man, such as being brave and strong 有男子氣概的; 勇敢而強壯的: *a deep manly voice* 低沉雄渾的嗓音 —**manliness** *n* [U]

man-made /ˌ· ˈ·◂/ *adj* produced by people; not natural 人造的, 人工的: *a man-made lake* 人工湖 | *man-made fibres* 人造纖維 —compare 比較 ARTIFICIAL, NATURAL¹

man·na /ˈmænə; ˈmænə/ *n* **1 manna from heaven** something that you need, which you suddenly or unexpectedly get or are given 天賜之物; 意外收穫 **2** [U] the food which, according to the Bible, was provided by God for the Israelites in the desert after their escape from

Egypt 嗎哪〔《聖經》中以色列人逃離埃及後在荒漠中獲得的神賜食物〕

man·ne·quin /ˈmænəkɪn; ˈmænɪkʒn/ *n* [C] **1** a model of the human body used for showing clothes in shop windows〔商店櫥窗中用以展示服裝的〕人體模型 **2** *old-fashioned* a woman whose job is to wear fashionable clothes and show them to people; MODEL[1] (2)【過時】女時裝模特

S3 W2 **man·ner** /ˈmænə; ˈmænə/ *n*

1 ▶WAY 方式◀ [singular] *formal* the way in which something is done or happens【正式】方式, 方法: **manner of doing sth** *This seems rather an odd manner of deciding things.* 這似乎是一種十分古怪的決定事情的方法。| **in a ... manner** *I felt stupid for reacting in such an impulsive manner.* 我以那樣一種衝動的方式作出反應我自己都感到愚蠢。| *The matter should be submitted to the accounts committee in the usual manner.* 此事應按通常的方式提交財務委員會解決。

2 ▶WAY OF SPEAKING/BEHAVING 説話/行事的方式◀ [singular] the way in which someone behaves towards or talks to other people 態度; 舉止: *She has a calm relaxed manner.* 她舉止鎮定而從容。| *I thought I noticed a certain coldness in his manner.* 我想我注意到他的態度有些冷淡。

3 manners [plural] **a)** polite ways of behaving in social situations 禮貌, 禮儀: **good/bad manners** *She has such good manners.* 她是那樣彬彬有禮。| **it's good/bad manners (to do sth)** *spoken* (=used to tell a child how to behave)【口】(做某事) 是有/沒有禮貌的 *It's bad manners to point at people.* 對人指指點點是不禮貌的。| **she/he has no manners** *spoken*【口】*"Vic and Lesley just got up and left." "Some people have no manners."* "維克和萊斯利站起來就走了。""有些人就是沒禮貌。" | **where are your manners?** *spoken* (=used to tell someone, especially a child, that they are behaving impolitely)【口】你的禮貌哪兒去了? | **table manners** (=the way that you behave at meals) 餐桌禮儀 **b)** *formal* the customs of a particular group of people【正式】習俗, 風俗: *a book on the life and manners of Victorian London* 一本關於維多利亞時期倫敦的生活和風俗的書

4 in a manner of speaking in some ways though not exactly 在某種意義上: *I suppose you could call us refugees in a manner of speaking.* 我想在某種意義上你可以稱我們為難民。

5 in the manner of in the style that is typical of a particular person or thing 體現…所特有的風格: *a painting in the manner of the early Impressionists* 一幅體現早期印象派風格的繪畫

6 all manner of *formal* many different kinds of things or people【正式】各種各樣的, 形形色色的: *We would discuss all manner of subjects.* 我們常常討論各種各樣的話題。

7 not by any manner of means *BrE spoken* not at all【英口】一點也不, 決不: *It's not over yet, by any manner of means.* 事情還沒有結束, 遠遠沒結束。

8 what manner of...? *literary* what kind of【文】甚麼樣的…?: *What manner of son would treat his mother in such a way?* 甚麼樣的兒子會這樣對待自己的母親?

9 (as) to the manner born in a natural confident way doing something, as if you have done it many times before 熟練得彷彿是與生俱來的 —see also 另見 COMEDY OF MANNERS

man·nered /ˈmænəd; ˈmænəd/ *adj* **1 well-mannered/bad-mannered/mild-mannered etc** polite, impolite etc in the way you behave in social situations 有禮貌的/沒禮貌的/態度謙和的等 **2** behaving or speaking in an unnatural way, because you want to impress people 做作的, 不自然的: *He gave a very mannered performance in the lead role.* 他演那個主角演得太矯揉造作。

man·ner·is·m /ˈmænəˌrɪzəm; ˈmænərɪzəm/ *n* **1** [C,U] a way of speaking or moving that is typical of a particular person〔某人所特有的説話或動作的〕習性, 習氣: *He has the same mannerisms as his father.* 他的小動作跟他父親的一樣。**2** [U] the use of a style in art that does not look natural〔藝術的〕矯飾風格

man·ni·kin /ˈmænɪkɪn; ˈmænɪkʒn/ *n* [C] a MANIKIN 人體模型; 侏儒

man·nish /ˈmænɪʃ; ˈmænɪʃ/ *adj* a woman who is mannish looks or behaves like a man, especially in a way that is considered unattractive〔女人長相或舉止〕像男人的, 男人氣的, 男子般的〔尤指被視為不美的〕: *She had strong, almost mannish features.* 她相貌粗獷, 幾乎像男人。—**mannishly** *adv*

ma·noeu·vra·ble *BrE*【英】, **maneuverable** *AmE*【美】/məˈnuvərəbl; məˈnuːvərəbəl/ *adj* easy to move or turn within small spaces 容易移動的, 轉動靈活的: *an easily manoeuvrable car* 容易操縱的汽車 —**manoeuvrability** /məˌnuvərəˈbɪlətɪ; məˌnuːvərəˈbɪlʒti/ *n* [U]

ma·noeu·vre[1] *BrE*【英】, **maneuver** *AmE*【美】/məˈnuvə; məˈnuːvə/ *n* **1** [C] a skilful or careful movement that you make, for example in order to avoid something or go through a narrow space 熟練[謹慎]的動作: *basic skiing manoeuvres* 滑雪的基本動作 **2** [C,U] a skilful or carefully planned action intended to deceive someone or achieve something 策略, 巧計, 花招: *They tried by diplomatic maneuvers to obtain an agreement.* 他們試圖利用外交策略達成協議。**3 manoeuvres** [singular] a military exercise like a battle done to train soldiers 軍事演習: **on manoeuvres** (=practising military exercises) 在演習中 *The regiment is abroad on manoeuvres.* 該團正在國外進行演習。**4 room for manoeuvre/freedom of manoeuvre** the possibility of changing your plans or decisions 迴旋的餘地: *They haven't left us much freedom of manoeuvre.* 他們沒有給我們留下多少迴旋的餘地。

manoeuvre[2] *BrE*【英】, **maneuver** *AmE*【美】*v* **1** [I always+adv/prep,T always+adv/prep] to move or turn skilfully or to move or turn something skilfully, especially something large and heavy 巧妙地移動[轉動]〔大而沉重的物件〕: *She managed to manoeuvre expertly into the parking space.* 她熟練地將車子駛進了停車位置。| **manoeuvre sth along/into/out etc** *Josh manoeuvred himself out of bed and hobbled to the door.* 喬希從牀上爬起來, 一瘸一拐地朝門口走去。**2** [I,T] to use cleverly planned and often dishonest methods to get the result that you want 策劃; 誘使: **manoeuvre sb into/out of sth** *It was a well-organized plan to maneuvre the President out of office.* 那是一個精心安排的計劃, 旨在使總統倒台。

ma·noeu·vring *BrE*【英】, **maneuvering** *AmE*【美】/məˈnuvərɪŋ; məˈnuːvərɪŋ/ *n* [C,U] the use of clever and sometimes dishonest methods to get what you want 策略, 花招: *diplomatic manoeuvrings* 外交手段

man of let·ters /ˌ· · ˈ··/ *n* [C] a male writer, especially one who writes NOVELs or writes about literature 男作家〔尤指小説家或文學評論家〕

man-of-war /ˌ· · ˈ·/ also 又作 **man-o'-war** *n* [C] *old use* a fighting ship in the navy【舊】戰艦

man·or /ˈmænə; ˈmænə/ *n* [C] **1** a big old house with a large area of land around it 莊園大宅 **2** the land that belonged to an important man, under the FEUDAL system〔封建領主的〕采邑, 領地; 莊園 **3** *BrE slang* an area that a particular POLICE STATION is responsible for【英俚】警察局的管轄區 —**manorial** /məˈnɔrɪəl; məˈnɔːriəl/ *adj*

manor house /ˈ· · / *n* [C] a big old house in the countryside with a large area of land around it 莊園大宅

man·pow·er /ˈmænˌpauə; ˈmænˌpauə/ *n* [U] all the workers available for a particular kind of work 勞動力; 人力: *a lack of trained manpower* 缺乏訓練有素的勞動力

man·qué /mɑnˈke; ˈmɒŋkeɪ/ *adj French*【法】**artist/actor/teacher manqué** someone who could have been successful as an artist etc, but never became one 本來可以成為藝術家/演員/教師卻並未如願以償

man·sard /ˈmænsɑrd; ˈmænsɑːd/ also 又作 **mansard roof** /ˈ·· ·/ *n* [C] a roof whose lower part slopes more steeply than its upper part 複斜屋頂〔下半部比上半部陡〕

manse /mæns; mæns/ *n* [C] a house that is lived in by a priest, in certain Christian churches〔某些基督教會中的〕牧師住宅

man·ser·vant /ˈmænˌsɝvənt; ˈmænˌsɜːvənt/ *n* [C] *old-fashioned* a male servant, especially a man's personal servant【過時】男僕〔尤指某男子的貼身僕人〕

-manship /mənʃɪp; mənʃɪp/ *suffix* [in U nouns 構成不可數名詞] the art or skill of a particular type of person〔某類人的〕技藝, 技能, 技術: *seamanship* (=sailing skill) 航海技術 | *statesmanship* 政治家才能 | *horsemanship* (=skill at horse-riding) 騎術, 馬術

man·sion /ˈmænʃən; ˈmænʃən/ *n* [C] a large impressive-looking house 富麗堂皇的房子; 大廈; 宅第; 公館

man-sized /ˈ· ·/ also 又作 **man-size** *adj* [only before noun 僅用於名詞前] large and considered suitable for a man 適於成年男子使用的, 成年男人尺寸的: *That's a man-sized breakfast!* 那一頓早餐足夠一個成年男人食用! | *man-sized paper handkerchiefs* 男用紙手巾

man·slaugh·ter /ˈmænˌslɔtɚ; ˈmænˌslɔːtə/ *n* [U] *law* the crime of killing someone illegally but not deliberately【法律】過失殺人; 誤殺 —compare 比較 MURDER[1] (1)

man·tel /ˈmæntl; ˈmæntl/ *n* [C] *especially AmE* a mantelpiece【尤美】壁爐架; 壁爐台; 壁爐面飾

man·tel·piece /ˈmæntlˌpis; ˈmæntlpiːs/ *n* [C] a frame surrounding a FIREPLACE, especially the top part that can be used as a shelf 壁爐架; 壁爐台; 壁爐面飾

man·tel·shelf /ˈmæntlˌʃɛlf; ˈmæntlʃelf/ *n* [C] *BrE* the top part of a mantelpiece that can be used as a shelf【英】壁爐台; 壁爐架

man·til·la /mænˋtɪlə; mænˈtɪlə/ *n* [C] a decorative piece of thin material that covers the head and shoulders, traditionally worn by Spanish women 連披肩的頭巾〔西班牙婦女的傳統服飾〕

man·tis /ˈmæntɪs; ˈmæntɪs/ *n* [C] a PRAYING MANTIS 螳螂

man·tle[1] /ˈmæntl; ˈmæntl/ *n* **1 take on/assume/wear the mantle of** *formal* to accept or have a particular duty or responsibility【正式】承擔/負有…的責任[義務]: *It is up to Europe to take on the mantle of leadership in environmental issues.* 在解決環境問題方面應由歐洲擔當起領導責任。**2 a mantle of snow/darkness etc** *literary* something such as snow or darkness that covers a surface or area【文】一層雪/一片黑暗等: *A mantle of snow lay on the trees.* 樹上覆蓋着一層雪。**3** [C] a loose piece of outer clothing without SLEEVES, worn in former times〔舊時穿的〕披風, 斗篷 **4** [C] a cover put over the flame of a gas or oil lamp to make it shine more brightly〔煤氣燈或油燈的〕白熾罩 **5** [C] *technical* the part of the Earth around the central CORE[1] (6)【術語】地幔

mantle[2] *v* [T] *literary* to cover the surface of something【文】覆蓋

man-to-man /ˌ· ·ˈ·◂/ *adv informal* if two men talk about something man-to-man, they discuss it in an honest, direct way【非正式】坦誠地, 開誠布公地: *You two need to discuss this man-to-man.* 你們兩個人需要坦率地討論一下這個問題。—**man-to-man** *adj*: *a man-to-man discussion* 坦誠的討論

man·tra /ˈmæntrə; ˈmæntrə/ *n* [C] **1** a piece of holy writing in the Hindu religion 曼特羅, 真言〔印度教中的一段經文〕 **2** a word or sound that is repeated as a prayer or to help people MEDITATE in the Hindu and Buddhist religions 曼特羅〔印度教和佛教中的禱文或咒語〕

man·u·al[1] /ˈmænjuəl; ˈmænjuəl/ *adj* **1** involving the use of the hands 手的; 手工的: *manual work* 手工[體力]活 | *manual skills* 手工技巧 **2** operated or done by hand or without the help of electricity, computers etc 用手操作的; 用手做的; 靠人工的: *a manual typewriter* 手動打字機 | *It would take too long to do a manual search of all the data.* 手工搜尋所有的資料將會花去太多的時間。—**manually** *adv*

manual[2] *n* [C] **1** a book that gives instructions about how to use a machine〔機器的〕說明書, 使用手冊: *an instruction manual* 說明手冊 **2 on manual** if a machine is on manual it can only be operated by using your hands and not by AUTOMATIC means〔機器〕手工操作的, 手動的

manual la·bour *BrE*【英】, **manual labor** *AmE*【美】/ˌ··· ˈ··/ *n* [U] work done with your hands that does not need much thought or skill 體力勞動 —**manual labourer** *n* [C]

manual work·er /ˈ··· ˌ··/ *n* [C] someone whose work involves using their hands rather than their mind 體力勞動者 —**manual work** *n* [U]

man·u·fac·ture[1] /ˌmænjəˋfæktʃɚ; ˌmænjʊˈfæktʃə/ *v* [T] **1** to make or produce large quantities of goods to be sold, using machinery〔用機器大量〕製造, 生產: *the company that manufactured the drug* 生產這種藥的公司 | *manufactured goods* 工業品, 製成品 **2** *technical* if your body manufactures a particular substance, it produces it【術語】〔人體〕生成: *Bile is manufactured by the liver.* 膽汁是由肝臟生成的。**3** to invent an untrue story, excuse etc 編造〔虛假情況、藉口等〕

manufacture[2] *n* **1** [U] *formal* the process of making or producing large quantities of goods to be sold【正式】〔大量的商品〕製造: *Cost will determine the methods of manufacture.* 成本將決定製造方法。**2 manufactures** [plural] *technical* goods that are produced in large quantities using machinery【術語】〔用機器大批量製造的〕商品

man·u·fac·tur·er /ˌmænjəˋfæktʃərɚ; ˌmænjʊˈfæktʃərə/ *n* [C] also 又作 **manufacturers** [plural] a company or industry that makes large quantities of goods 製造商; 製造公司, 製造廠: *Read the manufacturer's instructions before using your new dishwasher.* 使用新洗碗機之前請先閱讀廠家的說明書。| *The fridge was sent back to the manufacturers.* 那台冰箱被退給廠家了。

man·u·fac·tur·ing /ˌmænjəˋfæktʃərɪŋ; ˌmænjʊˈfæktʃərɪŋ/ *n* [U] the process or business of producing goods in factories 製造; 製造業: *Thousands of jobs had been lost in manufacturing.* 製造業中已失去了數千個工作崗位。

ma·nure /məˋnjur; məˈnjʊə/ *n* [U] waste matter from animals that is mixed with chemicals and put onto soil to produce better crops 糞肥 —**manure** *v* [T]

man·u·script /ˈmænjəˌskrɪpt; ˈmænjʊskrɪpt/ *n* [C] **1** a book or piece of writing before it is printed 手稿; 底稿: *I read his novel in manuscript.* 我讀過他小說的手稿。**2** a book or document written by hand before printing was invented 手抄本, 手寫本

Manx /mæŋks; mæŋks/ *adj* from or connected with the Isle of Man 馬恩島的

man·y /ˈmɛnɪ; ˈmeni/ *quantifier* **1** [used especially in formal English, or in ordinary written or spoken English when in questions and negative sentences 尤用於正式英語, 或在普通書面語或口語中用於疑問句和否定句] a large number of people or things 許多: **many people/things/places etc** *Many people find this kind of movie unpleasant.* 許多人覺得這類影片令人討厭。| *Rain has been forecast in many areas of the country.* 據預報那個國家許多地區有雨。| *Does she have many friends?* 她有許多朋友嗎? | **many of** *Many of our staff are actually part time workers.* 我們的許多職員實際上都是兼職人員。| *Thousands of soldiers were sent into battle, many of them killed outright.* 成千上萬的士兵被送上了戰場, 其中有許多當場戰死了。| **for many** *For many, the entrance exam proved too difficult.* 對許多人來說, 入學考試太難了。| **how many...?** *How many brothers and sisters do you have?* 你有幾個兄弟姐妹? | **not many** (=only a few) 不多 *There weren't many people at the party.* 那個聚會上人不多。| **the many people/things/places etc** *The committee would like to thank the many visitors who* *gave money so generously.* 委員會謹向慷慨解囊的眾多參觀者表示感謝。| **many a person/thing/place etc** *Through many a crisis it was his family that helped him survive.* 在很多危急關頭是他的家人幫他挺了過來。—compare 比較 LOT (1) **2 as many** the same number as another particular number 一樣多, 同樣數目: *Those cookies were great. I could eat as many again.* (=the same number again) 那些甜餅乾太好吃了, 我還能再吃那麼多。| **as many as** *Grandfather claimed to have as many medals as the general himself.* 祖父聲稱他擁有和將軍本人一樣多的勳章。| **in as many days/weeks etc** *A great trip! We visited five countries in as many days.* 一次多了不起的旅行啊! 我們五天裡參觀了五個國家。| **twice/three times etc as many** *The company now employs four times as many women as men.* 公司現在雇用的女工是男工的四倍。| **one/two etc too many** (=one more than necessary)〔比所需〕多出一個/兩個等 *You've bought one too many. There are only three of us who need tickets.* 你多買了一張。我們只有三個人需要票。**3 a) many a time** *old-fashioned* often【過時】時常, 常常: *I've sat here many a time and wondered what became of her.* 我時常坐在這兒, 想知道她後來怎麼樣了。**b) many's the time/day (that/when)** used to say that a particular thing happens often (有) 許多次/天〔用以表示某事經常發生〕: *Many's the time we've had to borrow money in order to get through the month.* 有許多次我們不得不借錢以撐到月底。**4 a good many** a fairly large number of people or things 相當多的: *Stop complaining! A good many people would be happy to have work.* 別發牢騷了! 很多人有工作做就感到滿足了。**5 a great many** a very large number of people or things 很多很多, 極多: *Most of the young men went off to the war, and a great many never came back.* 大多數年輕人走上了戰場, 好多人再也沒有回來。**6 have had one too many** *informal* to be drunk【非正式】喝醉了: *Don't pay any attention to him – he's had one too many.* 別理他 — 他喝醉了。**7 the many** *formal* a very large group of people, especially the public in general【正式】一大羣人〔尤指公眾〕: *This war is another example of the few sacrificing so much for the many.* 這場戰爭是少數人為多數人作出巨大犧牲的又一個例證。**8 be one too many for** *BrE old-fashioned* to be so clever that someone cannot gain advantage over you【英, 過時】勝過, 非某人能敵 —opposite 反義詞 FEW —compare 比較 MORE, MOST —see also 另見 MUCH, **in as many words** (WORD[1] (19))

many-sid·ed /ˌ‥ ˈ‥◂/ *adj* consisting of many different qualities or features〔性質或特徵等〕多方面的, 多樣的: *a complex many-sided personality* 複雜的多重性格

Mao·is·m /ˈmauˌɪzəm; ˈmaʊɪzəm/ *n* [U] the system of political thinking invented by Mao Zedong 毛澤東思想 —**Maoist** *n, adj*

Mao·ri /ˈmaurɪ; ˈmaʊri/ *n* **1** [C] someone who belongs to the race who first lived in New Zealand and who now form only a small part of the population 毛利人〔新西蘭土著〕**2** [U] the language of the Maori people 毛利語 —**Maori** *adj*: *a Maori tradition* 毛利人的傳統

2 2 **map[1]** /mæp; mæp/ *n* [C] **1** a drawing of an area of country showing rivers, roads, mountains, towns etc, or of a whole country or several countries 地圖: *According to the map we should turn left.* 根據地圖, 我們應該向左拐。| **[+of]** *a map of the world* 世界地圖 | **a street/road map** *a street map of Istanbul* 伊斯坦布爾市街道圖 | **read a map** (=understand the information it gives) 看地圖 **2 put sth on the map** to make a place famous, so that everyone knows it and talks about it 使〔某地〕出名: *It was the Olympic Games that really put Seoul on the map.* 真正使漢城出名的是那次奧運會。**3 off the map** *informal* a long way from towns or places where many people go【非正式】非常偏遠的 —see also 另見 **wipe sth off the map** (WIPE[1] (8))

map[2] *v* **mapped, mapping** [T] **1** to make a map of a particular area 繪製〔某地區〕的地圖: *Scientists have mapped the surface of the moon.* 科學家們已經繪製出了月球表面圖。**2** to discover or show the shape and arrangement of something 發現; 顯示〔某物的形狀和排列形式〕: *to map the part of the brain responsible for perception* 顯示大腦負責感知的部分

map sth ↔ **out** *phr v* [T] to plan something carefully 仔細計劃, 籌劃: *They had mapped out a demanding schedule for us.* 他們為我們精心制定了一個需費心費力才能完成的計劃。

ma·ple /ˈmepḷ; ˈmeɪpəl/ *n* **1** [C] a tree with pointed leaves that grows in northern countries such as Canada〔生長在加拿大等北方國家的〕槭樹, 楓樹 **2** [U] the wood from a maple 槭木, 楓木

maple syr·up /ˌ‥ ˈ‥/ *n* [U] a sweet sticky liquid, obtained from some kinds of maple tree 槭糖漿, 槭樹汁

map·ping /ˈmæpɪŋ; ˈmæpɪŋ/ *n* [C] *technical* a relationship between two mathematical sets in which a member of the first set is exactly matched by a member of the second【術語】〔數學中的〕函數, 映射

map-read·ing /ˈ· ˌ‥/ *n* [U] the practice of using a map to find which way you should go 地圖閱讀, 察看地圖 —**map-reader** *n* [C]

Mar the written abbreviation of 縮寫= MARCH

mar /mɑr; mɑː/ *v* **marred, marring** [T often passive 常用被動態] to make something less attractive or enjoyable; spoil 玷污; 損壞, 毀壞: *His appearance was marred by a scar on his left cheek.* 他的外貌因左頰上的一塊疤痕而受損。

mar·a·bou, marabout /ˈmærəˌbu; ˈmærəbuː/ *n* [C] a large African STORK (=a long-legged bird) 禿鸛〔非洲的一種大鸛〕

ma·ra·cas /məˈrɑkəz; məˈrækəz/ *n* [plural] a pair of hollow balls, filled with small objects such as stones, that are shaken and used as a musical instrument 沙球, 響葫蘆〔一種樂器〕

mar·a·schi·no /ˌmærəˈskino; ˌmærəˈskiːnəʊ/ *n* **1** [U] a sweet alcoholic drink made from a type of black CHERRY 黑櫻桃酒 **2** [C] a CHERRY that has been kept in maraschino and is used for decorating cakes, drinks etc〔浸泡於黑櫻桃酒中用以裝飾糕點、飲料等的〕酒浸櫻桃

mar·a·thon[1] /ˈmærəˌθɑn; ˈmærəθən/ *n* [C] **1** a long race of about 26 miles or 42 kilometres 馬拉松賽跑〔全程約 26 英里或 42 公里〕: *the Boston Marathon* 波士頓馬拉松賽跑 | **run a/the marathon** *Garcia ran the marathon in just under three hours.* 加西亞只用了不到三個小時就跑完了馬拉松。**2** an activity that lasts a long time and needs a lot of energy, patience, or determination〔需要很大精力、耐心或決心的〕持久活動, 馬拉松式的活動: *We finished the job but it was quite a marathon.* 我們完成了那項工作, 但它確實是一種費時耗力的活。

marathon[2] *adj* [only before noun 僅用於名詞前] a marathon event lasts a long time and needs a lot of energy, patience, or determination 馬拉松式的, 持久的, 需要很大精力[耐力, 決心]的: *After a marathon round of negotiations, the two leaders reached an agreement.* 在經過一輪馬拉松式的談判之後, 兩位領導人達成了一項協議。

ma·raud·ing /məˈrɔdɪŋ; məˈrɔːdɪŋ/ *adj* [only before noun 僅用於名詞前] a marauding person or animal moves around looking for something to destroy or kill〔人或動物〕四處破壞[殺戮]的: *Local residents live in fear of marauding street-gangs.* 當地居民生活在對街頭流氓四處搶劫的恐懼之中。—**marauder** *n* [C]

mar·ble /ˈmɑrbḷ; ˈmɑːbəl/ *n* **1** [U] a type of hard white rock that becomes smooth when polished, and is used for making buildings, STATUES etc 大理石: *The columns were of white marble.* 柱子是白色的大理石製成的。| *a marble statue* 大理石雕像 **2** [C] a very small, coloured glass ball that children roll along the ground as part of a game 玻璃彈子[彈珠] **3 marbles** [U] a children's game played with marbles〔兒童玩的〕彈子遊戲 **4 lose your**

M

marbles *informal* to start behaving in a crazy way【非正式】舉止開始失常 **5** [C] *technical* a STATUE or SCULPTURE made of marble【術語】大理石雕像; 大理石雕刻品

mar·bled /ˋmɑrbḷd; ˈmɑːbəld/ *adj* having an irregular pattern of lines and colours 有大理石花紋的: *a marbled book cover* 有大理石花紋的書皮

march¹ /mɑrtʃ; mɑːtʃ/ *v* **1** [I] to walk quickly and with firm, regular steps like a soldier 快速齊步行進: *Wellington's army marched until nightfall.* 威靈頓的部隊一直行軍到黃昏。| **[+across/along/through]** *They had to march across the desert.* 他們不得不行軍穿越沙漠。| **march 20km/40 miles etc** *We marched 50km across the foothills.* 我們行進50公里穿越了那片丘陵地帶。**2** [I always+adv/prep] to walk somewhere quickly and with determination, often because you are angry〔常指因生氣快速而毅然地〕走, 行走: **[+down/off etc]** *Brett marched out of the office, slamming the door behind him.* 布雷特快步走出辦公室, 砰的一聲摔上了門。**3** [I always+adv/prep] to walk somewhere slowly and in a large group to protest about something 遊行抗議, 遊行示威: *Hundreds of demonstrators are expected to march on the Council offices.* 預計數百名示威者將遊行到市政會辦公樓進行示威。**4** [T always+adv/prep] to force someone to walk somewhere with you, often pushing or pulling them roughly 迫使〔某人〕走〔常伴有推搡動作〕: **march sb to/along/into etc** *Mr Carter marched us to the principal's office.* 卡特先生將我們帶進校長辦公室。**5 be given/get your marching orders** *BrE informal* to be ordered to leave a particular place【英, 非正式】被命令離開某地 —**marcher** *n* [C]

march² *n* [C] **1** the act of walking with firm regular steps like a soldier 行進; 行軍: *The soldiers did a march around the parade ground.* 士兵們繞閱兵場齊步走了一圈。**2** an organized event in which many people walk together to protest about something 示威遊行, 抗議遊行: *a massive Civil Rights march in Washington* 在華盛頓舉行的一次大規模民權示威遊行 | **go on a march** *I went on a lot of peace marches when I was a student.* 學生時期我參加了好多次和平示威遊行。**3** a piece of music with a regular beat for soldiers to march to 進行曲 **4 a day's march/two weeks' march etc** the amount of time it takes to march somewhere 一天/兩週等的行軍路程: *Lake Van was still three days' march away.* 離〔土耳其的〕凡湖還有三天的路程。**5 marches** [plural] the area around the border of England and Wales or of England and Scotland 英格蘭與威爾斯[蘇格蘭]的交界地區 **6 on the march a)** an army that is on the march is marching somewhere〔軍隊〕在行軍中, 在行進中 **b)** a belief, idea etc that is on the march is becoming stronger and more popular〔信仰、觀念等〕越來越強烈, 越來越普遍: *Fascism is on the march again in some parts of Europe.* 在歐洲一些地區, 法西斯主義正在死灰復燃。**7 the march of time/history/events etc** *formal* the progress of time and of things happening that cannot be stopped【正式】時間的推移/歷史的發展/事件的進展等 —see also 另見 **steal a march on** (STEAL¹ (8))

March written abbreviation 縮寫為 **Mar** *n* [C,U] the third month of the year, between February and April 三月: **in March** *The theatre opened in March 1991.* 這家劇院1991年3月開業。| **last/next March** *She started work here last March.* 她去年3月開始在這兒工作。| **on March 6th/on 6th March** *The meeting will be on March 6th.* (spoken as 讀作: *on the sixth of March* or 或 *on March the sixth* (*BrE* 英) or 或 *on March sixth* (*AmE* 美)) 會議將於三月六日召開。

marching band /ˈ·· ˌ·/ *n* [C] a group of people who play musical instruments while they march 行進樂隊, 步操樂團

mar·chio·ness /ˋmɑrʃənɪs; ˌmɑːʃəˈnes/ *n* [C] **1** the wife of a MARQUIS 侯爵夫人 **2** a woman who has the rank of MARQUIS 女侯爵

march-past /ˈ· ·/ *n* [C] the march of soldiers past an important person during a ceremony〔受閱部隊從檢閱者前通過時的〕分列式

Mar·di Gras /ˋmɑrdɪ ˋgrɑ; ˌmɑːdi ˈgrɑː/ *n* [singular] the day before Lent, or the music, dancing etc that celebrate this day in some countries〔基督教〕大齋期的前一日; 懺悔節,〔慶祝大齋期前一日的〕狂歡活動

mare /mɛr; meə/ *n* [C] **1** a female horse or DONKEY 母馬; 母驢 —compare 比較 STALLION **2 mare's nest a)** a discovery that seems important but is actually of no value 似乎重要但實際上無價值的發現 **b)** a confused situation or a very untidy place 混亂的局勢; 亂糟糟的地方

mar·ga·rine /ˋmɑrdʒəˌrɪn; ˌmɑːdʒəˈriːn/ *n* [U] a yellow substance that is similar to butter but is not made from milk, which you eat with bread or use for cooking 麥淇淋, 人造黃油

mar·ga·ri·ta /ˌmɑrgəˋritə; ˌmɑːgəˈriːtə/ *n* [C] an alcoholic drink made with TEQUILA and LEMON or LIME juice 瑪格麗塔雞尾酒〔用龍舌蘭酒和檸檬汁或酸橙汁調成〕

marge /mɑrdʒ; mɑːdʒ/ *n* [U] *BrE spoken* margarine【英口】麥淇淋, 人造黃油

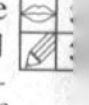

mar·gin /ˋmɑrdʒɪn; ˈmɑːdʒɨn/ *n* [C] **1** the empty space that goes down the side of a page 頁邊的空白, 頁邊, 白邊: **in the margin** *She scribbled some notes in the margin.* 她在頁邊上草草寫了一些評註。**2** the number of votes, or the amount of time or distance, by which an election or competition is won or lost〔選舉或競賽中勝方或負方在選票、時間或距離上的〕差數: **by a (wide/narrow) margin** *The election was won by a margin of only 200 votes.* 勝方僅以200票的優勢贏得選舉。**3** the difference between what a business pays for something and what they sell it for〔成本與售價間的〕差額, 利潤, 賺頭 —see also 另見 PROFIT MARGIN **4 on the margin(s)** not belonging to the main or central part of a society, group, or activity 處於〔社會、集團或活動〕的邊緣: *unemployed youths living on the margins of society* 生活在社會邊緣的失業青年 **5 margin of error** the degree to which a calculation can be wrong without affecting the final results 誤差幅度, 誤差值 **6** *literary* the edge of a forest, island, or other area【文】〔森林、島嶼或其他區域的〕邊緣

mar·gin·al /ˋmɑrdʒɪnḷ; ˈmɑːdʒɨnəl/ *adj* **1** too small to make a difference 微不足道的: *a marginal increase in the unemployment figures* 失業人數的略微增加 **2 marginal seat/constituency** *BrE* a SEAT¹ (5) in a parliament or similar institution, which can be won or lost by a small number of votes【英】〔議會或類似機構中〕以很小的票差就能贏得或失去的邊緣席位/選區 **3 marginal land** land that cannot produce good crops 貧瘠的土地 **4** written in a margin 寫在頁邊的: *marginal notes* 邊註, 旁註 —see also 另見 MARGINALLY

mar·gin·al·ize also 又作 **-ise** *BrE*【英】/ˋmɑrdʒɪnḷˌaɪz; ˈmɑːdʒɨnəlaɪz/ *v* [T] to make a group of people unimportant and powerless 使〔某羣體〕不重要並處於無權勢的地位; 使…邊緣化: *The decline of these industries marginalized the unions.* 這些行業的衰退把工會推向邊緣地位。

mar·gin·al·ly /ˋmɑrdʒɪnḷɪ; ˈmɑːdʒɨnəl-i/ *adv* not enough to make an important difference 稍微, 略微: *Gina's grades have improved marginally since last term.* 從上學期開始吉娜的成績略有提高。| **[+adj/adv]** *The new system is only marginally more efficient than the old one.* 新系統的效率比舊系統僅僅略高一點。

ma·ri·a·chi /ˌmɑrɪˋɑtʃɪ; ˌmæriˈɑːtʃi/ *n* [U] a kind of Mexican dance music 街頭音樂〔一種墨西哥舞曲〕

mar·i·gold /ˋmærəˌgold; ˈmærɨgəʊld/ *n* [C] a plant with golden-yellow flowers 萬壽菊 (花); 金盞花

mar·i·jua·na, marihuana /ˌmærəˋwɑnə; ˌmærɨˈwɑːnə/ *n* [U] an illegal drug smoked like a cigarette, made from the dried leaves of the HEMP plant 大麻煙; 大麻毒品

ma·rim·ba /məˋrɪmbə; məˈrɪmbə/ *n* [C] a musical instrument like a XYLOPHONE 馬林巴琴〔類似木琴的一種樂器〕

ma·ri·na /məˋrinə; məˈriːnə/ *n* [C] a small port or area of water where people keep boats that are used for pleasure〔供遊艇停泊的〕小港灣

mar·i·nade /ˌmærəˋned; ˌmærɪ̈ˈneɪd/ *n* [C,U] a mixture of oil, wine and SPICES in which meat or fish is put for a time before cooking 混合調味汁〔用油、酒和香料混合調製而成, 供肉或魚烹飪前浸泡調味用〕

mar·i·nate /ˋmærəˌnet; ˈmærɪ̈neɪt/ also 又作 **marinade** *v* [I,T] to put meat or fish in a marinade, or to be left in a marinade for some time 將〔肉或魚〕浸泡入調味汁中; 浸漬〔於調味汁中〕

Ma·rine /məˋrin; məˈriːn/ *n* [C] **1** a soldier who serves on a ship, especially a member of the Royal Marines or the Marine Corps 水兵; 英國皇家海軍陸戰隊士兵; 美國海軍陸戰隊士兵 —see also 另見 MERCHANT NAVY —see table on page C7 參見 C7 頁附錄 **2 the Marines a)** the Marine Corps 美國海軍陸戰隊 **b)** the Royal Marines 英國皇家海軍陸戰隊 **3 tell that to the Marines!** *spoken* used to say that you do not believe what someone has told you【口】鬼聽了才會相信!〔用以表示不相信某人對你講的話〕

marine *adj* [only before noun 僅用於名詞前] **1** connected with the sea and the creatures that live there 海洋的: *marine biology* 海洋生物學 **2** connected with ships or the navy 船舶的; 海軍的

Marine Corps /·ˈ· ·/ *n* [singular] one of the main parts of the US armed forces, consisting of soldiers who serve on ships 美國海軍陸戰隊

mar·i·ner /ˋmærənə; ˈmærɪ̈nə/ *n* [C] *literary* a SAILOR【文】水手, 海員

mar·i·o·nette /ˌmærɪəˋnɛt; ˌmæriəˈnet/ *n* [C] a PUPPET whose arms and legs are moved by pulling strings 牽線木偶

mar·i·tal /ˋmærətḷ; ˈmærɪ̈tl/ *adj* connected with marriage 婚姻的: *marital difficulties* 婚姻上的難題 | **marital bliss** *humorous* (=the state of being very happily married)【幽默】美滿婚姻 | **marital status** (=an expression used on official forms to ask if someone is married) 婚姻狀況〔正式表格中用語〕

mar·i·time /ˋmærəˌtaɪm; ˈmærɪ̈taɪm/ *adj* **1** connected with the sea or ships 海上的, 海事的; 與船舶有關的 **2** near the sea 近海的, 沿海的: *the Canadian maritime provinces* 加拿大各沿海省份

mar·jo·ram /ˋmɑrdʒərəm; ˈmɑːdʒərəm/ *n* [U] a HERB that smells sweet and is used in cooking 墨角蘭, 馬鬱蘭〔草本植物, 味香, 用於食品調味〕

3 2 **mark¹** /mɑrk; mɑːk/ *v*

1 ▶MAKE A MARK 留下痕跡◀ [I,T] to make a mark on something in a way that spoils its appearance, or to become spoiled in this way 留痕跡於, 弄污; 留下痕跡: *We were careful not to mark the paintwork.* 我們很小心, 避免在漆面上留下印跡。| *The disease had marked her face for life.* 這種病已在她臉上留下了一輩子去不掉的疤痕。| *It's a beautiful table, but it marks very easily.* 這是一張漂亮的桌子, 但桌面很容易留下印痕。

2 ▶SHOW POSITION 顯示位置◀ [T] to show where something is 標示〔某物的位置〕: *A simple wooden cross marked her grave.* 一個簡單的木十字架標出了她墳墓的位置。| *He had marked the route in red.* 他已用紅色標出了路線。| **mark your place** (=put something in a book to show the page you had reached) 在書中夾上某物標明已讀到那一頁

3 ▶CELEBRATE 慶祝◀ [T] to celebrate an important event 慶祝, 紀念〔重要事件〕: *a festival to mark the town's 200th anniversary* 慶祝該城市建立200週年的節日

4 ▶SHOW A CHANGE 顯示變化◀ [T] to be a sign of an important change or an important stage in the development of something 標誌〔重要變化或發展階段〕: *His third film marks a major advance in cinematic techniques.* 他的第三部電影標誌着電影技術的巨大進步。

5 be marked by to have a particular quality that is very typical of the way in which someone does something 具有…特徵: *Her writing is marked by a subtle irony.* 她的寫作特點是一種微妙的譏諷。

6 ▶STUDENT'S WORK 學生作業◀ [T] *especially BrE* to read a piece of written work and put a number or letter on it to show what standard it is【尤英】給〔學生作業〕打分數[評等級]; GRADE² (2) *AmE*【美】: *I've got a pile of exam papers to mark.* 我有一堆試卷要評閱打分。

7 ▶WRITE ON STH 在某物上寫◀ [T] to write or draw on something, so that someone will notice what you have written 寫[畫]…作記號, 在…上作記號: *I've marked the pages you need to look at.* 我已經在你需要閱讀的那幾頁上作了記號。| *a document marked 'private and confidential'* 標有"私人檔案, 不得公開"字樣的一份文件

8 ▶SPORT 體育運動◀ [T] *BrE* to stay close to a player of the opposite team during a game【英】〔比賽中〕釘住〔對方的隊員〕

9 (you) mark my words! *old-fashioned spoken* used to tell someone that they should pay attention to what you are saying【過時, 口】留心聽我的話!: *There'll be trouble, you mark my words.* 就要有麻煩了, 你留心我的話吧。

10 mark you *old-fashioned spoken* used to emphasize something you say【過時, 口】你聽着〔用於強調所說的某事〕: *Her uncle's just given her a car – given, mark you, not lent.* 她叔叔剛剛送給她一輛汽車。你聽好了, 是送給她, 不是借給她。

11 mark time a) *informal* to spend time not doing very much except waiting for something else to happen【非正式】混時間, 消磨時間; 等待時機: *I was just marking time until a better job came up.* 我只是在混時間, 直到有個更好的工作。**b)** if soldiers mark time, they move their legs as if they were marching, but remain in the same place〔士兵〕原地踏步

12 mark sb present/absent to write on an official list that someone is there or not there, especially in school〔尤指學校中〕記下某人出席/缺席 —see also 另見 MARKED

mark sb/sth ↔ **down** *phr v* [T] **1** to write something down, especially in order to keep a record 記下〔某事〕: *Mark down everything you eat on your daily chart.* 在你的日常記事表上記下你吃的每樣東西。| **mark sb down as absent/present** *The teacher marked him down as absent.* 教師將他登記為缺席。**2** to reduce the price of items that are being sold 降低〔正在出售商品〕的價格: *Winter coats have been marked down from $80 to $50.* 冬用大衣的價格已從80美元降到50美元。**3** to form an opinion about someone when you first meet them 對〔某人〕形成第一印象: **mark sb down as sth** *When I first saw Gilbert play I marked him down as a future England player.* 當第一次看到吉爾伯特踢球時, 我就認為他是未來的英格蘭隊球員。**4** to give someone a lower result in a test or exam because of something they have done wrong〔測驗或考試中〕給〔某人〕打較低的分數: *Write neatly as you can be marked down if your paper looks messy.* 寫得整齊些。如果考卷看起來亂糟糟的, 你就要被扣分。

mark sb/sth ↔ **off** *phr v* [T] **1** to make an area separate by drawing a line around it, putting a rope around it etc 劃線分隔出, 用繩子等隔開: *The competitors' arena had been marked off with cones.* 比賽場地已經用圓錐筒分隔出來了。**2** to make a person, period of time etc seem different from others 使某人[某段時間]看起來不同: *Sara's natural flair for languages marked her off from the other students.* 莎拉的語言天賦使得她在學生中非常突出。**3** to make a mark on a list to show that something has been done or completed〔在單子上〕標出…已經做完: *I've marked off all the places we've already tried.* 我已經標出了我們已試過的所有地方。

mark sb/sth ↔ **out** *phr v* [T] **1** to show the shape or position of something by drawing lines around it 劃線標出〔某物的形狀或位置〕: *A volleyball court had been marked out on the grass.* 排球場已經在草坪上劃了出來。**2** to make someone or something seem very different

from or much better than other people or things 使…看上去非常不同於[大大地好於]…: **mark sb out as sth** *His efficient manner marked him out as a professional.* 他辦事的麻利勁頭使他看起來一派內行模樣。| **mark sb out for sth** *She seemed marked out for success.* 看樣子她肯定會成功。

mark sb/sth ↔ **up** *phr v* [T] **1** to increase the price of something, so that you sell it for more than you paid for it 給〔某物的進價〕加價: *Compact disks may be marked up as much as 80%.* 光盤的標價可能比進價高 80%。—see also 另見 MARK-UP **2** to write notes or instructions on a piece of writing, music etc 在〔文章或樂譜〕上寫評註[說明]: *Someone had already marked up the alto part.* 有人已經給男高音部分寫了評註。

mark² *n*

1 ►DIRT 污物◄ [C] a spot or small area on a surface, piece of clothing etc which is darker or dirtier than the rest and spoils its appearance 污跡; 污點: *I can't get these marks out of my T-shirt.* 我無法把我T恤衫上這些污跡去掉。| *His feet left dirty marks all over the floor.* 地板上全是他的髒腳印。| **finger marks** *There were finger marks smeared on the window.* 窗子上沾着一些手指印。

2 ►DAMAGE 損壞◄ [C] a cut, hole, or other small sign of damage 〔劃破、小洞等毀損的〕痕跡: *a burn mark on the kitchen table* 廚房餐桌上的一塊燒痕 | **bite mark/scratch mark etc** *Her teeth left bite marks in the apple.* 她的牙齒在蘋果上留下了一些咬痕。

3 ►COLOURED AREA 帶顏色的地方◄ [C] a small area of darker or lighter colour on a plain surface such as a person's skin or an animal's fur 〔人皮膚或動物皮毛等上的〕斑點, 色斑; 胎記: *The kitten is mainly white with black marks on her back.* 那隻小貓主要是白色的, 背上有黑色斑點。—see also 另見 BIRTHMARK

4 ►SIGN 符號◄ [C] a shape or sign that is written or printed 符號; 記號; 標記: *What do those strange marks at the top mean?* 上面那些奇怪的符號表示甚麼意思? | **question mark/punctuation mark etc** *Her letter was full of exclamation marks.* 她的信滿是感嘆號。

5 ►STUDENT'S WORK 學生作業◄ [C] *especially BrE* a letter or number given by a teacher to show what standard a piece of work is【尤英】〔老師給學生的〕分數, 成績; GRADE¹ (5) *AmE*【美】: *The highest mark was a B+.* 最高分是 B+。| *Her marks have been a lot lower this term.* 她這學期的成績一落千丈。| **pass mark** (=the mark you needed in order to pass an exam) 〔考試的〕及格分數 *The pass mark was 50%.* 及格分數是(百分制) 50 分。| **full marks** (=the highest possible mark) 滿分

6 full marks for effort/trying etc *BrE* used to praise someone for trying hard to do something, even though they did not succeed【英】因努力嘗試等而給的滿分〔用於表揚某人已盡力做某事, 儘管沒有成功〕

7 mark 2/6 etc a) a particular type of a car, machine etc 2型/6型等〔指汽車、機器等的型號〕: *The Mark 4 gun is much more powerful than the old Mark 3.* 4型槍比舊式3型槍威力大得多。**b)** *BrE* a measurement of the temperature of a gas OVEN【英】〔煤氣烤箱的溫度〕擋: *Cook for 40 minutes at gas mark 6.* 將煤氣開到6擋加熱40分鐘。

8 ►MONEY 貨幣◄ [C] the former standard unit of money in Germany 馬克〔德國原標準貨幣單位〕

9 a mark of a sign that something is true or exists 〔某物真實或存在的〕跡象; 標誌; 表示: *She was carrying bags full of toys and clothes – the mark of a mother on the run.* 她手裡拿着一些裝滿玩具和衣服的袋子 —— 一個忙碌不停的母親模樣。| **a mark of respect** *There was a 2-minute silence as a mark of respect for the dead.* 向死者默哀兩分鐘。

10 hit/miss the mark a) to hit or miss the thing that you were shooting at 擊中/未中目標 **b)** to succeed or fail to have the effect you wanted 達到/未達到想要的效果: *His jibe had evidently hit the mark, for she laughed a little awkwardly.* 他的嘲諷顯然達到了他要的效果, 因為她笑起來有些不自然。

11 off the mark/wide of the mark not correct; INACCURATE 不正確; 不準確: *Our cost estimate was way off the mark.* 我們對成本的估計太離譜了。

12 make your mark to become successful or famous 成功; 成名: *Wilkins was quick to make his mark, scoring the touchdown.* 威爾金斯很快就取得先機, 持球觸地得分。| **[+on]** *Margaret Thatcher made an unforgettable mark on British politics.* 瑪格麗特·戴卓爾在英國政壇上取得的成功令人難忘。

13 leave its/their mark on to have an effect on someone or something that changes them in a permanent or very noticeable way 對某人產生持久[顯著]的影響: *The years of hardship and poverty had left their mark on her.* 那些艱難困苦的歲月給她留下了難以抹去的影響。

14 not up to the mark *BrE*【英】**a)** not good enough 不夠好; 不符合標準[要求]: *Her work just isn't up to the mark.* 她的工作根本不夠好。**b)** *old-fashioned* not well and healthy【過時】身體不適: *I'm not feeling quite up to the mark today.* 我今天感到不太舒服。

15 be quick/slow off the mark *informal* to be quick or slow to understand things or react to situations【非正式】對事情理解快/慢; 對局勢反應敏捷/遲鈍

16 reach the 60 second/two-mile/£20 etc mark to reach a particular time, distance, or amount 達到60秒/兩英里/20英鎊等: *Membership is approaching the two million mark.* 會員人數正接近二百萬。

17 the halfway mark the point in a race, journey, or event that is halfway between the start and the finish 〔賽跑、旅程或事件的〕中間點

18 on your marks, get set, go! *spoken* used to start a race【口】〔用於開始賽跑〕各就各位, 預備, 跑!

19 ►SIGNATURE 簽名◄ [C] *old use* a sign in the form of a cross, used by someone who is not able to write their name【舊】〔不會寫自己名字者用來代替簽名的〕十字畫押

20 ►CRIME 犯罪◄ [C] *AmE* someone that a criminal has decided to steal from or trick【美】被偷竊[欺騙]的對象 —see also 另見 EXCLAMATION MARK, **overstep the mark** (OVERSTEP (2)), PUNCTUATION MARK, QUESTION MARK, QUOTATION MARK, SPEECH MARKS

mark·down /ˈmɑrkˌdaʊn; ˈmɑːkdaʊn/ *n* [C] a reduction in the price of something 減價, 削價: *a markdown of $10* 減價 10 美元

marked /mɑrkt; mɑːkt/ *adj* **1** very clear and easy to notice 顯著的, 明顯的, 易見的: *He showed a marked lack of interest.* 他顯然缺乏興趣。| *a marked improvement in the patient's condition* 病人病情明顯的好轉 | **in marked contrast** *Sara wore red, in marked contrast to her sister's sombre colours.* 莎拉穿的是紅色衣服, 與她姐姐所穿的暗色衣服形成鮮明的對比。**2 a marked man** a man who is in danger because an enemy wants to harm him 因仇敵打算報復而處於險境的人 —**markedly** /ˈmɑrkɪdlɪ; ˈmɑːkɨ̣dli/ *adv*: *They have a markedly different approach to the problem.* 對於這個問題他們有明顯不同的處理方法。

mark·er /ˈmɑrkɚ; ˈmɑːkə/ *n* [C] **1** an object, sign etc that shows the position of something 標誌; 標示物 **2** a pen with a thick point made of FELT, used for marking or drawing things 記號筆〔做記號或繪畫用的粗氈頭筆〕—see picture at 參見 PEN¹ 圖 **3 put down a marker** to say or do something that makes your future intentions clear 顯示自己未來的意圖

marker pen /ˈ··· ·/ *n* [C] *BrE* a pen with a thick point made of FELT【英】記號筆

mar·ket¹ /ˈmɑrkɪt; ˈmɑːkɨ̣t/ *n*

1 ►PLACE TO BUY THINGS 購物場所◄ [C] **a)** a place where people buy and sell goods, especially in an open area or a large building 集市; 市場: *There's a good antiques market here on Sundays.* 每逢週日這裡都會有一個不錯的古董集市。| *I usually buy all my vegetables at* *the market.* 我所需要的蔬菜通常都是在菜市場裡購買。| **street market** (=with a lot of different people selling things from tables, STALLS etc in the street)〔各色人等在街上擺桌子或擺攤售貨的〕街市 **b)** *AmE* a shop that sells food and things for the home【美】食品雜貨店

2 the market a) the STOCK MARKET 證券市場: *Most analysts are forecasting a further downturn in the market.* 大多數分析家預測證券市場將會進一步下挫。| **play the market** (=risk money on the stock market) 在證券市場作風險投資; 在證券市場投機牟利 | **the markets** (=stock markets around the world) 全球證券市場 *The markets are nervous at the moment.* 全球證券市場眼下人心惶惶。**b)** the total amount of trade in a particular kind of goods〔某種貨物的〕市場總額; 總銷售量: *Honda is trying to increase its share of the market.* 本田公司正設法提高其市場總佔有率。| **the art/diamond/bond etc market** *The art market is rather depressed.* 藝術品市場非常不景氣。| **the market in** *the world market in aluminum* 全球鋁市場 **c)** the system in which all prices and wages depend on what goods people want to buy, how many they buy etc 市場機制; 市場情況: *a naive belief in leaving everything to the market* 將一切都交給市場的天真想法

3 on the market available for people to buy 在出售, 可買到: *There are thousands of different computer games on the market.* 在市場上可買到成千上萬套不同的電腦遊戲。| **put a house/business etc on the market** (=offer it for sale) 將房屋/企業等投放市場出售 *We put our house on the market at the wrong time.* 我們在一個錯誤的時候將自己的房子投放到市場上出售。| **come onto the market** (=become available for people to buy) 上市, 在市場上銷售 *a revolutionary new drug that has just come onto the market* 剛剛上市的一種全新藥物 | **on the open market** (=generally available for people to buy without any official restrictions) 在公開出售 *In some areas, handguns were freely available on the open market.* 在某些地區, 手槍曾可以隨意公開出售。

4 ►COUNTRY/AREA 國家/地區◄ [C] a particular country or area where a company sells its goods or where a particular type of goods is sold 商品銷售國家[地區]: *Our main overseas market is Japan.* 我們的主要海外市場是日本。| *cars intended for the domestic market* 供國內市場銷售的汽車 | **[+for]** *The main market for computer software is still in the US.* 電腦軟件的主要銷售市場仍然在美國。

5 ►PEOPLE WHO BUY 購買者◄ [singular] the number of people who want to buy something, or the kind of people who want to buy it 欲購買某物的人數; 欲購買某物的羣體; 銷路: **[+for]** *The market for specialist academic books is pretty small.* 專業學術著作的市場非常小。| **there is a market for** (=people want to buy a product)〔某商品〕有銷路 *There isn't much of a market for second-hand mainframe computers.* 二手主機電腦沒有多大的銷路。

6 be in the market for to be interested in buying something 有意購買…: *Several terrorist groups were believed to be in the market for nuclear technology.* 據信有幾個恐怖組織想購買核技術。

7 the job market/the labour market the number of jobs that are available 就業市場/勞務市場: *The job market has been badly hit by the recession.* 就業市場受到了經濟衰退的沉重打擊。

8 a buyer's/seller's market a time that is better for buyers because prices are low, or better for sellers because prices are high 買方/賣方市場 —see also 另見 BLACK MARKET, FLEA MARKET, **corner the market** (CORNER² (3)), **price yourself out of the market** (PRICE² (4))

market² *v* [T] **1** to try to persuade people to buy a product by advertising it in a particular way, using attractive packages etc 推銷: *The success of any beauty product depends on the way it is marketed.* 美容產品成功與否, 取決於它的推銷方式。**2** to make a product available in shops〔在店鋪〕出售: *The turkeys are marketed ready-to-cook.* 火雞是以即可烹調的形式銷售的。

mar·ket·a·ble /ˈmɑrkɪtəbəl; ˈmɑːkɪ̈təbəl/ *adj* marketable goods, skills etc can be sold easily because people want them 有銷路的, 暢銷的: *It's a very marketable qualification.* 這是一種非常符合市場需求的資歷。—**marketability** /ˌmɑrkɪtəˈbɪləti; ˌmɑːkɪ̈təˈbɪlɪ̈ti/ *n* [U]

market day /ˈ·· ˌ·/ *n* [C] *especially BrE* the day in the week when there is a market in a particular town【尤英】〔一週中〕有集市的日子, 集日

market-driv·en /ˌ·· ˈ··◂/ *adj* MARKET-LED 以市場(需求)為導向的

market e·con·o·my /ˌ·· ·ˈ···/ *n* [C] a system of producing wealth based on the free operation of business and trade without government controls 市場經濟

mar·ket·eer /ˌmɑrkɪˈtɪr; ˌmɑːkɪ̈ˈtɪə/ *n* [C] **anti-Marketeer/pro-Marketeer** *old-fashioned* someone who is against/in favour of Britain being a member of the European Union【過時】反對/支持英國成為歐盟成員的人 —see also 另見 BLACK MARKETEER, FREE MARKETEER

market forc·es /ˌ·· ˈ··/ *n* [plural] the free operation of business and trade without any government controls, which decides the level of prices and wages at a particular time 市場力量; 市場自由運作

market gar·den /ˌ·· ˈ··/ *n* [C] *BrE* an area of land where vegetables and fruit are grown so that they can be sold【英】〔種植蔬菜和水果供出售的〕商品果蔬園; TRUCK FARM *AmE*【美】—**market gardener** *n* [C]

mar·ket·ing /ˈmɑrkɪtɪŋ; ˈmɑːkɪ̈tɪŋ/ *n* [U] **1** the activity of trying to sell a company's products by advertising, using attractive packages etc〔藉助對產品作廣告宣傳、漂亮包裝等進行的〕市場營銷: *a marketing executive* 營銷經理 | *a clever marketing ploy* 聰明的營銷策略 **2 do the marketing/go marketing** *AmE old-fashioned* to go to the shops to buy things, especially food【美, 過時】去商店購物〔尤指食品〕 3 3

market lead·er /ˌ·· ˈ··/ *n* [C] the company that sells the most of a particular kind of product, or the product that is the most successful one of its kind 市場領導者〔佔有某產品最大市場份額的公司〕; 市場領導產品〔佔有最大市場份額的產品〕: *Kodak is still the market leader.* 柯達公司仍然處於市場的領導地位。

market-led /ˌ·· ˈ·◂/ *adj* market-led products, developments etc are a result of public demand for a particular product, service, or skill 以市場為導向的〔指根據公眾對產品、服務或技術的需求而提供產品、開發等〕

market mak·er /ˈ·· ˌ··/ *n* [C] *technical* someone who works on the STOCK MARKET buying and selling stocks (STOCK¹ (3)) and shares (SHARE² (5))【術語】證券市場中間人[莊家]

mar·ket·place /ˈmɑrkɪtˌples; ˈmɑːkɪ̈tpleɪs/ *n* [C] **1 the marketplace** the part of business activity which is concerned with selling goods 市場〔指涉及營銷的種種活動〕: *his uncanny ability to see new opportunities in the marketplace* 他那能在市場中看到新機會的神奇本領 **2** an open area in a town where a market is held 集市, 露天市場

market price /ˌ·· ˈ·/ *n* [singular] the price that people will actually pay for something at a particular time 市場價格, 市價, 時價

market re·search /ˌ·· ·ˈ·/ *n* [U] a business activity which involves collecting information about what goods people buy and why 市場調查

market town /ˈ·· ·/ *n* [C] *BrE* a town where there is an outdoor market, usually once or twice a week【英】〔通常每週有一次或兩次露天集市交易的〕集市城鎮

market val·ue /ˌ·· ˈ··/ *n* [singular] the value of a product, building etc based on the price that people are willing to pay for it rather than the cost of producing it or building it〔產品、建築物等的〕市場價值〔即以人們願意支付的價格而不以成本釐定的價值〕

mark·ing /ˈmɑrkɪŋ; ˈmɑːkɪŋ/ *n* **1** [C usually plural 一般用複數, U] the coloured patterns and shapes on an

animal's fur, on leaves etc〔動物皮毛、樹葉等上的〕斑紋, 斑點: *The leopard has beautiful markings.* 豹子身上有美麗的斑紋。**2** [C usually plural 一般用複數, U] colours and shapes painted on aircraft, army vehicles etc〔刷在飛機、軍車等上的〕彩色裝飾和圖形 **3** [U] *especially BrE* the activity of checking students' written work【尤英】批改學生作業: *I have to do a lot of marking tonight.* 今晚我有許多作業要批改。

marks·man /ˋmɑrksmən; ˈmɑːksmən/ *plural* **marksmen** /-mən; -mən/ *n* [C] someone who can shoot very well 神槍手, 神射手

marks·man·ship /ˋmɑrksmənʃɪp; ˈmɑːksmənʃɪp/ *n* [U] the ability to shoot very well 射擊術; 槍法

mark-up /ˈ· ·/ *n* [C] an increase in the price of something, especially from the price a shop pays for something to the price it sells it for 提價幅度〔尤指商店從進貨價到售出價的增加幅度〕: *The retailer's mark-up is 50%.* 零售商的提價幅度是50%。

mar·lin /ˋmɑrlɪn; ˈmɑːlɪn/ *n* [C] a large sea fish with a long sharp nose, which people hunt for sport 馬林魚, 槍魚

mar·ma·lade /ˋmɑrml̩ˌed; ˈmɑːməleɪd/ *n* [U] a JAM made from fruit such as oranges, LEMONs or GRAPEFRUIT, usually eaten at breakfast〔用橘子、檸檬或葡萄柚等製成的〕柑橘醬

mar·mo·re·al /mɑrˋmɔrɪəl; mɑːˈmɔːriəl/ *adj literary* like MARBLE【文】大理石似的

mar·mo·set /ˋmɑrməˌzɛt; ˈmɑːməzet/ *n* [C] a type of small monkey with long hair and large eyes that lives in Central and South America 狨猴, 絹猴〔一種生活在中南美洲的長毛大眼小猴〕

ma·roon¹ /məˋrun; məˈruːn/ *n* [U] a very dark red-brown colour 栗色, 褐紫紅色 —**maroon** *adj* —see picture on page A5 參見A5頁圖

maroon² *v* **be marooned** to be left in a place where there are no other people and where you cannot escape 被困於荒無人煙且無法脫身的地方: *The car broke down leaving us marooned in the middle of nowhere.* 汽車壞了, 我們被困在茫茫荒野中。

maroon³ *n* [C] a small ROCKET used as a signal by ships〔船舶用作信號的〕煙火; 鞭砲

marque /mɑrk; mɑːk/ *n* [C] the well-known name of a type of car or other product, especially an expensive one〔汽車或其他產品, 尤指名貴產品的〕牌子, 商標: *the prestigious Ferrari marque* 久負盛名的法拉利牌汽車

mar·quee /mɑrˋki; mɑːˈkiː/ *n* [C] **1** a large tent at an outdoor event or celebration, used especially for eating or drinking in〔大型戶外活動或慶祝活動時, 尤用作進餐或飲酒場所的〕大帳篷 **2** *AmE* a sign above the door of a theatre or cinema which gives the name of the play or film【美】〔戲院或電影院大門上方〕公佈劇名[影片名]的招牌

mar·quess /ˋmɑrkwɪs; ˈmɑːkwɪs/ *n* [C] *BrE* a MARQUIS【英】侯爵

mar·quet·ry /ˋmɑrkətrɪ; ˈmɑːkɪtri/ *n* [U] a pattern made of coloured pieces of wood fastened together, or the art of making these patterns〔用着色木片嵌接而成的〕鑲嵌圖案; 鑲嵌工藝

mar·quis /ˋmɑrkwɪs; ˈmɑːkwɪs/ *n* [C] a man who, in the British system of NOBLE titles, has a rank between DUKE and EARL〔英國的〕侯爵: *the Marquis of Bath* 巴斯侯爵

mar·riage /ˋmærɪdʒ; ˈmærɪdʒ/ *n* **1** [C] the relationship between two people who are married 婚姻: *They have a very happy marriage.* 他們的婚姻非常美滿。| *One in three marriages ends in divorce.* 三樁婚姻中就有一樁以離婚而告終。**2** [U] the state of being married 結婚: *My parents disapprove of sex before marriage.* 我父母不贊成婚前性行為。**3** [C] the ceremony in which two people get married; WEDDING 結婚儀式, 婚禮: *The marriage took place at St Bartholomew's church.* 婚禮是在聖巴梭羅繆教堂舉行的。**4 by marriage** if you are related to someone by marriage, they are married to someone in your family 通過姻親關係, 由於婚姻

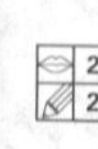

mar·riage·a·ble /ˋmærɪdʒəbl̩; ˈmærɪdʒəbəl/ *adj old-fashioned* suitable for marriage【過時】適合結婚的: *a young woman of marriageable age* 達到結婚年齡的年輕女子 —**marriageability** /ˌmærɪdʒəˋbɪlətɪ; ˌmærɪdʒəˈbɪləti/ *n* [U]

marriage bu·reau /ˈ·· ˌ··/ *n* [C] an organization that helps people find partners to marry 婚姻介紹所

marriage cer·tif·i·cate /ˈ·· ·ˌ···/ *n* [C] an official document that proves that two people are married 結婚證書

marriage guid·ance /ˌ·· ˈ··/ *n* [U] advice given to people who are having difficulties in their marriage 婚姻指導[諮詢]

marriage li·cence /ˈ·· ˌ··/ *n* [C] an official written document saying that two people are allowed to marry 結婚許可證

marriage lines /ˈ·· ·/ *n* [plural] *old-fashioned BrE* a MARRIAGE CERTIFICATE【過時, 英】結婚證書

marriage of con·ve·ni·ence /ˌ·· · ··ˈ···/ *n* [C] a marriage for political or economic reasons, not for love 基於政治[經濟]原因〔而非基於愛情〕的婚姻, 權宜婚姻

marriage vows /ˈ·· ·/ *n* [plural] the promises that you make during the marriage ceremony 結婚誓約, 婚誓

mar·ried /ˋmærɪd; ˈmærid/ *adj* **1** having a husband or a wife 已婚的, 有配偶的: *Are you married or single?* 你是已婚還是單身? | *They've been married for 28 years.* 他們已經結婚28年了。| *More and more married women were returning to the workplace.* 越來越多的已婚婦女開始重新就業。| [+to] *She's married to my brother.* 她嫁給了我哥哥。| **get married** *We're getting married next month.* 我們下個月結婚。| **married life** (=your life when you are married) 婚後生活; 婚姻生活 *How are you enjoying married life?* 你婚後過得怎麼樣? **2 be married to sth** to give most of your time and attention to a job or activity 專心致志於某事 —see also 另見 MARRY, YOUNG MARRIEDS

mar·row /ˋmæro; ˈmærəʊ/ *n* **1** [U] the soft fatty substance in the hollow centre of bones; BONE MARROW 骨髓: *a bone marrow transplant* 骨髓移植 **2** [C,U] a large long dark green vegetable that grows along the ground 西葫蘆, 食用葫蘆 —compare 比較 SQUASH² (3) —see picture on page A9 參見A9頁圖 **3 chilled/frozen/shocked to the marrow** very cold or shocked 冷得刺骨; 毛骨悚然: *She had walked all the way home, frozen to the marrow.* 她一路走着回了家, 感到全身寒冷刺骨。

marrow bone /ˈ·· ·/ *n* [C,U] a large bone that contains a lot of MARROW (1) 多髓的大骨, 髓骨

mar·ry /ˋmærɪ; ˈmæri/ *v* **marries, married, marrying 1** [I,T] to become someone's husband or wife 結婚; 娶; 嫁: **get married (to)** *I got married when I was 18.* 我18歲就結婚了。| *Billy got married to the first girl he went out with.* 比利和自己的初戀女友結了婚。| **marry sb** *one of those romances about a rich tycoon who marries his secretary* 大亨娶了女祕書為妻的那種浪漫故事中的一個 | **marry money** (=marry someone who is rich) 和有錢人結婚 **2** [T] to perform the ceremony at which two people get married 為…主持婚禮: *The priest who married us was really nice.* 為我們主持婚禮的那個牧師非常和藹可親。**3** [T] to find a husband or wife for one of your children 為自己的孩子找〔配偶〕: **marry sb to sb** *She's determined to marry all her daughters to rich men.* 她決心把她所有的女兒都嫁給有錢人。**4** [T] *formal* to combine two quite different ideas, designs, tastes etc together【正式】將〔兩個差別很大的想法、設計、品味等〕結合在一起: **marry sth with sth** *The design marries traditional styles with modern materials.* 這個設計把傳統風格和現代材料結合在一起。**5 not the marrying kind** not the kind of person who wants to get married 不是那種想結婚的人

marry into sth *phr v* [T] to join a family or social group by marrying someone who belongs to it 通過婚姻而加入〔配偶所屬的家庭或社會團體〕: *She married into a very* *wealthy family.* 她嫁進了一個非常富有的人家。

marry sb ↔ **off** *phr v* [T] to find a husband or wife for someone 為〔某人〕尋得配偶: **[+to]** *They married her off to the first young man who came along.* 他們把她嫁給了第一個出現的年輕人。

USAGE NOTE 用法説明: MARRY

GRAMMAR 語法

You *marry someone* or *get/are married to someone,* not *with* them. But you can be *married with four children.* 表示"與某人結婚", 要説 marry someone 或 get/are married to someone, 而不用 with。但可以説 married with four children (已婚, 有四個孩子)。

SPOKEN-WRITTEN 口語一書面語

Get married is more informal and more common in spoken English than **marry**. 在英語口語中, get married 比 marry 更通俗隨便, 更為常用: *Marti is getting married to Jeff next week.* 馬蒂下週和傑夫結婚。(compare 比較 *Marti is marrying Jeff next week.*)

In spoken English, speakers often avoid *to* with **married** by saying, for example 在口語中, 人們常常避免在 married 後面用 to, 例如: *Jeff and Marti got married/are married.* 傑夫和馬蒂結婚了。

Mars /mɑrz; mɑːz/ *n* [singular] the PLANET that is fourth in order from the sun, is nearest to the Earth, and is a red colour 火星 —see picture at 參見 SOLAR SYSTEM 圖

Mar·seil·laise /ˌmarsḷˋez; ˌmɑːsəˈleɪz/ *n* [singular] the national song of France 馬賽曲〔法國國歌〕

marsh /mɑrʃ; mɑːʃ/ *n* [C,U] an area of low flat land that is always wet and soft 沼澤, 濕地 —compare 比較 SWAMP[1], BOG[1] (1) —**marshy** *adj*: *marshy ground* 沼澤地

mar·shal¹ /ˋmɑrʃəl; ˈmɑːʃəl/ *n* [C] **1** an officer of the highest rank in an army or airforce〔陸軍或空軍〕元帥: *Marshal Zhukov* 朱可夫元帥 —see table on page C6 參見 C6 頁附錄 **2** *especially BrE* an official in charge of an important public event or ceremony【尤英】司禮官, 典禮官, 司儀〔主持重要公眾活動或典禮的官員〕**3** an official in charge of a race or sports event〔體育競賽等的〕主事官員 **4** *AmE* an official in a court of law; SHERIFF【美】執法官; 治安官 **5** *AmE* the officer in charge of a city's police force or fire-fighting department【美】警察局長; 消防隊長

marshal² *v* **marshalled, marshalling** *BrE*【英】, **marshaled, marshaling** *AmE*【美】[T] **1 marshal your arguments/ideas/facts etc** to organize your arguments, ideas etc so that they are effective or easy to understand 整理論據/想法/事實等: *Briggs paused for a moment as if to marshal his thoughts.* 布里格斯停頓了一會兒, 好像要整理一下思路。**2** to control or organize a large group 控制; 組織; 引領: *Extra stewards had to be employed to marshal the huge crowds.* 必須聘請額外的服務員來安頓這大羣大羣的人。**3 marshal your forces** to organize all the people and things that you need in order to be ready for a battle, election etc 組織力量, 集結力量

marshalling yard /ˈ··· ·/ *n* [C] *BrE* a place where railway WAGONS are brought together to form trains【英】〔鐵路上的〕調車場, 編組場

Marshal of the Roy·al Air·force /ˌ··· ·ˌ·· ˈ··/ *n* [C] an officer of high rank in the British airforce〔英國〕皇家空軍元帥

marsh gas /ˈ· ·/ *n* [U] gas formed from decaying plants under water in a MARSH; METHANE 沼氣, 甲烷

marsh·land /ˋmɑrʃlænd; ˈmɑːʃlænd/ *n* [U] an area of land where there is a lot of MARSH 沼澤地

marsh·mal·low /ˋmɑrʃˌmælo; ˌmɑːʃˈmæləʊ/ *n* [C,U] **1** a very soft light sweet that is white or pink 棉花糖 **2** a tall wild plant with pink flowers 沼澤蜀葵, 藥用蜀葵

mar·su·pi·al /mɑrˋsjupɪəl; mɑːˈsuːpiəl/ *n* [C] an animal such as a KANGAROO which carries its babies in a pocket of skin on its body 有袋動物〈如袋鼠〉

mart /mɑrt; mɑːt/ *n* [C] a market 市場: *the biggest cattle mart in the region* 該地區最大的牲畜市場

mar·ten /ˋmɑrtɪn; ˈmɑːtɪn/ *n* [C] a small flesh-eating animal that lives mainly in trees 貂

mar·tial /ˋmɑrʃəl; ˈmɑːʃəl/ *adj* [only before noun 僅用於名詞前] connected with war and fighting 軍事的; 戰爭的: *martial music* 軍樂

martial art /ˌ·· ˈ·/ *n* [C usually plural 一般用複數] a sport such as JUDO or KARATE, in which you fight with your hands and feet, and which was developed in Eastern countries〔東方國家的〕武術〈如柔道、空手道等〉

martial law /ˌ·· ˈ·/ *n* [U] a situation in which the army controls an area instead of the police, especially because of fighting against the government 軍事管制, 戒嚴: *Fighting in the capital led to the imposition of martial law.* 首都發生的戰鬥導致了戒嚴的實施。

Mar·tian /ˋmɑrʃən; ˈmɑːʃən/ *n* [C] an imaginary creature from the PLANET Mars〔假想的〕火星人 —**Martian** *adj*

mar·tin /ˋmɑrtɪn; ˈmɑːtɪn/ *n* [C] a small bird like a SWALLOW[2] (1) 聖馬丁鳥, 燕科小鳥〈如岩燕、雨燕等〉

mar·ti·net /ˌmɑrtnˋɛt; ˌmɑːtɪˈnet/ *n* [C] *formal* someone who is very strict and makes people obey rules exactly【正式】嚴格遵守紀律的人

mar·ti·ni /mɑrˋtinɪ; mɑːˈtiːni/ *n* [C,U] an alcoholic drink made by mixing GIN or VODKA with VERMOUTH 馬丁尼酒〔用杜松子酒或伏特加酒與苦艾酒混合而成的雞尾酒〕

mar·tyr¹ /ˋmɑrtɚ; ˈmɑːtə/ *n* [C] **1** someone who is killed or punished because of their religious or political beliefs 殉道者; 烈士 **2** someone who tries to get other people's sympathy by complaining about how hard their life is 訴説自己生活如何艱苦以博取他人同情者: *She's such a martyr!* 她就是這樣一個靠訴苦博取同情的人! **3 be a martyr to** *old-fashioned* to suffer a lot because of an illness【過時】〔因疾病〕受折磨, 受痛苦: *She's a martyr to her arthritis.* 她深受關節炎的折磨。

martyr² *v* **be martyred** to be killed or punished because of your religious beliefs〔因宗教信仰〕被處死; 受懲罰

mar·tyr·dom /ˋmɑrtɚdəm; ˈmɑːtədəm/ *n* [U] the death or suffering of a martyr 殉難; 殉道, 殉教; 受苦

mar·tyred /ˋmɑrtɚd; ˈmɑːtəd/ *adj* [only before noun 僅用於名詞前] a martyred look or expression is an unhappy one, as if you want to make other people feel sorry for you〔好像為博取他人同情而顯現的神色或表情〕痛苦的, 傷心的: *I wish you'd stop giving me those martyred looks.* 我希望你別再這麼傷心地看着我。

mar·vel¹ /ˋmɑrvḷ; ˈmɑːvəl/ *v* **marvelled, marvelling** *BrE*【英】, **marveled, marveling** *AmE*【美】[I,T] to feel great surprise or admiration for something, especially someone's behaviour〔尤指對某人的行為〕感到驚訝, 欽佩: **[+at]** *I marvelled at my mother's ability to remain calm in a crisis.* 我佩服我母親處事不驚的本領。| **marvel that** *I marvelled that anyone could be so stupid.* 我感到驚訝的是竟會有人如此愚蠢。

marvel² *n* [C] something or someone surprisingly useful or skilful, that you like and admire very much 十分有用[靈巧]的物[人]: *the marvels of modern science* 現代科學的奇跡 | *an electronic marvel* 奇妙的電子器件 | *I don't know how he did it – he's a bloody marvel!* 我不知道他是怎麼成功的 —— 他真是個非常了不起的人物!

mar·vel·lous *BrE*【英】, **marvelous** *AmE*【美】/ˋmɑrvḷəs; ˈmɑːvələs/ *adj* extremely good, enjoyable, or impressive etc 極好的; 絕妙的; 了不起的: *"How was your holiday?" "Marvellous!"* "假期過得好嗎?" "好極了!" | *It sounds like a marvellous idea.* 這個主意聽起來很不錯。| *It's marvelous what they can do with plastic surgery these days.* 如今他們能用整容手術做的事真是妙極了。—**marvellously** *adv* 

Marx·is·m /ˋmɑrksɪzəm; ˈmɑːksɪzəm/ *n* [U] the system of political thinking invented by Karl Marx, which explains changes in history as the result of a struggle between social classes 馬克思主義 —**Marxist** *n* [C]

M

mar·zi·pan /ˋmɑrzəˏpæn; ˈmɑːzə̩pæn/ *n* [U] a sweet food made from ALMONDs, sugar, and eggs, used to make sweets and for covering cakes 杏仁蛋白糖漿〔一種用杏仁、糖和蛋白混合而成的糖漿, 用於做糖果或澆在糕餅上〕

masc the written abbreviation of 縮寫= MASCULINE

mas·ca·ra /mæsˋkærə; mæˈskɑːrə/ *n* [U] a dark substance used by women to colour their EYELASHes and make them look thicker 睫毛膏, 睫毛油 —see picture at 參見 MAKE-UP 圖

mas·cot /ˋmæskət; ˈmæskət/ *n* [C] an animal, toy etc that represents a team or organization, and is thought to bring them good luck 吉祥物: *The team mascot is a grizzly bear.* 這支運動隊的吉祥物是大灰熊。

mas·cu·line /ˋmæskjəlɪn; ˈmæskjʊ̍lɪn/ *adj* **1** belonging to men, done by men, or considered to be typical of men 屬於男性的; 男人做的; 男子氣概的: *a masculine approach to the problem* 男人解決這一問題的方法 | *traditionally masculine subjects such as physics* 傳統上屬於男性的學科, 如物理學 | *a dark, masculine face* 一張黝黑的男子漢的臉 **2** if a woman's appearance or voice is masculine, it is like a man's〔女子外貌或嗓音〕像男人的 **3** belonging to the class of words for males〔詞〕陽性的〔此詞指雄性生物〕: *'Drake' is the masculine word for 'duck'.* drake (公鴨) 是 duck (鴨子) 的陽性詞。 **4** a masculine noun, PRONOUN etc belongs to a class of words that have different INFLECTIONs from FEMININE or NEUTER words〔名詞、代詞等〕陽性的〔此詞的詞形變化與語法中陰性或中性的詞不同〕: *The word for 'book' is masculine in French.* "書"這個詞在法語裡是陽性的。

mas·cu·lin·i·ty /ˏmæskjəˋlɪnətɪ; ˌmæskjʊ̍ˈlɪnə̩ti/ *n* [U] the characteristics and qualities considered to be typical of men 男性; 陽性; 男子氣: *Children's ideas of masculinity tend to come from their fathers.* 孩子們對於何謂男子氣的觀念往往來自他們的父親。

ma·ser /ˋmezɚ; ˈmeɪzə/ *n* [C] a piece of equipment that produces a very powerful electric force〔能產生極強電能的〕微波激射器 —compare 比較 LASER

mash¹ /mæʃ; mæʃ/ also 又作 **mash up** *v* [T] to crush something, especially a food that has been cooked, until it is soft and smooth 把〔某物, 尤指已做熟的食物〕搗成泥狀, 搗爛: *Mash the banana and add it to the batter.* 把香蕉搗成泥狀, 然後摻到麵糊裡。—**masher** *n* [C] —see picture on page A11 參見 A11 頁圖

mash² *n* [U] **1** *BrE informal* potatoes that have been boiled and then crushed until they are smooth; MASHED POTATO【英, 非正式】馬鈴薯泥, 土豆泥: *bangers and mash* 香腸和土豆泥 **2** a mixture of grain cooked with water to make a food for animals〔不同穀物混合煮成的〕糊狀飼料 **3** a mixture of MALT¹ (1) or crushed grain and hot water, used to make beer or WHISKY〔釀製啤酒或威士忌酒的〕麥芽漿

mashed po·ta·to /ˏ· ˋ··/ also 又作 **mashed potatoes** *n* [U] potatoes that have been boiled and then crushed until they are smooth 馬鈴薯泥, 土豆泥

mask¹ /mæsk; mɑːsk/ *n* [C] **1** something that covers all or part of your face, to protect or to hide it 面具; 面罩; 口罩: *a surgical face mask* 外科手術口罩 **2** something that covers your face, and has another face painted on it 假面具, 假面: *special masks used in Kabuki theater* 日本歌舞伎戲劇中專用的假面具 **3** [usually singular 一般用單數] an expression or way of behaving that hides your real emotions or character 偽裝; 掩飾: *Her sarcasm is only a mask for her insecurity.* 她說挖苦話只是為了掩飾她的焦慮不安。—see also 另見 DEATH MASK, GAS MASK

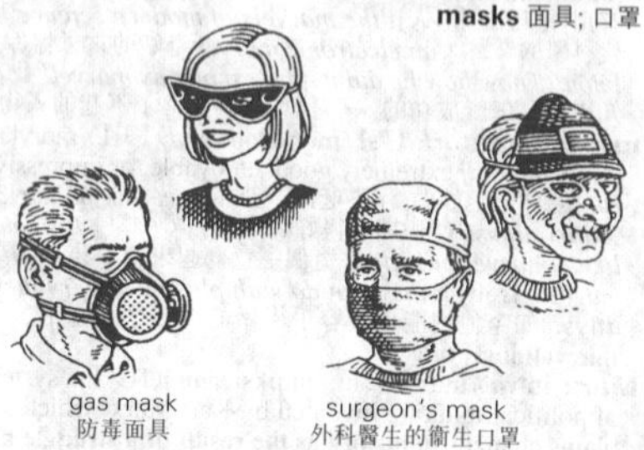

masks 面具; 口罩

mask² *v* [T] **1** to cover something so that it cannot be properly seen 遮蓋, 遮住: *an ugly concrete wall partially masked by straggling ivy* 一堵難看的水泥牆, 其中一部分被蔓生的常春藤所掩蓋 **2** a smell, taste, sound etc that is masked by a stronger one cannot be noticed because of it 蓋住〔氣味、味道、聲音等〕 **3** to hide the truth about a situation, about how you feel etc 掩飾, 隱瞞, 掩蓋: *His clownishness masks his loneliness.* 他滑稽的舉止掩蓋着他內心的孤寂。| *so-called democratic institutions that mask the reality of power in Britain* 掩蓋英國權力真相的所謂民主制度

masked /mæskt; mɑːskt/ *adj* wearing a mask 戴面具的; 戴面罩的; 戴口罩的

masked ball /ˏ· ˈ·/ *n* [C] a formal dance at which everyone wears masks 假面舞會; 化裝舞會

masking tape /ˈ·· ·/ *n* [U] long narrow paper that is sticky on one side, used especially to protect the edge of an area which you are painting〔繪畫或噴漆時用的〕遮蔽膠帶

mas·o·chis·m /ˋmæzəˏkɪzəm; ˈmæsəkɪzəm/ *n* [U] **1** enjoyment of being hurt or punished 受虐狂 **2** sexual behaviour in which you gain pleasure from being hurt 性受虐狂 —**masochist** *n* [C] —**masochistic** /ˏmæsəˋkɪstɪk; ˌmæsəˈkɪstɪk◂/ *adj*: *masochistic behavior* 受虐狂行為 —compare 比較 SADISM

ma·son /ˋmesn̩; ˈmeɪsən/ *n* [C] **1** a STONEMASON 石匠, 石工 **2** a FREEMASON 共濟會會員

Mason-Dix·on line /ˏmesn̩ ˋdɪksn̩ laɪn; ˌmeɪsən ˈdɪksən laɪn/ *n* [singular] the border between the American states of Pennsylvania and Maryland, considered as the dividing line between the northern and southern US 梅森—迪克森線〔美國賓夕法尼亞州和馬里蘭州之間的邊界線, 被認為是美國北部和南部的分界線〕

Ma·son·ic /məˋsɑnɪk; məˈsɒnɪk/ *adj* involved or connected with Freemasons 共濟會會員的: *a Masonic lodge* 共濟會地方分會集會處

Mason jar /ˈ·· ·/ *n* [C] *AmE* a glass pot with a tight lid used for preserving fruit and vegetables【美】梅森瓶〔一種帶密封蓋的玻璃瓶, 用於保存水果和蔬菜〕

ma·son·ry /ˋmesn̩rɪ; ˈmeɪsənri/ *n* [U] **1** the stones and MORTAR (=material which holds stones together) from which a building, wall etc is made〔蓋房屋、砌牆等用的〕石料和砂漿: *Several people had been buried under falling masonry.* 好幾個人被埋在墜落的磚石下面。**2** the skill of building with stone 砌石技藝 **3** FREEMASONRY 共濟會的制度; 共濟會儀式

masque /mæsk; mɑːsk/ *n* [C] a play written in the 16th and 17th centuries that was written in poetry and included music, dancing, and songs 假面劇〔16、17 世紀以詩歌形式寫成的戲劇, 有音樂和歌舞〕

mas·que·rade¹ /ˏmæskəˋred; ˌmæskəˈreɪd/ *n* **1** [C] a formal dance where people wear MASKs and unusual clothes 假面舞會, 化裝舞會 **2** [C,U] a way of behaving or speaking that hides your true thoughts or feelings 偽裝; 掩飾: *She didn't really love him, but she kept up the masquerade for years.* 她並不真正愛他, 但她卻一直偽裝了許多年。**3** [C] *AmE old-fashioned* a party at which people wear unusual clothes【美, 過時】穿奇裝異服參加的聚會

masquerade² *v* [I] to pretend to be something or someone different 假裝; 偽裝; 假扮: [+as] *secret police officers masquerading as demonstrators* 偽裝成示威者的祕密警察

Mass /mæs; mæs/ *n* **1** [C,U] the main ceremony in some Christian churches, especially the Roman Catholic Church 彌撒: **say/celebrate Mass** (=perform this ceremony as a priest) 做/主持彌撒 **2** [C] a piece of music written to be played at this ceremony 彌撒曲: *Mozart's Mass in C Minor* 莫扎特的《C 小調彌撒曲》

2 **mass[1]** *n*

1 ►LARGE AMOUNT 大量◄ a) [C] a large amount of a substance, liquid, or gas, that does not have a clear shape 團, 塊, 堆: *The food had all congealed into a sticky mass.* 食物全都凝結成了黏糊糊的一團。| **[+of]** *A mass of almost pure white cloud lay below us.* 一團近乎純白的雲朵飄浮在我們下面。**b) a mass of** a large amount or quantity of something 大量, 大宗: *a huge mass of data* 大量資料 | *The yard was just a mass of weeds.* 院子裡簡直是雜草叢生。**c) masses of** *BrE informal* a large amount of something, or a lot of people or things【英, 非正式】許多的, 大量的〔人或物〕: *Masses of books covered every surface in the room.* 大量的書籍攤滿了整個房間。| *We still had masses of time to spare.* 我們仍然可以抽出許多時間。

2 ►CROWD 人羣◄ [singular] a large crowd 一大羣人: **[+of]** *There was a mass of people around the club entrance.* 俱樂部門口聚集着一大羣人。| **a solid mass** *The road was blocked by a solid mass of protesters.* 道路被密密麻麻的抗議者阻塞了。

3 the masses all the ordinary people in society who do not have power or influence, and are thought of as not being very educated 羣眾, 平民

4 the mass of people/workers/the population etc most of the people in a group or society; the MAJORITY 人民/工人/人口等的大多數: *The mass of black children there have fewer educational opportunities than their white counterparts.* 那裡的大多數黑人孩子受教育的機會比當地的白人孩子都要少。

5 ►SCIENCE 科學◄ [U] *technical* in science, mass is the amount of material in something【術語】質量: *the mass of a star* 恒星的質量

3 **mass[2]** *adj* [only before noun 僅用於名詞前] **1** involving or intended for a very large number of people 民眾的, 羣眾的; 大量的: *Radio can reach mass audiences.* 無線廣播能夠覆蓋大量的聽眾。| *a mass protest* 羣眾抗議 **2 mass murderer** someone who has murdered a lot of people 殺了很多人的兇手

mass[3] *v* [I,T] to come together, or make people or things come together, in a large group 聚集, 集結, 集中: *grey clouds massing behind the mountains* 灰色雲團在羣山之後積聚 | *The country massed several divisions of troops along its border.* 該國沿其邊境地區集結了好幾個師的軍隊。

mas·sa·cre[1] /ˈmæsəkɚ; ˈmæsəkə/ *v* [T] **1** to kill a lot of people, especially people who cannot defend themselves 大規模屠殺: *The army massacred 642 French civilians.* 那支軍隊屠殺了 642 個法國平民。—see 見 KILL[1] (USAGE) **2** *informal* to defeat someone very badly in a game or competition【非正式】〔在比賽或競爭中〕徹底擊敗

massacre[2] *n* **1** [C,U] the killing of a lot of people, especially people who cannot defend themselves 大屠殺: *One man, the only survivor of the massacre, lived to tell the gruesome story.* 一個男人 —— 那次大屠殺的唯一倖存者 —— 活了下來講述當時發生的令人毛骨悚然的事。**2** [C] *informal* a very bad defeat in a game or competition【非正式】〔比賽或競爭中的〕慘敗: *United lost in a 9-0 massacre.* 聯隊以九比零慘敗。

mas·sage[1] /məˈsɑʒ; ˈmæsɑːʒ/ *n* [C,U] the action of pressing and rubbing someone's body with your hands, to help them relax or to reduce pain in their muscles 按摩; 推拿: *Massage helps ease the pain.* 按摩有助於緩解疼痛。| **give/have a massage** *She gave me a relaxing massage.* 她給我作了一次按摩, 讓我放鬆下來。

massage[2] *v* [T] **1** to press and rub someone's body with your hands, to help them relax or to reduce pain in their muscles 為…作按摩, 給…推拿: *Alex massaged Helena's aching back.* 亞歷克斯給海倫娜疼痛的脊背作了推拿。—see picture on page A20 參見 A20 頁圖 **2** to change official numbers or information in order to make them seem better than they are 篡改〔官方數字或資料〕: *massaging the unemployment statistics* 篡改失業統計數據 **3 massage sb's ego** to try to make someone feel that they are important, attractive, intelligent etc 對某人討好奉承, 拍某人的馬屁: *secretaries who are expected to drop everything to get coffee or massage their boss's ego* 被指望放下一切事情為老闆端來咖啡或對其討好奉承的秘書們

massage par·lour *BrE*【英】, **massage parlor** *AmE*【美】/ˈ·· ˌ··/ *n* [C] **1** a word meaning a BROTHEL (=place where people pay to have sex), used to pretend that it is not a brothel〔打着按摩院旗號以掩人耳目的〕妓院 **2** a place where you pay to have a MASSAGE 按摩院

masse —see 見 EN MASSE

massed /mæst; mæst/ *adj* **massed bands/choirs etc** a large number of musical groups playing together as one very large group 聯合大樂隊/大合唱團等

mas·seur /mæˈsɝ; mæˈsɜː/ *n* [C] someone who gives MASSAGE*s* 按摩師

mas·seuse /mæˈsɜz; mæˈsɜːz/ *n* [C] a woman who gives MASSAGE*s* 女按摩師

mas·sif /mæˈsif; ˈmæsiːf/ *n* [C] *technical* a group of mountains forming one large solid shape【術語】山巒, 山岳

mas·sive /ˈmæsɪv; ˈmæsɪv/ *adj* **1** very large, solid, and heavy 大而重的, 厚重的: *The bell is massive, weighing over 40 tons.* 那口鐘非常大, 重量超過 40 噸。| *the castle's massive walls* 城堡的高大圍牆 **2** unusually large, powerful, or damaging 巨大的; 強大的, 強烈的; 極具破壞力的: *a massive tax bill* 一張巨額稅單 | *I had a massive argument with Vicky yesterday.* 我昨天同維基進行了一場十分激烈的辯論。| **a massive stroke/heart attack etc** *He suffered a massive haemorrhage.* 他遭受了一次大出血。 2 3

mass me·di·a /ˌ· ˈ···/ *n* **the mass media** all the people and organizations that provide information and news for the public, including television, radio, and newspapers 大眾傳播媒介〔包括電視、廣播和報刊〕

mass-pro·duced /ˌ· ·ˈ·◂/ *adj* produced in large numbers using machinery, so that each object is the same and can be sold cheaply〔用機器〕大規模生產的, 大批量生產的: *mass-produced furniture* 大批量生產的家具 —**mass-produce** *v* [T] —**mass production** *n* [U]

mast /mæst; mɑːst/ *n* [C] **1** a tall pole on which the sails or flags on a ship are hung 船桅: **two/three masted** (=having two or three masts) 二/三桅的 —see picture at 參見 YACHT 圖 **2** *BrE* a tall metal tower that sends out radio and television signals【英】〔發射無線電和電視信號的〕發射塔, 天線塔 **3** a tall pole on which a flag is hung 旗桿 —see also 另見 HALF-MAST

mas·tec·to·my /mæsˈtɛktəmɪ; mæˈstektəmi/ *n* [C] *technical* a medical operation to remove a breast【術語】乳房切除手術

Mas·ter /ˈmæstɚ; ˈmɑːstə/ *n* [C] **1** *old-fashioned* a way of addressing or referring to young boys【過時】少爺〔對小男孩的稱呼或用於指小男孩〕: *How's young Master Toby today?* 托比小少爺今天好嗎? **2** a religious leader in some religions 宗教領袖: *a Sufi Master* 一位〔伊斯蘭教〕蘇非派領袖 **3** the person who is in charge of some British university colleges〔英國某些大學學院的〕院長: *the Master of Trinity College, Cambridge* 劍橋大學三一學院院長

master[1] *n* [C]

1 ►OWNER/LEADER 主人/領導◄ *old-fashioned* a man who has control or authority over other people, for example servants or workers【過時】主人; 雇主: *His staff were always very loyal to their master.* 他的所有雇員總

是對雇主忠心耿耿。| **be your own master** (=control your own work or life) 自己當老闆, 自己作主 *I started this business because I wanted to be my own master.* 我開這家公司是因為我想自己當老闆。—compare 比較 MISTRESS

2 be master of to be in complete control of a situation 完全控制, 掌握: *Without these changes, Africa cannot be master of its own economic destiny.* 沒有這些變化, 非洲就不能掌握自己的經濟命運。

3 ▶SKILLED 有技能的◀ someone who is very skilled at something 大師; 能手; 手工藝靈巧的人: *Runyon was a master of the short story.* 魯尼恩是一位短篇小說大師。| *learning from an acknowledged master* 向公認的大師學習

4 be a past master to be very good at doing something because you have done it a lot 擅長於, 善於, 精於: **[+at/in/of]** *He's a past master at getting free drinks out of people.* 他十分善於讓人家請他喝酒。

5 ▶ORIGINAL 原物◀ a document, record etc from which copies are made 原件; 原版; 母(磁)帶: *I gave him the master to copy.* 我把原件給他複製。

6 ▶TEACHER 教師◀ *BrE old-fashioned* a male teacher【英, 過時】男教師: *the maths master* 男數學教師 —see also 另見 HEADMASTER

7 ▶DOG OWNER 狗的主人◀ the male owner of a dog 狗的男主人: *a dog and its master* 狗和牠的男主人

8 ▶SHIP 船◀ someone who commands a ship 船長 —see also 另見 GRAND MASTER, OLD MASTER, QUIZ-MASTER

master² *v* [T] **1** to learn a skill or a language so well that you understand it completely and have no difficulty with it 掌握, 精通: *that well-known difficulty of mastering the Chinese writing system* 掌握漢語書寫系統那個眾所周知的難題 **2 master your fear/weakness etc** to manage to control a strong emotion 控制住你的恐懼/軟弱等

master³ *adj* [only before noun 僅用於名詞前] **1 master copy/list/tape etc** the original thing from which copies are made 原始拷貝/清單/磁帶等: *the master list of telephone numbers* 電話號碼表的原件 **2** most important or main 最重要的; 主要的: *the master control center at NASA* 〔美國〕太空總署的主要控制中心 **3 master craftsman/chef/plumber etc** someone who is very skilled at a particular job, especially a job that involves working with your hands 一流工匠/主廚/熟練水管工等

master-at-arms /,‥ · ˈ·/ *n* [C] an officer with police duties on a ship 船上的警衛官

master bed·room /ˈ‥ ,‥/ *n* [C] the largest bedroom in a house or apartment, often with its own bathroom 主臥室

master class /ˈ‥ ·/ *n* [C] a lesson, especially in music, given to very skilful students by someone famous 大師課〔由名家給優秀生講授的課, 尤指音樂課〕

mas·ter·ful /ˈmæstɚfəl; ˈmɑːstəfəl/ *adj* **1** controlling people or situations in a skilful and confident way 善於控制人[局勢]的: *We allowed him to take charge in his masterful way.* 我們讓他以他那把握十足的方式負責把事情抓起來。**2** done with great skill and understanding 老練高明的: *a masterful analysis of the text* 對課文透徹的分析 —**masterfully** *adv*

master key /ˈ‥ ,·/ *n* [C] a key that will open all the door locks in a building 萬能鑰匙

mas·ter·ly /ˈmæstɚlɪ; ˈmɑːstəli/ *adj* done or made very skilfully 熟練的; 巧妙的; 高明的: *a masterly analysis of the situation* 對局勢高明的分析

mas·ter·mind¹ /ˈmæstɚ,maɪnd; ˈmɑːstəmaɪnd/ *n* [singular] someone who plans and organizes a complicated operation, especially a criminal operation〔尤指犯罪活動的〕出謀劃策者: *the mastermind of an ingenious financial swindle* 一樁狡猾的金融詐騙案的謀劃者

mastermind² *v* [T] to think of, plan, and organize a large, important, and difficult operation 策劃, 組織〔重大而艱難的行動〕: *The election campaign was masterminded by Peter Walters.* 那次競選運動是由彼得·沃爾特斯策劃組織的。

Master of Arts /,‥ · ˈ·/ *n* [C] an MA 文學碩士; 文學碩士學位

master of ce·re·mo·nies /,‥ · ˈ‥‥/ *n* [C] someone who introduces speakers or performers at a social or public occasion 司儀; 典禮官; EMCEE *AmE*【美】: *the master of ceremonies for the Miss World Pageant* 世界小姐選美大賽的司儀

Master of Sci·ence /,‥ · ˈ‥/ *n* [C] an MSc 理學碩士; 理學碩士學位

mas·ter·piece /ˈmæstɚ,pis; ˈmɑːstəpiːs/ *n* [C] a work of art, piece of writing or music etc that is of very high quality or that is the best that a particular artist, writer etc has produced 傑作; 名作; 最佳作; 代表作: *Mary Shelley was just 18 when she wrote the horror masterpiece 'Frankenstein'.* 瑪麗·雪萊18歲時就寫出了恐怖小說名作《科學怪人》。| **a masterpiece of** (=a very good example of) 極好的例證 *His speech was a masterpiece of ambiguity.* 他的講話是含糊其辭的典範。

master plan /ˈ‥ ·/ *n* [C usually singular 一般用單數] a detailed plan for controlling everything that happens in a complicated situation 總體規劃: *an irrigation master plan* 灌溉總體規劃

mas·ter's /ˈmæstɚz; ˈmɑːstəz/ *n* [C] *informal* a MASTER'S DEGREE【非正式】碩士學位

master's de·gree /ˈ‥ ·,·/ *n* [C] a university degree such as an MA or an MSc, which you get by studying for one or two years after your first degree〔大學授予的文學或理學等〕碩士學位

mas·ter·stroke /ˈmæstɚ,strok; ˈmɑːstəstrəʊk/ *n* [C] a very clever, skilful, and often unexpected action that is completely successful 絕招, 高招; 妙舉: *a masterstroke of diplomacy* 高明的外交手腕

master switch /ˈ‥ ,·/ *n* [C] the SWITCH that controls the supply of electricity to the whole of a building or area〔電源的〕主控開關, 總開關

master·work /ˈmæstɚ,wɝk; ˈmɑːstəwɜːk/ *n* [C] a painting, SCULPTURE, piece of music etc that is the best that someone has done; MASTERPIECE〔油畫、雕塑、音樂作品等的〕傑作; 名作; 最佳作; 代表作

mas·ter·y /ˈmæstərɪ; ˈmɑːstəri/ *n* [U] **1** complete control or power over someone or something 完全控制; 控制權: **[+of/over]** *man's mastery over his environment* 人類對環境的控制 **2** thorough understanding or great skill 熟練; 精通: **[+of/over]** *She combines technical mastery of her instrument with great flair and originality.* 她把熟練的樂器演奏技巧與巨大的天賦和創造力結合在一起。

mast·head /ˈmæst,hɛd; ˈmɑːsthed/ *n* [C] **1** the name of a newspaper, magazine etc printed in a special design at the top of the first page〔以特別設計印在首頁上方的〕報刊[雜誌]名稱, 刊頭 **2** the top of a MAST on a ship〔船隻的〕桅頂

mas·tic /ˈmæstɪk; ˈmæstɪk/ *n* [U] a type of glue that does not crack or break when it is bent 瑪瑺脂; 膠黏劑, 膠合鋪料

mas·ti·cate /ˈmæstə,ket; ˈmæstɨkeɪt/ *v* [I,T] *technical* to CHEW (=crush food between the teeth)【術語】咀嚼 —**mastication** /,mæstəˈkeʃən; ,mæstɨˈkeɪʃən/ *n* [U]

mas·tiff /ˈmæstɪf; ˈmæstɨf/ *n* [C] a large, strong dog often used to guard houses〔常用於看家的〕大馴犬

mas·tur·bate /ˈmæstɚ,bet; ˈmæstəbeɪt/ *v* [I] to make yourself sexually excited by touching or rubbing your sexual organs 手淫, 自瀆, 自慰 —**masturbation** /,mæstɚˈbeʃən; ,mæstəˈbeɪʃən/ *n* [U]

mat¹ /mæt; mæt/ *n* [C] **1** a small piece of thick rough material which covers part of a floor 地墊; 地蓆; 小地毯: *Wipe your feet on the mat.* 在地墊上蹭蹭你的腳。**2** a small flat piece of wood, cloth etc which protects a surface, especially on a table〔尤指用以保護桌面的木質或布質〕小墊子 **3** a piece of thick soft material used in some sports for people to fall onto〔某些體育運動中用的〕厚軟墊 **4 a mat of hair/fur/grass etc** a thick mass of pieces of hair etc which are stuck together〔絞在一起的〕一簇頭髮/獸毛/草等 —see also 另見 MATTING

mat² *adj* another spelling of MATT matt的另一種拼法

mat·a·dor /ˋmætəˏdɔr; ˈmætədɔː/ *n* [C] a man who fights and kills BULLS during a BULLFIGHT 鬥牛士

matador 鬥牛士

3 3 **match¹** /mætʃ; mætʃ/ *n*

1 ►FIRE 火◄ [C] a small wooden or paper stick, used to light a fire, cigarette etc 火柴: *a box of matches* 一盒火柴 | **strike a match** (=rub a match against a surface to produce a flame) 劃火柴 | **put a match to** (=make something burn by using a match) 用火柴點燃 *I tore up the letter and put a match to it.* 我把信撕碎, 然後用火柴把它點着了。 —see picture at 參見 LABORATORY 圖

2 ►GAME 比賽◄ [C] *especially BrE* an organized sports event between two teams or people【尤英】比賽, 競賽: *a violent incident during Chelsea's match against Liverpool* 在車路士隊對利物浦隊的比賽中發生的暴力事件 | *a cricket match* 板球比賽

3 ►COLOURS/PATTERNS 顏色/圖案◄ [singular] something that is the same colour or pattern as something else, or looks attractive with it〔顏色或圖案上的〕相似[相配]之物: **[+for]** *That shirt's a perfect match for your blue skirt.* 那件襯衫和你的藍裙子完全相配。

4 be more than a match for to be much stronger, cleverer etc than an opponent 比…強[聰明]得多, 遠勝過

5 be no match for to be much less strong, clever etc than an opponent 根本不是…的對手: *Carlos was no match for the champion.* 卡洛斯遠遠不是那位冠軍的對手。

6 a slanging/shouting match a loud angry argument in which two people insult each other 相互高聲謾罵

7 be a perfect match if two people who love each other are a perfect match, they are very suitable for each other 天作之合, 非常般配的一對

8 make a good match *old-fashioned* to marry a suitable person【過時】結成良緣

9 ►SUITABILITY 適宜◄ [singular] a situation in which something is suitable for something else, so that the two things work together successfully 適合, 適應; 匹配: **[+between]** *We need to establish a match between students' needs and teaching methods.* 我們有必要使教學方法適應學生的需要。—see also 另見 **meet your match** (MEET¹ (16)), **mix and match** (MIX¹ (7))

2 2 **match²** *v*

1 ►LOOK GOOD TOGETHER 互相匹配, 相稱◄ [I,T] if one thing matches another, or if two things match, they look attractive together because they have a similar colour, pattern etc (與…) 相配, 相稱: *The towels match the color of the bathroom tiles.* 這些毛巾和浴室瓷磚的色調很匹配。| **sth to match** (=something which matches) 相配之物 *a dining table with four chairs to match* 餐桌和與之相配的四把椅子 —see also 另見 MATCHING —see 見 FIT¹ (USAGE)

2 ►LOOK THE SAME 看起來相同◄ [I,T] if one thing matches another or if two things match, they look the same (與…) 成對: *Your socks don't match.* 你那兩隻襪子不是一雙。

3 ►SEEM THE SAME 好像一樣, 相似◄ [I,T] if two reports or pieces of information match, or if one matches the other, there is no important difference between them (和…) 相似, (和…) 基本一致: *The witnesses' stories just didn't match.* 證人的證詞不能相互印證。| *Traces of blood on the knife matched the suspect's blood-type.* 刀上的血跡與嫌疑犯的血型一致。

4 ►PROVIDE WHAT IS NEEDED 提供所需之物◄ [T] to provide something that is suitable for a situation or enough for the people who need it 適應, 滿足: *creating sufficient employment to match the rising population* 創造足夠的就業機會以適應日益增長的人口的需要 | *teaching materials that match the individual needs of students* 適應學生各自所需的教材

5 ►FIND STH/SB SIMILAR 找到相似的物/人◄ [T] to find something that is similar to or suitable for something else 找到與…相似[相配]之物: **match sth/sb to** *We get the children to match the animal pictures to the correct sounds.* 我們讓孩子們把動物圖片與正確的聲音相配對。

6 ►BE AS GOOD AS 與…一樣好◄ [T] to be as skilful, intelligent etc as something or someone else 敵得過; 比得上: *No one can match Holden when it comes to winning an argument.* 說到在爭論中獲勝沒有人比得上霍爾登。| *I've never seen a goal to match that one.* 我從未見過哪一次進球堪與那次相媲美。

7 well-matched/ill-matched very suitable/very unsuitable for each other 很相配的/很不相配的: *a well-matched pair* 十分相配的一對

8 evenly matched if two competitors are evenly matched they are equal in strength, skill, speed etc 旗鼓相當的, 勢均力敵的

9 ►GIVE MONEY 提供資金◄ [T] to give a sum of money equal to a sum given by someone else 提供〔同等數額的資金〕: *The government has promised to match any private donations to the earthquake fund.* 政府已經承諾給防震基金提供與個人捐款等額的資金。

10 ►MAKE EQUAL 使相等◄ [T] to make something equal to or suitable for something else 使相等; 使相適應: **match sth to sth** *Match your spending to your income.* 你應該量入為出。

11 be matched with/against to be competing against someone else in a game or competition〔在體育運動或競賽中〕與…相較量: *Agassi will be matched against Sampras in the men's final.* 阿加斯在男子決賽中將與森柏斯對陣。

match up *phr v* **1** [I] if two reports or pieces of information match up, they seem the same〔兩則報道或消息〕相似 **2 [match sth up to sth]** to find something that is similar to or suitable for something else 把…和…配對起來 **3 match up to your hopes/expectations/ideals etc** to be as good as you expected, hoped etc 和所希望/期待/想像等的同樣好

match·book /ˋmætʃbʊk; ˈmætʃbʊk/ *n* [C] a small folded piece of thick paper containing paper matches 紙夾火柴

match·box /ˋmætʃˏbɑks; ˈmætʃbɒks/ *n* [C] a small box containing matches 火柴盒

match·ing /ˋmætʃɪŋ; ˈmætʃɪŋ/ *adj* having the same colour, style, or pattern as something else〔與某物顏色、風格或式樣〕相同的, 相配的: *pink cushions and a matching bedspread* 粉色的墊子和與之相配的牀罩

match·less /ˋmætʃlɪs; ˈmætʃləs/ *adj literary* more intelligent, beautiful etc than anyone or anything else【文】無可匹敵的, 無雙的: *the matchless beauty of the Parthenon* 巴特農神殿那無與倫比的美

match·mak·er /ˋmætʃˏmekɚ; ˈmætʃˏmeɪkə/ *n* [C] someone who tries to find a suitable partner for someone else to marry 媒人 —**matchmaking** *n* [U]

match point /ˏ· ˈ·/ *n* **1** [U] a situation in tennis when the person who wins the next point will win the match〔網球賽中再贏得一分即能勝出的〕決勝時刻 **2** [C] the point that a player must win in order to win the match 賽點, 決勝分 —compare 比較 GAME POINT

match·stick /ˋmætʃˏstɪk; ˈmætʃˏstɪk/ *n* [C] **1** a wooden

M

MATCH[1] (1) 火柴桿, 火柴棍 **2 matchstick men/figures** people drawn with thin lines to represent their arms, legs, and bodies, as if by a child〔似小孩所畫的〕火柴棍人/人形

match·wood /ˋmætʃˌwʊd; ˈmætʃwʊd/ *n* **break/splinter etc into matchwood** to be broken into very small pieces of wood 裂成碎木片: *Their boat hit the rocks and splintered into matchwood.* 他們的小船撞在岩石上, 裂成了碎片。

3 **mate[1]** /met; meɪt/ *n*
1 schoolmate/roommate/workmate etc someone you study with, live with etc 同學/同屋/同事等: *My flatmate and I aren't getting on very well!* 與我同住一套公寓的那個人跟我不大合得來! —see also 另見 RUNNING MATE, SOUL MATE
2 ►FRIEND 朋友◄ a) [C] *BrE informal* a friend【英, 非正式】朋友, 夥伴: *I'm going out with my mates tonight.* 今天晚上我要跟夥伴們出去。**b)** *BrE and AustrE informal* used by men as a friendly way to address a man【英和澳, 非正式】〔男人對男人友好的稱呼〕老兄: *What's the time, mate?* 老兄, 幾點了?
3 ►ANIMAL 動物◄ [C] the sexual partner of an animal〔動物的〕配偶
4 ►HUSBAND/WIFE 夫/妻◄ *especially AmE* a word meaning your husband or wife, used especially in magazines【尤美】〔尤用於雜誌中〕丈夫; 妻子; 配偶: *Does your mate snore?* 你愛人打呼嚕嗎?
5 ►PAIR OF OBJECTS 物體的一對◄ [C] *especially AmE* one of a pair of objects【尤美】一對中的一個, 配對物: *I can't find the mate to my glove.* 我找不到我的另一隻手套了。
6 ►SAILOR 海員◄ [C] a ship's officer who is one rank below the captain〔船上的〕大副
7 ►NAVY OFFICER 海軍軍官◄ [C] a US Navy PETTY OFFICER〔美國海軍的〕軍士
8 builder's mate/plumber's mate etc *BrE* someone who works with and helps a skilled worker; ASSISTANT【英】建築工/管子工等的助手
9 ►GAME 比賽◄ [C,U] CHECKMATE in the game of CHESS〔國際象棋比賽中王棋的〕將死

mate[2] *v* **1** [I+with] if animals mate, they have sex to produce babies〔動物〕交配 **2** [T] to put animals together so that they will have sex and produce babies 使〔動物〕交配 **3** [T] to achieve the CHECKMATE of your opponent in CHESS〔國際象棋中〕將死

ma·ter /ˋmetɚ; ˈmeɪtə/ *n* [C] *BrE old-fashioned or humorous* mother【英, 過時或幽默】母親, 媽媽 —compare 比較 PATER

1 **ma·te·ri·al[1]** /məˋtɪrɪəl; məˈtɪəriəl/ *n* **1** [C,U] cloth used
1 for making clothes, curtains etc; FABRIC (1) 料子, 衣料, 布料: *curtain material* 窗簾布 —see picture at 參見 CLOTHES 圖 **2** [C,U] a solid substance such as wood, plastic, or metal from which things can be made 材料, 原料〈如木材、塑料、金屬等〉: *building materials* 建築材料 **3** [U] also 又作 **materials** [plural] the things that are used for making or doing something 材料: *Videos often make good teaching material.* 錄像帶常常可用作很好的教學材料。| *artists' materials* 藝術家使用的材料 **4** [U] information or ideas used in books, films etc〔用於書本、電影等中的〕素材: *His act contains a lot of new material.* 他的表演中包含着許多新的素材。| **[+for]** *Anita is collecting material for her new novel.* 阿妮塔正在為她的新小說收集素材。**5 officer material/executive material etc** someone who is good enough for a particular job or position 當軍官/管理人員等的材料: *He's a good soldier, but not really officer material.* 他是個好士兵, 但不是當軍官的料。

3 **material[2]** *adj* [usually before noun 一般用於名詞前] **1** connected with people's money, possessions, living conditions etc, rather than the needs of their mind or soul 物質上的, 非精神上的: **material comforts/needs/well-being etc** *Improvements in health were linked to increasing material prosperity.* 健康水平的提高是與物質上的日益繁榮聯繫在一起的。**2** connected with the real world and physical objects 物質的, 實體的, 有形的: *material existence* 物質存在 **3** *law* important and needing to be considered when making a decision【法律】重要的, 需予以考慮的: *material evidence* 重要證據 | **[+to]** *facts material to the investigation* 對調查很重要的事實 **4** important and having a noticeable effect 重大並有顯著影響的: *material changes* 重大的變化 —see also 另見 MATERIALLY, RAW MATERIALS

ma·te·ri·al·is·m /məˋtɪrɪəlˌɪzəm; məˈtɪəriəlɪzəm/ *n* [U] **1** the belief that money and possessions are more important than art, religion, moral goodness etc 實利主義, 物質主義〔認為錢財比藝術、宗教、道德等更為重要的信仰〕**2** *technical* the belief that only physical things really exist【術語】唯物主義, 唯物論 —**materialist** *adj, n* [C]

ma·te·ri·a·lis·tic /məˌtɪrɪəlˋɪstɪk; məˌtɪəriəˈlɪstɪk◂/ *adj* caring only about money and possessions rather than things of the mind such as art or religion 實利主義的, 物質主義的: *People nowadays are so materialistic.* 現在的人太實利主義了。—**materialistically** /-klɪ; -kli/ *adv*

ma·te·ri·al·ize also 又作 **-ise** *BrE*【英】/məˋtɪrɪəlˌaɪz; məˈtɪəriəlaɪz/ *v* [I] **1** to happen or appear in the way that you planned or expected 成為現實, 實現;〔像計劃或預期的那樣〕發生, 出現: *The money we had been promised failed to materialize.* 答應給我們的錢並沒有兑現。**2** to appear in an unexpected and strange way 突然出現: *The figure of a man suddenly materialized in the shadows.* 在陰暗的地方突然出現了一個人影。—**materialization** /məˌtɪrɪələˋzeʃən; məˌtɪəriəlaɪˈzeɪʃən/ *n* [U]

ma·te·ri·al·ly /məˋtɪrɪəlɪ; məˈtɪəriəli/ *adv* **1** in a big enough or strong enough way to change a situation 極大地; 強有力地; 實質性地: *This would materially affect US security.* 這將會嚴重影響美國的安全。| *This improvement is not materially significant.* 這一改進在實質上並不重要。**2** in a way that concerns possessions and money, rather than the needs of a person's mind or soul 物質上: *Materially we are better off than ever before.* 在物質上我們比以前任何時候都好。

ma·té·ri·el /məˌtɪrɪˋɛl; məˌtɪəriˈel/ *n* [U] supplies of weapons used by an army〔供軍隊使用的〕武器裝備

ma·ter·nal /məˋtɝnḷ; məˈtɜːnl/ *adj* **1** typical of the way a good mother behaves or feels 母性的; 慈母似的: *I'm not maternal enough to have kids.* 我母性不夠, 不能要孩子。| *She kept a maternal eye on them all.* 她像母親似地照管着他們所有人。| **maternal instincts** (=the desire to have babies and take care of them) 母親的天性, 母性 **2** [only before noun 僅用於名詞前] of a mother or connected with being a mother 母親的; 與做母親有關的: *the relationship between maternal age and infant mortality* 生育年齡與嬰兒死亡率之間的關係 **3 maternal grandfather/aunt etc** your mother's father, sister etc 外祖父/姨母等〔母方的親戚〕—compare 比較 PATERNAL —**maternally** *adv*

ma·ter·ni·ty[1] /məˋtɝnətɪ; məˈtɜːnəti/ *adj* [only before noun 僅用於名詞前] **1 maternity clothes/dress etc** clothes etc used by women who are PREGNANT (=going to have a baby) 孕婦裝等 **2 maternity benefits/pay/allowance** the money that a woman is given by an employer or a government when she has a baby〔由雇主或政府支付的〕產婦津貼

maternity[2] *n* [U] the state of being a mother 母性; 母親身分

maternity leave /·ˈ··· ˌ·/ *n* [U] time that a mother is allowed to spend away from work when she has a baby 產假

maternity ward /·ˈ··· ˌ·/ *n* [C] a department in a hospital where women who are having babies are cared for 產科病房

mat·ey[1] /ˋmetɪ; ˈmeɪti/ *adj BrE informal* behaving as if you were someone's friend【英，非正式】友好的；親近的；親熱的：*She's been very matey with the boss recently.* 她近來跟老闆很親近。

matey² *n BrE* used by men as a very informal or disrespectful way of addressing other men【英】夥計〔男子之間十分隨便或不講禮貌的稱呼〕

2 **math** /mæθ; mæθ/ *n* [U] *AmE* mathematics【美】數學

math·e·mat·i·cal /ˌmæθəˋmætɪkl̩; ˌmæθɪ̇ˈmætɪkəl◂/ *adj* **1** connected with or using mathematics 數學的：*a mathematical equation* 數學方程 | *mathematical analysis* 數學分析 **2** calculating things in a careful, exact way 仔細而準確計算的：*The whole trip was planned with mathematical precision.* 整個旅行計劃得十分周密。**3 a mathematical certainty** something that is completely certain to happen 肯定會發生的事，確定無疑的事 **4 a mathematical chance (of)** a very small chance that something will happen 極小的可能性 —**mathematically** /-kl̩ɪ; -kli/ *adv*

math·e·ma·ti·cian /ˌmæθəməˋtɪʃən; ˌmæθɪ̇məˈtɪʃən/ *n* [C] someone who studies or teaches mathematics, or is a specialist in mathematics 數學家；數學教師

math·e·mat·ics /ˌmæθəˋmætɪks; ˌmæθɪ̇ˈmætɪks/ *n* [U] the science of numbers and of shapes, including ALGEBRA, GEOMETRY, and ARITHMETIC 數學

mathematical notations 數學符號

- = is equal to 等號
- ≠ is not equal to 不等號
- > is greater than 大於號
- < is less than 小於號
- ≥ is greater than or equal to 大於等於號
- ≤ is less than or equal to 小於等於號
- + add 加號
- − subtract 減號
- ÷ divide 除號
- × multiply 乘號

2 **maths** /mæθs; mæθs/ *n* [U] *BrE informal* mathematics【英，非正式】數學

mat·i·née /ˌmætn̩ˋe; ˈmætɪ̇neɪ/ *n* [C] a performance of a play or film in the afternoon〔戲劇或電影的〕下午場，午後的演出[放映]

matinée i·dol /ˈ··· ˌ··/ *n* [C] *old-fashioned* an actor who is very popular with women【過時】受女觀眾歡迎的男演員，女人的男偶像

matinée jack·et /ˈ··· ˌ··/ *n* [C] *old-fashioned BrE* a short coat for a baby【過時，英】嬰兒短外套

mat·ing /ˋmetɪŋ; ˈmeɪtɪŋ/ *n* [U] sex between animals〔動物的〕交配，交尾：*the mating season* 交配季節

mat·ins, mattins /ˋmætɪnz; ˈmætɪ̇nz/ *n* [U] the first prayers of the day in the Christian religion; MORNING PRAYER〔基督教的〕晨禱

matri- /metrɪ; meɪtrɪ/ *prefix* **1** concerning mothers 母親的：*matricide* (=killing one's own mother) 弒母 **2** concerning women 婦女的：*a matriarchal society* (=controlled by women) 女性統治的社會；母系社會 —compare 比較 PATRI-

ma·tri·arch /ˋmetrɪˌɑrk; ˈmeɪtriɑːk/ *n* [C] a woman, especially an older woman, who controls a family or a social group 女家長；女族長；〔社會團體的〕女統治者 —compare 比較 PATRIARCH (1)

ma·tri·ar·chal /ˌmetrɪˋɑrkl̩; ˌmeɪtriˈɑːkəl◂/ *adj* **1** ruled or controlled by women 婦女統治[控制]的：*a matriarchal society* 女權制社會；母系社會 **2** connected with or typical of a matriarch 女家長的；女族長的

ma·tri·ar·chy /ˋmetrɪˌɑrkɪ; ˈmeɪtriɑːki/ *n* [C,U] **1** a social system in which the oldest woman controls a family and its possessions 母權制，母系制 **2** a society in which women hold all the power 女權制社會；母系社會 —compare 比較 PATRIARCHY

mat·ri·cide /ˋmetrəˌsaɪd; ˈmætrɪ̇saɪd/ *n* [U] the crime of murdering your own mother 弒母罪 —compare 比較 PARRICIDE (1), PATRICIDE

ma·tric·u·late /məˋtrɪkjəˌlet; məˈtrɪkjʊ̈leɪt/ *v* [I] to officially start a course as a student at a university〔在大學〕註冊入學 —**matriculation** /məˌtrɪkjəˋleʃən; məˌtrɪkjʊ̈ˈleɪʃən/ *n* [U]

mat·ri·mo·ny /ˋmætrəˌmonɪ; ˈmætrɪ̇məni/ *n* [U] *formal* the state of being married【正式】婚姻；婚姻生活 —**matrimonial** /ˌmætrəˋmonɪəl; ˌmætrɪ̇ˈməʊniəl/ *adj*

ma·trix /ˋmetrɪks; ˈmeɪtrɪks/ *n plural* **matrices** /-trɪˌsiz; -trɪ̇siːz/ *or* **matrixes** [C] *technical*【術語】**1** an arrangement of numbers, letters, or signs on a GRID (=a background of regular lines) used in mathematics, science etc〔數學等的〕矩陣 **2** a situation from which a person or society can grow and develop〔人或社會的〕發源地，搖籃：*the cultural matrix* 文化發源地 **3** a living part in which something is formed or developed, such as the substance out of which the FINGERNAILs grow 基質；牀〈如指甲牀〉 **4** a MOULD (=a hollow container) into which melted metal, plastic, etc is poured to form a shape 鑄模，模子 **5** the rock in which hard stones or jewels have formed〔形成硬石或寶石的〕母岩，脈岩 —see also 另見 DOT-MATRIX PRINTER

ma·tron /ˋmetrən; ˈmeɪtrən/ *n* [C] **1** *BrE* a woman who works as a nurse in a school【英】〔學校的〕女護士，女總管 **2** *especially AmE* a woman who is in charge of women and children, for example in a prison【尤美】〔監獄等的〕女看守 **3** *BrE old-fashioned* a nurse who is in charge of the other nurses in a hospital【英，過時】護士長 **4** *especially literary* an older married woman【尤文】較年長的已婚婦女

ma·tron·ly /ˋmetrənlɪ; ˈmeɪtrənli/ *adj* a word to describe a woman who is fairly fat and no longer young, used to avoid saying this directly 發福的〔委婉語，用於較年長的女性〕

matron of hon·our *BrE*【英】, **matron of honor** *AmE*【美】/ˌ·· · ˈ··/ *n* [C] a married woman who helps the bride on her wedding day〔已婚的〕女儐相，伴娘 —compare 比較 BRIDESMAID

matt, mat, matte /mæt; mæt/ *adj* matt paint, colour, or photographs have a dull surface; not shiny〔油漆、顏色或照片〕表面無光澤的，暗淡的：*matt black* 無光黑色 —compare 比較 GLOSS¹ (4)

mat·ted /ˋmætɪd; ˈmætɪ̇d/ *adj* twisted or stuck together in a thick mass 纏結在一起的；亂成一團的：*matted fur* 纏結的亂毛 | *His hair was dirty and matted.* 他的頭髮很髒，而且亂蓬蓬的。

1
1 **mat·ter¹** /ˋmætɚ; ˈmætə/ *n*

① SUBJECT/SITUATION 事情/事態
② STH WRONG WITH ...出了問題
③ NO MATTER 無論
④ AS A MATTER OF 作為…的事
⑤ IT'S A MATTER OF 是…的問題
⑥ SMALL AMOUNT 少量
⑦ BOOKS/NEWSPAPERS 書籍/報紙
⑧ SUBSTANCE 物質
⑨ OTHER MEANINGS 其他意思

① SUBJECT/SITUATION 事情/事態

1 [C] a subject or situation that you have to think about or deal with 事情，情況：*You do realize this is a serious matter, don't you?* 你確實意識到這是一件嚴肅的事情，對吧？| *He wasn't particularly interested in financial matters.* 他對財務上的事不是特別感興趣。| **a matter of importance/concern/regret etc** (=a subject that is important, that people worry about etc) 重要／人們關

M

注/令人遺憾等的事情 *Wilson always consulted Landers on matters of importance.* 在重要問題上威爾遜總是和蘭德斯商量。| *The King's mental state was becoming a matter of concern.* 國王的精神狀況正成為一件人們關注的事。| **be a matter for** (=be something that a particular person or group should deal with) 是〔某人或團體〕應該處理的事 *If he was murdered, it's a matter for the police.* 如果他是被謀殺的, 那麼就該由警察來管了。| **the heart/crux of the matter** (=the most important part of a situation) 問題的核心 *The report didn't get to the heart of the matter.* 報告沒有觸及問題的核心。| **raise the matter with** (=discuss a subject with someone) 與〔某人〕討論問題; 向〔某人〕提出問題 *Have you raised the matter with your union representative?* 你與你們的工會代表討論過這個問題嗎? | **let the matter rest/drop** (=decide to stop worrying about something) 不再操心某事 *I'm prepared to let the whole matter drop if he apologizes.* 如果他道歉的話, 我準備讓整個事情到此為止。| **the matter at/in hand** (=the thing that you should be dealing with now) 目前需辦理的事情 *Could we please concentrate on the matter in hand?* 我們可以集中精力處理手頭上的事嗎?

2 subject matter the subject that is discussed or shown in a book, film, article etc〔書、電影、文章等的〕主題, 內容, 素材: *Because of its adult subject matter, the film is not suitable for under-16s.* 這部電影是成人題材的, 所以不適合 16 歲以下的少年兒童觀看。

3 it's no small/laughing matter used to say that something must be treated seriously 決不是小事/開玩笑的事〔用以表示某事必須嚴肅對待〕: *He ended up with a broken pelvis, which is no laughing matter, I can tell you.* 他最後弄得骨盆折斷了, 我可以告訴你, 這不是鬧着玩的事情。

4 that's the end of the matter/let that be an end to the matter *spoken* used to tell someone that you do not want to talk about something any more【口】此事到此為止〔用以表示不想再談論某事〕: *We will not let you date until you're 16, and that's the end of the matter.* 你 16 歲之前我們不會讓你約會的, 這事不要再談了。

5 be a different matter also 又作 **be quite another matter** *especially BrE* used to say that one situation or problem is much more serious than another【尤英】不是一回事, 完全是另一碼事〔用以表示某個情況或問題比另一個嚴重得多〕: *Having the occasional drink is one thing, but being drunk every night is quite another matter.* 偶爾喝點酒是一回事, 但每晚都喝醉就完全是另一碼事了。

6 matters *plural* a situation that you are in or have been describing 事態; 談到的情況: *Maybe some of these suggestions will help to improve matters.* 也許這些建議中有些將有助於事態的好轉。| **not help matters** *spoken* (=make a situation worse)【口】使情況更糟 *I had a headache when I took the test, which didn't help matters.* 測驗的時候我頭疼起來, 這使情況變得更糟了。

7 to make matters worse making a bad situation even worse 使不好的情況更糟: *The car had broken down, and to make matters worse, it was beginning to rain.* 車子壞了, 更糟糕的是, 天下起雨來了。

8 take matters into your own hands to deal with a problem yourself because other people have failed to deal with it〔因別人不能處理而〕把事情接過來親自處理: *Local people took matters into their own hands and hired their own security guards.* 當地人自己動手來解決問題, 雇用了他們自己的保安人員。

② STH WRONG WITH ...出了問題

9 what's the matter?/is anything the matter? *spoken* used when someone seems upset, unhappy, or ill and you are asking them why【口】怎麼了?/有甚麼麻煩嗎?〔用以詢問某人生氣、不高興或生病的原因〕: *What's the matter, Mary? Have you been crying?* 怎麼啦, 瑪麗? 你一直在哭嗎?

10 what's the matter with *spoken* used to ask why something is not working normally, someone seems upset or ill, or something looks wrong【口】...怎麼啦, ...出甚麼毛病了: *What's the matter with Bill?* 比爾怎麼了? | *"The television had to go back to the store." "Why, what's the matter with it?"* "那台電視機不得不退回了商店。" "為甚麼, 它出甚麼毛病了?"

11 there's something the matter with/something's the matter with *spoken* used to say that something is not working normally, someone is upset or ill, or something looks wrong【口】〔某物〕運行不正常[有問題];〔某人〕生氣[生病]: *There's something the matter with the washing machine – it keeps leaking.* 洗衣機有毛病了 —— 它漏水漏個不停。

12 there's nothing the matter with *spoken* used to say that someone is not ill or upset, or that something is working properly or looks good【口】〔某人〕沒生病[生氣];〔某物〕一切正常, 看起來不錯: *There was nothing the matter with it when I lent it to him.* 我借給他的時候它並沒有甚麼毛病。| *There's nothing the matter with your haircut – I really like it!* 你的髮型不錯 —— 我很喜歡!

③ NO MATTER 無論

13 no matter how/where/what etc used to say that something is always the same whatever happens, or in spite of someone's efforts to change it 不管怎樣/哪裡/甚麼等: *No matter how hard he tried, he couldn't get her to change her mind.* 不管他怎樣努力勸說, 也沒能使她改變主意。| *My parents always waited up for me, no matter what time I got home.* 無論我甚麼時候回家, 父母總是等着我。

14 no matter what (happens) *spoken* used to say that you will definitely do something【口】不管(發生)甚麼事; 無論如何: *I'll call you tonight no matter what.* 我今晚無論如何都會給你打電話。

15 no matter *spoken* used to say that something you have asked about is not important【口】不要緊, 無關緊要: *"She's not in her office." "No matter, I'll try and call her at home."* "她不在辦公室裡。" "沒關係, 我給她家裡打電話試試看。"

④ AS A MATTER OF 作為...的事

16 as a matter of fact *especially spoken*【尤口】**a)** used when saying something, especially something surprising, that is connected with what you are talking about 事實上, 其實: *I knew him when we were in college – as a matter of fact we were on the same course.* 我們在大學的時候我就認識他 —— 事實上我們那時在學同樣的課程。**b)** used when you do not agree with what someone has just said 事實恰恰相反〔表示不同意某人剛說過的話〕: *No, I wasn't annoyed. As a matter of fact I was very glad to see them.* 不, 我並不生氣。恰恰相反, 見到他們我非常高興。

17 as a matter of interest *BrE spoken* used when you want to ask or tell someone something that is not really necessary【英口】出於興趣: *Just as a matter of interest, Tony, how much did you pay for your house?* 托尼, 我只是好奇, 你買這棟房子花了多少錢?

18 as a matter of course/routine as the correct and usual thing to do in a particular situation 作為理所當然的事/常規: *We will contact your former employer as a matter of course.* 我們當然會與你以前的雇主聯繫。

19 as a matter of principle/belief/policy etc because of your personal beliefs about what you should do 由於原則/信念/政策等的緣故: *They're supporting him as a matter of principle.* 基於原則他們支持他。

20 as a matter of urgency/priority *formal* done as quickly as possible because it is very important【正式】作為緊急/優先之事〔來處理〕: *I want a full safety check* *as a matter of urgency.* 我要求進行一次全面的緊急安全檢查。

⑤ **IT'S A MATTER OF** 是…的問題

21 it's/that's a matter of opinion used to say that people have different opinions about a subject 這是看法因人而異的問題: *Personally I can't stand rock music, but I suppose it's all a matter of opinion.* 就個人來說我受不了搖滾樂, 但我認為這完全是個見仁見智的問題。

22 it's only/just a matter of time used to say that something will definitely happen eventually 只是時間的問題〔用於説明某事終究會發生〕: *It's only a matter of time before somebody gets hurt.* 有人會受到傷害, 這只是遲早的事。

23 it's a matter of life and death used to say that a situation is extremely serious or dangerous and something must be done immediately 這是關乎生死的問題〔用於説明情況十分危急〕: *We wouldn't usually operate on a pregnant woman, unless it's a matter of life and death.* 我們通常不會給一位孕婦做手術, 除非情況十分危急。

24 it's (just) a matter of (doing) sth *spoken* used to say that you only have to do a particular thing, or do something in a particular way, in order to be successful 【口】(只) 是個 (做) 某事的問題: *Anyone can take good photographs – it's just a matter of being in the right place at the right time.* 任何人都能拍出好照片 —— 問題只是你是否在合適的時間和合適的地點。

25 it's a matter of taste/cost/luck etc used to say that what happens or what you decide depends on your judgment, how much something costs, how lucky you are etc 這是個人愛好/成本/運氣等的問題: *I can't say which wine is best – it's a matter of personal taste.* 我説不上哪種酒最好 —— 這是個人口味的問題。

26 the fact/truth of the matter (is) used to say what you think is really true 事實/事情真相 (是): *The sad fact of the matter is that Alice is just not good enough for the job.* 令人遺憾的事實是艾麗絲做這個工作就是不夠資格。| *He doesn't love her any more – that's the truth of the matter.* 他不再愛她了 —— 這就是事情的真相。

⑥ **SMALL AMOUNT** 少量

27 a matter of seconds/months/metres etc only a few seconds, metres etc 僅僅數秒/幾個月/幾米等: *The ambulance was there in a matter of minutes.* 僅僅幾分鐘後救護車就到那裡了。| *In 1914 everyone expected the war to be over in a matter of months.* 1914 年, 每個人都以為戰爭會在幾個月後結束。

⑦ **BOOKS/NEWSPAPERS** 書籍/報紙

28 reading/printed etc matter things that are written for people to read 閱讀材料/印刷品等

⑧ **SUBSTANCE** 物質

29 waste/solid/organic/vegetable etc matter a substance that consists of waste material, solid material etc 廢棄物/固體物質/有機物/植物性物質等

30 [U] *technical* the material that everything in the universe is made of, including solids, liquids, and gases 【術語】〔構成宇宙萬物的〕物質〔包括固體、液體和氣體〕

31 [U] a yellow or white substance that is found in wounds or next to your eye〔傷口裡的〕膿; 眼屎

⑨ **OTHER MEANINGS** 其他意思

32 or ... for that matter *spoken* used to say that what you are saying about one thing is also true about something else 【口】對…同樣如此: *Ben never touched beer, or any kind of alcohol for that matter.* 本從來不沾啤酒, 其實他是滴酒不沾。

33 there's the little matter of *spoken* used jokingly to remind someone about something important that they may have forgotten 【口】還有這麼一件小事〔以開玩笑的方式提醒某人他可能已忘記的要事〕: *OK, that's settled – but there's still the little matter of my fee to discuss.* 好, 這事就解決了 —— 但還有我的服務費這點小事要討論。—see also 另見 GREY MATTER, **not mince matters** (MINCE¹ (3)), **mind over matter** (MIND¹ (50))

1 3 **matter²** *v* [I] **1** to be important, especially to be important to you personally or to have a big effect on what happens〔尤指對某人自己或對發生之事〕重要, 要緊, 有關係: **it doesn't matter/it won't matter etc** *"We've missed the train!" "It doesn't matter, there's another one in 10 minutes."* "我們已經誤了火車了!" "沒關係, 10分鐘以後還有一班。" | **matter if** *Will it matter if I'm a little late?* 我晚來一會兒不要緊吧? | **matter about** *It won't matter about the mess – I'll clear it up later.* 髒亂沒關係 —— 我過一會兒就收拾。| **matter who/why/what etc** *It doesn't matter what you wear, as long as you look neat and tidy.* 只要看起來乾淨整潔, 你穿甚麼都可以。| *Does it matter who goes first?* 誰先去有關係嗎? | **matter to sb** *It doesn't really matter to me if we don't see the film – I've seen it already anyway.* 我們不看那部電影對我確實無所謂 —— 反正我已經看過了。| **it matters a lot/a great deal** (=it is very important) …非常重要 *It mattered a great deal to her what other people thought of her.* 其他人怎麼看她對她來説極為重要。| **all that matters/the only thing that matters** (=the only thing that is important) 唯一要緊的 *All that matters is that you're safe.* 最要緊的是你平安無事。| *Money was the only thing that mattered to these people.* 對這些人來説金錢是唯一重要的東西。| **what matters is** *I don't care what it looks like – what matters is that it works.* 我不在乎它好看不好看 —— 要緊的是它要好用。| **nothing else matters** *He wanted to win the championship – nothing else really mattered to him.* 他想獲得冠軍 —— 除此之外沒有甚麼對他來説是重要的了。**2 it doesn't matter** *spoken* 【口】**a)** used to tell someone that you are not angry or upset about something, especially something that they have done 沒關係〔表示你並不生氣或介意〕: *"I've spilled some coffee on the carpet." "It doesn't matter."* "我把咖啡灑在地毯上了。" "沒關係。" **b)** used to say that you do not mind which one of two things you have 沒關係〔表示兩者中要哪個你都不會介意〕: *"Red or white wine?" "Oh, either. It doesn't matter."* "你要紅葡萄酒還是白葡萄酒?" "噢, 哪一種都行。沒有關係。" **3 what does it matter (if)** *spoken* used to say that something is not very important 【口】(即使) 又何妨〔表示某事不很重要〕: *What does it matter if he drinks a little, at least he's happy.* 即使喝一點酒又有甚麼關係, 至少他高興啊。

Frequencies of the verb **matter** in spoken and written English 動詞 matter 在英語口語和書面語中的使用頻率

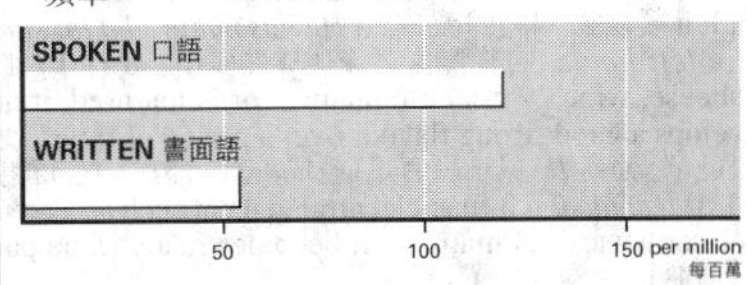

Based on the British National Corpus and the Longman Lancaster Corpus
據英國國家語料庫和朗文蘭卡斯特語料庫

This graph shows that the verb **matter** is much more common in spoken English than in written English. This is because it is used in a lot of common spoken phrases. 本圖表顯示, 動詞 matter 在英語口語中的使用頻率遠遠高於書面語, 因為它用於很多常見的口語片語中。

matter-of-fact /ˌ··ˈ·◄/ *adj* showing no emotion when you are talking about something exciting, frightening, upsetting etc 就事論事的; 不帶感情的; 實事求是的: *Jan was surprisingly matter-of-fact about her divorce.* 簡對待她的離婚出奇地淡然。—**matter-of-factly** *adv* —**matter-of-factness** *n* [U]

mat·ting /ˋmætɪŋ; ˈmætɪŋ/ *n* [U] strong rough material, used for making mats (MAT[1] (1))〔編席子用的〕編織材料: *straw matting* 編墊子用的麥秸[稻草]

mat·tins /ˋmætnz; ˈmætɨnz/ *n* [U] another spelling of MATINS matins的另一種拼法

mat·tock /ˋmætək; ˈmætək/ *n* [C] a tool used for digging, with a long handle and a metal blade 鶴嘴鋤

mat·tress /ˋmætrɪs; ˈmætrɨs/ *n* [C] the soft part of a bed that you lie on 牀墊, 褥墊: *an old, lumpy mattress* 凹凸不平的舊牀墊

ma·tu·ra·tion /ˌmætʃuˋreʃən; ˌmætʃʊˈreɪʃən/ *n* [U] *formal* the period during which something grows and develops【正式】成熟期, 成熟階段

ma·ture[1] /məˋtjur; məˈtʃʊə/ *adj*

1 ►SENSIBLE 理智的◄ a child or young person who is mature behaves in a sensible and reasonable way, as you would expect an older person to behave〔小孩或年輕人舉止〕成熟的, 理智的, 明白事理的: *She's very mature for her age.* 就她這個年齡來說她算是很成熟的。| *John has always shown a mature attitude to his work.* 約翰對工作總是表現出一種老成持重的態度。—opposite 反義詞 IMMATURE

2 ►FULLY GROWN 成年的◄ fully grown and developed 成年的; 成熟的: *The mature eagle has a wingspan of over six feet.* 成年的鷹翼展超過六英尺。

3 ►WINE/CHEESE ETC 酒/乾酪等◄ mature cheese, wine etc has a good strong flavour which has developed during a long period of time 製成的; 已釀成的: *mature cheddar* 成熟的切達乾酪

4 ►OLDER 較老的◄ a polite or humorous way of describing someone who is no longer young; MIDDLE-AGED 不再年輕的; 中年的〔禮貌或幽默的說法〕: *We design clothes for the maturer woman.* 我們為中年婦女設計服裝。| **of mature years** *a respectable gentleman of mature years* 一位已屆中年的體面紳士

5 ►NOVEL/PAINTING ETC 小說/油畫等◄ a mature piece of work by a writer or an artist shows a high level of understanding or skill 成熟的; 技巧嫺熟的; 老練的

6 on mature reflection/consideration *formal* after thinking about something carefully【正式】經過仔細考慮: *On mature reflection we have decided to decline their offer.* 經過慎重考慮, 我們已決定謝絕他們的建議。

7 ►FINANCIAL 金融的◄ *technical* a mature BOND[1] (1) or POLICY (2) is ready to be paid【術語】〔債券或保單〕到期應付的 —**maturely** *adv*

mature[2] *v* **matured, maturing 1** [I] to become fully grown or developed 變成熟; 完全長成: *A kitten matures when it is about a year old.* 小貓一歲左右就發育成熟了。**2** [I] to become sensible and start to behave like an adult 變理智;〔舉止〕變成熟: *He has matured a lot since he left home.* 自從離家之後他成熟多了。**3** [I,T] if a cheese, wine, WHISKY etc matures or is matured, it develops a good strong flavour over a period of time (使)〔乾酪、葡萄酒、威士忌酒等〕製成, (使) 釀成; (使) 釀熟 **4** [I] *technical* if a financial arrangement such as a BOND[1] (1) or POLICY (2) matures, it becomes ready to be paid【術語】〔債券或保單〕到期

mature stu·dent /ˌ·ˌ ˈ··/ *n* [C] *BrE* a student at a university or college who is over 25 years old【英】大齡學生〔年齡超過25歲的大學生〕

ma·tu·ri·ty /məˋtjurətɪ; məˈtʃʊərɨti/ *n* [U] **1** the quality of behaving in a sensible way like an adult 成熟: *Beth remained calm, showing a maturity way beyond her 16 years.* 貝思鎮定自若, 表現出一種超出她16歲年齡的成熟。**2** the time when a person, animal, or plant is fully grown or developed〔人、動物或植物的〕成熟期: **reach maturity** *These insects reach maturity after a few weeks.* 這些昆蟲幾週後就達到成熟期。**3** *technical* the time when a financial arrangement such as a BOND[1] (1) or POLICY (2) becomes ready to be paid【術語】〔債券或保單的〕到期時間, 到期日

mat·zo /ˋmɑtsə; ˈmɒtsə/ *n* [C] a type of flat bread eaten especially by Jewish people during PASSOVER 無酵餅〔尤指猶太人在逾越節期間吃的一種薄麵餅〕

maud·lin /ˋmɔdlɪn; ˈmɔːdlɪn/ *adj* talking or behaving in a sad, silly way, because you are drunk〔因醉酒〕言談[舉止]傷感的, 可笑的

maul /mɔl; mɔːl/ *v* [T] **1** to injure someone badly by tearing their flesh 撕裂…的皮肉, 抓裂: *The woman had been mauled by a panther.* 那個婦女被一隻豹撕裂了皮肉。**2** to write very unfavourable comments about a new book, play etc 抨擊〔新書、新戲劇等〕: *Her latest book was absolutely mauled by the critics.* 她的新書被評論家們批得體無完膚。**3** to touch someone in a rough sexual way which they think is unpleasant 對〔某人〕粗野地動手動腳: *Some guy came over and started mauling Jane.* 有個傢伙走了過來, 開始對簡粗野地動手動腳。

maun·der /ˋmɔndɚ; ˈmɔːndə/ *v* [I+on] *especially BrE* to talk or complain about something for a long time in a boring way【尤英】喋喋不休地說, 嘮叨: *What are you maundering on about, Sid?* 錫德, 你在嘮叨些甚麼?

Maun·dy Thurs·day /ˌmɔndɪ ˋθɝzdɪ; ˌmɔːndi ˈθɜːzdi/ *n* [U] the Thursday before Easter 濯足節〔復活節前的星期四〕, 聖星期四

mau·so·le·um /ˌmɔsəˋliəm; ˌmɔːsəˈliːəm/ *n* [C] a large stone building containing many graves or built over a grave 陵墓

mauve /mov; məʊv/ *n* [U] a pale purple colour 淡紫色 —**mauve** *adj* —see picture on page A5 參見A5頁圖

ma·ven /ˋmevən; ˈmeɪvən/ *n* [C] *AmE* someone who knows a lot about a particular subject【美】專家, 內行: *The café is a hangout for the cultural mavens.* 那家咖啡館是文化人常去的地方。

mav·e·rick /ˋmævrɪk; ˈmævərɪk/ *n* [C] an unusual person who has different ideas and ways of behaving from other people, and is often very successful 持不同意見者; 特立獨行者: *Charles was always a bit of a maverick, even at school.* 查爾斯總是有點特立獨行, 甚至在學校時也是如此。—**maverick** *adj*: *maverick tendencies* 特立獨行的傾向

maw /mɔ; mɔː/ *n* [C] **1** *formal* something which seems to swallow things completely【正式】似能吞噬他物的東西; 無底洞: *Millions of dollars were poured into the maw of defense spending.* 數百萬美元被投進了國防開支這個無底洞。**2** *literary* an animal's mouth or throat【文】動物的嘴[咽喉]

mawk·ish /ˋmɔkɪʃ; ˈmɔːkɪʃ/ *adj* showing too much emotion in a way that is embarrassing; SENTIMENTAL 情感過於外露的; 多愁善感的: *a mawkish love story* 感情淺露的愛情故事 —**mawkishly** *adv* —**mawkishness** *n* [U]

max[1] /mæks; mæks/ *n* [U] **1** an abbreviation of 縮寫= MAXIMUM **2** *informal* at the most【非正式】最大量; 最大值; 最大限度: *It'll cost about ten dollars max.* 它的價錢至多10美元左右。**3 to the max** *AmE slang*【美俚】**a)** an expression meaning extremely, used to emphasize how good, bad etc something is 極其, 極端〔用以強調好、壞等的程度〕: *"He's gorgeous, isn't he?" "To the max!"* "他很帥, 是吧?" "帥極了!" **b)** if you push yourself to the max, you try as hard as you can to succeed 最大程度地〔努力以取得成功〕

max[2] *v*

max out *phr v* [I] *AmE slang*【美俚】**1** to do something with as much effort and determination as you can 全力以赴, 竭盡全力: *Hilary maxed out on the campaign.* 希拉里在那次競選活動中使出了渾身解數。**2** to do too much, eat too much etc〔做、吃等〕過多: [+on] *"Want a beer?" "Nah, I maxed out on booze this weekend."* "要來杯啤酒嗎?" "不要了, 我這個週末喝多了。" —**maxed out** *adj*

max·im /ˋmæksɪm; ˈmæksɪ̣m/ *n* [C] a well-known phrase or saying, especially one that gives a rule for sensible behaviour 箴言, 格言

max·i·mal /ˋmæksəməl; ˈmæksɪ̣məl/ *adj technical* as much or as large as possible【術語】最多的; 最大的; 最大限度的: *the right conditions for a maximal increase in employment* 最大限度增加就業的合適條件 **—maximally** *adv*

max·i·mize also 又作 **-ise** *BrE*【英】/ˋmæksəˏmaɪz; ˈmæksɪ̣maɪz/ *v* [T] to increase something such as profit or income as much as possible 使增加到最大限度: *The company's main function is to maximize profit.* 該公司的主要職能是最大限度地增加利潤。—compare 比較 MINIMIZE **—maximization** /ˏmæksəməˋzeʃən; ˌmæksɪ̣maɪˈzeɪʃən/ *n* [U]

2 3 **max·i·mum¹** /ˋmæksəməm; ˈmæksɪ̣məm/ *adj* [only before noun 僅用於名詞前] the maximum amount, quantity, speed etc is the largest that is possible or allowed 最大量的, 最大限度的, 最大值的: *The car has a maximum speed of 120 mph.* 這輛汽車的最大速度為每小時120英里。| *The maximum number of students in each class is thirty.* 每個班學生人數的最高限額是三十名。| *We must make maximum use of the resources available.* 我們必須最大限度地利用可得到的資源。| **for maximum effect** (=to get the best possible results) 為得到最佳效果 *Display it under a strong light for maximum effect.* 把它放在強光下以產生最佳效果。—compare 比較 MINIMUM¹

maximum² *n plural* **maxima** /-mə; -mə/ *or* **maximums** [C] the largest number or amount that is possible or is allowed〔可能或可允許的〕最大量, 最大值: **[+of]** *Temperatures will reach a maximum of 45°C.* 氣溫最高將達到45攝氏度。| **the maximum** *40 students per class is the absolute maximum.* 每班40名學生是絕對的最高限額。

May /me; meɪ/ *n* [C,U] the fifth month of the year, between April and June 五月: **in May** *The theatre opened in May 1991.* 那家劇院開業於1991年5月。| **last/next May** *She started work here last May.* 她去年5月開始在這兒工作。| **on 6th May/on May 6th** *The meeting will be on 6th May.* (spoken as 讀作: *on the sixth of May* or 或 *on May sixth* (*AmE* 美) or 或 *on May the sixth* (*BrE* 英)) 會議將於5月6日召開。

1 1 **may¹** *modal verb negative short form* 否定縮略式為 **mayn't** *old-fashioned BrE*【過時, 英】

1 ►POSSIBILITY 可能性◄ if something may happen or may be true, there is a possibility that it will happen or be true but this is not certain 可能, 也許: *I may be late so start without me.* 我也許會晚來, 所以你們按時開始, 不要等我。| *Who knows what will happen. You may even have married by then.* 誰知道會發生甚麼呢? 到那時你甚至可能已經結婚了。| *It is feared that many workers may lose their jobs this winter.* 人們擔心這個冬天有許多工人會失業。| *£50 may not be enough.* 50英鎊可能不夠。| *Ian may be able to help.* 伊恩也許能幫忙。—compare 比較 MIGHT¹

2 ►PERMISSION 允許◄ **may I a)** *spoken* used to ask politely if you can do something【口】可以〔用以客氣地問是否可做某事〕: *May I speak to you for a moment in private, please?* 請問我可以跟您私下裡說幾句話嗎? | *I'd like to open a window, if I may.* 如果可以的話, 我想打開一扇窗子。**b)** *formal* used to say that someone is allowed to do something【正式】可以〔用以表示某人被允許做某事〕: *Thank you, you may go now.* 謝謝, 你現在可以走了。| *You may start writing now – the examination will finish in three hours.* 你們現在可以開始答題 —— 考試將在三小時後結束。| *Firearms may be used in an emergency.* 在緊急情況下可以開槍。**c) may I say/ask/suggest etc** *formal* used to say, ask, or suggest something politely【正式】〔禮貌說法〕我想(可否)說/詢問/建議等: *May I just add that Oliver was a pleasure to work with and will be missed by everyone in the team.* 我想補充一句: 和奧利弗一塊工作很愉快, 隊裡的每個人都會想念他。—compare 比較 CAN¹, MIGHT¹

3 may you/he/they etc do sth *formal* used to say that you hope that a particular thing will happen to someone【正式】祝你/他/他們等...〔用以表示希望、祝願〕: *May both the bride and groom have long and happy lives.* 祝新娘新郎幸福長壽。

4 may ... but ... used to say that although one thing is true, something else which seems very different is also true 儘管...但是...〔用以表示儘管某事是真實的, 但其他似乎與之非常不同的事也是真實的〕: *He may be lazy, but he can work very hard when he feels like it.* 他儘管懶惰, 但要是他願意的話, 也能很勤奮地工作。| *You may think you're smart but you don't understand this kind of work at all.* 你也許自認為很聰明, 但你對這種工作一點也不懂。—compare 比較 MIGHT¹

5 may well if something may well happen or may well be true, it is fairly likely to happen or be true 很可能, 極有可能: *These are excellent photographs and we may well be able to use them in our magazine.* 這些照片好極了, 我們很有可能把它們用在我們的雜誌上。—compare 比較 **might well** (MIGHT¹ (7))

6 may as well *spoken* used to say that you will do something that you do not really want to do, because you cannot think of anything better【口】還是...的好, 倒不如〔表示你要做你並不真正想做的事, 因為想不出更好的辦法〕: *I may as well go out tonight. There's nothing on television.* 我今晚還是出去的好, 電視上沒有甚麼好看的。| *If you're not going to eat that pizza I may as well throw it out.* 如果你不打算吃那塊比薩餅, 我還是把它扔掉的好。

7 ►PURPOSE 目的◄ *formal* used like 'can' after 'so that', to say that someone does something in order to make something else possible【正式】(以便) 能夠, (使) 可以〔與 can 一樣, 用於 so that 之後〕: *He gave up his life so that we may all live in a free and fair world.* 他獻出了自己的生命, 為了使我們所有的人能夠生活在一個自由、公平的世界上。—compare 比較 MIGHT¹

8 ►POSSIBLE TO DO STH 有可能做某事◄ if something may be done, completed etc in a particular way, that is how it is possible to do it 有可能〔做到〕: *The problem may be solved in a number of ways, but there is only one correct answer.* 這道題可以用多種方法來解, 但正確答案只有一個。—see 見 CAN (USAGE)

may² *n* [U] HAWTHORN flowers 山楂花

may·be /ˋmebɪ; ˈmeɪbi/ *adv* [sentence adverb 句子副詞] 1 2 **1** used like 'perhaps' to say that something may happen or may be true but you are not certain 也許, 大概, 可能〔和 perhaps 一樣用於表示某事可能會發生或可能真實, 但不肯定〕: *"Do you think he'll come back?" "Maybe."* "你認為他會回來嗎?" "也許會吧。" | *Maybe I was wrong about Karen; I don't know.* 或許我錯怪了卡倫; 我不知道。| *He said he'd finish the work soon – maybe tomorrow.* 他說他很快就會完成那個工作 —— 也許是在明天。**2** used to show that you are not sure of an amount or number 也許〔表示對某一數額或數目不能確定〕: *There were three, maybe four hundred people at the concert.* 音樂會上有三百人, 也許四百人。**3** used to make a suggestion you are not quite sure about 或許〔用以作出不十分確定的建議〕: *We thought maybe we should lower the price we were asking for our house.* 我們想或許應該降低對我們那幢房子的要價。**4** used when politely asking someone to do something or offering to help them 也許〔用於客氣地請某人做某事或表示願意幫助他們〕: *Maybe you could help me tidy the livingroom.* 也許你能幫我收拾一下客廳。**5** *spoken* used to reply to a suggestion or idea when either you are not sure if you agree with it, or you do not want to say 'yes' or 'no'【口】也許〔用於不明確自己是否同意某建議或想法, 或不願意明確表示同意與否之時〕: *"I think Sheila would be an excellent managing director." "Maybe."* "我想希拉會是一位優秀的總經理。" "也許是吧。" | *"Well,*

are you going to take the job or not?" "Maybe..." "我說，這份工作你到底要不要？" "也許啦…" **6 maybe ... but** *spoken* used to agree with someone but say that there are also other facts to be considered【口】也許…不過〔用於表示同意某人的看法，但說明同時也有其他因素要考慮〕: *"Mike should rent his own apartment and get away from home." "Maybe, but where would he get the money from?"* "邁克應該去租一套公寓房，離開家人自己生活。" "也許是該這樣，但是他從哪裡弄這筆錢呢？"

USAGE NOTE 用法說明: MAYBE
FORMALITY 正式程度
Maybe and **perhaps** mean the same thing, but **maybe** is more informal. maybe 和 perhaps 意思相同，但 maybe 更為隨便。To a friend you might say or write 對朋友可以這樣說或寫: *I'll maybe see you in August.* 我也許會在八月份見到你。To someone you do not know well you might say 而對一個不太熟悉的人你可以說: *Perhaps we could meet next week.* 或許我們能在下週見面。When you write a report or story you might put 寫報告或故事時可以說: *New York is perhaps the most interesting city in the US.* 紐約也許是美國最有趣的城市。In a speech you might say 在演講中，可能會說: *Perhaps in closing I could just thank everyone for coming.* 也許在結束我的講話時，我可以對各位的光臨表示感謝，but it would be less formal to say 但如果說 *Maybe...* 就不那麼正式了。
SPELLING 拼法
Maybe is always spelt as one word when it means 'perhaps'. maybe 的意思如果是"也許"，總是拼寫成一個詞: *Maybe it'll be fun.* 也許它會很有趣。Compare 比較 *It may be fun.*

may·bug /ˋmebʌg; ˈmeɪbʌg/ *n* [C] a COCKCHAFER 金龜子

May Day /ˋ· ·/ *n* [C,U] the first day of May, when LEFT-WING political parties have celebrations, and when people traditionally used to celebrate the arrival of spring 五一勞動節；五朔節〔過去傳統上人們在這一天慶祝春天的到來〕

may·day /ˋmeˌde; ˈmeɪdeɪ/ *n* [singular] a radio signal used to ask for help when a ship or plane is in serious danger〔船隻或飛機遇險時用的〕無線電求救信號 —compare 比較 SOS

may·est /ˋmeəst; ˈmeɪəst/ *v* **thou mayest** *old use*【舊】= you may

may·fly /ˋmeflaɪ; ˈmeɪflaɪ/ *n plural* **mayflies** [C] a small insect that lives near water, and only lives for a short time 蜉蝣

may·hem /ˋmehɛm; ˈmeɪhem/ *n* [U] an extremely confused situation in which people are very frightened or excited; CHAOS 極端混亂的局面，大混亂: *There was complete mayhem after the explosion.* 爆炸後到處一片混亂。

may·n't /ˋment; ˈmeɪənt/ *old-fashioned BrE*【過時，英】the short form of 縮略式= 'may not'

may·o /ˋmeo; ˈmeɪəʊ/ *n* [U] *AmE informal* mayonnaise【美，非正式】蛋黃醬

may·on·naise /ˋmeəˌnez; ˌmeɪəˈneɪz/ *n* [U] a thick white SAUCE eaten with cold SALADS, on CHIPS etc 蛋黃醬

mayor /ˋmeɚ; meə/ *n* [C] **1** someone who is chosen or elected each year in Britain to represent a town or city at official public ceremonies〔英國的〕市長 **2** the person who has been elected to lead the government of a town or city in the US〔美國的〕市長 —**mayoral** *adj*: *mayoral duties* 市長的職責

mayor·al·ty /ˋmeərəltɪ; ˈmeərəlti/ *n* [U] *formal* the position of mayor, or the period when someone is mayor【正式】市長的職位；市長的任期

mayor·ess /ˋmeərɪs; ˈmeərɪ̧s/ *n* [C] *BrE* the wife of a mayor, or a woman who shares the work of a mayor【英】市長夫人；女市長

may·pole /ˋmeˌpol; ˈmeɪpəʊl/ *n* [C] a tall pole around which people danced on May Day in England in the past 五月柱〔過去英國人在五朔節圍繞着這種柱子跳舞〕

mayst /mest; meɪst/ *v* **thou mayst** *old use*【舊】= you may

may've /ˋmeəv; ˈmeɪəv/ the short form of 縮略式= 'may have': *You may've heard this story before.* 你以前也許聽過這個故事。

maze /mez; meɪz/ *n* [C] **1 a maze of streets/paths/wires etc** a complicated and confusing arrangement of streets etc 迷宮似的街道/小路/電線等: *the maze of tiny streets in the old part of the city* 舊城區迷宮般的小街道 **2 a maze of rules/regulations/details etc** a large number of rules etc which are complicated and difficult to understand 一大堆複雜難懂的規則/規章/細節等 **3** a specially designed system of paths, often in a park or public garden, which is difficult to find your way through〔尤指公園中的〕迷宮，迷魂陣: *We got completely lost in the maze.* 我們在迷宮中徹底迷了路。**4** a children's game in which you draw a line through a complicated group of lines without crossing any of them 迷宮〔兒童畫線遊戲〕

MB /ˌɛm ˋbi; ˌem ˈbiː/ the abbreviation of 縮寫= Bachelor of Medicine 醫學士

MBA /ˌɛm bi ˋe; ˌem biː ˈeɪ/ *n* [C] Master of Business Administration; a university degree in the skills needed to be in charge of a business 工商管理學碩士

MBE /ˌɛm bi ˋi; ˌem biː ˈiː/ *n* [C] Member of the Order of the British Empire; a special honour given to some British people for things they have done for their country 英帝國普通勳章

MBSc /ˌɛm bi ɛs ˋsi; ˌem biː es ˈsiː/ the abbreviation of 縮寫= Master of Business Science 工商學碩士

MC /ˌɛm ˋsi; ˌem ˈsiː/ *n* [C] **1** the abbreviation of 縮寫= Master of Ceremonies —see also 另見 EMCEE **2** Military Cross; a MEDAL given to British army officers for bravery 軍功十字勳章〔授予表現勇敢的英軍軍官〕**3** *AmE*【美】the written abbreviation of 縮寫= Member of Congress

McCoy /məˋkɔɪ; məˈkɔɪ/ *n* **the real McCoy** *informal* something that is real and is not a copy, especially something valuable【非正式】真貨〔非複製品，尤指貴重物品〕: *"Is it a Rolex?" "Yes, it's the real McCoy."* "是一隻勞力士牌手錶嗎？" "不錯，是真貨。"

MD /ˌɛm ˋdi; ˌem ˈdiː/ *n* [C] **1** the written abbreviation of 縮寫= Doctor of Medicine 醫學博士 **2** *especially spoken* the MANAGING DIRECTOR of a company【尤口】總經理；董事總經理

ME /ˌɛm ˋi; ˌem ˈiː/ *n* [U] *BrE* myalgic encephalomyelitis; an illness that makes you feel very tired and weak and can last for a long time【英】肌痛性腦脊髓炎，ME 綜合徵; EPSTEIN-BARR VIRUS *AmE*【美】

me /mɪ; mi; *strong* 強讀 mi; miː/ *pron* the object form of I 我〔I 的賓格〕: *It fell off and hit me on the head.* 它掉下來砸在我的頭上。| *He bought me a drink.* 他給我買了一杯酒。| *Give that book to me.* 把那本書給我。| *She's two years older than me.* 她比我大兩歲。| *That's me, standing on the left of the bride.* 那是我，站在新娘子的左邊。

USAGE NOTE 用法說明: ME
FORMALITY 正式程度: **me, her, him, us, we, they, them**
When you are speaking you usually use **me, her, him, us,** and **them** after **as, than,** and the verb **to be,** and with **and** and **or** in a phrase that is the subject of a clause. 口語中在 as, than 和動詞 to be 之後，或者在由 and 或 or 連接、在句中作主語的詞組中通常用 me, her, him, us 和 them: *I'm not as pretty as her.* 我不如她漂亮。| *She's older than him.* 她比他年齡大。| *It's them.* 是他們。| *Tanya and*

me and Tanya are off to Acapulco（塔尼婭和我要去阿卡普爾科）, or even 甚至可以說 *Me and Tanya are off to Acapulco.*

In very formal or old-fashioned writing you may see **I, she, he, we** and **they** used instead. 在非常正式或過時的書面語中, 則會使用I, she, he, we 和 they: *None was as rich as he.* 沒有人像他那樣富有。You may also hear this in spoken English, but it often sounds much too formal or pompous. 在英語口語中你也會聽到這種用法, 但它常常聽起來過於正式或傲慢: *It was they.* 是他們。| *My husband and I are going to the opera.* 我丈夫和我要去聽歌劇。

You can avoid using either by rephrasing your sentence. 可以通過改變句子措辭來避免上述兩種用法: *No one was as rich as he was.* 沒有人像他那樣富有。| *They were the ones.* 就是他們。| *I am going to the opera with my husband.* 我要和我丈夫一起去聽歌劇。

me·a cul·pa /ˌmeə ˋkulpə; ˌmeɪə ˈkʊlpə/ *interjection Latin humorous* used to admit that something is your fault【拉丁, 幽默】是我的過失, 是我不好

mead /mid; miːd/ *n* **1** [U] an alcoholic drink made from HONEY 蜂蜜酒 **2** [C] *poetical* a meadow【詩】草地

mead·ow /ˈmɛdo; ˈmedəʊ/ *n* [C] a field with wild grass and flowers 草地 —see also 另見 WATER MEADOW

mead·ow·lark /ˋmɛdolɑrk; ˈmedəʊlɑːk/ *n* [C] a brown North American bird with a yellow front 草地鷚〔產於北美〕

mea·gre *BrE*【英】, **meager** *AmE*【美】/ˋmigɚ; ˈmiːgə/ *adj* a meagre amount of food, money etc is too small and is much less than you need〔食物、金錢等〕不足的, 貧乏的: *meagre wages* 微薄的工資 | *a meager diet* 簡單的飯食 —**meagrely** *adv* —**meagreness** *n* [U]

S2 W2 **meal** /mil; miːl/ *n* **1** [C] an occasion when you eat food, for example breakfast or lunch 餐, 飯: *Dinner is the main meal of the day for most people.* 對多數人來說晚飯是一天中的主餐。| *What time are you having your meal?* 你們甚麼時間吃飯? | **go (out) for a meal** *After the movie we went for a meal in a Chinese restaurant.* 看完電影後我們去一家中國餐館吃了一頓。| **take/ask sb out for a meal** *Why don't you ask her out for a meal?* 你為甚麼不請她出去吃頓飯? **2** [C] the food that you eat on a particular occasion 一餐吃的食物: *Michel cooked us a lovely French meal.* 米歇爾為我們做了一頓可口的法國餐。| *a five-course meal* 一頓五道菜的飯 —see also 另見 **square meal** (SQUARE¹ (7)) **3** [U] grain that has been crushed into a powder, for making flour or animal food〔穀類的〕粗磨粉 —see also 另見 BONE MEAL **4 make a meal of** *informal* to spend too much time or effort doing something【非正式】花費過多的時間[精力]〔做某事〕, 小題大做: *He made a real meal out of parking the car.* 他為了把車子停放好真肯花時間。

mea·lie /ˋmilɪ; ˈmiːli/ *n* [C,U] *SAfrE* MAIZE, or a piece of maize【南非】玉米, 玉蜀黍; 玉米穗

meal tick·et /ˈ· ˌ··/ *n* [C] **1** *informal* something or someone that you depend on to give you money or food【非正式】賴以為生的物[人] **2** a card that gives you the right to have free or cheaper meals at school or work in the US〔美國學校或工作場所的〕飯票, 餐券

meal·time /ˋmiltaɪm; ˈmiːltaɪm/ *n* [C] a time during the day when you have a meal 進餐[開飯]時間: *The only time I see them is at mealtimes.* 我只有在吃飯時間才見得到他們。

meal·y /ˋmilɪ; ˈmiːli/ *adj* **1** fruit or vegetables that are mealy are dry and do not taste good〔水果或蔬菜〕乾燥難吃的, 麵的: *mealy potatoes* 乾巴巴不好吃的馬鈴薯 **2** containing MEAL (3) 含粉的, 粉質的

mealy-mouthed /ˌ·· ˈ·◂/ *adj* not brave enough or honest enough to say clearly and directly what you really think 說話轉彎抹角的; 說話不真誠坦率的

mean¹ /min; miːn/ *v* [T] *past tense and past participle* **meant** /mɛnt; ment/ S1 W1

1 ►HAVE A PARTICULAR MEANING 有某種意思◄ [not in progressive 不用進行式] to have or represent a particular meaning 意思是, 表示…的意思: *"What does 'Konbanwa' mean in English?" "It means 'Good Evening'."* "Konbanwa 譯成英語是甚麼意思?" "它的意思是 Good Evening (晚上好)。" | *The red light means 'Stop'.* 紅燈表示"停"。| **what is meant by** (=what something means) …是甚麼意思, …的意思是甚麼 *What is meant by the term 'random access'?* "隨機存取"這個術語是甚麼意思? | **mean (that)** *This signal means your message has been received.* 這個信號表示你發送的信息已經收到了。

2 ►INTEND TO SAY STH 打算說某事◄ [not in progressive 不用進行式] to intend a particular meaning when you say something 意謂, 意思是說: **mean (that)** *I meant we'd have to leave early – that's all.* 我的意思是說我們必須早點離開 —— 沒有別的。| **what you mean/what she means etc** *So what he means is that we'll have to start the whole thing again.* 喏, 他的意思是說我們必須一切重新開始。

3 I mean *spoken*【口】**a)** used when explaining or giving an example of something, or when pausing to think about what you are going to say next 我的意思是〔用於進行解釋或舉例, 或停下來考慮下面說甚麼時〕: *He's really very rude – I mean he never even says 'Good Morning'.* 他確實很無禮 —— 我的意思是他甚至從來不說"早上好"。| *It's just not right. I mean it's unfair isn't it?* 這就不對。我是說這不公平, 你說呢? **b)** used to quickly correct something you have just said 我是說〔用以快速糾正剛說過的話〕: *She plays the violin, I mean the viola, really well.* 她的小提琴 —— 我是說中提琴 —— 拉得確實好。

4 do you know what I mean?/if you know what I mean *spoken* used when checking that someone has understood what you are saying【口】你明白我的意思嗎?/如果你明白我的意思〔用於核實某人是否已明白你正在說的話〕: *This year I want to buy her something really special. Do you know what I mean?* 今年我想給她買一件真正特殊的東西。你明白我的意思嗎?

5 (do) you mean …? *spoken* used when checking that you have understood what someone has said【口】你意思是說…?〔用於核實你確實聽懂了某人所說的話〕: *You mean we're supposed to tell you if we want to leave early?* 你意思是說如果我們想早些離開就該告訴你嗎?

6 I know what you mean *spoken* used to tell someone that you understand what they are talking about, because you have had the same experience yourself【口】我明白你的意思〔用以告訴某人你明白他所說的話, 因為你有過同樣的經歷〕: *Oh, I know exactly what you mean. Things like that drive me crazy too.* 噢, 我完全理解你的意思, 那樣的事情也會使我發瘋的。

7 I see what you mean *spoken* used to tell someone that you now understand what they have been saying【口】我明白你的意思〔用以告訴某人, 對他講的話你現在已經聽懂了〕: *Yes, I see what you mean. That would be the best way to do it.* 是的, 我明白你的意思。那將是做這件事的最好辦法。

8 see what I mean? *spoken* used when checking that someone has understood something you have said, often by showing them an example of it【口】懂我的意思嗎?〔用於核實某人是否已聽懂你說的話, 常通過舉例來說明〕: *See what I mean? Every time she calls me up she wants me to do something for her.* 懂我的意思嗎? 她每次給我打電話都是要我給她辦事。

9 that's what I mean *spoken* used when someone is saying the same thing that you were trying to say earlier【口】我就是這個意思〔用於表示某人說的話正是你剛才想說的〕: *"We might not have enough money." "That's what I mean, so we'd better find out the price first."* "我們也許錢不夠。" "我就是這個意思, 所以我們最好先弄清楚價錢。"

M

10 how do you mean? *spoken* used to ask someone to explain what they have just said or tell you more about it【口】你是甚麼意思?〔用以要求某人解釋剛說過的話或提供更多與之相關的信息〕: *"He says he finds it difficult at times." "How do you mean?"* "他說他有時覺得挺難的。" "你是甚麼意思?"

11 what do you mean ...? *spoken*【口】**a)** used when you do not understand what someone is trying to say ... 是甚麼意思?〔用於表示沒有聽懂某人正在說的話〕 **b)** used when you are very surprised or annoyed by what someone has just said 你是甚麼意思?〔用以表示對某人剛說過的話感到非常吃驚或不快〕: *What do you mean, you've cancelled the holiday?* 你說你取消了度假, 是甚麼意思? | *What do you mean by that?* 你那麼說是甚麼意思?

12 I mean to say *spoken* used when adding a reason or explanation for something you have just said, especially something you feel strongly about【口】我意思是說〔用以對自己剛剛說的話補充理由或解釋, 尤指你對之抱有強烈感情的某事〕: *Of course she wants to see the children, I mean to say, it's only natural isn't it?* 她當然想見到孩子們, 我的意思是說, 這不過是人之常情, 對吧?

13 ►SAY WHICH PERSON/THING 說的是哪個人/物◄ **I mean sb/sth** *usually spoken* used to say that a particular person or thing is the one that you are talking about, pointing to etc【一般口】我指的是某人/某物: *"Hey you!" "Do you mean me?"* "嗨, 你!" "你說的是我嗎?" | *I didn't mean that one, I meant this one.* 我說的不是那一個, 我指的是這一個。

14 ►INTEND (SB) TO DO (STH) 打算(讓某人)做(某事)◄ *especially spoken* to intend to do something or intend that someone else should do something【尤口】意欲, 打算: **mean to do sth** *I've been meaning to phone you all week.* 整整一星期以來我一直打算給你打電話。| *I didn't mean to interrupt your meal.* 我不是有意想打斷你們吃飯。| **mean sb to do sth** *Oh no! I never meant her to read those comments.* 真不應該! 我從來沒打算讓她看那些評論。| **mean for sb to do sth** *especially AmE*【尤美】*I didn't mean for her to get hurt.* 我並沒有讓她受到傷害的意思。—see also 另見 **mean no harm** (HARM¹ (3))

15 mean business to be determined to do something even if it involves hurting someone, or be very serious about something 決心做某事〔即使會傷害他人〕; 〔對某事〕是非常認真的: *We've got to show these gangsters we mean business.* 我們必須向這些歹徒表明我們是認真的。| *Get upstairs now! I mean business!* 現在就上樓去! 我可不是說着玩的!

16 he/she means well *spoken* used to say that someone intends to be helpful or kind, but often makes a situation worse【口】他/她用心是好的: *He may sound a bit rude at times, but he means well.* 他講話有時比較粗魯, 但他的用意是好的。—see also 另見 WELL-MEANING, WELL-MEANT

17 I/he etc meant it for the best *especially spoken* used to say that someone wanted to do something helpful, but their actions had the wrong effect【尤口】我/他本是出於好心: *I wasn't criticizing you, I really meant it for the best.* 我剛才並不是批評你, 我真的是出於好意。

18 mean mischief/trouble to intend to cause trouble 有意找麻煩: *I could tell from the look on his face that he meant mischief.* 從他的面部表情上我能看出他是存心搗亂。

19 what do you mean by doing sth? *spoken* used to tell someone that you are very annoyed because of what they have done【口】你怎麼竟然做某事?〔用以表示對某人做的事十分惱火〕: *What do you mean by calling me at this time of night?* 你怎麼竟然這麼晚還給我打電話?

20 ►SAY STH SERIOUSLY 嚴肅地說某事◄ [not in progressive 不用進行式] to have a serious purpose in something you say or write 當真, 說到做到: **mean it** *We've heard these threats before, but I think he means it this time.* 這些威脅我們以前也聽到過, 但我認為這次他會來真的。| **mean what you say** *She meant what she said – you'll have to watch out.* 她是會說到做到的 —— 你必須提高警惕。| **really mean** *You don't really mean that, do you?* 你並不當真是那個意思, 對吧?

21 I didn't mean it *spoken* used to say that you did not intend to upset or hurt someone【口】我不是有意的: *I'm sorry, I didn't mean it – it was just a stupid thing to say.* 對不起, 我不是有意的 —— 我剛才說的確實是一句蠢話。| *I'm sure she didn't mean it, really.* 我敢肯定她不是有意的, 真的。

22 ►RESULT IN STH 導致某事◄ [not in progressive 不用進行式] to have a particular result 引起, 導致, 造成: *The pit closures will mean a large rise in unemployment.* 關閉礦井將導致失業人數的大量增加。| **mean (that)** *His injury meant that he could no longer continue work.* 他的受傷意味着他不能再繼續工作了。

23 that doesn't mean used to say that something is not definitely true, or is not definitely going to happen, even though it may seem to be true because of something else you have mentioned 那並不意味着: *Just because he's been in prison that doesn't mean he's some kind of violent criminal.* 僅僅因為他坐過牢並不意味着他就是某種殘暴的罪犯。

24 ►INVOLVE DOING STH 包括做某事◄ [not in progressive 不用進行式] to involve having to do a particular thing 意味着: **mean doing sth** *I'm determined to solve this mystery even if it means traveling to New York myself.* 我決心解開這個祕密, 即使這意味着我要親自到紐約去一趟。

25 ►SHOW STH IS TRUE/WILL HAPPEN 表明某事真實/要發生◄ [not in progressive 不用進行式] to be a sign that something is true or will happen 表示; 預示着: *When the boss sends for me it usually means trouble.* 要是老闆派人叫我去見他, 這通常就是說我要有麻煩了。| **mean (that)** *If the sky is red in the evening, it usually means it'll be fine the next day.* 如果傍晚天空發紅, 這通常預示着第二天是個晴天。

26 sth means a lot to sb used to say something is very important to someone 某事對某人很重要: *Her job means a lot to her.* 她的工作對她來說十分重要。| **sth means everything/the world to sb** *Their grandchildren mean everything to them.* 對他們來說, 孫子孫女就是他們的一切。

27 mean nothing to sb a) to be unfamiliar to someone or impossible for them to understand 對某人完全陌生; 不可能為某人所理解: *"Who's that message for?" "No idea. It means nothing to me."* "那張便條是給誰的?" "不知道, 我完全看不懂。" **b)** to not be important to someone 對某人不重要: *Public honours mean nothing to her.* 榮譽對她來說是無所謂的。

28 mean something/anything to sb a) to be familiar to someone 為某人所熟悉: *Does the name 'Kanafani' mean anything to you?* 你熟悉 Kanafani 這個名字嗎? **b)** to be important to someone 對某人重要: *I spent years believing that I actually meant something to him.* 有許多年, 我以為自己對他來說還有一點甚麼重要性。

29 be meant to do sth a) if you are meant to do something, you should do it, especially because someone has told you to or because it is your responsibility〔尤因某人的吩咐或根據職責〕應該[必須]做某事: *We're meant to write our names at the top of the paper.* 按照規定我們應該把姓名寫在考卷上方。| *I thought the police were meant to protect people.* 我以為警察的職責就是保護人民。**b)** to be intended to do something 意在做某事: *The diagram is meant to show the different stages of the process.* 這個圖表意在顯示整個過程的各個不同階段。

30 be meant for to be intended for a particular person or purpose 為〔某人或某目的〕而準備的: *These chairs are meant for guests.* 這些椅子是為客人們準備的。

31 sb was never meant for sth/to be sth used to say that someone is not at all suitable for a particular job or activity 某人從來不是從事某種工作[活動等]的料: *I was*

never meant for the army. 我從來就不是當兵的料。
32 be meant for each other if two people are meant for each other, they are very suitable as partners for each other 彼此很合得來, 是天生的一對: *Monique and Didier were meant for each other.* 莫尼克和迪迪爾真是天生的一對。
33 sth was meant to be used to say that you think a situation was certain to happen and that no one had any power to prevent it 某事注定要發生: *They met in August, and were married within a month, so I guess it was just meant to be.* 他們在八月相遇, 一個月不到就結婚了, 所以我認為這完全是天意。
34 know/understand what it means to be sth to have experienced a particular situation, so that you know what it is like 知道/理解處於某種境況中意味着甚麼: *I understand your problems because I know what it means to be poor.* 我理解你的難處, 因為我知道貧窮意味着甚麼。

Frequencies of the verb **mean** in spoken and written English 動詞 mean 在英語口語和書面語中的使用頻率

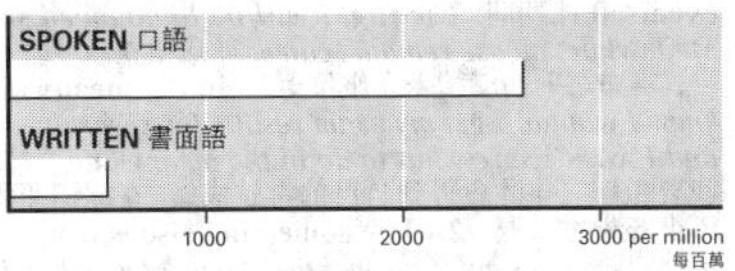

Based on the British National Corpus and the Longman Lancaster Corpus
據英國國家語料庫和朗文蘭卡斯特語料庫

This graph shows that the verb **mean** is much more common in spoken English than in written English. This is because it is used in a lot of common spoken phrases. 本圖表顯示, 動詞 mean 在英語口語中的使用頻率遠遠高於書面語, 因為口語中很多常用片語是由 mean 構成的。

mean² *adj* **1** unkind or nasty 不善良的; 卑鄙的; 刻薄的: *That was a mean thing to do.* 那是一件很卑鄙的事情。| [+to] *Don't be so mean to her!* 不要對她如此刻薄! **2** *BrE* unwilling to spend any money or share what you have with other people; CHEAP¹ (6), STINGY【英】吝嗇的, 小氣的: [+with] *He's always been mean with his money.* 他對錢總是很吝嗇。**3** *especially AmE* cruel and bad-tempered【尤美】兇惡的, 殘忍的; 脾氣暴躁的: *That's a mean dog. Be careful it doesn't bite you.* 那是條惡狗, 小心別讓牠咬着你。**4 no mean achievement/feat/task etc** something that is very difficult to do, so that someone who does it deserves to be admired 值得稱道的成就/業績/任務等: *Winning that competition was no mean feat.* 贏得那場競爭是了不起的成績。**5 be no mean performer/player etc** to be very good at doing something 是一位了不起的演員/運動員等: *He was no mean batsman in those days.* 在那時他是一位優秀的板球擊球手。**6** *AmE informal* very good and skilful【美, 非正式】很好的; 嫻熟的: *She's one mean tennis-player.* 她是一位技藝精湛的網球選手。| *Brock plays a mean game of poker.* 布羅克玩撲克牌很老道。**7** [only before noun 僅用於名詞前] *technical* average【術語】平均的: *the mean rate of consumption* 平均消耗速度 **8** [only before noun 僅用於名詞前] *literary* poor or looking poor【文】簡陋的, 難看的, 破舊的: *these mean streets* 這些簡陋的街道 **9** [only before noun 僅用於名詞前] *old use* belonging to a low social class【舊】〔社會地位〕低微的, 卑微的: *a man of mean birth* 出身低微的人 —**meanly** *adv* —**meanness** *n* [U]

mean³ *n* **1 the mean** *technical* the average amount, figure, or value【術語】平均數, 平均值: *The mean of 7, 9 and 14 is 10.* 7, 9 和 14 的平均數為 10。**2 the/a mean between sth and sth** a method or way of doing something which is between two very different methods, and better than either of them 中庸之道, 折中辦法〔介於兩種不同辦法之間而比兩者都好的做某事的一種辦法〕: *It's a case of finding the mean between firmness and compassion.* 這是一個在堅決和同情之間找出折中辦法的問題。—see also 另見 MEANS

me·an·der /mɪˈændə; miˈændə/ *v* [I] **1** if a river or stream meanders, it turns a lot as it flows〔河流〕蜿蜒流動: *a flat plain of meandering rivers* 河流蜿蜒其上的平原 **2** [always+adv/prep] to walk in a slow, relaxed way, not in any particular direction 漫步, 閒逛: **[+along/through etc]** *We meandered aimlessly along the lanes.* 我們沿着小巷漫無目的地閒逛着。**3** also 又作 **meander on** to talk for a long time in a way that is unclear or boring 嘮叨, 東拉西扯地講話: *Will meandered on for hours.* 威爾東拉西扯地談了好幾個小時。—**meanderings** *n* [plural] —**meander** *n* [C]

mean·ie, meany /ˈminɪ; ˈmiːni/ *n* [C] *spoken* a word meaning an unkind person, used especially by children【口】卑鄙的傢伙; 刻薄鬼〔尤作兒語〕: *Don't be such a meanie!* 別那麼刻薄!

mean·ing¹ /ˈminɪŋ; ˈmiːnɪŋ/ *n* 2 1
1 ▶OF A WORD/SIGN ETC 關於詞/符號等的◀ [C,U] the thing or idea that a word, expression, or sign represents 意義, 意思; 含義: **[+of]** *Can you explain the meaning of this word?* 你能解釋一下這個詞的意思嗎? | *The expression has two very different meanings in English.* 這個短語在英語中有兩個非常不同的含義。
2 ▶OF WHAT SB SAYS 某人所説的話的含義◀ [U] the things or ideas that someone wants you to understand from what they say〔某人的話的〕意思: **[+of]** *We couldn't work out the meaning of this last remark.* 我們搞不懂這最後一句話的意思。| **get/catch/understand sb's meaning** (=understand what they are trying to tell you) 明白某人的意思 *Barry could make things pretty unpleasant for us, if you get my meaning.* 巴里會給我們把事情搞得很糟糕的, 你明白我的意思嗎?
3 what's the meaning of this? *spoken* used to demand an explanation【口】這是甚麼意思?〔用以要求做出解釋〕: *What's the meaning of this? I asked you to be here an hour ago!* 這是甚麼意思? 我要求你一小時之前就要在這兒的!
4 ▶OF A BOOK/FILM ETC 關於書/電影等◀ [U] the ideas that a writer, artist etc wants to show in a book, picture, film etc〔書、圖畫、電影等的〕主題思想
5 ▶PURPOSE/SPECIAL QUALITY 目標/特殊品質◀ [U] the quality that makes something seem important and makes people feel that their life, work etc has a purpose and value 目標; 價值: **lose its meaning** *Life seemed to have lost its meaning since Janet's death.* 珍妮特去世以後生活似乎失去了意義。| **have meaning** *Her studies no longer seemed to have any meaning.* 她的研究似乎不再有任何意義了。
6 ▶TRUE NATURE 本質◀ [U] the true nature and importance of something 本質; 重要性: **[+of]** *I was starting to realize the full meaning of the night's events.* 我開始認識到晚上所發生事件的全部意義了。
7 (not) know the meaning of to (not) have experience and understanding of a particular situation or feeling 對...(沒)有體驗和了解, (不)知道...的含義: *Living in that area, they knew the meaning of fear.* 生活在那個地區, 他們知道甚麼叫恐懼。| *"Guilty, she doesn't know the meaning of the word!"* "愧疚, 她不知道這個詞的含義!"

meaning² *adj* **a meaning look/expression** a look that expresses a particular feeling strongly 意味深長的眼神/表情

mean·ing·ful /ˈminɪŋfl; ˈmiːnɪŋfəl/ *adj* **1** having a meaning that is easy to understand and makes sense 有意義的; 淺顯易懂的: *The statistics are not very meaningful when taken out of context.* 這些統計數據離開了上下文就看不太明白了。| *Standards must be specified in meaningful terms.* 標準必須用淺顯易懂的措辭寫清楚。
2 a meaningful look/glance/smile etc a look that clearly expresses the way someone feels, even though nothing is said 意味深長的眼神/一瞥/微笑等: *John gave*

us a meaningful look as if to say 'I told you so'. 約翰意味深長地看了我們一眼, 好像在說"我告訴過你們會是這個樣子"。**3 a meaningful relationship/experience/argument etc** a relationship etc that is serious, important, or useful 嚴肅[重要, 有用]的關係/經歷/辯論等 —**meaningfully** *adv*

mean·ing·less /ˈminɪŋlɪs; ˈmiːnɪŋləs/ *adj* **1** something that is meaningless has no purpose or importance and does not seem worth doing or having; FUTILE 無意義的; 無目的的; 無價值的; 不重要的: *a meaningless existence* 無意義的生活 **2** not having a meaning that you can understand or explain 〔意義〕不可理解的, 無法解釋的: *To me the marks on the page were just meaningless symbols.* 對我來說這一頁上的標記僅僅是一些沒有意義的符號。—**meaninglessness** *n* [U]

means /minz; miːnz/ *n plural* **means**
1 ►METHOD 方法◄ [C] a method, system, object etc that you use as a way of achieving a result 手段, 方法; 工具: [+of] *What would be the most effective means of advertising our product?* 宣傳我們產品的最有效手段是甚麼呢? | **means of transport** *BrE*【英】**/transportation** *AmE*【美】*We had no means of transport except for two bicycles.* 除了兩輛自行車以外, 我們沒有其他交通工具了。| **by honest/fair etc means** *The money was acquired by dishonest means.* 這些錢是用不正當手段獲得的。| **means of identification** (=something that shows your name and address) 身分證明文件
2 by means of using a particular method or system 以…方法[裝置]: *The blocks are raised by means of pulleys.* 那些大塊物件是用滑車吊起來的。
3 by all means *spoken* used to mean 'of course' when politely allowing someone to do something or agreeing with a suggestion【口】當然可以: *"Can I bring Alan to the party?" "By all means!"* "我能帶艾倫來參加聚會嗎?" "當然可以!" | *By all means try the jacket on, but I think it will be too big for you.* 當然可以試穿一下這件上衣, 但我覺得你穿太大了。
4 by no means/not by any means not at all 決不, 一點都不: *It is by no means certain that the game will take place.* 比賽是否會舉行完全不能肯定。| *She's not a bad kid, by any means.* 她不是個壞孩子, 絕對不是。
5 a means to an end something that you do only to achieve a result, not because you want to do it 達到目的的手段: *For Geoff, the job was simply a means to an end.* 對傑夫來說, 那份工作僅僅是達到目的的手段。
6 ►MONEY 錢◄ [plural] the money or income that you have 錢; 收入: **have the means to do sth** *I don't have the means to support a family.* 我沒有錢養活一家人。| **according to your means** *Each member contributes according to his or her means.* 每個成員根據自己的財力捐款。| **beyond your means** (=costing more than you can afford) 超出自己的財力, 負擔不起 *These medical costs are beyond the means of most working people.* 這些醫療費用大多數勞工階級都支付不起。| **within your means** (=not costing more than you can afford) 負擔[支付]得起 *The cost should be well within the means of the average family.* 費用應該完全不超出一般家庭的支付能力。
7 man/woman of means *literary* someone who is rich【文】富翁/富婆
8 the means of production *technical* the material, tools, and equipment that are used in the production of goods【術語】生產資料: *public ownership of the means of production* 生產資料公有制 —see also 另見 **by fair means or foul** (FAIR[1] (13)), **ways and means** (WAY[1] (3))

mean-spir·it·ed /,· ˈ···◄/ *adj* not generous or sympathetic 小氣的, 吝嗇的; 小心眼的; 無同情心的: *a mean-spirited, jealous man* 心胸狹窄、嫉妒心強的男子

means test /ˈ· ·/ *n* [C] an official check in order to find out whether someone is poor enough to need money from the state 經濟狀況調查〔用以確定某人是否很貧窮而需要國家救濟〕—**means-tested** *adj*: *means-tested benefits* 按經濟狀況調查結果而享受的補助

meant /mɛnt; ment/ *v* the past tense and past participle of MEAN[1]

mean·time /ˈmin,taɪm; ˈmiːntaɪm/ *adv* **1 in the meantime** in the period of time between now and a future event, or between two events in the past 在此期間; 與此同時: *The doctor will be here soon. In the meantime, try and relax.* 醫生很快就來, 你現在先設法放鬆一下。| *I didn't see her for another five years, and in the meantime she had got married and had a couple of kids.* 我又有五年沒見到她, 在此期間她結了婚並生了兩個孩子。**2 for the meantime** for the present time, until something happens 目前, 眼下: *The power supply should be back soon – for the meantime we'll have to use candles.* 應該很快就會恢復供電——眼下我們只好點蠟燭。**3** [sentence adverb 句子副詞] *spoken* in the present period, before something else happens【口】在目前這段時間裡: *Dinner will be at 7. Meantime, just make yourselves at home.* 七點鐘開飯。開飯前, 大家隨便些, 就像在自己家裡一樣。

mean·while /ˈmin,hwaɪl; ˈmiːnwaɪl/ *adv* [sentence adverb 句子副詞] **1** in the period of time between two events 在此期間: *The flight will be announced soon. Meanwhile, please remain seated.* 航班很快就要宣布登機。宣布之前請繼續坐在座位上。| **in the meanwhile** *I knew I wouldn't get my exam results for several weeks, and I wasn't sure what to do in the meanwhile.* 我知道我要數週以後才會得到自己的考試成績, 在此期間我拿不準該做點甚麼。**2** while something else is happening 與此同時: *Jim went to answer the phone. Meanwhile Pete started to prepare lunch.* 吉姆去接電話。皮特這時開始準備午飯。**3** used to compare two things that are happening at the same time 在這期間, 與此同時〔用以比較同時發生的兩件事〕: *The incomes of male professionals went up by almost 80%. Meanwhile, part-time women workers saw their earnings fall.* 男性專業人員的收入幾乎增加了 80%, 而與此同時兼職女性的收入卻下降了。

mean·y /ˈminɪ; ˈmiːni/ *n* [C] another way of spelling MEANIE meanie 的另一種拼法

mea·sles /ˈmizḷz; ˈmiːzəlz/ *n* [U] also 又作 **the measles** an infectious illness in which you have a fever and small red spots on your face and body 麻疹 —see also 另見 GERMAN MEASLES

meas·ly /ˈmizlɪ; ˈmiːzli/ *adj informal* very small and disappointing in size, quantity, or value【非正式】〔大小、數量或價值〕微不足道的, 小[少]得令人失望的: *All I got was a measly £5.* 我得到的只是區區五英鎊。

mea·su·ra·ble /ˈmɛʒrəbḷ; ˈmeʒərəbəl/ *adj* **1** large or important enough to have a definite effect 重大的, 重要的: *The tax will not have any measurable impact on the lives of most people.* 這種稅收將不會對大多數人的生活產生重大的影響。**2** able to be measured 可測量的, 可度量的: *measurable results* 可衡量的結果 —**measurably** *adv*: *His mood had improved measurably.* 他的情緒已經大大好轉了。

mea·sure[1] /ˈmɛʒɚ; ˈmeʒə/ *n*
1 ►OFFICIAL ACTION 正式行動◄ [C] an official action that is intended to deal with a particular problem 措施, 辦法: *Stronger measures are needed to combat crime.* 需要採取更強有力的措施來與犯罪作鬥爭。
2 half measures things done to deal with a difficult situation that are not effective or firm enough 〔處理困難情況效果不佳或不夠堅決的〕折衷辦法: *This was no time for half measures and compromises.* 這不是搞折衷和妥協的時候。
3 ►A CERTAIN AMOUNT 一定的量◄ **a measure of success/agreement/freedom etc** a certain amount of a good or useful quality 一定程度的成功/同意/自由等: *new legislation giving women a measure of economic independence* 給予婦女一定程度經濟獨立的新立法
4 ►UNIT OF MEASUREMENT 度量單位◄ [C] an amount or unit in a measuring system 計量[度量]單位: *A centimetre is a measure of length.* 厘米是長度計量單位。| *a table of weights and measures* 度量衡表

5 a measure of alcohol/whisky/etc a standard amount of an alcoholic drink 標準量的一杯酒/威士忌等

6 ▶SIGN/PROOF 標誌/證明◀ **be a measure of sth** *formal* to be a sign of the importance, strength etc of something【正式】是某事的標誌[證明]: *It is a measure of his popularity that he was able to travel around without a bodyguard.* 他能不帶保鏢到處旅行是他深得民心的證明。

7 ▶WAY OF JUDGING STH 判斷某事的方法◀ **a measure of** a way of testing or judging something 測試[判斷、評價]…的方法: *Exams are not necessarily the best measure of students' abilities.* 考試未必就是測試學生能力的最好方法。

8 beyond measure *formal* very great or very much【正式】非常大; 非常多; 極其: *The pride he felt was beyond measure.* 他感到無比的自豪。| *Her work has improved beyond measure.* 她的工作已大有進步。

9 for good measure in addition to what you have already done or given〔在已做好或已給出的某物之外〕再增加; 外加: *She tasted the mixture and added another glass of brandy for good measure.* 她嚐了嚐兑好的酒, 然後又加進去一杯白蘭地。

10 in large measure/in some measure to a great degree or to some degree 在很大/某種程度上: *The improvements are due in large measure to his leadership.* 這些改進在很大程度上是由於他領導有方。

11 in full measure if someone gives something back in full measure, they give back as much as they received 全部地〔回報所受之物〕: *They returned our hospitality in full measure.* 他們對我們報以同樣的熱情。

12 the full measure of *formal* the whole of something【正式】…的全部: *Ralph received the full measure of his mother's devotion.* 拉爾夫得到了母親全部的關愛。

13 get the measure of sb/take sb's measure to form a judgment of someone's abilities or character, so that you are able to deal with them or defeat them 估量某人的能力[性格], 掂某人的分量: *She soon got the measure of her opponent.* 她很快就掂出了對手的分量。

14 ▶THING USED FOR MEASURING 計量之物◀ [C] something such as a piece of wood or a container used for measuring 量具, 量器 —see also 另見 TAPE MEASURE

15 ▶SYSTEM FOR MEASURING 計量制◀ [U] a system for measuring amount, size, or weight 計量制, 度量法: *liquid measure* 液體量度, 液量

16 ▶MUSIC 音樂◀ [C] *AmE* one of a group of notes and rests (REST[1] (12)), separated by VERTICAL lines, into which a line of written music is divided【美】小節 —see also 另見 MADE-TO-MEASURE, **give sb short measure** (SHORT[1] (14))

measure 量, 測量

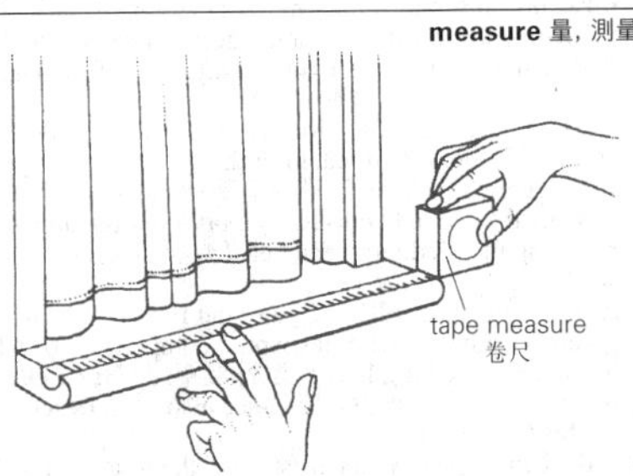

S2 W2 **measure**[2] *v* **1** [T] to find the size, length, or amount of something using standard units 量, 測量; 計量: *Could you measure the height of the wall for me?* 你能為我量一下牆的高度嗎? | *The rainfall was measured over a three-month period.* 對三個月內的降雨量進行了測量。| **measure sb for sth** (=measure someone in order to make clothes for them) 給某人量體裁衣 *She was being measured for her wedding dress.* 正在給她量尺寸做結婚禮服。**2** [T] to judge the importance, value, or true nature of something 估量, 衡量〔某物的重要性、價值或真正性質〕: *What criteria can we use to measure women's progress in the workforce?* 我們能用甚麼標準來衡量婦女在勞動大軍中的進步呢? | **measure sth by sth** *Education shouldn't be measured purely by examination results.* 教育不應該純粹用考試成績來衡量。**3** [linking verb 連繫動詞] to be a particular size, length, or amount〔某物的〕體積[長度, 數額]為…: *That old tree must measure at least 30 metres from top to bottom.* 那棵古樹從樹梢到地面至少有30米。| *an earthquake measuring 6.5 on the Richter scale* 黎克特制6.5級的地震 **4** [T] to show or record a particular kind of measurement 顯示, 記錄〔長度、高度、大小等〕: *an instrument for measuring tiny amounts of electrical current* 測微量電流的儀器 **5 measure your length** *old use* to fall down flat on the ground【舊】跌倒在地, 躺在地上

measure sb/sth **against** *phr v* [T] to judge someone or something by comparing them with another person or thing〔用與他人或他物相比較的方法〕評判: *When measured against the work of a professional, her efforts look unimpressive.* 當和專業人員的工作相比時, 她所作的努力看起來就不怎麼起眼了。

measure sth ↔ **off** *phr v* [T] to measure a length of material and cut it from a larger piece 量出並裁下: *The assistant measured off enough fabric for three dresses.* 助手量出並剪裁下足夠縫製三條連衣裙的衣料。

measure sth ↔ **out** *phr v* [T] to take a certain amount of liquid, powder etc from a larger amount 量出, 量取: *Measure out 100 grams of flour.* 量出100克麵粉。

measure up *phr v* **1** [I] to be good enough to do a particular job or to reach a particular standard 合格; 達到標準: **[+to]** *How will the Secretary General measure up to his new responsibilities?* 秘書長將如何才能勝任他的新職責呢? | *We'll give you a week's trial in the job to see how you measure up.* 我們將讓你在這個工作崗位試做一個星期, 看你是否合格。**2** [I,T] to measure something 計量〔某物〕: *I'd better measure up before I start laying the carpet.* 在開始鋪地毯之前我最好量一量。

mea·sured /ˈmɛʒɚd; ˈmeʒəd/ *adj* careful and slow or steady 慎重而緩慢的; 平穩的: *a calm measured voice* 平緩的聲音 | *a measured response* 慎重的答覆

mea·sure·less /ˈmɛʒɚlɪs; ˈmeʒələs/ *adj literary* too big to be measured【文】大得無法測量的, 無邊無際的: *falling through the measureless ocean* 在茫茫大海中下墜

mea·sure·ment /ˈmɛʒɚmənt; ˈmeʒəmənt/ *n* **1** [C usually plural 一般用複數] the length, height etc of something〔某物的〕長度; 高度; 大小: **waist/chest etc measurement** *What's your waist measurement?* 你的腰圍有多大? | **make/take measurements** (=measure something) 量尺寸, 測量 *The builders made careful measurements.* 建築人員仔細地進行了測量。| **take sb's measurements** (=measure someone in order to make or find clothes for them)〔為縫製或購買衣服〕給某人量尺寸 **2** [U] the act of measuring something 測量, 計量, 衡量: *the measurement of performance* 性能測試 W3

measuring cup /ˈ··· ˌ·/ *n* [C] *especially AmE* a cup used for measuring food or liquid when cooking【尤美】〔烹飪用的〕量杯

measuring jug /ˈ··· ˌ·/ *n* [C] *especially BrE* a glass or plastic container used for measuring liquid when cooking【尤英】〔烹飪用的〕玻璃[塑料]量壺 —see picture at 參見 JUG 圖

measuring tape /ˈ··· ˌ·/ *n* [C] a long piece of cloth or steel used for measuring; TAPE MEASURE 卷尺, 軟尺, 皮尺

meat /mit; miːt/ *n* **1** [U] the flesh of animals and birds eaten as food〔供食用的〕肉: *I gave up eating meat a few months ago.* 我幾個月以前就不吃肉了。| *meat pie* 肉 S2 W3

餡餅 **2** [C] a type of meat 一種肉: *a selection of cold meats* 各種冷盤肉 **3** [U] something that is interesting or important in a talk, book etc〔談話、書籍等中〕有趣[重要]的內容: *The lecture was well-delivered but there wasn't much meat in it.* 演講講得很好, 但沒有甚麼實質內容。| **the meat of** (=the main and most interesting part) …主要且最有趣的部分 *We then got down to the real meat of the debate.* 我們接下來就開始了辯論的主要部分。**4 sb doesn't have much meat on him/her** *informal* used to say that someone looks very thin【非正式】某人沒多少肉: *George doesn't have much meat on him, does he?* 喬治身上沒有幾兩肉, 是吧? **5 easy meat** *informal* someone who it is easy to deceive or hurt【非正式】易上當受騙的人; 易受傷害的人 **6 meat and drink to sb** something that someone enjoys doing or finds very easy to do 某人喜歡做的事; 某人認為很容易做的事: *The first five questions were on basketball, which was meat and drink to Larry.* 前五個問題是關於籃球的, 這對拉里來說輕而易舉。| *Repairing cars is meat and drink to him.* 修車是他喜歡做的事。**7 be the meat in the sandwich** *BrE informal* to be friendly with two people or groups who are quarrelling【英, 非正式】跟爭吵的雙方都友好 **8 one man's meat is another man's poison** used to say that something that one person likes may not be liked by someone else 甲之熊掌, 乙之砒霜; 一個人喜歡的另一個人未必喜歡 **9 the meat and potatoes** *AmE informal* the most important part of a discussion【美, 非正式】〔討論中〕最重要的部分: *Let's get down to the meat and potatoes; how much are you going to pay me for this?* 我們來討論最關鍵的問題: 你打算為此付我多少錢?

meat·ball /ˋmit͵bɔl; ˈmiːtbɔːl/ *n* [C] a small round ball made from thin pieces of meat pressed together 肉丸子

meat grind·er /ˈ· ͵··/ *n* [C] *AmE* a machine that cuts meat into very small pieces by forcing it through small holes【美】絞肉機; MINCER *BrE*【英】

meat·loaf /ˋmit͵lof; ˈmiːtləʊf/ *n* [C,U] a type of food made from meat and other foods which are mixed together in the shape of a LOAF and baked 肉糕〔一種用肉和其他食物攪拌在一起做成麵包形狀烤製而成的食物〕

meat-pack·ing /ˈ· ͵··/ *n* [U] *AmE* the preparation of dead animals so that they can be sold as meat【美】肉類加工: *the meat packing industry* 肉類加工業 —**meat-packer** *n* [C]

meat·y /ˋmitɪ; ˈmiːti/ *adj* **1** containing a lot of meat or tasting strongly of meat 多肉的; 肉味濃的: *a delicious meaty gravy* 味美肉多的肉汁 **2** *informal* big and fat, with a lot of flesh【非正式】大而肥胖的: *a tall guy with meaty shoulders* 身材高大、雙肩肥厚的男子 **3** *informal* containing a lot of interesting ideas or information【非正式】內容豐富的: *The lecture wasn't very meaty.* 這個講座內容不是很豐富。

mec·ca /ˋmɛkə; ˈmekə/ *n* [singular] **1** a place that many people want to visit for a particular reason 眾人想去參觀的地方, 眾人嚮往之勝地: **[+for]** *Florence is a mecca for students of Art History.* 佛羅倫薩是修藝術史的學生們嚮往的勝地。**2 Mecca** a city in Saudi Arabia which is the holiest city of Islam 麥加〔沙特阿拉伯城市, 伊斯蘭教的聖地〕

me·chan·ic /məˋkænɪk; mɪˈkænɪk/ *n* **1** [C] someone who is skilled at repairing motor vehicles and machinery 技工; 機械工; 機修工 **2 mechanics** [U] the science that deals with the effects of forces on objects 力學; 機械學 —see also 另見 QUANTUM MECHANICS **3 the mechanics of (doing) sth** the way in which something works or is done (做)某事的方法[技巧, 技術細節]: *I still don't understand the mechanics of transferring computer files onto a different machine.* 我仍然不懂怎樣把電腦文件轉到另一台電腦上去。

me·chan·i·cal /məˋkænɪkḷ; mɪˈkænɪkəl/ *adj* **1** using power from an engine to do a particular kind of work 機械操縱的: *a mechanical digger* 挖掘機 **2** affecting or involving a machine 機械方面的: *The pump shut off as a result of a mechanical failure.* 由於機械故障, 泵停住了。**3** a mechanical action, reply etc is done without thinking, and has been done many times before〔動作、回答等〕機械的, 不加思考的: *He was asked the same question so many times that the answer became mechanical.* 他被多次問到同樣的問題, 所以他的回答都變得機械起來。**4** *informal* someone who is mechanical understands how machines work【非正式】有機械方面知識的 **5** *technical* connected with or produced by physical forces【術語】物理的; 物理產生的: *the mechanical properties of solids* 固體的物理特性 —**mechanically** /-kḷɪ; -kli/ *adv*

mechanical en·gi·neer·ing /·͵··· ··ˈ··/ *n* [U] the study of the design and production of machines and tools 機械工程(學) —**mechanical engineer** *n* [C]

mechanically mind·ed /·͵··· ˈ··◂/ *adj* good at understanding how machines work and repairing them 精通機械的; 擅長機械修理的

mechanical pen·cil /·͵··· ˈ··/ *n* [C] *AmE* a pencil made of metal or plastic, with a thin piece of LEAD (=the part that you write with) inside【美】活動鉛筆, 自動鉛筆; PROPELLING PENCIL *BrE*【英】

mech·a·nis·m /ˋmɛkə͵nɪzəm; ˈmekənɪzəm/ *n* [C] **1** part of a machine that does a particular job 機械裝置, 機件, 工作部件: *the brake mechanism* 剎車裝置 **2** a system that is intended to achieve something or deal with a problem 機構; 結構; 機制; 體制: *mechanisms to stop the spread of nuclear weapons* 阻止核武器擴散的機制 | *The market system is an imperfect mechanism for achieving full employment.* 市場機制不是實現充分就業的最佳體制。**3** the way that something works 工作方式, 運行機制: *the mechanism of the brain* 大腦的運行機制 **4 defence/survival/escape mechanism** a way of behaving that helps you to avoid or deal with something that is difficult or dangerous 防衛/生存/逃避機制[手段]: *His aggression is actually a defence mechanism against rejection.* 他的好鬥其實是出於自衛, 以免被人排斥。

mech·a·nis·tic /͵mɛkəˋnɪstɪk; ͵mekəˈnɪstɪk◂/ *adj* tending to explain the actions and behaviour of living things as if they were machines 機械論的: *a mechanistic view of the universe* 對宇宙的機械論觀點 —**mechanistically** /-kḷɪ; -kli/ *adj*

mech·a·nize also 又作 **-ise** *BrE*【英】/ˋmɛkə͵naɪz; ˈmekənaɪz/ *v* [I,T] to change the way that something is made or done, so that the work is done by machines instead of people or animals (使)機械化: *Almost the entire process of car manufacturing has been mechanized.* 整個汽車製造過程已經幾乎完全機械化了。—**mechanized** *adj*: *mechanized farming* 機械化耕作 —**mechanization** /͵mɛkənəˋzeʃən; ͵mekənaɪˈzeɪʃən/ *n* [U]

M Econ *n BrE* Master of Economics; a university higher degree in ECONOMICS that you get after your first degree【英】經濟學碩士; 經濟學碩士學位

M Ed /͵ɛm ˋɛd; ͵em ˈed/ *n* Master of Education; a university higher degree in teaching that you get after your first degree 教育學碩士; 教育學碩士學位

Med /mɛd; med/ *n* **the Med** *BrE informal* the area surrounding the Mediterranean Sea【英, 非正式】地中海沿岸地區

med·al /ˋmɛdḷ; ˈmedl/ *n* [C] a round flat piece of metal given to someone who has won a competition or who has done something brave 獎牌; 獎章; 勳章: *an Olympic gold medal* 奧運會金牌 —see also 另見 **deserve a medal** (DESERVE (3))

med·al·ist /ˋmɛdḷɪst; ˈmedl-ɪ̵st/ *n* [C] the American spelling of MEDALLIST medallist的美式拼法

me·dal·li·on /mɪˋdæljən; mɪ̵ˈdæliən/ *n* [C] a piece of metal shaped like a large coin, worn as jewellery on a chain around the neck 圓形徽章〔形似大錢幣, 用鏈子戴於頸部的金屬飾物〕

med·al·list /ˋmɛdḷɪst; ˈmedl-ɪ̵st/ *n* [C] *BrE* someone who has won a medal in a competition【英】獎牌獲得者: *the*

Olympic silver medallist 奧運會銀牌得主

Medal of Hon·our /ˌ·· · ˈ··/ *n* [C] the highest award given by Congress to a soldier, sailor etc who has done something extremely brave〔美國〕榮譽勳章〔由美國國會授予士兵、水兵等的最高軍功勳章〕

med·dle /ˋmɛdḷ; ˈmedl/ *v* [I] **1** to deliberately become involved in a situation that does not concern you, or that you do not understand 干預, 干涉; 管閒事: **[+in/with]** *I wish you wouldn't meddle in my affairs.* 我希望你不要干涉我的事。**2** to touch something carelessly in a way that might break it 胡亂擺弄: **[+with]** *The kids are always meddling with the ornaments.* 孩子們總是亂動那些裝飾品。—**meddler** *n* [C]

med·dle·some /ˋmɛdḷsəm; ˈmedlsəm/ *adj* tending to become involved in situations that do not concern you, in a way that annoys people 好干預的; 愛管閒事的: *that meddlesome old woman* 那個愛管閒事的老太太

2 2 **me·di·a** /ˋmidɪə; ˈmiːdiə/ *n* **1 the media** all the organizations, such as television, radio, and the newspapers, that provide information for the public 新聞媒體, 傳媒, 大眾傳播媒介〈如電視、廣播、報紙等〉: *The letter was leaked to the media by a White House official.* 這封信被一名白宮官員透露給了新聞媒體。| [also+plural verb *BrE* 英] *The media have launched a bitter attack on the Health Minister.* 大眾傳媒向衛生部長發起了猛烈攻擊。| **media coverage** (=the amount of time or space given to an event by the media)〔新聞〕媒體報道量 *The war got massive media coverage.* 那次戰爭受到大眾傳媒的廣泛報道。| **media event** (=an event that the media give a lot of attention to) 傳媒矚目的事件 | **media hype** (=a lot of attention given to an event by the media, making it seem much more important than it really is) 傳媒宣傳[渲染] **2** the plural of MEDIUM —see also 另見 MASS MEDIA

med·i·ae·val /ˌmidɪˋivḷ; ˌmediˈiːvəl◂/ *adj* another spelling of MEDIEVAL medieval 的另一種拼法

me·di·an¹ /ˋmidɪən; ˈmiːdiən/ *n* **1** [C] *AmE* a thin area of land running down the middle of a road to keep traffic travelling in different directions apart【美】〔道路的〕中央分隔帶, 中央分道區, 中間安全區; CENTRAL RESERVATION *BrE*【英】**2** [C] the middle measurement in a set of measurements that are arranged in order 中位數 **3** [C] *technical* a line passing from one of the points of a TRIANGLE to the opposite side【術語】〔三角形的〕中線

median² *adj* [only before noun 僅用於名詞前] *technical*【術語】**1** in or passing through the middle 中間的; 穿過中點的 **2** *technical* related to a line passing from one of the points of a TRIANGLE to the opposite side【術語】〔三角形〕中線的

median strip /ˈ··· ˌ·/ *n* [C] *AmE* MEDIAN¹ (1)【美】〔道路的〕中央分隔帶, 中央分道區, 中間安全區 —see picture on page A3 參見 A3 頁圖

media stud·ies /ˈ··· ˌ··/ *n* [U] *BrE* the study of newspapers, radio and television【英】媒體研究

me·di·ate /ˋmidɪˌet; ˈmiːdieɪt/ *v* **1** [I,T] to try to end a quarrel between two people or groups 調停, 調解, 斡旋: **[+between]** *The U.N. attempted to mediate between the warring factions.* 聯合國試圖在兩個交戰派別之間進行斡旋。| **mediate sth** *The court was set up to mediate civil disputes.* 該法庭是為調解民事糾紛而成立的。**2** [T] to find an agreement or solution by talking to two people or groups who are quarrelling 通過調解促成〔協議等〕: *They've succeeded in mediating a ceasefire.* 他們通過斡旋成功地促成了停火。**3** [T usually passive 一般用被動態] *formal or technical* if the effect of something is mediated by another thing, it changes because of that other thing【正式或術語】使變化; 使受影響: *Child mortality is mediated by economic factors.* 兒童死亡率受經濟因素的影響。—**mediator** *n* [C] —**mediation** /ˌmidɪˋeʃən; ˌmiːdiˈeɪʃən/ *n* [U]

med·ic /ˋmɛdɪk; ˈmedɪk/ *n* [C] **1** *informal* a medical doctor【非正式】醫生 **2** *BrE* a medical student【英】醫科學生 **3** *AmE* someone in the army who gives medical treatment【美】隨軍衛生員

Med·i·caid /ˋmɛdɪˌked; ˈmedɪkeɪd/ *n* [U] a system in the US by which the government helps to pay the cost of medical treatment for poor people〔美國為窮人設立的〕醫療補助制度 —compare 比較 MEDICARE

med·i·cal¹ /ˋmɛdɪkḷ; ˈmedɪkəl/ *adj* connected with medicine and the treatment of disease or injury 醫學的; 醫術的; 醫療的: *The injury required urgent medical attention.* 那處傷口需要緊急治療。| *medical college* 醫學院 | *Poor people can only afford the most basic medical treatment.* 窮人只負擔得起最基本的醫療。| **the medical profession** (=doctors, nurses, and other people who treat people who are ill) 醫學界 —**medically** /-kḷɪ; -kli/ *adv* 2 2

medical² *n* [C] *BrE* an examination of your body by a doctor to see if you are healthy【英】體格檢查; PHYSICAL² *AmE*【美】: *You'll need to have a medical before starting the new job.* 在開始這項新工作以前你要進行體格檢查。

medical cer·tif·i·cate /ˈ··· ·ˌ···/ *n* [C] an official piece of paper signed by a doctor saying that you are too ill to work or that you are completely healthy〔證明病重不能工作的〕診斷書; 健康證明

medical prac·ti·tion·er /ˌ··· ·ˈ···/ *n* [C] *BrE formal* a doctor【英, 正式】醫生

medical school /ˈ··· ·/ *n* [C,U] a college or university where people study to become doctors 醫學院; 醫科大學

me·dic·a·ment /məˋdɪkəmənt; mɪˈdɪkəmənt/ *n* [C] *formal* a substance used on or in the body to treat a disease【正式】藥物, 藥劑

Med·i·care /ˋmɛdɪˌkɛr; ˈmedɪkeə/ *n* [U] a system by which the US government helps to pay for the medical treatment of old people〔美國由政府設立的〕老年人醫療保健制度 —compare 比較 MEDICAID

med·i·cat·ed /ˋmɛdɪˌketɪd; ˈmedɪkeɪtɪd/ *adj* medicated soap or SHAMPOO contains a substance to help small medical problems of your skin or hair〔香皂或洗髮劑〕含藥物成分的

med·i·ca·tion /ˌmɛdɪˋkeʃən; ˌmedɪˈkeɪʃən/ *n* [C,U] medicine or drugs given to people who are ill 藥物, 藥劑: **be on medication** *She's on medication for her heart.* 她正在服藥治療心臟病。

me·di·ci·nal /məˋdɪsṇḷ; mɪˈdɪsənəl/ *adj* **1** a medicinal substance can cure illness or disease (醫) 藥的; 藥用的; 有療效的: **medicinal properties** *Evening primrose oil is thought to have medicinal properties.* 夜來香油被認為有藥物效用。**2 for medicinal purposes** *humorous* used to say jokingly that you drink alcohol because it is good for your health【幽默】為了醫療目的, 為了治病〔用以開玩笑地說因對健康有益而飲酒〕: *I keep a bottle of brandy handy – purely for medicinal purposes.* 我手頭經常準備着一瓶白蘭地——純粹是為了治病。—compare 比較 MEDICAL¹ —**medicinally** *adv*

med·i·cine /ˋmɛdəsṇ; ˈmedsən/ *n* **1** [C,U] a substance used for treating illness, especially a liquid you drink 藥, 藥物〔尤指口服的藥水〕: **take medicine** *Have you taken your medicine?* 你服過藥了嗎? **2** [U] the treatment and study of illnesses and injuries 醫術; 醫學: *He studied medicine at Yale.* 他曾經在耶魯大學學醫。| *homeopathic medicine* 順勢療法 **3 the best medicine** the best way of making you feel better when you are sad 最好的藥〔憂傷時使你心情好一些的最佳辦法〕: *Laughter is the best medicine.* 大笑是最好的藥。**4 give someone a dose/taste of their own medicine** to treat someone as badly as they have treated you 以其人之道, 還治其人之身: *I love 'em and leave 'em, she said. I do it to give men a taste of their own medicine.* 我愛他們, 但不會跟他們長相廝守, 她說。我這樣對男人是以其人之道還治其人之身。**5 take your medicine (like a man)** to accept an unpleasant situation that you have caused, or a punishment, without complaining (像男子漢那樣) 認罰, 沒有怨言地忍受自己引起的不愉快的事情

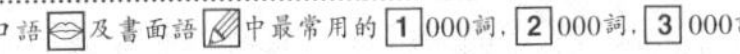

—see also 另見 ALTERNATIVE MEDICINE

medicine chest /ˈ‥ ˌ/ *n* [C] a small cupboard used to store medicines 藥櫃

medicine man /ˈ‥ ˌ/ or **medicine wom·an** /ˈ‥ ˌ‥ˌ/ *n* [C] a person in a Native American tribe who is considered to have the ability to cure illness and disease 巫醫〔美洲印第安人部落中被認為具有治病能力的人〕

med·i·co /ˈmɛdɪˌko; ˈmedɪkəʊ/ *n* [C] *informal* a MEDIC【非正式】醫生; 醫科學生; 隨軍衛生員

3 **med·i·e·val, mediaeval** /ˌmidɪˈivḷ; ˌmediˈiːvəl◂/ *adj* **1** connected with the Middle Ages (=the period between about AD 1100 and 1500) 中世紀的, 中古時期的: *medieval literature* 中世紀文學 | *medieval Europe* 中世紀的歐洲 **2** *humorous* very old or old-fashioned【幽默】古老的; 舊式的; 過時的: *The plumbing in this house is positively medieval!* 這個房子裡的水管實在太陳舊了!

me·di·o·cre /ˌmidɪˈokə; ˌmiːdiˈəʊkə◂/ *adj* not very good 不太好的; 平凡的, 平庸的: *I thought the film was pretty mediocre.* 我認為這部電影非常一般。| *a mediocre student* 普通學生 —**mediocrity** /ˌmidɪˈɑkrətɪ; ˌmiːdiˈɒkrɪ̵ti/ *n* [U]

med·i·tate /ˈmɛdəˌtet; ˈmedɪ̵teɪt/ *v* **1** [I] to empty your mind of thoughts and feelings, in order to relax completely or for religious purposes 默念, 默想; 冥想, 打坐: *I try to meditate for half an hour every evening.* 我每天晚上盡量默想半小時。**2** [I] to think seriously and deeply about something 思考, 沉思, 深思: **[+on/upon]** *She sat quietly, meditating on the day's events.* 她靜靜地坐着, 思考當天發生的事。**3** [T] to plan to do something, usually something unpleasant 策劃, 計劃〔不好的事〕: *Silently she meditated revenge.* 她默默地計劃復仇。

med·i·ta·tion /ˌmɛdəˈteʃən; ˌmedɪ̵ˈteɪʃən/ *n* **1** [U] the practice of emptying your mind of thoughts and feelings, in order to relax completely or for religious reasons 默念, 默想; 冥想; 打坐: *Try to set aside an hour each day for meditation.* 每天設法抽出一個小時來打坐冥想。**2** [C usually plural 一般用複數, U] the act of thinking deeply and seriously about something 沉思, 深思, 思考: *He stood gazing into the water, lost in meditation.* 他站在那兒凝望着水面, 陷入了沉思。| *Rob interrupted his father's meditations.* 羅布打斷了他父親的思考。**3** [C usually plural 一般用複數] serious thoughts about a particular subject〔關於某主題的〕感想; 沉思: **[+on]** *meditations on death and loss* 對於死亡和損失的沉思

med·i·ta·tive /ˈmɛdəˌtetɪv; ˈmedɪ̵tətɪv/ *adj* thinking deeply and seriously about something 深思的, 沉思的, 思考的: *Dr Wijk contemplated the picture in meditative silence.* 威克醫生凝視着那幅畫, 默默地沉思。—**meditatively** *adv*

Med·i·ter·ra·ne·an[1] /ˌmɛdətəˈrenɪən; ˌmedɪ̵təˈreɪniən◂/ *n* **the Mediterranean** the sea that is surrounded by the countries of southern Europe, North Africa, and the Middle East 地中海

Mediterranean[2] *adj* from or connected with the Mediterranean Sea, or typical of the area of Southern Europe around it 地中海的; 地中海地區的; 南歐環地中海地區特有的: *the Mediterranean way of life* 地中海地區的生活方式

3 **me·di·um**[1] /ˈmidɪəm; ˈmiːdiəm/ *adj* **1** of middle size between large and small, of middle height between tall and short etc〔大小、高矮等〕中等的; 中號的: *What size do you want – large, medium, or small?* 你想要多大尺寸的——大號、中號, 還是小號? | **medium sized/medium size** *a medium-sized onion* 中等大小的洋蔥 | **of medium height/length/build etc** *She's of medium height.* 她中等身材。| *The man is of medium build and is in his late 20s.* 那個男子中等身材, 年近30。| *hair of medium length* 中等長短的頭髮 | **medium to large** *medium to large companies* 大中型公司 | **medium heat/oven** (=at a temperature that is warm but not too high or low) 中等的熱度/溫度中等的烤爐 *Bake in a medium oven for 25 minutes.* 在溫度中等的烤爐裡烤25分鐘。**2 medium brown/blue etc** a colour which is neither light nor dark 中等色調的褐色/藍色等: *His jacket's a medium brown colour.* 他的夾克衫是中等色調的褐色。

medium[2] *n plural* **media** /-dɪə; -diə/ or **mediums** [C] **1** a way of communicating information and news to people, such as newspapers, television etc 傳播媒介〈如報紙、電視等〉: *Politicians prefer to use the medium of television.* 政治家們喜歡使用電視媒介。—see also 另見 MEDIA **2** a way of expressing your ideas, especially as a writer or an artist〔尤指作家或藝術家表達思想的〕方法, 手段; 藝術形式: **[+for]** *the novel as a medium for satire* 作為一種諷刺手段的小說 | *the visual media* 視覺媒介 **3 medium of instruction** a language that is used for teaching 教學語言: *English is still the main medium of instruction in Nigeria.* 在尼日利亞英語仍然是主要的教學語言。**4 medium of exchange** money or other ways of paying for things 交換媒介〔指金錢或其他的支付方法〕 **5** *technical* a substance or material in which things grow or exist【術語】培養基 **6** *technical* a substance through which a force travels【術語】媒質, 媒介物; 傳導體 —see also 另見 MAGNETIC MEDIA, **happy medium** (HAPPY (7))

medium[3] *n plural* **mediums** [C] someone who claims to have the power to receive messages from the spirits of the dead 靈媒, 巫師, 招魂者

medium term /ˈ‥ ˌ/ *n* [singular] the period of time a few weeks or months ahead of the present 中期: **in the medium term** *The company's prospects look good in the medium term.* 就中期而言, 公司的前景看好。| *medium term investments* 中期投資 —compare 比較 SHORT-TERM, LONG-TERM

medium wave /ˈ‥ ˌ/ *written abbreviation* 縮寫為 **MW** *n* [U] a system of radio broadcasting using radio waves (WAVE[1] (3)) that are between 100 and 1000 metres in length〔無線電廣播的〕中波

med·ley /ˈmɛdlɪ; ˈmedli/ *n* [C] **1** a group of songs or tunes sung or played one after the other as a single piece of music 集成曲, 組合曲; 一組聯唱[聯奏]的歌曲[樂曲]: *a medley of Eighties hits* 20世紀80年代走紅歌曲匯成的組合曲 **2** a swimming race in which the competitors swim using four different strokes (STROKE[1] (2b))〔游泳的〕個人四式比賽; 四式接力比賽 **3** [usually singular 一般用單數] a mixture of different kinds of the same thing which produces an interesting or unusual effect 混合物; 大雜燴: *a medley of architectural styles* 各種不同建築風格的大雜燴

meek /mik; miːk/ *adj* very quiet and gentle and unwilling to argue or express an opinion 溫順的, 馴服的: *a meek and obedient child* 一個溫順聽話的孩子 | **meek and mild** (=extremely quiet and gentle) 極其溫順的 *She'd never stand up for herself, she's too meek and mild.* 她從來不替自己爭辯, 她太溫順了。—**meekly** *adv*: *She smiled meekly.* 她溫順地笑了笑。—**meekness** *n* [U]

meet[1] /mit; miːt/ *v past tense and past participle* **met** /mɛt; met/

1 ►BE IN THE SAME PLACE 在同一地點◄ [I,T not in passive 不用被動態] **a)** to be in the same place as someone else because you have arranged to do this〔事先約好在某處〕會面, 碰頭: *Meet me at 8.00.* 八點鐘和我會面。| *We agreed to meet in front of the theatre.* 我們約好在劇院前碰頭。| *Why don't we meet for lunch on Friday?* 我們何不星期五一塊吃午飯? **b)** to see someone by chance and talk to them 偶然遇見, 碰到: *James and Tim met in the park.* 詹姆斯和蒂姆在公園相遇。| *You'll never guess who I met yesterday – my old teacher!* 你絕對猜不到我昨天遇見誰了——我過去的老師!

2 ►SEE SB FOR THE FIRST TIME 第一次見到某人◄ [I,T not in passive 不用被動態] to see and talk to someone for the first time, or be introduced to them 認識, 結識: *Diego and Susan met on vacation and were married six months later.* 迪哥和蘇珊度假時相識, 六個月後就結

婚了。| *Jane, come and meet Alan and Dave.* 簡, 過來認識一下艾倫和戴夫。| *I met my husband at University.* 我在大學認識了我丈夫。

3 nice/pleased/glad to meet you *spoken especially BrE*【口, 尤英】also 又作 **nice meeting you** *AmE spoken*【美口】used when meeting someone for the first time, especially when another person has introduced you to each other 認識你很高興〔第一次見面時用, 尤指有人介紹時〕: *"Farrah, this is Jean-Paul." "Nice to meet you."* "法拉, 這是讓－保羅。" "幸會!"

4 ►AT AN AIRPORT/STATION ETC 在機場/車站等◄ [T] to meet someone who has arrived at an airport, station etc 迎接: *Rob came to meet us at the airport.* 羅布來機場迎接我們。

5 ►COMMITTEE, GROUP ETC 委員會, 團體等◄ [I] to be together in the same place, usually in order to discuss something〔尤為商討某事而〕聚集開會: *The committee meets once a month.* 委員會每月開一次會。

6 ►OPPONENT 對手◄ [I,T not in passive 不用被動態] to play against another person or team in a competition, or to fight another army in a war〔在比賽中〕與對手交鋒;〔在戰爭中〕與敵軍交戰; 迎戰: *Manchester United will meet Blackburn Rovers in the sixth round of the Cup.* 曼徹斯特聯隊將在足總杯的第六輪中與布力般流浪隊交鋒。

7 ►RIVERS/ROADS/LINES ETC 河流/道路/線條等◄ [I,T not in passive 不用被動態] to join together at a particular place 相接; 相交, 交匯, 會合: *The two roads meet just north of Flagstaff.* 這兩條路就在弗拉格斯塔夫以北不遠處會合。| **meet sth** *You can see on the map where the land meets the sea.* 你可以在地圖上看到陸地和海洋的交匯處。

8 ►PROBLEM/ATTITUDE/SITUATION 問題/態度/情況◄ [T] to experience a particular kind of problem, attitude, or situation; ENCOUNTER[1] 經歷, 遭遇, 遭受: *I've never met this kind of problem before.* 我以前從來沒碰到過這類問題。

9 meet a demand/need/requirement to satisfy a demand etc 滿足需求/需要/要求: *The company is unable to meet these wage claims.* 該公司不能滿足這些增加工資的要求。

10 meet an aim/goal/target etc to achieve an aim etc 達到目的/目標/指標等: *It's virtually impossible to meet the weekly sales targets.* 要達到每週的銷售指標幾乎是不可能的。

11 meet debts/costs/expenses etc to pay debts etc 償付債務/支付費用/支付開銷等: *The firm has found itself unable to meet its debts.* 公司發現自己無力償債。

12 there's more to sb/sth than meets the eye used to say that someone or something is more interesting, intelligent etc than they seem to be 某人/某物比表面所看到的更為有趣[聰明等]

13 our/their eyes meet if two people's eyes meet they look at each other, because they are attracted to each other or because they are thinking the same thing 我們/他們的目光相遇: *Their eyes met across the crowded room.* 他們的目光越過擁擠的房間相遇了。

14 meet sb's eye/gaze/glance etc to look directly at someone who is looking at you 迎着[直視]某人的目光: *Martin met his father's accusing glance defiantly.* 馬丁不服氣地直視父親責備的目光。

15 meet your eye/ear to be heard or seen 被看見/聽見: *At the top of the mountain a scene of extraordinary beauty met our eyes.* 山頂上, 異常美麗的景色映入了我們的眼簾。

16 meet your match to have an opponent who is stronger or more skilful than you are 遇到對手: *I think he's finally met his match.* 我想他終於遇到對手了。

17 meet sb halfway to do some of the things that someone wants, in order to reach an agreement with them 與某人妥協, 遷就某人: *They won't pay all our expenses but they might be prepared to meet us halfway.* 他們不會支付我們的全部開銷, 但他們也許願意支付一部分。

18 ►TOUCH/HIT 接觸/碰撞◄ [I,T] to touch or hit another object〔與另一物體〕接觸, 碰撞: *Their hands met under the table.* 他們的手在桌子下面碰了一下。

19 meet (sth) head-on a) if two vehicles or people that are moving quickly towards each other meet head-on, they hit each other suddenly and violently〔車輛或人〕迎頭撞上(某物) **b)** if you meet a problem head-on, you deal with it directly without trying to avoid it 不迴避地直接處理〔某一問題〕

20 meet your death/end to die in a particular way〔以某種方式〕死去: *The general met a violent end at the hands of a paid assassin.* 將軍被一個雇傭殺手殘暴地殺害了。

21 meet your maker *informal humorous* to die【非正式, 幽默】去見上帝, 死

22 sb has met their Waterloo used to say that someone will be defeated 某人已[將]被擊敗, 某人遭遇了滑鐵盧 —see also 另見 **make ends meet** (END[1] (17))

meet up *phr v* [I] **1** to meet someone in order to do something together 碰頭, 相聚: *We often meet up after work and go for a drink.* 下班後我們常常一塊去喝一杯。| [+with] *Pete met up with us after the game.* 看完比賽後皮特和我們聚在一起。**2** if roads, paths etc meet up they join together at a particular place〔道路等〕相互連接, 相交, 交會: [+with] *The path eventually meets up with the main road.* 這條小路最終與大路交會。

meet with sb/sth *phr v* [T] **1** to have a meeting with someone 會見, 會晤: *Representatives of EC countries will meet with senior American politicians.* 歐共體國家的代表們將會晤美國高級政治人物。**2** to get a particular reaction or result 遭到, 遭受; 獲得: **meet with approval/disapproval/opposition** *The senator's suggestions met with widespread disapproval.* 參議員的建議遭到普遍反對。| **meet with success/failure** (=succeed or fail) 獲得成功/遭到失敗 *Our attempts at negotiation finally met with some success.* 我們談判中的努力最終獲得了一些成功。**3 meet with an accident/danger/death** *formal* to experience something by chance, often something unpleasant【正式】遭遇事故/危險/死亡: *Rizzio met with a fatal accident at Hollyrood Palace.* 里齊奧在霍利魯德宮遭遇意外事故身亡。

meet[2] *n* [C] **1 track/sports meet** *especially AmE* a sports competition, especially a competition between people running races【尤美】田徑/體育運動會 **2** *BrE* an occasion when a group of people riding horses go out to hunt foxes (FOX[1] (1))【英】集體騎馬獵狐

meet[3] *adj old use* right or suitable【舊】對的; 適合的

meet·ing /ˈmiːtɪŋ; ˈmiːtɪŋ/ *n* **1** [C] an event at which people meet to talk and decide things 會議; 集會: **attend a meeting** *Over a hundred people attended the meeting.* 一百多人參加了會議。| **be in/at a meeting** *Mrs Lavelle is in a meeting at the moment.* 拉韋爾夫人眼下正在開會。| **hold a meeting** *A meeting will be held in the City Hall on Thursday at 2pm.* 週四下午兩點鐘將在市政廳開會。**2 the meeting** *formal* all the people who attend a meeting【正式】所有參加會議的人, 全體與會者: *I'd like to put a few ideas before the meeting.* 我想向與會者提出幾點想法。**3** [usually singular 一般用單數] a situation of two or more people meeting each other by chance or because they have arranged to do this 會面, 會見: *I had felt drawn to Alice ever since our first meeting.* 自從第一次見面後我就被艾麗斯吸引住了。**4** [C] a sports competition or a set of races for horses 運動會; 賽馬會 **5 meeting of minds** a situation in which two people have very similar ideas and understand each other very well 彼此意見一致; 彼此非常理解: *There was a real meeting of minds between the composer and his young pupil.* 作曲家和他的年輕學生之間有一種真正的默契。**6** an event at which a group of Quakers (=a Christian religious group) worship together〔基督教貴格會教徒的〕宗教聚會, 祈禱會

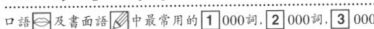

meeting-house /ˋ‥·/ *n* [C] a building where Quakers worship〔基督教貴格會的〕聚會所

meg·a /ˋmɛgə; ˈmegə/ *adj slang* very big and impressive or enjoyable【俚】非常大的; 給人深刻印象的; 十分令人愉快的: *a really mega party* 令人非常愉快的聚會 —**mega** *adv*: *a mega big rock star* 搖滾樂天王巨星

mega- /ˋmɛgə; megə/ *prefix* **1** a million times a particular unit of something 百萬倍: *a 100-megaton bomb* 一億噸級的炸彈 —see table on page C4 參見 C4 頁附錄 **2** *informal* much larger than usual in amount, importance, or size【非正式】〔數量、重要性或尺寸〕大得異乎尋常的: *Hollywood megastars* 好萊塢巨星 | *Frank told me her new boyfriend is megarich.* 弗蘭克告訴我她的新男友是一位巨富。

meg·a·bit /ˋmɛgəbɪt; ˈmegəbɪt/ *n* [C] *technical* a million bits (BIT[1](12))【術語】兆位, 兆比特

meg·a·bucks /ˋmɛgəbʌks; ˈmegəbʌks/ *n* [plural] *informal* a large amount of money【非正式】大量的錢: *She's earning megabucks now.* 她目前正在賺大錢。

meg·a·byte /ˋmɛgəbaɪt; ˈmegəbaɪt/ *n* [C] a million BYTEs 兆字節

meg·a·death /ˋmɛgədɛθ; ˈmegədeθ/ *n* [U] a word meaning one million deaths, used when talking about a NUCLEAR WAR 一百萬人的死亡〔用於談論核戰爭〕

meg·a·hertz /ˋmɛgəhɜts; ˈmegəhɜːts/ written abbreviation 縮寫為 **MHz** *n* a million HERTZ 兆赫

meg·a·lith /ˋmɛgə͵lɪθ; ˈmegəlɪθ/ *n* [C] a large tall stone put in an open place by people in ancient times, possibly as a religious sign〔古代人們可能作為宗教標誌豎立在空曠地上的〕巨石 —**megalithic** /͵mɛgəˋlɪθɪk; ͵megəˈlɪθɪk◂/ *adj*: *a megalithic monument* 巨石碑

meg·a·lo·ma·ni·a /͵mɛgələˋmenɪə; ͵megələʊˈmeɪniə/ *n* [U] the belief that you are extremely important and powerful, which makes you want to control other people's lives, and is often a kind of mental illness 誇大狂; 妄自尊大, 自高自大

meg·a·lo·ma·ni·ac /͵mɛgələˋmenɪ͵æk; ͵megələʊˈmeɪniæk/ *n* [C] someone who believes they are extremely important or powerful and tries to control other people's lives 患誇大狂的人; 妄自尊大的人 —**megalomaniac** *adj*

meg·a·phone /ˋmɛgə͵fon; ˈmegəfəʊn/ *n* [C] a piece of equipment like a large horn which you talk through to make your voice sound louder, when speaking to a crowd 擴音器, 喇叭筒

meg·a·star /ˋmɛgəstɑr; ˈmegəstɑː/ *n* [C] *informal* a very famous singer or actor【非正式】巨星, 超級明星〔指非常有名的歌手或演員〕: *rock megastar David Bowie* 搖滾巨星大衛寶兒

meg·a·ton /ˋmɛgə͵tʌn; ˈmegətʌn/ *n* [C] a measure of the power of an explosive that is equal to that of a million TONs of TNT (=a powerful explosive) 百萬噸級〔相當於一百萬噸黃色炸藥的爆炸威力〕: *a five megaton atomic bomb* 五百萬噸級的原子彈

mel·a·mine /ˋmɛləmin; ˈmeləmiːn/ *n* [U] a material like plastic used to make hard smooth surfaces on tables and shelves 密胺樹脂

mel·an·cho·li·a /͵mɛlənˋkolɪə; ͵melənˈkəʊliə/ *n* [U] *technical* a feeling of great sadness and lack of energy, often caused by mental illness; DEPRESSION (1)【術語】〔常由精神疾病所導致的〕憂鬱症, 抑鬱症

mel·an·chol·ic /͵mɛlənˋkɑlɪk; ͵melənˈkɒlɪk◂/ *adj formal* feeling or tending to be very sad, often because you are mentally ill【正式】憂鬱的, 憂鬱症的: *the cause of Emilia's melancholic condition* 伊米莉亞所患抑鬱症的原因

mel·an·chol·y[1] /ˋmɛlən͵kɑlɪ; ˈmelənkəli/ *adj* sad or making you feel sad 憂鬱的; 令人傷感的: *a melancholy expression* 憂鬱的表情 | *the seagulls' melancholy cry* 海鷗悽婉的叫聲

melancholy[2] *n* [U] *formal* a feeling of sadness for no particular reason【正式】憂鬱, 無名的傷感: *They sank into a mood of deep melancholy.* 他們陷入了深深的憂鬱之中。| *the lingering melancholy of "Gloomy Sunday"*《黑色星期日》那揮之不去的抑鬱之感

me·lange /meˋlɑnʒ; meɪˈlɑːnʒ/ *n* [singular] *French* a mixture of different things【法】混合物; 大雜燴: *a melange of sounds and smells* 各種聲音和氣味的混雜

mel·a·nin /ˋmɛlənɪn; ˈmelənɪn/ *n* [U] a natural dark brown colour in human skin, hair, and eyes〔人的皮膚、毛髮和眼睛的〕黑(色)素

mel·a·no·ma /͵mɛləˋnomə; ͵meləˈnəʊmə/ *n* [C] *technical* a TUMOUR on the skin which causes CANCER【術語】〔致癌的〕黑瘤, 黑素瘤

Mel·ba toast /͵mɛlbə ˋtost; ͵melbə ˈtəʊst/ *n* [U] a kind of thin toast which breaks easily into small bits 梅爾巴吐司〔一種易碎的薄片烤麵包〕

mel·ée /meˋle; ˈmeleɪ/ *n* [usually singular 一般用單數] a situation in which people rush around in a confused way〔人們四處亂竄的〕混亂局面: *Richard was thrown from his horse in the melée.* 在混亂中理查德從馬上被甩了下來。

mel·li·flu·ous /məˋlɪfluəs; mɪˈlɪfluəs/ *adj formal* having a pleasant musical sound【正式】聲音甜美的; 悅耳的, 動聽的: *a mellifluous voice* 悅耳的嗓音 —**mellifluously** *adv*

mel·low[1] /ˋmɛlo; ˈmeləʊ/ *adj* **1** a mellow colour or light looks soft, warm, and not too bright〔顏色或光線〕柔和的; 溫暖的; 不耀眼的: *the mellow, golden light of early evening* 傍晚時分柔和的金色光線 | *mellow shades of brown and orange* 棕色和橘黃色相間的柔和色調 **2** a mellow sound is pleasant and smooth〔聲音〕圓潤的, 悅耳的, 流暢的: *the mellow sound of a trombone* 長號悅耳的聲音 | *a friendly, mellow voice* 友善悅耳的聲音 **3** mellow wine or fruit has a smooth, ripe taste〔水果〕成熟香甜的;〔酒〕芳醇的: *a mellow red wine* 香醇的紅葡萄酒 **4** gentle, calm, and sympathetic because of age or experience〔因年齡或閱歷而〕溫和的, 平靜的, 有同情心的: *Tina's become more mellow since having children of her own.* 自從有了孩子之後, 蒂娜變得更加溫和了。**5** feeling calm and relaxed, especially after drinking alcohol〔尤指飲酒後〕感覺平和輕鬆的: *They were feeling pleasantly mellow.* 他們感到輕鬆愉快。—**mellowness** *n* [U]

mellow[2] *v* [I,T] **1** if colours mellow or are mellowed, they begin to look warm and soft (使)〔顏色〕變得溫馨而柔和 **2** if someone mellows or is mellowed, they become gentler and more sympathetic (使)變得平和而有同情心: *Paul's certainly mellowed over the years.* 這些年來保羅的確變得平和了。**3** if wine mellows or is mellowed it gets a smooth taste (使)〔酒〕變得芳醇

mellow out *phr v* [I,T] *AmE informal* to become relaxed and calm, or make someone relaxed and calm【美, 非正式】(使)變得輕鬆平靜: *Mellow out, OK? It's no big deal!* 放鬆一點, 好嗎? 沒甚麼大不了的!

me·lod·ic /məˋlɑdɪk; mɪˈlɒdɪk/ *adj* **1** *technical* concerned with the main tune in a piece of music【術語】旋律的: *the melodic structure of Beethoven's symphonies* 貝多芬交響樂的旋律結構 **2** having a pleasant tune or a pleasant sound like music 旋律優美的; 聲音悅耳的: *a sweet melodic voice* 甜美動聽的嗓音

me·lo·di·ous /məˋlodɪəs; mɪˈləʊdiəs/ *adj formal* having a pleasant tune or a pleasant sound like music【正式】旋律優美的; 聲音悅耳的, 動聽的: *The piece was melodious and simple.* 這支曲子旋律優美純樸。—**melodiously** *adv* —**melodiousness** *n* [U]

mel·o·dra·ma /ˋmɛlə͵drɑmə; ˈmelədrɑːmə/ *n* [C,U] **1** a story or play with many sudden exciting events, and very good or bad characters, who show feelings that are too strong or simple to seem real 情節劇 **2** a situation in which people behave with too much emotion and excitement 人們過於興奮和感情用事的局面: *Let's not make a melodrama out of this little problem.* 我們不要把這個小小的問題弄成一齣鬧劇。

M

mel·o·dra·mat·ic /ˌmɛlədrəˋmætɪk; ˌmelədrəˈmætɪk◂/ *adj* behaving or talking in an excited way with strong emotion 又哭又鬧的, 胡鬧的; 誇張的; 感情用事的: *Stop being so melodramatic!* 別再這麼胡鬧了! —**melodramatically** /-klɪ; -kli/ *adv*

mel·o·dy /ˋmɛlədɪ; ˈmelədi/ *n* **1** [C,U] a song or tune 歌曲, 曲調: *a haunting melody* 難以忘懷的曲子 **2** [C] the main tune in a complicated piece of music〔音樂的〕主旋律, 主調: *variations on the original melody* 以主旋律為依據的變奏曲 **3** [U] the arrangement of musical notes in a way that is pleasant to listen to 悅耳的音調, 美妙的音樂

mel·on /ˋmɛlən; ˈmelən/ *n* [C,U] a large round fruit with yellow, green, or red sweet juicy flesh 甜瓜, 香瓜 —see picture on page A8 參見 A8 頁圖

melt /mɛlt; melt/ *v* **1** [I,T] if something solid melts or if heat melts it, it becomes liquid (使) 融化; (使) 熔化: *The snow was melting in the early morning sun.* 雪在清晨的陽光下漸漸融化。| **melt sth** *Melt the butter and mix it with the eggs.* 把黃油化開, 然後和這些雞蛋混合攪拌。—compare 比較 FREEZE[1] (1), THAW[1] (1) **2** also 又作 **melt away** [I] to gradually disappear 逐漸消失: *Julie's anger slowly melted away.* 朱莉的怒氣漸漸地消了下去。| **melt into a crowd** *The man melted into the crowd and I lost sight of him.* 那個男子消失在人羣中, 我看不見他了。**3** [I,T] to become or make someone become more gentle and sympathetic than before (使) 變得心軟: **your heart melts** (=you suddenly feel very sympathetic) 心軟下來 *He shouted at the little girl, but his heart melted when he saw her crying.* 他衝着那個小女孩大喊大叫, 但看到她哭時, 他的心軟了。**4 melt into** if one sound, colour, or feeling melts into another one, it gradually becomes part of it until there is no difference between them〔聲音、顏色或情感〕逐漸融入: *The sound of the trumpet melted into the strains of the orchestra.* 小號的聲音逐漸融入了管弦樂隊演奏的旋律中。**5 melt in your mouth** if food melts in your mouth, it is soft and delicious〔食物〕入口即化; 鬆軟可口 —see also 另見 **butter wouldn't melt in sb's mouth** (BUTTER[1] (2))

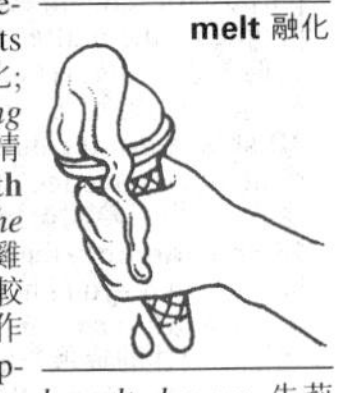

melt sth ↔ **down** *phr v* [T] to heat a metal object until it becomes a liquid, especially so that you can use the metal again 熔化〔金屬物件〕: *People were melting down coins to make earrings and ornaments.* 人們把硬幣熔化掉做成耳環和裝飾品。

melt·down /ˋmɛltdaʊn; ˈmeltdaʊn/ *n* [C,U] a very dangerous situation in which the material in a NUCLEAR REACTOR melts and burns through its container, allowing RADIOACTIVITY to escape〔造成放射性物質逸出的〕核反應堆堆芯熔毀

melt·ing /ˋmɛltɪŋ; ˈmeltɪŋ/ *adj* [usually before noun 一般用於名詞前] a melting look, voice, or expression makes you feel strong feelings of pity, love, or sympathy〔眼神、嗓音或表情〕令人愛憐的; 讓人同情的 —**meltingly** *adv*

melting point /ˋ‥ ˌ/ *n* [singular] the temperature at which a solid substance becomes a liquid 熔點

melting pot /ˋ‥ ˌ/ *n* [C usually singular 一般用單數] **1** a place where people from different races, countries, or social classes come to live together 大熔爐〔來自不同種族、國家或社會階層的人生活在一起的地方〕: *America has been a melting pot since the beginning of European immigration.* 從歐洲人向美洲移民時起美國就是一個融合不同種族的大熔爐。**2** a situation or place in which many different ideas are discussed 多種不同思想在一起討論的場面[地方] **3 in the melting pot** *BrE* still changing and not yet in a final state【英】仍在變化的, 尚未最後定型的

mem·ber /ˋmɛmbɚ; ˈmembə/ *n* [C] **1** someone who has joined a particular club, group, or organization 會員, 成員: *I'm a member of the local tennis club.* 我是本地網球俱樂部的會員。| **club/union/party etc members** *The strike was approved by a majority of union members.* 罷工得到了大多數工會會員的贊成。| **member states/countries/organizations etc** (=the states etc that have joined a particular group) 會員國/組織等 *UN member states* 聯合國會員國 | **full member** (=a member in the most complete way) 正式成員 *Turkey wants to become a full member of the EC.* 土耳其想成為歐共體的正式成員。**2** one of a particular group of people or things〔某一羣人或物中的〕一員: *Dogs and wolves are both members of the same species.* 狗和狼屬同一物種。| **member of a family** *The other members of his family were against the marriage.* 他家的其他成員反對這樁婚姻。| **member of staff** (=a worker at a particular company) 公司職員 *All members of staff must wear uniform.* 所有職員都必須穿制服。**3** *BrE* a Member of Parliament【英】下議院議員: *the member for Truro* 特魯羅地區的下議院議員 **4** *technical or humorous* the male sex organ; PENIS【術語或幽默】男性性器官; 陰莖 **5** *old use* a part of the body, especially an arm or leg【舊】身體的一部分〔尤指胳膊或腿〕 S1 W1

Member of Par·lia·ment /ˌ‥ ‥ ˋ‥/ *n* [C] an MP (1) 下議院議員

mem·ber·ship /ˋmɛmbɚˌʃɪp; ˈmembəʃɪp/ *n* **1** [U] the state of being a member of a club, group, organization, or system, and receiving the advantages of belonging to that group 會員身分[資格]: [+of] *Only full-time employees can apply for membership of the company pension plan.* 只有全職雇員才有資格申請成為該公司退休金計劃的會員。| [also+in *AmE* 美] *I forgot to renew my membership in the sailing club.* 我忘了重續我的航海俱樂部會員資格。| **membership card** (=a card that shows you are a member) 會員證 **2** [singular] all the members of a club, group, or organization 全體會員: *The membership voted to change the rules.* 全體會員投票贊成修改規章。**3** [U] the number of people who belong to a club, group, or organization 會員人數: *We're trying to increase our membership.* 我們正在努力增加我們的會員人數。 S2 W2

mem·brane /ˋmɛmbren; ˈmembreɪn/ *n* [C,U] **1** a very thin piece of skin that covers or connects parts of the body〔覆蓋或連接身體某些部分的〕膜, 薄膜: *a vibrating membrane in the ear which conveys sound* 耳朵中傳送聲音的振動膜 **2** a very thin piece of material that covers or connects something〔覆蓋或連接某物的〕膜狀物 —**membranous** /ˋmɛmbrənəs; ˈmembrənəs/ *adj*

me·men·to /mɪˋmɛnto; məˈmentəʊ/ *n plural* **mementos** [C] a small thing that you keep to remind you of someone or something 小紀念物, 小紀念品: [+of] *a memento of her time in Spain* 讓她回想起在西班牙那段時光的小紀念品

mem·o /ˋmɛmo; ˈmeməʊ/ *n plural* **memos** [C] a short official note to another person in the same company or organization〔致同一個公司或組織內部另一人的〕公務便條: *She dictated an urgent internal memo.* 她口授了一份緊急內部通知。 S3

mem·oir /ˋmɛmwar; ˈmemwɑː/ *n* **1 memoirs** [plural] an account written by someone, especially a famous person, about their life and experiences〔尤指名人〕回憶錄: *Lady Thatcher had just published her memoirs.* 戴卓爾夫人剛剛出版了她的回憶錄。**2** [C] *formal* a short piece of writing about someone or something that you know well【正式】傳略, 實錄

mem·o·ra·bil·i·a /ˌmɛmərəˋbɪlɪə; ˌmemərəˈbɪliə/ *n* [plural] things that you keep or collect because they are connected with a famous person, event, or time〔與某著名人物、事件或時代有關的〕紀念品, 收藏品: *Elvis Presley memorabilia* 有關皮禮士利的紀念品

mem·o·ra·ble /ˋmɛmərəbl̩; ˈmemərəbəl/ *adj* very good, enjoyable, or unusual, and worth remembering 極好的,

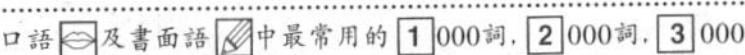

難忘的, 值得紀念的: *a truly memorable performance* 真正令人難忘的演出 | **[+for]** *The play was memorable for its beautiful costumes.* 那齣戲劇因其漂亮的戲裝而令人難忘。—**memorably** *adv*

mem·o·ran·dum /ˌmɛməˋrændəm; ˌmeməˈrændəm/ *n plural* **memoranda** *or* **memorandums** [C] **1** *formal* a MEMO【正式】公務便條 **2** *law* a short legal document recording the conditions of an agreement【法律】協議備忘錄

me·mo·ri·al[1] /məˋmɔrɪəl; məˈmɔːriəl/ *adj* [only before noun 僅用於名詞前] made, held, or done in order to remind people of someone who has died 紀念的, 追悼的: **memorial service/ceremony** *A memorial service will be held at 7 pm on Saturday.* 週六晚上七時將舉行一個追悼儀式。| **memorial prize/scholarship/fund etc** *the John Kobal memorial prize for best young photographer* 約翰·科貝爾最佳青年攝影師紀念獎

memorial[2] *n* **1** [C] something, especially a stone with writing on it, to remind people of someone who has died 紀念碑: *the Albert memorial* 艾伯特紀念碑 | **[+to]** *a memorial to the men who died in the war* 為在戰爭中犧牲的士兵而立的紀念碑 **2** [singular] an achievement that reminds people of someone who has died〔對死者成就的〕紀念: *The college is his true memorial.* 這所學院就是對他真正的紀念。—see also 另見 WAR MEMORIAL

mem·o·rize also 又作 **-ise** *BrE*【英】/ˋmɛməˌraɪz; ˈmeməraɪz/ *v* [T] to learn words, music etc 記住, 熟記

mem·o·ry /ˋmɛmərɪ; ˈmeməri/ *n*

1 ▶ABILITY TO REMEMBER 記憶力◀ [C,U] the ability to remember things, places, experiences etc 記憶力, 記性: *Grandpa was getting old and his memory wasn't so good.* 爺爺上年紀了, 記性不太好。| **have a good/bad memory for sth** (=be good or bad at remembering things of a particular kind) 對某事記憶力好/差 *I have a terrible memory for names.* 我特別不善於記名字。| **have a short/long memory** (=remember something for a short time or for a long time) 記性不好/好 | **do sth from memory** (=do something such as say a poem or play a piece of music by remembering it) 憑記憶做某事 *The cellist played the whole piece through from memory.* 大提琴手憑記憶從頭到尾演奏了那支曲子。

2 ▶STH YOU REMEMBER 記得的某事◀ [C usually plural 一般用複數] something that you remember from the past about a person, place, or experience 記憶, 回憶: **[+of]** *memories of the war* 對那場戰爭的回憶 | **happy/good/bad etc memories** *He has lots of happy memories of his stay in Japan.* 他對在日本逗留的那一段時光有許多美好的回憶。| **childhood memories** (=memories of the time when you were a child) 童年的記憶 *One of my earliest childhood memories is of my mother reading stories to me by the fire.* 我最早的童年記憶之一就是母親在爐火邊給我唸故事。| **bring back memories** (=to remind you of pleasant events) 引起對美好往事的回憶 *Those old songs bring back memories.* 那些老歌使人回想起美好的往事。

3 a) [C] the part of a computer in which information can be stored〔電腦的〕存儲器 **b)** [U] the amount of space that can be used for storing information on a computer〔電腦存儲器的〕存儲量: *30 megabytes of memory* 30兆字節的存儲量

4 if my memory serves me (well/correctly) used when you are almost sure that you have remembered something correctly 如果我沒有記錯的話: *We first moved here in 1962, if my memory serves me correctly.* 如果我沒有記錯的話, 我們最初搬到這裡是在1962年。

5 speaking from memory *spoken* used to say that you are telling someone what you remember about something【口】憑記憶; 就記憶所及

6 have a memory like a sieve *spoken* to be very bad at remembering things【口】記憶力極差

7 sb's memory is playing tricks on them *spoken* used to say that someone is remembering things incorrectly【口】某人的記性在和他開玩笑, 某人的記憶不準確: *My memory must be playing tricks on me; I'm sure I put that book on the desk.* 肯定是我的記憶出了問題, 我明明記得把那本書放在書桌上了。

8 take a walk/trip down memory lane spend some time remembering the past 追憶往事

9 in living memory since the earliest time that people now alive can remember 在活着的人的記憶中: *the hottest summer in living memory* 在世的人們記憶中最炎熱的夏天

10 within sb's memory during the time that someone can remember 就某人記憶所及: *There have been two world wars within the memory of my grandfather.* 兩次世界大戰都在我祖父腦海中留下記憶。

11 in memory of also 又作 **to the memory of** for the purpose of remembering someone and reminding other people of them after they have died 為了紀念〔已經故去的某人〕: *She set up a charitable fund in memory of her father.* 她設立了一項慈善基金以紀念她的父親。

12 sb's memory lives on used to say that people still remember someone after they have died or gone away 某人〔去世或離開後〕仍然留在人們的記憶中

13 sb's memory the way you think about someone who has died who you knew very well 對〔熟悉的〕亡故者的紀念[懷念]: *a rose garden dedicated to his memory* 為緬懷他而建的玫瑰花園 —see also 另見 **commit sth to memory** (COMMIT (6)), **jog sb's memory** (JOG[1] (3)), **lose your memory** (LOSE (4)), **photographic memory** (PHOTOGRAPHIC (2)), **refresh sb's memory** (REFRESH (2))

This graph shows some of the words most commonly used with the noun **memory**. 本圖表所示為含有名詞 memory 的一些最常用片語。

memory of
from memory
memory for
good memory
living memory
5 10 15 per million 每百萬

Based on the British National Corpus and the Longman Lancaster Corpus 據英國國家語料庫和朗文蘭卡斯特語料庫

memory bank /ˈ··· ˌ·/ *n* [C] the part of a big computer system that stores information〔大型電腦系統的〕存儲體, 數據總庫

mem·sahib /ˋmɛmˌsɑɪb; ˈmemˌsɑːb/ *n* [C] *IndE, PakE old-fashioned* a European woman【印, 巴, 過時】歐洲婦女

men /mɛn; men/ *n* the plural of MAN

men·ace[1] /ˋmɛnɪs; ˈmenəs/ *n* **1** [C] something or someone that is dangerous 危險的事物[人]: **[+to]** *hazardous chemicals that are a menace to public safety* 危害公共安全的危險化學品 | *That man's a menace to society!* 那個男子對社會是一個禍害! **2** [U] a threatening quality or manner 威脅, 恐嚇: *There was menace in her eyes as she spoke.* 她說話的時候目光中帶着恫嚇。**3** [C] a person, especially a child that is annoying or causes trouble; NUISANCE 討厭的人, 製造麻煩的人〔尤指小孩〕

menace[2] *v* [T] *formal* to threaten【正式】威脅, 恐嚇

men·ac·ing /ˋmɛnəsɪŋ; ˈmenəsɪŋ/ *adj* making you expect something unpleasant; THREATENING 威脅的, 不祥的, 凶兆的: *dark, menacing clouds* 預示着暴風雨的烏雲 | *a low, menacing laugh* 充滿恐嚇的一聲輕笑 —**menacingly** *adv*

mé·nage /meˋnɑʒ; ˈmeɪnɑːʒ/ *n* [C] *formal or humorous* all the people who live in a particular house; HOUSEHOLD[1]【正式或幽默】家庭

ménage à trois /meˋnɑʒ ɑ ˋtrwɑ; ˌmeɪnɑːʒ ɑː ˈtrwɑː/ *n* [singular] *French* a sexual relationship involving three people who live together【法】三角家庭, 三角性關係〔指居住在一起的三個人之間的性關係〕

me·na·ge·rie /mə`nædʒərɪ; mə̇'nædʒəri/ *n* [C] a collection of wild animals kept privately or for the public to see 私人豢養或向公眾展覽的野生動物

mend¹ /mɛnd; mend/ *v*

1 ►REPAIR 修理◄ [T] **a)** to repair a tear or hole in a piece of clothing 修補, 縫補〔布料上的裂口或破洞〕: *My father used to mend our shoes.* 我父親過去常為我們修補鞋子。**b)** *BrE* to repair something that is broken or not working; FIX¹ (1)【英】修理〔破損或有毛病的物件〕: *When are you going to mend that light in the hall?* 你甚麼時候修理一下廳裡的那盞燈?

2 ►BECOME HEALTHY 變得健康◄ [I] **a)** *informal* if a broken bone mends, it becomes whole again【非正式】〔斷骨〕癒合 **b)** [I] *old-fashioned* to become healthy again after being ill【過時】〔病後〕恢復健康, 痊癒

3 mend your ways to improve the way you behave after behaving badly for a long time 改正不良行為

4 mend (your) fences to talk to someone you have offended or argued with, and try to persuade them to be friendly with you again 消釋前嫌, 重修舊好

5 ►END A QUARREL 結束爭吵◄ [T] to end a quarrel or difficult situation by dealing with the problem that is causing it 結束爭吵[困境]: *I've tried to mend matters between us, but she's still very angry.* 我盡力去消除我們之間的不和, 但她仍然很生氣。—**mender** *n* [C] *BrE*【英】

mend² *n* [C] **1 be on the mend** to be getting better after an illness or after a difficult period〔病後或困難時期過後〕正在好轉: *He's had flu, but he's on the mend.* 他得了流感, 但正在痊癒。| *signs that the economy is on the mend* 經濟在好轉的跡象 **2** a place in something where it has been repaired 修補過的地方

men·da·cious /mɛn`deʃəs; men'deɪʃəs/ *adj formal* not truthful【正式】不真實的, 虛假的: *mendacious propaganda* 不真實的宣傳 —**mendaciously** *adv*

men·da·ci·ty /mɛn`dæsətɪ; men'dæsə̇ti/ *n* [U] *formal* the quality of being untruthful【正式】不真實, 虛假

men·di·cant /`mɛndɪkənt; 'mendə̇kənt/ *n* [C] *formal* someone who begs for money in order to live, usually for religious reasons【正式】〔常因宗教原因〕以乞討為生的人 —**mendicant** *adj*: *a mendicant monks' order such as the Franciscans* 化緣修士會, 如聖方濟各會

mend·ing /`mɛndɪŋ; 'mendɪŋ/ *n* [U] clothes that need to be mended 需縫補的衣服

men·folk /`mɛn,fok; 'menfəʊk/ *n* [plural] *old-fashioned* a word used by women meaning men, especially their male relatives【過時】男人們〔婦女指男人的用語, 尤指男性親屬〕: *Round up the menfolk for dinner, please.* 把男人們都請來吃飯吧。

me·ni·al¹ /`minɪəl; 'miːniəl/ *adj* menial work is boring, needs no skill, and is not important〔工作〕枯燥的; 無需技術的; 卑下的 —**menially** *adv*

menial² *n* [C] someone who does menial work, especially a servant in a house 幹粗活的人〔尤指家僕〕

men·in·gi·tis /,mɛnɪn`dʒaɪtɪs; ,menə̇n'dʒaɪtə̇s/ *n* [U] a serious illness in which the outer part of the brain becomes swollen 腦(脊)膜炎

men·o·pause /`mɛnə,pɔz; 'menəpɔːz/ *n* [U] the time when a woman stops menstruating (MENSTRUATE), which usually occurs around age 50〔婦女的〕絕經期, 更年期 —**menopausal** /,mɛno`pɔzəl; ,menəʊ'pɔːzəl◄/ *adj*

me·no·rah /mə`norə; mə'nɔːrə/ *n* [C] a Jewish CANDLESTICK that holds seven CANDLES〔猶太人用的〕七扦枝燭台

mensch /mɛnʃ; menʃ/ *n* [C] *AmE spoken* someone that you like and admire, especially because they have done something good for you【美口】讓人喜歡的人, 令人欽佩者〔尤因曾受過其恩惠〕: *You've been a real mensch.* 你是一個真正受愛戴的人。

men·ses /`mɛnsiz; 'mensiːz/ *n* [plural] *technical* the blood that flows out of a woman's body each month【術語】月經

men's room /'· ·/ *n* [C] *especially AmE* the men's toilet【尤美】男廁所, 男盥洗室; gents (GENT (2)) *BrE*【英】

men·stru·al /`mɛnstruəl; 'menstruəl/ *adj* connected with the time each month when a woman menstruates 月經的, 行經期的

menstrual pe·ri·od /'··· ,···/ *n* [C] *formal* the time each month when a woman menstruates; PERIOD¹ (4)【正式】月經期, 行經期

men·stru·ate /`mɛnstru,et; 'menstrueɪt/ *v* [I] *technical* when a woman menstruates, blood flows from her body every month【術語】行經, 來月經 —**menstruation** /,mɛnstru`eʃən; ,menstru'eɪʃən/ *n* [C,U]

mens·wear /`mɛnzwɛr; 'menzweə/ *n* [U] clothing for men 男士服裝: *a menswear shop* 男式服裝店

-ment /mənt; mənt/ *suffix* [in nouns 構成名詞] **1** the act, cause, means, or result of doing something〔表示做某事的〕動作; 原因; 手段; 結果: *the need for strong government* (=strong governing) 嚴格統治的必要性 | *the replacement* (=replacing) *of obsolete machinery* 陳舊機器的更換 | *some interesting new developments* 一些有趣的新進展 **2** the condition of being treated in a particular way〔表示遭受某種待遇的〕境況: *his confinement* (=being shut up) *in prison* 他被囚禁的境況 —**-mental** *suffix* [in adjectives 構成形容詞]: *governmental* 政府的

men·tal /`mɛntl; 'mentl/ *adj* S2 W2

1 ►MIND 精神◄ affecting the mind or happening in the mind 精神的; 智力的; 內心的: *mental health* 精神健康 | *a child's mental development* 兒童的智力發展 | **mental picture/image** (=a picture that you form in your mind) 在頭腦中勾畫出的形象 *I tried to get a mental picture of him from her description.* 我設法根據她的描述勾畫出他的形象。

2 ►MENTAL ILLNESS 精神病◄ [only before noun 僅用於名詞前] concerned with illnesses of the mind, or with treating illnesses of the mind 精神病的; 與精神病治療有關的: *Mental patients have to be kept under strict supervision.* 精神病人必須置於嚴格的監管之下。| *a mental institution* 精神病院 —see also 另見 MENTAL HOME, MENTAL HOSPITAL

3 mental block a difficulty in remembering something or in understanding something 心理阻隔; 記憶阻隔; 思維阻隔: *I got a complete mental block as soon as the interviewer asked me a question.* 考官剛問了我一個問題, 我的思維就完全阻斷了。| *Julie has a mental block when it comes to math.* 只要涉及數學, 朱莉就會產生心理阻隔。

4 make a mental note to make a special effort to remember something 記在腦子裡

5 ►CRAZY 發瘋的◄ [not before noun 不用於名詞前] *BrE slang* thinking or behaving in a way that seems crazy or strange【英俚】〔思維或行為〕瘋癲的, 不正常的: *He must be mental!* 他一定是瘋了!

6 go mental *BrE slang spoken*【英俚, 口】**a)** to get very angry 非常生氣: *She'll go mental if she finds out.* 她如果發現了會很氣憤的。**b)** to start behaving in a crazy way 行為失常, 發瘋: *I can't understand why she's doing this – has she gone mental or something?* 我無法理解她為甚麼做這種事 — 她是瘋了還是怎麼的? —**mentally** *adv*: *mentally ill* 精神上有病的, 患精神病的

mental age /,·· '·/ *n* [C] a measure of someone's ability to think, obtained by comparing their ability with the average ability of children at various ages 智力年齡, 心理年齡: *a 25-year-old man with a mental age of seven* 一個智力年齡為7歲的25歲男子 S3

mental a·rith·me·tic /,·· ·'···/ *n* [U] the act of adding numbers together, multiplying them etc in your mind, without writing them down 心算

mental home /'·· ·/ *n* [C] *BrE old-fashioned* a mental hospital【英, 過時】精神病院

mental hos·pi·tal /ˈ·· ˌ···/ *n* [C] a hospital where people with mental illnesses are treated; PSYCHIATRIC HOSPITAL 精神病院

men·tal·i·ty /mɛnˋtælətɪ; menˈtæləti/ *n* [C] a particular kind of attitude or way of thinking, especially one that you think is wrong or stupid〔尤指被視為錯誤或愚蠢的〕心態: *a get-rich-quick mentality* 快速致富的心態

mentally han·di·capped /ˌ··· ˈ···/ *adj* **1** a mentally handicapped person has a problem with their brain that affects their ability to think or control their body movements, usually from birth 弱智的 **2** [plural] **the mentally handicapped** people who are mentally handicapped 弱智者

men·thol /ˋmɛnθɑl; ˈmenθɒl/ *n* [U] a substance that smells and tastes of MINT to give cigarettes and sweets a special taste 薄荷腦, 薄荷醇

men·tho·la·ted /ˋmɛnθəˌletɪd; ˈmenθəleɪtɪd/ *adj* containing menthol 含薄荷醇的

S1 W1 **men·tion**[1] /ˋmɛnʃən; ˈmenʃən/ *v* [T] **1** to talk about something or someone in a conversation, piece of writing etc, especially without saying very much or giving details 提到, 說起, 談到: *As I mentioned earlier, this has been a very successful year for our company.* 正如我剛才提到的, 這是我們公司非常成功的一年。| *Jill mentioned something about a party on Saturday.* 吉爾提到了星期六舉行的一個聚會的事。| *Was my name mentioned at all?* 我的名字被提到過嗎? | **mention sth to sb** *I mentioned the idea to Joan, and she seemed to like it.* 我向瓊說起過這個想法, 她似乎很喜歡。| **mention (that)** *He mentioned that he was having problems, but he didn't explain.* 他說起過他碰到一些問題, 但沒作說明。| **it is worth mentioning that** (=this is a useful or important piece of information) 值得一提的是… *It's worth mentioning that the new regulations don't actually come into force until next year.* 值得一提的是新的規章制度要到明年才真正生效。**2 don't mention it** *spoken* used to say politely that there is no need for someone to thank you for helping them【口】不用謝: *"Thanks for the ride home!" "Don't mention it."* "謝謝你開車送我回家!" "不用客氣。" **3 not to mention** used to introduce an additional thing that makes a situation even more difficult, surprising, interesting etc 更不用說: *They already take pension and social security payments off my pay, not to mention state taxes.* 他們已經從我的工資裡扣除了養老金和社會保障金, 更不用說州稅了。**4 mention sth in passing** to mention something quickly without paying much attention to it 順便提到, 附帶說起: *Sue mentioned the party in passing, but I couldn't go.* 蘇順便提到那個聚會, 但我去不了。**5 above mentioned/mentioned above** mentioned earlier in a piece of writing 上述〔指在一篇文章前面提到過的〕**6 mentioned in dispatches** *BrE* honoured for being brave in a battle by being mentioned on an official list【英】〔因作戰勇敢而〕在正式通報上受到表揚

mention[2] *n* [C usually singular 一般用單數, U] the act of mentioning something or someone in a conversation, piece of writing etc 提及, 說起: *Just the mention of her name still upsets him.* 只要提起她的名字, 他現在還是會不高興。| **there's no mention** (=something is not mentioned) 沒有提到 *There was no mention of any trip to Holland in his diaries.* 他的日記中沒有提到過他曾經去過荷蘭。| **get a mention** (=be mentioned when someone is talking or writing about something)〔在口頭或文字中〕被提及, 被談到 *I didn't even get a mention in the list of contributors.* 我在捐贈者名單上甚至沒有被提到。| **make no mention** (=not say anything about) 沒提及, 沒說起 *He made no mention of his wife's illness to me.* 他沒有向我提起他妻子生病的事。—see also 另見 HONOURABLE MENTION

men·tor /ˋmɛntɚ; ˈmentɔː/ *n* [C] an experienced person who advises and helps a less experienced person 導師, 指導者

men·tor·ing /ˋmɛntɔrɪŋ; ˈmentɔːrɪŋ/ *n* [U] a system of using people with a lot of experience, knowledge etc to advise other people at work, or in their professional life 職業輔導制度: *Support for you in your new job will be provided by a system of mentoring.* 職業輔導制將在你新的工作中為你提供支持。

men·u /ˋmɛnju; ˈmenjuː/ *n* [C] **1** a list of all the kinds of food that are available for a meal, especially in a restaurant〔尤指餐館的〕菜單: *Is there any fish on the menu?* 菜單上有魚嗎? | *Could we have the menu, please?* 請把菜單給我們拿來, 好嗎? —see picture on page A15 參見A15頁圖 **2** a list of things that you can choose from or ask a computer to do, that is shown on the SCREEN of the computer〔電腦顯示器上顯示的〕功能選擇單, 選項單, 菜單: **menu-driven** (=operated by using a menu) 由菜單驅動的

me·ow /mɪˋaʊ; miˈaʊ/ *v* [I] the usual American spelling of MIAOW miaow的一般美式拼法 —**meow** *n* [C]

MEP /ˋɛm i ˋpi; ˌem iː ˈpiː/ *n* [C] Member of the European Parliament; someone who has been elected as a member of the Parliament of the European Union 歐洲議會議員

Meph·i·stoph·e·les /ˌmɛfəˋstɑfəˌliz; ˌmefɪˈstɒfɪliːz/ *n* the Devil, especially in the story of Faust 魔鬼〔尤指關於浮士德的傳說中的魔鬼〕, 靡菲斯特 —**Mephistophelean** /ˌmɛfɪstəˋfilɪən; ˌmefɪstəˈfiːliən◂/ *adj*

mer·can·tile /ˋmɝkənˌtil; ˈmɜːkəntaɪl/ *adj* [only before noun 僅用於名詞前] *formal* concerned with trade; COMMERCIAL[1] (1)【正式】貿易的, 商業的: *mercantile law* 商法

mercantile ma·rine /ˌ··· ·ˈ·/ *n* [singular] *BrE* the MERCHANT NAVY【英】〔一個國家的〕全部商船, 商船隊;〔一個國家的〕全體商船船員

Mer·ca·tor pro·jec·tion /mɝˌketɚ prəˋdʒɛkʃən; məˌkeɪtə prəˈdʒekʃən/ also 又作 **Mercator's projection** *n* [U] a way of drawing a map of the world so that it can be divided into regular squares, instead of getting thinner at the northern or southern edges 墨卡托投影(法)〔繪製世界地圖的一種方法〕

mer·ce·na·ry[1] /ˋmɝsn̩ˌɛrɪ; ˈmɜːsənəri/ *n* [C] a soldier who fights for any country or group that is willing to pay him 雇傭兵: *The Emperor hired an army of Saxon mercenaries.* 皇帝雇用了一支由撒克遜雇傭兵組成的軍隊。

mercenary[2] *adj* only interested in money, and not caring about whether your actions are right or wrong or about the effect of your actions on other people 只對錢感興趣的, 唯利是圖的: *It's a purely mercenary relationship, not a friendship.* 它純粹是一種金錢關係, 而不是友誼。

mer·cer·ized cot·ton /ˌmɝsəraɪzd ˋkɑtn̩; ˌmɜːsəraɪzd ˈkɒtn/ *n* [U] cotton that has been treated with chemicals to make it shiny and strong 絲光棉〔經過化學處理的棉花〕

mer·chan·dise[1] /ˋmɝtʃənˌdaɪz; ˈmɜːtʃəndaɪz/ *n* [U] goods that are produced in order to be sold, especially goods that are shown in a shop for people to buy 商品〔尤指在商店陳列供出售的貨物〕

merchandise[2] *v* [T] to try to sell goods or services using methods such as advertising〔用廣告等方式〕推銷〔商品或服務〕: *If the product is properly merchandised, it should sell very well.* 這種產品如果推銷得當, 應該會賣得很好。

mer·chan·dis·ing /ˋmɝtʃəndaɪzɪŋ; ˈmɜːtʃəndaɪzɪŋ/ *n* [U] toys, clothes, and other products based on a popular film, TV show etc and sold to make additional profits 文化衍生品〔指根據流行電影、電視節目等製作並銷售以獲取額外利潤的玩具、服裝及其他產品〕

mer·chant /ˋmɝtʃənt; ˈmɜːtʃənt/ *n* [C] **1** someone who buys and sells goods in large quantities 商人;〔大宗貨物〕批發商: *He's a wine merchant.* 他是個酒商。**2 con merchant/speed merchant etc** *BrE informal* someone who is involved in a particular activity, such as tricking people or driving very fast【英, 非正式】騙子/開快車者等

merchant bank /ˌ.. ˈ.ˌ/ *n* [C] a bank that provides banking services for business 商業銀行〔指為企業提供服務的銀行〕

mer·chant·man /ˈmɝtʃəntmən; ˈmɜːtʃəntmən/ *n* [C] *old-fashioned* a ship used for carrying goods【過時】商船

merchant na·vy /ˌ.. ˈ../ *BrE*【英】, **merchant ma·rine** *AmE*【美】/ˌ.. .ˈ./ *n* [singular] all of a country's ships that are used for trade, not war, and the people who work on these ships〔一個國家的〕全部商船, 商船隊; 〔一個國家的〕全體商船船員: *John worked as a chef in the merchant navy.* 約翰在商船隊裡當廚師。

merchant sea·man /ˌ.. ˈ../ *n* [C] a sailor in the merchant navy 商船船員

mer·ci·ful /ˈmɝsɪfəl; ˈmɜːsɪfəl/ *adj* **1 merciful death/end/release** a death that seems fortunate because it ends someone's suffering or difficulty 幸運的死亡/結束/解脫〔指結束了某人的痛苦或困境〕: *The final whistle came as a merciful relief.* 最後的哨聲成了幸運的解脫。**2** being kind to people and forgiving them rather than punishing them or being cruel 寬大的, 慈悲的, 仁慈的: *Merciful God, save us.* 仁慈的上帝, 救救我們吧。

mer·ci·ful·ly /ˈmɝsɪfəlɪ; ˈmɜːsɪfəli/ *adv* fortunately or luckily, because a situation could have been much worse 幸運地, 幸而, 幸虧〔指情況本來可能更糟〕: *Mercifully, I managed to stop the car just in time.* 幸運的是我及時煞住了車。

mer·ci·less /ˈmɝsɪlɪs; ˈmɜːsɪləs/ *adj* cruel and showing no kindness or forgiveness 冷酷無情的, 殘忍的: *a merciless attack on a defenceless village* 對沒有防衛能力的村莊進行的殘酷進攻 —**mercilessly** *adv* —**mercilessness** *n* [U]

mer·cu·ri·al /mɝˋkjʊrɪəl; mɜːˈkjʊəriəl/ *adj* **1** *literary* changing mood suddenly and unexpectedly【文】〔情緒〕變化無常的, 多變的: *an actor noted for his mercurial temperament* 以性情變化無常而著名的男演員 **2** *literary* quick and lively【文】敏捷的, 聰敏的; 活潑的: *her mercurial wit* 她的機智 **3** *technical* containing mercury【術語】含汞的, 含水銀的

Mer·cu·ry /ˈmɝkjərɪ; ˈmɜːkjəri/ *n* [singular] the PLANET that is nearest the sun 水星 —see picture at 參見 SOLAR SYSTEM 圖

mercury *n* [U] a heavy silver-white metal that is liquid at ordinary temperatures, and is used in THERMOMETERS 汞, 水銀〔在常溫下呈液態的銀白色重金屬, 用於溫度計〕

mer·cy /ˈmɝsɪ; ˈmɜːsi/ *n* **1** [U] kindness, pity, and a willingness to forgive, which you show towards someone that you have power over〔對自己有權力支配的人所表示的〕仁慈, 寬容, 憐憫: **show no mercy** *The terrorists showed no mercy to the hostages.* 恐怖分子對人質殘酷無情。| **have mercy (on)** *Oh Lord, have mercy on us sinners.* 主啊, 對我們這些罪人發發慈悲吧。**2 it's a mercy** *spoken* used to say that it is lucky that a worse situation was avoided【口】幸運的是, 幸虧〔用於表示更糟的情況得以避免總算是幸運〕: *It's a mercy the accident happened so near the hospital.* 幸虧事故發生在離醫院很近的地方。**3 at the mercy of** unable to do anything to protect yourself from someone or something 任憑…的擺佈〔而無力保護自己〕: *They were lost at sea, at the mercy of wind and weather.* 他們在海上迷失了方向, 任憑風和天氣的擺佈。| *a housing policy that leaves people at the mercy of unscrupulous landlords* 使人們完全受肆無忌憚的房東擺佈的住房政策 **4 leave sb to sb's (tender) mercies** *often humorous* to let someone be dealt with by another person, who may treat them very badly or strictly【常幽默】任憑某人受他人折磨[擺佈] **5 be thankful/grateful for small mercies** to be pleased that a bad situation is not even worse 慶幸一種壞的情況還沒有到更糟糕的地步 **6 mercy flight/mission etc** a journey taken to bring help to people 救援飛行/任務等: *a mercy dash to rescue stranded tourists* 快速救援被困遊客 **7 throw yourself on sb's mercy** to BEG someone to help you or not to punish you 懇求某人幫忙[寬恕]

mercy kill·ing /ˈ.. ˌ../ *n* [C,U] the act of killing someone who is very ill or old so that they do not have to suffer any more; EUTHANASIA 安樂死(術)

mere¹ /mɪr; mɪə/ *adj* [only before noun 僅用於名詞前, no comparative 無比較級] 3 **1** used to emphasize how small or unimportant something or someone is 僅僅, 只不過〔用於強調某事或某人小或微不足道〕: *She lost the election by a mere 20 votes.* 她以僅僅20票之差落選。| *He's a mere child.* 他只不過是個孩子。**2** also 又作 **the merest** used when something small or unimportant has a big effect 極小的, 極不重要的〔用於表示某物雖小或微不足道, 卻有很大的影響〕: *The merest little noise makes him nervous.* 一丁點兒聲音也會使他緊張。| *The mere presence of a police officer made him feel guilty.* 僅僅是有警察在場就會使他感覺有罪。

mere² *n* [C] *literary* a lake【文】湖

mere·ly /ˈmɪrlɪ; ˈmɪəli/ *adv* 2 2 **1** used to emphasize that something or someone is very small or unimportant, especially when compared with something else; ONLY 僅僅, 只不過: *It is an issue of merely local importance.* 它只不過是一個在本地有重要性的問題。| *This is merely the latest example of government interference.* 這僅僅是政府干預的最新例證。**2** *spoken* used to emphasize that you are doing something only for the reason you say【口】只是, 僅僅是: *I'm not trying to criticize you, I'm merely trying to find out how the accident happened.* 我不是在批評你, 我只是想弄清楚事故是如何發生的。

mer·e·tri·cious /ˌmɛrəˈtrɪʃəs; ˌmerɪ̌ˈtrɪʃəs◂/ *adj formal* seeming attractive but having no real value or not based on the truth【正式】華而不實的, 徒有其表的, 花哨的: *a meretricious argument* 華而不實的論據 —**meretriciously** *adv* —**meretriciousness** *n* [U]

merge /mɝdʒ; mɜːdʒ/ *v* **1** [I,T] to combine or join together to form one thing 合併; 融合: **[+with]** *Rover is to merge with BMW, the German car manufacturer.* 路華公司要和德國汽車製造商寶馬公司合併。| **merge sth** *The company plans to merge its subsidiaries in the US.* 該公司計劃合併其在美國的幾家子公司。| **[+together]** *The sounds of the wind and the water merged together.* 風聲和水聲融合在一起。**2 merge into sth** to seem to disappear into something and become part of it 慢慢融入某物; 逐漸消失在某物中: *As night fell, their outlines merged into the landscape.* 隨着夜幕降垂, 它們的輪廓慢慢消失在景色之中。**3 merge into the background** *BrE informal* to behave very quietly in social situations, so that people do not notice you【英, 非正式】社交場合中不顯露頭角; 隱入幕後

merg·er /ˈmɝdʒɚ; ˈmɜːdʒə/ *n* [C] the act of joining together two or more companies or organizations to form one larger one 公司[組織]的合併: *job losses as a result of the merger* (公司)合併導致的失業

me·rid·i·an /məˈrɪdɪən; məˈrɪdiən/ *n* **1** [C] an imaginary line drawn from the NORTH POLE to the SOUTH POLE over the surface of the Earth, used to show the position of places on a map 子午線, 經線 **2 the meridian** *technical* the highest point reached by the sun or another star, when seen from a point on the Earth's surface【術語】〔從地球表面某一點觀測到的太陽或其他星體達到的〕最高點

me·ringue /məˋræŋ; məˈræŋ/ *n* [C,U] a light sweet food made by baking a mixture of sugar and the white part of eggs 蛋白酥(糕餅)

me·ri·no /məˋrino; məˈriːnəʊ/ *n* [U] a kind of sheep with long wool, or cloth made from this wool 美利奴綿羊; 美利奴羊毛織物

mer·it¹ /ˈmɛrɪt; ˈmerɪ̌t/ *n* **1** [C usually plural 一般用複數] one of the good features of something such as a plan or system 長處, 優點: *The committee will look at the relative merits of the two proposals.* 委員會將會考慮這兩個提案相比之下各自的優點。—opposite 反義詞 DEMERIT (1) **2** [U] *formal* a good quality that makes something deserve praise or admiration【正式】〔使某物受讚揚或讚美的〕優秀品質: **have merit/be of merit** (=be good) 有可稱道之處 *The arguments for legalizing marijuana have considerable merit.* 贊成大麻合法化的論據大有可取之處。| **artistic/literary merit** *a film lacking any kind of artistic merit* 一部毫無藝術價值的電影 **3 judge sth on its (own) merits** to judge something only by how good it is, without considering anything else 就某物自身的品質對其作出判斷〔不考慮其他因素〕

merit² *v* [T not in progressive forms 不用進行式] *formal* to deserve something【正式】應得到, 值得: *Your suggestion merits serious consideration.* 你的建議值得認真考慮。

mer·i·toc·ra·cy /ˌmɛrəˋtɑkrəsɪ; ˌmerɪ̍ˈtɒkrəsi/ *n especially BrE*【尤英】**1** [C] a social system that gives the greatest power and highest social positions to people with the most ability 精英管理(制度), 賢能統治〔一種讓能者居高位、掌大權的社會制度〕**2** [singular] the people who have power in this kind of system 精英管理階層, 賢能統治者

mer·i·to·ri·ous /ˌmɛrəˋtɔrɪəs; ˌmerɪ̍ˈtɔːriəs◂/ *adj formal* very good and deserving praise【正式】極好而值得稱讚的 —**meritoriously** *adv*

mer·maid /ˋmɝˌmed; ˈmɜːmeɪd/ *n* [C] a woman in stories who has a fish's tail instead of legs〔傳說中的〕美人魚

mermaid 美人魚

mer·ri·ment /ˋmɛrɪmənt; ˈmerɪmənt/ *n* [U] *formal* laughter, fun, and enjoyment【正式】歡笑; 歡樂, 興高采烈: *His new hairstyle was the cause of much merriment.* 他的新髮型引來一片笑聲。

mer·ry /ˋmɛrɪ; ˈmeri/ *adj* **1 Merry Christmas!** used to say that you hope someone will have a happy time at Christmas 聖誕快樂! **2** cheerful and happy 歡快的: *He marched off, whistling a merry tune.* 他吹着歡快的口哨大步走了出去。**3 the more the merrier** *spoken* used to tell someone that you will be happy if they join you in something you are doing【口】〔人〕越多越好: *"Do you guys mind if I come with you?" "Sure – the more the merrier".* "如果我一塊去你們大家不介意吧?" "當然不會 —— 人越多越熱鬧嘛。" **4** [not before noun 不用於名詞前] *BrE informal* slightly drunk【英, 非正式】微醉的: *We were all quite merry at the party last night.* 在昨晚的聚會上我們都有些喝醉了。**5 make merry** *literary* to enjoy yourself by drinking, singing etc【文】飲酒唱歌, 尋歡作樂 **6** *old use* pleasant【舊】令人愉快的: *the merry month of June* 令人愉快的六月 —**merrily** *adv* —**merriness** *n* [U]

merry-go-round /ˈ·· ·ˌ·/ *n* **1** [C] a machine that turns around and around, and has model animals or cars for children to sit on〔供兒童玩耍的〕旋轉木馬; CAROUSEL *AmE*【美】**2** [singular] a series of similar events that happen very quickly one after another 快速發生的一連串類似事件: *the endless Washington merry-go-round of parties and socializing* 在華盛頓走馬燈似的聚會和應酬活動

merry-mak·ing /ˈ·· ˌ··/ *n* [U] *literary* fun and enjoyment, especially drinking, dancing, and singing【文】尋歡作樂〔尤指喝酒、跳舞、唱歌〕—**merry-makers** *n* [C]

me·sa /ˋmesə; ˈmeɪsə/ *n* [C] a hill with a flat top and steep sides, in the southwestern USA 方山, 平頂峭壁的山〔見於美國西南部地區〕

mes·ca·lin, mescaline /ˋmɛskəlɪn; ˈmeskəliːn/ *n* [U] a drug made from a CACTUS plant that makes people imagine that they can see things that do not really exist 墨斯卡靈, 仙人球毒鹼〔一種致幻劑〕

mesh¹ /mɛʃ; meʃ/ *n* [C,U] **1** a piece of material made of threads or wires that have been woven together like a net〔用線或金屬絲編織的〕網狀物: *Wire mesh covered all the windows to keep out flies.* 所有窗子都覆蓋有鐵絲紗網以防蒼蠅飛入。**2** a complicated situation that makes you feel confused and trapped〔令人感到困惑及無能為力的〕錯綜複雜的局面; 羅網: [+of] *He was caught in the mesh of emotions between the mother and her daughter.* 他陷入了那對母女間的感情糾葛之中。

mesh² *v* [I] **1** if two ideas or qualities mesh, they go well together and are suitable for each other〔想法或品性〕相合; 相配; 相互協調: *music in which classical harmonics mesh with the hypnotic rhythms of jazz* 古典和音與爵士音樂帶催眠作用的節奏融為一體的音樂 **2** *technical* if two parts of an engine or machine mesh, they fit closely together and connect with each other【術語】〔引擎或機器部件〕嚙合

mes·mer·ize also 又作 **-ise** *BrE*【英】/ˋmɛzməˌraɪz; ˈmezməraɪz/ *v* [T often passive 常用被動態] to make someone feel that they must watch or listen to something or someone, because they are so interested in it or attracted by it 使着迷, 使迷住: *He was mesmerized by her charm and beauty.* 他被她的魅力和美貌迷住了。—**mesmerizing** *adj*

mess¹ /mɛs; mes/ *n*

1 ►DIRTY/UNTIDY 髒的/凌亂的◄ [singular,U] a situation in which a place looks very untidy or dirty, with things spread all around 凌亂狀態, 髒亂情形: *Clean up this mess!* 把這髒亂的樣子收拾好! | *The house was an awful mess after the party.* 聚會之後屋裡一片狼藉。| **make a mess** *You can make cookies if you promise not to make a mess in the kitchen.* 如果你答應不把廚房搞得亂七八糟, 你就可以去做甜餅。

2 ►PROBLEMS/DIFFICULTIES 問題/困難◄ [singular] *informal* a situation in which there are a lot of problems and difficulties, especially as a result of mistakes or carelessness【非正式】〔尤指因錯誤或疏忽所造成的〕困難的局面: *We have to sort this problem out – the whole thing's a mess.* 我們必須解決這個問題 —— 一切都亂套了。| *You got us into this mess, Terry. You can get us out of it.* 特里, 你使我們陷入了這一困境, 你把我們解脱出來吧。

3 be in a mess to be very untidy or dirty, very disorganized or full of problems 髒亂不堪; 雜亂無章; 問題成堆: *The previous chairman had left the company in a terrible mess.* 前任董事長使公司成了一個爛攤子。| *My life was in a real mess and I didn't know what to do.* 我當時的境況狼狽不堪, 我也不知道該怎麼辦。

4 make a mess of *informal* to do something badly and make a lot of mistakes【非正式】把…搞得一塌糊塗: *I made a complete mess of that test.* 那次測驗我考得一團糟。| *They've made such a mess of the economy.* 他們把經濟搞得如此糟糕。

5 a mess of *AmE informal* a lot of【美, 非正式】許多: *The dress had a high neck with a mess of buttons coming down the back.* 那件連衣裙是高領的, 背部自上而下有許多鈕扣。

6 ►ARMY/NAVY 陸軍/海軍◄ [C] a room in which members of the army, navy etc eat and drink together 軍人食堂

7 ►WASTE MATTER 排泄物◄ [C,U] *informal especially BrE* solid waste material from a baby or animal【非正式, 尤英】〔嬰兒或動物的〕糞便: *The dog's made a mess on the carpet!* 狗把屎拉在地毯上啦!

mess² *v* [I] to have meals in a room where members of the army, navy etc eat together 在軍人食堂就餐

mess around also 又作 **mess about** *BrE*【英】*phr v informal*【非正式】**1** [I] to spend time lazily, doing things slowly and in a way that is not planned 無所事事, 漫無目的地度日: *He spent his vacation messing around on the farm.* 他在農場裡東遊西蕩, 無所事事地度過了假期。 **2** [I] to behave in a silly way when you should be working or paying attention 遊手好閒, 不務正業: *Stop messing around and help me move this furniture.* 不要遊手好閒了, 來幫我搬搬這些家具吧。 **3** [T **mess** sb **around/about**] to cause a lot of problems for someone, especially by changing your mind often or preventing them from getting what they want 對〔某人〕造成很多麻煩〔尤指不斷改變自己的主意或阻止他人得到他所要的東西〕: *Don't mess me about – I want the money you promised me.* 別擺弄我 — 我要你答應過我的那筆錢。

mess around with also 又作 **mess about with** *BrE*【英】*phr v* [T] *informal*【非正式】**1** to have a sexual relationship with someone that you should not have a sexual relationship with 與…有不正當的性關係: *She'd been messing around with another man.* 她一直在和另一個男人勾搭着。 **2** to spend time playing with something, repairing it etc 擺弄; 修理: *Dave likes messing around with old cars.* 戴夫喜歡擺弄舊汽車。

mess up *phr v informal*【非正式】**1** [T **mess** sth ↔ **up**] to spoil or ruin something, especially something important or something that has been carefully planned 弄壞, 毀掉〔尤指重要物品或精心策劃的事情〕: *It took me ages to get this right – I don't want some idiot to mess it up.* 我花了好長時間才把這東西弄好 — 我不想讓某個白痴把它毀掉。| *She felt she'd messed up her whole life.* 她感到她把自己整個生活都弄得一團糟。 **2** [T **mess** sth ↔ **up**] to make something dirty or untidy 弄髒, 弄亂: *Who messed up the kitchen?* 誰把廚房弄得又髒又亂? **3** [I,T **mess** sth ↔ **up**] to make a mistake and do something badly 出錯; 搞砸: *It doesn't matter if you mess it up, you can always try again.* 要是搞砸了也沒關係, 你總是可以再來一次的。| [**+on**] *I think I messed up on the last question.* 我想最後一個問題我答壞了。—see also 另見 MESSED UP, MESS-UP

mess with *phr v* [I,T] **don't mess with** *spoken*【口】**a)** used to warn someone not to annoy or argue with someone 別去招惹, 不要和…爭論: *Don't mess with me, buddy.* 喂, 你不要惹我。 **b)** used to warn someone not to get involved with something that is dangerous or harmful 不要沾染〔危險或有害之物〕: *Don't mess with illegal drugs. Just say no!* 不要去沾染非法毒品, 要對它們說不!

1 2 **mes·sage** /ˋmɛsɪdʒ; ˈmesɪdʒ/ *n* [C] **1** a spoken or written piece of information that you send to another person 消息; 口信; 信息: *Did you get my message?* 你收到我發給你的信息了嗎? | **leave a message** *He left a message saying he would probably be a little late.* 他留下口信說他可能會晚一會兒。| **can I take a message?** *spoken* (=used on the telephone when offering to give a message to someone)【口】我可以為你傳個話嗎?〔打電話時用〕 *I'm sorry, she's out right now, can I take a message?* 對不起, 她這會兒出去了, 我可以傳個話嗎? **2** [singular] the main or most important idea that someone is trying to tell people about in a film, book, speech etc〔電影、書籍、講話等的〕要旨, 主題思想; 寓意: *The message of the film is that good always triumphs over evil.* 這部電影的寓意是善良終會戰勝邪惡。 **3 get the message** *informal* to understand what someone means or what they want you to do【非正式】領會含意, 明白: *OK, I get the message – I'm going!* 好吧, 我明白了 — 我這就去!

messed up /ˌ· ˈ·/ *adj informal* someone who is messed up is very unhappy and has mental problems because of something that has happened to them【非正式】極不愉快的; 精神有毛病的: *He's been really messed up since his wife left him.* 自從妻子離開他以後, 他一直鬱鬱寡歡。

mes·sen·ger /ˋmɛsn̩dʒɚ; ˈmesɪndʒə/ *n* [C] **1** someone who takes messages to people 送信者, 信使; 通信員 **2 blame/shoot the messenger** to be angry with someone for telling you about something bad that has happened 責備/槍殺信使〔指遷怒於傳遞消息者〕

mess hall /ˈ· ·/ *n* [C] a large room where soldiers eat 軍人餐廳, 部隊食堂

mes·si·ah /məˋsaɪə; mɪ̍ˈsaɪə/ *n* [singular] **1 the Messiah a)** Jesus Christ, who is believed by Christians to be sent by God to save the world 救世主耶穌基督〔基督教徒認為上帝派他來拯救世界〕 **b)** a great religious leader who, according to Jewish belief, will be sent by God to save the world 彌賽亞〔在猶太人的信仰中, 指將被上帝派來拯救世界的一位偉大的宗教領袖〕 **2** someone who people believe will save them from great social or economic problems〔社會或經濟方面的〕救星: *He was seen as an economic messiah.* 他被視為經濟方面的救星。

mes·si·an·ic /ˌmɛsɪˋænɪk; ˌmesiˈænɪk◂/ *adj formal*【正式】**1** someone who has messianic beliefs or feelings wants to make very big social or political changes connected with the belief that the world should be completely changed 有救世的信仰[情感]的; 救世主似的: *messianic zeal* 救世主似的熱情 **2** connected with the Messiah 救世主耶穌的;〔猶太人期待的救世主〕彌賽亞的

Mes·srs *BrE*【英】, **Messrs.** *AmE*【美】/ˋmɛsɚz; ˈmesəz/ the plural of MR, used especially in the names of companies 先生〔Mr的複數, 尤用於公司名稱中〕: *Messrs Ford and Dobson* 福特和多布森先生

mess-up /ˈ· ·/ *n* [C] *informal* a situation in which someone has done something badly or made a lot of mistakes【非正式】混亂; 一團糟的局面: *The whole thing had been a mess-up from start to finish.* 這件事從始至終都是亂糟糟的。

mess·y /ˋmɛsɪ; ˈmesi/ *adj* **1** dirty or untidy 髒的; 不整潔的; 淩亂的: *messy saucepans* 髒兮兮的平底鍋 | *Sorry the place is so messy, I haven't had time to clear up.* 對不起, 我這個地方又髒又亂, 我一直沒時間整理。 **2** *informal* a messy situation is complicated and unpleasant to deal with【非正式】棘手的; 難辦的: *He's just been through a particularly messy divorce.* 他剛剛辦完了離婚手續, 過程十分崎嶇。 —**messily** *adv* —**messiness** *n* [U] 3

mes·ti·zo /mɛsˋtizo; meˈstiːzəʊ/ *n plural* **mestizos** [C] someone who has one Spanish parent and one Native American parent 梅斯蒂索混血兒〔父母一方為西班牙人, 一方為美洲土著人〕

Met /mɛt; met/ *n* **the Met** *informal*【非正式】**a)** the Metropolitan Opera Company; the main OPERA company in New York 大都會歌劇團〔紐約的主要歌劇團〕 **b)** the Metropolitan Police; the police force in London 都市警隊〔倫敦的警察部隊〕

met the past tense and past participle of MEET[1]

meta- /mɛtə; metə/ *prefix technical* beyond the ordinary or usual【術語】超越, 超出〔一般或通常情況〕: *metaphysical* (=beyond ordinary physical things) 形而上學的

me·tab·o·lis·m /məˋtæbl̩ˌɪzəm; mɪ̍ˈtæbəlɪzəm/ *n* [C,U] the chemical activity in your body that uses food to produce the energy you need to work and grow 新陳代謝 —**metabolic** /ˌmɛtəˋbɑlɪk; ˌmetəˈbɒlɪk◂/ *adj*: *An animal's lifespan is linked to its metabolic rate.* 動物的壽命與其新陳代謝速度是相聯繫的。

me·ta·bol·ize also 又作 **-ise** *BrE*【英】/məˋtæbl̩ˌaɪz; mɪ̍ˈtæbəlaɪz/ *v* [T] to break down food in the body by chemical activity and use it to produce energy 使發生新陳代謝

met·al /ˋmɛtl̩; ˈmetl/ *n* [C,U] a hard, usually shiny substance such as iron, gold, or steel 金屬〈如鐵、金或鋼〉: 2 2
The frame is made of metal. 這框架是用金屬做的。| *a metal box* 金屬盒子 | **precious metal** (=expensive metal used for making jewellery)〔用以製作首飾的〕貴金屬 —see also 另見 HEAVY METAL, METALLIC

met·a·lan·guage /ˋmɛtəˌlæŋgwɪdʒ; ˈmetəˌlæŋgwɪdʒ/ *n* [C,U] words used for talking about or describing language〔用以論述或描寫語言的〕元語言, 純理語言

metal de·tect·or /ˈ· · ˌ· ·/ *n* [C] **1** a machine used to find pieces of metal that are buried under the ground 金屬探測器 **2** a special frame that you walk through at an airport, used to check for weapons made of metal 金屬探測框〔機場中供旅客穿行的特製門框, 用以探測金屬製武器〕

metal fa·tigue /ˈ·· ·,·/ *n* [U] a weakness in metal that makes it likely to break, caused for example by frequent shaking over a long period 金屬疲勞

me·tal·lic /məˈtælɪk; məˈtælɪk/ *adj* **1** like metal in colour, appearance, or taste〔顏色、外觀或味道〕像金屬的, 金屬般的: *The sea was a dull metallic grey.* 大海呈現出昏暗的金屬灰色。**2** a metallic noise sounds like pieces of metal hitting each other〔聲音〕似金屬物件互相撞擊的: *The pans made a metallic clatter as they crashed to the floor.* 那些鍋噹啷一聲摔落在地板上。**3** made of or containing metal 金屬製的; 含金屬的: *metallic elements* 金屬元素

met·al·lur·gy /ˈmɛtḷ,ɝdʒɪ; məˈtælədʒi/ *n* [U] the scientific study of metals and their uses 冶金學 —**metallurgist** *n* [C] —**metallurgical** /,mɛtḷˈɝdʒɪkḷ; ,metəˈlɜːdʒɪkəl◂/ *adj*

met·al·work /ˈmɛtḷ,wɝk; ˈmetlwɜːk/ *n* [U] **1** the activity or skill of making metal objects 金屬加工; 金屬加工術; 金工: *metalwork classes* 金工課 **2** objects made by shaping metal 金屬製品 —**metalworker** *n* [C]

met·a·mor·pho·sis /,mɛtəˈmɔrfəsɪs; ,metəˈmɔːfəsɪs/ *n plural* **metamorphoses** [C,U] **1** *formal* a process in which something changes completely into something very different【正式】變化〔指由一物完全轉變成另一物〕: *the metamorphosis of China under Deng's economic reforms* 在鄧小平的經濟改革政策下中國的徹底變化 **2** a process in which a young insect, frog etc changes into another stage in its development〔幼蟲、幼蛙等的〕變態 —**metamorphose** /,mɛtəˈmɔrfoz; ,metəˈmɔːfəʊz/ *v* [I,T]

met·a·phor /ˈmɛtəfɚ; ˈmetəfə/ *n* [C,U] **1** a way of describing something by comparing it to something else that has similar qualities, without using the words 'like' or 'as' 隱喻, 暗喻〔將一物比喻為具有相似品質的另一物, 而不用"像"、"如"等字眼〕: *'The sunshine of her smile' is a metaphor.* "她微笑中的陽光"是一個隱喻。| *His poetry is brought alive by his masterful use of metaphor.* 他的詩歌由於對隱喻的巧妙運用而顯得生氣勃勃。—compare 比較 SIMILE **2 mixed metaphor** the use of two different metaphors at the same time to describe something, especially in a way that seems silly or funny 混雜隱喻〔指同時運用兩個不同的隱喻描寫某物, 尤指顯得笨拙或滑稽〕**3** [C,U] something in a book, painting, film etc that is intended to represent a more general idea or quality; SYMBOL〔書、畫、電影等中的〕象徵: **[+for]** *Their relationship is a metaphor for the failure of communication in the modern world.* 他們之間的關係是現代世界中溝通失敗的象徵。

met·a·phor·i·cal /,mɛtəˈfɔrɪkḷ; ,metəˈfɒrɪkəl◂/ *adj* using words to mean something different from their ordinary meaning when describing something in order to achieve an effect 隱喻的; 含有隱喻的 —**metaphorically** /-kḷɪ; -kli/ *adv*: *He's got a big head – metaphorically speaking of course!* 他有一個大腦袋——這當然是比喻的說法!

met·a·phys·i·cal /,mɛtəˈfɪzɪkḷ; ,metəˈfɪzɪkəl◂/ *adj* **1** concerned with the study of metaphysics 形而上學的, 玄學的 **2** *spoken* used to describe a complicated arrangement of words and ideas【口】難理解的, 深奧的; 抽象的 —**metaphysically** /-kḷɪ; -kli/ *adv*

met·a·phys·ics /,mɛtəˈfɪzɪks; ,metəˈfɪzɪks/ *n* [U] the part of the study of PHILOSOPHY that is concerned with trying to understand and describe the nature of reality 形而上學, 玄學

mete /mit; miːt/ *v*

mete sth ↔ **out** *phr v* [T] *formal* to give someone a punishment【正式】給予〔懲罰〕: *Judges are meting out increasingly harsh sentences for car theft.* 法官們對汽車盜竊罪給予越來越嚴厲的刑罰。

me·te·or /ˈmitɪɚ; ˈmiːtiə/ *n* [C] a piece of rock or metal that floats in space, and makes a bright line in the night sky when it falls through the Earth's ATMOSPHERE (1) 流星

me·te·or·ic /,mitɪˈɔrɪk; ,miːtiˈɒrɪk◂/ *adj* **1** happening very suddenly and quickly 突然而迅疾發生的: **meteoric rise/career** *her meteoric rise to fame* 她的迅速成名 **2** from a METEOR 流星的: *meteoric stones* 隕石 —**meteorically** /-kḷɪ; -kli/ *adv*

me·te·o·rite /ˈmitɪər,aɪt; ˈmiːtiəraɪt/ *n* [C] a piece of rock or metal that has come from space and has landed on Earth 隕星; 隕石; 隕鐵

me·te·o·rol·o·gy /,mitɪəˈrɑlədʒɪ; ,miːtiəˈrɒlədʒi/ *n* [U] the scientific study of weather conditions 氣象學 —**meteorologist** *n* [C] —**meteorological** /,mitɪərəˈlɑdʒɪkḷ; ,miːtiərəˈlɒdʒɪkəl◂/ *adj*

-meter[1] /mitɚ; miːtə/ *suffix* [in nouns 構成名詞] an instrument for measuring 測量儀器: *an altimeter* (=for measuring the height at which an aircraft is flying)〔飛機的〕高度計, 高度表

-meter[2] *suffix* the American spelling of -METRE -metre 的美式拼法

me·ter[1] /ˈmitɚ; ˈmiːtə/ *n* **1** [C] a machine that measures and shows the amount of something you have used or the amount of money that you must pay 計量器; 計價器: *The taxi driver turned off his meter.* 出租車司機關上了計價器。**2** [C,U] the American spelling of METRE metre 的美式拼法 —see also 另見 PARKING METER

meter[2] *v* [T] to measure something with a meter, or supply gas, electricity etc through a meter 用儀表計量[測量]; 通過計量器供應〔煤氣、電力等〕

meter maid /ˈ·· ·/ *n* [C] *AmE* a woman whose job is to make sure that cars are not parked in the wrong place or for longer than is allowed【美】〔監督汽車在允許的地點和時間內停放的〕女交通督導員; TRAFFIC WARDEN *BrE*【英】

meth·a·done /ˈmɛθədon; ˈmeθədəʊn/ *n* [U] a drug that is often given to people who are trying to stop taking HEROIN 美沙酮, 美散痛〔常供試圖戒除海洛因者使用〕

me·thane /ˈmɛθen; ˈmiːθeɪn/ *n* [U] a colourless gas with no smell that can be burned to give heat 甲烷, 沼氣

meth·a·nol /ˈmɛθənɔl; ˈmeθənɒl/ *n* [U] a poisonous alcohol that can be made from wood 甲醇

me·thinks /mɪˈθɪŋks; mɪˈθɪŋks/ *v past tense* **methought** /-ˈθɔt; -ˈθɔːt/ *old use or humorous* I think【舊或幽默】我想, 據我看來: *a holiday somewhere nice, Florida methinks* 在某個好地方休假, 我想是在佛羅里達

meth·od /ˈmɛθəd; ˈmeθəd/ *n* **1** [C] a planned way of doing something, especially one that a lot of people know about and use 方法, 辦法: *traditional teaching methods* 傳統教學法 | *I think we should try again using a different method.* 我想我們應該用不同的方法再試一次。| **[+of]** *There are several possible methods of payment.* 有好幾種可以使用的付款辦法。| **[+for]** *a new method for the early detection of cancer* 癌症早期診斷的新方法 **2** [U] *formal* proper planning of the way that something is done【正式】條理, 秩序: *There's no method in the way they do their accounts.* 他們記賬的方式沒有條理。**3 there's method in sb's madness** used to say that even though someone seems to be behaving strangely, there is a sensible reason for what they are doing 某人看起來舉止怪異, 但行事合乎情理

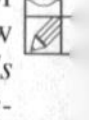

me·thod·i·cal /məˈθɑdɪkḷ; məˈθɒdɪkəl/ *adj* **1** done in a careful and well organized way 有條理的; 井然的: *a methodical piece of work* 一項井井有條的工作 **2** always doing things carefully, using an ordered system 做事有條不紊的, 辦事有條理的: *She's a very methodical person.* 她是個辦事很有條理的人。—**methodically** /-kḷɪ; -kli/ *adv*: *The detective went through the papers methodically, one by one.* 偵探有條不紊地、一份一份地檢查了那些文件。

Meth·o·dist /ˋmɛθədɪst; ˈmeθədɪ̣st/ *n* [C] someone who belongs to a Christian religious group that follows the teachings of John Wesley〔遵循約翰·衛斯理教義的〕循道公會教徒 —**Methodist** *adj* —**Methodism** *n* [U]

meth·o·dol·o·gy /ˌmɛθədˋɑlədʒɪ; ˌmeθəˈdɒlədʒi/ *n* [C, U] the set of methods and principles that are used when studying a particular subject or doing a particular kind of work 方法論; 方法學;〔某一學科的〕一套方法和原則: *teaching methodology* 教學法 —**methodological** /ˌmɛθədəˋlɑdʒɪkḷ; ˌmeθədəˈlɒdʒɪkəl◂/ *adj* —**methodologically** /-kḷɪ; -kli/ *adv*

me·thought /mɪˋθɔt; mɪˈθɔːt/ the past tense of METHINKS

meths /mɛθs; meθs/ *n* [U] *BrE informal* METHYLATED SPIRITS【英, 非正式】甲基化酒精

Me·thus·e·lah /məˋθjuzələ; məˈθjuːzɪ̣lə/ *n* **as old as Methuselah** very old 年紀非常大的

meth·yl al·co·hol /ˌmɛθəl ˋælkəˌhɔl; ˌmeθɪ̣l ˈælkəhɒl/ *n* [U] a poisonous alcohol that can be made from wood; METHANOL 甲醇 —compare 比較 ETHYL ALCOHOL

meth·yl·at·ed spir·its /ˌmɛθəˌletɪd ˋspɪrɪts; ˌmeθɪ̣leɪtɪ̣d ˈspɪrɪ̣ts/ *n* [U] a kind of alcohol that is burned in lamps, heaters etc〔燈盞、加熱器等用的〕甲基化酒精

me·tic·u·lous /məˋtɪkjələs; mɪ̣ˈtɪkjʊ̣ləs/ *adj* **1** very careful about small details, and always making sure that everything is done correctly 對細節十分注意的, 一絲不苟的: *He kept meticulous accounts.* 他記賬非常詳細準確。| *She pasted the cuttings into the scrapbook with meticulous care.* 她小心翼翼地把剪下的資料黏到剪貼簿上。**2** if you are meticulous about doing something, you are very careful to always do it 總是非常注意做到的: **[+in/about]** *He's meticulous about replying to correspondence.* 他非常注意做到有信必覆。—**meticulously** *adv* —**meticulousness** *n* [U]

met·i·er /meˋtje; ˈmetieɪ/ *n* [C usually singular 一般用單數] *formal* a kind of work or activity that you enjoy doing because you have a natural ability to do it well【正式】專長, 特長, 得心應手的工作: **not be sb's metier** *Modern music is not his metier.* 現代音樂不是他的專長。

-metre /mitɚ; miːtə/ *BrE*【英】, **-meter** *AmE*【美】*suffix* [in nouns 構成名詞] part of a metre, or a number of metres 一米的一部分; 若干米: *a millimetre* 一毫米 | *a kilometre* 一千米, 一公里

2 3 **me·tre** *BrE*【英】, **meter** *AmE*【美】/ˋmitɚ; ˈmiːtə/ *n* **1** [C] the basic unit for measuring length in the METRIC SYSTEM 米, 公尺〔公制長度的基本公制單位〕—see table on page C3 參見 C3 頁附錄 **2** [C,U] the arrangement of sounds in poetry into patterns of strong and weak beats〔詩的〕格律, 韻律 —compare 比較 RHYTHM (1)

met·ric /ˋmɛtrɪk; ˈmetrɪk/ *adj* **1** using or connected with the metric system of weights and measures 公制的, 米制的, 十進制的: *the metric tonne* 公噸 | *metric sizes* 公制尺碼 **2** metrical 用詩體寫的, 格律詩的 —compare 比較 IMPERIAL (2)

met·ri·cal /ˋmɛtrɪkḷ; ˈmetrɪkəl/ *adj technical* written in the form of poetry, with regular beats【術語】用詩體寫的, 格律詩的 —**metrically** /-kḷɪ; -kli/ *adv*

met·ri·ca·tion /ˌmɛtrɪˋkeʃən; ˌmetrɪˈkeɪʃən/ *n* [U] the change to using the metric system of weights and measures〔度量衡的〕公制化

metric sys·tem /ˈ·· ˌ··/ *n* [singular] the system of weights and measures that is based on the metre and the kilogram 公制, 米制

metric ton /ˌ·· ˈ·/ *n* [C] a unit for measuring weight equal to 1,000 kilograms 公噸, 米制噸〔重量計量單位, 等於 1,000 公斤〕

met·ro /ˋmɛtro; ˈmetrəʊ/ *n* [C] a railway system that runs under the ground below a city 地下鐵道系統, 地(下)鐵(道): *the Paris Metro* 巴黎地下鐵道系統

met·ro·nome /ˋmɛtrəˌnom; ˈmetrənəʊm/ *n* [C] a piece of equipment that shows the speed at which music should be played, by making a regular noise 節拍器〔顯示音樂應以甚麼速度演奏的設備〕

me·trop·o·lis /məˋtrɑplɪs; mɪ̣ˈtrɒpəlɪ̣s/ *n* [C] a very large city that is the most important city in a country or area〔一國或一地區的〕首要城市; 大都會

met·ro·pol·i·tan /ˌmɛtrəˋpɑlətn̩; ˌmetrəˈpɒlɪ̣tən◂/ *adj* **1** connected with or belonging to a very large city 大城市的, 大都會的: *the Los Angeles metropolitan area* 洛杉磯都市區 **2** *technical* connected with France, rather than its colonies (COLONY (1))【術語】法國本土〔而非其殖民地〕的: *metropolitan France* 法國本土

Metropolitan Po·lice /ˌ····· ·ˈ·/ *n* [singular] the police force that is responsible for London 都市警隊〔負責倫敦地區的警察部隊〕

met·tle /ˋmɛtḷ; ˈmetl/ *n* [U] **1** courage and determination to do something even when it is very difficult 勇氣, 奮鬥精神: *a man of mettle* 有奮鬥精神的人 | **show/prove your mettle** (=show that you can do something well, in spite of difficulties) 顯示出/證明你的勇氣[決心, 毅力] *It'll be a hard game, but it should give the team a chance to show their mettle.* 這將是一場艱苦的比賽, 但它會給隊員們一個顯示自己毅力的機會。**2 be on your mettle** to be ready to try as hard as possible because your abilities are being tested 準備盡最大努力: *You'll have to be on your mettle in the oral exam.* 口試中你必須全力以赴。

met·tle·some /ˋmɛtḷsəm; ˈmetlsəm/ *adj literary* full of energy and determination【文】精力充沛的; 剛毅的

mew /mju; mjuː/ *v* [I] to make the soft high crying sound that a cat makes 作貓叫聲 —**mew** *n*

mews /mjuz; mjuːz/ *n plural BrE* a small street or yard surrounded by houses in a city, where horses used to be kept【英】〔城市中為房屋環繞、過去用作馬廐的〕小街, 小院

Mex·i·can[1] /ˋmɛksɪkən; ˈmeksɪ̣kən/ *adj* from or connected with Mexico 墨西哥的

Mexican[2] *n* [C] someone from Mexico 墨西哥人

Mexican wave /ˌ··· ˈ·/ *n* [singular] *BrE* the effect that is made when all the people watching a game of football, BASEBALL etc stand up, move their arms up and down, and sit down again one after the other in a continuous movement【英】墨西哥人浪〔觀看足球、棒球等比賽時所有人依次站起上下揮動雙臂而後又坐下所形成的人浪〕

mez·za·nine /ˋmɛzəˌnin; ˈmezəniːn/ *n* [C] **1** a small floor that is built between two other floors in a building〔兩層樓之間的〕夾層樓面, 夾樓 **2** *AmE* the lowest BALCONY in a theatre, or the first few rows of seats in that balcony【美】〔劇院的〕最底層樓廳; 最底層樓廳的前幾排座位

mez·zo[1] /ˋmɛtso; ˈmetsəʊ/ *adv* **mezzo forte/piano etc** *technical* a word meaning quite or not very loud, softly etc, used in instructions for performing music【術語】中強/中弱等〔演奏音樂中用作說明的詞語〕

mezzo[2] *n* [C] a mezzo-soprano voice 女中音

mezzo-so·pra·no /ˌ·· ·ˈ··/ *n* [C] **1** a voice that is lower than a SOPRANO's but higher than an ALTO's 女中音 **2** a woman who sings with this kind of voice 女中音歌手

mez·zo·tint /ˋmɛtsəˌtɪnt; ˈmetsəʊˌtɪnt/ *n* [C,U] a picture printed from a metal plate that is polished in places to produce areas of light and shade 鏤刻金屬版印刷品

MFA /ˌɛm ɛf ˋe; ˌem ef ˈeɪ/ *n* [C] *AmE* Master of Fine Arts; a university degree in a subject such as painting or SCULPTURE【美】美術碩士; 美術碩士學位

mg the written abbreviation of 縮寫= MILLIGRAM

MHz the written abbreviation of 縮寫= MEGAHERTZ

mi /mi; miː/ *n* [singular] the third note in a musical SCALE[1] (8) according to the SOL-FA system 視唱法音階中的第三音

MI5 /ˌɛm aɪ ˋfaɪv; ˌem aɪ ˈfaɪv/ *n* [not with *the* 不與 the 連用] a secret British government organization whose job it is to keep Britain safe from attack by enemies inside the country, such as foreign spies (SPY[1]) or TERRORISTS MI5 局, 軍情五處〔英國祕密政府機構, 負責保衛英國不受國家內部敵人, 如外國間諜或恐怖分子的破壞〕

M

MI6 /ˌɛm aɪ ˋsɪks; ˌem aɪ ˈsɪks/ *n* [not with *the* 不與 the 連用] a secret British government organization that sends people to foreign countries to try and find out secret political and military information MI6局, 軍情六處〔英國祕密政府機構, 專司向外國派遣人員以搜集祕密的政治和軍事情報〕

MIA /ˌɛm aɪ ˋe; ˌem aɪ ˈeɪ/ *n* [C] *AmE* missing in action; a soldier who has disappeared in a battle and who may still be alive【美】戰鬥中失蹤人員

mi·aow, meow /mɪˋaʊ; miˈaʊ/ *v* [I] to make the crying sound that a cat makes 作貓叫聲 —**miaow** *n* [C]

mi·as·ma /maɪˋæzmə; miˈæzmə/ *n* [singular,U] *literary*【文】**1** a thick, unhealthy, unpleasant mist 瘴氣: *A foul miasma lay over the town.* 一陣難聞的瘴氣籠罩在城市上空。**2** an evil influence or feeling 有害的影響; 不良的感覺: *The miasma of defeat hung over them.* 失敗的氣氛彌漫在他們中間。

mi·ca /ˋmaɪkə; ˈmaɪkə/ *n* [U] a mineral that consists of small flat transparent pieces of rock, which is used to make electrical instruments 雲母

mice /maɪs; maɪs/ the plural of MOUSE

Mich·ael·mas /ˋmɪkḷməs; ˈmɪkəlməs/ *n* [C,U] 29th September, a Christian holy day in honour of Saint Michael 米迦勒節〔9月29日基督教紀念聖米迦勒的節日〕

mick /mɪk; mɪk/ *n* [C] *BrE* an insulting word for someone from Ireland【英】愛爾蘭人〔侮辱性詞語〕

mick·ey /ˋmɪkɪ; ˈmɪki/ *n* **1 take the mickey (out of sb)** *informal especially BrE* to make someone look silly often in a friendly way, for example by copying them or by pretending something is true when it is not【非正式, 尤英】戲弄〔指善意地捉弄某人, 如模仿他的動作、哄騙他等〕: *Why are people always taking the mickey out of Nigel?* 人們為甚麼總是捉弄奈傑爾? **2** also 又作 **Mickey Finn** [C] a type of drug that you give to someone to make them unconscious 麻醉藥; 蒙汗藥

Mickey Mouse /ˌ·· ˈ·◂/ *adj* **a Mickey Mouse operation/organization/outfit** a company or organization that is very small and unimportant, and not very good 無足輕重的企業/組織/機構

mi·cro /ˋmaɪkro; ˈmaɪkrəʊ/ *n* [C] *old-fashioned* a small computer; a PC[1]【過時】微型電腦; 個人電腦

micro- /ˋmaɪkro; ˈmaɪkrəʊ/ *prefix technical* extremely small【術語】極小的, 微小的: *a microcomputer* 微型電腦 | *microelectronics* 微電子學 —see table on page C4 參見 C4 頁附錄 —compare 比較 MACRO-, MINI-

mi·crobe /ˋmaɪkrob; ˈmaɪkrəʊb/ *n* [C] a living thing which is so small that it cannot be seen without a microscope, and which can sometimes cause disease 微生物; 病原體

mi·cro·bi·ol·o·gy /ˌmaɪkrobaɪˋɑlədʒɪ; ˌmaɪkrəʊbaɪˈɒlədʒi/ *n* [U] the scientific study of very small living things such as BACTERIA 微生物學 —**microbiologist** *n* [C] —**microbiological** /ˌmaɪkrobaɪəˋlɑdʒɪkḷ; ˌmaɪkrəʊbaɪəˈlɒdʒɪkəl/ *adj*

mi·cro·chip /ˋmaɪkrotʃɪp; ˈmaɪkrəʊˌtʃɪp/ *n* [C] a very small piece of SILICON containing a set of electronic parts which is used in computers and other machines; a CHIP[1] (4a) 微型集成電路片, 微晶片, 芯片

mi·cro·com·put·er /ˌmaɪkrokəmˋpjutɚ; ˌmaɪkrəʊkəmˈpjuːtə/ *n* [C] *old-fashioned* a small computer; a PC[1]【過時】微型電腦; 個人電腦

mi·cro·cos·m /ˋmaɪkrəˌkɑzəm; ˈmaɪkrəʊkɒzəm/ *n* [C] a small group, society, or place that has the same qualities as a much larger one 微觀世界; 縮影; 小天地, 小宇宙 —compare 比較 MACROCOSM —**microcosmic** /ˌmaɪkrəˋkɑzmɪk; ˌmaɪkrəʊˈkɒzmɪk◂/ *adj*

mi·cro·dot /ˋmaɪkrodɑt; ˈmaɪkrəʊdɒt/ *n* [C] a secret photograph of something such as a document, that is reduced to the size of a DOT so that it can easily be hidden 微粒照片〔指為便於藏匿而將文件等的機密照片縮小至微粒大小〕

mi·cro·e·lec·tron·ics /ˌmaɪkroɪlɛkˋtrɑnɪks; ˌmaɪkrəʊɪlekˈtrɒnɪks/ *n* [U] the practice or study of designing very small PRINTED CIRCUITS that are used in computers 微電子學 —**microelectronic** *adj*

mi·cro·fiche /ˋmaɪkrofiʃ; ˈmaɪkrəʊfiːʃ/ *n* [C,U] a sheet of film on which written information is stored in a very small form, and which can only be read using a special machine〔存儲文字資料的〕縮微膠片

mi·cro·film /ˋmaɪkrəˌfɪlm; ˈmaɪkrəʊfɪlm/ *n* [C,U] very small film for photographing maps, documents etc so that they can be easily stored〔供拍攝地圖、文件等以便存儲用的〕縮微膠卷 —**microfilm** *v* [T]

mi·cro·light /ˋmaɪkrəlaɪt; ˈmaɪkrəʊlaɪt/ *n* [C] a very light small aircraft for one or two people〔載一兩人的〕微型飛機

mi·crom·e·ter /maɪˋkrɑmətɚ; maɪˈkrɒmḷtə/ *n* [C] an instrument for measuring very small distances 測微計, 千分尺

mi·cron /ˋmaɪkrɑn; ˈmaɪkrɒn/ *n* [C] one millionth of a metre 微米〔百萬分之一米〕

mi·cro·or·gan·is·m /ˌmaɪkroˋɔrgənˌɪzəm; ˌmaɪkrəʊˈɔːgənɪzəm/ *n* [C] a living thing which is so small that it cannot be seen without a microscope 微生物

mi·cro·phone /ˋmaɪkrəˌfon; ˈmaɪkrəfəʊn/ *n* [C] a piece of equipment that you speak into to record your voice or make it louder when you are speaking or performing in public 麥克風, 話筒, 傳聲器, 擴音器

mi·cro·pro·ces·sor /ˋmaɪkroˋprɑsɛsɚ; ˈmaɪkrəʊˌprəʊsesə/ *n* [C] the central CHIP[1] (4a) in a computer, which controls most of its operations〔電腦的〕微處理器, 微處理機

mi·cro·scope /ˋmaɪkrəˌskop; ˈmaɪkrəskəʊp/ *n* [C] **1** a scientific instrument that makes extremely small things look larger 顯微鏡 —see picture at 參見 LABORATORY 圖 **2 put sth under the microscope** to examine a situation very closely and carefully 認真仔細地檢查某物

mi·cro·scop·ic /ˌmaɪkrəˋskɑpɪk; ˌmaɪkrəˈskɒpɪk◂/ *adj* **1** extremely small and therefore very difficult to see 極小的, 微小的, 小得難以看清的: *His handwriting is microscopic!* 他的字寫得極小! | *The insect's legs are covered with microscopic hairs.* 昆蟲的腿上覆有難以看到的細毛。**2** [only before noun 僅用於名詞前] using a microscope 用顯微鏡的: *The cells were identified through microscopic analysis.* 那些細胞通過顯微鏡分析被識別出來。—**microscopically** /-kḷɪ; -kli/ *adv*

mi·cro·sec·ond /ˌmaɪkroˋsɛkənd; ˌmaɪkrəʊˈsekənd/ *n* [C] one millionth of a second 微秒〔百萬分之一秒〕

mi·cro·wave[1] /ˋmaɪkrəˌwev; ˈmaɪkrəweɪv/ *n* [C] **1** also 又作 **microwave ov·en** /ˌ··· ˈ··/ a type of OVEN that cooks food very quickly using very short electric waves instead of heat 微波爐 —see picture on page A10 參見 A10 頁圖 **2** a very short electric wave that is used in cooking food, sending messages by radio, and in RADAR 微波

microwave[2] *v* [T] to cook something in a microwave oven 用微波爐烹調 —**microwaveable, microwavable** *adj*

mid /mɪd; mɪd/ *prep poetic* among or in the middle of【詩】在…中間

mid- /mɪd; mɪd/ *prefix* middle 中部, 中間, 當中: *She's in her mid-20s.* (=is about 25 years old) 她二十五歲左右。| *in mid-July* 在七月中旬 | *a cold midwinter night* 寒冷的仲冬之夜

mid·air /ˌmɪdˋɛr; ˌmɪdˈeə◂/ *n* **in midair** in the air or the sky, away from the ground 在空中, 在半空中: *The planes collided in midair.* 飛機在半空中相撞。—**midair** *adj*: *a midair collision* 空中相撞

mid At·lan·tic /ˌ· ·ˈ··◂/ *adj* **mid Atlantic accent** a way of speaking that uses a mixture of American and British English sounds and words 中大西洋口音〔在發音和用詞上混合使用美國英語和英國英語〕

mid·day /ˋmɪdˌde; ˌmɪdˈdeɪ◂/ *n* [U] the middle of the

day; twelve o'clock 中午, 正午: **at midday** *I'm meeting him at midday.* 我中午要見他。| **midday meal/sun etc** *the full heat of the midday sun* 正午的烈日 —compare 比較 MIDNIGHT (1)

mid·den /ˈmɪdn̩; ˈmɪdn/ *n* [C] *old use* a pile of something such as animal waste or rubbish【舊】糞堆; 垃圾堆

1 2 **mid·dle¹** /ˈmɪdl̩; ˈmɪdl/ *n* **1 the middle a)** the part that is furthest from the sides, edges, or ends 中間, 中央, 中部, 當中: *a seat in the middle of the front row* 前排中間的一個座位 | *Here's a photo of us on holiday – that's me in the middle.* 這是我們度假時拍的一張照片 — 中間的那個是我。| **right in the middle/right down the middle etc** *The other car was driving right in the middle of the road.* 另一輛汽車行駛在路的正中間。| *Going through the middle of Tokyo in the rushhour can be a nightmare.* 在交通高峯期穿越東京市中心會是一場噩夢。**b)** the part that is between the beginning and the end of an event, story, period etc〔事件、故事、階段等的〕中間部分: *Why don't we meet sometime in the middle of the week?* 我們何不在這個星期中間的某個時候碰頭呢? | *She started to feel sick in the middle of the exam.* 考試考到一半她開始感到身體不適。| *I arrived in Athens in the middle of a heatwave.* 我到達雅典時正逢酷暑。**c)** the position or rank that is between the highest and the lowest position in a list of people or things 中等, 中游: *Janine graduated top of the class and I finished somewhere around the middle.* 賈寧以全班第一名的成績畢業而我卻成績中等。**d)** the inside part of an object such as a ball, or piece of fruit〔球、水果等物體的〕內部, 裡邊: *Urgh! There's a maggot in the middle of this apple!* 哎呀! 這個蘋果裡頭有一條蛆! **2 be in the middle of (doing sth)** to be busy doing something 正忙於(做某事): *Can I call you back – I'm in the middle of a meeting.* 我過一會兒給你回電話好嗎 — 我正在開會。| *She was just in the middle of getting the dinner ready.* 她恰好正忙着準備晚飯。**3** [C usually singular 一般用單數] *informal* the waist and the part of the body around the stomach【非正式】腰; 腹部: *Nick seems to be getting a bit fat round his middle.* 尼克的腰部好像有點發胖了。**4 in the middle of nowhere** a long way from the nearest town or from any interesting places 在偏遠之地; 在茫茫蠻荒中: *So there we were, in the middle of nowhere, and out of gas.* 就這樣我們困在了茫茫荒野中, 而且汽油也用光了。**5 divide/split sth down the middle** to divide something into equal halves or groups 沿中間分開/劈開某物: *The votes are divided right down the middle on this issue.* 有關這一問題的贊成票數和反對票數恰好相等。—see also 另見 **piggy in the middle** (PIGGY¹ (2))

1 2 **middle²** *adj* [only before noun 僅用於名詞前] **1** nearest the centre, especially of a row, list, or group of things or people 居中的, 中央的, 中間的: *the middle house in a row of five* 一排五幢房子居中的那幢 | *Two of his middle front teeth were missing.* 他中間門牙有兩顆掉了。| *the middle drawer of the filing cabinet* 檔案櫃中間的抽屜 **2** halfway through an event or period of time〔事件或時間段〕中間部分的: *They spent the middle part of their vacation in Florida.* 假期的中期他們是在佛羅里達州度過的。**3 in your middle twenties/thirties etc** about 25, 35 etc years old 二十五/三十五歲等左右 **4 middle brother/child/daughter etc** the brother etc who is between the oldest and the youngest 排行中間的兄弟/孩子/女兒等 **5 middle course/way etc** a way of dealing with something that is between two opposite and often extreme ways 中庸之道, 中間路線: *The administration is trying to follow a middle course on health care reform.* 在醫療改革方面政府正在極力採取折衷的辦法。**6 Middle English/French etc** an old form of English, French etc, used in the Middle Ages (=between 1100 and 1500 AD) 中古英語/法語等〔使用於公元1100年至1500年之間〕—see also 另見 MIDDLE FINGER, MIDDLE NAME

middle age /ˌ·· ˈ·◂/ *n* [U] the period of your life when you are no longer young but are not yet old 中年: *The new technique allows women to have children well into middle age.* 那項新技術使婦女一直到中年都可以生育。

middle-aged /ˌ·· ˈ·◂/ *adj* **1** no longer young but not yet old 中年的: *a middle-aged businessman* 中年商人 **2** middle-aged attitudes or ways of behaving are rather boring or old-fashioned〔態度或行為方式〕有中年人特點的; 枯燥的; 過時的: *a middle-aged outlook on life* 中年人的人生觀 **3 middle-aged spread** an area of fat that many people develop around their waist as they grow older 中年發福

Middle Ag·es /ˌ·· ˈ··/ *n* **the Middle Ages** the period in European history between about 1100 and 1500 AD〔歐洲歷史上的〕中世紀〔約公元1100年至1500年〕

Middle A·mer·i·ca /ˌ·· ·ˈ···/ *n* [U] **1** the mid-western part of the United States 美國中西部 **2** Americans who are neither very rich nor very poor and who usually have traditional ideas about morality, education etc 美國中產階級

mid·dle·brow /ˈmɪdl̩ˌbraʊ; ˈmɪdlbraʊ/ *adj* middlebrow books, television programmes etc are not very difficult to understand〔書籍、電視節目等〕易讀的, 不難懂的 —compare 比較 HIGHBROW, LOWBROW

middle C /ˌmɪdl ˈsi; ˌmɪdl ˈsiː/ *n* [singular] the musical note C which is at the middle point of a piano KEYBOARD 中央C(音)

middle class /ˌ·· ˈ·◂/ *n* **the middle class** also 又作 **the middle classes** the social class that includes professional people such as teachers or managers, but does not include people who are very rich or people who work mainly with their hands 中產階級 —compare 比較 LOWER CLASS, UPPER CLASS, WORKING CLASS

middle-class *adj* **1** belonging to or typical of the middle class 中產階級的: *a middle-class suburb* 中產階級居住的郊區 | *She comes from a middle-class background.* 她來自中產階級家庭。**2** middle-class attitudes, values etc are typical of middle-class people and are often concerned with work, education, and possessions〔態度、價值觀等〕中產階級特有的

middle dis·tance /ˌ·· ˈ··/ *n* **the middle distance** the part of a picture or a view that is between the nearest part and the part that is farthest away〔圖畫或景色前景和背景之間的〕中景

middle-dis·tance /ˈ·· ··/ *adj* [only before noun 僅用於名詞前] a middle-distance race is neither very short nor very long, for example 800 or 1500 metres〔賽跑〕中距離的〈如800米或1500米〉

middle ear /ˌ·· ˈ·/ *n* [singular] the central part of the ear, between the outside part and the EARDRUM 中耳

Middle East /ˌ·· ˈ·◂/ *n* **the Middle East** the area including Iran and Egypt and the countries which are between them 中東 —compare 比較 FAR EAST —**Middle Eastern** *adj*

middle fin·ger /ˌ·· ˈ··/ *n* [C] the longest finger, which is the middle one of the five fingers on your hand 中指

middle ground /ˌ·· ˈ·/ *n* [U] something that two opposing groups can both agree about 中間觀點; 中間立場; 折衷辦法: *The negotiators could find no middle ground.* 談判人員找不到雙方都能接受的立場。

mid·dle·man /ˈmɪdl̩ˌmæn; ˈmɪdlmæn/ *plural* **middlemen** /-ˌmɛn; -men/ *n* [C] someone who buys things in order to sell them to someone else, or who helps to arrange business deals for other people 經紀人; 掮客; 中間人: *He acts as a middleman for British companies seeking contracts in the Gulf.* 他給在海灣地區尋找商機的英國公司當中間人。| **cut out the middleman** (=avoid having to use a middleman) 避開中間商 *Buy direct from the manufacturer and cut out the middleman.* 從廠家直接進貨, 繞開中間商。

middle man·age·ment /ˌ·· ˈ···/ *n* [U] managers who are in charge of small groups of people but do not take

M

the most important decisions 中層管理人員; 中級管理層 —**middle manager** *n* [C]

middle name /,·· ˈ·/ *n* [C] **1** the name that is between your first name and your family name 中間名〔名和姓之間的名字〕 **2 sth is sb's middle name** *informal* used to say that someone has a lot of a particular personal quality【非正式】某人在某方面有突出個性: *Generosity's her middle name.* 慷慨是她顯著的個性特徵。

middle-of-the-road /,·· · · ˈ·◂/ *adj* middle-of-the-road ideas, opinions etc are not extreme, and are similar to the ideas that most people have〔思想、看法等〕中間路線的, 中間派的; 温和(路線)的: *Her political views are fairly middle-of-the-road.* 她的政治觀點非常温和。

middle school /ˈ·· ·/ *n* **1** [C,U] a school in Britain for children between the ages of 8 and 12 中等學校〔英國8歲至12歲學生就讀的學校〕 **2** [C,U] a school in the US for children between the ages of 11 and 14 初中〔美國11歲至14歲學生就讀的學校〕

middle-sized /,·· ˈ·◂/ *adj* neither very large nor very small 中等大小的, 中號的: *a middle-sized house* 中等大小的房子

mid·dle·weight /ˋmɪdḷ,wet; ˈmɪdlweɪt/ *n* [C] a BOXER who is lighter than a LIGHT HEAVYWEIGHT and heavier than a WELTERWEIGHT 中量級拳擊手

Middle West /,·· ˈ·/ *n* **the Middle West** another form of the MIDWEST midwest 的另一種形式

mid·dling /ˋmɪdlɪŋ; ˈmɪdəlɪŋ/ *adj informal* not very good or bad, not very big or small etc; average【非正式】中等的, 一般的, 普通的: **fair to middling** (=about average) 過得去, 還算好 *"How are you?" "Oh, fair to middling."* "你好嗎?" "哦, 還好。"

mid·field /ˋmɪd,fild; ˈmɪdfiːld/ *n* [U] **1** the middle part of the area where a game such as football or BASEBALL is played〔足球場或棒球場等的〕中場: *a midfield player* 中場球員 **2** the members of a football team who play in this area〔足球隊的〕中場球員

mid·field·er /ˋmɪd,fildɚ; ˈmɪdfiːldə/ *n* [C] a player who usually plays in the midfield 中場隊員

midge /mɪdʒ; mɪdʒ/ *n* [C] a small flying insect that bites people 蠓; 搖蚊

midg·et[1] /ˋmɪdʒɪt; ˈmɪdʒɪ̈t/ *n* [C] **1** a very small person who will never grow tall because there is something wrong with their body 侏儒, 矮人 **2** *BrE informal* someone who is not very tall【英, 非正式】個子不很高的人

midget[2] *adj* **midget car/camera etc** a very small CAR etc 小型汽車/袖珍照相機等

Mid·lands /ˋmɪdləndz; ˈmɪdləndz/ *n* **the Midlands** *plural* the central part of England 英格蘭中部地區 —**Midland** *adj* —**Midlander** *n* [C]

mid·life cri·sis /,mɪdlaɪf ˋkraɪsɪs; ,mɪdlaɪf ˈkraɪsɪ̈s/ *n* [C] feelings of worry and lack of confidence, when you are between 40 and 50 years old 中年危機, 中年期心理危機〔指40歲至50歲的中年人所感受到的焦慮和缺乏自信〕

mid·night /ˋmɪd,naɪt; ˈmɪdnaɪt/ *n* [U] **1** 12 o'clock at night 半夜12點, 子夜, 午夜: *We close at midnight.* 我們晚上12點關門。| *the midnight train to Glasgow* 開往格拉斯哥的午夜火車 —compare 比較 MIDDAY **2 midnight feast** a secret meal eaten late at night, especially by children〔尤指孩子們偷偷舉行的〕午夜餐 —see also 另見 **burn the midnight oil** (BURN[1] (24))

midnight sun /,·· ˈ·/ *n* **the midnight sun** the sun seen in the middle of the night in summer in the far north or south of the world〔極地夏季見到的〕子夜太陽, 夜半太陽

mid·point /ˋmɪd,pɔɪnt; ˈmɪdpɔɪnt/ *n* [C usually singular 一般用單數] a point that is halfway through or along something 中點;〔時間、事件等進程的〕一半: **[+of]** *We are now at the midpoint of this government's term of office.* 我們這屆政府任期現在已經過半。

mid·riff /ˋmɪdrɪf; ˈmɪdrɪf/ *n* [C] the part of the body between your chest and your waist 腹部

mid·ship·man /ˋmɪd,ʃɪpmən; ˈmɪdʃɪpmən/ *n* [C] the rank of someone who is training to become an officer in the British Navy〔英國海軍〕候補少尉 —see table on page C6 參見C6頁附錄

midst[1] /mɪdst; mɪdst/ *n* **1 in the midst of a)** in the middle of a period, situation, or event 在…的中期; 正值…的時候: *in the midst of the Cold War* 在冷戰中期 **b)** in the middle of a place or a group of things 在〔某地〕中部; 在〔一堆事物〕中間 **2 in our/their midst** *formal* in a particular group【正式】在我們/他們當中: *We have a traitor in our midst.* 我們當中有個叛徒。

midst[2] *prep old use* in the middle of or among【舊】在…中間, 在…之中

mid·sum·mer /ˋmɪdˋsʌmɚ; ,mɪdˈsʌmə◂/ *n* [U] the middle of summer 仲夏: *one bright midsummer afternoon* 仲夏一個晴朗的下午

Midsummer Day /,·· ˈ·/ also 又作 **Midsummer's Day** *n* [singular] *BrE* the 24th of June【英】仲夏節; 施洗約翰節〔6月24日〕

mid·term[1] /,mɪdˋtɝm; ,mɪdˈtɜːm◂/ *n* **1** [U] the middle period of an elected government's time in power〔政府任期的〕中期: *Nixon was the first president to resign in midterm.* 尼克遜是第一位在任期中期辭職的總統。**2** [C] *AmE* an examination in the middle of one of the main periods in the year at university【美】〔大學的〕期中考試

mid·term[2] /ˋmɪd,tɝm; ˈmɪdtɜːm/ *adj* [only before noun 僅用於名詞前] during or in the middle of one of the main periods in the school year, or in the middle of an elected government's time in power〔學期〕期中的;〔政府任期〕中期的: *midterm tests* 期中測驗 —compare 比較 HALF-TERM

mid·town /,mɪdˋtaʊn; ,mɪdˈtaʊn◂/ *adj, adv AmE* in the area of a city that is near the centre but is not the main business area【美】靠近市中心區〔但不是主要商業區〕的; 在市中心附近(的) —compare 比較 DOWNTOWN, UPTOWN —**midtown** *n* [U]

mid·way /ˋmɪdˋwe; ,mɪdˈweɪ◂/ *adj, adv* **1** halfway between two places or along a line 在中途(的), 在半路(的); 在中間(的): **[+between/along]** *midway between Madagascar and the coast of Tanzania* 從馬達加斯加到坦桑尼亞海岸的半路上 **2** halfway through a period of time〔指一段時間〕在中間(的); 到一半(的): *Tyson knocked out his opponent midway through the third round.* 泰臣在第三個回合進行了一半時就擊倒了對手。

mid·week /ˋmɪdˋwik; ,mɪdˈwiːk◂/ *adj, adv* on one of the middle days of the week 一週中間(的), 在週中(的): *a midweek match against Liverpool* 週中與利物浦隊的比賽 | *I don't go out much midweek anymore.* 我週中不再經常出去了。

Mid·west /ˋmɪdˋwɛst; ,mɪdˈwest/ *n* **the Midwest** the central area of the United States〔美國的〕中西部 —**Midwestern** *adj*

mid·wife /ˋmɪd,waɪf; ˈmɪdwaɪf/ *n plural* **midwives** /-,waɪvz; -waɪvz/ [C] a specially trained nurse, usually a woman, whose job is to help women when they are having a baby 助產士, 接生員, 產婆

mid·wif·e·ry /ˋmɪd,waɪfərɪ; ˈmɪd,wɪfəri/ *n* [U] the skill or work of a midwife 助產(術)

mid·win·ter /ˋmɪdˋwɪntɚ; ,mɪdˈwɪntə◂/ *n* [U] the middle of winter 仲冬: *They crossed the Great Smoky Mountains in midwinter.* 他們在仲冬翻越了大煙山。

mien /min; miːn/ *n* [singular] *literary* someone's typical expression or way of behaving【文】儀表, 神態, 風度, 樣子: *a thoughtful and solemn mien* 沉思而又嚴肅的神態

miffed /mɪft; mɪft/ *adj spoken* slightly annoyed or upset【口】略微生氣的, 惱火的: *I was a bit miffed that you'd left without me.* 我有點生氣的是你不帶上我就離開了。

might[1] /maɪt; maɪt/ *modal verb negative short form* 否定縮略式為 **mightn't 1** if something might happen or might be true, there is a possibility that it may happen or be true but you are not certain 也許, 可能, 大概: *Who knows – England might win the next World Cup!* 誰知道呢 —— 英格蘭隊也許會贏得下一屆世界杯! | *"Are you going to write her a letter?" "I might, I might not."* "你打算給她寫封信嗎?" "也許會, 也許不會。" | *You might not have noticed but I've put up a 'no smoking' sign in here.* 你大概還沒注意到, 我已在這兒豎起了"禁止吸煙"的告示牌。| *Did you see the way he was driving? I might have been killed.* 你看見他是怎麼開車的嗎? 我差點喪了命。**2** the past tense of may 也許, 可能; 可以〔may 的過去式〕: *Thinking it might rain, I decided to go in the car.* 我當時以為會下雨, 所以決定開車去。| *She asked if she might open a window.* 她問是否可以打開窗子。**3** used to give advice or make a suggestion 可以〔用於提建議〕: *If the police can't help, you might try the Citizens Advice Bureau.* 如果警察幫不了忙, 你可以試一試市民諮詢局。| *I thought we might spend the lesson studying irregular verbs.* 我想我們可以用這節課學習不規則動詞。**4 a)** *spoken old-fashioned* used to ask politely if you can do something【口, 過時】可以〔用於禮貌地請求允許做某事〕: *Might I come in?* 我可以進來嗎? **b) might I say/ask/add etc** *spoken* used to politely give more information, ask a question, interrupt etc【口】我可否説/問/補充等〔用於禮貌地提供更多信息、問問題、插話等〕: *Might I just add that Miriam has been a pleasure to work with and we wish her every success in the future.* 請允許我補充一句: 與米麗亞姆一起工作是一種樂趣, 我們祝願她將來事事成功。**5** used when you are angry or surprised when someone has not done something that you think they should do 應該, 本該〔表示説話人因某人還沒做某事而生氣或驚奇〕: *You might have cleaned up before you left!* 離開之前你為甚麼不收拾一下! | *Don't you think he might at least say thank you?* 你不認為他至少應該説聲謝謝嗎? **6 I might have known/guessed etc** *spoken* used to say that you are not surprised at a situation【口】我早該知道/猜到等〔表示對某種情況不感到吃驚〕: *Jake Thompson! I might have known you'd be behind all this!* 傑克·湯普森! 我早該料到所有這一切都是你在幕後操縱! **7 might well** if something might well happen or might well be true you think it is fairly likely to happen or be true 很可能, 極有可能: *You might well find that you'll need more by the weekend.* 到週末你很可能會發現你需要更多的東西。**8 might (just) as well** *usually spoken* used to suggest doing something that you do not really want to do, because you have no better ideas【一般口】最好還是…, 還是…為好, 倒不如…: *It's no good waiting for the bus. We might as well walk.* 等公共汽車來沒用, 我們還不如步行呢。**9 might…but…** used to tell someone that although what they said is true, something else which seemed very different is also a fact 也許…但是…〔表示儘管某人所説是事實, 但與其似乎非常不同的事也真實〕: *You might be a strong swimmer but that doesn't mean you can win a triathlon.* 你也許在游泳上很有實力, 但這並不意味着你可以在三項全能中獲勝。**10** *formal* used to say why something happens or the reason why someone does something【正式】能, 會〔以表示原因〕: *Samuel left his children a letter, so that his family might understand why he had to go away.* 塞繆爾給孩子們留下了一封信, 以便家人能明白他為甚麼不得不離開。**11** *old-fashioned humorous* used to politely ask for information【過時, 幽默】〔用於客氣地詢問〕: *And who might you be, young man?* 你又是誰呢, 年輕人? —compare 比較 MAY¹

might² *n* [U] **1** great strength and power 力量; 威力; 權力: *the full might of the Russian army* 俄羅斯軍隊的全部軍力 | **with all your might** (=using all your strength and a lot of effort) 盡全力; 全力以赴 *He swung the ax with all his might.* 他用盡全身力氣掄起斧頭。| **with might and main** *literary* (=with a lot of strength)【文】竭盡全力地, 拚命地 **2 might is right** *BrE*【英】, **might makes right** *AmE*【美】used to say that powerful people and countries can do whatever they want 強權就是公理

might-have-beens /ˈ· · ˌ·/ *n* [plural] things that you wish had happened in the past but which never did 未遂心願的事, 本應發生的事

might·i·ly /ˋmaɪtɪlɪ; ˈmaɪtl̩i/ *adv especially literary*【尤文】**1** very 非常: *She seemed mightily impressed by his story.* 她好像被他的故事深深地打動了。**2** using great strength 用力地; 猛烈地: *Fred swung mightily at the ball.* 弗雷德使勁地揮棒擊球。

might·n't /ˋmaɪtn̩t; ˈmaɪtənt/ *informal, especially BrE*【非正式, 尤英】the short form of 縮略式= 'might not'

might·y¹ /ˋmaɪtɪ; ˈmaɪti/ *adj especially literary* very strong and powerful, or very big and impressive【尤文】強有力的, 強大的; 巨大的, 雄偉的: *the mighty Mississippi river* 浩淼的密西西比河 | *a mighty king* 權力很大的國王 —see also 另見 **high and mighty** (HIGH¹ (19))

mighty² *adv* [+adj/adv] *AmE informal* very【美, 非正式】非常, 很: *It's mighty good to see you.* 見到你太好了。

mi·graine /ˋmaɪgren; ˈmiːgreɪn/ *n* [C] an extremely bad headache, during which you feel sick and have pain behind your eyes 偏頭痛

mi·grant /ˋmaɪgrənt; ˈmaɪgrənt/ *n* [C] **1** someone who goes to another area or country, especially in order to find work〔尤指為了尋找工作而遷移的〕移民; 移居者: **migrant worker/labour/groups** *migrant workers in the depression of the 1930s* 20 世紀 30 年代經濟蕭條時期的流動工人 | **economic migrant** (=someone who goes to another country because living conditions are better there) 經濟移民 **2** a bird or animal that travels from one part of the world to another, especially in the autumn and spring 候鳥; 遷徙動物 —compare 比較 EMIGRANT, IMMIGRANT

mi·grate /ˋmaɪgret; maɪˈgreɪt/ *v* [I+**from/to**] **1** if birds or animals migrate, they travel from one part of the world to another, especially in the autumn and spring〔鳥或獸〕遷徙, 移棲 **2** to go to another area or coun-try, especially in order to find work〔尤指為找工作〕移居; 遷移 —compare 比較 EMIGRATE, IMMIGRATE

mi·gra·tion /maɪˋgreʃən; maɪˈgreɪʃən/ *n* [C] the movement from one place to another of a large group of people, birds, animals etc〔一大羣人的〕移居, 遷移;〔大量鳥、獸等的〕遷徙, 移棲: *the great migrations to America of the 19th century* 19 世紀湧向美國的移民潮 ⊜ 2

mike¹ /maɪk; maɪk/ *n* [C] *informal* a MICROPHONE【非正式】麥克風, 話筒, 傳聲器, 擴音器 —see also 另見 OPEN MIKE, **for the love of Mike** (LOVE² (14))

mike² *v*

mike sb **up** *phr v* [T] *informal* to put a MICROPHONE on someone so that their voice can be recorded or made louder【非正式】給〔某人〕安麥克風

mi·la·dy /mɪˋledɪ; mɪˈleɪdi/ *n* [singular] another spelling of M'LADY m'lady 的另一種拼法

milch cow /ˋmɪltʃ kaʊ; ˈmɪltʃ kaʊ/ *n* [C] another spelling of MILK COW milk cow 的另一種拼法

mild¹ /maɪld; maɪld/ *adj*

1 ►WEATHER 天氣◄ not too cold or wet, and sometimes pleasantly warm 温和的, 暖和的: *We had an exceptionally mild winter last year.* 去年我們過了一個異常暖和的冬天。

2 ►ILLNESS 疾病◄ a mild illness or health problem is not serious 不嚴重的, 輕微的: *It's nothing – just a mild throat infection.* 沒甚麼, 只是輕微的喉部感染。

3 ►FOOD/TASTE 食物/味道◄ not very strong or hot-tasting 不濃烈的, 淡的; 不辣的: *a mild curry* 淡味咖喱

4 ►PUNISHMENT/CRITICISM 懲罰/批評◄ not severe or strict 不嚴厲的; 婉轉的: *a mild rebuke* 温和的指責

5 ►SMALL EFFECT 小的影響◄ not serious enough to cause much suffering 不厲害的, 弱的, 輕的: *The recession in Germany has been comparatively mild.* 德國的衰退相對而言要輕一些。| *a mild earthquake* 輕微的地震

6 ►CHARACTER/MANNER 性格/舉止◄ having a

gentle character and not easily getting angry 温和的, 溫厚的: *Joe was a mild man who rarely raised his voice.* 喬是個性情温和的人, 極少大嗓門説話。

7 ►SOAP ETC 肥皂等◄ soft and gentle to your skin 軟性的; 柔性的: *a mild washing-up liquid* 柔性洗滌液 —see also 另見 MILDLY

mild² *n* [U] *BrE* dark beer with a mild taste【英】淡啤酒 —compare 比較 BITTER² (1)

mil·dew /ˈmɪlˌdju; ˈmɪldjuː/ *n* [U] a white or grey substance that grows on leaves, walls, or other surfaces in wet, slightly warm conditions 黴; 黴菌 **—mildewed** *adj*

mild·ly /ˈmaɪldlɪ; ˈmaɪldli/ *adv* **1** [+adj] slightly 輕微地, 稍微: ***The drug is** only mildly addictive.* 這種藥物只會使人略微有點上癮。**2 to put it mildly** *spoken* used when saying that you could use much stronger words to describe something【口】説得婉轉些: *The manager wasn't very happy, to put it mildly, when you came in two hours late for the meeting.* 説得婉轉些, 你開會遲到兩小時, 經理不太高興。**3** in a gentle way without being angry 温和地, 和善地: *"Of course I don't mind," she answered mildly.* 她和善地答道: "我當然不介意。"

mild-man·nered /ˌ· ˈ··◄/ *adj* gentle and polite 舉止温柔的; 有禮貌的: *She had always struck me as being mild-mannered and quiet.* 她給我的印象一直是温柔而文靜。

mile /maɪl; maɪl/ *n* [C] **1** a unit for measuring distance or length, equal to 1609 metres 英里〔距離或長度的計量單位, 等於 1609 米〕—see table on page C3 參見 C3 頁附錄 **2 the mile** a race that is a mile in length 一英里賽跑: *the world record holder in the mile* 一英里賽跑的世界記錄保持者 **3 miles** *informal* a very long distance【非正式】很長的距離: *We were miles from home, and very tired.* 我們離家很遠, 而且累透了。| **for miles** (=for a very long distance) 很遠 *You can see for miles from the top of the hill.* 你從那座小山頂上能看很遠。| **miles from anywhere/nowhere** (=a long way from the nearest town or city) 離最近的鎮[城]很遠; 在荒僻之地 *They lived in a little cottage miles from nowhere.* 他們住在茫茫荒野中的一間小屋裡。**4 go the extra mile** to try a little harder in order to achieve something, after you have already used a lot of effort 再加把勁〔以完成某事〕: *Neither of the negotiating teams seems willing to go the extra mile.* 談判雙方似乎都不願意再努力前進一步。**5 sth sticks out/stands out a mile** also 又作 **you can tell sth a mile away/off** *informal* used to say that something is very clear from someone's appearance or behaviour【非正式】某事物顯而易見, 某事物一目了然: *It's obvious she's English – you can tell it a mile away.* 她顯然是英國人 —— 這一眼就能看出來。**6 talk a mile a minute** to speak very quickly without stopping 快而不停地説話, 連珠砲般地説話 **7 be miles away** *spoken* to not be paying attention to anything that is happening around you【口】心不在焉: *"Kate!" "Sorry, I was miles away!"* "凱特!" "對不起, 我走神了!" **8 miles older/better/too difficult etc** *BrE informal* very much older, better, too difficult etc【英, 非正式】老很多/好很多/實在太難等: *You're going out with John? But he's miles older than you!* 你在和約翰戀愛嗎? 他年齡可比你大好多呢! **9 miles out** *BrE informal* a measurement, guess, or calculation that is miles out is completely wrong【英, 非正式】〔測量、猜測或計算〕差遠了 —see also 另見 NAUTICAL MILE, **run a mile** (RUN¹ (47)), **a miss is as good as a mile** (MISS² (8))

mile·age /ˈmaɪlɪdʒ; ˈmaɪlɪdʒ/ *n* **1** [C usually singular 一般用單數, U] the number of miles a vehicle has travelled since it was made〔車輛自出廠後的〕行駛里程: *For sale Red Ford Escort. Low Mileage.* 出售紅色福特護衛者。行駛里程少。**2** [C usually singular 一般用單數, U] the number of miles a vehicle can travel using one GALLON or litre of fuel〔耗油一加侖或一升所行駛的〕英里數 **3** [U] the amount of use or advantage you get from something 利益, 好處; 用處: *The newspapers have had a lot of mileage out of the Royal divorce story.* 各家報紙已從王室離婚報道中賺了一大筆。**4** [C usually singular 一般用單數, U] also 又作 **mileage allowance** an amount of money paid for each mile that is travelled by someone using a car for work〔按英里支付的〕交通補貼 **5** [U] a distance in miles that is covered by a country's roads or railways〔一國公路或鐵路的〕總英里里程

mile·om·e·ter, milometer /maɪˈlɑmətə; maɪˈlɒmɪ̣tə/ *n* [C] *BrE* an instrument in a car that shows how many miles it has travelled【英】〔汽車的〕里程表, 里程記錄器; ODOMETER *AmE*【美】—see picture on page A2 參見 A2 頁圖

mile·post /ˈmaɪlpost; ˈmaɪlpəʊst/ *n* [C] *especially AmE* a post next to a road or railway that shows the distance in miles to the next town【尤美】〔公路或鐵路旁用英里顯示下一城鎮距離的〕里程標

mil·er /ˈmaɪlə; ˈmaɪlə/ *n* [C] a person or horse that competes in one-mile races 參加一英里賽跑的選手[馬]

mile·stone /ˈmaɪlˌston; ˈmaɪlstəʊn/ *n* [C] **1** [usually singular 一般用單數] a very important event in the development of something 重大事件, 里程碑: **[+in]** *The agreement was a milestone in the history of US-Soviet relations.* 該協議是美蘇關係史上的轉折點。**2** a stone next to a road that shows the distance in miles to the next town〔路邊的〕里程標

mi·lieu /miˈlju; ˈmiːljɜː/ *n plural* **milieux** /-ˈljuz; -ljɜːz/ *or* **milieus** [C,U] *French formal* the things and people that surround you and influence the way you live and think【法, 正式】出身背景, 周圍環境: *Proust wrote exclusively about his own social and cultural milieu.* 普魯斯特專門描寫自己的社會和文化環境。

mil·i·tant /ˈmɪlətənt; ˈmɪlɪ̣tənt/ *adj* a militant organization or person is willing to use strong or violent action in order to achieve political or social change 好鬥的; 使用暴力的; 激進的: *militant trade unionists* 激進的工聯主義者 | *After the assassination of Martin Luther King, black leaders became more militant.* 馬丁·路德·金遇刺後, 黑人領袖變得更激進了。**—militant** *n* [C] **—militancy** *n* [U] **—militantly** *adv*

mil·i·ta·ris·m /ˈmɪlətəˌrɪzəm; ˈmɪlɪ̣tərɪzəm/ *n* [U] the belief that a country should build up its military forces and use them to get what it wants 軍國主義; 窮兵黷武主義 **—militarist** *n* [C] **—militaristic** /ˌmɪlətəˈrɪstɪk; ˌmɪlɪ̣təˈrɪstɪk◄/ *adj*

mil·i·ta·rized also 又作 **-ised** *BrE*【英】/ˈmɪlətəˌraɪzd; ˈmɪlɪ̣təraɪzd/ *adj* a militarized area is one that has a lot of soldiers and weapons in it〔地區〕軍事化的

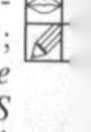

mil·i·ta·ry¹ /ˈmɪləˌtɛrɪ; ˈmɪlɪ̣təri/ *adj* used by or connected with war or the army, navy, or airforce 軍用的; 軍事的; 軍隊的: *a military helicopter* 軍用直升機 | *the use of military power* 使用軍事力量 | *the supreme US military commander in Europe* 美國駐歐洲最高軍事指揮官 **—militarily** *adv*

military² *n* **the military** the military forces of a country〔一國的〕武裝力量, 軍隊: [also+plural verb *BrE* 英] *The military have taken control of the government.* 軍方已控制了政府。| **in the military** *AmE* (=in the army, navy etc)【美】在部隊服役 *My brother is in the military.* 我兄弟在部隊服役。

Military A·cad·e·my /ˌ····ˈ···/ *n* [C] **1** a national college where people are trained to be officers in the military forces 軍事學院 **2** a private school in the US that gives students military training〔美國〕私立準軍事學校

Military Cross /ˌ···· ˈ·/ *n* [C] a MEDAL given to British army officers for being brave in battle〔授予英國陸軍軍官的〕英勇十字勳章

military po·lice /ˌ···· ·ˈ·/ *n* [singular] a special police force whose job is to deal with members of the army etc who break the rules 憲兵隊 —see also 另見 MP (2)

military ser·vice /ˌ···· ˈ··/ *n* [U] the system in which every adult man in a country has to be in the army, navy, or airforce, for a period of time 兵役(制) —compare 比較 DRAFT¹ (2)

M

mil·i·tate /ˋmɪlə͵tet; ˈmɪlɪteɪt/ *v*

militate against *phr v* [T] *formal* to prevent something or make it less likely to happen【正式】阻止; 妨礙: *Environmental factors militate against building the power station in this area.* 環境因素不利於在這一地區建設發電站。

mi·li·tia /məˋlɪʃə; mɪˈlɪʃə/ *n* [C] a group of people trained as soldiers, who are not part of the permanent army 民兵隊伍, 國民自衛隊

mi·li·tia·man /məˋlɪʃəmən; mɪˈlɪʃəmən/ *n* [C] a member of a militia 民兵

2 3 **milk¹** /mɪlk; mɪlk/ *n* [U] **1** a white liquid produced by cows or goats that is drunk by people 奶, 乳; 牛奶; 羊奶: *a bottle of milk* 一瓶牛奶 | *Would you like some milk in your tea?* 你的茶裡要加點牛奶嗎? **2** a white liquid produced by female animals and women for feeding their babies 奶汁, 母乳 **3** a liquid or juice produced by certain plants, especially the COCONUT (1)〔植物, 尤指椰樹產出的〕汁液 **4 the milk of human kindness** *literary* ordinary kindness and sympathy for other people【文】人類的善良天性; 惻隱之心 —see also 另見 EVAPORATED MILK, SKIMMED MILK, **cry over spilt milk** (CRY¹ (5)), **land of milk and honey** (LAND¹ (8))

milk² *v* [T] **1** to take milk from a cow or goat 擠〔牛或羊〕的奶 **2** *informal* to get as much money or as many advantages as you can from a situation, in a very determined and sometimes dishonest way【非正式】榨取, 勒索: **milk sb for sth** *Their landlord regularly milks them for extra money by claiming for damage to his property.* 他們的房東經常聲稱房產被損壞向他們榨取額外的錢財。| **milk sth for all it is worth** *Reporters were milking Nixon's resignation for all it was worth.* 記者們利用尼克遜辭職這件事大做文章。**3** to take the poison from a snake 取〔蛇的〕毒液

milk choc·o·late /͵· ˈ··◂/ *n* [U] chocolate made with milk and sugar 牛奶巧克力 —see also 另見 PLAIN CHOCOLATE

milk churn /ˈ· ·/ *n* [C] *BrE* a large metal container with a lid used to carry milk from farms【英】〔有蓋的金屬〕牛奶罐

milk cow /ˈ· ·/ also 又作 **milking cow** /ˈ·· ·/ *n* [C] a cow kept to give milk rather than for meat 奶牛

milk float /ˈ· ·/ *n* [C] *BrE* a vehicle used for delivering milk to people's houses, which is usually powered by electricity【英】送奶車

milking ma·chine /ˈ·· ·͵·/ *n* [C] a machine used for taking milk from cows 擠奶機, 擠奶器

milking par·lour *BrE*【英】, **milking parlor** *AmE*【美】/ˈ·· ͵··/ *n* [C] a building on a farm where milk is taken from the cows 擠奶房

milk loaf /ˈ· ·/ *n plural* **milk loaves** [C] *BrE* a LOAF of white bread made with milk【英】牛奶麵包

milk·maid /ˋmɪlk͵med; ˈmɪlkmeɪd/ *n* [C] *old use* a woman who gets milk from cows on a farm【舊】擠奶女工

milk·man /ˋmɪlk͵mæn; ˈmɪlkmən/ *n plural* **milkmen** /-͵mɛn; -mən/ [C] someone who delivers milk to houses each morning 送奶工

milk of mag·ne·sia /͵· · ·ˈ··/ *n* [U] a thick white liquid medicine used for stomach problems and CONSTIPATION 鎂乳, 氧化鎂乳劑〔用於醫治胃病和便祕的一種藥, 為白色濃稠液體〕

milk pud·ding /͵· ˈ··/ *n* [C] *BrE* a sweet food made of rice, TAPIOCA, or SAGO, baked in milk【英】牛奶布丁

milk round /ˈ· ·/ *n BrE*【英】**1** [C] the regular journey a milkman makes every day to deliver milk〔固定的〕送奶路線 **2 the milk round** *BrE* a series of visits to universities made each year by large companies to find people they may want to employ【英】〔大公司每年在各大學進行的〕巡迴招聘

milk run /ˈ· ·/ *n* [C] **1** *BrE informal* a familiar, easy journey that you do regularly【英, 非正式】例行的輕鬆差事 **2** *AmE informal* a train journey or regular plane flight that stops in many places【美, 非正式】〔在多處停留的〕火車線路; 定期航班

milk shake /͵· ˈ·/ *n* [C] **1** *BrE* a drink made of milk mixed with fruit or chocolate【英】奶昔〔牛奶與水果或巧克力混合的飲料〕**2** *AmE* a drink made of milk, ICE CREAM, and fruit or chocolate【美】泡沫牛奶〔牛奶與冰淇淋、水果或巧克力混合的飲料〕

milk·sop /ˋmɪlk͵sɑp; ˈmɪlksɒp/ *n* [C] *old-fashioned* a boy or man who is too gentle and weak, and who is afraid to do anything dangerous【過時】膽小懦弱的男孩[男人]; 懦夫

milk·toast /ˋmɪlk͵tost; ˈmɪlktəʊst/ *n* [C] another spelling of MILQUETOAST milquetoast 的另一種拼法

milk tooth /ˈ· ·/ *n plural* **milk teeth** [C] *BrE* one of the first set of teeth developed by young children; BABY TOOTH【英】乳牙, 乳齒

milk·weed /ˋmɪlk͵wid; ˈmɪlkwiːd/ *n* [U] a common North American plant that produces a bitter white substance when its stem is broken 馬利筋〔一種北美洲常見的植物〕

milk·y /ˋmɪlkɪ; ˈmɪlki/ *adj* **1** a drink that is milky contains a lot of milk〔飲料〕摻奶的, 多乳的: *milky coffee* 牛奶咖啡 **2** water or other liquids that are milky are not clear and look like milk〔水或其他液體〕不清的, 混濁的; 乳狀的 **3** milky skin is white and smooth〔皮膚〕白而滑的, 乳白色的 —**milkiness** *n* [U]

Milky Way /͵·· ˈ·/ *n* **the Milky Way** the pale white band of stars that can be seen across the sky at night 銀河(系)

mill¹ /mɪl; mɪl/ *n* [C] **1** a building containing a large machine for crushing grain into flour, or the machine itself 3
磨坊, 磨粉廠; 磨粉機: *an old mill with a ruined waterwheel* 水輪已壞的老磨坊 **2** a factory that produces materials such as cotton, cloth, steel〔生產布匹、鋼鐵等的〕工廠, 製造廠: *a woollen mill* 毛紡廠 **3 coffee/pepper mill** a small machine for crushing coffee or pepper 咖啡/胡椒研磨機 **4 go through the mill** to go through a time when you experience a lot of difficulties and problems 歷盡艱辛; 經受磨練: *Go easy on him – he's been through the mill lately.* 對他温和些 —— 他近來飽嘗了辛酸。**5 put sb through the mill** to make someone answer a lot of difficult questions or do a lot of difficult things in order to test them 使某人經歷嚴格的考查 **6** *AmE* a unit of money equal to 1/10 of a cent, used in setting taxes and for other financial purposes【美】密爾, 釐〔等於 1/10 美分, 用於定稅或其他金融用途〕—see also 另見 RUN-OF-THE-MILL, **(all) grist to the mill** (GRIST)

mill² *v* [T] **1** to produce flour by crushing grain in a mill 將〔穀物〕碾碎, 把…磨細 **2** to press, roll, or shape metal in a machine〔用機器〕碾[軋, 銑]〔金屬〕**3** to mark the edge of a coin with regular lines 在〔硬幣的邊緣〕軋齒邊, 軋凸緣

mill around/about *phr v* [I] *informal* if a lot of people mill around, they move around a place in different directions without any particular purpose【非正式】〔許多人〕無目的地亂轉, 亂兜圈子: *Crowds of students were milling around in the street.* 一羣羣的學生在街上轉來轉去。

mil·len·ni·um /məˋlɛnɪəm; mɪˈleniəm/ *n plural* **millennia** /-nɪə; -niə/ **1** [C] a period of 1000 years 1000 年, 千年期 **2** [C] the time when a new 1000-year period begins 新千年開始的時刻, 新千年開始之際: *plans for celebrating the millennium, in the year 2000* 在 2000 年慶祝新千年開始的計劃 **3 the millennium** the time in the future when Jesus Christ will return and rule on Earth for 1000 years 千禧年, 千年王國〔指耶穌基督將復臨並統治世界的 1000 年〕—**millennial** *adj*

mil·le·pede /ˋmɪlə͵pid; ˈmɪlɪpiːd/ another spelling of MILLIPEDE millipede 的另一種拼法

mill·er /ˋmɪlɚ; ˈmɪlə/ *n* [C] someone who owns or operates a mill which makes flour 磨坊主; 麵粉廠廠主

mil·let /ˋmɪlɪt; ˈmɪlɪt/ *n* [U] the small seeds of a plant similar to grass, used as food 粟, 小米

milli- /ˋmɪlɪ; ˈmɪlɪ̥/ *prefix* a 1000th part of a particular unit of something 千分之一: *a millilitre* (=0.001 litres) 一毫升 —see table on page C4 參見C4頁附錄

mil·li·bar /ˋmɪlɪ,bɑr; ˈmɪlɪ̥bɑː/ *n* [C] *technical* a unit for measuring the pressure of air【術語】毫巴〔氣壓單位〕

mil·li·gram /ˋmɪlə,græm; ˈmɪlɪ̥græm/ written abbreviation 縮寫為 **mg** *n* [C] a unit for measuring weight. There are 1000 milligrams in one gram. 毫克〔重量單位〕—see table on page C3 參見C3頁附錄

mil·li·li·tre *BrE*【英】, **milliliter** *AmE*【美】/ˋmɪlə,litɚ; ˈmɪlɪ̥,liːtə/ written abbreviation 縮寫為 **ml** *n* [C] a unit for measuring the amount of a liquid. There are 1000 millilitres in one litre. 毫升〔液體容量單位〕—see table on page C3 參見C3頁附錄

3 **mil·li·me·tre** *BrE*【英】, **millimeter** *AmE*【美】/ˋmɪlə,mitɚ; ˈmɪlɪ̥,miːtə/ written abbreviation 縮寫為 **mm** *n* [C] a unit for measuring length. There are 1000 millimetres in one metre. 毫米〔長度單位〕—see table on page C3 參見C3頁附錄

mil·li·ner /ˋmɪlənɚ; ˈmɪlɪ̥nə/ *n* [C] *old-fashioned* someone who makes and sells women's hats【過時】製做和銷售女帽的人, 女帽商

mil·li·ne·ry /ˋmɪlə,nɛrɪ; ˈmɪlɪ̥nəri/ *n* [U] **1** a word meaning hats, used in shops and in the fashion industry 女帽〔總稱〕 **2** the activity of making women's hats 女帽製作

mil·lion /ˋmɪljən; ˈmiljən/ *plural* **million** or **millions** *number, quantifier* **1** 1,000,000 百萬: *three million dollars* 三百萬美元 | *a population of 12 million people* 1200萬的人口 **2** also 又作 **millions** an extremely large number of people or things 極其龐大的數目; 許多, 無數: *Millions of people will see that film.* 數以百萬計的人將觀看那部電影。| *He made millions* (=a lot of money) *on that deal.* 他在那次交易中大賺了一筆。| *I've heard that excuse a million times.* 那個藉口我已聽過無數次了。**3 not/never in a million years** *spoken* used to emphasize that something is impossible or very unlikely to happen【口】一百萬年以後也不, 永遠也不: *I'd never marry him – not in a million years.* 我決不嫁給他 —— 永遠不會。**4 feel/look like a million dollars/bucks** *informal especially AmE* to feel or look very well or very attractive【非正式, 尤美】感覺很精神/看起來有吸引力: *Wow! You look like a million dollars tonight!* 哇!你今晚精神極了! **5 one in a million** also 又作 **a wife/teacher/writer etc in a million** *informal* one of the best possible wives, teachers etc【非正式】萬裡挑一的好妻子/好教師/好作家等 —**millionth** *determiner, n, pron, adv*

mil·lion·aire /,mɪljənˋɛr; ,mɪljəˈneə/ *n* [C] someone who is very rich and has at least a million pounds or dollars 富豪, 百萬富翁

mil·lion·air·ess /,mɪljənˋɛrɪs; ,mɪljəˈneərɪ̥s/ *n* [C] *old-fashioned* a woman who is very rich and has at least a million pounds or dollars【過時】女富豪, 女百萬富翁

mil·li·pede /ˋmɪlə,pid; ˈmɪlɪ̥piːd/ *n* [C] a long thin insect with a lot of legs 馬陸, 千足蟲

mill·pond /ˋmɪl,pɑnd; ˈmɪlpɒnd/ *n* [C] a very small lake that supplies water to turn the wheel of a WATERMILL 磨坊水池

mill·stone /ˋmɪl,ston; ˈmɪlstəʊn/ *n* [C] **1** one of the two large circular stones that crush grain into flour in a MILL[1] (1) 磨石, 磨盤 **2 a millstone around your neck** something that causes you a lot of problems and prevents you from doing what you would like to do 某人的沉重負擔[累贅, 包袱]: *His fame, so pleasant at first, became a millstone around his neck.* 他的名氣開始是那樣令人愜意, 後來卻成了他的一個包袱。

mill·wheel /ˋmɪlhwil; ˈmɪlwiːl/ *n* [C] *especially BrE* a large wheel that is turned by water flowing past it to provide power to the machinery in a MILL[1] (1)【尤英】〔磨坊的〕水車輪

mil·om·e·ter /maɪˋlɑmətɚ; maɪˈlɒmɪ̥tə/ *n* [C] another spelling of MILEOMETER mileometer的另一種拼法

milque·toast, milktoast /ˋmɪlktost; ˈmɪlktəʊst/ *n* [C] *AmE old-fashioned* a weak, quiet man with no courage; WIMP[1] (1)【美, 過時】膽小鬼, 懦夫

mime[1] /maɪm; maɪm/ *n* **1** [C,U] the use of actions or movements to express what you want to say without using words〔不用語言的〕比手畫腳, 做手勢 **2** [C] a simple play performed without using words 啞劇: *a mime artist* 啞劇藝術家 **3** [C] an actor who performs without using words 啞劇演員

mime[2] *v* [I,T] to act something using actions and movements without any words 以啞劇形式表演, 比手畫腳地表演: *The children mimed the whole story for the rest of the class.* 孩子們以啞劇形式為班上其他同學表演了整個故事。

mi·met·ic /mɪˋmɛtɪk; mɪ̥ˈmetɪk/ *adj technical* copying the movements or appearance of someone or something else【術語】模仿的, 模擬的; 擬態的

mim·ic[1] /ˋmɪmɪk; ˈmɪmɪk/ *v past tense and past participle* **mimicked** [T] **1** to copy the way someone speaks or behaves, especially in order to make people laugh 模仿〔某人的言行, 尤指為了逗樂〕, 學…的樣子: *Sally used to keep us entertained by mimicking the teacher.* 莎莉過去常常模仿老師逗我們樂。**2** to behave or operate in exactly the same way as something or someone else 學…的樣子; 模擬: *Will computers ever be able to mimic the way humans think?* 將來電腦能模擬人類思維嗎? **3** if an animal mimics something it tries to look or sound like something in order to protect itself〔動物為保護自己〕偽裝成〔另一事物〕: *an insect that mimics the appearance of a wasp* 擬態為黃蜂的昆蟲 —**mimicry** *n* [U]

mimic[2] *n* [C] **1** an entertainer who copies the way famous people speak or behave〔模仿名人言行的〕喜劇演員, 小丑 **2** a person or animal that is good at copying the movements, sound, or appearance of someone or something else 善於模仿的人[動物]

mimic[3] *adj* [only before noun 僅用於名詞前] **1** *technical* providing protection by looking exactly like something else【術語】擬態的 **2** imitating behaviour or movements 模仿的, 模擬的: *the mimic marching of the children playing soldiers* 扮演士兵的孩子們模仿行軍

mi·mo·sa /mɪˋmosə; mɪˈməʊzə/ *n* [C,U] a small tree that grows in hot countries and has small yellow flowers 含羞草

min 1 the written abbreviation of 縮寫= MINIMUM **2** the written abbreviation of 縮寫= minute or 或 minutes

min·a·ret /,mɪnəˋrɛt; ,mɪnəˈret/ *n* [C] a tall thin tower on a MOSQUE from which Muslims are called to prayer〔清真寺旁的〕宣禮塔, 尖塔

min·a·to·ry /ˋmɪnə,torɪ; ˈmɪnətəri/ *adj formal* threatening【正式】威脅性的, 恐嚇性的

mince[1] /mɪns; mɪns/ *v* **1** [T] to cut food, especially meat, into very small pieces, usually in a machine 切碎, 剁碎, 絞碎〔食物, 尤指肉〕: *minced lamb* 碎羔羊肉 **2** [I always+adv/prep] to walk in an unnatural way, taking short steps and moving your hips〔邁着碎步、擺着臀部〕扭扭捏捏地走: [+across/down/along etc] *She minced across the hall to her desk.* 她扭扭捏捏地邁着小步穿過大廳走到自己的辦公桌旁。**3 not mince matters/your words** to say exactly what you think even if this may offend people 直言不諱地說, 毫不遮掩地說: *He's a brash New Yorker who doesn't mince his words.* 他是個傲慢的紐約人, 說話直來直去。

mince[2] *n* [U] *BrE* meat, especially BEEF, that has been cut into very small pieces using a special machine【英】切[剁, 絞]碎的肉〔尤指牛肉〕, 肉末; GROUND BEEF *AmE*【美】

mince·meat /ˋmɪns,mit; ˈmɪns-miːt/ *n* [U] **1** a mixture of apples, RAISINS, SUET, and SPICES, but no meat, put inside PASTRY (1) and baked (百) 果餡〔蘋果、葡萄乾、板油、香料混合而成的果餅餡, 不含肉〕 **2 make mince-

meat of *informal* to completely defeat someone in an argument, fight, or game【非正式】〔在辯論、戰鬥或比賽中〕徹底擊敗, 駁倒〔某人〕: *They made mincemeat of the opposition's arguments.* 他們把反方的論點駁得體無完膚。

mince pie /ˌ· ˈ·/ *n* [C] **1** a small PIE filled with mincemeat that is eaten especially at Christmas〔尤指在聖誕節食用的〕百果餡餅 **2** *AmE* a large PIE filled with mincemeat【美】大百果餡餅

minc·er /ˈmɪnsə˞; ˈmɪnsə/ *n* [C] *BrE* a machine that cuts meat into very small pieces by forcing it through small holes【英】絞肉機; MEAT GRINDER *AmE*【美】

minc·ing·ly /ˈmɪnsɪŋli; ˈmɪnsɪŋlɪ/ *adv* with little short steps 邁着小碎步地

1 1

mind¹ /maɪnd; maɪnd/ *n*

① BRAIN/THINKING PROCESS 頭腦/思維過程
② DECIDE 決定
③ THINKING ABOUT STH 思考某事
④ WORRY/STOP WORRYING 擔心/停止擔心
⑤ CRAZY/MENTALLY ILL 發瘋的/有精神病的
⑥ FORGET 忘記
⑦ REMEMBER 記得
⑧ OPINION 看法
⑨ STRONG/DETERMINED 堅強的/堅決的
⑩ ATTENTION 注意(力)
⑪ IMAGINE 想像
⑫ INTEND/WANT 打算/想要
⑬ INTELLIGENCE 智力
⑭ OTHER MEANINGS 其他意思

① BRAIN/THINKING PROCESS 頭腦/思維過程

1 [C,U] the part of a person, usually considered to be their brain, that they use to think and imagine things 頭腦: *I have a picture of him in my mind – tall, blond and handsome.* 我心裡記着他的樣子 —— 高個子, 金髮, 很帥氣。| *I don't know what's going on in her mind.* 我不知道她腦子裡在想甚麼。

2 get sb/sth out of your mind to stop yourself thinking about someone or something 不再去想某人/某事: *I just can't seem to get her out of my mind.* 我就是無法不去想她。

3 go over sth/turn sth over in your mind to keep thinking about something because you are trying to understand it or solve a problem 反覆思考某事: *I kept turning the conversation over in my mind.* 我腦子裡一直思忖着那次談話。

② DECIDE 決定

4 make up your mind a) to decide which of two or more choices you want, especially after thinking for a long time 作出決定; 拿定主意: *I just couldn't make up my mind, so in the end I bought both.* 我就是拿不定主意, 最後兩個都買了。| *I wish you'd make your mind up whether you're coming or not.* 我希望你作出決定, 到底來不來。**b)** to become very determined to do something, so that you will not change your decision 下定決心, 決意: *I'm sorry but my mind's made up – I'm leaving.* 對不起, 我決心已下 —— 我要走了。| **make up your mind to do sth** *He's made his mind up to resign, and that's final.* 他已下決心辭職, 不會改變主意了。| **make up your mind that** *They made up their mind that they would buy a new house once Larry changed jobs.* 他們下定決心, 一旦拉里換了工作他們就買一座新房子。

5 change your mind to change your opinion or decision about something 改變主意[決定]: *I've changed my mind – I'll have a beer instead.* 我改變主意了 —— 給我來一杯啤酒。| [+about] *Try and get her to change her mind about coming with us.* 設法讓她改變主意, 不要和我們一起去。

6 be in two minds about *informal* to be unable to make a decision about something【非正式】三心二意, 拿不定主意, 猶豫不決: *We're in two minds about whether to sell the house or not.* 我們對該不該賣掉房子拿不定主意。

7 set your mind on (doing) sth to decide that you want to do something very much 決心要做某事: *Tom had set his mind on a trip to the Seychelles.* 湯姆已決定去塞舌爾羣島旅行。

③ THINKING ABOUT STH 思考某事

8 be the last thing on sb's mind to be the thing that someone is least likely to be thinking about 是某人最不可能在考慮着的事: *One thing was for sure, marriage was the last thing on Nick's mind.* 有一件事是肯定的 —— 結婚是尼克最不願意想的事。

9 come/spring to mind [not in progressive 不用進行式] if something comes to mind or springs to mind you suddenly think of it 突然想到, 猛然想起: *We needed someone to look after the kids, and your name sprang to mind.* 我們需要有個人照看孩子, 於是一下子就想到了你。

10 cross/enter your mind (that) [not in progressive 不用進行式] if something crosses or enters your mind, you have a particular thought or idea, especially for a short time 掠過/進入腦海: *It never crossed my mind that Lisa might be lying.* 我從來沒想過莉莎也許是在撒謊。

11 turn your mind to to begin to think about a subject after you have been thinking about something else 轉而開始考慮..., 把心思轉向...: *Let's now turn our minds to tomorrow's meeting.* 現在讓我們來考慮一下明天的會議。

④ WORRY/STOP WORRYING 擔心/停止擔心

12 take your mind off sth to make yourself stop thinking about something that is worrying you 不再想某事: *I decided to clean the car to take my mind off the events of the day.* 我決定去清洗一下汽車, 好讓自己不再去想那天發生的事。

13 set/put sb's mind at rest to make someone feel less worried or anxious 使某人放心, 使某人安心: *Call your mom and tell her you've arrived safely, just to set her mind at rest.* 給你媽打個電話, 告訴她你已經安全到達, 好讓她放心。

14 be out of your mind with grief/worry etc to be extremely worried, sad etc 極其悲傷/憂慮等: *Since her son was reported missing she's been out of her mind with worry.* 自從兒子被報失蹤以後, 她一直非常擔心。

15 be a load/weight off your mind *informal* to be something that you no longer need to worry about【非正式】不再需要憂慮; 心上的石頭落地: *The police said the accident wasn't my fault. Boy, was that a load off my mind.* 警察說那次事故不是我的錯。嘿, 我這才放下心上的大石頭。

M

16 on your mind if something is on your mind, you keep thinking about it and worrying about it 擔心: *You look worried, Sarah. Is there something on your mind?* 莎拉, 你看起來很焦慮。有甚麼心事嗎? | **have a lot on your mind** (=have a lot of problems to worry about) 有許多憂心事 *With Jim losing his job and her mother being sick, Michelle has had a lot on her mind lately.* 米雪兒近來有許多煩心事, 吉姆失業了, 而母親又在生病。

⑤ **CRAZY/MENTALLY ILL** 發瘋的/有精神病的
17 be out of your mind/not be in your right mind *informal* to behave in a way that is crazy or stupid【非正式】發狂, 發瘋; 犯傻: *Nobody in their right mind would go out on a night like this.* 精神正常的人不會在這樣的夜晚出去。| *She must be out of her mind to marry him.* 她要是嫁給他, 那準是瘋了。
18 go out of your mind/lose your mind *informal* to start to become mentally ill or behave in a strange way【非正式】精神失常; 失去理智: *I have so much to do – I feel like I'm going out of my mind.* 我有那麼多事情要做 —— 我覺得自己都要瘋了。
19 be of sound mind *law* to have the ability to think clearly and be responsible for your actions【法律】心智健全

⑥ **FORGET** 忘記
20 your mind goes blank *informal* if your mind goes blank, you suddenly cannot remember something【非正式】腦子裡突然一片空白, 突然甚麼也想不起來: *My mind went blank as soon as I went into the exam room.* 我一走進考場就突然大腦一片空白。
21 out of sight, out of mind used to say that if you cannot see someone or something, you stop thinking about them and forget about them 眼不見, 心不念
22 put sth out of your mind to deliberately try to forget about something unpleasant 把某事置於[拋諸]腦後: *Put the whole experience out of your mind and try to sleep.* 忘掉這一切, 試着睡覺吧。
23 go (right) out of your mind/slip your mind if something goes out of your mind, you forget it, especially because you are too busy doing other things〔通常指由於忙於做其他事情〕(完全) 忘記, 忘得乾乾淨淨: *Her birthday had gone right out of Jerry's mind.* 傑里把她的生日忘得一乾二淨。| **slip sb's mind that** *It slipped my mind that I'd agreed to meet him.* 我忘了自己已同意見他。

⑦ **REMEMBER** 記得
24 bring/call sth to mind a) to make yourself remember a name, fact etc 回想起某事: *I couldn't quite call his name to mind.* 我一時想不起他的名字了。**b)** to remind you of something 使回想起某事: *These violent scenes bring to mind the riots of last year.* 這些暴力場面使人想起去年的騷亂。
25 keep sth in mind to remember a fact or piece of information because it will be useful to you in the future 記住某事〔指將來對你有用的情況或信息〕: *It's a good idea – I'll keep it in mind.* 這是個好主意 —— 我要記在心裡。
26 bear sth in mind to remember a useful or important piece of information 記住某事〔指有用或重要的信息〕: *You should bear in mind that these exams affect your final result.* 你應該記住, 這些考試會影響到你的最後成績。
27 stick in your mind if a name, fact etc sticks in your mind, you remember it for a long time 對〔名字、事實等〕經久不忘: *For some reason the name really stuck in Joe's mind.* 由於某種原因, 那個名字深深地印在了喬的腦子裡。
28 at/in the back of your mind if something is at the back of your mind, you keep remembering it or feeling it, but you do not think about it directly 在內心深處: *At the back of his mind, Matt had been hoping that Beth would stay.* 在心底裡, 馬特一直希望貝思留下來。
29 put you in mind of [not in progressive 不用進行式] *old-fashioned* to remind you of a person or thing from your past【過時】使想起〔過去的人或事〕: *Seeing the movie put me in mind of my army days.* 這部電影讓我想起了自己當兵的日子。

⑧ **OPINION** 看法
30 to my mind *BrE spoken* used when you are giving your opinion about something【英口】照我的意見, 在我看來: *To my mind this is the finest building in Paris.* 依我看, 這是巴黎最漂亮的建築。
31 speak your mind to say exactly what you think about something, even when this might offend people 直言不諱
32 keep/have an open mind (about) to be willing to think about and accept new ideas or ways of doing things 思想開放, 能接受新事物: *My parents have a very open mind about sex before marriage.* 我父母對婚前性行為態度很開明。
33 have a closed mind (about) to refuse to think about or accept new ideas or ways of doing things 不易接受新事物, 守舊
34 be of one mind/of the same mind/of like mind to agree with someone about something 意見一致, 看法相似: *It's not often that I meet people who are of like mind in politics.* 我並不是經常會碰到政治觀點一致的人。| [+on/about] *We're all of the same mind on this issue.* 在這個問題上我們的看法都一致。

⑨ **STRONG/DETERMINED** 堅強的/堅決的
35 have a mind of your own to decide on your opinions and make your own decisions 有主見, 能自作決定: *Even at the age of two, Joey had a mind of his own.* 喬伊早在兩歲的時候, 就自己拿主意了。
36 know your own mind to be very clear about what your opinions or beliefs are and not be influenced by what other people think 有自己明確的見解[信念]; 有決斷
37 put your mind to to decide to do something or achieve something by thinking and working very hard at it 專心於: *It won't take long to sort it out once you put your mind to it.* 一旦你專心做, 用不了多長時間就能把它弄清楚。

⑩ **ATTENTION** 注意(力)
38 sb's mind is not on sth to not be thinking about what you are doing, because you are thinking or worrying about something else 某人的心思不在某事上: *Steve's mind just doesn't seem to be on the job these days. Is something wrong at home?* 史蒂夫這些天好像沒心思工作, 家裡出甚麼事了嗎?
39 keep your mind on to keep paying attention to something even if it is boring or if you want to think about something else 專心於, 把注意力集中於: *It was difficult to keep our minds on the job with all the talk of war.* 關於戰爭的議論那麼多, 我們難以專心工作。
40 pay sb/sth no mind *AmE* to not pay any attention to someone or something or not care about what they are saying or doing【美】不把某人/某事放在心上
41 your mind wanders if your mind WANDERS, you no longer pay attention to something, especially because you are bored〔尤因無聊而〕心不在焉, 走神

⑪ **IMAGINE** 想像
42 it's all in your mind used to tell someone that they have imagined something and it does not really exist 都是你自己想像出來的: *one of those doctors who say you're not really sick and it's all in your mind* 說你實際上沒病, 病都是你自己想出來的那些醫生中的一個
43 in your mind's eye if you see something in your mind's eye, you can imagine what it looks like because

you remember it 可以想像出, 在腦海中浮現: *She could see in her mind's eye the whitewashed cottage of her childhood.* 她兒時住的那座用石灰水粉刷過的小屋仍浮現在她腦海中。

⑫ **INTEND/WANT 打算/想要**

44 have sth/sb in mind to be thinking about or considering a particular person, plan etc for a particular purpose 考慮到某物/某人: *It's a nice house, but it wasn't quite what we had in mind.* 這是座不錯的房子, 但和我們心目中想要的不完全一樣。

45 have it in mind to do sth to intend to do something 打算做某事: *Once she had it in mind to win that trophy, nothing would have stopped her.* 一旦她想去贏得那座獎盃, 甚麼事也阻擋不了她。

46 have a good mind/half a mind to do sth a) used as a not very serious threat when you want to show your disapproval of what someone has done 很想/有點想做某事〔用來隨意嚇唬以示對某人的行為不贊同〕: *I've a good mind to phone him up and tell him exactly what I think.* 我很想給他打個電話, 告訴他我的確切想法。**b)** used when you are considering doing something but are not sure you will 很想/有點想做某事〔表示正在考慮做某事但拿不準是否會做〕: *I have half a mind just to take a cab home.* 我有點想坐出租車回家。

⑬ **INTELLIGENCE 智力**

47 [C usually singular 一般用單數] intelligence and ability to think rather than emotions; INTELLECT 思維能力; 智能, 心智: *Paul says he's doing the course to improve his mind.* 保羅說他正在學習那門課以提高思維能力。| *a bright child with an enquiring mind* 有求知慾的聰明孩子

48 [C] someone who is very intelligent, especially in a particular area of study or activity〔尤指在某一研究或活動領域〕有才智的人: *She is one of the finest political minds in the country.* 她是該國最具才華的政治家之一。

49 great minds think alike *spoken* used to say jokingly that you and someone else must be very intelligent because you both agree about something【口】智者所見略同

50 mind over matter an expression used when someone uses their intelligence to control a difficult situation 精神勝過物質〔指用智力控制物質世界的困難局面〕

⑭ **OTHER MEANINGS 其他意思**

51 frame/state of mind the way someone is thinking and feeling at a particular time 心情: *I'm not going to argue with you while you're in this frame of mind.* 你情緒這個樣子, 我不和你爭論了。

52 give sb a piece of your mind *informal* to tell someone how angry you are with them【非正式】責備某人; 向某人直陳不滿

53 bored out of your mind *informal* extremely bored【非正式】厭煩之至的

54 stoned/drunk etc out of your mind affected by drugs or alcohol so that you do not really know what you are doing 因吸毒/喝酒等而神志不清的

55 time out of mind more often than you can remember 無數次地: *I've told you time out of mind to close that door when you leave the room.* 我不知跟你講過多少次, 離開房間時要關上那道門。

56 ►CHARACTER 性格, 性情◄ [C] a particular way of thinking that is part of someone's character〔作為性格一部分的〕思維方式: *If you ask me O'Rourke has a very devious mind.* 在我看來, 奧羅克很狡猾。—see also 另見 ONE-TRACK MIND, **blow your mind** (BLOW[1] (17)), **the mind boggles** (BOGGLE (1)), **meeting of minds** (MEETING (5)), **peace of mind** (PEACE (4)), PRESENCE OF MIND, **read sb's mind** (READ[1] (12))

1 2 **mind²** *v*

1 ►FEEL ANNOYED 感到惱火◄ [I,T not in progressive or passive 不用進行式或被動態, usually in questions and negatives 一般用於疑問句和否定句] to feel annoyed or upset about something 介意, 反對: *We'll have to leave early. Do you mind?* 我們很早就得離開, 你介意嗎? | *I wouldn't have minded so much if he'd apologized.* 如果他道歉的話我就不會那麼在意了。| **mind sth** *He didn't mind the lie she'd told him, it was the fact that she'd made him look stupid.* 他並不在意她對他撒的謊, 他在意的是她使他看上去像個傻瓜。| **mind sb doing sth** *I hope you don't mind me bringing the dog with me.* 希望你不要介意我把狗帶在身邊。| **mind that** *She didn't mind that he was late as long as he got there.* 他既然趕到了那兒, 她就沒有計較他的遲到。

2 not mind doing sth to be willing to do something 願意做某事: *I don't mind driving if you're tired.* 如果你累了, 我願意開車。

3 ►NOT CARE WHICH ONE 不在乎哪一個◄ not mind [I,T not in progressive or passive 不用進行式或被動態] *especially BrE* to not care what is decided because you are equally happy with whatever is decided【尤英】不在乎, 無所謂: *I don't mind whether we see the film or not.* 我們看不看這個電影, 我都無所謂。

4 ►TAKE CARE OF 照看, 照料◄ [T] *BrE*【英】**a)** to be responsible for something for a short time; WATCH[1] (3)〔短期地〕看管, 照看〔某物〕: *Will you mind my bag while I buy my ticket?* 我買票的時候你照看一下我的行李好嗎? **b)** to take care of a child while their parents are not there; WATCH[1] (3) 照料, 照看〔孩子〕: *My sister minds the baby so I can go to my yoga class.* 我姐姐照料嬰兒, 所以我可以去上瑜伽課。

5 mind your own business to not get involved in or ask questions about other people's lives or personal details 管你自己的事, 別管閒事: *Why don't you just mind your own business and leave me in peace?* 你為甚麼就不能別管閒事, 讓我清靜一下呢?

6 mind the store *AmE informal* to be in charge of something, especially while the person who is usually in charge is not there【美, 非正式】料理事務〔尤指負責人不在時〕: *If the president didn't know about the arms sales to Iran, who is really minding the store?* 如果總統不知道向伊朗出售武器一事, 那麼究竟誰在管事呢?

7 mind your manners/language/p's and q's to be careful about what you say or how you behave so that you do not offend anyone 注意你的舉止/語言/禮貌

8 ►OBEY 服從◄ [T not in progressive 不用進行式] *AmE* to obey someone's instructions or advice【美】聽從, 服從: *Mind what your mother says, Anthony.* 安東尼, 要聽你媽媽的話。

Frequencies of the verb **mind** in spoken and written English 動詞 mind 在英語口語和書面語中的使用頻率

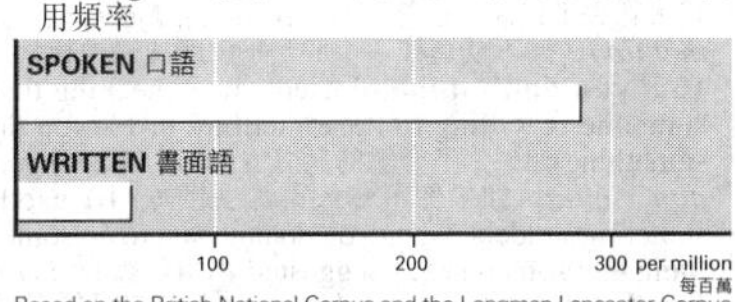

Based on the British National Corpus and the Longman Lancaster Corpus
據英國國家語料庫和朗文蘭卡斯特語料庫

This graph shows that the verb **mind** is much more common in spoken English than in written English. This is because it is used in a lot of common spoken phrases. 本圖表顯示, 動詞 mind 在英語口語中的使用頻率遠遠高於書面語, 因為口語中很多常用片語是由 mind 構成的。

mind (*v*) **SPOKEN PHRASES**
含 mind 的口語片語

9 never mind a) used to say that something is not

important or serious, especially when someone seems worried or is saying sorry to you 不要緊, 沒關係: *"I'm afraid I've broken the chair." "Never mind, I can easily get it fixed."* "恐怕我把椅子弄壞了。" "沒關係, 我可以輕而易舉地把它修好。" **b)** used to emphasize that something is impossible, because even something that should be easier is also impossible 更不用說, 更談不上: *I can't even explain the problem to my colleagues, never mind anyone else.* 我對同事也無法把這個問題解釋清楚, 更不用說對其他人解釋了。 **c)** used to emphasize that something else is also true, apart from the thing you have just mentioned 這還不算, 這還沒有把…考慮在內: *Cars kill thousands of people each year, never mind the damage they do to the environment.* 汽車每年要造成數千人死亡, 這還沒算上給環境造成的破壞。 **d)** used to tell someone not to do something now, because it is less important than something else, or because you will do it later yourself 別管, 不用管: **never mind sth** *Never mind the dishes – I'll do them later.* 別管那些盤子 —— 我過一會兒會洗的。| **never mind doing something** *Never mind looking at the boys, we're supposed to be playing tennis.* 別看着那些男孩子了, 我們應該專心打網球。 **e)** used to say that you do not really care about something because it is much less important than something else 不用擔心, 不必在乎: *I want the best, never mind the cost!* 我要最好的, 不計較費用! | **[+about]** *Let's get the economy right, never mind about the unemployed.* 讓我們先把經濟整頓好, 先不要為失業的人擔心。

10 never you mind *especially BrE* used to tell someone that you are not going to tell them something because it is private or secret【尤英】不關你的事: *"What's that you were saying to dad?" "Never you mind."* "你剛才跟爸爸說甚麼?" "不關你的事。"

11 mind you *BrE* used to say something that is the opposite of what you have just said, or that emphasizes it【英】儘管如此; 請注意, 聽着: *The photos look very old. Mind you, she did take them over 20 years ago.* 這些照片看起來很舊。要知道, 這是她在二十多年前拍攝的。

12 would/do you mind used to ask someone something politely 請你…好嗎, 倘若…你不介意吧: **would/do you mind doing sth** *Would you mind opening the window please?* 請你打開窗子好嗎? | **would/do you mind if** *Do you mind if I smoke?* 我抽煙你不介意吧?

13 I wouldn't mind used to politely ask for something 我想, 我願意〔用於客氣地索要某物〕: *I wouldn't mind a drink if you have one.* 如果你有酒的話我想喝一杯。

14 do you mind! used when you are annoyed at something that someone has done 不要這樣好不好! 你太冒失了!〔表示惱怒〕: *Do you mind! I just washed that floor!* 請不要這樣不小心! 我剛剛洗過地板!

15 if you don't mind a) used when checking that someone is willing to do something or let you do something 如果你不介意的話: *I'll come along if you don't mind.* 如果你不介意我就一起去。 **b)** used, sometimes rudely, when you do not want to do something that someone has suggested 不用你操心: *I can handle this myself, if you don't mind!* 我自己能處理這件事, 不用你操心!

16 if you don't mind my saying so used when you want to give advice or an opinion that you think might offend someone 如果我這麼說你不見怪的話: *I don't think you should ever hit a child, if you don't mind my saying so.* 如果你不介意我這麼說的話, 我認為你不應該打孩子。

17 mind! *BrE* used to warn someone to be careful because something bad or dangerous might happen【英】當心! 小心!: *Mind! That's my foot you're standing on.* 當心! 你踩在我腳上了。| **mind sth** *Mind the window! It's only just been repaired.* 小心窗子! 剛修好的呢。| **mind sb/sth doesn't do sth** *Mind you don't fall off the chair.* 小心別從椅子上掉下來。| **mind how/where/who etc** *Mind where you're walking. The floor's a bit slippery.* 注意腳下。地板有點滑。| **mind your head/back/fingers etc** *Mind your head. The ceiling's very low in here.* 小心別碰着頭。這個地方天花板很低。

18 mind out! *BrE*【英】**a)** used to warn someone that they are in danger 當心! 注意!: *Mind out! There's a car coming!* 當心! 有輛汽車開過來了! **b)** used to ask someone to move so that you can pass them 讓開! 閃開!: *Mind out! You're sitting right in front of the door.* 讓讓! 你剛好坐在門前面。

19 don't mind me used to tell someone not to pay any attention to you 別管我: *Just get on with your work, don't mind us!* 你幹你的活, 別管我們!

20 I don't mind if I do *humorous* used when politely accepting something such as food or drink that has been offered to you【幽默】好的〔用於客氣地接受餐飲等〕: *"Would you like a cigar?" "I don't mind if I do, thank you."* "來枝雪茄嗎?" "好的, 謝謝。"

mind-bend·ing /ˈ· ˌ··/ *adj informal* difficult to understand【非正式】令人費解的: *Filing letters is not exactly a mind-bending task.* 把信件存檔並不是一件費腦筋的工作。

mind-blow·ing /ˈ· ˌ··/ *adj informal* very exciting, shocking, or strange【非正式】令人極度興奮[震驚]的; 非常奇怪的: *The astronauts had mind-blowing views of planet Earth.* 宇航員們看到了美妙的地球景觀。| *a mind-blowing experience* 令人極度興奮的經歷 —see also 另見 **blow your mind** (BLOW[1] (17))

mind-bog·gling /ˈ· ˌ··/ *adj informal* difficult to imagine and very big, strange, or complicated【非正式】〔巨大、奇怪或複雜得〕令人難以想像的: *He's made a mind-boggling profit with his investments.* 他通過投資獲得了驚人的巨額利潤。

mind·ed /ˈmaɪndɪd; ˈmaɪndɪ̵d/ *adj* **1 serious-minded/evil-minded etc** having a particular attitude or way of thinking 性格嚴肅的/心術不正的等: *a very serious-minded girl who studies hard* 一個學習用功、不苟言笑的女孩 **2 safety-minded/efficiency-minded etc** believing in the importance of safety etc 注重安全/效率等的: *People need to be more safety-minded in the home.* 人們在家裡需要有更強的安全意識。 **3 be minded to do sth** *formal* to want or intend to do something【正式】想要[有意]做某事: *He has enough money to travel, if he were minded to do so.* 只要他想, 他有足夠的錢去旅遊。

mind·er /ˈmaɪndɚ; ˈmaɪndə/ *n* [C] *BrE*【英】**1** someone who is employed to protect another person 保鏢 **2 machine minder, child minder etc** a person whose job it is to look after a machine, a child etc 看管機器的人; 照看孩子的人

mind·ful /ˈmaɪndfəl; ˈmaɪndfəl/ *adj* **mindful of** behaving in a way that shows you remember a particular rule or fact 記着…的, 想着…的; 留神…的; 注意…的: *Mindful of the guide's warning they returned before dark.* 他們想着導遊的警告, 天黑前就回來了。

mind·less /ˈmaɪndlɪs; ˈmaɪndləs/ *adj* **1** completely stupid and without any purpose 愚笨的, 無知的; 毫無目標的: *mindless vandals* 愚昧的破壞公物者 **2** mindless work or a mindless activity can be done without intelligence or thought〔工作或活動〕無需動腦筋的: *a completely mindless task* 一項完全不需要動腦子的任務 | *mindless game shows on TV* 電視上無需動腦筋的遊戲節目 **3 mindless of** not paying attention to or thinking about danger or warnings; HEEDLESS 不注意[不考慮]…的, 不顧…的 —**mindlessly** *adv* —**mindlessness** *n* [U]

mind read·er /ˈ·,··/ *n* [C] *often humorous* someone who knows what someone else is thinking without being told 【常幽默】能看透別人心思的人

mind·set /ˈmaɪndset; ˈmaɪndset/ *n* [C] someone's way of thinking about things, which is often difficult to change 思維定式: *You need a logical mindset to develop computer programs.* 開發電腦程序需要邏輯思維定式。

1 **mine¹** /maɪn; maɪn/ *pron* [possessive form of 'I' I 的所有格形式] the one or the ones that belong to me 我的(東西): *"Whose is this coat?" "It must be mine."* "這大衣是誰的?" "一定是我的。" | *Can I borrow your CD player? Mine's broken.* 我可以借一下你的CD播放機嗎? 我的壞了。| **a friend/cousin etc of mine** *an old teacher of mine* 我以前的一位老師

2 3 **mine²** *n* [C] **1** a deep hole or series of holes under the ground that are dug in order to find coal, gold, tin etc 礦井, 礦: **coal/gold/copper mine etc** *He works in the coal mines.* 他在煤礦工作。—compare 比較 QUARRY¹ (1) **2** a type of bomb that is hidden just below the ground or under water and that explodes when it is touched 地雷; 水雷 **3 a mine of information/gossip etc** someone who knows a lot about something or a book that tells you a lot about a subject 大量信息/小道消息等的來源 **4** a passage dug beneath the place where an enemy army is 在敵人陣地下挖掘的坑道

mine³ *v* **mined, mining 1** [I,T] to make holes or passages under the ground in order to take out coal, gold etc, or to take coal, gold etc from these holes 挖掘礦井; 開採: [**+for**] *mining for coal* 採煤 **2** [T often passive 常用被動態] to hide bombs in the sea or under the ground 在…中佈水雷[地雷]: *All the roads leading to the city had been mined.* 通向該城市的所有道路都佈下了地雷。**3** [T] to dig a passage under the ground beneath the place where an enemy army is 在〔敵人陣地下面〕挖坑道

mine⁴ *determiner old use* a way of saying 'my', before a vowel sound or 'h', or after a noun 【舊】我的〔用於元音或 /h/ 之前, 或名詞之後〕: *mine host* 我的房東

mine·field /ˈmaɪn,fild; ˈmaɪnfiːld/ *n* **1** [C] an area where a lot of bombs have been placed just below the ground or under water 雷區 **2** [singular] something that has hidden dangers or difficulties 隱藏着危險[困難]的事物: *The legal system is a minefield for the ordinary person.* 法律體系對普通人來説隱藏着重重危險。

min·er /ˈmaɪnə; ˈmaɪnə/ *n* [C] someone who works under the ground in a MINE² (1) taking out coal, gold etc 礦工: *a coal miner* 煤礦工人

min·e·ral /ˈmɪnərəl; ˈmɪnərəl/ *n* [C] **1** a substance that is formed naturally in the earth, especially a solid substance such as coal, salt, stone, or gold 礦物: *an area rich in minerals* 礦藏豐富的地區 **2** a natural substance such as CALCIUM or iron that is present in some foods and that is important for good health 〔某些食物中的〕礦物質〈如鈣或鐵〉 **3** *BrE formal* a SOFT DRINK 【英, 正式】汽水

min·e·ral·o·gy /,mɪnəˈælədʒɪ; ,mɪnəˈrælədʒi/ *n* [U] the scientific study of minerals 礦物學 —**mineralogist** *n* [C]

mineral wa·ter /ˈ··· ,··/ *n* [C,U] water that comes from under the ground and contains minerals 礦泉水

min·e·stro·ne /,mɪnəˈstronɪ; ,mɪnɪ̵ˈstrəʊni/ *n* [U] an Italian soup containing vegetables and small pieces of PASTA 〔意大利式〕蔬菜濃湯

mine·sweep·er /ˈmaɪn,swipə; ˈmaɪn,swiːpə/ *n* [C] a ship that has equipment for removing bombs from under water 掃雷艦 —**minesweeping** *n* [U]

min·gle /ˈmɪŋgl; ˈmɪŋgəl/ *v* **mingled, mingling 1** [I,T] if two feelings, sounds, smells etc mingle, they combine with each other but can still be recognized separately (使)混合: [**+with**] *excitement mingled with nervousness* 既興奮又緊張 | [**+together**] *The smell of sweat and stale cigar smoke mingled together.* 汗臭味和污濁的雪茄煙味混雜在一起。**2** [I] to mix with different groups of people at a social occasion and talk to people that you do not already know; CIRCULATE (4) 〔在社交場合與不相識的人〕相交往; 來回應酬: *The cast and crew mingled as everyone started to relax.* 大家開始休息的時候, 演員和攝製組工作人員湊在一起交談起來。—**mingled** *adj*

min·gy /ˈmɪndʒɪ; ˈmɪndʒi/ *adj BrE informal* not at all generous; STINGY 【英, 非正式】小氣的, 吝嗇的: *Don't be so mingy.* 別這麼小氣。| *mingy portions* 極少量

min·i /ˈmɪnɪ; ˈmɪni/ *n* [C] **1** a very short skirt or dress; MINI-SKIRT 超短裙, 迷你裙 **2** a type of very small British car 〔英國〕微型汽車

min·i- /mɪnɪ; mɪni/ *prefix* very small compared with others of its kind 〔同類中〕極小的, 微型的; 極短的: *a mini-break* (=a short holiday) 短暫的休假 | *a miniskirt* (=very short) 超短裙, 迷你裙 —compare 比較 MICRO-

min·ia·ture¹ /ˈmɪnɪətʃə; ˈmɪnɪ̵tʃə/ *adj* **miniature camera/railway/garden etc** a camera etc that is much smaller than a normal one 微型照相機/鐵路/花園等

miniature² *n* **1 in miniature** exactly like something or someone but much smaller 縮影的, 微小模型的: *She's her mother in miniature.* 她是她母親的縮影。**2** [C] a very small painting, usually of a person 細密畫, 袖珍畫; 微型人像畫: *a collection of Victorian miniatures* 維多利亞時代的微型畫收藏品

miniature golf /,··· ˈ·/ *n* [U] *AmE* a GOLF game, played for fun, in which you hit a small ball through passages, over bridges and small hills etc 【美】小型高爾夫球(運動); CRAZY GOLF *BrE* 【英】

min·ia·tur·ist /ˈmɪnɪətʃərɪst; ˈmɪnɪ̵tʃərɪ̵st/ *n* [C] someone who paints very small pictures 微型畫畫家

min·ia·tur·ize also 又作 **-ise** *BrE* 【英】 /ˈmɪnɪətʃəraɪz; ˈmɪnɪ̵tʃəraɪz/ *v* [T] to make something in a very small size 使微型化, 使小型化 —**miniaturized** *adj* —**miniaturization** /,mɪnɪətʃərəˈzeʃən; ,mɪnɪ̵tʃəraɪˈzeɪʃən/ *n* [U]

min·i·bus /ˈmɪnɪbʌs; ˈmɪnibʌs/ *n* [C] *especially BrE* a small bus with seats for six to twelve people 【尤英】小型公共汽車, 麵包車, 小巴

min·i·cab /ˈmɪnɪkæb; ˈmɪnikæb/ *n* [C] *BrE* a taxi that you can call for on the telephone but cannot stop in the street 【英】〔可用電話預約但不能在街上截停的〕小型計程車

min·i·com·put·er /ˈmɪnɪkəm,pjutə; ˈmɪnikəm,pjuːtə/ *n* [C] a computer that is larger than a PERSONAL COMPUTER and smaller than a MAINFRAME, used by businesses and other large organizations 〔大於個人電腦但小於大型電腦的〕微型電腦

min·im /ˈmɪnɪm; ˈmɪnɪ̵m/ *n* [C] *BrE* a musical note that continues for half the length of a SEMIBREVE 【英】〔音樂中的〕二分音符; HALF NOTE *AmE* 【美】—see picture at 參見 MUSIC 圖

min·i·mal /ˈmɪnɪml; ˈmɪnɪ̵məl/ *adj* very small in degree or amount, especially the smallest degree or amount possible 極小的, 極少的; 〔尤指〕最小的, 最少的: *The storm caused only minimal damage.* 暴風雨只造成了輕微破壞。—**minimally** *adv*

min·i·mal·is·m /ˈmɪnɪmlɪzəm; ˈmɪnɪ̵məlɪzəm/ *n* [U] art, music etc that uses very simple ideas or patterns that are repeated often 〔美術、音樂的〕極簡主義; 極簡抽象派 —**minimalist** *n* [C]

min·i·mart /ˈmɪnɪmart; ˈmɪnimaːt/ *n* [C] *especially AmE* a small shop that stays open very late and that sells food, cigarettes etc 【尤美】〔營業到很晚的〕小商店

min·i·mize also 又作 **-ise** *BrE* 【英】 /ˈmɪnə,maɪz; ˈmɪnɪ̵maɪz/ *v* [T] **1** to reduce something to the smallest possible amount or degree 把…減至最小量[程度]: *We need to minimize disruptions to the schedule.* 我們需要盡可能降低對日程安排的干擾。**2** to make something seem less serious or important than it really is 對…的嚴重性[重要性]作最低估計; 極度輕視[貶低]: *a tendency to minimize the problem of sexual harassment in the workplace* 把工作場所中的性騷擾問題大事化小的傾向 —compare 比較 MAXIMIZE

M

min·i·mum¹ /ˋmɪnəməm; ˈmɪnɨməm/ *adj* [only before noun 僅用於名詞前] the minimum number, degree, or amount of something is the smallest or least that is possible, allowed, or needed 最小的, 最少的; 最低限度的: *The minimum requirements for the job are a degree and two years' experience.* 該工作的最低要求是要有學位和兩年的工作經歷。| *a minimum price* 最低價格 —compare 比較 MAXIMUM¹

minimum² *n* [singular] **1** the smallest amount, number, or degree of something that is possible, allowed, or needed 最少量, 最小數; 最低限度: **[+of]** *Looking after a horse costs a minimum of £2000 a year.* 照料一匹馬每年最少要花費2000英鎊。| **absolute/bare minimum** (=the very least amount or number) 絕對/僅夠的最少量 *Staffing levels at the hospital have been slashed to an absolute minimum.* 該醫院的職員人數已經減得不能再減了。**2 keep/reduce sth to a minimum** to limit something, especially something bad, to the smallest amount or degree possible 將某事物保持在/減少到最低限度: *The school manages to keep bullying to a minimum.* 學校設法最大限度地減少恃強凌弱的行為。

minimum se·cu·ri·ty pris·on /,··· ·ˈ··· ,··/ *n* [C] *AmE* a prison that does not restrict prisoners' freedom as much as ordinary prisons【美】〔對犯人自由比普通監獄限制少的〕不設防監獄; OPEN PRISON *BrE*【英】

minimum wage /,··· ˈ·/ *n* [C singular] the lowest amount of money that can legally be paid per hour to a worker〔法定每小時〕最低工資

min·ing /ˋmaɪnɪŋ; ˈmaɪnɪŋ/ *n* [U] the action or industry of getting minerals out of the earth 採礦(業) —see also 另見 STRIP MINING

min·ion /ˋmɪnjən; ˈmɪnjən/ *n* [C] a very unimportant person in an organization, who just obeys other people's orders〔某組織中〕順從聽話的小人物

mini-round·a·bout /,·· ˈ···/ *n* [C] *BrE* a white circle painted on the road that vehicles must drive around at a place where several roads meet【英】小環島圈〔道路交叉處塗在路面上的白色圓圈, 車輛須繞其行駛〕

min·is·cule /ˋmɪnɪskjul; ˈmɪnɨskjuːl/ *adj* another spelling of MINUSCULE minuscule的另一種拼法

min·i·se·ries /ˋmɪnɪˌsɪrɪz; ˈmɪniˌsɪəriz/ *n* [C] a television film that is divided into several parts, which are usually shown once a night for several days 電視連續短片[劇]

min·i·skirt /ˋmɪnɪskɝt; ˈmɪniskɜːt/ *n* [C] a very short skirt; MINI 超短裙, 迷你裙

min·is·ter¹ /ˋmɪnɪstɚ; ˈmɪnɨstə/ *n* [C] **1** a politician who is a member of the government and is in charge of a government department, in Britain and some other countries〔英國和其他一些國家的〕部長, 大臣: **[+of/for]** *the Minister of Education* 教育部長[大臣] —see also 另見 PRIME MINISTER **2** a priest in some Christian churches〔基督教的〕牧師 —see 見 PRIEST (USAGE) **3** someone whose job is to represent their country in another country, but who is lower in rank than an AMBASSADOR 公使 **4** a MINISTER OF STATE〔英國的〕國務大臣

minister² *v*

minister to sb/sth *phr v* [T] *formal* to give help to someone who needs it【正式】給以…幫助: *ministering to the sick* 幫助生病的人

min·is·ter·i·al /ˌmɪnəsˋtɪrɪəl; ˌmɪnɨˈstɪəriəl◂/ *adj* connected with or relating to a government minister or a minister in the Christian church 部長的, 大臣的;〔基督教〕牧師的: *ministerial duties* 部長的職責

minister of state /,··· · ˈ·/ *n* [C] a member of the government in Britain who has an important job in a government department but is not the chief minister〔英國的〕國務大臣

min·i·stra·tions /ˌmɪnəˋstreʃənz; ˌmɪnɨˈstreɪʃənz/ *n* [plural] *formal* the giving of help and service, especially to people who are ill or who need the help of a priest【正式】護理病人;〔牧師的〕行宗教儀式

min·is·try /ˋmɪnɪstrɪ; ˈmɪnɨstri/ *n* **1** [C] a government department that is responsible for one of the areas of government work, such as education, health, or defence〔政府的〕部: **[+of]** *the Ministry of Agriculture* 農業部 **2 the ministry** the profession of being a church leader, especially in the Protestant church〔尤指基督教新教的〕神職, 牧師職位: *James wants to join the ministry.* 詹姆斯想當牧師。**3** [U] the work done by a priest or other religious person 牧師[其他宗教人物]所做的工作: *the ministry of Jesus* 耶穌的傳道工作

min·i·van /ˋmɪnɪvæn; ˈmɪnivæn/ *n* [C] *AmE* a large car for up to eight people【美】〔可供八人乘坐的〕大轎車

mink /mɪŋk; mɪŋk/ *n plural* **mink** [C,U] a very valuable brown fur used to make coats, hats etc, or the animal from which this fur is obtained 水貂皮; 水貂

min·now /ˋmɪno; ˈmɪnəʊ/ *n* [C] **1** a very small fish that lives in rivers and lakes 米諾魚〔一種生活在河、湖中的極小的魚〕**2** an organization, company etc that is small and unimportant 微不足道的組織[公司等]: *one of the minnows of the computer industry* 電腦業中微不足道的公司之一

mi·nor¹ /ˋmaɪnɚ; ˈmaɪnə/ *adj* **1** small and not very important or serious, especially when compared with other things〔尤指與其他事物相比〕小的; 不很重要的; 不很嚴重的: *We have made some minor changes to the program.* 我們對那個計劃作了一些小改動。| *an issue of minor importance* 次要的問題 | **minor illness/operation/injury** (=one that is not very serious or dangerous) 小病/小手術/輕傷 *minor head injuries* 頭部輕傷 —opposite 反義詞 MAJOR¹ (1) **2** based on a musical SCALE¹ (8) in which the third note of the related MAJOR¹ (4) scale has been lowered by a SEMITONE〔音樂〕小調的; 小音階的: *a minor key* 小調 | *a symphony in D minor* D小調交響曲

minor² *n* [C] **1** *law* someone who is below the age at which they become legally responsible for their actions【法律】未成年人 **2** *especially AmE* a subject studied at university that has less importance and needs less work than your MAJOR (=main subject)【尤美】〔大學中的〕副修科目 **3 the minors** the MINOR LEAGUES〔美國棒球的〕小聯盟; 小企業, 小公司; 小的機構[組織]

minor³ *v*

minor in sth *phr v* [T] *especially AmE* to study an additional subject at university that is less important than your main subject【尤美】〔大學裡〕副修〔某課程〕—opposite 反義詞 MAJOR³

mi·nor·i·ty¹ /məˋnɔrətɪ; maɪˈnɒrɨti/ *n* **1** [singular] a small group of people or things within a much larger group 少數派; 少數: *Gaelic is still spoken in Ireland by a tiny minority.* 在愛爾蘭極少數人仍然說蓋爾語。| **[+of]** *It's only in a minority of cases that the illness is fatal.* 只有在少數情況下這種疾病才是致命的。| [also+plural verb *BrE* 英] *Only a minority support these new laws.* 只有少數人支持這些新法律。**2** [C usually plural 一般用複數] **a)** a group of people in a country who are different from the rest in race or religion 少數民族; 宗教少數派: *People from ethnic minorities often face prejudice and discrimination.* 來自少數民族的人們常常面臨偏見和歧視。**b)** *AmE* someone who belongs to a group like this【美】少數民族[宗教少數派](成員): *hiring minorities and women* 雇用少數民族和婦女 **3 be in the/a minority** to form less than half of a larger group 佔少數: *Boys are very much in the minority at the dance class.* 在舞蹈班上男孩子佔極少數。**4 be in a minority of one** to be the only person in a group who has a particular opinion 是孤家寡人, 得不到任何人的支持 **5** [U] *law* the period of time when someone is below the age at which they become legally responsible for their actions【法律】未成年期 —opposite 反義詞 MAJORITY

minority² *adj* [only before noun 僅用於名詞前] relating to people who form less than half of a larger group of people〔人〕少數的; 少數民族的: *a series of televi-*

sion programmes designed to appeal to minority interests 一系列迎合少數人趣味的電視節目 | *a minority language* 少數民族語言

minority gov·ern·ment /ˌ·ˌ···ˈ···/ *n* [C] a government that does not have enough politicians in parliament to control it without the support of other parties 少數黨政府

minority lead·er /ˌ·ˈ··· ˌ··/ *n* [C] *AmE* a leader of the political party that has fewer politicians in the law-making institutions than the leading party【美】(國會中的)少數黨領袖 —compare 比較 MAJORITY LEADER

minor league /ˈ·· ·/ *n* [C] **1** a group of professional BASEBALL teams in the US that are not as good as the teams in the MAJOR LEAGUES (美國棒球的)小聯盟(由水平低於職業棒球大聯盟的球隊組成) **2** *informal* small businesses and organizations, rather than large powerful ones【非正式】小企業, 小公司; 小的機構[組織] —**minor-league** *adj*

min·ster /ˈmɪnstə; ˈmɪnstə/ *n* [C] *BrE* a large or important church【英】大教堂: *York Minster* 約克大教堂

min·strel /ˈmɪnstrəl; ˈmɪnstrəl/ *n* [C] **1** a singer or musician in the Middle Ages (中世紀的)歌手; 樂師 **2** one of a group of singers and dancers who performed in popular shows in the 1920s (20世紀20年代的)歌舞團演員

mint[1] /mɪnt; mɪnt/ *n* **1** [C,U] a sweet that tastes of PEPPERMINT (=a strong tasting substance obtained from a plant) 薄荷糖 **2** [U] a small plant with leaves that have a fresh smell and taste and are used in cooking 薄荷屬植物 **3 in mint condition** looking new and in perfect condition 嶄新的; 完美的: *A copy in mint condition would fetch about £2,000.* 一份嶄新的拷貝大約能賣2,000英鎊。**4 a mint** *informal* a large amount of money【非正式】一大筆錢: *Lynn won a mint in that competition!* 林恩在那次競賽中贏了一大筆錢! **5** [C] a place where coins are officially made 鑄幣廠

mint[2] *v* [T] **1** to make a coin 鑄(幣) **2** to invent new words, phrases, or ideas 創造(新的詞、短語或思想), 發明: *a recently minted phrase* 一個新創短語

mint ju·lep /ˌ· ˈ··/ *n* [C] *AmE* a drink in which alcohol and sugar are mixed with ice and mint leaves are added【美】冰鎮薄荷酒, 薄荷朱利酒

mint·y /ˈmɪntɪ; ˈmɪnti/ *adj* tasting or smelling of mint 薄荷口味的; 薄荷氣味的

min·u·et /ˌmɪnjuˈɛt; ˌmɪnjuˈet/ *n* [C] a slow graceful dance of the 17th and 18th century, or a piece of music for this dance (17世紀和18世紀的一種緩慢優美的)小步舞, 米奴哀舞; 小步舞曲, 米奴哀舞曲

mi·nus[1] /ˈmaɪnəs; ˈmaɪnəs/ *prep* **1** used in mathematics when you SUBTRACT one number from another (數學中)減(去): *17 minus 5 is 12 (17–5 = 12).* 17減5等於12。 **2 minus 5, 20 etc** less than zero, especially less than zero degrees in temperature 零下5度, 20度等: *At night the temperature can go as low as minus 30.* 晚上氣溫能降至零下30度。**3** *informal* without something that would normally be there【非正式】沒有, 缺少: *He came back minus a couple of front teeth.* 他回來時門牙少了兩顆。 —opposite 反義詞 PLUS[1]

minus[2] *n* [C] **1** also 又作 **minus sign** a sign (–) showing that a number is less than zero, or that the second of two numbers is to be subtracted (SUBTRACT) from the first 負號; 減號 **2** something that is a disadvantage because it makes a situation unpleasant 不利條件; 不足; 缺點: *There are both pluses and minuses to living in a big city.* 住在大城市裡既有利也有弊。—opposite 反義詞 PLUS[2]

minus[3] *adj* **1 minus point/factor** *BrE* a quality that makes something or someone seem less good【英】弱點/不利因素: *Kirsten's very keen, but her inexperience is a definite minus factor.* 柯爾斯滕非常熱心, 但她沒有經驗卻是個明顯的弱點。**2 A minus, B minus etc** a mark used in a system of marking students' work, A minus is lower than A, but higher than B plus A減(A–), B減(B–)等(給學生打成績時用) —opposite 反義詞 PLUS[3]

min·us·cule, miniscule /mɪˈnʌskjul; ˈmɪnəskjuːl/ *adj* extremely small 極小的: *a minuscule amount* 極少量 | *Her office is miniscule.* 她的辦公室非常小。

min·ute[1] /ˈmɪnɪt; ˈmɪnət/ *n* [C] S1 W1

1 ▶TIME 時間◀ one of the 60 parts into which an hour is divided 分, 分鐘: *It takes me ten minutes to walk to work.* 我步行上班要用十分鐘。| *The train arrived at four minutes past eight.* 火車於八點零四分到達。

2 at the last minute at the last possible time, just before it is too late 在最後一刻; 在緊要關頭: *Clare changed her mind at the last minute and came with us.* 克萊爾在最後一刻改變了主意, 和我們一起來了。—see also 另見 LAST-MINUTE

3 by the minute also 又作 **every minute, minute by minute** *spoken* increasingly as time passes【口】每過一分鐘; 越來越: *"Do you still feel sick?" "No, I'm feeling better by the minute."* "你還覺得噁心嗎?" "不了, 我感覺越來越好了。"

4 love/enjoy/hate etc every minute of *informal* to love, enjoy etc all of something【非正式】特別喜歡/盡情享受/極其憎恨(某物): *I went camping for a week and enjoyed every minute of it.* 我去野營了一週, 盡情享受了一下。

5 within minutes very soon after something has happened 片刻後, 轉瞬間: *The ambulance was there within minutes.* 片刻之後救護車就到那兒了。

6 ▶MEETING 會議◀ minutes [plural] an official written record of what is said and decided at a meeting 會議記錄, 議事錄

7 ▶NOTE ON A REPORT 報告記錄◀ a short official note on or about a document 簡短的批示; 備忘錄

8 ▶MATHEMATICS 數學◀ *technical* one of the 60 parts into which a degree of angle is divided【術語】分(角的計量單位, 即六十分之一度) —see also 另見 UP-TO-THE-MINUTE

Frequencies of the noun **minute** in spoken and written English 名詞 minute 在英語口語和書面語中的使用頻率

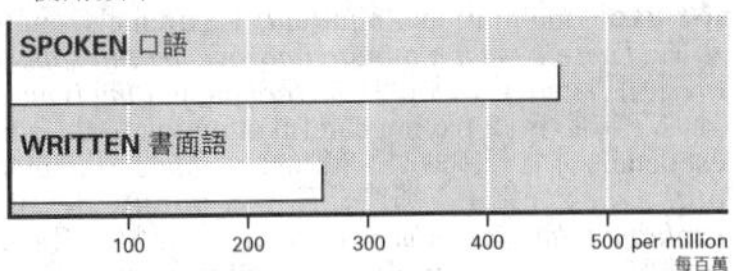

Based on the British National Corpus and the Longman Lancaster Corpus 據英國國家語料庫和朗文蘭卡斯特語料庫

This graph shows that the noun **minute** is much more common in spoken English than in written English. This is because it is used in a lot of common spoken phrases. 本圖表顯示, 名詞 minute 在英語口語中的使用頻率遠遠高於書面語, 因為口語中很多常用片語是由 minute 構成的。

minute (*n*) **SPOKEN PHRASES**
含 minute 的口語片語

9 a minute a very short period of time; MOMENT (2) 一會兒, 片刻: *He was there a minute ago.* 他剛才還在那兒。| *Stay there a minute.* 在那裡待一會兒。

10 in a minute very soon 很快, 立刻, 馬上: *All right, I'll do it in a minute.* 好吧, 我馬上就做。| *Mr Gregson will be with you in a minute.* 格雷格森先生很快就到。

11 wait a minute/just a minute/hold on a minute/hang on a minute a) used to tell someone you want them to wait for a short time while you do or say something else 稍等片刻: *Wait a minute, I have to turn off the cooker.* 稍等一會兒, 我得關掉爐具。| *Just a minute, I'll see if she's in.* 請等一下, 我看看她在不在。**b)** used to tell someone to stop speaking or doing something for a short time because they have

said or done something wrong 且慢: *Hold on a minute! That can't be right.* 且慢！那不可能是正確的。
12 any minute now used to say that something will happen extremely soon 隨時, 馬上, 在任何時刻: *We're expecting them any minute now.* 他們隨時會到。
13 have you got a minute? *BrE*【英】, **do you have a minute?** *AmE*【美】used to ask someone if it is convenient for you to talk to them for a short time 能耽誤你一點時間嗎?: *Have you got a minute? I've got a problem.* 能耽誤你一點時間嗎？我有一個問題。
14 one minute a) used to say that a situation suddenly changes 一會兒〔表示情況突然變化〕: *One minute they're madly in love and the next they've split up again.* 他們一會兒愛得發狂, 一會兒又分手了。**b)** used to ask someone to wait for a short time while you do something else 稍等一會兒: *One minute Stephen, let me finish this.* 斯蒂芬, 請稍等片刻, 讓我先把這個做完。
15 the minute sb does sth as soon as someone does something 某人一做某事就…: *Tell him I need to see him the minute he arrives.* 他一到就告訴他我要見他。
16 the next minute immediately afterwards 馬上, 立刻, 緊接着: *I put down the phone and the next minute it rang again.* 我剛放下電話, 電話鈴聲馬上又響了起來。
17 not think/believe etc for one minute used to say that you certainly do not think something, believe something etc 一點也不認為/相信等: *I don't think for one minute that he'll do it but I have to ask.* 我一點也不認為他會去做那件事, 但我必須問一下。
18 this minute used to tell someone, often angrily, to do something immediately 立刻, 馬上〔用於叫人馬上做某事, 常帶有怒意〕: *Johnny! Get inside, this minute!* 約翰尼！到裡面來, 馬上！

mi·nute² /mə`njut; maɪˈnjuːt/ *adj* **1** extremely small 極小的: *There's been a minute improvement in sales figures.* 銷售額有了一點上漲。| *Her handwriting is minute.* 她的字非常小。**2** paying careful attention to the smallest details 非常仔細的, 極詳細的: *a minute examination of the rock* 仔細檢查那塊岩石 | **in minute detail** *He explained the plan in minute detail.* 他非常詳細地解釋了那個計劃。—**minutely** *adv* —**minuteness** *n* [U]

min·ute³ /`mɪnɪt; ˈmɪnɪ̥t/ *v* [T] *especially BrE* to make an official note of something in the record of a meeting【尤英】將…記入議事錄[會議記錄]

minute hand /`mɪnɪt hænd; ˈmɪnɪ̥t hænd/ *n* [C] the long thin piece of metal that points to the minutes on a clock or watch〔鐘、錶的〕分針

min·ute·man /`mɪnɪtmæn; ˈmɪnɪ̥tmæn/ *n* [C] *AmE* one of a group of men in the past who were not official soldiers but who were ready to fight at any time【美】〔舊時〕隨時應召的民兵

mi·nu·ti·ae /mɪ`njuʃɪ,i; maɪˈnjuːʃiaɪ/ *n* [plural] very small and exact but unimportant details〔準確但不重要的〕微小細節, 細枝末節

minx /mɪŋks; mɪŋks/ *n* [C] *old-fashioned* a girl who is not RESPECTFUL and is very good at getting what she wants【過時】無禮而工於心計的女孩

mips /mɪps; mɪps/ *n* [plural] *technical* million instructions per second; a way of measuring how fast a computer works【術語】〔電腦運行速度〕每秒百萬條指令

mir·a·cle /`mɪrəkl̩; ˈmɪrəkəl/ *n* [C] **1** something lucky that you did not expect to happen or did not think was possible 意外的奇事, 不可思議的事; 奇跡: *By some miracle, we managed to catch the plane.* 令人有些不可思議的是, 我們竟然趕上了飛機。| **it is a miracle (that)** *It's a miracle you weren't killed!* 你沒有死真是奇跡！**2** an action or event that is impossible according to the ordinary laws of nature, believed to be done by God〔神創造的〕奇跡: *the miracles of Jesus* 耶穌創造的奇跡 **3 miracle cure/drug** a very effective medical treatment that cures even serious diseases 有奇效的療法/藥物 **4 work/perform miracles** to have a very good effect or result 創造奇跡; 有奇效: *Maybe you should try yoga – it worked miracles for me.* 也許你該試一試瑜伽 —— 它對我有驚人的效果。**5 a miracle of engineering/design etc** something that is produced or invented that is a very impressive example of a particular quality or skill 工程學/設計等上的奇跡: *This new electronic notebook is a miracle of miniaturization.* 這種新型電子筆記本是微型化技術的一項奇跡。

mi·rac·u·lous /mə`rækjələs; mɪˈrækjʊ̥ləs/ *adj* completely unexpected and usually resulting from extreme good luck 不可思議的; 神奇的; 非凡的: **miraculous recovery/escape/improvement** *It was thought she only had a month to live but she made a miraculous recovery.* 人們認為她只有一個月的壽命, 但她卻奇跡般康復了。—**miraculously** *adv*

mi·rage /mə`rɑʒ; ˈmɪrɑːʒ/ *n* [C] **1** a strange effect caused by hot air in a desert, in which you think you can see objects when they are not actually there〔沙漠裡的〕海市蜃樓 **2** a dream, hope, or wish that cannot come true 夢想; 幻想; 妄想

mire¹ /maɪr; maɪə/ *n* [U] *literary*【文】**1 drag sb's name through the mire** to talk about someone publicly in a way that brings shame on them 玷污某人的名聲, 辱沒某人 **2 in/into the mire** more and more deeply involved in problems 處於/陷入困境中: *The Party sank deeper into the mire of conflict.* 該黨在衝突的泥潭裡陷得更深了。**3** deep mud 泥潭, 泥坑

mire² *v* **be mired (down) in** *especially literary*【尤文】**a)** to be stuck in deep mud 陷入〔泥潭〕: *The plane's wheels were deeply mired in waterlogged ground.* 飛機的輪子深深地陷進泥沼地中。**b)** to be in a very difficult situation 陷入〔困境〕

mir·ror¹ /`mɪrɚ; ˈmɪrə/ *n* [C] **1** a piece of special flat glass that you can look at and see yourself in 鏡子: *Check your rearview and side mirrors before you drive away.* 開車之前檢查一下後視鏡和側視鏡。—see picture on page A2 參見A2頁圖 **2 a mirror of** something that gives a clear idea of what something else is like 清楚地反映…的東西: *We believe the polls are an accurate mirror of public opinion.* 我們認為這些民意測驗結果準確地反映了公眾的意見。

mirror² *v* [T] **1** if something mirrors a situation, fact, belief etc, it is very similar to it and gives a clear idea of what it is like 反映〔情況、事實、信念等〕: *The discussion mirrored the general attitudes prevalent in the local area.* 這一討論反映了當地人的普遍態度。**2** to be very similar to something or a copy of it 與…十分相似; 與…完全一樣: *Victor's expression mirrored her own, both of them staring in amazement.* 維克托的表情和她自己的一個樣, 兩個人都驚訝得傻了眼。

mirror im·age /`·· ,··/ *n* [C+of] **1** an image of something in which the right side appears on the left, and the left side appears on the right 鏡像 **2** something that is either very similar to something else or is the complete opposite of it 與…十分相似[完全相反]的事物: *Davy's messiness is the mirror image of his sister Dora's neatness.* 戴維的邋遢與他姐姐多拉的乾淨整潔形成了鮮明的對照。

mirth /mɝθ; mɜːθ/ *n* [U] *literary* happiness and laughter【文】歡樂; 歡笑: *Stifled laughter and cries of suppressed mirth issued from the next room.* 隔壁房間傳來了壓低的歡笑聲。—**mirthful** *adj* —**mirthfully** *adv*

mirth·less /`mɝθlɪs; ˈmɜːθləs/ *adj literary* mirthless laughter or a mirthless smile does not seem to be caused by real amusement or happiness【文】〔微笑等〕沒有歡樂的, 憂鬱的, 陰鬱的; 悲哀的: *Now it's your turn, he said* *with a mirthless grin.* 現在輪到你了，他咧着嘴苦笑地説道。—**mirthlessly** *adv*

mis- /mɪs; mɪs/ *prefix* **1** bad or badly 壞的[地]: *misfortune* (=bad luck) 不幸 | *He's been misbehaving.* 他一直行為不端。**2** wrong or wrongly 錯的; 錯誤地: *a miscalculation* 失算 | *I misunderstood what you said.* 我誤解了你的話。**3** shows an opposite or the lack of something 不; 相反; 缺少: *mistrust* 不信任

mis·ad·ven·ture /ˌmɪsədˋventʃɚ; ˌmɪsədˈventʃə/ *n* [C, U] **1 death by misadventure** *BrE law* the official name for an accidental death【英, 法律】意外致死[死亡] **2** *literary* bad luck or an accident【文】不幸, 災難; 事故

mis·al·li·ance /ˌmɪsəˋlaɪəns; ˌmɪsəˈlaɪəns/ *n* [C] *informal* a situation in which two people or organizations have mistakenly agreed to work together, marry each other etc, but are not suitable for each other【非正式】不適當的結合[聯合]; 不匹配的婚姻

mis·an·thro·pist /mɪsˋænθrəpɪst; mɪsˈænθrəpɪ̈st/ also 又作 **misanthrope** /ˋmɪsənˌθrop; ˈmɪsənθrəʊp/ *n* [C] *formal* someone who dislikes other people and prefers to be alone【正式】厭惡人類者; 性情孤僻的人, 遁世者 —**misanthropic** /ˌmɪsənˋθrɑpɪk; ˌmɪsənˈθrɒpɪk◂/ *adj* —**misanthropy** *n* [U]

mis·ap·ply /ˌmɪsəˋplaɪ; ˌmɪsəˈplaɪ/ *v* [T] to use a principle, rule etc incorrectly or for a wrong purpose 誤用; 用錯; 濫用 —**misapplication** /ˌmɪsæpləˋkeʃən; ˌmɪsæplɪ̈ˈkeɪʃən/ *n* [U+**of**]: *a misapplication of the law* 法律的誤用

mis·ap·pre·hend /ˌmɪsæprɪˋhɛnd; ˌmɪsæprɪˈhend/ *v* [T] *formal* to understand something wrongly【正式】誤解, 誤會

mis·ap·pre·hen·sion /ˌmɪsæprɪˋhɛnʃən; ˌmɪsæprɪˈhenʃən/ *n* [C] *formal* a mistaken belief or a wrong understanding of something【正式】誤會, 誤解: **(labour) under a misapprehension** (=believe something is true when in fact it is not) 誤認為 *I wonder if others are under the misapprehension that screwdrivers used to test electricity are infallible.* 我想知道其他人是否會錯誤地認為用螺絲刀來測試電流是絕對可靠的。

mis·ap·pro·pri·ate /ˌmɪsəˋproprɪˌet; ˌmɪsəˈprəʊprieɪt/ *v* [T] *formal* to dishonestly take something that you have been trusted to keep safe, for example to take money that belongs to your employer; EMBEZZLE【正式】侵吞; 私佔; 挪用; 盜用 —**misappropriation** /ˌmɪsəproprɪˋeʃən; ˌmɪsəprəʊpriˈeɪʃən/ *n* [U+**of**]: *the misappropriation of treasury funds* 盜用國庫資金

mis·be·got·ten /ˌmɪsbɪˋgɑtn̩; ˌmɪsbɪˈgɒtn◂/ *adj* [only before noun 僅用於名詞前] **1** a misbegotten plan, idea, etc is not likely to succeed because it is badly planned or not sensible〔計劃、想法等〕難以成功的; 不周詳的; 不合理的 **2** *formal or humorous* a misbegotten person is completely stupid or useless【正式或幽默】〔人〕非常愚蠢的; 完全無用的: *You misbegotten fool!* 你這個大笨蛋!

mis·be·have /ˌmɪsbɪˋhev; ˌmɪsbɪˈheɪv/ *v* [I] also 又作 **misbehave yourself** to behave badly, and cause trouble or annoy people 行為不端; 舉止不檢點: *William has been misbehaving himself at school.* 威廉在學校行為不端。

mis·be·ha·viour *BrE*【英】, **misbehavior** *AmE*【美】/ˌmɪsbɪˋhevjɚ; ˌmɪsbɪˈheɪvjə/ *n* [U] behaviour that is not acceptable to other people 不良行為; 不正當的舉止: *Even the most minor forms of misbehaviour were punished.* 即使最輕微的不良行為也受到了懲罰。

mis·cal·cu·late /mɪsˋkælkjəˌlet; ˌmɪsˈkælkjʊ̈leɪt/ *v* [I, T] **1** to make a mistake when deciding how long something will take to do, how much money you will need etc 誤算, 算錯: *The contractor miscalculated the costs of rebuilding.* 承包商算錯了重建所需的費用。**2** to make a wrong judgment about a situation 對〔局勢〕判斷錯誤

mis·cal·cu·la·tion /ˌmɪskælkjəˋleʃən; mɪsˌkælkjʊ̈ˈleɪʃən/ *n* [C] **1** a mistake made in deciding how long something will take to do, how much money you will need etc 誤算, 錯算 **2** a wrong judgment about a situation 錯誤判斷

mis·car·riage /mɪsˋkærɪdʒ; ˌmɪsˈkærɪdʒ/ *n* [C,U] the act of accidentally giving birth too early for the baby to live 流產, 小產: **have a miscarriage** *Unfortunately, she had a miscarriage at four months.* 不幸的是, 她在懷孕四個月的時候流產了。—compare 比較 ABORTION, STILLBIRTH

miscarriage of jus·tice /ˌ·ˌ·· · ˈ··/ *n* [C,U] a situation in which someone is wrongly punished by a court of law for something they did not do 誤判; 審判不公

mis·car·ry /mɪsˋkærɪ; mɪsˈkæri/ *v* [I] **1** to give birth to a baby too early for it to live 流產, 小產 —compare 比較 ABORT (3) **2** *formal* if a plan miscarries, it is not successful【正式】〔計劃〕失敗

mis·cast /mɪsˋkæst; ˌmɪsˈkɑːst/ *v past tense and past participle* **miscast** [T usually passive 一般用被動態] to choose an unsuitable actor to play a particular character in a play or film 選擇不合適的演員去演〔某個角色〕

mis·ce·ge·na·tion /ˌmɪsɪdʒəˋneʃən; ˌmɪsɪ̈dʒɪ̈ˈneɪʃən/ *n* [U] *formal* the act of having children by parents of different races, especially when one of the parents is white【正式】異族通婚生育子女〔尤指父母中一方為白種人〕

mis·cel·la·ne·ous /ˌmɪslˋenɪəs; ˌmɪsəˈleɪniəs◂/ *adj* [only before noun 僅用於名詞前] made up of many different things or people who do not seem to be connected with each other〔人或物〕各色各樣混在一起的, 混雜的; 多種多樣的: *a miscellaneous assortment of books* 各種各樣的書籍 | *miscellaneous expenses* 雜費, 雜項開支

mis·cel·la·ny /ˋmɪslˌenɪ; mɪˈseləni/ *n* [C] a collection of different things 大雜燴; 雜集, 雜錄: *a miscellany of American short stories* 美國短篇小説雜集

mis·chance /mɪsˋtʃæns; ˌmɪsˈtʃɑːns/ *n* [C,U] bad luck, or a situation that results from bad luck 不幸, 厄運; 不幸的事: *As mischance would have it we ran into Sue – just the person we wanted to avoid.* 倒霉的是我們遇上了蘇 — 就是那個我們想躲着的人。

mis·chief /ˋmɪstʃɪf; ˈmɪstʃɪ̈f/ *n* **1** [U] bad behaviour, especially by children, that causes trouble or damage, but no serious harm 惡作劇, 搗蛋, 胡鬧: **get into mischief** (=behave in a way that causes trouble) 胡鬧, 搗蛋 *Now run along, and don't get into mischief.* 好了, 走吧, 不要搗亂。| **be up to mischief** (=plan or do something you know you should not do) 搗鬼, 搞惡作劇 *If you can't see Nick, you can be sure he's up to some mischief.* 如果看不到尼克, 可以肯定他又在搗甚麼鬼。| **keep (sb) out of mischief** *They've got enough toys to keep them out of mischief for a while.* 他們有足夠的玩具使他們暫時不搗蛋。**2** [U] enjoyment of playing tricks on people or embarrassing them 頑皮, 調皮, 淘氣: *Helena's eyes flashed with amusement and mischief.* 海倫娜的眼裡閃現出快樂而頑皮的神情。**3 make mischief (between)** *informal* to deliberately cause quarrels or unfriendly feelings between people【非正式】(在…之間) 挑撥離間, 搬弄是非 **4 do yourself a mischief** *BrE humorous* to injure yourself slightly【英, 幽默】〔輕微地〕傷害自己: *If you try to lift that box, you'll do yourself a mischief.* 如果你試圖搬起那個箱子, 你會傷着自己。**5** [U] *formal* damage or harm that may or may not have been intended【正式】(有意[無心]的) 損壞[傷害]

mischief-mak·er /ˈ·· ˌ··/ *n* [C] someone who deliberately causes trouble or quarrels 惹是生非的人; 搬弄是非者, 挑撥離間者

mis·chie·vous /ˋmɪstʃɪvəs; ˈmɪstʃɪ̈vəs/ *adj* **1** liking to have fun, especially by playing tricks on people or doing things to annoy or embarrass them 調皮的, 淘氣的; 惡作劇的: *a mischievous boy* 淘氣的男孩 | **mischievous smile/expression etc** *Gabby looked at him with a mischievous grin.* 加貝看着他, 咧着嘴調皮地笑着。**2** causing trouble or quarrels deliberately 引起麻煩的; 造成不和的: *a mischievous remark* 挑撥離間的言論 —**mis-**

chievously *adv* —mischievousness *n* [U]

mis·con·ceived /ˌmɪskən`sivd; ˌmɪskənˈsiːvd◂/ *adj* **1** a misconceived plan will not succeed because it is stupid or has not been carefully thought about〔指計劃〕愚蠢的, 考慮不周的 **2** a misconceived idea is based on a wrong understanding of something〔指想法〕建立在對…誤解基礎上的; 設想錯誤的: *a misconceived notion of what acting really involves* 對演戲真正包含的內容的錯誤看法

mis·con·cep·tion /ˌmɪskən`sɛpʃən; ˌmɪskənˈsepʃən/ *n* [C,U] an idea which is wrong or untrue, but which people believe because they do not understand it properly 錯誤想法, 誤解; 錯誤印象: **[+that]** *the misconception that unemployment can be cured by government intervention* 認為政府干預能消除失業的錯誤想法 | **a popular/common misconception** (=a wrong idea that a lot of people believe) 普遍的/常見的誤解 *It is a popular misconception that eye problems result in headaches.* 認為眼病會引起頭痛是一個普遍的誤解。

mis·con·duct /mɪs`kɑndʌkt; ˌmɪsˈkɒndʌkt/ *n* [U] *formal* bad or dishonest behaviour by someone in a position of authority or trust【正式】不端行為; 不誠實行為; 胡作非為: *allegations of misconduct by council officials* 有關市政會官員濫用職權的指控 | **gross misconduct** (=very serious misconduct) 嚴重的不端行為 *One of the doctors had been dismissed for gross professional misconduct.* 其中一名醫生因職業上嚴重的不端行為已被免職。

mis·con·struc·tion /ˌmɪskən`strʌkʃən; ˌmɪskənˈstrʌkʃən/ *n* [C,U] *formal* an incorrect or mistaken understanding of something【正式】誤解, 曲解: **open to misconstruction** (=easy to misunderstand) 易被誤解 *A law must be worded so carefully that it is not open to misconstruction.* 法律措辭必須非常嚴謹以不致被人曲解。

mis·con·strue /ˌmɪskən`stru; ˌmɪskənˈstruː/ *v* [T] *formal* to misunderstand something that someone has said or done【正式】誤解

mis·count /mɪs`kaunt; ˌmɪsˈkaʊnt/ *v* [I,T] to count wrongly 算錯, 數錯: *Oops! Sorry, I miscounted – we need ten copies, not nine.* 哎喲! 對不起, 我數錯了——我們需要十份, 不是九份。

mis·cre·ant /`mɪskrɪənt; ˈmɪskriənt/ *n* [C] *old use* a bad person who causes trouble, hurts people etc【舊】壞蛋, 惡棍, 歹徒, 無賴

mis·deed /mɪs`did; ˌmɪsˈdiːd/ *n* [C] *formal* a wrong or illegal action【正式】錯誤行為; 違法行為; 罪行: *No one ever suspected the seriousness of his misdeeds.* 從來沒有人懷疑過他的違法行為的嚴重性。

mis·de·mea·nour *BrE*【英】, **misdemeanor** *AmE*【美】/ˌmɪsdɪ`minɚ; ˌmɪsdɪˈmiːnə/ *n* [C] **1** *formal* a bad or unacceptable action that is not very serious【正式】不很嚴重的惡劣行為: *Alfred beat his children for even the smallest misdemeanour.* 孩子們哪怕有最輕微的不端行為, 艾爾弗雷德也會打他們。**2** *law* a crime that is not very serious【法律】輕罪 —compare 比較 FELONY

mis·di·ag·nose /ˌmɪsdaɪəg`nos; ˌmɪsdaɪəgˈnəʊz/ *v* [T usually passive 一般用被動態] to give an incorrect explanation of an illness, a problem in a machine etc 誤診

mis·di·rect /ˌmɪsdə`rɛkt; ˌmɪsdɪˈrekt/ *v* [T usually passive 一般用被動態] **1** *formal* to use your efforts, energy or abilities in a wrong or unsuitable way【正式】誤用, 錯用〔精力或能力〕, 使用…不當: *We believe their efforts to prevent animal testing are misdirected.* 我們認為他們阻止動物實驗的努力是把精力用錯了地方。**2** if a judge misdirects a JURY (=the group of people who decide a legal case), he or she gives them incorrect information about the law〔法官對陪審團〕作錯誤引導 **3** *formal* to send someone or something to the wrong place【正式】把…送錯地方 —**misdirection** /-`rɛkʃən; -ˈrekʃən/ *n* [U]

mise-en-scène /ˌmizɑ̃`sɛn; ˌmiːz ɒn ˈsen/ *n* [C] *French*【法】**1** *technical* the arrangement of furniture and other objects used on the stage in a theatre play【術語】舞台佈置〔對道具等的佈局安排〕; 舞台調度 **2** *formal* the environment in which an event takes place【正式】〔事件的〕環境, 背景

mi·ser /`maɪzɚ; ˈmaɪzə/ *n* [C] someone who hates spending money and likes saving it 守財奴, 吝嗇鬼, 小氣鬼: *A typical miser, he hid his money in the house in various places.* 他是個典型的守財奴, 把錢藏在房子裡多個不同的地方。

mis·e·ra·ble /`mɪzərəbḷ; ˈmɪzərəbəl/ *adj* **1** extremely unhappy, for example because you feel lonely, cold, or badly treated 極不愉快的, 痛苦的: *You're making my life miserable!* 你使我的生活痛苦不堪! | *There's nothing like a bad cold to make you feel miserable.* 沒有甚麼能像重感冒那樣使人感到難受。| *You look miserable. What's up?* 你顯得愁眉苦臉的, 怎麼啦? **2** always unhappy, dissatisfied, or complaining 總是不高興[不滿意]的; 總是抱怨的: *He's a miserable old devil.* 他是個終日鬱鬱不樂的老傢伙。**3** [usually before noun 一般用於名詞前] making you feel very unhappy, uncomfortable etc 令人不愉快的; 令人不舒服的, 使人難受的: *They endured hours of backbreaking work in miserable conditions.* 他們忍受了數小時惡劣條件下繁重的勞動。**4** [only before noun 僅用於名詞前] very bad in quality, or very small in amount 質量極差的; 數量極少的: *I can hardly afford the rent on my miserable income.* 靠我微薄的收入我幾乎連房租都交不起。—**miserably** *adv*: *miserably cold and wet* 極度寒冷和潮濕

mi·ser·ly /`maɪzɚlɪ; ˈmaɪzəli/ *adj* **1** a miserly amount, salary etc is one that is much too small 小[少]得可憐的: *a miserly 4% pay rise* 區區4%的工資增長 **2** a miserly person is one who hates spending money 守財奴的, 吝嗇鬼的, 愛錢如命的 —**miserliness** *n* [U]

mis·e·ry /`mɪzərɪ; ˈmɪzəri/ *n* **1** [C,U] great suffering or discomfort, caused for example by being very poor or very sick 痛苦, 難受; 苦難: *the awful shantytowns, so full of human misery* 情況很糟的棚戶區, 充滿了如此之多人類的苦難 | **[+of]** *The cold increased the misery of the retreating army.* 寒冷使後撤部隊的狀況更加悲慘。**2** [C,U] great unhappiness 極大的不幸; 愁苦, 悲苦: *Her face was a picture of misery.* 她一臉苦相。**3 make sb's life a misery** to cause so much trouble for someone that they cannot enjoy their life 使某人的日子不好過, 使某人的生活充滿痛苦: *Competitive mothers can make their daughters' lives a misery.* 爭強好勝的母親會使自己的女兒日子不好過。**4 put sth/sb out of their misery a)** *informal* to make someone stop feeling worried, especially by telling them something they are waiting to hear【非正式】〔尤指通過告訴其想了解之事〕使某人不再感到憂慮[不安]: *Go on, put them out of their misery and announce the winner.* 說下去, 別再讓他們忐忑不安了, 宣布誰是獲勝者吧。**b)** to kill an animal in order to end its suffering 殺死動物以結束其痛苦 **5** [C] *BrE spoken* someone who is always complaining and never enjoys anything【英口】滿腹牢騷的人: *Don't be such a misery.* 別埋怨個沒完。| **misery guts** (=a name for someone who is like this) 牢騷包 *You don't want to be like old misery guts over there.* 你不會想成為那兒的一個老牢騷包吧?

mis·field /ˌmɪs`fild; ˌmɪsˈfiːld/ *v* [I,T] to make a mistake in catching or throwing the ball in some ball games, such as cricket〔板球等〕接[擲]球失誤 —**misfield** /`mɪsfild; ˈmɪsfiːld/ *n* [C]

mis·fire /mɪs`faɪr; ˌmɪsˈfaɪə/ *v* [I] **1** if a plan or joke misfires, it does not have the result that you intended〔計劃或笑話〕未達到預期的效果; 失敗 **2** if an engine misfires, the petrol mixture does not burn at the right time〔發動機〕不發火, 發動不起來 **3** if a gun misfires, the bullet does not come out〔槍〕發射不出子彈 —**misfire** /`mɪsfaɪr; ˈmɪsfaɪə/ *n* [C]

mis·fit /`mɪsˌfɪt; ˈmɪsˌfɪt/ *n* [C] someone who does not seem to belong in a place because they are very differ-

M

ent from the other people there 不適應環境的人: *a social misfit* 與社會格格不入的人

mis·for·tune /mɪsˋfɔrtʃən; mɪsˈfɔːtʃən/ *n* [C,U] very bad luck, or something that happens to you as a result of bad luck 不幸, 厄運; 不幸事故; 災難: *It seems the banks always profit from farmers' misfortunes.* 銀行似乎總是從農民的災禍中獲益。| **have the misfortune to do sth** *The French soldiers had the misfortune to be caught in the crossfire.* 那些法國士兵不幸受到了交叉火力的襲擊。

mis·giv·ing /mɪsˋgɪvɪŋ; ˌmɪsˈgɪvɪŋ/ *n* [C,U] a feeling of doubt, distrust, or fear about what might happen or about whether something is right 疑慮; 擔憂; 害怕: *She eyed Bert's pistol with misgiving.* 她恐懼地注視着伯特的手槍。| **have deep/serious misgivings** *Opponents of nuclear energy have deep misgivings about its safety.* 反核能人士對核能的安全性深感疑慮。

mis·guid·ed /mɪsˋgaɪdɪd; mɪsˈgaɪdʒd/ *adj* **1** intended to be helpful but in fact making a situation worse 幫倒忙的: *a well-meaning but misguided attempt to bring her parents back together* 想使她父母重歸於好卻幫了倒忙的好心嘗試 **2** a misguided idea or opinion is wrong because it is based on a wrong understanding of a situation〔基於對情況的誤解而觀點〕錯誤的: *They cling to the misguided belief that only big name managers can bring big time success.* 他們堅持只有大名鼎鼎的經理才能創造一流的業績這一錯誤的看法。—**misguidedly** *adv*

mis·han·dle /mɪsˋhændl̩; ˌmɪsˈhændl/ *v* [T] **1** to deal with a situation badly, because of a lack of skill or care 對…處理不當: *The Prime Minister admitted that the water privatisation had been mishandled.* 首相承認供水私營化的問題沒有處理好。**2** to treat something roughly, often causing damage 粗暴對待, 胡亂使用〔某物〕

mis·hap /ˋmɪsˌhæp; ˈmɪshæp/ *n* [C,U] a small accident or mistake that does not have very serious results 小事故; 小錯誤: *a slight mishap with the glasses* 眼鏡出的小問題 | **without mishap** *Only one horse finished the course without mishap.* 只有一匹馬一路平安地跑完了全程。

mis·hear /mɪsˋhɪr; ˌmɪsˈhɪə/ *v past tense and past participle* **misheard** /-ˋhɝd; -ˈhɜːd/ [I,T] to not properly hear what someone says, so that you think they said something different 聽錯, 誤聽: *It seemed a strange question; I wondered if I had misheard.* 這好像是一個古怪的問題; 我懷疑自己是不是聽錯了。

mis·hit /ˌmɪsˋhɪt; ˌmɪsˈhɪt/ *v* [T] to hit a ball badly, especially in GOLF〔尤指在打高爾夫球中〕誤擊〔球〕—**mishit** /ˋmɪshɪt; ˈmɪshɪt/ *n* [C]

mish·mash /ˋmɪʃˌmæʃ; ˈmɪʃmæʃ/ *n* [singular] *informal* a mixture with no particular order in its design or in the choice of what is included【非正式】混雜物, 大雜燴; HOTCHPOTCH *BrE*【英】: [**+of**] *The magazine is a jumbled mishmash of jokes, stories, and serious news.* 這本雜誌是笑話、故事和嚴肅新聞亂湊在一起的大雜燴。

mis·in·form /ˌmɪsɪnˋfɔrm; ˌmɪsɪnˈfɔːm/ *v* [T usually passive 一般用被動態] to give someone information that is incorrect or untrue 向〔某人〕提供錯誤信息, 向…誤報

mis·in·for·ma·tion /ˌmɪsɪnfɚˋmeʃən; ˌmɪsɪnfəˈmeɪʃən/ *n* [U] incorrect information, especially when deliberately intended to deceive people〔尤指故意騙人的〕錯誤信息, 錯誤情報 —compare 比較 DISINFORMATION

mis·in·ter·pret /ˌmɪsɪnˋtɝprɪt; ˌmɪsɪnˈtɜːprʒt/ *v* [T] to not understand the correct meaning of something that someone says or does, or to explain something wrongly to other people 對…誤解, 錯誤地解釋: *Liam misinterpreted her friendly offer of a lift home.* 利亞姆誤解了她友好地邀他搭車回家的用意。—**misinterpretation** /ˌmɪsɪnˌtɝprɪˋteʃən; ˌmɪsɪntɜːprʒˈteɪʃən/ *n* [C,U]: *a misinterpretation of the test results* 對檢驗結果的誤解

mis·judge /mɪsˋdʒʌdʒ; ˌmɪsˈdʒʌdʒ/ *v* [T] **1** to form a wrong or unfair opinion about a person or situation 對〔人或情況〕錯誤判斷: *The defeat showed how badly he'd misjudged the mood of the electorate.* 這次失敗表明他對選民的情緒判斷大錯特錯。**2** to guess an amount, distance etc wrongly 推測錯誤, 錯誤地估計〔數量、距離等〕: *I misjudged the turn and hit the sidewalk.* 我對拐彎處判斷錯誤, 駛上了人行道。—**misjudgment** or **misjudgement** *n* [C,U]

mis·lay /mɪsˋle; mɪsˈleɪ/ *v past tense and past participle* **mislaid** /-ˋled; -ˈleɪd/ [T] to put something somewhere, then forget where you put it; MISPLACE 忘記把…放在何處, 一時找不到〔某物〕: *I've mislaid my glasses again.* 我又忘記把眼鏡放在甚麼地方了。

mis·lead /mɪsˋlid; mɪsˈliːd/ *v past tense and past participle* **misled** /-ˋlɛd; -ˈled/ [T] to make someone believe something that is not true by giving them false or incomplete information 將…引入歧途, 誤導: *McFarlane admitted that he had misled Congress about aid to the Contra.* 麥克法蘭承認就向(尼加拉瓜)反政府勢力提供援助一事他誤導了國會。| **don't be misled by** *Don't be misled by appearances, he's a very competent worker.* 不要被表象迷惑, 他是一個非常能幹的工人。

mis·lead·ing /mɪsˋlidɪŋ; mɪsˈliːdɪŋ/ *adj* likely to make someone believe something that is not true 易使人誤信的; 誤導人的; 騙人的: *The article was misleading, and the newspaper has apologized.* 那篇文章誤導讀者, 那家報紙已致歉了。—**misleadingly** *adv*: *"You imply, misleadingly, that you knew nothing about it," accused the prosecutor.* "你, 以誤導人的方式, 暗示你對此一無所知。"檢控官指控道。

mis·man·age /mɪsˋmænɪdʒ; ˌmɪsˈmænɪdʒ/ *v* [T] if someone mismanages something they are in charge of, they deal with it badly 對…管理不善, 對…經營不當: *The nation's finances had been badly mismanaged.* 該國的財政管理非常紊亂。—**mismanagement** *n* [U]

mis·match /ˌmɪsˋmætʃ; ˈmɪsmætʃ/ *n* [C] a combination of things or people that do not work well together or are not suitable for each other 錯配; 不匹配; 不協調: *the mismatch between the demand for health care and the supply* 醫療保健供求之間的不協調 —**mismatched** /ˌmɪsˋmætʃt; ˌmɪsˈmætʃt◂/ *adj*: *a brilliant woman tragically mismatched with an incompetent, dull man* 不幸錯嫁了一個無能笨漢的才女

mis·no·mer /mɪsˋnomɚ; mɪsˈnəʊmə/ *n* [C] a wrong or unsuitable name 錯誤[使用不當]的名字: *The word 'new' in their New Development was now something of a misnomer given that building had not even started.* 那座樓都還沒有開工, 他們所說的"新建住宅區"中的"新"字用得有些不當。

mi·so·gy·nist /mɪˋsɑdʒənɪst; mʒˈsɒdʒʒnʒst/ *n* [C] a man who hates women 憎恨女人者, 厭惡女人者 —**misogyny** *n* [U] *formal*【正式】

mis·place /mɪsˋples; ˌmɪsˈpleɪs/ *v* [T] to lose something for a short time by putting it in the wrong place; MISLAY〔因放錯地方而〕暫時丟失, 一時找不到〔某物〕; 把…放在一時記不起的地方: *Oh dear, I seem to have misplaced the letter.* 哎呀, 我好像忘了把信放在甚麼地方了。

mis·placed /ˌmɪsˋplest; ˌmɪsˈpleɪst◂/ *adj* misplaced feelings of trust, love etc are wrong and unsuitable, because the person that you have these feelings for does not deserve them〔把信任、愛等感情〕錯給不值得的人的: *her misplaced sense of loyalty* 她那用於錯誤對象的忠誠感

mis·print /ˋmɪsˌprɪnt; ˈmɪs-prɪnt/ *n* [C] a mistake, especially a spelling mistake, in a book, magazine etc 印刷錯誤, 手民之誤

mis·pro·nounce /ˌmɪsprəˋnaʊns; ˌmɪsprəˈnaʊns/ *v* [T] to pronounce a word or name wrongly 唸錯, 發錯〔音〕—**mispronunciation** /ˌmɪsprəˌnʌnsɪˋeʃən; ˌmɪsprənʌnsiˈeɪʃən/ *n* [C,U]

mis·quote /mɪsˋkwot; ˌmɪsˈkwəʊt/ *v* [T] to make a mistake in reporting what someone else has said 錯誤地引

證, 誤引〔他人的話〕: *Dr Hall said he had been misquoted in the press.* 霍爾博士說新聞界錯誤地引用了他的話。—**misquotation** /ˌmɪskwoˋteʃən; ˌmɪskwəʊˈteɪʃən/ *n* [C,U]

mis·read /mɪsˋrid; ˌmɪsˈriːd/ *v past tense and past participle* **misread** /-ˋrɛd; -ˈred/ [T] **1** to make a wrong judgment about a person or situation 對…判斷錯誤: *Negotiators misread the clues as to the enemy's true intentions.* 談判者們對有關敵人真正意圖的線索判斷錯誤。**2** to read something incorrectly 讀錯, 唸錯; 看錯 —**misreading** *n* [C,U]: *a misreading of the situation* 對局勢的錯誤判斷

mis·re·port /ˌmɪsrɪˋpɔrt; ˌmɪsrɪˈpɔːt/ *v* [T usually passive 一般用被動態] to give an incorrect or untrue account of an event or situation 對…報道失實: *The facts of the story have been misreported.* 事情的真相被歪曲了。

mis·rep·re·sent /ˌmɪsrɛprɪˋzɛnt; ˌmɪsreprɪˈzent/ *v* [T] to deliberately give a wrong description of someone's opinions or of a situation 故意對…作錯誤的描述, 歪曲: *These statistics grossly misrepresent the reality.* 這些統計資料嚴重歪曲了事實真相。—**misrepresentation** /ˌmɪsrɛprɪzɛnˋteʃən; ˌmɪsreprɪzenˈteɪʃən/ *n* [C,U]

mis·rule /mɪsˋrul; ˌmɪsˈruːl/ *n* [U] *formal* bad government【正式】治理不當; 苛政, 暴政: *15 years of misrule by a weak and corrupt government* 一個無能、腐敗的政府15年的暴政

miss¹ /mɪs; mɪs/ *v*

① NOT DO STH/FAIL TO DO STH 不做某事/未能做到某事
② BE TOO LATE 太遲
③ FEEL SAD WITHOUT 因沒有…而難過
④ NOT NOTICE 不注意
⑤ AVOID STH 避免某事物
⑥ NOTICE STH ISN'T THERE 發現某物不在那兒
⑦ OTHER MEANINGS 其他意思

① NOT DO STH/FAIL TO DO STH 不做某事/未能做到某事

1 [T] to not go somewhere or do something, especially when you want to but cannot〔尤指想去或想做而〕未去[未做]: *I'm really hungry. I missed breakfast.* 我真的餓了, 我沒吃上早飯。| *Donna had to miss a week of school because of chickenpox.* 唐娜因出水痘只得缺了一週的課。

2 ►NOT HIT/GET HOLD OF 未擊中/抓住◄ [I,T] to not hit something or catch something 未擊中; 未抓住: *She fired at the target but missed.* 她朝目標開了槍, 但沒有擊中。| **miss sth** *He ran to catch the ball but missed it.* 他跑着去接球, 但沒接住。| **miss doing sth** *The car came screeching round the corner and just missed hitting a little boy who was crossing the road.* 汽車發出尖利的聲音從拐角開過來, 險些撞上一個正在過馬路的小男孩。—see picture on page A23 參見 A23 頁圖

3 miss a chance/opportunity to fail to use an opportunity to do something 錯過機會: *A free trip to Jamaica was an opportunity he couldn't miss.* 免費去牙買加旅遊是一個他不能錯過的機會。

4 I wouldn't miss it for the world *spoken* used to say that you really want to go to an event, see something etc【口】我無論如何也不想錯過

5 miss the boat/bus *informal* to fail to take an opportunity【非正式】錯過機會, 坐失良機: *You'll miss the boat if you don't buy these shares now.* 如果現在不買這些股票, 你會坐失良機。

② BE TOO LATE 太遲

6 [T] to be too late for something 未趕上: *By the time we got there we'd missed the beginning of the movie.* 我們趕到那兒的時候電影開頭已經放過去了。| **miss the train/bus etc** *I overslept and missed the train.* 我睡過了頭, 誤了火車。—opposite 反義詞 CATCH¹ (7)

③ FEEL SAD WITHOUT 因沒有…而難過

7 ►MISS SB 思念某人◄ [T] to feel sad because someone you love is not with you 思念, 想念; 懷念〔某人〕: *When George went away I really missed him.* 喬治走了後我確實想念他。| *Will you miss me?* 你會想我嗎?

8 ►MISS STH 留戀某物◄ to feel sad because you do not have something or cannot do something you had or did before 留戀, 思戀〔某物〕: *I miss the car, but the bus system is good.* 我留戀汽車, 但公共汽車系統也不錯。| *We really missed being able to go to the beach whenever we wanted.* 我們確實留戀甚麼時候想去海灘就能去的日子。

④ NOT NOTICE 不注意

9 [T] to not see, hear, or notice something, especially when it is difficult to notice 未看到; 未聽到; 未注意到〔某事物〕: *Grandpa Joe spoke very slowly so that Charlie wouldn't miss a word.* 喬爺爺說得非常慢, 這樣查利就不會漏聽一個字。| *J.D. noticed a design fault in the engine that everyone else had missed.* J.D.在發動機上發現了一個其他人都沒有注意到的設計上的缺陷。

10 you can't miss it/him etc *spoken* used to say that it is very easy to notice or recognize someone or something【口】你不會看不到[認不出]它/他等的: *He's the one in the red hat. You can't miss him.* 他是戴紅帽子的那個。你不會認不出來的。

11 sb doesn't miss much *spoken* used to say that someone is good at noticing things, even small details【口】某人很善於察覺事物, 明察秋毫: *Old Mr Staines doesn't miss much, does he?* 老斯坦斯先生對事情明察秋毫, 是吧?

12 sb doesn't miss a trick *spoken* used to say that someone notices every opportunity to get an advantage【口】某人很精明, 很善於把握機會: *The cunning old devil – he never misses a trick.* 這個狡猾的老傢伙 —— 他總是能把握住每次機會佔到上風。

⑤ AVOID STH 避免某事物

13 ►AVOID STH 避開某事◄ [T] to avoid doing something or going somewhere, especially deliberately〔尤指故意地〕避開, 躲開〔做某事或去某地〕: *If we leave now we should miss the traffic.* 如果我們現在走, 就能避開擁擠的車輛。| *They narrowly missed being killed in the fire.* 他們差點被那場火燒死。

⑥ NOTICE STH ISN'T THERE 發現某物不在那兒

14 [T] to notice that something or someone is not in the place you expect them to be 發覺〔某人或某物〕不在應在之處: *I didn't miss my wallet till it came to paying the bill.* 直到付賬時我才發現錢包沒了。

⑦ OTHER MEANINGS 其他意思

15 miss the point to not understand the main point of what someone is saying 沒有領會要點

16 sb's heart misses a beat used to say that someone is very excited, surprised, or frightened〔因激動、驚訝或害怕〕心跳停了一拍: *When I spotted Christophe my heart missed a beat.* 當我認出克里斯托弗時, 我激動得心跳都停了一拍。
17 without missing a beat if you do something without missing a beat, you do it without showing that you are very surprised or shocked 不露聲色地; 鎮定地: *"I hear you're a private detective," he said, without missing a beat.* "我聽說你是位私家偵探," 他若無其事地說道。
18 ▶ENGINE 發動機◀ [I] if an engine misses, it stops working for a very short time and then starts again 短時熄火

miss out *phr v* **1** [I] to not have the chance to do something that you enjoy 沒有做自己喜歡的事的機會: *Some children miss out because their parents can't afford to pay for school trips.* 一些孩子失去了機會, 因為他們的父母沒錢支付學校組織的旅行。| **[+on]** *She married young and felt she was missing out on life.* 她早早就結婚了, 因而感到失去享受生活的機會。**2** [T **miss** sb/sth ↔ **out**] *BrE* to not include someone or something【英】不包括, 漏掉: *Make sure you don't miss any details out.* 你要確保不漏掉任何細節。

2 **miss²** *n*
1 Miss Smith/Cleveland etc used in front of the family name of a woman who is not married to address her politely, to write to her, or to talk about her 史密斯/克利夫蘭小姐等〔用在未婚女子姓的前面, 作為禮貌的稱呼〕—compare 比較 MRS, MS —see 見 MR (USAGE)
2 ▶TEACHER 教師◀ *BrE* used by children when addressing a female teacher, whether she is married or not【英】老師〔兒童對女教師的稱呼〕: *I know the answer, Miss.* 老師, 我知道答案。—compare 比較 SIR (5)
3 Miss Italy/Ohio/World etc used before the name of a country, city etc which a woman represents in a beauty competition 意大利/俄亥俄/世界小姐等〔用在選美比賽中某女子所代表的國家、城市等名稱的前面〕
4 ▶YOUNG WOMAN 年輕女子◀ *old-fashioned* used as a polite way of addressing a young woman when you do not know her name【過時】小姐〔用來禮貌地稱呼不知其名的年輕女子〕: *Excuse me, miss, you've dropped your umbrella.* 對不起, 小姐, 您的傘掉了。—compare 比較 MADAM (1), SIR (1, 2)
5 ▶YOUNG GIRL 年輕姑娘◀ [C] *BrE* a young girl, especially one who has been naughty or rude【英】〔尤指頑皮或無禮的〕小姑娘, 女孩, 少女: *a cheeky little miss* 無禮的小姑娘
6 give sth a miss *informal especially BrE* to decide not to do something【非正式, 尤英】決定不做某事: *I think I'll give aerobics a miss this week.* 我想本週我不會去做有氧健身運動了。
7 ▶NOT HIT/CATCH 沒擊中/抓住◀ [C] a failed attempt to hit, catch, or hold something 未擊中; 未抓住; 沒接住: *an exciting game with three shots at goal and only two misses* 一場激動人心的比賽, 三次射門, 只兩次射失
8 a miss is as good as a mile used to say that although someone failed by only a small amount to do something, they were still unsuccessful 功敗垂成終是敗 —see also 另見 HIT-AND-MISS

mis·sal /ˋmɪsl̩; ˈmɪsəl/ *n* [C] a book containing all the prayers said during each Mass for a whole year in the Roman Catholic church〔羅馬天主教的〕彌撒經書

mis·shap·en /mɪsˋʃepən; ˌmɪsˈʃeɪpən/ *adj* not the normal or natural shape 畸形的: *Ballerinas often have blunted, misshapen toes.* 芭蕾舞女演員的腳趾常常會磨粗、變形。

mis·sile /ˋmɪsl̩; ˈmɪsaɪl/ *n* [C] **1** a weapon that can fly over long distances and that explodes when it hits the thing it has been aimed at 導彈, 飛彈: *a nuclear missile* 核導彈 **2** an object that is thrown at someone in order to hurt them〔用來傷人的〕投擲物: *Many of the hooligans were throwing missiles at the police.* 許多街頭惡棍在向警察投擲東西。

3 **miss·ing** /ˋmɪsɪŋ; ˈmɪsɪŋ/ *adj* **1** something that is missing is not in its usual place and you cannot find it 找不到的; 丟失的: *We found the missing piece of the jigsaw under the chair.* 我們在椅子下面發現了那塊丟失的拼圖塊。| **[+from]** *Fifty dollars were missing from my wallet.* 我的錢包裡少了五十美元。**2** if part of something is missing, it has been removed, destroyed etc and no longer exists 缺掉的, 缺少的, 缺損的: *Two of her front teeth were missing.* 她的兩顆門牙沒有了。**3** someone who is missing has disappeared, and no one knows where they are 下落不明的, 失蹤的: *The soldiers were reported missing, presumed dead.* 那些士兵據報失蹤, 估計已經死亡。**4** not included, although it ought to have been 漏掉的, 遺漏的: **[+from]** *Why is my name missing from the list?* 為甚麼名單上漏掉了我的名字? **5 go missing** *BrE* to disappear or become lost【英】失蹤, 走失; 丟失: *My cat's gone missing again.* 我的貓又不見了。

missing link /ˌ.. ˈ./ *n* [C] **1** a piece of information that you need in order to solve a problem 缺少的一環: *a discovery which could provide a new direction towards finding the missing link in the search for a cure for cancer* 為探索癌症治療方法找到所缺環節指明新方向的一項發現 **2 the missing link** an animal similar to humans that may have existed at the time when apes (APE[1] (1)) developed into humans 猿進化到人類的過程中或許存在過的一種過渡動物: *The race is on to find the missing link in our evolution.* 科學家正在進行競賽, 以找到那種被推定在人類進化過程中介於猿和人類之間的動物。

missing per·son /ˌ.. ˈ../ *n plural* **missing persons** [C] **1** someone who has disappeared and whose family has asked the police to try to find them 失蹤者 **2 Missing Persons** the police department responsible for trying to find people who have disappeared 失蹤人口調查部〔負責尋找失蹤者的警察部門〕

mis·sion /ˋmɪʃən; ˈmɪʃən/ *n* [C] 3
1 ▶AIRFORCE/ARMY ETC 空軍/陸軍等◀ an important job done by a member of the airforce, army etc, especially an attack on the enemy 任務, 使命: *He was sent on over 200 missions before being killed in action.* 在陣亡之前他奉命執行過二百多次軍事任務。| *a space mission* 航天任務
2 ▶GOVERNMENT/GROUP 政府/團體◀ a group of important people who are sent by their government to another country to discuss something or collect information 代表團, 工作團; 外交使團: *a British trade mission to Moscow* 派往莫斯科的英國貿易代表團
3 ▶JOB 工作◀ an important job that someone has been given to do especially when they are sent to another place〔尤指給予被派遣人員的〕重要任務, 使命: *His mission was to improve staff morale and output.* 他的任務是鼓舞員工的士氣, 提高產量。
4 ▶DUTY 職責◀ something that you feel you must do because it is your duty 職責, 天職; 使命: **mission in life** *He always felt that his mission in life was to help old people.* 他總是認為幫助老年人是他的天職。
5 ▶RELIGION 宗教◀ a) the work of a religious leader or organization, that has gone to a foreign country, in order to teach people about Christianity or help poor people〔在國外進行基督教的〕傳教, 佈道: *After he trained as a priest he went to work for the missions in Africa.* 在受過牧師培訓後, 他前往非洲進行傳教活動。**b)** a building where this kind of work is done 佈道所用的建築物
6 mission accomplished used when you have finished a job that someone has asked or told you to do 任務已完成

M

mis·sion·a·ry /ˈmɪʃən,ɛrɪ; ˈmɪʃənəri/ *n* [C] someone who has been sent to a foreign country to teach people about Christianity and persuade them to become Christians〔被派到國外傳教的〕基督教傳教士: *She spent 20 years in Africa as a missionary.* 她在非洲做了20年傳教士。

missionary po·si·tion /ˈ···· ·,··/ *n* [singular] the sexual position in which the woman lies on her back with the man on top of her and facing her 傳教士式姿勢〔指男上女下的面對面性交姿勢〕

mission con·trol /,·· ˈ··/ *n* [singular] the people on earth who control, communicate with and guide a group of people on a space flight 航天地面指揮中心

mission state·ment /ˈ·· ,··/ *n* [C] a clear statement about the aims of a company or organization 任務說明

mis·sis /ˈmɪsɪz; ˈmɪsɨz/ *n* another spelling of MISSUS missus的另一種拼法

mis·sive /ˈmɪsɪv; ˈmɪsɪv/ *n* [C] *humorous* a letter【幽默】書信, 信件: *An anonymous missive had been pushed under her door.* 一封匿名信被人從她的門下面塞了進去。

mis·spell /mɪsˈspɛl; ,mɪsˈspel/ *v past tense and past participle* **misspelt** /-ˈspɛlt; -ˈspelt/ or 或 **misspelled** [T] to spell a word wrongly 拼寫錯〔單詞〕—**misspelling** *n* [C,U]

mis·spend /mɪsˈspɛnd; ,mɪsˈspend/ *v past tense and past participle* **misspent** /-ˈspɛnt; -ˈspent◂/ [T] **1 misspent youth** *often humorous* someone who had a misspent youth wasted their time or behaved badly when they were young【常幽默】虛度的青春 **2** to use time, money, etc badly, and not carefully or effectively 濫用〔時間、金錢等〕, 使用…不當

mis·step /ˈmɪs-stɛp; ˈmɪs-step/ *n* [C] *AmE* a mistake, especially one that is caused by not understanding a situation correctly【美】〔尤指判斷上的〕錯誤; 失策: *He has made a number of missteps over health care.* 在保健方面他已犯了許多錯誤。

mis·sus, missis /ˈmɪsəz; ˈmɪsɨz/ *n* [singular] **1** *informal* a man's wife【非正式】妻子, 老婆: *How's the missus?* 老婆好嗎? **2** *spoken, especially BrE* used when addressing a woman whose name you do not know【口, 尤英】太太〔用以稱呼不知其名的婦女〕: *Hey, missus, are these your kids?* 喂, 太太, 這些孩子是你的嗎?

mist¹ /mɪst; mɪst/ *n* **1** [C,U] a light cloud low over the ground that makes it difficult for you to see very far 薄霧, 霧靄: *We could just see the outline of the house through the mist.* 透過薄霧我們只能看到房子的輪廓。—compare 比較 FOG¹ (1) —see picture on page A13 參見A13頁圖 **2** [singular] air that is filled with very small drops of a particular liquid 充滿霧狀液體的空氣: *a treatment for asthma in the form of an aerosol mist* 哮喘病的氣霧劑吸入療法 **3 lost in the mists of time** if something such as a fact or secret is lost in the mists of time, no one remembers it because it happened so long ago 淹沒在時間的迷霧中〔指某事因發生的時間太久已沒人能記起〕: *The real reasons for the war are now lost in the mists of time.* 那場戰爭爆發的真正起因現在已隨着時間的推移而被人遺忘了。

mist² *v* [T] to cover something with very small drops of liquid in order to keep it wet 使…蒙上霧氣〔以保持濕潤〕: *The plant has to be misted every day.* 這棵植物必須每天噴水。

mist over *phr v* [I] **1** if someone's eyes mist over, they become filled with tears〔眼睛因充滿淚水而〕變得模糊不清: *His eyes misted over at the memory of his wife.* 想起妻子, 他變得淚眼模糊。**2** to mist up 蒙上水蒸氣

mist up *phr v* [I,T] if a piece of glass mists up or if something mists it up, it becomes covered with very small drops of water so that you cannot see through it〔玻璃〕蒙上水蒸氣; 使〔玻璃〕蒙上水蒸氣: *I can't see where I'm going, the windows have misted up.* 我看不清我在往哪兒走, 車窗蒙上了水汽。

mis·take¹ /məˈstek; mɨˈsteɪk/ *n* [C]

1 ►INCORRECT ACTION/OPINION ETC 不正確的行為/看法等◄ something that has been done incorrectly, or an opinion or statement that is incorrect 錯誤的行為; 錯誤的看法[陳述]; 誤會: *Hitting the ball too hard in golf is a typical beginner's mistake.* 擊球過猛是高爾夫球初學者易犯的典型錯誤。| **make a mistake** *I think you've made a mistake – this isn't my coat.* 我想你弄錯了 — 這不是我的大衣。| **there must be some mistake** (=used when you think someone has made a mistake) 一定是弄錯了 *There must be some mistake – I already paid my hotel bill.* 一定是弄錯了 — 旅館的賬我已經付清了。| **learn from your mistakes** (=learn how to do something correctly by doing it the wrong way first) 從錯誤中吸取教訓 —see graph at 參見 ERROR 圖表

2 by mistake if you do something by mistake, you do it without intending to 錯誤地〔並非故意〕: *Someone must have left the door open by mistake.* 一定是有人疏忽忘了關門。

3 ►STUPID ACTION 愚蠢的行為◄ something unwise or stupid that someone does, which they regret doing afterwards 不明智的行為; 愚蠢的失誤[失策]: *Buying the house seemed a great idea at the time, but now I can see it was a mistake.* 買那座房子當時好像是一個很棒的主意, 但現在我才明白那是一次失策。| **make a mistake** *It's your decision, but I warn you – you're making a mistake.* 這是你的決定, 但我要警告你 — 你在做傻事。| **big mistake** *Marrying him was the biggest mistake she ever made.* 嫁給他是她最大的失誤。| **make the mistake of doing sth** *I stupidly made the mistake of giving them my phone number.* 我真蠢, 居然把我的電話號碼給了他們。| **it is a mistake to do sth** *It would be a mistake to underestimate the amount of support for his victims.* 低估他的受害者所得到的支持是不明智的。

4 ►IN SPEECH OR WRITING 在言語或文字中◄ something that is said or written incorrectly, for example in a piece of school work 錯誤: *Ivan's work is always full of mistakes.* 伊凡的作業總是錯誤滿篇。| **make a mistake** *At this level, students tend to make a lot of basic mistakes.* 學生在這個階段往往會犯許多基本錯誤。| **spelling mistake** *There are a lot of spelling mistakes in this letter.* 這封信中有許多拼寫錯誤。

5 we all make mistakes *spoken* used when telling someone not to be worried because they have made a mistake【口】我們都有出錯的時候, 人誰無過

6 make no mistake (about it) *spoken* used to emphasize what you are saying, especially when you are warning someone【口】(對這一點) 不要有半點懷疑, 完全可以肯定〔用以強調, 尤在警告某人時〕: *He'll get his revenge, make no mistake about it!* 他會報復, 這完全可以肯定!

7 and no mistake *spoken* used to show that you are very certain about something that you have just said【口】毫無疑問, 的確: *Miles was a heartbreaker, and no mistake!* 邁爾斯的確是一個令人傷心的人! —compare 比較 ERROR

mistake² *past tense* **mistook** /mɪsˈtʊk; mɨˈstʊk/ *past participle* **mistaken** /məˈstekən; mɨˈsteɪkən/ *v* [T] **1** to understand something wrongly 弄錯, 誤解, 誤會: *Ken mistook her concern, thinking she was interested in him for another reason.* 肯誤解了她的關心, 認為她對他感興趣是另有原因。| *She mistook my meaning entirely.* 她完全誤解了我的意思。**2 you can't mistake sb/sth** used to say that someone or something is very easy to recognize 你不會認錯某人/某物: *You can't mistake her. She's the one with the long red hair.* 你不會認錯人的, 她就是那個留着紅色長髮的人。**3 there is no mistaking sb/sth** used to say that you are certain about something 決不可能搞錯某人/某物: *There's no mistaking whose children they are – they all look just like Joe.* 他們是誰的孩子一清二楚 — 他們長得都很像喬。

mistake sb/sth **for** sb/sth *phr v* [T] to think that one person or thing is someone or something else 把〔某人/某物〕誤認為〔他人/他物〕: *I mistook the poor woman for my sister.* 我把那個可憐的女人誤認為是我姐姐。| *The doctor mistook the symptoms for blood poisoning.* (=and it was something else) 醫生把那些症狀誤診為血中毒。

mis·tak·en /məˋstekən; mɪ̇ˈsteɪkən/ *adj* **1** [not before noun 不用於名詞前] someone who is mistaken is wrong about something〔人〕弄錯的: **be mistaken** *I thought I saw her at the movies but I guess I was mistaken.* 我以為我在電影院裡看到了她, 但現在想來我是弄錯了。**2 mistaken idea/belief/impression etc** a mistaken belief etc is not correct or is based on bad judgment 錯誤[基於錯誤判斷]的想法/信念/印象等: *Marijuana has few withdrawal effects, and this has given rise to the mistaken belief that it is not addictive.* 由於脱癮症狀很少, 人們錯誤地認為大麻不會使人上癮。**3 a case of mistaken identity** a situation in which someone believes that they have seen a particular person taking part in a crime, when in fact it was someone else 認錯人的情況: *The police arrested her but it turned out to be a case of mistaken identity.* 警察逮捕了她, 但結果發現是張冠李戴, 弄錯了人。—**mistakenly** *adv*

mis·ter /ˋmɪstɚ; ˈmɪstə/ *n* **1 Mister** the full form of MR 先生〔Mr的全拼形式〕**2** *spoken especially AmE* used to address a man whose name you do not know【口, 尤美】先生〔用以稱呼不知其名的男子〕: *Hey, mister, you dropped your paper.* 喂, 先生, 你的報紙掉了。

mis·time /mɪsˋtaɪm; ˌmɪsˈtaɪm/ *v* [T] to do something at the wrong time or at an unsuitable time 在錯誤[不適當]的時候做: *We mistimed a scene where a door slams in my face and I ended up with a broken nose.* 門在我面前砰的關上的那個場景, 我們沒掌握好時間, 結果我的鼻子碰破了。

mis·tle·toe /ˋmɪslˌto; ˈmɪsəltəʊ/ *n* [U] a plant with small white berries, which grows over other trees, and is often used as a decoration at Christmas 槲寄生

mis·took /mɪsˋtʊk; mɪ̇ˈstʊk/ the past tense of MISTAKE (2)

mis·tral /ˋmɪstrəl; ˈmiːstrɑːl/ *n* [singular] a strong cold dry wind that blows from the north into the south of France 密史脱拉風〔從北方吹到法國南部的乾冷的強風〕

mis·tress /ˋmɪstrɪs; ˈmɪstrɪ̇s/ *n* [C] **1** a woman that a man has a sexual relationship with even though he is married to someone else 情婦: *The Prince had shocked society by living openly with his mistress.* 王子和他的情婦公開生活在一起, 使社會大為震驚。**2** *BrE old-fashioned* a female teacher【英, 過時】女教師: *the new English mistress* 新來的女英語教師 **3** the female owner of a dog, horse etc〔狗、馬等的〕女主人 **4** *old-fashioned* the female employer of a servant【過時】〔僕人的〕女雇主, 女主人: *You'll have to deal with the mistress of the house.* 你將不得不和家中的女主人打交道。**5 be mistress of** if a woman is a mistress of something she is in control of it, highly skilled at it etc〔婦女〕控制着…; 是…的能手: *She appeared to be very much the mistress of the situation.* 她似乎很好地控制着局面。**6 Mistress** *old use* used with a woman's family name as a polite way of addressing her【舊】夫人; 小姐〔對女子的禮貌稱呼, 置於女子的姓之前〕—compare 比較 MASTER¹ (1)

mis·tri·al /mɪsˋtraɪəl; ˌmɪsˈtraɪəl/ *n* [C] a trial during which a mistake in the law is made, so that a new trial has to be held 無效審判

mis·trust¹ /mɪsˋtrʌst; mɪsˈtrʌst/ *n* [U] the feeling that you cannot trust someone, especially because you think they may treat you unfairly or dishonestly 不信任: **[+of]** *He had a deep mistrust of the legal profession.* 他對司法界很不信任。—compare 比較 DISTRUST¹

mistrust² *v* [T] to not trust someone, especially because you think they may treat you unfairly or dishonestly 不信任, 不相信: *As a very small child she had learned to mistrust adults.* 她很小的時候就學會了不相信大人。—compare 比較 DISTRUST² —**mistrustful** *adj*: *Some people are very mistrustful of computerised banking.* 有些人非常信不過電腦化的銀行業務。—**mistrustfully** *adv*

mist·y /ˋmɪstɪ; ˈmɪsti/ *adj* **mistier, mistiest 1** misty weather is weather with a lot of mist 多霧的: *The forecast says it will be wet and misty tomorrow.* 天氣預報説明天潮濕、多霧。**2** *literary* full of tears【文】淚汪汪的: *Her eyes became misty.* 她雙眼變得淚汪汪的。**3** not clear or bright 不清楚的, 朦朧的, 模糊的: *Without my glasses everything is just a misty blur.* 如果我不戴眼鏡, 甚麼都是模模糊糊的。

mis·un·der·stand /ˌmɪsʌndɚˋstænd; ˌmɪsʌndəˈstænd/ *v past tense and past participle* **misunderstood** [I,T] to think that something means one thing when in fact it means something different 誤解, 誤會: *I don't think we should be seen travelling together – people might misunderstand.* 我認為我們不應該被人看到在一起旅行——人們會誤解的。

mis·un·der·stand·ing /ˌmɪsʌndɚˋstændɪŋ; ˌmɪsʌndəˈstændɪŋ/ *n* **1** [C,U] a problem caused by someone not understanding a question, situation, or instruction correctly 誤解, 誤會: *I think there must have been some misunderstanding. I didn't order all these books.* 我想準是出了點誤會, 我並沒有訂購所有這些書。**2** [C] an argument or disagreement that is not very serious 爭執; 不和: *We had a little misunderstanding with our neighbors last night.* 昨天晚上我們和鄰居發生了一點小爭執。

mis·use¹ /mɪsˋjuz; ˌmɪsˈjuːz/ *v* [T] **1** to use something in the wrong way or for the wrong purpose 錯用, 誤用; 把…派作不當的用途: *The term schizophrenia is often misused.* 精神分裂症這個術語經常被誤用。**2** to treat someone badly or unfairly 虐待, 苛待

mis·use² /mɪsˋjus; mɪsˈjuːs/ *n* [C,U] the use of something in the wrong way or for the wrong purpose 錯用, 誤用; 濫用: *a system designed to prevent credit card misuse* 為防止信用卡錯用而設計的系統 | *the misuse of power* 濫用權力

mite /maɪt; maɪt/ *n* [C] **1** a very small insect that lives in plants, carpets etc 螨蟲 **2** a small child, especially one that you feel sorry for〔尤指令人憐憫的〕小孩: *Poor mite! You must be starving!* 可憐的小傢伙！你一定是餓壞了！**3 a mite shy/boring/nervous etc** slightly shy, boring, nervous etc 有點害羞/枯燥/緊張等 **4 a mite of** *old-fashioned* a small amount【過時】一點點, 少量

mit·i·gate /ˋmɪtəˌget; ˈmɪtɪ̇geɪt/ *v* [T] *formal* to make a situation or the effects of something less unpleasant, harmful, or serious【正式】減輕, 緩解, 緩和: *Measures need to be taken to mitigate the environmental effects of burning more coal.* 需要採取措施以減輕燃燒更多的煤對環境造成的影響。

mit·i·gat·ing /ˋmɪtəˌgetɪŋ; ˈmɪtɪ̇geɪtɪŋ/ *adj* **mitigating circumstances/factors etc** facts about a situation that make a crime or bad mistake seem less serious 可使罪行[嚴重錯誤]減輕的情節/因素等: *a reduced prison sentence due to mitigating circumstances* 因情有可原而被縮短的刑期

mit·i·ga·tion /ˌmɪtəˋgeʃən; ˌmɪtɪ̇ˈgeɪʃən/ *n* [U] **1 in mitigation** *law* if you say something in mitigation, you try to make someone's crime or mistake seem less serious or show that they were not completely responsible【法律】為了減輕罪責: *The captain added, in mitigation, that the engines may have been faulty.* 船長為減輕罪責補充説, 也許發動機出了毛病。**2** *formal* a reduction in how unpleasant, harmful, or serious a situation is【正式】減輕, 緩和: *His marriage had brought slight mitigation of the monotony of his existence.* 結婚稍微緩解了一下他單調乏味的生活。

mi·tre *BrE*【英】, **miter** *AmE*【美】/ˋmaɪtɚ; ˈmaɪtə/ *n* [C] **1** a tall pointed hat worn by BISHOPS and ARCHBISHOPS 主教冠〔主教和大主教戴的一種尖頂高帽〕**2** also 又作 **mitre joint** a joint between two pieces of wood, in which each piece is cut at an angle 斜接口, 斜面接頭, 斜榫

mitt /mɪt; mɪt/ *n* [C] **1** a type of GLOVE that does not have separate parts for each finger; MITTEN 連指手套, 獨指手套 **2** a GLOVE made of thick material, worn to protect your hand 防護手套: *an oven mitt* 烤箱防護手套 | *ski mitts* 滑雪防護手套 **3** a type of leather GLOVE used to catch a ball in BASEBALL 棒球手套 —see picture on page A22 參見 A22 頁圖 **4** *informal, especially BrE* someone's hand【非正式, 尤英】手: *Robert's put his sticky mitts all over it.* 羅伯特用他黏乎乎的雙手捂了個嚴實。

mit·ten /ˈmɪtn̩; ˈmɪtn/ *n* [C] a type of GLOVE that does not have separate parts for each finger 連指手套, 獨指手套 —see picture at 參見 GLOVE 圖

2 3 **mix**[1] /mɪks; mɪks/ *v* **1** [I,T] if you mix two or more substances or if they mix, they combine to become a single substance, and they cannot be easily separated (使)混合, 拌和: *Mix the blue and yellow paint to make green.* 把藍色和黃色顏料混成綠色。| *Oil and water don't mix.* 油和水不交融。| **mix sth together/in etc** *First mix the butter and sugar together, then add the milk.* 先把黃油和糖攪拌好, 然後加牛奶。| **mix sth with sth** *Shake the bottle well so that the oil mixes with the vinegar.* 使勁兒晃動瓶子, 使油和醋混合。—see picture on page A11 參見 A11 頁圖 **2** [I,T] to combine two or more different activities, ideas, groups of things etc (使)結合: **mix sth with sth** *His books mix historical fact with fantasy.* 他的書把史實和想像結合在一起。| **mix business with pleasure** (=combine business and social activities at the same time) 使工作和娛樂相結合 **3 not mix** if two different ideas, activities etc do not mix, they are not suitable for each other and cause problems when they are combined 不相協調, 不相容: *We all know that drink, drugs and knives do not mix.* 我們都知道酒、毒品和刀子不能在一塊。**4** [T] to prepare something, especially food or drink, by mixing things together 調製, 配製: *Will you mix us some martinis, Bill?* 比爾, 給我們調製幾杯馬丁尼酒好嗎? **5** [I] to enjoy meeting, talking, and spending time with other people, especially people you do not know very well〔尤指與不相熟的人〕相處, 交往, 交際: **[+with]** *Charlie doesn't mix well with the other children.* 查利與其他孩子合不來。**6** [T] *technical* to control the balance of sounds in a record or film【術語】〔在製作唱片或影片時〕調諧, 混錄〔聲音〕**7 mix and match** to try wearing different pieces of clothing together to see whether they look good 混合着搭配〔不同的衣服〕**8 mix it (up) with** to argue or threaten to fight with someone 與…爭吵; 威脅要與…打架: *You don't want to mix it with him. He's been drinking since noon.* 你別去和他爭吵, 他從中午就一直在喝酒。

mix sb/sth ↔ **up** *phr v* [T] **1** [**mix** sb/sth ↔ **up**] to make the mistake of thinking that someone or something is another person or thing 混淆, 弄混〔人或物〕: **[+with]** *I always mix him up with his brother. They look so much alike.* 我總是把他和他的弟弟弄混, 他們長得太相像了。**2** [**mix** sth ↔ **up**] to change the way things have been arranged, often by mistake, so that they are no longer in the same order 弄亂〔某物〕: *Don't mix up those papers, or we'll never find the ones we need.* 別把那些文件搞亂了, 否則的話我們將永遠找不到所需要的文件。**3** [**mix** sb **up**] to make someone feel confused 使糊塗: *They kept trying to mix me up.* 他們一直想要把我弄糊塗。—see also 另見 MIXED UP, MIX-UP

mix[2] *n* **1** [singular] the particular combination of things or people that form a group 混合; 混合體: **[+of]** *There's a real mix of ethnic groups in that area of the city.* 在該城市的那個地區有許多不同民族雜居在一起。| *We have to come up with a mix of policies to please the voters.* 我們必須提出一套兼容並蓄的政策來取悅選民。**2** [C,U] a combination of substances that you mix together to make something such as a cake〔做蛋糕等用的〕混合配料: **cake/soup etc mix** *Add water to the cake mix and cook at 375°.* 往蛋糕混合料裡加水, 然後以375度的溫度烘烤。

2 **mixed** /mɪkst; mɪkst/ *adj* **1** [only before noun 僅用於名詞前] consisting of many different types of things or people 混合的, 混雜的: *The doctor suggested a mixed diet of fruits and vegetables.* 醫生建議水果蔬菜搭配着吃。| *a mixed race community* 不同種族混雜的居民區 **2 mixed reaction/response/reviews etc** if something gets a mixed reaction etc, some people say they like it or agree with it, but others dislike it or disagree with it 多種不同的反應/回應/評論等: *The film has had mixed reviews from the critics.* 這部電影得到了評論家們褒貶不一的評價。**3 have mixed emotions/feelings about** to be unsure about whether you like or agree with something or someone 對…懷有複雜[矛盾]的感情: *I must admit I have rather mixed feelings about my brother's new wife.* 我必須承認, 我對新嫂子確實說不上喜歡還是不喜歡。**4** *especially BrE* for both males and females【尤英】男女混合的: *a mixed school* 男女生兼收的學校 **5 a mixed blessing** something that is good in some ways but bad in others 利弊兼有的事物: *Having your parents living nearby is a mixed blessing.* 父母住在附近有利也有弊。**6 a mixed bag** a group of things or people that are all very different from each other 混合體, 大雜燴: **[+of]** *The concert was a mixed bag of classical and modern music.* 那場音樂會是古典音樂和現代音樂的大雜燴。**7 in mixed company** when you are with people of both sexes 在男女都有的場合: *It's not the sort of joke you tell in mixed company.* 這不是那種可以在男女都有的場合講的笑話。

mixed a·bil·i·ty /ˌ· ˈ····◂/ *adj* [only before noun 僅用於名詞前] a mixed ability school or class teaches all children of the same age together, even if they have different levels of ability〔學校或班級〕學生年齡相同但程度參差不齊的

mixed doub·les /ˌ· ˈ··/ *n* [U] a game in a sport such as tennis in which a man and a woman play against another man and woman 混合雙打

mixed e·con·o·my /ˌ· ·ˈ···/ *n* [C] *technical* an economic system in which some industries are owned by the government and some are owned by private companies【術語】〔包括公有制和私有制的〕混合經濟

mixed farm·ing /ˌ· ˈ··/ *n* [U] a system of farming in which you grow crops and keep animals〔既種莊稼又養牲畜的〕混合農業

mixed grill /ˌ· ˈ·/ *n* [C] *BrE* a dish consisting of meats such as SAUSAGE, BACON, LIVER etc which have all been grilled (GRILL[1] (1))【英】烤雜排, 什錦烤肉

mixed mar·riage /ˌ· ˈ··/ *n* [C,U] a marriage between two people from different races or religions 異族[異教]通婚

mixed up /ˌ· ˈ·◂/ *adj* **1 be mixed up in** to be involved in an illegal or dishonest activity 被捲入, 被牽連到…中: *He's the last person I'd expect to be mixed up in something like this.* 我認為他最不可能牽涉到這樣的事情中。**2 be mixed up with** to be involved with someone who has a bad influence on you 與〔行為不良者〕交往, 與…廝混: *When he left college he got mixed up with the wrong people.* 離開大學後, 他結交了一些不三不四的人。**3** [not before noun 不用於名詞前] confused, for example because you have too many different details to remember or think about 困惑的, 糊塗的, 頭腦混亂的: *I get all mixed up over the money whenever I travel abroad.* 每次在國外旅行, 對錢的事我總是弄不清楚。**4** *informal* confused and suffering from emotional problems【非正式】情感錯亂的, 感情迷茫的: *She's just a crazy mixed up kid.* 她只是一個瘋狂而迷茫的孩子。—see also 另見 **mix up** (MIX[1]), MIX-UP

mix·er /ˈmɪksɚ; ˈmɪksə/ *n* [C] **1** a piece of kitchen equipment used to mix flour, sugar, butter etc together 食品攪拌器, 攪拌機: *an electric food mixer* 電動食品攪拌器 **2** a drink that can be mixed with alcohol, especially to make a COCKTAIL 調酒〔尤指調製雞尾酒〕用的飲料: *We can use tonic water or orange juice as mixers.* 我們可以用奎寧水或橘子汁來調酒。**3 a good/bad mixer** someone who finds it easy or difficult to make friends with people and talk to strangers 善於/不善於交際的人 **4** someone whose job is to control the sound when making a record or tape of a piece of music, or to control the quality of the picture when making a film 調音技術員;〔電影〕畫面質量負責人 **5** *AmE old-fashioned* a party held so that people who have just met can get to know each other better【美, 過時】交誼會: *Are you going to the freshman mixer?* 你去參加新生交誼會嗎?

mix·ing bowl /ˈ·· ·/ *n* [C] a large bowl used for mixing things such as flour and sugar for making cakes 攪拌碗

3 3 **mix·ture** /ˈmɪkstʃɚ; ˈmɪkstʃə/ *n* **1** [C] a combination of two or more people, things, feelings, or ideas that are different 混合; 混合體: *People are a mixture of good and evil.* 人集善惡於一身。| *the mixture of different people living in a city* 生活在一個城市中的形形色色的人的混合體 | *He looked at her with a mixture of amusement and despair.* 他既開心又絕望地看着她。**2** [C,U] a liquid or other substance made by mixing several substances together 混合液, 混合料: *Pour the cake mixture into the pan slowly and then bake on a low heat.* 把蛋糕混合料慢慢倒進鍋裡, 然後用低溫烘烤。**3** [C] *technical* a combination of substances that are put together but do not mix with each other【術語】混合物 —compare 比較 COMPOUND[1] **4** [U] *formal* the action of mixing things or the state of being mixed【正式】混合動作; 混合狀態

mix-up /ˈ· ·/ *n* [C] *informal* a mistake that causes confusion about details or arrangements【非正式】〔引起混亂的〕錯誤: *There was a mix-up over the reservations and we had to share a room.* 旅館預訂出了差錯, 我們不得不合住一個房間。

miz·zen /ˈmɪzən; ˈmɪzən/ *n* [C] **1** also 又作 **mizzen mast** the MAST behind the main mast on a sailing ship 後桅 **2** also 又作 **mizzen sail** the main sail set lengthways on a mizzen on a sailing ship 後桅縱帆

Mk the written abbreviation of 縮寫= MARK[2] (7)

ml the written abbreviation of 縮寫= MILLILITRE(*s*)

m'lady, milady /mɪˈledɪ; mɪˈleɪdi/ *n old use* a word used by a servant to address a woman who belongs to a NOBLE family【舊】夫人, 太太〔僕人對貴婦人的稱呼〕: *Will that be all, m'lady?* 夫人, 還有甚麼吩咐?

MLitt /ˌɛm ˈlɪt; ˌem ˈlɪt/ Master of Letters; a university degree that you can get at some British universities by studying for two years after your first degree 文學碩士

M'lord /mɪˈlɔrd; mḷˈlɔːd/ *n* **1** a word used to address a judge 大人, 閣下〔對法官的稱呼〕 **2** *old use* a word used by a servant to address a man who belongs to a NOBLE family【舊】老爺, 大人〔僕人對貴族紳士的稱呼〕

M'lud /məˈlʌd; mḷˈlʌd/ *n* used to address a judge in a British court of law (short for 'my lord') 大人, 閣下〔英國法庭上對法官的稱呼〕

mm[1] /m; m/ *interjection spoken* used when someone else is speaking and you want to show that you are listening or that you agree with them【口】姆〔表示在聆聽或贊同〕

mm[2] the written abbreviation of 縮寫= MILLIMETRE(*s*)

mne·mon·ic /nɪˈmɑnɪk; nɪˈmɒnɪk/ *n* something, such as a poem, or a sentence that you use to help you remember a rule, a name etc 幫助記憶的東西〔如詩歌或句子〕 **—mnemonic** *adj* **—mnemonically** /-klɪ; -kli/ *adv*

MO /ˌɛm ˈo; ˌem ˈəʊ/ *n informal*【非正式】**1** [C] *especially BrE* medical officer; an army doctor【尤英】醫官, 軍醫 **2** [singular] modus operandi; a way of doing something that is typical of one person or a group 典型的做事方式, 一慣的做法; 慣技

mo /mo; məʊ/ *n* [singular] *BrE spoken* a very short period of time; MOMENT (2)【英口】極短的時間, 一會兒: *Wait a mo!* 等一會兒!

mo. *AmE*【美】the written abbreviation for 縮寫= MONTH

moan[1] /mon; məʊn/ *v* **1** [I] to make a long low sound expressing pain, unhappiness, or sexual pleasure 呻吟, 嗚咽, 哼哼: *The sick child moaned a little and then fell asleep.* 那個生病的小孩呻吟了一會兒後睡着了。**2** [I,T] *BrE informal* to complain in an annoying way, especially in an unhappy voice and without good reason【英, 非正式】抱怨, 發牢騷: *You've done nothing but moan all day.* 你甚麼也沒幹, 整天在發牢騷。| **[+at]** *My mum never stops moaning at me.* 我媽總是沒完沒了地對我發牢騷。| **[+that]** *He's always moaning that we use too much electricity.* 他總是抱怨我們用電太多。**3** [I] *literary* if the wind moans it makes a long low sound【文】〔風〕發出長而低的聲音, 發嗚咽聲: *She was awakened by the low moaning of the wind in the trees.* 樹林裡風聲嗚咽, 把她吵醒了。**—moaner** *n* [C]

moan[2] *n* [C] **1** a long low sound expressing pain, unhappiness, or sexual pleasure 呻吟聲; 嗚咽聲: *There was a moan of pain from the injured man.* 那個受傷的男子痛苦地呻吟了一聲。| **give a moan** *She gave a little moan of pleasure.* 她快活地輕輕呻吟了一聲。**2 have a moan** *BrE informal* to complain about something【英, 非正式】抱怨: *We were just having a moan about work.* 我們只是在抱怨工作。**3** *literary* a low sound made by the wind【文】〔風的〕嗚咽聲, 蕭蕭聲

moat /mot; məʊt/ *n* [C] **1** a deep wide hole, usually filled with water, around a castle or fort as a defence 護城河, 城壕 **2** a deep wide hole dug around an area used for animals in a zoo to stop them from escaping〔動物園為防止動物逃跑而在其場地四周挖的〕深溝 **—moated** *adj*

mob[1] /mɑb; mɒb/ *n* [C] **1** a large, noisy crowd, especially one that is angry and violent 成羣的暴民[亂民]; 烏合之眾: *a mob of demonstrators* 一幫示威者 | **mob rule** (=when a mob controls the situation rather than the government or the law) 暴民統治 **2** *informal* a group of people of the same type【非正式】同類的一羣人: *The usual mob of teenagers were standing on the corner.* 那幫常來的少年正站在拐角處。**3 the Mob** the MAFIA (=a powerful organization of criminals) 黑手黨 **4 the mob** *old use* an insulting expression meaning all the poorest and least educated people in society【舊】最窮且受教育最少的民眾, 下層民眾, 賤民〔侮辱性用詞〕**5 a mob of sheep/cattle** *AustrE, NZE* a large group of sheep or cattle【澳, 新西蘭】一大羣羊/牛

mob[2] *v* **mobbed, mobbing** [T] to form a crowd around someone in order to express admiration or to attack them 圍住; 圍攻: *The actress was mobbed by doting fans.* 那位女演員被崇拜她的影迷圍住了。

mob cap /ˈ· ·/ *n* [C] a light cotton hat with a decorative edge, worn by women in the 18th and 19th centuries〔18 和 19 世紀〕帶裝飾邊的女帽

mo·bile[1] /ˈmobḷ; ˈməʊbaɪl/ *adj* **1** able to move or travel easily 行動方便的: *She's more mobile now that she has her own car.* 有了自己的小汽車, 她現在行動方便多了。**2** not fixed in one position, and easy to move and use in different places 移動式的; 活動的; 可動的: *mobile air-conditioners* 移動式空調器 **3 mobile library/shop/clinic etc** *BrE* a shop etc that is kept in a vehicle and driven from place to place【英】流動圖書館/商店/診所等 **4** tending to move or able to move from one social class, job, or place to another〔在不同社會階層、職業或地區之間〕流動的: *People these days are much more socially mobile.* 如今人們的社會地位變化得快多了。**5 mobile face/features** a face that can change its expression quickly 表情多變的臉 —see also 另見 IMMOBILE, UPWARDLY MOBILE

mo·bile[2] /ˈmobil; ˈməʊbaɪl/ *n* [C] **1** a decoration made of small objects tied to wires or string and hung up so that the objects move when air blows around them〔懸掛在繩索等上的〕風動小飾物 **2** a MOBILE PHONE 移動電話

mobile home /ˌ·· ˈ·/ *n* [C] **1** *AmE* a type of house that looks like an ordinary house but can be moved to another place【美】活動房屋 **2** *BrE* a large CARAVAN which stays permanently in one place and is used as a house【英】〔永久地安置在某一地點的〕拖車式活動住房; TRAILER (1) *AmE*【美】

mobile phone /ˌ‥ ˈ·/ *n* [C] a telephone that you can carry with you and use in any place 流動電話, 移動電話

mobile phone
流動電話

mo·bil·i·ty /moˈbɪlətɪ; məʊˈbɪləti/ *n* [U] **1** the ability to move easily from one job, place to live, or social class to another 流動性; 易變性: **social/job mobility** *In America, social mobility is an everyday reality.* 在美國, 所屬社會階層的變動是很普通的事。**2** the ability to move easily from place to place 活動性, 機動性: *Arthritis restricted his mobility.* 關節炎限制了他的活動。| *The key to the Army's effectiveness is its increased mobility.* 增強軍隊戰鬥力的關鍵是提高其機動性。

mo·bil·ize also 又作 **-ise** *BrE*【英】/ˈmoblˌaɪz; ˈməʊbəlaɪz/ *v* **1** [T] to bring people together so that they can all work to achieve something important 調動, 鼓動起; 召集: *to mobilize the rural population in a drive for self-sufficiency* 動員農村人口開展自給自足運動 **2 mobilize support/resources etc** to bring together the supporters, resources etc that you need and prepare them for action 爭取支持/動用資源等: *Owen was trying to mobilize support for a new political party.* 歐文正為一個新政黨爭取支持。**3** [I,T] if a country mobilizes or mobilizes its army, it prepares to fight a war〔國家軍事力量〕動員起來; 動員〔軍隊〕—see also 另見 DEMOBILIZE —**mobilization** /ˌmobləˈzeʃən; ˌməʊbəlaɪˈzeɪʃən/ *n* [C,U]

mob·ster /ˈmɑbstɚ; ˈmɒbstə/ *n* [C] *especially AmE* a member of an organized criminal group; GANGSTER【尤美】犯罪集團成員, 匪徒, 歹徒

moc·ca·sin /ˈmɑkəsn̩; ˈmɒkəsɪn/ *n* [C] a flat comfortable shoe made of soft leather 莫卡辛鞋, 軟皮平底鞋 —see picture at 參見 SHOE[1] 圖

moch·a /ˈmokə; ˈmɒkə/ *n* [U] **1** a type of coffee 穆哈咖啡, 莫加咖啡 **2** *AmE* a combination of coffee and chocolate【美】咖啡巧克力調味料

mock- /mɑk; mɒk/ *prefix* **1** only pretendingly 假裝地: *a mock-serious expression* 假裝嚴肅的表情 **2** not real 非真實的, 假的; 仿製的: *a mock-Tudor fireplace* 仿都鐸式壁爐

mock[1] /mɑk; mɒk/ *v* **1** [I,T] *formal* to laugh at someone or something and try to make them look stupid by making unkind remarks about them or by copying them; make fun of【正式】嘲笑, 譏笑, 嘲弄;〔以模仿〕取笑: **mock sth/sb** *They have insulted us and mocked our religion.* 他們侮辱了我們, 還嘲笑我們的宗教。| ***It's easy for you to mock, but we put a lot of work into this play.*** 你講風涼話是不用費力氣的, 但我們卻在這齣戲中費了很大力氣。| *mocking laughter* 嘲弄的笑聲 **2** [T] *formal* to make something seem completely useless【正式】使無效; 使失敗, 挫敗: *His silence mocked her efforts to start a conversation.* 他的沉默使她搭訕的努力歸於失敗。—**mocker** *n* [C] —**mockingly** *adv*: *His lips twisted mockingly.* 他嘲弄地噘了噘嘴。

mock sth ↔ up *phr v* [T] to make a full-size model of something so that it looks real〔照原尺寸〕模仿, 仿製 —see also 另見 MOCK-UP

mock[2] *adj* [only before noun 僅用於名詞前] **1** not real, but intended to be very similar to a real situation, substance etc 非真實的; 模擬的: *war games with mock battles* 模擬戰爭的遊戲 | *a mock interview* 模擬面試 **2 mock surprise/horror/indignation etc** surprise etc that you pretend to feel, especially as a joke 假裝的吃驚/害怕/憤怒等〔尤指開玩笑〕: *He pulled at his hair in mock distress.* 他撕扯着頭髮, 假裝很痛苦。**3 mock Tudor/Georgian** copying the style of Tudor or Georgian buildings 仿都鐸/喬治王朝建築風格的

mock[3] *n* **1 mocks** [plural] *BrE* school examinations taken as practice before official examinations【英】模擬考試 **2 make mock of** *literary* to mock someone【文】嘲笑; 嘲弄: *He makes mock of my dreams.* 他嘲笑我的夢想。

mock·ers /ˈmɑkɚz; ˈmɒkəz/ *n* [plural] **put the mockers on** *BrE informal* to spoil an event or someone's plans【英, 非正式】挫敗, 使告吹, 使成功無望: *Oh well, if you've got the car that puts the mockers on my plans to go out!* 算了吧, 既然你買了那輛車, 我旅遊的計劃就吹了!

mock·e·ry /ˈmɑkərɪ; ˈmɒkəri/ *n* **1 make a mockery of** to make something such as a plan, system, or organization seem completely useless or ineffective 使…顯得無用[無效]: *The continued flouting of Security Council resolutions is making a mockery of the UN.* 繼續違反安理會決議的行為使聯合國形同虛設。**2** [U] a feeling or attitude of laughing at someone or something or of trying to make them seem completely stupid 嘲笑, 愚弄: *There was an element of mockery in the politeness he showed the inspector.* 他對那位督察員所表現出來的客套帶有一種嘲弄的成分。**3** [singular] something that is completely useless or ineffective 無用的東西; 無效的東西: *The driving test was a mockery as a test of real driving skill.* 那次駕駛測試根本不能測定實際駕駛技術。

mock·ing·bird /ˈmɑkɪŋˌbɝd; ˈmɒkɪŋbɜːd/ *n* [C] an American bird that copies the songs of other birds 嘲鶇〔一種產於美國的鳥, 能模仿其他鳥的叫聲〕

mock tur·tle /ˌ· ˈ‥/ *n* [C] *AmE* a shirt or SWEATER with a high, close-fitting band around the neck【美】高領衫; 高領毛衣; TURTLENECK *BrE*【英】—see picture on page A17 參見 A17 頁圖

mock-up /ˈ· ·/ *n* [C] a full-size model of something that is going to be made or built, which shows how it will look〔原尺寸〕實體模型: *a mock-up of the space shuttle* 航天飛機實體模型 —see also 另見 **mock up** (MOCK[1])

mod /mɑd; mɒd/ *n* [C] *BrE* a member of a group of young people in Britain in the 1960s who wore a particular type of neat clothes, listened to SOUL MUSIC, and drove MOTOR SCOOTERS【英】摩登派成員〔指英國20世紀60年代穿着整潔時髦、聽靈歌並騎小摩托車的青少年幫派成員〕—compare 比較 ROCKER (3)

mo·dal[1] /ˈmodl̩; ˈməʊdl/ *n* [C] a modal verb 情態動詞

modal[2] *adj technical*【術語】**1** [only before noun 僅用於名詞前] related to the MOOD (6) of a verb〔動詞〕語氣的 **2** related to or written in a musical MODE (5)〔音樂〕調式的 —**modally** *adv*

modal aux·il·ia·ry /ˌ‥ ·ˈ‥·/ *n* [C] a modal verb 情態動詞

modal verb /ˌ‥ ˈ·/ *n* [C] *technical* one of these verb forms: can, could, may, might, shall, should, will, would, must, ought to, used to, need, had better, and DARE. They are all used with other verbs to change their meaning by expressing ideas such as possibility, permission, or intention【術語】情態動詞 —see also 另見 AUXILIARY VERB

mod cons /ˌmɑd ˈkɑnz; ˌmɒd ˈkɒnz/ *n* **all mod cons** *BrE informal* all the things that are fitted in modern houses to make life easy and comfortable【英, 非正式】〔家中的〕現代化生活設施: *a property with many interesting features and all mod cons* 一處風格多樣而有趣、現代化生活設施一應俱全的房產

mode /mod; məʊd/ *n* [C] **1** *formal* a particular way or style of behaving, living or doing something【正式】方式, 方法, 做法: *They have a relaxed mode of life that suits them well.* 他們過着一種很適合自己的悠閒生活。| *a highly efficient mode of transport* 高效的運輸方式 **2** *technical* a particular way in which a machine operates when it is doing a particular job【術語】〔機器的〕運行方式; 狀態, 模式: *a spacecraft in re-entry mode* 處於重返大氣層狀態中的航天器 | *To get out of the 'auto' mode*

on the camera, turn the knob to 'M'. 要退出相機的"自動"模式, 將旋鈕轉向M。**3 be in work mode/holiday mode etc** *informal* to be in a particular state of mind【非正式】思想上處於工作狀態/休假狀態等: *With only 10 minutes to go, we were now in panic mode.* 僅僅還剩下十分鐘, 我們此刻心裡很驚慌。**4 be the mode** *formal* to be fashionable at a particular time【正式】流行, 時髦: *Long skirts were then the latest mode.* 長裙當時最時興。**5** *technical* one of various systems of arranging notes in music, such as MAJOR and MINOR in Western music【術語】〔音樂的〕調式 —see also 另見 À LA MODE, MODISH

2 1 **mod·el**[1] /ˈmadl̩; ˈmɒdl/ *n* [C]
1 ►SMALL COPY 小的仿製物◄ a small copy of a building, vehicle, machine etc, especially one that can be put together from separate parts 模型: *He enjoys making airplane models.* 他喜歡製作飛機模型。| **[+of]** *They brought us a little model of the Taj Mahal.* 他們帶給我們一個泰姬陵小模型。| **working model** (=one in which the parts move) 工作模型 *a working model of a steam engine* 蒸汽機的工作模型
2 ►FASHION 時裝◄ someone whose job is to show clothes, hair styles etc by wearing them and being photographed 時裝模特兒: *a top fashion model* 高級時裝模特兒 | *a male model* 男服裝模特兒
3 ►ART 藝術◄ someone who is employed by an artist or photographer to be painted or photographed〔繪畫或攝影〕模特兒
4 ►GOOD/SPECIAL PERSON 優秀/特殊人物◄ someone you should imitate because of their good qualities or behaviour 模範, 典範, 榜樣: **[+of]** *As a politician, she was a model of integrity and decency.* 作為一名政治家, 她是誠實、正派的典範。| **role model** (=someone that you try to copy because they have qualities you would like to have)〔具有令人崇拜的品質而被仿效的〕楷模 *A woman teacher can become a role model for female students.* 女教師會成為女學生的行為榜樣。
5 ►GOOD/SUCCESSFUL THING 好/成功的事物◄ a way of doing something that is successful or useful and therefore worth copying〔因成功或有用而〕值得效仿的做事方式, 典範: **[+of]** *Scarman's report is a model of fairness and clarity.* 斯卡曼的報告是公正和明確的模範。| *The science of astronomy was developed first and became a model for the other sciences.* 天文學成熟得最早並成為其他科學的典範。
6 ►DESCRIPTION 描述◄ a simple description of a system or structure that is used to help people understand similar systems or structures〔幫助理解用的〕模型: *a computer model of the main factors determining a company's market share* 對決定公司市場份額的主要因素進行分析的電腦模型
7 ►TYPE OF CAR ETC 汽車等的型號◄ a particular type or design of a vehicle or machine 樣式, 型號: *the cheapest model in the Volkswagen range* 大眾[福士]汽車公司生產的汽車系列中最便宜的型號 | **latest model** (=the newest design produced by a company) 最新型產品 *Our dishwasher is the latest model.* 我們的洗碗機是最新型產品。

model[2] *adj* **1 model airplane/train/car etc** a small copy of an airplane etc, especially one that a child can play with or put together from separate parts〔尤指兒童可玩或拼裝的〕模型飛機/火車/汽車等 **2 model wife/employee/student etc** someone who behaves like a perfect wife, employee etc 模範妻子/雇員/學生等: *His lawyers tried to show him as a model husband and father.* 他的律師們竭力想證明他是一個模範丈夫、模範父親。**3 model prison/farm/school etc** a prison etc that has been specially designed or organized to be as good as possible 模範監獄/農場/學校等

model[3] *v* **modelled, modelling** *BrE*【英】, **modeled, modeling** *AmE*【美】**1** [I,T] to wear clothes in order to show them to possible buyers 當模特兒, 做模特兒向顧客展示〔服裝〕: *She's modeling Donna Karan's fall collection of skirts.* 她在為唐娜·可倫的秋季系列女裙展覽當模特兒。**2 model yourself on** to try to be like someone else because you admire them 以…為榜樣: *Jim had always modelled himself on his great hero, Martin Luther King.* 吉姆總是以他心目中的大英雄馬丁·路德·金為榜樣。**3 be modelled on** to be designed in a way that copies another system or way of doing something 模仿, 效仿; 仿製: *Their education system is modelled on the French one.* 他們的教育體制是模仿法國的。**4** [T] to make small objects from materials such as wood or clay 用〔木頭或泥巴等材料〕製作小物品, 塑造: *She was modeling the plasticine into little animal figures.* 她正在用橡皮泥捏製一些小動物。

mod·el·ling *BrE*【英】, **modeling** *AmE*【美】/ˈmadlɪŋ; ˈmɒdlɪŋ/ *n* [U] **1** the work of a MODEL[1] (2) 模特兒的職業: *a career in modelling* 模特兒職業生涯 **2** the activity of making model ships, planes, figures etc〔船隻、飛機、人物等的〕模型製作

mo·dem /ˈmoˌdɛm; ˈməʊdəm/ *n* [C] a piece of electronic equipment that allows information from one computer to be sent along telephone wires to another computer 調制解調器 —see picture on page A14 參見A14頁圖

mod·e·rate[1] /ˈmadərɪt; ˈmɒdər̩t/ *adj* **1** neither very big nor very small, very hot nor very cold, very fast nor very slow etc 中等的, 適度的: *Bake the pie for 30 minutes in a moderate oven.* 把餡餅在烤爐裡用中溫烘烤30分鐘。| *We're looking for a house with a moderate-sized garden.* 我們正在找一所帶中型花園的住房。| *a moderate degree of success* 中等程度的成功 | *a student of only moderate ability* 能力一般的學生 **2** having opinions, or beliefs especially about politics, that are not extreme and that most people consider reasonable or sensible 不極端的, 溫和的; 穩健的: *Her views represent the moderate wing of the party.* 她的觀點代表着該政黨中溫和派的觀點。| *a moderate politician* 溫和派政治家 **3** staying within reasonable or sensible limits 有節制的, 不過分的: *a moderate smoker* 吸煙有節制的人 | *moderate wage demands* 適度的工資要求 —see also 另見 MODERATELY

mod·e·rate[2] /ˈmadəˌret; ˈmɒdəreɪt/ *v* [I,T] **1** *formal* to make something less extreme or violent, or to become less extreme or violent【正式】(使)和緩; (使)減輕; 節制, 克制: *The students moderated their demands.* 學生們降低了他們的要求。| *We couldn't leave the harbour until the storm moderated.* 在暴風雨減弱之前我們無法離開港口。**2** *BrE* to do the work of a MODERATOR【英】做調解人; 做考試監督員; 做〔比賽等〕主持人

mod·e·rate[3] /ˈmadərɪt; ˈmɒdər̩t/ *n* [C] someone whose opinions or beliefs, especially about politics, are not extreme and are considered reasonable by most people 持溫和觀點的人, 溫和派人士: *Carter appointed moderates to the Supreme Court.* 卡特任命了一些溫和派法官到最高法院任職。

mod·e·rate·ly /ˈmadərɪtlɪ; ˈmɒdər̩tli/ *adv* fairly but not very 適度地; 不過分地; 有限地: *a moderately successful film* 一部還算成功的電影

mod·e·ra·tion /ˌmadəˈreʃən; ˌmɒdəˈreɪʃən/ *n* [U] **1 in moderation** if you do something in moderation, such as drinking alcohol or smoking, you do not do it too much〔飲酒或吸煙等〕有節制地, 適度地: *Some people think drinking in moderation is healthy.* 有些人認為適度飲酒對健康有益。**2** *formal* control of your behaviour, so that you keep your actions, feelings, habits etc within reasonable or sensible limits【正式】節制, 克制: **[+in]** *Moderation in diet is the way to good health.* 飲食有節制是保持身體健康的方法。**3** *formal* reduction in force, degree, speed etc【正式】緩和, 減輕: *Even after sunset there was little moderation in the temperature.* 甚至在日落之後氣溫也幾乎沒有降低。

mod·e·ra·to /ˌmadəˈrato; ˌmɒdəˈrɑːtəʊ/ *adj, adv* a word meaning at an average speed, used as an instruction on how fast to play a piece of music〔音樂演奏〕中速的[地]

mod·e·ra·tor /ˈmɑdə͵retɚ; ˈmɒdəreɪtə/ *n* [C] **1** someone whose job is to control a discussion or argument and to help people reach an agreement 仲裁人; 調解人 **2** *BrE* someone who makes sure that an examination is fair, and that the marks given are fair and correct【英】〔保證考試公正、判分正確的〕考試監督員 **3** someone who asks questions and keeps the marks of competing teams in a spoken game or competition〔問答比賽中提問題並記錄參賽隊分數的〕主席, 主持人 **4** a religious leader who is in charge of the council of the Presbyterian and United Reformed Churches〔主持長老會和聯合歸正會會議的〕議長

S1 W1 **mod·ern** /ˈmɑdɚn; ˈmɒdn/ *adj* **1** [only before noun 僅用於名詞前] time belonging to the present time or most recent time 現代的, 近代的: *a book about modern history* 一本關於現代史的書 | *Traditional treatments, once shunned by modern medicine, are now being examined scientifically.* 傳統療法曾一度備受現代醫學的冷落, 但現在又被納入科學研究。| *The original supermarkets were small by modern standards.* 按現代的標準來看, 最初的超級市場很小。**2** made or done using the most recent methods; UP-TO-DATE 現代化的; 新式的: *Their offices are in a modern 25-storey skyscraper.* 他們的辦公室在一幢 25 層高的現代化摩天大樓中。| *modern surgical techniques* 現代外科技術 **3** using or willing to use very recent ideas, fashions, or ways of thinking〔思想、時裝或思維方式〕時髦的, 摩登的, 新潮的: *The school is very modern in its approach to sex education.* 這所學校在性教育方法上非常開放。**4** [only before noun 僅用於名詞前] modern art, music, literature etc uses styles that have been recently developed and are very different from traditional styles〔藝術、音樂、文學等〕當代風格的, 現代派的: *Modern dance looks more spontaneous than traditional ballet.* 現代派舞蹈看起來比傳統芭蕾更自由奔放、無拘無束。**5 Modern Greek/Hebrew/English** the form of the Greek etc language that is used today 現代希臘語/希伯來語/英語 —see also 另見 SECONDARY MODERN

modern-day /ˈ·· ·/ *adj* [only before noun 僅用於名詞前] existing in the present time, but considered in relation to someone or something else in the past 現代的, 當代的: *She's a modern-day Joan of Arc.* 她是當代的聖女貞德。| *The modern-day diet has too little fiber in it.* 現代人們的飲食含纖維太少。

mod·ern·is·m /ˈmɑdɚn͵ɪzəm; ˈmɒdənɪzəm/ *n* [U] a style of art, building etc that was popular especially from the 1940s to the 1960s, in which artists used simple shapes and modern artificial materials〔20 世紀 40 年代至 60 年代藝術、建築等的〕現代主義, 現代派 —compare 比較 POST-MODERNISM —**modernist** *adj, n* [C]: *the modernist school* 現代派

mod·ern·ist·ic /͵mɑdɚˋnɪstɪk; ͵mɒdəˈnɪstɪk◂/ *adj* designed in a way that looks very modern and very different from previous styles〔外觀〕非常現代化的; 現代派的: *a modernistic office building* 外觀非常現代化的辦公大樓

mo·der·ni·ty /məˋdɝnɪtɪ; mɒˈdɜːnəti/ *n* [U] *formal* the quality of being modern【正式】現代性; 現代狀態: *a conflict between tradition and modernity* 傳統與現代的衝突

mod·ern·ize also 又作 **-ise** *BrE*【英】/ˈmɑdɚn͵aɪz; ˈmɒdənaɪz/ *v* **1** [T] to change something so that it is more suitable for the present time by using new equipment or methods 使現代化: *NATO is determined to modernize its ground forces.* 北約決心使其地面部隊現代化。| *a tastefully modernized old farmhouse* 雅緻而現代化的舊農場住宅 **2** [I] to start using more modern methods and equipment 採用現代方法和設備, 現代化: *The business will lose money if it doesn't modernize.* 該企業如果不現代化的話就要賠錢。—**modernization** /͵mɑdɚnəˋzeʃən; ͵mɒdənaɪˈzeɪʃən/ *n* [C,U]

modern lan·gua·ges /͵· ˈ···/ *n* [plural] *BrE* modern European languages, such as French or Italian, studied as a subject at school or university【英】現代語言〔指作為中小學或大學課程的現代歐洲語言, 如法語或意大利語〕

mod·est /ˈmɑdɪst; ˈmɒdɪst/ *adj* **1** unwilling to talk proudly about your abilities and achievements 謙虛的, 謙遜的, 謙恭的: **[+about]** *He was always surprisingly modest about his role in the Everest expedition.* 他對自己在那次珠穆朗瑪峯探險中所起的作用總是謙虛得令人驚訝。**2** not very big, expensive etc, especially less big, expensive etc than you would expect 不太大的; 不很貴的: *quite a modest salary for such an important job* 對如此重要的工作而言一點也不算高的薪水 | *his modest ambitions* 他的小小的抱負 | **a modest amount/improvement etc** *House prices rose by a modest amount in the last quarter.* 房價在最近一個季度中有輕微的增長。**3** shy about showing your body or attracting sexual interest, because you are easily embarrassed 羞怯的, 靦腆的; 忸怩的: *Children often become very modest at around age 11.* 小孩子常常在 11 歲左右的時候變得非常靦腆。**4** *old-fashioned* modest clothing covers the body in a way that does not attract sexual interest【過時】〔衣服〕莊重的: *a modest knee-length dress* 長至膝部、顯得莊重的連衣裙 —**modestly** *adv*

mod·es·ty /ˈmɑdəstɪ; ˈmɒdɪsti/ *n* [U] **1** a modest way of behaving or talking 謙虛, 謙遜, 謙恭: *the great player's modesty* 那位優秀選手的謙遜 **2 in all modesty** *spoken* used to say that you do not want to seem too proud of something you have done, when in fact you are【口】〔用於不失謙遜地承認自己的功勞〕: *I think in all modesty that I can take some small credit for the team's success.* 我不是要為自己請功, 但我認為球隊的成功有我一份小小的功勞。**3** unwillingness to show your body or do anything that may attract sexual interest 羞怯; 端莊 **4 modesty forbids** *spoken* used when saying jokingly that you do not want to talk about your achievements【口】君子不自尚其功〔開玩笑地表示不想談論自己的成就〕—see also 另見 **false modesty** (FALSE (4))

mod·i·cum /ˈmɑdɪkəm; ˈmɒdɪkəm/ *n* **a modicum of** *formal* a small amount of something, especially a good quality【正式】〔尤指好的方面〕少量, 一點點: *a modicum of common sense* 一點兒常識

mod·i·fi·ca·tion /͵mɑdəfəˋkeʃən; ͵mɒdɪfɪˈkeɪʃən/ *n* **1** [C] a small change made in something such as a design, plan, or system 修改, 更改, 改變: *We've made one or two minor modifications to the original design.* 我們對原先的設計作了一兩處小小的修改。**2** [U] the act of modifying something, or the process of being modified 修改的行為[過程]; 改造: *The fuel can be used in diesel engines without modification.* 這種燃料柴油機無需改造就可使用。

mod·i·fi·er /ˈmɑdə͵faɪɚ; ˈmɒdɪfaɪə/ *n* [C] *technical* a word or group of words that give additional information about another word. Modifiers can be adjectives (such as 'fierce' in 'the fierce dog'), adverbs (such as 'loudly' in 'the dog barked loudly'), or phrases (such as 'with a short tail' in 'the dog with a short tail').【術語】修飾語〔可以是形容詞、副詞或片語〕

mod·i·fy /ˈmɑdə͵faɪ; ˈmɒdɪfaɪ/ *v* [T] **1** to make small changes to something in order to improve it and make it more suitable or effective〔略微地〕修改, 更改; 改進, 改造: *The present law needs to be modified.* 目前的法律需要稍作修改。**2** *technical* if an adjective, adverb etc modifies another word it describes it or limits its meaning【術語】〔形容詞、副詞等〕修飾〔另一詞〕: *In the phrase 'walk slowly', the adverb 'slowly' modifies the verb 'walk'.* 在片語 walk slowly 中, 副詞 slowly 修飾動詞 walk。

mod·ish /ˈmodɪʃ; ˈməʊdɪʃ/ *adj* modish ideas, designs etc are modern and fashionable 新潮的, 時髦的; 流行的 —**modishly** *adv*

mod·u·lar /ˋmɑdʒələ˞; ˈmɒdjʊ̈lə/ *adj* based on modules or made using modules 分單元的; 組合式的; 模塊化的: *a modular course in business studies* 商業課程中一門分單元進行的課程 | *modular furniture* 組合式家具

mod·u·late /ˋmɑdʒəˌlet; ˈmɒdjʊ̈leɪt/ *v* **1** [T] *formal* to change the sound of your voice or the strength of something【正式】改變〔音質或強度〕; 調整, 調節 **2** [**I+from/to**] *technical* to move from one KEY to another in a piece of music using a series of related chords (CHORD (1))【術語】〔音樂〕轉調; 變調 **3** [T] *technical* to change the form of a radio signal so that it can be broadcast more effectively【術語】調制〔無線電信號〕—**modulation** /ˌmɑdʒəˋleʃən; ˌmɒdjʊ̈ˈleɪʃən/ *n* [C]

2 **mod·ule** /ˋmɑdʒul; ˈmɒdjuːl/ *n* [C] **1** *especially BrE* one of the units that a course of study has been divided into, each of which can be studied separately【尤英】單元〔課程學習單位〕: *a module in mathematics* 數學課的一個單元 **2** a part of a SPACECRAFT that can be separated from the main part and used for a particular purpose〔宇宙飛船的〕分離艙 **3** one of several separate parts that can be combined to form a larger object, such as a machine or building〔機器、建築物等的〕組件, 模件, 模塊

mo·dus op·e·ran·di /ˋmodəs ˌɑpəˋrændaɪ; ˌməʊdəs ɒpəˈrændi/ *n* [singular] *Latin formal* a way of doing something that is typical of one person or group【拉丁, 正式】典型的做法; 一慣的做法

modus vi·ven·di /ˋmodəs vɪˋvɛndaɪ; ˌməʊdəs vɪˈvendi/ *n* [singular] *Latin formal* an arrangement between people with very different opinions or habits that allows them to live or work together without quarrelling【拉丁, 正式】〔矛盾雙方的〕妥協, 解決辦法, 權宜之計

mog·gy, moggie /ˋmɑgɪ; ˈmɒgi/ *n* [C] *BrE informal* a cat【英, 非正式】貓

mo·gul /ˋmogʌl; ˈməʊgəl/ *n* [C] **movie/record/tennis mogul etc** someone who has great power and influence in a particular industry or activity 電影業/唱片業/網球壇等泰斗

mo·hair /ˋmoˌhɛr; ˈməʊheə/ *n* [U] expensive wool made from the hair of the ANGORA goat〔用安哥拉羊毛製成的〕馬海毛毛線: *a mohair sweater* 馬海毛毛線衫 —see picture on page A16 參見 A16 頁圖

Mo·ham·me·dan /moˋhæmədən; məʊˈhæmʊ̈dən/ *n* [C] a word meaning Muslim, now considered offensive by most Muslims 穆斯林, 伊斯蘭教徒, 回教徒〔現在大多數伊斯蘭教徒認為此詞具冒犯性〕—**Mohammedan** *adj*

Mo·ham·me·dan·is·m /moˋhæmədənɪzəm; məʊˈhæmʊ̈dənɪzəm/ *n* [U] a word meaning the Muslim religion, now considered offensive by most Muslims; ISLAM 伊斯蘭教, 回教〔現在大多數伊斯蘭教徒認為此詞具冒犯性〕

moi /mwɑ; mwɑː/ *pron spoken humorous* me【口, 幽默】我〔賓格〕: *Difficult, moi?* 我難弄嗎?

moi·e·ty /ˋmɔɪətɪ; ˈmɔɪʊ̈ti/ *n* [**C+of**] *law or literary* a half share【法律或文】一半, 半份

moist /mɔɪst; mɔɪst/ *adj* slightly wet but not too wet, especially in a way that seems pleasant or suitable 潮濕的, 微濕的, 濕潤的: *Make sure the soil is moist before planting the seeds.* 播種之前要確保土壤濕潤。| *a moist chocolate cake* 鬆軟的巧克力蛋糕 —compare 比較 DAMP[1] (1) —**moistness** *n* [U]

moist·en /ˋmɔɪsn̩; ˈmɔɪsən/ *v* [I,T] to become slightly wet, or to make something slightly wet (使)潮濕, (使)濕潤: *Moisten the clay if it seems too dry.* 如果黏土看起來太乾, 就將其濕潤。

mois·ture /ˋmɔɪstʃə˞; ˈmɔɪstʃə/ *n* [U] small amounts of water that are present in the air, in a substance, or on a surface 水分, 水氣, 濕氣: *Plants use their roots to absorb moisture from the soil.* 植物利用根從土壤中吸收水分。

mois·tur·ize also 又作 **-ise** *BrE*【英】/ˋmɔɪstʃəˌraɪz; ˈmɔɪstʃəraɪz/ *v* [T] **1** to make your skin less dry by using special cream 使〔皮膚〕濕潤, 滋潤 **2 moisturizing cream/lotion/oil** cream, oil etc which you put on your skin to make it less dry 潤膚霜/潤膚露/潤膚油

mois·tur·iz·er also 又作 **-iser** *BrE*【英】/ˋmɔɪstʃəˌraɪzə˞; ˈmɔɪstʃəraɪzə/ *n* [C,U] cream that you put on your skin to make it less dry 潤膚膏, 潤膚霜

mo·lar /ˋmolə˞; ˈməʊlə/ *n* [C] one of the large teeth at the back of the mouth used for breaking up food 臼齒 —compare 比較 INCISOR —**molar** *adj* —see picture at 參見 TEETH 圖

mo·las·ses /məˋlæsɪz; məˈlæsʊ̈z/ *n* [U] *AmE* a thick dark sweet liquid that is obtained from raw sugar plants when they are being made into sugar【美】糖漿, 糖蜜; TREACLE *BrE*【英】

mold /mold; məʊld/ *n* [U] the American spelling of MOULD mould 的美式拼法 —**molding** *n* [C,U]

mol·der /ˋmoldə˞; ˈməʊldə/ *v* [I] the American spelling of MOULDER moulder 的美式拼法

mold·y /ˋmoldɪ; ˈməʊldi/ *adj* the American spelling of MOULDY mouldy 的美式拼法 —**moldiness** *n* [U]

mole /mol; məʊl/ *n* [C] **1** a small furry almost blind animal that usually lives under the ground 鼴鼠 **2** a small dark brown mark on the skin that is slightly higher than the skin around it 痣 **3** someone who works for an organization while secretly giving information to its enemies 內奸; 長期潛伏的間諜 **4** *technical* a scientific unit for measuring the quantity of a substance【術語】摩爾, 克分子(量)

mole 鼴鼠

mol·e·cule /ˋmɑləˌkjul; ˈmɒlɪkjuːl/ *n* [C] the smallest unit into which any substance can be divided without losing its own chemical nature, usually consisting of two or more atoms 分子 —**molecular** /məˋlɛkjələ˞; məˈlekjʊ̈lə/ *adj*: *molecular structure* 分子結構

mole·hill /ˋmolˌhɪl; ˈməʊlˌhɪl/ *n* [C] a small pile of earth made by a MOLE 鼴鼠丘 —see also 另見 **make a mountain out of a molehill** (MOUNTAIN (4)) —see picture at 參見 MOLE 圖

mole·skin /ˋmolˌskɪn; ˈməʊlˌskɪn/ *n* [U] **1** thick dark cloth 仿鼴鼠皮布料, 厚毛頭斜紋棉布 **2** the skin of a MOLE 鼴鼠皮

mo·lest /məˋlɛst; məˈlest/ *v* [T] **1** to attack or harm someone, especially a child, by touching them in a sexual way or trying to have sex with them〔尤指〕對〔兒童〕作性騷擾, 猥褻; 調戲: *men who molest young boys* 猥褻男童的男子 —compare 比較 ABUSE[2] (2) **2** *old-fashioned* to attack and physically harm someone【過時】襲擊; 傷害: *a dog that was molesting sheep* 一隻正在襲擾綿羊的狗 —**molester** *n* [C]: *a convicted child molester* 已被判猥褻兒童罪的犯人 —**molestation** /ˌmolɛsˋteʃən; ˌməʊleˈsteɪʃən/ *n* [U]

moll /mɑl; mɒl/ *n* [C] *old-fashioned, slang especially AmE* a criminal's girlfriend【過時, 俚, 尤美】罪犯的情人: *a gangster's moll* 匪徒的情人

mol·li·fy /ˋmɑləˌfaɪ; ˈmɒlʊ̈faɪ/ *v* [T] to make someone feel less angry and upset about something 撫慰, 使平靜; 使平息怒氣: *The old man seemed mollified by the flattery.* 老頭聽了那些恭維話好像氣消了。—**mollification** /ˌmɑləfɪˋkeʃən; ˌmɒlʊ̈fʊ̈ˈkeɪʃən/ *n* [U]

mol·lusc *BrE*【英】, **mollusk** *AmE*【美】/ˋmɑləsk; ˈmɒləsk/ *n* [C] a type of sea or land animal that has a soft body covered by a hard shell 軟體動物: *snails and other molluscs* 蝸牛和其他軟體動物

mol·ly·cod·dle /ˋmɑlɪˌkɑdl; ˈmɒliˌkɒdl/ *v* [T] to treat someone too kindly 溺愛; 嬌慣, 嬌養: *rather a weak young man who had always been mollycoddled as a boy* 小時候就一直嬌生慣養的、懦弱的青年男子

Mol·o·tov cock·tail /ˌmɑlətɔf ˋkɑktel; ˌmɒlətɒf

ˈkɒktɪl/ *n* [C] a simple bomb consisting of a bottle filled with petrol with a piece of cloth at the end 莫洛托夫燃燒彈, 莫洛托夫汽油彈〔用裝滿汽油的瓶子和塞在瓶口的引燃布條製成的一種簡易炸彈〕

molt /molt; məʊlt/ *v* [I] the American spelling of MOULT moult 的美式拼法

mol·ten /ˈmoltn̩; ˈməʊltən/ *adj* [usually before noun 一般用於名詞前] molten metal or rock has been made into a liquid by being heated to a very high temperature 熔化的, 熔融的: *molten lava* 熔岩

mol·to /ˈmolto; ˈmɒltəʊ/ *adv* a word used in music meaning 'very' 極, 甚〔音樂用語〕: *molto allegro* (=very fast) 極快

mo·lyb·de·num /məˈlɪbdənəm; məˈlɪbdənəm/ *n* [U] a pale-coloured metal used especially to strengthen steel 鉬

1 2 **mom** /mɑm; mɒm/ *n* [C] *AmE informal* mother【美, 非正式】媽媽; MUM[1] (1) *BrE*【英】: *fourteen-year-old girls and their moms and dads arguing about a moral issue* 一羣十四歲女孩和她們的爸爸媽媽正在爭論一個道德問題 | *"My mom got this for me." "Oh, isn't that pretty?"* "這個是我媽媽為我買的。" "哎呀, 真漂亮啊!"

mom-and-pop /ˌ· · ˈ·◂/ *adj* [only before noun 僅用於名詞前] *AmE* a mom-and-pop business is owned and operated by a family or a husband and wife【美】〔生意〕夫妻經營的, 家庭經營的: *a real mom-and-pop operation* 一家真正的夫妻企業

1 1 **mo·ment** /ˈmomənt; ˈməʊmənt/ *n*

1 ▶POINT IN TIME 時間點◀ [C] a particular point in time 某一時刻: *They've been arguing from the moment they walked in the door.* 他們從走進門的那一刻起就一直在爭論。| *There were a few worrying moments, but on the whole the play went well.* 儘管有一些令人擔心的時刻, 但總的說來那部劇演出得不錯。| **at the moment** *especially spoken BrE, formal AmE* (=used to say that something is happening or true now)【尤口, 英; 美, 正式】此刻, 目前, 眼下 *Julia's on holiday in Spain at the moment.* 朱莉婭目前在西班牙度假。|*At the moment, the situation in Haiti is very tense.* 眼下, 海地的局勢非常緊張。| **for the moment** (=used to say that something is happening or true now but will probably change in the future) 暫時, 目前 *Well, for the moment we're just friends.* 好吧, 目前我們僅僅是朋友。| *For the moment the troops had stopped firing and there was an eerie hush.* 部隊暫時停止了射擊, 四周一片死寂, 讓人可怕。| **at this/that moment** (=used to emphasize that something is happening now or at a particular time in the past) 在此/那時 *Just at that moment there was a knock on the door.* 就在那時有人敲門了。| *John's listening to the programme at this moment, in fact.* 事實上, 約翰此時正在收聽這個節目。| **at this moment in time** (=used especially by politicians, newspapers etc to mean now) 此時此刻〔尤為政治家、報紙等使用〕*At this moment in time it would be inappropriate to speculate on Castro's intentions.* 此時此刻推測卡斯特羅的意圖是不合適的。| **just this moment** (=used to emphasize that something has only just happened) 剛剛, 方才 *I just this moment arrived, and already Dan wants to know when I'm leaving.* 我剛剛到達, 而丹已急着想知道我甚麼時候要離開了。

2 ▶SHORT TIME 短時間◀ [C] a very short period of time 片刻, 瞬間, 刹那: *But you said a moment ago you weren't going to see him again!* 可你剛才還說你不再見他了呢! | *Can you spare a few moments to answer some questions?* 你能抽點時間回答幾個問題嗎? | **in a moment** (=very soon) 立刻, 馬上; 一會兒: *I'll come back to that point in a moment.* 我馬上就會再談那一點。| **for a moment** *It was quiet for a moment, then Rae asked what time he'd be back.* 靜默了一會兒, 然後雷問他甚麼時候會回來。| **wait/just a moment** (=used when you want someone to wait a short time while you do or say something) 請稍候, 稍等一下 *Just a moment, let me put these away first.* 請等一會兒, 讓我先把這些放起來。

3 the moment (that) sb does/says sth as soon as someone does something or says something 某人一做/一說…就…: *He said he'd phone you the moment he got home.* 他說他一到家就給你打電話。

4 the last moment if you do something at the last moment or wait until the last moment to do it, you do it at the last possible time 最後一刻: *How could you leave buying your wedding dress to the last moment?!* 你怎麼能到最後一刻才去買結婚禮服呢?!

5 not believe/think/do sth for a moment *especially spoken* used to say that you did not believe etc something at all【尤口】一點兒也沒相信/認識到/做某事: *He didn't fool me for a moment.* 他一點兒也騙不到我。

6 any moment extremely soon 馬上, 立刻: *The plumber should be here any moment now.* 水暖工現在應該就要到這兒了。| **at any moment** *The roof could collapse at any moment.* 屋頂隨時都會坍塌下來。

7 of the moment the job, person, event etc of the moment is the one that is most important or famous at the present time〔工作、人、事件等〕當前最重要[著名]的: *her boyfriend of the moment* 她那位眼下最親密的男友

8 ▶OPPORTUNITY 機會◀ [C usually singular 一般用單數] a particular period of time when you have a chance to do something 時機, 機會: **big moment** (=a time when you have a chance to show other people how skilled, intelligent etc you are) 大好機會, 絕佳時機 *It was André's big moment; he breathed deeply and began to play.* 這是安德烈大顯身手的好機會, 他深深地吸了口氣, 然後開始演奏起來。| **choose/pick your moment** (=an expression meaning to choose a good time to do something, often used if you choose a very bad time to do it) 選擇好時機〔常為反話〕

9 have its/your moments to have periods of being good or interesting 有好[有趣]的時刻: *a movie that had its moments* 一部局部可觀的電影

10 not a moment too soon almost too late 幾乎太遲, 險些遲到: *The ambulance finally arrived, and not a moment too soon.* 救護車終於到了, 但險些誤事。

11 the moment of truth the time when you will find out if something will work properly, be successful etc 發現真相[實情]的關鍵時刻[緊要關頭]

12 of great moment *old-fashioned* important【過時】重要的

mo·men·tar·i·ly /ˈmomənˌtɛrəlɪ; ˈməʊməntərəli/ *adv* **1** for a very short time 片刻地; 短暫地: *She paused momentarily and glanced over her shoulder.* 她停了片刻, 轉過頭看了一眼。**2** *AmE* very soon【美】馬上, 立刻: *Mr Johnson will be with you momentarily.* 約翰遜先生馬上就來見你。

mo·men·ta·ry /ˈmomənˌtɛrɪ; ˈməʊməntəri/ *adj* lasting for a very short time 短暫的, 瞬間的, 片刻的: *There was a momentary pause.* 停頓了片刻。

mo·men·tous /moˈmɛntəs; məʊˈmentəs/ *adj* a momentous event, occasion, decision etc is very important or serious, especially because it will have a great influence on the future 重大的, 重要的: *a momentous decision* 重大決定 | *1789 was a momentous year in European history.* 1789 年是歐洲歷史上非常重要的一年。

mo·men·tum /moˈmɛntəm; məʊˈmentəm/ *n* [U] **1** the ability to keep increasing, developing, or being more successful 動力, 勢頭: **lose momentum** (=stop increasing or developing) 失去〔增長或發展的〕勢頭 *The business did well at first but it seems to be losing momentum.* 該企業開始時很紅火, 但其發展勢頭現在好像正在減弱。| **gain/gather momentum** (=begin to increase or develop more quickly) 勢頭開始日益強勁 *The trend towards political change in South Africa was gathering momentum.* 南非政治變革的勢頭正變得日益強勁。**2** the force that makes a moving object keep moving〔使運動物體繼續運動的〕衝力, 推力, 動力: **gain/gather momentum**

(=move faster) 獲得動力; 加速 *The hill got steeper and the sled gained momentum.* 小山變得更陡了, 所以雪橇也滑得更快了。| **lose momentum** (=move more slowly) 失去動力; 減速 **3** *technical* the force or power contained in a moving object calculated by multiplying its weight by its speed【術語】動量

mom·ma /ˈmɑmə; ˈmɒmə/ *n* [C] *AmE*【美】another spelling of MAMA[1] mama[1] 的另一種拼法

3 **mom·my** /ˈmɑmɪ; ˈmɒmi/ *n* [C] *AmE* a word meaning mother, used by or to young children【美】〔兒語〕媽咪; MUMMY (1) *BrE*【英】

Mon the written abbreviation of 縮寫= MONDAY

mon·arch /ˈmɑnɚk; ˈmɒnək/ *n* [C] a king or queen 君主; 國王; 女王 —**monarchic** /məˈnɑrkɪk; məˈnɑːkɪk/ also 又作 **monarchical** *adj*: *monarchic rule* 君主統治

mon·arch·ist /ˈmɑnɚkɪst; ˈmɒnəkɪ̣st/ *n* [C] someone who supports the idea that their country should be ruled by a king or queen 君主主義者 —**monarchism** *n* [U]

mon·ar·chy /ˈmɑnɚkɪ; ˈmɒnəki/ *n* **1** [U] the system in which a country is ruled by a king or queen 君主政體, 君主制: *the abolition of the monarchy* 君主制的廢除 **2** [C] a country that is ruled by a king or queen 君主國: *Britain is a constitutional monarchy.* 英國是君主立憲國。—compare 比較 REPUBLIC

mon·as·tery /ˈmɑnəsˌtɛrɪ; ˈmɒnəstri/ *n* [C] a building or group of buildings in which MONKs live 寺院; 修道院 —compare 比較 CONVENT, NUNNERY

mo·nas·tic /məˈnæstɪk; məˈnæstɪk/ *adj* **1** concerned with or relating to MONKs or monasteries 修道院的, 寺院的; 修士的, 僧侶的: *monastic lands* 修道院的土地 **2** someone who has a monastic way of life lives alone and very simply 簡樸的; 遁世的 —**monastically** /-klɪ; -kli/ *adv* —**monasticism** *n* [U]

Mon·day /ˈmʌndɪ; ˈmʌndi/ *n* [C,U] the day between Sunday and Tuesday. In Britain, Monday is considered the first day of the week, and in the US, it is considered the second day of the week. 星期一〔在英國被認為是一週中的第一天, 而在美國則被認為是一週中的第二天〕: *It was raining on Monday.* 星期一天在下雨。| *I found it hard to get out of bed for work on Monday morning.* 我覺得星期一早上起牀上班很不容易。| *Sasha will arrive Monday.* 薩莎將於星期一到達。| **on Mondays** (=each Monday) 每個星期一 *We play football on Mondays.* 我們每個星期一都踢足球。| **a Monday** (=one of the Mondays in a year) 某個星期一 *Does Christmas fall on a Monday this year?* 今年聖誕節是在星期一嗎?

mon·e·ta·ris·m /ˈmɑnətəˌrɪzəm; ˈmʌnɪ̣tərɪzəm/ *n* [U] the belief that the best way to manage and control a country's economic system is to limit the amount of money that is available and being used 貨幣主義 —**monetarist** *adj, n* [C]

3 **mon·e·ta·ry** /ˈmʌnəˌtɛrɪ; ˈmʌnɪ̣təri/ *adj* concerned with or relating to money, especially all the money in a particular country 貨幣的, 金融的: *monetary growth* 貨幣增長 | *a monetary unit* 貨幣單位

1
1 **mon·ey** /ˈmʌnɪ; ˈmʌni/ *n* [U] **1** what you earn by working and what you spend in order to buy things 錢, 貨幣: *The repairs will cost a lot of money.* 這些修理要花不少錢。| **earn money** *She barely earns enough money to live on.* 她掙的錢勉強夠糊口。| **save money** *We're not going on holiday this year – we're trying to save money.* 我們今年不打算去度假了 —— 我們正在設法攢錢。| **get/be given your money back** *If it doesn't fit, just take it back to the shop and they'll give you your money back.* 如果不合適, 儘管拿回商店, 他們會把錢退給你。| **spend money** *I spent so much money at the weekend I can't afford to come.* 我那個週末花錢太多, 所以沒錢來了。| **borrow money** *Maybe you could borrow some money from the bank to pay for your course.* 也許你可以從銀行貸些款來支付你的學費。| **make money** (=earn money or make a profit) 賺錢, 掙錢, 贏利 *John's making a lot of money from his computer games.* 約翰靠他的電腦遊戲大把大把地賺錢。| *His business has finally started making money.* 他的企業終於開始賺錢了。| **charge money** *I said I didn't want it if they were going to charge me a lot of money for it.* 我說如果他們討價太高, 我就不要它了。| **good money** (=good wages for your work) 豐厚的薪水 *She's making about $40,000 a year, which is pretty good money.* 她每年掙大約4萬美元, 這可是一份很豐厚的薪水。| **raise money** (=collect money for a purpose) 集資, 籌款 *We're trying to raise money for the victims of the earthquake.* 我們正在設法為地震受災者籌集資金。| **birthday money/redundancy money etc** (=money you receive on a particular occasion or in a particular situation) 生日禮金/裁員費等 *They're using part of his redundancy money to go on a cruise.* 他們計劃動用他一部分裁員補償金去進行一次乘船遊覽。| **put money into** (=lend money or allow a business to use your money, especially in order to make a profit) 投資於 *George has decided to put some of his money into the business.* 喬治決定把他的一部分錢投到這家企業。| **put money on a race/ horse etc** (=risk money on the result of a race etc) 在比賽/〔參賽的〕馬等上下賭注 **2** money in the form of coins or notes; CASH[1] (1) 錢, 現款, 現金: *My bag came open, and all my money fell on the floor.* 我的包開了, 所有的錢都掉到了地上。| **have money on you** (=carry money with you) 隨身帶着現錢 *Do you have enough money on you to pay for the meal?* 你身上帶的錢夠付餐費嗎? **3 French/Japanese/Turkish money** the money that is used in a particular country; CURRENCY 法國/日本/土耳其貨幣: *Don't forget to get some French money before you leave.* 你走之前別忘了弄點法國貨幣。 **4** all the money that a person, organization, or country owns 資產, 財產, 財富: *The business collapsed and we lost all our money.* 企業倒閉了, 我們損失了所有的資產。| *She's only marrying him for his money.* 她只是為了他的財產才想跟他結婚。| **make your money** (=earn all your money) 發財 *I think he made his money in property speculation.* 我認為他靠房地產投機買賣發了財。 **5 pay good money for** *spoken* to spend a lot of money on something【口】為…花大筆的錢: *I paid good money for that sofa, so it should last.* 我買那張沙發花了不少錢, 想來應該經久耐用。 **6 there's money (to be made) in** *spoken* used to say that you can get a lot of money from a particular activity or from buying and selling something【口】在…中有錢可賺, 在…中有利可圖: *Apparently there's a lot of money in ostrich farming.* 據說飼養鴕鳥能賺大錢。 **7 be rolling in money/be rolling in it** *informal* to be very rich【非正式】非常富有, 財源滾滾: *They're always going on vacation – they must be rolling in money!* 他們總是去度假 —— 他們一定非常富有! **8 I'm not made of money** *spoken* used to say that you do not have a lot of money when someone asks you for some【口】我不是錢做的, 我沒有很多錢 **9 he/she must have money to burn** used when you think someone is wasting their money on unnecessary things 他/她錢多得燙手, 他/她一定是錢多得可以拿去燒 **10 get your money's worth** to get something worth the price that you paid 讓你的錢花得物有所值: *At that price you want to make sure you get your money's worth.* 價錢那麼貴, 你該弄清楚你的錢花得是否上算。 **11 be in the money** *informal* to have a lot of money, especially suddenly or when you did not expect to【非正式】〔尤指突然或出乎意料地〕發財, 擁有大筆的錢 **12 money is no object** *informal* used to say that you can spend as much money as you want to on something【非正式】錢不成問題: *Choose whatever you like, money is no object.* 喜歡甚麼你就選甚麼, 錢不成問題。 **13 for my money** *spoken* used when giving your opinion about something to emphasize that you believe it strongly【口】依我之見〔用於強調對自己的觀點非常有把握〕: *For my money, Torville and Dean were by far the best skaters.* 依我看, 托維爾和迪恩顯然是最好的滑冰者。 **14 I'd put money on it** *spoken* used to empha-

size that you are completely sure about something【口】我敢打賭, 我對此深信不疑: *"Do you really think that she'll get the gold medal?" "I'd put money on it."* "你真的認為她會獲得金牌嗎?" "我對此深信不疑。" **15 my money's on** *spoken* used to say that you think someone will probably win, or a situation will probably have a particular result【口】我認為…會…: *My money's on a draw – I don't think either team can win now.* 我想會打個平局 —— 我認為兩支球隊中哪一支現在也贏不了。**16 money for old rope/money for jam** *BrE spoken* money that you earn very easily【英口】很容易賺的錢 **17 put your money where your mouth is** *informal, often humorous* to show by your actions that you really believe what you say【非正式, 常幽默】以實際行動證明自己的觀點; 說話兌現 **18 money doesn't grow on trees** *spoken* used to tell someone that they should not waste money【口】錢不是樹上長的〔用以告誡某人不應亂花錢〕**19 money talks** *spoken* used to say that money is powerful, and people who have money can get what they want【口】金錢萬能 **20 be (right) on the money** *AmE spoken* used when something is perfect or exactly right for the situation【美口】(完全) 正確, 管用: *Her solution was right on the money – the clients loved it.* 她的解決辦法完全對路 —— 客戶很滿意。**21 marry (into) money** to marry someone whose family is rich 和富家人結婚 —see also 另見 BLOOD MONEY, HUSH MONEY, POCKET MONEY, **have a (good) run for your money** (RUN[2] (11)), **throw money at** (THROW[1] (20))

This graph shows some of the words most commonly used with the noun **money**. 本圖表所示為含有名詞 money 的一些最常用詞組。

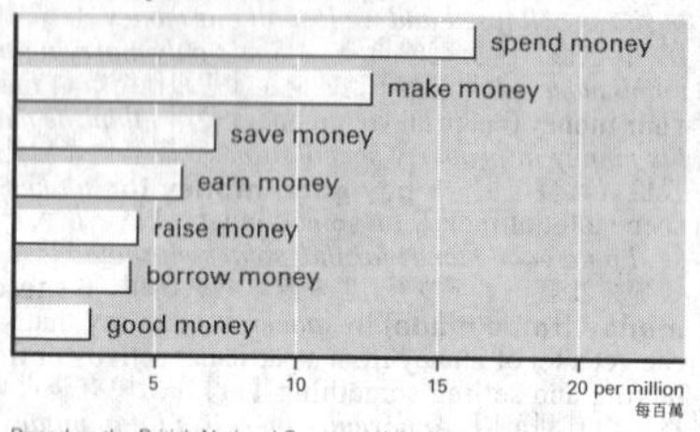

Based on the British National Corpus and the Longman Lancaster Corpus
據英國國家語料庫和朗文蘭卡斯特語料庫

USAGE NOTE 用法説明: MONEY

WORD CHOICE 詞語辨析: **money, cash, change, funds**

Money is the most general word. money 是表示 "錢" 的最通用的詞: *Where can I change money?* 我在哪兒可以兑換錢? | *How much money do you have?* 你有多少錢? | *taxpayers' money* 納稅人的錢

Cash usually means money in coins or notes rather than cheques or credit cards. cash 通常指現金、現鈔, 而不是支票或信用卡: *"May I pay by Visa?" "I'm sorry, we only take cash."* "我可以用維澤信用卡付款嗎?" "對不起, 我們只收現金。" But it can also mean money in any form that is available to be spent. 但它也可以指能夠用來消費的任何形式的錢: *We're going to Australia next year if we have the cash.* 如果有錢的話, 我們明年想去澳大利亞。

Change is used for the amount of money that is given back to you when you have given more for something than the amount it costs. change 用來指付款多於某物的價格時找回的錢: *three dollars fifty change* 三美元五十美分的找頭。**Change** can also mean money in low-value coins or notes. change 也可以指小面額的硬幣或紙幣, 即 "零錢": *Can you give me change for a ten pound note?* 你能換給我十英鎊的零錢嗎? | *I keep all my small change for the coffee machine.* 我留着所有的零錢以便在自動售咖啡機買咖啡用。

Money collected for a particular purpose may be called **funds**. 為某一特殊用途而籌集起來的錢可被稱作 funds (基金, 專款; 資金): *I need more funds if I'm to study abroad.* 我如果要到國外學習則需要更多的錢。| *We're short of funds at the moment.* 我們眼下缺少資金。

mon·ey·bags /ˈmʌnɪˌbægz; ˈmʌnibægz/ *n* [singular] *informal humorous* someone who has a lot of money【非正式, 幽默】富翁, 闊佬

mon·ey·box /ˈmʌnɪˌbɑks; ˈmʌnibɒks/ *n* [C] *especially BrE* a box for saving money in【尤英】儲錢盒, 儲錢罐

mon·ey·chang·er /ˈmʌnɪˌtʃendʒɚ; ˈmʌniˌtʃeɪndʒə/ *n* [C] someone whose business is to exchange one country's money for money from another country, sometimes unofficially〔有時指非官方的〕錢商, 貨幣兑換商

mon·eyed, monied /ˈmʌnɪd; ˈmʌnid/ *adj* [only before noun 僅用於名詞前] *formal* rich【正式】富有的: *the new moneyed classes* 新興有產階層

mon·ey·grab·bing /ˈmʌnɪgræbɪŋ; ˈmʌnigræbɪŋ/ also 又作 **moneygrubbing** /ˈmʌnɪgrʌbɪŋ; ˈmʌnigrʌbɪŋ/ *adj* [only before noun 僅用於名詞前] *informal* determined to get money, even by unfair or dishonest methods【非正式】財迷的, 貪財的 —**moneygrabber, moneygrubber** *n* [C]

mon·ey·lend·er /ˈmʌnɪˌlɛndɚ; ˈmʌniˌlendə/ *n* [C] someone whose business is to lend money to people, especially at very high rates of INTEREST[1] (4)〔尤指高息〕放款人, 放債人

mon·ey·mak·er /ˈmʌnɪˌmekɚ; ˈmʌniˌmeɪkə/ *n* [C] a product or business that earns a lot of money 賺大錢的產品[生意], 搖錢樹; MONEY-SPINNER *BrE*【英】: *The movie has turned into a real moneymaker.* 那部電影已變成了一棵真正的搖錢樹。

money mar·ket /ˈ‥ ˌ‥/ *n* [C] the banks and other institutions who buy, sell, lend, or borrow money, especially foreign money, for profit 金融市場, 貨幣市場, 資金市場

money or·der /ˈ‥ ˌ‥/ *n* [C] an official document that you buy in a post office or a bank and send to someone so that they can exchange it for money in a bank 匯票 —compare 比較 POSTAL ORDER

money-spin·ner /ˈ‥ ˌ‥/ *n* [C] *BrE* MONEYMAKER【英】賺大錢的產品[生意], 搖錢樹: *The hotel's a real money-spinner in the summer months.* 這家旅館在夏季是棵真正的搖錢樹。

money sup·ply /ˈ‥ ‥ˌ/ *n* [singular] *technical* all the money that exists in a country's economic system at a particular time【術語】貨幣供應量

-mon·ger /mɑŋgɚ; mʌŋgə/ *suffix* [in nouns 構成名詞] **1** someone who sells a particular thing 商人, 販子: *a fishmonger* 魚販 (子) **2** someone who likes to say or encourage something unpleasant 喜歡傳播[支持]壞事的人: *the rumour-mongers* (=people who say untrue things about other people) 好散布謠言的人, 好造謠的人 | *capitalist warmongers* 資本主義戰爭販子

mon·gol /ˈmɑŋgəl; ˈmɒŋgəl/ *n* [C] *old-fashioned* someone with DOWN'S SYNDROME【過時】唐氏綜合徵患者 —**mongolism** *n* [U]

mon·goose /ˈmɑŋgus; ˈmɒŋguːs/ *n plural* **mongooses** [C] a small furry tropical animal that kills snakes and rats 獴

mon·grel /ˈmʌŋgrəl; ˈmʌŋgrəl/ *n* [C] a dog that is a mix of several breeds of dog 雜種狗

mon·ied /ˈmʌnɪd; ˈmʌnid/ *adj* another spelling of MONEYED moneyed 的另一種拼法

mon·ies /ˈmʌniz; ˈmʌniz/ *n* [plural] *law* money【法律】錢, 貨幣

mon·i·ker /ˈmɑnɪkɚ; ˈmɒnɪkə/ *n* [C] *humorous* someone's name, signature, or NICKNAME【幽默】名字; 簽名; 綽號

3 3 **mon·i·tor¹** /ˈmɑnətɚ; ˈmɒnɪtə/ *v* [T] **1** to carefully watch and check a situation in order to see how it changes or progresses over a period of time 監視; 監測, 檢測; 監督: *British Aerospace has built a scanner that monitors damage to the ozone layer.* 英國航空航天工業公司已建起一座掃描站, 監測對臭氧層的破壞。| *Their job is to monitor healthcare costs.* 他們的工作是監督保健費用。**2** to secretly listen to other people's phone calls, foreign radio broadcasts etc 監聽: *The Security Police had monitored all of his phone calls.* 祕密警察對他所有的電話進行了監聽。

monitor² *n* [C] **1** a television that shows a picture of what is happening in a particular place 監視器: *a row of monitors covering key areas of the building* 覆蓋大樓關鍵區域的一排監視器 **2** the part of a computer that looks like a television and that shows information; VDU〔電腦的〕顯示器 —see picture on page A14 參見 A14 頁圖 **3** a piece of equipment that receives and shows information about what is happening inside someone's body〔人體內部〕檢測監視儀, 監護儀: *a monitor that shows the baby's heartbeat* 能顯示嬰兒心跳的監護儀 **4** a child who has been chosen to help the teacher in some way〔學校的〕班長, 級長, 值勤生: *the milk monitors*〔負責給同學分發牛奶的〕牛奶值勤生 **5** someone whose job is to listen to news, messages etc from foreign radio stations and report on them〔外國電台〕監聽員

monk /mʌŋk; mʌŋk/ *n* [C] a member of an all-male religious group that lives apart from other people in a MONASTERY 修道士, 僧侶 —compare 比較 NUN —**monkish** *adj*: *a monkish silence* 一片遠離俗世的寂靜

mon·key¹ /ˈmʌŋki; ˈmʌŋki/ *n* [C]

1 ►ANIMAL 動物◄ a small brown animal with a long tail, which uses its hands to climb trees and lives in hot countries 猴; 猿

2 ►CHILD 孩子◄ *informal* a small child who is very active and likes to play tricks【非正式】頑皮的兒童, 淘氣鬼, 搗蛋鬼: *Stop that, you little monkey!* 別搗亂了, 你這個淘氣鬼!

3 monkey business *informal* behaviour that may cause trouble or may be dishonest【非正式】惡作劇; 騙人把戲, 搗鬼: *The boys are awfully quiet – I think they're up to some monkey business.* 那些男孩子出奇地安靜 —— 我想他們在搗甚麼鬼。

4 make a monkey (out) of sb to make someone seem stupid 使某人出醜, 戲弄某人, 愚弄某人: *They got into the palace in broad daylight, and made monkeys out of the security men.* 他們在光天化日之下進入了皇宮, 讓保安人員出盡了醜。

5 I don't give a monkey's *BrE spoken* used to say that you do not care at all about something【英口】我一點都不在乎: *To be honest I don't give a monkey's what they do.* 說實話, 我一點都不在乎他們做甚麼。

6 a monkey on your back *AmE informal* a serious problem that makes your life very difficult, especially being dependent on drugs【美, 非正式】使生活艱難的沉重負擔〔尤指對毒品的依賴〕

monkey² *v*

monkey around also 又作 **monkey about** *phr v* [I] *BrE informal* to behave in a stupid or careless way【英, 非正式】胡鬧, 搗蛋, 調皮: *They were monkeying around in the playground and one of them got hurt.* 他們在操場上打鬧, 其中一個受了傷。| **[+with]** *I wish those kids would stop monkeying around with the remote control!* 我希望那些孩子別再亂動遙控器了!

monkey bars /ˈ·· ·/ *n* [plural] **1** *AmE* a structure for children to climb and play on【美】猴架〔一種供孩子攀爬玩耍的架子〕; CLIMBING FRAME *BrE*【英】**2** *BrE* bars fixed to the wall in a GYM (1)【英】〔體育館中固定在牆上的〕攀爬架

monkey nut /ˈ·· ·/ *n* [C] *BrE informal* a PEANUT in its shell【英, 非正式】帶殼花生

mon·key·shines /ˈmʌŋkiʃaɪnz; ˈmʌŋkiʃaɪnz/ *n* [plural] *AmE informal* tricks or jokes【美, 非正式】把戲, 惡作劇; 玩笑: *Jo's monkeyshines finally cost him his job.* 喬因搞惡作劇而最終失去了工作。

monkey suit /ˈ·· ·/ *n* [C] *old-fashioned* a formal suit, especially with black trousers and jacket and a BOW TIE【過時】男子禮服

monkey wrench /ˈ·· ·/ *n* [C] *AmE*【美】**1** a tool that is used to hold or turn things, especially nuts (NUT¹ (2)) 活動扳手, 活扳子; ADJUSTABLE SPANNER *BrE*【英】—see picture at 參見 TOOL¹ 圖 **2 throw a monkey wrench in the works** *AmE informal* to do something that will cause problems or spoil what someone else is planning【美, 非正式】阻撓; 破壞; 給…惹麻煩

mono- /mɑno; mɒnəʊ/ *prefix* one; single 一個, 單一: *a monoplane* (=plane with only one wing on each side) 單翼 (飛) 機 | *a monolingual dictionary* (=dealing with only one language) 單語詞典

mon·o¹ /ˈmɑno; ˈmɒnəʊ/ *n* [U] *informal*【非正式】**1** *AmE* an infectious illness that makes your LYMPH GLANDS swell and makes you feel weak and tired for a long time afterwards【美】傳染性單核細胞增多症, 腺熱; GLANDULAR FEVER *BrE*【英】**2** a system of recording or broadcasting sound, in which the sound comes from only one direction 單聲道錄[放]音系統 —compare 比較 STEREO¹

mono² *adj* using a system of recording or broadcasting sound in which all the sound comes from only one direction〔錄音或放音〕單聲道的: *a mono recording* 單聲道錄音 —compare 比較 STEREO²

mon·o·chrome /ˈmɑnəˌkrom; ˈmɒnəkrəʊm/ *adj* **1** in shades of only one colour, especially shades of grey 單色的〔尤指黑白的〕: *The landscape was dull, misty, and monochrome.* 那張風景畫灰暗、朦朧、色調單一。**2** using or appearing in only black, white, and grey 黑白的, 只用黑白灰三色的, 僅以黑白灰三色出現的: *a monochrome television* 黑白電視 **3** a monochrome computer MONITOR uses one colour as a background and only one other colour for the letters on the SCREEN〔電腦顯示器〕黑白的 —opposite 反義詞 COLOUR³

mon·o·cle /ˈmɑnəkḷ; ˈmɒnəkəl/ *n* [C] a single LENS (=ROUND PIECE OF GLASS) that you hold in front of one eye to help you to see better 單片眼鏡

mo·nog·a·my /məˈnɑgəmɪ; məˈnɒgəmi/ *n* [U] the custom or practice of being married to only one husband or wife 一夫一妻制 —compare 比較 BIGAMY, POLYGAMY —**monogamous** *adj* —**monogamously** *adv*

mon·o·gram /ˈmɑnəˌgræm; ˈmɒnəgræm/ *n* [C] two or more letters, usually the first letters of someone's names, that are put together to form a design 交織字母, 花押字〔兩個或兩個以上字母, 通常是姓和名的首字母, 放在一起構成的圖案〕—**monogrammed** *adj*

mon·o·graph /ˈmɑnəˌgræf; ˈmɒnəgrɑːf/ *n* [C+on] a serious article or short book about a subject 專題文章; 專題著作

mon·o·ling·ual /ˌmɑnəˈlɪŋgwəl; ˌmɒnəʊˈlɪŋgwəl◄/ *adj* speaking or using only one language 只說[使用]一種語言的, 單語的: *a monolingual dictionary* 單語詞典 —compare 比較 BILINGUAL, MULTILINGUAL

mon·o·lith /ˈmɑnḷˌɪθ; ˈmɒnəlɪθ/ *n* [C] **1** an organization, government etc that is very large and powerful and difficult to change 龐大而僵化的組織[政府等]: *the break-up of the Soviet monolith* 像鐵板一塊的蘇聯的解體 **2** a large tall block of stone, especially one that was put in place in ancient times, possibly for religious reasons〔尤指古代豎起、可能用於宗教目的的〕獨石柱[碑]

mon·o·lith·ic /ˌmɑnḷˈɪθɪk; ˌmɒnəˈlɪθɪk◄/ *adj* **1** very large, solid, and impressive 龐大結實的; 氣勢宏偉的; 磐石般的: *huge monolithic office buildings* 氣勢雄偉、堅

如磐石的辦公大樓 **2** a monolithic organization, political system etc is very large and powerful and difficult to change〔組織、政治制度等〕鐵板一塊的

mon·o·logue also 又作 **monolog** *AmE*【美】/ˈmɑnḷˌɔg; ˈmɒnəlɒg/ *n* [C] **1** *informal* a long period of talking by one person that prevents other people from taking part in a conversation【非正式】〔使別人無法插嘴的〕滔滔不絕的講話, 長篇大論: *Charles listened patiently to a fifteen-minute monologue before finally interrupting.* 查爾斯耐心地聽了持續十五分鐘之久的長篇大論後才插話打斷對方。**2** a long speech by one character in a play or film〔戲劇或電影的〕長篇獨白: *Hamlet's famous monologue* 哈姆雷特著名的獨白 —compare 比較 DIALOGUE, SOLILOQUY

mon·o·ma·ni·a /ˌmɑnəˈmenɪə; ˌmɒnəʊˈmeɪniə/ *n* [U] an unusually strong interest in a particular idea or subject; OBSESSION 單狂, 偏狂;〔對某一想法或問題的〕狂熱: *the victims of a computing monomania* 電腦偏狂症患者 —**monomaniac** /-nɪˌæk; -niæk/ *n adj*

mon·o·nu·cle·o·sis /ˌmɑnoˌnuklɪˈosɪs; ˌmɒnəʊnjuːkliˈəʊsɪ̣s/ *n* [U] *AmE technical* MONO[1] (1)【美, 術語】傳染性單核細胞增多症, 腺熱

mon·o·plane /ˈmɑnəˌplen; ˈmɒnəʊpleɪn/ *n* [C] a plane with only one wing on each side, like most modern planes 單翼(飛)機 —compare 比較 BIPLANE

mo·nop·ol·is·tic /məˌnɑpəˈlɪstɪk; məˌnɒpəˈlɪstɪk◂/ *adj* controlling or trying to control something completely, especially an industry or business activity 壟斷的, 壟斷性的: *monopolistic corporations* 壟斷公司

mo·nop·o·lize also 又作 **-ise** *BrE*【英】/məˈnɑpḷˌaɪz; məˈnɒpəlaɪz/ *v* [T] **1** to have complete control over something so that other people cannot share it 壟斷; 獨佔; 完全控制: *This small group monopolized the key positions in government for many years.* 這個小集團多年來一直佔據着政府中的關鍵職位。| *to monopolize a conversation* 壟斷談話 **2** to demand or need a lot of someone's time and attention 佔用〔時間和注意力〕: *Virtually all her time and energy is now monopolized by the children.* 現在她幾乎所有的時間和精力都被孩子佔去了。—**monopolization** /məˌnɑplə̩ˈzeʃən; məˌnɒpəlaɪˈzeɪʃən/ *n* [U]

mo·nop·o·ly /məˈnɑplɪ; məˈnɒpəli/ *n* **1** [C] the control of all or most of a business activity by a single company or by a government, so that other organizations cannot easily compete with them 壟斷; 獨佔; 專營: *Cigarette production is a state monopoly in China.* 在中國, 香煙生產是國家專營的。| **[+on/of]** *For years Bell Telephone had a monopoly on phone services in the US.* 過去許多年, 貝爾電話公司壟斷着美國的電話服務。**2** [singular] something that belongs to only one person, group, or organization, so that other people cannot share it 壟斷品, 被獨佔的東西: *Good healthcare shouldn't be the monopoly of the rich.* 良好的保健服務不應為富人所獨享。| **have/hold a monopoly on** *Universities do not hold a monopoly on intellectual life.* 知識生活不是大學所獨有的。

mon·o·rail /ˈmɑnəˌrel; ˈmɒnəʊreɪl/ *n* **1** [U] a railway system that uses a single RAIL[1] (3), usually high above the ground〔通常指高架的〕單軌鐵道 **2** [C] a train on this system 單軌火車

mon·o·sod·i·um glu·tam·ate /ˌmɑnəˈsodɪəm ˈglutəˌmet; ˌmɒnəʊˌsəʊdiəm ˈgluːtəmeɪt/ *n* [U] *technical* MSG【術語】穀氨酸一鈉〔味精的化學成分〕

mon·o·syl·lab·ic /ˌmɑnəsɪˈlæbɪk; ˌmɒnəsɪˈlæbɪk◂/ *adj* **1** someone who is monosyllabic or makes monosyllabic remarks seems rude because they do not say much〔說話〕簡短而無禮的: *Jim became more and more monosyllabic.* 吉姆說話越來越簡短無禮。**2** *technical* a monosyllabic word has only one SYLLABLE【術語】〔詞〕單音節的

mon·o·syl·la·ble /ˈmɑnəˌsɪləbḷ; ˈmɒnəˌsɪləbəl/ *n* [C] *technical* a word with one SYLLABLE【術語】單音節詞

mon·o·the·is·m /ˈmɑnəθiˌɪzəm; ˈmɒnəʊθiːɪzəm/ *n* [U] *technical* the belief that there is only one God【術語】一神論, 一神教 —compare 比較 POLYTHEISM —**monotheist** *n* [C] —**monotheistic** /ˌmɑnəθiˈɪstɪk; ˌmɒnəʊθiːˈɪstɪk◂/ *adj*: *Christianity is a monotheistic religion.* 基督教是一神教。

mon·o·tone /ˈmɑnəˌton; ˈmɒnətəʊn/ *n* [singular] a sound or way of speaking or singing that continues on the same note without getting any louder or softer, and therefore sounds very boring 單調的聲音; 單調: *Mr Major was talking in a flat, slow monotone.* 梅傑先生以一種平緩的單調聲音在說話。

mo·not·o·nous /məˈnɑtṇəs; məˈnɒtənəs/ *adj* boring because there is no variety 單調的, 乏味的: *He was speaking in a low monotonous voice.* 他以一種低沉而單調的聲音在說話。| *a monotonous factory job* 工廠裡單調乏味的工作 —**monotonously** *adv*: *The rain poured monotonously out of the grey sky.* 灰蒙蒙的天空中雨令人厭煩地下個不停。

mo·not·o·ny /məˈnɑtṇɪ; məˈnɒtəni/ *n* [U] a lack of variety that makes you feel bored 單調乏味, 無變化, 千篇一律: *A small group of houses relieved the monotony of the landscape.* 一小片房子為單調乏味的景色帶來生氣。

mon·ox·ide /mənˈɑksaɪd; məˈnɒksaɪd/ *n* [C,U] *technical* a chemical compound containing one atom of oxygen to every atom of another substance【術語】一氧化物: *carbon monoxide* 一氧化碳

Mon·sieur /məˈsjɝ; məˈsjɜː/ *n plural* **Messieurs** /meˈsjɝz; meɪˈsjɜːz/ [C] *French* a way of addressing or referring to a French-speaking man【法】先生: *Monsieur Bonnet* 邦尼先生

Mon·si·gnor /mɑnˈsinjɚ; mɒnˈsiːnjə/ *n* [C] a way of addressing or referring to a priest of high rank in the Roman Catholic Church 閣下〔對羅馬天主教高級教士的稱呼〕

mon·soon /mɑnˈsun; mɒnˈsuːn/ *n* [C] **1** [usually singular 一般用單數] the season, from about April to October, when it rains a lot in India and other southern Asian countries〔印度等南亞國家的〕季風季節, 雨季 **2** the rain that falls during this season or the wind that brings the rain 季風雨;〔帶來雨水的〕季風, 季雨風

mon·ster[1] /ˈmɑnstɚ; ˈmɒnstə/ *n* [C]

1 ►IN STORIES 在故事中◄ a large ugly frightening creature, especially an imaginary one 怪物; 怪獸; 妖怪: *the Kraken and other legendary sea monsters*〔挪威傳說中的〕北海巨妖克拉肯和其他傳說中的海妖 | *a prehistoric monster* 史前怪物

2 ►CRUEL PERSON 殘忍的人◄ someone who is very cruel and evil 殘忍的人; 惡人, 惡魔: *Only a monster could kill all those women and feel no remorse.* 只有惡魔才會把那些婦女殺光而毫無悔意。

3 ►CHILD 孩子◄ *often humorous* a small child, especially one who is behaving badly【常幽默】〔尤指不守規矩的〕小孩子; 調皮精, 搗蛋鬼: *I've got to get home and feed this little monster.* 我必須回家餵這個小搗蛋。

4 ►STH LARGE 巨大的東西◄ *informal* an object, animal etc that is unusually large【非正式】龐然大物: *That car of his is an absolute monster!* 他的那輛汽車簡直是個龐然大物!

5 a dangerous or threatening problem, especially one that develops gradually〔尤指漸漸惡化的〕危險[可怕]的問題: *It was years before people realized what a monster industrialization had created.* 人們經過多年後才認識到工業化帶來了多麼可怕的後果。

monster[2] *adj* [only before noun 僅用於名詞前] *informal* unusually large【非正式】異常大的, 龐大的, 巨大的: *the monster fortunes of the Mellons and DuPonts* 梅隆和杜邦家族巨大的財富

mon·stros·i·ty /mɑnˈstrɑsətɪ; mɒnˈstrɒsɪ̣ti/ *n* [C] something large and ugly, especially a building 巨大而醜陋的東西〔尤指建築物〕: *The office complex is yet another monstrosity in the very center of the city.* 那座綜合辦公大樓是市中心的另一個醜陋的大怪物。

mon·strous /ˋmɑnstrəs; ˈmɒnstrəs/ *adj* **1** very wrong, immoral, or unfair 極端錯誤的; 非常不道德的; 極不公正的: *It's monstrous to charge that much for a hotel room.* 一個旅館房間就要收那麼多錢真是太無理了。| *a monstrous injustice* 極端的不公正 **2** unusually large and ugly 巨大而醜陋的: *a monstrous castle* 一座醜陋的大城堡 —**monstrously** *adv*

mon·tage /mɑnˋtɑʒ; ˈmɒntɑːʒ/ *n* **1** [U] an art form in which a picture, film, piece of writing etc is made from parts of different pictures etc, that are combined to form a whole 蒙太奇〔圖像、電影、寫作等的藝術形式, 把不同的圖像等結合成整體〕, 剪輯 **2** [C] something made using this process 蒙太奇作品, 綜合[組合]式作品

1 1 **month** /mʌnθ; mʌnθ/ *n* [C] **1** one of the twelve named periods of time that a year is divided into 月, 月份: *It snowed heavily during the month of January.* 一月份雪下得很大。| *Phil is coming home for a visit next month.* 菲爾下個月要回家看看。| *She'll be thirteen this month.* 到這個月她就十三歲了。| *a tremendous article in this month's American Indian Review* 本月《美洲印第安人評論》雜誌中一篇精彩的文章 **2** a period of about four weeks 一個月: *She has an eight-month old daughter.* 她有一個八個月大的女兒。| *He'll be away for two months.* 他要離開兩個月。**3 once/twice etc a month** 每月一次/兩次等: *We update the schedule at least once a month.* 我們每月至少更新一次該時間表。**4 months** a long time, especially several months 很長一段時間〔尤指數月〕: *Redecorating the kitchen took months.* 重新裝修廚房用了好長時間。| **for/in months** (=for a long time) 好長時間, 很久 *I haven't seen him for months.* 我好長時間沒見到他了。**5 month after month** used to emphasize that something happens regularly or continuously for several months 一月又一月, 每月: *I felt I was doing the same old thing week after week, month after month.* 我感到我在一週復一週、一月復一月地幹着相同的事。**6 month by month** used when you are talking about a situation that develops over several months 逐月: *Unemployment figures are rising month by month.* 失業數字正在逐月增加。**7 never in a month of Sundays** *spoken* used to emphasize that something will definitely never happen【口】永遠也不會: *You'll never guess it in a month of Sundays.* 你永遠也猜不出來。

3 **month·ly**¹ /ˋmʌnθlɪ; ˈmʌnθli/ *adj* [only before noun 僅用於名詞前] **1** happening once a month 每月一次的: *The mortgage is payable in monthly instalments.* 該抵押借款按月償付。| *a monthly publication* 月刊 **2** a monthly income, figure etc is the total amount that is received, paid, measured etc in a month〔收入、數字等〕按月支付的, 按月計算的; 每月的: *a monthly salary of $850* 月薪850美元 | *Monthly rainfall in the area goes down from four inches in January to nothing at all in July.* 該地區的月降雨量從一月份的四英寸降到七月份的滴水全無。**3** a monthly ticket, PASS² (1) etc can be used for a period of one month〔票、通行證等〕有效期為一個月的 —**monthly** *adv*: *They meet monthly to discuss progress.* 他們每月碰一次頭討論進展情況。

monthly² *n* [C] **1** a magazine that appears once a month 月刊 **2 monthlies** *BrE old-fashioned* a woman's PERIOD (=flow of blood from the body each month)【英, 過時】月經

mon·u·ment /ˋmɑnjəmənt; ˈmɒnjʊmənt/ *n* [C] **1** a building or other large structure that is built to remind people of an important event or famous person 紀念碑, 紀念塔, 紀念館: [+of/to] *a monument to soldiers killed in battle* 陣亡將士紀念碑 | *The Victor Emmanuel monument was built to commemorate the unity of Italy.* 維克托·伊曼紐爾紀念碑是為紀念意大利的統一而建造的。**2** a very old building or place that is important historically 遺跡, 遺址, 名勝古跡: *The Alhambra is the last and most exquisite monument of Arab civilization in Europe.* 艾勒漢卜拉宮是阿拉伯文明在歐洲最後的也是建築得最精美的一處遺址。**3 be a monument to** to be a very clear example of what can happen as a result of a particular quality 是…的例證[見證]: *The house, built just before the stock market crash, was a monument to miscalculation.* 股票市場崩潰前不久建起的那幢房子是錯誤判斷的見證。

mon·u·ment·al /ˌmɑnjəˋmɛntl; ˌmɒnjʊˈmentl◂/ *adj* **1** [usually before noun 一般用於名詞前] a monumental achievement, piece of work, etc is very important and influential, and is usually based on many years of work 豐碑式的, 偉大的: *a monumental contribution to the field of medicine* 對醫學領域重大的貢獻 | *Charles Darwin's monumental study, 'The Origin of Species'* 查爾斯·達爾文的巨著《物種起源》**2** [only before noun 僅用於名詞前] extremely large, bad, good, impressive etc 極大[壞, 好, 令人難忘等]的: *There was a monumental traffic jam on the freeway.* 高速公路上出現了嚴重的交通阻塞。| *This is yet more evidence of his monumental incompetence.* 這將成為他極端無能的又一次證明。**3** [only before noun 僅用於名詞前] appearing on a monument or built as a monument 出現在紀念碑[塔]上的; 紀念性的: *a monumental temple* 紀念性神殿

mon·u·ment·al·ly /ˌmɑnjəˋmɛntlɪ; ˌmɒnjʊˈmentəli/ *adv* extremely 極端, 極其: [+adj/adv] *It was a monumentally stupid thing to do.* 那是一件極其愚蠢的事。

moo¹ /mu; muː/ *v* [I] to make the sound a cow makes 發牛叫聲, 發哞聲

moo² *n* [C] **1** the sound that a cow makes 哞〔牛叫聲〕**2** *BrE old-fashioned* a stupid woman【英, 過時】愚蠢的女人: *You silly old moo!* 你這個傻老太婆!

mooch /mutʃ; muːtʃ/ *v* [T] *AmE informal* to get something by asking someone to give you it, instead of paying for it; CADGE【美, 非正式】討要, 乞取: *He tried to mooch a drink from me.* 他想從我這兒討杯酒喝。

mooch around also 又作 **mooch about** *BrE*【英】*phr v* [I] *informal* to walk around without any purpose【非正式】閒蕩, 閒逛: *"Where've you been?" "Oh, just mooching around."* "你到哪兒去了?" "噢, 只是隨便逛了逛。"

mood /mud; muːd/ *n* 3 3

1 ▶WAY YOU FEEL 心情◀ [C] the way you feel at a particular time 心情, 心境, 情緒: *His moods change very quickly – one moment he's cheerful and the next he's sunk in despair.* 他的情緒變化無常——一會兒興高采烈, 一會兒又心灰意冷。| *It takes a couple of days to get into the holiday mood.* 進入假日氣氛需要幾天的時間。| **be in a good mood/bad mood etc** (=be happy, annoyed, angry etc) 心情好/壞等 *You're in a good mood this morning!* 你今天早晨心情不錯啊! | *The kids were in a really silly mood after the party.* 派對後那些年輕人感到很失落。| **be in a foul/filthy mood** (=be very angry or upset) 心情非常不好, 情緒很糟 *Don't talk to Jean; she's in a filthy mood!* 別跟瓊說話, 她情緒糟透了! | **put sb in a good/bad mood** (=make them feel happy or annoyed) 使某人心情愉快/不愉快 *I'd been stuck in the traffic for hours, which put me in a really bad mood.* 我被困在車流中好幾個小時, 心情都壞透了。

2 be in a mood to feel unhappy or angry 情緒不好: *She's been in a real mood all day.* 她整天在鬧情緒。| **be in one of your/his moods** (=used when someone often gets in a bad mood) 情緒不好

3 be in no mood for sth/to do sth to not want to do something, or be determined not to do something 不想做某事; 決心不做某事: *The boss is in no mood for compromise on this point.* 在這一點上老闆不想妥協。| *I was in no mood to argue any more.* 我不想再爭論了。

4 be/feel in the mood (for sth/to do sth) to want to do something or feel that you would enjoy doing something 有意(做某事), 有(做某事)的心情: *She was in the mood for a romantic walk in the woods.* 她想在樹林裡浪漫地走一走。| *I don't want to talk about it now. I'm not in the mood.* 我現在不想談論此事, 我沒心情。

5 ▶WAY PEOPLE FEEL 人們的情緒◀ [singular] the way a group of people feels about something or about

life in general 情緒; 心態: [+of] *The president had misjudged the mood of the people on this issue.* 總統在這個問題上錯誤地判斷了公眾的情緒。| *The novel captures the mood of postwar France.* 這部小説如實地呈現了戰後法國的社會氛圍。

6 ▶GRAMMAR 語法◀ [C] *technical* one of the sets of verb forms in grammar such as the INDICATIVE (=expressing a fact or action), the IMPERATIVE (=expressing a command) or the SUBJUNCTIVE (=expressing a doubt or wish)【術語】語氣〈如陳述、祈使和虛擬等語氣〉

mood mu·sic /ˈ· ˌ··/ *n* [U] music that is supposed to make you feel particular emotions, especially romantic feelings 氣氛音樂〔引起聽眾某種情感、尤指浪漫情感的音樂〕, 抒情樂曲

mood·y /ˈmudɪ; ˈmuːdi/ *adj* **moodier, moodiest 1** easily becoming annoyed or unhappy when there is no good reason to feel that way 易怒的; 情緒不好的: *She had been moody and difficult all day.* 她整天一直悶悶不樂、彆彆扭扭的。| *They kept apart in moody silence.* 他們悶悶不樂, 一言不發, 彼此保持着距離。**2** having moods that change often and quickly 喜怒無常的, 情緒多變的: *a moody child* 喜怒無常的孩子 **—moodily** *adv*: *She was staring moodily into the fire.* 她悶悶不樂地盯着爐火。**—moodiness** *n* [U]

moo·la, moolah /ˈmulə; ˈmuːlə/ *n* [U] *AmE slang* money【美俚】鈔票, 錢

3 **moon¹** /mun; muːn/ *n* **1 the moon** the round object that you can see shining in the sky at night, and that moves around the Earth every 28 days 月亮, 月球: *the first man on the moon* 第一個登上月球的人 **2** [singular] the shape of this object as it appears at a particular time〔特定時間出現的〕月亮, 月球的形狀: *a crescent moon* 新月, 娥眉月 | *There's no moon tonight.* (=it cannot be seen) 今晚沒有月光。**3** [C] a round object that moves around a PLANET other than Earth 衛星: *the moons of Saturn* 土星的衛星 **4 ask for the moon** also 又作 **cry for the moon** *BrE informal* to ask for something that is difficult or impossible to obtain【英, 非正式】要求得到難以[無法]得到的東西; 妄想, 異想天開 **5 over the moon** *BrE informal* very happy【英, 非正式】非常高興的: *She's over the moon about her new job.* 她對新工作非常滿意。**6 throw a moon** *BrE*【英】, **shoot the moon** *AmE*【美】*informal* to show your bare BUTTOCKs to someone as a joke or a way of insulting someone【非正式】〔開玩笑或侮辱性地〕露出光屁股 **7 many moons ago** *poetic* a long time ago【詩】很久以前: *It all happened many moons ago.* 那一切都發生在很久以前。—see also 另見 FULL MOON, HALF MOON, NEW MOON, **once in a blue moon** (BLUE¹ (4)), **promise sb the moon** (PROMISE¹ (3))

moon² *v* [I,T] *informal* to bend over and show your bare BUTTOCKs as a joke or a way of insulting someone【非正式】〔開玩笑或侮辱性地〕(對着...) 躬身露出光屁股

moon about/around *phr v* [I] *BrE informal* to spend your time lazily, moving around with no real purpose【英, 非正式】閒蕩; 閒混: *I wish you'd stop mooning about and do something useful!* 我希望你別再閒混, 做點有用的事吧!

moon over sb/sth *phr v* [T] *informal* to spend your time thinking and dreaming about someone or something that you love【非正式】為...出神, 如夢如痴地想念〔所愛的人或物〕: *She sits mooning over his photograph for hours.* 她連坐好幾個小時, 對着他的照片出神。

moon·beam /ˈmunˌbim; ˈmuːnbiːm/ *n* [C] a beam of light from the moon 一道[縷]月光

moon boot /ˈ· ·/ *n* [C] a thick warm cloth or plastic boot worn in snow and cold weather 月靴〔一種在雪中及寒冷天氣下所穿的厚而暖和的布靴或塑料靴〕

Moon·ie /ˈmunɪ; ˈmuːni/ *n* [C] a member of a religious group started by the Korean businessman Sun Myung Moon 統一教信徒〔韓國商人文鮮明所創始的一個宗教團體的成員〕

moon·less /ˈmunləs; ˈmuːnləs/ *adj* a moonless sky or night is dark because the moon cannot be seen 沒有月光的: *a cloudy, moonless night* 一個多雲、沒有月色的夜晚

moon·light¹ /ˈmunˌlaɪt; ˈmuːnlaɪt/ *n* [U] **1** the light of the moon 月光: *The hills were bathed in pale moonlight.* 羣山沐浴在淡淡的月光中。**2 do a moonlight** also 又作 **do a moonlight flit** *BrE* leave a place secretly in the middle of the night in order to avoid paying money that you owe【英】〔為躲債而〕夜間潛逃: *Two of the hotel guests had done a moonlight without paying their bills.* 旅館房客中有兩個沒有付賬, 於夜間偷偷地逃走了。

moonlight² *v past tense and past participle* **moonlighted** [I] *informal*【非正式】**1** to have a second job in addition to your main job, especially without the knowledge of the government tax department 從事第二職業〔尤指不為政府稅務部門所知〕, 兼職: *She's been moonlighting as a waitress in the evenings.* 她晚上一直兼職做女招待。**2** *BrE* to do paid work although you are getting money from the government because you do not officially have a job【英】〔在領取政府失業救濟金的同時〕做工賺錢; DOUBLE-DIP² *AmE*【美】**—moonlighter** *n* [C] **—moonlighting** *n* [U]: *He's been doing some moonlighting for another company.* 他一直在另一家公司做兼職。

moon·lit /ˈmunˌlɪt; ˈmuːnˌlɪt/ *adj* [only before noun 僅用於名詞前] made brighter by the light of the moon 月光照耀下的: *a moonlit garden* 月色下的花園

moon·scape /ˈmunˌskep; ˈmuːnskeɪp/ *n* [C] a bare empty area of land that looks like the surface of the moon〔如月球表面一樣的〕荒涼地帶, 荒山景色

moon·shine /ˈmunˌʃaɪn; ˈmuːnʃaɪn/ *n* [U] *informal*【非正式】**1** a stupid or impractical remark, idea, or plan 愚蠢[不切實際]的言辭[想法, 計劃]; 空談; 妄想: *He regarded her plans as romantic moonshine.* 他認為她的計劃不切實際。**2** *especially AmE* strong alcoholic drink that is produced illegally【尤美】非法釀造的烈性酒

moon·shot /ˈmunʃɑt; ˈmuːnʃɒt/ *n* [C] a SPACESHIP flight through space to the moon〔宇宙飛船的〕奔月飛行

moon·stone /ˈmunˌston; ˈmuːnstəʊn/ *n* [C,U] a milky-white stone used in making jewellery 月長石, 月光石: *a moonstone necklace* 月長石項鏈

moon·struck /ˈmunˌstrʌk; ˈmuːnstrʌk/ *adj informal* slightly mad【非正式】輕度神經錯亂的

moor¹ /mʊr; mʊə/ *n* [C] **1** usually 一般作 **moors** [plural] *especially BrE* a wild open area of high land, covered with rough grass or low bushes and HEATHER, that is not farmed because the soil is not good enough【尤英】漠澤, 高沼〔因土質差無法耕種的高地荒原〕; 荒野, 曠野: *They went grouse shooting up on the moors.* 他們去荒野射獵松雞。| *the Yorkshire moors* 約克郡漠澤 **2 Moor** one of the Muslim people of the Arab race who were in power in Spain from 711 to 1492 摩爾人〔公元711年至1492年統治西班牙的阿拉伯穆斯林〕

moor² *v* [I,T] to fasten a ship or boat to the land or to the bottom of the sea using ropes or an ANCHOR 停泊, 繫泊〔船隻〕: *We moored in the estuary, waiting for high tide.* 我們停泊在河口, 等待漲潮。

moor·hen /ˈmʊrˌhɛn; ˈmʊəhen/ *n* [C] a black bird that lives beside streams and lakes 澤雞; 黑水雞

moor·ing /ˈmʊrɪŋ; ˈmʊərɪŋ/ *n* [C] **1 moorings** [plural] the ropes, chains, ANCHORs etc used to moor a ship or boat〔船的〕繫泊用具〈如繩、鏈、錨等〉: *Several ships had broken their moorings during the storm.* 在暴風雨中好幾條船掙斷了纜繩。**2** the place where a ship or boat is moored〔船的〕繫泊處, 停泊地, 泊位: *a temporary mooring* 臨時繫泊處

Moor·ish /ˈmʊrɪʃ; ˈmʊərɪʃ/ *adj* connected with the MOORs 摩爾人的: *Moorish architecture in Spain* 西班牙的摩爾式建築

moor·land /ˈmʊrˌlænd; ˈmʊələnd/ also 又作 **moorlands** *n* [U] *especially BrE* wild open countryside covered with rough grass and low bushes【尤英】高沼地; 曠野, 荒原

—**moorland** *adj*: *a moorland cottage* 曠野中的小屋

moose /mus; muːs/ *n plural* **moose** [C] a large brown animal like a DEER that has very large flat ANTLERS (=horns that grow like branches), and lives in North America and northern Europe 麋, 駝鹿

moot¹ /mut; muːt/ *adj* **1 a moot point/question** something that has not yet been decided, and about which people have different opinions 爭論未決的論點/問題: *Whether these controls will really reduce violent crime is a moot point.* 這些控制措施能否真的減少暴力犯罪是一個尚有爭議的問題。**2** *AmE* a situation or possible action that is moot, is no longer likely to happen or exist 【美】〔某情況或行為〕不再會發生的, 不再會存在的: *The fear that airstrikes could endanger troops is moot now that the army is withdrawing.* 由於軍隊正在撤退, 人們不會再害怕空襲可能危及部隊的安全了。

moot² *v* [T] **be mooted** to be suggested for people to consider 被提出供考慮: *The question of changing the membership rules was mooted at the last meeting.* 修改會員章程的問題是在上一次會議上提出審議的。

moot court /ˈ· ·/ *n* [C] *AmE* a court in which law students practise holding trials 【美】〔法學院學生實習的〕模擬法庭, 假設法庭

mop¹ /mɑp; mɒp/ *n* [C] **1** a thing for washing floors with, consisting of a long stick with threads of thick string or a piece of SPONGE¹ (1) fastened to one end 拖把 **2** a thing for cleaning dishes with, consisting of a short stick with a piece of SPONGE¹ (1) fastened to one end 洗碗刷 **3** [usually singular 一般用單數] *informal* a large amount of thick, often untidy hair 【非正式】濃密(蓬亂)的頭髮: **[+of]** *a baby with a mop of golden curls* 長着一頭濃密的金色鬈髮的嬰兒

mop² *v* **mopping, mopped 1** [I,T] to wash a floor with a wet mop 用濕拖把拖(地板) —see picture at 參見 CLEAN² 圖 **2** [T] to dry your face by rubbing it with a cloth or something soft 擦乾〔臉〕, 揩乾: *It was so hot he had to keep stopping to mop his face.* 天氣太熱, 他只得不斷地停下來擦一擦臉。| **mop your brow** (=remove SWEAT² (1) from your forehead) 擦去額頭上的汗水 **3** [I,T] to remove liquid from a surface by rubbing it with a cloth or something soft 擦掉〔液體〕, 抹掉: **mop sth from sth** *The nurse gently mopped the blood from the wound.* 護士輕輕地抹去傷口上的血。| **mop sth away** *She mopped the tears away with a lacy handkerchief.* 她用一條花邊手絹擦去了淚水。**4 mop the floor with** *AmE* 【美】, **wipe the floor with** *BrE* 【英】 to completely defeat someone, for example in a game or argument 〔在比賽或辯論中〕徹底擊敗: *We mopped the floor with the team from Pomona High.* 我們徹底擊敗了來自波莫納中學的參賽隊。

mop sth ↔ **up** *phr v* [T] **1** to remove liquid with a mop, cloth, or something soft, especially in order to clean a surface 擦乾, 抹去〔液體〕: *Can you mop up the milk you've spilled?* 把你灑了的牛奶擦乾淨好嗎? | *Mop up the sauce with your bread.* 用你的麵包把調味汁抹乾淨。**2** to deal with the remaining members of a defeated army by killing them or making them prisoners 肅清〔殘敵〕, 掃蕩〔殘兵敗將〕: *mopping up isolated pockets of resistance* 掃蕩零星抵抗的敵人 | **mopping-up operations** *The rebellion has been crushed, but mopping-up operations may take several weeks.* 叛亂已被粉碎, 但肅清殘餘也許還要數週時間。**3** *BrE* to complete a piece of work or finish dealing with something or someone 【英】結束, 完成: *I've just got a couple of jobs to mop up before I go on holiday.* 在去休假之前我還有幾件工作要完成。

mope /mop; məʊp/ *v* [I] to feel sorry for yourself, without making any effort to be more cheerful 憂鬱, 悶悶不樂: *Don't lie there moping on a lovely morning like this!* 這麼美好的一個早晨, 你就別躺在那裡悶悶不樂了!

mope around also 又作 **mope about** *phr v* [I,T] *BrE* to move around a place in a sad, slow way 【英】(在...)沒精打采地閒蕩, 憂鬱地徘徊: *She spends her days moping around the house.* 她成天在房子裡沒精打采地瞎轉悠。

mo·ped /ˈmopɛd; ˈməʊped/ *n* [C] a small two-wheeled vehicle with an engine 機器腳踏車, 助動車 —compare 比較 MOTORCYCLE

mo·quette /moˈkɛt; mɒˈket/ *n* [U] a thick soft material used for covering furniture 〔包蓋家具的〕絨布織物: *a moquette armchair* 絨面扶手椅

mo·raine /moˈren; məˈreɪn/ *n* [C] *technical* a mass of earth or pieces of rock left in a line at the bottom or edge of a GLACIER 【術語】冰磧, 冰川堆石 —see picture on page A12 參見 A12 頁圖

mor·al¹ /ˈmɔrəl; ˈmɒrəl/ *adj* S3 W2

1 ►ABOUT RIGHT AND WRONG 有關對與錯◄ [only before noun 僅用於名詞前] connected with the principles of what is right and wrong behaviour, and with the difference between good and evil 道德(上)的: *a man of high moral standards* 道德高尚的人 | *You don't know the circumstances of the divorce, so don't make moral judgments about it.* 你不了解離婚的情況, 所以不要對此作道德上誰是誰非的判斷。| **moral dilemma/issue** (=a subject that involves morals) 道德上的困境/問題 *the abortion issue, one of the great moral dilemmas* 道德上的大難題之一 —— 墮胎問題 | **moral sense** (=ability to understand the difference between right and wrong) 道德感, 是非感 *Babies are born without a moral sense.* 嬰兒生下來並沒有道德感。

2 ►BASED ON WHAT IS RIGHT 基於是非感的◄ [only before noun 僅用於名詞前] based on your ideas about what is right, rather than on what is legal or practical 基於道德的, 道義上的: **moral responsibility/duty** *You have a moral responsibility to help people in need.* 你在道義上有責任幫助有困難的人。| **moral courage** (=the courage to do what you believe is right) 道義勇氣, 堅持正義的勇氣 *Does he have the moral courage necessary to lead the country?* 他具有國家領導人所需要的道義勇氣嗎? | **moral authority** (=influence that you have because people accept that your beliefs are right) 道義上的權力[權威, 影響力] *The UN feels that it has the moral authority to send troops to the area.* 聯合國認為它在道義上有權向該地區派遣部隊。| **moral fibre** *BrE* 【英】/ **fiber** *AmE* 【美】 (=the emotional strength to do what you believe is right) 道德力量, 正義感

3 moral support encouragement that you give by expressing approval or interest, rather than by giving practical help 道義上的支持, 精神支持: *He went along to give moral support.* 他前去給予道義上的支持。

4 moral victory a situation in which you show that your beliefs are right and fair, even if you do not win the argument 道義[精神]上的勝利: *We felt we had won a moral victory in the debate.* 我們感到在辯論中我們取得了道義上的勝利。

5 ►STORY 故事◄ a moral story, play etc is one that teaches or shows good behaviour 〔故事、戲劇等〕有教育意義的, 說教性的

6 ►PERSON 人◄ always behaving in a way that is based on strong principles about what is right and wrong 有道德的, 品行端正的 —compare 比較 AMORAL, IMMORAL —see also 另見 MORALLY

moral² *n* [C] **1 morals** [plural] principles or standards of good behaviour, especially in matters of sex 〔尤指男女關係上的〕道德準則[標準]; 道德, 倫理; 品行: *The novel reflects the morals and customs of the time.* 這部小說反映了當時的道德標準和社會習俗。| **public morals** (=the standards of behaviour, especially sexual behaviour, expected by society) 〔尤指性行為方面的〕公眾道德, 社會公德 *The sex shop was deemed a danger to public morals.* 性用品商店被認為有傷風化。| **loose morals** *old-fashioned or humorous* (=low standards of sexual behaviour resulting in someone having many sexual partners) 【過時或幽默】放蕩的品行, 不檢點的品行 **2** a practical lesson about what to do or how to behave, which you learn from a story or from something that

happens to you 寓意, 道德上的教訓; 教育意義: **the moral of sth is** *The moral of the film was that crime does not pay.* 這部電影的寓意是犯罪難逃法律制裁。| **draw a moral** (=understand what a story or event is teaching you) 明白〔故事或事件的〕寓意

mo·rale /məˈræl; məˈrɑːl/ *n* [U] the level of confidence and positive feelings, especially among a group of people who work together, belong to the same team etc 士氣, 鬥志; 精神面貌: *The team's morale was low after losing.* 比賽輸了之後, 球隊士氣低落。| *A few words of praise are always good for morale.* 幾句讚揚的話對提高士氣總是有用的。| **keep up/maintain morale** *the benefits of regular exercise in keeping up students' morale* 定期鍛鍊在保持學生良好的精神狀態方面所具有的好處 | **boost/raise/improve morale** *Churchill's visit did a great deal to boost morale among the troops.* 丘吉爾的到訪大大鼓舞了部隊的士氣。

mor·al·ist /ˈmɔrəlɪst; ˈmɒrəlɪst/ *n* [C] **1** someone who has very strong beliefs about what is right and wrong, and who tries to control other people's morals 說教者, 衛道士 **2** a teacher of moral principles 道德家; 德育家, 德育工作者

mor·al·ist·ic /ˌmɔrəˈlɪstɪk; ˌmɒrəˈlɪstɪk◂/ *adj* having very strong unchanging beliefs about what is right and wrong, especially when this makes you judge other people's behaviour 道德觀念強烈的; 道德說教的: *It's difficult to talk to teenagers about drugs without sounding too moralistic.* 跟青少年談論毒品, 很難做到聽起來不過於說教。—**moralistically** /-klɪ; -kli/ *adv*

mo·ral·i·ty /məˈrælətɪ; məˈræləti/ *n* **1** [U] beliefs or ideas about what is right and wrong and about how people should behave 道德; 道德觀: *traditional morality* 傳統道德觀 | *declining standards of morality* 日益低下的道德水平 **2** [U] the degree to which something is right or acceptable 道德性; 道義性; 正當性: **[+of]** *a discussion on the morality of abortion* 關於墮胎是否符合道德標準的討論 **3** [C,U] a system of beliefs and values concerning how people should behave, which is accepted by a particular person or group 道德體系; 道德規範: *Christian morality* 基督教的道德體系 | *a direct clash in moralities* 不同道德體系的直接衝突 —opposite 反義詞 IMMORALITY

mor·al·ize also 又作 **-ise** *BrE*【英】/ˈmɔrəlˌaɪz; ˈmɒrəlaɪz/ *v* [I] to tell other people your ideas about right and wrong behaviour, especially when they have not asked for your opinion 說教; 教化; 訓導: **[+about/on]** *politicians moralizing about people's sexual behaviour* 就人們的性態度進行說教的政治家 —**moralizer** *n* [C]

mor·al·ly /ˈmɔrəlɪ; ˈmɒrəli/ *adv* **1** according to moral principles about what is right and wrong 道德上, 道義上: *What you did wasn't illegal, but it was morally wrong.* 你做的事並不違法, 但從道義上講是錯誤的。| *The president is morally opposed to capital punishment.* 總統從道義上反對死刑。| **morally responsible** *He held himself morally responsible for the accident.* 他認為自己應為那次事故負道義上的責任。**2** in a way which is good or right 有道德地, 品行端正地: *one of the few politicians who always behaves completely morally* 行為一貫十分端正的極少數政治家之一 **3 morally certain** *old-fashioned* very probable【過時】很可能的: *It's morally certain that he'll be the next President.* 他很可能會成為下屆總統。

moral ma·jor·i·ty /ˌ.. .ˈ.../ *n* [singular] a group of people in the US with strong Christian principles, who have very traditional beliefs about the family, crime and punishment, people's sexual behaviour etc 道德多數派〔美國嚴格遵循基督教準則並對家庭、犯罪與懲罰及人們的性行為等抱有傳統觀念的團體〕

mo·rass /məˈræs; məˈræs/ *n* **1** [singular] a complicated and confusing situation that is very difficult to get out of 困境; 陷阱: **[+of]** *We were bogged down in a morass of detail.* 我們陷進了瑣碎細節的泥淖。**2** [C] *especially literary* a dangerous area of soft wet ground; MARSH【尤文】泥淖, 沼澤

mor·a·to·ri·um /ˌmɔrəˈtorɪəm; ˌmɒrəˈtɔːriəm/ *n* [C usually singular 一般用單數] **1** an official stopping of an activity for a period of time〔官方的〕暫停, 中止: **[+on]** *the proposed moratorium on nuclear testing* 擬議中的暫停核試驗 **2** a law or an agreement that gives people more time to pay their debts 允許延期償債的法律[協議]

mor·bid /ˈmɔrbɪd; ˈmɔːbɪd/ *adj* **1** having a strong and unhealthy interest in unpleasant subjects, especially death〔興趣、精神、思想等〕病態的, 不健康的: *He wanted to know all the morbid details about the accident.* 他想知道所有與那起事故有關的令人毛骨悚然的細節。| *a morbid fascination with instruments of torture* 對刑具的一種病態的迷戀 **2** *technical* connected with or caused by a disease【術語】疾病的; 疾病引起的; 致病的: *a morbid gene* 致病基因 —**morbidly** *adv* —**morbidity** *n* [U]

mor·dant /ˈmɔrdn̩t; ˈmɔːdənt/ *adj* **mordant criticism/wit/humour** *formal* cruel and insulting criticism, wit etc【正式】尖刻的批評/妙語/幽默

more[1] /mor; mɔː/ *adv* **1** [+adj/adv] having a particular quality or characteristic to a greater degree than someone or something else 更, 更加, 較為: **more interesting/expensive etc** *We can make the test more difficult by adding a time limit.* 我們可以通過加上時間限制使測試更難些。| *It could have been an infection but it's more likely to have been something you ate.* 這可能是由於感染, 但更可能是由於你吃的東西不合適。| **more interesting/expensive etc than** *Who knows if there are beings more advanced than ourselves out there on other planets?* 誰知道在其他行星上是否存在着比我們更高級的生物呢? | **much/a lot/far more** *Many of the children feel much more confident if they work in groups.* 許多孩子在集體協作時會感到自信得多。—opposite 反義詞 LESS[1] (1) **2** used to say that something happens more often or for a longer time than before or than something else 更〔經常地或長久地〕: *He's managed to master the basics of tennis but needs to practice a bit more.* 他已經設法掌握了網球的基本要領, 但還需要多加練習。| **more than** *Businesses use computers more than they used to.* 企業比過去更多地使用電腦。| **far/much/a lot more** *He goes out a lot more now he has the car.* 現在有了汽車, 他出去的次數多多了。—opposite 反義詞 LESS[1] (1) **3** used to say that something such as a feeling or opinion is felt or believed to a greater degree 更強烈; 更大程度地: *I couldn't agree more.* 我完全同意。| **more than** *It's her manner I dislike, more than what she actually says.* 我討厭的倒不是她實際上說些甚麼, 而是她的態度。| **much/far/a lot more** *She cares far more for her dogs than she does for me.* 她關心狗遠遠勝過關心我。—opposite 反義詞 LESS[1] (1) **4 more and more** if something happens or is done more and more it happens or is done more than before and is becoming common 越來越: *More and more I see young boys with no prospects turning to crime or drugs.* 我看到越來越多前途無望的男孩子走上犯罪或吸毒的邪路。**5 more and more tired/angry etc** increasingly tired, angry etc as time passes 越來越疲勞/生氣等: *As the disease worsened he found walking more and more difficult.* 隨着病情的惡化, 他感到走路越來越困難。**6 once more a)** if you do something once more you do it again and usually for the last time 再次〔通常為最後一次〕: *Can we rehearse the scene once more before the show starts?* 在演出開始之前我們把這場戲再排練一次好嗎? **b)** *especially literary* again【尤文】再一次, 又一次: *Once more the soldiers attacked and once more they were defeated.* 士兵們再次發動進攻, 但又一次被擊敗。**7 not any more** also 又作 **no more** *literary* no longer【文】不再: *Didn't you know? Paul and Ann aren't going out together any more.* 你不知道嗎? 保羅和安分手了。| *No more is it possible to stand on the football terraces and cheer on your local team.* 站在足

球場看台上, 為你們本地球隊歡呼吶喊, 這已是不再可能的事了。**8 more often than not** used to say that something usually happens 往往, 多半, 通常: *More often than not people don't realise what their rights are.* 人們往往不知道自己有哪些權利。**9 be more than pleased/sorry etc** used to emphasize that you are very pleased, very sorry etc 非常高興/難過等: *The store is more than happy to deliver goods to your home.* 本商店很樂意為您送貨上門。| *"I suppose you will be working late again tonight?" "More than likely, yes."* "我想今晚你又要工作到深夜, 是吧?" "是的, 極有可能。" **10 be more than a little angry/sad etc** used to emphasize how angry or sad you are 非常生氣/傷心等: *We're more than a little concerned about the state of his financial affairs.* 我們非常擔心他的財務狀況。**11 more...than...** used to emphasize that one thing is truer, more important etc than something 與其說…倒不如說…: *Don't be too hard on him. He's more misled than stupid.* 不要對他太苛刻。與其說他愚蠢, 倒不如說他被誤導了。| *She's known more for her wild private life than her acting ability.* 她很出名, 與其說她靠的是演技, 倒不如說是放蕩不羈的私生活。**12 a) no more than** used to say that something is needed or suitable 正是〔需要的或合適的〕: *It's no more than you deserve.* 這完全是你該得到的。**b)** also 又作 **little more than** used to say that someone or something is less important than they seem 只不過, 僅僅: *He's no more than a glorified accountant.* 他只不過是一個被美化了的會計而已。| *It was little more than a scratch.* 僅僅是一點擦傷而已。**13 (and) what's more** used to add more information that emphasizes what you are saying 而且, 更重要的是, 更有甚者: *He enjoyed the meal and what's more he ate the lot!* 他喜歡那頓飯, 而且把它全吃光了! **14 no more...than...** used to emphasize that something is not true, not suitable etc 不比…更…, 與…同樣不…: *He's no more fit to be a priest than I am!* 他和我一樣都不適合當牧師! **15 no more can she/no more do I etc** neither can she, neither do I etc 她也不能/我也沒有等: *I don't have time to do the filing and no more do you!* 我沒有時間把文件歸檔, 你也沒有! **16 (then) more fool you** *BrE* used to say that you think someone is being stupid【英】(那)你真是傻極了: *If you want to get up so early in the morning then more fool you!* 如果你想起得那麼早, 那你真是傻透了!

USAGE NOTE 用法說明: MORE

GRAMMAR 語法

More is used with an adjective instead of the *-er* form, not as well as it. more 後跟形容詞的原級形式而非其 -er 形式, 如: *This year's exam was harder for me* (NOT 不用 *more harder*). 今年的考試對我來說更難一些。

It is also used when an adjective does not have an *-er* form. 它後面也可跟沒有 -er 形式的形容詞: *This year's exam was more difficult than last year's.* 今年的考試比去年的難。

1 1 **more²** *quantifier comparative of many, much* many 和 much 的比較級 **1** used to say that a particular number or amount is larger than another 〔數量〕更大的, 更多的; 更大的數量: *"Do you want more cake?" "Uh, maybe. I'll get it."* "你還要點蛋糕嗎?" "唔, 也許吧。我會去拿的。" | **more people/things etc than...** *More cars are failing the emissions test than was anticipated.* 通不過尾氣排放測試的汽車比預計的多。| *She makes more phone calls in one day than anyone else I know.* 在我認識的所有人當中, 她每天打的電話最多。| **more than 10/100 etc** *More than 500 people had to be helped to safety when the stadium collapsed.* 體育館坍塌時, 有五百多人需要幫忙逃出險境。| **more than sth** *In some places bottled water costs more than a glass of beer.* 在有些地方一瓶瓶裝水比一杯啤酒還貴。| *It is possible to earn $100 a day, some days more.* 一天可能掙 100 美元, 有時還不止。| *I'd ask Veronica – she knows far more about it.* 我還是問問維朗妮卡 —— 她對此事知道得要多得多。| **[+of]** *We sell more of these maps because they're so colourful.* 這些地圖我們賣得多一些, 因為它們色彩非常鮮豔。| **much/far/a lot more** *Recent anti-smoking campaigns have driven a lot more smokers to give up.* 近來的反吸煙運動已經使更多的吸煙者戒了煙。—opposite 反義詞 LESS² or FEWER **2** used when you mean another number or amount in addition to what you have, expect, or have mentioned 〔數量〕另外的, 附加的, 額外的: *You'll have to pay more for a double room.* 住雙人間必須多付錢。| *A free trip to Jamaica? Tell me more!* 免費到牙買加旅遊? 跟我具體講講! | **2/10 etc more** *That was Jim on the phone. He needs two more tickets for the play.* 是吉姆來的電話。他還需要兩張戲票。| **some/any/a few etc more** *We have some wonderful people volunteering to help out but many more are needed.* 我們有一些很不錯的人志願幫忙, 但還需要更多的人。| **more people/things etc** *I think I'd need to know some more facts before I could agree to the trip.* 我想我還需要再了解一些情況, 才能同意作這次旅行。| *I'm sorry sir, your meal will be five minutes more, I'm afraid.* 對不起先生, 恐怕您的飯還要再等五分鐘。| **[+of]** *Can I have some more of that apple pie please?* 請問我可以再來一些那樣的蘋果餡餅嗎? | *You've had a week to do it. How much more time do you need?* 已經給了你一週時間了, 你還需要多少時間? —opposite 反義詞 LESS² **3 more and more** an increasing number of something 越來越多的: *More and more people are taking early retirement these days.* 現在越來越多的人提前退休。—opposite 反義詞 **less and less** (LESS¹ (2)) **4 more or less a)** almost 幾乎, 差不多: *By the time of the dress rehearsal she knew her lines more or less by heart.* 到最後彩排的時候, 她幾乎把台詞都背下來了。**b)** APPROXIMATELY 大致, 大約, 或多或少: *We're expecting 150 delegates at the conference, more or less.* 我們預計大約會有 150 名代表參加會議。**5 not/no more than** used to say that a price, distance etc is only a particular number or amount 〔價格、距離等〕不超過, 至多, 僅僅: *It's a beautiful cottage not more than five minutes from the nearest beach.* 那是一座漂亮的小屋, 離最近的海灘至多五分鐘的路程。**6 the more..., the more.../the less** used to say that when you do something or something happens, a particular situation will be the result of it 越…越…: *It's simple. The more preparation you do now, the less nervous you'll be before the exam.* 這很簡單。你現在準備得越充分, 考試前你就越不會緊張。—see also 另見 **more's the pity** (PITY¹ (5))

more·ish /ˈmɔrɪʃ; ˈmɔːrɪʃ/ *adj BrE spoken* food that is moreish tastes very good, and makes you want to eat more of it【英口】好吃的; 令人垂涎欲滴的

more·o·ver /mɔrˈovɚ; mɔːrˈəʊvə/ *adv* [sentence adverb 句子副詞] *formal* a word meaning 'in addition', used to introduce information that adds to or supports what has previously been said【正式】此外, 而且, 加之, 再者: *The rent is reasonable and, moreover, the location is perfect.* 房租合理, 而且地段極好。 2

USAGE NOTE 用法說明: MOREOVER

FORMALITY 正式程度

Moreover is very formal and not common in spoken English. But you may see it used in a report. moreover 非常正式, 口語中不常見, 但可見於報道中: *Local people would like a new road. Moreover, there are good economic reasons for building one.* 當地人希望修一條新公路。而且在經濟方面修路也有充足的理由。

Also is a less formal way of adding a reason or idea. It can be used at the beginning of a sentence to link it to the previous one. also 用以補充原因或想法,

正式程度比 moreover 低一些，此詞可用於句首把該句與前句連接起來：*You can stay at our house. Also, I can check the plane times for you.* 你可以住在我們這兒。另外，我能為你查一下班機的時間。Or it can be used within a sentence. 它也可以用於句中：*I can also check the plane times for you.* 我還能為你查一下班機的時間。

Besides (that) is more informal and used especially to add a reason. besides (that) 正式程度比 also 又低了一個層次，尤用以補充原因：*June isn't a good month to go there. Besides, I want to finish my exams first.* 六月份不是去那兒的好時候。而且，我還想先完成考試。

People also often add reasons and ideas within one sentence using **and** made stronger with **moreover/also/besides**. 人們也經常在句中用 and 與 moreover/also/besides 連用來補充原因和想法，後者加強前者的語氣：*You should switch to a healthier diet and moreover/also/besides that stop smoking.* 你應該轉向更有益於健康的飲食，除此之外，還要把煙戒掉。

mo·res /ˋmoriz; ˈmɔːreɪz/ *n* [plural] *formal* the customs, social behaviour, and moral values of a particular group【正式】習俗；慣例：*American social and sexual mores* 美國的社交和性習俗

morgue /mɔrg; mɔːg/ *n* [C] **1** a building or room, for example in a hospital, where dead bodies are kept until they are buried or cremated (CREMATE) 停屍房；陳屍所；太平間；MORTUARY[1] (1) *BrE*【英】**2** *often humorous* a quiet place where not much happens, so that you feel sad or bored【常幽默】死氣沉沉的地方

mor·i·bund /ˋmɔrəˌbʌnd; ˈmɒrɪ̣bʌnd/ *adj* **1** a moribund industry, institution, custom etc is no longer active or effective and therefore coming to an end〔行業、機構、風俗等〕沒有活力的，死氣沉沉的，行將消亡的：*The eastern region's heavy industry is inefficient and moribund.* 東部地區的重工業效率低下，已日落西山。**2** *literary* slowly dying【文】垂死的，奄奄一息的

Mor·mon /ˋmɔrmən; ˈmɔːmən/ *n* [C] a member of a religious organization formed in 1830 in the US, officially called The Church of Jesus Christ of Latter-day Saints 摩門教教徒 —**Mormon** *adj* —**Mormonism** *n* [U]

morn /mɔrn; mɔːn/ *n* [C usually singular 一般用單數] *poetic* morning【詩】早晨，黎明

morn·ing[1] /ˋmɔrnɪŋ; ˈmɔːnɪŋ/ *n* [C,U] **1** the early part of the day, from when the sun rises until the middle of the day 早晨；上午：*a sunny morning* 陽光燦爛的上午 | *six o'clock in the morning* 早上六點鐘 | *I had a letter from George this morning.* 我今天上午收到了喬治的一封信。| *We're leaving on Tuesday morning.* 我們週二早上動身。**2** the part of the day from midnight until the middle of the day 半夜至中午的時間：*The phone rang at three in the morning.* 電話在凌晨三點響了起來。**3 in the morning** tomorrow morning 明天早晨[上午]：*I'll deal with that in the morning.* 我明天上午會處理那件事。**4 mornings** during the morning each day 每天早晨[上午]：*She works mornings at the local school.* 她每天上午在當地的那所學校工作。**5 morning, noon, and night** used to emphasize that something happens a lot or continuously 白天黑夜地，夜以繼日：*That girl is on the phone morning, noon, and night!* 那個女孩子一天到晚不停地打電話！—see also 另見 COFFEE MORNING

morning[2] *interjection* used to greet someone in the morning 早上好，你好〔早上見面時的問候語〕：*Morning, Dave. How are you?* 早，戴夫，你好嗎？

morning-af·ter pill /ˌ·· ˈ·· ˌ·/ *n* [C] a drug that a woman can take after having sex to prevent her from having a baby〔女性房事後用的〕口服避孕藥，應急避孕藥

morning coat /ˈ·· ·/ *n* [C] a formal black coat with a long back that is worn as part of morning dress 常禮服的外套

morning dress /ˈ·· ·/ *n* [U] *especially BrE* men's formal clothes that include a morning coat, trousers, and a TOP HAT, worn at daytime ceremonies such as weddings【尤英】〔男式〕常禮服

morning glo·ry /ˌ·· ˈ··/ *n* [C,U] a plant that has white, blue, or pink flowers that open in the morning and close in late afternoon 牽牛花

Morning Prayer /ˌ·· ˈ·/ *n* [U] a morning church service in the Church of England and the Episcopal Church in the US; MATINS 晨禱

morning room /ˈ·· ·/ *n* [C] *old-fashioned* a comfortable room that is used in the morning, usually in a large house【過時】〔通常指大宅中的〕晨室

morning sick·ness /ˈ·· ˌ··/ *n* [U] a feeling of sickness that some women have before they have a baby 孕婦晨吐

morning star /ˌ·· ˈ·/ *n* [singular] a bright PLANET, usually Venus, you can see in the eastern sky when the sun rises 啟明星，晨星〔通常指金星〕—compare 比較 EVENING STAR

morning suit /ˈ·· ·/ *n* [C] a man's suit that is worn at formal ceremonies during the day, especially weddings〔男士在日間正式場合，尤指婚禮上穿的〕晨禮服

mo·roc·co /məˋrɑko; məˈrɒkəʊ/ *n* [U] fine soft leather used especially for covering books 摩洛哥皮革〔尤用來做書的封面〕

mo·ron /ˋmorɑn; ˈmɔːrɒn/ *n* [C] **1** *informal* someone who is very stupid【非正式】蠢人，傻子，笨蛋：*Don't leave it there, you moron!* 別把它放在那兒，你這個笨蛋！**2** *technical old use* someone whose intelligence has not developed to the normal level【術語，舊】痴愚者 —**moronic** /məˋrɑnɪk; məˈrɒnɪk/ *adj*: *a moronic grin* 傻笑，痴笑 —**moronically** /-kḷɪ; -kli/ *adv*

mo·rose /məˋros; məˈrəʊs/ *adj* bad-tempered, unhappy, and silent 脾氣不好的；悶悶不樂的；陰鬱的：*Daniel seems very morose and gloomy.* 丹尼爾好像非常乖僻，悶悶不樂。—**morosely** *adv* —**moroseness** *n* [U]

mor·pheme /ˋmɔrfim; ˈmɔːfiːm/ *n* [C] *technical* the smallest meaningful unit of language, consisting of a word or part of a word that cannot be divided without losing its meaning【術語】語素，詞素：*'Gun' contains one morpheme but 'gun-fight-er' contains three.* gun 含有一個詞素，但 gun-fight-er 卻含有三個詞素。

Mor·phe·us /ˋmɔrfɪəs; ˈmɔːfiəs/ *n* **in the arms of Morpheus** *literary* asleep【文】酣睡，在夢鄉中

mor·phi·a /ˋmɔrfɪə; ˈmɔːfiə/ *n* [U] *old-fashioned* morphine【過時】嗎啡

mor·phine /ˋmɔrfin; ˈmɔːfiːn/ *n* [U] a powerful and ADDICTIVE drug used for stopping pain and making people calmer 嗎啡

morph·ing /ˋmɔrfɪŋ; ˈmɔːfɪŋ/ *n* [U] a computer method that is used to make one image gradually change into a different one〔圖像的〕漸變〔一種電腦技術〕

mor·phol·o·gy /mɔrˋfɑlədʒɪ; mɔːˈfɒlədʒi/ *n technical*【術語】**1** [U] the study of the MORPHEMEs of a language and of the way in which they are joined together to make words〔語言〕詞法；形態學 —compare 比較 SYNTAX **2** [U] the scientific study of how animals, plants, and their parts are formed〔生物〕形態學 **3** [C,U] the structure of an object or system or the way it was formed 結構；形態 —**morphological** /ˌmɔrfəˋlɑdʒɪkəl; ˌmɔːfəˈlɒdʒɪkəl◂/ *adj*

mor·ris danc·ing /ˋmɔrɪs ˌdænsɪŋ; ˈmɒrɪ̣s ˌdɑːnsɪŋ/ *n* [U] traditional English country dancing performed by men wearing white clothes 莫里斯舞〔英國傳統鄉村舞〕—**morris dancer** *n* [C]

mor·row /ˋmɔro; ˈmɒrəʊ/ *n* **1 the morrow a)** the next day 次日，翌日，明日：*They were to arrive on the morrow.* 他們將於翌日到達。**b)** the future 將來，未來：*We wondered what the morrow would bring.* 我們想知道將來會發生甚麼。**2 the morrow of** *literary* the time immediately after a particular event【文】緊接〔某事件〕之後的時間: *the morrow of victory* 得勝之初 **3 good morrow** *old use* good morning【舊】早上好

Morse code /ˌmɔrs ˋkod; ˌmɔːs ˈkəʊd/ *n* [U] a system of sending messages in which the alphabet is represented by signals made of DOTs (=short signals) and DASHes (=long signals) in sound or light 莫爾斯電碼

mor·sel /ˋmɔrsəl; ˈmɔːsəl/ *n* [C] **1** a small piece of food〔食物的〕一小片, 一小塊: [+of] *a morsel of bread* 一小片麵包 | *tasty morsels* 一點可口的食物 **2 morsel of hope/wisdom/gossip etc** a small amount of hope etc 一點點希望/智慧/流言蜚語等: *That's the best morsel of scandal we've had for ages.* 那是我們多年來所聽到的最嚴重的一樁醜聞。

mor·tal[1] /ˋmɔrtḷ; ˈmɔːtl/ *adj* **1** not living for ever 凡人的, 不會長生不死的, 終有一死的: *Her father's death reminded her that she was mortal.* 父親的去世使她認識到她總會死的。| *mortal creatures* 最終會死的生物 —opposite 反義詞 IMMORTAL (1) **2 mortal blow/injuries/danger etc** causing death or likely to cause death 致命的打擊/傷害/危險等: *He was dealt a mortal blow in the battle.* 他在戰鬥中受了致命傷。| **mortal combat** (=fighting until one person kills the other) 殊死的戰鬥, 你死我活的搏鬥 *two gladiators locked in mortal combat* 陷入殊死搏鬥的兩個角鬥士 —compare 比較 LETHAL (1) **3 mortal enemy/foe** an enemy that you hate very much and always will hate 不共戴天的敵人, 死敵 **4 mortal fear/terror/dread** extreme fear 極度的恐懼: *She lives in mortal fear of her husband's anger.* 她成天生活在膽戰心驚之中, 生怕她丈夫發怒。**5** [only before noun 僅用於名詞前] *old-fashioned* used to emphasize the word that follows it, especially to show that you are annoyed【過時】〔用以強調後面的單詞, 尤表示惱怒〕: *Now I've lost every mortal thing I owned.* 現在我已失去了我所擁有的一切。**6** *poetic* belonging to a human【詩】人的; 凡人的: *a sight as yet unseen by mortal eyes* 凡胎肉眼所未見的景象 —see also 另見 MORTALLY

mortal[2] *n* [C] **1 lesser/ordinary/mere mortals** *humorous* ordinary people, as compared with people who are more important or more powerful【幽默】普通人, 草民, 平民百姓: *Of course, she dines in the executive suite, while we lesser mortals use the staff cafeteria.* 當然了, 她在經理套房用膳, 而我們這些小民在職工餐廳用餐。**2** *especially literary* a word meaning a human, used especially when comparing humans with gods, spirits etc【尤文】凡人〔與神相對〕

mor·tal·i·ty /mɔrˋtælətɪ; mɔːˈtælɪ̈ti/ *n* [U] **1** also 又作 **mortality rate** /ˌ·ˈ··· ·/ the number of deaths during a certain period of time among a particular type or group of people 死亡率; 死亡數: *Mortality from heart disease varies widely across the world.* 世界不同地區心臟病死亡率差異很大。| **infant mortality** (=the rate at which babies die) 嬰兒死亡率 **2** the condition of being human and having to die 必死性, 生死無常 —opposite 反義詞 IMMORTALITY

mor·tal·ly /ˋmɔrtḷɪ; ˈmɔːtəl-i/ *adv* **1** in a way that will cause death 致命地: *Arthur, mortally wounded, was attended by Sir Bedivere.* 亞瑟受了致命傷, 由貝德維爾爵士照料着。**2** extremely or greatly 極度地; 非常: *We hid, mortally afraid, in the cellar.* 我們藏在地下室裡, 害怕得要命。

mortal sin /ˌ·· ˈ·/ *n* [C] something that you do that is so bad, according to the Roman Catholic Church, that it will bring unending punishment to your soul after death unless it is forgiven〔天主教中的〕大罪〔天主教認為犯這種罪的人未得寬恕, 死後永遠受苦〕

mor·tar /ˋmɔrtɚ; ˈmɔːtə/ *n* **1** [U] a mixture of LIME[1] (3), sand, and water, used in building for joining bricks or stones together 砂漿, 灰漿 **2** [C] a heavy gun that fires bombs or shells (SHELL[1] (2)) in a high curve 迫擊砲 **3** [C] a hard bowl in which substances are crushed into powder with a PESTLE (=tool with a heavy round end) into very small pieces or powder 研缽; 臼: *Pound the garlic with a mortar and pestle.* 用臼和杵把蒜搗碎。—see picture at 參見 LABORATORY 圖

mor·tar·board /ˋmɔrtɚˌbord; ˈmɔːtəbɔːd/ *n* [C] a black cap with a flat square top worn by members of some universities on formal occasions 學士帽, 學位帽 —see picture at 參見 CAP[1] 圖

mort·gage[1] /ˋmɔrgɪdʒ; ˈmɔːgɪdʒ/ *n* [C] **1** a legal arrangement by which you borrow money from a bank or similar organization in order to buy a house, and pay back the money over a period of years 抵押借款, 按揭: *Your building society or bank will help arrange a mortgage.* 你們的購屋互助會或銀行將協助安排抵押借款。| **take out a mortgage** (=borrow money for a mortgage) 辦理抵押借款 *They've taken out a 30 year mortgage.* 他們已辦理了一筆30年期的抵押借款。| **pay off a mortgage** (=pay back all the money you borrowed for a mortgage) 償清抵押借款 | **mortgage rate/payment etc** *Mortgage interest rates are set to rise again in the spring.* 抵押貸款利率在春季又要上漲。**2** the amount of money you owe on a mortgage 抵押借款額: *a mortgage of $90,000* 一筆90,000美元的抵押借款 3

mortgage[2] *v* [T] **1** to give someone, usually a bank, the right to own your house, land, or property if you do not pay back the money they lent you within a certain period of time 抵押: *He's mortgaged all his assets to try and save the business.* 他抵押了他所有的資產, 試圖挽救那家企業。**2 be mortgaged to the hilt** to have everything that you own mortgaged 把全部家當抵押出去

mor·ti·cian /mɔrˋtɪʃən; mɔːˈtɪʃən/ *n* [C] *AmE* someone whose job is to arrange funerals and prepare bodies for burial【美】承辦喪葬者, 殯葬業者; UNDERTAKER *BrE*【英】

mor·ti·fy /ˋmɔrtəˌfaɪ; ˈmɔːtɪ̈faɪ/ *v* [T] **1 be mortified** to feel extremely embarrassed or ashamed 深感窘迫[丟臉]: *She was mortified to think that he had read her diary.* 想到他讀過她的日記, 她就感到很難堪。**2 mortify the flesh/yourself** *formal* to try to control your natural physical desires and needs by making your body suffer pain【正式】用苦行抑制〔身體的自然慾望〕, 用苦行禁慾 —**mortification** /ˌmɔrtəfəˋkeʃən; ˌmɔːtɪ̈fɪ̈ˈkeɪʃən/ *n* [U]: *To my utter mortification I could not remember his name.* 讓我十分尷尬的是, 我竟想不起他的名字了。

mor·ti·fy·ing /ˋmɔrtəfaɪ·ɪŋ; ˈmɔːtɪ̈faɪ-ɪŋ/ *adj* extremely embarrassing 令人極其難堪的: *The princess now faced further mortifying revelations in the tabloid press.* 王妃現在面臨着祕聞被通俗小報進一步曝光的尷尬局面。

mor·tise /ˋmɔrtɪs; ˈmɔːtɪ̈s/ *n* [C] *technical* a hole cut in a piece of wood or stone to receive the TENON (=the shaped end) of another piece and form a joint【術語】榫眼, 榫孔

mortise lock /ˈ·· ·/ *n* [C] *BrE* a lock that fits into a hole cut in the edge of a door【英】〔嵌入門裡的〕榫眼鎖, 插鎖, 嵌鎖, 暗鎖; DEAD BOLT *AmE*【美】

mor·tu·a·ry[1] /ˋmɔrtʃʊˌɛrɪ; ˈmɔːtʃuəri/ *n* [C] **1** *BrE* a building or room, for example in a hospital, where dead bodies are kept before they are buried or cremated (CREMATE); MORGUE (1)【英】停屍室, 太平間 **2** *AmE* the place where a body is kept before a funeral and where the funeral is sometimes held【美】殯儀館

mortuary[2] *adj* [only before noun 僅用於名詞前] *formal* connected with death or funerals【正式】死亡的; 喪葬的: *a mortuary urn* 骨灰甕

Mo·sa·ic /moˋze·ɪk; məʊˈzeɪ-ɪk/ *adj* connected with or relating to Moses, the great leader of the Jewish people in ancient times〔古代猶太人領袖〕摩西的: *Mosaic law* 摩西律法

mosaic *n* **1** [C,U] a pattern or picture made by fitting together small pieces of coloured stone, glass etc 馬賽克, 鑲嵌圖案: *a Roman stone mosaic* 古羅馬石子鑲嵌圖案 | *mosaic tiles* 馬賽克地磚 **2** [C usually singular 一般用單數] a group of various things that are seen or

M

considered together as a pattern 鑲嵌畫般的東西; 鑲嵌細工似的圖案: *The forest floor was a mosaic of autumn colours.* 森林裡落滿各色樹葉的地面是一幅秋色斑斕的鑲嵌畫。

Mo·ses bas·ket /ˋmozɪz ˏbæskɪt; ˈməʊzɨz ˏbɑːskɨt/ *n* [C] *BrE* a large basket with handles, in which a baby can sleep and be carried【英】手提搖籃

mo·sey /ˋmozi; ˈməʊzi/ *v* [I always+adv/prep] *AmE informal, often humorous*【美, 非正式, 常幽默】**1** to walk somewhere in a slow relaxed way 漫步, 溜達, 閒逛: [**+around/down etc**] *I guess I'll mosey on down to the store now.* 我想我可以溜達着去那家商店。**2 mosey along** to leave 離開, 離去: *I'd better mosey along – it's getting late.* 我還是走吧——天晚了。—**mosey** *n* [singular]

Mos·lem /ˋmɑzləm; ˈmɒzlɨm/ *n* [C] another spelling of MUSLIM, which is unacceptable to some Muslims Muslim 的另一種拼法〔這一拼法不為某些穆斯林所接受〕

mosque /mɑsk; mɒsk/ *n* [C] a building in which Muslims worship 清真寺: *the famous mosque in Regents Park* 〔倫敦〕攝政公園中著名的清真寺

mos·qui·to /məˋskito; məˈskiːtəʊ/ *n plural* **mosquitoes** or **mosquitos** [C] a small flying insect that sucks the blood of people and animals 蚊子

mosquito net /·ˈ·· ·/ *n* [C] a net placed over a bed as a protection against mosquitoes 蚊帳

moss /mɔs; mɒs/ *n* [C,U] a small flat green or yellow plant that grows in a thick furry mass on wet soil or rock 蘚, 苔蘚: *rocks covered in moss* 長滿苔蘚的岩石 —compare 比較 LICHEN —**mossy** *adj*

-most /most; məʊst/ *suffix* [in adjectives 構成形容詞] nearest to something 離〔某物〕最近的: *the northernmost town in Sweden* (=the town that is furthest to the north) 瑞典最北部的城鎮 | *the topmost branches of the tree* 那棵樹最頂上的樹枝

1 1 **most¹** /most; məʊst/ *adv* [+adj/adv] **1** used for forming the SUPERLATIVE of most adjectives and adverbs with more than two SYLLABLES, and many that only have two 最〔用以構成大多數具有兩個以上音節以及許多只有兩個音節的形容詞和副詞的最高級〕: *the most boring book I've ever read* 我所讀過的最乏味的書 | *She's one of the most experienced teachers in the district.* 她是該地區最有經驗的教師之一。| *The excuse I get told most often is that the train was late.* 我最常聽到的藉口是火車晚點了。| *In high school Kelly had been voted 'girl most likely to succeed'.* 在中學凱利被評選為"最有可能成功的女孩"。**2** more than anything else 比〔其他任何事物〕更多地, 最: *The food I eat most is pasta.* 我吃得最多的食物是麵食。| *What annoyed him most was the way she wouldn't even listen to his reasons.* 最使他惱怒的, 是她甚至不願意聽一聽他的理由。| **most of all** *Unfortunately they'd run out of the paint colour I liked most of all.* 遺憾的是我最喜歡的那種顏料賣完了。**3** *formal* very【正式】非常, 很: *I was most surprised to hear of your engagement.* 聽說你訂婚了, 我大為驚訝。| *Do you realise we'll most probably end up bankrupt?* 我們最終很可能會破產, 你明白嗎? | **a most interesting/expensive etc sth** *That really was a most illuminating lecture, Professer Jordan.* 那確實是一個很有啟發意義的講座, 喬丹教授。**4** *AmE informal* almost【美, 非正式】幾乎: *He plays poker most every evening.* 他幾乎天天晚上玩牌。

USAGE NOTE 用法說明: MOST

GRAMMAR 語法

Most meaning 'nearly all' is followed directly by a noun when you are speaking generally. most 意為"大多數"並在表示泛指時, 後面直接跟名詞: *Most cheese contains a lot of fat* (NOT 不用 *most of cheese*). 幾乎所有乾酪都含有大量的脂肪。| *Most Americans own cars.* 大多數美國人都有汽車。

You use **most of the** when you are talking about part of a particular thing, group, etc. 在談論某一特定事物或羣體等的一部分時用 most of the: *Greg has eaten most of the cheese that was in the fridge.* 格雷格把冰箱裡的大部分乾酪都吃了。| *Most of the Americans we asked owned cars.* 我們問到的美國人中大多數都有汽車。

You can also say: *Most Americans we asked own cars* without using **of the** to talk about that particular group. 也可以說 Most Americans we asked own cars, 這裡不用 of the, 指的是那個特定的羣體。

The most can be followed directly by a plural or uncountable noun, when it means 'more than any other(s)'. 當表示"在…中最多的"時, the most 後面可直接跟複數或不可數名詞: *The most damage was done to the houses nearest the cliff* 〔最靠近懸崖的房子受到的破壞最厲害〕 means more damage was done to those houses than any others 意思是最靠近懸崖的那些房子比其他房子遭受了更大的破壞。

You use **most** meaning 'more than anything else' in these ways. 在下列句子中 most 可用來表示"比其他任何事物更多地": *My swimming is the thing I most want to improve.* 我最想提高的是我的游泳水平。| *I want to improve my swimming most.* 我最想提高一下我的游泳水平。| *I most want to improve my swimming* (NOT 不用 *The most thing I want to improve is my swimming*). 我最想提高一下我的游泳水平。

Remember that most short adjectives have a form ending in *-est* that you usually use when you want to say 'more than any other', and you should not use **most** with them. 記住, 大多數音節少的形容詞其最高級形式以 -est 結尾, 不應在其前加 most: *Manhattan is the richest area in New York* (NOT 不用 *the most rich* or 或 *the most richest*). 曼哈頓區是紐約市最富有的地區。| *the dullest people I've ever met* (NOT 不用 *most dull*) 我所見到的最無聊的人

Note that you use the phrase 注意人們使用短語 **most of the time**, not 而不是 *the most time* or 或 *most of times*.

most² *quantifier* [superlative of **many, much** many, much 的最高級] **1** almost all of a particular group of people or things 大多數, 大部分, 幾乎全部: **most things/food etc** *These days most crime is against property, not people.* 如今大多數犯罪針對的是財物, 而不是人。| *Like most people, I try to take a vacation every year.* 像大多數人一樣, 我每年設法休一次假。| **most of** *It was afternoon and most of the shops were shut.* 當時是下午, 大多數商店都關門了。| *Tim spent most of his salary on alcohol and cigarettes.* 蒂姆把大部分工資都花在喝酒和抽煙上了。| **most** *Of all the money donated, most is spent on food and clothing for the refugees.* 捐款大部分都用在為難民提供食品和衣服上了。**2** more people or things than anyone else〔人或物〕在…中最多的: **the most people/food etc** *It's the best hotel in town and it also has the most rooms.* 這是鎮上最好的旅館, 客房也最多。| *This is the most votes any candidate has ever received.* 這是有史以來候選人獲得過的最高票數。| **the most** *It's unfair that you should have to pay the most when you earn so little.* 你掙得那麼少卻必須支付得最多, 這不公平。| **most** *Whoever scores most in the penalty competition will be awarded the trophy.* 誰在罰球比賽中得分最高, 誰就獲得獎盃。**3** the largest number or amount possible 最大數量, 最大部分: **most people/food etc** *How can we plan the campaign to reach most people?* 我們如何籌劃這次宣傳活動才能讓最多的人知道它? | **the most people/food etc** *To get the most use out of the machine, recharge the batteries overnight.* 為了最大限度地利用機器, 給電池充一晚上電。| **the most** *The most you can hope to achieve is to just get him to listen to your ideas.* 你能希望做到的充其量只是讓他聽

聽你的想法而已。**4 at (the) most** used to say that a number or amount could not be larger 至多, 不超過: *You could buy a good washing machine for about £350, £400 at most.* 350英鎊左右, 最多400英鎊, 就能買一台不錯的洗衣機。| **at (the) very most** *At the very most the temperature in summer goes up to about 38°C.* 夏天氣温最高上升到38攝氏度左右。—compare 比較 **at (the) very least** (LEAST[1] (1)) **5 for the most part** used when a statement or fact is generally true but not completely true 就絕大部分而言; 基本上, 大體上: *For the most part the relationship between private investment and government interests has not been a successful one.* 總的説來, 私人投資和政府利益之間的關係一直不太好。**6 make the most of sth** to get the most advantage from a good situation because it will not last a long time 最大限度地利用某物: *You should be outside making the most of the sunshine.* 你應該到戶外盡量多曬曬太陽。

2 3 **most·ly** /ˋmostlɪ; ˈməʊstli/ *adv* in most cases or most of the time 大部分; 主要地; 多半; 通常: *I mostly worked as a researcher, writer, or teacher.* 我主要從事研究、寫作或教學工作。| *More immigrants arrived, mostly Europeans.* 更多的移民到達, 大多是歐洲人。

MOT /ˌɛm o ˋti; ˌem əʊ ˈtiː/ *n* [C] a regular official examination in Britain of the condition and safety of cars that are more than three years old 〔英國對三年以上車齡的車輛的〕年檢: *Will the car pass its MOT?* 那輛汽車能通過車檢嗎?

mote /mot; məʊt/ *n* [C] *old-fashioned* a very small piece of dust【過時】微塵, 塵埃

mo·tel /moˋtɛl; məʊˈtel/ *n* [C] a hotel for people travelling, where you can park your car outside your room 汽車旅館

moth /mɔθ; mɒθ/ *n* [C] **1** an insect related to the BUTTERFLY that flies mainly at night and is attracted to lights 蛾 **2** also 又作 **clothes moth** a moth whose young eat holes in cloth 衣蛾

moth·ball[1] /ˋmɔθˌbɔl; ˈmɒθbɔːl/ *n* [C usually plural 一般用複數] **1** a small ball made of a strong-smelling chemical, used for keeping moths away from clothes 衛生球, 樟腦丸 **2 in mothballs** stored and not used for a long time 封存不用; 束之高閣: *With the end of the Cold War several warships were put into mothballs.* 隨着冷戰的結束, 數艘軍艦被封存起來了。

mothball[2] *v* [T] to close a factory or to decide not to use plans or machinery for a long time 長期關閉〔工廠〕; 把〔計劃〕束之高閣; 封存〔機器設備〕: *The company announced that plans to create new offices have been mothballed.* 公司宣布成立新辦事處的計劃已經擱置起來了。

moth-eat·en /ˋ· ˌ··/ *adj* **1** cloth that is moth-eaten has holes eaten in it by moths 蟲蛀的, 蛀壞的: *a moth-eaten sweater* 蛀壞了的羊毛衫 **2** old and in bad condition 破舊的: *a moth-eaten old sofa* 破舊的沙發

1 1 **moth·er[1]** /ˋmʌðɚ; ˈmʌðə/ *n* [C]

1 ►PARENT 母親◄ a female parent of a child or animal 母親, 媽媽: *His mother and father are both doctors.* 他的父母都是醫生。| *Can I borrow your car please, Mother?* 媽媽, 我能借用一下你的車嗎? | **mother hen/cat/dog etc** (=an animal that is a mother) 母雞/母貓/母狗等 —see picture at 參見 FAMILY 圖

2 be (like) a mother to to care for someone as if you were their mother 母親般照料

3 mother's boy *BrE*【英】, **mama's boy** *AmE*【美】a man or boy who allows his mother to protect him too much and is considered weak 過分依賴母親的男人[男孩], 嬌生兒

4 mother hen someone who tries to protect her children too much and worries about them all the time 老母雞〔過分保護子女並時時為他們操心的女人〕

5 learn/be taught sth at your mother's knee to learn something as a very young child 年幼時就學習某事: *She had learned to flirt at her mother's knee.* 她小時候就學會調情了。

6 ►BIG 大的◄ *spoken especially AmE* something very large and usually very good【口, 尤美】大傢伙〔通常指很好的事物〕: *a real mother of a car* 真正的大號汽車

7 ►SLANG 俚語◄ *AmE taboo spoken* MOTHERFUCKER【美, 諱, 口】不要臉的傢伙, 混賬東西

8 every mother's son *old-fashioned* an expression meaning every man, used for emphasis【過時】人人, 所有人: *I'd jail every mother's son of them.* 我要把他們全部監禁起來。

9 Mother a) used to address the woman who is head of a CONVENT 院長〔對女修道院院長的稱呼〕**b)** *old use* used by a man to address an old woman【舊】大娘, 大媽〔男子用以稱呼老年婦女〕

10 the mother of a) the origin or cause of something 根由, 根源: *Westminster is known as 'the mother of parliaments'.* 威斯敏斯特被公認為是"議會之母"。**b)** *informal* a very bad or severe type of something【非正式】糟糕的事; 艱難的事: *I woke up with the mother of all hangovers.* 我醒來後因宿醉而十分難受。

mother[2] *v* [T] to look after and protect someone as if you were their mother, especially by being too kind and doing everything for them 母親般照管; 〔尤指〕溺愛: *Tom was constantly mothered by his wife, and resented it.* 湯姆時時被妻子母親般呵護着, 他對此很反感。

moth·er·board /ˋmʌðɚbɔrd; ˈmʌðəbɔːd/ *n* [C] *technical* a board where all the circuits (CIRCUIT (4)) of a computer are placed【術語】〔電腦的〕母板, 主板

mother coun·try /ˋ·· ˌ··/ *n* [C usually singular 一般用單數] the country where you were born 祖國

Mother Earth /ˌ·· ˋ·/ *n* [U] the world considered as the place or thing from which everything comes 〔孕育萬物的〕大地, 大地母親

moth·er·fuck·er /ˋmʌðɚˌfʌkɚ; ˈmʌðəˌfʌkə/ *n* [C] *AmE taboo spoken* someone that you dislike very much or that you are very angry with【美, 諱, 口】不要臉的傢伙, 混賬東西 —**motherfucking** *adj*

moth·er·hood /ˋmʌðɚhʊd; ˈmʌðəhʊd/ *n* [U] the state of being a mother 母親身分: *teenage motherhood* 少女媽媽 | *She's enjoying motherhood.* 她喜歡做母親。

Mothering Sun·day /ˋ··· ˌ··/ *n* [C,U] *BrE old-fashioned* MOTHER'S DAY【英, 過時】母親節

mother-in-law /ˋ·· · ˌ·/ *n plural* **mothers-in-law** *or* **mother-in-laws** [C] the mother of your wife or husband 岳母; 婆婆 —see picture at 參見 FAMILY 圖

moth·er·land /ˋmʌðɚlænd; ˈmʌðəlænd/ *n* [C usually singular 一般用單數] the country where you were born or that you feel you belong to 祖國 —see also 另見 FATHERLAND, MOTHER COUNTRY

moth·er·less /ˋmʌðɚlɪs; ˈmʌðələs/ *adj* a motherless child is one whose mother has died 母親已去世的, 無母親的: *Alone and motherless, David set out to find fame and fortune.* 母親已亡且孑然一身, 戴維動身尋求名利去了。

mother lode /ˋ·· ·/ *n* [C usually singular 一般用單數] *AmE*【美】**1** a mine that is full of gold, silver etc 〔礦藏的〕母脈, 主脈 **2** a place where you can find a lot of a particular type of object 豐富的源泉: *The Sharper Image catalog has a mother lode of men's gadgets and toys.* 《時髦形象》的目錄列有許多男用小器具和小擺設。

moth·er·ly /ˋmʌðɚlɪ; ˈmʌðəli/ *adj* similar to or typical of a good mother 慈母般的, 母親一樣的: *a kind, motherly woman* 慈母般善良的婦女 —see also 另見 MATERNAL (1) —**motherliness** *n* [U]

Mother Na·ture /ˌ·· ˋ··/ *n* [U] an expression used to talk about the world and living creatures as a person 大自然〔擬人化用法〕: *We can hardly expect Mother Nature not to protest at the pollution we've been creating for the last half century.* 我們過去半個世紀一直在製造污染, 大自然對此不表示抗議才怪。

Mother of God /ˌ·· · ˋ·/ *n* [singular] a title for Mary, the mother of Jesus Christ, used in the Roman Catholic Church 聖母(馬利亞)〔羅馬天主教對耶穌基督母親的稱呼〕

mother-of-pearl /ˌ·· ·ˈ·/ *n* [U] a pale-coloured hard smooth shiny substance that forms the inside of some SHELLFISH, and is used for making buttons, jewellery etc 珍珠母

Mother's Day /ˈ·· ·/ *n* [C,U] a day on which people give cards and presents to their mother 母親節

mother ship /ˈ·· ·/ *n* [C] a large ship or SPACECRAFT from which smaller boats or spacecraft are sent out 母艦, 母船; 航天運載飛船

mother's ru·in /ˌ·· ˈ··/ *n* [U] *BrE old-fashioned humorous* GIN (=a strong alcoholic drink)【英, 過時, 幽默】杜松子酒

Mother Su·pe·ri·or /ˌ·· ·ˈ···/ *n* [C usually singular 一般用單數] the woman who is the leader of a CONVENT 女修道院院長

mother-to-be /ˌ·· ·ˈ·/ *n plural* **mothers-to-be** [C] a woman who is going to have a baby 準媽媽, 孕婦

mother tongue /ˌ·· ˈ·/ *n* [C] the first and main language that you learn as a child 母語: *Her mother tongue is French.* 她的母語是法語。

mo·tif /moˋtif; məʊˈtiːf/ *n* [C] **1** an idea, subject, or pattern that is regularly repeated and developed in a book, film, work of art etc〔書、電影、藝術品等的〕主題, 中心思想; 基本模式: *The theme of creation is a recurrent motif in Celtic mythology.* 天地萬物的創造是凱爾特神話中反覆出現的主題。**2** a small picture or pattern used to decorate something plain 裝飾圖畫[圖案]: *a cat motif on a child's pyjamas* 孩子睡衣褲上貓的圖案 **3** an arrangement of notes that is often repeated in a musical work〔音樂作品的〕樂旨, 動機

3 **mo·tion**¹ /ˋmoʃən; ˈməʊʃən/ *n*

1 ►MOVEMENT 移動◄ [U] the process of moving or the way that someone or something moves 動; 運動; 移動: *The rocking motion of the boat made Sylvia feel sick.* 小船晃來晃去, 使西維亞感到噁心。

2 ►MOVING YOUR HEAD OR HAND 動頭或手◄ [C] a single movement of your hand or head, especially done in order to communicate something〔手或頭的〕示意動作; 手勢; 姿勢: *He summoned the waiter with a motion of his hand.* 他做了個手勢, 召喚侍者。

3 ►SUGGESTION AT A MEETING 會議上的建議◄ [C] a proposal that is made formally at a meeting and then decided on by voting 提議, 動議: **motion to do sth/motion that** *We will now vote on the motion that membership charges should rise by 15%.* 我們現在將對會費提高 15% 這一動議進行投票表決。| **pass/carry a motion** (=accept it by voting)〔通過投票〕通過一項動議 *The motion was carried by 15 votes to 10.* 該動議以 15 票對 10 票通過。| **propose/put forward a motion** (=make a proposal) 提出一項動議 *I'd like to propose a motion to move the weekly meetings to Thursdays.* 我提議把每週的例會改到星期四。| **reject a motion** (=not accept it) 拒絕一項提議 | **motion denied** (=used by a judge in a law court to refuse a suggestion by one of the lawyers) 動議予以否決〔法官在法庭上說的話〕

4 in motion *formal or technical* moving from one place or position to another【正式或術語】運動中的: *a photograph of a frog in motion* 運動中的青蛙的照片

5 go through the motions to do something because you have to, even though you do not want to do it 裝樣子, 做姿態, 敷衍塞責地做: *The mayor said he enjoyed the party, but you could see he was only going through the motions.* 市長說他喜歡那個聚會, 但你能看出他只是在敷衍應付。

6 set/put sth in motion to start a process or series of events that will continue for some time 使某事開始: *The Church voted to set in motion the process allowing women to be priests.* 教會投票決定啟動允許婦女當牧師的程序。

7 in slow motion if a film is shown in slow motion, it is shown more slowly than usual so that all the actions can be clearly seen 以慢動作, 慢速地: *Let's look at that goal in slow motion.* 讓我們看一看那個進球的慢鏡頭。

8 ►BOWELS 腸◄ [C] *especially BrE* a word meaning an act of emptying your BOWELs, used especially by doctors and nurses【尤英】排便〔此詞尤為醫護人員所用〕— see also 另見 TIME AND MOTION STUDY

motion² *v* [I,T] to give someone directions or instructions by moving your hands 用手勢示意: **motion (for) sb to do sth** *The police officer motioned for me to pull over.* 警察招手示意我把車停在路邊。| **motion to sb to do sth** *He motioned to her to be quiet.* 他做手勢讓她安靜。| **motion sb in/out etc** *I saw her motioning me into the room.* 我看到她招手示意我進房間。

mo·tion·less /ˋmoʃənlɪs; ˈməʊʃənləs/ *adj* not moving at all 一動不動的, 靜止的: *Helen sat motionless and silent.* 海倫一動不動, 默默地坐着。—**motionlessly** *adv*

motion pic·ture /ˌ·· ˈ··◄/ *n* [C] *AmE* a film made for the cinema【美】電影: *the motion picture industry* 電影業

motion sick·ness /ˈ·· ˌ··/ *n* [U] *AmE* travel sickness (TRAVEL-SICK)【美】暈動病〈如暈車、暈船等〉: *I always get motion sickness when I sit in the back of a car.* 坐在車後部我總是暈車。

mo·ti·vate /ˋmotəˌvet; ˈməʊtɪ̵veɪt/ *v* [T] **1** to make someone want to achieve something and make them willing to work hard in order to do it 激發, 激勵, 促動: *A good teacher has to be able to motivate her students.* 好教師必須能激發學生積極學習。| **motivate sb to do sth** *The profit-sharing plan is designed to motivate the staff to work hard.* 制定利潤分紅計劃是為了激勵員工努力工作。**2** [often passive 常用被動態] to provide the reason why someone does something 為…的動機: *Would you say that he was motivated solely by a desire for power?* 你認為他僅僅是受權欲的驅使嗎?

mo·ti·va·ted /ˋmotəˌvetɪd; ˈməʊtɪ̵veɪtɪ̵d/ *adj* **1** very keen to do something or achieve something, especially because you find it interesting or exciting 積極的; 主動的: *They're a really good bunch of students – highly motivated and very intelligent.* 他們確實是一羣優秀的學生 —— 學習積極性高, 而且非常聰明。**2 politically/financially/commercially motivated etc** done for political, financial etc reasons 受政治/財政/商業等方面的原因所驅使的: *a politically-motivated decision* 有政治目的的決定 | *Police believe the attack was racially motivated.* 警察認為那次襲擊是由於種族仇恨。

mo·ti·va·tion /ˌmotəˋveʃən; ˌməʊtɪ̵ˈveɪʃən/ *n* **1** [U] eagerness and willingness to do something without needing to be told or forced to do it 動力; 積極性; 興趣: *Jack is an intelligent pupil, but he lacks motivation.* 傑克是一個很聰明的學生, 但他學習不夠主動。**2** [C] the reason why you want to do something 動機, 原因: [+for] *What was your motivation for becoming a teacher?* 你為甚麼做教師?

mo·tive¹ /ˋmotɪv; ˈməʊtɪv/ *n* [C] **1** the reason that makes someone do something, especially when this reason is kept hidden〔尤指隱藏的〕動機, 原因; 目的: *The police believe the motive for this murder was jealousy.* 警察認為這次謀殺的動機是嫉妒。**2** a MOTIF 主題; 裝飾圖畫;〔音樂作品的〕樂旨 —**motiveless** *adj*: *an apparently motiveless killing* 一起沒有顯然動機的殺人案

motive² *adj* [only before noun 僅用於名詞前] *technical* a motive power or force is one that causes movement【術語】引起運動的, 起推動作用的; 提供動力的

mot juste /ˌmo ˋʒust; ˌməʊ ˈʒuːst/ *plural* **mots justes** (*same pronunciation* 發音相同) *n* [C] *French* exactly the right word or phrase【法】最貼切的字眼, 最恰當的詞語: *How can I describe her? I'm searching for the mot juste ... Yes, that's it – slender.* 我怎麼形容她呢? 我在找一個最貼切的字眼…啊, 有了 —— 苗條。

mot·ley¹ /ˋmɑtlɪ; ˈmɒtli/ *adj* [only before noun 僅用於

名詞前] **1 a motley crew/bunch/assortment etc** a group of people of very different kinds, especially people that you do not approve of 形形色色的一夥／一幫／一批人等: *I looked at the motley bunch we were sailing with and began to feel uneasy about the trip.* 看到和我們一起航行這幫人當中三教九流的全有, 我開始對這次旅程感到不安起來。**2** a motley group of things contains objects that are all different in shape, size etc and that do not seem to belong together〔東西〕混雜的, 雜七雜八的: *His pockets contained a motley collection of coins, movie ticket stubs, and old peppermint candies.* 他的口袋裡亂七八糟, 有硬幣、電影票根和放了很久的薄荷糖。**3** *literary* having a strange mixture of many different colours【文】雜色的, 五顏六色的: *a court jester in motley garb* 穿着雜色花衣的宮廷小丑

motley² *n* [U] *technical* the clothes worn by a JESTER【術語】(小丑穿的) 雜色花衣

mo·to·cross /ˈmotoˌkrɔs; ˈməʊtəʊkrɒs/ *n* [U] the sport of racing MOTORCYCLE*s* over rough land, up hills, through streams etc 摩托車越野賽

mo·tor¹ /ˈmotɚ; ˈməʊtə/ *n* [C] **1** the part of a machine that makes it work or move, by changing power, especially electrical power, into movement 發動機; 電動機, 馬達: *The lawn-mower is powered by a small motor.* 這台割草機由一個小馬達提供動力。| *We had to replace the starter motor in the car's engine.* 我們不得不換掉汽車引擎上的起動電動機。**2** *BrE informal* a car【英, 非正式】汽車: *That's a nice motor you've got, Dave.* 戴夫, 你這輛汽車不錯。

motor² *adj* [only before noun 僅用於名詞前] **1** *especially BrE* connected with cars or other vehicles with engines【尤英】汽車的, 機動車輛的: *a motor accident* 汽車事故 | *the motor industry* 汽車工業 | *motor insurance* 汽車保險 **2** using power provided by an engine 機動的: *a motor scooter* 低座小摩托車 **3** *technical* related to a nerve that makes a muscle move【術語】運動神經的: *impaired motor function* 受到損傷的運動神經功能

motor³ *v* [I] *BrE old-fashioned* to travel by car【英, 過時】乘汽車旅行; 駕駛汽車: *Bertie is motoring down from London this weekend.* 本週末伯蒂要開車從倫敦南下。

motorbike 摩托車

motorbike/motorcycle *AmE*【美】摩托車 scooter 低座小摩托車

mo·tor·bike /ˈmotɚˌbaɪk; ˈməʊtəbaɪk/ *n* [C] *especially BrE* a fast two-wheeled vehicle with an engine【尤英】摩托車

mo·tor·boat /ˈmotɚˌbot; ˈməʊtəbəʊt/ *n* [C] a small fast boat with an engine 摩托艇, 汽艇; 汽船

mo·tor·cade /ˈmotɚˌked; ˈməʊtəkeɪd/ *n* [C] a group of cars and other vehicles that travel together and surround a very important person's car〔要人的〕車隊: *the President's motorcade* 總統車隊

motor car /ˈ·· ·/ *n* [C] *BrE formal or old-fashioned* a car【英, 正式或過時】汽車

mo·tor·cy·cle /ˈmotɚˌsaɪkḷ; ˈməʊtəˌsaɪkəl/ *n* [C] a fast, usually large, two-wheeled vehicle with an engine 摩托車 —see picture at 參見 MOTORBIKE 圖

mo·tor·drome /ˈmotɚˌdrom; ˈməʊtədrəʊm/ *n* [C] *AmE* a track where people can watch car or motorcycle races【美】汽車[摩托車]賽車場

motor home /ˈ·· ·/ *n* [C] a large vehicle with beds, a kitchen, toilet etc built into it, used for travelling and holidays〔有牀、廚房、衛生間等的〕旅宿汽車 —see also 另見 RV

mo·tor·ing /ˈmotərɪŋ; ˈməʊtərɪŋ/ *n* [U] *BrE old-fashioned* the activity of driving a car【英, 過時】開汽車: *a motoring enthusiast* 熱衷於開汽車的人

motor inn /ˈ·· ·/ *n* [C] *AmE* a MOTEL【美】汽車旅館

mo·tor·ist /ˈmotərɪst; ˈməʊtərɨst/ *n* [C] *especially BrE* someone who drives a car【尤英】汽車駕駛員: *12,000 motorists were stopped for speeding in the police crackdown.* 在警方懲治違章駕車的行動中, 12,000 名汽車司機因超速被攔截。

mo·tor·ized also 又作 **-ised** *BrE*【英】/ˈmotəˌraɪzd; ˈməʊtəraɪzd/ *adj* [only before noun 僅用於名詞前] **1** fitted with an engine, especially when something does not usually have an engine 裝發動機的, 機動的: *a motorized bicycle* 機動腳踏車, 助動車 **2** a motorized army or group of soldiers is one that uses motor vehicles〔軍隊或士兵〕摩托化的, 機動化的 —**motorize** *v* [T]

motor lodge /ˈ·· ·/ *n* [C] *AmE* a MOTEL【美】汽車旅館

mo·tor·mouth /ˈmotɚˌmaʊθ; ˈməʊtəmaʊθ/ *n* [C] *informal* someone who talks too much and too loudly【非正式】"馬達嘴", 喋喋不休大聲喧譁的人

motor neu·rone dis·ease /ˌmotɚ ˋnuron dɪˌziz; ˌməʊtə ˈnjʊərəʊn dɪˌziːz/ *n* [U] a disease that causes a gradual loss of control over the muscles and nerves of the body, resulting in death 運動神經元病

motor pool /ˈ·· ·/ *n* [C] *AmE* CAR POOL¹ (2)【美】〔公司等組織擁有的供其工作人員使用的多輛〕合夥用車

motor rac·ing /ˈ·· ˌ··/ *n* [U] the sport of racing fast cars on a special track 賽車運動

motor scoot·er /ˈ·· ˌ··/ *n* [C] a SCOOTER (1) 低座小摩托車

motor ve·hi·cle /ˈ·· ˌ···/ *n* [C] the official word for any vehicle which is powered by an engine, such as a car, bus, or TRUCK 機動車輛: *This road is closed to motor vehicles.* 這條路機動車禁止通行。

mo·tor·way /ˈmotɚˌwe; ˈməʊtəweɪ/ *n* [C] *BrE* a very wide road for travelling fast over long distances, especially between cities【英】高速公路 —compare 比較 EXPRESSWAY, FREEWAY, HIGHWAY (1) S2

mot·tled /ˈmɑtḷd; ˈmɒtld/ *adj* covered with patterns of light and dark colours of different shapes 雜色的; 斑駁的; 有花紋的; 雲紋狀的: *mottled like an owl's feathers* 像貓頭鷹的羽毛一樣斑斑駁駁的 | *His red, mottled face showed the effect of too much whiskey.* 他那張紅紅的、滿是斑點的臉表明, 他威士忌喝得太多了。

mot·to /ˈmɑto; ˈmɒtəʊ/ *n plural* **mottos** also 又作 **mottoes** [C] **1** a short statement giving a rule on how to behave, which expresses the aims or beliefs of a person, school, or institution 箴言, 格言, 座右銘: *'Be prepared' is the motto of the boy scouts.* "時刻準備着"是童子軍的格言。**2** *BrE* an amusing remark or joke printed on a piece of paper in a CHRISTMAS CRACKER【英】〔聖誕彩包爆竹中印在紙片上的〕俏皮話, 妙語

mould¹ *BrE*【英】, **mold** *AmE*【美】/mold; məʊld/ *n* **1** [U] a soft green or black substance that grows on food which has been kept too long, and on objects that are in warm, wet air 黴, 黴菌: *Throw that bread away, there's mold on it.* 把那塊麵包扔了吧, 上面長黴了。| *There was mould on the bathroom ceiling.* 浴室天花板發霉了。—see also 另見 LEAF MOULD **2** [C] a hollow container that you pour liquid into, so that when the liquid becomes solid, it takes the shape of the container 模子, 模具, 鑄模, 鑄型: *a jelly mould* 果凍模子 | *a candle mold* 蠟燭模子 **3** [singular] if someone is in, or fits into, a particular mould, they have all the attitudes, and qualities, typical of a certain type of person〔人的〕性格, 氣質, 類型: *a sex symbol in the traditional Hollywood mold* 具有傳統好萊塢氣質的性感偶像 | *She didn't quite fit into the*

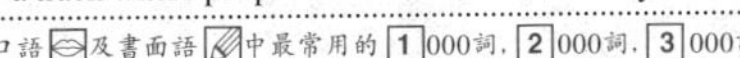

standard 'high-flying businesswoman' mould. 她並不完全屬於"雄心勃勃的女商人"那種類型。**4 break the mould** to change a situation completely, by doing something that has not been done before 徹底改變格局, 打破模式: *an attempt to break the mould of British politics* 打破英國政治模式的嘗試

mould² *BrE*【英】, **mold** *AmE*【美】*v* **1** [T] to shape a soft substance by pressing or rolling it or by putting it into a mould 使…成形; 用模子製作; 澆鑄: **mould sth into sth** *Mould the sausage meat into little balls.* 把灌香腸用的碎肉捏成丸子。| **mold sth** *moulded plastic piping* 模製塑料管材 **2** [T] to influence the way someone's character or attitudes develop 影響〔某人性格或態度〕的形成, 塑造: *I enjoy working with children, helping to mold their young minds.* 我喜歡和小孩子打交道, 幫着塑造他們稚嫩的頭腦。| *an attempt to mold public opinion* 影響輿論的企圖 **3** [I,T] to fit closely to the shape of something 與…的輪廓相符: *Her wet dress was moulded to her body.* 她的濕衣服緊貼在身上。

moul·der *BrE*【英】, **molder** *AmE*【美】/ˈmoldɚ; ˈməʊldə/ also 又作 **moulder away** *v* [I] to decay slowly and gradually 腐爛, 腐朽; 漸漸崩塌: *old papers mouldering away in the attic* 閣樓裡慢慢朽壞的舊報紙 | *the discovery of a dead body, mouldering in the woods* 在樹林中發現一具腐屍

mould·ing *BrE*【英】, **molding** *AmE*【美】/ˈmoldɪŋ; ˈməʊldɪŋ/ *n* **1** [C,U] a thin decorative line of stone or wood around the edge of a wall, a piece of furniture, a picture frame etc 裝飾線條, 線飾, 線腳 **2** [C] an object produced from a mould 模製件; 鑄造物

mould·y *BrE*【英】, **moldy** *AmE*【美】/ˈmoldɪ; ˈməʊldi/ *adj* **mouldier, mouldiest** covered with MOULD¹ (1) 發霉的: *mouldy cheese* 發霉的乾酪 | **go mouldy** *BrE* (=become mouldy)【英】發霉 *The bread's gone mouldy.* 麵包已發霉了。

moult *BrE*【英】, **molt** *AmE*【美】/molt; məʊlt/ *v* [I] when a bird or animal moults, it loses hair or feathers so that new ones can grow 〔鳥〕換羽; 〔動物〕脫毛 —**moult** *n* [C,U]

mound /maund; maʊnd/ *n* [C] **1** a pile of earth or stones that looks like a small hill 土[石]堆; 土岡, 土丘 **2** a large pile of something (大)堆, (大)垛: **[+of]** *There's a mound of papers on my desk.* 我辦公桌上有一大堆文件。| *The waiter appeared with a huge mound of spaghetti.* 服務生端着一大盤小山般高的意大利麵條出現了。**3** the small hill that the PITCHER stands on in the game of BASEBALL 〔棒球場中的〕投球區土墩 —see picture on page A22 參見A22頁圖

mount¹ /maunt; maʊnt/ *v*

1 ►INCREASE 增加◄ [I] to increase gradually, especially in a way that makes a situation worse 漸漸增加, 增長〔尤指朝着使情況更糟的方向〕: *The tension here is mounting, as we await the final result.* 我們等待着最終結果, 這裡的氣氛越來越緊張。| *For days after the accident, the death toll continued to mount.* 事故發生後的數日內死亡人數持續上升。—see also 另見 MOUNTING¹

2 mount a campaign/attack/exhibition etc to plan, organize, and begin an event or a course of action 發起戰役/發動進攻/舉辦展覽等: *Scott mounted an expedition to the South Pole.* 斯科特發起了去南極的探險。

3 ►HORSE/BICYCLE 馬/自行車◄ [I,T] to get on a horse, bicycle etc 騎上, 跨上: *She mounted and rode off.* 她騎上自行車走了。—opposite 反義詞 DISMOUNT (1)

4 ►CLIMB STAIRS 爬樓梯◄ [T] *formal* to go up something such as a set of stairs【正式】走上, 爬上, 登上: *We mounted some stone steps to a gallery.* 我們登上幾級石階, 來到一間陳列室。

5 be mounted to/on to be fixed to something and supported by it 被固定在…上: *The statue was mounted on a marble plinth.* 雕像被安放在一個大理石底座上。

6 ►PICTURE 圖畫◄ [T] to fix a picture or photograph to a larger piece of stiff paper so that it looks more attractive 裱貼〔圖畫或照片〕

7 ►SEX 性◄ [T] *technical* if a male animal mounts a female animal, he gets up onto her back to have sex【術語】〔雄性動物〕趴到〔雌性動物〕身上交配

8 mount guard (over) *formal* to guard a place, especially as a military duty【正式】擔任警衛; 站崗

mount up *phr v* [I] to gradually increase in size or amount 〔規模或數量〕逐漸增加, 增長: *Our debts are beginning to mount up again.* 我們的債務又開始增加了。

mount² *n* [C] **1 Mount** part of the name of a mountain …山, …峯〔山名的一部分〕: *Mount Everest* 埃佛勒斯峯〔即珠穆朗瑪峯〕**2** a horse that you ride on 被乘騎的馬, 坐騎 **3** *old use* a mountain【舊】山, 山岳

moun·tain /ˈmauntn̩; ˈmaʊntɪ̣n/ *n* [C] **1** a very high hill 高山, 山岳: *the Rocky Mountains* 落基山脈 | *a mountain rescue team* 山地救援隊 —see picture on page A12 參見A12頁圖 **2** also 又作 **mountains** *plural* a very large pile or amount of something 大堆; 大量: *My mother-in-law always gives me a mountain of potatoes from her garden.* 我岳母總是送給我一大堆她園子裡產的馬鈴薯。| *I've got mountains of washing to do.* 我有一大堆衣物要洗。**3 butter/grain etc mountain** a very large amount of food that is stored in order to prevent prices from becoming lower, especially by the European Union 〔尤指歐盟為防止價格下跌而〕大量積存的黃油/穀物等 —compare 比較 LAKE (2) **4 make a mountain out of a molehill** to treat a problem as if it was very serious when in fact it is not 小題大作

mountain ash /ˌ·· ˈ·/ *n* [C] a type of tree with red or orange-red berries; ROWAN 花楸樹

mountain bike /ˈ·· ˌ·/ *n* [C] a strong bicycle with a lot of GEARS and wide tyres, specially designed for riding up hills and on rough ground 山地(自行)車

moun·tain·eer /ˌmauntn̩ˈɪr; ˌmaʊntɪ̣ˈnɪə/ *n* [C] someone who climbs mountains as a sport 登山家, 登山運動員

moun·tain·eer·ing /ˌmauntn̩ˈɪrɪŋ; ˌmaʊntɪ̣ˈnɪərɪŋ/ *n* [U] the sport of climbing mountains 登山運動

mountain goat /ˈ·· ˌ·/ *n* [C] an animal with thick white fur which looks like a goat and lives in the western mountains of North America 石山羊〔生活在北美西部山區看似山羊的一種動物〕

mountain laur·el /ˌ·· ˈ··/ *n* [C] a bush with glossy leaves and pink or white flowers that grows in North America 山月桂

mountain li·on /ˈ·· ˌ··/ *n* [C] a COUGAR 美洲獅

moun·tain·ous /ˈmauntn̩əs; ˈmaʊntɪ̣nəs/ *adj* **1** having a lot of mountains 多山的: *the mountainous coast of Wales* 威爾斯多山的海岸 | *a mountainous region* 山區 **2** very large in amount or size 〔數量或規模〕巨大的; 龐大的: *a mountainous woman in a floral swimsuit* 穿着花泳衣的身材高大的女人

mountain range /ˌ·· ˈ·/ *n* [C] a long row of mountains that covers a large area 山脈

moun·tain·side /ˈmauntn̩ˌsaɪd; ˈmaʊntɪ̣nsaɪd/ *n* [C] the side of a mountain 山坡; 山腰: *Great rocks rolled down the mountainside.* 巨大的岩石順着山坡滾了下去。

moun·tain·top /ˈmauntn̩ˌtɑp; ˈmaʊntɪ̣ntɒp/ *n* [C] the top part of a mountain 山頂

moun·te·bank /ˈmauntəˌbæŋk; ˈmaʊntɪbæŋk/ *n* [C] *literary* a dishonest person who tricks and deceives people【文】江湖騙子

moun·ted /ˈmauntɪd; ˈmaʊntɪ̣d/ *adj* mounted soldiers or police officers ride on horses 〔士兵或警察〕騎馬的, 騎馬執行任務的: *the mounted police* 騎警(隊)

Mount·ie /ˈmauntɪ; ˈmaʊnti/ *n* [C] *informal* a member of the Royal Canadian Mounted Police【非正式】加拿大皇家騎警

mount·ing¹ /ˈmauntɪŋ; ˈmaʊntɪŋ/ *adj* [only before noun 僅用於名詞前] **1 mounting excitement/anger/violence** gradually increasing or becoming worse 越來越強烈的興奮/憤怒/暴力: *mounting violence in urban*

M

areas 城市地區越來越嚴重的暴力行為 | *With mounting excitement the children waited for Christmas morning.* 孩子們懷着越來越興奮的心情等待着聖誕早晨的到來。**2 mounting inflation/debts/losses** gradually increasing and causing serious problems 日益嚴重的通貨膨脹/不斷增加的債務/日漸增加的損失: *the mounting costs of the project* 該工程不斷增加的成本

mounting² *n* [C] an object to which other things, especially parts of a machine, are fastened to keep them in place 底座, 座架: *The engine is supported by four rubberized mountings.* 發動機由四個覆有橡膠層的座架支撐着。

mourn /mɔrn; mɔːn/ *v* [I,T] **1** to feel very sad because someone that you love has died, and show this in the way you behave 悼念, 哀悼, 為...哀痛: **mourn sb's death/loss** *She still mourns her son's death.* 她還在為兒子的死傷心。| **[+for]** *They mourned for their children, killed in the war.* 他們為自己死於戰爭的孩子們哀悼。**2** to feel very sad because something no longer exists or is no longer as good as it used to be 對...感到痛心[遺憾]: *The old steam trains were much-loved, and we all mourn their passing.* 那些老蒸汽火車曾深受人們的喜愛, 我們都為它們的消失而感到遺憾。

mourn·er /ˈmɔrnɚ; ˈmɔːnə/ *n* [C] someone who attends a funeral, especially a relative of the dead person 參加葬禮者, 送葬者〔尤指死者的親屬〕

mourn·ful /ˈmɔrnfl; ˈmɔːnfəl/ *adj* very sad 非常傷心的, 悲痛的, 悲傷的: *Durant was thin, mournful and silent.* 杜蘭特很消瘦, 神情悲傷, 默默不語。| *the slow, mournful music of the bagpipes* 風笛那緩慢、憂傷的音樂 —**mournfully** *adj* —**mournfulness** *n* [U]

mourn·ing /ˈmɔrnɪŋ; ˈmɔːnɪŋ/ *n* [U] **1** great sadness because someone has died〔因某人去世而感到的〕哀痛, 悲痛, 哀悼: *The drawn curtains and solemn hush told me that this was a house of mourning.* 拉上的窗簾和肅穆的寂靜告訴我這戶人家有喪事。**2** black clothes worn to show that you are very sad that someone has died 喪服: *She was recently widowed and wearing mourning.* 她失去丈夫不久, 所以穿着喪服。**3 be in mourning a)** to be very sad because of someone's death〔因某人去世而〕悲痛, 哀痛: *It was the custom to visit those in mourning and sit quietly with them.* 依照風俗, 要去拜訪那些因親人去世而處於悲痛中的人, 陪他們靜靜地坐些時候。**b)** to be dressed in black clothes to show that you are mourning 穿喪服, 戴孝

2 3 **mouse** /maus; maʊs/ *n* [C] **1** *plural* **mice** /maɪs; maɪs/ a small furry animal with a long tail that lives in people's houses or in fields, and that looks like a small rat 小(老)鼠, 家鼠, 耗子: *I think we have mice in the kitchen.* 我覺得我們的廚房裡有老鼠。| *a field mouse* 田鼠 **2** *technical* a small object connected to a computer by a wire, which you move with your hand to give commands to the computer【術語】鼠標, 滑鼠 —see picture on page A14 參見A14頁圖 **3** [usually singular 一般用單數] *informal* a quiet, nervous person【非正式】膽小的人 —see also 另見 **play cat and mouse with** (CAT (4))

mouse 鼠

mous·er /ˈmausɚ; ˈmaʊsə/ *n* [C] a cat that catches mice 捕鼠的貓

mouse·trap /ˈmausˌtræp; ˈmaʊs-træp/ *n* [C] a trap for catching mice 捕鼠器, 老鼠夾子

mous·sa·ka /muˈsɑkə; muːˈsɑːkə/ *n* [U] a Greek dish made from meat, cheese, and AUBERGINES 莫薩卡〔由肉、乾酪和茄子做成的一種希臘菜餚〕

mousse /mus; muːs/ *n* [C,U] **1** a sweet food made from a mixture of cream, eggs, and fruit or chocolate which is eaten when it is cold 奶油凍〔一種甜味食品〕: *chocolate mousse* 巧克力奶油凍 **2** a white slightly sticky substance that you put in your hair to make it look thicker or to hold it in place 定型髮膠, 摩絲

mous·tache also 又作 **mustache** *AmE*【美】/ˈmʌstæʃ; məˈstɑːʃ/ *n* [C] hair that grows on a man's upper lip 髭, 小鬍子: *He's shaved off his moustache.* 他剃去了小鬍子。—compare 比較 BEARD (1)

mous·tach·i·oed /məˈstæʃɪod; məˈstæʃiəʊd/ *adj* an American spelling of MUSTACHIOED mustachioed的美式拼法

mous·y, mousey /ˈmausɪ; ˈmaʊsi/ *adj* **1** mousy hair is a dull brown colour〔頭髮〕灰褐色的 **2** a mousy woman is quiet and unattractive〔女人〕沒有生氣的; 不引人注目的 —**mousiness** *n* [U]

mouth¹ /mauθ; maʊθ/ *n plural* **mouths** /mauðz; maʊðz/ 2 1

1 ►FACE 臉◄ [C] the part of your face which you put food into, or which you use for speaking 嘴, 口; 口腔: *Don't talk with your mouth full of food!* 嘴裡塞滿了吃的東西時別說話! —see picture at 參見 HEAD¹ 圖

2 keep your mouth shut *informal*【非正式】**a)** to not tell other people about a secret 保守祕密, 守口如瓶: *I don't want my parents finding out about this, so you'd better keep your mouth shut.* 我不想讓我父母知道這事, 所以你最好嘴嚴點。**b)** to not say anything because you might make a mistake, or annoy someone or upset them 保持緘默, 一聲不吭: *She started to cry, and I wished I'd kept my mouth shut.* 她開始哭了起來, 我真希望自己甚麼也沒說。

3 open your mouth to start to speak, especially in a situation where you feel you should not say anything 開口說話: *I didn't dare open my mouth in case I offended her.* 我不敢開口, 以免得罪她。

4 ►OPENING 口狀物◄ [C] **a)** the entrance to a large hole or CAVE〔洞穴等的〕入口 **b)** the open part at the top of a bottle or container〔瓶子或其他容器的〕開口處

5 ►RIVER 河流◄ [C] the part of a river where it joins the sea 入海口, 河口 —see picture on page A12 參見A12頁圖

6 big mouth *informal* someone who is a big mouth or has a big mouth is annoying because they cannot keep secrets or they often say things they should not say【非正式】嘴不嚴的人, 多嘴的人

7 me and my big mouth/you and your big mouth etc *spoken* used when you are annoyed with yourself or with someone else for telling other people a secret or saying something that should not be said【口】都怪我/你等多嘴

8 he/she is all mouth *spoken* used when you think that someone is not really brave enough, strong enough etc to do what they say they can do【口】他/她只是嘴上發發狠而已〔指某人只是嘴裡嚷着要做某事但實際上不敢付諸行動〕

9 mouth to feed someone who you must provide food for, especially one of your children 需要養活的人〔尤指孩子〕: *To these parents, a new baby is just another hungry mouth to feed.* 對這些父母來說, 新生一個嬰兒只不過是又添了一張嗷嗷待哺的嘴而已。

10 make your mouth water if food makes your mouth water, it looks so good you want to eat it immediately 使某人饞得流口水 —see also 另見 MOUTH-WATERING

11 down in the mouth *informal* looking very unhappy【非正式】垂頭喪氣的, 沮喪的: *Why's Tim so down in the mouth?* 蒂姆為甚麼這樣悶悶不樂?

12 open-mouthed/wide-mouthed etc with an open, wide etc mouth 張着嘴的/大嘴巴的等

13 out of the mouths of babes (and sucklings) *humorous* used when a small child has just said something clever or interesting【幽默】小孩子的話也有道理 —see also 另見 **by word of mouth** (WORD¹ (29)), **foam at the mouth** (FOAM² (2)), HAND TO MOUTH, **put your foot in your mouth** (FOOT¹ (12)), **shut your mouth** (SHUT¹ (3)), **shoot your mouth off** (SHOOT¹ (7))

mouth² /mauð; maʊð/ *v* [T] **1** to move your lips as if

you are saying words, but without making any sound 不出聲地說, 用口型默示: *Brook was waving and mouthing over the noise at the others to stand aside.* 在嘈雜聲中布魯克朝着其他人一邊擺手一邊用口形示意他們站到一邊去。**2** to say things that you do not really believe or that you do not understand 言不由衷地說;〔自己胡塗卻〕信口開河: *a third-rate politician, capable only of mouthing the current party line* 只會空談政黨當前路線的三流政客 | **mouth platitudes** (=give opinions that are not original) 信口重複一些陳詞濫調 *people at cocktail parties mouthing platitudes about the starving millions* 在雞尾酒會上信口說些數百萬人正在挨餓之類的老套話的人們

mouth off *phr v* [I+**at/about**] *informal* to complain angrily and noisily about something, or talk as if you know more than anyone else【非正式】憤怒而大聲地抱怨; 大發議論; 賣弄地說話

mouth·ful /ˈmauθˌful; ˈmaʊθfʊl/ *n* [C] **1** an amount of food or drink that you put into your mouth at one time〔食物或飲料的〕一口: *That was a great steak! I enjoyed every mouthful.* 牛排真是棒極了! 我吃得津津有味。**2 a mouthful** *informal* a long word or phrase that is difficult to say【非正式】冗長而拗口的詞[片語]: *Her real name is a bit of a mouthful, so we just call her Dee.* 她的真名長得有點兒拗口, 所以我們只叫她迪伊。**3 give sb a mouthful** *informal especially BrE* to speak angrily to someone, often swearing at them【非正式, 尤英】憤怒地對某人說; 咒罵某人 **4 say a mouthful** *AmE informal* to say a lot of true and important things about something in a few words【美, 非正式】幾句話說出許多真實而重要的事, 說到點子上; 話短而精

mouth or·gan /ˈ· ˌ··/ *n* [C] a small musical instrument which you hold close to your lips and blow or suck; HARMONICA 口琴

mouth·piece /ˈmauθˌpis; ˈmaʊθpiːs/ *n* [C] **1** [usually singular 一般用單數] a person, newspaper etc that expresses the opinions of a government or a political organization 代言人; 喉舌; 傳聲筒: *Pravda was the official mouthpiece of the Communist Party.*《真理報》曾是共產黨的官方喉舌。**2** the part of a musical instrument, telephone etc that you put in your mouth or next to your mouth〔樂器的〕吹口;〔電話的〕送話口

mouth-to-mouth re·sus·ci·ta·tion /ˌ· · ˌ· · ˌ· · ˈ· ·/ *n* [U] a method used to make someone start breathing again by blowing air into their mouth 口對口人工呼吸

mouth·wash /ˈmauθˌwɔʃ; ˈmaʊθwɒʃ/ *n* [C,U] a liquid used to make your mouth smell fresh or to get rid of infection in your mouth 漱口劑; 洗口藥

mouth-wa·ter·ing /ˈ· ˌ··/ *adj* food that is mouth-watering looks or smells extremely good〔食物〕令人饞涎欲滴的, 誘人的: *a mouth-watering aroma coming from the kitchen* 從廚房裡傳來的誘人的香味

mov·a·ble¹, moveable /ˈmuvəbḷ; ˈmuːvəbəl/ *adj* able to be moved and not fixed in one place or position 活動的; 可移動的: *a teddy bear with movable arms and legs* 四肢能活動的玩具熊

movable² also 又作 **moveable** *n* [C usually plural 一般用複數] *law* a personal possession such as a piece of furniture【法律】動產〈如家具〉

movable feast /ˌ··· ˈ·/ *n* [C] **1** *BrE informal* something that happens at different times, so that you are not sure exactly when it will happen【英, 非正式】發生時間不固定的事 **2** a special religious day, such as Easter, the date of which changes 日期因年而異的宗教節日〈如復活節〉

1 1 **move¹** /muv; muːv/ *v*

1 ▶CHANGE PLACE 改變地方◀ [I,T] to change your place or position, or to make something do this (使) 改變位置, 移動, 搬動: *Don't move or I'll shoot.* 不許動, 否則我就開槍了。| *You mustn't get off the train while it's still moving.* 火車還未停定的時候不得下車。| **move sth** *Can you move your car – it's blocking the road.* 你能不能移動一下你的汽車 —— 它擋着路。| *We'll have to move the bed closer to the wall.* 我們將不得不把牀移得靠牆更近一些。| **move about** *BrE*【英】**/around** *I could hear someone moving around upstairs.* 我能聽見有人在樓上來回走動。| **can't move** (=be stuck or trapped) 動彈不了, 被困住 *Get me out of here – I can't move.* 把我從這兒弄出去 —— 我動彈不了。

2 ▶NEW HOUSE/OFFICE 新房子/新辦公室◀ [I,T] to go to live or work in a different place 搬家; 搬遷; 遷移: [+**to**] *When are you moving to Memphis?* 你甚麼時候搬到孟菲斯去? | [+**into**] *They've moved into a bigger office.* 他們已搬進了一間大一些的辦公室。| **move house/home** *BrE* (=go to live in a different house)【英】搬家 *My parents kept moving house because of my dad's job.* 由於爸爸的工作需要, 我父母不斷地搬家。

3 ▶CHANGE JOB/CLASS ETC 換工作/班級等◀ [I,T] to change to a different job, class etc, or to make someone change to a different job, class etc (使) 改做〔不同工作〕; (把某人) 調到〔不同班級等〕: **move sb to/into** *His teacher wants him moved to a higher class.* 他的老師想把他調到高年級去。| **move to/from** *She's just moved from the sales department.* 她剛剛從銷售部調過來。

4 ▶CHANGE YOUR OPINION 改變看法◀ **a)** [I] to change from one opinion or way of thinking to another 改變看法: *Neither side is willing to move on the issue of territory.* 雙方都不願意在領土問題上讓步。| [+**towards/away from**] *The two political parties have moved closer towards each other in recent months.* 最近幾個月, 這兩個政黨的觀點已較為接近了。**b)** [T] to persuade someone to change their opinion 說服〔某人〕改變看法: *She won't be moved – it doesn't matter what you say to her.* 她是說不動的 —— 不管你對她說甚麼。

5 ▶MAKE SB SAD 使某人難過◀ [T] to make someone feel strong feelings, especially of sadness or sympathy 激起〔某人〕的強烈情感〔尤指難過或同情〕; 使感動: **be deeply/greatly moved** *I was deeply moved by their story.* 我被他們的故事深深地感動了。| **move sb to tears** *The child's suffering moved us to tears.* 那孩子受的苦使我們難過得流淚。—see also 另見 MOVING

6 ▶PROGRESS 進展◀ [I] to progress in a particular way or at a particular rate 進展, 前進; 發展: *Things moved quickly once the contract was signed.* 合同一簽, 事情進展得很快。| *The negotiations seem to be moving in the right direction.* 談判好像正在朝着正確的方向進展。

7 be/feel moved to do sth to want to do something because you feel angry, sad etc〔因感到生氣、難過等而〕想做某事: *Hearing so much nonsense talked, I felt moved to speak on the subject.* 聽到那麼多的廢話, 我想就那個話題說說自己的意見。

8 get moving *informal*【非正式】**a)** used when telling someone to hurry or when saying that you must hurry 趕緊; 趕快: *We'd better get moving if we're going to catch that plane.* 如果想趕上那班飛機, 我們最好趕緊出發。**b)** *spoken* used to tell someone that you need to leave a place【口】該走了: *It's time we got moving – I have to be up early tomorrow.* 我們該走了 —— 我明天得早起牀。

9 get things moving *informal* to make a process or event start happening【非正式】開始 (做) 某事, 取得進展

10 ▶CHANGE ARRANGEMENTS 改變安排◀ [T] to change the time or order of something 改變〔時間或順序〕: **move sth to/from** *Could we move the meeting to Thursday?* 我們可以把會議改到星期四嗎?

11 ▶CHANGE SUBJECT/ACTIVITY 改變話題/活動◀ [I] to change from one subject or activity to another 改變話題[活動]: [+**away from/off**] *We seem to be moving away from the main point of the discussion.* 我們好像偏離討論的要點了。—see also 另見 **move on**

12 ▶START DEALING WITH 開始處理◀ [I] to start doing something, especially in order to achieve something or deal with a problem 開始做某事, 開始採取行

動: **[+on/against etc]** *The governor has yet to move on any of the recommendations in the report.* 州長尚未處理報告中的任何建議。| **move fast/quickly** *You'll have to move fast if you want to get a place on the course.* 如果你想報名讀這門課程, 就得趕緊行動起來。
13 ▶LEAVE 離開◀ [I] *BrE especially spoken* to go somewhere or leave a place【英, 尤口】去某處; 離開某地: *It's time we were moving.* 我們該離開了。
14 ▶GAMES 遊戲◀ [I,T] to change the position of one of the pieces used to play a game such as CHESS 移動(棋子), 走(棋)
15 ▶AT A MEETING 在會上◀ [I,T] *formal* to officially make a proposal at a meeting【正式】提議, 提出〔動議〕: **move that** *The chairman moved that the meeting be adjourned.* 主席提議休會。| **move an amendment** *BrE* (=propose a change)【英】提出一項修正案 *They want to move an amendment to the bill.* 他們想提議修正該法案。
16 ▶GO FAST 快速行進◀ [I] *informal* to travel very fast【非正式】快速行進, 飛馳: *This car can really move!* 這輛小汽車跑得真快!
17 ▶SELL STH 賣掉某物◀ [I] *informal* to sell something quickly【非正式】快速銷售掉, 很快脱手: *You should watch these juggling kits move. The kids love 'em.* 你應該看看這些耍把戲用品賣得多快, 孩子們喜歡極了。
18 not move a muscle to stay completely still 一動不動, 紋絲不動
19 move with the times to change the way you think and behave, as the world changes around you 與時俱進
20 you can't move/you can hardly move *spoken* used to say that a place is very full and there is not much space【口】〔擠得〕動不了/幾乎無法動彈: *The bar was so crowded you could hardly move.* 酒吧非常擁擠, 人幾乎無法動彈。
21 you can't move for *spoken* used to say that a place is full of a particular kind of people or things【口】到處都是, 擠滿了〔某類人或物〕: *You couldn't move for police in town this morning.* 今天上午城裡到處都是警察。
22 move in a society/world/circle to spend a lot of time with a particular kind of people and know them well 與某一團體/社會/圈子的人長期交往: *Lady Olga moved in a different social world from me.* 奧爾加夫人出入的社交圈和我的不同。—see also 另見 **move the goalposts** (GOALPOST (2)), **move in for the kill** (KILL² (2)), **move heaven and earth** (HEAVEN (10)), **when the spirit moves you** (SPIRIT¹ (13))

move along *phr v* **1** [I] *BrE* to move further towards the back or front of something【英】向前[後]移動: *The bus-driver asked us all to move along.* 公共汽車司機要我們都往裡邊走。**2** [T **move** sb **along**] *especially BrE* to officially order someone to leave a public place【尤英】命令〔某人〕離開〔公共場所〕: *The police moved us along almost as soon as we started playing.* 我們剛開始玩, 警察就把我們趕走了。

move away *phr v* [I] to go to live in a different area 搬走: *Her children had moved away and she was left on her own.* 她的孩子都搬走了, 只剩她一個人獨自生活。

move in *phr v* [I] **1** to start living in a new house 搬進新居: *We decided not to move in until we'd finished decorating.* 我們決定裝修完後再搬進去。**2** to start living with someone in the same house 開始〔和某人〕同居; 搬來〔和某人〕一起居住: **[+with]** *She wants her boyfriend to move in with her.* 她想讓她的男朋友搬進來和她住在一起。**3** to take control of a situation, often using your power and influence unfairly 強行插手, 干預: *The big multinationals moved in and started pushing up prices.* 一些大的跨國公司插手進來, 開始抬高價格。**4** to go towards a place or group of people in order to attack them or take control of them〔為了進攻或控制而〕向…逼近, 進逼: **[+on]** *Already a special police task force was preparing to move in on the gang.* 一支特警隊已經在準備逼近那夥歹徒以採取行動。

move off *phr v* [I] if a vehicle or group of people moves off, they start to leave the place where they are〔車輛或人羣〕離開, 出發, 起程: *The conductor blew his whistle and the train slowly moved off.* 列車員吹響了哨子, 火車徐徐開動了。

move on *phr v*
1 ▶CONTINUE JOURNEY 繼續行程◀ [I] to leave the place where you have been staying and continue your journey 繼續前行: *That's enough rest – it's time to move on.* 休息夠了 —— 是繼續趕路的時候了。
2 ▶CHANGE SUBJECT 改變話題◀ [I] to start talking about a new subject in a discussion, book etc〔在討論、書籍等中〕開始談論新話題, 更換話題: *I think we've covered this topic – is it all right if we move on?* 我覺得這個話題我們都談過了 —— 我們換個話題好嗎?
3 ▶CHANGE JOB/CLASS 改換工作/班級◀ [I] to leave your present job, class, or activity and start doing another one 改換工作[班級, 活動]: **[+to]** *Children usually move on to secondary school at 11.* 兒童通常在11歲時升入中學。
4 ▶PROGRESS/DEVELOP 進步/發展◀ [I] **a)** to develop in your life, and become older and more experienced〔在生活中〕成長, 變得更成熟: **[+from]** *I felt that I'd moved on from my college days, and didn't want to go back.* 我感到自己與在大學時比較變得老成了, 不想再回到從前。**b)** to become more modern, advanced, or complicated than before 變得更現代[先進, 複雜], 有了新發展: *In my day you could only get them in black-and-white, but things have moved on since then.* 在我那個時候, 那些玩意兒只有黑白的, 現在和當時已大不一樣了。
5 move on to higher/better things *humorous* to get a better job or social position【幽默】高升: *I expect you'll be moving on to higher things now that you have your degree.* 你既然拿到了學位, 我認為你會高升的。
6 ▶TIME 時間◀ [I] if time moves on, the year moves on etc, the time passes〔歲月〕流逝
7 time is moving on *BrE spoken* used to say that you must leave soon or do something soon, because it is getting late【英口】時間不早了: *Time's moving on – we'd better get back to the car.* 時間不早了 —— 我們最好回到車上去。
8 ▶MAKE SB LEAVE 讓某人離開◀ [T **move** sb **on**] *BrE* to officially order someone to leave a public place【英】命令〔某人〕離開〔公共場所〕: *We got moved on by the police for making too much noise.* 我們太吵了, 警察要我們走開。

move out *phr v* [I] **1** to leave the house where you are living now in order to go and live somewhere else 搬出, 遷走: **[+of]** *They want to find a house somewhere and move out of their apartment.* 他們想在某個地方找棟房子, 然後搬出他們的公寓套房。**2** if a group of soldiers moves out, they leave a place〔部隊〕開拔, 撤出 **3** *AmE informal* to leave【美, 非正式】離開: *Is everything packed? Then let's move out.* 全都收拾好了嗎? 那咱們動身吧。

move over *phr v* [I] **1** to change position so that there is more space for someone else〔為騰出地方而〕挪動, 移動: *Move over so that we can all sit down.* 挪一挪, 讓我們都能坐下。**2** to change to a different system, opinion, group of people etc 轉變, 變更: **[+to]** *Most companies have moved over to computer-aided design systems.* 大多數公司已轉而採用電腦輔助設計系統。

move up *phr v* [I] **1** *BrE* to change position in order to make more space for other people or things, or to be near someone else【英】〔為騰出地方而〕挪動; 靠攏: *There's room for one more if everyone moves up a bit.* 如果大家都挪動一下, 那麼還會有一個人的地方。**2** to get a better job in a company, or move to a higher class in a school 升遷, 晉升; 升年級: *Everyone here's very ambitious – they all want to move up as quickly as possible.* 這兒所有的人都野心勃勃 —— 都想盡快升職。**3 move up in the world** *often humorous* to get a better job or social position【常幽默】升職, 高升: *John's moved up*

in the world since you knew him – he's a director now. 約翰在你認識他以後高升了 —— 他現在是總裁。

move² *n*

1 ▶ACTION 行動◀ [singular] something that you decide to do 步驟; 行動: *She's still thinking about her next move.* 她還在考慮她的下一步行動。| **a good/wise/smart etc move** *He said he was starting his own company, which sounded like a smart move.* 他說他要自己開公司, 這聽起來像是一着妙棋。

2 make a move a) to move in a particular direction, especially in order to attack someone or to escape〔尤指為襲擊某人或逃走而〕移動; 挪動: *If anyone makes a move, I'll shoot.* 誰動一下, 我就開槍。| **[+towards/for]** *He suddenly made a move towards the door.* 他突然朝門口走去。**b)** to do something to achieve a particular result 採取行動: *Neither side had made a move to resolve the dispute.* 雙方都沒有採取行動來解決爭端。**c)** *BrE informal* to leave a place【英, 非正式】離開, 出發: *It's getting late – we ought to make a move.* 時間不早了 —— 我們該走了。

3 be on the move a) to be travelling from one place to the next 在遷移; 在行進: *We have received reports that the rebel army is on the move.* 我們已接到報告, 說叛軍正在轉移。**b)** to be busy and active 忙碌; 活躍: *She's always on the move, isn't she?* 她總是閒不住, 是不是? **c)** to be changing and developing a lot 在發展變化; 在前進: *Georgian England was a society on the move.* 喬治王朝時期的英格蘭是一個正處於發展變化中的社會。

4 get a move on *spoken* used to tell someone to hurry【口】快點, 趕緊: *Get a move on or we'll be late!* 快點, 要不我們會遲到的!

5 make the first move to do something first, especially in order to end a quarrel or start a relationship〔尤指為了結束爭吵或建立關係而〕先邁出第一步, 先採取行動: *Neither was willing to make the first move towards reconciliation.* 雙方誰都不願意先邁出和解的第一步。

6 watch/follow sb's every move to carefully watch everything that someone does, especially because you think they are doing something illegal 注視某人的一舉一動: *I have three officers watching his every move.* 我讓三名警察監視着他的一舉一動。

7 make no move to do sth to make no attempt to prevent someone from doing something 沒有採取行動做某事: *They were staring, but made no move to stop us.* 他們瞪眼看着, 但沒有採取行動阻止我們。

8 ▶GOING TO A NEW PLACE 去新的地方◀ [singular] the process of leaving one house, office etc, and going to live or work in a different one 搬家; 搬遷, 遷移: *"How was the move?" "Exhausting!"* "搬家的滋味如何?" "累死人!"

9 ▶PROGRESS 進展◀ [C] something that is done to improve a situation〔使局面改觀的〕舉措: *It's a move in the right direction.* 這是一個方向正確的舉措。

10 ▶GAMES 遊戲◀ [C] **a)** an act of changing the position of one of the objects in a game such as CHESS〔下棋的〕一步, 一着 **b)** a way in which this may be done, according to the rules〔棋子的〕規定走法: *I'm learning all the different moves.* 我在學習棋的各種不同走法。**c)** the time when a player can move one of these objects〔輪到某一方的〕走棋: *It's your move.* 該你走了。

move·a·ble /ˈmuvəbḷ; ˈmuːvəbəl/ *adj* another spelling of MOVABLE movable的另一種拼法

move·ment /ˈmuvmənt; ˈmuːvmənt/ *n*

1 ▶GROUP 團體◀ [C] a group of people who share the same ideas or beliefs and work together to achieve a particular aim〔政治、社會方面的〕運動; 積極開展運動的團體: *the civil rights movement* 民權運動 | *The nationalist movement did not have widespread support.* 民族主義運動沒有得到廣泛的支持。

2 ▶MOVING 移動◀ **a)** [C,U] a change in the place or position of something or someone 移動; 調動: *reports of troop movement in the area* 該地區部隊動向的報道 **b)** [C] an act of moving your body, or the way someone moves their body 動作; 舉止, 風度: *the dancer's graceful movements* 舞蹈家優美的動作

3 ▶CHANGE/DEVELOPMENT 變化/發展◀ **a)** [U] a change that brings progress or improvement in a situation 改進, 改善; 進步, 發展: *There's been no movement in the dispute since Thursday.* 自週四以來, 爭端一直沒有緩和。**b)** [C] a gradual change or development in people's attitudes or behaviour〔態度或行為的〕逐漸變化, 趨勢, 傾向: *a growing movement among consumers away from buying processed foods* 消費者不再購買已加工食品這一日益增長的趨勢

4 sb's movements all of a person's activities over a certain period〔在某一期間內〕某人所有的活動: *Police are trying to trace Carter's movements over the last 48 hours.* 警方在設法追查卡特在過去48小時裡的活動。

5 ▶MUSIC 音樂◀ [C] one of the main parts into which a piece of music is divided, especially in a SYMPHONY〔尤指交響曲的〕樂章

6 ▶CLOCK/WATCH 鐘/錶◀ the moving parts of a piece of machinery, especially a clock or watch〔活動〕機件; 〔尤指鐘錶的〕機心

7 ▶BODY WASTE 人體的排泄物◀ [C] *formal* an act of getting rid of waste matter from the bowels (BOWEL (1))【正式】排便

mov·er /ˈmuvɚ; ˈmuːvə/ *n* [C] **1** someone who makes a formal proposal at a meeting〔會議上的〕提議人, 動議者: *The mover of the motion has a right of reply to the discussion.* 提出動議者有權對討論作出答覆。**2** someone or something that moves in a particular way〔以某種方式〕移動的人[物]: *Saturn is the slowest mover of all the planets.* 土星是所有行星中運行速度最慢的。**3** *especially AmE* someone whose job is to help people move from one house to another【尤美】搬家工人 **4 movers and shakers** powerful and influential people 有權勢的人: *The movers and shakers in the stock market predicted a rise in share-dealing.* 證券市場中有權勢的人物預測股票交易將會增加。—see also 另見 PRIME MOVER, **key mover/player** (KEY¹)

mov·ie /ˈmuvɪ; ˈmuːvi/ *n* [C] *especially AmE*【尤美】**1** a film made to be shown at the cinema 電影: *a Hollywood movie* 好萊塢影片 **2 the movies** the cinema 電影院: **go to the movies** (=go to watch a movie at the cinema) 去看電影

mov·ie·go·er /ˈmuvɪˌgoɚ; ˈmuːviˌgəʊə/ *n* [C] *especially AmE* someone who goes to see films, especially regularly【尤美】〔尤指經常〕看電影的人

movie star /ˈ·· ·/ *n* [C] *especially AmE* a famous film actor or actress【尤美】電影明星

movie thea·ter /ˈ·· ˌ··/ *n* [C] *AmE*【美】= CINEMA (1) *BrE*【英】

mov·ing /ˈmuvɪŋ; ˈmuːvɪŋ/ *adj* **1** making you feel strong emotions, especially sadness or sympathy 動人的, 感人的: *Jackson's speech was so moving, it made me cry.* 傑克遜的講話非常感人, 我感動得哭了。| **moving account/experience/story etc** *a moving account of life in the refugee camps* 對難民營生活的感人敘述 **2** [only before noun 僅用於名詞前] changing from one position to another 活動的, 移動的: *a moving stage* 活動舞台 | **fast/slow moving etc** *Be very careful when changing lanes in fast moving traffic.* 在快速行進的車流中換車道一定要非常小心。**3 the moving spirit** someone who makes something start to happen 發起人, 策動者: *Mr Arkwright was the moving spirit behind the founding of the union.* 阿克賴特先生是創建該協會的幕後發起人。—**movingly** *adv*: *the sufferings of the famine victims, so movingly described in Buerk's TV reports* 伯爾克的電視報道中描述得如此感人的飢民的苦難

moving part /ˌ·· ˈ·/ *n* [C] a part of a machine that moves when it is operating〔機器的〕活動部件: *Keep the moving parts well oiled.* 要使活動部件保持良好的潤滑狀態。

moving pic·ture /ˌ·· ˈ··◂/ *n* [C] *old-fashioned, espe-*

cially AmE a film made to be shown at the cinema【過時, 尤美】電影

moving stair·case /ˌ·· ˈ··/ *n* [C] *old-fashioned* an ESCALATOR【過時】自動扶梯

moving van /ˈ·· ˌ·/ *n* [C] *AmE*【美】搬家車, 搬運車; REMOVAL VAN *BrE*【英】

mow /mo; məʊ/ *v past participle* **mowed** *or* **mown** /mon; məʊn/ [I,T] **1** to cut grass or wheat using a machine or tool with special blades 刈, 割〔草或小麥〕: *It's time to mow the lawn again.* 又該修剪草坪了。**2 new-mown hay/grass etc** recently cut grass etc 新割的牧草／草等

mow sb ↔ **down** *phr v* [T] to kill large numbers of people at the same time, especially by shooting them 大量殺死〔尤指射殺〕; 掃殺: *The battalion was mown down by enemy tanks.* 那個營的士兵在敵軍坦克掃射下成片成片地倒下了。

mow·er /ˈmoɚ; ˈməʊə/ *n* [C] **1** a machine used for cutting grass; LAWNMOWER 割[刈]草機, 草坪修剪機 **2** *old use* someone who mows【舊】刈割者

mox·ie /ˈmɑksɪ; ˈmɒksi/ *n* [U] *AmE informal* courage and determination【美, 非正式】勇氣, 膽量; 決心: *He's always had plenty of moxie.* 他向來渾身是膽。

MP /ˋɛm ˋpi; ˌem ˈpiː/ *n* [C] **1** MEMBER OF PARLIAMENT; someone who has been elected to represent the people in a parliament 國會議員; 英國下議院議員: *She's the MP for Liverpool North.* 她是利物浦市北區的下議院議員。| *Ken Newton, MP* 肯·牛頓, 下議院議員 **2** *informal* a member of the MILITARY POLICE【非正式】憲兵隊隊員

mpg /ˌɛm pi ˋdʒi; ˌem piː ˈdʒiː/ the abbreviation of 縮寫= miles per GALLON, used to describe the amount of petrol used by a car 每加侖汽油所行英里數, 英里／加侖: *a car that does 35 mpg* 每加侖汽油行駛35英里的汽車

mph /ˌɛm pi ˋetʃ; ˌem piː ˈeɪtʃ/ the abbreviation of 縮寫= miles per hour, used to describe the speed of a vehicle 英里／小時: *speeding along at 100 mph* 以每小時100英里的速度飛馳

MPhil /ˌɛm ˋfɪl; ˌem ˈfɪl/ *n* [C] *BrE* Master of PHILOSOPHY; a university degree that you get after your first degree【英】哲學碩士; 哲學碩士學位

Mr *BrE*【英】, **Mr.** *AmE*【美】/ˋmɪstɚ; ˈmɪstə/ **1** a title used before a man's family name when you are speaking to him or writing to him and want to be polite 先生〔用於男子的姓之前的尊稱〕: *Mr Smith* 史密斯先生 | *Mr. John Smith* 約翰·史密斯先生 | *Mr and Mrs Smith* 史密斯先生及夫人 **2** a title used when addressing a man in an official position 先生〔對有官職的男子的稱呼〕: *Mr Chairman* 主席先生 | *Mr. President* 總統先生 —compare 比較 MADAM (3) **3 Mr Right** a man who would be the perfect husband for a particular woman 理想的丈夫, 如意郎君: *She's spent years waiting for Mr Right to come along.* 多少年來她一直在等着如意郎君的出現。**4 Mr Big** *informal* the leader or most important person in a group, especially a criminal group【非正式】〔尤指犯罪集團的〕頭兒, 最重要的人物 **5 Mr Clean** *informal* someone who is honest and always obeys the law【非正式】清白先生, 誠實守法的人 **6** *spoken* used before the name of a personal quality or kind of behaviour as a humorous name for a man who has that quality【口】…先生, …大王〔用於表示某種個人品質或行為的詞之前, 作為對具有該品質或行為的男子的幽默稱呼〕: *I don't think we need any comments from Mr Sarcasm here.* 我認為這裡我們不需要諷刺先生作任何評論。—see also 另見 **no more Mr Nice Guy!** (GUY[1] (5))

USAGE NOTE 用法說明: MR

COLLOCATION 搭配

Mr, Mrs, Miss, and **Ms** are only used with full names or last names (surnames). Mr, Mrs, Miss 及 Ms 只能與全名或姓連用: *Hello, Mr Gray.* 你好, 格雷先生。| *The next candidate for the job is Mrs Betty Schwarz* (NOT 不用 *Please Miss teacher* or 或 *Good morning Mr Jerry*). 該工作的下一個申請者是貝蒂·施瓦茨夫人。

When you are talking or writing to someone directly, you do not usually use their full name. 直接跟某人談話或通信時通常不用他的全名: *Hello, Mr Smith* (NOT 不用 *Hello, Mr Alan Smith*). 你好, 史密斯先生。

Usually **Mr, Ms** etc is not used with names of people you know well or who are famous. 通常情況下, 在很熟的人或名人的姓名之前不用Mr, Ms等: *This is my friend Annie Walker.* 這是我的朋友安妮·沃克。| *the defeat of Adolf Hitler* 阿道夫·希特勒的失敗 | *Clinton's health care policy* 克林頓的醫療保健政策 | *'The Wave' by Hokusai* 北齋畫的《神奈川沖浪裡》

POLITENESS 禮貌程度

Many women prefer to be addressed as **Ms** rather than **Miss** or **Mrs**, as **Ms** does not unnecessarily draw attention to whether or not the woman is married. 許多女性更喜歡被稱作Ms而不是Miss或Mrs, 因為Ms這一稱呼不會引起人們對其婚姻狀況的注意。

Mrs *BrE*【英】, **Mrs.** *AmE*【美】/ˋmɪsɪz; ˈmɪsəz/ **1** a title used before a married woman's family name when you are speaking or writing to her and want to be polite 夫人, 太太〔跟已婚婦女談話或通信時用於其姓之前的尊稱〕: *Mrs. Smith* 史密斯夫人 | *Mr and Mrs David Smith* 戴維·史密斯先生及夫人 —compare 比較 MISS[2], MS —see 見 MR (USAGE) **2** *spoken* used before the name of a personal quality or type of behaviour as a humorous name for a married woman who has that quality【口】夫人〔用於表示某種個人品質或行為的詞之前, 作為對具有該品質或行為的已婚女子的幽默稱呼〕: *Mrs Superefficiency* 超級效率夫人

MS /ˌɛm ˋɛs; ˌem ˈes/ *n* **1** [C] *AmE* Master of Science; a university degree in science that you get after your first degree【美】理科碩士; 理科碩士學位 **2** [U] multiple sclerosis; a serious illness that gradually destroys your nerves, making you weak and unable to move 多發性硬化(症)

Ms *BrE*【英】, **Ms.** *AmE*【美】/mɪz; mɪz/ a title used before a woman's family name because it is not important to say whether she is married or not, or when you do not know whether she is married or not 女士〔置於女子姓前的稱呼, 用在沒必要說明其婚姻狀況或其婚姻狀況不明時〕—compare 比較 MISS[2], MRS —see 見 MR (USAGE)

ms *n plural* **mss** the written abbreviation of 縮寫= MANUSCRIPT

MSc /ˋɛm ɛs ˋsi; ˌem es ˈsiː/ *n* [C] Master of Science; a university degree in science that you get after your first degree 理科碩士; 理科碩士學位; MS (1) *AmE*【美】—compare 比較 MA

MS-DOS /ˌɛm ɛs ˋdɑs; ˌem es ˈdɒs/ *n* [U] *trademark* one of the most common OPERATING SYSTEMs for a computer【商標】微軟磁盤操作系統

MSG /ˌɛm ɛs ˋdʒi; ˌem es ˈdʒiː/ *n* [U] MONOSODIUM GLUTAMATE; a chemical compound added to food 味精, 味素〔穀胺酸一鈉〕

Mt the written abbreviation of 縮寫= MOUNT[2] (1): *Mt Everest* 埃佛勒斯峯〔即珠穆朗瑪峯〕

much[1] /mʌtʃ; mʌtʃ/ *adv* **1 much taller/much more difficult etc** used especially before comparatives and superlatives to mean a lot taller, a lot more difficult 高得多／難得多等: *You get a much better view if you stand on a chair.* 站在椅子上看會清楚得多。| *She looks much fatter in real life than she does on TV.* 她在現實生活中看起來比在電視上胖得多。| **much too old/much too tall etc** *You can't marry him. He's much too old.* 你不能嫁給他, 他年齡實在太大了。| **much the bigger/much**

the more interesting *Her second novel was much the more exciting.* 她的第二部小說要令人激動得多。| **much the biggest/much the most interesting etc** *He is much the most handsome man I've ever met.* 他絕對是我所見過的最英俊的男子。| **much loved/much admired** *Maturity and wider experience are much sought after commodities in teaching these days.* 在現代教學中, 人們更注重追求的是成熟的處事態度和廣泛的經驗。**2 too much/so much/very much/how much etc** used to show the degree which someone does something or something happens 太多/如此多/很多/多麼地等: *If he didn't talk so much he'd do a lot better.* 如果他話不那麼多, 他會做得好很多。| *The divorce was messy and at the time upset her very much.* 那次離婚弄得亂糟糟的, 令她那時很苦惱。| *I've so much looked forward to your visit.* 我十分急切地期盼着你的來訪。| *However much you hate walking you still have to go to the top.* 不管你是多麼不喜歡走路, 你還是必須走到頂。**3 not much a)** only a little, only to a small degree etc 只一點點, 不多; 不怎麼: *"Did you enjoy the performance?" "Not much!"* "你喜歡那場演出嗎?" "不怎麼喜歡!" | *I haven't seen Tony for over 20 years. He hasn't changed much.* 我有二十多年沒見托尼了, 他變化不大。| *It was only a young dog – not much higher than my knee.* 那只是一條幼犬 —— 比我的膝蓋高不了多少。**b)** used to say that something does not happen often 不經常, 很少: *We don't go to the theatre much these days.* 我們如今不常去看戲。| *The new compact discs mean you don't see LPs in the shops as much.* 激光唱片的普及意味着你如今在商店裡不會 (像以前那樣) 經常地看到密紋唱片了。**4 much like/much as/much the same** used to say that something is very similar to something else 很像, 幾乎一樣: *The house was very much as I'd remembered it.* 那座房子和我記憶中的樣子幾乎完全一樣。| *It's easy to confuse us, we're much the same build and have the same coloured hair.* 很容易把我們弄混, 我們體型差不多, 而且頭髮的顏色也一樣。**5 not be much good at something** to not be able to do something such as play a sport, speak a foreign language etc very well 不太善於做某事, 對某事不太在行: *Brian's never been much good at understanding other people's feelings.* 布賴恩從來就不太善於理解別人的感情。**6 much less** used to say that one thing is even less true, possible etc, than another 更不用說, 更何況: *He can hardly afford beer, much less champagne.* 他幾乎連啤酒都買不起, 更不用說香檳了。**7 be too much/a bit much** *spoken* used to say that someone's behaviour is rude or impolite【口】太過分/有點過分: *I thought breaking your window and expecting you to pay for it was a bit much!* 打破了你的窗玻璃還指望你為此掏腰包, 我認為這有點過分! **8 not so much...as...** used to show that something is bigger, more difficult etc than people may think 與其說是…不如說是…: *In many cases nursing is not so much a job as a way of life.* 在許多情況下, 護理與其說是一件工作倒不如說是一種生活方式。**9 much as sb does sth** used to mean that although one thing is true, something else is also true 儘管某人做某事〔指儘管某一情況是事實, 而另一情況也是事實〕: *Much as I enjoy Shakespeare, I was glad when the play was over.* 儘管我喜歡莎士比亞, 但當那個戲劇演完時我還是很高興。**10 much to sb's surprise/disgust etc** *formal* used to say that someone was very surprised, very disgusted etc【正式】令某人非常吃驚/厭惡等的是: *Much to my displeasure some of the pupils in the school have been smoking outside the gates.* 令我非常不快的是, 有些小學生一直在校門外吸煙。**11 so much the better (for sb)** *especially spoken* used to say that you think a situation, idea etc is very good【尤口】那 (對某人來說) 更好: *If he wants to not drink and drive everyone home, so much the better for us!* 如果他打算不喝酒並開車把大夥都送回家, 那對我們來說就更好了。**12 Not much!** used to emphasize that you really do want to do something, that you really are excited about something etc 哪裡的話! 當然不是! 未必!〔用於強調確實想做某事或確實為某事感到興奮〕: *"You don't want any cake, do you Tom?" "Not much!"* "你不要蛋糕了, 是吧湯姆?" "我當然要了!"

USAGE NOTE 用法說明: MUCH

GRAMMAR POINTS 語法要點

Much, with or without *very*, is only used with nouns if they are uncountable, and then only with negative clauses or in questions. 不管帶very與否, much只能和不可數名詞連用, 而且只能用於否定句及疑問句中: *She doesn't get out much.* 她不大出門。| *Did you get very much work done?* 你做了很多很多的工作嗎? | *How much money do you have?* 你有多少錢?

For positive statements and with countable nouns, you use **a lot** or **many**. 在肯定句中或可數名詞之前要用a lot或many: *She's done a lot of work.* 她已做了很多工作。| *They visited many/a lot of countries.* 他們去過許多國家。| *Were there many people there?* 那裡人多嗎?

You often use **(very) much** with verbs in negative or question contexts. In questions, it usually comes at the end of a clause. 在否定或疑問語境中(very) much常和動詞連用, 在疑問句中通常位於句末: *Do you go to London much?* 你經常去倫敦嗎? In negative contexts, it may come before the verb, or, more often, at the end. 在否定語境中, 可以出現在動詞之前, 但更常見的是在句末。So you would say 所以人們會說: *I don't much like living in London.* | *I don't like living in London much* (NOT 不用 *I don't like living much in London*). 我不太喜歡住在倫敦。

So much, as much, much more and **too much** are often used in positive contexts with verbs and uncountable nouns. so much, as much, much more 和too much常用在肯定語境中, 修飾動詞或不可數名詞: *I go to restaurants so much I'm tired of them.* 我去飯館去得太多了, 我都感到厭煩了。| *She smokes too much!* 她吸煙吸得太兇了! | *Try to relax as much as possible.* 盡量放鬆。| *We'll need much more money than that.* 我們將需要比那多得多的錢。

With some verbs, especially with the general meaning 'like', **very much** can be used in positive contexts as well. Using **very much** before a verb is particularly common in British English. 當和某些動詞〔尤其和表示"喜歡"的動詞〕連用時, very much也可用於肯定句中。動詞前用very much在英國英語中特別常見: *Rhoda very much enjoys skiing* (NOT 不用 *Rhoda enjoys very much skiing*). 羅達非常喜歡滑雪。| *I love her very much.* 我很愛她。You also say 人們也說: *Thank you very much.* 非常感謝。

(Very) much is used with most adjectives only before **more** and **too**, or when they are in the **-er** form. You cannot use it simply instead of **very**. (very) much和大多數形容詞連用時只能用在more和too之前, 或者與形容詞的 -er 形式連用。它不能代替very: *This is much more/too difficult.* 這事困難得多/這事實在太難了。But note that you say 但注意可以說: *I am very sorry* (NEVER 永不用 *I am much sorry*, or 或 *I am sorry very much*). 我很抱歉。

Some adjectives end in **-ed** or **-ing** and look like forms of verbs, but they take **very** rather than **much** (unless **more** or **too** is there as well). 有些形容詞以 -ed 或 -ing 結尾, 看起來像動詞, 但它們卻用very而不是much作修飾語〔除非這些形容詞前有more或too〕。So you would use **much** in this sentence 所以在下面這個句子中人們會用much: *She was a* *much-loved colleague*（她是一個很受大家喜愛的同事）because **loved** is a passive verb, but you would use **very** in this one 因為 loved 是一個被動動詞，而在下句人們卻會用 very: *The kids are getting very tired*（孩子們很累了）because **tired** is an adjective. 因為 tired 是一個形容詞。

1 1 **much²** *quantifier* **1** used to mean a lot of something especially in spoken English in questions and negatives or in formal written English 很多（的），大量（的）〔尤用於口語裡的疑問句及否定句中，或用於正式的書面語中〕: *There isn't much time. Pack the bag quickly.* 時間不多了，趕快把包收拾好。| *He didn't say much about it but I think his wife left him.* 他對那事沒有多說，但我認為是他妻子離開了他。| *Do you get much chance to travel in your job?* 你到外地公幹的機會多嗎？| *After much deliberation the judges awarded the prize to Miss Venezuela.* 經過反覆研究，評委們把獎頒給了委內瑞拉小姐。| **how much?** *How much is the dress with the white collar?* 那件白領連衣裙多少錢？| **much of** *Much of the city was destroyed in the attack.* 在那次進攻中城市大部分被摧毀了。**2 so much/too much** used to talk about a particularly large amount of something, especially more than necessary 那麼多的/太多的: *I think it would taste nicer if you didn't use so much salt.* 我想如果你不放那麼多的鹽，味道會更好。| *There was too much work for one person.* 工作太多了，一個人幹不了。| **far/much etc too much** *Easy on the gin! You've put in much too much!* 少擱點杜松子酒吧！你已經加得過量了！**3 not much** mean that something is not important, interesting, worthy etc 並不那麼〔重要、有趣、有價值等〕: *The car may not be much to look at but it's very reliable.* 這輛汽車也許看上去不怎麼樣，但很靠得住。| *Spend the vacation decorating? I don't think much of that idea.* 把假期用在裝修上？我認為那並不是個好主意。| *I think we should leave. There's nothing much we can do to help.* 我想我們該走了。我們幫不了多大忙。| *The sequel was slightly better than the first movie but that's not saying much.* 這部影片的續集比第一部略好，但這並不是說續集就好。**4 not be up to much** *spoken especially BrE* to be fairly bad【口，尤英】很糟糕: *The restaurant's very grand but the food isn't up to much.* 那飯店很氣派，但飯菜卻非常糟糕。**5 not be much of a dancer/swimmer etc** to not be a good dancer, swimmer etc 不怎麼會跳舞/游泳等: *Greg's not much of a footballer but you can't fault his motivation.* 格雷格不太會踢足球，但他態度積極，無可挑剔。**6 it was as much as I/she etc could do** used to say that someone could only just manage to do something 我/她等盡最大努力也只能如此: *He looked so absurd, it was as much as I could do to keep a straight face.* 他看起來非常滑稽，我盡了最大努力才忍着沒笑出來。**7 be too much for sb** to be too difficult for someone to do 非某人力所能及: *Climbing the stairs is too much for her now that she's in her 90s.* 她九十多歲了，爬不動樓梯了。**8 think/say etc as much** to think or say what you have just mentioned 也這樣認為/說等: *She believed that the company should abandon such a risky proposal and said as much at the meeting.* 她認為公司應該放棄這樣一個有風險的計劃，她在會上也這麼說了。**9 make much of sb/sth a)** to treat information, a situation etc as though you think it is very important or serious 重視[認真對待]某人/某物: *The press didn't make as much of the discovery as they might have done.* 新聞界沒有像本該做到的那樣對這個發現大大宣傳一番。**b)** to think that something is very good or very impressive 高度評價: *I didn't make much of her latest novel.* 我對她最新寫的小說不敢恭維。**c)** to treat someone very kindly because you like them a lot 疼愛，溺愛: *A childless couple, they always made much of their nephews and nieces.* 那對夫婦沒有子女，總是寵愛他們的姪子和姪女。**10 not/without so much as** used when you are surprised or annoyed that someone did not do something 甚至沒有，連…都沒有: *He left without so much as saying goodbye.* 他甚至連一聲"再見"也沒說就走了。| *Sonia didn't so much as thank her for her help.* 對她的幫助，索尼婭甚至連謝都沒謝。**11 I'll say this/that much for** used to praise someone or something when they are being criticized a lot 我只能為…這麼說，起碼〔用以讚揚正遭受批評的人或事〕: *I'll say this much for Fiona – she has plenty of spirit!* 關於菲奧娜我只能這麼說 —— 起碼她勇氣十足！**12 so much for** used to say that it was not worth using something because it had little effect, it was useless etc …到此為止；…就談這些；…只好作罷: *So much for worrying she'd be lonely – she's having a party tonight!* 別再擔心她會寂寞了 —— 今晚她有聚會呢！**13 as much again** the same amount or number as the one mentioned before〔和前面提到的數量〕一樣多，同樣多: *The car only cost me £500 but it cost as much again to get it insured.* 那輛汽車只花了我 500 英鎊，但買保險也花了同樣多的錢。

much-her·ald·ed /ˌ· ˈ···◂/ *adj* [only before noun 僅用於名詞前] talked about a lot before it actually appears〔出現之前〕被廣為談論的；被看好的: *Ford's much-heralded new family saloon* 人們十分看好的福特新款家用轎車

much·ness /ˈmʌtʃnɪs; ˈmʌtʃnɪ̵s/ *n* **be much of a muchness** *BrE informal* to be very similar【英，非正式】很相像，差不多: *It was hard to choose between the candidates – they were all much of a muchness.* 很難在候選人之間作選擇 —— 他們各方面都不相上下。

mu·ci·lage /ˈmjusḷɪdʒ; ˈmjuːsɪ̵lɪdʒ/ *n* [U] a sticky liquid obtained from plants and used as a glue〔從植物中提取的〕黏液，黏膠 —**mucilaginous** /ˌmjusˈlædʒɪnəs; ˌmjuːsɪ̵ˈlædʒɪ̵nəs/ *adj*: *the mucilaginous fruit of the okra plant* 含黏液的秋葵果

muck¹ /mʌk; mʌk/ *n* [U] *informal*【非正式】**1** *especially BrE* something such as dirt, mud, or another sticky substance that makes something dirty【尤英】污物，污穢: *Come on, let's wipe that muck off your face.* 過來，讓我們把你臉上的髒東西擦掉。**2** *BrE* waste matter from animals, especially waste matter that is put on land to make plants grow better【英】糞便；糞肥: *dog muck* 狗糞 | *They were shovelling muck onto the fields.* 他們在把糞肥鏟到田裡去。**3** something that is unpleasant or of very bad quality 令人討厭的東西；劣質的東西: *How can you eat that muck? It looks disgusting.* 你怎麼能吃那玩意兒？看着就令人噁心。| *All that paper ever prints is muck about people's sex lives.* 那張報紙刊登的盡是些關於人們性生活的令人作嘔的東西。**4 as common as muck** *BrE old-fashioned* an insulting way of describing someone of a low social class【英，過時】舉止粗俗；沒有教養〔對低層社會的人侮辱性用語〕

muck² *v*

muck about/around *phr v BrE informal*【英，非正式】**1** [I] to behave in a silly way, especially when you should be working or paying attention to something; mess around (MESS²) 胡鬧；鬼混；閒蕩: *Stop mucking about and listen!* 別再胡鬧了，好好聽着！| *We spent the days mucking around on the beach.* 那些日子我們在海灘閒蕩。**2** [T **muck** sb/sth **about/around**] to cause trouble and inconvenience for someone, especially by changing your mind a lot; mess around (MESS²) 耍弄〔某人〕；瞎弄〔某物〕: *The travel agent has really been mucking me around over this holiday.* 這次休假，旅行社實在是耍弄我。

muck in *phr v* [I] *BrE informal*【英，非正式】**1** to work together with other people in order to get a job done; pitch in (PITCH²) 一起出力，一起幹活；參加: *Oh, stop moaning – we've all got to muck in!* 喂，別再抱怨了 —— 我們都得幹！**2** to share things with other people 分享: *We're a bit short of space. Do you mind mucking*

M

in with the other boys? 我們缺少點地方, 你和其他男孩子共用一處好嗎?

muck sth ↔ **out** *phr v* [I,T] to clean the place where an animal lives 打掃〔牲畜棚〕: *to muck out the stables* 打掃馬廄

muck sth ↔ **up** *phr v* [T] *BrE informal*【英, 非正式】**1** to do something wrong or badly, so that you fail to achieve something 弄糟; 弄砸: *I really mucked up those last two exams.* 最後兩門考試我確實考砸了。**2** to spoil something, especially an arrangement or plan 破壞, 打亂〔尤指安排或計劃〕: *The bad weather mucked up our plans for a picnic.* 壞天氣打亂了我們的野餐計劃。**3** to make something dirty 弄髒: *Don't muck up your shirt.* 別把你的襯衫弄髒了。

muck·heap /ˈmʌkˌhip; ˈmʌkhiːp/ *n* [C] *BrE* a pile of MANURE (=animal waste matter) in a farmyard【英】廐肥堆, 糞堆

muck·rak·ing /ˈmʌkˌrekɪŋ; ˈmʌk-reɪkɪŋ/ *n* [U] the practice of telling or writing unpleasant and perhaps untrue stories about people's private lives, especially famous people 收集和披露〔尤指名人的〕隱私: *low quality magazines specializing in muckraking* 專門揭人陰私的低級雜誌 —**muckraking** *adj* —**muckraker** *n* [C]

muck·spread·er /ˈmʌksprɛdə; ˈmʌkspredə/ *n* [C] *BrE* a machine used on a farm to spread MANURE (=animal waste matter) onto farm land【英】施糞肥機, 糞肥撒播機 —**muck-spreading** *n* [U]

muck·y /ˈmʌkɪ; ˈmʌki/ *adj BrE informal*【英, 非正式】**1** dirty, for example with mud or oil 骯髒的: *Your hands are all mucky.* 你的手骯髒不堪。**2** a mucky joke or story etc is slightly rude and about sex〔笑話等〕粗俗的, 下流的 **3** mucky weather is cold and wet〔天氣〕寒冷潮濕的

mu·cous mem·brane /ˌmjukəs ˈmɛmbren; ˌmjuːkəs ˈmembreɪn/ *n* [C] the thin surface that covers certain inner parts of the body, such as the inside of the nose, and produces mucus 黏膜

mu·cus /ˈmjukəs; ˈmjuːkəs/ *n* [U] a liquid produced in parts of your body such as your nose〔人體分泌的〕黏液〈如鼻涕〉—**mucous** *adj*

mud /mʌd; mʌd/ *n* [U] **1** wet earth that has become soft and sticky 泥, 爛泥: *His shoes were covered with mud.* 他的鞋沾滿了爛泥。**2 your name is mud** *spoken* if your name is mud, people are annoyed with you because you have caused trouble【口】某人名聲掃地: *His name is mud in the office after what happened.* 那事發生之後, 他在辦公室裡的名聲就臭了。**3** earth used for building〔建築用的〕泥土: *a mud hut* 一座小土屋 **4 here's mud in your eye** *spoken old-fashioned* used for expressing good wishes when having a drink with someone; CHEERS (1)【口, 過時】祝您健康; 乾杯 —see also 另見 **as clear as mud** (CLEAR[1] (19))

mud·bath /ˈmʌdbæθ; ˈmʌdbɑːθ/ *n* **1** [C] a health treatment in which heated mud is put onto your body, used especially to reduce pain 泥浴, 泥療 **2** [singular] a large area of mud 泥淖: *Heavy rain had turned the playing field into a mudbath.* 大雨把運動場變成了一片爛泥場。

mud·dle[1] /ˈmʌdḷ; ˈmʌdl/ *n* [C usually singular 一般用單數] **1** a state of confusion or untidiness, that results in things being done wrong 混亂, 雜亂: *There was a bit of a muddle over our reservations.* 我們所作的預訂有點混亂。| *We had to get an accountant in to sort out the muddle.* 我們不得不請了個會計, 整理那些亂糟糟的賬目。**2 be in a muddle a)** to be in an untidy and confused state 處於混亂狀態, 凌亂不堪: *The papers were all in a muddle.* 文件一團糟。**b)** to be confused because you have too much to do〔因事情多而〕糊塗: *I'm in such a muddle, I'd completely forgotten you were coming today.* 我真糊塗透了, 我完全忘了你今天要來。

muddle[2] *v* also 又作 **muddle up** [T] *especially BrE*【尤英】**1** to put something in the wrong order or mix something up 弄亂, 弄混: *Someone's muddled up all the papers on my desk.* 有人把我桌子上的文件全都弄亂了。| *Your invoice got muddled up with Mr Clark's.* 你的發票和克拉克先生的發票弄混了。**2 get muddled (up)** to get confused between one thing or person and another, and make a mistake 被弄糊塗: *Sorry, I got a bit muddled up over the dates.* 對不起, 我被這些日期弄得有點糊塗了。| **get sb/sth muddled (up)** *I'm not quite sure of their ages, I get them muddled up.* 我對他們的年齡説不太準, 我把他們弄混了。—**muddled** *adj*: *muddled thinking* 混亂的思維 —**muddling** *adj*

muddle along/on *phr v* [I] *BrE* to continue doing something without having any clear plan【英】混日子, 得過且過; 胡亂地幹下去: *We just seem to muddle along but never make any real progress.* 我們好像只是在混日子, 卻從來沒有取得任何真正的進展。

muddle through *phr v* [I] *especially BrE* to achieve something even though you do not have a clear plan or use the best methods or equipment【尤英】胡亂應付過去: *Jack got some difficult questions but he managed to muddle through.* 傑克遇上了一些難題, 但他設法稀里糊塗地應付過去了。

muddle-head·ed /ˌ.. ˈ..◂/ *adj BrE* confused or not able to think clearly【英】糊塗的, 頭腦混亂的 —**muddle-headedness** *n* [U]

mud·dy[1] /ˈmʌdɪ; ˈmʌdi/ *adj* **muddier, muddiest 1** covered with mud or containing mud 沾滿泥的; 泥濘的, 多泥的: *the muddy banks of the river* 泥濘的河岸 | *Take your boots off outside if they're muddy.* 如果你的靴子沾滿污泥, 就在門外脱掉。**2** colours that are muddy are dull〔顏色〕不亮的, 暗的 **3** confused and not clear 糊塗的, 混亂的; 不清晰的: *muddy thinking* 混亂的思維 —**muddiness** *n* [U]

muddy[2] *v* **muddied, muddying** [T] **1** to make something dirty with mud 使…沾上泥污: *She was taking care not to muddy her new shoes.* 她小心翼翼地走, 不讓新鞋沾上污泥。**2 muddy the waters/the issue** to make things more complicated or confusing in a situation that was simple before 把水攪渾, 使事情[問題]更加複雜

mud·flap /ˈmʌdflæp; ˈmʌdflæp/ *n* [C] *BrE* a piece of rubber that hangs behind the wheel of a vehicle to prevent mud from flying up【英】〔車輪後的〕擋泥膠皮, 擋泥板; SPLASH GUARD *AmE*【美】—see picture on page A2 參見 A2 頁圖

mud·flat /ˈmʌdflæt; ˈmʌdflæt/ *n* [C often plural 常用複數] **1** an area of muddy land, covered by the sea when it comes up at HIGH TIDE and uncovered when it goes down at LOW TIDE〔落潮時露出、漲潮時隱沒的〕泥灘, 潮泥灘 **2** *AmE* the muddy bottom of a dry lake【美】〔湖泊乾涸後的〕泥牀, 泥底

mud·guard /ˈmʌdˌgɑrd; ˈmʌdgɑːd/ *n* [C] *BrE* a curved piece of metal or plastic over the wheel of a bicycle that prevents the mud from flying up【英】〔自行車的〕擋泥板; FENDER (4) *AmE*【美】—see picture at 參見 BICYCLE[1] 圖

mud·pack /ˈmʌdˌpæk; ˈmʌdpæk/ *n* [C] a soft mixture containing clay that you spread over your face and leave there for a short time to improve your skin〔化妝或治療的〕泥膏

mud pie /ˌ. ˈ./ *n* [C] a little ball of wet mud made by children as a game〔兒童捏着玩的〕小泥餅

mud·sling·ing /ˈmʌdslɪŋɪŋ; ˈmʌdslɪŋɪŋ/ *n* [U] the practice of saying bad and often untrue things about someone in order to make other people have a low opinion of them 誹謗, 中傷: *There has been a lot of political mudslinging in the battle for votes.* 在選票爭奪戰中出現了大量的政治誹謗。—**mudslinger** *n* [C]

mues·li /ˈmjuzlɪ; ˈmjuːzli/ *n* [U] grains, nuts, and dried fruits, mixed together and eaten with milk as a breakfast food 穆兹利, 乾果全穀片〔一種把碾碎的穀物、堅

果、乾果混合後攙入牛奶吃的早餐食品〕; GRANOLA *AmE*【美】

mu·ez·zin /mju'ɛzɪn; muː'ezɪ̈n/ *n* [C] a man who calls Muslims to prayer from a MOSQUE 宣禮員〔清真寺中召喚信徒做禮拜的人〕

muff¹ /mʌf; mʌf/ *n* [C] a short tube of thick cloth or fur that you can put your hands into to keep them warm in cold weather〔禦寒用的〕手籠, 手筒 —see also 另見 EARMUFFS

muff² *v* [T] **1** also 又作 **muff up** *informal* to spoil a chance to do something well【非正式】錯過〔機會等〕; 把…弄糟: *I wanted to impress her with my efficiency but I muffed it up.* 我想讓她對我的辦事效率留個好印象, 但是我把事情搞砸了。**2 muff a catch/muff it** to fail to catch or hold a ball in a game or sport 漏接球, 接球失誤

muf·fin /'mʌfɪn; 'mʌfɪ̈n/ *n* [C] **1** *BrE* a small thick round kind of bread, usually eaten hot with butter【英】〔通常塗黃油趁熱吃的〕英式鬆餅; ENGLISH MUFFIN *AmE*【美】**2** *AmE* a small usually sweet cake that sometimes has bits of fruit in it【美】鬆餅: *blueberry muffins* 藍莓鬆餅

muf·fle /'mʌfl; 'mʌfəl/ *v* [T usually passive 一般用被動態] **1** to make a sound less loud and clear 使〔聲音〕減弱[低沉]: *The falling snow muffled the noise of the traffic.* 紛紛飄落的雪花減弱了車輛的噪音。**2** also 又作 **muffle up** to cover yourself with something thick and warm〔用保暖的衣物〕裹住: *He went out into the snow muffled up in his scarf and thick overcoat.* 他用圍巾和厚大衣把自己裹得嚴嚴實實, 走進雪中。

muf·fled /'mʌfld; 'mʌfəld/ *adj* muffled sounds or voices cannot be heard clearly, for example because they come from behind a door or wall〔聲音因隔着門或牆等〕聽不清楚的: *I heard the muffled thump of a car door slamming.* 我隱隱約約聽到了關汽車門的聲音。| *Muffled voices could be heard in the next room.* 能聽到隔壁房間裡隱隱約約的説話聲。

muf·fler /'mʌflɚ; 'mʌflə/ *n* [C] **1** a thick long piece of cloth worn to keep your neck warm 厚圍巾 **2** *AmE* SILENCER (2)【美】〔汽車引擎的〕消音器, 減聲器

muf·ti /'mʌftɪ; 'mʌfti/ *n* **1 in mufti** *old-fashioned* wearing ordinary clothes instead of a uniform【過時】穿着便服: *soldiers in mufti* 穿着便服的士兵 **2** [C] someone who officially explains Muslim law 穆夫提〔解釋伊斯蘭教法典的神職人員〕

mug¹ /mʌg; mʌg/ *n* [C] **1** a large cup with straight sides used for drinking tea, coffee etc〔喝茶或咖啡等用的〕圓筒形有柄大杯 —see picture at 參見 CUP¹ 圖 **2** a large glass with straight sides and a handle, used especially for drinking beer〔尤指喝啤酒用的〕圓筒形有柄大玻璃杯: *rugby players swilling mugs of beer at the bar* 在酒吧裡用大杯暢飲啤酒的橄欖球運動員 **3** also 又作 **mugful** a mug and the liquid inside it 一大杯(的量): *Two mugs of tea, please.* 請來兩大杯茶。**4** *BrE spoken* someone who is stupid and easy to deceive【英口】易上當受騙的傻瓜: *I expect they'll find some poor mug to buy their car.* 我預料他們會找到某個可憐的傻瓜買他們的汽車。**5** *spoken* a face【口】臉: *What an ugly mug!* 多醜陋的一張臉! **6 a mug's game** *BrE spoken* something that is not likely to be successful or profitable【英口】不易成功的事; 無利可圖的事: *Gambling is a mug's game, Jonah.* 喬納, 賭博是賭不來錢的。

mug² *v* **mugged, mugging 1** [T] to attack someone and rob them in a public place〔在公共場所〕行兇搶劫: *A lot of people won't go out alone at night for fear of being mugged.* 許多人因害怕被搶劫, 晚上不願單獨出門。**2** [I] *AmE informl* to make silly expressions with your face or behave in a silly way, especially in a photograph or a play【美, 非正式】〔尤指照相或演出時〕做鬼臉, 扮傻相: *Scotty's always mugging for the camera.* 斯科蒂照相時總是扮鬼臉。

mug up *phr v* [I,T] *BrE informal* to study something very hard, especially when preparing for an exam【英, 非正式】〔尤指為準備考試而〕用功, 攻讀: **mug sth ↔ up** *He's got to mug up some facts about pollution.* 他不得不拚命死記一些有關污染的情況。| **[+on]** *She's mugging up on Racine for her French paper.* 她正在為撰寫她的法語論文而攻讀拉辛的作品。

mug·ger /'mʌgɚ; 'mʌgə/ *n* [C] someone who attacks people and robs them in a public place〔在公共場所的〕行兇搶劫者

mug·ging /'mʌgɪŋ; 'mʌgɪŋ/ *n* [C,U] an attack on someone in which they are robbed in a public place〔在公共場所的〕行兇搶劫: *There has been an increase in muggings in the park.* 公園裡的搶劫案件增多了。

mug·gins /'mʌgɪnz; 'mʌgɪnz/ *n* [singular] *spoken BrE* used jokingly to mean yourself, when you know you have been stupid and let other people treat you unfairly【英口】傻瓜, 笨蛋〔用於自嘲〕: *Everyone disappeared after supper, leaving muggins here to do the washing-up.* 晚飯後大家都走光了, 把我這個傻子留在這兒洗碗碟。

mug·gy /'mʌgɪ; 'mʌgi/ *adj* **muggier, muggiest** *informal* muggy weather is unpleasantly warm and the air seems wet【非正式】〔天氣〕悶熱的: *The air was muggy and damp, threatening a storm later.* 空氣悶熱而潮濕, 預示着暴風雨即將來臨。—**mugginess** *n* [U]

mug·shot /'mʌgʃɑt; 'mʌgʃɒt/ *n* [C] *informal* a photograph of a criminal's face, taken by the police【非正式】〔警方拍攝的〕犯人面部照片: *Can you look through some mugshots to identify the man who attacked you?* 你能從這些照片辨認出襲擊你的那個男子嗎?

Mu·ham·ma·dan /mu'hæmədən; mʊ'hæmɪ̈dən/ *n, adj old-fashioned* a word meaning Muslim, now considered offensive by most Muslims【過時】穆斯林(的), 伊斯蘭教徒(的), 回教徒(的)〔現在大多數穆斯林認為此詞具冒犯性〕—**Muhammadanism** *n* [U]

mu·ja·hed·din /ˌmudʒəhɛ'din; ˌmuːdʒəhe'diːn/ *n* [plural] Muslim soldiers with strong religious beliefs〔具有強烈宗教信仰的〕穆斯林士兵

muk·luks /'mʌklʌks; 'mʌklʌks/ *n* [plural] *AmE* boots made of animal skin with a thick bottom, used for walking in snow【美】〔厚底〕雪地獸皮靴

mu·lat·to /mə'læto; mjuː'lætəʊ/ *n* [C] an insulting word for someone with one black parent and one white parent 穆拉托人〔侮辱性用語, 指黑人與白人的混血兒〕

mul·ber·ry /'mʌlˌbɛrɪ; 'mʌlbəri/ *n* **1** [C] a dark purple fruit that can be eaten, or the tree on which this fruit grows 桑椹; 桑樹 **2** [U] the dark purple colour of these fruit 桑椹色, 深紫紅色

mulch¹ /mʌltʃ; mʌltʃ/ *n* [singular] decaying leaves that are put on the soil to improve its quality, to protect the roots of plants, and to stop WEEDS (=unwanted plants) growing〔為改良土壤、護根及阻止雜草生長而覆在地表上的〕腐葉, 覆蓋料

mulch² *v* [T] to cover the ground with a mulch 用腐葉覆蓋〔地面〕

mule /mjul; mjuːl/ *n* [C] **1** an animal that has a DONKEY and a horse as parents 騾, 騾子 **2** [usually plural 一般用複數] a shoe or SLIPPER without a back, that has a piece of material across the toes to hold it on your foot 夾趾拖鞋 **3** *slang* someone who brings illegal drugs into a country by hiding them on or in their body【俚】體內攜帶毒品走私的人 —see also 另見 **stubborn as a mule** (STUBBORN (1))

mu·le·teer /ˌmjulə'tɪr; ˌmjuːlɪ̈'tɪə/ also 又作 **mule·skin·ner** *AmE*【美】/'mjulskɪnɚ; 'mjuːlskɪnə/ —*n* [C] someone who leads mules 趕騾人, 騾夫

mul·ish /'mjulɪʃ; 'mjuːlɪʃ/ *adj* refusing to do something or agree to something in an unreasonable way; STUBBORN 固執的, 執拗的, 犟的: *mulish obstinacy* 騾子般的倔強, 頑固透頂 —**mulishly** *adv* —**mulishness** *n* [U]

mull¹ /mʌl; mʌl/ *v* [T] to heat wine or beer with sugar and SPICES 將〔葡萄酒或啤酒〕放糖和香料後加熱

mull sth ↔ **over** *phr v* [T] to think about a problem, plan etc and consider it for a long time 仔細考慮〔問題、計劃等〕, 反覆思考: *Victor mulled over the idea and finally decided that it made sense.* 維克托仔細考慮了那個想法, 最後認為它很合理。

mull² *n* [C] *ScotE* an area of land that sticks out into the sea; PROMONTORY【蘇格蘭】岬, 海角: *Mull of Kintyre* 金泰爾角

mul·lah /ˋmʌlə; ˈmʌlə/ *n* [C] a Muslim teacher of law and religion 毛拉〔伊斯蘭法律及宗教教師〕

mulled wine /,· ˈ·/ *n* [U] wine that has been heated with sugar and SPICES〔放糖和香料後加熱而成的〕香甜熱葡萄酒: *mulled wine with lots of cloves and cinnamon* 加了大量乾丁香花苞和桂皮香料的香甜熱葡萄酒

mul·let /ˋmʌlɪt; ˈmʌlɪt/ *n* [C] a fairly small sea fish that can be eaten 鯔(魚)〔一種可食用的小海魚〕

mul·li·ga·taw·ny /ˌmʌlɪgəˋtɔnɪ; ˌmʌlɪgəˈtɔːni/ *n* [U] a soup that tastes hot because it contains hot SPICES 咖喱肉湯

mul·lion /ˋmʌljən; ˈmʌljən/ *n* [C] a piece of stone, metal, or wood that divides a window between the glass parts〔分隔窗扇的〕直欞, 豎框 —**mullioned** *adj*: *mullioned windows* 有直欞的窗

multi- /mʌltɪ; mʌltɪ/ *prefix* more than one; many 多於一的; 多的: *multicoloured* (=with many colours) 多色的 | *a multistorey office block* 多層寫字樓

mul·ti·choice /ˋmʌltɪtʃɔɪs; ˈmʌltitʃɔɪs/ *adj* MULTIPLE CHOICE〔試題〕多項選擇的

mul·ti·col·oured *BrE*【英】, **multicolored** *AmE*【美】/ˋmʌltɪˌkʌləd; ˈmʌltiˌkʌləd/ *adj* having many different colours 有多種不同顏色的, 雜色的: *a multicoloured sweatshirt* 雜色的圓領長袖運動衫

mul·ti·cul·tur·al /ˌmʌltɪˋkʌltʃərəl; ˌmʌltiˈkʌltʃərəl◂/ *adj* involving or including people or ideas from several different countries, races, or religions 多種文化的; 融合[具有]多種文化的: *a multicultural society* 融合多種文化的社會

mul·ti·cul·tu·ral·is·m /ˌmʌltɪˋkʌltʃərəlɪzəm; ˌmʌltiˈkʌltʃərəlɪzəm/ *n* [U] the belief that it is important and good to include people or ideas from many different countries, races, or religions 多元文化論 —**multiculturalist** *n* [C]

multi-faith /,·· ˈ·◂/ *adj* [only before noun 僅用於名詞前] including or involving people from several different religious groups 包括[涉及]不同宗教團體的: *a multi-faith service of thanksgiving* 由信仰不同宗教的人參加的感恩祈禱儀式

mul·ti·far·i·ous /ˌmʌltəˋfɛrɪəs; ˌmʌltɪˈfeəriəs◂/ *adj* of very many different kinds 多種多樣的, 五花八門的: *her multifarious business activities* 她的種種商業活動 —**multifariously** *adv* —**multifariousness** *n* [U]

multi-func·tion /,·· ˈ··◂/ **multi-func·tion·al** /,·· ˈ···◂/ *adj* [only before noun 僅用於名詞前] a multi-function machine, piece of equipment, building etc is designed to have several different uses〔機器、設備、建築等〕多功能的, 起多種作用的

mul·ti·lat·e·ral /ˌmʌltɪˋlætərəl; ˌmʌltɪˈlætərəl◂/ *adj* **multilateral agreements/trade etc** agreements, trade etc that involve the governments of several different countries 多邊協議/貿易等 —compare 比較 BILATERAL, UNILATERAL —**multilaterally** *adv*

mul·ti·lin·gual /ˌmʌltɪˋlɪŋgwəl; ˌmʌltɪˈlɪŋgwəl◂/ *adj* **1** able to speak several different languages 會說數種語言的: *a multilingual secretary* 會說好幾種語言的秘書 **2** written in several different languages 用數種語言寫的: *a multilingual phrasebook covering English, French, German, and Italian* 包括英語、法語、德語和意大利語的多語種常用語手冊 —compare 比較 BILINGUAL, MONOLINGUAL —**multilingualism** *n* [U]

M

mul·ti·me·di·a /ˌmʌltɪˋmidɪə; ˌmʌltiˈmiːdiə◂/ *adj* [only before noun 僅用於名詞前] using a mixture of sound, pictures, film, and writing to give information, especially with computers 多媒體的: *Encarta, the latest multimedia encyclopedia* 最新的多媒體百科全書《恩卡特》—**multimedia** *n* [U]

mul·ti·mil·lion /ˌmʌltəˋmɪljən; ˌmʌltiˈmɪljən◂/ *adj* **multimillion-pound/multimillion-dollar etc** worth or costing many millions of pounds, dollars etc〔值或花費〕數百萬英鎊/美元等的: *Gascoigne's multimillion-pound move to Lazio* 加斯居尼以數百萬英鎊的身價轉會到拉素

mul·ti·mil·lio·naire /ˌmʌltəˌmɪljənˋɛr; ˌmʌltɪˌmɪljəˈneə/ *n* [C] an extremely rich person, who has many millions of pounds or dollars 大富豪, 巨富, 千萬富翁

mul·ti·na·tion·al¹ /ˌmʌltɪˋnæʃənl; ˌmʌltɪˈnæʃənəl◂/ *adj* **1** a multinational company has factories, offices, and business activities in many different countries〔公司〕跨國的, 在多國經營的: *a multinational motor-manufacturing corporation* 跨國汽車製造公司 **2** involving people from several countries 由多個國家的人組成的, 多國的: *a multinational force sponsored by the UN* 由聯合國提供經費的多國部隊 —**multinationally** *adv*

multinational² *n* [C] a large company that has offices, factories etc in many different countries 跨國公司: *a giant food multinational* 龐大的跨國食品公司 | *the growth of the multinationals* 跨國公司的增長

mul·ti·ple¹ /ˋmʌltəpl̩; ˈmʌltɪpəl/ *adj* including or involving many things, people, events etc 包括[涉及]多個人[物, 事件等]的; 多的; 多種的: **multiple injuries/burns** *Baxter was rushed to the hospital with multiple stab wounds.* 巴克斯特因多處刺傷被急速送進了醫院。| **multiple collision/crash/accident** (=an accident involving many cars) 連環撞車事故 | **multiple birth** (=an occasion when several babies are born to the same mother at the same time) 多胎產

multiple² *n* [C] **1** a number that contains a smaller number an exact number of times〔數學中的〕倍數: *20 is a multiple of 5.* 20是5的倍數。—see also 另見 LOWEST COMMON MULTIPLE **2** a multiple store 連鎖商店

multiple choice /,··· ˈ·◂/ *adj* a multiple choice examination or question shows several possible answers and you have to choose the correct one〔試題〕多項選擇的

multiple scle·ro·sis /,··· ·ˈ··/ also 又作 **MS** —*n* [U] a serious illness that gradually destroys your nerves making you weak and unable to walk, often involving weakening eyesight and slow speech 多發性硬化(症)

multiple store /,··· ˈ·/ *n* [C] *BrE* a word used especially in business meaning a CHAIN STORE【英】連鎖商店

mul·ti·plex /ˋmʌltəˌplɛks; ˈmʌltɪpleks/ *adj* **1** a multiplex cinema shows several different films at the same time〔電影院〕同時放映多部電影的, 多放映場的 **2** *technical* having several different parts【術語】複合的

mul·ti·pli·ca·tion /ˌmʌltəpləˋkeʃən; ˌmʌltɪplɪˈkeɪʃən/ *n* [U] **1** a method of calculating in which you add the same number to itself a particular number of times 乘法; 乘法運算 **2** *formal* a large increase in the size or number of something【正式】〔大量〕增加; 增多: *the multiplication in the number of claim forms that have to be filled out* 需要填寫的索賠表格數量激增

multiplication sign /,····· ·/ *n* [C] a sign (×) showing that one number is multiplied by another 乘號(×) —see picture at 參見 MATHEMATICS 圖

multiplication ta·ble /,····· ,··/ *n* [C] a list showing the result of numbers between one and twelve that have been multiplied together, used by children in schools 乘法表

mul·ti·pli·ci·ty /ˌmʌltəˋplɪsətɪ; ˌmʌltɪˈplɪsɪti/ *n* [C,U] a large number or great variety of things 多, 大量; 多種

多樣, 多樣性: **[+of]** *the baffling multiplicity of courses available to language students* 學語言的學生可以選修的課程多得叫人不知選哪門好

mul·ti·ply /ˋmʌltəˏplaɪ; ˈmʌltɪ̯plaɪ/ *v* **1** [I,T] to increase greatly or make something increase greatly (使) 大大增加: *Our chances of success had multiplied several times over.* 我們成功的機會已增加了好幾倍。| *This vast stock of computerized images has multiplied the possibilities open to the artist.* 這一龐大的電腦圖像庫極大地增加了藝術家的創作潛力。**2** [I,T] to do a calculation in which you add a number to itself a particular number of times 乘, 乘以: **multiply sth by sth** *3 multiplied by 4 is 12.* 3 乘以 4 等於 12。—compare 比較 DIVIDE¹ (4) **3** [I] to breed 繁殖: *The bugs can easily multiply to give a nasty bout of food poisoning.* 這些病菌繁殖迅速, 容易引發嚴重的食物中毒。

mul·ti·pur·pose /ˏmʌltɪˋpɝpəs; ˌmʌltiˈpɜːpəs◂/ *adj* a multipurpose tool, building etc is designed to be used for many different purposes〔工具、建築等〕多用途的, 通用的

mul·ti·ra·cial /ˏmʌltɪˋreʃəl; ˌmʌltɪˈreɪʃəl◂/ *adj* including or involving several different races of people 多種族的: *a multiracial society* 多種族的社會

multi-sto·rey¹ /ˏ·· ˋ··◂/ *adj* [only before noun 僅用於名詞前] *BrE* a multi-storey building has many levels or floors【英】〔建築物〕多層的

multi-storey² *n* [C] *BrE spoken* a multi storey CAR PARK【英口】多層停車場

mul·ti·tude /ˋmʌltəˏtud; ˈmʌltɪ̯tjuːd/ *n* [C] **1 a multitude of** *formal or literary* a very large number of people or things【正式或文】眾多, 大量; 大批, 大羣: *The captain sat before a multitude of dials and levers.* 船長坐在一大堆儀表盤和操縱桿前面。| *a multitude of possible interpretations* 種種可能的解釋 **2 the multitude a)** ordinary people, especially when they are thought of as not being very well educated 大眾, 民眾, 羣眾: *Political power has been placed in the hands of the multitude.* 政治權力已交到羣眾手中。**b)** *literary or biblical* a large crowd of people【文或聖經】一大羣人 **3 cover/hide a multitude of sins** *especially humorous* to make faults or problems seem less clear or noticeable【尤幽默】掩蓋種種錯誤[問題]

mul·ti·tu·di·nous /ˏmʌltəˋtudṇəs; ˌmʌltɪ̯ˈtjuːdɪ̯nəs◂/ *adj formal* very many【正式】大量的, 眾多的: *language in all its multitudinous forms* 形式多種多樣的語言

1 2 **mum¹** /mʌm; mʌm/ *n* [C] **1** *BrE* mother【英】媽媽; MOM *AmE*【美】**2 mum's the word** used to tell someone that they must not tell other people about a secret 別聲張, 不要講出去; 要保密: *Remember, mum's the word! I don't want anyone else finding out about this!* 記住, 千萬別說出去! 我不想讓其他任何人知道這事!

mum² *adj* **keep mum** *informal* to not tell anyone about a secret【非正式】保密

mum·ble /ˋmʌmbḷ; ˈmʌmbəl/ *v* **mumbled, mumbling** [I,T] to say something too quietly and not clearly enough, so that it is difficult or impossible to hear 咕噥, 含糊地說: *The little boy mumbled something about wanting to go to the toilet.* 那個小男孩咕咕噥噥地說要去廁所。| *Stop mumbling and speak up!* 別咕咕噥噥的, 大聲說! —**mumbler** *n* [C] —**mumble** *n* [C]

mum·bo-jum·bo /ˋmʌmboˋdʒʌmbo; ˌmʌmbəʊ ˈdʒʌmbəʊ/ *n* [U] **1** talk or writing on a technical subject that is difficult to understand and seems to have no sense 晦澀難懂的文字; 莫名其妙的話: *Psychology books are often full of meaningless mumbo-jumbo.* 心理學書籍常常滿篇都是毫無意義、晦澀難懂的語言。**2** religious beliefs or activities that seem without sense or meaning 莫名其妙的宗教信仰[活動]

mum·mer /ˋmʌmɚ; ˈmʌmə/ *n* [C] an actor in a simple traditional play without words 啞劇演員 —**mumming** *n* [U]

mum·mi·fy /ˋmʌmɪˏfaɪ; ˈmʌmɪfaɪ/ *v* [T] to preserve a dead body by putting special oils on it and wrapping it with cloth 將〔屍體〕製成木乃伊 —**mummification** /ˏmʌmɪfəˋkeʃən; ˌmʌmɪfɪ̯ˈkeɪʃən/ *n* [U]

mum·my /ˋmʌmɪ; ˈmʌmi/ *n* [C] **1** *BrE* a word meaning mother, used by or to young children【英】媽咪〔兒語〕; MOMMY *AmE*【美】**2** a dead body that has been preserved by wrapping it in cloth, expecially in ancient Egypt〔尤指古埃及的〕木乃伊 2

mummy's boy /ˋ·· ·/ *n* [singular] *informal* a mother's boy (MOTHER¹ (3))【非正式】過分依賴母親的男人[男孩], 嬌生兒

mumps /mʌmps; mʌmps/ also 又作 **the mumps** *n* [U] an infectious illness which makes your neck swell and become painful, and is common among children 腮腺炎

mum-to-be /ˏ· · ˋ·/ *n* [C] *BrE informal* a MOTHER-TO-BE【英, 非正式】準媽媽, 孕婦

munch /mʌntʃ; mʌntʃ/ *v* [I,T] to eat something noisily 出聲地嚼; 用力嚼: *My father went on munching his toast.* 我爸爸繼續大嚼他的烤麵包片。| **[+on/at]** *She was busily munching on an apple.* 她正忙着咔哧咔哧地啃蘋果。

munch·ies /ˋmʌntʃɪz; ˈmʌntʃiz/ *n* [plural] *informal*【非正式】**1 have the munchies** to feel hungry 感到飢餓 **2** small pieces of food, that you can eat with drinks at a party〔晚會上邊喝飲料邊吃的〕小片食品, 小吃

mun·dane /ˋmʌnden; mʌnˈdeɪn/ *adj* **1** ordinary and uninteresting 平凡的; 平淡的; 乏味的: *Initially, the work was pretty mundane.* 剛開始, 該工作非常乏味。| *She led a mundane existence in the drab suburbs of Paris.* 她在巴黎了無生氣的郊區過着一種平淡的生活。**2** *formal* concerned with ordinary daily life rather than religious matters; WORLDLY (3)【正式】世俗的; 塵世間的, 人世間的 —**mundaneness** *n* [U] —**mundanely** *adv*

mung bean /ˏmʌŋ ˋbin; ˌmʌŋ ˈbiːn/ *n* [C] a small green bean, usually eaten as a BEANSPROUT 綠豆

mu·ni·ci·pal /mjuˋnɪsəpḷ; mjuːˈnɪsɪ̯pəl/ *adj* belonging to or concerned with the government of a town or city 市政府的; 市的; 市辦的: *the municipal waste dump* 城市垃圾場 | *municipal elections* 市級選舉 —**municipally** *adv*

mu·ni·ci·pal·i·ty /ˏmjunɪsəˋpælətɪ; mjuːˌnɪsɪ̯ˈpælɪ̯ti/ *n* [C] **1** a town, city, or other small area, which has its own government that makes decisions about local affairs 市, 自治市 **2** the government of a town, city etc, which makes decisions about local affairs 市政當局

mu·nif·i·cent /mjuˋnɪfəsṇt; mjuːˈnɪfɪ̯sənt/ *adj formal* very generous【正式】慷慨的, 大方的: *a munificent gift* 豐厚的禮物 —**munificence** *n* [U]: *She thanked the committee for their munificence.* 她感謝委員會成員的慷慨。—**munificently** *adv*

mu·ni·tions /mjuˋnɪʃənz; mjuːˈnɪʃənz/ *n* [plural] military supplies such as bombs and large guns 軍火〈如炸彈、大砲等〉: *a munitions factory* 兵工廠 —**munition** *adj* [only before noun 僅用於名詞前]: *munition workers* 兵工廠的工人

mu·ral /ˋmjurəl; ˈmjʊərəl/ *n* [C] a painting that is painted on a wall, either inside or outside a building 壁畫 —compare 比較 FRESCO —**mural** *adj* [only before noun 僅用於名詞前]

mur·der¹ /ˋmɝdɚ; ˈmɜːdə/ *n* **1** [C,U] the crime of deliberately killing someone 謀殺; 謀殺罪: *He is charged with the horrific murder of two young boys.* 他被指控以恐怖手段謀殺了兩個小男孩。| **commit (a) murder** *4600 murders were committed in the US in 1975.* 1975 年美國發生了 4600 宗謀殺案。| *the murder weapon* 謀殺用的兇器 —compare 比較 MANSLAUGHTER **2** [U] unnecessary loss of human life caused by stupidity, especially in war〔尤指戰爭中因愚蠢而導致的〕無謂的死亡: *Sending untrained men into the battle was sheer murder.* 把未經訓練的人送到戰場上純粹是讓他們去送死。**3 get**

away with murder *informal* if someone gets away with murder they are not punished for their actions and are allowed to do anything they want【非正式】犯了大錯而不受懲罰; 為所欲為: *She lets those kids get away with murder.* 她聽任那些孩子為所欲為。**4 it's murder** *spoken* used to say that something is very difficult or unpleasant【口】某事很難辦; 某事令人很不快: *It's murder trying to find somewhere to park in Cambridge these days.* 如今在劍橋找個地方停車簡直難死人。**5 it's murder on your feet/back etc** *spoken* used to say that something makes a part of your body feel very uncomfortable【口】腳/脊背等極難受: *It's murder on your feet wearing high-heels all day.* 整天穿着高跟鞋, 兩隻腳難受得要命。—see also 另見 **scream/yell blue murder** (BLUE¹ (5))

murder² *v* [T] **1** to kill someone deliberately and illegally 謀殺: *She murdered him for his money.* 她為得到他的錢而謀殺了他。| *Thousands of civilians have been brutally murdered by right-wing death squads.* 數以千計的平民遭到右翼殺手小組殘殺。| *the murdered man* 那個被謀殺的男子 —see 見 KILL¹ (USAGE) **2** *informal* to spoil a song, play etc completely by performing it very badly【非正式】〔因表演拙劣而〕糟蹋〔歌曲、劇本〕: *It's a beautiful song, but they murdered it.* 那是一首很美的歌曲, 但他們給唱糟蹋了。**3** *informal* to defeat someone completely【非正式】徹底擊敗: *They murdered us in the final.* 在決賽中他們徹底擊敗了我們。**4 I could murder a beer/pizza etc** *BrE spoken* used to say that you very much want to eat or drink something【英口】我能消滅一杯啤酒/一張比薩餅等〔表示極想吃或喝某物〕**5 sb will murder you** *spoken* used to tell someone that another person will be very angry with them【口】某人會宰了你〔表示某人會很生氣〕: *Your dad'll murder you when he hears about it.* 要是你爸聽説這事, 他會宰了你。

mur·der·er /ˈmɝdərɚ; ˈmɜːdərə/ *n* [C] someone who murders another person 謀殺犯, 兇手: *a convicted murderer* 已定罪的謀殺犯

mur·der·ess /ˈmɝdərɪs; ˈmɜːdərɪs/ *n* [C] *old-fashioned* a woman who murders another person【過時】女謀殺犯, 女兇手

mur·der·ous /ˈmɝdərəs; ˈmɜːdərəs/ *adj* **1** very dangerous and likely to kill people 殺氣騰騰的; 可能殺人的; 兇殘的: *Captain Bligh's murderous crew* 布萊船長的那幫殺人不眨眼的船員 | *murderous weapons of war* 殺人軍火 **2 murderous look/expression** an expression or look which shows that someone is very angry 氣勢洶洶的表情: *She kept giving me murderous looks every time I mentioned her husband.* 每次我提到她的丈夫, 她都是兇巴巴地看着我。—**murderously** *adv* —**murderousness** *n* [U]

murk /mɝk; mɜːk/ *n* [U] *literary* darkness caused by smoke, dirt, or cloud; GLOOM (1)【文】黑暗, 昏暗, 陰沉: *the misty murk of the lagoon* 環礁湖上霧蒙蒙的昏暗

murk·y /ˈmɝkɪ; ˈmɜːki/ *adj* **1** dark and difficult to see through 陰暗的, 黑暗的; 朦朧的: *the murky grey light of dawn* 黎明時分朦朦朧朧的灰色天光 | *He plunged into the murky waters of Honolulu harbour.* 他縱身跳進了火奴魯魯港渾濁的水中。**2** involving dishonest or illegal activities that are kept hidden or secret 不光彩的, 不可告人的, 不清白的: *It's a murky business.* 那是個見不得人的行當。| **a murky past** *a politician with a murky past* 歷史不清白的政客 —**murkily** *adv* —**murkiness** *n* [U]

mur·mur¹ /ˈmɝmɚ; ˈmɜːmə/ *v* **1** [I,T] to say something in a soft low voice which is difficult to hear clearly 小聲説, 咕噥: *He began stroking her hair and gently murmuring her name.* 他開始撫摸她的頭髮, 喃喃地呼喚她的名字。**2** [I] to complain to friends and people you work with, but not officially〔向朋友和同事〕私下抱怨, 發牢騷: **[+about/against]** *Within the city there was much murmuring against the new ruler.* 該城市的市民對那位新統治者非常不滿, 怨聲載道。**3** [I] to make a soft, low sound 發出輕柔的聲音: *The wind murmured through the trees.* 風穿過樹林發出沙沙聲。—**murmuring** *n* [C,U]: *vague murmurings of discontent* 表示不滿的嘰嘰咕咕聲

murmur² *n* [C] **1** a soft low sound made by people speaking quietly or from a long way away 輕輕的談話聲, 低語聲: *the murmur of voices from down the corridor* 從走廊那端傳來的絮絮低語聲 | *She replied in a low murmur.* 她輕聲作了回答。**2** a complaint, especially one made to friends and people you work with, but not officially〔尤指向朋友和同事的〕私下的抱怨, 怨言, 咕噥: *There have been some murmurs of discontent over new city taxes.* 對新的城市税已有一些不滿的言論。| **without a murmur** (=without complaining or opposing) 毫無怨言, 毫不反對 *Congress had accepted the treaty almost without a murmur.* 國會幾乎毫無異議地認可了那個條約。**3** the soft low sound made by a stream, the wind etc〔溪流、風等發出的〕細聲, 輕柔的聲音: *the murmur of the little brook* 小溪淙淙的流水聲 **4** [usually singular 一般用單數] an unusual sound made by the heart which shows that there may be something wrong with it〔心臟的〕雜音: *a heart murmur* 心臟雜音

Mur·phy's law /ˌmɝfɪz ˈlɔ; ˌmɜːfiz ˈlɔː/ *n* [singular] *especially AmE* a tendency for bad things to happen whenever it is possible for them to do so; SOD'S LAW【尤美】墨菲定律〔一種認為凡有可能出差錯的事終將出差錯的論斷〕

mus·ca·tel /ˌmʌskəˈtɛl; ˌmʌskəˈtel/ *n* [C,U] a sweet light-coloured wine, or the type of GRAPE that is used to make it 麝香葡萄酒; 麝香葡萄

mus·cle¹ /ˈmʌsl; ˈmʌsəl/ *n* **1** [C,U] one of the pieces of flesh inside your body that connects your bones together and that you use when you move 肌肉: *The next day the muscles in my arm felt sore.* 第二天我胳膊上的肌肉有些酸痛。| **arm/chest/stomach muscles** *bulging chest muscles* 隆起的胸肌 | **pull a muscle** (=injure a muscle so that it becomes painful) 拉傷肌肉 *My leg hurts – I think I've pulled a muscle.* 我腿疼——我想我把肌肉拉傷了。**2** [U] physical strength and power 體力, 力氣: *It must have taken a lot of muscle to get that piano up those stairs.* 把那架鋼琴沿着那些樓梯搬上去一定費了很大的力氣。| **put some muscle into it** *spoken* (=used to tell someone to try harder and use more effort)【口】再加把勁, 再努把力 **3** [U] military, political, or financial power or influence〔軍事、政治或財政的〕實力, 力量: *US military muscle* 美國的軍事實力 **4 not move a muscle** to remain completely still 一動不動: *I shouted at him, but he didn't move a muscle.* 我對着他大喊, 但他卻一動不動。**5** [U] *slang* strong men who are paid to protect or attack someone, especially by criminals【俚】保鏢; 打手; 暴徒 —see also 另見 **flex your muscles** (FLEX¹ (2))

muscle² *v* **muscled, muscling**

muscle in *phr v* [I] to use your strength, power, or influence to get control of someone else's business or to interfere in their affairs 強行控制[干預]: **[+on]** *Another gang was trying to muscle in on their territory.* 另一夥歹徒正企圖侵佔他們的地盤。

mus·cle·bound /ˈmʌslˌbaund; ˈmʌsəlbaʊnd/ *adj* having large stiff muscles because of too much physical exercise〔因運動過度而〕肌肉僵大的: *musclebound he-men with no imagination* 肌肉發達、頭腦簡單的強健男子

mus·cle·man /ˈmʌslˌmæn; ˈmʌsəlmæn/ *plural* **musclemen** /-ˌmɛn; -men/ *n* [C] **1** a man who has developed big strong muscles by doing exercises 肌肉發達的男子 **2** a strong man who is employed to protect someone, usually a criminal 保鏢; 打手; 暴徒

Mus·co·vite /ˈmʌskəˌvaɪt; ˈmʌskəvaɪt/ *n* [C] someone from Moscow 莫斯科人

mus·cu·lar /ˈmʌskjələ; ˈmʌskjʊ̈lə/ *adj* **1** having a lot of big muscles; strong-looking 肌肉發達的; 強壯的: *strong muscular arms* 肌肉發達而有力的雙臂 | *She liked men who were tall and muscular.* 她喜歡身材高大、體格健壯的男人。**2** concerning or affecting the muscles 肌肉的; 影響肌肉的: *muscular injuries* 肌肉損傷 **—muscularly** *adv* **—muscularity** /ˌmʌskjəˈlærɪtɪ; ˌmʌskjʊ̈ˈlærʊ̈ti/ *n* [U]

muscular dys·tro·phy /ˌmʌskjələ ˈdɪstrəfɪ; ˌmʌskjʊ̈lə ˈdɪstrəfi/ *n* [U] a serious illness in which the muscles become weaker over a period of time 肌肉萎縮(症)

muse¹ /mjuz; mjuːz/ *v* **1** [I] to think carefully about something for a long time 沉思, 冥想, 默想: **[+on/over]** *He lit a cigarette and sat musing over the problems of the world.* 他點上一枝煙, 坐着默默地思考世界上的種種問題。**2** [T] to say something in a thoughtful way, especially a question that you are trying to find the answer to 沉思着自語; 沉思着自問: *"I wonder why she was killed," mused Poirot.* "她為甚麼被殺呢?" 波洛沉思着自問。**—musingly** *adv*

muse² *n* [C] **1** someone's muse is the force or person that makes them want to write, paint, or make music, and helps them to have good ideas; INSPIRATION (3) 靈感(的源泉); 才氣: *She was the artist's lover and his creative muse.* 她是那位藝術家的情人, 也是他創作靈感的源泉。**2 the Muses** a group of ancient Greek goddesses, each of whom represented a particular art or a science 繆斯〔古希臘神話中掌管文藝、科學等的九位女神〕

3 2 **mu·se·um** /mjuˋziəm; mjuːˈziːəm/ *n* [C] a building where important cultural, historical, or scientific objects are kept and shown to the public 博物館, 博物院: *the Museum of Modern Art* 現代藝術博物館

museum piece /·ˈ·· ·/ *n* [C] **1** *often humorous* a very old-fashioned piece of equipment【常幽默】陳舊過時的設備, 老古董: *Some of the weapons used by the rebels are museum pieces.* 叛軍使用的一些武器都是老掉牙的過時貨。**2** an object that is so valuable or interesting that it should be in a museum 值得在博物館陳列的精品

mush¹ /mʌʃ; mʌʃ/ *n* **1** [singular, U] an unpleasant soft mass of a substance, especially food, which is partly liquid and partly solid 軟乎乎令人討厭的東西, 爛糊狀的東西〔尤指食物〕: *The cabbage had been boiled down into a flavourless mush.* 捲心菜被熬成了一團沒滋沒味的爛糊糊。**2** [U] *AmE* a thick PORRIDGE made from CORN MEAL【美】稠玉米粥 **3** [U] a book or film that is mush is about love and is SENTIMENTAL 談情説愛、感情淺露的書籍[電影等] **—mushy** *adj*

mush² /mʊʃ; mʊʃ/ *n* [singular] *BrE spoken* an angry and insulting way of addressing someone【英口】討厭鬼; 髒鬼〔對某人憤怒和侮辱的稱呼〕: *Oi, mush! Get your hands off my car!* 喂, 髒鬼! 把你的手從我車上拿開!

mush·room¹ /ˋmʌʃrum; ˈmʌʃruːm/ *n* [C] one of several kinds of FUNGUS with a flat top, some of which can be eaten 蘑菇: *mushroom soup* 蘑菇湯 —see also 另見 MAGIC MUSHROOM —see picture on page A9 參見A9頁圖

mushroom² *v* [I] **1** to grow and develop very quickly 快速成長; 迅速發展: *New housing developments mushroomed on the edge of town.* 在城郊雨後春筍般出現了一些新的住宅區。**2** [+adv/prep] to spread up into the air in the shape of a mushroom〔在空中〕呈蘑菇狀擴散

mushroom cloud /ˈ·· ˌ·/ *n* [C usually singular 一般用單數] a big cloud shaped like a mushroom, which is caused by a NUCLEAR explosion〔核爆炸後形成的〕蘑菇雲

mushy peas /ˌ·· ˈ·/ *n* [plural] *BrE* soft cooked PEAS, eaten especially in the north of England【英】〔尤指英格蘭北部人們食用的〕豌豆糊[泥]

mu·sic /ˋmjuzɪk; ˈmjuːzɪk/ *n* [U] **1** the arrangement of sounds made by instruments or voices in a way that is pleasant or exciting 音樂, 樂曲: *loud pop music* 響亮的流行音樂 | *I like all kinds of music.* 各種音樂我都喜歡。| **a piece of music** *The Moonlight Sonata is one of my favourite pieces of music.*《月光奏鳴曲》是我最喜歡的樂曲之一。| **write/compose music** *Nyman writes the music for most of Peter Greenaway's films.* 彼得·格里納韋的大多數電影是由尼曼作曲的。**2** the art of writing or playing music 音樂藝術: *studying music at college* 在大學學習音樂 | *music lessons* 音樂課 **3** a set of written marks representing music, or paper with the written marks on it 樂譜; 曲譜: **read music** (=understand the sounds that written music represents) 識譜 *Can you read music?* 你識樂譜嗎? | *organ/piano/pop music* 風琴/鋼琴/流行樂樂譜 **4 be music to your ears** if someone's words are music to your ears, they make you very happy or pleased〔某人的話〕聽起來順耳; 動聽 **5 set/put sth to music** to write music so that the words of a poem, play etc can be sung 為…譜曲 —see also 另見 **face the music** (FACE² (8))  1 1

mu·sic·al¹ /ˋmjuzɪkl; ˈmjuːzɪkəl/ *adj* **1** [only before noun 僅用於名詞前] connected with music or consisting of music 音樂的; 配樂的: *a musical entertainment* 音樂表演 | *We share the same musical tastes.* 我們有共同的音樂愛好。**2** good at or interested in playing or singing music 擅長音樂的; 對音樂感興趣的: *I wasn't very musical when I was at school.* 學生時代我不太喜歡音樂。**3** having a pleasant sound like music〔聲音〕音樂般好聽的, 悅耳的: *She had a sweet musical voice.* 她的嗓音甜美動聽。—see also 另見 MUSICALLY  3 3

musical² also 又作 **musical com·e·dy** /ˌ··· ˈ···/ *n* [C] a play or film that uses singing and dancing to tell a story 音樂劇, 音樂影片: *'West Side Story', a musical with music by Leonard Bernstein* 由倫納德·伯恩斯坦作曲的音樂劇《西城故事》

M

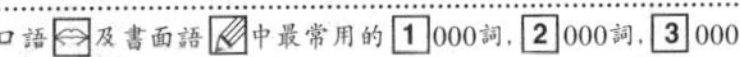

musical box /'··· ·/ *n* [C] *especially BrE* a box that plays a musical tune when you open it【尤英】音樂盒, 八音盒

musical chairs /,··· '·/ *n* [U] a children's game in which all the players must sit down when the music stops, but there are never enough chairs〔兒童玩的〕隨樂聲搶椅子遊戲

musical in·stru·ment /,··· '···/ *n* [C] something that you use for playing music, such as a piano or GUITAR 樂器

mu·sic·ally /ˈmjuzɪklɪ; ˈmjuːzɪkli/ *adv* **1** with regard to music 在音樂方面, 就音樂而言: *The band aren't much good musically, but they're very good-looking.* 這個樂隊在音樂方面的水平不是很高, 但他們人很漂亮。| *Musically speaking, the concert was only average.* 就音樂而言, 那次音樂會只是中等水平。**2** in a way that sounds like music 動聽地, 悦耳地: *Welsh people are supposed to pronounce English words musically.* 人們認為威爾斯人説英語悦耳動聽。

music box /'·· ,·/ *n* [C] *especially AmE* a musical box【尤美】音樂盒, 八音盒

music hall /'·· ·/ *n* **1** [U] a type of entertainment in the theatre, especially in the 19th and early 20th century consisting of singers, dancers, and people telling jokes〔尤指19世紀和20世紀初在劇院進行的包括唱歌、跳舞和講笑話的〕綜藝表演; VAUDEVILLE *AmE*【美】**2** [C] *BrE* a theatre used for this kind of entertainment【英】綜藝劇場, 歌舞雜耍劇院

mu·si·cian /mjuˋzɪʃən; mjuːˈzɪʃən/ *n* [C] a person who plays a musical instrument, especially very well or as a job 音樂家, 樂師: *a talented young musician* 有天賦的年輕音樂家

mu·si·cian·ship /mjuˋzɪʃənʃɪp; mjuːˈzɪʃənʃɪp/ *n* [U] skill in playing music 音樂演奏技巧: *His musicianship was superb, really beyond compare.* 他的音樂演奏技巧高超, 簡直是無與倫比。

mu·si·col·o·gy /,mjuzɪˋkɑlədʒɪ; ,mjuːzɪˈkɒlədʒi/ *n* [U] the study of music, especially the history of different types of music 音樂學 —**musicologist** *n* [C] —**musicological** /,mjuzɪkəˋlɑdʒɪkl; ,mjuːzɪkəˈlɒdʒɪkəl/ *adj*

music stand /'·· ·/ *n* [C] a metal frame for holding written music, so that you can read it while playing an instrument or singing 樂譜架

musk /mʌsk; mʌsk/ *n* [U] a strong smelling substance used to make PERFUME 麝香

mus·ket /ˈmʌskɪt; ˈmʌskʲt/ *n* [C] a type of gun used in former times〔舊時用的〕滑膛槍; 舊式步槍, 毛瑟槍

mus·ket·eer /,mʌskəˋtɪr; ,mʌskʲˈtɪə/ *n* [C] a soldier who uses a musket 火槍手, 滑膛槍手

musk mel·on /'· ,··/ *n* [C] a type of sweet MELON 甜瓜; 香瓜

musk·rat /ˈmʌskræt; ˈmʌskræt/ *n* [C] an animal which lives in water in North America and is hunted for its fur〔生長於北美洲水中的〕麝鼠

musk·y /ˈmʌskɪ; ˈmʌski/ *adj* like MUSK 麝香似的: *a musky smell* 麝香味 —**muskiness** *n* [U]

Mus·lim /ˈmʌzləm; ˈmʊzlʲm/ *n* [C] someone whose religion is Islam 穆斯林, 伊斯蘭教信徒 —**Muslim** *adj*

mus·lin /ˈmʌzlɪn; ˈmʌzlʲn/ *n* [U] a very fine thin cotton cloth used for making dresses and curtains, especially in past times〔尤指以前的〕麥斯林紗; 平紋細布

muss /mʌs; mʌs/ *v* [T+up] *informal especially AmE* to make something untidy, especially someone's hair【非正式, 尤美】把〔某物, 尤指頭髮〕弄亂, 使凌亂; 把…弄髒

mus·sel /ˈmʌsl; ˈmʌsəl/ *n* [C] a small sea animal, with a soft body that can be eaten and a black shell that is divided into two parts 貽貝, 殼菜, 淡菜 —see picture at 參見 SHELL[1] 圖

must[1] /məst; məst; *strong* 強讀 mʌst; mʌst/ *modal verb* [negative short form 否定縮略式為 **mustn't**] **1** [past usually 過去式一般作 **had to**] to have to do something because the situation forces you, because of a rule or law, or because you feel that you should 必須: *All passengers must wear seat belts.* 所有乘客都必須繫安全帶。| *You mustn't tell anyone about this – it's a secret.* 你不許跟任何人講這件事 —— 這是個祕密。| *I don't really want to make the appointment, but I suppose I must.* 我並不很想安排這次約會, 但看來我必須這樣做。| *Under no circumstances must any member of staff socialize with the patients.* 在任何情況下工作人員都不得與病人交往。| *Apologize? Must I? It was all her own fault.* 道歉? 我非得道歉嗎? 那完全是她自己的過錯。| **I must admit/say etc** *I must admit, I was surprised when he passed his driving test first time.* 我得承認, 他一次就通過了駕駛考試, 令我感到驚訝。—compare 比較 HAVE[3] —see graph at 參見 OBLIGE 圖表 **2** [past usually 過去式一般作 **must have**] used when you are guessing that something is true or that something has happened because there seems to be no other possibility 一定, 肯定: *Sam must be nearly 90 years old now.* 山姆現在肯定快90歲了。| *Buying roses? It must be love.* 買玫瑰花? 那一定是戀愛了。| *He must have been drunk to say that.* 他準是喝醉了才那樣説的。| *There must have been ten of them, all hiding in my attic.* 他們肯定有十個人, 都藏在我的閣樓上。**3 a)** used to suggest that someone does something, especially because you think they will enjoy it very much or you think it is a very good idea 應該: *You must go and see the new Spielberg movie, the special effects are amazing.* 你應該去看看史匹堡的那部新影片 —— 特技效果令人驚嘆。**b)** used when you want to do something and hope to do it soon 一定要: *We must come over and try out that new barbecue of yours.* 我們改天一定要來試試你那個新的烤肉架。**4 if you must** used to tell someone that they are allowed to do something but that you do not approve or agree with it 如果你硬要: *"Can I borrow your car, Mum?" "If you must."* "媽, 我可以借用一下你的汽車嗎?" "如果你非借不可那就借吧。" | **if you must do sth** *If you must smoke, do it outside please.* 如果你非要吸煙不可, 請到外面去吸。**5 you must be joking** used when you think someone's suggestion is silly or stupid 你準是在開玩笑〔用以表示某人的提議很愚蠢〕: *£2000 for that old car? You must be joking!* 花2000英鎊買那輛舊汽車? 你準是在開玩笑!

must[2] /mʌst; mʌst/ *n* **1 a must** something that you must do or must have 必須做的事; 必不可少的東西: *Warm clothes are a must in the mountains.* 禦寒衣服在山裡是必不可少的。**2** [U] the liquid from which wine is made; GRAPE juice〔釀酒用的〕葡萄汁

mus·tache /ˈmʌstæʃ; məˈstɑːʃ/ *n* [C] the usual American spelling of MOUSTACHE moustache的一般美式拼法

mustachioed, moustachioed /məˋstæʃɪod; məˈstæʃiəʊd/ *adj* having a large curly MOUSTACHE 留着〔大而彎的〕八字鬍的

mus·tang /ˈmʌstæn; ˈmʌstæŋ/ *n* [C] a small American wild horse〔產於美洲的〕小野馬

mus·tard /ˈmʌstəd; ˈmʌstəd/ *n* [U] **1** a yellow sauce that tastes hot, eaten especially with meat 芥末; 芥子醬 **2** a plant with yellow flowers whose seeds can be used to make the powder used to make this 芥菜 **3 not cut the mustard** to not be good enough for a particular job 不符合要求, 不符合條件: *He'll never cut the mustard as a manager.* 他永遠也不會是當經理的料。**4** a yellow-brown colour 芥末黃, 深黃色 —see also 另見 **keen as mustard** (KEEN[1] (8)) —see picture on page A5 參見A5頁圖

mustard gas /'·· ·/ *n* [U] a poisonous gas that burns the skin, which was used during the First World War 芥子氣〔一種毒氣〕

mus·ter[1] /ˈmʌstə; ˈmʌstə/ *v* **1 muster (up) courage/support/energy etc** to try to find as much courage, support etc as you can in order to do something difficult 鼓起勇氣/爭取支持/積蓄力量等: *Finally I mustered up the courage to ask her out.* 最後我鼓起了勇氣約她出來。| *Senator Newbolt has been trying to muster support for his proposals.* 參議員紐博爾特一直在盡力爭取

人們支持他的提議。**2** [I,T] to gather a group of people, especially soldiers, together in one place, or to come together as a group 召集〔人羣, 尤指士兵〕;〔人羣〕集合, 集結: *In April 1185 he began to muster an army.* 他於1185年4月開始召集軍隊。

muster² *n* **1 pass muster** to be accepted as good enough 被認為合格, 通過檢查: *Jackson wasn't a great player, but he just about passed muster.* 傑克遜不是一個優秀的運動員, 但還算過得去。**2** [C] *especially literary* a group of people, especially soldiers, that have been gathered together【尤文】集合在一起的一羣人〔尤指士兵〕

must·n't /ˈmʌsn̩t; ˈmʌsənt/ the short form of 縮略式='must not': *You mustn't tell Jerry what I've bought.* 不准你告訴傑里我買了甚麼。

must·y /ˈmʌstɪ; ˈmʌsti/ *adj* a musty room, house, or object has a damp and unpleasant smell, because it is old and has not had any fresh air for a long time〔房間、屋子或東西等〕霉臭的; 發霉的; 霉爛而潮濕的: *musty old books* 發霉臭味的舊書 | *the stale musty smell of the attic* 閣樓裡陳腐的霉臭味 —**mustiness** *n* [U]

mu·ta·ble /ˈmjutəbl̩; ˈmjuːtəbəl/ *adj formal* able or likely to change【正式】可變的; 易變的, 無常的 —**mutability** /ˌmjutəˈbɪlətɪ; ˌmjuːtəˈbɪlɨti/ *n* [U] —opposite 反義詞 IMMUTABLE

mu·ta·gen /ˈmjutədʒən; ˈmjuːtədʒən/ *n* [C] *technical* a substance that causes a living thing to mutate【術語】誘變劑, 致突變物

mu·tant /ˈmjutənt; ˈmjuːtənt/ *n* [C] an animal or plant that is different in some way from others of the same kind, because of a change in its GENETIC structure〔動物或植物的〕突變型, 突變體 —**mutant** *adj*

mu·tate /ˈmjutet; mjuːˈteɪt/ *v* [I] if a plant or animal mutates, it develops a feature that makes it different from other plants or animals of the same kind, because of a change in its GENETIC structure〔動物或植物〕突變

mu·ta·tion /mjuˈteʃən; mjuːˈteɪʃən/ *n* [C,U] **1** a change in the GENETIC structure of an animal or plant, that makes it different from others of the same type〔動物或植物的〕突變, 變異: *random mutation* 無規則突變 **2** *technical* a change in a speech sound, especially a vowel, because of the sound of the one next to it【術語】元音變化; 語音變異

mute¹ /mjut; mjuːt/ *adj* **1** not speaking or refusing to speak 緘默的, 不說話的; 拒絕說話的: *Helena glared at me in mute anger.* 海倫娜一聲不吭, 憤怒地瞪着我。**2** *old-fashioned* unable to speak; DUMB【過時】不會說話的, 啞的 **3** *technical* not pronounced【術語】〔語音中〕不發音的: *a mute 'e'* 不發音的 e —**mutely** *adv* —**muteness** *n* [U]

mute² *v* [T] **1** to make a sound quieter 使〔聲音〕減弱: *He placed a hand across her mouth to mute her screams.* 他用手捂住她的嘴, 把她的尖叫聲壓下去。**2** to make a musical instrument sound softer 使〔樂器〕聽起來柔和些, 使〔樂器聲音〕弱化

mute³ *n* [C] **1** something that is placed over or into a musical instrument to make it sound softer〔樂器上的〕弱音器 **2** someone who cannot speak 啞巴 —see also 另見 DEAF-MUTE

mut·ed /ˈmjutɪd; ˈmjuːtɨd/ *adj* **1 muted criticism/support/response etc** criticism etc that is not expressed strongly 温和的批評/有分寸的支持/有克制的反應等: *At first, criticism of the war was fairly muted.* 起初人們對戰爭的批評相當温和。**2** quieter than usual〔聲音〕減弱的, 比平常靜的: *We could hear the muted cries of newspaper-sellers in the street outside.* 我們能聽到外面街道上賣報人隱隱約約的叫賣聲。**3** a muted colour is not bright but soft and gentle〔顏色〕柔和的, 不耀眼的: *muted pinks and blues* 各種柔和的粉紅色和藍色

mu·ti·late /ˈmjutl̩ˌet; ˈmjuːtɨleɪt/ *v* [T often passive 常用被動態] **1** to severely and violently damage someone's body, especially by removing part of it 殘害〔某人的身體〕, 使斷肢, 使傷殘: *Many people were mutilated and maimed in the blast.* 許多人在那次爆炸中被炸得肢體殘缺不全。**2** to damage or change something so much that it is completely spoiled or ruined 完全損毀; 使支離破碎 —**mutilation** /ˌmjutl̩ˈeʃən; ˌmjuːtɨˈleɪʃən/ *n* [C,U]

mu·ti·neer /ˌmjutn̩ˈɪr; ˌmjuːtɨˈnɪə/ *n* [C] someone who is involved in a mutiny 叛變者, 反叛者

mu·ti·nous /ˈmjutn̩əs; ˈmjuːtɨnəs/ *adj* **1** behaving in a way that shows you do not want to obey someone; REBELLIOUS 抗命的, 反抗的; 桀驁不馴的: *There was a mutinous look in Rosie's eyes.* 在羅絲的目光裡有一種叛逆的眼神。| *mutinous teenagers* 桀驁不馴的青少年 **2** involved in a mutiny 叛變的, 反叛的: *mutinous soldiers* 叛亂的士兵 —**mutinously** *adv*

mu·ti·ny /ˈmjutn̩ɪ; ˈmjuːtɨni/ *n* [C,U] a situation in which people, especially sailors or soldiers, refuse to obey the person who is in charge of them, and try to take control for themselves〔尤指水手或士兵的〕反叛, 譁變, 叛亂: *There was already talk of mutiny among the crew.* 船員中間已經有譁變的傳言。—**mutiny** *v* [I]

mutt /mʌt; mʌt/ *n* [C] *informal*【非正式】**1** a dog that does not belong to any particular breed; MONGREL 雜種狗 **2** *BrE* a stupid person; fool【英】笨蛋, 傻瓜: *You dumb mutt – look what you've done now!* 你這個笨蛋 —— 瞧瞧你做了些甚麼!

mut·ter /ˈmʌtɚ; ˈmʌtə/ *v* **1** [I,T] to speak quietly or in a low voice, usually because you are annoyed about something, or because you do not want people to hear you 咕噥, 嘀咕; 悄聲説: *"I didn't even want to come in the first place," he muttered.* "我原來甚至都不想來的。" 他嘟噥着説。| *Mr Clarke left, muttering something about having to see a client.* 克拉克先生走了, 嘴裡咕噥着必須去見一個客戶甚麼的。**2** [I] to complain about something or express doubts about it, but without saying clearly and openly what you think 私下抱怨; 小聲質疑: **[+about]** *Some senators muttered darkly about the threat to national security.* 一些議員私下裡質疑對國家安全構成的威脅。—**mutter** *n* [singular]: *His voice subsided to a mutter.* 他的嗓音低了下來, 變成了輕輕的嘀咕聲。—**mutterer** *n* [C] —**muttering** *n* [C,U]

mut·ton /ˈmʌtn̩; ˈmʌtn/ *n* [U] **1** the meat from a sheep 羊肉 **2 mutton dressed as lamb** *BrE* an offensive expression meaning a woman who is trying to look younger than she really is【英】〔冒犯性説法〕設法使自己看起來年輕些的婦女

mutton chop /ˌ·· ˈ·/ *n* [C] **1** a piece of meat containing a bone, that has been cut from the RIBS of a sheep 羊排 **2 mutton chops** also 又作 **mutton chop whiskers** hair that grows only on the sides of a man's cheeks, not on his chin, in a style that was popular in the 19th century 羊排絡腮鬍子〔指僅在臉頰兩旁蓄的上窄下寬的絡腮鬍子, 盛行於19世紀〕

mu·tu·al /ˈmjutʃuəl; ˈmjuːtʃuəl/ *adj* **1 mutual respect/hatred/support** mutual feelings such as respect or hatred are felt equally by two people towards each other 相互尊重/仇恨/支持: *Mutual respect is necessary for the partnership to work.* 相互尊重是合作所必需的。| **the feeling is mutual** (=used to say that you have the same feeling about someone else as they have about you, especially when you dislike each other)〔感情方面〕彼此一樣, 彼此彼此 *I didn't like Dev, and the feeling seemed to be mutual.* 我不喜歡迪夫, 他好像也不喜歡我。—compare 比較 RECIPROCAL **2 mutual friend/interest** a friend or interest that two people both have 共同的朋友/興趣: *We discovered a mutual interest in gardening.* 我們在園藝方面找到了共同的愛好。**3 mutual admiration society** *humorous* a situation in which two people praise each other a lot【幽默】相互吹捧 —**mutuality** /ˌmjutʃuˈælətɪ; ˌmjuːtʃuˈælɨti/ *n* [U]

mutual fund /ˈ··· ·/ *n* [C] *AmE*【美】單位投資信託公司, 共同基金; a UNIT TRUST *BrE*【英】

mu·tu·al·ly /ˈmjutʃuəlɪ; ˈmjuːtʃuəli/ *adv* **1** done or experienced equally by two people 相互, 彼此: *a mutually*

beneficial arrangement 互利的安排 **2 mutually exclusive/contradictory** two ideas or beliefs that are mutually exclusive cannot both exist or be true at the same time 相互排斥/矛盾的

muu-muu /ˋmu mu; ˈmuː muː/ *n* [C] *AmE* a long loose dress【美】姆姆袍〔一種寬鬆的長袍〕

mu·zak /ˋmjuzæk; ˈmjuːzæk/ *n* [U] *trademark* recorded music that is played continuously in airports, shops, hotels etc【商標】背景音樂〔機場、商店、飯店等公共場所連續播放的錄製好的音樂〕

muz·zle¹ /ˋmʌzḷ; ˈmʌzəl/ *n* [C] **1** the nose and mouth of an animal such as a dog or horse〔狗或馬等動物的〕鼻口部, 吻: *a grey dog with a black muzzle* 嘴和鼻子呈黑色的灰狗 —see picture at 參見 HORSE¹ 圖 **2** something that you put over a dog's mouth to stop it from biting people〔狗的〕口套, 口絡 **3** the end of the BARREL of a gun 槍口, 砲口 —see picture at 參見 GUN¹ 圖

muzzle² *v* [T] **1** to prevent someone from speaking freely or expressing their opinions 使緘默, 封住…的嘴; 鉗制…的言論: *an attempt to muzzle the press and ban opposition newspapers* 限制新聞自由並取締反對派報紙的企圖 **2** to put a muzzle over a dog's mouth so that it cannot bite people 給〔狗〕戴口套

muz·zy /ˋmʌzɪ; ˈmʌzi/ *adj BrE*【英】**1** unable to think clearly, especially because you are ill or drunk; CONFUSED〔尤指因生病或醉酒而〕頭腦糊塗的, 昏昏沉沉的: *I was feeling a bit muzzy by that time, and decided to go home.* 我那時已感到頭腦有點昏沉, 所以決定回家。**2** not clear; BLURRED 不清楚的; 模糊的: *a muzzy TV picture* 不清晰的電視圖像 —**muzzily** *adv* —**muzziness** *n* [U]

MW a written abbreviation for 縮寫= MEDIUM WAVE

1 1 **my** /maɪ; maɪ/ *determiner* [possessive form of 'I' I的所有格形式] **1** of or belonging to me 我的: *Have you seen my car keys?* 你看到我的汽車鑰匙了嗎? | *My mother phoned last night.* 我母親昨天晚上來電話了。| *You should take my advice.* 你應該採納我的建議。| *I'm sure you don't want to listen to all my problems.* 我敢肯定你不想聽我所有的問題。**2** used when you are surprised about something 哎呀〔表示驚奇〕: *My! What a clever boy you are.* 哎呀! 你真是個聰明的孩子。**3** used when you are shocked or angry about something 天哪〔表示震驚或氣憤〕: *Oh my God! The house is on fire!* 天哪! 房子起火了! **4** used when addressing people who you love or like a lot 親愛的〔用於稱呼所愛或喜歡的人〕: *Good night, my dear. Sleep well.* 晚安, 親愛的。睡個好覺。

my·col·o·gy /maɪˋkɑlədʒɪ; maɪˈkɒlədʒi/ *n* [U] the study of fungi (FUNGUS) 真菌學

my·nah bird /ˋmaɪnə bɝd; ˈmaɪnə bɜːd/ also 又作 **mynah** *n* [C] a large dark Asian bird that can copy human speech 八哥, 鷯哥〔產於亞洲的一種能學說話的鳥〕

my·o·pi·a /maɪˋopɪə; maɪˈəʊpiə/ *n* [U] **1** inability to imagine what the results of your actions will be or how they will affect other people 目光短淺, 缺乏遠見 **2** *formal* inability to see things clearly that are far away【正式】近視

my·o·pic /maɪˋɑpɪk; maɪˈɒpɪk/ *adj* **1** unwilling or unable to think about the future results of your actions 目光短淺的, 缺乏遠見的: *the government's myopic refusal to take environmental issues seriously* 政府拒絕認真對待環境問題的短視行為 **2** *technical* unable to see things clearly that are faraway; SHORTSIGHTED (1)【術語】近視的 —**myopically** /-kḷɪ; -kli/ *adv*

myr·i·ad¹ /ˋmɪrɪəd; ˈmɪriəd/ *adj* [only before noun 僅用於名詞前] *literary* too many to count【文】無數的, 不計其數的: *Myriad bright stars shone in the sky above.* 無數明亮的星星在天空中閃耀。

myriad² *n* [C] *especially literary* a very large number of something【尤文】無數, 極大數量: **[+of]** *myriads of small islands* 無數的小島嶼

myrrh /mɝ; mɜː/ *n* [U] a sticky brown substance that is used for making PERFUME and INCENSE〔製香水和香用的〕沒藥 (樹脂)

myr·tle /ˋmɝtḷ; ˈmɜːtl/ *n* [C] a small tree with shiny green leaves and sweet-smelling white flowers 愛神木, 香桃木

my·self /maɪˋsɛlf; maɪˈself/ *pron* **1** [reflexive form of 'I' I的反身形式] 我自己: *I hurt myself.* 我把自己弄傷了。| *I passed the exam so I'm feeling pretty pleased with myself.* 我通過了考試, 所以對自己感到非常滿意。| *Those dishwashers are great. I think I'll get one for myself.* 那些洗碗機真棒, 我想給自己買一台。**2** used to emphasize the pronoun I 我本人, 我親自〔用以強調代名詞I〕: *Why do I always have to do everything myself?* 為甚麼我總是得親自做每一件事? | *I'm sorry, I'm a stranger here myself.* 對不起, 我自己也是新來這裡的。| *I myself might have done things differently.* 要是我自己也許會用不同的方式行事了。**3 not be/feel etc myself** to not feel or behave in the way you usually do because you are nervous or upset 自我感覺不正常: *I do apologise – I haven't been feeling myself lately.* 我真的表示道歉 —— 我近來一直心神恍惚。**4 (all) by myself a)** alone 獨自, 單獨: *If you don't mind, I'd like to be by myself for a while.* 如果你不介意的話, 我想獨自待一會兒。**b)** without help 獨力地; 獨自地: *It's hard to believe but I painted the house all by myself.* 真不敢相信我自己一個人刷完了房子。**5 (all) to myself** if you have something to yourself, you do not have to share it with anyone 獨自佔有的, 獨用的: *I always dreamt of having a room all to myself.* 我一直夢想着有一個完全屬於我自己的房間。—see also 另見 YOURSELF

mys·te·ri·ous /mɪsˋtɪrɪəs; mɪˈstɪəriəs/ *adj* **1** mysterious events, behaviour, or situations are difficult to explain or understand 神祕的, 難以解釋[理解]的: *His father died of a mysterious disease.* 他父親死於一種神祕的疾病。| *a mysterious smile* 神祕的微笑 | **in mysterious circumstances** *Benson later disappeared in mysterious circumstances.* 本森後來神祕地失蹤了。**2** a mysterious person is someone who you know very little about and who seems strange or interesting〔人〕神祕的: *Who was this mysterious stranger?* 這個神祕的陌生人是誰? **3** saying very little about what you are doing; SECRETIVE 故弄玄虛的; 詭祕的; 遮遮掩掩的: **[+about]** *Helen's being very mysterious about her plans.* 海倫在對她的計劃故弄玄虛。—**mysteriously** *adv* —**mysteriousness** *n* [U]

mys·te·ry /ˋmɪstrɪ; ˈmɪstəri/ *n* **1** [C] something that is impossible to understand or explain or about which little is known 神祕的事物, 無法理解[解釋]的事物, 謎: **remain a mystery** *Twenty years after the event, his death remains a mystery.* 事情過去二十年了, 他的死仍然是個謎。| **solve/unravel a mystery** (=find an explanation for it) 解開一個謎 *They never solved the mystery of Gray's disappearance.* 他們從來沒有解開格雷失蹤這個謎。| **a mystery phone call/lover/package etc** (=one that you know very little about, which therefore seems strange and interesting) 神祕的電話/情人/包裹等 *If I tell you the mystery ingredient, my recipe won't be a secret.* 如果我告訴你那種神祕的配料, 我的食譜就不會是個祕密了。| **be a mystery to** (=used to say that you do not know or understand much about something) 對…是個謎 *Jean's business affairs were always a mystery to him.* 吉恩生意上的事對他來說一直是個謎。**2 It's a mystery to me** *spoken* used to say that you cannot understand something at all【口】對我來說是個謎: *It's a mystery to me how she manages to work so fast.* 她怎麼能幹得那麼快, 這對我來說是個謎。**3** [U] a quality that makes someone or something seem strange, secret, or difficult to explain 神祕(性): **an air of mystery** *There was an air of mystery about him.* 他為人詭異難測。| **be shrouded/veiled in mystery** *The circumstances of his death were veiled in mystery.* 他的死籠罩着一層神祕的色彩。**4** [C] *formal* a quality that something has that cannot be explained in any practical or scientific way, especially because it is connected with God and religion【正式】(宗教的) 奧祕, 玄理: **[+of]** *the mystery of creation* 天地萬物的奧祕 **5** [C] a story about a murder, in which you are not told who the murderer is until the end 偵探[推理, 疑案]故事: *a murder mystery* 有關謀殺的偵探故事

mystery play /'··· ·/ *n* [C] a religious play from the Middle Ages based on a story from the Bible〔中世紀依據聖經故事編寫的〕神祕劇, 神蹟劇

mystery tour /'··· ·/ *n* [C] *BrE* a trip, usually by bus, in which people do not know where they will be taken【英】〔旅客事先不知道目的地、通常乘公共汽車進行的〕神祕旅遊

mys·tic¹ /ˋmɪstɪk; 'mɪstɪk/ *n* [C] someone who practises MYSTICISM 神祕主義者, 通靈論者, 通靈主義信奉者

mystic² *adj* another word for MYSTICAL mystical 的另一說法

mys·tic·al /ˋmɪstɪkḷ; 'mɪstɪkəl/ *adj* **1** involving religious, spiritual, or magical powers that people cannot understand 神祕的, 神奇的, 不可思議的: *a mystical union with nature* 與大自然的神祕結合 | *the mystical significance of names and numbers* 名字和數字的玄妙含義 **2** connected with mysticism 神祕主義的, 通靈(論)的 —**mystically** /-klɪ; -kli/ *adv*

mys·ti·cis·m /ˋmɪstəˏsɪzəm; 'mɪstɪ̵sɪzəm/ *n* [U] a religious practice in which people try to get knowledge of truth and to become united with God through prayer and MEDITATION 神祕主義, 通靈論, 通靈主義

mys·ti·fy /ˋmɪstəˏfaɪ; 'mɪstɪ̵faɪ/ *v* [T] to be impossible for someone to understand or explain; BAFFLE¹ 使困惑不解, 使迷惑; 難住: *a case that mystified the police* 使警方迷惑不解的案子 —**mystifying** *adj* —**mystification** /ˌmɪstəfəˋkeʃən; ˌmɪstɪ̵fɪ̵'keɪʃən/ *n* [U]

mys·tique /mɪsˋtik; mɪ'stiːk/ *n* [U] a quality that makes someone or something seem different, mysterious, or special 神祕性, 神祕色彩: *Hollywood has lost none of its mystique.* 荷里活絲毫也沒有失去其神祕色彩。

myth /mɪθ; mɪθ/ *n* **1** [C,U] an idea or story that many people believe, but which is not true〔許多人相信但不真實的〕荒誕傳說, 無根據的觀念: *the myth of male superiority* 沒有根據的男性優越論觀念 | *Most people think that bats are blind, but in fact this is a myth.* 大多數人認為蝙蝠看不見東西, 但事實上這是一個錯誤的觀念。| **popular myth** (=one that a lot of people believe) 許多人的誤解, 普遍的誤解 *Contrary to popular myth, there is no evidence that long jail sentences really deter young offenders.* 與人們的普遍看法相反, 沒有證據表明長期囚禁真的會嚇住年輕的罪犯。| **explode/dispel a myth** (=prove that it is not true) 戳穿謊言, 消除誤解 **2** [C] an ancient story, especially one invented in order to explain natural or historical events〔古代的〕神話: *the myth of Orpheus* 關於奧爾甫斯的(古希臘)神話 **3** [U] this kind of ancient story in general 神話故事: *the giants of myth and fairy-tale* 神話和童話故事中的巨人

myth·ic /ˋmɪθɪk; 'mɪθɪk/ *adj* like something or someone in a myth 像神話中人[物]的, 神話般的: *mythic powers* 神奇的力量 | *mythic beauty* 仙女般的美麗

myth·i·cal /ˋmɪθɪkḷ; 'mɪθɪkəl/ *adj* **1** connected with or only existing in an ancient story 神話的; 只存在於神話中的: *a mythical creature like the Minotaur* 神話中像彌諾陶洛斯〔古希臘神話中半人半牛的怪物〕一樣的動物 **2** imagined or invented; FICTITIOUS 想像中的; 虛構的; 非真實的: *all these mythical 'job prospects' he keeps talking about* 他一直在談論着的種種虛幻的"就業前景"

my·thol·o·gy /mɪˋθɑlədʒɪ; mɪ'θɒlədʒi/ *n* [C,U] **1** ancient myths in general, and the beliefs they represent 神話〔統稱〕; 神話學: *scenes from classical mythology* 古典神話中的場面 **2** ideas or opinions that many people believe, but that are wrong or not true〔許多人所持有的〕錯誤的想法, 不正確的看法: *popular mythology about the lives of the royal family* 公眾關於王室生活的錯誤想法 —**mythologist** *n* [C] —**mythological** /ˌmɪθəˋlɑdʒɪkḷ; ˌmɪθə'lɒdʒɪkəl◂/ *adj*: *a mythological hero* 神話中的英雄

myx·o·ma·to·sis /ˌmɪksəməˋtosɪs; ˌmɪksəmə'təʊsɪ̵s/ *n* [U] a disease that kills rabbits 多發性黏液瘤病, 兔瘟

N

N,n

N, n /ɛn; en/ *plural* **N's, n's** *n* [C] the 14th letter of the English alphabet 英語字母表的第十四個字母

n the written abbreviation of 縮寫= NOUN

N the written abbreviation of 縮寫= north or northern

n /ən; ən/ a short form of 縮略式= 'and': *rock 'n' roll* 搖滾樂

N/A not applicable; written on a form to show that you do not need to answer a question 不適用〔寫在表格中表示某項無必要填寫〕

NAACP /ˌɛn e e si ˋpi; ˌen eɪ eɪ siː ˈpiː/ *n* [singular] the National Association for the Advancement of Colored People; an American organization that works for the rights of African-American people〔美國〕全國有色人種協進會

Naaf·i /ˋnæfɪ; ˈnæfi/ *n* [C] a shop or eating place in a British military establishment〔英國軍營中的〕小吃部, 小賣部; 小食堂

naan /nɑn; nɑːn/ *n* [U] another spelling of NAN[2] nan[2] 的另一種拼法

nab /næb; næb/ *v* **nabbed, nabbing** [T] *informal*【非正式】**1** to catch someone doing something illegal; ARREST[1] (1) 當場抓住; 逮捕 **2** to get something quickly 快速得到; 猛然抓住; 搶: *See if you can nab a seat.* 看你能不能搶個座位。

na·bob /ˋnebɑb; ˈneɪbɒb/ *n* [C] an Englishman in the 18th or 19th century who became rich in India and returned to Europe〔18或19世紀〕在印度發財後回到歐洲的英國人

nach·os /ˋnætʃoz; ˈnætʃəʊz/ *n* [plural] hot-tasting Mexican food consisting of small pieces of TORTILLAs covered with cheese, beans etc 辣味乳酪玉米〔墨西哥食物〕

na·cre /ˋnekɚ; ˈneɪkə/ *n* [U] MOTHER-OF-PEARL 珍珠母: *Buzz's gift, a nacre box, lay on the table.* 桌子上放着布茲的禮物——一個珍珠母做的盒子。—**nacreous** *adj*

na·dir /ˋnedɚ; ˈneɪdɪə/ *n* [singular] *literary* the time when a situation is at its worst【文】最低點, 最糟的時刻: *By 1932, the depression had reached its nadir.* 經濟大蕭條在1932年到了最糟的時刻。

naff[1] /næf; næf/ *adj BrE slang* silly, especially in a way that shows a lack of good judgement about style, fashion etc【英俚】愚蠢的; 低級的: *a really naff film* 荒唐透頂的影片

naff[2] *v* **naff off** *BrE spoken* used to tell someone rudely to go away【英口】滾開

nag[1] /næg; næg/ *v* **nagged, nagging** [I,T] **1** to keep complaining to someone about their behaviour or asking them to do something, in a way that is very annoying 嘮叨; 不停地抱怨; 跟…糾纏不休: *I wish you'd stop nagging!* 我希望你別再嘮叨了! | **nag sb to do sth** *Nadia's been nagging me to fix the lamp.* 納迪亞一直在嘮叨着要我修理那盞燈。| **nag sb for** *The kids are always nagging me for new toys.* 孩子們總是纏着要我買新玩具。**2** to make someone feel continuously worried or uncomfortable 困擾, 煩擾: **[+at]** *a problem that had been nagging at him for days* 已經困擾他多日的一個問題 | **nagged by doubts/worries/fears** *Karen lay awake all night, nagged by doubts.* 卡倫滿心疑慮, 一整夜都沒有睡着。

nag[2] *n* [C] *informal*【非正式】**1** a person who nags continuously 愛嘮叨的人 **2** a horse, especially one that is old or in bad condition 馬〔尤指老馬或駑馬〕

nag·ging /ˋnægɪŋ; ˈnægɪŋ/ *adj* [only before noun 僅用於名詞前] making you worry or feel pain all the time 無法擺脱的; 煩人的; 讓人頭痛的: **nagging doubt/fear/feeling etc** *It was a week before the wedding, and there was still the nagging doubt in the back of her mind.* 尚有一星期就舉行婚禮, 但她的內心卻仍然無法擺脱疑慮。| **nagging toothache/headache/pain etc** *Lee had a nagging pain in her back.* 李的背一直痛個不停。

nai·ad /ˋneæd; ˈnaɪæd/ *n* [C] a female spirit who, according to ancient Greek stories, lived in a lake, stream, or river〔古希臘神話故事中的〕水精; 水泉女神

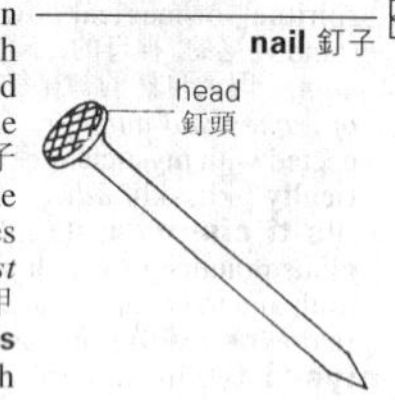

nail[1] /nel; neɪl/ *n* [C] **1** a thin pointed piece of metal which you force into a piece of wood with a hammer to fasten the wood to something else 釘子 **2** the hard smooth layer on the ends of your fingers and toes 指甲; 趾甲: *Damn! I've just broken a nail.* 該死!我的指甲斷了。**3 a nail in sb's/sth's coffin** something bad which will help to destroy someone's success or hopes 促使某人/某事物失敗的因素: *This latest scandal was one more nail in the coffin of Manley's ambitions.* 最近這宗醜聞是對曼利雄心壯志的又一次致命打擊。**4 on the nail a)** *BrE* if you pay money on the nail, you pay it immediately【英】當即, 當場〔付款〕**b)** *AmE* completely correct in what you say or when you guess something【美】準確(地): *Ed was right on the nail when he guessed Sue's age.* 埃德猜蘇的年齡猜得真準。—see also 另見 **as hard as nails** (HARD[1] (27)), **hit the nail on the head** (HIT[1] (24))

nail[2] *v* [T] **1** [always+adv/prep] to fasten something to something else with a nail or nails 釘, 將…釘牢: **nail sth to/together/down etc** *A sign saying 'No Fishing' had been nailed to the tree.* 樹上釘着一塊牌子, 上面寫着"禁止釣魚"。| *The lid was nailed down.* 蓋子被釘牢了。**2** *informal* to catch someone and prove that they are guilty of a crime or something bad【非正式】抓住, 逮住: *It took us 10 years to nail the bastard who killed our daughter.* 我們花了10年時間, 終於將殺害我們女兒的那個雜種抓捕歸案。| **nail sb for** *The state police finally nailed him for fraud.* 州警方最終以詐騙罪逮捕了他。**3 nail sb to the wall/cross** *especially AmE* to punish someone severely【尤美】嚴懲某人 **4 nail your colours to the mast** *BrE* to say clearly and publicly which ideas or which people you support【英】明確表態 **5 nail a lie/rumours** *informal* to prove that what someone has said is a lie【非正式】揭穿謊言/謠言

nail sb/sth ↔ **down** *phr v* [T] *informal*【非正式】**1** to force someone to say clearly what they want or what they intend to do 強迫〔某人〕表明意圖: **nail sb down to sth** *Before they repair the car, nail them down to a price.* 在他們修車前, 先讓他們把價錢講明白。**2** *AmE* to reach a final and definite decision about something【美】最終確定, 對…作出定論: *Two days isn't enough time to nail down the details of an agreement.* 要把協議的所有細節都確定下來, 兩天的時間是不夠的。

nail-bit·er /ˈ· ˌ··/ *n* [C] *informal* a very exciting story, film etc【非正式】非常刺激的故事[影片]

nail-bit·ing /ˈ· ˌ··/ *adj* [only before noun 僅用於名詞前] extremely exciting because you do not know what is going to happen next 非常刺激的; 充滿懸念的: *a nail-biting finish to the tennis final* 網球決賽中令人緊張的最後時刻

nail·brush /ˈ· ·/ *n* [C] a small, stiff brush for cleaning your fingernails 指甲刷 —see picture at 參見 BRUSH 圖

nail file /ˈ· ·/ *n* [C] a thin piece of metal with a rough surface used for making your fingernails a nice shape 指甲銼

nail pol·ish /ˈ· ˌ··/ also 又作 **nail e·nam·el** /ˈ· ·ˌ··/, **nail var·nish** /ˈ· ˌ··/ *BrE*【英】*n* [U] coloured or transparent liquid which is painted on women's fingernails or toenails to make them look attractive 指[趾]甲油: *pink nail polish* 粉紅色指甲油

nail scis·sors /ˈ· ˌ··/ *n* [plural] a small pair of scissors for cutting fingernails or toenails 指[趾]甲剪 —see picture at 參見 SCISSORS 圖

na·ive /nɑˋiv; naɪˈiːv/ *adj* not having much experience of how complicated life is so that you trust people too much and believe that good things will always happen 無經驗的, 幼稚的, 天真的: *a group of young, naive revolutionaries* 一羣年輕幼稚的革命者 | *You really believe him? How can you be so naive?* 你竟然相信他?你怎麼會這麼天真呢? —**naively** *adv*: *I had naively imagined that he was in love with me.* 我一直天真地以為他愛我。—**naivety** /nɑˋivtɪ; naɪˈiːvəti/ also 又作 **naiveté** /nɑˋivte; naɪˈiːvəteɪ/ *n* [U]: *dangerous political naivety* 危險的政治幼稚性

3 **na·ked** /ˈnekɪd; ˈneɪkɪ̣d/ *adj* **1** not wearing clothes or not covered by clothes; NUDE¹ 裸體的, 赤條條的: *The children swam naked in the lake.* 孩子光着身子在湖裡游泳。| **stark naked** also 又作 **buck naked/naked as a jaybird** *AmE* (=completely naked)【美】一絲不掛的 **2 with the naked eye** without the help of any instrument 憑肉眼: *Bacteria can't be seen with the naked eye.* 細菌是肉眼無法看到的。**3 naked sword/light/flame etc** a sword etc that is not enclosed by a cover 無鞘劍/無罩燈/沒有遮擋的火焰: *The naked light bulb glared in her eyes.* 無罩燈泡刺得她的雙眼很不舒服。**4 naked truth/self-interest/aggression etc** truth etc that is not hidden and is shocking 明擺着的事實/明顯的私利/赤裸裸的侵略: *Their claim was based on naked self-interest.* 他們的要求是建立在赤裸裸的利己主義基礎上的。—**nakedly** *adv* —**nakedness** *n* [U]

nam·by-pam·by /ˈnæmbɪ ˋpæmbɪ; ˌnæmbi ˈpæmbi◂/ *adj informal* too weak and gentle and lacking determination【非正式】柔弱的; 無決斷的: *To these soldiers writing poetry must have seemed a namby-pamby sort of occupation.* 對這些士兵來說, 寫詩一定是件婆婆媽媽的事。—**namby-pamby** *n* [C]

1 1 **name¹** /nem; neɪm/ *n* **1** [C] the word that someone or something is called or known by 姓名; 姓; 名字; 名稱: *What's the name of that river?* 那條河的名稱是甚麼? | *Her name is Mandy Wilson.* 她的姓名是曼迪·威爾遜。| **first name/Christian name** *Her first name is Mandy.* 她的名字叫曼迪。| **last name/surname/family name** *Her surname is Wilson.* 她姓威爾遜。| **middle name** *Lots of girls have Elizabeth as their middle name.* 很多女孩的中名都叫伊麗莎白。| **full name** (=complete name) 全名 *Please leave your full name and address with reception.* 請在接待處留下您的全名和地址。| **know sb by name** (=know what someone is called) 知道某人叫甚麼名字 *It's a big school but the principal knows everyone by name.* 儘管這所學校很大, 但校長叫得上每個人的名字。| **by the name of** (=whose name is...) 名叫… *Is there anyone here by the name of Sommerville?* 這裡有人叫薩默維爾嗎? | **go by the name of** (=call yourself a particular name which may not be your real name) 自稱名叫 *a wrestler who went by the name of Mazambula* 一位自稱名為馬贊布拉的摔跤手 | **under the name (of)** (=using a name that is different from your own) 用…為別名; 以…為筆名 *H. H. Munro wrote under the name Saki.* H. H. 芒羅以筆名薩基從事寫作。**2 call sb names** to say something nasty or insulting about someone 罵某人: **call sb all the names under the sun** (=say rude and insulting things about someone) 謾罵[辱罵]某人 **3** [singular] the opinion that people have about a person or organization; REPUTATION 名聲; 名譽: **have a name for** (=be known by people to have a particular quality) 以…著稱 *The company has a name for reliability.* 這家公司享有可靠的名聲。| **get a good/bad name** *The restaurant got a bad name for slow service.* 這家餐館因服務效率低而名聲不好。| **make a name for yourself** (=become known and admired by many people) 出名, 聞名, 揚名 *Manyac made a name for himself in the Parisian art world.* 馬尼亞克在巴黎藝術界出了名。**4 big/famous/household name** *informal* someone who is famous【非正式】名人, 名家, 知名人士: *some of the biggest names in show business* 演藝界中一些最出名的人物 **5 not have a penny to your name** *informal* to be very poor【非正式】一文不名, 十分貧窮 **6 in sb's name** if an official document, a hotel room etc is in someone's name it officially belongs to them or is for them 屬於某人; 以某人的名義: *The mortgage is in my husband's name.* 抵押是以我丈夫的名義申請的。**7 do sth in the name of science/religion etc** to do something that is wrong and believe that you are doing it to support the work of science etc 借科學/宗教等的名義做某事: *cruel experiments on animals carried out in the name of science* 借科學名義進行的殘忍的動物試驗 **8 in the name of sb** doing something as someone else's representative 代表某人: *I claim this land in the name of the King!* 我代表國王宣布擁有這塊土地! **9 in name only** if something exists in name only it does not really exist although it is officially said to 只是在名義上: *a democracy in name only* 有名無實的民主國家 **10 in all but name** if a situation exists in all but name, it is the real situation but people do not admit that it is 既成事實地, 不承認但已成事實地: *She was his wife in all but name.* 她雖無妻子的名分, 但事實上已經是他的妻子了。**11 I can't put a name to it** *spoken* used when you cannot remember what something is called【口】我忘了它叫甚麼, 我叫不出它的名字: *I know the tune but I can't put a name to it.* 我知道這首曲子, 但說不出曲名來。**12 take sb's name in vain** *often humorous* to talk about someone without showing respect【常幽默】以不尊重的方式談論某人, 在背後說某人的閒話 **13 the name of the game** *informal* the most important thing or quality needed for a particular activity【非正式】〔從事某種活動所需的〕最重要的東西[元素]: *In fishing, patience is the name of the game.* 就釣魚而言, 有耐性是最重要的。**14 sb's name is mud** *informal* used to say that people are angry with someone because of something he or she has done【非正式】某人聲名狼藉 —see also 另見 PEN NAME, **clear sb's name** (CLEAR² (3))

name² *v* [T] 2 2

1 ►GIVE SB A NAME 給某人取名◄ to give someone or something a particular name 給…取名, 給…命名: **name sb John/Ann etc** *We named our daughter Sarah.* 我們給女兒取名為薩拉。| *I name this ship 'Arcadia'.* 我把這艘船命名為"世外桃源"。| **name sb after** *BrE*【英】**/name sb/sth for** *AmE*【美】(=give someone the same name as) 以…的名字給某人/某物命名 *Bill is named after his father.* 比爾以其父親的名字命名。| *The college is named for George Washington.* 這所大學以喬治·華盛頓的名字命名。

2 ►SAY SB'S OR STH'S NAME 說出某人或某物的名字[名稱]◄ to say what the name of someone or something is 說出…的名字: *Can you name this tune?* 你能說出這首曲子的名字嗎? | *The two murder victims have yet to be named.* 這兩個被謀殺者的姓名尚未公佈。| **name names** (=name the people who were involved in something, especially something bad or illegal) 點名揭發 *She has secret information and is threatening to name names.* 她掌握着祕密情報, 並恐嚇要把相關人員的名字捅出來。

3 ►CHOOSE SB 選擇某人◄ to officially choose someone or something 選定; 指定; 任命: **name sb as** *Gerry's been named as successor to the present manager.* 傑里已被選定接替現任經理。| **name sb to sth** *AmE*【美】*Fitzgerald was named to the committee by the chairman.* 菲茨傑拉德被主席選定進入該委員會。

4 to name but a few used after a short list of things or people to say that there are many more you could mention 略舉幾例: *Gina Fratini, David Neil and Benny Ong, to name but a few, became famous when the Princess wore their designs.* 略舉幾個例子, 吉納·弗拉提尼、戴維·尼爾和本尼·翁都因王妃穿了他們所設計的時裝而出了名。

5 you name it *spoken* used after a list of things to mean that there are many more you could mention【口】凡是你說得出的, 應有儘有: *Clothes, furniture, books – you name it, they sell it!* 服裝、家具、書籍——凡是你說得出的, 他們都賣!

6 name the day to decide on a date for your wedding 選定結婚日期

7 name your price used to mean that you can decide how much money you want to buy or sell something for (自己)出個價錢

name-call·ing /ˈ· ˌ·· / *n* [U] the act of saying nasty things about someone 辱罵, 罵人〔行為〕: *children subjected to jibes and name-calling* 遭受嘲諷和辱罵的孩子們

name day /ˈ· ·/ *n* [C] the day each year when the Christian church gives honour to the particular SAINT (=holy person) whose name you have been given 命名日〔基督教教會紀念某聖徒的日子〕

name·drop /ˈnemˌdrɑp; ˈneɪmdrɒp/ *v* [I] *informal* to mention famous or important people's names to make it seem that you know them personally【非正式】〔在言談中〕提及名人[要人]的名字〔表示和他們相識, 以抬高自己的身價〕—**namedropping** *n* [U]

name·less /ˈnemlɪs; ˈneɪmləs/ *adj* **1** not known by name; ANONYMOUS 不知名的; 匿名的: *the work of a nameless 13th century writer* 13世紀一位不知名作家的作品 **2 a)** [only before noun 僅用於名詞前] *literary* difficult to describe【文】難以名狀的, 難以形容的: *Nameless fears made her tremble.* 不可名狀的恐懼使她全身顫抖。**b)** too terrible to name or describe 壞得說不出口的: *nameless crimes* 難以言喻的罪行 **3** having no name 無名的, 未取名的: *hundreds of nameless canyons* 數百個無名峽谷 **4 who shall remain nameless** *spoken* used when you want to say that someone has done something wrong but without mentioning their name【口】不便說出其名字的: *A certain person, who shall remain nameless, forgot to lock the front door.* 某位我不便說出名字的人忘了鎖上前門。

name·ly /ˈnemlɪ; ˈneɪmli/ *adv* used to introduce additional information which makes it clear exactly who or what you are talking about 即, 也就是(說): *Three students were mentioned, namely John, Sarah and Sylvia.* 有三位學生被提到, 他們是約翰、莎拉和西爾維亞。

name·plate /ˈnempleт; ˈneɪmpleɪt/ *n* [C] a piece of metal or plastic fastened to something, showing the name of the owner or maker, or the person who lives or works in a place 姓名牌; 名稱牌

name·sake /ˈnemˌsek; ˈneɪmseɪk/ *n* [C] **sb's namesake** another person, especially a more famous person, who has the same name as someone〔尤指較著名的〕同(姓)名的人: *Like his famous namesake, young Nelson had a brave, adventurous spirit.* 像與他同名的那位名人一樣, 小納爾遜具備勇敢、冒險的精神。

name tag /ˈ· ·/ *n* [C] a small sign with your name on it that you wear〔胸前佩帶的〕姓名牌

name-tape /ˈ· ·/ *n* [C] *BrE* a small piece of cloth with your name on it that is sewn onto clothes【英】〔縫在衣服上的〕標有姓名的布條; LABEL[1] (1) *AmE*【美】

nan[1] /næn; næn/ *n* [C] *BrE informal* a word meaning grandmother, used by children【英, 非正式】奶奶; 外婆〔兒語〕

nan[2], naan /nɑn; nɑːn/ *n* [U] a type of bread made without YEAST and eaten with Indian food〔未經發酵的〕印度式麵包

nan·ny /ˈnænɪ; ˈnæni/ *n* [C] **1** a woman whose job is to take care of the children in a family, usually in the children's own home〔照看小孩的〕保姆 **2** *BrE informal* a word meaning grandmother, used by children【英, 非正式】奶奶; 外婆〔兒語〕: *It's my Nanny's birthday.* 今天是我奶奶的生日。**3 the nanny state** *especially BrE* a government which tries to control the lives of citizens too much【尤英】保姆國家; 保姆政府〔指過分干涉國民生活的政府〕

nanny goat /ˈ·· ·/ *n* [C] a female goat 雌山羊

nano- /næno; nænəʊ/ *prefix* one thousand millionth of a particular unit 納, 毫微, 10^{-9}: *nanometre* (=one thousand millionth of a metre) 納米, 10^{-9} 米 —see table on page C4 參見 C4 頁附錄

nan·o·sec·ond /ˈnænoˌsɛkənd; ˈnænəʊˌsekənd/ *n* [C] a unit for measuring time. There are one thousand million nanoseconds in a second 毫微秒, 十億分之一秒

nap[1] /næp; næp/ *n* **1** [C] a short sleep, especially during the day〔尤指白天的〕小睡, 打盹: **have/take a short nap** *I usually take a nap after lunch.* 我午飯後通常要小睡一會兒。**2** [singular] the soft surface on some cloth and leather, made by brushing the short, fine threads or hairs in one direction〔布或皮革上的〕絨面, 絨毛 —compare 比較 PILE[1] (4) **3** [C] information about the horse likely to win a race〔賽馬中的〕獲勝預測

nap[2] *v* **napped, napping 1** [I] to sleep for a short time during the day〔在白天〕小睡, 打盹 **2 be caught napping** *informal* to not be ready to deal with something when it happens, although you should be ready for it【非正式】措手不及, 沒有防備 **3** [T] to give advice about which horse is likely to win a race〔在賽馬中〕作獲勝預測

na·palm /ˈnepɑm; ˈneɪpɑːm/ *n* [U] a thick liquid made from petrol, which is used in bombs〔炸彈中使用的〕凝固汽油

nape /nep; neɪp/ *n* [singular] the back of your neck 頸背, 後頸: *He nuzzled the soft, warm nape of her neck.* 他緊貼着她那柔軟溫暖的後頸。

naph·tha /ˈnæfθə; ˈnæfθə/ *n* [U] a chemical compound like petrol 石腦油

nap·kin /ˈnæpkɪn; ˈnæpkɪ̍n/ *n* [C] **1** a square piece of cloth or paper used for protecting your clothes and for cleaning your hands and lips during a meal〔布或紙質的〕餐巾 —see picture on page A10 參見 A10 頁圖 **2** SANITARY PAD *AmE*【美】衞生巾

napkin ring /ˈ·· ˌ·/ *n* [C] a small ring in which a napkin is put and kept for someone to use at the next meal 餐巾套環

nap·py /ˈnæpɪ; ˈnæpi/ *n* [C] *BrE* a piece of soft cloth or paper worn by a baby between its legs and fastened around its waist to hold its liquid and solid waste【英】尿布; DIAPER *AmE*【美】

nappy rash /ˈ·· ·/ *n* [U] *BrE* sore skin between a baby's legs and on its BUTTOCKS caused by a wet or dirty nappy【英】尿布疹; DIAPER RASH *AmE*【美】

narc[1] /nɑrk; nɑːk/ *n* [C] *AmE informal* a police officer who deals with the problem of illegal drugs【美, 非正式】緝毒警察

narc[2] *v* [I+on] *AmE slang* to secretly tell the police about someone else's criminal activities, especially activities involving illegal drugs【美俚】告密〔尤指向警方透露有關販毒的情報〕

nar·cis·sis·m /nɑrˈsɪsˌɪzəm; ˈnɑːsɪ̍sɪzəm/ *n* [U] a tendency to admire your own physical appearance or abilities 自我陶醉; 自戀: *He went to the gym to train every day, driven purely by narcissism.* 他每天都去健身房健身, 純粹出於自我欣賞。—**narcissist** *n* [C] —**narcissistic** /ˌnɑrsɪˈsɪstɪk; ˌnɑːsɪ̍ˈsɪstɪk◂/ *adj*

nar·cis·sus /nɑrˈsɪsəs; nɑːˈsɪsəs/ *n* [C] a white or yel-

N

low spring flower, such as the DAFFODIL 水仙花

nar·cot·ic[1] /nɑrˋkɑtɪk; nɑːˈkɒtɪk/ *n* **1** **narcotics** [plural] *especially AmE* illegal drugs that affect the mind in a harmful way【尤美】毒品: **narcotics agent** (=a police officer who deals with the problems of narcotics) 緝毒警察 **2** [C] a type of drug which makes you sleep and reduces pain 安眠藥; 麻醉劑

narcotic[2] *adj* **1** [only before noun 僅用於名詞前] *especially AmE* connected with illegal drugs【尤美】(有關) 毒品的: *narcotic addiction* 毒癮 **2** a narcotic drug takes away pain or makes you sleep 麻醉(性)的; 催眠(用)的

nark[1] /nɑrk; nɑːk/ *n* [C] *BrE slang* someone who is friendly with criminals and who secretly tells the police about their activities【英俚】〔混入罪犯中向警方提供情報的〕線人, 密探, 臥底; STOOLPIGEON *AmE*【美】

nark[2] *v BrE slang*【英俚】**1** **be/get narked** to be angry or get angry about something someone has done 生氣, 發火: *I was really narked when she wouldn't listen to me.* 她不聽我的話時, 我真的非常生氣。**2** [I+on] to secretly tell the police about someone else's criminal activities〔向警方〕告密

nark·y /ˋnɑrkɪ; ˈnɑːki/ *adj BrE slang* bad-tempered【英俚】脾氣壞的, 暴躁的

nar·rate /nǽˋret; nəˈreɪt/ *v* [T] *formal* to tell a story by describing all the events in order【正式】講〔故事〕; 敍述, 描述: *a wild life film narrated by David Attenborough* 一部由〔英國極具盛名的自然歷史影片拍攝者〕大衛·艾登堡解說的野生動物影片

nar·ra·tion /nǽˋreʃən; nəˈreɪʃən/ *n* [C,U] *formal*【正式】**1** the act of telling a story 講故事 **2** a spoken description or explanation which is given during a film, play etc〔電影、戲劇等的〕旁白; 解說

nar·ra·tive /ˋnærətɪv; ˈnærətɪv/ *n* **1** [C,U] *formal* something that is told as a story【正式】敍述, 記敍: *The last chapter of the book brings the narrative of his journey to an end.* 書的最後一章結束了對他旅途的敍述。**2** [U] the art of telling a story 敍述(藝術) —**narrative** *adj*: *a narrative poem* 敍事詩

nar·ra·tor /nǽˋretɚ; nəˈreɪtə/ *n* [C] a person in some books, plays etc who tells the story〔書、戲劇等中的〕敍述者, 講解人, 解說人

[3] [2] **nar·row**[1] /ˋnæro; ˈnærəʊ/ *adj*

1 ▶NOT WIDE 不寬的◀ not wide, especially in comparison with length or with what is usual 狹窄的: *a narrow winding valley* 狹長蜿蜒的山谷 | *a long narrow room* 窄長形房間 | *There are plans to widen the narrowest sections of the road.* 有計劃要拓寬該道路最狹窄的部分。—compare 比較 BROAD[1] (1) —opposite 反義詞 WIDE[1] (1) —see picture at 參見 THIN[1] 圖

2 narrow escape a situation in which you only just avoid danger, difficulties, or trouble 死裡逃生, 險些遇險: *Peter had a narrow escape from drowning when he fell overboard.* 彼得從船上掉入水中, 險些淹死。

3 narrow majority/victory/defeat etc one that is only just achieved or happens by only a small amount 微弱多數/險勝/勉強擊敗

4 by a narrow margin if you win or lose by a narrow margin, you do it by only a small amount 幅度有限地, 相差不多地

5 ▶IDEAS/ATTITUDES 觀點/態度◀ a narrow attitude or way of looking at a situation is too limited and does not consider enough possibilities 狹隘的; 不夠全面的: *The company takes too narrow a view of possible export markets.* 公司對潛在出口市場的看法十分狹隘。| *Each group has their own narrow economic interest.* 每個羣體都有自己狹隘的經濟利益。—see also 另見 NARROW-MINDED

6 narrow squeak *informal* a situation in which you only just escape from danger or avoid an accident【非正式】死裡逃生; 勉強避過危險

7 *formal* careful and thorough【正式】精細而嚴密的: *a narrow examination of events* 對所有事件進行的嚴密審查 —see also 另見 NARROWLY, NARROWS, **keep to/stray from the straight and narrow** (STRAIGHT[3] (4)) —**narrowness** *n* [U]

narrow[2] *v* [I,T] **1** to become narrower or make something narrower (使) 變窄: *The river narrows at this point.* 河在這裡變窄了。| *He narrowed his eyes against the sun.* 他對着太陽眯起了雙眼。**2** also 又作 **narrow down** to become less or make something less in range, difference etc 縮小…的範圍: *The police have narrowed down their list of suspects.* 警方已經縮小了嫌疑犯的範圍。| *New tax laws will narrow the gap between rich and poor.* 新稅法將會縮小貧富差距。| *The choice of goods available is narrowing.* 可供選擇的商品越來越少。

narrow boat /ˈ·· ˌ·/ *n* [C] *BrE* a long, narrow boat for use on CANALS【英】〔運河中的〕狹長小船

narrow gauge /ˈ·· ˌ·/ *n* [C] a size of railway track of less than standard width 窄軌(鐵路) —see also 另見 GAUGE[1] (3)

nar·row·ly /ˋnærolɪ; ˈnærəʊli/ *adv* **1** only by a small amount 勉強地, 差一點兒: *We narrowly missed hitting the other car.* 我們差一點撞上另一輛汽車。| *The amendment was narrowly defeated.* 修正案差了幾票未獲通過。**2** looking at or considering only a small part of something 狹隘地, 不全面地: *The law is being interpreted too narrowly.* 對該法律的詮釋過於狹隘。**3** *formal* in a thorough way, looking for detail【正式】徹底地, 仔細地: *The teacher questioned the boy narrowly about why he was late.* 老師追根究底地盤問那男孩為甚麼遲到。

narrow-mind·ed /ˌ·· ˈ··◂/ *adj* unwilling to accept or understand new or different ideas or customs; PREJUDICED 心胸狹窄的, 氣量小的; 不開放的; 有偏見的 —opposite 反義詞 BROADMINDED —**narrow-mindedness** *n* [U] —**narrow-mindedly** *adv*

nar·rows /ˋnæroz; ˈnærəʊz/ *n* [plural] **1** also 又作 **Narrows** a narrow passage of water between two pieces of land which connects two larger areas of water 海峽; 江峽 **2** *AmE* a narrow part of a river, lake etc【美】〔江、湖等的〕狹窄處

na·ry /ˋnɛrɪ; ˈneəri/ *adv old use* not one【舊】一個也沒有: *They said nary a word.* 他們一個字也沒有說。

NASA /ˋnæsə; ˈnæsə/ *n* [singular] National Aeronautics and Space Administration; a US government organization that controls space travel and the scientific study of space 美國航空航天局, 美國太空總署

na·sal[1] /ˋnezḷ; ˈneɪzəl/ *adj* **1** related to the nose 鼻(子)的: *the nasal passage* 鼻腔 —see picture at 參見 RESPIRATORY 圖 **2** a sound or voice that is nasal comes mainly through your nose 有鼻音的: *He spoke in a high nasal voice.* 他說話鼻音很重。**3** *technical* a nasal CONSONANT or vowel such as /n/ or /m/ is one that is produced wholly or partly through your nose【術語】〔發音〕鼻音的 —**nasally** *adv*

nasal[2] *n* [C] *technical* a particular speech sound, such as /m/, /n/, or /ŋ/ that is made through your nose【術語】鼻音

na·sal·ize also 又作 **-ise** *BrE*【英】/ˋnezḷˌaɪz; ˈneɪzəl-aɪz/ *v* [T] to make a sound partly through your nose 使…鼻音化; 將…發成鼻音: *nasalized vowels* 鼻元音

nas·cent /ˋnæsṇt; ˈnæsənt/ *adj formal* coming into existence or starting to develop【正式】初生的, 新生的; 開始發展的: *South Africa's nascent democracy* 南非剛剛開始發展的民主

nas·tur·tium /næˋstɝʃəm; nəˈstɜːʃəm/ *n* [C] a garden plant with orange, yellow, or red flowers and circular leaves 旱金蓮

[2] **nas·ty** /ˋnæstɪ; ˈnɑːsti/ *adj*

1 ▶BEHAVIOUR 行為◀ nasty behaviour or remarks are extremely unkind and unpleasant; MALICIOUS 不友善的; 不好的; 惡毒的: *a nasty temper* 壞脾氣 | *That's a nasty*

thing to say! 說這話真惡毒! | *There's a nasty streak in her character.* 她性格中有壞的一面。| **be nasty to** (=treat someone in an unkind way) 對…不友善 *Don't be so nasty to your mum.* 別對你媽媽這麼兇。| **get/turn nasty** *especially BrE* (=suddenly start behaving in a threatening way)【尤英】突然變兇 *Don't tease the dog. He might turn nasty.* 別逗那條狗, 牠會變得很兇的。

2 ►SIGHT/SMELL ETC 景象/氣味等◄ having a bad appearance, smell, taste etc 難看的; 難聞的; 難吃的: *The medicine tastes nasty, but it works.* 這藥雖然難吃, 但很管用。| **cheap and nasty** *cheap and nasty furniture* 廉價而難看的家具

3 nasty illness/cut/wound etc an illness etc that is severe or very painful 嚴重的疾病/割傷/傷口等: *a nasty cut on the head* 頭部嚴重的傷口

4 ►EXPERIENCE/SITUATION 經歷/情況◄ a nasty experience, feeling or situation is unpleasant 令人不快的, 糟糕的: *nasty weather* 惡劣的天氣 | *It gave me a nasty shock.* 這使我非常震驚。| *I have a nasty suspicion that he's going to make us pay for everything.* 我有個不祥的感覺, 他會讓我們為這一切付出代價。| **leave a nasty taste in the mouth** (=make you feel upset or angry afterwards) 使人事後懊惱不已 *When you feel you've been cheated, it always leaves a nasty taste in the mouth.* 你感覺受騙時, 總會有一種懊惱的感覺。

5 ►OFFENSIVE 冒犯人的◄ morally bad or offensive; OBSCENE (1) 不道德的; 下流的, 猥褻的: *nasty language* 下流話 | *You've got a nasty mind.* 你的思想很骯髒。

6 a nasty piece of work *BrE* someone who is dishonest, violent, or likely to cause trouble【英】不誠實的人; 兇暴的人; 易惹麻煩的人 —see also 另見 VIDEO NASTY —**nastily** *adv* —**nastiness** *n* [U]

na·tal /ˈnetl; ˈneɪtl/ *adj technical* connected with birth【術語】出生的: *the salmon's natal stream* 鮭魚出生的河流

natch /nætʃ; nætʃ/ *adv* [sentence adverb 句子副詞] *slang* used to say that something is exactly as you would expect【俚】當然: *"What does he drive?" "A BMW, natch."* "他開甚麼車?" "當然是寶馬。"

na·tion /ˈneʃən; ˈneɪʃən/ *n* [C] **1** a country, considered especially in relation to its people and its social or economic structure 國家: *the President's radio broadcast to the nation* 總統對全國的廣播講話 | *the world's leading industrial nations* 世界上的主要工業國 **2** a large group of people of the same race and language 民族: *the Cherokee nation* 切羅基民族 —see 見 RACE[1] (USAGE)

na·tion·al[1] /ˈnæʃənḷ; ˈnæʃənəl/ *adj* **1** related to a whole nation as opposed to any of its parts 國家的, 全國性的: *national and local news* 全國及地方新聞 **2** related to a nation as opposed to other nations 國內的, 本國的: *We refuse to sign any treaty that is against our national interests.* 我們拒絕簽署任何違反本國利益的條約。| *selling to national and international markets* 銷往國內外市場 **3** [only before noun 僅用於名詞前] owned or controlled by the central government of a country 國有的; 國立的: *a national bank* 國有銀行 | *the National Health Service* 〔英國〕國民保健制度 —see also 另見 NATIONALLY

national[2] *n* [C] someone who is a citizen of a particular country but is living in another country 〔僑居國外的〕(某國)國民, 僑民: *Foreign nationals were advised to leave the country.* 建議外國僑民離開該國。—compare 比較 ALIEN[2] (1), CITIZEN (2), SUBJECT[1] (6)

national an·them /,··· ˈ··/ *n* [C] the official song of a nation that is sung or played on certain formal occasions 國歌

national cos·tume /,··· ˈ··/ *n* [C,U] special clothing traditionally worn by the people of a particular country; NATIONAL DRESS 民族服裝: *folk dancers in national costume* 身穿民族服裝的民間舞蹈演員

national debt /,··· ˈ·/ *n* [C] the total amount of money owed by the government of a country 國債

national dress /,··· ˈ·/ *n* [U] national costume 民族服裝

national grid /,··· ˈ·/ *n* [C] the system of numbered squares printed on a map to show the exact position of a place 地圖坐標網格

National Guard /,··· ˈ·/ *n* [singular] a military force in each state of the US which can be used when it is needed by the state or the US government 〔美國的〕國民警衛隊

National Health Ser·vice /,··· ˈ· ,··/ *n* [singular] the NHS 〔英國〕國民保健制度

National In·sur·ance /,··· ·ˈ··/ *n* [U] a system of insurance organized by the British Government into which workers and employers make regular payments, and which provides money for people who are unemployed, old, or ill 〔英國的〕國民保險制度〔由英國政府經管的一項保險制度, 雇主和雇員必須按時繳納錢款, 以幫助失業者、老年人或病人〕

na·tion·al·ise /ˈnæʃənḷ,aɪz; ˈnæʃənəlaɪz/ *v* [T] *BrE* another spelling of NATIONALIZE【英】nationalize 的另一種拼法

na·tion·al·is·m /ˈnæʃənḷ,ɪzəm; ˈnæʃənəlɪzəm/ *n* [U] **1** desire by a group of people of the same race, origin, language, etc to form an independent country 民族主義: *Scottish nationalism* 蘇格蘭民族主義 **2** the belief that your own country is better than any other country 本國優越感; 民族自豪感: *the rise of nationalism in Eastern Europe* 東歐民族主義的興起

na·tion·al·ist[1] /ˈnæʃənḷɪst; ˈnæʃənəlɪst/ *adj* [only before noun 僅用於名詞前] a nationalist organization, party etc wants to get or keep political independence for their country and people 國家主義的; 民族主義的

nationalist[2] *n* [C] someone who is involved in trying to gain or keep political independence for their country 國家主義者; 民族主義者: *Welsh nationalists* 威爾斯民族主義者

na·tion·al·is·tic /,næʃənḷˈɪstɪk; ,næʃənəˈlɪstɪk◄/ *adj* someone who is nationalistic believes that their country is better than other countries, and often has no respect for people from other countries 有民族[國家]主義情緒的; 民族[國家]主義的 —**nationalistically** /-klɪ; -kli/ *adv*

na·tion·al·i·ty /,næʃənˈælətɪ; ,næʃəˈnæləti/ *n* **1** [C,U] the legal right of belonging to a particular country 國籍: *people of the same nationality* 同國籍的人 | **French/Brazilian etc nationality** *He has British nationality.* 他有英國國籍。| **dual nationality** (=the legal right of being a citizen of two countries) 雙重國籍 **2** [C] a large group of people with the same race, origin, language etc 民族: *the different nationalities within the former USSR* 前蘇聯的各個民族

na·tion·al·ize also 又作 **-ise** *BrE*【英】/ˈnæʃənḷ,aɪz; ˈnæʃənəlaɪz/ *v* [T] if a government nationalizes a very large industry or service such as water, gas or electricity, it buys or takes control of it 使國有化, 把…收歸國有: *The British government nationalized the railways in 1948.* 英國政府在 1948 年將鐵路國有化。| *a nationalised industry* 國有化工業 —compare 比較 PRIVATIZE —**nationalization** /,næʃənḷaɪˈzeʃən; ,næʃənəlaɪˈzeɪʃən/ *n* [C,U]

National League /,··· ˈ·/ *n* [singular] one of the two organizations that arranges professional BASEBALL games in the US 〔美國〕全國棒球聯盟

na·tion·al·ly /ˈnæʃənḷɪ; ˈnæʃənəli/ *adv* by or to everyone in the nation 全國性地; 全民地: *The programme will be broadcast nationally.* 該節目將向全國播出。

national mon·u·ment /,··· ˈ···/ *n* [C] a building, special feature of the land etc that is kept and protected by a government for people to visit 〔受政府保護、供參觀的〕名勝古蹟, 名勝區: *the Death Valley National Monument in California* 加利福尼亞州的死亡谷名勝區

national park /,··· ˈ·/ *n* [C] an area of natural, historical, or scientific interest which is kept and protected by a

N

government for people to visit 國家公園: *Yosemite National Park*〔加州〕約塞米蒂國家公園

national se·cu·ri·ty /,⋯ ·'⋯/ *n* [U] the idea that a country must keep its secrets safe and its army strong in order to protect its citizens 國家安全: *a matter of national security* 涉及國家安全的事

national ser·vice /,⋯ '⋯/ *n* [U] *BrE* the system of making all men serve in the army for a limited time, whether the country is involved in a war or not【英】國民義務兵役制

National Trust /,⋯ '·/ *n* [singular] a British organization which owns and takes care of many beautiful places and historic buildings in England and Wales〔英國的〕全國名勝古蹟託管協會

nation state /,·· '·/ *n* [C] a nation that is a politically independent country〔政治上獨立的〕民族國家: *European union is seen as a threat to the sovereignty of the nation state.* 歐盟被視為是對民族國家主權的一種威脅。

na·tion·wide /ˌneʃənˋwaɪd; ˌneɪʃən'waɪd◂/ *adj* happening or existing in every part of the country 全國性的, 全國各地的: *a nationwide radio broadcast* 全國性電台廣播 | *a nationwide search for the criminals* 全國性的搜捕罪犯行動 —**nationwide** *adv*: *We have 350 sales outlets nationwide.* 我們在全國各地有 350 個銷售點。

3 **na·tive¹** /ˋnetɪv; 'neɪtɪv/ *adj* [only before noun 僅用於名詞前]

1 ▶COUNTRY 國家◀ your native country, town etc is the place where you were born 出生地的: *a visit by the Pope to his native Poland* 教皇對他出生地波蘭的訪問 | *They never saw their native land again.* 他們從此再也沒見到自己的故土。

2 native New Yorker/Londoner/Californian etc a person who has always lived in New York, London etc 土生土長的紐約人/倫敦人/加州人等

3 native language/tongue the language you spoke when you first learned to speak 本國語, 本地語; 母語: *Lara's native language is Swedish.* 拉臘的母語是瑞典語。

4 ▶PLANT/ANIMAL 植物/動物◀ growing, living, produced etc in one particular place; INDIGENOUS 土產的, 當地的: **[+to]** *The oregano plant is native to Italy.* 牛至是意大利的一種土生植物。| *the region's native birds* 該地區的本地鳥類

5 ▶ART/CUSTOM 藝術/風俗◀ related to the people of a country who were the earliest people to live there 土著的: *the native art of Peru* 祕魯的土著藝術

6 native intelligence/wit etc a quality that you have naturally from birth 天生的才智/智慧等: *native genius* 天才

7 go native *humorous* to behave, dress, or speak like the people who live in the country where you have come to stay or work【幽默】入鄉隨俗, 過當地人的生活: *I once knew an anthropologist who went native and married a Masai warrior.* 我曾經認識一位人類學家, 她入鄉隨俗, 還與一位馬薩伊族的鬥士結了婚。

native² *n* [C] **1** a person who was born in a particular place 出生於某地的人: **[+of]** *a native of Texas* 一個出生在德克薩斯州的人 **2** someone who lives in a place all the time or has lived there a long time 本地人, 當地人; 久居某地的人: **[+of]** *Are you a native of these parts?* 你是本地人嗎? **3** [often plural 常用複數] a word that is now considered offensive, in former times used by Europeans to mean one of the people who lived in Africa, S. Asia etc before Europeans arrived 土著, 土人〔昔日歐洲人用來指居住在非洲、南亞等地的當地人, 現在一般認為此詞具冒犯性〕**4** a plant or animal that grows or lives naturally in a place 當地土生的植物[動物]: **[+of]** *The bear was once a native of Britain.* 熊曾是英國的土生動物。

Native A·mer·i·can /,·· ·'⋯/ *n* [C] one of the people who were living in N. America before white people arrived there 北美土著居民, 印第安人

native speak·er /,·· '··/ *n* [C] someone who has learned a particular language as their first language, rather than as a foreign language 以某種語言為母語的人, 說本族語的人: *a native speaker of English* 以英語為母語的人

Na·tiv·i·ty /nəˋtɪvətɪ; nə'tɪvəti/ *n* **1** [singular] the birth of Jesus Christ 耶穌的誕生 **2** [C] a picture or model of the baby Jesus Christ and his parents in the place where he was born 耶穌誕生圖[模型]

Nativity play /·'⋯ ,·/ *n* [C] a play telling the story of the birth of Jesus Christ performed by children at Christmas〔由孩子們在聖誕節時表演的〕關於耶穌降生的短劇

NATO /ˋneto; 'neɪtəʊ/ *n* [singular] the North Atlantic Treaty Organization; a group of countries including the US and several European countries, which give military help to each other 北大西洋公約組織: *our allies in NATO* 我們在北約中的盟國 | *a NATO country* 北約成員國

nat·ter¹ /ˋnætɚ; 'nætə/ *v* [I] *BrE informal* to talk continuously about unimportant things【英, 非正式】嘮叨, 喋喋不休: *Lynne's been nattering on about the wedding for weeks.* 林恩幾週來一直在嘮叨婚禮的事。

natter² *n* [singular] *BrE informal* the act of talking about unimportant things for fun【英, 非正式】閒聊, 閒談: **have a natter** *Come round after work and we'll have a natter.* 下班後到我家來, 我們聊聊。

nat·ty /ˋnætɪ; 'næti/ *adj informal* very neat and fashionable in appearance【非正式】〔外表〕整潔而時髦的: *a natty suit* 時髦的套裝 —**nattily** *adv*

nat·u·ral¹ /ˋnætʃərəl; 'nætʃərəl/ *adj* S2 W1

1 ▶NORMAL 正常的◀ normal and what you would expect in a particular situation or at a particular time 平常的, 正常的: *Don't worry – it's a perfectly natural reaction.* 別擔心, 這完全是正常反應。| **it's only natural** *spoken*【口】*It's only natural to be afraid sometimes.* 人有時會害怕的心理是正常的。| **it is natural for sb to do sth** *It's not natural for a child of his age to be so quiet.* 像他這個年齡的孩子這麼安靜不太正常。—opposite 反義詞 UNNATURAL (1), ABNORMAL

2 ▶NOT ARTIFICIAL 非人為的◀ not caused, made, or controlled by human beings 自然的, 天然的; 非人為的: *an area of spectacular natural beauty* 自然風景秀麗的地區 | *natural disasters* 自然災害 | *death from natural causes* 自然死亡 —compare 比較 ARTIFICIAL, MAN-MADE

3 ▶TENDENCY/ABILITY 傾向/能力◀ a) a natural tendency or type of behaviour is part of your character when you are born, rather than one that you learn later; INNATE 天生的, 生來的; 固有的: *Cats have a natural aversion to water.* 貓生來就討厭水。**b)** [only before noun 僅用於名詞前] having a particular quality or skill without needing to be taught and without needing to try hard 有天賦的; 無需教導的: *a natural musician* 天生的音樂家 | *Cheryl has a natural elegance about her.* 徹麗爾具有一種天生的高雅氣質。

4 ▶NOT PRETENDING 不假裝的◀ behaving in a way that is normal and shows you are relaxed and not trying to pretend 表現自然的; 不做作的: *Try to look natural for your photograph.* 拍照時你要自然些。

5 natural parent/mother etc the parent from whom a child is born 生身父母/母親等: *John was adopted; he never knew his natural parents.* 約翰是領養來的, 他從不知道自己的生身父母是誰。

6 ▶NOT MAGIC 非神怪的◀ not connected with gods, fairies, or spirits 與神仙鬼怪無關的: *I'm sure there's a perfectly natural explanation.* 我相信一定有一種純自然的解釋。—opposite 反義詞 SUPERNATURAL¹

7 ▶FOOD 食物◀ with nothing added to change the taste 天然的, 沒有添加其他成分的: *natural yoghurt* 原味酸乳酪

8 a musical note that is natural has been raised from a FLAT² (3) by one SEMITONE or lowered from a SHARP³ (1)

N

by one semitone〔音符〕本位(音)的, 標明本位號的 **9 natural child/son/daughter** *old use* a child whose parents are not married【舊】私生子/兒子/女兒 —**naturalness** *n* [U]

natural² *n* [C] **1 be a natural** to be good at doing something without having to try hard or practise 是天生具有某種才能的人; 是天才: *Look how he swings that bat – he's a natural.* 瞧他揮動球棒的樣子, 他是個天生的高手。**2 a)** a musical note that has been changed from a FLAT² (3) to be a SEMITONE higher, or from a SHARP³ (1) to be a semitone lower〔音樂中的〕本位音 **b)** the sign (♮) in written music that shows this〔音樂中的〕本位號 —see picture at 參見 MUSIC 圖

natural-born /ˈ··· ·/ *adj* **natural-born fool/singer etc** *AmE informal* someone who has always had a particular quality or skill without having to try hard【美, 非正式】天生的傻瓜/歌手等

natural child·birth /ˌ··· ˈ··/ *n* [U] a method of giving birth to a baby in which a woman chooses not to use drugs 自然分娩(法)

natural gas /ˌ··· ˈ·/ *n* [U] gas used for heating and lighting, taken from under the earth or under the sea 天然氣

natural his·to·ry /ˌ··· ˈ···/ *n* [U] the study of plants, animals, and minerals 博物學: *the Natural History Museum* 自然博物館

nat·u·ral·is·m /ˈnætʃərəlˌɪzəm; ˈnætʃərəlɪzəm/ *n* [U] a style of art or literature which tries to show the world and people exactly as they are〔藝術或文學的〕自然主義

nat·u·ral·ist /ˈnætʃərəlɪst; ˈnætʃərəl̩ɪst/ *n* [C] **1** someone who studies plants or animals, especially outdoors 博物學家〔尤指在野外研究動植物者〕**2** someone who believes in naturalism in art or literature〔藝術或文學的〕自然主義者

nat·u·ral·is·tic /ˌnætʃərəlˈɪstɪk; ˌnætʃərəˈlɪstɪk/ also 又作 **naturalist** *adj* painted, written, etc according to the ideas of naturalism 自然主義的 —**naturalistically** /-klɪ; -kli/ *adv*

nat·u·ral·ize also 又作 **-ise** *BrE*【英】/ˈnætʃərəlˌaɪz; ˈnætʃərəlaɪz/ *v* **be naturalized a)** if someone who was born outside a particular country is naturalized, they become a citizen of that country 使歸化, 使〔外國人〕入國籍 **b)** if a foreign word or phrase is naturalized in another language, it has become part of it 採納, 吸收〔外來詞語〕—**naturalization** /ˌnætʃərəlaɪˈzeʃən; ˌnætʃərəlaɪˈzeɪʃən/ *n* [U]

2 3 **nat·u·ral·ly** /ˈnætʃərəlɪ; ˈnætʃərəli/ *adv* **1** [sentence adverb 句子副詞] used to mean that the fact you are mentioning is just what you would have expected 當然; 自然: *Naturally, you'll want to discuss this with your wife.* 自然你一定想和你妻子商量一下這件事的。| *"How do you feel about it?" "Well, naturally, we're very disappointed, but ..."* "你對此感覺如何?" "嗯, 我們當然很失望, 不過..." —see 見 SURELY (USAGE) **2** *spoken* used to say 'yes' when you think the person who asked the question should know that your reply will be yes【口】當然了: *"You'll write to me, won't you?" "Naturally."* "你會給我寫信的, 是嗎?" "當然了!" —see 見 OF COURSE (USAGE) **3** as a natural feature or quality 生來; 天然地: *My hair is naturally curly.* 我的頭髮生來就是鬈的。| **come naturally (to)** (=be easy for you to do because you have a natural ability) 天生就會... *Speaking in public seems to come quite naturally to her.* 她似乎天生就會在公眾面前講話。**4** in a relaxed manner without trying to look or sound different from usual 表現自然地, 不做作地: *Just speak naturally and pretend the microphone isn't there.* 自然地說就行, 就當麥克風根本不存在。

natural phi·los·o·phy /ˌ··· ·ˈ···/ *n* [U] *old use* science【舊】科學, 自然哲學

natural re·sourc·es /ˌ··· ·ˈ··/ *n* [plural] all of the land, minerals, natural energy etc that exist in a country 自然資源: *a country rich in natural resources* 自然資源豐富的國家

natural sci·ence /ˌ··· ˈ··/ *n* [C,U] chemistry, BIOLOGY, and PHYSICS considered together as subjects for study, or one of these subjects 自然科學〔指化學、生物和物理〕

natural se·lec·tion /ˌ··· ·ˈ··/ *n* [U] *technical* the process by which only plants and animals that are naturally suitable for life in their environment will continue to live, while all others will die【術語】自然淘汰, 自然選擇 —see also 另見 **survival of the fittest** (SURVIVAL (2))

natural wast·age /ˌ··· ˈ··/ *n* [U] a reduction in the number of people employed by an organization, which happens when people leave their jobs and the jobs are not given to anyone else〔由退職引起的〕自然減員

na·ture /ˈnetʃɚ; ˈneɪtʃə/ *n*

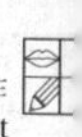

1 ►PLANTS/ANIMALS ETC 植物/動物等◄ also 又作 **Nature** [U] everything in the physical world that is not controlled by humans, such as wild plants and animals, earth and rocks, and the weather 大自然, 自然界: *We grew up in the countryside, surrounded by the beauties of nature.* 我們在鄉村長大, 周圍是美麗的大自然。| *the fundamental forces of nature* 自然界的基本力量

2 ►SB'S CHARACTER 某人的性格◄ [C,U] someone's character 本性, 天性: *Eric's got a lovely easy-going nature.* 埃里克為人可愛隨和。| **be in sb's nature** *Jana wouldn't lie, it's not in her nature.* 賈娜不會說謊, 這不是她的本性。| **by nature** *He was, by nature, a man of few words.* 他生來就是個寡言少語的人。| **sb's better nature** (=your feelings of kindness) 某人性格中善良的一面 *I've tried appealing to her better nature, but she still refuses to help.* 我竭力想喚起她善良的一面, 但她還是拒絕幫忙。| **human nature** (=the feelings and natural qualities that everyone has) 人類的天性 *Of course she's jealous – it's only human nature.* 她當然嫉妒, 這是人的天性。

3 ►CHARACTER OF STH 某物的特性◄ [C,U] a particular combination of qualities that makes something what it is and makes it different from other things 特性, 性質: *the true nature of their difficulties* 他們那些困難的真正性質 | **by its very nature** *Companies are, by their very nature, conservative.* 就本質而言, 公司都是保守的。

4 ►TYPE 類型◄ [singular] a particular kind of thing 類別, 種類: **of a personal/political/difficult nature** *books of an erotic nature* 色情書籍 | *The support being given is primarily of a practical nature.* 提供的支持主要是實用性的。| **of that nature** (=of that kind) 那類的, 那種的 *I never trouble myself with affairs of that nature.* 我從不關心那類事情。| **be in the nature of sth** (=to be like something) 屬於某一類的, 與某事物類似 *The cruise was to be in the nature of a 'rest cure'.* 這次乘船出遊是屬於"休養療法"一類的。

5 in the nature of things according to the natural way things happen 按照事物的規律: *In the nature of things, there is bound to be the occasional accident.* 按照事物的規律, 偶爾發生事故是必然的。

6 let nature take its course to allow events to happen without doing anything to change the results 順其自然, 任其自然發展: *Sometimes the best cure is just to let nature take its course.* 有時最好的辦法就是順其自然。

7 in a state of nature a) in a natural state, not having been affected by the modern world 處於未開化的自然狀態 **b)** *humorous* not wearing any clothes【幽默】一絲不掛, 裸體

8 back to nature a style of living in which people try to live more simply 返璞歸真, 回歸自然(的生活方式) —see also 另見 SECOND NATURE, **the call of nature** (CALL² (12))

nature re·serve /ˈ·· ·ˌ·/ *n* [C] an area of land in which animals and plants, especially rare ones, are protected 自然保護區

nature stud·y /ˈ·· ˌ··/ *n* [U] the study of plants, animals etc as a school subject〔學校裡的〕自然課

na·tur·ist /ˈnetʃərɪst; ˈneɪtʃərɪst/ *n* [C] someone who enjoys not wearing any clothes because they believe it is natural and healthy; NUDIST 裸體主義者 —**naturism** *n* [U]

na·tu·ro·path /ˈnetʃərəˌpæθ; ˈneɪtʃərəpæθ/ *n* [C] someone who tries to cure illness using natural things such as plants, rather than drugs〔使用植物等代替藥物治病的〕自然療法者 —**naturopathy** /ˌnetʃəˈrɑpəθɪ; ˌneɪtʃəˈrɒpəθi/ *n* [U] —**naturopathic** /ˌnetʃərəˈpæθɪk; ˌneɪtʃərəˈpæθɪk◂/ *adj*

naught /nɔt; nɔːt/ *n* [U] *old use* nothing【舊】無; 沒有甚麼東西; 不存在: *He cared naught for public opinion.* 他一點也不在乎公眾輿論。| **come to naught** (=fail) 失敗 *All their plans came to naught.* 他們的所有計劃都泡了湯。

naugh·ty /ˈnɔtɪ; ˈnɔːti/ *adj* **1** a naughty child behaves badly and is rude and disobedient〔孩子〕淘氣的, 頑皮的; 沒有規矩的; 不聽話的: *You're a very naughty boy! Look what you've done!* 你真是個淘氣鬼! 瞧你幹了些甚麼! **2** *especially BrE* used jokingly about an adult when you are pretending to disapprove of their behaviour【尤英】〔開玩笑地説成年人〕不聽話的; 不守規矩的: **it's naughty of sb to do sth** *spoken*【口】*It was a bit naughty of me to stay out so late last night.* 我昨天晚上很晚才回家, 真是有點不聽話。**3 naughty jokes/magazines/pictures etc** *BrE* naughty jokes etc deal with sex in a rude but not very serious way【英】黃色笑話/雜誌/圖片等 —**naughtily** *adv* —**naughtiness** *n* [U]

nau·se·a /ˈnɔʒə; ˈnɔːziə/ *n* [U] *formal* the feeling that you have when you think you are going to VOMIT (=bring food up from your stomach through your mouth)【正式】噁心; 嘔吐感: *Early pregnancy is often accompanied by nausea.* 懷孕早期常帶有噁心。—see also 另見 AD NAUSEAM

nau·se·ate /ˈnɔʒɪˌet; ˈnɔːzieɪt/ *v* [T] to make someone feel NAUSEA 使噁心, 使作嘔; 使厭惡: *Even clear fluids were making him feel nauseated.* 連清水都會使他感到噁心。| *It nauseates me the way Keith bullies you.* 基思欺侮你的樣子讓我覺得噁心。

nau·se·a·ting /ˈnɔʒɪˌetɪŋ; ˈnɔːzieɪtɪŋ/ *adj* **1** making you feel NAUSEA 令人噁心的, 令人作嘔的: *In summer the smell of the farmyard was nauseating.* 夏天農場裡的氣味讓人作嘔。**2** making you feel angry 使人生氣的: *It's nauseating how the coach always picks his favorites.* 教練總是挑他最喜歡的隊員上場, 真讓人生氣。—compare 比較 DISGUSTING —**nauseatingly** *adv*

nau·se·ous /ˈnɔʒəs; ˈnɔːziəs/ *adj* **1** *especially AmE* feeling nausea【尤美】感到噁心的, 有嘔吐感的: *I awoke from my drunken stupor feeling nauseous.* 我醉酒後醒來, 感到很噁心。**2** *formal* making you feel NAUSEA【正式】令人噁心的, 令人作嘔的: *the nauseous stench of the durian fruit* 榴槤果令人噁心的氣味 —**nauseously** *adv* —**nauseousness** *n* [U]

nau·ti·cal /ˈnɔtɪkḷ; ˈnɔːtɪkəl/ *adj* connected with ships or sailing 船舶的; 航海的 —**nautically** /-klɪ; -kli/ *adv*

nautical mile /ˌ··· ˈ·/ *n* [C] a measure of distance used at sea, equal to 1,853 metres; SEA MILE 海里〔相當於1,853米〕—see table on page C4 參見C4頁附錄

na·val /ˈnevḷ; ˈneɪvəl/ *adj* [only before noun 僅用於名詞前] connected with or used by the navy 海軍的: *a naval officer* 海軍軍官 | *naval battles* 海戰

nave /nev; neɪv/ *n* [C] the long central part of a church〔教堂的〕中殿

na·vel /ˈnevḷ; ˈneɪvəl/ *n* [C] **1** the small hollow or raised place in the middle of your stomach 肚臍, 臍 —see picture at 參見 BODY 圖 **2 gaze at/contemplate your navel** *humorous* to spend too much time thinking about your own problems【幽默】過多地考慮自己的問題

nav·i·ga·ble /ˈnævəgəbḷ; ˈnævɪgəbəl/ *adj* a river, lake etc that is navigable is deep and wide enough for ships to travel on〔水域〕可通航的, 可航行的: *The St Lawrence River is navigable from the Great Lakes to the Atlantic.* 聖勞倫斯河自五大湖區至大西洋的整段河道都可通航。—**navigability** /ˌnævəgəˈbɪlətɪ; ˌnævɪgəˈbɪlɪti/ *n* [U]

nav·i·gate /ˈnævəˌget; ˈnævɪgeɪt/ *v* **1** [I,T] to find the way to a place, especially by using maps〔尤指用地圖〕導航; (為…) 指引方向: *I'll drive, you take the map and navigate.* 我來開車, 你拿着地圖指方向。| **navigate by the stars/sun** *Early explorers used to navigate by the stars.* 早期的探險家往往靠星辰確定方向。**2** [T] to sail all the way across or along an area of water〔海上〕航行

nav·i·ga·tion /ˌnævəˈgeʃən; ˌnævɪˈgeɪʃən/ *n* [U] **1** the science of planning the way along which you travel from one place to another 航行學; 航海術; 航空術: *compasses and other instruments of navigation* 羅盤等導航儀器 **2** the act of sailing a ship or flying a plane along a particular line of travel 航行; 航海; 航空: *Navigation becomes more difficult further up the river.* 越往河上游, 航行就越困難。**3** the movement of ships or aircraft〔船或飛機的〕航行: *open to navigation* 可通航 —**navigational** *adj*

nav·i·ga·tor /ˈnævəˌgetɚ; ˈnævɪgeɪtə/ *n* [C] an officer on a ship or aircraft who plans the way along which it is travelling〔船或飛機的〕領航員

nav·vy /ˈnævɪ; ˈnævi/ *n* [C] *BrE* an unskilled worker who does tiring physical work, such as building roads【英】〔從事築路等的〕幹粗活的工人

na·vy /ˈnevɪ; ˈneɪvi/ *n* [C] **1** the part of a country's military forces that is organized for fighting a war at sea 海軍: *My father joined the Navy during the war.* 戰時我父親參加了海軍。**2** the war ships belonging to a country〔某國的〕軍艦, 艦隊: *demands for a larger navy* 擴大艦隊規模的要求 S3

navy blue /ˌ·· ˈ·◂/ also 又作 **navy** *adj* very dark blue 深藍色的, 藏青色的 —**navy blue** *n* [U] —see picture on page A5 參見A5頁圖

nay[1] /ne; neɪ/ *adv* **1** [sentence adverb 句子副詞] *literary* used when you are adding something to emphasize what you have just said【文】不但如此, 而且: *a bright – nay, a blinding light* 不只明亮, 還令人目炫的一道光 **2** *old use or dialect* used to say no【舊或方言】不, 否: *Nay, lad. It's not that bad.* 不, 小伙子。沒有那麼糟。

nay[2] *n* [C] a vote against or someone who votes against an idea, plan, etc 反對票; 投反對票者 —opposite 反義詞 AYE[1] (1), YEA[2]

Na·zi /ˈnɑtsɪ; ˈnɑːtsi/ *n plural* **Nazis** [C] **1** a member of the National Socialist Party of Adolf Hitler which controlled Germany from 1933 to 1945〔1933年到1945年德國的〕納粹黨員, 納粹分子 **2** someone who likes to use their authority in an unreasonably strict way 獨斷專橫者: *Some of the traffic wardens are real Nazis.* 有些交通管理員真霸道。—**Nazi** *adj* —**Nazism** *n* [U]

NB, nb *Latin* nota bene; used to make a reader pay attention to an important piece of information【拉丁】注意, 留心〔用於提醒讀者留意某個重要信息〕

NBA /ˌɛn bi ˈe; ˌen biː ˈeɪ/ *n* [singular] National Basketball Association; the American organization which arranges BASKETBALL games〔美國〕全國籃球協會

NBC /ˌɛn bi ˈsi; ˌen biː ˈsiː/ *n* [U] National Broadcasting Company; one of three main American television companies〔美國〕全國廣播公司

NCO /ˌɛn si ˈo; ˌen siː ˈəʊ/ *n* [C] noncommissioned officer; a soldier such as a CORPORAL or SERGEANT 軍士

-nd /nd; nd/ *suffix* forms written ORDINAL numbers with 2 構成以2結尾的序數詞: *the 2nd* (=second) *of March* 3月2日 | *her 22nd birthday* 她的22歲生日

NE the written abbreviation of 縮寫= northeast or northeastern 東北; 東北的: *NE Scotland* 蘇格蘭東北部

ne·an·der·thal /nɪˈændɚˌtɑl; niˈændəˌtɑːl/ *n* [C] **1** *humorous* a big, ugly, stupid man【幽默】體形巨大、相貌醜陋的蠢人, 傻大粗 **2** someone who opposes all change without even thinking about it 反對變革的人; 守舊的

人, 思想保守的人 **3** a Neanderthal man 尼安德特人 —**Neanderthal** *adj*

Neanderthal man /ˈ···· ·/ *n* an early type of human being who lived in Europe during the STONE AGE 尼安德特人〔石器時代住在歐洲的原始人〕

nea·pol·i·tan /ˌniəˋpɑlətn̩; nɪəˈpɒlɪ̵tən/ *adj* neapolitan ICE CREAM has layers of different colours and tastes〔冰淇淋〕各層味道、顏色不同的

neap tide /ˋnip taɪd; ˈniːp taɪd/ *n* [C] a very small rise and fall of the level of the sea at the times of the first and third quarters of the moon〔上弦或下弦時的〕小潮

near¹ /nɪr; nɪə/ *adv, prep* **1** only a short distance from a person or thing 接近（地）, 靠近（地）; 離…很近（地）: *Bob was standing near enough to hear what they said.* 鮑勃站得很近, 能聽到他們的談話。| *Why don't you move your chair nearer mine?* 你為甚麼不把你的椅子挪得離我近一些呢? | **near to** *Don't sit too near to the screen.* 別坐得離屏幕太近。| **go/come/get etc near** (=to move near someone or something) 靠近/接近 *Don't come any nearer – I have a gun.* 別再過來, 我手裡有槍。| *As the car drew nearer I realized the man was a stranger.* 車子駛近的時候, 我發現那是個陌生人。**2 come/be near (to) sth** to almost do something or almost be in a particular state 差不多, 幾乎: *She had what came near to a perfect singing voice.* 她的歌喉幾近完美。| **come/be near (to) tears/death etc** *Sarah was trembling, and near to tears.* 莎拉全身發抖, 都快哭出來了。| **come/be near to doing sth** *especially BrE*【尤英】*Samuel came very near to rejecting the award before accepting graciously.* 塞繆爾差點拒絕接受獎項, 但最後還是很有風度地接受了。**3** soon before a particular time or event 接近〔某時間或事件〕: *Near the day of the wedding she started to have second thoughts.* 臨近婚禮之日時, 她又開始改變想法了。| *Remind me nearer the time of the meeting.* 快到開會的時候提醒我一下。| **draw near** *As my birthday drew near, I began to dread being fifty.* 臨近生日的時候, 我開始害怕自己五十歲了。**4 near perfect/impossible etc** almost perfect etc 近乎完美/不可能等: *The dye left a near transparent liquid on the surface of her skin.* 染劑在她的皮膚表面留下了一層幾乎透明的液體。**5 (as) near as dammit** *BrE spoken* used to say that something is very nearly true or correct【英口】幾乎一點不差: *The repairs will cost us £1,000, as near as dammit.* 修理費用將高達 1,000 英鎊。

near² *adj* **1** only a short distance away from someone or something〔距離〕近的, 接近的: *It's a beautiful house but it's 20 miles away from the nearest town.* 這是一幢漂亮的房子, 但離最近的城鎮也有 20 英里。| *We can meet at the pub or in the restaurant, whichever's nearer for you.* 我們可以在酒吧或餐館見面, 看哪個離你近一些。| **[+to]** *Of course I've heard of the Littleton sports centre – it's near to my college.* 我當然聽說過利特爾頓體育中心, 那兒離我就讀的大學不遠。**2** if something is near something else, it is similar to it 相似的, 近似的, 接近的: **[+to]** *It seems that his diaries are as near to the truth as we'll ever get.* 看來他的日記和我們掌握的事實真相很接近。| *Hyde Park is the nearest thing we have to the countryside round here.* 海德公園是附近最具鄉村風情的地方了。| *It may not be an exact replica but it's pretty damn near.* 這也許說不上是完美的複製品, 但的確已經十分相似了。**3 a near disaster/collapse etc** almost a disaster, a collapse etc 險些發生的災難/幾乎崩潰等: *The factory has seen a near doubling of its output this year alone.* 該廠今年的產量幾乎增長了一倍。**4 be a near thing a)** if something you succeed in doing is a near thing, you manage to succeed but you nearly failed 險勝: *They won the championship, but it was a near thing.* 他們得了冠軍, 但是險些輸掉。**b)** used to say that you just managed to avoid a dangerous or unpleasant situation 好險〔表示剛好躲過危險或不愉快的情況〕: *That was a near thing – that truck was heading straight for us.* 剛才好險啊, 那輛卡車朝着我們直衝過來。**5 be a near miss** if a bomb, shot etc is a near miss it seemed as if it would hit something but did not〔炸彈、子彈等〕幾乎打中 **6 in the near future** soon 在不久的將來: *They promised to contact us again some time in the near future.* 他們答應不久將和我們再聯繫。**7 to the nearest £10/hundred etc** an amount to the nearest £10, hundred etc is the number nearest to it that can be divided by £10, a hundred etc 以十英鎊/一百等略算: *Give me the car mileage to the nearest thousand.* 告訴我以千位數略算, 這車行駛了多少英里。**8 a) near relative/relation** a relative who is very closely related to you such as a parent 近親: *You are only allowed time off if the funeral is for a near relative.* 你只能在參加近親葬禮時才允許請假。**b) sb's nearest and dearest** *humorous* someone's family【幽默】某人的家人[親人]; 某人的至愛 **9** [only before a noun, no comparative 僅用於名詞前, 無比較級] **a)** used to describe the side of something that is closest to where you are 離得較近的〔一側〕: *the near bank of the river* 較近的河岸 **b)** used when talking about the wheels on a vehicle to mean the one on the left side〔車輛〕左側的: *the near wheel of a car* 汽車的左輪 —opposite 反義詞 OFF³ (3) —see also 另見 NEARLY, **nowhere near** (NOWHERE (4)) —**nearness** *n* [U]

near³ *v* **1** [T] to come closer to a particular place, time, or state; APPROACH¹ 靠近, 接近: *Work is nearing completion.* 工作快完成了。| *The ship was nearing harbour.* 船正在向港口靠近。**2** [I] if a time nears, it gets closer and will come soon〔時間〕臨近: *He got more and more nervous as the day of his departure neared.* 隨着自己離開的日子一天天臨近, 他變得越來越緊張。

near·by /ˋnɪrˋbaɪ; ˈnɪəbaɪ/ *adj* [only before noun 僅用於名詞前] not far away 附近的: *Lucy was staying in the nearby town of Hamilton.* 露西當時住在附近的漢密爾頓鎮。—**nearby** /nɪrˋbaɪ; nɪəˈbaɪ/ *adv*: *Dan found work on one of the farms nearby.* 丹恩在附近的一個農場裡找到了工作。

Near East /ˌ· ˈ·/ *n* **the Near East** the Middle East 近東〔即中東〕—**Near Eastern** *adj*: *Ancient Near Eastern literature* 古代近東文學

near·ly /ˋnɪrlɪ; ˈnɪəli/ *adv* **1** *especially BrE* almost, but not quite or not completely【尤英】幾乎, 差不多, 將近: *It took nearly two hours to get here.* 花了將近兩個小時才到這裡。| *Michelle's nearly twenty.* 米歇爾快二十歲了。| *Is the job nearly finished?* 這工作快幹完了嗎? | *He's nearly always right.* 他幾乎永遠都是對的。| *Louise is nearly as tall as her mother.* 路伊絲幾乎和她母親一樣高。| **very nearly** *He very nearly died.* 他幾乎死了。| **not nearly enough** (=much less than enough) 遠遠不夠 *I can earn some money, but not nearly enough to live on.* 我能賺一點錢, 但還遠遠不夠養活我自己。—see 見 ALMOST (USAGE) **2** *old use* closely【舊】密切地: *a problem which concerns me nearly* 一個和我密切相關的問題

near·side /ˋnɪrˌsaɪd; ˈnɪəsaɪd/ *adj* [only before noun 僅用於名詞前] *BrE* on the side of a vehicle that is nearest the edge of the road【英】〔車輛〕左側的, 左邊的: *a scratch on the nearside front wing of the car* 汽車左前側的一道劃痕 —**nearside** *n* [singular] —opposite 反義詞 OFFSIDE²

near·sight·ed /ˋnɪrˋsaɪtɪd; ˌnɪəˈsaɪtɪ̵d◂/ *adj* unable to see things clearly unless they are close to you 近視的; SHORTSIGHTED *BrE*【英】—**nearsightedly** *adv* —**nearsightedness** *n* [U]

neat /nit; niːt/ *adj* **1** tidy and carefully arranged 整齊的; 整潔的: *neat handwriting* 工整的筆跡 | *She wears her hair short and neat.* 她的頭髮剪得又短又齊。| *He folded his clothes in a neat pile on the chair.* 他把自己的衣服在椅子上摺成了整齊的一疊。| **neat and tidy** *Can't you keep your bedroom neat and tidy?* 難道你不能把臥室保持得整潔一點嗎? **2** *AmE spoken* very nice or pleasant

【美口】很好的, 美妙的: *The party was really neat – we had a good time.* 那晚會美妙極了, 我們玩得很開心。| *I liked working for him – he was a neat guy.* 我喜歡為他工作, 他是個好人。**3** simple and effective 簡潔的, 簡明的; 巧妙的: *a neat turn of phrase* 簡潔的措詞 | *There are no neat solutions to this problem.* 這個問題沒有簡捷的解決辦法。**4** neat alcoholic drinks have no ice or water or any other liquid added; STRAIGHT² (12)〔酒〕純的〔不加冰、水或其他酒的〕: *She likes her whisky neat.* 她喜歡喝純威士忌。**5** someone who is neat likes to keep things tidy〔人〕愛整潔的: *The new lodger was fortunately a neat person.* 幸虧新房客是個愛整潔的人。—**neatly** *adv*: *He arranged the books neatly on the shelf.* 他把書整齊地排放在架子上。—**neatness** *n* [U]

neath /niθ; niːθ/ *prep poetic* below【詩】在…之下: *neath the stars* 在星空下

neb·u·la /`nɛbjələ; 'nebjɪ̈lə/ *n* [C] **1** a mass of gas and dust among the stars, often appearing as a bright cloud in the sky at night 星雲 **2** a GALAXY (=mass of stars) which has this appearance 星雲狀的星系 —**nebular** *adj*

neb·u·lous /`nɛbjələs; 'nebjɪ̈ləs/ *adj formal*【正式】**1** an idea that is nebulous is not at all clear or exact; VAGUE 模糊不清的, 含糊的: *The reasons he gave were rather nebulous.* 他提出的理由很含糊。**2** a shape that is nebulous is misty and has no definite edges 朦朧的, 輪廓不清的: *a nebulous ghostly figure* 鬼影般朦朧的身影 —**nebulously** *adv* —**nebulousness** *n* [U]

1 2 **ne·ces·sar·i·ly** /`nɛsə,sɛrəlɪ; 'nesɪ̈sərɪ̈li/ *adv* **1 not necessarily** possibly but not certainly 不一定: *Expensive restaurants are not necessarily the best.* 昂貴的餐館不一定是最好的。| *"We'll need to employ another engineer, then." "Not necessarily."* "那麼我們需要再雇用一名工程師。" "不一定。" | *It does not necessarily follow that a larger workforce will be more productive.* 人越多不一定生產效率就越高。**2** in a way that cannot be different or be avoided; INEVITABLY 必然, 必定: *Testing criteria are necessarily subjective.* 測試標準必定是主觀的。

1 1 **ne·ces·sa·ry¹** /`nɛsə,sɛrɪ; 'nesɪ̈səri/ *adj* **1** something that is necessary is what you need to have or need to do; ESSENTIAL 必要的, 必需的, 必不可少的: *I'll leave it to you to make all the necessary arrangements.* 所有必要的準備工作我就讓你來負責了。| **[+for]** *Food is necessary for life.* 食物是生命所必需的。| **it is necessary (for sb) to do sth** *It's not necessary to wear a tie.* 不一定要打領帶。| *The doctor says it may be necessary for me to have an operation.* 醫生說也許我有必要做手術。| **make it necessary (for sb) to do sth** *The heavy rain made it necessary to close several roads.* 大雨使得有必要關閉幾條道路。| **is it really necessary to do sth?** *spoken* (=used to complain about something that someone is doing)【口】真的必須做某事嗎?〔表示抱怨〕*Is it really necessary to make all that noise!* 真有必要那麼吵鬧嗎? | **if necessary** (=if it is necessary) 如果必要 *I'll stay up all night, if necessary, to get it finished.* 如果必要, 我會熬個通宵把這事做完。| **hardly necessary** (=almost not necessary) 幾乎沒有必要 *Taking notes was hardly necessary – she had a brilliant memory.* 她記憶力很好, 幾乎沒有必要記筆記。**2 necessary connection/consequence etc** a connection, result etc that must exist 必然的聯繫/結果等: *the necessary connection between wage rates and the price of food* 工資水平和食物價格之間的必然聯繫 **3 a necessary evil** something bad or unpleasant that you have to accept in order to achieve what you want〔為實現目的不得不接受的〕不得已的事; 難免的壞事: *Mr Hurst regarded work as a necessary evil.* 赫斯特先生把工作看成一件不得已的事情。

necessary² *n* **1 the necessaries** things that you need, such as food or money, especially for a journey〔尤指旅行的〕必需品 **2 do the necessary** *spoken* to do what is necessary【口】做必要的事: *Leave it to me – I'll do the necessary.* 交給我吧, 我會把該辦的事都辦好的。

ne·ces·si·tate /nə`sɛsə,tet; nɪ̈'sesɪ̈teɪt/ *v* [T] *formal* to make it necessary for you to do something【正式】使成為必需; 需要: *Lack of money necessitated a change of plan.* 由於缺乏資金, 只能改變計劃。| **necessitate doing sth** *This change would necessitate starting all over again.* 這樣一變動, 就得從頭幹起。

ne·ces·si·tous /nə`sɛsətəs; nə'sesɪ̈təs/ *adj* a word meaning 'poor' used when people are trying to sound important or want to avoid saying 'poor' directly〔誇張或委婉用語〕貧困的, 貧窮的 —**necessitously** *adv*

ne·ces·si·ty /nə`sɛsətɪ; nɪ̈'sesɪ̈ti/ *n* **1** [C] something that you need to have 必需品: *A telephone is an absolute necessity for this job.* 電話是做這項工作絕對必需的。| *We went to buy the basic necessities for our stay.* 我們去購買了逗留期間用的基本必需品。| **bare necessities** (=basic things that you must have) 基本必需品 *Food and clothing are the bare necessities of life.* 食物和衣服是生活的基本必需品。—compare 比較 LUXURY (2) **2** [U] the fact of something being necessary 必要; 需要: **[+for]** *the necessity for decent, affordable housing* 對舒適而經濟的住屋的需要 | **necessity of doing sth** *Martell Bakeries was faced with the necessity of firing many of its employees.* 馬特爾麵包房不得不大規模裁員。| **necessity to do sth** *There's no necessity to buy tickets in advance.* 沒有必要提前買票。**3** [C] something that must happen, even if it is unpleasant or undesirable 無奈的事物; 不好卻必要的東西: *Taxes are a regrettable necessity.* 稅收是令人遺憾而又必要的東西。| *The treaty is considered a diplomatic necessity.* 該條約被認為是外交上的必要手段。**4** [U] the condition of urgently needing money or food 貧窮, 窘迫: *He was forced by necessity to steal a loaf of bread.* 他迫於貧困偷了一條麵包。| **dire necessity** (=great need) 極為需要 **5 of necessity** used when something happens in a particular way because that is the only possible way it can happen 勢必, 必定: *The summary of his findings is, of necessity, very brief.* 他研究成果的總結必定很簡短。**6 necessity is the mother of invention** used to say that if someone really needs to do something they will find a way of doing it 需要乃發明之母

neck¹ /nɛk; nek/ *n* 2 2

1 ►**PART OF THE BODY** 人體部位◄ [C] the part of your body that joins your head to your shoulders 頸, 脖子: *She wore a string of pearls around her neck.* 她脖子上戴了一串珍珠。—see picture at 參見 HEAD¹ 圖

2 ►**CLOTHING** 衣服◄ [C] the part of a piece of clothing that goes around your neck 衣領, 領口: *the neck of the shirt* 襯衫的領子 | *The colour's all right, but the neck's a bit low.* 顏色還不錯, 只是領口低了點。—see also 另見 **crew neck, polo neck, scoop neck, turtleneck, V-neck** —see picture on page A17 參見A17頁圖

3 ►**BOTTLE** 瓶子◄ [C] the narrow part of a bottle 瓶頸

4 be up to your neck in to be in a difficult situation, or to be very busy doing something 深深陷入〔困境中〕; 忙於〔做某事〕: *Jim's always up to his neck in debt.* 吉姆總是債台高築。| *I've been up to my neck in paperwork all week.* 我整個星期都在處理文件, 忙得不可開交。

5 breathe down sb's neck to watch what someone is doing very carefully, in a way that makes them nervous or annoyed 密切監視某人: *How can I concentrate with you breathing down my neck all the time?* 你總是盯着我, 我怎能集中精神?

6 V-necked/open-necked etc also 又作 **V-neck/open-neck etc** if a piece of clothing is V-necked etc, it has that type of neck V字領/開領等的: *a navy V-necked sweater* 深藍色的V形領套頭毛衣

7 I'll break/wring your neck *spoken* used to tell someone that you are so angry with them you feel like hurting them【口】我會扭斷你的脖子〔表示生氣〕

N

8 (hanging) around your neck if a problem or difficult situation is hanging around your neck, you are responsible for it, and this makes you worry〔問題或困難〕纏着令人煩惱

9 get it in the neck *BrE spoken* to be severely punished【英口】受到嚴懲: *You'll really get it in the neck if you lose that watch!* 你要是把錶丟了, 就會受到嚴厲的懲罰!

10 ►MEAT 肉◄ [U] the neck of an animal, used as food〔動物的〕頸肉: *neck of lamb* 羊頸肉

11 neck and neck *informal* if two things are neck and neck in a competition or race, they both have an equal chance of winning【非正式】〔在比賽中〕不相上下; 並駕齊驅

neck and neck 並駕齊驅

12 in this neck of the woods *informal* in this area or part of the country【非正式】在這一帶, 在這地區: *What are you doing in this neck of the woods?* 你在這一帶幹甚麼?

13 by a neck *informal* if a race is won by a neck, the winner is only a very short distance in front【非正式】〔比賽中〕以些微之差〔獲勝〕: *Our horse won by a neck.* 我們的馬以一頸之差獲勝。—see also 另見 **a pain in the neck** (PAIN¹ (4)), **risk your neck** (RISK² (1)), **save sb's skin/neck/bacon etc** (SAVE¹ (10)), **stick your neck out** (STICK¹)

14 ►LAND 土地◄ a narrow piece of land that comes out of a wider part 狹長地帶

neck² *v* [I] *informal* if two people neck, they kiss for a long time in a sexual way【非正式】摟脖子深吻, 擁吻 —**necking** *n* [U]

neck·band /ˈnɛkˌbænd; ˈnekbænd/ *n* [C] a narrow piece of material around the neck of a piece of clothing〔衣服上的〕領圈: *a velvet neckband* 絲絨領圈

neck·er·chief /ˈnɛkɚtʃɪf; ˈnekətʃiːf/ *n* [C] a square piece of cloth that is folded and worn tied around the neck 圍巾, 領巾

neck·lace /ˈnɛklɪs; ˈnek-lɪ̈s/ *n* [C] a string of jewels, BEADs etc or a thin gold or silver chain 項鏈, 頸鏈: *a diamond necklace* 鑽石項鏈 | *a pearl necklace* 珍珠項鏈 —see picture at 參見 JEWELLERY 圖

neck·let /ˈnɛklɪt; ˈnek-lɪ̈t/ *n* [C] a short necklace 短項鏈, 短頸鏈

neck·line /ˈnɛkˌlaɪn; ˈnek-laɪn/ *n* [C usually singular 一般用單數] the shape made by the upper edge of a piece of woman's clothing around or below the neck〔女裝的〕領口: *a flattering scoop neckline* 使人顯得更漂亮的湯匙領 | **low/plunging neckline** (=leaving part of the chest uncovered) 低開口領, 低胸 *Her evening gown had a plunging neckline.* 她的晚禮服領口開得很低。

neck·tie /ˈnɛkˌtaɪ; ˈnektaɪ/ *n* [C] *AmE formal* a man's TIE【美, 正式】領帶

nec·ro·man·cy /ˈnɛkrəˌmænsɪ; ˈnekrəmænsi/ *n* [U] **1** magic, especially evil magic 魔法;〔尤指〕妖術 **2** *literary* the practice of claiming to talk with the dead【文】召亡魂問卜的巫術 —**necromancer** *n* [C]

nec·ro·phil·i·a /ˌnɛkroˈfɪlɪə; ˌnekrəʊˈfɪliə/ *n* [U] sexual interest in dead bodies 戀屍癖

nec·tar /ˈnɛktɚ; ˈnektə/ *n* [U] **1** the sweet liquid that BEEs collect from flowers 花蜜: *The sunbird feeds on nectar.* 太陽鳥以花蜜為食。**2** the drink of the gods, in the stories of ancient Greece〔古希臘神話中〕眾神飲的酒; 瓊漿玉液 **3** thick juice made from certain fruits〔未經沖淡的〕水果原汁: *mango nectar* 芒果汁

nec·ta·rine /ˈnɛktəˌrin; ˈnektəriːn/ *n* [C] a type of fruit like a PEACH that has a smooth skin, or the tree that produces this fruit 蜜桃(樹) —see picture on page A8 參見A8頁圖

née /ne; neɪ/ *adj* a word used after a woman's married name and before the family name that she had when she was born〔已婚婦女〕婚前原名為…的; 娘家姓…的: *Mrs Carol Cook née Williams* 卡羅爾·庫克太太, 娘家姓威廉斯

need¹ /nid; niːd/ *v* [T not in progressive 不用進行式] 1

1 ►MUST 必須◄ to feel that you must have something or must do something; REQUIRE 需要〔做某事〕: **need sth** *That was what I needed – strong, hot coffee.* 那才是我要的——一杯又濃又熱的咖啡。| *I don't need your approval, thank you very much.* 我不需要你的批准, 謝謝! | **need to do sth** *I need to think about this before I make a decision.* 在決定之前我需要想一想。| **need sth for** *He said he needed the information for an article he was writing.* 他說他正在寫的文章需要那些資料。| **need sb to do sth** *We need volunteers to clean up after the performance.* 我們需要志願者在演出結束後打掃衛生。| **need sth badly** *Money was tight and he needed a job badly.* 他手頭很緊, 急需找份工作。—see graph at 參見 REQUIRE 圖表 1

2 to have to do something because you feel you should do it or because you think it is necessary 必須〔做某事〕: **need (to) do sth** *Do you think I need to go to the meeting?* 你認為我必須去開會嗎? | *You need to work harder if you're going to pass those exams.* 如果你想通過那些考試, 你就必須加倍努力。| *Nobody need feel jealous.* 誰也不必妒嫉。| **need not do sth** *BrE*【英】*You needn't worry. I've taken care of it.* 你不必擔心, 我已經把這事處理好了。| **do not need to do sth** *Honestly, you don't need to get changed. You look fine as you are.* 說實話, 你不必換衣服。你現在穿的就不錯。| **need not have done sth** *BrE* (=used when someone does something that was not necessary)【英】本來不必做某事 *Terence has done so little work, he needn't have bothered to come to school today.* 特倫斯幾乎甚麼也沒做, 他今天其實就不用來學校! | **did not need to do sth** *What a beautiful day! I didn't need to bring my umbrella after all.* 天氣真好!我根本不必帶雨傘! | **need sb do sth?** *BrE old-fashioned*【英, 過時】*Need we leave so soon? I'm having a wonderful time.* 我們一定要這麼快就走嗎? 我正玩得開心呢!

3 need cleaning/mending/fixing etc if something needs cleaning or needs to be cleaned, someone should clean it because it is dirty 需要清潔/修補/修理等: *That fence needs fixing.* 那個柵欄需要修理。| **need washing/mending etc** *The children need collecting at 4 o'clock.* 孩子們需要在4點鐘接回。| **need to be washed/to be mended etc** *I think these potatoes need to be cooked a little longer.* 我認為這些馬鈴薯需要多煮一會兒。| **need a wash/a mend etc** *He looked tired and looked like he needed a shave.* 他看起來很疲憊, 好像還需要刮一刮臉。

4 if a job or activity needs a particular quality, you need to have that quality in order to do it well 要求, 需要〔某種素質〕: *A job like nursing needs patience and understanding.* 做護理工作需要有耐心和通情達理。

5 I need hardly say/tell/remind etc used when you think that people should already know what you are going to say 不用我說/告訴/提醒等: *I need hardly remind you that people will judge the school by the way you behave.* 不用我說你也知道, 人們會根據你的表現對學校作出判斷。

6 need you ask/need I ask *spoken* used to say that someone already knows what they are asking about【口】這還用問: *"Who did it?" "Need you ask? It was Joe, of course."* "這是誰幹的?" "那還用問? 當然是喬。"

7 who needs it? *spoken* used to say you are not interested in something【口】才沒人想要呢?: *To hell with enlightenment, who needs it?* 去他的開導, 才沒有人需要呢!

This graph shows how common different grammar patterns of the verb **need** are. 本圖表所示為動詞 need 構成的不同語法模式的使用頻率。

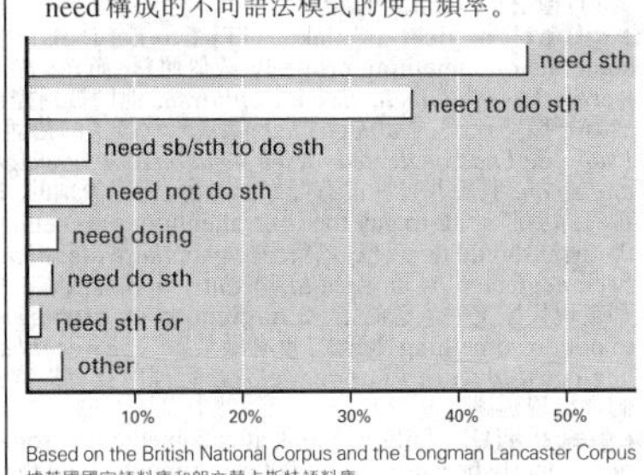

Based on the British National Corpus and the Longman Lancaster Corpus
據英國國家語料庫和朗文蘭卡斯特語料庫

1 1 **need²** *n*
1 ▶WHEN STH IS NECESSARY 需要某事物時◀ [singular] a situation in which something is necessary, especially something that is not happening yet or is not yet available 需要, 需求: **[+for]** *the need for stricter safety regulations* 對更嚴格安全條例的需要 | *There's a growing need for new housing in many rural areas.* 許多農村地區對新住屋的需求不斷增長。| **the need to do sth** *We fully recognize the need to improve communications.* 我們充分意識到改善溝通的需要。| *Don't you ever feel the need to take a vacation?* 你難道從未想過要休假嗎? | **as the need arises** (=whenever it is necessary) 有必要時 *We draw money from the account as the need arises.* 必要時我們從賬戶上提款。| **if need be** (=if it is necessary) 如果需要的話 *I'll work all night if need be.* 如果需要, 我將通宵工作。
2 there's no need (for sb) to do sth a) used to say that someone does not have to do something〔某人〕不必做某事: *There's no need for you to come if you don't want to.* 如果你不想來, 就不必來了。**b)** *spoken* used to tell someone to stop doing something【口】別做某事了: *There's no need to shout; I'm not deaf!* 不用大聲喊, 我不是聾子!
3 be in need of a) to need to be cleaned, repaired, or given attention in some way 需要〔清潔、修理或照料〕: *The whole house is in need of decorating.* 整座房子都需要裝修。**b)** to need help, advice, money etc, because you are in a difficult situation 需要〔幫助、建議、金錢等〕: *I felt lonely and in need of some companionship.* 我覺得孤獨, 需要有人作伴。| **be in dire need of** (=need something urgently) 急需... *Many of the refugees are in dire need of medical treatment.* 許多難民急需醫治。
4 have no need of to not need something 不需要: *Japan has its own space technology and has no need of American help.* 日本擁有自己的太空技術, 不需要美國的幫助。
5 ▶WHAT YOU NEED 所需要的◀ [C usually plural 一般用複數] what someone needs to have in order to live a normal healthy comfortable life〔生活上的〕需求, 需要的東西: **sb's needs** *We must look after the needs of the elderly.* 我們必須照顧老年人的需要。| **meet/answer/fill a need** (=provide something that people want or need) 滿足需求 *meeting the educational needs of every child* 滿足每個兒童的教育需求 | **your every need** *a service that caters for your every need* 滿足你各種需求的服務
6 ▶LACK OF MONEY 缺錢◀ [U] the state of not having enough food or money〔食物或金錢的〕短缺; 困窘: *cases of severe need in the inner cities* 舊城區中出現的嚴重食物短缺現象 | **in need** (=not having enough food or money) 缺〔食物或錢〕 *Our aim is to provide adequate food for those families in need.* 我們的目標是為有困難的家庭提供足夠的食物。
7 in your hour of need when you are in trouble 處於困境時, 患難時: *a friend you can turn to in your hour of need* 患難時會向你伸出援手的朋友

need·ful /ˈnidfəl; ˈniːdfəl/ *adj formal* necessary【正式】必要的, 需要的: *needful expenditure* 必要的開支 — **needfully** *adv*

needles 針

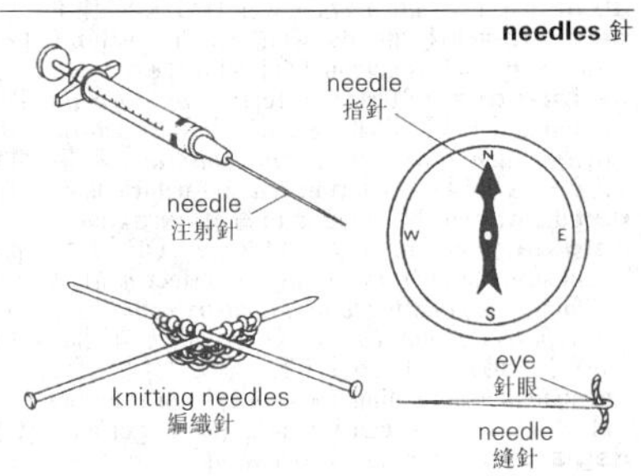

nee·dle¹ /ˈnidl; ˈniːdl/ *n* [C]
1 ▶SEWING 縫紉◀ **a)** a small thin piece of steel, with a point at one end and a hole in the other, used for sewing 縫針: *a needle and thread* 穿了線的針 **b)** a KNITTING NEEDLE 編織針
2 ▶DRUGS 藥◀ a very thin, pointed steel tube at the end of a SYRINGE, which is pushed into your skin to put a drug or medicine into your body or to take out blood 注射針
3 ▶POINTING 指示◀ a long thin piece of metal on a scientific instrument, that moves backwards and forwards and points to numbers or directions〔儀器上的〕指針
4 ▶FROM A TREE 樹上的◀ a small needle-shaped leaf, especially from a PINE tree〔尤指松樹的〕針葉: *pine needles* 松樹的針葉
5 ▶FOR PLAYING RECORDS 播放唱片用◀ the very small, pointed part in a RECORD PLAYER that picks up sound from the records; STYLUS (1) 唱針
6 like looking for a needle in a haystack *informal* used to say that something is almost impossible to find【非正式】如同海底撈針
7 a needle match *BrE* a game in which both teams are determined to win because they do not like each other【英】充滿火藥味的比賽

needle² *v* [T] *informal* to deliberately annoy someone by continuously making unkind remarks or stupid jokes【非正式】〔用話〕刺激; 激怒: *She's always needling me about my accent.* 她老是嘲笑我的口音。

nee·dle·point /ˈnidl̩ˌpɔɪnt; ˈniːdlpɔɪnt/ *n* [U] pictures made by covering a piece of material with small stitches 刺繡畫; 刺繡品

need·less /ˈnidlɪs; ˈniːdləs/ *adj* **1** needless troubles, suffering, loss etc are unnecessary because they could easily have been avoided 不必要的; 不需要的: *the needless loss of life* 不必要的犧牲 | *needless expense* 不必要的開支 | *a lot of needless worry* 許多不必要的憂慮 **2 needless to say** used when you are telling someone something that they probably know or expect 不用說, 當然: *Needless to say, we'll pay your expenses.* 當然了, 我們會支付你的費用。—**needlessly** *adv*: *Thousands of women die needlessly every year because of poor medical care.* 每年成千上萬的婦女因為醫療條件欠佳而白白死去。

nee·dle·wom·an /ˈnidl̩ˌwʊmən; ˈniːdlˌwʊmən/ *n* [C] a woman who is good at sewing 精於縫紉的婦女; 縫紉女工

nee·dle·work /ˈnidl̩ˌwɝk; ˈniːdlwɜːk/ *n* [U] the activity or art of sewing, or things made by sewing 縫紉; 刺繡; 針線活

N

need·n't /ˋnidnt; ˈniːdnt/ *especially BrE*【尤英】the short form of 縮略式= 'need not': *I needn't have put on this thick coat.* 我原本不必穿上這件厚外套的。

need·y /ˋnidɪ; ˈniːdi/ *adj* **1** having very little food or money 缺食物[錢]的; 貧困的; : *a needy family* 貧窮家庭 **2 the needy** needy people 窮人: *money to help the needy* 用來幫助窮人的錢 —**neediness** *n* [U]

ne'er /nɛr; neə/ *adv poetic* never【詩】永不, 決不

ne'er-do-well /ˋnɛr du ˌwɛl; ˈneə duː ˌwel/ *n* [C] *old use* a lazy useless person【舊】無用的懶人

ne·far·i·ous /nɪˋfɛrɪəs; nɪˈfeəriəs/ *adj formal* evil or criminal【正式】惡毒的, 邪惡的; 罪惡的: *nefarious activities such as drug trafficking and fraud* 販毒和詐騙之類的犯罪活動 —**nefariously** *adv* —**nefariousness** *n* [U]

neg the written abbreviation of 縮寫= NEGATIVE

ne·gate /nɪˋget; nɪˈgeɪt/ *v* [T] *formal*【正式】**1** to prevent something from having any effect 取消, 使無效: *Efforts to expand the tourist industry could be negated by reports that the sea is highly polluted.* 有關海洋受到嚴重污染的報道可能會使拓展旅遊業的努力完全白費。**2** to state that something does not exist or is untrue; DENY (1) 否認; 否定 —**negation** /nɪˋgeʃən; nɪˈgeɪʃən/ *n* [U]

2 2 **neg·a·tive¹** /ˋnɛgətɪv; ˈnegətɪv/ *adj*

1 ►EFFECT 效果◄ bad or harmful 不好的, 有害的: *socialist policies that have had a negative effect on the country's economy* 對該國經濟產生不良影響的社會主義政策 | *I think our relationship was very negative and destructive.* 我認為我們的關係很差, 並帶有破壞性。—opposite 反義詞 POSITIVE (7)

2 ►ATTITUDE 態度◄ considering only the bad qualities of a situation, person etc and not the good ones 消極的; 負面的: *Her negative attitude really annoys me.* 她的消極態度令我十分惱火。| *The play was criticized for its violence, and its bleak, negative message.* 該劇因帶有暴力內容並宣揚悲觀消極的思想而受到批評。| **be negative (about)** *Don't be so negative – of course you can win!* 別那麼消極, 你當然能贏! —opposite 反義詞 POSITIVE (2)

3 ►NO/NOT 不◄ a) saying or meaning no 拒絕的; 不; 否定的: *a negative response to our request* 對我們的要求說不 **b)** containing one of the words 'no', 'not', 'nothing', 'never' etc; for example 'cannot' and 'can't' are the negative forms of 'can' 否定式的 —opposite 反義詞 AFFIRMATIVE (1)

4 ►SCIENTIFIC TEST 科學試驗◄ not showing any sign of the chemical or medical condition that was being looked for〔結果〕陰性的: *The pregnancy test was negative.* 妊娠試驗結果為陰性。—opposite 反義詞 POSITIVE (6)

5 ►ELECTRICITY 電◄ *technical* of the type that is carried by ELECTRONS【術語】陰性的, 負的 —opposite 反義詞 POSITIVE (11)

6 ►NUMBER/QUANTITY 數字/數量◄ less than zero 負的: *a negative return to our investment* (=a loss) 我們投資的負收益[虧損]

7 ►BLOOD 血液◄ *technical* not having RHESUS FACTOR in your blood【術語】不含獼[Rh]因子的 —opposite 反義詞 POSITIVE (13) —**negatively** *adv*

negative² *n* [C] **1** a statement or expression that means 'no' 否定; 不: **in the negative** *formal* (=saying 'no')【正式】否定; 不 *He answered in the negative.* 他作出了否定的回答。—opposite 反義詞 AFFIRMATIVE(2) **2** a photographic image that shows dark areas as light and light areas as dark, from which the final picture is printed〔照相〕底片

negative 底片

negative³ *v* [T] *formal*【正式】**1** to refuse to accept a proposal or request 否決; 拒絕 **2** to prove something to be untrue 否定; 否認; 證明…錯誤

negative pole /ˌ... ˈ./ *n* [C] *technical*【術語】**1** the end of a MAGNET which turns naturally to the south〔磁鐵的〕負極 **2** a CATHODE 陰極

ne·glect¹ /nɪˋglɛkt; nɪˈglekt/ *v* [T] **1** to not look after someone or something properly 疏於照料; 疏忽: *They were accused of neglecting the children.* 他們被指控沒有好好照顧孩子。| *a neglected garden* 荒廢了的花園 | *I suppose I had neglected myself – put on a bit of weight and so on.* 我想我可能沒有好好照料自己, 不說別的, 我都有點發胖了。**2** to pay too little attention to something that you should do 忽視; 忽略: *Many of these ideas have been neglected by modern historians.* 這些想法有許多都被現代歷史學家忽略了。**3 neglect to do sth** *formal* to not do something【正式】沒有做某事: *The agent had neglected to warn us about delays.* 代理商沒有提醒我們會出現延誤。

neglect² *n* [U] **1** failure to look after something or someone properly because you do not care enough about them 忽視; 疏忽; 忽略: **[+of]** *Tenants are complaining about the landlord's neglect of the property.* 住戶在抱怨屋主疏忽了物業的維修。**2** the condition of not being properly looked after 被忽略的狀況: *Grass grew on the sidewalk. The whole district had an air of abandonment and neglect.* 人行道上長滿了草。整個地區給人一種荒涼的氣氛。

ne·glect·ful /nɪˋglɛktfəl; nɪˈglektfəl/ *adj formal* not looking after something properly, or not giving it enough attention【正式】疏忽的; 不注意的: **[+of]** *She became more and more neglectful of her responsibilities.* 她越來越無視自己的責任。—**neglectfully** *adv* —**neglectfulness** *n* [U]

neg·li·gee /ˌnɛglɪˋʒe; ˈneglɪʒeɪ/ *n* [C] a very thin, pretty coat, worn over a NIGHTDRESS〔套在睡衣上的〕薄料寬鬆室內服

neg·li·gence /ˋnɛglədʒəns; ˈneglɪdʒəns/ *n* [U] failure to take enough care over something that you are responsible for 疏忽; 玩忽職守: *negligence in carrying out safety procedures* 在執行安全程序中的疏忽 | *The bridge's architect was sued for criminal negligence.* 該橋的建築師被控犯玩忽職守罪。

neg·li·gent /ˋnɛglədʒənt; ˈneglɪdʒənt/ *adj* **1** not taking enough care over something that you are responsible for, with the result that serious mistakes are made 疏忽的, 粗心大意的; 玩忽職守的: *The report stated that Dr Brady had been negligent in not giving the patient a full examination.* 這份報告稱布雷迪醫生粗心大意, 未給病人作全面的身體檢查。**2** a negligent manner or way of dressing is careless, but in a pleasantly relaxed way〔態度、穿着〕不拘泥的; 不計較的; 隨便的: *He dresses with negligent grace.* 他穿着隨便而又自然大方。—**negligently** *adv*

neg·li·gi·ble /ˋnɛglədʒəbl̩; ˈneglɪdʒəbəl/ *adj* too slight or unimportant to have any effect 可以忽視的, 無足輕重的, 微不足道的: *The damage done to his property was negligible.* 對他財產造成的損失十分輕微。—**negligibly** *adv*

ne·go·ti·a·ble /nɪˋgoʃɪəbl̩; nɪˈgəʊʃiəbəl/ *adj* **1** an offer, price, contract etc that is negotiable can be discussed and changed before being agreed on 可談判的, 可協商的: *Part-time barman required. Hours and salary negotiable.* 招聘兼職酒吧男服務員, 工作時間及薪金面議。**2** a road, path etc that is negotiable can be travelled along〔道路〕可通行的: *The road is only negotiable in the dry season.* 這條路只有在旱季才可通行。**3** *technical* a cheque that is negotiable can be exchanged for money【術語】〔支票〕可兌現的

ne·go·ti·ate /nɪˋgoʃɪˌet; nɪˈgəʊʃieɪt/ *v* **1** [I,T] to discuss something in order to reach an agreement, especially in business or politics〔尤指商業或政治〕談判, 協商: **[+with]** *The government refuses to negotiate with terrorists.* 政府拒絕和恐怖分子談判。| **negotiate an**

agreement/contract etc *Union leaders have negotiated an agreement for a shorter working week.* 工會領袖已經商定了一份縮短每週工作時間的協議。| **come to the negotiating table** (=start official discussions) 開始正式談判 *The French have brought new proposals to the negotiating table.* 法國人在談判桌上提出了幾項新提議。**2** [T] to succeed in getting past or over a difficult place on a path, road etc 順利通過: *Eliot negotiated the steep stairs and walked across the courtyard.* 艾略特順利走下陡峭的樓梯, 然後穿過了院子。—**negotiator** *n* [C]

2 2 **ne·go·ti·a·tion** /nɪˌgoʃɪˋeʃən; nɪˌgəʊʃiˈeɪʃən/ *n* [C usually plural 一般用複數, U] official discussions between the representatives of opposing groups, who are trying to reach an agreement, especially in business or politics〔尤指正式的商業或政治〕談判, 協商: *The treaty was a result of long and complex negotiations.* 該條約是漫長而複雜的談判的結果。| *Through negotiation we were able to reach a compromise.* 通過談判我們達成了妥協。| **be open to negotiation** (=can be negotiated and changed) 可以協商(修改) *The terms of the contract are still open to negotiation.* 合同條款仍可協商。| **enter into negotiation** (=start negotiation) 開始[進入]談判

Ne·gress /ˋnigrɪs; ˈniːgrɪ̈s/ *n* [C] *old-fashioned* a word meaning a black woman, which is now usually considered offensive【過時】女黑人〔現在被視為具有冒犯性〕

Ne·gro /ˋnigro; ˈniːgrəʊ/ *plural* **Negroes** *n* [C] *old-fashioned* a word meaning a black person, which is now usually considered offensive【過時】黑人〔現在被視為具有冒犯性〕—**negro** *adj*

USAGE NOTE 用法說明: NEGRO

POLITENESS 禮貌程度

People of African origin (recent or long ago) usually prefer to be called **black**, or in the US, often **African-American**. In the UK the term **Afro-Caribbean** is often used. 非洲血統的人(最近或過去)通常都願意被稱作black, 在美國則喜歡被稱作African-American。在英國, 他們經常被稱作Afro-Caribbean。

Some people think that it is polite to use the word **coloured** but this is now considered to be offensive and unacceptable. 有人覺得用 coloured 一詞較為禮貌, 但現在這種說法被認為是不禮貌和難以接受的。

ne·groid /ˋnigrɔɪd; ˈniːgrɔɪd/ *adj technical* having the physical features of a black person from Africa【術語】帶有黑人生理特徵的

Negro spir·i·tu·al /ˌ·· ˈ····/ *n* [C] a religious song of the type sung by the black people of the US〔美國黑人唱的帶有宗教色彩的〕黑人靈歌

neigh /ne; neɪ/ *v* [I] if a horse neighs, it makes a long loud noise〔馬〕嘶 —**neigh** *n* [C]

2 2 **neigh·bour** *BrE*【英】, **neighbor** *AmE*【美】/ˋnebɚ; ˈneɪbə/ *n* [C] **1** someone who lives next to you or near you 鄰居; 鄰人: **next-door neighbour** (=in the house next to you) 隔壁鄰居 *Our next-door neighbours are so noisy we can hardly sleep some nights.* 我們隔壁的鄰居愛吵鬧, 有時我們晚上幾乎無法睡覺。**2** someone who is sitting or standing next to you 身邊的人: *The teacher saw Bobby passing a note to his neighbour.* 老師看到博比給坐在他旁邊的人遞了一張條子。**3** a country's neighbour is the country next to it 鄰國: *The USA is Canada's only neighbour.* 美國是加拿大唯一的鄰國。

neigh·bour·hood *BrE*【英】, **neighborhood** *AmE*【美】/ˋnebɚˌhʊd; ˈneɪbəhʊd/ *n* [C] **1** a small area of a town, or the people who live there 社區, 住宅小區; 四鄰, 街坊: *You're going to wake up the whole neighbourhood with that noise.* 你發出這麼大的聲音, 會把街坊鄰居全都吵醒的。| *I grew up in a quiet neighborhood of Boston.* 我是在波士頓一個寧靜的住宅區裡長大的。| *a neighbourhood school* 社區裡的學校 **2 in the neighbourhood** in the area around you or around a particular place 在附近地區: *Are there any hotels in the neighbourhood?* 附近有旅館嗎? | **[+of]** *somewhere in the neighbourhood of Chester* 在切斯特附近的某個地方 **3 in the neighbourhood of** either a little more or a little less than a particular number or amount; APPROXIMATELY 大約, 左右: *I'm hoping to buy one for something in the neighbourhood of £500.* 我希望能以500英鎊左右的價錢買下。

neighbourhood watch /ˌ··· ˈ·/ *n* [U] a system for preventing crime by which people living in an area watch each other's houses 居民區防盜制度

neigh·bour·ing *BrE*【英】, **neighboring** *AmE*【美】/ˋnebərɪŋ; ˈneɪbərɪŋ/ *adj* [only before noun 僅用於名詞前] near the place where you are or the place you are talking about; NEARBY 鄰近的, 附近的: **neighbouring country/town/house etc** *The fair attracted hundreds of people from the neighbouring towns and villages.* 集市吸引了鄰近城鎮及村莊的好幾百人前來。

neigh·bour·ly *BrE*【英】, **neighborly** *AmE*【美】/ˋnebɚlɪ; ˈneɪbəli/ *adj* friendly and helpful towards your neighbours 睦鄰的; 友好的, 友善的: *Since we've moved in people have been very neighbourly.* 自我們搬來時起, 這兒的人一直對我們十分友善。—**neighbourliness** *n* [U]

nei·ther[1] /ˋniðɚ; ˈnaɪðə/ *determiner, pron* not one or the other of two people or things 兩者都不(的); 兩者中無一(的): **neither person/thing etc** *Neither parent cares what happens to the child.* 父母都不關心這孩子。| **neither of them/the people etc** *Both players have been warned, but neither of them seem to take it seriously.* 兩名運動員都受到了警告, 但他們好像都不把它當回事。| **neither** *"Would you like tea or coffee?" "Neither, thanks."* "你喝茶還是咖啡?" "都不喝, 謝謝。" | *We went to see a couple of houses, but neither was suitable.* 我們去看了兩所房子, 但都不合適。—compare 比較 EITHER, NONE[1] —see 見 EACH (USAGE) 3

neither[2] *adv* **1** used to add a negative statement to one that has just been mentioned 也不: **neither can I/neither does John etc** *"I have never been to Paris before." "No, neither have we."* "我從未去過巴黎。" "我們也沒去過。" | *Tom didn't believe a word she said and neither did the police.* 湯姆根本不相信她說的話, 警方也不相信。| **me neither/John neither etc** *"I don't like horror movies." "Me neither."* "我不喜歡恐怖電影。" "我也不喜歡。" —see 見 ALSO (USAGE) **2** *formal* used to emphasize or add information to a negative statement【正式】更不: *The authorities were not sympathetic to the students' demands, neither would they tolerate any disruption.* 當局沒有對學生提出的要求表示同情, 他們更不會容忍任何擾亂行為。—compare 比較 ANY, EITHER[4] 2 3

neither[3] *conjunction* **1 neither... nor...** used when two states, facts, actions etc are mentioned and both are not true or not possible 既不…也不…, 不…也不…, …和…都不: *The equipment is neither accurate nor safe.* 這種設備既不精確也不安全。| *She was expressionless, neither laughing nor crying.* 她毫無表情, 既不哭也不笑。**2 be neither here nor there** *especially spoken* used to say that something is not important because it does not affect or change another fact or situation【尤口】一點都不重要: *The fact that she needed the money for her children is neither here nor there, it's still stealing.* 儘管她偷錢是為了孩子, 可是畢竟還是偷竊。

nel·ly, nellie /ˋnɛlɪ; ˈneli/ *n* **not on your nelly** *BrE spoken* used to tell someone humorously or rudely that you are definitely not going to do something【英口】〔幽默或粗魯口氣〕絕不可能, 當然不

nem con /ˌnɛm ˋkɑn; ˌnem ˈkɒn/ *adv Latin law* without any opposition【拉丁, 法律】無異議地; 全體一致地: *The motion was passed nem con.* 該動議得到一致通過。

nem·e·sis /ˋnɛməsɪs; ˈnemɪ̈sɪ̈s/ *n* [singular] *literary* a punishment that is deserved and cannot be avoided【文】天罰; 不可逃避的懲罰; 報應

neo- /nio; niːəʊ/ *prefix* [in nouns and adjectives 構成名

N

詞和形容詞] a recent or later kind of a former system, style etc; new 新的: *neoclassical architecture* (=copying that of ancient Greece and Rome) 新古典主義建築 | *neo-colonialism* (=the control of other countries by large modern states) 新殖民主義

ne·o·clas·sic·al /ˌnioˋklæsɪkḷ; ˌniːəʊˈklæsɪkəl◂/ *adj* neoclassical art copies the style of ancient Greece or Rome 新古典主義的

ne·o·co·lo·ni·al·is·m /ˌniokəˋlonɪəˌlɪzəm; ˌniːəʊkəˈləʊniəlɪzəm/ *n* [U] the economic and political influence which a powerful country uses to control another country 新殖民主義

ne·o·lith·ic /ˌnioˋlɪθɪk; ˌniːəˈlɪθɪk◂/ *adj* connected with the latest period of the STONE AGE about 10,000 years ago, when people began to settle in villages and make stone tools and weapons 新石器時代的: *the discovery of a Neolithic burial mound* 發現一處新石器時代的墳堆

ne·ol·o·gis·m /niˋɑləˌdʒɪzəm; niːˈɒlədʒɪzəm/ *n* [C] a new word or expression, or a word used with a new meaning 新詞; 舊詞新義

ne·on /ˋniɑn; ˈniːɒn/ *n* [U] gas that produces a bright light when electricity is passed through it 氖

neon light /ˌ.. ˈ./ *n* [C] a glass tube filled with neon that produces a bright light when electricity is passed through it 氖光燈; 霓虹燈: *the neon lights of Las Vegas* 拉斯維加斯的霓虹燈

neon sign /ˌ.. ˈ./ *n* [C] an electric advertising sign consisting of neon lights in the form of shapes and words 霓虹燈廣告牌

ne·o·phyte /ˋnioˌfaɪt; ˈniːəfaɪt/ *n* [C] *formal*【正式】**1** someone who has just started to learn a particular skill, art, trade etc 初學者; 新手 **2** a new member of a religious group 新入教者

neph·ew /ˋnɛfju; ˈnefjuː/ *n* [C] the son of your brother or sister, or the son of your husband's or wife's brother or sister 姪子; 外甥: *I've got one nephew. He's two.* 我有一個姪子, 他兩歲了。—see picture at 參見 FAMILY 圖 —compare 比較 NIECE

nep·o·tis·m /ˋnɛpəˌtɪzəm; ˈnepətɪzəm/ *n* [U] the practice of giving the best jobs to members of your family when you are in a position of power 任人唯親; 重用親戚; 裙帶關係 —**nepotistic** *adj*

Nep·tune /ˋnɛptʃun; ˈneptjuːn/ *n* [singular] the PLANET eighth in order from the sun 海王星 —see picture at 參見 SOLAR SYSTEM 圖

nerd /nɝd; nɜːd/ *n* [C] *informal*【非正式】**1** someone who is boring and unfashionable 乏味落伍的人 **2** someone who is extremely interested in computers 電腦迷 —**nerdy** *adj*: *nerdy glasses* 難看落伍的眼鏡

ner·e·id /ˋnɪrɪɪd; ˈnɪəri-ɪd/ *n* [C] a female spirit who lives in the sea according to ancient Greek stories〔古希臘神話中的〕海中仙女

3 3 **nerve¹** /nɝv; nɜːv/ *n*

1 ▶FEELINGS 情緒◀ nerves [plural] the feeling of being nervous because you are worried or a little frightened 焦慮; 緊張: *"What's wrong?" "It's just nerves. He's got his exams tomorrow."* "怎麼了?" "只是緊張。他明天要考試。" | **be a bundle/bag of nerves** *informal* (=be extremely worried or frightened)【非正式】極度焦慮[害怕] *I remember you were a bundle of nerves on your wedding day.* 我記得你在婚禮那天緊張極了。| **calm/steady your nerves** (=stop yourself feeling worried or frightened) 定神/穩住情緒 *Sean drank a large glass of brandy to calm his nerves.* 肖恩喝了一大杯白蘭地, 好讓自己定定神。| **live on your nerves** (=be always worried) 常常感到憂慮 *He's the type of person who lives on his nerves.* 他是那種一天到晚老是擔驚受怕的人。

2 get on sb's nerves *informal* to annoy someone, especially by repeatedly doing something【非正式】煩擾某人, 使人心煩不安: *She's always moaning. It really gets on my nerves.* 她老是在呻吟, 真令我心煩。

3 ▶COURAGE 勇氣◀ [U] the ability to stay calm and confident in a dangerous, difficult or frightening situation 鎮定; 勇氣; 意志力: **have the nerve to do sth** *Not many people have the nerve to stand up and speak in front of a large audience.* 不是很多人都有勇氣站在一大羣人面前講話的。| **it takes a lot of nerve to do sth** *spoken*【口】*It takes a lot of nerve to report a colleague for sexual harassment.* 要舉報同事的性騷擾行為需要很大的勇氣。| **lose your nerve** *He'd have won if he hadn't lost his nerve.* 要不是他失去勇氣, 他就贏了。

4 have a nerve *spoken* to be surprisingly rude without seeming ashamed or embarrassed【口】厚顏無恥; 放肆: *He's got a nerve asking for more money.* 他居然有臉要更多的錢。| **have the nerve to do sth** *She lets me do all the work, and then she has the nerve to criticise my cooking.* 她讓我做所有的工作, 居然還有臉挑剔我的廚藝。| **what a nerve!** *What a bloody nerve! Telling me how to do something I've been doing for years!* 真是不要臉! 居然指手畫腳告訴我怎樣做, 要知道我都幹了多少年了。

5 ▶BODY PART 身體部分◀ [C] one of the thin parts like threads inside your body, along which feelings and messages are sent to the brain 神經: *The dentist was drilling and he hit a nerve. The pain was incredible!* 牙醫在鑽我的牙齒時碰到了我的神經, 真是疼死了! —see picture at 參見 TEETH 圖

6 hit/touch a raw nerve to say something that someone else is very sensitive about especially accidentally〔尤指無心地〕觸到敏感話題; 觸到痛處 —see also 另見 **touch a raw nerve** (RAW¹ (6)), **strain every nerve** (STRAIN² (7))

nerve² *v* **nerve yourself** to force yourself to be brave enough to do something difficult or dangerous 鼓起勇氣: **[+for]** *The parachutist nerved himself for the jump.* 跳傘者鼓足勇氣準備往下跳。

nerve cen·tre *BrE*【英】, **nerve center** *AmE*【美】/ˈ. ˌ../ *n* [C] the place from which a system, activity, organization etc is controlled 中樞, 核心; 控制中心: *The bridge is the ship's nerve center.* 駕駛台是這艘船的控制中心。

nerve gas /ˈ. ./ *n* [U] a poisonous gas that is used in war and that damages your CENTRAL NERVOUS SYSTEM 神經性毒氣〔一種破壞人體中樞神經系統的毒氣, 於戰時使用〕

nerve·less /ˋnɝvlɪs; ˈnɜːvləs/ *adj* nerveless fingers, feet, hands etc have no strength or feeling in them〔手、腳等〕無力的; 神經麻木的

nerve-wrack·ing, nerve-racking /ˈ. ../ *adj* a nerve-wracking situation makes you feel very nervous because it is difficult or frightening 令人心煩的, 使人緊張的: *Your first appearance on stage is always a nerve-wracking experience.* 初次上台總是讓人緊張不安。

3 3 **ner·vous** /ˋnɝvəs; ˈnɜːvəs/ *adj* **1** worried or frightened about something that may happen so that you cannot relax 神經緊張的; 焦慮不安的; 害怕的, 膽怯的: **[+about]** *I was so nervous about my exams that I couldn't sleep.* 考試讓我緊張得睡不着覺。| **[+of]** *Jill's always been a little nervous of dogs.* 吉爾一直有點怕狗。**2** often becoming worried or frightened and easily upset 神經脆弱的, 神經質的: *She's a nervous, sensitive child.* 她是一個神經脆弱而且敏感的孩子。| **nervous wreck** (=someone whose health and confidence have been destroyed by worry, fear etc)〔因焦慮或恐懼〕身心極度受損的人 *This job is turning me into a nervous wreck.* 這份工作快使我神經崩潰了。| **of a nervous disposition** *This film is unsuitable for people of a nervous disposition.* 這部影片不適合性格焦慮的人看。**3 nervous exhaustion/strain etc** a mental condition in which you feel very tired, usually caused by working too hard or by difficult emotional problems 精神極度疲勞/緊張 **4** related to the nerves in your body 神經系統的, 神經方面的: *a nervous disorder* 神經系統紊亂 —**nervously** *adv*: *She smiled nervously.* 她緊張地笑了一

N

笑。—**nervousness** *n* [U]: *Minelli's nervousness showed in his voice.* 米內里的聲音裡透着他的緊張不安。

USAGE NOTE 用法說明: NERVOUS

WORD CHOICE 詞語辨析: **nervous, uneasy, concerned, anxious, worried**

You are **nervous** about something difficult or strange that you are doing, or when you are worried and a little frightened about something that might happen or is going to happen, so that you cannot relax. 當你做一件困難或陌生的事情, 或者對某件可能發生或即將發生的事感到擔心或害怕時, 你會感到 nervous: *Don't drive so fast – you're making me nervous!* 別把車開那麼快, 這使我有些緊張。| *She gets nervous about walking home alone late at night.* 她對深夜獨自一人走回家感到害怕。You are **uneasy** when you are unable to relax because you think but do not know for certain that something bad is happening or is going to happen. 當你猜想有不祥的事正在發生或即將發生而無法放鬆時, 你會感到 uneasy: *When Jody didn't call for the next three days I started to get uneasy.* 在接下來的三天裡喬迪一直沒有來電話, 這使我開始變得不安。

You are **concerned** when there is a problem or when someone has a problem that you wish you could do something about 當出現某個問題, 或某人遇到問題而你想幫助解決時, 你會感到 concerned: *I'm rather concerned about Harvey's health.* 我對哈維的健康感到相當憂慮。**Worried** is stronger. If you are **worried** you are unhappy and cannot stop thinking about a problem or about something bad that might happen. worried 一詞較為強烈。如果你感到 worried, 就說明你不開心, 總是為某個問題或可能發生的不祥之事而擔心: *Martha's very worried about her son's disappearance.* 瑪莎因為兒子失蹤而十分擔心。**Anxious** is stronger still. You are **anxious** when you are very worried and frightened about something that is happening or might happen. anxious 則更為強烈。當你為正在發生或可能發生的某事感到十分擔心和害怕時, 你會感到 anxious: *the little girl's anxious face as she searched the crowds for her mother* 在人羣中尋找母親時小女孩那充滿憂慮的臉。

nervous break·down /ˌ·· ˈ··/ *n* [C] *not technical* a mental illness in which someone becomes extremely anxious and tired and cannot deal with the things they usually do【非術語】精神崩潰

nervous sys·tem /ˈ·· ˌ··/ *n* [C] the parts of your body, including your nerves, brain, and SPINAL CORD, by means of which you feel pain, heat etc and control your movements 神經系統

nerv·y /ˈnɜvɪ; ˈnɜːvi/ *adj* **1** *informal* nervous and easily frightened【非正式】神經質的; 緊張不安的 **2** *AmE informal* brave and confident【美, 非正式】勇敢自信的

-ness /nɪs; nəs/ *suffix* [in nouns 構成名詞] the condition, quality, or degree of being something (…的) 狀態; 性質; 程度: *loudness* 響度 | *sadness* 悲傷 | *warm-heartedness* 熱心 | *the many kindnesses you've done me* 你給我的許多幫助

nest¹ /nɛst; nest/ *n* [C] **1** a hollow place made or chosen by a bird to lay its eggs in and to make its home in 鳥巢, 鳥窩 **2** a place where insects or small animals live 〔昆蟲或小動物的〕窩; 穴: *a field mouse's nest* 田鼠穴 **3 a nest of spies/criminals/vice etc** a place where there are many bad people or evil activities 間諜/罪犯/罪惡等的老巢[溫牀] **4 leave the nest** to leave your parents' home 搬出父母家, 離家獨立 **5 nest of tables/ boxes** a set of tables etc that fit inside one another 〔可依大小套放的〕一套桌子/盒子 —see also 另見 **feather your nest** (FEATHER² (1)), **stir up a hornets' nest** (HORNET (2)), **mare's nest** (MARE (2)), **love nest** (LOVE² (15))

nest² *v* [I] to build or use a nest 築巢; 巢居: *gulls nesting on the cliffs* 在懸崖上築巢的海鷗

nest egg /ˈ· ·/ *n* [C] an amount of money that you have saved 個人儲蓄金, 儲備金

nes·tle /ˈnɛsl; ˈnesəl/ *v* **1** [I always+adv/prep, T always+adv/prep] to move into a comfortable position, pressing your head or body against someone or against something soft (使) 舒適地安頓下來; (使) 偎依, (使) 依靠: **nestle against/beside/by etc** *Sarah lay there peacefully, the child nestling by her side.* 莎拉安靜地躺在那兒, 孩子偎依在她身邊。| **nestle sth against/beside etc** *He nestled his head against her shoulder.* 他把頭靠在她的肩膀上。**2** [I always+adv/prep] to be in a position that seems to be protected by the hills etc around 坐落在〔山間〕: [**+among/between etc**] *several small villages nestling among the mountains* 羣山環抱的幾個小村落

nest·ling /ˈnɛslɪŋ; ˈnestlɪŋ/ *n* [C] a very young bird 雛鳥

net¹ /nɛt; net/ *n* **1** [C,U] a piece of material consisting of strings, threads, or wires woven across each other with regular spaces in between, used, for example, for catching fish, protecting vegetables etc 網: *a fishing net* 魚網 **2 the net a)** a long net used in games such as tennis that the players must hit the ball over 〔網球等的〕球網 —see picture at 參見 TENNIS 圖 **b)** a net forming an enclosure at the back of the GOAL in football, HOCKEY etc 〔足球、曲棍球等的〕球門網: *Cole slammed the ball into the back of the net.* 科爾將球狠狠地踢進網窩。**3** [U] very thin material made from fine threads woven together with very small spaces between 網眼織物; 網紗: *net curtains* 網紗窗簾 **4** [C] a bag made of net on the end of a stick used for catching butterflies (BUTTERFLY (1)) etc 〔捕昆蟲等的〕網〈如捕蝶網〉**5** [C] a communications or computer network 〔通訊、電腦〕網絡 **6 the Net** *technical* the Internet; a system that allows millions of computer users around the world to exchange information【術語】互聯網 —see also 另見 **cast your net wide** (CAST¹ (18)), HAIRNET, SAFETY NET 3

net² *v* **netted, netting** [T] **1** to catch a fish in a net 用網捕〔魚〕: *We netted three fish in under an hour.* 不到一小時我們就網住了三條魚。**2** *especially AmE* to earn a particular amount of money as a profit after tax has been paid【尤美】獲得淨收入, 淨賺: *I was netting around $64,000 a year.* 我每年淨賺約 64,000 美元。**3** *informal* to hit or kick the ball into the net in sport【非正式】擊〔球〕入網; 踢〔球〕入網 **4** to succeed in getting something by using your skill 〔靠技能〕成功獲取: *a company that has netted several large contracts* 成功獲取幾個大合同的公司 2

net³ also 又作 **nett** *BrE*【英】—*adj* [only before noun 僅用於名詞前] **1** a net amount of money is the amount that remains after everything has been taken away from it 〔錢〕淨得的: **net profit** (=profit after tax, rent etc are paid) 純利, 淨利潤 *He took 50% of the net revenue.* 他拿走了淨收入的 50%。—compare 比較 GROSS¹ (1) **2 net weight** the weight of something without its container 淨重: **21b/500g etc net** *jars of coffee weighing 450 grams net* 淨重 450 克的瓶裝咖啡 **3 net result (of)** the final result of something (…的) 最後結果: *The net result of this policy was even worse inflation.* 這項政策的最後結果是更為嚴重的通貨膨脹。

net·ball /ˈnɛtbɔl; ˈnetbɔːl/ *n* [U] a game similar to BASKETBALL played in Britain especially by girls 〔英國女子玩的〕無板籃球

neth·er /ˈnɛðɚ; ˈneðə/ *adj* [only before noun 僅用於名詞前] *literary or humorous* lower down【文或幽默】下面的, 下部的: *the nether regions* 地獄, 陰間

neth·er·most /ˈnɛðɚˌmost; ˈneðəməʊst/ *adj literary* lowest【文】最下面的, 最低的: *the nethermost fiery pit of hell* 烈火熊熊的地獄最深處

nett /nɛt; net/ *adj* a British spelling of NET³ net³ 的英式拼法

N

net·ting /ˈnɛtɪŋ; ˈnetɪŋ/ *n* [U] material consisting of string, wire etc that has been woven into a net 網; 網狀物: *a fence of wire netting* 鐵絲網圍欄

net·tle¹ /ˈnɛtl̩; ˈnetl/ *n* [C] a wild plant with rough leaves that sting you 蕁麻 —see also 另見 **grasp the nettle** (GRASP¹ (4))

nettle² *v* [T] **be nettled** *informal* to be annoyed by someone's behaviour【非正式】被惹怒: *She was nettled by Holman's remark.* 她被霍爾曼的話激怒了。

nettle rash /ˈ·· ·/ *n* [C,U] *BrE* a condition that causes areas of red spots on your skin【英】蕁麻疹, 風疹塊

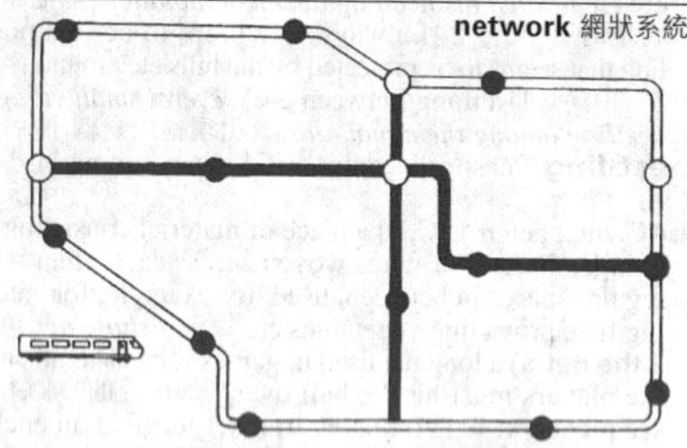
network 網狀系統

3 **net·work¹** /ˈnɛtˌwɝk; ˈnetwɜːk/ *n* [C] **1** a group of radio or television stations, which broadcast many of the same programmes, but in different places 廣播網; 電視網 **2** a system of lines, tubes, wires, roads etc that cross each other and are connected to each other 網絡, 網狀系統: **[+of]** *an elaborate network of canals* 四通八達的運河網 | *the network of blood vessels in the body* 人體內的血管網 **3** a group of people, organizations etc that are connected or that work together 人際關係網, 聯絡網: **[+of]** *It's important to build up a network of professional contacts.* 建立一個專業聯繫網是很重要的。**4** a set of computers that are connected to each other and can be used to send information or messages 電腦網絡

net·work² *v* [I,T] **1** to broadcast a radio or television programme on several different channels (CHANNEL¹ (1, 2)) at the same time 通過〔電台、電視〕網絡播出 **2** to connect several computers together so that you can send information between them (使)〔電腦〕聯網

net·work·ing /ˈnɛtwɝkɪŋ; ˈnetwɜːkɪŋ/ *n* [U] the practice of meeting other people involved in the same kind of work, to share information, support each other etc 聯網(技術)〔指與同行建立聯繫, 旨在共享資料或相互支援〕

neur- /njʊr; njʊə/ *prefix* another form of the prefix NEURO- 前綴 neuro- 的另一種形式

neu·ral /ˈnjʊrəl; ˈnjʊərəl/ *adj technical* related to a nerve or the NERVOUS SYSTEM【術語】神經的, 神經系統的: *neural networks* 神經網絡

neu·ral·gia /njʊˈrældʒə; njʊˈrældʒə/ *n* [U] a sharp pain along the length of a nerve 神經痛 —**neuralgic** *adj*

neuro- /ˈnjʊrə; ˈnjʊərəʊ/ *prefix* also 又作 **neur-** *technical* concerning the nerves【術語】(關於)神經的: *neuropathology* 神經病理學 | *a neurosurgeon* (=who specializes in the body's nervous system) 神經外科醫生

neu·rol·o·gy /njʊˈrɑlədʒɪ; njʊˈrɒlədʒi/ *n* [U] the scientific study of the NERVOUS SYSTEM and its diseases 神經(病)學 —**neurologist** *n* [C]: *consultant neurologist David Hart* 神經病科顧問[會診]醫生大衛·哈特 —**neurological** /ˌnjʊrəˈlɑdʒɪkəl; ˌnjʊərəˈlɒdʒɪkəl◂/ *adj*

neu·ro·sis /njʊˈrosɪs; njʊˈrəʊsɪs/ *n plural* **neuroses** /-siz; -siːz/ [C,U] a mental illness that makes someone unreasonably worried or frightened 神經機能病; 神經官能症

neu·rot·ic /njʊˈrɑtɪk; njʊˈrɒtɪk/ *adj* **1** unreasonably anxious or afraid 神經質的, 神經過敏的; 極度害怕的: *He seemed a neurotic, self-obsessed character.* 他看起來像個神經質、自我陶醉的人。**2** connected with or affected by neurosis 神經官能症的: *neurotic disorders* 神經機能失調 —**neurotically** /-klɪ; -kli/ *adv* —**neurotic** *n* [C]

neu·ter¹ /ˈnjutɚ; ˈnjuːtə/ *adj* **1** plants or animals that are neuter have undeveloped sex organs or no sex organs〔動植物〕生殖器發育不完全的; 無性的; 無生殖器的 **2** *technical* a neuter noun, PRONOUN etc belongs to a class of words that have different inflections (INFLECTION (1)) from MASCULINE (4) or FEMININE (2) words【術語】〔名詞、代名詞等〕中性的

neuter² *v* [T] to remove part of the sex organs of an animal so that it cannot produce babies 閹割〔動物〕: *a neutered tomcat* 已閹割的雄貓

neu·tral¹ /ˈnjutrəl; ˈnjuːtrəl/ *adj*

1 ▶**IN AN ARGUMENT ETC** 在爭吵中等◀ not supporting either of the people or groups involved in an argument or disagreement 中立的, 不偏不倚的: *I always tried to remain neutral when they started arguing.* 他們開始爭吵時我總是努力保持中立。

2 ▶**IN A WAR** 在戰爭中◀ a country that is neutral does not support any of the countries involved in a war〔國家在戰時〕中立的: *During the Second World War, Sweden was neutral.* 在第二次世界大戰期間, 瑞典是中立國。| **neutral territory/waters** (=land or sea that is not controlled by any of the countries involved in a war) 中立國的領土/海域

3 be on neutral ground if two opposing teams or representatives are on neutral ground they are in a place that is not favourable to either of them〔對手間〕旗鼓相當, 沒有一方佔優勢

4 ▶**LANGUAGE** 語言◀ language, words etc that are neutral are deliberately chosen to avoid expressing any strong opinion or feeling 中性的; 不帶感情色彩的: *the neutral language of an official news report* 官方新聞報道採用的中性語言

5 ▶**COLOUR** 色彩◀ a neutral colour is not very strong or bright, for example grey or light brown 暗淡的; 不鮮豔的〈如灰色或淺棕色〉

6 ▶**WIRE** 電線◀ *technical* a neutral wire has no electrical CHARGE¹ (7)【術語】不帶電的

7 ▶**CHEMICAL** 化學品◀ *technical* a neutral substance is neither acid nor ALKALI【術語】中性的 —**neutrally** *adv*

neutral² *n* **1** [U] the position of the gears (GEAR¹ (1)) of a car or machine in which the engine does not turn the wheels〔汽車或機器的〕空擋位置: **in/into neutral** *When you start the engine, be sure the car's in neutral.* 你在發動引擎時, 一定要讓汽車處於空擋。**2** [C] a country or person that is not fighting for or helping any of the countries involved in a war〔戰時的〕中立國; 中立人士

neu·tra·list /ˈnjutrəlɪst; ˈnjuːtrəlɪst/ *adj AmE* tending not to support either side in a war, quarrel etc【美】中立的 —**neutralist** *n* [C]

neu·tral·i·ty /njuˈtrælətɪ; njuːˈtræləti/ *n* [U] the state of not supporting either side in an argument or war 中立; 中立地位

neu·tral·ize also 又作 **-ise** *BrE*【英】/ˈnjutrəlˌaɪz; ˈnjuːtrəlaɪz/ *v* [T] **1** to prevent something from having any effect 使失效; 抵消: *Rising prices tend to neutralize increased wages.* 不斷上漲的物價往往會抵消工資的增長。**2** *technical* to make a substance chemically NEUTRAL【術語】(使)中和: *a medicine that neutralizes the acid in the stomach* 能中和胃酸的藥物 **3** to make a country or population NEUTRAL in war〔在戰爭期間〕使〔國家或人民〕中立 —**neutralization** /ˌnjutrələˈzeʃən; ˌnjuːtrəlaɪˈzeɪʃən/ *n* [U]

neu·tron /ˈnjutrɑn; ˈnjuːtrɒn/ *n* [C] a part of an atom that has no electrical CHARGE¹ (7) 中子

neutron bomb /ˈ·· ˌ·/ *n* [C] a kind of NUCLEAR bomb which kills people but which does not cause much damage to property 中子彈

nev·er /ˈnɛvɚ; ˈnevə/ *adv*
1 ▶NOT AT ANY TIME 任何時候都不◀ not once or not at any time 從來沒有; 決不, 永不: *We've never been to Paris.* 我們從未去過巴黎。| *I'll never forget what my mother said.* 我永遠不會忘記母親的話。| **never... again** *Never let me hear you use that word again!* 永遠別讓我再聽到你用那個詞! | **never in all my life** *spoken* (=used to emphasize how bad something was)【口】我這輩子從沒 *Never in all my life have I felt so humiliated.* 我這輩子從未感到如此受辱。| **never ever** *spoken* (=used to emphasize 'never')【口】永不 *I'll never ever forgive him for leaving me.* 我永遠不會原諒他離開我。| **never once** *spoken* (=used when you are annoyed because someone never did something although they had many opportunities)【口】一次也沒有…過 *Never once did she offer to look after the children.* 她一次也沒有提出過要照顧孩子們。| **never for one moment** *especially spoken* (=used to emphasize that you never thought, imagined, or doubted something)【尤口】一刻都沒有 *Never for one moment did I think that we were going to encounter so many problems.* 我從未想過我們會遇到這麼多問題。| **sb/sth has never been known to do something** (=used to mean that something is strange because it has never happened before) 從未聽說某人/某物做某事 *Max had never been known to leave home without telling someone.* 從未聽說過馬克斯不跟任何人說一聲就出家門。—see picture at 參見 FREQUENCY 圖
2 never mind *spoken* used to tell someone that something is not important or serious, so that there is no need to worry or feel sorry【口】別擔心; 沒關係, 不要緊: *"We've missed the train." "Never mind, there's another one in ten minutes."* "我們沒趕上火車。" "別擔心, 十分鐘後還有一班。"
3 never you mind *spoken* used to tell someone not to ask questions about something because you do not want to tell them about it【口】不關你的事: *"What were you talking about just now?" "Never you mind."* "你們剛才在談論甚麼呢?" "不關你的事。"
4 you never know *spoken* used to say that something which seems unlikely may happen【口】說不定: *Try it! You never know, you might be lucky.* 試試看!說不定你會有好運。
5 that would never do *spoken* used to say that you would not want something to happen【口】那就糟了: *Someone might discover our secret and that would never do.* 也許會有人發現我們的祕密, 那就糟了。
6 I never knew (that) *spoken* used to mean that you did not know something until now【口】以前我一直不知道: *I never knew Texas was so big.* 我一直不知道得克薩斯州這麼大。| *I've just learned something I never knew before.* 我剛聽說了一件我以前一直不知道的事。
7 well, I never (did)! *spoken* used to say that you are very surprised【口】啊, 真沒想到!: *Well, I never! I wouldn't have thought she was that old.* 啊, 真出乎意料!我沒想到她有那麼大年紀了。
8 never! *BrE spoken* used when you are surprised by something, because you think it is not possible【英口】不可能!: *He's never going to cycle all the way to Manchester!* 他不可能一路騎腳踏車去曼徹斯特! | *Never! I don't believe it!* 不可能! 我不相信!
9 never so much as not even 甚至沒有: *The thought that Laura might be having an affair had never so much as crossed his mind.* 他腦子裡從未出現過勞拉可能有外遇的想法。
10 no I never! *BrE spoken* used by a child to say that they did not do something bad when someone else is saying that they did【英口】〔兒童申辯用語〕我沒幹過!: *"You cheated, didn't you?" "No, I never."* "你騙人了, 是嗎?" "不, 我沒有。"
11 never fear *old-fashioned* used to tell someone not to worry【過時】別怕, 別擔心: *She'll be back, never fear.* 別擔心, 她會回來的。
12 never say die used to encourage someone when they are losing hope 別放棄, 別輕言放棄

never-end·ing /ˌ.. ˈ..◂/ *adj* seeming to continue for a very long time 永遠不會完結的; 不斷的: *The work is never-ending.* 這工作永無休止。

nev·er·more /ˌnɛvɚˈmɔr; ˌnevəˈmɔː/ *adv poetic* never again【詩】永不再, 決不再

never-never /ˌ.. ˈ../ *n* **on the never-never** *BrE humorous* if you buy something on the never-never, you buy it on HIRE PURCHASE (=by making small regular payments)【英, 幽默】分期付款 (購買)

never-never land /ˌ.. ˈ.. ./ *n* [U] an imaginary place where everything is perfect〔想像中的〕世外桃源, 理想樂土

nev·er·the·less /ˌnɛvɚðəˈlɛs; ˌnevəðəˈles/ *adv* [sentence adverb 句子副詞] *formal* in spite of a fact that you have just mentioned【正式】然而, 不過; 儘管如此: *What you said was true. It was, nevertheless, a little unkind.* 你說的都是實話, 只不過有點刻薄。| *He insisted that everything would be alright. Nevertheless, I could not help feeling anxious.* 他堅持說一切都會好。儘管如此, 我還是放心不下。

new /nju; njuː/ *adj*
1 ▶RECENTLY MADE 新造的◀ recently made, built, or invented 新造的; 新建的; 新發明的: *the city's new hospital* 市裡新建的醫院 | *Renault's new GTI hatchback* 雷諾新推出的 GTI 後開門小轎車 | *the new issue of 'Time' magazine* 新一期《時代週刊》| *the new fashions* 新的時裝款式 | *a new way of organizing data* 數據整理的新方法
2 ▶RECENTLY BOUGHT 新買的◀ recently bought 新買的: *Do you like my new dress?* 你喜歡我新買的連衣裙嗎? | *That's a nice bag – is it new?* 這個手提袋不錯, 是新買的嗎?
3 ▶NOT THERE BEFORE 以前沒有的◀ having just developed 新出現的: *new buds on the trees* 樹上的新芽 | *a young woman with new ideas* 擁有新觀念的女青年 | *the new nations of Africa* 非洲的新興國家 | **new hope/confidence/optimism etc** (=hope etc that you have only just started to feel) 新的希望/信心/樂觀態度等 *a medical breakthrough that offers new hope to cancer patients* 給癌症患者帶來新希望的醫學突破
4 ▶NOT USED BEFORE 以前未用過的◀ [no comparative 無比較級] not used or owned by anyone before 未用過的, 嶄新的: *New and second hand books for sale.* 出售新書及二手書。| **buy sth new** *I got a used video camera for £300 – it would have cost £1,000 if I'd bought it new.* 我花 300 英鎊買了一台二手攝影機, 如果買新的要花 1,000 英鎊。| **brand new** (=completely new) 嶄新的 *When did you buy this sofa? It looks brand new.* 這張沙發你甚麼時候買的? 看起來像是全新的。
5 like new/as good as new in excellent condition 跟新的一樣: *Your watch just needs cleaning and it'll be as good as new.* 你的手錶該清潔一下了, 之後會跟新的一樣。| *We polished the car till it looked like new.* 我們把汽車擦亮, 直到它看起來跟新的一樣。
6 ▶UNFAMILIAR 不熟悉的◀ not recognized or not experienced before 不認識的; 未體驗過的: *learning a new language* 學習新的語言 | *Living in the city was a new experience for Philip.* 在城市裡生活對菲利普來說是一種新的經歷。| **be new to sb** *The fruit had a delicate taste that was completely new to me.* 這種水果帶有一種我從未嚐過的鮮美味道。| **that's a new one on me** *spoken* (=used to say that you have never heard a particular word, name etc before)【口】我第一次聽說
7 ▶RECENTLY ARRIVED 最近到達的◀ having recently arrived in a place, joined an organization, or started a new job 新來的; 新加入的; 剛開始的: *You're new here, aren't you?* 你是新來的, 是嗎? | **be new to sth/be new at sth** *Don't worry if you make mistakes you're still new to the job.* 別怕犯錯, 你才剛剛開始幹這份工作呢! | **new member/employee/student etc** (=people who are not

already members) 新成員／新雇員／新生等 *training for new employees* 對新員工的培訓 | *The party is anxious to recruit new members.* 該黨正在急切地招募新成員。| **new arrival** (=someone who has recently arrived in a place) 新來的人 *As a new arrival, Maria was obviously going to have problems with the language.* 作為一名新來的人，瑪麗亞肯定會在語言方面遇到問題。| **be the new kid on the block** *AmE informal* (=be the newest person in a job, school etc)【美，非正式】新雇員；新生 *It's not always easy being the new kid on the block.* 做新生並非總是件輕鬆的事。| **be the new boy/girl** *BrE humorous* (=be the newest person in a job, organization etc)【英，幽默】新雇員；新成員

8 new owner/address/job etc the owner etc that has recently replaced the previous one 新業主／地址／工作等: *Have you met Keith's new girlfriend?* 你見過基思的新女朋友嗎？| *I'll let you have my new phone number.* 我會告訴你我的新電話號碼。

9 ▶RECENTLY DISCOVERED 新發現的◀ recently discovered 新發現的: *the discovery of a new planet* 一顆新行星的發現 | *new oilfields in Alaska* 阿拉斯加的新油田 | *important new evidence that may prove her innocence* 可能證明她是清白的重要新證據

10 new life/day/era a period that is just beginning and seems to offer better opportunities 新的生活／一天／紀元: *They went to Australia to start a new life there.* 他們去澳大利亞開始新的生活。

11 feel (like) a new man/woman to feel much healthier and have a lot more energy than before 感到自己煥然一新

12 new blood new members of a group or organization who will bring new ideas and be full of energy〔團體或組織中的〕新血液，新成員，新生力量: *What we need in this company is some new blood.* 我們這個公司需要的是新生力量。

13 new broom someone who has just become the leader or manager of an organization and is eager to make changes〔急於變革的〕新上任官員[領導人]

14 what's new? *spoken especially AmE* used as a friendly greeting to mean 'how are you?'【口，尤美】〔招呼語〕怎麼樣？你好嗎？

15 the new unfamiliar ideas or changes in society 新觀念；新變化: *the shock of the new* 新觀念帶來的震撼

16 new-made/new-formed etc recently made, formed etc 新造的／新建立的等 —see also 另見 **a new lease of life** (LEASE[1] (2)), **turn over a new leaf** (LEAF[1] (3)) —**newness** *n* [U]: *Philip was bewildered by the newness of his surroundings.* 菲利普對他四周的全新環境感到迷茫。

New Age /ˌ· ˈ·◂/ *adj* concerning the belief in SPIRITUAL ideas, cures, and ways of life which became popular in Britain and the US in the late 20th century 新時代的〔形容20世紀晚期在英國和美國十分流行的一種關於精神信念、療法和生活方式的信仰〕

New Age trav·el·lers /ˌ· · ˈ···/ *n* [plural] people in Britain who refuse to live the way other people live in ordinary society, and go from place to place living in vehicles〔新時代中以車為家四處漫遊的〕新潮一族，新時代旅行者

new·born /ˈnjuˌbɔrn; ˈnjuːbɔːn/ *adj* **newborn child/baby/son etc** a child that has just been born 新生兒／嬰兒／兒子等: *He took his newborn baby in his arms.* 他把自己的新生寶寶抱到懷裡。—**newborn** *n* [C]

new·com·er /njuˈkʌmɚ; ˈnjuːkʌmə/ *n* [C] someone who has only recently arrived somewhere or only recently started a particular activity 新來的人；新手: **[+to]** *I'm a relative newcomer to the retail business.* 我在零售行業相對來說還是個新手。| *Promising newcomer Gillespie won outright.* 前途無量的新秀吉萊斯皮大獲全勝。

new·fan·gled /ˌnjuˈfæŋgl̩d; ˌnjuːˈfæŋgəld◂/ *adj* newfangled ideas, machines etc have been recently invented but you think they are too complicated or unnecessary〔主意、機器等〕新而無價值的，新奇而無意義的；新花樣的: *newfangled ideas about education* 關於教育的異想天開的新想法

new-found /ˌ· ˈ·◂/ *adj* **newfound confidence/freedom/happiness etc** confidence, freedom etc that someone has only recently gained 新獲得的信心／自由／幸福等: *At first Mozart enjoyed his new-found freedom, earning enough to rent a big apartment.* 剛開始時，莫扎特賺到足夠的錢租了一套大公寓，享受着新的自由。

new-laid /ˌ· ˈ·◂/ *adj* a new-laid egg is fresh〔蛋〕新下的，新鮮的

new-look /ˈ· ·/ *adj* recently made more modern or more attractive 新面孔的，新面貌的: *the new-look Labour Party* 以新面貌出現的工黨

new·ly /ˈnjulɪ; ˈnjuːli/ *adv* **newly formed/created/appointed/married etc** formed etc very recently 新成立／新創造／新任命／新婚等的: *the newly appointed director* 新任命的董事 | *newly fallen snow* 新下的雪 3

new·ly·weds /ˈnjulɪˌwɛdz; ˈnjuːliwedz/ *n* [plural] a man and a woman who have recently got married 新婚夫婦，〔一對〕新人 —**newlywed** *adj*

New Man /ˌ· ˈ·/ *n* [C] a man who is considered to be very modern because he enjoys looking after his children and helping his partner with the care of the home〔樂於照料子女及做家務的〕新男性，新派男子: *He is a New Man, freely admitting to doing cleaning in place of his career-woman wife.* 他是個新派男子，坦率地承認替自己事業型的妻子打掃房子。

new maths /ˌ· ˈ·/ *BrE*【英】, **new math** *AmE*【美】*n* [U] a way of teaching and understanding mathematics, first used in schools in the early 1970s 新數學〔20世紀70年代初引入學校的一種數學教學和理解的新方法〕，基礎數學集論教學法

new mon·ey /ˌ· ˈ··/ *n* [U] people who have recently or suddenly become very rich, as opposed to people whose families have always been rich 暴發戶

new moon /ˌ· ˈ·/ *n* **1** [C] the moon when it first appears in the sky as a thin CRESCENT〔月牙形的〕新月 **2** [C,U] the time of the month at which this is first seen 新月出現的時候 **3** [C] *technical* the time when the moon is between the Earth and the sun, and cannot be seen【術語】新月期 —compare 比較 FULL MOON, HALF MOON

new-mown /ˌ· ˈ·◂/ *adj* **new-mown hay/grass** grass that has recently been cut 新割的飼草／新剪的草坪: *the sweet smell of new-mown grass* 新剪草坪的清香

new po·ta·to /ˌ· ·ˈ··/ *n* [C] a potato from one of the first crops of a year 新收穫的馬鈴薯

new rich /ˌ· ˈ·◂/ *n* **the new rich** *AmE* people who have recently or suddenly become very rich, as opposed to people whose families have always been rich【美】新貴；暴發戶 —**new rich** *adj*

news /njuz; njuːz/ *n* [U] **1** information about something 1
that has happened recently（新）消息: *That's great news!* 1
那是個好消息！| *Sit down and tell me all your news.* 坐下來給我說說你最新的消息。| **[+about/of]** *There hasn't been any news of him since he left home.* 自從他離開家後，一直都沒有他的消息。| **[+that]** *Our delegates returned with the news that negotiations had broken down.* 我們的代表團回來時帶來了談判破裂的消息。| **good/bad news** *You're looking upset – not bad news, I hope?* 你看起來很不高興，我想不會有甚麼壞消息吧？| **hear news** (=receive news) 聽到消息，得到消息 *Have you heard any news from Emily yet?* 你有艾米莉的任何音訊嗎？| **piece of news** *Your brother's just told me an interesting piece of news.* 你兄弟剛告訴我一則有趣的消息。| **have news for** *I've some good news for you – they've signed the contract.* 告訴你一個好消息，他們已經簽了合同。| **I've got news for you** (=some bad news) 我有壞消息要告訴你 *You may think you've fooled him, but I've got news for you – he's wise to your little trick.* 你以為你騙過了他，告訴你，他早已識破了你的小把戲。| **break the news to** (=tell someone some bad news) 告

N

訴〔某人〕壞消息, 向〔某人〕透露實情 *I don't know how to break the news to her.* 我不知道該怎樣告訴她這個壞消息。**2** reports of recent events in the newspapers or on the radio or television 新聞 (報道) : **[+of/about]** *News is coming in of a major explosion at the World Trade Centre.* 有報道稱世界貿易中心發生了大爆炸。| *We'll bring you more news about the election at 11 o'clock.* 我們將在 11 點報道更多有關選舉的新聞。| **news that** *Several evening papers carried the news that a cabinet minister was about to resign.* 好幾家晚報報道了一名內閣部長將要辭職的消息。| **latest news** *the latest news from the Olympic stadium* 來自奧林匹克運動場的最新消息 | **local/national etc news** *a programme bringing you national and international news* 國內外新聞報道 | **make the news** (=be considered important enough to be in the news) 成為新聞 *Twenty years ago environmental issues rarely made the news.* 二十年前, 環境問題很少被傳媒報道。| **be in the news** *I see Michael Jackson's in the news again.* 我看到米高積遜又在新聞中出現了。| **be front page news** (=be interesting enough to be on the front page of a newspaper) 成為頭版新聞 *Wallace's resignation was front page news.* 華萊士的辭職成了頭版新聞。| **news story/report** *Wilks had been paid by journalists to simply invent bogus news stories.* 記者們付錢給威爾克斯為他們憑空杜撰新聞。**3 the news** a regular television or radio programme that gives you reports of recent events〔電視或電台的〕新聞報道, 新聞節目: **on the news** *It must be true – I heard it on the news last night.* 這肯定是真的, 我昨晚在新聞節目中聽到的。**4 be good/bad news for** if the facts about something are good or bad news for someone, they are likely to make life better or worse for them 對〔某人〕是個好/壞消息: *House prices are very low at the moment, which is good news for first-time buyers.* 目前房價很低, 這對首次置業人士來說是個好消息。**5 he's/she's bad news** *informal* used to say that someone is likely to cause trouble【非正式】他/她不是好東西〔指某人可能會帶來麻煩〕: *Stay away from that guy, he's bad news.* 離那傢伙遠一點, 他不是個好東西。**6 that's news to me!** *spoken* used when you are surprised or annoyed because you have not been told something earlier【口】我一點都不知道!: *So, the meeting's been cancelled? Well, that's news to me!* 這麼說, 會議被取消了? 啊, 我一點都不知道呢! **7 no news is good news** *spoken* used when you have not received any news about someone and you hope this means that nothing bad has happened【口】沒有消息就是好消息, 不聞凶訊便是吉

This graph shows some of the words most commonly used with the noun **news**. 本圖表所示為含有名詞 news 的一些最常用的詞組。

the news
good/bad news
news of/about
news story/report
local/national news
10
20
30 per million
每百萬

Based on the British National Corpus and the Longman Lancaster Corpus
據英國國家語料庫和朗文蘭卡斯特語料庫

news a·gen·cy /ˈ· ˌ···/ *n* [C] a company that supplies information to newspapers, radio and television 新聞社, 通訊社

news·a·gent /ˈnjuzedʒənt; ˈnjuːzˌeɪdʒənt/ *n* [C] *BrE* someone who owns or works in a shop that sells newspapers and magazines【英】報刊經銷人: **newsagent's** (=a newsagent's shop) 報刊銷售店

news bul·le·tin /ˈ· ˌ···/ *n* [C] **1** *BrE* a short news programme on radio or television, reporting only the most important information【英】〔電台或電視的〕新聞簡報 **2** *AmE* a very short news programme on radio or television, broadcast suddenly in the middle of another programme when something very important has happened【美】新聞快訊〔指插在電台或電視其他節目中播出的重要新聞〕; NEWSFLASH *BrE*【英】

news·cast /ˈnjuzˌkæst; ˈnjuːzkɑːst/ *n* [C] *AmE* a news programme on radio or television【美】〔電台或電視的〕新聞廣播[報道]

news·cast·er /ˈnjuzˌkæstɚ; ˈnjuːzˌkɑːstə/ *n* [C] someone who reads the news on radio or television〔電台或電視的〕新聞播音員; NEWSREADER *BrE*【英】

news con·fer·ence /ˈ· ˌ···/ *n* [C] a PRESS CONFERENCE 記者招待會

news·flash /ˈnjuzˌflæʃ; ˈnjuːzflæʃ/ *n* [C] *especially BrE* a very short news programme on radio or television, broadcast suddenly in the middle of another programme when something very important has happened【尤英】新聞快訊〔指插在電台或電視其他節目中播出的重要新聞〕; NEWS BULLETIN *AmE*【美】: *We interrupt this programme to bring you a newsflash from the Malabar front.* 我們暫時中斷本節目, 向大家報道來自馬拉巴爾前線的新聞快訊。

news·hound /ˈnjuzˌhaʊnd; ˈnjuːzhaʊnd/ *n* [C] *informal* someone who writes for a newspaper and is always looking for exciting new stories but sometimes upsets people by being too eager【非正式】無孔不入的新聞記者

news·let·ter /ˈnjuzˌlɛtɚ; ˈnjuːzˌletə/ *n* [C] one or several sheets of printed news sent regularly to a particular group of people〔給特定讀者定期寄發的〕通訊; 簡報; 業務通訊: *Have you seen the church newsletter?* 你看到教會的通訊了嗎?

news·pa·per /ˈnjuzˌpepɚ; ˈnjuːsˌpeɪpə/ *n* **1** [C] a set of large folded sheets of paper containing news, articles, pictures, advertisements etc printed and sold daily or weekly 報(紙): *a national newspaper* 一份全國性的報紙 **2** [U] sheets of paper from old newspapers〔舊〕報紙: *Wrap the plates in newspaper to stop them from breaking.* 用舊報紙把盤子包起來, 免得它們被打破。**3** [C] a company that produces a newspaper 報社: *I think he works for a local newspaper.* 我認為他在一家本地報社工作。 2 2

newspaper stand /ˈ··· ˌ·/ *n* [C] a NEWSSTAND 書報攤; 報刊亭

news·print /ˈnjuzˌprɪnt; ˈnjuːzˌprɪnt/ *n* [U] *technical* cheap paper used mostly for printing newspapers on【術語】新聞紙, 白報紙

news·read·er /ˈnjuzˌridɚ; ˈnjuːzˌriːdə/ *n* [C] *especially BrE* someone who reads the news on television or radio【尤英】〔電視或電台的〕新聞播音員, 新聞廣播員

news·reel /ˈnjuzˌril; ˈnjuːzriːl/ *n* [C] a cinema film of news 新聞片

news re·lease /ˈ· ·ˌ·/ *n* [C] a PRESS RELEASE 新聞稿

news·room /ˈnjuzrum; ˈnjuːzrʊm/ *n* [C] the office in a newspaper or broadcasting company where news is received and news reports are written〔報社、廣播公司的〕新聞編輯室

news·stand /ˈnjuzˌstænd; ˈnjuːzstænd/ *n* [C] a place on a street where newspapers and magazines are sold 書報攤; 報刊亭

news ven·dor /ˈ· ˌ··/ *n* [C] *especially BrE* someone who sells newspapers【尤英】報販

news·wor·thy /ˈnjuzˌwɝðɪ; ˈnjuːzˌwɜːði/ *adj* important or interesting enough to be reported as news 有新聞價值的, 值得報道的: *The reporter's task is to report what is newsworthy about an event.* 記者的職責是將事件中有新聞價值的內容報道出來。

news·y /ˈnjuzɪ; ˈnjuːzi/ *adj* a newsy letter is from a friend or relative and contains a lot of news about them〔信件〕消息豐富的

newt /njut; njuːt/ *n* [C] a small animal with a long body, four legs and a tail, that lives in water 蠑螈, 水螈

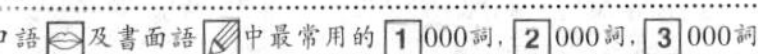

New Tes·ta·ment /ˌ· ˈ···/ *n* **the New Testament** the part of the Bible which includes the four Gospels describing the life of Jesus Christ and what he taught〔《聖經》的〕《新約全書》〔其中包括四部福音書, 講述耶穌的生平與傳教的事跡〕—compare 比較 OLD TESTAMENT

New·toni·an /njuˋtonɪən; njuːˈtəʊniən/ *adj* related to the laws of PHYSICS that were discovered by the scientist Isaac Newton 牛頓學説的: *Newtonian mechanics* 牛頓力學

new town /ˈ· ·/ *n* [C] one of several towns built in Britain since 1946, each designed and built according to a plan that included houses, shops, and factories〔英國自1946年以來建立的〕新市鎮: *A new town may not be very attractive but is certainly a very convenient place to live.* 新市鎮也許不太吸引人, 但肯定是一個生活十分方便的地方。

new wave /ˌ· ˈ·◂/ *n* [C] a group of people making a conscious effort to introduce new ideas in music, films, art, politics etc〔在音樂、電影、藝術、政治等方面引入新觀念的〕新浪潮; 新潮派 —**new wave** *adj*: *new wave music* 新潮派音樂

New World /ˌ· ˈ·◂/ *n* **the New World** North, Central, and South America 新大陸, 新世界〔指美洲〕—**New World** *adj*: *New World wines* 新大陸出產的葡萄酒

New Year, new year /ˌ· ˈ·◂/ *n* [U] **1** the time at the beginning of the year when you celebrate 新年: *We're going to spend Christmas and New Year with my parents.* 我們打算和父母一起過聖誕節和新年。| **Happy New Year** (=used as a greeting) 新年快樂 | **see in the new year** (=celebrate the beginning of the year) 慶祝新年, 迎接新年 *Our neighbours invited us round to see in the new year.* 鄰居邀請我們去他們家慶祝新年。**2 the new year** the first few weeks of the year 新年伊始: *Let's hope things will begin to improve in the new year.* 希望在新的一年情況會有所好轉。| **new year resolution** (=a decision to improve yourself in the new year) 新年的決心 *I haven't made any new year resolutions – I never stick to them anyway.* 我沒有下定任何新年的決心, 反正我從未照辦過。

New Year's Day /ˌ· · ˈ·/ *n* [singular, U] 1st January, the first day of the year 元旦

New Year's Eve /ˌ· · ˈ·/ *n* [singular, U] 31st December, the last day of the year 除夕

1 1 **next¹** /nɛkst; nekst/ *determiner* **1** the next house, room etc is the one that is closest to you〔位置〕離得最近的; 隔壁的: *I asked the woman at the next table what time it was.* 我向鄰桌的女人打聽幾點鐘了。| *They could be heard arguing from the next room.* 能聽到他們在隔壁的房間爭吵。**2** the next event, day, time etc is the one that happens after the present one〔時間〕緊接着來到的; 下次的: **the next train/meeting/class etc** *The next episode was watched by over 10 million anxious viewers.* 接下來的一集吸引了一千多萬名焦急的觀眾收看。| *If they win the next election they have promised to reform the health service.* 如果他們在下次大選中獲勝, 他們承諾要改革醫療制度。| *I've just missed the flight to Chicago, what time's the next one?* 我沒趕上飛往芝加哥的航班, 下一班是幾點? | **the next few weeks/three years etc** *Over the next couple of months, try to relax more and take more exercise.* 在今後幾個月裡, 要試着多放鬆, 多運動。| **next Monday/July/year etc** *We're hoping to reopen the factory some time next year.* 我們希望能在明年某個時候重開工廠。| **(the) next day** *She called me and we arranged to meet the next day.* 她給我打了電話, 我們約好第二天見面。| **(the) next time** *Next time I take a cab, I'll be more careful.* 下次坐計程車時, 我會更加小心。—compare 比較 LAST¹ (1) **3** the next person or thing in a list, a series, a line of people etc is the one that you come to after the one that you are dealing with at the present time〔次序〕下一個的: *The letter continues on the next page.* 此信未完, 見下頁。| *The next interviewee has a degree in geography and plenty of work experience.* 下一位應試人擁有地理學學位, 還有豐富的工作經驗。| *The cottage is just around the next bend in the road.* 那間小屋就在公路的下一個拐彎處附近。**4 a) the next biggest/smallest etc** the one that is a bit bigger, smaller etc than the one you are talking about 第二大/小等: *The hotel was full and the next nearest was over 20 miles away.* 這家旅館已經客滿, 離此地最近的下一家旅館在20英里以外。**b) the next best thing** the thing that is almost as good as something else 僅次於…的東西: *If butter is too expensive use the next best thing – margarine.* 如果黃油太貴的話, 就退而求其次用人造黃油。—see also 另見 **next of kin** (KIN (2))

next² *adv* **1** immediately afterwards 緊接下來地; 下一步; 然後: *Being a doctor is a great life, you never know what will happen next.* 做醫生的生活很奇妙, 你永遠無法預料下一步會發生甚麼事情。| *The mixture is heated to a temperature of 40°C. Next, it is poured into a mould and left to cool.* 將混合物加熱至攝氏40度, 然後把它倒進模子裡冷卻。| *Where do you think you'll travel next?* 你接下來要去哪兒旅行呢? **2 next to a)** situated very close to someone or something with nothing in between 緊挨着, 緊靠着: *There was a little girl sitting next to him.* 有一個小女孩坐在他旁邊。| *The church is on the left, next to the school.* 教堂在左邊, 緊靠着學校。—see picture on page A1 參見 A1 頁圖 **b)** used when giving a list of things you like or prefer etc in order to say what is first in the list 僅次於, 在…之後: *Next to soccer, squash is the sport I'm best at.* 我最擅長的運動是足球, 其次是壁球。**3 next to nothing** very little 幾乎沒有: *He knows next to nothing about antiques.* 他對古董幾乎一竅不通。**4** the next time 下次, 再次: *When I next saw her she completely ignored me.* 我再次見到她時, 她壓根兒沒有理我。 1 1

next³ *pron* **1** the person or thing in a list, a series, a line of people etc that you come to after the one that you are dealing with at the present time 下一個〔人或事物〕: *Un, deux, trois...what comes next?* 一、二、三…, 下面是甚麼? | *You're next, Mrs Williams. The doctor will be ready in a moment.* 威廉斯太太, 下一位輪到您了。醫生很快就會準備好。**2 the day/week etc after next** the day, week etc that follows the next one 後天/下下個星期等: *Have you remembered it's Susie's birthday the week after next?* 你還記得下下星期是蘇西的生日嗎? **3 the next to last** the one before the last one 倒數第二: *We'll need to buy some more ink. I'm on the next to last bottle at the moment.* 我們得買些墨水了。我正在用倒數第二瓶。**4 next (please)** used to tell someone that it is now their turn to speak or their turn to do something 下一位(請) **5 be next in line** to be the next person to become king, a leader etc〔王位、領袖等的〕下一位繼任人

next door¹ /ˌ· ˈ·/ *adv* **1** in the house, room etc next to yours or someone else's 在隔壁: *the boy next door* 住在隔壁的男孩 | *the people who've just moved in next door* 隔壁剛搬來的那家人 | *Her office is just next door.* 她的辦公室就在隔壁。**2 next door to a)** next to another building, room etc 在…的隔壁: *He runs that small restaurant next door to the theatre.* 他經營在劇院隔壁的那家小餐館。**b)** almost the same as 幾乎等於, 和…差不多: *Leaving a man to die is next door to murder.* 見死不救簡直和謀殺差不多。

next door² *n* [U] *BrE informal* the people living in the house or apartment next to yours【英, 非正式】隔壁鄰居: *Have you seen next door's new car?* 你看到隔壁鄰居的新車了嗎?

next-door³ /ˌ· ˈ·◂/ *adj* **1 next-door neighbour** the person who lives in the house or apartment next to yours 隔壁鄰居: *I met my new next-door neighbour for the first time last night.* 我昨晚首次見到隔壁新搬來的鄰居。**2 next door apartment/office etc** the apartment etc that is next to yours 隔壁房間/辦公室等

nex·us /ˈnɛksəs; ˈneksəs/ *n plural* **nexus** [C+of] *formal* a connection or network of connections between a num-

ber of people, things or ideas【正式】〔人、事物、思想等之間的〕關係, 關聯, 聯繫, 連結: *Beneath the apparent certainty was a nexus of contradictions.* 在表面的確定性底下是一連串矛盾。

NHS /ˌen etʃ ˋɛs; ˌen eɪtʃ ˈes/ *n* **the NHS** the National Health Service; the British system that provides free medical treatment for everyone, paid for by taxes 國民保健制度〔英國的一種免費醫療制度〕: *NHS hospitals* 國民保健制度所屬的醫院 | **on the NHS** (=paid for by the NHS) 由國民保健制度支付 *Can I get my glasses on the NHS?* 我配眼鏡可以享受國民醫療保健嗎?

nib /nɪb; nɪb/ *n* [C] **1** the pointed metal part at the end of a pen 鋼筆尖 **2 his/her nibs** *old-fashioned* someone of a higher social rank than you or someone who thinks they are important【過時】上司; 要人; 自以為了不起的人: *His nibs has wine with his meal – we get water.* 那位大人物吃飯有酒喝, 我們只有水。

nib·ble¹ /ˋnɪbl̩; ˈnɪbəl/ *v* **1** [I,T] to eat small amounts of food by taking very small bites 啃; 一點一點地咬[吃]: *He nibbled the biscuit cautiously.* 他小心地啃着餅乾。| [+at] *She nibbled at her sandwich.* 她小口小口地吃着三明治。**2** [I+at] to show slight interest in an offer or suggestion 對〔提議、建議〕略表興趣

nibble away at sth *phr v* [T] to keep reducing a large amount by taking smaller amounts from it 一點一點地減少[耗掉]; 蠶食: *All these expenses are nibbling away at our savings.* 所有這些開支在一點一點地耗掉我們的積蓄。

nibble² *n* [C] **1** a small bite of something 一小口: *taking tiny nibbles of a biscuit* 一小口一小口地啃餅乾 **2 nibbles** [plural] *informal* small things to eat, especially at a party【非正式】〔尤指聚會上的〕小吃; 少量食品 **3** an expression of slight interest in an offer or suggestion 略有興趣的表示: *We've had the house on the market for a month and not even a nibble yet.* 我們的房子上市已有一個月了, 但至今連略表興趣的人都沒有。

1 2 **nice** /naɪs; naɪs/ *adj*

1 ►ENJOYABLE/ATTRACTIVE 令人愉快/吸引人的◄ pleasant, attractive or enjoyable 令人愉快的; 吸引人的, 美好的: *That's a nice dress.* 那條裙子很漂亮! | *We had a really nice day at the beach.* 我們在海灘度過了愉快的一天。| *not too hot, just a nice temperature* 不太熱, 溫度正好 | *"We could take a picnic." "Yes, that'd be nice."* "我們可以去野餐。" "對, 好主意。" | **it is nice to do something** *It's nice to have a sit down.* 能坐一會兒真好。| *It's really nice to see you again.* 能再見到你真高興。| **look/taste/smell nice** *You look nice in that suit.* 你穿那套西服看起來很不錯。| *If it doesn't taste nice, don't eat it.* 如果味道不好, 就別吃了。| **nice big/new/long etc** *spoken*【口】*I had a nice long letter from your mother.* 我收到你母親的一封長信。| **nice and warm/nice and sweet etc** *Have one of these oranges – they're nice and juicy.* 吃個橙吧, 汁很多的。| **one of the nice things about...** *One of the nice things about Christmas is having all the family together.* 聖誕節的一個好處是全家團聚在一起。

2 ►FRIENDLY 友好的◄ friendly or kind 友好的; 友善的, 和善的: *Dave's a really nice guy.* 戴夫是個很友善的人。| *He told me, in the nicest possible way, that I was interfering too much.* 他以最友善的方式告訴我, 我干涉得太多了。| *Did she really say all those nice things about me?* 她真的說了我那麼多好話嗎? | **be nice to** *Be nice to Grandad. He's not feeling very well today.* 對爺爺好些, 他今天有點不舒服。| **it is nice of sb (to do sth)** *It was nice of you to help.* 你幫了忙, 真好。

3 it's nice to know (that) *spoken* used to mean that you feel happier when you know something【口】知道…真好: *I still haven't heard any news – it would be nice to know what's happening.* 我還是沒有得到任何消息, 要是能知道在發生甚麼事就好了。

4 ►NOT NICE AT ALL 一點也不好◄ *spoken* used when you think that something or someone is not nice at all【口】壓根兒不好的; 令人不快的: *That's a nice way to treat a friend, I must say!* 我說, 你這樣對待朋友太不像話了! | *You've got us into a nice old mess, haven't you?* 你使我們陷入了這種困境, 不是嗎?

5 be as nice as pie *spoken* if someone is as nice as pie, they are very nice to you when you were expecting them to be angry【口】〔出乎意料地〕極好: *I told her about the broken window and she was as nice as pie about it.* 我告訴她打破窗子的事, 但她卻絲毫沒有生氣。

6 have a nice day! *spoken especially AmE* used to say goodbye to someone, especially to customers in shops and restaurants when they are leaving【口, 尤美】祝你今天過得愉快!〔尤用作商店店員、餐廳侍應向顧客告別時的用語〕

7 nice to meet you *spoken* used as a friendly greeting when you meet someone for the first time【口】很高興認識你〔初次見面時的禮貌用語〕: *Hello. It's nice to meet you at last.* 你好。終於見到你, 我真高興!

8 it's been nice meeting you *spoken* used when you say goodbye to someone you have just met【口】能認識你真高興〔初次見面後的告別用語〕

9 nice one! *BrE spoken* used to say that you think someone has just said or done something clever, amusing, helpful etc【英口】真聰明! 真好笑! 好極了!: *"Dad said he'd give us some money to help pay for it." "Nice one!"* "爸爸說他會給我們一些錢, 幫我們付賬。" "太棒了!"

10 nice work! *BrE spoken* used to praise someone when they have succeeded in doing something【英口】幹得好!: *"I've traced those missing files, sir." "Nice work, Cardew!"* "先生, 我找到丟失的文件了!" "幹得好, 卡迪尤!"

11 ►DETAIL 細節◄ *formal* involving a very small difference or detail【正式】細微的; 微妙的: *a nice point of law* 一項微妙的法律條款

12 ►RESPECTABLE 正派的◄ *old-fashioned* having high standards of moral and social behaviour【過時】高尚的; 正派的: *the kind of nightclubs nice people don't go to* 正派人不去的那種夜總會 —**niceness** *n* [U] —see also 另見 **no more Mr Nice Guy!** (GUY¹ (5))

USAGE NOTE 用法說明: NICE

GRAMMAR 語法

Nice is often joined to another adjective by *and* when it follows **is, seems** etc without a noun. (But you do not use 'nice and' before a noun) 當 nice 用在 is, seems 等詞之後, 後面又沒有名詞時, 往往要用 *and* 將其與另一形容詞連接 (但 nice and 不用於名詞前) : *Your new house looks nice and big.* 你的新房子看起來真大! Compare 比較: *This is a nice big house!* 這房子真大!

SPOKEN-WRITTEN 口語－書面語

Nice is very frequent in spoken English, but many people feel you should not use it too much in writing. Often it is better to think of a word that describes what you mean more exactly. nice 在英語口語中的使用頻率很高, 但很多人認為書面語中不宜用得過多, 而應使用一些更加具體的詞來描述確切含義。For example, look at this sentence 如下句: *That area of France is really nice.* 法國的那個地區真不錯! Here you could make your meaning clearer by using more specific adjectives such as **interesting** or **beautiful**. 這裡可使用一些更加具體的形容詞, 如 interesting (有意思的) 或 beautiful (美麗的) 將意思表達得更清楚。

nice-look·ing /ˌ· ˈ··/ *adj* attractive 美麗的, 漂亮的; 英俊的: *Do you really think he's nice-looking?* 你真的認為他長得英俊嗎?

nice·ly /ˋnaɪslɪ; ˈnaɪsli/ *adv* 

1 ►WELL 很好地◄ in a satisfactory or pleasing way 很好地; 令人滿意地; 令人愉快地: *The car seems to be running nicely now it's been fixed.* 汽車修理過以後好像跑

得很不錯。| *We were managing quite nicely till you started interfering.* 你沒有插手以前我們本來進展得很順利。| *My legs are getting nicely tanned.* 我把雙腿曬成漂亮的棕褐色。

2 ▶IN A FRIENDLY/PLEASANT WAY 友好/適宜地◀ in a pleasant, polite, or friendly way 友好地; 禮貌地; 適宜地: *I hope you thanked Mrs Deville nicely.* 我希望你已經好好謝過德維爾夫人了。

3 be doing nicely (for yourself) to be successful and be earning a lot of money (為自己) 幹得很出色, 幹得很成功: *I've heard Malcom's doing very nicely for himself out in Japan.* 我聽說馬爾科姆在日本幹得很出色。

4 will do nicely *spoken* if something will do nicely, it is suitable for a particular purpose【口】非常好用: *"Is this knife big enough?" "Yes, it'll do nicely."* "這把刀子夠大嗎?" "夠大, 它非常好用。"

5 ▶EXACTLY 確切地◀ *formal* exactly or carefully【正式】精確地; 仔細地: *a nicely calculated distance* 精確計算出的距離

ni·ce·ty /ˈnaɪsətɪ; ˈnaɪsəti/ *n* **1** [C usually plural 一般用複數] a small and exact point of difference or detail 細微區別; 細微之處; 細節: *legal niceties* 法律細節 | **[+of]** *the niceties of etiquette* 禮節的細微之處 **2 to a nicety** *formal* exactly【正式】精確地, 精細入微地

niche /nɪtʃ; nɪtʃ/ *n* **1** [C] a job or activity that is perfect for someone 合適的工作[活動]: *She's found a niche for herself in the book trade.* 她在圖書行業找到了一份非常適合自己的工作。**2** [C] a hollow place in a wall, often made to hold a STATUE〔用來放雕像的〕壁龕 **3** [singular] *technical* all the people who buy a particular product or use a particular service【術語】〔特定產品或服務的〕用戶羣

niche mar·ket·ing /ˈ· ˌ···/ *n* [U] the practice of trying to sell a product to a particular group of people 針對特定羣體的銷售法, 目標羣體銷售法

nick¹ /nɪk; nɪk/ *n* **1 in the nick of time** just before it is too late or just before something bad happens 在緊要關頭; 正是時候: *Luckily, help arrived in the nick of time.* 幸運的是援兵及時來了。**2** [C] a very small cut made on the edge or surface of something 刻痕; 裂口 **3 in good nick/in bad nick etc** *BrE informal* in good condition or in bad condition【英, 非正式】狀態良好/不好等: *It's an old car but it's in good nick.* 這是輛舊汽車, 但性能良好。**4 the nick** *BrE informal* prison or a POLICE STATION【英, 非正式】監獄; 警察局

nick² *v* [T] **1** to make a small cut in the surface or edge of something, usually by accident〔意外地〕刻痕於; 擦傷: *A bullet nicked his leg.* 一顆子彈擦傷了他的腿。**2** *BrE informal* to steal something【英, 非正式】偷: *Someone's nicked my bike.* 有人偷了我的腳踏車。**3** *BrE informal* if the police nick you, they catch you and charge you with a crime; ARREST¹ (1)【英, 非正式】抓獲, 逮捕, 拘捕

nick·el /ˈnɪkl; ˈnɪkəl/ *n* **1** [U] a hard silver-white metal that is an ELEMENT (=a simple substance) and is used in the production of other metals 鎳 **2** [C] a coin in the US or Canada that is worth five cents〔美國、加拿大的〕五分硬幣

nickel-and-dime /ˌ···ˈ·◂/ *adj AmE* unimportant and not costing a lot of money【美】不重要的; 不值錢的

nick·nack /ˈnɪk ˌnæk; ˈnɪk næk/ *n* [C] another spelling of KNICK-KNACK knick-knack 的另一種拼法

nick·name /ˈnɪkˌnem; ˈnɪkneɪm/ *n* [C] a name given to someone, especially by their friends or family, that is not their real name and is often connected with what they look like or something they have done〔尤指給朋友或家人取的〕綽號, 外號; 諢名 —**nickname** *v* [T]: *Frank Sinatra, nicknamed 'Old Blue Eyes'*〔美國歌手兼電影演員〕法蘭仙納杜拉, 外號"老藍眼"

nic·o·tine /ˈnɪkəˌtin; ˈnɪkətiːn/ *n* [U] a substance in tobacco which makes it difficult for people to stop smoking 尼古丁, 煙鹼

nicotine patch /ˈ··· ˌ·/ *n* [C] a small piece of material containing nicotine which you stick on your skin to help you stop smoking〔貼在某人皮膚上幫助戒煙的〕尼古丁貼片, 戒煙貼

niece /nis; niːs/ *n* [C] the daughter of your brother or sister, or the daughter of your wife's or husband's brother or sister 姪女; 外甥女 —compare 比較 NEPHEW —see picture at 參見 FAMILY 圖

niff /nɪf; nɪf/ *n* [singular] *BrE informal* a bad smell【英, 非正式】難聞的氣味 —**niffy** *adj*

nif·ty /ˈnɪftɪ; ˈnɪfti/ *adj informal* very good, fast, or effective【非正式】極好的; 極快的; 極有效的: *a nifty little gadget for squeezing oranges* 精巧的榨橙汁的小玩意兒 | *a nifty little car* 跑得極快的小汽車

nig·gard·ly /ˈnɪgɚdlɪ; ˈnɪgədli/ *adj* **1** unwilling to spend money or be generous; STINGY 小氣的, 吝嗇的: *The landlord was niggardly about repairs.* 房東在維修方面很吝嗇。**2** a niggardly gift, amount, salary etc is not worth very much and is given unwillingly 很少的, 勉強給的: *niggardly wages* 微薄的工資 —**niggard** *n* [C] —**niggardliness** *n* [U]

nig·ger /ˈnɪgɚ; ˈnɪgə/ *n* [C] *taboo* an extremely offensive word for a black person【諱】黑鬼〔對黑人極具冒犯性的用語〕—see 見 NEGRO (USAGE)

nig·gle¹ /ˈnɪgl; ˈnɪgəl/ *v* **1** [T] if something niggles you, it worries or annoys you slightly and you cannot forget about it 惹惱, 煩擾: *Something's been niggling her all day.* 有件事一整天都在煩擾着她。**2** [I] to argue or make criticisms about small unimportant details 挑剔, 吹毛求疵: **[+about/over]** *She niggled over every detail of the bill.* 她在這賬單上處處挑毛病。—**niggle** *n* [C] —**niggler** *n* [C]

nig·gling /ˈnɪglɪŋ; ˈnɪgəlɪŋ/ *adj* **niggling doubt/worry/suspicion etc** a doubt etc that keeps worrying you slightly and that you cannot stop thinking about 使人心煩的疑慮/擔心/懷疑等: *A niggling doubt about Marlow's motives suddenly entered his mind.* 他心裡突然懷疑起馬洛的動機。

nigh /naɪ; naɪ/ *adv* **1 nigh on** *old-fashioned* almost【過時】幾乎: *There were nigh on 40 people there.* 那裡有近40個人。**2** *literary* near【文】接近, 臨近: **draw nigh** (=come near or be about to happen soon) 接近; 即將來臨 *Winter draws nigh.* 冬天快要來了。—see also 另見 **well-nigh**

night /naɪt; naɪt/ *n*

1 ▶WHEN IT IS DARK 黑夜時◀ [C,U] the dark part of each 24-hour period when the sun cannot be seen 夜晚, 夜間: *a starry night* 星夜 | **at night/by night** (=when it is dark) 在夜裡 *At night the temperature drops below zero.* 溫度在夜間降至零度以下。| *They travelled by night and slept during the day.* 他們夜間旅行, 白天睡覺。| **all night (long)** (=through the whole night) 整夜; 通宵 *In New York, some stores stay open all night long.* 在紐約, 有些商店通宵營業。| *The party went on all night.* 晚會持續了一整夜。| **night train/flight/bus** (=a train, plane, bus etc that travels at night) 夜班火車/航班/公共汽車 *We took the night train to Glasgow.* 我們坐夜班火車去格拉斯哥。| **the night sky/air** *the cold night air* 夜間寒冷的空氣 | **at dead of night** (=in the middle of the night when it is quiet) 夜深人靜時 *Their meetings were held in secret at dead of night.* 他們的會議是在夜深人靜時祕密召開的。| **night falls** (=it becomes dark) 夜幕降臨 *Night was beginning to fall as we sailed into Vera Cruz.* 當我們駛入維拉克魯斯港時, 夜幕開始降臨。

2 ▶WHEN YOU SLEEP 睡覺時◀ the time when most people are in bed 夜晚, 晚上: *I didn't sleep too well last night.* 我昨晚睡得不太好。| *We had to get up in the middle of the night.* 我們不得不在半夜裡起牀。| *14 nights in a 5 star hotel* 在一家五星級酒店住的14夜 | **at night** (=when it is night) 在夜裡 *She's so worried she can't sleep at night.* 她擔心得晚上無法入睡。| **in**

N

the night (=during the night) 在夜間 *The baby woke up twice in the night.* 嬰兒夜裡醒了兩次。| **spend the night** *We spent the first two nights of our vacation in a cheap motel.* 我們度假的頭兩個晚上住在一家廉價的汽車旅館裡。| **spend the night with sb** (=and have sex with someone) 與某人過夜(並發生性關係) | **stay the night** (=sleep at someone's house) 借宿 *If you miss the last bus home, you can always stay the night.* 如果你沒趕上末班車回家, 你可以隨時來借宿。| **a good night's sleep** (=when you sleep well all night) 一夜好覺 *You look exhausted! What you need is a good night's sleep.* 你看起來累壞了！你需要好好睡一夜。| **have a bad night** *BrE* (=not sleep much)【英】沒睡好覺

3 ►EVENING 傍晚◄ [C,U] the time during the evening until you go to bed 傍晚, 黃昏; 晚上: *Most nights we just stay at home and watch television.* 大多數晚上我們只是留在家裡看電視。| **last night** *Where did you go last night?* 昨晚你去哪兒了？| **at night** *Do you mean 9:30 in the morning or 9:30 at night?* 你是說上午九點半還是晚上九點半？| **tomorrow night** *My parents are coming for dinner tomorrow night.* 我父母明晚要過來吃晚飯。| **the other night** *spoken* (=a few nights ago)【口】幾天前的一個晚上 *Did I tell you I saw Nicky Ansell the other night?* 我有沒有告訴你我前幾天晚上看到了尼基·安塞爾？| **Friday night/Saturday night etc** *There's a party at Ben's place on Saturday night.* 星期六晚上班恩的家裡有個聚會。| **a night out** (=a night when you go to a party, restaurant, theatre etc) 外出的一晚 *Let's go see a band – I could do with a night out.* 我們去看樂隊演出吧 —— 我想晚上出去玩玩。| **late at night** *Anna doesn't like him walking home late at night.* 安娜不想他深夜走路回家。

4 nights *especially AmE* if you do something nights, you do it regularly or often at night【尤美】每晚; 晚上經常: *I lie awake nights.* 我晚上躺在牀上總是睡不着。| **work nights** *I'd hate to work nights – it's so antisocial.* 我討厭晚上工作, 那太不合生活常規。

5 night! *spoken* used to say goodbye to someone when it is late in the evening or when they are going to bed【口】晚安!: *Night! See you tomorrow!* 晚安!明天見!

6 night night! *spoken* used to say goodbye to someone, especially a child, when they are going to bed【口】晚安!〔尤用於對兒童說〕

7 night after night every night for a long period〔長期以來〕每晚; 一夜又一夜地: *He's out drinking night after night.* 他每天晚上都出去喝酒。

8 night and day/day and night all the time 夜以繼日地, 日夜不停地: *The store is guarded day and night.* 這家商店日夜都有保安人員看守。

9 late night a night when you go to bed later than usual 比通常晚睡的晚上: *You're looking sleepy this morning. Too many late nights!* 你今天上午看起來很睏。熬夜太多了! —see also 另見 LATE-NIGHT

10 have an early night to go to bed earlier than usual 睡得早,〔比平常〕早睡覺: *I'm exhausted – I think I'll have an early night.* 我累極了, 我想我要早點睡覺。

11 last thing at night just before you go to bed 臨睡之前: *You should never eat cheese last thing at night.* 臨睡之前千萬不要吃乳酪。

12 at this time of night! *spoken* used when you are surprised because something happens late at night【口】夜這麼深了!: *Who on earth could be calling at this time of night?* 誰會這麼晚打電話來呢?

13 first night/opening night the first performance of a play or show 首場演出; 首映: *We saw 'Miss Saigon' on its opening night.* 我們看了《西貢小姐》的首場演出。

14 make a night of it to stay out late drinking, dancing etc 在外痛快地玩一個晚上 —see also 另見 NIGHTLY

night·cap /ˈnaɪtˌkæp; ˈnaɪtkæp/ *n* [C] **1** an alcoholic drink that you have just before you go to bed 臨睡前喝的酒 **2** a soft cap that people in the past used to wear in bed〔舊時的〕睡帽

night·clothes /ˈnaɪtkloðz; ˈnaɪtkləʊðz/ *n* [plural] clothes that you wear in bed 睡衣

night·club /ˈnaɪtˌklʌb; ˈnaɪtklʌb/ *n* [C] a place of entertainment open late at night where people can dance and drink 夜總會

night·club·bing /ˈnaɪtˌklʌbɪŋ; ˈnaɪtˌklʌbɪŋ/ *n* [U] **go nightclubbing** *BrE* to spend an evening at a nightclub【英】去夜總會

night de·pos·it·o·ry /ˈ· ·,··· ·/ *n* [C] *AmE* NIGHT SAFE【美】夜用保險箱

night·dress /ˈnaɪtˌdrɛs; ˈnaɪtdres/ *n* [C] a piece of clothing, like a thin dress, that women wear in bed 女睡袍

night·fall /ˈnaɪtˌfɔl; ˈnaɪtfɔːl/ *n* [U] the time when it begins to get dark in the evening; DUSK 黃昏, 傍晚: *We rushed to reach home before nightfall.* 我們在黃昏之前趕回了家。

night·gown /ˈnaɪtˌgaʊn; ˈnaɪtgaʊn/ *n* [C] a nightdress 女睡袍

night·hawk /ˈnaɪtˌhɔk; ˈnaɪthɔːk/ *n* [C] *especially AmE informal* someone who enjoys staying awake all night【尤美, 非正式】夜貓子, 喜歡熬夜的人

night·ie /ˈnaɪtɪ; ˈnaɪti/ *n* [C] *informal* a NIGHTDRESS【非正式】女睡袍

nigh·tin·gale /ˈnaɪtɪŋˌgel; ˈnaɪtɪŋgeɪl/ *n* [C] a small bird that sings very beautifully, especially at night 夜鶯

night·life /ˈnaɪtlaɪf; ˈnaɪtlaɪf/ *n* [U] entertainment in the evening 夜生活, 夜間娛樂活動: *It's a beautiful place but there's not much nightlife.* 這是個美麗的地方, 但沒有多少夜生活。

night·light /ˈnaɪtlaɪt; ˈnaɪtlaɪt/ *n* [C] a small electric light that you put in a child's room at night〔兒童房中的〕小夜燈

night·long /ˈnaɪtˌlɔŋ; ˈnaɪtlɒŋ/ *adj* [only before noun 僅用於名詞前] *literary* lasting all night【文】徹夜的, 通宵的: *a nightlong vigil* 通宵守夜

night·ly /ˈnaɪtlɪ; ˈnaɪtli/ *adv* every night 每晚, 每夜: *The band performed nightly.* 樂隊每晚都演出。—**nightly** *adj*: *nightly news broadcasts* 晚間新聞廣播

night·mare /ˈnaɪtˌmɛr; ˈnaɪtmeə/ *n* [C] **1** a very frightening dream 惡夢, 夢魘: *Years after the accident I still have nightmares about it.* 事故發生很多年之後, 我依然做惡夢。**2** a very unpleasant or frightening experience 不愉快的[可怕的]經歷: *He kept trying to hold my hand all the time – it was a real nightmare!* 他一直想要握住我的手, 真是可怕極了!| **nightmare journey/situation etc** (=the worst journey etc you can imagine) 可怕的旅程/情景等 *a nightmare sea voyage in a raging storm* 狂風暴雨中一次可怕的海上航行 **3** something terrible that you fear may happen in the future 可能發生的恐怖事件: **[+of]** *the nightmare of a nuclear war* 核戰爭的恐怖 | **nightmare scenario** (=the worst or most frightening situation that you can imagine) 最壞[恐怖]的設想 —**nightmarish** *adj*

night owl /ˈ· ·/ *n* [C] *informal* someone who enjoys staying awake all night【非正式】夜貓子, 喜歡熬夜的人

night por·ter /ˈ· ˌ··/ *n* [C] someone who works at the main entrance of a hotel during the night〔旅館門口的〕夜班服務員

night safe /ˈ· ·/ *n* [C] *BrE* a special hole in the outside wall of a bank into which a customer can put money or documents when the bank is closed【英】夜用保險箱〔銀行關門後, 其外牆上供顧客存放錢物的安全存放器〕; NIGHT DEPOSITORY *AmE*【美】

night school /ˈ· ·/ *n* [U] classes that take place in the evening for people who work during the day 夜校

night shift /ˈ· ·/ *n* [C] **1** a period of time at night during which people regularly work, especially in a factory 夜班: *She's on the night shift this week.* 她這星期上夜班。**2** the group of people who work at this time 上夜班的人: *The night shift was just arriving.* 上夜班的人正在陸續到來。

N

night·shirt /ˈnaɪtˌʃɝt; ˈnaɪt-ʃɜːt/ *n* [C] a long loose shirt that people, especially men, wear in bed〔男用〕襯衫式長睡衣

night soil /ˈ· ·/ *n* [U] *technical* human waste used in growing crops【術語】〔人的〕糞便

night spot /ˈ· ·/ *n* [C] a place people go to at night for entertainment 夜間娛樂場所; 夜總會: *my favourite New York night spot* 紐約我最喜歡的一個夜間娛樂場所

night·stand /ˈnaɪtˌstænd; ˈnaɪtstænd/ *n* [C] *AmE* a small table beside a bed【美】牀頭櫃

night·stick /ˈnaɪtˌstɪk; ˈnaɪtˌstɪk/ *n* [C] *AmE* a short thick stick carried as a weapon by police officers【美】警棍; TRUNCHEON *BrE*【英】

night·time /ˈnaɪtˌtaɪm; ˈnaɪtˌtaɪm/ *n* [U] the time during the night 夜間: **at nighttime** *animals that hunt at nighttime* 夜間獵食的動物 —opposite 反義詞 DAYTIME

night watch /ˈ· ·/ *n* **the night watch** a kind of police force in the past, who looked after a town at night〔舊時的〕巡夜警察; 值夜警衛(隊)

night watch·man /ˌ· ˈ·· / *n* [C] someone whose job is to guard a building at night〔大樓的〕夜間守衛

night·wear /ˈnaɪtˌwɛr; ˈnaɪtweə/ *n* [U] clothes that you wear in bed at night 睡衣

nig·nog /ˈnɪg ˌnɑg; ˈnɪg nɒg/ *n* [C] *BrE old-fashioned taboo* an extremely offensive word for a black person【英, 過時, 諱】黑鬼〔對黑人極具冒犯性的用語〕

ni·hil·is·m /ˈnaɪəlˌɪzəm; ˈnaɪḷlɪzəm/ *n* [U] **1** the belief that nothing has any meaning or value 虛無主義〔認為一切都沒有意義或價值〕**2** the idea that all social and political institutions should be destroyed 政治虛無主義〔主張摧毀一切社會和政治機構的思想〕—**nihilist** *n* [C] —**nihilistic** /ˌnaɪəˈlɪstɪk; ˌnaɪḷˈlɪstɪk◂/ *adj*

-nik /nɪk; nɪk/ *suffix* [in nouns 構成名詞] *informal* someone who is connected with something or enjoys something【非正式】與…有關的人; 愛好…的人: *a computernik* (=someone who works with or is very keen on computers) 用電腦工作的人; 電腦迷 | *a peacenik* (=someone who supports peace) 和平愛好者

3 **nil** /nɪl; nɪl/ *n* [U] **1** nothing 無; 零: *The new machine reduced labour costs to almost nil.* 新機器把人工成本幾乎降到零。**2** *BrE* the number zero, used in sports results【英】〔體育比賽比分中的〕零: *Our team won by two goals to nil.* 我隊以二比零獲勝。

nim·ble /ˈnɪmbḷ; ˈnɪmbəl/ *adj* **1** able to move quickly and easily with light neat movements 敏捷的, 靈活的: *a nimble climber* 敏捷的爬山者 | *nimble fingers* 靈巧的手指 **2 a nimble mind/brain/wit** an ability to think quickly or understand things easily 敏捷的思維/頭腦/才智: *They liked his nimble mind – his ability to come up with original ideas.* 他們喜歡他敏捷的頭腦, 他常常都能提出一些新穎的想法。—**nimbly** *adv* —**nimbleness** *n* [U]

nim·bus /ˈnɪmbəs; ˈnɪmbəs/ *n* **1** [C,U] a dark cloud that may bring rain or snow 雨雲 **2** [C] a HALO〔神像等頭上的〕光輪, 光環

nim·by /ˈnɪmbɪ; ˈnɪmbi/ *n* [C] not in my backyard; someone who does not want a particular activity or building near their home 反對自家附近有某種活動或建築的人—**nimby** *adj*: *nimby attitudes* 反對在附近建樓或舉行活動的態度

nin·com·poop /ˈnɪŋkəmˌpup; ˈnɪŋkəmpuːp/ *n* [C] *old-fashioned* a stupid person【過時】笨人, 傻瓜

nine /naɪn; naɪn/ *number* **1** 9 九(個) —see table on page C1 參見 C1 頁附錄 **2 nine times out of ten** almost always 十之八九, 幾乎總是, 幾乎每次: *Nine times out of ten it's careless driving that causes an accident.* 事故十之八九是由於駕駛不謹慎造成的。**3 nine days' wonder** a thing or event that makes people very excited for a short time 轟動一時(即被遺忘)的事物; 曇花一現的新鮮事 —see also 另見 **dressed up to the nines** (DRESSED (5)), **be on cloud nine** (CLOUD[1] (4))

nine·pins /ˈnaɪnˌpɪnz; ˈnaɪnˌpɪnz/ *n* [U] a game in which you roll a ball at nine bottle-shaped objects to try to knock them down 九柱滾球戲

nine·teen /ˌnaɪnˈtin; ˌnaɪnˈtiːn◂/ *number* **1** 19 十九(個) —see table on page C1 參見 C1 頁附錄 **2 nineteen to the dozen** if you talk nineteen to the dozen, you talk very quickly and without stopping 說個不停, 喋喋不休 —**nineteenth** *adj*

nine·teenth /ˈnaɪnˈtinθ; ˌnaɪnˈtiːnθ◂/ *number* [singular] *humorous* an expression used by GOLF players meaning the bar where they drink after playing【幽默】第十九穴〔指高爾夫球員在打球後喝酒聊天的酒吧〕

nine-to-five /ˌ· · ˈ·◂/ *adv* **work nine-to-five** to work from 9 o'clock until 5 o'clock; the normal working hours of an office worker 從早上 9 點工作到下午 5 點〔早上 9 點至下午 5 點是辦公室工作人員正常的工作時間〕—**nine-to-five** *adj*: *a nine-to-five job* 一份朝九晚五的工作

nine·ty /ˈnaɪntɪ; ˈnaɪnti/ *number* **1** 90 九十(個) —see table on page C1 參見 C1 頁附錄 **2 the nineties** also 又作 **the '90's, the 1990's;** the years from 1990 to 1999 20 世紀 90 年代 **3 be in your nineties** to be aged from ninety to ninety-nine 九十多歲: *My grandparents are both in their nineties.* 我的祖父母都九十多歲了。—**ninetieth** *number*

nin·ja /ˈnɪndʒə; ˈnɪndʒə/ *n* [C] a member of a Japanese class of professional killers in former times〔舊時的〕忍者, 日本武士: *a ninja warrior* 日本武士

nin·ny /ˈnɪnɪ; ˈnɪni/ *n* [C] *old-fashioned* a silly person【過時】笨人, 傻瓜

ninth[1] /naɪnθ; naɪnθ/ *number* 9th 第九 —see table on page C1 參見 C1 頁附錄

ninth[2] *number* [C] one of nine equal parts of something 九分之一

nip[1] /nɪp; nɪp/ *v* **nipped, nipping 1** [T] to bite someone or something lightly 輕咬: *The dog nipped my ankles.* 那隻狗輕輕地咬了一下我的腳踝。**2** [I always+adv/prep] *BrE informal* to go somewhere quickly or for a short time【英, 非正式】快走; 急忙離去; 去一會兒: **[+in/down/out etc]** *I'm just nipping out to the shops – I'll be back in five minutes.* 我只是去一下商店, 五分鐘後就回來。| *Another car nipped in* (=nipped into a space) *in front of me.* 又一輛車突然插到我前面。**3 nip sth in the bud** to prevent something from becoming a problem by stopping it as soon as it starts 把某事物消滅在萌芽狀態; 對某事物一開始即加以阻止: *If you feel a cold coming on try to nip it in the bud by keeping warm and getting a lot of sleep.* 如果你感覺要感冒了, 就穿暖些, 多睡覺, 不讓它進一步惡化。**4** [T] *BrE* to suddenly and accidentally press something tightly between two edges or surfaces【英】夾; 鉗; 掐; 捏: *He nipped his finger in the door.* 他的手指被門夾了一下。

nip sth ↔ **off** *phr v* [T] to remove a small part of something, especially a plant, by pressing it tightly between your finger and thumb 掐掉, 摘去〔尤指植物〕: *She nipped off a dead flower.* 她掐掉了一朵凋謝的花。

nip[2] *n* [C] **1** the act or result of pressing something between two edges or biting it lightly 夾; 鉗; 掐; 捏; 輕咬 **2** a small amount of strong alcoholic drink 少量的烈性酒: **[+of]** *a nip of brandy* 一點兒白蘭地酒 **3 a nip in the air** coldness in the air 寒氣, 寒冷 **4 nip and tuck** *AmE informal*【美, 非正式】**a)** if two competitors are nip and tuck in a race or competition, they are doing equally well; **neck and neck** (NECK[1] (11)) 並駕齊驅, 不相上下: *They were nip and tuck in the last lap of the race.* 他們比賽到最後一圈時仍難分高低。**b)** equally likely to happen or not happen 概率相等, 均有可能: *I might just make it to the airport, but it'll be nip and tuck.* 我也許能及時趕到機場, 但這很難說。

nipp·er /ˈnɪpɚ; ˈnɪpə/ *n* [C] *BrE informal* a child, especially a small boy【英, 非正式】小孩〔尤指男孩〕

nip·ple /ˈnɪpḷ; ˈnɪpəl/ *n* [C] **1** the small dark circular part of a woman's breast, through which a baby sucks milk

〔女人的〕乳頭 —see picture at 參見 BODY 圖 **2** one of the two small dark circular parts on a man's chest〔男人的〕乳頭 —see picture at 參見 BODY 圖 **3** *AmE* the rubber part on a baby's bottle that a baby sucks milk through【美】〔奶瓶的〕橡皮奶嘴; TEAT (1) *BrE*【英】**4** a small thing shaped like a nipple on a machine, with a hole in it which you pour oil through〔機器上的〕(乳頭狀) 注油口; 加油嘴

nip·py /ˈnɪpɪ; ˈnipi/ *adj informal*【非正式】**1** weather that is nippy is slightly cold〔天氣〕有點冷的, 冷颼颼的: *It's rather nippy out there.* 外面有點冷颼颼的。**2** *BrE* moving quickly or able to move quickly【英】敏捷的, 動作快的: *a nippy little car* 一輛快速的小汽車 —**nippiness** *n* [U] —**nippily** *adv*

nir·va·na /nɪrˋvɑnə; nɪəˈvɑːnə/ *n* [U] **1** *technical* a state of knowledge or understanding that is beyond life and death, suffering, and change, and is the aim of believers in Buddhism【術語】〔佛教的〕涅槃; 解脫 **2** *informal* a condition of great happiness and a feeling of peace【非正式】極樂世界, 無憂無慮的境界

ni·si /ˈnaɪsaɪ; ˈnaɪsaɪ/ *n* —see 見 DECREE NISI

nit /nɪt; nɪt/ *n* [C] **1** an egg of a LOUSE (=a small insect that sucks blood), that is sometimes found in people's hair 虱卵, 蟣子 **2** *BrE informal* a silly person【英, 非正式】笨蛋, 傻瓜

nit·pick·ing /ˈnɪt͵pɪkɪŋ; ˈnɪt͵pɪkɪŋ/ *n* [U] *informal* the annoying habit of arguing about unimportant details, especially in someone's work【非正式】〔尤指對某人的工作〕挑剔, 吹毛求疵 —**nitpicking** *adj* —**nitpicker** *n* [C]

ni·trate /ˈnaɪtret; ˈnaɪtreɪt/ *n* [C,U] a chemical compound that is mainly used to improve the soil for growing crops 硝酸鹽〔主要用作肥料〕

ni·tre *BrE*【英】, **niter** *AmE*【美】/ˈnaɪtɚ; ˈnaɪtə/ *n* [U] one of several natural nitrates, including SALTPETRE 硝石

nitric ac·id /͵naɪtrɪk ˋæsɪd; ͵naɪtrɪk ˈæsɪd/ *n* [U] a powerful acid that is used in explosives and other chemical products 硝酸

ni·tro·gen /ˈnaɪtrədʒən; ˈnaɪtrədʒən/ *n* [U] a gas that is an ELEMENT (=a simple substance) without colour or smell, that forms most of the Earth's air 氮 (氣)

ni·tro·gly·ce·rine, nitroglycerin /͵naɪtrəˋglɪsərɪn; ͵naɪtrəʊˈglɪsərɪn/ *n* [U] a powerful liquid explosive 硝化甘油

nit·ty-grit·ty /ˈnɪtɪ ˋgrɪtɪ; ͵nɪti ˈgrɪti/ *n informal*【非正式】**the nitty-gritty** the basic and practical facts of a subject or activity 基本內容; 實質性部分: **get down to the nitty-gritty** *Let's get down to the nitty-gritty and work out the costs, shall we?* 讓我們來談談實質性問題, 把成本計算出來, 好嗎?

nit·wit /ˈnɪt͵wɪt; ˈnɪt-wɪt/ *n* [C] *informal* a silly person【非正式】笨蛋, 傻瓜

nix¹ /nɪks; nɪks/ *adv AmE old-fashioned* no【美, 過時】不, 不行

nix² *v* [T] *AmE old-fashioned* to answer no to something or FORBID something【美, 過時】拒絕, 否決; 禁止: *They nixed the idea of filming in Ireland.* 他們否決了在愛爾蘭拍攝的建議。

no *plural* **nos.** the written abbreviation of 縮寫= NUMBER

no¹ /no; nəʊ/ *adv* [S1] [W1] **1** *spoken* used to give a negative reply to a question, offer, or request【口】不, 不行〔對問題、提議或請求表示否定或拒絕〕: *"Are you Italian?" "No, I'm Spanish."* "你是意大利人嗎?" "不, 我是西班牙人。" | *"Do you want any more?" "No thanks."* "你還要再來點兒嗎?" "不要了, 謝謝。" | *"Could you help me write this?" "No, sorry, I haven't got time at the moment."* "你能幫我寫嗎?" "抱歉, 不行, 我現在沒時間。" | **say no** *Would you be terribly offended if I said no?* 如果我拒絕的話, 你會很生氣嗎? | **the answer's no** *If she asks to borrow any money, the answer's no!* 要是她想借錢, 休想! —opposite 反義詞 YES¹ (1) **2** *spoken* used to say that you disagree with a statement【口】不, 不是〔表示不同意〕: *"You're always complaining about things." "No, I'm not!"* "你總是愛發牢騷。" "不, 我沒有。" **3** *spoken* used to say that you agree with a negative statement【口】是, 對〔對否定陳述表示贊同〕: *"They shouldn't be charging such high prices." "No, it's ridiculous!"* "他們不該要這麼高的價錢。" "沒錯, 太離譜了!" **4 won't take no for an answer** if someone won't take no for an answer, they say firmly that you must do something 不能接受否定的回答: *You simply must come to dinner, and I won't take no for an answer.* 你必須來吃晚飯, 非來不可。**5** *spoken* used to show that you are shocked, surprised, annoyed, or disappointed by what someone has just told you, or by what has just happened【口】不會吧, 不可能〔表示驚訝、生氣或失望〕: *"This skirt cost me £7." "No!"* "這條裙子花了我 7 英鎊。" "不會吧!" | **Oh no** *Oh no, not another false alarm?* 哦, 不會又是一次假警報吧? **6 no good/no use etc** not at all good, not at all useful etc 沒有任何好處/沒有用等: *This map's no use – it's out of date.* 這張地圖毫無用處, 早就過時了。| *I'm no good at physics.* 我的物理很差。**7 no better/no more/no less etc** not better, not more etc 不比…好/不多於/不少於等: *They've written no fewer than ten letters of complaint and still nothing's been done.* 他們已經寫了不少於十封投訴信, 但甚麼問題也沒解決。**8 no small part/no great matter etc** *formal* a large part, a small matter etc【正式】大作用/小事等: *a question of no great importance* (=of little importance) 無關緊要的問題 | *She had no small part* (=had a large part) *in its success.* 此事成功她大有功勞。

no² *determiner* [S1] [W1] **1** not one or not any 沒有, 無: *Do you mind having black coffee? There's no milk.* 喝清咖啡你介意嗎?沒有牛奶了。| *There're no buses in this part of town.* 城裡這一帶沒有公共汽車。| *a house with no central heating* 沒有中央暖氣系統的房子 | **be no reason why** *There's no reason at all why Jenny shouldn't come along too.* 珍妮不一起來完全沒有理由。**2** used on a notice to say that something is forbidden 不准, 不許〔用於告示中表示禁止某事〕: *No parking* 禁止停車 | *No smoking* 禁止吸煙 **3 in no time** *informal* very soon or very quickly【非正式】很快, 馬上: *We're almost home now – we'll be there in no time.* 我們快到家了, 轉眼就到。**4 there's no knowing/telling/saying etc** *spoken* used to say that it is impossible to guess what will happen or what is true【口】誰也說不準, 不可能知道[說清]: *He's such a strange person – there's no knowing what he'll do next.* 他這人很怪, 誰也說不準他下一步會做甚麼。**5 be no fool/expert/friend etc** to be not at all stupid etc 根本不是傻瓜/專家/朋友等: *Larry's no friend of mine.* 拉里根本不是我的朋友。

USAGE NOTE 用法說明: NO

GRAMMAR 語法

No is used before nouns and adjectives when it means 'not any'. no 用在名詞和形容詞前表示"沒有"、"並不": *No problem.* 沒問題。| *That's no good – it's broken.* 那沒有用, 已經破了。| *He's no slimmer than he was before.* 他跟以前一樣胖。

Otherwise **not** is used, especially before *a, all, many, much,* and *enough.* 其他情況下則用 not, 尤其是在 *a, all, many, much* 和 *enough* 之前: *Not many tourists come here.* 來這兒的遊客不多。| *not enough food for all of us* 食物不夠大家吃 | *She's not stupid.* 她不笨。| *The news was not good.* 這不是一個好消息。

SPELLING 拼法

Nobody meaning 'no one' is always spelt as one word. 表示"沒有人"的 nobody 是連在一起拼寫的一個單詞: *There was nobody there* (=no person). 那裡沒有人。Compare 比較: *There was no body there* (=there was not a dead body there). 那裡沒有屍體。

N

no³ *n plural* **noes 1** [singular] a negative answer or decision 不, 拒絕; 否定, 否認: *The answer was a definite no.* 答覆是明確的拒絕。**2 noes** [plural] votes against a proposal in parliament〔議會中的〕反對票

No.10 /ˌnʌmbɚ ˋtɛn; ˌnʌmbə ˈten/ *n* [singular] No. 10 Downing Street; the address of the official home of the British Prime Minister 唐寧街十號〔英國首相官邸〕

no-ac·count /ˈ· ·ˌ·/ *adj AmE*【美】another form of the word NO-COUNT no-count 的另一種形式: *a series of no-account boyfriends who drank too much* 一個接一個沒出息的酗酒男友

No·ah's ark /ˌnoəz ˋɑrk; ˌnəʊəz ˈɑːk/ *n* [singular] the large boat which Noah built, according to the Bible, to save his family and two of every type of animal from a flood sent by God〔《聖經》中的〕挪亞方舟

nob /nɑb; nɒb/ *n* [C] *BrE old-fashioned* a rich person with a high social position【英, 過時】有錢有勢的人, 上流人物: *They watched the nobs in their satin and feathers.* 他們注視着穿着華麗的上流人物。

no ball /ˈ· ·/ *n* [C] an act of bowling (BOWL² (1, 2)) the ball, in games such as CRICKET, in a way not allowed by the rules〔板球等球類運動中的〕投球犯規

nob·ble /ˋnɑbl; ˈnɒbəl/ *v* [T] *BrE informal*【英, 非正式】**1** to get someone's attention, especially in order to persuade them to do something〔尤指為說服某人做某事而〕引起〔某人〕的注意: *I'll try to nobble Jim and ask him if he'll help us.* 我會努力接近吉姆, 問他能不能幫助我們。**2** to make someone do what you want by offering them money or threatening them 收買; 要挾 **3** to prevent a horse from winning a race, especially by giving it drugs〔尤指給賽馬服藥〕使不能取勝

No·bel Prize /ˋnoˌbɛl ˋpraɪz; nəʊˌbel ˈpraɪz/ *n* [C] a prize given in Sweden each year to people from any country for important work in science, medicine, literature, economics, or work towards world peace 諾貝爾獎

no·bil·i·ty /noˋbɪlətɪ; nəʊˈbɪlɨti/ *n* **1 the nobility** the group of people in some countries who belong to the highest social class and have titles such as Duke or Countess; the ARISTOCRACY 貴族〔階層〕**2** [U] the quality of being noble in character or appearance 崇高, 高貴: *For him, true nobility is found in hard work.* 對他來說, 真正的高尚在於勤奮。

no·ble¹ /ˋnobḷ; ˈnəʊbəl/ *adj* **1** someone who is noble behaves in a morally good or generous way that should be admired 高尚的, 崇高的; 豁達的: *It's very noble of you to spend all your weekends helping the old folk.* 你心地真好, 把週末時間全部用來幫助老人。| *noble ideals* 崇高的理想 **2** something that is noble is very impressive and beautiful 宏偉的, 堂皇的, 壯麗的: *this noble monument to our war heroes* 宏偉的戰爭英雄紀念碑 **3** belonging to the nobility 貴族的, 顯貴的: *a man of noble birth* 貴族出身的人 **4** a noble metal, such as gold or silver, is not affected chemically by the air〔金、銀等貴金屬〕不〔與空氣〕起化學變化的, 不易鏽蝕的 —compare 比較 BASE METAL

noble² *n* [C] a member of the highest social class with a title such as Duke or Countess, especially in the past〔尤指舊時的〕貴族〈如公爵或女伯爵〉: *a vast gathering of kings and nobles* 一大羣王公貴族 —compare 比較 COMMONER

no·ble·man /ˋnobḷmən; ˈnəʊbəlmən/ *n plural* **noblemen** /-mən; -mən/ [C] a man who is a member of the highest social class and has a title such as Duke〔男〕貴族〈如公爵〉

no·blesse o·blige /noˋblɛs oˋbliʒ; nəʊˌbles əˈbliːʒ/ *n French* used to mean that people who belong to a high social class should be generous and behave with honour【法】位高則任重; 貴人行為理應高尚

no·ble·wom·an /ˋnobḷˌwʊmən; ˈnəʊbəlˌwʊmən/ *n plural* **noblewomen** /-ˌwɪmɪn; -ˌwɪmɨn/ [C] a woman who is a member of the highest social class with a title such as Duchess 女貴族〈如女公爵或公爵夫人〉

no·bly /ˋnoblɪ; ˈnəʊbli/ *adv* **1** in a morally good or generous way that should be admired 崇高地, 高尚地; 豁達地: *great pain nobly borne* 從容地承受巨大的痛苦 **2 nobly born** *literary* having parents who are members of the NOBILITY (1)【文】出身於貴族的

no·bod·y¹ /ˋnoˌbɑdɪ; ˈnəʊbədi/ *pron* no one 沒有人, 無人, 誰也不: *I knocked on the door but nobody answered.* 我敲了敲門, 但沒人來開。—see also 另見 **like nobody's business** (BUSINESS (24)), **be nobody's fool** (FOOL¹ (3)) —see 見 NO² (USAGE)

nobody² *n* [C] someone who is not important and has no influence 無名小卒, 小人物, 無足輕重的人: *I'm tired of being a nobody!* 我再也不想當無名小卒了!

no-claims bo·nus /·ˈ· ˌ··/ *n* [C] *BrE* a reduction in the amount that you have to pay for car insurance, because you have not made any claims【英】無索償折扣, 無索償獎勵, 無賠款回扣〔指汽車保險, 如在保險期間未有任何賠款要求, 可以給予一定回扣〕

no-count /ˈ· ·/ *adj* [only before noun 僅用於名詞前] *AmE* a no-count person never achieves very much because they are very lazy【美】沒出息的, 混日子的, 不長進的: *my no-count good-for-nothing nephew* 我那個一無所長沒出息的姪子

noc·tur·nal /nɑkˋtɝnəl; nɒkˈtɜːnl/ *adj* **1** *technical* an animal that is nocturnal is active at night【術語】〔動物〕夜間活動的: *Hamsters are nocturnal creatures.* 倉鼠是夜間出沒的動物。**2** *formal* happening at night【正式】夜間發生的: *nocturnal visits* 夜訪 —**nocturnally** *adv*

noc·turne /ˋnɑktɝn; ˈnɒktɜːn/ *n* [C] a piece of music, especially a soft beautiful piece of piano music〔尤指用鋼琴彈奏的〕夜曲

nod 點頭

The lady nodded her head. 那位女士點了點頭。 Sam shook his head. 山姆搖了搖頭。

nod¹ /nɑd; nɒd/ *v* **nodded, nodding** [I,T] **1** to move your head up and down, especially in order to show agreement or understanding〔尤指表示贊同或理解而〕點頭: *I asked her if she was ready to go, and she nodded.* 我問她是否已準備好出發, 她點了點頭。| **nod your head** *Jane nodded her head sympathetically.* 簡同情地點了點頭。| **nod your approval/agreement etc** (=show your approval etc by nodding) 點頭表示贊成/同意等 **2** to move your head down and up again once in order to greet someone or give someone a sign to do something 點頭〔打招呼或示意〕: **[+at/to]** *The judge nodded at the foreman to proceed.* 法官點頭示意陪審團團長繼續說下去。| *She nodded to us as she walked by.* 她從我們身邊走過時向我們點了點頭。**3 be on nodding terms (with)/have a nodding acquaintance (with)** to know someone slightly or know a little about a subject〔與某人〕只是點頭之交;〔對某事〕略知一二: *Burke was already on nodding terms with a number of senators.* 伯克已經與一些參議員有了點頭之交。| *a nodding acquaintance with local history* 對當地歷史略知一二

nod off *phr v* [I] to begin to sleep, when you do not intend to 打盹, 打瞌睡: *I missed the movie because I'd nodded off.* 我打了個盹, 結果沒看到電影。

nod² *n* **1** [C] an act of nodding 點頭: *The woman greeted*

N

us with a nod of the head. 那個女人向我們點點頭打招呼。| **give a nod** *I showed the doorman my card and he gave a friendly nod.* 我向門衛出示證件, 他友善地點了一下頭。**2 give sb the nod** *BrE informal* to give someone permission to do something【英, 非正式】點頭同意某人〔做某事〕: *We're waiting for the boss to give us the nod on this one.* 我們都在等着老闆的同意。**3 a nod's as good as a wink** *humorous* used to tell someone that you have understood something, although it was said in an indirect way【幽默】不用明說, 不用多說; 一暗示就明白 **4 on the nod** *BrE informal* by general agreement and without discussion【英, 非正式】無異議地; 無反對地: *The chairman's proposals are usually passed on the nod.* 主席的提議通常在無人反對的情況下一致通過。—see also 另見 **the land of nod** (LAND[1] (9))

no·dal /ˋnodəl; ˈnəʊdl/ *adj technical* connected with nodes【術語】節的; 結的: *nodal root systems* 莖節的根系

nod·dle /ˈnɑdḷ; ˈnɒdl/ *n* [C] *BrE old-fashioned* your head or brain【英, 過時】頭; 頭腦; NOODLE *AmE*【美】: *It's easy enough to do if you just use your noddle.* 這事很容易, 你只要動動腦筋就行了。

node /nod; nəʊd/ *n* [C] **1** the place on the stem of a plant from which a leaf or branch grows 莖節〔植物莖上生葉的部分〕**2** a place where lines in a network, GRAPH etc meet or join〔線條的〕交點; 結點 **3** a LYMPH NODE 淋巴結

nod·ule /ˋnɑdʒul; ˈnɒdjuːl/ *n* [C] a small round raised part, especially a small swelling on a plant or someone's body〔植物的〕小結節;〔人體的〕小瘤 —**nodular** *adj*

No·el /noˋɛl; nəʊˈel/ *n* [U] a word used in songs, on cards etc meaning CHRISTMAS 聖誕節〔常用於歌詞、賀卡中〕

noes /noz; nəʊz/ the plural of NO[3]

no-fly zone /ˌ· ˈ· ˌ·/ *n* [C] an area that no airplane is allowed to enter, and in which it would be attacked 禁飛區

nog·gin /ˋnɑgɪn; ˈnɒgɨn/ *n* [C] *old-fashioned*【過時】**1** a small amount of an alcoholic drink 一小杯酒 **2** *informal* your head or brain【非正式】頭; 腦袋: *Use your noggin. Don't light a match in here.* 動動腦子, 別在這裡點火柴。

no-go ar·e·a /ˌ· ˈ· ˌ···/ *n* [C] **1** an area in a city that is controlled by a violent group and is dangerous for anyone else to enter〔城市裡由暴力分子控制的〕危險地帶; 禁區: *They had taken a wrong turning and now found themselves in one of the most dangerous no-go areas in the city.* 他們拐錯了彎, 結果進入了市內最危險的地區之一。**2** a subject that cannot be discussed because it may offend people 忌諱的話題

no·how /ˋnoˌhaʊ; ˈnəʊhaʊ/ *adv usually humorous* not in any way or in any situation【通常幽默】決不; 毫不, 一點也不: *I never liked her nohow.* 我從未喜歡過她。

2 **noise**[1] /nɔɪz; nɔɪz/ *n*

2 **1 ▶SOUND 聲音◀** [C,U] sound, especially a loud or unpleasant sound 噪音, 雜音; 嘈雜聲, 喧鬧聲: *the noise of the traffic* 交通噪音 | *a loud cracking noise* 巨大的爆裂聲 | **make (a) noise** *Try not to make a noise when you go upstairs.* 上樓時盡量不要弄出聲。| *Stop making so much noise.* 別吵了。

2 make polite/encouraging etc noises to talk in a way that sounds polite, encouraging etc 說客氣/鼓勵等的話: *My teacher made encouraging noises when I told her I wanted to go to university.* 我告訴老師我想上大學時, 她連聲鼓勵。| **make the right noises** (=pretend to be concerned about or interested in what someone is saying) 隨聲附和;〔對某人所說的話〕假裝感興趣

3 make a noise about to complain a lot about something so that other people will notice 對…不停地抱怨

4 ▶ELECTRICAL 電的◀ [U] *technical* unwanted signals produced by an electrical CIRCUIT【術語】雜音; 干擾

5 ▶COMPUTERS 電腦◀ [U] *technical* pieces of unwanted information that can prevent a computer from working effectively【術語】噪聲 —see also 另見 BIG NOISE

USAGE NOTE 用法說明: NOISE

WORD CHOICE 詞語辨析: **noise, sound, racket, voice**

A **sound** is anything that you hear. sound 指人所聽到的任何聲音: *I love the sound of the sea.* 我喜歡聽大海的聲音。| *the sound of voices/a guitar/breaking glass* 人聲/結他聲/打碎玻璃的聲音

A **noise** is usually an unpleasant sound, often not made by a person. noise 通常指難聽的聲音, 往往不是由人發出的: *"What's that noise?" she asked nervously.* "那是甚麼聲音?"她緊張地問道。| *They had to shout to make themselves heard above the noise of the machines.* 他們不得不大聲叫喊, 這樣才能壓過機器的噪聲讓別人聽到自己說話。

A **voice** is the sound of a person speaking or singing. voice 指人說話或唱歌的聲音: *We heard voices outside.* 我們聽到外面有人聲。| *She has rather a high-pitched voice.* 她的嗓音很尖。

Racket is an informal word for a loud unpleasant noise. racket 是表示音量大而難聽的噪音的非正式用詞: *They're making a hell of a racket next door.* 他們在隔壁發出很大的噪音。

noise[2] *v* **be noised abroad/about/around** *old-fashioned, especially BrE* if news or information is noised abroad people are talking about it【過時, 尤英】〔消息〕傳播出去: *Rumours of an election are being noised abroad.* 有關要進行一場選舉的謠言到處傳開了。

noise·less·ly /ˋnɔɪzlɪslɪ; ˈnɔɪzləsli/ *adv* without making any sound 無聲無息地, 靜悄悄地: *We crept noiselessly down the hall.* 我們悄悄地穿過大廳。—**noiseless** *adj*: *noiseless tears* 無聲的眼淚 —**noiselessness** *n* [U]

noise pol·lu·tion /ˈ· ·ˌ··/ *n* [U] very loud or continuous loud noise which is considered to be harmful to people 噪音污染

noi·some /ˋnɔɪsəm; ˈnɔɪsəm/ *adj literary* extremely unpleasant【文】極糟的; 十分令人不快的: *The workers lived in noisome slums.* 工人們生活在條件十分惡劣的貧民窟裡。

nois·y /ˋnɔɪzɪ; ˈnɔɪzi/ *adj* making a lot of noise, or full of noise 噪音大的, 嘈雜的, 喧鬧的: *The kids have been really noisy today.* 孩子們今天實在很吵鬧。| *The bar was too noisy and crowded.* 酒吧太吵太擠了。| *a noisy engine* 噪音大的發動機 —**noisily** *adv*: *The children chattered noisily.* 孩子們在哇啦哇啦地聊天。—**noisiness** *n* [U] 3

no·mad /ˋnomæd; ˈnəʊmæd/ *n* [C] a member of a tribe that travels from place to place, especially to find grass for their animals 遊牧民, 遊牧部落中的一員 —**nomadic** /noˋmædɪk; nəʊˈmædɪk/ *adj*: *a nomadic people* 遊牧民族

no-man's-land /ˈ· · ˌ·/ *n* [singular, U] an area of land that no one owns or controls, especially an area between two borders or opposing armies〔尤指邊界處或敵對陣地間的〕無人地帶; 真空地帶

nom de plume /ˌnɑmdəˌplum; ˌnɒm də ˈpluːm/ *n* [C] a name used by a writer instead of their real name 筆名

no·men·cla·ture /ˋnomənˌkletʃɚ; nəʊˈmeŋklətʃə/ *n* [C, U] *formal* a system of naming things, especially in science【正式】〔尤指科學上的〕命名法: *medical nomenclature* 醫學命名法

nom·i·nal /ˋnɑmənḷ; ˈnɒmɨnəl/ *adj* **1 nominal head/leader etc** someone who has the title of leader etc but is not really doing that job 名義上的負責人/領導人等: *Longo was the real power in the Communist Party while Togliatti was merely the nominal head.* 朗哥是〔意大利早期〕共產黨中的真正掌權人物, 而陶格里亞蒂只是名義上的領袖。**2** a nominal sum of money is very small, especially when compared with the usual amount that

N

would be paid for something〔金額〕極小的, 微不足道的, 象徵性的: *Golfers may play this course for a nominal fee in the off-peak season.* 打高爾夫球者在淡季只需付象徵性的一點費用就可以在這塊球場上打球。**3** *technical* connected with or used as a noun【術語】名詞性的, 作名詞用的: *nominal endings such as 'ness' and 'ation'* 諸如 ness 和 ation 等的名詞性詞尾

nom·i·nal·ly /ˈnɑmənḷɪ; ˈnɒmɪnəli/ *adv* officially described as something when this is not really true 名義上: *Although Banda is nominally a Christian island, few of its inhabitants actually attend church.* 雖然班達名義上是個基督教島嶼, 但居民中很少有人去教堂做禮拜。

nom·i·nate /ˈnɑməˌnet; ˈnɒmɨneɪt/ *v* [T] **1** to officially suggest someone for an important position, duty, or prize 提名, 推薦: **nominate sb for sth** *He was nominated for the Nobel Prize.* 他獲得諾貝爾獎提名。| **nominate sb as** *BrE*【英】*I wish to nominate Jane Morrison as president of the club.* 我想提名簡·莫里森為本俱樂部的主席。| **nominate sb to do sth** *I nominate John to represent us at the meeting.* 我推薦約翰代表我們出席會議。**2** to choose someone for a particular job 任命, 委任, 指定: **nominate sb as** *The director nominated me as her official representative at the conference.* 那位董事指定我為她的正式代表出席會議。| **nominate sb to sth** *She was nominated to the legislative council.* 她被任命為立法委員會委員。

nom·i·na·tion /ˌnɑməˈneʃən; ˌnɒmɨˈneɪʃən/ *n* **1** [C,U] the act of officially suggesting someone for a position, honour or prize, or the fact of being suggested for it (被) 提名: **[+for]** *Who will get the Republican nomination for president?* 誰會被共和黨提名競逐總統呢? | *All the committee's nominations were approved.* 該委員會的所有提名均獲得批准。**2** [C] the name of a book, film, actor etc that has been suggested to receive an honour or prize〔書、電影、演員等的〕(被) 提名〔獲獎〕: *'Schindler's List' was an obvious nomination for an Oscar.*《舒特拉的名單》顯然是角逐奧斯卡獎的提名影片。**3** [C,U] the act of choosing someone for a particular job, or the fact of being chosen (被) 任命, (被) 指定: **[+as]** *O'Neil's nomination as chief executive* 任命奧尼爾為行政總裁

nom·i·na·tive /ˈnɑmənətɪv; ˈnɒmɨnətɪv/ *n* [C] *technical* a particular form of a noun in some languages, such as Latin and German, which shows that the noun is the SUBJECT[1] (5) of a verb【術語】主格 —**nominative** *adj*

nom·i·nee /ˌnɑməˈni; ˌnɒmɨˈniː/ *n* [C] someone who has been suggested for a prize, duty, or honour 被提名者: *Oscar nominee Whoopi Goldberg* 獲得奧斯卡提名的胡比·高拔〔美國著名黑人女影星〕

non- /nɑn; nɒn/ *prefix* **1** in some adjectives and nouns, shows a negative; not 非, 不 (是), 無〔用在形容詞、名詞前表示"否定"之意〕: *a nonalcoholic drink* 非酒精飲料 | *a nonsmoker* (=someone who does not smoke) 不吸煙的人 | *a nonstick frying pan* (=which food does not stick to) 不粘鍋底的平底煎鍋 **2** *informal* in some nouns, means something not deserving a particular name【非正式】名不符實的, 與名稱不相符的〔用於某些名詞中〕: *a non-event* (=something boring) 枯燥無味的活動

no·na·ge·nar·i·an /ˌnɑnədʒəˈnɛrɪən; ˌnəʊnədʒɨˈneəriən/ *n* [C] someone between 90 and 99 years old 90 至 99 歲的人

non-ag·gres·sion /ˌ· ·ˈ··/ *n* [U] the idea that countries should not attack each other〔國與國之間的〕互不侵犯: *a policy of non-aggression* 互不侵犯政策 | **non-aggression pact/treaty** *In 1939 Stalin and Hitler signed a non-aggression pact.* 史太林和希特拉於 1939 年簽訂了一項互不侵犯條約。

non-al·co·hol·ic /ˌ· ··ˈ··◂/ *adj* a drink that is non-alcoholic does not contain alcohol 不含酒精的

non-a·ligned /ˌ· ·ˈ·◂/ *adj* a non-aligned country does not support, or is not dependent on, any of the powerful countries in the world〔國家〕不結盟的 —**non-alignment** *n* [U]

nonce[1] /nɑns; nɒns/ *adj technical* a nonce word or phrase is only invented once for a particular occasion【術語】〔詞或片語〕臨時造的

nonce[2] *n* **for the nonce** *literary or humorous* for the present time or for this particular occasion【文或幽默】目前, 暫時

non·cha·lant /ˈnɑnʃələnt; ˈnɒnʃələnt/ *adj* behaving calmly and seeming not to worry or care about anything 若無其事的; 毫不在乎的: *He was leaning on the bar, trying to look nonchalant.* 他靠在酒吧台上, 裝出若無其事的樣子。—**nonchalance** *n* [U] —**nonchalantly** *adv*

non-com·ba·tant /ˌ· ˈ···/ *n* [C] someone who is in the army, navy etc during a war but who does not actually fight, for example an army doctor〔軍隊中的〕非戰鬥人員〈如軍醫〉

non-commis·sioned of·fi·cer /ˌ· ··· ˈ···/ *n* [C] an NCO 軍士

non·com·mit·tal /ˌnɑnkəˈmɪtḷ; ˌnɒnkəˈmɪtl◂/ *adj* not expressing a definite opinion or intention 不表明意見的, 不表態的, 態度曖昧的: **[+about]** *The doctor was noncommittal about his chances of making a full recovery.* 醫生對他是否可以完全康復沒有明確表態。| *a noncommittal answer* 模棱兩可的回答 —**noncommittally** *adv*

non com·pos men·tis /ˌnɑn ˈkɑmpəs ˈmɛntɪs; ˌnɒn ˌkɒmpəs ˈmentɨs/ *adj* [not before noun 不用於名詞前] *Latin* unable to think clearly or be responsible for your actions【拉丁】神智不清的; 不能為自己的行為負責的

Non·con·form·ist[1] /ˌnɑnkənˈfɔrmɪst; ˌnɒnkənˈfɔːmɨst◂/ *adj* belonging to one of the Protestant Christian churches that have separated from the Church of England 不信奉英國國教的 —**Nonconformist** *n* [C] —**Nonconformism** *n* [U]

nonconformist[2] *n* [C] someone who does not follow ways of living, thinking, or behaving accepted by most people 不遵守規範的人, 不遵循常規的人; 不落俗套的人: *a political nonconformist* 政治主張上不隨俗的人 —**nonconformist** *adj*: *nonconformist attitudes* 不順應傳統規範的態度 —**nonconformity** *n* [U]

non·con·trib·u·to·ry /ˌnɑnkənˈtrɪbjəˌtorɪ; ˌnɒnkənˈtrɪbjɨtəri◂/ *adj* a noncontributory PENSION or insurance plan is paid for by the employer only, and not by the worker〔退休金、保險金計劃〕由雇主支付的, 非分擔的

non-co·op·e·ra·tion /ˌ· ··ˈ··/ *n* [U] the refusal to do any more than you officially have to, as a protest 不合作〔作為抗議〕

non·cus·to·di·al /ˌnɑnkʌsˈtodɪəl; ˌnɒnkʌˈstəʊdiəl◂/ *adj* **noncustodial sentence** a form of punishment which does not involve being kept in prison 不涉及監禁的判決

non·de·script /ˈnɑndɪˌskrɪpt; ˈnɒndɨˌskrɪpt/ *adj* very ordinary looking and without any interesting or unusual qualities or features 沒有獨特之處的; 平凡無奇的: *a nondescript suburban house* 平平常常的郊區房子

none[1] /nʌn; nʌn/ *pron* **1** not any of something 全無, 沒有一點兒: *I was going to offer you some cake but there's none left.* 我本來想請你吃些蛋糕, 但一點也沒剩。| **none of** *Everyone was talking about it – it did not matter to them that none of it was true.* 所有人都在談論這件事, 全然不顧這事根本不是真的。| *She had inherited none of her mother's beauty.* 她絲毫也沒有遺傳她母親的美貌。| **none at all/none whatsoever** *"Any mail arrive today?" "None whatsoever."* "今天有信嗎?" "一封也沒有。" **2** not any of a number of people or things〔幾個人或幾樣東西中〕沒有一個: **none of** *None of my friends phone me anymore.* 我的朋友全都不再給我打電話了。| *None of you need worry.* 你們全都不用擔心。| *None of their promises were kept.* 他們所作的承諾沒有一個兌現的。| **none** *Of all the movies Hepburn made none is more memorable than 'Breakfast at Tiffany's'.* 在柯德莉夏萍拍攝的所有影片中, 沒有哪部像《珠光寶氣》那樣令人難忘。| *Perhaps none felt the effects more than Peter.* 也

許沒有哪個人受的影響有彼得那麼深。**3** not one thing or person 沒有任何一個〔人或物〕: *Even an old car is better than none.* 即使是一輛舊車也比沒有車好。| **none at all** *It'd be better to make some sort of decision than none at all.* 作出某種決定總比甚麼決定都沒有強。**4 have none of sth** to not allow someone to do something or to not allow someone to behave in a particular way 不允許〔做〕某事; 不接受〔做〕某事: *This time I'll have none of her tears and tantrums.* 這一次我不會再容忍她大哭大鬧。| *We offered to pay our half of the cost but Charles would have none of it.* 我們提出支付一半的費用, 但查理斯不答應。**5 none but** *literary* only 【文】只有: *None but she would have been capable of such strength and courage.* 只有她才有這樣的力量和勇氣。**6 none other (than)** used when you are surprised that a particular person, especially someone famous, has done something〔表示驚奇〕不是別的, 正是...: *The mystery guest turned out to be none other than Cher herself.* 神祕嘉賓不是別人, 正是雪兒她本人。—see also 另見 NONETHELESS, **be second to none** (SECOND[1] (6)), **bar none** (BAR[3] (2))

USAGE NOTE 用法說明: NONE
FORMALITY 正式程度
When **none of** is followed by a plural noun, it usually takes a plural verb in ordinary spoken English. 在日常英語口語中, 當none of後面跟複數名詞時, 動詞常用複數形式: *None of us are ready yet.* 我們還沒有人準備好。
In formal writing a singular verb is used. 在正式的書面語中則用動詞的單數形式: *None of our factories is in operation yet.* 我們的工廠還沒有一個運作起來。Some people believe the singular is the only correct form. 有些人認為只有單數形式才是正確的。

none[2] *adv* **1 none the worse/better etc** not at all worse, better etc than before 一點也沒有變得更差/更好: *She seems none the worse for her experience.* 這次經歷後她似乎一點也沒有變壞。| **none the wiser** (=not knowing any more about something than you did at the beginning) 仍然不明白 *I've read the instruction book from cover to cover, but I'm still none the wiser.* 我已經將說明書從頭看到尾, 但仍然不明白。**2 none too** *informal* not at all 【非正式】一點也不: *I was none too pleased to have to take the exam again.* 我要重考一次, 一點也高興不起來。

non·en·ti·ty /nɑnˋɛntətɪ; nɒˈnentɪ̮ti/ *n* [C] someone who has no importance, power, or ability, and who you have no respect for 無足輕重的人; 無能力的人: *Chomsky was the only speaker of any importance – the rest were nonentities.* 喬姆斯基是唯一有份量的發言人, 其餘的全是無足輕重的人。

non-es·sen·tial /ˌ· ·ˈ··◂/ *adj* not completely necessary 非必要的, 非必需的: *The US has imposed a ban on non-essential aerosols.* 美國已經禁止使用非必要的噴霧器。

none·such, nonsuch /ˋnʌnˌsʌtʃ; ˈnʌnsʌtʃ/ *n* [singular] *old use* a person or thing that is better than all the others of the same kind 【舊】無以匹敵的人[物], 完美無比的人[物]

none·the·less /ˌnʌnðəˋlɛs; ˌnʌnðəˈles◂/ *adv* [sentence adverb 句子副詞] *formal* in spite of the fact that has just been mentioned; NEVERTHELESS 【正式】然而, 但是; 儘管如此, 雖然如此: *These islands are not a popular holiday destination, but are worth considering nonetheless.* 雖然這些島嶼算不上甚麼熱門的度假去處, 但值得考慮。| *The region was extremely beautiful. Nonetheless Gerard could not imagine spending the rest of his life there.* 這個地方非常漂亮, 然而傑拉德卻無法想像自己要在那裡度過餘生。

non-e·vent /ˌ· ·ˈ·/ *n* [C usually singular 一般用單數] an event that is disappointing because it is much less interesting and exciting than you expected 遠不如預料中那麼有趣[興奮]的事: *The conference was a bit of a non-event – hardly anyone turned up for it.* 會議令人大失所望, 幾乎沒有人來參加。

non-ex·ec·u·tive di·rec·tor /ˌ· ···· ·ˈ··/ *n* [C] one of the directors (DIRECTOR (1)) of a company who gives advice, but does not have any responsibility for how the company is managed 非執行董事, 非常務董事

non·ex·ist·ent /ˌnɑnɪgˋzɪstənt; ˌnɒnɪgˈzɪstənt/ *adj* not existing at all, or not present in a particular place 不存在的: *We were expected to sit on non-existent chairs.* 要讓我們坐在根本不存在的椅子上。| *Their sex life was practically nonexistent.* 他們實際上沒有甚麼性生活。—**non-existence** *n* [U]

non-fic·tion /ˌ· ˈ··◂/ *n* [U] books, articles etc about real facts or events, not imagined ones 非小說類文學作品, 寫實作品 —**non-fiction** *adj*

non-fi·nite /ˌ· ˈ··/ *adj* **1** a non-finite verb is not marked to show a particular tense or subject, and is either the INFINITIVE or the PARTICIPLE form of the verb, for example 'go' in the sentence 'Do you want to go home?'〔動詞〕非限定形式的, 非限定的 **2** not having an end or limit; INFINITE 無限的, 無窮無盡的 —opposite 反義詞 FINITE

non·flam·ma·ble /nɑnˋflæməbḷ; ˌnɒnˈflæməbəl/ *adj* nonflammable materials or substances do not burn easily or do not burn at all 不易燃的; 不燃的 —opposite 反義詞 FLAMMABLE, INFLAMMABLE

non-in·ter·ven·tion /ˌ· ··ˈ··/ *n* [U] the practice by a government of not trying to influence or become involved in the affairs of other countries or organizations 不干涉: *a policy of non-intervention in internal affairs* 不干涉內政的政策

non-i·ron /ˌ· ˈ··◂/ *adj* non-iron materials do not need to be ironed (IRON[2]) after washing 免熨的, 不需熨燙的

non-ne·go·ti·a·ble /ˌ· ·ˈ····/ *adj* **1** rights and conditions that are non-negotiable are parts of a law or contract that cannot be discussed or changed 不可談判的, 無商量餘地的; 不能更改的 **2** a cheque that is non-negotiable can only be exchanged for money by the person whose name is on it〔支票〕不可轉讓的

no-no /ˈ· ·/ *n* [C] *informal* something that you must not do because it is considered to be unacceptable behaviour 【非正式】不准幹的事: *Colouring your hair was a distinct no-no at that time.* 染髮在那時是絕對不能做的事。

no-non·sense /ˌ· ˈ··◂/ *adj* [only before noun 僅用於名詞前] very practical and direct, without wasting time on unnecessary and unimportant things 實事求是的, 務實的; 直截了當的, 不繞彎子的: *His clients admired his straightforward no-nonsense attitude to business.* 他的客戶欣賞他那種直截了當、實事求是的經營態度。

non·pa·reil /ˌnɑnpəˋrɛl; ˈnɒnpərəl/ *n* **1 nonpareils** [plural] *AmE* very small pieces of coloured sugar used to decorate cakes 【美】〔裝飾蛋糕用的〕彩色珠子糖 **2** [C] *AmE* a piece of chocolate covered with nonpareils 【美】沾有彩色珠子糖的巧克力 **3** [singular] *literary* someone or something that is much better than all the others 【文】無可匹敵的人[物]: *reviews by film critic nonpareil Pauline Kael* 無與倫比的〔美國〕影評家波琳·凱爾所寫的影評 —**nonpareil** *adj*

non-par·ti·san /ˌ· ··ˈ·◂/ *adj* not supporting the ideas of any political party or group 不支持任何黨派的, 無黨派的: *a non-partisan approach to the housing problem* 在住屋問題上不支持任何一派的態度

non-pay·ment /ˌ· ˈ··/ *n* [U] failure to pay money that you owe in tax, rent etc 未能[無力]支付: **[+of]** *nonpayment of rent* 付不起房租

non·plussed also 又作 **nonplused** *AmE* 【美】/ˌnɑnˋplʌst; ˌnɒnˈplʌst/ *adj* so surprised by something that you do not know what to say or do 驚訝不已的; 不知所措的: *He stood, nonplussed, the letter still in his hand.* 他不知所措地站在那裡, 手裡還捏着那封信。

non-prof·it·mak·ing /ˌnɑn ˋprɑfɪtmekɪŋ; ˌnɒn

N

'prɒfɪ̯tmeɪkɪŋ/ *BrE*【英】, **non-prof·it** /ˌ· '··/ *AmE*【美】 *adj* a non-profitmaking organization uses the money it earns to help people〔機構〕非營利性的, 非牟利的

non-pro·lif·e·ra·tion /ˌ· ···'··/ *n* [U] the aim of limiting the number of NUCLEAR OR CHEMICAL WEAPONS in the world, especially by stopping countries that do not yet have them from developing them 防止核[化學]武器擴散: *the nuclear non-proliferation treaty* 防止核擴散條約

non-re·new·a·ble /ˌ· ·'···◂/ *adj* non-renewable types of energy such as coal or gas cannot be replaced after they have been used〔能源〕不可再生的: *the diminishing non-renewable resource of coal* 不斷減少、不可再生的煤資源

non-res·i·dent /· '···/ *n* [C] **1** someone who is not staying in a particular hotel〔旅館的〕非住客: *The hotel restaurant is open to non-residents.* 那家旅館的餐廳對非住客開放。**2** someone who is not living in a particular place or country 非本地居民, 非本國居民 —**non-resident** *adj*

non-res·i·den·tial /ˌnɑnrɛzə'dɛnʃəl; ˌnɒnrezɪ̯'denʃəl◂/ *adj* not providing somewhere for people to live or stay at night 不提供住宿的: *The course is nonresidential.* 那個課程不提供住宿。| *nonresidential care for the elderly* 對老人的日間護理

non-re·strict·ive /ˌ· ·'··◂/ *adj technical* a non-restrictive RELATIVE CLAUSE gives additional information about a particular person or thing rather than saying which person or thing is being mentioned, for example in the sentence 'Perry, who is 22, was arrested yesterday.', the phrase 'who is 22' is a non-restrictive clause【術語】〔從句〕非限制性的

3 **non·sense** /'nɑnsɛns; 'nɒnsəns/ *n* [U]

1 ►STUPID/UNTRUE 愚蠢/不真實的◄ ideas, opinions, statements etc that are untrue or stupid 荒謬的話[想法]; 胡說, 廢話: *all this nonsense about health foods* 有關健康食品的一派胡言 | *"She says she's 39." "Nonsense!"* "她說她 39 歲。" "胡說!" | **a load of nonsense** (=a lot of nonsense) 一派胡言 *If you ask me, these modern teaching methods are a load of nonsense.* 要我說, 這些現代化的教學方法全是一派胡言。| **talk nonsense** *He was talking utter nonsense as usual.* 他像平常一樣又在胡說八道了。| **be a nonsense** *The whole idea's a complete nonsense.* 這整個想法真是太荒謬了。

2 ►WITHOUT MEANING 毫無意義的◄ speech or writing that has no meaning or cannot be understood 無意義的話[字句]: *Computer programs look like complete nonsense to me.* 在我看來, 電腦程式像是毫無意義的東西。

3 nonsense poems/verse poetry that is humorous because it does not have a normal sensible meaning 打油詩

4 ►ANNOYING BEHAVIOUR 令人不快的行為◄ behaviour that is stupid and annoying 愚蠢的行為; 胡鬧: *I wish they'd stop all this nonsense and be nice to each other for a change.* 我希望他們別再胡鬧, 而是相互之間變得友好一些。| **not stand any nonsense** (=be very strict) 十分嚴格, 不允許胡鬧 *She won't stand any nonsense from the kids in her class.* 她不允許孩子們在她的課上胡鬧。

5 make (a) nonsense of *BrE* to show that a previous action or idea was useless and had no meaning【英】使…失去作用[意義]: *Having the army still in power makes a nonsense of last year's democratic elections.* 讓軍隊繼續掌權使得去年的民主選舉失去意義。

non·sen·si·cal /nɑn'sɛnsɪkl; nɒn'sensɪ̯kəl/ *adj* not reasonable or sensible 無意義的; 愚蠢的; 荒謬的: *nonsensical ideas* 荒謬的想法 —**nonsensically** /-klɪ; -kli/ *adv*

non seq·ui·tur /nɑn 'sɛkwɪtɚ; ˌnɒn 'sekwɪ̯tə/ *n* [C] a statement which does not seem to be connected in a reasonable or sensible way with what was said before 前後不連貫的陳述, 不根據前提的推論

non-shrink /ˌ· '·◂/ *adj* non-shrink materials do not become smaller when they are washed 不縮水的

non-smok·er /ˌ· '··/ *n* [C] someone who does not smoke 不抽煙的人

non-smok·ing /ˌ· '··◂/ *adj* a non-smoking area is one where you are not allowed to smoke 禁煙的, 不准吸煙的

non-stan·dard /ˌ· '··◂/ *adj* **1** not the usual size or type〔尺寸等〕不標準的, 不規則的: *a non-standard disk size* 不標準的磁碟尺寸 **2** non-standard words, expressions, or pronunciations are not usually considered to be correct by educated speakers of a language, for example 'gotta' in the sentence 'I gotta go.'〔用詞、發音等〕不標準的, 不規範的

non·start·er /ˌnɑn'stɑrtɚ; ˌnɒn'stɑːtə/ *n* [C] **1** [usually singular 一般用單數] *informal* a person, idea, or plan that has no chance of success【非正式】無成功機會的人[想法、計劃]: *The whole thing sounds like a nonstarter to me.* 這件事在我聽來不可能成功。**2** a horse that is supposed to take part in a race but does not run 參加了比賽, 但沒有上場跑的馬

non-stick /ˌ· '·◂/ *adj* a non-stick cooking pan has a special inside surface which prevents food from sticking to it〔鍋〕不粘食物的

non·stop /ˌnɑn'stɑp; ˌnɒn'stɒp◂/ *adj, adv* without stopping 不停頓的[地], 不斷的[地]: *She talked nonstop for over an hour.* 她一刻不停地講了一個多小時。| *a nonstop flight to Los Angeles* 直飛洛杉磯的航班

non·such /'nʌnsʌtʃ; 'nʌnsʌtʃ/ *n* [singular] another spelling of NONESUCH nonesuch 的另一種拼法

non-u·nion /ˌ· '··◂/ *adj* [usually before noun 一般用於名詞前] **1** not belonging to a TRADE UNION (=official organization for workers) 不屬於工會的: *non-union members* 非工會成員 **2** not officially accepting TRADE UNIONS, or not employing their members 不承認工會的; 不雇用工會會員的: *nonunion factories* 不雇用工會會員的工廠 —**non-unionized** *adj*

non·ver·bal /ˌnɑn'vɝbl; ˌnɒn'vɜːbəl◂/ *adj* not using words 不用言辭表達的: *non-verbal communication* 不用言語的交流 —**nonverbally** *adv*

non·vi·o·lence /ˌ· '···/ *n* [U] political opposition without fighting, shown especially by not obeying laws or orders 非暴力反抗; 非暴力主義: *Gandhi's policy of non-violence and negotiation* 甘地提出的非暴力和協商的政策 —**non-violent** *adj*: *non-violent protests* 非暴力抗議 —**non-violently** *adv*

non-white /ˌ· '·/ *n* [C] *especially SAfrE* someone who does not belong to a white race【尤南非】非白種人 —**non-white** /ˌ· '·◂/ *adj*

noo·dle /'nudl; 'nuːdl/ *n* **1 noodles** [plural] long thin pieces of food made from a mixture of flour, water, and eggs, usually cooked in soup or boiling water 麵條: *egg noodles* 雞蛋麵 **2** [C] *old-fashioned* a silly person【過時】笨人, 傻瓜 **3** [C] *AmE old-fashioned* your head or brain【美, 過時】頭; 頭腦: *Use your noodle!* 動動腦子!

nook /nʊk; nʊk/ *n* [C] **1** a small quiet place which is sheltered by a rock, a big tree etc 隱蔽處: *a shady nook* 陰涼的隱蔽處 **2** a small space in a corner of a room〔房間的〕角落: *a cozy little nook next to the fireplace* 壁爐旁舒適的一隅 **3 nook and cranny** every part of a place 到處, 四處: *We searched every nook and cranny.* 我們搜遍了每個角落。

nook·ie /'nʊkɪ; 'nʊki/ *n* [U] *humorous* the activity of having sex【幽默】性交

noon /nun; nuːn/ *n* [U] 12 o'clock in the daytime; MIDDAY 正午, 中午: *We left home at noon.* 我們在中午離開了家。| *He rarely gets up before noon.* 他很少在中午之前起牀。—see also 另見 **morning, noon and night** (MORNING[1] (5))

noon·day /'nunˌde; 'nuːndeɪ/ *adj literary* happening or appearing at noon【文】正午的: *in the heat of the noonday sun* 在正午的驕陽下

no one /'· ·/ *pron* not anyone; NOBODY 沒人, 無人: *No one likes being criticized.* 沒有人喜歡受到批評。| *There's no one else I really want to invite apart from*

N

you. 除你之外, 我不想再邀請別人了。| *I see no one new has joined the department in my absence.* 我發現我不在期間系裡沒有增加新人。| *No one can say I didn't warn you.* 沒有人能説我沒有警告過你。—see 見 EACH[1] (USAGE)

noose /nus; nuːs/ *n* **1** [C] a ring formed by the end of a piece of rope or string, which closes more tightly as it is pulled 活繩結, 繩套 **2 the noose** punishment by hanging 絞刑: *The outlaws managed to escape the hangman's noose.* 犯人們逃脱了絞刑。

3 **nope** /nop; nəʊp/ *adv spoken* used to say 'no' when you answer someone【口】不, 不是: *"Hungry?" "Nope, I just ate."* "餓嗎?" "不餓, 我剛吃過了。"

no place /'· ·/ *adv informal especially AmE* nowhere【非正式, 尤美】無處: *There's no place left to hide.* 已經無處可藏了。

nor'- /nɔr; nɔː/ *prefix* a prefix meaning 'north', used especially by sailors 表示"北", 尤為海員所用: *nor'east* 東北 | *nor'west* 西北

2 1 **nor**[1] /nɔr; nɔː/ *conjunction* **1 neither... nor...** used when two states, facts, actions etc are mentioned and both are not true or not possible 既不…也不…: *He can neither read nor write.* 他既不會讀也不會寫。| *Hilary was neither shocked nor surprised by the news.* 希拉里對這個消息既沒有感到震驚也沒有覺得意外。**2** *formal* used after a negative statement to mean 'and not something else too'【正式】也不〔用於否定句之後〕: *I wasn't very impressed by his replies, nor his reasons.* 我對他的回答不太滿意, 對他的理由也是一樣。

nor[2] *adv* **1 nor can I/nor does John etc** *especially BrE* used to add a negative statement to one that has just been mentioned【尤英】我也不會/約翰也不等: *She couldn't work out the answer, and nor could I.* 她算不出答案, 我也算不出。**2** *formal* used to emphasize or add information to a negative statement【正式】〔表示強調或增加信息〕也不: *I don't expect children to be rude, nor do I expect to be disobeyed.* 我不希望孩子們沒禮貌, 也不希望他們不聽話。| *I am not, nor have I ever been a wealthy man.* 我現在不是, 也從來不是一個富人。—see also 另見 NEITHER

Nor·dic /'nɔrdɪk; 'nɔːdɪk/ *adj* from or connected with the Northern European countries of Denmark, Norway, Sweden, Iceland, and Finland 來自北歐的; 北歐國家的: *Nordic beauty* 北歐美人

norm /nɔrm; nɔːm/ *n* **1** [C] the usual or normal situation, way of doing something etc 標準; 準則; 規範: *Joyce's style of writing was a striking departure from the literary norm.* 喬伊斯的寫作風格與傳統的文學風格大相徑庭。| **be the norm** *Short term contracts are now the norm with some big companies.* 簽訂短期合同是目前一些大公司的慣常做法。**2 norms** [plural] generally accepted standards of social behaviour 社會準則: *terrorists who violate the norms of civilized society* 違反文明社會準則的恐怖分子

1 1 **nor·mal** /'nɔrml; 'nɔːməl/ *adj* **1** not unusual in any way, but happening just as you would expect 正常的; 平常的; 意料之中的: *normal working hours* 正常工作時間 | **it is normal for sb to do sth** *In the West it's becoming quite normal for couples to live together before they are married.* 在西方, 婚前同居正在變得十分平常。| **back to normal** *Train services are back to normal again after the strike.* 罷工結束後火車服務已回復正常。| **above/below normal** *The rainfall has been below normal for this time of year.* 這個時期的降雨量低於正常水平。**2** a normal person, especially a child, is physically and mentally healthy and does not behave strangely〔尤指兒童〕發育正常的, 身心健康的: *a normal healthy baby* 發育正常的健康嬰兒 | **perfectly normal** *He seems a perfectly normal little boy.* 他看起來是個發育完全正常的小男孩。—compare 比較 ABNORMAL

nor·mal·i·ty /nɔr'mælətɪ; nɔː'mæləti/ also 又作 **nor·mal·cy** /'nɔrmḷsɪ; 'nɔːməlsi/ *AmE*【美】*n* [U] a situation in which things happen in the usual or expected way 正常狀態: *a return to normality* 恢復正常 | *a comforting sense of normality* 一種一切如常的令人安心的感覺

nor·mal·ize also 又作 **-ise** *BrE*【英】/'nɔrmḷ,aɪz; 'nɔːməlaɪz/ *v* [I,T] if you normalize a situation, or if it normalizes, it becomes normal again（使）變得正常;（使）正常化: **normalize relations** (=start having a normal friendly relationship with a country again after a period of war or disagreement)（使）〔國家〕關係正常化,（使）邦交正常化 —**normalization** /,nɔrmḷə'zeʃən; ,nɔːməlaɪ'zeɪʃən/ *n* [U]

nor·mal·ly /'nɔrmlɪ; 'nɔːməli/ *adv* **1** *especially BrE* usually, or under normal conditions【尤英】通常, 平常, 一般地: [sentence adverb 句子副詞] *Normally, I get home about 6 o'clock.* 我通常六點左右回到家。| *The illness normally lasts about a week or ten days.* 這種病通常持續約七到十天。**2** in a normal ordinary way 正常地: *The patient started breathing normally again.* 病人又開始正常呼吸了。 1 2

Nor·man /'nɔrmən; 'nɔːmən/ *adj* **1** built in the style that was popular during the 11th and 12th centuries in Europe〔建築〕諾曼式的; 諾曼風格的〔指11至12世紀時的北歐建築風格〕: *a Norman church* 一座諾曼式教堂 **2** connected with the Normans, the northern French people who took control of England in the 11th century 諾曼(人)的

nor·ma·tive /'nɔrmətɪv; 'nɔːmətɪv/ *adj formal* describing or establishing a set of rules or standards of behaviour【正式】合乎規範的; 按規定準則的: *a normative social structure* 合乎規範的社會結構

Norse /nɔrs; nɔːs/ *adj* connected with the people of ancient Scandinavia or their language 古代斯堪的納維亞人的; 古代斯堪的納維亞語的: *Norse legends* 古代斯堪的納維亞人的傳奇故事

Norse·man /'nɔrsmən; 'nɔːsmən/ *n* [C] *literary* a VIKING【文】古代斯堪的納維亞人, 北歐海盜

north[1], **North** /nɔrθ; nɔːθ/ written abbreviation 縮寫為 **N** *n* [singular, U] **1** the direction that is at the top of a map of the world, above the EQUATOR, and is on the left of a person facing the rising sun 北, 北方: *Which way is north?* 哪邊是北方? | **from/towards the north** *A strong wind was blowing from the north.* 一陣狂風從北方吹來。| **to the north (of)** *Cheshunt is a few miles to the north of London.* 切森特位於倫敦以北幾英里處。| **in the north** *A strange light appeared in the north.* 一道奇特的光在北方出現。| *The wind is in the north.* (=is coming from the north) 風從北面吹來。**2 the North a)** the northern part of a country〔一國的〕北部, 北方: *The North will be dry and bright.* 北部地區的天氣將是乾燥而晴朗的。| *in the north of England* 在英格蘭北部 **b)** the north-eastern states of the US, which fought against the South in the American Civil War〔美國南北戰爭中的〕北方各州 **c)** the richer countries of the world, especially Europe and N America 北方富裕國家〔尤指歐洲和北美的一些國家〕 1 2

north[2] written abbreviation 縮寫為 **N** *adj* **1** in the north or facing the north 北方的, 北部的; 朝北的: *The north side of the building doesn't get much sun.* 該建築物朝北的一面很少曬到太陽。| *He lives in North Wales.* 他住在威爾斯北部。**2** a north wind comes from the north〔風〕來自北面的

north[3] written abbreviation 縮寫為 **N** *adv* **1** towards the north 向北, 朝北: *The birds fly north in summer.* 夏季鳥兒向北飛。| *Chicago is four hours north of Indianapolis.* 芝加哥位於印第安納波利斯以北四小時路程處。| *a north-facing window* 朝北的窗戶 **2 up north** *informal* to or in the north of the country【非正式】往〔國家的〕北部; 在〔國家的〕北部: *They've moved up north.* 他們搬到北部去了。

north·bound /'nɔrθ,baund; 'nɔːθbaʊnd/ *adj* travelling or leading towards the north 向北行的; 往北的: *a north-*

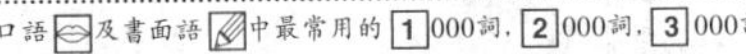

口語 及書面語 中最常用的 1 000詞, 2 000詞, 3 000詞

N

bound bus 北行的公共汽車 | *the northbound lane of the A1* A1號公路的北行車道

north·east¹ /ˌnɔrθˋist; ˌnɔːθˈiːst◂/ written abbreviation 縮寫為 **NE** *n* [U] **1** the direction that is exactly between north and east 東北, 東北方向 **2 the northeast** the northeastern part of a country 〔一國的〕東北部 —**northeast** *adv*: *This road goes northeast.* 這條路通往東北方向。

northeast² written abbreviation 縮寫為 **NE** *adj* **1** a northeast wind comes from the northeast 〔風〕來自東北的 **2** in the northeast of a place 東北部的: *the northeast outskirts of Las Vegas* 拉斯維加斯東北部的郊區

north·east·er /ˌnɔrθˋistɚ; ˌnɔːθˈiːstə/ *n* [C] a strong wind or storm coming from the northeast 東北大風[風暴]

north·east·er·ly /ˌnɔrθˋistɚlɪ; ˌnɔːθˈiːstəli/ *adj* **1** towards or in the northeast 向東北方的; 在東北方的: *They set off in a northeasterly direction.* 他們向着東北方出發。**2** a northeasterly wind comes from the northeast 〔風〕來自東北的

north·east·ern /ˌnɔrθˋistɚn; ˌnɔːθˈiːstən/ *adj* in or from the northeast part of a country or area 東北部的; 來自東北部的: *the northeastern states of the US* 美國東北部各州

north·east·wards /ˌnɔrθˋistwɚdz; ˌnɔːθˈiːstwədz/ also 又作 **northeastward** *adv* towards the northeast 向東北方向 —**northeastward** *adj*

nor·ther·ly /ˋnɔrðɚlɪ; ˈnɔːðəli/ *adj* **1** towards or in the north 向北的; 在北方的: *a northerly direction* 向北的方向 **2** a northerly wind comes from the north 〔風〕來自北方的

nor·thern /ˋnɔrðɚn; ˈnɔːðən/ *adj* in or from the north of a country or area 北部的; 來自北部的: *a man with a northern accent* 帶有北方口音的男子 | *Northern Europe* 北歐

nor·thern·er /ˋnɔrðənɚ; ˈnɔːðənə/ *n* [C] someone who comes from the northern part of a country 北方人

northern hem·is·phere /ˌ‥ ˈ‥·/ *n* [singular] the half of the world that is north of the EQUATOR 北半球 —see picture at 參見 EARTH 圖

Northern Lights /ˌ‥ ˈ·/ *n* [plural] bands of coloured light that are seen in the night sky in the most northern parts of the world; AURORA BOREALIS 北極光

nor·thern·most /ˋnɔrðɚnˌmost; ˈnɔːðənməʊst/ *adj* furthest north 最北端的, 極北的: *the northernmost tip of the island* 島嶼的最北端

North Pole /ˌ· ˈ·/ *n* [singular] the most northern point on the surface of the earth, or the area around it 北極; 北極地區 —see also 另見 SOUTH POLE —see picture at 參見 EARTH 圖

north·wards /ˋnɔrθwɚdz; ˈnɔːθwədz/ also 又作 **northward** *adv* towards the north 向北方: *We sailed northward.* 我們向北航行。—**northward** *adj*

northwest¹ /ˌnɔrθˋwɛst; ˌnɔːθˈwest◂/ written abbreviation 縮寫為 **NW** *n* [U] **1** the direction that is exactly between north and west 西北, 西北方 **2 the northwest** the northwestern part of a country 〔一國的〕西北部 —**northwest** *adv*: *The house faces northwest.* 房子面向西北。

northwest² written abbreviation 縮寫為 **NW** *adj* **1** a northwest wind comes from the northwest 〔風〕來自西北的 **2** in the northwest of a place 在西北部的: *the northwest suburbs of the city* 城市西北部的郊區

north·west·er /ˌnɔrθˋwɛstɚ; ˌnɔːθˈwestə/ *n* [C] a strong wind or storm coming from the northwest 西北大風[風暴]

north·west·er·ly /ˌnɔrθˋwɛstɚlɪ; ˌnɔːθˈwestəli/ *adj* **1** towards or in the northwest 向西北的; 在西北方的 **2** a northwesterly wind comes from the northwest 〔風〕來自西北的

north·west·ern /ˌnɔrθˋwɛstɚn; ˌnɔːθˈwestən/ *adj* in or from the northwest part of a country or area 西北部的; 來自西北部的: *northwestern Canada* 加拿大西北部

north·west·wards /ˌnɔrθˋwɛstwɚdz; ˌnɔːθˈwestwədz/ also 又作 **northwestward** *adv* towards the northwest 向西北方向

nos. the written abbreviation of 縮寫= numbers: *nos. 17–33* 17至33號

nose¹ /noz; nəʊz/ *n*

1 ►ON YOUR FACE 在臉上◄ [C] the part of your face that you smell with and breathe through 鼻子: *a broken nose* 破損了的鼻子 | *Marty punched him on the nose.* 馬蒂一拳打在他鼻子上。| **blow your nose** (=clear it by blowing strongly into a piece of cloth or soft paper) 擤鼻子 *Here, take this hanky and blow your nose.* 拿去, 用這條手帕擤擤鼻子。—see picture at 參見 HEAD¹ 圖

2 red-nosed/long-nosed etc having a nose that is red, long etc 紅鼻子/長鼻子等的

3 (right) under sb's nose so close to someone that they ought to notice, but they do not 就在某人眼前, 當着某人的面; 公然地: *The drugs were smuggled in right under the noses of security guards.* 毒品就在保安人員的眼皮底下被走私進來。

4 stick/poke your nose into to show too much interest in private matters that do not concern you 多管〔閒事〕, 干涉〔別人的私事〕: *She always has to stick her nose into everything, doesn't she?* 她老是愛管閒事, 是嗎? — see also 另見 NOSY

5 keep your nose out (of) *spoken* to stop showing too much interest in private matters that do not concern you 【口】別管〔閒事〕: *I'd prefer you to keep your nose right out of my business!* 我寧願你別過問我的事!

6 turn your nose up (at) *informal* to refuse to accept something because you do not think it is good enough for you 【非正式】瞧不起, (對…) 嗤之以鼻: *My children turn their noses up at home cooking.* 我的孩子們看不上家裡做的飯菜。

7 look down your nose at *informal* to behave as if you think someone or something is not good enough for you 【非正式】瞧不起, 對…嗤之以鼻: *The Taggarts have always looked down their noses at their neighbours.* 塔格特一家人一向瞧不起他們的鄰居。

8 with your nose in the air behaving as if you are more important than other people and not talking to them 目中無人地; 瞧不起人地: *Maria flounced past with her nose in the air.* 瑪麗亞目中無人地大步走了過去。

9 have a nose round *BrE spoken* to look around a place or to look for something 【英口】四處觀看; 四處尋找: *Let's have a nose round while there's no one here.* 趁這兒沒人的時候, 讓我們四處找找吧!

10 have a (good) nose (for) a) to be naturally good at finding and recognizing something 天生擅長尋找[識別]〔某物〕: [+**for**] *a reporter with a nose for a story* 擅長發掘題材的新聞記者 **b)** to be good at recognizing smells 嗅覺靈敏: *a dog with a good nose* 嗅覺靈敏的狗

11 get up sb's nose *BrE spoken* to annoy someone very much 【英口】使某人非常生氣: *His manner really gets up my nose.* 他的態度着實惹惱了我。

12 follow your nose to keep going straight ahead 一直向前走: *Turn left at the post office and then just follow your nose.* 在郵局那兒向左轉, 然後一直向前走。

13 keep your nose clean *spoken* to make sure you do not get into trouble, or do anything wrong or illegal 【口】遵紀守法; 行為檢點; 不捲入是非

14 on the nose *AmE spoken* exactly 【美口】確切地, 精確地: *Guess how much I paid. That's right; $50 on the nose!* 猜猜我付了多少錢。沒錯, 50元整!

15 keep your nose to the grindstone *informal* to work very hard, without stopping to rest 【非正式】努力工作, 一刻不停地苦幹

16 have your nose in a book to be giving all your attention to what you are reading 埋頭苦讀

17 by a nose if a horse wins a race by a nose, it only just wins 〔賽馬〕險勝

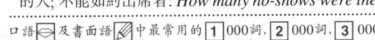

18 put sb's nose out of joint *informal* to annoy someone, especially by attracting everyone's attention away from them【非正式】〔尤指通過搶奪眾人的注意力〕使某人氣歪鼻子; 使某人眼紅

19 nose to tail *especially BrE* cars, buses etc that are nose to tail are moving very slowly without much space between them【尤英】〔車輛〕首尾相接〔指交通擠塞〕: *Traffic was nose to tail for three miles.* 汽車首尾相接堵了三英里長。

20 ▶PLANE 飛機◀ [C] the pointed front end of a plane, ROCKET etc〔飛機、火箭等的〕頭部, 機首, 前端; 突出部分 —see picture at 參見 AIRCRAFT 圖 —see also 另見 HARD-NOSED, BROWN-NOSE, **cut off your nose to spite your face** (CUT OFF (9)), NOSE JOB[1], **pay through the nose (for sth)** (PAY[1] (13)), **powder your nose** (POWDER[2] (3)), **thumb your nose at** (THUMB[2] (2))

nose² *v* **1** [I always+adv/prep] *informal* to try to find out things about other people in a way that is annoying【非正式】窺探; 探聽; 四處查看: **nose about** *BrE*【英】/ **around/into** *The landlady was nosing around the house while we were out.* 女房東在我們外出時在屋裡四處查看。| *Stop nosing into my affairs!* 別管我的事! **2** [I always+adv/prep, T always+adv/prep] if a vehicle, boat etc noses forward, or if you nose it forward, it moves forward slowly〔車輛、船隻等〕緩慢地前行; 將〔車輛、船隻等〕緩慢地向前開: **[+out/through etc]** *The boat nosed out into Nantucket Sound.* 船徐徐駛進了楠塔基特灣。| **nose sth out/through etc** *She carefully nosed the car forward through the traffic.* 她小心地在車流中將車慢慢向前開。

nose sth ↔ **out** *phr v* [T] *informal* to discover information by searching carefully for a long time【非正式】〔經長時間仔細查找而〕發現, 察覺: *The reporters have nosed out some interesting facts about the politician's past life.* 記者們找到了這位政治家舊日的一些趣事。

nose·bag /ˈnozbæg; ˈnəʊzbæg/ *n* [C] a bag that holds food and can be hung around a horse's head〔掛在馬頭上的〕飼料袋; FEEDBAG *AmE*【美】

nose·bleed /ˈnozˌblid; ˈnəʊzbliːd/ *n* [C] **have a nosebleed** to have blood coming out of your nose 鼻出血

nose·cone /ˈnozkon; ˈnəʊzkəʊn/ *n* [C] the pointed front part of a MISSILE〔導彈的〕頭部, 前錐體

nose·dive¹ /ˈnozˌdaɪv; ˈnəʊzdaɪv/ *n* [C] **1** a sudden drop in amount, price, rate etc〔數量、價格、比率等的〕猛跌, 急降: *The pound took a nosedive on the foreign exchange market today.* 英鎊今天在外匯交易市場上出現暴跌。**2** a sudden steep drop made by a plane with its front end pointing towards the ground〔飛機的〕垂直俯衝: *Everyone screamed as the plane suddenly went into a nosedive.* 當飛機突然垂直俯衝下來時, 大家都尖叫起來。

nosedive² *v* [I] **1** if a price, rate, amount etc nosedives, it becomes smaller or reduces in value suddenly〔價格、比率、數量等〕猛跌, 急降 **2** if a plane nosedives, it drops suddenly and steeply with its front end pointing towards the ground〔飛機〕垂直俯衝

nose·gay /ˈnozˌge; ˈnəʊzgeɪ/ *n* [C] *old-fashioned* a small arrangement of flowers【過時】小花束

nose job /ˈ· ·/ *n* [C] *informal* a medical operation on someone's nose to improve its appearance【非正式】鼻子整形手術

nos·ey /ˈnozɪ; ˈnəʊzi/ *adj* another spelling of NOSY nosy 的另一種拼法

nosh /nɑʃ; nɒʃ/ *n informal*【非正式】**1** [U] *BrE* food【英】食物: *They serve good nosh there.* 那裡的食物不錯。**2** [singular] *BrE* a meal【英】一頓飯 **3** [singular] *AmE* a small amount of food eaten between meals; SNACK【美】〔正餐之外的〕小吃, 零食

nosh² *v* [I] *informal* to eat【非正式】吃

no-show /ˌ· ˈ·/ *n* [C] someone who is expected to arrive somewhere, for example at a restaurant or plane, but does not arrive 已預訂〔餐館坐位或飛機航班等〕但未到的人; 不能如約出席者: *How many no-shows were there?* 有多少客人沒來? —**no-show** *v* [I,T] *AmE*【美】

nosh-up /ˈ· ·/ *n* [singular] *BrE informal* a big satisfying meal【英, 非正式】盛宴; 美餐

nos·tal·gia /nɑˈstældʒɪə; nɒˈstældʒə/ *n* [U] the slightly sad feeling of remembering happy events or experiences from the past 對往昔事物的留戀, 懷舊情緒: *He thought with nostalgia of his carefree childhood.* 他懷念地想起那無憂無慮的童年。| **[+for]** *nostalgia for the good old days* 對美好過去的留戀

nos·tal·gic /nɑˈstældʒɪk; nɒˈstældʒɪk/ *adj* feeling or expressing a slight sadness when remembering happy events or experiences from the past 留戀過去的, 懷舊的: *Seeing those old school photographs has made me quite nostalgic.* 看到那些上學時拍的舊照片, 我不禁產生了懷舊之情。| *a nostalgic look back at the 1950s* 對20世紀50年代的懷念 —**nostalgically** /-klɪ; -kli/ *adv*

nos·tril /ˈnɑstrəl; ˈnɒstrəl/ *n* [C] one of the two openings at the end of your nose, through which you breathe and smell things 鼻孔 —see picture at 參見 HEAD[1] 圖

nos·trum /ˈnɑstrəm; ˈnɒstrəm/ *n* [C] **1** *formal* an idea that someone thinks will solve a problem easily, but probably will not help at all【正式】〔實際上也許並無用處的〕妙計, 妙策: *an economic nostrum* 經濟上的靈丹妙藥 **2** *old-fashioned* a medicine that is probably not effective and is not given by a doctor【過時】祕藥; 騙人的假藥

nos·y, nosey /ˈnozɪ; ˈnəʊzi/ *adj* always wanting to find out things that do not concern you, especially other people's private affairs 好管閒事的, 愛打聽別人事情的: *Don't be so nosy! It's none of your business.* 別這麼愛管閒事! 這不關你的事。—**nosiness** *n* [U]

nosy park·er /ˌ·· ˈ··/ *n* [C] *BrE informal* a nosy person【英, 非正式】愛管閒事的人

not /nɑt; nɒt/ *adv* **1** used to make a word or expression negative 不, 沒, 不是〔表示否定的意思〕: *"Can we go to the park?" "No, not today, dear."* "我們可以去公園嗎?" "不, 今天不去, 親愛的。" | *Lorna was not a tidy child and left toys everywhere.* 洛娜不是一個整潔的孩子, 把玩具丟得到處都是。| *The store is open all week but not on Sundays.* 這家店每天都開, 但星期天不開。| *Sally will not eat meat.* 莎莉不吃肉。| *You were wrong not to inform the police.* 你沒有通知警方是不對的。| **not at all easy/difficult etc** *I was not at all surprised to see her at the meeting.* 在會上看到她, 我一點也不感到驚訝。| **not at all** *I don't like his attitude at all.* 我一點也不喜歡他的態度。—compare 比較 NO[1] —see also 另見 -N'T —see 見 NO[2] (USAGE) **2** used instead of a word or expression to mean the opposite of something that has been mentioned before it〔用來代替前面提到的整個語句, 表示與其相反的意思〕: *Are you ready to eat or not?* 你準備好吃飯了沒有? | *I hope to see you tomorrow, but if not, leave me a message.* 我希望明天能見到你, 如果不行的話, 你給我留個口。| **hope/think/be afraid etc not** *"Is Fiona coming?" "I hope not, she's so boring."* "菲奧娜要來嗎?" "我希望她不要來, 她實在煩人。" | *I asked if she would be able to help out but she said not.* 我問她能不能幫忙, 她說不能。—compare 比較 SO[1] (3) **3** used to give a word or expression the opposite meaning 不, 不是〔表示相反的意思〕: *"Will the journey take much longer?" "Oh, it's not far now."* "路途還很遠嗎?" "哦, 現在不遠了。" | *Madeline is such a caring person, not without problems of her own.* 馬德琳真是個熱心的人, 儘管她自己也不是沒有困難。| *In the war years diphtheria was not an uncommon disease.* 戰爭年代白喉是常見病。| *They want a cheap service but they're not slow to complain if the trains break down.* 他們想要廉價服務, 但火車壞了他們又會急着抱怨。| **not very tall/expensive etc** (=fairly short, cheap etc) 不太高/昂貴等 *These teabags aren't very good, are they?* 這些茶包不太好喝, 是嗎? | **not a little/a few etc** (=quite a lot) 很多, 不少: *He drank not a little of the wine.* 他喝了不少酒。| **not a lot/much/many etc** (=only a few/a little etc) 不

N

多, 很少 *It's a new remedy for hay fever which not many people have heard of.* 這是一種鮮為人知的治療花粉病的新方法。**4 not a/not one** not any person or thing 一個也沒有: *Since she went abroad she hasn't even written a letter, not one word!* 她出國後一封信也沒寫過, 一個字也沒有! | **not even a** *Her face was stony, not even a smile.* 她臉上毫無表情, 連一點笑容也沒有。| **not a single** *He has none of his savings left, not a single penny!* 他的積蓄一點也沒剩下, 一分錢都沒有了! **5 not at all** *especially BrE* used to be polite when someone has thanked you or asked you to do something【尤英】別客氣; 一點不介意: *"Would you mind helping me with my suitcase?" "Not at all."* "你能幫我提一下行李箱嗎?" "沒問題。" **6 not only** used to say that besides someone doing one thing they have also done something else 不僅, 不但: **not only...but (also)...** *Shakespeare was not only a writer but also an actor.* 莎士比亞不僅是個作家, 而且還是個演員。| **not only do/will/can etc** *Not only do the nurses want a pay increase, they want reduced hours as well.* 護士們不僅要求提高工資, 還要求縮短工作時間。**7 not that I care/not that it is important etc** used to mean that you do not care, that it is not important etc 我並不在乎/那並不重要: *Sarah's found herself a new boyfriend – not that I care about it.* 莎拉找了個新的男朋友, 不過我並不在乎。**8 –not!** *spoken* used, especially by young people, to say that you really mean the opposite of what you have just said【口】才不是呢! 〔年輕人常用〕: *I really like spending my Saturday afternoons tidying the house – not!* 我很喜歡在星期六下午整理房子 —— 才不是呢! —see also 另見 **not half** (HALF[3] (5)), **not to say** (SAY[1] (43))

USAGE NOTE 用法說明: NOT

FORMALITY 正式程度

In spoken English and informal writing **not** is usually shortened to **n't** with *is, are, was, were, has, have, had, do, does etc. Shall not* becomes *shan't,* and *will not* becomes *won't.* (Note however that **shan't** is only used in British English). 在英語口語和非正式的書面語中, not 與 is, are, was, were, has, have, had, do, does 等連用時通常縮略為 n't。shall not 變成 shan't, 而 will not 則變成 won't。(注意 shan't 只在英國英語中使用)。

SPELLING 拼法

The short form of **not** is **n't** not *'nt.* not的縮略形式是 n't, 而不是 'nt。

Can with the full form **not** is written as one word. can和not的非縮略形式連寫時為一個單詞: *The two sides in the dispute still cannot reach an agreement.* 糾紛的雙方仍未能達成協議。| *I simply cannot understand what he's talking about.* 我完全聽不懂他在說甚麼。

no·ta·bil·i·ty /ˌnotəˈbɪlətɪ; ˌnəʊtəˈbɪləti/ *n* [C usually plural 一般用複數] *formal* an important person【正式】要人; 名人

no·ta·ble /ˈnotəbl̩; ˈnəʊtəbəl/ *adj* important, interesting, excellent, or unusual and therefore deserving to be noticed or mentioned 顯要的; 顯著的; 值得注意的: *a notable achievement* 顯著的成就 | *a notable lack of enthusiasm* 明顯的熱情不足 | **[+for]** *The book is notable for its striking illustrations.* 該書以引人注目的插圖著稱。| **a notable example/exception etc** *Most birds sing only in daylight, one notable exception being the nightingale.* 多數鳥類只在白天鳴叫, 而夜鶯顯然是個例外。

no·ta·bles /ˈnotəbl̩z; ˈnəʊtəbəlz/ *n* [plural] important or famous people 顯要人物; 著名人士

3 **no·ta·bly** /ˈnotəblɪ; ˈnəʊtəbli/ *adv* **1** particularly; especially 格外地; 特別地: *Some early doctors, notably Hippocrates, thought that diet and hygiene were important.* 一些早期的醫生, 如〔古希臘醫學家〕希波克拉底, 認為飲食和衛生是很重要的。**2** in a way that is noticeably different, important, or unusual 明顯地, 顯著地: *Emigration has notably increased.* 移居國外的人明顯增加。

no·ta·rize also 又作 **-ise** *BrE*【英】/ˈnotəˌraɪz; ˈnəʊtəraɪz/ *v* [T often passive 常用被動態] if a notary notarizes a document or written statement they make it official〔公證人〕對...作公證, 公證

no·ta·ry /ˈnotərɪ; ˈnəʊtəri/ also 又作 **notary pub·lic** /ˌ··· ˈ··/ *n* [C] someone, especially a lawyer, who has the legal power to make a signed statement or document official 公證人, 公證員

no·ta·tion /noˈteʃən; nəʊˈteɪʃən/ *n* [C,U] a system of written marks or signs used to represent something such as music, mathematics, or scientific ideas 記號, 符號; 記法

notch¹ /nɑtʃ; nɒtʃ/ *n* [C] **1** a V-shaped cut in a surface or edge〔V字形的〕切口, 凹口; 刻痕: *He made three notches in the stick.* 他在棍子上刻了三個V字形切口。**2** a degree or level on a scale of achievement, social position etc 等級, 水平: *Her new book is several notches above anything else she has written.* 她的新書比她以前的作品要高出好幾個等級。**3** *AmE* a passage between two mountains or hills【美】山峽, 峽谷 —see also 另見 TOP-NOTCH

notch² *v* [T] to cut a usually V-shaped mark into something, especially as a way of showing the number of times something has been done〔尤指為記錄次數而〕在...上刻下V字形切口, 在...上開V形槽口

notch sth ↔ **up** *phr v* [T] to achieve something, especially a victory or a particular total or SCORE 贏得, 獲取: *The Houston Astros have notched up another win.* 休斯敦太空人隊又贏了一場比賽。

note¹ /not; nəʊt/ *n*

1 ►TO REMIND YOU 用於提醒自己◄ [C] something that is written down to remind you of something you need to do, say, or remember 筆記, 記錄: *I'll write myself a note so I don't forget to ring the bank.* 我會用筆記下來, 這樣就不會忘了給銀行打電話。| *She gave a brilliant speech – and without any notes.* 她作了個精彩的演講, 連講稿都沒有用。| **make a note of sth** (=write something down so that you can look at it later) 將某事記下來 *I made a note of her address and phone number.* 我記下了她的地址和電話號碼。

2 ►SHORT LETTER 短信◄ [C] a short, usually informal letter〔通常指非正式的〕短箋, 便條: *There was a note on the table – 'Gone to movies – Back about 11:30.'* 桌上有張便條 ——"我看電影去了, 大約11點半回來。" | **thank-you note** (=a note to thank someone for a present etc) 感謝信

3 ►FOR STUDYING 為了學習◄ **notes** [plural] pages written by a student containing information from a book, lesson etc〔學生的〕筆記: *There is no textbook, so you must rely on your lecture notes.* 沒有教科書, 因此你們必須依靠課堂筆記。| **take/make notes** (=write notes) 記筆記 *She sat quietly in the corner making careful notes.* 她靜靜地坐在角落裡仔細地做筆記。

4 ►MUSIC 音樂◄ [C] **a)** a particular musical sound or PITCH[1] (3a) 樂音; 音調: *She has a good voice but has trouble hitting the high notes.* 她的嗓音很好, 但唱高音時有困難。**b)** a sign in a piece of music that represents a particular musical sound or pitch and that is of a particular length 音符 —see picture at 參見 MUSIC 圖 **c) the black/white notes** the black or white KEYs of a piano〔鋼琴的〕黑/白鍵

5 ►MONEY 錢◄ [C] *BrE* a piece of paper that is used as money【英】紙幣, 鈔票; BILL[1] (3) *AmE*【美】: *Alice took out a ten-pound note.* 愛麗斯拿出一張十英鎊的鈔票。

6 ►VOICE 聲音◄ [singular] if there is a particular note in someone's voice, they show what they are thinking or feeling by the way their voice sounds 口氣, 調子: *There was a strained note in Fischer's normally relaxed voice.*

費舍爾一貫輕鬆的說話聲中帶有一點緊張的口氣。| **a note of anger/jealousy/anxiety etc** *I detected a note of jealousy in his voice.* 我從他的聲音裡聽出了嫉妒的口氣。
7 ▶PARTICULAR QUALITY 特徵◀ [singular] something that adds a particular quality to a situation, statement, or event 特徵, 特點; 色彩: *Her story brought a personal note to the debate on child care.* 她的故事給這場關於育兒的爭論添加了一絲個人色彩。| **a note of humour/sadness/dissent etc** *We need to add a note of caution to such optimism.* 我們需要給這種樂觀的態度添加一點謹慎。
8 ▶ADDITIONAL INFORMATION 附加資料◀ [C] a short piece of writing at the bottom of a page or at the end of a book, that gives more information about something written in the main part〔頁尾或書後的〕註釋, 註解; 評註: *the notes at the back of the book* 書後的註釋
9 ▶LETTER 信◀ [C] a formal letter between governments〔外交上的〕照會; 通牒: *a diplomatic note* 外交照會
10 of note important or famous 重要的; 著名的: *The school has produced several architects of note.* 這所學校培養了幾位著名的設計師。
11 worthy/deserving of note important or interesting and deserving to be noticed 值得注意的: *History has been called 'the record of what one age finds worthy of note in another'.* 歷史被稱為"某一時代對自己認為值得後世注意的事件的記錄"。
12 take note to pay careful attention to something 注意(到), 留意(到): **[+of]** *People were beginning to take note of her talents.* 人們開始注意到她的才能。
13 hit/strike the right/wrong note to succeed or not succeed in being right and suitable for a particular occasion 做對/錯事 —see also 另見 **compare notes** (COMPARE¹ (6))

note² *v* [T] *formal*【正式】**1** to notice or pay careful attention to something 注意, 留意: **note that** *Please note that the bill must be paid within ten days.* 請注意本賬單必須在十天以內付清。| **note sth** *The children should be encouraged to note the colours and textures of the fabrics.* 應該鼓勵孩子們注意織物的顏色和質地。| **note who/what/how etc** *I noted how her face reddened every time Ben's name was mentioned.* 我注意到每次一提到本的名字, 她就會臉紅。**2** to mention something because it is important or interesting 特別提到; 指出: *The report noted a complete disregard for the safety regulations.* 報告特別提到人們對安全規定的漠視。| **note that** *We have already noted that soybeans are a good source of protein.* 我們已經說過, 大豆含有豐富的蛋白質。**3** also 又作 **note down** to write something down so that it will be remembered 記下來: *Note any adverse reaction to the medication on the chart.* 把對藥物的任何不良反應都記在這張表上。

note·book /ˈnotˌbʊk; ˈnəʊtbʊk/ *n* [C] **1** a book made of plain paper on which you can write notes 筆記本 **2** a very small PERSONAL COMPUTER that is the size of a book 筆記本電腦, 手提電腦 —see picture on page A14 參見A14頁圖

note card /ˈ· ·/ *n* [C] *AmE* a NOTELET【美】郵簡

not·ed /ˈnotɪd; ˈnəʊtɪ̈d/ *adj* well known, especially because of some special quality or ability〔尤指因有特別之處而〕著名的, 知名的: *restaurants noted for the excellence of their cuisine* 以精美菜餚著稱的餐館

note·let /ˈnotlɪt; ˈnəʊtlɪ̈t/ *n* [C] *BrE* a small folded piece of paper with a picture on it, for writing a short letter【英】〔用來寫短信的卡式〕郵簡, 便箋; NOTE CARD *AmE*【美】

note·pad /ˈnotpæd; ˈnəʊtpæd/ *n* [C] a number of sheets of paper fastened together at the top, used for writing notes 便條簿, 記事本

note·pa·per /ˈnotˌpepə; ˈnəʊtˌpeɪpə/ *n* [U] paper used for writing letters etc 信紙, 信箋; 便條紙: **headed notepaper** (=with someone's address printed on it) 印有抬頭的信箋

note·wor·thy /ˈnotˌwɝðɪ; ˈnəʊtˌwɜːði/ *adj* something such as an event that is noteworthy deserves attention because it is important, interesting, or unusual 值得注意的; 顯著的: *a noteworthy achievement* 顯著的成就 | *a noteworthy piece of architecture* 值得注意的建築

not-for-prof·it /ˌ· ·ˈ··/ *adj AmE* NON-PROFITMAKING【美】非營利性的

noth·ing¹ /ˈnʌθɪŋ; ˈnʌθɪŋ/ *pron* **1** not anything; no thing 沒有任何東西; 沒有事: *Nothing ever happens in this town.* 這個城鎮從來都不會發生甚麼特別的事。| *There's nothing in this box. Throw it away.* 這盒子裡甚麼也沒有, 扔掉吧。| *He said nothing about it to me.* 這件事他甚麼都沒對我說。| **nothing new/bad etc** *Why are you still in bed when there's nothing wrong with you?* 既然你沒有甚麼不舒服, 為甚麼還不起牀呢? | **nothing to do/to eat etc** *If you have nothing to do how about helping me in the garden?* 如果你沒事幹, 能不能來花園幫我呢? | **nothing else** (=nothing more) 沒有別的東西 *I had nothing else to say so I signed the letter.* 我沒有別的甚麼要說, 所以就在信上簽了名。| **nothing at all** (=absolutely nothing) 甚麼也不; 根本沒有 *You must eat nothing at all before the operation.* 手術前你甚麼都不能吃。**2** something which is considered unimportant, not interesting or not worth worrying about 微不足道的事, 小事: *A harmless kiss. It meant nothing.* 只是一個沒有惡意的親吻, 別當回事。| *It's nothing, just a scratch.* 沒甚麼, 只是一點擦傷。| *There's nothing on television tonight.* 今晚電視上沒有甚麼好節目。| *It was nothing for a family to have ten children in those days.* 那時一家有十個孩子不算甚麼。**3** *especially AmE* zero【尤美】零: *We beat them ten to nothing.* 我們以十比零擊敗了他們。**4 for nothing a)** without paying for something or being paid for something 不要錢; 不交錢; 免費: *Why pay a plumber when my brother will do it for nothing?* 我弟弟可以免費幹, 何必花錢去雇一個管子工呢? | *She knows the club manager so we always get in for nothing.* 她認識俱樂部的經理, 所以我們總是不花錢就能入場。**b)** without having a good reason or purpose 平白無故地, 白白地: *We went all that way for nothing.* 我們白白地走了那麼多路。| *They don't call him Babyface Dickson for nothing!* 他們並非無緣無故地叫他"娃娃臉迪克森"的。**5 have/be nothing to do with sb/sth** [not in progressive 不用進行式] **a)** if something has nothing to do with a particular fact or situation it is not connected with that fact or situation 與某事無關: *Our decision has nothing to do with the fact that her father is on the committee.* 我們的決定與她父親是委員會成員沒有關係。**b)** if a situation has nothing to do with someone, it is personal and private 不關某人的事: *It's nothing to do with you. Mind your own business.* 這事與你無關。別管閒事。**6 have/want nothing to do with** to not be involved in something, especially because you disapprove〔尤指因不贊同而〕不想牽連在內, 不想涉足〔某事〕: *He told the police that he had wanted nothing to do with the whole thing.* 他告訴警方他一直不想與那件事有任何瓜葛。**7 nothing special** not very bad and not very good; average 沒甚麼特別之處的, 普通的: *The meal was nothing special, just a little fish with a cheese sauce.* 這頓飯很普通, 只不過是一點魚加上乾酪汁罷了。**8 nothing but** *formal* only【正式】只不過: *He's nothing but a common criminal.* 他只不過是個普通的罪犯。**9 nothing much** very little 很少, 沒有甚麼: *"What did you do last weekend?" "Oh, nothing much."* "你上個週末幹了些甚麼?" "噢, 沒幹甚麼。" **10 there's nothing like** used to say that something is very good 甚麼都比不上…: *There's nothing like a long hot bath after a day's climbing.* 爬了一天山以後, 甚麼都比不上好好泡個熱水浴。**11 there's nothing in/to sth** used to say that what people are saying about someone else's personal life is not true 某事是捏造的: *It seems there's nothing in the rumours that she's pregnant.* 看來關於她懷孕的謠言是毫無根據的。**12 there's nothing for it but to do sth** used when

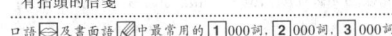

there is only one thing you can do in a particular situation 除了做某事以外別無他法: *With the bridge destroyed there was nothing for it but to swim.* 橋被毀壞了, 除了游過去別無他法。**13 nothing doing** *spoken* used to refuse to do something【口】不行, 我不幹: *Lend you £500? Nothing doing!* 借給你 500 英鎊? 不行! **14 be nothing if not** used to emphasize a particular quality that someone or something has〔用於強調〕極其, 非常: *You've got to admit – he's nothing if not persistent.* 你必須承認, 他非常執着。**15 nothing to it** *spoken* used when something is easy to do【口】〔做某事〕沒有困難, 很容易: *Anyone can use a computer. There's nothing to it!* 任何人都能用電腦, 很容易的! **16 it was nothing/think nothing of it** *spoken* used when someone has thanked you a lot for something you have done for them【口】〔用於回答他人的感謝〕別放在心上, 沒甚麼: *"You really shouldn't have gone to so much trouble." "Oh, think nothing of it."* "讓你這麼麻煩真不好意思。" "噢, 沒甚麼。" **17 nothing of the sort** *spoken* used to strongly refuse to do something or when you feel strongly that something is not true【口】〔用於嚴詞拒絕或否認〕絕對不行; 絕對不可能: *What do you mean you're going to borrow my car? You'll do nothing of the sort!* 你說要借用我的汽車? 那絕對不行! —see also 另見 **sweet nothings** (SWEET[1] (12)), **to say nothing of** (SAY[1] (47)), **nothing on earth** (EARTH[1] (11))

nothing² *adv* **1 be nothing like sb/sth** to have no qualities or features that are similar to someone or something else 一點都不像某人/某物: *She's nothing like her brother. He's dark and she's fair.* 她一點都不像她的哥哥。她哥哥皮膚黑, 她皮膚白。**2 be nothing short of sth** if someone's behaviour is nothing short of something such as laziness, corruption etc, they are extremely lazy or corrupt 完全…, 確實…: *His behaviour was nothing short of rudeness.* 他的行為非常不禮貌。

noth·ing·ness /ˈnʌθɪŋnɪs; ˈnʌθɪŋnəs/ *n* [U] **1** empty space or the complete absence of everything 無; 空: *Natalie found him standing very still, looking into nothingness.* 納塔莉發現他一動不動地站着, 目光茫然。**2** the state of not existing 不存在: *Is there only nothingness after death?* 人死後一切便化為烏有嗎?

no·tice¹ /ˈnotɪs; ˈnəʊtəs/ *v* [I, T not in progressive 不用進行式] **1** to see, hear, or feel something 看到; 聽到; 感覺到; 注意(到): *He spilled the tea, but Miss Whitley did not notice.* 他把茶潑出來了, 但惠特利小姐沒有注意到。| **notice sth/sb** *You may notice a numb feeling in your fingers.* 你可能會感覺到手指有點麻木。| **notice that** *Catherine noticed that Isabella was restless.* 凱瑟琳注意到伊莎貝拉有點坐立不安。| **notice who/what/how etc** *He was too tired even to notice how hungry and thirsty he was.* 他太累了, 甚至沒有意識到自己有多餓多渴。| **notice sb/sth doing sth** *Did you notice him leaving the party early?* 你注意到他提前離開了聚會嗎? **2 be/get noticed** to get attention from someone 引起注意: *a young actress trying to get herself noticed* 一心想引人注目的年輕女演員

This graph shows how common different grammar patterns of the verb **notice** are. 本圖表所示為動詞 notice 構成的不同語法模式的使用頻率。

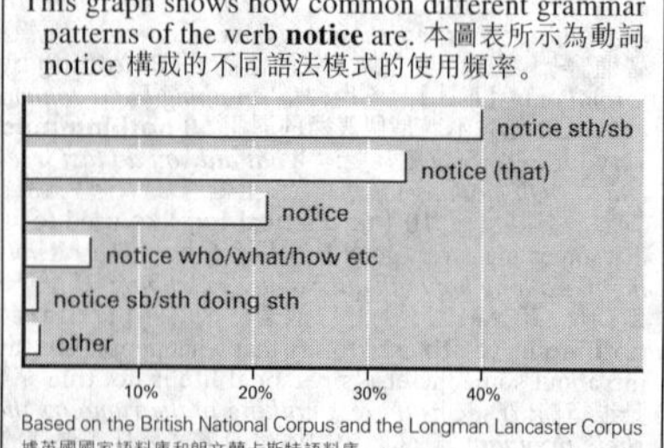

Based on the British National Corpus and the Longman Lancaster Corpus
據英國國家語料庫和朗文蘭卡斯特語料庫

notice² *n*
1 take notice (of) to pay attention to something or someone and let them affect or influence you 注意(到): **not take any notice/take no notice** *I keep complaining but nobody takes any notice.* 我不斷地抱怨, 但沒有人理我。| *Take no notice of Henry – he's just being silly.* 別理亨利, 他在發傻。| *I hope you'll take notice of what I'm going to tell you.* 我希望你注意我下面要講的話。
2 ►ON PAPER 在紙上◄ [C] a written or printed statement that gives information or a warning to people 佈告; 通告; 啟事: *That notice on the wall says 'No smoking'.* 牆上的告示寫着 "禁止吸煙"。| *I'll put up a notice about the meeting.* 我會貼一張開會通告的。
3 ►WARNING/TIME TO PREPARE 警告/準備時間◄ [U] information or a warning about something that is going to happen 通知, 預告: *These rules are subject to change without notice.* 這些規則可不經通知便進行更改。| **ten days' notice/three months' notice etc** (=a warning ten days etc before) 提前十天/三個月通知等 *Either party may terminate the contract upon three months' notice.* 任何一方可在提前三個月通知對方後終止合同。| **at short notice/at a moment's notice** (=allowing only a short time to prepare for something) 在短時間內 *You can't expect me to produce a meal at a moment's notice.* 別指望一告訴我我馬上就能做出一頓飯。| **give sb some notice** *If they'd given me more notice, I'd have had everything ready.* 如果他們能更詳細地通知我, 我早就把一切都準備妥當了。| **serve notice** *formal* (=officially warn someone that something is going to happen)【正式】正式通知
4 give sb notice a) to tell someone that they must leave their job in a week, a month etc 向某人發出解雇通知: *They closed the factory, giving the workers only a week's notice.* 他們只提前一週通知工人, 就關閉了工廠。**b)** to tell someone officially that they must leave the place they are renting by a particular date 正式向某人發出停租通知: **give sb notice to quit/leave** *BrE*【英】*I've been given notice to leave my flat.* 我接到通知, 要我搬出所住的套房。
5 hand in/give in your notice to inform your employer that you will be leaving your job soon, especially by writing a formal letter〔正式〕遞交辭呈
6 come to sb's notice *formal* if a fact, problem etc comes to your notice, you notice it or find out about it【正式】引起某人的注意; 為某人察覺: *It has come to my notice that your account is overdrawn by £200.* 我注意到你的賬戶已透支了 200 英鎊。| **bring sth to sb's notice** (=tell someone about something) 提醒某人注意某事 *There are several important matters I'd like to bring to your notice.* 我想提醒你注意幾件重要的事。| **escape sb's notice** (=not be noticed by someone) 沒有被某人注意到 *It may have escaped your notice but your father is much too ill to travel.* 你可能沒有注意到, 你父親病得很嚴重, 已無法旅行了。
7 until further notice from now until another change is announced 直至另行通知: *The office is closed until further notice.* 辦事處將一直關閉, 直到另行通知時為止。
8 ►BOOK/PLAY ETC 書/戲等◄ [C usually plural 一般用複數] a statement of opinion, especially one written for a newspaper or magazine, about a new play, book, film etc; REVIEW[1] (2)〔尤指報刊上對新劇、新書、新電影等的〕評價; 評論; 短評: *The new play got mixed notices* (=some good, some bad) *in the newspapers.* 報紙對那齣新劇的評價褒貶不一。—see also 另見 **make sb sit up (and take notice)** (SIT)

no·tice·a·ble /ˈnotɪsəbl; ˈnəʊtəsəbəl/ *adj* easy to notice 容易注意到的; 明顯的, 顯著的: *However much he drank it had no noticeable effect on him.* 不管他喝了多少酒, 看起來都沒有甚麼明顯的影響。| *There was a noticeable lack of interest in the idea.* 對這個想法大家顯然沒有興趣。| **it is noticeable that** *It was noticeable that she invited everybody except Gail.* 顯而易見, 除了蓋爾外,

所有人都收到了她的邀請。—**noticeably** *adv*: *The atmosphere at the dinner table was noticeably less relaxed.* 飯桌上的氣氛顯然不像以前那麼輕鬆。

no·tice·board /ˈnotɪsˌbɔrd; ˈnəʊtɪ̈sˌbɔːd/ *n* [C] *BrE* a special board on a wall which notices can be fixed to【英】佈告牌, 佈告欄; BULLETIN BOARD *AmE*【美】—see picture at 參見 BOARD[1] 圖

no·ti·fi·a·ble /ˈnotəˌfaɪəbl̩; ˈnəʊtɪ̈faɪəbəl/ *adj BrE technical* a notifiable disease is one that by law must be reported to an office of public health【英, 術語】〔疾病〕須報告衛生當局的, 應具報的

no·ti·fi·ca·tion /ˌnotəfəˈkeʃən; ˌnəʊtɪ̈fɪ̈ˈkeɪʃən/ *n* [C, U] *formal* an act of officially informing someone about something【正式】通知, 告知: **[+of]** *Notification of any changes should be in writing.* 任何變更均應以書面形式告知。

no·ti·fy /ˈnotəˌfaɪ; ˈnəʊtɪ̈faɪ/ *v* [T] to formally or officially tell someone about something; inform〔正式地〕通知, 告知: **notify sb of** *You will be notified of any changes in the system.* 系統中如有任何變化都會通知你。

3 **no·tion** /ˈnoʃən; ˈnəʊʃən/ *n* [C] **1** an idea, belief or opinion, especially one that is false or not very clear〔尤指錯誤或模糊的〕概念; 觀點; 看法: **[+of]** *misguided notions of male superiority* 男尊女卑的錯誤觀念 | *We haven't the faintest notion of her whereabouts.* 我們一點也想不出她在哪兒。| **notion that** *the notion that human beings are basically good* 認為人本質上是好的這一觀念 **2** a sudden desire to do something; WHIM 突然的念頭, 奇想: **notion to do sth** *At midnight she had a sudden notion to go to the beach.* 半夜裡她突發奇想要去海灘。**3 notions** [plural] *AmE* small things used for sewing【美】小件縫紉用品

no·tion·al /ˈnoʃənl̩; ˈnəʊʃənəl/ *adj* existing only in the mind as an idea or plan, and not existing in reality 概念上的; 理論上的: *Their calculations were based on a notional minimum wage.* 他們的計算是以假定的最低工資為依據的。

no·to·ri·e·ty /ˌnotəˈraɪətɪ; ˌnəʊtəˈraɪəti/ *n* [U] the state of being famous or well-known because of something bad 臭名昭著, 聲名狼藉: *His affairs with young actresses earned him great notoriety.* 他和幾位年輕女演員的風流韻事使他聲名狼藉。

no·to·ri·ous /noˈtorɪəs; nəʊˈtɔːriəs/ *adj* famous or well-known for something bad 臭名遠揚的, 聲名狼藉的: *a notorious bandit* 臭名昭著的歹徒 | **[+for]** *The region is notorious for its terrible snowstorms.* 該地區因可怕的暴風雪而壞名遠揚。—**notoriously** *adv*: *a notoriously inefficient company* 一家人人都知道效率奇低的公司 —see 見 FAMOUS (USAGE)

not·with·stand·ing /ˌnɑtwɪθˈstændɪŋ; ˌnɒtwɪθˈstændɪŋ/ *prep formal* in spite of something【正式】儘管: *The government is determined to proceed with the housing policies, notwithstanding public opposition.* 儘管公眾反對, 政府仍決心繼續執行其房屋政策。| *The EU nations embarked upon the trade agreement, a few exceptions notwithstanding.* 儘管有幾個國家例外, 多數歐盟國家都開始執行這項貿易協定。—**notwithstanding** *adv*

nou·gat /ˈnugət; ˈnuːgɑː/ *n* [U] a sticky pink or white sweet made of sugar, nuts, and small pieces of fruit 鳥結糖, 牛軋糖, 果仁糖

nought /nɔt; nɔːt/ *n* **1** [C] *BrE* the number 0; zero【英】零: *A billion is 1 with 9 noughts after it.* 十億是1後面加9個零。**2** [U] *old use* nothing【舊】無

noughts and cross·es /ˌ· · ˈ··/ *n* [U] *BrE* a game in which two players write 0 or X in a pattern of nine squares, trying to win with a row of three 0s or three Xs【英】畫圈打叉遊戲, 劃井遊戲〔在"井"字的九個方格內, 由兩人輪流填寫, 誰能先把三個X或O列成一行即取勝〕; TICK-TACK-TOE *AmE*【美】

noun /naun; naʊn/ *n* [C] a word or group of words that represent a person (such as 'Michael' or 'teacher' or 'police officer'), a place (such as 'France' or 'school'), a thing or activity (such as 'coffee' or 'football'), or a quality or idea (such as 'danger' or 'happiness'). Nouns can be used as the subject or object of a verb (as in 'The teacher arrived' or 'We like the teacher') or as the object of a PREPOSITION (as in 'good at football') 名詞 —see also 另見 COMMON NOUN, COUNT NOUN, PROPER NOUN, VERBAL NOUN

nour·ish /ˈnɝɪʃ; ˈnʌrɪʃ/ *v* [T] **1** to give a person or other living thing the food they need in order to live, grow, and stay healthy 滋養; 給…營養: *a well nourished baby* 營養良好的嬰兒 **2** *formal* to keep a feeling, idea, or belief strong or help it to grow stronger【正式】保持, 懷有; 培養〔感情、觀念等〕: *The beauty of the region has nourished the imagination of countless artists.* 該地區的美景激發了無數藝術家的想像力。

nour·ish·ing /ˈnɝɪʃɪŋ; ˈnʌrɪʃɪŋ/ *adj* food that is nourishing makes you strong and healthy〔食物〕有營養的, 滋養人的

nour·ish·ment /ˈnɝɪʃmənt; ˈnʌrɪʃmənt/ *n* [U] *formal* food that is needed to live, grow, and stay healthy【正式】食物; 滋養品; 營養: *The child has taken no nourishment all day.* 這孩子已經一整天沒吃東西了。

nous /nus; naʊs/ *n* [U] *BrE informal* intelligence and the ability to make good practical decisions; COMMON SENSE【英, 非正式】良好的判斷力; 常識: *She did have the nous to ring and tell us she'd be late.* 她很明事理, 打電話告訴我們她要晚到。

nou·veau riche /nuvo ˈriʃ; ˌnuːvəʊ ˈriːʃ/ *plural* **nouveaux riches** (*same pronunciation* 讀音相同) *n* [C] someone who has only recently become rich and spends a lot of money 暴發戶 —**nouveau riche** *adj*

nou·velle cui·sine /ˌnuvɛl kwɪˈzin; ˌnuːvel kwɪˈziːn/ *n* [U] a style of cooking from France that uses fresh fruit and vegetables cooked in a simple way and attractively served 新式烹飪〔一種源自法國的烹飪法, 它注重保持新鮮蔬果的原有風味, 並講究食物的外觀〕

Nov. the written abbreviation of 縮寫= NOVEMBER

no·va /ˈnovə; ˈnəʊvə/ *plural* **novas** *or* **novae** /-vi; -viː/ *n* [C] a star which explodes and suddenly becomes much brighter for a short time 新星

nov·el[1] /ˈnɑvl̩; ˈnɒvəl/ *n* [C] a long written story in which 3
the characters and events are usually imaginary〔長篇〕小說: *an Agatha Christie novel*〔英國偵探小說作家〕阿嘉莎·克里斯蒂的小說

novel[2] *adj* not like anything known before and often thought of as new, unusual, and interesting 新的; 新穎的; 新奇的: *That's a novel idea – opening an English restaurant in France.* 在法國開一家英國式餐館, 那真是個新奇的想法。

nov·el·ist /ˈnɑvl̩ɪst; ˈnɒvəlɪ̈st/ *n* [C] someone who writes novels 小說家

no·vel·la /noˈvɛlə; nəʊˈvelə/ *n* [C] a story that is shorter than a novel, but longer than a SHORT STORY 中篇小說

nov·el·ty /ˈnɑvl̩tɪ; ˈnɒvəlti/ *n* **1** [C] something new and unusual which attracts people's attention and interest 新奇的事物: *Cars were still something of a novelty at the beginning of the century.* 世紀初期汽車仍是一種新奇的東西。**2** [U] the quality of being new, unusual, and interesting 新穎; 新奇性: *I was intrigued by the novelty of her ideas.* 我被她想法的新奇之處深深吸引。| **the novelty wears off** (=used to say that something gradually loses its novelty) 新奇感慢慢消失 *I enjoyed living in Paris at first but the novelty soon wore off.* 起初我很喜歡住在巴黎, 但這種新鮮感很快就消失了。**3** [C *often plural* 常用複數] an unusual, small, cheap object, suitable to be given as a present 新穎小巧而價廉的物品: *Christmas novelties* 聖誕小飾物 | *a novelty key ring* 一個小巧的鑰匙圈

No·vem·ber /noˈvɛmbɚ; nəʊˈvembə/ written abbreviation 縮寫為 **Nov.** *n* [C,U] the 11th month of the year, between October and December 十一月: **in November**

N

This office opened in November 1991. 這個辦事處是在1991年11月開業的。| **last/next November** *He started work here last November.* 他去年11月開始在這裡工作。| **on November 6th** (also 又作 **on 6th November** *BrE*【英】) *It happened on November 6th.* (spoken as 讀作 *on the sixth of November* or 或 *AmE*【美】: *on November the sixth* or 或 *on November sixth*) 這件事發生在11月6日。

nov·ice /ˋnɑvɪs; ˈnɒvɪ̣s/ *n* [C] **1** someone who has no experience in a skill, subject, or activity; beginner 新手, 生手; 初學者: *You'll have to show me what to do – I'm a complete novice.* 你得教我怎麼做, 我完全是個新手。| **a novice skier/driver etc** *The novice pilot had to take the controls.* 新飛行員不得不握住操縱器。**2** someone who has recently joined a religious group to become a MONK or NUN 見習修道士; 見習修女

no·vi·ti·ate, noviciate /noˋvɪʃɪɪt; nəʊˈvɪʃiɪ̣t/ *n* [C] *technical* the period of being a novice【術語】見習期

No·vo·cain /ˋnovəˏken; ˈnəʊvəkeɪn/ *n* [U] *AmE trademark* a drug used for stopping pain during a small operation, especially on your teeth【美, 商標】奴佛卡因〔一種局部麻醉藥, 尤用於牙齒〕

S1 W1 **now¹** /naʊ; naʊ/ *adv* **1** at the present time 現在, 此刻, 目前: *If we leave now we'll be there before dark.* 如果我們現在出發, 天黑之前就能到那兒。| *They now live in the city centre.* 他們目前住在市中心。| **right now** (=exactly now) 此刻, 目前 *Right now I couldn't give a damn about your broken window.* 我此刻可顧不上你的破窗戶。| **just now** *especially BrE* (=at the present time)【尤英】此刻, 目前 *There are a lot of bargains in the shops just now.* 商店裡現在有許多便宜貨賣。| **up to now/until now** *It's been a good game up to now but it would be nice to see a few more goals.* 這場比賽到目前為止還算不錯, 但要是能再進幾個球就更好了。| **by/before now** (=before the present time) 到現在 *Sonia should be home by now. Do you think she's had an accident?* 索妮亞這個時候該到家了, 你說她會不會出甚麼事了? | **from now on/as of now** (=starting from now) 從現在開始 *From now on Bill wishes to be addressed as Mr Wilson by all the staff.* 從現在開始, 比爾希望全體員工稱他為威爾遜先生。| **for now** (=used when something is happening at the present time but may change in the future) 目前; 暫時 *That's enough talk for now. Take a break and we'll try again after lunch.* 暫時說到這裡。休息一下, 我們午飯後再繼續。**2** immediately 馬上, 立刻: *I've already told you to clean up. I said now and I mean now.* 我告訴過你要整理乾淨。我說馬上, 還不快去! | *The bell has rung – stop writing now.* 鈴聲已經響了, 立即停筆。**3** used when you know or understand something because of something you have just seen, just been told etc 這下, 一來: *Having met the rest of the family, she now saw where he got his temper from.* 見到他家裡的其他成員之後, 她這才明白他的脾氣是從哪兒來的。**4 3 weeks/2 years etc now** starting 3 weeks, 2 years etc ago and continuing into the future 至今3週/2年等: *They've been going out together for a long time now.* 他們至今已經來往很長一段時間了。| *It's been over five years now since I started working here.* 自從我開始在這兒工作至今已經五年多了。| **it is now 3 weeks/2 years etc** *It's now a month since we bought the car and it's broken down three times already.* 這輛車我們買了才一個月時間, 就已壞過三次了。**5 any day/minute etc now** very soon 很快, 不久, 隨時: *The guests will arrive any minute now.* 客人馬上就會到。**6 (every) now and then/now and again** sometimes 時而, 有時, 不時: *I try to buy myself something every now and then.* 我偶爾會試着給自己買點東西。**7** used in stories when you mean at the time that the event or story is happening 這時候, 當時〔用於講述故事時〕: *She blew out the candle. Now she could hear the sound of the wind howling in the trees outside.* 她吹滅了蠟燭, 這時她聽到了外面樹林裡呼嘯的風聲。**8 now... now...** *literary* used to say that at one moment someone does one thing and immediately after they do something else【文】時而…時而…; 忽而…忽而…: *The eagle glided through the sky, now rising, now swooping.* 鷹在天空中翱翔, 時而向上急衝, 時而向下猛撲。

Frequencies of the adverb **now** in spoken and written English 副詞 now 在英語口語和書面語中的使用頻率

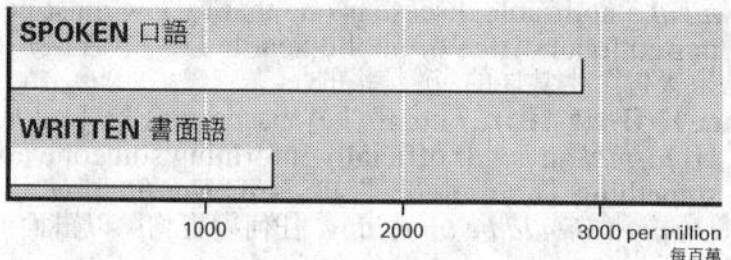

Based on the British National Corpus and the Longman Lancaster Corpus
據英國國家語料庫和朗文蘭卡斯特語料庫

This graph shows that the adverb **now** is much more common in spoken English than in written English. This is because it has some special uses in spoken English and is used in a lot of common spoken phrases.
本圖表顯示, 副詞 now 在英語口語中的使用頻率要遠遠高於書面語, 這是因為它在英語口語中有一些特殊的用法, 而且口語中很多常用片語是由now構成的。

now (*adv*) **SPOKEN PHRASES**
含 now 的口語片語

9 a) used when pausing or getting someone's attention before continuing what you are saying or changing the subject 好了〔用於停頓或引起別人的注意, 然後才繼續說話或改變話題〕: *Now, what did you say your name was?* 呃, 你剛才說你叫甚麼名字? | *Now, let's move on to the question of payment.* 好了, 我們下面來談付款的問題吧。**b)** used when pausing when you are thinking what to say next 好, 嗯〔在說話過程中停下來思索時用〕: *Now, let's see, oh yes – they wanted to know what time you'll be back on Friday.* 嗯, 讓我想想, 噢, 對了, 他們想知道你星期五甚麼時候回來。**c)** used to say that if the situation was different, something different would happen 反過來, 不過〔用於假設〕: *Now, if I'd been in charge there's no way I'd have let them use the van.* 如果我負責的話, 我絕不會讓他們用那輛小貨車的。**d)** used to make someone calm or comfort them when they are angry, upset etc 好了, 好了〔用於安慰別人〕: *Come on now, don't cry.* 好了, 別哭了。**e)** used when telling or reminding someone to do something 這下〔用於告訴或提醒某人做某事〕: *Don't forget now – put the keys in the right hand drawer.* 這下可別忘了, 把鑰匙放在右手邊的抽屜裡。| *Now hurry up! I haven't got all day.* 好了, 快點! 我沒有太多時間。**10 right now** at the moment 此刻, 現在: *I'm really busy right now, can I call you back?* 我現在正忙着, 過一會再給你打電話好嗎? **11 just now** *especially BrE*【尤英】**a)** at the moment 此刻, 目前: *I can't do it just now, I'm busy.* 我現在不行, 我正忙着呢。**b)** a moment ago 剛才: *Where have I put that pen? I was using it just now.* 我把那枝鋼筆放在哪兒了? 我剛才還在用呢。**12 now then** used to get someone's attention before telling them to do something or asking them a question 喂, 聽着〔用於引起別人的注意〕: *Now then, what's the matter?* 喂, 怎麼了? **13 well now** used when giving an opinion or asking someone to tell you something 聽着; 說吧〔用於發表意見或要求別人告知某事〕: *Well now, what's all this I hear about you getting married?* 說吧, 我聽別人說你要結婚了, 這到底是怎麼回事? **14 now for** used when saying what you are going to do next 接下來, 下面: *That's that done. Now for a nice cup of coffee.* 那事就這麼辦了, 接下來喝杯咖啡吧。**15 and now a)** used when introducing the next activity, performer etc 接下來, 下面〔用於介紹下一個活動或表演者等〕: *And now, live from New York, Diana Ross.* 下面請看來自紐約的直播, 黛安娜·羅絲。**b)** to ask someone what the situation is like at the moment when they have been telling you what it was like in the past 那現在呢〔在聽了別人敘述某事的經過後用於詢問目前情況〕: *"It was terrible, she nearly died." "And now?" "Oh, she's back to normal now."* "當時情況很糟糕, 她差點死了。" "那現在呢?" "噢, 她現在又恢復正常了。" **16 now now a)** used to make someone calm or comfort them when they are angry, upset etc 好了, 好了〔用於安慰別人〕: *Now now, don't worry, everything will be okay.* 好了, 好了, 別擔心, 一切都會好的。**b)** *especially BrE* used when telling someone not to behave badly【尤英】行了, 得了〔用於勸阻別人〕: *Now now, leave her alone, it's not fair to blame her.* 行了, 行了, 放過她吧, 責備她是不公平的。**17 not now** used to tell someone that you do not want to talk to them or do something now, because you are busy, tired etc 現在不行: *"Tell me a story." "Not now, Daddy's working."* "給我講個故事吧。" "現在不行, 爸爸在工作呢。" **18 it's now or never** used to say that if someone does not do something now, they will not get another chance to do it 機不可失, 莫失良機 **19 now's the time** used to say that someone should do something now, because it is the right time to do it 現在是〔做某事〕的時候, 正是時候: *Now's the time to buy a suit, while there are still sales on.* 趁現在還在減價, 正是買一套西裝的時候。**20 now I know** used when you have just found out something you didn't know before 我現在明白了: *Okay, now I know. I won't do it again, I'm sorry.* 好了, 我現在明白了。我不會再這樣做, 對不起。**21 what is it now?** used when you are annoyed because someone keeps interrupting you or asking you things 又怎麼了?〔表示因受到煩擾而生氣〕: *What is it now? I wish you'd leave me alone!* 又怎麼了? 讓我清靜一會兒吧! **22 now you tell me!** used when you are annoyed or amused because someone has just told you something they should have told you before 為甚麼不早告訴我?: *Now she tells me! After I spent hours waiting for you all to arrive!* 她為甚麼不早說? 害我在這裡等了你們半天!

S1 W3 **now²** *conjunction* also 又作 **now that** because of something or as a result of something 既然, 由於: *Now that they've got to know each other a little better, they get along just fine.* 由於彼此之間有了進一步了解, 他們相處得不錯。| *Now you're here, why not have a drink.* 既然你來了, 就喝一杯吧。

S2 **now·a·days** /ˈnauəˌdez; ˈnauədeɪz/ *adv* now, compared with what happened in the past〔與過去相比〕現今, 現時: *Nowadays young people are much more aware of ecological issues than they used to be.* 如今, 年輕人比以往更加注意生態問題。

S2 **no way** /ˌ· ˈ·/ *adv spoken* certainly not【口】不行, 決不: *"Are you going to offer to work over the weekend?" "No way!"* "你願意週末加班嗎?" "不行!" | *No way will we be finished by five o'clock.* 我們決不可能在五點鐘前結束。| **there's no way...** *There's no way I'm going to pay £300 just for a weekend in Paris.* 我決不會花 300 英鎊就為了在巴黎度個週末。

S2 **no·where** /ˈnoˌwɛr; ˈnəuweə/ *adv* **1** also 又作 **no place** *AmE informal*【美, 非正式】not in any place or to any place 甚麼地方都不, 無處: *I have no job and nowhere to live.* 我沒有工作, 也沒有地方住。| **nowhere else** (=no other place) 沒有別的地方 *You've got to help me. I've nowhere else to go.* 你一定要幫我。我沒有別處可去了。**2 get nowhere** to have no success or make no progress 沒有結果; 沒有進展: *It's a good idea but it will get nowhere without more financial support.* 這個主意不錯, 但如果沒有更多的資金支持它是不會成功的。| **get sb nowhere** *Taking that kind of attitude will get us nowhere.* 採取那種態度對我們沒好處。| **get nowhere with** *Flaherty was getting nowhere with the Americans, and decided on a different approach.* 弗萊厄蒂與那些美國人在一起並沒有甚麼進展, 因此決定採用另一種方式。| **get nowhere fast** *I soon realized that being tough was getting me nowhere fast.* 不久我發現, 態度強硬對我沒甚麼幫助。**3 be nowhere to be seen/found/heard** not to be seen, found, or heard anywhere 哪兒也見/找/聽不到: *Typical – another street crime and the police are nowhere to be seen.* 很典型, 又是一宗街頭罪案, 而警察則哪兒也找不到。**4 nowhere near a)** far from a particular place 離〔某地方〕很遠: *He swore he was nowhere near her house on the night she died.* 他發誓說在她死的當夜他離她家很遠。**b)** not at all 遠沒有, 遠不及: **nowhere near ready/full/finished etc** *The building's nowhere near finished.* 這棟大樓還遠沒有建好。| **nowhere near as good as etc** *Sarah's nowhere near as fit as I am.* 莎拉遠不及我健康。**5 out of/from nowhere** happening or appearing suddenly and without warning 突然發生; 突然出現: *In the last few seconds Gunnell came from nowhere to win another gold medal.* 在最後幾秒鐘裡, 岡內爾不知從哪兒突然冒出來, 又贏得了一枚金牌。| *From out of nowhere he asks me to marry him!* 他突如其來地向我求婚!

no-win sit·u·a·tion /ˌ· ˈ· ··ˌ·/ *n* [C] a situation which will end badly whatever you decide to do 無法取勝的狀況; 注定的敗局

no·wise /ˈnoˌwaɪz; ˈnəuwaɪz/ *adv old use* not at all【舊】一點也不, 決不

nox·ious /ˈnakʃəs; ˈnɒkʃəs/ *adj formal* harmful or poisonous【正式】有害的; 有毒的: *noxious gases* 有毒氣體

noz·zle /ˈnazl̩; ˈnɒzəl/ *n* [C] a short tube fitted to the end of a HOSE, pipe etc to direct and control the stream of liquid or gas pouring out 管嘴; 噴嘴

nozzle 管嘴; 噴嘴

nr *BrE* the written abbreviation of 縮寫= 'near', used in addresses【英】在…附近〔用於書寫地址〕

NSPCC /ˌɛn ɛs ˌpi si ˈsi; ˌen es ˌpiː siː ˈsiː/ *n* the National Society for the Prevention of Cruelty to Children; a British organization that protects children who are being badly treated 全國防止虐待兒童協會〔英國機構, 旨在保護受虐待的兒童〕

NSU /ˌɛn ɛs ˈju; ˌen es ˈjuː/ *n* [U] non-specific urethritis; an infection of the URETHRA 非特異性尿道炎

n't /nt; ənt/ the short form of 縮略式= 'not': *hadn't* | *didn't* | *wouldn't* | *isn't* —see 見 NOT (USAGE)

nth /ɛnθ; enθ/ *adj* **1** [only before noun 僅用於名詞前] *informal* the most recent of a long series of similar things that have happened【非正式】無數次的, 多次的: *Even after I'd reminded him for the nth time, he forgot.* 儘管我已提醒過他無數次, 但他還是忘了。**2 to the nth degree** *informal* extremely, or as much as possible【非正式】極度地; 無窮地: *It was boring to the nth degree.* 那事令人厭煩透頂。

nu·ance /njuˈans; ˈnjuːɑːns/ *n* [C,U] a very slight, hardly noticeable difference in manner, colour, meaning etc〔方式、顏色、意義等的〕細微差別: *He was aware of every nuance in her voice.* 他聽得出她聲音中所有細微的變化。

nub /nʌb; nʌb/ *n* **the nub of the problem/matter/argument etc** the main point of a problem etc 問題/事情/爭論等的焦點[要點]: *Differing social attitudes lie at the nub of the dispute.* 不同的社會態度是這場爭議的關鍵。

nu·bile /ˈnubl̩; ˈnjuːbaɪl/ *adj formal or humorous* a woman who is nubile is young and sexually attractive【正式或幽默】〔女子〕年輕性感的

3 **nu·cle·ar** /ˈnjuklɪɚ; ˈnjuːkliə/ *adj* **1** using or connected with nuclear energy 核能的, 核動力的: *a nuclear power station* 核電站 | *a nuclear-powered submarine* 核動力潛艇 **2** concerning the NUCLEUS (1) of an atom（原子）核的: *nuclear fission* 核裂變 **3** connected with or involving the use of NUCLEAR WEAPONS 核武器的: **nuclear bomb/war** *the threat of nuclear war* 核戰的威脅 | **nuclear tests** (=for testing nuclear bombs) 核試驗 | **nuclear disarmament** (=getting rid of nuclear weapons) 核裁軍, 裁減核軍備 | **the nuclear deterrent** (=nuclear weapons used as a threat to stop an enemy attacking) 核武器威脅

nuclear en·er·gy /ˌ··· ˈ···/ *n* [U] the powerful force that is produced when the NUCLEUS (=central part) of an atom is either split or joined to another atom 核能

nuclear fam·i·ly /ˌ··· ˈ···/ *n* [C] a family unit that consists only of husband, wife and children〔僅由夫妻與子女組成的〕核心家庭, 小家庭

nuclear fis·sion /ˌ··· ˈ··/ *n* [U] the splitting of the NUCLEUS (=central part) of an atom which results in a lot of power being produced 核裂變

nuclear-free /ˌ··· ˈ·◂/ *adj* places that are nuclear-free do not allow NUCLEAR materials to be carried, stored or used in that area〔地區〕無核的: *a nuclear-free zone* 無核區

nuclear fu·sion /ˌ··· ˈ··/ *n* [U] a NUCLEAR (2) reaction in which the nuclei (NUCLEUS (1)) of light atoms join with the nuclei of heavier atoms, which produces power without producing any waste 核聚變

nuclear phys·ics /ˌ··· ˈ··/ *n* [U] the area of PHYSICS which is concerned with the structure and features of the NUCLEUS (=central part) of atoms 核物理學〔研究原子核的結構和屬性的科學〕

nuclear pow·er /ˌ··· ˈ··/ *n* [U] power, usually in the form of electricity, from NUCLEAR ENERGY 核動力; 核電

nuclear re·ac·tion /ˌ··· ·ˈ··/ *n* [C] a process in which the parts of the NUCLEUS (=central part) of an atom are rearranged to form new substances 核反應

nuclear re·ac·tor /ˌ··· ·ˈ··/ *n* [C] a large machine that produces NUCLEAR ENERGY, especially as a means of producing electricity〔尤指用於發電的〕核反應堆

nuclear waste /ˌ··· ˈ·/ *n* [U] waste material from NUCLEAR REACTORS, which is RADIOACTIVE 核廢料〔核反應堆中核燃料使用後的放射性廢棄物〕: *There are no easy solutions to the problems of nuclear waste disposal.* 有關核廢料的處理問題並無簡單的解決方法。

nuclear weap·on /ˌ··· ˈ··/ *n* [C] a very powerful weapon which uses atomic power to cause death and destruction over a large area 核武器: *the controversy over nuclear weapons testing* 有關核武器試驗的爭議

nu·cle·ic ac·id /njuˌkliɪk ˈæsɪd; njuːˌkliːɪk ˈæsɪd/ *n* [C,U] one of the two acids, DNA and RNA, that exist in the cells of all living things 核酸

nucleus 核心

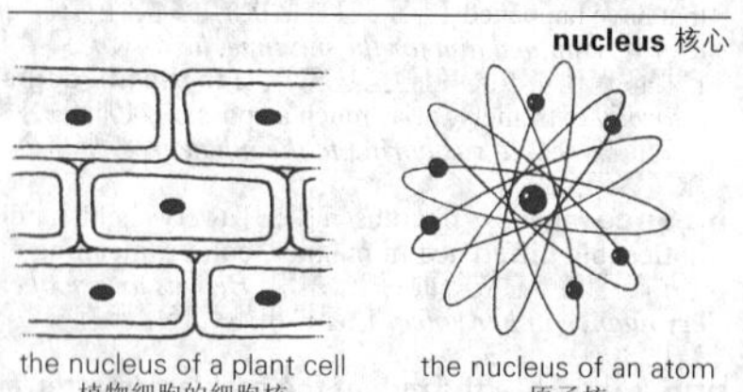

the nucleus of a plant cell 植物細胞的細胞核

the nucleus of an atom 原子核

nu·cle·us /ˈnjuklɪəs; ˈnjuːkliəs/ *n plural* **nuclei** /-klɪaɪ; -kliaɪ/ [C] **1** the central part of an atom, made up of NEUTRONS, PROTONS, and other ELEMENTARY PARTICLES（原子）核 **2** the central part of almost all the cells of living things 細胞核 **3** a small, important group at the centre of a larger group or organization 核心, 中心: *the nucleus of an effective team* 高效團隊的核心

nude[1] /njud; njuːd/ *adj* **1** not wearing any clothes; NAKED 赤裸的, 裸體的 **2** done by or involving people who are not wearing any clothes 裸體者的: *There are several nude scenes in the film.* 影片中有幾個裸體鏡頭。

nude[2] *n* **1** [C] a painting, STATUE etc of someone not wearing clothes 裸體藝術品〈如人體畫、人體雕塑等〉**2 in the nude** not wearing any clothes 裸體的[地], 赤裸的[地]: *He was standing there in the nude.* 他光着身子站在那裡。

nudge /nʌdʒ; nʌdʒ/ *v* **1** [T] to push someone gently, usually with your elbow, in order to get their attention〔通常用肘〕輕推〔以引起某人的注意〕: *"Look!" Benjamin nudged his mother. "There's my teacher, Miss Watts."* "看!"班傑明輕輕碰了一下母親。"那是我的老師沃茨小姐。"—see picture on page A21 參見A21頁圖 **2** [T always+adv/prep] to move something or someone a short distance by gently pushing 輕推移動, 推開: **nudge sth/sb towards/away etc** *She nudged the glass towards me.* 她將杯子輕輕推向我。| *David nudged me out of the way.* 大衛把我擠到一邊。**3** also 又作 **nudge your way** [I always+adv/prep] to move forward slowly by pushing gently 往前擠: **[+to/through/forward etc]** *I started to nudge my way to the front of the crowd.* 我慢慢地擠到人羣前面。**4** [T always+adv/prep] to gently persuade or encourage someone to take a particular decision or action 勸説; 鼓勵: **[+into/towards]** *We're trying to nudge them towards a practical solution.* 我們正在努力促使他們找到一種切實可行的解決方法。**5** [T usually in progressive 一般用進行式] to almost reach a particular level or amount 接近, 靠近〔某程度或數量〕: *For the first time in my life I was nudging 80kg.* 我這輩子第一次體重接近80公斤。—**nudge** *n* [C]: *Hannah gave me a sharp nudge.* 漢納突然推了我一下。

nud·ist /ˈnjudɪst; ˈnjuːdɪst/ *n* [C] someone who enjoys not wearing any clothes because they believe it is natural and healthy; NATURIST 裸體主義者 —**nudist** *adj*: *a nudist camp* 裸體營 —**nudism** *n* [U]

nu·di·ty /ˈnjudətɪ; ˈnjuːdɪti/ *n* [U] the state of not wearing any clothes 裸體, 赤裸, 裸露

nug·get /ˈnʌgɪt; ˈnʌgɪt/ *n* [C] **1** a small rough piece of a valuable metal found in the earth〔天然〕塊金; 礦塊: *gold nuggets* 天然金塊 **2** a small, round piece of food〔食物〕小圓塊: *chicken nuggets* 雞塊 **3 nugget of information/wisdom etc** a piece of valuable information, advice etc 有價值的資料/幾句至理名言等: *It took ages to extract that nugget of information from him.* 費了好長時間才從他那兒套出一點資料來。

nui·sance /ˈnjusn̩s; ˈnjuːsəns/ *n* **1** [C usually singular 一般用單數] a person, thing, or situation that annoys you or causes problems 討厭或麻煩的人[事物, 情況]: *Those dogs next door are a thorough nuisance.* 隔壁的那幾隻狗真是討厭極了。| **What a nuisance!** *spoken*【口】*What a nuisance! I've forgotten my ticket.* 真討厭!我忘了帶票。| **make a nuisance of yourself** (=behave in a way that annoys other people) 惹人討厭 *Stop making a nuisance of yourself.* 別那樣惹人討厭。**2** [C,U] *law* the use of a place or property in a way that causes public annoyance【法律】妨害公共利益的行為: *She was charged with causing a nuisance in a public place.* 她被控在公共場所滋擾他人。**3 nuisance value** *BrE* something that has nuisance value is useful because it causes problems for your opponents【英】給對手造成麻煩的價值, 阻擾[騷擾]作用 

nuke[1] /njuk; njuːk/ *v* [T] *informal* to attack a place using NUCLEAR WEAPONS【非正式】用核武器攻擊

nuke[2] *n* [C] *informal* a NUCLEAR WEAPON【非正式】核武器

null /nʌl; nʌl/ *adj* **null result/effect etc** *technical* a result etc that is zero or nothing【術語】零結果/無效等

null and void /ˌ· · ˈ·/ *adj law* having no legal effect; INVALID[1] (1)【法律】無效的: *The contract was declared* *null and void.* 該合同被宣布無效。

nul·li·fy /ˋnʌlə͵faɪ; ˈnʌlɪ̵faɪ/ *v* [T] **1** *law* to officially state that something has no legal force【法律】宣布…在法律上無效: *The claim was nullified by the court.* 法庭宣布該要求無效。**2** *formal* to make something lose its effect or value【正式】使無效; 使無價值: *Inflation has nullified the recent wage increases.* 通貨膨脹抵消了最近的工資增長。—**nullification** /͵nʌləfəˋkeʃən; ͵nʌlɪ̵fɪ̵ˈkeɪʃən/ *n* [U]

nul·li·ty /ˋnʌlətɪ; ˈnʌlɪ̵ti/ *n* [U] *law* the fact that a marriage or contract no longer has any legal force【法律】〔婚姻或合約等〕法律上無效: *a decree of nullity* 宣布在法律上無效的判決

null set /,· ˈ·/ *n* [C] *technical* a mathematical set with no members, usually written { }【術語】〔數學中通常用 {} 表示的〕零集; 空集

numb¹ /nʌm; nʌm/ *adj* **1** a part of your body that is numb is unable to feel anything, for example because you are very cold〔身體部位〕麻木的; 失去感覺的: *My fingers were so numb I could hardly write.* 我的手指都麻木了, 幾乎不能寫字。| *The anaesthetic had made his whole face go numb.* 麻醉劑使他整個臉部都失去了知覺。**2** unable to think, feel, or react in a normal way〔思維、感覺、反應〕遲鈍的; 麻木的: **numb with shock/fear/terror etc** *I just sat there, numb with terror.* 我只是坐在那兒, 嚇呆了。—**numbly** *adv* —**numbness** *n* [U]

numb² *v* [T] **1** to make someone unable to feel pain or other sensations 使麻木; 使失去感覺: *fingers numbed with cold* 凍僵了的手指 | *the numbing effect of the drug* 藥物的麻醉作用 **2** to make someone unable to think, feel, or react in a normal way 使遲鈍; 使麻木: *He was numbed by the shock of his wife's death.* 他受到妻子去世的打擊而變得麻木。

S1 W1 **num·ber¹** /ˋnʌmbɚ; ˈnʌmbə/ *n*

1 ▶NUMBER 數字◀ [C] a word or sign which represents an amount or a quantity 數; 數字: *Add together the following numbers: 1027, 643, and 378.* 將下列數字相加: 1027、643 和 378。| **high/low number** *Choose a fairly low number – under 100, say.* 選擇一個較小的數字, 比如低於100的。| **even number** (=2, 4, 6, 8, 10 etc) 偶數 | **odd number** (=1, 3, 5, 7, 9 etc) 奇數 | **round number** (=a number ending in 0) 整數 *I'll give her £17 – no, make it £20. That's a good round number.* 我要給她17英鎊, 不, 20英鎊吧。那是個吉利的整數。| **be good/no good etc with numbers** *informal* (=to be good, bad etc at calculating things using numbers)【非正式】擅長/不擅長計算 —see also 另見 CARDINAL NUMBER, ORDINAL NUMBER, PRIME NUMBER, WHOLE NUMBER

2 ▶IN A SET/LIST 在系列/清單中◀ [C] a number used to show the position of something in an ordered set or list 號碼; …號, 第…號: *We live at number 107 Castle Street.* 我們住在城堡街107號。| *Answer question number 4.* 回答第4題。| *a number 17 bus* 17路公共汽車 —see also 另見 E NUMBER, NO. 10, NUMBER ONE

3 model/account/fax etc number a number used to communicate with someone, to find information about someone or something etc 型號/賬號/傳真號碼等: *What is your account number, please?* 請問你的賬號是多少? —see also 另見 BOX NUMBER, PIN, SERIAL NUMBER

4 ▶TELEPHONE 電話◀ [C] a telephone number 電話號碼: *My new number is 502655.* 我的新電話號碼是502655。| **sb's home/office/work number** *I gave him my home number.* 我給了他我家的電話號碼。| **wrong number** *"Is that 70348?" – "No, I'm afraid you have the wrong number."* "你這裡的電話號碼是70348嗎?" "不是, 你打錯電話了。"

5 ▶CAR 汽車◀ [C] *BrE* the official series of numbers and letters shown on a motor vehicle; REGISTRATION NUMBER【英】車牌號碼, 登記號碼: *Did you get the number of the car?* 你記下那輛車的車牌號碼了嗎?

6 ▶AMOUNT 數量◀ [singular] also 又作 **numbers** *plural* an amount of something that can be counted; a QUANTITY 數目; 數量: *The number of cars on our roads rose dramatically last year.* 去年道路上的汽車數量劇增。| *Estimates put the number of deaths at between three and five thousand.* 估計死亡人數在三千到五千之間。| **a large/great/small etc number of** also 又作 **large/great/small etc numbers of** *Doctors believe only a tiny number of people are at risk.* 醫生們認為只有極少數人有危險。| **in large/great/small etc numbers** *They were printed in limited numbers.* 印數有限。| **bring the number of sth to five/ten etc** *This latest bomb brings the number of terrorist attacks this year to seven.* 最近一次爆炸事件使今年的恐怖襲擊次數達到七次。| **ten/twelve etc in number** *formal*【正式】*A small number of protesters, about 20 in number, gathered outside.* 一羣為數不多、大約 20 人的抗議者聚集在外面。—see 見 AMOUNT¹ (USAGE)

7 numbers [plural] how many people there are, especially people attending an event or doing an activity together〔尤指參加某一活動的〕人數: *Can you give me some idea of numbers?* 你能告訴我一個大致的人數嗎? | **student/client etc numbers** *Visitor numbers increase in the summer.* 遊客人數在夏季有所增加。

8 by (sheer) force/weight of numbers if a group of people is defeated by force of numbers, it is defeated because many more people are attacking or opposing it (純粹) 靠數量上的優勢〔取勝〕

9 a number of *formal* several【正式】幾個, 若干(個): *She has written a number of articles for the local paper.* 她為當地報紙寫過幾篇文章。| **a good number of/quite a number of** (=a lot of) 許多 *Darke knew a good number of people with government connections.* 達克認識不少和政府有聯繫的人。| **a number of ways/reasons/factors etc** (=various different ways etc) 幾個不同的方式/原因/因素等 *These paintings differ from his earlier ones in a number of ways.* 這些畫與他以前的作品相比有好幾個不同之處。| **any number of** *There could be any number of reasons why she's late.* 她遲到的原因有很多。

10 some/none/20 etc of sb's number *formal* some etc of a group of people【正式】一羣人中的一些/一個也沒有/20個等: *Only three of our number could speak Italian.* 我們當中只有三人會講意大利語。

11 ▶MUSIC 音樂◀ [C] a piece of popular music that forms part of a longer performance 一首流行樂曲: *Madonna sang several numbers from her latest album.* 麥當娜唱了她最新的唱片集中的幾首歌曲。—see also 另見 PRODUCTION NUMBER

12 a recent/an old/last month's number *BrE* a copy of a magazine printed recently, a long time ago etc【英】最新一期/過期/上月的雜誌; ISSUE¹ (2) *AmE*【美】: **back number** (=an old copy of a magazine) 過期的雜誌

13 have sb's number *informal* to understand something about someone that helps you deal with them【非正式】對某人心中有數, 摸透某人的底: *You'll never fool her, Mike – she's got your number!* 你是騙不了她的, 邁克——她對你瞭如指掌。

14 sb's number is up/has come up *informal* someone will suffer or be punished【非正式】輪到某人遭殃[受罰]: *Your number's up, Hanks!* 你會受到懲罰的, 漢克斯!

15 black/elegant etc (little) number *informal* a black etc dress【非正式】黑色/高貴等的禮服: *Sue turned up in a very elegant number.* 蘇穿着一件十分高貴的禮服出現。

16 sb's number comes up someone has the winning number in a competition 某人的號碼中了

17 the number of times I've... *spoken* used to say that you have done something many times, without any result【口】我已經說過無數次…: *Honestly, the number of times I've told that girl not to walk home alone.* 說實話, 我已多次告訴過那個女孩不要獨自一人步行回家。

18 the numbers an illegal game in the US in which

people risk money on the appearance of a combination of numbers in a newspaper〔美國的〕數字(彩票)賭博〔通常是非法的, 就報紙上出現的某種數字組合下賭注〕: *playing the numbers* 賭數字
19 beyond/without number *literary* if things are beyond number, there are so many of them that no one could count them all【文】數不勝數
20 ►GRAMMAR 語法◄ [U] *technical* the form of a word, depending on whether one thing or more than one thing is being talked about【術語】數: *'Horses' is plural in number, 'horse' is singular.* horses 是複數, horse 是單數。

number² *v* **1** [T] to give a number to something that is part of an ordered set or list 給…編號: *They haven't numbered the pages of the report.* 他們還未給報告編頁碼。| *All the seats in the theatre are numbered.* 劇場裡的所有座位都編了號。| **number sth (from) 1 to 10/100 etc** *Number the questions 1 to 25.* 把這些問題從 1 到 25 編號。| *a numbering system* 編號系統 **2 his/their/its days are numbered** someone or something cannot live or continue much longer 生命垂危; 活着[存在]的日子屈指可數 **3 number several thousands/almost a million etc** to be several thousands etc 數量有幾千/近一百萬等: *The crowd numbered at least 7,000.* 聚集的人羣至少有 7,000 人。| *The men on strike now number 5% of the workforce.* 罷工人數目前約佔工人總數的 5%。**4 number among/be numbered among** *formal* to be included as one of a particular group【正式】被認為; 被算作: *Amis numbers among the best of our younger writers.* 埃米斯被視為當代最優秀的年輕作家之一。**5** [T] *literary* to count【文】計算, 數: *Who can number the stars?* 誰能數清星星有多少?

number off *phr v* [I] *BrE technical* if soldiers number off, they call out their number when their turn comes【英, 術語】〔士兵〕報數; COUNT off *AmE*【美】

number crunch·er /'·· ,··/ *n* [C] *informal humorous*【非正式, 幽默】**1** someone who works with numbers, such as an ACCOUNTANT 搗弄數字者〈如會計師〉**2** a computer designed to work with numbers and calculate results〔運算用的〕計算機, 電腦

number crunch·ing /'·· ,··/ *n* [U] *informal humorous* the process of working with numbers and calculating results【非正式, 幽默】數字搗弄 —**number-crunching** *adj*

num·ber·less /ˋnʌmbɚlɪs; 'nʌmbələs/ *adj* too many to be counted; INNUMERABLE 數不勝數的, 多到數不清的, 無數的: *numberless possibilities* 無數種可能

number one¹ /,·· '·◄/ *n* [singular] **1** the most important or successful person or thing 最重要的人物[事物], 頭號人物[事物]: *George is number one in this organization.* 喬治是這個組織的頭號人物。| *Kline had so many great plans – number one being to star in a movie.* 克蘭有許多重大的計劃, 最重要的就是要在某部影片中擔任主角。**2** the musical record that is the most popular at a particular time 最熱門的唱片: *number one in the charts* 排行榜榜首的唱片 **3 look out for number one/look after number one** *spoken* to look after yourself and not worry about other people【口】只顧自己: *Suzanne's only bothered about looking after number one.* 蘇珊娜只知道顧自己。

number one² /,·· '·◄/ *adj* **1** most important or successful in a particular situation 頭號的; 最重要的; 最成功的: *Obedience was the organization's number one priority.* 服從是該組織最為看重的事情。| *Sweden's number one model* 瑞典的頭號模特兒 **2** first on a list of several things to be considered, done etc 首要的; 第一的: *item number one on the agenda* 議程上的第一項

num·ber·plate /ˋnʌmbɚ,plet; 'nʌmbəpleɪt/ *n* [C] *BrE* one of the signs at the front and back of a car showing its REGISTRATION NUMBER【英】〔汽車的〕牌照, 號碼牌; LICENSE PLATE *AmE*【美】—see picture on page A2 參見 A2 頁圖

Number Ten /,·· '·/ *n* [singular] —see 見 NO. 10

numb·skull /ˋnʌm,skʌl; 'nʌmskʌl/ *n* [C] another spelling of NUMSKULL numskull 的另一種拼法

nu·me·ral /ˋnjumərəl; 'nju:mərəl/ *n* [C] a written sign that represents a number 數字 —**numeral** *adj*

nu·me·rate /ˋnjumə,ret; 'nju:mərɪ̣t/ *adj* able to do calculations and understand simple mathematics 會計算的; 能做算術的: *We need someone who's numerate.* 我們需要一個懂計算的人。—opposite 反義詞 INNUMERATE —compare 比較 LITERATE (1) —**numeracy** *n* [U]

nu·me·ra·tion /,njuməˋreʃən; ,nju:mə'reɪʃən/ *n* [C,U] *technical* a system of counting or the process of counting【術語】命數法, 讀數法; 計算法; 計算

nu·me·ra·tor /ˋnjumə,retɚ; 'nju:məreɪtə/ *n* [C] *technical* the number above the line in a FRACTION (2), for example 5 is the numerator in ⁵/₆【術語】〔分數的〕分子 —compare 比較 DENOMINATOR

nu·mer·i·cal /njuˋmɛrɪkḷ; nju:'merɪkəl/ *adj* expressed or considered in numbers 用數字表示的; 數字的; 數值的: *a numerical code* 數字密碼 | *the numerical superiority of the government forces* (=the fact that they were greater in number) 政府軍在數量上的優勢 —**numerically** /-klɪ; -kli/ *adv*: *numerically equal* 數字上相等的

nu·me·rous /ˋnjumərəs; 'nju:mərəs/ *adj formal* many【正式】許多的, 很多的: *Numerous attempts have been made to hide the truth.* 為掩蓋事實作了很多嘗試。| *on numerous occasions* 很多次

nu·mi·nous /ˋnjumənəs; 'nju:mɪ̣nəs/ *adj literary* having a mysterious and holy quality, which makes you feel that God is present【文】神祕的; 神聖的

nu·mis·mat·ics /,njumɪzˋmætɪks; ,nju:mɪ̣z'mætɪks/ *n* [U] *technical* the activity of collecting and studying coins and MEDALS【術語】錢幣[徽章]收集; 古錢學, 錢幣學; 徽章學 —**numismatic** *adj* —**numismatist** /njuˋmɪzmətɪst; nju:'mɪzmətɪ̣st/ *n* [C]

num·skull, numbskull /ˋnʌm,skʌl; 'nʌmskʌl/ *n* [C] *informal* a very stupid person; IDIOT【非正式】笨蛋, 傻瓜, 白痴: *Look what you've done now, you numskull!* 看看你幹了些甚麼, 你這個笨蛋!

nun /nʌn; nʌn/ *n* [C] a member of an all female religious group who live together in a CONVENT 修女; 尼姑 —compare 比較 MONK

nun·ci·o /ˋnʌnʃɪ,o; 'nʌnsiəʊ/ *n* [C] *plural* **nuncios** a representative of the Pope in a foreign country 羅馬教皇的使節; 教廷大使

nun·ne·ry /ˋnʌnərɪ; 'nʌnəri/ *n* [C] *literary* a CONVENT【文】女修道院; 尼姑庵

nup·tial /ˋnʌpʃəl; 'nʌpʃəl/ *adj formal or humorous* connected with marriage or the marriage ceremony【正式或幽默】婚姻的, 結婚的; 婚禮的: *the nuptial day* 結婚日 | *nuptial bliss* 美滿婚姻

nup·tials /ˋnʌpʃəlz; 'nʌpʃəlz/ *n* [plural] *formal or humorous* a wedding【正式或幽默】婚禮

nurse¹ /nɝs; nɜ:s/ *n* [C] **1** someone who is trained to look after people who are ill or injured, usually in a hospital〔通常指醫院裡的〕護士: *The nurse is coming to give you an injection.* 護士很快會來給你打針。| *a student nurse* (=someone learning to be a nurse) 實習護士 | *Nurse Jones* 瓊斯護士 | *a male nurse* 男護士 **2** *old-fashioned* a woman employed to look after a young child; NANNY (1)【過時】保姆 —see also 另見 WET NURSE

nurse² *v*
1 ►SICK PEOPLE 病人◄ **a)** [T] to look after someone who is ill or injured 護理; 照顧, 照料: *nursing an elderly relative* 照料一位年老的親戚 | **nurse sb back to health** (=nurse someone until they are well again) 照料某人直至其康復 **b)** [I usually in progressive 一般用進行式] to work as a nurse 當護士: *She spent several years nursing in a military hospital.* 她在一家陸軍醫院裡當了幾年護士。
2 ►YOUR FEELINGS 情感◄ [T not in passive 不用被動態] to secretly have a feeling or idea in your mind for

a long time, especially an angry feeling 懷有〔憤恨等〕: **nurse a grudge/grievance/ambition etc** *For years he had nursed a grievance against his former employer.* 多年來他一直對自己的前任雇主懷恨在心。
3 ▶YOUR ILLNESS/INJURY 疾病/損傷◀ [T not in passive 不用被動態] to rest when you have an illness or injury so that it will get better 養病, 休養: *Andrea was at home, nursing a cold.* 安德烈亞在家休養以醫治感冒。
4 ▶TAKE CARE OF STH 照料某事物◀ [T] to take special care of something especially during a difficult situation〔尤指在困難時期〕精心照料, 打理: **nurse sth through/along etc** *Royton succeeded in nursing the company through a financially difficult period.* 羅伊頓使公司成功地渡過了財政困難時期。
5 ▶HOLD 抱◀ [T] to hold something carefully in your hands or arms close to your body 小心地捧[抱]着; 愛惜地摟抱: *a child nursing a kitten* 摟着小貓的孩子 | *Frank sat there nursing his glass of beer.* 弗蘭克坐在那裡, 手裡捧着一杯啤酒。
6 ▶FEED A BABY 餵嬰兒◀ a) [I,T] if a woman nurses a baby, she feeds it with milk from her breasts; BREASTFEED 哺乳, 給〔嬰兒〕餵奶 **b)** [I] if a baby nurses, it sucks milk from its mother's breast〔嬰兒〕吃〔母親的〕奶

nurse·ling /ˈnɝslɪŋ; ˈnɜːslɪŋ/ *n* [C] another spelling of NURSLING nursling 的另一種拼法

nurse·maid /ˈnɝsˌmed; ˈnɜːsmeɪd/ *n* [C] *old-fashioned* a woman employed to look after young children【過時】保姆

nur·se·ry /ˈnɝsərɪ; ˈnɜːsəri/ *n* [C] **1** a place where young children are taken care of during the day while their parents are at work, shopping etc 托兒所 —see also 另見 DAY CARE CENTRE (1) **2 nursery education/school/unit/teacher etc** education etc for young children from three to five years old 幼兒園教育/幼兒園/幼兒園機構/幼兒園教師等 —see also 另見 KINDERGARTEN **3** *old-fashioned* a baby's bedroom or a room where young children play, in a private house【過時】〔私人住宅中的〕嬰兒房; 兒童活動室 **4** a place where plants and trees are grown and sold 苗圃; GARDEN CENTRE *BrE*【英】

nur·se·ry·man /ˈnɝsərɪmən; ˈnɜːsərimən/ *n* [C] *plural* **nurserymen** /-mən; -mən/ someone who grows plants and trees in a nursery 苗圃工人; 苗木培養工

nursery nurse /ˈ··· ˌ·/ *n* [C] *BrE* someone who has been trained to work with and look after young children【英】〔受過訓練的〕保育員

nursery rhyme /ˈ··· ·/ *n* [C] a short traditional song or poem for children 童謠, 兒歌

nursery slope /ˈ··· ˌ·/ *n* [C] *BrE* a slope that is not very steep, where people are taught to SKI【英】〔供初學滑雪者使用的〕練習坡地; BUNNY SLOPE *AmE*【美】

nurs·ing /ˈnɝsɪŋ; ˈnɜːsɪŋ/ *n* [U] the job or skill of looking after people who are ill, injured, or old 護士[護理]工作; 護士[護理]技巧: *I'd love to go into nursing.* 我很樂意加入護理行業。

nursing home /ˈ·· ·/ *n* [C] a type of small private hospital for old people who cannot look after themselves 私立護老院, 私立療養院

nursing moth·er /ˌ·· ˈ··/ *n* [C] a mother who is feeding her baby from her breast 哺乳期婦女

nurs·ling, nurseling /ˈnɝslɪŋ; ˈnɜːslɪŋ/ *n* [C] *old use* a baby who is being fed from the breast, or who is being looked after by a nurse【舊】乳嬰;〔由保姆照料的〕嬰兒

nur·tur·ance /ˈnɝtʃərəns; ˈnɜːtʃərəns/ *n* [U] *AmE* loving care and attention that you give to someone【美】關愛, 關懷; 養育: *the feminine virtue of nurturance* 女性關愛的美德 —**nurturant** *adj*

nur·ture¹ /ˈnɝtʃɚ; ˈnɜːtʃə/ *v* [T often passive 常用被動態] *formal*【正式】**1** to feed and take care of a child or a plant while it is growing 養育; 培育: *children nurtured in an overprotective environment* 在過分保護的環境下養育出來的孩子 | *plants nurtured in the greenhouse* 在溫室裡培育的植物 **2** to help a plan, idea, feeling etc to develop 發展〔計劃、想法等〕; 培養〔感情等〕: *European union is an ideal that has been nurtured since the post-war years.* 建立歐盟是戰後多年來一直發展的一個理想。

nurture² *n* [U] *formal* the education and care that you are given as a child, and the way it affects your later development and attitudes【正式】〔兒時所受的〕教育; 教養; 培育

nut¹ /nʌt; nʌt/ *n* [C] [spoken] 3
1 ▶FOOD 食物◀ a dry brown fruit inside a hard shell, that grows on a tree 堅果; 堅果仁: *crack a nut* 砸開堅果 | *a cashew nut* 腰果
2 ▶TOOL 工具◀ a small piece of metal with a hole through the middle which is screwed onto a BOLT¹ (2) to fasten things together 螺母, 螺帽
3 ▶CRAZY PERSON 瘋子◀ *informal especially AmE* someone who is crazy or behaves strangely【非正式, 尤美】瘋子; 怪人: *He's kind of a nut, but I like him.* 他是個怪人, 但我喜歡他。
4 a golf/opera etc nut *informal* someone who is very interested in golf etc【非正式】高爾夫球迷/歌劇迷等: *She's a Clark Gable nut.* 她是〔美國著名影星〕奇勒基寶的忠實影迷。
5 ▶SEXUAL ORGAN 性器官◀ *slang* a man's testicles【俚】睾丸: *He got kicked in the nuts.* 他被人踢中了睾丸。
6 the nuts and bolts of *informal* the practical details of a subject or job【非正式】基本要點, 實質性要點: *the nuts and bolts of the project* 該計劃的基本要點
7 a tough/hard nut *informal* someone who is difficult to deal with【非正式】難對付的人: *Johnny Stone was a tough nut.* 約翰尼·史東是個難對付的傢伙。
8 a hard/tough nut to crack a difficult problem or situation 棘手的問題; 難辦的事: *Saturday's match will be a tough nut to crack.* 週六的比賽將是場硬仗。
9 ▶HEAD 頭◀ *BrE spoken* your head or brain【英口】頭; 頭腦: *Oh come on, use your nut!* 加油, 動動腦筋吧!
10 be off your nut *BrE spoken* to be crazy【英口】發瘋: *You must be off your nut!* 你一定是瘋了!
11 do your nut *BrE spoken* to become very angry or worried【英口】大發雷霆; 極度憂慮: *I didn't get home till three – my Mum did her nut!* 我三點鐘才到家, 媽媽都擔心壞了!
12 sb can't... for nuts *spoken* used to say that someone is completely unable to do something【口】某人對…一竅不通: *She can't sing for nuts.* 她一點也不會唱歌。—see also 另見 NUTS¹

nut² *v* [T] *BrE informal* to hit someone with your head; HEADBUTT【英, 非正式】用頭撞: *He just turned round and nutted me!* 他乾脆轉過身來用頭撞我!

nut·case /ˈnʌtˌkes; ˈnʌtkeɪs/ *n* [C] *informal humorous* someone who is crazy or mentally ill【非正式, 幽默】瘋子: *That man's a complete nutcase.* 那個男人完全是個瘋子。

nut·crack·er /ˈnʌtˌkrækɚ; ˈnʌtˌkrækə/ *n* [C] also 又作 **nutcrackers** [plural] *BrE* a tool for cracking the shells of nuts【英】夾碎堅果的鉗子, 胡桃鉗

nut·house /ˈnʌtˌhaus; ˈnʌthaʊs/ *n* [C] *slang* an offensive word for a PSYCHIATRIC HOSPITAL【俚】瘋人院〔對精神病醫院的冒犯性用語〕

nut·meg /ˈnʌtmɛg; ˈnʌtmeg/ *n* **1** [U] a brown powder used as a SPICE¹ (1) to give a particular taste to food 肉豆蔻粉〔用作調味品〕**2** [C] the seed of a tropical tree from which this powder is made 肉豆蔻

nu·tri·ent /ˈnjutrɪənt; ˈnjuːtriənt/ *n* [C] a chemical or food that provides what is needed for plants or animals to live and grow 養分, 營養物: *The plant absorbs nutrients from the soil.* 植物從土壤中吸取養分。—**nutrient** *adj*

nu·tri·ment /ˈnjutrəmənt; ˈnjuːtrɪmənt/ *n* [U] *formal* substances that plants and animals need in order to live and grow; NOURISHMENT【正式】養分; 營養

N

nu·tri·tion /nju`trɪʃən; njuː'trɪʃən/ *n* [U] the process of giving or getting the right kind of food for good health and growth 營養(作用); 滋養: *Nutrition and exercise are essential to fitness and health.* 營養和運動是保持健康所必不可少的。—**nutritional** *adj*: *the nutritional value of fresh vegetables* 新鮮蔬菜的營養價值 —**nutritionally** *adv*

nu·tri·tious /nju`trɪʃəs; njuː'trɪʃəs/ *adj* food that is nutritious is full of the natural substances that your body needs to stay healthy or to grow properly; NOURISHING 〔食物〕有營養的, 滋養的, 營養價值高的: *Wholemeal bread is more nutritious than white bread.* 全麥麵包比白麵包更有營養。

nu·tri·tive /`njutrətɪv; 'njuːtrətɪv/ *adj* **1** [no comparative 無比較級] *technical* relating to nutrition【術語】有關營養的 **2** *formal* nutritious【正式】有營養的, 營養價值高的

nuts[1] /nʌts; nʌts/ *adj* [not before noun 不用於名詞前] *informal*【非正式】**1** crazy 發瘋的, 發狂的: **go nuts** (=become crazy) 發瘋 *I'll go nuts if I have to wait any longer.* 再等下去我會發瘋的。| **drive sb nuts** (=annoy someone very much) 使某人發瘋 *Turn that radio off. It's driving me nuts.* 把那個收音機關掉, 吵得我快發瘋了。**2 be nuts about/on/over** to like someone or something very much 對…着迷; 熱衷於…: *She's nuts about the boy next door.* 她迷戀上了隔壁的男孩。

nuts[2] *interjection AmE old-fashioned* used when you are angrily refusing to listen to someone【美, 過時】去你的; 混蛋〔表示生氣、拒絕〕: *"Nuts to you, wise guy," he sneered.* "去你的, 自作聰明的人。"他譏笑道。

nut·shell /`nʌt,ʃɛl; 'nʌt-ʃel/ *n* [C] **1 (to put it) in a nutshell** *spoken* used when you are stating the main facts about something in a short, clear way【口】一言以蔽之, 簡括地說, 用一句話概括: *To put it in a nutshell, the show was a total disaster.* 概括說來, 這場演出糟糕透了。**2** the hard outer part of a nut 堅果的外殼

nut·ter /`nʌtə; 'nʌtə/ *n* [C] *BrE informal* a crazy person【英, 非正式】瘋子: *an absolute nutter* 十足的瘋子

nut·ty /`nʌtɪ; 'nʌti/ *adj* **1** tasting like nuts 有堅果味的: *This coffee has a rich nutty flavour.* 這種咖啡帶有濃郁的堅果味道。**2** containing or filled with nuts 含堅果的, 放了很多堅果的: *a nutty cake* 果仁蛋糕 **3** *informal* crazy【非正式】發瘋的: *another of his nutty ideas* 他又一個古怪的主意 | **nutty as a fruitcake** (=completely crazy) 徹底瘋掉的 —**nuttiness** *n* [U]

nuz·zle /`nʌzl; 'nʌzəl/ also 又作 **nuzzle up** *v* [I always+adv/prep, T] to gently rub or press your nose or head against someone to show you like them〔為表示喜愛〕用鼻子觸碰; 用頭挨擦; 把頭緊挨在: *The horses were nuzzling up against each other.* 馬用鼻子相互蹭來蹭去。| *Tim nuzzled Clare's neck.* 蒂姆把頭緊挨在克萊爾的脖子上。

NW the written abbreviation of 縮寫= NORTHWEST or NORTHWESTERN

ny·lon /`naɪlɑn; 'naɪlɒn/ *n* [U] **1** a strong artificial material that is used to make plastics, clothes, rope etc 尼龍; 耐綸: *shirts made of nylon* 尼龍襯衫 | *nylon thread* 尼龍線 **2 nylons** *old-fashioned* women's STOCKINGS or TIGHTS made of nylon【過時】〔婦女的〕尼龍長襪; 連褲襪

nymph /nɪmf; nɪmf/ *n* [C] **1** one of the spirits of nature, who, according to ancient Greek and Roman stories, appeared as young girls living in trees, mountains, streams etc〔希臘和羅馬神話中居於山林水澤中的〕仙女 **2** *poetic* a girl or young woman【詩】少女; 少婦

nym·phet /nɪm`fɛt; nɪm'fet/ *n* [C] *humorous* a young girl who is very sexually attractive【幽默】性感少女

nym·pho·ma·ni·ac /,nɪmfə`menɪæk; ,nɪmfə'meɪniæk/ also 又作 **nympho** *informal*【非正式】*n* [C] a woman who always wants to have sex, with a lot of different men 慕男狂; 患色情狂的女子 —**nymphomaniac** *adj*: *nymphomaniac tendencies* 慕男狂傾向 —**nymphomania** /-nɪə; -niə/ *n* [U]

NZ the written abbreviation of 縮寫= New Zealand

O,o

O

O, o /o; əʊ/ *plural* **O's, o's 1** the 15th letter of the English alphabet 英語字母表的第十五個字母 **2** *spoken* a zero【口】零

O /o; əʊ/ *interjection* **1** *poetic* used when addressing someone or something【詩】啊〔用於稱呼前〕: *O Death, where is thy sting?* 啊! 死亡, 你的毒鉤在哪裡? **2** another form of OH oh 的另一種形式

o' /ə; ə/ *prep* **1** a way of writing 'of' as it is usually said in speech〔口語中通常所說的 of 的書寫形式〕: *a pint o' beer* 一品脫啤酒 **2** *literary*【文】= on

oaf /of; əʊf/ *n* [C] a stupid awkward man or boy 蠢人, 呆子〔指男性〕: *You clumsy oaf!* 你這個笨手笨腳的蠢貨! —**oafish** *adj* —**oafishly** *adv* —**oafishness** *n* [U]

3 **oak** /ok; əʊk/ *n* [C,U] a large tree that is common in northern countries, or the hard wood of this tree 櫟樹, 橡樹; 櫟木, 橡木: *ancient oaks* 古老的橡樹 | *an oak door* 橡木做的門 | *polished oak* 拋光的櫟木

oak ap·ple /ˈ· ,··/ *n* [C] a raised part on the leaf or stem of an oak tree, caused by an insect 櫟癭, 櫟五倍子〔櫟樹葉或樹幹上由昆蟲引致的瘤狀物〕

oak·en /ˈokən; ˈəʊkən/ *adj especially literary* made of oak【尤文】櫟[橡]木製的

oa·kum /ˈokəm; ˈəʊkəm/ *n* [U] small pieces of old rope used for filling up small holes in the sides of wooden ships 麻絮, 填絮〔用於填塞木船幫上的小洞〕

OAP /ˌo e ˈpi; ˌəʊ eɪ ˈpiː/ *n* [C] *BrE* Old Age Pensioner; a person who is old enough to receive a PENSION from the state【英】領取養老金者

oar /ɔr; ɔː/ *n* [C] **1** a long pole with a wide flat blade at one end, used for rowing a boat 櫓, 槳 —compare 比較 PADDLE[1] (1) **2 put/shove/stick your oar in** *BrE informal* to join in a discussion without being asked to【英, 非正式】多嘴, 插嘴

oar·lock /ˈɔrˌlɑk; ˈɔːlɒk/ *n* [C] *AmE* a ROWLOCK【美】槳叉, 槳架

oars·man /ˈɔrzmən; ˈɔːzmən/ *n plural* **oarsmen** /-mən; -mən/ [C] someone who rows a boat, especially in races〔尤指划船比賽中的〕划手, 槳手

oars·wom·an /ˈɔrzˌwʊmən; ˈɔːzˌwʊmən/ *n plural* **oarswomen** /-ˌwɪmɪn; -ˌwɪmɪn/ [C] a woman who rows a boat, especially in races〔尤指划船比賽中的〕女划手, 女槳手

o·a·sis /oˈesɪs; əʊˈeɪsɪs/ *n plural* **oases** /-siz; -siːz/ [C] **1** a place with water and trees in a desert〔沙漠中的〕綠洲 **2** a peaceful or pleasant place that is very different from everything around it 寧靜宜人的地方: *the one oasis of calm in the war-torn city* 飽經戰禍之城市中的一片寧靜之地

oast house /ˈost ˌhaus; ˈəʊst haʊs/ *n* [C] *BrE* a round building with a pointed top, built for drying HOPS[2] (4)【英】〔烘烤啤酒花的〕尖頂圓形烘房

oat cake /ˈot ˌkek; ˈəʊt keɪk/ *n* [C] a flat cake made of oatmeal 燕麥餅

oath /oθ; əʊθ/ *n* [C] *plural* **oaths** /oðz; əʊðz/ **1** a formal and very serious promise 誓言, 誓約, 誓詞: **swear/take an oath** *The knights swore an oath of loyalty to their king.* 騎士們宣誓效忠於國王。**2 be on/under oath** *law* to have made a formal promise to tell the truth in a court of law【法律】〔在法庭上〕已發誓要講真話, 在宣誓的約束下: *evidence given under oath* 宣誓後提供的證詞[證據] **3 take the oath** to make an official promise to tell the truth in a court of law〔在法庭上〕宣誓, 立誓, 發誓 **4** an expression of strong feeling that uses religious or sexual words in an offensive way 詛咒, 咒罵: *He shouted oaths and curses as they took him away.* 他們把他帶走時, 他大聲地詛咒謾罵。

oat·meal /ˈotˌmil; ˈəʊtmiːl/ *n* [U] **1** crushed OATS used for making cakes and PORRIDGE (1) 燕麥片 **2** *AmE* a soft breakfast food made by boiling crushed oats【美】燕麥片粥; PORRIDGE (1) *BrE*【英】

oats /ots; əʊts/ *n* [plural] **1** a grain that is eaten by people and animals 燕麥 **2** oatmeal 燕麥片 **3 feel your oats** *informal* to feel full of energy【非正式】精力充沛, 精神飽滿 **4 get your oats** *BrE informal* to have sex regularly【英, 非正式】定期行房 **5 be off your oats** *BrE informal* to have lost the desire to eat【英, 非正式】食慾不振, 胃口不好

ob·du·ra·cy /ˈɑbdjərəsɪ; ˈɒbdjʊrəsi/ *n* [U] *formal* an unreasonable refusal to change your beliefs or feelings【正式】執拗, 倔強, 頑固

ob·du·rate /ˈɑbdjərɪt; ˈɒbdjʊrɪt/ *adj formal* unreasonably determined not to change your beliefs or feelings; STUBBORN【正式】執拗的, 倔強的, 頑固的: *She remained obdurate despite their pleas.* 不管他們怎樣懇求, 她依然倔強如初。—**obdurately** *adv*

o·be·di·ence /əˈbidɪəns; əˈbiːdiəns/ *n* [U] obedient behaviour; doing what you are told to do by your parents etc 服從, 順從; 遵從: **[+to]** *obedience to her father's wishes* 遵從她父親的意願 | **demand obedience** *a master who demanded absolute obedience from his servants* 要求僕人絕對服從的主人

o·be·di·ent /əˈbidɪənt; əˈbiːdiənt/ *adj* **1** always doing what you are told to do by your parents, by someone in authority etc 服從的, 順從的, 聽話的: *an obedient and dutiful child* 聽話而孝順的孩子 **2 your obedient servant** *old use* used to end a very formal letter【舊】您恭順的僕人〔正式信尾用語〕—opposite 反義詞 DISOBEDIENT —**obediently** *adv*: *She obediently did as she was told.* 她順從地按吩咐做了。

o·bei·sance /oˈbesn̩s; əʊˈbeɪsəns/ *n* [C,U] *formal* an act of showing respect and obedience, by bending your head or the upper part of your body【正式】敬禮〈如鞠躬等〉

ob·e·lisk /ˈɑblˌɪsk; ˈɒbəlɪsk/ *n* [C] **1** a tall pointed stone PILLAR (1) 方尖碑; 方尖塔 **2** a DAGGER (1) sign used in printing〔印刷品中的〕劍號

o·bese /oˈbis; əʊˈbiːs/ *adj technical* very fat in a way that is unhealthy【術語】肥胖的; 臃腫的 —see 見 FAT[1] (USAGE)

o·be·si·ty /oˈbisətɪ; əʊˈbiːsɪti/ *n* [U] *technical* the condition of being too fat in a way that is dangerous to your health【術語】肥胖症

o·bey /əˈbe; əʊˈbeɪ/ *v* [I,T] to do what someone in a position of authority tells you to do, or to do what a law or rule says you must do 服從〔權威等〕; 遵守〔法規等〕: *The men always obey him.* 他手下的人總是聽命於他。| *"Stand still!" he bellowed. Only a few obeyed.* "站着別動!" 他大聲喝道, 但只有幾個人服從。| **obey an order/command** *Soldiers are expected to obey orders.* 軍人必須服從命令。| **obey the law/laws/rules** *You'll have to obey the rules if you want to live here.* 要想在這裡住, 你就得守規矩。—opposite 反義詞 DISOBEY

ob·fus·cate /ˈɑbfəsˌket; ˈɒbfəskeɪt/ *v* [T] *formal* to deliberately make something unclear or difficult to understand【正式】〔有意地〕使模糊, 使費解 —**obfuscation** /ˌɑbfəsˈkeʃən; ˌɒbfəsˈkeɪʃən/

ob/gyn /ˌo bi ˌdʒi waɪ ˈɛn; ˌəʊ biː ˌdʒiː waɪ ˈen/ *n* [U] *informal, especially AmE* OBSTETRICS and GYNAECOLOGY

【非正式, 尤美】婦產科 (學)

o·bit·u·ar·y /ə`bɪtʃʊˌɛrɪ; ə'bɪtʃuəri/ *n* [C] a report in a newspaper about the life of someone who has just died〔報紙上的〕訃告, 訃聞, 訃文

3 **ob·ject¹** /`ɑbdʒɪkt; 'ɒbdʒɪkt/ *n*
2 **1 ►THING 東西◄** [C] a solid thing, especially something that you can hold or touch 實物, 物體: *some kind of heavy blunt object* 某種笨重的東西

2 an object of pity/desire/contempt etc someone or something that is pitied, desired etc 讓人憐憫/渴望/鄙視等的對象: *Once famous, he was now a mere object of pity.* 他曾經名噪一時, 但現在不過是一個讓人憐憫的對象。—see also 另見 SEX OBJECT

3 ►AIM 目的◄ [singular] the intended result of a plan, action, or activity 目的, 目標; 宗旨: **[+of]** *The object of the game is to score 100 points.* 這個遊戲的目標是得到100分。| *His primary object was to gain publicity.* 他的主要目的是想出名。| **the object of the exercise** (=the object of whatever you are doing) 做事的目的 *The customer will benefit most, and that after all is the object of the exercise.* 客戶將是最大的得益者, 說到底, 這正是此舉的目的。

4 money/expense is no object used to say that you are willing to spend a lot of money 錢/費用不成問題

5 object lesson an event or story that shows you the right or wrong way of doing something 有教誨的事件[故事]; 可引以為訓的事例: *The whole weekend was an object lesson in how not to attract a woman.* 這整個週末可引以為訓, 像那樣做吸引不了女人。

6 ►IN GRAMMAR 語法◄ [C] a noun, noun phrase, or PRONOUN representing **a)** the person or thing that something is done to, for example 'the house' in 'We built the house.'; DIRECT OBJECT 直接受詞[賓語]〈如 We built the house 中的 the house〉 **b)** the person who is concerned in the result of an action, for example 'her' in "I gave her the book.'; INDIRECT OBJECT 間接受詞[賓語]〈如 I gave her the book 中的 her〉 **c)** the person or thing that is joined by a PREPOSITION to another word or phrase, for example 'table' in 'He sat on the table.' 介詞受詞[賓語]〈如 He sat on the table 中的 table〉

2 **ob·ject²** /əb`dʒɛkt; əb'dʒekt/ *v* **1** [I] to complain or protest about something, or to feel or say that you oppose it or disapprove of it 反對, 不贊成: *Do you think anyone would object if I park my car here?* 如果我把車停在這裡, 你認為會有人反對嗎? | **[+to]** *My mother objected to every boy I brought home.* 我帶回家的男孩, 我母親一個都不喜歡。| **object to being called/being told etc** *I object to being spoken to like that.* 我不喜歡別人那樣對我說話。| **I object** (=used in formal arguments) 我反對〔用於正式辯論中〕 *Mr. Chairman, I object. That is an unfair allegation.* 主席先生, 我反對。這是不公正的指控。**2** [T+that] to state a fact or opinion as a way of opposing something or complaining 提出…作為反對的理由; 反對說: *Mom objected that we were too young to go on vacation alone.* 媽媽表示反對, 說我們年紀太小, 不能單獨去度假。| *"My name's not Sonny," the child objected.* "我的名字不叫小傢伙。"那孩子反駁道。—see also 另見 OBJECTOR

object code /'·· ˌ·/ *n* [U] MACHINE CODE〔電腦中的〕目標代碼

3 **ob·jec·tion** /əb`dʒɛkʃən; əb'dʒekʃən/ *n* [C] **1** something that you say to show that you oppose or disapprove of an action, idea etc 反對, 不贊成; 異議: **[+to]** *objections to the Governor's plan* 對州長計劃的反對意見 | **have an objection** *If no one has any objection, I'll declare the meeting closed.* 如果沒有人反對的話, 我將宣布會議結束。| **raise/voice an objection** (=state an objection) 提出反對 (意見) **2** a reason against doing something 反對的原因: **[+to/against]** *The only objection to hiring him is that he can't drive.* 反對雇用他的唯一理由是他不會開車。

ob·jec·tion·a·ble /əb`dʒɛkʃənəbl; əb'dʒekʃənəbəl/ *adj* unpleasant and likely to offend people; offensive 令人不快的; 可能得罪人的; 討厭的: *a most objectionable remark* 很令人討厭的說話 | *What an objectionable man he is!* 他真討厭! —**objectionably** *adv*

ob·jec·tive¹ /əb`dʒɛktɪv; əb'dʒektɪv/ *n* [C] **1** an aim that 3
you are trying to achieve, especially in business or politics〔尤指生意或政治方面的〕目的, 目標: *The main objective of this policy is to reduce unemployment.* 這項政策的主要目的是減少失業。**2** a place that you are trying to reach, especially in a military attack 出擊目標〔尤指軍事攻擊目標〕: *The valley was our primary objective.* 這山谷是我們主要的出擊目標。

objective² *adj* **1** not influenced by your own feelings 3
or opinions, when you have to make a judgment or decision 客觀的, 公正的: *I need an objective opinion from someone who's not involved.* 我需要一個與此事沒有牽連的人的客觀看法。—opposite 反義詞 SUBJECTIVE (1) **2** *formal* existing outside the mind; real【正式】客觀存在的; 真實的: *objective facts* 客觀事實 **3** *technical* connected with the object【術語】受格的, 賓格的 —**objectivity** /ˌɑbdʒɛk`tɪvətɪ; ˌɒbdʒek'tɪvəti/ *n* [U]

ob·jec·tive·ly /əb`dʒɛktɪvlɪ; əb'dʒektɪvli/ *adv* if you consider something objectively, you try to think about it without being influenced by your own feelings or opinions 客觀地

ob·jec·tor /əb`dʒɛktɚ; əb'dʒektə/ *n* [C] someone who states or shows that they oppose something 反對者: *objectors to the new motorway* 反對修建這條新公路的人

ob·jet d'art /ˌɑbʒe `dɑr; ˌɒbʒeɪ 'dɑː/ *plural* **objets d'art** (*same pronunciation* 發音相同) *n* [C] a small object, used for decoration, that has some value as art 小藝術[工藝、裝飾]品

ob·la·tion /əb`leʃən; ə'bleɪʃən/ *n* [C,U] *formal* a gift that is offered to God or a god, or the act of offering the gift【正式】〔給上帝或神的〕祭品, 供物; 供奉

ob·li·gat·ed /`ɑbləˌgetɪd; 'ɒblɪgeɪtɪd/ *adj especially AmE*【尤美】**1 be obligated (to do something)** to have to do something or have a duty to do it 不得不 (做某事); 有義務 (做某事): *IBM's European customers will be obligated to make more drastic cutbacks in mainframe expenditure.* 國際商業機器公司的歐洲客戶將不得不更大幅度地縮減在大型電腦主機方面的開支。**2 be/feel obligated to someone** to owe someone loyalty, thanks, or money, because they have done something for you 欠某人人情, 對某人感恩圖報

ob·li·ga·tion /ˌɑblə`geʃən; ˌɒblɪ'geɪʃən/ *n* [C,U] **1** a
moral or legal duty to do something〔道義或法律上的〕義務, 職責, 責任: **obligation to do sth** *You can look at the books without any obligation to buy.* 你可以看看這些書, 不一定非要買。| **[+to]** *I have certain obligations to my family.* 我對自己的家庭負有一定的義務。| **meet/fulfil an obligation** (=do something that is your duty) 履行義務[職責] *Have the employers met their contractual obligations?* 雇主履行合同規定的義務了嗎? | **a sense of obligation** (=feeling that you ought to do something) 責任感 *I helped you because I wanted to, not out of any sense of obligation.* 我幫你是因為我想這樣做, 而不是出於甚麼責任感。**2 be under an obligation a)** to have to do something because it is a legal or moral duty 有義務〔做某事〕: **be under no obligation to do sth** *We are invited but we are under no obligation to go.* 我們接到了邀請, 但我們沒有義務一定要去。| **place sb under an obligation** *Signing a contract places you under a long-term obligation.* 簽署一項合同就使人在很長一段時期內負有責任。**b)** to owe someone loyalty, thanks, or money because they have done something for you 欠〔某人〕人情: **[+to]** *I don't want to be under an obligation to anyone.* 我不想欠任何人的人情。

ob·lig·a·to·ry /ə`blɪgəˌtorɪ; ə'blɪgətəri/ *adj* **1** *formal* something that is obligatory must be done because of a law, a rule etc; COMPULSORY, MANDATORY【正式】〔因法律、規定等〕必須履行的, 有義務的; 強制性的: *Attendance* *is obligatory.* 必須出席。**2** *often humorous* used to describe something that is usually done, worn, or included because many people also do it, or you have always done it in the past【常幽默】慣常的, 習慣上的: *Paula was smartly dressed in a new tweed suit with the obligatory matching bag and shoes.* 保娜穿得很時髦, 一身新花呢套服以及當然少不了與之相配的手提袋和鞋子。

Frequencies of **be obliged to**, **must**, and **have to/have got to** in spoken and written English 英語口語和書面語中be obliged to, must和have to/have got to 的使用頻率

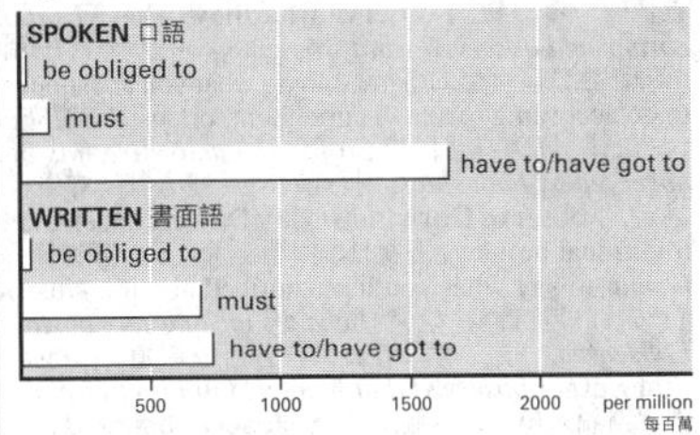

Based on the British National Corpus and the Longman Lancaster Corpus 據英國國家語料庫和朗文蘭卡斯特語料庫

This graph shows that the expressions **have to** and **have got to** are much more common in spoken English than **must** or **be obliged to**. **Have got to** is only used in British English. **Must** is more common in written English. **Be obliged to** is much less common than the others and is only used to say that someone must do something because of a rule or law, or because the situation forces them to do it. 本圖表顯示, 在英語口語中have to和have got to的使用頻率遠遠高於must或be obliged to。have got to僅用於英國英語。must更多用於書面語。be obliged to的使用頻率要低得多, 且僅用於表示某人因受某規定或法律所約束, 或因為情況所迫而必須做某事。

3 **o·blige** /əˋblaɪdʒ; əˈblaɪdʒ/ *v formal*【正式】**1** [T usually passive 一般用被動態] to make it necessary for someone to do something 使〔某人〕非做...不可, 迫使; 責成: **be obliged to do sth** *As a result of falling profits we were obliged to close the factory.* 由於利潤下降, 我們被迫關閉這家工廠。| **feel obliged to do sth** (=feel that you have a duty to do something) 覺得有義務做某事 *Don't feel obliged to play if you don't want to.* 你不想玩就不要勉強。**2** [I,T] to do something that someone has asked you to do 幫忙; 答應〔某人的〕請求: *Would you oblige me by taking this letter to the Director?* 勞駕你幫我把這封信捎給主任好嗎? | **happy/glad/ready to oblige** *If you need a ride home, I'd be happy to oblige.* 如果你需要搭車回家, 我很樂意效勞。**3 I'd be obliged if** *spoken* used to make a polite request【口】多謝〔請別人幫忙時的客氣話〕: *I'd be obliged if you'd treat this matter as strictly confidential.* 此事如你能嚴格保密, 我將非常感激。**4 (I'm) much obliged (to you)** *spoken* used to thank someone very politely【口】(我) 非常感謝 (你)〔用於有禮貌地向某人致謝〕

o·blig·ing /əˋblaɪdʒɪŋ; əˈblaɪdʒɪŋ/ *adj* willing and eager to help 樂於助人的, 熱心相助的: *What an obliging child!* 一個多麼熱心助人的孩子呀! —**obligingly** *adv*: *"Of course I'll do it," she said obligingly.* "這事我當然要做。" 她熱情地說。

o·blique[1] /əˋblik; əˈbliːk/ *adj* **1** not expressed in a direct way 間接的, 不直截了當的: *oblique references to his drinking problems* 拐彎抹角地提及他的酗酒問題 **2** not looking or pointing directly at something 斜的, 傾斜的: *an oblique glance* 睥視 **3 oblique line/stroke etc** a sloping line etc 斜線 **4 oblique angle** *technical* an angle that is not 90°, 180°, or 270°【術語】斜角 —**obliquely** *adv* —**obliqueness** *n* [U]

oblique[2] *n* [C] a mark (/) used for writing FRACTIONS (2) or for separating numbers, letters, words etc; SLASH[2] (2) 斜線符號

o·blit·er·ate /əˋblɪtə͵ret; əˈblɪtəreɪt/ *v* [T] **1** to destroy something so completely that no sign of it remains 完全毀滅〔不留痕跡〕: *The entire village was obliterated by incendiary bombs.* 整個村子被燃燒彈夷為平地。**2** to cover something completely so that it cannot be seen 塗抹; 遮蔽 **3** to remove a thought, feeling, or memory from someone's mind 忘卻, 抹去〔想法、感情或記憶〕: *Nothing could obliterate the memory of those tragic events.* 甚麼也不能讓人忘卻對那些悲慘事件的記憶。—**obliteration** /ə͵blɪtəˋreʃən; ə͵blɪtəˈreɪʃən/ *n* [U]

o·bliv·i·on /əˋblɪvɪən; əˈblɪviən/ *n* [U] **1** the state of being completely forgotten 被完全忘卻 (的狀態); 遺忘: *The loser's name is consigned to oblivion.* 那敗者的姓名湮沒無聞了。**2** the state of being unconscious or of not noticing what is happening 無感覺[知覺]的狀態; 漠視: *the oblivion of sleep* 睡眠中的無知覺狀態

o·bliv·i·ous /əˋblɪvɪəs; əˈblɪviəs/ *adj* [not before noun 不用於名詞前] not knowing about, or not noticing, something that is happening around you; UNAWARE 不在意的, 未覺察到的: **[+of/to]** *Mallory set off, utterly oblivious of the danger.* 馬洛里出發了, 全然沒有覺察到有危險。—**obliviousness** *n* [U]

ob·long /ˋɑblɔŋ; ˈɒblɒŋ/ *adj* **1** *AmE* an oblong shape is much longer than it is wide【美】長橢圓形的: *an oblong leaf* 長橢圓形的葉子 **2** *BrE* an oblong shape has four straight sides at 90° to each other, two of which are much longer than the other two【英】長方形的: *an oblong frame* 長方形的框架 —compare 比較 RECTANGLE —**oblong** *n* [C]

ob·lo·quy /ˋɑbləkwɪ; ˈɒbləkwi/ *n* [U] *formal*【正式】**1** very strong, offensive criticism 辱罵, 痛責 **2** loss of respect and honour 喪失尊嚴, 恥辱

ob·nox·ious /əbˋnɑkʃəs; əbˈnɒkʃəs/ *adj* extremely unpleasant or rude 可憎的, 討厭的; 粗暴無禮的: *You obnoxious little creep!* 你這個煩人的小討厭鬼! | *an obnoxious smell* 難聞的氣味 —**obnoxiously** *adv* —**obnoxiousness** *n* [U]

o·boe /ˋobo; ˈəʊbəʊ/ *n* [C] a wooden musical instrument, shaped like a narrow tube, which you play by blowing air through a REED (2) 雙簧管

o·bo·ist /ˋoboɪst; ˈəʊbəʊɪst/ *n* [C] someone who plays the oboe 雙簧管吹奏者

ob·scene /əbˋsin; əbˈsiːn/ *adj* **1** dealing with sex in a socially unacceptable and offensive way; INDECENT (1) 猥褻的, 淫猥的, 下流的: *The condemned man made an obscene gesture at the jury.* 被判罪者向陪審團做了個下流的手勢。| *obscene publications* 淫穢刊物 | **obscene phone calls** (=from an unknown person saying obscene things)〔來自陌生人的〕下流電話 **2** extremely immoral and unfair in a way that makes you angry 令人震怒的, 使人震驚的: *an obscene indifference to the needs of the poor* 對貧民的需求無動於衷, 令人震怒 —**obscenely** *adv*

ob·scen·i·ty /əbˋsɛnətɪ; əbˈsenəti/ *n* **1** [U] sexually offensive language or behaviour, especially in a book, play, film etc〔尤指書籍、戲劇、電影等中的〕猥褻語言; 下流舉動 **2** [C usually plural 一般用複數] a sexually offensive word or action 淫話; 淫行: *He ran off, shouting obscenities at them.* 他跑開了, 對他們大聲說着淫話。

ob·scu·ran·tis·m /əbˋskjurənt͵ɪzəm; ͵ɒbskjʊˈræntɪzəm/ *n* [U] *formal* the practice of deliberately stopping ideas and facts from being known【正式】蒙昧主義, 愚民政策 —**obscurantist** *adj*

ob·scure[1] /əbˋskjur; əbˈskjʊə/ *adj* **1** not at all well known and usually not very important 無名的; 微賤的: *an obscure poet* 沒有名氣的詩人 | *The exact origin of the paisley design is obscure.* 佩兹利渦旋紋圖案的確

切起源不明。**2** difficult to understand 難理解的, 晦澀的: *obscure legal phrases* 費解的法律詞語 **—obscurely** *adv*

obscure² *v* [T] **1** to make something difficult to know or understand 搞混, 使難理解: **obscure the fact/issue etc** *Recent successes obscure the fact that the company is still in trouble.* 近來的一些成功使人看不清公司依然處於困境。**2** to prevent something from being seen or heard clearly 遮蔽, 使朦朧; 使聽不清: *Thick cloud obscured the stars from view.* 厚厚的雲層遮住了星星。

ob·scu·ri·ty /əb`skjurətɪ; əb'skjʊərəti/ *n* **1** [U] the state of not being known or remembered 無名, 默默無聞: **[+in]** *O'Brien retired from politics and died in obscurity.* 奧布賴恩退出政壇後默默無聞地死去。**2** [C,U] something that is difficult to understand, or the quality of being difficult to understand 費解的事物; 費解, 晦澀: *After years of analysis, a great many obscurities remain in the text.* 雖經多年分析探討, 文中仍存有大量難解之處。**3** [U] *literary* darkness【文】黑暗

ob·se·quies /`ɑbsɪkwɪz; 'ɒbsəkwiz/ *n* [plural] *formal* a funeral ceremony【正式】葬禮, 喪禮

ob·se·qui·ous /əb`sikwɪəs; əb'siːkwiəs/ *adj* too eager to serve people and agree with them; SERVILE (1) 諂媚的, 奉承的; 奴顏婢膝的: *The salesman's obsequious manner was beginning to irritate me.* 那推銷員逢迎的樣子讓我惱怒起來。**—obsequiously** *adv* **—obsequiousness** *n* [U]

ob·ser·va·ble /əb`zɝvəbl; əb'zɜːvəbəl/ *adj* something that is observable can be seen or noticed 看得見的, 能觀察到的: *unemployment and other observable effects of the recession* 失業及其他可看得到的經濟衰退帶來的影響 **—observably** *adv*

ob·ser·vance /əb`zɝvəns; əb'zɜːvəns/ *n* **1** [U] the practice of obeying a law or doing what is expected according to a custom or ceremony〔對法律、風俗或儀式的〕遵守, 奉行: **[+of]** *strict observance of the rules* 對規則的嚴格遵守 | *the observance of Chinese New Year* 奉行過中國農曆新年的習俗 **2** [C] a part of a religious ceremony 宗教的典禮, 儀式: *ritual observances* 例行的宗教儀式

ob·ser·vant /əb`zɝvənt; əb'zɜːvənt/ *adj* **1** good or quick at noticing things 觀察力敏銳的, 機警的: *Luckily, an observant passerby spotted the broken cable.* 幸虧一位機警的過路人發現了那根斷裂的電纜。| **[+of]** *Artists tend to be more observant of their surroundings.* 藝術家往往對他們周圍的環境更為留意。**2** **[+of]** obeying laws, religious rules etc 遵守法律[宗教教規等]的

3 **ob·ser·va·tion** /ˌɑbzɚ`veʃən; ˌɒbzə'veɪʃən/ *n* **1** [C,U] the process of watching something or someone carefully for a period of time 觀察, 注意; 監視: *a study based on detailed observation of a group of 20 patients* 基於對一組20位患者詳細觀察的研究 | *a result of scientific observation* 科學觀察的結果 | **under observation** (=being watched continuously by police, doctors etc) 受〔警方或醫生等的〕監視[觀察] *She's in hospital under observation.* 她在醫院接受觀察。| *Detectives are keeping the place under observation.* 偵探們監視着這個地方。**2** [C] a spoken or written remark about something you have noticed〔對所注意到的事物的〕評述, 評論: **[+on]** *Darwin's observations on the habits of certain birds* 達爾文對某些鳥類習性的評述 | **make an observation** *I'd like to make a few observations about the current style of management.* 我想對當前的管理方式提出一些看法。**3 powers of observation** a natural ability to notice what is happening around you 觀察力 **4 escape observation** to avoid being noticed 避免被人看見 **5** [U] the act of obeying a law etc; OBSERVANCE (1)〔對法律等的〕遵守, 奉行 **—observational** *adj*

observation post /.,..'.. ./ *n* [C] a position from which an enemy can be watched 監視哨, 瞭望哨

ob·ser·va·to·ry /əb`zɝvəˌtorɪ; əb'zɜːvətəri/ *n* [C] a special building from which scientists watch the moon, stars, weather etc 天文台; 觀象台; 氣象台: *the Greenwich Observatory* 格林尼治天文台

ob·serve /əb`zɝv; əb'zɜːv/ *v* [T] **1** [not in progressive 2 不用進行式] *formal* to see and notice something【正式】看到, 注意到: **observe sb doing sth** *Ben knew that someone had observed him meeting Ryan.* 本知道有人看到他和瑞安見面了。| **[+that]** *She observed that the pond was drying up.* 她注意到池塘日漸乾涸。| **observe sth** *The car I had observed earlier was no longer there.* 我早些時候看到的那輛汽車不在那裡了。**2** to watch something or someone carefully 觀察, 監視, 觀測: *The police have been observing his movements.* 警方一直監視着他的一舉一動。| **observe what/how/where** *I sat in a corner and observed what was going on.* 我坐在一個角落裡觀察當時發生的事情。**3** to do what you are supposed to do according to a law, agreement, or custom 遵守, 奉行〔法律、協議或習俗〕: *So far the ceasefire has been observed by both sides.* 到目前為止, 雙方都遵守着停火協定。| **observe Christmas/May Day etc** (=celebrate a traditional holiday) 慶祝[紀念]聖誕節/五一勞動節等 **4** *formal* to say what you have noticed about a situation【正式】評述, 評論, 說: *"Michael's looking very anxious," I observed.* "邁克爾看上去很着急。"我說道。| **observe that** *Keynes observed that humans fall into two classes.* 凱恩斯說人類分為兩個階級。**5 closely observed** a play, character etc that is closely observed is very like a situation, character etc in real life〔戲劇、人物等〕與現實生活非常相似的, 逼真的

ob·serv·er /əb`zɝvɚ; əb'zɜːvə/ *n* [C] **1** someone who sees or notices something 目擊者: *Shocked observers told police about the robbery.* 震驚的目擊者將搶劫案的情況告知了警方。| **casual observer** (=one who is not specially interested) 漫不經心的目擊者 *To a casual observer she may have seemed fine, but I knew better.* 對於不是很留意她的人來說, 她也許看上去不錯, 但我知道得更清楚。**2** someone who regularly watches or pays attention to particular things 觀察者, 觀測員: **[+of]** *an impartial observer of the current political scene* 對當今政治局面不帶偏見的觀察者 | *an observer of nature* 自然界的觀察者 **3** someone who attends meetings, classes etc to check what is happening〔會議等的〕觀察員;〔課程的〕旁聽者: *The UN sent a team of observers to the peace talks.* 聯合國派出一個觀察員小組出席和平會談。

ob·sess /əb`sɛs; əb'ses/ *v* **1** [T usually passive 一般用被動態] if something or someone obsesses you, you think about them all the time and you cannot think of anything else 使着迷; 使纏繞; 使心神不寧: **be obsessed with** *You've always been obsessed with making money.* 你總是心心念念想着掙錢。| *He had become obsessed with another man's wife.* 他迷戀上一名有夫之婦。| **obsess sb** *Minute details seem to obsess lawyers.* 律師似乎總糾纏於細節問題。**2** [I] *AmE* to think about something or someone much more than is necessary or sensible【美】過分擔心: **[+over/about]** *Stop obsessing about your weight. You look fine.* 不要過於擔心你的體重, 你看上去很好。

ob·ses·sion /əb`sɛʃən; əb'seʃən/ *n* [C] an unreasonably strong and continuous interest in something, or worry about something, which stops you from thinking about anything else 困擾人的想法; 無法擺脱的意念; 着迷, 着魔: *He's convinced he was unfairly treated and it's become an obsession.* 他認為自己受到了不公正的對待, 這想法一直困擾着他。| **[+with/about]** *an unhealthy obsession with death* 一種總是想到死的不健康的念頭 **—obsessional** *adj*: *She had an almost obsessional desire to win.* 她有一種接近無法擺脱的想赢的慾望。

ob·ses·sive¹ /əb`sɛsɪv; əb'sesɪv/ *adj* an obsessive feeling, interest or attitude makes you think all the time about a particular thing or person 着迷的; 纏住不放的;〔在某方面〕過分的: *an obsessive need for excitement* 對刺激感着魔般的需求 | *She's becoming obsessive about hygiene.* 她變得有潔癖了。**—obsessively** *adv*

obsessive² *n* [C] *technical* someone whose behaviour is obsessive【術語】着迷的人; 強迫觀念症患者

ob·sid·i·an /əbˋsɪdɪən; əbˈsɪdiən/ *n* [U] a type of dark rock which looks like glass 黑曜岩

ob·so·les·cence /ˌɑbsəˋlɛsəns; ˌɒbsəˈlesəns/ *n* [U] **1** the state of becoming old-fashioned and no longer useful, because something else that is newer and better has been invented 過時; 淘汰, 廢棄 **2 planned/built-in obsolescence** the practice of making a product in such a way that it will soon become unfashionable or impossible to use〔商品等〕計劃報廢, 有計劃的淘汰〔指讓產品具有不久就會過時或淘汰的特徵〕

ob·so·les·cent /ˌɑbsəˋlɛsənt; ˌɒbsəˈlesənt◂/ *adj* becoming obsolete 逐漸被廢棄的; 即將過時的

ob·so·lete /ˋɑbsəˌlit; ˈɒbsəliːt◂/ *adj* no longer useful because something newer and better has been invented 廢棄的, 淘汰的; 過時的: *obsolete weapons* 老式的武器 | **render sth obsolete** (=make it obsolete) 使某物變過時 *Current production methods will soon be rendered obsolete.* 現在的生產方法將很快被淘汰。

ob·sta·cle /ˋɑbstəkḷ; ˈɒbstəkəl/ *n* [C] **1** something that makes it difficult for you to achieve your aim 障礙, 阻礙, 妨礙: **[+to]** *Fear of change is the greatest single obstacle to progress.* 害怕變革是進步的一個最大障礙。| **put obstacles in the way (of)** (=try to prevent something by causing difficulties) 設法阻撓, 設置障礙 *They tried to put obstacles in the way of our marriage.* 他們想阻撓我們的婚姻。**2** an object which blocks your way, so that you must try to go around it 障礙物

obstacle course /ˈ··· ˌ·/ *n* [C] **1** a line of objects which runners in an OBSTACLE RACE have to jump over, climb through etc 障礙賽跑道 **2** a series of difficulties which must be dealt with to achieve a particular aim 重重困難 **3** *AmE* an ASSAULT COURSE【美】突擊訓練場, 軍事訓練場地

obstacle race /ˈ··· ˌ·/ *n* [C] a type of race in which runners have to jump over or climb through various objects 障礙賽跑

ob·ste·tri·cian /ˌɑbstɛˋtrɪʃən; ˌɒbstəˈtrɪʃən/ *n* [C] a doctor who has special training in obstetrics 產科醫生

ob·stet·rics /əbˋstɛtrɪks; əbˈstetrɪks/ *n* [U] the part of medical science concerned with the birth of children 產科學 —**obstetric** *adj*

ob·sti·na·cy /ˋɑbstənəsɪ; ˈɒbstənəsi/ *n* [U] an unreasonable determination not to change your mind 固執, 頑固; 倔強

ob·sti·nate /ˋɑbstənɪt; ˈɒbstənət/ *adj* **1** unreasonably refusing to change your ideas of behaviour, even though people try to persuade you 固執的, 頑固的; 倔強的: *Harry was obstinate and wouldn't admit he was wrong.* 哈里很固執, 不肯承認他錯了。| *a sulky, obstinate child* 愛生悶氣的倔強孩子 | *an obstinate refusal to face facts* 頑固地拒絕面對事實 **2** [only before noun 僅用於名詞前] difficult to deal with or get rid of 難以對付的; 難以去除的; 難治的: *strong enough to remove the most obstinate stains* 效力很強, 足以去除最難對付的污漬 | *an obstinate cough* 難治的咳嗽 —**obstinately** *adv*

ob·strep·e·rous /əbˋstrɛpərəs; əbˈstrepərəs/ *adj* obstreperous behaviour is noisy and cheerful or angry 喧嘩的, 喧鬧的; 吵嚷的 —**obstreperously** *adv* —**obstreperousness** *n* [U]

ob·struct /əbˋstrʌkt; əbˈstrʌkt/ *v* [T] **1** to block a road, passage etc 阻塞, 堵塞〔道路、通道等〕: *A small aircraft now obstructed the runway.* 一架小型飛機現在堵塞了跑道。| *an accident obstructing northbound traffic* 一宗堵塞了北行交通的事故 | *Our view was obstructed by a high wall.* 我們的視線被一堵高牆擋住了。**2** to try to prevent someone from doing something by making it difficult for them 阻撓, 妨礙, 阻止: *A small minority obstructed policies that would help the majority of people.* 一小撮人阻撓了將對大多數人有益的若干政策。| *obstructing a police officer in the course of his duty* 妨礙警官執行公務

ob·struc·tion /əbˋstrʌkʃən; əbˈstrʌkʃən/ *n* **1** [U] the act of trying to prevent or delay a legal or political process〔對立法或議事等的〕阻撓; 拖延: **[+of]** *obstruction of vital legislation* 對重要立法的阻撓 **2** [U] the act of blocking a road, passage, tube etc〔道路、通道、管道等的〕阻塞, 堵塞: **[+of]** *obstruction of the public highway* 阻塞公共交通幹線 **3** [C] something that blocks a road, passage, tube etc〔堵塞道路、通道、管道等的〕障礙物: *There's an obstruction in the fuel pipe.* 燃料管道中有阻塞物。**4** [C] an offence in football, HOCKEY etc in which a player gets between an opponent and the ball〔足球、曲棍球等中的〕阻擋行為 —see picture on page A23 參見 A23 頁圖

ob·struc·tion·is·m /əbˋstrʌkʃənɪzṃ; əbˈstrʌkʃənɪzəm/ *n* [U] the practice of trying to prevent or delay a legal or political process〔對立法或議事等的〕蓄意阻撓; 故意拖延 —**obstructionist** *n* [C]

ob·struc·tive /əbˋstrʌktɪv; əbˈstrʌktɪv/ *adj* trying to prevent someone from doing something by deliberately making it difficult for them 蓄意阻撓的; 故意妨礙的: *an obstructive official* 蓄意阻撓的官員 | *obstructive tactics* 故意妨礙的策略 —**obstructively** *adv* —**obstructiveness** *n* [U]

ob·tain /əbˋten; əbˈteɪn/ *v formal*【正式】**1** [T] to get something that you want, especially through your own effort, skill, or work〔尤指通過自身的努力、技能或工作等〕獲得, 得到: *Further information can be obtained from head office.* 詳細資料可從總辦事處得到。| *They've extended the growing season to obtain a larger crop.* 他們延長了作物的生長期以獲得更好的收成。| *the difficulty of obtaining credit* 得到信任的困難 **2** [I not in progressive 不用進行式] if a situation, system, or rule obtains, it continues to exist〔情況、系統、規則等〕繼續存在, 通用: *These conditions no longer obtain.* 這些條件已不復存在。

USAGE NOTE 用法說明: OBTAIN

WORD CHOICE 詞語辨析: **obtain, get, get hold of, find out, achieve, receive**

Obtain is formal and often sounds unnatural in spoken English or in a personal letter. obtain 屬正式用語, 用於口語或私人信函時常會令人感覺不自然: *Where can I obtain a list of restaurants?* 我從哪裡能得到一份各餐館的名錄? | *Fresh fruit and vegetables were especially difficult to obtain.* 新鮮的水果和蔬菜尤其難以買到。

Get is the most common word in spoken English and informal writing meaning to come to have something. However, some people feel that **get** should not be used too often in writing. get 是口語及非正式書面語中最常用的詞, 意為"得到某物"。但有人認為 get 不應過多地用於書面語中: *Where did you get that painting?* 你從哪裡得到那幅畫的? | *He gets about $200 a week at the textile mill.* 他在紡織廠工作, 週薪為 200 美元左右。

You can also **get hold of** things, or information, especially after some difficulty (informal). get hold of〔非正式〕也可用來表示得到東西或資料, 尤指在經歷了困難之後: *I need to get hold of a powerful computer.* 我需要弄到一台功能強大的電腦。| *At last I managed to get hold of her address.* 最終我設法得到了她的地址。

You **find out** information. find out 指查獲資料: *I need to find out where my classes are.* 我需要搞清楚我的課都在哪裡上。

If you get yourself into a better situation through your own efforts, you **achieve** something. achieve 指通過個人努力改善自身的狀況: *We are working to achieve better results/equality/independence.* 我們正在努力以爭取更好的成績/平等/獨立。| *Regular exercise helps people achieve better health.* 經常鍛鍊使人身體更健康。

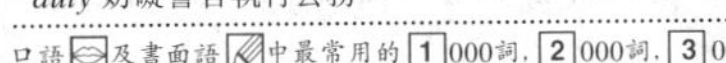

If what you get comes naturally or is given to you, you can use the word **receive** (slightly formal). receive〔稍正式〕指所得之物是自然而來的或是饋贈的: *The charity receives most of its money through private donations.* 那個慈善機構收到的善款大多來自私人捐贈。

ob·tain·a·ble /əbˋtenəbḷ; əbˈteɪnəbəl/ *adj* something that is obtainable can be obtained 能得到的, 可獲得的: *Most of the ingredients for Chinese cooking are obtainable at the supermarket.* 中式菜餚的配料大部分都能在超級市場裡買到。

ob·trude /əbˋtrud; əbˈtruːd/ *v* [I,T] *formal*【正式】**1** if something obtrudes, or you obtrude something, it becomes noticed where it is not wanted (使) 強行進入[闖入]; 強加: **[+into/upon]** *Personal taste is bound to obtrude into a book about wine.* 評酒的書中肯定摻有個人的喜好。—compare 比較 INTRUDE (1), PROTRUDE **2** to stick out or make something stick out (使) 凸出, (使) 伸出

ob·tru·sive /əbˋtrusɪv; əbˈtruːsɪv/ *adj* noticeable in a way that is unpleasant 過分突出而難看[討人嫌]的, 突兀的: *large obtrusive TV antennas* 高聳刺眼的電視天線 | *He was here just now, being kind of obtrusive and polite at the same time.* 他剛才還在這裡, 表現得既有點惹眼又彬彬有禮。—opposite 反義詞 UNOBTRUSIVE —**obtrusively** *adv* —**obtrusiveness** *n* [U]

ob·tuse /əbˋtus; əbˈtjuːs/ *adj* **1** slow to understand things, in a way that is annoying 遲鈍的, 愚笨的: *an obtuse lout of a man* 遲鈍的笨人 | **be obtuse** (=pretend to not understand something) 裝傻 *Is he being deliberately obtuse?* 他在故意裝傻嗎? **2 obtuse angle** *technical* an angle between 90 and 180 degrees【術語】鈍角 —**obtusely** *adv* —**obtuseness** *n* [U] —see picture at 參見 ANGLE[1]圖

ob·verse /ˋɑbvɝs; ˈɒbvɜːs/ *n* **1** *formal* the opposite of a particular situation or feeling【正式】對立面; 對應物: **[+of]** *Defeat is the obverse of victory.* 與失敗相對的是勝利。**2 the obverse** *technical* the front side of a coin or MEDAL【術語】〔硬幣或獎章的〕正面 —opposite 反義詞 REVERSE[2] (6)

ob·vi·ate /ˋɑbvɪˌet; ˈɒbvieɪt/ *v* [T] **1 obviate the need** *formal* to make something unnecessary【正式】使成為不必要, 避免: *The use of a credit card obviates the need to carry a lot of money.* 使用信用卡就不必隨身攜帶大量現金。**2** to remove a difficulty 排除, 消除〔困難〕

ob·vi·ous /ˋɑbvɪəs; ˈɒbviəs/ *adj* **1** easy to notice or understand 顯然的, 顯而易見的, 明白的: *the obvious advantages of co-operation* 合作的明顯好處 | *For obvious reasons we have had to cancel tonight's performance.* 基於顯而易見的原因, 我們不得不取消了今晚的演出。| *"Why is she leaving?" "Well, it's pretty obvious isn't it?"* "她為甚麼要走?" "哦, 這很明白, 不是嗎?" | **it is obvious (to sb) that** *It was obvious to everyone that Gina was lying.* 大家都很清楚吉娜在撒謊。**2 obvious statement/remark etc** a statement that is unnecessary because it states what is obvious to everyone 明顯多餘的說明/話語等 **3 the obvious choice** the person or thing that you would expect everyone to choose 明擺着的選擇: *Nicholson was the obvious choice for team leader.* 尼科爾森是明擺着的隊長人選。**4 the obvious thing (to do)** what clearly seems the best thing to do 最好的做法: *The obvious thing would have been to travel with her husband, but she couldn't.* 明顯地最好的做法是她和丈夫一起去旅遊, 但她不能去。**5 state the obvious** to say something that is already obvious and is therefore unnecessary 說出明擺着的大實話 —**obviousness** *n* [U]

ob·vi·ous·ly /ˋɑbvɪəslɪ; ˈɒbviəsli/ *adv* used to mean that a fact can easily be noticed or understood 明顯地, 顯而易見地, 明白地: [sentence adverb 句子副詞] *We're obviously going to need more help.* 顯然我們將需要更多的幫助。| *"Is she sorry?" "Obviously not! Look at her."* "她難過嗎?" "顯然不! 你看她那個樣子。" | **[+adj/adv]** *The woman was lying across the chairs, obviously unwell.* 那女子橫躺在椅子上, 顯然是身體不舒服。—see 見 OF COURSE (USAGE) —compare 比較 APPARENTLY, EVIDENTLY

oc·ca·sion[1] /əˋkeʒən; əˈkeɪʒən/ *n*

1 ▶TIME 時間◀ a) [C] a time when something happens〔某事發生的〕時刻, 時候, 時節: **on an occasion** *She had met Zahid on an earlier occasion.* 她早些時候曾見過扎希德。| *I've seen Jana with them on several occasions.* 我幾次看見亞娜和他們在一起。**b)** [singular] a suitable or favourable time〔合適的〕機會, 〔有利的〕時機: **[+for]** *We used the meeting as an occasion for announcing the restructuring.* 我們把握這次會議的機會宣布重組。

2 ▶SPECIAL EVENT 特殊活動◀ [C] an important social event or ceremony 重要的社交活動, 盛會: *I'm saving this bottle of champagne for a special occasion.* 我要把這瓶香檳酒留到特殊場合用。| **quite an occasion** (=a very exciting or impressive occasion) 重大場合, 盛大的場面 *The opening of the new library turned out to be quite an occasion.* 新圖書館的開幕典禮成了一次令人難忘的盛事。

3 ▶CAUSE/REASON 起因/緣由◀ [singular] *formal* a direct cause or reason【正式】直接的原因[誘因]: **be the occasion of** *His remark was the occasion of a bitter quarrel.* 他的話引起了一場激烈的爭吵。| **have occasion to do sth** (=need to do something) 有必要做某事 *More than once Dr Standish had occasion to warn his son about his irresponsible behaviour.* 對兒子不負責任的行為, 斯坦迪什博士不得不多次向他提出告誡。

4 if (the) occasion arises *formal* if a particular action ever becomes necessary【正式】如有必要, 必要時: *I am ready to defend our policies if the occasion arises.* 必要時, 我準備為我們的政策進行辯護。

5 on occasion sometimes but not often 有時, 間或, 偶爾: *I have on occasion visited her at home.* 有時我去登門拜訪她。

6 on the occasion of *formal* at the time of an important event【正式】在〔重要事件〕之際: *on the occasion of her 50th birthday* 在她 50 歲生日之際

7 rise to the occasion to deal well with an unexpected and difficult situation 隨機應變, 善於應付突如其來的困難局面 —see also 另見 **sense of occasion** (SENSE[1] (20))

occasion[2] *v* [T] *formal* to cause something【正式】引起, 惹起: *disputes occasioned by greed and intolerance* 因貪婪和偏狹引起的糾紛 | **occasion sb sth** *Your behaviour has occasioned us a great deal of anxiety.* 你的行為讓我們極為不安。

oc·ca·sion·al /əˋkeʒənḷ; əˈkeɪʒənəl/ *adj* **1** happening sometimes but not often 偶爾的, 偶然的, 不經常的: *Expect occasional showers today.* 今天偶爾有陣雨。| *He smokes an occasional cigar.* 他偶爾抽一支雪茄煙。**2** *formal* written or intended for a special occasion【正式】為特殊場合寫作[使用]的, 應景的: *occasional poems* 應景詩

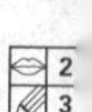

oc·ca·sion·al·ly /əˋkeʒənḷɪ; əˈkeɪʒənəli/ *adv* sometimes, but not regularly and not often 偶爾, 偶然, 間或: *Occasionally Alice would look up from her books.* 艾麗絲偶爾從書本中抬起頭來。| **very occasionally** (=rarely) 難得, 不常 *We only see each other very occasionally.* 我們極少見面。—see picture at 參見 FREQUENCY 圖

occasional ta·ble /ˌ·ˈ··· ˌ··/ *n* [C] *BrE* a small light table that can be easily moved【英】〔易於挪動的〕輕便小桌, 備用小桌

Oc·ci·dent /ˋɑksədənt; ˈɒksədənt/ *n* **the Occident** *literary* the western part of the world, especially Europe and the Americas【文】西方, 西方國家, 西半球〔尤指歐洲和美洲〕—compare 比較 ORIENT[2]

oc·ci·den·tal /ˌɑksəˋdɛntḷ; ˌɒksəˈdentəl◂/ *n* [C] *formal* someone from the western part of the world【正式】西

方人, 西洋人, 歐美人 —compare 比較 ORIENTAL² — **occidental** *adj*

oc·cult¹ /əˋkʌlt; ˈɒkʌlt/ *n* **the occult** mysterious practices and powers involving magic and spirits 神祕學; 神祕儀式; 魔法: *He was a strange man who dabbled in the occult.* 他是個怪人, 懂一點魔法。

occult² *adj* magical and mysterious 玄妙的; 奧祕的; 神祕的; 超自然的: *the occult powers* 魔力, 超自然力量

oc·cu·pan·cy /ˋɑkjəpənsɪ; ˈɒkjʊpənsi/ *n* [U] *formal* someone's use of a building, piece of land, or other space, for living or working in【正式】〔對房產、土地等的〕佔有, 佔用; 居住: *their occupancy of the apartment* 他們對那套公寓的佔用

oc·cu·pant /ˋɑkjəpənt; ˈɒkjʊpənt/ *n* [C] *formal*【正式】**1** someone who lives in a house, room etc, though without necessarily owning it 居住者, 住戶: *furniture left by the previous occupants* 先前的住戶留下的家具 **2** someone who is in a room, vehicle etc at a particular time〔房間、汽車等某一時期的〕使用者, 佔有人: *Neither of the car's two occupants was injured.* 車裡的兩個人都沒有受傷。

3 3 **oc·cu·pa·tion** /ˌɑkjəˋpeʃən; ˌɒkjʊˈpeɪʃən/ *n* **1** [C] a job or profession 工作, 職業: *Please state your name, address and occupation.* 請說明你的姓名、地址和職業。—see 見 JOB (USAGE) **2** [C] a way of spending your time; PASTIME 消遣, 業餘活動: *Marcus regarded stamp-collecting as a childish occupation.* 馬庫斯把集郵視為一種幼稚的消遣。**3** [U] the act of living or staying in a building or place 居住; 佔用: *In many of the caves there is evidence of human occupation.* 其中許多洞穴有人類居住過的痕跡。**4** [U] the act of entering a place in a large group and keeping control of it, especially by military force〔尤指用軍事力量的〕佔領, 佔據, 控制: **[+of]** *the German occupation of France* 德軍佔領法國 | *Demonstrators are continuing their occupation of the building.* 示威者繼續佔據着那棟大樓。

oc·cu·pa·tion·al /ˌɑkjəˋpeʃənl; ˌɒkjʊˈpeɪʃənəl◂/ *adj* [only before noun 僅用於名詞前] related to, or caused by your job 職業的, 工作的; 由職業引起的: *an occupational disease* 職業病 | **occupational hazard** (=a risk that always exists in a particular job) 職業上的風險 —**occupationally** *adv*

occupational ther·a·py /ˌ····· ˈ···/ *n* [U] a form of treatment for helping people to get back their health after illness by giving them special work 職業[作業]療法 —**occupational therapist** *n* [C]

oc·cu·pi·er /ˋɑkjəˌpaɪɚ; ˈɒkjʊpaɪə/ *n* [C] *especially BrE* someone who lives in or uses a particular house, piece of land etc, especially temporarily【尤英】〔房屋、土地等的暫時〕佔用者, 居住者 —see also 另見 OWNER-OCCUPIER

3 2 **oc·cu·py** /ˋɑkjəˌpaɪ; ˈɒkjʊpaɪ/ *v* [T]

1 ▶STAY IN A PLACE 住在某處◀ *formal* to live or stay in a place【正式】佔居, 居住: *The Jackson family have occupied this apartment for the past six months.* 過去半年中, 傑克遜一家住在這套公寓裡。

2 be occupied if a room, seat, or bed is occupied, someone is in it or using it〔房間、座位、牀位等〕有人使用, 被佔用

3 ▶SEIZE AND CONTROL 佔據並控制◀ to enter a place in a large group and keep control of it, for example by military force〔被軍隊等〕佔領, 佔據: *Bosnian Serb forces have occupied the city for 8 months.* 波斯尼亞的塞爾維亞軍隊佔領該城市已有八個月。| *an occupying army* 佔領軍

4 ▶FILL TIME/SPACE 佔時間/空間◀ to fill a space or period of time 佔用〔空間或一段時間〕: *Soccer occupies most of my leisure time.* 足球佔去了我大部分的閒暇時間。| *Traditional paintings occupy most of the wall-space in the gallery.* 傳統繪畫佔去了美術館的大部分牆面。

5 occupy sb's mind/thoughts/attention if something occupies your mind etc, you think about that thing more than anything else 佔據某人的頭腦/思想/注意力

6 ▶BUSY 忙碌◀ **a) occupy sb/keep sb occupied** to keep someone busy 使某人忙碌: *I've invented a game that will keep the kids occupied for hours.* 我發明了一種遊戲, 夠孩子們玩上幾個小時的。| *Hannah gets so bored – she needs something to occupy her.* 漢娜很是膩煩 — 她需要點東西使自己忙碌起來。**b) be occupied with** to be busy doing something 忙於〔做某事〕: *Helen was fully occupied with business matters, so we didn't want to bother her.* 海倫公務纏身, 所以我們不想打擾她。

7 ▶OFFICIAL POSITION 正式職位◀ to have an official position or job 擔任〔正式職位或工作〕: *Before becoming prime minister, Mrs Thatcher had already occupied several cabinet posts.* 在成為首相之前, 戴卓爾夫人曾出任過好幾個內閣職位。

oc·cur /əˋkɝ; əˈkɜː/ *v* **occurred, occurring** [I] *formal* 1 1【正式】**1** to happen 發生: *Many accidents occur in the home.* 許多事故都在家中發生。| *Climatic changes have occurred at intervals throughout the millenium.* 整個千年中, 氣候變化時有發生。**2** [always + adv/prep] to happen or exist in a particular place or situation〔在特定地點或情況下〕發生; 存在: **[+in/among etc]** *Whooping cough occurs mainly in young children.* 百日咳多發於幼兒。

occur to sb *phr v* [T not in passive 不用被動態] if an idea or thought occurs to you, it suddenly comes into your mind〔主意或想法突然〕浮現於腦中; 被想起, 被想到: **it occurs to sb that** *Didn't it occur to you that your husband might be late?* 你當時沒有想到你丈夫也許會晚到嗎? | *The possibility that she might be wrong never occurred to her.* 她壓根兒沒想到自己可能會錯。| **it occurs to sb to do sth** *I suppose it never occurred to you to phone the police?* 我想你根本就沒想到打電話報警吧?

USAGE NOTE 用法說明: OCCUR

WORD CHOICE 詞語辨析: **occur to, strike, occur, there is, happen, take place, arise, crop up**

If a thought comes into your mind it **occurs to** you or **strikes** you. 倘有一個想法出現在某人腦海中, 可用 occur to 或 strike (某人): *It suddenly occurred to/struck me I hadn't seen Peter all day.* 我突然想到, 我一整天都沒看見彼得。

Occur meaning 'happen' is rather formal and not common in spoken English. occur 作"發生"解時, 是相當正式的用語, 且很少用於口語: *The court will decide what really occurred.* 法庭會判定到底發生了甚麼事。**Occur to** is not used in this sense: *A problem occurred to me* means 'I thought of a problem' NOT 'I had a problem'. occur to 則不用於此意: A problem occurred to me 意為"我想到了一個問題", 而不是"我有一個問題"。

Usually people use **there is...** 人們通常使用 there is ...: *There was a loud bang from outside.* 外面傳來砰的一聲巨響。| *There's been an accident.* 發生了一宗事故。| *There's going to be a meeting next Tuesday.* 下週二有個會議。When the person who something happens to is mentioned, you use **have**. 當提及某人遭遇某事時, 則用 have: *He had an interview last week.* 上週他去了面試。| *She's bound to have trouble with the customs officials.* 她肯定要和海關官員鬧糾紛。

Events and processes **happen** or **happen to** you, especially if they are not planned. happen 或 happen to 用以指某事情和過程發生, 或某事件和過程發生在某人身上, 尤其是未經計劃的事情: *All sorts of unexpected things might happen.* 甚麼樣的意外都有可能發生。| *The Industrial Revolution happened in the eighteenth century.* 工業革命發生在

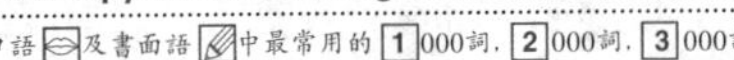

十八世紀。| *What's happening to us?* 我們這是怎麼啦?

If you are talking about something that is planned or arranged, you often use **take place**. 在談論有計劃或預先安排的事情時, 常使用take place: *The wedding will take place in St Peter's Church.* 婚禮將在聖彼得教堂舉行。

Problems or difficulties **arise** (formal) and something that happens suddenly and unexpectedly **crops up** (informal). 問題或困難的"出現"用arise〔正式〕, 某事"突然發生"則用crop up〔非正式〕: *Let's consider what kind of difficulties might arise from the situation.* 讓我們考慮一下, 這種情況下可能會出現哪些困難。| *I have to go home early – something's cropped up.* 我得早點回家 — 出了點事。

SPELLING 拼法

Remember that there are two 'r's in *occurred* and *occurring*. 切記 occurred 和 occurring 中都有兩個 r。

oc·cur·rence /ə`kɝəns; əˈkʌrəns/ *n* **1** [C] something that happens 發生的事, 事件: **a common/rare/regular occurrence** *Flooding under this bridge is a common occurrence.* 這橋下經常洪水氾濫。| *Laughter was a rare occurrence in his classroom.* 他的課堂上難得有笑聲。**2** [U] the fact of something happening〔事件的〕發生, 出現: *the frequent occurrence of violent storms in the area* 該地區強風暴的頻繁發生

o·cean /`oʃən; ˈəʊʃən/ *n* **1 the ocean** *especially AmE* the great mass of salt water that covers most of the Earth's surface【尤美】海洋, 大海: *She stood on the beach, gazing at the ocean.* 她站在海灘上, 凝視着大海。**2** [C] one of the very large areas of sea on the Earth's surface ...洋: *the Pacific Ocean* 太平洋 **3 oceans of** *informal* a great mass or amount of something【非正式】大量, 許多 —see also 另見 **a drop in the ocean** (DROP[2] (8)) —**oceanic** /ˌoʃɪ`ænɪk; ˌəʊʃiˈænɪk◂/ *adj*

o·cean·go·ing /`oʃənˌgoɪŋ; ˈəʊʃənˌgəʊɪŋ/ *adj* an oceangoing ship is designed to sail across the sea〔船隻〕用於越洋的, 遠洋航行的; 行駛外洋的: *an oceangoing tanker* 遠洋油輪

o·cean·og·ra·phy /ˌoʃɪən`ɑgrəfɪ; ˌəʊʃənˈɒgrəfi/ *n* [U] the scientific study of the ocean 海洋(地理)學 —**oceanographer** *n* [C]

oc·e·lot /`ɑsəˌlɑt; ˈɒsɪ̣lɒt/ *n* [C] a large American wild cat that has a pattern of spots on its back〔美洲的一種背部有斑點的大型〕豹貓

och /ɑk; ɒk/ *interjection ScotE* used to express surprise or to emphasize a remark; OH (3)【蘇格蘭】啊, 呀, 哎喲〔用於表示驚訝或加強語氣〕

o·chre usually 一般作 **ocher** *AmE*【美】/`okɚ; ˈəʊkə/ *n* [U] **1** a reddish-yellow earth used in paints 赭石〔用作顏料〕**2** the colour of ochre 赭色, 黃褐色 —**ochre** *adj*

ock·er /`ɑkɚ; ˈɒkə/ *n* [C] *AustrE, NZE* a word for an Australian man, also used in Australia by men speaking to or about each other【澳, 新西蘭】澳大利亞人; 老兄〔澳大利亞男人互相稱呼對方的用語〕: *G'day Ocker – how's it going?* 你好, 老兄! 過得怎麼樣?

o'clock /ə`klɑk; əˈklɒk/ *adv* **one o'clock/two o'clock etc** one of the times when the clock shows the exact hour as a number from 1 to 12 一點鐘/兩點鐘等: *"What time is it?" "It's 9 o'clock."* "現在幾點鐘?" "九點鐘。"

USAGE NOTE 用法說明: O'CLOCK

UK-US DIFFERENCE 英國英語和美國英語的差異

O'clock is used only when you are talking about the exact hour. o'clock 只用於表示正點時間: *nine o'clock* 九點鐘。Compare 比較: *ten to nine* 8點50分

Minutes after the hour are expressed with **past** (usually **after** in American English). 說幾點過幾分可用past〔美國英語中通常用after〕: *five/a quarter/ten past nine* 9點5分/15分/10分。Compare 比較: *five/ten/a quarter after nine* (American English only 只用於美國英語) 9點5分/10分/15分。In British English you can say 'half past' the hour, but it is not possible in American English to say 'half after' the hour. 在英國英語中, 可說 half past (the hour)〔幾點半〕, 但在美國英語中則不能說 half after (the hour)。

You talk about minutes before the hour using **to** (and also **of** in American English). e.g. 說幾點差幾分可用to〔美國英語中也用of〕, 如: *twenty/a quarter to eight.* 8點差20分/15分。Compare 比較: *It's five minutes of two/a quarter of eight* (American English only 只用於美國英語). 現在是2點差5分/8點差15分。

Time can also be expressed by using the numbers alone. 時間也可以單用數字表示: *The meeting is at 10.15.* 會議定於10點15分召開。| *I'll pick you up about 3.20.* (=said 口語中說 three-twenty). 我將在3點20分來接你。

-oc·ra·cy /ɑkrəsɪ; ɒkrəsi/ also 又作 **-cracy** *suffix* [in nouns 構成名詞] **1** government by a particular sort of people or according to a particular principle〔由某一類人或根據某一原則管理的〕政府, 政體; 統治; 政治: *democracy* (=government by the people) 民主政府; 民主政體 | *mobocracy* 暴民統治; 暴民政治 **2** a society or country governed in this way 有...政體的社會[國家]: *the Western democracies* (=countries governed by their people) 西方的民主國家 | *a meritocracy* 精英管理的社會; 精英領導[統治]集團 **3** the powerful social class made up of a particular sort of people〔由特定的某類人組成的強大的〕社會階層: *the aristocracy* (=people with noble titles) 貴族

-o·crat /əkræt; əkræt/ also 又作 **-crat** *suffix* [in nouns 構成名詞] **1** a believer in a particular principle of government 某種政體的信奉者: *a democrat* (=someone who believes in government by the people) 民主主義者 **2** a member of a powerful or governing social class or group 有權勢的社會階層或統治階級的一分子: *a technocrat* (=scientist who controls organizations etc) 技術專家官員 —**-ocratic** /əkrætɪk; əkrætɪk/ *suffix* —**-ocratically** /əkrætɪkḷɪ; əkrætɪkli/ *suffix*

Oct the written abbreviation of 縮寫= October

oc·ta·gon /`ɑktəˌgɑn; ˈɒktəgən/ *n* [C] a flat shape with eight sides and eight angles 八邊形, 八角形 —**octagonal** /ɑk`tægənḷ; ɒkˈtægənəl/ *adj*: *an octagonal room* 八角形的房間

oc·tane /`ɑkten; ˈɒkteɪn/ *n* [U] **high octane petrol/fuel etc** petrol etc of the highest quality 辛烷值高的汽油/燃料等

oc·tave /`ɑktɪv; ˈɒktɪ̣v/ *n* [C] **a)** the range of musical notes between the first note of a SCALE[1] (8) and the last one 八度, 八度音程 **b)** the first and last notes of a musical SCALE[1] (8) played together 八度和音

oc·tet /ɑk`tɛt; ɒkˈtet/ *n* [C] **1** eight singers or musicians performing together 八重唱[八重奏]演出小組 **2** a piece of music for an octet 八重唱(曲), 八重奏(曲)

Oc·to·ber /ɑk`tobɚ; ɒkˈtəʊbə/ written abbreviation 縮寫為 **Oct** *n* [C,U] the tenth month of the year, between September and November 十月: *It happened on October the third.* 事情在10月3日發生。| *on the third of October* 在10月3日 | *on October third* 在10月3日 | *in October 1991* 在1991年10月

oc·to·ge·nar·i·an /ˌɑktədʒə`nɛrɪən; ˌɒktəʊdʒɪ̣ˈneəriən/ *n* [C] a person who is between 80 and 89 years old 80至89歲之間的人, 八旬老人

oc·to·pus /ˈɑktəpəs; ˈɒktəpəs/ *n plural* **octopuses** [C] a sea creature with eight TENTACLES (=arms) 章魚, 八爪魚

octopus 章魚, 八爪魚

tentacle 觸鬚

oc·u·lar /ˈɑkjələ; ˈɒkjʊ̈lə/ *adj technical* related to the eyes【術語】眼睛的, 視覺的: *ocular muscles* 眼部肌肉

oc·u·list /ˈɑkjəlɪst; ˈɒkjʊ̈lɪ̈st/ *n* [C] *old-fashioned* a doctor who examines and treats people's eyes【過時】眼科醫生[醫師]

OD /ˌo ˈdi; ˌəʊ ˈdiː/ *v* **[I+on]** *slang*【俚】**1** to take too much of a dangerous drug; OVERDOSE 服用過量的毒品 **2** to see, hear too much of something 沉溺〔於看、聽某物〕—**OD** *n* [C]

o·da·lisque /ˈodl̩ˌɪsk; ˈəʊdəlɪsk/ *n* [C] *literary* a beautiful female slave in former times【文】〔古時貌美的〕女奴

1 3 **odd** /ɑd; ɒd/ *adj*

1 ▶STRANGE 奇怪的◀ different from what is normal or expected 奇特的, 異常的, 古怪的: *an odd character* 古怪的人 | *Isn't that odd? She's never done that before.* 難道這不奇怪嗎? 她以前可從來沒這樣做過。| *An odd thing happened last night!* 昨晚發生了一件怪事! | **it is odd (that)** *It's odd that Diana never answered your letter.* 很奇怪, 戴安娜從不回你的信。| **the odd thing is...** *The odd thing is no one seems to know who actually bought the picture.* 奇怪的是好像沒有人知道到底是誰買那幅畫的。

2 odd-looking/sounding looking or sounding strange or unusual 看上去/聽上去奇特[異常]的: *He was an odd-looking bloke.* 他是個模樣古怪的傢伙。

3 the odd drink/word/moment etc *especially BrE* a few drinks etc at various times but not often and not regularly; OCCASIONAL (1)【尤英】偶爾喝酒/得到消息/有時間等: *We get the odd complaint from customers.* 我們偶爾會收到客戶的投訴。| *We have the odd drink together now and again.* 我們偶爾一起去喝上幾杯。

4 ▶VARIOUS 各種各樣的◀ [only before noun 僅用於名詞前] not specially chosen or collected 非特意挑選[收集]的, 零碎的: *He'd written the addresses on odd scraps of paper.* 他把地址寫在零零碎碎的紙片上。| **odd jobs** (=many different small pieces of work) 零工, 雜活 *He sometimes does odd jobs around the estate.* 他有時在這一區幹點零活。

5 ▶NOT IN A PAIR/SET 不成對/套◀ [only before noun 僅用於名詞前] separated from its pair or set〔一雙、一套中〕單隻的, 不成對的: *an odd shoe* 單隻鞋 | **odd socks/gloves etc** (=not a matching pair of socks etc) 不配對的襪子/手套等

6 odd number a number that cannot be divided exactly by two, for example 1, 3, 5, 7 etc 奇數, 單數〔不能被2整除的數, 如1、3、5、7等〕—opposite 反義詞 EVEN[2] (4)

7 20-odd/30-odd etc *spoken* a little more than 20 etc【口】二十多一點/三十多一點等: *I have 20-odd years to work before I retire.* 我還要工作二十多年才退休。

8 odd man out/odd one out a) *especially BrE* someone or something that is different from the rest of the group【尤英】與眾不同的人/物: *Which of these three shapes is the odd one out?* 這三種形狀中哪一個是不一樣的? **b)** *BrE informal* someone who is not usually included in groups of people or friends【英, 非正式】與集體或朋友不合的人, 不合羣的人: *I was always the odd one out in my class at school.* 在學校我總是跟班上的同學合不來。—see also 另見 ODDLY —**oddness** *n* [U]

odd·ball /ˈɑdˌbɔl; ˈɒdbɔːl/ *n* [C] *especially AmE informal* someone who behaves in a strange or unusual way【尤美, 非正式】舉止古怪的人 —**oddball** *adj*: *Ernest, the odd-ball comedian in 'Ernest goes to Jail'* 歐內斯特, 在《歐內斯特入獄》中那個怪模怪樣的喜劇演員

odd·i·ty /ˈɑdətɪ; ˈɒdɪ̈ti/ *n* **1** [C] a strange or unusual person or thing 怪人; 怪事, 奇特的東西: *He was something of an oddity in the neighborhood with his neat suits.* 他穿着筆挺的西裝, 在街坊四鄰中有點像個怪人。**2** [C,U] a strange quality in someone or something 奇怪, 古怪, 奇特: *fashions that are remembered for their oddity* 因款式怪異而讓人記得的時裝

odd-job man /ˈ· · ·/ *n* [C] a man who does various jobs in or around people's houses〔在他人家裡或周圍〕打零工的人

odd·ly /ˈɑdlɪ; ˈɒdli/ *adv* **1** in a strange or unusual way 奇怪地, 古怪地; 異常地: *Brenda's been acting oddly this week.* 布倫達這一週表現得相當古怪。**2** also 又作 **oddly enough** [sentence adverb 句子副詞] used to say that something seems strange or surprising 奇怪的是; 令人驚訝的是: *Oddly enough, her anger made her seem more attractive.* 說也奇怪, 她一生氣倒使她顯得更迷人了。**3 oddly matched/assorted** very different and looking strange together 不相配的/配搭怪異的

odd·ments /ˈɑdmənts; ˈɒdmənts/ *n* [plural] small things of no value, or pieces of stuff that were not used when something was made 零頭, 碎屑, 零碎物件; 殘剩物

odds /ɑdz; ɒdz/ *n* [plural] 3

1 ▶PROBABILITY 可能性◀ how likely it is that something will or will not happen, especially when this can be stated in numbers〔事物發生的〕可能性, 機會〔尤用於可用數字表示時〕: *If you are male, the odds are about 1 in 12 of being colour-blind.* 如果你是男性, 患色盲的可能性在十二分之一左右。| **the odds are (that)** (=it is likely) 可能會… *Invest now – the odds are that the share prices will rise after the budget.* 現在就投資吧 —— 預算案完成後股價可能會上漲。| **odds in favour of** *The odds are in favour of a Russian victory.* 俄羅斯獲勝的機會居多。| **odds against** *The odds against you getting killed in a plane crash are around a million to one.* 死於空難的可能性極小, 大約為百萬分之一。

2 ▶DIFFICULTIES 困難◀ **a) enormous/heavy odds** difficulties which make a good result seem very unlikely 巨大的困難/非常不利的條件: *Theresa has overcome enormous odds to get where she is today.* 特麗莎克服了巨大的困難才取得今天這樣的成就。**b) against all (the) odds** in spite of great difficulties 儘管困難重重: *Against all the odds, racing driver Lauda recovered from his terrible injuries.* 儘管非常困難, 賽車手勞德從嚴重的受傷中康復過來。

3 be at odds (with) a) to disagree (與…) 不合, 爭吵: *Briggs found himself at odds with his colleagues at NASA.* 布里格斯發現自己與太空總署的同事們意見不合。**b)** if two statements, descriptions, actions etc are at odds with each other, they are different although they should be the same〔說法、描述、行為等〕不一致: *Burt's latest evidence is at odds with his earlier statements.* 伯特的最新證據與他早前的說法有矛盾。

4 ▶HORSE RACING ETC 賽馬等◀ numbers based on the probability of a horse winning a race, or a particular result in any competition, which show by how much you can increase your money if you BET[1] (1) on the one that wins〔打賭時用數字表示的〕可能性; 賠率: *I bet £10 on Broadway Flyer with the odds at 6-1.* 我在"百老匯飛人"上押注10英鎊, 賠率為6比1。| **lay/offer (sb) odds** *I laid him odds of 7-2.* 我向他提出以7比2的賠率打賭。| **long/short odds** (=odds based on a high or low risk of losing) 贏面不大的/較大的押注

5 it makes no odds/what's the odds? *BrE spoken* it makes no difference【英口】沒有多大差別[無關緊要]/那有甚麼關係?: *You can pay me now or later – it makes no odds.* 你可以現在或以後付我錢 —— 沒關係的。

6 pay/charge over the odds *BrE informal* to pay or charge a higher price than is usual or reasonable【英, 非正式】花高價/索要高價: *There's always somebody ready to pay over the odds for a designer jacket.* 總有人樂意花高價買一件專門設計師設計的夾克。—see also 另見

have the odds stacked against you (STACK[2] (3))
odds and ends /ˌ· · ˈ·/ *n* [plural] small things of various kinds without much value 瑣碎物品, 零星雜物: *He didn't keep much in his desk – just odds and ends.* 他書桌裡沒放多少東西, 只是些零碎物品。
odds and sods /ˌ· · ˈ·/ *n* [plural] *BrE informal* odds and ends【英, 非正式】瑣碎物品, 零星雜物
odds-on /ˌ·ˈ·◂/ *adj* **1 the odds-on favourite** a competitor that is very likely to win, especially a horse in a race 大有希望赢[大熱門]的競賽者〔尤指參賽的賽馬〕**2** *informal* **it's odds-on (that)** used to say that something is very likely to happen【非正式】很有可能〔發生的〕: *It's odds-on that she won't come.* 她很可能不來。
ode /od; əʊd/ *n* [C] a long poem addressed to a person or thing 頌詩, 頌歌: *Keats' 'Ode to A Grecian Urn'* 濟慈的《希臘古甕頌》
o·di·ous /ˈodɪəs; ˈəʊdiəs/ *adj formal* extremely unpleasant【正式】十分討厭的, 可憎的, 醜惡的: *an odious and conceited little man* 醜惡而又自負的小個子男人 —**odiously** *adv*
o·di·um /ˈodɪəm; ˈəʊdiəm/ *n* [U] *formal* hatred that a lot of people feel for someone【正式】反感, 憎恨, 公憤
o·dom·e·ter /oˈdɑmətə·; əʊˈdɒmɪ̩tə/ *n* [C] *AmE*【美】〔汽車等的〕里程計; MILEOMETER *BrE*【英】
o·do·rif·er·ous /ˌodəˈrɪfərəs; ˌəʊdəˈrɪfərəs◂/ *adj old use* odorous【舊】有氣味的; 有香味的, 芳香的
o·do·rous /ˈodərəs; ˈəʊdərəs/ *adj literary* having a smell, especially a pleasant one【文】有氣味的;〔尤指〕有香味的, 芳香的
o·dour *BrE*【英】, **odor** *AmE*【美】/ˈodə·; ˈəʊdə/ *n* [C] **1** a smell, especially an unpleasant one 氣味;〔尤指〕臭氣: *Get rid of unpleasant household odours with new Fleur!* 請使用全新的Fleur, 消除室內的異味! **2 be in bad odour (with)** if you are in bad odour with someone, they are not pleased with something you have done 不得寵; 不受(…的)青睞[歡迎] —see also 另見 BODY ODOUR
o·dour·less *BrE*【英】, **odorless** *AmE*【美】/ˈodələs; ˈəʊdələs/ *adj* not having a smell 沒有氣味的: *Water is a colorless, odorless liquid.* 水是一種無色、無味的液體。
od·ys·sey /ˈɑdəsɪ; ˈɒdɪ̩si/ *n* [C] *literary* a long journey with lots of adventures【文】漫長的歷險旅程
OECD /ˌo i si ˈdi; ˌəʊ iː siː ˈdiː/ *n* **the OECD** the Organization for Economic Cooperation and Development; a group of rich countries who work together to develop trade and economic growth 經濟合作與發展組織〔一些發達國家致力於發展貿易和經濟增長的組織〕
oe·di·pal /ˈɛdəpəl; ˈiːdɪ̩pəl/ *adj* related to an Oedipus complex 俄狄普斯的, 戀母情結的: *oedipal fantasies* 戀母幻想
Oe·di·pus com·plex /ˈɛdəpəs ˌkɑmplɛks; ˈiːdɪ̩pəs ˌkɒmpleks/ *n* an unconscious sexual desire that a son feels for his mother, combined with a hatred for his father, according to Freudian PSYCHOLOGY〔弗洛伊德心理學中所說的〕戀母情結
o'er /or; əʊə/ *adv, prep poetic* over【詩】在…之上: *o'er vales and hills* 在溪谷和羣山之上
oe·soph·a·gus *especially BrE*【尤英】, usually 一般作 **esophagus** *AmE*【美】/iˈsɑfəgəs; ɪˈsɒfəgəs/ *n* [C] the tube from your mouth to your stomach, down which food passes 食道, 食管 —see picture at 參見 DIGESTIVE SYSTEM 圖
oes·tro·gen *BrE*【英】, **estrogen** *AmE*【美】/ˈɛstrədʒən; ˈiːstrədʒən/ *n* [U] a substance that is produced in a woman's ovaries (OVARY), and causes changes in her body that prepare it for having babies 雌激素
oeu·vre /ˈɜvrə·; ˈɜːvrə/ *n* [C] *French* all the works of an artist, such as a painter or writer【法】〔畫家、作家等的〕全部作品

of /əv; əv; *strong* 強讀 ɑv; ɒv/ *prep* **1 a)** used to show a feature or quality that something has …的〔表示某物的特徵或品質〕: *the colour of her dress* 她裙子的顏色 | *the width of the road* 馬路的寬度 | *the size of John's overdraft* 約翰透支的數額 **b)** used to say that something is part of something else …的一部分: *the leg of the table* 桌子的腿 | *the roots of her hair* 她的頭髮根 | *the last scene of the movie* 電影的最後一幕 **2** used to show that something belongs to someone〔屬於某人〕的: *a friend of my parents* 我父母的一個朋友 | *a computer of her own* 她自己的電腦 | *a habit of his* 他的習慣 **3** used to talk about a group or collection of particular people or things〔說明一組或一類特定的人或物〕: *a herd of elephants* 一羣大象 **4** used to talk about a particular amount or measurement of something〔說明某物的特定數量〕: *two kilos of sugar* 兩公斤糖 | *lots of money* 許多錢 | *a drop of water* 一滴水 | *a cup of coffee* 一杯咖啡 **5** used to talk about a particular person or thing from a larger group of the same people or things〔用於指一個同類的羣體中的某一人或物〕: *a member of the soccer team* 足球隊的一個隊員 | *both of us* 我們倆 | *The Mona Lisa is one of his finest works.*《蒙娜·麗莎》是他最優秀的作品之一。| *the leading brand of shampoo* 洗髮劑的頭號品牌 **6 a)** used in dates〔用於日期〕: *the 27th of July* 7月27日 **b)** *AmE* used in giving the time to mean before【美】在…之前〔用於報時〕: *a quarter of seven* (=6.45) 七點差一刻 **7** used when giving the name of something or being more specific about something that is very general〔用於某物的名稱, 或表明泛指事物的具體範疇〕: *the city of New York* 紐約市 | *the art of painting* 繪畫藝術 | *the age of eight* 八歲 | *the problem of unemployment* 失業問題 **8 a)** used after nouns describing actions, to show who the action is done to〔用於說明動作的名詞之後, 表示動作的對象〕: *the killing of innocent children* (=the children are killed) 對無辜兒童的殺害 **b)** used after nouns describing actions, to show who does the action〔用於說明動作的名詞之後, 表示動作的發出者〕: *the barking of the dogs* (=the dogs bark) 狗的吠叫 **9** used to say what subject, person, thing etc another subject, person or thing is connected with or deals with 關於…的, 與…有關的〔用於說明論題之間、人物之間、事物之間等的相互關係〕: *the Queen of England* 英國女王 | *disease of the liver* 肝病 | *the results of the meeting* 會議的結果 | *the advantages of using a computer* 使用電腦的好處 **10** used to say what something is made from 用…製的〔用於說明某物是由何種材料製作的〕: *a dress of pure silk* 真絲連衫裙 | *These bowls are made of plastic.* 這些碗是塑料做的。**11 a) the day/year etc of** the day, year etc that something happened〔某事發生的〕那天/那年等: *the day of the accident* 出事那天 | *the week of the festival* 節日的那週 **b) of the day/year etc** the best or most important person or thing on a particular day or year 某日/某年等最佳的[最重要的]: *She has been voted 'Woman of the Year'.* 她被選為"年度最傑出女性"。**c) of an evening/of a weekend** used to say that you often do something in the evenings, at weekends etc 晚上/週末經常…: *We always like to walk by the river of an evening.* 我們總喜歡傍晚到河邊去散步。**12** used to show that something is the result of something else 因, 由〔用於表示事物之間的因果關係〕: *She left of her own free will.* 她是自願離開的。| *He died of cancer.* 他死於癌症。| *the effects of radiation* 輻射的影響 **13 a)** used to say who writes a play, who paints a painting etc 由…著作的; 由…畫的〔用於說明誰寫的劇本、誰畫的畫等〕: *the plays of Shakespeare* 莎士比亞的戲劇 | *The building is the work of a great artist.* 這幢建築是一位藝術大師的作品。**b)** used to show what a picture, story etc is about or who is in it 關於…的, 以…為主題的〔用於說明圖片、故事等是何內容, 或是有關何人的〕: *a photo of Elizabeth* 伊莉莎白的照片 | *a map of Indonesia* 印度尼西亞的地圖 | *a story of love and loss* 有關愛情與迷惘的故事 **14** about 關於: *He's never heard of John Lennon.* 他從未聽說過約翰連儂。| *Rumours of his infidelity filled the newspapers.* 報上滿是關於他不忠行為的傳聞。**15** used to show where something is or how far something is from something else〔用於表示某物的方位或與另一物之間的距離〕: *east of Suez* 蘇伊士以東 | *I live within a mile of here.* 我住的

地方距離這裡不到一英里。**16** used to describe a particular person or thing〔用於描述某人或物〕: *a woman of tremendous spirit* 一名具有無比勇氣的女子 | *a matter of no importance* 無關緊要的事 **17** *especially literary* used to say where someone comes from【尤文】來自…的〔用於說明某人來自何方〕: *Jesus of Nazareth* 拿撒勒的耶穌 | *the people of China* 中國人民 **18 it is kind of/it was wrong of etc** used to say that something that someone has done shows that they are kind, wrong etc〔某人做某事〕是仁慈的/錯誤的: *It was silly of him to think he could cheat.* 他以為他可以作弊, 這是很愚蠢的。

USAGE NOTE 用法說明: OF
GRAMMAR 語法
You use **'s** or plural **s'** rather than **of** to mean 'belonging to someone'. 常用 's 或複數的 s', 而不用 of, 來表示"屬於某人"之意: *the students' grades* 學生的成績 | *my friend's car* 我朋友的汽車 | *Clive's new hairstyle* 克萊夫的新髮型
When you talk about something that belongs to or is part of something, you can use **of**. 表示某物屬於另一物或是其部分時, 可用 of: *the corner of the street* 街角 | *the top of the mountain* 山頂 | *the street corner* 街角 | *the mountain top* 山頂
You also use **'s and s'** to talk about periods of time, for example 表示一段時間也可用 's 和 s', 如: *a day's work* 一天的工作 | *three weeks' vacation* 三週的假期
's is increasingly used with the names of places, especially in newspapers and American English. 's 越來越多地用於地名, 尤其是在報紙上和美國英語中: *Chicago's favorite son* 芝加哥的寵兒 | *China's recent history* 中國近代史
When you use words like **a, some, the, this** etc with the word for something that belongs to someone, or the person you are talking about in connection with them, you can use both **of** and **'s** together. 當 a, some, the, this 等與表示屬於某人之物的詞, 或與某人有關之人的詞連用時, 可同時使用 of 和 's: *that old bike of Cathy's* 卡西的那輛舊腳踏車 | *a friend of Terry's* 特里的一位朋友

1 1 **of course** /· '·/ *adv* **1** certainly 當然: *Of course I'll give you your money back.* 我當然要還你錢。| *"Were you glad to leave?" "Of course not!"* "你願意離開嗎?" "當然不願意!" | *Of course you must make a profit, but not if it involves exploiting people.* 當然你得賺取利潤, 但是這要以不剝削人為前提。**2** used when you think that someone should know something, or should not be surprised by something 理當, 自然: *You should of course keep copies of all correspondence.* 所有信件你自然都該留底存檔。| *Well, she won, of course.* 嗯, 她贏了, 當然嘍。

USAGE NOTE 用法說明: OF COURSE
POLITENESS 禮貌程度
You use **of course** as a polite and friendly way of agreeing to something or agreeing to do something someone has asked you. 可用 of course 作為一種禮貌而友好的方式來表示同意某事或同意做某人要求你做的事: *"May I borrow this book?" "Of course you can."* "我可以借這本書嗎?" "當然可以。" | *"Do you think I was wrong?" "Of course not."* "你認為我錯了嗎?" "當然沒有。"
It is not usually polite to use **of course** or **of course not** as a reply to a request for information. If for example someone asked you 用 of course 或 of course not 來回答查詢資料, 通常是不禮貌的: *"Is this the way to the station?"* and you replied *"Of course (it is)"*, this would sound as if you think the answer to the question is very clear and you think the person is stupid to need to ask you. 如某人問你: "這是去車站的路嗎?" 而你回答說: "當然(是啦)", 這聽上去好像你認為答案十分明顯, 那人這樣問很愚蠢和多餘。
STYLE 文體
Except when you are answering questions, **of course** is not usually used at the beginning of a sentence. 除了在回答問題時, of course 通常不用在句首。Instead of saying 我們不說: *We play a lot of tennis and polo. Of course we have our own swimming pool,* you would say 而說: *We also have our own swimming pool, of course* or 或 *...and of course we have our own swimming pool.* 我們經常打網球和馬球。當然嘍, 我們還有自己的游泳池。

off¹ /ɔf; ɒf/ *adv, adj* [not before noun 不用於名詞前] **1** away or from where something is 離開, 離去: *Travis got into his car and drove off.* 特拉維斯上汽車後就開走了。| *Suddenly they turned off and parked in a side road.* 突然他們轉向停在一條岔路上。| **be off** (=to leave) 離開 *We're off now. Thanks for the meal!* 我們要走了。謝謝你的飯菜款待! | **be off to** (=to go to a particular place) 去, 前往〔某處〕 *They're off to Jamaica for a hard-earned vacation.* 他們要去牙買加度一個來之不易的假期。**2** out of a bus, train, car etc 下〔公共汽車、火車、汽車等〕: *I'll get off at the next stop.* 我將在下一站下車。**3** removed; no longer connected or fastened to something 脱落, 脱離, 脱掉: *Can anyone get the lid off?* 誰能掀開這個蓋子? | *Take off your shoes.* 把你的鞋子脱掉。| *Waxing the table is a really good way of keeping the dust off.* 給桌子上蠟的確是一種保持潔淨的好辦法。**4** a machine, piece of equipment etc that is off is not working or operating〔機器、設備等〕不在工作; 不在運轉; 停止: *Will someone switch the radio off?* 誰把收音機關掉好嗎? —opposite 反義詞 ON²(6) **5** not at work, school etc because you are ill or on holiday〔因病或假日〕不工作; 不上學; 休息: *You look tired. Why don't you take tomorrow off?* 你看上去很疲憊, 為甚麼明天不休息一天呢? | **day/afternoon etc off** *I'm entitled to 25 days off a year.* 我每年可享受25天的年假。| **be off** (=to be absent) 缺席 *Mary is off with the flu today.* 瑪麗因患流感今天沒來。**6 a) be/go off** *especially BrE* food that is off is beginning to decay【尤英】〔食品〕腐壞, 變質: *Ugh! This milk is off.* 呀, 這牛奶酸掉了! **b) be off** not be available to be eaten in a restaurant〔餐館裡〕不供應的: *The fish is off today, sir.* 今天沒有魚了, 先生。**7 a) 4 kilometres/3 days' walk etc off** a particular distance away 離開有四公里/三天的步行距離: *The hostel is at least two more miles off.* 旅舍至少還有兩英里路。**b) 4 hours/10 years etc off** a particular amount of time away in the future 相隔四小時/十年等: *The game is only two days off and our top player has been injured.* 距離比賽只有兩天, 而我們最好的隊員受傷了。**8** a particular amount of money off is how much the price has been reduced by 扣除, 減掉: *If you buy more than ten, they knock 10% off.* 如果你買十個以上, 他們會打九折。**9** *BrE* behaviour that is off is rude or not what is expected【英】〔行為〕粗魯; 失常: *I thought it was a little off when he said he wished he'd never been invited.* 我認為, 他說但願自己永遠沒受到邀請時是有點失常了。| *Look, I know when someone's being off with me. OK?* 聽着, 別人對我不客氣時我是知道的, 明白嗎? **10** an arranged event that is off will no longer happen 不再舉行, 取消了的: *The wedding's off!* 婚禮取消了! —compare 比較 ON²(8) **11 a) be badly/well off** to be poor or rich 貧窮的/富有的: *They have to be fairly well off to have that big a house.* 擁有那麼大的一棟房子, 他們得相當有錢才行。**b) be badly/well off for sth** *informal* to have a small amount or large amount of something【非正式】少量/大量擁有某物: *The school's fairly well off for books these days.* 學校如今擁有很多書。| **how are you off for sth?** *How are you* *off for jeans?* (=do you have enough pairs of jeans?) 你有足夠的牛仔褲嗎? **12 be better off** *especially spoken* to be in a situation where you would gain more advantage【尤口】處於較有利的境況: **be better off with** *I always said she was better off with a boyfriend of her own age.* 我總是說, 她找個同齡的男朋友會好一些。| **be better off doing sth** *You'd be better off resigning and working part time.* 你辭去工作幹兼職會好些。**13 off and on** also 又作 **on and off** for short periods but not regularly, over a long period of time 斷斷續續地: *We've been going out together for five years, off and on.* 我們兩人交往斷斷續續有五年了。**14 right off/straight off** *especially BrE informal* immediately【尤英, 非正式】立即, 立刻, 馬上 **15** not on the stage but still able to be heard in the theatre; OFFSTAGE (1) 幕後的, 舞台後面的: *noises off* 幕後的噪音

1 1 **off²** *prep* **1** not on something or not touching something 離開; 不觸及: *Keep off the grass.* 勿踩草地。| *Get off your backside and start digging.* 別坐着了, 開始挖吧。| *I hope your dirty feet are off my clean floor.* 我希望你的髒腳不要踩我乾淨的地板。—opposite 反義詞 ON¹(1) **2** away from a particular person or thing 離開〔某人或某物〕: *Once we were off the main freeway the trip felt more like a vacation.* 我們一駛離了高速幹道, 這趟旅行感覺更像是一次度假。| *The referee ordered three players off the field.* 裁判命令三名球員離場。**3** taken from someone or something 從〔某人處〕拿走; 從〔某物中〕去掉: *Tom borrowed £500 off his sister.* 湯姆從他姐姐那裡借了 500 英鎊。| *I got this necklace off a woman outside the market.* 我從市場外的一位女子那裡買了這條項鏈。| *What do you plan to live off while you're studying?* 在學習期間你打算靠甚麼生活呢? **4** out of a bus, train, car etc 離開〔公共汽車、火車、汽車等〕: *Both robbers jumped off the train while it was still moving.* 搶劫者雙雙跳離了還在行駛的火車。**5** no longer held or supported by a particular thing 從…上脫落[脫離]: *Take your coat off the hook.* 把你的外套從鈎上取下來。| *Suddenly the trophy fell off the platform.* 獎杯突然從台上掉了下來。**6** no longer connected or fastened to something; REMOVED 從…分開, 從…去掉: *A button has come off my shirt.* 我襯衫上的一顆鈕扣掉了。| *Cut about an inch off my bangs please.* 請把我的劉海剪短一英寸左右。**7 a)** at a particular distance from something; REMOVED 與〔某物〕相隔; 離…: *My house is about 50 yards off Main Street.* 我的房子離大街約有 50 碼。**b)** in the sea but near the land 在〔陸地附近〕的海面: *an island off the coast of France* 法國海岸附近的一個島嶼 | *The ship began to sink 30 miles off Portsmouth.* 那艘船在距離樸次茅斯 30 英里的海面上開始沉沒。**8** if one room is off another, you get to the second room by passing through the first 穿過〔某屋〕到〔另一屋〕, 經由〔某處〕到〔另一處〕: *Off the main bedroom was a beautiful en suite bathroom.* 穿過主臥室是一個漂亮的配套的浴室。**9** *informal* not in a particular building, area etc【非正式】不在〔某建築物或地區內〕: *Smoking is only allowed off the hospital premises.* 只准在醫院外面吸煙。**10 a)** no longer interested in something 不再對…感興趣: *Toby's been off his food for a few days.* 托比有幾天不想吃東西了。| **go right off** *BrE*【英】*I've gone right off her books.* 我已不再喜歡看她的書了。**b)** no longer taking something such as medicine 不再吃〔藥等〕: *The operation was a success, and she's off the morphine.* 手術很成功, 她已不再服用嗎啡了。**11 off the top of your head** if you say something off the top of your head, you are guessing 猜測, 猜想

off³ *adj* [only before noun, no comparative 僅用於名詞前, 無比較級] **1 off day/ week etc** a day, week etc when you are not doing something as well as you usually do 發揮不正常的[失水準的]一天/一個星期等: *Brian never forgets the words – he must be having one of his off days.* 布賴恩從來都不會忘記台詞——今天他肯定是狀態不好。**2 off period/season etc** a period or season which is not as busy as other times of the year 淡靜的時期/淡季等: *In the off season there's hardly anyone in the hotel at all.* 在淡季, 這家旅館幾乎沒甚麼人。**3** used when talking about a pair of things such as wheels on a car, to mean the one on the right〔一對之中〕右邊的, 右側的 —opposite 反義詞 NEAR² (9)

off⁴ *n* **the off** the start, especially of a race or a journey〔尤指比賽或旅程的〕開始; 出發: *The horses were in line, ready for the off.* 賽馬已站成一排, 準備出開。

off⁵ *v* [T] *AmE slang* to kill someone【美俚】殺死〔某人〕

of·fal /ˈɔfl; ˈɒfəl/ *n* [U] the inside organs of an animal, for example the heart, LIVER, and KIDNEYS used as food〔用作食物的〕動物內臟, 下水, 雜碎

off-bal·ance /ˌ· ˈ··/ *adj* [not before noun 不用於名詞前] **1** in an unsteady position so that you are likely to fall 不平衡的, 不穩定的: **throw/knock/push sb off-balance** *Lee caught hold of my wrist and pulled me off-balance.* 李抓住我的手腕, 拽得我失去了平衡。**2** unprepared for something, so that it surprises or shocks you 突然的, 冷不防的: **catch sb off-balance** *This time poor old Simpson had been caught off-balance by events.* 這一次可憐的老辛普森猝不及防。

off·beat /ˈɔfˌbit; ˌɒfˈbiːt◂/ *adj informal* unusual and not what people normally expect【非正式】不尋常的; 異常的; 不落俗套的: *a slightly offbeat lifestyle* 有點別具一格的生活方式

off-cen·tre *BrE*【英】, **off-center** *AmE*【美】/ˌ· ˈ··◂/ *adj* not exactly in the centre of something 偏離中心的, 中心錯位的: *Here, the photo is slightly off-centre.* 這兒, 照片稍微有點偏離了中心。

off-chance /ˈ· ·/ *n* **on the off-chance** hoping that something will happen, although it is unlikely 懷有萬分之一的希望: *I just stopped by on the off-chance that Pippa might be here.* 我懷着萬分之一的希望來這裡看看, 心想或許皮帕會在這兒。

off-col·our *BrE*【英】, **off-color** *AmE*【美】/ˌ· ˈ··◂/ *adj* **1** sexually offensive 下流的, 有傷風化的, 猥褻的: *Lou followed that up with some fairly off-color jokes.* 盧隨後又講了一些相當下流的笑話。**2** [not before noun 不用於名詞前] *especially BrE* slightly ill【尤英】稍有不適的, 臉色不好的: *She's been feeling a bit off-colour lately.* 近來她一直感到身體有點不舒服。

off-cut /ˈ· ·/ *n* [C] a piece of wood, paper etc that is left after the main piece has been cut and removed〔木頭、紙張等的〕邊料

off day /ˈ· ·/ *n* [C] **have an off day** to not do things as well as you usually do on a particular day 發揮失常, 狀態不好

off-du·ty /ˌ· ˈ··◂/ *adj* someone such as a policeman, nurse, or soldier is off-duty during the hours when they are not working 不在值班的, 下了班的: *an off-duty guard* 不當班的警衛 | *Sorry, I'm off-duty now.* 對不起, 我現在已下了班。

of·fence *BrE*【英】, usually 一般作 **offense** *AmE*【美】/əˈfɛns; əˈfens/ *n* **1** [C] an illegal action or a crime 違法行為, 違例; 犯罪: *Driving while drunk is a serious offence.* 醉酒駕車屬嚴重違例。| *a parking offense* 停車違例 | **[+against]** *sexual offences against children* 對兒童的性犯罪 | **commit an offence** (=do something that is an offence) 犯罪 | **first offence** (=the first illegal thing that someone has done) 初犯 | **criminal offence** *Possession of stolen property is a criminal offence.* 私藏贓物屬刑事犯罪。| **serious offence** *serious offences under the Prevention of Terrorism Act* 嚴重觸犯《反恐怖主義法案》| **capital offence** (=a crime for which death is the punishment) 死罪 | **minor offence** (=one that is not very serious) 輕微犯罪[違例] **2** [U] behaviour which offends someone 得罪, 冒犯行為: **cause/give offence** (=offend someone) 得罪, 使傷感情 *The problem was how to get rid of her without causing offence.* 問題是怎樣擺脫她而又不得罪她。| **mean no offence** (=have no

intention of offending someone) 並無冒犯某人之意 *Don't be upset by what he said; he meant no offence.* 不要為他的話感到生氣, 他沒有冒犯你的意思。**3 no offence** *spoken* used to tell someone that you do not want to offend them by what you are saying【口】請別見怪, 沒有冒犯你的意思: *No offense, but this cheese tastes like rubber.* 請別見怪, 這乳酪吃起來像是嚼橡膠。**4 take offence** to feel offended because of something someone has said or done 對...生氣, 因...見怪: *She's always quick to take offence.* 她老是動不動就生氣。**5** [U] *formal* the act of attacking【正式】進攻, 攻擊行為: *It depends on whether it was used as a weapon of offence or defence.* 那要看這武器是用來攻擊的還是用來防衛的。**6** [U] *BrE* the part of a game such as football concerned with getting points and winning【英】〔足球等比賽中的〕進攻 —see also 另見 OFFENSE

of·fend /əˋfɛnd; əˈfend/ *v* **1** [T usually passive 一般用被動態] to make someone angry or upset 使生氣, 使惱火: **be offended** *Richard was deeply offended that people thought he'd faked the story.* 人們認為理查德說的事情是編造的, 這使他大為惱火。| *I hope you won't be offended if I leave early.* 我如果早走, 希望你不要生氣。| **offend sb** *I'm sorry; have I done something to offend you?* 對不起, 我做甚麼事讓你生氣了? **2** [T] to seem bad or unpleasant to someone 使反感, 使不快; 冒犯: *Cruelty to animals offends many people.* 許多人對虐待動物很反感。| **offend the eye/ear** (=look very ugly or sound very bad) 刺眼/刺耳 **3** [I] to do something that is a crime 犯罪: *Many criminals offend again within a year of their release from prison.* 許多罪犯出獄不到一年又再犯罪。**4** [I,T] *formal* to go against people's feelings of what is morally right【正式】違背, 有失〔道德準則〕: **[+against]** *behaviour that offends against common decency* 有悖日常禮節的行為

of·fend·er /əˋfɛndɚ; əˈfendə/ *n* [C] **1** someone who is guilty of a crime 罪犯, 有罪者: *an institute for young offenders* 青少年罪犯教養院 | **first offender** (=one who has done a criminal action for the first time) 初犯 **2** someone or something that is the cause of something that is bad 引發壞事的人[事物]: *Among causes of air pollution, car exhaust fumes may be the worst offender.* 在造成空氣污染的多種原因中, 汽車排放的廢氣可能是罪魁禍首。

of·fend·ing /əˋfɛndɪŋ; əˈfendɪŋ/ *adj* **the offending ...** *often humorous* the thing that is causing a problem【常幽默】引起問題的..., 造成不便的...: *I decided to have the offending tooth removed.* 我決定把這顆討厭的牙拔掉。

of·fense¹ /əˋfɛns; əˈfens/ *n* [C,U] the usual American spelling of OFFENCE offence 的一般美式拼法

of·fense² /ˋɔfɛns; əˈfens/ *n* [U] *AmE* the part of a game such as football concerned with getting points and winning【美】〔足球等比賽中的〕進攻: *The Bears are going to have to work on their offense this season.* 本賽季熊隊將不得不加強進攻。—opposite 反義詞 DEFENSE²

of·fen·sive¹ /əˋfɛnsɪv; əˈfensɪv/ *adj* **1** very rude or insulting and likely to upset people 無禮的, 冒犯的, 令人惱火的: *I found her remarks deeply offensive.* 我發現她的話令人非常惱火。| **[+to]** *crude jokes that are offensive to women* 冒犯女士的粗鄙笑話 —opposite 反義詞 INOFFENSIVE¹ (1) **2** *formal* unpleasant【正式】令人不快的: *an offensive smell* 令人討厭的氣味 **3** [only before noun 僅用於名詞前] for attacking 攻擊的, 進攻性的: *offensive weapons* 攻擊性武器 | *The troops took up offensive positions.* 部隊已準備發動攻擊。—opposite 反義詞 DEFENSIVE **4** *AmE* concerned with getting points and getting a game, as opposed to stopping the other team from getting points【美】〔體育比賽中〕進攻的, 攻勢的: *offensive play* 進攻型打法 | *an offensive coach* 進攻型教練 —opposite 反義詞 DEFENSIVE —**offensively** *adv*: *His clothes smelled slightly, but not offensively.* 他的衣服有點發臭, 但不是臭得令人作嘔。| *The planes were too few to be used offensively.* 飛機太少, 難以展開攻勢。—**offensiveness** *n* [U]

offensive² *n* [C] **1** a planned military attack involving large forces over a long period〔軍事〕進攻, 攻勢: *On March 6th they launched a full-scale offensive.* 3月6日他們發起了全面進攻。**2 be on the offensive** to be ready to attack or criticize people 採取攻勢, 出擊; 批評 **3 take the offensive/go on the offensive** to be the first to make an attack or strong criticism 率先攻擊; 先發制人 **4 sales/charm/PR offensive** a planned set of actions intended to influence a lot of people 銷售/魅力/公關攻勢

O

of·fer¹ /ˋɔfɚ; ˈɒfə/ *v* **1** [T] to say that you are willing to give someone something, or to hold something out to them so that they can take it 提出, 提供: **offer sb sth** *You haven't offered Grandma any ice cream.* 你沒給奶奶吃冰淇淋。| *They offered him a very good job but he turned it down.* 他們給他提供了一份很好的工作, 但他拒絕了。| **offer sth to sb** *Offer some coffee to the guests.* 端些咖啡給客人。**2** [T] to say that you are willing to pay a particular amount of money 出價, 開價: **offer (sb) sth for** *They've offered us £75,000 for the house.* 他們已向我們出價75,000英鎊買這幢房子。| *The police are offering a reward for any information.* 警方在懸賞獎金給提供情報的人。**3** [I,T] to say that you are willing to do something 願意〔做某事〕: *I don't need any help, but it was nice of you to offer.* 我不需要任何幫助, 但是我很感激你的好意。| **offer to do sth** *My dad has offered to pick us up.* 我爸爸表示願意開車來接我們。| *Shelly didn't even offer to help.* 雪莉甚至都不願意幫忙。**4** [T] to provide something that people need or want 提供, 給予: *He offered no explanation for his actions.* 他對自己的行為未作任何解釋。| **offer sth to sb** *Senator Joseph's speech will have offered little comfort to bankrupt businessmen.* 參議員約瑟夫的講話不會對破產的商人有多大安慰。| **have sth to offer (to sb)** *Edinburgh has a great deal to offer to visitors in the way of entertainment.* 愛丁堡能給遊客提供大量的娛樂活動。**5 offer (up) a prayer/sacrifice etc** to pray to God or give something to God 作禱告/獻祭等 **6 offer itself** *formal* if an opportunity offers itself, it happens for you【正式】〔機會〕出現: *I shall be ready to raise the matter with him when a suitable occasion offers itself.* 等有合適的機會, 我會樂意向他提出這個問題的。**7 offer your hand to sb** to hold out your hand in order to shake hands with someone 向某人伸出手來〔握手〕

offer² *n* [C] **1** a statement that you are willing to give someone something or do something for them〔願給某人某物或願為某人做某事的〕提議; 提供: **[+of]** *an offer of assistance* 願提供幫助的建議 | **offer to do sth** *an offer to help* 願意幫忙的提議 | **turn down/refuse/decline an offer** (=say no to an offer) 拒絕提議[建議] *He turned down the offer of a free trip to Milan.* 他拒絕了免費去米蘭的提議。**2** an amount of money that you are willing to pay for something 出價, 開價, 報價: **make (sb) an offer (for)** *I'm prepared to make you a generous offer for the house.* 這幢房子我願意給你出一個高價。| **accept an offer** *They've accepted our offer of £50,000.* 他們已接受了我們50,000英鎊的報價。| **be open to offers** (=be ready to consider people's offers) 願意考慮還價 *We're asking £2,500, but we're open to offers.* 我們要價2,500英鎊, 但允許還價。**3** a reduction of the price of something in a shop for a short time 特價〔售貨〕: **special offer** *They have a special offer on this week – buy two, get one free.* 本週他們特價售貨, 買二贈一。**4 on offer a)** available to be bought or used 供購買的; 供使用的: *a whole range of services on offer* 提供的一整套服務 **b)** *BrE* for sale at a very cheap price for a short time【英】〔短期〕削價[特價]出售的: *Olive oil is on offer this week.* 橄欖油本週削價出售。**5 be under offer** *BrE* if a house that is for sale is under offer, someone has offered money for it【英】〔待售房屋〕已有人出價要買

of·fer·ing /ˋɔfərɪŋ; ˈɒfərɪŋ/ *n* **1** [C] a book, play, piece

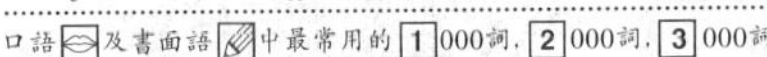

of music etc that someone has written recently 新近完成的作品: *the latest offering from Nancy Griffith* 南希·格里菲思的最新作品 **2** something that is given to God or given as a present to please someone 供品, 祭品; 贈品 —see also 另見 **burnt offering** (BURNT² (2)), PEACE OFFERING

of·fer·to·ry /ˋɔfəˏtɔrɪ; ˈɒfətəri/ *n plural* **offertories** [C] **1** the money people give during a religious ceremony in church 宗教儀式上的獻金 —see also 另見 COLLECTION (2a) **2** the offering of the bread and wine to God at COMMUNION (2)〔聖餐禮中向上帝奉上麵包和酒的〕奉獻儀式

off-guard /ˏ· ˈ·◄/ *adj* [not before noun 不用於名詞前] not expecting something surprising or dangerous to happen, and not prepared to deal with it 未加提防的, 措手不及的: **catch/take sb off-guard** *Caught off-guard, Paul blushed and looked away in embarrassment.* 措手不及之下, 保羅臉紅了, 尷尬地移開了目光。

off·hand¹ /ˏɔfˋhænd; ˌɒfˈhænd◄/ *adj* not giving people much time or attention, when you are talking to them 說話漫不經心的, 簡慢的: *She said you were a bit offhand with her this afternoon.* 她說你今天下午對她有點簡慢無禮。—**offhandedly** *adv* —**offhandedness** *n* [U]

offhand² *adv* immediately, without time to think about it or find out about something 立刻, 不假思索地: *I can't remember offhand what shifts I'm working next week.* 我一時記不起來下週我上甚麼班。

of·fice /ˋɔfɪs; ˈɒfɪs/ *n*

1 ►BUILDING 建築物◄ [C] the building that belongs to a company or organization, with a lot of rooms where people work〔公司或組織的〕辦公樓, 辦事處: *The company is moving to new offices in central London.* 公司準備遷往倫敦市中心的新辦事處。| **head office** (=main office) 總部 | **the office** *Did you go to the office today?* 你今天去辦公了嗎? | **at the office** *I must have left my keys at the office.* 我準是把鑰匙忘在辦公室了。| **work in an office** *I'd hate to work in an office, but I could use a regular income.* 我討厭在辦公室裡工作, 但倒是能有一份固定的收入。

2 ►ROOM 房間◄ [C] a room where you do work that involves writing, calculating, or talking to people 辦公室: *the manager's office* 經理辦公室 | *My office gets really hot and sticky in the summer.* 夏天時我的辦公室真的又熱又悶。—see picture on page A14 參見A14頁圖

3 office hours the time between about nine in the morning and five in the afternoon, when the people in offices are working 辦公時間〔大約為上午九點至下午五點〕: *You can contact us during office hours.* 你可以在辦公時間跟我們聯繫。

4 information/ticket etc office a room or building where people go to ask for information 詢問處/售票處等 —see also 另見 BOX OFFICE, POST OFFICE

5 ►IMPORTANT JOB 要職◄ [C,U] an important job or position with power, especially in government〔尤指政府中擁有權力的〕重要職位: *the office of President* 總統的職位 | **in office** (=in an important position) 執政 *His decision to resign after 30 years in office came as a great shock.* 他在執政30年後作出退職的決定, 令人大為震驚。| **hold office** *She had previously held office as Minister of Education.* 她曾擔任過教育部長一職。| **take office** (=start an important job) 就職, 上任

6 Office used in the names of British government departments〔英國政府的〕部, 局, 處: *the Foreign Office* 外交部

7 sb's good offices *formal* help given by someone who has authority or can influence people【正式】某人的得力相助: *I managed to get a visa through the good offices of a friend in the Service.* 我得到政府部門裡一個朋友的大力幫助而獲得了簽證。

office block /ˈ·· ·/ *n* [C] *BrE* a large building with many offices in it【英】辦公大樓; OFFICE BUILDING *AmE*【美】

office build·ing /ˈ·· ˌ··/ *n* [C] *AmE* a large building with many offices in it【美】辦公大樓; OFFICE BLOCK *BrE*【英】

office girl /ˈ·· ·/ *n* [C] a young woman who does unimportant work in an office〔擔任的工作相對不重要的〕辦公室小姐

office hold·er /ˈ·· ˌ··/ *n* [C] someone who has an official position, especially in the government 政府官員, 任公職者, 公務員

office par·ty /ˈ·· ˌ··/ *n* [C] a party just before Christmas in the office of a company, government department etc for the people who work there〔聖誕節前夕在辦公室為員工舉辦的〕辦公室派對, 聯歡會

of·fi·cer /ˋɔfəsə; ˈɒfɪsə/ *n* [C] **1** someone who is in a position of authority in the army, navy etc 軍官: *a naval officer* 海軍軍官 | *Report to your commanding officer.* 去向你的指揮官報告。**2** someone who has an important position in an organization, such as a government, company etc〔政府的〕高級官員;〔公司等的〕高級職員: *a local government officer* 地方政府官員 | *a personnel officer* 人事部主管 **3** a policeman or policewoman 警察, 警官: *What's the problem, officer?* 甚麼問題, 警官? | *the officer in charge of the murder inquiry* 負責調查謀殺案的警察 **4 Officer** *AmE* a title for a policeman or policewoman【美】警官〔用於對男女警察的稱呼〕: *Officer Maloney will help you.* 馬洛尼警官會幫助你。

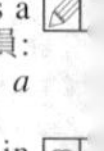

of·fi·cial¹ /əˋfɪʃəl; əˈfɪʃəl/ *n* [C] someone who has a responsible position in an organization 官員; 高級職員: *trade union members and officials* 工會會員和幹事 | *a government official* 政府官員

official² *adj* **1** approved of or done by someone in authority, especially the government 官方的, 正式的: *You have to get official permission to build a new house.* 你要蓋一幢新房必須得到官方的許可。| *an official inquiry* 官方調查 | *The official languages of Canada are English and French.* 加拿大的官方語言是英語和法語。**2** done as part of your job and not for your own private purposes 公務上的, 公職的: *Are you here in your official capacity?* 你是以官方身分來這裡的嗎? | *the Queen's official visit to the Bahamas* 女王對巴哈馬的官式訪問 **3** official information, reasons etc are given formally and publicly, but may not always be true 正式公布的, 公開宣稱的〔但並非總是事實〕: *The official motive for his resignation was that he wanted to spend more time with his children.* 官方公布他辭職的原因是想多花些時間和孩子在一起。| *The news is not yet official.* (=has not been publicly announced) 這消息尚未正式公布。**4** chosen to represent someone or an organization, or do something for them 被正式選用的: *official photographer to the Royal Family* 皇家專職攝影師 | *their official logo* 他們選用的標誌 **5** an official event is a formal, public event〔事件〕正式的, 公開的; *the official opening of the new store* 新商店的正式開張

of·fi·cial·dom /əˋfɪʃəldəm; əˈfɪʃəldəm/ *n* [U] a word meaning government departments or the people who work in them, used when you think they are unhelpful 官場; 官僚

of·fi·cial·ese /əˏfɪʃəˋliz; əˌfɪʃəlˈiːz/ *n* [U] *informal* a way of talking or writing used by government officials, that is unnecessarily difficult to understand【非正式】官話; 官場公文體

of·fi·cial·ly /əˋfɪʃəlɪ; əˈfɪʃəli/ *adv* **1** publicly and formally 官方地; 正式地: *They have officially announced their engagement.* 他們已正式宣布訂婚。| *The new clinic was officially opened this morning.* 新診所今天上午正式開業。| *The two countries are still not officially at war.* 兩國尚未正式交戰。**2** [sentence adverb 句子副詞] according to what you say publicly, even though this may not be true 根據公布所說〔不一定是事實〕: *Officially, he's on vacation, but there's a rumor that he's very ill.* 據公布所說, 他正在休假, 但傳言說他病得很重。

official re·ceiv·er /ˌ·,·· ·ˈ··/ *n* [C] someone whose job is to take care of the financial affairs of a company or a person that is BANKRUPT〔負責處理公司或私人破產事務的〕官方接管人, 破產管理人

of·fi·ci·ate /əˈfɪʃɪˌet; əˈfɪʃieɪt/ *v* [I+at] to do official duties, especially at a religious ceremony 行使職責; 主持宗教儀式

of·fi·cious /əˈfɪʃəs; əˈfɪʃəs/ *adj* too eager to tell people what to do 愛發號施令的, 好管閒事的: *An officious little guard came and told me not to whistle in the museum.* 一位好用權威的小警衞走過來, 叫我不要在博物館裡吹口哨。—**officiously** *adv* —**officiousness** *n* [U]

off·ing /ˈɔfɪŋ; ˈɒfɪŋ/ *n* **be in the offing** to be about to happen or to be possible 即將發生, 即將來到: *Everything's topsy-turvy at the moment with this big trip in the offing.* 這次大規模的旅行活動即將開始, 此刻一切都很混亂。

off·ish /ˈɔfɪʃ; ˈɒfɪʃ/ *adj informal* behaving in a slightly unfriendly or impolite way【非正式】(有點)冷淡的, 疏遠的: *I don't know why but she seemed a bit offish to me.* 我不知道為甚麼, 她好像對我有點冷淡。

off-key /ˌ·ˈ·◂/ *adj* music that is off-key sounds unpleasant because it is played slightly above or below the correct PITCH[1] (3)〔音樂〕走調的, 不和諧的: *The band sounds slightly off-key.* 樂隊的演奏稍有點走調。—**off-key** *adv*: *Someone upstairs was singing off-key.* 樓上有人唱歌走調了。

off-li·cence /ˈ· ··/ *n* [C] *BrE* a shop that sells wine, beer, and other alcoholic drinks, in bottles or cans【英】出售瓶裝或罐裝含酒精飲料的商店; LIQUOR STORE *AmE*【美】

off lim·its /ˌ· ˈ··/ *adj* **be off limits** if a place is off limits, you are not allowed to go there 禁止入內: [+to] *Under the proposal, the Antarctic would be declared off-limits to whalers.* 根據這項提議, 南極洲將被宣布為捕鯨船禁入區。

off·line /ˈɔflaɪn; ˈɒflaɪn/ *adj* not directly connected to a computer or directly controlled by it〔電腦〕脱機的; 離線的: *an offline terminal* 離線終端 | *offline storage of data* 脱機數據儲存 —opposite 反義詞 ONLINE —**offline** *adv*

off-load /ˌ· ˈ·/ *v* **1** [T] to get rid of something that you do not need by giving it to someone else〔通過送給別人來〕清除〔不需要之物〕: **off-load sth onto sb** *We managed to off-load all those old typewriters onto a friend of mine.* 我們設法將那些舊打字機全都清理給了我的一個朋友。**2 off-load your problems/guilt/troubles etc** to tell someone about your problems etc in order to make yourself feel better〔為了減輕心理負擔而〕傾訴困難/愧疚/麻煩等

off-peak /ˌ· ˈ·◂/ *adj* **1** off-peak hours or periods are times when fewer people want to do or use something 非高峯時間的, 非繁忙的: *Telephone charges are lower during off-peak periods.* 非繁忙時間電話收費要低一些。**2** off-peak travel, electricity etc is cheaper because it is done or used at these times 非繁忙時間所做[用]的

off·print /ˈɔfprɪnt; ˈɒfprɪnt/ *n* [C] an article from a magazine that is printed and sold separately〔雜誌中選出的文章的〕單印本, 選印本

off-put·ting /ˈ· ˌ··/ *adj* if someone's behaviour or the appearance of something is off-putting, it is strange or unpleasant and stops you from liking or being interested in them〔某人的舉止或某物的外觀〕令人氣惱的, 令人討厭的: *Jack's aggressiveness is really off-putting.* 傑克的挑釁行為的確很令人討厭。—see also 另見 **put sb/sth off** (PUT) —**off-puttingly** *adv*

off-ramp /ˈ· ·/ *n* [C] *AmE* a road for driving off a HIGHWAY (1)【美】〔主要公路或高速公路上的〕駛出坡道, 駛出匝道

off-road ve·hi·cle /ˌ· · ˈ···/ *n* [C] a vehicle that is built very strongly so that it can be used on rough ground 越野車輛, 非道路車輛

off-screen /ˌ· ˈ·◂/ *adv* when a film actor is not acting〔電影演員〕在銀幕外, 在私人生活中: *What's he like off-screen?* 他在銀幕外是甚麼模樣的? —**off-screen** *adj*: *The fan magazines are full of her off-screen romances.* 各種影迷雜誌中滿是她銀幕外的風流韻事。

off-sea·son /ˌ· ˈ··◂/ *n* **the off-season** the time of the year when there is not much work or activity, especially in farming or the tourist industry〔尤指農業或旅遊業的〕淡季: *Most hotels are closed in the off-season.* 在淡季時, 大多數旅館都關門停業。—**off-season** *adj, adv*: *Take advantage of our special off-season fares.* 我們提供淡季特惠票價, 請莫失良機。

O

off·set[1] /ɔfˈsɛt; ˈɒfset/ *v past tense and past participle* **offset** *present participle* **offsetting** [T] **1** if something such as a cost or sum of money offsets another cost, sum etc or is offset against it, it has an opposite effect so that the situation remains the same 補償, 抵銷: **be offset by** *In 1992 the cost of the layoffs was offset by the savings on the payroll.* 在1992年, 裁員的成本費用因工資總額的減少而得以彌補。| **offset sth against sth** *He was able to offset his travel expenses against tax.* 他用旅費抵銷了他的税。**2** to make something look better by being close to it and different 襯托出: *Streaks of blond in his hair offset his deep tan.* 他頭髮中一縷縷的金色襯托出了他黝黑的膚色。

off·set[2] /ˈɔfsɛt; ˈɒfset/ *n* [C,U] a method of printing in which ink is put onto rollers (ROLLER (1)) and the paper then passes between the rollers 膠印法 —**offset** *adj*

off·shoot /ˈɔfˌʃut; ˈɒfʃuːt/ *n* [C] **1** an organization, system of beliefs etc which has developed from a larger or earlier one〔組織、信仰等的〕分支, 衍生事物: *Marxism-Leninism and its various offshoots* 馬列主義及其諸多不同的分支 | [+of] *The company was originally an offshoot of Bell Telephones.* 該公司原本是貝爾電話公司的一家分支機構。**2** a new stem or branch on a plant〔植物的〕新莖, 分枝, 分株

off·shore /ˌɔfˈʃor; ˌɒfˈʃɔː/ *adj* **1** connected with work that is done on or under the sea 海上[海下]作業的: **offshore fishing/oil rig/exploration etc** *more than 10,000 offshore workers based in Orkney* 以奧克尼為基地的一萬多海上作業的工人 **2 offshore bank/company/investment etc** a bank etc that is based abroad in a country where you pay less tax than in your home country 境外[海外]銀行/公司/投資等 **3 offshore wind/current etc** a wind etc that is blowing or moving away from the land 從陸地吹向海面的風/離岸的水流 —compare 比較 INSHORE, ONSHORE —**offshore** *adv*: *a boat anchored offshore* 在近海岸錨泊的船

off·side[1] /ˌɔfˈsaɪd; ˌɒfˈsaɪd◂/ *adj, adv* in a position where you are not allowed to play the ball in sports such as football〔足球等運動中〕越位(的) —opposite 反義詞 ONSIDE

offside[2] /ˈɔfsaɪd; ˈɒfsaɪd/ *n* **the offside** *BrE* the side of a car that is nearest to the middle of the road when you are driving it【英】〔汽車的〕右側, 右邊 —opposite 反義詞 NEARSIDE —**offside** *adj*: *the offside headlight* 右邊的前燈

off·spring /ˈɔfˌsprɪŋ; ˈɒfˌsprɪŋ/ *n plural* **offspring** [C] **1** someone's child or children〔某人的〕子女, 子孫, 後代: *one of her numerous offspring* 她眾多兒女中的一個 **2** an animal's baby or babies〔動物的〕崽

off·stage /ˌɔfˈstedʒ; ˌɒfˈsteɪdʒ◂/ *adv* **1** just behind or to the side of a stage in a theatre, where the people watching a play cannot see 幕後, 舞台後, 舞台旁: *There was a loud crash offstage.* 後台發出很大的碰撞聲。**2** when an actor is not acting〔演員〕在台下, 在私生活中: *Offstage Peter always seemed a quiet, shy sort of person.* 舞台後, 彼得總像是那麼文靜靦腆。—**offstage** *adj*

off-street /ˈ· ·/ *adj* **off-street parking** places for parking that are not on main streets 離開主要街道的停車處

off-the-cuff /ˌ· · ˈ·◂/ *adj* [usually before noun 一般用於名詞前] an off-the-cuff remark, reply etc is one that you make without thinking about it first 未經準備的, 隨口作出的, 當場的, 即席的 —**off-the-cuff** *adv*

off-the-peg /ˌ· · ˈ·/ *adj BrE* off-the-peg clothes are not made to fit one particular person but are made in standard sizes【英】〔衣服〕現成的, 非訂製的; OFF-THE-RACK

O

AmE【美】—compare 比較 MADE-TO-MEASURE —**off-the-peg** *adv*: *It was only a cheap suit, bought off-the-peg.* 這不過是一套便宜的西服，是現成買來的。

off-the-rack /ˌ· · ˈ·◂/ *adj AmE* OFF-THE-PEG【美】〔衣服〕現成的，非訂製的

off-the-rec·ord /ˌ· · ˈ··◂/ *adj* an off-the-record remark is unofficial and is not supposed to be made public 非正式的，不准公開的: *The Prime Minister's remarks were strictly off-the-record.* 首相的講話是非正式的，嚴禁發表。—**off-the-record** *adv*

off-the-shelf /ˌ· · ˈ·◂/ *adj, adv* already made and available in shops 現成的[地]: *off-the-shelf database software* 現成的數據庫軟件

off-the-wall /ˌ· · ˈ·◂/ *adj informal* a little strange or unusual【非正式】有點古怪的，異乎尋常的: *an off-the-wall idea* 古怪的想法

off·track /ˋɔftræk; ˈɒftræk/ *adj AmE* away from a place where horses race【美】〔賽馬賭博等〕場外進行的: *Few states allow offtrack betting.* 只有幾個州允許場外賽馬賭博。

off-white /ˌ· ˈ·◂/ *n* [U] a white that has some yellow or grey in it 黃白色，灰白色，米色 —**off-white** *adj*: *an off-white blouse* 一件黃白色的女襯衫

off-year /ˈ· ·/ *n* [C usually singular 一般用單數] **1** a year when something is not as successful as usual 情況較差的年頭，小年: **[+for]** *an off-year for car sales* 汽車滯銷的一年 **2** *AmE* a year in which no elections happen【美】非選舉年

oft /ɔft; ɒft/ *adv poetical or formal* often【詩或正式】經常，時常: **oft-repeated/quoted etc** *oft-repeated advice* 多次重複的忠告

1 1 **of·ten** /ˋɔfən; ˈɒfən/ *adv* **1** if something happens often, or you do something often, it happens regularly or many times 經常，時常，多次: *Rosi often works till 7 or 8 o'clock in the evening.* 羅西經常工作到晚上七八點鐘。| *If you wash your hair too often, it tends to make it greasy.* 如果洗頭過勤，會使頭髮變得油光光的。| **how often?** *How often do you go to the movies?* 你多久去看一次電影？| **very/quite often** *Tom quite often goes to his Mum's on Saturday for tea.* 湯姆星期六常去他媽媽家喝茶。| **not often** *It's not often that you meet people who are so willing to help.* 這樣樂於助人的人不是經常能遇到的。—see picture at 參見 FREQUENCY 圖 **2** [sentence adverb 句子副詞] if something happens often, it happens in many situations or cases 在許多情況下: *It's often difficult to translate poetry.* 詩歌大部分都不容易翻譯。| **very/quite often** *Very often you find that children with behavioral problems come from broken homes.* 你會發現行為有問題的孩子大都來自破裂的家庭。**3 all too often** also 又作 **only too often** used to say that something sad, disappointing, or annoying happens too much 過於頻繁，屢次三番: *All too often victims of bullying are too frightened to ask for help.* 往往都是這樣，受欺侮的人因太害怕而不敢求助。| *These loopholes in the tax laws are exploited only too often.* 這些稅法中的漏洞屢屢被人利用。**4 every so often** sometimes 有時，偶爾: *An inspector would come round every so often to check the premises.* 偶爾有檢查員來查看這地方的情況。**5 as often as not** also 又作 **more often than not** *spoken* usually【口】通常: *More often than not he'll come and apologize within minutes of shouting at us.* 他跟我們吵嚷過後通常沒幾分鐘就會來道歉。

of·ten·times /ˋɔfənˌtaɪmz; ˈɒfəntaɪmz/ *adv old use* often【舊】經常，時常

o·gle /ˋogḷ; ˈəʊgəl/ *v* [I,T] to look at someone in an offensive way that shows you think they are sexually attractive 色迷迷地看着，盯視: *A small fat man sat there most days, ogling girls' legs.* 一個矮胖的男子在那裡每天要坐上老半天，色迷迷地盯着姑娘們的腿看。

O grade /ˋo gred; ˈəʊ greɪd/ *n* [C] an examination in a particular subject, taken in Scotland, usually at the age of 16 O級考試〔蘇格蘭地區對某一特定科目的考試，考生年齡通常在16歲〕—see also 另見 O LEVEL

o·gre /ˋogɚ; ˈəʊgə/ *n* [C] **1** a large character in children's stories who eats people〔童話中的〕吃人大妖魔 **2** someone who seems fierce, cruel, and frightening 兇殘可怕的人: *My boss is a real ogre.* 我們老闆真是可怕。

oh /o; əʊ/ *interjection* **1** used to make a slight pause, especially before replying to a question or giving your opinion on something 噢〔用於稍作停頓，尤其是在回答問題或對某事發表看法時〕: *"What time are you going into town?" "Oh, I haven't decided yet."* "你甚麼時候去城裡？" "噢，我還沒決定呢。" | *"I don't like the new boss." "Oh, I think she's quite nice."* "我不喜歡新來的老闆。" "噢，我認為她很不錯呀。" **2** used to get or keep someone's attention so that you can ask them a question or continue what you are saying 喂，啊〔用於讓人注意〕: *Oh, Janet, could you get me a paper while you're out?* 喂，珍妮特，外出時給我買份報紙好嗎？| *Milk, cereal, juice – oh, and put lettuce on the list too.* 牛奶、麥片、果汁 — 啊，把生菜也加到購物單上去。**3** used to express a strong emotion or to emphasize what you think about something 啊，呀〔用於表示強烈的情感或強調對某事的看法〕: *Oh, aren't those flowers gorgeous!* 呀，那些花可真漂亮！| *Oh, how awful!* 啊，真糟糕！| *She got the job? Oh great!* 她得到那份工作啦？啊，太好了！**4 oh, did he?/oh, are you?/oh, was she? etc** used to show that you did not previously know what someone has just told you 哦，真的嗎？〔用於表示以前不知道剛聽說的事〕: *"Frances has left her husband, you know." "Oh, has she?"* "你知道，弗朗西絲跟她丈夫分手了。" "哦，真的嗎？"

ohm /om; əʊm/ *n* [C] *technical* the standard unit of electrical RESISTANCE (5) which allows one AMP (1) to flow under a pressure of one VOLT【術語】歐姆〔電阻單位〕

o·ho /oˋho; əʊˈhəʊ/ *interjection old-fashioned* used to show surprise or satisfaction【過時】哦嗬，嗳喲，嘿嘿〔用於表示驚訝或滿意〕

-oid /ɔɪd; ɔɪd/ *suffix technical* [in adjectives 構成形容詞] like or in the form of something【術語】像…的，似…的: *humanoid creatures* (=similar to humans) 類人動物 | *ovoid* (=egg shaped) 卵型的

oik /ɔɪk; ɔɪk/ *n* [C] *BrE slang* a rude unintelligent man who is likely to cause trouble【英俚】蠢人，笨人；鄉巴佬；舉止粗魯的人 —**oikish** *adj*

oil¹ /ɔɪl; ɔɪl/ *n* **1** [U] a smooth thick mineral liquid that is burned to produce heat, or used to make machines run easily 油；燃料油；潤滑油: *Check the oil level in your car every week.* 每週檢查一下你汽車的油量。| **oil-burning/oil-fired** *oil-fired central heating* 燃油集中供暖系統 **2** [U] the thick, dark liquid from under the ground from which oil and petrol are produced; PETROLEUM 石油: *the oil industry* 石油工業 **3** [C,U] a smooth, thick liquid made from plants or animals, used in cooking or for making beauty products〔用於烹調或生產美容用品的〕植物油，動物油: *olive oil* 橄欖油 | *coconut oil shampoo* 椰子油洗髮劑 **4 oils** [plural] paints that contain oil; OIL PAINTS 油漆；油性塗料；油畫顏料: **in oils** *Mostly I paint in oils.* 大多數情況下，我都用油畫顏料作畫。—see also 另見 **burn the midnight oil** (BURN¹ (24)), **pour oil on troubled waters** (POUR (8))

oil² *v* [T] **1** to put oil into or onto something, such as a machine, in order to make it work more smoothly 加油於…；給…加潤滑油: *Isabel went upstairs to oil the attic lock and door hinges.* 伊莎貝爾上樓去給閣樓的鎖和門合葉上油。**2 oil the wheels** to help something to be done in business, politics etc successfully and easily 使某事順利進行

oil-bear·ing /ˈ· ˌ··/ *adj* oil-bearing rock contains oil〔岩石〕含油的

oil·cake /ˋɔɪlkek; ˈɔɪlkeɪk/ *n* [C] a type of food for cattle〔作牛飼料用的〕油渣餅

oil-can /ˈ· ·/ *n* [U] a metal container for oil with a long thin tube for pouring 油壺，加油罐

oil·cloth /ˈɔɪlˌkloθ; ˈɔɪlklɒθ/ *n* [U] cloth treated with oil to give it a smooth surface 油布

oiled /ɔɪld; ɔɪld/ *adj* **well oiled** *BrE informal* very drunk【英, 非正式】爛醉的

oil·field /ˈɔɪlˌfild; ˈɔɪlfiːld/ *n* [C] an area of land or sea under which there is oil 油田

oil-fired /ˈ· ·/ *adj* an oil-fired heating system burns oil to produce heat〔供暖系統〕燃油的, 燒油的

oil·man /ˈɔɪlmæn; ˈɔɪlmæn/ *n plural* **oilmen** /-mən; -mən/ [C] someone who owns an oil company or works in the oil industry 石油商; 石油工人

oil paint /ˈ· ·/ *n* [C,U] paint that contains oil 油漆; 油性塗料; 油畫顏料

oil paint·ing /ˈ· ˌ··/ *n* **1** [C] a picture painted with oil paint 油畫 **2** [U] the art of painting with oil paint 油畫藝術 **3 he's/she's no oil painting** *BrE humorous* used to say that someone is unattractive or ugly【英, 幽默】某人一點都不漂亮

oil pan /ˈ· ·/ *n* [C] *AmE* a part of an engine that holds the supply of oil【美】〔發動機底部的〕油盤, 潤滑油箱; SUMP (2) *BrE*【英】

oil plat·form /ˈ· ˌ··/ *n* [C] an oil rig 石油鑽台[塔]

oil rig /ˈ· ·/ *n* [C] a large structure with equipment for getting oil from under the ground, especially from under the sea bottom〔尤指從海底取油的〕石油鑽台[塔]; 油井設備

oil·seed rape /ˌɔɪlsid ˈrep; ˌɔɪlsiːd ˈreɪp/ *n* [U] RAPE² (3) 歐洲油菜

oil·skin /ˈɔɪlˌskɪn; ˈɔɪl-skɪn/ *n* **1** [U] cloth treated with oil so that water will not pass through it 防水油布 **2 oilskins** [plural] a coat and trousers made of oilskin 油布[防水布]衣褲

oil slick /ˈ· ·/ *n* [C] a layer of oil floating on water〔水面上的一層〕浮油

oil tank·er /ˈ· ˌ··/ *n* [C] a ship that has large containers for carrying oil 油輪, 運油船

oil well /ˈ· ·/ *n* [C] a hole that is dug in the ground to obtain oil 油井

oil·y /ˈɔɪlɪ; ˈɔɪli/ *adj* **1** covered with oil or containing a lot of oil 塗油的; 含油的; 油膩的: *oily skin* 油性皮膚 | *oily rags* 油膩的抹布 **2** looking or feeling like oil 似油的, 油質的: *an oily liquid* 油質液體 **3** unpleasantly polite 圓滑的, 會奉承人的, 討好的 —**oiliness** *n* [U]

oink /ɔɪŋk; ɔɪŋk/ *interjection* used to represent the sound that a pig makes 哼哼〔豬的叫聲〕—**oink** *n* [C]

oint·ment /ˈɔɪntmənt; ˈɔɪntmənt/ *n* [C,U] a soft substance made of solid oil that you rub into your skin, especially as a medical treatment 油膏, 軟膏, 藥膏 —see also 另見 **fly in the ointment** (FLY³ (5))

OJ /ˈo dʒe; ˈəʊ dʒeɪ/ *n* [U] *AmE informal* orange juice【美, 非正式】橙汁, 橘子汁

o·ka·pi /oˈkɑpɪ; əʊˈkɑːpi/ *n* [C] an African animal like a GIRAFFE, but with a shorter neck 獾加狓〔產於非洲, 類似長頸鹿, 但頸短〕

1 **o·kay¹, OK** /oˈke; əʊˈkeɪ/ *adj spoken*【口】**1** [not before noun 不用於名詞前] not ill, injured, unhappy etc 身體好的; 未受傷的; 愉快的: *Do you feel OK now?* 現在你感覺好嗎? **2** used to say that something is acceptable 行的, 可以的: *"Sorry I'm late." "That's okay."* "對不起, 我來晚了。" "沒關係。" | *Does my hair look OK?* 我的頭髮看上去行嗎? **3** [not before noun 不用於名詞前] satisfactory but not extremely good 不錯的, 還算滿意的: *Well, it was OK, but I liked the other one better.* 嗯, 這個不錯, 但我更喜歡那一個。**4 is it OK...?/...OK?** used to ask if you can do something or to tell someone they can do it ...好嗎?/...行嗎?〔用於徵求同意或表示允許〕: *Is it OK if I take Monday off?* 我星期一休假, 行嗎? | *I'll go first, OK?* 我先走, 行嗎? | **it is okay for sb to do sth** *It's okay for you to go home now.* 你現在可以回家了。| **it is okay with/by sb** *If it's OK with your mom, it's OK by me.* 如果你媽同意, 我也就沒意見。**5** *especially AmE* nice, helpful, honest etc【尤美】很好的; 有用的; 誠實的: *Dwight's OK – you can trust him.* 德懷特是好人, 你可以信任他。| *an OK kind of guy* 一個挺好的小夥子 —**okay, OK** *adv*: *Mum's doing OK now.* 媽現在過得不錯。| *Yeah, the TV's working okay.* 對, 這電視機性能不錯。

okay², OK *interjection* **1** used when you start talking about something else, or when you pause before continuing 好(了)〔用於轉換話題或停頓〕: *OK, let's go on to item B.* 好, 我們接着做B項吧。| *OK, any questions so far?* 好, 到現在為止有甚麼問題嗎? **2** used to express agreement or give permission 行, 可以〔用於表示同意或給予許可〕: *"Can I take the car today?" "Okay."* "今天我能用這車嗎?" "可以。" **3** used to stop people arguing with you 行了, 好了〔用於停止他人與你爭吵〕: *OK, OK, so I made a mistake, I've told you I'm sorry.* 好了, 好了, 是我出了錯, 我已經跟你説對不起了。**4** used when you think people are being unreasonable 難道不是, 還要怎樣〔用於認為他人不近情理時〕: *Look, I'm doing my best, OK?* 瞧, 我正拚命幹着呢, 不是嗎? 1

okay³, OK *v* **okayed, okaying** [T] *informal* to say officially that you will agree to something or allow it to happen【非正式】〔正式表明〕對...同意; 批准, 允許: *Has the bank okayed your request for a loan?* 銀行批准你的貸款申請了嗎?

okay⁴, OK *n informal* **give (sb) the okay/get the okay** to give or get permission to do something【非正式】給(某人)以批准/獲得批准: *I got the OK to leave early today.* 我獲准今天早走。

Frequencies of the word **okay** in spoken and written English 單詞okay在英語口語和書面語中的使用頻率

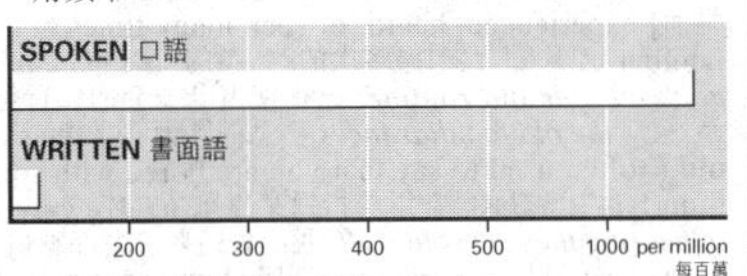

Based on the British National Corpus and the Longman Lancaster Corpus
據英國國家語料庫和朗文蘭卡斯特語料庫

This graph shows that the word **okay** is much more common in spoken English than in written English. 本圖表顯示, 單詞okay在英語口語中的使用頻率遠遠高於書面語。

o·key-doke /ˌokɪ ˈdok; ˌəʊki ˈdəʊk/ also 又作 **okey-do·key** /-ˈdokɪ; -ˈdəʊki/ *adj, adv spoken* used like 'okay' to express agreement【口】行, 好〔用法同okay, 表示同意〕

o·kra /ˈokrə; ˈɒkrə/ *n* [U] a green vegetable used in cooking in Asia and the southern US 秋葵〔亞洲和美國南部用於烹調的一種綠色蔬菜〕—see picture on page A9 參見A9頁圖

old /old; əʊld/ *adj* 1 1

1 ►USED OR NOT NEW 用過的或舊的◄ having existed for a long time, or having been used a lot before 古老的, 年代久遠的; 用舊了的: *an old winter coat* 冬天穿的舊大衣 | *a big old house* 很大的老房子 | *an old saying* 老話, 古老的格言 | *My car's older than yours.* 我的汽車比你的舊。| **be (as) old as the hills** (=be extremely old) 極老的, 陳年老舊的

2 ►NOT YOUNG 不年輕的◄ having lived for a long time 年老的, 年邁的: *an old man* 老人 | **get/grow old** (=become old) 變老, 上年紀 *The next time Robbie saw Mrs Dawes he thought she had grown very old.* 再次見到道斯夫人時, 羅比認為她已變得很老了。

3 the old old people 老(年)人: *taking care of the old and the sick* 照料老人和病人

4 ►AGE 年齡◄ **be ... old** to be a particular age 有...歲: *How old are you?* 你多大年紀? | **be 5/10/50 etc years**

old *Our house is 60 years old.* 我們的房子有60年了。| **5-year-old/10-year-old etc** *our 12-year-old son* 我們12歲大的兒子 | *a six-week-old baby* 六星期大的寶寶 | **old enough/too old** *I think you're old enough to make your own decisions.* 我認為你已經到了自己拿主意的年齡了。
5 old house/job/teacher etc a house, job etc that you had before but do not have now 從前的房子/工作/老師等: *I saw Phil with one of my old girlfriends.* 我看見菲爾和我以前的一個女朋友在一起。| *My old car didn't have air conditioning.* 我從前的那輛汽車沒有空調。
6 he's old enough to be your father/she's old enough to be your mother *informal* used to say that someone is too old for someone to have a sexual relationship with【非正式】他都能當你爸了/她都能當你媽了〔用於表示某人年齡過大, 不適合成為性伴侶〕
7 be old beyond your years to be wiser or more sensible than most people your age 比你的實際年齡來得聰明[明智]
8 be old before your time to behave like someone much older than you, because bad things have happened to you〔因有過不好的經歷而〕比你的實際年齡來得老成, 未老先衰的, 老氣橫秋的
9 sb is old enough to know better used to say that you think someone should have behaved more sensibly 某人已經長大該知好歹了
10 an old friend/enemy etc someone you have known for a long time 老朋友/夙敵等: *Bob's an old friend of mine.* 鮑勃是我的一個老朋友。
11 an old head on young shoulders a young person who seems to think and behave like an older person 少年老成
12 ►FAMILIAR 熟悉的◄ [only before noun 僅用於名詞前] experienced, heard, or seen many times before; familiar 已經歷[見聞]過多次的; 熟悉的: *It's good to get back into the old routine.* 還是恢復老一套的例行做法為好。| *the old familiar faces* 熟悉的老面孔 | **the same old** (=often used to say that you are bored with something) 老生常談的〔常用於指對某事厭煩〕*We get tired of hearing the same old stuff.* 我們對這老一套都聽煩了。—see also 另見 **it's the same old story** (STORY (10))
13 old flame someone with whom you used to have a romantic relationship 老相好, 舊情人
14 the old country *especially AmE* the country that you were born in, but that you no longer live in, used especially to mean Europe【尤美】〔移民等的〕祖國, 故國〔尤指歐洲國家〕
15 the old days times in the past 舊日的時光, 以前: *In the old days people used to fetch water from the pump.* 過去, 人們都用抽水泵來打水。
16 the good old days/the bad old days an earlier time in your life, or in history, when things seemed better or worse than now 過去的好/壞日子: *We like to chat about the good old days.* 我們喜歡聊聊過去的好時光。
17 of old a) *literary* long ago in the past【文】往日的, 從前的: *in days of old* 在古時, 在從前的日子 **b)** if you know someone of old you know them from a long time ago 從前, 很久以前〔便認識某人〕
18 for old times' sake if you do something for old times' sake, you do it to remind yourself of a happy time in the past 看在舊日的情份上; 為了老交情; 為懷念往日之故
19 be/feel/look like your old self to feel or look better again after you have been ill or very unhappy 感覺/看上去恢復了正常狀態: *Glad to see you looking more like your old self again.* 很高興看到你又恢復過去的老樣子。
20 Old English/Old Icelandic etc an early form of English, Icelandic etc 古英語/古冰島語等
21 good old/poor old/silly old etc *spoken* used to talk to or about someone you are fond of【口】〔與喜歡之人說話或談論喜歡之人的用語〕: *Good old Keith!* 老友基思! | *You poor old thing!* 你這個可憐的老東西!
22 the old... used to talk about something that you often use or are very familiar with 用慣了的; 很熟悉的: *So I got the old paint brushes out and set to work.* 於是, 我拿出那些用慣了的漆刷, 開始幹活。
23 you old .../the old ... used to show that you are surprised or amused by what someone has said or done〔表示對某人所說或所做的事情感到吃驚或好笑的用語〕: *You told her that? You old liar!* 你跟她那麼說的? 你這個老騙子! | *Don't ask him, the old miser.* 別求他, 這個吝嗇鬼!
24 old fool/old cow etc *spoken* used to talk about someone you do not like【口】老糊塗/討厭鬼等〔用於談論不喜歡之人〕: *the old bastard* 老雜種 | *silly old fool* 老糊塗
25 a good old also 又作 **a right old** *BrE spoken* used to talk about something you enjoy【英口】〔用於談論欣賞之事〕: *We had a good old talk.* 我們暢快地聊了一陣子。
26 any old thing/hat/place etc *informal* used to say that it does not matter which thing, place etc you choose【非正式】隨便哪個東西/帽子/地方等都行: *Oh, just wear any old thing.* 噢, 就隨便穿一件吧。| *You can't just turn up at any old time, you know.* 你知道, 你不能隨便找個時間就來。
27 any old how/way *informal* untidily or carelessly【非正式】不整潔地; 粗心地: *Put these away properly, don't shove them in any old how.* 把這些收拾利索, 不要亂塞亂放。
28 pay/settle an old score to punish someone for something wrong that they did to you in the past 清算舊仇, 了結宿怨
29 of the old school old-fashioned and believing in old ideas and customs 老派的, 守舊的: *a real English lady of the old school* 地道的老派英國女士
30 old wives' tale a belief based on old ideas that are now considered to be untrue 無稽之談; 愚蠢的信仰; 迷信
31 be an old hand at to have a lot of experience of something 是…的老手, 在…方面經驗老到: *I'm an old hand at this game.* 我是玩這種把戲的老手。
32 the old guard a group of people within an organization or club who do not like changes or new ideas〔機構、俱樂部等內的〕守舊派, 保守派, 保守分子: *The old guard will vote against letting women into the club.* 那些保守派將投票反對婦女加入俱樂部。
33 the Old Bill *BrE informal* the police【英, 非正式】警察, 警察當局 —see also 另見 **the old school tie** (SCHOOL TIE (2))

USAGE NOTE 用法說明: OLD
WORD CHOICE 詞語辨析: **older, elder, elderly, senior citizen, OAP**
You can use **older** to describe either people or things. **Elder** means the same thing but you only use it to talk about people and usually only your close family. 可用 older 來描述人或事物。elder 意思相同, 但只可用於人, 而且通常只用於關係密切的家庭成員: *My elder/older daughter is at university.* 我的大女兒在上大學。| *Shane is the elder brother of the two.* 沙恩是兩人中的哥哥。But you can also say 但也可以說: *elder members of the community* 社區中的年長成員
Older but not **elder** can be used with **than**. older 可與 than 連用, 而 elder 則不能: *Shane is older than Mark* (NOT 不用 *elder than*). 沙恩比馬克年齡大。
When you are talking about people, **elderly** (NOT 不用 *elder*) is a polite way of saying **old**. 當講到人時, elderly (上了年紀的) 比 old (老的) 更有禮貌。Compare 比較 *an old church* (一座古老的教堂) and 和 *an old/elderly lady* (一位年老/上了年紀的婦人)。Most people however now prefer to be called **senior citizens**, and this is the most common,

polite, and acceptable expression to use. 但現在, 大多數人更樂意被叫作 senior citizen (年長的公民), 這是最普遍、最禮貌和最能被接受的叫法。
In British English, especially in official notices, you might see OAP, which is short for 'old age pensioner'. 在英國英語中, 尤其是在官方通告中, 還可能會見到 OAP 一詞, 這是 old age pensioner (領取養老金者) 的縮寫。

old age /ˌ· ˈ·◂/ *n* [U] the part of your life when you are old 老年, 晚年: *the effects of old age* 因年老而出現的問題 | **in your old age** *My aunt needed to be cared for in her old age.* 我姨母在晚年時需要照顧。

old age pen·sion /ˌ· · ˈ··/ *n* [U] *BrE* money paid regularly by the state to old people【英】〔政府付給的〕養老金; SOCIAL SECURITY (1) *AmE*【美】

old age pen·sion·er /ˌ· · ˈ···/ *n* [C] *BrE* someone who does not work any more and who receives an old age pension【英】領取養老金者 —see also 另見 OAP

old boy /ˈ· · (for 適用於義項 1, 2), ˌ· ˈ· (for 適用於義項 3, 4)/ *n* [C] **1** *BrE* a man who used to be a student at a particular school【英】男校友, 老同學: *an old boys' reunion* 男校友聚會 **2 the old-boy network** the system by which men from rich families, men who went to the same school, belong to the same club etc, use their influence to help each other 男校友關係網, 男校友會 **3** *BrE spoken* an old man【英口】老漢, 老頭兒: *the old boy from down the road* 沿路走來的那位老頭兒 **4** *BrE old-fashioned* a way of addressing a male friend【英, 過時】老朋友, 老兄〔對男性朋友的一種稱呼〕: *How are you, old boy?* 你好嗎, 老朋友。—compare 比較 OLD GIRL

old·e /ˈoldɪ; ˈəʊldi/ *adj* another spelling of old, used in the names of shops, products etc to make them seem traditional 老的〔old 的另一種拼寫形式, 用於商號、產品等名稱, 以示傳統悠久〕: *ye olde tea shoppe* 老 (字號) 茶莊

old·en /ˈoldn̩; ˈəʊldən/ *adj* **in olden days/times** a long time ago 往昔, 從前: *In olden times life was simpler.* 從前的生活比較簡樸。

Old En·glish Sheep·dog /ˌ· ·· ˈ··/ *n* [C] a large dog with long thick grey and white hair 老英國牧羊犬〔體型大, 有長而密的灰白相間的毛髮〕

olde-world·e /ˌoldɪ ˋwɜldɪ; ˌəʊldi ˈwɜːldi◂/ *adj BrE informal* a place that is olde-worlde has been decorated so that it looks old-fashioned【英, 非正式】古色古香的, 古老奇趣的: *an olde-worlde country pub* 一家古色古香的鄉村小酒館

old-fash·ioned¹ /ˌ· ˈ··◂/ *adj* **1** not modern and considered not to be fashionable any more 舊式的, 老式的, 過時的: *Gwen's clothes are so old-fashioned!* 格温的衣服太過時了! | *'Wireless' is an old-fashioned word for 'radio'.* wireless (無線電) 是 radio (收音機) 的舊稱。**2** someone who is old-fashioned believes in ways of doing things that are not usual any more 〔人〕老派的, 守舊的: *Dad's kind of old-fashioned in his views on sex before marriage.* 老爸對婚前性行為的看法有點守舊。**3 an old-fashioned look/expression** *BrE old use* a disapproving look or expression【英舊】不以為然的目光/表情

old-fashioned² *n* [C] *AmE* an alcoholic drink made with WHISKEY【美】古典雞尾酒〔用威士忌等調製的含酒精飲料〕

old fo·gey /ˌold ˋfogɪ; ˌəʊld ˈfəʊgi/ *n* [C] *informal* someone who is old, or has old-fashioned ideas about things【非正式】老傢伙; 極守舊的人, 老頑固: *Oh come on, it's only 10 o'clock, don't be such an old fogey!* 喂, 得啦! 才 10 點鐘, 別那麼死板嘛!

old folk /ˈ· ˌ·/ *BrE*【英】also 又作 **old folks** *especially AmE*【尤美】*n* [plural] an expression meaning old people, used especially when speaking of them in a kind way 老人, 長輩: *We always try to do something for the old folk at Christmas.* 聖誕節時, 我們總想着為老人家們做點事。

old folks' home /ˌ· ˈ· ˌ·/ *n* [C] *informal* an OLD PEOPLE'S HOME【非正式】養老院

old girl /ˈ· · (for 適用於義項 1), ˌ· ˈ· (for 適用於義項 2)/ *n* [C] *BrE*【英】**1** a woman who is a former student of a particular school 女校友 **2** *spoken* an old woman【口】老婦人: *Don't tell me the old girl still drives!* 那老太太不至於還開車吧! —compare 比較 OLD BOY

Old Glo·ry /ˌ· ˈ··/ *n* [U] *AmE* the flag of the US【美】美國國旗

Old Har·ry /ˌ· ˈ··/ *n BrE old-fashioned* the devil【英, 過時】魔鬼; 撒旦

old hat /ˌ· ˈ·/ *adj* [not before noun 不用於名詞前] familiar or old-fashioned, and therefore boring 舊式的, 過時的, 老套的: *Most of this is probably old hat to you, isn't it?* 對你來說, 這其中大部分很可能是陳年老套了, 是嗎?

old·ie /ˈoldɪ; ˈəʊldi/ *n* [C] *informal* someone or something that is old【非正式】老人; 古老的東西, 陳舊之物: **oldie but goodie** *It's all nostalgia – they play the oldie-but-goodie records.* 這全是懷舊情愫 —— 他們愛放那些經典的老唱片。—see also 另見 **golden oldie** (GOLDEN (6))

old·ish /ˈoldɪʃ; ˈəʊldɪʃ/ *adj* not very old, but not young or new either 有點老的; 稍舊的

old la·dy /ˌ· ˈ··/ *n slang*【俚】**1** an expression meaning someone's wife 老婆, 妻子: *Gotta go home to my old lady, I guess.* 我想我要回家去會老婆了。**2** an expression meaning your mother 老娘, 母親

old lag /ˌ· ˈ·/ *n BrE old-fashioned* someone who has been in prison many times【英, 過時】慣犯, 多次坐牢的人

old maid /ˌ· ˈ·/ *n* [C] **1** an offensive expression meaning a woman who has never married and is not young any more 老姑娘, 老處女〔具冒犯性的稱呼〕**2** *informal* someone who pays too much attention to unimportant matters and has old-fashioned ideas【非正式】斤斤計較的人; 思想保守的人; 謹小慎微的人 —**old-maidish** *adj*

old man /ˌ· ˈ·/ *n* [C] **1** *slang* an expression meaning someone's husband【俚】老公, 丈夫: *I heard her old man beats her.* 我聽說她老公經常打她。**2** *slang* an expression meaning your father【俚】老爹, 父親 **3** *BrE old-fashioned* used to address a male friend【英, 過時】老兄, 夥計, 老朋友〔用於稱呼男性朋友〕: *Could I have a word with you, old man?* 我可以和你談一下嗎, 老兄?

old mas·ter /ˌ· ˈ··/ *n* [C] a famous painter, especially from the 15th to 18th century, or a painting by one of these painters〔尤指 15 至 18 世紀的〕古典名畫家 (作品): *a priceless collection of old masters* 一批古典名畫家的珍貴收藏品

Old Nick /ˌ· ˈ·/ *n BrE old-fashioned* the devil【英, 過時】魔王, 魔鬼

old peo·ple's home /ˌ· ˈ·· ˌ·/ *n* [C] a place where old people live together and are cared for 養老院, 老人院

old salt /ˌ· ˈ·/ *n* [C] *old-fashioned* a SAILOR who has had a lot of experience of sailing【過時】有經驗的老水手

old·ster /ˈoldstɚ; ˈəʊldstə/ *n* [C] *informal* an old person【非正式】老傢伙, 老年人

Old Tes·ta·ment /ˌ· ˈ···◂/ *n* **the Old Testament** the first part of the Christian Bible containing ancient Hebrew writings about the time before the birth of Christ〔《聖經》的〕《舊約全書》—compare 比較 NEW TESTAMENT

old tim·er /ˌ· ˈ··/ *n* [C] **1** someone who has been in a particular job, place etc for a long time and knows a lot about it 老資格的人, 老前輩, 老手 **2** *especially AmE* an old man【尤美】老人, 上了年紀的人

old wom·an /ˌ· ˈ··/ *n BrE slang*【英俚】**1 the old woman** an offensive expression meaning someone's wife or mother 老婆; 老娘〔具冒犯性的說法〕**2** [C] a man who pays too much attention to unimportant details 斤斤計較[婆婆媽媽]的男人 —**old womanish** *adj*

Old World /ˌ· ˈ·◂/ *n* **the Old World** *old use* the Eastern Hemisphere, especially Europe, Asia and Africa【舊】

舊世界, 東半球〔尤指歐洲、亞洲和非洲〕—compare 比較 NEW WORLD

old-world /ˈ· ·/ *adj* [only before noun 僅用於名詞前] an old-world place or quality is attractive because it is old or reminds you of the past〔地方、品質等〕老式的, 古色古香的: *the old-world charm of the village* 那村莊古樸的魅力

ole /ol; əʊl/ *adj* used in written English to represent the way some people say 'old' 老的〔英語書面語中用以表示一些人說 old 的方式〕: *The poor ole guy!* 可憐的老傢伙!

o·le·ag·i·nous /ˌolɪˈædʒənəs; ˌəʊliˈædʒənəs/ *adj technical* containing, producing, or like oil【術語】含油的; 產油的; 油質的

o·le·an·der /ˌolɪˈændɚ; ˌəʊliˈændə/ *n* [C,U] a green bush with white, red, or pink flowers 夾竹桃

O lev·el /ˈo ˌlɛvl̩; ˈəʊ ˌlevəl/ *n* **1** [U] Ordinary level; an examination taken in schools in England and Wales before 1988, usually at the age of 16 O 級; 普通級 (考試)〔指英格蘭和威爾斯在 1988 年前對中學生進行的考試, 考生年齡通常在 16 歲〕**2** [C] one of these examinations in a particular subject〔某一學科的〕O 級證書考試, 普通級證書考試: *He left school with five O levels.* 他畢業時通過了五門學科的普通級證書考試。| *O level German* 普通級證書的德語考試 —compare 比較 A LEVEL, GCSE

ol·fac·to·ry /ɑlˈfæktərɪ; ɒlˈfæktəri/ *adj technical* connected with the sense of smell【術語】嗅覺的: *the olfactory ducts* 嗅覺管

ol·i·gar·chy /ˈɑlɪˌɡɑrkɪ; ˈɒləɡɑːki/ *n* **1** [U] government or control by a small group of people 寡頭政治; 寡頭統治 **2** [C usually singular 一般用單數] a state governed by a small group of people, or the group who govern such a state 寡頭統治的國家; 寡頭政治集團 **—oligarch** *n* [C]

ol·ive /ˈɑlɪv; ˈɒləv/ *n* **1** [C] a tree grown in Mediterranean countries that has small bitter egg-shaped fruits, usually black or green 橄欖樹: *an olive grove* 一片橄欖樹林 **2** [C] the fruit of this tree, used for food and also for its oil〔作食品或榨油用的〕橄欖 **3** a deep yellowish green colour 黃綠色, 橄欖色, 茶青色 —see picture on page A5 參見 A5 頁圖 **4 olive skin/complexion** skin colour that is yellowish brown 橄欖色的皮膚 / 膚色 **5 offer/hold out/extend the olive branch** to do something to show that you want to end an argument 伸出橄欖枝〔做某事以表示願意和解〕**—olive** *adj*: *an olive sweatshirt* 橄欖色的圓領長袖運動衫

olive drab /ˌ·· ˈ·/ *n* [U] *especially AmE* a greyish green colour, used especially in military uniforms【尤美】草綠色〔尤指軍服顏色〕**—olive drab** *adj*

olive oil /ˌ·· ˈ·/ *n* [U] a pale yellow or green oil obtained from olives and used in cooking 橄欖油

-ol·o·gist /ɑlədʒɪst; ɒlədʒəst/ also 又作 **-logist** *suffix* [in nouns 構成名詞] a person who studies or specializes in a particular kind of science ...學家: *a biologist* 生物學家

-ology /ɑlədʒɪ; ɒlədʒi/ also 又作 **-logy** *suffix* [in nouns 構成名詞] **1** the scientific study of something ...學: *geology* (=the study of rocks and the Earth) 地質學 | *climatology* (=the study of CLIMATE) 氣候學 | *Egyptology* (=the study of ancient Egypt) 古埃及學 **2** *informal* something that is done or talked about as though it was a scientific study【非正式】...學科[學說]〔把某物說成是一門學說似的〕: *futurology* (=the practice of trying to say how the future will develop) 未來學 **3** the things studied by a particular science〔某種科學研究的〕對象: *The geology of north Devon is particularly interesting* (=it has interesting rocks, etc). 德文郡北部的地質格外有意思。**—-ological** /əlɑdʒɪkl; əlɒdʒɪkəl/ *suffix* [in adjectives 構成形容詞] **—-ologically** /əlɑdʒɪklɪ; əlɒdʒɪkli/ *suffix* [in adverbs 構成副詞]: *geologically interesting* 地質上有趣的

O·lym·pi·ad /əˈlɪmpɪˌæd; əˈlɪmpi-æd/ *n* [C] *formal* a particular occasion of the modern Olympic Games【正式】〔現代〕奧林匹克運動會: *Welcome to the games of the 23rd Olympiad.* 歡迎光臨第 23 屆奧運會。

O·lym·pi·an¹ /əˈlɪmpɪən; əˈlɪmpiən/ *n* one of the ancient Greek Gods 奧林匹斯山諸神之一

Olympian² *adj* **1** like a god, especially by being calm and not concerned about ordinary things 神仙般逍遙自在的, 超脫世俗的: *to view the world with an Olympian detachment* 以一種超然的態度看待世界 **2** connected with the ancient Greek gods 奧林匹斯山諸神的

O·lym·pic /əˈlɪmpɪk; əˈlɪmpɪk/ *adj* [only before noun 僅用於名詞前] connected with the Olympic Games 奧運會的: *an Olympic runner* 奧運會賽跑選手

Olympic Games /·ˌ·· ˈ·/ *n* [plural] **1** an international sports event held every four years in different countries 奧林匹克運動會〔每四年一次在不同國家舉行〕**2** a sports event held at Olympia in Greece every four years in ancient times〔古希臘〕奧林匹克競技會〔每四年在奧林匹亞城舉行一次〕

O·lym·pics /əˈlɪmpɪks; əˈlɪmpɪks/ *n* [plural] the Olympic Games 奧林匹克運動會

OM /ˌo ˈɛm; ˌəʊ ˈem/ *n* [C] the Order of Merit; a special HONOUR¹ (4) given to someone by the Queen of England 功績勳章〔英國女王授予的特殊榮譽〕

om·buds·man /ˈɑmbudzmən; ˈɒmbʊdzmən/ *n* [C] someone who deals with complaints made by ordinary people against the government, banks, insurance companies etc 民情調查員, 巡視官, 申訴專員〔專門處理民眾對政府、銀行、保險公司等投訴的人〕

o·me·ga /oˈmɛɡə; ˈəʊməɡə/ *n* [C] the last letter of the Greek alphabet 希臘字母表的最後一個字母

ome·lette also 又作 **omelet** *AmE*【美】/ˈɑmlɪt; ˈɒmləṭ/ *n* [C] **1** eggs mixed together and cooked in hot fat, sometimes with other foods added 煎蛋 (卷), 奄列: *a cheese omelette* 乳酪煎蛋卷 **2 you can't make an omelette without breaking eggs** used to say that it is impossible to do something important without causing problems 要煎蛋卷就得打破雞蛋, 有失才有得〔指要做大事必會引起一些問題〕

o·men /ˈomən; ˈəʊmən/ *n* [C] a sign of what will happen in the future 前兆, 預兆, 兆頭: **a good/bad/ill omen** *The sudden change in weather seemed to Frank to be a good omen.* 對弗蘭克來說, 天氣突變似乎是個好兆頭。—see also 另見 ILL-OMENED

om·i·nous /ˈɑmənəs; ˈɒmənəs/ *adj* making you feel that something bad is going to happen〔使人感到〕不吉的, 不祥的: *The car is making an ominous rattling sound.* 汽車在發出一種不祥的卡嗒卡嗒聲。**—ominously** *adv*: *The sky looked ominously dark.* 天空黑沉沉的, 像要變天。

o·mis·sion /oˈmɪʃən; əʊˈmɪʃən/ *n* **1** [U] the act of not including or not doing something 省略; 刪節; 遺漏: *The omission of her name was not a deliberate act.* 她的名字不是故意遺漏的。**2** [C] something that has been omitted 省略的東西; 遺漏的東西: *It was one of many errors and omissions pushing up the cost of the road works.* 有許多失誤和疏漏造成了道路施工費用的增加, 而這只是其中之一。| **a glaring omission** (=one that is very bad and easily noticed) 顯而易見的嚴重疏忽

o·mit /oˈmɪt; əʊˈmɪt/ **omitted, omitting** *v* [T] **1** to not include someone or something, either deliberately or because you forget to do it; **leave out** (LEAVE¹) 省去, 略去, 刪去; 遺漏: *Please don't omit any details, however trivial they may seem.* 請勿省略任何細節, 不管這些細節看似多麼瑣碎。**2 omit to do sth** *formal* to not do something, either because you forgot or deliberately【正式】忘記做某事; 故意不做某事: *Oliver omitted to mention that he was married.* 奧立弗沒有提及他已結婚。

om·ni- /ɑmnɪ; ɒmnɪ/ *prefix* everything or everywhere; all 一切; 到處; 全部: *an omnivore* (=animal that eats all sorts of food) 雜食動物

om·ni·bus /ˈɑmnɪbəs; ˈɒmnɪbəs/ *n* [C] *especially BrE*【尤英】**1** a book containing several stories, especially by one writer, that have already been printed separately〔尤指某作家的〕選集, 文集; 匯編 **2** a radio or television programme made of several programmes that have previously been broadcast separately 節目薈萃, 多集節目的一次播出〔由曾分別播出過的幾個節目組成的廣播或電視節目〕: *the Brookside omnibus* 布魯克塞德節目薈萃 **3** *old use* a bus【舊】公共汽車

om·nip·o·tent /ɑmˋnɪpətənt; ɒmˈnɪpətənt/ *adj formal* able to do everything【正式】全能的 —**omnipotence** *n* [U]: *God's omnipotence* 上帝的全能

om·ni·pres·ent /ˌɑmnɪˋprɛznt; ˌɒmnɪˈprezənt◂/ *adj formal* present everywhere at all times【正式】〔任何時候都〕無所不在的; 普遍存在的 —**omnipresence** *n* [U]

om·nis·ci·ent /ɑmˋnɪʃənt; ɒmˈnɪʃənt/ *adj formal* knowing everything【正式】無所不知的, 全知的: *Only God is omniscient.* 唯有上帝是無所不知的。—**omniscience** *n* [U]

om·ni·vore /ˋɑmnɪvɔr; ˈɒmnɪvɔː/ *n* [C] *technical* an animal that eats both meat and plants【術語】雜食動物, 肉草兼食的動物

om·niv·o·rous /ɑmˋnɪvərəs; ɒmˈnɪvərəs/ *adj technical*【術語】**1** an animal that is omnivorous eats both meat and plants〔動物〕雜食性的, 肉草兼食的 **2** interested in everything, especially in all books 對甚麼都感興趣的; 〔尤指〕甚麼書都看的: *an omnivorous reader* 甚麼書都讀的人

1 1 **on¹** /ɑn; ɒn/ *prep* **1** touching or being supported by a particular surface 在…上〔表示接觸或由某一表面支撐着〕: *The plate's on the table.* 盤子在桌上。| *You have mud on your shoes.* 你的鞋子上有泥。| *The answer is written on page 25.* 答案在第25頁上。—see picture on page A1 參見A1頁圖 **2** hanging from, supported by or connected to a particular thing 自…懸下; 由…支持; 與…連接[有聯繫]: *Stand on one foot.* 用單腳站立。| *pictures stuck on the wall* 貼在牆上的圖畫 | *a ball on a string* 吊在繩上的球 **3 a)** in a particular place, building or area of land 在〔某個場所、建築物或地區〕內: *Several bombs landed on the runway.* 幾顆炸彈落在跑道上。| *He grew up on a ranch in California.* 他在加利福尼亞的一個大牧場上長大。**b)** *AmE* in a particular road【美】在〔某條道路、街道〕上: *We live on Mulberry Drive.* 我們住在馬爾伯里大道。| *I met Amy on the street the other day.* 前幾天我在街上遇到了艾美。**4** in a particular direction 向…, 朝…方向: *On my right sat the Chancellor.* 我的右邊坐着校長。| *As the troops marched on the city, the leaders planned their escape.* 大軍向該城市進發時, 那些頭腦人物已籌劃好逃跑了。**5** used to show the person or thing affected by an action or someone's behaviour 受〔某種行動或某人行為〕的影響: *a tax on cigarettes* 煙草稅 | *The divorce has had a particularly bad effect on the children.* 離婚已對孩子們造成了極壞的影響。**6** on one of the sides of something such as a river or road 在〔河流或道路等的〕一邊: *a cafe on the river* 河邊的咖啡館 | *a beautiful village on the Austrian border* 位於奧地利邊界的美麗村莊 | *trees on both sides of the street* 街道兩旁的樹 **7 on Friday/August 2nd/my birthday** at some time during a particular day 在星期五/8月2日/我的生日: *They arrive on Tuesday.* 他們於星期二到達。| *I was born on July 1st.* 我出生於7月1日。**8** about a particular subject 關於〔某一主題〕: *a book on India* 一本關於印度的書 | *advice on what to wear* 關於衣着方面的建議 **9** in a bus, train, aircraft etc 乘坐〔公共汽車、火車、飛機等〕: *Everyone on the plane was frightened.* 飛機上所有的人都很驚慌。| *He managed to be on the first train back to London.* 他設法坐上了返回倫敦的頭班火車。—see also 另見 **on foot** (FOOT¹(2)), **on horseback** (HORSEBACK) **10** used to say what food someone needs to survive, what FUEL¹(1) something needs to operate etc 以〔某種食物〕為生; 靠〔某種燃料〕運轉: *We can't live on rice and water forever.* 我們不能總以大米和水來過日子。| *Many cars nowadays run on lead free petrol.* 如今許多汽車都用無鉛汽油(為燃料)來行駛。**11** used to say what money people use to live, the amounts of money someone earns etc 靠〔某種錢財〕為生; 賺〔錢的數額〕: *Some families in the ghettos have been on welfare all their lives.* 貧民區的一些家庭終生靠福利救濟金過活。| *People on high salaries should pay more tax.* 高薪人士應該多納稅。**12** *informal* used to say that someone takes a particular drug or medicine【非正式】吸食〔毒品〕; 服用〔藥物〕: *Since she's been on Prozac she's been a different person.* 自服用"百憂解"〔一種抗抑鬱藥〕以來, 她完全變了一個人。**13 on the radio/telephone** using a radio or telephone 使用收音機/電話: *Shut up! I'm on the phone.* 別說話! 我在打電話呢。**14 on a trip/journey etc** during a trip, journey etc 在旅途中: *I met several people on the voyage.* 在這次旅行中, 我結識了好幾個人。| *On my way to work the car broke down.* 在去上班的路上, 我的汽車壞了。**15** used to say what has been used to do something 使用…〔做某事〕: *Phil had torn his shirt on a nail.* 菲爾的襯衫被釘子掛破了。| *It's amazing what you can do on these new word processors.* 這些新的文字處理機的功能真讓人不可思議。**16** *formal* immediately after something has happened or after someone has done something【正式】一…就, 在…後立即: **on doing sth** *On hearing the news of the air attack most foreigners headed for the border.* 一聽到空襲的消息, 大多數外國人便湧到邊境去。| **on arrival/sb's return etc** *On arrival at reception, guests should sign the visitors' book.* 客人一到接待處就要在來賓簽名簿上簽名。| **on sth** *On the general's command, all soldiers must salute.* 一聽到將軍的口令, 全體士兵必須立即敬禮。**17** used to say that someone is a member of a team, organization etc 是…的成員: *What team did you say your boyfriend was on?* 你說你的男朋友是甚麼球隊的? **18** compared with another person or thing 與〔其他人或東西〕相比較: *This essay is a definite improvement on your last one.* 與上一篇相比, 你這篇文章有了明顯的改進。| *Sales are 10% up on last year.* 銷量比去年增加了10%。**19 have/carry etc sth on you** *informal* to have a particular thing in your pocket, your bag etc【非正式】有/攜帶某物在身上: *How much cash do you have on you?* 你身上帶了多少現金? **20** *spoken* used to say that someone will pay for something such as a drink, a meal etc【口】由某人支付〔飲料、飯菜等的費用〕: *Drinks are on Harold!* 喝酒由哈羅德請客! **21** *informal* if a machine stops, breaks etc on you, it stops or breaks while you are using it【非正式】在〔某人〕使用時出現故障: *Suddenly the telephone went dead on me.* 我的電話突然斷了。

on² *adj, adv* [not before noun 不用於名詞前] **1** used to say that someone continues to do something or something continues to happen, without stopping 繼續, 不停的[地]: **play/read/talk etc on** (=to continue playing, reading etc) 繼續玩耍/閱讀/談話等 *Both teams managed to play on into overtime, despite the blistering heat.* 儘管天氣炎熱, 兩隊都堅持不懈, 進入了加時賽。| **carry/keep/go on etc doing sth** *If you keep on eating like that you'll need to diet.* 如果照那樣吃下去, 你就得節食了。| **carry/keep/go on etc** *Carry on. You're doing very well.* 堅持下去, 你幹得很好。**2** if you move, walk etc on, you move forward to a particular place (再)往前, 向前: *If you walk on a little, you can see the coast.* 再往前走一點, 你就會看見海岸了。| *You can have your letters sent on to you at your new address.* 你可以把信件轉到你的新地址。| **straight on** *Keep straight on and turn left at the bank.* 一直往前走, 到了銀行向左拐彎。**3** used to say that something happens at a time that is before or after another time〔指某事發生的時間〕早於或晚於另一時間: **earlier/later on** *Later on we learned that he got back to France safely.* 後來我們得知, 他平安回到了法國。| **from then on/from that day on etc** *From that moment on I never believed a word she told me.* 自那一刻起, 我不再相信她跟我說的任何一句話。**4** if you have something on, you are wearing it 穿[戴]上: *Put your coat on. It's freezing outside.* 穿上大衣吧, 外面冷極了。| *The*

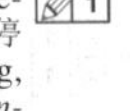

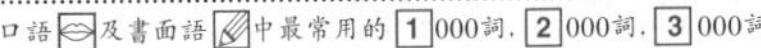

poor child had absolutely nothing on. 那可憐的孩子身上一絲不掛。**5** in a bus, train, aircraft etc 上〔汽車、火車、飛機等〕: *The bus stopped and everyone rushed to get on.* 公共汽車停下來後, 人們一擁而上。**6** if a machine, light etc is on, it is operating〔機器、燈等〕工作[運轉]着的: *Who left the hot water faucet on?* 誰把熱水龍頭開着? | *The TV's on but nobody seems to be watching it.* 電視開着, 但好像沒人在看。—opposite 反義詞 OFF[1] (4) **7** if a film, TV programme etc is on, it is being broadcast or shown at a theatre〔電影、電視節目等〕正在播放[放映]的: *That new sitcom is on tonight.* 那部新拍的情境喜劇將於今晚播映。**8** if an event is on, it is happening or will still happen 正在[將要]發生: *There's a jazz festival on in Vancouver this week.* 爵士音樂節於本週在溫哥華舉行。| *Are you sure the party's on for tonight?* 你肯定聚會是今晚舉行嗎? **9 have a lot on** *informal* to be very busy【非正式】十分忙碌: *We don't have much on at the moment. I could see you tomorrow.* 我們現在不怎麼忙, 明天我可以見你。**10 be on at sb** *informal* to keep asking someone to do something, so that they become annoyed【非正式】向某人嘮叨, 不停地催促某人〔做某事〕: *Mildred's been on at him to fix that cupboard for weeks now.* 米爾德麗德要他修理那個碗櫃, 都嘮叨了好幾個星期了。**11 be/go on about sth** *informal BrE* to keep talking about something, in a way that is boring【非正式, 英】〔令人生厭地〕不斷談論某事物: *Will you stop going on about that goal! It was definitely a penalty.* 你別再嘮叨那個進球啦! 那肯定是個罰球。**12 on and off** also 又作 **off and on** if you do something during a period of time on and off, you do it for several short periods in that time but not continually 斷斷續續地, 間歇地: *He's been smoking for 10 years now, on and off.* 到現在, 他斷斷續續地吸煙有十年了。**13 it's not on** *spoken BrE* used to say that you do not think something is socially acceptable or reasonable【口, 英】這不可以, 這不能接受, 這不合理: *It's not on, is it? Leaving your children alone like that.* 這是說不過去的, 不是嗎? 就那樣把你的孩子撇下不管。**14 head on/full on** if two things hit each other head on, they hit the front part of each other, usually very hard 迎面地, 迎頭地: *Both cars skidded, crashing head on at 80 miles an hour.* 兩輛車都打滑了, 以每小時80英里的速度迎頭相撞。**15** if an actor is on, they are performing〔演員〕正在演出, 在表演中的: *You're on in two minutes.* 你兩分鐘後上場。

on-air /ˈ· ·/ *adj* [only before noun 僅用於名詞前] broadcast while actually happening 現場直播的: *an on-air interview* 現場採訪

once[1] /wʌns; wʌns/ *adv*

1 ▶ONE TIME 一次◀ on one occasion 一次, 一回: *I've only met her once.* 我只見過她一面。| **once before** *Paul's been to Wexford once before.* 保羅曾去過韋克斯福德一次。

2 once a week/year etc one time every week etc as a regular activity 每週/每年等一次: *We do aerobics once a week.* 我們每週做一次有氧健身操。

3 at once a) immediately or without delay 立刻, 馬上: *Young lady, get upstairs and clean your room at once!* 小姐, 趕快上樓去打掃你的房間! **b)** at the same time, together 同時; 一起: *Don't all talk at once.* 不要同時都發言。

4 all at once if something happens all at once, it happens suddenly when you do not expect it 一下子; 突然: *All at once there was a loud banging on the door.* 突然傳來一記重重的敲門聲。

5 once more one more time or again 再一次: *Can we go please Daddy, just once more!* 請讓我們去吧, 爸爸, 就再去一次嘛!

6 once again/once more again, after happening several times before〔像從前那樣〕再次, 又一次: *Once again she's refusing to help.* 她再一次拒絕幫忙。

7 once or twice a few times 一兩次, 幾次: *I've driven down here once or twice before.* 我以前開車來過這裡幾次。

8 once in a while sometimes, although not often 偶爾, 有時, 間或: *It'd be nice if you'd write to me once in a while.* 你要是能偶爾給我來封信就好了。

9 ▶IN THE PAST 從前◀ at some time in the past, but not now 過去, 以前: *Franklyn had obviously been handsome once.* 顯然富蘭克林以前挺英俊的。| **once-great/beautiful etc** *It was sad to see the once-great man looking so frail.* 看見那個曾經叱咤一時的人如此虛弱, 真令人難過。

10 once in a blue moon *informal* very rarely【非正式】極為罕見, 難得一次

11 (just) for once *spoken* used to say that something hardly ever happens, although it should happen often【口】難得一次, 就這一回: *Just for once I'd like to see him cook dinner.* 我就想看看他做一次飯。| *Well, for once he's being nice to me.* 嗯, 他就這一回對我好。

12 (just) this/the once *spoken* used to emphasize that this is the only time that you will let someone do something, or ask someone to do something【口】僅這一回, 就這一次: *Go on, lend me the car, just this once.* 來吧, 把車借給我吧, 就這一次。

13 once and for all a) if you deal with something once and for all, you deal with it definitely and finally 一勞永逸地: *Let's settle this matter once and for all.* 讓我們一勞永逸地解決這個問題吧。**b)** *spoken* used to say that you are asking someone to do something for the last time, and they must do it【口】最後一次〔要求某人必須做某事〕: *Once and for all, will you switch off that television!* 最後說一次, 把那電視關掉!

14 once upon a time a) used at the beginning of children's stories 從前, 很久以前〔用於兒童故事的開頭〕**b)** *spoken* at a time in the past that you think was much better than now【口】那時候〔指比現在好得多的過去某一時期〕: *Once upon a time you used to be able to leave your front door unlocked.* 那時候, 你的前門總是可以不上鎖。

15 do sth once too often to be hurt because of something dangerous or stupid that you have done 某事做得太多〔而遭殃〕

16 the once *spoken* on one particular occasion【口】一次, 一回: *I've only met her the once.* 我就見過她那麼一次。

17 once bitten, twice shy used to say that people will not do something again if it has been a bad experience 一遭被咬, 下次膽小; 一朝被蛇咬, 十年怕草繩

once[2] *conjunction* from the moment that something happens 一…便, 一旦, 一經: *Once she arrives, we can start.* 她一到, 我們就可以開始。| *Once in bed, the children usually stay there.* 小孩子一上牀一般就不再下來。

once-o-ver /ˈ· ˌ··/ *n* **give sb/sth the once-over** to look at someone or something quickly to check who they are or what they are like 粗略地看某人/某物一眼, 草草過目: *A guard gave us the once-over before letting us in the door.* 警衛掃了一眼就讓我們進門了。

on-com-ing /ˈɑnˌkʌmɪŋ; ˈɒnˌkʌmɪŋ/ *adj* **oncoming car/traffic etc** a car etc that is coming towards you 迎面而來的汽車/車流等

one[1] /wʌn; wʌn/ *number* **1** the number one〔數字〕1, 一: *one hundred and twenty one pounds (£121)* 121英鎊 | *The answer is on page forty-one.* 答案在第四十一頁上。| *Can I have one coffee and two milkshakes please?* 請給我一杯咖啡、兩杯奶昔好嗎? **2 one or two** a small number of people or things 一兩個, 很少的: *There are one or two things to sort out before I leave.* 我在走之前還要處理一兩件事。**3 in ones and twos** if people do something in ones and twos they do it on their own or in small groups 三三兩兩地, 零零落落地: *Guests arrived in ones and twos.* 客人三三兩兩地到來了。**4 a)** *AmE* a one dollar bill【美】一張一美元的紙幣 **b)** *BrE* a one pound coin【英】一個一英鎊的硬幣 **5 for one thing** *spoken* used to introduce the first of several reasons【口】其中一個理由是，一則: *You can't see in that fridge, for one thing the light's gone and for another the button's broken.* 你看不清那個冰箱裡的東西，一是燈不亮，二是開關壞了。**6 one-armed/one-eyed/one-legged etc** having only one arm, eye, leg etc 獨臂的／獨眼的／一條腿的

1 1 **one²** *determiner* **1** a person or thing, especially when there are other people or things of the same type or kind〔尤指同類中的〕一個人；一樣東西，一件事: *Sam's just heard that one of his houses has caught fire.* 山姆剛得知他的其中一棟房子着火了。| *If there's one thing I can't stand it's people who bite their nails.* 如果說有一件事讓我無法忍受，那就是有些人咬自己的指甲。| *There's one person I really must thank.* 有一個人我真的要感謝。**2 one day/afternoon/year etc a)** a particular day, afternoon etc in the past 過去的某一天／某個下午／某一年等: *We first met one cloudy day last July.* 我們初次見面是在去年七月的一個陰天。| *One morning I was sitting at my desk when a policeman knocked at my door.* 一天上午我正坐在書桌旁，突然有個警察敲門。**b)** any day, afternoon etc at any time in the future 未來的任何一天／一個下午／一年等: *One evening you and I should go out for a drink.* 哪天晚上我和你去外面喝一杯。**3 sb's one fear/worry/concern etc** someone's main fear, worry etc 某人主要的擔心／憂慮／掛慮等: *My one fear is that her nerves will get the better of her.* 我最擔心的是她會神經緊張。**4 the one man/place etc** the only man, place etc 唯一的人／地方等: *Claire is the one person I can trust.* 克萊爾是我唯一能信任的人。| *I'm sorry madam, we've only the one ticket left.* 對不起，夫人，我們只剩下這一張票。**5** used to talk about one person or thing in comparison with other similar or connected people or things〔一羣類似的或有關的人或物中的〕某一個: *It's impossible to tell one child from another in that family.* 那家的孩子讓人難以分清誰是誰。| *One of the gang broke into the safe while the other was keeping watch.* 歹徒中的一人撬開保險箱，另一人在把風。| **It's one thing... but...** *It's one thing passing your driving test but being a good driver is another.* 通過駕車考試是一回事，但成為一個好司機則是另一回事。**6** *formal* used before the name of someone who you do not know well【正式】某位〔用於不太熟悉之人的姓名之前〕: *It seems the inheritance went to an old family friend, one Joseph Nelson.* 繼承權似乎歸於家族的一位老朋友，一個叫約瑟夫·納爾遜的人。**7 one wonderful woman/one interesting job etc** *spoken especially AmE* a very wonderful woman, a very interesting job etc【口，尤美】一位非常出色的女性／一份很有趣的工作等: *Hey, your brother is one amazing guy!* 嗨，你兄弟真是個不尋常的傢伙！**8 one by one/one after another** if people do something one by one, first one person does it, then the next, then the next etc 一個接一個地／依次地: *One by one each soldier approached the coffin and gave a final salute.* 士兵一個個地依次走到靈柩跟前，致以最後的敬禮。**9 I/John etc for one** used to emphasize that you are doing something, believe something etc and hope others will do the same 拿我／約翰等來說〔用於強調某人會怎麼做、怎麼認為等，並希望別人也會如此〕: *If they continue to abuse civil rights, I for one will be boycotting any food they produce.* 如果他們繼續濫用公民權，我首先就會罷買他們生產的任何食品。**10 (all) in one** if someone or something is many different things all in one, they are all of those things 合為一體，一起，兼: *She's president, secretary and treasurer all in one.* 總裁、祕書和會計都由她一個人兼任。**11 be one up (on sb)** to have an advantage over someone 比(某人)佔優勢，佔(某人的)上風，略勝一籌 —see also 另見 ONE-UPMANSHIP **12 put one over on sb** *informal* to trick someone【非正式】哄騙某人: *No one's going to put one over on me!* 誰也別想哄騙我！**13 get one over on sb** *informal* to get an advantage over someone【非正式】勝[強]過某人: *The easiest way to get one over on bullies is to answer them back.* 打敗霸道者最簡單的辦法就是以牙還牙。**14 the one and only** *informal* used to emphasize that someone is very famous【非正式】真正的〔用於強調某人非常有名〕: *"That wasn't George Best I saw you talking to, was it?" "The one and only!"* "我看到和你在說話的不會是喬治·貝斯特吧？""正是他！" **15 be at one with sb/sth a)** to feel very calm or relaxed because of the calm situation or environment you are in〔在安詳的環境中〕感到很鎮定[放鬆]: *a weekend in the country, when you can feel at one with nature* 在鄉村度過的一個週末，有一種與大自然融為一體的感覺 **b)** *formal* to agree with someone about something【正式】與某人意見一致: **16 a) be as one** *formal* to agree about something【正式】贊同〔某事〕: *The whole committee is as one on this – no women are allowed on the golf course.* 委員會全體贊同這一點 —— 女子不得進入高爾夫球場。**b) as one** if many people do something as one they all do it at the same time〔許多人〕同時，一起〔做某事〕: *The whole team stood up as one and marched out of the room.* 全隊同時站立起來，邁着大步走出房間。**17 got it in one!** *spoken* used to say that someone has guessed correctly【口】猜對了!: *"You're not painting the house again are you?" "Got it in one!"* "你不會又要刷房子吧？""猜對了！" **18 have one for the road** *informal* to have an alcoholic drink, especially the last one before you leave a place【非正式】喝一杯酒〔尤指離開某處前的最後一杯〕**19 you are/he is a one** *old-fashioned especially BrE* used to tell someone that they are being rude, foolish etc【過時，尤英】你／他真是粗魯[愚蠢]: *The patient in the end bed is a real one, I can tell you.* 最裡頭那張牀上的病人真是粗魯，我能肯定。—see also 另見 ONE-TO-ONE

one³ *pron plural* **ones 1** used instead of a noun that has already been mentioned or which the person you are talking to already knows about〔用於代替已提及的某個名詞或對方已知道的某個名詞〕: *I've always wanted a CD player and I've just saved enough money to buy one.* 我一直想要一個雷射唱機，現在我剛攢夠了買一個的錢。| *The train was crowded so we decided to catch a later one.* 這班火車太擠了，我們決定乘坐下一班。| **the one that/who/which etc** *Soufflés are so hard to cook. Why is it that the ones I make always sink?* 蛋奶酥真是難做，為甚麼我做的那些總是塌下去？| **this one/that one/these ones/those ones** *I'll take that one, the one with all the chocolate on top.* 我要那個，就是上頭全是巧克力的那個。**2** *formal* used when you mean YOU (2), especially when you do not mean any one person in particular【正式】任何人〔尤用於泛指時〕: *One asks oneself where children learn to behave so badly.* 誰都該問問自己，孩子是從哪裡學壞的。**3 the one about ...** *especially spoken* a joke or humorous story【尤口】關於…的笑話[幽默故事]: *Have you heard the one about the dog that thought it was a cat?* 你聽過那個關於狗把自己當作貓的笑話嗎？**4 a...one** a particular kind of problem, question, story etc 一個…的難題[問題、故事等]: *"Excuse me, can you tell me the way to the bank?" "Oh, that's a hard one, it's either the second or the third road on the left."* "對不起，你能告訴我去銀行的路嗎？""噢，這有點難說，該是左邊第二條或是第三條馬路。" **5 not be one to do sth/not be one who does sth** *informal* to never do a particular thing, especially something that annoys people【非正式】決不做某事〔尤指讓人生氣的事〕: *I'm never one to complain, as you know, but I do think you could come and visit me more often.* 你知道，我這人從來不愛抱怨，但我真的認為你可以多來看看我。**6 be one for** *informal* to enjoy doing a particular sport, subject etc【非正式】喜愛〔某種體育運動、學科等〕: *I've never been (a great) one for watersports.* 我一向都不(很)喜歡水上運動。**7 one and the same** the same person or thing 同一個人[物]: *Muhammad Ali and Cassius Clay are one and the same.* 穆罕默德·阿里和凱薩斯·克萊是同一個人。**8 one and all** *old-fashioned* everyone【過

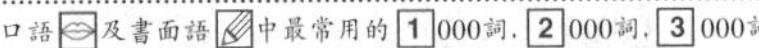

時】每個人，全體: *The bride was welcomed by the family, one and all.* 新娘受到全家所有人的歡迎。**9 be one of the family/the boys** to be accepted as a member of a particular group of people 接納為家庭/男孩中的一員: *It took me a while to settle in but I just feel like one of the family now.* 我過了一段時間才適應，但現在感覺就像是家庭中的一員了。**10 one of us** *especially spoken* used to say that someone is a member of the same group that you are in and has the same ideas, beliefs etc【尤口】我們自己人: *You can talk in front of Terry – he's one of us.* 你可以在特里面前說話，他是我們自己人。**11 the little/young ones** *humorous or old-fashioned* children, especially young children【幽默或過時】孩子，小傢伙〔尤指小孩子〕

O

USAGE NOTE 用法說明: ONE
FORMALITY 正式程度

One meaning 'people in general' is very formal. Most people usually use **you** with the same meaning. one 作"任何人"解時是非常正式的詞。大多數人通常用 you 來表示同樣的意思。Compare 比較: *One can do what one likes here.* | *You can do what you like here.* 在這裡，人們愛幹甚麼就幹甚麼。

You use **one** instead of repeating a noun phrase in both spoken and written English. 在英語口語和書面語中，都可以用 one 來避免重複一個名詞片語: *The reason is basically an economic one.* 原因主要是經濟方面的。

You can use **ones** when two adjectives are used to compare things, but it is best to avoid this in formal written English. 當兩個形容詞用於比較複數之物時，可以用 ones，但在正式書面語中最好避免這種用法: *He buys German rather than British cars* (formal 正式). 他買德國汽車而非英國汽車。| *He buys German cars rather than British ones* (informal 非正式). 他買德國汽車而不買英國的。

S3 W3 **one an·oth·er** /ˌ· ˈ··/ *pron* each other 互相，彼此: *Liz and I have known one another for years.* 我和利茲相識好多年了。| *They often stay at one another's houses.* 他們經常住在彼此的家裡。—compare 比較 EACH OTHER

one-armed ban·dit /ˌ· · ˈ··/ *n* [C] a machine with a long handle, into which you put money in order to try to win more money 吃角子老虎，獨臂強盜〔指用一臂狀桿操縱放入硬幣賭博的機器〕; FRUIT MACHINE *BrE*【英】; SLOT MACHINE *AmE*【美】

one-horse /ˈ· ·/ *adj* **1 one-horse town** *informal* a small and boring town【非正式】沉悶的小鎮: *I can't wait to get out of this one-horse town!* 我恨不得馬上就能離開這個死氣沉沉的鄉下小鎮! **2** pulled by one horse 由一匹馬拉的: *a one-horse plough* 單匹馬拉的犁

one-lin·er /ˌ· ˈ··/ *n* [C] a very short joke or humorous remark 很短的笑話; 俏皮話，打趣話

one-man /ˈ· ·/ *adj* [only before noun 僅用於名詞前] performed, operated, controlled etc by one person 由一人表演[經營、控制]的: *He does a one-man show in Las Vegas.* 他在拉斯維加斯表演獨角戲。| *a one-man business* 一人經營的生意

one-man band /ˌ· · ˈ·/ *n* [C] **1** *informal* an organization or activity in which one person does everything【非正式】唱獨腳戲式的組織[活動]: *The company is really a one-man band.* 這家公司其實只有一個人在唱獨腳戲。**2** a street musician who plays several instruments at the same time 單人樂隊〔一個同時演奏多種樂器的街頭藝人〕

one-night stand /ˌ· · ˈ·/ *n* [C] **1** *informal*【非正式】**a)** an occasion when two people have sex, but do not intend to meet each other again 一夜情，一宿風流: *I'm not into one-night stands.* 我對一夜情不感興趣。**b)** a person that you have sex with once and do not see again 一夜情人〔有過一夜性關係後再未見過的人〕**2** a performance of music or a play that is given only once in a particular place 在某地僅表演一次的（巡迴）演出: *The band had a series of one-night stands around the country.* 這支樂隊在全國各地巡迴演出，每個地方只表演一場。

one-off¹ /ˌ· ˈ·◂/ *adj* [only before a noun 僅用於名詞前] *BrE* happening or done only once, not as part of a regular series【英】只發生一次的; 一次完成的; ONE-SHOT *AmE*【美】: *Yours for a one-off payment of only £200.* 只要一次付完 200 英鎊，這東西就是你的了。

one-off² *n* [C] *BrE*【英】**1** something that is done or made only once 只做過一次的事; 一次性事物: *I missed my chance. The deal was a one-off.* 我錯過了機會，這種事情只有一次。**2** *informal* someone who is completely different from anyone else【非正式】與他人完全不同者

one-pa·rent fam·i·ly /ˌ·· ˈ···/ *n* [C] a family in which there is only one parent who looks after the children 單親家庭

one-piece /ˈ· ·/ *adj* [only before noun 僅用於名詞前] consisting of only one piece, not separate parts 單件的，上下連身的: *a one-piece bathing suit* 連衣褲泳裝

o·ner·ous /ˈɑnərəs; ˈɒnərəs/ *adj formal* work or RESPONSIBILITY that is onerous is difficult and worrying or makes you tired【正式】繁重的，艱巨的，困難的: *an onerous task* 艱巨的任務 | *onerous duties* 繁重的職責 —**onerously** *adv* —**onerousness** *n* [U]

one·self /wʌnˋsɛlf; wʌnˈself/ *pron formal* the reflexive form of ONE³ (2)【正式】自己，自身〔one 的反身代詞〕: *It is only through study that one really begins to know oneself.* 人只有通過學習才能逐漸認識自己。—see 見 ONE (USAGE)

one-shot /ˈ· ·/ *adj AmE* happening or done only once【美】只發生一次的; 一次完成的; ONE-OFF *BrE*【英】: *It's a one-shot deal. You don't get any second chances.* 這次交易只此一回，不會有第二次機會。

one-sid·ed /ˌ· ˈ··◂/ *adj* **1** considering or showing only one side of a question, subject etc in a way that is unfair 片面的，偏頗的，偏於一方的，不公正的: *The newspapers give a very one-sided account of the war.* 報紙對這場戰爭作了非常片面的報道。**2** an activity or competition that is one-sided is one in which one person or side does what they want and the other can do nothing〔活動、比賽等〕一面倒的; 不均衡的: *a very boring, one-sided game* 一場很乏味的雙方實力懸殊的比賽 | *I'd say the conversation was pretty one-sided.* 我說這次對話很不對等。—**one-sidedly** *adv* —**one-sidedness** *n* [U]

one-star /ˈ· ·/ *adj* **one-star hotel/restaurant etc** a hotel etc that is not of a very high standard 一星級酒店/餐館等〔指質量不高〕

one-stop /ˈ· ·/ *adj AmE* **one-stop shop/store etc** a shop where you can buy many different things【美】一站式[綜合性]商店

one-time /ˈ· ·/ *adj* [only before noun 僅用於名詞前] former 從前的，一度的: *Neil McMurtry, a one-time busdriver, is the lead singer.* 內爾·麥克默特里以前是公共汽車司機，現在成了領唱歌手。

one-to-one /ˌ· · ˈ·◂/ *adj* **1** between only two people 只在兩人之間的，一對一的: *tuition on a one-to-one basis* 一對一的輔導 **2** matching each other exactly 完全對應的: *a one-to-one correlation* 完全對應的相互依存關係 —**one-to-one** *adv*: *I need to discuss it with him one-to-one.* 我需要和他面對面地商討此事。

one-track mind /ˌ· · ˈ·/ *n* **have a one-track mind** to be continuously thinking about one particular thing 腦子裡只想着一件事: *All you ever talk about is sex! You've got a one-track mind.* 你講的都是關於性的問題! 你滿腦子只有這一樣東西。

one-two /ˌ· ˈ·/ *n* [C] a movement in which a BOXER hits his opponent with one hand and then quickly with the other〔拳擊中〕連續左右猛擊: *Ali gives his opponent the old one-two, and it's all over.* 阿里左右開弓，向對手施展出他那一貫的二連擊，比賽就此結束了。

one-up·man·ship /ˌwʌnˋʌpmənˌʃɪp; wʌnˈʌpmənʃɪp/

n [U] the skill of making yourself seem better than other people 勝人一籌的本領

one-way /ˌ· ˈ·◂/ *adj* [usually before noun 一般用於名詞前] **1** moving or allowing movement in only one direction 單向的, 單行的: *one-way traffic* 單向交通 | *a one-way street* 單行街道 **2** *especially AmE* a one-way ticket is for travelling from one place to another but not back again【尤美】單程的; SINGLE[1] (6) *BrE*【英】—opposite 反義詞 RETURN[3], ROUND-TRIP **3** a one-way process, relationship etc is one in which only one person makes any effort 單方面的

one-way mir·ror /ˌ· · ˈ··/ *n* [C] a mirror which can be used as a window by people secretly watching from the other side of it 單向玻璃鏡

one-wom·an /ˈ· ··/ *adj* [only before noun 僅用於名詞前] performed, operated, controlled etc by only one woman 只有一個女子表演[經營、控制等]的: *a one-woman show* 女子獨腳戲

on·go·ing /ˈɑnˌgoɪŋ; ˈɒnˌgəʊɪŋ/ *adj* [usually before noun 一般用於名詞前] continuing, or continuing to develop 繼續進行的; 不斷發展中的: *an ongoing search for a new director* 繼續尋找一位新主管 | *ongoing negotiations* 還在進行的談判

3 **on·ion** /ˈʌnjən; ˈʌnjən/ *n* [C,U] **1** a round white vegetable with a brown skin and many layers, that has a strong taste and smell 洋葱(頭) —see picture on page A9 參見A9頁圖 **2 know your onions** *BrE informal* to know a lot about something【英, 非正式】精通某事

on·ion·skin /ˈʌnjənskɪn; ˈʌnjənskɪn/ *n* [U] *AmE* very thin light paper, used especially for writing letters on【美】〔尤用於寫信的〕薄光澤紙

on·line /ˈɑnˌlaɪn; ˈɒnlaɪn/ *adj* directly connected to or controlled by a computer〔電腦〕聯機的;〔與電腦〕聯線的: *an online printer* 聯機打印機 —**online** *adv*

on·look·er /ˈɑnˌlʊkɚ; ˈɒnˌlʊkə/ *n* [C] someone who watches something happening without being involved in it 旁觀者, 觀看者: *A crowd of onlookers had gathered at the scene of the accident.* 一羣旁觀者圍聚在事故現場。—see also 另見 **look on** (LOOK[1])

1 1 **on·ly**[1] /ˈonlɪ; ˈəʊnli/ *adv* **1** not more than a particular amount, number, age etc 僅僅, 才: *Naomi was only 17 when she got married.* 尚美結婚時才17歲。| *Only five minutes more, and then we can go home.* 只要再過五分鐘, 我們就可以回家了。**2** nothing or no one except 只限, 只有: *Only the president can authorize a nuclear attack.* 只有總統才能授權發動核攻擊。| *Get me some peaches, but only pick the ones that are ripe.* 給我弄些桃子來, 但只能摘那些熟了的。| **staff/women/men etc only** *The car park is for staff only.* 那個停車場只限員工使用。**3** not better, worse, or more important than 只不過, 只是: *I didn't mean what I said. It was only a joke.* 我說的並不算數, 那不過是一個玩笑。| *It's no good asking me. I'm only the cleaner.* 問我沒有用, 我只是一個清潔工。**4** in one place, situation, or way and no other, or for one reason and no other 只在; 只因為: *a plant that is only found in Madagascar* 一種只產於馬達加斯加的植物 | *I only did it for the money.* 我做這事只是為了那筆錢。| *I'll tell you, but only if you promise not to tell anyone else.* 如果你保證不告訴任何人, 我就告訴你。—see 見 UNIQUE (USAGE) **5** no earlier than a particular time 不早於: *I only got here last night.* 我昨晚才到這裡。| **only yesterday/last week/recently** *They got married five weeks ago but I only heard about it yesterday.* 他們五週前已經結了婚, 但我只是昨天才聽說。| **only then** (=at that moment and not before) 只在那時 *Trevor sat in the dark, and it was only then that he realised how unhappy he was.* 特里沃坐在一片漆黑中, 直到那時他才意識到自己是多麼的不快樂。**6 only just** *especially BrE*【尤英】**a)** a moment ago 剛剛, 剛才: *No wonder she looks sleepy – she's only just got up.* 難怪她看上去睡眼惺忪的——她剛剛才起牀。**b)** almost not; hardly 幾乎不: *There's only just room for the two of us on the back seat.* 我們倆勉強才能擠在後座上。| *The dress fits her, but only just.* 這連衣裙她能穿上, 不過很勉強。**7 I only wish/hope** *spoken* used to express a strong wish or hope【口】但願/希望: *"What's going to happen after the divorce?" "I only wish I knew."* "離婚後會發生甚麼事?" "但願我能知道。" **8 if only** used to express a strong wish 但願, 真希望, 要是...就好了〔表示強烈的願望〕: *If only I had a car, I could get out of this place.* 要是我有輛車, 我就能離開這個地方了。**9 you'll only ...** used to tell someone that what they want to do will have a bad effect 你只會...: *Don't interfere, you'll only make things worse.* 別插手, 你只會把事情弄得更糟。**10 you only have to read/look at/listen to etc** *spoken* used to mean that it is easy to realise that something is true because you can see or hear things that prove it【口】你只要讀一讀/看一看/聽一聽等〔就會明白〕: *The situation's getting worse – you only have to look at the crime statistics.* 情況在惡化——你只要看看這犯罪的統計數字就會明白。**11 I can only assume/suppose etc** used to say that you can only think of one explanation for something surprising or disappointing 我只能認為: *I can only assume that there has been some kind of mistake.* 我只能認為出現了某種差錯。**12 only to...** used to say that someone did something, with a disappointing or surprising result 結果只是...: *Scott arrived at the South Pole on January 18th, only to find that Amundsen had got there before him.* 斯科特於1月18日到達南極, 結果卻發現阿蒙森已先於他到了那裡。**13 only too** very or completely 很, 非常; 完全: *Mark was only too ready to agree with her.* 馬克非常同意她。| **only too true/likely etc** (=used when something unpleasant is true etc)〔某件令人不快的事〕完全是事實/完全有可能等 *"Is it true that there's going to be a war?" "Only too true, I'm afraid."* "真的會發生一場戰爭嗎?" "恐怕很有可能。" —see also 另見 **not only...but (also)** (NOT (6)), **only have eyes for sb** (EYE[1] (25))

only[2] *adj* [only before noun 僅用於名詞前] **1 the only thing/person/way etc a)** the one single thing, person etc that there is when there are no others 唯一的東西/人/方法等: *Dan's the only guy in this office who smokes.* 丹是這個辦公室裡唯一抽煙的人。| *The only reason I came here was to see you.* 我來這裡的唯一原因是看望你。**b)** the best 最好的東西/人/方法等: *She's the only person for this job.* 她是擔任這一工作的最佳人選。| *I'd recommend Kensington. Honestly – it's the only place to live.* 我會推薦肯辛頓區。說實話, 這是最好的居住地點。**2 the only thing is...** *spoken* used when you are going to mention a problem or disadvantage about something【口】唯一的問題是...: *I'd be happy to take you to the airport. The only thing is I think my mother needs the car.* 我很樂意送你去機場, 唯一的問題是我想我母親要用這輛車。**3 an only child** a child who has no brothers or sisters 獨生子[女] — see also 另見 **the one and only** (ONE[2] (14)), **(only) time will tell** (TIME[1] (66)) 1 1

only[3] *conjunction informal* used like 'but' to introduce the reason why something is not possible【非正式】只是, 但是, 可是: *I'd offer to help you, only I'm really busy just now.* 我是想幫你的, 但眼下我實在很忙。

o.n.o *BrE* the written abbreviation of 縮寫= 'or nearest offer', used in advertisements to show that you may be willing to sell something for slightly less money than you have asked for【英】或最接近的價格〔廣告用語〕: *Bicycle for sale; £60 ono* 有腳踏車出售; 價格60英鎊, 可還價

on·o·mat·o·poe·ia /ˌɑnəˌmætəˈpiə; ˌɒnəmætəˈpiːə/ *n* [U] *technical* the use of words that sound like the thing that they are describing, like 'hiss' or 'boom'【術語】擬聲法構詞, 擬聲詞〈如hiss, 蛇、沸水等嘶嘶作聲; boom, 砲、雷等的隆隆聲〉—**onomatopoeic** *adj*

on-ramp /ˈ· ·/ *n* [C] *AmE* a road for driving onto a HIGHWAY(1)【美】〔高速公路的〕駛入坡道[匝道], 高速公路的支路 —see picture on page A3 參見A3頁圖

on·rush /ˈɑnˌrʌʃ; ˈɒnrʌʃ/ *n* [singular] a strong fast movement forward 向前猛衝, 急衝: **[+of]** *the second onrush of demonstrators* 示威者的第二次向前猛衝 —**onrushing** *adj*: *the onrushing tide* 洶湧的潮水

on-screen /ˌ· ˈ·◂/ *adv* if information appears or is written on-screen, it appears on the SCREEN of a computer 在電腦屏幕上: *I prefer to edit on-screen rather than on paper.* 我喜歡在屏幕上修改, 不喜歡在紙上。—**on-screen** *adj*

on·set /ˋɑnsɛt; ˈɒnset/ *n* **the onset of** the beginning of something, especially something unpleasant〔尤指某種不好事情的〕開始, 發作: *The enemy had to withdraw before the onset of winter.* 敵人不得不在冬季到來前撤退。

on·shore /ˋɑnˌʃɔr; ˌɒnˈʃɔː◂/ *adj* **1** on or near the land rather than in the sea 在陸地上的, 在岸上的, 在近岸處的: *onshore oil production* 近海石油生產 **2** moving towards the land 向陸地的, 朝着岸的: *strong onshore winds* 吹向陸地的強風 —**onshore** *adv*

on·side /ˌɑnˋsaɪd; ˌɒnˈsaɪd◂/ *adj, adv* in a position where you are allowed to play the ball in sports such as football〔足球等運動中〕沒有越位(的) —opposite 反義詞 OFFSIDE[1]

on·slaught /ˋɑnˌslɔt; ˈɒnslɔːt/ *n* [C] a very strong attack against someone or something 猛攻, 猛擊, 攻擊: *He was confident his armies could withstand the Allied onslaught.* 他有信心他的軍隊能夠抵擋盟軍的猛攻。| **[+on]** *an onslaught on their whole culture and way of life* 對他們整個文化和生活方式的猛烈抨擊

on-stream /ˌ· ˈ·◂/ *adv* in operation or ready to begin operation 投入生產; 處於開工狀態: *More hotel developments are due to come on-stream for the 1998-99 season.* 更多新開發的酒店要在 1998 年至 1999 年的季度投入使用。—**on-stream** *adj*

on·to /ˋɑntu; ˈɒntu; *before consonants* 子音前 ˋɑntə; ˈɒntə/ *prep* **1** used with verbs expressing movement meaning in or on a particular place 在…中; 到…之上: *The men managed to jump onto the train while it was moving.* 那些人設法跳上了正在行駛的火車。| *Some paint was dripping off the ceiling onto the floor.* 一些油漆正由天花板滴落到地板上。**2 a) be onto sb** *informal* to know who did something wrong, committed a crime etc【非正式】知道某人的錯事[罪行等]: *The police are onto him.* 警察盯上他了。**b) be/get onto sb** *especially BrE* to get in contact with someone【尤英】與某人聯絡: *Get onto the hospital and see if they can spare extra nurses.* 與這家醫院聯絡, 看他們能不能抽調一些額外的護士。**3 be onto a good thing/a winner** *informal* to be in a very good situation that gives you many advantages【非正式】處境不錯, 找到了一個有利可圖的位置: *She's onto a real winner with that job.* 有了那份工作, 她就是一個真正的贏家。**4** if something such as a room looks or gives onto another room, a view etc, that is what you can see from that room or where that room leads〔房間等〕面向, 面對; 通向: *The main sitting area looked out onto a beautiful view of the hills.* 主要的起居室面對着一片峯巒疊嶂的美景。

on·tol·o·gy /ɑnˋtɑlədʒɪ; ɒnˈtɒlədʒi/ *n* [U] a subject of study in PHILOSOPHY that is concerned with the nature of existence〔哲學中的〕本體論, 實體論 —**ontological** /ˌɑntəˋlɑdʒɪkl; ˌɒntəˈlɒdʒɪkəl◂/ *adj*

o·nus /ˋonəs; ˈəʊnəs/ *n* **the onus** the responsibility for something〔對某事的〕責任, 義務: **the onus is on sb (to do sth)** *The onus is on the prosecution to provide proof of guilt.* 控方有責任提供(疑犯)有罪的證據。

on·ward /ˋɑnwəd; ˈɒnwəd/ *adj* [only before noun 僅用於名詞前] **1** moving forward or continuing 向前的; 繼續的: *the onward journey* 繼續向前的旅程 **2** developing over a period of time〔在某一時期內〕發展的, 進步的: *the onward march of scientific progress* 科學發展的前進步伐

on·wards /ˋɑnwədz; ˈɒnwədz/ usually 一般作 **onward** *AmE*【美】*adv* **1** forwards 向前: *The ship sailed majestically onwards.* 那艘船威風凜凜地向前駛去。**2 from... onwards** beginning at a particular time and continuing after that time 從…起: *I'm on call at the hospital from midnight onwards.* 我從半夜起在醫院值班。

on·yx /ˋɑnɪks; ˈɒnɪks/ *n* [U] a stone with lines of different colours in it, often used in jewellery 縞瑪瑙〔常用於珠寶首飾〕

oo·dles /ˋudl̩z; ˈuːdlz/ *n* [plural] *informal* a large amount of something【非正式】大量, 許多: **[+of]** *Give me oodles of cream. I love it.* 給我多來些奶油, 我愛吃。

oof /uf; uːf/ *interjection* the sound that you make when you have been hit, especially in the stomach 哎喲, 哎唷〔挨打時發出的聲音, 尤被打中肚子時〕

ooh /u; uː/ *interjection* used when you think something is very beautiful, unpleasant, surprising etc 嗬〔用於覺得某事物很美麗、很討厭、很令人驚訝等時〕: *"Look what I've bought." "Ooh!"* "看我買了甚麼。" "嗬!"

ooh la la /ˌu lɑ ˋlɑ; ˌuː lɑː ˈlɑː/ *interjection French humorous* used when you think that something or someone is surprising, unusual, or sexually attractive【法, 幽默】嗬啦啦〔覺得某事或某人令人驚訝、異乎尋常或漂亮性感時的用語〕

oomph /ʊmf; ʊmf/ *n* [U] *informal*【非正式】**1** energy 精力, 活力: *It's not a bad song, but it needs more oomph.* 這是一首不錯的歌曲, 但還要更強勁些。**2** sexual attractiveness 性感, 魅力

oops /ʊps; ʊps/ *interjection* used when someone has fallen, dropped something, or made a small mistake 哎喲, 啊呀〔某人摔倒、掉了某物或出了點小差錯時的用語〕: *Oops! Sorry, Calvin, I didn't mean to bump into you like that.* 啊呀, 對不起, 卡爾文, 我不是故意這麼撞你的。

oops-a-dai·sy /ˋ· · ˌ··/ *interjection* used when someone has fallen, especially a child 一, 二, 三, 起來了〔用於某人摔倒時, 尤指小孩〕

ooze[1] /uz; uːz/ *v* **1** [I always+adv/prep, T] if a liquid oozes from something or if something oozes a liquid, liquid flows from it very slowly 滲出; 慢慢地冒出; 分泌出: **[+from/out]** *Great tears oozed out from between her tight-shut eyelids.* 淚水從她那緊閉的雙眼中滲出。| **ooze sth** *The stone walls of the cottage oozed moisture.* 小屋的石牆上滲出水分。**2** [I,T] to show a lot of a particular quality or feeling 顯示出〔特質或情感〕: *oozing charm from every pore* 每一個毛孔都散發着魅力 | **[+with]** *oozing with sexuality* 顯示性徵

ooze[2] *n* **1** [U] very soft mud, especially at the bottom of a lake or the sea〔尤指湖底或海底的〕淤泥, 軟泥 **2** [singular] a very slow flow of liquid〔液體的〕緩緩流動, 流淌

ooz·y /ˋuzɪ; ˈuːzi/ *adj* soft and wet like mud 泥濘的, 淤泥的

Op the written abbreviation of 縮寫= OPUS

op /ɑp; ɒp/ *n* [C] *BrE informal* a medical operation【英, 非正式】醫療手術

o·pac·i·ty /oˋpæsɪtɪ; əʊˈpæsəti/ *n* [U] **1** the quality of being difficult to understand 難解, 晦澀 **2** the quality of being difficult to see through 不透明性[度]: *different degrees of opacity and translucence* 不同程度的不透明性和半透明性

o·pal /ˋopl̩; ˈəʊpəl/ *n* [C,U] a type of white stone with changing colours in it, or a piece of this stone used in jewellery 蛋白石

o·pa·les·cent /ˌoplˋɛsn̩t; ˌəʊpəˈlesənt◂/ *adj* having colours that shine and seem to change 乳白的, 乳色的; 發乳光的: *The sky shone a pale, opalescent blue.* 天空發出一種朦朧的乳光藍。—**opalescence** *n* [U]

o·paque /oˋpek; əʊˈpeɪk/ *adj* **1** glass, liquid etc that is opaque is too thick or too dark to see through〔玻璃、液體等〕不透明的: *There was a shower with an opaque glass door.* 有一個淋浴間裝着不透明的玻璃門。**2** speech or writing that is opaque is difficult to understand〔演講或文章〕難理解的, 晦澀的: *very opaque style of writing* 晦澀的寫作風格 —**opaquely** *adv* —**opaqueness** *n* [U]

—compare 比較 TRANSPARENT —see also 另見 OPACITY

op art /'· ·/ *n* [U] a form of art using patterns that seem to move or to produce other shapes as you look at them 歐普藝術, 視幻藝術, 光效應藝術

op cit an abbreviation used in formal writing to refer to a book that has been mentioned before 在前面所引用的書中〔用於正式的文章中〕

ope /op; əʊp/ *v* [I,T] *poetic* to open【詩】打開; 把…張開

OPEC /ˈopɛk; ˈəʊpek/ *n* [U] Organization of Petroleum Exporting Countries; an organization of nations that produce and sell oil and which fixes the price of the oil 石油輸出國組織, 歐佩克

op-ed /,· '·/ *adj AmE informal* **op-ed page** the page in a newspaper that has articles containing opinions on various interesting subjects【美, 非正式】〔報紙的〕專欄版, 特寫稿版

1 1

o·pen¹ /ˈopən; ˈəʊpən/ *adj*

① NOT CLOSED 未關閉的
② NOT ENCLOSED 敞開的, 開曠的
③ NOT UNDER A ROOF/COVER 無遮蓋的/未覆蓋的
④ READY FOR SERVICE 準備好提供服務的
⑤ AVAILABLE 現成可使用的
⑥ NOT RESTRICTED 不受限制的
⑦ NOT DECIDED 未決定的
⑧ NOT HIDING ANYTHING 不加隱瞞的
⑨ OTHER MEANINGS 其他意思

open 開着的

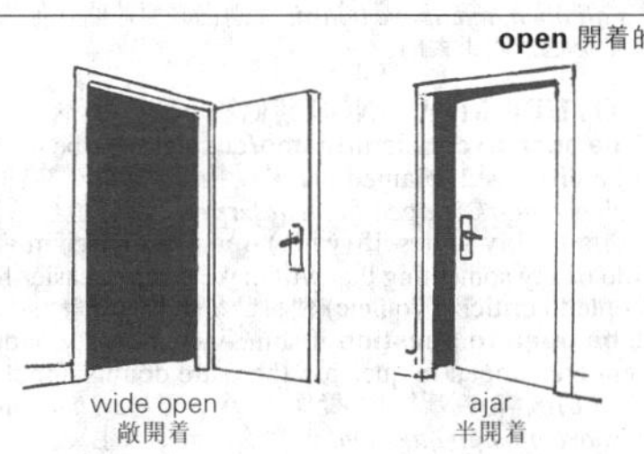

① NOT CLOSED 未關閉的

1 ▶DOOR/CONTAINER 門/容器◀ not closed, so that you can go through, take things out, or put things in 開着的: *an open window* 開着的窗子 | *I guess I did leave the door open.* 我想我的確沒關門。| *I can't get this milk open.* 我打不開這瓶牛奶。| **wide open** (=completely open) 敞開着 *The door was wide open and we could hear everything she said.* 門大開着, 她說甚麼我們都能聽見。| **fly/blow/burst open** *A suitcase fell off the cart and burst open.* 箱子掉下馬車, 一下子撞開了。| **push/slide/throw sth open** *Fran flung the window open and screamed.* 弗蘭猛地推開窗子, 尖叫起來。| **tear/rip sth open** *He snatched the envelope from me and ripped it open.* 他從我手中搶過信去撕開了。

2 ▶EYES/MOUTH 眼睛/嘴巴◀ not closed 未合上的, 張開的: *I was so sleepy, I couldn't keep my eyes open.* 我睏得眼睛都睜不開了。| **wide open** (=completely open) 大張着 *Ben gaped at me, his mouth wide open.* 本愣愣地看着我, 大張着嘴巴。

3 ▶BOOK 書◀ a book that is open has its pages moved apart so that you can read it 打開的: *A book lay open on the table.* 桌上放着一本打開的書。

4 ▶NOT BLOCKED 無障礙的◀ if a road or line of communication is open, it is not blocked and can be used 可通行的: *We try to keep the mountain roads open all through the winter.* 我們要盡力保證那些山路在整個冬季都暢通無阻。

5 ▶CLOTHES 衣服◀ not fastened 未繫好的; 未扣上的: *His shirt was open at the neck.* 他襯衫的領口敞開着。

② NOT ENCLOSED 敞開的, 開曠的

6 [only before noun 僅用於名詞前] not behind a cover or surrounded by a structure 敞開的; 未被圍起的: *goods displayed on the open shelves* 開架陳列的商品 | *An open fire is cosier than central heating.* 明火比集中供暖系統更暖和舒服。

7 open country/fields/space countryside where there are no buildings, walls etc 空曠[開闊]的郊野/田野/地方: *To the east, through miles of suburban streets, lay the open country.* 往東穿過數英里的市郊大街就是空曠的郊外。

8 the open sea sea that is far from any land 外海, 外洋; 公海: *The battered boat slowly drifted out towards the open sea.* 那艘撞壞的船隻緩慢地漂向外海。

9 the open road roads that you can travel on freely or quickly 暢通無阻的道路: *The thought of the open road is already making my feet itch.* 想起那條快捷的公路我就腳板發癢, 躍躍欲試。

③ NOT UNDER A ROOF/COVER 無遮蓋的/未覆蓋的

10 in the open air/(out) in the open outdoors 在戶外, 在露天: *In the summer we have our meals in the open air.* 夏天我們在戶外吃飯。| *It was too cold to spend the night out in the open.* 在露天過夜太冷了。—see also 另見 OPEN-AIR

11 ▶NOT COVERED 未覆蓋的◀ without a roof or cover 無頂的, 無遮蓋的: *an open limousine* 敞篷豪華大轎車 | *an open sewer* 排污明溝 | **open to the sky/elements** (=without a roof) 無頂的, 露天的

④ READY FOR SERVICE 準備好提供服務的

12 ▶SHOP/BANK ETC 商店/銀行等◀ [not before noun 不用於名詞前] allowing customers to enter and ready to serve them 準備好營業的: *The bank is open until 12:00 on Saturdays.* 這家銀行星期六一直營業到12點。

13 declare sth open to officially state that a building is ready to be used, or that an organized event is ready to start 宣布大樓落成; 宣布活動開始: *I now declare the exhibition open.* 我現在宣布展覽會正式開幕。

⑤ AVAILABLE 現成可使用的

14 ▶OPPORTUNITY 機會◀ **be open to sb** if an opportunity or possible action is open to you, you have the chance to do it 對某人開放: *training opportunities open to science graduates* 面向理科畢業生的培訓機會 | *There is only one course of action open to me.* 我可採取的行動只有一個。

15 ▶JOB 工作◀ [not before noun 不用於名詞前] a job that is open is available〔職位〕空額的, 空缺的: *Is the vacancy still open?* 這職位還空缺着嗎?

⑥ NOT RESTRICTED 不受限制的

16 an open competition, discussion etc is one that anyone can join in〔競賽、討論等〕公開的: *the British Open Squash Championships* 英國壁球公開錦標賽 | **[+to]** *The competition is open to men and women of all ages.* 這項

比賽男女都可以參加，年齡不限。| **throw sth open to sb** *The discussion was thrown open to the studio audience.* 現場觀眾可自由參加討論。

17 be open to the public/be open to visitors etc if a place is open to the public etc, anyone can enter or visit it 向公眾/參觀者等開放: *The bar is open to non-residents.* 那家酒吧對非住客開放。

18 on the open market if something is sold on the open market, it is made available for anyone to buy 在公開市場上〔任何人都可購買〕: *This house would sell for £300,000 on the open market.* 這所房子在公開市場上會賣到30萬英鎊。

19 an open invitation a) an invitation to visit someone whenever you like 隨時歡迎的邀請 **b)** something that makes it easier for criminals to steal, cheat etc 給罪犯以方便之門的東西: *An unlocked car is an open invitation to thieves.* 汽車沒上鎖等於是請盜賊來偷。

⑦ **NOT DECIDED 未決定的**

20 a choice or question that is open has been considered but not finally decided〔選擇或問題〕未決定的，懸而未決的: *Who will lead the new party is still an open question.* 誰將領導這個新黨派還是個懸而未決的問題。| **leave it open** (=not decide yet) 暫不作決定

21 keep/leave your options open to delay any decision so that you can choose later 留有選擇餘地: *a flexible fare package for executives who need to keep their options open* 一整套靈活的票價，讓主管自由選擇

22 be open to discussion/negotiation if something is open to discussion etc, you can discuss it and suggest changes 尚可討論/談判: *The terms are open to negotiation.* 這些條款還可以談判。

23 keep/have an open mind to deliberately not make a decision or form a definite opinion about something 有意不作決定；不對某事存先入之見: *Try to keep an open mind on the subject until you've heard all the evidence.* 對這個問題先不要作定論，聽完所有的證詞再說吧。

24 be open to suggestions/offers to be ready to consider people's suggestions, or prices that people offer to pay 願意考慮建議/接受報價: *We're always open to suggestions about how we can improve our service.* 我們隨時歡迎你對於如何改進我們的服務提出建議。

⑧ **NOT HIDING ANYTHING 不加隱瞞的**

25 [only before noun 僅用於名詞前] actions, feelings, or intentions that are open are not hidden or secret〔行為、感情或目的〕公開的: *open threats against the president* 對總統公開的威脅 | *Ralph was looking at her in open admiration.* 拉爾夫不加掩飾地以欣賞的目光看着她。| **open hostility/rivalry/rebellion** *open rivalry between two of the big TV channels* 其中兩個主要電視頻道之間的公開競爭 | **open government** (=a system of government where information is freely available) 公開的政府 | **in open court** (= in a court of law where everything is public) 在公開法庭上 *allegations made in open court* 在公開法庭上所作的指控 | **(out) in/into the open** (=no longer secret) 公開(出來) *The public has a right to know what has been happening. Let's get it out in the open.* 公眾有權知道發生了甚麼事。我們把情況公開出來吧。| **an open secret** (=something that is supposed to be secret but that most people know about) 公開的祕密 *It was an open secret that he had links with far-right extremists.* 他與極右翼極端分子有瓜葛是公開的祕密。

26 ►HONEST 誠實的◄ honest and not wanting to hide any facts from other people 坦率的，坦誠的: **[+with]** *Let's be completely open with each other.* 讓我們彼此完全坦誠相對吧。| *frank and open discussions* 真誠坦率的討論 | *a friendly open smile* 友好坦誠的微笑 | **open and above board** (=done in a completely honest and legal way) 光明正大的 *We don't have to bribe anyone. It's all open and above board.* 我們沒必要賄賂任何人，這完全是光明正大的。

⑨ **OTHER MEANINGS 其他意思**

27 be open to criticism/blame/suspicion to be likely to be criticized, blamed etc 易受批評/指責/懷疑的: *Such a remark is open to misinterpretation.* 這種話易受曲解。| **lay yourself (wide) open to criticism etc** (=do or say something that will make it much easier for people to criticize you etc) 使自己易遭受批評等

28 be open to question if someone's honesty, judgment etc is open to question there are doubts about it〔某人的誠信、判斷等〕有疑問的，令人懷疑: *Their motives are open to question.* 他們的動機令人生疑。

29 keep your eyes/ears open to keep looking or listening so that you will notice anything that is important, dangerous etc 留心看着/聽着

30 greet/welcome sb with open arms to be very pleased to see someone 熱情地迎接/歡迎某人: *Wealthy investors are usually welcomed with open arms.* 有錢的投資者通常都很受歡迎。

31 be an open book to be something that you know and understand very well 是一目了然的事物: *The natural world was an open book to him.* 他對自然界瞭如指掌。

32 open weave/texture cloth with an open weave or texture has wide spaces between the threads 粗疏的織法/質地 — see also 另見 **keep your eyes open** (EYE[1] (15)), **with your eyes open** (EYE[1] (38)), OPEN-EYED

open² *v*

① OPEN (打)開
② START 開始
③ SPREAD/UNFOLD 展開/打開
④ OTHER MEANINGS 其他意思

① **OPEN (打)開**

1 ►DOOR/WINDOW ETC 門/窗等◄ a) [T] to move a door, window etc so that people, things, air etc can pass through 打開，開啟: *Open all the windows and let some fresh air in.* 打開所有的窗子，讓新鮮空氣進來。**b)** [I] to be moved in this way 開: *The bus doors open and close automatically.* 公共汽車的門是自動開關的。

2 ►CONTAINER/PACKAGE 容器/包裝盒◄ [T] to unfasten or remove the lid, top, or cover of a container, package etc 開；撕開；揭開: *I've asked the waiter to open a bottle of champagne.* 我叫了服務員開一瓶香檳。| *She opened the letters one by one and read them in silence.* 她把信一封一封地拆開，默默地看。

3 ►EYES 眼睛◄ a) open your eyes to raise your EYELIDS so that you can see 睜開眼睛 **b) open sb's eyes (to)** to make someone realize something that they had not realized before 使某人認清[了解]...: *Dan's remarks opened my eyes to the fact that he was only interested in my money.* 丹的話使我看清了這一事實: 他只是對我的錢財感興趣。

4 ►MOUTH 嘴巴◄ open your mouth to move your lips apart 張開嘴巴

5 ►BOOK 書◄ [T] to turn the covers and pages of a book so that you can read it 翻開, 打開: *Open your books to page 29.* 把書翻到第29頁。

6 ►OPEN A WAY THROUGH 開出一條通道◄ [T] to make it possible for cars, goods etc to pass through a place 開通, 打通: *They were clearing away snow to open the tunnel.* 他們在清掃積雪以開通隧道。| **open a border/frontier (to)** *The new republic has opened its borders to foreign trade.* 新的共和國已開放其邊境地區進行外貿。

② START 開始

7 ►SHOP/RESTAURANT ETC 商店/餐館等◄ a) [I] if a shop or office opens at a particular time, it starts business at that time 開始營業: *What time do the banks open?* 銀行甚麼時候開門(營業)? **b)** [I,T] if a new business such as a shop or restaurant opens or is opened, someone starts it〔商店、餐館等〕開業, 開張: *A new supermarket has opened.* 一家新的超級市場開張了。| *plans to open a chain of restaurants* 開辦連鎖式餐館的計劃

8 ►START AN ACTIVITY 開始一項活動◄ a) open an inquiry/investigation to start gathering information or opinions from a lot of people 展開調查: *Police have opened an investigation into the girl's disappearance.* 警方對那女孩的失蹤展開了調查。

9 ►MEETING/EVENT 會議/事情◄ [I,T] if a meeting etc opens or is opened in a particular way, it starts in that way〔會議等〕開幕, (使) 開始: *Our chairman opened the conference by welcoming new delegates.* 我們的主席以歡迎新代表來宣布大會揭幕。| **[+with]** *The concert opens with Beethoven's Egmont Overture.* 音樂會以貝多芬的《埃格蒙特序曲》開場。

10 ►FILM/PLAY ETC 電影/戲劇等◄ [I] to start being shown to the public 開始公演[公映]: *Bertolucci's new film opens in London on March 15th.* 貝托魯奇的新電影於3月15日在倫敦首映。

11 ►OFFICIAL CEREMONY 正式儀式◄ [T] to perform a ceremony in which you officially state that a building is ready to be used 為〔大樓等〕舉行揭幕典禮; 宣布…落成

12 open an account to start an account at a bank or other financial organization by putting money into it 開立賬戶

③ SPREAD/UNFOLD 展開/打開

13 [I,T] if something that is folded opens or you open it, you make it spread out into a wide shape (使) 展開, 打開: *His parachute failed to open.* 他的降落傘無法打開。| *I opened my umbrella.* 我打開了雨傘。

14 ►FLOWER/LEAF 花/葉◄ [I] if a flower or BUD opens, it spreads out wide 綻開, 綻放: *The buds are starting to open.* 花蕾開始綻放。

15 open your arms to stretch your arms wide apart 張開雙臂: *Marcus opened his arms in a welcoming gesture.* 馬庫斯張開雙臂以示歡迎。

④ OTHER MEANINGS 其他意思

16 open sth to the public to let people come and visit a house, garden etc 向公眾開放〔房屋、花園等〕: *For the first time, Buckingham Palace has been made open to the public.* 白金漢宮破天荒第一次向公眾開放。

17 open the door/way to to make an opportunity for something to happen 給…以機會, 給…敞開方便之門: *a joint venture that opens the way to wider international co-operation* 開拓更廣闊的國際合作之路的合資企業 | **open doors** *A degree no longer opens doors in the way it used to.* 學位不再像以前那樣使人無往而不利了。

18 open fire (on) to start shooting at someone or something (向…) 開火: *Troops opened fire on the rioters.* 軍隊向暴徒開火了。

19 open your mind to to be ready to consider or accept new ideas 樂於考慮[接受]〔新觀念〕

20 the heavens opened it started to rain heavily 天開始下大雨

21 open your heart (to) to tell someone your real thoughts and feelings because you trust them (對…) 敞開心扉, (向…) 傾吐心事 —see also 另見 **open the floodgates** (FLOODGATE (1))

open onto/into sth *phr v* [T] if a room, door etc opens onto or into another place, you can enter that other place directly through it〔房間、門等〕通往, 通向: *The living room opens into the dining room.* 起居室通往飯廳。| *patio doors opening onto the garden* 通向花園的露台門

open out *phr v* [I] **1** if a road, path, or passage opens out, it becomes wider〔道路或通道〕變寬, 變開闊: **[+into]** *Beyond the forest the path opened out into a track.* 過了森林, 這條小徑就拓寬成了小路。**2** *BrE* if someone opens out, they become less shy【英】變得不羞怯: *As she got to know us better, Lizzie gradually started to open out.* 莉齊跟我們熟了之後, 漸漸地就放開了。

open up *phr v*

1 ►LAND 土地◄ [I,T] if someone opens up an area of land, they make it easier to reach and ready for development 開發, 開拓, 開闢: **open sth ↔ up** *They saw the new railroad as a means of opening up the far west of the country.* 他們把這條新鐵路視為開發國家大西部的一種途徑。

2 ►SHOP/RESTAURANT ETC 商店/餐館等◄ a) [I,T] if a shop, restaurant etc opens up or is opened up, someone starts it (使) 開張, 開辦, 開設 **b)** [I] if a shop, office etc opens up at a particular time, it starts business at that time〔商店、辦公室等〕開始營業[辦公]

3 ►DOOR/BOX 門/箱子◄ [I,T] an expression meaning to open a door or something such as a box or case, often used to order someone to do this 開門, 打開, 開啟〔常用於命令某人〕: *Open up, this is the police.* 開門, 我們是警察。| **open sth ↔ up** *Is this your suitcase? Right, open it up.* 這是你的行李箱嗎? 好, 把它打開。

4 ►OPPORTUNITY 機會◄ [I,T] if an opportunity opens up or is opened up, it develops 展現, (使) 顯現, 開拓: *A new life was opening up before her.* 新生活展現在她面前。| **open sth ↔ up** *A move to New York would open up all kinds of exciting new possibilities.* 遷到紐約也許會帶來各種令人振奮的新機遇。

5 ►WITH A GUN 用槍砲◄ [I] to start shooting 開火, 射擊: *The enemy opened up with machine guns.* 敵人的機關槍開火了。

6 ►DISAGREEMENT 分歧, 不一致◄ [I,T] if a disagreement opens up or is opened up between people, it starts to divide them (使) 產生分歧, (使) 分裂: *A rift has opened up, splitting the committee down the middle.* 分歧出現了, 使委員會分裂成兩派。| **open sth ↔ up** *The abortion issue may open up a split in the Democratic party.* 人工流產的問題可能會在民主黨中引起分歧。

7 ►TALK 講話◄ [I] to stop being shy and say what you really think〔不拘束地〕暢談, 傾吐心事: *Once she knew she could trust me, Melissa started to open up.* 梅莉莎知道可以信任我之後, 便開始沒有顧忌地談了起來。

8 ►HOLE/CRACK ETC 洞/隙縫等◄ [I,T] if a hole, crack etc opens up or is opened up, it appears and becomes wider (使) 變寬, (使) 擴大

USAGE NOTE 用法說明: OPEN
WORD CHOICE 詞語辨析: **open, shut, close, undo, do up, turn on/off, switch on/off, open up**

You **open**, **shut** or **close** your mouth, eyes, doors, windows, boxes, bottles, and shops. 張開或閉上嘴巴、眼睛, 打開或關上門、窗、箱子、瓶子, 使商店開

門或關門用 open, shut 或 close。

You **open** meetings and debates, but you can only **close** (NOT **shut**) them. 開始會議和辯論用 open, 但結束只能用 close (不用 shut) : *Madam Chair, I think we should close the meeting at eight.* 主席女士, 我想我們應該在八點結束會議。

You **undo** or **do up** clothes. 解開或扣上衣服用 undo 和 do up: *She did up her boots/shirt.* 她繫上靴子/扣上襯衫。

You **turn** water or gas **on** or **off**. 開關水或煤氣用 turn on 和 turn off。

You **turn** or **switch** electrical things **on** or **off**. 開關電器用 turn/switch on 和 turn/switch off: *Turn that radio off.* 把那收音機關掉。| *She opened her laptop and switched it on.* 她打開手提電腦, 按下了啟動的開關。

You **open up** new opportunities or possibilities. 開闢新的機會和可能性用 open up: *plans to open up the world of higher education to people from poor backgrounds* 將高等教育的天地向來自貧窮家庭的人開放的計劃

open³ *n* **1 the open** outdoors 戶外, 野外: **in the open** *It must be wonderful to be able to take your meals in the open every day.* 每天都能在戶外吃飯一定很快活。**2 in the open** not hidden or secret 公開的[地]: *It was a great relief to know that it was all in the open at last.* 得知最後一切都公布於眾, 真讓人大鬆了一口氣。| **bring sth (out) into the open** *an opportunity to bring all your gripes out into the open* 傾訴所有苦惱的機會 **3 the Open** a national GOLF competition 全國高爾夫球公開賽: *the US Open* 美國高爾夫球公開賽

open-air /ˌ·· ˈ·◂/ *adj* [usually before noun 一般用於名詞前] happening or existing outdoors, not in a building 戶外的, 露天的: *open-air concerts* 露天音樂會 | *an open-air swimming pool* 室外游泳池

open-and-shut case /ˌ···· ˈ·/ *n* [C] a law case that is easy to prove and will not take a long time in court 昭然若揭[容易證明]的案子

open bar /ˌ·· ˈ·/ *n* [C] *AmE* a bar at an occasion such as a wedding, where drinks are served free【美】〔在婚禮等場合提供飲料的〕免費酒櫃[吧台]

o·pen·cast /ˈopənˌkæst; ˈəʊpənkɑːst/ *adj BrE* **opencast mine/mining** mines where minerals, especially coal, are dug from large open holes in the ground【英】露天礦山/採礦〔尤指煤礦〕

open-cut /ˈ·· ·/ *adj AmE* opencast【美】露天開採的

open day /ˈ·· ·/ *n* [C] *BrE* a day or time when a school, organization etc allows anyone to come in and see the work that is done there【英】〔學校、機構等允許公眾參觀的〕開放日; 開放時間; OPEN HOUSE (2) *AmE*【美】

open door pol·i·cy /ˌ·· ˈ· ˌ···/ *n* [C] **1** the principle of allowing people and goods to move into your country 〔國家的〕對外開放政策 **2** the principle of allowing anyone to come and talk to you while you are working 對外〔指公眾〕接待政策

open-end·ed /ˌ·· ˈ··◂/ *adj* **1** without a fixed ending time 無最終限期的, 無時間限制的: *hiring workers on open-ended contracts* 按沒固定期限的合同雇用工人 **2** not having rules that limit or restrict anything 無限制的, 無拘束的: *These interviews are fairly open-ended in format.* 這些訪問在形式上是相當輕鬆隨意的。

o·pen·er /ˈopənɚ; ˈəʊpənə/ *n* [C] **1** a tool or machine used to open letters, bottles, or cans〔拆信或開啟瓶罐等用的〕開具: *an electric can opener* 電動開罐器 **2** the first of a series of things such as sports competitions〔體育比賽的〕首場比賽: *the opener against the 49ers* 與"49 人"隊的首場賽事 **3 for openers** as a beginning or first stage 首先, 作為開始: *Well, for openers, it would be nice to know your name.* 嗯, 首先, 請告知您的尊姓大名。

open-eyed /ˌ·· ˈ·◂/ *adj, adv* **1** awake, or with your eyes open 醒着的[地], 睜着眼睛的[地] **2** accepting or taking notice of all the facts of a situation 警覺的[地], 留神的[地], 警惕的[地]: *clear, open-eyed reasoning* 清晰而嚴謹的推論

open-faced sand·wich /ˌ·· · ˈ··/ *n* [C] *AmE*【美】〔露餡的〕單片[開口]三明治; an OPEN SANDWICH *BrE*【英】

open-hand·ed /ˌ·· ˈ··◂/ *adj* generous and friendly 慷慨的, 〔出手〕大方的; 友好的: *an open-handed offer of help* 慷慨地提供幫助 —**openhandedness** *n* [U]

open-heart·ed /ˌ·· ˈ··◂/ *adj* kind and sympathetic 和善的, 富同情心的

open-heart sur·ge·ry /ˌ·· ˌ· ˈ···/ *n* [U] a medical operation in which doctors operate on someone's heart 心臟直視手術, 開心 (外科) 手術

open house /ˌ·· ˈ·/ *n* **1** [U] a situation in which visitors are welcome at any time 熱情好客: *It's always open house at Beryl's.* 貝里爾一家一向都熱情好客。**2** [C] *AmE* an occasion when a college, factory, or organization allows the public to come in and see the work that is done there【美】〔大學、工廠或機構的〕對外開放參觀日, 開放日; OPEN DAY *BrE*【英】**3** [C] *AmE* an occasion on which someone who is selling their house lets everyone who is interested in buying it come to see it【美】售房參觀日

o·pen·ing¹ /ˈopənɪŋ; ˈəʊpənɪŋ/ *n* **1** [C] a hole or space in something through which air, light, objects etc can pass 洞, 孔, 開口, 〔空氣、光、物體等進出的〕通路: *There was another opening to the cave.* 這個洞穴另有一條通路。**2** [C] an occasion when a new business, building, road etc starts working or being used〔新的公司、大樓、公路等的〕開張; 開業; 啟用: **[+of]** *the opening of the new theatre* 新劇院的開幕 **3** [C usually singular 一般用單數] the beginning or first part of something 開始, 開端: **[+of]** *The opening of the novel is dull.* 這部小說的開頭部分很乏味。| *at the opening of each school day* 每天上學的開始時 **4** [C] a good chance for someone to do or say something〔某人做或說某事的〕良機, 機遇: **[+for]** *His question left an opening for me to say exactly what I thought.* 他的提問給了我一個確切地表述自己想法的好機會。**5** [C] a job or position that is available 空缺, 空額: *Are there any openings for computer programmers?* 電腦程序員有空缺嗎? **6** [U] the act of opening something 開, 啟: **[+of]** *the opening of markets in Eastern Europe* 打開東歐的市場

opening² *adj* [only before noun 僅用於名詞前] first or beginning 首先的; 開始的: *the opening speech of the debate* 辯論會的開場白

opening hours /ˈ··· ˌ·/ *n* [plural] the hours during which a shop, building etc is open to the public〔商店、建築物的〕營業時間; 對外開放時間

opening night /ˌ··· ˈ·/ *n* [C] the first night that a new play, film etc is shown to the public〔新戲劇或新電影等的〕首演之夜, 首映之夜

opening time /ˈ··· ˌ·/ *n* [C] the time that a business opens to the public, especially the time a PUB begins serving drinks〔尤指酒館的〕開始營業時間: *It was nearly an hour till opening time.* 離開門營業的時間差不多還有一小時。

opening up /ˌ··· ˈ·/ *n* [singular] **1** the process of making something, especially land, available for use or development〔尤指土地的〕開發, 開拓, 開闢: *The opening up of new land brought a rush of immigrants.* 開發新土地引起了一陣移民潮。**2** the process of becoming less restricted or limited 開放〔限制〕: *the opening up of jobs for women* 為婦女開放就業機會

open let·ter /ˌ·· ˈ··/ *n* [C] a letter to an important person, which is printed in a newspaper or magazine in order to protest or complain about something〔刊於報章上的〕公開信

o·pen·ly /ˈopənlɪ; ˈəʊpənli/ *adv* in a way that does not hide your feelings or opinions 公開地, 公然地: *Sarah talked openly about her abusive parents.* 莎拉公開談起了虐待她的父母。| *He was openly contemptuous of his colleagues.* 他公然蔑視自己的同事。

open mike /ˌ·· ˈ·/ *n* [U] *AmE* a time when anyone is allowed to tell jokes, sing etc in a bar or NIGHTCLUB【美】〔酒吧或夜總會裡〕自願者的即興表演〈如講笑話或唱歌等〉

open-mind·ed /ˌ·· ˈ··◂/ *adj* willing to consider and accept other people's ideas, opinions etc 願意考慮他人觀點的, 思想開放的: *I'm quite open-minded about this subject.* 對於這個問題我是相當開通的。—**openmindedly** *adv* —**openmindedness** *n* [U]

open-mouthed /ˌ·· ˈ·◂/ *adj, adv* with your mouth wide open, because you are very surprised or shocked〔因驚訝或震驚而〕張大嘴的[地], 吃驚的[地]: *They stared open-mouthed at the extraordinary spectacle.* 他們張着大嘴凝視着那奇妙的壯觀景象。

open-necked /ˌ·· ˈ·◂/ *adj* an open-necked shirt is one on which the top button has not been fastened〔襯衫〕開領的 —see picture on page A17 參見 A17 頁圖

o·pen·ness /ˈopənnɪs; ˈəʊpən-nɪ̧s◂/ *n* [U] **1** the quality of being honest and not keeping things secret 公開, 坦率: *dealing based on honesty and openness* 以坦誠為本的買賣 **2** the quality of being willing to accept new ideas or people 開明, 思想開通: *his openness to new experience* 他樂於體驗新事物的開明態度 **3** the quality of being open and not enclosed 開闊, 敞開, 空曠: *the openness of the landscape* 景色的壯闊

open-plan 敞開式的

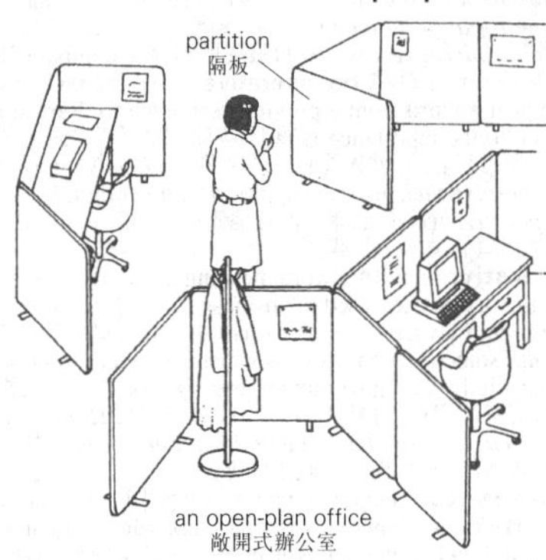

an open-plan office
敞開式辦公室

open-plan /ˌ·· ˈ·◂/ *adj* an open-plan office, school etc does not have walls dividing it into separate rooms〔辦公室、學校等〕敞開式的, 無隔牆的

open pri·ma·ry /ˌ·· ˈ···/ *n* [C] a PRIMARY ELECTION in the US in which any voter may vote for someone from any party〔美國的〕開放預選

open pris·on /ˌ·· ˈ··◂/ *n* [C] *BrE* a prison that does not restrict the actions or freedom of prisoners as much as ordinary prisons【英】〔對囚犯行動限制較少的〕開放式監獄; MINIMUM SECURITY PRISON *AmE*【美】

open sand·wich /ˌ·· ˈ··/ *n* [C] *BrE* a single piece of bread with meat, cheese, etc on top【英】〔露餡的〕單片[開口]三明治; OPEN-FACED SANDWICH *AmE*【美】

open sea·son /ˈ·· ˌ··/ *n* [singular] **1** the period of time each year when it is legal to kill certain animals or fish as a sport〔漁獵的〕開禁期, 狩獵期: **[+for/on]** *open season for deer* 允許獵鹿的季節 —opposite 反義詞 CLOSE SEASON (1) **2 open season (on sb)** a time when a lot of people take the opportunity to criticize someone〔對某人的〕自由批評期〔指許多人同時批評某人的一段時期〕: *The CNN broadcast, in effect, declared open season on Lester Coleman.* 實際上, 美國有線新聞電視網的廣播節目已宣布對萊斯特·科爾曼開始自由批評。

open ses·a·me /ˌ·· ˈ···/ *n* [singular] a way to achieve something that is nearly impossible 開門咒; 訣竅, 法寶: *A degree isn't an open sesame to a good job.* 大學學位並非是獲得一份好工作的敲門磚。

open sys·tem /ˈ·· ˌ··/ *n* [C] *technical* a computer system that is made so that it can be connected with similar computer systems made by other companies【術語】〔電腦〕開放系統〔根據已設定的標準所開發的電腦系統, 可與其他公司開發的類似系統相連接〕

Open U·ni·ver·si·ty /ˌ·· ··ˈ···/ *n* [singular] a British university that teaches adult students mainly in their own homes by means of radio and television programmes and courses of study sent by mail〔英國採用廣播、電視和函授對成人學生進行教學的〕開放大學, 公開進修大學

open ver·dict /ˌ·· ˈ··/ *n* [C] a decision of a JURY (1) in a British court that the cause of someone's death is not known〔陪審團作出的〕死因未定裁決: *Johnson returned an open verdict.* 約翰遜裁決死因不詳。

open vow·el /ˌ·· ˈ··/ *n* [C] *technical* a vowel that is pronounced with your tongue flat on the bottom of your mouth【術語】開元音〔發音時舌位較低〕

o·pen·work /ˈopənˌwɝk; ˈəʊpənˌwɜːk/ *adj* [only before noun 僅用於名詞前] using or containing a pattern that has spaces in between metal bars, pieces of thread etc〔金屬條、細紗等上的〕透雕細工; 網狀細工; 透孔樣式: *a beautiful openwork screen* 漂亮的鏤雕屏風 —**openwork** *n* [U]

op·e·ra /ˈɑpərə; ˈɒpərə/ *n* **1** [C] a musical play in which all of the words are sung 歌劇: **go to the opera** (=go to a performance of an opera) 去看歌劇 *Helena had never been to the opera until that night.* 海倫娜直到那天晚上才看過歌劇。**2** [U] these plays considered as a form of art 歌劇藝術: *Do you enjoy opera?* 你喜歡歌劇嗎? | *an opera lover* 歌劇愛好者 —see also 另見 COMIC OPERA, GRAND OPERA, SOAP OPERA —compare 比較 OPERETTA —**operatic** *adj* —**operatically** *adv*

op·e·ra·ble /ˈɑpərəbl; ˈɒpərəbəl/ *adj* a medical condition that is operable can be treated by an operation〔疾病〕可施手術的, 可開刀的

opera glass·es /ˈ··· ˌ··/ *n* [plural] a small pair of special glasses used at the theatre for making things seem closer〔看戲用的〕小型雙筒望遠鏡

opera house /ˈ··· ·/ *n* [C] a theatre where operas are performed 歌劇院: *the Sydney Opera House* 悉尼歌劇院

op·e·rate /ˈɑpəˌret; ˈɒpəreɪt/ *v* S3 W2

1 ►MACHINE 機器◄ a) [T] to use and control a machine or equipment 使用, 操作, 操縱〔機器或設備〕: *If affected by drowsiness, do not drive or operate heavy machinery.* 犯睏時不要開車或操作重型機器。| *instructions for operating the central heating* 集中供暖設備的操作說明 **b)** [I always+adv/prep] if a machine operates in a particular way, it works in that way; FUNCTION[2] 運轉, 運行: **[+in/at]** *a motor operating at high speeds* 高速運轉的電動機

2 ►SYSTEM/PROCESS/SERVICE 制度/程序/服務◄ a) [I] if a system, process etc operates, it works in a particular way or for a particular purpose 運作; 有效, 起作用: *How well does your company's decision-making system operate in practice?* 你們公司的決策系統實際效果如何? | *The new law doesn't operate in our favour.* 這項新法規對我們不利。**b)** [T] if you operate a system, service etc, you make it work 實行, 實施: *St. Mark's School operates a system of rewards and punishments.* 聖馬可學校實行獎懲制度。

3 ►MEDICAL 醫學的◄ [I] to cut open someone's body in order to remove or repair a part that is damaged 開刀, 動手術: *It's serious. We'll have to operate immediately.* 情況嚴重, 我們得馬上動手術。| **[+on/for]** *Doctors had to operate on his spine.* 醫生不得不給他做脊椎手術。

4 ►BUSINESS/ORGANIZATION 公司/機構◄ [I always+adv/prep] to work in a particular place or way 經營, 做生意; 活動: **[+in/within/from]** *rival gangs that*

operate in the south side of the city 在城南一帶活動的幾個敵對匪幫 | *a small company operating out of a converted barn* 在一家改頭換面的倉庫裡經營業務的小公司

5 ►WORK 工作◄ [I] to do your job or try to achieve things in a particular way 行事; 行使職責: *Soldiers cannot operate effectively without good food.* 士兵吃不好就不能好好作戰。| *That's just the way she operates.* 那就是她做事的方法。

6 operate as to have a particular purpose 起…作用, 作…用: *The word 'onward' can operate as an adjective and an adverb.* onward一詞可用作形容詞和副詞。| *Our consciences operate as a check on our behaviour.* 我們的行為受控於自己的良知。

7 ►LAWS/PRINCIPLES 定律/原理◄ [I] to have an effect on something 起作用; 發生影響: *evolutionary principles operating in the physical world* 在物質世界起作用的進化原理

op·e·rat·ing room /'···· ,·/ *n* [C] *AmE* an OPERATING THEATRE【美】手術室

operating sys·tem /'···· ,··/ *n* [C] a system in a computer that helps all the programs (PROGRAM[1] (1)) in it to work together〔電腦的〕操作系統

operating ta·ble /'···· ,··/ *n* [C] a special table that you lie on to have a medical operation 手術台

operating thea·tre /'···· ,··/ *n* [C] *BrE* a room in a hospital where operations are done【英】手術室; OPERATING ROOM *AmE*【美】

op·e·ra·tion /,ɑpə`reʃən; ,ɒpə'reɪʃən/ *n*

1 ►MEDICAL 醫學的◄ [C] the process of cutting into someone's body to repair or remove a part that is damaged 手術: *a heart bypass operation* 心臟搭橋手術 | *She had a bad operation, she had a hysterectomy.* 她動了個大手術, 被切除了子宮。| **[+on/for]** *She's going to have an operation on her knee.* 她準備去醫院接受膝部手術。| **perform an operation** *an operation only the most skilled surgeon could perform* 只有最老練的外科醫生才能做的手術

2 ►SET OF ACTIONS 整個行動◄ [C] a set of planned actions or activities for a particular purpose〔為達到某一目的而計劃好的〕整個行動[活動]: *The whole operation should only take about ten minutes to perform.* 整個行動應該只要十分鐘左右就完成。| *a search and rescue operation, expertly performed* 一次搜救行動, 幹得很專業

3 ►MACHINE/SYSTEM 機器/系統◄ [U] **a)** the way the parts of a machine or system work together 運轉, 運作: *to maintain proper engine operation* (=working) 維持引擎正常運轉 | **in operation** (=working) 運轉着, 操作中 *Protective clothing must be worn when the machine is in operation.* 操作這機器時必須穿着防護服。**b)** the process of making a machine or system work 操作: *Operation of the system is automatic.* 該系統的操作是自動的。

4 ►BUSINESS 經營◄ **a)** [C] a business, company, or organization, especially one with many parts〔尤指有許多分支的〕商號, 公司, 機構: *Their huge interstate operation reportedly brings in $20 million a year.* 據報道, 他們龐大的州際公司每年掙得2000萬美元的收益。**b)** [C,U] the work or activities done by a business, organization etc, or the process of doing this work 經營; 業務: *Many small businesses fail in the first year of operation.* 許多小商行在經營的第一年常常虧本。| **be in operation** *Chris's courier service has only been in operation for two months.* 克里斯的快遞服務才經營了兩個月。

5 ►PRINCIPLE/LAW/PLAN ETC 原理/定律/計劃等◄ [U] the way something such as a principle, law etc works or has an effect 作用, 效力: *the operation of the laws of gravity* 萬有引力定律的作用 | **in operation** *a clear example of Murphy's law in operation* 墨菲定律起了作用的明顯例子 | **come/go into operation** (=begin to have an effect) 開始生效 *The Act will come into operation later this year.* 這項法令將於今年晚些時候實施。| **put/bring sth into operation** (=make something start to work) 使…開始工作[生效]

6 ►MILITARY/POLICE ACTION 軍事的/警方的行動◄ [C] a planned military or police action, especially one that involves a lot of people〔尤指涉及眾多人員的〕軍事行動; 警方行動: *an espionage operation* 諜報行動

7 ►COMPUTERS 電腦◄ [C] *technical* an action done by a computer【術語】運算: *a multitasking machine performing millions of operations per second* 每秒運算數百萬次的多任務處理機

op·e·ra·tion·al /,ɑpə`reʃənl; ,ɒpə'reɪʃənəl◄/ *adj* **1** working and ready to be used 工作着的, 即可使用的: *The new vehicle could be operational as early as 1994.* 這種新車早在1994年就可使用。| **fully operational** *The new laboratory is fully operational and open for business.* 新實驗室已經全面投入使用, 並對外開放。—compare 比較 OPERATIVE[1](1) **2** [only before noun 僅用於名詞前] related to the operation of a business, government etc〔公司、政府等〕運作的, 操作上的, 經營上的: *operational and budgetary planning officer* 運作及預算規劃官員 —**operationally** *adv*

operational re·search /,····· ·'·/ *n* [U] *technical* the study of how best to build and use machines or plan organizations【術語】運籌學

op·e·ra·tive[1] /`ɑpə,retɪv; 'ɒpərətɪv/ *adj* **1** working and able to be used 運作中, 工作着的; 可使用的: *We had only one radar station operative.* 我們只有一個雷達站在工作。| *operative missiles* 可發射的導彈 —compare 比較 OPERATIONAL (1) **2 the operative word** used when you repeat a word from a previous sentence to draw attention to its importance 最重要[關鍵]的詞〔用於重複前一句中的某個詞, 使人注意其重要性〕: *He is supposed to supervise their work. 'Supposed', unfortunately, is the operative word.* 他應該監督他們的工作。不幸的是"應該", 這個詞才是關鍵。

operative[2] *n* [C] **1** a word meaning a worker, especially a factory worker, used in business 工人, 技工: *increased productivity from the operatives* 由工人提高的生產力 **2** *AmE* someone who does work that is secret in some way, especially for a government organization【美】〔尤指為政府部門服務的〕特工, 特務; 間諜; 密探: *Hunt was no ordinary consultant, but a political operative.* 亨特不是個普通的顧問, 而是個政治間諜。

op·e·ra·tor /`ɑpə,retɚ; 'ɒpəreɪtə/ *n* [C] **1** someone who works on a telephone SWITCHBOARD, who you can call for help when you have problems 電話接線員: *Ask the operator to put you through.* 讓接線員接通你的電話。—see 見 TELEPHONE (USAGE) **2** someone who operates a machine or piece of equipment〔機器或設備的〕操作員: *a tow truck operator* 拖車司機 | *a computer operator* 電腦操作員 **3** a person or company that operates a particular business 經營者: *a tour operator* 旅行社經營者 | *the largest road haulage operator in Alaska* 阿拉斯加最大的公路運輸公司 **4** a disapproving word for someone who is able to get what they want by persuading people 善於擺佈他人的人; 精明圓滑的人: *a supreme operator in congressional politics* 議會政治事務中的頭號大騙子 | **a smooth/sharp operator** *He's a smooth operator with the women.* 他是欺騙婦女的老手。

op·e·ret·ta /,ɑpə`rɛtə; ,ɒpə'retə/ *n* [C] a short or romantic musical play in which some of the words are spoken and some are sung 小歌劇, 輕歌劇: *Strauss's operetta Die Fledermaus* 斯特勞斯的小歌劇《蝙蝠》—compare 比較 OPERA (1)

oph·thal·mi·a /ɑf`θælmɪə; ɒf'θælmiə/ *n* [U] *technical* an illness of the eyes that makes them red and swollen【術語】眼炎

oph·thal·mic /ɑf`θælmɪk; ɒf'θælmɪk/ *adj* related to the eyes and the illnesses that affect them 眼的; 眼炎的: *an ophthalmic surgeon* 眼外科醫生

oph·thal·mol·o·gist /ˌɑfθælˋmɑlədʒɪst; ˌɒfθæl-ˈmɒlədʒɪst/ *n* [C] a doctor who treats people's eyes and does operations on them 眼科醫生[師] —compare 比較 OPTICIAN (1), OPTOMETRIST

oph·thal·mol·o·gy /ˌɑfθælˋmɑlədʒɪ; ˌɒfθælˈmɒlədʒi/ *n* [U] *technical* the study of the eyes and diseases that affect them【術語】眼科學

o·pi·ate /ˋopɪˌet; ˈəʊpiɪt/ *n* [C] a type of drug that contains OPIUM and makes you want to sleep〔用以安眠的〕鴉片製劑

o·pine /oˋpaɪn; əʊˈpaɪn/ *v* [T+that] *formal* to say that you think something is true【正式】認為, 以為, 發表意見: *"She did right, if you ask me," opined Moreau.* "要是問我的話, 她做對了。"莫羅發表意見說。

S1 W2 **o·pin·ion** /əˋpɪnjən; əˈpɪnjən/ *n* **1** [C] your ideas or beliefs about a particular subject 意見, 看法, 主張: **[+about]** *Sarah's parents have strong opinions about divorce.* 莎拉的父母強烈反對離婚。| **[+on]** *I went to my boss to ask him for his opinion on the matter.* 我問老闆對此事的看法。| **[+of]** *What's your opinion of her as a teacher?* 你認為她這個老師怎麼樣? | **the general opinion** (=what most people believe) 普遍的看法 *The general opinion is that the new working hours are a good thing.* 人們普遍認為實行新的工作時間是件好事。—compare 比較 VIEW[1] (1) **2** [C] judgement or advice from a professional person about something 專家意見, 專業意見: *When choosing an insurance policy it's usually best to get an independent opinion.* 選擇保險時, 通常最好去聽聽(專家)獨立的意見。| **a second opinion** (=advice from a second person to make sure that the first advice is right) 他人的忠告[意見] *My doctor says I need an operation, but I've asked for a second opinion.* 我的醫生說我需要開刀, 不過我又徵詢了其他醫生的意見。**3 have a high/low/good/bad etc opinion of** to think that someone or something is very good or very bad 對…評價很高/很低/很好/很差等: *They seem to have a very high opinion of Paula's work.* 他們似乎對保娜的工作評價很高。**4 in my opinion/if you want my opinion** used to tell someone what you think about a particular subject 依我看/如果要聽我的意見: *If you want my opinion, Phil's gone crazy.* 我的意見是, 菲爾發瘋了。**5 be of the opinion (that)** to think that something is true 認為, 主張: *Aristotle was of the opinion that there would always be rich and poor in society.* 亞里士多德認為, 社會上總有貧富存在。—see also 另見 **a difference of opinion** (DIFFERENCE (4)), **it's/that's a matter of opinion** (MATTER[1](21)), PUBLIC OPINION

o·pin·ion·at·ed /əˋpɪnjənˌetɪd; əˈpɪnjəneɪtɪd/ *adj* expressing very strong opinions about things 固執己見的, 武斷的: *an opinionated old fool* 固執的老糊塗

opinion-mak·ers /ˌ·ˈ·· ˌ··/ *n* [plural] people who have great influence over the way other people think 觀念製造者〔指對他人的思維方式有巨大影響的人〕

opinion poll /ˌ·ˈ·· ˌ·/ *n* [C] an attempt to find out what the public thinks about something, especially politics, by asking many people the same questions 民意測驗[調查]: *The latest opinion polls show the Social Democrats leading by 10%.* 最新的民意測驗顯示, 社會民主黨領先10%。

o·pi·um /ˋopɪəm; ˈəʊpiəm/ *n* [U] a powerful illegal drug made from POPPY seeds, that used to be used legally as a PAINKILLER 鴉片 —see also 另見 HEROIN

o·pos·sum /əˋpɑsəm; əˈpɒsəm/ also 又作 **possum** *n* [C] one of various small animals from America and Australia that has fur and climbs trees 負鼠〔產於美洲和澳大利亞〕

opp. the written abbreviation of 縮寫= OPPOSITE

W3 **op·po·nent** /əˋponənt; əˈpəʊnənt/ *n* [C] **1** someone who tries to defeat another person in a competition, game, fight, or argument〔競爭、比賽等的〕對手, 敵手: *Tyson knocked his opponent out in the first round.* 泰臣在第一回合中把對手擊倒了。| *Rumpole was a formidable opponent in court.* 在法庭上, 朗波爾是個令人生畏的對手。**2** someone who disagrees with a plan, idea etc, and wants to try and stop it 反對者: **[+of]** *opponents of the Administration's plans to cut the Federal budget* 反對政府削減聯邦預算的人

op·por·tune /ˌɑpɚˋtjun; ˈɒpətjuːn/ *adj formal*【正式】**1 an opportune moment/time** a time that is suitable for doing something 合適的時機/時間: *Deborah was waiting for an opportune moment to ask for a raise.* 黛博拉在等待合適的時機要求加薪。**2** done at a very suitable time 適時的, 及時的: *an opportune remark* 合時宜的話 —opposite 反義詞 INOPPORTUNE —**opportunely** *adv*

op·por·tun·is·m /ˌɑpɚˋtjunɪzəm; ˌɒpəˈtjuːnɪzəm/ *n* [U] trying whenever possible to gain power or unfair advantages over other people 機會主義; 投機取巧: *a blatant piece of political opportunism* 一宗無恥的政治投機事件

op·por·tun·ist /ˌɑpɚˋtjunɪst; ɒpəˈtjuːnɪst/ *n* [C] someone who uses every chance to gain power or unfair advantage over others 機會主義分子 —**opportunist** *adj*: *the opportunist policies of war-time leaders* 戰時領導人的機會主義政策 —**opportunistic** /ˌɑpɚtjuˋnɪstɪk; ˌɒpətjuːˈnɪstɪk/ *adj*: *A recent police video reflects the increasing number of opportunistic thefts from drivers in heavy urban traffic.* 警方最近的一份錄像顯示, 在城市交通繁忙之時, 伺機向駕車者下手的盜竊案數目在增加。

op·por·tu·ni·ty /ˌɑpɚˋtjunətɪ; ˌɒpəˈtjuːnɪti/ *n* **1** [C,U] S1 W1 a chance to do something or an occasion when it is easy for you to do something 機會, 時機: *I just thought it was too good an opportunity to miss.* 我認為這是個不可錯過的好機會。| **opportunity to do sth** *You have had plenty of opportunity to observe our way of doing things.* 你已有很多機會觀察我們如何辦事。| **[+for]** *When you're in school there are lots of opportunities for meeting people of the opposite sex.* 上學時, 你會有很多機會接觸異性。| **take the opportunity to do sth** (=use a chance to say something you want to) 借機做某事 *I'd like to take this opportunity to wish you a good trip.* 我想借此機會祝你旅途順利。| **at the earliest/first opportunity** (=as soon as possible) 一有機會〔就…〕*He must have got rid of the body at the first opportunity.* 他準是一有機會便把那屍體棄掉了。| **at every opportunity** (=whenever possible) 利用一切機會 *I try to speak French at every available opportunity.* 我努力抓住各種機會講法語。—CHANCE[1] (USAGE) **2** [C] a chance to get a job 就業機會: *There are fewer opportunities for new graduates this year.* 對今年新畢業的大學生來說, 就業機會要少一些。—see also 另見 **equal opportunities** (EQUAL[1] (2))

opposable thumb /ˌ·ˌ··· ˈ·/ *n* [C] a thumb that human beings, MONKEYs etc have that can be used for holding things〔人類、猴等的〕拇指

op·pose /əˋpoz; əˈpəʊz/ *v* [T] **1** to disagree with something such as a plan or idea and try to prevent it from happening or succeeding 反對; 阻礙: *Congress is continuing to oppose the President's healthcare budget.* 國會繼續反對總統的衛生保健預算。| **be opposed to sth** *Most of us are opposed to the death penalty.* 我們大多數人反對死刑。**2** to fight or compete against another person or group in a battle, competition, or election 與…對抗, 與…較量: *He is opposed by two other candidates.* 還有兩名候選人和他較量。 W3

op·posed /əˋpozd; əˈpəʊzd/ *adj* [not before noun 不用於名詞前] **1** two ideas that are opposed to each other are completely different from each other 相反的, 對立的: **[+to]** *The principles of capitalism and socialism are diametrically opposed to each other.* 資本主義與社會主義的原理彼此截然相反。**2 as opposed to** used to compare two things and show that they are different from each other 與…對照之下, 而非: *Students discuss ideas,*

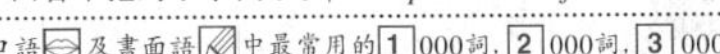

as opposed to just copying from books. 學生一起討論想法，而不是單純抄襲課本。| *his private as opposed to his public life* 他的私生活而非他的社會生活

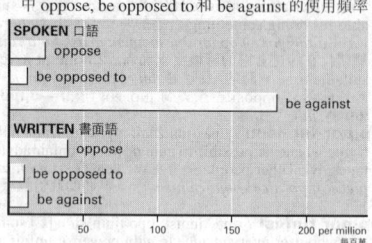

Frequencies of **oppose, be opposed to** and **be against** in spoken and written English 英語口語和書面語中 oppose, be opposed to和 be against的使用頻率

SPOKEN 口語
oppose
be opposed to
be against
WRITTEN 書面語
oppose
be opposed to
be against
50 100 150 200 per million 每百萬

Based on the British National Corpus and the Longman Lancaster Corpus 據英國國家語料庫和朗文蘭卡斯特語料庫

This graph shows that it is much more usual in spoken English to say that you **are against** something, rather than to say that you **oppose** it or **are opposed to** it. This is because **be against** is more informal and more general than **oppose** and **be opposed to**, which often suggest not only disagreeing with and disapproving of something, but also taking action to prevent it. 本圖表顯示，英語口語中說"反對某事"時，大多使用 are against，而少用 oppose 或 are opposed to。這是因為相比而言，be against 比較非正式且較為通用，而 oppose 和 be opposed to 常不僅表示不同意和不贊成某事，而且還含有採取行動加以阻止的意思。

op·pos·ing /ə'pozɪŋ; ə'pəʊzɪŋ/ *adj* **1** opposing teams, groups, forces etc are competing, arguing, or fighting against each other 對抗的，對立的，反對的，敵對的: *The opposing armies were already preparing for war.* 敵對雙方的軍隊已經在備戰了。| *The Socialist Party has split into two opposing camps.* 社會黨分裂成兩個對立的陣營。**2** opposing ideas, opinions etc are completely different from each other〔觀點、意見等〕相反的，相對立的，截然不同的: *Bobbie and Jo have opposing views on abortion.* 鮑比和喬對人工流產持截然相反的觀點。

2 2 **op·po·site**[1] /'ɑpəzɪt; 'ɒpəzɪt/ *prep* if one thing or person is opposite another, they are facing each other 在…的對面: *The people sitting opposite us looked very familiar.* 坐在我們對面的人看上去很面熟。| *It's easy to find – there's a church just opposite my house.* 我家很容易找，正對面有座教堂。

opposite[2] *adj* **1** as different as possible from something else 對立的，截然相反的，完全不同的: *I thought the medicine would make him sleep, but it had the opposite effect.* 我以為這藥會使他入睡，但效果卻完全相反。| *two parties at opposite ends of the political spectrum* 政治派別中截然對立的兩個黨派 **2** the opposite direction, way etc is directly away from someone or something〔方向〕相反的: *The woman turned and walked off in the opposite direction.* 那婦女轉身朝着相反的方向走了。**3** one thing that is opposite another is on the other side of the same area, often directly across from it（在…）對面的，相對的: *The grocery store was on the opposite side of the street.* 雜貨店在街對面。| *the houses opposite* 對面的房子 —see 見 FRONT[1] (USAGE) **4 at opposite ends of the city/country etc** on different sides of a city etc, and a long way apart 在城市/國家等的兩端: *We live at opposite ends of the city, so it's not always easy to meet.* 我們住在城市的兩頭，所以見面總是不容易。**5 the opposite sex** the other sex 異性: *He doesn't feel comfortable with the opposite sex.* 與異性相處時，他覺得不自在。**6 opposite number** someone who has the same job in another similar organization〔在別的機構中〕居相同職位的人，職務對等的人: *his opposite number in the KGB* 在克格勃中與他的職務對等的人

opposite[3] *n* [C] **1** a person or thing that is as different as possible from someone or something else 相反的人[事物]，對立物: *The colors 'black' and 'white' are opposites.* 黑色與白色相反。| **be the opposite (of)** *She's tall and slim, and he's the complete opposite.* 她高挑而苗條，他則全然相反。**2 not ... just/quite the opposite** used to say that something is completely different from what has just been said 不…，正好/完全相反: *Martha's not shy at all – just the opposite in fact.* 瑪莎一點都不靦腆，事實上正好相反。

opposite[4] *adv* in a position on the other side of the same area 在對面，對過: *The Browns live just opposite.* 布朗家就住在對面。

op·po·si·tion /ˌɑpə'zɪʃən; ˌɒpə'zɪʃən/ *n* [U] **1** strong disagreement with, or protest against, something such as a plan, law, or system etc 反對；反抗: **opposition to sth** *There was a great deal of opposition to the war.* 對這場戰爭有很多反對意見。| **strong/fierce opposition** *Plans to build a new airport met with fierce opposition from local farmers.* 興建新機場的計劃遭到當地農民的強烈反對。| **in opposition to (sth)** *The party was founded in opposition to the more moderate policies of the government.* 該黨的成立是為了反對政府較為溫和的政策。**2** [also+plural verb *BrE* 英] the people who you are competing against 對手，對抗者: *He passed the ball to the opposition by mistake.* 他把球誤傳給了對方。—see also 另見 RIVAL[1] (1) **3 the opposition** the main political party in a country's parliament that is not part of the government 反對黨，在野黨: *the leader of the Opposition* 反對黨的領袖 | *protests from the opposition* 反對黨的抗議 **4 in opposition** a political party that is in opposition is in parliament, but is not part of the government〔政黨〕在野的: *The Socialists were elected to power after 10 years in opposition.* 在野十年後，社會黨人當選執政。

op·press /ə'prɛs; ə'pres/ *v* [T often passive 常用被動態] **1** to treat a group of people unfairly or cruelly, and prevent them from having the same rights that other people in society have 壓迫，壓制: *Native tribes had been oppressed by the government and police for years.* 多年來，土著部落一直受到政府和警方的壓迫。**2** to make someone feel unhappy by restricting their freedom in some way 使壓抑，使煩惱: *The solitude of her little apartment oppressed her.* 獨居於那套小公寓房使她感到壓抑。

op·pressed /ə'prɛst; ə'prest/ *adj* **1** a group of people who are oppressed are treated unfairly or cruelly and prevented from having the same rights as other people have 受壓迫的，受壓制的: *oppressed minorities* 受壓迫的少數民族 | **the oppressed** (=people who are oppressed) 受壓迫者，被壓迫的人民 **2** someone who is oppressed feels unhappy because their freedom has been restricted in some way〔因受壓制而〕煩惱的，憂鬱的

op·pres·sion /ə'prɛʃən; ə'preʃən/ *n* [U] the act of oppressing a group of people, or the state of being oppressed 壓迫，壓制: *immigrants taking refuge from the oppression of a dictatorship* 為了躲避專制壓迫而尋求避難的難民

op·pres·sive /ə'prɛsɪv; ə'presɪv/ *adj* **1** powerful, cruel, and unfair 暴虐的，殘酷的；不公平的: *an oppressive military regime* 暴虐的軍事政權 **2** weather that is oppressive is unpleasantly hot with no movement of air〔天氣〕悶熱的，令人煩悶的: *The evening gradually grew more and more oppressive.* 夜晚漸漸變得越來越悶熱。**3** a situation that is oppressive makes you feel too uncomfortable to do or say anything 難以忍受的，鬱悶的: *The silence in the meeting was becoming oppressive.* 會場上一片寂靜，讓人開始難以忍受。—**op-**

pressively *adv* —**oppressiveness** *n* [U]

op·pres·sor /əˋprɛsɚ; əˈpresə/ *n* [C] a person or group that oppresses people 暴君, 壓迫者: *They rose up against their colonial oppressors.* 他們奮起反抗殖民地的暴君。

op·pro·bri·ous /əˋprobrɪəs; əˈprəʊbriəs/ *adj formal* showing great disrespect【正式】極無禮的, 鄙俗的; 表示輕蔑的 —**opprobriously** *adv*

op·pro·bri·um /əˋprobrɪəm; əˈprəʊbriəm/ *n* [U] *formal* strong public criticism, hatred, or shame【正式】公眾強烈的批評; 羞辱; 恥辱: *in the face of public opprobrium* 面對公眾猛烈的批評

opt /ɑpt; ɒpt/ *v* [I] to choose one thing or one course of action instead of another 選擇, 挑選: **[+for]** *GM workers opted for job security over pay increases.* 〔美國〕通用汽車公司的工人寧願選擇就業保障, 而不要加薪。| **opt to do sth** *Many young people are opting to go on to further education.* 許多年輕人都在選擇繼續學習深造。

opt out *phr v* [I] **1** to avoid doing a duty 躲避盡責: **[+of]** *You can't just opt out of all responsibility for the child!* 你不能對孩子全然撒手不管! **2** to decide not to join in a group or system 決定不參與: *Britain wants to opt out of the European Social Chapter.* 英國不想加入歐洲社會憲章。**3** if a school or hospital in Britain opts out, it decides to control its own money, that it is given by the government, instead of being controlled by local government〔英國學校或醫院〕自主管理政府撥給的經費〔而非由地方政府來管理〕

op·tic¹ /ˋɑptɪk; ˈɒptɪk/ *adj* [only before noun 僅用於名詞前] concerning the eyes 眼睛的; 視覺的: *the optic nerve* 視覺神經 —see picture at 參見 EYE¹ 圖

optic² *n* **1 optics** [U] the scientific study of light 光學 **2** [C] *BrE* a small plastic object on a bottle of alcohol that measures the amount to be poured into a glass【英】奧普蒂克量杯〔一種烈酒量杯, 罩在酒瓶上〕

op·ti·cal /ˋɑptɪkḷ; ˈɒptɪkəl/ *adj* **1** used for seeing images and light 視覺的, 有助於視力的; 光學的: *microscopes and other optical instruments* 顯微鏡和其他光學儀器 **2** concerned with the way light is seen 光像的: *an optical diagram* 光學圖像 **3** using light, especially for the purpose of sending or storing information for use in a computer system 光學的, 利用光的〔尤指為電腦系統所使用發送或儲存信息〕: *optical character recognition* 光字符識別 (技術), 感光字元辨識 —**optically** /-kḷɪ; -kli/ *adv*

optical fi·bre /ˌ··· ˈ··/ *n* [U] a thread-like piece of glass or plastic which is used for sending information, for example in a telephone or computer system 光學纖維

optical il·lu·sion /ˌ··· ·ˈ··/ *n* [C] a picture or image that tricks your eyes and makes you see something that is not actually there 視錯覺, 光幻覺

op·ti·cian /ɑpˈtɪʃən; ɒpˈtɪʃən/ *n* [C] **1** *BrE* someone who tests people's eyes and sells SPECTACLES in a shop【英】〔眼鏡店的〕驗光配鏡技師 **2** *AmE* someone who makes lenses (LENS (1)) for SPECTACLES【美】鏡片製造商

op·ti·mal /ˋɑptəməl; ˈɒptɪ̈məl/ *adj* the best or most suitable; OPTIMUM (1) 最佳的; 最適宜的

op·ti·mis·m /ˋɑptəˌmɪzəm; ˈɒptɪ̈mɪzəm/ *n* [U] a tendency to believe that good things will always happen 樂觀; 樂觀主義: *the optimism of the postwar years* 戰後幾年的樂觀 (情緒) —opposite 反義詞 PESSIMISM

op·ti·mist /ˋɑptəmɪst; ˈɒptɪ̈mɪst/ *n* [C] someone who always believes that good things will happen 樂觀者, 樂觀主義者: *I'm a born optimist.* 我是個天生的樂天派。—opposite 反義詞 PESSIMIST

op·ti·mis·tic /ˌɑptəˋmɪstɪk; ˌɒptɪ̈ˈmɪstɪk◂/ *adj* **1** believing that good things will happen in the future 樂觀的; 樂觀主義的: **[+about]** *Foreign bankers are cautiously optimistic about the country's economic future.* 外國銀行家對該國的經濟前景持謹慎樂觀的態度。**2** thinking that things will be better, easier or more successful than is actually possible〔對未來〕(過於) 有信心的, (過分) 樂觀的: **over-optimistic** *They're being over-optimistic if they think that car can make an 800 mile trip.* 如果他們以為那輛車能勝任一趟 800 英里的旅行, 那他們想得過於樂觀了。—**optimistically** /-kḷɪ; -kli/ *adv* —opposite 反義詞 PESSIMISTIC

op·ti·mize also 又作 **-ise** *BrE*【英】/ˋɑptəˌmaɪz; ˈɒptɪ̈maɪz/ *v* [T] to make the way that something is done or used as effective as possible 使最優化, 使盡可能完善, 使盡量有效: *The company is seeking to optimize its use of financial resources by introducing performance-related pay.* 公司正尋求採取將薪酬與業績掛鉤的方式來盡力優化資金的使用。

op·ti·mum /ˋɑptəməm; ˈɒptɪ̈məm/ *adj* [only before noun 僅用於名詞前] **1** the best or most suitable for a particular purpose 最優的, 最有利的, 最適宜的: *the optimum temperature for keeping wine* 儲存酒的最適宜溫度 **2 the optimum** the best possible situation, conditions, amount of time etc for something to happen 最佳條件, 最佳狀況

op·tion /ˋɑpʃən; ˈɒpʃən/ *n* [S1] [W2]

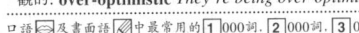

1 ▶A CHOICE 選擇◀ [C] a choice you can make in a particular situation 選擇: *As I see it, we have two options – either we sell the house or we rent it out.* 依我看, 我們有兩種選擇 —— 或是賣掉房子, 或是出租。| *I usually choose the vegetarian option in restaurants.* 我在餐館裡通常都點素菜。| **the option of doing sth** *I always had the option of going back to Canada.* 我當時隨時都可以選擇回加拿大。| **have no option but to do sth** (=be forced to do something because there are no other choices) 不得不做某事, 除做某事外別無選擇 *Teenage mothers often have no option but to live with their parents.* 少女媽媽經常只能與父母同住, 別無選擇餘地。

2 keep/leave your options open to wait before making a decision 暫不作決定, 留有選擇餘地: *We should keep our options open until Jim can study the results of the survey.* 我們暫且不作決定, 等吉姆對調查結果研究過以後再說。

3 ▶RIGHT TO BUY/SELL 買/賣的選擇權◀ [C] the right to buy or sell something in the future〔將來〕買賣某物的選擇權利: **[+on]** *The Saudi government has agreed to buy 20 planes, with an option on a further 10.* 沙特政府已同意購買 20 架飛機, 並擁有再買 10 架的選購權。

4 ▶COMPUTERS 電腦◀ [C] one of the possible choices you can make when using a computer PROGRAM¹ (1)〔使用電腦程式時〕可能的選擇之一: *Press 'P' to select the print option.* 按 P 鍵選擇打印。

5 ▶STH THAT IS ADDITIONAL 附件, 配件◀ [C] something that is offered in addition to the standard equipment when you buy something new, especially a car〔購買新商品, 尤指汽車時〕標準設備之外提供的附件

6 ▶AT COLLEGE/UNIVERSITY 在大學◀ [C] *BrE* a subject that you can choose to study as part of a course【英】選修課: *I did an option in Korean Studies.* 我選了一門朝鮮語研究課程。

7 first option the chance to buy or get something before anyone else 優先權: *They've agreed to give us the first option on their apartment.* 他們同意給予我們那套房子的優先購買權。

8 the soft/easy option the course of action that needs the least effort, chosen because you are being lazy 最輕鬆/最容易的選擇: *Some people consider studying Expressive Arts to be a soft option.* 一些人認為選修表現藝術最容易及格。

op·tion·al /ˋɑpʃənḷ; ˈɒpʃənəl/ *adj* if something is optional, you do not have to do it or use it, but you can choose to if you want to 可選擇的, 非強制的: *Woodwork was an optional subject at our school.* 木工手藝在我們學校是一門選修課。| **an optional extra** (=something that you can choose to have in addition to what you would normally get) 可選的額外之物 *Leather seats are an optional extra in the hatchback.* 這款裝有後車門的小轎車另有皮革座椅可供選擇。

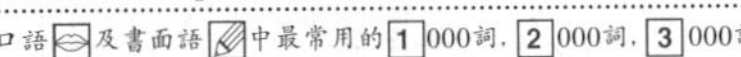

op·tom·e·trist /ɑpˋtɑmətrɪst; ɒpˈtɒmɪ̆trɪ̆st/ *n* [C] someone who tests people's eyes and orders SPECTACLES for them 驗光師, 配鏡師

op·u·lence /ˋɑpjələns; ˈɒpjʊ̆ləns/ *n* [U] great wealth 富裕; 財富: *the opulence of ancient Rome* 古羅馬的富足

op·u·lent /ˋɑpjələnt; ˈɒpjʊ̆lənt/ *adj* **1 a)** very beautiful, highly decorated, and made from expensive materials; LUXURIOUS 華麗的, 豪華的, 奢侈的: *the opulent splendour of the Sultan's palace* 蘇丹王宮的金碧輝煌 **b)** very rich 闊綽的, 非常富有的: *opulent officials in large limousines* 坐着大型豪華轎車的富有官員 **2** growing healthily and in large amounts; LUXURIANT 繁茂的; 大量的; 濃密的

o·pus /ˋopəs; ˈəʊpəs/ *n* [usually singular 一般用單數] **1** a piece of music by a great musician, numbered according to when it was written〔根據創作時間先後〕編號的音樂作品: *Beethoven's Opus 95 quartets* 貝多芬的四重奏, 作品第 95 號 **2** an important work of art by a famous writer, painter etc〔著名作家、畫家等的〕大作, 傑作, 主要作品: *Verdi's Requiem, his greatest opus* 威爾第的《安魂曲》, 他最偉大的作品 —see also 另見 MAGNUM OPUS

-or /ɚ; ə/ *suffix* [in nouns 構成名詞] the form used for -ER in certain words〔在某些詞中用以代替 -ER 的(後綴)形式〕: *an actor* (=someone who acts) 演員 | *an inventor* 發明家; 創造者

or /ɚ; ə; *strong* 強讀 ɔr; ɔː/ *conjunction* **1** used between two things or before the last in a list of possibilities, things that people can choose from etc 或, 或者; 還是: *Do you want to leave now or would you rather set off later?* 你想現在動身還是願意晚點出發? | *Was it London, Paris or Rome where you first met Maxim?* 你初次見到馬克西姆是在倫敦、巴黎還是羅馬? | **or anything/something** *spoken* (=or something of the same kind)【口】或其他甚麼的, 諸如此類的甚麼 *Would you like a coffee or something?* 你想來杯咖啡或別的甚麼飲料? | *I wasn't trying to push in or anything.* 我並不想擠進去或怎麼的。| **either... or...** *If either Lennie or Miranda calls, I'm not at home.* 如果倫尼或米蘭達來電話就說我不在家。—compare 比較 EITHER[1] **2** used after a negative verb when you mean not one thing and also not another thing 也不〔用於含否定意思的動詞後〕: *He doesn't have a television or a video.* 他沒有電視機, 也沒有錄像機。| *Sonia never cleans or even offers to wash the dishes.* 索尼婭從不收拾整理, 連主動提出洗碗碟也沒有。**3** used to warn or advise someone that if they do not do something, something they do not want will happen 否則, 要不然: *Wear your coat or you'll catch cold.* 穿上外套, 要不你會着涼的。| **or else** *You have to roll the clothes very tightly or else they won't all fit in the rucksack.* 你得把衣服裹緊, 要不沒法全都塞進帆布包裡。| *You'd better be there, or else.* (=used to threaten someone) 你最好去那裡, 要不夠你受的。**4** used to correct something that you have said or to give more specific information 即, 那就是, 或者說〔用於更正說法或給予更確切的信息〕: *It's going to snow tomorrow, or that's what the forecast says.* 明天將要下雪, 確切地說, 氣象預報是這樣說的。| *She was born in Saigon, or Ho Chi Minh City as it is now called.* 她出生於西貢, 即現在所稱的胡志明市。| **or rather** *The computer software is old, or rather very out of date.* 這個電腦軟件很老了, 更確切地說是早就過時了。**5** used to explain why something happens or to show that something must be true 要不然〔用以解釋某事發生的原因或說明某事必定是真的〕: *He must be very drunk or he wouldn't keep falling down.* 他準是喝得爛醉了, 要不然他不會老是摔倒。| **or else** *It's either a coincidence they're so alike, or else they are related in some way.* 要不就是他們碰巧這麼相像, 要不就是他們有某種血緣關係。**6 a minute/a mile/twenty etc or so** a particular amount or a little more 一分鐘/一英里/二十等左右: *They had to wait an hour or so for the police to arrive.* 他們得等上一小時左右警察才到來。**7 a minute/a dollar etc or two** a small amount or number of something 大約一兩分鐘/一兩塊錢等: *I saw Nigel leaving a second or two ago.* 我看見奈傑爾一兩秒鐘前剛離開。

or·a·cle /ˋɔrəkl; ˈɒrəkəl/ *n* [C] **1** someone the ancient Greeks believed could communicate with the gods, who gave advice to people or told them what would happen〔古希臘時〕宣示神諭的人, 傳神諭者: *Spartans would consult the oracle before going into battle.* 斯巴達人總要先請示神諭後再去打仗。**2** a message given by an oracle 神諭 **3** *humorous* a person or book that gives advice and information【幽默】提供意見[信息]的人[書籍]

o·rac·u·lar /ɔˋrækjəlɚ; ɒˈrækjʊ̆lə/ *adj* **1** said by an oracle 神諭的 **2** difficult to understand 難解的; 玄妙深奧的

o·ral[1] /ˋɔrəl; ˈɔːrəl/ *n* [C] **1** *BrE* a spoken test, especially in a foreign language【英】〔尤指外語的〕口試: *I've got my French oral tomorrow* 我明天有法語口試。**2** *AmE* a spoken test for a MASTER'S DEGREE【美】碩士學位中的口試

oral[2] *adj* **1** spoken, not written 口頭的, 口述的: *oral history* 口述的歷史 | *a brief oral report* 簡短的口頭報告 **2** concerned with or involving the mouth 口的, 口腔的: *oral hygiene* 口腔衛生 —**orally** *adv*

oral con·tra·cep·tive /,·· ··ˈ··/ *n* [C] a drug that a woman takes by mouth, so that she can have sex without having a baby; the PILL (2) 口服避孕藥

oral ex·am /ˈ·· ·,·/ *n* [C] an ORAL 口試

oral sex /,·· ˈ·/ *n* [U] touching someone's sex organs with the lips and tongue, to give sexual pleasure 口交, 舐淫

oral sur·geon /ˈ·· ,··/ *n* [C] **1** a DENTIST who performs operations in the mouth 口腔外科醫生 **2** *AmE* a DENTIST【美】牙醫

or·ange /ˋɔrɪndʒ; ˈɒrɪ̆ndʒ/ *n* [C] **1** a round fruit that has a thick orange skin and is divided into parts inside 柑橘, 橙 —see picture on page A8 參見 A8 頁圖 **2** a colour that is between red and yellow 橘黃色, 橙色: *The sky turned a brilliant orange.* 天空轉而呈現出鮮豔的橙色。—**orange** *adj*: *Carrots are orange.* 胡蘿蔔是橘黃色的。—see picture on page A5 參見 A5 頁圖

or·ange·ade /,ɔrɪndʒˋed; ,ɒrɪ̆ndʒˈeɪd/ *n* [U] a drink that tastes like oranges 橘子水, 橙汁飲料

or·an·ge·ry /ˋɔrɪndʒrɪ; ˈɒrɪ̆ndʒəri/ *n* [C] a place where orange trees are grown 柑橘園

orange squash /,·· ˈ·/ *n* [U] *BrE* a drink that tastes like oranges, made by adding water to a strong tasting liquid【英】橙子水, 鮮橘水, 橘子汽水

o·rang·u·tang /əˋræŋə,tæŋ; ɔː,ræŋuːˈtæŋ/ also 又作 **o·rang·u·tan** /-tæn; -tæn/ *n* [C] a large APE[1] (1) with long arms and long orange hair 猩猩

o·ra·tion /ɔˋreʃən; əˈreɪʃən/ *n* [C] a formal public speech〔正式的〕演說, 演講

or·a·tor /ˋɔrətɚ; ˈɒrətə/ *n* [C] someone who makes speeches and is good at persuading people 演講者, 演說家

or·a·to·ri·o /,ɔrəˋtorɪo; ,ɒrəˈtɔːriəʊ/ *n* [C] a long piece of music in which a large group of people sing 清唱劇, 神劇

or·a·tory /ˋɔrə,torɪ; ˈɒrətri/ *n* **1** [U] the skill of making powerful and persuasive speeches 演講術, 雄辯術: *a dazzling display of oratory* 表現出令人讚嘆的口才 **2** [U] language that includes long and formal words〔含長而正式詞語的〕華麗的言辭 **3** [C] a small building or part of a church where people can go to pray 小禮拜堂, 祈禱室 —**oratorical** /,ɔrəˋtɔrɪkḷ; ,ɒrəˈtɒrɪkəl◂/ *adj*: *Churchill's formidable oratorical skills* 丘吉爾令人欽佩的雄辯才能 —**oratorically** /-klɪ; -kli/ *adv*

orb /ɔrb; ɔːb/ *n* [C] **1** *literary* a bright ball-shaped object, especially the sun or the moon【文】明亮的球體〔尤指太陽或月亮〕: *the red orb of the sun* 紅彤彤的太陽球體

2 a ball decorated with gold, carried by a king or queen on formal occasions as a sign of power〔國王或女王在正式場合作為王權標誌攜帶的〕寶球

or·bit¹ /ˈɔrbɪt; ˈɔːbɪ̣t/ *v* [I,T] to travel in a circle around a much larger object such as the Earth, the sun etc 環繞…軌道運行: *The satellite orbits the Earth every 48 hours.* 那顆人造衛星每 48 小時繞地球軌道運行一周。

orbit² *n* [C] **1** the path travelled by an object which is moving around another much larger object such as the Earth, the sun etc〔環繞地球或太陽等運行的〕軌道: *the Moon's orbit around the Earth* 月球環繞地球運行的軌道 | **in orbit** (=travelling in this kind of path) 在軌道上運行 *The Space Shuttle is now in orbit.* 太空穿梭機已進入軌道飛行。**2** an area of power and influence 勢力範圍: *brought within orbit of the Central Office* 納入總局的勢力範圍

or·bit·al /ˈɔrbɪtḷ; ˈɔːbɪtl/ *adj* **1** concerned with the orbit of one object around another 軌道的: *the Earth's orbital path* 地球的運行軌道 **2** *BrE* an orbital road goes around a large city【英】〔公路〕環城的: *the London orbital motorway* 倫敦外環高速公路 —**orbital** *n* [C]

or·chard /ˈɔrtʃɚd; ˈɔːtʃəd/ *n* [C] a place where fruit trees are grown 果園: *a cherry orchard* 櫻桃園

or·ches·tra /ˈɔrkɪstrə; ˈɔːkɪ̣strə/ *n* [C also+plural verb *BrE* 英] a large group of musicians playing many different kinds of instruments and led by a CONDUCTOR (1)〔大型的〕管弦樂隊

or·ches·tral /ɔrˋkɛstrəl; ɔːˈkestrəl/ *adj* concerned with or written for an orchestra 管弦樂隊(演奏)的; 為管弦樂隊創作的: *orchestral music* 管弦樂

orchestra pit /ˈ··· ·/ *n* [C] the space below the stage in a theatre where the musicians sit〔劇場舞台前凹陷的〕樂池 —see picture at 參見 THEATRE 圖

or·ches·trate /ˈɔrkɪsˌtret; ˈɔːkɪ̣streɪt/ *v* [T] **1** to organize an important event or a complicated plan, especially secretly〔尤指祕密地〕精心策劃: *The coup was orchestrated by the CIA.* 這次政變是中央情報局一手策劃的。**2** to arrange a piece of music so that it can be played by an orchestra 將〔樂曲〕編成管弦樂曲 —**orchestrated** *adj* —**orchestration** /ˌɔrkɪˋstreʃən; ˌɔːkɪ̣ˈstreɪʃən/ *n* [C, U]

or·chid /ˈɔrkɪd; ˈɔːkɪ̣d/ *n* [C] a plant that has flowers with three parts, the middle one being shaped like a lip 蘭花

or·dain /ɔrˋden; ɔːˈdeɪn/ *v* [T] **1** to officially make someone a priest or religious leader 正式任命〔某人〕為牧師, 授予〔某人〕聖職: *Desmond Tutu was ordained in 1960.* 德斯蒙德·圖圖於1960年被任命為牧師。| **ordain sb (as) sth** *Paulson was ordained deacon.* 保爾森被任命為執事牧師。—see also 另見 ORDINATION **2** *formal* to order that something should happen【正式】命令, 規定; 判定: *a duty ordained by God* 上帝規定的職責 | **[+that]** *The King ordained that a feast should be prepared.* 國王命令準備一場盛宴。

or·deal /ɔrˋdil; ɔːˈdiːl/ *n* [C] a terrible or painful experience 可怕的經歷, 痛苦的折磨: **[+of]** *the ordeal of having your child kidnapped* 孩子遭綁架的痛苦經歷 | **it is an ordeal to do sth** *Some people find it an ordeal to appear before the TV camera.* 有些人覺得面對電視攝像機是一種煎熬。

S1 W1 **or·der¹** /ˈɔrdɚ; ˈɔːdə/ *n*

1 ►FOR A PURPOSE 為某一目的◄ **a) in order to do sth** for the purpose of doing something 為了做某事: *politicians who make promises simply in order to win more votes* 純粹為了贏得更多選票而作出種種承諾的政客 | *In order to understand how the human body works, you need to have some knowledge of chemistry.* 為了了解人體是如何運作的, 你需要學一些化學知識。**b) in order for/that** *formal* so that something can happen or so that someone can do something【正式】為了, 以便: **in order for sb/sth to do sth** *Sunlight is needed in order for photosynthesis to take place.* 需要陽光來進行光合作用。| **in order that** *I locked the door in order that we might continue our discussions undisturbed.* 我鎖上門以便我們能不受干擾地繼續商談。

2 ►ARRANGEMENT 安排◄ [C,U] the way that several things, events etc are arranged or put on a list, showing whether something is first, second, third etc; SEQUENCE 順序, 次序: *The programme shows the order of events for the day.* 節目表列出這天節目的順序。| **in order** (=arranged in a particular way) 整齊, 有條理 *You should keep the files in order.* 你應當把文件都歸放整齊。| *What order are these videos supposed to be in?* 這些錄像節目應該怎樣排序? | **do sth in order** (=do things one after another, according to a plan) 做事有條不紊 *Then they call out our names in order and we answer yes or no.* 隨後, 他們依次點我們的名字, 我們則回答到與否。| **out of order** (=in the wrong order) 次序顛倒, 不按順序 | **in chronological/alphabetical/numerical order** *Let us examine these events in chronological order.* 我們按年代順序來考察一下這些事件吧。| **in the right/wrong order** *Wait a minute, we've got these photos in the wrong order.* 等一下, 我們把這些照片的順序弄錯了。| **in order of importance/preference/appearance etc** *Characters are listed in order of appearance.* 人物是按出場順序排列的。| **in reverse order** (=in the opposite order to what is usual) 次序顛倒 | **in ascending/descending order** (=starting with the lowest or highest number) 按遞增/遞減的順序

order 順序

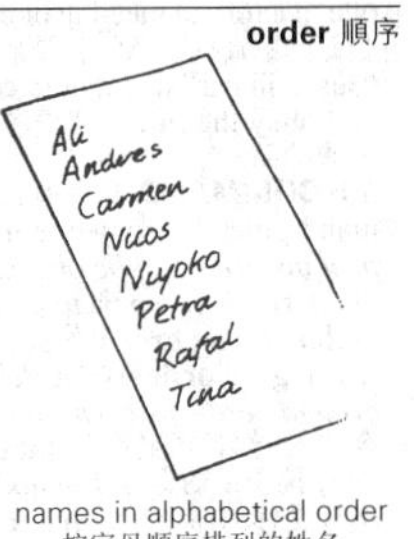

names in alphabetical order
按字母順序排列的姓名

3 ►REQUEST FOR GOODS 訂貨◄ [C] a request by a customer for a company to supply goods or for a meal in a restaurant 訂貨; 訂購; 點菜: **place an order** (=make an order) 訂貨, 下訂單 *The Canadian Air Force has placed a large order for electronic equipment.* 加拿大空軍訂購了一大批電子設備。| **order form** (=special piece of paper for writing orders on) 訂單, 訂購表格 *Have you filled out the order form?* 你填好訂單了嗎? | **on order** (=ordered but not yet received) 訂購中的, 已訂購但尚未交貨的 *It's on order – it should be in next week.* 貨已訂購, 下週該到了。| **have sth on order** (=be waiting for something you have ordered) 等待着已訂購之物的交貨 | **take sb's order** (=write down what a customer in a restaurant wants) 記下顧客點的飯菜 *The waiter came over to take my order.* 服務員過來請我點菜。| **make/supply sth to order** (=produce something especially for a particular customer) 按訂貨要求生產/供應貨物 *We supply hand-made shoes to order.* 我們供應手工訂做的鞋。

4 ►GOODS/MEAL 貨物/飯菜◄ [C] goods or a meal that a customer has asked for〔客戶訂的〕貨物; 點的飯菜: *Your order has arrived – you can collect it from the store any time.* 你訂的貨已經到了, 你可以隨時來店鋪提取。| **side order** (=a small plate of food in addition to your main meal) 主菜以外另點的小菜

5 ►NO TROUBLE OR CRIME 無動亂或犯罪◄ [U] a situation in which rules are obeyed and authority is respected 治安, 秩序; 規矩: **law and order** *the work of the police in maintaining law and order* 警方在維持法律和秩序方面的工作 | **public order** *Their speeches were clearly a threat to public order.* 他們的言論無疑是對社會治安的一種威脅。| **keep order/keep sb in order** (=stop people from behaving badly) 維持秩序/使某人守規矩 *Some of the new teachers can't keep order.* 年輕老師中有一些人無法維持課堂秩序。| *Don't worry, I'll* *keep them in order.* 別擔心，我會讓他們規規矩矩的。| **restore order** *The army was called in to restore order.* 軍隊被召來恢復秩序。| **call sb to order** (=order someone in a formal meeting or court of law to obey the rules) 〔在正式會議或法庭上〕要某人遵守秩序 | **Order! Order!** (=used in parliament or in court to tell people to be quiet and obey the rules) 守秩序！守秩序！〔在議會裡或法庭上說的話〕

O

6 ▶COMMAND 命令◀ also 又作 **orders** [C] a command given by someone in authority 命令；指示：*I expect my orders to be obeyed.* 我希望大家能服從我的命令。| *You will report to me at eight o'clock tomorrow – and that's an order.* 你要在明天八點向我報到，這是命令。| **give orders** *I'm the one who gives the orders around here – just remember that.* 在這裡我才是發號施令的人，你們要記着。| **take orders from** (=obey someone) 接受…的命令 *I'm not taking orders from you!* 我不接受你的命令！| **order to do sth** *General Bradley gave the order to advance.* 布拉德利將軍下令前進。| **have orders to do sth** (=have been commanded to do something) 奉命做某事 *I have orders to search your house.* 我奉命搜查你的房子。| **by order of/on the orders of** (=because of someone's order) 奉…之命 *On Stalin's orders the target for the five year plan was raised once again.* 奉史太林之命，五年計劃的目標又一次提高了。| **under orders to do sth** (=having been commanded to do something) 奉命做某事 *A warship was dispatched, under orders to sail directly to Georgetown.* 軍艦奉命出發，直駛喬治敦。

7 ▶LEGAL DOCUMENT 法律文件◀ [C] an official statement from a court of law that something must be done; COURT ORDER 法院決議；法院指令

8 be out of order a) if a machine or piece of equipment is out of order, it is not working 〔機器或設備等〕發生故障，失靈：*The phone at the street corner is out of order again.* 街角的電話又壞了。**b)** if things on a list or in a series are out of order, they are not correctly arranged 次序顛倒[紊亂]；排列錯誤：*Some of the pages in this book are out of order.* 這本書的一些書頁次序顛倒了。**c)** *BrE informal* if someone's behaviour is out of order it is unacceptable【英，非正式】舉止不當；OUT OF LINE (LINE¹ (32)) *AmE*【美】**d)** to be breaking the rules in a committee, court, parliament etc 違反〔委員會、法庭、議會等的〕規程：*The MP's remarks were ruled out of order.* 該議員的意見被裁定為違反章程。

9 be in order a) if things on a list or in a series are in order they are correctly arranged 〔排列〕順序正確 **b)** if an official document is in order it is legal and correct 〔正式文件等〕合法，無誤，妥當：*Is your passport in order?* 你的護照有效嗎？**c)** if something that you do is in order, it is allowed by the rules in a committee, court, parliament etc 符合〔委員會、法庭、議會等的〕規程 **d)** to be a suitable thing to do or say on a particular occasion 適宜，合適，恰當：*I hear congratulations are in order.* 聽說該向你道喜了。

10 be in (good) working/running order if a vehicle or machine is in good working or running order, it is working well 〔車輛或機器等〕狀況良好：*a 1927 Model A Ford, still in good running order* 一輛1927年的A型福特汽車，車況依然良好

11 ▶WELL-ORGANIZED STATE 井然有序的狀態◀ [U] a situation in which everything is controlled, well organized, and correctly arranged 有條理，整齊：*Let's have some order in here. Someone put those desks straight.* 我們把這裡整理一下，誰去把那些書桌擺擺整齊吧。| **put sth in order** (=organize or arrange something properly) 把某事安排妥當 *Uncle Bob put his business affairs in order before he died.* 鮑勃大叔在去世前把生意方面的事情都安排妥當了。| **in apple-pie order** *AmE informal* (=very tidy and correctly arranged)【美，非正式】井然有序，有條不紊 *Tim's room was in apple-pie order.* 蒂姆的房間井然不紊。

12 leave/retreat/retire in good order to leave in a controlled way, when people are angry or attacking you 〔在他人生氣或攻擊時〕以克制的方式離開/退出/離去

13 ▶POLITICAL/SOCIAL SITUATION 政治/社會的模式◀ [singular] the political, social, or economic situation at a particular time 〔某一時期政治、社會或經濟的〕模式，制度：*the present economic order* 當前的經濟模式 | **the established order** (=the traditional rules and customs of society) 現存制度；傳統社會習俗 *The gay rights movement emerged to challenge the established order.* 同性戀者爭取權益的運動對現存制度發起了挑戰。| **the new order** (=the new situation after an important change in politics or society) 〔重大政治或社會變革之後的〕新模式 *the new world order since the end of the Cold War* 自冷戰結束以來的世界新秩序

14 the (natural) order of things the way that life and the world are organized and intended to be 事物的正常秩序：*People accepted the class system as part of the natural order of things.* 人們曾把等級制度看作是自然而然的事。

15 of a high/the highest/the first order of a very good or of the best kind 優秀的/最高級的/一流的：*an achievement of the highest order* 最出色的成就

16 be the order of the day a) to be suitable for a particular occasion or situation 〔在某場合或情況中〕適宜的，恰當的：*Casual clothes are the order of the day.* 休閒服裝很合時宜。**b)** to be very common at a particular time 在某一時期變得很尋常，非常普遍：*Sexual explicitness seems to be the order of the day.* 現在人們公然地討論性的話題，這似乎已成為尋常之事。

17 in the order of/of the order of also 又作 **on the order of** *AmE*【美】a little more or a little less than a particular amount; APPROXIMATELY 大約：*a figure in the order of $7 million* 大約700萬美元的一筆數字

18 in short order *especially AmE* immediately【尤美】立即，毫不耽擱地：*The crisis was resolved in relatively short order.* 這場危機很快就化解了。

19 ▶RELIGIOUS GROUP 宗教團體◀ [C] a society of MONKS or NUNS (=people who live a holy life according to religious rules) 修道會，修士[修女]會：*the Benedictine Order* 本篤會 | **[+of]** *the order of Jesuits* 耶穌會

20 take (holy) orders to become a priest 擔任聖職

21 ▶SECRET SOCIETY 祕密會社◀ [C] an organization or society whose members meet for secret ceremonies 祕密組織[會社]：*a Masonic order* 共濟會 | *the Royal Ancient Order of Boars* 皇家古野豬會

22 ▶OFFICIAL HONOUR 正式榮譽◀ [C] **a)** a group of people who have received a special official reward from a king, president etc for their services or achievements 獲得勳位的一批人，勳爵士團：*the Order of the Garter* 獲得嘉德勳位的勳爵士團 **b)** a special piece of metal, silk etc that members of the order wear at ceremonies 〔獲勳位者佩戴的〕勳章

23 ▶MONEY 錢財◀ [C] an official piece of paper that can be exchanged for money 匯票，匯單 —see also 另見 POSTAL ORDER, BANKER'S ORDER, MONEY ORDER

24 the lower orders *BrE old-fashioned* people who belong to the lowest social class【英，過時】低下階層

25 ▶OF ANIMALS/PLANTS 動物的/植物的◀ [C] *technical* a group of animals or plants that are considered together because they are descended from the same plant or animal in EVOLUTION (1)【術語】〔動、植物分類用的〕目 —compare 比較 CLASS¹ (6), KINGDOM (3), SPECIES

26 ▶COMPUTER 電腦◀ [C] *AmE technical* a list of jobs that a computer has to do in a particular order【美，術語】任務排序；等待隊列；QUEUE *BrE*【英】—see also 另見 POINT OF ORDER, **tall order** (TALL (3)), STANDING ORDER, PECKING ORDER, **be given/get your marching orders** (MARCH¹ (5)), **under starter's orders** (STARTER (3)), **set/put your own house in order** (HOUSE¹ (7))

This graph shows some of the words most commonly used with the noun **order**. 本圖表所示為含有名詞 order 的一些最常用詞組。

in order
first/highest/high order
out of order
give orders
good/working order
take orders
chronological/alphabetical order
right/wrong order

10 20 30 40 50 60 70 80 90 100 per million 每百萬

Based on the British National Corpus and the Longman Lancaster Corpus
據英國國家語料庫和朗文蘭卡斯特語料庫

order² *v* **1** [I,T] to ask for goods or services 點菜; 訂購: *Have you ordered yet, madam?* 夫人, 您點過菜了嗎? | **order sth** *She ordered a double brandy.* 她要了一杯雙份白蘭地。| **order sb sth** *We'll order you a taxi from the station.* 我們會為你在車站預訂一輛計程車。| **order sth for sb/sth** *I've ordered new curtains for the living room.* 我已經為起居室訂購了新窗簾。**2** [T] to tell someone to do something, using your authority or power 命令, 指令; 囑咐: *"Stay right there," she ordered.* "就待在這裡。"她命令道。| **order sb in/out etc** *If you make any more noise I'll order you out of the room.* 要是你再吵, 我就要你離開這個房間。| **order sb to do sth** *The commandant ordered them to line up against the wall.* 指揮官命令他們靠牆排成一行。| **order sth** *Only the king has the power to order the release of the prisoners.* 只有國王有權下令釋放囚犯。| **[+that]** *A grand jury has ordered that Schultz be sent for trial.* 大陪審團已下令將舒爾茨送審。**3** [T] to arrange something in an order 安排, 整理: *The diamonds are ordered according to size.* 這些鑽石是按規格大小整理排列的。**4** [T] *old use* to arrange things neatly or effectively【舊】將…收拾整齊; 有效地安排

order sb **about/around** *phr v* [T] *BrE* to continuously give someone orders in an annoying or threatening way【英】不斷地支使〔某人〕,〔專橫地〕將〔某人〕差來遣去: *Keith's older brother is always ordering him around.* 基思的大哥總是支使他幹這幹那。

order sb ↔ **out** *phr v* [T] to order soldiers or police to go somewhere to stop violent behaviour by a crowd 下令出動〔軍警等〕: *The Governor decided to order out the National Guard.* 州長決定出動國民警衛隊。

or·dered /ˈɔrdɚd; ˈɔːdəd/ also 又作 **well-ordered** *adj* well arranged or controlled 有條理的, 有秩序的: *a well-ordered household* 井然有序的家庭 | *an ordered existence* 安排得很好的生活 —compare 比較 DISORDERED (1)

or·der·ly¹ /ˈɔrdɚlɪ; ˈɔːdəli/ *adj* **1** arranged or organized in a sensible or neat way 有條理的, 整齊的: *an orderly household* 整潔的家庭 | *an orderly mind* 有條理的頭腦 **2** peaceful or well-behaved 守秩序的: *An orderly crowd assembled at the gate.* 一羣守秩序的人聚集在大門口。—**orderliness** *n* [U]

orderly² *n* [C] **1** someone who does unskilled jobs in a hospital〔醫院裡從事簡單工作的〕護理員, 勤雜人員 **2** a soldier who does unskilled jobs 勤務兵

order pa·per /ˈ·· ˌ··/ *n* [C] a list of subjects to be discussed in the British Parliament〔英國議會的〕議事日程表

or·di·nal¹ /ˈɔrdṇəl; ˈɔːdɪnəl/ *adj* showing a position in a set of numbers 順序的, 依次的

ordinal² *n* [C] an ordinal number 序數

ordinal num·ber /ˌ··· ˈ··/ *n* [C] one of the numbers such as first, second, third etc which show the order of things 序數〈如第一、第二、第三等〉—compare 比較 CARDINAL NUMBER

or·di·nance /ˈɔrdṇəns; ˈɔːdɪnəns/ *n* [C] **1** an order given by a ruler or governing organization 條例, 法令, 法規: *a Royal ordinance* 敕令, 聖旨 **2** *AmE* a law, usually of a city or town, that forbids or restricts an activity【美】〔城鎮頒布的〕法規, 條例: *contravening city ordinances* 違反城市法規

or·di·na·ri·ly /ˌɔrdṇˈɛrɪlɪ; ˈɔːdənərɪli/ *adv* **1** [sentence adverb 句子副詞] usually 通常: *Ordinarily, the process of buying clothes irritates me.* 買衣服的過程通常都使我感到煩躁。| *It is ordinarily possible to predict the results with some accuracy.* 準確預測結果通常是可能的。**2** in an ordinary or normal way 平常地, 普普通通地: *He was walking along quite ordinarily.* 他很平常地走着。

or·di·na·ry /ˈɔrdṇˌɛrɪ; ˈɔːdənəri/ *adj* **1** average, common, or usual, not different or special 普通的, 平常的, 通常的: *part of a politician's ordinary routine* 政治家例行公事的一部分 | *The new taxes came as a shock to ordinary Americans.* 新稅費使美國的普羅大眾大為震驚。| **out of the ordinary** (=unusual or unexpected) 不尋常的; 例外的 *Nothing out of the ordinary had happened.* 沒發生甚麼意外之事。| **in the ordinary way** *BrE* (=normally)【英】一般, 通常 *Jim was not in the ordinary way a romantic, but he decided to bring Joanna some roses.* 吉姆通常並不是一個浪漫的人, 但他決定送一些玫瑰花給喬安娜。**2** not particularly good or impressive 平淡無奇的: *I thought the paintings were pretty ordinary.* 我認為這些畫是泛泛之作。—see also 另見 EXTRAORDINARY (1,2) —**ordinariness** *n* [U]

ordinary sea·man /ˌ··· ˈ··/ *n* [C] a low rank in the British Navy〔英國海軍的〕二等水兵, 見習水兵 —see table on page C6 參見 C6 頁附錄

ordinary shares /ˌ··· ˈ·/ *n* [plural] *technical* the largest part of a company's CAPITAL¹ (2), which is owned by people who have the right to vote at meetings and to receive part of the company's profits【術語】普通股〔公司資本的最大一部分。擁有普通股的股東可在股東會上投票及在公司贏利時分享紅利〕

or·di·na·tion /ˌɔrdṇˈeʃən; ˌɔːdɪˈneɪʃən/ *n* [C,U] the act or ceremony making someone a priest 授聖職(禮): *the ordination of women* 授予婦女聖職

ord·nance /ˈɔrdnəns; ˈɔːdnəns/ *n* [U] **1** large guns with wheels; ARTILLERY (1) 大砲 **2** weapons, explosives, and vehicles used in fighting 軍械〈如武器、彈藥、軍車等〉

ordnance sur·vey map /ˌ·· ˈ··· ·/ *n* [C] *BrE* a map which shows all the roads, paths, hills etc of an area in detail【英】〔精細準確的〕地形測量圖

or·dure /ˈɔrdʒɚ; ˈɔːdjʊə/ *n* [U] *formal* dirt, especially waste matter from the body【正式】污物; 排泄物, 糞便

ore /ɔr; ɔː/ *n* [C,U] rock or earth from which metal can be obtained 礦石, 礦砂: *iron ore* 鐵礦石 | *veins of rich ore* 富礦脈

o·reg·a·no /əˈrɛgəno; ˌɔrɪˈgɑːnəʊ/ *n* [U] a plant used in cooking, especially in Italian cooking 牛至〔可用作調味品的植物, 尤用於意大利烹調〕

or·gan /ˈɔrgən; ˈɔːgən/ *n* [C]

1 ▶BODY PART 人體部位◀ **a)** a part of the body, such as the heart or lungs, that has a particular purpose 器官: *inflammation affecting the internal organs* 影響內臟的炎症 | *an organ transplant* 器官移植 **b)** a word meaning PENIS, used because you want to avoid saying this directly〔委婉語〕陰莖

2 ▶MUSICAL INSTRUMENT 樂器◀ a large musical instrument used especially in churches, with one or more keyboards (KEYBOARD¹ (1)) and large pipes out of which the sound comes 管風琴: *an organ recital in Westminster Cathedral* 西敏寺大教堂的管風琴獨奏會

3 ▶ORGANIZATION 機構◀ an organization that is part of, or works for, a larger organization or group 部門, 機關, 機構: **[+of]** *Giving too much power to any organ of government should be avoided.* 應避免給予任何一個政府部門過多的權力。

4 ▶NEWSPAPER/MAGAZINE 報紙/雜誌◀ *formal* a

newspaper or magazine which gives information, news etc for an organization【正式】機關報刊, 宣傳工具, 喉舌: [+of] *This publication is the organ of the Conservative Party.* 這份刊物是保守黨的機關報。
5 ▶PLANT 植物◀ a part of a plant, such as a leaf or stem, that has a special purpose 植物器官〈如葉子、莖等〉

or·gan·die also 又作 **organdy** *AmE*【美】/ˈɔrgəndɪ; ˈɔːgəndi/ *n* [U] very thin, stiff cotton, used as dress material〔做女裝用的〕蟬翼紗, 玻璃紗

organ grind·er /ˈ·· ˌ··/ *n* [C] a musician who plays a BARREL ORGAN in the street〔街頭的〕手搖風琴師

or·gan·ic /ɔrˈgænɪk; ɔːˈgænɪk/ *adj*
1 ▶LIVING THINGS 生物◀ living, or produced by or from living things 生物的, 有機物的: *Peat is decomposed organic matter.* 泥炭是已分解的有機物。—opposite 反義詞 INORGANIC (1)
2 ▶BODY ORGANS 人體器官◀ concerning the organs of the body 器官的: *organic diseases* 器官疾病
3 ▶PART OF STH 某物的部分◀ a) made up of many parts that all depend on each other 有組織[系統]的: *an organic system* 有組織的系統 | *an organic link between the music and the meaning* 音樂與含義之間的有機聯繫 **b)** connected with the relationship between these parts 有機的, 不可分割的
4 ▶FARMING 農業◀ using farming or gardening methods without artificial chemicals, or produced or grown by these methods 不使用化肥[農藥]生產的, 施用有機肥料的: *organic vegetables* 有機蔬菜 | *an organic farmer* 用有機肥料耕作的農民
5 ▶DEVELOPMENT 發展◀ change or development which is organic happens in a natural way, without anyone planning it or forcing it to happen 自然發展的 —**organically** /-klɪ; -kli/ *adv*

organic chem·is·try /·ˌ·· ˈ···/ *n* [U] the study of CARBON (1) compounds 有機化學 —compare 比較 INORGANIC CHEMISTRY

S3 **or·gan·is·m** /ˈɔrgənˌɪzəm; ˈɔːgənɪzəm/ *n* [C] **1** an animal, plant, human, or any other living thing 生物, 有機體: *the human organism* 人體組織 | *a microscopic organism living in the cow's stomach* 寄生在牛胃裡的微生物 **2** a system made up of parts that are dependent on each other 有機組織[體系]: *A society is essentially an organism.* 就本質而言, 社會是一個有機整體。

or·gan·ist /ˈɔrgənɪst; ˈɔːgənᵻst/ *n* [C] someone who plays the ORGAN (2) 管風琴手, 管風琴演奏家: *a church organist* 教堂的管風琴手

S2 W1 **or·gan·i·za·tion** also 又作 **organisation** *BrE*【英】/ˌɔrgənəˈzeʃən; ˌɔːgənaɪˈzeɪʃən/ *n* **1** [C] a group such as a club or business that has formed for a particular purpose 組織, 團體, 機構: *a charitable organization* 慈善機構 **2** [U] the act of planning and arranging things effectively 統籌安排, 組織, 協調: *Organisation's never been my strong point.* 做組織工作向來不是我的長處。| [+of] *The organization of the fund raisers has been left to Ellen.* 募捐活動的籌備工作交給了埃倫。**3** [U] the way in which the different parts of a system are arranged and work together 結構, 體制: [+of] *the social organization of primitive cultures* 各種原始文化的社會結構 —**organizational** *adj*: *organizational ability* 組織能力 —**organizationally** *adv*

S1 W2 **or·gan·ize** also 又作 -ise *BrE*【英】/ˈɔrgənˌaɪz; ˈɔːgənaɪz/ *v* **1** [T] to make the necessary arrangements so that an activity can happen 籌劃, 籌辦: *They organized a protest march.* 他們籌劃了一次抗議遊行。| *Who's going to organise the party this year?* 誰來籌辦今年的聚會? **2** [T] to arrange information, work, a group etc so that it works correctly 組織; 安排; 將...编組: *Organize your thoughts before you begin to speak.* 把思緒理清楚再說話。| *A team of professionals will organize the volunteers.* 一個專家小組將給志願人員編隊。| **be organized in/along/around** *The political system is organized along party lines.* 這個政治體制是按照政黨的路線建立的。| *industrial towns organized around places of work* 環繞工作場所建立的工業城鎮 **3** [I,T] *especially AmE* to form a TRADE UNION (=an organization that protects workers' rights) or persuade people to join one; UNIONIZE【尤美】組織工會; 使加入工會

or·gan·ized also 又作 **organised** *BrE*【英】/ˈɔrgənˌaɪzd; ˈɔːgənaɪzd/ *adj* **1** achieving aims in an effective, ordered, and sensible way 有序的, 有組織[條理]的: *I'm sorry I forgot – I'm not very organized these days.* 對不起我忘了 —— 我這些天腦子有點亂。| *You can be sure the conference will be well organised if Barb is in charge.* 如果由巴布來負責, 你可以肯定大會將組織得有條不紊。| **get organized** *spoken*【口】*I have to get organized and get some things done.* 我得讓自己清醒一下, 做掉一些事情。| **highly organized** (=very well organized) 高度組織化的, 很有條理的 *a highly organized social system* 高度組織化的社會體系 —opposite 反義詞 DISORGANIZED **2** an organized activity is arranged for and done by many people〔活動〕有組織的, 安排有序的; 由多人參與的: *organized religion* 有組織的宗教 | *organized sports* 安排有序的體育活動 S3

organized crime /ˌ··· ˈ·/ *n* [U] a large and powerful organization of criminals 有組織罪行, 集團犯罪; 犯罪集團: *moves to combat terrorism, drug trafficking and organized crime* 打擊恐怖主義、販毒及有組織罪行的行動

or·gas·m /ˈɔrgæzəm; ˈɔːgæzəm/ *n* [C,U] the greatest point of sexual pleasure 性高潮

or·gas·mic /ɔrˈgæzmɪk; ɔːˈgæzmɪk/ *adj* **1** *technical* related to orgasm【術語】性高潮的 **2** *slang* extremely exciting or enjoyable【俚】極度興奮的; 令人非常愉快的

or·gy /ˈɔrdʒɪ; ˈɔːdʒi/ *n* [C] **1** a wild party with a lot of eating, drinking, and sexual activity〔縱慾的〕狂歡宴會, 縱酒宴樂 **2** sexual activity in a group 集體縱慾, 羣交 **3 an orgy of** a short time spent doing too much of an activity in a way that is not sensible or controlled 無節制的〔行為、活動〕: *an orgy of shopping* 無節制的購物 —**orgiastic** *adj*

o·ri·el win·dow /ˈɔrɪəl ˌwɪndo; ˈɔːriəl ˌwɪndəʊ/ *n* [C] *technical* an upper window that is built out from a wall【術語】凸肚窗

o·ri·ent[1] /ˈɔrɪɛnt; ˈɔːriənt/ also 又作 **orientate** *BrE*【英】*v* **1 be oriented to/towards** to be developed, trained, made etc for a particular purpose 針對, 面向; 以...為方向; 為...設計: *an English language course oriented towards the needs of businessmen* 針對商務人士需要而開設的英語課程 **2 be oriented around** if something is oriented around a particular idea, that idea is very important to it 圍繞, 以...為重點: *Wanda's whole life has been oriented around the children.* 温達的一生全是在為孩子們操心。**3 orient yourself a)** to find your position with a map or a COMPASS (1)〔依據地圖或指南針〕確定自己的方位: *The climbers stopped to orientate themselves.* 登山者停下來確定自己所在的位置。**b)** to become familiar with a new situation 使自己熟悉新環境[新情況]: *I'll need a few days to orient myself.* 我需要幾天時間來熟習新環境。

o·ri·ent[2] *n* **the Orient** *old-fashioned* the eastern part of the world, especially China and Japan and the countries near them【過時】東方 (世界)〔尤指中國和日本及鄰近國家〕—compare 比較 **the East** (EAST (1a)), OCCIDENT

orient[3] *adj poetic*【詩】**1** eastern 東方的 **2 orient star/sun** a rising star or sun 正在升起的星星/太陽

o·ri·en·tal[1] /ˌɔrɪˈɛntl; ˌɔːriˈentl◂/ *adj* concerning or from the East or South-East Asia 東方的; 東南亞的: *oriental countries* 東方國家 | *oriental culture* 東方文化

oriental[2] *n* [C] *old-fashioned* a word meaning someone from an oriental country, which is now usually considered offensive【過時】東方人〔現通常視為具冒犯性〕—compare 比較 OCCIDENTAL

o·ri·en·tal·ist /ˌɔrɪˈɛntlɪst; ˌɔːriˈentəlᵻst/ *n* [C] someone who studies the languages and culture of oriental countries〔研究東方國家語言、文化等的〕東方學專家, 東方通

o·ri·en·tate /ˈɔriɛn͵tet; ˈɔːriənteɪt/ *v BrE* another form of the word ORIENT¹【英】orient¹ 的另一種形式: *an English language course orientated towards the needs of businessmen* 針對商務人士需要而開設的英語課程 | *The climbers stopped half way up the mountain to orientate themselves.* 登山者在半山腰停下來確定自己所在的位置。| *I'll need a few days to orientate myself.* 我需要幾天時間來熟習新環境。

o·ri·en·ta·tion /͵ɔriɛnˋteʃən; ͵ɔːriənˈteɪʃən/ *n* [C,U] **1** the aims or interests of a particular activity or organization 目標, 目的; 興趣: **[+towards/to]** *an orientation to world affairs* 對世界事務的興趣 | **[+of]** *the orientation of post-war policy* 戰後政策的目標 **2 political/religious orientation** the political views or religious beliefs that you have 政治/宗教傾向 **3 sexual orientation** the fact that someone is HETEROSEXUAL or HOMOSEXUAL 性取向〔指某人是異性戀還是同性戀〕: *questions about race and sexual orientation* 有關種族和性取向的問題 **4** [U] *especially AmE* training and preparation for a new job or activity【尤美】〔為熟悉新工作或活動的〕培訓, 準備: *This is orientation week for all the new students.* 這是讓全體新生熟悉情況的迎新周。**5** [C] the angle or position of an object in relation to another object or a direction 定向; 定位

o·ri·ent·ed /ˈɔriɛntɪd; ˈɔːriəntɪ̣d/ also 又作 **o·ri·en·ta·ted** /ˈɔriɛn͵tetɪd; ˈɔːriənteɪtɪ̣d/ *BrE*【英】*adj* **politically oriented/family oriented etc** giving a lot of time, effort, or attention to politics, family etc 重視政治的/家庭的等: *The new generation doesn't seem to be politically oriented at all.* 新一代人好像對政治全無興趣。

o·ri·en·teer·ing /͵ɔriənˋtɪrɪŋ; ͵ɔːriənˈtɪərɪŋ/ *n* [U] a sport in which people have to find their way quickly across unknown country using a map and a COMPASS (1) 定向運動, 越野識途比賽〔一種靠地圖和指南針快速尋找目的地的運動〕

or·i·fice /ˈɔrəfɪs; ˈɒrɪ̣fɪ̣s/ *n* [C] **1** *technical or humorous* one of the holes in your body, such as your mouth, nose etc【術語或幽默】〔身體上的〕孔, 洞: *the dental orifice* 牙洞 **2** *formal* a hole or entrance【正式】孔, 洞; 入口

o·ri·ga·mi /͵ɔrəˋgɑmɪ; ͵ɒrɪˈgɑːmi/ *n* [U] the Japanese art of folding paper to make attractive objects〔日本的〕摺紙藝術, 摺紙手工

2 **or·i·gin** /ˈɔrədʒɪn; ˈɒrɪ̣dʒɪ̣n/ *n* **1** also 又作 **origins** [plural] the situation, place, or physical matter from which something begins 起源, 開端: **[+of]** *the origins of language* 語言的起源 | **have your/its origin in sth** (=begin in a particular place, situation etc) 起源於… *Many of the problems had their origin in post-war Europe.* 其中的許多問題起源於戰後的歐洲。**2** also 又作 **origins** [plural] the country, race or class from which someone or their family comes 出身, 血統; 來歷: *They are proud of their aristocratic origins.* 他們因出身於名門望族而感到自豪。**3** [C] *technical* the point where two axes (AXIS (3)) cross on a GRAPH【術語】〔曲線圖上兩根軸線相交處的〕原點

1 1 **o·rig·i·nal¹** /əˋrɪdʒənl̩; əˈrɪdʒɪ̣nəl/ *adj* **1** [only before noun 僅用於名詞前] existing or happening first, before being changed or replaced by something or someone else 原先的, 最早的, 最初的: *The land was returned to its original owner.* 這塊土地被歸還給原主。| *We still have the original stone floor.* 我們還保留着原先的石頭地面。**2** completely new and different from anything that anyone has thought of before 新穎的, 獨特的; 與眾不同的, 獨創的: *a highly original style* 極為獨特的風格 | *an original thinker* 富有創見的思想家 | *What an original idea!* 多麼別出心裁的主意啊! **3** [only before noun 僅用於名詞前] not copied 原版的, 非抄襲的, 非模仿的: *an original Holbein drawing* 霍爾拜因的原畫

original² *n* [C] **1** a painting, document, etc that is not a copy, but is the one produced by the writer or artist〔繪畫、文件等的〕原件, 原物, 原稿, 原作品: *The colour was paler in the original.* 原作的色彩要淡一些。| *I'll keep a copy, and give you the original.* 我將留一份副本, 把原件給你。**2 in the original** in the language that a book, play etc was first written in, before it was translated 原著的語言, 原文: *I read it in the original.* 我讀過它的原著。**3** *informal* someone whose behaviour, clothing etc is unusual and amusing【非正式】〔舉止、服飾等〕怪異滑稽的人

o·rig·i·nal·i·ty /ə͵rɪdʒəˋnælətɪ; ə͵rɪdʒɪ̣ˈnælɪ̣ti/ *n* [U] the quality of being completely new and different from anything that anyone has thought of before 獨創性; 創見; 創造力; 新穎: *poems of great originality* 非常新穎獨特的詩

o·rig·i·nal·ly /əˋrɪdʒənl̩ɪ; əˈrɪdʒɪnəli/ *adv* in the beginning 最初, 原先: *The family originally came from France.* 那個家族最初來自法國。| *The book was originally conceived as an autobiography, but it became a novel.* 該書最初的構思是一部自傳, 但後來卻寫成了一本小說。| [sentence adverb 句子副詞] *Originally, we had planned a tour of Scotland but we never got further than Edinburgh.* 我們原先計劃周遊蘇格蘭, 但最後最遠的只去到了愛丁堡。 2 2

original sin /· ͵··· ˈ·/ *n* [U] the state of disobedience to God which everyone is in from birth, according to some Christian teaching 原罪〔基督教教義中的指人類與生俱來的罪孽〕

o·rig·i·nate /əˋrɪdʒə͵net; əˈrɪdʒɪ̣neɪt/ *v* **1** [I always+adv/prep, not in progressive 不用進行式] *formal* to start to develop in a particular place or from a particular situation【正式】發源; 開始; 起因: **[+in/from/with]** *a custom originating in Chinese culture* 源自中國文化的一種習俗 | *How did the idea originate?* 這主意是怎麼來的? **2** [T] to have the idea for something and start it 創始; 創造; 發起: *Who originated the present complaints procedures?* 誰最先創建了現在這套投訴程序?

o·rig·i·nat·or /əˋrɪdʒə͵netɚ; əˈrɪdʒɪ̣neɪtə/ *n* [C] the person who first has the idea for something and starts it 創始人; 發明者: **[+of]** *the originator of a whole genre of detective fiction, Edgar Allan Poe*〔美國作家〕埃德加·艾倫·坡, 偵探小說體裁的創始者

or·i·ole /ˈɔrɪ͵ol; ˈɔːriəʊl/ *n* [C] **1** a N. American bird that is black with a red and yellow stripe on its wing 擬黃鸝〔產於北美洲, 黑色羽毛, 翅膀帶紅黃色條紋〕**2** a European bird with black wings and a yellow body 金黃鸝〔產於歐洲, 黃色羽毛, 翅膀為黑色〕

or·i·son /ˈɔrɪzn̩; ˈɒrɪ̣zən/ *n* [C] *old use* a prayer【舊】祈禱

or·mo·lu /ˈɔrmə͵lu; ˈɔːməluː/ *n* [U] a gold-coloured mixture of metals, not containing real gold 鍍金用金箔, 仿金箔(塗料): *an ormolu clock* 鍍金的時鐘

or·na·ment¹ /ˈɔrnəmənt; ˈɔːnəmənt/ *n* **1** [C] an object that you keep in your house because it is beautiful rather than useful 裝飾品, 點綴物, 飾物, 擺設: *china ornaments* 瓷器飾品 **2** [U] decoration that is added to something 裝飾, 點綴: *plain architecture with very little ornament* 樸實無華的建築風格 **3 be an ornament to** *old-fashioned* to add honour, importance, or beauty to something【過時】給…增加光彩[重要性、美麗]: **[+to]** *She is an ornament to her profession.* 她為同業增了光。

ornament² *v* **be ornamented with** to be decorated with something 用…裝飾, 裝飾有…: *a silver goblet ornamented with pearls* 綴有珍珠的銀製高腳酒杯

or·na·men·tal /͵ɔrnəˋmɛntl̩; ͵ɔːnəˈmentl◂/ *adj* designed to decorate something 裝飾(用)的, 觀賞(用)的: *ornamental gardens* 觀賞用的花園 | *These buttons are only ornamental.* 這些扣子只是用作裝飾。—**ornamentally** *adv*

or·na·men·ta·tion /͵ɔrnəmɛnˋteʃən; ͵ɔːnəmenˈteɪʃən/ *n* [U] decoration 裝飾, 修飾; 裝飾性: *the Victorian love of ornamentation* 維多利亞時代對裝飾的喜愛

or·nate /ɔrˋnet; ɔːˈneɪt/ *adj* a lot of decoration, or too much decoration, especially with many complicated details 裝飾華美的, 華麗的, 過分修飾的: *a heavy ornate gold cigarette case* 一個很重的華麗的金質煙盒 —**or-**

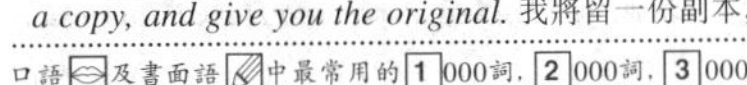

nately *adv* —**ornateness** *n* [U]

or·ne·ry /ˈɔrnərɪ; ˈɔːnəri/ *adj humorous AmE* behaving in an unreasonable and angry way【幽默, 美】脾氣壞的, 執拗的

or·ni·thol·o·gist /ˌɔrnɪˈθɑlədʒɪst; ˌɔːnɪ̇ˈθɒlədʒɪ̇st/ *n* [C] someone who studies birds 鳥類學家

or·ni·thol·o·gy /ˌɔrnəˈθɑlədʒɪ; ˌɔːnɪ̇ˈθɒlədʒi/ *n* [U] the scientific study of birds 鳥類學 —**ornithological** /ˌɔrnɪθəˈlɑdʒɪkḷ; ˌɔːnɪ̇θəˈlɒdʒɪkəl◂/ *adj*

o·ro·tund /ˈɔrəˌtʌnd; ˈɒrəʊtʌnd/ *adj formal*【正式】**1** an orotund sound or voice is strong and clear〔聲音〕洪亮的, 嘹亮的, 高昂的 **2** orotund speech or writing is trying to sound important and impressive〔演說、文筆等〕做作的, 浮誇的, 誇張的

or·phan¹ /ˈɔrfən; ˈɔːfən/ *n* [C] a child whose parents are both dead 孤兒: *the plight of thousands of war orphans* 數以千計的戰爭孤兒的困境

orphan² *v* **be orphaned** to become an orphan 成為孤兒: *She was orphaned when her parents died in a plane crash.* 父母死於空難後, 她便成了孤兒。

or·phan·age /ˈɔrfənɪdʒ; ˈɔːfənɪdʒ/ *n* [C] a place where orphan children live 孤兒院: *He was raised in a Catholic orphanage.* 他是在一家天主教會辦的孤兒院裡長大的。

or·tho·don·tics /ˌɔrθəˈdɑntɪks; ˌɔːθəˈdɒntɪks/ *n* [U] the practice or skill of making teeth grow straight when they have not been growing correctly 正牙術; 畸齒矯正術 —**orthodontic** *adj*: *orthodontic treatment* 畸齒矯正治療

or·tho·don·tist /ˌɔrθəˈdɑntɪst; ˌɔːθəˈdɒntɪ̇st/ *n* [C] a DENTIST who is a specialist in making teeth grow straight when they have not been growing correctly 正牙醫生

or·tho·dox /ˈɔrθəˌdɑks; ˈɔːθədɒks/ *adj* **1** ideas or behaviour that are orthodox are considered by most people to be normal, correct and acceptable 傳統的, 正統的: *orthodox theories of medicine* 傳統醫學理論 —see also 另見 UNORTHODOX **2** believing in and following all the traditional beliefs, laws, and practices of a religion〔宗教觀念〕正統的, 信奉宗教觀念的; 循規蹈矩的: *an orthodox Jew* 正統派猶太教徒 **3** believing in or following the usual form of a particular set of ideas 正統觀念的: *orthodox monetarism* 正統貨幣主義

Orthodox Church /ˌ··· ˈ·/ *n* [U] one of the Christian churches in eastern Europe and parts of Asia〔東歐及亞洲部分地區的〕正教(會), 東正教(會)

or·tho·dox·y /ˈɔrθəˌdɑksɪ; ˈɔːθədɒksi/ *n* **1** [C,U] an idea or set of ideas considered by most people to be normal, correct and acceptable 正統觀念: *The early feminists challenged the social and political orthodoxy of their time.* 早期的女權主義者對他們那個時代的社會及政治方面的正統觀念提出了挑戰。**2** the traditional ideas and beliefs of a group or religion, or the practice of following these strictly〔團體或宗教的〕傳統觀念[信仰]; 傳統習俗

or·thog·ra·phy /ɔrˈθɑgrəfɪ; ɔːˈθɒgrəfi/ *n* [U] *technical*【術語】**1** the spelling of words 拼字法 **2** correct spelling 正確拼字法 —**orthographic** /ˌɔrθəˈgræfɪk; ˌɔːθəˈgræfɪk◂/ *adj* —**orthographically** /-klɪ; -kli/ *adv*

or·tho·pe·dic, orthopaedic /ˌɔrθəˈpidɪk; ˌɔːθəˈpiːdɪk◂/ *adj* **1** connected with or providing medical treatment for problems affecting bones, muscles etc 矯形學的, 矯形外科的: *an orthopaedic surgeon* 矯形外科醫生 **2 orthopedic bed/chair/shoe etc** one that is designed to cure or prevent medical problems affecting your bones, muscles etc 矯形牀 / 矯形椅 / 矯形鞋等 —**orthopedically** /-klɪ; -kli/ *adv*: *orthopedically designed seats* 為矯形設計的座椅

or·tho·pe·dics, orthopaedics /ˌɔrθəˈpidɪks; ˌɔːθəˈpiːdɪks/ *n* [U] the area of medical science or treatment that deals with problems, diseases, or injuries of bones, muscles etc 矯形學; 矯[整]形外科

or·tho·pe·dist, orthopaedist /ˌɔrθəˈpidɪst; ˌɔːθəˈpiːdɪ̇st/ *n* [C] a doctor with special training in orthopedics 矯形外科醫生

-ory¹ /ɔrɪ; əri/ *suffix* [in nouns 構成名詞] a place or thing used for doing something 作…之用的場所[東西]: *an observatory* (=where people look at things, especially the stars) 天文台, 觀測台 | *a directory* 號碼簿

-ory² *suffix* [in adjectives 構成形容詞] describes something that does a particular thing 作…之用的: *an explanatory note* (=that gives an explanation) 注釋 | *a congratulatory telegram* (=that CONGRATULATES) 賀電

Os·car /ˈɑskɚ; ˈɒskə/ *n* [C] an American prize given each year for the best film, actor etc in the film industry 奧斯卡金像獎〔一年一度的美國電影獎〕: *the Oscar for best actress* 奧斯卡最佳女主角獎

os·cil·late /ˈɑsḷˌet; ˈɒsɪ̇leɪt/ *v* [I] **1** *technical* to keep moving regularly from side to side, between two limits【術語】〔兩點間有規律地〕來回擺動, 振動 **2** *formal* to keep changing between one feeling or attitude and another; VACILLATE【正式】搖擺不定, 躊躇: **[+between]** *Her attitude towards her husband oscillated between tender affection and deep mistrust.* 她對丈夫時而溫柔體貼, 時而疑慮重重, 態度飄忽。**3** if an electric current oscillates, it changes direction very regularly and very frequently〔電流很有規律並很頻繁地〕來回振蕩 —**oscillatory** /ˈɑsələˌtorɪ; ˈɒsɪ̇lətəri/ *adj*

os·cil·la·tion /ˌɑsḷˈeʃən; ˌɒsɪ̇ˈleɪʃən/ *n technical*【術語】**1** [U] the regular movement of something from side to side between two limits〔兩點間有規律的〕來回擺動 **2** [C] a single movement from side to side of something that is oscillating〔來回搖擺的〕一次擺動, 振幅

os·cil·la·tor /ˈɑsḷˌetɚ; ˈɒsɪ̇leɪtə/ *n* [C] a machine that produces electrical oscillations 振蕩器

-oses /osiz; əʊsiːz/ *suffix* the plural form of the suffix -OSIS 後綴 -osis 的複數形式

o·si·er /ˈoʒɚ; ˈəʊziə/ *n* [C] a type of WILLOW tree whose branches are used for making baskets 杞柳〔枝條可編筐籃〕

-osis /osɪs; əʊsɪ̇s/ *suffix plural* **-oses** /osiz; əʊsiːz/ [in nouns 構成名詞] **1** *technical* a diseased condition【術語】病, 病變狀態: *silicosis* (=a lung disease) 矽肺 | *neuroses* (=disorders of the mind) 神經機能病 **2** a condition or process 狀態; 過程: *a metamorphosis* (=change from one state to another) 變形; 變態 —**-otic** /ɑtɪk; ɒtɪk/ [in adjectives 構成形容詞]: *neurotic* 神經機能病的 | *hypnotic* 催眠(術)的 —**-otically** /ɑtɪklɪ; ɒtɪkli/ [in adverbs 構成副詞]

os·mo·sis /ɑzˈmosɪs; ɒzˈməʊsɪ̇s/ *n* [U] **1 by osmosis** if you learn facts or receive ideas by osmosis, you gradually learn them by hearing them often 通過耳濡目染, 靠潛移默化: *I must have learnt it by osmosis.* 這事我準是靠耳濡目染慢慢學會的。**2** *technical* the gradual process of liquid passing through a MEMBRANE (2)【術語】滲透(作用) —**osmotic** /ɑzˈmɑtɪk; ɒzˈmɒtɪk/ *adj* —**osmotically** /-klɪ; -kli/ *adv*

os·prey /ˈɑsprɪ; ˈɒspri/ *n* [C] a type of large bird that eats fish 鶚, 魚鷹

os·si·fy /ˈɑsəˌfaɪ; ˈɒsɪ̇faɪ/ *v* **1** [I] to become unwilling to consider new ideas or change your behaviour 墨守陳規; 僵化 **2** [I,T] *technical* to change into bone or to make something change into bone【術語】(使)骨化 —**ossification** /ˌɑsəfəˈkeʃən; ˌɒsɪ̇fɪ̇ˈkeɪʃən/ *n* [U]: *the rapid ossification of the Soviet hardline position* (前)蘇聯強硬立場的急速僵化

os·ten·si·ble /ɑsˈtɛnsəbḷ; ɒˈstensɪ̇bəl/ *adj* seeming to be the reason for or the purpose of something but usually hiding the real reason or purpose〔指理由或動機〕表面上的, 貌似真實的, 詭稱的: *The ostensible purpose of the war was to liberate a small nation from tyranny.* 這場戰爭的目的表面上是要把一個小國從專制政權解放出來。

os·ten·si·bly /ɑsˈtɛnsəblɪ; ɒˈstensɪ̇bli/ *adv* if something is done ostensibly for a particular reason, it is not really done for this reason but people pretend that it is 表面上, 假裝地: *The big bosses went to Hawaii, ostensibly* *to launch the new project.* 大老闆都去了夏威夷，表面上是要開展那個新項目。

os·ten·ta·tion /ˌɑstənˋteʃən; ˌɒstənˈteɪʃən/ *n* [U] an unnecessary show of wealth or knowledge intended to make people admire you〔財富或學識的〕炫耀，賣弄: *Their simple style of dress and complete lack of ostentation made me like them even more.* 他們簡樸的衣着和全無炫耀賣弄的作風令我更加喜歡他們。

os·ten·ta·tious /ˌɑstənˋteʃəs; ˌɒstənˈteɪʃəs◂/ *adj* **1** something that is ostentatious is large, looks expensive and is designed to make people think that its owner must be very rich 擺闊氣的，講排場的，鋪張的: *The hotel loomed huge and ostentatious above the street.* 那家飯店隱隱出現在街道前方，顯得又大又排場。**2** someone who is ostentatious likes to show everyone how rich they are 誇示的，炫耀的，賣弄的: *I was vaguely annoyed by his generosity which seemed almost ostentatious.* 他大方得幾乎就像在炫耀，讓我隱隱地感到一絲不快。—**ostentatiously** *adv*

osteo- /ɑstɪə; ɒstiəʊ/ *prefix technical* concerning bones【術語】骨的

os·te·o·ar·thri·tis /ˌɑstɪoɑrˋθraɪtɪs; ˌɒstiəʊɑːˈθraɪtɪ̠s/ *n* [U] *technical* a condition which makes your knees and other joints stiff and painful【術語】骨關節炎

os·te·o·path /ˋɑstɪəˌpæθ; ˈɒstiəpæθ/ *n* [C] someone trained in osteopathy 整骨醫士，按骨醫士

os·te·op·a·thy /ˌɑstɪˋɑpəθɪ; ˌɒstiˈɒpəθi/ *n* [U] the practice or skill of treating physical problems such as back pain by moving and pressing muscles and bones 整骨術，按骨術

os·tler /ˋɑslɚ; ˈɒslə/ also 又作 **hostler** *AmE*【美】*n* [C] a man who, in former times, took care of guests' horses at a hotel〔舊時旅店照料客人馬匹的〕馬夫

os·tra·cize also 又作 **-cise** *BrE*【英】/ˋɑstrəˌsaɪz; ˈɒstrəsaɪz/ *v* [T] if a group of people ostracize someone, they stop accepting them as a member of the group〔一夥人〕把…排除在外，排斥: *Reg was ostracized by the whole squadron, who cursed his actions.* 雷格遭到整個中隊的排斥，他們咒罵他的一舉一動。—**ostracism** /-sɪzəm; -sɪzəm/ *n* [U]

os·trich /ˋɔstrɪtʃ; ˈɒstrɪtʃ/ *n* [C] **1** a large African bird with long legs, that runs very quickly but cannot fly 鴕鳥 **2** *informal* someone who refuses to accept that unpleasant problems exist instead of dealing with them【非正式】鴕鳥般的人，不願正視不快現實的人

OT the written abbreviation of 縮寫= OLD TESTAMENT

OTC /ˌo ti ˋsi; ˌəʊ tiː ˈsiː◂/ the abbreviation of 縮寫= OVER-THE-COUNTER (2)

S1 W1 **oth·er** /ˋʌðɚ; ˈʌðə/ *determiner, adj, pron* **1** used when there are two people, things etc to mean the one that is not being used, the one that you do not already have etc〔兩者中的〕另一個，其他的人[東西]: **the other** *She was driving the car with one hand and wiping the window with the other.* 她一隻手開車，另一隻手擦車窗。| *I've got mud all over my trousers – are my others clean?* 我褲子上全是泥，我的另一條乾淨嗎? | **the other person, thing etc** *On weekends I do all my housework on one day so the other day I'm free to relax.* 週末我把所有的家務一天幹完，另一天就有空放鬆一下。| **the other one** *I recognize one of the guitarists but who's the other one?* 我認得其中一個結他手，但另一個是誰? **2** used to mean all the people, things etc that are not the particular one you are talking about 所有其他的，其餘的: **the other people/things etc** *Olivia is cleverer than all the other children in the class.* 奧莉維亞比班上別的孩子都聰明。| *The museum may be closed but the other tourist places are open.* 博物館可能已經關門，但其他旅遊景點還開着。| **the others** *The wine glasses got broken but some of the others are alright.* 葡萄酒杯都破了，但其他的一些還是完好的。| **other ones** *I bought this dress on sale. There were other ones that were nicer but I could only afford this one.* 這裙子我是在減價時買的，還有幾條比它好看，但我只買得起這一條。**3** used to mean more people or things in addition to the ones you already have or are talking about 更多的，另外的: **other people/things etc** *I know you've met Peter but I have two other brothers as well.* 我知道你見過彼得，但我還有兩個兄弟呢。| *I'm sure if you asked other people they would say the same.* 我敢肯定，如果你問別的人，他們也都會這麼說。**4** used to mean the people or things which are different from the ones you already have or are talking about 不同的: *Making omelettes is one way to cook eggs but there are others you know.* 蛋的一種做法是煎蛋卷，但你知道，還有別的做法呢。| **some/any/no etc other thing** *I'm busy – we'll have to meet some other time.* 我很忙，我們只能改天見面了。| *Do you know of any other job where you get as many benefits as this one?* 你知道還有甚麼工作有這麼多的福利待遇嗎? **5 others** [plural] other people or things 其他的人[物]: *Some of these lapel microphones are better than others.* 這些微型麥克風中有部分的質量比其他的更好。**6 other than** apart from a particular person or thing; except 除了: *You should get a little stiffness but other than that there should be no side effects.* 你會有一點僵硬的感覺，但除此之外應該不會有別的副作用。| *How can you say that religion is anything other than a way of controlling people?* 你怎麼能說宗教不是一種擺佈人的手段呢? **7 none other than** used when saying who someone is when you are surprised or shocked to find out exactly who they are 不是別人而正是: *The winner of 'journalist of the year' was none other than the editor's daughter.* 贏得"年度最佳記者"稱號的不是別人，正是主編的女兒。**8 a) on the other side/bank etc** on the opposite side of the road, river etc, facing you 在對面/對岸等: *There is a book store on the other side of the road.* 馬路對面有一家書店。**b) the other way/direction etc** in the opposite direction to the one you are moving in already 相反的方向等: *She thought it unusual that all the traffic was going the other way.* 所有車輛都跟她反向而行，她覺得很奇怪。**9 the other end/side etc** the end, side etc of something that is furthest away from where you are now 另一端/另一邊等: *My car broke down on the other side of town.* 我的汽車在城的另一邊出故障了。| *The woman on the other end of the phone didn't really understand what I'd asked for.* 電話另一端的女士不太明白我要些甚麼。**10 the other way around/round** *BrE* if the situation is the other way around, it is actually the opposite of how you thought it was【英】相反地，倒過來，以相反方式: *If you look at it the other way around, the soldiers were only trying to protect themselves.* 如果你反過來看，士兵們其實只是為了自衛而已。**11 the other day/morning etc** *especially spoken* on a recent day, morning etc【尤口】前幾天/前幾天早上等: *I saw Rufus the other day.* 前些天我看見了魯弗斯。**12 something/someone etc or other** used to mean a particular thing, person etc or anything or person that is similar 諸如此類的事/人等: *Don't worry, we'll get the money somehow or other.* 別擔心，我們會想個甚麼辦法弄到錢的。**13 in other words** used to express an idea or opinion in a way that is easier to understand 換句話說: *The company claims it's got to rationalize its workforce, in other words many of the staff will lose their jobs.* 公司宣稱必須合理配置勞動力，換言之，許多員工將失去工作。—compare 比較 ANOTHER —see also 另見 EACH OTHER, **every other** (EVERY (7)), **on the one hand ... on the other hand** (HAND[1] (36))

oth·er·ness /ˋʌðɚnɪs; ˈʌðənɪ̠s/ *n* [U] the quality of being strange or different 另一性；不同性；特異性

oth·er·wise /ˋʌðɚˌwaɪz; ˈʌðəwaɪz/ *adv* **1** [sentence adverb 句子副詞] a word meaning 'if not', often used when there will be a bad result if something does not happen 否則，要不然: *You'll have to go now, otherwise you'll miss your bus.* 你現在得走了，要不然就趕不上公共汽車了。| *They got two free tickets to Canada, otherwise they'd never have been able to afford to go.* 他們得 S1 W2

到了兩張去加拿大的免費機票，否則他們絕對出不起旅費的。| *A surveyor's inspection of the building revealed faults that might otherwise have been overlooked.* (=if there had not been an inspection) 檢視員檢查大樓時找出了一些毛病，要不然的話，這些毛病可能就被忽視了。**2 say/think/decide etc otherwise** to say, think etc something different from what has been mentioned 説/認為/決定等並非如此: *The government claims that the economy is improving, but this survey suggests otherwise.* 政府宣稱經濟狀況在好轉，但這份調查顯示情況並非如此。**3** [sentence adverb 句子副詞] except for what has just been mentioned 除此之外; 在其他方面: *I could hear the distant rumbling of traffic. Otherwise all was still.* 我能聽見遠處車輛的隆隆聲，除此之外，萬籟俱寂。| *He was tired but otherwise in good health.* 他很疲倦，但除此之外身體很健康。| [+adj/adv] *a few mistakes in an otherwise excellent piece of work* 瑕不掩瑜的一件作品 **4 or otherwise** *especially BrE* or not【尤英】或相反，或其反面: *We welcome any comments from viewers, favourable or otherwise.* 觀眾的任何意見，無論是褒是貶，我們都歡迎。**5 otherwise engaged** *formal* busy doing something else【正式】忙於別的事情: *I was unable to attend the conference because I was otherwise engaged.* 我無法出席會議，因為我在忙別的事情。**6 otherwise known as** also called 又稱，也叫: *Albert DeSalvo, otherwise known as the Boston strangler* 阿爾伯特·德薩爾沃，又稱波士頓扼殺者 **7 it cannot be otherwise/how can it be otherwise?** used to mean that it is impossible for something to be different from the way it is 不可能是別的/怎麼可能會是別的?: *Life in the military is hard – how can it be otherwise?* 軍隊生活是艱苦的，怎麼可能不艱苦呢?

oth·er·world·ly /ˋʌðɚˋwɝldlɪ; ˌʌðəˈwɜːldli◂/ *adj* more concerned with religious or SPIRITUAL[1] (1) thoughts than with normal daily life 超俗的，超脱塵世的

o·ti·ose /ˋoʃɪˌos; ˈəʊʃiəʊs/ *adj formal* ideas or words that are otiose are unnecessary; REDUNDANT (2)【正式】〔想法或言辭等〕不必要的，多餘的

OTT /ˌo ti ˋti; ˌəʊ tiː ˈtiː/ *adj BrE informal* OVER-THE-TOP【英，非正式】〔言行等〕過於誇張的，荒唐的

ot·ter /ˋɑtɚ; ˈɒtə/ *n* [C] a swimming animal that has smooth brown fur and eats fish 水獺

ot·to·man /ˋɑtəmən; ˈɒtəmən/ *n* [C] **1** a piece of furniture like a big box with a soft top, used as a seat and for storing things 褥榻，〔可存放東西的〕軟墊椅 **2** *AmE* a soft piece of furniture shaped like a box, used to rest your feet on when you are sitting down【美】軟墊擱腳櫈

OU /ˌo ˋju; ˌəʊ ˈjuː/ the abbreviation of 縮寫= OPEN UNIVERSITY

ou·bli·ette /ˌublɪˋɛt; ˌuːbliˈet/ *n* [C] a small room or prison in an old castle where prisoners were kept〔古堡中關押囚犯的〕土牢，地牢

ouch /aʊtʃ; aʊtʃ/ *interjection* a sound that you make when you feel sudden pain 哎唷!〔突然感到疼痛時的叫聲〕: *Ouch! That hurt!* 哎唷！那好疼!

ought /ɔt; ɔːt/ *modal verb* **1** used to say that someone should do something because it is the best or most sensible thing to do 應該〔指做最好或最明智的事〕: **ought to do sth** *I think you ought to make more time for yourself to relax.* 我認為你應該多給自己一些放鬆的時間。| *What you ought to have done is call the police.* 你當時應該報警。| *If Veronica's trying to get to college she ought to study more.* 要是維羅妮卡想上大學，她就應該多學習。**2** used to say that someone should do something because it is right 應該〔指做正確的事〕: **ought to do sth** *You ought to be ashamed of yourself.* 你應該感到羞恥。| *I don't care what you say – I still think he ought to have apologised.* 我不在乎你説甚麼 —— 我還是認為他本該道歉的。| **ought (to)** *"I can't decide whether to tell him the truth." "Well you ought to."* "我無法決定是否要告訴他真相。" "哦，你應該告訴他。" **3** used to say that you think something will probably happen, probably be true etc 可能會，預料會: **ought to do sth** *He left 2 hours ago so he ought to be there by now.* 他兩小時前動身的，現在該到那裡了。| *They ought to win, they've trained hard enough.* 他們應該能贏，他們訓練夠刻苦的。| *This ought to be good.* 這應該不錯。—see also 另見 SHOULD

oughtn't /ˋɔtn̩t; ˈɔːtnt/ the short form of 縮略式= 'ought not' 不應該: *You oughtn't to drive if you are feeling so drowsy.* 你要是感到這麼睏倦的話就不該開車。

Oui·ja board /ˋwidʒə ˌbord; ˈwiːdʒə bɔːd/ *n* [C] *trademark* a board with letters and signs on it, used to try to receive messages from the spirits of dead people【商標】靈應牌，靈乩板〔一種上有字母和符號，用於接收亡靈信息的乩板〕

ounce /aʊns; aʊns/ *n* **1** [C] written abbreviation 縮寫為 **oz** a unit for measuring weight equal to 28.35 grams 盎司，安士，英兩〔相等於 28.35 克〕—see table on page C3 參見 C3 頁附錄 —see also 另見 FLUID OUNCE **2 not an ounce of sense/truth/decency** no sense etc at all 毫無頭腦/真實性/禮節: *If you had an ounce of sense you wouldn't believe these stupid rumors!* 你要是有一點頭腦就不會相信這些愚蠢的謠言! **3 every (last) ounce of courage/energy/ strength** all the courage etc that you have (最後) 全部的勇氣/精力/力量: *He clung to the rock with every last ounce of strength in his body.* 他用體內最後一點兒力氣緊抓着岩石。

our /aʊr; aʊə/ *determiner* [possessive form of **we** we 的所有格] **1** of or belonging to us (屬於) 我們的: *Our daughter is in France at the moment.* 我們的女兒目前在法國。| *Winning the Grand Prix was one of our finest sporting achievements.* 贏得格蘭披治大賽是我們最傑出的體育成就之一。| *It is important that we preserve our natural resources.* 保護我們的自然資源很重要。**2** *N Eng spoken* used to show that the person mentioned is your child, brother, or sister【英格蘭北部，口】我們的，我家的: *Our Sharon did really well in her exams.* 我家莎倫各科考試都考得非常好。

Our Fa·ther /ˌ· ˈ··/ *n* [singular] the LORD'S PRAYER〔基督教的〕主禱文

Our La·dy /ˌ· ˈ··/ *n* [singular] Mary, the mother of Christ 聖母馬利亞

Our Lord /ˌ· ˈ·/ *n* [singular] Jesus Christ〔基督教的〕耶穌

ours /aʊrz; aʊəz/ *pron* [possessive form of **we** we 的所有格] the one or the ones that belong to us or that are of us (屬於) 我們的 (人、物): *I'll show you to your room. Ours is the one next door.* 我帶你去你的房間，我們的房間在你的隔壁。| *We wouldn't dream of wasting your time, so don't waste ours.* 我們不會想着去浪費你的時間，所以你也別浪費我們的。

our·selves /aʊrˋsɛlvz; aʊəˈselvz/ *pron* **1** the reflexive form of 'we'〔we 的反身代詞〕我們自己: *It was strange seeing ourselves on television.* 在電視上看到我們自己很奇怪。| *We all introduced ourselves before the meeting started.* 會議開始前我們都作了自我介紹。**2** used to emphasize the pronoun we, a plural noun etc 我們親自，我們自己〔用於強調〕: *Not many people realise we built the house ourselves.* 沒多少人知道這座房子是我們自己蓋的。| *As we are parents ourselves we can understand what you've gone through.* 我們自己也是父母，所以我們能理解你所經受的艱辛。**3 (all) by ourselves a)** alone 我們獨自地: *Our teacher left us by ourselves for over an hour.* 老師讓我們獨自呆了一個多小時。**b)** without help 我們獨力地，無他人幫助地: *My sister and I learnt to use the computer all by ourselves.* 我和妹妹完全是自己學會使用電腦的。**4 to ourselves** if we have something to ourselves, we do not have to share it with any other people 歸我們單獨使用，非合用: *Once Sam left town we had the house to ourselves.* 山姆一離開城裡，房子就歸我們單獨使用了。—see also 另見 YOURSELF

-ous /əs; əs/ *suffix* [in adjectives 構成形容詞] describes something that causes or has a particular quality 具有...

的; 有…特性的: *dangerous* (=full of danger) 危險的 | *spacious* (=with much space) 寬敞的

oust /aʊst; aʊst/ *v* [T] to force someone out of a position of power, especially so that you can take their place 強迫〔某人〕放棄職權, 把…攆走〔以取代之〕: **oust sb from** *an attempt to oust the Conservatives from power* 把保守黨人攆下台的企圖

ous·ter /ˈaʊstɚ; ˈaʊstə/ *n* [C] *AmE* an act of moving someone from a position of power in order to take their place【美】撤職, 罷黜, 攆走

out¹ /aʊt; aʊt/ *adv, adj* [adv only after verb 作副詞僅用於動詞後, adj not before noun 作形容詞不用於名詞前]

1 ▶NOT INSIDE STH 不在某物裡面◀ from the inside of something 由〔某物〕裡面出來, 到外面: *She opened the envelope and took the letter out.* 她打開信封取出信來。| **[+of]** *The diary must have fallen out of her pocket.* 日記本準是從她的口袋裡掉出來的。| *Someone has torn the last page out of the book I'm reading.* 有人把我在看的這本書的最後一頁撕掉了。

2 ▶LEAVE A PLACE 離開某處◀ from the inside part of something such as a building to the outside part 由〔建築物等的〕內部到外部: *Lock the door on your way out.* 外出時鎖好門。| **[+of]** *I don't think I'd have the courage to jump out of a plane.* 我想我沒有膽量跳出飛機。| **out jumped/walked etc** *The plane door slid open, and out walked the princess.* 飛機艙門拉開後, 公主邁步而出。—see picture on page A1 參見 A1 頁圖

3 ▶NOT HOME 不在家◀ away from your home, especially because you are in a restaurant, party etc 在外面(的)〔尤指因在餐館或參加聚會等而不在家〕: *Let's go out to eat tonight.* 我們今晚去外面吃吧。| *That guy she likes has finally asked her out.* 她喜歡的那個男人終於約她出去了。

4 ▶ABSENT 不在的◀ not in the place where you usually are, especially for a short time〔尤指短暫〕外出(的), 不在通常的地方(的): *I'm sorry, my mother is out at the moment.* 對不起, 我母親這會兒出去了。| *He went out at 11 o'clock.* 他 11 點外出的。

5 ▶OUTSIDE 外面◀ outside 在[到]外面, 在[到]室外: *Many of the homeless have been sleeping out for years.* 許多無家可歸者常年露宿街頭。| *Billy was out playing in the street.* 比利在外面街上玩耍。—see 見 OUTSIDE (USAGE)

6 ▶GIVEN TO MANY PEOPLE 給許多人◀ used to say that something is given to many people, a situation affects many people etc〔分發〕出去; 向四面八方: *The examination will start when all the question papers have been handed out.* 試卷全部分發完後考試就開始。

7 ▶GET RID OF STH 去除某物◀ used to say that something no longer exists or that someone has got rid of something 去除; 不再存在: *These eggs are old, throw them out.* 這些雞蛋不新鮮, 把它們扔了吧。| **[+of]** *There's this stuff you can buy to get the stains out of delicate fabrics.* 你可以買這種東西來去除精細織物上的污漬。

8 ▶NOT INCLUDED 排除在外◀ used to say that someone or something has not been included, not allowed to enter somewhere etc 不包括在內的; 不允許進入的: *The house had a 'Keep Out' sign in front.* 房子前面有一塊"禁止入內"的標牌。| **[+of]** *Daniels has been left out of the team due to injury.* 丹尼爾斯因受傷而被排除在隊外。

9 ▶FIND STH 發現某物◀ used to say that someone finds or discovers something 發現, 弄明白: **[+of]** *If she knows what the plan is I'll soon get it out of her.* 如果她知道計劃的內容, 我會很快讓她說出來的。

10 ▶PRODUCE STH 製造某物◀ used to say that someone or something produces something 製造出來: *factories throwing out pollution into the atmosphere* 向大氣中排放污染物的工廠 | **[+of]** *A lot of good music came out of the hippy culture in the 1960s.* 許多好的音樂來源於 20 世紀 60 年代的嬉皮士文化。

11 ▶STICK OUT 突出◀ used to say that something is very easy to see, feel etc because it is not part of the main part of something 伸出(的), 顯眼(的): **[+of]** *the nail sticking out of the chair* 椅子上凸出的釘子 | *a small peninsula jutting out into the sea* 伸進海中的小半島

12 ▶CHOOSE STH 選擇某物◀ used to say that one person or thing is chosen or taken from a larger group〔從一組人或東西中〕挑選, 選出: *Pick out something to wear.* 找件衣服穿上吧。| *singled out for punishment* 挑出來加以懲罰

13 ▶DO STH COMPLETELY 徹底地做某事◀ used to say that something is done carefully and completely 徹底地, 完全地: *When the cupboard was cleared out I found some of my old books.* 我在清理櫃子時發現了自己的一些舊書。| *The work rota is a little confused but we'll sort it out.* 工作輪值表有點混亂, 但我們會排好的。

14 ▶PRODUCT 產品◀ used to say that a product is available to be bought 上市的, 問世的, 推出: *When's Archer's new book out?* 阿切爾的新書甚麼時候出版? | *Sony have brought out a new portable music system.* 新力公司推出了一種新的便攜式音響設備。

15 ▶FREE 自由的◀ used to say that someone is no longer in prison or locked in a place against their will 不再囚禁的, 不再關起來的: *Once he was out it was only a matter of time till he reoffended.* 他出獄以後必定會再次犯罪, 這是遲早的事。| **[+of]** *I like to let my parrots out of their cage once in a while.* 我喜歡偶爾把鸚鵡放出籠子來。

16 ▶NOT FASHIONABLE 不時髦◀ used to say that something is no longer fashionable 不再時興(的), 過時(的): *You can't wear that, maxi skirts have been out for years.* 你不能穿那條超長裙, 它已經多年不時興了。

17 ▶SECRET 祕密◀ used to say that some information is no longer a secret 暴露(的), 泄漏(的): *Her secret was out.* 她的祕密泄露了。| *The word's out that Mel Gibson is in town.* 有消息傳出, 米路·吉遜在城裡。

18 ▶APPEAR 出現◀ used to say that someone or something has suddenly appeared (突然)顯露出來(的): *You don't often see daffodils out at this time of year.* 在一年的這個時候, 你很少見到水仙花開放的。| *The house looks so much better when the sun comes out.* 太陽出來一照, 這房子看上去要漂亮很多。

19 read/shout etc sth out (loud) to say something in a voice that is loud enough for others to hear 大聲唸出/叫出某物: *The teacher made Ben read the note out to the whole class.* 老師讓本把筆記大聲地唸給全班聽。| *As I call out the winners' names, will you please approach the stage?* 我宣讀獲勝者名字時, 請你們走到台前來好嗎?

20 watch/listen/mind etc out *especially spoken* used to tell someone to be careful【尤口】當心, 小心: *Look out! There's a van coming.* 當心!有輛小貨車開過來了。

21 a fire or light that is out is no longer burning or shining〔火或燈等〕熄滅(的); 燃盡(的): *Blow the candles out.* 把蠟燭吹滅。| *Suddenly the lights went out.* 燈突然滅了。

22 ▶NOT AWAKE 未醒的◀ **a)** used to say that someone is asleep 沉睡(的), 酣睡(的): **be/go out like a light** *The poor kid's exhausted. He went out like a light.* 那可憐的孩子累壞了, 一下子就睡着了。| **flat out** *Ray spent the whole afternoon flat out on the sofa.* 雷整個下午都在沙發上沉睡。**b)** used to say that someone is no longer conscious 昏迷(的), 失去知覺(的): *He was out for about 10 minutes.* 他昏迷了大約 10 分鐘。| **be out cold** *How hard did you hit him? He's out cold.* 你使了多大勁打他?他都昏過去了。

23 ▶DISTANT PLACE 遙遠之處◀ used to say that someone goes to a place that is a long way away, very difficult to get to etc 去很遠的地方, 去很難到達之處: *They've just moved out to a farm in Massachusetts.* 他們剛搬走, 去了馬薩諸塞州的一個農場。| *He went out to Africa.* 他出遠門去非洲了。

24 wear/tire etc out to make someone feel extremely tired 使精疲力竭: *By the time she'd tidied up she was*

worn out. 她拾掇完後已經疲憊不堪。

25 be/run/sell etc out to not have something because you have used it all, sold it all etc 沒有了/用完/售完等: *The album was sold out within minutes.* 專輯幾分鐘就銷售一空。| **[+of]** *We've run out of coffee.* 我們沒有咖啡了。

26 think/plan etc it out to think, plan etc something very carefully before you do it 周詳地考慮/計劃等: *It would be wiser to work it out with your financial advisors.* 較明智的做法是和你的財務顧問一起來細商此事。

27 ►NOT WORKING 出了毛病的◄ *especially AmE* if a machine, piece of equipment etc is out it is not working 【尤美】〔機器、設備等〕出了毛病(的),發生故障(的): *I don't believe it – the elevator's out again!* 我真不敢相信 —— 電梯又壞了! —see also 另見 **out of order** (ORDER[1] (8))

28 before the day/year etc is out before the day, year etc has ended 在一天/一年等過去之前: *Don't cry, I'll be back before the week's out.* 別哭,我不出一週就回來。

29 ►MEASUREMENT 計量◄ if a measurement, result etc is out, it is wrong because the numbers have not been calculated correctly 錯誤的,不正確的: *He was out in his calculations, so there was a lot of carpet left over.* 他計算錯了,所以地毯還剩下很多。| **be out by £4/$5 etc** *The bill was out by over £10.* 賬單算錯了十多英鎊。| **be way out** *These accounts are way out – the tax people will never accept them.* 這些賬目差錯嚴重,稅務人員絕不會認可的。

30 be out for sth/be out to do sth *informal* to have a particular intention 【非正式】試圖得到某物/力圖做某事: *Mark my words – he's only out for one thing and that's her money.* 你聽着 —— 他只想得到一樣東西,那就是她的錢。| *These salesmen are out to trick you into buying something you just don't need.* 這些推銷員是想哄騙你買下你根本就不需要的東西。

31 ►NOT IN POWER 下台◄ used to say that someone, especially a political party, no longer has power or authority 在野(的),下台的: *It's time we voted the Republicans out.* 該是我們把共和黨人選下台的時候了。

32 be the stupidest/silliest etc person out *BrE* to be extremely stupid, silly etc 【英】最愚蠢/最呆笨等的人: *You've got to be the luckiest man out!* 你得算是所有人中最走運的了!

33 ►OFFICIAL PROTEST 正式抗議◄ *BrE* used to say that someone has stopped working as a way of protesting about something 【英】罷工: *The doctors have come out in sympathy with the miners.* 醫生罷診以聲援礦工。

34 ►HOMOSEXUAL 同性戀者◄ if a homosexual is or comes out, they tell people that they are homosexual 公開承認自己是同性戀者

35 sth's out used to say that a suggestion is not possible (做)某事不行[不可能]: *"What are we going to do?" "Well bowling's out because my wrist is killing me."* "我們去做甚麼?" "噢,打保齡球不行,我的手腕正痛得厲害呢。"

36 ►SEA 大海◄ if the sea, the TIDE[1] (1) etc is out, it is at its lowest level〔海水、潮汐等〕最低水位的,落[退]潮(的)

37 ►SPORT 體育◄ **a)** a player or team that is out in a game such as cricket or baseball is no longer allowed to play in the game〔板球或棒球等比賽中選手或球隊〕出局(的): *Sussex were all out for 365.* 蘇塞克斯隊得了365分後便全部出局了。**b)** a ball that is out in a game such as tennis or basketball is outside the line〔網球或籃球等比賽中的球〕出界(的)

38 out with it! used to tell someone to say something that they are having difficulty saying 說出來!〔要某人說出難以啟齒的事〕: *OK, out with it! What really happened?* 好啦,說出來吧!到底出了甚麼事?

39 out you go! used to order someone to leave a room 滾出去!

40 be out of luck/condition etc used to say that someone or something is no longer in a particular state or situation 不走運/健康狀況不好等: *She's not completely cured but at least she's out of danger.* 她還未痊癒,但至少已經脫離了危險。| *This whole situation is getting out of control.* 整個局面越來越失控了。

41 be out of earshot/sight to be so far away from someone that they cannot hear you, see you etc 在聽覺/視線所及的範圍之外: *I thought she was out of earshot or I wouldn't have said that.* 我以為她聽不見的,否則我就不說了。

42 out of curiosity/interest etc because you are curious, interested etc 出於好奇/興趣等: *Just out of curiosity, why did you take that job?* 我只是有點好奇,你為甚麼接受那份工作?

43 out of wood/metal etc used to say what substance a particular thing is made of 由木頭/金屬等製成: *a little box made out of wood and decorated with flowers* 用花裝飾的木製小盒子

44 9 out of 10/4 out of a hundred etc used to say that there are ten people or things and you are talking about nine of them 十個中有九個/一百個中有四個等: *Apparently they've lost three games out of seven already.* 很明顯,他們七盤比賽已輸了三盤。

45 be out of work/a job etc to not have a job 失業: *those who have been out of work for over 6 months* 那些已失業超過半年的人

46 ►MONEY 金錢◄ used to say where the money has come from to pay for something or buy something 從…取錢〔來付賬或購物〕: *Can you believe he used money out of our bank account to pay for his trips with another woman?* 你能相信他動用我們的銀行存款去和別的女人遊山玩水嗎?

47 out of the way a) a place that is out of the way is fairly far from any town 偏僻的,人煙稀少的: *The camp site is a little out of the way but the views are magnificent.* 營地有點偏僻,但景色壯麗。**b)** if you get a problem out of the way you solve it so that you can do something else 解決〔難題〕: *So, that's got the salary thing out of the way, let's move on to productivity.* 那麼,薪水的問題就這麼定了。我們接下來談生產率的問題吧。

48 be out of your head/mind *informal* 【非正式】**a)** to be very worried 非常焦慮: *His parents were out of their minds with worry when he didn't come home.* 他沒有回家,使父母急得團團亂轉。**b)** to be very drunk 爛醉,神志不清: *By the time I got to the party most people were out of their heads.* 等我到達晚會上時,大多數人已喝得醉醺醺的。

49 be/feel out of it (all) a) *informal* to feel different from the rest of a group of people 【非正式】感到格格不入: *It was nice but I felt really out of it because I was the only one who couldn't speak French.* 活動搞得很不錯,但我感到很像個局外人,因為我是唯一不會說法語的人。**b)** *informal* to be drunk 【非正式】喝醉: *You were really out of it last night. What were you drinking?* 昨晚你真的醉了,你喝了甚麼?

50 ►HORSE 馬◄ *technical* having a particular horse as a mother 【術語】生自〔特定的母馬〕: **[+of]** *Golden Trumpet, by Golden Rain out of Silver Trumpet* 由"金雨"和"銀喇叭"交配所生的"金喇叭" —compare 比較 BY[1] —see also 另見 **out of the blue** (BLUE[2] (4)), **out of the question** (QUESTION[1] (8)), **out of sorts** (SORT[1] (5)), **out of this world** (WORLD[1] (13))

out[2] *prep informal* 【非正式】**a)** *AmE* used to say that someone or something is removed from inside something, leaves somewhere etc 【美】從…裡面出去;離開〔某處〕: **[+of]** *When I first came out of the army I worked in a drug store.* 我剛離開軍隊時,去了一家藥店工作。**b)** *BrE* used in a way which some people think is incorrect, to say that someone or something is removed from inside something, leaves somewhere etc 【英】從…裡面出去;離開〔某處〕〔有人認為這一用法不正確〕: *Get* *out the car and push with the rest of us!* 下車, 跟我們一起推車!

out³ *v* **1** [T usually passive 一般用被動態] to publicly say that someone is homosexual when that person would prefer to keep it private 揭發〔某人〕為同性戀者; 使〔同性戀者〕曝光: *Several gay politicians have been outed in recent months.* 近幾個月來, 數名政客的同性戀身分被揭發了。**2 truth/murder etc will out!** used to say that it is difficult to hide the truth, a murder etc 真相/謀殺案等終將水落石出!

out⁴ *n* **1** [singular] an excuse for not doing an activity or to avoid being blamed for something 推託的藉口, 逃脱的託辭: *I have tons of work to do. At least that gives me an out.* 我有大量的工作要做, 起碼這可以給我一個推託的藉口。**2** [C] the state of no longer being allowed to take part in a particular game in a sport such as baseball〔棒球等的〕出局 —see also 另見 INS AND OUTS

out- /aut; aʊt/ *prefix* **1** used to form nouns and adjectives from verbs followed by 'out'〔與後接 out 的動詞構成名詞和形容詞〕: *an outbreak of flu* (=from 'break out') 流感的爆發 | *outspoken comments* (=from 'speak out') 直言不諱的評論 **2** in some nouns and adjectives, means outside; beyond 在外; 超過〔與某些名詞及形容詞合用〕: *an outhouse* (=small additional building)〔附屬於正屋的〕外屋 | *outlying areas* (=far from the centre) 邊緣地區 **3 a)** beyond; further 超過; 更進一步: *She outlived her brother.* (=he died before her) 她比她哥哥活得長。| *He's outgrown his clothes.* (=become too big for them) 他個子長得衣服穿不下了。**b)** better than someone, so that you defeat them 強於…, 勝過…: *I can outargue you any day.* 我任何時候都能辯過你。

out·age /ˋautɪdʒ; ˈaʊtɪdʒ/ *n* [C] *AmE* a period when a service such as the electricity supply is not provided【美】〔電力等的〕斷供期: *a power outage* 停電期

out-and-out /ˌ· · ˈ·◂/ *adj* [only before noun 僅用於名詞前] having all the qualities of a particular kind of person or thing; complete 十足的, 徹頭徹尾的: *an out-and-out villain* 十足的惡棍

out·back /ˋautbæk; ˈaʊtbæk/ *n* **the outback** the Australian countryside far away from cities, where few people live〔澳大利亞遠離城市、人煙稀少的〕內地

out·bid /autˋbɪd; aʊtˈbɪd/ *v past tense* **outbid** *present participle* **outbidding** [T] to offer a higher price than someone else, especially at an AUCTION¹〔尤指在拍賣中〕出價高過〔別人〕

out·board mo·tor /ˋautˌbord ˋmotɚ; ˌaʊtbɔːd ˈməʊtə/ *n* [C] a motor fixed to the back end of a small boat〔小船的〕舷外[尾掛]發動機

out·bound /ˌautˋbaund; ˈaʊtbaʊnd/ *adj* moving away from you or away from a town, country etc 向外去的; 向城外的; 向國外的: *outbound traffic* 駛向城外的車流

out·break /ˋautˌbrek; ˈaʊtbreɪk/ *n* [C] a sudden appearance or start of war, fighting, or serious disease〔戰爭、戰鬥、惡疾的〕突然發生, 爆發: *a cholera outbreak* 霍亂的爆發 | **[+of]** *renewed outbreaks of fighting* 戰鬥的持續爆發 | *the outbreak of World War II* 第二次世界大戰的爆發 —see also 另見 **break out** (BREAK¹)

out·build·ing /ˋautˌbɪldɪŋ; ˈaʊtˌbɪldɪŋ/ *n* [C] a building such as a BARN (1) or SHED¹ (1) near a main building〔主要建築物旁如穀倉或棚屋的〕附屬建築, 外屋: *the farm and its outbuildings* 農場及其附屬建築物

out·burst /ˋautˌbɝst; ˈaʊtbɜːst/ *n* [C] **1** a sudden powerful expression of strong emotion〔感情的〕突然爆發: *He later came to apologize to me for his outburst.* 他後來為自己亂發脾氣而向我道歉。| **[+of]** *I was surprised by this outburst of resentment.* 我對這突然爆發的怨恨感到吃驚。**2** a sudden temporary increase in activity〔活動的〕突發, 激增: *an outburst of creative energy* 創作力的勃發

out·cast /ˋautˌkæst; ˈaʊtkɑːst/ *n* [C] someone who is not accepted by the people they live among, or has been forced out of their home 被〔家庭、社會等〕遺棄[排斥]的人; 被逐出者: *In these health-conscious times smokers are often treated as social outcasts.* 在如今注重健康的時代, 吸煙者在社會上常常成了被排斥的一羣。—**outcast** *adj*

out·caste /ˋautˌkæst; ˈaʊtkɑːst/ *n* [C] someone who does not belong to or who has been forced out of a CASTE (=a traditional social class) in India〔印度〕被逐出種姓者; 賤民

out·class /autˋklæs; aʊtˈklɑːs/ *v* [T often passive 常用被動態] to be much better than someone at doing something, or to be much better than something else 遠遠勝過; 比…等級高: *The Pittsburgh Steelers were completely outclassed by their rivals.* 匹茲堡鋼人隊完全敵不過對手。| *There's never been a jet engine to outclass the Rolls Royce Avon.* 從未有哪種噴氣引擎能超過勞斯萊斯艾文郡牌的。

out·come /ˋautˌkʌm; ˈaʊtkʌm/ *n* [singular] the final result of a meeting, discussion, war etc, especially when no-one knows what it will be until it actually happens〔尤指未發生前無人知曉的〕結果; 後果: **[+of]** *We are anxiously awaiting the outcome of the negotiations.* 我們急切地等待着談判的結果。 3

out·crop /ˋautˌkrɑp; ˈaʊtkrɒp/ *n* [C] a rock or group of rocks above the surface of the ground 露出地面的岩石[岩層], 露頭

out·cry /ˋautˌkraɪ; ˈaʊtkraɪ/ *n* [singular] an angry protest by a lot of ordinary people 公眾的強烈抗議[反對], 吶喊: *The closure of our local hospital has caused a huge public outcry.* 我們當地醫院的關閉激起了大規模的公開抗議。| **[+against]** *an outcry against this waste of public money* 反對如此浪費公帑

out·dat·ed /autˋdetɪd; ˌaʊtˈdeɪtɪd◂/ *adj* **1** unsuitable for the modern world and no longer used much; old-fashioned 不適合現代社會的; 過時的, 陳舊的: *outdated teaching methods* 不合時宜的教學方法 | *We reject outdated notions of national sovereignty.* 我們拒絕過時的國家主權概念。**2** a document that is outdated cannot be used because it is no longer effective〔文件等〕過期的, 失效的: *an outdated passport* 過期的護照

out·did /autˋdɪd; aʊtˈdɪd/ the past tense of OUTDO

out·dis·tance /autˋdɪstəns; aʊtˈdɪstəns/ *v* [T] to run, ride etc faster than other people, especially in a race, so that you are far ahead〔尤指在賽跑、賽車等中〕遙遙領先於, 超過: *Laura quickly outdistanced her pursuers.* 勞拉很快就把追趕者遠遠地拋在後面。

out·do /autˋdu; aʊtˈduː/ *v past tense* **outdid** /-ˋdɪd; -ˈdɪd/, *past participle* **outdone** /-ˋdʌn; -ˈdʌn/, *3rd person singular present tense* **outdoes** [T] **1** to be better or more successful than someone else at doing something 勝過, 超過; 比…更成功: *The economies of South East Asia are already outdoing Western competitors.* 東南亞的經濟已超越了西方的競爭對手。| **outdo sb in** *skaters trying to outdo the others in grace and speed* 想在動作的優美程度及速度上勝過他人的滑冰者 **2 not to be outdone** in order not to let someone else do better than you (為了) 不讓別人超過自己: *Not to be outdone by the rival country-clubs, the Glen Hills golf club put in a new swimming pool.* 格倫·希爾高爾夫球俱樂部建了一個新的游泳池, 為的是不讓對手的鄉村俱樂部超過自己。

out·door /ˋautˌdor; ˈaʊtdɔː/ *adj* **1** [only before noun 僅用於名詞前] existing, happening, or used outside, not inside a building (在) 戶外的; 用於戶外的: *outdoor activities* 戶外活動 | *outdoor clothing* 戶外活動服裝 | *a healthy outdoor life* 有益健康的戶外生活 —opposite 反義詞 INDOOR **2 outdoor type** a person who enjoys camping, walking in the countryside etc 野外活動愛好者

out·doors¹ /ˌautˋdorz; ˌaʊtˈdɔːz/ *adv* outside, not inside a building; OUT OF DOORS 在戶外, 在野外: *I reckon it's warm enough to eat outdoors this evening.* 我想今晚夠暖和, 可以在室外吃飯。—opposite 反義詞 INDOORS

outdoors² *n* **the (great) outdoors** the countryside far away from buildings and cities〔遠離建築物和城市的〕野外: *a love of the great outdoors* 對野外大自然的喜愛

O

out·door·sy /aʊt`dɔrzɪ; aʊt'dɔːzi/ *adj informal* enjoying outdoor activities【非正式】愛好野外活動的: *She's a real outdoorsy type.* 她是真正愛好野外活動的一類人。

out·draw /aʊt`drɔ; aʊt'drɔː/ *v* [T] to pull a gun out faster than someone else 比〔他人〕更快地拔出手槍: *The kid could outdraw any man in Texas.* 那小子拔槍的速度快過德克薩斯州的任何男子。

out·er /`aʊtɚ; 'aʊtə/ *adj* [only before noun 僅用於名詞前] **1** on the outside of something 在外的, 外面的: *Remove the tough outer leaves before cooking.* 煮之前先把外面的老葉子去掉。**2** further from the centre of something 遠離中心的: *the outer suburbs* 遠郊 —opposite 反義詞 INNER (1)

out·er·most /`aʊtɚ,most; 'aʊtəməʊst/ *adj* [only before noun 僅用於名詞前] furthest outside or furthest from the middle 最外面的, 離中心最遠的: *the outermost stars* 最遠的星球 —opposite 反義詞 INMOST (2), INNERMOST (2)

outer space /,·· '·/ *n* [U] the space outside the Earth's air, where the PLANET*s* and stars are 外太空

out·er·wear /`aʊtɚ,wɛr; 'aʊtəweə/ *n* [U] clothes, such as coats, that are worn over ordinary clothes 外衣, 外套

out·face /aʊt`fes; aʊt'feɪs/ *v* [T] to deal bravely with a difficult situation or opponent 勇敢地面對〔困境或對手〕

out·fall /`aʊt,fɔl; 'aʊtfɔːl/ *n* [C] a place where water flows out, especially from a DRAIN[2] (1) or river 排水口; 河口: *a sewage outfall* 污水排出口

out·field /`aʊt,fild; 'aʊtfiːld/ *n* **the outfield a)** the part of a cricket or BASEBALL field furthest from the player who is batting (BAT[2] (1))〔板球或棒球場的〕外野, 外場 **b)** the players in this part of the field 外場手 —compare 比較 INFIELD —**outfielder** *n* [C]

3 **out·fit**[1] /`aʊt,fɪt; 'aʊtfɪt/ *n* [C] **1** a set of clothes worn together, especially for a special occasion〔尤指在特殊場合穿着的〕全套服裝: *She bought a new, elegant two-piece outfit in shades of apricot for the wedding.* 她為婚禮買了一身兩件套的新禮服, 款式雅致, 顏色是有深有淺的杏黃色。**2** *informal* a group of people who work together as a team or organization【非正式】〔一起工作的〕一羣人, 全班人馬: *a small advertising outfit* 廣告業務小組 **3** a set of equipment that you need for a particular purpose or job〔為特定目的或工作所需的〕全套設備: *a tyre repair outfit* 修理輪胎用的整套工具

outfit[2] *v* **outfitted, outfitting** [T] to provide someone with a set of clothes or equipment for a special purpose 為…提供全套服裝[設備], 配備, 裝備

out·fit·ter /`aʊt,fɪtɚ; 'aʊtfɪtə/ *n* [C] **1** *BrE old-fashioned* a shop that sells men's clothes【英, 過時】男式服裝商店: *a firm of gentlemen's outfitters* 銷售男子全套服裝的商行 **2** *AmE* a shop that sells equipment for outdoor activities such as camping【美】〔出售戶外活動所需裝備的〕旅行用品商店

out·flank /aʊt`flæŋk; aʊt'flæŋk/ *v* [T] **1** to go around the side of an enemy during a battle and attack them from behind 包抄〔敵人〕, 迂迴攻擊 **2** to gain an advantage over an opponent, especially in politics〔尤指在政治上〕出奇制勝, 智勝: *The Tories found themselves outflanked by Labour on the issue of law and order.* 保守黨人發現他們在法律和秩序的問題上被工黨佔了上風。

out·flow /`aʊt,flo; 'aʊtfləʊ/ *n* [C,U] **1** the process in which money, goods etc leave a bank, country etc〔錢、貨物等從銀行、國家等的〕外流: *the outflow of gold from the US Federal Reserve* 黃金由美國聯邦儲備銀行外流出去 **2** the flow of water or air from something〔水或空氣由某物中的〕流出: *an outflow of gas escaping from the main duct* 從主管道泄漏的煤氣 | *the outflow valve* 外流閥, 排放閥

out·fox /aʊt`fɑks; aʊt'fɒks/ *v* [T] to gain an advantage over someone by being cleverer than they are; OUTWIT 智勝, 以計謀勝過; 比…更狡猾

out front /,· '·/ *adv AmE informal*【美, 非正式】**1** honest, in a way that other people can clearly see 坦誠地, 直率地: *I just want you to know, out front, that I can't stand the guy, and I don't like spending time with him.* 我就是要坦率地讓你知道, 我實在不能忍受那傢伙, 而且我也不願意費時間和他待在一起。**2** taking a leading position 帶頭, 擔起領導職責: *The President has to be out front, not ducking responsibility for important issues.* 總統必須作出表率, 對重大問題不逃避責任。—**out front** *adj*

out·go·ing /`aʊt,goɪŋ; ,aʊt'gəʊɪŋ◂/ *adj* **1** liking to meet and talk to new people 好交際的, 外向的: *She's got a warm, outgoing personality.* 她具有一種熱心、外向的個性。**2 the outgoing president/chancellor etc** someone who is finishing their time as a president etc 即將離任的總統/總理等 **3** [only before noun 僅用於名詞前] going out or leaving a place 外出的, 離開的: *the tray for outgoing mail* 放置外發郵件的公文格 | *outgoing phone calls* 外撥電話

out·go·ings /`aʊt,goɪŋz; 'aʊt,gəʊɪŋz/ *n* [plural] *especially BrE* amounts of money that you spend, especially money that you have to spend regularly【尤英】支出, 開銷〔尤指定期的必要花費〕: *My monthly outgoings come to about £500.* 我每月的開支在500英鎊左右。

out·grow /aʊt`gro; aʊt'grəʊ/ *v past tense* **outgrew** /-`gru; -'gruː/, *past participle* **outgrown** /-`gron; -'grəʊn/ [T] **1** to grow too big for something; GROW OUT OF 長得太大而不適用…: *You've outgrown that coat; I'll have to buy you another one.* 你已長大, 穿不下這件外套了; 我得給你再買一件。**2** to change as you become older, and no longer enjoy the things that you used to do 年長而放棄…, 隨年長而改變…: *Callahan had outgrown the radical idealism of his younger days.* 卡拉漢長大了, 也改變了自己少年時的激進理想主義。**3** to grow faster than someone or something else 長得比…快: *a population outgrowing its resources* 增長速度超過資源開發的人口 **4 outgrow your strength** *BrE* to grow too quickly when you are a child, so that you become weak or unhealthy【英】個子長得太快而營養跟不上

out·growth /`aʊt,groθ; 'aʊtgrəʊθ/ *n* [C] **1** a natural result of something, especially an unpleasant one〔尤指令人不悅的〕自然結果; 後果; 副產品: *Crime is often an outgrowth of poverty.* 犯罪往往是貧困的產物。**2** *technical* something that grows out of something else【術語】〔某物上的〕生長物, 長出物

out·house /`aʊt,haʊs; 'aʊthaʊs/ *n* [C] **1** *BrE* a small building which is near to and belongs to a larger main building【英】〔主建築物外面的〕附屬建築物, 外屋 **2** *AmE* an outside toilet【美】戶外廁所

out·ing /`aʊtɪŋ; 'aʊtɪŋ/ *n* **1** [C] a short pleasure trip for a group of people〔一羣人的〕短途旅遊, 遠足: **a school/church/class etc outing** *a class outing to the ballet* 班級組織外出觀看芭蕾舞 **2** [C,U] the practice of publicly naming people as HOMOSEXUAL*s*, when they do not want anyone to know this 公開指出某些人為同性戀者的行為

out·land·ish /aʊt`lændɪʃ; aʊt'lændɪʃ/ *adj* strange and unusual 古怪的, 奇異的: *He used to play guitar and wear outlandish costumes in a punk band.* 他以前常在一支龐克搖滾樂隊中身着奇裝異服彈結他。—**outlandishly** *adv* —**outlandishness** *n* [U]

out·last /aʊt`læst; aʊt'lɑːst/ *v* [T] to continue to exist for a longer time than something else 比…經久[持久] —compare 比較 OUTLIVE

out·law[1] /`aʊt,lɔ; 'aʊtlɔː/ *n* [C] someone who has done something illegal, and who is not protected by the law 不法之徒, 逃犯, 不受法律保護的罪犯

outlaw[2] *v* [T] **1** to completely stop something by making it illegal or socially unacceptable 將〔某事〕定為非法, 全面禁止: *Certain counties have outlawed the sale of alcohol.* 一些郡已禁止售酒。**2** to officially state that someone is an outlaw 宣布〔某人〕為不法之徒

out·lay /`aʊt,le; 'aʊtleɪ/ *n* [C,U] the amount of money that you have to spend in order to start a new business, activity etc〔用於開設新商號、進行某活動等的〕花費; 開支: *For a relatively small outlay you can start manufacturing T-shirts.* 如果可用的資金相對較少, 你可以先開始

生產T恤。| [+on/for] *House buyers usually have a large initial outlay on carpets and furniture.* 購房者通常先要為買地毯和家具花去一大筆錢。

out·let /ˈaʊtˌlɛt; ˈaʊtlet/ *n* [C] **1** a way of expressing or getting rid of strong feelings〔強烈情感的〕發泄途徑[方法]: [+for] *I play racquet ball as an outlet for stress.* 我用打壁球來排解壓力。**2** a shop, company, or organization through which products are sold 批發商店, 商行; 銷售公司: **retail outlet** *Benetton has retail outlets in every major European city.* 貝納通公司在歐洲各主要城市都有零售店。**3** a way through which something such as a liquid or gas can flow out〔液體或氣體的〕出口; 排水口; 通風口 **4** *AmE*【美】電源插座; a POWER POINT *BrE*【英】

out·line¹ /ˈaʊtˌlaɪn; ˈaʊtlaɪn/ *n* [singular] **1** the main ideas or facts about something, without the details 綱要, 梗概, 要點: *I'd like to see the proposal outline.* 我想看看這份建議書的概要。| *an outline of world history* 世界史綱 | **broad/rough outline** (=a very general outline) 大致的/粗略的綱要 | **in outline** (=giving an outline) 扼要地 *Chapter I describes in outline the way money circulates through the economy.* 第一章扼要地講述了貨幣在經濟中的流通方式。**2** a line around the edge of something which shows its shape 外形; 輪廓: *the outline of a footprint in the snow* 雪中腳印的輪廓 | **outline map/sketch etc** *an outline map of Europe* 歐洲略圖 **3** *especially AmE* a plan for a report, story etc in which each new idea is separately recorded【尤美】〔報告、故事等的〕設想, 草案

outline 外形, 輪廓

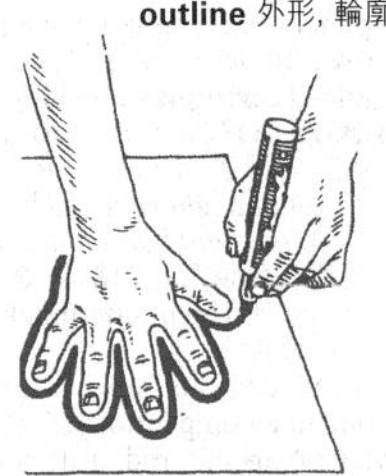

She is drawing an outline of her hand. 她在勾畫自己手的輪廓。

outline² *v* [T] **1** to describe something in a general way, giving the main points but not the details 概述; 提出…的綱要: *The President outlined his peace plan for the Middle East.* 總統概述了他的中東和平計劃。**2** [often passive 常用被動態] to make the outline of a shape very clear 畫…的輪廓, 描…的外形: *a map of the area with our property outlined in red* 用紅色勾畫出我們的物業所在的地圖

out·live /aʊtˈlɪv; aʊtˈlɪv/ *v* [T] **1** to live longer than someone else 比…活得長: *She outlived her husband by twenty years.* 她比她丈夫多活了二十年。**2** to continue to exist after something else has ended or disappeared 比…經久: *The military regime has outlived its statutory term by three years.* 這一軍事政權的存在已超過法定期限三年。| **outlive its usefulness** (=become no longer useful) *As a commuter service the Seacombe Ferry had outlived its usefulness.* 作為通勤服務設施, 西庫姆渡輪已不再有用了。

out·look /ˈaʊtˌlʊk; ˈaʊtlʊk/ *n* [C] **1** your general attitude to life and the world〔對生活、世界的〕看法, 觀點, 態度: [+on] *He's got a very positive outlook on life.* 他持有一種非常積極的人生觀。| *The farmers were narrowly provincial in their outlook.* 這些農民觀念偏狹, 見識不廣。**2** what is expected to happen in the future 前景, 遠景: [+for] *The weather outlook for the weekend is bad.* 本週末的天氣情況不佳。| *The outlook for sufferers from this disease is not good.* 這種疾病的患者希望渺茫。**3** a view from a particular place〔從某處望見的〕景色; 風光: *a very pleasing outlook from the bedroom window* 從臥室窗戶看到的非常宜人的景色

out·ly·ing /ˈaʊtˌlaɪɪŋ; ˈaʊtˌlaɪ-ɪŋ/ *adj* [only before noun 僅用於名詞前] far from the centre of a city, town etc or from a main building 邊遠的; 遠離市中心的; 遠離主要建築物的: *one of the outlying suburbs* 邊遠郊區之一 | *the outlying barns* 外圍的穀倉

out·ma·noeu·vre *BrE*【英】, **outmaneuver** *AmE*【美】/ˌaʊtməˈnuvɚ; ˌaʊtməˈnuːvə/ *v* [T] to gain an advantage over someone by using cleverer plans or methods than they do 智勝〔對手〕, 比〔對手〕計高一籌, 使〔對手〕處於下風: *a woman who could outmanoeuvre even the Prime Minister* 一個甚至能比首相計高一籌的女人

out·mod·ed /aʊtˈmodɪd; aʊtˈməʊdʒd/ *adj* no longer fashionable or useful 過時的, 不再流行的; 廢棄的: *an outmoded set of values* 一套過時的價值觀

out·most /ˈaʊtˌmost; ˈaʊtməʊst/ *adj* furthest outside or furthest from the middle; OUTERMOST 最外面的, 離中心最遠的

out·num·ber /aʊtˈnʌmbɚ; aʊtˈnʌmbə/ *v* [T usually passive 一般用被動態] to be more in number than another group 比…多, 在數量上勝過: *We were completely outnumbered by the enemy.* 在數量上我們完全被敵人壓倒。| *In the nursing profession women still outnumber men by four to one.* 在護理行業, 女性依然多於男性, 人數比例為四比一。

out-of-bod·y /ˌ· · ˈ··◂/ *adj* **out-of-body experience** the feeling that sometimes happens when someone is close to death that they are outside of their body and can look down on it from above 游離體外的感覺, 靈魂出竅的感覺〔人臨死前有時產生的一種游離於體外俯視自己身體的感覺〕

out-of-court /ˌ· · ˈ·◂/ *adj* **out-of-court settlement** an agreement to settle a legal argument, in which one side agrees to pay money to the other so that the problem is not brought to court 庭外和解 —see also 另見 **settle sth out of court** (COURT¹ (1))

out-of-date /ˌ· · ˈ·◂/ *adj* no longer useful, correct or fashionable 過時的, 不再正確的, 不再流行的: *out-of-date theories on education* 陳腐的教育理論 | *The information in last year's tourist guide is already out of date.* 去年的旅遊指南上的資料已經過時。

out of doors /ˌ· · ˈ·/ *adv* outside, not in a building; OUTDOORS 在戶外, 在室外; 在野外 —see 見 OUTSIDE (USAGE)

out-of-pock·et ex·pens·es /ˌ· · ·· ·ˈ··/ *n* [plural] small amounts of money that you have to spend as part of your job, and get back from your employer 自掏腰包的開銷〔指在工作上須先行支付但可向雇主報銷的小額開支〕

out-of-sight /ˌ· · ˈ·/ *adj AmE* an amount of money that is out-of-sight is extremely large【美】金額極大的, 非常昂貴的: *The hotel bill was out-of-sight.* 旅館的賬單數額極大。—see also 另見 **out of sight, out of mind** (SIGHT¹ (18))

out-of-the-way /ˌ· · · ˈ·◂/ *adj* **1** far from other towns and villages and often difficult to find 邊遠的, 偏僻的, 人跡罕至的: *Don't you find it inconvenient living in such an out-of-the-way place?* 你住在這樣荒僻的地方難道不覺得不方便嗎? **2** *BrE* unusual or strange【英】不尋常的; 怪異的: *Her taste in music is a bit out-of-the-way.* 她對音樂的品味有點怪異。

out-of-work /ˌ· · ˈ·◂/ *adj* unemployed 失業的, 未受雇用的: *out-of-work actors* 未受聘用的演員

out·pa·tient /ˈaʊtˌpeʃənt; ˈaʊtˌpeɪʃənt/ *n* [C] someone who goes to a hospital for treatment but does not stay there 門診病人 —compare 比較 INPATIENT

out·per·form /ˌaʊtpɚˈfɔrm; ˌaʊtpəˈfɔːm/ *v* [T] to perform better than someone or something else 做得比…好; 勝過: *The new Pentium computers outperform our 486s.* 新的奔騰電腦比我們的 486 好。

out·place·ment /ˈaʊtˌplesmənt; ˈaʊtˌpleɪsmənt/ *n* [C, U] the process of a company helping people to find new jobs after asking them to leave their employment〔公司解雇員工後的〕新職介紹, 再就業服務

out·play /aʊtˈple; aʊtˈpleɪ/ *v* [T] to beat an opponent in a game by playing with more skill than they do〔比賽中〕勝過〔對手〕, 擊敗

out·point /aʊtˈpɔɪnt; aʊtˈpɔɪnt/ *v* [T] to defeat an opponent in BOXING by gaining more points〔拳擊賽中〕以得分多而擊敗〔對手〕

out·post /ˈaʊtˌpost; ˈaʊtpəʊst/ *n* [C] a small town or group of buildings in a distant lonely place, usually established as a military camp or a place for trade〔通常作為軍營或貿易點而建的〕邊遠村落, 偏遠居民區

out·pour·ing /ˈaʊtˌpɔrɪŋ; ˈaʊtpɔːrɪŋ/ *n* **1 outpourings** [plural] continuous expressions of strong feeling 強烈感情的不斷流露: **[+of]** *outpourings of grief* 悲傷的傾吐 **2** [C,U] a lot of something that is produced suddenly 迸發; 湧出（物）; 瀉出（物）: *an outpouring of creative energy* 創造力的迸發

O

2 **out·put¹** /ˈaʊtˌpʊt; ˈaʊtpʊt/ *n* [C,U] **1** the amount of goods or work produced by a person, machine, factory etc 產量; 產品: *Output is up 30% on last year.* 產量比去年增加了 30%。**2** *technical* the information produced by a computer【術語】〔電腦的〕輸出信息 **3** *technical* the amount of electricity produced by a GENERATOR【術語】〔發電機的〕發電量, 輸出功率 —compare 比較 INPUT¹

output² *v past tense and past participle* **output** [T] if a computer outputs information, it produces it〔電腦〕輸出〔信息〕

out·rage¹ /ˈaʊtˌredʒ; ˈaʊtreɪdʒ/ *n* **1** [U] a feeling of great anger and shock 憤慨, 義憤; 震怒: *The injustice of the situation filled him with a sense of outrage.* 這種不公正的情況使他滿腔憤慨。**2** [C] a very cruel, violent, and shocking action or event 殘忍的行徑, 暴行; 令人震驚的事情: **[+against]** *These terrorist attacks are an outrage against society.* 這些恐怖襲擊是一種反社會的暴行。

outrage² *v* [T usually passive 一般用被動態] to make someone feel very angry and shocked 激起〔某人〕的義憤; 使〔某人〕震怒: *People were outraged at the idea of the murderer Hindley being released.* 人們對釋放兇手欣德利的主意義憤填膺。

out·ra·geous /aʊtˈredʒəs; aʊtˈreɪdʒəs/ *adj* **1** very shocking and extremely unfair or offensive 駭人的; 極不公正的; 蠻橫的: *outrageous prices* 駭人的價格 | *I can't believe he's been allowed to spread such outrageous lies!* 我無法相信竟然會允許他散布這種聳人聽聞的謊言! | **it is outrageous that** *It's outrageous that the poor should have to pay such high taxes.* 窮人得繳納這麼高的稅額, 真是令人駭然。**2** extremely unusual and slightly amusing or shocking 極不尋常的; 有點可笑[嚇人]的: *an outrageous hairstyle* 怪裡怪氣的髮型 | *Mark will say the most outrageous things, especially when he's supposed to be polite.* 馬克常會出言不遜, 尤其是在要他講究禮貌時。

out·ran /aʊtˋræn; aʊtˈræn/ the past tense of OUTRUN

out·rank /aʊtˋræŋk; aʊtˈræŋk/ *v* [T] **1** to have a higher rank than someone else in the same group 級別高於〔同一團體中的某人〕; 地位高於 **2** to be more important than something else 重要性超過〔某物〕

ou·tré /uˋtre; ˈuːtreɪ/ *adj French* strange, unusual, and slightly shocking【法】怪誕的, 異常的, 有點嚇人的: *the genius of artists as outré as Beardsley or Toulouse-Lautrec* 像〔英國插圖畫家〕比爾茲利或〔法國畫家〕土魯斯－勞特累克一樣怪誕的藝術家之天賦

out·reach /ˈaʊtritʃ; ˈaʊtriːtʃ/ *n* [U] *especially AmE*【尤美】**1** services based close to people's homes to help those who cannot easily come to an office, hospital etc〔靠近人們家庭, 以幫助不便上班或去醫院看病等的人為主要業務的〕擴大範圍的服務, 外展服務: **outreach service/center etc** *outreach centers for drug addicts* 戒毒外展中心 **2** the work a church does to teach or serve people who are not its members〔教堂為非教民所做的〕佈道; 善事

out·ride /aʊtˋraɪd; aʊtˈraɪd/ *v past tense* **outrode** /-ˋrod; -ˈrəʊd/ *past participle* **outridden** /-ˋrɪdn̩; -ˈrɪdn/ [T] to ride faster or further than someone or something else 騎得比…快[遠]

out·rid·er /ˈaʊtˌraɪdɚ; ˈaʊtˌraɪdə/ *n* [C] a guard or police officer who rides on a MOTORCYCLE or horse beside or in front of a vehicle in which an important person is travelling〔為重要人物的車輛開路的〕駕摩托車的警衛, 騎馬的警官

out·rig·ger /ˈaʊtˌrɪgɚ; ˈaʊtˌrɪgə/ *n* [C] **1** a piece of wood shaped like a small narrow boat which is fixed to the side of a boat, especially a CANOE¹, to prevent it from turning over in the water〔尤指獨木舟的〕舷外浮木〔形如一小船的木頭, 固定在船側以防船在水中翻轉〕**2** a boat fitted with one of these 裝有舷外浮木的小艇

out·right¹ /ˌaʊtˋraɪt; aʊtˈraɪt/ *adv* **1** without trying to hide your feelings or intentions 直率地, 無掩飾地, 痛快地: *They laughed outright at my suggestion.* 他們聽了我的建議後爽快地笑了。| *Tell him outright exactly what you think.* 把你的想法坦白告訴他。**2** completely 完全地, 徹底地: *The town was destroyed outright.* 城鎮被徹底毀掉了。| *She won outright.* 她大獲全勝。**3 buy/own sth outright** to own something such as a house completely because you have paid the full price with your own money 一次性付款買下某物/完全擁有某物 **4 be killed outright** to be killed immediately 當場殺死

out·right² /ˈaʊtˌraɪt; ˈaʊtraɪt/ *adj* [only before noun 僅用於名詞前] **1** clear and direct 明白無誤的; 直截了當的: *an outright refusal* 斷然拒絕 **2** complete 徹底的, 完全的: *outright ban on the sale of pornographic films* 徹底禁止色情影片的銷售 **3 outright winner/victor** someone who has definitely and easily won 毫無疑問的輕鬆獲勝者

out·ri·val /aʊtˋraɪvl̩; aʊtˈraɪvəl/ *v* [T] to defeat someone in a competition〔在競爭中〕擊敗, 勝過

out·rode /aʊtˋrod; aʊtˈrəʊd/ the past tense of OUTRIDE

out·run /aʊtˋrʌn; aʊtˈrʌn/ *v past tense* **outran** /-ˋræn; -ˈræn/ *past participle* **outrun** *present participle* **outrunning** [T] **1** to run faster or further than someone 比…跑得快[遠], 跑得比…更快[更遠] **2** to develop more quickly than something else 發展快於…, 比…發展得更快: *The Reverend believes that technological progress has outrun our moral development.* 那位牧師認為科技發展已經超過了人類道德的進化。

out·sell /aʊtˋsɛl; aʊtˈsel/ *v past tense and past participle* **outsold** /-ˋsold; -ˈsəʊld/ [T] **1** to be sold in larger quantities than something else 賣得比…多, 銷量勝過: *a detergent that outsells every other brand* 銷量超過其他任何牌子的洗滌劑 **2** to sell more goods or products than a competitor 比〔競爭對手〕銷售得多

out·set /ˈaʊtˌsɛt; ˈaʊtset/ *n* **at/from the outset** at or from the beginning of an event or process 在開頭時/從一開始: *It was clear right from the outset that there were going to be problems.* 從一開始就很清楚, 會有問題出現的。

out·shine /aʊtˋʃaɪn; aʊtˈʃaɪn/ *v past tense and past participle* **outshone** /aʊtˋʃon; aʊtˈʃɒn/ *present participle* **outshining** [T] **1** to be better at something than someone else 優於; 使…黯然失色: *Vera's flowers outshone all the others in the competition.* 在比賽中, 維拉的花讓別的花都黯然失色。**2** to shine more brightly than something else 照耀得比…更亮

out·side¹ /aʊtˋsaɪd; aʊtˈsaɪd/ *prep* **1** out of a particular building or room 到〔建築物或房間〕的外面, 由…向外: *As soon as we were outside the door we burst out laughing.* 我們一出門就大笑起來。—opposite 反義詞 INSIDE¹ (2) **2** out of a building but still close to it 在〔離建築物不遠〕的外邊: *I'll meet you outside the hardware store at 2 o'clock.* 我兩點鐘會在五金商店外邊見你。**3** beyond the limits of a city, country etc 超出〔城市、鄉村等的〕界限: *Add the area code 212 if you are calling from outside the New York area.* 如果在紐約市範圍以外打電話, 要加上地區號 212。| **just outside** *Bolton is a beautiful mill town just outside Manchester.* 博爾頓是一座美麗的磨坊之城, 就在曼徹斯特邊上。**4** beyond the limits or range of a situation, activity etc 超出〔情況、活動等的〕界限, 在…範圍之外: *It's outside my experience I'm afraid.* 恐怕我沒有這方面的經驗。| *I don't care who you see outside working hours.* 我並不在意你在上班時間以外見甚麼人。—opposite 反義詞 WITHIN —compare 比較 BEYOND¹ **5** if someone is outside a group of people, an organization etc they do not have the same ideas and beliefs 與〔團體、組織等的想法、看法〕不一致: *Outside the party the official story was that he needed to spend more time with his family.* 該黨對外的官方口徑是, 他需要多花些時間和家人在一起。

1 3 **out·side[2]** /ˋaʊtˋsaɪd; aʊtˈsaɪd/ *adv* **1** not inside a building 在外面, 在戶外: *Can't you kids go and play outside?* 你們這幾個小傢伙不能去外頭玩嗎? | *What do you want to go out for? It's still dark outside.* 你想出去幹甚麼?外面天還黑着呢。**2** not in a room or building but close to it 在〔房屋、建築物附近的〕外面, 在室外: *I don't have time to chat, my husband's waiting outside.* 我沒時間聊天, 我丈夫在外面等着呢。| *What's happening at the stadium? There are lots of people standing outside.* 體育場有甚麼活動?好多人在外頭站着。**3 outside of** *informal especially AmE*【非正式, 尤美】**a)** apart from a particular person or thing; except 除...以外, ...除外: *What else can we do, outside of tearing the work up and starting from the beginning?* 除了推翻一切重來之外, 我們還能做甚麼? **b)** outside a particular place, building etc 在〔某處、某建築物等〕的外面: *It was decided to run a campaign outside of Washington.* 已決定在華盛頓附近舉行一場(競選)活動。

USAGE NOTE 用法說明: OUT

WORD CHOICE 詞語辨析: **out, outside, outdoors/out of doors**

If you are **outside** a room or building, you are not in it but are close to it. outside 指在房間或建築物外面, 但相距很近: *You have to go outside if you want to smoke.* 你如果想吸煙, 就得到外面去。| *It's cold outside.* 外面很冷。

If you are **out**, you are away from a building, especially somewhere you live or spend a lot of time. out 指離開某建築物, 尤指居住或待很長時間的地方: *Let's go out for a meal/drive.* 我們出去吃飯吧/我們開車出去兜兜風吧。| *I'm sorry, Mr. Davies is out at the moment.* 對不起, 戴維斯先生這會兒外出了。

You use **outdoors** (or **out of doors**) more informally to mean being out of any building. outdoors〔或 out of doors〕為較非正式的用語, 意指在任何建築物之外: *I'd like a job where I can work outdoors.* 我想找一份能在室外幹活的工作。

GRAMMAR 語法

People or things go or come **out of** somewhere. 人或物由某處出來用 out of: *He comes out of prison next week.* (NOT 不用 *out from prison*) 他下週出獄。| *Water poured out of the pipe.* 水從管道中流出。(Also *out the pipe* in American English and informal spoken British English. 美國英語及非正式的英國口語中也用 out the pipe。)

You go/are **out of** *the house*, but **away from** *home*. 出屋用 out of the house, 離家用 away from home。

Outside may be used alone or with **of** (especially in spoken and American English). outside 可以單用, 也可與 of 連用〔尤在口語和美國英語中〕: *He lives outside (of) Miami.* (NOT 不用 *outside from...*) 他住在邁阿密附近。

2 2 **out·side[3]** /ˋaʊtˋsaɪd; ˈaʊtsaɪd/ *adj* [only before noun 僅用於名詞前] **1 outside wall/toilet etc** a wall, toilet etc that is not inside a building 外牆/在外面的廁所等: *Most apartments have outside staircases in case of emergency.* 大多數公寓都有供緊急情況用的室外樓梯。| *The house will need a lot of outside repairs before we can sell it.* 房子外部要好好修繕才能出售。—opposite 反義詞 INSIDE[4] (1) —see also 另見 OUTDOORS[1], OUTER **2 outside help/interest etc** help etc from people who do not belong to the same group or organization as you 外援/外界的關注等: *My family solved its problems without any outside interference.* 我家沒靠外人干預, 自己解決了問題。**3 outside expert/consultant etc** an expert, consultant etc who does not work for your company or organization but who you pay to do some work for you 外聘專家/顧問等: *A firm of outside caterers were brought in especially for the function.* 這次宴會請了一家對外承辦酒席的公司來專門供應酒食。**4 outside interests/experiences etc** interests, experiences etc that are different from those that you have in your job 業餘愛好/工作以外的經歷等: *Ex-scientists can bring their outside knowledge into the teaching profession.* 曾經當過科學家的人可以把他們獨到的知識用於教學。**5 the outside world** the rest of the world which is unknown to you because you have no communication with it, you are not involved in it etc 外界: *Since the attack the city has been cut off from the outside world.* 那個城市自遭受襲擊以來, 與外界的聯繫已被隔絕。**6 an outside chance** a very small possibility that something will happen 極小的可能性, 不大可能的機會: *There's an outside chance that Regis might be sent to Uganda on business.* 派里吉斯去烏干達出差的可能性不大。**7 an outside figure/estimate etc** a number or amount that is the largest something could possibly be 最大限度的數字/估計等 **8 outside line/call etc** a telephone line or telephone call which is to or from someone not inside a building 外線/外線電話等 **9 the outside lane** the LANE (2) that is nearest the middle of the road 外車道 —see picture on page A3 參見 A3 頁圖

out·side[4] /ˋaʊtˋsaɪd; aʊtˈsaɪd/ *n* **the outside 1** the outer walls, windows etc of something such as a building or vehicle〔某物的〕外牆; 外層窗; 外面: **[+of]** *We've decided to paint the outside of the house brown.* 我們決定把房子的外牆刷成棕色。**2** the area of land around something such as a building, vehicle etc〔建築物、車輛等的〕周圍, 周邊地帶, 外圍: *From the outside the hotel looked fairly rundown.* 從外面看, 這家旅館已經相當破舊。**3** the outer part or surface of something〔某物的〕外部; 表面: **[+of]** *The outside of the cheese is red but this is just a protective wax.* 乳酪的外表呈紅色, 但這只是一層保護蠟而已。—opposite 反義詞 INSIDE[3] (1a) **4** someone who is on or from the outside is not involved in an activity or does not belong to a particular group, organization etc 局外〔人士〕; 外界〔人士〕: *To anyone on the outside our discipline methods may seem a little severe.* 對任何局外人而言, 我們的訓練方法看來也許有些嚴厲。**5 on the outside a)** used to describe the way someone appears to be or to behave 表面上, 由表面來看: *On the outside she appeared gentle and kind but really she was the meanest person I ever met.* 從表面上看, 她溫柔可親, 但實際上她是我所遇到的最卑鄙的人。**b)** not in prison 在監獄外(的): *Life on the outside was not as easy as he'd first thought.* 出獄後的生活並非像他原來想的那樣輕鬆。**6 at the (very) outside** used to say that a particular number or amount could be the largest something, and it might be less 最多, 充其量: *It's only a 20 minute walk, half an hour at the outside.* 那只是 20 分鐘的路程, 最多半個小時。**7** the LANE (2) on a road that is nearest to the middle of the road 外車道: *In some countries it is only permissible to overtake on the outside.* 有些國家只允許在外車道超車。—opposite 反義詞 INSIDE[3] (1b)

out·sid·er /aʊtˋsaɪdɚ; aʊtˈsaɪdə/ *n* [C] **1** someone who is not accepted as a member of a particular social group〔不被某一社會團體接受的〕局外人, 外人; 非成員: *We felt like complete outsiders when we first moved here.* 剛搬來這裡時, 我們感到自己完全像外人。**2** someone who does not seem to have much chance of winning a race or competition〔比賽中〕贏面不大的人: *The champion was knocked out by an outsider.* 冠軍被一位不被看好的拳擊手擊倒了。**3** someone who does not belong to a particular company or organization 公司[組織]外的人: *The firm was obliged to seek the help of outsiders.* 該商行被迫尋求外援。

out·size /ˋaʊtˌsaɪz; ˈaʊtsaɪz/ *adj* also 又作 **out·sized**

/-ˌsaɪzd; -saɪzd/ **1** larger than normal 超過正常尺寸的, 特大號的: *peering through outsize spectacles* 透過特大號眼鏡凝視 **2** made for people who are very large 為非常高大的人裁製的, 超大號的: *outsize clothes* 超大號服裝

out·skirts /ˈaʊtˌskɝts; ˈaʊtskɜːts/ *n* [plural] the parts of a town or city that are furthest from the centre 遠離城市中心的地區; 市郊; 郊區: **on the outskirts** *They live on the outskirts of Paris.* 他們住在巴黎的郊區。

out·smart /aʊtˋsmɑrt; aʊtˈsmɑːt/ *v* [T] to gain an advantage over someone using tricks or clever plans; OUTWIT 比…更精明, 智勝…: *The lizard can outsmart any predators by leaving its tail behind to confuse them.* 蜥蜴比任何食肉動物都機靈, 牠會甩掉自己的尾巴來迷惑其他動物。

out·sour·cing /ˈaʊtˌsɔrsɪŋ; ˈaʊtˌsɔːsɪŋ/ *n* [U] the practice of using workers from outside a company 外包, 外判〔使用公司外聘員工的做法〕

out·spo·ken /aʊtˋspokən; aʊtˈspəʊkən/ *adj* expressing your opinions honestly, even when it is not popular to do so 坦率的, 直言不諱的: *an outspoken critic of the country's human rights policies* 對該國人權政策直言不諱的評論家 —**outspokenly** *adv* —**outspokenness** *n* [U]

out·spread /ˈaʊtˌsprɛd; ˌaʊtˈspred◂/ *adj* spread out flat or completely 張開的, 伸開的: *He was lying on the beach with arms outspread.* 他兩臂攤開躺在沙灘上。

3 **out·stand·ing** /aʊtˋstændɪŋ; aʊtˈstændɪŋ/ *adj* **1** extremely good 傑出的, 優秀的, 出色的: *an area of outstanding natural beauty* 極佳的自然風景區 | *an outstanding performance* 出色的表演 **2** not yet done, solved, or paid 未完成的; 未解決的; 未付款的: *We've got quite a few debts still outstanding.* 我們尚有好多欠債未曾償還。| *an outstanding problem* 懸而未決的問題

out·stand·ing·ly /aʊtˋstændɪŋlɪ; aʊtˈstændɪŋli/ *adv* extremely well 出色地, 極好地: *Varese played outstandingly.* 瓦雷塞打得很出色。| [+adj/adv] *an outstandingly talented musician* 一位才華出眾的音樂家

out·stare /aʊtˋstɛr; aʊtˈsteə/ *v* [T] to look at someone for so long that they feel too uncomfortable to look at you 以目光逼視; 盯得…侷促不安

out·stay /aʊtˋste; aʊtˈsteɪ/ *v* [T] to stay somewhere longer than someone else 停留較〔他人〕長久, 比〔他人〕待得久: *As usual she outstayed all the other guests at the party.* 晚會上, 她照例比其他客人都待得久。—see also 另見 **outstay your welcome** WELCOME[3] (3)

out·stretched /aʊtˋstrɛtʃt; ˌaʊtˈstretʃt◂/ *adj* stretched out to full length 張開的, 伸開的: *She ran to meet them with outstretched arms.* 她張開雙臂跑過去迎接他們。

out·strip /aʊtˋstrɪp; aʊtˈstrɪp/ *v* **outstripped, outstripping** [T] **1** to do something better than someone else 比…做得好, 勝過: *We outstripped all our competitors in sales last year.* 去年我們在銷售方面超過了所有的競爭對手。**2** to be greater in quantity than something else 數量上大於…: *Demand for energy is outstripping the supply.* 能源目前求大於供。**3** to run or move faster than someone or something else 跑步[移動]快於…, 把…拋在後面: *Dawson outstripped the other runners on the last lap.* 道森在最後一圈超越了其他賽跑者。

out·take /ˈ· ·/ *n* [C] a piece of a film or television show that is removed before it is broadcast, especially because it contains a mistake〔尤指因內容有錯而在播放前〕被臨時撤掉的電影[電視節目]片段

out tray /ˈ· ·/ *n* [C] a box on an office desk to hold work and letters which are ready to be sent out or put away〔辦公桌上存放已處理或待發文件的〕發文匣[格] —compare 比較 IN TRAY

out·vote /aʊtˋvot; aʊtˈvəʊt/ *v* [T] to defeat a person or an idea by voting against them 以票數多擊敗…, 比…得到更多選票

out·ward /ˈaʊtwɚd; ˈaʊtwəd/ *adj* **1** [only before noun 僅用於名詞前] concerning how someone seems to other people, rather than what they are actually like 外表的, 表面上的: *She managed to maintain her outward composure.* 她保持着外表的鎮靜。| *His house shows few outward signs of worldly success.* 他的房子看不出他有取得世俗成就的跡象。| **to all outward appearances** (=as much as you can judge by the way things seem) 從外表上看 *To all outward appearances, Jayne seems to be dealing with the tragedy well.* 從外表看, 傑恩似乎對那件慘事應付得很好。**2 outward journey/voyage etc** a journey in which you are travelling away from home 外出旅行/出航等 **3** [only before noun 僅用於名詞前] directed towards the outside or away from something 往外的, 向外的: *an outward movement of the arm* 手臂的向外運動 **4 outward bound** a train, ship, etc that is outward bound is leaving a place that it will return to later〔列車、船隻等〕開往外地的; 出海的

out·ward·ly /ˈaʊtwɚdlɪ; ˈaʊtwədli/ *adv* according to the way things seem 外表上, 從表面上看: *Calvin remained outwardly calm but inside he was seething.* 卡爾文表面上仍不露聲色, 但內心卻激動不已。| [sentence adverb 句子副詞] *Outwardly, nothing seemed to have changed.* 從表面上看, 似乎一無變化。

out·wards /ˈaʊtwɚdz; ˈaʊtwədz/ also 又作 **outward** *AmE*【美】*adv* towards the outside or away from the centre of something 往外, 向外: *The door opens outwards.* 這門是朝外開的。

out·weigh /aʊtˋwe; aʊtˈweɪ/ *v* [T] to be more important or valuable than something else 比…更重要; 比…更有價值: *The advantages of this plan far outweigh the disadvantages.* 該計劃的利遠大於弊。

out·wit /aʊtˋwɪt; aʊtˈwɪt/ *v* **outwitted, outwitting** [T] to gain an advantage over someone using tricks or clever plans 智勝, 以計謀擊敗: *My father spent years trying to build a bird feeder that would outwit the squirrels.* 我父親花了數年的時間, 想造一個讓松鼠無計可施的餵鳥器。

out·work /ˈaʊtˌwɝk; ˈaʊtwɜːk/ *n* [U] work for a business that is done by people at home〔由人們在家中完成的〕外包活 —**outworker** *n* [C]

out·worn /ˌaʊtˋwɔrn; ˌaʊtˈwɔːn◂/ *adj* [only before noun 僅用於名詞前] old-fashioned, and no longer useful or important 過時的, 廢棄了的; 不再重要的: *A lot of schools have abolished these outworn traditions.* 許多學校已廢除了這些過時的傳統習俗。

ou·zo /ˈuzo; ˈuːzəʊ/ *n* [U] a Greek alcoholic drink that is drunk with water〔希臘的〕茴香烈酒

o·va /ˈovə; ˈəʊvə/ *n* the plural form of OVUM

o·val /ˈovl; ˈəʊvəl/ *n* [C] a shape like a circle, but longer than it is wide 卵形, 橢圓形 —**oval** *adj*: *an oval mirror* 橢圓形的鏡子 —see picture at 參見 SHAPE[1] 圖

Oval Of·fice /ˌ·· ˈ··/ *n* the office of the US president, in the White House, Washington DC〔美國華盛頓白宮內的〕橢圓形辦公室, 總統辦公室: *We're waiting for a reaction from the Oval Office.* 我們在等候總統辦公室的反應。

o·var·i·an /oˋvɛrɪən; əʊˈveəriən/ *adj* related to the ovary 卵巢的; 子房的: *ovarian cancer* 卵巢癌

o·va·ry /ˈovərɪ; ˈəʊvəri/ *n plural* **ovaries** [C] **1** the part of a female that produces eggs〔雌性動物的〕卵巢 **2** the part of a female plant that produces seeds〔植物的〕子房

o·va·tion /oˋveʃən; əʊˈveɪʃən/ *n* [C] *formal* if a group of people give someone an ovation they CLAP[1] (1) to show approval【正式】〔以鼓掌表示的〕贊同; 歡呼, 喝采: *60,000 fans gave the rock group a thunderous ovation.* 60,000名歌迷向搖滾樂隊報以雷鳴般的掌聲。| **standing ovation** (=one in which people stand) 起立鼓掌

ov·en /ˈʌvən; ˈʌvən/ *n* [C] **1** a thing inside which food is cooked, shaped like a box with a door on the front 烘箱; 烤箱, 烤爐: **a medium/moderate oven** (=an oven that has not been made very hot) 溫度調在中擋的烘箱 *Bake in a medium oven for 40 minutes.* 用中擋溫度在烘箱內烤40分鐘。**2 like an oven** *informal* uncomfortably hot【非正式】很熱的: *It's like an oven in here! Open the* *window.* 這裡熱得像火爐！快把窗戶打開吧。—see also 另見 **have a bun in the oven** (BUN (4))

ov·en·proof /ˈʌvən,pruf; ˈʌvənpruːf/ *adj* a dish, plate etc that is ovenproof will not be harmed by the high temperatures in an oven〔碟子、盤子等〕耐熱的，經得起烘箱溫度而不致碎裂的

oven-read·y /ˌ.. ˈ..◂/ *adj* oven-ready food is already prepared when you buy it, so you only have to cook it〔購買時已加工好的食物〕即可入爐烤製的

ov·en·ware /ˈʌvən,wɛr; ˈʌvənweə/ *n* [U] cooking pots that can be put in a hot oven without cracking〔經得起烘箱高溫烘烤的〕耐熱器皿

1 1 **over[1]** /ˈovə; ˈəʊvə/ *prep* **1** above or higher than something, without touching it 在…上面[上方]〔但未觸及〕，在…上空: *A lamp hung over the table.* 桌子上方懸吊着一盞燈。| *She leaned over the desk to answer the phone.* 她俯身靠在書桌上接電話。| *The sign over the door said 'Mind your head'.* 門上方的警示牌寫着"小心碰頭"。—opposite 反義詞 UNDER[1] (1) —see also 另見 ABOVE[1], ACROSS[1]—see picture at 參見 ABOVE[1] 圖 **2** on something, so that it is covered 蒙在…上，覆蓋在…的上面: *Over the body lay a thin white sheet.* 屍體上蓋着一層薄薄的白布單。| *She wore a large jacket over her sweater.* 她在毛衣外面穿了件寬大的夾克。—opposite 反義詞 UNDER[1] (1) **3** from one side of something to the other side of it 從〔某物〕的一邊到另一邊: *Somehow the sheep had jumped over the fence.* 不知怎麼地，那隻羊跳過了圍欄。| *The road over the mountains is steep and dangerous.* 這條翻越山區的路陡峭而危險。**4 over on** also 又作 **over** *BrE*【英】on the opposite side of something from where you already are 在〔所在之處〕的另一邊: *We live over on the other side of town.* 我們住在城鎮的那一邊。**5** down from the edge of something 從…邊緣上掉下: *Apparently the car fell over a cliff.* 汽車顯然是從懸崖邊上掉下去的。| *The shirt was hanging over the back of the chair.* 襯衫搭在椅子的靠背上。**6** in many parts of a particular place, organization etc 遍及〔某一地方、組織等〕，到處: *I've travelled over most of Europe but my favourite place was Austria.* 我遊歷了歐洲的大多數地方，最喜歡之處是奧地利。| **all over** (=in every part) 到處，各處 *They said they had cleaned up but there were bottles all over the place.* 他們說已經清掃過了，但那裡到處都是瓶子。**7 be over sth** to feel better after an illness or bad situation 從〔疾病或困境之後〕恢復過來: *I think I'm over the worst of it now.* 我想我現在已經熬過了最困難的時候。**8** in control of someone or having authority to give orders to someone 控制；統治；支配: *He rules over a large kingdom.* 他統治着一個疆域遼闊的王國。| *In this office there is one manager over a staff of 15 workers.* 在這個辦公室裡每一位經理都管理着 15 名員工。—opposite 反義詞 UNDER[1] (9) **9** more than a particular number, amount or level 超出〔某一數目、數額或程度〕，比…多: *I've lost over 3 kilos in weight.* 我的體重已減了三公斤多。| *Children over 12 are not allowed in the swimming area.* 12 歲以上的兒童不得進入本游泳區。| *The driver was found to have over the legal alcohol limit in his blood.* 司機被查出血液裡的酒精含量超出了法律許可之限度。| **the over-30s/the over-50s etc** (=people who are more than a particular age) 30 歲/50 歲等以上者 *a social club for the over-60s* 為 60 歲以上者而設的聯誼俱樂部 **10** during 在…期間: *Will you be home over the Christmas vacation?* 聖誕節期間你在家嗎？| *Over a period of ten years he stole a million pounds from the company.* 他在十年間從公司偷走了一百萬英鎊。| *Can we talk about this over dinner?* 我們能否邊吃飯邊談這問題？**11** using something such as a telephone or radio 使用〔電話或收音機等〕: *I don't want to talk about this over the telephone.* 我不想在電話裡談這件事。**12** about a particular subject, person or thing 與…有關，關於: *He's having problems over his income tax.* 他在所得稅方面出了問題。| *a row over public expenditure* 有關公共開支的爭論 **13 over and above** an amount that is over and above another is an extra amount 除…外(還): *He gets a travel allowance over and above his existing salary.* 他除目前的薪水以外，還有一份出差補助。—see also 另見 **all over** (ALL[2] (6))

over[2] *adv* **1 fall over/knock sth over etc** to fall etc so that you are lying down or knock something etc so that it is flat on a surface after being upright 摔倒/弄倒某物等: *He was so drunk he fell over in the road.* 他喝得爛醉，跌倒在馬路上。| *A lot of work is being done to prevent the tower from toppling over.* 正在進行大量工作以避免塔樓倒塌。 1 1
2 bend over/fold sth over etc to bend etc so that you are no longer upright or fold something etc so that it is no longer straight or flat and is folded in the middle 彎腰/摺疊某物等: *As Sheila bent over, a sudden pain shot up her back.* 希拉彎腰時，背部突然一陣疼痛。| *He silently folded the paper over and put it in his pocket.* 他默默地把紙摺疊起來放入口袋。**3** [only after verb 僅用於動詞後] from one side of something to the other side 從…的一邊到另一邊，穿越: *There are only 3 canoes so some people will have to swim over.* 僅有三艘獨木舟，所以一部分人得游過去。| *I went over to say hello but Vincent didn't recognize me.* 我走過去打招呼，但文森特沒有認出是我。| **over to/from** *We flew over to the US to visit my Aunt Polly.* 我們飛往美國去探望我的姨母波莉。| *I took her over to Saginaw because she had a doctor's appointment.* 我帶她去薩吉諾，因為她約好了醫生。**4** [only after verb 僅用於動詞後] to or in a particular house, city etc 到，在〔某處〕: *You really should come over and see our new house.* 你真的該過來看看我們的新房子。**5 hand over/sign over etc** to give something to another person 移交/簽字轉讓等: *The attacker was ordered to hand over his weapon and lie on the ground.* 襲擊者被命令交出武器並就地趴下。| *Most of the money has been signed over to his children.* 大部分錢已簽字過戶給了他的孩子。**6 change over/swap over** if you change two things over you put one of the things in the place of the other 交換/對調: *The vases had been swapped over and nobody had spotted the fake.* 花瓶被人調包了，誰也沒認出那個贋品。| *The guards change over at midnight.* 衛兵午夜時換崗。**7 turn over/roll over** if you turn something over you move it so that the side of it which could not be seen can now be seen 翻轉/翻滾: *Turn the page over.* 把這一頁翻過去。| *The children spent hours rolling over and over in the sand.* 孩子們在沙地裡打滾玩耍了幾個小時。**8 twelve years/90% etc and over** more than 12 years, 90% etc 十二歲/90% 等以上: *The film is suitable for people of 18 and over.* 這部影片適合 18 歲及 18 歲以上人士觀看。| *Sorry, this agency only deals with properties worth $200,000 and over.* 對不起，本事務所只接手財產價值在 20 萬美元以上的生意。—opposite 反義詞 UNDER **9** a particular amount of something that is over is what remains after some of it has been used 剩下，餘下: *We were over by about $300!* 我們還剩下大約 300 美元！| **left over** *We had so much food left over we donated it to charity.* 我們剩了很多食品，都贈給了慈善機構。**10 covered over/painted over etc** covered with a particular substance or material 覆蓋/塗抹等: *Most of the windows have been boarded over.* 大部分窗戶都用木板封死了。| [+with] *The door had been painted over with a bright red varnish.* 門用鮮紅的清漆刷過了。**11 read/think/talk etc sth over** to read something, think about something etc very carefully before deciding what to do 仔細地閱讀/思考/商量某事: *After talking it over with my wife, I've decided to retire.* 我和妻子仔細商量之後，決定退休。**12 over and over (again)** repeatedly 再三地，重複地: *The only way to learn the script is to say it to yourself over and over again.* 要背熟劇本唯一的辦法是自己反覆地唸。**13 over to sb** used to say that it is now someone else's turn to do something, to speak etc 輪到某人: *I've done my best. Now it's over to the profes-*

sionals. 我已經盡了全力, 現在該到專家們出手了。| *We're going over live to our correspondent at the scene of the explosion.* 我們現在轉給在爆炸現場的記者作進一步的報道。**14 over!** *spoken* used when using a radio to show that you have finished speaking【口】〔無線電通話用語〕完畢! **15 over against** compared to someone or something else 與…相比, 與…成對照 —see also 另見 **all over** (ALL² (6))

over³ *adj* [not before noun 不用於名詞前] **1** if an event or period of time is over, it has finished〔指一件事或一段時間〕完結的, 結束的: *When the game was over all the players shook hands.* 比賽結束時, 所有球員都互相握手。**2 be over (and done) with** if an unpleasant situation or experience is over with, it has finished〔不快之事或經歷〕已了結, 已過去: *We don't have to mention the court case again! It's all over and done with now.* 我們不要再提這樁官司! 事情已經了結了。| **get sth over (and done) with** (=to do something so that the situation no longer exists) 把某事了結掉 *The sooner you get it over with the better so phone up and make the appointment.* 這事你早了早好, 所以打電話預約一下吧。

over⁴ *n* [C] the period of time in the game of CRICKET (2) during which six or eight balls are thrown by the same BOWLER (1) in one direction〔板球比賽中投球手連續投出六次或八次的〕一輪投球數

over- /ovə; əʊvə/ *prefix* **1** too much 過多, 過頭, 過分: *overpopulation* 人口過剩 | *overcooked cabbage* 煮過頭的洋白菜 **2** above; beyond; across 在上面; 超過; 橫越: *overhanging branches* 懸垂的樹枝 | *the overland route* (=not by sea or air) 陸路 **3** outer; covering 外面的; 覆蓋的: *an overcoat* 外套 **4** additional 額外的: *working overtime* (=beyond the usual time) 加班[超時]工作

over·a·chiev·er /ˌ·· ·ˈ··/ *n* [C] someone who works very hard to be successful and is very unhappy if they do not achieve everything they want to 成就慾望過強者〔指非常努力地工作以獲取成功的人, 他們如未能獲得想要的一切便會非常惱怒〕—**over-achieve** *v* [I]

o·ver·act /ˌovəˋækt; ˌəʊvərˈækt/ *v* [I,T] to act a part in a play with too much emotion or movement 把〔角色〕演得過火[過於誇張]

o·ver·ac·tive /ˋovəˋæktɪv; ˌəʊvərˈæktɪv◂/ *adj* too active, in a way that produces a bad result 過度活躍的: *Paul's illness was due to an overactive thyroid.* 保羅的病是因甲狀腺過於活躍而引起的。| **have an overactive imagination** (=tend to imagine things that are untrue) 有過於豐富的想像力 *The rumor is probably just the result of someone's overactive imagination.* 這謠言或許只是某些人想像力過於豐富的結果。

over-age /ˌ·· ˈ·◂/ *adj* too old for a particular purpose or activity 過老的; 超齡的: *He looked like an over-age drummer from some sixties band.* 他看上去像一個老去的來自60年代某個樂隊的鼓手。—compare 比較 UNDERAGE

S3 W2 **o·ver·all¹** /ˌovəˋɔl; ˌəʊvərˈɔːl◂/ *adj* including everything 包括一切的, 全部的: *My overall impression of his work is good.* 我對他的作品總的印象是良好的。| *What's the overall cost of repairs?* 修理費用總共是多少?

overall² *adv* **1** including everything 全部地; 總共: *The fish measures 1.7 metres overall.* 那條魚全長為1.7米。| *What will it cost, overall?* 這總共要花多少錢? **2** [sentence adverb 句子副詞] generally 一般地, 總體上: *Overall, prices are still rising.* 總的來說, 價格仍在上漲。

o·ver·all³ /ˋovəɔl; ˈəʊvərɔːl/ *n* **1** [C] *BrE* a loose-fitting piece of clothing like a coat, that is worn over clothes to protect them【英】〔穿在其他衣服外面的〕寬大罩衫 **2 overalls** [plural] *especially AmE* heavy cotton trousers with a piece covering your chest and held up by pieces of cloth that go over your shoulders【尤美】粗布工裝褲; DUNGAREES (1) *BrE*【英】**3 overalls** [plural] *BrE*【英】also 又作 **overall** [C] *AmE*【美】a piece of clothing like a shirt and trousers in one piece worn over other clothes to protect them〔上下連身的〕工作服

overall ma·jor·i·ty /ˌ··· ·ˈ···/ *n* [C] **1** more votes than all the other political parties together 壓倒多數票〔指得票數多於所有其他政黨的總和〕**2** *BrE* the difference between this number of votes and the total votes gained by all the other parties【英】總合多數票〔指得票數與所有其他政黨得票數總和之間的差額〕

o·ver·arch·ing /ˌovəˋartʃɪŋ; ˌəʊvərˈɑːtʃɪŋ◂/ *adj* **1** including or influencing every part of something 包羅萬象的; 支配一切的: *The project's overarching aim is the improvement of education.* 這項計劃的宗旨在於提高教育水平。**2** forming a curved shape over something 在…上成圓拱形的: *the overarching sky* 蒼穹

o·ver·arm /ˋovəˌarm; ˈəʊvərɑːm/ *adj, adv especially BrE* an overarm throw in a sport is when you throw the ball with your arm high above your shoulder【尤英】〔運動中擲球或投球時〕揮臂[舉手]過肩的[地]; OVERHAND *AmE*【美】—see picture on page A23 參見A23頁圖

o·ver·awe /ˌovəˋɔ; ˌəʊvərˈɔː/ *v* [T] to make someone feel respect or fear so that they become very quiet 使敬畏, 使懾服: *overawed by the great man's booming voice* 被那偉人深沉的嗓音所鎮服

o·ver·bal·ance /ˌovəˋbæləns; ˌəʊvəˈbæləns/ *v* [I,T] **1** *especially BrE* to shake and start to fall because you lose balance, or to make someone or something do this【尤英】(使) 失去平衡而歪倒: *The horse reared, overbalanced, and fell.* 馬用後腿直立起來, 失去平衡而倒下了。**2** *AmE* OUTWEIGH【美】比…更重要, 重要性超過…: *The lack of social life is overbalanced by the amount of money I'll save living here.* 比起住在這裡我將攢下的錢數, 缺少社交生活就不那麼重要了。

o·ver·bear /ˌovəˋbɛr; ˌəʊvəˈbeə/ *v* [T usually passive 一般用被動態] *past tense* **overbore**, *past participle* **overborne** to defeat someone or something 擊敗; 戰勝

o·ver·bear·ing /ˌovəˋbɛrɪŋ; ˌəʊvəˈbeərɪŋ◂/ *adj* always trying to control other people without considering their wishes or feelings; DOMINEERING 專橫的, 好指使人的; 飛揚跋扈的: *self-important overbearing attitudes of these high-up doctors* 這些高級醫生那自視甚高且盛氣凌人的態度 —**overbearingly** *adv*

o·ver·bid /ˌovəˋbɪd; ˌəʊvəˈbɪd/ *v* **1** [I +**for**] to offer too high a price for something, especially at an AUCTION¹〔尤指在拍賣中〕出價太高 **2** [I,T] to offer more than the value of your cards in a card game such as BRIDGE¹ (4)〔在橋牌賽中〕叫牌超過〔自己的實力〕

o·ver·bite /ˋovəˌbaɪt; ˈəʊvəbaɪt/ *n* [C] a condition in which someone's upper jaw is too far forwards beyond their lower jaw〔牙齒的〕覆咬合

o·ver·blown /ˌovəˋblon; ˌəʊvəˈbləʊn◂/ *adj* **1** *formal* made to seem greater or more impressive; EXAGGERATED (1)【正式】誇張的; 過分渲染的: *overblown news stories* 誇大的新聞報道 **2** overblown flowers have opened too wide and become less beautiful〔指花〕已過盛期的, 開得太大的

o·ver·board /ˋovəˌbord; ˈəʊvəbɔːd/ *adv* **1** over the side of a ship or boat into the water 從船舷掉入水中: *One of the crew fell overboard and drowned.* 船員中有一人從船邊跌入水中淹死了。| *Man overboard!* 有人落水了! **2 go overboard** *informal* to do or say too much because you are too eager or excited【非正式】〔因太急切或激動而〕做事[說話]過分, 走極端: *Dean knew he had gone overboard by sending six dozen roses.* 迪安知道自己送六打玫瑰是做過頭了。**3 throw sth overboard** to get rid of an idea etc that is useless or unnecessary 拋棄某物, 去除某物

o·ver·book /ˌovəˋbuk; ˌəʊvəˈbʊk/ *v* [I,T] to sell more tickets for a theatre, plane etc than there are seats available 超量售出〔戲票、機票等〕, 超額訂出[預訂]

o·ver·bur·den /ˋovəˋbɝdn̩; ˌəʊvəˈbɜːdn/ *v* [T usually passive 一般用被動態] to give someone or a system too much work or too many problems to deal with 使負擔過多; 使負荷過重: *an overburdened donkey* 負載過重的驢 |

[+with] *a student overburdened with essays* 因作文繁多而不堪重負的學生

o·ver·came /ˌovɚˋkem; ˌəʊvəˈkeɪm/ *v* the past tense of OVERCOME

o·ver·cap·i·tal·ize also 又作 **-ise** *BrE*【英】/ˋovɚˌkæpətḷˌaɪz; ˌəʊvəˈkæpɪ̣tl-aɪz/ *v* [I,T] **1** to supply too much money for a business 對〔企業〕投資過多 **2** to put too high a value on a business 對〔企業的〕資本估價過高 —**overcapitalization** /ˋovɚˌkæpətḷəˋzeʃən; ˌəʊvəkæpɪ̣tl-aɪˈzeɪʃən/ *n* [U]

o·ver·cast /ˌovɚˋkæst; ˌəʊvəˈkɑːst◂/ *adj* dark with clouds 陰天的, 多雲的: *an overcast day* 多雲的日子 | *an overcast sky* 陰沉沉的天空 —see picture on page A13 參見 A13 頁圖

o·ver·charge /ˋovɚˋtʃɑrdʒ; ˌəʊvəˈtʃɑːdʒ/ *v* **1** [I,T] to charge someone too much money for something 對〔某人〕索價過高: **overcharge sb** *The cashier overcharged me by at least $2.00.* 收銀員至少多收了我兩美元。**2** too full of emotion or excitement 充滿〔過度的〕感情[激情]: *The atmosphere in the stadium was overcharged with excitement.* 體育場裡的氣氛充滿了激情。**3** [T] to put too much power into a BATTERY (1) or electrical system 使〔電池〕充電過度; 使〔電路系統〕超負荷

o·ver·cloud /ˌovɚˋklaʊd; ˌəʊvəˈklaʊd/ *v* [T usually passive 一般用被動態] **1** to cover the sky, sun etc with clouds〔天空、太陽等〕佈滿雲層, 給雲遮蓋 **2** to fill someone or a situation with unhappy or worried feelings 使悲傷, 使憂鬱: *a look of fear suddenly overclouding his face* 突然籠罩在他臉上的恐懼神色

o·ver·coat /ˋovɚˌkot; ˈəʊvəkəʊt/ *n* [C] a long, thick, warm coat worn over other clothes in cold weather 大衣

3 3 **o·ver·come** /ˌovɚˋkʌm; ˌəʊvəˈkʌm/ *v past tense* **overcame** /-ˋkem; -ˈkeɪm/ *past participle* **overcome** **1** to control a feeling or problem that prevents you from achieving something 控制〔感情〕; 克服〔困難〕: *He struggled to overcome his shyness.* 他努力克服自己的羞怯。**2** [I, T] to fight and win against someone or something 征服, 戰勝: *They overcame the enemy after a long battle.* 經過一場漫長的戰鬥, 他們擊敗了敵人。| *We shall overcome!* 我們一定會勝利! **3** [T usually passive 一般用被動態] to have such a strong effect on someone that they become weak, unconscious, or unable to control their feelings 被〔感情〕制服; 使無能為力: *She was overcome by emotion.* 她激動得難以自持。| *Those who died in the fire were overcome by the gas fumes.* 那些死於大火的人是被煤氣熏倒的。

o·ver·com·pen·sate /ˌovɚˋkɑmpənset; ˌəʊvəˈkɒmpənseɪt/ *v* [I] to try to correct a weakness or mistake by doing too much of the opposite thing〔為彌補缺陷或過失而〕矯枉過正, 過度補償: *Zoe overcompensates for her shyness by talking a lot.* 佐伊為克服自己的羞怯而說話過多, 真是矯枉過正。—**overcompensation** /ˌovɚkɑmpənˋseʃən; ˌəʊvəkɒmpənˈseɪʃən/ *n* [U]

o·ver·crowd /ˌovɚˋkraʊd; ˌəʊvəˈkraʊd/ *v* [T] to fill a space or period of time with too many things or people 使〔某處〕過分擁擠; 使〔某段時間〕安排過滿: **[+with]** *The courts overcrowd their calendars with too many trials.* 法庭安排了過多的庭審, 日程表排得太滿了。

o·ver·crowd·ed /ˌovɚˋkraʊdɪd; ˌəʊvəˈkraʊdɪ̣d◂/ *adj* filled with too many people or things 過分擁擠的: *an overcrowded room* 擁擠不堪的房間

o·ver·crowd·ing /ˌovɚˋkraʊdɪŋ; ˌəʊvəˈkraʊdɪŋ/ *n* [U] the condition of living or working too close together, with too many people in a small space 過度擁擠

o·ver·de·vel·oped /ˋovɚdɪˋvɛləpt; ˌəʊvədɪˈveləpt◂/ *adj* too great or large 過度的; 過大的: *Ryan has an overdeveloped sense of his own importance.* 瑞安自視過高。

o·ver·do /ˋovɚˋdu; ˌəʊvəˈduː/ *v past tense* **overdid** /-ˋdɪd; -ˈdɪd/ *past participle* **overdone** /-ˋdʌn; -ˈdʌn/ [T] **1** to do something more than is suitable or natural 把〔某事〕做得過火[過於誇張]: *Don't overdo the praise. She wasn't that good.* 不要過分讚揚, 她沒那麼好。| **overdo it** *I think Trudy's overdone it with all the lace and frills in the bedroom.* 特魯迪在臥室裡弄了那麼多飾帶和花邊, 我認為有點過火。**2** to use too much of something 使用…過多: *I think I overdid the salt.* 我想是鹽放多了。**3 overdo it** to work too hard or be too active so that you become tired 工作過度; 過於勞碌: *She's been overdoing it lately.* 近來她勞碌過度。

o·ver·done /ˋovɚˋdʌn; ˌəʊvəˈdʌn◂/ *adj* cooked too much 煮得過度的, 燒得太久的: *The beef was overdone.* 牛肉煮過頭了。—compare 比較 UNDERDONE

o·ver·dose /ˋovɚˌdos; ˈəʊvədəʊs/ *n* [C] too much of a drug taken at one time〔藥物的〕使用過量: *a massive overdose of heroin* 過量服用海洛因 —**overdose** /ˌovɚˋdos; ˌəʊvəˈdəʊs/ *v* [I+on] *He overdosed on heroin.* 他服用了過量的海洛因。

o·ver·draft /ˋovɚˌdræft; ˈəʊvədrɑːft/ *n* [C] the amount of money you owe to a bank when you have taken out more money than you had in your bank account 透支額: *I have to find the money to pay off this overdraft.* 我得弄點錢來償還這筆透支款。

overdraft fa·cil·i·ty /ˈ‥ ·ˌ‥/ *n* [C] *BrE* an agreement with the bank that a customer may take more money from the bank than they have in their account, up to a certain amount【英】透支服務〔銀行按協議允許客戶提取超出其賬戶存款一定數目的錢款〕

o·ver·drawn /ˋovɚˋdrɔn; ˌəʊvəˈdrɔːn/ *adj* **be overdrawn** if your bank account is overdrawn you have spent more than is in it and you owe the bank money〔存款賬戶〕透支的: *I'm overdrawn at the moment.* 我現已透支了。| **be overdrawn by £50/$600 etc** *My account is overdrawn by £300.* 我的存款賬戶透支了 300 英鎊。—**overdraw** *v* [I]

o·ver·dressed /ˋovɚˋdrɛst; ˌəʊvəˈdrest◂/ *adj* dressed in clothes that are too formal for the occasion〔對某種場合來說〕穿着過於正式的: *I felt distinctly overdressed beside all those young people in jeans.* 與那些全是穿着牛仔褲的年輕人相比, 我感覺自己顯然穿得過於隆重。—**overdress** *v* [I]

o·ver·drive /ˋovɚˋdraɪv; ˈəʊvədraɪv/ *n* [U] **1** an additional GEAR[1] (2) which allows a car to go fast while its engine produces the least power necessary〔汽車的〕加速擋, 加速轉動齒輪: *Put the car in overdrive when you hit 50 mph.* 你開到每小時 50 英里的速度時, 把車掛到加速擋。**2 go into overdrive** to become very excited or active 變得非常激動[活躍]: *You could see his imagination go into overdrive at the thought.* 你能看出來, 他一想到這個, 想像力就會變得十分活躍。

o·ver·due /ˋovɚˋdju; ˌəʊvəˈdjuː◂/ *adj* **1** a payment that is overdue should have been paid earlier 過期未付的: *an overdue gas bill* 逾期未付的煤氣賬單 **2 be overdue for** to have needed something done for a long time 早就需要, 早該: *The car is overdue for a tune-up.* 這輛汽車早該檢修了。**3** something that is overdue should have happened or been done a long time ago 早該發生的; 早該完成的; 期待已久的: **long overdue** *This is a major, but long overdue reform which will benefit around 4 million low-paid people.* 這是一項早該實行的重大改革, 它將會使約 400 萬低收入人士獲益。**4** [not before noun 不用於名詞前] a baby that is overdue was not born at the time that it was expected〔嬰兒〕超過預產期的: *Collette's baby is a week overdue.* 科利特的胎兒已超過預產期一週了。**5** a library book that is overdue was not returned to the library when it should have been〔圖書館的書〕逾期未還的

o·ver·eat /ˋovɚˋit; ˌəʊvərˈiːt/ *v past tense* **overate** /-ˋet; -ˈet/ *past participle* **overeaten** /-ˋitṇ; -ˈiːtn/ [I] to eat too much, or eat more than is healthy 吃得過飽, 暴食: *Pete's gained so much weight because he can't stop overeating.* 皮特體重增加了那麼多, 是因為他不停地暴食。

o·ver·egg /ˌovɚˋɛg; ˌəʊvərˈeg/ *v* **overegg the pudding** *BrE informal* to do more than is necessary, or add something that is not needed【英, 非正式】做不必要的事; 畫蛇添足

o·ver·es·ti·mate[1] /ˈovɚˋɛstə͵met; ˌəʊvərˈestɨmeɪt/ *v* **1** [T] to judge something to be better than it really is 對〔某事〕估計過好, 估計過高: *I'm afraid we overestimated his abilities.* 恐怕我們對他的能力評價過高。**2** [I,T] to guess an amount or value that is too high 對〔數額或價值〕估計過高: *We overestimated the number of people who would come.* 我們高估了到場的人數。| **[+by]** *I think Jo's overestimated by about 300.* 我認為喬多估了 300 左右。—compare 比較 UNDERESTIMATE[1]

o·ver·es·ti·mate[2] /ˈovɚˋɛstəmɪt; ˌəʊvərˈestɨmɨt/ *n* [C] a calculation, judgment, or guess that is too large 過高的估計[評價]

o·ver·ex·cit·ed /ovərɪkˋsaɪtɪd; əʊvərikˈsaɪtɨd/ *adj* children who are overexcited are too excited to behave sensibly〔指兒童〕過於激動的, 過度興奮的

o·ver·ex·pose /ˈovərɪkˋspoz; ˌəʊvərɪkˈspəʊz/ *v* [T] **1** to allow too much light to reach the film when taking or developing a photograph 使〔底片或照片〕過度感光[曝光] **2 be overexposed** become less popular because of appearing too many times on television, in the newspapers etc 曝光率過高〔指在電視、報紙等上面出現次數過多而使受歡迎程度下降〕—opposite 反義詞 UNDEREXPOSE

over·ex·po·sure /͵‥ ·ˋ··/ *n* [U] the state of having received too much light, sunlight, RADIATION etc, that is harmful to someone's skin, a photographic film etc〔皮膚、膠片等受光線、陽光、輻射等的〕過度照射; 過度曝光

o·ver·ex·tend /ˈovərɪkˋstɛnd; ˌəʊvərɪkˈstend/ *v* [T] to try to do or use too much of something, causing problems, illness, or damage 把…做得過分; 把…使用過頭: *The accountants have advised us not to overextend our resources.* 會計師告誡我們不要過度動用我們的財力。| **overextend yourself** *Be careful not to overextend yourself. You've been very ill!* 注意不要讓自己操勞過度, 你已經重病在身了!

o·ver·flow[1] /͵ovɚˋflo; ˌəʊvəˈfləʊ/ *v* **1** [I,T] if a river, lake, or container overflows, it is so full that the water, material etc inside flows over its edges 從…溢出; 氾濫: *The toilet's just overflowed again.* 馬桶的水剛才又溢出來了。| **[+with]** *a trash can overflowing with papers* 被報紙塞得滿出來的垃圾箱 | **overflow sth** *The river had overflowed its banks.* 河水溢出河堤了。**2 overflow with love/gratitude etc** to have a very strong feeling of love etc 充滿愛意/感激等: *My heart was overflowing with gratitude for the old man.* 我心裡充滿了對那位老人的感激之情。**3** [I,T] if people overflow a place, there are too many of them to fit into it〔人〕多得使…無法容納, 擠出: **[+into/onto]** *The crowd overflowed into the street.* 人羣湧到了大街上。

overflow 溢出

o·ver·flow[2] /ˈovɚ͵flo; ˈəʊvəfləʊ/ *n* [C] **1** [singular] the amount of something or the number of people that cannot be contained in a place because it is already full 容納不下的東西[人]; 溢出物; 超出的數額: *The overflow will be accommodated in another hotel.* 接納不下的人將安排下榻另一家旅館。| **[+of]** *the overflow of water from the lake* 由湖裡外溢的水 **2** [U] an act of overflowing something 溢流, 氾濫 **3** [C] a pipe through which water flows out of a container when it becomes too full 排水管; 溢流道

o·ver·fly /͵ovɚˋflaɪ; ˌəʊvəˈflaɪ/ *v* [T] to fly over an area or country in an aircraft 在〔某地區或國家的〕上空飛行

o·ver·grown /ˈovɚˋgron; ˌəʊvəˈgrəʊn◂/ *adj* **1** covered with plants that have grown in an uncontrolled way 長滿〔野生植物等〕的: **[+with]** *The garden will be overgrown with weeds by the time we get back.* 我們回來的時候, 花園裡將長滿雜草。**2 overgrown child/schoolboy/baby** used to describe an adult who behaves like a child 長得太大[太快]的小孩/男生/嬰兒〔用於形容孩子氣的成人〕: *Stop acting like an overgrown schoolboy.* 不要表現得像個大孩子似的。

o·ver·growth /ˈovɚ͵groθ; ˈəʊvəgrəʊθ/ *n* [U] plants and branches of trees growing above your head, usually in a forest 蔓生的植物〔通常指森林裡長得比人高的植物或樹枝〕

o·ver·hand /ˈovɚ͵hænd; ˈəʊvəhænd/ *adj, adv AmE* an overhand throw in a sport is when you throw the ball with your arm above the level of your shoulder【美】〔體育運動中投擲球時〕舉手過肩的[地]; OVERARM *especially BrE*【尤英】—opposite 反義詞 UNDERHAND[2]

o·ver·hang[1] /͵ovɚˋhæŋ; ˌəʊvəˈhæŋ/ *v past tense and past participle* **overhung** /-ˋhʌŋ; -ˈhʌŋ/ [I,T] to hang over something 懸在…的上方: *Our apple trees overhang the neighbors' yard.* 我們的蘋果樹俯臨着鄰居的院子。

o·ver·hang[2] /ˈovɚ͵hæŋ; ˈəʊvəhæŋ/ *n* [usually singular 一般用單數] **1** a rock, roof etc that hangs over something else 懸垂物〈如岩石、屋頂等〉: *We stood under the overhang while it rained.* 下雨時我們站在懸伸的遮蔽物之下。**2** the amount by which something hangs over something else 懸伸量, 伸出量

o·ver·haul[1] /͵ovɚˋhɔl; ˌəʊvəˈhɔːl/ *v* [T] **1** to repair or change all the parts that need it, in a machine, system etc that is not working correctly 徹底檢修; 全面改革[革新]: *overhaul an engine* 檢修引擎 **2** to move up to a vehicle, ship, or person from behind and pass them; OVERTAKE (1) 趕上並超過〔車輛、船或人〕

o·ver·haul[2] /ˈovɚ͵hɔl; ˈəʊvəhɔːl/ *n* [C] necessary changes or repairs made to a machine or system〔對機器的〕大檢修;〔對體制的〕徹底改革: *The Chevy needs a complete overhaul.* 這輛雪佛萊汽車需要徹底檢修一下。| *an overhaul of civil court procedures to speed up and simplify cases* 徹底改革民事法庭的辦案程序以加快並簡化案件的審理

o·ver·head[1] /ˈovɚ͵hɛd; ˌəʊvəˈhed◂/ *adv* above your head 在頭頂上, 在空中: *A plane flew overhead.* 一架飛機從空中飛過。| *Bullets whizzed overhead.* 子彈颼颼地掠過頭頂。—**overhead** *adj*: *overhead wires* 架空電線 —see picture on page A1 參見 A1 頁圖

o·ver·head[2] /ˈovɚ͵hɛd; ˈəʊvəhed/ *n* **1** [singular] *especially AmE*【尤美】also 又作 **overheads** [plural] *especially BrE*【尤英】money spent regularly on rent, insurance, electricity, and other things that are needed to keep a business operating 企業經常性支出, 管理費用〈如租金、保險費、電費等〉: *Their offices are in London so the overheads are very high.* 他們的辦事處在倫敦, 所以經常性開支非常大。**2** [C] a piece of transparent material used with an overhead projector to show words, pictures etc〔用於投影儀顯示文字、圖片等的〕透明膠片

overhead pro·jec·tor /͵‥ ·ˋ··/ *n* [C] a piece of electrical equipment used for making words, pictures etc look larger by showing them on a wall or large SCREEN[1] (1) so that many people can see 投影儀, 高射投影器 —see picture on page A14 參見 A14 頁圖

o·ver·hear /͵ovɚˋhɪr; ˌəʊvəˈhɪə/ *v past tense and past participle* **overheard** /-ˋhɝd; -ˈhɜːd/ [T] to accidentally hear what other people are saying, when they do not know that you have heard 無意中聽到, 偶然聽到: *I overheard part of their conversation.* 我無意中聽到了他們的一些談話。| **overhear sb saying sth** *Christie overheard the men saying they were going to rob the bank!* 克里斯蒂不經意間聽到那幾個人說要去搶劫銀行! | **overhear sb say (that)** *We overheard the teacher say there would be a pop quiz today.* 我們無意中聽到老師說今天有突擊測驗。—compare 比較 EAVESDROP

o·ver·heat /͵ovɚˋhit; ˌəʊvəˈhiːt/ *v* [I,T] to become too hot, or to make something too hot 變得過熱; 使…太熱: *I think the engine's overheating again.* 我想引擎又過熱了。| **overheat sth** *Try not to overheat the sauce.* 注意別把調味汁熱過頭了。

o·ver·heat·ed /͵ovɚˋhitɪd; ˌəʊvəˈhiːtɨd◂/ *adj* **1** too hot

過熱的: *the overheated waiting room* 過熱的等候室 **2** full of angry feelings 充滿憤怒的: *an overheated quarrel that turned into a fight* 最終演變成打架的激烈口角 **3** an ECONOMY[1] (1) that is overheated is too active to work properly〔指經濟〕過熱的, 發展過快的

o·ver·hung /ˌovɚˋhʌŋ; ˌəʊvəˈhʌŋ/ *v* the past tense and past participle of OVERHANG[1]

o·ver·in·dulge /ˈovərɪnˋdʌldʒ; ˌəʊvərɪnˈdʌldʒ/ *v* **1** [I] to eat or drink too much 吃喝過度: *I'm getting too fat, so I mustn't overindulge.* 我變得太胖了, 所以決不能大吃大喝。**2** [T] to let someone have everything they want, or always let them do what they want 過分放任〔某人〕: *Penny was overindulged by her parents.* 彭妮被她的父母寵壞了。—**overindulgence** *n* [U]

o·ver·joyed /ˈovɚˋdʒɔɪd; ˌəʊvəˈdʒɔɪd/ *adj* [not before noun 不用於名詞前] extremely pleased or happy 極為高興的, 十分開心的: **overjoyed to hear/find/see sth** *We were overjoyed to hear that they were safe.* 聽到他們都安全, 我們感到非常高興。| **[+at]** *Richard was overjoyed at the prospect of becoming a father.* 理查德為將要成為父親而欣喜若狂。

o·ver·kill /ˈovɚˌkɪl; ˈəʊvəkɪl/ *n* [U] **1** more of something than is necessary or desirable 過分, 過火: *I thought 24 hours of television coverage of the election verged on overkill.* 我認為對大選作 24 小時電視實況報道有點過分。**2** more than enough weapons, especially NUCLEAR (3) weapons, to kill everyone in a country〔尤指核武器〕過量的殺傷力

o·ver·la·den /ˌovɚˋledn̩; ˌəʊvəˈleɪdn/ *v* a past tense and past participle of OVERLOAD

o·ver·laid /ˌovɚˋled; ˌəʊvəˈleɪd/ *v* the past tense and past participle of OVERLAY[1]

o·ver·land /ˈovɚˌlænd; ˌəʊvəˈlænd◂/ *adv* across land, not by sea or air 經陸路的, 陸上的: *travelling overland to China* 從陸路去中國 —**overland** *adj*

o·ver·lap¹ /ˌovɚˋlæp; ˌəʊvəˈlæp/ *v* **overlapped, overlapping** [I,T] **1** if two or more things overlap, part of one thing covers part of another thing 與〔某物〕部分重疊, 交搭, 疊蓋: *One of Jilly's front teeth overlaps the other.* 吉里的一顆門牙與另一顆有些交疊。| *The tiles on the roof overlap.* 屋頂的瓦片相互交搭在一起。**2** if two sets, subjects, ideas etc overlap, they include some but not all of the same things〔兩種傾向、學科、觀念等〕部分交叉: **[+with]** *This is where sociology overlaps with economics.* 這就是社會學與經濟學在內容上的交叉之處。| **overlap sth** *Maxwell's responsibilities overlap yours, so you will be sharing some of the work.* 馬克斯韋爾的職責中有一部分與你重疊, 所以你得分擔一些工作。**3** if two events or activities overlap, the first one finishes a short time after the second one starts〔時間上〕重疊, 與…部分同時發生: **[+with]** *My vacation overlaps with yours, so we won't see each other for a month or so.* 我的假期和你的假期前後挨着, 所以我倆將有一個月左右見不着面。| **overlap sth** *The first shift overlaps the second.* 第一班次與第二班次之間有一段交接的時間。

overlap 交搭, 重疊

overlapping roof tiles
交搭的瓦片

o·ver·lap² /ˈovɚˌlæp; ˈəʊvəlæp/ *n* [C,U] the amount by which two things, activities etc overlap〔兩種事物、活動等〕交搭的數量, 重疊: **[+between]** *The overlap between the two subjects is considerable.* 這兩門學科間重疊的內容極多。

o·ver·lay¹ /ˌovɚˋle; ˌəʊvəˈleɪ/ *v past tense and past participle* **overlaid** /-ˋled; -ˈleɪd/ [T] *technical*【術語】**1 be overlaid with** to be thinly covered with something 在…上塗[蓋、包、貼]薄薄的一層: *wood overlaid with silver* 包着一層薄銀的木料 **2** [usually passive 一般用被動態] to add an outer appearance to something that hides its real character 遮蓋〔某物的本質〕: **[+with]** *His ordinarily cheerful face was overlaid with gloom.* 他臉上沒有了平日的開朗, 卻添了一層憂鬱。

o·ver·lay² /ˈovɚˌle; ˈəʊvəleɪ/ *n* [C] **1** something laid over something else 覆蓋物 **2** a transparent sheet with a picture or drawing on it which is put on top of another picture to change it〔上有圖片或畫樣, 用於覆蓋在另一圖片上對其進行修改的〕套圖塑料膜 **3** an additional quality or feeling 附加的特性[情感]: *sad stories with an overlay of humour* 幽默掩蓋下的悲慘故事

o·ver·leaf /ˈovɚˌlif; ˌəʊvəˈliːf/ *adv* on the other side of the page 在一頁的另一面, 在一頁的背面: *See the diagram overleaf.* 參見背頁的示意圖。

o·ver·lie /ˌovɚˋlaɪ; ˌəʊvəˈlaɪ/ *v* [T] *technical*【術語】**1** to lie over something 躺在〔某物〕上面: *A thick layer of soil overlies the rocks.* 一層厚厚的泥土壓在岩石上。**2** if a parent animal overlies its young it kills them by lying on them 壓在〔幼小動物〕上面使悶死, 使窒息

o·ver·load /ˌovɚˋlod; ˌəʊvəˈləʊd/ *v past participle* **overloaded** *or* **overladen** /-ˋledn̩; -ˈleɪdn/ [T] **1** to load something with too many things 使過量載重, 使超載: **[+with]** *The bus was overloaded with tourists and their luggage.* 公共汽車因遊客和行李過多而超載。**2** to put too much electricity through an electrical system or piece of equipment 使〔電路系統或設備〕超過負荷: *Don't overload the outlet by plugging in too many appliances.* 不要同時使用太多的電器而使電源插座超過負荷。**3** to give someone too much work 給〔某人〕過多的工作: **[+with]** *All the staff are overloaded with work.* 所有的員工都已是超負荷工作了。—**overload** /ˈovɚˌlod; ˈəʊvələʊd/ *n* [C,U]

o·ver·long /ˈovɚˋlɔŋ; ˌəʊvəˈlɒŋ/ *adj* continuing for too long 持續過久的, 時間太長的: *an overlong performance* 表演時間過長的節目

o·ver·look /ˌovɚˋlʊk; ˌəʊvəˈlʊk/ *v* [T] **1** to not notice something 沒有注意到, 忽視: *It is easy to overlook a small detail like that.* 那樣的細枝末節很容易被忽略。**2** to ignore and forgive someone's mistake, bad behaviour etc 不計較, 寬恕〔某人的過錯、不良舉止等〕: *I'll overlook your mistake this time.* 這次我會原諒你的過失。**3** if a building, room, or window overlooks a place, you can look down on that place from it 俯視, 俯瞰: *Our room overlooks the ocean.* 從我們的房間能眺望大海。| *My garden is overlooked by the neighbours.* 我的花園被居高臨下的鄰居看得一清二楚。

o·ver·lord /ˈovɚˌlɔrd; ˈəʊvəlɔːd/ *n* [C] a lord who ruled over other lords in the past〔昔日的〕封建君主; 大領主

o·ver·ly /ˈovɚlɪ; ˈəʊvəli/ *adv* [often in negatives 常用於否定句] too or very 太, 非常, 極為: *I wasn't overly impressed with her performance.* 我認為她的表演不太出色。| *You're being overly critical.* 你過於吹毛求疵了。

o·ver·manned /ˌovɚˋmænd; ˌəʊvəˈmænd◂/ *adj* having more workers than are needed for a job; OVERSTAFFED 人手過多的, 人員配備太多的 —**overmanning** *n* [U]

o·ver·mas·ter /ˌovɚˋmæstɚ; ˌəʊvəˈmɑːstə/ *v* [T] *literary* to gain control or power over someone【文】控制, 壓倒〔某人〕

o·ver·much /ˈovɚˋmʌtʃ; ˌəʊvəˈmʌtʃ◂/ *adv literary or humorous* too much【文或幽默】太多, 過多: *It is unwise to indulge overmuch in strong drink.* 過度飲用烈酒是不明智的。| **not overmuch** *We didn't like each other overmuch.* 我們彼此不大喜歡對方。

o·ver·night¹ /ˈovɚˋnaɪt; ˌəʊvəˈnaɪt/ *adv* **1** for or during the night 夜裡, 在夜間: **stay overnight** *Pam's staying overnight at my house.* 帕姆將在我家過夜。**2** *informal* suddenly【非正式】突然, 一下子: *Logan became famous overnight.* 洛根一夜之間成名了。

o·ver·night² /ˈovɚˋnaɪt; ˈəʊvənaɪt/ *adj* **1** continuing all night 持續整夜的: *an overnight flight from Boston to London* 從波士頓到倫敦的一整夜飛行 **2** done in one night 一夜間完成的: *an overnight delivery service* 隔夜就能送達的快遞服務 **3 an overnight success** something that suddenly becomes very popular or successful 突如其來的成功: *The show was an overnight success on Broadway.* 這場表演在百老匯一舉成功。

o·ver·night·er /ˌ·· ˈ··/ *n* [C] a bag or small case which holds a few clothes and other things you need for a short trip〔短途旅行用的〕小旅行包, 小提箱

over-op·ti·mis·tic /ˌ·· ···ˈ··◂/ *adj* expecting that things will be better than is possible or likely 過分樂觀的, 盲目樂觀的: *over-optimistic forecasts of economic growth* 對經濟增長過於樂觀的預測

o·ver·pass /ˈovɚˌpæs; ˈəʊvəpɑːs/ *n* [C] *AmE* FLYOVER (1)【美】立交橋, 高架公路 —see picture on page A3 參見 A3 頁圖

o·ver·pay /ˈovɚˈpe; ˌəʊvəˈpeɪ/ *v past tense and past participle* **overpaid** /-ˈped; -ˈpeɪd/ [T] to pay someone too much 多付給〔某人〕錢; 給〔某人〕過高的報酬: *I think lawyers are overpaid for what they do.* 我認為律師所幹的工作報酬過高。

o·ver·play /ˌovɚˈple; ˌəʊvəˈpleɪ/ *v* [T] **1** to make something seem more important than it is 誇大…的重要性, 把…做得過頭: *The poet's importance is overplayed by his biographer.* 該詩人的重要性被其傳記作者誇大了。—opposite 反義詞 UNDERPLAY (1) **2 overplay your hand** to try to gain more advantage than you know you can reasonably expect 不自量力, 試圖獲取應得之外的更多好處: *If you're asking for more vacation time, don't overplay your hand by bringing salary into it too.* 你要是想得到更多的假期, 就別太貪心還要提薪水的問題。

o·ver·pop·u·lat·ed /ˌovɚˈpɑpjəˌletɪd; ˌəʊvəˈpɒpjəleɪtɪd◂/ *adj* a city or country that is overpopulated has too many people〔城市或國家等〕人口過密[過多]的: *a programme of resettlement from the most overpopulated areas* 從人口最過於稠密的地區重新安置居民的計劃 —**overpopulation** /ˌovɚpɑpjəˈleʃən; ˌəʊvəpɒpjəˈleɪʃən/ *n* [U]

o·ver·pow·er /ˌovɚˈpauɚ; ˌəʊvəˈpaʊə/ *v* [T] **1** to defeat someone because you are stronger〔以更強的力量〕打敗, 制服〔某人〕: *The policeman and a dog handler struggled to overpower the man.* 警察和警犬訓練員努力想制服那名男子。**2** if a smell, task, emotion etc overpowers someone or something it is too strong; OVERCOME (3)〔氣味、任務、情感等〕使…無法忍受; 壓倒, 壓服: *a full flavour slightly overpowered by saltiness* 鹹味略重的醇厚風味

o·ver·pow·er·ing /ˌovɚˈpauərɪŋ; ˌəʊvəˈpaʊərɪŋ◂/ *adj* **1** very strong; INTENSE (1) 很強的, 強烈的; 不可抗拒的: *an overpowering smell* 濃烈的氣味 | *an overpowering desire to slap her* 要掌摑她的強烈慾望 **2** someone who is overpowering has such a strong character that they make other people feel uncomfortable or afraid; OVERBEARING〔人〕個性強的; 專橫的 —**overpoweringly** *adv*

o·ver·priced /ˌovɚˈpraɪst; ˌəʊvəˈpraɪst◂/ *adj* too expensive 過於昂貴的, 定價過高的: *The patisserie has good food, but it's overpriced.* 這家法式糕點店的糕點很好, 但價錢太貴。

o·ver·print /ˌovɚˈprɪnt; ˌəʊvəˈprɪnt/ *v* [T+**with/on**] to print additional words over a document, stamp etc that already has printing on it 在〔已印的文件、郵票等〕上加印〔文字〕

o·ver·proof /ˈovɚˈpruf; ˌəʊvəˈpruːf/ *adj* **10%/15% overproof** containing 10% etc more alcohol than PROOF SPIRIT does 酒精含量超標 10%/15% 以上的

o·ver·pro·tec·tive /ˌovɚprəˈtɛktɪv; ˌəʊvəprəˈtektɪv◂/ *adj* so anxious to protect someone from harm, danger etc that you restrict their freedom〔對某人〕過分保護的, 溺愛的: *I suppose I've been overprotective, but Mike's my only son.* 我相信我是過分保護孩子, 但邁克畢竟是我的獨生子。

o·ver·qual·i·fied /ˌovɚˈkwɑləfaɪd; ˌəʊvəˈkwɒlɪfaɪd◂/ *adj* having so much experience or training that people do not want to employ you for particular jobs〔對某職位而言〕資歷過高的: *The firm told me not to bother applying because I was overqualified.* 那家公司叫我不必費心去應徵, 因為我的資歷過高。

o·ver·ran /ˌovɚˈræn; ˌəʊvəˈræn/ *v* the past tense of OVERRUN

o·ver·rate /ˈovɚˈret; ˌəʊvəˈreɪt/ *v* [T] to think that something is better or more important than it is 對…評價過高: *'Titus Andronicus' is an overrated play in my opinion.* 我認為人們對《泰特斯·安德洛尼克斯》這部戲劇評價過高了。—opposite 反義詞 UNDERRATE

o·ver·reach /ˌovɚˈritʃ; ˌəʊvəˈriːtʃ/ *v* [T] **overreach yourself** to try to do more than you have the ability or money to do 試圖做能力[財力]不及之事: *The company overreached itself financially.* 該公司的做法超過了自己的經濟實力。

o·ver·re·act /ˌovɚrɪˈækt; ˌəʊvəriˈækt/ *v* [I] to react to something with too much emotion, especially anger 對〔某事〕反應過火〔尤指憤怒〕: [+**to**] *You always overreact to criticism.* 你對待批評總是反應過激。—**overreaction** /-rɪˈækʃən; -riˈækʃən/ *n* [C,U]

o·ver·ride /ˌovɚˈraɪd; ˌəʊvəˈraɪd/ *v past tense* **overrode** /-ˈrod; -ˈrəʊd/ *past participle* **overridden** /-ˈrɪdn̩; -ˈrɪdn/ [T] **1** to ignore a decision or order made by someone with less authority than you 無視, 不顧〔下屬的決定或命令〕: *The principal overrode the teacher's rule and let the children stay outside.* 校長不顧那位老師的規定, 讓孩子們待在外面。**2** to be regarded as more important than something else 視為比…更重要: *The needs of the mother should not override the needs of the child.* 母親的需要不應優先於孩子的需要。

o·ver·rid·ing /ˌovɚˈraɪdɪŋ; ˌəʊvəˈraɪdɪŋ/ *adj* [only before noun 僅用於名詞前] more important than anything else 最重要的; 壓倒一切的: *a question of overriding importance* 壓倒一切的重要問題 | *Our overriding obligation is to prepare our graduates for their future.* 我們最重要的職責是要為畢業生的前途着想。

o·ver·rule /ˌovɚˈrul; ˌəʊvəˈruːl/ *v* [T] to change someone's order, or decision that you think is wrong, using your official power〔用職權〕推翻, 否決, 駁回〔認為是錯誤的命令或決定〕: *Parliament overruled the local authorities.* 議會否決了地方政府的意見。

o·ver·run /ˌovɚˈrʌn; ˌəʊvəˈrʌn/ *v past tense* **overran** /-ˈræn; -ˈræn/ *past participle* **overrun 1** [T] if something unwanted overruns a place or area, it spreads over it in great numbers〔討厭的事情在某地〕大量蔓延; 侵擾: *Rats had overrun the barn in the few years since we'd been there.* 我們初到那兒的幾年間, 穀倉裡老鼠成災。| **overrun by/with** *a tiny island overrun with tourists* 佈滿遊客的小島 **2** [I,T] to continue longer than intended 超越, 超出〔預期的時間〕: *The final speaker overran by at least half an hour.* 最後那位演講者至少多用了半個小時。

o·ver·seas¹ /ˈovɚˈsiz; ˌəʊvəˈsiːz◂/ *adv* to or in a foreign country somewhere across the sea 向國外, 在海外, 在外國: *Carmen is going to work overseas.* 卡文打算去國外工作。| *Most applications came from overseas.* 申請大部分來自海外。

o·ver·seas² /ˈovɚˈsiz; ˈəʊvəsiːz/ *adj* [only before noun 僅用於名詞前] coming from or happening abroad 來自海外的, 外國來的; 發生在國外的: *overseas students* 外國留學生 | *overseas trade* 海外貿易

o·ver·see /ˌovɚˈsi; ˌəʊvəˈsiː/ *v past tense* **oversaw** /-ˈsɔ; -ˈsɔː/ *past participle* **overseen** /-ˈsin; -ˈsiːn/ [T] to be in charge of a group of workers and check that a piece of work is done satisfactorily 監管, 監察, 監督: *A team leader was appointed to oversee the project.* 任命了一位組長來監管該工程。| *overseeing the workers* 監督工人

o·ver·seer /ˈovɚˌsiɚ; ˈəʊvəsɪə/ *n* [C] someone in charge of a group of workers, who checks that their work is done properly 監工; 工頭; 監督人

o·ver·sell /ˌovɚˈsɛl; ˌəʊvəˈsel/ *v past tense and past participle* **oversold** /-ˈsold; -ˈsəʊld/ [T] to praise someone or something too much 對〔某人或某事〕讚揚過多; 過分吹噓

o·ver·sen·si·tive /ˋovɚˋsɛnsɪtɪv; ˌəʊvəˈsensɪ̇tɪv◂/ *adj* easily upset or offended 易於煩惱[生氣]的, 過分敏感的: *I didn't mean that. Rod's just being oversensitive.* 我不是那個意思, 羅德過於敏感了。

o·ver·sexed /ˌovɚˋsɛkst; ˌəʊvəˈsekst◂/ *adj* having too much interest in or desire for sex 性慾過強的

o·ver·shad·ow /ˌovɚˋʃædo; ˌəʊvəˈʃædəʊ/ *v* [T] **1** to make someone or something else seem less important 使〔別的人或事〕顯得較不重要, 使相形見絀[黯然失色]: *Her success has been overshadowed by her fears for her daughter, Maggie.* 她對女兒瑪吉的擔憂使她的成功顯得無足輕重。**2** if a tall building, mountain etc overshadows a place, it is very close to it〔高樓、高山等〕使〔周圍某處〕陰暗, 使暗淡不明: *a dark valley overshadowed by towering peaks* 被高聳的山峯遮蔽的陰暗山谷 **3** to make an occasion or period of time less enjoyable by making people feel sad or worried 給〔某一場合或某段時間〕蒙上陰影, 使感到難過[憂慮]: *The threat of war overshadowed the summer of 1939.* 戰爭的威脅給1939年的夏天蒙上了一層陰影。

o·ver·shoe /ˋovɚˌʃu; ˈəʊvəʃuː/ *n* [C] a rubber shoe that you wear over an ordinary shoe to keep your feet dry〔穿在普通鞋子外面的〕橡膠套鞋; 罩靴

o·ver·shoot /ˌovɚˋʃut; ˌəʊvəˈʃuːt/ *v past tense and past participle* **overshot** /-ˋʃɑt; -ˈʃɒt/ [I,T] **1** to drive past the place where you intended to stop or turn 駛過〔原想停下或拐彎之處〕: *I didn't see the sign and overshot the turning.* 我沒看見標誌, 駛過了拐彎處。**2 overshoot the mark** to make the mistake of going higher or further than the amount or distance you had aimed for 超過原定高度[距離]: *We realized after a half hour that we'd overshot the mark, and had to turn back.* 半小時後我們意識到我們走過頭了, 只得掉頭而行。

o·ver·sight /ˋovɚˌsaɪt; ˈəʊvəsaɪt/ *n* [C,U] **1** a mistake that you make by not noticing something or by forgetting to do something 失察; 疏忽: *I assure you that this was purely an oversight on my part.* 我向你保證, 這純粹是我的一個疏忽。**2 have oversight of** to be in charge of a piece of work and check that it is satisfactory 監管, 監督: *The works manager will have general oversight of the project.* 廠長將全面監督這項工程。

o·ver·sim·pli·fy /ˌovɚˋsɪmpləˌfaɪ; ˌəʊvəˈsɪmplɪ̇faɪ/ *v* [I,T] to make a situation or problem seem less complicated than it really is, by ignoring important facts〔以忽略重要事實〕使〔情況或問題〕看似比實際簡單, 使…過於簡單化: *My research has been grossly oversimplified in your account.* 在你的報道中, 我的研究在很大程度上被過於簡單化了。—**oversimplification** /ˋovɚˌsɪmpləfəˋkeʃən; ˌəʊvəsɪmplɪ̇fɪ̇ˈkeɪʃən/ *n* [C,U]

over-six·ties /ˌ‥ ˈ‥/ *n* [plural] people who are over sixty years old 六十歲以上的人: *holidays for the over-sixties* 針對六十歲以上人士的度假安排

o·ver·size /ˋovɚˋsaɪz; ˌəʊvəˈsaɪz◂/ also 又作 **o·ver·sized** /-ˋsaɪzd; -ˈsaɪzd◂/ *adj* bigger than usual or too big 大於一般的; 太大的: *His features were dwarfed by a pair of oversize spectacles.* 他戴了一副大號的眼鏡, 相比之下五官便顯得十分玲瓏了。

o·ver·sleep /ˋovɚˋslip; ˌəʊvəˈsliːp/ *v past tense and past participle* **overslept** /-ˋslɛpt; -ˈslept/ [I] to sleep for longer than you intended 睡過頭, 睡得過久: *I had overslept that morning, and was late for work.* 那天早上我睡過了頭, 所以上班遲到了。—compare 比較 **sleep in** (SLEEP[1])

o·ver·spend /ˋovɚˋspɛnd; ˌəʊvəˈspend/ *v past tense and past participle* **overspent** /-ˋspɛnt; -ˈspent/ [I] to spend more money than you can afford 支出超過〔自己的財力〕, 超支: *Credit cards have encouraged people to overspend.* 信用卡鼓勵人們透支消費。—**overspend** /ˋovɚspɛnd; ˈəʊvəspend/ *n* [C]: *an overspend of £200,000* 20萬英鎊的超支額

o·ver·spill /ˋovɚˌspɪl; ˈəʊvəˌspɪl/ *n* [U] *BrE* people who move out of a big city because there are too many people living there, and go to live in new houses outside the city【英】〔因城市人口過多而遷移到市外新居的〕過剩人口: *a new town built to accommodate London's overspill* 為容納倫敦的過剩人口而建的一座新城鎮

o·ver·staffed /ˌovɚˋstæft; ˌəʊvəˈstɑːft◂/ *adj* a company, organization etc that is overstaffed has more workers than it needs〔公司、機構等〕人員過多的 —opposite 反義詞 UNDERSTAFFED

o·ver·state /ˋovɚˋstet; ˌəʊvəˈsteɪt/ *v* [T] to talk about something in a way that makes it seem more important, serious etc than it really is; EXAGGERATE 把…講得過分; 誇大, 誇張: *We must not frighten people by overstating the dangers.* 我們決不能誇大這些危險來嚇唬人。—opposite 反義詞 UNDERSTATE

o·ver·state·ment /ˋovɚˋstetmənt; ˌəʊvəˈsteɪtmənt/ *n* [C,U] the act of talking about something in a way that makes it seem more important, serious etc than it really is, or an example of this; EXAGGERATION 言過其實; 誇張, 大話: *It's a bit of an overstatement to say that the man's a fool, but he's not brilliant.* 說這個人蠢是有點過分, 不過他不很聰穎是對的。

o·ver·stay /ˋovɚˋste; ˌəʊvəˈsteɪ/ *v* [T] to stay somewhere longer than you intended or longer than you should〔在某處〕逗留超過時限, 待得時間過久 —see also 另見 **overstay your welcome** (WELCOME[3] (3))

o·ver·step /ˌovɚˋstɛp; ˌəʊvəˈstep/ *v* **overstepped, overstepping** [T] **1 overstep the rules/limits etc** to behave in a way that is not polite or not allowed by the rules〔行為〕超越規定/限度等 **2 overstep the mark** to do or say more than you should, and offend people or make them angry 言行過分〔得罪人或讓人生氣〕: *I've been very patient with him so far, but he's really overstepped the mark this time!* 迄今為止我已經夠能忍耐的了, 但他這次也確實太過分了!

o·ver·stock /ˌovɚˋstɑk; ˌəʊvəˈstɒk/ *v* [I,T] to obtain more of something than is needed for a shop, hotel etc〔商店、旅館等〕進貨過多; 使存貨過多

o·ver·sub·scribe /ˌovɚsəbˋskraɪb; ˌəʊvəsəbˈskraɪb/ *v* [T] **be oversubscribed** if an activity, sale, service etc is oversubscribed, people are asking for more places, tickets etc than there are available〔活動、銷售、服務等〕被超額預訂, 被過量訂購: *Hostels for single people are normally oversubscribed.* 單身客人住的旅舍通常供不應求。

o·vert /ˋovɝt; ˈəʊvɜːt/ *adj formal* actions that are overt are done publicly, without trying to hide anything【正式】〔行動〕公開的, 不加隱瞞的: *an overt attempt to silence their political opponents* 想讓他們的政敵閉嘴的明顯企圖 | *overt discrimination* 公然的歧視 —opposite 反義詞 COVERT —**overtly** *adv*

o·ver·take /ˌovɚˋtek; ˌəʊvəˈteɪk/ *v past tense* **overtook** /-ˋtʊk; -ˈtʊk/ *past participle* **overtaken** /-ˋtekən; -ˈteɪkən/ **1** [I,T] to go past a moving vehicle or person because you are going faster than them and want to get in front of them 追上; 趕上並超過〔汽車或人〕: *He pulled out to overtake the red van.* 他開出車道去超越那輛紅色的貨車。—see picture on page A3 參見A3頁圖 **2** [T] if something bad overtakes you, it happens to you suddenly and prevents you from doing what you had planned to do〔不愉快的事〕突然降臨〔使人不能按計劃行事〕, 意外侵襲: [+by] *We'd both been overtaken by sheer fatigue.* 我們倆都累壞了。**3** [T] to develop or increase more quickly than someone or something else and become bigger, better, or more advanced than them〔發展或增長〕趕超: *By 1970 the Americans had overtaken the Russians in space technology.* 到1970年, 美國人在太空技術方面已領先於俄羅斯人。**4 be overtaken by events** if you are overtaken by events, the situation changes, so that your plans or ideas are not useful any more 因情況有變而不再有用: *His last years were spent working from a theory that was rapidly being overtaken by events.* 他在生命最後的幾年應用了一套很快就被淘汰的理論。

o·ver·tax /ˋovɚˋtæks; ˌəʊvəˈtæks/ *v* [T] **1** to make someone do more than they are really able to do, so that they become very tired 使〔某人〕負擔過重[過度疲勞]: **overtax yourself** *Don't overtax yourself!* 別讓自己過於勞累！**2** to make people pay too much tax 對〔人民〕徵稅過重

O

over-the-coun·ter /ˌ·· · ˈ··◂/ *adj* [only before noun 僅用於名詞前] **1** over-the-counter drugs can be obtained without a PRESCRIPTION (=a written order) from a doctor〔藥品〕無醫生處方也可買到的, 非處方的 **2** *AmE* abbreviation 縮寫為 **OTC** over-the-counter business shares are ones that do not appear on an official STOCK EXCHANGE (2) list【美】〔股票買賣〕場外的, 買賣雙方直接交易的, 非掛牌的

over-the-top /ˌ·· · ˈ·◂/ *adj* abbreviation 縮寫為 **OTT** *BrE informal* remarks, behaviour etc that are over-the-top are so exaggerated (EXAGGERATE) or unreasonable that they seem stupid or offensive【英, 非正式】〔言行等〕過於誇張的, 荒唐的: *It's a bit over-the-top to call him a fascist.* 把他叫作法西斯分子有點誇張了。

o·ver·throw[1] /ˌovɚˋθro; ˌəʊvəˈθrəʊ/ *v past tense* **overthrew** /-ˋθru; -ˈθruː/ *past participle* **overthrown** /-ˋθron; -ˈθrəʊn/ [T] **1** to remove a leader or government from a position of power 顛覆, 推翻〔某領導或政府〕: *Rebels were already plotting to overthrow the government.* 反叛者已在密謀顛覆政府。**2** to get rid of the rules of a society 背棄, 摒棄〔社會制度〕: *a social revolution that has overthrown basic standards of morality* 摒棄了基本道德標準的社會變革

o·ver·throw[2] /ˋovɚˌθro; ˈəʊvəθrəʊ/ *n* [U] the defeat and removal from power of a leader or government, especially by force〔尤指用武力〕打倒, 推翻〔某領導或政府〕: **[+of]** *The organization was dedicated to the overthrow of capitalism.* 該組織致力於推翻資本主義。| *the overthrow of Mussolini* 推翻墨索里尼政府

o·ver·time /ˋovɚˌtaɪm; ˈəʊvətaɪm/ *n* [U] **1** time that you spend working in your job in addition to your normal working hours 超時工作, 加班時間, 額外工作時間: *six hours' overtime* 六小時的加班 | *overtime pay* 加班費 | **work overtime** *They're working overtime to get the job finished.* 他們正在加班以完成那項工作。**2** the money that you are paid for working more hours than usual 加班費: *A miner could earn £250 a week, including overtime.* 連加班費在內, 礦工一週能掙 250 英鎊。**3 be working overtime** *informal* to be very active【非正式】變得非常活躍: *After nine months of pregnancy your hormones are working overtime.* 懷孕九個月後, 你體內的荷爾蒙會變得異常活躍。**4** *AmE*【美】〔足球比賽等的〕加時, 延長時間; EXTRA TIME *BrE*【英】

o·ver·tone /ˋovɚˌton; ˈəʊvətəʊn/ *n* **1 overtones** [plural] signs of an emotion or attitude that is not expressed directly〔情感或態度〕含蓄的表示, 暗示; 弦外之音: *His words were polite, but there were overtones of anger in his voice.* 他的話很客氣, 但聲音裡卻暗含怒氣。| *heavy moral overtones* 濃重的說教意味 **2** [C] *technical* a higher musical note that sounds together with the main note: HARMONIC【術語】〔高於主音並與之合為一個單音的〕泛音 —see also 另見 UNDERTONE

o·ver·took /ˌovɚˋtʊk; ˌəʊvəˈtʊk/ the past tense of OVERTAKE

o·ver·top /ˌovɚˋtɑp; ˌəʊvəˈtɒp/ *v* **overtopped, overtopping** [T] *formal* to be higher or more important than something【術語】高於〔某物〕; 比…更重要; 勝過, 超過

o·ver·ture /ˋovɚtʃɚ; ˈəʊvətjʊə/ *n* **1** [C] a short piece of music written as an introduction to a long piece of music, especially an OPERA〔尤指歌劇的〕前奏曲, 序曲 **2 overtures** an attempt to begin a friendly relationship with a person, country etc〔試圖與某人、某國等開始友好關係的〕主動表示; 姿態: **[+of]** *overtures of friendship* 希望友好的表示 | **make overtures to** *They began making overtures to the Irish government in the hope of gaining their support.* 他們主動向愛爾蘭政府表示友好, 希望獲得他們的支持。**3 be an overture** if an event is an overture to a more important event, it happens just before it and makes you expect it 是一個序幕〔表示某事是另一更為重要之事的開端〕: *This encounter was a sort of overture to their first real meeting.* 這次見面是他們首次正式會談的一個序幕。

o·ver·turn /ˌovɚˋtɝn; ˌəʊvəˈtɜːn/ *v* **1** [I,T] if you overturn something or if it overturns, it turns upside down or falls over on its side (使) 翻倒, (使) 傾覆; 打翻: *Leslie leapt to her feet, overturning her chair.* 萊斯麗一躍而起, 弄倒了椅子。| *One of the boats had overturned.* 有一艘船翻了。**2** [T] **overturn a decision/verdict etc** to change a decision or result so that it becomes the opposite of what it was before 推翻決定/裁決等: *The decision was finally overturned by the Supreme Court last year.* 這項判決去年最終被最高法院推翻了。**3** [T] to suddenly remove a government from power, especially by using violence; OVERTHROW[1] (1)〔尤指用暴力突然〕推翻, 顛覆〔政府〕

o·ver·val·ue /ˌovɚˋvælju; ˌəʊvəˈvæljuː/ *v* [T] to believe or say that something is more valuable or more important than it really is 對…估價過高; 高估…的重要性 —**overvaluation** *n* [U]

o·ver·view /ˋovɚˌvju; ˈəʊvəvjuː/ *n* [C] a short description of a subject or situation that gives the main ideas without explaining all the details 概述; 概要: **[+of]** *an overview of the issues involved* 對所涉及問題的概述 | **give an overview** *Professors often give an overview of the subject at the start of the lecture.* 教授經常在講課開始時先扼要介紹一下主要內容。

o·ver·ween·ing /ˋovɚˋwinɪŋ; ˌəʊvəˈwiːnɪŋ◂/ *adj formal* too proud and confident; ARROGANT【正式】過於傲慢的, 過分自信的; 傲慢無禮的: *overweening vanity* 妄自尊大的虛榮心 —**overweeningly** *adv*

o·ver·weight /ˋovɚˋwet; ˌəʊvəˈweɪt◂/ *adj* **1** someone who is overweight is too heavy and fat〔人〕體重超常的, 過重的, 肥胖的: **10 kilos/20 lbs etc overweight** *Sally was three stone overweight.* 莎莉體重超了 42 磅。**2** something such as a package that is overweight weighs more than it is supposed to weigh〔包裹等〕超重的: *My luggage was overweight by five kilos.* 我的行李超重五公斤。—compare 比較 UNDERWEIGHT —see 見 FAT[1] (USAGE)

o·ver·whelm /ˌovɚˋhwɛlm; ˌəʊvəˈwelm/ *v* [T]

1 ▶EMOTION 感情◀ if someone is overwhelmed by an emotion, they feel it so strongly that they cannot think clearly〔感情上〕使〔某人〕感到不能自持, 使不知所措: *He was suddenly overwhelmed by a strong feeling of his insignificance.* 一股強烈的卑微感突然襲上他的心頭。| *Grief overwhelmed me.* 我不勝悲傷。

2 ▶SURPRISE SB 使某人吃驚◀ to surprise someone very much, so that they do not know how to react 使〔某人〕非常驚訝: *I was completely overwhelmed by his generosity.* 他的慷慨教我驚訝萬分。

3 ▶DEFEAT SB 擊敗某人◀ to defeat an army completely 徹底擊敗, 擊潰〔軍隊〕: *In 1532 the Spaniards finally overwhelmed the armies of Peru.* 1532 年, 西班牙人最終打垮了祕魯軍隊。

4 ▶PROBLEM 問題◀ if a problem overwhelms someone or something, it has such a great effect that nothing can be done to deal with it 使不可解決, 毀壞, 摧毀: *Decades of war and natural catastrophes had overwhelmed the city's finances.* 幾十年的戰爭和自然災害摧毀了這座城市的經濟。

5 ▶WATER 水◀ *literary* if water overwhelms an area of land, it covers it completely and suddenly【文】突然淹沒〔某地〕

o·ver·whelm·ing /ˌovɚˋhwɛlmɪŋ; ˌəʊvəˈwelmɪŋ/ *adj* **1** having such a great effect on you that you feel confused and do not know how to react 令人迷惘而不知所措的: *The sheer size of the place will seem overwhelming and confusing at first.* 一開始的時候, 單是這地方的幅員廣大已令人感到勢不可擋, 不知所措。| *overwhelm-*

ing generosity 極其寬宏大量[慷慨] **2 overwhelming numbers/majority/odds etc** very large numbers etc 壓倒性的數字/多數/差距等: *An overwhelming majority of the members were against the idea.* 反對這項主張的成員佔壓倒多數。—**overwhelmingly** *adv*: *Congress voted overwhelmingly in favor of the bill.* 國會表決時, 這項提案得到壓倒性的支持。

o·ver·win·ter /ˌovɚˋwɪntɚ; ˌəʊvəˈwɪntə/ *v* [I,T] to live through the winter, or to make it possible for something to live through the winter 過冬; (使) 越冬: *These birds generally overwinter in tropical regions.* 這些鳥通常在熱帶地區過冬。

o·ver·work[1] /ˌovɚˋwɝk; ˌəʊvəˈwɜːk/ *v* [I,T] to work too much, or to make someone work too much (使) 過度工作, (使) 過分勞累: *Batson overworked his staff mercilessly.* 巴特森冷酷無情地讓員工承擔過於繁重的工作。| *You've been overworking – why don't you take a week off?* 你已經勞累過度了 —— 為甚麼不休息一週呢?

overwork[2] *n* [U] too much hard work 過於繁重的工作; 過分勞累: *a heart attack brought on by overwork* 因過度勞累導致的心臟病

o·ver·worked /ˌovɚˋwɝkt; ˌəʊvəˈwɜːkt◂/ *adj* **1** made to work too hard 操勞過度的: *an overworked doctor* 勞累過度的醫生 **2** a word or phrase that is overworked is used too much and has become less effective〔詞語〕使用過度的, 陳詞濫調的: *overworked metaphors* 用得過濫的比喻

o·ver·wrought /ˋovɚˋrɔt; ˌəʊvəˈrɔːt◂/ *adj* very upset, nervous, and worried 非常煩惱的; 神經很緊張的; 十分憂慮的: *Clara was tired and overwrought after the upheavals of the last few days.* 經歷了過去幾天的劇變之後, 克拉拉既疲憊又緊張。

o·vi·duct /ˋovɪˌdʌkt; ˈəʊvɪdʌkt/ *n* [C] *technical* one of the two tubes in a female through which eggs pass to the WOMB【術語】輸卵管

o·vip·a·rous /oˋvɪpərəs; əʊˈvɪpərəs/ *adj technical* an animal, fish, bird etc that is oviparous produces eggs that develop outside its body【術語】〔動物、鳥、魚等〕卵生的; 產卵的

o·void /ˋovɔɪd; ˈəʊvɔɪd/ *adj* shaped like an egg 卵形的—**ovoid** *n* [C]

ov·u·late /ˋɑvjulet; ˈɒvjʊleɪt/ *v* [I] when a woman or female animal ovulates, she produces eggs inside her body 排卵; 產卵 —**ovulation** /ˌɑvjuˋleʃən; ˌɒvjʊˈleɪʃən/ *n* [U]

o·vum /ˋovəm; ˈəʊvəm/ *n plural* **ova** /ˋovə; ˈəʊvə/ [C] *technical* an egg, especially one that develops inside the mother's body【術語】卵 (子), 卵細胞

ow /aʊ; aʊ/ *interjection* used to express sudden pain 哎唷〔用於表示突然的疼痛〕: *"Ow, that hurts!"* "哎唷, 好痛!"

2 3 **owe** /o; əʊ/ *v* [T]

1 ▶MONEY 錢◀ to have to pay someone for something that they have done for you or sold to you, or to have to give someone back money that they have lent you 欠〔錢〕; 負債: **owe sb sth** *I owe my brother $50.* 我欠我弟弟 50 美元。| **owe sb for sth** *We still owe the garage for those repairs.* 我們還沒有付給汽車修理廠那筆修理費呢。| **owe sth** *How much do you owe?* 你欠了多少錢?

2 ▶STH DONE/GIVEN 做過的事情/已給的東西◀ to feel that you should do something for someone, give someone something etc because they have done something for you or given something to you 應該做; 應給予; 對…負有…的義務: **owe sb a drink/letter etc** *I'll write and tell Marie, I owe her a letter anyway.* 我將寫信告訴瑪麗; 不管怎樣, 我該給她寫封信了。| **owe sb a favour** *One of the neighbours owes me a favor, I'm sure they'll take care of the cat.* 鄰居中有一家曾讓我幫過忙, 我肯定他們會幫我照料這隻貓的。| **I owe you one** (=used when saying thank you, when they have helped you and you are willing to help them) 我得報答你〔用於別人幫助你後, 你願意回報並表示感謝之時〕*Thanks a lot for being so understanding about all this – I owe you one!* 非常感謝你對這一切這麼通情達理 —— 我得報答你! | **owe sb** *informal* (=be in a position in which someone has helped you, so that you should help them)【非正式】報答某人 *Let's go and see Joe – he owes me!* 我們去看看喬 —— 他該報答我!

3 owe sb an explanation/apology to feel that you should give someone an explanation of why you did something, or say you are sorry 該向某人解釋/致歉: *"I owe you an apology, Margaret," he said sheepishly.* "我得向你道歉, 瑪格利特。" 他靦腆地說道。

4 ▶STH YOU HAVE/ACHIEVE 你所擁有/獲得的東西◀ **a)** to have something or achieve something because of what someone else has done 把…歸功於, 有…是由於: **owe sth to sb** *Helena probably owed her rapid recovery to her husband's devoted care.* 海倫娜的迅速痊癒也許應歸功於她丈夫的悉心照料。| **owe sb sth** *I knew that I owed Shanklin my life.* 我知道我能活下來全虧了尚克林。**b)** to know that someone's help has been important to you in achieving something 感激: **owe sb a lot/owe sb a great deal** *"I owe my parents a lot," he admitted.* "我非常感激我的父母。" 他承認道。| *He owes a great deal to his publishers.* 他對他的出版商感激涕零。| **owe it all to/owe everything to** *I owe it all to you.* 我把這一切都歸功於你。| **owe sb a debt (of gratitude)** *the debt that we owe to our teachers* 我們對老師們的感激之情

5 owe it to sb to do sth to feel you should do something for someone because they have helped you or given you support 認為應該為某人做某事: *You owe it to your supporters not to give up now.* 為了你的支持者, 你現在不應該放棄。

6 owe it to yourself to do sth to feel you should try to achieve something because it is what you deserve 認為自己應該做某事: *You owe it to yourself to take some time off.* 你該讓自己休息一下了。

7 ▶GOOD EFFECT 良好的作用◀ to be successful because of the good effect of something 歸功〔於某事〕: *Their success owes more to good luck than to careful management.* 他們的成功靠的是好運氣, 而不是苦心經營。

8 owe loyalty/allegiance etc to have a duty to obey someone 負有盡忠的義務: *From then on English and Scottish citizens owed allegiance to the same king.* 自那時起, 英格蘭和蘇格蘭的公民便效忠於同一個國王。

9 think that the world owes you a living to be unwilling to work in order to get things, and expect them to be provided for you 認為生來就該過舒服的日子

ow·ing /ˋo·ɪŋ; ˈəʊɪŋ/ *adj* **1** [not before noun 不用於名詞前] *especially BrE* if money is owing, it has not yet been paid to the person who should receive it【尤英】未付的, 欠着的: *There's still over £100 owing to the bank.* 還欠着銀行一百多英鎊。**2 owing to** because of 因為, 由於: *Owing to a lack of funds, the project will not continue next year.* 由於缺乏資金, 該項目明年將停止進行。

USAGE NOTE 用法説明: OWING

WORD CHOICE 詞語辨析: **owing to, due to, because of, thanks to**

Owing to is less common in spoken English than **due to**, but both are slightly formal and are often used in official notices or public statements. owing to 在英語口語中不如 due to 那麼常用, 但二者都略為正式, 並經常用於正式的通告或公開聲明中: *All flights into London Heathrow have been delayed due to/owing to thick fog.* 所有進入倫敦希斯路機場的航班均因大霧而延誤。

You would usually use **because of** in spoken English. 英語口語中通常用 because of: *All the flights have been delayed because of fog.* 因為有霧, 所有的航班都延誤了。

Thanks to is not formal and is used especially to

explain why or how something good has happened. thanks to 是非正式用語, 尤用於解釋某件好事發生的原因或過程: *Thanks to the public's generosity, we've been able to build two new schools in the area.* 多虧公眾慷慨解囊, 我們才得以在該地區建造了兩所新學校。

GRAMMAR 語法

You do not use **owing to** directly after the verb **to be**, but with other verbs. owing to 不能直接用於動詞 be 之後, 而要和別的動詞連用。

Some people think **due to** should only be used after the verb **to be**, but many people use it with other verbs as well. 有些人認為 due to 只能用於 be 動詞之後, 但許多人也將其與別的動詞連用: *The accident was largely due to human error.* 這次事故主要是由人為錯誤造成的。| *Prices have risen due to an increase in demand.* 價格是因需求增加而上漲的。

owl /aʊl; aʊl/ *n* [C] a bird with large eyes that hunts at night 鴞, 貓頭鷹

owl·et /ˈaʊlɪt; ˈaʊlɪ̥t/ *n* [C] a young owl 小鴞, 小貓頭鷹

owl·ish /ˈaʊlɪʃ; ˈaʊlɪʃ/ *adj* looking like an owl and seeming serious and clever 像貓頭鷹的; 看似嚴肅而聰明的: *Professor Jay looked owlish in his hornrimmed spectacles.* 傑伊教授戴着角質鏡架的眼鏡, 看上去嚴肅而富有智慧。—**owlishly** *adv*

own¹ /on; əʊn/ *determiner, pron* **1** belonging to you and no one else 自己的, 屬於自己的: **your own house/car etc** *He was so drunk he even forgot his own name.* 他醉得竟然忘了自己的名字。| *He tells people how to bring up their children but is so lenient with his own.* 他常教導人們該怎樣教育孩子, 但對自己的孩子卻非常寬容。| **a house/car etc of your own** *He left the company to start a business of his own.* 他離開公司去開辦自己的企業。| **your very own** (=used to add emphasis) 完全屬於自己的〔用於加強語氣〕*When you grow up you can have your very own room.* 等你長大以後你便會有一間完全屬於自己的房間。**2** done or caused without the help or influence of someone else 自己做[造成]的: *Why buy clothes when you can make your own more cheaply?* 既然你自己會做衣服, 還更便宜, 為甚麼還要買衣服呢? | *You've got to learn to make your own decisions.* 你得學會自己作決定。| *It's your own fault for leaving the window open.* 讓窗戶開着是你自己的過錯。**3 get your own back (on sb)** *informal* to get REVENGE¹ (1) for something someone has done to you【非正式】(向某人)復仇, 報復(某人): *All I wanted was to get my own back on my stepfather for punishing me.* 我想做的一切就是要報復繼父對我的懲罰。**4 (all) on your own a)** alone 單獨地, 獨自地: *I've been living on my own for four years now.* 我獨自生活迄今已四年了。**b)** without anyone's help 無援地, 獨立地: *I made this wardrobe all on my own.* 這個衣櫃是我自己打造的。—see graph at 參見 ALONE¹ 圖表 **5 be your own man/woman** to have your opinions and not be influenced by others〔不受他人影響〕自己拿主意, 自己做主 —see also 另見 **come into your own** (COME INTO (5)), **hold your own** (HOLD¹ (39))

USAGE NOTE 用法説明: OWN

GRAMMAR 語法

You use **own** only after possessive words like *my, John's, the company's,* etc. own 只能用在如 *my, John's, the company's* 等表示所屬關係的詞之後: *He has his own room/a room of his own.* 他有他自己的房間。

Own can be made stronger by adding **very**. 加上 very 可使 own 的語氣更強: *He has his very own room/a room of his very own.* 他有一間完全屬於自己的房間。

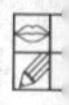

own² *v* [T not in progressive 不用進行式] **1** to have something when it is legally yours, especially because you have bought it, been given it etc〔尤指因購買或贈與等而合法地〕擁有〔某物〕: *Who owns that beautiful house?* 誰擁有那幢漂亮的房子? | *Mr Silver owned a large printing firm.* 西爾弗先生擁有一家大型印刷公司。**2 behave as if you own the place** also 又作 **act like you own the place** *informal* to behave in a way that is too confident and upsets other people【非正式】弄得好像是這裡的主人似的〔指表現過於自信而令他人不快〕: *She's only been here five minutes and she's already acting like she owns the place!* 她到這裡不過五分鐘, 但卻表現得像這裡的主人! **3** *old-fashioned* to admit that something is true【過時】承認: **own (that)** *I own that I judged her harshly at first.* 我承認原先我對她的評價很苛刻。| **[+to]** *I must own to a feeling of anxiety.* 我得承認有焦慮感。

own up *phr v* [I] to admit that you have done something wrong, especially something that is not serious 承認〔犯錯誤, 尤指小錯〕: *Unless the guilty person owns up, the whole class will be punished.* 除非犯錯者自己認錯, 否則全班都要受罰。| **own up to sth/to doing sth** *No one owned up to breaking the window.* 沒人承認打碎了窗子。

own brand /ˌ· ˈ·◂/ *adj BrE* own brand goods are specially produced and sold by particular shops and have the name of the shop on them【英】本店商標的, 自己商標的〔指產品由店家自產自銷並標有店家名稱的〕; STORE BRAND *AmE*【美】: *Sainsbury's own brand tomato sauce* 塞恩斯伯里商店以自己商標出品的番茄醬

own·er /ˈonə; ˈəʊnə/ *n* [C] someone who owns something 所有人, 物主, 業主: **[+of]** *I met the owner of the local hotel.* 我碰見了那家當地旅館的業主。| **the proud owner of** *the proud owner of a bright red sports car* 大紅跑車那位得意的車主 | **car-owner/dog-owner etc** *Dog-owners have been warned to keep their animals under control.* 狗主已被告誡要看管好自己的狗。| **home-owner** (=someone who owns their house) 住宅擁有者, 房主

owner-oc·cu·pied /ˌ·· ˈ···◂/ *adj* houses, apartments etc that are owner-occupied are lived in by the people who own them〔房子等〕業主居住的, 業主自用的: *Most of these properties are owner-occupied.* 這些房產大部分都是業主自用的。

owner-oc·cu·pi·er /ˌ·· ˈ····/ *n* [C] someone who owns the house or apartment etc that they live in 業主居住者

own·er·ship /ˈonəˌʃɪp; ˈəʊnəʃɪp/ *n* [U] the fact of owning something 所有權: *a dispute over the ownership of the land* 關於土地所有權的糾紛

own goal /ˌ· ˈ·/ *n* [C] *BrE*【英】**1** a GOAL that you accidentally SCORE² (1) against your own team without intending to in a game of football, HOCKEY etc 烏龍球〔足球、曲棍球等比賽中誤入自己球門的一球〕**2** *informal* an action or remark that has the opposite effect from what you intended【非正式】〔不利於自己的〕錯事, 蠢話, 自打嘴巴: *the minister's spectacular own goal when he admitted that his own department had leaked the document* 那位部長承認是他的部門泄漏文件內容, 這顯然是在自打嘴巴

own la·bel /ˌ· ˈ··◂/ *adj BrE* OWN BRAND【英】自己商標的, 本店商標的

ox /ɑks; ɒks/ *n plural* **oxen** /ˈɑksn̩; ˈɒksən/ [C] **1** a BULL whose sex organs have been removed, often used for working on farms etc〔常用於幹農活的〕閹牛 **2** a large cow or BULL 牛〔指大的母牛或公牛〕

Ox·bridge /ˈɑksˌbrɪdʒ; ˈɒksˌbrɪdʒ/ *n* [U] the universities of Oxford and Cambridge 牛津大學和劍橋大學 —compare 比較 REDBRICK

ox·cart /ˈɑksˌkɑrt; ˈɒkskɑːt/ *n* [C] a vehicle pulled by oxen 牛車

ox-eye /ˈ· ·/ *n* [C] a yellow flower like a DAISY 牛眼菊, 春白菊

Ox·fam /ˋɑksfæm; ˈɒksfæm/ *n* [singular] the Oxford Committee for Famine Relief; a British CHARITY organization that aims to help people in poor countries 樂施會, 牛津饑荒救濟委員會〔英國專門幫助貧困國家人民的慈善機構〕

ox·ford /ˋɑksfɚd; ˈɒksfəd/ *n AmE*【美】**1** [C] a type of shirt made of thick cotton 牛津襯衫〔一種用厚棉布做的襯衫〕 **2 oxfords** [plural] a type of leather shoes that fasten with SHOELACES 牛津鞋〔一種縛帶的男式皮鞋〕

ox·ide /ˋɑksaɪd; ˈɒksaɪd/ *n* [C,U] *technical* a chemical compound in which another substance is combined with oxygen【術語】氧化物: *iron oxide* 氧化鐵

ox·i·dize also 又作 **-ise** *BrE*【英】/ˋɑksəˌdaɪz; ˈɒksɪ̣daɪz/ *v* [I,T] *technical* to combine with oxygen, or make something combine with oxygen, especially in a way that causes RUST【術語】(使) 氧化; (使) 生鏽 —**oxidation** /ˌɑksəˋdeʃən; ˌɒksɪ̣ˈdeɪʃən/ also 又作 **oxidization** /ˌɑksədəˋzeʃən; ˌɒksɪ̣daɪˈzeɪʃən/ *n* [U]

Ox·on /ˋɑksɑn; ˈɒksɒn/ used after the title of a degree from Oxford University 牛津大學的〔用於學位名稱之後〕: *David Jones, BA (Oxon)* 大衛·瓊斯, 文學士 (牛津大學)

ox·tail /ˋɑksˌtel; ˈɒksteɪl/ *n* [U] the meat from the tails of cattle, used especially in soup〔尤指做湯用的〕牛尾: *oxtail soup* 牛尾湯

ox·y·a·cet·y·lene /ˌɑksɪəˋsɛtl̩ˌin; ˌɒksiəˈsetəliːn◂/ *n* [U] *technical* a mixture of oxygen and ACETYLENE that produces a hot white flame that can cut steel【術語】氧 (乙) 炔

ox·y·gen /ˋɑksədʒən; ˈɒksɪdʒən/ *n* [U] a gas with no colour, smell, or taste, that is present in air and is necessary for most animals and plants to live 氧, 氧氣

ox·y·gen·ate /ˋɑksədʒənˌet; ˈɒksɪdʒəneɪt/ *v* [T] *technical* to add oxygen to something【術語】充氧於 —**oxygenation** /ˌɑksədʒənˋeʃən; ˌɒksɪdʒɪ̣ˈneɪʃən/ *n* [U]

oxygen mask /ˈ··· ·/ *n* [C] a piece of equipment that fits over someone's mouth and nose to provide them with oxygen 氧氣面罩, 氧幕

oxygen tent /ˈ··· ·/ *n* [C] a piece of equipment shaped like a tent that is put around people who are very ill in hospital, to provide them with oxygen〔給醫院病人用的〕氧氣帳

ox·y·mo·ron /ˌɑksɪˋmɔrɑn; ˌɒksiˈmɔːrɒn/ *n* [C] *technical* a deliberate combination of two words that seem to mean the opposite of each other, such as 'cruel kindness'【術語】矛盾修辭法, 逆喻〈如殘酷的善良〉

o·yez /ˋojɛz; əʊˈjez/ *interjection* a word used by law officials or by TOWN CRIERs in the past to get people's attention 肅靜! 靜聽!〔法官或過去的城鎮公告員在街上宣布要事時要人注意聽的喊聲〕

oy·ster /ˋɔɪstɚ; ˈɔɪstə/ *n* [C] **1** a type of SHELLFISH that can be eaten cooked or uncooked, and that produces a jewel called a PEARL (1) 牡蠣, 蠔 —see picture at 參見 SHELL[1] 圖 **2 the world is your oyster** used to tell someone that they can achieve whatever they want 你可以隨心所欲; 想要甚麼就能得到甚麼

oyster bed /ˈ·· ·/ *n* [C] an area at the bottom of the sea where oysters live〔海底〕牡蠣養殖場

oyster-catch·er /ˈ·· ˌ··/ *n* [C] a black and white bird that eats SHELLFISH 蠣鷸〔一種捕食水生有殼動物的海鳥〕

Oz /ɑz; ɒz/ *n BrE, AustrE informal* Australia【英, 澳, 非正式】澳大利亞

oz the written abbreviation of 縮寫= OUNCE or ounces

o·zone /ˋozon; ˈəʊzəʊn/ *n* [U] **1** *technical* a poisonous blue gas that is a type of oxygen【術語】臭氧〔有毒的藍色氣體, 氧的同素異形體〕 **2** *informal* air near the sea, thought to be fresher and healthier【非正式】〔近海處的〕清新空氣

ozone-friend·ly /ˌ·· ˈ··◂/ *adj* not containing chemicals that damage the ozone layer 不含破壞臭氧層的化學物的, 對臭氧層無害的: *an ozone-friendly aerosol* 對臭氧層無害的噴霧劑

ozone lay·er /ˈ·· ˌ··/ *n* [singular] a layer of gases that prevents harmful RADIATION (2) from the sun from reaching the Earth 臭氧層: *CFCs, the chemicals responsible for the hole in the ozone layer* 含氯氟烴, 造成臭氧層空洞的化學物

P,p

P, p /pi; piː/ *plural* **P's, p's** *n* [C] the 16th letter of the English alphabet 英語字母表的第十六個字母 —see also 另見 **mind your p's and q's** (MIND[2] (7))

p 1 the written abbreviation of 縮寫= page **2** *BrE* pence or PENNY【英】便士: *'The Times' now costs only 30p.* 《泰晤士報》現在只售30便士。**3** the written abbreviation of 縮寫= PARTICIPLE **4** the written abbreviation of 縮寫= POPULATION **5** used in written music to show that a part should be played or sung quietly 柔聲地, 輕輕地〔用於樂譜中表示該部分演奏或演唱時應用輕聲〕

p & p the written abbreviation of 縮寫= **postage and packing**: *Please send 20p to cover p & p.* 請寄20便士支付郵資和包裝費。

PA /ˌpi ˋe; ˌpiː ˈeɪ/ *n* **1** [C, usually singular 一般用單數] public address system; a set of electronically controlled pieces of equipment that makes someone's voice loud enough to be heard by large groups of people 有線廣播系統; 擴音系統 **2** [C] *BrE* personal assistant; a special secretary who looks after the affairs of just one person【英】私人助理

p.a. the written abbreviation of 縮寫= PER ANNUM

pa /pɑ; pɑː/ *n* [C] *old-fashioned* a word meaning 'father' used by or to children【過時】爸爸〔兒語〕

3 **pace[1]** /pes; peɪs/ *n*

1 ▶WALK/RUN 走/跑◀ [singular] the speed at which you walk or run 步速, 走[跑]的速度: *They've run the first mile in under six minutes – can they keep up this pace?* 他們不到六分鐘就跑完了頭一英里 —— 他們能保持這個速度嗎? | **at a steady/gentle/brisk pace** *The troops marched at a steady pace.* 部隊穩步行進。

2 ▶SPEED STH HAPPENS 某事發生的速度◀ [singular] the rate or speed at which something happens or at which someone does something 速度, 進度: **[+of]** *The pace of change in Eastern Europe has been breathtaking.* 東歐的變化速度是驚人的。| **at your own pace** (=at the pace that suits you) 以適合自己的速度 *He liked to work at his own pace.* 他喜歡以自己的進度工作。

3 ▶A STEP 一步◀ [C] a single step when you are running or walking, or the distance moved in one step〔跑或走的〕一步; 一步之距: *I moved forward a couple of paces.* 我向前移動了幾步。

4 force the pace to make something happen or develop more quickly than it would do normally 使加快速度, 使加速發展: *Gorbachev favoured gradual reform and felt it was dangerous to force the pace.* 戈爾巴喬夫支持循序漸進的改革, 並認為採用加速改革是很危險的。

5 keep pace (with) to move or change as fast as someone or something else (與…) 並駕齊驅, 齊頭並進; 跟上…: *She followed Bobby, barely keeping pace with him.* 她跟着博比, 只能勉強跟上他。| *Pensions and benefits have failed to keep pace with the rate of inflation.* 養老金和救濟金的增加跟不上通貨膨脹的速度。

6 put sb/sth through their paces to make a person or a machine show how well they can do something 測試某人/某物的本領[性能]; 使某人/某物展示本領[性能]: *a series of tests to put candidates through their paces* 考察候選人能力的一連串測試

7 set the pace a) to establish a speed at which others try to do something, or a quality they try to achieve 起帶頭作用, 樹立榜樣: *Japanese firms have been setting the pace in electronic engineering.* 日本公司一直在電子工程方面處於領先地位。**b)** to run at a speed that other runners try to keep to, at the beginning of a race〔在比賽開始時〕定步速〔使其他賽跑者跟從〕

8 stand the pace to be able to deal with situations where you are very busy and have to think and act very quickly 能夠適應緊張的節奏: *If you can stand the pace, working in advertising pays well.* 要是你能適應緊張的工作節奏, 在廣告行業工作報酬很高。

9 show your paces to show your skill or speed in an activity 顯示自己的本領[才能], 顯身手; 展示自己的速度

10 the pace of life the amount of activity in people's lives and how busy they are 生活節奏: *The pace of life in the village was slow and restful.* 這個鄉村的生活節奏緩慢而悠閒。

11 ▶HORSE 馬◀ [C] one of the ways that a horse walks or runs〔馬的〕步法, 溜蹄

pace[2] *v* **1** [I always+adv/prep,T] to walk with slow, regular, steady steps, usually backwards and forwards 慢步走(於), 踱步; 以規律的步伐行走: **pace up and down** *He paced nervously up and down the hospital room, waiting for news.* 他緊張不安地在醫院的房間裡踱來踱去, 等待消息。| **pace the floor/room etc** *Ben stood up and paced the floor, deep in thought.* 本站起來踱來踱去, 陷入了沉思。—see picture on page A24 參見A24頁圖 **2 pace yourself a)** to set a controlled regular speed for yourself, especially in a race〔尤指在比賽中〕控制自己的步速: *I paced myself so that I was not too far ahead of the others.* 我控制好自己的速度, 以使自己不領先別人太多。**b)** to do something at a steady speed without rushing 以平穩的速度做某事; 掌握速度 **3 pace someone** to set a speed for someone running or riding, especially in a race〔尤指在比賽中〕為某人定步速 **4** also 又作 **pace off, pace out** [T] to measure a distance by taking steps of an equal length 用腳步測量, 步測: *The director paced out the length of the stage.* 那位導演用步子測量了舞台的長度。

pace·mak·er /ˋpesˌmekɚ; ˈpeɪsˌmeɪkə/ *n* [C] a small machine that is fixed inside someone's chest in order to make weak or irregular beats of the heart regular〔心臟〕起搏器

pace·set·ter /ˋpesˌsɛtɚ; ˈpeɪs-setə/ *n* [C] **1** a team that is ahead of others in a competition〔比賽中〕領先隊伍 **2** someone or something that sets an example for others 帶頭人, 榜樣: *Industry is the pacesetter of modern life.* 工業是現代生活的先導。**3** someone who runs at the front at the beginning of a race and sets the speed at which others must run〔賽跑中其他參賽者跟隨其速度的〕領跑者, 定步速者

pach·y·derm /ˋpækəˌdɝm; ˈpækɪdɜːm/ *n* [C] *technical* a thick-skinned animal such as an elephant or a RHINOCEROS【術語】厚皮動物〈如象或犀牛〉

pa·cif·ic /pəˋsɪfɪk; pəˈsɪfɪk/ *adj literary*【文】**1** peaceful or loving peace 平靜的, 安寧的; 愛好和平的: *a normally pacific community* 通常很平靜的社區 **2** helping to cause peace 求和的, 和解的; 息事寧人的 —**pacifically** /-klɪ; -kli/ *adv*

Pacific Rim /ˌ·ˌ·· ˈ·/ *n* **the Pacific Rim (countries)** the countries or parts of countries that border the Pacific Ocean, such as Japan, Australia, and the west coast of the US, considered as an economic group 太平洋沿岸國家[地區]〔如日本、澳大利亞和美國西海岸, 被視為一個經濟羣體〕

pac·i·fi·er /ˋpæsəˌfaɪɚ; ˈpæsɪfaɪə/ *n* [C] **1** *AmE* a specially shaped rubber object that you give a baby to suck so that it does not cry【美】〔哄嬰孩用的〕橡皮奶頭[奶

嘴]; DUMMY[1] (3) *BrE*【英】**2** something that makes people calm 鎮靜劑; 使人安定的東西

pac·i·fis·m /ˈpæsəˌfɪzəm; ˈpæsɨfɪzəm/ *n* [U] the belief that all wars and all forms of violence are wrong 和平主義; 反戰主義

pac·i·fist /ˈpæsəfɪst; ˈpæsɨfɨst/ *n* [C] someone who believes that all wars are wrong and who refuses to use violence 和平主義者; 反戰主義者

pac·i·fy /ˈpæsəˌfaɪ; ˈpæsɨfaɪ/ *v* [T] **1** to make someone calm, quiet, and satisfied after they have been angry or upset 使平靜, 使安靜, 安撫: *Gregory knew his wife would be furious and he was trying to think how to pacify her.* 格雷戈里知道妻子會大發雷霆的, 所以他在想如何安撫她。**2** to bring peace to an area or to end war in a place 給〔某個地區〕帶來和平; 使〔某地〕結束戰爭, 平定, 綏靖: *It was hoped the new ruler could pacify the region.* 人們希望這位新的統治者能給這一地區帶來和平。—**pacification** /ˌpæsəfəˋkeʃən; ˌpæsɨfɨˈkeɪʃən/ *n* [U]

pack (把…)裝箱

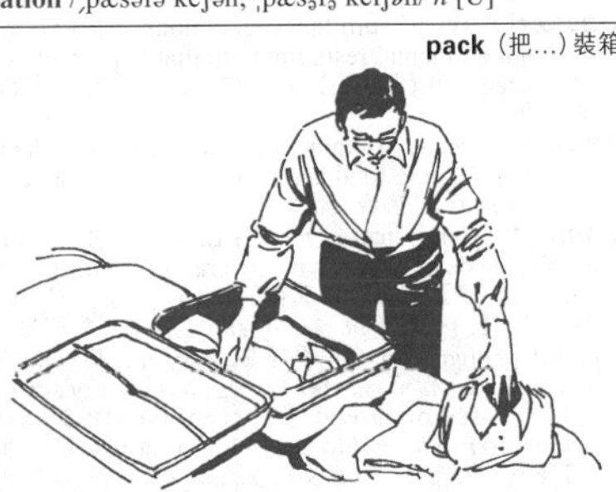

2 3 **pack¹** /pæk; pæk/ *v*

1 ▶IN BOXES, CASES ETC 在箱子、盒子等中◀ also 又作 **pack up** [I,T] to put things into cases, boxes etc for taking somewhere or storing (把…)打包; (把…)裝箱: *I forgot to pack my razor.* 我忘記把剃鬚刀放入行李包。| *They packed up the contents of their house.* 他們把屋子裡的東西打好捆。| *We're off to Greece tomorrow and I haven't even started packing yet.* 我們明天就動身去希臘, 但我還沒有開始收拾行李呢。| **pack sb sth** *Have you packed the kids a lunch?* 你為孩子們備好盒裝午餐了嗎?

2 pack a bag/case etc to put things into a bag, case etc 把東西裝入袋[包]/箱[盒]等: *She packed her suitcase and headed for the airport.* 她把東西裝入手提箱, 然後動身去機場。—opposite 反義詞 UNPACK (1)

3 ▶CROWD OF PEOPLE 人羣◀ [I always+adv/prep, T always+adv/prep] to go in large numbers into a space that is not big enough, or to make a lot of people or things do this 擠進, 湧進; 塞滿, 使擠滿: **[+into/in/onto]** *When the door was opened people began to pack into the hall.* 門一打開, 人們就開始湧入大廳。| *They packed as many people as possible onto the bus.* 他們盡量讓多些人擠上那輛公共汽車。

4 ▶PROTECT STH 保護某物◀ [T] to cover, fill, or surround an object closely with a protective material〔用保護材料〕把…裹[包]起來: *Pack the newspaper around the china so that it doesn't break.* 用報紙把瓷器包起來以免打破。| **[+in/with]** *china cups packed with paper* 用紙包起來的瓷杯

5 pack your bags *informal* to leave a place and not return, especially because of a disagreement【非正式】〔尤指由於意見不合而〕離開: *Why don't you pack your bags and find another job?* 你為甚麼不離開再找一份工作呢?

6 ▶SNOW/SOIL ETC 雪/土壤等◀ [T] to press soil, sand etc into a firm mass 把〔土壤、沙等〕結實地堆積起來; 壓緊; 搗固: *pack soil firmly around the stem* 把土壤結實地堆積在樹幹周圍

7 ▶MEAT ETC 肉等◀ [T] to prepare food and put it into containers for preserving or selling 把〔食品〕裝罐[製成罐頭]

8 pack a committee/jury/meeting etc [T] to secretly and dishonestly arrange for a committee etc to be filled with people who support you〔祕密及不正當地〕在委員會/陪審團/會議等中安插[安排]支持自己的人

9 pack a gun *AmE* to regularly carry a gun【美】攜帶槍支

10 pack a (hard) punch *informal*【非正式】**a)** to be able to hit another person hard in a fight〔在打鬥中〕能有力地擊拳, 用力出拳 **b)** to be able to speak very effectively in an argument or discussion〔在辯論或討論中〕措辭有力 —see also 另見 **send sb packing** (SEND (9))

pack sth ↔ **away** *phr v* [T] to put something back in a box, case etc where it is usually kept 將〔某物〕收拾起來: *We packed away the picnic things.* 我們把野餐用的東西收拾起來。

pack sb/sth ↔ **in** *phr v* [T] **1** *informal* to attract people in large numbers【非正式】吸引〔大批的人〕: *'Pulp Fiction' is really packing them in.*〔電影〕《危險人物》〔又譯《低俗小說》〕確實把他們吸引住了。**2** also 又作 **pack** sth **into** sth to fit a lot of something into a space, place, or period of time 把〔太多事物〕塞入, 擠入: *They packed so much into their holiday, they returned exhausted.* 他們把假期安排得太緊密, 結果回來時筋疲力盡。**3** *informal especially BrE* to stop doing something, especially a job that you find unpleasant or annoying【非正式, 尤英】停止〔尤指不愉快或令人討厭的工作〕: *At times like this I feel like packing it all in and going off travelling.* 像這種時候我就想丟下所有的事情去旅行。**4 pack it in** *spoken* used to tell someone to stop doing something that is annoying you【口】〔用於告訴別人〕停止〔做令人討厭的事〕: *Pack it in you two. I'm tired of hearing you arguing.* 你們兩個別爭了, 我都聽厭了。**5** *BrE informal* to end a romantic relationship with someone【英, 非正式】結束與…的戀情, 與…分手

pack sb/sth **off** *phr v* [T] *informal* to send someone away quickly, to avoid trouble or because you want to get rid of them【非正式】〔為避免麻煩或擺脫某人而〕把…打發走, 攆走: *My parents packed us off to camp every summer.* 我的父母每到夏天就打發我們去夏令營。

pack up *phr v* **1** [I] *informal* to finish work【非正式】完成工作, 停工, 收工: *Business was slack and she packed up early.* 由於生意清淡, 她早早就收工了。**2** [I] *informal especially BrE* if a machine packs up it stops working【非正式, 尤英】〔機器〕停止運轉, 出故障, 失靈: *The engine's packed up!* 引擎壞了! **3** [T] *informal BrE* to stop doing something such as a job【非正式, 英】停止〔做某事〕; 停止工作: *He's packed up his job after only three months.* 僅三個月後他就放棄了自己的工作。

pack² *n* [C] 2 3

1 ▶THINGS WRAPPED TOGETHER 包在一起的東西◀ several things wrapped or tied together or put in a case, to make them easy to carry, sell, or give to someone 包, 捆, 包裹: *Send away for your free information pack today.* 今天就寫信索取免費資料包。—see also 另見 SIX-PACK

2 ▶SMALL CONTAINER 小容器◀ *especially AmE* a small container, usually made of paper, with a set of things in it; PACKET (1,2)【尤美】〔一般用紙造的〕小盒, 小包: **[+of]** *a pack of cigarettes* 一包香煙 | *a pack of gum BrE*【英】一包口香糖 —see picture at 參見 CONTAINER 圖

3 ▶BAG 包◀ [C] *BrE* a bag carried by a climber, walker, or soldier, that is fastened to their shoulders and is used to carry equipment, clothes etc【英】背包

4 ▶ANIMALS 動物◀ a group of wild animals that hunt together, or a group of dogs trained together for hunting

〔野獸或獵犬的〕一羣: *a wolf pack* 狼羣 | *a pack of hounds* 一羣獵狗

5 ▶GROUP OF PEOPLE 一羣人◀ a group of people who do something together, especially a group who you do not approve of 一幫, 一夥: *a pack of thieves* 一夥賊 | *the Hollywood brat pack* 一幫荷里活的青年名演員

6 ▶MILITARY 軍事◀ a group of aircraft, SUBMARINES, etc that fight the enemy together〔作戰飛機或潛艇的〕一隊, 一羣

7 be a pack of lies *informal* to be completely untrue【非正式】一派謊言: *Don't you believe what it says in the paper – it's a pack of lies.* 別相信報紙上說的 —— 那全是一派謊言。

8 ▶CARDS 紙牌◀ a complete set of PLAYING CARDS〔紙牌的〕一副: *Please shuffle the pack and deal.* 請洗牌並發牌。

9 Cub/Brownie pack a group of children belonging to a children's organization 一隊幼年男/女童子軍 —see 見 CUB SCOUT, BROWNIE

10 ▶ON A WOUND 在傷口上◀ a thick mass of soft cloth that you press on a wound to stop the flow of blood; COMPRESS² 〔壓在傷口上止血用的〕敷布, 裹布, 繃帶 —see also 另見 ICE PACK

11 ▶BEAUTY TREATMENT 美容◀ a substance, often a special mud or clay, that you put on your skin to make you feel better 美容敷劑 —see also 另見 FACE PACK, MUDPACK

2 2 **pack·age¹** /ˈpækɪdʒ; ˈpækɪdʒ/ *n* [C] **1** an amount of something, or several things, packed together firmly and wrapped in paper etc; PARCEL¹ (1) 包, 包裹: **[+of]** *Can you deliver a large package of books?* 你能遞送一大包書嗎? **2** *AmE* the box, bag etc that foods are put in for selling【美】〔包裝食物的〕盒, 包 **3** a set of related things or services sold or offered together〔出售或提供的相關東西或服務的〕一套, 一攬子: *a new software package* 一套新的軟件包 | *The bank is offering a special financial package for students.* 這家銀行正給學生提供一整套特殊的金融服務。

package² also 又作 **package up** *v* [T] **1** to make something into a package or tie it up as a package 把...包成一包[紮成一捆]: *She packaged up the clothes to send to her daughter.* 她把衣服包成一包寄給她的女兒。**2** to put something in a special package ready to be sold 將...包裝〔以備出售〕

pack·aged /ˈpækɪdʒd; ˈpækɪdʒd/ *adj* specially wrapped and put in a container for selling〔作銷售用途〕包裝的, 裝盒的: *The soap was beautifully packaged in a special gift box.* 那塊肥皂被放在一個特製的禮品盒裡, 包裝非常精美。

package deal /ˈ·· ·/ *n* [C] an offer or agreement that includes several things that must all be accepted together 一攬子交易, 整批交易

package hol·i·day /ˈ·· ˌ···/ *n* [C] *BrE* a package tour【英】包辦旅遊, 包價旅遊

package store /ˈ·· ·/ *n* [C] *AmE old-fashioned* a store where alcohol is sold【美, 過時】銷售酒的商店; OFF LICENCE *BrE*【英】

package tour /ˈ·· ·/ *n* [C] a completely planned holiday arranged by a company at a fixed price, which includes travel, hotels, meals etc〔一切由旅行社安排且費用固定的〕包辦旅遊, 包價旅遊

pack·ag·ing /ˈpækɪdʒɪŋ; ˈpækɪdʒɪŋ/ *n* [U] **1** material used to cover a product that is sold in a shop 包裝材料: *Packaging adds to the cost of food.* 包裝材料增加了食品的成本。**2** [U] the process of wrapping food for sale 包裝; 打包: *Prepacked bacon carries the date of packaging.* 預先包裝好的熏肉均有包裝日期。**3** a way of making a plan or a politician seem better than they are〔對某項計劃或某個政客進行的〕包裝, 美化: *the imaginative packaging of an unacceptable tax* 對於一項難以接受的稅收進行的富於想像力的包裝

pack an·i·mal /ˈ· ˌ···/ *n* [C] an animal, such as a horse, used for carrying heavy loads 馱畜〈如馬〉

packed /pækt; pækt/ *adj* **1** extremely full of people 擠滿人的, 非常擁擠的: *a packed dance floor* 擠滿人的舞池 **2 packed with/packed full of** containing a lot of a particular kind of thing 充滿...的; 含有很多...的: *a new magazine packed with exciting recipes* 內有很多誘人食譜的新雜誌 **3** [not before noun 不用於名詞前] if you are packed, you have put everything you need into boxes or cases before going somewhere 收拾好行李的 **4 loosely packed** packed without being pressed closely together 包裝鬆散的: *loosely packed cigarettes* 包裝鬆散的香煙 **5 tightly packed** pressed into a small space 包裝密實的; 壓得緊密的: *tightly packed fibres* 壓得結實的纖維

packed lunch /ˌ· ˈ·/ *n* [C] *BrE* a cold meal of SANDWICHes, fruit etc packed into a box【英】〔三明治、水果等〕盒裝午餐

packed out /ˌ· ˈ·/ *adj* [not before noun 不用於名詞前] *informal* a cinema, restaurant etc that is packed out is completely full【非正式】〔電影院、餐館等〕擠得滿滿的, 滿座的

pack·er /ˈpækə; ˈpækə/ *n* [C] someone who works in a factory, preparing food and putting it into containers 包裝工, 打包工; 裝罐頭食品的工人

pack·et /ˈpækɪt; ˈpækɪt/ *n* [C] **1** *BrE* a small container, usually made of paper, with several things of the same kind in it【英】〔通常用紙製作的〕小包, 小盒, 小袋; PACK *AmE*【美】: **[+of]** *a packet of envelopes* 一紮信封 | *a packet of cigarettes* 一包香煙 **2** a very small packet like an envelope〔像信封一樣的〕小包: *a packet of seeds* 一包種子 —see picture at 參見 CONTAINER 圖 **3 cost a packet** *BrE informal* to cost a lot of money【英, 非正式】花費一大筆錢: *That car cost me a packet.* 那輛汽車花了我一大筆錢。**4** a packet boat 定期郵船, 班輪 **5 catch/cop/get/stop a packet** *BrE old-fashioned* to get into serious trouble or receive a severe punishment【英, 過時】陷入嚴重困境; 受到嚴厲懲罰 2

packet boat /ˈ·· ·/ *n* [C] *old-fashioned* a boat that carries mail and usually passengers at regular times【過時】定期郵船, 班輪

packet-switch·ing /ˈ·· ˌ··/ *n* [C] a method of sending DATA (=information stored on a computer) on telephone lines, that breaks long messages into pieces and puts them together again when they are received 小包交換法; 封包交換, 分封交換〔一種通過電話線傳送電腦數據的方法, 即把長信息分割成片斷傳送, 在信息收到之後再組合在一起〕

pack horse /ˈ· ·/ *n* [C] a horse used for carrying heavy loads〔用來馱重物的〕馱馬

pack ice /ˈ· ·/ *n* [U] sea ice in a large floating mass〔海上的〕大片浮冰, 浮冰羣

pack·ing /ˈpækɪŋ; ˈpækɪŋ/ *n* [U] **1** the act of putting things into cases or boxes so that you can send or take them somewhere 包裝, 打包, 裝箱; 收拾行李: **do the packing** *I'll do my packing the night before we leave.* 我會在我們動身前一晚收拾行李。**2** paper, plastic, cloth etc used for packing things 包裝材料〈如紙、塑料、布等〉

packing case /ˈ·· ·/ *n* [C] a large strong wooden box in which things are packed to be sent somewhere or stored 粗板箱, 裝貨大木箱

pack rat /ˈ· ·/ *n* [C] *AmE* someone who collects and stores things that they do not really need【美】收藏無用東西的人

pack sad·dle /ˈ· ˌ··/ *n* [C] a SADDLE¹ (1) that you fasten bags to so that a horse or other animal can carry them 馱鞍

pack trip /ˈ· ·/ *n* [C] *AmE* a trip through the countryside on horses, for fun or as a sport【美】〔為消遣或運動的〕鄉間騎馬旅行; PONY-TREKKING *BrE*【英】

pact /pækt; pækt/ *n* [C] a formal agreement between two groups, nations, or people, especially to help each other or fight together against an enemy〔尤指團體、國家之間為互相援助或共同抗擊敵人而訂的正式〕條約, 協定, 協議: **make/sign a pact** *The two countries signed a non-aggression pact.* 這兩個國家簽署了互不侵犯條約。| **a pact to do sth** *an electoral pact to keep out the Fascists* 為排擠法西斯主義者而訂立的選舉協議 —see also 另見 SUICIDE PACT

3 **pad**[1] /pæd; pæd/ *n* [C]
1 ▶SOFT MATERIAL 柔軟材料◀ something made of or filled with soft material, that is used to protect something or make it more comfortable 墊, 襯墊; 護墊: *She put a sterile pad of cotton over the wound.* 她把一團消過毒的棉花敷在傷口上。| *a foam rubber pad* 泡沫橡膠襯墊 | **knee/elbow/shoulder pad** (=a pad sewn into someone's clothes to protect their knee etc or make them look bigger) 護膝/護肘/護[墊]肩
2 ▶PAPER 紙◀ several sheets of paper fastened together, used for writing letters, drawing pictures etc 便箋本, 拍紙簿: *a writing pad* 拍紙簿
3 ▶ANIMAL'S FOOT 動物的足◀ the flesh on the bottom of the foot of a cat, dog, etc〔貓、狗等動物的〕肉趾, 爪墊
4 ▶APARTMENT 公寓◀ *informal* a room or apartment where someone lives【非正式】住所, 房間, 公寓: *a bachelor pad in Mayfair* 在〔倫敦〕梅爾菲區的單身人士公寓
5 ▶QUIET SOUND 輕聲◀ [singular] a soft sound made by someone walking quietly 輕輕走路的聲音: *I heard the pad and squeak of footsteps in the snow.* 我聽到走在雪地裡低沉而吱吱作響的腳步聲。
6 ▶WATER PLANT 水生植物◀ *technical* the large floating leaf of some water plants such as the WATER LILY【術語】〔睡蓮等水生植物的〕浮葉
7 ▶FOR WOMEN 供婦女用的◀ a soft material like paper, worn by a woman during her PERIOD[1] (4) to take up the blood〔婦女經期使用的〕衛生巾
8 ▶FOR INK 盛墨水用的◀ a piece of material that has been made wet with ink and is used for covering a STAMP[1] (1) with ink; INK PAD 印色盒, 印 (泥) 台 —see also 另見 LAUNCH PAD, HELICOPTER PAD

pad[2] *v* **padded, padding 1** [I always+adv/prep] to walk softly and quietly 輕輕地走, 放輕腳步走: *The boy's dog padded after him.* 那個男孩的狗輕輕地跟在他後面。**2** [T] to protect something, shape it, or make it more comfortable by covering or filling it with soft material 給…裝襯墊; 用軟物覆蓋[填塞] **3** [T] *AmE* to dishonestly make bills more expensive than they really are【美】虛報, 誇大〔賬目〕: *padding the bills of medicare patients* 虛報醫療保健病人的賬目

pad sth ↔ **out** *phr v* [T] to make a sentence, speech etc longer by adding unnecessary words〔用增加不必要的空話來〕拉長, 充斥〔句子、演講等〕: *The last two chapters are padded out with boring stories.* 最後兩章被加進乏味的故事而拉長了。

pad·ded /ˈpædɪd; ˈpædɪd/ *adj* something that is padded is filled or covered with a soft material to make it thicker or more comfortable 裝有襯墊的, 有護墊的: *a jacket with padded shoulders* 裝墊肩的短上衣

padded cell /ˌ·· ˈ·/ *n* [C] a special room with thick, soft walls in a MENTAL HOSPITAL, used to stop people who are being violent from hurting themselves〔精神病院裡牆上裝有護墊以防病人自傷的〕軟牆病房, 軟壁小室

pad·ding /ˈpædɪŋ; ˈpædɪŋ/ *n* [U] **1** soft material used to fill or cover something to make it softer or more comfortable 襯料, 襯墊, 填料 **2** unnecessary words that are added to make a sentence, speech etc longer 湊篇幅的詞句, 冗詞贅句

pad·dle[1] /ˈpædl; ˈpædl/ *n* [C] **1** a short pole that is wide and flat at one end or both ends, used for moving a small boat along〔小船的〕短槳, 槳 —compare 比較 OAR —see picture at 參見 CANOE 圖 **2** [singular] *BrE* the action of walking about in water which is not very deep【英】涉水, 蹚水: **have a paddle/go for a paddle** *I'm just going for a quick paddle to cool my feet down.* 我正要去蹚一蹚水使我的腳涼快下來。**3** *AmE* a small round BAT[1] (2b) with a short handle, used for hitting the ball in TABLE TENNIS【美】〔乒乓球的〕球拍 **4** one of the wide blades on the wheel of a PADDLE STEAMER〔明輪船的〕輪葉, 明輪翼 **5** a tool like a flat spoon, used for mixing food〔平匙狀〕攪拌器: *a paddle for making the butter* 製作黃油的攪拌棒 **6** *AmE* a piece of wood with a handle, used for hitting a child to punish them【美】〔用於懲罰孩子的〕帶柄木板 —see also 另見 DOG PADDLE

paddle[2] *v* **paddled, paddling 1** [I,T] to move a small light boat through water, using one or more paddles 用槳划〔小船〕: **[+along/upstream/towards]** *We got out the canoe and paddled upstream.* 我們取出獨木舟向上游划去。| **paddle sth** *They paddled the canoe across the lake.* 他們划着獨木舟過了那個湖。—compare 比較 ROW[3] **2** [I] *BrE* to walk about in water that is not very deep【英】涉水, 蹚水: *The children paddled in the sea.* 孩子們在海邊蹚水。—see picture on page A24 參見 A24 頁圖 **3** [I] to swim by moving your hands and feet up and down〔游泳時用手腳〕撥水 **4** [T] *AmE informal* to hit a child with a piece of wood as a punishment【美, 非正式】用木板打孩子〔作為懲罰〕 **5 paddle your own canoe** *informal* to depend on yourself and no one else【非正式】獨立自主; 自力更生

paddle boat /ˈ·· ·/ *n* [C] a paddle steamer 明輪船

paddle steam·er /ˈ·· ˌ··/ *n* [C] *BrE* a STEAMBOAT (=a large boat driven by steam) which is pushed forward by two large wheels at the sides【英】明輪船; SIDE-WHEEL *AmE*【美】

paddle ten·nis /ˈ·· ˌ··/ *n* [U] *AmE* TABLE TENNIS【美】乒乓球

paddling pool /ˈ·· ·/ *n* [C] *BrE*【英】**1** a small pool, which is not very deep, for children to play in〔供孩子玩水用的〕嬉水池 **2** a plastic container that is filled with water, for small children to play in〔灌水供孩子在裡面玩的〕塑料嬉水池; WADING POOL *AmE*【美】

pad·dock /ˈpædək; ˈpædək/ *n* [C] **1** a small field near a house or STABLE in which horses are kept or exercised〔住宅或馬廐附近的〕小牧場; 練馬場 **2** a place where horses are brought together before a race so that people can look at them〔賽馬前的〕馬匹檢閱場 **3** *AustrE, NZE* a field, especially one with grass【澳, 新西蘭】牧場, 草場

Pad·dy /ˈpædɪ; ˈpædi/ *n* [C] *informal* a joking word for an Irishman, that is often considered offensive【非正式】愛爾蘭人〔常被認為具冒犯性的戲稱〕

pad·dy /ˈpædɪ; ˈpædi/ *n* [C] **1 be in a paddy** *BrE* to be in a bad temper【英】發脾氣, 大怒 **2** a paddy field 水稻田

paddy field /ˈ·· ·/ *n* [C] a field in which rice is grown in water; RICE PADDY 水稻田

paddy wag·on /ˈ·· ˌ··/ *n* [C] *AmE informal* a police vehicle【美, 非正式】警車

pad·lock /ˈpædˌlɑk; ˈpædlɒk/ *n* [C] a small lock that you can put on a door, cupboard, bicycle etc〔用於鎖門、櫃櫥、腳踏車等的〕掛鎖, 扣鎖 —**padlock** *v* [T]

pa·dre /ˈpɑdrɪ; ˈpɑːdri/ *n* [C] *informal* a priest, especially one in the army【非正式】牧師,〔尤指〕隨軍牧師 —see 見 PRIEST (USAGE)

pae·an /ˈpiən; ˈpiːən/ *n* [C] *literary* a happy song of praise, thanks, or victory【文】讚歌; 感恩歌; 凱歌

paed·e·rast *BrE*【英】, **pederast** *AmE*【美】/ˈpɛdəˌræst; ˈpedəræst/ *n* [C] *technical* a man who has sex with a boy【術語】雞姦者 —**paederasty** *n* [U]

pae·di·a·tri·cian *BrE*【英】, **pediatrician** *AmE*【美】/ˌpidɪəˈtrɪʃən; ˌpiːdiəˈtrɪʃən/ *n* [C] a doctor who looks after children and treats their illnesses 兒科醫生

pae·di·at·rics *BrE*【英】, **pediatrics** *AmE*【美】/ˌpidɪˈætrɪks; ˌpiːdiˈætrɪks/ *n* [U] the branch of medicine connected with children and their illnesses 兒科學 —**paediatric** *adj*: *a paediatric hospital* 兒科醫院

pae·do·phile *BrE*【英】, **pedophile** *AmE*【美】/ˈpidəfaɪl; ˈpiːdəfaɪl/ *n* [C] someone who is sexually attracted to young children 戀童癖患者

pa·el·la /pɑˋɛlə; paɪˈelə/ *n* [U] a Spanish dish of rice cooked with pieces of meat, fish, and vegetables〔用肉、魚和蔬菜烹製的〕西班牙肉菜飯, 西班牙什錦飯

pa·gan¹ /ˋpegən; ˈpeɪgən/ *adj* pagan religious beliefs and customs do not belong to any of the main religions of the world, and may come from a time before these religions 異教的: *Christmas is held around the time of an old pagan festival.* 聖誕節是在一個舊的異教節日前後。

P

pagan² *n* [C] **1** someone who believes in a pagan religion 異教徒 **2** *humorous* someone who has few or no religious beliefs【幽默】無宗教信仰的人 —**paganism** *n* [U]

1 1 **page¹** /pedʒ; peɪdʒ/ *n* [C]

1 ▶PAPER 紙◀ one side of a sheet of paper in a book, newspaper etc, or the sheet of paper itself〔書、報紙等的〕頁;〔紙的〕一張: *There's a picture on the next page.* 下一頁有一幅圖畫。| *I've made several pages of notes.* 我已經做了好幾頁筆記。| *an eight-page booklet* 一本八頁的小冊子 | **front/back page** (=of a newspaper)〔報紙的〕頭版/末版 *The story was all over the front page.* 這篇報道佔據了整個頭版。| **see/turn to page 5/20 etc** *See page 5 for further details.* 詳情見第五頁。| **turn a page** *idly turning the pages* 懶洋洋地翻閱 | **the opposite/facing page** *the diagram on the facing page* 在對面那頁上的示意圖 | **over the page** (=on the next page) 在下頁 | **the sports pages/the fashion page etc** (=part of a newspaper)〔報紙的〕體育版/時尚版等 | **a blank page** (=a page that is empty) 空白頁

2 ▶COMPUTER 電腦◀ a) a piece of TEXT (=writing) or a picture on a computer screen that will fill one side of a piece of paper when it is printed 頁〔指電腦屏幕上可打滿一頁紙的文本或圖片〕**b)** all the text that can be seen at one time on a computer screen 頁面〔指電腦屏幕上一次所見的所有文本內容〕

3 ▶BOY 男孩◀ a PAGEBOY (1,2) 男侍童

4 ▶MIDDLE AGES 中世紀◀ a boy who served a KNIGHT during the Middle Ages as part of his training to become a knight himself〔中世紀為接受騎士訓練並服侍某個騎士的〕學習騎士

5 ▶STUDENT 學生◀ *AmE* a student who works as a helper to a member of the US Congress【美】〔美國國會成員的〕青年聽差

6 page in history an important event or period of time 歷史上的一頁〔指某重要事件或某段重要時期〕: *a significant page in our country's history* 我們國家歷史上重要的一頁

7 ▶SERVANT 侍從, 僕人◀ *old use* a boy who is a servant to a person of high rank【舊】高層人員的男侍從

page² *v* [T] **1** to call someone's name out in a public place, especially using a LOUDSPEAKER, in order to find them〔尤指用擴音器在公共場合〕呼喊找〔人〕: *I couldn't find Jenny at the airport, so I had her paged.* 我在機場找不到詹妮, 只好通過擴音器呼叫她。**2** to call someone by sending a message to their PAGER (=a small machine they carry that receives signals)〔透過傳呼機〕傳呼〔某人〕: *If you need me for anything, just page me.* 如果你需要我做甚麼, 就傳呼我。

page through sth *phr v* [T] *AmE* to look at a book, magazine etc【美】翻閱〔書本、雜誌等〕: *paging through old newspapers* 翻看舊報紙

pag·eant /ˋpædʒənt; ˈpædʒənt/ *n* **1** [C] a public show or ceremony, often performed outdoors, with people dressed in beautifully decorated clothes or actors acting historical scenes〔歷史性場面的〕(露天) 演出; 盛大慶典; 盛裝的遊行 **2** [singular] *literary* history or a continuous series of events that are interesting and impressive【文】歷史場景; 一系列有趣而難忘的事件: *the dramatic pageant of life in the upland valleys* 高地山谷中富有戲劇性的生活場景 **3** [C] *AmE* a public competition for young women in which their appearance, and sometimes other qualities, are compared and judged; BEAUTY CONTEST【美】選美 (競賽) **4** [U] behaviour or ceremonies which look impressive or grand, but have no real meaning〔無實際意義的〕炫耀; 虛飾

pag·eant·ry /ˋpædʒəntrɪ; ˈpædʒəntri/ *n* [U] impressive ceremonies or events, involving many people wearing special clothes〔許多人穿着特殊服裝的〕盛大慶典; 盛況: *the pageantry of a military ceremony* 軍事典禮的盛況

page·boy /ˋpedʒbɔɪ; ˈpeɪdʒbɔɪ/ *n* [C] **1** *BrE* a boy chosen to help a BRIDE as part of a wedding ceremony【英】〔婚禮中陪伴新娘的〕男侍童, 男小儐相 **2** *old-fashioned* a boy or young man employed in a hotel, club, theatre etc to deliver messages, carry bags etc【過時】〔酒店、俱樂部、劇院等雇用的〕侍童, 門童; 青年男侍 **3** a style of cutting women's hair in which the hair is cut fairly short and has its ends turned under 娃娃頭〔一種髮梢向內捲曲的女式短髮型〕

pag·er /ˋpedʒɚ; ˈpeɪdʒə/ *n* [C] a small machine that you carry in a pocket, that makes short high noises to tell the person who is wearing it that they must telephone someone 傳呼機〔可放入口袋, 會發出短促而高的聲響提醒你給某人回電話的一種小裝置〕

pa·gi·na·tion /ˌpædʒəˋneʃən; ˌpædʒɪ̇ˈneɪʃən/ *n* [U] *technical* the process of giving a number to each page of a book, magazine etc【術語】〔書、雜誌等的〕頁碼標註 —**paginate** /ˋpædʒəˌnet; ˈpædʒɪ̇neɪt/ *v* [T]

pa·go·da /pəˋgodə; pəˈgəʊdə/ *n* [C] a Buddhist TEMPLE that has several levels with a decorated roof at each level (佛) 塔

pah /pɑ; pɑː/ *interjection* used to show that you disapprove strongly of something 呸, 哼〔表示強烈的不贊同〕

paid /ped; peɪd/ the past tense and past participle of PAY —see also 另見 **put paid to** (PUT (19)) 2

paid-up /ˌ· ˈ·◂/ *adj* **1 paid-up member** someone who has paid the money necessary to be a member of a club, political party etc 已繳納會[黨]費的會[黨]員 **2 a fully paid-up** used when saying that someone who is definitely a particular kind of person or a member of a particular group 十足的, 絕對的; 忠實的〔用於表示某人確屬某種人或某個團體的成員〕: *a fully paid-up heavy metal fan* 十足的重金屬音樂迷

pail /pel; peɪl/ *n* [C] *especially AmE*【尤美】**1** a container with a handle for carrying liquids or used by children when playing on the beach〔用來運送液體或供孩子在海灘上玩耍的〕桶: *a milk pail* 牛奶桶 | *The kids brought shovels and pails to the beach.* 孩子們把鏟子和桶帶到沙灘上。**2** also 又作 **pail·ful** /-ˌful; -fʊl/ the amount a pail will hold 一桶的量: *It takes about ten pails of water to fill the trough.* 要裝滿這條槽需要十桶水。

pail·lasse /ˌpælˈjæs; ˈpæliæs/ *n* [C] another spelling of PALLIASSE palliasse 的另一種拼法

pain¹ /pen; peɪn/ *n*  2 2

1 ▶PHYSICAL 肉體的◀ [C,U] the feeling you have when part of your body hurts〔肉體上的〕疼, 痛, 疼痛: **be in pain** (=having a pain in part of your body) 疼痛 *Take these tablets if you're in pain.* 要是疼痛就服下這些藥片。| **feel pain** *We've given him an anaesthetic so he shouldn't feel any pain.* 我們已給他用了麻醉劑, 所以他不會感到任何疼痛。| **be in great pain** *Her face was contorted and she was clearly in great pain.* 她臉部都扭曲了, 顯然在經受着劇烈疼痛。| **severe pain** *She started getting severe back pains and had to stay off work.* 她背部開始劇烈疼痛, 只得停止工作。| **relieve pain** (=stop pain) 緩解疼痛; 止痛 *drugs to relieve the pain* 緩解疼痛的藥物, 止痛藥 | **ease the pain** (=reduce the pain) 減輕疼痛 | **a sharp pain** (=one that you feel very severely, usually for a short time) 劇烈的疼痛 | **a dull pain** (=one that is not very strong but which continues for a long time) 鈍痛 | **have a pain in your chest/leg/back etc** *I've got a terrible pain in my left side.* 我的左肋非常疼。| **labour pains** (=pain felt by women beginning to have a baby)〔分娩時的〕陣痛 —see also 另見 GROWING PAINS (1)

2 ►MENTAL 精神的◄ [C,U] emotional or mental suffering, or a particular experience of this suffering〔感情或精神上的〕痛苦; 痛苦經歷: *life with its pleasures and pains* 充滿歡樂和痛苦的人生 | **cause (sb) pain/inflict pain on sb** *She hated to say the words, for fear of causing pain.* 她不願説那些話, 怕引起悲痛之情。

3 a pain in the ass/butt *AmE*【美】also 又作 **pain in the arse/backside** *BrE*【英】*spoken* an impolite expression meaning someone or something extremely annoying【口】令人極其討厭的人[事物]〔不禮貌的説法〕: *What's wrong with Dave? He's becoming a total pain in the ass.* 戴夫怎麼了? 他變得十分令人討厭。

4 a pain also 又作 **a pain in the neck** *spoken* someone or something that you have to do that is very annoying【口】令人非常討厭的人[事物]: *My commute to work is a real pain.* 我每天乘車上下班真煩人。| *He's such a pain in the neck.* 他是個非常討厭的傢伙。

5 aches and pains many small pains in various parts of your body 各種各樣的疼痛, 周身不適: *everyday aches and pains increase* 每天全身疼痛加劇

6 take pains to do sth also 又作 **take pains with/over sth** to make a special effort to do something, or to be very careful in doing something 煞費苦心[盡心竭力]做某事; 小心謹慎地做某事: *Take pains to present a smart, efficient appearance.* 費盡心思表現出聰明能幹的樣子。

7 be at pains to do sth to be especially careful to do something, or try very hard to do something 小心翼翼地做某事; 費盡苦心[盡心竭力]做某事: *Major and Clinton were clearly at pains to avoid a row.* 很明顯, 梅傑和克林頓在盡力避免爭吵。

8 for your pains used when saying that you got something, especially an unfairly small payment, as a reward for your efforts 作為辛勞的報酬〔尤指少量報酬〕: *I drive them sixty miles, and I only get a fifty-cent tip for my pains!* 我開車載他們行駛了六十英里, 到頭來卻只得到五十美分的小費作為酬勞!

9 on/under pain of death at the risk of being killed as punishment 違則處死: *You are sworn to keep the secret, on pain of death.* 你要發誓保守祕密, 違則處死。

This graph shows some of the words most commonly used with the noun **pain**. 本圖表所示為含有名詞 pain 的一些最常用詞組。

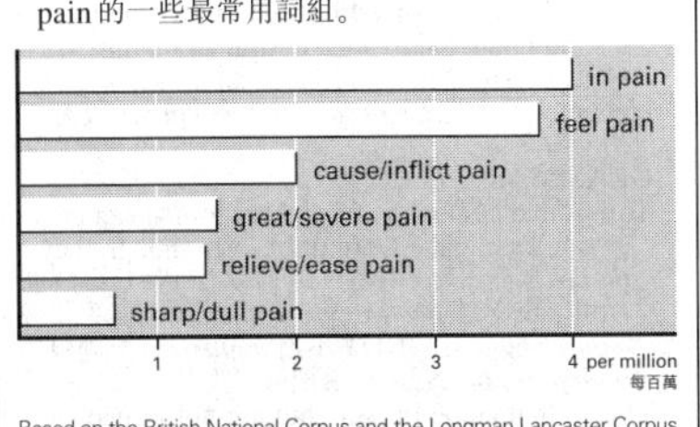

Based on the British National Corpus and the Longman Lancaster Corpus
據英國國家語料庫和朗文蘭卡斯特語料庫

pain² *v* [T] **1 it pains sb to do sth** *formal* it is very difficult and upsetting for someone to have to do something【正式】必須做某事使某人難受: *It pains me to leave you.* 離開你使我感到痛苦。**2** *old use* if a part of your body pains you, it hurts【舊】〔身體某一部分〕疼痛

pained /pend; peɪnd/ *adj* worried and upset 痛苦的, 難過的: *Every time she saw us smoking, my mother got a pained look on her face.* 媽媽每次看到我們在抽煙, 臉上就露出難過的樣子。

pain·ful /ˈpenfəl; ˈpeɪnfəl/ *adj* **1** making you feel very upset, or very difficult and unpleasant for you 令人痛苦[難受]的; 困難的, 令人不快的: **be painful for sb (to do sth)** *It's still painful for her to talk about the divorce.* 她談到離婚仍然覺得心裡不好受。| **painful memories/experience** *Hearing about the war again brings back painful memories for many people.* 再次聽到有關那場戰爭的事勾起許多人痛苦的回憶。| **painful decision/choice/task etc** *Wendy took the painful decision to switch off their son's life support system.* 溫迪痛苦地決定切斷他們兒子的生命維持系統。| **painful to watch/hear etc** *It was painful to hear those words.* 聽到那樣的話真令人痛心。**2** if part of your body is painful, you feel pain in it〔身體某個部位〕疼痛的: *My leg's still really painful.* 我的腿還很痛。**3** causing physical pain 引起疼痛的, 痛苦的: *painful cosmetic surgery* 痛苦的整容手術 | *Brynner's excrutiatingly painful death from cancer.* 布琳納極痛苦地死於癌症。**4** very bad and embarrassing for other people to watch, hear etc 難看的; 不好聽的;〔看着或聽着〕令人難堪的: *The poor script and bad acting make the film painful to watch.* 拙劣的劇本和糟糕的表演讓那部電影十分難看。| *the boy's painful shyness* 那個男孩讓人看着難受的羞怯 —**painfulness** *n* [U]

pain·ful·ly /ˈpenfəlɪ; ˈpeɪnfəli/ *adv* **1** with pain or causing pain 疼痛地; (令人) 痛苦地: *The prince walked slowly and painfully.* 王子緩慢而痛苦地走着。| *The ball hit him painfully on the shin.* 那個球打在他的脛部使他很痛。**2 painfully obvious/clear/evident** easy to see and disappointing or embarrassing 明顯地令人失望; 顯而易見地令人尷尬: *It was becoming painfully obvious that I would never be a singer.* 越來越清楚我永遠成不了一名歌手, 這真叫人痛心。**3** with a lot of effort and trouble 費力地, 困難地: *all the knowledge that he had so painfully acquired* 他盡心竭力地獲得的所有知識 | **painfully slow** *Progress in the negotiations has been painfully slow.* 談判的進程吃力而緩慢。**4** in a way that makes you sad or upset 令人傷心地, 令人痛苦地: *the painfully early death of someone who was very close to her* 她某個至親令人痛心的早逝

pain·kill·er /ˈpenˌkɪlɚ; ˈpeɪnˌkɪlə/ *n* [C] a medicine which reduces or removes pain 止痛藥, 祛痛藥

pain·less /ˈpenlɪs; ˈpeɪnləs/ *adj* **1** causing no pain 無痛的: *A visit to the dentist should be quite painless.* 看牙醫應該沒甚麼痛苦。**2** *informal* needing no effort or hard work【非正式】不費力的: *a painless way to learn a foreign language* 一種不費力的學習外語的方法 —**painlessly** *adv*

pains·tak·ing /ˈpenzˌtekɪŋ; ˈpeɪnzˌteɪkɪŋ/ *adj* very careful and thorough 小心的; 費盡心思的; 精心的: *fourteen months of painstaking investigation* 十四個月的艱苦調查 —**painstakingly** *adj*

paint¹ /pent; peɪnt/ *n* **1** [U] a liquid that you put on a surface to make it a particular colour 油漆; 塗料; 顏料: 2 3 *a can of blue paint* 一罐藍色油漆 | **a coat of paint** (=a layer of paint) 一層油漆[塗料] *The whole house could do with a fresh coat of paint.* 整個房子需要塗一層新的油漆。| **wet paint** (=used as a warning on a sign) 油漆未乾 **2 paints** [plural] a set of small tubes or dry blocks of coloured substance, used for painting pictures〔繪畫用的呈管狀或塊狀的〕(一套) 顏料: *oil paints* 油畫顏料 **3** [U] *old-fashioned* MAKE-UP【過時】化妝品

paint² *v* **1** [I,T] to put paint on a surface 給…上油漆; 2 給…塗顏料: *I wear old clothes when I'm painting.* 我油 3 漆東西時穿上舊衣服。| *The ceiling needs painting.* 天花板需要上油漆了。| **paint sth blue/red/green etc** *We painted the door blue.* 我們把那扇門漆成藍色。**2 a)** [T] to make a picture, design etc using paint〔用顏料〕畫; 給…上色: **paint a picture/portrait etc** *Turner is famous for painting landscapes.* 特納以畫風景畫而聞名。**b)** [I] to use paint to make pictures or designs〔用顏料〕繪畫: **paint in oils/watercolours etc** (=using a particular kind of paint) 畫油畫/水彩畫等 *Jana likes to paint in watercolours.* 買娜喜歡畫水彩畫。**c)** [T] to make a picture of someone or something using paint〔用顏料〕畫像, 描繪: *I'll paint the view from the window.* 我要畫窗外的風景。**3** [T] to put a coloured substance on part of your face or body to make it more attractive〔用化妝品〕塗, 搽, 擦: **paint your lips/fingernails etc** *Her lips and fingernails were painted bright red.* 她把嘴唇和指甲塗成了鮮紅色。**4 paint a picture of sth** to describe something in a particular way〔以某種方式〕描繪[描寫]某物: **paint a grim/rosy/gloomy picture of sth** *Dickens painted a grim picture of Victorian factory conditions.* 狄更斯描繪了一幅維多利亞時代工廠環境的陰暗畫面。**5 paint sth with a broad brush** to describe something without giving many details 對某事物作概括[大致]的描述 —see also 另見 BROADBRUSH **6 paint the town red** *informal* to go out to bars, clubs etc to enjoy yourself【非正式】〔到酒吧、夜總會等處〕痛飲[狂歡]作樂, 尋歡作樂 **7** [T] to put medicine on a part of your body with a brush〔用小刷子〕搽藥於 —see also 另見 **not be as black as you are painted** (BLACK[1] (7))

paint sth ↔ **in** *phr v* [T] to fill a space in a picture or add more to it using paint〔用顏料〕在畫上加繪, 補畫: *The additional figures were painted in at a later date.* 另外的一些人物是後來補畫上去的。

paint sth ↔ **out** *phr v* [T] to remove a design, figure etc from a picture or surface by covering it with more paint 用漆[顏料]塗掉, 覆蓋: *On the side of the van the company name had been painted out.* 貨車側面的公司名稱已用顏料塗掉了。

paint sth ↔ **over** *phr v* [T] to cover a picture or surface with new paint 用新的顏料[塗料]覆蓋…的畫面[表面]

paint·box /ˈpentˌbɑks; ˈpeɪntbɒks/ *n* [C] a small box containing dry blocks of paint that can be mixed with water 顏料盒

paint·brush /ˈpentˌbrʌʃ; ˈpeɪntbrʌʃ/ *n* [C] a brush for spreading paint on a surface 漆刷; 畫筆 —see picture at 參見 BRUSH[1] 圖

paint·er /ˈpentɚ; ˈpeɪntə/ *n* [C] **1** someone who paints pictures; ARTIST 畫家: *a landscape painter* 風景畫家 | *a portrait painter* 肖像畫家 **2** someone whose job is painting houses, rooms etc 油漆工 **3** a rope for tying a small boat to a ship or to a post on land 纜索; 繫船索

paint·er·ly /ˈpentəlɪ; ˈpeɪntəli/ *adj* typical of painters or painting 畫家的; 美術的; 繪畫藝術的: *painterly images* 美術形象

3 2 **paint·ing** /ˈpentɪŋ; ˈpeɪntɪŋ/ *n* **1** [C] a painted picture 圖畫; 水彩畫; 油畫: *A large painting hung in the hallway.* 一幅巨大的油畫掛在門廳裡。**2** [U] the act of making a picture using paint 繪畫: *I've always admired O'Keefe's style of painting.* 我一向敬慕〔美國著名女畫家〕歐姬芙的繪畫風格。**3** [U] the act of covering a wall, house etc with paint〔給牆壁、房屋等〕(上)油漆: *painting and decorating* 油漆和裝修

paint strip·per /ˈ· ˌ··/ *n* [U] a substance used to remove paint from walls, doors etc〔用以清除牆壁、門等上塗料的〕脫漆劑

paint·work /ˈpentˌwɝk; ˈpeɪntwɜːk/ *n* [U] paint on a car, house etc〔汽車、房子等上的〕油漆: *the drab office with its faded paintwork and nicotine-stained ceiling* 油漆褪色、天花板染有尼古丁污跡的色調灰暗的辦公室

2 2 **pair[1]** /pɛr; peə/ *n plural* **pairs** or **pair** [C]

1 ▶TROUSERS ETC 褲子等◀ a single thing made of two similar parts that are joined together〔由連在一起的相同兩部分構成的〕一副, 一把, 一條: **a pair of jeans/trousers/scissors/glasses etc** *Go put on a clean pair of jeans.* 去穿上一條乾淨的牛仔褲。| *a new pair of sunglasses* 一副新的太陽鏡

2 ▶SHOES ETC 鞋子等◀ two things of the same kind that are used together〔由兩個一起使用的同類東西組成的〕一雙, 一對: **a pair of shoes/socks/gloves etc** *three pairs of socks* 三雙襪子 | *a pair of candlesticks* 一對燭台 | **a matching pair** (=two things that are exactly alike) 匹配的一雙[對]

3 in pairs in groups of two 兩個一組地, 成對地, 成雙地: *OK class, get in pairs for the next activity.* 好, 同學們, 分成兩人一組進行下一個活動。| *earrings sold in pairs* 成對出售的耳環

4 ▶TWO PEOPLE 兩個人◀ [singular] two people who are standing or doing something together, or are connected with each other in some way〔站在一起或合做某事或相互關聯的〕兩個, 一對〔人〕: **[+of]** *a pair of dancers* 一對舞伴 | *a pair of scruffy kids* 兩個邋遢的孩子

5 the pair of you/them *BrE spoken* used when you are angry or annoyed【英口】你們/他們兩個〔用於生氣或厭煩時〕: *Oh get out, the pair of you.* 滾出去, 你們兩個。| *They're crooks, the pair of them.* 他們是一對騙子。

6 ▶TWO ANIMALS 兩個動物◀ [singular] **a)** two animals, one male and one female, that come together to have sex 雌雄成對的動物: **[+of]** *a pair of doves* 一對鴿子 | *the mating pair* 交配的一對 **b)** *old use* two horses that work together【舊】〔一起幹活的〕兩匹馬, 雙套馬: *a carriage and pair* 雙駕馬車

7 I've only got one pair of hands *spoken* used to say that you are busy and cannot do any more than you are doing【口】我只有一雙手〔意指幹不了更多的工作〕

8 ▶CARDS 紙牌◀ two PLAYING CARDS which have the same value 兩張同點的牌, 〔牌的〕一對: **[+of]** *a pair of jacks*〔牌中的〕一對傑克

9 the happy pair two people who have just become married 新婚夫婦

USAGE NOTE 用法說明: PAIR

WORD CHOICE 詞語辨析: **pair, couple**

A **pair** is a set of two things which are joined or normally used together, or two people who work or do something together. pair 指兩件連在一起或通常一起使用的物品, 或指兩個一起工作或合做某事的人: *a pair of jeans/slippers* 一條牛仔褲/一雙拖鞋 | *Drug dealers often work in pairs.* 毒品販子常常兩個一組地工作。

A **couple** is two or a few things of the same kind. couple 指同類的兩個或幾個物品: *I've found two/a couple of socks but they aren't a pair.* 我找到了兩隻襪子, 但它們不是一對。| *Can you lend me a couple of dollars (=a few dollars)?* 你能借給我幾塊錢嗎?

Note that two married people or two people in a lasting relationship are a **couple** not a **pair**. 注意, 結了婚的兩個人或持續保持關係的兩個人是 a couple, 而不是 a pair: *a childless couple* 沒有孩子的一對夫婦

GRAMMAR 語法

Things that come in pairs and are joined can only be counted using the word **pair**, even though they are plural. 成對出現並連在一起的物品即使是複數也只能用 pair 來表示: *two pairs of jeans* 兩條牛仔褲 | *a pair of glasses* (NOT 不用 *a glasses*) 一副眼鏡 | *both pairs of scissors* 兩把剪刀

Things that come in pairs but are not joined can be counted either in pairs or separately. 成對出現但不連在一起的物品可以成對地數, 也可以單個地數: *one shoe* 一隻鞋 | *two/both shoes* 兩隻鞋 | *a pair of shoes* 一雙鞋

pair[2] also 又作 **pair up** *v* [I,T usually passive 一般用被動態] to form groups of two or be put into groups of two (使) 結成一對; (使) 配成一對: **be paired with sb** *We were each paired with a newcomer to help with training.*

我們被安排每人和一名新手組成一對，以幫助他們訓練。

pair off *phr v* [I,T] to come together or bring two people together to have a romantic relationship（使）結成一對，（使）結合，（使）結婚：*All the others were pairing off and I was left on my own.* 其他人都在出雙入對，就剩我獨身一人。| **pair sb off with sb** *They want to pair their daughters off with rich men.* 他們想讓自己的女兒都嫁給有錢的男人。

pair up *phr v* [I] **1** to become friends and start to have a relationship 成對，成搭檔 **2** to agree to start to work together with someone 同意〔與某人〕一起開始工作，同意〔與某人〕結成搭檔

pais·ley /ˋpezlɪ; ˈpeɪzli/ *adj* made from cloth that is covered with a pattern of shapes that look like curved drops of rain 佩茲利渦旋紋花呢的：*a paisley shawl* 佩茲利紋呢披肩 —see picture on page A16 參見 A16 頁圖

pa·ja·mas /pəˋdʒæməz; pəˈdʒɑːməz/ *n* [plural] the usual American spelling of PYJAMAS pyjamas 的一般美式拼法 —**pajama** *adj*

Pa·ki /ˋpækɪ; ˈpæki/ *n* [C] *BrE taboo* a very offensive word for a person from Pakistan, or a person born in Britain whose parents were from Pakistan【英諱】〔嚴重冒犯用語〕巴基斯坦佬，老巴；生在英國但父母來自巴基斯坦的人

Pak·i·sta·ni /ˌpækɪˋstænɪ; ˌpækɪˈstɑːni◂/ **1** *n* [C] someone from Pakistan 巴基斯坦人 **2** *adj* from or connected with Pakistan 巴基斯坦的；來自巴基斯坦的

pal[1] /pæl; pæl/ *n* [C] **1** *informal* a close friend【非正式】密友，好友：*an old pal of mine* 我的一位老朋友 | *We just weren't pals any more.* 我們只是不再是好朋友了。**2** *spoken* used to address a man in an unfriendly way【口】老兄，小子〔對男性不友好的稱呼〕：*Listen, pal, I don't want you hanging around my sister any more.* 聽着，小子，我不許你再糾纏我妹妹。

pal[2] *v*

pal around *phr v* [I+with] *AmE* to go to places and do things with someone as a friend【美】〔與某人〕結伴〔去某地或做某事〕：*It was nice having someone to pal around with.* 有人作伴真好。

pal up *phr v* [I+with] *BrE* to become someone's friend【英】〔與某人〕結成朋友：*They palled up while travelling round Europe.* 他們在歐洲旅行時結成朋友。

3 **pal·ace** /ˋpælɪs; ˈpæləs/ *n* [C] **1** often 常作 **Palace** a large grand house where a ruling king or queen, or a British BISHOP or ARCHBISHOP, officially lives 皇宮，宮殿；〔主教或大主教的〕宅邸：*Buckingham Palace* 白金漢宮 **2** a large, grand, beautifully decorated house 富麗堂皇的大房子，豪宅：*The nobles of Florence built splendid palaces.* 佛羅倫斯的貴族建造了許多富麗堂皇的住宅。

palace rev·o·lu·tion /ˌ·· ··ˈ··/ *n* [C] a situation in which a ruler or an important person in a large organization, has their power taken away by the less important people who work with them 宮廷政變

pal·a·din /ˋpælədɪn; ˈpælədɪn/ *n* [C] **1** *literary* a respected person who strongly supports a particular action or opinion; CHAMPION[1] (2)【文】〔強烈支持某項行動或某種看法的〕衞士；捍衞者，擁護者 **2** a KNIGHT (=a soldier of high rank) in the Middle Ages who fought loyally for his prince〔中世紀親王的〕武士，騎士

palaeo- /pelɪə; pæliəʊ/ *prefix* another spelling of PALEO- paleo- 的另一種拼法

pal·ae·o·lith·ic /ˌpelɪəˋlɪθɪk; ˌpæliəʊˈlɪθɪk◂/ *adj* the British spelling of PALEOLITHIC paleolithic 的英式拼法

pal·ae·on·tol·o·gy /ˌpelɪɑnˋtɑlədʒɪ; ˌpæliɒnˈtɒlədʒi/ *n* [U] the British spelling of PALEONTOLOGY paleontology 的英式拼法

pal·ais /ˋpæle; ˈpæleɪ/ also 又作 **palais de danse** /ˌpæle də ˋdɑns; ˌpæleɪ də ˈdɑːns/ *n* [C] *BrE* a large public building used for dancing in the past【英】〔舊時的〕大舞廳

pal·an·quin, palankeen /ˌpælənˋkin; ˌpælənˈkiːn/ *n* [C] a box-shaped container with a seat or bed inside it for one person, carried on poles by other people 轎子

pal·a·ta·ble /ˋpælətəbl̩; ˈpælətəbəl/ *adj* **1** having a pleasant or acceptable taste 美味的，可口的：*a palatable wine* 美味的葡萄酒 **2** something such as an idea, suggestion etc that is palatable is acceptable or pleasant〔主意、建議等〕合意的，受歡迎的：**[+to]** *We need to find a compromise that's more palatable to the voters.* 我們需要尋求一種更合選民心意的折衷方案。—opposite 反義詞 UNPALATABLE —**palatably** *adv*

pal·a·tal /ˋpælətl; ˈpælətl/ *n* [C] *technical* a CONSONANT[1] (1) sound made by putting your tongue against or near your HARD PALATE【術語】〔輔音中的〕腭音 —**palatal** *adj*

pal·ate /ˋpælɪt; ˈpælɪ̥t/ *n* **1** [C] the ROOF (=top inside part) of the mouth 腭〔口腔的頂蓋〕—see also 另見 CLEFT PALATE, HARD PALATE, SOFT PALATE **2** [C,U] the sense of taste 味覺：*a crisp salad to refresh the palate* 鮮嫩爽口的沙律[色拉] | *too spicy for my palate* 就我的口味來說太辣

pa·la·tial /pəˋleʃəl; pəˈleɪʃəl/ *adj* very large and beautifully decorated, like a palace 豪華的，富麗堂皇的，宮殿似的：*a palatial home* 富麗堂皇的住宅 —**palatially** *adv*

pa·lat·i·nate /pəˋlætn̩ɪt; pəˈlætɪ̥nɪ̥t/ *n* [C] an area which in past times was ruled over by a man of high rank who was the representative of a higher ruler 巴拉丁領地〔舊時指享有特權的貴族或伯爵的領地〕

pa·la·ver /pəˋlævɚ; pəˈlɑːvə/ *n* **1** [U, singular] *informal* unnecessary trouble and anxiety over small matters; BOTHER[2] (1); FUSS[1] (1)【非正式】〔不必要的〕麻煩，不便，〔瑣事引起的〕煩惱：*all the palaver of booking a flight and getting a passport* 訂機票和領取護照的麻煩（手續）| *What a palaver!* 真麻煩！**2** [U] *informal* a lot of silly and meaningless talk【非正式】廢話，空談：*What's all the palaver about?* 這些廢話都在說些甚麼？**3** [C] *old use* a long talk about something important【舊】〔重要事件的長時間〕談判，交涉，商談

pale[1] /pel; peɪl/ *adj* **1** having a much whiter skin colour than usual, especially because you are ill, worried etc〔尤指由於生病、憂慮等而造成膚色〕蒼白的：*She suddenly noticed how pale and drawn he looked.* 她突然注意到他看起來那麼蒼白又憔悴。| *a pale complexion* 蒼白的臉色 —see picture on page A6 參見 A6 頁圖 **2** a pale colour is much lighter than the standard colour〔顏色〕淺的，淡的：**pale blue/pink/green etc** *pale blue curtains* 淡藍色的窗簾 —compare 比較 DEEP[1] (7), LIGHT[2] (1) **3** pale light is not bright〔光線〕微弱的，暗淡的：*the pale light of early morning* 晨曦的微光 —**palely** *adv* —**paleness** *n* [U] 3

pale[2] *v* [I] **1** if your face pales, it becomes much whiter than usual because you have had a shock〔臉色〕變蒼白：*Kent's face paled when he saw Rob had a knife.* 肯特看到羅布有把刀子，頓時面無血色。**2 pale into insignificance** to seem much less important when compared to something else, especially something much worse that has happened〔尤指與更糟的事情相比〕顯得微不足道[無足輕重]：*All her anger, her jealousy, paled into insignificance beside this momentous news.* 與這一重大新聞比起來，她所有的憤怒、嫉妒都顯得微不足道了。**3 pale in/by comparison** to seem small or unimportant compared to something else 與…相比顯得微不足道，相形見絀：*This year's profits pale in comparison to last year's.* 今年的利潤與去年的相比顯得大為遜色。

pale[3] *n* **1 beyond the pale** behaviour that is beyond the pale is offensive or unacceptable〔行為〕不可容忍的，越軌的 **2** [C] a PALING〔做柵欄用的〕尖板條，樁

pale ale /ˌ· ˈ·/ *n* [C,U] a type of beer that does not contain much ALCOHOL and is sold in bottles〔酒精含量低的〕淡啤酒

pale·face /ˋpelˌfes; ˈpeɪlfeɪs/ *n* [C] an insulting word for a white person used by Native Americans in films 白人〔電影中美洲土著印第安人對白人的侮辱性用語〕

paleo-, palaeo- /pelɪo; pæliəʊ/ *prefix technical* extremely ancient, before historical times【術語】非常古老的，史前的：*paleobotany* 古植物學

pal·e·o·lith·ic, palaeolithic, often 常作 **Paleolithic** /ˌpelɪo`lɪθɪk; ˌpæliəʊˈlɪθɪk◂/ *adj* connected with the earliest period of the STONE AGE (=the period thousands of years ago when people made stone tools and weapons) 舊石器時代的: *a paleolithic axe* 舊石器時代的石斧 —compare 比較 NEOLITHIC

pal·e·on·tol·o·gy, palaeontology /ˌpelɪɑn`tɑlədʒɪ; ˌpæliɒnˈtɒlədʒi/ *n* [U] the study of FOSSIL*s* (=ancient animals and plants that have been preserved in rock) 古生物學, 化石學 —**paleontologist** *n* [C]

pal·ette /`pælɪt; ˈpælɪ̈t/ *n* [C] **1** a board with a curved edge and a hole for your thumb, on which a painter mixes colours〔畫家用的〕調色板 **2** [usually singular 一般用單數] *technical* the particular colours used by a painter or for a picture【術語】〔畫家或一幅畫所用的〕一組顏色; 一套顏料

palette knife /`·· ·/ *n* [C] a thin knife that bends easily and has a rounded end, used in cooking and by painters〔烹調用的〕圓頭刀;〔畫家用的〕調色刀

pal·frey /`pɔlfrɪ; ˈpɔːlfri/ *n* [C] *old use* a horse trained to be ridden, especially by a woman【舊】〔尤指供婦女騎的〕馴馬

pa·li·mo·ny /`pælɪmonɪ; ˈpælɪ̈məni/ *n* [U] *AmE* money that someone is ordered to pay regularly to a former partner, when they have lived together without being married【美】〔非婚同居者分居後一方被判令付給另一方的〕同居生活費

pal·imp·sest /`pælɪmpˌsɛst; ˈpælɪ̈mpsest/ *n* [C] an ancient written document which had its original writing rubbed out, not always completely, so that it could be used again〔古時可擦去原有文字供再次使用的〕羊皮紙

pal·in·drome /`pælɪnˌdrom; ˈpælɪ̈ndrəʊm/ *n* [C] a word or phrase such as 'deed' or 'level', which is the same when you read it backwards 迴文〔指順讀和倒讀都一樣的詞或短語, 如 deed 或 level〕

pal·ing /`pelɪŋ; ˈpeɪlɪŋ/ *n* **1** [C usually plural 一般用複數] a pointed piece of wood used with other pointed pieces in making a fence〔做柵欄用的〕尖板條, 樁 **2 palings** [plural] a fence made out of palings 柵欄, 圍籬

pal·i·sade /ˌpælə`sed; ˌpælɪ̈ˈseɪd/ *n* [C] **1** a fence made of strong pointed poles, used for defence in past times〔古時用於防禦的堅固的〕尖木柵; 柵欄 **2** [plural] also 又作 **palisades** *especially AmE* a line of high straight cliffs, especially along a river or beside the sea【尤美】〔尤指河邊或海邊的〕一排陡崖

pal·ish /`pelɪʃ; ˈpeɪlɪʃ/ *adj* slightly pale 略帶蒼白的

pall¹ /pɔl; pɔːl/ *v* [T+on/upon] if something palls on you, it becomes uninteresting or unpleasant, because you have done, used, heard, or seen it too often or for too long〔因過多、過久而〕失去吸引力, 令人發膩: *Gradually the novelty of city life began to pall.* 漸漸地, 城市生活的新奇之處開始失去它的吸引力。

pall² *n* **1 a pall of smoke/dust etc** something heavy or dark, which covers something else, like a cloud 一層煙/灰塵等: *A pall of grey smoke hung over the buildings.* 那些建築物的上空籠罩着一層灰色的煙幕。**2 cast a pall on/over** to spoil an event or occasion that should have been happy and enjoyable 給〔原本應該高興和愉快的事情〕蒙上一層陰影: *The drugs scandal cast a pall over the athletics championships.* 違禁藥醜聞給那次田徑錦標賽蒙上了一層陰影。**3** [C] a large piece of cloth spread over a COFFIN (=box in which a dead body is carried) 棺罩; 柩衣 **4** [C] a COFFIN with a body inside〔內有屍體的〕棺材

pall·bear·er /`pɔlˌbɛrɚ; ˈpɔːlˌbeərə/ *n* [C] someone who walks beside a COFFIN (=a box with a dead body inside) or helps to carry it at a funeral〔葬禮中的〕護柩者, 扶靈人, 抬棺者

pal·let /`pælɪt; ˈpælɪ̈t/ *n* [C] **1** a large metal plate or flat wooden frame on which heavy goods can be lifted, stored, or moved〔供提起、儲存或移動重物用的金屬或木製〕托盤, 托板, 貨板, 集裝架 **2** *old-fashioned* a temporary bed, or a cloth bag filled with STRAW (1a) for sleeping on【過時】臨時牀鋪; 草墊

pal·li·asse, paillasse /ˌpæl`jæs; ˈpæliæs/ *n* [C] *old use* a cloth bag filled with STRAW (1a) for sleeping on【舊】草褥, 草墊

pal·li·ate /`pælɪˌet; ˈpælieɪt/ *v* [T] *formal*【正式】**1** to reduce the unpleasant effects of illness, pain etc without curing them 減輕, 緩和〔病痛等〕**2** to make a bad situation seem better than it really is by giving excuses 掩飾; 為…找藉口 —**palliation** /ˌpælɪ`eʃən; ˌpæliˈeɪʃən/ *n* [U]

pal·li·a·tive /`pælɪˌetɪv; ˈpæliətɪv/ *n* [C] *formal*【正式】**1** an action taken to make a bad situation seem better, but which does not solve the problem 緩和(之舉): *Promises of reform are mere palliatives.* 改革的承諾只不過是緩兵之計。**2** a medical treatment that will not cure a problem but will reduce the pain 治標之藥, 舒緩劑 —**palliative** *adj*: *palliative surgery* 治標手術

pal·lid /`pælɪd; ˈpælɪ̈d/ *adj* **1** unusually or unhealthily pale 蒼白的, 無血色的: *Paul was still pallid and sick.* 保羅仍然臉色蒼白, 一副病容。**2** boring, without any excitement 乏味的, 無趣的; 無生氣的 —**pallidly** *adv* —**pallidness** *n* [U]

pal·lor /`pælɚ; ˈpælə/ *n* [singular] unhealthy paleness of the skin or face〔膚色或臉色〕蒼白: *Her skin had a deathly pallor.* 她的膚色如死一般地蒼白。

pal·ly /`pælɪ; ˈpæli/ *adj* [not before noun 不用於名詞前] *informal* very friendly with someone【非正式】與…非常友好的, 親密的: *She's getting very pally with the boss these days.* 這些日子她與老闆相處得很好。| **be pally with sb** *I didn't know you were pally with her.* 我不知道你和她要好。

palm¹ /pɑm; pɑːm/ *n* [C] **1** the inside surface of your hand between the base of your fingers and your wrist 手掌, 掌部: *He held the pebble in the palm of his hand.* 他把那顆卵石握在手中。**2** a palm tree 棕櫚樹 **3 hold/have sb in the palm of your hand** to have a strong influence on someone, so that they do what you want them to do 把某人攥在手心裡, 完全掌握[控制]某人: *She's got the whole committee in the palm of her hand.* 她已完全控制了整個委員會。**4 read sb's palm** to tell someone what is going to happen to them by looking at their hand 看某人的手相 —see also 另見 **itchy palm** (ITCHY (6)), **cross sb's palm (with silver)** (CROSS¹ (17)), **grease sb's palm** (GREASE² (2))

palm² *v* [T] to hide something in the palm of your hand, especially when performing a magic trick or stealing something〔尤指變戲法或偷東西時〕把…藏在手心裡[藏於手中]

palm off *phr v* [T **palm** sth/sb ↔ **off**] to persuade someone to accept or buy something, especially by deceiving them 哄騙某人接受…, 把…騙賣給: **palm sth off on/onto sb** *The fruit seller palmed some damaged apples off onto an old lady.* 那個水果販子把一些壞蘋果騙賣給了那位老太太。| **palm sth off as** *He tried to palm it off as a real Renoir.* 他企圖把那幅畫冒充雷諾瓦的真跡騙賣出去。| **palm sb off with sth** *They palmed her off with an obsolete computer.* 他們騙她買下了一台已過時的電腦。

pal·met·to /pæl`mɛto; pælˈmetəʊ/ *n* [C] a small PALM TREE that grows in the south-eastern US〔生長於美國東南部的〕扇形葉矮棕櫚, 蒲葵

palm·ist /`pɑmɪst; ˈpɑːmɪ̈st/ *n* [C] *BrE* someone who claims they can tell what a person is like or what will happen to them, by looking at the palm of their hand【英】看手[掌]相者 —compare 比較 FORTUNE-TELLER

palm·ist·ry /`pɑmɪstrɪ; ˈpɑːmɪ̈stri/ *n* [U] the art of looking at the palm of a person's hand to tell what they are like or what will happen to them 手[掌]相術

palm oil /`· ·/ *n* [U] the oil obtained from the nut of an African PALM TREE〔非洲油棕櫚的〕棕櫚油

palm read·ing /`· ˌ··/ *n* [U] palmistry 手[掌]相術 —**palm reader** *n* [C]

Palm Sun·day /ˌ· `··/ *n* the Sunday before Easter in the

Christian Church〔基督教的〕棕櫚主日〔指復活節前的星期日〕

palm·top /ˈpɑmtɑp; ˈpɑːmtɒp/ *n* [C] a very small computer that you can hold in your hand 掌上型電腦

palm tree /ˈ· ·/ *n* [C] a tropical tree which typically grows near beaches or in deserts, with a long straight trunk and large pointed leaves at the top 棕櫚樹

palm·y /ˈpɑmɪ; ˈpɑːmi/ *adj* used to describe a period of time when people have money and life is good 繁榮的, 興旺的: *in the palmy days of Elizabeth I* 在伊莉莎白一世時的興盛時期

pal·o·mi·no /ˌpæləˋmino; ˌpæləˈmiːnəʊ◂/ *n* [C] a horse of a golden or cream colour, with a white MANE and tail 帕洛米諾馬〔毛呈金黃或淡黃色, 有白色鬃毛和尾毛〕

pal·pa·ble /ˋpælpəbḷ; ˈpælpəbəl/ *adj formal*【正式】**1** easily and clearly noticed; OBVIOUS (1) 明顯的, 顯而易見的: *a palpable lie* 明顯的謊言 **2** able to be touched or physically felt; TANGIBLE (2) 可觸知的, 摸得到的: *an almost palpable atmosphere of mistrust* 幾乎一下就能察覺出的不信任氣氛 —opposite 反義詞 IMPALPABLE —**palpably** *adv*: *What he said was palpably false.* 他的話顯然是假的。

pal·pate /ˋpælpet; pælˈpeɪt/ *v* [T] *technical* to give someone a medical examination by touching their body【術語】〔檢查身體時〕摸, 觸: *The doctor palpated his abdomen.* 醫生摸查他的腹部。—**palpation** /pælˋpeʃən; pælˈpeɪʃən/ *n* [C,U]

pal·pi·tate /ˋpælpəˌtet; ˈpælpɪ̈teɪt/ *v* [I] **1** if your heart palpitates, it beats quickly and irregularly〔心臟〕急速而不規則地跳動, 悸動 **2** to tremble 顫抖, 發抖: **[+with]** *He was positively palpitating with excitement.* 他興奮得全身發顫。

pal·pi·ta·tions /ˌpælpəˋteʃənz; ˌpælpɪ̈ˈteɪʃənz/ *n* [plural] irregular or extremely fast beating of your heart, caused by illness or too much effort〔因疾病或勞累引起的〕心悸, 心跳不規則[過速]

pal·sied /ˋpɔlzɪd; ˈpɔːlzid/ *adj not technical* suffering from an illness that makes your arms and legs shake because you cannot control your muscles【非術語】〔因患病而〕四肢顫抖的; 麻痹的, 癱瘓的

pal·sy /ˋpɔlzɪ; ˈpɔːlzi/ *n* [U] **1** *old use* PARALYSIS (1)【舊】麻痹, 癱瘓 **2** an illness that makes your arms and legs shake because you cannot control your muscles 麻痹性震顫(症) —see also 另見 CEREBRAL PALSY

pal·sy-wal·sy /ˋpɔlzɪ ˋwɔlzɪ; ˌpælzi ˈwælzi/ *adj BrE spoken* very friendly, especially in a way that seems insincere【英口】親密的, 友好的〔尤指顯得不真誠〕; 僞善的

pal·try /ˋpɔltrɪ; ˈpɔːltri/ *adj* **1** a paltry amount of something such as money is too small to be useful or important〔錢等〕太少的, 微不足道的: *The management offered us a paltry 3% pay increase.* 資方提出給我們的加薪幅度是微不足道的3%。**2** worthless and silly 無價值的; 愚蠢的: *paltry excuses* 拙劣的藉口 | *her paltry little observations on Russia* 她對俄羅斯的毫無價值的評論

pam·pas /ˋpæmpəz; ˈpæmpəz/ *n* **the pampas** the large wide flat areas of land covered with grass in some parts of South America 潘帕斯草原, 南美大草原

pampas grass /ˈ·· ·/ *n* [U] a kind of tall grass with silver-white feathery flowers 蒲葦

pam·per /ˋpæmpɚ; ˈpæmpə/ *v* [T] to look after someone too kindly or very kindly 寵, 嬌慣, 過分呵護: *a pampered cat* 被嬌養的貓 | *Pamper yourself with a long, luxurious bath.* 好好地泡一個舒適的浴善待一下自己。

pam·phlet /ˋpæmflɪt; ˈpæmflɪ̈t/ *n* [C] a very thin book with paper covers, giving information about something 小冊子

pam·phle·teer /ˌpæmflɪˋtɪr; ˌpæmflɪ̈ˈtɪə/ *n* [C] someone who writes pamphlets giving political opinions〔涉及政治見解的〕小冊子作者

pan-, Pan- /pæn; pæn/ *prefix* including all 全, 總, 泛: *pan-African unity* 泛非團結 | *Pan-Arabism* (=political union of all Arabs) 泛阿拉伯主義

pans 鍋

frying pan〔長柄的〕平底煎鍋　cake tin *BrE*【英】/ cake pan *AmE*【美】蛋糕烤盤　saucepan〔長柄有蓋的〕深平底鍋

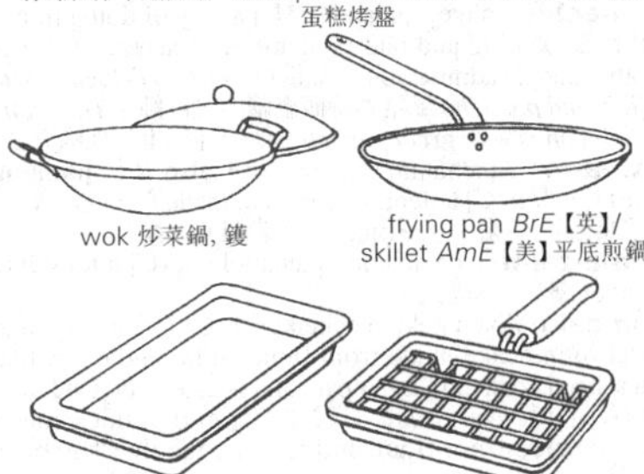
wok 炒菜鍋, 鑊　frying pan *BrE*【英】/ skillet *AmE*【美】平底煎鍋

roasting tin *BrE*【英】/ roasting pan *AmE*【美】烤盤　grill pan *BrE*【英】/ broiler pan *AmE*【美】焙盤

pan¹ /pæn; pæn/ *n* [C]
1 ▶FOR COOKING 用於烹飪◀ a round metal container used for cooking usually, with one long handle and a lid; SAUCEPAN〔長柄有蓋的〕鍋, 平底鍋: *Cook the pasta in a large pan of boiling salted water.* 在大鍋鹽開水裡煮意大利麵。
2 ▶FOR BAKING CAKES ETC 用於烘烤糕餅等◀ *AmE* a metal container for baking things in【美】蛋糕烤盤; TIN *BrE*【英】: *a 9" cake pan* 9英寸的蛋糕烤盤
3 ▶FOR WEIGHING 用於量重◀ one of the two dishes on a pair of SCALES (=a small weighing machine)〔天平的〕秤盤
4 ▶TOILET 廁所◀ *especially BrE* the bowl of a toilet【尤英】抽水馬桶, 便池
5 ▶DRUM 鼓◀ a metal drum that is played in a STEEL BAND〔鋼鼓樂隊中的〕鋼鼓
6 ▶FOR FINDING GOLD 用於淘金◀ *AmE* a container used to separate gold from other substances, by washing them in water【美】淘(金)盤
7 go down the pan *BrE slang* to be wasted or become useless or ruined【英俚】被破壞[糟蹋], 變得無用 —see also 另見 FRYING PAN, SKIDPAN, WARMING PAN, **a flash in the pan** (FLASH² (8))

pan² *v* **panned, panning**
1 ▶CRITICIZE 批評◀ [T] *informal* to strongly criticize a film, play etc in a newspaper or on television or radio【非正式】〔在報紙、電視或廣播上〕嚴厲批評〔電影、戲劇等〕: *a production that was panned by the critics* 受到評論家嚴厲批評的一部作品
2 ▶CAMERA 攝影[像]機◀ **a)** [I always+adv/prep] if a film or television camera pans in a particular direction, it moves and follows the thing that is being filmed〔製作電影或電視時攝影機隨着被拍攝對象移動而〕搖動拍攝, 移動拍攝: *The camera panned slowly across the crowd.* 攝影機鏡頭慢慢移動搖向那羣人。**b)** [I,T] to move a camera in this way 使〔攝影機〕搖攝, 移動拍攝
3 ▶GOLD 金子◀ **a)** [I,T] to wash soil in a pan to separate gold from it 用淘金盤淘洗〔含金砂礫〕: **[+for]** *panning for gold* 淘金 **b)** also 又作 **pan out, pan off** to get or separate gold in this way〔用淘金盤淘洗的方法〕淘出金子

pan out *phr v* [I] to happen or develop in a particular way〔以某種方式〕發生, 進展: *I wonder how it will all* pan out. 我想知道其結果會怎麼樣。

pan·a·cea /ˌpænəˋsɪə; ˌpænəˈsɪə/ *n* [C] **1** something that people think will make everything better and solve all their problems〔解決所有問題的〕萬全之策, 解決一切弊病的方法: *Battery-powered cars are not a panacea for the pollution problem.* 以電池為動力的汽車不是解決污染問題的萬全之策。**2** a medicine or form of treatment that is supposed to cure any illness 包治百病的藥, 萬靈藥

pa·nache /pəˋnæʃ; pəˈnæʃ/ *n* [U] a way of doing things that is exciting and makes them seem easy, and makes other people admire you 神氣活現, 瀟灑: *a designer with flair and panache* 風格獨特而瀟灑的設計師 | *They sang their songs with great panache.* 他們神氣十足地唱着歌。

P

pan·a·ma /ˌpænəˋmɑ; ˌpænəˈmɑː◂/ also 又作 **panama hat** /ˌ··· ˈ·/ *n* [C] a light hat for men, made from STRAW 巴拿馬(式)草帽 —see picture at 參見 HAT 圖

pan·a·tel·la /ˌpænəˋtɛlə; ˌpænəˈtelə/ *n* [C] a long thin CIGAR 細長雪茄煙

pan·cake /ˋpænˌkek; ˈpænkeɪk/ *n* **1** [C] *BrE* a very thin, flat round cake made from flour, milk, and eggs, that has been cooked in a flat pan, and is eaten hot【英】薄烤[煎, 烙]餅; CREPE *AmE*【美】**2** [C] *AmE* a thick round cake made from flour, milk, and eggs that has been cooked in a flat pan and is eaten for breakfast, often with MAPLE SYRUP; FLAPJACK (2); HOT CAKE【美】〔當早點吃的〕厚煎餅〔通常和楓糖漿一起食用〕**3** [U] very thick MAKE-UP for the face〔化妝用的〕粉餅

Pancake Day /ˈ·· ·/ *n* [C,U] *BrE informal* SHROVE TUESDAY, when people in Britain traditionally eat pancakes【英, 非正式】〔按傳統吃薄煎餅的〕薄煎餅日〔即懺悔星期二〕

pancake land·ing /ˌ·· ˈ··/ *n* [C] an act of bringing an aircraft down to the ground in such a way that it drops flat from a low height〔飛機的〕平墜着陸, 平降

pancake roll /ˌ·· ˈ·/ *n* [C] *BrE* a SPRING ROLL【英】春卷

Pancake Tues·day /ˌ·· ˈ··/ *n* [C,U] Pancake Day 薄煎餅日〔即懺悔星期二〕

pan·cre·as /ˋpæŋkrɪəs; ˈpæŋkriəs/ *n* [C] a GLAND inside your body, near your stomach, that produces INSULIN and a liquid that helps your body to use the food that you eat 胰, 胰腺 —**pancreatic** /ˌpæŋkrɪˋætɪk; ˌpæŋkriˈætɪk◂/ *adj* —see picture at 參見 DIGESTIVE SYSTEM 圖

pan·da /ˋpændə; ˈpændə/ *n* [C] **1** a large black and white animal that looks like a bear and lives in the mountains of China; GIANT PANDA 大熊貓, 大貓熊 **2** a small animal with red-brown fur and a long tail, living in the south-eastern Himalayas〔產於喜馬拉雅山東南部的〕小熊貓, 小貓熊

Panda car /ˈ·· ·/ *n* [C] *BrE* a small police car used by local police; PATROL CAR【英】巡邏警車

pan·dem·ic /pænˋdɛmɪk; pænˈdemɪk/ *n* [C] *technical* an illness or disease that affects the population of a large area【術語】廣泛地區流行的病 —**pandemic** *adj* —compare 比較 ENDEMIC

pan·de·mo·ni·um /ˌpændɪˋmonɪəm; ˌpændɪˈməʊniəm/ *n* [U] a situation in which there is a lot of noise because people are angry, confused or frightened〔人們因感到憤怒、迷惑或恐懼而引起的〕大混亂, 嘈雜, 騷亂: *Pandemonium broke out when the results were announced.* 結果公布之後一片混亂。

pan·der /ˋpændɚ; ˈpændə/ *v*

pander to sth/sb *phr v* [T] to give someone what they want, when you know it is not good for them 迎合〔不良需求〕: *newspapers that pander to people's interest in sex* 迎合人們性趣味的報紙

pan·dit /ˋpʌndɪt; ˈpʌndɪt/ *n* [C] a title of respect for a wise man, used in India 博學之士, 學者〔在印度對智者、賢人的尊稱〕: *Pandit Nehru* 博學之士尼赫魯

Pan·do·ra's box /pænˌdorəz ˋbɑks; pænˌdɔːrəz ˈbɒks/ *n* **open Pandora's box** to cause a lot of problems that did not exist before 打開潘多拉的盒子, 引發種種禍患

pane /pen; peɪn/ *n* [C] a sheet of glass used in a window or door〔窗或門上的〕一塊玻璃 —see also 另見 WINDOWPANE —see picture on page A7 參見 A7 頁圖

pan·e·gyr·ic /ˌpænəˋdʒɪrɪk; ˌpænɪˈdʒɪrɪk/ *n* [C+**on**/**upon**] *formal* a speech or piece of writing that praises someone or something very highly【正式】頌詞; 頌文

pan·el[1] /ˋpænḷ; ˈpænl/ *n* [C]

1 ►PART 部分◄ **a)** a flat piece of wood, glass etc with straight sides, which forms part of a door, wall, fence etc〔門、牆、柵欄等的〕鑲板, 嵌板; 窗玻璃片: *a stained glass panel* 一塊染色玻璃板 **b)** a piece of metal that forms part of the outer structure of a vehicle〔車身的〕金屬板 **c)** a piece of material that forms part of a piece of clothing〔衣服上的〕鑲條, 飾片

2 ►GROUP OF PEOPLE 一組人◄ **a)** a group of people with skills or specialist knowledge who have been chosen to give advice or opinions on a particular subject〔由選定人員組成的〕專門小組; 專題討論小組: *A panel of experts was consulted.* 專家小組接受了諮詢。| *a crime prevention panel* 防止犯罪專門小組 **b)** a group of well-known people who answer questions on a radio or television programme〔由知名人士組成在廣播或電視節目中回答問題的〕答問小組: *Let me introduce tonight's panel.* 讓我介紹一下今晚的答問小組。—see also 另見 PANELLIST **c)** a group of people who are chosen to listen to a case in a court of law and to decide the result; JURY 陪審團

3 instrument/control panel a board in a car, plane, boat etc on which the controls are fixed〔汽車、飛機、船等的〕儀表板/控制面板

4 ►PICTURE 圖畫◄ a thin board with a picture painted on it 畫板 —see also 另見 SOLAR PANEL

panel[2] *v* **panelled, panelling** *BrE*【英】, **paneled, paneling** *AmE*【美】[T usually passive 一般用被動態] to cover or decorate something with flat pieces of wood, glass etc〔用木頭、玻璃鑲板等〕覆蓋; 裝飾〔某物〕: **be panelled with** *The walls were panelled with oak.* 這些牆壁都鑲着橡木板。| **oak-panelled/glass-panelled etc** *an oak-panelled library* 鑲有橡木板的圖書館

panel-beat·er /ˈ·· ˌ··/ *n* [C] *BrE* someone whose job is to repair the outer structure of cars, for example after an accident, by beating the metal with a hammer【英】汽車板金工

pan·el·ling *BrE*【英】, **paneling** *AmE*【美】/ˋpænḷɪŋ; ˈpænəl-ɪŋ/ *n* [U] wood, especially in long or square pieces, used to decorate walls etc〔用於裝飾牆壁的〕嵌板, 鑲板: *oak panelling* 橡木鑲板

pan·el·list *BrE*【英】, **panelist** *AmE*【美】/ˋpænḷɪst; ˈpænəl-ɪst/ *n* [C] one of a group of well-known people who answer questions on a radio or television programme 答問小組成員〔在廣播或電視節目中回答問題的一組知名人士之一〕

panel pin /ˈ·· ·/ *n* [C] a short, thin nail used for fastening thin pieces of wood together〔用來把薄木板釘在一起的短而細的〕鑲板釘

panel truck /ˈ·· ·/ *n* [C] *AmE* a small motor vehicle used for delivering goods【美】小型貨車

pang /pæŋ; pæŋ/ *n* [C] a sudden feeling of pain, sadness etc 一陣劇痛; 一陣傷心: [**+of**] *pangs of jealousy* 一陣陣忌妒 | *hunger pangs* 飢餓引起的陣陣劇痛

pan·han·dle[1] /ˋpænˌhændḷ; ˈpænˌhændl/ *n* [C] *AmE* a thin piece of land that is joined to a larger area like the handle of a pan【美】〔鍋柄狀的〕狹長地帶: *the Alaskan panhandle* 阿拉斯加狹長地帶

panhandle[2] *v* [I] *especially AmE* to ask for money in the streets【尤美】在街上行乞, 乞討: *a ban on panhandling in New York's subway* 紐約地鐵裡禁止行乞 —**panhandler** *n* [C]

pan·ic[1] /ˋpænɪk; ˈpænɪk/ *n* **1** [C usually singular 一般用單數, U] a sudden strong feeling of fear or nervousness that makes you unable to think clearly or behave sensibly 惶恐, 驚恐, 驚慌: **get into a panic/be thrown into (a)**

panic *She got into a real panic when she thought she'd lost the tickets.* 她十分驚慌，以為自己把入場券丟了。| **in (a) panic** *Shoppers fled the street in panic after two bombs exploded in central London.* 兩枚炸彈在倫敦市中心爆炸之後，購物者驚慌失措地逃離了那條街。| **panic attack** *Philip sometimes gets panic attacks and can't breathe properly.* 菲利普有時會突然恐慌起來，不能正常呼吸。**2** [C usually singular 一般用單數, U] a situation in which people are suddenly made very anxious, and make quick decisions without thinking carefully 大恐慌: *the recent panic over the contamination of food by listeria and salmonella* 最近對於食物受到李氏桿菌和沙門氏菌污染的恐慌 | **panic buying/selling** *A wave of panic selling in Hong Kong shook the city yesterday.* 昨天香港的恐慌性拋售浪潮震動了整個城市。**3** [singular] *especially BrE* a situation in which there is a lot to do and not much time to do it in【尤英】忙亂，慌亂: *There was the usual last minute panic just before the deadline.* 在截止時間到來之前的最後一刻，通常總是一陣忙亂。**4 press/push the panic button** *BrE* to do something quickly without thinking enough about it, because something unexpected or dangerous has suddenly happened【英】驚慌失措，在緊急情況下慌亂行事 **5 panic stations** *BrE* a state of confused anxiety because something needs to be done urgently【英】緊急慌亂的狀態，驚慌: *It was panic stations here on Friday.* 星期五這裡是一片慌亂。

panic² *v* **panicked, panicking** [I, T] to suddenly become so frightened that you cannot think clearly or behave sensibly, or to make someone do this（使）恐慌，（使）驚慌失措: *The crowd panicked at the sound of the gunfire.* 砲火聲一響，羣眾便驚慌失措。| *He panicked thinking it was a shark.* 他以為那是一條鯊魚，因而驚慌起來。| **Don't panic!** (=used to tell people to stay calm) 別慌！| **panic sb into doing sth** *The protests became more violent and many landowners were panicked into leaving the country.* 抗議變得更加激烈，許多地主慌忙地離開了那個國家。

pan·ic·ky /ˋpænɪkɪ; ˈpænɪki/ *adj informal* very nervous or anxious【非正式】驚惶的，緊張不安的: *Emily always gets panicky about exams.* 埃米莉總是害怕考試。

panic-strick·en /ˋ·· ˌ··/ *adj* so frightened that you cannot think clearly or behave sensibly 驚惶失措的，恐慌萬分的: *the panic-stricken faces of the hostages* 那些人質惶恐萬分的表情

pan·ni·er /ˋpænɪɚ; ˈpæniə/ *n* [C] **1** one of a pair of baskets or bags carried one on each side of an animal or a bicycle〔掛在動物或腳踏車兩邊的〕馱籃，掛籃；掛包 **2** a basket used to carry a load on someone's back 背簍

pan·ni·kin /ˋpænəkɪn; ˈpænɪkɪn/ *n* [C] *BrE old use* a small metal drinking cup【英舊】金屬小杯

pan·o·ply /ˋpænəplɪ; ˈpænəpli/ *n* [U+**of**] **1** an impressive show of special clothes, decorations etc, especially at an important ceremony 盛裝；盛大的場面: *the whole panoply of a royal wedding* 王室婚禮的整個盛大場面 **2** a large amount of equipment, weapons etc 大量裝備[武器等] —**panoplied** *adj*

pan·o·ra·ma /ˌpænəˋræmə; ˌpænəˈrɑːmə/ *n* [C usually singular 一般用單數] **1** an impressive view of a wide area of land 風景的全貌，全景: *A breathtaking panorama of mountains and lakes spread out in front of them.* 一大片令人驚嘆的湖光山色展現在他們面前。| [+**of**] *a vast panorama of roof tops* 一大片屋頂的全景 **2** a description or series of pictures that shows all the features of a subject, historical period etc 概述，概論；概觀；概貌: [+**of**] *a panorama of life in England 400 years ago* 400年前英格蘭生活的概貌 —**panoramic** /ˌpænəˋræmɪk; ˌpænəˈræmɪk◂/ *adj*: *a panoramic view of the valley* 山谷的全景 —**panoramically** /-klɪ; -kli/ *adv*

pan·pipes /ˋpænˌpaɪps; ˈpænpaɪps/ *n* [plural] a simple musical instrument made of several short wooden pipes of different lengths, that are played by blowing across their open ends 排簫；潘神簫

pan·sy /ˋpænzɪ; ˈpænzi/ *n* [C] **1** a small garden plant with flat brightly coloured flowers 三色堇，三色紫羅蘭 **2** *informal* an insulting word for a man who seems weak and too much like a woman【非正式】脂粉[女人]氣的男子〔稱呼男子的侮辱性詞語〕

pant /pænt; pænt/ *v* **1** [I] to breathe quickly with short noisy breaths because you have been running, climbing etc or because it is very hot〔累得或熱得〕氣喘，喘息: *He was panting after his exertions.* 他在用力之後累得氣喘吁吁。| *The dog lay panting on the doorstep.* 那隻狗躺在門階上喘着氣。**2** [T] to say something while panting 喘着氣說: *"I can't run any farther," she panted.* 她氣喘吁吁地說："我實在跑不動了。"

pant for sth *phr v* [T] to want something very much 渴望…，迫切想要…: *He was panting for a chance to speak.* 他渴望得到說話的機會。—**pant** *n* [C]

pan·ta·loons /ˌpæntḷˋunz; ˌpæntəˈluːnz/ *n* [plural] long trousers with wide legs, which are gathered in again at the ankles〔褲腿寬大、腳踝處收緊的〕燈籠褲

pan·tech·ni·con /pænˋtɛknɪˌkɑn; pænˈteknɪkən/ *n* [C] *BrE old-fashioned* a REMOVAL VAN【英，過時】搬運車

pan·the·is·m /ˋpænθiˌɪzəm; ˈpænθi-ɪzəm/ *n* [U] the religious idea that God and the universe are the same thing and that God is present in all natural things 泛神論 —**pantheist** *n* [C] —**pantheistic** /ˌpænθiˋɪstɪk; ˌpænθi-ˈɪstɪk◂/ *adj*

pan·the·on /ˋpænθɪən; ˈpænθiən/ *n* [C] **1** all the gods of a particular people or nation〔某一民族所信奉的〕諸神，眾神: *the Roman pantheon* 羅馬眾神 **2** *literary* a group of famous and important people【文】〔一批〕名人；要人: *a leading figure in the pantheon of 20th century designers* 20世紀著名設計師中的領導人物 **3** a TEMPLE built in honour of all gods 萬神殿，萬神廟

pan·ther /ˋpænθɚ; ˈpænθə/ *n plural* **panthers** or **panther** [C] **1** a black LEOPARD 黑豹 **2** *AmE* a COUGAR or JAGUAR【美】美洲獅；美洲豹

pan·ties /ˋpæntɪz; ˈpæntiz/ *n* [plural] a piece of women's underwear that covers the area between their waist and the top of their legs〔婦女的〕短襯褲，內褲；KNICKERS *BrE*【英】: *a pair of lacy panties* 一條帶花邊的短襯褲 —see picture at 參見 UNDERWEAR 圖

pan·ti·hose /ˋpæntɪˌhoz; ˈpæntihəʊz/ *n* [plural] *AmE*【美】another spelling of PANTYHOSE pantyhose 的另一種拼法

pan·tile /ˋpænˌtaɪl; ˈpæntaɪl/ *n* [C usually plural 一般用複數] a curved roof TILE〔屋頂的〕波形瓦

pan·to /ˋpænto; ˈpæntəʊ/ *n* [C] *BrE informal* pantomime【英，非正式】童話劇

pan·to·graph /ˋpæntəˌgræf; ˈpæntəgrɑːf/ *n* [C] **1** an instrument used to make a smaller or larger exact copy of a drawing, plan etc〔繪畫、製圖等使用的〕縮放儀 **2** the metal structure on top of an electric train that takes power from the wires above the track〔電氣列車頂上的〕導電弓架，受電弓

pan·to·mime /ˋpæntəˌmaɪm; ˈpæntəmaɪm/ *n* **1** [C,U] a type of play for children that is performed in Britain around Christmas, in which traditional stories are performed with jokes, music, and songs〔英國在聖誕節前後演出，用笑話、音樂和歌曲演繹傳統故事的〕童話劇 **2** [C,U] a method of performing using only actions and not words, or a play performed using this method; MIME¹ (1) 啞劇[默劇]表演藝術；啞劇，默劇

pan·try /ˋpæntrɪ; ˈpæntri/ *n plural* **pantries** [C] **1** a very small room in a house where food is kept; LARDER〔家庭中的〕食品儲藏室 **2** a room in a big house, hotel etc where glasses, dishes etc are kept〔大宅第、酒店等的〕餐具室

pants /pænts; pænts/ *n* [plural] **1** *AmE* a piece of clothing that covers you from your waist to your feet and has a separate part for each leg【美】(長) 褲子；TROUSERS *especially BrE*【尤英】—see graph at 參見 TROUSERS 圖表 —see picture on page A17 參見A17頁圖 **2** *BrE* a S3 piece of underwear that covers the area between your waist and the top of your legs【英】短襯褲, 內褲 **3 bore/charm/beat etc the pants off** *spoken* to make you feel very bored, very frightened etc【口】使…厭煩透頂/把…迷倒/把…徹底打敗等: *She always bores the pants off me.* 她總是讓我厭煩透頂。**4 he/she puts his/her pants on one leg at a time** *AmE spoken* used to say that someone is just like everyone else【美口】他/她也是個普通人: *Go on, ask him for his autograph – he puts his pants on one leg at a time just like you do.* 去吧, 問他要一個親筆簽名——他和你一個樣子, 沒甚麼特別的。**5 be in short pants** *informal* to still be a very young boy【非正式】還是小孩, 未成年: *I've known Eric since he was in short pants.* 埃里克還是小孩子時我就認識他了。—see also 另見 **by the seat of your pants** (SEAT[1] (9)), **catch sb with their pants down** (CATCH[1] (3)), **wear the pants/trousers** (WEAR[1] (8))

pant·suit /ˈpæntsut; ˈpæntsuːt/ *n* [C] *AmE*【美】女式褲套裝; a TROUSER SUIT *BrE*【英】

pan·ty·hose, pantihose /ˈpæntɪˌhoz; ˈpæntihəʊz/ *n* [plural] *AmE* a very thin piece of women's clothing that covers their legs from the toes to the waist and is usually worn with dresses or skirts【美】〔女用〕連褲襪; TIGHTS *BrE*【英】

pan·ty·lin·er /ˈpæntɪˌlaɪnɚ; ˈpæntilaɪnə/ *n* [C] a very thin SANITARY PAD〔薄型的〕衛生護墊

pap /pæp; pæp/ *n* [U] **1** books, television programmes etc that people read or watch for entertainment but which have no serious value〔無甚價值的〕消遣性讀物; 娛樂節目: *Telly snobs dismiss the show as lightweight pap.* 自以為對電視在行的人輕率地把這個節目視為思想淺薄的娛樂節目。**2** very soft food eaten by babies or sick people〔嬰兒或病人吃的〕軟食, 半流質食物 —see also 另見 PAP SMEAR

pap·a /ˈpɑpə; pəˈpɑː/ *n* [C] *AmE or old-fashioned BrE* a way of talking about your father【美或過時, 英】爸爸: *Good morning, Papa!* 早上好, 爸爸!

pa·pa·cy /ˈpepəsɪ; ˈpeɪpəsi/ *n* **1 the papacy** the position and authority of the POPE 教皇的職位; 教皇的職權 **2** [U] the time during which a particular POPE is in power 教皇的任期

pap·a·dum /ˈpæpədəm; ˈpæpədəm/ *n* [C] another spelling of POPADUM popadum 的另一種拼法

pa·pal /ˈpepl; ˈpeɪpəl/ *adj* [only before noun 僅用於名詞前] connected with or belonging to the POPE 教皇的: *papal authority* 教皇的權威

pap·a·raz·zi /ˌpɑpəˈrɑtsɪ; ˌpæpəˈrætsi/ *n* [plural] newspaper writers or photographers who follow famous people 追逐名人的 (攝影) 記者, 狗仔隊

pa·pa·ya /pəˈpaɪə; pəˈpaɪə/ *n* [C] the large yellow-green fruit of a tropical tree 番木瓜, 木瓜 —see picture on page A8 參見A8頁圖

1 **pa·per[1]** /ˈpepɚ; ˈpeɪpə/ *n*
1 **1 ►FOR WRITING ON** 用於在上面書寫◄ [U] material in the form of thin sheets that is used for writing on, wrapping things etc 紙: *a piece of paper* 一張紙 | *wrapped in brown paper* 用棕色紙包起來 | **writing/wrapping/drawing paper** *sheets of writing paper* 幾張信紙

2 ►NEWSPAPER 報紙◄ [C] a newspaper 報紙: *Have you seen today's paper?* 你看到今天的報紙了嗎? | *Why don't you put an ad in the local paper?* 你為甚麼不在當地報紙上刊登一則廣告呢? | **daily/evening/Sunday paper** *The story was all over the Sunday papers.* 這則報道刊登在週日的所有報紙上。

3 ►DOCUMENTS/LETTERS 文件/信件◄ **a) papers** [plural] pieces of paper with writing on them that you use in your work, at meetings etc〔工作、會議等上用的〕文件, 文獻: *I left some important papers in my briefcase.* 我把一些重要的文件遺了在公文包裡。**b)** documents and letters concerning someone's private or public life〔私人的〕文件; 書信: *I found this photograph among his private papers.* 我在他的私人書信裡找到了這張照片。**c)** official documents such as your PASSPORT, IDENTITY CARD etc 公文文件; 證件〈如護照、身分證等〉: *After checking our papers, the border guards let us through.* 邊境衛兵檢查了我們的證件之後便讓我們通過了。—see also 另見 WHITE PAPER, GREEN PAPER, ORDER PAPER

4 on paper a) if you put ideas or information on paper, you write them down 在紙上: *As soon as you have an idea, get it down on paper so you don't forget it.* 一有想法就把它寫下來, 這樣就不會忘記了。**b)** if something seems true on paper, it seems to be true as an idea, but may not be true in a real situation 理論上: *It's a nice idea on paper, but you'll never get it to work.* 這在理論上是個好主意, 但你永遠無法把它付諸實踐。

5 ►EXAMINATION 考試◄ **a)** [C] *BrE* a set of printed questions used as an examination in a particular subject【英】試卷〔指未做的考卷〕: *an exam paper* 考卷 | **history/French etc paper** *The history paper was really easy.* 那份歷史試卷真容易。**b)** the answers that have been written to these questions 試卷〔指已完成的答卷〕: *I have a stack of papers to mark.* 我有一疊試卷要批改。

6 ►ABOUT A SUBJECT 關於某個主題◄ [C] **a)** a piece of writing or a talk by someone who has made a study of a particular subject〔研究〕論文; 講話: *a scientific paper* 科學論文 | **give a paper on** (=give a talk about) 就…發表講話, 談一談… *Professor Usborne gave a paper on recent developments in the field of cognitive psychology.* 厄斯本教授就認知心理學領域的新動態發表了講話。| **working paper** (=an official document that makes suggestions about a subject or problem) 建議書〔關於一個題目或問題提出建議的正式文件〕**b)** *especially AmE* a piece of writing that is done as part of a course at school or university【尤美】文章, 論文〔學生的作業〕: **[+on]** *I have a paper to write on the Civil War.* 我有一篇關於南北戰爭的文章要寫。

7 ►FOR WALLS 用於牆壁◄ [C,U] paper for covering and decorating the walls of a room; WALLPAPER 牆紙, 壁紙: *We've chosen a floral paper for Pauline's bedroom.* 我們為葆琳的臥室選了一種有花卉圖案的牆紙。

8 not worth the paper it is written on/printed on if something such as a contract is not worth the paper it is written on, it has no value because whatever is promised in it will not happen〔合同等〕毫無價值的, 不會兌現的 —see also 另見 **put/set pen to paper** (PEN[1] (3)), TOILET PAPER, WASTE PAPER

paper[2] *adj* [only before noun 僅用於名詞前] **1** made of paper 用紙做的, 紙製的: *a paper cup* 紙杯 **2 paper qualifications** an expression meaning documents showing that you have passed certain examinations, used specially when you think that someone's experience and knowledge of a subject are more important 紙上資歷〔尤用在你認為某人的經驗及對某一學科的了解更重要時〕**3** existing only as an idea but not having any real value 紙上的, 有名無實的: *paper profits* 紙上盈利, 賬面利潤 | *paper promises* 一紙空文的保證 **4 paper tiger** an enemy or opponent who seems powerful but actually is not 紙老虎〔指外強中乾的敵人或對手〕

paper[3] *v* [T] **1** to decorate the walls of a room by covering them with special paper 用牆紙裱糊〔牆壁〕**2 paper over the cracks/a problem etc** to try to hide disagreements or difficulties 隱瞞[掩蓋]分歧/困難等

pa·per·back /ˈpepɚˌbæk; ˈpeɪpəbæk/ *n* [C] a book with a stiff paper cover 平裝書, 簡裝書: *a shelf full of paperbacks* 放滿了平裝書的書架 | **in paperback** *His first novel sold over 20,000 copies in paperback.* 他的第一部小說賣了20,000 冊平裝本。—compare 比較 HARDBACK

pa·per·boy /ˈpepɚˌbɔɪ; ˈpeɪpəbɔɪ/ *n* [C] a boy who delivers newspapers to people's houses 送報的男孩, 報童

paper chase /ˈ‥ ˌ/ *n* [C] **1** *especially BrE* a game in which someone runs ahead of a group of people dropping pieces of paper which they have to follow【尤英】逐紙

遊戲〔跑在前面的人沿途撒下紙屑供後面的一羣人循蹤追逐〕 **2** *AmE* an attempt to gain a university degree【美】追逐文憑

pa·per·clip /ˈpepɚˌklɪp; ˈpeɪpəklɪp/ *n* [C] a small piece of curved wire used for holding sheets of paper together 紙夾, 回形針

paper doll /ˌ·· ˈ·/ *n* [C] a piece of stiff paper cut in the shape of a person〔用硬紙剪出的〕紙人; 紙娃娃

paper fas·ten·er /ˈ·· ˌ···/ *n* [C] *BrE* a small metal object like a button used to hold several pieces of paper together【英】圓形紙夾, 曲頭釘, 平頭釘; BRAD *AmE*【美】

paper girl /ˈ··· ·/ *n* [C] a girl who delivers newspapers to people's houses 送報的女孩, 女報童

pa·per·hang·er /ˈpepɚˌhæŋɚ; ˈpeɪpəˌhæŋə/ *n* [C] someone whose job is to decorate rooms with WALLPAPER 裱糊工人, 糊牆紙工人

paper knife /ˈ·· ·/ *n* [C] *BrE* a knife for opening envelopes【英】拆信刀

paper mon·ey /ˈ·· ˌ··/ *n* [U] money consisting of small sheets of paper, not coins 紙幣

paper-push·er /ˈ·· ˌ··/ *n* [C] someone whose job is doing unimportant office work〔辦公室中處理瑣事的〕文書, 辦事員

paper round /ˈ·· ·/ *n* [C] *BrE* the job of delivering newspapers to a group of houses【英】挨戶送報: *Harry used to do a paper round before breakfast.* 哈里過去常常在早餐之前挨家挨戶送報。

paper route /ˈ·· ·/ *n* [C] *AmE* a paper round【美】送報路線

paper shop /ˈ·· ·/ *n* [C] *BrE* a shop that sells newspapers and magazines【英】報刊店; NEWSAGENT *AmE*【美】

paper-thin /ˌ·· ˈ·◂/ *adj* very thin 薄如紙的, 極薄的

paper tow·el /ˌ·· ˈ··/ *n* [C] a sheet of soft thick paper that you use to dry your hands (擦手) 紙巾

pa·per·weight /ˈpepɚˌwet; ˈpeɪpəweɪt/ *n* [C] a small heavy object used to hold pieces of paper in place 鎮紙, 壓紙器

pa·per·work /ˈpepɚwɝk; ˈpeɪpəwɜːk/ *n* [U] **1** work such as writing letters or reports, which must be done but is not very interesting 日常文書工作〈如寫信或寫報告等〉: *The job involves a lot of paperwork.* 這項工作需要大量的文書工作。**2** the documents that you need for a business deal, a journey etc〔商貿、旅行等所需的〕資料, 文件: *I'm leaving the solicitors to sort out the paperwork.* 我把整理資料的工作留給律師們去做。

pa·per·y /ˈpepərɪ; ˈpeɪpəri/ *adj* something such as skin or leaves that is papery is very dry and thin and a little stiff〔皮膚、樹葉等〕像紙的, 紙一樣的, 質地似紙的: *the papery skin of her hands* 她雙手像紙一般又乾又硬的皮膚

pap·ier-mâ·ché /ˈpepɚ məˈʃe; ˌpæpieɪ ˈmæʃeɪ/ also 又作 **paper-mâché** *AmE*【美】*n* [U] a soft substance made from a mixture of paper, water, and glue, which becomes hard when it dries and is used for making boxes, pots etc〔製紙箱等用的〕混凝紙漿

pa·pist /ˈpepɪst; ˈpeɪpɨst/ *n* [C] an insulting word for a member of the Roman Catholic Church 羅馬天主教徒〔侮辱性詞語〕

pa·poose /pæˈpus; pəˈpuːs/ *n* [C] **1** a type of bag fixed to a frame, used to carry a baby on your back〔揹負幼兒用的〕有框架的背袋 **2** *old use* a Native American baby or young child【舊】北美土著嬰[幼]兒

pap·py /ˈpæpɪ; ˈpæpi/ *n* [C] *AmE old-fashioned* a father【美, 過時】爸爸

pap·ri·ka /pəˈprikə; ˈpæprɪkə/ *n* [U] a red powder made from a type of SWEET PEPPER, used to give a strong taste to food 辣椒粉

Pap smear /ˈ· ·/ *n* [C] *AmE* a medical test that takes cells from a woman's CERVIX and examines them for signs of CANCER【美】帕氏塗片試驗〔一種探查早期癌變的子宮頸塗片檢查〕; SMEAR TEST *BrE*【英】

pa·py·rus /pəˈpaɪrəs; pəˈpaɪərəs/ *n plural* **papyruses** or **papyri** /-raɪ; -raɪ/ **1** [U] a plant like grass that grows in water 紙莎草 **2** [C,U] a type of paper made from this plant and used in ancient Egypt, or a piece of this paper〔古埃及人用的〕紙莎草紙

par /pɑr; pɑː/ *n* [U] **1 be on a par (with)** to be at the same level or standard (與…) 水平[標準]相同: *The wages of clerks were on a par with those of manual workers.* 文員的工資和體力勞動者的工資是一樣的。**2 be below/under par a)** to feel a little ill or lacking in energy 感覺有些不舒服, 健康狀況欠佳; 沒精神: *I've been feeling a little under par the last couple of weeks.* 幾個星期以來我一直感覺有些不舒服。**b)** also 又作 **not be up to par** to be less good than usual or below the proper standard 在一般水平以下; 達不到標準: *None of the people who'd auditioned were really up to par.* 試演過的人中沒有一個真的達到標準。**3 be par for the course** to be what you would normally expect to happen 不出所料, 意料之中: *The train's late again – I guess that's about par for the course.* 火車又晚點了——我想這幾乎是意料中的事。**4** the number of STROKES a player should take to hit the ball into a hole in the game of GOLF〔高爾夫球擊球入洞的〕標準桿數 **5** also 又作 **par value** the value of a STOCK or BOND that is printed on it when it is first sold〔證券或債券的〕票面價值, 面值: *a par value of $40 million* 4000 萬美元的票面價值 —see also 另見 PAR EXCELLENCE

para- /pærə; pærə/ *prefix* **1** beyond 超: *the paranormal* (=strange unnatural events) 超自然現象 **2** very similar to something 和…相似[接近]: *terrorists wearing paramilitary uniforms* 穿着準軍事部隊制服的恐怖分子 | *paratyphoid* 副傷寒 **3** connected with a profession and helping more highly trained people 輔助: *paramedical workers such as ambulance drivers* 如救護車司機等醫務輔助人員

par·a[1] /ˈpærə; ˈpærə/ *n BrE informal* a PARATROOPER【英, 非正式】傘兵

para[2] also 又作 **par** the written abbreviation of 縮寫= PARAGRAPH

par·a·ble /ˈpærəbl; ˈpærəbəl/ *n* [C] a short simple story that teaches a moral or religious lesson, especially one of the stories told by Jesus in the Bible〔道德或宗教〕說教寓言 (故事)〔尤指《聖經》中耶穌所講的故事〕

pa·rab·o·la /pəˈræbələ; pəˈræbələ/ *n* [C] *technical* a curve in the shape of the imaginary line a ball makes when it is thrown high in the air and comes down a little distance away【術語】拋物線 —**parabolic** /ˌpærəˈbɑlɪk; ˌpærəˈbɒlɪk◂/ *adj*

par·a·ce·ta·mol /ˌpærəˈsitəmɑl; ˌpærəˈsiːtəmɒl/ *n* [C, U] *BrE* a common drug used to reduce pain, which does not contain ASPIRIN【英】撲熱息痛, 止痛退熱藥, 對乙酰氨基酚〔一種不含阿斯匹林的常用鎮痛藥〕

par·a·chute[1] /ˈpærəˌʃut; ˈpærəʃuːt/ *n* [C] the thing that you wear fastened to your back to make you fall through the air slowly when you jump out of a plane 降落傘: *a parachute jump* 跳傘

parachute[2] *v* **1** [I always+adv/prep] to jump from a plane using a parachute 跳傘: **[+into/on]** *We parachuted into Vietnam in September 1968.* 我們於1968年9月跳傘降落在越南境內。**2** [T always+adv/prep] to drop something from a plane with a parachute〔用降落傘〕空投: **parachute sth to/into** *It may be possible to parachute supplies to the garrison.* 或許可以給衛戍部隊空投補給品。

parachute 跳傘

pa·ra·chut·ist /ˈpærəˌʃutɪst; ˈpærəʃuːtɨst/ *n* [C] someone who jumps from a plane with a parachute 跳傘員; 傘兵

pa·rade¹ /pəˋred; pəˈreɪd/ *n* [C] **1** a public celebration when musical bands, brightly decorated vehicles etc move down the street〔慶祝〕遊行; 列隊行進: *a victory parade* 慶祝勝利的遊行 **2** a military ceremony in which soldiers stand or march together so that important people can examine them 閱兵式: *a passing-out parade* 軍校學生畢業閱兵式 | **be on parade** (=be standing or marching in a parade) 在接受檢閱; 在列隊行進 **3** a line of people moving along so that other people can watch them 列隊表演, 展示: **fashion parade** (=a show of different styles of clothes) 時裝表演 **4** *especially BrE* a street with a row of small shops【尤英】商業街 —see also 另見 IDENTIFICATION PARADE, HIT PARADE

parade² *v*

1 ►CELEBRATE/PROTEST 慶祝/抗議◄ [I always+adv/prep] to walk or march together to celebrate or protest about something 遊行; 列隊行進: **[+around/past etc]** *The marchers paraded peacefully through the center of the capital.* 遊行者有秩序地列隊穿過首都中心。

2 ►SHOW STH 展示某物◄ [T] to show your possessions, knowledge etc in order to make people admire you 誇示, 炫耀〔財產、知識等〕: *He loves to parade his knowledge in front of his students.* 他喜歡在學生面前賣弄自己的知識。

3 ►WALK AROUND 四處走動◄ [I always+adv/prep] to walk around, especially in a way that shows that you want people to notice and admire you 炫耀地走來走去, 招搖而過: **[+around/past etc]** *A trio of girls in extremely brief bikinis paraded up and down.* 三個女孩穿着極暴露的比基尼泳裝招搖地走來走去。

4 ►SHOW SB 展示某人◄ [T always+adv/prep] to proudly show someone to other people, often to prove that you have control over them 使示眾: *The prisoners were paraded in front of the TV cameras.* 囚犯在電視攝影機前曝光。

5 ►SOLDIERS 士兵◄ [I,T] if soldiers parade or if an officer parades them, they march together so that an important person can watch them (使) 列隊行進接受檢閱: *Two thousand of his warriors paraded before him.* 他的兩千名武士在他面前列隊行進接受檢閱。

6 parade as/be paraded as if something parades as something else that is better, someone is pretending that it is the other better thing 冒充為/被冒充為: *It's just self-interest parading as concern for your welfare.* 這只是假裝關心你幸福的利己表現。

parade ground /ˈ·· ˌ·/ *n* [C] a large flat area where soldiers practise marching or standing together in rows 閱兵場, 練兵場

par·a·digm /ˋpærəˌdaɪm; ˈpærədaɪm/ *n* [C] **1** *formal* a very clear or typical example of something【正式】示例, 範例, 樣式: **[+of]** *The Holocaust, to me, is a paradigm of evil.*〔第二次世界大戰期間〕納粹對猶太人的大屠殺在我看來是邪惡的典型。**2** *technical* a model or example that shows how something works or is produced【術語】〔展示工作或製作方法的〕模型, 例子 **3** *technical* an example or pattern of a word, showing all its forms in grammar, like child's, children, children's【術語】詞形變化 (表) —**paradigmatic** /ˌpærədɪgˋmætɪk; ˌpærədɪgˈmætɪk◄/ *adj* —**paradigmatically** /-kl̩ɪ; -kli/ *adv*

par·a·dise /ˋpærəˌdaɪs; ˈpærədaɪs/ *n* **1** [U] a place or situation that is extremely pleasant, beautiful, or enjoyable 極樂 (世界); 至美, 至福: *the beautiful Thai holiday paradise of Phuket* 美麗的泰國度假樂園布吉島 | *The hotel felt like paradise after two weeks of camping.* 兩個星期的野營之後, 那酒店讓人感覺像是天堂。**2** [singular] a place that has everything you need for doing a particular activity〔所需物一應俱全的〕樂園, 樂土: *The market is a shopper's paradise.* 這個市場是購物者的天堂。| **[+for]** *Hawaii is a paradise for surfers.* 夏威夷是衝浪者的理想去處。**3 Paradise** [singular] **a)** Heaven, thought of as the place where God lives and where there is no illness, death, or evil 天堂, 天國 **b)** the garden where Adam and Eve lived (=the first humans, according to the Bible)〔《聖經》中人類始祖亞當和夏娃居住的〕伊甸園 —see also 另見 BIRD OF PARADISE, **be living in a fool's paradise** (FOOL¹ (8))

par·a·dox /ˋpærəˌdɑks; ˈpærədɒks/ *n* **1** [C] a situation that seems strange because it involves two ideas or qualities that are very different 自相矛盾 (的情況): *It's a paradox that in such a rich country there can be so much poverty.* 在如此富有的國家卻有這麼多的貧窮現象, 真是自相矛盾。**2** [C] a statement that seems impossible because it contains two opposing ideas that are both true 反論, 似非而是的說法[雋語] **3** [U] the use of such statements in writing or speech 反論運用, 似是而非的雋語運用 —**paradoxical** /ˌpærəˋdɑksɪkl̩; ˌpærəˈdɒksɪkəl◄/ *adj*

par·a·dox·i·cally /ˌpærəˋdɑksɪkl̩ɪ; ˌpærəˈdɒksɪkli/ *adv* in a way that is surprising because it is the opposite of what you would expect 自相矛盾地; 反常地: [sentence adverb 句子副詞] *Paradoxically, the prohibition of liquor caused an increase in alcoholism.* 十分矛盾的是, 禁酒反而導致了酗酒的增加。

par·af·fin /ˋpærəfɪn; ˈpærəfɪ̣n/ *n* [U] **1** *BrE* an oil used for heating and in lamps, made from PETROLEUM or coal【英】〔取暖、點燈用的〕煤油; KEROSENE *AmE*【美】**2** paraffin wax 石蠟

paraffin wax /ˈ··· ˌ·/ *n* [U] a soft white substance used for making CANDLEs, made from PETROLEUM or coal 石蠟

par·a·glid·ing /ˌpærəˋglaɪdɪŋ; ˈpærəˌglaɪdɪŋ/ *n* [U] a sport in which you jump off a hill and use a PARACHUTE to float back down to the ground 乘降落傘滑翔運動, 翼傘滑翔運動

par·a·gon /ˋpærəˌgɑn; ˈpærəgən/ *n* [C] someone who is perfect or is extremely brave, good etc 完 (美的) 人; 典範, 模範: **[+of]** *a paragon of virtue* 美德的典範

par·a·graph /ˋpærəˌgræf; ˈpærəgrɑːf/ *n* [C] a group of several sentences in a piece of writing, the first sentence of which starts on a new line〔文章的〕段, 段落 —**paragraph** *v* [T]

par·a·keet /ˋpærəˌkit; ˈpærəkiːt/ *n* [C] a small brightly coloured bird with a long tail 長尾 (小) 鸚鵡

par·a·le·gal /ˌpærəˋligl̩; ˌpærəˈliːgəl/ *n* [C] *AmE* LEGAL EXECUTIVE【美】法律事務助理; 律師助手

par·al·lel¹ /ˋpærəˌlɛl; ˈpærəlel/ *n* [C] **1** a connection between two things, especially things that exist or happen in different places or at different times〔尤指不同地點或不同時間的兩事物之間的〕聯繫, 相似 (之處): **[+between]** *There are certain parallels between Europe today and 100 years ago.* 今天的歐洲和100年前的歐洲存在某些相似之處。| **[+with]** *The study of philosophy has close parallels with the study of linguistics.* 哲學研究和語言學研究非常相似。| **draw a parallel between** (=show that two things are similar) 在…之間作比較〔以顯示其相似處〕*The book draws a parallel between ancient and modern theories of education.* 這本書把古代和現代的教育理論作了比較。**2** something that is very similar to something else 和…相似的事物: *Modern styles of painting have their parallels in music and literature.* 現代繪畫風格與現代音樂和現代文學的風格有相似之處。| **have no parallel/be without parallel** (=be greater, better, worse etc than anything else) 沒有可相比擬的事物; 無可匹敵 *a social revolution without parallel in history* 歷史上獨一無二的社會革命 **3 in parallel with** together with and at the same time as something else 和…一起, 和…同時; 並行: *private organizations working in parallel with the state education system* 與國家教育體制平行運作的私人機構 **4** an imaginary line drawn on a map of the Earth, that is parallel to the EQUATOR 緯線, 緯度圈: *the 38th parallel* 38 度緯線 **5 be in parallel** *technical* if two electrical CIRCUITs (=complete circular paths) are in parallel, they are connected so that any electric current is divided equally between them【術語】〔電路的〕並聯

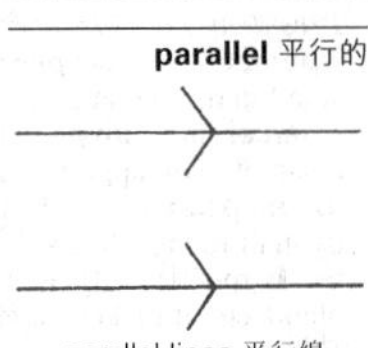

parallel² *adj* **1** two lines that are parallel to each other are the same distance apart along their whole length 平行的, 並行的: *Lines AB and CD are parallel.* AB 線和 CD 線平行。| **[+to/with]** *Parallel with the old fence was a new one of barbed wire.* 和舊柵欄平行的是一排新的帶刺鐵絲柵欄。| *The road runs parallel to the railway.* 這條公路與鐵路(線)相平行。**2** *formal* similar and happening at the same time【正式】相似的; 同時發生的: *Social changes in Britain are matched by parallel trends in other countries.* 在英國發生社會變革的同時, 其他國家也出現了相似的趨勢。

parallel³ *v* [T] *formal*【正式】**1** to be as good as something else 與…相當, 與…相匹敵: *a level of economic prosperity paralleled by few other countries* 只有少數幾個國家能比得上的經濟繁榮水平 **2** to be similar to something else 與…相似: *Does the geology of Mars parallel in any way that of Earth?* 火星和地球的地質狀況有甚麼相似之處嗎?

parallel bars /ˌ… ˈ·/ *n* [plural] two wooden bars that are held parallel to each other on four posts, used in GYMNASTICS (1)〔體操的〕雙槓

par·al·lel·is·m /ˋpærəlɛlˌɪzəm; ˈpærəlelɪzəm/ *n* **1** [U] the state of being PARALLEL with something 平行; 類似; 對應 **2** [C] a similarity 相似; 相似點

par·al·lel·o·gram /ˌpærəˋlɛləˌgræm; ˌpærəˈleləgræm/ *n* [C] a flat shape with four sides in which each side is the same length as the side opposite it and parallel to it 平行四邊形 —see picture at 參見 SHAPE¹ 圖

parallel pro·cess·ing /ˌ… ˈ…/ *n* [U] *technical* the method of using several computers to work on a single problem at one time【術語】〔電腦〕並行處理(技術)〔用多台電腦一次處理一個問題的方法〕

par·a·lyse *BrE*【英】, **paralyze** *AmE*【美】/ˋpærəˌlaɪz; ˈpærəlaɪz/ *v* [T] **1** to make someone lose the ability to move part or all of their body, or to feel anything in it 使癱瘓; 使麻痹: *Mrs Burrows had been paralysed by a stroke.* 伯羅斯夫人因中風癱瘓了。**2 be paralysed** to be unable to move, or to deal with a situation, because you are frightened or surprised〔因害怕或驚嚇而〕無法動彈; 不知所措: *She was paralysed by shock and disbelief.* 她由於震驚和懷疑而不知所措。**3** to make something unable to operate normally 使不能正常運作, 使陷入癱瘓: *The electricity failure paralysed the city.* 停電使這個城市陷於癱瘓。

par·a·lysed *BrE*【英】, **paralyzed** *AmE*【美】/ˋpærəˌlaɪzd; ˈpærəlaɪzd/ *adj* **1** unable to move part or all of your body or feel things in it 癱瘓的; 麻痹的: *The accident left him permanently paralysed.* 那次意外事故使他永久癱瘓了。**2** unable to think clearly or deal with a situation 不知所措的: *paralysed in the face of danger* 面對危險不知所措

pa·ral·y·sis /pəˋræləsɪs; pəˈræləsəs/ *n* [U] **1** the loss of the ability to move all or part of your body or feel things in it 癱瘓; 麻痹: *He suffered a stroke and partial paralysis.* 他患了中風, 身體局部癱瘓。**2** a state of being unable to take action, make decisions, or operate normally 不知所措;〔行動、決策、運行等〕癱瘓, 停頓 —see also 另見 INFANTILE PARALYSIS

par·a·lyt·ic¹ /ˌpærəˋlɪtɪk; ˌpærəˈlɪtɪk◂/ *adj* **1** [not before noun 不用於名詞前] *BrE informal* very drunk【英, 非正式】酩酊大醉的 **2** [only before noun 僅用於名詞前] suffering from PARALYSIS 癱瘓的; 患麻痹的 —**paralytically** /-klɪ; -kli/ *adv*

paralytic² *n* [C] someone who is PARALYSED 麻痹症患者; 癱瘓病人

par·a·lyze /ˋpærəˌlaɪz; ˈpærəlaɪz/ the American spelling of PARALYSE paralyse 的美式拼法

par·a·med·ic /ˌpærəˋmɛdɪk; ˌpærəˈmedɪk/ *n* [C] someone who has been trained to help people who are hurt or to do medical work, but who is not a doctor or nurse〔非醫生或護士的〕護理人員, 醫務輔助人員

par·a·med·i·cal /ˌpærəˋmɛdɪkḷ; ˌpærəˈmedɪkəl◂/ *adj* helping or supporting doctors, nurses, or hospitals 輔助醫務的: *paramedical staff* 醫務輔助人員

pa·ram·e·ter /pəˋræmətɚ; pəˈræmətə/ *n* [C usually plural 一般用複數] a set of fixed limits that control the way that something should be done 起限定作用的因素; 界限, 範圍: **establish/set/lay down parameters** *The inquiry has to stay within the parameters laid down by Congress.* 調查要局限在國會設定的範圍之內。

par·a·mil·i·ta·ry /ˌpærəˋmɪlɪˌtɛrɪ; ˌpærəˈmɪlətəri◂/ *adj* [usually before noun 一般用於名詞前] **1** a paramilitary organization fights and kills people illegally in order to achieve political aims 準軍事的: *extremist paramilitary groups* 極端分子的非法準軍事組織 **2** connected with or helping a military organization 與正規軍有聯繫的; 輔助正規軍的: *Their police have paramilitary duties.* 他們的警察有輔助正規軍的職責。—**paramilitary** *n* [C]

par·a·mount /ˋpærəˌmaunt; ˈpærəmaʊnt/ *adj* more important than anything else 至高無上的, 最重要的: *The interests of the consumer should be paramount.* 消費者的利益應是至高無上的。| **of paramount importance** *A balanced budget is of paramount importance.* 保持預算平衡是最重要的。—**paramountcy** *n* [U]

par·a·mour /ˋpærəˌmur; ˈpærəmʊə/ *n* [C] *literary* someone who you have a romantic or sexual relationship with, but who you are not married to; LOVER (2)【文】情人, 情婦[夫]

par·a·noi·a /ˌpærəˋnɔɪə; ˌpærəˈnɔɪə/ *n* [U] **1** an unreasonable belief that you cannot trust other people, or that they are trying to harm you or saying bad things about you 多疑, 瞎猜疑: *No one's blaming her – it's pure paranoia!* 沒有人會責怪她——那純粹是瞎猜疑! **2** *technical* a serious mental illness that makes someone believe that people hate them and treat them badly【術語】偏執狂; 妄想狂

par·a·noi·ac /ˌpærəˋnɔɪæk; ˌpærəˈnɔɪæk◂/ *adj* paranoid 多疑的; 患偏執狂的; 患妄想狂的 —**paranoiac** *n* [C]

par·a·noid /ˋpærənɔɪd; ˈpærənɔɪd/ *adj* **1** believing unreasonably that you cannot trust other people, or that they are trying to harm you or are saying bad things about you 多疑的, 疑神疑鬼的: *You think I'm just being paranoid, but something's going on!* 你認為我只是多疑, 但是確實發生了一些事! | *She's getting paranoid about being burgled.* 她總是疑神疑鬼, 怕有人入室盜竊。**2** *technical* suffering from a mental illness that makes you believe that other people are trying to harm you【術語】患偏執狂的; 患妄想狂的

par·a·nor·mal /ˌpærəˋnɔrməl; ˌpærəˈnɔːməl◂/ *adj* **1** paranormal events cannot be explained by science and seem strange and mysterious 不能用科學解釋的; 超自然的, 神祕的: *ESP and other paranormal phenomena* 超感知覺及其他超自然現象 **2 the paranormal** these events in general 超自然現象, 超自然事件 —compare 比較 SUPERNATURAL¹

par·a·pet /ˋpærəpɪt; ˈpærəpət/ *n* [C] **1** a low wall at the edge of a high roof, bridge etc〔屋頂、橋梁等邊上的〕矮牆, 護牆 **2** a protective wall of earth or stone built in front of a TRENCH (2) in a war〔塹壕前作掩護用的〕胸牆

par·a·pher·na·li·a /ˌpærəfɚˋnelɪə; ˌpærəfəˈneɪliə/ *n* [U] **1** a lot of small things that belong to someone, or are needed for a particular activity 個人隨身物品;〔某項活動所需的〕用具, 裝備: *camping paraphernalia* 野營用品 **2** the things and events that are connected with a particular activity〔與某項活動有關的〕煩瑣手續, 複雜程序: *all the usual paraphernalia of bureaucracy* 官僚作風那照常的一整套繁文縟節

par·a·phrase¹ /ˋpærəˌfrez; ˈpærəfreɪz/ *v* [T] to express in a shorter or clearer way what someone has written or said〔把書面或口頭的文字以簡短、清晰的方式〕意譯, 釋義; 改述: *To paraphrase Finkelstein: mathematics is a language, like English.* 芬克爾斯坦所説的意思是: 數學就像英語一樣是一門語言。

paraphrase² *n* [C] a statement that expresses in a shorter or clearer way what someone has said or written〔對一段口頭或書面文字的〕意譯, 釋義; 改述

par·a·ple·gi·a /ˌpærəˋplidʒɪə; ˌpærəˈpliːdʒiə/ *n* [U] inability to move your legs and the lower part of your body 截癱, 下身癱瘓[麻痹]

par·a·ple·gic /ˌpærəˋplidʒɪk; ˌpærəˈpliːdʒɪk◂/ *n* [C] someone who is unable to move the lower part of their body including their legs 截癱患者, 下身癱瘓[麻痹]者 —**paraplegic** *adj*

par·a·psy·chol·o·gy /ˌpærəsaɪˋkɑlədʒɪ; ˌpærəsaɪˈkɒlədʒi/ *n* [U] the scientific study of mysterious abilities that some people claim to have, such as knowing what will happen 通靈學, 心理玄學〔對於某些人所聲稱具有的神奇能力的科學研究〕

par·a·quat /ˋpærəˌkwɑt; ˈpærəkwɒt/ *n* [U] a strong poison used to kill WEEDs 百草枯〔一種強力除草劑〕

par·a·sail·ing /ˋpærəˌselɪŋ; ˈpærəˌseɪlɪŋ/ *n* [U] a sport in which you wear a PARACHUTE and are pulled behind a motor boat so that you sail through the air〔由汽船拖引在空中滑翔的〕帆傘運動, 水上拖傘運動

par·as·cend·ing /ˋpærəˌsɛndɪŋ; ˈpærəˌsendɪŋ/ *n* [U] a sport in which you wear a PARACHUTE, go up into the sky by being pulled along behind a car, and float back down to the ground〔由汽車拖引升到空中然後飄降地面的〕拖引式降落傘運動

par·a·site /ˋpærəˌsaɪt; ˈpærəsaɪt/ *n* [C] **1** a plant or animal that lives on or in another plant or animal and gets food from it 寄生植物; 寄生動物, 寄生蟲 **2** a lazy person who does not work but depends on other people 靠他人為生的人, 寄生者: *He thinks students are just parasites.* 他認為學生只是靠他人為生的人。

par·a·sit·ic /ˌpærəˋsɪtɪk; ˌpærəˈsɪtɪk◂/ also 又作 **parasitical** /-ˋsɪtɪkḷ; -ˈsɪtɪkəl/ *adj* **1** living in or on another plant or animal and getting food from them 寄生的: *parasitic fungi* 寄生真菌 **2** a parasitic person is lazy, does no work, and depends on other people〔人〕寄生蟲似的, 靠他人為生的 **3** a parasitic disease is caused by parasites〔疾病〕由寄生蟲引起的 —**parasitically** /-klɪ; -kli/ *adv*

par·a·sol /ˋpærəˌsɔl; ˈpærəsɒl/ *n* [U] a type of UMBRELLA used to provide shade from the sun (太) 陽傘

par·a·troop·er /ˋpærəˌtrupɚ; ˈpærəˌtruːpə/ *n* [C] a soldier who is trained to jump out of a plane using a PARACHUTE 傘兵

par·a·troops /ˋpærəˌtrups; ˈpærətruːps/ *n* [plural] a group of paratroopers that fights together as a military unit 傘兵部隊

par·a·ty·phoid /ˌpærəˋtaɪfɔɪd; ˌpærəˈtaɪfɔɪd/ *n* [U] a disease that causes fever and severe pain in your INTESTINE 副傷寒〔可引起高熱和劇烈的腸痛〕

par·boil /ˋpɑrˌbɔɪl; ˈpɑːbɔɪl/ *v* [T] to boil something until it is partly cooked 把…煮到半熟

3 **par·cel¹** /ˋpɑrsḷ; ˈpɑːsəl/ *n* [C] **1** *especially BrE* an object that has been wrapped in paper or put in a special envelope, especially so that it can be sent by mail【尤英】(小) 包裹; 郵包; PACKAGE¹ (1) *AmE*【美】: *She tied up the parcel with string.* 她用繩子把包裹綁緊。**2** an area of land that is part of a larger area which has been divided up〔土地的〕一塊, 一片〔指已被分割的較大塊土地的一部分〕: *a parcel of farmland* 一塊農田 **3** *BrE* a small quantity of food that has been wrapped up, usually in PASTRY (1)【英】〔通常指油酥點心的〕餡: *parcels of cod* 鱈魚餡 —see also 另見 **be part and parcel of** (PART¹ (25))

parcel² *v* **parcelled, parcelling** *BrE*【英】, **parceled, parceling** *AmE*【美】

parcel sth ↔ **out** *phr v* [T] to divide or share something among several people 把…分成; 分配: *Government posts have already been parcelled out among the President's friends.* 政府職位已分給了總統的朋友。

parcel sth ↔ **off** *phr v* [T] to divide something into small parts so that it can be sold 把…分成小份〔待售〕

parcel sth ↔ **up** *phr v* [T] *BrE* to make something into a parcel by wrapping it up【英】把…包起來, 把…打包

parcel post /ˈ·· ·/ *n* [U] the system of sending parcels by mail in the US〔美國〕包裹郵遞系統

parch /pɑrtʃ; pɑːtʃ/ *v* [T] if sun or wind parches land, plants etc, it makes them very dry 曬[吹]乾; 使焦乾[乾枯]

parched /pɑrtʃt; pɑːtʃt/ *adj* **1** very dry, especially because of hot weather〔尤指由於天氣炎熱而〕焦乾的, 乾枯的: *the parched African landscape* 乾燥的非洲地貌 | *He raised the water bottle to his parched lips.* 他把水瓶舉到自己乾裂的嘴唇邊。—see picture on page A13 參見 A13 頁圖 **2 be parched** *informal* to be very thirsty【非正式】渴得要命

Par·chee·si /pɑrˋtʃizi; pɑːˈtʃiːzi/ *n* [U] *AmE trademark* a children's game in which you move a small piece of plastic around a board after throwing DICE【美, 商標】巴棋戲〔一種兒童遊戲, 擲骰子後在板上移動一小塊塑料的棋戲〕; LUDO *BrE*【英】

parch·ment /ˋpɑrtʃmənt; ˈpɑːtʃmənt/ *n* **1** [U] a material used in the past for writing on, made from the skin of a sheep or a goat〔古時寫字用的〕羊皮紙 **2** [U] thick yellow-white writing paper, sometimes used for official documents〔用於書寫正式文件的〕仿羊皮紙 **3** [C] a document written on this paper or material 羊皮紙文件; 仿羊皮紙文件

pard·ner /ˋpɑrdnɚ; ˈpɑːdnə/ *n AmE humorous spoken* a way of addressing someone you know well【美, 幽默, 口】夥伴, 老兄: *Howdy, pardner!* 你好, 朋友!

par·don¹ /ˋpɑrdṇ; ˈpɑːdn/ *interjection especially BrE*【尤英】**1** used when you want someone to repeat something because you did not hear it 請重複一遍, 請再説一遍〔沒聽清對方的話希望重複一遍時的用語〕: *Pardon, you'll have to talk louder, I can't hear you.* 請再説一遍, 你得大聲點説, 我聽不見。| *"Is it hanging up in your bedroom?" "Pardon?" "I said is it in your bedroom?"* "那東西是不是掛在你的臥室裡?" "請原諒, 你説甚麼?" "我説那東西是不是在你的臥室裡?" **2** used to say 'sorry' after you have made an impolite sound such as a BURP or YAWN 對不起, 請原諒〔在發出不禮貌的聲音如打嗝或打呵欠後的道歉語〕

pardon² *v* [T] **1** to officially allow someone to be free without being punished, although a court has proved that they are guilty of a crime 赦免: *The governor pardoned the two offenders.* 州長赦免了那兩名罪犯。**2** [not in progressive 不用進行式] *old-fashioned* to forgive someone for behaving badly【過時】寬恕, 原諒: *I hope you will pardon my son's little outburst at dinner.* 我希望你能原諒我兒子在晚餐時耍的小脾氣。**3 sb may be pardoned for doing sth** used to say that it is easy to understand why someone has done something or why they think something 某人做某事情有可原: *Anyone reading the advertisement might be pardoned for thinking that the offer was genuine.* 無論誰看了那則廣告認為那個開價名符其實, 也許都是情有可原的。

Frequencies of the verb **pardon** in spoken and written English 動詞 pardon 在英語口語和書面語中的使用頻率

SPOKEN 口語

WRITTEN 書面語

5 10 15 per million 每百萬

Based on the British National Corpus and the Longman Lancaster Corpus 據英國國家語料庫和朗文蘭卡斯特語料庫

This graph shows that the verb **pardon** is much more common in spoken English than in written English. This is because it is used in a lot of common spoken phrases. 本圖表顯示, 動詞 pardon 在英語口語中的使用頻率遠遠高於書面語, 因為口語中很多常用片語是由 pardon 構成的。

pardon (*v*) **SPOKEN PHRASES**
含 pardon 的口語片語

4 a) pardon me used to say 'sorry' politely when you have accidentally pushed someone, interrupted them etc 對不起, 請原諒〔無意中碰到某人、打斷某人等時的禮貌用語〕: *Oh, pardon me, I didn't mean to disturb you.* 噢, 對不起, 我不是有意要打擾你。**b)** used to say 'sorry' politely after you have made an impolite sound such as a BURP (1) or a YAWN[2] (1) 對不起, 很抱歉〔在發出不禮貌的聲音如打嗝、打呵欠後的道歉用語〕 **c)** used before you politely correct someone or disagree with them 對不起, 不好意思〔在糾正或不同意某人時的禮貌用語〕: *Pardon me, but I think you've got your facts wrong.* 對不起, 我想你把事情搞錯了。**d)** *old-fashioned, especially AmE* used to politely get someone's attention in order to ask them a question【過時, 尤美】對不起, 勞駕〔為問問題而吸引別人注意力時的禮貌用語〕: *Pardon me, can you direct me to City Hall?* 勞駕, 你能告訴我去市政廳怎麼走嗎? **5 pardon me for interrupting/asking/saying** *especially BrE* used to politely ask if you can interrupt someone, ask something etc【尤英】請原諒我打斷/問/説: *Pardon me for saying so, but you're doing that all wrong.* 請原諒我這麼説, 但是你全做錯了。**6 pardon my ignorance/rudeness etc** used when you think that you may seem not to know enough, not to be polite enough etc 請原諒我的無知/無禮等: *Pardon my ignorance, but what does OPEC stand for?* 請原諒我的無知, OPEC 代表甚麼? **7 if you'll pardon the expression** used when you are saying sorry for using a slightly impolite phrase 請原諒我用這個詞語: *It was a bit of a cock-up, if you'll pardon the expression.* 這事搞得有點兒一團糟, 請原諒我用這個詞。**8 pardon my French** *humorous* used to say sorry after you have said an impolite word【幽默】請原諒我講了這樣的話〔説了無禮的話之後使用〕 **9 pardon me for breathing/living** used when you are annoyed because you think someone has answered you angrily for no good reason 請原諒我活着讓你受氣了〔表示對當別人無緣無故氣沖沖地回答你時讓你感到惱火〕

pardon[3] *n* **1 (I) beg your pardon a)** *spoken* used when politely saying sorry because you have just made a mistake【口】對不起, 請原諒〔用於對自己的過錯表示歉意〕: *I beg your pardon, I meant the green one.* 對不起, 我説的是綠色的那個。| *I do beg your pardon, I thought you were someone else.* 請原諒, 我認錯人了。**b)** used to politely ask someone to repeat something because you did not hear it 對不起, 你説甚麼?〔用於禮貌地請求別人重複説過的話〕: *"I think the radiator's leaking." "Beg your pardon?" "The radiator, I think it's leaking."* "我想散熱器在漏水。" "對不起, 你説甚麼?" "那散熱器, 我想它在漏水。" **c)** used to politely say sorry because you have accidentally touched someone, stepped on their foot, burped (BURP (1)) etc 對不起, 很抱歉〔無意中碰到別人、踩了別人的腳、打嗝等時的道歉用語〕 **d)** used when you are strongly or angrily disagreeing with what someone has just said 對不起〔用於對某人所説的話感到強烈反對〕: *I beg your pardon, I never said that at all.* 對不起, 我從來沒有那樣説過。**e)** used when you are surprised or shocked by what someone has just said 對不起, 不好意思〔對別人剛説過的話表示驚奇或震驚時的用語〕: *"I'm ready to pay £20,000." "I beg your pardon, are you serious?"* "我準備付 20,000 英鎊。" "對不起, 你是認真的嗎?" —see 見 EXCUSE[1] (USAGE) **2** [C] an official order allowing someone to be free and stopping their punishment, although a court has proved them guilty of a crime 赦免令, 赦免狀: **grant/give sb a pardon** *Tyler was convicted but was granted a royal pardon.* 泰勒被判有罪, 但得到了國王的赦免。**3** [U] *old-fashioned* the act of forgiving someone【過時】寬恕, 原諒: **ask/beg sb's pardon (for)** (=ask someone to forgive you) 請求某人的原諒 *Walter begged her pardon for all the pain he had caused her.* 沃爾特請求她原諒自己給她造成的所有痛苦。

par·don·a·ble /ˋpɑrdn̩əbl̩; ˈpɑːdənəbəl/ *adj formal* pardonable behaviour or mistakes are not very bad and can be forgiven; EXCUSABLE【正式】〔行為或過失〕可寬恕的, 可原諒的 —**pardonably** *adv*

pare /pɛr; peə/ *v* [T] **1** to cut off the thin outer part of something using a sharp knife〔用刀子〕削去...的皮: *Pare the onions then cut them.* 先削去洋蔥的外皮, 然後再將其切開。**2** to cut your nails so that they look neat 修剪〔指甲〕

pare sth **down** *phr v* [T] to gradually reduce an amount or number〔逐步〕削減, 減少: *The workforce has been pared down from 1,400 to 700.* 職工總數已從 1,400 人裁減至 700 人。| **pare sth down to the bone** (=reduce an amount or number as much as possible) 盡可能地削減某物, 將某物減到極限[最低] —**pared-down** *adj*

par·ent /ˋpɛrənt; ˈpeərənt/ *n* [C] **1** the father or mother of a person or animal〔人的〕父; 母;〔動物的〕親體, 母體: *I don't really get on with my boyfriend's parents.* 我和我男朋友的父母相處得不怎麼好。| *a parent substitute, such as an aunt* 代替母親的人如姨媽 —see picture at 參見 FAMILY 圖 **2** something that produces other things of the same type 母體, 母公司: *Shares in Mercury parent Cable and Wireless went up by 3p.* 默庫里的母公司英國大東電報局的股價上漲了三便士。—see also 另見 ONE-PARENT FAMILY, SINGLE PARENT (S1 W1)

par·ent·age /ˋpɛrəntɪdʒ; ˈpeərəntɪdʒ/ *n* [U] someone's parents and the country and social class they are from 出身, 身世: *a child of unknown parentage* (=we do not know who its parents are) 身世不明的孩子

pa·rent·al /pəˋrɛntl̩; pəˈrentl/ *adj* connected with one parent or both parents 父親的; 母親的; 父母的: *parental responsibilities* 父母的責任

parent com·pa·ny /ˈ·· ˌ···/ *n* [C] a company that controls a smaller company or organization 母公司, 總公司

pa·ren·the·sis /pəˋrɛnθəsɪs; pəˈrenθɪ̣sɪ̣s/ *n plural* **parentheses** /-ˌsiz; -siːz/ [usually plural 一般用複數] *especially AmE* a round BRACKET【尤美】圓括號: **in parentheses** *The figures in parentheses refer to page numbers.* 圓括號內的數字指的是頁碼。—see picture at 參見 PUNCTUATION MARK 圖

par·en·the·t·ical /ˌpærənˋθɛtɪkl; ˌpærənˈθetɪkəl◂/ also 又作 **parenthetic** *adj* said or written as an extra remark about something you are talking about 補充性質的, 附帶[加]説明的 —**parenthetically** /-klɪ; -kli/ *adv*

par·ent·hood /ˋpɛrəntˌhʊd; ˈpeərənthʊd/ *n* [U] the state of being a parent 父母的身分

par·ent·ing /ˋpɛrəntɪŋ; ˈpeərəntɪŋ/ *n* [U] the skill or activity of looking after children as a parent 父母對孩子的養育[照顧]

par ex·cel·lence /pɑr ˋɛksəˌlɑns; ˌpɑːr ˈeksəlɑːns/ *adj* [only after noun 僅用於名詞後] *French* the very best【法】最卓越的, 出類拔萃的: *Auguste Escoffier, master-chef par excellence* 奧古斯特·埃斯克菲爾, 技藝超羣的廚師長

par·fait /pɑrˋfe; pɑːˈfeɪ/ *n* [U] *AmE* a sweet food made of layers of ICE CREAM and fruit【美】冰淇淋水果凍〔由多層冰淇淋和水果製成的甜點〕

pa·ri·ah /pəˋraɪə; pəˈraɪə/ *n* [C] **1** someone who is hated and avoided by other people 被痛恨和排斥的人, 被遺棄的人: *a social pariah* 為社會遺棄者 **2** *old use* a member of a very low social class in India【舊】〔古印度社會下層的〕賤民

par·i·mu·tu·el /ˋpærɪˋmjutʃuəl; ˌpæriˈmjuːtʃʊəl/ *n French*【法】**1** [U] a system in which the money that people have risked on a horse race is shared between the people who have won〔賽馬賭博中由贏家分享全部賭金的〕同注分彩賭博法 **2** [C] *AmE* a machine used to calculate the amount of money people can win by risking it on horse races【美】〔計算賽馬賭金的〕賭金計算器, 同注分彩計算器; TOTE[2] *BrE*【英】

par·ings /ˋpɛrɪŋz; ˈpeərɪŋz/ *n* [plural] thin pieces of something that have been cut off 削下的薄片: *nail parings* 剪下的指甲 | *cheese parings* 削下的乳酪片

P

par·ish /ˋpærɪʃ; ˈpærɪʃ/ *n* [C] **1** the area that a priest is responsible for〔由一名牧師管理的〕教區: *a parish priest* 教區牧師 **2** *BrE* a small area, especially a village, that has its own local government【英】〔有其地方政府的〕郡以下的小行政區〔尤指村莊〕: *a parish boundary* 小行政區邊界 **3 the parish** the people who live in a particular area, especially those who go to church〔尤指參加教區教堂活動的〕教區居民 **4 sb's parish** *BrE old-fashioned* something which someone knows a lot about or which they are responsible for【英, 過時】某人的知識領域[職責範圍]

parish church /ˌ‥ ˈ·/ *n* [C] the main church in a particular area 教區教堂

parish clerk /ˌ‥ ˈ·/ *n* [C] an official who works for a church in a particular town or area 教區執事

parish coun·cil /ˌ‥ ˈ‥/ *n* [C] a group of people who are responsible for taking decisions about a small area, especially a village 教區管理委員會

pa·rish·io·ner /pəˋrɪʃənɚ; pəˈrɪʃənə/ *n* [C] someone who lives in a parish, especially someone who regularly goes to the church there〔尤指定期參加教區教堂活動的〕教區居民

parish pump /ˌ‥ ˈ·/ *adj* [only before noun 僅用於名詞前] *BrE old-fashioned* concerned only with a small local area【英, 過時】區域性的, 地方性的: *parish pump politics* 區域性政治

parish re·gis·ter /ˌ‥ ˈ‥·/ *n* [C] an official record of the births, deaths, and marriages in a parish〔有關教區居民出生、死亡、婚姻的〕教區記事錄

Pa·ris·i·an /pəˋrɪʒən; pəˈrɪziən/ *adj* coming from or connected with Paris 來自巴黎的; 巴黎的 —**Parisian** *n* [C]

par·i·ty /ˋpærətɪ; ˈpærəti/ *n* [U] **1** the state of being equal, especially having equal pay, rights, or power〔尤指薪金、權利、權力的〕相同, 相等, 同等: **[+with]** *Women workers are demanding parity with their male colleagues.* 女職工在要求與男同事享有同等的待遇。**2** *technical* equality between the units of money from two different countries【術語】〔兩個不同國家的貨幣單位的〕平價, 等價: *until the time the pound has parity with the dollar* 直到英鎊和美元等價的時候 **3** *technical* a system for finding mistakes in the sending of information from one computer to another【術語】〔在兩台電腦之間發送信息時發現錯誤的〕奇偶校驗, 同位核對: *parity checking* 奇偶校驗

1 2 **park**[1] /park; pɑːk/ *n* [C] **1** a large open area with grass and trees, especially in a town, where people can walk, play games etc 公園: *Let's go for a walk in the park.* 我們去公園散步吧。| *a park bench* 公園長椅 **2** a large enclosed area of land, with grass and trees, around a big house in the countryside〔鄉村別墅周圍的〕庭園, 園林 **3 the park** *BrE informal* the field where a game of football or RUGBY is played【英, 非正式】足球場; 橄欖球場 **4** *AmE informal* the field where a game of BASEBALL is played【美, 非正式】棒球場 —see also 另見 AMUSEMENT PARK, BALL PARK, CAR PARK, NATIONAL PARK, SAFARI PARK, SCIENCE PARK, THEME PARK, TRAILER PARK

2 **park**[2] *v* **1** [I,T] to put a car or other vehicle in a particular place for a period of time 停放〔汽車或其他車輛〕: *You can't park here – it's private property.* 這裡不能停車——這是私人地產。| **park sth** *We couldn't find anywhere to park the van.* 我們找不到地方停放那輛小型貨車。| *There's a police car parked outside our house.* 一輛警車停在我們的房子外面。| *parked cars* 停放的汽車 | *I'm parked over there.* (=I've parked my car over there) 我的汽車停在那邊。**2** [T] *spoken* to put something in a particular place for a period of time, in a way that is inconvenient or annoying【口】〔引起不便或令人討厭地〕把〔某物〕放在〔某處〕: **park sth in/on/here etc** *He parked a load of papers on my desk.* 他把一大摞文件放在我桌上。**3 park yourself** *spoken* to sit or stand in a particular place, that is inconvenient for other people【口】〔給別人帶來不便地〕坐在某處; 站在某處: *Alma parked herself in the hotel lobby and refused to budge.* 阿爾瑪站在酒店大廳裡不肯動。

par·ka /ˋparkə; ˈpɑːkə/ *n* [C] a thick warm JACKET with a HOOD 風雪大衣, 派克大衣〔帶兜帽的禦寒夾克〕—see picture at 參見 COAT[1] 圖

park and ride /ˌ· · ˈ·/ *n* [U] a system in which you leave your car just outside a town or city and then take a special bus to the centre of the town 換車通勤〔一種把汽車停在城外, 換乘公共汽車進城的交通體制〕

par·kin /ˋparkɪn; ˈpɑːkɪn/ *n* [U] *BrE* a type of cake made with OATMEAL and GINGER【英】〔用燕麥片和薑製成的〕燕麥薑餅

park·ing /ˋparkɪŋ; ˈpɑːkɪŋ/ *n* [U] **1** the act of parking a car or other vehicle〔車輛等的〕停放: *No Parking.* 禁止停車。| *a parking fine* 違章停車罰款 | *a parking space* 停車位 **2** spaces in which you can leave a car or other vehicle 停車處, 停車位: *There's plenty of parking at the shopping mall.* 那個購物中心有許多停車位。

parking ga·rage /ˈ‥ ˌ‥/ *n* [C] *AmE* MULTISTOREY CAR PARK【美】公共停車庫, 多層停車場

parking light /ˈ‥ ˌ·/ *n* [C] *AmE* SIDELIGHT【美】側燈; 旁燈, 停車信號燈 —see picture on page A2 參見 A2 頁圖

parking lot /ˈ‥ ·/ *n* [C] *AmE* an open area for cars to park in【美】露天停車場[區]; CAR PARK *BrE*【英】

parking me·ter /ˈ‥ ˌ‥/ *n* [C] a machine which you put money into when you park your car next to it 停車計時收費器 —see picture on page A3 參見 A3 頁圖

parking tick·et /ˈ‥ ˌ‥/ *n* [C] an official notice fixed to a vehicle, saying that you have to pay money because you have parked your car in the wrong place or for too long 違章停車罰款通知單

Par·kin·son's dis·ease /ˋparkɪnsənz dɪˌziz; ˈpɑːkənsənz dɪˌziːz/ also 又作 **Parkinson's** *n* [U] a serious illness in which your muscles become very weak and your arms and legs shake 帕金森(氏)病, 震顫性麻痹

Parkinson's law /ˈ‥· ˌ·/ *n* [singular] the idea that the amount of work you have to do increases to fill the amount of time you have to do it in 帕金森定律〔指工作量隨工作時限延長而增加的一種觀點〕

park keep·er /ˈ· ˌ‥/ *n* [C] *BrE* someone whose job is to look after a park【英】公園管理員

park·land /ˋparkˌlænd; ˈpɑːk-lænd/ *n* [U] **1** *BrE* an area of land with grass and trees, surrounding a big house in the countryside【英】〔環繞鄉村宅邸的〕邸園, 草木區 **2** land with grass and trees which is used as a park〔用作公園的〕公園用地, 公共綠地

park ran·ger /ˈ· ˌ‥/ *n* [C] *AmE* a RANGER (1)【美】公園管理員

park·way /ˋparkˌwe; ˈpɑːkweɪ/ *n* [C] *AmE* a wide road with an area of grass and trees in the middle or along the sides【美】〔中間或兩旁有草地和樹木的〕林園式大路, 林蔭大路

par·ky /ˋparkɪ; ˈpɑːki/ *adj BrE informal* cold【英, 非正式】寒冷的: *It's a bit parky outside today.* 今天外面有點兒冷。

par·lance /ˋparləns; ˈpɑːləns/ *n* **in common/medical/advertising etc parlance** expressed in words that most people, or a particular group of people, would use 用一般的／醫學上的／廣告上等的說法[用語]等: *This is called a unique selling proposition in advertising parlance.* 在廣告用語中, 這叫做獨特的銷售主張。

par·lay /ˋparlɪ; ˈpɑːli/ *v* [T] *AmE* to increase the value of something that you have, especially your abilities, previous success, or money, by using all your opportunities well【美】使增值, 使更有價值; 成功地利用〔尤指才能、以往的成功或金錢等〕: **parlay sth into** *He parlayed his athletic achievements into a successful sports broadcasting career.* 他利用自己的體育成就成為了一名成功的體育播音員。

par·ley /ˋparlɪ; ˈpɑːli/ *n* [C] *old-fashioned* a discussion in which enemies try to achieve peace【過時】〔與敵人謀求和平的〕和談, 會談 —**parley** *v* [I]

2 **par·lia·ment** /ˋparləmənt; ˈpɑːləmənt/ *n* [C] **1** the group of people who are elected to make a country's laws and discuss important national affairs 議會, 國會 **2 Parliament** the main law-making institution in the United Kingdom, which consists of the HOUSE OF COMMONS and the HOUSE OF LORDS 英國議會〔由上議院和下議院組成〕: **enter Parliament/get into Parliament** (=be elected as a member of Parliament) 被選為議員 **3** the period during which this institution meets 一屆議會[國會]: *We expect to get these laws passed during the present parliament.* 我們期望這些法律能在本屆議會中通過。

par·lia·men·tar·i·an /ˌparləmɛnˋtɛrɪən; ˌpɑːləmənˈteəriən/ *n* [C] a skilled and experienced member of a parliament 有經驗的議員

3 **par·lia·men·ta·ry** /ˌparləˋmɛntərɪ; ˌpɑːləˈmentəri◂/ *adj* connected with or governed by a parliament 議會的, 國會的; 由議會[國會]支配的: *the world's oldest parliamentary democracy* 世界上最古老的議會民主制

par·lor /ˋparlɚ; ˈpɑːlə/ *n* [C] the American spelling of PARLOUR parlour 的美式拼法

parlor car /ˈ·· ·/ *n* [C] *AmE* a special railway carriage which has comfortable seats【美】豪華型列車車廂 —compare 比較 PULLMAN

par·lour *BrE*【英】, **parlor** *AmE*【美】/ˋparlɚ; ˈpɑːlə/ *n* [C] **1 ice cream/massage/funeral etc parlour** a shop or type of business that provides a particular service 冰淇淋店／按摩院／殯儀館等〔專門提供某種服務的店〕 **2** *old-fashioned* a room in a house which has comfortable chairs and is used for meeting guests【過時】〔家庭的〕起居室, 會客室, 客廳 —see also 另見 MILKING PARLOUR

parlour game *BrE*【英】, **parlor game** *AmE*【美】/ˈ·· ·/ *n* [C] *old-fashioned* a game that can be played indoors, such as a guessing game or a word game【過時】室內遊戲〈如猜謎或文字遊戲〉

parlour maid *BrE*【英】, **parlor maid** *AmE*【美】/ˈ·· ·/ *n* [C] a female servant who was employed in former times in a large house to clean the rooms, serve guests etc〔舊時受雇清理房間、服侍客人等的〕客廳女僕

par·lous /ˋparləs; ˈpɑːləs/ *adj formal* in a very bad or dangerous condition【正式】糟糕的; 危險的: *the parlous state of the country* 該國的危險狀況

Par·me·san /ˌparməˋzæn; ˌpɑːmɪ̈ˈzæn◂/ also 又作 **Parmesan cheese** /ˌ··· ˈ·/ *n* [U] a hard strong-tasting Italian cheese 帕爾馬乾酪〔一種味道很重的意大利硬牛奶乾酪〕

pa·ro·chi·al /pəˋrokɪəl; pəˈrəʊkiəl/ *adj* **1** only interested in the things that affect you and your local area, and not interested in more important matters〔興趣、視野等〕偏狹的, 狹隘的: *Local newspapers tend to be very parochial.* 地方報紙一般視野很狹隘。**2** [only before noun 僅用於名詞前] concerned with a PARISH 教區的 —**parochialism** *n* [U] —**parochially** *adv*

parochial school /ˈ··· ˈ·/ *n* [C] *especially AmE* a private school which is run by or connected with a church【尤美】〔由教會興辦或與教會有關的〕教區學校, 教會學校

par·o·dy¹ /ˋpærədɪ; ˈpærədi/ *n* **1** [C,U] a piece of writing or music that copies a particular well-known style in an amusing way〔文章或音樂的〕詼諧性模仿作品, 滑稽的模仿作品: **[+on/of]** *The play is a parody of James Joyce's book 'Ulysses'.* 該劇是對詹姆斯·喬伊斯作品《尤利西斯》的滑稽模仿。**2** [C] something that is so bad that it seems like a very bad copy of another thing 拙劣的模仿: *a grotesque parody of her former self* 對她自己以前樣子的怪誕模仿 **3 a parody of justice** something that is extremely unfair 極不公平的事, 對正義的嘲弄

parody² *v* [T] to copy someone's style or attitude 模仿〔某人的風格或態度〕: *East end working class attitudes have been parodied by the TV character Alf Garnett.* 電視人物阿爾夫·加尼特滑稽地模仿了倫敦東區工人階層的態度。—**parodist** *n* [C]

pa·role¹ /pəˋrol; pəˈrəʊl/ *n* [U] permission for someone to leave prison, on the condition that they promise to behave well 假釋(出獄), 有條件釋放: **on parole** *He was released on parole after serving 2 years.* 服刑兩年後他獲假釋出獄。| **break parole** (=not behave as you are supposed to when you are on parole) (假釋期間) 違誓

parole² *v* [T] to allow someone to leave prison on the condition that they promise to behave well 准許假釋; 使獲假釋

par·ox·ys·m /ˋpærəksˌɪzəm; ˈpærəksɪzəm/ *n* [C] **1 a paroxysm of rage/jealousy/laughter etc** a sudden uncontrollable expression of strong feeling 勃然大怒／頓生妒嫉／一陣狂笑等: *Joshua suddenly broke out into a paroxysm of sobbing.* 喬舒亞突然一陣啜泣。**2** a sudden, short attack of pain, coughing, shaking etc〔疼痛、咳嗽、顫抖等的〕發作, 陣發: **[+of]** *paroxysms of coughing* 一陣咳嗽 —**paroxysmal** /ˌpærəkˋsɪzml; ˌpærəkˈsɪzməl◂/ *adj*

par·quet /parˋke; ˈpɑːkeɪ/ *n* [U] small flat blocks of wood fitted together in a pattern that cover the floor of a room 鑲木地板: *a parquet floor* 鑲木地板

par·ri·cide /ˋpærəˌsaɪd; ˈpærɪ̈saɪd/ *n* **1** [U] *formal* the crime of killing your father, mother, or any other close relative【正式】弒父[母]罪; 弒近親罪 **2** [C] *technical* someone who is guilty of this crime【術語】弒父[母]者; 弒近親者 —compare 比較 MATRICIDE, PATRICIDE

par·rot¹ /ˋpærət; ˈpærət/ *n* [C] **1** a tropical bird with a curved beak and brightly coloured feathers that can be taught to copy human speech 鸚鵡 **2 parrot fashion** *BrE* repeating what someone has just said without understanding it【英】鸚鵡學舌般地, 重複而不解其義地: *reciting poems parrot-fashion* 鸚鵡學舌般地背誦詩歌 —see also 另見 **sick as a parrot** (SICK¹ (8))

parrot² *v* [T] to repeat someone else's words or ideas without really understanding what you are saying 不加思索[不解其義]地重複, 鸚鵡學舌般地重複, 機械地模仿

par·ry /ˋpærɪ; ˈpæri/ *v* [T] **1** to avoid answering a difficult question 迴避〔難以回答的問題〕: *White House spokesmen tired of parrying journalists' questions.* 白宮發言人對迴避記者的問題感到厭倦。**2** to defend yourself against someone who is attacking you by pushing their weapon or hand to one side; DEFLECT 擋開, 避開〔武器、手〕—**parry** *n* [C]

parse /pars; pɑːz/ *v* [T] *technical* to describe the grammar of a word when it is in a particular sentence, or the grammar of the whole sentence【術語】對〔句中的詞或句子〕作語法分析 —**parser** *n* [C]: *a powerful parser that analysed errors in word processed letters* 對以文字處理的信件中的錯誤進行分析的強大語法分析程式

Par·see, Parsi /ˋparsi; pɑːˈsiː/ *n* [C] a member of an ancient Persian religious group in India 帕西人, 印度袄教徒 —**Parsee** *adj*

par·si·mo·ni·ous /ˌparsəˋmonɪəs; ˌpɑːsɪ̈ˈməʊniəs◂/ *adj formal* extremely unwilling to spend money; MEAN² (2)【正式】過分節儉的, 吝嗇的, 小氣的 —**parsimoniously** *adv* —**parsimony** /ˋparsəˌmonɪ; ˈpɑːsɪ̈məni/ *n* [U]

pars·ley /ˋparslɪ; ˈpɑːsli/ *n* [U] a small plant with curly leaves that have a strong taste, used in cooking or as decoration on food 歐芹〔可供食用或作食品上的裝飾〕

pars·nip /ˈparsnɪp; ˈpɑːsnɪp/ *n* [C,U] a plant with a thick white or yellowish root that is eaten as a vegetable 歐防風〔其根部可食用, 呈白色或淡黃色〕—see picture on page A9 參見A9頁圖

par·son /ˈparsn̩; ˈpɑːsən/ *n* [C] *old-fashioned* a Christian priest or minister responsible for a small area, especially in the Church of England【過時】〔尤指英國國教的〕教區牧師

par·son·age /ˈparsnɪdʒ; ˈpɑːsənɪdʒ/ *n* [C] the house where a parson lives 教區牧師住宅

parson's nose /,·· ˈ·/ *n* [C] *BrE informal* the piece of flesh at the tail end of a bird, usually a chicken, that has been cooked【英, 非正式】〔烹調過的禽類的, 通常指雞的〕尾部[屁股]肉; POPE'S NOSE *AmE*【美】

S1 W1 **part¹** /part; pɑːt/ *n*

1 ►PIECE OF 部分◄ [C,U] a piece of something such as an object, area, event, or period of time ...的(一)部分: **[+of]** *The front part of the car was badly damaged.* 這輛汽車的前部損壞嚴重。| *In parts of Canada, French is the first language.* 在加拿大的部分地區, 法語是第一語言。| *What part of America do you come from?* 你來自美國的哪個地區? | *I only saw the first part of the programme.* 我只看了那個節目的第一部分。| **be (a) part of** *Falling over is part of learning how to ski.* 學滑雪少不了要摔倒。| **late/early part** *She spent the early part of her life in Belfast.* 她的早年是在貝爾法斯特度過的。| **best/worst part** *The best part of the holiday was the trip to the Islands.* 假期中最開心的一段是去那座島上旅行。| **hard/easy part** *Getting dad to agree will be the hard part.* 讓爸爸同意會是很難的。

2 ►MACHINE/OBJECT 機器/物體◄ [C] one of the separate pieces that something such as a machine, object etc is made of〔機器、物體等的〕零件, 部件: *I've glued it back together, but this part won't fit properly.* 我已重新用膠把它黏好了, 但這一塊不怎麼合適。| *They send you the parts and you build it yourself.* 他們寄給你部件, 你要自己組裝。| **spare part** (=kept for when a part breaks, needs replacing etc) 備用零件

3 ►NOT ALL 不是全部◄ [C,U] some but not all of a particular thing or group of things〔東西的〕部分, 局部: **[+of]** *Part of the castle was destroyed in the fire.* 這個城堡的一部分毀於火災。| **in parts** *The film is very violent in parts.* 這部電影有些片段是非常暴力的。| **(only) part of the story/problem/explanation etc** *Poor working conditions are only part of the problem.* 惡劣的工作條件僅僅是問題的一方面。

4 play a part a) if something plays a part in something, it is one of the several causes that make it happen or be successful 起作用, 有影響: **[+in]** *This innovation has played a part in the company's success.* 這項革新對於公司的成功起了作用。| **play a big/important part in** *Besides dieting, exercising plays an important part in losing weight.* 除節食之外, 鍛鍊對減肥也起着重要的作用。**b)** to perform the actions, words etc of a particular character in a play, film etc 扮演...角色: **play the part of** *Kenneth Brannagh played the part of Henry V.* 肯尼斯·布拉納扮演亨利五世。**c)** to be involved in something 參與, 參加: *Britain should play its full part in these negotiations.* 英國應充分參與這些談判。

5 take part to be involved in an activity, sport, event etc together with other people 參加, 參與: **[+in]** *About 400 students took part in the protest.* 大約400名學生參加了抗議活動。| *She wanted to take part but she was too ill.* 她想參加, 但她病得太厲害了。| **take an active/leading part** *At college I took an active part in student politics.* 在大學裡我積極參與學生政治活動。

6 the best/better part of nearly all of something 絕大部分/大部分, 大半: *We waited for the best part of an hour.* 我們等了近一個小時。

7 a good/large part of a lot or more than half of something 多半, 大半: *A large part of the budget will be spent on advertising.* 大部分預算將花費在廣告上。

8 in large part/for the most part mostly, to a great extent, or in most places 多半, 在很大程度上; 在大多數地方: *The team, for the most part, was confident of success.* 這個隊的隊員大多有獲勝的信心。| *The money was in large part raised by sponsorship.* 這些錢多半是籌集得來的贊助費。

9 form part of/form a part of to be one of the things that together make up something larger or more important 組成...的(一)部分: *Practical work forms an integral part of the course.* 實習是這門課必不可少的部分。

10 ►HAIR 頭髮◄ *AmE* a PARTING【美】〔頭髮的〕分縫

11 ►ACTING 表演◄ [C] the words and actions of a particular character in a play, film etc, performed by an actor〔角色的〕台詞和動作: *I have to learn the part of Romeo by Tuesday.* 我必須在星期二之前背熟羅密歐這一角色的台詞。

12 part of the body a particular piece or area of a body 身體部位: *More heat is lost through the head than through any other part of the body.* 身體熱量通過頭部散發比通過其他部位散發來得多。—see also 另見 PRIVATE PARTS

13 ►BOOK 書◄ [C] the different parts of something written such as a book, sometimes used as a title〔書等的〕部分, 篇, 章: **first/last part** *Please turn to the first part of the report.* 請翻到報告的第一部分。| **Part One/Three/Six etc** *The first chapter of Part Two begins at the funeral.* 第二部分的第一章是從葬禮開始的。

14 ►MUSIC 音樂◄ [C] a tune that a particular type of instrument or voice within a group plays or sings〔樂器或聲音的〕部, 聲部, 音部: *The tenor part carried the melody.* 男高音部唱主旋律。

15 take/have/play/want no part in not be involved in something, because you do not agree with or approve of it〔因不同意或不贊成而〕不(想)參與; 和...沒有關係: *I played no part in leaking the information to the press.* 我沒有把消息泄露給新聞界。

16 ►YOUR PART IN 某人在...中的作用◄ what you yourself did, in an activity that was shared by several people, especially something bad〔尤指壞事中的〕份兒; 責任; 作用: *They were sentenced for their part in a £14 million fraud.* 他們因參與1,400萬英鎊的詐騙活動而被判刑。

17 in/round these parts in the particular area, part of a country etc that you are in 在這一帶: *We don't get many tourists in these parts.* 我們這一帶沒有多少遊客。

18 part of me/him etc used when you have many different feelings or thoughts about something, so it is difficult to decide what you feel or what you should do 我/他等有點...〔用於表示你無法斷定自己的想法或感覺〕: *Part of me just wants to leave, but I know I will be unhappy if I do.* 我有點想一走了之, 但我知道如果我走了, 我會不開心的。

19 take sb's part to support someone when they are being criticized or attacked 站在某人一邊, 支持[袒護]某人: *The school took the teacher's part and told Jamie to leave.* 校方支持那位老師, 並要傑米退學。

20 ►QUANTITY 數量◄ [C] a particular quantity of a substance used when measuring different substances together into a mixture ...中的一份, ...分之一: *Prepare the glue with one part powder to three parts water.* 用一份粉末和三份水來配製膠水。

21 for the part of/for his part etc used to say what someone's opinions are, when compared to someone else's opinions 就...而言[對...來說]/就他而言[對他來說]等: *For my part I prefer living in the country.* 對我來說, 我寧願住在鄉下。

22 on sb's part/on the part of sb used to say that someone has done something or feels something 由某人所作出的; 就某人而言: *It was probably just a mistake on her part.* 這可能只是她的一個失誤。| *There has never been any jealousy on my part.* 我從沒有感到嫉妒。

23 in part to some degree, but not completely 在某種程度上; 部分地: *The accident was due in part to my own carelessness.* 這次事故在某種程度上是由於我的粗心大意造成的。

24 take sth in good part *old-fashioned* to be able to laugh at a joke, which is about you or affects you【過時】對某事一笑置之, 對某事物並不見怪

25 be part and parcel of included in something else or connected with it 是…的一部分, 是…不可或缺的部分: *Working irregular hours is all part and parcel of being a journalist.* 工作時間無規律是從事記者工作的基本特徵。

part[2] *v* **1** [T] to pull the two sides of something apart, making a space in the middle 使分開, 使分離: *The sunlight flooded the room when he parted the curtains.* 他拉開窗簾, 陽光灑滿了整個房間。| **parted lips** (=your mouth open) 張開的嘴 *Ralph's lips parted into a delighted smile.* 拉爾夫咧開嘴, 露出了開心的笑容。**2** [I] to separate from someone, or end a relationship with them 分手, 分別; 斷絕關係: *They parted on amicable terms.* 他們友好地分手了。| *I hope we will never part.* 我希望我們永不分離。| **be parted** *They were hardly ever parted in thirty years of marriage.* 在三十年的婚姻生活中, 他們幾乎從沒有分開過。**3 part company a)** to separate from someone, or end a relationship with them 分手, 分別; 斷絕關係: *The two women parted company outside their rooms.* 那兩個女人在她們的屋外分了手。**b)** to no longer agree with or think the same as someone else (和…)意見不合, 有分歧: *He parted company with Lloyd George over post-war diplomacy.* 他和〔英國前首相〕勞埃德·喬治在戰後外交問題上意見不合。**4** [T] if you part your hair you separate it into two parts with a comb so that it looks tidy 用梳子給〔頭髮〕分縫

part with sth *phr v* [T] to unwillingly give something to someone else or stop having it yourself〔不情願地〕放棄, 捨棄: *I'm reluctant to part with any of the kittens, but we need the money.* 我不願賣掉任何一隻小貓, 但是我們需要錢。

part[3] *adv* **part sth, part sth** if something is part one thing, part another, it consists of both of those things 部分是某物, 部分是某物; 既有某物, 又有某物: *The medical exams are part written, part practical.* 醫學考試部分是筆試, 部分是考實踐。| *The room is really part sitting room, part bedroom.* 這個房間實際上既是起居室, 又是臥室。

part[4] *adj* **part owner/payment etc** only owning, paying etc a bit of something, not all of it 共同所有者/部分付款等: *I gave them £10 in part payment.* 我給了他們10英鎊作為部分付款。

par·take /pɑrˋtek; pɑːˈteɪk/ *v past tense* **partook** /-ˋtʊk; -ˈtʊk/ *past participle* **partaken** /-ˋtekən; -ˈteɪkən/ [I] *formal*【正式】**1** to eat or drink something that is offered to you 吃; 喝: **[+of]** *Will you partake of a glass of wine?* 你要喝杯酒嗎? **2** to take part in an activity or event; PARTICIPATE 參加, 參與: **[+in]** *I like to partake in the festivities.* 我想參加這次慶祝活動。

partake of sth *phr v* [T] *formal* to have a certain amount of a particular quality【正式】有點…, 帶有幾分〔某種性質或特徵〕: *a self-confident manner that partakes of arrogance* 自信中帶有幾分傲慢的態度

par·terre /pɑrˋtɛr; pɑːˈteə/ *n* [C] a part of a garden with flat areas of grass and flowers that make a formal pattern〔庭園的〕花壇, 花圃

part-ex·change /ˌ· ·ˈ·/ *n* [C,U] *BrE* a way of buying a new car, television etc in which you give your old car, television etc as part of the payment【英】以舊換新, 部分抵價交易(法); TRADE-IN *AmE*【美】

par·the·no·gen·e·sis /ˌpɑrθənoˋdʒɛnəsɪs; ˌpɑːθənəʊˈdʒenəsəs/ *n* [U] *technical* the production of a new plant or animal from a female without the sexual involvement of the male【術語】孤雌生殖, 單性生殖

par·tial /ˋpɑrʃəl; ˈpɑːʃəl/ *adj* **1** not complete 部分的, 不完全的: *a partial success* 部分成功 | *The patient may only make a partial recovery.* 那病人或許只能部分復原。**2 be partial to sth** *formal* to like something very much【正式】特別喜歡某物, 偏愛某物: *I'm very partial to cream cakes.* 我特別喜歡吃奶油蛋糕。**3** unfairly supporting one person or one side against another 偏向一方的, 偏袒的, 不公平的 —opposite 反義詞 IMPARTIAL

par·ti·al·i·ty /ˌpɑrʃɪˋælətɪ; ˌpɑːʃiˈæləti/ *n* [U] **1** unfair support of one person or one side against another; BIAS[1] (1) 偏袒, 偏向; 不公平: *Councillors were accused of partiality on land issues.* 市政委員們被指控在土地問題上有失公正。**2 partiality for** *formal* a special liking for something【正式】對…的特別喜愛, 偏愛, 癖好: *a partiality for Moorish architecture* 對摩爾式建築的偏愛

P

par·tial·ly /ˋpɑrʃəlɪ; ˈpɑːʃəli/ *adv formal*【正式】**1** not completely; partly 不完全地; 部分地: *He was only partially to blame for the accident.* 他對這次事故只應負部分責任。**2** in a way that shows you unfairly support one person, side etc against another 偏向一方地, 偏袒地

par·tic·i·pant /pɑrˋtɪsəpənt; pɑːˈtɪsəpənt/ *n* [C] someone who is taking part in an activity or event 參加者, 參與者: **[+in]** *Would participants in the next race come forward?* 下個項目參賽者請到前面來好嗎? W3

par·tic·i·pate /pɑrˋtɪsəˌpet; pɑːˈtɪsəpeɪt/ *v* [I] *formal* to take part in an activity or event【正式】參加, 參與: **[+in]** *Everyone in the class is expected to participate in these discussions.* 希望全班同學都參加這些討論。—see 見 JOIN[1] (USAGE) W3

par·ti·ci·pa·tion /pɑrˌtɪsəˋpeʃən; pɑːˌtɪsəˈpeɪʃən/ *n* [U] the act of taking part in an activity or event 參加, 參與: **[+in]** *We want more participation in the decision-making.* 我們想更多地參與決策。| *entertainment with plenty of audience participation* 有許多觀眾參與的娛樂活動 W3

par·ti·ci·pa·tory /pɑrˋtɪsəˌpətorɪ; pɑːˌtɪsəˈpeɪtəri◂/ *adj formal* a way of making decisions that is participatory involves everyone who is affected by the decisions【正式】〔決策〕眾人參與的: *a participatory democracy* 公眾參與決策的民主

par·ti·cip·i·al /ˌpɑrtəˋsɪpɪəl; ˌpɑːtəˈsɪpiəl/ *adj technical* using a participle, or having the form of a participle【術語】分詞的; 有分詞形式的 —**participially** *adv*

par·ti·ci·ple /ˋpɑrtəˌsɪpl; ˈpɑːtəsɪpəl◂/ *n* [C] *technical* the form of a verb, usually ending in -ing or -ed, which is used to make compound forms of the verb or as an adjective【術語】分詞 —see also 另見 PAST PARTICIPLE, PRESENT PARTICIPLE

par·ti·cle /ˋpɑrtɪkl; ˈpɑːtɪkəl/ *n* [C] **1** a very small piece of something 微粒, 粒子: *dust particles* 塵埃 —see also 另見 ELEMENTARY PARTICLE **2 not a particle of truth/evidence etc** no truth etc at all 沒有一點真實性/證據等: *There's not a particle of truth in what he says.* 他所說的沒有半點是真的。**3** *technical* a type of word in grammar, such as a CONJUNCTION (3) or PREPOSITION, that is usually short and is not as important in a sentence as the subject or verb【術語】〔語法中的〕質詞, 小品詞, 虛詞〈如連詞、介詞〉

particle ac·cel·e·ra·tor /ˈ··· ·ˌ····/ *n* [C] *technical* an ACCELERATOR (2)【術語】粒子加速器

particle phys·ics /ˈ··· ˌ··/ *n* [U] the study of the way ELEMENTARY PARTICLES (=very small bits of substance inside atoms) develop and behave 粒子物理學

par·ti·col·oured /ˋpɑrtɪˌkʌləd; ˌpɑːtiˈkʌləd◂/ *adj* having different colours in different parts 雜色的, 斑駁的

par·tic·u·lar[1] /pəˋtɪkjələ; pəˈtɪkjələ/ *adj* **1** [only before noun 僅用於名詞前] a particular thing or person is the one that you are talking about, and not any other 特定的, 特指的: *Fred hasn't seen that particular film.* 弗雷德還沒看過那部電影。| *We expect budget pressures in this particular area.* 我們預計這一地區會出現經費緊張。**2** special or important enough to mention separately 特殊的, 特別的; 值得特別一提的: *You should pay particu-* S1 W1 *lar attention to spelling.* 你應特別注意拼寫。| *There was nothing of particular interest in the letter.* 這封信中沒有甚麼特別需要注意的事。| *Is there any particular thing that's worrying you?* 有甚麼特別的事讓你煩惱嗎? **3** very careful about choosing exactly what you like and not easily satisfied 講究的; 挑剔的, 吹毛求疵的: [+about] *Marty's very particular about his food.* 馬迪吃東西非常挑剔。**4 I'm not particular** *spoken* used to say that you do not care what is decided【口】我不在意, 我不管: [+what/how/where etc] *I'm not particular how you do it, as long as it gets done.* 你怎麼做我不管, 只要把它做完就行。**5** *formal* giving exact details【正式】詳細的, 詳盡的; 細緻的: *She gave us a full and particular account of what had happened.* 她全面而詳盡地向我們敘述了所發生的事情。

particular² *n* **1 in particular** especially 尤其, 特別: *It was a good concert – I enjoyed the last song in particular.* 那是一場不錯的音樂會 —— 我尤其喜歡最後一首歌。| **anything/anyone in particular** *Was there anything in particular that you wanted to talk about?* 你有甚麼特別想談的嗎? | **nothing/no one in particular** *"What did you want?" "Oh, nothing in particular."* "你想要甚麼?" "噢, 沒甚麼特別的。" **2 particulars** [plural] the facts and details 細節, 詳情: [+of] *I am not familiar with the particulars of the case.* 我對這個案子的詳細情況並不熟悉。| **sb's particulars** (=details such as their name, address, profession etc) 某人的詳細資料〈如名字、地址、職業等〉 **3 in every particular/in all particulars** *formal* in every detail【正式】在每個/所有細節上: *The documents were identical in almost every particular.* 這些文件幾乎在每個細節上都是完全一樣的。

par·tic·u·lar·i·ty /pɚˌtɪkjəˋlærətɪ; pəˌtɪkjʊˈlærɪti/ *n formal*【正式】**1** [U] the quality of being exact and paying attention to details 詳細, 詳盡, 仔細, 細緻 **2** [C] a detail 細節

par·tic·u·lar·ize also 又作 -ise *BrE*【英】/pɚˋtɪkjələˌraɪz; pəˈtɪkjʊləraɪz/ *v* [I,T] *formal* to give the details of something; ITEMIZE【正式】詳述; 具體列出, 列舉 —**particularization** /pəˌtɪkjələrəˋzeʃən; pəˌtɪkjʊləraɪˈzeɪʃən/ *n* [U]

par·tic·u·lar·ly /pɚˋtɪkjələlɪ; pəˈtɪkjʊləli/ *adv* **1** more than usual or more than others; ESPECIALLY 特別, 尤其: *Steve was in a particularly bad mood when he got back.* 史蒂夫回來時情緒特別差。| *The restaurant is particularly popular with young people.* 那家餐館尤其受到年輕人的歡迎。| *We are hoping to expand our business, particularly in Europe.* 我們希望擴大我們的業務, 尤其是在歐洲。**2 not particularly a)** not very 不太, 不是非常: *I'm not particularly impressed with their performance.* 我對他們的表演印象不太深。**b)** *spoken* not very much【口】不(是)特別…: *"Do you want to come to the party?" "Not particularly."* "你想去參加聚會嗎?" "不是特別想。"

par·tic·u·lates /pɚˋtɪkjəlets; pəˈtɪkjʊləts/ *n* [plural] substances that consist of very small separate parts, especially substances in the air that come from car engines and seriously damage your health〔尤指空氣中由汽車引擎排出的對人體十分有害的〕微粒, 顆粒

part·ing¹ /ˋpɑrtɪŋ; ˈpɑːtɪŋ/ *n* **1** [C,U] an occasion when two people leave each other 分離, 分開, 離別: *It had been a melancholy parting in the rain.* 那曾是一場令人傷感的雨中別離。**2** [C] *BrE* the line on your head made by dividing your hair with a comb【英】〔頭髮的〕分縫; PART *AmE*【美】: *a centre parting*〔頭髮的〕中間分界 —see picture on page A6 參見 A6 頁圖 **3 the parting of the ways** the point at which two people or organizations decide to separate〔兩個人或組織〕決定分手的時刻, 決定分道揚鑣的時刻; (十字) 路口

parting² *adj* **1 a parting kiss/gift/glance etc** a kiss etc that you give someone as you leave 臨別的一吻/禮物/一瞥等 **2 parting shot** an unpleasant remark that you make just as you are leaving, especially at the end of an argument 臨別時說的令人不快的話;〔尤指〕爭論結束時的尖刻話: *As her parting shot, she told me never to phone her again.* 臨別時, 她居然告訴我再也不要打電話給她。

par·ti·san¹ /ˋpɑrtəzn̩; ˌpɑːtɪˈzæn/ *adj* **1** supporting a particular party, plan or leader and disliking all others 黨派的, 幫派性的;〔對某個政黨、計劃或領導〕熱忱(而盲目)支持的: *a partisan report* 黨派性的報告 **2 partisan struggle/conflict** the continuing fight of an armed group against an enemy that has defeated its country 游擊鬥爭/衝突

partisan² *n* [C] **1** someone who supports a party, plan, or leader〔某個政黨、計劃或領導人的〕盲目支持者; 黨徒, 黨羽 **2** a member of an armed group that continues to fight against an enemy that has defeated its country〔抗擊佔領者的〕游擊隊員

par·ti·tion¹ /pɑrˋtɪʃən; pɑːˈtɪʃən/ *n* **1** [C] a thin wall that separates one part of a room from another 隔牆, 隔板 —see picture at 參見 OPEN-PLAN 圖 **2** [U] the division of a country into two or more independent countries〔國家的〕分裂, 分割: *the partition of India* 印度的分裂

partition² *v* [T+into] to divide a country, building, or room into two or more parts 分割; 把…分成部分; 分隔

partition sth ↔ **off** *phr v* [T] to divide part of a room from the rest by using a partition〔用隔牆、隔板〕將…隔開, 分隔: *They partitioned off part of the living room to make a study.* 他們把客廳隔出一部分做書房。

par·ti·tive /ˋpɑrtətɪv; ˈpɑːtɪtɪv/ *n technical* a word which comes before a noun and shows that part of something is being described, not the whole of it, for example the word 'some' in the phrase 'some of the cake'【術語】表示部分的詞〈如片語 some of the cake 中的 some〉 —**partitive** *adj*

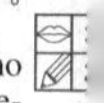
part·ly /ˋpɑrtlɪ; ˈpɑːtli/ *adv* to some degree, but not completely 在某種程度上; 部分地: *It was partly my fault.* 那件事部分是我的錯。| *The company's problems are partly due to bad management.* 那家公司的問題部分是由於管理不善造成的。| *The track was partly covered by long grass.* 那條小路有一部分被長長的草覆蓋住了。

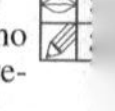
part·ner¹ /ˋpɑrtnɚ; ˈpɑːtnə/ *n* [C]

1 ►MARRIAGE ETC 婚姻等◄ one of two people who are married, or who live together and have a sexual relationship 配偶; (性) 伴侶; 情人

2 ►BUSINESS 生意◄ one of the owners of a business, who share the profits and losses 合夥人, 股東: *She's a partner in a law firm.* 她是一家法律事務所的合股人。—see also 另見 SLEEPING PARTNER

3 ►DANCING/GAMES ETC 跳舞/遊戲等◄ someone you do a particular activity with, for example dancing or playing a game against two other people〔跳舞、玩遊戲等的〕搭檔, 同伴: *Clare's my tennis partner.* 克萊爾是我的網球搭檔。

4 ►COUNTRY 國家◄ a country that your country has an agreement with 夥伴: *Britain's new trading partners in Eastern Europe* 英國在東歐的新貿易夥伴

5 partners in crime *humorous* two people who have planned and done something together, especially something that slightly annoys other people【幽默】〔尤指惡作劇的〕同夥, 共犯

partner² *v* [T] to be someone's partner in a dance, game etc〔在跳舞、遊戲等中〕做…的同伴[搭檔]: *I used to partner him in tennis matches.* 我過去常在網球比賽中做他的搭檔。

partner up also 又作 **partner off** *phr v* [I,T] to become or make people become partners (使) 成為夥伴[搭檔]: **partner sb ↔ up with sb** *The host tried to partner me up with Janice.* 主人設法讓我和賈妮絲成為舞伴。

part·ner·ship /ˋpɑrtnɚˌʃɪp; ˈpɑːtnəʃɪp/ *n* **1** [U] the state of being a partner in business〔生意中的〕合夥(關係): **be in partnership** *We've been in partnership for five years.* 我們合夥經營已經五年了。| **go into partnership** *She's gone into partnership with two local doctors.* 她

已和當地的兩名醫生合夥開業。**2** [C] a business owned by two or more partners who share the profits and losses 合夥企業, 合股公司: *It's one of the most profitable partnerships in the country.* 那是該國最賺錢的合夥企業之一。**3** [C] a relationship between two people, organizations, or countries that work together regularly〔兩個人、組織或國家之間的〕合作關係; 夥伴關係: *Laurel and Hardy – a comedy partnership that lasted all through the 1930s* 勞萊和哈代── 整個20世紀30年代一直合作的一對喜劇搭檔

part of speech /ˌ· ˈ·/ *n* [C] *technical* one of the types into which words are divided in grammar according to their use, such as noun, verb, or adjective【術語】詞類, 詞性

par·took /pɑrˋtuk; pɑːˈtʊk/ the past tense of PARTAKE

par·tridge /ˋpɑrtrɪdʒ; ˈpɑːtrɪdʒ/ *n* [C] a fat bird with a short tail which is shot for sport and food 山鶉, 鷓鴣

part-sing·ing /ˈ· ˌ··/ *n* [U] the singing of part-songs 多聲部合唱

part-song /ˋpɑrtsɔŋ; ˈpɑːtsɒŋ/ *n* [C] a song that consists of three or more musical lines that are sung together〔三個或三個以上聲部的〕多聲部合唱歌曲

3 **part-time** /ˌ· ˈ·◂/ *adj* [only before noun 僅用於名詞前] a part-time worker works regularly for a part of the usual working time 部分時間的, 兼職的: *Mattie had a part-time job in the evenings.* 馬蒂有一份在晚上兼職的工作。—compare 比較 FULL-TIME —**part-time** *adv*: *She'll work part-time after she's had the baby.* 她生完孩子以後將做兼職工作。—**part-timer** *n* [C] *informal*【非正式】: *A part-timer helps us out in the mornings.* 一名兼職人員每天早上過來幫我們的忙。

part·way /ˋpɑrtˋwe; ˈpɑːtweɪ/ *adv informal* some of the way into a space, or after some of a period of time has passed【非正式】(到) 中途; 一段時間過後: *She slid partway into the room.* 她中途悄悄地溜進了房間。| *He came in partway through the presentation.* 他在演出[演講]進行到一半時進來了。

1 **par·ty**[1] /ˋpɑrtɪ; ˈpɑːti/ *n plural* **parties** [C]

1 **1 ▶FOR FUN** 為娛樂◀ an occasion when people meet together, to enjoy themselves by eating, drinking, dancing etc〔社交或娛樂性的〕聚會, 宴會: *a birthday party* 生日聚會 | *a garden party* 遊園會 | *Want to come to a party on Saturday?* 星期六想來參加聚會嗎? | *Let's have a party here before we move out.* 我們搬出去之前在這裡舉行一次聚會吧。| **give/throw a party** *Robin threw a party while his parents were away.* 羅賓趁他父母不在時舉行了一次聚會。| **party dress/clothes/hat** (=worn at a party) 宴會裝/禮服/宴會[禮]帽 | **party game/trick** (=played or done at a party) 晚會遊戲/把戲 | **party animal** *informal* (=someone who enjoys parties)【非正式】熱衷於社交聚會的人 | **party house/school** *AmE informal* (=a place that often has noisy parties)【美, 非正式】經常舉行聚會的場所/學校 —see also 另見 HEN PARTY, HOUSE PARTY, STAG PARTY

2 ▶IN POLITICS 政治上◀ an organization of people with the same political beliefs and aims, that you can vote for in elections 政黨: *The Democratic Party increased its majority.* 民主黨擴大了自己的多數優勢。| [also+plural verb] *BrE*【英】*The Labour party have launched their manifesto.* 工黨已發表了他們的宣言。| *an all-party committee* 由所有政黨組成的委員會 | **party leader/member** *Party leaders met to discuss their housing policy.* 黨領導人開會討論他們的房屋政策。| **the party faithful** (=its most loyal members) 忠誠的黨員 —see also 另見 PARTY LINE (1)

3 ▶GROUP OF PEOPLE 一組人◀ a group of people that someone has formed in order to go somewhere or do something in an organized way〔共同去某地或做某事的〕一組, 一隊, 一羣: *a search party* 搜索隊 | *a rescue party* 援救小組 | *The bus was rented by a party of tourists.* 一羣遊客租用了那輛公共汽車。—see also 另見 WORKING PARTY

4 ▶IN AN ARGUMENT/LAW 在爭論中/法律上◀ one of the people or groups involved in an argument, agreement etc, especially a legal one〔法律上爭論、協議等的〕一方; 當事人: *The two parties are having difficulty agreeing.* 雙方爭執不下。—see also 另見 THIRD PARTY

5 the guilty party the person who has done something illegal or wrong 有罪的一方; 有錯的一方

6 be (a) party to sth *formal* to be involved in or have your name connected with an activity【正式】參與某事, 參加; 與某事有牽連: *I insist on being a party to this discussion.* 我堅持要求參與這次討論。

party[2] also 又作 **party down** *v* [I] *informal especially AmE* to enjoy yourself, especially by drinking alcohol, eating, dancing etc【非正式, 尤美】〔尤指飲酒、吃飯、跳舞等〕盡情歡樂: *All right! Let's party!* 好吧! 大家盡興吧!

P

party fa·vors /ˈ·· ˌ··/ *n* [plural] *especially AmE* small gifts such as paper hats or toys given to children at a party【尤美】〔社交聚會上送給孩子的〕聚會小禮物〈如紙帽或玩具〉

party line /ˈ·· ˌ·/ *n* [C] **1** the official opinion of a political party, which its members are expected to agree with and support 政黨的路線: *He follows the party line fairly closely.* 他相當嚴格地遵循黨的路線。—see also 另見 **toe the line** (TOE[2]) **2** a telephone line connected to two or more telephones belonging to different people 電話合用線

party piece /ˈ·· ˌ·/ *n* [C] something that you usually do to entertain people at a party, for example a song that you sing〔某人〕經常在社交聚會上表演的節目〈如唱歌〉

party po·lit·i·cal /ˌ·· ·ˈ···◂/ *adj* [only before noun 僅用於名詞前] *especially BrE* related to party politics【尤英】黨派政治的: *party-political conflict* 黨派政治衝突 | *a party political broadcast* 黨派政治的廣播[電視]節目

party pol·i·tics /ˌ·· ˈ···/ *n* [U] activities that are concerned with getting support for a political party rather than with doing things to improve the situation in a country 黨派政治

party poop·er /ˋpɑrtɪ ˌpupɚ; ˈpɑːti ˌpuːpə/ *n* [C] *informal* someone who spoils other people's fun【非正式】社交聚會上令人掃興[煞風景]的人

party wall /ˌ·· ˈ·/ *n* [C] a dividing wall between two houses, apartments etc which belong to both owners〔兩座房屋或公寓等之間的〕界牆, 共有牆

par·ve·nu /ˋpɑrvəˌnu; ˈpɑːvənjuː/ *n* [C] *formal* someone from a low social position who suddenly becomes rich or powerful【正式】暴發戶; 新貴: *Aristocratic families found themselves associating with parvenus.* 貴族家庭發現他們自己在與新貴們來往。—**parvenu** *adj*

PASCAL /pæˋskæl; ˈpæskæl/ *n* [U] a computer language that works well on small computer systems and is used in teaching PASCAL語言〔一種用於教學的電腦語言〕

pas·chal /ˋpæskḷ; ˈpæskəl/ *adj* **1** related to the Jewish holiday of Passover〔猶太人〕逾越節的 **2** related to the Christian holiday of Easter〔基督教〕復活節的

pas de deux /ˌpɑ də ˋdu; ˌpɑː də ˈdɜː/ *n* [C] a dance in BALLET performed by a man and a woman〔芭蕾〕雙人舞

pass[1] /pæs; pɑːs/ *v* 1

1 ▶GO PAST 通過◀ [I,T] to come up to a particular point or object and go past it 經過, 越過: *The crowd parted to let the truck pass.* 人羣散開讓卡車通過。| *They kept quiet until the soldiers had passed.* 他們在士兵走過之前一直保持安靜。| **pass sb/sth** *We passed each other on the staircase.* 我們在樓梯上擦肩而過。| *I pass the sports centre on the way to work.* 我去上班的路上經過體育中心。 1

2 ▶MOVE/GO 移動/行進◀ **a)** [I always+adv/prep] to move, go, or travel from one place to another, following a particular direction 前行, 穿過: **[+through/into/from etc]** *We saw her arrive, passing through the little gate into the garden.* 我們看見她到了, 穿過那道小門進了花園。| *A few seconds later, I heard his footsteps pass*

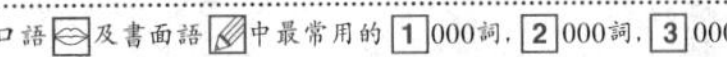

along the deck above my head. 幾秒鐘後，我聽到他沿着我頭頂上的甲板走過的腳步聲。| *Light bends as it passes from air to water.* 光從空氣進入水中時會彎曲。| **be (just) passing through** *spoken* (=be travelling through a place)【口】(恰好) 經過 *We were just passing through and thought we'd call in and see you.* 我們正好經過，於是就想到你家看看你。**b)** [T always+adv/ prep] to move something or place something across, through, around etc something else 使通過，使穿過；使環繞：**pass sth around/along/across etc** *Pass the rope around the tree.* 把繩子繞在樹上。

3 ►ROAD/RIVER ETC 道路/河流等◄ [I always+adv/ prep] if a road, river, railway line etc passes through a place, it goes through that place〔道路、河流、鐵路線等〕經過，通過，穿過：*The new road passes immediately behind the theatre.* 那條新公路緊挨着劇院後面經過。

4 ►TIME 時間◄ **a)** [I] if time passes, it goes by〔時間〕過去，流逝：*The days passed slowly.* 日子慢慢地過去。| *Several years passed before she realized the truth.* 好幾年過去了，她才知道事情的真相。| **with each day that passes/with every passing day** *The situation seems to get worse with each day that passes.* 情況好像一天比一天糟。| **not a day/hardly a day passes without** *Hardly a day passes without me thinking about Ian.* 我幾乎沒有一天不想念伊恩。**b)** [T] if you pass time or pass your life in a particular way, you spend it in that way 度過〔時間〕：*We passed the winter pleasantly enough.* 我們非常愉快地度過了那個冬天。| **pass the time** (=when you are bored or waiting for something) 消磨時間 *We played cards to pass the time until morning.* 我們打牌消磨時光，直到次日凌晨。

5 ►EXAM/TEST 考試/測試◄ [I,T] **a)** to succeed in an examination or test 考試及格；通過〔考試〕：*Do you think you'll pass?* 你覺得你考試會及格嗎？| *I passed my driving test first time.* 我第一次駕駛考試就通過了。| **pass (sth) with flying colours** (=get very high marks) 以優異成績通過 (某事) **b)** [T] to officially decide that someone has passed an examination or test 讓〔某人〕通過考試[測試]：*The examiners finally passed her.* 考官們最終還是讓她通過了。

6 ►LAW/PROPOSAL 法律/提案◄ **a)** [T] to officially accept a law or proposal, especially by voting〔尤指以投票方式〕通過〔法律或提案〕：**pass a law/motion/resolution etc** *Parliament passed a series of important measures in 1994.* 議會在1994年通過了一系列重要舉措。| *The motion was passed unanimously.* 那項動議獲一致通過。**b)** [I,T] if a law or proposal passes an official group, it is officially accepted by that group〔法律、提案等〕被…接受，被…通過：*The bill failed by 17 votes to pass the House of Representatives.* 那項法案以17票之差沒有被眾議院通過。

7 ►GIVE 給◄ [T] to take something and put it in someone's hand, especially because they cannot reach it 傳遞，遞給：*Pass the salt, please.* 請把鹽遞過來。| **pass sb sth** *Can you pass me that bag that's on the floor by your feet?* 你能把地板上你腳邊的那個包遞給我嗎？| **pass sth to sb** *I passed the note back to her.* 我把便條遞還給她。—see also 另見 **pass around**

8 ►SAY/COMMUNICATE 說/交流◄ **a)** [I always+adv/ prep] if words, looks, or signs pass between two or more people, they exchange them with one another 交流；交換〔眼色、信號等〕：**[+between/through etc]** *A glance of understanding passed between them.* 他們會意地互相看了一眼。| *The news passed quickly through the crowd outside the palace.* 那消息在王宮外的人羣中傳得很快。**b) pass a remark/comment/opinion etc** to say something or give your opinion 發表評論/意見等：*She sat and watched the game, passing the occasional witty comment.* 她坐在那裡觀看比賽，時而發表一些言辭風趣的評論。

9 let sth pass to deliberately not say anything or not react when someone says or does something that you do not like 對某事物不予理會[不加追究]：*Carla made some comment about my work but I decided to let it pass.* 卡拉對我的工作作了一些評論，但我決定不予理會。

10 ►END 結束◄ [I] to gradually come to an end 漸漸終止[消失]：*The storm soon passed.* 暴風雨很快就過去了。| *You may feel a little stiff, but it'll pass.* 你會感到有點兒僵硬，但這種感覺會漸漸消失。

11 ►SPORT 體育運動◄ [I,T] to kick, throw, or hit a ball etc to a member of your own team〔給己方隊員〕傳〔球〕：*Maradona quickly passed to Jaires.* 馬勒當拿迅速把球傳給雅爾伊。| **pass sth** *Pass the baton, you idiot!* 把接力棒傳過來，你這個蠢貨！—see picture on page A22 參見A22頁圖

12 pass 600/pass the $5,000 mark etc to go past a particular number or amount, as a total gradually increases or is added to 超過600/超過5,000美元大關等：*Contributions to the disaster fund have already passed the $2 million mark.* 救災捐款已超過二百萬美元大關。

13 pass unnoticed to happen without anyone noticing or saying anything 不被注意地發生

14 pass the time of day (with sb) to talk to someone for a short time in order to be friendly (與某人) 寒暄

15 ►CHANGE CONTROL 改變控制◄ [I] *formal* to go from one person's control or ownership to someone else's【正式】〔控制權或所有權〕轉移；轉讓：**[+to/into]** *On his death his lands passed to his son.* 他死後，土地傳給了兒子。

16 ►CHANGE 變化◄ [I] *formal* if a substance passes from one condition into another, it changes into another condition【正式】轉變，轉化：**[+from/to]** *Ice passes from a solid to a liquid state.* 冰從固態變成液態。

17 ►FALSE MONEY 假幣◄ [T] to use false money to pay for something 使用〔假幣〕付款：*She tried to pass a counterfeit $100 bill.* 她企圖使用一張100美元的假鈔付款。

18 ►PROBLEM 問題◄ [T always+adv/prep] to send a problem or question to another person or group so that they can deal with it 把〔難題或問題〕轉給：**pass sth (across/back/on) to sb** *They passed your enquiry over to us.* 他們把你詢問的事轉給了我們。

19 pass (a) sentence (on sb) to officially decide how a criminal will be punished, and to announce what the punishment will be (對某人) 宣判，宣布判決

20 pass judgment (on sb) to give your opinion about someone's behaviour (對某人) 作出評論

21 ►GIVE NO ANSWER 不予回答◄ [I] to give no answer to a question because you do not know the answer〔因不知問題答案而〕不予回答；略過：*"Who won the Cup in 1966?" "Pass."* "1966年誰贏了那獎杯？" "過。"

22 pass urine/stools/blood etc *formal or technical* to send out something as waste material or in waste material from your BLADDER or BOWELS【正式或術語】排尿/大便/便血等

23 pass water *technical* to send out URINE (=liquid waste) from your body【術語】排尿，小便

24 pass understanding/comprehension/belief *formal* to be impossible to understand or believe【正式】難以理解/相信

25 come to pass *literary or biblical* to happen【文或聖經】發生 —see also 另見 PASSING, **pass the buck** (BUCK¹ (2)), **pass muster** (MUSTER² (1))

pass as sb/sth *phr v* [T] **pass for** (PASS¹)〔錯誤地〕被看[當]作，被認為是

pass sth ↔ **around** *phr v* [T] **1** to offer something to each person in a group 分發〔某物〕：*Pass the cookies around, would you?* 請把小甜餅分發給大家，好嗎？**2** to give something to one person in a group for them to give to the person next to them 傳遞〔某物〕：*He took a cigar and passed the box around.* 他拿了一支雪茄，然後把盒子傳下去。—see also 另見 **pass the hat round** (HAT (5))

pass away *phr v* [I] an expression meaning to die,

used because you want to avoid upsetting someone by saying this directly 去世〔委婉說法〕

pass by *phr v* **1** [I, T] to move past or go past a person, place, vehicle etc 經過: *I'd lie on my back and look at the clouds passing by.* 我常常仰面躺着, 看片片的雲彩掠過。| **pass by sb/sth** *Call in and see us if you're ever passing by the house.* 如果你甚麼時候經過我家, 就來看看我們。—see also 另見 PASSERBY **2** [T **pass** sb ↔ **by**] if something passes you by, it is there but you do not get any profit or advantage from it〔某人〕沒有從中受益[獲益]; 忽視, 忽略: *She felt that life was passing her by.* 她覺得自己從未受到生活的眷顧。

pass sth ↔ **down** *phr v* [T often passive 常用被動態] to give or teach something, such as knowledge or traditions, to people who are younger than you or live after you 把〔知識、傳統等〕傳給後人; 把…往下傳: **pass sth down (from sb) to sb** *They pass their knowledge down from one generation to the next in stories and rhymes.* 他們把自己的知識以故事和韻詩的形式一代一代地傳下去。

pass for sb/sth *phr v* [T] if someone or something passes for something, people think that they are that thing, although they are not really〔錯誤地〕被看[當]作, 被認為是: *With my hair cut short I could have passed for a boy.* 我要是把頭髮剪短, 或許會被當作是一個男孩。| **what passes for** *Davis then encountered the police, or what passed for the police in those peculiar conditions.* 就在那時, 戴維斯遇到了警察, 或者說在那種特定條件下被當作是警察的人。

pass off *phr v* **1** [T **pass** sb/sth **off as** sth] to try to make people think that something or someone is something that it is not, especially something valuable 把…冒充為, 假稱…是: *There is rarely any attempt to pass these copies off as originals.* 很少有人試圖把這些複製品冒充為原作。**2 pass off well/badly etc** if an event passes off well, badly etc, it happens and is completed in that way 進行順利/不順利等: *The presidential tour passed off without a hitch.* 總統的巡訪非常成功。

pass on *phr v* **1** [T **pass** sth ↔ **on**] to tell someone a piece of information that someone else has told you 把〔信息〕傳給〔其他人〕: **pass sth on to sb** *She said she'd pass the message on to the other students.* 她說她會把口信傳給其他學生。**2** [T **pass** sth ↔ **on**] **a)** to give something, especially a disease, to your children through your GENES〔尤指把疾病〕遺傳給 **b)** to give a slight illness to someone else 傳染〔疾病〕: *I stayed off work, as I didn't want to pass my cold on to anyone.* 我沒有去上班, 因為我不想把感冒傳給別人。**3** [T **pass** sth ↔ **on**] to make someone else pay the cost of something 把〔費用〕轉嫁給…: *Any increase in wage costs is bound to be passed on to the consumer.* 增加工資的成本必然會轉嫁到消費者的頭上。**4** [I] **pass away** (PASS[1]) 去世

pass out *phr v* **1** [I] to faint 昏過去, 暈倒, 失去知覺: *He always passes out at the sight of blood.* 他總是一見到血就暈過去。**2** [T **pass** sth ↔ **out**] to give something to each one of a group of people 分[散]發〔某物〕: *Their teacher passed out the dictionaries.* 老師把詞典分發給他們。**3** [I] *especially BrE* to finish a course of study at a military school or police college【尤英】〔從軍校或警校〕畢業

pass over *phr v* [T] **1** [**pass** sb ↔ **over** usually passive 一般用被動態] if you pass someone over for a job, you choose someone else who is younger or lower in the organization than them〔就某項工作〕對〔某人〕不加考慮: **be passed over for promotion** (=someone else got the promotion) 不被考慮提升 **2** [**pass over** sth] if you pass over a remark or a subject in a conversation, you do not spend any time discussing it〔談話中〕忽略…, 對…不加理會: *I think we'd better pass over that last remark.* 我想我們最好不理會最後那句話。

pass sth ↔ **round** *phr v* [T] *BrE* to pass something around【英】分發〔某物〕; 傳遞〔某物〕

pass up *phr v* **pass up a chance/opportunity/offer** to not make use of a chance to do something 放過[放棄, 錯過]機會: *Why did you pass up the opportunity to go to university?* 你為甚麼放棄了上大學的機會?

pass² *n* [C] **1** an official piece of paper which shows that you are allowed to enter a building, travel on something without paying, etc 出入證, 通行證; (免費) 乘車證: *The guard checked our passes.* 警衛檢查了我們的通行證。| **bus pass/train pass etc** *She issued us with a one-day bus pass.* 她給我們發了一天有效的公共汽車免費乘車證。**2** a successful result in an examination (考試) 及格: **a pass in** *delighted with her pass in geography* 為她地理考試及格感到高興 | **pass mark** (=the mark you need to succeed in an examination) 及格分數 **3** a single act of kicking, throwing, or hitting a ball etc to another member of your team 傳球: *Holden intercepted a short pass by Maradona.* 霍爾登攔截了馬勒當拿的一個短距離傳球。**4 make a pass at** *informal* to try to kiss or touch another person with the intention of starting a sexual relationship with them【非正式】向…調情, 勾引… **5** a road or path which goes through a place that is difficult to cross 山道, 山口, 要隘: *The road wound over a narrow mountain pass.* 那條路蜿蜒越過狹窄的山道。| *at the top of the pass into Italy* 在進入意大利的要隘的頂端 —see picture on page A12 參見 A12 頁圖 **6 this pass/the first etc pass** this, the first etc stage in a process, especially one which involves separating unwanted things out from a group 這一輪/第一輪篩選, 這一個/第一個回合: *On the second pass we eliminated all the candidates with less than a year's experience.* 在第二輪篩選中, 我們淘汰了所有經驗不足一年的候選人。**7 a pretty/sorry/fine etc pass** *old-fashioned informal* an unpleasant situation【過時, 非正式】令人不快的處境, 困境: **come to a pretty pass** *Things have come to a pretty pass if we can't even afford to get a newspaper!* 如果我們連一張報紙都買不起, 那情況就糟透了! **8 a)** a single movement of your hands or of a WAND over something〔用手或魔杖做的〕遮掩動作, 障眼法動作 **b)** a single movement of an aircraft over a place which it is attacking〔飛機等對攻擊目標的〕一次俯衝

pass·a·ble /ˈpæsəbl; ˈpɑːsəbəl/ *adj* **1** just good enough to be acceptable, but not very good 過得去的, 尚可的, 還好的: *a passable piece of work* 還可以接受的一項工作 **2** a road or river that is passable is not blocked, so you can travel along or across it〔道路、河流〕可通行的, 能通過的: *The mountain path is not passable in winter.* 這條山路冬天不能通行。—**passably** *adv*: *passably well* 還不錯

pas·sage /ˈpæsɪdʒ; ˈpæsɪdʒ/ *n*

1 ►IN A BUILDING 建築物內◄ [C] a long narrow way with walls on either side which connects one room or place to another; CORRIDOR (1) 過道, 走廊: *Vaughan's room is just along the passage.* 沃恩的房間就在過道前邊。| *an underground passage* 地下通道

2 ►A WAY THROUGH 穿行的路◄ [singular] a way through something 通道, 通路: **[+through]** *We forced a passage through the crowd.* 我們從人羣中擠出一條通道。

3 ►FROM A BOOK ETC 來自一本書等◄ [C] a short part of a book, poem, speech, piece of music etc〔書、詩、演講、樂曲等的〕一段, 一節

4 ►OF A LAW 關於一項法律◄ [U] the process of getting a BILL through a parliament or Congress so that it can become law〔法案的〕通過: **[+through]** *The bill was amended several times during its passage through Congress.* 那項法案在國會通過期間作過幾次修正。

5 ►MOVEMENT 移動◄ [U] *formal* the action of going across, over, along etc something【正式】穿過; 越過; 經過: *The bridge isn't strong enough to allow the passage of heavy vehicles.* 那座橋不夠堅固, 無法讓重型車輛通過。

6 the passage of time the passing of time 時間的流

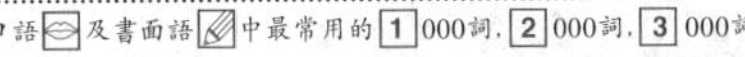

逝: *With the passage of time, things began to look more hopeful.* 隨着時間的流逝, 事情開始顯得更有希望。
7 ▶INSIDE A BODY 體內◀ a tube in your body that air or liquid can pass through〔人體的〕管道: *nasal passages* 鼻道
8 ▶JOURNEY 旅行◀ [singular] the cost of a journey on a ship 乘船旅行的費用, 船費: **[+to]** *My parents couldn't afford the passage to America.* 我父母付不起去美國的船費。| **work your passage** (=pay for a journey by working on the ship) 在船上做工以支付船費 —see also 另見 **rite of passage** (RITE (2))

pas·sage·way /ˈpæsɪdʒˌwe; ˈpæsɪdʒweɪ/ *n* [C] a PASSAGE (1) 過道, 走廊

pas·sant /pɑˋsɑn; ˈpæsɒŋ/ *adv* —see 見 EN PASSANT

pass·book /ˈpæsˌbuk; ˈpɑːsbʊk/ *n* [C] **1** a book in which a record is kept of the money you put into and take out of a BUILDING SOCIETY or SAVINGS AND LOAN ASSOCIATION〔房屋互助協會或儲蓄貸款協會的〕存款提款記錄簿, 存摺 **2** *AmE* a BANK BOOK【美】〔銀行〕存摺

pas·sé /pæˋse; ˈpæseɪ/ *adj* no longer modern or fashionable 過時的, 老式的, 陳舊的: *passé colours typical of the 80s* 過時的80年代典型色彩

pas·sel /ˈpæsəl; ˈpæsəl/ *n* [C+of] *AmE old-fashioned* a group of people or things【美, 過時】一羣; 一批: *a whole passel of kids* 一大羣孩子

3 2 **pas·sen·ger** /ˈpæsn̩dʒɚ; ˈpæsɪndʒə/ *n* [C] **1** someone who is travelling in a vehicle, plane, boat etc, but is not driving it or working on it〔車輛、飛機、船舶等的〕乘客, 旅客: *Neither the driver nor the passengers were hurt.* 司機和乘客均未受傷。| **passenger train/carriage/car** (=for people, not for goods)〔火車〕客車 **2** *BrE* someone in a team who does not do their share of the group's work【英】〔團體中〕不做分內事的成員, 不幹活的人

passenger seat /ˈ···ˌ·/ *n* [C] the seat in the front of a vehicle next to the driver〔汽車駕駛員旁邊的〕乘客座位

pass·er·by /ˈpæsɚˋbaɪ; ˌpɑːsəˈbaɪ/ *n plural* **passersby** [C] someone who is walking past a place by chance〔過〕路人: *A few passersby witnessed the accident.* 有幾個過路人目擊了那次事故。

pas·sim /ˈpæsɪm; ˈpæsɪm/ *adv technical* used in the notes to a book or article to show that a particular word or name appears many times【術語】多處, 到處, 各處〔用於書籍或文章後面的註釋, 表示某個詞或名稱在書中或文章中出現多次〕

pass·ing[1] /ˈpæsɪŋ; ˈpɑːsɪŋ/ *n* [U] **1 the passing of time/the years** the process of time going by 時間/歲月的流逝: *With the passing of years, he grew more bad-tempered.* 隨着歲月的流逝, 他的脾氣更壞了。**2 mention/note in passing** if you say something in passing, you mention it while you are mainly talking about something else〔在談論別的事情時〕順便〔說起〕, 附帶〔提及〕: *He did mention his brother's wife, but only in passing.* 他確實提到了他的弟媳, 但只是順帶而已。**3** the fact of something ending or disappearing 終止; 消失: *The old regime was defeated, and few people mourned its passing.* 舊政權被打垮, 但很少有人對其消失感到痛惜。**4** a word meaning death, used when you want to avoid saying this directly 去世, 逝世〔委婉說法〕

passing[2] *adj* [only before noun 僅用於名詞前] **1** going past 經過的, 通過的: *Michael watched the passing cars.* 邁克爾望着來往的汽車。**2 with each passing day/week/year** *literary* continuously as time passes【文】隨着一天天/一週週/一年年的過去: *With each passing day she grew stronger.* 她一天天變得更加強健[堅強]。**3** short, or disappearing after only a short time; BRIEF[1] (1) 短暫的; 一時的: *He didn't even give the matter a passing thought.* 他對那件事甚至連想都沒想一下。| *a passing reference* 順帶提及

passing[3] *adv old use* very【舊】很, 非常: *passing strange* 很奇怪

3 **pas·sion** /ˈpæʃən; ˈpæʃən/ *n* **1** [C,U] a very strong, deeply felt emotion, especially of sexual love, of anger, or of belief in an idea or principle 強烈的情感, 激情〔尤指性愛、憤怒或對某種思想、原則的信念〕: *a sermon full of passion and inspiration* 充滿激情和靈感的佈道 | **[+for]** *Paolo's burning passion for an older woman* 保羅對一位比他年長的女子燃燒的激情 | **fly into a passion** (=suddenly become very angry) 勃然大怒 **2** [C] a strong liking for something 對…的強烈愛好, 熱愛: **[+for]** *the Cubans' passion for baseball* 古巴人對棒球的熱愛 **3 the Passion** *technical* the suffering and death of Christ【術語】耶穌的受難 —see also 另見 **crime of passion** (CRIME (5)) —**passionless** *adj*

pas·sion·ate /ˈpæʃənɪt; ˈpæʃənət/ *adj* **1** having or involving very strong feelings of sexual love 情慾強烈的; 多情的: *a passionate kiss* 充滿激情的親吻 **2** having or expressing a very strong feeling, especially belief in an idea or principle〔尤指對某種思想、原則〕具有[表現出]強烈感情的; 激昂的: *Lewis is a passionate supporter of women's rights.* 劉易斯是女權運動的狂熱支持者。**3** very eager; INTENSE 熱切的; 強烈的: *Brian is passionate about football.* 布賴恩酷愛足球。—**passionately** *adv*: *Peter is passionately involved in environmental issues.* 彼得熱烈地參與有關環境的議題。

pas·sion·flow·er /ˈpæʃənˌflauɚ; ˈpæʃənˌflaʊə/ *n* [C] a climbing plant with large flowers 西番蓮〔一種攀緣植物〕

passion fruit /ˈ·· ·/ *n* [C,U] a small fruit that grows on some types of passionflower 西番蓮果實 —see picture on page A8 參見A8頁圖

passion play /ˈ·· ·/ *n* [C] a play telling the story of the suffering and death of Christ 耶穌受難〔復活〕劇

pas·sive[1] /ˈpæsɪv; ˈpæsɪv/ *adj* **1** tending to accept situations or things that other people do, without attempting to change or fight against them; SUBMISSIVE 被動的; 消極的; 順從的: *They accepted their defeat with passive resignation.* 他們以無可奈何的消極心態接受了失敗。| *Kathy seems to take the passive role in the relationship.* 凱西在這一關係中似乎扮演着被動的角色。**2** *technical* a verb or a sentence that is passive has as its subject the person or thing to which an action is done, as in 'The boy was thrown from his horse.'【術語】〔動詞或句子〕被動的 —compare 比較 ACTIVE[1] (7) —see also 另見 —**passively** *adv* —**passiveness, passivity** *n* [U]

passive[2] *n* **the passive** *technical* the passive form of a verb, for example 'was kicked' in the sentence 'The ball was kicked by the boy.'【術語】〔動詞的〕被動式; 被動語態〈如句子'The ball was kicked by the boy.'中的'was kicked'〉—compare 比較 ACTIVE[2]

passive re·sis·tance /ˌ·· ·ˈ··/ *n* [U] a way of opposing or protesting against something without using violence 消極抵抗, 非暴力抵抗: *Gandhi's campaign of passive resistance* 甘地的非暴力抵抗運動

passive smok·ing /ˌ·· ˈ··/ *n* [U] the act of breathing in smoke from someone else's cigarette, PIPE etc 被動吸煙, 吸二手煙

passive voice /ˈ·· ˌ·/ *n* [singular] the PASSIVE[2]〔動詞的〕被動式; 被動語態

pas·siv·ize also 又作 **-ise** *BrE*【英】/ˈpæsɪˌvaɪz; ˈpæsɪvaɪz/ *v* [I,T] *technical* to make a verb PASSIVE, or to become passive【術語】〔使〕變成被動式 —**passivization** /ˌpæsɪvəˈzeʃən; ˌpæsɪvaɪˈzeɪʃən/ *n* [U]

pass·key /ˈpæsˌki; ˈpɑːs-kiː/ *n* [C] **1** a key given to a few people for a door that only they are allowed to use〔只有少數人擁有的〕專用鑰匙 **2** a key that will open a number of different locks〔能開啟若干不同鎖的〕萬能鑰匙

Pass·o·ver /ˈpæsˌovɚ; ˈpɑːsəʊvə/ *n* [singular] an important Jewish religious holiday when the escape of the Jews from Egypt is remembered〔猶太教紀念猶太人逃離埃及的〕逾越節

pass·port /ˈpæsˌport; ˈpɑːspɔːt/ *n* [C] **1** a small official book given by a government to a citizen that proves who that person is and allows them to leave the country and enter other countries 護照 **2 a passport to success/romance/a good job etc** something that makes success, romance etc possible and likely 獲取成功/愛情/好工作等的手段: *Erin saw marriage as a passport to happiness.* 埃琳把婚姻看作是獲取幸福的一個手段。

passport con·trol /ˈ·· ·,·/ *n* [U] the place where your passport is checked when you leave or enter a country 護照檢查處

pass·word /ˈpæs,wɜd; ˈpɑːswɜːd/ *n* [C] **1** a secret word or phrase that someone has to speak before they are allowed to enter a place such as a military camp〔進入某地如軍營的〕口令 **2** a secret group of letters or numbers that must be put into a computer before you can use a system or PROGRAM〔使用電腦系統或程式所用的〕通行密碼

1 1 **past¹** /pæst; pɑːst/ *adj*

1 ►PREVIOUS 以前的◄ [only before noun 僅用於名詞前] done, used, or experienced before now 以前的, 過去的, 曾經的: *Judging by her past performance, I'd say Rowena should do very well.* 從羅伊娜以往的表現來看, 我要說她會幹得很好的。| *From past experience she knew not to ask him where he'd been.* 根據過去的經驗, 她知道不能問他去了哪裡。| *Study some past exam papers to get an idea of the questions.* 研究一些以前的考卷, 大致了解一下所考的問題。

2 ►RECENTLY 最近◄ a little earlier than the present or up until now 剛過去的: **in the past 24 hours/year/few weeks etc** *In the past year Shane's changed jobs 3 times.* 在過去一年裡, 莎恩更換了三次工作。| **for the past 24 hours/year/few weeks etc** *Ben hasn't been feeling too good for the past week.* 這一星期來本一直感到不太舒服。

3 ►FINISHED 完成的◄ finished or having come to an end 完成的, 結束的: *Winter is past and spring has come at last.* 冬天過去了, 春天終於來臨。| *Sarah's eyes shone with memories of past happiness.* 薩拉的眼睛閃耀着對以往幸福的回憶。| **past life** (=part of your life that you have no connection with any more) 昔日的生活 *a sleep filled with dreams of my past life in the East* 夢境中盡是昔日我在東方的生活

4 ►FORMER 以往的◄ [only before noun 僅用於名詞前] achieving something in the past, or holding a particular important position in the past 以往的; 前任的: **past president/champion/heroes etc** *celebrating in honour of all our nation's past heroes* 紀念我們以往所有的民族英雄

5 be past it *spoken* to be too old to do something【口】年紀太大幹不了甚麼; 太舊而不能用: *Talbot's past it – they should have dropped him.* 塔爾博特年紀太大——他們本該把他除名的。

6 ►GRAMMAR 語法◄ [only before noun 僅用於名詞前] *technical* being the form of a verb that is used to show a past action or state【術語】〔動詞形式〕過去的: *the past tense* 過去時[式]

1 2 **past²** *prep* **1** further than 在…的更遠處: *The hospital's just up this road about a mile past the school on your left.* 醫院就在這條路上離你左手邊的學校大約一英里外的地方。| **just past** (=a little further than) 比…遠一點 *There are parking spaces over there, just past the garage.* 那邊有停車的地方, 就在那個車庫過去一點兒。—see picture on page A1 參見 A1 頁圖 **2** up to and beyond 越過: *Will you be going past my house on your way home?* 你回家的路上會經過我家嗎? | **straight past** (=directly past without stopping) 徑直經過 *Eva had changed so much I walked straight past her and didn't recognize her.* 伊娃變化太大了, 我從她旁邊徑直走過竟沒有認出她來。**3 I wouldn't put it past sb (to do sth)** *spoken* used to say that you would not be surprised if someone did something bad or unusual because it is typical of them to do that type of thing【口】我認為某人很有可能〔做壞事或不尋常的事〕: *I'm not sure if he actually did cheat in the exams, but I wouldn't put it past him!* 我不能肯定他考試是否真的作弊了, 但我認為他會做出這種事來的! **4 be past caring/being interested/hope etc** to not care any more, be interested in something any more etc 不再在乎/感興趣/抱希望等: *I used to get really upset when he wouldn't see me, but I'm past caring now.* 當他不願見我, 我曾一度非常傷心, 但我現在已不再在乎了。

past³ *n* **1 the past a)** the time that existed before the present 過去, 以前, 昔日: *James has done many things in the past, but he's happiest now in his job as a teacher.* 詹姆斯以前做過很多工作, 但他對現在當教師感到最開心。| **a thing of the past** (=something that does not exist any more) 往事 *Good manners seem to have become a thing of the past.* 以禮待人似乎已成了往事。**b)** the form of a verb that shows that the action or state described by the verb happened or existed some time before the present time〔動詞的〕過去式: *Change the following verbs into the past.* 把以下動詞改變成過去式。**2 it's all in the past** *spoken* used to say that an unpleasant experience has ended and can be forgotten【口】一切都已過去了: *You mustn't think about it. It's all in the past now.* 你千萬不要再想那件事, 現在一切都已過去了。**3 sb's/sth's past** all the things that have happened to someone or something in the past 某人/某物的過去: *There were certain things in his past which were very painful for Neil to remember.* 奈爾的一些往事對他來說是非常痛苦的記憶。**4** [singular] part of someone's life that they try to keep secret because they did things that are considered to be wrong〔某人做過錯事而試圖保密的〕經歷: **a shady past** *There was something odd about him which suggested he had a shady past.* 他有點怪, 這表明他有見不得人的過去。 1 2

past⁴ *adv* **1** up to and beyond a particular place 經過: *Hal and his friends came running past at top speed.* 哈爾和他的朋友以最快的速度跑了過去。**2 go past** if a period of time goes past, it passes〔一段時間〕過去: *Weeks went past without any news of them.* 幾個星期過去了, 一點關於他們的消息也沒有。 2

P

pasta 意大利麵食

spaghetti 意大利麵條

tagliatelle 意大利扁麵條

rigatoni 波紋管狀通心粉

macaroni 通心粉

vermicelli 意大利細麵條

ravioli 意大利式方形小餃子

pasta shapes 花色麵食

pas·ta /ˈpɑstə; ˈpæstə/ *n* [U] an Italian food made from flour, eggs, and water and cut into various shapes, usually eaten with a sauce〔常拌以調味汁的〕意大利麵食

paste¹ /pest; peɪst/ *n* **1 meat/fish/tomato etc paste** a soft mixture made from crushed solid food that is used in cooking or is spread on bread〔用於烹調或塗麵包的〕肉醬/魚醬/番茄醬等 **2** [C,U] a soft thick mixture that can easily be shaped or spread 糊狀物; 膏: *Mix the powder with enough water to make a smooth paste.* 把粉末

和足夠的水混合調成均勻的糊狀。**3** [C,U] a kind of glue that is used for sticking paper onto things 漿糊: *wallpaper paste* 貼牆紙用的漿糊 **4** [U] artificial diamonds 人造鑽石

paste² *v* **1** [T always+adv/prep] to stick paper to a surface using paste〔用漿糊〕黏貼〔紙〕: **[+on/over/down etc]** *A notice had been pasted to the door.* 一張告示貼在門上。| *Paste down the edges of the label.* 用漿糊把標籤的邊黏牢。**2** [I,T] to make words appear in a new place on a computer SCREEN〔在電腦屏幕上〕貼上〔詞語〕—see also 另見 PASTE-UP, PASTING

paste·board /ˋpest͵bɔrd; ˈpeɪstbɔːd/ *n* [U] flat stiff CARDBOARD made by sticking sheets of paper together (硬) 紙板

pas·tel¹ /pæsˋtɛl; ˈpæstl/ *n* **1 a)** [C,U] a small coloured stick for drawing pictures with, made of a substance like CHALK 彩色粉筆[蠟筆] **b)** [C] a picture drawn with pastels 彩色粉筆畫; 蠟筆畫 **2** [C usually plural 一般用複數] a soft pale colour, such as pale blue or pink 淡而柔和的色彩〈如淡藍色或粉紅色〉

pastel² *adj* [only before noun 僅用於名詞前] **1** a pastel colour is pale and light〔色彩〕淺的, 淡的, 柔和的: *pastel blue* 淡藍色 **2** drawn using pastels 用彩色粉筆畫的; 用蠟筆畫的

pas·tern /ˋpæstɚn; ˈpæstɜːn/ *n* [C] *technical* the narrow upper part of a horse's foot, just above the HOOF【術語】〔馬腳的〕骹 —see picture at 參見 HORSE¹ 圖

paste-up /ˋ· ·/ *n* [C] a piece of paper with writing and pictures stuck on it that show what a page will look like when a book or magazine is produced 拼貼版樣〔用於看書頁或雜誌頁的效果〕

pas·teur·ize also 又作 **-ise** *BrE*【英】/ˋpæstə͵raɪz; ˈpɑːstʃəraɪz/ *v* [T] to heat a liquid in a special way that kills any BACTERIA in it 用巴斯德[巴氏]殺菌法給〔液體〕消毒: *pasteurized milk* 消毒牛奶 —**pasteurization** /͵pæstərəˋzeʃən; ͵pɑːstʃəraɪˈzeɪʃən/ *n* [U]

pas·tiche /pæsˋtiʃ; pæˈstiːʃ/ *n* **1** [C] a piece of writing, music etc that is deliberately made in the style of another artist〔文章、音樂等的〕模仿作品: *The concert was a weird mixture of traditional classics and slightly embarrassing Beatles pastiches.* 這場音樂會是傳統的經典作品和有點令人難堪的披頭四模仿作品的奇怪混合。**2** [C] a work of art that consists of a variety of different styles put together 拼湊的藝術作品, 混成作品, 集錦 **3** [U] the style or practice of making works of art in either of these ways 模仿[混成]的藝術風格[手法, 實踐]

pas·tille /pæsˋtil; pæˈstiːl/ *n* [C] *especially BrE* a small round sweet, sometimes containing medicine for a sore throat; LOZENGE (1)【尤英】〔含治喉疾藥物的〕錠劑; 潤喉糖: *fruit pastilles* 水果潤喉糖

pas·time /ˋpæs͵taɪm; ˈpɑːstaɪm/ *n* [C] something that you do because you find it enjoyable or interesting 消遣; 娛樂: *Reading was her favourite pastime.* 閱讀是她最喜愛的消遣。

past·ing /ˋpestɪŋ; ˈpeɪstɪŋ/ *n* **1 give sb a pasting** *informal especially BrE*【非正式, 尤英】**a)** to punish someone by hitting them hard 痛打[毒打]某人: *You'll get a pasting if your dad finds out.* 如果被你爸爸發現, 你會挨一頓痛打的。**b)** to defeat someone easily in a game or other competition〔在比賽或其他競賽中〕輕易擊敗某人 **2** [U] the activity of moving words from one place to another on a computer screen〔詞語在電腦屏幕上的〕貼上: *cutting and pasting* 剪下和貼上

pas·tor /ˋpæstɚ; ˈpɑːstə/ *n* [C] a Christian priest in some protestant churches〔某些新教教會的〕牧師

pas·tor·al /ˋpæstərəl; ˈpɑːstərəl/ *adj* **1** connected with the duties of a priest, minister etc towards the members of their religious group 牧師的; 牧師職責的: *The Rabbi makes pastoral visits on Tuesdays.* 拉比每星期二作履行神職的訪問。**2** *literary* typical of the simple peaceful life in the country【文】田園生活的; 田園式的: *a charming pastoral scene* 迷人的田園景象 **3** connected with the duties of a teacher in advising students about their personal needs outside of lessons 精神上指導的〔指教師在課外對學生個人需求提供諮詢的〕

past par·ti·ci·ple /͵· ˋ····/ *n* [C] *technical* a participle that can be used in compound forms of a verb to show the PASSIVE or the PERFECT tenses (for example 'broken' in 'I have broken my leg'), or sometimes as an adjective (for example 'broken' in 'a broken leg')【術語】過去分詞

past per·fect /͵· ˋ··/ *n* [singular] *technical* the form of a verb that shows that the action described by the verb was completed before a particular time in the past, formed in English with 'had' and a past participle【術語】過去完成時[式] —**past perfect** *adj*

pas·tra·mi /pəˋstrɑmɪ; pəˈstrɑːmi/ *n* [U] smoked BEEF that contains a lot of SPICES 五香煙熏牛肉

pas·try /ˋpestrɪ; ˈpeɪstri/ *n* **1** [U] a mixture of flour, fat, and milk or water, used to make the outer part of baked foods such as PIES〔用來做烘烤食物外層的〕油酥麵團 **2** [C] a small sweet cake, made using this substance 油酥點心[糕餅]: *a Danish pastry* 丹麥油酥糕餅

pas·tur·age /ˋpæstʃərɪdʒ; ˈpɑːstʃərɪdʒ/ *n* [U] **1** *technical* the right to use an area of land for feeding your sheep, cattle, horses etc【術語】放牧權 **2** pasture 牧場

pas·ture¹ /ˋpæstʃɚ; ˈpɑːstʃə/ *n* [C,U] **1** land or a field that is covered with grass and is used for cattle, sheep etc to feed on 牧場: *Stone walls divided pasture from arable land.* 道道石牆把牧場和可耕地分隔開了。| *the rolling pastures of southern England* 英格蘭南部綿延起伏的牧場 **2 put sth/sb out to pasture a)** to move cattle, horses etc into a field to feed on the grass 放〔牛、馬等〕到牧場吃草 **b)** *informal* to make someone leave their job because you think they are too old to do it properly【非正式】〔認為某人年紀太大而〕使離職, 使退休 **3 pastures new/greener** *humorous* a new and exciting or better job, place or activity【幽默】更刺激[更好]的新職位[活動, 地方]: *"I'd like to say goodbye to Paul who leaves us for pastures new."* "我想向保羅道別, 他要離開我們奔更好的前程去了。"

pasture² *v* **1** [T] to put animals outside in a field to feed on the grass 放牧 **2** [I+on] if animals pasture on a particular area of land, they eat the grass that is growing there〔牛、羊等〕在草地上吃草

pas·ture·land /ˋpæstʃɚ͵lænd; ˈpɑːstʃəlænd/ *n* [U] pasture 牧場

past·y¹ /ˋpestɪ; ˈpeɪsti/ *adj* a pasty face looks very pale and unhealthy〔臉色〕蒼白的; 不健康的

past·y² /ˋpæstɪ; ˈpæsti/ *n* [C] *BrE* a small case of PASTRY (1) filled with meat, vegetables etc and baked【英】〔用肉、蔬菜等做餡的〕肉餡餅: *a Cornish pasty* 康沃爾肉餡餅

pasty-faced /ˋpestɪ ˋfest; ˈpeɪsti feɪst/ *adj* having a very pale face that looks unhealthy 臉色蒼白的

pat¹ /pæt; pæt/ *v* **patted, patting** [T] **1** to repeatedly touch someone or something lightly with your hand flat, especially to give comfort 輕拍〔尤指給予安慰〕: *He patted the dog affectionately as he spoke.* 他邊說邊疼愛地輕輕拍了拍那隻狗。**2 pat sb/yourself on the back** to praise someone or yourself for doing something well〔因幹得好而〕讚揚某人/自己: *You can pat yourselves on the back for a job well done.* 你們可以因為工作幹得出色而讚揚一下自己。—see picture on page A21 參見 A21 頁圖

pat² *n* [C] **1** a friendly act of touching someone with your hand flat〔表示友善的〕輕拍: *Mrs Dodd gave the child a pat on the head.* 多德夫人輕輕地拍了拍那個孩子的頭。**2** the sound made by hitting something lightly with a flat object〔用扁平物輕輕擊打某物時發出的〕輕拍聲 **3 a pat of butter** a small flat lump of butter 一小塊黃油 **4 a pat on the back** *informal* praise for something that you have done well【非正式】稱讚, 讚揚: *Alex deserves a pat on the back for all his hard work.* 亞列克斯幹活十分賣力, 應該受到表揚。—see also 另見 COWPAT

pat³ *adj* [usually before noun 一般用於名詞前] a pat answer or explanation is made quickly and sounds as if it has been used before〔回答或解釋〕脱口而出的, 預先準備好似的: *Don't give me any of your pat answers.* 我不想聽你那早有準備的回答。

pat⁴ *adv* **1 have sth off pat** *BrE*【英】, **have sth down pat** *AmE*【美】to know something thoroughly so that you can say it, perform it etc immediately without thinking about it 對…瞭如指掌, 對…熟悉得可隨口說出[隨即表演等] **2 stand pat** *especially AmE* to refuse to change your opinion or decision【尤美】堅持自己的意見[決定]

patch¹ /pætʃ; pætʃ/ *n* [C]

1 ▶PART OF AN AREA 小塊, 小片◀ a part of an area that is different or looks different from the parts that surround it〔與周圍部分不同的〕斑; 小塊: *Lost: a small dog, white with brown patches.* 尋動物啟事: 一隻小狗, 白色帶有棕色斑點。| **patch of dirt/grease/damp etc** *Watch out for icy patches on the roads.* 小心路上結冰的地方。| **patch of light/sky etc** *Patches of blue sky peeked through the clouds.* 片片藍天從雲層中顯露出來。

2 ▶OVER A HOLE 在破洞上◀ a small piece of material used to cover a hole in something 補片, 補丁: *a jacket with leather patches at the elbows* 肘部有皮革補丁的短上衣

3 ▶FOR GROWING STH 用於種植某物◀ a small area of ground for growing fruit or vegetables〔用於種水果或蔬菜的〕小塊土地: *a strawberry patch* 一小塊草莓地

4 ▶ON YOUR EYE 在眼睛上◀ a piece of material that you wear over your eye to protect it when it has been hurt〔保護受傷眼睛的〕眼罩

5 ▶DECORATION 裝飾◀ a small piece of cloth with words or pictures on it that you can stitch onto clothes〔用於縫在衣服上的帶有文字或圖畫的〕小布片

6 a bad/difficult/sticky patch *informal especially BrE* a period of time when you are having a lot of difficulty【非正式, 尤英】〔碰到許多困難的〕倒霉時期: *Gemma's going through a bad patch right now.* 吉瑪目前正處於困難時期。

7 sb's patch *BrE informal* an area that someone knows very well because they work or live there【英, 非正式】某人的地盤[管轄區]〔指某人因在某處工作或生活而對之非常了解〕; TURF¹ (4) *AmE*【美】: *The boss knows everything that's going on in our patch.* 那位老闆對發生在我們這裡的任何事情都瞭如指掌。

8 not be a patch on *BrE informal* to be much less attractive, good etc than something or someone else【英, 非正式】遠不如, 比…差得遠: *She's no great beauty – not a patch on Maria.* 她根本算不上大美人 —— 比瑪麗亞差遠了。

9 good/interesting/boring etc in patches *especially BrE* good etc in some parts, but not all the time【尤英】有些部分不錯/有趣/乏味

patch² *v* [T] to put a piece of cloth over a hole, especially in a piece of clothing〔尤指用布塊〕修補〔衣服〕

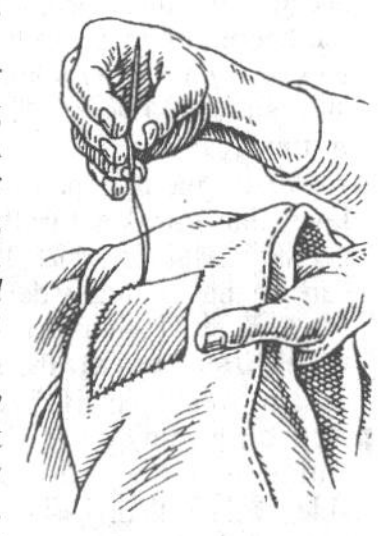
patch 修補

patch sth ↔ **together** *phr v* [T] to make something quickly or carelessly from a number of different pieces or ideas〔用碎料〕倉促拼製;〔把不同的觀點〕草草拼湊: *A new plan was quickly patched together.* 一項新計劃被匆匆拼湊起來了。

patch sth/sb ↔ **up** *phr v* [T] **1** to end an argument because you want to stay friendly with someone 平息〔爭吵〕; 解決〔分歧〕: *Try to patch up your differences before he leaves.* 在他離開之前努力解決你們之間的分歧。| **patch it up (with)** *I've patched it up with the landlord.* 我已和房東和解了。**2** to repair something by adding a new piece of material to it 修補: *We'd better patch up the roof – we can't afford a new one.* 我們最好把屋頂修一下 —— 我們沒有錢蓋新的。**3** to give quick and basic medical treatment to someone who is hurt〔給傷者〕草草包紮: *We just patch up the wounded as best we can.* 我們只是盡可能地給傷者草草包紮一下。

patch pock·et /ˌ· ˈ··/ *n* [C] a pocket made by SEWING a square piece of cloth onto a piece of clothing〔縫在衣服外面的〕貼袋

patch·work /ˈpætʃˌwɝk; ˈpætʃwɜːk/ *n* [U] **1** a type of needlework in which many coloured squares of cloth are stitched together to make one large piece〔由各色方形布片拼縫而成的〕拼布工藝(品); 拼縫物: *a patchwork quilt* 用各色布片拼縫的被子, 百衲被 —see picture on page A16 參見 A16 頁圖 **2 a patchwork of fields/villages etc** a pattern that fields and villages seem to make when you see them from far above 片片田野/村莊等〔自空中俯看時似由田野和村莊等拼綴而成的圖案〕**3 a patchwork of ideas/techniques etc** a combination of many different ideas etc 不同觀念/技術等的拼湊物: *a patchwork of architectural styles* 各種建築風格的拼湊物

patch·y /ˈpætʃɪ; ˈpætʃi/ *adj* **1** happening or existing irregularly in a number of small separate areas 局部地區的; 零散的, 斑駁的: *patchy fog* 零散薄霧 **2** not complete enough to be useful 不完整的, 零零碎碎的: *His knowledge of French remained pretty patchy.* 他對法語仍然是一知半解。| *patchy evidence* 零零碎碎的證據 **3** *especially BrE* good in some parts but bad in others【尤英】只有部分好的: *I thought the performance was patchy.* 我認為那場演出只有部分是不錯的。—**patchiness** *n* [U]

pate /pet; peɪt/ *n* [C] *old use* the top of your head【舊】頭頂: *his bald pate* 他的禿頭頂

pâ·té /pɑˋte; ˈpæteɪ/ *n* [C,U] a smooth, soft substance made from meat or fish that can be spread on bread〔可塗抹在麵包上的〕肉醬; 魚醬

pa·tel·la /pəˋtɛlə; pəˈtelə/ *n* [C] *technical* your KNEE CAP【術語】髕骨, 膝蓋骨 —see picture at 參見 SKELETON 圖

pa·tent¹ /ˈpetn̩t; ˈpeɪtnt/ *n* **1** [C] a special document that says that you have the right to make or sell a new INVENTION or product and that no one else is allowed to do so 專利證書; 許可證: *When does the patent expire?* 這項專利甚麼時候到期? | **take out a patent on sth** (=get one officially) 獲得某物的專利 **2** [U] the right given by this document to make or sell something that no one else is allowed to copy 專利, 專利權: *The machine is protected by patent.* 這種機器受專利保護。

patent² *adj* [only before noun 僅用於名詞前] **1** a patented INVENTION or product is protected by a patent, so that nobody else can copy it〔發明或產品〕受專利保護的; 專利的: *a patent lock* 專利鎖 **2 patent lie/nonsense/impossibility etc** *formal* something that is clearly a lie etc; OBVIOUS (1)【正式】明顯的謊言/胡說/不可能等 —see also 另見 PATENTLY

patent leath·er /ˌpetn̩t ˋlɛðɚ; ˌpeɪtnt ˈleðə◂/ *n* [U] thin shiny leather, usually black 漆皮〔通常為黑色〕: *patent leather shoes* 漆皮鞋

pa·tent·ly /ˈpetn̩tlɪ; ˈpeɪtntli/ *adv formal* a word meaning clearly, used about something that is so clearly bad that no reasonable person could disagree with that fact【正式】〔指壞事〕顯然地, 明顯地: *The treatment is patently not working.* 這種療法顯然沒有甚麼效果。| **patently false/impossible/absurd/obvious etc** *Her denial was swift and patently false.* 她的否認來得那麼快, 顯然是虛假的。

patent medi·cine /ˌ·· ˈ···/ *n* [C] a medicine which can be bought without a PRESCRIPTION (=a written order from your doctor) 專賣藥; 成藥〔指不要處方就能買到的藥〕

pa·ter /ˈpetɚ; ˈpeɪtə/ *n* [C] *BrE old-fashioned* father【英, 過時】父親, 爸爸

pa·ter·fa·mil·ias /ˌpetɚfəˋmɪlɪˌæs; ˌpeɪtəfəˈmiːliæs/ *n* [C] *formal* a father or a man who is the head of a family【正式】父親;〔男性〕家長, 戶主

pa·ter·nal /pəˋtɝnḷ; pəˈtɜːnl/ *adj* **1** paternal feelings or behaviour are like those of a father for his children〔感情或行為〕父親(般)的: *Dan took a paternal interest in my work.* 丹像父親般關注我的工作。**2 paternal grandmother/uncle etc** your father's mother, brother etc 祖母/叔叔等〔父方的親戚〕—compare 比較 MATERNAL —**paternally** *adv*

pa·ter·nal·is·m /pəˋtɝnḷˌɪzəm; pəˈtɜːnəl-ɪzəm/ *n* [U] a system of controlling people or organizations in which people are protected, and their needs are satisfied, but they do not have any freedom or responsibility 家長式統治[管理]—**paternalist, paternalistic** /pəˌtɝnḷˋɪstɪk; pəˌtɜːnəlˈɪstɪk◂/ *adj*

pa·ter·ni·ty /pəˋtɝnətɪ; pəˈtɜːnəti/ *n* [U] *law* the fact of being the father of a particular child, or the question of who the child's father is【法律】父親的身分, 生父: *The paternity of the child is in dispute.* 這個孩子的生父是誰尚在爭論之中。

paternity leave /·ˈ··· ˌ·/ *n* [U] a period of time away from work that a father of a new baby is allowed〔父方享有的〕陪產假

paternity suit /·ˈ··· ˌ·/ *n* [C] a legal action in which a mother asks a court of law to say that a particular man is the father of her child 生父確認訴訟程序

pa·ter·nos·ter /ˋpætəˋnɑstə; ˌpætəˈnɒstə/ *n* [C] the LORD'S PRAYER 主禱文

path /pæθ; pɑːθ/ *n plural* **paths** /pæðz; pɑːðz/ [C]
1 ▶TRACK 小徑◀ a track that people walk along over an area of ground〔人走出來的〕小徑;〔人走的〕小道: *I walked nervously up the path towards the front door.* 我提心吊膽地沿着小道向前門走去。| *A path had been worn across the grass.* 草地上被踩出了一條小徑。
2 ▶WAY THROUGH STH 通道◀ a way through something, that is made by opening a space to allow you to move forward〔開出的〕通道: *The crowd moved aside to make a path for them.* 人們挪往一旁給他們讓路。| **[+through]** *They used axes to clear a path through the jungle.* 他們用斧頭開闢出一條穿過密林的小道。
3 ▶DIRECTION 方向◀ the direction or line along which someone or something moves〔人或事物移動的〕方向; 路線; 軌道: *Sherman's army burned and looted everything that lay in its path.* 謝爾曼的軍隊燒毀並劫掠了所經之地的一切東西。| *the orbital path of the moon around the earth* 月亮繞地球的軌道
4 ▶PLAN 計劃◀ what you intend to do over a long period of time 道路; 途徑: *a career path* 職業發展途徑 | **[+to]** *Shamira saw a college degree as her path to independence.* 沙米拉把大學學位看作是她走向獨立的一條途徑。
5 sb's paths cross if two people's paths cross, they meet by chance〔兩個人〕不期而遇: *Our paths did not cross again until 1941.* 我們直到1941年才再次相遇。—see also 另見 **beat a path (to sb's door)** (BEAT[1] (23)), **lead sb up the garden path** (LEAD[1] (18)), **stand in sb's way/path** (STAND[1] (42))

pa·thet·ic /pəˋθɛtɪk; pəˈθetɪk/ *adj* **1** something or someone that is pathetic is so useless, unsuccessful, or badly done that they annoy you 無用的; 差勁的; 令人生厭的: *You're pathetic! Here, let me do it.* 你真沒用! 讓我來做吧。| *It's a pretty pathetic computer, basically.* 這實際上是一台很差勁的電腦。| *Vic made a pathetic attempt to apologise.* 維克很不像樣地試圖道歉。**2** making you feel pity or sympathy 招人憐憫的, 可憐的: *a pathetic sight* 悲慘的景象 —**pathetically** /-klɪ; -kli/ *adv*

pathetic fal·la·cy /·ˌ·· ˈ···/ *n* [U] *technical* the idea of describing the sea, rocks, weather etc in literature as if they were human【術語】感情的誤置〔文學中對大海、石頭、氣候等的擬人化描述〕

path·find·er /ˋpæθˌfaɪndə; ˈpɑːθˌfaɪndə/ *n especially AmE*【尤美】**1** [C] a person who goes ahead of a group and finds the best way through unknown land 探路者, 開路先鋒 **2** a person who discovers new ways of doing things; TRAILBLAZER 先驅, 開拓者, 探索者

path·o·gen /ˋpæθədʒən; ˈpæθədʒən/ *n* [C] *technical* something that causes disease in your body【術語】病原體, 致病菌 —**pathogenic** /ˌpæθəˋdʒɛnɪk; ˌpæθəˈdʒenɪk◂/ *adj*

path·o·log·i·cal /ˌpæθəˋlɑdʒɪkḷ; ˌpæθəˈlɒdʒɪkəl◂/ *adj* **1** pathological behaviour or feelings happen regularly, are unreasonable, and impossible to control〔行為或感情〕非理智的, 無法控制的, 病態的: *a pathological liar* 病態說謊者 | *a pathological hatred of women* 對女人的病態的憎恨 **2** a mental or physical condition that is pathological is caused by disease 由疾病引起的, 病理的 **3** *technical* connected with pathology【術語】病理學的 —**pathologically** /-klɪ; -kli/ *adv*: *pathologically jealous* 病態妒忌的

pa·thol·o·gy /pəˋθɑlədʒɪ; pəˈθɒlədʒi/ *n* [U] the study of the causes and effects of illnesses 病理學 —**pathologist** *n* [C]

pa·thos /ˋpeθɑs; ˈpeɪθɒs/ *n* [U] the quality that a person or a situation has that makes you feel pity and sadness〔人或境況具有的〕激起憐憫[傷感]的性質, 傷感力: *a scene full of pathos* 充滿傷感的場面

path·way /ˋpæθˌwe; ˈpɑːθweɪ/ *n* [C] a path 小道, 小徑

pa·tience /ˋpeʃəns; ˈpeɪʃəns/ *n* [U] **1** the ability to wait calmly for a long time and accept delays without becoming angry or anxious〔忍受長時間等待的〕耐心, 忍耐(性): *You'll need patience if you want to be served in this shop.* 如果你想在這家商店得到服務, 你需要有耐心。| *Marianna listened to his story with patience.* 瑪利安娜耐心地傾聽他的敘述。**2** the ability to accept trouble and other people's annoying behaviour without complaining or becoming angry〔忍受麻煩事或他人討厭行為的〕耐心, 耐性, 忍受力, 克制力: **have no patience with** *She has no patience with time-wasters.* 她對浪費時間的人沒有耐性。| **lose patience (with)** (=stop being patient and get angry) (對…)失去耐心 *I'm beginning to lose patience with you people.* 我開始對你們這些人失去耐心了。| **the patience of Job/the patience of a saint** (=very great patience when someone is annoying you) 約伯/聖人的耐心〔指極大的耐心〕| **try sb's patience** (=make someone lose their patience) 使…失去耐心, 使…無法忍受 *Henry began to try Isabel's patience with his negative attitude.* 亨利消極的態度開始讓伊莎貝爾無法忍受了。**3** the ability to continue to give your attention to work that is difficult or tiring 堅忍; 韌性; 毅力: **have the patience to do sth** *I wouldn't have the patience to sit sewing all day.* 我可沒有整天坐着做針線活的毅力。**4** *BrE* a card game for one player【英】單人紙牌戲; SOLITAIRE (3) *AmE*【美】

pa·tient¹ /ˋpeʃənt; ˈpeɪʃənt/ *n* [C] someone receiving medical treatment from a doctor 病人, 患者

patient² *adj* able to wait calmly for a long time or to accept difficulties, people's annoying behaviour etc without becoming angry 有耐心的; 忍耐的: **[+with]** *Louise was very patient with me when I was ill and crabby.* 在我生病而且脾氣乖戾的日子裡, 路易絲對我很有耐心。—**patiently** *adv*

pat·i·na /ˋpætɪnə; ˈpætɪnə/ *n* [singular, U] **1** a greenish layer that forms naturally on the surface of copper or BRONZE〔銅或青銅表面的〕銅綠, 銅鏽 **2** a smooth, shiny surface that gradually develops on wood, leather etc〔木頭、皮革等表面因年久而產生的〕光澤 **3 the patina of wealth/success etc** the attractive or impressive appearance of wealth etc 有錢人/成功者等的神采[氣派]

pat·i·o /ˋpɑtɪˌo; ˈpætiəʊ/ *n plural* **patios** [C] a flat area with a stone floor next to a house, used for sitting outside〔與房屋相連並鋪有石頭地面的、作戶外歇息用的〕露台, 平台

patio doors /ˈ··· ˌ·/ *n* [plural] *especially BrE* glass doors that open from a living room onto a patio【尤英】〔起居室通往露台的〕玻璃門

pa·tis·se·rie /pəˋtisərɪ; pəˈtiːsəri/ *n* [C] *French* a shop that sells French cakes and pies, or the cakes it sells【法】法式糕點店; 法式糕點

pa·tois /ˋpætwa; ˈpætwɑː/ *n plural* **patois** /-twaz; -twɑːz/ [C,U] a spoken form of a language used by the people of a small area and different from the national or standard language 方言; 土語

patri- /petrɪ; peɪtrɪ/ *prefix* **1** concerning fathers 父親的: *patricide* (=killing one's father) 弒父(罪) **2** concerning men 男人的: *a patriarchal society* (=controlled by men) 男人統治的社會, 父權制社會 —compare 比較 MATRI-

pa·tri·al /ˋpetrɪəl; ˈpeɪtriəl/ *n* [C] *BrE technical* someone who has a legal right to come to live in the United Kingdom because their parents, grandfather, or grandmother were born there【英, 術語】〔因父母或祖父母在英國出生而〕有英國居留權的人

pa·tri·arch /ˋpetrɪˌɑrk; ˈpeɪtriɑːk/ *n* [C] **1** an old man who is respected as the head of a family or tribe〔年長而受人尊敬的〕家長; 族長; 年高德劭的人 —compare 比較 MATRIARCH **2** a BISHOP (1) in the early Christian church〔早期基督教的〕主教 **3** a chief BISHOP (1) of the Orthodox Christian churches〔東正教的〕大主教

pa·tri·arch·al /ˌpetrɪˋɑrkḷ; ˌpeɪtriˈɑːkəl◂/ *adj* **1** ruled or controlled only by men 由男性控制[統治]的: *a patriarchal system* 父權制 **2** connected with being a patriarch, or typical of a patriarch 家長的; 族長的; 家長[族長]特有的: *patriarchal attitudes* 家長式的態度

pa·tri·arch·y /ˋpetrɪˌɑrkɪ; ˈpeɪtriɑːki/ *n* [C,U] **1** a social system in which the oldest man rules his family and passes power and possessions on to his sons 父權制(社會) **2** a social system in which men have all the power 男權至上的社會制度; 男性政體 —compare 比較 MATRIARCHY

pa·tri·cian /pəˋtrɪʃən; pəˈtrɪʃən/ *adj* **1** typical of a member of the highest class in society; ARISTOCRATIC 貴族的; 貴族似的: *a patrician face* 高貴的面容 **2** belonging to the governing classes in ancient Rome〔屬於古羅馬〕統治階層的 —compare 比較 PLEBEIAN —**patrician** *n* [C]

pat·ri·cide /ˋpætrɪˌsaɪd; ˈpætrɪsaɪd/ *n* [U] the crime of murdering your father 弒父(罪) —compare 比較 MATRICIDE, PARRICIDE (1)

pat·ri·mo·ny /ˋpætrəˌmonɪ; ˈpætrɪməni/ *n* [U, singular] *formal* property given to you after the death of your father, which was given to him by your grandfather etc; INHERITANCE (1)【正式】祖傳的財產; 遺產 —**patrimonial** /ˌpætrəˋmonɪəl; ˌpætrɪˈməʊniəl◂/ *adj*

pat·ri·ot /ˋpetrɪət; ˈpætriət/ *n* [C] someone who loves their country and is willing to defend it 愛國者: *Mr Bush praised Weinburger as 'a true American patriot'.* 布殊先生稱讚溫伯格為"美國真正的愛國者"。

pat·ri·ot·ic /ˌpetrɪˋɑtɪk; ˌpætriˈɒtɪk◂/ *adj* having or expressing a great love of your country 愛國的, 有愛國心的: *good patriotic Americans* 正直愛國的美國人 | *patriotic songs* 愛國歌曲 —**patriotism** /ˋpetrɪətɪzəm; ˈpætriətɪzəm/ *n* [U]

pa·trol¹ /pəˋtrol; pəˈtrəʊl/ *v* **patrolled, patrolling** [I always+adv/prep, T] **1** to go around the different parts of an area or building at regular times to check that there is no trouble or danger 巡邏, 巡查: *waters patrolled by enemy submarines* 敵方潛水艇巡邏的水域 | *Armed guards with dogs patrolled the exhibition.* 武裝衛兵帶着狗在展覽會上巡邏。**2** to drive or walk repeatedly around an area in a threatening way 以威脅性的架勢在〔某地帶〕走來走去[駕着車轉來轉去]: *Gangs of youths patrolled the streets at night.* 晚上一幫幫的年輕人在街上擺出威脅性的架勢走來走去。

patrol² *n* **1** [C,U] the act of going around different parts of an area at regular times to check that there is no trouble or danger 巡邏, 巡查: *Security guards carry out regular patrols of the factory premises.* 保安人員對廠房進行定時巡查。| *patrol duty* 巡邏任務 | **on patrol** *submarines on patrol in the North Atlantic* 在北大西洋巡邏的潛水艇 | **patrol boat/car** (=used by the army or police)〔軍隊或警察用的〕巡邏船/巡邏車 **2** [C] a group of police, soldiers, vehicles, planes etc sent out to search a particular area 巡警隊; 巡邏兵; 巡邏車; 巡邏機隊: *the US border patrol* 美國邊境巡邏隊 **3** [C] a small group of BOY SCOUTS or GIRL GUIDES 童子軍小隊 —see also 另見 HIGHWAY PATROL

patrol car /·ˈ· ·/ *n* [C] a police car that drives around the streets of a city 巡邏警車

pa·trol·man /pəˋtrolmən; pəˈtrəʊlmən/ *n* [C] **1** *AmE* a police officer who regularly walks or drives around a particular area to prevent crime from happening【美】巡警 **2** someone employed by a car owners' association in Britain who drives along roads to give help to drivers〔由英國車主協會雇用、在道路上駕車巡邏給司機提供幫助的〕流動汽車修理工

patrol wag·on /·ˈ· ˌ··/ *n* [C] *AmE* a police vehicle used to move prisoners【美】囚車; BLACK MARIA *BrE*【英】

pa·tron /ˋpetrən; ˈpeɪtrən/ *n* [C] **1** someone who supports the activities of an organization, for example by giving money; BENEFACTOR 贊助者, 資助人: *a patron of the arts* 藝術的贊助者 | *patron companies* 贊助公司 **2** *formal* someone who uses a particular shop, restaurant or hotel【正式】〔商店、餐館、酒店的〕(老)顧客, (老)主顧 —compare 比較 CUSTOMER (1)

pat·ron·age /ˋpetrənɪdʒ; ˈpætrənɪdʒ/ *n* [U] **1** the support, especially financial support, that is given to an organization or activity by a patron 贊助, 資助 **2** *AmE* the support that you give a particular shop, restaurant etc by buying their goods or using their services【美】〔對商店、餐館等的〕惠顧, 光顧; CUSTOM (3) *BrE*【英】: *Thank you for your patronage.* 感謝您的惠顧。**3** a system by which someone in a powerful position gives people generous help or important jobs in return for their support〔有權勢者為回報人們的支持而給予慷慨幫助或重要職位的〕恩惠制; 任命權

pat·ron·ize /ˋpetrənˌaɪz; ˈpætrənaɪz/ *v* [T] **1** to talk to someone as if they are stupid when in fact they are not 以高人一等的態度對待: *Don't patronize me – I'm not a fool.* 別對我擺出高人一等的臭架子——我不是傻瓜。**2** *formal* to use or visit a shop, restaurant etc【正式】光顧, 惠顧〔商店、餐館等〕: *tourists who patronize the shopping and recreational facilities* 光顧購物和娛樂場所的遊客 **3** to support or give money to an organization or activity 贊助, 資助〔機構或活動〕

pat·ro·niz·ing /ˋpetrənˌaɪzɪŋ; ˈpætrənaɪzɪŋ/ *adj* someone who is patronizing talks to you as if they think you are less intelligent or important than them〔說話時〕高人一等的, 屈尊俯就的: *Try not to sound so patronizing when you talk to the students.* 和學生談話時, 儘量不要用這種高人一等的口吻。| *a patronizing attitude* 屈尊俯就的態度 —**patronizingly** *adv*

patron saint /ˌ·· ˈ·/ *n* [C+of] a Christian SAINT (=very holy person) who is believed to give special protection to a particular place, activity, or person〔某個地方、某種活動、某個人的〕守護神, 主保聖人: *St. Christopher, patron saint of travellers* 聖克里斯托弗, 旅行者的守護神

pat·ro·nym·ic /ˌpætrəˋnɪmɪk; ˌpætrəˈnɪmɪk/ *n* [C] *technical* a name formed from the name of your father, grandfather etc【術語】源自父名[祖父名等]的名字 —**patronymic** *adj*

pat·sy /ˋpætsɪ; ˈpætsi/ *n* [C] *AmE informal* someone who is easily tricked or deceived, especially into taking the blame for someone else's crime【美, 非正式】易上當受騙的人, 〔尤指〕替罪羊, 替死鬼

pat·ten /ˋpætn̩; ˈpætn/ *n* [C] a wooden shoe with pieces of iron on the bottom〔底部釘有鐵片的〕木套鞋

pat·ter¹ /ˋpætɚ; ˈpætə/ *v* [I] **1** to make the quiet sound of something hitting a surface lightly, quickly, and repeatedly 發出急速的輕拍聲: *rain pattering on the window panes* 雨啪嗒啪嗒地打在窗玻璃上 **2** [always+adv/prep] to walk or run with light steps making this sound 以輕快的腳步走[跑], 篤篤地跑: [**+around/along etc**] *I can hear the dog pattering around downstairs.* 我能聽到狗兒在樓下嗒啦嗒啦地到處走動。

patter² *n* **1** [singular] the repeated sound of something hitting a surface lightly and quickly 急速的輕拍聲: [+of] *the patter of hooves on the street* 大街上嗒嗒的馬蹄聲 **2** [U, singular] very fast, continuous, and usually amusing talk, used by someone telling jokes or trying to sell something〔講笑話等時的〕急口詞, 順口溜;〔推銷物品時〕喋喋不休的叫賣語: *It's difficult to look at the cars without getting the sales patter.* 看汽車時總免不了要聽推銷員喋喋不休的花言巧語。**3 the patter of tiny feet** *humorous* used to mean that someone is going to have a baby【幽默】將要有小寶寶了: *Are we going to hear the patter of tiny feet?* 我們要有小寶寶了嗎?

3 1 **pat·tern¹** /ˈpætɚn; ˈpætən/ *n* [C]
1 ►OF EVENTS 關於事件◄ the regular way in which something happens, develops, or is done〔事情發生、發展、完成的〕模式; 方式, 形式: *Watch for changes in her breathing pattern.* 注意她呼吸模式的變化。| *a strange pattern of events* 事件發生的奇特方式 | **follow a set pattern** (=always happen or develop in the same fixed way) 遵循固定的模式 *Romantic novels tend to follow a set pattern.* 浪漫愛情小說趨向於遵循一定的模式。
2 ►DESIGN 設計◄ **a)** a regularly repeated arrangement of shapes, colours, or lines on a surface usually intended as decoration 圖案, 花樣, 式樣: *a cotton dress with a flowery pattern* 帶有花卉圖案的棉布連衣裙 | *tracing an intricate pattern in the sand* 追尋沙地上一個錯綜複雜的圖形 **b)** a regularly repeated arrangement of sounds or words〔聲音或詞彙有規則排列的〕模式: *A sonnet has a fixed rhyming pattern.* 十四行詩有固定的押韻模式。
3 ►EXAMPLE 範例◄ [usually singular 一般用單數] a thing, form, or person that is an example to copy 模範, 典範, 榜樣: **set a pattern (for)** (=become a pattern) 為…樹立典範[榜樣] *a successful course that set a pattern for the training of all new employees* 為所有新雇員的培訓樹立典範的成功課程
4 ►MAKING THINGS 製造東西◄ a shape used as a guide for making something, especially a thin piece of paper used when cutting material to make clothing〔用以製作某物的〕模型;〔服裝的〕紙樣: *a dress pattern* 連衣裙的紙樣
5 ►CHOOSING 選擇◄ a small piece of cloth, paper etc that shows what a larger piece will look like; SAMPLE¹〔布、紙等的〕樣品

pattern² *v* **be patterned on** to be designed or made in a way that is copied from something else 仿製; 模仿: *a planned economy patterned on the Stalinist model* 仿效史太林模式的計劃經濟

pat·terned /ˈpætɚnd; ˈpætənd/ *adj* decorated with a pattern 有圖案裝飾的: *a patterned carpet* 有圖案的地毯 | *wallpaper patterned with roses* 有玫瑰圖案的壁紙

pat·tern·ing /ˈpætɚnɪŋ; ˈpætənɪŋ/ *n* [U] **1** *technical* the development of fixed ways of behaving, thinking, doing things etc as a result of copying and repeating actions, language etc【術語】〔行為、思維等的〕模式(化): *cultural patterning* 文化的模式化 **2** patterns of a particular kind, especially on an animal's skin〔尤指動物毛皮上的〕圖案結構

pat·ty /ˈpætɪ; ˈpæti/ *n plural* **patties** [C] **1** *especially AmE* small, flat pieces of cooked meat or other food【尤美】小肉餅; 餅狀食品: *a hamburger patty* 一塊牛肉餅 **2** *BrE dialect* a PASTY【英, 方言】肉餡餅

patty melt /ˈ·· ·/ *n* [C] a flat round piece of BEEF that is cooked with cheese on top and served on bread in the US〔美國的〕扁圓形牛肉餅

pau·ci·ty /ˈpɔsətɪ; ˈpɔːsɪ̈ti/ *n* **a paucity of** *formal* less than is needed of something【正式】(…的) 不足; 缺乏: *a paucity of information* 缺乏資料[信息]

paunch /pɔntʃ; pɔːntʃ/ *n* [C] *often humorous* a man's fat stomach【常幽默】〔男人的〕大肚子 —**paunchy** *adj*

pau·per /ˈpɔpɚ; ˈpɔːpə/ *n* [C] *old-fashioned* someone who is very poor【過時】窮人, 貧民

pau·per·ize also 又作 **-ise** *BrE*【英】/ˈpɔpəˌraɪz; ˈpɔːpəraɪz/ *v* [T] *technical* to make people poor【術語】使貧窮, 使貧困 —**pauperization** /ˌpɔpərəˈzeʃən; ˌpɔːpəraɪˈzeɪʃən/ *n* [U]

pause¹ /pɔz; pɔːz/ *v* [I] to stop speaking or doing something for a short time before starting again 暫停, 停頓: *I paused for breath, almost choking with rage.* 我停下來喘口氣, 憤怒得幾乎說不出話來。| *Please pause to consider the matter.* 請停下來考慮一下這個問題。

pause² *n* [C] **1** a short time during which someone stops speaking or doing something before starting again 暫停, 停頓: *"Yes," said Philip after a moment's pause.* "是的。"菲利普停頓了一下說。| [+in] *an awkward pause in the conversation* 談話中令人尷尬的停頓 **2** a mark (⌒) over a musical note, showing that the note is to be played or sung longer than usual〔音樂中的〕延長記號〔標在音符上, 表示該音符應比通常演奏或唱得長一些〕**3 give sb pause (for thought)** to make someone stop and consider carefully what they are doing 使某人停下來〔仔細考慮〕: *an avoidable accident that should give us all pause for thought* 值得我們都停下來仔細考慮的一次可以避免的事故

pa·vane /pəˈvɑn; pəˈvæn/ *n* [C,U] a formal dance of the 16th and 17th centuries, or the music for this dance 帕凡舞; 帕凡舞曲〔16 和 17 世紀很正式的舞蹈或舞曲〕

pave /pev; peɪv/ *v* [T usually passive 一般用被動態] **1** to cover a path, road, area etc with a hard level surface such as blocks of stone or CONCRETE〔用石板或混凝土板〕鋪〔路、地面等〕, 鋪砌, 鋪築: *The road was only paved last year.* 這條路是去年剛鋪成的。| *a paved courtyard* 地面鋪砌過的院子 **2 pave the way for** to make a later event or development possible by producing the right conditions 為…鋪平道路; 為…創造條件: *The Supreme Court decision paved the way for further legislation on civil rights.* 最高法院的這個決定為人權的進一步立法鋪平了道路。**3 the streets are paved with gold** used to say that it is easy to become rich quickly in a particular place〔某地〕遍地是黃金〔表示在某地很容易快速變富〕

pave·ment /ˈpevmənt; ˈpeɪvmənt/ *n* **1** [C] *BrE* a hard level surface or path at the side of a road for people to walk on【英】人行道; SIDEWALK *AmE*【美】—see picture on page A4 參見 A4 頁圖 **2** [U] *AmE* the hard surface of a road【美】〔道路的〕硬路面 **3** [C,U] paved surface or area of any kind; PAVING (2) 鋪過的地面[路面]

This graph shows how common the nouns **pavement** and **sidewalk** are in British and American English.
本圖表所示為名詞 pavement 和 sidewalk 在英國英語和美國英語中的使用頻率。

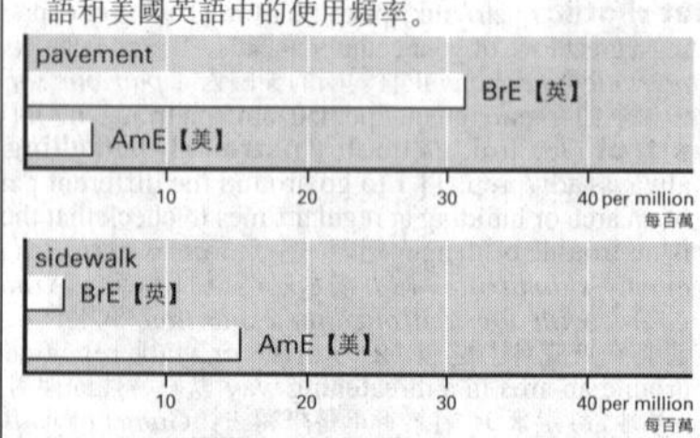

Based on the British National Corpus and the Longman Lancaster Corpus
據英國國家語料庫和朗文蘭卡斯特語料庫

In British English the word **pavement** means the path for people to walk on at the side of a road. Americans use the word **sidewalk** for this meaning. In American English, **pavement** is used to mean the hard surface of a road, or a paved surface. 在英國英語中, pavement 一詞意為"〔路邊的〕人行道", 美國人則用 sidewalk 表示這種意思。在美國英語中, pavement 用於表示"硬路面"或"鋪過的地面"。

pavement art·ist /'·· ,··/ *n* [C] *BrE* someone who draws coloured pictures on a pavement, hoping that people passing will give them money【英】馬路畫家〔在人行道上畫彩色圖畫, 以此向路人討錢的人〕; SIDEWALK ARTIST *AmE*【美】

pa·vil·ion /pə`vɪljən; pə'vɪljən/ *n* [C] **1** a large, light structure that is built to be used for only a short time especially for public entertainments or EXHIBITIONS〔尤用於公共娛樂或展覽的〕臨時建築物; 亭子; 大帳篷: *the German pavilion at the World Trade Fair* 世界貿易博覽會的德國展覽館 **2** *especially BrE* a building beside a sports field, especially a CRICKET field, used by the players and people watching the game【尤英】〔尤指板球場旁供運動員和觀眾使用的〕選手席; 看台

pav·ing /`pevɪŋ; 'peɪvɪŋ/ *n* **1** [U] material used to form a hard, level surface on a path, road, area etc 鋪築材料, 鋪面材料 **2** [U] any kind of paved (PAVE) surface 鋪過的路面[地面] **3** [C] a paving stone 鋪路石(板)

paving stone /'·· ·/ *n* [C] one of the flat square pieces of stone that are used to make a hard surface to walk on 鋪路石板

pav·lo·va /pæv`lovə; pæv'ləʊvə/ *n* [C,U] a light cake made of MERINGUE, cream, and fruit〔用蛋白酥、奶油和水果做成的〕奶油蛋白餅

paw[1] /pɔ; pɔː/ *n* [C] **1** an animal's foot that has nails or CLAWS〔動物的〕爪子: *a lion's paw* 獅爪 **2** *informal* someone's hand【非正式】〔人的〕手: *Keep your filthy paws off me!* 別用你的髒爪子碰我!

paw[2] *v* [I,T] **1** if an animal paws a surface, it touches or rubs one spot repeatedly with its paw 用爪子[前足、蹄等]抓[觸, 扒, 刨]: **[+at]** *The dog's pawing at the door again – let him out.* 那隻狗又在扒門了——讓牠出去吧。 **2** *informal* to feel or touch someone in a rough or sexual way that is offensive【非正式】〔粗魯或放肆地〕摸弄: *First he drank too much, then he started pawing me.* 他先是喝多了酒, 然後開始對我動手動腳。

paw·ky /`pɔkɪ; 'pɔːki/ *adj especially ScotE* humorous in a quiet clever way that could be intended to be either funny or serious【尤蘇格蘭】俏皮的; 狡詐的; 冷面滑稽的: *a pawky sense of humour* 俏皮的幽默感

pawn[1] /pɔn; pɔːn/ *n* [C] **1** one of the eight smallest and least valuable pieces in the game of CHESS〔國際象棋中的〕兵, 卒 **2** someone who is used by a more powerful person or group〔被更有權勢的人或團體利用的〕馬前卒, 爪牙: **[+in]** *We're just pawns in the director's power game.* 在那位主管的權力遊戲中, 我們只是一批小卒子。

pawn[2] *v* [T] to leave something valuable with a pawnbroker in order to borrow money from them 典當; 抵押

pawn·bro·ker /`pɔn,brokɚ; 'pɔːn,brəʊkə/ *n* [C] someone whose business is to lend people money in exchange for valuable objects 當鋪老闆

pawn·shop /`pɔn,ʃɑp; 'pɔːnʃɒp/ *n* [C] a pawnbroker's shop 當鋪

paw·paw /`pɔ,pɔ; 'pɔːpɔː/ *n* [C] *especially BrE and CarE* the large yellow-green fruit of a tall tropical tree; PAPAYA【尤英和加勒比】番木瓜, 木瓜

pax /pæks; pæks/ *interjection* a word used by children when they want to end an argument or fight 別吵了! 別打了! 算了吧!〔小孩在勸別人停止爭吵或打架時的用語〕

1 1 **pay**[1] /pe; peɪ/ *v past tense and past participle* **paid** /ped; peɪd/

1 ►GIVE MONEY 付錢◄ [I,T] to give someone money for something you have bought, or for something they have done for you 給〔某人〕付款; 付錢給〔某人〕: *They ran off without paying.* 他們沒有付錢就逃走了。| *Didn't pay 'em a penny, just asked 'em to do it.* 沒付給他們一個子兒, 只是讓他們去幹活。| **[+for]** *Mum and Dad paid for my driving lessons.* 媽媽和爸爸支付了我學駕駛所需的費用。| **pay sb for sth** *When can you pay me for the work?* 你甚麼時候付給我工錢? | **pay sb sth** *I paid her $200 for this painting.* 我付給她 200 美元買這幅畫。| **pay sb to do sth** *Ray paid some kids to wash the car.* 雷尹花錢雇一些孩子洗車。| **pay (in) cash** *You'd get a discount for paying cash.* 用現金付款你可以享有折扣。| **pay by cheque/credit card** *May I pay by credit card?* 我可以用信用卡付款嗎?

2 ►DEBT/BILL/TAX 債務/賬單/稅◄ [T] to pay money that you owe to a person, company etc 償還; 交付; 繳納: *I forgot to pay the gas bill!* 我忘記交煤氣費了! | *How much tax did you pay last year?* 去年你交了多少稅?

3 ►WAGE/SALARY 工資/薪水◄ [I,T] to give someone money for the job they do 付給〔某人〕報酬: *How much do they pay you?* 他們付給你多少報酬? | *Home workers are very poorly paid.* 在家工作的人工資很低。| **pay sb $100 a day/£200 a week etc** *Programmers are paid about £200 a day.* (電腦) 程式編製員每天的報酬約為 200 英鎊。

4 pay attention (to) to give your attention to something (對…) 注意: *I'm sorry, I wasn't paying attention to what you were saying.* 對不起, 我沒有仔細聽你説的話。

5 pay a call/visit on sb or **pay sb a call/visit** to visit someone 拜訪某人

6 pay the penalty/price to experience something unpleasant because you have done something wrong, made a mistake etc〔因做壞事、犯錯誤等而〕吃苦頭, 付出代價: **pay the price for (doing) sth** *You'll pay the price for drinking so much tomorrow.* 你喝酒太多, 明天你將會為此吃苦頭。

7 ►GOOD RESULT 好的結果◄ [I] if a particular action pays, it brings a good result or advantage for you 合算, 值得, 有利, 有好處: *Crime doesn't pay.* 犯罪不會有好結果。| **it pays to do sth** *It usually pays to tell the truth.* 講真話通常有好處。| **it would/it might pay (you) to do sth** *It would pay you to ask if there are any jobs going at the London office.* 問一下倫敦分公司是否有工作做或許對你有好處。| **pay dividends** *Getting some qualifications now will pay dividends in the long term.* 現在取得一些資格證明將會給你帶來長期的好處。

8 ►PROFIT 利潤◄ [I] if a shop or business pays, it makes a profit〔商店或公司〕有利可圖, 有收益: *If the pub doesn't start to pay, we'll have to sell it.* 如果這家酒館還沒有開始贏利, 我們將不得不把它賣掉。

9 pay sb a compliment to say nice things about someone's appearance, behaviour etc 恭維[讚揚]某人: **pay sb the compliment of doing sth** *Gretta paid me the compliment of saying I was a good judge of character.* 格利塔恭維説我很擅長識別人品。

10 pay your respects (to sb) *formal* to send polite greetings to someone or to visit them【正式】(向某人) 表示敬意; 問候[拜訪] (某人): **pay your last respects** (=go to someone's funeral)〔向某人〕致以最後的敬意, 參加某人的葬禮

11 pay for itself if something you buy pays for itself, it makes you save as much money as you bought it for 省下相當於購買某物的錢: *A new boiler would pay for itself within two years.* 一台新鍋爐兩年內就可以為你省下買它的錢。

12 pay your way to pay for everything that you want without having to depend on anyone else for money 支付自己應付的費用, 不負債

13 pay through the nose (for sth) *spoken* to pay far too much for something【口】(為某物) 付費過高; (為某事) 花代價過大: *I had to pay through the nose for these tickets.* 我得花高價去買這些票。

14 pay tribute to to say how much you admire or respect someone or something 對…表示讚賞[敬佩]; 稱讚: *Doctors paid tribute to her courage at the end.* 最後, 醫生們對她的勇氣表示讚賞。

15 pay court to sb *old-fashioned* to treat someone, especially a woman, with great respect and admiration【過時】向某人〔尤指女人〕大獻殷勤, 討好某人 —see also 另見 **pay lip service to** (LIP SERVICE), **pay your dues** (DUE[2] (2))

pay sb/sth ↔ **back** *phr v* [T] **1** to give someone the money that you owe them; REPAY 償還〔欠款〕: **pay sb back** *Can you lend me £10 and I'll pay you back on Friday?* 你能借給我十英鎊嗎？我星期五就還你。| **pay sth ↔ back** *We're paying back the loan over 15 years.* 我們要在15年內償還貸款。| **pay sb back sth** *Did I pay you back that £5?* 我把那五英鎊還給你了嗎？**2** to make someone suffer for doing something wrong or unpleasant 向…報復: **pay sb back for sth** *I'll pay Jenny back for what she did to me!* 珍妮這樣對待我，我一定要向她報復！

pay for sth *phr v* [T] to suffer or be punished for something you have done 為…而受苦；因…而受懲罰: *These people should pay for their crimes.* 這些人應為他們的罪行受到懲罰。| *You'll pay for that!* 你一定會為那事而受到懲罰的！| **pay for doing sth** *I'll make her pay for ruining my chances.* 她毀了我的機會，我要她為此吃苦頭。| **pay dearly** *Nick's paid dearly for his unfaithfulness to his wife.* 尼克因對妻子不忠而付出了巨大的代價。

pay sth ↔ **in/into** *phr v* [T] to put money in your bank account etc 把〔錢〕存入〔銀行賬戶〕: *Did you remember to pay that cheque in?* 你記得把那張支票存入銀行賬戶了嗎？| **pay sth into sth** *I've paid $250 into my account.* 我已把250美元存入了我的賬戶。

pay off *phr v* **1** [T **pay** sth ↔ **off**] to give someone all the money you owe them 付清，還清〔債務〕: *I've paid off the balance on the dishwasher.* 我已付清了那台洗碗機的餘款。**2** [T **pay** sb ↔ **off**] to pay someone their wages and dismiss them from their job 付清工資解雇〔某人〕: *Two hundred workers have been paid off.* 兩百個工人已被結清工資後解雇了。**3** [T **pay** sb ↔ **off**] to pay someone to keep quiet about something illegal or dishonest 用錢封住〔某人〕的嘴〔使其對非法或不誠實的事情保持沉默〕，付捂口費 **4** [I] if a plan or something that you try to do pays off, it is successful〔計劃等〕取得成功: *They took a hell of a risk but it paid off.* 他們冒了很大的風險，但事情成功了。—see also 另見 PAYOFF

pay out *phr v* **1** [I,T **pay** sth ↔ **out**] to pay a lot of money for something 為〔某事〕付出大筆款項: *Why is it always me who has to pay out?* 為甚麼總是得我付款？| **pay out sth for sth** *I paid out a lot of money for that car.* 我為那輛汽車花了很多錢。**2** [T **pay** sth ↔ **out**] to let a piece of rope be unwound 放出，鬆開〔繩索〕—see also 另見 PAYOUT

pay sth ↔ **over** *phr v* to make an official payment of money 正式付款: **pay sth over to** *The solicitor arranged for Clancy's share of the inheritance to be paid over to him.* 律師安排正式支付克蘭西應得的那份遺產。

pay up *phr v* [I] to pay money that you owe, especially when you do not want to or you are late〔尤指不情願地或遲遲地〕付清，償還〔欠款〕—see also 另見 PAID-UP

USAGE NOTE 用法說明: PAY

GRAMMAR 語法

You **pay** the cost of something. pay 表示支付某物的費用: *pay $100/the bill/postage/the cost of removal* 支付100美元/賬款/郵資/搬遷費 | *Will they pay my traveling expenses/accommodation costs?* 他們會支付我的旅行費/住宿費嗎？

You **pay for** something you buy. pay for 表示為所買的東西付款: *I'll pay for the tickets.* 我會付買這些票的錢。| *You'll have to pay for any stationery you use.* 你必須為你所使用的任何文具付錢。You also say **pay for** when both the cost and what is bought are mentioned. 當同時提到所買的東西及其費用時，也用 pay for: *She paid $200 for the use of the room.* 她為使用那個房間花了200美元。

You **pay** a person etc. pay 後可接人等: *Could you pay the taxi driver?* 你來付錢給計程車司機可以嗎？

You also pay someone something, or pay something to someone. 也可以用 pay someone something 或 pay something to someone: *He paid the assistant £30.* 他付給助手30英鎊。| *He has to pay half his salary to his ex-wife every month.* 他得把每月一半的薪水付給他的前妻。

You **pay by** cheque/credit card etc. pay by 表示用支票/信用卡等支付: *Can I pay by Visa?* 我可以用維薩卡付款嗎？

SPELLING 拼法

The past tense of **pay** is **paid** (NOT 不用 *payed*). pay 的過去式為 paid

This graph shows how common the different grammar patterns of the verb **pay** are. 本圖表所示為動詞 pay 構成的不同語法模式的使用頻率。

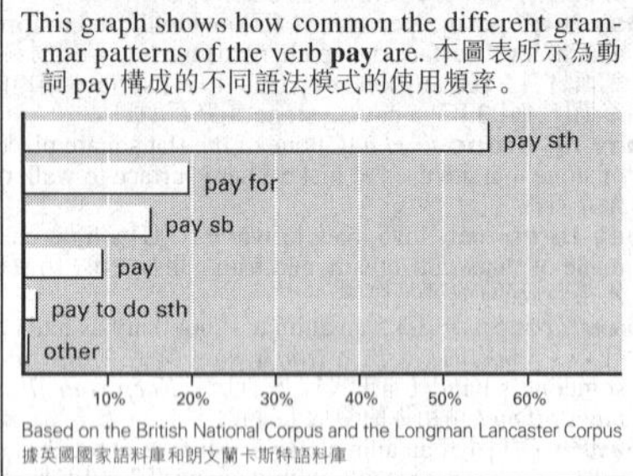

Based on the British National Corpus and the Longman Lancaster Corpus
據英國國家語料庫和朗文蘭卡斯特語料庫

pay² *n* [U] **1** money that you are given for doing your job; SALARY 工資，薪金: *Wayne gets his pay every Friday.* 韋恩每星期五領工資。| *I like the work but the pay's terrible.* 我喜歡這份工作，但報酬太低了。| **holiday/sick pay** (=money your employer gives you when you are on holiday or are ill) 節假日/病假工資 | **a pay rise/increase** *I've been promised a pay rise in January.* 我已得到許諾一月份給我加薪。**2 in the pay of** someone who is in someone else's pay is working for them, often secretly〔多指祕密地〕受雇於〔某人〕: *an informer in the pay of the police* 一名受警察雇用的線人[告密者]

USAGE NOTE 用法說明: PAY

WORD CHOICE 詞語辨析: **pay, salary, wages, fee, income**

Money given to someone in return for work is called **pay**. pay 表示支付給某人的工資、薪金: *Truck drivers are demanding higher pay.* 卡車司機正在要求增加工資。| *a compaign against low pay* 反對低薪酬的運動

A **salary** is paid to someone once a month, especially to professional people, managers etc and usually goes directly into their bank account. salary 指每月發給某人〔尤指專業人員、經理等〕的薪金，通常直接存入其銀行賬戶: *a salary of $100,000 a year* 每年10萬美元的薪金

Wages are paid weekly, usually in the form of coins and notes, especially to people whose job is not professional, in management etc. wages 指每週付給某人〔尤指非專業人員、非管理人員等〕的報酬，通常以現金形式支付: *Wages at the cannery are very low.* 那家罐頭食品廠的工資很低。

A **fee** is money that some professions charge for a particular service they have done. fee 指從事某些職業的人收取的服務費: *doctor's/lawyer's fees* 醫生的診金/律師費

Income means any money you receive regularly, from work or anywhere else. income 意為從工作或其他地方得到的經常性收入: *Unearned income* (=money you get but not from work) *is taxed at a higher rate.* 對於非工作所得的收入，所徵的稅更高。

pay·a·ble /ˋpeəbḷ; ˈpeɪəbəl/ *adj* [not before noun 不用於名詞前] **1** a bill, debt etc that is payable must be paid 〔賬單、債務等〕應支付的: *payable in advance* 可預付的 **2 payable to** a cheque etc that is payable to someone has that person's name written on it and should be paid to them 〔支票等〕寫明給〔某人〕的, 應付給…的

pay·bed /ˋpebɛd; ˈpeɪbed/ *n* [C] a hospital bed in a publicly owned hospital in Britain, used by someone who is paying to have better conditions, such as a private room 〔英國公立醫院中的〕自費病牀

pay·cheque *BrE*【英】, **paycheck** *AmE*【美】/ˋpetʃɛk; ˈpeɪ-tʃek/ *n* [C] **1** a cheque that pays someone's wages 支付工資的支票: *a weekly paycheque* 支付週薪的支票 **2** *especially AmE* the amount of wages someone earns【尤美】薪金, 工資; PAY PACKET *BrE*【英】: *a nice fat paycheck* 豐厚的工資

pay·day /ˋpeˌde; ˈpeɪdeɪ/ *n* [U] the day on which you get your wages 發放工資日, 發薪日: *When's payday?* 哪一天是發薪日?

pay·dirt /ˋpedɝt; ˈpeɪdɜːt/ *n* [U] *AmE*【美】**1 hit paydirt** *informal* to make a valuable or useful discovery【非正式】作出有價值[有用]的發現 **2** earth found to contain valuable minerals such as gold 貴金屬砂土〔含有金等的礦砂〕

PAYE /ˌpi e waɪ ˋi; ˌpiː eɪ waɪ ˈiː/ *n* [U] pay as you earn; a system in Britain by which tax is taken away from your wages before you are paid 〔英國的〕所得稅預扣法〔未發工資前預先從工資中扣除所得稅〕

pay·ee /peˋi; peɪˈiː/ *n* [C] *technical* the person to whom money, especially a cheque, should be paid【術語】〔錢, 尤指支票的〕受款人, 收款人

pay en·ve·lope /ˈ· ˌ···/ *n* [C] *AmE* an envelope containing your wages【美】工資袋; PAY PACKET *BrE*【英】

paying guest /ˌ·· ˈ·/ *n* [C] someone who lives in someone else's house with them and pays them rent; LODGER 〔私人家中的〕房客

paying-in book /ˌ·· ˈ· ·/ *n* [C] *BrE* a book of forms that you use when you pay money into your bank account【英】〔銀行〕存款單簿

paying-in slip /ˌ·· ˈ· ·/ *n* [C] *BrE* a form that you use to pay money into your bank account【英】〔銀行〕存款單; DEPOSIT SLIP *AmE*【美】

pay·load /ˋpelod; ˈpeɪləʊd/ *n* **1** [C,U] the amount of goods or passengers carried by a vehicle or aircraft, for which payment is received 〔車輛或飛機的〕收費載重, 酬載 **2** [C] the instruments and equipment carried in a SPACECRAFT 有效載重〔宇宙飛船攜帶的儀器設備〕: *The shuttle had a maximum payload of 65,000 pounds.* 這架太空穿梭機的最大載重量為65,000磅。**3** [C] the amount of explosive that a MISSILE can carry 〔導彈的〕有效載荷, 炸藥量

pay·mas·ter /ˋpeˌmæstɚ; ˈpeɪˌmɑːstə/ *n* [C] **1** an official in a factory, the army etc, who gives people their wages 〔工廠、軍隊等發放工資、軍餉的〕出納員; 軍需官 **2** someone who pays someone else to do something, especially something illegal 〔雇用別人做非法勾當的〕操縱者: *The assassin's paymasters were never identified.* 那位刺客的幕後操縱者始終沒有查出來。

2 1 **pay·ment** /ˋpemənt; ˈpeɪmənt/ *n* **1** [C] an amount of money that has been or must be paid 已[應]支付的金額: *discounts offered for cash payments* 給予現金付款的折扣 | *Tom's gotten into arrears with his mortgage payments.* 湯姆已開始拖欠抵押貸款了。| **make a payment** *Interest payments are made quarterly.* 利息是按季度支付的。**2** [U] the act of paying 支付, 付款: *We expect prompt payment.* 我們期望即時付款。| *payment by instalments* 分期支付 | **in payment of** (=to pay) 支付 *I enclose a cheque in full payment of my account.* 我(隨信)附上一張支付我全部欠賬的支票。| **on payment of** (=when an amount has been paid) 支付…之後 *Any item can be reserved on payment of a small deposit.* 付一小筆訂金後就可以預訂任何物品。**3** [U] someone's reward for doing something 報償: [+for] *All the payment I got for my troubles was insults.* 我辛苦了一番, 結果還要受辱。**4 payment in kind** a way of paying for something with goods or services instead of money 以貨物[服務]代替錢款的支付方式 —see also 另見 BALANCE OF PAYMENTS, DOWN PAYMENT

pay·off /ˋpeˌɔf; ˈpeɪɒf/ *n* [C] *informal*【非正式】**1** a payment that you make to someone in order to stop them from causing you any trouble, or when you make them leave their job 〔為使某人不來找麻煩而付的〕賄賂款; 〔辭退某人時的〕付款: *A network of police payoffs was discovered.* 賄賂警察的網絡被發現了。| *The redundancies were bought by offering massive payoffs.* 以巨額的遣散費解雇冗員。**2** the good result of a particular series of actions 〔一系列行動的〕良好結果 —see also 另見 **pay off**

pay·o·la /peˋolə; peɪˈəʊlə/ *n informal, especially AmE*【非正式, 尤美】**1** [singular] a secret or indirect payment made to someone who uses their influence to make people buy what your company is selling 〔暗中付給某人以利用其影響推銷公司產品的〕賄賂 —compare 比較 BRIBE[2] **2** [U] the practice of giving or taking these payments 行賄; 受賄

pay·out /ˋpeˌaʊt; ˈpeɪ-aʊt/ *n* [C] *informal* a large payment of money in an insurance claim, competition etc or the act of making this payment【非正式】〔保險索賠、競賽等中的〕大筆付款: *a big payout on this month's lottery* 本月彩票派發的大筆彩金 —see also 另見 **pay out**

pay pack·et /ˈ· ˌ··/ *n* [C] *BrE*【英】**1** the amount of money someone earns; PAYCHEQUE (2) 工資 **2** an envelope containing your wages 工資袋; PAY ENVELOPE *AmE*【美】

pay phone /ˈ· ·/ *n* [C] a public telephone that you can use when you put in a coin or a CREDIT CARD 〔投幣式或插卡式〕公用電話

pay rise /ˈ· ·/ *BrE*【英】, **pay raise** *AmE*【美】*n* [C] an increase in the amount of money you are paid for doing your job 增加工資, 加薪: *Some company directors have awarded themselves huge pay rises.* 一些公司董事已給他們自己大幅加薪了。

pay·roll /ˋpeˌrol; ˈpeɪrəʊl/ *n* **1** [C] a list of people who are employed by a company and the amount of wages each of them is paid 〔公司員工的〕在職人員名冊, 發薪員工表: **be on the payroll** (=be employed by a company) 被雇用 *Nathan's still on the company payroll.* 內森仍受雇於這家公司。**2** [singular] the total amount of wages paid to all the people working for a particular company 〔某家公司的〕發放工資總額

payroll tax /ˈ·· ˌ·/ *n* [C,U] a tax that an employer must pay to the government in the US, and that is a PERCENTAGE of the total wages they pay 〔在美國雇主必須向政府繳納的〕薪金稅, 工資稅〔佔雇主所付工資總額的一定比例〕

pay set·tle·ment /ˈ· ˌ···/ *n* [C] an agreement, after a long argument, between managers and a union, on how much workers should be paid 〔管理者和工會經過長時間爭論之後達成的〕工人工資協議

pay·slip /ˋpeslɪp; ˈpeɪslɪp/ *n* [C] a piece of paper that shows how much money an employed person has been paid and how much has been taken away for tax etc 〔顯示工資額、扣稅額等的〕工資單

P.C. /ˌpi ˋsi; ˌpiː ˈsiː◂/ *n* [C] *BrE* police constable; a policeman of the lowest rank【英】警員〔職級最低的警察〕: *P.C. Williams* 警員威廉斯 | *Two P.C.s were attacked.* 兩名警員遭到了襲擊。—see also 另見 WPC

PC[1] /ˌpi ˋsi; ˌpiː ˈsiː◂/ *n* [C] a personal computer; a small computer that is used by one person at a time, in business or at home 個人電腦

PC[2] *adj* POLITICALLY CORRECT 政治上正確的

pcm per calendar month; used when stating the amount of rent to be paid each month 每月〔用於說明每月應付的房租〕: *£500 pcm* 每月500英鎊

PCP /ˌpi si ˋpi; ˌpiː siː ˈpiː/ *n* [U] phencyclidine

hydrochloride; an ANAESTHETIC that is also taken as an illegal drug 苯環己哌啶〔別稱"天使粉"，一種被當作毒品使用的麻醉劑〕

pd the written abbreviation of 縮寫= paid

pdq /ˌpi di ˋkju; ˌpiː diː ˈkjuː/ *adv slang* pretty damn quick; used to say that something should be done immediately【俚】馬上，立刻: *If Jeff doesn't get back here pdq there's going to be trouble.* 傑夫如果不馬上回到這裡，就要有麻煩了。

PDT /ˌpi di ˋti; ˌpiː diː ˈtiː/ the abbreviation of 縮寫= PACIFIC DAYLIGHT TIME

PE /ˌpi ˋi; ˌpiː ˈiː/ *n* [U] physical education; sport and physical activity taught as a school subject 體育(課); PT *BrE*【英】

pea /pi; piː/ *n* [C] **1** a large round green seed that is cooked and eaten as a vegetable〔作為蔬菜食用的〕豌豆: *frozen peas* 冰凍豌豆 | *garden peas* 庭園豌豆 | *pea soup* 豌豆湯 | **shell peas** (=take them out of their seed container) 剝豌豆 —see picture on page A9 參見A9頁圖 **2** a plant that produces long green PODs that contain these seeds 豌豆〔一種植物〕 **3 like two peas in a pod** *informal* exactly the same in appearance, behaviour etc【非正式】〔容貌、行為等〕一模一樣 —see also 另見 SPLIT PEA, SWEET PEA

2 2 **peace** /pis; piːs/ *n*

1 ▶NO WAR 沒有戰爭◀ **a)** [U] a situation in which there is no war between countries or in a country 和平: **world peace** *a dangerous situation that threatens world peace* 威脅世界和平的危險局面 | **peace agreement/treaty etc** *the Geneva peace talks* 日內瓦和談 | **be at peace with** *Germany has been at peace with France for fifty years.* 德國已與法國和平相處了五十年。**b)** [singular] a period of time in which there is no war 和平時期: *a lasting peace* 持久和平 **c) peace movement/campaign etc** organized efforts to prevent war 和平運動

2 ▶AGREEMENT 協議◀ [singular] an agreement that ends a war 和約: *the Peace of Nijmegen* 奈梅亨和約 | *a negotiated peace* 談判後達成的和約

3 ▶NO NOISE 無噪聲◀ [U] a peaceful situation with no unpleasant noise 安靜，平靜: *A single gunshot shattered the peace of the May afternoon.* 一聲槍響劃破了五月那個下午的寧靜。| **in peace** (=without being interrupted) 安靜地；不被打斷地 *I wish you'd leave me in peace – I've got work to do.* 我希望你不要打擾我——我有工作要做。| **peace and quiet** *We're going to the countryside for some peace and quiet.* 我們打算去鄉下過一些清靜的日子。

4 ▶CALMNESS 平靜◀ [U] a feeling of calmness and lack of worry and problems 平靜，安寧: *the search for inner peace* 尋求內心的平靜 | **peace of mind** (=to stop you from worrying) 心境的平靜，安心 *Ann had to check the baby every few minutes for her own peace of mind.* 為使自己安心，安不得不每隔幾分鐘就查看一下嬰兒。| **at peace with yourself** (=calm and happy) 平靜而快樂 *Lynn never seems to be at peace with herself.* 林恩好像永不會平靜下來似的。

5 [U] a situation in which there is no quarrelling between people who live or work together 和睦〔相處〕: *peace and stability in industrial relations* 勞資關係的和睦穩定 | **keep the peace** (=stop people from quarrelling, fighting, or causing trouble) 維持治安

6 disturb the peace *law* to behave in a noisy and unpleasant way in public【法律】擾亂治安: *Macklin was charged with disturbing the peace.* 麥克林被指控擾亂治安。—see also 另見 BREACH OF THE PEACE, JUSTICE OF THE PEACE

7 hold/keep your peace to keep quiet even though there is something you would like to say 保持緘默: *In spite of John's provocative remarks, I held my peace.* 不管約翰說甚麼挑釁的話，我都保持緘默。

8 make (your) peace with to end your quarrel with someone, especially by telling them you are sorry 與〔某人〕和解〔尤指主動表示道歉〕: *Ann wanted to make her peace with her father before he died.* 安想在她父親死之前與他和解。

9 at peace an expression meaning dead, used when you want to say this in a gentle way 長眠〔"死"的委婉說法〕

10 rest in peace a prayer for someone who has died, said during a funeral service or written on a GRAVESTONE 安息吧〔在葬禮上說的或刻在墓碑上的禱辭〕

peace·a·ble /ˋpisəbl̩; ˈpiːsəbəl/ *adj* **1** a situation or way of doing something that is peaceable is calm, without any violence or fighting 平和的；太平的，和平的 **2** someone who is peaceable dislikes arguing 不愛爭吵的，溫和的，和睦的 —**peaceably** *adv*: *The two tribes live peaceably together.* 這兩個部落和睦相處。

peace div·i·dend /ˋ· ˌ···/ *n* [singular] the money saved on weapons and available for other purposes, when a government reduces its military strength〔政府通過削減軍費而節省下來用於其他用途的〕和平紅利，和平效益

peace·ful /ˋpisfəl; ˈpiːsfəl/ *adj* **1** quiet and calm without any worry or excitement 平靜的，安寧的，寧靜的: *We had a peaceful afternoon without the children.* 孩子們不在，我們度過了一個寧靜的下午。| *into a deep and peaceful sleep* 進入安詳的熟睡 **2** without war 沒有戰爭的，和平的: *a state of peaceful coexistence between nations* 國家之間和平共處的狀態 **3** deliberately avoiding any violence 有意避免暴力的: *a peaceful demonstration* 和平示威 —**peacefully** *adv* —**peacefulness** *n* [U]

peace·keep·ing /ˋpisˌkipɪŋ; ˈpiːskiːpɪŋ/ *adj* **peacekeeping force/troops etc** soldiers that are sent to a place where the people are fighting, to try to stop more violence 維持和平部隊

peace-lov·ing /ˋ· ˌ··/ *adj* believing strongly in peace rather than war 愛好和平的

peace·mak·er /ˋpisˌmekɚ; ˈpiːsmeɪkə/ *n* [C] someone who tries to persuade other people or nations to stop fighting 調解人，調停者: *Eisenhower was anxious to play the role of peacemaker in his last year in office.* 艾森豪威爾在他執政的最後一年渴望扮演調解人的角色。

peace march /ˋ· ·/ *n* [C] a march by people who are protesting against violence or military activities 反戰[反暴力]遊行

peace of·fer·ing /ˋ· ˌ···/ *n* [C] *informal* something you give to someone to show them that you are sorry and want to be friendly, after you have annoyed or upset them【非正式】〔為表示歉意和友好而贈送的〕和平禮物，謝罪禮: *I took along a box of chocolates as a peace offering.* 我帶了一盒巧克力作為謝罪禮。

peace pipe /ˋ· ·/ *n* [C] a pipe which Native Americans use to smoke tobacco, which is shared in a ceremony as a sign of peace; PIPE OF PEACE〔美洲土著用作和平象徵的〕長桿煙斗，和平煙斗

peace·time /ˋpisˌtaɪm; ˈpiːstaɪm/ *n* [U] a period of time when a nation is not fighting a war 和平時期 —opposite 反義詞 WARTIME

peach /pitʃ; piːtʃ/ *n* **1** [C] a round fruit with soft yellow or red skin, that has sweet juicy flesh, and a large seed in its centre, or a tree that produces this fruit 桃(子)；桃樹 —see picture on page A8 參見A8頁圖 **2** [U] a pale pinkish-orange colour 桃紅色 —see picture on page A5 參見A5頁圖 **3** [singular] *old-fashioned* someone or something that you think is attractive or like very much【過時】有吸引力的人[物]，特別惹人喜愛的人[物]: *a peach of a hat* 漂亮的帽子 | *Jan's a real peach.* 簡真是個美人兒。**4 a peaches and cream complexion** skin with an attractive pink colour 白皙紅潤的膚色

Peach Mel·ba /ˌpitʃ ˋmɛlbə; ˌpiːtʃ ˈmelbə/ *n* [C,U] half a peach served with ice cream and RASPBERRY juice〔澆以懸鉤子汁的〕蜜桃加冰淇淋

pea·cock /ˋpiˌkɑk; ˈpiːkɒk/ *n* [C] a large male bird which has long tail feathers that it can spread out, showing their beautiful blue and green colours and patterns (雄)孔雀

peacock blue /ˌ·· ˈ·◂/ *n* [U] a deep greenish-blue colour 孔雀藍(色) —**peacock blue** *adj*

pea·fowl /ˈpiˌfaʊl; ˈpiːfaʊl/ *n* [C] a peacock or peahen 〔雄或雌的〕孔雀

pea green /ˌ· ˈ·◂/ *n* [U] a light green colour, like that of PEAS 青豆色, 嫩綠色 —**pea green** *adj*

pea·hen /ˈpiˌhɛn; ˈpiːhen/ *n* [C] a large, brownish bird, the female peafowl 雌孔雀

peak 高峯

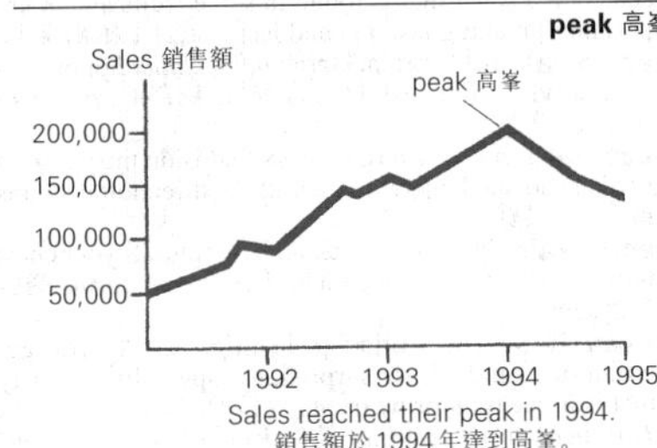

Sales reached their peak in 1994.
銷售額於 1994 年達到高峯。

3 **peak¹** /pik; piːk/ *n* [C]
1 ▶TIME 時間◀ [usually singular 一般用單數] the time when something or someone is strongest, most successful, or best 高峯, 頂點: *Her career was at its peak.* 她的事業正處於鼎盛時期。| *Sales have reached a new peak.* 銷售額達到了新的最高點。| **be at your peak/reach your peak** *Most athletes have reached their peak by the time they're 20.* 大多數運動員在 20 歲時已達到巔峯時期。—compare 比較 OFF-PEAK
2 ▶MOUNTAIN 山◀ **a)** the sharply pointed top of a mountain 山頂, 山峯: *peaks covered with snow all the year round* 終年被白雪覆蓋的山峯 —compare 比較 SUMMIT (1) —see picture on page A12 參見 A12 頁圖 **b)** a whole mountain with a pointed top 有尖峯的山: *K2 is one of the world's highest peaks.* 喬戈里峯是世界上最高的山峯之一。
3 ▶POINT 尖◀ a part that curves to a point above a surface 尖端, 尖頂: *Whisk the egg whites until they form stiff peaks.* 把蛋白打到發稠並頂端聳起為止。
4 ▶CAP 帽子◀ the flat curved part of a cap that sticks out in front above your eyes 帽簷, 帽舌 —see picture at 參見 CAP 圖

peak² *v* [I] to reach the highest point or level 達到頂峯, 達到最高水平: *Sales peaked in August, then fell sharply.* 銷售額於八月份達到最高點, 然後急劇下降。| [+at] *Around 1950 Chicago's population peaked at about 3.6 million.* 在 1950 年左右, 芝加哥的人口達到高峯, 約有 360 萬之多。

peak³ *adj* **1 peak level/rate/value** the highest level etc of something 最高水平/(速)率/值: *The factory is running at peak productivity.* 這家工廠的生產能力正處於最高峯。**2** *BrE* the peak time or period is when the greatest number of people are doing the same thing, using the same service etc【英】〔時間、階段〕高峯的: *the peak time for electricity consumption* 用電的高峯時間 | *Extra buses run at peak times.* 交通高峯期有加開的公共汽車。

peak·ed¹ /ˈpikɪd; ˈpiːkɪd/ *adj especially AmE* pale and ill【尤美】蒼白的, 有病容的; peaky *BrE*【英】: *You're looking a bit peaked this morning.* 今早你看起來有點憔悴。

peaked² /pikt; piːkt/ *adj* a peaked cap has a flat curved part at the front above the eyes 有帽簷的 —see picture at 參見 CAP 圖

pea·ky /ˈpikɪ; ˈpiːki/ *adj informal especially BrE* pale or ill【非正式, 尤英】蒼白的, 有病容的, 不適的: *Jane's feeling a bit peaky today.* 簡今天感到有點不舒服。

peal¹ /pil; piːl/ *n* [C] **1** a sudden loud sound of laughter or thunder 洪亮的笑聲; 隆隆的雷聲: [+of] *Peal of laughter came from the other room.* 陣陣笑聲從另一個房間傳來。**2** the sound of the loud ringing of bells 響亮的鐘聲[鈴聲]: [+of] *a joyous peal of bells* 歡快的鈴聲 **3** *technical*【術語】**a)** a musical pattern made by ringing a number of bells one after the other 鐘樂 **b)** a set of bells 編鐘

peal² *v* also 又作 **peal out** [I] if bells peal, they ring loudly〔鐘或鈴〕發出響亮的聲音, 鳴響: *The bells pealed out across the churchyard.* 教堂墓地對面的鐘聲噹噹地響起。

pea·nut /ˈpiˌnʌt; ˈpiːnʌt/ *n* **1** [C] a nut which grows in a soft shell under the ground and which can be eaten (落)花生: *salted peanuts* 鹹花生 **2 peanuts** [U] *informal* a sum of money that is so small that it is hardly worth mentioning【非正式】微不足道的一小筆錢: *The hotel workers get paid peanuts.* 酒店工人的報酬十分微薄。

peanut but·ter /ˌ·· ˈ··/ *n* [U] a soft substance made from crushed peanuts, eaten on bread or used in cooking 花生醬

peanut gal·ler·y /ˈ·· ˌ···/ *n* [C] *AmE humorous* the cheap rows of seats at the back of a theatre or cinema【美, 幽默】〔劇院或影院裡票價較低的〕後排座位

pear /pɛr; peə/ *n* [C] a sweet juicy fruit that has a round base and becomes thinner nearer the top, or the tree that produces this fruit 梨; 梨樹 —see also 另見 PRICKLY PEAR—see picture on page A8 參見 A8 頁圖 3

pearl /pɝl; pɜːl/ *n*
1 ▶JEWEL 首飾◀ [C] **a)** a small round hard white object with a silvery shine, that is formed inside the shell of an OYSTER, and is very valuable as a jewel 珍珠: *a string of pearls* 一串珍珠 | *a pearl necklace* 珍珠項鏈 **b)** an artificial copy of this jewel 人造珍珠
2 ▶LIQUID 液體◀ [C] *literary* a small round drop of some liquid【文】〔液體的〕珠狀物: *Pearls of dew sparkled on the grass.* 草地上露珠閃爍。
3 ▶HARD SUBSTANCE 堅硬物質◀ [U] a hard shiny, variously coloured substance formed inside some SHELLFISH, which is used for decorating objects; MOTHER-OF-PEARL 珍珠母: *a knife with a pearl handle* 一把帶珍珠母柄的小刀
4 ▶EXCELLENT THING/PERSON 出色的東西/人◀ [C usually singular 一般用單數] someone or something that is especially good or valuable 極其優秀的人; 特別珍貴的東西: *a pearl among women* 女中俊傑 | **a pearl beyond price** *Good health is a pearl beyond price.* 健康的身體是無價之寶。
5 cast pearls before swine to give something valuable to someone who does not understand its value 把貴重的東西給不懂其價值的人; 明珠暗投
6 pearls of wisdom an expression meaning wise remarks, often used jokingly to mean slightly stupid remarks 有見識的評說, 智慧的結晶〔常用於開玩笑, 表示其中略有點愚蠢〕: *Have you any more pearls of wisdom you'd like to share with us?* 你還有甚麼"至理名言"要與我們分享嗎?

pearl bar·ley /ˌ· ˈ··/ *n* [U] small grains of BARLEY that have been polished smooth 珍珠大麥

pearl div·er /ˈ· ˌ··/ *n* [C] someone who swims underwater in the sea, looking for shells that contain pearls (潛水)採珠人

pearl·y /ˈpɝlɪ; ˈpɜːli/ *adj* like pearls or having the colour of pearls 珍珠似的; 珍珠色的: *pearly white teeth* 珍珠般潔白的牙齒

pearly gates /ˌ·· ˈ·/ *n* [plural] *often humorous* the entrance to heaven【常幽默】天國之門

pear-shaped /ˈ· ·/ *adj* someone who is pear-shaped is larger around their waist and HIPS than around their chest〔人的體形〕梨形的〔指腰部和臀部寬, 胸部窄的體形〕

peas·ant /ˈpɛznt; ˈpezənt/ *n* [C] **1** someone who works in a poor country or in former times, who does farm work on the piece of land where they live〔貧窮國家的或從前的〕農

民，農夫: *He was born into a peasant family during the 1930s.* 他於20世紀30年代出生於一個農民家庭。**2** *informal* someone who does not have good manners or much education【非正式】鄉下人，土包子; 缺乏教養的人: *Don't be such a peasant!* 別這麼沒有教養!

peas·ant·ry /ˋpɛzn̩trɪ; ˈpezəntri/ *n* **the peasantry** all the peasants of a particular country〔某一國家的〕農民〔總稱〕

pease pud·ding /ˌpiz ˋpʊdɪŋ; ˌpiːz ˈpʊdɪŋ/ *n* [U] *BrE* a dish made of dried PEAS, boiled with ham to make a thick yellow substance that is eaten with bread【英】豌豆布丁

pea·shoot·er /ˋpiˌʃutɚ; ˈpiːˌʃuːtə/ *n* [C] a small tube used by children to blow small objects, especially dried PEAS, at someone or something 射豆槍〔一種兒童用來吹射豆子等的玩具槍〕

pea soup·er /ˌpi ˋsupɚ; ˌpiː ˈsuːpə/ *n* [C] a very thick FOG 濃霧

peat /pit; piːt/ *n* **1** [U] a substance formed from decaying plants under the surface of the ground in some areas, which can be burned instead of coal, or mixed with soil to help plants grow well 泥炭，泥煤: *a peat bog* 泥炭沼澤 **2** [C] a piece of this used for burning on a fire〔用作燃料的〕泥炭[泥煤]塊 —**peaty** *adj*: *brown peaty water* 泥炭似的黑水

peb·ble /ˋpɛbl̩; ˈpebəl/ *n* [C] **1** a small smooth stone found on the beach or on the bottom of a river〔見於海灘或河底等的〕卵石，小圓石，礫石 **2 you're not the only pebble on the beach** used to say that someone is not the only person who has to be considered or who deserves attention 你並非絕無僅有的人，除了你還大有人在 —**pebbly** *adj*: *a pebbly beach* 多卵石的海灘

peb·ble·dash /ˋpɛbl̩ˌdæʃ; ˈpebəldæʃ/ *n* [U] *BrE* a surface for the outside walls of houses, made of CEMENT with a lot of very small pebbles set into it【英】〔房屋外牆面上的〕灰泥卵石塗層 —**pebbledash** *v* [T]

pe·can /pɪˋkɑn; pɪˈkæn/ *n* [C] a long thin nut with a dark red shell, or the tree that it grows on 山核桃; 山核桃樹: *pecan pie* 山核桃餡餅

pec·ca·dil·lo /ˌpɛkəˋdɪlo; ˌpekəˈdɪləʊ/ *n* [C] a small unimportant thing that someone does wrong 小錯誤，小過失: *Bernard's wife had learnt to put up with his little peccadillos.* 伯納德的妻子已學會了忍受他的小過失。

pec·ca·ry /ˋpɛkərɪ; ˈpekəri/ *n* [C] a wild animal like a pig that lives in Central and South America〔生活在中、南美洲的〕西貒

peck[1] /pɛk; pek/ *v* **1** [I,T] if a bird pecks something, it makes quick repeated movements with its beak to try to bite it〔鳥〕啄; 啄食: **[+at]** *sparrows pecking at breadcrumbs* 啄食麵包屑的麻雀 | **peck sth** *A bird flew down and pecked my hand.* 一隻鳥飛下來啄了我的手。| *It had pecked a hole in the bottom of its cage.* 牠在籠底啄了一個洞。**2 peck sb on the cheek** to kiss someone quickly and lightly 匆匆地輕吻某人的面頰 —see also 另見 HENPECKED

peck at sth ↔ *phr v* [T] to eat only a little bit of a meal because you are not hungry; **pick at** (PICK[1])〔因不餓而〕吃一點點

peck[2] *n* [C] **1 give sb a peck** to kiss someone quickly and lightly 匆匆地輕吻某人 **2** an act of pecking 啄 **3** a measure of amount for dry substances such as fruit or grain 配克〔水果、穀物等的計量單位〕

peck·er /ˋpɛkɚ; ˈpekə/ *n* [C] **1 keep your pecker up** *BrE spoken* used to tell someone to stay cheerful even when it is difficult to do so【英口】打起精神，振作起來 **2** *AmE slang* PENIS【美俚】陰莖

pecking or·der /ˋ‥ ˌ‥/ *n* [C] *often humorous* the social system of a particular group of people or animals, in which each one knows who is more important and less important than themselves【常幽默】〔人或動物特定羣體中的〕社羣等級，權勢等級: *Patients seem to be very low down in the pecking order as far as making changes to hospital policy is concerned.* 就改變醫院的政策而言，病人好像處於最無足輕重的地位。

peck·ish /ˋpɛkɪʃ; ˈpekɪʃ/ *adj BrE informal* slightly hungry【英，非正式】有點餓的

pecs /pɛks; peks/ *n* [plural] *informal* PECTORALS【非正式】胸肌

pec·tic /ˋpɛktɪk; ˈpektɪk/ *adj technical* containing pectin【術語】果膠的; 含果膠的

pec·tin /ˋpɛktɪn; ˈpektɪn/ *n* [U] *technical* a chemical substance like sugar that is found in some fruits and is important in making JAM[1] (1) and JELLY (1,2)【術語】果膠

pec·to·ral /ˋpɛktərəl; ˈpektərəl/ *adj technical* of or connected with the chest【術語】胸的; 胸部的: *pectoral muscles* 胸肌

pectoral fin /ˌ‥ ˈ‥/ *n* [C] the FIN that is on the side of a fish's head and helps it to control the direction it swims in〔魚的〕胸鰭

pec·to·rals /ˋpɛktərəlz; ˈpektərəlz/ *n* [plural] your chest muscles 胸肌: *strong men with bulging pectorals* 胸肌發達的強壯男人

pe·cu·li·ar /pɪˋkjuljɚ; pɪˈkjuːliə/ *adj* **1** strange, unfamiliar, and a little surprising, especially in a way that is unpleasant or worrying 奇怪的; 異常的; 乖僻的: *This meat tastes peculiar.* 這肉味道很古怪。| *It seems very peculiar that no one noticed Kay had gone.* 沒有人注意到凱已經走了，這好像很奇怪。**2 be peculiar to** if something is peculiar to a particular person, place, or situation, it is a feature that only belongs to that person etc〔某人、某地方或某情況所〕特有的: *The problem of racism is not peculiar to this country.* 種族歧視問題並不是這個國家才有。**3** behaving in a strange and slightly crazy way〔行為〕怪癖的; 有點瘋狂的: *Auntie May's gone a bit peculiar lately.* 梅姑媽最近有點古怪。**4 feel peculiar** *informal* to feel slightly ill【非正式】感到有點不舒服

pe·cu·li·ar·i·ty /pɪˌkjulɪˋærətɪ; pɪˌkjuːliˈærəti/ *n* **1** [C] something that is a feature of only one particular place, person, or situation〔僅為某人、某地方或某情況所獨有的〕特點，獨特性: **[+of]** *The lack of a written constitution is a peculiarity of the British political system.* 沒有一部成文憲法是英國政治制度的一大特點。**2** [C] a strange or unusual habit, quality etc 奇異的性質; 怪癖: *It took some time for Theresa to get used to her husband's peculiarities.* 特里薩花了好一段時間才習慣了她丈夫的怪癖。**3** [U] the quality of being strange or unfamiliar 奇特; 怪異; 古怪

pe·cu·li·ar·ly /pɪˋkjuljɚlɪ; pɪˈkjuːliəli/ *adv* **1** especially 特別; 尤其(是): *a peculiarly difficult question* 特別難的問題 **2** in a strange or unusual way 奇怪地，古怪地: *Theo had been behaving most peculiarly.* 西奧的舉止一直很古怪。**3 peculiarly British/middle-class/Christian etc** something that is peculiarly British etc is a feature only of British people etc 英國人/中產階級/基督教徒等特有的: *a peculiarly American phenomenon* 美國特有的一種現象

pe·cu·ni·a·ry /pɪˋkjunɪˌɛrɪ; pɪˈkjuːniəri/ *adj formal* connected with or consisting of money【正式】錢的; 金錢上的: *a pecuniary advantage* 金錢上的優勢

ped·a·go·gi·cal /ˌpɛdəˋgɑdʒɪkl̩; ˌpedəˈgɒdʒɪkəl/ *adj technical* concerning teaching methods or the practice of teaching【術語】教學(法)的: *training in pedagogical skills* 教學技巧的培訓 —**pedagogically** /-kl̩ɪ; -kli/ *adv*

ped·a·gogue /ˋpɛdəˌgɑg; ˈpedəgɒg/ *n* [C] **1** a teacher who cares too much about rules 過分拘泥條條框框的老師，學究 **2** *old use* a teacher【舊】老師

ped·a·go·gy /ˋpɛdəˌgɑdʒɪ; ˈpedəgɒdʒi/ *n* [U] *technical* the practice of teaching or the study of teaching【術語】教學(法); 教育學

ped·al[1] /ˋpɛdl̩; ˈpedl/ *n* [C] **1** one of the two parts of a bicycle that you push round with your feet to make the bicycle go forward〔腳踏車的〕踏板，腳蹬 —see picture at 參見 BICYCLE[1] 圖 **2** a part in a car or on a machine that you press with your foot to control it〔汽車或機器的〕踏板: *the accelerator pedal* 油門踏板 **3** a part on a piano or organ that you press with your foot to change the quality of the sound〔鋼琴或風琴的〕踏板

pedal² *v* **pedalled, pedalling** *BrE*【英】, **pedaled, pedaling** *AmE*【美】[I, T] **1** [always+adv/prep] to ride a bicycle 騎〔腳踏車〕: [**+up/along/down etc**] *Andrew pedalled up the road towards the town centre.* 安德魯騎着腳踏車在通往市中心的路上行駛。—see also 另見 SOFT PEDAL **2** to turn or push the pedals on a bicycle or other machine 踩動〔腳踏車或機器的〕踏板: *pedalling furiously on her exercise bike* 飛快地踏着她的訓練車

pedal bin /ˈ·· ·/ *n* [C] a container for waste that has a lid which is opened by pressing a pedal with your foot〔用腳一踩蓋子即開啟的〕腳踏式垃圾桶

ped·ant /ˋpɛdn̩t; ˈpednt/ *n* [C] someone who pays too much attention to rules and details 過分注重規則和細節的人, 學究, 迂夫子: *She is something of a pedant when it comes to intellectual argument.* 說到知性的討論時, 她多少有點像一個迂夫子。—**pedantry** *n* [U]

pe·dan·tic /pɪˋdæntɪk; pɪˈdæntɪk/ *adj* paying too much attention to rules and details 過分注重規則和細節的; 學究式的; 書呆子氣的: *He was meticulous, but never pedantic.* 他非常謹慎, 但決不迂腐。—**pedantically** /-kl̩ɪ; -kli/ *adv*

ped·dle /ˋpɛdl̩; ˈpedl/ *v* [T] **1** to go from place to place, trying to sell something 沿街叫賣, 挨戶兜售: *An old woman was peddling goods on a street corner.* 一位老婦人正在街角處兜售物品。| **peddle drugs** (=sell illegal drugs) 販賣毒品 **2** to try to get people to accept opinions, false information etc 散播, 兜售〔觀點、假信息等〕: *a magazine that peddles scandal and gossip* 散播醜聞和流言的雜誌 **3** *informal, especially AmE* to sell goods that are of low quality【非正式, 尤美】兜售〔劣質貨物〕

ped·dler /ˋpɛdlɚ; ˈpedlə/ *n* [C] **1** the American form of the word PEDLAR pedlar 的美式拼法 **2** *old-fashioned* someone who sells illegal drugs【過時】販賣毒品的人: *a dope peddler* 毒品販子 —compare 比較 PUSHER

ped·e·rast /ˋpɛdəræst; ˈpedəræst/ *n* [C] a man who has sex with a boy 雞姦者, 與男童發生性行為的男子

ped·es·tal /ˋpɛdɪstl̩; ˈpedɪstəl/ *n* [C] **1** the base on which a PILLAR or STATUE stands〔柱子或雕像的〕基座, 台座, 柱腳: *a Grecian bust on a pedestal* 放在基座上的古希臘半身人像 **2 pedestal basin/table** *especially BrE* a BASIN or table that is supported by a single COLUMN【尤英】〔只有一根支柱支撐的〕支柱式洗臉盆/獨腳桌子 **3 put/place sb on a pedestal** to admire someone so much that you treat them or talk about them as though they are perfect 非常敬慕某人, 把某人當作偶像崇拜: *You shouldn't put him on a pedestal – he doesn't deserve it.* 你不應把他當作偶像崇拜——他不值得你那樣做。

pe·des·tri·an¹ /pəˋdɛstrɪən; pɪˈdestriən/ *n* [C] someone who is walking, especially in a street or other place used by cars 行人, 步行者 —see picture on page A3 參見 A3 頁圖

pedestrian² *adj* **1** ordinary and uninteresting and without any imagination 平淡無奇的; 乏味的; 缺乏想像力的: *a pedestrian description* 單調乏味的描述 | *a rather pedestrian student* 相當平凡的學生 **2 pedestrian walkway/footbridge etc** a path, bridge etc used by pedestrians 人行道/步行橋等

pedestrian cross·ing /ˌ·,··· ˈ··/ *n* [C] *BrE* a special place for people to cross the road【英】人行橫道; CROSSWALK *AmE*【美】

pe·des·tri·a·nize also 又作 **-ise** *BrE*【英】/pɪˋdɛstrɪənˌaɪz; pɪˈdestriənaɪz/ *v* [T] to change a street or shopping area into a place where vehicles are not allowed 使成為行人專用區, 使成為步行購物區 —**pedestrianization** /pɪˌdɛstrənəˋzeʃən; pɪˌdestrənaɪˈzeɪʃən/ *n* [U]

pedestrian pre·cinct /ˌ·,··· ˈ··/ *BrE*【英】, **pedestrian mall** /ˌ·,··· ˈ·/ *AmE*【美】*n* [C] a shopping area in the centre of a town where traffic cannot go〔市中心禁止車輛通行的〕步行購物區, 行人區

pe·di·a·tri·cian /ˌpidɪəˋtrɪʃən; ˌpiːdiəˈtrɪʃən/ *n* [C] the American spelling of PAEDIATRICIAN paediatrician 的美式拼法

pe·di·at·rics /ˌpidɪˋætrɪks; ˌpiːdiˈætrɪks/ *n* [U] the American spelling of PAEDIATRICS paediatrics 的美式拼法

ped·i·cel /ˋpɛdəsl̩; ˈpedɪsel/ *n* [C] *technical* a long thin part of a plant below each flower【術語】花梗

ped·i·cure /ˋpɛdɪkˌjʊr; ˈpedɪkjʊə/ *n* [C, U] treatment for feet and toenails, to make them more comfortable or beautiful 足部治療; 修腳指甲 —**pedicurist** *n* [C]

ped·i·gree¹ /ˋpɛdəˌgri; ˈpedəgriː/ *n* [C, U] the past family, especially the parents, grandparents etc, of a person or animal, or an official written record of this 血統; 家系, 家譜; 〔動物的〕純種系譜

pedigree² *adj* [only before noun 僅用於名詞前] a pedigree animal comes from a family that has been recorded for a long time and is considered to be of a very good breed〔動物〕純種系譜的: *a pedigree greyhound* 純種靈䴕 —compare 比較 PUREBRED, THOROUGHBRED (1)

ped·i·ment /ˋpɛdəmənt; ˈpedəmənt/ *n* [C] a three-sided piece of stone or other material placed above the entrance to a building, especially in the buildings of ancient Greece〔尤指古希臘建築門頂上的〕三角頂飾[楣飾]

ped·lar /ˋpɛdlɚ; ˈpedlə/ *n* [C] *BrE* someone who used to walk from place to place selling small things【英】流動小販, 貨郎; PEDDLER *AmE*【美】

pe·dom·e·ter /pɪˋdɑmətɚ; pɪˈdɒmɪtə/ *n* [C] an instrument used for measuring how far you walk 計步器, 步程計

pe·do·phile /ˋpidəfaɪl; ˈpiːdəfaɪl/ *n* [C] the American spelling of PAEDOPHILE paedophile 的美式拼法

pee¹ /pi; piː/ *v* [I] *informal* to pass liquid waste from your body; URINATE【非正式】撒尿

pee² *n informal*【非正式】**1** [singular] an act of passing liquid waste from your body 撒尿: **go for a pee/have a pee** *Have I got time to go for a pee before we leave?* 在我們離開前我有時間去小便嗎? **2** [U] liquid waste passed from your body; URINE 尿

peek /pik; piːk/ *v* [I] to look quickly at something, especially something that you are not supposed to see 偷看, 窺視: *The children were peeking from behind the wall.* 孩子們在從牆後面偷看。—compare 比較 PEEP¹ —**peek** *n* [C]: *I noticed Diane taking a quick peek at herself in the mirror.* 我注意到戴安娜快速地照了一下鏡子。

peek·a·boo /ˋpikəˌbu; ˌpiːkəˈbuː/ *interjection, n* [U] a game played to amuse babies, in which you repeatedly hide your face and then show it again, or the word you say when you play this game 躲躲貓〔把臉一隱一現地逗小孩的一種遊戲〕; 做躲躲貓時所說的話

peel¹ /pil; piːl/ *v* **1** [T] to remove the skin from fruit or vegetables 剝去, 削去〔水果、蔬菜〕的皮: *peeling potatoes* 削馬鈴薯皮 —see picture on page A11 參見 A11 頁圖 **2 peel sth from/away/off etc** [T always+adv/prep] to remove the outer layer from something 除去[剝去]...的外皮: *Jessie peeled the wrapper from the sweet.* 傑西把糖紙剝掉了。**3** [I] **a)** to lose an outer layer or surface〔外層或表面〕脫落, 剝落: *The walls were peeling with the damp.* 牆面因受潮而正在剝落。**b)** if skin, paper, or paint peels, it comes off, usually in small pieces〔皮膚、紙或油漆〕脫皮, 剝落: *My skin always peels when I've been in the sun.* 我的皮膚在曬了太陽後總要脫皮。—see picture on page A18 參見 A18 頁圖 —see also 另見 **keep your eyes open/peeled** (EYE¹ (15))

peel off *phr v* **1** [I,T **peel** sth ↔ **off**] to take your clothes off 脫去〔衣服〕: *The children peeled off their clothes and leapt into the pool.* 孩子們脫去衣服, 跳進了水池。**2** [I] to leave a moving group of vehicles, aircraft etc and go in a different direction〔車輛、飛機等〕離隊, 離

P

晕: *The last two motorcycles peeled off from the convoy.* 最後的兩輛摩托車離開了車隊。

peel² *n* [U] the outer layer of some fruits, especially the ones that you usually peel before you eat them〔尤指某些水果在吃前要剝掉的〕外皮: *orange peel* 橙皮

peel·er /ˈpilɚ; ˈpiːlə/ *n* [C] **1** a special type of knife for removing the skin from fruit or vegetables〔水果或蔬菜的〕削皮刀, 剝皮器 —see picture on page A11 參見A11頁圖 **2** *BrE old-fashioned* a police officer【英, 過時】警官

peel·ings /ˈpilɪŋz; ˈpiːlɪŋz/ *n* [plural] pieces of skin that have been removed from fruit or vegetables〔水果或蔬菜〕剝下[削下]的皮

P

peep¹ /pip; piːp/ *v* [I] **1** to look at something quickly and secretly, especially through a hole〔尤指從小孔〕窺視, 偷看: [+into/through etc] *I caught him peeping through the keyhole.* 他從鑰匙孔偷看時, 我當場抓住了他。**2** [always+adv/prep] if something peeps from somewhere, it is just possible to see it 隱約出現, 微現: [+through/from etc] *The sun peeped briefly through the clouds.* 太陽從雲中短暫地露了一會。—compare 比較 PEEK, PEER²

peep² *n* [C] **1** a quick or secret look at something 一瞥; 偷看; 窺視: **take a peep** *Mike had taken a peep at the answers.* 邁克偷偷看了一下答案。**2 not hear a peep out of** *spoken* to not hear a sound from someone【口】聽不到…的說話聲: *I don't want to hear a peep out of you until you've done your homework.* 在你完成作業之前, 我不想聽到你在說話。**3** *BrE* a word meaning the sound of a car's horn, used especially by or to children【英】汽車的喇叭聲〔尤用於兒語〕**4** a short weak high sound like the sound a mouse or a young bird makes〔老鼠或幼鳥發出的〕吱吱聲, 啾啾聲

peep·bo /ˈpipbo; ˈpiːpbəʊ/ *interjection, n* [U] PEEKABOO 躲躲貓; 做躲躲貓時所說的話

peep·ers /ˈpipɚz; ˈpiːpəz/ *n* [plural] *old-fashioned* your eyes【過時】眼睛

peep·hole /ˈpipˌhol; ˈpiːphəʊl/ *n* [C] a small hole in a door or wall that you can see through〔門或牆上的〕窺視孔

peeping Tom /ˌpipɪŋ ˈtɑm; ˌpiːpɪŋ ˈtɒm/ *n* [C] someone who secretly watches people, especially when they are undressing, having sex etc 窺視者〔尤指偷看別人脫衣服、性交等〕

peep·show /ˈpipˌʃo; ˈpiːpʃəʊ/ *n* [C] **1** a type of show in which a man pays for a woman to take her clothes off while he watches〔男人付錢讓女人在面前脫去衣衫的〕脫衣表演 **2** a box containing moving pictures that you look at through a small hole or LENS 西洋景; 西洋鏡

peer¹ /pɪr; pɪə/ *n* [C] **1** someone of the same age, social class etc as you 同齡人; 社會地位相同的人: *Children compete to win the approval of their peers.* 孩子互相競爭以贏得同齡人的認同。| *The jury system gives you the right to be judged by your peers.* 陪審團制度使你有權利接受與自己地位相同的人的審判。—see also 另見 PEER GROUP, PEER PRESSURE **2** a member of the British NOBILITY, who has the right to sit in the House of Lords〔英國可出席上議院的〕貴族 —see also 另見 LIFE PEER

peer² *v* [I always+adv/prep] to look very carefully or hard, especially because you are having difficulty in seeing〔尤指因看起來費勁而〕盯着看, 凝視: [+at/across/through etc] *Every few paces they stopped to peer ahead into the gloom.* 每走幾步, 他們就停下來張望着黑暗的前方。

peer·age /ˈpɪrɪdʒ; ˈpɪərɪdʒ/ *n* **1 the peerage** all the British peers (PEER¹ (2)) considered as a group 貴族〔總稱〕**2** [C] the rank of a British PEER¹ (2) 貴族爵位: *After ten years in the government she was given a peerage.* 她在政府工作十年後獲授予貴族爵位。

peer·ess /ˈpɪrɪs; ˈpɪərɪ̈s/ *n* [C] **1** a woman who is a member of the British NOBILITY and has the right to sit in the House of Lords; a female peer (PEER¹(2))〔英國可出席上議院的〕女貴族; 上議院女議員 **2** the wife of a British PEER¹ (2) 上議院議員夫人

peer group /ˈ· ·/ *n* [C] a group of people, especially young people of the same age, social class etc as yourself 同輩羣體, 年齡、社會地位等相同的一羣人〔尤指年輕人〕: *Establishing good peer group relationships is very important.* 同齡人之間建立良好的關係是非常重要的。

peer·less /ˈpɪrlɪs; ˈpɪələs/ *adj* better than any other 無與匹敵的; 無雙的: *Torvill and Dean's peerless performances in ice dancing* 托維爾和迪安無與倫比的冰上舞蹈表演

peer pres·sure /ˈ· ˌ··/ *n* [C] a strong feeling that you must do the same things as other people of your age if you want them to like you 同輩間的壓力, 同齡人間的壓力: *Teenagers often start smoking because of peer pressure.* 青少年通常由於同齡人的壓力而開始吸煙。

peeve /piv; piːv/ *n* [C] *informal* something that annoys you【非正式】令人氣惱的事情: **pet peeve** *Car alarms going off at night is one of my pet peeves.* 夜間響起的汽車警報聲是最令我頭痛的事情之一。

peeved /pivd; piːvd/ *adj informal* annoyed【非正式】生氣的, 惱怒的: *Ranulf felt peeved that she had not thanked him properly for his help.* 拉諾夫感到生氣的是她沒有好好感謝自己對她的幫助。

peev·ish /ˈpivɪʃ; ˈpiːvɪʃ/ *adj* easily annoyed by small and unimportant things; bad-tempered 易動怒的, 脾氣壞的: *The kids were peevish after so long in the car.* 孩子們坐了這麼長時間的汽車, 脾氣很急躁。—**peevishly** *adv* —**peevishness** *n* [U]

pee·wit /ˈpiwɪt; ˈpiːwɪt/ *n* [C] a LAPWING 田鳧, (鳳頭)麥雞

pegs 釘, 栓, 短樁

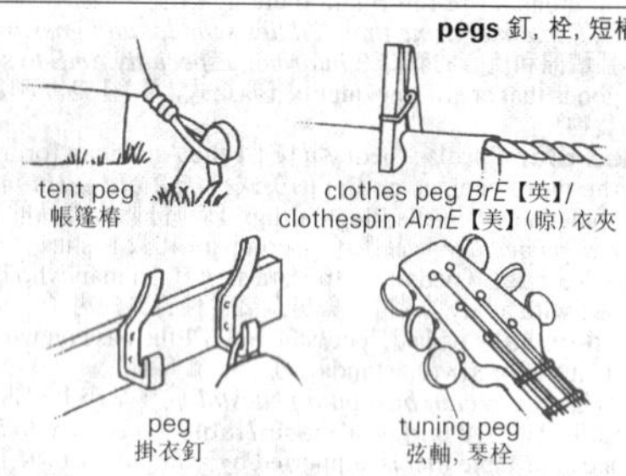

peg¹ /pɛg; peg/ *n* [C]

1 ►CLOTHES 衣服◄ **a)** a short piece of wood, metal etc fixed to a wall or door, used for hanging things on, especially clothes〔木頭或金屬製的〕短釘; 掛衣釘: *Hang your coat up on the peg.* 把你的外套掛在掛衣釘上。**b)** *BrE* a small piece of plastic or wood used for fastening wet clothes to a line to dry; CLOTHES PEG【英】〔晾衣服用的塑料或木製〕衣夾 **c) off the peg** *BrE* clothes that are off the peg are made to a standard size and have not been specially made to fit you【英】〔衣服〕現成的, 非訂做的; OFF-THE-RACK *AmE*【美】—see also 另見 OFF-THE-PEG

2 take/bring sb down a peg (or two) to make someone realize that they are not as important or as good at something as they think they are 煞某人的威風, 挫某人的傲氣: *It's time that young man was brought down a peg or two.* 是時候煞煞那個年輕人傲氣了。

3 ►FOR A TENT 用於帳篷◄ a pointed piece of wood or metal that you push into the ground in order to keep a tent in the correct position〔用於固定帳篷的木製或金屬〕樁

4 ►MUSICAL INSTRUMENT 樂器◄ a wooden screw used to tighten or loosen the strings of a VIOLIN, GUITAR etc; TUNING PEG〔用於調節小提琴、結他等弦線鬆緊的〕弦軸, 琴栓

5 a peg to hang sth on something that is used as a reason or excuse when you are trying to prove or explain something〔做〕某事的理由[藉口]
6 ►DRINK 飲料◄ *BrE old-fashioned* a small amount of strong alcoholic drink, especially WHISKY or BRANDY【英, 過時】少量威士忌[白蘭地]—see also 另見 **square peg in a round hole** (SQUARE[1] (11))

peg[2] **pegged, pegging** *v* [T] **1** to fasten something somewhere with a peg 用釘或椿等固定〔某物〕, 把…釘牢 **2** to fix prices, wages etc at a particular level, or fix them in relation to something else 把〔價格、工資等〕固定在一定水平, 限定: **peg sth to** *Most industrial countries stopped pegging their currencies to the US dollar in the early 1970s.* 在20世紀70年代早期, 大部分工業化國家不再把他們的貨幣與美元掛鈎而"釘住"。**3 have sb pegged as** *especially AmE* to regard someone's character in a particular way【尤美】認定某人為〔某種性格的人〕: *I never had you pegged as an idler.* 我從來沒有認定你是遊手好閒的人。**4 peg it** *AmE slang* to die【美俚】死

peg away at sth *phr v* [T not in passive 不用被動態] *BrE informal* to work hard and with determination【英, 非正式】堅持不懈地努力工作: *Vicky's been pegging away at her books all week.* 整個星期維基都在苦讀她的那些書。

peg out *phr v* **1** [I] *BrE informal* to die, or fall down because you are tired【英, 非正式】死; 〔因筋疲力盡而〕倒下 **2** [T **peg** sth ↔ **out**] *BrE* to fasten wet clothes to a washing line to dry【英】把〔濕衣服〕夾在晾衣繩上晾曬 **3** [T **peg** sth ↔ **out**] to mark a piece of ground with wooden sticks 用木樁標明〔某塊土地〕

peg·board /ˋpɛgbɔrd; ˈpegbɔːd/ *n* **1** [C] a small piece of board with holes in it, used to record the players' points in some games, especially card games〔在某些遊戲中, 尤指紙牌戲中記錄選手得分的〕插孔記分板 **2** [U] thin board with holes in it, into which you can put PEGS or hooks to hang things on〔有孔眼可裝掛物釘的〕配掛板

peg leg /ˈ··/ *n* [C] *informal* an artificial leg, especially a wooden one【非正式】〔尤指木製的〕假腿

pe·jo·ra·tive /pɪˋdʒɔrətɪv; pɪˈdʒɒrətɪv/ *adj formal* a word or expression that is pejorative expresses disapproval or criticism【正式】〔單詞或片語〕貶義的: *'Spinster' is a pejorative word for an unmarried woman.* spinster〔老處女〕是對未婚婦女的貶抑言詞。—**pejoratively** *adv*

peke /pik; piːk/ *n* [C] *informal* a pekinese【非正式】北京狗, 獅子狗

pe·kin·ese /ˌpikɪnˋiz; ˌpiːkɪˈniːz◄/ *n* [C] a very small dog with a short flat nose and long silky hair 北京狗, 獅子狗 —see picture at 參見 DOG[1] 圖

pe·lag·ic /pəˋlædʒɪk; pɪˈlædʒɪk/ *adj technical* connected with or living in the deep sea, far from shore【術語】深海的, 遠洋的: *pelagic fish* 深海魚類

pel·i·can /ˋpɛlɪkən; ˈpelɪkən/ *n* [C] a large water bird that catches fish for food and stores them in a deep bag under its beak 鵜鶘, 塘鵝〔一種食魚鳥〕

pelican cross·ing /ˌ··· ˈ··/ *n* [C] a place on some roads in Britain, where someone who wants to cross the road can stop the traffic by pushing a button that makes TRAFFIC LIGHTS change to red〔行人想橫過馬路時可按下按鈕使交通燈轉為紅色的〕自控人行橫道 —compare 比較 ZEBRA CROSSING

pel·lag·ra /pəˋlægrə; pɪˈlægrə/ *n* [U] a disease caused by a lack of a type of B VITAMIN, that makes you feel tired and causes problems with your skin and CENTRAL NERVOUS SYSTEM 陪拉格病, 糙皮病〔因缺乏維生素B而引起的一種病。患者會感到疲倦, 皮膚和中樞神經系統均會出毛病〕

pel·let /ˋpɛlɪt; ˈpelɪt/ *n* [C] **1** a small ball of any soft substance, sometimes made by rolling it between your fingers〔軟的〕小丸; 〔用手指搓成的〕小球, 小丸 **2** a small ball of metal made to be fired from a gun〔槍中射出的〕小彈丸, 子彈

pell-mell /ˋpɛl ˋmɛl; ˌpel ˈmel◄/ *adv old-fashioned* rushing very quickly, and in a way that seems uncontrolled【過時】匆忙地, 忙亂地: *The children ran pell-mell out of school.* 孩子一窩蜂地跑出學校。

pel·lu·cid /pəˋlusɪd; pɪˈluːsɪd/ *adj literary* very clear; TRANSPARENT (1)【文】清澈的; 透明的: *a pellucid stream* 清澈的小溪 —**pellucidly** *adv*

pel·met /ˋpɛlmɪt; ˈpelmɪt/ *n* [C] *BrE* a narrow piece of wood or cloth above a window that hides the rod that the curtains hang on【英】〔窗簾上方用以遮蔽簾子拉桿的〕窗簾盒; 布帷幔; VALANCE *AmE*【美】

pelt[1] /pɛlt; pelt/ *v* **1** [T] to attack someone by throwing a lot of things at them 向…連續投擲: **pelt sb with sth** *The Senator was pelted with rotten eggs.* 那位參議員遭人投擲臭雞蛋。**2 it is pelting down/it is pelting with rain** used to mean that it is raining very heavily〔雨〕傾盆而下 **3** [I always+adv/prep] *informal* to run somewhere very fast【非正式】向…飛快地跑去: **[+along/into/past etc]** *Three huge dogs came pelting out into the street.* 三條大狗飛快地跑到街上。

pelt[2] *n* [C] **1 a)** the skin of a dead animal with the fur or hair still on it〔死動物的〕生皮, 帶毛的獸皮 **b)** the skin of a dead animal with the fur or hair removed and ready to be prepared as leather〔清理掉毛準備做皮革用的〕獸皮 **2** the fur or hair of a living animal〔活動物身上的〕毛皮 **3 (at) full pelt** moving as fast as possible 全速地, 開足馬力地; 盡快地: *Nancy drove her car at full pelt down the road.* 南希駕着汽車全速地沿大路駛去。

pel·vic /ˋpɛlvɪk; ˈpelvɪk/ *adj* in or connected with the pelvis 骨盆內的; 盆腔的

pel·vis /ˋpɛlvɪs; ˈpelvɪs/ *n* [C] the large frame of bones at the base of your SPINE, to which your legs are joined 骨盆 —see picture at 參見 SKELETON 圖

pem·mi·can /ˋpɛmɪkən; ˈpemɪkən/ *n* [U] dried meat, beaten into small pieces and pressed into flat round shapes 乾肉餅

pens〔用墨水的〕筆

marker 記號筆

biro *BrE*【英】/ ballpoint pen *AmE*【美】圓珠筆 | felt tip 氈頭筆 | fountain pen/ ink pen 自來水筆 | ballpoint pen 圓珠筆

pen[1] /pɛn; pen/ *n* [C] **1** an instrument for writing or drawing with ink〔用墨水的〕筆: *a ballpoint pen* 圓珠筆 | *a fountain pen* 自來水筆 | *a felt-tip pen* 氈頭筆 **2** a small piece of land enclosed by a fence, used for keeping farm animals in〔圍養家畜的〕欄, 圈, 棚: *a sheep pen* 羊圈 —see also 另見 PLAYPEN **3 put/set pen to paper** to begin to write 開始書寫 **4** *AmE slang* PENITENTIARY; a prison【美俚】監獄 S2

pen[2] *v* **penned, penning** [T] *formal to* write a letter or note with a pen【正式】用筆寫〔信或便條〕

pen sb/sth ↔ **up/in** *phr v* [T] **1** to shut an animal in a small enclosed area 把〔動物〕關入圍欄中 **2 be penned in** to be restricted, as if you are being kept in a small place 被約束的, 被束縛的: *They were penned in watching TV with their parents all night.* 他們被管束着, 與父母看了一整夜電視。

pe·nal /ˋpinḷ; ˈpiːnl/ *adj* **1** [only before noun 僅用於名詞前] connected with the legal punishment of criminals, especially in prisons〔尤指在獄中〕刑罰的, 懲戒(性)的: *penal reform* 刑罰改革 | *the penal system* 刑罰制度 | **penal colony/settlement** (=a special area of land where prisoners are kept) 罪犯流放地 | **penal servitude** *law* (=a period of being kept in prison with hard physical work)【法律】勞役監禁 **2** [only before noun 僅用於名詞前] a penal offence can be punished by the law 當受處罰的, 當受刑罰的 **3** very severe 非常嚴厲的: *penal rates of taxation* 極苛刻的稅率

penal code /ˈ· ˌ·/ *n* [C] a system of laws and statements of the punishments for breaking those laws 刑法典

pe·nal·ize also 又作 **-ise** *BrE*【英】/ˈpinḷˌaɪz; ˈpiːnəl-aɪz/ *v* [T] **1** to treat someone unfairly or make them have a disadvantage 對待…不公平; 使…處於不利地位: *The whole class is being penalized just because one student behaved badly.* 只因一位學生行為惡劣, 全班同學都要受到不公平的對待。| *Sales taxes penalize the consumer.* 銷售稅對消費者不利。**2** to punish a team or player in sports by giving an advantage to the other team〔在運動中〕對…處罰: *In one game the All Blacks were penalized for wasting time.* 在一場比賽中, 全黑隊因拖延時間而受罰。—**penalization** /ˌpinḷɪˈzeʃən; ˌpiːnəlaɪ-ˈzeɪʃən/ *n* [U]

3 3 **pen·al·ty** /ˈpɛnḷtɪ; ˈpenlti/ *n plural* **penalties** [C] **1** a punishment for breaking a law, rule, or legal agreement〔因違反法律、規則或合約而受到的〕懲罰, 處罰: *No littering. Penalty $500.* 不要亂扔東西, 違者罰款500元。| **[+for]** *The penalty for murder was death.* 對謀殺罪的刑罰是死刑。| **impose a penalty** (=force someone to accept a penalty) 對…施加懲罰 *the highest penalty the court can impose* 法庭能夠施加的最重處罰 | **stiff/heavy penalty** (=a severe penalty) 嚴厲的懲罰[處罰] | **the death penalty** *Some MPs are calling for the death penalty to be brought back.* 一些下議院議員正在要求恢復死刑。**2** something unpleasant that happens to you because of something unwise that you have done or because of the situation you are in〔行為或處境所造成的〕不利結果; 苦惱: **[+of]** *One of the penalties of being famous is the loss of privacy.* 成名的麻煩之一是失去個人隱私。| **pay the penalty (for)** (=suffer the penalty for something) (為…)受到懲罰 *They never insured their property and now they're paying the penalty for their foolishness.* 他們從不為自己的財產投保, 現在他們正為自己的愚蠢而自食苦果。**3** a disadvantage in sports given to a player or team for breaking a rule〔體育運動中對犯規者的〕處罰 **4** a chance to kick the ball into the GOAL (3) in a game of football, given because the other team has broken a rule〔足球中因一方犯規而給予對方的〕罰球

penalty ar·e·a /ˈ··· ˌ···/ also 又作 **penalty box** /ˈ··· ˌ·/ *n* [C] the area in front of the GOAL (3) in football, in which the breaking of a rule means that the opposing team gets a PENALTY (4)〔足球的〕罰球區 —see picture on page A23 參見A23頁圖

penalty clause /ˈ··· ˌ·/ *n* [C] the part of a contract which says what someone will have to pay or do if they break the agreement, for example if they fail to complete work on time〔合同中對違約方的〕懲罰條款

penalty kick /ˈ··· ˌ·/ *n* [C] a penalty (PENALTY (4)) 罰(點)球

penalty point /ˈ··· ˌ·/ *n* [C] *BrE* a note made on a driver's LICENCE to show that they have done something wrong while they were driving【英】〔對違章司機的〕處罰記分

penalty shoot-out /ˌ··· ˈ· ·/ *n* [C] a series of penalty kicks used as a way of deciding which team has won a football game (罰)點球決勝賽〔足球中決定勝負的一種方式〕

pen·ance /ˈpɛnəns; ˈpenəns/ *n* **1** [C,U] the action of willingly making yourself suffer, especially for religious reasons, to show you are sorry for having done something wrong〔表示懺悔的〕自我懲罰: **do penance (for)** *Bianca has confessed and done penance for her sins.* 比安卡已悔過, 並為贖罪而自我懲罰。**2** [singular] something that you have to do but do not enjoy doing 不喜歡做而又不得不做的事情, 苦差: *Visiting old Uncle Edgar had become more of a penance than a pleasure.* 去探望老埃德加叔叔已成為一件苦差而不是樂事。

pence /pɛns; pens/ abbreviation 縮寫為 **p** *BrE*【英】the plural of PENNY (4): *a few pence* 幾便士 | *a 13 pence stamp* 一枚面值13便士的郵票

pen·chant /ˈpɛntʃənt; ˈpɒnʃɒn/ *n* [C] *French* a liking for something, especially something that is slightly disapproved of by other people【法】嗜好, 愛好〔尤指別人有點不贊成的事物〕: **[+for]** *a penchant for fast cars* 對高速汽車的強烈愛好

pen·cil¹ /ˈpɛnsḷ; ˈpensəl/ *n* [C, U] **1** a narrow pointed wooden instrument, used for writing or drawing, containing a thin stick of a black or coloured substance 鉛筆; 顏色鉛筆: *written in pencil* 用鉛筆書寫的 | *drawn with a pencil* 用鉛筆畫的 | *a pencil sketch* 鉛筆速寫畫 **2 a pencil of light** a narrow beam of light beginning from or ending in a small point 一束光 —see also 另見 EYEBROW PENCIL 2

pencil² *v* **pencilled, pencilling** *BrE*【英】, **penciled, penciling** *AmE*【美】[T] to write something or make a mark with a pencil 用鉛筆寫[標記]〔某物〕: *Mark pencilled a note to his wife.* 馬克用鉛筆寫了一張便條給他妻子。

pencil sb/sth ↔ **in** *phr v* [T] to include someone or something in a list or an arrangement, knowing that this might have to be changed later〔在清單或安排中〕暫時添入, 暫時填入; 暫定: *Let's pencil in Friday at 10 for the meeting.* 讓我們暫定星期五早上10點開會。

pencil push·er /ˈ·· ˌ··/ *n* [C] *AmE* PEN PUSHER【美】文員, 文書

pencil sharp·en·er /ˈ·· ˌ···/ *n* [C] a small thing with a blade inside, used for sharpening pencils 削鉛筆器, 捲筆刀[器], 鉛筆刨

pencil skirt /ˈ·· ˌ·/ *n* [C] a long narrow straight skirt 直筒長裙, 筆桿裙(一種窄而直的長裙)

pen·dant, pendent /ˈpɛndənt; ˈpendənt/ *n* [C] a piece of jewellery hanging from a thin chain that you wear around your neck〔項鏈上的〕垂飾, 掛件, 墜子: *a ruby pendant* 紅寶石墜子

pen·dent /ˈpɛndənt; ˈpendənt/ *adj literary or technical*【文或術語】**1** hanging from something 懸掛着的, 下垂的, 吊着的: *a pendent lamp* 吊燈 **2** sticking out beyond a surface 向外伸出的, 突出的: *pendent ledges of rocks* 突出的岩礁

pend·ing¹ /ˈpɛndɪŋ; ˈpendɪŋ/ *prep formal* while waiting for something, or until something happens【正式】在等待…之際; 直到…時: *A decision has been delayed pending further inquiries.* 在進一步調查之前暫不作出決定。

pending² *adj* **1** [not before noun 不用於名詞前] *formal* not yet decided or settled【正式】未定的, 未決的; 待定的, 待決的: *As my divorce was pending, I had to stay where I was.* 因為我的離婚訴訟還未判決, 我不得不待在原來的地方。**2 pending file/tray** a container for keeping papers, letters etc that have not yet been dealt with 待處理文件夾/格 **3** *formal* something that is pending is going to happen soon【正式】將要發生的, 迫近的: *a pending criminal trial* 待審的刑事案件

pen·du·lous /ˈpɛndʒələs; ˈpendjələs/ *adj literary* hanging down loosely and swinging freely【文】鬆垂的, 懸垂而自由擺動的: *pendulous breasts* 鬆垂的乳房 —**pendulously** *adv*

pen·du·lum /ˈpɛndʒələm; ˈpendjələm/ *n* [C] **1** a rod with a weight at the bottom that swings regularly from side to side to control the working of a clock 鐘擺 **2 the pendulum of opinion/fashion etc** something that tends to change regularly from one position to an opposite one 搖擺不定的觀點/時尚等: *The pendulum of public opin-*

ion has swung back. 搖擺不定的輿論已轉過來了。

pen·e·trate /ˈpɛnəˌtret; ˈpenǝtreɪt/ *v*

1 ▶GO THROUGH 穿過◀ [I,T] to enter something or pass through it, especially when this is difficult 進入; 滲入; 刺入; 穿過, 穿透: *shells that penetrate thick armour plating* 穿過厚厚裝甲層的砲彈 | **[+into]** *Explorers penetrated into unknown regions.* 探險者深入了未知的區域。

2 ▶BUSINESS 生意◀ [T] to start to sell things to an area or country, or to have an influence there 打進〔某地區或國家的市場〕: *Their goal is to penetrate undeveloped markets in the Third World.* 他們的目標是打入第三世界國家的未開發市場。

3 ▶ORGANIZATION 組織◀ [T] to get yourself accepted into a group or an organization in order to find out their secrets 〔為發現祕密而〕滲入〔某團體或組織〕: *KGB agents had penetrated most of their intelligence services.* 克格勃特工人員已滲透到他們的大部分情報部門。

4 ▶SEE THROUGH 看穿◀ [T] to see into or through something even though it is difficult 透過…看見, 看穿: *My eyes couldn't penetrate the gloom.* 我的眼睛在黑暗裡看不見。

5 ▶UNDERSTAND 理解◀ **a)** [T] to succeed in understanding something 洞察, 了解: *Science has penetrated the mysteries of nature.* 科學已揭開了大自然的奧祕。**b)** [I] *informal* to be fully understood by someone【非正式】被完全理解: *I heard what you said but it didn't fully penetrate.* 你的話我聽見了, 但沒有完全明白。

6 ▶SEX 性◀ [T] *technical* if a man penetrates a woman, he puts his PENIS into her VAGINA when having sex【術語】〔性交時〕把陰莖插入…的陰道 —see also 另見 IMPENETRABLE —**penetration** /ˌpɛnəˈtreʃən; ˌpenǝˈtreɪʃən/ *n* [U]: *the CIA's penetration of left wing organizations* 〔美國〕中央情報局對左翼組織的滲透 —**penetrable** /ˈpɛnətrəbl̩; ˈpenǝtrəbəl/ *adj* —**penetrability** /ˌpɛnətrəˈbɪlətɪ; ˌpenǝtrəˈbɪlǝti/ *n* [U]

pen·e·trat·ing /ˈpɛnəˌtretɪŋ; ˈpenǝtreɪtɪŋ/ *adj* **1 penetrating look/ eyes/gaze** a look etc which makes you feel uncomfortable and seems to see inside your mind 銳利的目光/眼睛/凝視: *an attempt to avoid her husband's penetrating gaze* 試圖避開她丈夫犀利的目光 **2** a penetrating sound is loud, clear, and often unpleasant 〔聲音〕響亮的, 刺耳的, 尖銳的: *a penetrating whistle* 尖得刺耳的汽笛聲 **3** showing an ability to understand things quickly and completely 有洞察力的, 思維敏銳的: *Parker had prepared some penetrating questions.* 帕克準備了一些尖銳的問題。**4** spreading and reaching everywhere 彌漫的; 滲透的: *penetrating dampness* 無孔不入的潮氣 —**penetratingly** *adv*

pen·e·tra·tive /ˈpɛnəˌtretɪv; ˈpenǝtrətɪv/ *adj* **1** able to get into or through something easily 容易穿透的 **2** showing an ability to understand things quickly and completely 思想敏銳的, 有洞察力的: *penetrative observations* 敏銳的觀察

pen friend /ˈ· ·/ *n* [C] *BrE* someone you make friends with by writing letters, especially someone in another country whom you have never met; PEN PAL【英】筆友

pen·guin /ˈpɛŋgwɪn; ˈpeŋgwǝn/ *n* [C] a large black and white Antarctic sea bird, which cannot fly but uses its wings for swimming 企鵝

pen·i·cil·lin /ˌpɛnɪˈsɪlɪn; ˌpenǝˈsɪlǝn/ *n* [U] a substance used as a medicine to destroy bacteria; an ANTIBIOTIC 青黴素, 盤尼西林

pe·nile /ˈpinaɪl; ˈpiːnaɪl/ *adj technical* relating to the penis【術語】陰莖的

pe·nin·su·la /pəˈnɪnsələ; pǝˈnɪnsjǝlǝ/ *n* [C] a piece of land almost completely surrounded by water but joined to a large mass of land 半島 —**peninsular** *adj*

pe·nis /ˈpinɪs; ˈpiːnǝs/ *n* [C] the outer sex organ of men and male animals that is used for urinating (URINATE) and in sexual activity 陰莖

pen·i·tent¹ /ˈpɛnətənt; ˈpenǝtǝnt/ *adj formal* feeling sorry because you have done something wrong, and intending not to do anything wrong again; REPENTANT【正式】後悔的; 悔過的; 懺悔的: *He knelt and put his head on her knee like a penitent dog.* 他像一隻悔罪的狗般跪了下來, 把頭放在她的膝上。—**penitently** *adv* —**penitence** *n* [U]

penitent² *n* [C] someone who is doing religious PENANCE 悔過者; 懺悔者; 告解者; 苦行贖罪者

pen·i·ten·tial /ˌpɛnəˈtɛnʃəl; ˌpenǝˈtenʃǝl◀/ *adj formal* connected with being sorry for having done something wrong【正式】後悔的, 懺悔的: *penitential journeys to famous shrines* 去著名聖地以示悔過的旅行 —**penitentially** *adv*

pen·i·ten·tia·ry /ˌpɛnəˈtɛnʃərɪ; ˌpenǝˈtenʃǝri/ *n* [C] a prison, especially in the US〔尤指美國的〕監獄: *the North Carolina state penitentiary* 北卡羅來納州監獄

pen·knife /ˈpɛnˌnaɪf; ˈpen-naɪf/ *n plural* **penknives** /-ˌnaɪvz; -naɪvz/ [C] a small knife with blades that fold into the handle, usually carried in your pocket 摺疊式小刀 —see picture at 參見 KNIFE¹ 圖

pen·man·ship /ˈpɛnmənˌʃɪp; ˈpenmǝnʃɪp/ *n* [U] *formal* the art of writing by hand, or skill in this art【正式】書法; 書寫技巧

pen name /ˈ· ·/ *n* [C] a name used by a writer instead of their real name; PSEUDONYM 筆名

pen·nant /ˈpɛnənt; ˈpenǝnt/ *n* [C] **1** a long narrow pointed flag used on ships or by schools, sports teams, etc〔船隻, 學校, 運動隊等用的〕三角旗 **2 the pennant** the prize given to the best team in the American and National BASEBALL competitions〔發給美國國家棒球比賽中最好球隊的〕錦旗, 獎旗

pen·nies /ˈpɛnɪz; ˈpeniz/ *n* the plural of PENNY

pen·ni·less /ˈpɛnɪlɪs; ˈpenɪlǝs/ *adj* having no money 一文不名的, 一貧如洗的: *The old lady died penniless.* 那位老婦人死的時候一貧如洗。

pen·non /ˈpɛnən; ˈpenǝn/ *n* [C] a long narrow pointed flag, especially one carried on the end of a long pole by soldiers on horses in the Middle Ages〔尤指中世紀騎士長矛上的〕三角矛旗; 小三角旗

pen·n'orth /ˈpɛnəθ; ˈpenǝθ/ *n* [singular+**of**] *BrE old-fashioned* a PENNYWORTH【英, 過時】一便士的價值; 值一便士的東西

pen·ny /ˈpɛnɪ; ˈpeni/ *n plural* **pennies** or **pence** /pɛns; pens/ *BrE*【英】[C] **1** a small BRONZE coin, used in Britain since 1971, worth one hundredth (1/100th) of a pound〔英國 1971 年起使用的〕一便士銅幣〔值 1/100 英鎊〕: *a bag of pennies* 一袋一便士的硬幣 **2** *plural* **pence** abbreviation 縮寫為 **p** a unit of money used in Britain since 1971 便士〔英國 1971 年起使用的貨幣單位〕: *There are 100 pence in one pound.* 一英鎊等於 100 便士。| *It only costs a few pence.* 這東西只要幾便士。| *a 20 pence piece* 一枚 20 便士的硬幣 **3** *AmE* a coin worth a CENT in the US or Canada【美】〔美國或加拿大的〕一分錢硬幣: *I only have pennies and nickels in my pocket.* 我口袋裡只有一分和五分的硬幣。**4** written abbreviation 縮寫為 **d** *plural* **pence** a unit of money in Britain before 1971, equal to one 12th (1/12th) of a SHILLING〔英國 1971 年前使用的〕便士〔等於 1/12 先令〕: *pounds, shillings and pence* 鎊、先令和便士 | **twopence/threepence etc** *a book costing only sixpence* 只賣六便士的書 **5 fourpenny/sixpenny etc** worth or costing fourpence, sixpence etc of the money used in Britain before 1971〔英國 1971 年前的〕值四便士/六便士等的: *a sixpenny piece* 一枚六便士的硬幣 **6 not a penny** no money at all 一個便士也沒有, 一文不名: *Not a penny of the money came to me.* 我一個便士也沒有拿到。| *She'll never get a penny from me.* 她一個便士也別想從我這兒拿走。**7 every penny** all of an amount of money 一筆錢的全部, 全部的錢: *You'd better pay it back – every penny!* 你最好還錢——一便士都不能少! **8 the/your last penny** the only money that is left 僅剩的錢: *She had given away her last penny.* 她把最後一個便士都送掉了。**9 a penny for your thoughts/**

a penny for them *spoken* used to ask someone what they are thinking about when they are silent【口】告訴我你在想甚麼〔用於對沉默不語的人說〕**10 the penny (has) dropped** *BrE informal* used to mean that someone has finally understood something that had been said【英, 非正式】最後終於明白了 **11 be two/ten a penny** *BrE* to be very cheap and easy to obtain, and therefore of little value【英】廉價而易得的; 多得不值錢的: *Computer experts are two a penny nowadays.* 如今電腦專家多的是。**12 not have two pennies/half-pennies to rub together** *BrE informal* to be very poor【英, 非正式】非常窮的 **13 in for a penny, in for a pound** *BrE* used to mean that if something has been started, it should be finished, whatever the cost may be【英】一不做, 二不休; 一旦開始就幹到底 **14 turn up like a bad penny** *BrE* if someone you dislike turns up like a bad penny, they keep appearing in situations where they are not wanted【英】〔不喜歡的人〕又來了 —see also 另見 HALFPENNY, **spend a penny** (SPEND (5)), **cost a pretty penny** (PRETTY² (7))

P

penny an·te /ˈ·· ,·/ *adj AmE informal* involving very small sums of money【美, 非正式】涉及金額很小的, 沒甚麼價值的: *his penny ante schemes to make money* 他的蠅頭小利的賺錢計劃

penny can·dy /ˈ·· ,··/ *n* [C,U] *AmE old-fashioned* a sweet that costs one cent for a piece【美, 過時】一便士一塊的糖果

penny dread·ful /,·· ˈ··/ *n* [C] *BrE* a cheap and badly written book about violent crime【英】〔描寫暴力犯罪的〕廉價低劣的小說

penny-far·thing /,·· ˈ··/ *n* [C] a bicycle with a very large front wheel and a very small back wheel, used in the late 19th century〔19 世紀晚期使用的〕前輪大後輪小的腳踏車

penny-half·penny /,·· ˈ···/ *n BrE* one and a half old pence【英】〔舊便士的〕一個半便士

penny-pinch·ing /ˈ·· ,··/ *adj* unwilling to spend or give money 吝嗇的, 小氣的 —**penny pinching** *n* [U] —**penny pincher** *n* [C]

penny whis·tle /,·· ˈ··/ *n* [C] a simple musical instrument shaped like a tube that you blow down 六孔小笛〔一種簡單的管狀吹奏樂器〕

pen·ny·worth /ˈpɛnɪ,wɝθ; ˈpenɪwəθ/ *n* [singular+**of**] *old-fashioned* as much as you can buy with a penny【過時】一便士的價值; 值一便士的東西

pe·nol·o·gy /piˈnɑlədʒɪ; piːˈnɒlədʒi/ *n* [U] the scientific study of the punishment of criminals and the operation of prisons 刑罰學; 監獄 (管理) 學 —**penologist** *n* [C]

pen pal /ˈ· ·/ *n* [C] *especially AmE* someone you make friends with by writing letters, especially someone in another country whom you have never met【尤美】筆友; PEN FRIEND *BrE*【英】

pen push·er /ˈ· ,··/ *n* [C] *BrE* someone who has a boring unimportant job in an office【英】〔在辦公室做枯燥而不重要工作的〕文員, 文書; PENCIL PUSHER *AmE*【美】

S3 W2 **pen·sion¹** /ˈpɛnʃən; ˈpenʃən/ *n* [C] an amount of money paid regularly by a government or company to someone who is officially considered to be too old or too ill to earn money by working 養老金; 退休金; 撫恤金: *They both have their pensions to live on now that they've retired.* 由於已經退休, 他們倆都靠退休金生活。| *a disability pension* 殘疾撫恤金 | **draw a pension** *BrE* (=receive or collect a pension)【英】領取退休金 | **pension rights/plan/scheme** *a company pension plan* 公司退休金計劃 | **occupational/company pension** (=one that you get from your former employer)〔從前雇主那裡獲得的〕職業退休金 / 公司退休金 | **old age pension** *BrE* (=paid regularly by the government to old people; SOCIAL SECURITY *AmE*【美】)【英】養老金, 社會保險金

pension² *v* [T] *BrE*【英】

pension sb/sth ↔ **off** [T] **1** *informal* to make someone leave their job, especially because of old age or illness, and pay them a pension【非正式】〔尤指由於年老或疾病而〕發給〔某人〕養老金使其 (提早) 退休: *Jean was pensioned off at 55.* 吉恩在 55 歲時被迫領養老金退休。**2** *informal* to get rid of something because it is too old or not useful any more【非正式】〔因太舊或不再有用而〕丟棄某物

pension³ *n* [C] a house like a small hotel, where you can get a room and meals, in France or some other European countries〔在法國或其他歐洲國家的〕膳宿公寓 —compare 比較 BOARDING HOUSE

pen·sion·a·ble /ˈpɛnʃənəbl̩; ˈpenʃənəbəl/ *adj* **1** giving someone the right to receive a pension 有享受養老金 [退休金、撫恤金] 資格的: *a pensionable age* 領取養老金的年齡 | *appointments that were not pensionable* 不能領取養老金的職位 **2 pensionable pay/salary** pay from which money is regularly taken for a pension 扣除養老金的報酬 / 薪水

pen·sion·er /ˈpɛnʃənɚ; ˈpenʃənə/ *n* [C] *BrE* someone who is receiving a pension, especially an OLD AGE PENSION【英】領取退休金〔尤指養老金〕的人

pension fund /ˈ·· ·/ *n* [C] a sum of money which is invested (INVEST (1)) and used to pay PENSIONS to those people who have regularly paid money into it 退休 [養老, 撫恤] 基金

pension plan /ˈ·· ·/ *n* [C] a system by which your employer, insurance company etc provides you with a pension after you have made regular payments to them over many years 退休金 [養老金] 計劃 —compare 比較 RETIREMENT PLAN

pension scheme /ˈ·· ·/ *n* [C] *BrE* a pension plan【英】退休金 [養老金] 計劃

pen·sive /ˈpɛnsɪv; ˈpensɪv/ *adj* thinking deeply about something and seeming a little sad 沉思的; 鬱鬱不樂的: *Jan was pensive.* 簡心事重重。| *a pensive expression* 憂傷的表情 —**pensively** *adv* —**pensiveness** *n* [U]

penta- /pɛntə; pentə/ *prefix* five 五 (個) : *a pentagon* (=shape with five sides) 五邊形, 五角形

Pent·a·gon /ˈpɛntə,gɑn; ˈpentəgən/ *n* **the Pentagon** the building in Washington DC from which the army, navy etc of the US are controlled, or the military officers who work in this building 美國五角大樓, 美國國防部; 美國國防部軍事官員

pen·ta·gon *n* [C] a flat shape with five, usually equal, sides and five angles 五邊形, 五角形 —**pentagonal** *adj*

pen·ta·gram /ˈpɛntə,græm; ˈpentəgræm/ *n* [C] a five-pointed star, used as a magic sign 五角星形 (符號)〔巫術的標記〕

pen·tam·e·ter /pɛnˈtæmətɚ; penˈtæmɪtə/ *n* [C] a line of poetry with five main beats 五音步詩行 —see also 另見 IAMBIC PENTAMETER

pen·tath·lon /pɛnˈtæθlən; penˈtæθlən/ *n* [singular] a sports event involving five different sports〔體育中的〕五項全能運動

Pen·te·cost /ˈpɛntɪ,kɔst; ˈpentɪkɒst/ *n* [singular] **1** a Jewish religious holiday 50 days after Passover〔猶太教的〕五旬節〔為逾越節後第 50 日〕**2** the seventh Sunday after Easter when Christians celebrate the coming of the Holy Spirit〔基督教的〕聖靈降臨節〔復活節後第七個星期日〕; WHITSUN *BrE*【英】

Pen·te·cos·tal /,pɛntɪˈkɔstl̩; ,pentɪˈkɒstəl◂/ *adj* **1** belonging to or connected with a group of Christian churches with particular interest in the gifts of the HOLY SPIRIT 五旬節派教會的〔注重聖靈的恩賜〕**2** connected with the holiday of Pentecost〔猶太人的〕五旬節的;〔基督教的〕聖靈降臨節的

Pen·te·cos·tal·ist /,pɛntɪˈkɔstl̩ɪst; ,pentɪˈkɒstəlɪst/ *n* [C] someone who belongs to a Pentecostal church 五旬節派教會的教徒 —**Pentecostalist** *adj* —**Pentecostalism** *n* [U]

pent·house /ˈpɛnt,haus; ˈpenthaʊs/ *n* [C] a very expensive and comfortable apartment or set of rooms built on top of a tall building〔建在大廈屋頂的昂貴舒適的〕樓頂公寓[套房]: *a magnificent penthouse apartment* 一套豪華的樓頂公寓

pent up /ˌpɛnt ˋʌp; ˌpent ˈʌp◂/ *adj* pent up emotions are not freely expressed〔感情〕被壓抑的: *She began to cry, letting her pent up grief come out.* 她哭了起來, 讓自己鬱結的悲痛發泄出來。

pe·nul·ti·mate /pɪˋnʌltəmɪt; peˈnʌltɪmɪt/ *adj* [only before noun 僅用於名詞前] *literary* next to the last【文】倒數第二的: *the penultimate chapter* 倒數第二章

pe·num·bra /pɪˋnʌmbrə; pɪˈnʌmbrə/ *n* [C] *technical* a slightly dark area between full darkness and full light【術語】半陰影; 半影

pe·nu·ri·ous /pəˋnurɪəs; pɪˈnjʊəriəs/ *adj formal* very poor【正式】非常貧窮的

pen·u·ry /ˋpɛnjərɪ; ˈpenjʊri/ *n* [U] *formal* the state of being very poor; POVERTY【正式】貧窮, 貧困: *families living in penury* 生活非常貧困的家庭

pe·on /ˋpiən; ˈpiːən/ *n* [C] **1** *AmE usually humorous* someone who works at a boring or physically hard job for low pay【美, 通常幽默】〔從事枯燥或重體力工作、報酬很低的〕勞工, 苦工 **2** *AmE* someone in Mexico or South America who works as a kind of slave to pay his debts【美】〔墨西哥或南美的〕抵債苦工, 抵債奴 **3** an office messenger in India〔印度的〕辦公室信差

pe·o·ny /ˋpiənɪ; ˈpiːəni/ *n* [C] a garden plant with large round flowers that are dark red, white, or pink 牡丹, 芍藥

1 1 **peo·ple¹** /ˋpipl; ˈpiːpəl/ *n*

1 [plural] persons 人: *Were there many people at the meeting?* 開會的人多嗎? | *Most people in our neighborhood drive to work.* 我們家附近的人大多開車去上班。| *a retirement home for elderly people* 老年人之家 —see 見 PERSON (USAGE)

2 ►PEOPLE IN GENERAL 人的總稱◄ [plural] people in general, or people other than yourself 人們: *Sometimes people think we're sisters.* 有時候人們認為我們是姐妹。| *People enjoy reading about the rich and famous.* 人們喜歡閱讀有關富人和名人的書。| **theatre/business etc people** *Computer people are notoriously bad at arithmetic.* 搞電腦的人算術差是出了名的。

3 the people [plural] all the ordinary people in a country or a state who do not have special rank or position 平民, 民眾, 老百姓: *Abraham Lincoln spoke of 'government of the people, by the people, for the people'.* 亞伯拉罕·林肯曾講到"民有, 民治, 民享的政府"。| *the common people* 老百姓 | **man of the people** *a politician who was regarded as a man of the people because his father had been a miner* 因為父親曾是礦工而被視為平民政治家

4 [C] a race or nation 種族; 民族: *the national heritage of the American people* 美國的民族遺產 | *the peoples of Africa* 非洲各民族 | *The Chinese people share a common written language.* 中國人使用的是同一種書面語言。—see 見 RACE¹ (USAGE)

5 sb's people [plural] **a)** the people that God, a king, or a leader rules or leads〔上帝、國王的〕臣民;〔領袖的〕擁護者: *the exaltation of God's people* 上帝子民的狂喜 **b)** your parents, grandparents etc 家族: *His people have lived in this valley for centuries.* 他的家族已在這山谷中生活了幾個世紀。**c)** *old-fashioned* your close relatives, especially parents【過時】家屬, 親屬〔尤指父母〕: *Come home with me to meet my people.* 跟我回家見見我的父母。

6 of all people *spoken* used to say that someone is the one person who you would not have expected to do something【口】在所有人中偏偏: *Why should he, of all people, get a promotion?* 在所有人中為甚麼偏偏是他獲得晉升呢? | *You of all people should have known better.* 在所有人中尤其是你本應該更明智一些。

7 *AmE spoken* used to get the attention of a group of people【美口】諸位〔用於引起一羣人的注意〕: *Listen up, people!* 注意聽, 各位! —compare 比較 FOLK¹ (3) —see also 另見 LITTLE PEOPLE, PERSON

people² *v* **1 be peopled with/by** *literary* to be filled with people or things of a particular type【文】充滿〔某種類型的人或物〕; 充斥: *Her little world was peopled with imaginary friends.* 她的小世界裡滿是假想的朋友。**2** [T] *technical* to live in a place; INHABIT【術語】居住於: *the tribes who first peopled the peninsula* 最早居住在該半島上的部落

pep¹ /pɛp; pep/ *v* **pepped, pepping**

pep sb/sth ↔ **up** *phr v* [T] *informal* to make something or someone more active, interesting or full of energy【非正式】使〔某人[物]〕更活躍[更有意思, 充滿活力]: *You need something to pep you up – how about a drink?* 你需要點東西讓自己振作起來 —— 來杯酒怎麼樣? | *Pep up the dish with some curry powder.* 給這份菜加點咖喱粉提提味。

P

pep² *n* [U] *informal* physical energy; VIGOUR【非正式】精力, 活力: *His exercise routine keeps him full of pep.* 他的日常鍛鍊使他充滿活力。—see also 另見 PEP TALK

pep·per¹ /ˋpɛpɚ; ˈpepə/ *n* **1** [U] a grey or pale yellow powder used to add a slightly hot taste to food 胡椒粉: *Pass the salt and pepper, please.* 請把鹽和胡椒粉遞過來。—see also 另見 BLACK PEPPER, WHITE PEPPER **2** a red powder like this, especially CAYENNE PEPPER or PAPRIKA 辣椒粉 **3** [C] a hollow red, green or yellow vegetable that is used in hot or cold dishes 辣椒 —see also 另見 BELL PEPPER, SWEET PEPPER —see picture on page A9 參見 A9 頁圖 3

pepper² *v* [T] **1** to scatter things all over or all through something 在…上撒; 使…佈滿: **be peppered with** *a report peppered with statistics* 滿篇都是統計數字的報告 **2** to hit something repeatedly with many bullets〔用許多子彈〕連續射擊, 猛擊: **pepper sth with** *He peppered the side of the barn with buckshot.* 他用大號鉛彈猛擊穀倉的一側。**3** to add pepper to food 給〔食物〕加胡椒粉

pepper-and-salt /ˌ·· · ˈ·◂/ *adj* coloured with small areas of black and white mixed together 花白的, 黑白相間的: *a pepper-and-salt beard* 花白鬍子

pep·per·corn /ˋpɛpɚˌkɔrn; ˈpepəkɔːn/ *n* [C] the small dried fruit from a tropical plant which is crushed to make pepper 胡椒粒[子]

peppercorn rent /ˌ··· ˈ·/ *n* [C] *BrE* a very small amount of rent, much less than you would expect to pay【英】象徵性租金, 極少的租金

pep·per mill /ˈ·· ·/ *n* [C] a small piece of kitchen equipment which is used to crush peppercorns into pepper 胡椒研磨器

pep·per·mint /ˋpɛpɚˌmɪnt; ˈpepəˌmɪnt/ *n* **1** [U] a MINT plant with a strong taste which is often used in sweets and medicine〔常用來做成糖果和藥的〕胡椒薄荷 **2** the taste of this plant 薄荷味: *peppermint candy* 薄荷糖 **3** [C] a sweet with the taste of peppermint 薄荷糖

pep·pe·ro·ni /ˌpɛpəˋronɪ; ˌpepəˈrəʊni/ *n* [C,U] an Italian spicy dry SAUSAGE 意大利辣香腸

pepper pot /ˈ·· ·/ *BrE*【英】, **pepper shak·er** /ˈ·· ˌ··/ *AmE*【美】*n* [C] a small container with little holes in the top used for shaking pepper onto food〔蓋子上有小孔的〕胡椒(粉)瓶

pep·per·y /ˋpɛpərɪ; ˈpepəri/ *adj* **1** tasting of pepper 胡椒味的, 辛辣的 **2** easily made angry; IRRITABLE 易怒的, 暴躁的

pep pill /ˈ· ·/ *n* [C] *informal* a PILL containing a drug that gives you more energy or makes you happier for a short time; STIMULANT (1)【非正式】興奮藥丸[片]

pep ral·ly /ˈ· ˌ··/ *n* [C] *AmE* a meeting of all the students at a school before a sports event when CHEERLEADERS lead students in encouraging their team to win【美】〔全體學生參加的〕學校運動會賽前動員大會

pep·sin /ˋpɛpsɪn; ˈpepsɪn/ *n* [U] a liquid in your stomach that changes food into a form that can be used by your body 胃蛋白酶

pep talk /ˈ· ·/ *n* [C] *informal* a speech that is intended to encourage you to work harder, win a game etc【非正式】鼓舞士氣的講話, 激勵性講話: *The manager gave his team a pep talk at half time.* 經理在半場休息時給隊員作了鼓舞士氣的講話。

pep·tic ul·cer /ˌpɛptɪk ˋʌlsɚ; ˌpeptɪk ˈʌlsə/ *n* [C] a sore painful place inside the stomach caused by the action of pepsin 消化性潰瘍

per /pɚ; pə; strong 強讀 pɝ; pɜː/ *prep* **1** for each 每: **per kilo/gallon/metre etc** (=for each kilo etc) 每公斤/每加侖/每米等 *Apples are 60 cents per pound.* 蘋果每磅60美分。| *My car does about 12 miles per litre* (=for each litre of petrol). 我的汽車每升汽油大約跑12英里。| **per head** (=for or by each person) 每人 *How much food should we allow per head?* 我們應允許每人吃多少食物? **2 per hour/day/week etc** during each hour etc 每小時/每天/每星期等: *How many calls do you make per day?* 你每天打多少個電話? | **miles/kilometres per hour** (=used for measuring speed) 每小時…英里/公里〔用以測量速度〕*a train travelling at 150 miles per hour* 每小時行駛150英里的火車 **3** according to 按照: **as per sth** *work carried out as per your instructions* 按照你的指示完成的工作 **4 as per usual** *spoken* used when something annoying happens which has often happened before【口】〔令人討厭的事情〕照常, 照舊: *Hardy was late, as per usual.* 哈迪同往常一樣遲到了。—see also 另見 PER ANNUM, PER CAPITA

per·ad·ven·ture /ˌpɝədˋvɛntʃɚ; ˌperədˈventʃə/ *adv old use*【舊】**1** perhaps 也許; 或許 **2** by chance 偶然; 碰巧: *if peradventure we should meet* 如果我們碰巧相遇的話

per·am·bu·late /pəˋæmbjəˌlet; pəˈræmbjʊleɪt/ *v* [I,T] *old-fashioned* to walk around or along a place without hurrying【過時】徘徊於; 漫步於 —**perambulation** /pəˌæmbjəˋleʃən; pəˌræmbjʊˈleɪʃən/ *n* [C,U]

per·am·bu·la·tor /pəˋæmbjəˌletɚ; pəˈræmbjʊleɪtə/ *n* [C] *old-fashioned especially BrE* a PRAM【過時, 尤英】嬰兒車

per an·num /pɚ ˋænəm; pər ˈænəm/ written abbreviation 縮寫為 **p.a.** *adv formal* for or in each year【正式】每年: *a salary of $20,000 per annum* 二萬美金的年薪

per·cale /pɚˋkel; pəˈkeɪl/ *n* [C,U] *AmE* cotton cloth, used especially for making sheets【美】〔尤指用來做牀單的〕棉布

per cap·i·ta /pɚ ˋkæpɪtə; pə ˈkæpɪtə/ *adj, adv formal* for or by each person in a particular place【正式】〔某個特定地方〕每人(的), 人均(的): *What is the average per capita income in this country?* 這個國家的人均收入是多少?

per·ceive /pɚˋsiv; pəˈsiːv/ *v* [T not in progressive 不用進行式] **1** to understand or think of something in a particular way〔以某種方式〕理解, 領悟: **perceive that** *People now perceive that green issues are important to our future.* 人們現在認識到環境問題對我們未來很重要。| **perceive sth as sth** *Holly began to perceive her father as a loser.* 霍莉開始認為她父親是一個失敗者。| **perceive sth to be sth** *The past is often perceived to be better than the present.* 過去常常被認為比現在好。| **perceive what/where/who etc** *We were able to perceive where the problem lay.* 我們能夠看出問題出在何處。**2** to notice something that is difficult to notice 察覺, 注意到, 發覺: *That morning, he perceived a change in Franca's mood.* 那天早上, 他發覺弗蘭卡的情緒有些變化。| **perceive that** *Jill could just perceive that someone was inside the house.* 吉爾只能注意到有人在房子裡。

percent¹ also 又作 **per cent** *BrE*【英】/pɚˋsɛnt; pəˈsent/ *adj, adv* **1 5 percent (5%)/10 percent (10%) etc** equal to 5, 10 etc parts out of a total that consists of 100 parts 5%/10%等: *Leave the waitress a 15 percent (=15%) tip.* 留給服務員15%的小費。**2 a/one hundred percent** completely, totally 百分之百地, 完全地: *I agree with you a hundred percent.* 我百分之百地同意你的看法。

percent² also 又作 **per cent** *BrE*【英】*n* **5 percent (5%)/10 percent (10%) etc** an amount equal to 5, 10 etc parts out of a total that consists of 100 parts 5%/10%等: *30 percent (=30%) of our profits* 我們利潤的30% | *The bank charges interest at fourteen per cent* (=14%). 銀行收取百分之十四的利息。

per·cen·tage /pɚˋsɛntɪdʒ; pəˈsentɪdʒ/ *n* **1** [C,U] *technical* an amount stated as if it is part of a whole which is 100【術語】百分比, 百分率: *"What percentage of school leavers go to university?" "About five per cent."* "離校畢業生上大學的百分比是多少?" "大約百分之五。" | **high/low percentage** *A high percentage of married women have part-time jobs.* 已婚婦女擁有兼職工作的比例很高。| **in percentage terms** *The numbers are small in percentage terms, but significant.* 按百分比來說, 這些數目並不大, 但意義重大。**2** [C usually singular 一般用單數] a share of profits 利潤分成: *She gets a percentage for every record sold.* 每賣一張唱片她都可得到一份利潤。**3 there is no percentage in** *informal* used to say that there is no advantage or profit in doing something【非正式】〔做某事〕沒有好處[利益]

per·cep·ti·ble /pɚˋsɛptəbl; pəˈseptəbəl/ *adj formal* something that is perceptible can just be noticed, although it is small【正式】可察覺的: *a barely perceptible sound* 幾乎察覺不出的聲響 | *a small but perceptible change* 微小但可以察覺的變化 —opposite 反義詞 IMPERCEPTIBLE —**perceptibly** *adv*

per·cep·tion /pɚˋsɛpʃən; pəˈsepʃən/ *n* **1** [C] the way you regard something and your beliefs about what it is like 認識, 觀念; 看法: *Parents' views influence their children's perceptions of the world.* 父母的觀點影響其孩子對世界的看法。**2** [U] the way that you notice things with your senses 感覺, 感知方式: *This drug alters perception.* 這種藥物會改變感知方式。**3** [U] the natural ability to understand or notice something quickly 感知能力; 認識能力; 洞察力: *Ross shows unusual perception for a boy of his age.* 羅斯所表現出的洞察力對於他這個年紀的男孩來說是非凡的。

per·cep·tive /pɚˋsɛptɪv; pəˈseptɪv/ *adj approving* good at noticing and understanding what is happening or what someone is thinking or feeling【褒】觀察敏銳的, 洞察力強的: *a perceptive woman* 一位洞察力強的女士 | *perceptive comments* 頗有見地的評論 —**perceptively** *adv* —**perceptiveness** *n* [U]: *trust in their own powers of perceptiveness and intuition* 相信他們自己的理解力和直覺力

perch¹ /pɝtʃ; pɜːtʃ/ *n* [C] **1** a branch, stick, rod etc where a bird sits, especially in a bird cage〔尤指鳥籠中的〕棲木, 棲枝 **2** *informal* a high place where a person sits or where a building is placed【非正式】〔人或建築物所處的〕高位, 高處: *From our perch on the hill, we can see the whole city.* 從這山崗的高處, 我們能鳥瞰全市。**3** a fish that lives in lakes and rivers〔生活在湖和河中的〕鱸魚

perch² *v* **1 be perched on/upon/over etc** to be in a position on top of, or on the edge of something 處在…的頂上[邊上]: *a house perched on a cliff above the town* 一幢位於懸崖之上俯瞰城鎮的房屋 **2 perch (yourself) on** to sit on top of, or on the edge of, something〔使自己〕坐在…的上面[邊上]: *Linda perched herself on a bar stool.* 琳達坐在酒吧的櫈子上。**3** [I+on] if a bird perches on something, it flies down and sits on it〔鳥〕落, 歇

per·chance /pɚˋtʃæns; pəˈtʃɑːns/ *adv old use or literary*【舊或文】**1** perhaps 或許, 也許 **2** by chance 偶然, 碰巧: *Leave now, lest perchance he should find you.* 現在就離開, 以免他碰巧找到你。

per·cip·i·ent /pɚˋsɪpɪənt; pəˈsɪpiənt/ *adj formal* quick to notice and understand things; PERCEPTIVE【正式】目光敏銳的, 洞察[理解]力強的 —**percipience** *n* [U]

per·co·late /ˋpɝkəˌlet; ˈpɜːkəleɪt/ *v* **1** [I always+adv/prep] if liquid, light etc percolates somewhere, it passes slowly through a material that has very small holes in it

〔液體、光等〕滲透, 濾出: [+through/down] *Water percolated down through the rock.* 水從岩石中滲漏下來。**2** [I always+adv/prep] if information percolates among people, it is passed gradually from one person to another〔信息〕逐漸傳播開來: **[+through/down]** *News of the war percolated through to us after a few days.* 幾天後, 戰爭的消息逐漸傳到我們這裡。**3 a)** [I] if coffee percolates, it is made in a special pot in which hot water is passed through crushed coffee beans〔咖啡在滲濾式咖啡壺中〕濾煮 **b)** [T] to make coffee by this method〔用滲濾式咖啡壺〕濾煮〔咖啡〕—**percolation** /ˌpɝkəˋleʃən; ˌpɜːkəˈleɪʃən/ *n* [C,U]

per·co·la·tor /ˈpɝkəˌletɚ; ˈpɜːkəleɪtə/ *n* [C] a pot in which coffee is percolated 咖啡滲濾壺, 煮咖啡壺

per·cus·sion /pɚˋkʌʃən; pəˈkʌʃən/ *n* **1** [U, singular] musical instruments, especially drums, that are played by being hit with an object such as a stick or hammer, or the group of people who play these instruments in an ORCHESTRA 打擊樂器〔尤指鼓〕;〔管弦樂隊中的〕打擊樂器演奏組: *The percussion is too loud.* 打擊樂器聲音太響。**2** [U] the sound or effect of two things hitting each other with great force〔兩物猛烈相撞產生的〕撞擊聲; 振動, 震動

per·cus·sion·ist /pɚˋkʌʃənɪst; pəˈkʌʃənɪst/ *n* [C] someone who plays percussion instruments 打擊樂器演奏者

per di·em¹ /pɚ ˋdiəm; pə ˈdiːəm/ *n* [C] *especially AmE* money paid by an employer to workers who are paid by the day【尤美】〔雇主付給工人的〕日工資: *What's the per diem for the job?* 這份工作每日的報酬是多少?

per diem² *adv* happening every day or from one day to another 每日地, 按日: *We are paid per diem.* 我們按日計酬。

per·di·tion /pɚˋdɪʃən; pəˈdɪʃən/ *n* [U] *formal*【正式】**1** punishment after death 死後的懲罰, 永劫; 惡報 **2** *old use* complete destruction【舊】徹底毀滅: *He had gambled his way to perdition.* 他因賭博走上了滅亡之路。

per·e·gri·na·tion /ˌpɛrəgrɪˋneʃən; ˌperɪgrɪˈneɪʃən/ *n* [C] *literary or humorous* a long journey, especially in foreign countries【文或幽默】〔尤指在外國的〕旅行; 遊歷: *His peregrinations took him to India and China.* 他遊歷到了印度和中國。

per·e·grine fal·con /ˈpɛrəgrɪn ˋfælkən; ˌperɪgrɪn ˈfɔːlkən/ also 又作 **peregrine** *n* [C] a hunting bird with a black and white spotted front 游隼

pe·remp·to·ry /pəˋrɛmptərɪ; pəˈremptəri/ *adj formal*【正式】**1** peremptory behaviour, speech etc is not polite or friendly and shows that the person speaking expects to be obeyed at once〔行為、說話等〕專橫的, 霸道的; 盛氣凌人的: *a peremptory tone of voice* 專橫的語調 **2** a peremptory command must be obeyed〔命令〕強制性的, 必須服從的, 不容抗拒的 —**peremptorily** *adv*

pe·ren·ni·al¹ /pəˋrɛnɪəl; pəˈreniəl/ *adj* **1 perennial problem/concern/struggle etc** a problem etc that people are concerned with all the time 長期存在的問題/擔憂/鬥爭等: *The film addresses the perennial theme of marital discord.* 這部電影關注的是夫妻不和這個永恒的主題。**2** a plant that is perennial lives for more than two years〔植物〕多年生的 —**perennially** *adv*

perennial² *n* [C] a plant that lives for more than two years〔兩年以上的〕多年生植物 —see also 另見 HARDY PERENNIAL

per·e·stroi·ka /ˌpɛrəˋstrɔɪkə; ˌperɪˈstrɔɪkə/ *n* [U] a Russian word meaning rebuilding, used to describe the policies of social, political, and economic change started by Mikhail Gorbachev in the former USSR 重建, 改革〔俄語詞, 用於指前蘇聯米哈伊爾·戈爾巴喬夫開始的社會、政治和經濟變革的政策〕

2 2 **per·fect¹** /ˈpɝfɪkt; ˈpɜːfɪkt/ *adj* **1** of the very best possible kind or standard 完美的, 理想的: *It's a perfect day for a picnic.* 這是個適合野餐的理想日子。| *a perfect example of Gothic architecture* 哥德式建築的極好例子 | *a perfect marriage* 美滿的婚姻 | **the perfect crime** (=one in which the criminal is never discovered) 掩蓋得天衣無縫的罪行 *There is no such thing as the perfect crime.* 沒有甚麼永不敗露的罪行。**2** complete, without any faults or weaknesses 完整的, 完好的, 完美的: *a perfect performance* 完美的演出 | *a perfect set of teeth* 一口完好無缺的牙齒 | *in perfect condition* 狀況完好的 | **nobody's perfect** *spoken* (=used when you are answering someone who has criticized you)【口】人無完人〔用來回答批評你的人時用〕*So I did the wrong thing! Well nobody's perfect.* 我確是做錯事了! 嗯, 人無完人嘛。**3** exactly right and just what is needed for a particular purpose; IDEAL¹ (1) 完美的, 最適當的; 理想的: *That's perfect! – just the way I wanted it to look.* 那太完美了——正是我想要的樣子。| *"D'you want some more soup?" "No, this is perfect."* (=enough; plenty) "你再要點湯嗎?" "不要啦, 這些足夠了。" | *We've found the perfect actor to play the part.* 我們找到了最適合扮演這個角色的演員。| **[+for]** *The house is perfect for our family.* 這房子對我們家來說是最合適不過的。**4** completely correct and accurate 完全正確的, 精確的: *Your English is perfect.* 你的英語說得很地道。| *a perfect copy of the original* 與原件一字不差的副本 | **perfect timing** (=when something happens at exactly the right time) 精確的時間掌握 *"Have you been waiting?" "No, it was perfect timing. I've just arrived."* "你一直在等嗎?" "沒有, 是時間算得好。我剛到。" **5 the perfect gentleman/wife/host** someone who behaves exactly as a typical gentleman etc ought to behave 十足的紳士/理想的妻子/完美(待客)的主人 **6 a perfect stranger/fool/angel etc** complete stranger etc 完全陌生的人/十足的傻瓜/十足的好人等: *I felt a perfect idiot.* 我感到自己是個十足的傻瓜。—see also 另見 PERFECTLY, **practice makes perfect** (PRACTICE (11)), PRESENT PERFECT, PAST PERFECT

per·fect² /pɚˋfɛkt; pəˈfekt/ *v* [T] to make something perfect or as good as you are able to 使…完美[完善]: *It's just a working model; we haven't perfected it yet.* 這只是個工作模型, 我們還沒有使它完善。

per·fect³ /ˈpɝfɪkt; ˈpɜːfɪkt/ *n technical*【術語】**the perfect** the form of a verb which shows a period of time up to and including the present, and in English is usually formed with 'have' and the past participle; PRESENT PERFECT〔動詞的〕完成式 —see also 另見 PAST PERFECT

per·fec·ti·ble /pɚˋfɛktəbḷ; pəˈfektɪbəl/ *adj* something that is perfectible can be improved or made perfect 可臻完美的, 可完善的, 可改進[改善]的 —**perfectibility** /pɚˌfɛktəˋbɪlətɪ; pəˌfektɪˈbɪlɪti/ *n* [U]

per·fec·tion /pɚˋfɛkʃən; pəˈfekʃən/ *n* [U] **1** the state of being perfect 完美, 完善: **to perfection** (=perfectly) 完美地, 恰到好處 *The meat was cooked to perfection.* 這肉煮得恰到好處。**2** the process of making something perfect 達到完美的過程: *the perfection of his technique* 他的技術的完善過程 **3** a perfect example of something〔某物的〕完美典型: *Her performance was pure perfection.* 她的表演達到了盡善盡美的地步。

per·fec·tion·ist /pɚˋfɛkʃənɪst; pəˈfekʃənɪst/ *n* [C] someone who is not satisfied with anything unless it is completely perfect 力求完美者, 完美主義者, 凡事求全者: *You did fine! Don't be such a perfectionist.* 你做得不錯了! 不要苛求盡善盡美。—**perfectionist** *adj* —**perfectionism** *n* [U]

per·fect·ly /ˈpɝfɪktlɪ; ˈpɜːfɪktli/ *adv* **1** in a perfect way 完美地; 極佳地: *She speaks English perfectly.* 她說得一口地道的英語。| *The colors match perfectly.* 這些顏色搭配得非常好。**2** a word meaning very or completely, used especially when you are annoyed about something 十分地, 完全地〔尤用於表示對某事討厭時〕: *We want to make our position perfectly clear!* 我們想把我們的立場完全說清楚! | *You know perfectly well what I mean.* 你完全知道我是甚麼意思。 2 3

perfect par·ti·ci·ple /ˌ‥ ˈ‥‥/ *n* [C] the PAST PARTICIPLE 過去分詞

perfect pitch /ˌ‥ ˈ‧/ *n* [U] the ability to correctly name

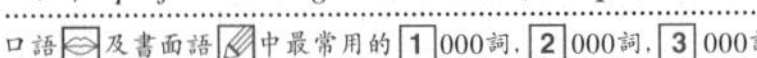

any musical note that you hear, or to sing any note at the correct PITCH without the help of an instrument 完全音高(感), 絕對音高(感)〔不借助樂器而正確地說出或唱出任何一個樂音的能力〕

per·fid·i·ous /pɚˋfɪdɪəs; pəˈfɪdiəs/ *adj literary* someone who is perfidious is disloyal and cannot be trusted; TREACHEROUS (1)【文】不忠實的, 背信棄義的 —**perfidiousness** *n* [U]

per·fi·dy /ˈpɝfədɪ; ˈpɜːfɪdi/ *n* [U] *literary* disloyalty to someone who trusts you; TREACHERY【文】不忠, 背信棄義

per·fo·rate /ˈpɝfəˌret; ˈpɜːfəreɪt/ *v* [T] **1** to make a hole or holes in something 在…上打洞[穿孔]: *A broken rib had perforated her lung.* 一根折斷的肋骨把她的肺刺穿了。**2** [usually passive 一般用被動態] to make a line of small holes in a piece of paper so that a part of it can be torn off easily 在〔紙〕上打孔眼線〔以便撕開〕—**perforated** *adj*: *a perforated sheet of paper* 一張打有齒孔的紙

per·fo·ra·tion /ˌpɝfəˈreʃən; ˌpɜːfəˈreɪʃən/ *n* **1** [C usually plural 一般用複數] a small hole in something, or a line of holes made in a piece of paper so that it can be torn easily 孔; 〔紙上的〕孔眼線: *the perforations in a sheet of stamps* 整版郵票上的齒孔 **2** [U] the making of a hole or holes in something 穿孔; 打齒孔

per·force /pɚˋfɔrs; pəˈfɔːs/ *adv literary* because it is necessary【文】由於需要, 不得已: *He fell sick and had perforce to stay at home.* 他感到不舒服, 所以不得不待在家裡。

S3 W2 **per·form** /pɚˋfɔrm; pəˈfɔːm/ *v* **1** [I,T] to do something to entertain people, for example by acting a play, or playing a piece of music 表演, 演出〈如演戲、演奏〉: *I've never seen 'Othello' performed so brilliantly.* 我從未看過《奧賽羅》這齣戲表演得如此精彩。| *Chris will be performing in public next week.* 克里斯下星期將進行公開演出。**2** [T] to do something such as a piece of work, a duty, or a ceremony, especially according to a usual or established method 做; 執行; 履行; 實行: *an operation performed by surgeons at Guy's Hospital* 蓋伊醫院的外科醫生進行的一個手術 | *The advice service performs a useful function.* 諮詢服務發揮了有益的作用。| **perform miracles** (=do things that seem impossible) 創造奇蹟 **3 perform well/badly** to work or do something well, badly etc 表現得好/差: *Our team performed very well on Saturday.* 我們隊星期六表現得很好。| *The car performs badly in the wet.* 這輛汽車在下雨天不好開。

S3 W1 **per·form·ance** /pɚˋfɔrməns; pəˈfɔːməns/ *n* **1 a)** [C] an act of performing a play or a piece of music 表演; 演出; 演奏: **[+of]** *Stern's performance of the Bruch concerto* 斯特恩演奏的布魯赫協奏曲 | **give a performance** *The orchestra will give two more performances this week.* 這個管弦樂隊本週將加演兩場。**b)** an occasion on which a play, piece of music etc is performed〔戲劇、音樂等的〕表演, 演出: *This evening's performance will begin at 8:00 pm.* 今晚的演出八點開始。**2** [U] **a)** the act of doing a piece of work, duty etc 履行, 執行: *the performance of his official duties* 履行他的公務 **b)** how well or badly you do a particular job or activity〔工作或活動中的〕表現: *Jodie's performance in the exams was disappointing.* 喬迪考試的成績令人失望。**3** [U] how well a car or other machine works〔汽車或機器的〕性能: *The car's performance on mountain roads was impressive.* 這輛汽車在山路上表現出的性能給人留下深刻的印象。| *high-performance cars* (=very powerful cars) 性能很好的汽車 **4 a) a performance** *spoken* a process that takes too much time and effort【口】費時費力的事: *What a performance!* 真是麻煩事! **b)** an example of bad behaviour that involves angry shouting〔帶有憤怒叫喊的〕糟糕的行為[舉止]

performance-re·lat·ed pay /ˈ·ˌ·· ˌ·ˌ·· ˈ·/ *n* [U] money that you earn which increases if you work well and decreases if you work badly 與工作表現掛鉤的報酬

per·form·er /pɚˋfɔrmɚ; pəˈfɔːmə/ *n* [C] **1** an actor, musician etc, who performs to entertain people 表演者; 演奏者; 演員: *circus performers* 馬戲演員 **2 skilful/brilliant/poor etc performer** someone who does a particular job or activity well or badly 技術嫻熟的/才華橫溢的/表演欠佳的演奏者[演員]: **star performer** (=the best performer) 明星演員

performing arts /·ˌ·· ˈ·/ *n* **the performing arts** arts such as dance, music, or DRAMA, which are performed to entertain people 表演藝術〈如舞蹈、音樂或戲劇〉

per·fume[1] /ˈpɝfjum; ˈpɜːfjuːm/ *n* [C,U] **1** a liquid that has a strong pleasant smell, that you put on your skin or clothing to make yourself smell nice 香水: *She never wears perfume.* 她從來不用香水。**2** a sweet or pleasant smell 香味: *the rose's heady perfume* 令人陶醉的玫瑰香味

per·fume[2] /pɚˋfjum; ˈpɜːfjuːm/ *v* **1** *literary* to fill something with a sweet, pleasant smell【文】使充滿香氣: *The flowers in her garden perfumed the evening air.* 她花園裡的鮮花使夜間的空氣充滿了香味。**2** to put perfume on something 噴[擦]香水於: *Use lavender oil to perfume your handkerchiefs.* 把薰衣草油灑在你的手絹上。—**perfumed** *adj*: *perfumed soap* 香皂

per·fum·er·y /pɚˋfjumərɪ; pəˈfjuːməri/ *n* **1** [C] a place where perfumes are made or sold 香水製造廠; 香水商店: *the store's perfumery counter* 商店中的香水(經銷)櫃台 **2** [U] the process of making perfumes 香水調製法

per·func·to·ry /pɚˋfʌŋktərɪ; pəˈfʌŋktəri/ *adj formal*【正式】**1** a perfunctory action is done quickly, and is only done because people expect it〔行動〕草率的, 馬虎的; 敷衍的: *Olivia dismissed him with a perfunctory nod.* 奧利維亞敷衍地點了點頭, 把他打發走了。| *a perfunctory kiss on the cheek* 在臉頰上漫不經心的一吻 **2** someone who is perfunctory does things in this way〔指人〕做事敷衍塞責的 —**perfunctorily** *adv*: *The two men shook hands perfunctorily.* 那兩個人敷衍地握了握手。

per·go·la /ˈpɝgələ; ˈpɜːgələ/ *n* [C] a structure made of posts built for plants to grow over in a garden〔花園中的〕藤架, 蔓棚

per·haps /pɚˋhæps; pəˈhæps/ *adv* **1** possibly; MAYBE 也許, 可能: *This is perhaps her finest novel yet.* 這或許是她迄今為止寫得最好的一部小說。| *Perhaps she's next door.* 也許她住在隔壁。| *"Do you think Mark's upset?" "Perhaps."* "你覺得馬克很難過嗎?" "也許是吧。" | **perhaps not** *"Do you think I dare ask him?" "Perhaps not."* "你認為我敢問他嗎?" "也許不敢。" **2** used to say that a number is only a guess 也許, 可能〔用於表示某個數字僅僅是猜測〕: *The room was large, perhaps twenty feet square.* 這個房間很大, 可能有二十平方英尺。**3** *spoken* used to politely ask or suggest something【口】也許, 或許〔用於表示禮貌的請求或建議〕: *I thought perhaps we'd have lunch in the garden.* 我想或許我們可以在花園裡吃午餐。| *Perhaps you'd like to join us?* 也許你願意加入我們吧? **4** *spoken formal* used to say what you are going to do, or what someone else should do【口, 正式】也許〔用於表示你自己要做或別人應該做的事情〕: *Perhaps in closing I could repeat a statement from our Chairman's opening address.* 在結束時, 我也許可以重複我們的主席在開幕詞中說的一句話。—see 見 MAYBE (USAGE)

per·il /ˈpɛrəl; ˈperɪl/ *n* **1** [U] *literary* great danger, especially of being harmed or killed【文】〔尤指遭傷害或殺害的〕巨大的危險: **in peril** *a prayer for those in peril on the sea* 為遇上海難的人祈禱 **2 the perils of a)** *literary* things that can cause great danger【文】可招致極大危險的事物: *Cook faced the perils of the Atlantic seas.* 庫克面臨着充滿危險的大西洋。**b)** things that might cause you problems in life 可能招致麻煩的事物: *Her mother had warned her about the perils of living alone.* 她母親告誡過她獨居的難處。**3 you do sth at your peril** used to warn someone that what they intend to do is very dangerous 你做某事要自擔風險〔用於告誡某人他們打算做的事情很危險〕: *Those who ignore the gale warning do so at their peril.* 那些無視大風警告的人這樣做要自擔風險。

per·il·ous /ˋpɛrələs; ˈperɨləs/ *adj especially literary* very dangerous【尤文】非常危險的: *a perilous journey across the mountains* 穿越羣山的危險旅程 —**perilously** *adj*: *perilously close to the precipice* 離懸崖太近, 十分危險 —**perilousness** *n* [U]

pe·rim·e·ter /pəˋrɪmətɚ; pəˈrɪmɨtə/ *n* [C] **1** the border around an enclosed area such as a military camp〔軍營等的〕四周, 周圍; 周邊, 邊緣: *the perimeter of the airfield* 機場的四周 | *a perimeter fence* 環形的籬笆圍牆 **2** the whole length of the border around an area or shape 周長: *Calculate the perimeter of this rectangle.* 計算這個長方形的周長。—compare 比較 CIRCUMFERENCE

pe·ri·na·tal /ˌpɛrəˋnetl̩; ˌperɨˈneɪtl◂/ *adj technical* at or around the time of birth【術語】圍產期的, 接近出生時期的: *a high rate of perinatal mortality* 很高的圍產期死亡率

3 1 **pe·ri·od¹** /ˋpɪrɪəd; ˈpɪəriəd/ *n* [C]

1 ▶LENGTH OF TIME 時間長度◀ a particular length of time with a beginning and an end 一段時間; 時期: *Tomorrow's weather will be dry with sunny periods.* 明天天氣乾燥, 間或有太陽。| *the period 1910–1917* 1910–1917 年間 | *a period of six weeks* 六週的時間 | *a six-week period* 六週的時間 | **trial period** (=a period of testing) 試用期 *Helen has been taken on for a three month trial period.* 海倫已被錄用, 試用期為三個月。

2 ▶IN DEVELOPMENT 發展中的◀ a particular period in the development of a country or a person〔國家或個人發展的〕時期; 階段: *Van Gogh's early period* 梵谷的早期階段

3 ▶IN HISTORY 歷史上的◀ a particular period in history〔歷史上的〕時期; 階段; 時代: *Which period are you studying?* 你在學哪一段歷史?

4 ▶WOMAN 婦女的◀ the MONTHLY flow of blood from a woman's body 月經 (期)

5 ▶DOT 點◀ *AmE* a DOT (.) in a piece of writing that shows the end of a sentence or an ABBREVIATION【美】句號; FULL STOP *BrE*【英】—see picture at 參見 PUNCTUATION MARK 圖

6 ▶FOR EMPHASIS 用於強調◀ **period!** *AmE spoken* used to say that you have made a decision and that you do not want to discuss the subject any more【美口】到此為止, 就這樣定了〔用於表示已做出決定, 不想再討論某話題〕: *I'm not going, period!* 我不去, 就這樣決定了!

7 ▶SCHOOL 學校◀ one of the equal parts that the school day is divided into; lesson 課時, 學時, 一節 (課): *What class do you have first period?* 你第一節課上甚麼? | *a double period of Science* 理科課程的雙節課時

period² *adj* **period costume/furniture** clothes or furniture in the style of a particular time in history 具有特定歷史時期特點的服裝/家具: *actors dressed in period costume* 穿着當時式樣的服裝的演員

pe·ri·od·ic /ˌpɪrɪˋɑdɪk; ˌpɪəriˈɒdɪk◂/ also 又作 **periodical** *adj* [only before noun 僅用於名詞前] happening repeatedly, usually at regular times 週期 (性) 的; 定期的: *periodic bouts of depression* 抑鬱症的定期發作 —compare 比較 SPASMODIC (1) —**periodically** /-kl̩ɪ; -kli/ *adv*: *Teachers meet periodically to discuss progress.* 教師定期開會討論進展情況。

pe·ri·od·i·cal /ˌpɪrɪˋɑdɪkl̩; ˌpɪəriˈɒdɪkəl/ *n* [C] a magazine, especially one about a serious or technical subject, that comes out at regular times such as once a month 期刊, 雜誌

periodic ta·ble /ˌ···· ˋ··/ *n* [singular] a list of ELEMENTS (=simple chemical substances) arranged according to their ATOMIC STRUCTURE (元素) 週期表

period pain /ˋ··· ·/ *n* [U] pain that a woman gets when she has her PERIOD¹ (4) 月經痛, 痛經; CRAMPS¹ (2) *AmE*【美】

period piece /ˋ··· ·/ *n* [C] **1** something that was very modern when it was first made, written etc, but now seems old-fashioned 一度時新但現已過時的物品[作品] **2** a typical example of something, such as a piece of furniture or work of art, from a particular period in history 具有某一歷史時期特點的東西〈如家具或藝術品〉

per·i·pa·tet·ic /ˌpɛrəpəˋtɛtɪk; ˌperɨpəˈtetɪk◂/ *adj formal* travelling from place to place, especially in order to do your job【正式】〔尤指為工作而〕到處旅行的, 到處走的: *a peripatetic music teacher* 巡迴音樂教師 —**peripatetically** /-kl̩ɪ; -kli/ *adv*

pe·riph·e·ral¹ /pəˋrɪfərəl; pəˈrɪfərəl/ *adj* **1** connected to the main idea, question or activity, but much less important, and given much less attention 次要的, 非主要的: *Can we leave the peripheral issues till later?* 我們能不能把這些次要問題留待以後再說? | **[+to]** *The love interest is peripheral to the main plot of the movie.* 對愛情的關注相對整部電影的主要情節來說是次要的。**2** in the outer area of something or related to this area 外圍的, 周邊的, 邊緣的: *the city's peripheral suburbs* 這個城市的市郊住宅區 **3** peripheral equipment can be connected to a computer and used with it〔電腦設備〕周邊的, 外圍的, 外部的: *peripheral software* (電腦) 周邊軟件 —**peripherally** *adv*

peripheral² *n* [C] a piece of equipment that is connected to a computer and used with it, for example a PRINTER¹〔電腦的〕周邊[外圍]設備〈如打印機〉

pe·riph·e·ry /pəˋrɪfərɪ; pəˈrɪfəri/ *n* **1** [C usually singular 一般用單數] the outer area or edge that surrounds a place 外圍, 邊緣: **[+of]** *a residential area on the periphery of the city* 位於城市邊緣的住宅區 —compare 比較 OUTSKIRTS **2** **be on the periphery** to be only slightly involved in a group or activity〔與某團體或活動〕稍有牽連的, 處於…外圍的: *extremists on the periphery of the animal rights movement* 與動物權利運動稍有牽連的極端分子

pe·riph·ra·sis /pəˋrɪfrəsɪs; pəˈrɪfrəsɨs/ *n plural* **periphrases** [C,U] *formal*【正式】**1** the unnecessary use of long words or phrases or unclear expressions 迂說 (法)〔指不必要地使用較長的單詞、短語或不清晰的表達法〕**2** *technical* the use of AUXILIARY words instead of inflected (INFLECT (1)) forms【術語】迂說法〔用助動詞而不用屈折變化的表達法〕—**periphrastic** /ˌpɛrəˋfræstɪk; ˌperɨˈfræstɪk◂/ *adj*

per·i·scope /ˋpɛrəˌskop; ˈperɨskəʊp/ *n* [C] a long tube with mirrors fitted in it used to look over the top of something, especially to see out of a SUBMARINE〔尤指潛水艇上用的〕潛望鏡

per·ish /ˋpɛrɪʃ; ˈperɪʃ/ *v* **1** [I] *especially literary* to die, especially in a terrible or sudden way【尤文】死亡〔尤指慘死或猝死〕: *Hundreds perished when the ship went down.* 輪船沉沒, 數百人遇難。**2** [I,T] *BrE, technical in AmE* if a material such as rubber or leather perishes, it decays and loses its natural strength【英, 美術語】〈如橡膠或皮革的〉損壞, 腐爛, 老化 **3** **Perish the thought!** *spoken* used as a reply to an unacceptable idea or suggestion, to say that you hope this never happens【口】但願這事永遠不會發生! 死了心吧!〔用來答覆不能接受的觀點或建議〕

per·ish·a·ble /ˋpɛrɪʃəbl̩; ˈperɪʃəbəl/ *adj* food that is perishable is likely to decay if it is not kept in the proper conditions〔食品〕易腐爛的, 易變質的: *perishable goods such as butter, milk, fruit and fish* 牛油、牛奶、水果和魚等易變質的商品 —**perishables** *n* [plural]

per·ished /ˋpɛrɪʃt; ˈperɪʃt/ *adj* **1** *BrE spoken* feeling very cold【英口】感到很冷的: *I wish I'd brought a jacket – I'm perished!* 我真希望帶了件夾克來——我現在冷得要命! **2** *BrE,technical in AmE* material such as rubber that is perished has lost its strength and become useless【英, 美語術語】〔橡膠等〕老化的; 無用的: *The rubber hoses were found to be perished and had to be replaced.* 這些橡皮軟管已經老化, 需要更換。

per·ish·er /ˋpɛrɪʃɚ; ˈperɪʃə/ *n* [C] *BrE old-fashioned* a child that behaves badly【英, 過時】淘氣的小孩: *Come here, you little perisher!* 到這兒來, 你這個小淘氣鬼!

per·ish·ing /ˋpɛrɪʃɪŋ; ˈperɪʃɪŋ/ *adj spoken especially BrE*【口, 尤英】**1** weather that is perishing is very cold〔天氣〕非常冷的: *It's really perishing this morning!* 今天早上簡直冷死了! **2** feeling very cold 感到非常冷的: *Let's go indoors. I'm perishing!* 我們進屋去吧 —— 我冷死了! **3** *old-fashioned* used to describe someone or something that is annoying you【過時】討厭的; 該死的〔用於描述令人討厭的人或事〕: *Tell those perishing kids to shut up!* 叫那些該死的孩子別吵了! **—perishingly** *adv*: *perishingly cold* 冷得要命

P

per·i·style /ˋpɛrə͵staɪl; ˈperɨstaɪl/ *n* [C] *technical* a row of PILLARS around an open space in a building or the open space itself【術語】周柱廊; 周柱中庭

per·i·to·ni·tis /͵pɛrətəˋnaɪtɪs; ˌperɨtəˈnaɪtɨs/ *n* [U] *technical* a poisoned and sore condition of the inside wall of your ABDOMEN (=part around and below your stomach)【術語】腹膜炎

per·i·wig /ˋpɛrə͵wɪg; ˈperɪwɪg/ *n* [C] a white WIG with rolls or curls at the sides, worn in the 18th century〔18世紀戴的白色〕假髮

per·i·win·kle /ˋpɛrə͵wɪŋkḷ; ˈperɪwɪŋkəl/ *n* **1** [C] a small plant with light blue or white flowers that grows close to the ground 長春花 **2** [C] a small sea animal that lives in a shell and can be eaten; WINKLE[2] 濱螺, 玉黍螺 **3** [U] a light blue colour 淡藍色

per·jure /ˋpɝdʒɚ; ˈpɜːdʒə/ *v* [I] **perjure yourself** to tell a lie after promising to tell the truth in a court of law〔在法庭上〕作偽證; 起[發]假誓

per·jur·er /ˋpɝdʒərɚ; ˈpɜːdʒərə/ *n* [C] someone who tells a lie after promising to tell the truth in a court of law〔在法庭上〕作偽證者; 發假誓者

per·ju·ry /ˋpɝdʒərɪ; ˈpɜːdʒəri/ *n* [C,U] the crime of telling a lie after promising to tell the truth in a court of law, or a lie told in this way 偽證罪; 偽誓: *Hall was found guilty of perjury.* 霍爾被發現犯有偽證罪。

perk[1] /pɝk; pɜːk/ *n* [C usually plural 一般用複數] something that you get legally from your work in addition to your wages such as goods, meals, or a car〔工資以外的〕額外收入〈如實物、膳食或汽車〉, 津貼: *With all the perks, she's really earning over £20,000 a year.* 加上她的全部津貼, 她每年實際上的工資超過兩萬英鎊。| **one of the perks of the job** *I get a company car – it's one of the perks of the job.* 我得到公司的一輛汽車 —— 這是該項工作的額外津貼之一。

perk[2] *v* [I,T] *informal* to percolate (PERCOLATE (3))【非正式】濾煮〔咖啡〕

perk up *phr v informal*【非正式】**1** [I,T] to become more cheerful and interested in what is happening around you, or to make someone feel this way (使)快活[振作]起來: *Zara perked up when her boyfriend's letter arrived.* 薩拉收到男朋友的來信後, 精神為之一振。| **perk sb ↔ up** *Have a cup of tea – that'll perk you up.* 喝杯茶 —— 那會幫你提提神。**2** [T **perk sb/sth ↔ up**] to make someone or something look brighter, neater etc 使看起來較為鮮亮[整潔]: *You can soon perk the room up with a coat of paint.* 刷一層油漆, 一下子就能使這個房間煥然一新。

perk·y /ˋpɝkɪ; ˈpɜːki/ *adj informal* confidently cheerful and interested in what is happening around you【非正式】自信而愉快的; 活潑的, 生氣勃勃的: *You're very perky today!* 你今天看起來很精神! **—perkily** *adv* **—perkiness** *n* [U]

perm[1] /pɝm; pɜːm/ *n* [C] a process of putting curls into straight hair, by chemical treatment〔用化學劑的〕燙髮: *I'm going to have a perm to give my hair more body.* 我要把頭髮燙一下, 讓它增添豐滿感。

perm[2] *v* [T] **1** to put curls into straight hair by means of a chemical treatment 燙〔髮〕: *I'm having my hair permed today.* 我今天要去燙髮。**2** *BrE* to choose and combine a number of football games from the list given in the FOOTBALL POOLS【英】〔足球賽賭博中〕選定並組合〔數字〕

per·ma·frost /ˋpɝmə͵frɔst; ˈpɜːməfrɒst/ *n* [U] a layer of soil, in very cold countries, that is always frozen〔寒冷國家的〕永久凍土

per·ma·nence /ˋpɝmənəns; ˈpɜːmənəns/ also 又作 **per·ma·nen·cy** /-nənsɪ; -nənsi/ *n* [U] the state of being permanent 持久(性); 永久(性), 永恒(性): *There's no feeling of permanence about our relationship.* 我們的關係不會長久。

per·ma·nent[1] /ˋpɝmənənt; ˈpɜːmənənt/ *adj* continuing to exist for a long time or for all future time 長久的; 永久的, 永恆的: *a paint that gives woodwork permanent protection against the weather* 長久保護木製品不受風雨侵蝕的塗料 | *I need a permanent job.* 我需要一份固定的工作。| *Natalie seems to have a permanent grin on her face.* 納塔莉臉上好像永遠掛着笑容。| **permanent fixture** (=someone or something that is always there) 總是在某處的人[物] *Dan seems to have become a permanent fixture in her life now.* 丹恩現在好像已成為她生活中的一部分了。—compare 比較 TEMPORARY **—permanently** *adv*: *The accident left him permanently disabled.* 那次意外事故使他永久殘廢了。

permanent[2] *n* [C] *AmE* a PERM[1]【美】〔用化學劑的〕燙髮

permanent wave /͵… ˈ·/ *n* [C] *formal* a PERM[1]【正式】〔用化學劑的〕燙髮

permanent way /͵… ˈ·/ *n* [C] *BrE* a railway track and the stones and beams on which it is laid【英】鐵路路基, 軌道

per·man·ga·nate /pɚˋmæŋgə͵net; pəˈmæŋgənɨt/ also 又作 **permanganate of potash** *n* [U] a dark purple chemical compound used for killing BACTERIA 高錳酸鉀

per·me·a·ble /ˋpɝmɪəbḷ; ˈpɜːmiəbəl/ *adj formal or technical* material that is permeable allows water, gas etc to pass through it【正式或術語】可滲透的, 具滲透性的: *a fine-grained permeable rock* 紋理細密的滲水岩 —opposite 反義詞 IMPERMEABLE **—permeability** /͵pɝmɪəˋbɪlətɪ; ˌpɜːmiəˈbɪlɨti/ *n* [U]

per·me·ate /ˋpɝmɪ͵et; ˈpɜːmieɪt/ *v* **1** [I always+adv/prep, T] if liquid, gas etc permeates something, it enters it and spreads through every part of it〔液體、氣體等〕滲透, 滲入; 瀰漫(於): *Toxic chemicals may permeate the soil, threatening the environment.* 有毒化學品會滲入土壤, 威脅環境。| **[+through/into]** *Water had permeated through cracks in the wall.* 水從牆縫裡滲了進來。**2** [T] if ideas, beliefs, emotions etc permeate something, they are present in every part and have an effect on all of it〔觀點、信念、感情等〕充滿於: *A feeling of sadness permeates all his music.* 他的音樂都充滿着悲哀的情緒。**—permeation** /͵pɝmɪˋeʃən; ˌpɜːmiˈeɪʃən/ *n* [U]

per·mis·si·ble /pɚˋmɪsəbḷ; pəˈmɪsɨbəl/ *adj formal* allowed by law or by the rules【正式】〔根據法律或規定〕允許的, 許可的, 准許的: *maximum permissible levels of radiation* 允許的最大輻射強度 **—permissibly** *adv*

per·mis·sion /pɚˋmɪʃən; pəˈmɪʃən/ *n* [U] an act of officially allowing someone to do something 允許, 許可, 准許: **permission to do sth** *I applied to the authorities for permission to cross the frontier.* 我向當局申請批准我越過邊境。| **give sb permission (to do sth)** *Who gave you permission to leave class early?* 誰准許你提早離開課堂的? | **ask permission (from sb)** *If you want to take photographs, you must ask permission from the warden.* 要想拍照必須徵得管理員的許可。| **with your permission** *spoken* (=used to politely ask someone for permission to do something)【口】如果你准許的話〔用於禮貌地徵求某人的許可〕*With your permission, I'll send a copy of this letter to the doctor.* 如果你准許的話, 我就把這封信的副本寄給那位醫生。—see also 另見 PLANNING PERMISSION

per·mis·sive /pɚˋmɪsɪv; pəˈmɪsɪv/ *adj* allowing behaviour, especially sexual behaviour, that many other people disapprove of〔尤指對許多人反對的性行為〕縱容的, 寬容的: *parents who are too permissive* 過分縱容的父母 | *the permissive society of the 1960s* 20世紀60年代性開放的社會 —**permissiveness** *n* [U]: *permissiveness in education* 教育上的放任 —**permissively** *adv*

3 **per·mit¹** /pəˋmɪt; pəˈmɪt/ *v* **permitted, permitting** [T] **1** *formal* to allow something to happen, especially by an official order or decision【正式】〔尤指根據正式命令或決定〕允許, 准許, 許可: *Smoking is only permitted in the public lounge.* 只允許在公共休息室裡抽煙。| **permit sb sth** *You are not permitted access to confidential files.* 你不准翻查機密檔案。| **permit sb to do sth** *I am afraid I cannot permit my daughter to marry you.* 恐怕我不會允許我的女兒嫁給你。| **permit sth in/near etc** *Dogs are not permitted inside the shop.* 狗不准進入店內。**2** [I] to make it possible for something to happen 容許, 許可: *I'll see you after the meeting, if time permits.* (=if it finishes early enough) 如果時間許可的話, 我開完會去見你。| **weather permitting** (=if the weather is good enough) 如果天氣允許的話, 假如天氣好的話 *We'll have a picnic in the woods, weather permitting.* 如果天氣好, 我們將在樹林裡野餐。**3** also 又作 **permit of** [T] *formal* to make something possible【正式】容許有; 允許有: *The facts permit of no other explanation.* 這些事實不容有其他解釋。

Frequencies of the verbs **let**, **allow** and **permit** in spoken and written English 動詞let, allow和permit在英語口語和書面語中的使用頻率

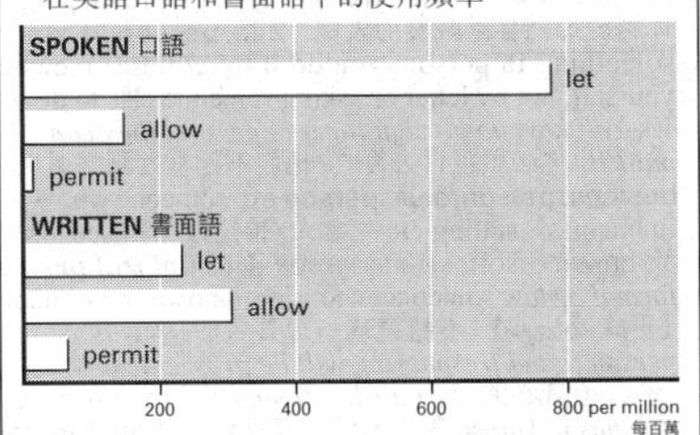

Based on the British National Corpus and the Longman Lancaster Corpus
據英國國家語料庫和朗文蘭卡斯特語料庫

This graph shows that **let** is much more common in spoken English than **allow** and **permit**. **Allow** is more common in written English. **Permit** is a formal word meaning to officially let someone do something. 本圖表顯示, let在英語口語中的使用頻率遠遠高於allow和permit。allow在書面語中較常用。permit較正式, 意思為正式地准許某人做某事。

per·mit² /ˋpɝmɪt; ˈpɜːmɪt/ *n* [C] an official written statement giving you the right to do something 許可證: *You're not allowed to park here unless you have a permit.* 除非你有許可證, 否則不許在這兒停車。| **a travel/work/export etc permit** *The authorities may refuse to issue an export permit.* 當局可以拒絕簽發出口許可證。—see also 另見 WORK PERMIT

per·mu·ta·tion /ˌpɝmjəˋteʃən; pɜːmjʊˈteɪʃən/ *n* [C] one of the different ways in which a number of things can be arranged in order〔數學的〕排列, 置換: *The six possible permutations of two letters chosen from ABC are AB, BA, CB, BC, AC, and CA.* 從ABC中取兩個字母有六組可能的排列, 即AB, BA, CB, BC, AC及CA。—compare 比較 COMBINATION —**permute** *v* [T]

per·ni·cious /pəˋnɪʃəs; pəˈnɪʃəs/ *adj formal* very harmful or evil, often in a way that you do not notice easily【正式】很有害的; 惡性的: *the pernicious effect of horror videos on children* 恐怖錄影帶對兒童的極壞影響 | *a pernicious lie* 惡毒的謊言 —**perniciously** *adv* —**perniciousness** *n* [U]

pernicious a·nae·mi·a /·ˌ··ˈ··/ *n* [U] *technical* a form of severe ANAEMIA (=too few red blood cells in the blood) that will kill the sick person if it is not treated【術語】惡性貧血

per·nick·e·ty /pəˋnɪkɪtɪ; pəˈnɪkəti/ *adj BrE informal*【英, 非正式】**1** worrying too much about small and unimportant things; FUSSY (1)【英】吹毛求疵的; 愛挑剔的; PERSNICKETY *AmE*【美】**2** difficult to do because you have to deal with a lot of small objects; FIDDLY (1) 精細的, 需要仔細的: *Changing this fridge lightbulb is a pernickety job.* 更換這個冰箱的燈泡是一項精細的工作。

per·o·ra·tion /ˌpɛroˋreʃən; ˌperəˈreɪʃən/ *n* [C] *technical*【術語】**1** the last part of a speech, especially a part in which the main points are repeated〔演說的〕結束語, 總結 **2** *formal* a long speech that sounds impressive but does not have much meaning【正式】誇誇其談的長篇演說

per·ox·ide /pəˋrɑksaɪd; pəˈrɒksaɪd/ *n* [U] a chemical liquid used to make dark hair lighter or to kill BACTERIA 過氧化氫〔用作漂染頭髮劑或防腐劑〕

peroxide blonde /·ˌ·· ˈ·/ *n* [C] *old-fashioned* a woman who has changed the colour of her hair to very light yellow by using peroxide【過時】用過氧化氫把頭髮漂染成金黃色的女人

per·pen·dic·u·lar¹ /ˌpɝpənˋdɪkjələ; ˌpɜːpənˈdɪkjələ◂/ *adj* **1** not leaning to one side or the other but exactly upright; VERTICAL¹ (1) 直立的, 垂直的: *a perpendicular line* 垂直線 | *a perpendicular wall of rock* 筆直的石牆 **2 be perpendicular to** if one line is perpendicular to another line, they form an angle of 90 degrees〔線〕與…成直角 **3 Perpendicular** in the style of 14th and 15th century English churches which are decorated with straight, upright lines〔14、15世紀英國教堂〕垂直式裝飾風格的 —**perpendicularly** *adv* —**perpendicularity** /ˌpɝpəndɪkjəˋlærətɪ; ˌpɜːpəndɪkjəˈlærəti/ *n* [U]

perpendicular² *n* **the perpendicular** an exactly upright position or line 直立姿勢; 垂直線: *at an angle to the perpendicular* 與垂直線成一定角度

per·pe·trate /ˋpɝpəˌtret; ˈpɜːpətreɪt/ *v* [T] *formal* to do something that is morally wrong or criminal【正式】做〔錯事〕; 犯〔罪〕: *crimes that have been perpetrated in the name of religion* 以宗教名義犯下的罪行 —**perpetrator** *n* [C]: *We'll bring the perpetrators to justice.* 我們將把罪犯緝拿歸案。—**perpetration** /ˌpɝpəˋtreʃən; ˌpɜːpəˈtreɪʃən/ *n* [U]: *the perpetration of crime* 犯罪

per·pet·u·al /pəˋpɛtʃuəl; pəˈpetʃuəl/ *adj* **1** continuing all the time without stopping, especially in a way that is worrying 連續不斷的, 無休止的: *the perpetual noise of the machines* 不絕於耳的機器噪音 | *His wife lived in perpetual fear of his fiery temper.* 他的妻子一直生活在對他暴躁脾氣的恐懼之中。**2** repeated many times in a way that annoys you〔令人討厭地〕一再重複的: *Ella's perpetual moaning nearly drove me mad.* 艾拉沒完沒了的抱怨幾乎把我逼瘋了。**3** *literary* permanent【文】永久的, 永恆的: *the perpetual snows of the mountaintops* 終年積雪的山峯 —**perpetually** *adv*

per·pet·u·ate /pəˋpɛtʃuˌet; pəˈpetʃueɪt/ *v* [T] to make something continue to exist for a long time 使長存; 使永恆: *an education system that perpetuates the divisions in our society* 使我們的社會長期分化的一種教育制度 —**perpetuation** /pəˌpɛtʃuˋeʃən; pəˌpetʃuˈeɪʃən/ *n* [U]

per·pe·tu·i·ty /ˌpɝpəˋtuətɪ; ˌpɜːpəˈtjuːəti/ *n* **in perpetuity** *law* for all future time【法律】永久; 永恆; 永遠: *The community does not own land in perpetuity.* 公眾對土地並沒有永久的擁有權。

per·plex /pəˋplɛks; pəˈpleks/ *v* [T usually passive 一般用被動態] if something perplexes you, it makes you feel worried and confused because it is difficult to understand 使困惑, 使茫然, 使費解: *I was somewhat perplexed by his response.* 我有點兒被他的回答弄糊塗了。| *a perplexing problem* 一個令人困惑的問題

per·plexed /pəˋplɛkst; pəˈplekst/ *adj* confused and worried by something that you do not understand 困惑的, 茫然的; 糊塗的: *She looked up at me with a perplexed stare.* 她抬起頭迷惑地盯着我。—**perplexedly** /pə-ˋplɛkstlı; pəˈpleksɨdli/ *adv*: *Florian was examining her perplexedly.* 弗洛里安正迷惑地打量着她。

per·plex·i·ty /pəˋplɛksətı; pəˈpleksɨti/ *n* **1** [U] the feeling of being confused or worried by something you cannot understand 困惑, 茫然 **2** [C usually plural 一般用複數] something that is complicated or difficult to understand 複雜的事物; 使人困惑的事物; 令人費解的事物: *moral perplexities* 道德上的複雜性

per·qui·site /ˋpɝkwəzıt; ˈpɜːkwɨzıt/ *n* [C] *formal* a PERK[1] 【正式】〔工資以外的〕額外收入, 津貼

per·ry /ˋpɛrı; ˈperi/ *n* [U] *especially BrE* an alcoholic drink made from PEARS 【尤英】梨子酒

per se /ˋpɝ ˋsi; ˌpɜː ˈseı/ *adv Latin* a word meaning 'in itself' or 'by itself', used to say that something is being considered alone, not in connection with other things 【拉丁】本身; 就本身而言: *The music per se was not very good, but it did help to create the right atmosphere.* 這音樂本身並不太好, 但它的確幫助營造了合適的氣氛。

per·se·cute /ˋpɝsıˌkjut; ˈpɜːsıkjuːt/ *v* [T] **1** to treat someone cruelly over a period of time, especially because of their religious or political beliefs〔尤指因宗教、政治信仰不同而在一段時期中〕迫害: *Puritans left England to escape being persecuted.* 清教徒離開了英國以躲避受到迫害。**2** to deliberately cause trouble for someone by continually annoying them; HARASS 騷擾, 煩擾; 糾纏: *Actors complained of being persecuted by the press.* 演員抱怨說受到新聞界的糾纏。—**persecutor** *n* [C] —**persecution** /ˌpɝsıˋkjuʃən; ˌpɜːsıˈkjuːʃən/ *n* [C,U]: *the persecution of writers who criticize the government* 對批評政府的作家的迫害

persecution com·plex /ˌ··ˈ·· ˌ··/ *n* [C] a mental illness in which someone believes that other people are continually trying to harm them 受迫害妄想症, 被迫害情結症

per·se·ver·ance /ˌpɝsəˋvırəns; ˌpɜːsɨˈvıərəns/ *n* [U] *approving* determination to keep trying to achieve something in spite of difficulties 【褒】不屈不撓, 堅持不懈: *Beth has shown great perseverance in trying to overcome her handicap.* 貝思在努力克服殘疾的過程中表現出堅忍的毅力。

per·se·vere /ˌpɝsəˋvır; ˌpɜːsɨˈvıə/ *v* [I] *approving* to continue trying to do something in a very determined way in spite of difficulties 【褒】堅忍不拔, 堅持不懈: [+at/in/with] *Rob keeps persevering in his efforts to learn French.* 羅伯堅持不懈地學習法語。—**persevering** *adj*

Per·sian[1] /ˋpɝʒən; ˈpɜːʃən/ *n* **1** [U] the language of Iran; FARSI 波斯語, 伊朗語 **2** [C] someone from Iran 波斯人, 伊朗人

Persian[2] *adj* from or connected with Iran, which used to be known as Persia 波斯的, 伊朗的: *a Persian carpet* 波斯地毯

Persian cat /ˌ·· ˈ·/ *n* [C] a cat with long silky hair 波斯貓

per·si·flage /ˋpɝsıˌflɑʒ; ˈpɜːsıflɑːʒ/ *n* [U] *formal* amusing talk, which usually includes laughing at other people 【正式】〔通常含有嘲弄別人意味的〕打趣; 玩笑; 挖苦

per·sim·mon /pəˋsımən; pəˈsımən/ *n* [C] a soft orange-coloured fruit that grows in hot countries 柿, 柿子 —see picture on page A8 參見 A8 頁圖

per·sist /pəˋzıst; pəˈsıst/ *v* **1** to continue to do something, although this is difficult, or other people warn you not to do it 堅持; 執意: **persist in (doing) sth** *If you persist in causing trouble, the company may be forced to dismiss you.* 如果你堅持製造麻煩, 公司可能不得不解雇你。| *"I'm sorry, I just don't think it's right," John persisted.* "我很抱歉, 我只是認為那不對。" 約翰堅持說道。**2** [I] to continue to exist or happen 繼續存在[發生]: *Despite official denials, the rumours persisted.* 儘管官方否認, 謠言仍在繼續流傳。

per·sis·tent /pəˋsıstənt; pəˈsıstənt/ *adj* **1** continuing to do something, although this is difficult, or other people warn you not to do it 堅持的; 執意的: *Paul is amazingly persistent in trying to get Gina to go out with him.* 保羅以驚人的執着在追求吉娜。| *Persistent attempts to interview Garbo were fruitless.* 試圖採訪嘉寶的不懈努力毫無結果。| **persistent offender** (=someone who continually breaks the law) 慣犯 **2** continuing to exist or happen, especially for longer than is usual or desirable 持續存在[發生]的: *the persistent bad weather* 持續的壞天氣 | *persistent headaches* 持續的頭疼 —**persistently** *adv*: *He persistently called her at home.* 他不斷地往她家裡打電話。—**persistence** *n* [U]

per·snick·e·ty /pəˋsnıkıtı; pəˈsnıkɨti/ *adj AmE* PERNICKETY 【美】吹毛求疵的; 愛挑剔的

per·son /ˋpɝsn̩; ˈpɜːsən/ *n* **1** [C] *plural* **people** a human being, especially considered as someone with their own particular character 人: *Tessa's a very intense person.* 特莎是個非常熱情的人。| *Hank's not the sort of person I find easy to talk to.* 漢克不是那種我覺得容易交談的人。| *I like her as a person, but not as a boss.* 她本人我是喜歡的, 但她作為老闆我就不喜歡了。| *What nice young people!* 多好的年輕人啊! | *The person I need to speak to isn't here.* 我要找他[她]談的那個人不在這兒。—see 見 MAN[1] (USAGE) | **a city/cat etc person** (=someone who likes a particular thing or activity) 喜歡城市/貓等的人 *Are you one of those drama people?* 你屬於那種喜歡戲劇的人嗎? **2 in person** if you do something in person, you do it by going somewhere yourself, not by letter or asking someone else to do it 親自: *You have to go sign for it in person, they can't just mail it.* 你必須親自去簽收, 他們不能直接郵寄過來。**3 businessperson/salesperson etc** someone who works in business, selling etc 生意人/推銷員等 —see also 另見 CHAIRPERSON, SPOKESPERSON **4** [C] *plural* **persons** *formal or law* someone who is not known or not named 【正式或法律】〔不認識或不知其名的〕人; 法人: *Any person found trespassing will be prosecuted.* 禁止非法侵入, 違者必究。| *murder committed by a person or persons unknown* 兇手不明的謀殺案 **5 about/on your person** *formal* on your body or hidden in your clothes 【正式】在你身上; 藏在你衣服裡: *Customs Officers found a gun concealed about his person.* 海關人員發現他身上藏有一支槍。**6 first/second/third person** one of the three special forms of verbs or PRONOUNs that show the speaker (first person), the one who is being spoken to (second person), or the one who is being spoken about (third person) 第一/第二/第三人稱: *The third person singular of the verb 'go' is 'goes'.* 動詞 go 的第三人稱單數是 goes。| *'I', 'me', and 'we' are all first person pronouns.* I, me 和 we 都是第一人稱代(名)詞。—see also 另見 FIRST PERSON **7 in the person of** *formal* used before someone's name to emphasize that this is the person who represents a particular group 【正式】名叫…的; 即; 那就是〔用在某人的名字前強調此人代表某個團體〕: *I was met by the police in the person of Sergeant Black.* 前來接我的是布萊克警官。—see also 另見 MISSING PERSON, PERSON-TO-PERSON

USAGE NOTE 用法說明: PERSON

GRAMMAR 語法

The usual plural of **person** is **people**. person 通常的複數形式是 people: *Only one person turned up.* 僅有一個人露面。| *A lot of people replied to our advert.* 很多人對我們的廣告作出了回應。| *young people* 年輕人

People meaning 'more than one person' is already plural and cannot form a plural with 's'. It always takes a plural verb. people 表示"人們", 是複數形

式，故不能再加s構成複數。它總是與複數動詞連用：*Most people are basically honest.* 大多數人基本上是誠實的。| *People are dying of starvation every day* (NOT 不用 *...is dying*). 每天都有人死於飢餓。

People meaning 'race' or 'nation' is countable and you can add 's' in the normal way. people 表示"種族"或"民族"時是可數的，可以用通常的方式加s構成複數：*the peoples of South East Asia* 東南亞各民族

Persons is very formal and used, for example, in official language. persons 非常正式，可用於譬如官方語言中：*He was murdered by a person or persons unknown.* 他被不知姓名的人殺害了。You may also see it on offical notices. 也可見於正式公告：*This elevator may only carry eight persons.* 本電梯限乘八人。

per·so·na /pəˋsonə; pəˈsəʊnə/ *n plural* **personae** /-ni; -niː/ [C] the way you behave when you are with other people, that makes them think that you are a particular type of person〔在公開場合裝出的〕偽裝外表，表面形象：*Joel has a very cheerful public persona but in private he's very different.* 喬爾在公開場合顯得很開朗，但私下裡就很不一樣了。

per·son·a·ble /ˋpɝsn̩əbl̩; ˈpɜːsənəbəl/ *adj* having an attractive appearance and a pleasant, polite way of talking and behaving 英俊的；有風度的，有魅力的：*a very personable young man* 一位英俊瀟灑的年輕人

per·son·age /ˋpɝsn̩ɪdʒ; ˈpɜːsənɪdʒ/ *n* [C] *formal*【正式】**1** a famous or important person 名人，要人：*a royal personage* 皇室要人 **2** a character in a play or book, or in history〔戲劇、書籍或歷史中的〕人物，角色

1 1 **per·son·al¹** /ˋpɝsn̩l; ˈpɜːsənəl/ *adj*

1 ▶DONE YOURSELF 本人做的◀ [only before noun 僅用於名詞前] done, learned, or experienced by you yourself 親自的，親身的：*I know from personal experience that you can't trust Ralph.* 從我的親身經歷來說，我認為你不能相信拉爾夫。| *The Mayor promised to give the matter his personal attention.* 市長答應親自處理此事。| *I'll take personal responsibility if this doesn't work.* 如果這行不通，由我本人負責任。| **personal contact** (=meeting and dealing with people yourself directly) 直接與人接觸，親自與人打交道 *As you get promoted in a firm you lose that personal contact.* 當你在公司裡得到提升，你就失去了與人直接接觸的機會。

2 ▶PRIVATE 私人的◀ concerning only you, especially the private areas of your life 個人的：*May I ask you a personal question?* 我可以問你一個私人問題嗎？| *personal problems* 個人隱私問題 | *personal letters* 私人信件 | *I'd tell you what's wrong, but it's a bit personal.* 我會告訴你問題出在哪裡，但那有點涉及隱私。| **personal details** (=where you live, how old you are etc)〔住址、年齡等〕個人資料 *You will have to fill out a form giving your personal details.* 你必須要填一張表格提供你的個人資料。

3 ▶YOUR OWN 你自己的◀ yours and no one else's 個人的：*Well, that's my personal view, anyway.* 好吧，不管怎樣，那是我的個人觀點。| *Modern art isn't to my personal taste.* 我個人不喜歡現代藝術。| **my/their etc own personal** *They paid for everything and then he was given his own personal chauffeur to drive him home.* 他們包下了他的一切開支，而且還給他派了一名私人司機送他回家。| **personal possessions/property/belongings** (=things belonging only to you) 私人財物 | **personal effects** *formal* (=small possessions)【正式】隨身物品，私人物品 *personal effects scattered all around the wreckage of an aircraft* 散落在飛機殘骸周圍的私人物品

4 ▶CRITICIZING 批評◀ involving rude or upsetting criticism of someone 人身攻擊的：*It's unprofessional to make such personal remarks.* 進行這樣的人身攻擊是違反職業準則的。| **get personal** *You don't have to get so personal!* 你不必進行人身攻擊！| **(it's) nothing personal** *spoken* (=used to tell someone that you do not intend to be rude to them)【口】無意冒犯〔用於告訴某人你無意對他們無禮〕*It's nothing personal, I just have to go home now.* 我無意冒犯，我只是現在必須回家了。

5 personal friend someone that you know well, especially a famous or important person 私人朋友〔尤指名人或要人〕：*Apparently the director is a personal friend of hers.* 顯然，那位主任是她的私人朋友。

6 ▶NOT OFFICIAL 非公務的◀ not concerned with your work, business, or official duties 與公務無關的，私人的：*Please try not to make personal phone calls at work.* 上班時請盡量不要打私人電話。| **sb's personal life** *I don't answer questions about my personal life.* 我不回答有關我私生活的問題。

7 ▶YOUR BODY 你的身體◀ [only before noun 僅用於名詞前] concerning your body or the way you look 身體的；容貌的：*Grant was always fussy about his personal appearance.* 格蘭特總是過於講究自己的外表。| *personal hygiene* 個人衛生

8 personal touch something you do to make something special, or that makes someone feel special 個人風格[特色]：*It's those extra personal touches that make our service better.* 正是那些額外的個性化特點使得我們的服務更出色。

9 personal development the improvements in your character that come from your experiences in life 個性發展：*the role of physical activities in the child's personal development* 體育活動在孩子個性發展中所起的作用

personal² *n* [C] *AmE* a short advertisement put in a newspaper or magazine by someone who wants a friend or LOVER【美】〔報紙或雜誌上的〕徵友[婚]廣告

personal al·low·ance /ˌ··· ˈ··/ *n* [C] *BrE* the amount of money that you are allowed to earn each year before you start to pay INCOME TAX【英】〔計算所得稅時的〕個人免稅額；EXEMPTION *AmE*【美】

personal as·sis·tant /ˌ··· ·ˈ··/ *n* [C] a PA; a special secretary who works for one person 私人助理，私人祕書

personal col·umn /ˈ··· ˌ··/ *n* [C] a part of a newspaper in which people can have private or personal messages printed〔報紙上的〕人事欄，私人廣告欄

personal com·pu·ter /ˌ··· ·ˈ··/ *n* [C] a PC; a small computer that is used by one person for business or at home 個人電腦

personal i·den·ti·fi·ca·tion num·ber /ˌ··· ····ˈ·· ˌ··/ *n* [C] a PIN 個人身分識別碼，私人密碼

per·son·al·i·ty /ˌpɝsn̩ˋælətɪ; ˌpɜːsəˈnælə̇ti/ *n* **1** [C,U] someone's character, especially the way they behave towards other people 個性；性格：*Iain has a very dynamic personality.* 伊恩是個精力很充沛的人。| *Childhood experiences have a strong influence on forming personality.* 童年經歷對個性的形成有很大的影響。| **personality clash** (=when two people find it impossible to work together in a friendly way) 性格衝突 **2** [U] the qualities that make someone interesting, friendly and enjoyable to be with〔使某人有趣、友好、受人喜愛的〕品質；個性：*The boss likes people with personality.* 那位老闆喜歡有個性的人。**3** [C] someone who is well known to the public, because they are often in the newspapers, on television etc〔因常出現在報紙、電視等上而知名的〕名人：*a TV personality* 電視名人 | *a sports personality* 體育名人 **4 personalities** [plural] *BrE old-fashioned* unkind or rude remarks about someone's appearance, character etc【英，過時】人身攻擊，誹謗：*Let's keep personalities out of the conversation, shall we!* 我們談話時不要帶有人身攻擊好嗎？**5** [C usually singular 一般用單數] the qualities which make a place or thing special〔地方或事物的〕特色：*It's partly the architecture* S3 W3 *which gives the town its personality.* 這個城鎮具有特色一部分原因在於它的建築。

personality cult /˙˙ˈ˙˙˙ ˙/ *n* [C] the officially encouraged practice of giving too much admiration, praise, love etc to a political leader〔對政治領袖的〕個人崇拜

per·son·al·ize also 又作 **-ise** *BrE*【英】/ˈpɝsn̩l͵aɪz; ˈpɜːsənəlaɪz/ *v* [T usually passive 一般用被動態] **1** to put your name or INITIALS on something, or decorate it in your own way to show that it belongs to you 在…上標出個人的姓名[姓名的首字母], 使個性化: *Why not do something to personalize your office?* 為甚麼不佈置一下使你的辦公室具有個性呢? **2** to make something suitable for someone's particular needs or desires 使〔某物〕符合某人的特定需求: *The bank is trying to personalize its service to customers.* 這家銀行在努力使自己的服務滿足客戶的個性化需求。**3** to change the subject of your remarks, arguments etc so that they are more concerned with personal matters or relationships than with facts 使〔評論、爭論等〕針對個人, 使個人化: *In the later stages the campaign became highly personalized.* 這項運動在後期變成了過分針對個人的運動。—**personalized** *adj*: *personalized license plates* 個性化車牌 —**personalization** /͵pɝsn̩lə`zeʃən; ͵pɜːsənəlaɪˈzeɪʃən/ *n* [U]

2 **per·son·al·ly** /ˈpɝsn̩lɪ; ˈpɜːsənəli/ *adv*

1 ▶**IN YOUR OPINION** 以你的觀點◀ [sentence adverb 句子副詞] *especially spoken* used to emphasize that you are only giving your own opinion about something【尤口】就個人而言; 就自己的看法而言: *Personally, I don't think much of the idea.* 就我本人而言, 我認為這個主意不怎麼樣。

2 ▶**DIRECTLY** 直接地◀ doing or having done something yourself rather than through someone else 本人直接地, 親自地: *I'm holding you personally responsible for this mess!* 出了這樣的亂子, 我要唯你是問! | *The managing director wrote personally to thank me.* 那位總經理親自寫信向我表示感謝。

3 take sth personally to let yourself get upset or hurt by the things other people say or do 為某人的言行感到不快: *Don't take it personally; she's rude to everyone.* 不要為此感到不高興, 她對每個人都沒有禮貌。

4 ▶**CRITICISM** 批評◀ directed against someone's character or appearance in an unpleasant way 攻擊人地: *Sue didn't mean those criticisms personally you know.* 你知道, 蘇所作的那些批評並不是針對某個人的。

5 ▶**FRIEND** 朋友◀ as a friend, or as someone you have met 作為一個朋友, 作為熟人: *I don't know her personally, but I like her work.* 我並不認識她本人, 但我喜歡她的作品。

personal or·ga·niz·er /͵˙˙ ˈ˙˙˙˙/ *n* [C] a small book with loose sheets of paper, or a very small computer, for recording information, addresses, meetings etc〔記錄資料、地址、會議等的活頁〕記事本;〔記事用的〕掌上型電腦

personal pro·noun /͵˙˙ ˈ˙˙/ *n* [C] *technical* a PRONOUN used for the person who is speaking, being spoken to, or being spoken about, such as 'I', 'you', and 'they'【術語】人稱代(名)詞〈如I, you 和 they〉

personal ster·e·o /͵˙˙ ˈ˙˙˙/ *n* [C] a small CASSETTE PLAYER which you carry around with you and listen to through small HEADPHONES; WALKMAN〔可隨身攜帶, 使用耳機的〕小型音機, 隨身聽

personal stereo 小型放音機, 隨身聽

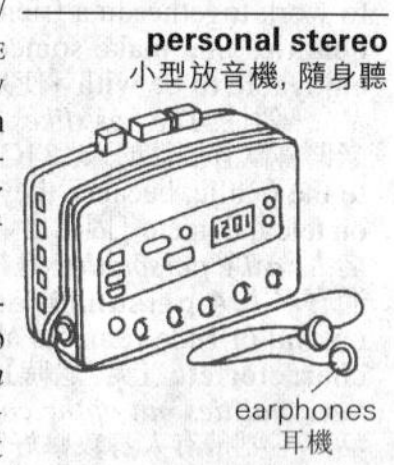

earphones 耳機

persona non gra·ta /pɚ`sonə ͵nɑn `gretə; pə͵səunə nɒn ˈgrɑːtə/ *n* [U] *Latin* someone who is not acceptable to a government or not welcome in someone's house【拉丁】不受歡迎的人: *He was declared persona non grata.* 他被宣布為不受歡迎的人。

per·son·i·fi·ca·tion /pɚ͵sɑnəfəˋkeʃən; pə͵sɒnɪ̥fɪ̥ˈkeɪʃən/ *n* **1 the personification of** someone who is a perfect example of a quality because they have a lot of it …的化身: *the personification of evil* 罪惡的化身 **2** [C, U] the representation of a thing or a quality as a person, in literature or art〔文學或藝術中的〕擬人化, 人格化: *the personification of Justice as a woman* 用一位女性象徵正義

per·son·i·fy /pɚˋsɑnə͵faɪ; pəˈsɒnɪ̥faɪ/ *v* [T] **1** to think of or represent a quality or thing as a person 把…擬人化[人格化]: *Time is often personified as an old man with a scythe.* 時間經常被擬人化地表現為一位拿着一把長柄鐮刀的老人。**2** to represent a particular quality or thing by having a lot of that quality or by being a typical example of that thing 是…的化身[典型]: *Our son is laziness personified.* 我們的兒子是懶惰的典型。| *The President seemed to personify American people in general.* 總統好像代表了整個美國人民。

per·son·nel /͵pɝsn̩ˋɛl; ͵pɜːsəˈnel/ *n* **1** [plural] the people who work in a company or organization, or in the army, navy etc〔公司、組織或軍隊等中的〕全體人員; 員工, 全體職員: *medical personnel* 醫療人員 | *All personnel are to receive security badges.* 所有人員都將收到安全徽章。**2** [U] the department in an organization that appoints people to jobs and deals with their complaints, problems etc; HUMAN RESOURCES 人事部門: *Fay finally decided to take her grievance to Personnel.* 費伊最後決定把她的不滿向人事部門申訴。

person-to-person /͵˙˙ ˙ ˈ˙˙◂/ *adj* **person-to-person call** *AmE* a telephone call that is made to one particular person and does not have to be paid for if they are not there【美】指定受話人的電話, 叫人電話〔如果指定受話人不在則不必付電話費〕

perspective 透視圖

a chessboard drawn in perspective
用透視法繪製的國際象棋棋盤

per·spec·tive /pɚˋspɛktɪv; pəˈspektɪv/ *n* **1** [C] a way of thinking about something which is influenced by the kind of person you are or by your experiences〔思考問題的〕角度; 觀點; 想法: **[+on]** *His father's death gave him a whole new perspective on life.* 他父親的死使他對生活有了全新的看法。| **from the perspective of** *The novel is written from the perspective of a child.* 這部小說是從一個孩子的視角寫的。| **from a…perspective** *From a white male perspective, it's hard to understand oppression.* 從一個白人男性的角度來看, 很難理解甚麼是壓迫。**2** [C,U] a sensible way of judging and comparing situations so that you do not imagine that something is more serious than it really is〔對事物的〕合理判斷, 正確認識: *I think Viv's lost all sense of perspective.* 我認為維夫已不能明察事理。| **get/keep sth in perspective** (=judge the importance of something correctly) 正確判斷某物的重要性 **3** [U] a method of drawing a picture that makes objects look solid and shows distance and depth, or the effect this method produces in a picture 透視(畫)法; 透視效果, 透視感: *Children's drawings often have no perspective.* 兒童畫通常沒有透視感。| **in perspective/out of perspective** (=drawn with or without the effect of perspective) 有透視感/沒有透視感 *The background is all out of perspective.* 這背景整個沒有透

視感。**4** [C] a view, especially one that stretches into the distance〔尤指由近而遠的〕景, 遠景

per·spex /ˋpɝspɛks; ˈpɜːspeks/ *n* [U] *BrE* a strong plastic material that can be seen through and is used instead of glass【英】珀斯佩有機玻璃〔一種高強度透明塑膠〕; PLEXIGLASS *AmE*【美】

per·spi·ca·cious /ˌpɝspɪˋkeʃəs; ˌpɜːspɪˈkeɪʃəs◂/ *adj formal* good at judging and understanding people and situations【正式】判斷力強的; 敏鋭的; 有洞察力的: *a perspicacious literary critic* 睿智的文學評論家 | *a perspicacious remark* 有見地的評論 —**perspicaciously** *adv* —**perspicacity** /-ˋkæsətɪ; -ˈkæsɪ̥ti/ *n* [U]

per·spi·ra·tion /ˌpɝspəˋreʃən; ˌpɜːspəˈreɪʃən/ *n* [U] **1** liquid that appears on your skin when you are hot; SWEAT[2] (1) 汗, 汗水 **2** the process of perspiring 出汗, 流汗

per·spire /pəˋspaɪr; pəˈspaɪə/ *v* [I] to become wet on parts of your body, especially because you are hot or have been doing hard work; SWEAT[1] (1) 出汗, 流汗

2 2 **per·suade** /pəˋswed; pəˈsweɪd/ *v* [T] **1** to make someone decide to do something, especially by repeatedly asking them or telling them reasons why they should do it 說服; 勸服: **persuade sb to do sth** *I finally managed to persuade her to go out for a drink with me.* 我最後終於想法子説服她跟我一起出去喝一杯。| **persuade sb** *Leo wouldn't agree, despite our efforts to persuade him.* 儘管我們努力説服利奧, 他還是不同意。| **persuade sb into doing sth** *Don't let yourself be persuaded into buying things you don't really want.* 不要讓別人説服你去買那些根本不想要的東西。**2** to make someone believe something or feel sure about something; CONVINCE 使相信, 使信服: *I was persuaded by the sheer strength of this argument.* 我被這個極具説服力的論點勸服了。| **persuade sb of sth** *We finally persuaded Ben of the wisdom of this decision.* 我們最終使班恩相信這項決定是明智的。| **persuade sb (that)** *Carla failed to persuade us that she was innocent.* 卡拉沒能使我們相信她是無辜的。

per·sua·sion /pəˋsweʒən; pəˈsweɪʒən/ *n* **1** the act or skill of persuading someone to do something 説服; 勸服: *After a little gentle persuasion, Debbie agreed to let us in.* 經過一小會兒温和的勸説, 黛比同意讓我們進去。| **powers of persuasion** (=skills used for persuading) 説服的技巧 **2** [C] *formal* a particular kind of belief, especially a political or religious one【正式】〔尤指政治或宗教的〕信仰; 信念: *people of all political persuasions* 各種政治信仰的人們 **3** [singular] *formal* a strongly held belief or opinion【正式】堅定的信念[看法]: *It has always been my persuasion that capital punishment is wrong.* 我一直堅定地認為死刑是錯誤的。**4 of the... persuasion** *formal or humorous* of a particular kind【正式或幽默】...種類的, ...派別的: *an artist of the modern persuasion* 一位現代派的藝術家

per·sua·sive /pəˋswesɪv; pəˈsweɪsɪv/ *adj* good at influencing other people to believe or do what you want 有説服力的: *They used some very persuasive arguments.* 他們用了一些很有説服力的論據。—**persuasively** *adv* —**persuasiveness** *n* [U]

pert /pɝt; pɜːt/ *adj* **1** a girl or woman who is pert is amusing, but slightly disrespectful〔女孩或婦女〕俏皮的; 有點不規矩但有趣的: *Angie gave him one of her pert little glances.* 安吉調皮地瞥了他一眼。**2** clothing that is pert is neat and attractive in a cheerful way〔衣服〕別緻的; 俏麗的: *a pert little red hat set well back on her head* 戴在她頭頂後面的一頂俏麗的小紅帽 —**pertly** *adv* —**pertness** *n* [U]

per·tain /pəˋten; pəˈteɪn/ *v*

pertain to sth *phr v* [T] *formal* to be directly connected with something【正式】與...直接相關; 有關, 關於: *legislation pertaining to employment rights* 與就業權利有關的立法

per·ti·na·cious /ˌpɝtn̩ˋeʃəs; ˌpɜːtɪ̥ˈneɪʃəs◂/ *adj formal* continuing to believe something or to do something in a very determined way; TENACIOUS【正式】固執的; 堅持的; 頑固的 —**pertinaciously** *adv* —**pertinacity** /-n̩ˋæsətɪ; -ˈnæsɪ̥ti/ *n* [U]

per·ti·nent /ˋpɝtn̩ənt; ˈpɜːtɪ̥nənt/ *adj formal* directly concerned with something that is being considered: RELEVANT【正式】直接相關的, 有關的: *The investigator asked several highly pertinent questions.* 那位調查員問了幾個高度相關的問題。| [+to] *Your remarks are not pertinent to today's discussion.* 你的話與今天的討論不相干。—**pertinently** *adv* —**pertinence** *n* [U] —see also 另見 IMPERTINENT

per·turbed /pəˋtɝbd; pəˈtɜːbd/ *adj* worried or annoyed because of something that has happened〔由於發生某事而〕憂慮的, 不安的, 煩惱的: *Fritz did not seem unduly perturbed when asked to change rooms.* 當弗里茨被要求更換房間時, 他好像並沒有過分不安。—**perturbation** /ˌpɝtəˋbeʃən; ˌpɜːtəˈbeɪʃən/ *n* [U] —**perturb** /pəˋtɝb; pəˈtɜːb/ *v* [T]

pe·ruse /pəˋruz; pəˈruːz/ *v* [T] *formal or humorous* to read something, especially in a careful way【正式或幽默】〔尤指仔細〕閱讀, 精讀: *I'll give you the leaflet so you can peruse it at your leisure.* 我會把小冊子給你, 以便你可以在閒暇時仔細閱讀。—**perusal** *n* [C,U]

perv /pɝv; pɜːv/ *n* [C] *BrE spoken* a PERVERT[2]【英口】性行為反常者, 性變態者 —**pervy** *adj*

per·vade /pəˋved; pəˈveɪd/ *v* [T] if a feeling, idea, or smell pervades a place, it spreads through every part of it〔感覺、想法或氣味〕彌漫於, 遍及, 充滿: *After the war a spirit of hopelessness pervaded the country.* 戰爭過後, 全國普遍存在着一種絕望的情緒。

per·va·sive /pəˋvesɪv; pəˈveɪsɪv/ *adj* existing or spreading everywhere 到處存在的; 到處彌漫着的, 遍佈的: *the pervasive influence of television* 電視無所不在的影響 | **all-pervasive** (=extremely pervasive) 無所不在的, 極其普遍的 *the all-pervasive mood of apathy* 無處不在的冷漠情緒 —**pervasiveness** *n* [U] —**pervasively** *adv*

per·verse /pəˋvɝs; pəˈvɜːs/ *adj* continuing to behave in an unreasonable way, especially by deliberately doing the opposite of what people want you to do 任性的; 不合情理的, 一意孤行的: *He gets some kind of perverse satisfaction from embarrassing people.* 他有一種不正常的心態, 以使別人難堪而獲得某種滿足。—**perversely** *adv* —**perverseness** *n* [U]

per·ver·sion /pəˋvɝʒən; pəˈvɜːʃən/ *n* **1** [C,U] a type of sexual behaviour that is considered unnatural and unacceptable 性反常行為, 性變態 **2** [C,U] the process of changing something that is natural and good into something that is unnatural and wrong, or the result of such a change 歪曲, 曲解; 墮落, 變壞: *a perversion of the true meaning of democracy* 對民主的真正含義的歪曲

per·ver·si·ty /pəˋvɝsətɪ; pəˈvɜːsɪ̥ti/ *n* [U] the quality of being perverse 任性, 執拗; 反常; 執迷不悟: *Max refused the money out of sheer perversity.* 馬克斯拒收那些錢完全是出於任性。

per·vert[1] /pəˋvɝt; pəˈvɜːt/ *v* [T] **1** to change something in an unnatural and often harmful way〔以不合自然規律且通常有害的方式〕改變: *Genetic scientists are often accused of perverting nature.* 遺傳學家經常被指責破壞了自然狀態。**2** to influence someone so that they begin to think or behave in an immoral way; CORRUPT[2] (1) 使走上邪路, 使墮落, 使變壞; 腐蝕: *TV sex and violence perverts the minds of young children.* 電視上的性和暴力鏡頭腐蝕了青少年的心靈。**3 pervert the course of justice** *law* to deliberately prevent a fair examination of the facts about a crime【法律】妨礙司法公正

per·vert[2] /ˋpɝvɝt; ˈpɜːvɜːt/ *n* [C] someone whose sexual behaviour is considered unnatural and unacceptable 性行為反常者, 性變態者: *What are you, some kind of pervert?* 你是甚麼? 性變態者嗎?

per·vert·ed /pəˋvɝtɪd; pəˈvɜːtɪ̥d/ *adj* **1** perverted ways of thinking and behaving, especially sexual behaviour, are unacceptable and unnatural〔思維和行為方式〕反常

的;〔尤指性行為〕反常的, 變態的 **2** morally wrong or unnatural 道德上錯誤的; 有悖常理的: *the perverted logic of Nazi propaganda* 納粹宣傳的荒謬邏輯

pe·se·ta /pəˋsɛtə; pəˈseɪtə/ *n* [C] the standard unit of money in Spain 比塞塔〔西班牙貨幣單位〕

pes·ky /ˋpɛskɪ; ˈpeski/ *adj informal especially AmE* annoying and causing trouble【非正式, 尤美】令人討厭的, 惹麻煩的: *Those pesky kids!* 那些令人討厭的孩子!

pe·so /ˋpeso; ˈpeɪsəʊ/ *n* [C] the standard unit of money in Mexico, Colombia and Cuba 比索〔墨西哥、哥倫比亞和古巴的貨幣單位〕

pes·sa·ry /ˋpɛsərɪ; ˈpesəri/ *n* [C] **1** a solid medicine or CONTRACEPTIVE chemical which is put into a woman's VAGINA〔治療或避孕的〕陰道栓(劑) **2** an instrument put into a woman's VAGINA to support her WOMB or as a CONTRACEPTIVE 子宮帽, 子宮托

pes·si·mist /ˋpɛsəmɪst; ˈpesɪ̣mɪst/ *n* [C] someone who always expects that the worst thing will happen 悲觀主義者: *Don't be such a pessimist – you're not going to fail.* 別這麼悲觀——你不會失敗的。—opposite 反義詞 OPTIMIST —**pessimism** *n* [U]

pes·si·mis·tic /ˌpɛsəˋmɪstɪk; ˌpesɪ̣ˈmɪstɪk◂/ *adj* expecting that bad things will happen in the future or that a situation will have a bad result 悲觀的; 悲觀主義的: **[+about]** *He remains deeply pessimistic about the peace process.* 他對和平進程仍持極度悲觀的態度。—opposite 反義詞 OPTIMISTIC —**pessimistically** /-klɪ; -kli/ *adv*

pest /pɛst; pest/ *n* [C] **1** a small animal or insect that destroys crops or food supplies〔毀壞莊稼或食物的〕有害小動物[昆蟲]; 害蟲: *a chemical used in pest control* 用於防治蟲害的化學品 **2** *informal* an annoying person, especially a child【非正式】令人討厭的人〔尤指孩子〕; 害人精: *Giles was being a thorough pest.* 賈爾斯是個十足的害人蟲。

pes·ter /ˋpɛstɚ; ˈpestə/ *v* [T] to annoy someone repeatedly, especially by asking them to do something 不斷煩擾, 糾纏〔尤指不斷要求某人做某事〕: **pester sb for sth** *Beggars kept pestering us for money.* 乞丐糾纏着我們要錢。| **pester sb to do sth** *The kids have been pestering me to buy them new trainers.* 孩子一直纏着我, 要我給他們買新運動鞋。

pes·ti·cide /ˋpɛstɪsaɪd; ˈpestɪ̣saɪd/ *n* [C] a chemical substance used to kill insects and small animals that destroy crops 殺蟲劑, 農藥

pes·ti·lence /ˋpɛstləns; ˈpestɪ̣ləns/ *n* [C,U] *literary* a disease that spreads quickly and kills large numbers of people【文】瘟疫

pes·ti·lent /ˋpɛstlənt; ˈpestɪ̣lənt/ also 又作 **pes·ti·len·tial** /ˌpɛstlˋɛnʃəl; ˌpestɪ̣ˈlenʃəl◂/ *adj* **1** *literary or humorous* extremely unpleasant and annoying【文或幽默】特別令人討厭的; 極其令人不快的 **2** *old use* causing a pestilence【舊】引起瘟疫的

pes·tle /ˋpɛsl; ˈpesəl/ *n* [C] a short stick with a heavy round end, used for crushing things in a MORTAR (=a special bowl)〔搗研用的〕杵, 搗錘 —see picture at 參見 LABORATORY 圖

pet¹ /pɛt; pet/ *n* [C] **1** an animal such as a cat or a dog which you keep and look after at home 供玩賞的動物, 寵物〈如貓、狗〉: *Rabbits can make very good pets.* 兔子可以成為很好的寵物。| *a pet tortoise* 寵物烏龜 —see also 另見 TEACHER'S PET **2** *BrE spoken* a way of addressing someone who you like or love【英口】寶貝兒〔用於稱呼你喜歡[愛]的人〕**3 be in a pet** *BrE old-fashioned* to be annoyed【英, 過時】煩惱的, 不痛快的

pet² *v* [T] **1** to touch and stroke someone, especially a child or an animal, in a kind loving way 撫弄; 愛撫: *Our cat loves being petted.* 我們的貓喜歡被人愛撫。**2** to kiss and touch someone as part of a sexual activity〔兩性間〕親吻, 愛撫 —see also 另見 HEAVY PETTING

pet³ *adj* **1 pet theory/project/subject** a plan, idea, or subject that you particularly like or are interested in 特別喜愛的理論/計劃/主題 **2 pet hate** *BrE*【英】, **pet peeve** *AmE*【美】something that you strongly dislike because it always annoys you 特別討厭的事物; 極可惡的事物: *TV game shows are one of my pet hates.* 電視遊戲節目是我最討厭的節目之一。

pet·al /ˋpɛtl; ˈpetl/ *n* [C] **1** the coloured part of a flower that is shaped like a leaf 花瓣: *rose petals* 玫瑰花瓣 | *Each of these flowers has seven petals.* 這些花每朵有七個花瓣。**2 eight-petalled, blue-petalled etc** *BrE*【英】, **-petaled** *AmE*【美】having eight petals, blue petals etc 有八瓣的/有藍色花瓣的等

pe·tard /pɪˋtɑrd; pɪ̣ˈtɑːd/ *n* —see 見 **be hoist with your own petard** (HOIST¹ (2))

Peter —see 見 **rob Peter to pay Paul** (ROB (3))

pet·er /ˋpitɚ; ˈpiːtə/ *v*

peter out *phr v* [I] to gradually become smaller or happen less often and then come to an end 逐漸變小; 逐漸減少; 逐漸消失: *The road became narrower and eventually petered out.* 那條路變得越來越窄, 最後消失了。| *Public interest in the environment is in danger of petering out.* 公眾對環境的興趣面臨逐漸消失的危險。

pet·it bour·geois /ˌpɛtɪ ˋburʒwa; ˌpeti ˈbʊəʒwɑː/ *adj* another spelling of PETTY BOURGEOIS petty bourgeois 的另一種拼法

pe·tite /pəˋtit; pəˈtiːt/ *adj* a woman who is petite is short and attractively thin〔女子〕嬌小的

petit four /ˋpɛtɪ ˋfɔr; ˌpeti ˈfʊə/ *n* [C] *French* a small sweet cake or BISCUIT served with coffee【法】〔配咖啡吃的〕小蛋糕; 小餅乾

pe·ti·tion¹ /pəˋtɪʃən; pɪ̣ˈtɪʃən/ *n* [C] **1** a written request signed by a lot of people, asking someone in authority to do something or change something 請願(書): **[+against]** *They wanted me to sign a petition against experiments on animals.* 他們要我在反對用動物做實驗的請願書上簽名。| **draw up a petition** *Local residents have drawn up a petition to protest the hospital closure.* 當地居民已草擬了抗議醫院關閉的請願書。**2** an official letter to a law court, asking for a legal case to be considered〔向法院遞交的〕陳情書, 訴狀: *She is threatening to file a petition for divorce.* 她在威脅說要提起離婚訴訟。**3** *formal* a formal prayer or request to someone in authority or to God or to a ruler【正式】〔向當局、上帝或統治者的〕正式請求; 祈求; 祈禱

petition² *v* [I,T] **1** to ask the government or an organization to do something by sending it a petition 向〔政府或組織〕請願, 請求: **petition sb to do sth** *Villagers petitioned the local authority to provide better bus services.* 村民請求地方當局提供更好的公共汽車服務。| **[+against/for]** *Residents are petitioning against the new road.* 居民正在請願反對修建這條新路。**2** to make a formal request to someone in authority, to a court of law, or to God〔向當權者、法庭或上帝〕正式請求, 祈求

pe·ti·tion·er /pəˋtɪʃənɚ; pɪ̣ˈtɪʃənə/ *n* [C] **1** someone who writes or signs a petition 請願人; 請願書簽名人 **2** *law* someone who asks for their marriage to be legally ended【法律】離婚申請人, 離婚訴訟原告

petit mal /ˌpɛtɪ ˋmɑl; ˌpeti ˈmæl/ *n* [U] *technical* a form of EPILEPSY which is not very serious【術語】〔癲癇〕小發作 —compare 比較 GRAND MAL

pet name /ˌ· ˈ·/ *n* [C] a name you call someone you like very much 愛稱, 昵稱

pet·rel /ˋpɛtrəl; ˈpetrəl/ *n* [C] a black and white sea bird; STORMY PETREL 海燕

pet·ri·fied /ˋpɛtrəˌfaɪd; ˈpetrɪ̣faɪd/ *adj* **1** extremely frightened, especially so frightened that you cannot move or think 嚇呆的, 驚呆的: *She stood there, petrified at the thought of the crowds waiting outside.* 一想到在外面等待的人羣, 她嚇得一動不動地站在那裡。**2 petrified wood/trees/insects etc** wood, trees etc that have changed into stone over a long period of time 石化木/樹/昆蟲等 —**petrify** *v* [T]: *My new boss absolutely petrifies me.* 我的新老闆簡直把我嚇呆了。—**petrifaction**

/ˌpɛtrəˋfækʃən; ˌpetrəˈfækʃən/ *n* [U]

pet·ro·chem·i·cal /ˌpɛtroˋkɛmɪkl̩; ˌpetrəʊˈkemɪkəl/ *n* [C] a chemical substance obtained from PETROLEUM or natural gas 石(油)化(學)產品: *the petrochemical industry* 石(油)化(學)工業

pet·ro·dol·lar /ˋpɛtroˌdɑlɚ; ˈpetrəʊˌdɒlə/ *n* [C] a dollar earned by the sale of oil 石油美元〔出售石油所得的美元〕: *in search of petrodollars from Iran* 從伊朗尋求石油美元

3 **pet·rol** /ˋpɛtrəl; ˈpetrəl/ *n* [U] *BrE* a liquid that is used to supply power to the engine of cars and other vehicles, which is obtained from PETROLEUM【英】汽油; GASOLINE *AmE*【美】

pet·ro·la·tum /ˌpɛtrəˋletəm; ˌpetrəˈleɪtəm/ *n* [U] *AmE* VASELINE【美】凡士林, 礦脂

petrol bomb /ˈ·· ·/ *n* [C] *BrE* a simple bomb consisting of a bottle filled with petrol with a lighted cloth in the end【英】汽油彈, 燃燒彈

pe·tro·le·um /pəˋtrolɪəm; pəˈtrəʊliəm/ *n* [U] oil that is obtained from below the surface of the Earth and is used to make petrol, PARAFFIN and various chemical substances 石油: *petroleum-based products* 石油產品

petroleum jel·ly /·ˌ··· ˈ··/ *n* [U] *especially BrE* VASELINE【尤英】凡士林, 礦脂, 石油凍

petrol sta·tion /ˈ·· ˌ··/ *n* [C] *BrE* a place where you can take your car and fill it with petrol【英】汽車加油站; GAS STATION *AmE*【美】

pet·ti·coat /ˋpɛtɪˌkot; ˈpetikəʊt/ *n* [C] **1** *especially BrE* a piece of women's underwear that hangs from your shoulders or waist; SLIP² (6)【尤英】〔從雙肩或腰部垂下的〕襯裙 **2** a long skirt that was worn under a skirt or dress by women in the past〔過去婦女穿在外衣內的〕長襯裙

pet·ti·fog·ging /ˋpɛtɪˌfɑgɪŋ; ˈpetiˌfɒgɪŋ/ *adj BrE old-fashioned*【英, 過時】**1** too concerned with small details 過分關注細節的; 吹毛求疵的 **2** too unimportant to be worth considering 無足輕重的, 微不足道的; 瑣碎的

pet·ti·ness /ˋpɛtɪnɪs; ˈpetinəs/ *n* [U] behaviour and attitudes that are ungenerous and are too much concerned with unimportant matters 小心眼; 心胸狹窄: *the jealousy and pettiness of Hollywood* 荷里活的妒嫉和狹隘

petting zoo /ˈ·· ·/ *n* [C] *AmE* part of a zoo which has baby animals in it for children to touch【美】〔有供兒童撫摸的小動物的〕愛畜動物園

pet·tish /ˋpɛtɪʃ; ˈpetɪʃ/ *adj* PETULANT 任性的; 耍孩子脾氣的; 脾氣暴躁的 —**pettishly** *adv* —**pettishness** *n* [U]

pet·ty /ˋpɛtɪ; ˈpeti/ *adj* **1** a problem, detail, worry etc that is petty is small and unimportant〔問題、細節、擔心等〕小的, 瑣碎的, 不重要的: *He said he wasn't interested in petty details.* 他說他對細枝末節不感興趣。| *petty squabbles* 小事引起的口角 **2** not generous and caring only about small unimportant things 小氣的, 小心眼的, 心胸狹窄的; 只關注瑣事的: *petty jealousy and spitefulness* 心胸狹窄的嫉妒和怨恨 —see also 另見 PETTINESS **3 petty tyrant/dictator etc** someone who is not really important but uses their power as if they were important 小暴君/小獨裁者等: *Some petty bureaucrat wanted all the documents in triplicate.* 一些小官僚想要所有的文件一式三份。**4 petty crime** a crime that is not serious, for example stealing things that have little value 輕罪〈如小偷小摸〉: **petty criminal/thief etc** *Big-time gangsters despise petty thieves.* 大牌匪徒看不起那些小偷小摸的賊子。

petty bour·geois /ˌ·· ˈ··/ also 又作 **petit bourgeois** *adj* **1** paying too much attention to unimportant matters concerning social position, private possessions etc 小資產階級的〔過分注重社會地位和個人財物, 過分注重名利〕: *a petty bourgeois mentality* 小資產階級心理 **2** belonging to the group of MIDDLE CLASS people who own small businesses, shops etc 小資產階級的 —**petty bourgeois** *n* [C]

petty cash /ˌ·· ˈ·/ *n* [U] an amount of money in coins or notes that is kept in an office for making small payments 零用現金; 小額現金[備用金]

petty lar·ce·ny /ˌ·· ˈ···/ *n* [U] *law* the crime of stealing things that are only worth a small amount of money【法律】輕微盜竊罪, 小偷小摸

petty of·fi·cer /ˌ·· ˈ···◂/ *n* [C] an officer of low rank in the Navy 海軍軍士 —see table on page C6 參見C6頁附錄

pet·u·lant /ˋpɛtʃələnt; ˈpetʃələnt/ *adj* behaving in an impatient and angry way for no reason at all, like a child 任性的; 耍孩子脾氣的; 脾氣暴躁的: *Kara stamped her foot and frowned petulantly.* 卡拉暴躁地跺着腳, 皺着眉。—**petulantly** *adv* —**petulance** *n* [U]

pe·tu·ni·a /pəˋtunɪə; pəˈtjuːniə/ *n* [C] a garden plant which has pink, purple, or white TRUMPET-shaped flowers 矮牽牛

pew¹ /pju; pjuː/ *n* [C] **1** a long wooden seat in a church〔教堂裡的〕長條木座椅 **2 take a pew** *BrE spoken* used to invite someone to sit down【英口】請坐下

pew² *interjection AmE spoken* used when there is a very unpleasant smell【美口】呸!〔用來表示氣味非常難聞〕; POOH *BrE*【英】

pew·ter /ˋpjutɚ; ˈpjuːtə/ *n* [U] **1** a grey metal made by mixing LEAD and TIN 白鑞〔鉛和錫的合金〕: *a pewter tankard* 一個用白鑞製作的有柄大酒杯 **2** objects made from this metal 白鑞製品

pey·o·te /peˋotɪ; peɪˈəʊti/ *n* **1** [U] a drug made from a Mexican CACTUS, which makes people imagine that strange things are happening to them; MESCALIN 佩奧特鹼〔取自一種墨西哥仙人掌的致幻藥〕**2** [C] the plant that produces this drug〔提取這種致幻藥的〕佩奧特掌

pfen·nig /ˋfɛnɪg; ˈfenɪg/ *n* [C] a unit of money worth 1/100th of a German MARK² (8) 芬尼〔德國貨幣單位, 相當於 1/100 馬克〕

PG /ˌpi ˋdʒi; ˌpiː ˈdʒiː/ *adj* parental guidance; a film that is PG may include parts that are unsuitable for children under 15 需在家長指導下觀看的, 家長指引級影片〔指電影部分鏡頭不適宜15歲以下的兒童觀看〕: *Jurassic Park (PG)*《侏羅紀公園》(家長指引級) —compare 比較 G, U, R, X-CERTIFICATE

pH /ˋpi ˋetʃ; piː ˈeɪtʃ/ also 又作 **pH val·ue** /· ˈ· ˌ··/ *n* [singular] a number on a scale of 0 to 14 which shows how acid or ALKALINE a substance is pH值, 酸鹼度

phae·ton /ˋfeətn̩; ˈfeɪtn/ *n* [C] a light open carriage used in the past, usually pulled by two horses〔舊時用的通常由兩匹馬拉的〕輕便敞篷馬車

phag·o·cyte /ˋfægəˌsaɪt; ˈfægəsaɪt/ *n* [C] a blood cell that protects your body by destroying harmful BACTERIA etc 吞噬細胞〔殺死有害細菌保護身體的血液細胞〕

pha·lanx /ˋfelæŋks; ˈfælæŋks/ *plural* **phalanxes** *n* [C] **1** a large group of people who stand close together so that it is difficult to go through them 密集的人羣; 密集隊形: *A solid phalanx of policemen blocked the road.* 警察排成密集的隊形封鎖了那條道路。**2** a group of soldiers who stand or move closely together in battle〔作戰時的〕士兵方陣

phal·lic /ˋfælɪk; ˈfælɪk/ *adj* like or related to the phallus 陰莖狀的; 陰莖的: *phallic symbols* 陰莖的象徵

phal·lus /ˋfæləs; ˈfæləs/ *n* [C] **1** a model of the male sex organ, used to represent sexual power〔用來象徵生殖力的〕男性生殖器形像 **2** *technical* the male sex organ; PENIS【術語】陰莖

phan·tas·m /ˋfæntæzəm; ˈfæntæzəm/ *n* [C,U] *literary* something that exists only in your imagination; an ILLUSION【文】幻像; 幻影; 幻覺 —**phantasmal** /fænˋtæzml̩; fænˈtæzməl/ *adj*

phan·tas·ma·go·ri·a /ˌfæntæzməˋgorɪə; ˌfæntæzməˈgɔːriə/ *n* [C] *literary* a confused, changing strange scene like something from a dream【文】如夢般變幻無常的情景, 夢幻景象 —**phantasmagorical** /-ˋgɑrɪkl̩; -ˈgɒrɪkəl/ *adj*

phan·ta·sy /ˋfæntəsɪ; ˈfæntəsi/ *n* [C,U] an old spelling of FANTASY fantasy 的舊式拼法

phan·tom /ˋfæntəm; ˈfæntəm/ *n* [C] *literary*【文】**1** a frightening and unclear image, especially of a dead person; GHOST[1] (1) 可怕而模糊的影像〔尤指鬼魂〕; 幽靈: **phantom horseman/hound/ship etc** *The phantom hound loomed suddenly out of the mist.* 那隻幽靈獵犬突然從霧中隱現。**2** something that exists only in your imagination 幻象; 幻覺; 幻影: *the phantoms that troubled his dreams* 困擾他夢境的幻影 **3** *humorous* used to describe an unknown person that you blame for something annoying【幽默】幽靈〔用來描述做了令人討厭的事又不為人知的人〕: *The phantom pen stealer strikes again!* 那個偷筆的幽靈又出動了!

phantom preg·nan·cy /ˌ·· ˈ···/ *n* [C] a medical condition in which a woman seems to be PREGNANT, but in fact is not 精神性假妊娠

pha·raoh /ˋfɛro; ˈfeərəʊ/ *n* [C] a ruler of ancient Egypt 法老〔古埃及統治者的稱號〕

phar·i·see /ˋfærəˌsi; ˈfærɨsiː/ *n* [C] **1** someone who pretends to be religious or to be concerned about morals〔假裝虔誠或關注道德的〕偽善者 **2 Pharisee** a member of a group of Jews who lived at the time of Christ and who believed in strictly obeying religious laws 法利賽人〔生活在耶穌基督時代, 相信應嚴守宗教法規的猶太人〕—**pharisaic** /ˌfærəˋse·ɪk; ˌfærɨˈseɪ-ɪk/ *adj*

phar·ma·ceu·ti·cal /ˌfɑrməˋsutɪkl; ˌfɑːməˈsjuːtɪkəl◂/ *adj* concerned with the production of drugs and medicine 製藥的: *the large pharmaceutical companies* 大型製藥公司

phar·ma·ceu·ti·cals /ˌfɑrməˋsutɪklz; ˌfɑːməˈsjuːtɪkəlz/ *n* [plural] drugs and medicines 藥物, 藥品

phar·ma·cist /ˋfɑrməsɪst; ˈfɑːməsɨst/ *n* [C] someone who is trained to prepare drugs and medicines and who works in a shop or in a hospital〔藥店或醫院的〕藥劑師 —compare 比較 CHEMIST

phar·ma·col·o·gy /ˌfɑrməˋkɑlədʒɪ; ˌfɑːməˈkɒlədʒi/ *n* [U] the scientific study of drugs and medicines 藥理學, 藥物學 —**pharmacologist** *n* [C] —**pharmacological** /ˌfɑrməkəˋlɑdʒɪkl; ˌfɑːməkəˈlɒdʒɪkəl◂/ *adj*

phar·ma·co·poe·ia /ˌfɑrməkəˋpiə; ˌfɑːməkəˈpiːə/ *n* [C] *technical* an official book giving information about medicines【術語】藥典

phar·ma·cy /ˋfɑrməsɪ; ˈfɑːməsi/ *n* **1** [C] *especially AmE* a shop or a part of a shop where medicines are prepared and sold【尤美】藥店; 藥房; 〔商店的〕藥品部: *an all-night pharmacy* 通宵營業的藥房 **2** [U] the study or practice of preparing drugs and medicines 藥劑學; 製[配]藥(學)

phar·yn·gi·tis /ˌfærɪnˋdʒaɪtɪs; ˌfærɪnˈdʒaɪtɨs/ *n* [U] a medical condition in which you have a sore swollen pharynx 咽喉炎

phar·ynx /ˋfærɪŋks; ˈfærɪŋks/ *n plural* **pharynxes** [C] the tube that goes from the back of your mouth to where the separate passages for food and air divide 咽 —see picture at 參見 RESPIRATORY 圖

2 **phase**[1] /fez; feɪz/ *n* [C] **1** a part of a process of development or growth〔發育或生長的〕階段; 時期: *a transitional phase before democratic elections are held* 舉行民主選舉前的過渡階段 —compare 比較 STAGE[1] (1) **2 in phase/out of phase (with)** *BrE* working together in a way that produces the right effect, or not working together in this way【英】同相/異相的; 協調/不協調的; 同步/不同步的: *The traffic lights were out of phase with each other.* 交通信號燈是不同步的。**3** one of a fixed number of changes in the appearance of the moon or a planet when it is seen from the Earth〔月亮、行星的〕位相

phase[2] *v* [T] to make something happen gradually in a planned way 使…逐步進行, 使…分階段進行: *a phased withdrawal of military forces* 軍隊的分階段撤出

phase sth ↔ **in** *phr v* [T] to introduce something such as a new law, rule etc gradually 逐步採用[實施]〈如新的法律、規定等〉: *The government is going to phase in the new pension system over the next five years.* 在今後的五年中, 政府將逐步實施新的退休金計劃。

phase sth ↔ **out** *phr v* [T] to gradually stop using or providing something 逐步停止使用[提供]; 逐步淘汰: *Leaded gas was phased out in the 1970s.* 含鉛汽油在20世紀70年代就被逐漸淘汰了。

PhD /ˌpi etʃ ˋdi; ˌpiː eɪtʃ ˈdiː/ *n* [C] Doctor of Philosophy; a university degree of very high rank, above an MA or an MSc, which involves doing RESEARCH, or someone who has this degree 哲學博士學位; 哲學博士: *Jacqueline Hope, PhD* 哲學博士傑奎琳·霍普 —see also 另見 DOCTORATE

pheas·ant /ˋfɛznt; ˈfezənt/ *n* [C,U] a large bird with a long tail, often shot for food, or the meat of this bird 雉, 野雞; 野雞肉

phe·no·bar·bi·tone /ˌfinoˋbɑrbɪˌton; ˌfiːnəʊˈbɑːbɨtəʊn/ *BrE*【英】, **phe·no·bar·bi·tal** /-bɪˌtɔl; -bɨtl/ *AmE*【美】*n* [U] a powerful drug that helps you to sleep 苯巴比妥〔一種強效安眠藥〕

phe·nom·e·nal /fəˋnɑmənl; fɪˈnɒmɨnəl/ *adj* very unusual and impressive 非凡的; 驚人的: *phenomenal strength* 驚人的力氣 | *phenomenal economic growth* 不尋常的經濟增長 —**phenomenally** *adv*: *phenomenally successful* 極成功的

phe·nom·e·non /fəˋnɑməˌnɑn; fɪˈnɒmɨnən/ *n plural* **phenomena** [C] **1** something that happens or exists, especially something that is studied because it is not understood〔尤指因不理解而加以研究的〕現象: **[+of]** *the phenomenon of international terrorism* 國際恐怖主義現象 | *violent natural phenomena such as hurricanes* 諸如颶風之類猛烈的自然現象 **2** something or someone that is very unusual because of a rare quality or ability that they have 非凡的人[事物]; 奇才; 奇跡 3

phew /fju; fjuː/ *interjection* used when you feel tired, hot, or RELIEVED 啊!唷!唉!〔表示疲倦、炎熱或放心〕

phi·al /ˋfaɪəl; ˈfaɪəl/ *n* [C] a small bottle, especially for liquid medicines〔尤指盛藥水的〕小藥瓶: *a phial of morphine* 一小瓶嗎啡

Phi Be·ta Kap·pa /ˌfaɪ ˌbitə ˋkæpə; ˌfaɪ ˌbiːtə ˈkæpə/ *n* [singular] an American society for university and college students who have reached a high level in their studies〔美國的〕大學優秀生聯誼會

-phil /fɪl; fɪl/ *suffix* another form of the suffix -PHILE 後綴 -phile 的另一種形式

phi·lan·derer /fəˋlændərə; fɨˈlændərə/ *n* [C] *old-fashioned* a man who has sex with many women, without intending to have any serious relationships【過時】玩弄女性的男人 —**philandering** *adj* —**philandering** *n* [U]

phil·an·throp·ic /ˌfɪlənˋθrɑpɪk; ˌfɪlənˈθrɒpɪk◂/ *adj* a philanthropic person or institution gives money and help to people who are poor or in trouble〔人或機構〕慈善的; 仁慈的 —**philanthropically** /-klɪ; -kli/ *adv*

phi·lan·thro·pist /fəˋlænθrəpɪst; fɨˈlænθrəpɨst/ *n* [C] a rich person who gives a lot of money to help poor people 慈善家, 樂善好施者

phi·lan·thro·py /fəˋlænθrəpɪ; fɨˈlænθrəpi/ *n* [U] the practice of giving money and help to people who are poor or in trouble 慈善行為

phi·lat·e·ly /fəˋlætlɪ; fɨˈlætəli/ *n* [U] the activity of collecting stamps for pleasure 集郵 —**philatelic** /ˌfɪləˋtɛlɪk; ˌfɪləˈtelɪk◂/ *adj* —**philatelist** /fəˋlætlɪst; fɨˈlætəlɪst/ *n* [C]

-phile /faɪl; faɪl/ *suffix* also 又作 **-phil** [in nouns 構成名詞] someone who likes something 喜愛…的人; 愛好…的人: *a bibliophile* (=who likes books) 書籍愛好者 | *an Anglophile* (=who likes England or Britain) 親英者, 崇英者

Phil·har·mon·ic /ˌfɪləˋmɑnɪk; ˌfɪləˈmɒnɪk◂/ *adj* used in the names of ORCHESTRAS 愛樂的〔用於管弦樂隊的名稱中〕

-philia /fɪlɪə; fɪliə/ *suffix* [in nouns 構成名詞] **1** *technical* a tendency to feel sexually attracted in a way that is not approved of, that may be part of a mental illness【術語】〔病態地〕愛戀…的傾向,〔不正常的〕癖好: *necrophilia* (=a sexual attraction to dead bodies) 戀屍癖 **2** *technical* a diseased or unhealthy tendency to do something【術語】〔不健康地〕做…的傾向, 癮癖: *haemophilia* (=a tendency to bleed) 血友病 **3** a tendency to like something 喜愛…的傾向, 愛好…的傾向, 親…: *Francophilia* (=liking France) 親法

-philiac /fɪliæk; fɪliæk/ *suffix technical*【術語】[in nouns 構成名詞] **1** someone who feels sexually attracted in a way that is not approved of〔不正常地〕愛戀…的人: *a necrophiliac* 戀屍癖者 **2** someone who has a particular illness 患某種病的人: *a haemophiliac* 血友病患者

phi·lip·pic /fəˋlɪpɪk; fɨˈlɪpɪk/ *n* [C] *literary* a strong angry speech publicly attacking someone【文】猛烈的抨擊性演說; 痛斥

phil·is·tine /ˋfɪləsˏtin; ˈfɪlɨstaɪn/ *n* [C] someone who does not like or understand art, literature, music etc 不喜歡[懂]藝術、文學或音樂等的人; 沒有教養的人 —**philistine** *adj* —**philistinism** *n* [U]

phi·lol·o·gy /fɪˋlɑlədʒɪ; fɨˈlɒlədʒi/ *n* [U] *old-fashioned* the study of words and of the way words and languages develop【過時】語文學 —compare 比較 LINGUISTICS —**philologist** *n* [C] —**philological** /ˌfɪləˋlɑdʒɪkḷ; ˌfɪləˈlɒdʒɪkəl◂/ *adj* —**philologically** /-kḷɪ; -kli/ *adv*

phi·los·o·pher /fəˋlɑsəfɚ; fɨˈlɒsəfə/ *n* [C] **1** someone who studies and develops ideas about the nature and meaning of existence and reality, good and evil etc 哲學家: *Plato, Aristotle, and other Greek philosophers* 柏拉圖、亞里士多德和其他希臘哲學家 **2** someone who thinks deeply about the world, life etc 思想深刻的人, 思想家

philosopher's stone /ˋ·ˌ··· ˋ·/ *n* [singular] an imaginary substance that was thought in the past to have the power to change any other metal into gold 點金石〔舊時被認為能使任何金屬變成黃金的物質〕

phil·o·soph·i·cal /ˌfɪləˋsɑfɪkəl; ˌfɪləˈsɒfɪkəl◂/ also 又作 **phil·o·soph·ic** /ˌfɪləˋsɑfɪk; ˌfɪləˈsɒfɪk◂/ *adj* **1** related to philosophy 哲學的: *the philosophical writings of Sartre* 沙特的哲學著作 **2** someone who is philosophical calmly accepts a difficult or unpleasant situation because they know it cannot be changed 豁達的, 達觀的: [+about] *Robert was surprisingly philosophical about losing his job.* 羅拔對於失去工作表現得驚人地達觀。—**philosophically** /-kḷɪ; -kli/ *adv*: *Marne took her defeat philosophically.* 瑪內以豁達的態度對待失敗。

phi·los·o·phize also 又作 **-ise** *BrE*【英】/fəˋlɑsəˌfaɪz; fɨˈlɒsəfaɪz/ *v* [I+about] to make remarks about the nature and meaning of things as if you were a philosopher 像哲學家似地談論〔事物的本質和意義〕

3 **phi·los·o·phy** /fəˋlɑsəfɪ; fɨˈlɒsəfi/ *n* **1** [U] the study of the nature and meaning of existence and reality, good and evil, etc 哲學 **2** [C] one of the many systems of thought that has this study as its base〔以哲學為基礎的〕思想體系; 哲學體系: *the philosophy of Kant* 康德的哲學體系 **3** [C] a rule you follow in living your life, doing your job etc 人生哲學; 生活[工作]準則: *current management philosophy* 目前的管理準則 —see also 另見 NATURAL PHILOSOPHY

phil·tre also 又作 **philter** *AmE*【美】/ˋfɪltɚ; ˈfɪltə/ *n* [C] *literary* a magic drink or object that makes someone fall in love【文】催情藥, 春藥

phiz·og /ˋfɪzɑg; ˈfɪzɒg/ *n* [C] *BrE old-fashioned* your face【英, 過時】臉, 面孔; 容貌

phle·bi·tis /flɪˋbaɪtɪs; flɪˈbaɪtɨs/ *n* [U] a swollen condition of the VEINS (=tubes that carry blood through your body) 靜脈炎

phlegm /flɛm; flem/ *n* [U] **1** the thick yellowish substance produced in your nose and throat, especially when you have a cold; MUCUS 痰 **2** unusual calmness in worrying, frightening, or exciting situations 冷靜, 沉着; 不衝動

phleg·mat·ic /flɛgˋmætɪk; flegˈmætɪk/ *adj* calm and not easily excited or worried 冷靜的; 沉着的; 鎮定的: *Even the most phlegmatic individual would get stressed out under such pressure.* 即使最鎮靜的人在這樣的壓力下也會變得很緊張。—**phlegmatically** /-kḷɪ; -kli/ *adv*

phlox /flɑks; flɒks/ *n* [C] **1** a tall garden plant with red, purple, or white flowers 福祿考〔一種園藝植物, 開紅色、紫色或白色的花〕**2** *AmE* a low, spreading plant with pink or white flowers【美】叢生福祿考〔一種低矮蔓生植物, 開粉色或白色的花〕

-phobe /fob; fəʊb/ *suffix* [in nouns 構成名詞] a person who dislikes or hates something 憎惡…的人, 仇視…的人: *an Anglophobe* (=someone who hates England or Britain) 仇英者 | *a xenophobe* (=someone who hates foreigners) 憎惡外國人的人

pho·bi·a /ˋfobɪə; ˈfəʊbiə/ *n* [C] a strong unreasonable fear of something〔對某物無端的〕強烈恐懼: **[+about]** *Owen has a phobia about heights.* 歐文有畏高症。—**phobic** *adj*

-phobia /fobɪə; fəʊbiə/ *suffix* [in nouns 構成名詞] **1** a dislike or hatred of something 憎惡, 仇視: *Anglophobia* (=dislike of England or Britain) 仇英 **2** *technical* a strong dislike or fear of something, that is unusual and may be part of a mental illness; a phobia【術語】〔不正常的〕憎惡, 恐懼: *claustrophobia* (=fear of being in a small enclosed space) 幽閉恐懼〔症〕| *aquaphobia* (=fear of water) 畏水〔症〕

-phobic /fobɪk; fəʊbɪk/ *suffix technical*【術語】**1** [in nouns 構成名詞] someone suffering from a particular phobia 患…恐懼症的人: *He's a claustrophobic.* 他是一個患有幽閉恐懼症的人。**2** [in adjectives 構成形容詞] suffering from or connected with a particular phobia 患恐懼症的, 懼怕…的: *I'm a bit agoraphobic.* 我有點恐曠症。—**-phobically** /fobɪkḷɪ; fəʊbɪkli/ [in adverbs 構成副詞]

phoe·nix /ˋfinɪks; ˈfiːnɪks/ *n* [C] **1** a magic bird that is born from a fire according to ancient stories 鳳凰〔古代傳說中一種生於火中的神奇的鳥〕**2 rise like a phoenix from the ashes** to become successful again after seeming to have failed completely 在看似徹底失敗後取得成功; 起死回生

phon- /fən; fən; *strong* 強讀 fon; fəʊn/ *prefix* another form of the prefix PHONO- 前綴 phono- 的另一種形式

-phone /fon; fəʊn/ *suffix* **1** [in nouns 構成名詞] an instrument or machine connected with sound or hearing, especially a musical instrument 與聲音[聽力]有關的樂器[機器]: *earphones* (=for listening to a radio, etc) 耳機 | *a saxophone* 薩克斯管 **2** *technical* [in nouns 構成名詞] someone who speaks a particular language【術語】講某種語言的人: *a Francophone* (=who speaks French) 講法語的人 **3** [in adjectives 構成形容詞] speaking a particular language 講某種語言的: *Francophone nations* (=where French is spoken) 講法語的國家

phone¹ /fon; fəʊn/ *n* [C] **1** a telephone 電話: *Could you* 1
answer the phone, please? 請你接一下電話, 好嗎? | *a* 2
long-distance phone call 長途電話 | *What's your phone number?* 你的電話號碼是幾號? | **by phone/over the phone** (=using a telephone) 用電話, 通過電話 *I made a booking by phone.* 我打電話進行了預訂。**2** the part of a telephone into which you speak; RECEIVER (1)〔電話的〕聽筒: *Greg slammed down the phone angrily.* 格雷格生氣地把電話聽筒砰地放下。**3 be on the phone a)** to be making a telephone call 在通電話: *Turn down the TV! I'm on the phone!* 把電視音量關小! 我正在打電話! **b)** *BrE* to have a telephone in your home or office【英】〔在家或辦公室〕裝有電話: *Are you on the phone?* 你安裝了電話沒有?

phone² also 又作 **phone up** *v* [I,T] to speak to someone 1
by telephone; TELEPHONE² 給…打電話: *Has Anna phoned yet?* 安娜打電話了嗎? | *I bet they'll phone up with some excuse.* 我敢肯定他們會打電話來為自己找藉口。| **phone sb (up)** *I phoned Jim up last night.* 昨晚我給吉姆打了電話。—see graph at 參見 TELEPHONE 圖表

phone in *phr v* [I,T] **1** to telephone the place where you work, especially to report something〔尤指為報告某事而〕打電話到自己的工作處: *Why don't you phone in and say you are ill?* 為甚麼你不給單位打電話說你病了? | **phone** sth ↔ **in** *How many salespeople have phoned in their figures so far?* 到目前為止, 有多少推銷員已打電話回來匯報了他們的銷售額? **2** to telephone a radio or television show to give your opinion or ask a question〔給無線電台或電視節目〕打電話〔發表意見或提問〕: *We encourage viewers to phone in during the program.* 我們鼓勵觀眾在節目進行期間打電話進來。—see also 另見 PHONE-IN

phone book /ˈ· ·/ *n* [C] a book that contains an alphabetical list of the names, addresses, and telephone numbers of all the people who have a telephone in a particular area; TELEPHONE DIRECTORY 電話 (號碼) 簿

phone booth /ˈ· ·/ *n* [C] *AmE* a small structure that is partly or completely enclosed, containing a public telephone【美】〔公用〕電話亭

phone box /ˈ· ·/ *n* [C] *BrE* a small structure that is partly or completely enclosed, containing a public telephone【英】〔公用〕電話亭

phone·card /ˈfonkɑrd; ˈfəʊnkɑːd/ *n* [C] a plastic card that can be used in some public telephones instead of money〔在公用電話上使用的〕電話卡

phone-in /ˈ· ·/ *n* [C] a radio or television programme in which you hear ordinary people expressing opinions or asking questions over the telephone 公眾打電話參與的電台[電視]節目, 聽眾[觀眾]來電話參加的直播節目

pho·neme /ˈfonim; ˈfəʊniːm/ *n* [C] *technical* the smallest unit of speech that can be used to make one word different from another word, such as the 'b' and the 'p' in 'big' and 'pig'【術語】音素; 音位 —**phonemic** /foˈnimɪk; fəˈniːmɪk/ *adj* —**phonemically** /-kl̩ɪ; -kli/ *adv*

pho·ne·mics /fəˈnimɪks; fəˈniːmɪks/ *n* [U] *technical* the study and description of the phonemes of languages【術語】音位學

phone-tap·ping /ˈ· ,··/ *n* [U] the activity of listening secretly to other people's telephone conversations using special ELECTRONIC equipment〔利用特殊電子設備進行的〕電話竊聽

pho·net·ic /fəˈnɛtɪk; fəˈnetɪk/ *adj technical*【術語】**1** related to the sounds of human speech 語音的 **2** using special signs, often different from ordinary letters, to represent the sounds of speech 使用音標代表語音的, 表示發音的: *a phonetic alphabet* 音標 | *phonetic symbols* 音標符號

pho·net·ics /fəˈnɛtɪks; fəˈnetɪks/ *n* [U] the science and study of speech sounds 語音學 —**phonetician** /ˌfonəˈtɪʃən; ˌfəʊnɪ̩ˈtɪʃən/ *n* [C]

pho·ney also 又作 **phony** *AmE*【美】/ˈfonɪ; ˈfəʊni/ *adj informal*【非正式】**1** false or not real, and intended to deceive someone; FAKE 假冒的, 偽造的: *a phoney British accent* 假冒的英國口音 | *I gave the police a phoney address.* 我給了警察一個假地址。**2** someone who is phoney pretends to be good, clever, kind etc when they are not 偽善的; 假裝聰明的; 騙人的 —**phoney** *n* [C]: *Grant's such a phoney!* 格蘭特是個大騙子! —**phoniness** *n* [U]

phoney war /ˌ·· ˈ·/ *n* [singular] a period during which a state of war officially exists but there is no actual fighting 戰爭中的暫時息戰

phon·ic /ˈfɑnɪk; ˈfɒnɪk/ *adj technical*【術語】**1** related to sound 聲音的 **2** related to speech sounds 語音的

phon·ics /ˈfɑnɪks; ˈfɒnɪks/ *n* [U] a method of teaching people to read in which they are taught to recognize the sounds that letters represent 讀音法〔一種教人閱讀的方法〕

phono- /fono; fəʊnəʊ/ *prefix* also 又作 **phon-** *technical*【術語】**1** concerning the voice or speech 音, 語音: *phonetics* (=science of speech sounds) 語音學 **2** concerning sound 聲: *a phonoreceptor* (=hearing organ) 感聲器

pho·no·graph /ˈfonəˌgræf; ˈfəʊnəgrɑːf/ *n* [C] *AmE old-fashioned* a RECORD PLAYER【美, 過時】留聲機, 唱機

pho·nol·o·gy /foˈnɑlədʒɪ; fəˈnɒlədʒi/ *n* [U] *technical* the study of the system of speech sounds in a language, or the system of sounds itself【術語】音系學; 音韻學; 語音體系 —**phonologist** *n* [C] —**phonological** /ˌfonəˈlɑdʒɪkl; ˌfəʊnəˈlɒdʒɪkəl◂/ *adj* —**phonologically** /-kl̩ɪ; -kli/ *adv*

pho·ny /ˈfonɪ; ˈfəʊni/ *adj* the usual American spelling of PHONEY phoney 的一般美式拼法

phoo·ey /ˈfuɪ; ˈfuːi/ *interjection* used to express strong disbelief or disappointment 呸, 啐〔用於表示強烈的不信任或失望〕

phos·gene /ˈfɑzdʒin; ˈfɒzdʒiːn/ *n* [U] a poisonous gas used in war and in industry〔戰爭或工業中使用的〕光氣, 碳酰氯

phos·phate /ˈfɑsfet; ˈfɒsfeɪt/ *n* [C,U] **1** one of the various forms of a SALT[1] (3) of PHOSPHORUS, widely used in industry 磷酸鹽 **2** [usually plural 一般用複數] a substance containing a phosphate used for making plants grow better 磷肥

phos·pho·res·cence /ˌfɑsfəˈrɛsn̩s; ˌfɒsfəˈresəns/ *n* [U] a slight steady light that can only be noticed in the dark 磷光, 磷火

phos·pho·res·cent /ˌfɑsfəˈrɛsn̩t; ˌfɒsfəˈresənt◂/ *adj* shining slightly in the dark but producing little or no heat 發磷光的: *a strange phosphorescent light at night* 夜晚奇異的磷光 —**phosphorescently** *adv*

phos·pho·rus /ˈfɑsfərəs; ˈfɒsfərəs/ *n* [U] a poisonous yellowish ELEMENT (=simple substance) that starts to burn when brought out into the air 磷 —**phosphoric** /fɑsˈfɔrɪk; fɒsˈfɒrɪk/ *adj*

pho·to /ˈfoto; ˈfəʊtəʊ/ *n plural* **photos** [C] *informal* a photograph【非正式】照片, 相片: *the family photo album* 家庭相冊 | **take a photo** *Let's take a photo of the hotel.* 讓我們拍一張酒店的照片。

photo- /foto; fəʊtəʊ/ *prefix technical*【術語】**1** concerning light 光的: *photosensitive paper* (=that changes when light acts on it) 感光紙 **2** concerning photography 照相的, 攝影的: *photojournalism* (=use of photographs in reporting news) 攝影新聞 (工作)

photo booth /ˈ·· ·/ *n* [C] a small structure in which you can sit to have photographs taken by a machine〔立等可取的〕自助照相亭

pho·to·cop·i·er /ˈfotoˌkɑpɪɚ; ˈfəʊtəʊˌkɒpiə/ *n* [C] a machine that quickly makes photographic copies of documents 影印機, 複印機; 攝影複製機 —see picture on page A14 參見 A14 頁圖

pho·to·cop·y[1] /ˈfotoˌkɑpɪ; ˈfəʊtəʊˌkɒpi/ *n* [C] a photographic copy, especially of something printed, written, or drawn 影印本, 複印件: *Make three photocopies of the report, please.* 請把這份報告影印三份。

photocopy[2] *v* [T] to make a photographic copy of something 影印, 複印: *Could you get this photocopied in the office?* 你把這個在辦公室影印一下好嗎?

pho·to·e·lec·tric /ˌfoto·ɪˈlɛktrɪk; ˌfəʊtəʊ-ɪˈlektrɪk◂/ *adj* using an electrical effect that is controlled by light 光電的

photoelectric cell /ˌ····· ˈ·/ *n* [C] **1** an electronic instrument that changes light into electricity 光電池 **2** an electronic instrument that uses light to start an electrical effect, often used in BURGLAR ALARMS〔常用於防盜警報器的〕光電管, 電眼

photo fin·ish /ˌ·· ˈ··/ *n* [C] the end of a race in which the leading runners finish so close together that a photograph has to be taken to decide which is the winner 攝影定勝負〔參賽者到達終點時非常接近, 需藉照片決定勝負〕

Pho·to·fit /ˈfotofɪt; ˈfəʊtəʊfɪt/ *n* [U] *BrE trademark* a way of making a picture of a face using a collection of photographs of parts of different faces, used to help the police catch a criminal【英, 商標】〔由多張照片拼成, 用於幫助警方捉拿罪犯的〕拼圖像法

pho·to·gen·ic /ˌfotəˈdʒɛnɪk; ˌfəʊtəʊˈdʒenɪk◂/ *adj* always looking attractive in photographs 上鏡的, 上照的: *Helen is very photogenic.* 海倫非常上照。

2 2 **pho·to·graph¹** /ˈfotə,græf; ˈfəʊtəgrɑːf/ also 又作 **photo** *informal*【非正式】*n* [C] a picture obtained by using a camera and film that is sensitive to light 照片, 相片: *a passport photograph* 護照照片 | *wedding photographs* 結婚照 | *an old black-and-white photograph of the city* 一張這個城市的黑白舊照片 | **take a photograph** *Visitors are not allowed to take photographs inside the museum.* 遊客不許在博物館內拍照。| **sb's photograph** (=a photograph of someone) 某人的照片 *Did you see Leo's photograph in the newspaper?* 你在報紙上看到利奧的照片了嗎?

photograph² *v* **1** [T] to make a picture of someone or something by using a camera and film sensitive to light 給…拍照, 拍攝: *Michelle doesn't like being photographed.* 米雪兒不喜歡被拍照。**2 photograph well/badly** to always look attractive or unattractive in photographs 上照/不上照

pho·tog·ra·pher /fəˈtɑgrəfə; fəˈtɒgrəfə/ *n* [C] someone who takes photographs, especially as a professional or as an artist 攝影者〔尤指專業攝影師或藝術攝影師〕: *a fashion photographer* 時裝攝影師

pho·to·graph·ic /,fotəˈgræfɪk; ,fəʊtəˈgræfɪk◂/ *adj* **1** connected with photographs, using photographs, or used in producing photographs 攝影的; 使用照片的; 攝影用的: *a photographic history of the West* 西方歷史畫冊 | *photographic equipment* 攝影器材 **2 photographic memory** the ability to remember exactly every detail of something you have seen 準確得驚人的記憶力 —**photographically** /-klɪ; -kli/ *adv*

pho·tog·ra·phy /fəˈtɑgrəfɪ; fəˈtɒgrəfi/ *n* [U] the art, profession, or method of producing photographs or the scenes in films 攝影業; 攝影術: *a documentary with marvellous wildlife photography* 有精彩的野生動物鏡頭的紀錄片

pho·ton /ˈfotɑn; ˈfəʊtɒn/ *n* [C] *technical* a unit of energy (ENERGY (2)) that carries light and has zero MASS【術語】光子, 光量子

photo-op·por·tu·ni·ty /ˈ·· ··,···/ *n* [C] a chance for someone such as a politician to be photographed for a newspaper in a way that will make them look good〔政治家等〕接受宣傳媒體拍照的時間

pho·to·sen·si·tive /,fotəˈsɛnsətɪv; ,fəʊtəʊˈsensɪ̈tɪv◂/ *adj* sensitive to the action of light, for example by changing colour or form 感光的: *photosensitive paper* 感光紙

pho·to·sen·si·tize also 又作 **-ise** *BrE*【英】/,fotəˈsɛnsə,taɪz; ,fəʊtəʊˈsensɪ̈taɪz/ *v* [T] to make something photosensitive 使具感光性

photo shoot /ˈ·· ·/ *n* [C] an occasion during which a professional PHOTOGRAPHER takes pictures of a fashion model or an actor for advertisements〔由職業攝影師進行拍攝的〕時裝拍照會; 明星廣告照

pho·to·stat /ˈfotə,stæt; ˈfəʊtəstæt/ *n* [C] *trademark* a type of machine used for making photographic copies, or the copy itself【商標】影[複]印機; 影[複]印件 —**photostat** *v* [T] —**photostatic** /,fotəˈstætɪk; ,fəʊtəˈstætɪk◂/ *adj*

pho·to·syn·the·sis /,fotəˈsɪnθəsɪs; ,fəʊtəʊˈsɪnθɪ̈sɪ̈s/ *n* [U] the production by a green plant of special substances like sugar that it uses as food, caused by the action of sunlight on CHLOROPHYLL (=the green substance in leaves) 光合作用

phras·al /ˈfrezl̩; ˈfreɪzəl/ *adj* consisting of or connected with a phrase or phrases 詞組的; 短語的; 片語的

phrasal verb /,·· ˈ·/ *n* [C] a group of words that is used like a verb and consists of a verb with an adverb or PREPOSITION, such as 'set off', 'look after', 'put up with'. In this dictionary phrasal verbs are marked *phr v.* 片語動詞, 短語動詞〔在本辭典中片語動詞以 *phr v* 表示〕

3 **phrase¹** /frez; freɪz/ *n* [C] **1** a group of words that together have a particular meaning, especially when they express the meaning well in a few words〔尤指簡潔的〕說法, 用語, 警句: *He said the President was – what was the phrase he used? – 'trigger happy'.* 他說總統——他用甚麼詞來着?——"好戰"。| *Mrs Thatcher was, in Gorbachev's phrase, 'the iron lady'.* 用戈巴喬夫的說法, 戴卓爾夫人是個"鐵娘子"。**2** *technical* a group of words without a FINITE verb, especially when they are used to form part of a sentence, such as 'walking along the road' and 'a bar of soap'【術語】短語, 片語 —compare 比較 CLAUSE (2), SENTENCE¹ (1) **3** a short group of musical notes that is part of a longer piece 樂句 —see also 另見 **to coin a phrase** (COIN² (2)), **a turn of phrase** (TURN² (10))

phrase² *v* [T] **1** to express something in a particular way 以某種方式表達, 以…措辭表達: *Criticisms were phrased in careful terms.* 對批評的用詞十分謹慎。| *a politely-phrased refusal* 婉言拒絕 **2** to perform music so as to produce the full effect of separate musical phrases 把〔樂曲〕分成短句演奏〔以充分表現每個樂句的效果〕

phrase·book /ˈfrezbʊk; ˈfreɪzbʊk/ *n* [C] a book that explains phrases of a foreign language, for people to use when they travel to other countries〔供遊客到國外旅行時用的〕(外語) 常用語手冊

phra·se·ol·o·gy /,frezɪˈɑlədʒɪ; ,freɪziˈɒlədʒi/ *n* [U] the way that words and phrases are chosen and used in a particular language or subject 專門用語; 術語

phras·ing /ˈfrezɪŋ; ˈfreɪzɪŋ/ *n* [U] **1** the way that something is said 措詞, 說法; 用語: *I don't remember her exact phrasing.* 我不記得她原話是怎麼說的了。**2** a way of playing music, reading poetry etc that separates the notes, words, or lines into phrases〔演奏音樂時的〕樂句劃分; 〔朗誦詩歌時的〕分句法

phre·nol·ogy /frəˈnɑlədʒɪ; frəˈnɒlədʒi/ *n* [U] the study of the shape of the human head as a way of showing someone's character and abilities, which was popular especially in the 19th century 顱相學〔通過研究頭顱的形狀來判斷一個人的性格和能力, 尤在19世紀流行〕—**phrenologist** *n* [C]

phut /fʌt; fʌt/ *n* [singular] *BrE informal*【英, 非正式】**1 go phut** to stop working completely 停止運作, 出故障, 壞了: *The microwave's gone phut.* 微波爐壞了。**2** a sound like air suddenly escaping from something 啪〔氣體突然排出的聲音〕: *The engine gave a phut, and stopped.* 引擎發出啪的一聲響, 然後就停止運轉了。

phy·lum /ˈfaɪləm; ˈfaɪləm/ *n plural* **phyla** /-lə; -lə/ [C] *technical* one of the main groups into which scientists divide plants, animals, and languages, above a CLASS【術語】〔動植物分類的〕門; 〔語言的〕語系, 語羣

physi- /fɪzɪ; fɪzi/ *prefix* another form of the prefix PHYSIO- 前綴 physio- 的另一種形式

phys·ic /ˈfɪzɪk; ˈfɪzɪk/ *n* [C,U] *old use* medicine【過時】藥品

phys·i·cal¹ /ˈfɪzɪkl̩; ˈfɪzɪkəl/ *adj* 2 1

1 ►BODY NOT MIND 身體而非精神的◄ related to someone's body rather than their mind or soul 身體的, 肉體的: *physical exercise* 體育活動, 體操 | *physical abuse* 肉體上的虐待 | *people with mental or physical disabilities* 精神或身體有殘疾的人

2 ►REAL/SOLID 真實的/固體的◄ related to real objects or structures that can be touched, seen, felt, etc 物質的, 有形的: *man's domination of his physical environment* 人類對物質環境的主宰 | *They were kept in appalling physical conditions.* 他們被困在物質條件極差的地方。

3 ►NATURAL 自然的◄ related to or following natural laws 自然的; 按照自然規律的: *There must be a physical explanation for the strange lights in the sky.* 天空中這些奇怪的光一定可以根據自然規律作出解釋。

4 ►PERSON 人◄ *informal* someone who is physical likes touching people a lot【非正式】〔人〕喜歡動手動腳的

5 ►VIOLENT 粗暴的◄ a word meaning violent, used to avoid saying this directly 粗暴的, 粗野的: *That was a very physical tackle!* 那是個非常粗暴的擒抱動作!

6 ►SCIENCE 科學◄ [only before noun 僅用於名詞前]

a physical science is the part of an area of scientific study that is connected with PHYSICS 物理學的: *physical chemistry* 物理化學 —see also 另見 PHYSICALLY

physical² also 又作 **physical ex·am·i·na·tion** /,··· ···'··/ *n* [C] a thorough examination of someone's body and general health by a doctor, especially to decide whether they are fit to do a particular job〔尤指決定是否適合做某種工作的〕身體[體格]檢查

physical ed·u·ca·tion /,··· ··'··/ *n* [U] sport and physical exercise taught as a school subject 體育教育; 體育課

physical ge·og·ra·phy /,··· ·'···/ *n* [U] the study of the Earth's surface and of its rivers, mountains etc rather than of the countries it is divided into 自然地理學 —compare 比較 POLITICAL GEOGRAPHY

physical jerks /,··· '·/ *n* [plural] *BrE old-fashioned* physical exercises such as bending and stretching etc【英, 過時】體操

3 **phys·i·cally** /ˋfɪzɪkḷɪ; 'fɪzɪkli/ *adv* **1** in relation to the body rather than the mind or soul 身體上, 體格上: *She is young and physically fit.* 她年輕而且身體健康。| *He's all right physically, but he's still very confused.* 他身體並沒有問題, 但仍然十分糊塗。**2 physically impossible** not possible according to the laws of nature or what is known to be true〔根據自然法則或已知事實〕不可能的; 完全不可能的: *Surely it's physically impossible to go a week without water?* 當然, 在沒有水的情況下堅持一個星期是完全不可能的?

physically chal·lenged /,··· '··/ *adj especially AmE* a word meaning physically HANDICAPPED, used when you want to avoid offending people【尤美】身體殘疾的〔避免冒犯人的委婉說法〕

physical sci·ence /,··· '··/ *n* [U] also **the physical sciences** [plural] the sciences, such as CHEMISTRY, PHYSICS etc, that are concerned with things that are not living 自然科學〈如化學、物理等非生命科學〉

phy·si·cian /fəˋzɪʃən; fɪ̆'zɪʃən/ *n* [C] *AmE formal* a doctor【美, 正式】(內科)醫生

phys·i·cist /ˋfɪzəsɪst; 'fɪzɪ̆sɪ̆st/ *n* [C] someone who studies or works in PHYSICS 物理學家

phys·ics /ˋfɪzɪks; 'fɪzɪks/ *n* [U] the science concerned with the study of physical objects and substances, and of natural forces such as light, heat and movement 物理學

phys·i·o /ˋfɪzɪo; 'fɪziəʊ/ *n plural* **physios** [C] *informal* a PHYSIOTHERAPIST【非正式】理療家, 物理治療師

physio- /fɪzɪo; fɪziəʊ/ *prefix* also 又作 **physi-** *technical*【術語】**1** concerning nature and living things 關於自然和生物的: *physiology* (=study of how the body works) 生理學 **2** physical 物理的: *physiotherapy* (=treatment using exercises etc) 物理療法

phys·i·og·no·my /,fɪzɪˋɑgnəmɪ; ,fɪzi'ɒnəmi/ *n* [C] *technical or humorous* the general appearance of a person's face【術語或幽默】相貌, 容貌

phys·i·ol·o·gy /,fɪzɪˋɑlədʒɪ; ,fɪzi'ɒlədʒi/ *n* [U] **1** the science concerned with the study of how the bodies of living things work 生理學 **2** the way the body of a person or an animal works and looks〔人或動物的〕生理機能; 生理: *A newborn's physiology is not the same as an older baby's.* 新生兒的生理機能和大一些的嬰兒是不一樣的。—compare 比較 ANATOMY —**physiologist** *n* [C] —**physiological** /,fɪzɪəˋlɑdʒɪkḷ; ,fɪziə'lɒdʒɪkəl◂/ *adj*: *The doctors could find no physiological cause for his illness.* 醫生們找不出他患病的生理方面的原因。

phys·i·o·ther·a·pist /,fɪzɪoˋθɛrəpɪst; ,fɪziəʊ'θerəpɪ̆st/ *n* [C] someone whose job is to give PHYSIOTHERAPY as a treatment for medical conditions 理療醫師; 理療學家

phys·i·o·ther·a·py /,fɪzɪoˋθɛrəpɪ; ,fɪziəʊ'θerəpi/ *n* [U] a treatment for illnesses and problems with muscles which uses special exercises, rubbing, heat etc 物理療法, 理療

phy·sique /fɪˋzik; fɪ̆'ziːk/ *n* [C] the shape and appearance of a human body, especially a man's body〔尤指男人的〕體格, 體形: *exercises designed to improve your physique* 為改善你的體形而設計的運動

pi /paɪ; paɪ/ *n* [U] *technical* a number that is represented by the Greek letter (π) and is equal to the distance around a circle, divided by its width【術語】圓周率 (π)

pi·a·nist /pɪˋænɪst; 'piːənɪ̆st/ *n* [C] someone who plays the piano, especially very well 鋼琴演奏者, 鋼琴家

pi·an·o¹ /pɪˋæno; pi'ænəʊ/ *n* [C] a large musical instrument that you play by sitting in front of it and pressing the KEYS (=narrow black and white bars) 鋼琴 3

piano² *adj, adv* played or sung quietly〔彈或唱時〕輕柔的[地]

pi·a·no·la /,piəˋnolə; ,piːə'nəʊlə/ *n* [C] a PLAYER PIANO 自動鋼琴

piano stool /·'·· ·/ *n* [C] a small seat for sitting on while you play the piano〔彈奏鋼琴時坐的〕琴櫈

pi·az·za /pɪˋæzə; pi'ætsə/ *n* [C] a public square (=large open area in a city) or market place, especially in Italy〔尤指意大利的〕廣場; 市場

pic·a·dor /ˋpɪkə,dɔr; 'pɪkədɔː/ *n* [C] a man in a BULLFIGHT who rides a horse, and annoys and weakens the BULL by sticking a long spear into it〔鬥牛中用長矛刺牛使之發怒並變弱的〕騎馬鬥牛士

pic·a·resque /,pɪkəˋrɛsk; ,pɪkə'resk◂/ *adj* a picaresque story or NOVEL tells the adventures and travels of a character whose behaviour is not always moral but who is still likeable〔指故事或小說〕以流浪漢冒險事跡為題材的

pic·a·yune /,pɪkəˋjun; ,pɪkə'juːn/ *adj AmE* small and unimportant【美】微不足道的, 無關緊要的, 瑣細的: *the picayune squabbling of party politicians* 政黨的政客為瑣事進行的爭論

pic·ca·lil·li /,pɪkəˋlɪlɪ; ,pɪkə'lɪli/ *n* [U] a hot-tasting sauce made with small pieces of vegetables and eaten with cold meat 辣泡菜

pic·co·lo /ˋpɪkə,lo; 'pɪkələʊ/ *n plural* **piccolos** [C] a musical instrument that looks like a small FLUTE 短笛

pick¹ /pɪk; pɪk/ *v* [T]

1 ▸CHOOSE STH 選擇某物◂ to choose someone or something good or suitable from a group or range of people or things 挑選; 選擇: *Students have to pick three courses from a list of 15.* 學生必須從十五門學科中選修三門。| *Let me pick a few examples at random.* 讓我隨便選取幾個例子。| **pick your words** (=be careful about what you say) 斟酌詞句 *Trevor was picking his words with great care.* 特雷弗正在小心地斟字酌句。| **pick sb as** *The group picked me as their spokesperson.* 這個組選我作為他們的發言人。| **pick sb/sth for** *Harris was picked for the England team.* 哈里斯被選進了英格蘭隊。| **pick sb to do sth** *She has been picked to represent us in Rome.* 她已被挑選為我們在羅馬的代表。—see also 另見 PICKED, **pick out** (PICK¹)

2 ▸FLOWERS/FRUIT ETC 花/水果等◂ to pull off or break off a flower, fruit, nut etc from a plant or tree 採, 摘〔花果等〕: *The cotton was picked by teams of men.* 棉花是由男隊採摘的。| *We picked some blackberries to eat on the way.* 我們採了一些黑莓以供在路上吃。| **pick sb sth** *He picked her a single red rose.* 他採了一朵紅玫瑰給她。| **pick a bunch/a basketful etc** *Amy picked a small bunch of wild flowers.* 艾美採了一小束野花。| **newly/freshly picked** *Runner beans should be eaten young and freshly picked.* 紅花菜豆應趁幼嫩新鮮的時候吃。| **go grape/strawberry etc picking** (=pick something either for your own use or as a part-time job) 去摘葡萄/採草莓等

3 ▸SMALL THINGS/PIECES 小東西/小碎片◂ to remove small things from something, or pull off small pieces of something 挖, 剔: **pick sth from/off/out of** *Ahmed picked the melon pips from his teeth.* 阿米德剔去牙縫裡的瓜子。| *She was nervously picking bits of fluff off her sweater.* 她正在緊張地拔去毛衣上的小絨毛。| **pick a hole in sth** (=make a hole in something by repeatedly pulling off small pieces of it) 在某物上挖[鑿,

掘]出一個洞

4 pick your teeth to remove bits of food from between your teeth, with your fingers or something pointed 剔牙齒

5 pick your nose to take MUCUS from your nose with your finger〔用手〕挖鼻孔

6 pick sth clean to take all the meat from a bone 把骨頭剔[啃]乾淨

7 pick your way through/across/among etc to move slowly and carefully, choosing exactly where to put your feet down 小心翼翼地穿過: *She picked her way between the piles of books.* 她小心翼翼地走在書堆中間。

8 pick and choose to choose only the people or things you really like 仔細挑選〔真正喜歡的人或物〕, 挑挑揀揀: *We can't pick and choose, we'll have to take what they give us.* 我們不能挑挑揀揀, 只能是他們給甚麼, 我們就要甚麼。

9 pick a quarrel/fight (with sb) to deliberately start a quarrel or fight with someone〔故意〕(向某人) 挑釁, 找岔兒: *He got drunk one night and picked a quarrel with his girlfriend.* 有一天晚上他喝醉了, 就向女朋友找岔吵架。

10 pick sb's brains to ask someone who knows a lot about something for information and advice about it 請教某人: *Have you got a minute? I need to pick your brains.* 你有時間嗎? 我需要向你請教請教。

11 pick a lock (with) to use something that is not a key to unlock a door, drawer etc〔用鑰匙之外的東西〕打開[撬開]鎖: *She picked the lock with a hairpin.* 她用髮夾把鎖打開了。

12 pick holes (in) to criticize a plan, an idea etc 批評〔計劃、觀點等〕; 挑...的毛病; 找...的漏洞: *I had no trouble picking holes in her theory.* 我毫不費事地找出了她理論中的漏洞。| *Stop picking holes! I bet you couldn't do any better.* 別再挑毛病了! 我敢肯定要你做也好不到哪裡去。

13 pick sb's pocket to quietly steal something from someone's pocket〔從口袋裡〕偷, 扒竊: *When all the fuss died down I found my pocket had been picked.* 當所有的忙亂平息下來時, 我發現口袋裡的東西被扒竊了。—see also 另見 PICKPOCKET

14 pick a winner *informal* an expression meaning to make a very good choice, sometimes used jokingly when you think someone has made a very bad choice【非正式】挑選得極好〔有時戲謔地用作反話〕

15 pick sb/sth to pieces *informal* to criticize someone or something very severely and in a very detailed way【非正式】把某人/某物駁得體無完膚; 對某人/某物吹毛求疵

16 ►MUSICAL INSTRUMENT 樂器◄ *AmE* to play a musical instrument by pulling at its strings with your fingers; PLUCK¹ (5)【美】彈撥〔琴弦〕; 彈奏〔弦樂器〕—see also 另見 **have a bone to pick with sb** (BONE¹ (2))

pick at sth *phr v* [T] **1** to eat something taking small bites and without much interest, for example because you feel unhappy〔因不高興而〕一點一點地吃, 挑挑揀揀地吃: *He picked gloomily at his lamb chop.* 他沮喪地一點一點吃着羊排。**2** to touch something repeatedly with your fingers, often pulling it slightly 拉扯: *The little boy was picking at his mother's sleeve, trying to get her attention.* 這個小男孩正在拉扯他媽媽的袖子, 試圖引起她的注意。

pick sb/sth ↔ **off** *phr v* [T] to shoot people or animals that are some distance away one at a time, by taking careful aim 逐個地仔細瞄準射殺〔人或動物〕: *The sniper was picking off our men one by one.* 那個狙擊手正在把我們的人逐個瞄準打死。

pick on sb/sth *phr v* [T] *spoken*【口】**1** to choose someone to do an unpleasant job or blame someone for something, especially unfairly 選中〔某人做不愉快的工作〕;〔尤指不公平地〕責備〔某人〕: *Why does the boss always pick on me?* 為甚麼老闆總是跟我過不去? | *You big bully – pick on someone your own size!* 你這個恃強凌弱的大壞蛋——挑一個跟你個頭一樣大的人欺負呀! **2** to decide to choose someone or something 選中〔某人或某物〕: *First, pick on some daily task that you all share.* 首先, 挑選出某項你們都要分擔的日常工作。

pick sb/sth ↔ **out** *phr v* [T] **1** to choose someone or something carefully 認真挑選〔人或物〕: *Pick out all the words in the poem that suggest despair.* 挑出這首詩中所有表示絕望的詞。**2** to recognize someone or something in a group of people or things 分辨出, 辨認出: *It was easy to pick out Bob's father.* 鮑勃的父親很容易被認出來。| *I could just pick out a few landmarks in the gloom.* 在黑暗中我只能分辨出幾處地標。**3 a)** if you pick out a shape, letter etc in a particular colour, you make it that colour so that it can be clearly seen〔用某種顏色〕把...襯托出來: *Every name on the memorial was picked out in scarlet edged with gold.* 紀念碑上的每個名字都以紅色鑲金邊襯托得十分顯眼。**b)** if a light picks someone or something out, it shines directly on it〔光〕直接照射在...上: *The searchlight picked out a figure on the roof.* 探照燈照在屋頂的一個人身上。**4** to play a tune on a stringed musical instrument slowly or with difficulty 憑記憶〔緩慢或困難地在弦樂器上〕彈奏〔曲調〕: *He picked out a moody chord on his guitar.* 他緩慢地撥動結他, 憑記憶彈奏起憂傷的和弦。

pick over sth ↔ *phr v* [T] to examine a group of small things very carefully in order to choose the ones you want 仔細檢查...以選出想要的東西, 甄選, 精選: *He turned the drawer upside-down and picked over the spilled contents.* 他把抽屜翻個底朝天, 仔細從倒出來的東西中挑選。

pick through sth *phr v* [T] to search through a pile or group of things, and take the one that you want 在...裡搜尋〔以發現想要的東西〕

pick up 撿起, 拿起, 拾起

Steve is picking up the can.
斯蒂夫正在撿起罐子。

Mom picked up her jacket from the dry cleaner's.
媽媽從乾洗店取回她的短上衣。

The truck driver picked up a hitchhiker.
卡車司機接載了一個搭便車的人。

pick up *phr v*

1 ►LIFT STH UP 撿起, 拿起, 拾起◄ [T pick sth ↔ up]

P

to lift something up from a surface 撿起, 拿起, 拾起: *She kept picking up magazines and putting them down again.* 她不斷地把那些雜誌拿起來又放下。| *My wife picks the baby up whenever it cries.* 每次嬰兒一哭, 我妻子就把他抱起來。| *The phone rang and I picked it up.* 電話響起, 我拿起了話筒。| *The vacuum cleaner won't pick this stuff up.* 吸塵器不能把這東西吸起來。| **pick sth up by sth** *The lioness picked up her cub by its neck.* 母獅咬住幼獅的脖子把牠銜起來。| **bend/stoop (down) and pick sth up** *Seth bent to pick up the papers.* 塞思彎腰撿起文件。| **pick your feet up** (=used to tell someone to walk properly) 把你的腳提起來〔用於告訴別人好好走路〕

P

2 pick yourself up to get up from the ground after a fall〔跌倒後〕再站起來: *Carol picked herself up and dusted herself off.* 嘉露跌倒後爬了起來, 拍去自己身上的灰塵。

3 ►TIDY STH 整理某物◄ [T **pick** sth ↔ **up**] **a)** to put toys, magazines etc away neatly 把〔玩具、雜誌等〕收拾起來; 整理〔某物〕: *Please pick up your slippers.* 請把你的拖鞋收拾好。**b)** *AmE* to make a place tidy【美】整理, 收拾某個地方: *Connie had made some effort to pick up the apartment.* 康妮費了一些功夫才把公寓收拾乾淨。

4 pick up after sb *informal especially AmE* to tidy things that someone else has left untidy【非正式, 尤美】跟在某人後面收拾[整理]東西: *Who wants to get married and spend their life picking up after some man?* 誰願意結了婚就一輩子跟在某個男人後面收拾東西?

5 ►GET STH 獲得某物, 得到某物◄ [T **pick** sth ↔ **up**] *informal*【非正式】**a)** to find or get something, especially unexpectedly〔尤指無意中〕發現, 得到: *I picked up a bug on holiday.* (=became ill) 我度假時染上了病。| *Hill only picked up four points from the two races.* 希爾兩次賽跑只得了四分。| *We picked up some nice souvenirs.* 我們買到一些很不錯的紀念品。| *Where can I pick up a cheap video camera?* 我到哪裡可以買到一台廉價的攝像機? **b)** to get or buy something, while you are going somewhere or doing something〔去某地或做某事時〕得到, 買到〔某物〕: *I picked up an evening paper on the way home.* 我在回家的路上買了一份晚報。| *For more details, pick up a leaflet in your local post office.* 要了解更多細節, 你可以在當地的郵局取得一份小冊子。

6 ►COLLECT SB/STH 接某人/取某物◄ [T **pick** sth ↔ **up**] to collect someone who is waiting for you or something that you have left somewhere or need 接〔某人〕, 取〔某物〕: *I'll pick my things up later.* 我過一會兒來取我的東西。| *She just dropped by to pick up her mail.* 她只是順便過來取她的郵件。| *My husband will pick you up in the car.* 我丈夫會開車來接你。| *Pick me up at 8:00.* 八點來接我。

7 ►SKILL/INFORMATION ETC 技術/信息等◄ [T **pick** sth ↔ **up**] to get a skill, language, habit, idea or piece of information by chance rather than by deliberately trying to get it〔偶然、無意間〕學會〔技術、語言〕; 染上〔習慣〕; 想到〔主意〕; 得到〔信息〕: *"Where did you study Greek?" "I didn't, I just sort of picked it up when I lived there."* "你在哪裡學希臘語的?" "我沒學, 只是在希臘生活時偶然學了一點。" | *If you sing it several times, your children will begin to pick up the words.* 如果你把它唱上幾遍, 你的孩子就會不知不覺地學會歌詞。| *There's a tip I picked up from a professional model.* 我偶然從一位職業模特兒那裡學到了一個小竅門。

8 ►RADIO/RECORDING 無線電/錄音◄ if a machine picks up a sound, a movement or the presence of something, it is able to receive it, record it, or TRANSMIT (1) it 收看[收聽]到; 記錄; 傳送: *The sensors pick up faint vibrations in the Earth.* 這些傳感器可記錄地球內部微弱的振動。| *I managed to pick up an American news broadcast.* 我設法收聽到一檔美國的新聞廣播節目。

9 ►LET SB INTO A VEHICLE 讓某人進入車輛◄ [T **pick** sb ↔ **up**] to stop and let someone get into your car, boat etc 搭載, 接載: *They were picked up by a fishing boat.* 他們被一艘漁船接走了。| *It is an offence to pick up or set down a hitchhiker on a motorway.* 在高速公路上讓搭便車的人上下車是違規的。

10 ►BECOME FRIENDLY WITH SB 與某人關係變得友好起來◄ [T **pick** sb ↔ **up**] to become friendly with someone you have just met because you find them sexually attractive 結識, 勾搭上〔某人〕; 結識: *I wish I could just go out and pick up a nice man.* 我希望我能夠走出去就結識一位好男人。| *Are you trying to pick me up?* 你在設法勾搭我嗎?

11 ►NOTICE STH 注意到某事物◄ [T **pick** sth ↔ **up**] **a)** [U] to smell a slight smell or hear a quiet sound 聞到〔輕微的味道〕; 聽到〔輕微的聲音〕: *Then he picked up the even fainter aroma of apple pie.* 然後他聞到一點更弱的蘋果派的香味。| *The dogs picked up the scent and raced off.* 那些狗嗅出了氣味, 飛快地跑了。**b)** to see something that you are looking for 發現[找到]〔某事物〕: *She picked up a flicker of movement just beyond the fence.* 她發現籬笆那邊晃動了一下。| *We picked up the car again within a block.* 我們在一個街區內又發現了那輛轎車。| **pick up the track/trail/traces** *Cody picked up the track of their horses but lost it again.* 科迪發現了他們的馬的足跡, 但過後又找不到了。

12 ►START AGAIN 重新開始◄ [I,T **pick** sth ↔ **up**] **a)** if a conversation, meeting etc picks up or if you pick it up, it starts again from the point where it was interrupted〔談話、會議等〕重新開始, 繼續: **pick up where you left off** *informal*【非正式】*He left her for two years and then came back expecting to pick up where they had left off!* 他離開她兩年後又回來了, 希望重新開始兩人的關係! **b)** if you pick up a point or an idea that has been mentioned, you return to it and develop it further 回過頭來進一步闡述〔某觀點〕: *Tocqueville picks up this theme in his later works.* 托克維爾在他後來的著作中進一步闡述了這個主題。

13 ►IMPROVE 改進, 提高◄ [I] **a)** if business, your social life etc picks up, it improves〔生意、社交生活等〕改進, 提高, 好轉: *Trade is picking up nicely.* 生意很有起色。| *The economy is finally beginning to pick up again.* 經濟最終又開始有所好轉。**b)** [T **pick** sb ↔ **up**] if a medicine, drink etc picks you up, it makes you feel better〔藥物、飲料等〕使感覺好些, 使好轉 —see also 另見 PICK-ME-UP

14 sb's speed/the wind/the beat etc picks up if someone's speed etc picks up, it increases or grows stronger 某人的速度/風力/節拍等增加[增強]: *The breeze had now picked up considerably.* 微風現在已颳得大起來了。

15 pick up speed/steam to go faster 加快速度: *The train was gradually picking up speed.* 火車逐漸加快了速度。

16 pick up the bill/tab (for sth) *informal* to pay for something【非正式】(為某物)付款: *Why should the taxpayer pick up the tab for a private company's mistakes?* 為甚麼納稅人要為一家私人公司的過錯所造成的損失付賬呢?

17 ►A COLOUR 顏色◄ [T **pick** sth ↔ **up**] if a colour or a piece of furniture picks up the colour of something else, it has small amounts of that colour in it〔顏色或家具〕有少量的…顏色: *I like the way the curtains pick up the red and yellow in the rug.* 我喜歡那些窗簾帶一點地毯中的紅色和黃色。

18 ►A CRIMINAL 罪犯◄ [T **pick** sb ↔ **up**] if the police or another organized group of people pick someone up, they find them and take them somewhere, to answer questions or to be locked up 逮捕; 拘捕: *The coastguard picked him up at Dover.* 海岸警衛隊員在多佛爾逮捕了他。| *She was picked up on prostitution charges.* 她因被控賣淫而遭拘捕。

19 pick up the pieces (of sth) if you pick up the pieces

of a business, relationship etc that has gone seriously wrong, you try to get it back to the point where it was before 重整旗鼓; 恢復正常; 重修舊好: *Small agricultural communities are picking up the pieces after the long depression.* 長時間的蕭條之後, 小型的農業社區正在重整旗鼓。
20 pick up the threads (of sth) if you pick up the threads of a relationship, a way of life, or an idea that has been interrupted, you try to return to it again 恢復〔被中斷的關係、生活方式、觀念〕: *When I got home after the war it wasn't so easy to pick up the threads of my ordinary life again.* 戰後我回到家中, 要重新過起普通人的生活可不那麼容易。

pick up on *phr v* [T] **1 [pick up on** sth] **a)** to notice something that other people do not notice 注意到〔別人沒有注意到的事物〕: *It was very smart of you to pick up on the undercurrents between those two.* 你注意到了那兩人之間潛在的不滿, 真是很聰明。**b)** to notice something and react to it 理解並作出反應: *I was trying to indicate that I didn't want to go, but they didn't pick up on it.* 我試圖暗示我不想去, 但他們沒有會意到這點。**c)** to return to a point or an idea that has been mentioned and discuss it further 重新回到〔已被提到的論點或觀點〕並作進一步討論: *Can I just pick up on your objections to the project?* 我能否回過頭來進一步談談你反對這項計劃的問題呢? **2 [pick** sb **up on** sth] to criticize someone slightly for something they have said〔因某人說了某種話而〕指責, 責備: *The Senator picked him up on his use of the word 'deception'.* 那位參議員因他使用了"欺騙"一詞而批評了他。

pick² *n* **1** [U] choice 挑選, 選擇: **take your pick** (=choose) 選擇, 挑選 *You can have any one you like – take your pick!* 你想要哪一個都行——自己挑吧! | **have your pick of** (=to be able to choose any one of a group of things) 任意挑選 *Sarah could have had her pick of any university in the country, but she chose her local college.* 莎拉原本可以挑選全國任何一所大學, 但她選擇了當地的一所大學。**2 the pick of sth** *informal* the best thing or things of a group【非正式】某物中的精華[最好的東西]: *It's the pick of this month's new movies.* 這是本月上映的新影片中最好的。| **the pick of the bunch** (=the best in the group) 一批中最好的, 出類拔萃者 *It's not much good, but it's the pick of the bunch.* 它雖不特別好, 但它是這一批中的佼佼者。**3** [C] *AmE informal* someone or something that is chosen from among other people or things【美, 非正式】挑選出來的人[物]: *Reno was able to name his own pick for the Criminal Division.* 雷諾可以自行挑選任命刑事組人員。**4** [C] a pickaxe 鎬, 鶴嘴鋤: *He put his pick and shovel over his shoulder.* 他把鎬和鏟扛在自己的肩膀上。**5** [C] *AmE informal* a small, flat object for pulling at the strings of an instrument such as a GUITAR; PLECTRUM【美, 非正式】〔撥結他等弦樂器用的〕撥子 —see also 另見 ICE PICK

pick·a·nin·ny /ˌpɪkəˈnɪnɪ; ˌpɪkəˈnɪni/ *n* [C] word for a small African child, used in the past but now considered very offensive 黑人小孩〔過去使用、現被認為是冒犯用語〕

pick·axe *BrE*【英】, **pickax** *AmE*【美】/ˈpɪkˏæks; ˈpɪkæks/ *n* [C] a large tool used for breaking up roads, which consists of a curved iron bar with a sharp point on each end and a long handle 鎬, 鶴嘴鋤

picked /pɪkt; pɪkt/ *adj* [only before noun 僅用於名詞前] chosen as being very suitable for a particular job or purpose 仔細挑選的, 精選的: *The assault group consisted of six picked men.* 突擊隊由六名精選出來的男子組成。—see also 另見 HANDPICKED

pick·er /ˈpɪkɚ; ˈpɪkə/ *n* [C] **cotton picker/fruit picker etc** a person or machine that picks things, especially crops 摘棉工[機]/摘水果工[機]: *Orange pickers are on strike in California.* 加利福尼亞的柑橘採摘工在罷工。

pick·et¹ /ˈpɪkɪt; ˈpɪkɪt/ *n* [C] **1** also 又作 **picket line** a group or line of people who stand or march in front of a shop, factory, government building etc to protest about something or to stop people from going in during a STRIKE〔罷工時設置的〕糾察隊; 糾察線: *a picket on the steps of the Federal court building* 聯邦法院大樓樓梯上的糾察隊 | *None of the workers crossed the picket lines.* 沒有一個工人越過糾察線。**2** one person in a picket 糾察隊員: *The pickets persuaded some drivers not to enter the factory.* 罷工糾察隊員勸阻一些司機不要進入工廠。—see also 另見 FLYING PICKET **3** a soldier or a group of soldiers with the special duty of guarding a military camp 警戒哨; 警戒隊: **picket duty** *Hanks, you're on picket duty tonight.* 漢克斯, 今晚該你放哨。

picket² *v* **1** [I,T] to stand or march in front of a shop, factory, government building etc to protest about something or to stop people from going in during a STRIKE 在…設置糾察隊, (派…) 擔任糾察隊員: *protesters picketing outside the White House gates* 在白宮門外擔任糾察員的抗議者 | **picket sth** *Miners picketed every pit for months.* 礦工已有好幾個月在每個礦井設置糾察隊了。**2** [T] to place soldiers around or near a place as guards 派士兵擔任警戒哨

picket fence /ˈ·· ˌ·/ *n* [C] *AmE* a fence made up of a line of strong pointed sticks fixed in the ground【美】〔用尖板條連成的〕尖樁籬柵, 柵欄, 籬笆 —see picture on page A4 參見 A4 頁圖

pick·ings /ˈpɪkɪŋz; ˈpɪkɪŋz/ *n* [plural] *informal*【非正式】**rich/easy pickings** money or profits that you can get easily 容易得來的錢[利潤]: *There were rich pickings to be had if you played the stock market.* 如果你玩股票, 就可輕而易舉地賺到許多錢。

pick·le¹ /ˈpɪkḷ; ˈpɪkəl/ *n* **1** [U] a strong-tasting liquid made with VINEGAR, used to preserve vegetables〔腌菜用的〕醋漬液 **2** [U] *BrE* a thick cold sauce eaten with food, made from pieces of vegetables preserved in VINEGAR【英】腌菜, 泡菜: *sweet pickle* 甜味泡菜 | *cheese and pickle sandwiches* 乾酪和腌菜三明治 **3** [C,U] *AmE* a CUCUMBER preserved in VINEGAR or salt water, or a slice of this【美】腌黃瓜 (片), 醋漬黃瓜 (片): *Would you like pickle on your cheeseburger?* 你的乾酪漢堡包上要配些腌黃瓜嗎? **4 be in a (pretty) pickle** *old-fashioned* to be in a difficult or confusing situation【過時】處於困境; 處於混亂境地

pickle² *v* [T] to preserve food in VINEGAR or salt water〔用醋或鹽水〕腌製〔食物〕; 腌漬: *pickled onions* 腌洋蔥

pick·led /ˈpɪkḷd; ˈpɪkəld/ *adj old-fashioned informal* drunk【過時, 非正式】醉的

pick-me-up /ˈ·· ˌ·/ *n* [C] *informal* something that makes you feel more cheerful and gives you more energy, especially a drink or medicine【非正式】興奮飲料, 提神的飲料[食品]; 興奮劑

pick·pock·et /ˈpɪkˌpɑkɪt; ˈpɪkˌpɒkɪt/ *n* [C] someone who steals things from people's pockets, especially in a crowd 扒手

pick-up /ˈ· ·/ *n* **1** [C] *especially AmE* a small open motor vehicle with low sides, used for carrying goods【尤美】敞篷小貨車: *We used the pick-up to carry the lumber to the building site.* 我們用敞篷小貨車把木材運到了建築工地。**2** [C] *informal* a stranger that you meet in a bar, at a party etc and spend a short time with, often in order to have sex【非正式】〔在酒吧、派對等中為調情而〕偶然結識的人; 勾搭的人 **3** [U] *AmE* the rate at which a vehicle can increase its speed; ACCELERATION【美】〔汽車的〕加速能力: *It was a tiny car, but it had good pick-up.* 這是一部很小的汽車, 但它有很好的加速能力。**4** [C] the part of a record player that receives and plays the sound from a record〔唱機的〕拾音器, 電唱頭

pick-up truck /ˈ·· ˌ·/ *n* [C] *AmE* a PICK-UP (1)【美】敞篷小貨車

pick·y /ˈpɪkɪ; ˈpɪki/ *adj AmE informal* someone who is picky only likes very particular things【美, 非正式】挑剔的: *a picky eater* 挑食的人 | *She's so picky about her clothes.* 她對穿甚麼衣服很挑剔。

picnic 野餐

pic·nic¹ /pɪknɪk; ˈpɪknɪk/ *n* [C] **1** an occasion when people take food and eat it outdoors, especially in the country 野餐: *We're having a picnic in the park this afternoon.* 今天下午我們要在公園野餐。| *a picnic basket* (=for carrying food for a picnic) 野餐食品籃 **2 be no picnic** *informal* to be difficult or unpleasant and need a lot of work【非正式】不是件輕鬆愉快的事: *Taking 60 kids to the museum will be no picnic!* 帶60個孩子去博物館不會是件輕鬆愉快的事! **3 picnic lunch/supper** *especially AmE* the food you take for a picnic【尤美】野外午餐/晚餐: *Vera packed a picnic lunch and headed for the river.* 薇拉把野外午餐裝好, 朝河邊走去。**4** *BrE* the food you take for a picnic【英】野餐用的食物: *We'll take a picnic with us.* 我們會帶野餐食物。

picnic² *v* **picnicked, picnicking** [I] to have a picnic 舉行野餐; 去郊遊野餐: *holidaymakers picnicking on the grass* 在草地上野餐的度假者 —**picnicker** *n* [C]

picnic ar·e·a /ˈ·· ˌ···/ *n* [C] an area near a road where people in cars can stop and have a picnic〔公路附近供開車的人停下野餐的〕野餐區

pic·to·ri·al /pɪkˋtɔrɪəl; pɪkˈtɔːriəl/ *adj* related to paintings, drawings, or photographs 畫的; 圖畫的; 圖片的

S1 W1 **pic·ture¹** /ˋpɪktʃɚ; ˈpɪktʃə/ *n*

1 ►IMAGE 影像◄ [C] a painting, drawing, or photograph 畫, 圖畫; 照片: *A picture of a waterfall hung on the wall.* 一幅瀑布畫掛在牆上。| *Get the children to draw a picture of their dream house.* 讓孩子畫出夢想中房子的圖畫。| *Gary got his picture in the papers.* 加里的照片上了報紙。

2 ►SITUATION 情況◄ [singular] the general situation in a place, organization etc〔某地方、組織等的〕情況, 局面: *The general picture appears to be of low levels of union membership.* 總體情況好像是工會會員的人數處於較低水平。| *the wider political picture* 更廣泛的政治局面

3 ►DESCRIPTION 描述◄ [C usually singular 一般用單數] a description that gives you an idea of what something is like 描述, 描繪; 描寫: [+of] *Archaeologists are trying to build up a picture of life in Mayan cities.* 考古學家正試圖再度呈現瑪雅人的城市生活。| **paint a picture** (=describe something in a particular way)〔以某種方式〕描述[繪] *Lee's film paints a bleak picture of life in the inner city.* 李的電影描繪了市中心的黯淡生活。

4 ►TELEVISION 電視◄ [C usually singular 一般用單數] the image that appears on a television or cinema SCREEN〔電視或電影的〕圖像, 畫面: *Something's wrong with the TV – the picture is blurry.* 這台電視機出毛病了——畫面模糊不清。

5 ►MENTAL IMAGE 頭腦中的形象◄ [C usually singular 一般用單數] an image or memory that you have in your mind〔腦中的〕形象; 印象: *I still have a vivid picture of the first time I saw Paris.* 我還清晰地記得我第一次見到巴黎時的情形。

6 take a picture to use a camera to take a photograph 拍一張照片: *Dad took a picture of us standing by a huge redwood tree.* 父親拍了一張我們站在一棵巨大紅杉樹旁的照片。

7 put sb in the picture to give someone information about something, so that they can understand it 使某人明白[了解]實情: *I've been away for a month so you'll have to put me in the picture.* 我離開了一個月, 所以你必須告知我詳情。

8 get the picture *especially spoken* to understand a situation【尤口】了解情況: *"Her parents are separated and she's being raised by her sister." "I get the picture."* "她的父母分居了, 她目前由她姐姐撫養。" "我明白了。"

9 out of the picture if someone is out of the picture, they are not involved in a situation 不相干; 不知情: *"Is Pam still with Eric?" "No, he's out of the picture."* "帕姆還和艾力克在一起嗎?" "不, 他已經和她不相干了。"

10 ►FILM 電影, 影片◄ **a)** [C] a word meaning a film, used especially by people in the film industry 電影〔尤被電影界人士使用〕: *It was voted the year's best picture.* 它被選為本年度最佳影片。**b) the pictures** *old-fashioned* the cinema【過時】電影院: *Do you want to go to the pictures on Saturday?* 星期六你想去電影院看電影嗎? | **be in pictures** (=act in films or work in making films) 從事電影[表演; 製作]工作

11 be the picture of health/innocence/despair etc to look very healthy, innocent etc 看上去很健康/天真/絕望等: *Head bowed and sobbing, she was the picture of misery.* 她低頭啜泣, 看上去非常痛苦。

12 the big picture *AmE informal* a situation considered as a whole, rather than its details【美, 非正式】整體情況, 大局: *Try and get an idea of the big picture before you suggest any changes.* 在你建議進行任何改變前, 盡量了解一下整體情況。

13 be/look a picture *especially BrE* to be beautiful or unusual to look at【尤英】美麗如畫, 漂亮; 看起來不尋常: *Madge's garden is a picture in the summer.* 瑪奇的花園在夏季美不勝收。—see also 另見 **pretty as a picture** (PRETTY² (8))

picture² *v* [T] **1** to imagine something, especially by creating an image in your mind 想像, 設想: **picture sb/sth as sth** *Rob had pictured her as kind of serious, but she wasn't like that at all.* 羅伯想像她有些嚴肅, 但她根本不是那樣。| **picture sb doing sth** *I really can't picture him skiing. He's so clumsy!* 我真的無法想像他滑雪的樣子, 他那麼笨拙! | **picture my surprise/horror/annoyance etc** (=used when saying how surprised, annoyed etc you were) 想像我有多麼驚奇/恐懼/煩惱等〔用於表示你有多麼驚奇、煩惱等〕*Picture my surprise on finding everyone had left!* 想像一下, 當我發現每個人都離開了, 我有多麼驚訝! **2** to show something or someone in a photograph, painting, or drawing 畫, 繪; 拍攝: *The billboard pictured a handsome, thirtyish man smoking a cigarette.* 在這個廣告牌上是一位三十歲左右的英俊男子在抽煙的照片。**3** [often passive 常用被動態] to describe something clearly〔清楚地〕描繪, 描述: *This situation is realistically pictured in the first chapter.* 第一章真實地描繪了這一狀況。

picture book /ˈ·· ·/ *n* [C] a children's book that has a lot of pictures and usually a simple story〔兒童看的〕圖畫書

picture card /ˈ·· ·/ *n* [C] a FACE CARD 花牌, 人頭牌

picture pal·ace /ˈ·· ˌ··/ *n* [C] *old-fashioned, especially BrE* a large building used for showing films to the public; CINEMA【過時, 尤英】電影院

picture-per·fect /ˌ·· ˈ··◄/ *adj AmE* exactly right in appearance or quality【美】外表[品質]完美的: *Doesn't the bride look picture-perfect?* 新娘子真是太漂亮了, 對嗎?

picture post·card /ˌ·· ˈ··/ *n* [C] *BrE* a POSTCARD with a photograph or picture on the front of it【英】〔印有照片或圖畫的〕明信片

picture-postcard /ˌ·· ˈ··◄/ *adj* [only before noun 僅用於名詞前] *BrE* very pretty【英】非常漂亮的: *picture-postcard villages* 風景如畫的村莊

picture rail /ˈ··· ·/ *n* [C] a long narrow piece of wood fixed high on a wall, from which pictures can be hung〔固定在牆的高處用來懸掛圖畫的〕掛鏡線, 畫鏡線

pic·tur·esque /ˌpɪktʃəˋrɛsk; ˌpɪktʃəˈresk◂/ *adj* **1** a place that is picturesque is pretty and interesting, especially in an old-fashioned way〔某個地方〕美麗的, 風景如畫的: *a picturesque New England village in the fall* 秋天風景如畫的新英格蘭村莊 **2** language that is picturesque uses unusual, interesting, or sometimes rude words to describe things〔語言〕生動的, 形象化的, 繪聲繪色的: *He gave a picturesque account of his trip to New York.* 他繪聲繪色地敍述了他的紐約之行。**3** someone who is picturesque looks or behaves in an interesting, unusual, or slightly strange way〔人的外表或行為〕奇特的, 獨特的, 不同尋常的: *a picturesque character with a long beard and a large pipe* 一個蓄着長鬍鬚、叼着大煙斗的奇人 —**picturesquely** *adv* —**picturesqueness** *n* [U]

picture win·dow /ˈ·· ˌ··/ *n* [C] a large window made of a single piece of glass〔一整塊大玻璃做的〕觀景窗

pid·dle /ˋpɪdḷ; ˈpɪdl/ *v* [I] *informal* to URINATE【非正式】撒尿

piddle around also 又作 **piddle about** *BrE*【英】*phr v* [I] *informal* to waste time doing unimportant things【非正式】做無關緊要的事情浪費時間; 混日子 —**piddle** *n* [U]

pid·dling /ˋpɪdlɪŋ; ˈpɪdlɪŋ/ *adj* small and unimportant 無關緊要的, 微不足道的; 瑣碎的: *I can't be bothered with all these piddling details.* 我不想為那些瑣碎的細節操心。

pid·gin /ˋpɪdʒɪn; ˈpɪdʒɨn/ *n* [C,U] **1** a language that is a mixture of two other languages and is used especially between people who do not speak each other's languages well〔兩種語言混合在一起的〕混雜語言, 洋涇浜語 **2** **pidgin English/French etc** English, French etc that is either not very good or is mixed with the words or grammar of another language 洋涇浜英語/法語等

2 **pie** /paɪ; paɪ/ *n* [C,U] **1** a sweet food usually made with fruit baked inside a PASTRY covering 水果餡餅: *apple pie* 蘋果餡餅[派] | *a slice of pie* 一塊餡餅 —compare 比較 TART[1] (1) **2** *especially BrE* a food made of meat or vegetables baked in a PASTRY covering【尤英】肉餡餅; 蔬菜餡餅: *He bought a pie for lunch.* 他買了個肉餡餅當午餐。| *steak and kidney pie* 牛排和腰子餡餅 **3** **slice/share/piece of the pie** a share of something such as money, profits etc〔錢、利潤等的〕一份: *The smaller companies want a bigger share of the pie.* 那些較小的公司想分到更大的一杯羹。**4** **pie in the sky** something good that someone is promising or suggesting, but which you do not think will happen 天上的餡餅, 不大可能實現的允諾[建議]: *The idea of full employment is just pie in the sky.* 充分就業的想法只不過是空中樓閣。—see also 另見 MUD PIE, PIE CHART, **easy as pie** (EASY[1] (1)), **eat humble pie** (HUMBLE[1] (6)), **have a finger in every pie** (FINGER[1] (11)), **be as nice as pie** (NICE (5))

pie·bald /ˋpaɪˌbɔld; ˈpaɪbɔːld/ *adj* a piebald animal has large areas of skin of two different colours, usually black and white〔動物〕有花斑的〔通常指有黑白斑點的〕—**piebald** *n* [C]

1 1 **piece**[1] /pis; piːs/ *n* [C]

1 ►**SEPARATE PART** 分離的部分◄ a part of something that has been separated, broken, or cut from the rest of it 碎塊, 碎片; 斷片, 切片: *She cut the cake into 8 pieces.* 她把蛋糕切成8塊。| **[+of]** *How many pieces of toast would you like?* 你想要幾片烤麪包? | *pieces of broken glass* 碎玻璃片 | **in pieces** (=broken into many pieces) 摔成碎片 *The vase had slipped and lay in pieces on the floor.* 那隻花瓶滑動了一下, 摔到地板上碎了。

2 ►**OBJECT** 物體◄ a single thing of a particular type, often one that is part of a set of things 一塊, 一片, 一件, 一張, 一首: *Each piece of clothing had her name written in it.* 每件衣服都寫上了她的名字。| *Can I have another piece of paper?* 再給我一張紙, 好嗎? | *a beautifully made piece of furniture* 做得很漂亮的一件家具 | **24-piece/60-piece etc** (=with 24, 60 etc pieces in the set) 24件/60件等的 *an 80-piece orchestra* 80人[80件樂器]組成的管弦樂隊

3 ►**CONNECTED PART** 相關聯的部分◄ one of several different parts that must be joined together to make something 部件, 部分: *Some of the jigsaw pieces are missing.* 這套拼圖的一些部分找不到了。| **in pieces** (=separated into pieces) 拆成部分 *The shelves are sold in pieces that you have to assemble.* 這些架子是以散件賣的, 你必須自己安裝。| **take sth to pieces** (=separate it into pieces) 把某物拆開 *We'll have to take the whole engine to pieces to fix it.* 我們必須把整個引擎拆開才能修理。| **come to pieces** (=be designed to be separated into pieces)〔被設計成〕可以拆開的 *The table comes to pieces so it's easy to deliver.* 那張桌子可以拆卸, 所以它很容易運送。

4 **piece of advice/information/gossip etc** some advice, information etc 一條建議/消息/流言蜚語等: *Let me give you a piece of advice – sell the car.* 讓我給你一點忠告——把那輛汽車賣掉吧。| *a juicy piece of gossip* 繪聲繪色的小道消息

5 **piece of luck/stupidity/willfulness etc** something lucky, stupid etc 幸運/愚蠢/任性等的事情: *Finding that store sure was a piece of luck.* 找到那家商店確實是件幸運的事。

6 ►**LAND** 土地◄ an area of land 一片土地: *The factory had been built on a piece of waste ground.* 該工廠建在一片廢棄的土地上。

7 **fall to pieces** to become very old and damaged 變舊並損壞: *All my clothes are falling to pieces.* 我所有的衣服都破損了。

8 **go to pieces** to be so upset or nervous that you cannot think or behave normally〔因傷心、緊張不安而〕崩潰, 垮掉: *We're looking for someone who won't go to pieces in a crisis.* 我們在尋找一個在危機時刻不會垮下來的人。

9 **smash/rip/tear sth to pieces** to damage something very severely 把某物摔成/撕成碎片; 徹底毀壞某物: *The city had been shot to pieces in the air strike.* 這個城市在空襲中遭到徹底的摧毀。| *In a rage, I tore the letter to pieces.* 我一怒之下把信撕得粉碎。

10 **pull/rip/tear sb to pieces** to criticize someone or their ideas very severely 把某人駁得體無完膚, 嚴厲批評某人[某人的觀點]: *After she had finished speaking, Hayes tore her to pieces.* 她説完之後, 海斯把她駁得一無是處。

11 **(all) in one piece** not damaged or injured 完好無損的: *Luckily the parcel arrived all in one piece.* 所幸的是, 那個包裹完好無損地送到了。| *The car was a wreck, but we got out in one piece.* 雖然那輛汽車受到嚴重損壞, 我們卻安然無恙地出來了。

12 **give sb a piece of your mind** *informal* to tell someone that you are very angry with them【非正式】告訴某人你很生他們的氣, 責備[申斥]某人

13 **be a piece of cake** *informal* to be very easy to do【非正式】很容易做的, 輕鬆的: *Learning to drive was a piece of cake for me.* 學開車對我來説是件很容易的事。

14 **a piece of the action** *informal* a share of the profits from a business activity, especially an illegal one【非正式】〔尤指從非法的商業活動中獲得的〕一份收益

15 **be (all) of a piece a)** to be the same as something else〔與...〕相似的,〔與...〕一樣的: *The testimony was all of a piece with Mandeville's version of events.* 那份證詞和曼德維爾對事件的敍述一致。**b)** to be the same in all parts 完全一樣: *The style of the book is all of a piece, both in illustrations and text.* 這本書無論是插圖還是文字, 都是統一的風格。

16 ►**MONEY** 錢◄ **a)** a coin of a particular value〔某種幣值的〕硬幣: **ten pence/fifty-cent etc piece** *Does anyone have change for a 50 pence piece?* 有誰能給我換50便士的零錢嗎? **b)** *old use* a coin【舊】硬幣: *30 pieces of silver* 30塊銀元

17 ►ART/MUSIC ETC 藝術/音樂等◄ something that has been produced by an artist, musician, or writer〔藝術家、音樂家或作家創作的〕作品: *The 1812 Overture is one of Tchaikovsky's finest pieces.*《1812序曲》是柴可夫斯基最好的作品之一。
18 ►IN A NEWSPAPER 報紙上◄ a short written ARTICLE (2) in a newspaper or magazine〔報紙或雜誌上的〕文章, 短文: *Did you see that piece in the Observer about censorship?* 你看到《觀察家》報上那篇有關審查制度的文章了嗎?
19 ►IN GAMES 遊戲中◄ a small object or figure used in playing games such as CHESS〔棋類遊戲等中的〕棋子
20 ►GUN 槍◄ *AmE slang* a small gun【美俚】小型的槍
21 be a piece of shit/crap *spoken* a rude way of saying that something is of very low quality【口】是一件廢物〔表示某物質量非常低劣的粗魯說法〕: *Why did you buy that car? It's a piece of crap!* 你為甚麼買那輛汽車? 那是一件廢物!
22 piece of ass *AmE* an offensive expression meaning a woman, used by men when they are talking about sex【美】女人, 雌兒〔男人談論性時的冒犯用語〕
23 a piece *AmE old-fashioned* a short distance away【美, 過時】〔路程的〕一小段: *The store is down the road a piece.* 沿着這條路往前走一小段就到那個商店了。—see also 另見 MUSEUM PIECE, PARTY PIECE, SET PIECE, **a nasty piece of work** (NASTY (6)), **pick up the pieces** (PICK UP (19)), **say your piece** (SAY[1] (2)), **the villain of the piece** (VILLAIN (3))

piece² *v*
piece sth ↔ **together** *phr v* [T] **1** to use all the facts or information you have about a situation in order to understand it〔把所有事實或信息〕拼湊起來: *Police are still trying to piece together his movements before the murder.* 警方還在設法拼湊他在謀殺案前的行動。**2** to put all the separate parts of an object into the correct order or position〔把物體的部件〕拼合起來: *He was slowly piecing together torn fragments of a letter.* 他正在慢慢地把撕碎的信拼起來。

pi·èce de ré·sis·tance /ˌpjɛs də ˌrezisˈtɑ̃s; piˌes də reziːˈstɑːns/ *n* [C] *French* the best or most important thing or event in a series, especially when it comes after all the others【法】最佳項目; 最重要的事件: *The pièce de résistance was an enormous birthday cake with 21 candles.* 最重要的東西是一個巨大的插着21支蠟燭的生日蛋糕。

piece·meal /ˈpisˌmil; ˈpiːsmiːl/ *adj* a process that is piecemeal happens slowly in separate unconnected stages and is not planned 一步一步的, 逐漸的, 逐個的: *The airport had been developed in a piecemeal fashion.* 這個機場是逐步發展起來的。—**piecemeal** *adv*: *The house was filled with odd furniture they'd bought piecemeal.* 那屋子裡滿是他們一件一件買來的不配套的家具。

piece rate /ˈ· ·/ *n* [C] an amount of money that is paid for each thing a worker produces 計件工資; 按件計酬: *The piece rate was $2.00 per skirt.* 每條裙子的計件工資為2美元。

pieces of eight /ˌ·· ˈ·/ *n* [plural] silver coins used in the past in Spain 西班牙古銀幣

piece·work /ˈpisˌwɝk; ˈpiːswɜːk/ *n* [U] work that is paid according to the number of things you complete or produce rather than the number of hours you work 按件計酬的工作, 計件工作

pie chart /ˈ· ˌ·/ *n* [C] a circle divided into several parts that shows how something such as an amount of money or the population is divided 圓形統計圖, 餅分圖〔以大小扇形表示比例〕—see picture at 參見 CHART[1] 圖

pie crust /ˈ· ·/ *n* [C,U] the PASTRY (1) that is underneath and sometimes covering the meat or fruit in a PIE 餡餅皮

pied /paɪd; paɪd/ *adj* [only before noun 僅用於名詞前] a pied animal, especially a bird, has two colours on its feathers or fur, usually black and white〔尤指某些鳥〕雜色的;〔通常為〕黑白的

pied-à-terre /ˌpjed ɑ ˈtɛr; ˌpjeɪd æ ˈteə/ *n* [C] *French* a small apartment or house that is not your main home but which you own and stay in sometimes【法】備用小公寓, 臨時寓所: *The Maines keep a pied-à-terre in London for theatre evenings.* 梅因一家在倫敦有一所備用房屋供看戲時過夜。

pie-eyed /ˈpaɪ ˌaɪd; ˌpaɪ ˈaɪd◄/ *adj old-fashioned* very drunk【過時】喝醉了的

pier /pɪr; pɪə/ *n* [C] **1** a structure that is built out into the water so that boats can stop next to it〔伸向海中的〕突堤碼頭; 凸式碼頭: *The troop transport ship docked at Pier Five.* 運兵船停靠在五號碼頭。—compare 比較 JETTY **2** *especially BrE* a structure that is built out into the sea and has small buildings on it where people can eat, play games, and enjoy themselves【尤英】〔伸入海中, 上面有小型建築物供人們遊樂的〕突堤, 長堤: *Brighton pier* 布賴頓長堤 | *a concert on the pier* 在長堤上舉行的音樂會 —compare 比較 BOARDWALK **3** a thick post of stone, wood, or metal used to support something such as a bridge〔石頭、木頭或金屬的〕橋墩, 支柱

pierce /pɪrs; pɪəs/ *v* [T] **1** to make a small hole in or through something using an object with a sharp point 刺入, 刺穿, 刺破: *Maybe you can pierce another hole in your belt.* 也許你可以在皮帶上再穿一個洞。| *Steam the corn until it can easily be pierced by a fork.* 把玉米蒸到可以用叉子一扎就破的程度。**2 have your ears/nose etc pierced** to have a small hole made in your ears, nose etc so that you can wear jewellery 給耳朵/鼻子等穿孔 **3** if sound, light, pain etc pierces something you can suddenly hear it, see it, or feel it〔聲音、光、痛苦等〕被突然聽到〔看到、感覺到〕: *The sun finally pierced the haze and the day was beautiful.* 太陽終於劃破了陰霾, 天色很美。| *A sudden scream pierced the air.* 突然一聲尖叫劃破了長空。**4 pierced ear/nose etc** a part of your body that has had small holes made in it so that you can wear jewellery 穿了孔的耳朵/鼻子等

pierc·ing /ˈpɪrsɪŋ; ˈpɪəsɪŋ/ *adj*
1 ►SOUND 聲音◄ high, sharp, and usually unpleasant 尖銳的, 刺耳的: *Raimundo grinned and let out a piercing whistle.* 雷蒙多咧嘴一笑, 接着發出一聲刺耳的口哨聲。
2 ►COLD/WIND 寒冷/風◄ very cold and seeming to cut through your clothes 凜冽的, 刺骨的: *The wind whipped off the water with a piercing bite.* 凜冽刺骨的寒風掠過水面。
3 ►EYES/LOOK 眼睛/目光◄ seeming to examine things and notice and understand more than other people would 敏銳的, 銳利的, 有洞察力的: *Her piercing brown eyes scanned their faces.* 她犀利的棕色眼睛掃視了他們的臉。
4 ►REMARK/QUESTION 評論/問題◄ piercing questions, criticisms etc seem to notice and express the main point of something very clearly 深刻的, 尖銳的, 直指要害的
5 ►EMOTION 感情◄ affecting your emotions very much, especially in a sad way 強烈的〔尤指傷心的〕: *She had a piercing vision of what life would be like without David.* 她很擔心沒有大衛生活將會怎麼過。—**piercingly** *adv*

pier·rot /ˈpiəro; ˈpɪərəʊ/ *n* [C] a CLOWN with white clothes and a white painted face〔穿白衣、塗白臉的〕丑角, 小丑

pi·e·ty /ˈpaɪətɪ; ˈpaɪəti/ *n* [U] respect for God and religion, often shown in the way you behave 虔誠, 虔敬 —opposite 反義詞 IMPIETY —see also 另見 PIOUS

pie·zo·e·lec·tric /paɪˌizo·ɪˈlɛktrɪk; ˌpiːzəʊ-ɪˈlektrɪk◄/ *adj* operated by electricity which is produced by pressure on a CRYSTAL 壓電的

pif·fle /ˈpɪfl; ˈpɪfəl/ *n* [U] *BrE old-fashioned* nonsense【英, 過時】廢話, 無聊話; 胡說

pif·fling /ˈpɪflɪŋ; ˈpɪflɪŋ/ *adj BrE old-fashioned* unimportant or useless【英, 過時】不重要的; 無用的: *Even these sums seem piffling in comparison.* 相比之下, 甚至這些錢也顯得微不足道。

pig[1] /pɪg; pɪg/ *n* [C]
1 ▶ANIMAL 動物◀ a farm animal that is usually pink or black and has short legs, a fat body, and a curved tail 豬 —see also 另見 GUINEA PIG (1)
2 ▶PERSON 人◀ *spoken*【口】**a)** someone who eats too much or eats more than their share 貪吃的人: *Greedy pig, you ate all the candy!* 貪吃的傢伙, 你把所有的糖果都吃了! **b)** someone who is very dirty or untidy 不整潔的人, 骯髒的人: *How can you live in this mess? You're such a pig!* 你怎麼能住在這麼亂的地方? 你可真髒! **c)** someone who is unpleasant or offensive 令人討厭的人; 無禮的人: *You're a selfish pig.* 你是個自私鬼。| **male chauvinist pig** (=unpleasant man who thinks women are not equal to men) 大男子主義者
3 ▶POLICE 警察◀ *slang* an insulting word meaning a police officer【俚】警察豬玀〔對警察的侮辱性稱呼〕
4 a pig (of a...) *BrE spoken* something that is very difficult or unpleasant to do【英口】困難的事情; 討厭的事: *Stripping wallpaper is a pig of a job.* 撕去牆紙是件令人討厭的工作。
5 make a pig's ear of *BrE spoken* to do something very badly【英口】把…弄糟: *Jon's made a complete pig's ear of the decorating.* 喬恩把裝修完全搞砸了。—see also 另見 **in a pig's eye** (EYE[1] (21))

pig[2] *v* [I,T] *BrE spoken* to eat a lot of food, even when you are not very hungry【英口】狼吞虎嚥, 貪婪地吃: *There's no ice cream left, Tony pigged the lot.* 冰淇淋沒有了, 東尼把它全吃了。
pig out *phr v* [I] *informal* to eat a lot of food【非正式】大吃大喝, 狼吞虎嚥: *We pigged out on pizza and beer.* 我們大吃比薩餅, 大喝啤酒。

pi·geon /ˋpɪdʒən; ˈpɪdʒɨn/ *n* **1** [C] a grey bird with short legs that is common in cities 鴿子 **2 sb's pigeon** *BrE old-fashioned* something that a particular person is responsible for【英, 過時】某人的職責[事務]: *It's not my pigeon – someone else can deal with it.* 那不是我的事, 別人會處理的。—see also 另見 CARRIER PIGEON, CLAY PIGEON SHOOTING, HOMING PIGEON

pigeon-chest·ed /ˌ‥ ˈ‥◂/ *adj* someone who is pigeon-chested has a narrow chest that sticks out〔人〕雞胸的

pi·geon·hole[1] /ˋpɪdʒənˌhol; ˈpɪdʒɨnhəʊl/ *n* [C] **1** one of a set of small boxes built into a desk or into a frame on a wall, in which letters or papers can be put〔辦公桌上或牆上的〕鴿籠式分類架, 信件格, 文件格 **2 put sb/sth into a pigeonhole** to have a very fixed idea about a person, activity etc, which is too simple and therefore unfair 把某人/某物簡單分類

pigeonhole[2] *v* [T] to consider a person, activity etc as belonging to a particular type or group, in a way that is too simple and therefore unfair; CATEGORIZE 把〔某人或某活動等〕簡單分類, 把…歸檔: *People tend to pigeonhole her just because she's a feminist.* 只因為她是個女權主義者, 人們往往將她簡單地對號入座。

pigeon-toed /ˈ‥ ˌ/ *adj* someone who is pigeon-toed has feet that point inwards rather than straight forwards〔人〕腳向內彎的, 內八字的

pig·ge·ry /ˋpɪgərɪ; ˈpɪgəri/ *n* [C] *BrE*【英】**1** a pig farm 養豬場 **2** a place where pigs are kept, usually with a building and an outdoor area; PIGSTY (1) 豬圈, 豬欄

pig·gish /ˋpɪgɪʃ; ˈpɪgɪʃ/ *adj* someone who is piggish eats too much or is dirty, or is unpleasant 貪吃的; 骯髒的, 邋遢的; 令人討厭的: *piggish behaviour* 令人生厭的行為 —**piggishly** *adv* —**piggishness** *n* [U]

pig·gy[1] /ˋpɪgɪ; ˈpɪgi/ *n* [C] **1** a word meaning a pig, used especially by or to children 豬仔, 小豬〔尤用作兒語〕**2 piggy in the middle** *BrE*【英】**a)** *informal* someone who is between two opposing groups or people and is unable to influence either side【非正式】〔夾在對立雙方之間而又無法影響任何一方的〕夾在中間的人 **b)** a game in which a ball is thrown between two people who try to prevent a third person in the middle from catching it 擲球遊戲〔兩個人互相擲球盡量不讓中間的第三人接到球的遊戲〕; KEEP-AWAY *AmE*【美】

piggy[2] *adj* **1** like a pig 豬似的: *little piggy eyes* 豬似的小眼睛 **2** *informal* wanting or taking more food than you really need; GREEDY【非正式】貪婪的, 貪吃的: *Don't be so piggy, Ed.* 別這麼貪吃, 艾德。

pig·gy·back[1] /ˋpɪgɪˌbæk; ˈpɪgibæk/ *n* [C] a ride on someone's back or shoulders 騎在…的背[肩]上, 馱, 扛: *Please, Uncle Jack, give me a piggyback!* 求求你了, 傑克叔叔, 揹我一下嘛! —**piggyback** *adv*

piggyback 騎在…的背[肩]上

piggyback[2] *v* [I] *AmE informal* to join or be joined with something that is larger, more important or more effective【美, 非正式】〔與更大、更重要、更有效的東西〕連接起來, 附帶出現[發生]: [+on/onto] *videos that simply piggyback onto the success of proven TV programs* 僅隨公認成功的電視節目而附帶出現的錄影帶

piggy-bank /ˈ‥ ˌ/ *n* [C] a small container, usually in the shape of a pig, in which children can save coins〔豬形〕儲錢罐, 撲滿

pig·head·ed /ˋpɪgˋhɛdɪd; ˌpɪgˈhedɨd◂/ *adj* determined to do things the way you want and refusing to change your mind, even when there are good reasons to do so; STUBBORN 頑固的, 固執的: *Stop being so pigheaded and admit that you were wrong!* 別再這麼固執了, 承認你錯了吧! —**pigheadedly** *adv* —**pigheadedness** *n* [U]

pig i·ron /ˈ· ˌ‥/ *n* [U] a form of iron that is not pure, obtained directly from a BLAST FURNACE 生鐵

pig·let /ˋpɪglɪt; ˈpɪglɨt/ *n* [C] a young pig 小豬, 豬仔

pig·ment /ˋpɪgmənt; ˈpɪgmənt/ *n* [C,U] **1** a dry coloured powder that is mixed with oil, water etc to make paint 顏料(粉) **2** one of the natural substances in humans, plants, and animals that gives colour to skin, blood, hair etc〔人和動植物的〕天然色素

pig·men·ta·tion /ˌpɪgmənˋteʃən; ˌpɪgmənˈteɪʃən/ *n* [U] **1** the colouring of plant or animal cells caused by too much pigment 色素沉着 **2** the colouring of living things〔生物的〕天然顏色: *Pigmentation is biologically inherited.* 生物體的天然顏色是遺傳的。

pig·my /ˋpɪgmɪ; ˈpɪgmi/ *n* [C] another spelling of PYGMY pygmy 的另一種拼法

pig·pen /ˋpɪgpɛn; ˈpɪgpen/ *n* [C] *AmE*【美】**1** a place where pigs are kept, usually with a building and an outdoor area; PIGSTY 豬圈, 豬欄 **2** *informal* a very dirty or untidy place; PIGSTY (2)【非正式】非常骯髒的地方

pig·skin /ˋpɪgˌskɪn; ˈpɪgˌskɪn/ *n* **1** [U] leather made from the skin of a pig 豬皮(革) **2** [singular] *AmE informal* the ball used in American football【美, 非正式】橄欖球: *tossing the pigskin around* 把橄欖球擲來擲去

pig·sty /ˋpɪgˌstaɪ; ˈpɪgstaɪ/ *n* [C] **1** a place where pigs are kept, usually with a building and an outdoor area 豬圈, 豬欄 **2** a very dirty or untidy place 非常骯髒的地方: *Clean up your room. It's a pigsty!* 清掃一下你的房間, 簡直太髒了!

pig·swill /ˋpɪgˌswɪl; ˈpɪgˌswɪl/ *n* [U] *BrE* **1** food that is given to pigs 豬食, 泔水, 潲水 **2** tasteless or unpleasant food 無味的食物; 難吃的食物

pig·tail /ˋpɪgˌtel; ˈpɪgteɪl/ *n* [C] **1** one of two lengths of hair that have been pulled together on either side of the head and usually plaited (PLAIT[1]), worn especially by very young girls 女孩垂在頭兩側的長髮〔通常編着〕, 髮辮: **in pigtails** *Jenny wore her hair in pigtails.* 珍妮梳着辮子。

2 all of the hair pulled to the back of the head and plaited so that it hangs down 辮子〔指獨辮〕; BRAID[1] (2) *AmE* 【美】—compare 比較 BUNCH[1] (5), PLAIT[2], PONYTAIL —see picture at 參見 HAIRSTYLE 圖

pike /paɪk; paɪk/ *n* [C] **1** a large fish that eats other fish and lives in rivers and lakes 狗魚 **2** a TURNPIKE（收費）高速公路 **3** a long-handled weapon used in the past by soldiers〔古時士兵使用的〕長矛, 長槍 **4** *NEngE* a mountain or hill with a pointed top【英格蘭北】尖峯: *Scafell Pike* 斯科費爾峯

pike·man /ˋpaɪkmən; ˈpaɪkmən/ *n* [C] a soldier who fought in the past with a pike〔舊時的〕長矛兵

pike·staff /ˋpaɪkˌstæf; ˈpaɪkstɑːf/ *n* [C] the long wooden handle of a pike (PIKE (3)) 長矛柄, 長槍柄

pi·laff, pilaf /pəˋlɑf; ˈpiːlæf/ *n* [C,U] a pilau（菜）肉飯

pi·las·ter /pəˋlæstɚ; pḭˈlæstə/ *n* [C] a square COLUMN that sticks out partly beyond the wall of a building and is usually only a decoration〔裝飾性的〕壁柱, 半露柱

pi·lau /pɪˋlo; ˈpiːlaʊ/ *n* [C,U] a dish made from rice mixed with vegetables and often meat（菜）肉飯〔由大米加蔬菜和肉煮成〕: *mushroom pilau* 磨菇肉飯

pil·chard /ˋpɪltʃɚd; ˈpɪltʃəd/ *n* [C] a small fish that lives in the sea and can be eaten 沙丁魚: *pilchards in tomato sauce* 番茄醬沙丁魚

2 **pile¹** /paɪl; paɪl/ *n*

1 ►LARGE AMOUNT/MASS 大量◄ [C] **a)** a tidy collection of several things of the same kind placed on top of each other; STACK[1] (1)〔由同類東西堆成的整齊的〕堆, 疊, 摞: *We put the newspapers in piles on the floor.* 我們把報紙在地板上堆疊起來。| *The record I want is at the bottom of the pile.* 我要的那張唱片在這一摞的最底層。| **[+of]** *a pile of blankets* 一疊毯子 —compare 比較 HEAP[1] (1) **b)** a large mass of things collected together 一大堆: *big pile of brushwood* 一大堆柴枝

2 a pile of also 又作 **piles of** *informal* a lot of something【非正式】一大堆, 大量: *I've got piles of work to do this evening.* 我今晚有一大堆事情要做。

3 at the bottom of the pile in a very weak position in society or in an organization 處於〔社會或組織的〕底層: *At the bottom of the pile are young people in their first jobs.* 處於底層的是那些剛開始工作的年輕人。

4 ►CLOTH/CARPETS 布料/地毯◄ [C,U] the soft surface of short threads on a CARPET or some types of cloth, especially VELVET〔地毯、某些布料上的, 尤指天鵝絨〕絨面: *a deep pile carpet* 厚絨地毯 —compare 比較 NAP[1] (2)

5 ►POST 柱; 樁◄ [C] a heavy post made of wood, stone, or metal, pushed into the ground as a support for a building, bridge etc〔建築物、橋梁等的〕柱, 樁

6 make a/your pile *informal* to make a lot of money【非正式】賺很多錢, 發財: *He made his pile in the antiques business.* 他做古董生意賺了大錢。

7 ►BUILDING 建築物◄ [C] *especially BrE* a large tall old building or group of buildings【尤英】高大的古建築物; 建築羣: *They live in a rambling Victorian pile.* 他們居住在佈局零亂的維多利亞式建築羣中。

8 ►MEDICAL 醫藥的◄ **piles** *BrE not technical* HAEMORRHOIDS【英, 非術語】痔(瘡)

pile² *v* **1** also 又作 **pile up** [T] to make a pile by collecting things together; STACK[2] (1) 把…堆積[堆疊]起來: *Ma stacked the cups and piled the plates.* 媽媽把杯子和盤子摞好。| *We piled the books up on the table.* 我們把書堆放在桌子上。| **pile sth high** (=make a tall pile) 高高地堆起 *Clothes were piled high on the chair.* 衣服高高地堆放在椅子上。**2** [T] to fill something or cover a surface with a lot of something 把…堆放在; 塞滿, 堆滿: *Anna piled spaghetti onto her plate.* 安娜把意大利麵條堆在她的碟子裡。| **be piled (high) with** *The cart was piled high with fruit and vegetables.* 馬車上堆滿了水果和蔬菜。

pile in/into sth *phr v* [T] to go quickly into a place or vehicle in a disorganized way 擁進, 擠進, 蜂擁進入: *We all piled into the back of his car.* 我們一窩蜂地擠進他車子的後座。

pile on *phr v* [T] *informal*【非正式】**1 pile on the praise/criticism etc** also 又作 **pile it on** to talk about something in a way that makes it seem much better or much worse than it really is; EXAGGERATE 過分地稱讚/批評等: *Mitch was really piling on the compliments!* 米奇確實恭維得過分了！| *It can't be that bad – Nellie tends to pile it on.* 情況不可能那麼糟 — 內莉往往誇大其詞。**2 pile on the agony** *BrE* to enjoy making something seem worse than it really is【英】大肆渲染壞的情況, 過分誇大壞的情況

pile out *phr v* [I] to quickly leave a place or get out of a vehicle in a rather disorderly way 擠出, 蜂擁而出: **[+of]** *As soon as the bell went the kids piled out of the building.* 鈴聲一響, 孩子們就一窩蜂地從大樓裡出來了。

pile up *phr v* [I,T] to become much larger in quantity or amount, or to make something do this; ACCUMULATE（使）堆積,（使）積累: *Work is really piling up.* 工作確實越積越多。| **pile** sth **↔ up** *Greg has managed to pile up enormous debts.* 格雷格已負債累累。—see also 另見 PILE-UP

pile driv·er /ˈ· ˌ··/ *n* [C] **1** a machine for pushing heavy posts into the ground 打樁機 **2** *informal* a very hard PUNCH[2] (1), especially in BOXING【非正式】〔尤指拳擊中的〕重(重一)擊

pile-up /ˈ· ·/ *n* [C] *informal* a road traffic accident in which several vehicles crash into each other【非正式】多車相撞, 連環撞車: *There had been several motorway pile-ups in the fog.* 霧中高速公路上發生了幾起連環撞車事故。

pil·fer /ˋpɪlfɚ; ˈpɪlfə/ *v* [I,T] to steal small amounts of things, or things that are not worth much, especially from the place where you work〔尤指從工作的地方〕偷竊〔少量或不值錢的東西〕, 小偷小摸: *They'd been caught pilfering building materials from the construction site.* 他們在從建築工地偷竊建築材料時被當場抓住。—**pilferer** *n* [C] —**pilfering** *n* [U]

pil·grim /ˋpɪlgrɪm; ˈpɪlgrḭm/ *n* [C] someone who travels a long way to a holy place for a religious reason 朝聖者, 香客: *pilgrims at Lourdes* 盧爾德的朝聖者

pil·grim·age /ˋpɪlgrəmɪdʒ; ˈpɪlgrḭmɪdʒ/ *n* [C,U] **1** a journey to a holy place for religious reasons 朝聖者的旅程: *a pilgrimage to Mecca* 去麥加朝聖 **2** a journey to a place connected with someone or something famous〔去因某人或某物而有名的地方〕旅行: *Elvis Presley's home has become a place of pilgrimage.* 艾爾維斯·皮禮士利的家已成了人們參觀的地方。

Pilgrim Fa·thers /ˌ·· ˈ··/ *n* **the Pilgrim Fathers** the group of English people who arrived to settle at Plymouth, Massachusetts in the US in 1620 清教徒前輩移民〔1620年到達美洲創立普利茅斯殖民地的英國移民〕

pill /pɪl; pɪl/ *n* **1** [C] a small solid piece of medicine, that 3
you swallow whole 藥丸; 藥片: *He has to take pills to control his blood pressure.* 他必須服藥控制他的血壓。| *sleeping pills* 安眠藥 **2 the Pill** a pill taken regularly by some women in order to prevent them having babies〔女用〕口服避孕藥: **on the Pill** *My doctor advised me to go on the Pill.* 我的醫生建議我口服避孕藥。**3 sugar the pill** *BrE*【英】, **sweeten the pill** *AmE*【美】to do something to make an unpleasant job or situation less unpleasant for the person who has to accept it 給藥丸加糖衣, 使不愉快的工作[局面]變得較易接受 **4** *AmE informal* someone who annoys you, often a child【美, 非正式】令人討厭的人〔通常指小孩〕: *Luke can be a real pill sometimes.* 路加有時候確實很討厭。—see also 另見 **a bitter pill (to swallow)** (BITTER[1] (7)), MORNING-AFTER PILL

pil·lage /ˋpɪlɪdʒ; ˈpɪlɪdʒ/ *v* [I,T] if an army pillages a place, it uses violence to steal from and damage a place that it has taken control of in a war; PLUNDER[1]〔軍隊〕搶劫, 劫掠, 掠奪 —compare 比較 LOOT[2] —**pillage** *n* [U] —**pillager** *n* [C]

pil·lar /ˈpɪlɚ; ˈpɪlə/ *n* [C] **1 a)** a tall upright round post used as a support for a roof 房柱, 柱子: *Huge pillars support the cathedral roof.* 巨大的柱子支撐着大教堂的屋頂。—see picture on page A4 參見A4頁圖 **b)** a tall upright round post, usually made of stone, put up to remind people of an important person or event〔通常為石製的〕紀念柱 **2 pillar of the community/church etc** an active and important member of a group, organization etc 社區/教會等的活躍而重要的成員[棟梁、中堅分子] **3** a very important part of a system of beliefs, especially religious beliefs〔尤指宗教信仰的〕非常重要部分: *These tenets are the pillars on which our faith is founded.* 這些信條是我們信仰得以建立的基礎。**4 be driven/passed from pillar to post** to go from one difficult situation to another without achieving much 到處碰壁, 走投無路 **5 pillar of dust/smoke/flame etc** a tall upright mass of dust, smoke, flame etc 一縷灰塵/煙柱/火柱等

pillar box /ˈ·· ·/ *n* [C] *old-fashioned* a large red tube-shaped box for posting letters that stands on streets in Britain【過時】〔英國的〕郵筒, 信筒 —compare 比較 LETTERBOX (2)

pill·box /ˈpɪl͵bɑks; ˈpɪlbɒks/ *n* [C] **1** a small round box for holding pills (PILL (1))〔圓形〕藥丸盒, 藥片盒 **2** a small, strong, usually circular shelter with a gun inside it, built as a defence 碉堡, 堅固的機槍掩體 **3** also 又作 **pillbox hat** /͵·· ˈ·/ a small round hat for a woman〔女人的〕圓形小帽

pil·lion /ˈpɪljən; ˈpɪljən/ *n* [C] **1** a seat for a second person behind the driver of a motorcycle or a rider on a horse 摩托車後座;〔馬鞍後的〕附座, 加鞍 **2 ride pillion** to sit behind someone who is driving a motorcycle or riding a horse 騎在摩托車後座上; 騎在馬的後鞍上

pil·lock /ˈpɪlək; ˈpɪlək/ *n* [C] *BrE slang* a very stupid person【英俚】非常愚蠢的人

pil·lo·ry¹ /ˈpɪlərɪ; ˈpɪləri/ *v* [T usually passive 一般用被動態] if someone is pilloried, they are publicly criticized by a lot of people 使〔某人〕受公眾責備: *The education secretary was pilloried by the press for his latest proposals.* 教育部長因他最近的提議而受到新聞界公開的批評。

pillory² *n* [C] a wooden frame with holes for the head and hands to be locked into, used in the past as a way of publicly punishing someone 頸手枷〔將罪犯的頸和手枷住示眾的古代刑具〕—compare 比較 **the stocks** (STOCK¹ (14))

S3 **pil·low¹** /ˈpɪlo; ˈpɪləʊ/ *n* [C] **1** a cloth bag filled with soft material, that you put your head on when you are sleeping 枕頭 —compare 比較 CUSHION¹ (1) **2** any object used to support your head while you are sleeping 用作枕頭的東西: *Paula used her rucksack as a pillow.* 柏拉把背包當作枕頭。**3 pillow fight** a game in which children hit each other with pillows 枕頭戰〔小孩玩的遊戲, 即用枕頭互相打鬧〕**4 pillow talk** *informal* conversation between lovers in bed【非正式】〔情人間的〕枕邊話

pillow² *v* [T] to rest your head somewhere, especially so that you can go to sleep〔尤指為睡覺而〕把〔頭〕枕在…: **pillow your head on sth** *Don fell asleep with his head pillowed on a sack.* 唐把頭枕在一個麻袋上睡着了。

pil·low·case, pillow case /ˈpɪlo͵kes; ˈpɪləʊkeɪs/ *n* [C] a cloth cover for a pillow 枕頭套

S3 **pi·lot¹** /ˈpaɪlət; ˈpaɪlət/ *n* [C] **1** someone who operates the controls of an aircraft or spacecraft〔飛機、宇宙飛船上的〕駕駛員, 飛行員: *an airline pilot* 航空公司機師 **2** someone with a special knowledge of a particular area of water, who is employed to guide ships across it〔船舶的〕領航員: *a harbour pilot* 海港領航員 **3** a television programme that is made in order to test whether people like it and would watch it〔為測試觀眾是否喜歡和觀看的〕電視試播節目 **4 pilot test/project/scheme etc** a test that is done to see if an idea, product etc will be successful 小規模試驗/試點項目/試驗性計劃等: *If the pilot survey goes well, we'll go into full production.* 如果這次試銷調查順利的話, 我們將投入全面生產。—see also 另見 AUTOMATIC PILOT

pilot² *v* [T] **1** to guide an aircraft, spacecraft, or ship as its pilot 駕駛〔飛機或宇宙飛船〕; 給〔船舶〕領航 **2** to help someone to go to a place 引領, 帶領, 指引: **pilot sb toward/out etc** *He took my hand and piloted me through the corridors.* 他拉着我的手領着我穿過走廊。**3** to be responsible for making sure that a new law or plan is officially approved 使〔新的法律、計劃〕順利通過: **pilot sth through** *I'm relying on your skill in piloting this through Parliament.* 我要靠你的技巧使它得以在議會順利通過。**4** to test a new idea, product etc on people to find out whether it will be successful 試用〔新想法、新產品等〕, 試行: *They are piloting parts of the book in language schools.* 他們正在語言學校試用這本書的一些部分。

pilot light /ˈ·· ·/ also 又作 **pilot burner** *n* [C] **1** a small gas flame that burns all the time and is used for lighting larger gas burners〔用於點燃大煤氣用具的〕常燃引火小火苗 **2** a small electric light on a piece of electrical equipment that shows when it is turned on〔電器上顯示通電的〕指示燈, 信號燈

pilot of·fi·cer /ˈ·· ͵···/ *n* [C] a middle rank in the Royal Air Force, or someone who has this rank 英國皇家空軍少尉(軍階) —see table on page C7 參見C7頁附錄

pi·men·to also 又作 **pimiento** /pɪˈmɛnto; pɪ̩ˈmentəʊ/ *n* [C,U] a small red PEPPER often used for putting inside OLIVES 甜辣椒, 番椒

pimp /pɪmp; pɪmp/ *n* [C] a man who makes money by controlling PROSTITUTES (=women who have sex with men for money) 拉皮條的男子, 妓院男老闆 —**pimp** *v* [I]

pim·per·nel /ˈpɪmpɚ͵nɛl; ˈpɪmpənel/ *n* [C] a small wild plant with flowers that are blue, white, or especially red 海綠〔矮小野生植物, 開藍色白色、尤其是紅色的花〕

pim·ple /ˈpɪmpl̩; ˈpɪmpəl/ *n* [C] a small raised red spot on your skin, especially on your face〔尤指長在臉上的〕丘疹, 小膿疱, 粉刺 —see also 另見 GOOSE PIMPLES —**pimpled** *adj* —**pimply** *adj*

PIN /pɪn; pɪn/ also 又作 **PIN num·ber** /ˈ· ͵··/ *n* [C] Personal Identification Number; a number that you use when you get money from a CASHPOINT using a plastic card 個人身分識別號碼, 私人密碼〔用銀行卡在自動提款機上取款時的密碼〕

pins 針

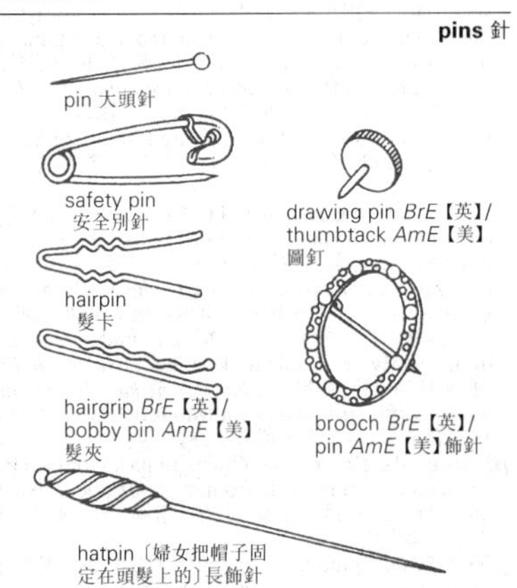

S3 **pin¹** /pɪn; pɪn/ *n* [C]
1 ►FOR CLOTH 用於布料◄ a short thin piece of metal

with a sharp point at one end, used especially for fastening together pieces of cloth while making clothes〔尤在做衣服時固定布料用的〕別針, 大頭針

2 ▶JEWELLERY 首飾◀ a) *AmE* an attractively shaped piece of metal, sometimes containing jewels, that you fasten to your clothes and wear as a decoration【美】胸針; BROOCH *BrE*【英】**b)** *BrE* a short thin piece of metal with a decoration at one end, used as jewellery【英】〔一端有裝飾的〕飾針

3 ▶ELECTRICAL 電的◀ one of the pieces of metal that sticks out of an electric PLUG〔電器插頭的〕插腳: *a three-pin plug* 三腳插頭

4 ▶FOR SUPPORT 用於支撐◀ a thin piece of metal or wood used as a support for something, or to fasten things together〔用於支撐或固定物品的〕釘, 楔, 銷, 栓: *When I broke my leg, I had to have a pin inserted.* 我把腿折斷後, 需植入一根鋼釘。

5 ▶GAMES 遊戲◀ one of the bottle-shaped objects that you try to knock down in a game of BOWLING〔保齡球運動中的〕球柱

6 you could hear a pin drop *spoken* used to say that it is very quiet and no one is speaking【口】靜得可以聽到針掉下來的聲音〔用於表示非常安靜〕

7 for two pins I'd ... *BrE old-fashioned* used to say that you would like to do something to someone because they have annoyed you【英, 過時】恨不得, 巴不得〔用於表示你想要對惹惱你的人做某事〕: *For two pins, I'd tell him to get lost.* 我真想叫他滾開。

8 pins [plural] *BrE informal* legs【英, 非正式】腿 —see also 另見 DRAWING PIN, PIN MONEY, PINS AND NEEDLES, ROLLING PIN, SAFETY PIN

pin² *v* **pinned, pinning 1** [T always+adv/prep] to fasten something somewhere, or to join two things together, using a pin〔用別針〕把…別住,〔用釘〕把…釘住; 固定住: **pin sth together** *Pin the pieces together before sewing them.* 把布片用別針別在一起, 然後再縫起來。| **pin sth to/on/onto** *Can you pin this to the notice board?* 你能把這釘在佈告板上嗎? **2 pin your hopes on** to hope that something will happen or someone will help you, because all your plans depend on this 把你的希望寄託在…上, 指望: *Chris is pinning his hopes on getting into Yale.* 基斯正寄望於進入耶魯大學。**3 pin the blame on** to blame someone for something, often unfairly〔通常不公平地〕把某事歸罪於〔某人〕, 把責任加在〔某人〕身上: *It's your fault – don't try to pin the blame on me!* 這是你的錯——別想把過錯推在我身上! **4** [T always+adv/prep] to make someone unable to move by putting a lot of pressure or weight on them 按住, 壓住; 使不能動: **pin sb to/under** *In the accident she was pinned under the car.* 在那次事故中, 她被壓在汽車底下, 動彈不得。**5 pin your ears back!** *BrE spoken* used to tell someone to listen carefully【英口】注意聽! 豎起耳朵聽!〔用於告訴別人仔細聽〕

pin sb/sth ↔ **down** *phr v* [T] **1** to make someone give clear details or make a definite decision about something 使〔某人〕詳細說明, 使〔某人〕明確表態: *I've been trying to pin him down all week, but he won't say what's going on.* 我一整個星期都在努力讓他把事情說個明白, 但他就是不肯說發生了甚麼事。**2** to understand something clearly or be able to describe it exactly 清楚地知道, 確切地描述, 確定: *We know someone's been stealing, but it's difficult to pin down who it is.* 我們知道有人一直在偷竊, 但難以確定那人是誰。

pi·ña co·la·da /ˌpinjə koˈlɑdə; ˌpiːnə kəˈlɑːdə/ *n* [C,U] an alcoholic drink made from COCONUT juice, PINEAPPLE juice, and RUM¹ 椰子菠蘿雞尾酒〔用椰子汁、菠蘿汁和朗姆酒攙雜而成〕

pin·a·fore /ˈpɪnəˌfɔr; ˈpɪnəfɔː/ *n* [C] **1** also 又作 **pinafore dress** /ˈ··· ˌ·/ *BrE* a dress that does not cover your arms and under which you wear a shirt or BLOUSE【英】無袖連衣裙〔一般穿在襯衫外面〕; JUMPER (2) *AmE*【美】**2** a loose piece of clothing that does not cover your arms, worn over your clothes to keep them clean 連胸圍裙

pin·ball /ˈpɪnˌbɔl; ˈpɪnbɔːl/ *n* [U] a game played on a machine with a sloping board down which a ball rolls, which the player has to prevent reaching the bottom 彈球戲, 玩彈子機

pince-nez /ˈpæns ˌne; ˌpæns ˈneɪ/ *n* GLASSES worn in the past that were held in position on the nose by a spring, instead of by pieces fitting round the ears〔從前使用的〕夾鼻眼鏡

pin·cer /ˈpɪnsə; ˈpɪnsə/ *n* **1** [C usually plural 一般用複數] one of the pair of claws (CLAW¹ (3)) that some SHELLFISH and insects have, used for holding and cutting food, and for fighting〔一些甲殼類動物和昆蟲的〕螯(鉗) —see picture at 參見 LOBSTER 圖 **2 pincers** [plural] a tool made of two crossed pieces of metal used for holding things tightly 鉗子 —see picture at 參見 TOOL¹ 圖

pincer move·ment /ˈ·· ˌ··/ *n* [C] a military attack in which two groups of soldiers come from opposite directions in order to trap the enemy between them〔軍事進攻中的〕鉗形攻勢[運動]

pinch¹ /pɪntʃ; pɪntʃ/ *v* **1** [T] to press a part of someone's flesh very tightly between your finger and thumb, especially so that it hurts 捏, 掐, 擰; 夾: *Mum, he pinched me!* 媽媽, 他擰我! —see picture on page A20 參見 A20 頁圖 **2** [T] *informal* to steal something, especially something small or not very valuable【非正式】偷竊〔尤指小的物品或不很值錢的東西〕: *Someone's pinched my coat!* 有人偷了我的大衣! **3** [I,T] if something you are wearing pinches you, it presses painfully on your flesh, because it is too tight〔穿的東西〕夾痛, 擠痛: *Her head was aching and her new shoes pinched dreadfully.* 她感到頭痛, 新買的鞋子又夾腳夾得很厲害。**4 I had to pinch myself** *especially spoken* used to say that you needed to make sure a situation was real and that you were not imagining it【尤口】我不得不擰自己一下〔以證實某情況是真的〕 **5 pinch and scrape** to be very careful about how much money you spend, because you do not have very much 盡量節省, 省吃儉用 —see also 另見 PENNY-PINCHING **6** [T usually passive 一般用被動態] *old-fashioned BrE* to ARREST¹ (1) someone【過時, 英】逮捕, 拘留

pinch² *n* **1 pinch of salt/pepper etc** a small amount of salt, pepper etc that you can hold between your finger and thumb 一撮鹽/胡椒粉等: *Add a pinch of cayenne pepper.* 加一撮辣椒粉。**2** [C] an act of pressing someone's flesh between your finger and thumb 捏, 擰, 掐; 夾: *She gave him a playful pinch.* 她鬧着玩地擰了他一把。**3 at a pinch** *BrE*【英】, **in a pinch** *AmE*【美】if necessary in a particularly difficult or urgent situation 必要時; 在緊要關頭: *We can squeeze one more person in the car, at a pinch.* 如果有必要, 我們的轎車裡可以再擠一個人。| *In a pinch, I could manage $60.* 必要時我能夠拿得出60美元。**4 take sth with a pinch of salt** to not completely believe what someone says to you 對所說的事半信半疑, 對某事不完全相信 **5 feel the pinch** to have financial difficulties, especially because you are not making as much money as you used to make〔尤指因賺錢不如以前多而〕感到拮据: *Local stores and businesses are beginning to feel the pinch.* 本地的商店和公司開始感到資金短缺。

pinched /pɪntʃt; pɪntʃt/ *adj* a pinched face looks thin and unhealthy, for example because the person is ill, cold, or tired〔臉〕消瘦的, 不健康的: *Years of working in the mine had left their faces pinched and haggard.* 多年的礦井下工作使他們形容枯槁。

pinch-hit /ˈ· ·/ *v* [I+for] *AmE*【美】**1** to do something for someone else because they are unexpectedly not able to do it〔緊急時〕代替某人做某事 **2** to HIT¹ (4a) for someone else in BASEBALL (1)〔在棒球運動中〕替補擊球 — **pinch-hitter** *n* [C]: *Mark is sick – we're sending Jim as a pinch-hitter.* 馬克病了——我們要安排吉姆為替補擊球員。

pin·cush·ion /ˈpɪnˌkuʃən; ˈpɪnˌkʊʃən/ *n* [C] a soft filled bag for sticking pins in until you need to use them〔供插縫紉針用的〕針墊

pine¹ /paɪn; paɪn/ *n* **1** [C,U] a tall tree with long hard sharp leaves that do not fall off in winter 松樹: *a pine forest* 松樹林 **2** the soft pale-coloured wood of this tree, used to make furniture, floors etc 松木: *a pine table* 松木桌子

pine² also 又作 **pine away** *v* [I] to gradually become weaker, less active, and less healthy, especially because you feel very unhappy〔尤指因不開心而逐漸〕衰弱, 憔悴: *After my grandfather died, my grandmother just pined away.* 祖父死後, 祖母就一天比一天憔悴了。

pine for sth/sb *phr v* [T] to become unhappy or ill because you cannot be with someone you love or in a place you love 想念〔某人或某地〕, 苦苦思念〔某人或某地〕: *She won't touch her food. I think she's pining for home.* 她不願吃一點東西, 我想她在想家。

pin·e·al gland /ˈpaɪnɪəl glænd; ˈpɪniəl ˌglænd/ *n* [C] a part of the brain that is thought to be sensitive to light in some way〔腦部的〕松果腺, 松果體

pine·ap·ple /ˈpaɪnˌæpl; ˈpaɪnæpəl/ *n* [C,U] a large yellow-brown tropical fruit or its sweet juicy yellow flesh 菠蘿, 鳳梨: *pineapple chunks* 菠蘿塊 | *pineapple juice* 菠蘿汁 —see picture on page A8 參見 A8 頁圖

pine·cone /ˈpaɪnkon; ˈpaɪnkəʊn/ *n* [C] a fruit of the PINETREE 松果, 松球

pine mar·ten /ˈ· ˌ··/ *n* [C] a small European animal that lives in forests 松貂〔一種生活在森林中的歐洲小動物〕

pine nee·dle /ˈ· ˌ··/ *n* [C] a leaf of the pinetree, that is thin and sharp like a needle 松針; 松葉

pine·tree /ˈpaɪntri; ˈpaɪnˌtriː/ *n* [C] a tall tree with long hard sharp leaves that do not fall off in winter; a PINE¹ (1) 松樹

pine·wood /ˈpaɪnwʊd; ˈpaɪnwʊd/ *n* **1** [C] a forest of pinetrees 松林 **2** [U] the wood from a pinetree 松木

ping¹ /pɪŋ; pɪŋ/ *n* [C] a short high ringing sound 砰, 乒; 鐺: *The bell on the counter let out a sharp ping.* 櫃枱上的鈴發出鐺的一聲響。

ping² *v* **1** [I] to make a short high ringing sound 發出砰[鐺鐺]的聲響 **2** [I] *AmE* PINK³【美】〔汽車引擎有毛病時〕格登格登地響

ping-pong /ˈ· ·/ *n* [U] an indoor game played on a table top by two people with a small plastic ball and two BATS; TABLE TENNIS 乒乓球運動

pin·head /ˈpɪnˌhɛd; ˈpɪnhed/ *n* [C] the head of a pin〔大頭針的〕針頭, 釘頭

pin·ion¹ /ˈpɪnjən; ˈpɪnjən/ *v* **1** [T always+adv/prep] to hold or tie up someone's arms or legs very tightly, so that they cannot move freely 捆住〔手臂或腿〕: *Her arms were pinioned tightly behind her.* 她的雙臂被緊緊地反綁在背後。**2** [T usually passive 一般用被動態] *technical* to cut off the big strong feathers from a bird's wings so that it cannot fly【術語】剪去〔鳥的〕飛羽

pinion² *n* **1** [C] a small wheel, with teeth on its outer edge, that fits into a larger wheel and turns it or is turned by it 小齒輪 —compare 比較 COGWHEEL **2** [C] *literary* a bird's wing【文】〔鳥的〕翅膀, 翼 **3** [C] *technical* the outer part of a bird's wing, where the strongest flying feathers grow【術語】〔鳥的〕翼梢, 翼尖, 前翼

S2 W3 **pink¹** /pɪŋk; pɪŋk/ *adj* **1** pale red 粉紅色的: *a wedding cake with pink and white icing* 用粉紅色和白色糖霜做的結婚蛋糕 | *The western sky was glowing pink.* 西邊的天空閃着粉紅色的光。**2** [only before noun 僅用於名詞前] a word used to talk about HOMOSEXUAL people 同性戀的: *a campaign aimed at the pink consumer* 面向同性戀消費者的活動 —see also 另見 **be tickled pink** (TICKLE¹ (3))

pink² *n* **1** [C,U] a pale red colour 粉紅色 —see picture on page A5 參見 A5 頁圖 **2** [C] a garden plant with pink, white, or red flowers 石竹〔一種園藝植物, 開粉紅色、白色或紅色的花〕**3 in the pink** *old-fashioned* in very good health【過時】非常健康(的), 身體很好(的)

pink³ *v* [I] *BrE* if a car engine pinks, it makes knocking sounds because it is not working properly【英】〔汽車引擎有毛病時〕格登格登地響; PING² *AmE*【美】

pink-col·lar /ˌ· ˈ··◂/ *adj* **pink-collar jobs/workers/industries etc** *especially AmE* low-paid jobs done mainly by women, for example in offices and restaurants, or the women who do these jobs【尤美】粉領工作/工人/行業等〔指主要由婦女做的報酬很低的工作, 如辦公室和餐館工作〕—compare 比較 WHITE-COLLAR, BLUE-COLLAR

pink gin /ˌ· ˈ·/ *n* [C,U] an alcoholic drink made of GIN and ANGOSTURA which gives it a pink colour 紅杜松子酒

pink·ie, pinky /ˈpɪŋkɪ; ˈpɪŋki/ *n* [C] *especially AmE or ScotE* the smallest finger of the human hand【尤美或蘇格蘭】小(手)指

pink·ing shears /ˈ·· ·/ also 又作 **pinking scissors** /ˈ·· ˌ··/ *n* [plural] a special type of scissors with blades that have V-shaped teeth, used for cutting cloth〔用於剪布的〕鋸齒剪刀, 齒邊布樣剪刀 —see picture at 參見 SCISSORS 圖

pink·ish /ˈpɪŋkɪʃ; ˈpɪŋkɪʃ/ *adj* slightly pink 淺粉紅色的: *a pinkish tinge* 淡淡的粉紅色

pink·o /ˈpɪŋko; ˈpɪŋkəʊ/ *n* [C] **1** *AmE* an insulting word for a SOCIALIST or COMMUNIST² (1)【美】赤色分子〔稱呼社會主義者或共產主義者的冒犯用語〕**2** *BrE* someone who supports LEFT WING ideas, but is not a strong believer in SOCIALISM【英】準左傾分子, 略帶左傾色彩的人 —compare 比較 RED¹ (4) —**pinko** *adj*

pink·y /ˈpɪŋkɪ; ˈpɪŋki/ *n* [C] a PINKIE 小(手)指

pin mon·ey /ˈ· ˌ··/ *n* [U] a small amount of money that you can spend on yourself rather than on necessary things 零用錢

pin·na·cle /ˈpɪnəkl; ˈpɪnəkəl/ *n* **1** [singular] the most successful, powerful, exciting etc part of something〔某事物最成功、最強大、最激動人心的〕部分; 頂點, 頂峯: [+of] *By the age of 40, she had reached the pinnacle of her political career.* 到了40歲, 她已達到了政治生涯的頂峯。**2** [C] a pointed stone decoration, like a small tower, on a building such as a church or castle〔教堂或城堡等上作裝飾用的〕尖頂, 小尖塔 **3** [C] *especially literary* a high mountain top【尤文】山峯; 山頂

pin·nate /ˈpɪnet; ˈpɪneɪt/ *adj technical* a pinnate leaf is made of two rows of little leaves arranged opposite each other along a stem【術語】〔葉〕羽狀的

pin·ny /ˈpɪnɪ; ˈpɪni/ *n* [C] *BrE informal* a PINAFORE (2)【英, 非正式】連胸圍裙

pin·point¹ /ˈpɪnˌpɔɪnt; ˈpɪnpɔɪnt/ *v* **1** [T] to say exactly what the facts about something really are 準確地說出, 描述〔事實真相〕: *This new report pinpoints the failings of the welfare system.* 這份新的報告準確地指出了福利制度的缺點。| **pinpoint what/how/why etc** *When children have learning difficulties, it's often difficult to pinpoint what the problem really is.* 當兒童有學習困難時, 往往很難確定問題到底是甚麼。**2** [T] to find or show the exact position of something 準確地找出〔某物的位置〕; 為…準確定位: *The team went behind enemy lines to pinpoint the exact locations of missile launchers.* 那一隊人到了敵人的後方, 以確定導彈發射器的精確位置。

pinpoint² *n* [C] **1** a very small point or dot of something 極小的點: [+of] *tiny pinpoints of light* 點點亮光 **2 with pinpoint accuracy/precision** very exactly 非常精確地: *Radar can locate an underwater target with pinpoint accuracy.* 雷達可以非常精確地確定水下目標的位置。

pin·prick /ˈpɪnˌprɪk; ˈpɪnˌprɪk/ *n* [C] **1** [C] a very small area or DOT of something〔某物的〕極小區域[點]: [+of] *a pinprick of light* 一絲亮光 **2** a very small hole in something, similar to one made by a pin〔似針刺的〕小孔 **3** something that slightly annoys you 小煩惱

pins and nee·dles /ˌ· · ˈ··/ *n* **1** [U] the uncomfortable prickly feeling you get in a part of your body when a full supply of blood comes back to it after having been partly blocked 酸痛, 發麻, 針刺感: **get pins and needles** *If you sit like that for too long you'll get pins and needles.* 如果你那樣坐太久了就會感到發麻。**2 be on pins and needles** *AmE* to be very nervous and unable to relax, especially because you are waiting for something important【美】〔尤指等待重要事情時〕如坐針氈, 坐立不安: *I wish Billy would give her a call. She's been on pins and needles all day.* 我希望比利會給她打個電話。她一整天都坐立不安。

pin·stripe /ˈpɪn͵straɪp; ˈpɪnstraɪp/ *n* [C] **1** one of the thin light-coloured lines that forms a pattern on cloth against a darker background〔織物上的〕細條花紋 —see picture on page A16 參見A16頁圖 **2 pinstripe suit** a man's suit made from cloth with a pinstripe pattern, worn especially by business people〔尤指商界人士穿的〕細條紋布西裝: *a navy-blue pinstripe suit* 一套海軍藍色細條紋布西裝 —**pin-striped** *adj*

2 **pint** /paɪnt; paɪnt/ *n* **1** [C] a unit for measuring an amount of liquid, especially beer or milk, in the US and Britain. In the US a pint contains 16 ounces of liquid, and in Britain it contains 20 ounces 品脫〔美國和英國的液量單位, 尤指啤酒或牛奶。在美國, 一品脫等於16盎司, 而在英國, 一品脫等於20盎司〕: *Add two pints of water to the mixture.* 在混合物中加入兩品脫的水。| *half a pint of milk* 半品脫牛奶—see table on page C3 參見C3頁附錄 **2** [C] *BrE* a pint of beer, especially one that you drink in a bar【英】〔尤指在酒吧喝的〕一品脫啤酒: *He's gone down the pub for a quick pint.* 他去小酒館喝一品脫啤酒。| *My dad remembers when a pint cost sixpence.* 我爸爸還記得買一品脫啤酒才花六便士的時候。—compare 比較 HALF[2] (1)

pin·ta·ble /ˈpɪn͵tebl̩; ˈpɪn͵teɪbəl/ *n* [C] *BrE* a machine for playing PINBALL on【英】彈球機, 彈子機

pin·to /ˈpɪnto; ˈpɪntəʊ/ *n* [C] *AmE* a horse with irregular markings of two or more colours【美】雜色馬; 花斑馬; PIEBALD *BrE*【英】

pinto bean /ˈ·· ·/ *n* [C] a small light brown bean 斑豆

pint-size /ˈ· ·/ also 又作 **pint-sized** *adj* [only before noun 僅用於名詞前] small, and unimportant or unsatisfactory 微小的; 無足輕重的; 不能令人滿意的

pin-up /ˈ· ·/ *n* **1** [C] a picture of an attractive person, often a woman with not many clothes on, that is put up on a wall to be looked at and admired〔被釘[掛]在牆上供欣賞的〕半裸美女圖片 **2** [C] someone who appears in one of these pictures 這類圖片中的人物

pin·wheel /ˈpɪn͵hwil; ˈpɪnwiːl/ *n* [C] *AmE* WINDMILL (2) 玩具風車

pi·o·neer[1] /͵paɪəˈnɪr; ͵paɪəˈnɪə/ *n* **1** [C] one of the first people to do something that other people will later develop or continue to do 先驅, 先鋒, 創始人: **[+of]** *the pioneers of the Women's Liberation movement* 婦女解放運動的先驅 | **[+in]** *Hans Richter, a pioneer in experimental cinema* 漢斯·李希特, 實驗電影的創始人 | **pioneer photographer/geologist etc** (=one of the first people to develop photography etc) 攝影術/地質學等的創始人 **2** [C] one of the first people to travel to a new country or area and begin living there, farming etc 拓荒者, 開拓者, 開發者: *the early pioneers of the Dakota territory* 達科他地區的早期拓荒者

pioneer[2] *v* [T] to be the first person to do, invent or use something 開創, 開發; 倡導: *The new cancer treatment was pioneered in the early eighties by Dr Sylvia Bannerjee.* 這種新的癌症治療方法是由西爾維亞·班納基醫生在八十年代初期開創的。

pi·o·neer·ing /͵paɪəˈnɪrɪŋ; ͵paɪəˈnɪərɪŋ◂/ *adj* [only before noun 僅用於名詞前] introducing new and better methods or ideas for the first time 開創性的, 先驅的: *the pioneering work of NASA scientists* 美國太空總署科學家們的開創性工作 | *his pioneering discoveries in the field of dynamics* 他在動力學領域的開創性發現

pi·ous /ˈpaɪəs; ˈpaɪəs/ *adj* **1** having strong religious beliefs, and showing this in the way you behave〔對宗教〕虔誠的 **2** pretending to have sincere religious feelings in order to make people think you are better than you really are 假虔誠的, 虛偽的, 偽善的: *Don't believe any of his pious talk.* 不要相信他那些虛偽的話。**3 pious hope/wish** something that you want to be true or to happen, but that probably will not 不大可能實現的希望/願望 —see also 另見 PIETY —**piously** *adv* —**piousness** *n* [U]

pip[1] /pɪp; pɪp/ *n* [C] *BrE*【英】**1** a small seed from a fruit such as an apple or orange〔蘋果、柑橘等水果的〕果核, 種子, 籽 **2** a high note that is part of a series of short sounds, used for example on the radio to show the time, or in the operation of public telephones 短而尖的聲音;〔電台的〕報時信號;〔電話中的〕嗶嗶聲; BEEP[2] (1) *AmE*【美】**3** *old-fashioned* one of the stars on the shoulders of the coats of army officers that shows their rank【過時】〔軍官肩章上表示等級的〕星 **4 give sb the pip** *old-fashioned* to annoy someone【過時】使某人惱怒[煩惱]

pip[2] **pipped, pipping** *v* [T] *BrE informal*【英, 非正式】**1 pip sb at the post** to beat someone at the last moment in a race, competition etc, when they were expecting to win 在最後關頭擊敗某人: *I nearly got the job, but was pipped at the post by the other candidate.* 我幾乎得到了這份工作, 但在最後關頭敗在了另一位應聘者手裡。**2** to beat someone in a race, competition etc, by only a small amount〔在比賽、競爭等中〕險勝, 以微弱優勢擊敗〔對手〕

pi·pal /ˈpipəl; ˈpiːpəl/ *n* [C] a large Indian tree〔印度的〕菩提樹

pipe[1] /paɪp; paɪp/ *n* [C]

1 ►**TUBE** 管子◄ a tube through which a liquid or gas flows, often under the ground〔通常埋在地下的〕管, 管子, 管道: *A pipe had burst in the kitchen and flooded the floor.* 廚房的一根管道爆裂了, 弄得滿地都是水。| *Workmen were laying pipes under the road.* 工人正在道路下面鋪設管道。| *The pipe's blocked again!* 管道又堵塞了! | *a gas pipe* 煤氣管

2 ►**FOR SMOKING** 用於抽煙◄ a thing used for smoking tobacco, consisting of a small tube with a container shaped like a bowl at one end 煙斗: *Peters filled and lit his pipe.* 彼得斯裝上煙斗, 然後把它點着。| *pipe tobacco* 煙斗用的煙絲

3 ►**MUSIC** 音樂◄ **a)** a simple musical instrument shaped like a tube and played by blowing 笛(子); 管樂器 **b)** one of the metal tubes through which air passes when an ORGAN (2) is played〔管風琴的〕音管, 風管 **c) the pipes** *BrE informal* BAGPIPES【英, 非正式】〔蘇格蘭的〕風笛

4 pipe dream a hope, idea, plan etc that is impossible or will probably never happen 白日夢, 幻想, 空想: *Arsenal lost 4-0, making winning the league something of a pipe dream.* 阿仙奴隊以0比4輸了, 這使他們獲得聯賽冠軍的好夢成空。

5 Put that in your pipe and smoke it! *spoken* used to say that someone must accept what you have just said, even though they do not like it【口】不管喜歡不喜歡你都得接受我所說的!

6 the pipes BAGPIPES 蘇格蘭風笛

pipe[2] *v*

1 ►**SEND LIQUID/GAS** 輸送液體/氣體◄ [T usually passive 一般用被動態] to send a liquid or gas through a pipe to another place 用管道輸送〔液體或氣體〕: *a piped water supply* 管道供水 | **pipe sth into/to** *Eighty per cent of sewage is piped directly into the sea.* 百分之八十的污水通過管道被直接排入海中。

2 ►**SPEAK/SING** 説話/唱歌◄ [I,T] to speak or sing in a high voice 用尖嗓子説話; 尖聲唱; 高聲鳴叫: *A moorhen piped suddenly from the lake.* 一隻黑水雞突然從湖中發出鳴叫聲。

3 ►**MAKE MUSIC** 演奏音樂◄ [I,T] to make a musical sound using a pipe 吹奏〔管樂〕: *He piped a jaunty tune* *for us to dance to.* 他吹奏了一支輕快的曲子讓我們隨之跳舞。

4 ▶FOOD 食物◀ to decorate food, especially a cake, with thin lines of ICING or cream 用糖霜[奶油]細線條裝飾食物〔尤指蛋糕〕

5 pipe sb aboard *technical* to welcome someone important onto a ship by blowing a special whistle【術語】〔通過吹特殊的哨子〕歡迎...上船

pipe down *phr v* [I] *spoken* to stop talking or making a noise, and become calmer and less excited【口】停止講話[吵鬧]; 安靜下來: *Pipe down! I'm trying to listen to the news.* 別吵！我想聽新聞呢。

pipe up *phr v* [I] *informal* to begin to say something or start speaking, especially when you have been quiet until then【非正式】突然開始說話〔尤指之前一直很安靜〕: *The smallest child suddenly piped up with the answer.* 最小的那個孩子突然說出了答案。

pipe clean·er /ˈ· ˌ··/ *n* [C] a length of wire covered with soft material, used to clean the inside of a tobacco pipe〔清理煙斗用的〕煙斗通條

piped mu·sic /ˌ·ˈ··/ *n* [U] quiet recorded music played continuously in shops, hotels, restaurants etc〔商店、旅店、餐館等地〕不斷播放的輕音樂

pipe fit·ter /ˈ· ˌ··/ *n* [C] someone who puts in and repairs pipes for water, gas etc 管道安裝修理工

pipe·line /ˋpaɪpˋlaɪn; ˈpaɪp-laɪn/ *n* [C] **1** a line of connecting pipes, often under the ground, used for taking gas, oil etc over long distances〔用來長距離輸送氣、油等的地下〕管道, 管線 **2 be in the pipeline** if a plan, idea or event is in the pipeline, it is still being prepared, but it will happen or be completed soon〔計劃、觀點或事件〕在準備中; 在進行中: *We've made several changes lately, and there are more in the pipeline.* 我們最近做了一些改動, 但還有一些改動正在進行之中。

pipe of peace /ˌ· ··ˈ·/ *n* [C] a PEACE PIPE 長桿煙斗, 和平煙斗

pip·er /ˋpaɪpɚ; ˈpaɪpə/ *n* [C] a musician who plays a PIPE[1] (3) or the BAGPIPES 吹笛人, 風笛吹奏者

pipe rack /ˈ· ·/ *n* [C] a small frame for holding several tobacco pipes 煙斗架

pi·pette /pɪˋpɛt; pɪˈpet/ *n* [C] a thin glass tube for sucking up exact amounts of liquid, used especially in chemistry〔尤指化學試驗用的〕吸量管, 移液管 —see picture at 參見 LABORATORY 圖

pip·it /ˋpɪpɪt; ˈpɪpɪt/ *n* [C] a small brown or grey singing bird 鷚〔一種棕色或灰色的鳴禽〕

pip·pin /ˋpɪpɪn; ˈpɪpɪn/ *n* [C] a small sweet apple〔一種小而甜的〕蘋果

pip·squeak /ˋpɪpˌskwik; ˈpɪpskwiːk/ *n* [C] someone that you think is not worth attention or respect, especially because they are small or young 無足輕重的人, 小人物: *Shut up, you little pipsqueak!* 閉嘴, 你這個小東西！

pi·quant /ˋpikənt; ˈpiːkənt/ *adj* **1** having a pleasantly sharp taste or flavour 辛辣的; 開胃的: *a piquant tomato sauce* 辣味番茄醬 **2** interesting and exciting; INTRIGUING 有趣的; 激動人心的: *The disappearance of the letter made the situation all the more piquant.* 那封信的消失使情況更加令人感興趣。—**piquantly** *adv* —**piquancy** *n* [U]

pique[1] /pik; piːk/ *n* [U] **1** a feeling of being annoyed or upset, especially because someone has ignored you or made you look stupid〔尤指因被人忽視或被人愚弄而〕不悅, 生氣: **a fit of pique** (=sudden anger) 一怒之下 *Greta stormed off in a fit of pique.* 格麗塔一賭氣, 氣沖沖地離開了。**2** also 又作 **piqué** a type of material made of cotton, silk, or RAYON 一種用棉花、絲或人造絲製成的織物

pique[2] *v* **1** [T usually passive 一般用被動態] to make someone feel annoyed or upset, especially by ignoring them or making them look stupid〔尤指因忽視或愚弄而〕使〔某人〕生氣, 激怒: **be/feel piqued** *We did feel a little piqued when nobody even bothered to ask us.* 甚至都沒有人詢問我們一下, 我們的確感到有點生氣。**2 pique your interest/curiosity** *especially AmE* to make you feel interested in something or someone【尤美】激起你的興趣／好奇心

pi·ra·cy /ˋpaɪrəsɪ; ˈpaɪərəsi/ *n* [U] **1** the illegal copying and sale of books, TAPES, VIDEOS etc 非法翻印〔書籍等〕; 非法翻錄〔磁帶、錄影帶等〕, 盜版: *software piracy* 軟件的非法複製 **2** the crime of attacking and stealing from ships at sea 海上搶劫, 海盜行為

pi·ra·nha /pɪˋrɑnjə; pḷˈrɑːnjə/ *n* [C] a South American fish with sharp teeth that lives in rivers and eats flesh 鋸脂鯉〔南美一種有尖利牙齒的食肉河魚〕

pirate 海盜

pi·rate[1] /ˋpaɪrət; ˈpaɪərət/ *n* [C] **1** someone who dishonestly copies and sells another person's work 剽竊者; 侵犯版權者, 非法翻印者; 侵犯專利權者 **2 pirate radio/TV (station)** illegal radio or television broadcasts, or the station sending them out 非法無線電廣播[台]／非法電視[台]: *a pirate channel* 非法電視頻道 **3** someone who sails on the seas, attacking other boats and stealing things from them 海盜 —**piratical** /paɪˋrætɪkḷ; paɪˈrætɪkəl/ *adj* —**piratically** /-kḷɪ; -kli/ *adv*

pirate[2] *v* [T] to illegally copy and sell another person's work such as a book, design, or invention 剽竊, 盜用; 非法翻印; 非法仿製 —**pirated** *adj*: *pirated video tapes* 非法翻錄的錄影帶

pir·ou·ette /ˌpɪruˋɛt; ˌpɪruˈet/ *n* [C] a very fast turn made on one toe or the front part of one foot, especially by a BALLET dancer〔尤指芭蕾舞演員的〕足尖旋轉, 單足旋轉 —**pirouette** *v* [I]

pis·ca·to·ri·al /ˌpɪskəˋtorɪəl; ˌpɪskəˈtɔːriəl◂/ *adj formal* connected with fishing or fishermen【正式】捕魚業的; 漁民的

Pis·ces /ˋpaɪsiz; ˈpaɪsiːz/ *n* **1** [singular] the twelfth sign of the ZODIAC, represented by two fish, and believed to affect the character and life of people born between February 21 and March 20 雙魚座, 雙魚宮〔黃道第十二宮〕: *Nick's a Pisces.* 尼克是雙魚座。**2** [C] someone who was born between February 21 and March 20 出生於雙魚座時段〔2月21日至3月20日〕的人

pish /pɪʃ; pɪʃ/ *interjection old use* used to express annoyance or impatience【舊】呸！〔表示不愉快或不耐煩〕

piss[1] /pɪs; pɪs/ *v* **1** [I] *informal* an impolite word meaning to URINATE【非正式】撒尿〔不禮貌的說法〕**2 piss all over sb** *spoken* an impolite expression meaning to thoroughly defeat a person or a team【口】把某人打得屁滾尿流〔不禮貌的說法〕**3 piss in the wind** *spoken* an impolite expression meaning to waste time or effort trying to do something that is impossible【口】浪費時間[精力]做不可能的事〔不禮貌的說法〕**4 be pissing (it) down (with rain)** *BrE informal* to rain very heavily【英, 非正式】下大雨: *By the time we got there, it was absolutely pissing down!* 我們到那裡時, 天下起了傾盆大雨！**5 piss yourself (laughing)** *BrE spoken* an impolite expression meaning to laugh uncontrollably【英口】笑得尿都出來了〔不禮貌的說法〕: *When Michelle fell in that puddle we absolutely pissed ourselves.* 當米雪跌倒在那個水坑裡時, 我們都笑得不得了。**6 go piss up a rope!** *AmE spoken* a very impolite expression used to tell someone to go away【美口】滾開！滾蛋！〔非常不禮貌的說法〕**7 not have a pot to piss in** *AmE spoken* a very impolite expression meaning to be extremely poor【美口】窮得連個尿壺都沒有〔非常不禮貌的說法〕

piss about/around *phr v BrE spoken*【英口】**1** [I] an impolite expression meaning to waste time doing stupid things with no purpose or plan 胡鬧, 浪費時間, 遊手好閒〔不禮貌的說法〕: *Stop pissing about and get some work done!* 別再瞎混了, 找些事幹幹吧! **2** [T **piss** sb **about/around**] an impolite expression meaning to treat someone badly by not doing what you have promised to do, or by not being honest with them〔不禮貌的說法, 以不履行承諾或不坦誠的方式〕愚弄, 欺騙: *I wish he'd say yes or no – he's been pissing me around for weeks.* 我希望他能給予明確的答覆 —— 他已經愚弄我好幾個星期了。

P

piss sth ↔ **away** *phr v* [T] *spoken* a very impolite expression meaning to waste something very stupidly【口】〔不禮貌的說法〕非常愚蠢地浪費〔某物〕, 糟蹋: *Jean inherited a load of money, but she pissed it all away.* 吉恩繼承了一大筆錢, 但她全揮霍掉了。

piss off *phr v* [I] *spoken*【口】**1** [usually imperative 一般用於祈使句] an offensive expression meaning to go away 滾開, 滾蛋〔冒犯用語〕: *Why don't you just piss off and leave me alone!* 你為甚麼不滾開, 讓我一個人待着! **2** an offensive expression used to say no or to refuse to do something 沒門兒, 不行〔不禮貌的說法; 用以說不或拒絕做某事〕: *"Johnny, will you do the dishes?" "Piss off!"* "約翰尼, 你去洗碗好嗎?" "不行!"

piss sb ↔ **off** *phr v* [T] *spoken* an impolite expression meaning to annoy someone very much【口】激怒〔某人〕, 使〔某人〕非常惱火〔不禮貌的說法〕: *It really pisses me off when my car won't start in the morning.* 早上要是汽車發動不了, 那真會把我氣死。

piss² *n* **1** [singular] *spoken* an impolite word for an act of urinating (URINATE)【口】撒尿〔不禮貌的說法〕: **have/take a piss** *I need to have a piss.* 我需要去撒尿。**2** [U] *spoken* an impolite word meaning URINE【口】尿〔不禮貌的說法〕**3 take the piss (out of sb/sth)** *BrE spoken* to make fun of someone, especially by copying them or trying to make them believe something untrue【英口】〔尤指通過模仿某人或使某人相信不真實的事情而〕取笑〔某人〕: *Stop taking the piss out of Dave!* 別捉弄戴夫了! | *£900 for that stereo? You're taking the piss!* 900英鎊買那台立體聲音響? 你在開玩笑吧! **4 be on the piss** *BrE spoken* to be drinking a lot of alcohol【英口】在大量喝酒: *"Where's Jo?" "Out on the piss somewhere."* "喬在哪裡?" "在外面某個地方喝酒呢。" **5 a piece of piss** *BrE spoken* something very easy【英口】非常容易的事: *That test was a piece of piss!* 那考試非常容易! **6 full of piss and vinegar** *AmE spoken* full of energy【美口】充滿活力, 精力充沛

piss³ *adv spoken*【口】**piss poor/piss easy etc** an impolite expression meaning very poor, very easy etc 非常蹩腳[貧窮]/非常容易等〔不禮貌的說法〕: *"You'd make a piss-poor lawyer," he replied.* "你只能當一個非常蹩腳的律師。" 他回答道。

piss-ant¹, pissant /ˈpɪsænt; ˈpɪsænt/ *adj* [only before noun 僅用於名詞前] *AmE informal* an impolite word meaning of very low value, quality, or importance【美, 非正式】沒甚麼價值的; 質量低劣的, 無足輕重的〔不禮貌的說法〕: *I get really fed up doing these piss-ant little jobs.* 我對於幹這些無足輕重的瑣碎工作真的感到煩透了。

piss-ant², pissant *n AmE informal* an impolite word meaning an annoying person with a weak character【美, 非正式】令人討厭的膽小鬼〔不禮貌的說法〕: *The stupid little piss-ant!* 那個愚蠢的膽小鬼!

piss ar·tist /ˈ· ,··/ *n* [C] *BrE informal* an impolite word for someone who drinks a lot of alcohol【英, 非正式】酒鬼〔不禮貌的說法〕

piss-ass /ˈ· ·/ *adj AmE spoken* [only before noun 僅用於名詞前] a very impolite word meaning not at all important, or very silly【美口】一點也不重要的; 非常愚蠢的〔非常不禮貌的說法〕: *Seth thinks his piss-ass little job makes him somebody!* 賽思居然以為就憑他那個不值一提的工作會讓他成為甚麼大人物呢!

pissed /pɪst; pɪst/ *adj* **1** *BrE spoken* drunk【英口】喝醉的: *They rolled in pissed at three in the morning.* 他們早上三點醉醺醺地擁進來。| **pissed as a newt/pissed out of your head** (=extremely drunk) 酩酊大醉的 **2** *AmE spoken* an impolite word meaning annoyed, disappointed, or unhappy【美口】生氣的, 惱火的, 失望的〔不禮貌的說法〕: *Oh God, I'm really pissed, I screwed up on my exam.* 噢上帝, 我真的很煩, 我考試考糟了。| [+with/at] *Are you still pissed at me?* 你還在生我的氣嗎? **3 pissed off** *especially BrE* annoyed, disappointed, or unhappy【尤英】生氣的, 惱火的, 失望的, 不快的: [+with] *I'm a bit pissed off with my job at the moment.* 我現在對我的工作感到有點厭煩。

pis·ser /ˈpɪsə; ˈpɪsə/ *n* [C] *spoken*【口】**1** an impolite word meaning a difficult job or activity, or a bad or annoying situation 難事, 苦差事; 糟糕的情況, 令人討厭的局面〔非常不禮貌的說法〕: *"I'm grounded." "What a pisser."* "我被罰不准出去。" "真糟糕。" **2** an impolite word meaning a toilet 茅(屎)坑〔不禮貌的說法〕**3** *AmE* a very impolite word meaning a good situation【美】好的情況; 好事〔非常不禮貌的說法〕: *I got the job! What a pisser!* 我得到了那份工作! 真太好了!

piss·head /ˈpɪs,hɛd; ˈpɪshed/ *n* [C] *BrE spoken* an impolite word for someone who drinks a lot of alcohol【英口】酒鬼〔不禮貌的說法〕

pis·soir /piˈswar; ˈpɪswaː/ *n* [C] *French* a public toilet【法】公共廁所

piss-take /ˈ· ·/ *n* [C usually singular 一般用單數] *BrE spoken* a joke in which you try to make fun of someone, for example by copying them or laughing at them【英口】嘲弄[取笑]某人的玩笑 —see also 另見 **take the piss out of** (PISS² (3))

piss-up /ˈ· ·/ *n* [C] *BrE spoken* an occasion when several people drink a lot of alcohol together【英口】痛飲, 狂飲: *I'm not going to the party – it sounds like just a piss-up to me.* 我不會去參加聚會 —— 它聽起來像是一場狂歡痛飲。

pis·sy /ˈpɪsɪ; ˈpɪsi/ *adj spoken* an impolite word meaning small or unimportant and annoying【口】微小的, 瑣碎的; 令人討厭的〔不禮貌的說法〕

pis·ta·chi·o /pɪsˈtæʃɪ,o; pɪˈstɑːʃiəʊ/ *plural* **pistachios** *n* [C] a small green nut 阿月渾子(核果), 開心果: *pistachio ice cream* 阿月渾子[開心果]冰淇淋

piste /pist; piːst/ *n* [C] a snow-covered slope which has been prepared for people to SKI² down 滑雪道

pis·til /ˈpɪstl; ˈpɪstl/ *n* [C] *technical* the female seed-producing part of a flower【術語】雌蕊

pis·tol /ˈpɪstl; ˈpɪstl/ *n* [C] a small gun you can use with one hand 手槍

pistol-whip /ˈ·· ·/ *v* [I,T] to hit someone many times with a pistol 用手槍多次毆打〔某人〕

pis·ton /ˈpɪstn; ˈpɪstən/ *n* [C] a part of an engine consisting of a short solid piece of metal inside a tube, that moves up and down to make the other parts of the engine move 活塞

piston ring /ˈ·· ·/ *n* [C] a circular metal spring used to stop gas or liquid escaping from between a piston and the tube that it moves in 活塞環

pit¹ /pɪt; pɪt/ *n*

1 ▶HOLE 洞◀ [C] **a)** a hole in the ground, especially one made by digging〔尤指在地上挖出的〕坑: *Dig a pit and bury the rubbish in it.* 挖一個坑, 然後把垃圾埋進去。| *a sand pit* 沙坑 | *a barbecue pit* 燒烤坑 **b)** a large hole in the ground from which stones or minerals have been dug〔地上採掘石頭或礦物的〕大坑; 礦坑: *a gravel pit* 砂礫採掘場, 砂礫坑

2 ▶MARK 痕跡◀ [C] **a)** a small hollow mark in the surface of something〔某物表面的〕微小凹痕: *There are tiny scratches and pits on the windshield.* 擋風玻璃上有微小的刮痕和凹痕。**b)** a small hollow mark that is left on your face by some diseases, especially SMALLPOX〔某

些疾病，尤指天花留下的〕疤痕，麻子
3 ▶MINE 礦井◀ [C] a mine, especially a coal mine 礦井〔尤指煤礦〕: *We have no choice but to close unprofitable pits.* 我們別無選擇，只得關閉無利可圖的礦井。
4 ▶UNTIDY PLACE 不潔的地方◀ [C] *spoken* a house or room that is dirty, untidy, or in bad condition【口】很髒的房屋[房間]; 狀況很差的房屋[房間]: *No, we decided not to rent it – the place is an absolute pit!* 不，我們決定不租了 —— 那屋子狀況太差了！
5 be the pits *usually spoken* used to say that something is extremely bad【通常口】極差，極糟糕: *Rap music? That stuff is the pits!* 說唱樂？那東西是最糟糕的。
6 in/at the pit of your stomach if you feel nervous, frightened etc at the pit of your stomach, you experience these emotions strongly, often as an unpleasant feeling in your stomach 在你的胸口[心窩]: *a knot of fear in the pit of my stomach* 我心中的一陣恐慌
7 ▶CAR RACING 賽車◀ **the pit** *AmE*【美】, **the pits** *BrE*【英】the place beside the track in car RACES[1] (1) where cars can come in during a race to be quickly repaired〔賽車時設在車道邊的〕汽車快修站
8 ▶IN A GARAGE 在汽車修理廠◀ [C] a hole in the floor of a garage that lets you get underneath a car to repair it〔修車處的〕檢修坑
9 ▶IN FRUIT 在水果中◀ [C] *AmE* the single, large hard seed in some fruits; STONE[1] (4)【美】〔某些水果的〕核: *a peach pit* 桃核
10 ▶IN A THEATRE 在劇院裡◀ [C] **a)** an ORCHESTRA PIT〔劇場舞台前面的〕樂池 **b)** *BrE old use* the seats at the back of the ground floor of a theatre【英舊】〔劇院裡的〕(樓下) 正廳後座
11 the pit of despair/dismay/depression etc *literary* a situation in which you feel extremely sad and without hope【文】極其絕望/驚愕/沮喪等
12 ▶BUSINESS 交易◀ [C] *AmE* the area of a STOCK EXCHANGE where people buy and sell shares (SHARE[2] (5))【美】證券交易所的交易區; FLOOR[1] (8) *BrE*【英】
13 ▶BODY PART 身體部位◀ [C] *AmE informal* an ARMPIT【美，非正式】腋窩
14 the pit *biblical* HELL[1] (3)【聖經】地獄: *cast into the pit of eternal damnation* 投入永受詛咒的地獄

pit² *v past tense and past participle* **pitted 1 pit your wits against** to compete with someone or something in a situation in which you need all your intelligence 絞盡腦汁與〔某人〕較量，用盡智慧對付〔某事物〕: *Pit your wits against the Double or Dare computer!* 與挑戰者電腦遊戲鬥智去吧！**2** [T] *AmE* to take out the single, hard seed inside some fruits; STONE[2] (2)【美】除去…的核 **3** [T usually passive 一般用被動態] to put small marks or holes in the surface of something 使留下疤痕; 使有凹陷: *Heavy rain had pitted and blurred the trail.* 大雨使小徑變得坑坑窪窪，都有些看不清了。—see also 另見 PITTED

pit sb/sth **against** sb/sth *phr v* [T] to test your strength, ability, power etc against someone else 使與…競爭，使相鬥: *a chance to pit our strength against pro ball players* 一次讓我們與職業球員比實力的機會

pit sth ↔ **out** *phr v* [T] *AmE informal* to SWEAT so much that your clothes become wet under your arms【美，非正式】汗濕〔腋下的衣服〕

pit·a bread /ˈpitə brɛd; ˈpɪtə bred/ *n* [U] the American spelling of PITTA BREAD pitta bread 的美式拼法

pit-a-pat /ˈ· · ˌ·/ *adv informal* PITTER-PATTER【非正式】劈劈啪啪地 —**pit-a-pat** *n* [singular]

pit bull ter·ri·er /ˌ· · ˈ···/ also 又作 **pit bull** /ˌ· ˈ·◀/ *n* [C] a small but extremely strong and sometimes violent fighting dog 鬥牛㹴狗〔一種體小但極其強壯、有時兇猛的鬥犬〕—see picture at 參見 DOG[1] 圖

3 **pitch¹** /pɪtʃ; pɪtʃ/ *n*
1 ▶SPORTS FIELD 運動場地◀ [C] *BrE* a specially marked out area of ground on which a sport is played【英】比賽場地; FIELD[1] (4) *AmE*【美】: *The crowd invaded the pitch at the end of the match.* 比賽結束時，人羣湧入了球場。| *a cricket pitch* 板球場
2 ▶STRONG FEELINGS 強烈的感情◀ [singular, U] the strength of your feelings or opinions about something〔感情、意見的〕程度，強度: *Disagreement reached such a pitch that we thought a fight would break out.* 分歧達到如此程度，以致於我們認為會爆發一場打鬥。| **at fever pitch** (=with a lot of excited feeling) 高度興奮，狂熱程度 *Speculation about the election was at fever pitch.* 有關選舉的各種推測已達到了高潮。
3 ▶MUSIC 音樂◀ **a)** the highness or lowness of a musical note 音調; 音高 —see also 另見 PERFECT PITCH **b)** the ability of a musician to play or sing a note at exactly the correct pitch 樂感; 音樂家以精確的音高演奏[演唱]的能力: *She's got good pitch.* 她樂感很好。
4 ▶SELLING 銷售◀ [C] *informal* what a sales person says about a product to persuade people to buy it; SALES PITCH【非正式】〔推銷員的〕叫賣語，廣告語
5 ▶BASEBALL 棒球◀ [C] a throw of the ball, or a way in which it can be thrown 投球; 投球姿式: *His first pitch went wide.* 他的第一球投偏了。
6 ▶BLACK SUBSTANCE 黑色物質◀ [U] a black, sticky substance that is used on roofs, the bottoms of ships etc to stop water coming through 瀝青: **as black as pitch** (=very dark) 漆黑的 —see also 另見 PITCH-BLACK, PITCH-DARK
7 ▶SHIP/AIRCRAFT 船/飛機◀ [C] a backward and forward movement of a ship or an aircraft〔船或飛機的〕顛簸 —compare 比較 ROLL[2] (4)
8 ▶SLOPE 斜坡◀ [singular, U] the degree to which a roof slopes〔屋頂的〕斜度，坡度
9 ▶STREET/MARKET 街道/市場◀ [C] *BrE* a place in a public area where a street trader or entertainer goes to sell things or perform【英】〔街道小商販的〕擺攤處;〔街頭藝人的〕表演場地 —see also 另見 **queer sb's pitch** (QUEER[3])

pitch² *v*
1 ▶THROW 扔，投，擲◀ [T] to throw something with a lot of force, often aiming carefully〔通常仔細瞄準後〕用力投，扔，拋，擲: *Men slouched on the corner, pitching pennies.* 男人們懶洋洋地坐在一角，擲錢幣賭博。| **pitch sth over/into/through etc** *Fran screwed up the letter and pitched it into the fire.* 弗蘭把信揉成一團，扔進火中。
2 ▶BALL GAMES 球類運動◀ **a)** [I,T] to aim and throw a ball in BASEBALL〔棒球中〕投(球) —see picture on page A22 參見 A22 頁圖 **b)** [I] if a ball pitches in CRICKET or GOLF, it hits the ground〔板球或高爾夫球中〕(球) 落地，擊地 **c)** [T] to hit the ball in a high curve in golf〔高爾夫球中〕把〔球〕擊成下旋高球 **d)** [T] to make the ball hit the ground when you are bowling (BOWL[2] (2)) in cricket〔板球中〕使球擊地[觸地]
3 ▶FALL 跌倒◀ [I always+adv/prep, T always+adv/prep] to fall suddenly and heavily in a particular direction, or to make someone or something fall in this way (使) 突然重重地跌倒: **pitch forward/backward/over etc** *Jim pitched forward as the train jerked to a halt.* 火車突然停下，吉姆向前栽倒了。
4 ▶SHIP/AIRCRAFT 船/飛機◀ [I] if a ship or an aircraft pitches, it moves along with the back and front going up and down 顛簸: *The old frigate pitched violently on the massive waves.* 那艘舊護航艦在巨浪中劇烈地顛簸着。—compare 比較 ROLL[2] (4), YAW
5 ▶SET A LEVEL 確定水平◀ [T always+adv/prep] **a)** if you pitch an examination, explanation, speech etc at a particular level of difficulty, you make sure that it can be understood by people at that level 把〔考試、解釋、演說等〕定於某一特定難度: *Pitch the test at your average students' level of ability.* 按照普通學生的能力水平確定考試的難度。| *They're a young audience, so don't pitch it too high.* 他們是年輕的聽眾，所以別講得太深了。**b)** to set prices at a particular level 把價格定在某個水平:

Prices for the new hatchbacks are pitched very competitively. 這種新型倉門式後背車身小客車售價定得很有競爭力。

6 ▶MUSIC 音樂◀ [T always+adv/prep] if you pitch your voice or another sound at a particular level, the sound is produced at that level 為…定音高, 為…定調: **pitch sth high/low etc** *This song is pitched too high for my voice.* 對我的嗓子來說, 這首歌的音定得太高了。—see also 另見 HIGH-PITCHED, LOW-PITCHED

7 pitch camp/pitch a tent to set up a tent or a camp for a short time 紮營/搭帳篷: *We pitched our tents beside a stream.* 我們在一條小溪邊搭起帳篷。

8 ▶BUSINESS DEALS 交易◀ [I,T] *informal, especially AmE* to try to make a business agreement, or to sell something by saying how good it is【非正式, 尤美】竭力推銷: *sales reps pitching the latest gadgets* 竭力推銷最新小玩意的銷售代表 | [+for] *Jack's trying to pitch for a deal.* 為達成交易, 傑克正在竭力推銷。

9 ▶SLOPE 斜坡◀ [I always+adv/prep] to slope downwards 向下傾斜: **pitch gently/steeply etc** *The roof pitches sharply to the rear of the house.* 屋頂向屋頂後部大幅度傾斜。—see also 另見 PITCHED

10 pitch sb a line/yarn *AmE informal* to tell someone a story or give them an excuse that is difficult to believe【美, 非正式】給某人編造荒誕無稽的故事, 給某人編造令人難以相信的藉口: *She pitched me some yarn about a bomb scare on the metro.* 她向我大談有關地鐵上炸彈恐慌的騙人故事。

pitch in *phr v* [I] *informal*【非正式】**1** to start to work eagerly as a member of a group〔作為小組中的一員〕開始大幹特幹, 拚命地幹起來: *If we all pitch in, we'll have it finished in no time.* 我們如果都全力投入地幹起來, 那麼立刻就可以把它完成。**2** to add your help or support 提供幫助[支持]: **pitch in with sth** *The local council pitched in with the offer of a free van.* 當地市議會免費提供輕型貨車予以協助。**3** to start to eat hungrily 開始狼吞虎嚥, 開始大吃特吃: *Pitch in – there's plenty for everyone.* 放開肚子吃吧 — 足夠每個人吃的。

pitch into sb *phr v* [T] *spoken* to attack someone by hitting them or insulting them【口】〔武力或口頭〕攻擊〔某人〕

pitch up *phr v* [I] *BrE spoken* to arrive somewhere; TURN UP【英口】出現; 到達: *Guess who just pitched up on Saturday night?* 猜猜星期六晚上誰來了?

pitch-and-putt /ˌ· · ˈ·/ *n* [U] *BrE* a game of GOLF played on a very small course【英】在小型高爾夫球場進行的比賽

pitch-black /ˌ· ˈ·◂/ *adj* completely black or dark 烏黑的; 漆黑的: *Night in the city is never pitch-black.* 這個城市的夜晚從來不會漆黑一片。

pitch·blende /ˈpɪtʃˌblɛnd; ˈpɪtʃblend/ *n* [U] a dark shiny substance dug from the earth, from which URANIUM and RADIUM are obtained 瀝青鈾礦

pitch-dark /ˌ· ˈ·◂/ *adj* completely dark 漆黑的

pitched /pɪtʃt; pɪtʃt/ *adj* a roof that is pitched is sloping rather than flat〔屋頂〕傾斜的, 有坡度的

pitched bat·tle /ˌ· ˈ··/ *n* [C] **1** an angry and usually long quarrel or argument 激烈的長期爭執[辯論]: *We had a pitched battle with the council before they'd agree to repair the road.* 在市議會同意修路之前, 我們曾有過長期激烈的爭論。**2** a battle between armies who have already chosen and prepared their positions〔佈好陣式的〕陣地戰, 對陣戰 —compare 比較 SKIRMISH[1] (1)

pitch·er /ˈpɪtʃɚ; ˈpɪtʃə/ *n* [C] **1** *AmE or BrE old-fashioned* a container for holding and pouring liquids with a handle and a SPOUT (=shaped part for pouring); JUG[1] (1)【美或英, 過時】〔帶柄和嘴的〕壺, 罐: *a pitcher of water* 一壺水 —see picture at 參見 JUG[1] 圖 **2** *BrE* a large container for holding and pouring liquids, usually made of clay, with two handles【英】有兩個柄的陶製大水壺 **3** the player in BASEBALL who throws the ball〔棒球運動中的〕投手 —see picture on page A22 參見 A22 頁圖

pitch·fork[1] /ˈpɪtʃˌfɔrk; ˈpɪtʃfɔːk/ *n* [C] an old-fashioned farm tool with a long handle and two long curved metal points, used especially for lifting HAY (=dried cut grass) 乾草叉, 長柄草耙〔一種老式農具〕—see picture at 參見 FORK[1] 圖

pitchfork[2] *v* [T+into/in/onto] to put someone suddenly into a situation for which they are not properly prepared 使…突然處於某種境地: *She was pitchforked into this predicament by her husband's early death.* 她丈夫的早逝使她突然陷入這種困境。

pitch·out /ˈpɪtʃaut; ˈpɪtʃaʊt/ *n* [C] a ball in BASEBALL that the PITCHER deliberately throws too far to the side for it to be hit〔棒球〕投手故意投的壞球, 戰術性壞球

pitch pine /ˈ· ·/ *n* [C,U] a type of PINETREE that grows in North America, or the wood from this tree 北美油松; 北美油松木

pit·e·ous /ˈpɪtɪəs; ˈpɪtiəs/ *adj especially literary* expressing suffering and sadness in a way that makes you feel pity【尤文】可憐的, 讓人憐憫的: *piteous sobs* 可憐的抽泣聲 —**piteously** *adv*

pit·fall /ˈpɪtˌfɔl; ˈpɪtfɔːl/ *n* [C] a problem or difficulty that is likely to happen in a particular job, course of action, or activity 可能出現的問題[困難], 隱患, 陷阱: *English spelling presents many pitfalls for foreign learners.* 英語拼寫有很多意想不到的難點, 外國學生很容易出錯。| **avoid a pitfall** *This little booklet will help you avoid the more obvious pitfalls of travelling alone.* 這本小冊子將幫助你在單獨旅行時避開那些較明顯的陷阱。

pith /pɪθ; pɪθ/ *n* [U] **1** a white substance just under the outside skin of oranges and similar fruit 柑橘等外皮之下的海綿層, 中果皮 **2** a soft white substance that fills the stems of some plants〔某些植物莖中的〕木髓 **3 the pith of an argument/issue etc** the most important and necessary part of an argument etc 論証/問題等的核心[精髓, 最重要部分]

pit·head /ˈpɪtˌhɛd; ˈpɪt-hed/ *n* [C] the entrance to a coal mine and the buildings around it 礦井口[煤礦和周圍建築物的入口]

pith hel·met /ˌ· ˈ··/ *n* [C] a large light hat worn especially in the past in hot countries, to protect your head from the sun; TOPEE〔尤指從前在熱帶地區戴的〕遮陽帽 —see picture at 參見 HELMET 圖

pith·y /ˈpɪθɪ; ˈpɪθi/ *adj* **pithy comments/saying/advice etc** strongly and cleverly stated, without wasting any words 簡練的評論/諺語/忠告等 —**pithily** *adv* —**pithiness** *n* [U]

pit·i·a·ble /ˈpɪtɪəbḷ; ˈpɪtiəbəl/ *adj formal* making you feel pity【正式】令人憐憫的, 可憐的: *refugees living in pitiable conditions* 生活條件可憐的難民 —**pitiably** *adv*

pit·i·ful /ˈpɪtɪfəl; ˈpɪtɪfəl/ *adj* **1** someone or something that is pitiful looks so sad and unfortunate that you feel very sorry for them〔人或物〕令人同情的, 可憐的: *The animals were a pitiful sight, in their small cages.* 那些動物在小小的籠子裡, 看着令人可憐。**2** not good enough to deserve respect or serious consideration 可鄙的, 可恥的, 不值得認真考慮的: *You don't expect me to believe that pitiful excuse.* 你別指望我會相信那個拙劣的藉口。—**pitifully** *adv*: *pitifully thin* 瘦得可憐的

pit·i·less /ˈpɪtɪlɪs; ˈpɪtɪləs/ *adj* **1** showing no pity; cruel 沒有憐憫心的, 冷酷的, 無情的: *a pitiless tyrant* 冷酷無情的暴君 **2** pitiless wind, rain, sun etc is very severe and shows no sign of changing〔風、雨、太陽等〕嚴酷的, 無情的: *the pitiless desert sun* 無情的沙漠烈日 —**pitilessly** *adv* —**pitilessness** *n* [U]

pi·ton /ˈpitɑn; ˈpiːtɒn/ *n* [C] a piece of metal used in climbing, that you fix into the rock to hold the rope〔攀登用的〕鋼錐

pit po·ny /ˈ· ˌ··/ *n* [C] a small horse that was used in the past for moving coal in a mine〔過去在煤礦中運煤的〕小馬

pit prop /ˈ· ·/ *n* [C] a support for the roof of an underground passage in a coal mine〔支撐礦井巷道頂用的〕坑柱, 支柱

pit stop /ˈ· ·/ *n* [C] **1** a time when you stop in the pits (PIT[1] (7)) during a car race to get more petrol or have repairs done〔汽車賽中的〕加油時間, 停車維修時間 **2 make a pit stop** *AmE informal* to stop when driving on a long journey, for food, petrol etc【美, 非正式】〔駕車長途旅程中旨在用餐或加油等的〕中途停車

pit·ta bread *BrE*【英】, **pita bread** *AmE*【美】/ˈpitə brɛd; ˈpɪtə bred/ *n* [C,U] a type of bread which is flat and hollow〔扁平且中空的〕圓麵包

pit·tance /ˈpɪtn̩s; ˈpɪtəns/ *n* [singular] a very small or unfairly small amount of money 少量的錢, 少得可憐的錢: *She gets paid a pittance.* 她的收入少得可憐。

pit·ted /ˈpɪtɪd; ˈpɪt̬ɪd/ *adj* **1** having small marks or holes in the surface 有麻點的, 有凹陷的, 有坑窪的: *His skin was pitted like orange peel.* 他的皮膚像橙皮一樣滿是麻點。| **[+with]** *The cylinders were pitted with corrosion.* 這些鋼瓶鏽跡斑斑。**2** a pitted fruit has had the single, hard seed removed from it〔水果〕去核的: *pitted cherries* 去核櫻桃 | *pitted olives* 去核橄欖

pit·ter·pat·ter /ˈpɪtɚ ˌpætɚ; ˈpɪtə ˌpætə/ *adv* **go pitter-patter** to make a sound consisting of many quick light beats or sounds 發出劈劈啪啪的聲音, 發出噗噗的聲音: *Anna's heart went pitter-patter as she opened the letter.* 安娜打開信時, 心噗噗直跳。—**pitter-patter** *n* [singular]: *the pitter-patter of rain on the roof* 雨落在屋頂上劈劈啪啪的聲音

pi·tu·i·ta·ry /pɪˈtuəˌtɛrɪ; pɪ̆ˈtjuːɪ̆təri/ also 又作 **pituitary gland** /·ˈ···· ˌ·/ *n* [C] the small organ at the base of your brain which produces HORMONES that control the growth and development of your body (腦) 垂體 —**pituitary** *adj*

3 **pit·y[1]** /ˈpɪtɪ; ˈpɪti/ *n* **1 (it's a) pity** *spoken* used to show that you are disappointed about something and you wish things could happen differently【口】真可惜, 真遺憾: **[+(that)]** *Ralph's a really nice guy – pity he's not better looking.* 拉爾夫真是個好人 —— 遺憾的是他長得不怎麼好看。| *It's a pity that Jan and George can't make it to the party.* 真可惜, 簡和喬治不能來參加這次聚會。| *Pity they didn't think of that earlier.* 可惜的是他們沒有早想到那點。| **a pity to do sth** *It seems a pity to waste it.* 把它浪費掉似乎可惜。| **what a pity** *"Did you know the concert was cancelled?" "No, what a pity."* "你知道音樂會取消了嗎?" "不知道, 真遺憾。" | **a great pity** *There were very few locals at the meeting, which is a great pity.* 會上沒有幾個當地人, 真是一大遺憾。**2** [U] sympathy for someone who is suffering or unhappy 憐憫, 同情: *London's homeless need more than pity – they need practical help.* 倫敦的無家可歸者需要的不僅僅是憐憫, 他們需要的是實實在在的幫助。| *Poor man, she thought with pity, he's given up.* 真可憐, 她滿懷同情地想, 他已經放棄了。**3 for pity's sake** *spoken* used to show that you are very annoyed and impatient【口】請發發慈悲吧, 請可憐可憐吧〔用於表示非常煩惱和不耐煩〕: *For pity's sake just shut up and let me drive!* 請發發慈悲, 閉上嘴讓我開車! **4 take pity on** to feel sorry for someone and do something to help them 同情, 可憐: *We walked on through the pouring rain until a kind driver took pity on us.* 我們走在傾盆大雨中, 直到一位好心的司機對我們發了善心。**5 more's the pity** *spoken* used after describing a situation, to show that you wish it was not true【口】太不幸了, 太可惜了〔用於描述某個情況並希望那不是真的〕: *The new staff are all women, more's the pity.* 新的工作人員都是女性, 太可惜了。**6 have pity on** *formal* to forgive someone or treat them sympathetically【正式】原諒; 同情, 憐憫

pity[2] *v* [T not usually in progressive 一般不用進行式] to feel sorry for someone because they are in a very bad situation 同情, 憐憫; 可憐: *I pity anyone who has to feed a family on such a low income.* 我同情所有那些須以如此微薄的收入養活全家的人。| *I pity Sophie having to live with that awful woman.* 我很同情蘇菲, 她不得不和那個可惡的女人住在一起。

piv·ot[1] /ˈpɪvət; ˈpɪvət/ *n* [C] **1** a fixed central point or pin on which something balances or turns 樞, 樞軸, 支點, 支軸 **2** the one central thing that a whole plan depends on, and that everything is arranged around 核心, 中心: **[+of]** *The village chapel was the pivot of community life.* 這個村子的小禮拜堂是社區生活的中心。

pivot[2] *v* **1** [I,T] to turn or balance on a central point, or to make something do this (使) 在樞軸上轉動[平衡]: **[+on]** *The table-top pivots on two metal pins.* 那個桌面以兩個金屬釘為支軸旋轉。**2** [I] to turn quickly on your feet so that you face in the opposite direction〔以腳為支點〕轉身

pivot on sth *phr v* [T] to depend on or be planned around a particular event, or to have a particular idea as the central one 依靠, 依賴; 以...為中心: *This meeting with the board is crucial – our entire project pivots on it.* 與董事會的這次見面至關重要 —— 我們整個項目都取決於此了。

piv·ot·al /ˈpɪvətl̩; ˈpɪvətəl/ *adj* **1 a pivotal event/role/moment etc** an event etc that has a very important effect on the way something develops 關鍵事件/作用/時刻等: *Mandela's release was a pivotal event in South Africa's history.* 曼德拉的獲釋是南非歷史上的一個關鍵事件。| *The Small Business Act had a pivotal role in job creation.*《小型企業法案》在創造就業機會方面起了關鍵作用。**2** like or being a pivot 似樞軸的; 以樞軸為支點的: *a pivotal movement* 旋轉動作

pix /pɪks; pɪks/ *n* [plural] *slang* pictures or photographs【俚】圖片; 照片

pix·el /ˈpɪksl̩; ˈpɪksəl/ *n* [C] *technical* the smallest unit of an image on a computer SCREEN[1] (1)【術語】像素, 像點〔電腦屏幕上圖像最小的單元〕

pix·ie, pixy /ˈpɪksɪ; ˈpɪksi/ *n* [C] an imaginary creature that looks like a very small human being, has magical powers, and likes to play tricks on people 小妖精, 小精靈〔一種想像中的生物, 身材矮小、有法術且喜愛捉弄人〕

piz·za /ˈpitsə; ˈpiːtsə/ *n* [C,U] a thin flat round bread, baked with tomato, cheese, and sometimes vegetables or meat on top 比薩餅, 意大利薄餅〔餅上放番茄、乳酪, 有時加蔬菜或肉等烘烤而成〕 2

pizza par·lor /ˈ·· ˌ··/ *n* [C] *AmE* a restaurant that serves pizza; PIZZERIA【美】比薩餅餐廳, 意大利薄餅店

piz·zazz /pəˈzæz; pəˈzæz/ *n* [U] *informal* an exciting strong quality or style【非正式】活力, 激情, 生氣: *This song and dance show needs more pizzazz.* 這場歌舞表演需要更多點活力。

piz·ze·ri·a /ˌpitsəˈriə; ˌpiːtsəˈriːə/ *n* [C] a restaurant that serves pizza 比薩餅餐廳, 意大利薄餅店

piz·zi·ca·to /ˌpɪtsɪˈkato; ˌpɪtsɪˈkɑːtəʊ/ *n* [U] musical notes played by pulling on the strings (STRING[1] (4a)) of an instrument 撥奏; 撥奏曲

pj's /ˌpi ˈdʒez; ˌpiː ˈdʒeɪz/ *n* [plural] *AmE informal* PYJAMAS【美, 非正式】(一套) 睡衣褲

Pk the written abbreviation of 縮寫= PARK

pkt the written abbreviation of 縮寫= PACKET

Pl the written abbreviation of 縮寫= PLACE

pl the written abbreviation of 縮寫= PLURAL

plac·ard /ˈplækɑrd; ˈplækɑːd/ *n* [C] a large notice or advertisement put up or carried in a public place 廣告; 廣告牌; 佈告; 標語牌; 招貼: *The demonstrators carried placards attacking the government.* 示威者拿着攻擊政府的標語牌。

pla·cate /ˈpleket; pləˈkeɪt/ *v* [T] *formal* to make someone stop feeling angry; APPEASE【正式】使息怒, 使平靜; 安撫, 撫慰: *I tried to placate her by offering to pay for the repairs.* 我提出支付修理費, 試圖讓她平靜下來。—**placatory** /ˈplekəˌtorɪ; pləˈkeɪtəri/ *adv*: *placatory words* 安撫的話 —**placation** /pləˈkeʃən; pləˈkeɪʃən/ *n* [U]

place¹ /ples; pleɪs/ *n* [C]

① **PLACE, POSITION, OR AREA** 地方, 位置, 地區
② **TAKE PLACE** 發生, 舉行
③ **IN PLACE** 在適當的位置
④ **FIRST/SECOND PLACE** 第一/第二名
⑤ **OTHER MEANINGS** 其他意思

place 位置

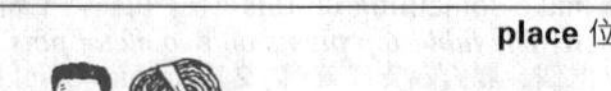

There are two places at the back.
There's still some room at the back.
後面有兩個位置。後面還有一些空位。

① PLACE, POSITION, OR AREA 地方, 位置, 地區

1 ▶POINT/POSITION 地點/位置◀ **a)** any area, point, or position in space 地方, 地點, 〔空間的〕位置: *This is the place where the accident happened.* 這就是事故發生的地方。| *Make sure you keep it in a safe place.* 一定要把它存放在安全的地方。| *We kept moving from place to place.* 我們不停地搬家。| *The whole place was covered in dust.* 整個地方滿是灰塵。**b)** a particular point in a larger area 〔較大區域的〕部位; 地方; 處: *a sore place on my shoulder* 肩膀的傷痛處 | *There's a place on the wall where the paint's coming off.* 牆上有塊地方的漆脫落了。—see 見 POSITION (USAGE) —see graph at 參見 LOCATION 圖表

2 ▶PLACE FOR DOING STH 做某事的地方◀ a place that is used for, or is suitable for, a particular purpose or activity 〔適合特定用途或活動的〕地方, 場所: **place to live/eat/park etc** *What they need is a decent place to live.* 他們所需要的是一個像樣的住處。| *I couldn't find a place to park.* 我找不到一個停車的地方。| **place for** *It's a great place for a vacation.* 這是度假的很好去處。| **sth's place** (=where something is usually kept) 某物常處的[原來的]位置 *Put it back in its place when you've finished with it.* 你用完以後把它放回原處。

3 ▶BUILDING/TOWN/COUNTRY ETC 建築物/城鎮/國家等◀ a particular place such as a shop, factory, town, or country 場所; 地區; 地方〈如商店、工廠、城鎮、國家〉: *They've just bought a little place in Wales.* 他們剛在威爾斯買了一所小房子。| *We were living then in a place called Alberiga.* 那時候我們正住在一個叫阿爾伯里格的地方。| *I got it at that big furniture place on the ring road.* 我是在環城路上的那個大家具店買到的。| *a nice Korean place* (=restaurant) *on the corner* 拐角處一家很好的朝鮮餐館

4 ▶SB'S HOUSE 某人的家◀ **your place/my place etc** *informal* the house, apartment, or room where you live, I live etc【非正式】你的住所/我的住所等: *Do you want to come back to our place for coffee?* 你想回到我們家喝咖啡嗎?

5 be no place for to be a completely unsuitable place 完全不適合…的地方[場所]: *A damp bedsit was no place for a baby.* 潮濕的臥室兼起居室完全不適合嬰兒。

6 place of work *formal* a factory, office etc where you work【正式】工作的地方〈如工廠、辦公室等〉

7 place of worship *formal* a building such as a church, where people have religious ceremonies【正式】做禮拜的場所〈如教堂〉

② TAKE PLACE 發生, 舉行

8 take place to happen, especially after being planned or arranged 〔尤指經過計劃或安排後〕發生, 舉行: *The next meeting will take place on Thursday.* 下次會議將在星期四舉行。| *the changes taking place in Indian society* 印度社會發生的變化

9 take the place of to exist or be used instead of someone or something else; REPLACE 代替, 取代: *Electric trains have now taken the place of steam ones.* 電氣化火車現在已取代了蒸汽機火車。| *No-one could take the place of her mother.* 沒有人能夠代替她的母親。

10 take second place to to be less important than someone or something else 處於次要地位: *Our personal wishes must take second place to the needs of the children.* 和孩子的需要相比較, 我們的個人願望必須置於次要地位。

11 take your place a) to go to a particular position that you need to be in for an activity 站好位置, 就位: *Take your places for the next dance.* 各就各位, 準備跳下一個舞。**b)** to join, and form an important part of, a group of people or things 佔據一席之地, 躋身於: *This new work will take its place among the most important paintings of the century.* 這一新作將躋身於本世紀最重要的繪畫作品之列。

③ IN PLACE 在適當的位置

12 in place in the correct or usual position 在適當[通常]的位置: *Have you got all the lights in place yet?* 你把所有的燈都放好了嗎?

13 in place of instead of 代替: *In place of our advertised programme, we will be showing a film.* 我們將放映一部電影來代替廣告節目。

14 in sb's place a) if you do something in someone's place, you do it because they were supposed to but could not 代替某人: *Jane was ill, so I went to the conference in her place.* 簡生病了, 所以我代替她出席了這次會議。**b)** *spoken* used when talking about what you would do if you were in someone else's situation【口】處於某人的處境[情況]: *What would you do in my place?* 你要是處於我的地位, 你會怎麼做?

15 in places in some parts or areas, but not everywhere 在一些地方, 有幾處: *In places, there was even mould on the walls.* 牆上有些地方甚至長了黴。

④ FIRST/SECOND PLACE 第一/第二名

16 first/second/third etc place first, second etc position in a race or competition 第一/第二/第三名等: *I finished in fifth place.* 我得了第五名。

17 in the first place a) used to introduce a series of points in an argument, discussion etc 首先, 第一: *Well, in the first place, I can't afford it, and in the second place I'm not really interested.* 首先我沒錢, 其次我也不怎麼感興趣。**b)** *spoken* used when talking about what was done, or should have been done, at the start of a situation【口】一開始, 起初: *I should never have gone in the first place!* 當初我壓根兒就不該去!

⑤ **OTHER MEANINGS** 其他意思

18 ▶AT COLLEGE ETC 在大學等◀ an opportunity to take part in a course, activity, event etc〔修讀課程、參加活動、項目等的〕機會, 名額: *He's been offered a place at York University.* 他已被約克大學錄取。| *There are only two places left on the word-processing course.* 文字處理課程只剩兩個名額了。

19 ▶AVAILABLE SPACE 可利用的空間◀ a seat on a bus, room in a hotel etc that is available for someone to use〔公共汽車上的〕座位, 位子;〔酒店裡的〕房間: *There are still a few places left on the coach.* 長途公共汽車上還有幾個空位。

20 all over the place *informal*【非正式】**a)** everywhere 到處: *There were policemen all over the place.* 這個地方到處都有警察。**b)** in a very untidy state 淩亂, 雜亂: *Her hair was all over the place.* 她的頭髮亂蓬蓬的。

21 ▶AT A TABLE 在桌子上◀ a knife, fork, spoon, plate etc arranged on a table for one person to use〔餐桌上供一人使用的〕餐具; 餐位: *Shall I lay places for five or for six?* 我要擺五個人的餐具還是六個人的?

22 put sb in their place to show someone that they are not as clever or important as they think they are 使某人明白自己的地位; 煞某人的氣焰: *A few curt remarks from the chairperson soon put Bates in his place.* 主席幾句冷淡無禮的話很快就使貝茨明白了他自己是誰。

23 out of place a) not suitable for a particular situation or occasion 不適當的; 不相稱的: *I felt completely out of place among all those smart rich people.* 在那些精明的富人中間, 我覺得完全格格不入。**b)** not in the correct or usual position 不在適當[通常]的位置上: *Nothing was ever out of place in Kitty's house.* 在吉蒂的家裡, 每樣東西都擺放得整整齊齊。

24 not your place if it is not your place to do something, it is not your responsibility to do it, especially because you do not have enough power 你無權..., 你沒有責任...: *It's not my place to tell the directors what to do!* 我無權吩咐董事們做甚麼!

25 lose your place to not know what point you had reached in a book, speech etc 找不到剛才讀到[講到]的地方: *The lecturer seemed to have lost his place.* 那位講師好像想不起剛才講到哪兒了。

26 save/keep sb a place to make sure that people do not sit in a particular chair that you want to save for someone else 給某人留位置/佔位置: *I might arrive a bit late, so could you save me a place?* 我可能會晚來一會兒, 你能給我留個位置嗎?

27 have no place *formal* to be completely unacceptable【正式】完全不能接受的: *People with racist views have no place in this union.* 帶有種族主義觀點的人該工會是不吸納的。

28 fall into place a) if things fall into place in your mind, you suddenly realize and understand what is really happening〔情況〕變得清楚: *When I found out who he was, everything suddenly fell into place.* 當我查明他是誰時, 一切都突然變得豁然開朗。**b)** if plans or events fall into place, they start to happen in the way that you hoped they would〔計劃或事件〕按所希望的方式發生, 變得有條不紊: *Eventually I got a job, moved house, and my life began to fall into place.* 最後我得到了一份工作, 搬了家, 我的生活開始步入正軌。

29 be going places *informal* to start becoming successful in your life【非正式】開始取得成功: *He's really going places as an actor.* 作為演員, 他真的開始走紅了。

30 know your place *often humorous* to behave in a way that shows that you know which people are more important than you【常幽默】知道你自己的位置〔指你知道哪些人比你更重要〕, 有自知之明: *I'll get back to the kitchen then – I know my place!* 我會回廚房去——我知道自己的位置! —see also 另見 DECIMAL PLACE, **have/take pride of place** (PRIDE[1] (6))

USAGE NOTE 用法說明: PLACE

WORD CHOICE 詞語辨析: **room, space, place, somewhere, anywhere**

The uncountable nouns **room** and **space** can both mean an empty area that can be used for any purpose. 不可數名詞 room 和 space 兩者都能用來指可作任何用途的空間: *Is there (any) room/space for me/us to sit down in here?* 這裡有我/我們坐的地方嗎? | *Is there room/space for more books on this shelf?* 書架上有可以放更多書的地方嗎? | *There's not enough room/space to move in here!* 這裡沒有足夠的活動空間!

A place or **a space** [C] is a single piece of space that can be used for something. However, **a place** in this sense often has a planned or official purpose, while **a space** may be unplanned and smaller. a place 或 a space 指用於做某事的單個空間, 但 a place 用於此意時常指有計劃好的或正式的用途, 而 a space 可能沒有計劃, 而且很小: *I need a place to work* (=an office, a study, or desk). 我需要一個工作的地方〔指辦公室、書房或書桌〕。| *I need a space to work* (=a part of a room or table). 我需要一個工作的空間〔屋子或桌子的一部分〕。You say *a public place* but usually *a parking space* (=for one car) and, *an open/green space.* 人們可以說 a public place (公共場所), 但通常說 a parking space (停車位) 和 an open/green space (一塊空地/綠地)。

In spoken English people often use **somewhere** or **anywhere** 在英語口語中人們常用 somewhere 或 anywhere: *I can't find anywhere to park.* 我找不到停車的地方。| *He's looking for somewhere to park his car.* 他正在找停車的地方。

GRAMMAR 語法

Place is singular, with the plural **places**. place 是單數形式, 複數形式是 places: *I visited a lot of different places* (NOT 不用 *place*). 我參觀過很多不同的地方。

place² *v*

1 ▶POSITION 位置◀ [T always+adv/prep] to put something somewhere, especially with care〔尤指小心地〕放置: **place sth in/on/under etc** *He placed the book back on the shelf.* 他把那本書放回到了書架上。| *She had placed a tape recorder in front of her on the table.* 她把一台錄音機放在自己面前的桌子上。

2 ▶SITUATION 處境◀ [T always+adv/prep] to put someone or something in a particular situation 使...處於某種境地: *Her request places me in a very difficult position.* 她的要求使我非常為難。

3 ▶HOW IMPORTANT 多重要◀ [T] to decide how good or important something is, as compared to something else〔按好壞或重要性〕排列, 安排: *Place the wines in order of preference.* 把這些葡萄酒按口味偏好排列好。| **place value/importance etc on sth** *The company places emphasis on training its staff.* 這家公司很重視對員工的培訓。

4 ▶IN A JOB 在工作中◀ [T] *formal* to find a suitable job for someone【正式】為...找到合適的工作; 安插; 安排; 任命: *The agency had placed her with a local firm.* 該介紹所為她在當地一家公司找到了一份工作。

5 can't place sb to be unable to remember why you recognize someone, what their name is etc 不能想起[不記得]某人的詳情〈如為甚麼自己會認出某人或知道其名字等〉: *I'm sure I've met that girl before somewhere,* but I can't quite place her. 我肯定以前在甚麼地方見過那個女孩, 但她的具體情況我就想不起來了。

6 place a bet to risk money by guessing the result of a future event 下賭注

7 place an order to ask a shop or business to provide a product that you need 下定單, 訂購: *We placed an order with Whiteley's for 200 shirts.* 我們向懷特利商店訂購了200件襯衫。

8 be placed to do sth/be placed for sth to be in a situation where you have the ability or opportunity to do or have something 處於有能力[機會]做某事[擁有某物]的境地: *You're better placed to arrange the meeting than I am.* 你比我更有能力籌備這次會議。| *How are you placed for money?* (=do you have enough money?) 你的資金情況怎麼樣?

9 ►RACES 比賽◄ **a) be placed first/second etc** to be first, second etc in a race or competition〔在賽跑或競賽中〕得第一/第二名等 **b)** [T] *BrE* if a horse is placed in a race, it comes second or third【英】〔賽馬中〕得第二或第三名 **c)** [I] *AmE* if a horse places in a race, it comes second【美】〔賽馬中〕得第二名

pla·ce·bo /plə`sibo; plə'siːbəʊ/ *n* [C] a substance given to a patient instead of medicine, without telling them it is not real, so that they get better because they think they are taking medicine〔用來代替真的藥物使病人誤以為自己是在服藥而病情好轉的〕安慰劑: **placebo effect** (=the positive effect achieved by this) 安慰劑效應〔服用安慰劑後病情好轉〕

place card /'· ·/ *n* [C] a small card with someone's name on it, put on a table to show where they are going to sit〔放在桌子上、寫明名字的〕座位卡[牌]

place kick /'· ·/ *n* [C] a kick at a ball, especially in RUGBY or American football, when the ball is placed or held on the ground〔尤在橄欖球或美式足球中的〕定位踢

place mat /'· ·/ *n* [C] a mat that you put on a table for each person who is eating there〔餐桌上用餐人面前的〕餐具墊(子)

place·ment /`plesmənt; 'pleɪsmənt/ *n* **1** [U] the act of finding a place for someone to live or work 安置; 就業安排 **2** [C] *especially BrE* a job, usually as part of a course of study, which gives you experience of a particular type of work【尤英】〔通常作為學習一部分的〕工作; 實習職位 **3** [C,U] the act of placing something in position 放置, 佈置, 擺放

pla·cen·ta /plə`sɛntə; plə'sentə/ *n* [C] a thick mass of flesh that joins an unborn child to its mother in the WOMB 胎盤

place set·ting /'· ˌ··/ *n* [C] an arrangement of knives, forks, spoons, glasses etc to be used by one person〔進餐前〕餐位餐具的擺放

plac·id /`plæsɪd; 'plæsɪ̈d/ *adj* **1** a placid person or animal does not easily get angry or excited〔人或動物〕平和的, 溫和的: *He had a placid nature, well-suited to teaching.* 他天性溫和, 非常適合教書。**2** calm and peaceful 平靜的, 寧靜的: *The lake was placid and still under the moonlight.* 月光下, 湖面上水平如鏡。—**placidly** *adv*: *Dobbs stood at the entrance, placidly smoking his pipe.* 多布斯站在入口處, 平靜地抽着煙斗。—**placidity** /plə`sɪdətɪ; plə'sɪdɪ̈ti/ *n* [U]

pla·gia·ris·m /`pledʒəˌrɪzəm; 'pleɪdʒərɪzəm/ *n* **1** [U] the act of using someone else's words, ideas, or work and pretending they are your own 剽竊, 抄襲: *He was accused of plagiarism in his doctoral thesis.* 他被指責在博士論文中有剽竊行為。**2** [C] an idea, phrase, story etc that has been copied from someone else's work, without stating that this is where it came from 剽竊物〈如觀點、短語、故事等〉: *an article full of plagiarisms* 一篇東抄西拼的文章 —**plagiarist** *n* [C]

pla·gia·rize also 又作 **-ise** *BrE*【英】/`pledʒəˌraɪz; 'pleɪdʒəraɪz/ *v* [I,T] to take words, ideas etc from someone else's work and use them in your work, as if they were your own ideas 剽竊, 抄襲〔別人的作品〕: *Half the ideas in his talk were plagiarized from an article I wrote last year.* 他講話中有一半的觀點是從去年我寫的一篇文章中剽竊來的。

plague[1] /pleg; pleɪg/ *n* **1** [C,U] an attack of a disease that causes death and spreads quickly to a large number of people 瘟疫, 傳染病, 疫病: *Europe suffered many plagues in the Middle Ages.* 歐洲在中世紀遭受過多次瘟疫。**2** [U] also 又作 **the plague** a very infectious disease that produces high fever and swellings on the body, and often leads to death, especially BUBONIC PLAGUE 瘟疫, 鼠疫〔尤指淋巴腺鼠疫〕: *an outbreak of plague* 鼠疫的爆發 —see also 另見 BLACK DEATH **3 a plague of rats/locusts etc** an uncontrollable and harmful increase in the numbers of a particular animal or insect 鼠災/蝗災等 **4 a plague on** *literary* used to show that you are extremely annoyed with someone or something【文】願上天降禍於〔表示非常氣惱〕—see also 另見 **avoid sb/sth like the plague** (AVOID (2))

plague[2] *v* [T usually passive 一般用被動態] **1** to cause continual discomfort, suffering, or trouble to someone 不斷困擾, 折磨, 使苦惱: *Nick was plagued by ill health throughout his short life.* 尼克短暫的一生中一直遭受着疾病的折磨。| *street crime, riots, and other social problems plaguing our community* 困擾我們社區的馬路犯罪、騷亂以及其他社會問題 **2** [T] to annoy someone, especially by continually asking them for something 使煩惱[生氣], 打攪: **plague sb with sth** *The kids have been plaguing me with questions.* 孩子們一直纏着問我問題。

plaice /ples; pleɪs/ *n plural* **plaice** [C,U] a flat sea fish that is a popular food 鰈〔頗受歡迎的一種食用海魚〕

plaid /plæd; plæd/ **1** [U] thick cloth with a pattern of squares, especially of a type (TARTAN) originally from Scotland〔尤指起源於蘇格蘭的〕彩格呢, 格子花呢 —see picture on page A16 參見A16頁圖 **2** [C] a piece of plaid worn over the shoulder and across the chest by people from Scotland as part of their NATIONAL COSTUME〔作為蘇格蘭民族服裝一部分的〕彩格呢披肩

plain[1] /plen; pleɪn/ *adj*

1 ►CLEAR 清楚的◄ very clear, and easy to understand or recognize; OBVIOUS (1) 清楚的, 明白的, 顯而易見的, 明顯的: *He spoke in Russian, but his message was plain enough.* 他雖是用俄語說的, 但意思表達得十分清楚。| **it is plain (that)** *It was plain that management policies would have to change.* 顯然, 管理方針將不得不加以改變。| **as plain as day/as plain as the nose on your face** (=very clear) 極為明顯(的), 非常清楚(的) *Phil loves her – that's as plain as day.* 菲爾愛她 —— 這是顯而易見的。

2 ►SIMPLE 簡單的◄ without anything added or without decoration; simple 無裝飾的, 簡單的, 樸素的, 單純的: *a plain white blouse* 一件樸素的白襯衫 | *It's just a plain wooden table but it looks just right in this room.* 這只是一張普通的木頭桌子, 但它放在這個房間正合適。| *plain food* 清淡的食物 | *a plain gold wedding ring* 一枚純金的結婚戒指 —see picture on page A16 參見A16頁圖

3 ►HONEST 誠實的◄ showing clearly and honestly what you think about something, without trying to hide anything; FRANK[1] (1) 坦白的, 直率的, 爽快的: *Let's have some plain, truthful answers.* 讓我們聽聽坦率而真實的回答吧。

4 make sth plain/make yourself plain to state something very clearly, in a way that cannot be misunderstood 把某事/自己的意思說明白: *They made their position plain from the start.* 他們一開始就表明了自己的立場。| *Let me make myself plain – we are not prepared to accept the deal as it stands.* 讓我把自己的立場說清楚 —— 我們不準備接受目前的這個協議。—see also 另見 PLAINLY

5 the plain truth/fact is *especially spoken* used to say what you think is the simple and honest truth about a situation【尤口】簡單的事實是, 明顯的事實是: *The plain*

truth is he's just not good enough. 簡單的事實是, 他就是不夠好。

6 plain stupidity/greed etc stupidity etc, and nothing else 十足的愚蠢/貪婪等: *His motive was plain greed.* 他的動機純粹是貪婪。

7 ▶NOT BEAUTIFUL 不漂亮的◀ a word meaning ugly or unattractive, often used because you want to avoid saying this directly 不好看的, 不漂亮的, 相貌平平的〔醜陋、難看的委婉說法〕: *Mrs Cookson was a rather plain woman.* 庫克森夫人是個相貌平庸的女人。

8 ▶PAPER 紙◀ plain paper does not have lines on it 不劃線的, 空白的

9 (just) plain Mr/Mrs etc used to say that someone does not have a title, rank, or special name (僅僅是) 不帶頭銜[稱號]的先生/夫人等〔用來表示某人沒有頭銜、特殊名稱等〕: *No, it's not Doctor, just plain Mister.* 不, 不是博士, 直接稱呼先生就行了。

10 in plain English simply or clearly expressed, especially without using technical language 用簡單的英語: *The computer system is explained in plain English.* 電腦系統是用簡單的英語解釋的。

11 in plain clothes police officers in plain clothes are not wearing uniform〔警察〕穿便衣的

12 be plain sailing to be very easy to do or achieve 一帆風順, 非常順利 —**plainness** *n* [U]

plain² *n* **1** also 又作 **plains** [C] a large area of flat dry land (大)平原: *The grassy plain gave way to an extensive swamp.* 青草覆蓋的草原被廣闊的沼澤地所取代。| *the vast plains of central China* 華中地區的廣闊平原 **2** [U] the ordinary stitch in knitting; KNIT (2)〔編織的〕平針

plain³ *adv* **plain stupid/wrong/rude etc** *informal* simply or completely stupid etc【非正式】簡直愚蠢/完全錯誤/十分粗魯: *It's just plain crazy to spend all your pay as soon as you get it.* 報酬一拿到手就花光, 簡直是瘋了。

plain·chant /ˋplentʃænt; ˈpleɪntʃɑːnt/ *n* [U] PLAINSONG〔昔日教堂中齊唱而無伴奏的〕素歌, 單旋律聖歌

plain choc·olate /ˌ· ˈ···/ *n* [U] *BrE* chocolate made without milk and with very little sugar【英】〔不加牛奶只加少量糖的〕黑[素, 純]巧克力; DARK CHOCOLATE *AmE*【美】

plain-clothes /ˌ· ˈ·◂/ *adj* plain-clothes police are police who wear ordinary clothes so that they can work without being recognised〔警察〕穿便衣的: *plain-clothes detectives* 便衣偵探

plain flour /ˌ· ˈ·/ *n* [U] *BrE* flour that contains no BAKING POWDER【英】無發酵粉的麵粉: *sift 6 oz plain flour* 篩六盎司不含發酵粉的麵粉 —compare 比較 SELF-RAISING FLOUR

plain·ly /ˋplenlɪ; ˈpleɪnli/ *adv* **1** in a way that is easy to hear, see etc 清楚地〔聽見、看見等〕: *We could hear Tom's voice plainly over the noise of the crowd.* 在人羣的喧鬧聲中, 我們可以清楚地聽到湯姆的聲音。| *The mountains were plainly visible from our window.* 從我們的窗戶望去, 羣山清晰可見。**2** speaking honestly, and without trying to hide the truth 坦白地, 直率地: *She told him plainly that she had no intention of marrying him.* 她坦率地告訴他自己不打算嫁給他。**3** if something is plainly true, necessary, correct etc it is easy to see that it is true etc; OBVIOUSLY很清楚, 顯然 [sentence adverb 句子副詞]: *Plainly an investigation into the tragedy would be necessary.* 顯然有必要對這場悲劇進行調查。**4** simply or without decoration 簡單地, 簡樸地, 樸素地: *a plainly dressed young girl* 穿着簡樸的年輕女孩

plain sail·ing /ˌ· ˈ··/ *n* [U] **be plain sailing** to be easy and not cause any trouble 一帆風順, 非常順利

plain·song /ˋplenˌsɔŋ; ˈpleɪnsɒŋ/ *n* [U] a type of old Christian church music in which a group of people sing a simple tune together, without musical instruments〔昔日教堂中齊唱而無伴奏的〕素歌, 單旋律聖歌

plain·spo·ken /ˋplenˋspokən; ˌpleɪnˈspəʊkən◂/ *adj* saying exactly what you think, especially in a way that people think is honest rather than rude 直言不諱的, 坦率的, 不客氣的

plain·tiff /ˋplentɪf; ˈpleɪntɪf/ *n* [C] someone who brings a legal action against someone in a court of law; COMPLAINANT 起訴人, 原告 [W3]

plain·tive /ˋplentɪv; ˈpleɪntɪv/ *adj* a plaintive sound is high, like someone crying, and sounds sad〔聲音〕淒厲的, 哀傷的: *the plaintive cry of the seagull* 海鷗淒厲的叫聲 —**plaintively** *adv*

plait¹ /plet; plæt/ *v* [T] *BrE* to twist 3 long pieces of hair, rope etc over and under each other to make one long piece【英】把…編成辮[繩]; BRAID² *AmE*【美】: *a plaited leather belt* 編成辮狀的皮帶 | *She plaited her hair hurriedly.* 她匆匆地把頭髮編成辮子。—see picture at 參見 HAIRSTYLE 圖

P

plait² *n* [C] *BrE* a length of something, especially hair, made by plaiting【英】髮辮, 辮子; 辮繩; BRAID¹ (2) *AmE*【美】: *Jenni wore her hair in plaits.* 珍妮梳着辮子。

plan¹ /plæn; plæn/ *n* [C] [S1] [W1]

1 ▶INTENTION 意圖◀ something you have decided to do or achieve 計劃, 打算, 目標: *His plan is to get a degree in economics and then work abroad for a year.* 他的計劃是取得一個經濟學學位, 然後去國外工作一年。| **sb's best plan** *BrE* (=the best course of action)【英】某人最好的辦法 *Your best plan would be to catch a taxi – it's much too far to walk.* 你最好的辦法是乘計程車——走路太遠了。| **change your plans/a change of plan** *There's been a change of plan – we're going on Monday instead.* 計劃有變——我們打算星期一去。| **have plans (for)** (=intend to do something) 有安排[打算] *We don't have any plans for the weekend – why don't you come over?* 我們週末沒有甚麼安排——你為何不過來呢? | **make plans (for)** (=prepare for something that you intend to do) 為…製訂計劃 *Julia's been busy making plans for her wedding.* 朱莉婭一直在忙於籌劃她的婚禮。

2 ▶METHOD/ARRANGEMENT 方法/安排◀ a set of actions for achieving something in the future, especially one that has been considered carefully and in detail〔尤指經過仔細考慮的〕規劃, 計劃, 方案: *the government's five-year economic plan* 政府的五年經濟計劃 | **plan for** *NASA announced plans for a new space station to be launched in 1998.* 美國太空總署公布了1998年發射新太空站的計劃。| **plan to do sth** *Have you heard about the plan to build a new science park?* 你聽說過要建造一個新的科技園的計劃嗎? | **keep to/stick to a plan** *If we keep to the plan the work should be completed in two weeks.* 如果我們按照計劃去做, 這項工作應該在兩週內完成。| **work out/draw up/devise a plan** *They devised a plan to reduce costs.* 他們製訂了一個降低成本的計劃。| **a plan falls through** (=it becomes impossible because something unexpected happens) 計劃落空 | **go according to plan** (=happen in the way that was expected or arranged) 按計劃進行 *If everything goes according to plan the first stage will be completed by December.* 如果一切按計劃進行, 第一期將在十二月之前完成。

3 ▶MAP 地圖◀ a drawing similar to a map, showing roads, towns, and buildings〔顯示道路、城鎮和建築物的〕詳圖: *a street-plan of London* 倫敦街道圖

4 ▶DRAWING 圖畫◀ **a)** *technical* a drawing of a building, room, or machine as it would be seen from above, showing the shape, measurements, position of the walls etc【術語】〔建築物、房間等的〕平面圖; 〔機器的〕圖樣, 圖紙 —compare 比較 ELEVATION (4), SECTION¹ (6) —see also 另見 GROUND PLAN (1) **b)** a drawing that shows exactly how something will be arranged〔顯示如何安排某物的〕示意圖: *I have to organise a seating plan for the dinner.* 我得為這次宴會設計一個座位示意圖。

5 plan of action/campaign a series of actions that you plan to carry out in order to achieve a particular thing 行動/活動計劃[方案]: *Get your team around a table and*

agree a plan of action to reach this season's targets. 讓你的小組集中起來商定一套能實現本季度目標的行動計劃。

6 Plan A your first plan, which you will use if things happen as you expect 第一方案〔指事情按預料的情況發展時用的計劃〕

7 Plan B your second plan, which you can use if things do not happen as you expect 第二方案, 備用方案〔指事情超出預期時用的計劃〕

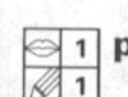

plan² *v* **planned, planning 1** [I,T] to think carefully about something you want to do in the future, and decide exactly how you will do it 計劃; 籌劃, 策劃: *We've been planning this visit for months – you can't cancel now.* 這次參觀我們已經計劃了好幾個月 —— 你不能現在就把它取消。| *The whole operation went exactly as planned.* 整個行動嚴格按計劃進行。| **[+on]** *We hadn't planned on having so many guests – we'll never have enough food for them all!* 我們沒料到會來這麼多客人 —— 我們根本沒有足夠的食物給他們吃! | **plan ahead** (=make plans for a long time in the future) 事先計劃 *Now that you're pregnant, you'll have to plan ahead.* 你既然懷孕了, 就必須預先把事情都安排妥當。**2** [T] to intend to do something, especially when you have definite plans for how you will do it 打算: **plan to do sth** *Josie planned to work until she had saved enough money to go to nursing school.* 喬茜打算先工作, 等儲足錢了再去上護士學校。**3** [T] to think about something you are going to make, and decide what it will be like; DESIGN² 設計: *Planning a small garden is often difficult.* 設計一個小花園常常都很困難。

plan sth ↔ out *phr v* [T] to plan something carefully, considering all the possible problems〔周密地〕計劃: *I'll get the maps so we can plan out our route.* 我去拿地圖, 讓我們來設計一下路線。

2 3 **plane¹** /plen; pleɪn/ *n* [C]

1 ►AIRCRAFT 飛機◄ a vehicle that flies in the air and has wings and at least one engine 飛機; AEROPLANE *BrE*【英】, AIRPLANE *AmE*【美】: *The next plane to New York departs in 20 minutes.* 下一班飛往紐約的航班將於 20 分鐘後起飛。| *It's quicker to go by plane.* 乘飛機去會快一些。

2 ►LEVEL 水平◄ a level or standard of thought, conversation etc〔思想、談話等的〕水平, 程度; 標準: *You can't really compare the two newspapers – they're on completely different intellectual planes.* 你實在無法比較這兩份報紙, 它們提供的知識層次完全不一樣。

3 ►TOOL 工具◄ a tool that has a flat bottom with a sharp blade in it, used for making wooden surfaces smooth 刨子, 平刨 —see picture at 參見 TOOL¹ 圖

4 ►TREE 樹◄ a PLANE TREE 懸鈴木

5 ►SURFACE 表面◄ *technical* a completely flat surface in GEOMETRY【術語】〔幾何學中的〕平面

plane² *adj* [only before noun 僅用於名詞前] *technical* completely flat and smooth【術語】平的, 平面的: *a plane surface* 平面

plane³ *v* [T] to use a PLANE¹ (3) on a piece of wood to make it smooth 用刨子把…刨平: *He planed the edge of the door.* 他把門的邊緣刨平。

plane ge·om·e·try /ˈ· ·ˌ···/ *n* [U] the study of lines, shapes etc that are TWO-DIMENSIONAL (=with measurements in only two directions, not three) 平面幾何學

plan·er /ˈplenɚ; ˈpleɪnə/ *n* [C] an electric tool for making wooden surfaces smooth 刨機, 刨牀 —see picture at 參見 TOOL¹ 圖

plan·et /ˈplænɪt; ˈplænɪ̣t/ *n* [C] **1** a very large round object in space that moves around the sun or another star; Earth is a planet 行星〈如地球〉: *Pluto is the smallest of all the planets.* 冥王星是所有行星中最小的。| *Is there life on other planets?* 在其他行星上有生命嗎? | *Planet Earth* 地球 **2 be (living) on another planet/what planet is sb on?** *spoken* humorous expressions used to say that someone's ideas are not at all practical or sensible【口】異想天開〔一種幽默的說法, 表示某人的想法毫不實際或不明智〕 **3 the planet** an expression meaning the world, used when talking about the environment 世界, 地球〔用於談論環境〕: *the future of the planet* 地球的未來 —**planetary** *adj*

plan·e·tar·i·um /ˌplænəˈtɛrɪəm; ˌplænɪ̣ˈteəriəm/ *n* [C] a building where lights on a curved ceiling show the movements of planets and stars 天文館, 天象館, 太空館

plane tree /ˈ· ·/ *n* [C] a large tree with broad leaves that is often planted along streets; PLANE¹ (4) 懸鈴木

plan·gent /ˈplændʒənt; ˈplændʒənt/ *adj literary* a plangent sound is loud and deep and sounds sad【文】〔聲音〕淒切的, 悲戚的, 如泣如訴的 —**plangently** *adv* —**plangency** *n* [U]

plank /plæŋk; plæŋk/ *n* [C] **1** a long narrow, usually heavy piece of wooden board, used especially for making structures to walk on (厚) 木板: *a small bridge made of planks* 用厚木板搭成的小橋 **2 plank of an argument/agenda/programme etc** one of the main features or principles of an argument etc 論證/議程/計劃等的要點: *The main plank of their election strategy is to reduce taxes on business.* 他們競選策略的主要一條是降低企業的稅收。—see also 另見 **walk the plank** (WALK¹ (12))

plank·ing /ˈplæŋkɪŋ; ˈplæŋkɪŋ/ *n* [U] planks when they are put together to make a floor 板材; 地板

plank·ton /ˈplæŋktən; ˈplæŋktən/ *n* [U] the very small forms of plant and animal life that live in water, especially the sea, and are eaten by fish〔尤指海中被魚類吞食的〕浮游生物

planned ob·so·les·cence /ˌ· ··ˈ··/ *n* [U] the practice of making products that will soon become unfashionable or less advanced than the newest ones, so that people will have to buy new ones more often 計劃報廢〔指生產很快就會過時或落後的產品, 以使人們不得不經常購買新的產品〕

plan·ner /ˈplænɚ; ˈplænə/ *n* [C] someone who plans something, especially someone whose job is to plan the way towns grow and develop 策劃者, 設計者; 〔尤指城市發展的〕規劃者

planning per·mis·sion /ˈ·· ·ˌ··/ *n* [U] official permission to build a new building or change an existing one〔興建或改建建築物的〕建築許可

plant¹ /plænt; plɑːnt/ *n* 2 1

1 ►LIVING THING 生物◄ [C] a living thing that has leaves and roots and grows in earth, especially one that is smaller than a tree〔尤指比樹小的〕植物; 樹秧: *Don't forget to water the plants.* 別忘記給植物澆水。| *a potato plant* 一棵馬鈴薯苗 | *plant pots* 花盆 —see also 另見 HOUSEPLANT

2 ►FACTORY 工廠◄ [C] a factory or building where an industrial process happens 工廠; 車間: *a huge chemical plant* 一座龐大的化工廠 —see also 另見 POWER PLANT

3 ►MACHINERY 機械◄ [U] *BrE* heavy machinery that is used in industrial processes【英】重型機械, 機械設備: *We are investing in new plant for the factory.* 我們正為工廠投資購置新的機械設備。| *a plant hire business* 出租重型機械的公司

4 ►STH ILLEGAL 非法的東西◄ [C usually singular 一般用單數] something illegal or stolen that is hidden in someone's clothes or possessions to make them seem guilty〔陷人入罪的〕贓物, 被栽的贓物

5 ►PERSON 人◄ [C] someone who is put somewhere or sent somewhere secretly to find out information 線人; 間諜

plant² *v* [T]

1 ►PLANTS/SEEDS 植物/種子◄ to put plants or seeds in the ground to grow 種植, 栽種; 播種: *to plant a tree* 種一棵樹 | *We've planted tomatoes and carrots in the garden.* 我們在花園裡種了番茄和胡蘿蔔。

2 plant a field/garden/area etc (with sth) to plant

seeds, plants, or trees in a field etc 在田地裡/花園裡/某地方種植[栽種]（某物）: *a hillside planted with fir trees* 種滿杉樹的山坡

3 ▶PUT STH SOMEWHERE 把某物放在某處◀ [always +adv/prep] *informal* to put something firmly in or on something else【非正式】牢牢插進; 安置: **plant sth in/on etc** *My grandmother planted a big wet kiss on my cheek.* 祖母在我的臉頰上使勁地印上一個大大的濕吻。| *She planted her feet firmly to the spot and refused to move.* 她雙腳穩穩地站在那裡, 拒絕移動。

4 ▶ILLEGAL GOODS 非法物品◀ *informal* to hide stolen or illegal goods in someone's clothes, bags, room etc in order to make them seem guilty【非正式】栽〔贓〕: **plant sth on sb** *Someone must have planted the drugs on her.* 一定是有人把這些毒品栽贓於她。

5 plant a bomb *informal* to put a bomb somewhere【非正式】放置炸彈: *Two men are accused of planting a bomb on the plane.* 兩名男子被控在飛機上放置炸彈。

6 ▶PERSON 人◀ [T] to put or send someone somewhere, especially secretly, so that they can find out information〔尤指祕密地〕安插〔線眼、密探等以獲取信息〕: **plant sb in/at etc** *The police had planted undercover detectives at every entrance.* 警方在每個入口處都安插了密探。

7 plant an idea/doubt/suspicion (in sb's mind) to make someone begin to believe an idea, especially so that they do not realize it was you who gave them the idea 把思想/懷疑/猜疑注入（某人的頭腦）,（給某人）灌輸思想/懷疑/猜疑

plant sth ↔ **out** *phr v* [T] to put a young plant into the soil outdoors, so that it has enough room to grow 把〔幼苗〕移植到戶外

plan·tain /ˈplæntɪn; ˈplæntɨn/ *n* **1** [C,U] a kind of BANANA that is cooked before it is eaten, or the plant on which it grows 大蕉（果實）—see picture on page A8 參見A8頁圖 **2** [C] a common wild plant with small green flowers and wide leaves 車前草

plan·ta·tion /plænˋteʃən; plænˈteɪʃən/ *n* [C] **1** a large area of land in a hot country, where crops such as tea, cotton, and sugar etc are grown〔熱帶國家的〕種植園[場]: *a rubber plantation* 橡膠園 **2** a large group of trees grown to produce wood 造林地, 林場

plant·er /ˈplæntɚ; ˈplɑːntə/ *n* [C] **1** a decorative container for growing plants in 花盆 **2** someone who owns or is in charge of a plantation 種植園主; 種植園管理者: *a tea planter* 茶場主, 茶葉種植園園主 **3** a machine used for planting 種植機, 播種機

plaque /plæk; plɑːk/ *n* **1** [C] a piece of flat metal or stone with writing on it that is fixed to a building and reminds people of an event or person connected with the place〔用金屬或石板製的、刻有紀念文字的〕飾板, 匾: *The mayor unveiled a special commemorative plaque.* 市長為一塊有特別意義的紀念牌匾揭幕。**2** [U] a substance which forms on your teeth, which BACTERIA can live and breed in〔牙齒上的〕牙斑

plas·ma /ˈplæzmə; ˈplæzmə/ *n* [U] **1** the yellowish liquid part of the blood that contains blood cells 血漿 **2** the living substance inside a cell; PROTOPLASM 原漿, 原生質 **3** a gas at a very high temperature inside stars, in flashes of electricity etc 等離子體

plas·ter[1] /ˈplæstɚ; ˈplɑːstə/ *n* **1** [U] a substance used to cover walls and ceilings and give a smooth surface, consisting of LIME, water, and sand〔塗抹牆壁、天花板等用的〕灰泥 **2** [U] PLASTER OF PARIS 熟石膏 **3** [C,U] *BrE* a piece of thin material that is stuck on to the skin to cover cuts and other small wounds【英】膏藥;（窄條）橡皮膏; BANDAID *AmE*【美】**4 in plaster** *BrE* if you have a leg, arm etc in plaster you have a PLASTER CAST around a bone that is broken to keep it in place while it mends【英】打了石膏（的）

plaster[2] *v* [T usually passive 一般用被動態] **1** to spread or stick something all over a surface so that it is thickly covered 在…上厚厚地塗抹; 覆蓋: **plaster sth with sth** *Her face was plastered with makeup.* 她的臉上塗着厚厚的化妝品。**2** to cover the pages of a newspaper with a particular story or report〔新聞報道等〕覆蓋, 佔滿〔報紙的版面〕: *The news of the wedding was plastered all over the morning papers.* 有關這場婚禮的新聞覆蓋了所有早報。**3** to put wet plaster on a wall or ceiling 在〔牆或天花板〕上塗灰泥 **4** to make your hair lie flat or stick to your head 使〔頭髮〕緊貼, 黏貼: **[+down/to etc]** *His hair was plastered to his forehead with sweat.* 他的頭髮沾了汗水, 緊貼在前額上。

plaster sth **over** *phr v* [T] to cover a hole or an old surface by spreading plaster over it〔通過塗灰泥〕覆蓋〔洞或舊的表面〕

plas·ter·board /ˈplæstɚˌbɔrd; ˈplɑːstəbɔːd/ *n* [U] board made of large sheets of cardboard held together with plaster, which is used to cover walls and ceilings 灰泥板, 石膏板

plaster cast /ˌ·· ˈ·/ *n* [C] **1** a cover made from plaster of Paris used to keep a broken bone in place while it mends; CAST[2] (2)〔用熟石膏製成的〕石膏繃帶, 石膏夾 **2** a copy of a STATUE made of plaster of Paris 石膏模型

plas·tered /ˈplæstɚd; ˈplɑːstəd/ *adj* [not before noun 不用於名詞前] *informal* very drunk【非正式】爛醉的: *Chris was plastered after five beers.* 克里斯喝了五瓶啤酒後就爛醉如泥了。

plas·ter·er /ˈplæstərɚ; ˈplɑːstərə/ *n* [C] someone whose job is to cover walls and ceilings with PLASTER[1] (1) 泥水匠, 塗灰泥工人

plaster of Par·is /ˈplæstɚ əv ˈpærɪs; ˌplɑːstər əv ˈpærɨs/ *n* [U] a quick-drying mixture of a white powder and water used for making plaster casts and to decorate buildings 熟石膏, 燒石膏

plas·tic[1] /ˈplæstɪk; ˈplæstɪk/ *n* **1** [C,U] a light strong material that is chemically produced, which can be made into different shapes when soft and is used to make many things 塑料, 塑膠: *children's toys made of plastic* 塑料製的兒童玩具 | *the plastics industry* 塑料工業 **2** [singular,U] *informal* small plastic cards that are used to pay for things instead of money; CREDIT CARDS【非正式】信用卡: *"I haven't got any cash." "Don't worry, I'll stick it on the plastic."* "我沒帶現金。" "別擔心, 給你記在信用卡上。" S2 W2

plastic[2] *adj* **1** made of plastic 塑料製的: *a plastic spoon* 塑料湯匙 | *plastic bags* 塑料袋 **2** *technical* a plastic substance can be formed into many different shapes and keeps the shape【術語】〔物質〕可塑的, 塑性的 **3** something that is plastic looks or tastes artificial or unnatural 人造的; 非自然的: *plastic food* 人造食品 | *I hate that plastic smile of hers.* 我討厭她那做作的笑容。

plastic art /ˌ·· ˈ·/ *n* [C,U] *technical* art which shows things in ways in which they can be clearly seen, especially painting or SCULPTURE【術語】造型藝術〔尤指繪畫或雕塑〕

plastic bul·let /ˌ·· ˈ··/ *n* [C] a large bullet made of hard plastic that is intended to injure but not kill, and is used for controlling violent crowds 塑料[塑膠]子彈〔用於控制暴亂人羣〕

plastic ex·plo·sive /ˌ·· ·ˈ··/ *n* [C,U] an explosive substance that can be shaped by hand, or a small bomb made from this 可塑炸藥;〔由可塑炸藥製成的〕可塑炸彈

plas·ti·cine /ˈplæstəˌsin; ˈplæstɨsiːn/ *n* [U] *BrE trademark* a soft substance like clay made in many different colours, used by young children for making models or shapes【英, 商標】〔兒童用以製作模型的〕橡皮泥, 塑膠黏土

plas·tic·i·ty /plæsˋtɪsətɪ; plæˈstɪsɨti/ *n* [U] *technical* the quality of being easily made into any shape【術語】可塑性

plastic mac /ˌ·· ˈ·/ *n* [C] a cheap coat made of plastic, used to keep you dry in the rain〔廉價的〕塑料雨衣

plastic sur·ge·ry /ˌ·· ˈ···/ *n* [U] the medical practice of changing the appearance of people's faces or bodies, either to improve their appearance or to repair injuries 整形外科, 整容手術 —**plastic surgeon** /ˌ‥ ˈ‥/ *n* [C]

plastic wrap /ˌ‥ ˈ‥/ *n* [U] *AmE* CLINGFILM【美】〔食物的〕保鮮塑料薄膜

plat du jour /ˌplɑ də ˈʒur; ˌplɑː duː ˈʒʊə/ *n* [C] *French* a dish that a restaurant prepares specially on a particular day in addition to its usual food【法】〔餐廳的〕當日特製菜, 當日推薦菜

plate¹ /plet; pleɪt/ *n*

1 ▶**FOOD** 食物◀ **a)** [C] a flat and usually round dish that you eat from or serve food from 盤, 碟: *The plates were piled high with rice.* 盤子裡盛滿了米飯。| *a dinner plate* 菜盤, 餐碟 | **clear/empty your plate** (=eat everything on your plate) 把盤子裡的東西吃乾淨 **b)** also 又作 **plateful** [C] the amount of food that is on a plate 〔食物〕一滿盤[碟]: [+of] *He's eaten a whole plate of french fries.* 他吃了一整盤炸薯條。

2 ▶**SIGN** 標牌◀ **a)** [C] a flat piece of metal with words or numbers on it, for example on a door or a car 〔印有文字或數字的〕金屬牌, 牌子, 名牌〈如門牌、車牌等〉: *The plate on the door said 'Dr Rackman'.* 門牌上寫着"雷克曼博士"。| *A plate below the statue indicated that it had been donated by the artist.* 塑像下面的牌子寫着它是由這位藝術家捐贈的。| **number/licence/registration plate** (=on a car) 汽車的牌照[號碼牌] *Did anyone see the car's license plate?* 有人看見那輛汽車的牌照嗎? —see also 另見 L-PLATE, NAMEPLATE **b) plates** [plural] the flat pieces of metal on a car which give information about who the car belongs to or which country it is from 〔顯示汽車歸誰所有或來自哪個國家等資料的〕車牌

3 have a lot on your plate *informal* to have a lot of problems to deal with or a lot of things to worry about【非正式】要應付的問題很多, 要操心的事情很多

4 hand sth to sb on a plate *informal* to let someone have what they want without making them work to achieve it【非正式】把某事物奉送給某人; 讓某人輕易獲得某事物: *Liverpool virtually handed the game to United on a plate.* 利物浦隊幾乎是拱手將這場比賽讓給了曼聯隊。

5 ▶**PROTECTIVE COVERING** 保護性覆蓋物◀ [C] **a)** *technical* one of the thin sheets of bone, horn etc that covers and protects the outside of an animal【術語】〔骨質、角質等的〕盾片, 鱗甲: *The reptile's body is covered with horny protective plates.* 爬蟲的身體表面覆蓋着保護性的角質鱗甲。**b)** a thin sheet of metal used to protect something 〔用於保護某物的〕金屬板[片]: *steel plates used in the construction of ships* 造船用的鋼板

6 ▶**EARTH'S SURFACE** 地球表面◀ [C] *technical* one of the very large sheets of rock that form the surface of the Earth【術語】板塊 —see also 另見 PLATE TECTONICS

7 ▶**GOLD/SILVER ETC** 金/銀等◀ **a) gold/silver etc plate** ordinary metal with a thin covering of gold, silver etc 鍍金/鍍銀等的金屬 **b)** [U] articles such as plates, cups, forks or knives made of gold or silver 金銀器具[餐具]

8 ▶**FOR COOKING** 用於烹飪◀ [C] *especially BrE* a metal ring on an electric COOKER that you put pans on when cooking【尤英】〔電爐上用於放鍋的〕金屬灶眼[爐板]

9 ▶**PICTURES/PHOTOS** 圖片/照片◀ [C] **a)** a sheet of metal that has been cut or treated in some way so that words or pictures can be printed from its surface 〔印刷用的〕金屬版, 印版, 圖版 **b)** a picture in a book, printed on good-quality paper and usually coloured 〔書中的〕整頁〔彩色〕插圖 **c)** *technical* a thin sheet of glass used especially in the past in photography, with chemicals on it that are sensitive to light【術語】〔尤指過去攝影用的〕感光板[片]

10 ▶**IN CHURCH** 在教堂裡◀ **the plate** a small plate or container, used to collect money in a Christian church 〔教堂中的〕捐獻盤[箱]

11 ▶**BASEBALL** 棒球◀ HOMEPLATE 本壘板

12 ▶**TEETH** 牙齒◀ [C] **a)** a thin piece of plastic shaped to fit inside a person's mouth, into which false teeth are fixed 假牙牀, 假牙托 **b)** a thin piece of plastic with wires fixed to it, that people wear to straighten their teeth; BRACE² (1) 牙箍, 牙齒矯正器

plate² *v* [T] **be plated with a)** to be covered with a thin covering of gold, silver etc 用〔金、銀等〕覆鍍, 鍍上〔金、銀等〕: *a beautiful necklace, plated with 22 carat gold* 一條漂亮的22開鍍金項鏈 | **gold-plated/silver-plated** *a gold-plated bracelet* 鍍金手鐲 **b)** to be covered in sheets of a hard material such as metal or bone 用〔金屬板或骨頭等堅硬材料〕覆蓋: *The ship had been heavily plated with protective sheets.* 那艘船有厚厚的保護性金屬板覆蓋着。

plat·eau /plæˈto; ˈplætəʊ/ *n plural* **plateaus** or **plateaux** /-ˈtoz; -təʊz/ [C] **1** a large area of flat land that is higher than the land around it 高原 —see picture on page A12 參見A12頁圖 **2** a period during which the level of cost, achievement etc does not change, especially after a period when it was increasing 平穩時期, 穩定狀態; 停滯時期: *Inflation rates have reached a plateau.* 通貨膨脹率已趨平穩。| *learning plateaus among 14-year-olds* 14歲孩子的學習停滯期

plate·ful /ˈpletful; ˈpleɪtfʊl/ *n* [C] all the food that is on a plate 一整盤[碟]〔食物〕

plate glass /ˌ· ˈ·◂/ *n* [U] big pieces of glass made in large thick sheets for use especially in shop windows 〔尤用於商店櫥窗的〕厚玻璃板, 平板玻璃

plate·lay·er /ˈ· ˌ‥/ *n* [C] *BrE* someone whose job is to make or repair railway tracks【英】〔鐵路的〕鋪路工; 〔維修軌道的〕養路工; TRACKLAYER *AmE*【美】

plate·let /ˈpletlɪt; ˈpleɪtlɪ̣t/ *n* [C] one of the very small plate-shaped cells in your blood that help it become solid when you bleed 血小板

plate tec·ton·ics /ˌ· ·ˈ‥/ *n* [U] the study of the forming and movement of the large sheets of rock that lie under the surface of the Earth 板塊構造學

plat·form /ˈplætˌfɔrm; ˈplætfɔːm/ *n* [C]

1 ▶**TRAIN** 火車◀ the raised place beside a railway track where you get on and off a train in a station 站台, 月台: *The Edinburgh train will depart from platform six.* 開往愛丁堡的火車將從六號站台開出。

2 ▶**FOR SPEECHES** 用於演講◀ a raised floor or stage for people to stand on when they are making a speech, performing etc 講台; 戲台, 舞台: *He climbed on to the platform and began to address the crowd.* 他登上講台開始向羣眾講話。| *Please address your comments to the platform.* (=the people on the platform) 請把你的意見向台上的講者提出來。| *a popular platform speaker* 一位受歡迎的公開演講者

3 ▶**STRUCTURE** 結構◀ a tall or high structure built so that people can stand or work above the surrounding area 高台, 平台: *an oil exploration platform* 石油勘探平台

4 ▶**POLITICS** 政治◀ **a)** [usually singular 一般用單數] the main ideas and aims of a political party, especially the ones that they state just before an election 〔尤指政黨競選之前發表的〕政綱, 綱領: *He's running for mayor on a platform of low taxation.* 他正以低稅收的政綱競選市長。—see also 另見 PLANK (2) **b)** a chance for someone to express their opinions, especially their political opinions 發表觀點的機會〔尤指政治觀點〕: *The conference provides a platform for people on the left wing of the party.* 這次會議給該黨的左翼人士提供了發表意見的機會。

5 ▶**BUS** 公共汽車◀ *BrE* the open part at the back of a DOUBLE-DECKER bus, where passengers get on and off the bus【英】〔雙層公共汽車後部的〕出入口平台

6 ▶**SHOES** 鞋子◀ also 又作 **platform shoe** a shoe that has a thick layer of wood, leather etc underneath the front part and the heel 厚底鞋

7 ►COMPUTERS 電腦◄ used to describe the type of computer system or SOFTWARE that you are using 平台〔指使用中的電腦系統或軟件〕: *We're changing from an IBM to a Macintosh platform.* 我們正在把IBM操作平台換成Macintosh平台。

plat·form game /'·· ˌ·/ *n* [C] a computer game in which the action happens against a background that does not move 平台遊戲〔背景不動的電腦遊戲〕

plat·ing /ˋpletɪŋ; 'pleɪtɪŋ/ *n* [U] a thin layer of metal that covers another metal surface 金屬鍍層: *gold plating* 鍍金層

plat·i·num /ˋplætṇəm; 'plætɪ̣nəm/ *n* [U] a silver-grey metal that does not change colour or lose its brightness, used in making expensive jewellery and in industry. Platinum is an ELEMENT (1) 鉑, 白金〔一種化學元素〕: *a platinum ring* 白金戒指 | *jewellery made of platinum* 白金首飾

platinum blonde /ˌ··· '·/ *n* [C] *informal* a young woman whose hair is a silver-white colour, especially one whose hair has been coloured with chemicals【非正式】(染)銀白色頭髮的年輕女子

plat·i·tude /ˋplætəˌtud; 'plætɪ̣tjuːd/ *n* [C] a statement that has been made many times before and is not interesting or clever 老生常談, 陳詞濫調: *a typical politician's speech, full of platitudes* 充滿陳詞濫調的典型政客演講 —**platitudinous** /ˌplætəˋtudṇəs; ˌplætɪ̣'tjuːdɪ̣nəs◄/ *adj*

pla·ton·ic /pləˋtɑnɪk; plə'tɒnɪk/ *adj* a relationship that is platonic is just friendly or affectionate, not a sexual relationship〔關係〕親密而無性愛的, 柏拉圖式的, 純精神戀愛的, 純友誼的 —**platonically** /-klɪ; -kli/ *adv*

pla·toon /pləˋtun; plə'tuːn/ *n* [C] a small group of soldiers which is part of a COMPANY and is commanded by a LIEUTENANT〔士兵的〕排

plat·ter /ˋplætɚ; 'plætə/ *n* [C] **1** *especially AmE* a large plate from which food is served【尤美】大淺盤 **2 chicken/seafood etc platter** chicken etc and other foods arranged on a plate and served in a restaurant〔餐館裡的〕雞肉/海鮮等拼盤 **3** *BrE old use* a large plate, usually made of wood【英舊】〔一般為木製的〕淺盤 **4** *AmE old-fashioned* a RECORD¹ (3)【美, 過時】唱片

plat·y·pus /ˋplætəpəs; 'plætɪ̣pəs/ *n* [C] a small, furry Australian animal that has a beak and feet like a duck, lays eggs, and gives milk to its young; DUCKBILLED PLATYPUS 鴨嘴獸

plau·dits /ˋplɔdɪts; 'plɔːdɪ̣ts/ *n* [plural] *formal* praise and admiration【正式】喝采, 讚揚, 讚美: *Her performance won the plaudits of the critics.* 她的表演贏得了評論家的讚揚。

plau·si·ble /ˋplɔzəbḷ; 'plɔːzɪ̣bəl/ *adj* **1** a statement that is plausible is reasonable and seems likely to be true 似乎是真的, 貌似有理的: *His explanation sounds fairly plausible to me.* 他的解釋我聽起來似乎頗有道理。**2** someone who is plausible is good at talking in a way that sounds reasonable and truthful, although they may in fact be lying〔人〕花言巧語的, 能言善辯的, 能說會道的: *a plausible rogue* 花言巧語的無賴 —opposite 反義詞 IMPLAUSIBLE —**plausibly** *adv*: *It could plausibly be argued that these improvements are due to government policy.* 有人可能會爭辯說這些進步都歸功於政府的政策, 這似乎有點兒道理。—**plausibility** /ˌplɔzəˋbɪlətɪ; ˌplɔːzɪ̣'bɪlɪ̣ti/ *n* [U]

1 1 **play¹** /ple; pleɪ/ *v*

1 ►CHILDREN 兒童◄ [I,T] when children play, they do things that they enjoy, often together or with toys 玩, 玩耍: *The children ran off to play on the beach.* 孩子跑到海灘上玩耍。| **play sth** *The boys were playing soldiers.* 孩子們假裝成士兵在玩。| *I don't want to play that game!* 我不想玩那個遊戲! | **[+with]** *play with your new toys* 玩你的新玩具 | *He loves playing with his grandchildren.* 他喜歡和孫兒一起玩。

2 ►SPORTS/GAMES 運動/比賽◄ [I,T] to take part in a game or sport 參加〔比賽或運動〕: **play sth** *Do you play a lot of golf?* 你常打高爾夫球嗎? | *I enjoy playing chess.* 我喜歡下棋。| **[+against]** *They're a terrible team to play against.* 他們是一支很難對付的球隊。| **[+for]** *He has played for England fifteen times now.* 他現在已為英格蘭隊打了十五場比賽。| **play sb** *She's playing Helen Evans in the semi-final.* (=playing against her) 她將在半決賽中與海倫·埃文斯交鋒。

3 play a ball to hit a ball in a game or sport〔在比賽或運動中〕擊球, 打球: *She played the ball low, just over the net.* 她把球打得很低, 剛剛過網。

4 play games to hide your real feelings or wishes in order to achieve something in a clever or secret way 與...耍花招, 耍手段〔指為獲得某物而隱藏真實的感情或願望〕

5 play the game to behave in a fair and honest way 辦事公道, 行動光明正大

6 ►MUSIC 音樂◄ [I,T] **a)** to perform a piece of music on a musical instrument 演奏, (用...)演[彈]奏〔樂曲〕: *I've always wanted to learn to play the piano.* 我一直想學彈鋼琴。| *She tried to play a Bach Prelude.* 她試着演奏了巴赫的一首前奏曲。| *Please play a tune on your concertina for me.* 請用你的六角形手風琴為我彈奏一曲吧。**b)** to produce music 播放[演奏]〔音樂〕: *The bedside radio played softly.* 牀邊的收音機輕柔地播放着音樂。| *I could hear a violin playing a waltz in the background.* 我可以聽到背景中有小提琴在演奏華爾茲舞曲。| **play a record/tape/CD** (=produce music from it) 播放唱片/錄音帶/雷射唱片 *He just sits in his bedroom all day playing records.* 他只是整天坐在臥室裡放唱片。

7 ►THEATRE/ACTING 劇院/表演◄ **a)** [T] to perform the actions and say the words of a particular character in a theatre performance 扮演〔角色〕: *He had always wanted to play Hamlet.* 他一直想扮演哈姆雷特。| **play a role/part** *The role of Mrs Goodfire was played by Jane Easton.* 古德費爾太太這個角色是由簡·伊斯頓扮演的。**b)** [I] if a play is playing at a particular theatre, it is being performed there〔戲劇〕上演: *'Macbeth' is now playing at the Theatre Royal in York.*《麥克白》目前正在約克皇家劇院上演。**c)** [T] if actors play a theatre, they perform there in a play〔演員〕在...演出

8 play a part/role in sth to have an effect or an influence on something 在某事中起作用, 在某事中有影響: *The press plays an important role in the life of a democracy.* 新聞界在民主國家的生活中起着很重要的作用。

9 ►PRETEND 假裝◄ [linking verb 連繫動詞] to behave as if you are a particular kind of person or have a particular feeling or quality, even though it is not true 假裝, 裝扮: **play dumb/dead etc** *The snake fools predators by playing dead.* 蛇以裝死來欺騙捕獵者。| **play the idiot/the teacher etc** *If he is captured, he must play the idiot and reveal nothing.* 如果他被抓獲, 就必須裝成白痴, 不透露任何事情。| **play policeman/soldier etc** *These are ordinary people who think they'll play policeman for a while.* 這些是自認為可以扮一會兒警察的普通人。| **play the fool** (=behave in a silly way) 做蠢事

10 play hard to get to pretend that you are not sexually interested in someone so that they will become more interested in you 對〔異性〕欲擒故縱〔故意裝出對某人不感興趣的樣子以吸引對方〕

11 ►BEHAVE 表現◄ [T always+adv/prep] to behave in a particular way in a situation in order to achieve the result or effect that you want〔以某種方式〕表現, 行事: *We always discuss how the event will be played.* 我們總是討論這件事將會如何發展下去。| **play it carefully/cool etc** *I think he might offer me the job, but I must play it carefully.* 我想他可能會給我這份工作, 但我必須謹慎對待。| **play (it) safe** (=avoid taking any risks) 穩重[謹慎]行事, 不冒險 | **play it by ear** (=decide what to do according to the way a situation develops) 見機行事, 隨機應變 *Let's just play it by ear.* 我們見機行事吧。

12 play a joke/trick on sb to do something to some-

one as a joke or trick 跟某人開玩笑/捉弄某人: *I was trying to play a joke on you.* 我本想跟你開個玩笑。
13 ►CARDS 紙牌◄ [T] to show a card in a game of cards by putting it down on the table 出〔牌〕: *She couldn't decide which card to play.* 她無法決定出哪一張牌。| *He played his ace and won the game.* 他出了張A牌贏了那一局。
14 play your cards right to behave in a clever or skilful way in a situation so that you gain as much as possible from it 做事精明, 處理得當: *If I play my cards right, I should do very well out of the deal.* 如果我處理得當的話, 應該可以從這項交易中大賺一筆。
15 play second fiddle (to sb) to be in a lower position or rank than someone else (給某人)當第二把手[副手], 居次要地位
16 play for time to try to delay something so that you have more time to prepare for it or prevent it from happening 為爭取時間而拖延: *He was playing for time until the others arrived.* 在其他人到齊之前, 他一直在拖延時間。
17 ►SMILE 笑容◄ [I always+adv/prep] if a smile plays over someone's lips, they smile quickly and only a little 〔嘴唇〕露出〔一絲微笑〕
18 ►LIGHT 光線◄ [I always+adv/prep] if light plays on something, it shines on it and moves about on it 〔在…上〕閃爍, 移動: *She watched the sunlight playing on the water.* 她注視着水面上閃爍的陽光。
19 play the system to use the rules of a system in a clever way, to gain advantage for yourself 鑽制度的空子〔使自己得益〕: *These accountants know how to play the tax system.* 這些會計知道如何鑽稅制的空子。
20 play the market to risk money on the STOCK MARKET as a way of trying to earn more money 〔在證券市場〕買賣證券謀利
21 play hooky *AmE* 【美】**/play truant** *BrE* 【英】 to stay away from school without permission 逃學; 曠課
22 play with fire to do something that could have a very dangerous or harmful result 做危險的事, 玩火
23 play a hose/light on sth to direct a HOSE or light towards something so that water or light goes onto it 把水龍頭[光線]對着某物噴射[照射]
24 not play ball to refuse to do something that someone else wants you to do 拒絕做〔別人要你做的事〕, 拒絕合作: *She wanted Dean to lend her the money, but he wouldn't play ball.* 她想迪安借錢給她, 但他拒絕了。
25 play the field to have sexual relationships with a lot of different people 與很多異性發生性關係, 濫交
26 play sb for a sucker *AmE* to show by the way that you behave towards someone that you think they are stupid 【美】把某人當成傻瓜: *It seems to me they are playing me for a sucker in this hotel.* 在我看來, 他們好像把我當作這酒店裡的傻瓜。
27 play fast and loose with sb *old-fashioned* to treat someone in a selfishly careless way 【過時】玩弄某人, 輕率地對待某人

play about/around with sb/sth *phr v* [T] **1** to have a sexual relationship with someone that is not serious or not intended to last very long 玩弄〔某人〕; 與〔某人〕有不正當性關係, 跟…亂搞[廝混]: *Her husband accused her of playing around with other men.* 她的丈夫指控她與別的男人鬼混。**2** to keep moving something around in your hands 〔在手中〕擺弄, 把玩: *Stop playing around with that knife!* 別再擺弄那把刀子了!

play along *phr v* **1** [I+with] to pretend that you agree with someone's ideas because you want to gain an advantage for yourself or to avoid a quarrel 假裝同意〔某人的觀點以獲得好處或避免爭吵〕, 暫且附和 **2** [T] **play sb along** to tell someone something that is not true because you need their help in some way 〔為取得某人的幫助而〕對某人撒謊, 欺騙某人

play at sth *phr v* [T] **1** if you play at doing something, you do not do it properly or seriously 不認真地幹, 對…敷衍了事: *He just plays at being an artist.* 他當藝術家只是玩玩而已。**2** if children play at doctors, soldiers etc, they pretend to be doctors or soldiers 〔小孩〕假扮…玩 **3 What is he/she etc playing at?** used when you do not understand what someone is doing or what they are trying to achieve 他/她等在幹甚麼?: *What do you think you're playing at?* 你到底在搞甚麼鬼? | *I don't know what on earth he's playing at.* 我不知道他究竟在幹甚麼。

play sth ↔ **back** *phr v* [T] to play something that has been recorded on a machine so that you can listen to it or watch it 重新播放〔已錄製的錄音帶、錄像帶等〕: *I recorded my brother singing a song then played it back to him.* 我把弟弟唱的歌錄下來然後放給他聽。

play sth ↔ **down** *phr v* [T] to try to make something seem less important than it really is 使…看起來不那麼重要, 貶低…, 對…輕描淡寫: *The government has tried to play down its defeat in the local elections.* 政府極力淡化它在地方選舉中的失敗。

play sb **off against** sb *phr v* [T] if you play one person off against another, you encourage them to argue or quarrel with each other so that you can gain something 〔為漁利而〕挑撥離間, 使…相鬥[對立, 爭吵]

play on sth *phr v* [T] to use a feeling or an idea in order to gain an advantage for yourself 利用〔別人的感情、觀點等〕: *They are playing on the fact that we don't like to appear ignorant.* 他們在利用我們不喜歡顯得無知這一事實。

play sth ↔ **out** *phr v* [T] if you play out an event, you take part in it in a way that seems to have been planned or thought about before 實際參加, 親身體驗: *The weekend gives you a chance to play out your fantasies.* 週末使你有機會親身實踐你所幻想的事情。| *She watched the farce that was being played out before her.* 她看着正在自己面前上演的鬧劇。

play up *phr v* **1** [T **play** sth ↔ **up**] if you play something up, you make it seem more important than it really is 誇大…的重要性; 抬高; 大肆渲染: *She knew the newspapers would try to play it up.* 她知道各家報紙將極力渲染這件事。**2** [I,T **play** sb ↔ **up**] if children play up, they behave badly 〔孩子〕搗蛋; 使〔某人〕惱火, 給〔某人〕製造麻煩: *The children have really been playing up this afternoon.* 今天下午孩子們一直在調皮搗蛋。| *I hope the kids don't play you up.* 我希望孩子們不會給你搗亂。**3** [I,T **play** sb ↔ **up**] to hurt you or cause problems for you 使〔某人〕感到痛苦; 給〔某人〕造成麻煩: *My leg's been playing me up recently.* 我的腿最近老是疼。| *The car's playing up again.* 這輛汽車又出毛病了。

play up to sb *phr v* [T] to behave in a very polite or kind way to someone because you want something from them 投〔某人〕所好, 逢迎, 討好, 巴結: *politicians playing up to popular opinion* 迎合公眾輿論的政客

play with sb/sth *phr v* **1** [T] to keep touching something or moving it about 擺弄, 玩弄: *Stop playing with the light switch!* 別再亂摸電燈開關了! **2 play with the idea of doing sth** to consider the possibility of doing something (不大認真地)考慮做某事: *I'm playing with the idea of writing a novel.* 我正在考慮寫部小說。**3 play with yourself** to touch your own sex organs for pleasure 手淫 **4 play with words** to use words in a clever or amusing way 玩文字遊戲, 玩弄詞藻 **5 have time/money to play with** to have extra time or money that is available to be used 有多餘的時間[金錢]可用: *The budget is very tight; there isn't much money to play with.* 經費很緊, 沒有很多錢可用。

play² *n*
1 ►THEATRE 劇院◄ [C] a piece of writing performed in a theatre or on television or radio, consisting of speeches and conversations between several characters 劇本; 戲劇; 電視[廣播]劇: *one of Shakespeare's best-known plays* 莎士比亞最著名的戲劇之一 | *When he retired, he wrote plays.* 他退休後開始寫劇本。| **put on**

a play (=perform a play) 上演戲劇 *The school will be putting on a play in the summer term.* 這所學校將在夏季學期上演一齣戲劇。

2 ▶AMUSEMENT 娛樂◀ [U] things that people, especially children, do for amusement rather than as work〔尤指兒童的〕遊戲, 玩耍; 娛樂: *Soon Henry tired of his play, and wandered off along the beach.* 亨利很快就玩厭了, 他於是沿着海灘漫無目的地走去。| **at play** (=playing) 在玩耍, 玩耍時 *the happy laughter of children at play* 孩子玩耍時快樂的笑聲 | **in play** (=done only for amusement, not seriously) 開玩笑地, 鬧着玩地 *She had hidden his books, in play.* 她鬧着玩地把他的書藏了起來。

3 ▶ACTION IN A GAME OR SPORT 比賽或體育活動中的動作◀ [U] the actions that form part of a game or a sport〔比賽或體育活動中的〕動作; 比賽: *The changes in rules were agreed upon before the next day's play began.* 在第二天的比賽開始之前, 人們一致同意對比賽規則的修改。| *The match began on time, but rain stopped play after only an hour.* 比賽準時開始, 但僅僅進行了一小時便因下雨而中止。| *We have seen some very good play this afternoon.* 今天下午我們看了一些很精彩的比賽。

4 in play/out of play if a ball is in play or out of play, it is inside or outside the area allowed by the rules of the game 界內/界外: *He kicked the ball out of play.* 他把球踢出界外。

5 bring sth into play to use something or make it have an effect 利用某物; 使某物發揮作用: *A whole complex system of muscles is brought into play for each movement of the body.* 身體的每個動作都要運用全身複雜的肌肉系統。

6 come into play to be used or have an effect 被利用[運用]; 起作用, 產生影響: *Several factors came into play to make this possible.* 幾個因素同時發揮作用使此事變得可能。

7 the play of light the pattern made by light as it moves gently over a surface 光的閃爍[掩映]: *the play of light on the water* 水面上光的閃動

8 play on words a use of a word that is interesting or amusing because it can be understood as having two very different meanings 說[用]雙關語

9 ▶LOOSENESS 鬆動◀ [U] if there is some play in something, it is loose and can be moved 鬆動: *There's too much play in that rope.* 那根繩子太鬆了。

10 make a play for sth to make an attempt to gain something 設法得到某物: *He made a play for the leadership last year.* 他去年費盡心機想當領導。

play·a·ble /ˈpleəbl; ˈpleɪəbəl/ *adj* **1** a piece of ground used for sports that is playable is in good condition and suitable for playing on〔場地〕可用於運動比賽的 **2** a piece of music that is playable is not too difficult to be played〔樂曲〕可演奏的, 不難演奏的

play-act·ing /ˈ· ˌ··/ *n* [U] behaviour that is not serious or sincere but is made to look as if it is 裝腔作勢, 假裝, 裝扮 —**play-act** *v* [I]

play·back /ˈpleˌbæk; ˈpleɪbæk/ *n* [C] *especially BrE* a recording of something that you play as soon as it is made, so that you can study it carefully; REPLAY[2] (2)【尤英】〔錄音、錄影等供仔細再聽再看的〕重放, 回放

play·bill /ˈplebɪl; ˈpleɪbɪl/ *n* [C] a printed notice advertising a play 戲劇海報

play·boy /ˈpleˌbɔɪ; ˈpleɪbɔɪ/ *n* [C] a rich man who does no work and spends his time enjoying himself with beautiful women, fast cars etc 花花公子, 尋歡作樂的有錢男子: *a middle-aged playboy* 一個中年的花花公子

play-by-play /ˌ· · ˈ·◂/ *n* [C usually singular 一般用單數] *AmE* a report on what is happening in a game of sport, given at the same time as the game is being played【美】〔體育比賽的〕實況報道

Play-Doh /ˈ· ·/ *n* [U] *trademark* a soft substance like clay made in many different colours, used by children for making models or shapes【商標】培樂多牌橡皮泥[黏土]

played-out /ˌ· ˈ·◂/ *adj* **1** someone who is played-out is not as strong, powerful etc as they used to be〔人〕衰竭的; 筋疲力盡的; 已喪失權力的 **2** old-fashioned and no longer useful 過時的, 陳舊的: *played-out ideas* 過時的觀念 —see also 另見 **play out** (PLAY[1])

play·er /ˈpleɚ; ˈpleɪə/ *n* [C] **1** someone who takes part in a game or sport 運動員, 選手, 球員: *a basketball player* 籃球運動員 **2** one of the important people or companies involved in a new or competitive type of business〔新型或競爭性商業的〕重要參與者: *Murdoch is one of the major players in the multimedia industry.* 梅鐸是多媒體產業的巨頭之一。**3** someone who plays a musical instrument〔樂器的〕演奏者 **4** *old-fashioned* an actor【過時】演員—see also 另見 **key mover/player** (KEY[1]) S2 W1

player pi·an·o /ˌ·· ·ˈ··/ *n* [C] a piano that is played by machinery, with the music controlled by a continuous roll of paper with holes cut into it for the notes 自動鋼琴 —see also 另見 PIANOLA

play·fel·low /ˈpleˌfɛlo; ˈpleɪˌfeləʊ/ *n* [C] *old-fashioned* someone that you play with when you are a child【過時】〔兒時〕一起玩耍的朋友, 玩伴

play·ful /ˈplefəl; ˈpleɪfəl/ *adj* **1** happily active and full of fun 活潑可愛的; 愛玩的: *a playful little dog* 活潑可愛的小狗 **2** not intended in a serious way 鬧着玩的, 開玩笑的, 不認真的: *a playful kiss on the cheek* 在面頰上鬧着玩地吻一下 | *She tried to sound playful.* 她極力用開玩笑的語氣說。—**playfully** *adv* —**playfulness** *n* [U]

play·go·er /ˈpleˌgoɚ; ˈpleɪˌgəʊə/ *n* [C] someone who often goes to see plays 經常看戲的人, 戲迷

play·ground /ˈpleˌgraund; ˈpleɪgraʊnd/ *n* [C] **1** a piece of ground for children to play on, especially at a school or in a park〔學校的〕操場, 運動場;〔公園的〕遊樂場 **2** a place where a particular group of people go to enjoy themselves 娛樂的地方, 享樂的地方: *the playground of the rich* 有錢人享樂的地方

play·group /ˈplegrup; ˈpleɪgruːp/ *n* [C,U] *BrE* a kind of school where children aged 2-5 meet to learn and play【英】〔二至五歲孩子的〕幼兒遊戲班; 幼兒園; PRESCHOOL *AmE*【美】: *Robert's at playgroup today.* 羅伯特今天上幼兒園了。

play·house /ˈpleˌhaus; ˈpleɪhaʊs/ *n* [C] **1** a word meaning a theatre used in its name 劇場, 戲院: *the Oxford Playhouse* 牛津戲院 **2** a small structure like a little house for children to play in〔像房子一樣的〕兒童遊戲屋

playing card /ˈ·· ·/ *n* [C] *formal* a CARD[1] (7)【正式】紙牌, 撲克牌

playing field /ˈ·· ·/ *n* [C] a large piece of ground with particular areas marked out for playing football, cricket etc〔足球、板球等的〕運動場 —see also 另見 LEVEL PLAYING FIELD

play·mate /ˈpleˌmet; ˈpleɪmeɪt/ *n* [C] *old-fashioned* someone who you play with when you are a child【過時】〔兒時〕一起玩耍的朋友, 玩伴

play-off /ˈ· ·/ *n* [C] an additional game played to decide who will win after a game has ended with no winner〔因不分勝負而進行的〕加時賽, 延長賽

play·pen /ˈpleˌpɛn; ˈpleɪpen/ *n* [C] a frame made of bars or a net that provides an area for a small child to play safely in〔讓幼兒安全地在其中玩耍的〕遊戲圍欄

play·room /ˈpleˌrum; ˈpleɪrʊm/ *n* [C] a room for children to play in 兒童遊戲室

play·school /ˈpleskul; ˈpleɪskuːl/ *n* [C] *BrE* another word for PLAYGROUP【英】playgroup的另一種說法

play·thing /ˈpleˌθɪŋ; ˈpleɪˌθɪŋ/ *n* [C] **1** a person that you treat like a toy, using them only for your own amusement and not caring about them 玩物, 被玩弄的人: *I'm not just your plaything, you know.* 你要知道我可不是你的玩物。| *Humanity has become the plaything of scientists, engineers and planners.* 人類已成了科學家、工程師和規劃者的玩物。**2** *formal* a toy【正式】玩具

play·time /ˈple͵taɪm; ˈpleɪtaɪm/ *n* [U] a period of time at a school, when children can go outside and play〔學校裡的〕遊戲[娛樂]時間

play·wright /ˈple͵raɪt; ˈpleɪraɪt/ *n* [C] someone who writes plays 劇作家

pla·za /ˈplæzə; ˈplɑːzə/ *n* [C] **1** a public square or market place, especially in towns in Spanish-speaking countries〔尤指講西班牙語國家的城市中的〕廣場; 集市場所 **2** a group of shops and other business buildings in a town〔城市的〕購物區; 商業區: *Central Plaza* 中心商業區 —compare 比較 MALL

plc /͵pi ɛl ˋsi; ͵piː el ˈsiː/ *n* PUBLIC LIMITED COMPANY; a large company in Britain which has shares that the public can buy〔英國的〕公共有限公司: *Marks & Spencer plc* 馬莎公共有限公司

plea /pli; pliː/ *n* **1** [C] an urgent, serious or emotional request 懇求, 請求: **make a plea (for)** *The missing girl's parents made a desperate plea for her to contact them.* 那個失蹤女孩的父母絕望地祈求女兒與他們聯絡。**2** [C usually singular 一般用單數] a statement by someone in a court of law saying whether they are guilty or not〔法庭上所作的〕答辯, 辯護, 抗辯: **make/enter a plea** *Your Honor, we enter a plea of 'not guilty'.* 法官大人, 我們作"不承認有罪"的抗辯。**3** [singular] an excuse for something 藉口, 託詞, 口實

plea bar·gain·ing /ˈ· ͵···/ *n* [U] the practice of agreeing to admit in a court that one is guilty of a small crime, in exchange for not being charged with a more serious crime〔為避免受到較重處罰而在法庭上承認輕罪的〕認罪求情協議

plead /plid; pliːd/ *v past tense* **pleaded** *or* **pled** /plɛd; pled/ *especially AmE*【尤美】**1** [I] to ask for something that you want very much, in a sincere and emotional way 懇求, 祈求, 央求: *"Don't go!" Robert pleaded.* "別走!"羅伯特央求道。| **[+for]** *The hostages' families pleaded for their safe return.* 人質的家屬祈求他們能平安回來。| **plead with sb to do sth** *Moira pleaded with her mother to let her go out.* 莫伊拉懇求母親讓她出去。| *a pleading voice* 懇求的聲音 **2** [I,T not in passive 不用被動態] *law* to state in a court of law whether or not you are guilty of a crime【法律】〔在法庭上〕認罪; 不認罪; 申辯, 答辯: *You are charged with grand theft. How do you plead?* 你被控犯有嚴重的盜竊罪, 你認罪嗎? | **plead guilty/not guilty/innocent** *Henderson pled not guilty to the charge of murder.* 亨德森不承認謀殺的指控。| *The accused is mentally unstable, and unfit to plead.* 被告精神不穩定, 不適合出庭申辯。—see graph at 參見 GUILTY 圖表 **3 plead ignorance/illness/insanity etc** to give a particular excuse for your actions 以不知情/生病/精神錯亂等為理由[藉口]: *Well, if a cop stops you for speeding, you can always plead ignorance.* 如果你因超速而被警察攔下, 你總是可以以不知道作為藉口。| *She left early, pleading a headache.* 她以頭痛為由提早離開了。**4** [T] to speak or argue in support of something 為…爭辯[辯護, 說話], 發表見解支持: **plead that** *Politicians pleaded that raising teachers' salaries would make the job more attractive.* 政客辯解說提高教師工資將使這項工作更有吸引力。

plead·ing·ly /ˈplidɪŋli; ˈpliːdɪŋli/ *adv* if you say something pleadingly, or look at someone pleadingly, you speak to them or look at them as though you are asking them to do something in a sincere and emotional way 懇求地, 乞求地

S3 W3 **pleas·ant** /ˈplɛzn̩t; ˈplezənt/ *adj* **1** enjoyable and making you feel happy; nice 令人愉快的, 愜意的, 舒適的: *Well, do have a pleasant weekend.* 好啦, 週末愉快。| *Nora! What a pleasant surprise to see you!* 諾拉!見到你真讓人驚喜! | *Yes, the cider's sweet, but it's pleasant.* 是的, 這蘋果酒很甜, 但它喝起來味道不錯。**2** friendly, polite, and easy to talk to 禮貌而友善的, 和藹可親的: *I know you don't like her, but at least try to be pleasant.* 我知道你不喜歡她, 但至少盡量對她友善一點。| *Nick seemed very pleasant on the phone.* 尼克在電話裡好像非常友善。**3** weather that is pleasant is dry and not too hot or cold〔天氣〕好的, 宜人的: *It's overcast, but quite pleasant.* 天雖然陰沉, 但相當宜人。—opposite 反義詞 UNPLEASANT —**pleasantly** *adv*: *pleasantly surprised* 又驚又喜

pleas·ant·ry /ˈplɛzn̩trɪ; ˈplezəntri/ *plural* **pleasantries** *n* [C usually plural 一般用複數] a funny or not very serious remark, made in order to be polite〔為表示禮貌而說的〕打趣的話, 客氣話: *A couple of old men stopped to exchange pleasantries in the street.* 幾位老人在大街上停下來互相寒暄一番。

please[1] /pliz; pliːz/ *interjection* **1** used when you want to ask for something politely 請, 好嗎〔用於禮貌地請求〕: *I'd like a cup of coffee, please.* 請給我來杯咖啡。| *Please can we go now?* 我們現在就走, 好嗎? | *"Would you like some more?" "Yes please."* "你想再來一點嗎?" "好的, 謝謝。" **2** used to emphasize a request or wish 好嗎, 請〔用於加強請求或願望的語氣〕: *"May I have some water?" "Please do."* "我可以喝點水嗎?" "請吧。" | *Please don't be too long, because I have to go out soon.* 請別待得太久, 因為我很快就得出去。| *Will you children please be quiet!* 你們這些孩子安靜些好嗎! **3** used when you want to accept something that someone has offered you and show that you are grateful 好, 行, 謝謝〔用於接受別人的好意並表示感謝〕: *"Would you like a cup of tea?" "Please, I'd love one."* "你想來杯茶嗎?" "好的, 請給我來一杯。" **4 Please!** *informal, often humorous* used to ask someone to stop behaving badly【非正式, 常幽默】夠了〔用於要求別人停止做某事〕: *Alison! Please!* 艾莉森!夠了! | *Please, John, this isn't the time to discuss it!* 好了, 約翰, 現在不是談論這件事的時候! **5 please Sir/Mrs Towers etc** *spoken* used by children to get an adult's attention【口】請聽我說, 先生/托爾斯太太等〔小孩用來引起成人的注意〕

please[2] *v* [not in progressive 不用進行式] **1** [I,T] to make someone happy or satisfied (使)高興, (使)歡喜, (使)滿意, 討好: **please sb** *I only got married to please my parents.* 我是為了讓父母高興才結婚的。| *The child is very eager to please.* 那個孩子非常熱衷於討好人。| **be hard/ easy etc to please** *Mark's a hard one to please.* 馬克是個難以取悅的人。—opposite 反義詞 DISPLEASE **2 please yourself a)** *spoken* used to tell someone that they can do whatever they like because you are annoyed and do not care what they do【口】〔表示不耐煩〕隨你的便, 我不在乎: *Well I'm going to the party – you can please yourself!* 那麼我要去參加聚會了——隨你的便吧! **b)** to do whatever you like because you do not have to obey anyone or follow any rules 願意怎樣就怎樣, 隨自己的便去做: *We don't have to be back in the hotel by any particular time, we can just please ourselves.* 我們不必一定要在某個時間以前回到旅館去, 我們想甚麼時候回去就甚麼時候回去。**3 as sb pleases a)** doing whatever you want to do 想做甚麼就做甚麼; 隨意: *He just does as he pleases and never thinks of anyone else.* 他只是想做甚麼就做甚麼, 從不考慮別人。**b)** *formal* used to tell someone that they will have to decide something and you do not mind what they do【正式】願意怎麼做都行〔用於表示不介意別人做甚麼〕**4 whatever/however etc sb pleases** whatever, however etc someone wants 某人喜歡的任何…: *They can appoint whoever they please.* 他們喜歡任命誰就可以任命誰。**5 bold/cool as you please** *spoken* used to express surprise about someone's behaviour, when they have done something strange as if it is completely normal【口】竟然若無其事地〔表示驚訝〕: *He was walking down the road carrying a rifle, as bold as you please.* 他竟若無其事地拿着一支步槍在大路上走。**6 if you please a)** *formal* used to make a polite request【正式】請, 勞駕〔用於禮貌地提出請求〕: *Close the door, if you please.* 請關上門。**b)** *old-fashioned* used to say that you find something difficult to believe, or are very surprised or angry about it【過時】

真奇怪; 真是豈有此理; 真令人難以置信〔用於表示難以置信、驚訝或氣憤〕: *And now she says she needs yet another new dress, if you please!* 她現在竟然說還需要一件新衣服, 真是豈有此理! **7 please God** used to express a very strong hope or wish 但願, 希望〔用於表示非常強烈的願望〕: *They should have got back by now – please God they're OK.* 他們現在應該已經回去了, 但願他們平安無事。

2 3 **pleased** /plizd; pli:zd/ *adj* **1** *especially BrE* happy or satisfied【尤英】快樂的, 高興的; 滿意的: *I was so pleased when they said they'd be able to stay another week.* 當他們說能多留一星期, 我非常高興。| **[+about]** *Are you pleased about the results?* 你對結果感到滿意嗎? | **pleased (with)** *Di seems pleased with her new car.* 迪好像對她的新車很滿意。| **pleased (that)** *I'm pleased you decided to come.* 我很高興你決定來。| **very/really pleased** *We asked our lawyer to check the contract, and we're really pleased we did.* 我們要求律師檢查一下合同, 我們非常高興自己那樣做了。| **be pleased to hear/see/report etc** *I'm pleased to hear about your new job.* 聽說你找到新工作, 我感到很高興。**2 be pleased to help/assist** to be very willing or happy to help 非常樂意幫助: *If there's anything we can do, we'd be pleased to help.* 如果我們可以做些甚麼, 我們將非常樂意幫忙。**3 (I'm) pleased to meet you** *spoken* used as a polite greeting when you meet someone for the first time【口】幸會, 很高興見到[認識]你〔初次會面時的禮貌說法〕**4 pleased with yourself** feeling unreasonably proud or satisfied because you think you have done something clever 自鳴得意: *She was looking very pleased with herself so I guessed she'd passed her driving test.* 她顯得非常得意, 我猜她是通過了駕駛考試。**5 not very pleased** *informal, often humorous* rather annoyed【非正式, 常幽默】相當生氣的: *She wasn't very pleased when she found out about the dent in her car.* 她發現自己的汽車上有凹痕後很不高興。

pleas·ing /ˈplizɪŋ; ˈpli:zɪŋ/ *adj formal*【正式】**1** giving pleasure or enjoyment; pleasant 使人愉快的; 愜意的: **[+to]** *The painting is very pleasing to the eye.* 那幅畫非常悅目。**2** making you feel pleased and satisfied 使人高興的, 令人滿意的: *He has made pleasing progress in French this year.* 今年他在法語方面取得了令人滿意的進步。—**pleasingly** *adv*

plea·sur·a·ble /ˈplɛʒərəbl; ˈpleʒərəbəl/ *adj formal* enjoyable【正式】令人愉快的, 令人快樂的, 舒適的: *a pleasurable feeling of anticipation* 愉快的期待心情 —**pleasurably** *adv*

2 2 **plea·sure** /ˈplɛʒɚ; ˈpleʒə/ *n*

1 ▶ENJOYMENT 愉快, 樂趣◀ [U] the feeling of happiness or satisfaction that you get from an experience you enjoy 愉快, 快樂; 滿足: *The children used to get a lot of pleasure out of that game when they were young.* 這些孩子小時候從那個遊戲中得到過很多樂趣。| **give/bring pleasure** *Small gifts give pleasure and don't cost much.* 小禮物使人得到很多樂趣而且花費不多。| **great pleasure** *a film that has given great pleasure to millions* 一部給數百萬人帶來無窮歡樂的電影

2 ▶ENJOYABLE EXPERIENCE 令人愉快的經歷◀ [C, U] an activity or experience that you enjoy very much 愉快的活動[經歷], 樂事: *the simple pleasures of life* 簡單的生活樂趣 | **it is a pleasure to do sth** *It's been a great pleasure to meet you.* 見到你真是一大樂事。

3 take pleasure in to be pleased about and proud of something 以…為樂; 為…感到驕傲: *He took great pleasure in his grandchildren's achievements.* 他為孫輩的成就感到驕傲。

4 take pleasure in doing sth to enjoy doing something bad to other people 喜歡做某事〔指對別人不好的事〕: *Charlie seems to take pleasure in bullying the younger kids.* 查利似乎很喜歡欺負比自己小的孩子。

5 (it's) my pleasure *spoken* used when someone has thanked you for doing something and you want to say that you were glad to do it【口】別客氣, 不用謝〔表示樂意做某事〕

6 with pleasure *spoken* used to say politely that you are happy to do something that someone has just asked you to do【口】非常願意, 非常樂意: *"Will you come?" "With pleasure madam."* "你願意來嗎?" "非常願意, 夫人。"

7 have the pleasure of (doing) sth a) *formal* to enjoy the experience of something【正式】有幸(做), 榮幸: *I don't think I've had the pleasure of meeting your wife.* 我想我還未有幸見到你的妻子。**b)** *humorous* used when you do not think something is enjoyable【幽默】有幸[福氣](做)…〔用於表示某事令人不愉快〕: *We had the pleasure of Rob's company last week.* 我們上星期真榮幸有羅布做伴〔反話〕。

8 at his/her Majesty's pleasure *BrE law* if someone is put in prison at his or her Majesty's pleasure, there is no fixed limit to the time they have to spend there【英, 法律】犯人被監禁沒有固定的期限, 隨意在押

9 at your pleasure if you can do something at your pleasure, you can do it when and as you want to 隨你的便, 隨你的意願

10 sb's pleasure *formal* what someone wants【正式】某人的意願[願望]: *You can go there if that's your pleasure.* 你如果想去那裡就可以去。

pleasure seek·er /ˈ‥ ˌ‥/ *n* [C] someone who does things just for enjoyment without considering other people〔不考慮他人的〕尋歡作樂者, 玩樂的人

pleat[1] /plit; pli:t/ *n* [C] a flat narrow fold in cloth〔布料上的〕褶 —see picture on page A17 參見A17頁圖

pleat[2] *v* [T] to make a lot of flat narrow folds in a piece of cloth 使打褶 —**pleated** *adj*: *a pleated skirt* 百褶裙

pleb /plɛb; pleb/ *n* [C usually plural 一般用複數] *informal or humorous* an insulting word meaning someone who is from a low social class【非正式或幽默】下層平民〔侮辱性說法〕: *Plebs like me can never aspire to such perfect manners.* 像我這樣的下層平民永遠不會追求如此完美的禮儀。—**plebby** *adj*

plebe /plib; pli:b/ *n* [C] *AmE informal* a first year student at a military or naval college or university【美, 非正式】〔美國陸軍或海軍學院的〕一年級新生

ple·be·ian /plɪˈbiən; plɪˈbi:ən/ *n* [C] **1** an insulting word for someone who is from a low social class 下層平民〔侮辱性說法〕**2** an ordinary person who had no special rank in ancient Rome〔古羅馬的〕平民, 庶民 —compare 比較 PATRICIAN —**plebeian** *adj*

pleb·is·cite /ˈplɛbəˌsaɪt; ˈplebɪ̈sɪ̈t/ *n* [C,U] a system by which everyone in a country votes to decide a matter of national importance 公民投票(制): *The choice of whether to join the federation was decided by plebiscite.* 是否加入聯邦是由公民投票決定的。—compare 比較 REFERENDUM

plec·trum /ˈplɛktrəm; ˈplektrəm/ *n* [C] a small thin piece of plastic, metal, or wood, that you hold and use for playing some stringed musical instruments such as a GUITAR; PICK[2] (5)〔彈奏結他等弦樂器用的〕撥子, 琴撥

pled /plɛd; pled/ *ScotE and AmE*【蘇格蘭和美】the past tense and past participle of PLEAD

pledge[1] /plɛdʒ; pledʒ/ *n* [C]

1 ▶PROMISE 保證, 諾言◀ *formal* a firm promise or agreement, especially one made publicly or officially【正式】〔尤指公開或正式作出的〕誓言, 誓約; 保證: *Industrial conflicts continued in spite of a no-strike pledge by the unions.* 儘管各工會都作出了不罷工的承諾, 但是勞資衝突仍在繼續。| **a pledge to do sth** *the government's pledge to make no deals with terrorists* 政府不向恐怖分子妥協的保證 | **fulfil a pledge** (=do what you promised) 履行諾言 *Eisenhower fulfilled his election pledge to end the war in Korea.* 艾森豪威爾履行了他競選時所作的結束韓戰的承諾。

2 sign/take the pledge *old-fashioned* to promise never to drink alcohol, for religious or moral reasons【過時】

〔出於宗教或道德原因而〕發誓戒酒
3 a pledge of love/friendship etc a serious promise of love etc made by two people 發誓相愛/友好等
4 ►SOMETHING VALUABLE 有價值的東西◄ something valuable that you leave with someone else as proof that you do what you have agreed to do, pay back what you owe etc 抵押物: *She borrowed £50 and left her gold bracelet as a pledge.* 她借了 50 英鎊, 並留下她的金手鐲作抵押品。
5 ►AT US COLLEGES 在美國的大學裡◄ someone who has promised to become a member of a university FRATERNITY or SORORITY in the US but must pass a test before they can join〔美國大學的〕宣誓加入男生[女生]聯誼會的人〔他們在成為正式會員前須先通過一些測試〕

pledge[2] *v* [T] **1** to make a formal, usually public, promise that you will do something 發誓, 作保證: **pledge to do sth** *They have pledged to fight any changes to the abortion laws.* 他們已發誓竭力阻止對墮胎法所作的任何改動。| **pledge that** *The UK government has pledged that the wishes of the minority community in Northern Ireland will be respected.* 英國政府已作出允諾, 北愛爾蘭少數民族的意願都將受到尊重。| **pledge support/loyalty/solidarity etc** (=promise to give your support etc) 發誓支持/效忠/團結等 **2** to make someone give a firm promise 使〔某人〕發誓[保證, 許諾]: *75% of members were pledged in advance to vote for the labor program.* 75% 的成員事先被要求發誓投票支持工會的計劃。| **pledge yourself to sth** *The Republicans pledged themselves to a tough stand against crime.* 共和黨已保證會採取強硬態度抵制罪案。**3** to leave something with someone as a PLEDGE[1] (4) 抵押, 典當 **4** to promise to become a member of a university FRATERNITY or SORORITY in the US〔在美國的大學〕宣誓加入男生[女生]聯誼會

pleis·to·cene /ˈplaɪstəˌsin; ˈplaɪstəsiːn/ *adj* belonging to the period in the Earth's history that started about a million years ago and lasted about 800,000 years, when much of the Earth was covered with ice 更新世的〔地球上大約一百萬年前開始並持續了約八十萬年的一段時期, 那時地球表面大部分被冰覆蓋〕

ple·na·ry /ˈplinərɪ; ˈpliːnəri/ *adj* [only before noun 僅用於名詞前] *formal*【正式】**1** a plenary meeting is one that is attended by everyone who has a right to attend〔會議〕全體出席的: *The conference ended with a plenary debate.* 這次會議以一場全體出席的辯論結束。**2** plenary power or authority is complete and has no limit〔權力或權威〕全權的, 充分的, 無限制的: *The envoy was given plenary powers to negotiate with the rebels.* 該特使被授予全權同反叛者談判。—**plenary** *n* [C]

plen·i·po·ten·tia·ry /ˌplɛnəpəˈtɛnʃərɪ; ˌplenɪ̱pəˈtenʃəri/ *n* [C] *formal or technical* someone who has full power to take action or make decisions, especially as a representative of their government in a foreign country【正式或術語】〔尤指在外國代表本國政府的〕全權大使, 全權代表 —**plenipotentiary** *adj*: *plenipotentiary powers* 全權

plen·i·tude /ˈplɛnəˌtjud; ˈplenɪ̱tjuːd/ *n literary*【文】**1** [U] completeness or fullness 完全, 充分 **2 a plenitude of** a large amount of something 大量的, 豐富的, 充足的: *a plenitude of sunshine* 充足的陽光

plen·te·ous /ˈplɛntɪəs; ˈplentiəs/ *adj poetic* plentiful【詩】豐富的, 充足的, 富裕的 —**plenteously** *adv* —**plenteousness** *n* [U]

plen·ti·ful /ˈplɛntɪfəl; ˈplentɪfəl/ *adj* more than enough in quantity 豐富的, 充足的: *a plentiful supply of food and wine* 食物和(葡萄)酒的大量供應 | *Opportunities to practice the language are plentiful.* 練習該語言的機會很多。—**plentifully** *adv*

S1 W2 **plen·ty[1]** /ˈplɛntɪ; ˈplenti/ *pron* a large quantity that is enough or more than enough 豐富, 充足, 眾多, 大量: *If you want some more chairs, there are plenty more in here.* 如果你還想要椅子, 這裡多的是。| [+of] *Make sure she eats well and gets plenty of fresh air.* 要確保她吃得好並多吸新鮮空氣。| *You've got plenty of time.* 你有充足的時間。| *I don't want any more work, I already have plenty to do.* 我不想再做甚麼工作了, 我要做的已經夠多了。—compare 比較 FEW, LOT

plenty[2] *adv informal*【非正式】**1 plenty big enough, plenty bright enough etc** more than big enough, bright enough etc 非常[足夠]大/明亮等: *This apartment's plenty big enough for two.* 這套公寓非常大, 足夠兩個人住。**2** *AmE* to a large degree; a lot【美】十分, 非常; 很多: *I sleep plenty, but I always wake up feeling tired.* 雖然我睡得很多, 但醒來後總是感到疲倦。

plenty[3] *n* [U] *formal*【正式】**1** a situation in which there is a large supply of something, especially something that is needed for life〔尤指生活所需東西的〕充裕, 富足: *In years of plenty everyone has enough to eat.* 豐年時人人都吃得飽。**2 in plenty** in large supply; more than enough 供應充足, 多得很: *There was food and wine in plenty.* 食物和(葡萄)酒都很充足。—see also 另見 HORN OF PLENTY

ple·o·nas·m /ˈpliəˌnæzəm; ˈpliːənæzəm/ *n* [C,U] *technical* the use of more words than are needed to express an idea【術語】冗筆, 贅述, 冗詞[句]: *The phrase 'an apple divided into two halves' is a pleonasm.* 片[短]語 an apple divided into two halves (分成兩個一半的蘋果) 是贅述。—**pleonastic** /ˌpliəˈnæstɪk; ˌpliːəˈnæstɪk◂/ *adj*

pleth·o·ra /ˈplɛθərə; ˈpleθərə/ *n* **a plethora of** *formal* an amount of something that is larger than is needed or more than you can deal with【正式】過多, 過剩, 過量: *a plethora of suggestions* 一大堆建議 | *a plethora of paperwork* 過多的文書工作

pleu·ri·sy /ˈplurəsɪ; ˈplʊərɪ̱si/ *n* [U] a serious illness which affects your lungs, causing severe pain in your chest and sides 胸膜炎, 肋膜炎

plex·i·glass /ˈplɛksɪˌglæs; ˈpleksiˌglɑːs/ *n* [U] *AmE trademark* the name of a particular type of plastic, that is often just used to mean any plastic【美, 商標】珀斯佩有機玻璃; 透明塑膠; PERSPEX *BrE*【英】

plex·us /ˈplɛksəs; ˈpleksəs/ *n* —see 見 SOLAR PLEXUS

pli·a·ble /ˈplaɪəbl̩; ˈplaɪəbəl/ *adj* **1** easy to bend without breaking or cracking 柔韌的, 易彎的; 柔軟的: *The clay should be moistened regularly to keep it soft and pliable.* 這黏土應定期弄濕使之保持柔軟易塑。**2** able and willing to change and accept new ideas and ways of doing things; ADAPTABLE 能夠變通的, 樂意接受新思想[方法]的; 適應力強的: *The committee would benefit from having members who are more pliable.* 委員會擁有適應力強的成員將大有好處。**3** too easily influenced by other people 易受影響的; 順從的 —**pliability** /ˌplaɪəˈbɪlətɪ; ˌplaɪəˈbɪlɪ̱ti/ *n* [U]

pli·ant /ˈplaɪənt; ˈplaɪənt/ *adj* pliable 易彎的; 柔韌的; 能夠變通的; 適應力強的; 易受影響的; 順從的 —**pliantly** *adv* —**pliancy** *n* [U]

pli·ers /ˈplaɪɚz; ˈplaɪəz/ *n* [plural] a small tool made of two crossed pieces of metal, used to hold small things or to bend and cut wire 鉗子, 手鉗, 老虎鉗 —see picture at 參見 TOOL[1] 圖

plight[1] /plaɪt; plaɪt/ *n* [usually singular 一般用單數] a bad, serious, or sad condition or situation〔壞的、嚴重的或悲傷的〕境況, 困境, 苦境: *the plight of homeless children* 無家可歸的兒童的苦況

plight[2] *v* **plight your troth** *old use* to make a promise to someone that you will marry them【舊】答應結婚, 訂婚

plim·soll /ˈplɪmsl̩; ˈplɪmsəl/ *n* [C] a light shoe with a top made of thick cotton cloth and a flat rubber SOLE[2] (2) 橡皮底帆布鞋, 膠底運動鞋; SNEAKER *AmE*【美】—see picture at 參見 SHOE 圖

Plimsoll line /ˈ·· ·/ also 又作 **Plimsoll mark** *n* [C] a line painted on the outside of a ship, showing the depth to which it can safely be allowed to float in the water when it is loaded〔船的〕載重線標誌, 載重吃水線

plinth /plɪnθ; plɪnθ/ *n* [C] a square block, usually made of stone, that is used as the base for a PILLAR OR STATUE〔石柱或雕像的〕柱基; 底座

Pli·o·cene /ˈplaɪəˌsin; ˈplaɪəsiːn/ *adj* belonging to the period in the Earth's history that started about thirteen million years ago and lasted about twelve million years 上新世的〔地球上始於約一千三百萬年前並持續了約一千二百萬年的一段歷史時期〕

plod /plɑd; plɒd/ *v* **plodded, plodding 1** [I always+adv/prep] to walk along slowly, especially with difficulty and great effort; TRUDGE[1] 沉重緩慢地走, 步履艱難地走: **[+through/along etc]** *The children were plodding through the snow.* 孩子們正步履艱難地走過雪地。| *The mule plodded up the hill.* 那頭騾子艱難緩慢地往山上走。 **2 plod on/along** to keep working steadily, especially at something that is uninteresting or difficult 孜孜不倦地幹, 埋頭苦幹: *I'll just plod on for another hour or so.* 我再埋頭苦幹一小時左右。

plod·der /ˈplɑdɚ; ˈplɒdə/ *n* [C] someone who works slowly and is not very clever 工作很慢且不太聰明的人: *I've always been a bit of a plodder.* 我一向是個慢慢苦幹的人。

plonk[1] /plɑŋk; plɒŋk/ *v* [T] *informal*【非正式】**1** to put something down somewhere, especially noisily and carelessly 重重地放下: **plonk sth in/on etc** *Just plonk those bags anywhere in my room.* 把那些袋隨便放在我房間裡就行了。**2 plonk yourself (down)** to sit down heavily and then relax 重重地坐下放鬆: *We plonked ourselves in front of the telly.* 我們咚的一聲坐在電視機前。

plonk[2] *n* [U] *BrE informal* cheap wine【英, 非正式】廉價酒

plonk·er /ˈplɑŋkɚ; ˈplɒŋkə/ *n* [C] *BrE slang*【英俚】**1** a stupid person 愚蠢的人 **2** a PENIS 陰莖

plop[1] /plɑp; plɒp/ *n* [C] a sound like something solid dropping into liquid〔物體掉入液體中的〕撲通聲, 啪嗒聲: *The soap fell into the bath with a loud plop.* 肥皂撲通一聲掉進了浴缸。

plop[2] *v* **plopped, plopping 1** [I always+adv/prep] to fall somewhere making a sound like a plop 撲通[啪嗒]地落下: **[+on/down etc]** *A few drops of rain began to plop on to the roof.* 幾滴雨開始啪嗒啪嗒地落到屋頂上。**2** [T] to put something into a liquid so that it makes a sound like a plop 把…撲通[啪嗒]一聲放入[液體裡]: **[+into]** *I plopped a couple of ice cubes into the drink.* 我把幾塊冰啪嗒一聲放入飲料之中。**3 plop (yourself) down** to sit down or lie down heavily 重重地坐下[躺下]: *She plopped down on a chair.* 她撲通一聲坐在椅子上。

plo·sive /ˈplosɪv; ˈpləʊsɪv/ *n* [C] *technical* a CONSONANT sound that is made by completely stopping the flow of air out of your mouth and then suddenly letting it out, done, for example, when saying /b/ or /t/【術語】〔輔音〕爆破音〈如 /b/ 和 /t/ 音〉—**plosive** *adj*

plot[1] /plɑt; plɒt/ *n* [C]
1 ►STORY/FILM 故事/電影◄ the set of connected events that a story, film etc is based on〔故事、電影等的〕情節: *The plot of 'Twin Peaks' was so complicated that I couldn't follow it.*《雙峯》的情節太複雜了, 我跟不上。
2 ►PLAN 計劃◄ a secret plan, involving several people, to do something harmful or illegal 密謀, 陰謀, 祕密計劃: **[+to]** *There have been rumors of a plot to overthrow the President.* 謠傳說有人密謀推翻總統。| **hatch a plot** (=start making a plan) 策劃陰謀
3 the plot thickens *spoken humorous* used to say that events seem to be becoming more complicated and difficult to understand【口, 幽默】情況開始複雜起來; 事情越來越糾纏不清了
4 ►PIECE OF LAND 一塊土地◄ **a)** a small piece of land for building or growing things on〔建築或種植用的〕小塊土地[地皮] **b)** a piece of land that a particular family owns in a CEMETERY, in which members of the family are buried when they die〔屬於某家族的〕一塊墓地
5 ►DRAWING 圖畫◄ *AmE* a drawn plan of a building at ground level; GROUND PLAN【美】樓層平面圖

plot[2] *v* **plotted, plotting 1** [I,T] to make a secret plan to harm a person or organization, especially a political leader or government 密謀, 策劃, 圖謀: *We spent all week plotting our revenge.* 我們花了整整一星期策劃報復行動。| **[+against]** *They were plotting against the government.* 他們正在密謀反對政府。| **plot to do sth** *It was alleged that they had plotted to blow up the White House.* 據說他們密謀要炸毀白宮。**2** [T] to draw a line or curve that shows facts, figures etc 繪製…的圖表[平面圖, 曲線圖]: *We plotted a graph to show the increase in sales figures this year.* 我們繪製了一個圖表來顯示今年銷售額的增長。**3** [T] to mark, calculate, or follow the position of a moving aircraft or ship 標繪[計算, 追蹤]〔移動中的飛機或船隻的〕位置: *He was already bent over the table, plotting a new course.* 他已經趴在桌子上繪製新航線了。—**plotter** *n* [C]

plough[1] *usually* 一般作 **plow** *AmE*【美】/plaʊ; plaʊ/ *n* [C] **1** a large piece of farm equipment used to turn over the earth so that seeds can be planted 犁 **2 under the plough** used for growing crops 用於種植莊稼; 在耕種中 **3 the Plough** *especially BrE* the group of seven bright stars seen only from the northern part of the world【尤英】北斗七星; BIG DIPPER (2) *AmE*【美】—see also 另見 SNOW PLOUGH

plough[2] *usually* 一般作 **plow** *AmE*【美】*v* **1** [I,T] to turn over the earth using a plough so that seeds can be planted 犁(地), 耕(地): *a ploughed field* 犁過的地 **2** [I always+adv/prep] to move with a lot of effort or force 奮力前進: **[+along/across etc]** *The ship ploughed slowly across the bay.* 那艘船緩慢地破浪前進, 駛過海灣。

plough sth ↔ **back** *phr v* [T] to put money that you have earned back into a business in order to make the business bigger and more successful 把〔賺來的錢〕再投資: *Profits from ticket sales are ploughed back into further conservation projects.* 售票所得的利潤被再投放到更多的(自然)保護項目之中。

plough into sb/sth *phr v* [T] to hit something hard, especially while driving, because you are going too fast or not paying attention〔尤指駕車過快或不留神而〕猛撞上〔某物〕: *I ploughed into the car in front.* 我猛地撞上了前面的一輛車。

plough on *phr v* [I] to continue doing something that is difficult or boring 繼續做〔困難或枯燥的事情〕: *Julia ploughed on through the endless exam papers.* 朱莉婭繼續批改那些沒完沒了的考卷。

plough through *phr v* [T] to read all of something, even though it is boring and takes a long time 費力地堅持讀[看]完: *After ploughing through all those textbooks, it was a relief to read a novel.* 費力地看完那些課本之後, 讀本小說是一種放鬆。

plough sth ↔ **up** *phr v* [T] to break up the surface of the ground by repeatedly travelling over it 犁〔地〕, 翻〔土〕; 使有溝脊: *Horses plough up the paths and make them muddy for walkers.* 馬匹把條條小路踏出許多溝脊, 使行路者走起來泥濘不堪。

plough·boy /ˈplaʊˌbɔɪ; ˈplaʊbɔɪ/ *n* [C] *old use* a boy who led a horse that pulled a PLOUGH【舊】耕童, 牽耕畜的男孩

plough·man /ˈplaʊmən; ˈplaʊmən/ *n* [C] *old use* a man whose job was to guide a PLOUGH that was being pulled by a horse【舊】把[扶]犁人, 駕着馬拉犁的人

plough·man's lunch /ˌ·· ˈ·/ *n* [C] *BrE* a simple meal that people eat especially in PUBs, consisting of bread, cheese, onion, and PICKLE【英】〔尤指在小酒館吃的〕簡單午餐〔通常是麵包、乳酪、洋蔥和泡菜〕

plough·share *BrE*【英】*usually* 一般作 **plowshare** *AmE*【美】/ˈplaʊˌʃɛr; ˈplaʊʃeə/ *n* [C] the broad curved metal blade of a PLOUGH, which turns over the soil 犁頭, 犁鏵

plov·er /ˈplʌvɚ; ˈplʌvə/ *n* [C] a small bird that lives near the sea〔棲於海邊的〕鴴

plow /plaʊ; plaʊ/ *n, v* the usual American spelling of PLOUGH plough 的一般美式拼法

ploy /plɔɪ; plɔɪ/ *n* [C] a clever method of getting an advantage, especially by deceiving someone〔尤指欺騙性的〕計策, 手段, 花招: *His usual ploy is to pretend he's ill.* 他慣用的花招是裝病。| *a cynical ploy to win votes* 為博取選票而耍的不正當手段

pluck¹ /plʌk; plʌk/ *v*

1 ►TAKE STH 拿, 取某物◄ [T] to take hold of something and remove it from somewhere by pulling it 拔; 扯, 拉: **pluck sth from/off etc** *She bent forward to pluck a thread off the lapel of his jacket.* 她俯下身從他上衣的翻領上扯去一根線。

2 pluck up (the) courage to force yourself to be brave and do something you are afraid of doing 鼓起勇氣, 振作精神: *He finally plucked up enough courage to ask her out on a date.* 他終於鼓足勇氣約她出去。

3 ►CHICKEN ETC 雞等◄ [T] to pull the feathers off a dead chicken or other bird before cooking it 拔去〔死雞或其他禽類〕的毛〔準備烹調〕

4 ►FLOWER 花◄ *literary* to pick a flower or fruit【文】採, 摘, 掐〔花或果實〕: *Eve plucked an apple and offered it to Adam.* 夏娃摘了一個蘋果給亞當。

5 ►MUSIC 音樂◄ [I,T] to pull sharply at the strings of a musical instrument 撥〔弦〕, 彈奏: **[+at]** *Someone was plucking at the strings of an old guitar.* 有人在撥弄一把舊結他的弦。

6 ►TAKE SB AWAY 帶某人離開◄ [T always+adv/prep] to take someone away from a place or situation 帶〔某人〕離開〔某地或某處境〕: **pluck sb from/off/away etc** *She was plucked from obscurity by a film producer.* 一位電影製片人使她從無名之輩中脱穎而出。

7 pluck sth out of the air to say or suggest a number, name etc that you have just thought of without thinking about it carefully〔未經仔細考慮〕隨口說出〔一個數字或名字等〕: *I'm just plucking a figure out of the air here, but let's say it'll cost about $15,000.* 我只是隨口說一個數字, 比如說這東西要花大約 15,000 美元。

8 pluck your eyebrows to pull out hairs from the edges of your EYEBROWS 拔眉毛

pluck at sth *phr v* [T] to pull something quickly and repeatedly with your fingers〔用手指〕猛揪[拉, 扯]: *The little boy plucked at her sleeve.* 那個小男孩不停地拉她的袖子。| *Sally was staring into space, plucking nervously at her pearl choker.* 莎莉凝視着天空, 緊張不安地扯着她那條貼頸的珍珠項鏈。

pluck² *n* [U] *old-fashioned* courage and determination【過時】勇氣, 膽量; 决心: *I really admire him for cycling to Paris on his own – it must have taken a lot of pluck.* 他獨自一人騎車去巴黎, 我真的很佩服他——那一定需要極大的勇氣。

pluck·y /ˈplʌkɪ; ˈplʌki/ *adj* **pluckier, pluckiest** *informal* brave and determined【非正式】勇敢的, 有勇氣的, 有膽量的: *It took guts to stand up to those bullies – she's a plucky kid.* 站起來反抗那些恃強凌弱者需要勇氣——她是個很勇敢的孩子。—**pluckily** *adv* —**pluckiness** *n* [U]

S3 **plug¹** /plʌg; plʌg/ *n* [C]

1 ►ELECTRICITY 電◄ **a)** a thing used for connecting a piece of electrical equipment to the main supply of electricity〔電〕插頭: *a two-pin plug* 雙腳插頭 **b)** *BrE informal* a piece of plastic, usually on a wall, where electrical equipment is connected to the main electricity supply; SOCKET (1)【英, 非正式】〔電〕插座: *Make sure you turn the television off at the plug.* 記緊從插座處關掉電視機。**c)** an object used for connecting a wire from one piece of electrical equipment such as a computer to another〔連接兩台電器的〕接頭

2 ►BATH 浴缸◄ a round flat piece of rubber or plastic used for stopping the water flowing out of a bath or SINK² 〔浴缸、洗滌槽的〕塞子, 栓

3 ►ADVERTISEMENT 廣告◄ *informal* an attempt to persuade people to buy a book, see a film etc, by talking about it publicly, especially on television or radio【非正式】〔尤指電視或電台上的〕推銷廣告; 推薦: **give sth a plug** *She appeared on all the talk shows to give her new book a plug.* 她在所有的清談節目中出現, 極力推銷她的新書。

4 ►IN AN ENGINE 在引擎中◄ *informal* the part of a petrol engine that makes a SPARK and explodes the petrol mixture; SPARK PLUG【非正式】火花塞: *Change the plugs every 10,000 miles.* 每 10,000 英里換一下火花塞。

5 pull the plug (on sth) to prevent a plan or business from being able to continue, especially by deciding not to give it any more money〔尤指通過不再提供資金〕使〔某事物〕不能繼續, 突然中斷[停止]: *We were doing fine until the bank pulled the plug on us.* 在銀行中止給我們提供資金以前, 我們一直幹得還是不錯的。

6 ►PIECE 塊◄ a piece of something pressed tightly together〔緊緊壓在一起的〕塊: *a cotton wool plug* 藥棉塊 | *a plug of tobacco* 煙草塊

7 ►FOR HOLDING SCREWS 用於固定螺釘◄ [C] a small plastic tube put in a hole to hold a screw tightly〔置於孔內使螺釘固定的〕塑料螺釘襯套

plug in 插上

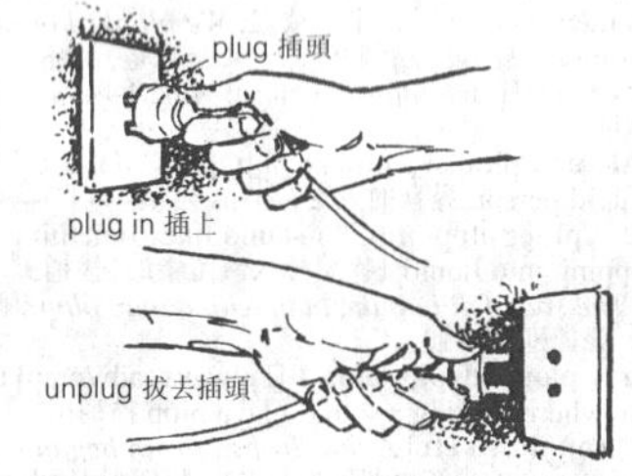

plug² *v* [T]

1 also 又作 **plug up** to fill or block a small hole 把…塞住, 堵塞; 填塞: *I used cement to plug the holes in the plaster.* 我用水泥填補灰泥上的洞。**2** to try to persuade people to buy a book, see a film etc by talking about it on television or radio〔在電視或電台上〕為…做廣告, 宣傳, 推銷: *Arnold was only on the show to plug his new movie.* 阿諾上節目只是為了宣傳他的新影片。**3 plug the gap/gaps** to provide more of something that is needed 填補空缺: *With so few trained doctors, paramedics were brought in to plug the gap.* 由於受過訓練的醫生寥寥無幾, 所以引進了醫務輔助人員以填補空缺。**4** *AmE old-fashioned* to shoot someone【美, 過時】射擊, 槍擊〔某人〕

plug away *phr v* [I] to keep working hard at something 堅持努力做〔某事〕, 拚命地幹: **[+at]** *I'm sure if you keep plugging away at it, your English will improve.* 我相信只要你堅持下去, 你的英語水平就會提高。

plug sth ↔ **in** *phr v* [T] to connect a piece of electrical equipment to the main supply of electricity, or to another piece of electrical equipment 給〔電器〕接通電源; 把〔一電器與另一電器〕接上, 插上: *I don't think the antenna's plugged in right.* 我覺得天線沒接好。

plug into sth *phr v* [T] **1** to connect one piece of electrical equipment to another〔把一台電器與另一電器〕連接起來, 接通: **plug sth into sth** *The TV was plugged into the stereo system.* 電視與立體聲系統接通了。**2** to connect your computer to a big computer system〔把電腦與大的電腦系統〕接通

plug·hole /ˈplʌgˌhol; ˈplʌghəʊl/ *n* [C] *BrE*【英】**1** a hole in a bath or SINK² where water can flow out, which you can put a PLUG¹ (2) into〔浴缸或洗滌槽中可用塞子

堵住的〕排水孔; DRAIN² (2) *AmE*【美】**2 go down the plughole a)** if work or effort goes down the plughole it is completely wasted〔工作或努力〕完全白費, 付諸東流: *Two years of hard work went right down the plughole.* 兩年來的努力工作全都白費了。**b)** if a business goes down the plughole, it fails〔企業〕失敗; 破產

plum¹ /plʌm; plʌm/ *n* **1** [C] a small round juicy fruit which is dark red or yellow and has a hard part in the middle, or the tree that produces this fruit 李(子), 梅子; 李樹: *stewed plums and custard* 燜李子牛奶蛋糊 | *plum blossoms* 李花 —see picture on page A8 參見 A8 頁圖 **2** [U] a dark red colour, like a plum 李子色, 深紅色 —see also 另見 PLUM PUDDING

plum² *adj* **1 a plum job** *BrE informal* a good,well-paid, and often easy job that other people wish they had【英, 非正式】輕鬆而報酬豐厚的工作, 優差 **2** having a dark red colour, like a plum 李子色的, 深紅色的

plum·age /ˈpluːmɪdʒ; ˈpluːmɪdʒ/ *n* [U] the feathers covering a bird's body〔鳥的〕全身羽毛, 羽衣: *the parrot's brilliant blue plumage* 那隻鸚鵡亮麗的藍色羽毛

plumb¹ /plʌm; plʌm/ *v* [T] **1 plumb the depths of despair/misery/bad taste etc** to express a bad quality or feel an unpleasant emotion in a very extreme way 陷入絕望[痛苦]的深淵; 趣味低級到了極點: *When his wife left him Matt plumbed the very depths of despair.* 妻子離他而去, 馬特絕望極了。**2** to succeed in understanding something completely; FATHOM² 查明, 探明, 完全理解: *Psychologists are trying to plumb the deepest mysteries of the human psyche.* 心理學家正努力探究人類心理最深層的奧祕。

plumb sth ↔ **in** *phr v* [T] to connect a piece of equipment such as a washing machine to the water supply 將〔洗衣機等電器〕與水源接通

plumb² *adv* **1** [always+adv/prep] *informal* exactly【非正式】精確地, 正, 恰恰: *The bullet hit him plumb between the eyes.* 子彈不偏不倚地擊中他的兩眼之間。**2** *AmE informal, often humorous* completely【美, 非正式, 常幽默】完全地: *I'm plumb tuckered out.* (=very tired) 我累極了。| *The whole idea sounds plumb crazy to me.* 整個想法在我聽起來簡直是瘋了。

plumb³ *adj technical*【術語】**1** exactly upright or level 垂直的; 水平的 **2 out of plumb** not exactly upright or level 不垂直[水平]的, 傾斜的

plumb·er /ˈplʌmɚ; ˈplʌmə/ *n* [C] someone whose job is to repair water pipes, baths, SINKs etc 管子工, 水暖工, 鉛管工

plumb·ing /ˈplʌmɪŋ; ˈplʌmɪŋ/ *n* [U] **1** the pipes that water flows through in a building〔建築物內的〕管道設備, 水管: *We keep having problems with the plumbing.* 我們的水管老是出問題。**2** the work of fitting and repairing water pipes, baths etc 水管[浴缸等]安裝及修理工作

plumb line /ˈ· ·/ *n* [C] a piece of string with a piece of LEAD tied to one end, used for measuring the depth of water or for finding out if a wall is built exactly upright 鉛錘線, 鉛垂線

plume¹ /plum; pluːm/ *n* [C] **1** a small cloud of smoke, dust etc which rises up into the air 升上空中的羽狀物〈如煙、塵等〉: **[+of]** *After the explosion, a plume of black smoke hung over the horizon.* 爆炸過後, 一道黑煙懸在地平線上方。**2** a large feather or bunch of feathers, especially one that is used as a decoration on a hat〔尤指用於裝飾帽子的〕羽毛, 大羽; 羽飾 —see also 另見 NOM DE PLUME

plume² *v* **1** [T] if a bird plumes its feathers, it cleans them and makes them smooth〔鳥〕整理〔羽毛〕**2 plume yourself on** *literary* to feel proud about a quality you have【文】為〔自己的某種品性〕感到驕傲[自豪]: *Meg plumed herself on her superior virtue.* 梅格為自己高尚的品德感到驕傲。

plumed /plumd; pluːmd/ *adj* [only before noun 僅用於名詞前] having or decorated with feathers 有[飾有]羽毛的: *the knights' plumed helmets* 飾有羽毛的騎士頭盔

plum·met /ˈplʌmɪt; ˈplʌmɪ̣t/ *v* [I] **1** to suddenly and quickly go down in value or amount〔價值或數量〕驟然跌落, 暴跌: *House prices have plummeted.* 房價已經暴跌。**2** to fall very suddenly and quickly from a great height〔從高處突然而迅速地〕墜落, 墮下: *The plane plummeted towards the earth.* 那架飛機直向地面墜落。—compare 比較 PLUNGE¹

plum·my /ˈplʌmɪ; ˈplʌmi/ *adj* **1** a plummy British voice sounds very upper-class and old-fashioned〔英國發音〕拿腔拿調的, 上層階級腔調的: *the plummy Oxford tones of the newsreader* 新聞廣播員拿腔拿調的牛津音 **2** tasting of or containing a lot of PLUMs 李子味的; 含有很多李子的

plump¹ /plʌmp; plʌmp/ *adj* **1** a word meaning pleasantly fat, often used when you want to avoid saying the word fat 豐滿的, 胖乎乎的: *The nurse was a cheerful plump woman.* 那位護士是一位性格開朗、體形豐滿的女人。| *Dad's getting a bit plump – he needs to go on a diet.* 爸爸有點兒發胖了 — 他需要節食。—see picture on page A6 參見 A6 頁圖 **2** having a full, round shape 圓鼓鼓的: *plump, soft pillows* 圓鼓鼓的柔軟枕頭 | *plump juicy tomatoes* 圓鼓鼓的多汁的番茄 —compare 比較 CHUBBY, PORTLY —**plumpness** *n* [U] —see 見 FAT¹ (USAGE)

plump² *v* **1 plump sth in/on etc** to put something down suddenly and carelessly 把某物突然重重地放進…裡面/扔在…上面等: *Otto plumped a sheaf of papers on my desk and told me to get on with it.* 奧托把一疊文件重重地扔在我的桌子上, 告訴我快點兒處理。| *You can plump the bags down anywhere you like.* 你可以把袋子隨便放下。**2 plump (yourself) down** to sit down suddenly and heavily 突然重重地坐下

plump for sth *phr v* [T] *informal* to choose something after thinking carefully about it【非正式】〔經過仔細考慮後〕選擇; 選定: *We finally plumped for a bottle of pink champagne.* 我們最後選定了一瓶粉紅色的香檳酒。

plump sth ↔ **up** *phr v* [T] to make CUSHIONs, PILLOWs etc bigger and softer by shaking them〔用手輕拍〕使〔軟墊、枕頭等〕鬆軟鼓起, 把…拍鬆

plum pud·ding /ˌ· ˈ··/ *n* [C,U] *BrE* CHRISTMAS PUDDING【英】聖誕布丁

plum to·ma·to /ˈ· ·ˌ··/ *n* [C] a type of tomato which is shaped like a PLUM¹ (1) and is used in cooking〔烹調用〕李形番茄

plun·der¹ /ˈplʌndɚ; ˈplʌndə/ *v* [I,T] to steal large amounts of money or property from somewhere, especially in a violent way that causes damage〔尤指以暴力〕竊取; 侵佔; 掠奪, 搶劫: *The rich provinces of Asia Minor were plundered by the invaders.* 小亞細亞的富饒地區遭到侵略者的劫掠。| *greedy tycoons who plunder their companies' pension funds* 侵吞了公司的退休基金的貪婪大亨 | *plundered treasures* 搶劫得來的財寶 —**plunderer** *n* [C]

plunder² *n* [U] **1** things that have been stolen during a violent attack, especially during a war 贓物;〔尤指戰時的〕戰利品; 掠奪物: *Henry's army returned loaded down with plunder.* 亨利的部隊滿載戰利品而歸。**2** the act of plundering 掠奪, 搶劫: *the plunder of Africa by the European nations* 歐洲國家對非洲的掠奪

plunge¹ /plʌndʒ; plʌndʒ/ *v* **1** [I, T always+adv/prep] to move, fall, or be thrown suddenly forwards or downwards (使)突然向前倒下[跌落]: **[+off/into etc]** *Her car swerved and plunged off the cliff.* 她的車突然轉向衝下了懸崖。| **plunge to your death** *The rope broke and both the climbers plunged 500 feet to their death.* 繩子斷了, 兩名登山者從 500 英尺的高處跌下來摔死了。| **plunge sb/sth forward/through etc** *The car stopped suddenly and he was plunged forward through the windshield.* 汽車突然停下, 他被猛地拋出了擋風玻璃。**2** [I] if a price, value, or rate plunges it suddenly goes down by a large amount〔價格、價值等〕暴跌, 驟降: *The price* *of oil has plunged to a new low.* 石油價格已跌至新低。 **3** [I] if a ship plunges, it moves violently up and down, usually because of high waves 〔船〕猛烈地顛簸

plunge in *phr v* [I] to start talking, doing sth etc quickly and confidently, without worrying 〔迅速而自信地〕開始談論[做]〔某事〕: *Zoe plunged in and started chatting happily.* 佐伊開始愉快地聊了起來。

plunge into *phr v* [T] **1 plunge sth into sth** to push something firmly and deeply into something else 把某物投[插, 刺]入某物中: *Plunge the asparagus into boiling water.* 把蘆筍投入沸水中。| *Jill plunged her hands deep into her pockets.* 吉爾把雙手深深地插入口袋中。 **2 plunge sb/sth into sth** to make someone or something experience a particular type of situation, especially one that is difficult or unpleasant 使某人/某物陷入[遭受]某種情況: *This latest scandal has plunged the Administration into controversy.* 最近的醜聞已使政府陷入爭議之中。| *The hall was suddenly plunged into darkness.* 大廳突然陷入一片黑暗之中。| **be plunged into gloom/despair etc** (=suddenly experience great unhappiness) 突然陷入憂傷/絕望等之中 *The whole regiment was plunged into despair by this news.* 這個消息使全團陷入絕望之中。**3 plunge into sth** to begin to do something suddenly, without thinking about the possible results 突然[倉促]地開始做某事: *Stuart was always plunging into risky ventures.* 斯圖爾特總是貿然地參與一些冒險的投資項目。

plunge[2] *n*

1 take the plunge to decide finally to do something, especially after delaying it or worrying about it for a long time 〔尤指經過拖延或躊躇之後〕最終決定做某事, 決定冒險一試: *In 1990 Pam took the plunge and set up her own business.* 1990年帕姆毅然決定設立她自己的公司。

2 ►DOWNWARD MOVEMENT 向下移動◄ [C usually singular 一般用單數] a sudden quick downward movement 突降; 俯衝: *Without warning, the plane began a plunge towards the Earth.* 那架飛機沒有發出警告就開始向地面俯衝下來。

3 ►INTO WATER 進入水中◄ [C usually singular 一般用單數] a DIVE[2](1) or jump into water, or a quick swim 跳水; 〔短時間的〕游泳: *Sue felt refreshed after a quick plunge in the lake.* 蘇在湖中游了一會兒泳後感到精神煥發。

4 ►DECREASE 降低◄ [C] a sudden large fall in the value of property, SHARES[2](5) etc 〔財產、股票等價值的〕暴跌, 驟降: *a dramatic plunge in house prices* 房價的突然暴跌

plung·er /ˋplʌndʒɚ; ˈplʌndʒə/ *n* [C] **1** a rubber cup on the end of a rod used for unblocking kitchen or bathroom pipes 〔用於疏通廚房或浴室水管的〕搋子, 橡膠吸盤 **2** *technical* a part of a machine that moves up and down 【術語】〔機器的〕活塞, 柱塞 **3** *AmE informal* someone who GAMBLES a lot 【美, 非正式】賭徒

plung·ing neck·line /ˌ‥ ˈ‥/ *n* [C] a very low curve or V shape on the top edge of the front of a woman's dress 〔女服的〕低領口, V形領

plu·per·fect /pluˋpɝfɪkt; pluːˈpɜːfɪkt/ *n* **the pluperfect** *technical* the PAST PERFECT tense of a verb 【術語】〔動詞的〕過去完成式[時]

plu·ral[1] /ˋplurəl; ˈplʊərəl/ *n* [C] a word or form that shows you are talking about more than one object, person etc. For example, 'dogs' is the plural of 'dog' 複數(形式)

plural[2] *adj* **1** a plural word or form shows you are talking about more than one object, person etc. For example 'we' is a plural pronoun 複數的〈如 we 是複數代名詞〉 **2** *formal* involving more than one person or thing or different kinds of people or things 【正式】〔人或事物〕多種的; 多元的: *plural cultures* 多元文化 | *plural marriage* 一夫多妻制, 一妻多夫制

plu·ral·is·m /ˋplurəlɪzm; ˈplʊərəlɪzəm/ *n* [U] *formal* 【正式】 **1** the principle that people of different races, religions, and political beliefs can live together peacefully in the same society 多元主義, 多元文化〔在同一社會中不同民族、宗教和政治信仰的人和平共處的原則〕 **2** the holding of more than one job at a time, especially in the Church 〔尤指在教會中的〕兼職, 兼任 **—pluralist** *n* [C] **—pluralistic, pluralist** /ˌplurəˋlɪstɪk; ˌplʊərəˈlɪstɪk◄/ *adj*: *living in a pluralist society* 生活在多元主義的社會中

plu·ral·i·ty /pluˋrælətɪ; plʊˈræləti/ *n* **1** [C] *formal* a large number of different things 【正式】大量不同事物: [+of] *a plurality of cultures* 多元文化 **2** [C,U] *especially AmE technical* the largest number of votes in an election, especially when this is less than the total number of votes that all the other people or parties have received 【尤美, 術語】〔尤指選舉中未超過半數的〕相對多數(票) **3** [U] *technical* the state of being plural 【術語】複數(形式)

plus[1] /plʌs; plʌs/ *prep* **1** used when one number or amount is added to another 加: *Three plus six equals nine. (3+6=9)* 三加六等於九。| *The book has 250 pages, plus 28 pages of appendices.* 這本書有250頁, 另有28頁附錄。| *All employees are paid $3 an hour plus $1.50 for time worked on the weekend.* 所有雇員的報酬都是每小時3美元, 週末工作每小時另加1.5美元。**2** and also 和, 加上: *The unit deals with all lung and heart conditions, plus many other lesser ailments.* 該科治療所有的肺部和心臟疾病, 還有各種較輕微的疾病。**3 plus four/six etc** *technical* four, six etc more than zero 【術語】正(數)4/6等 —opposite 反義詞 MINUS[1]

plus[2] *n* [C] **1** *informal* something that gives you an advantage in a situation 【非正式】有利因素[條件]: *Knowledge of French and Spanish could be a plus in this job.* 懂法語和西班牙語可能是做這份工作的有利條件。**2** a sign (+) showing that you should add two or more numbers together, or that a number is more than zero 加號; 正號

plus[3] *adj* **1 plus factor/point** an advantage or favourable feature that something has 有利因素[條件]/優點: *Another plus point for the VHS system is that you can record three or four hours of material onto one tape.* 家用錄像系統的另一優點是你可以把三四小時的材料錄製到一盤帶子上。**2 10/50 etc plus** more than a particular amount, number or level 多於10/50等: *She earns $50,000 a year plus.* 她一年多一點掙了五萬美元。| *All the children in the class are six plus.* (=more than six years old) 這班裡所有的孩子都在六歲以上。**3** [only before noun 僅用於名詞前] greater than zero 大於零的, 在零以上的, 正的: *Daytime temperatures vary between minus 5° and plus 12°.* 日間的氣溫介乎零下五度至零上十二度。

plus[4] *conjunction* and also 並且, 而且: *He's been studying for the exams all week, plus he's been working in a bar at night.* 他整個星期都在為應考溫習, 而且晚上還在一家酒吧裡工作。| *It's an old, draughty house. Plus the plumbing's not fixed yet.* 這是一座透風的破舊房子, 而且裡面的水管還沒有安裝。

plus fours /ˌ‧ ˈ‧/ *n* [plural] trousers with loose wide legs that are fastened just below the knee, worn by men especially in the 1920s when playing GOLF 〔尤指20世紀20年代打高爾夫球時穿的〕燈籠褲

plush[1] /plʌʃ; plʌʃ/ also 又作 **plush·y** /ˋplʌʃɪ; ˈplʌʃi/ *adj informal* expensive, comfortable, and of good quality 【非正式】昂貴而舒適的; 高級的; 豪華的: *a plush hotel* 豪華酒店

plush[2] *n* [U] silk or cotton cloth with a surface like short fur 長毛絨: *plush curtains* 長毛絨窗簾

plus sign /ˋ‧ ‧/ *n* [C] the sign (+) 加號; 正號

Plu·to /ˋpluto; ˈpluːtəʊ/ *n* [singular] the most distant PLANET, ninth in order from the Sun 〔九大行星中距離太陽最遠的〕冥王星 —see picture at 參見 SOLAR SYSTEM 圖

plu·toc·ra·cy /pluˋtɑkrəsɪ; pluːˈtɒkrəsi/ *n* [C] a ruling class of rich people, or a country ruled by such people, or a government that consists of them 富豪[財閥]統治

階層; 由財閥統治的國家; 由財閥組成的政府

plu·to·crat /ˋplutə͵kræt; ˈpluːtəkræt/ *n* [C] someone who has power because they are rich 有錢有勢的人, 財閥, 富豪: *bloated plutocrats who exploit the workers* 剝削工人的趾高氣揚的財閥 —**plutocratic** /͵plutəˋkrætɪk; ˌpluːtəˈkrætɪk◂/ *adj*

plu·to·ni·um /pluˋtonɪəm; pluːˈtəʊniəm/ *n* [U] an element (=simple substance) that is used in the production of NUCLEAR power〔用於生產核能的〕鈈, 鈽

ply[1] /plaɪ; plaɪ/ *v past tense and past participle* **plied 1** [I always+adv/prep, T] *literary* if a vehicle or boat plies between two places or across a place it makes that journey regularly【文】〔車、船〕定期地來回[往返]: [**+between/across etc**] *Small fishing boats plied to and fro across the harbor.* 小漁船定期往返於港口之中。| **ply sth** *a regular boat service that plies the lake* 定期在湖上往返的船運服務 **2 ply your trade** *literary* to work at your job or business【文】從事工作, 經營生意: *Flower sellers were plying their trade in the marketplace.* 賣花者在市場上做生意。**3** [T] *old use or literary* to use or work skilfully with a tool【舊或文】使用〔工具〕; 熟練地用〔工具〕工作 **4 ply for hire** *BrE* if a taxi driver plies for hire, they drive around or wait somewhere looking for passengers【英】〔計程車司機〕候客, 等生意, 攬客

ply sb **with** sth *phr v* [T] **1** to keep giving someone large quantities of food and drink 不斷地給〔某人大量食物和飲料〕: *They plied us with sandwiches and mugs of strong coffee.* 他們不停地給我們三明治和一杯又一杯的濃咖啡。**2 ply sb with questions** to keep asking someone questions 不斷地向某人提問題

ply[2] *n* [U] **two/three etc ply a)** used as a measurement of the thickness of thread, rope etc, according to the number of single threads it is made from〔線、繩等的〕股 **b)** used as a measurement of the thickness of plywood according to the number of thin sheets of wood it is made from〔夾板的〕層片

Plym·outh Breth·ren /͵plɪməθ ˋbrɛðrən; ˌplɪməθ ˈbreðrən/ *n* [plural] a Christian organization that has very strict moral rules and is opposed to religious ceremony 普利茅斯兄弟會〔一個基督教組織, 有非常嚴格的道德準則, 並反對宗教儀式〕

ply·wood /ˋplaɪ͵wud; ˈplaɪwʊd/ *n* [U] a material made of several thin sheets of wood stuck together to form a strong board 膠合板, 夾板

PM /͵pi ˋɛm; ˌpiː ˈem/ *n* [C] *informal, especially BrE* the PRIME MINISTER【非正式, 尤英】首相: *an urgent meeting with the PM* 與首相的緊急會議

pm /͵pi ˋɛm; ˌpiː ˈem/ *Latin* post meridiem; used after numbers expressing the time to show that it is after midday【拉丁】下午〔用於表示鐘點的數字之後〕: *The meeting starts at 2.30 pm.* 會議下午兩點半開始。

PMS /͵pi ɛm ˋɛs; ˌpiː em ˈes/ *n* [U] *AmE* premenstrual syndrome; unpleasant physical and emotional feelings felt by many women just before their PERIOD【美】經前綜合徵; PMT *BrE*【英】

PMT /͵pi ɛm ˋti; ˌpiː em ˈtiː/ *n* [U] *BrE* premenstrual tension【英】經前緊張症; PMS *AmE*【美】

pneu·mat·ic /nuˋmætɪk; njuːˈmætɪk/ *adj* **1** *technical* filled with air【術語】充氣的: *pneumatic tyres* 充氣輪胎 **2** worked by air pressure 由壓縮空氣推動的: *a pneumatic pump* 氣壓泵 —**pneumatically** /-klɪ; -kli/ *adv*

pneumatic drill /·͵·· ˈ·/ *n* [C] *especially BrE* a large powerful tool worked by air pressure which is used for breaking up hard materials, especially road surfaces【尤英】〔尤指用於打破路面的〕風鑽; JACKHAMMER *AmE*【美】—see picture at 參見 DRILL[1] 圖

pneu·mo·ni·a /nuˋmonjə; njuːˈməʊniə/ *n* [U] a serious disease of the lungs that makes it difficult for you to breathe 肺炎

PO /͵pi ˋo; ˌpiː ˈəʊ/ **1** the written abbreviation of 縮寫= POST OFFICE **2** the written abbreviation of 縮寫= PETTY OFFICER **3** the written abbreviation of 縮寫= POSTAL ORDER

poach /potʃ; pəʊtʃ/ *v*

1 ►COOK 烹調◄ [T] **a)** to cook eggs in a special pan over boiling water 用沸水煮〔荷包蛋〕: *poached eggs on toast* 烤麵包片上的水煮荷包蛋 **b)** to cook fish or meat in boiling water or other liquid 在沸水或其他液體中煮〔魚或肉〕: *Salmon is usually poached in a fish kettle.* 鮭魚通常在煮魚鍋中炖煮。

2 ►ANIMALS 動物◄ [I,T] to catch or shoot animals, birds, or fish illegally, especially on private land without permission〔尤指未經允許在私人土地上〕偷獵, 偷捕: *the poaching of elephants and the illegal trading of ivory* 偷獵大象和非法買賣象牙

3 ►PEOPLE/IDEAS 人/想法◄ [I,T] **a)** to persuade someone to leave a team or company and join yours 挖走〔球隊或公司的成員〕: *Foreign football clubs seem to be poaching all our best players.* 國外的球會似乎要挖走我們所有優秀的球員。**b)** to unfairly or illegally use someone else's ideas 剽竊; 竊取〔他人的想法〕: *screenwriters poaching from literature* 剽竊文學作品的電影劇本作家

4 poach on sb's territory/preserve to do something that is someone else's responsibility, especially when they do not want you to do it 越權行事

poach·er /ˋpotʃɚ; ˈpəʊtʃə/ *n* [C] **1** someone who catches or shoots animals, birds, or fish on private land without permission 偷獵者, 偷捕者 **2** a pan with small containers shaped like cups for poaching eggs 荷包蛋鍋, 煮鍋〔內有數個杯形煮蛋容器的平底鍋〕 **3 poacher turned gamekeeper** *BrE* someone who was previously a criminal and now has responsibility for stopping crime【英】由罪犯搖身一變成為執法者的人

PO Box /͵pi o ˋbɑks; ˌpiː əʊ ˈbɒks◂/ *n* [C] a numbered box in a post office to which someone's mail can be sent and from which they can collect it 郵政信箱: *For further information, write to PO Box 714, Key Largo, Florida.* 欲知詳情, 請函寄佛羅里達州基拉戈島 714 號郵政信箱。

pocked /pɑkt; pɒkt/ *adj* covered with small holes or marks; POCKMARKED 佈滿小洞的; 滿是麻點的: *His face was pocked with scars.* 他的臉上佈滿了疤痕。

pock·et[1] /ˋpɑkɪt; ˈpɒkɨt/ *n* [C] S2 W2

1 ►IN CLOTHES 衣服上的◄ a small bag sewn onto or into a coat, trousers etc so that you can put things such as money or keys into it 衣袋, 口袋: *Joseph always stands with his hands in his pockets.* 約瑟夫總是把雙手插在衣袋裡站着。| **coat/trouser/jacket etc pocket** *The keys are in my coat pocket.* 鑰匙在我的外衣口袋裡。| **turn out your pockets** (=empty your pockets) 把口袋翻出來 —see picture on page A17 參見 A17 頁圖

2 ►MONEY 金錢◄ the amount of money available for you to spend 錢; 收入; 財力: *When will the new taxes start hitting people's pockets?* 新稅收會在甚麼時候開始影響人們的收入? | **suit every pocket** *We offer a range of repayment plans to suit every pocket.* 我們提供一系列還款計劃以適應各種收入人士的需求。| **from/out of your own pocket** (=using your own money instead of money from your company, the government etc) 自掏腰包, 用自己的錢〔而不是公司、政府等的錢〕*The prince offered to pay for the restoration out of his own pocket.* 王子提出自掏腰包支付修復所需的費用。| **have deep pockets** (=have a lot of money) 財力充足, 有很多錢

3 ►IN A BAG/DOOR ETC 袋子裡/門上等◄ a small bag or piece of material fastened to an object so that you can put small things into it〔固定於某物上用於容納小東西的〕小袋: *All passengers should read the air safety card in the pocket of the seat in front.* 所有的乘客都應該讀一下放在前面座位的袋裡的飛行安全卡。

4 ►SMALL AREA/AMOUNT 小的區域/數量◄ **a)** a small area where the situation is very different from the area surrounding it〔與周圍區域情況不同的〕一小片[小塊]區域: *Apart from a few pockets of resistance, the new*

government is firmly established. 除了一些零星的抵抗之外，新政府已穩固地建立起來。| *a poor country dotted with pockets of wealth* 有着零星富裕地區的貧窮國家 **b)** a small amount of something that is different from what surrounds it〔與周圍事物不同的〕少量: *The mine has a few remaining pockets of iron ore.* 那個礦井有少量殘留的鐵礦石。

5 be/live in each other's pockets *informal, especially BrE* if two people are in each other's pockets, they are together too much【非正式，尤英】〔兩人〕經常在一起，形影不離

6 have sb/sth in your pocket a) to be able to control someone such as a police officer or politician, by threatening them, paying them money etc〔通過威脅、收買等手段〕控制[支配]某人: *a powerful organization with many local politicians in its pockets* 操縱着許多本地政客的強大組織 **b)** to be very sure that you are going to win something such as a competition or election〔在比賽或選舉中〕穩操勝券: *It looks like the Democrats have this election in their pockets already.* 看來民主黨在這次選舉中已穩操勝券。

7 be out of pocket *BrE informal* to have less money than you should have, after some form of exchange or business deal【英，非正式】賠錢的: *Unless you handle the deal carefully, you could be badly out of pocket.* 如果你不小心處理這筆交易，你會賠大錢的。| **£10/£50 etc out of pocket** *Selling the car so cheaply left her £100 out of pocket.* 這麼便宜賣掉那部車使她賠了100英鎊。

8 pick sb's pocket to steal from someone by taking money from their pocket without them realizing〔從某人的口袋裡〕扒竊，偷竊

9 put your hand in your pocket to give money to someone who needs it or in order to help someone 出錢〔幫助某人〕: *I hope everyone will put their hands in their pockets and give generously to the fund.* 我希望每個人都慷慨解囊，捐款給這個基金。

10 ►FOR BALLS 用於裝球◄ a small net bag fastened to a BILLIARD or SNOOKER table which you have to hit the ball into〔桌球桌上的〕球囊，球袋 —see also 另見 AIRPOCKET, **line your own pockets** (LINE² (4))

pocket² *v* [T] **1** to put something into your pocket 把…裝入口袋[衣袋]中: *Roy pocketed his wallet and car keys and left the house.* 羅伊把他的錢包和汽車鑰匙放進衣袋裡，然後離開了房子。**2 a)** to steal money, especially money that you are responsible for 竊取，盜用，侵吞〔公款〕: *The society's treasurer was accused of pocketing some of the profits.* 該協會的財務主管被控侵吞了部分利潤。**b)** to get money in a slightly dishonest way 撈取〔錢財〕: *It's simple – we buy them for $5, sell them for $8, and pocket the difference.* 這很簡單——我們以五美元買進，以八美元賣出，撈取其中的差價。**3** to hit a ball into a pocket in games such as BILLIARDS〔桌球等〕擊〔球〕落袋

pocket³ *adj* [only before noun 僅用於名詞前] small enough to be carried in your pocket 可放在衣袋內的，袖珍的: *a pocket dictionary* 袖珍詞典

pocket bat·tle·ship /ˌ·· ˈ···/ *n* [C] a fairly small fighting ship 袖珍[小型]戰艦

pock·et·book /ˈpɑkɪtˌbʊk; ˈpɒkə̇tbʊk/ *n* [C] **1** *AmE* a small flat case for holding papers and paper money; WALLET【美】皮夾，錢包 **2** a small NOTEBOOK 小筆記本 **3** *AmE old-fashioned* a woman's HANDBAG, especially one without a STRAP¹【美，過時】〔尤指無肩帶的〕女用手袋

pocket cal·cu·lat·or /ˌ·· ˈ····/ *n* [C] a small piece of electronic equipment which you use to do calculations 袖珍計算器

pock·et·ful /ˈpɑkɪtˌfʊl; ˈpɒkə̇tfʊl/ *n* [C] the amount that a pocket will hold 一口袋，一袋之量: [+of] *a pocketful of pebbles* 一口袋卵石

pocket hand·ker·chief /ˌ·· ˈ···/ *n* [C] *old-fashioned* a handkerchief made of cloth not of paper【過時】手帕

pocket-handkerchief *adj informal, especially BrE* small and square in shape【非正式，尤英】又小又方的: *a pocket-handkerchief garden* 一小片花園

pocket knife /ˈ·· ·/ *n plural* **pocket knives** /-ˌnaɪvz; -naɪvz/ [C] a small knife with one or more blades that fold into the handle〔有一個或幾個刀片、可摺疊的〕小刀 —see picture at 參見 KNIFE¹ 圖

pocket mon·ey /ˈ·· ˌ··/ *n* [U] **1** *especially BrE* money given regularly to a child by its parents to spend on small things【尤英】〔父母定期給小孩的〕零花錢; ALLOWANCE (4) *AmE*【美】: *Sophie spends her pocket money on sweets and magazines.* 索菲把零花錢用在買糖果和雜誌上。**2** *informal* a small amount of money that you can use to buy small things【非正式】零用錢: *Gavin gives private lessons to earn himself a bit of pocket money.* 加文給私人授課為自己賺點零用錢。

pocket ve·to /ˌ·· ˈ··/ *n* [C] a method used by the US President to stop a BILL (=proposal for a new law), by keeping it without signing it until Congress is no longer working 袋中否決，擱置否決〔美國總統把議案擱置起來不予簽署直到國會休會從而阻止議案通過的一種方法〕

pock·mark /ˈpɑkˌmɑrk; ˈpɒkmɑːk/ *n* [C] a hollow mark on someone's skin left by a disease such as SMALLPOX〔由於天花之類的疾病而留在皮膚上的〕痘痕，麻子，麻點

pock·marked /ˈpɑkˌmɑrkt; ˈpɒkmɑːkt/ *adj* covered with pockmarks; POCKED 有麻子[麻點]的: *a pockmarked face* 有麻子的臉

pod¹ /pɑd; pɒd/ *n* [C] **1** a long narrow seed container that grows on various plants, especially PEAS and beans 豆莢: *a pea pod* 豌豆莢 **2** a part of a space vehicle that can be separated from the main part〔太空船的〕可分離艙 **3** a long narrow container for petrol or other substances, especially one carried under an aircraft wing〔尤指飛機翼下的〕容器，箱; 吊艙 **4** a container which holds the eggs of some types of insects〔某些昆蟲的〕卵囊

pod² *v* [T] to take beans, PEAS etc from their POD¹ (1) before cooking them 把〔豆等〕剝出莢

podg·y /ˈpɑdʒɪ; ˈpɒdʒi/ *adj* another form of PUDGY pudgy 的另一種形式

po·di·a·trist /pəˈdaɪətrɪst; pəˈdaɪətrə̇st/ *n* [C] *especially AmE* someone who looks after people's feet and treats foot diseases【尤美】足病醫生; CHIROPODIST *especially BrE*【尤英】—**podiatry** *n* [U]

po·di·um /ˈpodɪəm; ˈpəʊdiəm/ *n* [C] **1** a small raised area for a performer, speaker, or musical CONDUCTOR to stand on 表演台; 講台; 樂隊指揮台 **2** *AmE* a tall sloping desk for putting an open book, notes for a speech etc on; LECTERN【美】〔用於放置打開的書或演講筆記等的〕斜面高桌

po·dunk /ˈpodʌŋk; ˈpəʊdʌŋk/ *adj AmE informal* a podunk place is small and unimportant【美，非正式】〔地方〕小的; 不重要的; 藉藉無名的: *Brad comes from some podunk town east of the mountains.* 布拉德來自該山區以東某個無名小鎮。

p.o.ed /piˈod; piːˈəʊd/ *adj AmE informal* very annoyed【美，非正式】非常煩惱的，很生氣的: *She was really p.o.ed when she didn't get the job.* 她因沒有得到那份工作而感到非常惱怒。

po·em /ˈpo·ɪm; ˈpəʊə̇m/ *n* [C] a piece of writing arranged in patterns of lines and of sounds which often RHYME, expressing thoughts, emotions, and experiences in words that excite your imagination 詩，韻文

po·e·sy /ˈpo·ɪsɪ; ˈpəʊə̇zi/ *n* [U] *old use* poetry【舊】詩歌

po·et /ˈpo·ɪt; ˈpəʊə̇t/ *n* [C] someone who writes poems 詩人

po·et·as·ter /ˈpo·ɪtˌæstɚ; ˌpəʊə̇ˈtæstə/ *n* [C] *literary* someone who writes bad poems【文】蹩腳詩人

po·et·ess /ˈpoətɪs; ˌpəʊə̇ˈtes◂/ *n* [C] *old-fashioned* a female poet【過時】女詩人

po·et·ic /poˈɛtɪk; pəʊˈetɪk/ also 又作 **poetical** /poˈɛtɪkl̩; pəʊˈetɪkəl/ *adj* **1** concerning poetry or typical of poetry 詩（一般）的，詩歌特有的: *poetic drama* 詩體戲劇 | *po-*

etic imagery 詩的意象 **2** having qualities of deep feeling or graceful expression 富有詩意的; 表達優雅的; 詩一般的: *Their dancing has a kind of poetic intensity.* 他們的舞蹈有一種如詩一般的激情。—**poetically** /-klɪ; -kli/ *adv*

poetic jus·tice /·,·· '··/ *n* [U] a situation in which someone is made to suffer for something bad they have done, in a way that seems perfectly suitable or right 惡有惡報, 應得的懲罰: *After being bullied by her for so long, it struck me as poetic justice that she was now being victimized.* 我被她欺負了這麼久之後, 現在她成了受害者, 我覺得真是惡有惡報。

poetic li·cence /·,·· '··/ *n* [U] the freedom to change facts, not to obey the usual rules etc, that is allowed to poets and other artists 詩或其他藝術形式的破格

Poet Lau·re·ate /,·· '···/ *n* [C] a poet who is appointed by the king or queen in Britain to write poems on important occasions〔英國的〕桂冠詩人

3 **po·et·ry** /'po·ɪtrɪ; 'pəʊɪ̮tri/ *n* [U] **1** poems 詩, 詩歌: *Wordsworth's poetry* 華茲華斯的詩 **2** the art of writing poems 寫詩的藝術, 作詩法: *the art of poetry* 詩歌藝術 **3** *approving* a quality of beauty, grace, and deep feeling【褒】詩意, 詩情; 詩一般的美: *The way Martina moves around the court is sheer poetry.* 馬蒂娜在球場上移動的姿態如詩一般的優美。

po-faced /,po 'fest; ,pəʊ 'feɪst◂/ *adj BrE informal* having an unfriendly disapproving expression on your face【英, 非正式】板起面孔的, 面無表情的, 一本正經的: *That po-faced woman behind the bar refused to serve us.* 吧台後面那個板着臉的女人拒絕招待我們。

po·go stick /'pogo ,stɪk; 'pəʊgəʊ stɪk/ *n* [C] a pole with a spring near the bottom and a bar which you can stand on while holding the top in order to jump about for fun〔底部裝有腳踏彈簧跳躍用的〕彈簧單高蹺

pog·rom /po'grɑm; 'pɒgrəm/ *n* [C] a planned killing of large numbers of people, especially Jews, usually done for reasons of race or religion〔有組織的〕大屠殺, 集體迫害〔尤指屠殺猶太人〕

poi·gnant /'pɔɪnjənt; 'pɔɪnjənt/ *adj* making you feel sad or full of pity 令人傷心的, 令人充滿同情[惋惜]的: *I was struck by the poignant contrast between his lively mind and his old frail body.* 他活躍的思想和老弱的身體之間的對比使我感到無限惋惜。—**poignancy** *n* [U] —**poignantly** *adv*: *The road between Hué and Danang was poignantly named 'Street without Joy'.* 越南順化和峴港之間的路被命名為"無歡樂街", 真令人傷感。

poin·set·ti·a /pɔɪn'sɛtɪə; pɔɪn'setiə/ *n* [C] a tropical plant with groups of large bright red leaves that look like flowers 一品紅〔熱帶植物, 其鮮紅色葉子似花瓣〕

1 1 **point¹** /pɔɪnt; pɔɪnt/ *n*

1 ▶IDEA 想法◀ [C] a single fact, idea, or opinion that is part of an argument or discussion 某一事實; 某一想法; 某一觀點: *There was one point on which everyone agreed.* 有一點大家都同意。| *She had brought a list of points for discussion.* 她列出了一些討論要點。| *One important point must be borne in mind.* 有很重要的一點必須記住。| *That's a very interesting point.* 那一點很有趣。| **make a point** (=give a fact, idea, or opinion) 提出一個想法[論點、意見] *John made an interesting point about the role of the artist in society.* 約翰就藝術家在社會中的作用提出了有趣的看法。| **sb's point** *I agree with Jane's point that we need to look more closely at the costs.* 我同意簡關於我們需要更仔細地審查成本的看法。| **make/prove your point** (=show that your idea or opinion is right) 證明你的觀點[主張]正確 *He brought along a handful of documents to help prove his point.* 他帶來了一些文件以幫助證實他的觀點。| **the finer points** (=details that are difficult to understand) 難以理解的細節 *the finer points of political theory* 政治理論的微妙難解之處

2 ▶MAIN MEANING/IDEA 主要的意思/觀點◀ the point the main idea in something that is said or done which gives meaning to all of it 要點, 重點; 中心意思, 主要含意; 核心問題: **the point is...** (=the most important thing is) 最重要的是..., 問題是... *The point is that you should have told me where you were going.* 問題是你應該告訴我你要去哪兒。| **beside the point** (=not important) 不重要的, 不相干的, 離題的 *She is young, but that's beside the point.* 她很年輕, 但這並不要緊。| **come/get to the point** (=used to tell someone to reach the most important part of what they want to say) 談正題, 談關鍵問題 *I wish you would get to the point!* 我希望你能進入正題! | **miss the point** (=not understand the main meaning of something) 不理解[明白]要點 *Was I hearing him right, or had I completely missed the point?* 我是聽明白了他說的話呢, 還是完全沒有領會他的意思? | **to the point** (=saying something important about the matter being dealt with) 切題的; 中肯的 *The message was short and to the point.* 這消息簡短扼要。

3 ▶PLACE 地方◀ [C] an exact place or position〔確切的〕地方, 地點; 位置: *Line A crosses line B at point C.* A線和B線於C點相交。| *a border crossing point* 跨越邊境處

4 ▶IN TIME/DEVELOPMENT 在時間上/在發展中◀ [C] an exact moment, time, or stage in something's development 時候, 時刻;〔發展的〕階段; 程度; 地步: **at this point** *It was at this point the surgeon realized things were going wrong.* 那位外科醫生就在這時意識到情況不妙。| **at this point in time** (=now) 現在, 此時 *It is impossible to give a definite answer at this point in time.* 現在不可能給予一個明確的答覆。| **starting point** (=a time or stage from which something can start) 起點, 開頭 *We can use this document as a starting point for our discussions.* 我們可以以這份文件為出發點來進行討論。| **to the point of** (=to a particular stage) 到...的階段[程度, 地步] *The beams had weakened to the point of being dangerous.* 那些橫梁已經老化到危險的地步。| **if it comes to the point** (=if a particular situation is reached when a decision has to be made) 到了關鍵時刻, 到必須作出決定的時候 *If it comes to the point, I am prepared to resign over this.* 必要時我願為此辭職。

5 boiling point/freezing point/melting point etc the temperature at which something boils, freezes, melts etc 沸點/冰點/熔點等

6 the high/low point of the best or worst stage, or best or worst moment of something 最佳/最糟[差]階段[時期, 時刻]: *The firework display was the high point of the evening.* 煙火表演是當晚的高潮。| *This was the low point of his teaching career.* 這是他教學生涯的低谷。

7 the point of no return a stage in a process or activity when it becomes impossible to stop it or do something different 有進無退[欲罷不能]的地步

8 be on the point of (doing) something to be going to do something very soon 正要做某事: *I was on the point of leaving when the phone rang.* 我正要走時, 電話鈴響了。

9 ▶QUALITY/FEATURE 特質/特點◀ [C] a particular quality or feature that something or someone has 特點, 特質, 特徵: *She tried to remind herself of his good points.* 她極力使自己想起他的種種優點。| *What are the points to look out for when buying a new computer?* 在買一台新電腦時需要特別注意哪些特殊性能? | **the finer points of** (=the small details of quality) 細節 *He went on to educate us all on the finer points in choosing champagne.* 他繼續教我們在選擇香檳酒時應注意的細節。| **it has its points** (=used to say that something has some good features or qualities) 它自有它的優點[好處] *It's not a car that I would buy, but it does have its points.* 我不會買那輛車, 但它確實有自己的優點。| **selling point** (=a feature that will help to sell sth) 賣點 *The main selling point of the product is its price.* 該產品的主要賣點是它的價格。| **strong/weak point** (=a part of someone or something that is good or bad) 長處, 優點; 短處, 缺[弱]點 *Neatness is not his strong point.* 他這個人不大注重整潔。

10 ►PURPOSE 目的◄ [U] the purpose or aim of something 目的; 目標; 意義: *The whole point of this experiment is to show how the chemicals react in water.* 這項實驗的目的是要顯示這些化學品在水中是如何起反應的。| **there is no point** *I could see that there was no point in arguing with him.* 我覺得與他爭論沒有甚麼意義。| **not see the point** *I couldn't see the point of trying to explain.* 我看不出極力解釋有甚麼用處。| **what is the point?** *What was the point in working to pass exams if there were no jobs available?* 如果沒有空缺的職位, 努力通過考試還有甚麼意思呢?

11 up to a point to some extent, but not completely 在某程度上: *I agree with you up to a point.* 我不完全同意你的看法。

12 ►SHARP END 尖端◄ [C] a sharp end of something 〔某物的〕尖(端): *a knife with a very sharp point* 很尖的刀子

13 at the point of a gun/at gun point if you do something at gun point, you do it while someone is pointing a gun towards you 在槍口(威逼)之下

14 ►GAMES/SPORT 比賽/運動◄ [C] a unit used to show the score in a game or sport 〔比賽或運動中的〕分數, 得分: *Steve Jones is 15 points ahead.* 史提夫·瓊斯領先15分。| **win/lose a point** *She lost three points for that fall.* 她因為那次摔倒而丟了三分。| **beat sb on points/win on points** (=win a boxing match by gaining more points than your opponent rather than by defeating them completely) 〔拳擊比賽中〕以點數擊敗某人/以點數獲勝

15 ►NUMBERS 數字◄ [C] a sign (.) used to separate a whole number from any decimals that follow it 小數點

16 ►MEASURE ON A SCALE 刻度表上的測量單位◄ [C] a mark or measure on a scale 點; 度: *The cost of living has risen by three percentage points.* 生活指數已增長了三個百分點。

17 ►SMALL SPOT 小點◄ [C] a very small spot 一小點: *The stars shone like tiny points of light in the sky.* 星星像一個個小光點一樣在天空中閃爍。

18 ►DIRECTION 方向◄ [C] one of the marks on a COMPASS that shows direction 羅盤(方位)點: *the points of the compass* 羅盤上的方位點

19 ►PIECE OF LAND 一塊土地◄ [C] a long thin piece of land that stretches out into the sea 尖岬, 岬角

20 ►ELECTRICITY 電◄ [C] a piece of plastic with holes in it which is fixed to a wall and to which electrical equipment can be connected 插座

21 make a point (of doing sth) to do something deliberately so that people notice 特意做某事〔以使人注意〕: *I always make a point of introducing new members to the chairman.* 我總是特意把新成員介紹給主席。

22 ►RAILWAYS 鐵路◄ **points** [plural] a piece of railway track that can be moved to allow a train to cross over from one track to another 〔鐵路上的〕道岔, 轉轍器

23 ►DANCING 跳舞◄ **points** [plural] *technical* the ends of a dancer's feet, on which they balance when they are dancing in BALLET 【術語】〔芭蕾舞中的〕足尖

Frequencies of the noun **point** in spoken and written English 名詞point在英語口語和書面語中的使用頻率

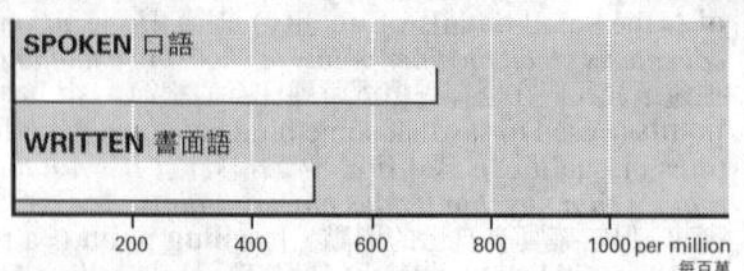

Based on the British National Corpus and the Longman Lancaster Corpus
據英國國家語料庫和朗文蘭卡斯特語料庫

This graph shows that the noun **point** is more common in spoken English than in written English. This is because it is used in a lot of common spoken phrases. 本圖表顯示, 名詞 point 在英語口語中的使用頻率遠遠高於書面語, 因為口語中很多常用片語是由point構成的。

point (*n*) **SPOKEN PHRASES**
含point的口語片語

24 what's the point?/there's no point used to say that you do not think something is worth doing 有甚麼意義[用處]呢?/沒有意義[用處]: *I could try to help but what's the point? He never listens to anyone.* 我可以盡力幫忙, 但有甚麼用呢? 他根本不聽任何人的說話。| **what's the point in doing sth?/there's no point in doing sth** *There's no point in lying, I'll find out anyway.* 撒謊沒有甚麼用, 無論如何我都會發現的。

25 I can't see any point in used to say that you do not think something has any real purpose 我看不出…有甚麼意義[用處]: *I've got no time for politics – I can't see any point in it.* 我沒有時間勾心鬥角——我看不出那有甚麼意義。| **I can't see any point in doing sth** *I can't see any point in going there when we can just call instead.* 既然我們打個電話就行了, 我看不出去那裡還有甚麼意義。

26 that's the point used when emphasizing what the main fact, idea or purpose of something is 那才是重要的, 那才是問題所在: *It costs me more but it lasts much longer, you see. That's the point.* 這東西昂貴多了, 但你瞧它也耐用多了。這才是最重要的。| **that's the whole point** *But that's the whole point – the richer you are, the more you should pay.* 但問題是——你越富有, 你應付的錢就越多。

27 that's a good point used when someone mentions an important fact or detail that you had not thought of 說得對(我沒有想到這一點), 所言極是: *"But how will you get there?" "That's a good point, I won't have the car, will I?"* "但你如何到那裡去呢?""說的也是, 我拿不到那輛車, 不是嗎?"

28 that's not the point used to tell someone that the fact or reason they are mentioning is not at all important 那並不重要, 那並不是問題所在: *Maybe you were trying to be helpful, but that's not the point, is it?* 或許你極力想幫忙, 但那並不重要, 是嗎?

29 (that's) more to the point used to say that a particular fact or reason is more important than the one that was just mentioned 那才更重要: *Yes, she has stolen the money, but why? That's more to the point.* 對, 她是偷了錢, 但是為了甚麼? 這才是更重要的問題。

30 I see your/his point used to say that you can understand why someone has a particular idea or opinion 我明白你/他的意思: *He thought the meeting was a waste of time, and I could see his point.* 他認為那次會議是浪費時間, 我能明白他的意思。

31 I take your point used to tell someone you accept that their idea or opinion is correct 我接受你的看法, 你說的是: *I take your point about that picture. It does look better here.* 我認為你對那幅畫的看法很正確, 它在這裡看起來確實更好一些。

32 point taken used to tell someone that you accept that you were wrong and they were right about something 我承認我是錯了, 你說的是: *OK, point taken. I won't interfere any more.* 好吧, 你說得對。我不會再干預了。

33 you/they have a point used to say that someone has an idea or opinion that is right 你(們)/他們說得有道理: *Sue thinks it would be better to go by train, and I think she has a point.* 蘇認為乘火車去更好, 我認為她說得有道理。

34 not to put too fine a point on it used when you are saying something in a very direct way that might upset someone 直言不諱地說, 直話直說, 說句老實話: *She was being a real pain in the ass, not to put too fine a point on it.* 直話直說, 她真是個令人討厭的傢伙。

1 1 **point**² *v*

1 ►SHOW STH WITH YOUR FINGER 用手指向某物◄ [I] to show someone something by holding up one of your fingers or a thin object towards it〔用手指或細物〕指, 指向: *"Look!" said a soldier, and pointed.* "看!" 一個士兵指着說。| *John leaned over her and pointed ahead.* 約翰向她俯過身來, 指着前方。| **[+at]** *I could see him pointing at me and telling the other guests what I had said.* 我看見他一邊指着我, 一邊告訴其他客人我說過的話。| **[+to]** *He shook his head, and pointed to a gate at the bottom of the field.* 他搖搖頭, 指向田地盡頭的一個大門。| **[+with]** *The driver pointed with his whip.* 馬車夫用他的鞭子指着。

2 ►BE AIMED 對着◄ [I always+adv/prep] to be aimed in a particular direction 面向, 對着: *The arrow always points north.* 箭頭總是指向北方。| **[+at]** *There were TV cameras pointing at us.* 有電視攝像機對着我們。| **[+to]** *The hands of the clock pointed to a quarter past one.* 時鐘的指針指向一點一刻。

3 ►AIM STH 瞄準某物◄ [T] to hold something so that it is aimed towards a person or thing 用〔某物〕對準〔某人或某物〕, 使指向: **point sth at** *I wish you'd stop pointing that gun at men.* 我希望你別再用那支槍對着人們。| *Lionel had stood up and was pointing an accusing finger at his brother.* 萊昂內爾站了起來, 用手指着弟弟加以責罵。

4 ►SHOW SB WHERE TO GO 為某人指明方向◄ [T always+adv/prep] to show someone which direction they should go in 為〔某人〕指明方向, 指路: **point sb down/along/to etc** *The receptionist pointed her down the corridor to the manager's office.* 接待員指引她沿着走廊去經理辦公室。| *He pointed Mrs Morel to a large armchair.* 他指引莫雷爾太太坐上一把大扶手椅。

5 ►WALLS/BUILDINGS 牆/建築物◄ [T] to put new CEMENT between the bricks of a wall〔用水泥〕勾嵌〔牆的砌縫〕

6 point your toes to stretch the ends of your feet downwards when you are dancing〔跳舞時〕向下繃直腳尖

7 point the finger at to blame someone or say that they have done something wrong 指責〔某人〕, 責怪: *I don't want to point the finger at anyone in particular – I think we are all to blame for this.* 我不想指責某個人——我認為我們所有人對此都有責任。

8 point the way a) to show the direction that something is in 指明方向: *A line of buildings pointed the way to the village.* 一排建築物指明了村子的所在。**b)** to show how something could change or develop successfully 指明如何改變[成功地發展], 指明方向: *We feel that this report points the way forward for the water industry.* 我們覺得這份報告為水工業的發展指明了方向。

point sth ↔ **out** *phr v* **1** [T] to show something to someone by pointing at it 把〔某物〕指出來(給某人看), 指出: *They walked into the car park and Cook pointed out his new car.* 他們走進停車場, 庫克指出了他的新車。| *My mother pointed him out to me.* 媽媽把他指給我看。**2** [T] to tell someone something that they did not already know or had not thought about 指出, 指明: *He pointed out the dangers of setting out without proper equipment.* 他指出了沒有適當的裝備就出發的種種危險。| **point out that** *The officer pointed out that the story was somewhat hard to believe.* 那位官員指出, 那個故事有點令人難以置信。| **point sth out to sb** *Mr Rogers had pointed out to us that we should keep well away from the lake.* 羅傑斯先生向我們指出我們應遠離那個湖。

point to sth *phr v* [T] to mention something because you think it is important〔因認為重要而〕提到〔某事物〕: *Many politicians have pointed to the need for a written constitution.* 很多政客都提出需要一部成文憲法。

point to/towards sb/sth *phr v* [T] if something points to a fact, it makes it seem very likely that it is true 表明…大有可能: *All the evidence pointed to Blake as the murderer.* 所有的證據都表明布萊克很可能是兇手。

point sth ↔ **up** *phr v* [T] *formal* to make something seem more important or more noticeable【正式】使〔某事〕顯得更重要[明顯], 清楚地表明, 強調: *The latest economic figures point up the failure of the government's policies.* 最近的經濟數字表明了政府政策的失敗。

point-blank /ˌ· ˈ·◂/ *adv* **1** if you say or refuse something point-blank, you do it directly and without trying to explain your reasons 直截了當地, 乾脆地, 斷然地: *I told him point-blank that I did not want to be involved in the deal.* 我直截了當地告訴他我不想捲入這宗交易。**2** a gun fired point-blank is fired very close to the person or thing it is aimed at 近距離平射地, 直射地: *Dodds fired both barrels point-blank at his former lover.* 多茲雙管齊發, 近距離向他的舊情人射擊。—**point-blank** *adj*: *shot at point-blank range* 近距離中彈

point du·ty /ˈ· ˌ··/ *n* [U] *BrE* a police officer who is on point duty stands at a place where two roads cross and controls the traffic passing through【英】〔交通警察在十字路口的〕崗位值勤

point·ed /ˈpɔɪntɪd; ˈpɔɪntɨd/ *adj* [usually before noun 一般用於名詞前] **1** having a point at the end 尖的: *Poirot was a dapper little man with a pointed beard.* 普瓦羅是一個矮小精悍、留着尖鬍子的男人。—see picture on page A6 參見A6頁圖 **2 a pointed comment/look/remark** something you say or do in a deliberately direct and noticeable way, in order to show your annoyance or disapproval 尖銳的評論/犀利的目光/一針見血的話: *Mark's father made a pointed remark about his hair just as we were leaving.* 我們正要離開時, 馬克的父親就他的頭髮說了句尖刻的話。—**pointedly** *adv*: *He looked at his watch pointedly. "Are you ready to go or not?"* 他故意看了看自己的手錶。"你準備走還是不走?"

point·er /ˈpɔɪntə; ˈpɔɪntə/ *n* [C]

1 ►SHOWS NUMBER/DIRECTION ETC 顯示數字/方向等◄ a thin piece of metal that points to a number or direction on a piece of equipment, for example on a measuring instrument〔儀器等的〕指針: *The pointer is halfway between 105 and 110 pounds.* 指針指在105和110磅中間。

2 ►STICK 棍棒◄ a long stick used to point at things on a map, board etc 指物棒, 教鞭

3 ►ADVICE 忠告◄ a useful piece of advice or information that helps you do or understand something 提示; 忠告; 點子: **[+on]** *Ralph gave me some pointers on my golf swing.* 拉爾夫就我打高爾夫球的揮桿姿勢提出了一些建議。

4 ►SIGN 標誌◄ something that shows how a situation is developing, or is a sign of what might happen in the future 標誌; 線索; 暗示: **[+to]** *A pointer to the growing interest in healthy eating has been the rise in sales of fresh fish.* 鮮魚銷售量的增長表明人們對健康飲食日益關注。

5 ►DOG 狗◄ a hunting dog that stands very still and points with its nose to where birds or animals are hiding〔能站着不動用鼻子指示獵物所在處的〕指示獵犬

poin·til·lis·m /ˈpwæntəlɪzm; ˈpwæntɪlɪzəm/ *n* [U] a style of painting popular in the late 19th century that uses small spots of colour all over the painting, rather than brush strokes 點彩派, 點彩畫法〔19世紀晚期流行的一種繪畫風格〕—**pointillist** *adj* —**pointillist** *n* [C]

point·less /ˈpɔɪntlɪs; ˈpɔɪntləs/ *adj* **1** without any purpose or meaning 無目的的; 無意義的: *a pointless waste of money* 無意義地浪費金錢 | *Life just seemed so pointless.* 人生好像沒有甚麼意義。**2** not likely to have any useful result 無益的, 無用的: *a pointless quarrel* 無用的爭吵 | **it is pointless to do sth** *I think it would be pointless to discuss this issue again.* 我認為再討論這個問題沒有甚麼用處。| **it is pointless doing sth** *It's pointless telling her to clean her room – she'll never do it.* 叫她打掃自己的房間是沒有用的 —— 她決不會幹的。—**pointlessly** *adv* —**pointlessness** *n* [U]

point man /ˈ· ·/ *n* [C] *AmE* a soldier who goes ahead of a group to see if there is any danger【美】先頭偵察兵

point of or·der /ˌ· · ˈ··/ *n* [C] *formal* a rule connected with the organization of an official meeting【正式】〔正式會議的〕議事程序問題: *One MP raised an objection on a point of order.* 一名下議院議員就議事程序問題提出反對意見。

point of ref·er·ence /ˌ· · ˈ···/ *n* [C] something you already know about that helps you understand a situation 參照依據, 參照標準

point of sale /ˌ· · ˈ·◂/ *n* [C] the place or shop where a product is sold 銷售處[點]: *an advertising campaign in which posters and leaflets would be displayed at the point of sale* 於銷售點張貼海報和派發小冊子的宣傳攻勢

point of view /ˌ· · ˈ·/ *n* [C] **1** a particular way of thinking about or judging a situation 視角, 角度: *From a purely environmental point of view, this is not a good decision.* 從純粹環保的角度來看, 這不是一個好決定。**2** someone's own personal opinion or attitude about something 觀點, 看法, 意見: *I respect your point of view, but I really don't agree with you.* 我尊重你的觀點, 但是我真的不敢苟同。| *My parents never seem to be able to see my point of view.* 我的父母好像從來都不能理解我的觀點。

points·man /ˈpɔɪntsmən; ˈpɔɪntsmən/ *n* [C] *BrE* someone who operates the short RAILS that move so that a train can change from one set of tracks to another【英】鐵路扳道工

point-to-point /ˌ· · ˈ·◂/ *n* [C] *BrE* a race for horses that goes across country areas【英】定點越野賽馬

poise[1] /pɔɪz; pɔɪz/ *n* [U] **1** a calm, confident way of behaving, combined with an ability to control your feelings or reactions in difficult situations 鎮定, 自信, 泰然自若, 沉着: *Travelling around Europe by herself seems to have given Louisa more poise and confidence.* 路易莎隻身一人遍遊歐洲, 這好像使她變得更加沉着自信。**2** a graceful way of moving or standing, so that your body seems balanced and not awkward〔優雅的〕體態, 姿態: *the poise of a dancer* 舞蹈者優美的體態

poise[2] *v* [T always+adv/prep] to put or hold something in a carefully balanced position, especially above something else 使平衡, 使平穩: **poise sth over/above etc** *Benjamin poised the bottle over the second glass and glanced at Consuela to see if she wanted a drink.* 本傑明把那個瓶子平穩地放在第二個玻璃杯上, 然後瞥了孔敍埃拉一眼, 看她是否想喝點甚麼。

poised /pɔɪzd; pɔɪzd/ *adj* **1** [not before noun 不用於名詞前] not moving but ready to move or do something at any moment (擺好姿勢) 準備行動的: [+for/on etc] *She saw Matthew poised on the board for a swift, controlled racing dive.* 她看見馬休在跳板上作好姿勢準備來一個敏捷而且控制得很好的跳水動作。| **poised to do sth** *He was waiting with the door open, poised to jump, as the train pulled into the station.* 火車進站時, 他開着門等着, 準備隨時跳下車去。**2** [not before noun 不用於名詞前] completely ready to do or achieve something, and about to do it 準備就緒的, 完全作好準備的: **poised to do sth** *At this point, Spain was poised to become the dominant power in Europe.* 這時, 西班牙作好了成為歐洲主導大國的一切準備。**3** [not before noun 不用於名詞前] not moving and seeming to hang in the air 似懸着不動的: **[+over/above etc]** *Noriko was holding her chopsticks poised in the air, as though waiting for me to say something.* 諾里科拿着筷子懸在空中, 似乎在等我說些甚麼。| *Stanley's hand remained poised over the open box as the footsteps came closer.* 隨着腳步的臨近, 史坦利的手懸在打開了的箱子上面。**4** [not before noun 不用於名詞前] in a position in which two things have an equally strong influence 平衡的; 介乎兩者的: **[+between]** *The tone of the book is poised between comedy and moral seriousness.* 這本書的格調介乎喜劇和道德教訓之間。**5** behaving in a calm, confident way, and able to control your feelings and reactions 鎮定的, 自信的, 泰然自若的, 沉着的: *Abbey walked to the microphone, poised and smiling.* 阿比泰然自若、笑容滿面地走向麥克風。

poi·son[1] /ˈpɔɪzn̩; ˈpɔɪzən/ *n* **1** [C,U] a substance that can cause death or serious illness if you eat it, drink it etc 毒, 毒物, 毒藥: *These fruits contain a deadly poison.* 這些水果含有劇毒。| *Joanna committed suicide by swallowing poison.* 喬安娜服毒自殺了。**2** [C,U] something such as an emotion or idea that makes you behave badly or become very unhappy 使人不愉快的事物, 有危害的東西: *Anger and hatred are poisons that destroy a person's emotional life.* 憤怒和仇恨是毀掉一個人的感情生活的毒素。**3 what's your poison?** *spoken* a humorous way of asking someone which alcoholic drink they would like【口】〔幽默說法〕你想喝甚麼酒? —see also 另見 **one man's meat is another man's poison** (MEAT (8))

poison[2] *v* [T] **1** to harm or kill someone by giving them poison 毒害; 毒殺: *The whole family had been poisoned with strychnine.* 這家人全被馬錢子鹼毒死了。**2** to add poison to something 放毒於, 下毒於: *Germanicus feared that someone had poisoned his food.* 傑曼尼克斯害怕有人在他的食物中下了毒。| *poisoned arrows* 毒箭 **3** to make land, rivers, air etc impure, especially by the use of harmful chemicals〔尤指通過使用有害化學品而〕污染〔土地、河流、空氣等〕: *We are poisoning our rivers with pesticides and toxic waste.* 我們以殺蟲劑和有毒廢棄物污染着我們的河流。**4** to have very harmful and unpleasant effects on someone's mind and emotions 毒害, 對...有不良的影響, 危害: *Her father's tyranny had poisoned her childhood.* 她父親的專制對她的童年產生了不良影響。| *these violent videos that poison the minds of the young* 這些毒害年輕人思想的暴力錄影帶 **5 poison sb's mind against sb** to make someone dislike another person by saying bad and untrue things〔通過說壞話、撒謊〕使某人對另一人產生厭惡感 **6** *especially BrE* to infect a part of the body【尤英】使〔身體的某部分〕受感染 **7 poisoned chalice** an important job that someone is given, which is likely to cause them a lot of trouble 可能帶來很多麻煩的重要工作 —**poisoner** *n* [C]

poison gas /ˌ·· ˈ·/ *n* [U] gas that causes death or serious injury, used especially against an enemy in a war〔尤指戰爭中使用的〕毒氣

poi·son·ing /ˈpɔɪzn̩ɪŋ; ˈpɔɪzənɪŋ/ *n* [C,U] illness caused by swallowing, touching, or breathing in a poisonous substance 中毒: *Several cases of poisoning have been reported.* 已接獲數宗中毒事件的報告。| **alcohol/mercury/radiation poisoning** (=caused by a particular substance) 酒精/水銀/輻射中毒 —see also 另見 FOOD POISONING

poison i·vy /ˌ·· ˈ··/ *n* [U] a bush or VINE that causes pain on your skin when you touch it 毒漆, 氣根毒藤〔觸碰會引起皮膚疼痛〕

poison oak /ˌ·· ˈ·/ *n* [U] a North American plant that causes painful spots on your skin when you touch it 毒櫨楊; 櫟葉漆樹〔北美植物〕

poi·son·ous /ˈpɔɪzn̩əs; ˈpɔɪzənəs/ *adj* **1** containing poison or producing poison 有毒的; 引起中毒的: *poisonous mushrooms* 有毒蘑菇 | *poisonous snakes* 毒蛇 **2** full of unpleasant and unfriendly feelings 充滿敵意的, 令人很不愉快的: *There was a poisonous atmosphere in the household that made Bonita feel very uneasy.* 家裡充滿了敵意, 這使博尼塔感到很不自在。**3** someone who is poisonous seems to get pleasure from causing arguments, unhappiness etc〔人〕以引起爭論[不快]而取樂的; 討厭的; 惡毒的: *That poisonous bastard Lucett told Morris I was seeing his wife.* 那個搬弄是非的壞蛋盧塞特告訴莫里斯我在和他的妻子約會。—**poisonously** *adv*

poison-pen let·ter /,·· '· ,··/ *n* [C] a letter that is not signed and that says nasty and unpleasant things about the person it has been sent to 匿名(誹謗)信

poke¹ /pok; pəʊk/ *v*

1 ▶WITH A FINGER/STICK ETC 用手指/棒等◀ [T] to quickly push into something or someone with your finger, a stick, or something pointed 戳, 捅, 刺: *Andy poked the fish to see if it was still alive.* 安迪戳了戳那條魚, 看牠是否還活着。| *Be careful with that umbrella, or you'll poke someone in the eye.* 小心那把傘, 否則你會戳到別人的眼睛。—see picture on page A21 參見A21頁圖

2 ▶THROUGH A SPACE/HOLE 通過空隙/洞◀ **a)** [T always+adv/prep] to move or push something through a space or opening 插; 伸出; 探出: *He poked his hands deep into his pockets.* 他把雙手深深地插進口袋裡。| **poke your head around the door/through the window etc** *One of the nurses poked her head around the door.* 一名護士從門裡探出頭來。**b) ▶BE SEEN** 被看見◀ [I always+adv/prep] if something is poking through or out of something else, you can see part of it but not all of it 從…中露出[伸出, 探出]: *Ella looked at the tiny face poking out of the wool blanket.* 埃拉看着那張從毛毯裡露出的小臉。| *Weeds had started poking through the cracks in the path.* 雜草已開始從小徑的縫隙中鑽了出來。

3 poke a hole to make a hole or hollow area in something by pushing something pointed into or through it〔在某物上〕戳出[捅出]一個洞: *Poke a hole in the dough and form it into a doughnut shape.* 在麵團上戳一個洞, 把它做成麵包圈的形狀。

4 poke fun at make fun of someone in an unkind way 嘲弄, 取笑: *Some of the kids were poking fun at Judy because of the way she dressed.* 一些孩子因茱迪的衣着而取笑她。

5 poke your nose into *informal* to take an interest or get involved in someone else's private affairs【非正式】干預[插手]〔別人的私事〕; 管閒事: *I don't want him poking his nose into our marriage.* 我不想讓他插手我們的婚姻。

6 poke the fire to move coal or wood in a fire with a stick to make it burn better〔用棍棒〕撥[捅]火〔使之燒得更旺〕

7 ▶SEX 性◀ [T] *slang taboo* to have sex with a woman【俚, 諱】與〔女人〕性交

poke around/about *phr v* [I] *BrE informal*【英, 非正式】**1** to look for something by moving a lot of things around 到處尋找, 亂翻: *James began poking about in the cupboard, looking for the sugar.* 詹姆斯開始在櫥櫃中亂翻, 希望能找到些糖。**2** to try to find out information about other people's private lives, business etc, in a way that annoys them 打聽, 刺探〔別人的私事〕: *I don't want you poking around in my business.* 我不想你管我的閒事。

poke at sth *phr v* [T] to keep pushing something by making repeated movements with something pointed 反覆地戳[輕推]〔某物〕; 撥弄: *He was poking at the dust with his stick, making little patterns.* 他用拐杖撥弄灰塵, 劃出一些小圖案來。

poke² *n* **1 give sb/sth a poke** to quickly push your fingers, a stick etc into something or someone 戳, 刺: *Vanessa gave me a poke in the ribs.* 瓦內莎碰了一下我的肋骨。**2** [C] *AmE old-fashioned slang* a WALLET containing money【美, 過時, 俚】裝有錢的錢包

pok·er /ˈpokɚ; ˈpəʊkə/ *n* **1** [U] a card game that people usually play for money〔通常指賭錢的〕撲克牌戲, 紙牌戲 **2** [C] a metal stick used to move coal or wood in a fire to make it burn better 撥火棒

poker-faced /,·· '·◂/ *adj* showing no expression on your face 面無表情的, 不動聲色的, 一本正經的: *Melanie waited poker-faced for their next offer.* 梅拉妮面無表情地等着他們下一次出價。—**poker face** *n* [singular]

po·ker·work /ˈpokɚ,wɝk; ˈpəʊkəwɜːk/ *n* [U] pictures or patterns burned onto the surface of wood or leather with hot tools, or the art of making these pictures〔在木頭或皮革上的〕烙畫(藝術)

po·key /ˈpokɪ; ˈpəʊki/ *n* [C] *AmE old-fashioned* a jail【美, 過時】監獄

pok·y, pokey /ˈpokɪ; ˈpəʊki/ *adj* **1** too small and not very pleasant or comfortable 簡陋的, 不舒適的, 狹小的: *The whole family was crammed into two poky little rooms.* 全家人擠在兩間狹小的房間裡。**2** *AmE* doing things very slowly, especially in a way that you find annoying【美】慢吞吞的, 緩慢的, 磨磨蹭蹭的: *I got behind some poky driver on the freeway.* 在高速公路上, 我落在了一些慢吞吞的司機後面。

pol /pɑl; pɒl/ *n* [C] *AmE informal* a politician【美, 非正式】政客

Po·lack /ˈpolæk; ˈpəʊlæk/ *n* [C] *AmE* an insulting word for someone from Poland【美】波蘭佬〔侮辱性詞語〕

po·lar /ˈpolɚ; ˈpəʊlə/ *adj* **1** close to, or connected with the North Pole and the South Pole 近南極[北極]的, 極地的: *As our climate warms up, the polar ice caps will begin to melt.* 隨着我們的氣候逐漸變暖, 極地的冰冠也將融化。**2** *technical* related to one of the POLES of a MAGNET【術語】磁極的 **3 polar opposite/extreme** something exactly or completely opposite in character or nature〔性格或性質〕完全相反, 正好相反

polar bear /,·· '·/ *n* [C] a large white bear that lives near the North Pole 北極熊

po·lar·ise /ˈpolə,raɪz; ˈpəʊləraɪz/ *v* a British spelling of POLARIZE polarize 的英式拼法

po·lar·i·ty /pəˈlærətɪ; pəˈlærɪ̀ti/ *n* [C,U] **1** *formal* the fact of people, opinions, or ideas being completely different or opposite to each other【正式】〔人、意見或觀點的〕截然相反, 截然對立, 分歧: **[+between]** *the supposed polarity between the intellect and the emotions* 理智和感情之間假定的對立 **2** *technical* the state of having either a positive or negative electric charge【術語】〔電的〕極性; 正負極

po·lar·ize also 又作 **-ise** *BrE*【英】/ˈpolə,raɪz; ˈpəʊləraɪz/ *v* [I,T] *formal* to divide into clearly separate groups with opposite beliefs, ideas, or opinions, or to make people do this【正式】(使)兩極分化: *a highly controversial issue that has polarized the country* 使該國兩極分化的極具爭議的問題 | *Patterns of political support had become polarized between the north and south.* 南北之間政治支持模式已變得兩極化了。—**polarization** /,polərəˈzeʃən; ,pəʊləraɪˈzeɪʃən/ *n* [U]

Po·lar·oid /ˈpolə,rɔɪd; ˈpəʊlərɔɪd/ *n trademark*【商標】**1** [C] a camera that uses a special film to produce a photograph very quickly 寶麗來一次成像照相機, 拍立得照相機, 即影即有相機 **2** [C] a photograph taken with a Polaroid camera 寶麗來一次成像照片, 即影即有照片 **3** [U] a special material which is put on the glass in SUNGLASSES, car windows etc to make the sun seem less bright〔用於太陽鏡、汽車玻璃等的〕偏振片, 寶麗來偏光薄膜 **4 Polaroids** [plural] dark glasses with Polaroid material on them〔含有偏振材料的〕太陽眼鏡, 柔光眼鏡

pole¹ /pol; pəʊl/ *n* [C] W3

1 ▶STICK/POST 棒/桿◀ a long stick or post usually made of wood or metal, often set upright in the ground to support something 桿, 柱, 竿: *a telephone pole* 電話線桿 | *a flagpole* 旗桿 | *The dusty curtains hung from unpolished brass poles.* 滿是灰塵的窗簾掛在未磨光的黃銅桿上。

2 ▶NORTH/SOUTH POLE 北極/南極◀ the most northern or most southern point on a PLANET, especially the Earth〔尤指地球的〕南[北]極; 地極: *Amundsen's expe-*

dition was the first to reach the pole. 阿蒙森的探險隊是第一支到達南極的隊伍。

3 be poles apart two people or things that are poles apart are as different from each other as it is possible to be〔兩人或兩事物〕截然相反, 大相徑庭: *Both brilliant pianists, Powell and Monk are poles apart in style.* 兩位卓越的鋼琴家——鮑威爾和蒙克——在風格上截然不同。

4 ►OPPOSITE IDEAS/BELIEFS 相反的觀點/信仰◄ one of two situations, ideas, or opinions that are the complete opposite of each other〔兩種情況、觀點或意見〕截然相反的兩極之一; 極端: *We have the accumulation of wealth at one pole and poverty and misery at the other.* 在一端, 我們有財富堆積如山的人, 而在另一端卻又有貧苦不堪的人。

P

5 ►ELECTRICAL 電的◄ **a)** one of two points at the ends of a MAGNET where its power is the strongest 磁極 **b)** one of the two points at which wires can be fixed onto a BATTERY (1) in order to use its electricity 電極

6 ►IN THE SKY 天空中◄ one of the two points in the sky, one to the north of the Earth and one to the south, around which the stars appear to turn 天空中的南[北]極

Pole² *n* [C] someone who comes from Poland 波蘭人

pole³ *v* [I,T] to push a boat along in the water using a pole 用篙撐(船)

pole·axed /ˈpolˌækst; ˈpəʊlækst/ *adj* [not before noun 不用於名詞前] **1** *informal* very surprised and shocked【非正式】非常驚訝的, 目瞪口呆的, 震驚的: *I was poleaxed when I heard I'd passed the exam.* 我聽到自己通過考試的消息時簡直驚呆了。**2** unable to stand because something has hit you very hard〔因受重擊而〕不能站立的, 被擊倒的: *The big Texan staggered and collapsed as if poleaxed.* 那個大塊頭德克薩斯人搖搖晃晃, 最後像猛挨了一下似的癱倒在地。

pole·cat /ˈpolˌkæt; ˈpəʊlkæt/ *n* [C] **1** a small dark brown wild animal that lives in northern Europe and can defend itself by producing an unpleasant smell〔北歐產的〕艾鼬, 臭貂 **2** *AmE informal* a SKUNK【美, 非正式】臭鼬

po·lem·ic /poˈlɛmɪk; pəˈlemɪk/ *n formal or technical*【正式或術語】**1** [C] a written or spoken statement that strongly criticizes or defends a particular idea, opinion, or person〔口頭或書面的〕爭辯, 辯論, 論戰 **2** [U] also 又作 **polemics** the practice or skill of making such statements 爭辯, 辯論; 辯論術, 辯論法: *Before long, the dispute had degenerated into heated polemics.* 不久, 分歧就演變成激烈的爭辯。

po·lem·i·cal /poˈlɛmɪkl̩; pəˈlemɪkəl/ also 又作 **polemic** *adj formal or technical* using strong arguments to criticize or defend a particular idea, opinion, or person【正式或術語】爭辯的, 辯論的, 論戰的: *The health reforms were attacked in a highly polemical piece in the 'New Yorker'.* 醫療改革在《紐約人》的一篇措辭強烈的文章中遭到了抨擊。—**polemically** /-klɪ; -kli/ *adv*

pole po·si·tion /ˈ· ·ˌ··/ *n* [C,U] the front position at the beginning of a car or bicycle race〔汽車或腳踏車賽開始時的〕竿位, 前排位置, 有利位置

Pole Star /ˈ· ·/ *n* **the Pole Star** a star that is almost directly over the North Pole and that can be seen from the northern part of the world 北極星

pole vault /ˈ· ·/ *n* **the pole vault** the sport of jumping over a high bar using a long pole 撐竿跳高 —**pole vaulter** *n* [C]

S1 W1 **po·lice¹** /pəˈlis; pəˈliːs/ *n* [plural] **1 the police** an official organization whose job is to make sure that people obey the law, to catch criminals, and to protect people and property 警察機關, 警方: *I heard the sound of a window breaking and called the police.* 我聽到一扇窗戶被打破的聲音就叫了警察。| *Accidents involving injuries must be reported to the police.* 傷亡事故必須報警。| *a police car* 警車 **2** the people who work for this organization 警察: *Armed police surrounded the courthouse.* 武警包圍了法院。| *Several police were injured when violence broke out.* 暴力事件發生後, 有幾名警察受了傷。—see also 另見 MILITARY POLICE, SECRET POLICE

police² *v* [T] **1** to keep control over a particular area in order to make sure that laws are obeyed and people and property are protected, using a police or military force〔動用警察或軍隊對某地區〕實施管制, 維持治安, 管治: *The army was brought in to police the riot-torn city.* 軍隊受命對這個遭受騷亂蹂躪的城市實施管制。| *new methods of policing the neighborhood* 維持社區治安的新方法 **2** to control a particular activity or industry by making sure that people follow the correct rules concerning what they do 控制, 監督〔某活動或行業〕: *The agency was set up to police the nuclear power industry.* 設立這個機構是為了監督核電工業。—**policing** *n* [U]: *policing in rural areas* 農村地區的治安維持

police con·sta·ble /·ˌ· ˈ···/ *n* [C] *BrE formal* a police officer of the lowest rank【英, 正式】(普通)警員〔最低一級的警察〕

police court /ˈ·· ·/ *n* [C,U] *AmE* a court of law for small crimes【美】警察法庭〔審理輕微違法行為的法庭〕

police de·part·ment /ˈ·· ·ˌ··/ *n* [C] *AmE* the official police organization in a particular area or city【美】〔某地區或城市的〕警察局, 警察部門

police dog /ˈ·· ·/ *n* [C] a dog trained by the police to find hidden drugs or catch criminals 警犬

police force /ˈ·· ·/ *n* [C] the official police organization in a country or area 警隊, 警察部門: *Marshall joined the police force in 1983.* 馬歇爾於1983年加入了警隊。

po·lice·man /pəˈlismən; pəˈliːsmən/ *n plural* **policemen** /-mən; -mən/ [C] a male police officer 男警察 S2 W3

police of·fi·cer /ˈ·· ˌ···/ *n* [C] a member of the police 警察, 警員

police state /ˈ·· ·/ *n* [C] a country where the government strictly controls people's freedom to meet, write or speak about politics, travel where they like etc 警察國家; 極權國家

police sta·tion /ˈ·· ˌ··/ *n* [C] the local office of the police in a town, part of a city etc〔城鎮等的〕警察(分)局, 派出所

po·lice·wom·an /pəˈlisˌwʊmən; pəˈliːsˌwʊmən/ *n plural* **policewomen** /-ˌwɪmɪn; -ˌwɪmɪn/ [C] a female police officer 女警察

pol·i·cy /ˈpɑləsɪ; ˈpɒlɪ̈si/ *n* **1** [C,U] a course of action that has been officially agreed and chosen by a political party, business, or other organization 政策, 方針: *the government's disastrous economic policies* 政府災難性的經濟政策 | **[+on]** *The company operates a very strict policy on smoking.* 這家公司在抽煙方面有非常嚴格的規定。| **defence/housing/foreign etc policy** *the President's new health policy* 總統的新保健政策 | **policy maker** (=someone who helps to decide what an organization's policies will be) 政策制定者, 決策人 **2** [C] a contract with an insurance company, or an official written statement giving all the details of such a contract 保險單: *You should obtain a separate policy covering valuable household items.* 你應該給家裡的貴重物品另外投保。**3** [C,U] a particular principle that you believe in and that influences the way you behave〔處事〕原則, 策略: *Well, it's always been my policy not to talk behind people's backs.* 不在背後談論別人是我一貫的做人原則。| *You know what they say – honesty is the best policy.* 人們常言道——人貴乎誠。 S3 W1

po·li·o /ˈpolɪo; ˈpəʊliəʊ/ also 又作 **po·li·o·my·e·li·tis** /ˌpolɪoˌmaɪəˈlaɪtɪs; ˌpəʊliəʊmaɪəˈlaɪtɪ̈s/ *technical*【術語】*n* [U] a serious infectious disease of the nerves in the SPINE, often resulting in permanent PARALYSIS (=complete inability to move particular muscles) 脊髓灰質炎, 小兒麻痹症

pol·i sci /ˌpɑlɪ ˈsaɪ; ˌpɒli ˈsaɪ/ *n* [U] *AmE informal* political science【美, 非正式】政治學

pol·ish¹ /ˈpɑlɪʃ; ˈpɒlɪʃ/ *v* [T] to make something smooth, bright, and shiny by rubbing it 擦亮, 擦光: *The floor had* *been polished to a satiny sheen.* 地板已被擦得光亮如緞。| *It was my duty to polish the silver on Saturdays.* 我的職責是每星期六把銀器擦亮。—**polisher** *n* [C]: *an electric floor polisher* 電動地板磨光機[打蠟機] —**polishing** *n* [U] —see picture at 參見 CLEAN 圖

polish sth ↔ **off** *phr v* [T] *informal* to finish food, work etc, quickly or easily【非正式】快速[輕易]做完〔工作等〕; 很快吃完〔食物〕: *At lunch, Rowan polished off six sandwiches!* 吃午飯時, 羅旺一轉眼就吃掉了六份三文治!

polish sb ↔ **off** *phr v* [T] *AmE informal* to kill or defeat someone【美, 非正式】殺死〔某人〕; 擊敗〔某人〕: *Mather was polished off with a shotgun in another gangland killing.* 馬瑟在另一次黑社會仇殺中被人用獵槍打死了。

polish sth ↔ **up** *phr v* [T] **1** to improve a skill or an ability by practising it〔通過練習〕提高, 改善〔技術、能力〕: *I need to polish up my Spanish before we go on vacation.* 我們去度假前, 我需要練習一下我的西班牙語。**2** to polish something 擦亮, 擦光

polish[2] *n* **1** [C,U] a liquid, powder, or other substance used for rubbing into a surface to make it smooth and shiny 上光劑; 擦光劑; 上光蠟; 鞋油; 亮漆: *pine panelling gleaming with wax polish* 用上光蠟擦得閃閃發亮的松木鑲板 | *furniture polish* 家具上光劑 | *shoe polish* 鞋油 —see also 另見 FRENCH POLISH **2** [U] a special quality of great skill and style in the way someone performs, writes, or behaves 優美, 高雅, 精緻, 完善: *Carla's writing has potential, but it lacks polish.* 卡拉的文章很有潛力, 但不夠優美。**3** [singular] a smooth shiny surface produced by polishing〔因摩擦而產生的〕光亮的表面 **4** [singular] an act of polishing a surface to make it smooth and shiny 擦亮, 磨光: *An occasional wipe and polish with a soft cloth will keep wall tiles looking good.* 偶爾用軟布擦拭能使牆磚保持美觀。—see also 另見 SPIT AND POLISH

Pol·ish[3] /ˋpolɪʃ; ˈpəʊlɪʃ/ *adj* from or connected with Poland, its people, or their language 來自波蘭的; 波蘭的; 波蘭人的; 波蘭語的

Pol·ish[4] *n* [U] the language of Poland 波蘭語

pol·ished /ˋpɑlɪʃt; ˈpɒlɪʃt/ *adj* **1** shiny because of being rubbed, usually with polish〔通常使用上光劑來〕擦亮的, 磨光的: *highly polished boots* 擦得很亮的靴子 **2** a polished performance, piece of writing etc is done with great skill and style〔表演、作品等〕完美的, 優雅的, 精緻的 **3** polished social behaviour, speech etc is polite, confident, and graceful〔行為、言談等〕彬彬有禮的, 文雅的

po·lit·bu·ro /ˋpɑlɪtbjʊro; ˈpɒlɪtbjʊərəʊ/ *n* [C] the chief decision-making committee of a Communist party or Communist government〔共產黨或其政府的〕政治局

[S3] **po·lite** /pəˋlaɪt; pəˈlaɪt/ *adj* **1** behaving or speaking in a way that is correct for the social situation you are in, and showing that you are careful to consider other people's needs and feelings 有禮貌的, 客氣的: *a polite refusal* 婉言謝絕 | *What polite well-behaved children!* 多麼懂禮貌的乖孩子! | **it is polite to do sth** *We left as soon as it was polite to do so.* 我們在不失禮節的情況下提早離開了。| *It's not polite to talk with your mouth full.* 嘴裡塞滿了食物講話是不禮貌的。—opposite 反義詞 RUDE (1), IMPOLITE **2** polite conversation, remarks etc are made because it is considered socially correct to do this 客套的, 出於禮貌的: *a few polite remarks about the weather* 幾句談論天氣的客套話 | *Nathaniel's sexual exploits are hardly the subject of polite conversation.* 納撒內爾的豔遇不能作為優雅談話的話題。**3 in polite society/circles/company** *often humorous* among people who are considered to have a good education and correct social behaviour【常幽默】上流社會, 上流階層: *You can't use words like that in polite company.* 在上流階層你不能使用那樣的詞語。**4 just/only being polite** *spoken* saying something you may not really believe or think, in order to avoid offending someone【口】只是出於禮貌: *I know Ian said he liked her singing, but he was just being polite.* 我知道伊恩說他喜歡她唱的歌, 但這只是出於禮貌。—**politely** *adv* —**politeness** *n* [U]

pol·i·tic /ˋpɑlə,tɪk; ˈpɒlɪ̩tɪk/ *adj formal* sensible and likely to bring advantage; PRUDENT【正式】明智的, 精明的; 考慮周到的, 深謀遠慮的; 慎重的: *It would not be politic to ignore the reporters.* 忽視記者是不明智的。—see also 另見 POLITICS, BODY POLITIC

po·lit·i·cal /pəˋlɪtɪkḷ; pəˈlɪtɪkəl/ *adj* **1** [no comparative 無比較級] connected with the government or public affairs of a country and its relations with other countries 政治(上)的; 政府的; 政權的; 有關行政的: *a loss of political freedom* 喪失政治上的自由 | *a long period of political stability* 長期的政治穩定 | *The UN is seeking a political solution rather than a military one.* 聯合國正在尋求政治上的而不是軍事上的解決方法。| *Cuba's political structure* 古巴的政治架構 | *one of the main political parties* 主要政黨之一 **2** [no comparative 無比較級] connected with the ideas, activities, or advantage of a particular party or group in politics 與(政黨)政治有關的, 黨派的: *a decision that was taken for purely political reasons* 純粹出於政治原因而作出的決定 | *There were obvious political advantages in cutting taxes.* 減稅在政治上有明顯的好處。| *political propaganda* 政治宣傳 **3** [no comparative 無比較級] a political offence or crime is harmful to a government〔罪行等〕危害政府的: *the summary execution of a political offender* 對一名政治犯的即時處決 **4** interested in or active in politics 對政治感興趣的, 政治上活躍的: *Most students these days aren't very political.* 如今大多數學生對政治都不怎麼感興趣。**5 political football** *especially BrE* a difficult problem which opposing politicians argue about or which each side deals with in a way that will bring them advantage【尤英】政治皮球〔對立的政客互相爭議的難題。他們各以對自己有利的方式處理這問題〕: *It is unfortunate that education has become something of a political football.* 不幸的是教育在某程度上已成了被踢來踢去的政治皮球。—see also 另見 POLITICALLY [S3] [W1]

political ac·tion com·mit·tee /·,··· ˈ·· ·,··/ *n* [C] *AmE* an organization formed by a business, union, or INTEREST GROUP to help raise money so that people who support their ideas can try to be elected for Congress; PAC【美】政治行動委員會〔由某個企業、工會或利益集團等組織的機構, 旨在籌集資金幫助支持其想法的人競選國會議員〕

political a·sy·lum /·,··· ·ˈ··/ *n* [U] the right to remain safely in another country if you cannot live safely in your own because of the political situation there 政治避難(權), 政治庇護: *refugees seeking political asylum* 尋求政治庇護的難民

political e·con·o·my /·,··· ·ˈ···/ *n* [U] the study of the way nations organize the production and use of wealth 政治經濟學

political ge·og·ra·phy /·,··· ·ˈ···/ *n* [U] the study of the way the Earth's surface is divided up into different countries, rather than the way it is marked by rivers, mountains etc 政治地理學

po·lit·ic·ally /pəˋlɪtɪkḷɪ; pəˈlɪtɪkli/ *adv* in a political way 政治上: *Women were becoming more politically active.* 婦女在政治上變得愈來愈活躍。| *a politically motivated strike* 出於政治動機的罷工 | [sentence adverb 句子副詞] *Politically, the organization was still very divided.* 從政治上來說, 該組織仍然四分五裂。

politically cor·rect /·,··· ·ˈ·/ *adj* language, behaviour, and attitudes that are politically correct are regarded as right and acceptable because they are careful to avoid offending women, black people, DISABLED people etc〔語言、行為、態度〕政治上正確的〔即避免冒犯婦女、黑人、殘疾人士等的〕: *It's not politically correct to say 'handicapped' anymore.* 政治上已不再使用"殘廢"這種說法。—see also 另見 PC[2] —**political correctness** /·,··· ·ˈ··/ *n* [U]

political ma·chine /ˌ··· ·ˈ·/ *n* [singular] *AmE* the system used by people with the same political interests to make sure that political decisions bring advantage to themselves or to their group【美】政治機器〔政治利益相同的人為確保政治決策給自己或自己的團體帶來好處而採用的體制〕

political pris·on·er /ˌ··· ˈ···/ *n* [C] someone who is put in prison because they oppose and criticize the government of their own country 政治犯〔因反對或批評本國政府而被投入監獄的人〕

political sci·ence /ˌ··· ˈ··/ *n* [U] the study of politics and government 政治學 —**political scientist** *n* [C]

2 **pol·i·ti·cian** /ˌpɑləˋtɪʃən; ˌpɒlɪ̈ˈtɪʃən/ *n* [C] **1** someone who works in politics, especially an elected member of a parliament or similar institution 政治家〔尤指議員等〕 **2** someone who is skilled at dealing with people or using the situation in an organization to bring advantage to themselves 政客, 善於玩弄權術者: *You really have to be a politician to succeed in this place.* 你要在這個地方獲得成功, 就一定得有政客的手腕。

po·li·ti·cize also 又作 **-ise** *BrE*【英】/pəˋlɪtəˌsaɪz; pəˈlɪtɪ̈saɪz/ *v* [T] to make something more political or more involved in politics 使政治化, 使具有政治性: *an attempt to politicise the police* 使警察部門政治化的嘗試

po·lit·i·cized also 又作 **-ised** *BrE*【英】/pəˋlɪtəˌsaɪzd; pəˈlɪtɪ̈saɪzd/ *adj* having become involved in or interested in politics 捲入政治的, 政治化的; 關心政治的: *The public-sector unions are the most politicized.* 公營部門的工會政治化程度最高。—**politicization** /pəˌlɪtəsəˋzeʃən; pəˌlɪtɪ̈saɪˈzeɪʃən/ *n* [U]

pol·i·tick·ing /ˋpɑlətɪkɪŋ; ˈpɒlɪ̈tɪkɪŋ/ *n* [U] political activity, usually done only for your own advantage〔通常為了個人利益而進行的〕政治活動: *the politicking behind the scenes at the party conference* 政黨大會上的幕後政治活動

po·lit·i·co /pəˋlɪtɪˌko; pəˈlɪtɪkəʊ/ *n* [C] a disapproving word meaning a politician or someone who is active in politics 政客, 政治上活躍的人〔帶有貶義〕: *east-coast politicos seeking Irish-American votes* 尋求愛爾蘭裔美國人選票的東岸政客

politico- /pəlɪtɪko; pəlɪtɪkəʊ/ *prefix* political and 政治和…的: *politico-scientific* 政治和科學的

2
2 **pol·i·tics** /ˋpɑləˌtɪks; ˈpɒlɪ̈tɪks/ *n* **1** [U] ideas and activities that are concerned with the gaining and using of power in a country, city etc 政治; 政治活動[事務]: *Most people are fairly cynical about politics.* 大多數人對政治都抱譏諷的態度。| *She became quite active in student politics.* 她變得很熱衷於學生的政治活動。| [also+plural verb *BrE* 英] *Politics have always interested Anita.* 阿尼塔對政治一直感興趣。**2** [U] the profession of being a politician 政治事業: *Flynn retired from politics in 1986.* 弗林於1986年退出政壇。| **go into politics** (=become a politician) 從政 *Smith went into politics in his early twenties.* 史密斯二十歲出頭就進入了政界。**3** [U] the activities of people in a group, organization etc that are concerned with gaining personal advantage〔某組織內的〕爭權活動; 權術; 派別之爭: *Try not to get involved in office politics.* 盡量不要捲入辦公室內的派別之爭。| *sexual politics* 性政治; 美人計 **4** [plural] someone's political beliefs and opinions 政治信仰; 政治觀點; 政見: *I've always been open about my politics.* 我從不隱瞞自己的政見。**5** [U] the study of political power and systems of government 政治學: *Tom is studying for a degree in politics.* 湯姆正在攻讀政治學的學位。

pol·i·ty /ˋpɑlətɪ; ˈpɒlɪ̈ti/ *n* [C,U] *formal* a particular form of political or government organization, or a condition of society in which political organization exists【正式】政治[政府]組織; 政體; 國體

pol·ka /ˋpolkə; ˈpɒlkə/ *n* [C] a very quick, simple dance for people dancing in pairs, or a piece of music for this dance 波爾卡舞(曲) —**polka** *v* [I]

polka dot /ˈ·· ·/ *n* [C] one of a number of DOTS (spots) that form a pattern, especially on material for clothing〔尤指衣料上的〕圓點圖案: *a white scarf with red polka dots* 有紅色圓點圖案的白色圍巾 —**polka-dot** *adj*: *a polka-dot dress* 有圓點圖案的連衣裙 —see picture on page A16 參見A16頁圖

poll[1] /pol; pəʊl/ *n* **1** [C] **a)** an attempt to find out what 3
the public think about something, especially about a political subject, done by questioning a large number of people; OPINION POLL 民意調查, 民意測驗: *Another poll asked respondents if they favoured nuclear power.* 另一項民意調查詢問被訪者是否贊成利用核能。| **carry out/conduct a poll** *MORI carried out a poll among senior managers to get their views on taxation.* 英國國際市場與輿論研究中心在高級經理中間進行了一項民意調查, 以收集他們對稅收的看法。**b)** a record of the result of this; OPINION POLL 民意測驗[調查]的結果: *Recent polls show Labour well in the lead.* 最近的民意調查結果顯示工黨遙遙領先。—see also 另見 DEED POLL, EXIT POLL, STRAW POLL **2 the poll** also 又作 **the polls** an election to choose a government or political representative 選舉: *a fourth successive defeat at the polls* 連續第四次在選舉中失利 | *The result of the poll won't be known until around midnight.* 選舉投票結果要到午夜前後方能揭曉。| **go to the polls** (=vote in an election) 參加投票 *It's only one more week until the country goes to the polls.* 距離全國進行選舉投票僅有一星期。**3** [singular] the number of votes recorded at an election 選票數: *In most constituencies the largest party can pull 40% of the poll.* 在大多數選區中, 最大的政黨可以拉到40%的選票。**4 the polls** *especially AmE* the place where you can go to vote in an election【尤美】投票處, 投票地點: *The polls won't close for another hour.* 投票處再過一小時才會關閉。

poll[2] *v* [T] to try to find out what the public thinks about a subject by questioning a large number of people 對…進行民意測驗[調查]: *18% of the women we polled said their husbands had a drinking problem.* 我們調查的婦女當中有18%的人說她們的丈夫有嗜酒的毛病。

pol·lard[1] /ˋpɑləd; ˈpɒləd/ *n* [C] a tree that has had the top cut off to make the lower branches grow more thickly 截去樹梢的樹, 截頭樹

pollard[2] *v* [T] to cut the top off a tree in order to make the lower branches grow more thickly〔為使枝葉更繁茂而〕截去〔樹的〕樹梢 —**pollarded** *adj*

pol·len /ˋpɑlən; ˈpɒlən/ *n* [U] a fine powder produced by flowers, which is carried by the wind or by insects to other flowers of the same type making them produce seeds 花粉

pollen count /ˈ·· ·/ *n* [C] a measure of the amount of pollen in the air, usually given as a guide for people who are made ill by it 散佈在空中的花粉量, 花粉計數〔通常用作花粉過敏症者的指引〕: *an unusually warm day with a very high pollen count* 花粉計數很高的不尋常的熱天

pol·li·nate /ˋpɑləˌnet; ˈpɒlɪ̈neɪt/ *v* [T] to make a flower or plant produce seeds by giving it pollen 給〔花、植物〕傳授花粉: *flowers pollinated by bees* 由蜜蜂傳授花粉的花 —**pollination** /ˌpɑləˋneʃən; ˌpɒlɪ̈ˈneɪʃən/ *n* [U]

poll·ing /ˋpolɪŋ; ˈpəʊlɪŋ/ *n* [U] the activity of voting in a political election〔在政治選舉中的〕投票: *Polling started at 8.00 this morning.* 投票於今早八點鐘開始。| **heavy/light polling** (=with many/few people voting) 投票人數很多/很少

polling booth /ˈ·· ·/ *n* [C] *especially BrE* a small partly enclosed space in a polling station where you can vote secretly in an election【尤英】〔投票站裡供祕密寫選票用的〕投票亭, 寫票處; VOTING BOOTH *AmE*【美】

polling day /ˈ·· ·/ *n* [C] *BrE* the day on which people vote in an election【英】投票日, 選舉日

polling sta·tion /ˈ·· ˌ··/ *especially BrE*【尤英】**polling place** *AmE*【美】*n* [C] the place where people go to vote in an election 投票站

pol·li·wog, pollywog /ˋpɑlɪˏwɑg; ˈpɒliwɒg/ *n* [C] *AmE* a TADPOLE【美】蝌蚪

poll·ster /ˋpolstɚ; ˈpəʊlstə/ *n* [C] someone who prepares and asks questions to find out what people think about a particular subject 民意調查者, 民意測驗者

poll tax /ˋ· ·/ *n* **1** [C] a tax of a fixed amount collected from every citizen of a country 人頭稅 **2 the poll tax** a British tax of a fixed amount which was paid by each person during the late 1980s and early 1990s〔英國20世紀80年代晚期至90年代初期的〕人頭稅, 國民稅, 丁稅

pol·lut·ant /pəˋlutn̩t; pəˈluːtənt/ *n* [C,U] a substance that makes air, water, soil etc dangerously dirty, and is caused by cars, factories etc 污染物, 污染物質: *emissions of chemical pollutants* 化學污染物的排放

pol·lute /pəˋlut; pəˈluːt/ *v* [T] **1** to make air, water, soil etc dangerously dirty and not suitable for people to use 污染〔空氣、水、土壤等〕: *beaches polluted by raw sewage* 被未經處理的污水污染的海灘 | *industrial emissions that pollute the air* 污染空氣的工業排放物 **2 pollute sb's mind** to give someone immoral thoughts and spoil their character 毒害[荼毒]某人的思想: *fears that Lawrence's novels would pollute young minds* 害怕勞倫斯小說會毒害年輕人思想 —**polluted** *adj*: *polluted rivers* 受污染的河流 —**polluter** *n* [C]

W2 **pol·lu·tion** /pəˋluʃən; pəˈluːʃən/ *n* [U] **1** the process of making air, water, soil etc dangerously dirty and not suitable for people to use 污染: *California's tough anti-pollution laws* 加利福尼亞州嚴厲的反污染法 | *chronic pollution of the atmosphere* 長期的大氣污染 **2** substances that make air, water, soil etc dangerously dirty 污染物: *industries and other sources of pollution* 工業及其他污染源| *a national programme to cut sulphur dioxide pollution* 減少二氧化硫污染物的全國性計劃

Pol·ly·an·na /ˏpɑlɪˋænə; ˌpɒliˈænə/ *n* [C usually singular 一般用單數] someone who is always cheerful and always thinks something good is going to happen 一貫樂觀的人, 盲目樂觀者

po·lo /ˋpolo; ˈpəʊləʊ/ *n* [U] a game played between two teams of players riding horses, who hit a small ball with long-handled wooden hammers 馬球(運動) —see also 另見 WATER POLO

pol·o·naise /ˏpɑləˋnez; ˌpɒləˈneɪz/ *n* [C,U] a slow Polish dance popular in the 19th century, or the music for this dance 波洛奈兹舞〔19世紀盛行的一種波蘭慢步舞〕; 波洛奈兹舞曲

polo neck /ˋ·· ·/ *n* [C] *BrE* a shirt or SWEATER with a high, close-fitting band around the neck that is rolled down【英】高圓領襯衫[羊毛衫]; TURTLENECK *AmE*【美】—**polo-neck** *adj*: *a polo-neck sweater* 高圓領羊毛衫 —see picture on page A17 參見A17頁圖

polo shirt /ˋ·· ·/ *n* [C] a shirt with short SLEEVES and a collar, made out of soft cotton material 馬球襯衫〔棉製開領短袖襯衫〕

pol·ter·geist /ˋpoltɚˏgaɪst; ˈpɒltəgaɪst/ *n* [C] a spirit that makes objects move around and causes strange noises 捉弄人的鬼怪〔使物體到處移動並製造奇怪噪聲的鬼怪〕

pol·troon /pɑlˋtrun; pɒlˈtruːn/ *n* [C] *old use* a COWARD【舊】懦夫, 膽小鬼

pol·y /ˋpɑlɪ; ˈpɒli/ *n* [C] *BrE informal* a POLYTECHNIC【英, 非正式】綜合性理工學院, 工藝專科學校

poly- /pɑlɪ; pɒlɪ/ *prefix* many 多: *polysyllabic* (=with three or more SYLLABLES) 多音節的 | *polyandry* 一妻多夫(制)

pol·y·an·dry /ˋpɑlɪˏændrɪ; ˌpɒliˈændri/ *n* [U] *technical* the custom or practice of having more than one husband at the same time【術語】一妻多夫(制) —compare 比較 BIGAMY, POLYGAMY —**polyandrous** /ˏpɑlɪˋændrəs; ˌpɒliˈændrəs◂/ *adj*

pol·y·an·thus /ˏpɑlɪˋænθəs; ˌpɒliˈænθəs/ *n* [C,U] a small garden plant with a group of round brightly-coloured flowers at the top of each stem 西洋櫻草

pol·y·es·ter /ˏpɑlɪˋɛstɚ; ˈpɒliestə/ *n* [U] a man-made material used to make cloth 聚酯纖維

pol·y·eth·y·lene /ˏpɑlɪˋɛθɪlin; ˌpɒliˈeθəliːn/ *n* [U] *AmE* a strong light plastic used to make bags, sheets for covering food, small containers etc【美】聚乙烯; POLYTHENE *BrE*【英】

po·lyg·a·my /pəˋlɪgəmɪ; pəˈlɪgəmi/ *n* [U] *technical* the custom or practice of having more than one husband or wife at the same time in a society where this is allowed【術語】多配偶(制); 一夫多妻(制); 一妻多夫(制) —compare 比較 BIGAMY, MONOGAMY —**polygamous** *adj*

pol·y·glot /ˋpɑlɪˏglɑt; ˈpɒliglɒt/ *adj formal* speaking or using many languages; MULTILINGUAL【正式】使用[通曉]多種語言的 —**polyglot** *n* [C]

pol·y·gon /ˋpɑlɪˏgɑn; ˈpɒlɪgən/ *n* [C] *technical* a flat shape with three or more sides【術語】多邊形, 多角形 —**polygonal** /pəˋlɪgənl; pəˈlɪgənəl/ *adj*

pol·y·graph /ˋpɑlɪˏgræf; ˈpɒligrɑːf/ *n* [C] *technical* a piece of equipment that is used by the police to find out whether someone is telling the truth; LIE DETECTOR【術語】測謊器[儀]

pol·y·he·dron /ˏpɑlɪˋhidrən; ˌpɒlɪˈhiːdrən/ *n* [C] a solid shape with many sides 多面體

pol·y·math /ˋpɑlɪˏmæθ; ˈpɒlɪmæθ/ *n* [C] *formal* someone who has a lot of knowledge about many different subjects【正式】博學之士, 博學的人

pol·y·mer /ˋpɑlɪmɚ; ˈpɒlɪmə/ *n* [C] a chemical compound that has a simple structure of large MOLECULES 聚合物[體]

pol·y·mor·phous /ˏpɑlɪˋmɔrfəs; ˌpɒlɪˈmɔːfəs◂/ also 又作 **pol·y·mor·phic** /-fɪk; -fɪk◂/ *adj technical* having many forms, styles etc during different stages of growth or development【術語】〔生長或發展等過程中〕多種形式的, 多形(態)的

pol·yp /ˋpɑlɪp; ˈpɒl$_{\rm ɪ}$p/ *n* [C] **1** a very simple sea animal that has a body like a tube 水螅體 **2** a small lump that grows inside someone's body and is caused by an illness 息肉

po·lyph·o·ny /pəˋlɪfənɪ; pəˈlɪfəni/ *n* [U] a kind of music in which several different tunes or notes are sung or played together at the same time 複調音樂(作品) —**polyphonic** /ˏpɑlɪˋfɑnɪk; ˌpɒlɪˈfɒnɪk◂/ *adj*

pol·y·pro·py·lene /ˏpɑlɪˋpropəlin; ˌpɒlɪˈprəʊp$_{\rm ə}$liːn/ *n* [U] a hard light plastic material 聚丙烯

po·lys·e·mous /pəˋlɪsɪməs; pəˈlɪs$_{\rm ɪ}$məs/ *adj technical* a polysemous word has two or more different meanings【術語】(一詞)多義的 —**polysemy** *n* [U]

pol·y·sty·rene /ˏpɑlɪˋstaɪrin; ˌpɒlɪˈstaɪriːn◂/ *n* [U] *especially BrE* a soft light plastic material that prevents heat or cold from passing through it, used especially for making containers【尤英】聚苯乙烯; STYROFOAM *AmE trademark*【美, 商標】

pol·y·syl·la·ble /ˋpɑləˏsɪləbl̩; ˈpɒlɪˌsɪləbəl/ *n* [C] *technical* a word that contains more than three SYLLABLES【術語】多音節詞〔含有三個以上音節〕—**polysyllabic** /ˏpɑləsɪˋlæbɪk; ˌpɒlɪsɪˈlæbɪk◂/ *adj*

pol·y·tech·nic /ˏpɑləˋtɛknɪk; ˌpɒlɪˈteknɪk/ *n* [C] a kind of British college similar to a university, which provided training and degrees in many subjects, and existed until 1993〔1993年以前英國的〕綜合性理工學院, 工藝專科學校

pol·y·the·is·m /ˋpɑləθiˏɪzəm; ˈpɒlɪθiːɪzəm/ *n* [U] the belief that there is more than one god 多神論[主義]; 多神教 —compare 比較 MONOTHEISM —**polytheistic** /ˏpɑləθiˋɪstɪk; ˌpɒlɪθiːˈɪstɪk◂/ *adj*

pol·y·thene /ˋpɑlɪθin; ˈpɒl$_{\rm ɪ}$θiːn/ *n* [U] *BrE* a strong light plastic used to make bags, sheets for covering food, small containers etc【英】聚乙烯; POLYETHYLENE *AmE*【美】

pol·y·un·sat·u·rate /ˏpɑlɪʌnˋsætʃərɪt; ˌpɒliʌnˈsætʃər$_{\rm ɪ}$t/ *n* [C] a FATTY ACID (=chemical that helps your body produce energy) that is POLYUNSATURATED 多重不飽和物, 多重不飽和脂肪酸

P

pol·y·un·sat·u·ra·ted /ˌpɑlɪʌnˋsætʃəretɪd; ˌpɒliʌnˈsætʃəreɪtɪ̣d/ *adj* polyunsaturated fats or oils come from vegetables and plants, and are considered to be better for your health than animal fats〔脂肪或油脂〕多重不飽和的 —compare 比較 SATURATED FAT

pol·y·u·re·thane /ˌpɑlɪˋjurəθen; ˌpɒlɪˈjʊərɪ̣θeɪn/ *n* [U] a plastic used to make paints and VARNISH 聚氨酯

pom /pɑm; pɒm/ *n* [C] *AustrE, NZE slang* an insulting word for an English person, especially one who has gone to live in Australia or New Zealand【澳, 新西蘭, 俚】英國佬〔侮辱性説法, 尤指遷居澳大利亞或新西蘭的英國人〕

po·made /poˋmed; pəˈmeɪd/ *n* [U] a sweet-smelling oily substance rubbed on men's hair to make it smooth, which was used especially in former times〔尤指舊時的〕男用潤髮油, 男用頭油

po·man·der /ˋpomændə; pəʊˈmændə/ *n* [C] a box or ball that contains dried flowers and HERBS and is used to make clothes or a room smell pleasant〔用於放出香味的〕香盒, 香球, 香丸

pom·e·gran·ate /ˋpɑmˌgrænɪt; ˈpɒmɪ̣grænɪ̣t/ *n* [C] a round fruit that has a lot of small seeds, red juicy flesh, and a thick reddish skin 石榴

pom·mel¹ /ˋpʌml̩; ˈpʌməl/ *n* [C] **1** the high, rounded part at the front of a SADDLE¹ (1) on a horse〔馬鞍的〕前橋, 鞍頭 —see picture at 參見 HORSE¹ 圖 **2** the round end of a sword handle〔刀劍柄上的〕圓頭

pommel² *v* [T] *especially AmE*【尤美】another spelling of PUMMEL pummel 的另一種拼法

pommel horse /ˈ·· ·/ *n* [C] a piece of equipment used in GYMNASTICS with two handles on top, which you hold onto and jump over 鞍馬〔體操運動器械〕

pom·my /ˋpɑmɪ; ˈpɒmi/ *n* [C] *AustrE, NZE slang* a POM【澳, 新西蘭, 俚】英國佬

pomp /pɑmp; pɒmp/ *n* [U] *formal* all the impressive clothes, decorations, music etc that are traditional for an important official or public ceremony【正式】〔典禮等的〕盛況, 壯觀場面: *all the usual pomp that surrounds occasions such as the royal wedding* 諸如皇家婚禮之類場合常見的壯觀場面

pom·pom /ˋpɑmˌpɑm; ˈpɒmpɒm/ also 又作 **pom·pon** /-pɑn; -pɒn/ *n* [C] **1** a small woollen ball used as a decoration on clothing, especially hats〔尤指裝飾帽子用的〕小絨球 **2** a large round ball of loose plastic strings connected to a handle, used by CHEERLEADERS〔啦啦隊用的〕塑料線球, 絲球 —see picture at 參見 CHEERLEADER 圖

pom·pous /ˋpɑmpəs; ˈpɒmpəs/ *adj* trying to make people think you are important, especially by using very formal and important-sounding words 自命不凡的, 自高自大的; 浮華的, 虛誇的: *The principal gave a very pompous speech about 'the portals of learning'.* 那位校長誇誇其談地發表了關於"知識之門"的演講。—**pompously** *adv* —**pompousness, pomposity** /pɑmˋpɑsətɪ; pɒmˈpɒsɪ̣ti/ *n* [U]

ponce¹ /pɑns; pɒns/ *n* [C] *BrE informal*【英, 非正式】**1** a PIMP 拉皮條的男子, 淫媒 **2** an offensive word meaning a man who is too concerned about his appearance 過分注重外表的男人, 女人氣的男人, 脂粉氣十足的男人〔不禮貌的説法〕

ponce² *v*

ponce about/around *phr v* [I] *BrE informal*【英, 非正式】**1** to waste time doing silly things 瞎混, 閒逛, 遊手好閒: *At least I haven't been poncing about all day with theatre people.* 至少我没有整天和那些搞戲劇的人瞎混。**2** if a man ponces about, he behaves in a way that is thought to be how a woman behaves〔男人〕矯揉造作, 舉止似女人

ponce off sb *phr v* [T] *BrE* to ask someone to give you something such as a cigarette or drink without offering to pay【英】向〔某人〕要〔煙、飲料等〕: *I'd no money, you know, so I ponced off him.* 你知道的, 我沒有錢嘛, 所以我就向他要。

pon·cho /ˋpɑntʃo; ˈpɒntʃəʊ/ *n plural* **ponchos** [C] **1** a coat consisting of one large piece of thick wool cloth like a BLANKET, with a hole in the middle for your head 披風, 斗篷〔形似氈子, 中間有領口〕**2** *AmE* a coat that keeps out rain and is made of one large piece of material with a cover for your head【美】雨披

ponc·y, poncey /ˋpɑnsɪ; ˈpɒnsi/ *adj BrE informal* poncy clothes or behaviour are typical of a man who is too concerned about his appearance【英, 非正式】〔衣服、行為〕女人氣的, 脂粉氣的, 娘娘腔的

pond /pɑnd; pɒnd/ *n* [C] **1** a small area of still water, especially one that has been artificially made〔尤指人工的〕池塘: *a duck pond* 養鴨池 **2 across the pond/on the other side of the pond** *informal* on the other side of the Atlantic Ocean in the US or in Britain【非正式】在大西洋的另一邊〔指美國或英國〕 3

pon·der /ˋpɑndə; ˈpɒndə/ *v* [I,T] *formal* to spend time thinking carefully and seriously about a problem, a difficult question, or something that has happened【正式】仔細考慮, 深思, 默想: *Lisa pondered for a while before answering.* 莉莎仔細考慮了一會兒才回答。| **[+on/over/about]** *As I pondered over the whole business, an idea struck me.* 我在思考整件事情的時候, 突然想到了一個主意。| **ponder how/what/whether etc** *His critics might well ponder what would happen if he quit.* 批評他的人很可能會充分考慮他一旦辭職將會發生甚麼事。| **ponder sth** *Esteban sat pondering the state of his marriage.* 埃斯特班坐了下來, 細細地思考着他的婚姻狀況。

pon·der·ous /ˋpɑndərəs; ˈpɒndərəs/ *adj* **1** moving slowly or awkwardly because of being very big and heavy 行動遲緩的, 笨拙的: *an elephant's ponderous walk* 大象笨拙的行走方式 **2** boring and too serious 嚴肅而乏味的, 呆板的; 生硬的: *a ponderous and difficult book, intended for experts* 一本為專家寫的沉悶而又難懂的書 **3** very big and heavy 大而重的, 笨重的: *Calvin's way was blocked by the ponderous body of his host.* 卡爾文被主人龐大的身軀擋住了去路。—**ponderously** *adv* —**ponderousness** *n* [U]

pone /pon; pəʊn/ *n* [U] *AmE informal* CORN PONE【美, 非正式】玉米餅

pong¹ /pɑŋ; pɒŋ/ *n* [C usually singular 一般用單數] *BrE informal* an unpleasant smell【英, 非正式】難聞的氣味: *There's an awful pong in the fridge!* 冰箱裡有股可怕的氣味!

pong² *v* [I] *BrE informal* to have a strong and unpleasant smell【英, 非正式】有強烈的異味, 發出難聞的氣味: *Ugh! Your socks really pong!* 哎呀!你的襪子真難聞! —**pongy** *adj*

pon·iard /ˋpɑnjəd; ˈpɒnjəd/ *n* [C] a small pointed knife used as a weapon in former times〔舊時用作武器的〕匕首, 短劍

pon·tiff /ˋpɑntɪf; ˈpɒntɪ̣f/ *n* [C] *technical* the POPE【術語】教皇, 教宗

pon·tif·i·cal /pɑnˋtɪfɪkl̩; pɒnˈtɪfɪkəl/ *adj formal*【正式】**1** speaking as if you think your judgment or opinion is always right〔説話〕武斷的, 專橫的, 自負的 **2** connected with the POPE 教皇的, 教宗的 —**pontifically** /-klɪ; -kli/ *adv*

pon·tif·i·cate¹ /pɑnˋtɪfɪket; pɒnˈtɪfɪ̣keɪt/ *v* [I] to give your opinion about something in a way that shows you think you are always right 武斷地談論, 自以為是地發表意見: **[+about/on]** *He's always pontificating about the evils of modern society.* 他總是自以為是地對現代社會的種種弊病大發議論。

pon·tif·i·cate² /pɑnˋtɪfɪkɪt; pɒnˈtɪfɪkɪ̣t/ *n* [C] *technical* the position or period of being POPE【術語】教皇的職位[任期]

pon·toon /pɑnˋtun; pɒnˈtuːn/ *n* [C] **1** *BrE* a card game, usually played for money【英】〔通常用來賭錢的〕紙牌遊戲, 二十一點牌戲; BLACKJACK *AmE*【美】**2** one of several metal containers or boats that are fastened together to support a floating bridge〔架設浮橋用的〕浮舟, 平底

船 **3** one of two hollow metal containers fastened to the bottom of a plane so that it can come down onto water and float〔固定在飛機底部的〕浮筒

pontoon bridge /'·· ·/ *n* [C] a floating bridge which is supported by several pontoons 浮橋

po·ny /ˈponɪ; ˈpəʊni/ *n* [C] a small horse 小馬, 駒; 矮種馬 —see also 另見 PIT PONY, SHETLAND PONY

po·ny·tail /ˈponɪˌtel; ˈpəʊniteɪl/ *n* [C] hair tied in a bunch at the back of your head and falling like a horse's tail 馬尾辮, 馬尾髮 —see picture at 參見 HAIRSTYLE 圖

pony-trek·king /'·· ,··/ *n* [U] *BrE* the activity of riding through the countryside on ponies【英】鄉間騎馬旅行; PACK TRIP *AmE*【美】

poo /pu; puː/ *n informal*【非正式】**1** [U] a word meaning solid waste from your BOWEL*s*, used especially by children 屎, 大便〔尤兒語〕; POOP[1] (3) *AmE*【美】**2** [C usually singular 一般用單數] a word meaning the act of passing waste from your BOWEL*s*, used especially by children 拉屎, 大便〔尤兒語〕; POOP[1] (4) *AmE*【美】—**poo** *v* [I,T] *informal*【非正式】

pooch /putʃ; puːtʃ/ *n* [C] *informal often humorous* a dog【非正式, 常幽默】狗

poo·dle /ˈpudl; ˈpuːdl/ *n* [C] **1** a dog with thick curly hair 長鬈毛狗, 貴婦狗 —see picture at 參見 DOG[1] 圖 **2 be sb's poodle** *BrE humorous* if someone is another person's poodle, they always do what the other person tells them to do【英, 幽默】當某人的走狗[走卒]

poof[1] /pʊf; pʊf/ also 又作 **poof·ter** /ˈpʊftɚ; ˈpʊftə/ *n* [C] *BrE* an offensive word for a HOMOSEXUAL man【英】搞同性戀的男人, 男同性戀者〔具冒犯性的說法〕—**poofy** *adj* —compare 比較 POUF

poof[2] *interjection* **1** used when talking about something that happened suddenly 噗!〔表示某事突然發生〕: *Then poof! She was gone.* 於是, 噗!她消失了。**2** used to show that you do not agree with or believe what someone has said 呸! 啐!〔用於表示不同意或不相信〕: *Poof! He doesn't know what he's talking about.* 呸!他不知道自己在說些甚麼。

pooh /pu; puː/ *interjection BrE spoken* used when there is a very unpleasant smell【英口】哼! 呸!〔表示對難聞氣味的厭惡〕; PEW[2] *AmE*【美】

pooh-pooh /,· '·/ *v* [T] *informal* to say that you think that an idea, suggestion, effort etc is silly or not very good【非正式】對〔主意、建議、努力等〕嗤之以鼻[不以為然]: *Critics pooh-poohed the idea at first.* 評論家起初對這觀點嗤之以鼻。

2 2 **pool**[1] /pul; puːl/ *n*

1 ►WATER 水◄ [C] **a)** a SWIMMING POOL or PADDLING POOL 游泳池; 嬉水池: *Does the hotel have a pool?* 這家酒店有游泳池嗎? | *an inflatable rubber wading pool* 可充氣的橡皮嬉水池 **b)** a small area of still water in a hollow place 水窪, 水坑, 水池: *The children hunted for crabs in the pools between the rocks.* 孩子們在岩石間的水坑裡尋找螃蟹。| *where the stream formed a shallow pool* 溪流形成一個淺水池的地方

2 a pool of water/blood/light etc a small area of liquid or light on a surface 一攤水/一攤血/一小片光等: *Trautman lay unconscious in a pool of blood.* 特勞特曼躺在血泊之中, 不省人事。| *His desk lamp cast a pool of light on the documents.* 他的枱燈在文件上投下一小片光。

3 ►GAME 遊戲◄ [U] a game in which you use a stick to knock numbered balls into holes around a table, which is often played in bars 落袋撞球戲 —compare 比較 SNOOKER

4 ►FOOTBALL 足球◄ **the pools** a system in Britain in which people try to win money each week by guessing the results of football games 足球賭博〔英國的一種賭博方式, 通過競猜足球比賽的結果以贏錢〕

5 ►GROUP OF THINGS/PEOPLE 一組事物/人◄ [C] **a)** a number of things or an amount of money that is shared by a group of people 合夥使用的錢[物品] **b)** a group who are available to work when they are needed 可招之即來的人員, 備用人員: *a pool of volunteers for community projects* 一批為社區項目提供服務的志願者 —see also 另見 CAR POOL, GENE POOL, TYPING POOL

pool[2] *v* [T] to combine your money, ideas, skills etc with those of other people so that you can all use them 合夥[集中]使用, 共用: **pool your resources** *Investors agreed to pool their resources to develop the property.* 投資者同意集資開發房地產。

pool hall /'· ·/ *n* [C] *AmE* a building where people go to practise playing pool【美】撞球室, 彈子房

pool·room /ˈpulˌrum; ˈpuːlruːm/ *n* [C] a room used for playing pool, especially in a bar〔尤指酒吧裡的〕撞球室, 彈子房, 桌球房

poop[1] /pup; puːp/ *n* **1** [C] *technical* the raised part at the back end of an old sailing ship【術語】〔舊帆船的〕船尾樓甲板 **2 the poop** *AmE informal* the latest news about something that has happened, which is told to you unofficially by someone; LOWDOWN【美, 非正式】小道消息, 最新消息, 內幕: *Come on, Dan, what's the poop? Are they hiring Collins?* 來吧, 丹, 有甚麼內幕消息嗎?他們要雇用柯林斯嗎? **3** [U] *AmE informal* a word meaning solid waste from your BOWEL*s*, used especially by children【美, 非正式】大便, 屎〔尤兒語〕; POO (1) *BrE*【英】**4** [singular] *AmE informal* a word meaning the act of passing waste from your BOWEL*s*, used especially by children【美, 非正式】大便, 拉屎〔尤兒語〕; POO (2) *BrE*【英】

poop[2] *v* [I,T] *AmE informal* a word meaning to pass solid waste from your BOWEL*s*, used especially by children【美, 非正式】拉屎, 大便〔尤兒語〕; POO *BrE*【英】—see also 另見 PARTY POOPER

poop out *phr v* [I] *AmE informal*【美, 非正式】**1** to stop trying to do something because you are tired, bored etc〔由於勞累、厭煩等而〕停止做〔某事〕: *Ouida pooped out about halfway through the race.* 維達在賽跑中跑到中途就筋疲力盡停了下來。**2** to decide not to do something you have already said you would do, because you are tired or not interested〔由於勞累或沒有興趣而〕決定不做〔已經說好要做的事〕: **poop out on sb** *"Is Bill coming along?" "Nah, he's pooping out on us."* "比爾要來嗎?" "不, 他又決定不跟我們去了。"

poop deck /'· ·/ *n* [C] the floor on the raised part at the back of an old sailing ship〔舊帆船的〕船尾樓甲板

pooped /pupt; puːpt/ also 又作 **pooped out** /,· '·/ *adj* [not before noun 不用於名詞前] *AmE informal* very tired; EXHAUSTED (1)【美, 非正式】很累的, 筋疲力盡的

poop·er scoop·er /ˈpupɚ ˌskupɚ; ˈpuːpə ˌskuːpə/ *n* [C] *informal* a small SPADE and a container, used by dog owners for removing their dogs' solid waste from the streets【非正式】〔供狗主撿狗糞用的〕長柄糞鏟及盛糞容器

poo-poo /'· ·/ *n* [U] POO 屎, 大便

poop sheet /'· ·/ *n* [C] *AmE informal* written official instructions or information【美, 非正式】〔書面的〕詳細指示; 〔官方的〕書面材料

poor /pur; pɔː/ *adj* 1 1

1 ►NO MONEY 無錢◄ having very little money and not many possessions 貧窮的, 貧困的: *Her family were so poor they couldn't afford to buy her new clothes.* 她家很窮, 買不起新衣服給她。| *Ethiopia is one of the poorest countries in the world.* 埃塞俄比亞是世界上最貧困的國家之一。| *a poor neighborhood* 貧困居民區, 貧民區

2 the poor people who are poor 窮人: *state subsidies to help the poor buy basic foods* 幫助窮人購買基本食品的國家補助

3 ►NOT GOOD 不好的◄ not as good as it could be or should be; INFERIOR[1] (1) 不佳的, 差的, 次等的, 低劣的: *Poor sanitation can lead to the spread of diseases.* 衛生狀況不佳會導致疾病的傳播。| *The soil in this area is very poor.* 這地區的土壤很貧瘠。| *poor rates of pay* 很低的報酬 | **poor hearing/eyesight/memory** *You'd bet-*

ter read it to me – my eyesight's pretty poor. 你最好讀給我聽——我的視力很不好。

4 poor boy/girl/Joe etc *especially spoken* used to show pity for someone because they are so unlucky, unhappy etc【尤口】可憐的[不幸的]男孩/女孩/喬等: *Poor kid, he's had a rough day.* 可憐的孩子, 他度過了倒霉的一天。| *I feel sorry for the poor horse with me riding it.* 這匹可憐的馬要由我來騎, 我為牠感到難過。| **poor thing** *You poor thing, you've had a hard time of it, haven't you?* 可憐的東西, 你吃了不少苦頭, 是嗎? | **poor old** *Poor old Lou, having to work at weekends.* 可憐的老盧, 週末還得工作。

5 ►NOT GOOD AT STH 不善於某事的◄ not good at doing something 不善於…的, 對…不熟練的, 差的: *a poor public speaker* 不善於演講的人 | **[+at]** *poor at spelling* 拼寫很差

6 make a poor job of to do something badly 把〔某事〕做得很糟: *The builders have made a really poor job of fixing our roof.* 那些建築工人把我們的屋頂修得很糟糕。

7 ►HEALTH 健康◄ someone whose health is poor is ill or weak for a long period of time〔身體〕虛弱的, 衰弱的: **be in poor health** *My parents are both in rather poor health.* 我父母的身體都不好。

8 poor in sth lacking things that people need 缺乏某物: *fatty snacks that are poor in nutrients* 缺乏營養的高脂肪小食

9 poor loser someone who behaves badly if they lose a game 輸不起的人

10 be a poor second/third etc to finish a race, competition etc a long way behind the person ahead of you〔在比賽中〕被遠遠拋在後面的第二名/第三名等

11 poor man's *spoken often humorous*【口, 常幽默】**a)** used to say that someone is like a very famous performer, writer etc but is not as good as they are 稍遜一籌的, 較差的, 無實的: *He's a kind of poor man's Richard Gere.* 他的樣子跟李察基爾很相像, 但其他的都及不上他。**b)** used to say that something can be used for the same purpose as something else, and is much cheaper〔可作同樣用途但〕價格較低廉的, 次等的: *The abacus is the poor man's pocket calculator.* 算盤算是廉價的袖珍計算器。

12 poor relation someone or something that is not treated as well as other members of a group or is much less successful than they are 同類中較次者: *Theatre musicians tend to be the poor relations of the musical profession.* 劇院樂師往往被看作是音樂界中地位稍低的人。—see also 另見 **be in bad/poor taste** (TASTE[1] (6)), POORLY, POORNESS

poor boy /ˈ· ·/ *n* [C] *AmE* a long bread roll that is cut open and filled with meat, cheese etc; SUBMARINE SANDWICH【美】〔切開後中間夾肉、乾酪等的〕長麵包卷, 大型三明治

poor·house /ˈpʊrˌhaʊs; ˈpɔːhaʊs/ *n* [C] a building in former times where people could live and be fed, which was paid for with public money〔舊時的〕濟貧院

poor law /ˈ· ·/ *n* **the Poor Law** a group of British laws which controlled the help given to poor people in former times〔英國舊時的〕濟貧法, 恤貧法令

poor·ly¹ /ˈpʊrlɪ; ˈpɔːli/ *adv* badly 糟糕地, 不好地, 拙劣地, 蹩腳地: *poorly paid* 報酬很低 | *Jana's doing poorly in school.* 簡娜在學校裡的成績很差。| *a poorly written article* 一篇寫得很差的文章

poorly² *adj* [not before noun 不用於名詞前] *informal especially BrE* ill【非正式, 尤英】身體不舒服的, 健康不佳的: *Matt's wife's been feeling poorly.* 馬特的妻子一直感到身體不適。

poorly off /ˌ·· ˈ·/ *adj* [not before noun 不用於名詞前] **1** someone who is poorly off does not have very much money 貧困的, 貧窮的 **2 be poorly off for** to not have enough of something 不夠…的, 缺…的: *We have enough textbooks but we're poorly off for lab equipment.* 我們有足夠的教科書, 但是缺少實驗室設備。

poor·ness /ˈpʊrnɪs; ˈpɔːnɪs/ *n* [U] *formal* lack of skill or good qualities【正式】差, 拙劣, 低劣: **[+of]** *the poorness of my German accent* 我那蹩腳的德語口音—compare 比較 POVERTY

poor-spir·it·ed /ˌ· ˈ···◄/ *adj literary* having no confidence or courage【文】缺乏信心的, 膽怯的, 懦弱的 —**poor-spiritedly** *adv*

poo·tle /ˈputl; ˈpuːtl/ *v* [I+about/around] *BrE spoken* to spend time pleasantly, doing things that are not very important【英口】玩, 愉快地度過

pop¹ /pɑp; pɒp/ **popped, popping** *v* S3

1 ►GO SOMEWHERE QUICKLY 迅速去某處◄ [I always+adv/prep] *spoken* to go somewhere quickly, suddenly, or unexpectedly【口】迅速[突然, 出人意料]地去〔某處〕: **[+in/out/round/to etc]** *Could you pop round to the store for some bread?* 你能不能快去商店買些麵包回來? | *Pat's just popped next door for ten minutes.* 帕特剛去了隔壁十分鐘。

2 ►COME OUT OF STH 從某物中出來◄ [I always+adv/prep] to come suddenly or unexpectedly out of or away from something 突然[出人意料]地從〔某物〕中出來, 蹦出, 離開, 脱落: **[+out/off/up etc]** *A button popped off my shirt when I sneezed.* 我打噴嚏時, 一顆鈕扣突然從我的襯衫上掉了下來。| **out/up popped** *The egg cracked open and out popped a tiny head.* 那隻蛋裂開了, 裡面冒出一個小腦袋來。

3 ►PUT STH SOMEWHERE 把某物放在某處◄ [T always+adv/prep] *informal* to put something somewhere quickly for a short time【非正式】迅速地把〔某物〕放在〔某處〕一會兒: **pop sth in/round/over etc** *I'll just pop these cakes into the oven.* 我來把這些蛋糕放到烤箱裡烤一會兒。| *Barry popped his head round the door to say hello.* 巴里從門口探進頭來問好。

4 ►SHORT SOUND 短促的聲音◄ [I,T] to make a short sound like a small explosion, or to make something make this sound (使) 噼啪作響: *Champagne corks were popping.* 香檳酒的瓶塞砰的一聲爆了出來。| **pop sth** *Please don't pop all the balloons before the party starts.* 請不要在聚會開始前就把所有的汽球都噼啪弄破。

5 ►EARS 耳朵◄ [I] if your ears pop, you feel the pressure in them suddenly become less when you go quickly up or down in a plane, lift etc〔在飛機、電梯等中迅速升降時〕耳朵內發出'噗'的一聲〔因耳內壓力降低〕

6 sb's eyes popped (out of their head) used to say that someone looked extremely surprised or excited〔極度驚訝或興奮〕某人的眼睛都瞪出來了

7 pop the question *informal* to ask someone to marry you【非正式】求婚: *Hasn't Bill popped the question yet?* 比爾還沒有求婚嗎?

8 pop pills *informal* to take PILLS too often【非正式】過度地服藥

9 pop your clogs *BrE humorous* to die【英, 幽默】死, 死亡

10 ►CORN 玉米◄ [I,T] to cook corn until it swells and bursts open, or to be cooked in this way 爆玉米花;〔玉米〕爆成玉米花

11 ►BORROWING MONEY 借錢◄ [T] *BrE old-fashioned* to PAWN² something【英, 過時】典當, 抵押

pop off *phr v* [I] *informal* to die suddenly【非正式】突然死掉, 猝死

pop sth ↔ on *phr v* [T] *spoken*【口】**1** to quickly put on a piece of clothing 迅速穿上〔衣服〕: *Just pop this jacket on and we'll see if it fits.* 快把這件短上衣穿上, 我們看合不合身。**2** to quickly turn on a piece of electrical equipment 迅速打開〔電器〕: *Pop the kettle on, would you.* 把水壺開關打開, 好嗎?

pop up *phr v* [I] **1** to appear suddenly and unexpectedly 突然[意外]地出現, 冒出來: *Mushrooms tend to pop up overnight.* 蘑菇往往會在一夜之間長出來。| *She popped up in Munich after all that time.* 經過那麼長的時間以後, 她突然在慕尼黑出現。—see also 另見 POP-UP

2 to hit a ball into the air in a game of BASEBALL so that it only travels a short distance〔棒球比賽中〕擊出小騰空球: *O'Malley popped up to first base.* 奧馬利朝一壘擊出個小騰空球。

S3 W3 **pop²** *n* **1** [U] modern music that is popular with young people, and usually consists of simple tunes with a strong beat 流行音樂, 流行歌曲: **pop singer/concert/festival etc** *a pop record* 流行音樂唱片 | *pop culture* 通俗文化 **2** [singular] *AmE informal* a word meaning your father, used especially to address him【美, 非正式】爸爸: *Can I borrow the car, Pop?* 爸爸, 我可以借用一下汽車嗎? **3** [U] *informal* a sweet FIZZY drink such as LEMONADE【非正式】蘇打水, 汽水; SODA (2) *AmE*【美】: *a bottle of pop* 一瓶汽水 **4** [C] a sudden short sound like a small explosion 砰[啪、噗]的一聲: *the pop of a champagne cork* 香檳酒瓶塞發出的砰的一聲 | **go pop** (=make this sound) 發出砰[啪]的一聲 *The balloon went pop.* 汽球砰的一聲破了。—see picture on page A19 參見A19 頁圖

pop³ the written abbreviation of 縮寫=POPULATION

pop·a·dum, poppadum /ˈpɑpədəm; ˈpɒpədəm/ *n* [C] a large circular piece of very thin flat Indian bread cooked in oil〔印度的〕油煎薄餅

pop art /,· ˈ·◂/ *n* [U] a kind of art that was popular in the 1960s, which shows ordinary objects, such as advertisements, or things you see in people's homes〔反映日常生活事物的〕波普藝術, 通俗藝術, 大眾藝術〔20 世紀 60 年代流行的一種藝術〕

pop·corn /ˈpɑpˌkɔrn; ˈpɒpkɔːn/ *n* [U] a kind of corn that swells and bursts open when heated, and is usually eaten warm with salt or sugar 爆玉米花, 爆穀

Pope /pop; pəʊp/ *n* [C] **1** the leader of the Roman Catholic church〔羅馬天主教的〕教皇, 教宗: *The Pope will visit El Salvador this year.* 教皇今年將訪問薩爾瓦多。| *Pope John XXIII* 教皇約翰[若望]二十三世 —see also 另見 PAPAL **2 Is the Pope (a) Catholic?** *informal humorous* used to say that something is clearly true or certain【非正式, 幽默】教皇是天主教徒嗎? 這還用問?〔用於表示某事毫無疑問是真實的或確定的〕: *"Do you think they'll win?" "Is the Pope Catholic?"* "你認為他們會贏嗎?" "這還用問?"

pope's nose /,· ˈ·/ *n* **the pope's nose** *AmE, IrishE, ScotE* the piece of flesh at the tail end of a cooked bird, such as a chicken【美, 愛爾蘭, 蘇格蘭】〔煮熟的〕雞[禽類]的尾部[屁股]肉; PARSON'S NOSE *BrE*【英】

pop-eyed /,· ˈ·◂/ *adj informal* having your eyes wide open, because you are surprised or excited【非正式】〔由於驚訝或興奮而〕目瞪口呆的, 瞪大眼睛的

pop fly /ˈ· ·/ *n* [C] a type of hit in BASEBALL in which the ball is hit straight up into the air and only travels a short distance〔棒球的〕小騰空球 —see picture on page A22 參見A22 頁圖

pop group /ˈ· ·/ *n* [C] a group of people who sing and play POP MUSIC 流行樂隊, 流行音樂組合

pop-gun /ˈ· ·/ *n* [C] a toy gun that fires small objects, such as corks (CORK¹ (2)), with a loud noise〔發射軟木塞等的〕玩具汽槍

pop·in·jay /ˈpɑpɪnˌdʒe; ˈpɒpɪndʒeɪ/ *n* [C] *old use* a young man who is too proud of his appearance【舊】講究衣着的年青男人, 花花公子〔過分以外貌為榮的年輕人〕

pop·lar /ˈpɑplə; ˈpɒplə/ *n* [C] a very tall straight thin tree 楊樹

pop·lin /ˈpɑplɪn; ˈpɒplɪn/ *n* [U] a strong shiny cotton cloth 毛葛, 府綢

pop mu·sic /ˈ· ˌ··/ *n* [U] modern music that is popular with young people and usually consists of simple tunes with a strong beat 流行音樂

pop·o·ver /ˈpɑpˌovə; ˈpɒpəʊvə/ *n* [C] *AmE* a light, hollow cake made with eggs, milk, and flour【美】空心酥脆餅, 膨鬆餅〔用雞蛋、牛奶和麵粉製成〕

pop·pa /ˈpɑpə; ˈpɒpə/ *n* [singular] *AmE informal* father【美, 非正式】爸爸

pop·pa·dum /ˈpɑpədəm; ˈpɒpədəm/ *n* [C] another spelling of POPADUM popadum 的另一種拼法

pop·per /ˈpɑpə; ˈpɒpə/ *n* [C] *informal especially BrE* a small metal thing used for fastening a piece of clothing which consists of two parts, one of which is pressed into the hollow part of the other; SNAP² (6)【非正式, 尤英】按扣, 揿扣, 子母扣 —see picture at 參見 FASTENER 圖

pop·pet /ˈpɑpɪt; ˈpɒpɪt/ *n* [C] *BrE spoken* a way of talking to or about a child or animal you are fond of【英口】寶寶, 寶貝兒, 乖乖〔指寵愛的小孩或動物〕: *Isn't he a poppet?* 他真是個小寶貝, 不是嗎? | *Come here, poppet.* 到這兒來, 寶寶。

pop·py /ˈpɑpɪ; ˈpɒpi/ *n* [C] **1** a plant that has brightly coloured, usually red, flowers and small black seeds 罌粟 **2** a red colour 深橘紅色 —see picture on page A5 參見 A5 頁圖

pop·py·cock /ˈpɑpɪˌkɑk; ˈpɒpikɒk/ *n* [U] *old-fashioned* nonsense【過時】廢話, 胡扯: *He's talking absolute poppycock!* 他完全是在胡說八道!

pop·py·seed /ˈpɑpɪsid; ˈpɒpisiːd/ *n* [U] the small black seeds of the poppy plant used in cakes, bread etc 罌粟籽〔用於做糕點、麵包等〕

pop quiz /ˈ· ·/ *n* [C] *AmE* a short test which is given without any warning in order to check that students have been studying【美】突擊測驗, 突擊考試

pops /pɑps; pɒps/ *adj* **pops concert/orchestra** *AmE* a concert or ORCHESTRA which performs CLASSICAL and popular music【美】〔演奏古典和流行音樂的〕通俗音樂會/管弦樂團: *the Boston Pops Orchestra* 波士頓大眾管弦樂團

Pop·si·cle /ˈpɑpsɪkḷ; ˈpɒpsɪkəl/ *n* [C] *AmE trademark* a piece of ice, usually tasting of fruit, that you suck on a stick【美, 商標】冰棍, 冰棒, 雪條; ICE LOLLY *BrE*【英】

pop star /ˈ· ·/ *n* [C] a famous and successful entertainer who plays or sings POP MUSIC 流行樂歌星

pop·u·lace /ˈpɑpjələs; ˈpɒpjʊləs/ *n* [singular] *formal* the ordinary people who live in a country【正式】平民, 百姓, 大眾: *breaking the news to a joyful populace* 把這消息透露給歡樂的老百姓

pop·u·lar /ˈpɑpjələ; ˈpɒpjʊlə/ *adj* **1** liked by a lot of people 受大眾喜愛的, 受歡迎的: *Hilary was popular at school.* 希拉莉在學校裡很受歡迎。| **[+with]** *Video games are very popular with children.* 電子遊戲很受孩子的喜愛。| *a popular holiday resort* 人們喜歡的度假勝地 —opposite 反義詞 UNPOPULAR **2 popular belief/view/misconception** a belief etc that a lot of people have 普遍的信念/觀點/誤解: **contrary to popular belief** *Contrary to popular belief, gorillas are basically shy, gentle creatures.* 與人們普遍的看法相反, 大猩猩其實是一種羞怯、溫和的動物。**3** [only before noun 僅用於名詞前] popular entertainment, newspapers, programmes etc are intended to be suitable for ordinary people〔娛樂、報紙、節目等〕通俗的, 大眾(化)的: *pilloried by the popular press* 受到通俗報刊的嘲笑 **4** [only before noun 僅用於名詞前] done by a lot of people in a society, group etc 由〔社會、團體等中〕多數人做的, 公眾的: *popular protest* 公眾的抗議 | *It was decided by popular vote.* 這是由公眾投票決定的。**5 you'll be popular** *spoken* used when telling someone that other people will be annoyed with them【口】你會"走紅"的〔用於告訴某人別人將會生他們的氣〕: *You'll be popular when they find out you've lost their tickets.* 他們一旦知道你把他們的票丢了, 你可就要"走紅"了。 S2 W1

pop·u·lar·i·ty /ˌpɑpjəˈlærətɪ; ˌpɒpjʊˈlærɪti/ *n* [U] the quality of being liked or supported by a large number of people 流行, 普及, 受歡迎; 聲望: **gain in popularity** (=start to be liked by many people) 開始流行 *Western music is steadily gaining in popularity.* 西方音樂逐漸流行起來。| *The president's popularity has declined considerably.* 總統的受歡迎程度已大大降低。

pop·u·lar·ize /ˈpɑpjələˌraɪz; ˈpɒpjʊləraɪz/ also 又作

P

-ise *BrE*【英】*v* [T] **1** to make something well known and liked 使〔某物〕受歡迎; 宣傳, 推廣: *Reggae music was popularized by Bob Marley in the 1970s.* 雷蓋音樂由鮑勃·馬利在 20 世紀 70 年代推廣開來。**2** to make a difficult subject or idea easily understandable for ordinary people who have no special knowledge about it 使〔困難的學科或觀點〕通俗化, 使大眾化, 使易懂, 普及: *books aimed at popularizing modern science* 致力於普及現代科學的書籍 —**popularization** /ˌpɑpjələrəˈzeʃən; ˌpɒpjʊləraɪˈzeɪʃən/ *n* [U]

P

pop·u·lar·ly /ˈpɑpjələ·lɪ; ˈpɒpjʊləli/ *adv* **popularly believed/thought/known etc** believed, thought, known etc by many people (人們) 普遍相信/認為/知道等: *Vitamin C is popularly believed to prevent colds.* 人們普遍認為維生素 C 有預防感冒的作用。

pop·u·late /ˈpɑpjəˌlet; ˈpɒpjʊleɪt/ *v* **be populated** if an area is populated by a particular group of people, they live there 〔某地區〕居住着: **[+by]** *The Central Highlands are populated mainly by peasant farmers.* 在中部高地居住的主要是農民。| **densely/heavily/highly/thickly populated** (=a lot of people live in that place in relation to its size) 人口密集的 *densely populated urban areas* 人煙稠密的市區 | **thinly/sparsely populated** (=few people live in that place in relation to its size) 人煙稀少的 *The northern islands are very sparsely populated.* 北部各島人煙稀少。

2 1 **pop·u·la·tion** /ˌpɑpjəˈleʃən; ˌpɒpjʊˈleɪʃən/ *n* [U] **1** the number of people living in a particular area, country etc 人口: *a city with a population of over two million* 一個有兩百多萬人口的城市 | *What is the population of Mexico?* 墨西哥有多少人口? **2** [C usually singular 一般用單數] all of the people who live in a particular area 〔某一地區的〕全體居民: *The whole population had turned out to welcome us home.* 所有居民都出來歡迎我們回家。| *Most of the world's population don't get enough to eat.* 世界上大多數人都吃不飽。| **the white/French/urban etc population** (=part of the group of people who live in a particular area who are white, French etc) 白人/法國人/城市等的人口 *By the middle of the 19th century, the urban population of England exceeded the rural population.* 到 19 世紀中期, 英格蘭的城市人口已經超過了農村人口。**3 population explosion** a rapid increase in the population of an area or the whole planet 人口爆炸 **4 centre of population/population centre** a city, town etc 城市, 城鎮: *far from most centres of population* 遠離大多數城市

pop·u·list /ˈpɑpjəlɪst; ˈpɒpjʊlɪst/ *adj* claiming to represent ordinary people 聲稱代表人民的, 平民主義的: *a populist leadership* 聲稱代表民眾利益的領導人 —**populist** *n* [C] —**populism** *n* [U]: *the switch from Marxism to populism* 從馬克思主義到平民主義的轉變

pop·u·lous /ˈpɑpjələs; ˈpɒpjʊləs/ *adj formal* a populous area has a large population in relation to its size【正式】人口稠密的: *Hong Kong is one of the most populous areas in the world.* 香港是世界上人口最稠密的地區之一。—**populousness** *n* [U]

pop-up /ˈ· ·/ *adj* **pop-up book/card/toaster etc** a book, card, TOASTER etc that is designed to make something suddenly spring out of it 〔可以將內部的東西突然彈出的〕彈出式書籍/賀卡/烤麵包機等

porce·lain /ˈpɔrslɪn; ˈpɔːslɪn/ *n* [U] **1** a hard shiny white substance that is used for making expensive plates, cups etc 瓷 **2** plates, cups etc made of this 瓷器

porch /pɔrtʃ; pɔːtʃ/ *n* [C] **1** an entrance covered by a roof outside the front door of a house or church 〔房子或教堂前門外有頂的〕入口處, 門廊 **2** *AmE* an open area with a floor and a roof, often made of wood, fixed to the side of a house on the ground floor; VERANDA【美】〔房屋側面有屋頂和地板的〕遊廊, 走廊; 陽台: *sitting out on the porch* 坐在外面的遊廊上 —see picture on page A4 參見 A4 頁圖

por·cu·pine /ˈpɔrkjəˌpaɪn; ˈpɔːkjʊpaɪn/ *n* [C] an animal with long, sharp, needle-like parts growing all over its back and sides which it can make point upwards 豪豬, 箭豬

pore¹ /pɔr; pɔː/ *n* [C] one of the small holes in your skin that liquid, especially SWEAT can pass through, or a similar hole in the surface of a plant 〔皮膚的〕毛孔; 〔植物表面的〕氣孔, 細孔: *Witch-hazel can help to unblock greasy pores.* 金縷梅酊劑有助於疏通含油脂的毛孔。

pore² *v*

pore over sth *phr v* [T] to read or look at something very carefully for a long time 仔細閱讀; 凝視, 注視: *They expected to find him poring over his notes the night before the exam.* 他們原以為會發現他在考試的前一天晚上仔細地研讀筆記。

pork /pɔrk; pɔːk/ *n* [U] **1** the meat from pigs 豬肉: *pork chops* 豬排 **2** *AmE slang* government money spent in a particular area in order to get political advantages【美俚】政治恩惠〔為獲得政治上的好處而撥給某一地區的政府資金〕

pork bar·rel /ˈ· ˌ··/ *n* [singular, U] *AmE slang* a government plan to increase the amount of money spent in a particular area in order to gain political advantage【美俚】〔政府為爭取選票而給予地方的〕國庫撥款, 政治分肥: *the pork barrel politics of military production contracts* 軍用生產合同方面的政治分肥

pork·er /ˈpɔrkə; ˈpɔːkə/ *n* [C] **1** a young pig that is made fat before being killed for food 〔宰殺前經過催肥的〕食用小豬 **2** *informal* an insulting word for a fat person【非正式】肥豬, 胖豬〔對肥胖者的侮辱性稱呼〕**3** *slang* a lie【俚】謊言, 謊話

pork pie /ˌ· ˈ·◂/ *n* [C,U] *BrE* a small round PIE which contains pieces of cooked pork【英】豬肉餡餅

pork rinds /ˌ· ˈ·/ *n* [plural] *AmE* SCRATCHINGS【美】豬肉皮

pork·y¹ /ˈpɔrkɪ; ˈpɔːki/ *adj informal* an insulting word meaning fat【非正式】肥的, 肥胖的〔侮辱性詞語〕

porky² /ˈpɔrkɪ; ˈpɔːki/ *n* [C] also 又作 **porky pie** /ˌ·· ˈ·/ *BrE slang* a lie【英俚】謊言, 謊話

porn /pɔrn; pɔːn/ *n* [U] *informal* pornography【非正式】色情作品; 色情描寫: *the porn industry* 色情業 | *Computer porn is the latest threat.* 電腦色情是最新的威脅。—see also 另見 HARD PORN, SOFT PORN

porn·o /ˈpɔrno; ˈpɔːnəʊ/ *adj* [usually before noun 一般用於名詞前] *informal* PORNOGRAPHIC【非正式】色情的: *a porno movie* 色情電影

por·nog·ra·phy /pɔrˈnɑgrəfɪ; pɔːˈnɒgrəfi/ *n* [U] **1** magazines, films etc that show sexual acts and images in a way that is intended to make people feel sexually excited 色情作品[雜誌、電影等]: *a major campaign against pornography* 一場反對色情作品的重大運動 **2** the treatment of sexual acts in pictures, film or writing in a way that is intended to make people feel sexually excited 〔圖片、電影或文字作品中的〕色情描繪 —**pornographer** *n* [C] —**pornographic** /ˌpɔrnəˈgræfɪk; ˌpɔːnəˈgræfɪk◂/ *adj*: *The script was condemned as pornographic.* 這個劇本被指責為淫穢作品。—**pornographically** /-klɪ; -kli/ *adv*

po·rous /ˈporəs; ˈpɔːrəs/ *adj* porous rock or soil allows liquid, air etc to pass through slowly 〔岩石或土壤〕能滲透的, 透水[氣]的 —**porousness** *n* [U]

por·phy·ry /ˈpɔrfərɪ; ˈpɔːfəri/ *n* [U] a type of hard dark red or purple rock containing CRYSTALS 斑岩

por·poise /ˈpɔrpəs; ˈpɔːpəs/ *n* [C] a sea animal rather like a DOLPHIN, that swims in groups 鼠海豚

por·ridge /ˈpɔrɪdʒ; ˈpɒrɪdʒ/ *n* [U] **1** a soft breakfast food made by boiling OATMEAL (=crushed grain) in milk or water 燕麥片[麥片]粥; OATMEAL *AmE*【美】**2** *BrE slang* a period of time spent in prison【英俚】關押, 監禁 (期): **do porridge** (=spend time in prison) 坐牢, 服刑

port /pɔrt; pɔːt/ *n*

1 ►WHERE SHIPS STOP 輪船停泊的地方◄ [C,U] a place where ships can load and unload people or things;

HARBOUR[1] 港, 港口, 海港: **come into port/leave port** *The ferry was just about to leave port.* 那艘渡船正要離港。| **in port** *We're going to have two days ashore while the ship is in port.* 輪船在港口停靠時, 我們將有兩天的上岸時間。

2 ▶TOWN 城鎮◀ [C] a town or city with a HARBOUR[1] or DOCKS 港口城市, 港市; 口岸: *Britain's largest port* 英國最大的港口城市 | *the Israeli port of Haifa* 以色列海法港市

3 ▶WINE 葡萄酒◀ [C,U] strong sweet Portuguese wine, usually drunk after a meal 波爾圖葡萄酒〔葡萄牙產的一種葡萄酒, 通常在飯後飲用〕: *port and Stilton* 波爾圖葡萄酒和斯提爾頓乳酪

4 ▶LEFT OF SHIP 輪船的左側◀ [U] the left side of a ship or aircraft when you are looking towards the front 〔輪船或飛機航行方向的〕左舷: *on the port side* 在左舷一邊 | **to port** *After the collision, the ship began leaning over to port.* 碰撞之後, 那艘輪船開始向左舷傾斜。—opposite 反義詞 STARBOARD

5 ▶COMPUTER 電腦◀ [C] *technical* a part of a computer where you can connect another piece of equipment such as a PRINTER【術語】端口, 埠〔電腦與其他設備的接口〕

6 any port in a storm *usually spoken* an expression meaning that you should take whatever help you can when you are in trouble, even if it has some disadvantages【一般口】〔即使有不利之處也應接受的〕擺脱困境的任何幫助, 窮途之策 —see also 另見 FREE PORT, PORT OF ENTRY

por·ta·ble /ˋpɔrtəbḷ; ˈpɔːtəbəl/ *adj* light and able to be carried or moved easily 手提式的, 便攜式的, 輕便的: *a portable typewriter* 便攜式打字機 —**portable** *n* [C]: *We swapped the colour television for a black and white portable.* 我們用彩色電視機換了一台手提式黑白電視機。—**portability** /ˌpɔrtəˋbɪlətɪ; ˌpɔːtəˈbɪlɪ̣ti/ *n* [U]

por·ta·crib /ˋpɔrtəkrɪb; ˈpɔːtəkrɪb/ *n* [C] *AmE trademark* a small bed with handles in which a baby lies and can be carried【美, 商標】手提式嬰兒牀; CARRYCOT *especially BrE*【尤英】—see picture at 參見 BED[1] 圖

port·age /ˋpɔrtɪdʒ; ˈpɔːtɪdʒ/ *n* [U] the act of carrying boats over land from one river to another〔兩條河之間的〕路運, 陸運〔將船從一條河經陸地運至另一條河的動作〕

Por·ta·kab·in /ˋpɔrtəkæbɪn; ˈpɔːtəkæbɪ̣n/ *n* [C] *trademark* a small hut that can be used as a temporary office, classroom etc, and can be moved by TRUCK【商標】活動房屋〔一種可裝上大卡車搬運的臨時房屋, 可用作臨時辦公室、教室等〕

por·tal /ˋpɔrtḷ; ˈpɔːtl/ *n* [C usually plural 一般用複數] *literary* a tall and impressive gate or entrance to a building【文】〔建築物高大壯觀的〕大門, 正門: *the carved Gothic portals of the college* 這所學院帶有雕飾的哥德式大門

port·cul·lis /pɔrtˋkʌlɪs; pɔːtˈkʌlɪ̣s/ *n* [C] a strong iron gate that can be lowered over the entrance of a castle〔城堡的〕吊門, 吊閘

por·tend /pɔrˋtɛnd; pɔːˈtend/ *v* [T] *literary* to be a sign that something is going to happen, especially something unpleasant【文】預示〔不祥之事〕, 為…的凶兆: *strange events that portend some great disaster* 預示着巨大災難的奇怪事件

por·tent /ˋpɔrtɛnt; ˈpɔːtent/ *n* [C] *literary* a sign or warning that something is going to happen【文】跡象, 徵兆, 預兆: **[+of]** *This was a striking portent of things to come.* 這明顯地預示着即將發生的事情。—compare 比較 OMEN

por·ten·tous /pɔrˋtɛntəs; pɔːˈtentəs/ *adj* **1** *literary* events that are portentous are very important, especially because they show that something unpleasant is going to happen【文】預示未來的; 凶兆的, 徵兆不祥的: *portentous events that boded ill* 預示凶兆的不祥事件 **2** trying to appear important and serious 自命不凡的, 擺架子的, 自大的: *The book is portentous and badly edited.* 這本書煞有介事, 編得很差勁。—**portentously** *adv* —**portentousness** *n* [U]

por·ter /ˋpɔrtɚ; ˈpɔːtə/ *n* **1** [C] someone whose job is to carry travellers' bags at railway stations, airports etc〔火車站、機場等的〕行李搬運工人, 腳夫: *I hailed a porter and then a cab.* 我叫了一名搬運工人, 然後又叫了一輛計程車。**2** [C] *especially BrE* someone in charge of the entrance to a hotel, hospital etc【尤英】〔酒店、醫院等的〕守門人 **3** [C] someone whose job is to carry heavy goods at markets〔在市場搬運重物的〕貨物搬運工 **4** [C] *AmE* someone whose job is to look after a sleeping carriage in a train【美】〔火車臥鋪車廂的〕服務員 **5** [U] *old-fashioned* a dark brown bitter beer【過時】黑啤酒, 深褐色苦啤酒

por·ter·house steak /ˌpɔrtɚhaus ˋstek; ˌpɔːtəhaʊs ˈsteɪk/ *n* [C,U] a thick, flat piece of high quality BEEF[1] (1) 上等牛排

port·fo·li·o /pɔrtˋfolɪˌo; pɔːtˈfəʊliəʊ/ *n* [C] **1** a large flat case used especially for carrying drawings, documents etc 公事包, 文件夾 **2** a collection of drawings, paintings or other pieces of work by an artist, photographer etc〔藝術家、攝影師等的〕畫作[相片]選輯, 作品選輯 **3** a collection of shares (SHARE[2] (5)) owned by a particular person or company〔某人或某公司持有的〕有價證券組合; 資產組合; 投資搭配: *an investment portfolio* 投資組合 **4** *formal, especially BrE* the area of responsibility of a particular government minister【正式, 尤英】部長[大臣]的職責[職務]: *the foreign affairs portfolio* 外交部長職務

port·hole /ˋpɔrtˌhol; ˈpɔːthəʊl/ *n* [C] a small round window on the side of a ship or plane〔輪船或飛機的〕舷窗: *a row of illuminated portholes* 一排張燈結彩的舷窗

por·ti·co /ˋpɔrtɪˌko; ˈpɔːtɪkəʊ/ *n* [C] a covered entrance to a building, consisting of a roof supported by PILLARS (有圓柱的) 門廊, 柱廊: *Above the portico is an commemorative plaque.* 門廊上面是一塊紀念匾.

por·tion[1] /ˋpɔrʃən; ˈpɔːʃən/ *n* [C] **1** a part of something larger, especially a part that is different from the other parts〔東西的〕一部分〔尤指與其他部分不同〕: **[+of]** *The front portion of the rocket breaks off.* 火箭的前部脱落了。| *The factory represents only a small portion of the company's interests.* 這家工廠只佔公司股份的一小部分。**2** an amount of food for one person, especially served in a restaurant〔尤指餐館中食物的〕一份, 一客: *They're good-sized portions.* 它們是大份的。| **[+of]** *Another portion of chips?* 再來一份薯條好嗎? **3** [usually singular 一般用單數] a share of something, such as responsibility, blame, or profits that is divided between a small number of people〔責任、利潤等的〕一份, 一部分: **[+of]** *The other driver must bear a portion of the blame for the accident.* 另一位司機必須對這次事故承擔部分責任。**4 sb's portion** *formal or literary* something that happens in your life that you cannot avoid; FATE (1)【正式或文】某人的命運: *Sorrow has always been her portion.* 她命中注定悲傷不斷。

portion[2] *v*

portion sth ↔ **out** *phr v* [T] to divide something into parts and give them to several people 分配: **portion sth out among** *The money was portioned out among them.* 那筆錢被他們分了。

port·ly /ˋpɔrtlɪ; ˈpɔːtli/ *adj* someone who is portly, especially a rather old man, is fat and round〔尤指年長男子〕肥胖的, 發福的: *a portly old gentleman* 一位發福的老先生 —**portliness** *n* [U]

port·man·teau[1] /pɔrtˋmænto; pɔːtˈmæntəʊ/ *n* [C] *old-fashioned* a very large SUITCASE that opens into two parts【過時】〔對開的〕手提箱, 皮箱

portmanteau[2] *adj* [only before noun 僅用於名詞前] *formal* a portmanteau word is made by combining the sound and meaning of two other words【正式】由兩個詞的詞義和讀音合併組成的, 混合的, 緊縮的:

'Edutainment' is a portmanteau word meaning education by entertainment. edutainment是一個緊縮詞，意思為寓教於樂。

port of call /ˌ· ·ˈ·/ *n* [C usually singular 一般用單數] **1** *informal* one of a series of places that you visit【非正式】旅途中的落腳點[停留地]；沿途要拜訪的地方：*My next port of call was the City Records Department.* 我下一個要去的地方是市檔案局。**2** a port where a ship stops on a journey from one place to another〔船的〕沿途停靠港：*Our next port of call was Istanbul.* 我們下一個要停泊的港口是伊斯坦布爾。

P

port of en·try /ˌ· · ˈ··/ *n* [C] a place, such as a port or airport, where people or goods can enter a country〔人或貨物的〕入口港，進口港，入境地點

por·trait /ˈpɔrtrɪt; ˈpɔːtrɪ̇t/ *n* **1** [C] a painting, drawing, or photograph of a person〔人的〕畫像；照片；肖像：**[+of]** *a portrait of Lenin* 列寧的畫像 | *She's been commissioned to paint Andrew's portrait.* 她已受託畫安德魯的肖像。**2** [C] a description or representation of something〔對某物的〕描繪，描述，表現：**[+of]** *The article's portrait of Owen's career was very interesting.* 這篇文章對奧雲職業生涯的描述非常有趣。**3** [U] *informal* portrait mode【非正式】縱向格式 —see also 另見 SELF-PORTRAIT

portrait mode /ˈ·· ·/ *adj* a photograph, picture, book, or page that is portrait has the longer edges at the sides〔照片、圖片、書或頁〕豎排的，縱向的 —opposite 反義詞 LANDSCAPE

por·trai·ture /ˈpɔrtrɪtʃɚ; ˈpɔːtrɪ̇tʃə/ *n* [U] the art of painting or drawing pictures of people 肖像畫技法

por·tray /pɔrˈtre; pɔːˈtreɪ/ *v* [T] **1** to describe or represent something or someone 描繪，描寫，描述：*His most famous painting portrayed the death of Nelson.* 他最出名的一幅畫描繪了納爾遜死時的情景。| *Levi portrays the sheer horror of the concentration camps very powerfully.* 利瓦伊將集中營的恐怖描繪得極有感染力。**2 portray sb/sth as sth** to describe or show someone or something in a particular way, according to your opinion of them 把某人/某物描寫為[刻畫為]某物：*women portrayed as sex objects in Hollywood movies* 在荷里活電影中被刻畫成性對象的女人 | *Joan Crawford's daughter portrayed her as a maniac.* 瓊·克勞福德的女兒把她說成是個瘋子。**3** to act the part of a character in a play 扮演〔角色〕：*She portrayed a doomed woman in the TV film 'Right to Die'.* 她在電視電影《死的權利》中扮演一位遭遇厄運的女性。

por·tray·al /pɔrˈtreəl; pɔːˈtreɪəl/ *n* [C,U] the action of portraying someone or something 描繪，描寫，描述；扮演；表現：*Does the film give an accurate portrayal of life under Stalin?* 這部電影如實地表現了史太林統治下的生活嗎？

Por·tu·guese /ˈpɔrtʃəˌgiz; ˌpɔːtʃʊˈgiːz◂/ *n* [U] **1** the language of Portugal, Brazil, and some other countries 葡萄牙語：*Do you speak Portuguese?* 你說葡萄牙語嗎？**2 the Portuguese** the people of Portugal 葡萄牙人 —**Portuguese** *adj*: *Portuguese wine* 葡萄牙的葡萄酒

Portuguese man-of-war /ˌ··· · ·ˈ·/ *n* [C] a very large JELLYFISH, which has long poisonous parts hanging down from its body 僧帽水母，葡萄牙軍艦水母

3 **pose**¹ /poz; pəʊz/ *v* **1 pose a problem/threat/challenge etc** to cause a problem, danger, difficulty etc 引起問題/造成威脅/提出挑戰：*Newton's challenge poses no threat to the leadership.* 牛頓的挑戰對領導層造不成任何威脅。| *Rising unemployment is posing serious problems for the administration.* 不斷上升的失業率正給政府造成嚴重的困難。**2** [I,T] to sit or stand in a particular position in order to be photographed or painted, or to make someone do this〔為照相或畫像而〕(使)擺好〔某種〕姿勢：**[+for]** *We posed for photographs after the graduation ceremony.* 畢業典禮之後，我們排好拍照。**3 pose a question** to ask a question, especially one that needs to be carefully thought about 提出問題〔尤指需要仔細考慮的問題〕：*The first chapter poses the question: What constitutes a democracy?* 第一章提出的問題是：民主國家是由甚麼構成的？**4 pose as sb** to pretend to be someone else, in order to deceive people 假裝成某人，假扮成某人：*Bryce was caught posing as a lawyer.* 布賴斯因冒充律師而被捕。**5** [I] *especially BrE* to dress or behave like a fashionable, rich etc person in order to make other people notice you or admire you【尤英】裝腔作勢

pose² *n* [C] **1** the position in which someone stands or sits, especially in a painting, photograph etc〔為畫像、拍照而擺的〕姿勢，姿態：**in a pose** *a painting of the Duchess in a dramatic pose* 擺着演戲般的姿勢的公爵夫人畫像 | **strike a pose** (=stand or sit in a particular position) 擺個姿勢 **2** *especially BrE* behaviour in which someone pretends to behave like a fashionable, rich, intelligent etc person in order to make other people notice them or admire them【尤英】做作；裝腔作勢的舉止：**it's just a pose** *He's always talking about his deep interest in philosophy – it's just a pose.* 他總在談論他對哲學有濃厚的興趣——那只是裝腔作勢罷了。

pos·er /ˈpozɚ; ˈpəʊzə/ *n* [C] **1** *informal* someone who tries to behave like a fashionable, rich, intelligent etc person to make people notice or admire them【非正式】裝腔作勢的人：*Kate's such a poser.* 凱特真會裝腔作勢。**2** *old-fashioned* a difficult question or problem【過時】難題，棘手的問題

po·seur /poˈzɝ; pəʊˈzɜː/ *n* [C] *French* a POSER (1)【法】裝腔作勢的人

posh /pɑʃ; pɒʃ/ *adj* **1** a posh restaurant, hotel, car etc is expensive and looks as if it is used or owned by rich people〔餐館、酒店、汽車等〕高檔的，豪華的，時髦的：*a posh nightclub in Mayfair*（倫敦）梅菲爾區的高級夜總會 **2** *BrE* behaving or speaking in a way which is typical of upper class people【英】〔行為或說話方式〕上流社會的：*My mum has a really posh voice when she's on the phone.* 我媽媽打電話時有一口上流社會的口音。—**posh** *adv*: *Doesn't he talk posh?* 他說話時難道沒有上流社會的腔調嗎？

pos·it /ˈpɑzɪt; ˈpɒzɪ̇t/ *v* [T] *formal* to suggest that a particular idea should be accepted as a fact; POSTULATE¹【正式】假定，假設：*positing the existence of even smaller particles* 假定存在更小的粒子

po·si·tion¹ /pəˈzɪʃən; pəˈzɪʃən/ *n*

1 ►STANDING/SITTING/POINTING ETC 站/坐/指等◄ [C] the way someone stands or sits, or the direction in which an object, SWITCH etc is pointing〔人的〕姿態，姿勢；〔物體等的〕所指方向，位置：*I had to work in an uncomfortable position, lying under the car.* 我只得不舒服地躺在汽車底下工作。| **a sitting/kneeling/standing position** *The prisoners were kept in a kneeling position.* 那些囚犯被迫跪着。| **a vertical/upright/horizontal position** *Make sure the container remains in an upright position.* 要確保那個容器保持直立。| *She turned the switch to the 'on' position.* 她把開關扭到"開"的位置。

2 ►SITUATION 情況，狀況◄ [C usually singular 一般用單數] the situation that someone is in, or the situation concerning a particular subject 處境，狀況，狀態；形勢：*What's the present position with regard to import restrictions?* 有關進口限制的現狀如何？| **in a good/strong/enviable etc position** *Reuters are now in an enviable position in the news and current affairs industry.* 路透社目前在新聞和時事行業中處於令人羨慕的地位。| **in your/her etc position** *I'm not sure what I'd do if I were in your position.* 我不能肯定如果我身在你的處境會怎麼辦。| **put sb in a difficult/awkward position** *You're putting me in rather a difficult position.* 你讓我陷入一個相當困難的處境。

3 ►LEVEL/RANK 水平/級別◄ [C] someone's or something's level or rank in a society or organization 地位，級別，身分：**[+in]** *the position of women in society* 婦女在社會中的地位 | **position of authority/influence**

You need to ask someone in a position of authority. 你需要問一位權威人士。| **position of trust/responsibility** (=a position in which people depend on you to be honest or careful) 責任重大的職務 | **abuse your position** (=use your authority wrongly) 濫用職權

4 ▶OPINION 觀點, 看法◀ [C] an opinion or judgment on a particular subject, especially the official opinion of a government, party, or someone in authority; ATTITUDE〔尤指政府、政黨、當權者的〕立場, 態度: **[+on]** *What's the party's position on tax reform?* 該黨對於稅制改革持甚麼態度? | **take the position that** *The principal took the position that the students didn't need music classes.* 那位校長認為學生不需要上音樂課。| **reconsider your position** *The administration should reconsider its position.* 政府應重新考慮自己的立場。

5 ▶PLACE WHERE SB/STH IS 某人/某物的位置◀ [C] the place where someone or something is, especially in relation to other objects and places 位置, 方位: *I checked our position by the compass.* 我用指南針查看我們的方位。| *the position of the sun in the sky* 太陽在天空中的位置 | **a strategic position** (=one that is suitable for a particular purpose) 戰略位置,〔適合某一目的的〕有利位置 *He placed himself in a strategic position next to the doorway.* 他使自己處於靠近門口的有利位置。

6 ▶CORRECT PLACE 適當的位置◀ [U] the place where someone or something is supposed to be 適當的位置: **in position/out of position** *After the shelves were in position we realized we'd forgotten to paint them.* 我們把那些架子放好之後才意識到忘了給它們上漆。| *One of the legs was out of position.* 其中的一條支架錯位了。

7 take up (your) position to move to a particular place so that you are ready to take part in a planned activity 站好位置〔準備參加活動〕, 就位: *Police marksmen took up their positions around the bank.* 警方的神射手在銀行周圍站好了位置。

8 ▶JOB 工作◀ [C] your job 職位, 職務, 工作: *Richard had to give up his position with the company.* 理查德不得不放棄在這家公司的工作。| **hold a position** (=have a particular job) 擔任某個職務 *She held the position of sales manager.* 她擔任銷售經理的職務。| **the position has been filled** (=the company has found someone to do the job) 這職位已經有人遞補了 —see 見 JOB (USAGE)

9 be in a position to do sth to be able to do something because you have the ability, money, or power to do it〔因為有能力、金錢或權力而〕能夠做某事: *When I know all the facts, I'll be in a position to advise you.* 在我了解所有的事實之後, 我就能給你提出建議了。

10 be in no position to do sth to be unable to do something because you do not have the ability, money or power to do it〔因為沒有能力、金錢或權力而〕不能夠做某事: *While I'm unemployed, I'm in no position to support a family.* 在我沒有工作時, 我沒有能力養家。

11 sb is in no position to talk *spoken* used to say that someone should not criticize another person, because they have made the same mistakes【口】某人沒有資格説話[批評別人]〔因為他們犯有同樣的錯誤〕

12 ▶RACE/COMPETITION 賽跑/比賽◀ [C,U] the place of someone or something in a race, competition, list etc 名次: **2nd/3rd/4th position** *Alesi has moved up into 3rd position.* 阿列希已經升至第三名。

13 ▶SPORT 體育運動◀ [C] the place where someone plays in a game of football, HOCKEY etc〔足球、曲棍球等運動中〕球員的位置: *"What position do you play?"* "你打甚麼位置?"

14 be in a position of strength to be in a situation in which you should be able to succeed or win 處於能夠成功[獲勝]的境況, 處於優勢地位: *workers bargaining from a position of strength* 談判中處於優勢的工人

15 jockey/manoeuvre/jostle for position to try to get an advantage over other people who are all trying to succeed in doing the same thing 想盡辦法使自己處於有利的位置[地位]: *On the eve of the election the candidates were all jockeying for position.* 在大選前夕, 各候選人都在盡力爭取有利的地位。

16 ▶ARMY 軍隊◀ [C] a place where an army has put soldiers, guns etc 陣地: *UN forces attacked Serb military positions around Sarajevo.* 聯合國部隊襲擊了塞爾維亞人在薩拉熱窩的軍事陣地。

17 ▶SEX 性◀ [C] one of the ways in which two people can have sex〔性交〕姿勢: *Most people prefer face-to-face positions.* 大多數人都喜歡臉對臉的正面性交姿勢。

USAGE NOTE 用法説明: POSITION

WORD CHOICE 詞語辨析: **place, position, location, spot, where**

Place is the usual word you use to talk about where something is or happens. place 是談論某物所在或某事所發生的地點常用的詞: *the place where I was born* 我出生的地方 | *one of the coldest places in the world* 世界上最寒冷的地方之一

Position is used to talk about the place where something is in relation to other things or places. position 用來表示相對於其他事物或地點而言的某個位置: *Plant the flowers in a sunny position.* 把花種在有陽光的地方。| *a plan that shows the position of everything in the room* 顯示房間內所有東西的位置的平面圖

Location is a more formal word for a place where someone works or lives, or where something is built. It may be used, for example, in business English or in advertising. location 表示某人工作或生活的地方, 或某建築物所在的位置, 較為正式。例如, 它可用在商業英語或廣告中: *The company has found a new location for its offices.* 這家公司已找到了新的辦公地點。| *a hotel in an extremely attractive location* 一家位置優越的酒店

Spot is a more informal word used especially for a pleasant place. spot 比較非正式, 尤用於表示令人愉快的地方: *This part of the beach is my favourite spot.* 沙灘的這部分是我最喜歡的地方。

In spoken English you usually use **where, anywhere, somewhere, someplace** etc instead of these words. 在英語口語中, 通常用 where, anywhere, somewhere, someplace 等來代替上述的詞語: *I'll show you where I was born.* 我帶你去看我出生的地方。| *She looked everywhere, but still couldn't find the letter.* 她到處都找遍了, 但還是沒有找到那封信。| *Can we put the TV someplace else?* 我們能把電視放在其他地方嗎? | *It depends on where they are from.* 這視乎他們是從哪裡來的。

position² *v* [T] to put something in a particular position 把〔某物〕放在〔某個位置上〕, 安置: *Position the cursor before the letter you want to delete.* 把光標放在你想刪去的字母前。

position pa·per /·'·· ,··/ *n* [C] a written statement that shows how a department, organization etc intends to deal with something〔部門、組織等關於處理某事的〕立場聲明

pos·i·tive /ˈpɑzətɪv; ˈpɒzɪ̈tɪv/ *adj* S2 W2

1 ▶SURE 確信的, 肯定的◀ [not before noun 不用於名詞前] very sure, with no doubt at all that something is right or true 確信的, 肯定的, 有把握的: *"Are you sure?" "Positive."* "你能肯定嗎?" "我能肯定。" | **positive (that)** *Are you absolutely positive you locked the door?* 你能絕對肯定你已把門鎖好嗎? | **[+of/about]** *It was definitely his fault – James was positive of that.* 那一定是他的錯 —— 詹姆斯對那點很有把握。

2 ▶CONFIDENT 有信心的◀ believing that you will be successful or that a situation will have a good result 有信心的, 積極的, 樂觀的: *You've got to be more positive about your work.* 你必須更積極地對待自己的工作。| **positive attitude/approach/outlook etc** *She started to have a more positive outlook on life.* 她開始擁有更積極

的人生觀。| **think positive** *Think positive and all your problems will be solved.* 往積極的方面去想，你所有的問題都會迎刃而解。—compare 比較 NEGATIVE[1] (2)

3 ▶LIKELY TO BE SUCCESSFUL 可能成功的◀ showing that something is likely to succeed or improve 很可能成功[改善]的: *All the signs are extremely positive – he'll be well again soon.* 所有跡象都表示非常良好——他將很快恢復健康。

4 ▶AGREEMENT/SUPPORT 同意/支持◀ showing that someone agrees with you, supports what you are doing, and wants you to succeed 予以肯定的，表示贊同的，支持的；有建設性的: *The response we've had so far from the public has been very positive.* 到目前為止，公眾對我們一直十分支持。| **positive criticism/feedback** (=criticism which includes praise for things done well, and encourages you to do better) 建設性的批評/積極的反饋意見

5 positive proof/evidence/identification etc proof, EVIDENCE etc that shows that there is no doubt that something is definitely true 確鑿的證據/確切的證明: *The fingerprints are positive proof that Elliott is the murderer.* 那些指紋是證明埃利奧特就是兇手的確實證據。

6 ▶SCIENTIFIC TEST 科學試驗◀ showing signs of the chemical or medical condition that was being looked for 陽性的: *The test results came back positive.* 測試結果呈陽性。—opposite 反義詞 NEGATIVE[1] (4)

7 ▶GOOD/USEFUL 好的/有用的◀ having a good or useful effect 有用的，有助益的: *At least something positive has come out of the situation.* 至少這個情況也產生了一些積極的東西。| *a very positive experience* 非常有益的經歷

8 ▶MORALLY GOOD 道德上好的◀ [usually before noun 一般用於名詞前] showing or encouraging someone, especially a child, to behave in a way that is morally good 導人向善的，正面的: *a positive social environment* 良好的社會環境 | *positive role models* 正面的榜樣

9 a positive miracle/delight/thrill etc *spoken* used to emphasize how good, surprising, exciting etc something is【口】絕對是奇蹟/享受/令人興奮的事等: *It was a positive miracle that she survived.* 她能生存下來簡直是奇蹟。

10 ▶MATHEMATICS 數學◀ *technical* a positive number is more than zero【術語】正的，正數的: *+ is the positive sign* +是正號

11 ▶ELECTRICITY 電◀ [no comparative 無比較級] *technical* having the type of electrical charge that is carried by PROTONS【術語】正的，陽性的: *a positive charge* 正電荷 —opposite 反義詞 NEGATIVE[1] (5)

12 positive pole the end of a MAGNET which turns naturally towards the Earth〔磁鐵的〕北極

13 ▶BLOOD 血液◀ *technical* having RHESUS FACTOR in your blood【術語】〔血液〕含 RH 因子的，含獼因子的 —opposite 反義詞 NEGATIVE[1] (7) —**positiveness** *n* [U]

positive di·scrim·i·na·tion /,··· ···'··/ *n* [U] the practice of giving a certain number of jobs, places in universities etc to a group of people who are often treated unfairly because of their race or sex; AFFIRMATIVE ACTION 逆向歧視〔提供一定數量的工作、大學學位等給那些由於種族或性別原因而常常受到不公平對待的人〕

pos·i·tive·ly /ˈpɑzətɪvlɪ; ˈpɒzɪtɪvli/ *adv* **1** *spoken* used to emphasize that something is true about someone or something, or when saying something surprising about them【口】確實，事實上: *Gabi isn't pretty, she's positively beautiful!* 加比不是漂亮，而是美貌絕倫！| *Some patients positively enjoy being in hospital.* 一些病人確實喜歡呆在醫院裡。**2** *spoken* used to emphasize that you really mean what you are saying, especially when it may seem surprising【口】〔用以加強語氣〕真的，確實: *This is positively the last time you'll hear me say this.* 這確確實實將是你最後一次聽到我說這些話。**3** in a way that shows you agree with something or want it to succeed 表示贊同地，肯定地: *The mayor spoke positively about the work that had been done so far.* 市長對於到目前為止已做的工作給予了積極的評價。**4 think positively** to believe that you are going to be successful or that a situation is going to have a good result 持積極[樂觀]的態度 **5** in a way that leaves no possibility of doubt 確信地，肯定地，有把握地: *Otto said quite positively that he would come.* 奧托十分肯定地說他會來。**6 positively charged** *technical* having the type of electrical charge that is carried by PROTONS【術語】帶正電的

pos·i·tiv·is·m /ˈpɑzətɪv,ɪzəm; ˈpɒzɪtɪvɪzəm/ *n* [U] a kind of PHILOSOPHY that is based only on real facts which can be scientifically proved, rather than on ideas〔哲學中的〕實證主義，實證論 —**positivist** *n* [C]

poss /pɑs; pɒs/ **1** *BrE*【英】the written abbreviation of 縮寫= possible: *Please send a photo if poss.* 如果可能的話寄張照片來。**2** the written abbreviation of 縮寫= POSSESSIVE[1] (3)

pos·se /ˈpɑsɪ; ˈpɒsi/ *n* [C] **1 a posse of** a large group of the same kind of people〔同類人的〕一羣，一隊，一批: *I was surrounded by a posse of photographers.* 我被一羣攝影師圍住了。**2** a group of men gathered together by a SHERIFF (=local law officer) in the US in past times to help catch a criminal〔美國舊時由縣治安官召集的幫助抓捕罪犯的〕民防團 **3** *slang* someone's group of friends【俚】〔某人的〕一羣朋友

pos·sess /pəˋzɛs; pəˈzes/ *v* [T not in progressive 不用進行式] **1** *formal* to own or have something, especially something valuable or important, something illegal, or an ability or quality【正式】擁有，具有，持有〔尤指貴重或重要的東西、非法物品、某種能力或品質〕: *Campbell was found guilty of possessing heroin.* 坎貝爾被判犯有持有海洛因罪。| *The prison inmates possess a considerable degree of autonomy.* 獄中犯人有相當大的自主權。**2** *formal* a word meaning to own or have something, used especially when you are surprised that someone does not have something, or when saying that this is all they have【正式】擁有，具有〔尤用來表示某人居然沒有某物或某物竟是他們的全部所有〕: *I don't think Joe possesses a suit.* 我想喬沒有一套正經的西服。| *They used all the money they possessed.* 他們用盡了所有的錢。**3 what (on earth) possessed you to...?** used to say that you cannot understand why someone did something stupid（究竟）甚麼驅使你...〔表示不明白某人為何做傻事〕: *What on earth possessed her to do such a thing?* 究竟是甚麼使她鬼迷心竅做了這樣的事呢？**4** *literary* if a feeling possesses you, you suddenly feel it very strongly and it affects your behaviour【文】〔感覺〕纏住，控制，支配，影響: *A sense of fear possessed him as he walked into the old house.* 他走進那所老房子時感到非常恐懼。

pos·sessed /pəˋzɛst; pəˈzest/ *adj* [not before noun 不用於名詞前] **1** if someone is possessed, their mind is controlled by an evil spirit 着了魔的，鬼迷心竅的: *Her family believed that she was possessed, and called in a priest.* 她的家人認為她着了魔，就把牧師請來了。| **like a man possessed/like one possessed** (=violently or with a lot of energy) 猛烈地，拚命地，着了魔似地 *He threw himself around like a man possessed.* 他發了瘋似地四處亂撞。**2 be possessed of** *literary* to have a particular quality, ability etc【文】具有〔某種品質、能力等〕: *Charles was possessed of a sound intellect and a happy manner.* 查爾斯具有健全的智力和得體的舉止。—see also 另見 SELF-POSSESSED

pos·ses·sion /pəˋzɛʃən; pəˈzeʃən/ *n*

1 ▶STH YOU OWN 個人擁有的東西◀ [C usually plural 一般用複數] something that someone owns and keeps or uses themselves 所有物；財產，財物: *The police went through all the dead girl's possessions.* 警方檢查了那個死去的女孩的所有財物。| *I packed my remaining possessions into the trunk.* 我把剩下的財物裝進箱子裡。

2 ▶STATE OF HAVING STH 擁有某物的狀態◀ [U] *formal* the state of having or owning something, especially a valuable object, piece of information etc【正

式】擁有, 持有, 佔有〔尤指貴重物品、資料等〕: **be in sb's possession** *The house has been in the family's possession since the 1500s.* 這所房子自16世紀以來一直歸這個家族所有。| **be in possession of sth/have sth in your possession** (=have something) 擁有[佔有, 持有]某物 *She was found in possession of stolen goods.* 她被發現藏有贓物。| *I have in my possession a number of secret documents.* 我掌握着一些祕密文件。| **come into sb's possession** (=if something comes into your possession, you get it) 為某人所得到[佔有], 落入某人手中 *How did the painting come into your possession?* 你是怎麼得到那幅畫的? | **have possession of** (=to own or have something, after you have bought it or taken it from someone else) 擁有〔指買來或從別人那裡拿來〕 *The finance company now has possession of the house.* 該金融公司現在擁有這所房子的所有權。

3 take possession of sth if you take possession of a house, car, or valuable object, you get it after it has become yours 擁有[佔有]某物, 拿到某物: *We didn't take possession of the car until a few days after the auction.* 拍賣會過後幾天, 我們才實際拿到了那輛汽車。

4 ►DRUGS/GUN 毒品/槍支◄ [U] *law* the crime of having illegal drugs or a gun with you or in your home【法律】〔毒品或槍支的〕私藏, 持有, 管有: *He faces trial on charges of possession of a loaded firearm.* 他因被控持有裝上子彈的槍支而面臨審判。

5 ►COUNTRY 國家◄ [C] a country controlled or governed by another country 領地, 屬地, 殖民地: *Britain's former overseas possessions* 英國過去的海外領地

6 ►BALL 球◄ [U] the state of having control of the ball in some sports〔一些體育運動中對球的〕控制: **get/lose possession** *Waddell gets possession, and he scores!* 沃德爾控制着球, 他得分了!

7 ►AMERICAN FOOTBALL 美式足球◄ [C] a period of time in American football when one team is playing OFFENSE[2] and has control of the ball〔進攻一方球隊的〕控球時間

8 ►EVIL SPIRITS 魔鬼◄ [U] a situation in which someone's mind is being controlled by an evil spirit 鬼魂附體, 着魔: *tales of possession and poltergeists and exorcisms* 有關魔鬼附體、惡作劇鬼和驅魔的傳説

9 in (full) possession of your faculties/senses able to think in a clear and intelligent way and not crazy, or affected by old age 神智[頭腦](非常)清醒: *She's over 80 now, but she's still in full possession of all her faculties.* 她八十多歲了, 但頭腦仍然非常清醒。

10 possession is nine-tenths of the law used to mean that someone who has something is likely to keep it 現實佔有, 敗一勝九〔實際佔有者在財產訴訟中十有九勝〕

pos·ses·sive¹ /pəˋzɛsɪv; pəˈzesɪv/ *adj* **1** wanting someone to have feelings of love or friendship only for you〔愛情或友情上〕佔有慾強的, 自私的: *Men are very protective and sometimes possessive towards their daughters.* 男人對女兒很有保護之心, 有時還有很強的佔有慾。**2** unwilling to let other people use something you own 不願與別人分享的, 佔有慾強的: **[+about]** *He's so possessive about his new car.* 他不願讓別人用他的新汽車。**3 possessive adjective/pronoun/form** used in grammar for words such as 'my', 'its', 'their' etc, which mean belonging to someone or something〔語法中的〕所有格形容詞/代(名)詞/形式 —**possessively** *adv* —**possessiveness** *n* [U]

possessive² *n* [C] *technical* a possessive adjective, pronoun, or form of a word【術語】所有格形容詞[代(名)詞, 形式]

pos·ses·sor /pəˋzɛsɚ; pəˈzesə/ *n* **be the proud possessor of** *often humorous* to have or own something【常幽默】擁有, 持有: *He's now the proud possessor of two satellite dishes.* 他現在擁有兩個衛星接收器, 這使他引以為榮。

2 2 **pos·si·bil·i·ty** /ˌpɑsəˋbɪlətɪ; ˌpɒsəˈbɪləti/ *n* **1** [C,U] something that may happen or may be true 可能的事; 可能性: **[+of]** *the possibility of an enemy attack* 敵人進攻的可能性 | **a distinct/real possibility** (=something that is quite likely to happen) 很可能發生的事 *A peace settlement now looks like a real possibility.* 和平解決現在看來很有可能。| **there's a possibility (that)** (=used to say that you think something might happen or be TRUE) 有可能...: *There's always a possibility that he might go back to Seattle.* 他隨時可能會回到西雅圖去。**2** [usually plural 一般用複數] something that gives you an opportunity to do what you want 餘地; 潛力: **[+for]** *The possibilities for improvement are endless.* 改善的餘地是無限的。| **a world of possibilities** (=many opportunities) 許多機遇 *China's economic expansion has opened up a new world of possibilities for Western companies.* 中國的經濟擴張為西方公司打開了一個充滿機遇的新天地。**3 exhaust all the possibilities** to try every possible way of doing something 試盡了所有可能的辦法 **4 have possibilities** if something has possibilities it could be made into something much better 有改善的餘地, 有潛力, 有發展的可能性: *The house has great possibilities!* 那所房子有極大的潛在價值! —see also 另見 **within the realms of possibility** (REALM (2))

P

pos·si·ble¹ /ˋpɑsəbḷ; ˈpɒsəbəl/ *adj* **1** able to be done or likely to happen or exist 可能的; 可能做到的; 可能發生的; 可能存在的: *Accidents are always possible in this kind of situation.* 在這種情況下, 事故隨時可能發生。| *Sony and Showscan are discussing possible joint projects.* 新力和休斯堪公司正在討論可能的合資項目。| **it is possible to do sth** *Is it possible to predict what will happen in Russia?* 有可能預測俄羅斯將會發生甚麼事嗎? | **it is possible (that)** (=used to say that you think something might happen or be true) 可能..., 也許... *It's possible that she might have got lost on the way home.* 她有可能在回家的路上迷路了。| **it is possible for** (=used to say that someone is able to do something)〔某人〕能做... *It should soon be possible for most people to work from home.* 讓大多數人在家裡辦公應該是很快就能實現的事。| **if (at all) possible** (=if it is possible to do it) 如果可能的話 *I want to avoid the rush hour traffic if possible.* 如果可能的話, 我想避開高峯時間的交通。**2 would it be possible** *spoken* used when asking politely if you can do or have something【口】可以嗎?〔用於禮貌地詢問某人是否能做某事或擁有某物〕: **would it be possible (for sb) to do sth** *Would it be possible to have brown bread instead of white?* 可不可以要黑麵包而不要白麵包呢? **3** acceptable or suitable 可接受的, 合適的: *This is only one of many possible answers to the problem of air pollution.* 這僅僅是解決空氣污染問題的眾多可行辦法之一。**4 as long/much/soon as possible** as long, soon, quickly etc as you can 盡可能長/多/快: *I need the money as soon as possible.* 我需要盡快拿到這筆錢。| *Sharon always does as little work as possible.* 莎朗總是盡可能少做事。**5 the best/biggest/fastest possible** the best that can exist or be achieved 盡可能好/大/快的: *Try to get the best possible price.* 盡可能獲得最好的價格。**6 where/wherever/whenever possible** every time you have an opportunity to do something 一有機會: *I send a donation whenever possible.* 我一有機會就捐款。

possible² *n* [C] someone or something that might be suitable or acceptable for a particular purpose 可能適合的人[事物]: *Frank's a possible for the job.* 弗蘭克是那份工作的一個可能人選。

pos·si·bly /ˋpɑsəblɪ; ˈpɒsəbli/ *adv* **1** used when saying that something may be true or likely, although you do not know exactly; perhaps 可能, 也許, 或許: *"Are you coming with us tomorrow?" "Possibly. I'm not sure yet."* "你明天要和我們一起去嗎?" "可能吧, 我還不能肯定。" | *This novel is his most accessible, and possibly his most beautiful, book.* 這本小説是他的作品中最易懂、而且可能是最美的一本。| **quite possibly** (=used to say that something is very likely) 很有可能 *"Do you think it*

was murder?" "Quite possibly." "你認為這是謀殺嗎?" "很可能是。" **2 could you possibly/can you possibly** *spoken* used when making a polite request【口】請你…可以嗎?〔用於禮貌地請求〕: *Could you possibly lend me another $20 till Monday?* 你能再借給我 20 美元到星期一嗎? **3** *spoken* used to say that you are very surprised or shocked by something, or you cannot understand it【口】究竟; 怎麼〔用於表示驚訝、震驚或不理解〕: **can/could sb possibly** *What on earth can she possibly mean?* 她究竟是甚麼意思呢? | *How could anyone possibly do such a thing?* 怎麼會有人做出這樣的事呢? **4** used to emphasize that someone tried as hard as they could to achieve something〔用於強調某人為獲得某物盡了最大努力〕: **do everything you possibly can/could** *Doctors did everything they possibly could to save the little boy's life.* 醫生盡了一切可能來挽救這個小男孩的生命。**5 sb can't/couldn't possibly** used to say strongly that you refuse to do something or that someone cannot do something 某人不可能〔用於強烈地表示拒絕做某事或某人不能做某事〕: *I can't possibly allow you to go home in this weather.* 我不可能讓你在這種天氣下回家。

P

pos·sum /ˈpɑsəm; ˈpɒsəm/ also 又作 **opossum** *especially BrE*【尤英】*n* [C] **1** one of various types of small furry animals that climb trees and live in America or Australia〔產於美洲或澳洲的〕負鼠; 袋貂 **2 play possum** *informal* to pretend to be asleep or dead so that someone will not annoy or hurt you【非正式】〔為避免某人打擾或傷害而〕假裝睡着; 裝死

post- /post; pəʊst/ *prefix* later than; after 在…之後: *postwar* (=after a war) 戰後 | *We'll have to postpone the meeting.* (=make it later) 我們不得不把會議延期。—compare 比較 ANTE-

3 3 **post¹** /post; pəʊst/ *n*

1 ►POSTAL SYSTEM 郵政系統◄ **the post** *especially BrE* the official system for carrying letters, parcels etc from one place to another【尤英】郵政, 郵遞; MAIL¹ (1) *especially AmE*【尤美】: *The letter must have got lost in the post.* 那封信一定是在郵遞過程中丟了。| **be in the post** *Your cheque is in the post.* 你的支票已寄出。| **by post** *If you send the book by post it should get there by Friday.* 如果郵寄這本書, 它應該在星期五之前寄到。

2 put sth in the post to send something to someone 把某物寄給〔某人〕: *I'll put a copy in the post to you today.* 我今天將給你寄上一本。

3 ►COLLECTING/DELIVERING LETTERS 收集/投遞信件◄ [C,U] *especially BrE* the time when letters are collected or delivered, or the act of collecting or delivering them【尤英】信件收集[投遞]時間; 收信; 投遞信件; MAIL¹ *especially AmE*【尤美】: **first/second post** (=the first collection or delivery of letters each day)〔每天的〕第一次/第二次收信[投遞] *The parcel arrived in the second post.* 那包裹是隨第二批郵件送到的。| **catch/miss the post** *If you hurry, you should catch the last post.* 你如果快一點, 應該能趕上最後一次收信。—see also 另見 **by return (of post)** (RETURN² (8))

4 ►LETTERS 信件◄ [U] *especially BrE* letters, parcels etc delivered to someone's house, office etc【尤英】郵件〈如信件、包裹等〉; MAIL¹ (2) *especially AmE*【尤美】: *Was there any post for me today?* 今天有寄給我的郵件嗎?

5 ►PIECE OF WOOD/METAL 一塊木頭/金屬◄ [C] a strong upright piece of wood, metal etc that is fixed into the ground, especially to support something 柱, 桿, 樁: *a fence post* 柵欄柱

6 ►JOB 工作◄ [C] *formal especially BrE* a job, especially an important one; POSITION¹ (8)【正式, 尤英】〔尤指重要的〕工作; 職位: *She has been offered the post of ambassador to India.* 她獲委任為駐印度大使。| **take up a post** (=start doing an important job) 開始擔任一個職務 *When he took up his present post at the BBC he was only 33.* 他到英國廣播公司出任目前的職位時才 33 歲。| **resign (from) your post** *As a result of the scandal, Profumo was forced to resign his post.* 由於這宗醜聞, 普洛夫姆被迫辭職。—see 見 JOB (USAGE)

7 ►SOLDIER/GUARD ETC 士兵/衛兵等◄ **sb's post** the place where someone is expected to be in order to do their duty 崗位, 哨位: *The guard was punished for falling asleep at his post.* 那個衛兵由於站崗時睡覺而受到了處罰。

8 ►FOOTBALL/HOCKEY ETC 足球/曲棍球等◄ [C] one of the two upright pieces of wood which players try to kick or hit the ball between in football, HOCKEY etc; GOALPOST 球門柱

9 ►RACE 競賽◄ **the post** also 又作 **the finishing post** the place where a race finishes, especially a horse race〔競賽, 尤指賽馬的〕終點標誌: *Dandyboy fell ten yards from the post.* 馬匹"花花公子"在離終點十碼的地方摔倒了。—see also 另見 **deaf as a post** (DEAF (1)), **pip sb at the post** (PIP² (1)), **second-class post** (SECOND-CLASS (3)), LAST POST, STAGING POST, TRADING POST

post² *v* [T] 

1 ►LETTER 信件◄ *especially BrE* to send a letter, parcel etc by post【尤英】郵寄, 寄出〔信件、包裹等〕; MAIL² *AmE*【美】: *She's just gone to post a letter.* 她剛出去寄信了。| **post sb sth/post sth to sb** *I posted John the cheque last Friday.* 我上星期五把支票寄給約翰了。| *I must post a card to Clara today.* 我今天必須寄張賀卡給克拉拉。

2 keep sb posted to keep telling someone the latest news about something 不斷向某人提供有關某事的最新消息: *Please, keep us posted about your financial situation, and let us know if we can help.* 請隨時告訴我們你的經濟狀況, 看看我們能否幫上忙。

3 ►GUARD 衛兵◄ to send someone somewhere, to guard a building, check who enters or leaves a place, watch something etc; STATION² 設置〔崗哨等〕: *Two National Guardsmen had been posted at the gate.* 兩名國民警衛隊隊員被安排在大門口站崗。

4 ►JOB 工作◄ [usually passive 一般用被動態] *especially BrE* to send someone to a different country or place to work for a company or to do a period of duty for the army, navy, or government【尤英】派駐, 調派; STATION² *AmE*【美】: **post sb abroad/overseas etc** *Roger's been posted overseas for a few years.* 羅傑被派往國外工作了幾年。| **post sb to** *Two years later he was posted to Buenos Aires.* 兩年後他被派往布宜諾斯艾利斯。—see 見 JOB (USAGE)

5 ►PUBLIC NOTICE 公告◄ also 又作 **post up** to put up a public notice about something on a wall or notice board 張貼, 貼出〔公告〕: *The exam results were posted on the bulletin board yesterday.* 昨天佈告板上張貼了考試成績。

6 be posted missing if someone is posted missing, it is announced officially that they have disappeared〔某人〕被正式宣布失蹤

post·age /ˈpostɪdʒ; ˈpəʊstɪdʒ/ *n* [U] the money charged for carrying a letter, parcel etc by post 郵資, 郵費: *Please enclose $9.99, including $1.00 for postage.* 請在信中附上 9.99 美元, 其中包括 1 美元的郵資。| **postage and packing** (=charge for packing and sending something you have bought) 包裝加郵寄費 *Yours for only £16.95 plus postage and packing!* 你的只需 16.95 英鎊, 另加包裝和郵費。

postage me·ter /ˈ·· ˌ··/ *n* [C] *AmE* a machine used by businesses which puts a mark on letters and packages to show that postage has been paid【美】郵資機〔在信封或包裹上蓋印以示郵資已付〕

postage stamp /ˈ·· ·/ *n* [C] *formal* a stamp【正式】郵票

post·al /ˈpostl; ˈpəʊstl/ *adj* [only before noun 僅用於名詞前] connected with the official system which takes letters from one place to another 郵政的: *postal workers* 郵政工人 | *an increase in postal charges* 郵資的上漲

postal or·der /ˈ·· ˌ··/ *n* [C] *BrE* an official paper that you buy at a post office as a safe way of sending money through the post【英】郵政匯票: *a £2.00 postal order* 一張兩英鎊的郵政匯票 —compare 比較 MONEY ORDER

postal ser·vice /'·· ,··/ *n* [C] *especially AmE* the public service for carrying letters, parcels etc from one part of a country or the world to another【尤美】郵政服務

postal vote /'·· ,·/ *n* [C] *BrE* a vote sent through the post, especially by someone who cannot be present to vote on the day of an election【英】郵寄投票; ABSENTEE VOTE *AmE*【美】

post·bag /ˋpost,bæg; 'pəʊstbæg/ *n BrE*【英】**1** [singular] *informal* all the letters received by an important person, television programme etc on a particular occasion【非正式】〔要人、電視節目等的〕一次收到的郵件: *We've had an enormous postbag on the recent programme changes.* 我們就最近的節目變更收到了大批來信。**2** [C] a bag for carrying letters, used by the person who delivers them〔郵遞員的〕郵袋; MAILBAG *AmE*【美】

post·box /ˋpost,bɑks; 'pəʊstbɒks/ *n* [C] *BrE* a box in a public place, into which you put letters you want to send【英】〔投寄信件用的〕郵箱, 郵筒; MAILBOX (2) *AmE*【美】—see also 另見 LETTERBOX, PILLAR BOX

post·card /ˋpost,kɑrd; 'pəʊstkɑːd/ *n* [C] a card that can be sent in the post without an envelope, especially one with a picture on it 明信片: *Don't forget to send us a postcard!* 別忘了給我們寄張明信片!

post·code /ˋpost,kod; 'pəʊstkəʊd/ *n* [C] *BrE* a group of letters or numbers which shows the exact area where a house is, so that letters, parcels etc can be delivered more quickly【英】郵政編碼; ZIP CODE *AmE*【美】

post·date /,postˋdet; ,pəʊst'deɪt/ *v* [T] **1** to write a cheque with a date that is later than the actual date, so that it cannot be used or become effective until that time〔在支票上〕填寫比實際晚的日期, 把…的日期填遲 **2** to happen, live, or be made later in history than something else 發生於…之後; 生活在…之後; 在歷史上發生的時間後於…: *The mosaic postdates this period, although the style is quite similar.* 儘管風格很相似, 但這種鑲嵌圖案是晚於這個時期的作品。—compare 比較 ANTEDATE, BACKDATE

post doc /,· '·/ *n* [C] *informal especially AmE* someone who is studying after they have finished their PHD【非正式, 尤美】博士後研究人員

post doc·tor·al /,· '···◂/ *adj* connected with study done after a PHD 博士後的

3 **post·er** /ˋpostɚ; 'pəʊstə/ *n* [C] a large printed notice, picture, or photograph, used to advertise something or as a decoration 招貼(畫); 海報; 廣告(畫): *the bedroom wall was covered in posters* 臥室的牆壁上貼滿了海報

poste res·tante /,post rɛsˋtɑnt; ,pəʊst 'restɒnt/ *n* [U] *BrE* a post office department which keeps letters for people who are travelling, until they arrive to collect them【英】〔郵局的〕郵件存局候領處; GENERAL DELIVERY *AmE*【美】

pos·te·ri·or¹ /pɑsˋtɪrɪɚ; pɒ'stɪəriə/ *n* [C] *humorous* the part of the body you sit on; BOTTOM¹ (7)【幽默】臀部, 屁股: *plonking his substantial posterior down on the bench* 他肥大的臀部重重地坐在長櫈上

posterior² *adj* [only before noun 僅用於名詞前] *technical* near or at the back of something【術語】(靠近)後部的, 後端的; 後面的, 背部的: *the posterior end of the abdomen* 下腹部 —opposite 反義詞 ANTERIOR (1)

pos·ter·i·ty /pɑsˋtɛrətɪ; pɒ'sterɪ̣ti/ *n* [U] people who will live after you are dead 後裔, 後代, 子孫: **preserve sth for posterity** *We must preserve these songs for posterity.* 我們必須把這些歌曲保存下來傳給子孫後代。

poster paint /'·· ·/ *n* [C, U] *BrE* brightly coloured paint that contains no oil, used especially by children to paint pictures【英】〔尤指供兒童畫畫用的不含油的〕廣告顏料

post-free /,· '·◂/ *adv BrE* a letter sent post-free has no charge for the person who sends it【英】郵資免付地; 郵資已付地; POSTPAID *AmE*【美】—**post-free** *adj*

post-grad /,· '·◂/ *n* [C] *informal* a postgraduate【非正式】研究生 —**post-grad** *adj*

post·grad·u·ate¹ /postˋgrædʒʊɪt; ,pəʊst'grædjuɪ̣t/ *n* [C] **1** *especially BrE* someone who is studying at a university to get a MASTER'S DEGREE or a PHD【尤英】〔碩士或博士〕研究生 **2** *AmE* someone who is studying after finishing a PHD【美】博士後研究人員

postgraduate² *adj* **1** *BrE* connected with studies done at a university after completing a first degree【英】研究生的; GRADUATE² *AmE*【美】: *postgraduate qualifications* 研究生資格 **2** *AmE* connected with studies done after completing a PHD【美】博士後的

post-haste /,· '·/ *adv literary* very quickly【文】很快地, 盡快地, 急忙地: *departing post-haste* 匆匆離開

post hoc /,· '·/ *adj formal* a post hoc explanation, argument etc make a connection between two events that have happened simply because one happened after the other【正式】〔解釋、論證等〕僅僅因為一件事發生在另一件事之後, 即把二者聯繫起來的: *spurious post hoc analyses of the causes of the war* 錯誤地根據發生在其後必然是其結果來分析戰爭的原因

post horn /'· ·/ *n* [C] a horn used in the 18th and 19th centuries as a warning by people riding on a carriage〔18和19世紀馬車上用的〕驛車號

post·hu·mous /ˋpɑstʃʊməs; 'pɒstjʊ̣məs/ *adj* happening after someone's death, or given to someone or printed after their death 死後發生的; 死後獲得的; 死後出版的 —**posthumously** *adv*: *The medal was awarded posthumously.* 這枚勳章是死後頒予的。

post·ie /ˋpostɪ; 'pəʊsti/ *n* [C] *informal* a POSTMAN【非正式】郵遞員, 郵差

post-in·dus·tri·al /,· ·'···◂/ *adj* connected with the period in the late 20th century when the older types of industry became less important, and computers became more important 後工業化的, 工業化之後的〔指20世紀晚期舊的工業類型的重要性日漸下降, 而電腦工業的重要性則與日俱增〕: *work patterns in post-industrial society* 後工業化社會的工作模式

post·ing /ˋpostɪŋ; 'pəʊstɪŋ/ *n* [C] *especially BrE* the act of sending someone to a place to do their job, especially a soldier【尤英】〔尤指士兵的〕任命, 派任: **[+to]** *still waiting for a posting to France* 還在等待去法國的任命

Post-it /'· ·/ *n* [C] *trademark* a small piece of sticky coloured paper, used for leaving notes to people【商標】〔用於留便條的〕告示貼

post·man /ˋpostmən; 'pəʊstmən/ *n plural* **postmen** /-mən; -mən/ [C] *especially BrE* someone whose job is to collect and deliver letters【尤英】郵遞員, 郵差; MAILMAN *AmE*【美】

post·mark /ˋpost,mɑrk; 'pəʊstmɑːk/ *n* [C] an official mark made on a letter, parcel etc that shows the place and time it was sent〔信件、郵包等上的〕郵戳 —**postmark** *v* [T]: *The letter was postmarked Iowa.* 這封信上蓋着衣阿華州的郵戳。

post·mas·ter /ˋpost,mæstɚ; 'pəʊst,mɑːstə/ *n* [C] the person who is in charge of a post office 郵局局長

post·mis·tress /ˋpost,mɪstrəs; 'pəʊstmɪstrɪ̣s/ *n* [C] a woman who is in charge of a post office 郵局女局長

post-mod·ern·is·m /,· '····/ *n* [U] a style of building, painting etc which uses an unusual mixture of old and new styles and was popular in the 1980s 後現代主義〔建築、繪畫等的一種風格, 盛行於20世紀80年代, 特徵為新舊形式的奇妙混合〕—**post-modernist** *adj*: *a post-modernist painting* 後現代主義繪畫 —**post-modernist** *n* [C]

post-mor·tem /,postˋmɔrtəm; ,pəʊst'mɔːtəm/ *n* [C] **1** also 又作 **postmortem examination** *formal* an examination of a dead body to discover why the person died; AUTOPSY【正式】屍體檢驗, 驗屍, 屍體解剖: *The post-mortem revealed that Mills had been strangled.* 屍體檢驗顯示米爾斯是被勒死的。**2** an examination of a plan or event that failed, in order to discover why it failed〔對失敗的計劃或事件進行的〕事後剖析, 事後檢討: *a post-mortem on the company's poor results* 對公司業績不佳所作的事後剖析

post·na·tal /ˌpostˋnetl̩; ˌpəʊstˈneɪtl◂/ *adj technical* connected with the time after a baby is born【術語】產後的, 分娩後的: *postnatal care* 產後護理 —compare 比較 ANTENATAL, PRENATAL

postnatal de·pres·sion /ˌ··· ·ˈ··/ *n* [U] an illness in which a woman feels DEPRESSED (1) after her baby has been born 產後抑鬱症

P

post of·fice /ˈ· ˌ··/ *n* **1** [C] a place where you can buy stamps, send letters and parcels etc 郵(政)局 **2 the Post Office** *BrE* the national organization which is responsible for collecting and delivering letters【英】〔英國〕郵政總局: *a Post Office van* 郵政貨車

post office box /ˈ· ·· ,·/ *n* [C] *formal* a PO BOX【正式】郵政信箱

post·paid /ˋpostˋped; ˌpəʊstˈpeɪd◂/ *adv AmE* a letter sent postpaid has no charge for the person sending it【美】郵資已付; POST-FREE *BrE*【英】—**postpaid** *adj*

post·pone /posˋpon; pəʊsˈpəʊn/ *v* [T] to change an event, action etc to a later time or date 使〔事件、行動等〕延期, 延遲, 推遲: *The match had to be postponed.* 比賽不得不延期舉行。| **postpone sth until** *We're postponing our holiday until we have some more money.* 我們把度假日期推遲到我們有較多錢的時候。| **postpone doing sth** *Gail and Jim have decided to postpone having a family for a while.* 蓋爾和吉姆決定暫緩成家。—**postponement** *n* [C,U]

post·pran·di·al /postˋprændɪəl; ˌpəʊstˈprændiəl◂/ *adj formal* happening just after dinner【正式】飯後的: *a post-prandial nap* 飯後小睡

post·script /ˋpos·skrɪpt; ˈpəʊsˌskrɪpt/ written abbreviation 縮寫為 **PS** *n* [C] **1** a message written at the end of a letter below the place where you sign your name〔信末簽名後的〕附筆, 附言, 又及: *The postscript at the end said, 'See you soon'.* 信末的附言寫道, "希望很快見到你。" **2** something that you add at the end of a story or account that you have been telling someone〔加在故事、敍述等末尾的〕附言, 補充說明: *an interesting postscript to this tale* 對這個故事有趣的補述

post-trau·mat·ic stress dis·or·der /ˌ· ···ˈ·· ·ˈ··/ *n* [U] *technical* a mental illness which can develop after a very bad experience such as a plane crash【術語】創傷後壓力[緊張]症〔遭遇創傷性事件如飛機失事後患上的精神疾病〕

pos·tu·late¹ /ˋpɑstʃəˌlet; ˈpɒstjʊleɪt/ *v* [T] *formal* to suggest that something might have happened or be true【正式】假定…是真的, 假設…發生過: **[+that]** *One theory postulates that the ancient Filipinos came from India and Persia.* 一種理論假設古代菲律賓人來自印度和波斯。—**postulation** /ˌpɑstʃəˋleʃən; ˌpɒstjʊˈleɪʃən/ *n* [C, U]

pos·tu·late² /ˋpɑstʃəlɪt; ˈpɒstjʊlɪt/ *n* [C] *formal* something believed to be true, but not proven, on which an argument or scientific discussion is based【正式】假定, 假設: *the basic postulates of Marxism* 馬克思主義的基本假設

pos·ture¹ /ˋpɑstʃɚ; ˈpɒstʃə/ *n* **1** [C,U] the position you hold your body in when you sit or stand 姿勢; 姿態: *Poor posture can lead to muscular problems in later life.* 不良的姿勢可能導致以後生活中肌肉的障礙。**2** [singular] the way you behave or think in a particular situation 態度, 立場: *the administration's posture towards China* 該政府對中國的態度

posture² *v* [I] **1** to stand or behave in a way that you hope will make other people notice and admire you 擺姿勢〔以引起注意和讚賞〕: *Alexi stood posturing in front of the mirror.* 亞力克西在鏡子面前站着擺姿勢。**2** to pretend to have a particular opinion or attitude 假裝持某種觀點[態度], 故作姿態: *pseudo-intellectual posturing* 偽知識分子的裝腔作勢 —**posturing** *n* [C,U]

post-vi·ral syn·drome /ˌ· ˌ·· ˈ··/ *n* [U] an illness that lasts for a long time and causes weakness, tiredness, and pain in your muscles; ME 肌痛性腦脊髓炎

post-war /ˌ· ˈ·◂/ *adj* [only before noun 僅用於名詞前] happening or existing after a war, especially the Second World War 戰後的;〔尤指〕第二次世界大戰之後的: *economic conditions in post-war Britain* 戰後英國的經濟狀況 —**post-war** *adv* —compare 比較 PRE-WAR

po·sy /ˋpozɪ; ˈpəʊzi/ *n* [C] *especially literary* a small BUNCH of flowers【尤文】小花束: *a posy of African violets* 一小束非洲紫羅蘭

pot¹ /pɑt; pɒt/ *n* 2 3

1 ▶TEA/COFFEE 茶/咖啡◀ [C] a container with a handle and a small tube for pouring, used to make tea or coffee 壺

2 ▶COOKING 烹飪◀ [C] a container used for cooking which is round, deep, and usually made of metal〔圓而深的〕鍋: *The sink was full of dirty pots and pans.* 洗滌槽裡滿是骯髒的鍋碗瓢盆。

3 ▶STORING FOOD 儲存食物◀ [C] a glass or clay container used for storing food 用於儲存食物的容器, 罐: *a jam pot* 果醬罐 | *a pot of honey* 一罐蜂蜜

4 ▶FOR A PLANT 用於植物◀ [C] a container for a plant, usually made of plastic or baked clay 花盆

5 ▶BOWL 碗◀ [C] a dish, bowl, plate or other container that is made by shaping clay and then baking it 陶罐, 陶壺, 陶盆

6 have pots of *BrE informal* to have a lot of something, especially money【英, 非正式】有很多〔尤指錢〕: *Julie's Dad's got pots of money!* 朱莉的爸爸有很多錢!

7 go to pot *informal* if something such as a place or an organization goes to pot, it becomes much worse because no one is interested in looking after it or making it work【非正式】衰落; 荒蕪; 垮掉: *This government has let the whole country go to pot.* 該政府已使整個國家垮了。

8 ▶DRUG 毒品◀ [U] *old-fashioned* MARIJUANA【過時】大麻

9 ▶STOMACH 肚子◀ [singular] *informal* a large rounded stomach that sticks out; POTBELLY【非正式】大肚子

10 ▶CARD GAMES 撲克牌戲◀ **the pot** all the money that people have risked in a game of cards, especially POKER (1)〔尤指撲克牌戲中一局的〕賭注總額

11 the pot calling the kettle black *informal* used to say that you should not criticize someone for a fault that you also have【非正式】鍋笑壺黑, 五十步笑百步

12 take a pot at *informal* to shoot at something without aiming carefully【非正式】胡亂朝…開槍 —see also 另見 CHAMBER POT, MELTING POT

pot² *v* **potted, potting** [T] **1** to shoot at animals in order to kill them 射殺〔動物〕: *Giles was out with his gun, potting rabbits.* 賈爾斯帶着槍出去打野兔。—see also 另見 POT SHOT **2** to put a plant in a pot filled with soil 把〔植物〕栽種在花盆中 —see also 另見 POTTED (1) **3** [T] to hit a ball into one of the bags at the edge of the table in games such as BILLIARDS, POOL¹ (3), and SNOOKER 把〔枱球〕打進袋中

pot sth ↔ **on** *phr v* [T] *BrE* to move a plant into a large pot because it has grown too big for the pot it is in【英】把〔植物〕移栽到大盆中

po·ta·ble /ˋpotəbl̩; ˈpəʊtəbəl/ *adj formal* water that is potable is suitable for drinking【正式】〔水〕可飲用的

pot·ash /ˋpɑtˌæʃ; ˈpɒtæʃ/ *n* [U] a sort of potassium used especially in farming to make the soil better 鉀鹼, 碳酸鉀

po·tas·si·um /pəˋtæsɪəm; pəˈtæsiəm/ *n* [U] a silver-white soft metal that is an ELEMENT (1) and usually exists in compounds formed with other substances 鉀

po·ta·to /pəˋteto; pəˈteɪtəʊ/ *n plural* **potatoes 1** [C,U] a round white vegetable with a brown skin, that grows as 2 a root 馬鈴薯, 土豆: *mashed potato* 馬鈴薯[土豆]泥 | *roast potatoes* 烤馬鈴薯[土豆] —see picture on page A9 參見A9頁圖 **2** [C] a plant that has potatoes growing at its roots 馬鈴薯植株 —see also 另見 SWEET POTATO

potato chip /ˈ·ˈ·· ˌ·/ *n* [C] *AmE* a thin piece of fried potato which is sold in packets【美】炸馬鈴薯片; CRISP[1] *BrE*【英】

potato peel·er /ˈ·ˈ·· ˌ··/ *n* [C] a small tool like a knife, used for removing the skin of a potato 馬鈴薯削皮器

pot·bel·lied /ˈpɑtˌbɛlɪd; pɒtˈbelid/ *adj* having a large stomach that sticks out 肚子大的, 大腹便便的: *naked potbellied children begging for food* 赤身裸體討飯的大肚皮孩子

pot·bel·ly /ˈpɑtˌbɛlɪ; ˈpɒtˌbeli/ *n* [C] a large round stomach that sticks out 大肚子

pot·boil·er /ˈpɑtˌbɔɪlɚ; ˈpɒtˌbɔɪlə/ *n* [C] a book that is written quickly to make money〔為賺錢而〕粗製濫造的書

pot·bound /ˈpɑtˌbaund; ˈpɒtbaʊnd/ *adj BrE* a plant that is potbound cannot grow any more because its roots have grown to fill the pot it is in【英】〔盆栽植物〕根滿盆的, 盆縛的; ROOTBOUND *AmE*【美】

po·teen /poˈtin; pəˈtʃiːn/ *n* [U] Irish WHISKY made secretly and illegally to avoid paying tax〔為逃税而〕私釀的愛爾蘭威士忌酒

po·ten·cy /ˈpotn̩sɪ; ˈpəʊtənsi/ *n* [U] **1** the power that an idea, argument, action etc has to influence people 力量, 威力; 影響力: *The spectre of mass unemployment had lost none of its political potency.* 大規模失業的恐懼絲毫沒有失去它的政治影響力。**2** the strength of the effect of a drug, medicine, alcohol etc on your mind or body〔藥物、酒等的〕效力, 效能: *a high potency drug* 強效藥 **3** the ability of a man to have sex〔男子的〕性交能力

po·tent /ˈpotn̩t; ˈpəʊtənt/ *adj* **1** having a powerful effect or influence on your body or mind 有效力的, 效力大的; 有影響力的: *a particularly potent cider* 特別濃烈的蘋果酒 | *The film is full of potent images of war.* 這部電影充滿了震撼人心的戰爭場面。**2** powerful and effective 強有力的, 有威力的; 有説服力的: *a potent new weapons system* 有強大威力的新武器系統 —**potently** *adv* —see also 另見 IMPOTENT

po·ten·tate /ˈpotn̩ˌtet; ˈpəʊtənteɪt/ *n* [C] *literary* a ruler with direct power over his people【文】〔直接統治民眾的〕君主, 統治者: *Eastern potentates* 東方君主

3 2 **po·ten·tial¹** /pəˈtɛnʃəl; pəˈtenʃəl/ *adj* [only before noun 僅用於名詞前] a potential customer, problem, effect etc is not a customer, problem etc yet, but may become one in the future 潛在的, 可能的: *The agents were eager to impress potential buyers.* 這些代理商急於給潛在的買主留下深刻的印象。| *a potential threat to national security* 對國家安全的潛在威脅

3 **potential²** *n* [U] **1** the possibility that something will develop in a certain way, or have a particular effect 可能性, 潛在性: **[+for]** *The potential for abuse in such a system is enormous.* 在這樣的體制下, 濫用職權的可能性極大。| *sales potential* (=the amount of something that is likely be sold) 銷售潛力 **2** natural ability that could develop to make you very good at something 潛力, 潛能: *a young player with great potential* 有很大潛力的年輕選手 | **have/show potential** (=to be likely to be successful) 有潛力/表現出潛力 | **achieve/fulfil/realize your potential** (=succeed in doing as well as you possibly can) 發揮你的潛力 *We want each student to realize their full potential.* 我們想讓每一位學生發揮他們最大限度的潛力。**3** *technical* the difference in VOLTAGE between two points on an electrical CIRCUIT (4)【術語】電勢, 電位, 電壓

po·ten·ti·al·i·ty /pəˌtɛnʃɪˈælətɪ; pəˌtenʃiˈælɪ̈ti/ *n* [C,U] *formal* the possibility that something may develop in a particular way【正式】潛力, 可能性

po·ten·tial·ly /pəˈtɛnʃəlɪ; pəˈtenʃəli/ *adv* [+adj/adv] something that is potentially dangerous, useful etc is not actually dangerous etc at the present time but is likely to become so 潛在地, 可能地: *I knew that I was in a potentially dangerous situation.* 我知道我處於潛在的危險之中。| *The benefits of computerised ordering are potentially very great.* 電腦訂貨有很大的潛在好處。

pot·ful /ˈpɑtful; ˈpɒtfʊl/ *n* [C] the amount that a pot can contain 一(滿)罐, 一(滿)壺; 一(滿)鍋

pot·head /ˈpɑthɛd; ˈpɒthed/ *n* [C] *informal* someone who smokes a lot of MARIJUANA【非正式】吸大麻者

pot·hold·er /ˈpɑtˌholdɚ; ˈpɒthəʊldə/ *n* [C] a piece of thick material used for holding hot cooking pans〔用於端熱鍋等的〕防燙厚布墊

pot·hole /ˈpɑtˌhol; ˈpɒthəʊl/ *n* [C] **1** a hole in the surface of a road that makes driving difficult or dangerous〔路面上的〕凹坑, 坑洞: *swerving to avoid the potholes* 突然轉向避開地面的凹坑 **2** a long hole that goes deep under the ground, formed by natural processes 鍋穴, 壺穴, 甌穴 —**potholed** *adj*

pot·hol·ing /ˈpɑtˌholɪŋ; ˈpɒtˌhəʊlɪŋ/ *n* [U] the sport of climbing down inside holes under the ground 地下洞穴探險〔一種體育運動〕—**pothole** *v* [I] —**potholer** *n* [C]

po·tion /ˈpoʃən; ˈpəʊʃən/ *n* [C] **1** *literary* a drink intended to have a special or magic effect on the person who drinks it【文】〔有特效或魔力的〕飲劑: *a love potion* 春藥飲劑 **2** *humorous* a medicine, especially one that seems strange, old-fashioned, or unnecessary【幽默】藥物〔尤指看上去奇怪、過時或不必要的藥物〕: *treating herself with pills and potions* 用各種藥劑給她自己治療

pot luck /ˌ· ˈ·/ *n* **take pot luck a)** to choose something without knowing very much about it and hope that it will be what you want 碰運氣: *We hadn't booked a hotel so we had to take pot luck.* 我們沒有預訂酒店, 所以只能碰碰運氣。**b)** to have a meal at someone's home in which you eat whatever they have available 吃家常便飯: *I'm not sure what there is in the fridge – you'll have to take pot luck.* 我不清楚冰箱裡有甚麼 —— 你只能有甚麼吃甚麼。

pot·luck /ˈpɑtˌlʌk; ˌpɒtˈlʌk◂/ *n AmE* a meal made up of dishes of food brought by many different people【美】〔多人帶食物拼成的〕百樂餐

pot plant /ˈ· ·/ *n* [C] **1** *BrE* a plant that is grown indoors in a pot as a decoration【英】盆栽植物; POTTED PLANT *AmE*【美】**2** *informal* a MARIJUANA plant【非正式】大麻植株

pot·pour·ri /pɑtˈpʊrɪ; pəʊˈpʊri/ *n* **1** [U] a mixture of pieces of dried flowers and leaves kept in a bowl to make a room smell pleasant 百花香〔放在鉢內的乾花和葉子, 能使室內空氣芳香〕**2** [C] a mixture of things that are not usually put together, for example different pieces of music or writing〔音樂或文學作品等的〕集錦; 集錦曲; 雜集: *a potpourri of literary styles* 多種文學風格的雜集

pot roast /ˈ· ·/ *n* [C] a dish that consists of a piece of meat cooked in a pan with potatoes or other vegetables 罐燉肉菜〔用一塊肉和馬鈴薯或其他蔬菜一起燉成〕

pot·sherd /ˈpɑtˌʃɝd; ˈpɒt-ʃɜːd/ *n* [C] *technical* a piece of a broken clay pot from long ago【術語】〔時代久遠的〕陶器碎片: *Roman coins and potsherds* 古羅馬時代的錢幣和陶器碎片

pot shot /ˈ· ·/ *n* **take a pot shot at** to shoot at someone or something without aiming very carefully 對…任意射擊[盲目射擊, 亂射]

pot·ted /ˈpɑtɪd; ˈpɒtɪ̈d/ *adj* [only before noun 僅用於名詞前] **1** a potted plant grows indoors in a pot 盆栽的: *a potted palm* 盆栽棕櫚 **2 a potted history/version** *especially BrE* a short explanation or description of something that gives only the main facts【尤英】簡史/節本: *short potted histories of all the teams in the league* 俱樂部聯合會所有球隊的簡史 **3** *BrE* potted meat or fish has been made into a PASTE for spreading on bread【英】〔肉、

魚〕製成醬的

potted plant /ˌ·· ˈ·/ *n* [C] a plant that is grown indoors in a pot as a decoration 盆栽植物; POT PLANT *BrE*【英】

pot·ter[1] /ˈpɑtɚ; ˈpɒtə/ *n* [C] **1** someone who makes pots, dishes etc out of clay 陶工, 製陶工人 —see also 另見 POTTERY **2 have a potter/go for a potter** *spoken* to move around a place in a slow unhurried way【口】隨便走走, 閒逛

potter[2] also 又作 **potter about/around** *v* [I] *BrE* to spend time doing pleasant things that are not important without hurrying【英】悠然地做些輕鬆的工作[瑣碎的事情]; PUTTER[2] *AmE*【美】: *I spent the morning pottering about in the garden.* 我花了一個上午在花園裡隨便幹了些瑣碎的事。—**potterer** *n* [C]

potter's wheel /ˌ·· ˈ·/ *n* [C] a special round flat object that spins around very fast, onto which wet clay is placed so that it can be shaped into a pot 陶輪, 拉坯輪

pot·ter·y /ˈpɑtərɪ; ˈpɒtəri/ *n* **1** [U] objects made out of baked clay 陶器: *a fine collection of medieval pottery* 精美的中世紀陶器收藏品 **2** [U] clay that has been shaped and baked in order to make pots,dishes etc 陶: *a pottery dish* 陶碟 **3** [U] the activity of making pots, dishes etc out of clay 製陶: *Pottery and basket-making were usually done by the women.* 製陶和編籃子通常由婦女來做。| *a pottery class* 製陶手工學習班 **4** [C] a factory where pottery objects are made 陶瓷廠

pot·ting shed /ˈ·· ·/ *n* [C] *BrE* a small building, usually made of wood, where garden tools, seeds etc are kept【英】〔存放園藝工具、種子等的〕小木屋, 園圃棚

pot·ty[1] /ˈpɑtɪ; ˈpɒti/ *adj BrE informal*【英, 非正式】**1** crazy or silly 瘋狂的; 愚蠢的: *What a potty idea!* 多麼愚蠢的主意! | **drive sb potty** (=make someone crazy) 使某人發瘋 *Your radio is driving me potty.* 你的收音機吵得我快發瘋了。**2 potty about** extremely interested in something, or liking someone very much 迷戀…的, 對…着迷的: *Gemma's potty about riding.* 吉瑪迷上了騎馬。| *He's completely potty about her.* 他完全迷上了她。—**pottiness** *n* [U]

potty[2] *n* [C] *informal* a container shaped like a bowl, used by very young children as a toilet【非正式】小孩用的便盆

potty-train /ˈ·· ·/ *v* [T] to teach a child to use a potty or toilet 訓練〔小孩〕使用便盆[廁所] —**potty-training** *n* [U] —**potty-trained** *adj*

pouch /pautʃ; paʊtʃ/ *n* [C] **1** a small leather bag used for keeping things such as tobacco or money in〔儲物的皮製〕小袋; 小煙袋; 小錢袋: *a rucksack with pouches on the sides* 兩側有小袋的帆布揹包 **2** a pocket of skin which KANGAROOS use for carrying their babies〔袋鼠的〕育兒袋 **3** a fold of skin like a bag which animals such as SQUIRRELS have inside each cheek to carry and store food〔松鼠等的〕頰囊, 頰袋〔用於攜帶和儲存食物〕**4** *AmE* an area of loose skin under someone's eyes【美】眼袋

pouf /puf; puːf/ *n* [C] *BrE*【英】**1** a round soft piece of furniture used to sit on or rest your feet on 坐墊, 腳墊; HASSOCK *AmE*【美】**2** *BrE informal* an insulting word for a male HOMOSEXUAL【英, 非正式】男同性戀者〔侮辱性詞語〕—compare 比較 POOF[1]

pouffe /puf; puːf/ *n* [C] *BrE* a POUF (1)【英】坐墊, 腳墊

poul·ter·er /ˈpoltərɚ; ˈpəʊltərə/ *n* [C] *BrE old-fashioned* someone who sells poultry【英, 過時】家禽商販

poul·tice /ˈpoltɪs; ˈpəʊltʒs/ *n* [C] something that is put on someone's skin to make it less swollen or painful, often made of bread and milk〔常由麵包和牛奶製成的〕泥敷劑, 泥罨劑

poul·try /ˈpoltrɪ; ˈpəʊltri/ *n* **1** [plural] birds that are kept on farms for supplying eggs and meat 家禽: *large-scale poultry farms* 大型家禽飼養場 **2** [U] meat from birds such as chickens, ducks etc 家禽肉

pounce /pauns; paʊns/ *v* [I] to suddenly jump on an animal or person after waiting to attack them 猛撲, 突然襲擊: *crouching, ready to pounce* 弓着身子準備猛撲過去 | **[+on]** *The cat pounced on an unsuspecting mouse.* 那隻貓猛然撲向一隻絲毫沒有戒備的老鼠。—**pounce** *n* [C]

pounce on sb/sth *phr v* [T] **1** to notice a mistake and immediately criticize or disagree with it 發現錯誤並立即批評[反對]: *The boss was quick to pounce on any error in her work.* 老闆能夠一眼看出她工作中的任何錯誤。**2** to accept an offer or invitation eagerly 欣然接受〔提議、邀請〕

pound[1] /paund; paʊnd/ *n*

1 ►WEIGHT 重量◄ written abbreviation 縮寫為 **1b** [C] a unit for measuring weight, equal to 16 OUNCES or about 0.454 kilograms 磅〔重量單位, 相當於 16 盎司或 0.454 千克〕: *a pound of apples* 一磅蘋果 | *Moira weighs about 130 pounds.* 莫伊拉重約 130 磅。| *The grapes cost $2 a pound.* 葡萄的價格是 2 美元一磅。—see table on page C3 參見 C3 頁附錄

2 ►MONEY 錢◄ [C] **a)** written abbreviation 縮寫為 **£** the standard unit of money in Britain, which is divided into 100 pence 英鎊〔英國標準貨幣單位, 等於 100 便士〕: *a five pound note* 五英鎊的鈔票 | *They spent over a thousand pounds on their holiday.* 他們度假花了一千多英鎊。| *a multi-million pound business* 價值數百萬英鎊的企業 **b)** the standard unit of money in various other countries, such as Egypt and the Sudan 鎊〔埃及、蘇丹等國的標準貨幣單位〕**c)** a coin or note worth this amount 一英鎊的硬幣[紙幣]: *Can you change a pound?* 你能把一英鎊換成零錢嗎?

3 the pound the value of British money in relation to the money of other countries 英鎊兌換其他國家貨幣的比值: *There was pressure on the pound in the foreign exchange markets.* 外匯市場上英鎊的壓力很大。

4 ►PLACE 地方◄ [C] a place where lost dogs and cats, or cars that have been illegally parked, are kept until the owner claims them〔走失的狗、貓的〕待領場; 〔違規停放車輛的〕臨時扣押場

5 a quarter/half pounder a HAMBURGER with a quarter or half pound of meat in it 四分之一磅肉的/二分之一磅肉的漢堡(包): *a quarter-pounder with cheese* 四分之一磅肉的加乳酪漢堡

6 get your pound of flesh to get something that is legally yours from someone, even though it makes them suffer and you do not really need it 要回合法但不合情理的東西: *merciless creditors, demanding their pound of flesh* 要求如數償還欠款的無情債主

7 a 3-pounder/24-pounder etc a) animal, or fish that weighs 3 pounds, 24 pounds etc 3 磅/24 磅重的獸[魚] **b)** a gun that fires a SHELL[1] (2) that weighs 3 pounds, 24 pounds etc 發射 3 磅/24 磅等重砲彈的大砲

pound[2] *v*

1 ►HIT 擊打◄ [I,T] to hit something several times, making a lot of noise 連續重擊, 猛打: **[+against/on]** *A heavy sea pounded against the pier.* 巨浪猛烈地拍擊着碼頭。| **pound sth** *Thomas pounded the door with his fist.* 湯瑪斯用拳頭猛烈地敲打着門。

2 ►MOVE 移動◄ [I always+adv/prep] to walk or run quickly with heavy, loud steps 腳步重重地快走[快跑]: **[+along/through/down]** *He pounded up the stairs in front of her.* 他嗵嗵嗵地跑上樓來到她的面前。

3 ►HEART 心臟◄ [I] if your heart pounds, it beats very quickly〔心臟〕劇烈地跳動: *Patrick rushed to the door, his heart pounding with excitement.* 帕特里克衝到門口, 他的心激動得怦怦直跳。

4 ►BREAK 弄碎◄ [T] to hit something many times with a tool in order to break it into pieces or make it flat 搗碎, 舂爛: *Pound the almonds and mix with breadcrumbs.* 把杏仁搗碎與麵包屑混在一起。

5 ►MUSIC 音樂◄ also 又作 **pound out, pound away** [T] to play music loudly by hitting your piano, drum etc very hard 猛烈地敲打〔鋼琴、鼓等〕, 彈奏出: *Mrs Jones pounded out the hymns on the old piano.* 瓊斯太太在那

架舊鋼琴上重重地彈奏出聖歌。
6 ►ARMY 軍隊◄ [T] to attack a place continuously for a long time with bombs or shells (SHELL[1] (2)) 猛烈襲擊, 向…猛烈開火: *Enemy forces have been pounding the city for over two months.* 敵軍兩個多月來一直在猛烈襲擊那個城市。
7 pound the beat *BrE* if a policeman pounds the beat, he walks regularly around the area he is responsible for 【英】〔警察〕在轄區作例行徒步巡邏

pound·age /ˈpaʊndɪdʒ; ˈpaʊndɪdʒ/ *n* [U] **1** *technical* an amount charged for every pound in weight, or for every British £1 in value 【術語】每磅重量的收費額; 每英鎊收費額 **2** *informal* weight 【非正式】重量: *trying to shed that extra poundage* 極力想減掉多餘的重量

pound cake /ˈ· ·/ *n* [C] *AmE* a heavy cake made from flour, sugar, and butter 【美】磅蛋糕, 重奶油蛋糕

pound·ing /ˈpaʊndɪŋ; ˈpaʊndɪŋ/ *n* **1** [singular, U] the action or the sound of something repeatedly hitting a surface very hard, or of your heart beating 猛擊(聲); 猛跳(聲); 沉重的腳步(聲): *The pounding of hooves was getting nearer.* 隆隆的馬蹄聲越來越近了。**2 take a pounding a)** to be completely defeated 被徹底擊敗: *Our football team took a real pounding.* 我們的足球隊遭到慘敗。**b)** to be hit many times by a lot of bombs or shells (SHELL[1] (2)) 遭到猛烈襲擊

pound ster·ling /ˌ· ˈ··/ *n* [singular] *technical* the standard unit of money in Britain, which is divided into 100 pence 【術語】英鎊〔英國標準貨幣單位, 等於 100 便士〕

2 3 **pour** /pɔr; pɔː/ *v*
1 ►LIQUID 液體◄ [T] to make a liquid or a substance such as salt or sand flow out of or into a container 灌, 注, 倒: **pour sth into/out/down etc** *Kim poured some water into a glass.* 金往一隻玻璃杯裡倒了些水。| *You might as well pour the oil down the drain.* 你還是把油倒進排水管吧。| **pour sb sth** *Why don't you pour yourself another drink?* 你為甚麼不給自己再倒一杯酒呢?

pour 灌, 注, 倒

2 ►TEA 茶◄ also 又作 **pour out** [I] *BrE* to fill cups with tea 【英】倒茶, 斟茶: *Shall I pour or will you?* 我來給你倒茶還是你自己來?
3 ►LIQUID/SMOKE 液體/煙◄ [I always+adv/prep] to flow quickly and in large amounts 傾瀉, 大量湧出: **[+from/down/out]** *Smoke was pouring out of the chimney.* 那煙囱正冒出濃煙。
4 ►ARRIVE/LEAVE 到達/離開◄ [I always+adv/prep] if people or things pour into or out of a place, a lot of them arrive or leave at the same time 湧進[出]: **[+into/from/through]** *The men poured into the hall for the meeting.* 男人們湧進大廳開會。| *Offers of help poured in from all over the country.* 全國上下紛紛伸出援助之手。
5 ►RAIN 雨◄ also 又作 **pour down** [I] to rain heavily without stopping 〔雨〕傾盆而下: *The rain poured down endlessly.* 傾盆大雨下個不停。| **it's pouring/it poured** *It poured all night.* 傾盆大雨下了一整夜。| **It's pouring rain/hail etc** *AmE* 【美】: *It's pouring rain out there!* 外面正下着傾盆大雨!
6 pour money/aid/dollars into to provide a lot of money over a period of time to pay for something 提供大筆的錢/大量援助/大量美元給…: *pouring millions of dollars into education* 把上百萬美元投入到教育中
7 pour cold water over/on to spoil someone's plan, idea or keenness to do something by criticizing them 對…潑冷水: *pouring cold water on suggestions that he might resign* 對認為他可能會辭職的提法潑冷水
8 pour oil on troubled waters to try to stop a quarrel by talking to people and making them calmer 平息風波, 調解爭端, 息事寧人
9 pour scorn on to say that something or someone is stupid and not worth considering 鄙夷地談論〔某物或某人〕, 對…嗤之以鼻: *The press is pouring scorn on the 'do nothing' Congress.* 報界正以鄙夷的口氣談論“毫無作為”的國會。
10 pour well if a container pours well, you can pour liquid easily from it 〔容器〕倒起來容易
11 pour it on *informal* to tell someone about a situation in a way that makes it seem much worse than it really is, in order to make them feel sorry for you 【非正式】〔為獲得同情而〕誇大其辭, 極力渲染: *She was really pouring it on.* 她實際上在誇大其辭。

pour sth ↔ **out** *phr v* [T] if you pour out your thoughts, feelings etc, you tell someone everything about them, especially because you feel very unhappy 傾吐, 傾訴, 盡情地訴說: **pour sth out to sb** *Liam poured out his feelings of loneliness to Laura.* 利亞姆向勞拉傾訴了自己的孤獨感。| **pour out your heart/soul** (=tell someone all your feelings including your most secret ones) 訴說心裡話

pout /paʊt; paʊt/ *v* [I,T] to push out your lips because you are annoyed or to look sexually attractive 撅起〔嘴唇〕, 撅嘴〔表示不高興或顯得性感〕: *The child pouted, cried, and went into a tantrum.* 那孩子撅起嘴哭着喊着, 然後是大發脾氣。—**pout** *n* [C] —**pouty** *adj*

pov·er·ty /ˈpɑvɚtɪ; ˈpɒvəti/ *n* **1** [U] the situation or experience of being poor 貧窮, 貧困: **dire/abject/grinding poverty** (=very bad poverty) 極其貧困, 赤貧 *Thousands of children live in dire poverty.* 成千上萬的兒童生活極為貧困。**2 the poverty line/level** the income below which a person or a family is officially considered to be very poor and in need of help 貧困線: *More than 20% of American families now live below the poverty line.* 現在有超過 20% 的美國家庭生活在貧困線以下。**3** [singular,U] *formal* a lack of a particular quality 【正式】缺少, 貧乏: **[+of]** *a surprising poverty of imagination* 驚人地缺乏想像力 —compare 比較 POORNESS 3

poverty-strick·en /ˈ··· ˌ··/ *adj* extremely poor and having problems because of this 極度貧窮[貧困]的: *a poverty-stricken area* 貧困不堪的地區

poverty trap /ˈ··· ˌ·/ *n* [C] a situation in which a poor person will not get any advantage from taking a job because they would then lose their payments from the government 貧困陷阱〔因窮人找到了工作就會失去政府救濟款, 以致從工作中並無得到好處的情況〕

POW /ˌpi o ˈdʌblju; ˌpiː əʊ ˈdʌbəljuː/ *n* [C] a PRISONER OF WAR 戰俘: *Thousands of POWs died in the camps.* 成千上萬的戰俘死在戰俘營裡。

pow /paʊ; paʊ/ *interjection* used to represent the sound of a gun firing, an explosion, or someone hitting another person hard, especially in children's COMICS 〔尤指在兒童連環漫畫中〕啪! 砰!〔表示射擊聲、爆炸聲或某人猛打另一人的聲音〕

pow·der[1] /ˈpaudɚ; ˈpaʊdə/ *n* **1** [C,U] a dry substance in the form of very small grains 粉, 粉末: *Grind the sugar into a powder.* 把糖碾成粉末。| *Zara put down some insect powder to kill the ants.* 薩拉放了一些殺蟲粉以殺死螞蟻。| **milk/custard etc powder** (=food that is stored as a powder and which you add water to in order to make it back into a liquid) 奶粉/蛋奶醬汁粉等 **2 take a powder** *AmE informal* to leave a place quickly, especially to avoid a difficult situation 【美, 非正式】〔尤指為避免困難局面而〕匆忙離去: *When she shows up I'll take a powder.* 她一到, 我就會趕快離開。**3 a powder keg** a dangerous situation or place where violence or trouble could suddenly start 火藥庫〔比喻暴力或麻煩隨時可能發生的危險局面或地方〕: *Since the riot the city has been a powder keg waiting to blow.* 這個城市自騷亂以來已變成一個隨時會爆發的火藥庫。**4 powder snow** snow consisting of extremely small pieces 粉狀雪

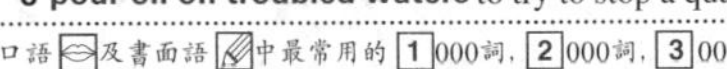

powder² *v* **1** [T] to put powder on something, especially your skin 給〔某物, 尤指皮膚〕塗粉: *Dana took out her compact and began powdering her cheeks.* 戴娜拿出她的小粉盒開始往臉頰上抹粉。**2 be powdered with** to be covered with small pieces of something 撒滿; 鋪滿〔某種粉狀東西〕: *Their shoulders were powdered with snow.* 他們的肩膀上落滿了雪。**3 powder your nose** an expression meaning to go to the TOILET, used by women to avoid saying this directly 上廁所〔女士使用的委婉說法〕

powder blue /ˌ‥ ˈ‥◂/ *n* [U] pale blue 淡藍色: *a powder blue dress* 淡藍色的服裝

P

pow·dered /ˈpaʊdəd; ˈpaʊdəd/ *adj* **1** produced or sold in the form of a powder (製成) 粉狀的, 以粉狀出售的: *powdered milk* 奶粉 **2** covered with powder 佈滿粉的: *powdered hair* 搽了粉的頭髮

powder puff /ˈ‥ ·/ *n* [C] a small piece of soft material used by women to spread POWDER on their face or body 粉撲

powder room /ˈ‥ ·/ *n* [C] **1** an expression meaning a toilet for women in a theatre, hotel, restaurant etc, used to avoid saying this directly〔劇院、酒店、餐館等內的〕女廁所〔委婉說法〕**2** *AmE* a small room with a toilet and WASHBASIN next to the main living room in a house or apartment【美】〔主起居室旁的〕盥洗室

pow·der·y /ˈpaʊdərɪ; ˈpaʊdəri/ *adj* **1** like powder or easily broken into powder 粉末狀的; 易碎成粉末的: *The snow was dry and powdery.* 雪乾乾的而且像粉末一樣。**2** covered with powder 佈滿粉的; 搽了粉的

S1 W1 **pow·er¹** /ˈpaʊə; ˈpaʊə/ *n*

1 ▶CONTROL 控制◀ [U] the ability or right to control people or events 權力, 權勢; 支配力: *We all felt that the chairman had too much power.* 我們都覺得主席的權力太大了。| *He was motivated by greed, envy, and the lust for power.* 他受貪婪、嫉妒、權力慾的驅使。| **[+over]** *She has a lot of power over the people in her team.* 她對她隊裡的人有很大的影響力。| **power struggle** (=a situation in which groups or leaders try to defeat each other and get complete control) 權力鬥爭 *engaged in a bitter power struggle against Chairman Sir George Scott* 捲入反對議長喬治·史考特爵士的殘酷的權力鬥爭中

2 ▶CONTROL OF A COUNTRY 對一個國家的控制◀ [U] the position of having political control of a country or government 政權: **be in power** *The dictator had been in power for seven years.* 那個獨裁者已執政七年了。| **come/rise to power** (=start having political control) 開始掌權, 上台 *De Gaulle came to power in 1958.* 戴高樂是1958年上台的。| **return to power** *The Labour Party returned to power after 13 years.* 工黨於13年之後重新執政。| **get into power** *If the Social Democrats got into power, they would change the whole system of local government.* 如果社會民主黨上台, 他們就會改變地方政府的整個體制。| **take/sieze power** *The Communists seized power in 1962.* 共產黨於1962年奪取了政權。| **lose power** *Left-wing parties lost power in several European countries last year.* 去年左翼政黨在幾個歐洲國家都垮台了。

3 ▶INFLUENCE 影響◀ [U] the ability to influence people or give them strong feelings 影響力, 感染力: **[+of]** *We were stunned by the power of his speech.* 我們驚嘆於他演講的感染力。| *the immense power of television* 電視的巨大影響力

4 ▶RIGHT/AUTHORITY 權利/權威◀ [C,U] the right or authority to do something 職權, 權限: *The police have been given special powers to help them in the fight against terrorism.* 警方被賦予特殊的權力以幫助他們打擊恐怖主義。| **the power to do sth** *She was the one who had the power to hire or fire people.* 有權雇用或解雇人的是她。| **the power of** *The chairman has the power of veto on all decisions.* 議長對所有的決定都有否決權。

5 ▶ABILITY 能力◀ [C,U] a natural or special ability to do something 能力, 本領: **[+of]** *After the accident she lost the power of speech.* 那次事故之後, 她失去了語言的能力。| **the power to do sth** *Local people believe that the plant has the power to cure all kinds of ailments.* 當地人相信這種植物具有治癒各種疾病的效能。

6 earning/purchasing/bargaining power the ability to earn money, buy things etc 賺錢能力/購買力/議價能力: *Average earning power has shot up by more than 50%.* 平均賺錢能力已迅速增長了超過50%。

7 student power/black power/parent power etc the political or social influence that an organized group has 學生/黑人/家長的勢力: *another victory for student power* 學生勢力的又一次勝利

8 ▶STRENGTH 力量◀ the strength of something such as an explosion, animal or natural force and its ability to move or destroy things 力量, 威力: *the sheer power and majesty of the elephant* 大象的力量和威嚴 | *the power of the explosion* 爆炸的威力

9 ▶ENERGY 能量◀ [U] energy that can be used to make a machine work or to make electricity 能, 動力: **nuclear/wind/solar etc power** *Many people are opposed to the use of nuclear power.* 很多人反對使用核動力。| **under its own power** (=without help from another machine, ship etc) 靠它自己的動力 *The cruiser was able to leave port under its own power.* 這艘巡洋艦能靠自己的動力離港。| **lose/run out of power** *It keeps losing power when I take a sharp bend.* 我急轉彎時它老是熄火。

10 ▶ELECTRICITY 電◀ [U] electricity that is used in houses, factories etc 電, 電力: *She plugged the machine in and switched the power on.* 她把機器的插頭插上, 並打開電源開關。| *Power is provided by a small 9 volt battery.* 電是由一節小小的9伏特電池提供的。| **power cut/failure/outage** (=a short time when the electricity supply is not working) 斷電, 停電 *Parts of the country have had power cuts because of the storms.* 這個國家的部分地區由於暴風雨而停電了。

11 ▶STRONG COUNTRY 強國◀ [C] a country that is strong and important, or has a lot of military strength 強國; 軍事強國: *Egypt is still an important power in the Middle East.* 埃及仍然是中東地區一個重要的強國。| **world power** (=a very important country that can influence events in different parts of the world) 世界強國

12 air/sea power ships or aircraft that help an army in the air or on the sea 空軍/海軍力量: *The outcome will be decided by air power.* 結果將取決於空軍實力。

13 be in sb's power to be in a situation in which someone has complete control over you 在某人的控制下

14 be in sb's power to do sth if it is in someone's power to do something, they have the authority or ability to do it 某人有權[有能力]做某事: *It is not in my power to tell you the results of the exam.* 我無權告訴你考試的結果。

15 be beyond/outside sb's power to do sth if it is beyond someone's power to do something, they do not have the authority or ability to do it 某人無權[無能力]做某事: *I am afraid it is beyond my power to do what you are asking.* 我恐怕無力做你要求做的事。

16 do everything in your power to do everything that you are able or allowed to do 盡你的所能: *The ambassador promised to do everything in his power to get the hostages released.* 那位大使答應盡他所能使人質獲釋。

17 do sb a power of good *BrE informal* to make someone feel more healthy, happy, and hopeful about the future【英, 非正式】對某人大有好處: *It looks as if your holiday has done you a power of good.* 看起來你的假期對你大有好處。

18 the powers of good/evil spirits or magical forces that are believed to influence events in a good or evil way 正義/邪惡的力量

19 ▶MATHEMATICS 數學◀ [C] if a number is increased to the power of three, four, five etc, it is multiplied by itself three, four, five etc times 冪, 乘方

20 high-powered/low-powered etc having a motor that is very powerful, not very powerful etc 高功率的/低功率的等: *irresponsible young men in high-powered sports cars* 開着大馬力賽車的不負責任的青年人
21 a power in the land *old-fashioned* someone who has a lot of power and influence in a country【過時】有權勢的人物
22 the power behind the throne someone who is able to secretly control and influence decisions made by the leader or government of a country, but does not have an official government position themselves 太上皇, 幕後掌權者
23 the powers that be *informal* the unknown people who have important positions of authority and power, and whose decisions affect your life【非正式】掌權者; 當權派: *The powers that be have decided that smoking is a Bad Idea.* 權威人士已斷定抽煙不好。
24 be on a power trip *informal* to be enjoying the new power or authority that you have been given, in a way that other people find unpleasant【非正式】過權力癮 —see also 另見 STAYING POWER, BALANCE OF POWER, HIGH-POWERED

power² *v* **1** [T usually passive 一般用被動態] to supply power to a vehicle or machine 給〔車輛或機器〕提供動力, 以動力驅動: *The motor is powered by a solar battery.* 這台發動機是由太陽能電池驅動的。**2** [I+adv/prep] to move powerfully and quickly 飛速行駛, 快速行進: **[+through/up/down]** *His strong body powered through the water.* 他強壯的身體在水中快速地游動。**3 battery-powered/nuclear-powered etc** working or moving by means of power from a BATTERY, NUCLEAR energy etc 電池驅動的/核能驅動的等: *an atomic-powered ship* 原子能動力輪船 —see also 另見 HIGH-POWERED

power³ *adj* **1** driven by a motor 電動機驅動的: *power tools* 電動工具 **2** *informal* showing that you are important in a business organization【非正式】〔顯示某人在企業組織中是〕重要的: *a power lunch* 由重要商業人士參加的商務午餐

power base /ˈ·· ·/ *n* [C] an area or group of people whose support gives a politician or leader their power 權力基礎, 支持某人的勢力[地區]: *Texas remained Johnson's political power base.* 得克薩斯州一直是約翰遜的政治權力基礎所在。

pow·er·boat /ˈpauɚˌbot; ˈpaʊəbəʊt/ *n* [C] a powerful MOTORBOAT that is used for racing 摩托賽艇; 汽艇, 快艇

power bro·ker /ˈ·· ˌ··/ *n* [C] someone who controls who should have political power in an area〔操縱某地區政治勢力的〕權力掮客

power cut /ˈ·· ·/ *n* [C] a period of time when there is no electricity supply 停電, 斷電

power dres·sing /ˈ·· ˌ··/ *n* [U] a way of dressing in which the colour and style of your clothes is intended to emphasize how important your job is 突顯工作重要性的穿着方式; 職業強人裝束: *Eighties power dressing at its brashest* 二十世紀八十年代極其花哨的職業裝

power drill /ˈ·· ·/ *n* [C] a tool for making holes that works by electricity 電鑽

2 **pow·er·ful** /ˈpauɚfəl; ˈpaʊəfəl/ *adj*
1 ▶IMPORTANT 重要的◀ a powerful person, organization, group etc is able to control and influence events and other people's actions 權力強大的, 有勢力的: *The president is the most powerful man in America and probably the world.* 總統是美國而且很可能是世界上權力最大的人。| *a powerful consortium of European companies* 強大的歐洲企業集團
2 ▶AFFECTING SB'S FEELINGS/IDEAS 影響某人的感情/觀念◀ having a strong effect on someone's feelings or on the way they think 強有力的, 有影響[感染]力的: *Jealousy is such a powerful emotion.* 嫉妒是一種如此強烈的感情。| *a powerful speech* 有感染力的演講 | *The film uses a powerful blend of images and words.* 這部電影將圖像和語言很有感染力地融合在一起。| **powerful reasons/arguments** (=reasons that make you think that something must be true) 有說服力的推理/論證
3 ▶MACHINE/WEAPON ETC 機器/武器等◀ a powerful machine, engine, weapon etc works very effectively and quickly or with great force〔機器、引擎、武器等〕功率大的, 效能大的: *a new generation of more powerful PCs* 更高效的新一代個人電腦 | *The Jaguar XJ12 features a powerful 24 valve engine.* "美洲虎 XJ12" 型汽車的特點是有一個大功率的 24 閥引擎。
4 ▶MEDICINE 藥◀ a powerful medicine or drug has a very strong effect on your body〔藥物〕強效的: *The drug is a thousand times more powerful than LSD.* 這種藥比 LSD (迷幻藥) 的效力高一千倍。
5 ▶PHYSICALLY STRONG 身體強壯的◀ physically strong 強壯的, 強健的: *Jed was a powerful, well-built man.* 傑德是個強壯結實的男人。| *powerful jaws that can kill in seconds* 可在數秒鐘之內咬死獵物的強有力的嘴
6 ▶TEAM/ARMY ETC 球隊/部隊等◀ a powerful team, army etc is very strong and can easily defeat other teams or armies 強大的: *The Allies had assembled a powerful fighting force.* 同盟國集結了一支強大的戰鬥隊伍。
7 ▶LIGHT/SOUND/TASTE/SMELL 光/聲/味道/氣味◀ very strong, bright, loud etc 非常強的, 濃烈的, 強烈的: *The alarm emits a powerful high-pitched sound.* 警報器發出很響的高聲。
8 ▶EXPLOSION/KICK/PUNCH ETC 爆炸/踢/猛擊等◀ a powerful blow, explosion etc hits someone with a lot of force or has a lot of force 猛烈的, 用力的: *an explosion ten times more powerful than Hiroshima* 比廣島原子彈爆炸威力大十倍的爆炸 | *a powerful header just over the bar* 打在橫木上方的有力的頭球 —**powerfully** *adv*: *Christie is very powerfully built.* 克利斯蒂身材魁梧。—see also 另見 ALL-POWERFUL

pow·er·house /ˈpauɚˌhaus; ˈpaʊəhaʊs/ *n* [C] *informal*【非正式】**1** an organization or place that produces a lot of ideas and has a lot of influence 很有影響力的機構[地方]: *In the 60s, MIT was an intellectual powerhouse.* 在 20 世紀 60 年代, 麻省理工學院是一個具有很大影響力的學術機構。**2** someone who is very strong and has a lot of energy 身強力壯的人, 精力充沛的人: *a powerhouse of a man* 精力充沛的男人

pow·er·less /ˈpauɚlɪs; ˈpaʊələs/ *adj* [not before noun 不用於名詞前] unable to stop or control something because you do not have the power, strength, or legal right to do so 無權力的; 無力量的; 無能為力的: **powerless to do sth** *The fire was so big that firefighters were powerless to prevent it from spreading.* 火勢如此大, 以致消防人員沒有能力阻止它蔓延。| **[+against]** *The Hungarians were powerless against the might of the Red Army.* 匈牙利人無力對抗蘇聯紅軍的力量。—**powerlessly** *adv* —**powerlessness** *n* [U]

power line /ˈ·· ·/ *n* [C] a large wire carrying electricity above or under the ground 電力線, 輸電線: *overhead power lines* 架空輸電線

power of at·tor·ney /ˌ·· · ·ˈ··/ *n* [C,U] *law* the legal right to do things for another person in their personal or business life, or a document giving this right【法律】〔法律上的〕委任權, 代理權; 委任書[狀], 授權書

power plant /ˈ·· ·/ *n* [C] **1** *technical* the machine or engine that supplies power to a factory, plane, car etc【術語】動力設備, 發電裝置 **2** *AmE* a building where electricity is produced to supply a large area; POWER STATION【美】發電廠, 發電站

power point /ˈ·· ·/ *n* [C] *especially BrE* a place on a wall where electrical equipment can be connected to the electricity supply; SOCKET【尤英】〔牆上的〕電源插座

power pol·i·tics /ˈ·· ˌ···/ *n* [U] the use or threat of armed force in international politics〔國際上的〕強權政治: *mere pawns in a game of international power politics* 世界強權政治遊戲中的區區走卒

power sta·tion /ˈ·· ˌ··/ *n* [C] a building where electricity is produced to supply a large area 發電站, 發電廠

power steer·ing /ˈ·· ˌ··/ *n* [U] a system for steering (STEER[1] (1)) a vehicle which uses power from the vehicle's engine and so needs less effort from the driver〔汽車的〕動力轉向裝置〔利用引擎動力減輕司機操縱方向盤時的力的裝置〕

power tool /ˈ·· ·/ *n* [C] a tool that works by electricity 電動工具

pow·wow /ˈ· ·/ *n* [C] **1** *humorous* a meeting or discussion【幽默】會議, 討論會 **2** a meeting or council of Native Americans 北美印第安人的議事會

pox /pɑks; pɒks/ *n old use*【舊】**1 the pox** the disease SYPHILIS 梅毒 (病) **2** [U] the disease SMALLPOX 天花 (病) **3 a pox on** *old use* used to show that you are angry or annoyed with someone【舊】讓…倒大霉, 叫…見鬼去, 降災禍於…〔表示生氣或厭煩〕—see also 另見 CHICKENPOX

pox·y /ˈpɑksɪ; ˈpɒksi/ *adj BrE slang* used to show that you do not like someone or something【英俚】令人討厭的: *Keep your poxy money.* 收好你的臭錢!

pp 1 the written abbreviation of 縮寫= pages: *See pp 15–17.* 見第15–17頁。**2** written before the name of another person when you are signing a letter for them 代表…〔代別人簽署信件時寫在別人名字前〕

PPS /ˌpi pi ˋɛs; ˌpiː piː ˈes/ *n* [C] **1** a note added after a PS in a letter or message〔信末附言後的〕再附言 **2** Parliamentary Private Secretary; a member of the British parliament who is appointed to help a minister〔英國的〕議會私人祕書〔指定協助一位大臣工作的議員〕

PR /ˌpi ˋɑr; ˌpiː ˈɑː/ *n* [U] **1** PUBLIC RELATIONS; the work of persuading people to think that a company or organization is a good one 公共關係: *a leading PR agency in the city* 該市一家主要的公關公司 | *It's not very good for your PR, is it?* 這不利於你的公共關係, 是嗎? **2** PROPORTIONAL REPRESENTATION〔議會選舉中的〕比例代表制

prac·ti·ca·ble /ˈpræktɪkəbl̩; ˈpræktɪkəbəl/ *adj* an idea or way of doing something that is practicable is able to be used successfully in a particular situation〔觀點、方法〕可行的, 行得通的: *The only practicable course of action is to sell the company.* 唯一可行的做法是賣掉這家公司。—**practicably** *adv* —**practicability** /ˌpræktɪkəˋbɪlətɪ; ˌpræktɪkəˈbɪlɪ̣ti/ *n* [U]

3 2 **prac·ti·cal[1]** /ˈpræktɪkl̩; ˈpræktɪkəl/ *adj*

1 ►CONCERNED WITH REAL SITUATIONS 與實際情況相關的◄ concerned with real situations and events rather than ideas 實踐 (中) 的, 實際的: *How much practical experience do you have of working with computers?* 你有多少操作電腦的實踐經驗? | *a practical knowledge of simple medicine* 關於簡單藥物的實用知識 | *Most of the things you learn at school have no practical value in the real world.* 在學校裡學的大多數東西在現實生活中並沒有實際的價值。—compare 比較 THEORETICAL

2 ►SENSIBLE 明智的◄ sensible and basing your decisions on what is possible and what will really work 注重實際的, 務實的: *Be practical! We can't afford the car and the vacation!* 實際點吧! 我們沒有足夠的錢既去買車又去度假。—opposite 反義詞 IMPRACTICAL (1)

3 ►LIKELY TO WORK 可行的◄ practical plans, methods, advice etc are likely to succeed or be effective in a situation〔計劃、方法、建議等〕可行的, 行得通的: *The only practical solution is to sell the company.* 唯一可行的解決辦法是把公司賣掉。| *The agency provides practical advice and support to pregnant teenagers.* 這家機構為懷孕的少女提供切實可行的建議和支持。| **practical alternative** (=another way of doing something that is likely to work) 可行的其他方案 —opposite 反義詞 IMPRACTICAL (1)

4 ►USEFUL 有用的◄ designed to be useful rather than attractive 講求實用的: *Majorie always gets us practical Christmas presents – last year we got a kettle.* 梅傑里總是給我們買實用的聖誕禮物 —— 去年我們得到一個水壺。

5 ►SUITABLE 合適的◄ suitable for a particular purpose or for normal life 切合實際的, 實用的: *I always wanted a Ferrari, but it's not a very practical car.* 我一直想要一輛法拉利車, 但那不是一種很實用的車。| *Jeans would be the most practical thing to wear.* 牛仔褲將是最適於穿着的衣服。—opposite 反義詞 IMPRACTICAL (1)

6 ►GOOD AT REPAIRING/MAKING THINGS 擅長修理/製作東西◄ good at repairing or making things 心靈手巧的: *I'm not very practical – I don't know the first thing about cars.* 我動手能力不強 —— 我對汽車一竅不通。

7 a practical certainty/disaster/sell-out etc something that is almost certain, almost a DISASTER etc 幾乎確定無疑/是災難/滿座: *Sampras looks a practical certainty to win Wimbledon this year.* 桑普拉斯看起來幾乎確定無疑會贏得今年溫布頓網球賽的冠軍。

8 for/to all practical purposes used when saying what the real effect of a situation is 實際上, 事實上: *For all practical purposes the federation no longer exists.* 實際上該聯盟已不存在了。

practical[2] *n* [C] *BrE* a lesson or examination in science, cooking etc in which you have to do or make something yourself rather than write or read about it【英】〔科學、烹飪等的〕實驗課, 實習課; 實用知識考試: *We have chemistry practicals after Christmas.* 聖誕節過後我們要上化學實驗課。

prac·ti·cal·i·ty /ˌpræktɪˋkælətɪ; ˌpræktɪˈkælɪ̣ti/ *n* **1 practicalities** [plural] the real facts of a situation rather than ideas about how it might be 實際的事情, 實際問題: *concerned with the practicalities of planning lessons and courses* 關注課程設計的實際問題 **2** [U] how suitable an idea, method, or plan is for a situation, and whether or not it will work 可行性, 實用 (性): *doubts about the practicality of your suggestion* 對於你所提建議的可行性表示的懷疑 **3** [U] the quality of being sensible and basing your plans on what you know will work 實際, 務實

practical joke /ˌ··· ˈ·/ *n* [C] a trick that is intended to give someone a surprise or shock and make other people laugh 惡作劇 —**practical joker** *n* [C]

prac·ti·cally /ˈpræktɪklɪ; ˈpræktɪkli/ *adv* **1** *especially spoken* almost【尤口】幾乎, 差不多: *The hall was practically empty.* 這個大廳幾乎空無一人。| *Practically all my friends are gay.* 我的朋友幾乎全是同性戀者。**2** in a sensible way which takes account of problems 講究實際地; 從實際出發: *"But how can we pay for it?" said John practically.* "但我們如何付款呢?" 約翰講究實際地問道。

prac·tice /ˈpræktɪs; ˈpræktɪ̣s/ *n*

1 a) ►A SKILL 技能◄ [U] regular activity that you do in order to improve a skill 練習: *It takes hours of practice to learn to play the guitar.* 學會彈結他需要練習好長時間。| *With a little more practice you should be able to pass your test.* 再進行一些練習, 你應該能通過考試。**b)** [C] a period of time you spend training to improve your skill in doing something 進行練習的一段時間, 練習期間: *choir practice* 唱詩班合唱練習 | *We have two rugby practices a week.* 我們一星期進行兩次橄欖球訓練。

2 in practice used when saying what really happens rather than what should happen or what people think happens 實際上; 在實踐中: *In practice women receive much lower wages than their male colleagues.* 實際上婦女所得的工資比她們的男同事低得多。

3 ►CUSTOM 習俗◄ [C] something that you do often because of your religion or your society's tradition 慣常做法, 慣例; 習俗: *religious beliefs and practices* 宗教信仰和習俗 | **the practice of doing sth** *The Navy has abandoned the practice of serving rum to the men.* 海軍終止了給士兵供應朗姆酒的慣例。—see also 見 HABIT (USAGE)

4 ►STH DONE OFTEN 經常做的事◄ [C,U] something that people do often, especially a particular way of doing something 習慣做法: *the widespread practice of under-declaring taxable income* 低報應納稅收入的普遍

做法｜*unsafe sexual practices* 不安全的性習慣｜*dangerous working practices* 危險的工作方法
5 ▶DOCTOR/LAWYER 醫生/律師◀ [C] the work of a doctor or lawyer or the place where they work〔醫生或律師的〕業務; 診所; 律師事務所: **medical/legal practice** *Mary Beth had a busy legal practice in Los Angeles.* 瑪麗·貝思在洛杉磯有一家業務繁忙的律師事務所。—see also 另見 GENERAL PRACTICE, PRIVATE PRACTICE
6 common/standard/general/normal practice the usual and accepted way of doing something 普遍[通常, 一般]的做法: *In Scandinavian countries it is common practice for the husband to stay at home to look after the baby.* 在斯堪的納維亞國家, 丈夫待在家裡照料嬰兒是很普遍的做法。
7 good/bad practice an example of a good or very bad way of doing something, especially in a particular job〔尤指工作中〕良好的/不好的習慣做法: *It's not considered good practice to reveal clients' names.* 泄露客戶的姓名被認為是不好的做法。
8 be out of practice to have not done something for a long time so that you are unable to do it well〔因久不練習而〕荒廢, 生疏
9 be in practice if you are in practice you have practised something regularly and are able to do it well 經常練習, 熟練
10 put sth into practice if you put an idea, plan etc into practice, you start to use it and see if it is effective 把某物付諸實施: *The hard part is putting it all into practice.* 困難的是將它全部付諸實施。
11 practice makes perfect used to say that if you do an activity regularly, you will become very good at it 熟能生巧

S3 W3 **prac·tise** *BrE*【英】, **practice** *AmE*【美】/ˋpræktɪs; ˈpræktɨs/ *v* **1** [I,T] to do an activity regularly in order to improve your skill or to prepare for a test 練習, 實踐, 實習: **practise (doing) sth** *John's practising the violin.* 約翰在練習拉小提琴。| *Today we're going to practise parking.* 今天我們要練習停車。| **practise for sth** *She's practising for her driving test.* 她正在為駕駛考試進行練習。| **practise sth on sb** *Everybody wants to practise their English on me.* 每個人都想與我練習英語。| **practise hard** (=practise a lot) 刻苦練習 *If you practise hard you might be the next Carl Lewis.* 你如果刻苦練習, 或許會成為下一個卡爾·劉易斯。**2** [T] to use a particular method or custom 實行, 奉行: *Polyandry is still practised in some parts of the world.* 世界上一些地區仍然實行着一妻多夫制。**3** [I,T] to work as a doctor or lawyer〔醫生、律師〕執業, 從業: **[+as]** *Gemma is now practising as a dentist.* 吉瑪現在執業當一名牙醫。| **practise sth** *He went on to practise law.* 他繼續當律師。**4** [T] if you practise a religion, system of ideas etc, you live your life according to its rules 遵照〔教義、觀念等〕行事 **5 practise what you preach** to do the things that you advise other people to do 躬行己說, 以身作則: *The Green candidate should practise what she preaches and sell her car.* 那位綠黨候選人應該身體力行, 賣掉她的汽車。

prac·tised *BrE*【英】, **practiced** *AmE*【美】/ˋpræktɪst; ˈpræktɨst/ *adj* **1** someone who is practised in a particular job or skill is good at it because they have done it many times before 老練的, 有經驗的; 熟練的: *a practised hunter* 有經驗的獵人｜**practised in (doing) sth** *Kate became practised in the art of disguising her emotions.* 凱特變得很善於掩飾自己的感情。| **to the practised eye** (=to someone who has seen something many times and knows a lot about it) 對於目光老練的人, 對於見多識廣的人 **2** [only before noun 僅用於名詞前] a practised action has been done so often that it now seems very easy〔動作〕嫻熟的: *With practised ease he slit open the sack.* 他熟練輕鬆地拆開了袋子。

prac·tis·ing *BrE*【英】, **practicing** *AmE*【美】/ˋpræktɪsɪŋ; ˈpræktɨsɪŋ/ *adj* **1 a practising Catholic/Muslim/Jew etc** someone who follows the rules and customs of a particular religion 虔誠的天主教徒/穆斯林/猶太教徒等 **2 a practising doctor/lawyer/teacher etc** someone who is working as a doctor, lawyer etc 執業醫生/律師/教師等: *Few practising teachers have time for such research.* 很少正在從事教學工作的教師有時間做這樣的研究。

prac·ti·tion·er /prækˋtɪʃənɚ; prækˈtɪʃənə/ *n* [C] **1** W3 **medical/legal practitioner** someone who works as a doctor or a lawyer 執業醫生/律師 **2** someone who regularly does a particular activity 從事者, 實踐者: *skilful public relations practitioners* 老練的公關人員｜**[+of]** *a practitioner of Taoist philosophy* 道家哲學的實踐者 —see also 另見 GENERAL PRACTITIONER

prae·sid·i·um /prɪˋsɪdɪəm; prɪˈsɪdiəm/ *n* [C] another spelling of PRESIDIUM presidium 的另一種拼法

prag·mat·ic /prægˋmætɪk; prægˈmætɪk/ *adj* dealing with problems in a sensible, practical way instead of strictly following a set of ideas 講求實際的, 務實的, 重實效的: *a pragmatic approach to politics* 對政治的務實態度 —**pragmatically** /-klɪ; -kli/ *adv*

prag·mat·ics /prægˋmætɪks; prægˈmætɪks/ *n* [U] *technical* the study of how words and phrases are used with special meanings in particular situations【術語】語用學

prag·ma·tis·m /ˋprægmə͵tɪzəm; ˈprægmətɪzəm/ *n* [U] a way of dealing with problems in a sensible, practical way instead of following a set of ideas 實用主義; 務實的方法: *conditioned more by political pragmatism than religious zeal* 較多取決於政治實用性而不是宗教狂熱 —**pragmatist** *n* [C]

prai·rie /ˋprɛrɪ; ˈpreəri/ *n* [C] a wide open area of land in North America which is covered in grass or wheat〔北美洲的〕大草原

prairie dog /ˋ·· ·/ *n* [C] a small animal with a short tail, which lives in holes on the prairies 草原犬鼠

praise[1] /prez; preɪz/ *v* [T] **1** to say that you admire and approve of someone or something, especially publicly〔尤指公開地〕稱讚, 讚揚, 表揚: *The play was praised by the critics when it was first shown on Broadway.* 該劇首次在百老匯上演時就受到了評論家的讚揚。| **praise sb/sth for sth** *The Mayor praised the rescue team for their courage.* 市長讚揚救援隊的勇氣。| **praise sb/sth highly** *a highly praised novel* 備受稱道的小說｜**praise sb/sth to the skies** (=to praise someone or something very much) 對某人/某事讚嘆不已, 把某人/某事捧上天 **2** to give thanks to God and show your respect to him, especially by singing in a church〔尤指在教堂以唱讚美詩〕讚美〔上帝〕 **3 God/Heaven be praised** also 又作 **Praise the Lord** used to say that you are pleased something has happened and thank God for it 謝天謝地, 感謝上帝

praise[2] *n* [U] **1** words that you say or write in order to praise someone or something 讚揚; 讚美: **be full of praise for** (=praise something a lot) 對…大加讚揚 *Mrs George was full of praise for her nurses' caring attitude.* 喬治太太對照顧她的護士們充滿愛心的態度大加讚揚。| **high praise** (=a lot of praise) 高度的讚揚 *Bork received high praise for his efforts to cut spending.* 勃克由於為削減開支所做的努力而受到了高度的讚揚。| **win praise** (=receive praise) 受到讚揚 *The film has won praise from audiences and critics alike.* 這部電影贏得了觀眾和評論家的一致讚揚。**2** the expression of respect and thanks to God〔對上帝的〕崇拜, 讚頌: *Let us give praise unto the Lord.* 讓我們讚美上帝吧。**3 praise be!** *old-fashioned* used when you are very pleased about something that has happened【過時】謝天謝地! 感謝上帝! —see also 另見 **sing sb's praises** (SING (5))

praise·wor·thy /ˋprez͵wɝðɪ; ˈpreɪzwɜːði/ *adj* deserving praise, especially when not completely successful 值得讚揚的, 精神可嘉的〔尤用於未取得徹底成功時〕: *the Italian team's praiseworthy attempts to reach a draw* 意大利隊為打成平局所作出值得讚揚的努力 —**praiseworthiness** *n* [U]

pra·line /ˈprɑlin; ˈprɑːliːn/ *n* [C,U] a sweet food made of nuts cooked in boiling sugar 果仁糖

prams (四輪手推) 嬰兒車

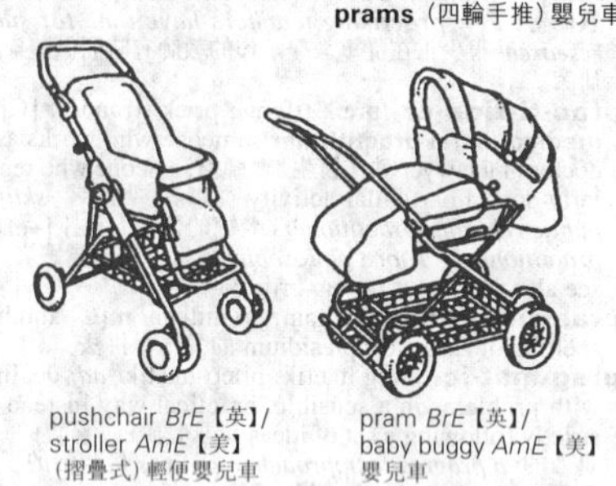

pushchair *BrE*【英】/ stroller *AmE*【美】(摺疊式) 輕便嬰兒車

pram *BrE*【英】/ baby buggy *AmE*【美】嬰兒車

3 **pram** /præm; præm/ *n* [C] *BrE* a small vehicle with four wheels in which a baby can lie down while being pushed【英】〔嬰兒可躺在裡面的〕(四輪手推) 嬰兒車; BABY CARRIAGE *AmE*【美】—compare 比較 BUGGY (3)

prance /præns; prɑːns/ *v* [I] **1** [always+adv/prep] to walk moving your body in a confident way in order to make people notice and admire you 趾高氣揚地走, 昂首闊步: [+around/in/up] *Leo's always prancing around as if he owns the place.* 利奧總是神氣十足地走來走去, 好像那地方是他的。**2** if a horse prances, it moves with high steps〔馬〕騰跳, 騰躍

prang /præŋ; præŋ/ *v* [T] *BrE informal* to damage a vehicle in an accident【英, 非正式】〔在事故中〕撞毀〔車輛〕, 損壞 —**prang** *n* [C]

prank /præŋk; præŋk/ *n* [C] a trick, especially one which is played on someone to make them look silly〔尤指使人難堪的〕玩笑, 惡作劇: *a childish prank* 孩子的胡鬧

prank·ster /ˈpræŋkstɚ; ˈpræŋkstə/ *n* [C] someone who plays tricks on people to make them look silly 惡作劇者

prat /præt; præt/ *n* [C] *BrE informal* a stupid person【英, 非正式】傻瓜, 愚蠢的人: *Don't be such a prat.* 別這麼愚蠢。—**prattish** *adj*

prate /pret; preɪt/ *v* [I+on/about] *old-fashioned* to talk in a meaningless, boring way about something【過時】嘮叨; 瞎扯

prat·fall /ˈprætfɔl; ˈprætfɔːl/ *n* [C] an embarrassing accident or mistake 令人尷尬的事故[失誤]: *another one of the Vice-President's pratfalls* 副總統的另一次令人尷尬的失誤

prat·tle /ˈprætl; ˈprætl/ *v* [I] to talk continuously about silly and unimportant things 喋喋不休, 閒扯, 嘮叨: **prattle on (about)** *What's Sarah prattling on about?* 莎拉在喋喋不休地講甚麼? —**prattle** *n* [U] —**prattler** *n* [C]

prawn /prɔn; prɔːn/ *n* [C] a small pink SHELLFISH that is used for food 對蝦, 明蝦, 大蝦: *a prawn salad sandwich* 明蝦沙拉三明治

3 **pray**[1] /pre; preɪ/ *v* **1** [I,T] to speak to God in order to ask for help or give thanks 祈禱; 禱告: *They went to the mosque to pray.* 他們去清真寺做禱告。| [+for] *Let us pray for peace.* 讓我們為和平祈禱吧。| [+to] *Martha prayed to God every night.* 瑪莎每晚都向上帝祈禱。| **pray sth** *"Dear Lord, show me my duty," she prayed.* "親愛的主, 請向我指明我的義務," 她祈禱道。**2** [I,T] to wish or hope very strongly that something will happen 強烈地希望, 祈望, 祈求: **pray that** *Paul was praying that no one had noticed his absence.* 保羅正在祈求沒有人注意到他的缺席。| [+for] *We're praying for a fine day tomorrow.* 我們正在祈望明天是個好天氣。

pray[2] *adv* [sentence adverb 句子副詞] *old-fashioned* used when politely asking a question or telling someone to do something【過時】請, 懇請〔用於禮貌地問問題或叫某人做某事〕: *Pray be seated.* 請坐下。| *And who, pray, is this?* 請問是誰?

prayer /prɛr; preə/ *n* **1** [C] words that you say when praying to God, especially a fixed form of words 祈禱文, 禱辭: *We all had to say our prayers before going to bed.* 上牀睡覺前我們都得做禱告。| [+for] *a prayer for the deceased* 為死者所做的禱告 **2** [U] the act of praying or the regular habit of praying 祈禱(的習慣): *the power of prayer* 祈禱的力量 | *a prayer meeting* 祈禱會 | **in prayer** (=praying) 在祈禱 *The congregation knelt in prayer.* 教堂的會眾跪下祈禱。**3** [C] a wish or hope that something will happen 願望, 希望, 祈望: *Nadia's one prayer is that the children won't suffer.* 娜迪亞的一個願望是孩子們不要受罪。**4 prayers** [plural] a regular religious meeting in a church, school etc, at which people pray together〔教堂、學校等的〕祈禱式: *Prayers are at 9 o'clock.* 祈禱式在9點鐘舉行。**5 not have a prayer** *informal* to have no chance of succeeding【非正式】沒有成功的機會: *I hadn't done any work for the exam, and I knew I didn't have a prayer.* 我沒有為考試做任何功課, 所以我知道我過不了。**6 sb's prayers are answered** *informal* used to say that someone has got something that they wanted very much【非正式】某人的禱告應驗了: *I thought all my prayers were answered when I got that job.* 當我得到那份工作時, 我覺得我所有的祈求都應驗了。—see also 另見 LORD'S PRAYER

prayer book /ˈ· ·/ *n* [C] a book containing prayers used in some Christian church services〔基督教的〕祈禱書

prayer mat /ˈ· ·/ also 又作 **prayer rug** *n* [C] a small mat which Muslims kneel on when praying〔穆斯林祈禱時用的〕跪墊, 跪毯

prayer wheel /ˈ· ·/ *n* [C] a piece of wood or metal that is shaped like a drum and turns around on a pole, on which prayers are written, used in Tibet〔西藏用的上面刻有祈禱文的〕轉經筒, 祈禱輪

pray·ing man·tis /ˌ·· ˈ··/ *n* [C] a large insect that eats other insects 螳螂

pre- /pri; priː/ *prefix* **1** before someone or something 在…之前: *prewar* (=before a war) 戰前的 **2** in preparation 預先: *a prearranged signal* 預定的信號 | *Preset the video.* 預先設置好錄影機。—compare 比較 ANTE-

preach /pritʃ; priːtʃ/ *v* **1** [I,T] to give a talk in public about a religious subject, especially about the correct moral way for people to behave 佈道, 講道: [+to/on/about] *Christ began preaching to large crowds.* 基督開始向大批羣眾佈道。| **preach sth** *The pastor preached a sermon on brotherly love.* 牧師在佈道會上宣講兄弟之愛。**2** [T] to talk about how good or important something is and try to persuade other people about this 宣揚, 鼓吹: **preach the virtues of** *Imran's always preaching the virtues of a healthy outdoor life.* 艾姆蘭一直在宣揚健康戶外生活的好處。**3** [I] to give someone advice in a way that they think is boring or annoying 嘮叨地勸誡: *I'm sorry, I didn't mean to preach.* 對不起, 我無意說教。**4 preach to the converted** to talk about what you think is right or important to people who already have the same opinions as you 對已持有相同觀念的人作宣傳 —see also 另見 **practise what you preach** (PRACTISE (5))

preach·er /ˈpritʃɚ; ˈpriːtʃə/ *n* [C] someone who gives talks at religious meetings but who is not actually a priest〔實際上本身並不是牧師的〕說教者, 講道者

preach·y /ˈpritʃɪ; ˈpriːtʃi/ *adj informal* trying too much to persuade people to accept a particular opinion【非正式】愛說教的

pre·am·ble /ˈpriæmbl; priˈæmbəl/ *n* [C] *formal* a statement at the beginning of a book, document, or talk, explaining what it is about【正式】〔書、文件、講話的〕前言; 序言; 開場白: **without preamble** (=immediately and without any explanation) 開門見山地 *"Murder," he said, without preamble. "No doubt about it."* "謀殺," 他開門見山地說, "毫無疑問是謀殺。"

pre·arranged /ˌpriəˈrendʒd; ˌpriːəˈreɪndʒd◂/ *adj* planned in advance 預先安排的, 預定的: *At a prearranged signal, everyone stood up.* 一見到預定的信號, 大家都站了起來。 —**prearrangement** *n* [U]

pre·car·i·ous /prɪˋkɛrɪəs; prɪˈkeəriəs/ *adj* **1** a precarious situation or state is likely to become very dangerous〔局勢、情況〕不穩定的, 不安全的; 危險的: *The refugees live a precarious existence in shanty towns.* 難民在城市貧民窟過着不安定的生活。| *a precarious peace* 不穩固的和平 **2** someone or something precarious is likely to fall 可能倒的, 不穩的, 不牢靠的 —**precariously** *adv*: *a cup of tea balanced precariously on her knee* 她膝蓋上放置不穩的一杯茶 —**precariousness** *n* [U]

pre·cast /priˈkæst; ˌpriːˈkɑːst◂/ *adj* precast CONCRETE is already formed into blocks ready for use to make buildings〔混凝土〕預澆的, 預製的

pre·cau·tion /prɪˋkɔʃən; prɪˈkɔːʃən/ *n* [C usually plural 一般用複數] something you do in order to prevent something dangerous or unpleasant from happening 預防措施: *Fire precautions were neglected.* 防火措施被忽視了。| *elaborate precautions to avoid detection* 為避免被發現而採取的精心預防措施 | **[+against]** *You should save your work often as a precaution against computer failure.* 你要經常保存所做的工作以防電腦發生故障。| **take the precaution of doing sth** *I took the precaution of insuring my camera.* 我把我的照相機投了保以防萬一。

pre·cau·tion·a·ry /prɪˋkɔʃənˌɛrɪ; prɪˈkɔːʃənəri/ *adj* **precautionary measures/steps etc** things that you do in order to prevent something dangerous or unpleasant from happening 預防措施: *The ward will be closed for a week as a precautionary measure.* 作為預防措施, 該病房將關閉一星期。

3 **pre·cede** /prɪˋsid; prɪˈsiːd/ *v* [T] *formal*【正式】**1** to happen or exist before something or someone or to come before something else in a series 先於...(發生、存在); 位於...之前: *The numbers on the license plate are preceded by a letter.* 汽車車牌的號碼前面有一個英文字母。| *He was a much stronger leader than the man who preceded him.* (=was leader before him) 比起他的前任, 他是個強得多的領導人。**2** to go somewhere before someone else 在...之前去[到]: *John preceded his guests into the lounge.* 約翰進入大廳, 隨後客人也到了。**3** to say or write something as an introduction to a speech, book etc 在...前先說; 給...加上引言: *The author preceded his speech with a few words of welcome.* 這位作者在演講之前先說了幾句表示歡迎的話作為開場白。

pre·ce·dence /ˋprɛsədəns; ˈpresɪ̈dəns/ *n* [U] **1 take/have precedence over** to be considered more important than someone or something else and therefore come or be done before them 優先於, 〔重要性〕高於: *Saving the child's life took precedence over everything else.* 救這個孩子的命比其他任何事情都重要。**2** the relative importance of different things or people and the need to deal with the most important first, then the second most important, and so on 優先權; 地位先後, 級別高低: **in order of precedence** *Arrange the tasks in order of precedence.* 按輕重緩急安排這些任務。

pre·ce·dent /ˋprɛsədənt; ˈpresɪ̈dənt/ *n* **1** [C] an action or official decision which can be used to give legal support to later actions or decisions〔可援引的〕先例; 判例: **set/create a precedent** *The invasion of Panama set a dangerous precedent.* 對巴拿馬的入侵開了一個危險的先例。**2** [C,U] something of the same type that has happened or existed before 先例, 前例: **[+for]** *Is there any precedent for this?* 這事有先例嗎? | **without precedent** (=never happening before) 無先例的 *An epidemic on this scale is without precedent.* 如此規模的流行病以前從未發生過。**3** [U] the way that things have always been done 慣例: **break with precedent** (=to do something in a new way) 打破慣例

pre·ced·ing /prɪˋsidɪŋ; prɪˈsiːdɪŋ/ *adj* [only before noun 僅用於名詞前] *formal* happening or coming before the time, place, or part mentioned【正式】在前的, 在先的; 前面的: *We made more money this month than in the whole of the preceding quarter.* 我們本月賺的錢比前一整個季度還多。—opposite 反義詞 FOLLOWING

pre·cept /ˋprisɛpt; ˈpriːsept/ *n* [C] *formal* a rule on which a way of thinking or behaving is based【正式】戒律, 格言, 準則: *basic moral precepts* 基本的道德準則

pre·cinct /ˋprisɪŋkt; ˈpriːsɪŋkt/ *n* **1** [C] *AmE* an area within a town or city that has its own police force, local government representatives etc【美】〔城鎮中擁有自己的警隊、地方政府代表等的〕分區: *the 44th Precinct* 第44分區 **2** [C] *AmE* the main police station in a particular area of a town or city【美】〔城鎮分區的〕警察分局: *Book him and take him down to the precinct.* 將他記錄在案並把他帶到警察分局。**3** [C] **shopping/pedestrian precinct** *BrE* an area of a town where people can walk and cars are not allowed【英】商業/行人專用區 **4 precincts** [plural] the area that surrounds an important building〔某主要建築物的〕周圍地區: *the precincts of the cathedral* 大教堂周圍地區

pre·ci·os·i·ty /ˌprɛʃɪˋɑsətɪ; ˌpreʃiˈɒsɪ̈ti/ *n* [U] *literary* the attitude of being too concerned about style or detail in your writing or speech, so that it sounds unnatural【文】〔寫作或講話的〕矯揉造作; 故作風雅

pre·cious¹ /ˋprɛʃəs; ˈpreʃəs/ *adj* **1** precious memories or possessions are important to you because they are connected with people you like or events in your life〔記憶或財物〕珍貴的; 寶貴的: *The doll is very precious to me because it was my mother's.* 這個玩具娃娃對我來說很珍貴, 因為它是我媽媽的。**2** something that is precious is valuable and important and should not be wasted or used without care 寶貴的: *Don't waste precious time talking to him, he's not worth it.* 別浪費寶貴的時間跟他交談, 他不值得。**3** rare and worth a lot of money 貴重的; 珍貴的: *a precious jewel* 貴重的首飾 **4** [only before noun 僅用於名詞前] *spoken* used to show that you are annoyed that someone seems to care too much about something【口】"寶貴"的, 寶貝似的〔用於對某人似乎太過注重某事表示討厭〕: *Your precious career is becoming more important than your family.* 你"寶貴"的事業正變得比家庭還重要。**5** someone who is precious is formal and unnatural because they are trying too hard to be perfect〔某人〕矯揉造作的, 過分講究的 —**preciously** *adv* —**preciousness** *n* [U]

precious² *adv informal*【非正式】**precious little/few** very little or very few 非常少: *He has precious little experience of computing.* 他沒有多少電腦方面的經驗。

precious met·al /ˌ.. ˈ../ *n* [C,U] a rare and valuable metal such as gold or silver 貴金屬〈如指金、銀等〉

precious stone /ˌ.. ˈ./ *n* [C] a rare and valuable jewel such as a DIAMOND or an EMERALD¹ 寶石 —compare 比較 SEMIPRECIOUS

pre·ci·pice /ˋprɛsəpɪs; ˈpresɪ̈pɪ̈s/ *n* [C] a very steep side of a high rock, mountain or cliff 懸崖, 峭壁: *towards the edge of the precipice* 向懸崖邊緣

pre·cip·i·tate¹ /prɪˋsɪpəˌtet; prɪ̈ˈsɪpɪ̈teɪt/ *v* **1** [T] *formal* to make something serious happen more quickly than was expected; HASTEN【正式】促成, 加速: *The economic crisis was precipitated by the US's inability to deal with the budget deficit.* 美國無力應付預算赤字, 這加速了經濟危機。**2** [T] to force someone or something into a particular state or condition 使陷入〔某種狀態〕: *The rise in the value of oil precipitated a world economic crisis.* 油價的上升引發了世界經濟危機。**3 precipitate sb somewhere** *formal* to make someone fall forwards or downwards with great force【正式】把某人猛摔[猛拋]到某處 **4** [I,T+out] *technical* to separate a solid substance from a liquid by chemical action, or to be separated in this way【術語】(使) 沉澱, (使) 澱析

pre·cip·i·tate² /prɪˋsɪpətɪt; prɪ̈ˈsɪpɪ̈tɪ̈t/ *n* [C,U] *technical* a solid substance that has been chemically separated from a liquid【術語】沉澱物

precipitate[3] *adj formal* done too quickly, especially without thinking carefully enough【正式】倉促的; 貿然的, 輕率的 —**precipitately** *adv*

pre·cip·i·ta·tion /prɪˌsɪpə`teʃən; prɪ̈ˌsɪpɪ̈ˈteɪʃən/ *n* **1** [C, U] *technical* rain, snow etc that falls on the ground, or the amount of rain, snow etc that falls【術語】〔雨、雪等的〕降落; 降水量 **2** [C,U] *technical* a chemical process in which a solid substance is separated from a liquid【術語】沉澱 **3** [U] *formal* the act of doing something too quickly in a way that is not sensible【正式】倉促, 魯莽, 輕率

pre·cip·i·tous /prɪ`sɪpətəs; prɪ̈ˈsɪpɪ̈təs/ *adj* **1** dangerously high or steep 險峻的, 陡峭的: *A precipitous path led down the cliff.* 一條陡峭的小路沿懸崖而下。**2** PRECIPITATE[3] —**precipitously** *adv* —**precipitousness** *n* [U]

pré·cis /pre`si; ˈpreɪsiː/ *n plural* **précis** /`presiz; ˈpreɪsiːz/ [C] a statement which gives the main ideas of a piece of writing, speech etc〔文章或演說等的〕摘要; 梗概; 概要: *a concise and accurate précis* 簡明而精確的概要 —**précis** *v* [T]

3 **pre·cise** /prɪ`saɪs; prɪˈsaɪs/ *adj* **1** precise details, costs, measurements etc are exact 精確的, 準確的: *The precise details of the sale have not yet been released.* 這次銷售的精確細節還沒有發佈。**2** [only before noun 僅用於名詞前] used to emphasize that something happens exactly in a particular way or that you are describing something correctly and exactly 恰好的, 正是的: *Just at that precise moment her husband walked in.* 恰恰就在那個時候, 她的丈夫走了進來。| *The precise nature of the job will be made clear when you start.* 這項工作的確切性質將在你開始進行時明確地告知你。**3 to be precise** used to show that you are giving more exact details relating to something you have just said 精確地說, 確切地說: *My parents live abroad – in North Borneo to be precise.* 我父母生活在國外, 確切地說, 生活在北婆羅洲。**4** someone who is precise is very careful about small details or about the way they behave〔人〕周密的, 細心的, 一絲不苟的 —**preciseness** *n* [U]

2 3 **pre·cise·ly** /prɪ`saɪslɪ; prɪˈsaɪsli/ *adv* **1** exactly 精確地, 確切地, 準確地: **precisely what/how/where etc** *I won't know precisely what the job involves until I actually start.* 直到我真正開始做時, 我才會確切地知道這項工作所涉及的內容。| *Be there at precisely 4 o'clock.* 4點正到那裡。**2** used to emphasize that a particular thing is completely true or correct 恰好, 正是〔表示強調〕: *I didn't go precisely because I thought he might be there.* 我沒有去正是因為我認為他可能在那兒。| *She's precisely the kind of person we're looking for.* 她正是我們要找的那種人。**3** *spoken* used to say that you agree completely with someone【口】對, 確實如此〔表示同意〕: *"Roberts should resign." "Precisely."* "羅伯茨應該辭職。" "的確如此。"

pre·ci·sion[1] /prɪ`sɪʒən; prɪˈsɪʒən/ *n* [U] the quality of being very exact 精確(性), 準確(性)

precision[2] *adj* [only before noun 僅用於名詞前] **1** made or done in a very exact way 精確的, 精密的: *precision grinding* 精磨 **2 precision tool/ instrument** a precision tool or instrument is used for making or measuring something in a very exact way 精密工具/儀器

pre·clude /prɪ`klud; prɪˈkluːd/ *v* [T] *formal* to prevent something or make something impossible【正式】阻止, 防止, 使不可能; 排除, 消除: **preclude sb from doing something** *Age alone will not preclude him from standing as a candidate.* 單是年齡不會妨礙他作為候選人參加競選。—**preclusion** /-`kluʒən; -ˈkluːʒən/ *n* [U]

pre·co·cious /prɪ`koʃəs; prɪˈkəʊʃəs/ *adj often spoken* a precocious child behaves more like an adult than a child, for example by asking difficult and intelligent questions【常口】早熟的, 智慧超前的: *At school he revealed precocious talents as a painter and writer.* 在學校他表現出作為畫家和作家的超前才能。—**precociously** *adv* —**precociousness** also 又作 **precocity** /prɪ`kɑsətɪ; prɪˈkɒsɪ̈ti/ *n* [U]

pre·cog·ni·tion /ˌprikɑg`nɪʃən; ˌpriːkɒgˈnɪʃən/ *n* [U] *formal* the knowledge that something will happen before it does【正式】預知, 預感

pre·con·ceived /ˌprikən`sivd; ˌpriːkənˈsiːvd◂/ *adj* [only before noun 僅用於名詞前] preconceived ideas, opinions etc are formed before you really have enough knowledge or experience〔思想、觀點等〕預先形成的, 先入為主的: *preconceived notions about art* 對於藝術的先入之見

pre·con·cep·tion /ˌprikən`sɛpʃən; ˌpriːkənˈsepʃən/ *n* [C] a belief or opinion you have already formed before you know the actual facts 事先形成的看法[想法]; 先入之見, 成見: *widely held but largely unexamined preconceptions about girls' attitudes towards science* 人們普遍持有但大多未經驗證的關於女孩對科學的態度的成見

pre·con·di·tion /ˌprikən`dɪʃən; ˌpriːkənˈdɪʃən/ *n* [C] something that must happen or exist before something else can happen 前提, 先決條件: **[+of/for]** *A ceasefire is a precondition for talks.* 停火是對話的先決條件。

pre·cooked /ˌpri`kukt; ˌpriːˈkʊkt◂/ *adj* precooked food has been partly or completely cooked in advance so that it can be quickly heated up later〔食物〕預先煮過[熟]的 —**precook** *v* [T]

pre·cur·sor /prɪ`kɝsɚ; prɪˈkɜːsə/ *n* [C] *formal* something that happened or existed before something else and influenced its development【正式】〔事物的〕前身, 初期形式: **[+of/to]** *a precursor of modern jazz* 現代爵士樂的早期形式

pre·date /pri`det; priːˈdeɪt/ *v* [T] to happen or exist earlier in history than something else 在歷史上早於: *The kingdom predates previously known African cultures by over 3,000 years.* 該王國比先前所知道的非洲文化早三千多年。

pred·a·tor /`prɛdətɚ; ˈpredətə/ *n* [C] **1** an animal that kills and eats other animals 食肉動物, 捕食其他動物的動物 **2** someone who tries to use another person's weakness to get advantages 利用別人的弱點謀取利益的人, 損人利己的人

pred·a·to·ry /`prɛdəˌtorɪ; ˈpredətəri/ *adj* **1** a predatory animal kills and eats other animals for food 以捕食其他動物為生的, 食肉的 **2** trying to use someone's weakness to get advantages for yourself 利用別人的弱點謀取利益的, 損人利己的: *predatory share-buying by large foreign companies* 大型外國公司損人利己的股票收購

pre·de·ces·sor /ˌprɛdɪ`sɛsɚ; ˈpriːdɪ̈sesə/ *n* [C] **1** someone who had your job before you started doing it 前任, 前輩: *The President inherited his economic problems from his predecessor.* 該總統的前任遺留給他很多經濟問題。**2** a machine, system etc that existed before another one in a process of development〔被取代的〕原有事物, 前身: *The Julian calendar was more accurate than its predecessor.* 儒略曆〔公曆〕比其前身較為精確。— opposite 反義詞 SUCCESSOR

pre·des·ti·na·tion /prɪˌdɛstə`neʃən; prɪˌdestɪ̈ˈneɪʃən/ *n* [U] the belief that God has decided everything that will happen and that people cannot change this 宿命論〔認為上帝決定萬事萬物, 人無力改變〕

pre·des·tined /prɪ`dɛstɪnd; prɪˈdestɪ̈nd/ *adj* something that is predestined is certain to happen because it has been decided by God or FATE (命中) 注定的: **predestined to do sth** *All our plans seemed predestined to fail.* 我們所有的計劃好像都注定要失敗。

pre·de·ter·mined /ˌpridɪ`tɝmɪnd; ˌpriːdɪˈtɜːmɪ̈nd/ *adj formal* if something is predetermined, it has been formed or arranged before it happens, and does not happen by chance【正式】預先決定[確定]的: *The colour of your eyes is predetermined by those of your parents.* 你眼睛的顏色是由父母眼睛的顏色決定的。| *a predetermined location* 預先確定的地點 —**predetermination** /ˌpridɪˌtɝmə`neʃən; ˌpriːdɪtɜːmɪ̈ˈneɪʃən/ *n* [U]

pre·de·ter·min·er /ˌpridɪˋtɝmɪnɚ; ˌpriːdɪˈtɜːmɪ̈nə/ *n* [C] *technical* a word that is used before a DETERMINER (=a word such as 'the', 'that', 'his' etc). In the phrases 'all the boys' and 'both his parents', the words 'all' and 'both' are determiners【術語】前置限定詞〈如 the, that, his 等〉

pre·dic·a·ment /prɪˋdɪkəmənt; prɪˈdɪkəmənt/ *n* [C] a difficult or unpleasant situation in which you do not know what to do, or you have to make a difficult choice 困境, 窘況, 尷尬的處境: *There is no painless way out of America's current economic predicament.* 美國要擺脱當前的經濟困境可沒有輕而易舉的方法。

pred·i·cate¹ /ˋprɛdɪkɪt; ˈpredɪkɪ̈t/ *n* [C] the part of a sentence that makes a statement about the subject, such as 'swim' in 'Fishes swim' and 'is an artist' in 'She is an artist'〔語法中的〕謂語 —compare 比較 SUBJECT¹ (5)

pred·i·cate² /ˋprɛdɪˌket; ˈpredɪkeɪt/ *v* [T] *formal*【正式】**be predicated on** to be based on something as the reason for doing something else 基於, 取決於: *The company's decision to take on more staff was predicated on the belief that the recession was over.* 該公司雇用更多員工的決定是基於經濟衰退已經結束的看法。

pre·dic·a·tive /ˋprɛdɪˌketɪv; prɪˈdɪkətɪv/ *adj* a predicative adjective or phrase comes after a verb, for example 'happy' in the sentence 'She is happy.' 謂語性的, 表語的 —**predicatively** *adv*

3 3 **pre·dict** /prɪˋdɪkt; prɪˈdɪkt/ *v* [T] to say that something will happen or that something will happen in a particular way 預言, 預料; 預測: *Economists are predicting a fall in interest rates.* 經濟學家預言利率將會下降。| **predict (that)** *The report predicted that more jobs would be lost in the coal industry.* 這項報告預言煤炭業將失去更多的工作職位。| **predict whether/what/how etc** *It is difficult to predict what the long-term effects of the accident will be.* 很難預料這次事故會有甚麼長期的後果。

pre·dic·ta·ble /prɪˋdɪktəbḷ; prɪˈdɪktəbəl/ *adj* **1** if the result of something is predictable, you know what it will be before it happens 可預言[預料]的: *The outcome of these experiments is not always entirely predictable.* 這些實驗的結果並非經常完全可以預料的。**2** behaving or happening in the way that you expect, especially when this seems boring or annoying 不出所料的; 墨守成規的; 按老一套辦事的: *I used to be interested in politics, but now it's all getting very predictable.* 我過去對政治感興趣, 但現在它整個變得完全是老一套了。| *You're just so predictable!* 你太墨守成規了! —**predictably** *adv* [sentence adverb 句子副詞]: *Predictably it was the demonstrators who were blamed for the violence.* 不出所料, 暴力行為的責任推到了示威者身上。—**predictability** /prɪˌdɪktəˋbɪlətɪ; prɪˌdɪktəˈbɪlɪ̈ti/ *n* [U]

pre·dic·tion /prɪˋdɪkʃən; prɪˈdɪkʃən/ *n* [C,U] something that you say is going to happen, or the act of saying what you think is going to happen 預言的事物; 預言, 預告: **[+of]** *Earlier predictions of a Republican victory began to look increasingly unlikely.* 對於共和黨獲勝的早期預測開始顯得越來越不可能了。| **make a prediction** *I'd find it very hard to make a prediction.* 我發現這非常難以預料。—**predictive** /-tɪv; -tɪv/ *adj*

pre·di·gested /ˌpridəˋdʒɛstɪd; ˌpriːdaɪˈdʒestɪ̈d/ *adj* predigested new information etc has been put in a simple form and explained so that it is easy to understand 簡化的

pre·di·lec·tion /ˌprɛdḷˋɛkʃən; ˌpriːdɪˈlekʃən/ *n* [C] *formal* if you have a predilection for something, especially something rather unusual, you like it very much【正式】偏愛, 偏好

pre·dis·pose /ˌpridɪsˋpoz; ˌpriːdɪsˈpəʊz/ *v* [T] to make someone more likely to behave or think in a particular way or suffer from a health problem 使預先傾向於; 使易於感染

pre·dis·posed /ˌpridɪsˋpozd; ˌpriːdɪsˈpəʊzd/ *adj* **predisposed to/towards** tending to behave in a particular way, or to have a particular health problem 對…預先有傾向的; 易感染…的: *Men are more likely to be predisposed towards violence than women.* 男人比女人較有實施暴力的傾向。

pre·dis·po·si·tion /ˌpridɪspəˋzɪʃən; ˌpriːdɪspəˈzɪʃən/ *n* [C] a tendency to behave in a particular way or suffer from a particular illness〔以某種方式行事的〕傾向; 易患某疾病的傾向: **[+to/towards]** *a predisposition towards seasickness* 容易暈船

pre·dom·i·nance /prɪˋdɑmənəns; prɪˈdɒmɪ̈nəns/ *n* **1** [singular] if there is a predominance of one type of person or thing in a group, there are more of that type than of any other type〔數量的〕優勢: **[+of]** *the predominance of white people in the audience* 觀眾中佔絕大多數的是白人 **2** [U] someone or something that has predominance has the most power or importance in a particular group or area 主導地位, 支配地位: *The company has finally achieved predominance in Asia.* 該公司最終獲得了在亞洲的主導地位。

pre·dom·i·nant /prɪˋdɑmənənt; prɪˈdɒmɪ̈nənt/ *adj* more powerful, more common, or more easily noticed than others 佔優勢的; 佔主導地位的; 最普遍[顯著]的, 突出的: *the predominant group in society* 社會中的主導羣體

pre·dom·i·nant·ly /prɪˋdɑmənəntlɪ; prɪˈdɒmɪ̈nəntli/ *adv* mostly or mainly 絕大多數, 主要地: *The city's population is predominantly Irish.* 該城市的人口絕大多數是愛爾蘭人。

pre·dom·i·nate /prɪˋdɑməˌnet; prɪˈdɒmɪ̈neɪt/ *v* [I] **1** to have the most importance or influence, or to be most easily noticed 佔主導地位, 佔支配地位: *The views of the leftwing have tended to predominate within the party.* 左翼的觀點趨向於在該黨內部佔支配地位。**2** if one type of person or thing predominates in a group or area, there are more of this type than any other〔數量上〕佔優勢, 佔絕大多數: *Pine trees predominate on the west coast.* 西海岸以松樹居多。

pree·mie /ˋprimɪ; ˈpriːmi/ *n* [C] *AmE informal* a PREMATURE (2) baby【美, 非正式】早產兒

pre·em·i·nent /prɪˋɛmənənt; priˈemɪ̈nənt/ *adj* much more important, more powerful, or much better than any others of its kind 卓越的, 傑出的, 超羣的: *Hollywood's pre-eminent role in the film industry* 荷里活在電影業中超羣的角色 —**pre-eminently** *adv* —**pre-eminence** *n* [U]

pre·empt /prɪˋɛmpt; priˈempt/ *v* [T] to make what someone has planned to do or say unnecessary or ineffective by saying or doing something first 搶在…之前行動; 先發制人: *I didn't want to pre-empt what you were about to say.* 我不想搶先説出你要説的話。—**pre-emption** /-ˋɛmpʃən; -ˈempʃən/ *n* [U]

pre·emp·tive /prɪˋɛmptɪv; priˈemptɪv/ *adj* a pre-emptive action is done to harm someone else before they can harm you, or to prevent something bad from happening〔行動〕搶先的, 先發制人的: **pre-emptive strike/attack** *a series of pre-emptive strikes on guerilla bases* 對游擊隊根據地一系列先發制人的打擊 —**pre-emptively** *adv*

preen /prin; priːn/ *v* **1** [I,T] if a bird preens or preens itself, it cleans itself and makes its feathers smooth using its beak〔鳥〕用喙整理〔羽毛〕**2** [I] to look proud because of something you have done 為…感到驕傲 **3** **preen yourself a)** to spend a lot of time in front of a mirror making yourself look tidier and more attractive 精心打扮 **b)** to be very pleased with yourself 得意洋洋, 沾沾自喜

pre·ex·ist /ˌpriɪgˋzɪst; ˌpriːɪgˈzɪst/ *v* [I,T] *formal* to exist before something else【正式】先存在; 先於…存在: *Inform your doctor of any pre-existing medical condition, eg, diabetes.* 要告知醫生原先就有的任何內科疾病, 如糖尿病。—**pre-existing** *adj*

pre·fab /ˋpriˋfæb; ˈpriːfæb/ *n* [C] *informal* a small prefabricated building【非正式】預製裝配式小房屋

pre·fab·ri·cate /priˋfæbrəˌket; priːˈfæbrɪkeɪt/ *v* [T] to make the parts of a building, ship etc in a factory in

P

standard sizes, so that they can be fitted together somewhere else 預製〔房屋、船等的構件〕—**prefabricated** *adj: a prefabricated building* 預製裝配式房屋 —**prefabrication** /priˌfæbrəˋkeʃən; priːˌfæbrɪˈkeɪʃən/ *n* [U]

pref·ace¹ /ˋprɛfɪs; ˈprefɪ̥s/ *n* [C] an introduction at the beginning of a book or speech〔書籍的〕序言, 前言, 緒言;〔演講的〕開場白

preface² *v* [T] *formal* to say or do something before the main part of what you are going to say【正式】作為…的開端, 作為…的開場白: *I'd like to preface my remarks by saying a little about myself.* 我先簡單介紹一下我自己, 作為我講話的開場白。

P

pref·a·to·ry /ˋprɛfəˌtorɪ; ˈprefətəri/ *adj formal* forming a preface or introduction【正式】序言的, 引言的; 作為開場白的: *a few prefatory remarks* 幾句開場白

pre·fect /ˋprifɛkt; ˈpriːfekt/ *n* [C] **1** an older student in some British schools, who has special duties and helps to control younger students〔英國某些學校中幫助管理年幼學生的〕級長 **2** a public official in France, Italy etc who is responsible for a particular area〔法國、意大利等負責某個地區的〕地方行政長官, 省長

pre·fec·ture /ˋprifɛktʃɚ; ˈpriːfektʃʊə/ *n* [C] a large area which has its own local government in France, Italy, Japan etc〔法國、意大利等的〕省;〔日本的〕縣: *Saitama prefecture*〔日本〕崎玉縣

2 2 **pre·fer** /prɪˋfɝ; prɪˈfɜː/ *v* **preferred, preferring** [T not in progressive 不用進行式] **1** to like someone or something more than someone or something else 更喜歡: *"What kind of music do you like?" "These days I prefer classical music."* "你喜歡甚麼樣的音樂?" "這些日子我更喜歡古典音樂。" | **prefer sb/sth to sb/sth** *I much prefer dogs to cats.* 貓和狗兩者之中我更喜歡狗。| **prefer to do sth** *Many people living in cities would actually prefer to live in the country.* 很多生活在城市的人實際上寧願生活在鄉下。| **prefer doing sth** *Chantal prefers travelling by train.* 錢特爾較喜歡乘火車旅行。**2 would prefer** if you would prefer to do something, you want to do it more than another thing you could do instead, or that you are doing now 更願意, 更希望, 寧願: **would prefer to do sth** *We would prefer to live in the US, but I can't get a visa.* 我們更願意生活在美國, 但我得不到簽證。**3 I would prefer it if** *spoken*【口】**a)** used to say that you wish a situation was different 我更願意[希望]: *Of course, I'd prefer it if I didn't have to do so much work.* 當然我更希望我不必做那麼多工作。**b)** used when telling someone politely not to do something〔用於禮貌地告訴別人不要做某事〕我希望: *I'd prefer it if you didn't smoke in front of the children.* 我希望你不要在孩子面前抽煙。**4 prefer charges** *law* to make an official statement that someone has done something illegal【法律】起訴, 提出控告

pref·e·ra·ble /ˋprɛfrəbḷ; ˈprefərəbəl/ *adj* better or more suitable 更好的, 更合適的, 更可取的: **preferable to (doing) sth** *I think France would be preferable to Majorca in August.* 我認為八月份的法國比馬約卡島更好。| **infinitely preferable** (=much better or much more suitable) 好得多, 可取得多, 適合得多 *Leah finds novels infinitely preferable to poetry.* 利厄覺得小說比詩歌好得多。—**preferably** *adv*: *Can you tidy your room please – preferably today?* 你能整理一下你的房間嗎? 最好是今天。

3 **pref·e·rence** /ˋprɛfərəns; ˈprefərəns/ *n* **1** [C,U] if you have a preference for something, you like it more than another thing〔兩者之中〕較喜歡的東西; 偏愛, 偏好: **have a preference** *We could eat Chinese, Italian, or Indian – do you have any preference?* 我們可以吃中餐、意大利餐或印度餐——你有甚麼偏愛的嗎? | **have a preference for** *I must admit I have a preference for younger men.* 我必須承認我更喜歡年輕一些的男人。| **have no strong/particular preference** (=not prefer one thing more than anything else) 沒有特別的偏好 | **express a preference** (=say that you like one person or thing more than others) 表示對…的偏愛 *I asked her where she wanted to go on vacation, but she didn't express any preference.* 我問她假期想去哪裡, 但她沒有表示較喜歡去哪裡。**2** [C] the thing that you like best in a group of things〔一組東西中〕最喜歡的東西, 偏愛的事物: *Taste both drinks and make a note of your preference.* 嚐一下兩種酒並記下你最喜歡哪種。**3 give/show preference to** to treat someone more favourably than you treat other people 偏愛…; 給予…優先權; 流露出對…的偏愛: *In allocating housing, preference is given to those who have young children.* 在分配房屋時, 有小孩的人有優先權。**4 in preference to** if you choose one thing in preference to another, you choose it instead because you think it is better 優先於…: *Many people choose the train in preference to driving.* 很多人寧願乘火車而不願自己駕車。

pref·e·ren·tial /ˌprɛfəˋrɛnʃəl; ˌprefəˈrenʃəl◂/ *adj* [only before noun 僅用於名詞前] preferential treatment, rates etc are deliberately different in order to give an advantage to particular people 優先的; 優待的; 優惠的: *preferential credit terms* 優惠的貸款條件 —**preferentially** *adv*

pre·fer·ment /prɪˋfɝmənt; prɪˈfɜːmənt/ *n* [U] *formal* appointment to a more important job【正式】提升, 晉升

pre·fig·ure /priˋfɪgjɚ; ˌpriːˈfɪgə/ *v* [T] *formal* to be a sign that shows that something will happen later【正式】預示; 成為…的預兆 —**prefiguration** /ˌprifɪgjəˋreʃən; ˌpriːfɪgəˈreɪʃən/ *n* [C,U]

pre·fix¹ /ˋpriˌfɪks; ˈpriːfɪks/ *n* [C] **1** a group of letters that is added to the beginning of a word to change its meaning and make a new word, such as 'un' in 'untie' or 'mis' in 'misunderstand' 前綴 —compare 比較 AFFIX, SUFFIX **2** a title such as 'Ms' or 'Dr' used before someone's name〔人名前的〕稱謂〈如 Ms, Dr〉

prefix² *v* [T] **1** to add a prefix to a word, name or set of numbers 在…前加前綴 **2** *formal* to say something before the main part of what you have to say【正式】加…作為前言[開場白]

preg·nan·cy /ˋprɛgnənsɪ; ˈpregnənsi/ *n* [C,U] the condition of being pregnant or the period of time when a woman is pregnant 懷孕(期), 妊娠(期): *This drug should not be taken during pregnancy.* 這種藥不應在妊娠期間服用。| *her third pregnancy* 她的第三次懷孕 | *teenage pregnancies* 少女懷孕

preg·nant /ˋprɛgnənt; ˈpregnənt/ *adj* **1** having an unborn baby growing inside your body 懷孕的, 妊娠的: *On the same day I started the job I found out I was pregnant.* 我開始工作的那一天, 發現自己已經懷孕了。| **twenty weeks/three months etc pregnant** *She went skiing when she was 7 months pregnant!* 她懷孕7個月時還去滑雪! | **get pregnant** *It came as a shock – I thought I was too old to get pregnant.* 這是個令人震驚的消息——我以為自己老得不能懷孕了。| **get sb pregnant** (=make a woman pregnant by having sex with her) 使某人懷孕 *I didn't mean to get her pregnant.* 我沒打算使她懷孕。| **fall pregnant** *old-fashioned* (=become pregnant)【過時】懷孕 | **heavily pregnant** (=having a baby inside your body that is almost ready to be born) 懷孕後期的, 快臨產的 **2 a pregnant pause/silence** a pause or silence which is full of meaning or emotion, even though no one says anything 耐人尋味[意味深長]的停頓/沉默: *Dave's outburst was followed by a pregnant pause.* 戴夫的衝動之後是一段耐人尋味的停頓。**3 pregnant with** *formal* containing a lot of a quality or feeling【正式】包含, 孕育着: *Every phrase in this poem is pregnant with meaning.* 這首詩的每一組詞語都富含着意義。 3

pre·heat /priˋhit; ˌpriːˈhiːt/ *v* [T] to heat an OVEN to a particular temperature before it is used to cook something 預熱〔爐灶等到一定的溫度以便進行烹調〕: *Preheat the oven to 375°.* 把烤箱預熱到375°。

pre·hen·sile /prɪˋhɛnsḷ; prɪˈhensaɪl/ *adj technical* a prehensile tail, foot etc can curl round things and hold on to them【術語】〔尾巴、腳等〕能捲纏和抓牢〔某物〕的

pre·his·tor·ic /ˌprihɪsˋtɔrɪk; ˌpriːhɪˈstɒrɪk◂/ *adj* **1** connected with the time in history before anything was written down 史前的, 有歷史記載以前的: *prehistoric burial grounds* 史前墓地 | *prehistoric animals* 史前動物 **2** *often humorous* very old-fashioned【常幽默】非常陳舊的, 老掉牙的: *Keith's ideas about educating girls are positively prehistoric.* 基思關於教育女孩的觀念實在太陳舊了。—**prehistorically** /-klɪ; -kli/ *adv*

pre·his·to·ry /priˋhɪstərɪ; priːˈhɪstəri/ *n* [U] the time in human history before anything was written down〔有歷史記載以前的〕史前時期

pre·judge /priˋdʒʌdʒ; ˌpriːˈdʒʌdʒ/ *v* [T] to form an opinion about someone or something before you know or have considered all the facts 對〔人或事〕預先判斷, 過早判斷: *Try not to prejudge the issue.* 不要過早對這個問題下判斷。—**prejudgment** *n* [C,U]

prej·u·dice[1] /ˋprɛdʒədɪs; ˈpredʒədəs/ *n* **1** [C,U] an unreasonable dislike and distrust of people who are different from you in some way, especially because of their race, sex, religion etc 偏見, 成見; 歧視: *Women still have to face a great deal of prejudice in the workplace.* 女性在工作場所仍然必須面對很多的偏見。| **[+against]** *Prejudice against black people is common in many parts of America.* 在美國很多地方仍普遍存在着對黑人的偏見。| **racial/sexual prejudice** (=prejudice against people who belong to a different race or sex) 種族/性別歧視 *victims of racial prejudice* 種族歧視的受害者 **2** [U] **to the prejudice of** *formal* having a harmful effect or influence on something else【正式】對…不利; 有損於: *Harry continued to smoke, to the prejudice of his health.* 哈里繼續抽煙, 這不利於他的健康。**3 without prejudice** *law* without harming or affecting something else【法律】〔對…〕沒有不利; 無損〔於〕

prejudice[2] *v* [T] **1** to influence someone so that they have an unfair or unreasonable opinion about someone or something 使有偏見, 使有成見; 使不公正地偏向: **prejudice sb against sth** *My own schooldays prejudiced me against all formal education.* 我自己的學生時代使我對所有的正規教育產生了偏見。| **prejudice sth/sb in sb's favour** *Johnson's pleasant manner prejudiced the jury in his favour.* 約翰遜令人愉快的舉止使陪審團對他產生了偏心。**2** to have a bad effect on your opportunities, chances etc of succeeding in doing something 損害, 不利於: *I don't want to do anything that would prejudice my chances of getting the job.* 我不想做任何不利於我得到這份工作的事情。

prej·u·diced /ˋprɛdʒədɪst; ˈpredʒədəst/ *adj* **1** having an unreasonable dislike of a particular group of people who are different from you in some way, especially because they belong to a different race, sex, or religion 有偏見的, 有成見, 歧視的: **[+against]** *He denied being prejudiced against black people.* 他否認對黑人存有偏見。**2** having an unreasonable dislike of something 反感的: **[+against]** *I don't know why they're all so prejudiced against the idea.* 我不知道他們為何全都對這個想法如此反感。

prej·u·di·cial /ˌprɛdʒəˋdɪʃəl; ˌpredʒəˈdɪʃəl◂/ *adj formal* having a bad effect on something【正式】不利的, 有損害的

prel·ate /ˋprɛlɪt; ˈprelət/ *n* [C] *technical* a BISHOP, CARDINAL, or other important priest in the Christian church【術語】高級教士〈如主教、紅衣主教〉

pre·lim·i·na·ry[1] /prɪˋlɪməˌnɛrɪ; prɪˈlɪmənəri/ *adj* [only before noun 僅用於名詞前] happening before something that is more important, often in order to prepare for it 初步的; 預備的: *the preliminary rounds of the competition* 比賽的預賽 | *a preliminary draft* 初稿 | **[+to]** *Speeches are preliminary to the real debate.* 演講是為真正的辯論作準備。

preliminary[2] *n* [C usually plural 一般用複數] **1** something that is done first, to introduce or prepare for something else 初步行動, 準備工作: *After the usual preliminaries, we made a start on the food.* 在通常的客套之後, 我們開始吃飯。**2 the preliminaries** the first part of a competition, when it is decided who will go on to the main competition 預賽, 預試

pre·lit·e·rate /priˋlɪtərɪt; priːˈlɪtərət/ *adj technical* a society that is preliterate has not developed a written language【術語】無文字的, 尚未使用文字的 —compare 比較 ILLITERATE

prel·ude /ˋprɛljud; ˈpreljuːd/ *n* [C] **1 be a prelude to** if an event is a prelude to a more important event, it happens just before it and makes people expect it 是…的序幕[前奏, 開端]: *The fighting in the streets may be a prelude to more serious trouble.* 街頭打鬥可能是更嚴重事端的序幕。**2** *technical* a short piece of music for piano or ORGAN【術語】〔鋼琴或風琴的〕短篇作品 **3** a short piece of music at the beginning of a large musical piece〔音樂作品的〕序曲: *Chopin's preludes* 蕭邦的序曲

pre·mar·i·tal /priˋmærətl; priːˈmærətəl/ *adj* happening or existing before marriage 婚前的: *premarital sex* 婚前性行為 —**premaritally** *adv*

pre·ma·ture /ˌpriməˋtjur; ˈpremətʃə/ *adj* **1** happening before the natural or proper time 過早的, 提早的: *His premature death at the age of 32 is a great loss.* 他32歲就早逝是一大損失。| *premature ageing of the skin* 皮膚的早衰 **2** PREGNANCY a premature baby is born before the usual time of birth〔嬰兒〕早產的: *a premature birth* 早產 | *The baby was six weeks premature.* 那嬰兒早產了六個星期。**3** done too early or too soon〔做事〕過早的, 過快的; 倉促的, 草率的; 不成熟的: *I think your criticism of the new law is a bit premature, as we don't yet know all the details.* 我認為你對這項新法律的批評未免太早了一點, 因為我們還不了解其全部細節。—**prematurely** *adv*: *The baby was born prematurely.* 這嬰兒早產了。

pre·med·i·tat·ed /prɪˋmɛdəˌtetɪd; priːˈmedəteɪtəd/ *adj* a premeditated crime or attack is planned in advance and done deliberately〔犯罪、襲擊〕預謀的, 預先策劃的: *The defense claim that the killing was not premeditated.* 被告方聲稱謀殺不是預先策劃好的。

pre·med·i·ta·tion /ˌprimɛdəˋteʃən; priːˌmedəˈteɪʃən/ *n* [U] the act of thinking about something and planning it before you actually do it 預先考慮; 預先策劃, 預謀: *cold-blooded premeditation* 冷酷的預謀

pre·men·stru·al /priˋmɛnstruəl; priːˈmenstruəl/ *adj technical* happening just before a woman's PERIOD (=the time each month when blood flows from her body)【術語】月經前的

premenstrual syndrome /·ˌ··· ˈ··/, **premenstrual tension** *BrE*【英】*n* [U] the tiredness, headache, bad temper etc experienced by many women in the days before their PERIOD[1] (4) 經前(期)綜合徵〔緊張症〕

prem·i·er[1] /ˋprimɪɚ; ˈpremiə/ *n* [C] a PRIME MINISTER 總理, 首相: *the Irish Premier* 愛爾蘭總理

premier[2] *adj formal* [only before noun 僅用於名詞前] best or most important【正式】最好的; 最重要的: *the Shelbourne, one of Dublin's premier hotels* 謝爾本, 都柏林最好的酒店之一

prem·i·ere, première /prɪˋmɪr; ˈpremieə/ *n* [C] the first public performance of a film or play〔電影的〕首映,〔戲劇的〕首演: **world premiere** (=the first performance in the world) 世界首演 *Spielberg's new movie gets its world premiere tonight.* 史匹堡的新電影今晚進行世界首映。—**premiere** *v* [I,T]: *Her film was premiered in New York.* 她的電影在紐約首次上映。

prem·i·ere·ship /prɪˋmɪəʃɪp; ˈpremiəʃɪp/ *n* [C,U] the period when someone is PRIME MINISTER 首相[總理]的任期

prem·ise /ˋprɛmɪs; ˈpreməs/ *n* [C] **1 premises** the buildings and land that a shop, restaurant, company etc uses〔商店、餐館、公司等使用的〕房屋及土地: *We hope to be moving to new premises shortly.* 我們希望很快搬到新址。| *business premises* 企業經營場所 | **off the premises** *The manager escorted him off the premises.* 那位經理把他送出門外。| **on the premises** *No food or drink is* 3

P

to be consumed on the premises. 場內禁止飲食。**2** also 又作 **premiss** *BrE* a statement or idea that you accept as true and use as a base for developing other ideas【英】前提: *American justice works on the premise that an accused person is innocent until they are proved guilty.* 美國司法運作的前提是被告在被證明有罪之前是清白的。

P

pre·mi·um /ˈprimɪəm; ˈpriːmiəm/ *n* **1** [C] the cost of insurance, especially the amount to pay each year〔尤指每年支付的〕保險費: *Insurance premiums are set to rise again.* 保險費很有可能再次上漲。| *the annual premium* 每年的保險費 **2** [U] *especially AmE* HIGH-OCTANE (=good quality petrol)【尤美】優質汽油 **3 premium quality** very high quality 優質: *premium quality British potatoes* 優質英國馬鈴薯 **4** [C] an additional amount of money, above a standard rate or amount 加付款; 額外費用; 津貼; 花紅; 獎金: *Farmers are being offered a premium for organically grown vegetables.* 人們出高價購買農民種植的有機蔬菜。| *premium payments for weekend work* 週末工作津貼 **5 at a premium a)** if something is at a premium, there is little of it available or it is difficult to get 奇缺, 難以取得: *Foldaway furniture is the answer where space is at a premium.* 對於空間很小的地方, 可摺疊家具是個好的解決辦法。**b)** if something is sold at a premium, it is sold at a higher price than usual 以高價, 以超出一般的價格 **6 put/place a premium on** to consider one quality as being much more important than others 高度重視: *The new management puts a premium on efficiency.* 新的管理人員十分注重效率。**7 premium prices** prices that are higher than usual, especially because there is not much of something available〔尤指因某物稀罕而超過一般價格的〕高價

premium bond /ˈ··· ˌ·/ *n* [C] a document that you buy from the government in Britain, giving you the chance to win a large prize each month〔英國〕政府發行的有獎債券

pre·mo·ni·tion /ˌpriməˋnɪʃən; ˌpreməˈnɪʃən/ *n* [C] a strange and unexplainable feeling that something, especially something unpleasant, is going to happen〔尤指不祥的〕預感, 預兆: **have a premonition** *When Anne didn't arrive, Paul had a premonition that she was in danger.* 當安妮沒有到達時, 保羅預感到她有危險。| **[+of]** *a premonition of death* 死亡的預感

pre·mon·i·to·ry /prɪˋmɑnəˌtorɪ; prɪˈmɒnɪ̀təri/ *adj formal* giving a warning that something unpleasant is going to happen【正式】給予警告的; 預兆的: *a disease with few premonitory symptoms* 幾乎沒有甚麼先兆的疾病

pre·na·tal /priˋnetl; ˌpriːˈneɪtl◂/ *adj* [only before noun 僅用於名詞前] concerning unborn babies and the care of PREGNANT women 產前的; 孕期的; ANTENATAL *BrE*【英】: *prenatal care* 產前保健[護理] —compare 比較 POSTNATAL —**prenatally** *adv*

pre·oc·cu·pa·tion /priˌɑkjəˋpeʃən; priːˌɒkjʊ̀ˈpeɪʃən/ *n* **1** [singular, U] a strong interest in something, usually because you are worried about it, with the result that you do not pay attention to other things 全神貫注; 入神: **[+with]** *the Bundesbank's preoccupation with keeping down inflation* 德意志聯邦銀行對於控制通貨膨脹的關注 **2** [C] something that you give all your attention to 使人全神貫注的事物, 使人入神的事物: *Brad's main preoccupations were eating and sleeping.* 布萊德主要關心的事情就是吃和睡。

pre·oc·cu·pied /priˋɑkjəˌpaɪd; priːˈɒkjʊ̀paɪd/ *adj* thinking about something a lot, with the result that you do not pay attention to other things 全神貫注的, 入神的: *I tried to speak to Bella, but she seemed a little preoccupied.* 我試圖和貝拉說話, 但她好像有點若有所思。| **[+with]** *Rod's completely preoccupied with all the wedding preparations at the moment.* 羅德此時整個心思想的就是婚禮的所有準備工作。

pre·oc·cu·py /priˋɑkjəˌpaɪ; priːˈɒkjʊ̀paɪ/ *v* [T] *formal* if something preoccupies someone, they think or worry about it a lot【正式】使對...全神貫注, 使專心於; 佔據〔某人的思想〕: *Something's been preoccupying you – what is it?* 你心裡老是在想着甚麼事情——是甚麼事呢?

pre·or·dain /ˌpriorˋden; ˌpriːɔːˈdeɪn/ *adj* [not before noun 不用於名詞前] *formal* if something is preordained, it is certain to happen in the future because God or FATE has decided it【正式】命中注定的, 預先注定的

prep¹ /prɛp; prep/ *n* [U] *BrE informal* school HOMEWORK【英, 非正式】〔學校安排的〕家庭作業

prep² **prepped, prepping** *v* [T] *AmE informal*【美, 非正式】**1** to prepare someone for an operation or an examination 使〔某人〕作好進行手術[考試]的準備 **2** to prepare food for cooking in a restaurant〔在餐館中〕為〔烹調〕作好準備

prep³ *n* [C] the written abbreviation of 縮寫= PREPOSITION

pre·packed /ˌpriˋpækt; ˌpriːˈpækt◂/ also 又作 **pre·pack·aged** /-ˋpækɪdʒd; -ˈpækɪdʒd◂/ *adj* prepacked or prepackaged food or other goods are already wrapped or are sold ready to use〔食物等〕預先包裝好的: *prepacked fresh fruit and vegetables* 預先包裝好的新鮮果蔬

pre·paid /ˌpriˋped; ˌpriːˈpeɪd◂/ *adj* a prepaid envelope does not need a stamp because the cost of posting it has already been paid by the person who will receive it〔信封〕郵資預付的

prep·a·ra·tion /ˌprɛpəˋreʃən; ˌprepəˈreɪʃən/ *n* **1** [U] the act or process of preparing something 預備, 準備: **[+for]** *Business training is a good preparation for any career.* 商業培訓對任何職業都是良好的基礎。| **[+of]** *Richard's currently involved in the preparation of the budget.* 理查德當前在忙於編製預算。| **in preparation for** (=in order to prepare for something) 為...作準備 *Justin had opened several bottles of wine in preparation for the party.* 賈斯廷已開了好幾瓶葡萄酒為聚會作準備。| **be in preparation** (=being prepared) 在準備中 *Plans for the new school are now in preparation.* 建造新校舍的圖則正在繪製之中。**2 preparations** [plural] arrangements for something that is going to happen 準備工作, 籌備工作: **[+for]** *preparations for the Queen's visit* 女王訪問的準備工作 | **make preparations** *The army is making preparations for a full-scale invasion.* 軍隊正在為全面侵略作準備。**3** [C] a medicine, COSMETIC etc 配製劑; 藥劑: *a new preparation for cleansing the skin* 清潔皮膚的新護膚劑

pre·par·a·to·ry /prɪˋpærəˌtorɪ; prɪˈpærətəri/ *adj* **1** [only before noun 僅用於名詞前] done in order to get ready for something 預備的, 準備的: *preparatory talks to clear the way for a peace settlement* 為和平解決問題掃清道路的預備性會談 **2 preparatory to** *formal* before something else and in order to prepare for it【正式】作為...的準備; 在...之前: *The partners held several meetings preparatory to signing the agreement.* 合夥人在簽訂協議之前舉行了幾次預備性會議。

preparatory school /-ˈ····· ˌ·/ *n* [C] **1** a private school in Britain for children between the ages of 8 and 13〔英國供8至13歲孩子讀書的〕私立小學 **2** a private school in the US that prepares students for college〔美國為學生上大學作準備的〕私立預備學校

pre·pare /prɪˋpɛr; prɪˈpeə/ *v*

1 ►MAKE STH READY 使某事物作好準備◄ to make something such as a machine, a place, or a piece of writing ready to be used 把...準備好, 使...作好準備: *Mansell's team were up all night preparing the car for the race.* 曼塞爾車隊整夜未眠準備比賽用車。| *I'd better go upstairs and prepare her room.* 我最好上樓去把她的房間整理好備用。| *Have you prepared your speech yet?* 你準備好演講稿了嗎?

2 ►MAKE PLANS/ARRANGEMENTS 製訂計劃/作出安排◄ [I,T] to make plans or arrangements for something that will happen in the future 籌備, 進行各項準備工作: *Olympus is preparing to launch a new range of* cameras. 奥林巴斯正在籌備將一批新照相機投放市場。| [+for] *We only heard about the meeting yesterday, so we haven't started preparing for it yet.* 我們昨天才剛聽說這次會議, 所以我們還沒有開始籌備呢。| **prepare sth** *They've prepared a special surprise party for him.* 他們已為他籌備了一次讓他感到驚喜的特別聚會。| *The airlines have prepared contingency plans in case the strike goes ahead.* 各航空公司已準備了應急計劃以防罷工繼續下去。| **prepare to do sth** *Her parents were busy preparing to go on holiday.* 她的父母正忙於為度假進行各項準備工作。

3 ►MAKE YOURSELF READY 使自己準備好◄ [T] to make yourself mentally or physically ready for something that you expect to happen soon 使〔某人〕在思想上[身體上]作好準備: **prepare yourself (for)** *Prepare yourself for a shock.* 有件事會讓你大吃一驚, 你得作好心理準備。| *They prepared themselves for a long wait.* 他們作好了長時間等待的思想準備。| *Can you just give me a couple more moments to prepare myself?* 你能否再給我一點時間讓我作好心理準備? | **prepare for action** *The captain told the men to prepare for action.* 上尉命令士兵準備戰鬥。

4 ►TRAINING/EXPERIENCE 培訓/經歷◄ [T] to provide someone with the training, skills, experience etc that they will need to do something or to deal with an unpleasant situation 〔通過提供培訓、技能、經驗等〕使〔某人〕作好準備: **prepare sb for sth** *a course that prepares students for English examinations* 為學生參加英語考試而開設的課程 | *Schools should do more to prepare children for the world of work.* 學校應該為培養孩子適應職業場合做更多的事情。| **prepare sb to do sth** *Nothing in his life had prepared him for this ordeal.* 他一生中沒有經歷過這樣的嚴酷考驗。

5 ►FOOD 食物◄ [T] to make food or a meal ready to eat 準備〔食物、飯菜〕: *Prepare the sauce while the pasta is cooking.* 在煮麵食的同時準備好調味汁。| **prepare sth for sb** *John's preparing supper for us.* 約翰正在為我們準備晚餐。| **prepare sb sth** *Helen had prepared us a wonderful meal.* 海倫為我們準備了一頓豐盛的飯菜。

6 prepare the way for/prepare the ground for to provide the conditions that make it possible for something to be achieved, or for someone to succeed in doing something 為…準備條件, 為…打好基礎: *Curie's research prepared the way for the work of modern nuclear scientists.* 居里的研究為現代核科學家的工作打下了基礎。

7 ►MEDICINE/CHEMICAL 藥物/化學品◄ [T] to make a medicine or chemical ready to be used, usually by mixing several substances 製作; 調製; 配製: *Preparing herbal medicines requires a lot of skill and knowledge about different kinds of herbs.* 配製草藥需要很多技能和有關各種藥草的知識。

Frequencies of **prepare**, **get ready** and **make preparaions** in spoken and written English 英語口語和書面語中prepare, get ready 和 make preparations 的使用頻率

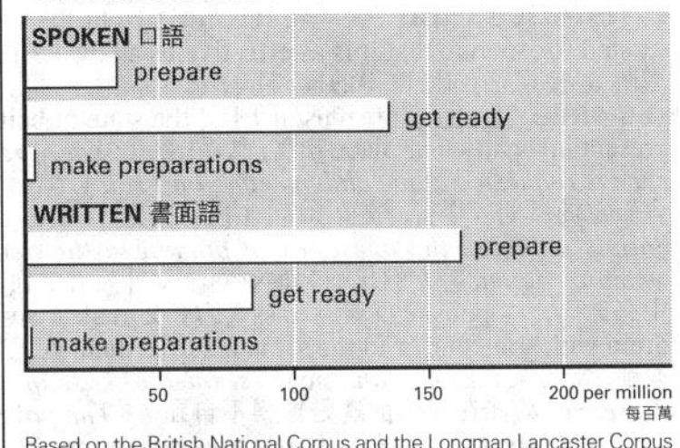

Based on the British National Corpus and the Longman Lancaster Corpus
據英國國家語料庫和朗文蘭卡斯特語料庫

This graph shows that **get ready** is more common in spoken English than **prepare** or **make preparations**. However, in written English, **prepare** is the most common of the three. **Make preparations** is the least common in both spoken and written English. It is less general, and suggests making a lot of arrangements for something that is going to happen. 本圖表顯示, get ready 在英語口語中的使用頻率遠遠高於 prepare 和 make preparations。但是在書面語中, prepare 是三者中最常用的。make preparations 在口語和書面語中都是最不常用的。它較少使用, 表示為將要發生的某事作很多安排。

pre·pared /prɪˋpɛrd; prɪˈpeəd/ *adj* S2

1 be prepared to do sth to be willing to do something, especially something difficult or something that you do not usually do 願意做某事〔尤指難做或通常不做的事〕: *You have to be prepared to take risks in this kind of work.* 你必須自願承擔做這種工作的風險。| *How much is she prepared to pay?* 她願意付多少錢?

2 I'm not prepared to do sth *spoken* used when saying strongly that you refuse to do something【口】我不願意做某事: *I'm not prepared to sit here and listen to this rubbish!* 我不願意坐在這裡聽這些廢話!

3 ►READY TO DEAL WITH STH 準備應付某事◄ [not before noun 不用於名詞前] ready to do something or deal with a situation because you were expecting it to happen or because you have made careful and thorough preparations 有準備的, 準備好的: [+for] *I wasn't prepared for all their questions.* 對於他們所有的問題我都沒有準備。| **well/badly prepared** *Luckily we were well prepared for the storm.* 幸運的是我們為這次暴風雨作好了準備。| **ill-prepared** (=not prepared to deal with a difficult situation) 沒有準備好的 *The country was ill-prepared to fight another war.* 該國並沒有作好再打一場戰爭的準備。| **be prepared for the worst** (=expect that something very bad may happen and be ready for it) 作最壞的打算 *There was no news and we were prepared for the worst.* 由於沒有任何消息, 我們作好了最壞的打算。

4 ►READY TO BE USED 準備被使用◄ [not before noun 不用於名詞前] arranged and ready to be used 安排好的, 配備好的: *The boss is due any minute – is everything prepared?* 老闆隨時會到——一切都準備好了嗎? | **get sth prepared** *By the time we'd got all our stuff prepared it was time to go on stage.* 我們把所有東西準備好時, 也該上台了。

5 ►MADE EARLIER 事先做好的◄ planned, made, or written at an earlier time 事先準備好的: *The president read out a prepared statement.* 總統宣讀了一份事先準備好的聲明。| **hastily prepared** (=prepared very quickly because you were not expecting something) 倉促[匆忙]準備的 *Hastily prepared arrangements were made to welcome the new visitor.* 為歡迎新的訪客, 進行了一些倉促的準備。

pre·pared·ness /prɪˋpɛrɪdnɪs; prɪˈpeədnɪ̥s/ *n* [U] the state of being ready for something 有準備(的狀態), 作好準備: *the country's lack of military preparedness* 該國在軍事上的準備不足

pre·pon·de·rance /prɪˋpɑndərəns; prɪˈpɒndərəns/ *n formal* **a preponderance of** if there is a preponderance of people or things of a particular type in a group, there are more of that type than of any others【正式】…數量上的優勢: *There is a preponderance of female students in the music department.* 在音樂系中女學生佔大多數。

pre·pon·de·rant /prɪˋpɑndərənt; prɪˈpɒndərənt/ *adj formal* main or most important【正式】主要的; 最重要的 —**preponderantly** *adv*

pre·pon·de·rate /prɪˋpɑndəˌret; prɪˈpɒndəreɪt/ *v* [I] *formal* to be more important or frequent than something else【正式】〔重要性或頻率上〕佔優勢, 勝過

prep·o·si·tion /ˌprɛpəˋzɪʃən; ˌprepəˈzɪʃən/ *n* [C] a word that is used before a noun, PRONOUN, or GERUND to show that word's connection with another word, such as 'of' in 'a house made of wood', and 'by' in 'We open it by breaking the lock' 介(系)詞, 前置詞 —**prepositional** *adj* —**prepositionally** *adv*

prepositional phrase /ˌ····ˈ·/ *n* [C] *technical* a phrase consisting of a preposition and the noun following it, such as 'in bed' or 'on the table'【術語】介詞片語, 前置詞短語

pre·pos·sess·ing /ˌpripəˋzɛsɪŋ; ˌpriːpəˈzesɪŋ◂/ *adj formal* looking attractive or pleasant【正式】有吸引力的, 給人好感的: *a prepossessing smile* 動人的微笑

pre·pos·ter·ous /prɪˋpɑstərəs; prɪˈpɒstərəs/ *adj formal*【正式】**1** completely unreasonable; ABSURD 反常的, 荒謬的, 荒唐的: *The whole idea sounds absolutely preposterous!* 整個想法聽起來荒謬透頂! **2** extremely unusual and silly 極異常且可笑的: *Look at that preposterous car!* 看那輛荒謬可笑的汽車! —**preposterously** *adv* —**preposterousness** *n* [U]

prep·py /ˋprɛpɪ; ˈprepi/ *adj AmE informal* typical of students who go to expensive private schools in the US, especially by dressing very neatly【美, 非正式】私立學校學生的, 衣着講究[整潔]的: *preppy clothes* 講究而又整潔的學生裝

prep school /ˈ· ·/ *n* [C] *informal* a PREPARATORY SCHOOL【非正式】私立小學；私立預備學校

pre·pu·bes·cent /ˌpripjuˋbɛsənt; ˌpriːpjuːˈbesənt◂/ *adj formal* concerned with the time just before a child reaches PUBERTY【正式】青春期前的

pre·quel /ˋprikwəl; ˈpriːkwəl/ *n* [C] a book, television programme, etc that tells you what happened before the story that is told in a popular book or film〔故事的〕前篇, 先行篇

Pre-Raph·ae·lite /priˋræfəˌlaɪt; priːˈræfəlaɪt/ *n* [C] a member of a group of late 19th century English painters and artists〔英國 19 世紀晚期的〕拉斐爾前派畫家[藝術家] —**Pre-Raphaelite** *adj*

pre·re·cord /ˌprirɪˋkɔrd; ˌpriːrɪˈkɔːd/ *v* [T] to record music, a radio programme etc on a machine so that it can be used later 將〔音樂、電台節目等〕預先錄下, 預先錄製 —**prerecorded** *adj*: *prerecorded videos* 預先錄製的錄影[像]帶 —**prerecording** *n* [C,U]

pre·req·ui·site /priˋrɛkwəzɪt; priːˈrekwɪzɪt/ *n* [C] *formal* something someone must have before they can be allowed to do something, or which must exist before something else can happen【正式】先決條件, 前提; 必備條件: [+for/to/of] *A reasonable proficiency in English is a prerequisite for the course.* 掌握適當程度的英語是學習這門課程的先決條件。

pre·rog·a·tive /prɪˋrɑgətɪv; prɪˈrɒgətɪv/ *n* [C, usually singular 一般用單數] a right that someone has because of their importance or position 獨有的權利[權力], 特權: *the royal prerogative* 皇家的特權

pres 1 the written abbreviation of 縮寫= present **2** the written abbreviation of 縮寫= president

pres·age /prɪˋsedʒ; ˈpresɪdʒ/ *v* [T] *literary* to be a warning or a sign that something is going to happen especially something bad【文】預示, 預兆: *A chill breeze blows, presaging winter.* 冷風吹起, 預示着冬天的來臨。—**presage** *n* [C]

Pres·by·te·ri·an /ˌprɛzbəˋtɪrɪən; ˌprezbɪˈtɪəriən/ *n* [C] a member of the Presbyterian church, one of the largest churches in the US and the national church of Scotland 長老會教友〔長老會為美國最大的教會之一, 並為蘇格蘭國教〕—**Presbyterian** *adj* —**Presbyterianism** *n* [U]

pres·by·ter·y /ˋprɛzbəˌtɛrɪ; ˈprezbɪtəri/ *n* [C] **1** a local court or council of the Presbyterian church or the area controlled by that church〔長老會的〕教務評議會 (管區) **2** a house in which a Roman Catholic priest lives〔天主教的〕神父住宅 **3** the eastern part of a church, behind the area where the CHOIR (=trained singers) sit〔教堂內的〕司祭席〔位於教堂東側, 唱詩班席之後的神職人員座席〕

preschool /ˋpriskul; ˈpriːskuːl/ *n* [C] *AmE* a school for young children between two and five years of age, where they learn such things as numbers, colours, and letters【美】學齡前學校, 〔二到五歲孩子的〕幼兒園; **nursery school** (NURSERY (2)) *BrE*【英】

pre-school /priˋskul; ˌpriːˈskuːl◂/ *adj* connected with the time in a child's life before they are old enough to go to school 學齡前的: *a pre-school playgroup* 學齡前的幼兒遊戲班

pre-school·er /ˌpri ˋskulɚ; ˌpriː ˈskuːlə/ *n* [C] *AmE* a child who does not yet go to school【美】學齡前兒童

pre·sci·ent /ˋprɛʃɪənt; ˈpreʃiənt/ *adj formal* able to imagine or know what will happen in the future【正式】有預知能力的, 能預知未來的 —**prescience** *n* [U]

pre·scribe /prɪˋskraɪb; prɪˈskraɪb/ *v* [T] **1** to say what medicine or treatment a sick person should have (給…) 開藥, 開處方; 指示〔療法〕: **prescribe sb sth** *If these don't work I may have to prescribe you something stronger.* 如果這些藥無效, 我也許得給你開一些藥效更強的。| **prescribe sth for sth** *one of the most commonly prescribed drugs for treating depression* 治療抑鬱症最常見的處方藥之一 **2** to state officially what someone can and cannot do, or what should be done in a particular situation 規定, 指定: *What punishment does the law prescribe for this crime?* 按照法律規定, 這種罪該怎麼處罰? | **prescribe who/how/what etc** *You have no right to prescribe how others should behave.* 你無權規定別人的行為舉止。

pre·scribed /prɪˋskraɪbd; prɪˈskraɪbd/ *adj* decided by a rule 規定的: *a prescribed number of hours* 規定的小時數

pre·script /ˋpriskrɪpt; ˈpriːˌskrɪpt/ *n* [C] *formal* an official order or rule【正式】規定, 命令, 條例

pre·scrip·tion /prɪˋskrɪpʃən; prɪˈskrɪpʃən/ *n* **1** [C] a piece of paper on which a doctor writes what medicine a sick person should have, so that they can get it from a PHARMACIST 處方, 藥方 **2** [C] a particular medicine or treatment ordered by a doctor for a sick person〔醫生開的〕處方藥; 治療方法: *Prescriptions used to be free when the National Health Service started.* 在國民保健服務剛啟動時, 處方藥一度是免費的。| **prescription charges** (=the fixed amount of money you have to pay in Britain for drugs which your doctor has ordered) 處方費 **3 on prescription** a drug that you get on prescription can only be obtained with a written order from the doctor 憑處方的, 根據藥方的 —compare 比較 **over the counter** (COUNTER[1] (2)) **4** [C usually singular 一般用單數] an idea or suggestion about how to make a situation, activity etc successful 解救方法, 訣竅: [+for] *Her prescription for the advancement of women was education.* 她為婦女進步提出的訣竅是教育。**5** [U] the act of prescribing a medicine or drug 開處方, 開藥; 指示療法

pre·scrip·tive /prɪˋskrɪptɪv; prɪˈskrɪptɪv/ *adj* **1** stating or ordering how something should be done or what someone should do 規定的, 指定的: *prescriptive teaching methods* 規定的教學方法 **2** *technical* stating how a language should be used, rather than describing how it is used【術語】〔語言〕規定性的, 指定的; 規範的: *prescriptive grammar* 規定性語法 —**prescriptively** *adv*

prescriptive right /ˌ·ˌ·· ˈ·/ *n* [C] *law* a right that has existed for so long that it is as effective as a law【法律】因時效[長期存在]而取得的權利

pres·ence /ˋprɛzn̩s; ˈprezəns/ *n* **1** [U] the state of being present in a particular place 出席; 到場; 存在: *Your presence is requested at the club meeting on Friday.* 俱樂部會議定於星期五舉行, 敬請出席。| [+of] *The police scientists detected the presence of poison in the dead woman's blood.* 警方的化驗師檢測到該女性死者的血液中有毒藥。—opposite 反義詞 ABSENCE (1) **2 in sb's presence** with someone or in the same place as them 在某人面前, 當着某人的面: *John never seemed at ease in my presence.* 約翰在我面前總是顯得不自在。| *The police will only interview a child in the presence of an adult.* 警方只有在成人在場時才能向孩子提出詢問。**3** [U] the ability to impress people and make them believe you 儀態, 風度; 風采: *a man of great presence* 很有風度的男子 **4** [singular] a group of people from another country, an army, or the police, who are in a place to watch and influence what is happening〔某國在外國的〕勢力;〔部隊或警察的〕駐紮; 存在: *the American presence in the war zone* 戰區的美國人 | *a strong police presence at the march* 在遊行現場的大批警察 **5** [C usually singular 一般用單數] a spirit or influence that cannot be seen but is felt to be near〔看不見的〕靈氣, 鬼怪: *They felt a strange presence in the deserted house.* 他們感到在那所廢棄的房屋裡有奇特的幽靈。**6 make your presence felt** to have a strong and obvious effect on the people around you or the situation you are in 使周圍的人感到你的重要: *Since Webb joined the team he has really made his presence felt.* 韋伯加入這個隊以來, 他就使人感到他是個舉足輕重的隊員。

presence of mind /,·· · '·/ *n* [U] the ability to deal with a dangerous situation calmly and quickly 鎮定自若, 沉着冷靜: **have the presence of mind to do sth** *Luckily Isabel had the presence of mind to take down the car's registration number.* 所幸的是, 伊莎貝沉着鎮定地記下了那輛汽車的車牌號碼。

2 2 **pres·ent¹** /ˈprɛzn̩t; ˈprezənt/ *adj* **1 be present a)** to be in a particular place 出席的, 到場的; 存在的: *How many people were present at the meeting yesterday?* 昨天出席會議的有多少人? | *small amounts of gas present in the atmosphere* 大氣中存在的少量氣體 **b)** to be felt strongly or remembered for a long time 強烈感覺到的; 歷歷在目的: *The memory of her brother's death a year ago is still present in her mind.* 她哥哥一年前去世時的情景仍留在她腦海中。**2** [only before noun 僅用於名詞前] happening or existing now 現存的; 目前的, 現在的: *What is your present address?* 你現在的住址在哪裡? | *Usually I'd advise you to wait, but in the present situation I think it's best to act without delay.* 通常情況下我會建議你等着, 但在目前的情況下, 我認為最好是立即採取行動。**3** [only before noun 僅用於名詞前] *technical* related to a verb that shows an existing state or action【術語】〔動詞〕現在式[時]的: *'He wants' and 'They are coming' are examples of verbs in the present tense.* He wants 和 They are coming 是動詞現在式的例子。**4 all present and correct** *BrE*【英】also 又作 **all present and accounted for** *AmE*【美】used to say that everyone who is supposed to be in a place, at a meeting etc is now here 所有該到的都到了, 如數到齊 **5 present company excepted** used when you are saying something rude about someone to tell the people you are with that you do not mean to include them in the statement 在座者除外: *Women are never satisfied with anything! Present company excepted, of course.* 女人總是對甚麼事都不滿足! 當然在座者除外。—see also 另見 PRESENTLY

Frequencies of **present** (*adj*), **now** and **at the moment** in spoken and written English 英語口語和書面語中 present (adj), now 和 at the moment 的使用頻率

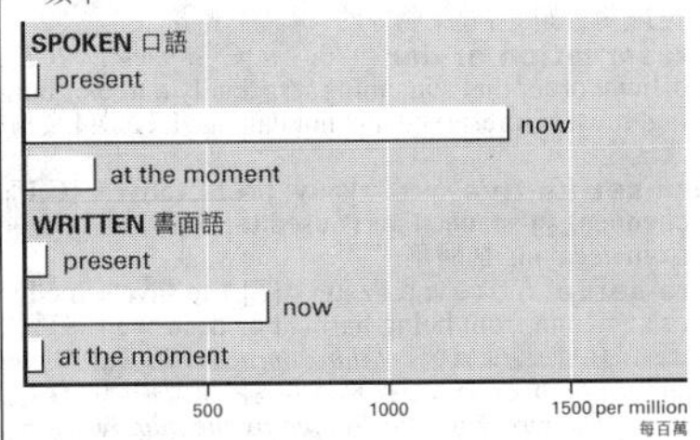

Based on the British National Corpus and the Longman Lancaster Corpus
據英國國家語料庫和朗文蘭卡斯特語料庫

This graph shows that **now** is much more common than **present** and **at the moment** in both spoken and written English. **At the moment** is more common in spoken English than in written English. **Present** is the least common of the three. It is formal, and is only used before a noun, for example in expressions such as 'the present situation', 'the present leader' etc. 本圖表顯示, now 在英語口語和書面語中的使用頻率遠遠高於 present 和 at the moment。at the moment 在英語口語中的使用頻率遠遠高於書面語。present 是三個中最不常用的, 它較為正式, 而且只用於名詞前, 譬如在 the present situation (目前情況), the present leader (現任領導人) 等之類的表達法中。

pres·ent² /prɪˈzɛnt; prɪˈzent/ *v* [T] 2 1

1 ►GIVE 給予◄ to give something to someone, especially at a formal or official occasion〔尤指在正式場合〕頒發, 授予, 贈送; 呈獻; 呈遞: **present sb with sth** *David's manager presented him with the award for best sales in the region.* 由於大衛在這一地區的銷售業績最出色, 他的經理向他頒了獎。

2 ►CAUSE STH TO HAPPEN 使某事發生◄ to cause something to happen or exist 使發生[存在], 引起, 造成: *Slippery floors in the work area present a hazard to employees.* 工作區很滑的地板對雇員是一種危險。| **present sb with sth** *His resignation presents us with a tricky situation.* 他的辭職給我們造成一個尷尬的局面。| **present a problem/difficulty** *This equation should present no problems if you know some basic trigonometry.* 如果你懂一些三角學的基本知識的話, 這個方程式應該不會造成甚麼困難。

3 ►SHOW 呈現◄ to offer or show information about something in a particular way 呈現; 展現; 表現: *The movie presents its characters in a way that I find difficult to believe in.* 我覺得這部電影表現人物的方式很難讓人相信。| *Tobacco companies are trying to present a more favorable image.* 煙草公司正試圖展現出較取悅人的形象。

4 ►A SPEECH 講話◄ to give a speech in which you offer an idea, plan etc to be considered or accepted 提出〔觀點、計劃等〕; 陳述: **present sth to sb** *The team is presenting its report to the board on Tuesday.* 該工作組將在星期二向董事會提出報告。

5 ►DOCUMENT/TICKET 文件/入場券◄ to show something such as an official document or ticket to someone in an official position 呈遞, 出示: *You must present your passport to the customs officer.* 你必須向海關人員出示護照。

6 ►THEATRE/CINEMA 劇院/電影院◄ to give a performance in a theatre, cinema, etc, or broadcast a programme on television or radio 上演; 演出; 上映; 播出〔廣播或電視節目〕: *This evening PBS presents the first of a six-part historical drama about the Civil War.* 今晚公共廣播公司播出有關內戰的六集歷史劇的第一集。

7 ►TELEVISION/RADIO 電視/廣播◄ *BrE* if you present a television or radio programme, you introduce its different parts【英】主持〔廣播或電視節目〕: *Tonight's edition of Newsnight, presented by Jeremy Paxman.* 今晚的晚間新聞由傑里米·派克斯曼主持。

8 sth presents itself if a situation, opportunity etc presents itself, it suddenly happens or exists〔情況、機會等〕出現, 發生: *As soon as the opportunity presents itself, I'm going to talk to Mr Boyer about that job.* 一旦機會來了, 我就會找博耶先生談那份工作。

9 ►FORMALLY INTRODUCE SB 正式介紹某人◄ to introduce someone formally, especially to someone of a very high rank〔正式地〕介紹; 引見〔尤指向地位極高者〕: *I was presented to the Queen in 1964.* 我有幸於 1964 年被引見給女王。

10 present arms a command to soldiers to hold their weapons upright in front of their bodies as a greeting to a person of high rank 舉槍〔於胸前〕敬禮〔用於軍令〕

11 present your apologies/compliments etc *formal* used to greet someone, apologize to them etc very politely【正式】致歉/致意等: *Mrs Gottlieb presents her apologies and regrets she will not be able to attend.* 哥特利布夫人表達歉意, 並為她不能出席感到遺憾。

pres·ent³ /ˈprɛznt; ˈprezənt/ *n* [C] something you give someone on a special occasion or to thank them for something; gift 禮物, 贈品: *One of my Japanese students gave me a beautiful fan as a present.* 我的一位日本學生送給我一把漂亮的扇子作為禮物。| **birthday/Christmas present** *Christmas presents under the tree* 樹下的聖誕禮物

present⁴ *n* [singular] **1** the time that we are experiencing now 現在, 目前: *You have to stop worrying about the past and start thinking about the present!* 你必須停止為過去擔憂, 而開始為現在考慮! | **no time like the present** (=used to say that if you are going to do something at all, you should do it now) 沒有比現在更合適的時機 *"I was thinking of asking Maura to marry me." "Do it! There's no time like the present!"* "我正想向莫拉求婚。" "去啊! 沒有比現在更合適的時機了。" **2** *technical* the form of a verb that shows what exists or is happening now【術語】〔動詞的〕現在式[時]形式 —see also 另見 HISTORIC PRESENT **3 at present** at this time; now 現在, 目前: *Ms Hellman is busy at present, can she ring you later?* 赫爾曼女士現在正忙着, 過一會兒她給你回電話好嗎? —see 見 PRESENTLY (USAGE)

pre·sen·ta·ble /prɪˋzɛntəbl; prɪˈzentəbəl/ *adj* tidy and attractive enough to be introduced or shown to someone 拿得出手的; 像樣的; 體面的: *a presentable piece of work* 擺得出去的作品 | **make yourself presentable** *I must go and make myself presentable before the guests arrive.* 客人來以前, 我得去把自己打扮得像樣一點。—**presentably** *adv*

pre·sen·ta·tion /ˌprɛznˋteʃən; ˌprezənˈteɪʃən/ *n*
1 ►PROOF 證據◄ [C,U] the act of showing someone something so that it can be checked or considered 提出; 出示: **[+of]** *On presentation of the relevant identity documents you may collect your property.* 在出示相關身分證件之後, 你就可以領走你的財物。
2 ►APPEARANCE 外貌◄ [U] the way in which something is said, offered, shown, explained etc to others 講述, 描繪; 外觀, 外貌: *This word processor is excellent for presentation and layout of complex documents.* 這種文字處理機非常適於處理複雜文件的外觀和版式。| *The presentation of food can be as important as the taste.* 食物的外觀和味道同樣重要。
3 ►PRESENT PRIZE 頒獎◄ [C] the act of giving someone a prize or present at a formal ceremony 授予, 頒發: **[+of]** *The presentation of prizes will begin at three o'clock.* 頒獎儀式將在三點鐘開始。
4 ►TALK 講話◄ [C] an event at which a new product or idea is described and explained 報告; 〔新產品的〕介紹; 〔觀點的〕陳述, 說明: **give a presentation** *I've been asked to give a short presentation on the aims of the project.* 我被要求簡短地介紹一下該項目的目標。
5 ►PERFORMANCE 表演◄ [C] the act of performing something in front of an audience 表演, 演出: **[+of]** *There are two presentations of the cabaret every night.* 每晚有兩場卡巴萊歌舞表演。
6 ►BABY 嬰兒◄ [C,U] *technical* the position in which a baby is lying in its mother's body just before it is born【術語】〔胎兒的〕先露位置, 產位: *a breech presentation* 臀產位 —**presentational** *adj*

presentation cop·y /ˌ··ˈ·· ˌ··/ *n* [C] a book that is given to someone, especially by the writer or PUBLISHER〔尤指作者或出版者提供的〕贈(閱)本

pres·ent-day /ˋprɛznt ˋde; ˌprezənt ˈdeɪ◄/ *adj* modern or existing now 現代的; 當今的, 當前的: *present-day Sicily* 當今的西西里

pre·sent·er /prɪˋzɛntə; prɪˈzentə/ *n* [C] *BrE* someone who introduces the different parts of a television or radio show【英】〔電視或廣播節目的〕主持人, 主播; ANNOUNCER *AmE*【美】: *radio presenter, Libby Purves* 廣播節目主持人: 利比·珀維斯

pre·sen·ti·ment /prɪˋzɛntəmənt; prɪˈzentɪmənt/ *n* [C] *formal* a strange and uncomfortable feeling that something is going to happen; PREMONITION【正式】〔尤指不祥的〕預感: **[+of]** *a presentiment of danger* 有危險的預感

pres·ent·ly /ˋprɛzntlɪ; ˈprezəntli/ *adv formal*【正式】**1** in a short time; soon 馬上, 一會兒, 不久, 很快: *The doctor will be here presently.* 醫生一會兒就到。| *Presently a bell rang and they all trooped into school.* 很快鈴響了, 他們全都成羣地湧入學校。**2** *especially AmE and ScotE* now; at this time【尤美和蘇格蘭】現在, 目前, 此刻: *Scientists are presently working on identifying the cause of the disease.* 科學家正致力於確認該病的病因。

> **USAGE NOTE 用法說明: PRESENTLY**
> UK-US DIFFERENCE 英美差別
> In both British and American English **presently** can mean the same as **soon**, but is a little old-fashioned. 在英語和美語中, presently 都可表示 soon (馬上、很快), 但有點過時: *If you take a seat, the doctor will see you presently.* 請坐, 醫生一會兒就來看你。
> In American English, and formal British English, it can also be used to mean 'at the present time' or to talk about something that is happening now. 在美語和正式英語中, 該詞也可用來表示"目前, 現在"或談論目前正在發生的事情: *He is presently living in Seoul.* 他現在住在漢城。| *District councils are presently making good progress on the development plans.* 區委員會目前在發展規劃方面進展順利。

present par·ti·ci·ple /ˌ·· ˈ····/ *technical* a PARTICIPLE that is formed in English by adding 'ing' to the verb, as in 'sleeping'. It can be used in COMPOUND¹ (4) forms of the verb to show PROGRESSIVE tenses, as in 'she's sleeping', or as an adjective, as in 'the sleeping child'【術語】現在分詞

present per·fect /ˌ·· ˈ··/ *n technical* the form of a verb that shows a period of time up to and including the present, formed in English with the present tense of the verb 'have', as in 'he has gone' and a PAST PARTICIPLE【術語】現在完成式[時]

pres·er·va·tion /ˌprɛzəˋveʃən; ˌprezəˈveɪʃən/ *n* [U] **1** the act of keeping something unharmed or unchanged 維護; 保護; 保持, 維持: **[+of]** *The police are responsible for the preservation of law and order.* 警察負責維護治安。**2** the degree to which something has remained unchanged or unharmed by weather, age etc 保養(程度): *The old building is in a good state of preservation.* 這所老房子保養得很好。—see also 另見 SELF-PRESERVATION

pres·er·va·tion·ist /ˌprɛzəˋveʃənɪst; ˌprezəˈveɪʃənɪst/ *n* [C] *especially AmE* someone who works to prevent historical places, buildings etc from being destroyed【尤美】〔對古蹟、古建築物等的〕保護主義者

preservation or·der /··ˈ·· ˌ··/ *n* [C] *especially BrE* an official order that something, especially a tree or building, must be preserved and not damaged【尤英】文物保護法令

pre·ser·va·tive /prɪˋzɝvətɪv; prɪˈzɜːvətɪv/ *n* [C,U] a chemical substance that is used to stop food or wood from decaying 防腐劑

pre·serve¹ /prɪˋzɝv; prɪˈzɜːv/ *v* [T] **1** to save something or someone from being harmed or destroyed 維護, 保護; 保存〔使免受破壞〕: *I think these traditional customs should be preserved.* 我認為這些傳統習俗應該保存下去。| *The wreck was preserved by the muddy sea bed.* 失事船隻的殘骸被泥濘的海牀保護了起來。| **preserve sb/sth from sth** *They were determined to preserve their* *leader from humiliation.* 他們決心保護他們的領導人免受侮辱。**2** to store food for a long time after treating it so that it will not decay 醃製; 保存〔食物〕: *figs preserved in brandy* 用白蘭地浸漬的無花果 **3** to make something continue without changing 保持, 維持: *The Baroness had managed to preserve her good looks.* 那位男爵夫人設法留駐了自己姣好的面容。—see also 另見 WELL-PRESERVED —**preservable** *adj*

preserve² *n* **1** [C, U] a substance made from boiling fruit or vegetables with sugar, salt, or VINEGAR 果醬 **2** [singular] an activity that is only suitable or allowed for a particular group of people 〔某羣體〕獨有[專有]的活動: *Banking used to be a male preserve.* 銀行業過去是男人獨佔的領域。| **[+of]** *Gardening is sometimes considered the preserve of the elderly.* 園藝有時被認為是老年人獨有的活動。**3** [C] an area of land or water that is kept for private hunting or fishing 私人漁獵區

pre-set /pri ˋsɛt; priː ˈset/ *present participle* **pre-setting** *past tense and past participle* **pre-set** *v* [T] to set a piece of electrical equipment, so that it will start to work 預先設置, 預先調好

pre-shrunk /ˌpri ˋʃrʌŋk; ˌpriː ˈʃrʌŋk◂/ *adj* clothes that are pre-shrunk are made to SHRINK (=became smaller when washed) before they are sold 〔衣服在出售之前〕已預縮的, 縮過水的: *pre-shrunk Levis* 預先縮過水的利維斯牌牛仔褲

pre·side /prɪˋzaɪd; prɪˈzaɪd/ *v* [I] to be in charge of a formal ceremony, meeting etc 〔在正式儀式、會議等〕擔任主持, 負責: *They could find no clergyman who would agree to preside at the funeral.* 他們找不到願意主持葬禮的牧師。

preside over *phr v* [T] **1** to be in charge of a situation over which you do not have much control 負責〔無力控制的局面〕: *The president found himself presiding over the worst economic depression in the history of the US.* 該總統發現自己無可奈何地面臨美國歷史上最嚴重的經濟蕭條。**2** to be the head of a company or organization 掌管, 管轄, 領導 **3** to be in charge of a meeting or a formal meal 主持

pres·i·den·cy /ˋprɛzədənsɪ; ˈprezɪdənsi/ *n* [C] **1** the job of president 總統[主席、校長等]的職位: *Roosevelt was elected four times to the presidency of the US.* 羅斯福四次當選美國總統。**2** the period of time for which a person is president 總統[主席、校長等]的任期: *During his presidency he undertook a great initiative towards world peace.* 在他擔任總統期間, 他積極地倡導世界和平。

2 1 **pres·i·dent** /ˋprɛzədənt; ˈprezɪdənt/ *n* [C] **1** the official leader of a country that does not have a king or queen 總統: *the President of France* 法國總統 | *President Kennedy* 甘迺迪總統 **2** the person in charge of a club, college, government department etc 〔俱樂部〕會長; 〔大學〕校長; 〔政府部門〕首長 **3** *AmE* the head of a business, bank etc 【美】〔公司〕董事長; 〔銀行〕行長; 總裁: *the president of General Motors* 通用汽車公司總裁

president-e·lect /ˌ··· ·ˈ·/ *n* [singular] someone who has been elected as a new president, but who has not yet started the job 〔尚未就職的〕當選總統

pres·i·den·tial /ˌprɛzəˋdɛnʃəl; ˌprezɪˈdenʃəl◂/ *adj* connected with a president 總統的: *a presidential election* 總統大選 | *the party's presidential candidate* 該黨的總統候選人

pre·sid·i·um, praesidium /prɪˋsɪdɪəm; prɪˈsɪdiəm/ *n plural* **presidia** [C] a committee chosen to represent a large political organization, especially in a COMMUNIST country 〔尤指共產黨執政國家的〕常務委員會, 主席團

2 2 **press¹** /prɛs; pres/ *n*

1 ▶NEWS 新聞◀ a) [U] also 又作 **the press** people who write reports for newspapers, radio, or television 〔報紙、電台、電視台的〕記者們; 新聞界: *the freedom of the press* 新聞自由 | [also+plural verb *BrE* 英] *In August the press are desperate for news.* 八月份記者們不顧一切地捕捉新聞。| *press photographers* 新聞攝影記者 **b)** [singular,U] reports in newspapers and on radio and television 〔報紙、電台、電視台的〕新聞報道: *To judge from the press, the concert was a great success.* 據新聞報道來看, 這次音樂會取得了巨大成功。| *press clippings* 剪報 | **press coverage** (=the reports written about something in newspapers) 〔報紙上有關某事的〕新聞報道

2 get/be given a bad press to be criticized in the newspapers or on radio or television 受到輿論界的批評: *The police have been getting a bad press in the last few months.* 在過去的幾個月裡, 警方一直受到輿論界的批評。

3 get/be given a good press to be praised in the newspapers or on radio or television 受到輿論界的好評: *Our recycling policy is getting a good press.* 我們的回收利用政策正獲得新聞輿論的好評。

4 ▶PRINTING 印刷◀ [C] **a)** a business that prints and sometimes also sells books 出版社: *the Clarendon Press* 克拉倫登出版社 **b)** also 又作 **printing press** a machine that prints books, newspapers, or magazines 印刷機

5 trouser/flower/wine press a piece of equipment used to put weight on something to make it flat or to force liquid out of it 褲子熨燙機/壓花器/葡萄榨汁機: *You can still buy old cheese presses in some areas.* 在一些地區, 你仍可以買到舊的壓酪機。

6 ▶PUSH 推◀ a light steady push against something small 按, 揿: *Give the button another press.* 再按一下這個按鈕。

7 go to press if a newspaper, magazine, or book goes to press, it is printed 付印, 開印

8 ▶CROWD 人羣◀ a crowd of people pushing against each other 擁擠的人羣

1 2 **press²** *v*

press 按, 揿

1 ▶AGAINST STH 靠着某物◀ [T always+adv/prep] to push something firmly against a surface 按; 壓: *The little boys pressed their noses against the glass.* 那些小男孩把他們的鼻子貼在玻璃上。| *Viv tried to press himself back against the wall.* 維夫盡量往後緊貼牆壁。| *The old man pressed a coin into her hand.* 老人把一枚硬幣塞進她的手裡。

2 ▶BUTTON 按鈕◀ [T] to push something with your finger to make a machine start, a bell ring etc 按, 揿: *What happens if I press the reset button?* 要是我按 reset (重新設置) 按鈕, 會發生甚麼事呢?

3 ▶CLOTHES 衣服◀ [T] to make clothes smooth using heat; IRON 熨平〔衣物〕: *I'll need to press my suit.* 我需要燙一下我的西裝。

4 ▶CROWD 人羣◀ [I always+adv/prep] to move in a particular direction by pushing 擁擠着移動, 擠着走: *The crowds pressed around her, hoping for her autograph.* 人羣圍擠在她身旁, 希望得到她的簽名。

5 ▶PERSUADE 勸說◀ [T] to try hard to persuade someone to do something 極力勸說, 敦促, 催促: *Please don't press me on this point, I have no more to say.* 在這一點上請不要逼我, 我無話可說了。| **press sb to do sth** *Katie pressed me to stay a little longer.* 凱蒂極力勸我再多留一會兒。| **press sb for sth** *The bank is pressing us for a quick decision.* 銀行催促我們迅速作出決定。

6 ▶FOR JUICE 為取得果汁◀ [T] to put a heavy weight on something to get liquid from it 擠取, 榨取: *The grapes must be pressed to extract the juice.* 葡萄必須經壓榨才能提取葡萄汁。

7 ▶MAKE STH FLAT 使某物平整◀ [T] to put pressure or a weight on something to make it flat 把…壓平[壓扁]: *pressing flowers* 把花壓平

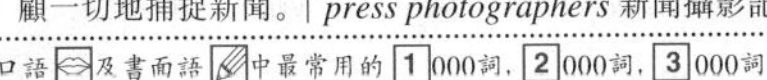

8 ►HOLD SB/STH CLOSE 抱緊某人/某物◄ [T] to hold someone or something close to you because you feel upset, are protecting them etc 使緊貼; 緊抱, 緊握: **press sb/sth to you** *Prue pressed the photograph to her chest and wept.* 普魯把照片緊貼在她胸前哭了。

9 press sb's hand/arm to hold someone's hand or arm tightly for a short time, to show friendship, sympathy etc 緊握某人的手/手臂〔表示友好、同情等〕: *Frank pressed my hand warmly when we met.* 我們見面時法蘭克熱情地緊握我的手。

10 press charges to say officially that someone has done something illegal and must go to court 提出訴訟: *Police are often reluctant to press charges in such cases.* 在這些情況下, 警方常常不願提出訴訟。

11 ►CLAIM/STATEMENT 聲稱/聲明◄ [T] to continue to try to make someone accept a claim or statement that you are making 堅持, 竭力要求: *We shall not press our claim for compensation.* 我們將不再堅持賠償要求。| *I don't want to press the point, but we are late.* 我不想老提這一點, 但我們遲到了。

12 press sb/sth into service to use someone or something not completely suitable, because of an unexpected problem〔因意外問題而〕將就使用[暫用]某人/某物: *My scarf was pressed into service as a bandage.* 我的圍巾被臨時用作了繃帶。

13 press sth home a) to push something into its place 把某物推入[壓入, 按入, 塞入]適當的位置: *Jane slammed the door and pressed the bolt home.* 簡砰地把門關上並插好插銷。**b)** to repeat or emphasize something, so that people remember it 重複[強調]某事物〔以使人們記住它〕: *We must press home the case for action.* 我們必須令人信服地闡明這件案子以便採取行動。

14 press home your advantage to try to succeed completely, using an advantage that you have gained 盡量利用優勢大獲成功

15 press the flesh *humorous* to shake hands with a lot of people【幽默】與許多人握手: *politicians pressing the flesh* 與眾人握手的政客

16 ►RECORD 唱片◄ [T] to make a copy of a GRAMOPHONE record etc 壓製〔唱片〕

press (sb) **for** sth *phr v* [I,T] to keep asking for something or to try hard to achieve something 敦促, 催促; 迫切要求; 努力取得: *The firm is pressing me for a decision on their offer.* 該公司正催我對他們的提議作出決定。| *We must continue to press for full equality.* 我們必須繼續爭取完全平等。

press on *phr v* **1** [I] also 又作 **press ahead** to continue doing something, especially working, in a determined way 繼續堅定做某事〔尤指工作〕: **[+with]** *Shall we stop here, or press on to the next town?* 我們是在這裡停下還是繼續趕往下一個城鎮? | *Let's press on with our work.* 我們繼續工作吧。**2** [T **press** sth **on** sb] to try hard to give something to someone, so that it is hard for them to refuse it 硬給, 強迫〔某人〕接受〔某物〕: **press sth on sb** *Nick was pressing yet another drink on me.* 尼克硬要我再喝一杯酒。

press a·gent /ˈ· ˌ··/ *n* [C] someone whose job is to supply photographs or information about a particular actor, musician etc to newspapers, radio or television〔為演員、音樂家等作宣傳的〕宣傳員 —**press agency** *n* [C]

press bar·on /ˈ· ˌ··/ *n* [C] *informal, especially BrE* someone who owns and controls one or more important national newspapers【非正式, 尤英】報業巨頭, 報業大王

press box /ˈ· ·/ *n* [C] an enclosed area at a sports ground used by people from newspapers, radio, or television〔運動場上的〕記者席

press con·fer·ence /ˈ· ˌ···/ *n* [C] a meeting at which someone makes an official statement to people who write news reports and answers questions 記者招待會: *The Green Party held a press conference the next day.* 綠黨第二天召開了一個記者招待會。

press corps /ˈ· ·/ *n* [C] a group of people who write news reports, at a place where something important is happening 記者團, 聯合報道組

press cut·ting /ˈ· ˌ··/ also 又作 **press clipping** *n* [C] a short piece of writing or a picture, cut out from a newspaper or magazine 剪報

pressed /prɛst; prest/ *adj* **be pressed for time/money etc** to not have enough time, money etc 時間緊迫/缺錢等: *I'm a bit pressed for time – could you call back tomorrow?* 我現在沒有時間——你能明天打電話過來嗎?

press gal·le·ry /ˈ· ˌ···/ *n* [C] an area above or at the back of a hall, used by news reporters 新聞記者席

press-gang[1] /ˈ· ·/ *n* [C] a group of sailors employed in the past to take men away by force to join the navy〔過去為海軍強抓壯丁的〕徵兵隊, 招募水手隊

press-gang[2] *v* [T] **press-gang sb into doing sth** *informal* to force someone to do something【非正式】強迫某人做某事: *I was press-ganged into doing the dishes.* 我是被強行拉去洗碗的。

pre·ssie, prezzie /ˈprɛzɪ; ˈprezi/ *n* [C] *BrE spoken* a present【英口】禮物, 贈品: *Did you get some nice pressies?* 你收到一些精美的禮品沒有?

press·ing[1] /ˈprɛsɪŋ; ˈpresɪŋ/ *adj* **1** needing to be discussed or dealt with very soon; URGENT 緊迫的; 迫切的: *There is a pressing need for reform in this area.* 這一地區迫切需要改革。**2** demanding something in a way that is hard to refuse 懇切要求的, 堅持的: *a pressing invitation* 懇切的邀請 —**pressingly** *adv*

pressing[2] *n* [C] **1** a number of GRAMOPHONE records made at one time 同一批壓製的唱片 **2** an act of pressing 按, 壓, 擠, 推; 壓平; 壓榨

press·man /ˈprɛsmæn; ˈpresmæn/ *plural* **pressmen** /-mɛn; -men/ *n* [C] *BrE informal* someone who writes news reports【英, 非正式】記者

press of·fice /ˈ· ˌ··/ *n* [C] the office of an organization or government department which gives information to the newspapers, radio, or television〔組織或政府部門的〕新聞處 —**press officer** *n* [C]

press re·lease /ˈ· ·ˌ·/ *n* [C] an official statement giving information to the newspapers, radio, or television 新聞稿

press sec·re·ta·ry /ˈ· ˌ····/ *n* [C] a secretary to an important organization or person, who gives information about them to the newspapers, radio, or television 新聞祕書

press-stud /ˈ· ·/ *n* [C] *BrE* a small metal FASTENER for a piece of clothing, in which one part is pressed into a hollow part in the other【英】摁扣, 子母扣; SNAP[2] (6) *AmE*【美】

press-up /ˈ· ·/ *n* [C] *especially BrE* a type of exercise in which you lie facing the ground, and push your body up with your arms【尤英】俯臥撐, 伏地挺身, 掌上壓; PUSH-UP *especially AmE*【尤美】

pres·sure[1] /ˈprɛʃɚ; ˈpreʃə/ *n*

1 ►FORCE 力◄ [U] the act of force or weight being put on to something 壓, 按, 擠, 榨: *The pressure of the water turns the wheel.* 水壓使輪子轉動。| *factors such as temperature and pressure* 諸如溫度和壓力之類的因素

2 ►STRENGTH 力量◄ [C,U] the strength of the force or weight put on something 壓力: **high/low pressure** *The gas containers burst at high pressures.* 在高壓下這些瓦斯容器會爆炸。| *Low atmospheric pressure often brings rain.* 低氣壓常常帶來降雨。—see also 另見 BLOOD PRESSURE

3 ►STRONG 有力的◄ [U] an attempt to persuade someone by using influence, arguments, or threats〔利用影響、辯論、威脅施加的〕壓力: **[+for]** *pressure for change inside the party* 黨內要求變革的壓力 | **pressure to do sth** *There was great pressure to conform to existing standards.* 要求遵循現行標準的壓力很大。| **under pressure from** *John only agreed to go under pressure from his parents.* 約翰是在父母的壓力下才同意去的。|

be/come under pressure (to do sth) *The company is under pressure to improve pay and conditions.* 該公司面臨提高工資並改善工作條件的壓力。| **give in to pressure** (=agree to do something that someone has persuaded you to do) 屈服於壓力 | **put pressure on** (=to try to persuade someone to do something because it is their duty) 向…施加壓力 *Their parents were putting pressure on them to get married.* 他們的父母在對他們施加壓力, 要求他們結婚。| **exert pressure on/bring pressure to bear on** *formal*【正式】*Special interest groups can bring great pressure to bear on legislation.* 一些特殊利益集團會給立法施加很大的壓力。

4 ►PROBLEMS/DEMANDS 問題/要求◄ [C,U] conditions of work or a way of living that cause anxiety or difficulties〔工作或生活的〕壓力: *Paul changed jobs because he couldn't stand the pressure.* 保羅因受不了這種壓力而換了工作。| **[+on]** *There are a lot of pressures on young people today.* 如今的年輕人有很多的壓力。| **under pressure** *You need to be able to work accurately under pressure.* 你必需能夠在壓力下準確無誤地進行工作。| **pressure of work** *Lou couldn't stay long because of pressure of work.* 盧因為工作壓力而不會待得很久。

5 pile on the pressure to increase the amount of pressure on someone 增加〔某人的〕壓力: *Just when she was at her weakest, Martin started piling on the emotional pressure.* 就在她最脆弱的時候, 馬丁開始增加她感情上的壓力。

pressure² *v* [T] to try to make someone do something by making them feel it is their duty to do it 對…施加壓力; PRESSURIZE *BrE*【英】: **pressure sb into doing sth** *I've been pressured into helping with the decorating.* 我被迫幫助裝修。| **pressure sb to do sth** 對某人施加壓力使其做某事

pressure cook·er /ˈ·· ˌ··/ *n* [C] a tightly covered cooking pot in which food is cooked very quickly by the pressure of hot steam 壓力鍋, 高壓鍋

pres·sured /ˈprɛʃɚd; ˈpreʃəd/ *adj* feeling worried, or making you feel worried because of the number of things you have to do (感到) 有壓力的; PRESSURIZED (2) *BrE*【英】: *This is the most pressured job I've ever had.* 這是我做過的壓力最大的一份工作。

pressure group /ˈ·· ·/ *n* [C] a group or organization that tries to influence the opinions of ordinary people and persuade the government to do something 壓力集團〔為影響輿論或政府行為而開展活動的團體〕: *environmental pressure groups* 環境保護壓力集團 —see also 另見 INTEREST GROUP

pressure point /ˈ·· ·/ *n* [C] **1** a point on the body where an ARTERY (=a tube that carries blood) that runs near a bone can be pressed and closed off, to stop blood loss〔身體上按之即可止血的〕壓迫點, 加壓止血點 **2** a place on the body that is massaged (MASSAGE² (1)) or used in treatments such as REFLEXOLOGY or ACUPUNCTURE〔指壓按摩中的〕壓(覺)點, 穴位 **3** a place or situation that may involve trouble or problems 可能有麻煩[問題]的地方[局面]: *a pressure point for racial tension* 會出現種族間緊張局勢的地方[局面]

pres·sur·i·za·tion /ˌprɛʃərəˈzeʃən; ˌpreʃəraɪˈzeɪʃən/ *n* [U] the quality of being (PRESSURIZED (1)) or the degree to which something is pressurized 增壓, 加壓; 加壓[增壓]的程度

pres·sur·ize also 又作 **-ise** /ˈprɛʃəˌraɪz; ˈpreʃəraɪz/ *v* [T] *BrE* to try to make someone do something by making them feel it is their duty to do it; PRESSURE²【英】對…施加壓力: **pressurize sb into doing sth** *They would have enjoyed the party more if they hadn't been pressurised into going.* 如果他們不是被逼迫去的, 他們在聚會上可能會玩得更好。| **pressurize sb to do sth** *Normally apathetic members were pressurized to vote.* 通常漠不關心的成員都會被迫進行投票。

pres·sur·ized also 又作 **-ised** *BrE*【英】/ˈprɛʃərˌaɪzd; ˈpreʃəraɪzd/ *adj* **1** containing air that has controlled pressure 耐壓的, 密封的: *a pressurized container* 密封容器 | *pressurised high altitude aircraft* 耐高壓的高空飛行器 **2** *BrE* feeling worried or making you feel worried, because of the amount of things you have to do; PRESSURED【英】〔感到〕有壓力的: *today's pressurized society* 如今壓力重重的社會

pres·tige /prɛsˈtiʒ; preˈstiːʒ/ *n* [U] **1** the respect and importance a person, organization, or profession has, because of their high position in society, or the quality of their work 威望, 聲望, 威信: *striving for prestige, status and power* 為聲望、地位和權力而努力奮鬥 | *The teaching profession has lost the prestige it used to have.* 教學職業已失去以往具有的那種威望。**2 prestige car/position/neighbourhood etc** a car etc that is expensive and important-looking in a way that other people admire 有氣派的汽車/令人羨慕的職位/有氣派的住宅區 —compare 比較 STATUS (2)

pres·ti·gious /prɛˈstɪdʒəs; preˈstɪdʒəs/ *adj* admired as one of the best and most important 有威望[聲望, 威信]的: *a prestigious job* 受人尊敬的工作 | *a prestigious award* 享有盛名的獎項

pres·to¹ /ˈprɛsto; ˈprestəʊ/ *adj, adv technical* played or sung very quickly【術語】〔演奏或演唱〕急板的[地]

presto² *n* [C] *technical* a piece or section of music played or sung very quickly【術語】急板; 急板樂段[樂章, 樂曲]

presto³ *interjection spoken* used when you show someone something unbelievable or magical【口】嘿〔用於給人看令人難以置信或不可思議的東西時〕; HEY PRESTO *BrE*【英】: *And presto! The rabbit disappears.* 嘿! 那隻兔子不見了。

pre-stressed /ˌpri ˈstrɛst; ˌpriː ˈstrest◄/ *adj* pre-stressed CONCRETE has been made stronger by having wires put inside it〔混凝土〕預加應力的, 加了鋼筋的

pre·sum·a·bly /prɪˈzuməblɪ; prɪˈzjuːməbli/ *adv* [sentence adverb 句子副詞] used to say that you think something is likely to be true 可能, 大概, 據推測: *If you're eating beforehand, presumably you won't want to go to a restaurant.* 如果你要提前吃, 看來你就不想去餐館了。| *Presumably you've all seen this notice now.* 現在你們大概都已看到這則告示了。 S1 W3

pre·sume /prɪˈzum; prɪˈzjuːm/ *v* **1** [T] to think you can be sure of something because it is likely, although there is no proof〔沒有證據地〕相信, 認為; 推測: *Each of you will make a speech, I presume?* 我想你們每個人都要演講, 是嗎? | **presume (that)** *I presume we'll be there by six o'clock.* 我想我們將在六點之前到達那裡。| **presume sb/sth to be sb/sth** *From the way they talked I presumed them to be married.* 從他們談話的樣子看, 我想他們已經結婚了。| **be presumed to do sth** *The temple is presumed to date from the first century BC.* 這座寺廟被認為建於公元前一世紀。**2** [T] to accept something as true until it is proved untrue, especially in law 認定, 視為, 推定〔尤用於法律〕: *We must presume innocence until we have evidence of guilt.* 除非我們有罪證, 否則我們應作無罪推定。| **be presumed dead/ innocent etc** *Their nephew was missing, presumed dead.* 他們的姪子失蹤了, 據推定已經死亡。**3** [I] *formal* to behave without respect or politeness by doing something that you have no right to do【正式】冒昧做某事, 放肆, 擅作主張: **presume to do sth** *Are you presuming to tell me how to treat my family?* 如何對待我的家人難道我還要你來教嗎? **4** [T usually in present tense 一般用現在式] *formal* to accept something as being true and base something else on it; PRESUPPOSE【正式】意味着, 以…為先決條件: *The statement that everyone is free presumes equality of opportunity.* 人皆自由這一說法意味着機會是平等的。| **presume that** *Our recommendations presume that a capable person is in charge.* 我們推薦的先決條件是要有一個有能力的人來負責。 W3

presume on/upon sth *phr v* [T] *formal* to use someone's kindness, or a relationship, to ask them for more than you should【正式】濫用, 不正當地利用〔某種關係、某人的好心〕: *I felt it would be presuming on our friendship to ask him to lend me that much money.* 我覺得向他借那麼多錢是在利用我們的友情。

pre·sump·tion /prɪ`zʌmpʃən; prɪˈzʌmpʃən/ *n* **1** [C] an act of thinking that something is true because it is very likely 假定; 推測; 設想: *the presumption that she would leave* 關於她要離開的推測 **2** [U] disrespectful or impolite behaviour that shows you are too confident 放肆, 冒昧; 自以為是: *Ryan's presumption in telling her when they would meet* 瑞恩自作主張地告訴她他們將在甚麼時候見面 **3** [C,U] *law* the act of thinking something is true because it is very likely, although there is no certain proof【法律】〔無證據的〕推定, 認定: *the presumption of innocence* 無罪認定

pre·sump·tive /prɪ`zʌmptɪv; prɪˈzʌmptɪv/ *adj formal or technical* based on a reasonable belief about what is likely to be true【正式或術語】推定的, 假定的: *a presumptive diagnosis* 推定的診斷 —**presumptively** *adv* —see also 另見 HEIR PRESUMPTIVE

pre·sump·tu·ous /prɪ`zʌmptʃuəs; prɪˈzʌmptʃuəs/ *adj* showing disrespect as a result of being too confident 專橫的, 自以為是的; 冒失的; 放肆的: *She found Conrad charming but rather presumptuous.* 她發現康拉德長得迷人, 只是頗為專橫。—**presumptuously** *adv* —**presumptuousness** *n* [U]

pre·sup·pose /ˌprisə`poz; ˌpri:səˈpəʊz/ *v* [T] *formal*【正式】**1** to depend on something that is thought to be true; ASSUME 預先假定, 假設, 預料: **presuppose that** *The plans presuppose that people usually respond to calls for help.* 這些計劃是預先假定人們通常會對呼救作出反應。**2** to depend on something in order to exist or be true 以…為先決條件, 意味着: *Every form of human society presupposes some kind of division of labour.* 每一種人類社會形式都以某種分工為先決條件。

pre·sup·po·si·tion /ˌprisʌpə`zɪʃən; ˌpri:sʌpəˈzɪʃən/ *n formal*【正式】**1** [C] something that someone thinks is true without proof; ASSUMPTION 預先假定(的事), 預想(的事), 假設(的事): **[+that]** *the presupposition that crime is just another form of sickness* 對於犯罪只是另一種形式的病態的假設 **2** [U] the act of thinking something is true without proof 預先假定, 假設

pre·teen /ˌpri`tin; ˌpri:ˈti:n◂/ *adj* connected with, or made for children who are 11 or 12 years old 青春期前兒童的; 為青春期前兒童製造的: *preteen clothing* 青春期前的童裝 —**preteen** *n* [C] *AmE*【美】

pre·tence also 又作 **pretense** *AmE*【美】/prɪ`tɛns; prɪˈtens/ *n* [singular, U] **1** an attempt to pretend that something is true 假裝, 作假, 做作: **[+that]** *Susie abandoned the pretence that she didn't want to go to the party.* 蘇茜不再假裝不想去參加聚會了。| **keep up the pretence of being/doing sth** *How long are you going to keep up the pretence of being ill?* 你裝病還要裝多久呢? | **under (the) pretence of sth** *John waited for her under pretence of tying his shoelaces.* 約翰假裝在繫鞋帶等着她。| **make a pretence of doing sth** *Tollitt made no pretence of hiding his surprise.* 托里特沒有假裝掩飾他的驚訝。**2 under/on false pretences** if you do something under false pretences, you do it by pretending that something is true 以欺詐手段, 以虛假的藉口: *Mellors obtained credit under false pretences.* 梅勒斯以欺詐手段騙得了貸款。**3 no pretence to superiority/faith/education etc** no claim that you are SUPERIOR[1] (4) etc 不自稱高人一等/信仰上帝/受過教育等: *a simple man, with little pretence to education* 不自吹受過教育的純樸的人

pre·tend[1] /prɪ`tɛnd; prɪˈtend/ *v* **1** [I,T] to behave as if something is true when in fact you know it is not 假裝, 佯稱: *We're not really sisters; we were just pretending.* 我們不是真姐妹, 我們只是裝着是姐妹。| **pretend (that)** *The candidate pretended she had worked for a newspaper before.* 這位候選人佯稱她以前在一家報社工作過。| **pretend to do sth** *Sarah pretended to be cheerful and said nothing about the argument.* 莎拉假裝很開心, 沒有說起爭吵的事。| **pretend sth** *Dennis often pretends deafness when you ask him an awkward question.* 當被問及難以回答的問題時, 丹尼斯經常裝聾作啞。**2** [T, usually in questions and negatives 一般用於疑問句及否定句] to claim that something is true, especially something that cannot be shown to be true 聲稱, 自稱, 自命: **pretend (that)** *I can't pretend I understand these technical terms.* (=I admit I do not understand them) 我不能假裝懂這些專業用語。| **pretend to sth** *I can't pretend to much expertise in computing.* 我不敢自命有很多電腦方面的專門知識。**3** [I,T] to imagine something is true as a game〔作為遊戲〕裝扮, 假裝: **pretend (that)** *Let's pretend we're on the moon.* 讓我們假裝成是在月亮上吧。

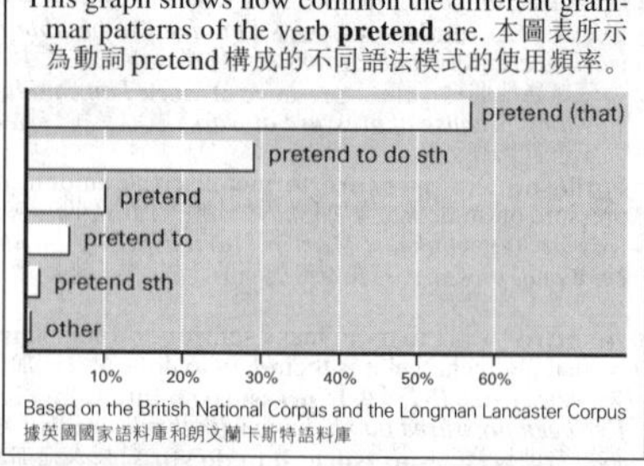

pretend[2] *adj* a word meaning imaginary, used especially by or with children〔尤兒語〕假裝的, 想像的, 假想的: *We sang songs around a pretend campfire.* 我們圍在假想的營火旁唱歌。

pre·tend·ed /prɪ`tɛndɪd; prɪˈtendɪ̈d/ *adj* false or unreal, in spite of seeming to be true or real 假裝的; 虛假的: *pretended sorrow* 假裝的悲傷

pre·tend·er /prɪ`tɛndɚ; prɪˈtendə/ *n* [C] someone who claims a right to be king, leader etc, that many people do not accept 覬覦高位[王位]者: *the pretender to the English throne* 覬覦英國王位者

pre·tense /prɪ`tɛns; prɪˈtens/ *n* [singular, U] an American spelling of PRETENCE pretence 的美式拼法

pre·ten·sion /prɪ`tɛnʃən; prɪˈtenʃən/ *n* [C usually plural 一般用複數] an attempt to seem richer, more important etc than you really are 自命不凡; 虛榮; 炫耀: **[+to]** *a man with pretensions to grandeur* 妄自尊大的男人 | *an area with upper-class pretensions* 具有上流社會虛榮的地區

pre·ten·tious /prɪ`tɛnʃəs; prɪˈtenʃəs/ *adj* trying to seem more important, clever etc than you really are 自以為是的, 自我炫耀的, 矯飾的: *It's pretentious of him to keep the complete works of Proust on full display.* 為了炫耀他把普魯斯特全集都擺了出來。| *a pretentious movie* 狂妄的影片 —opposite 反義詞 UNPRETENTIOUS —**pretentiously** *adv* —**pretentiousness** *n* [U]

pret·er·ite also 又作 **preterit** *AmE*【美】/`prɛtərɪt; ˈpretərɪ̈t/ *n* **the preterite** *technical* the tense or verb form that expresses a past action or condition【術語】過去式[時] —**preterite** *adj*

pre·ter·nat·u·ral /ˌpritɚ`nætʃərəl; ˌpri:təˈnætʃərəl◂/ *adj formal*【正式】**1** beyond what is usual or normal 超乎尋常的, 異常的: *He felt possessed of a preternatural strength and fearlessness.* 他感到擁有異乎尋常的力量和勇氣。**2** strange, mysterious, and unnatural 奇特的; 神祕的; 超自然的: *twisted images emerging through the preternatural green light* 從神祕的綠光中現出的扭曲的影像 —**preternaturally** *adv*: *preternaturally strong* 異常強壯的

pre·text /`pritɛkst; ˈpri:tekst/ *n* [C] a reason given for an action, in order to hide the real intention; EXCUSE² (1, 2) 藉口: **[+for]** *The riots were used as a pretext for banning all political activity.* 騷亂被利用來作為禁止一切政治活動的託辭。| **on/under the pretext of doing sth** *Tom called at her apartment on the pretext of asking for a book.* 湯姆藉口要一本書到她的公寓去。—see 見 EXCUSE² (USAGE)

pret·ti·fy /ˋprɪtɪˏfaɪ; ˈprɪtɪfaɪ/ *v* [T] to change something with the intention of making it pretty, but often with the effect of spoiling it 裝飾, 美化; 粉飾: *The new owners have prettified the house.* 新的主人給那所房子進行了裝飾。

2 3 **pret·ty¹** /ˋprɪtɪ; ˈprɪti/ *adv* [+adj/adv] *spoken*【口】**1** fairly, though not completely 頗, 相當: *I'm pretty sure he'll say yes.* 我相當肯定他會說行。| *Life on the farm was pretty tough.* 農場的生活相當艱苦。—see 見 RATHER (USAGE) **2** very 很, 非常: *It's pretty hard to see how we'll manage.* 很難想像我們將如何應付。**3 pretty well** also 又作 **pretty much** very nearly; almost 差不多, 幾乎: *I'd say that's pretty well impossible.* 我要說那幾乎是不可能的。| *"How is he feeling today?" "Pretty much the same."* "他今天覺得怎麼樣?" "差不多還是老樣子。" **4 pretty near** *especially AmE* almost【尤美】幾乎, 差不多: *That bout of pneumonia pretty near killed Roy.* 那次肺炎發作幾乎致羅伊於死地。—see also 另見 **be sitting pretty** (SIT⁶)

3 3 **pretty²** *adj* **prettier, prettiest 1** a woman or child who is pretty is good-looking in an ordinary way 漂亮的, 好看的, 標致的: *Susan's certainly a pretty girl, but I wouldn't call her beautiful.* 蘇姍確實是一個標致的女孩, 但我認為她稱不上美麗。| *Maria looks much prettier with her hair cut short.* 瑪麗亞把頭髮剪短看起來好看得多。**2** something that is pretty is pleasant to look at or listen to without being very beautiful or impressive 悅目的; 悅耳的, 優美的: *a pretty dress* 漂亮的裙子 | *a pretty tune* 優美的曲調 | *What a pretty little garden!* 多麼好看的小花園! **3** a boy who is pretty looks attractive in a way that is typical of a girl〔男孩〕俊俏的, 女孩子氣的: *She said, "Oh Nick's the pretty one really."* 她說, "噢, 尼克確實是長得俊俏的那個。" **4 not a pretty sight** *often humorous* very unpleasant to look at【常幽默】讓人看起來非常不舒服: *After a night's drinking, Al was not a pretty sight.* 喝了一整夜酒之後, 艾爾看上去糟透了。**5 not just a pretty face** *humorous spoken* to have qualities or abilities as well as an attractive appearance【幽默, 口】不僅相貌好〔還有其他優點〕: *I'm not just a pretty face, you know!* 你知道的, 我不僅僅徒有其表。**6 come to a pretty pass** *old-fashioned* used to say that a very bad situation has developed【過時】情況變得很糟糕: *Things have come to a pretty pass, if you can't say what you think without causing a fight.* 如果你說出自己的想法就會引起爭吵的話, 情況就很糟糕了。**7 cost a pretty penny** *old-fashioned* to cost a lot of money【過時】花費很多錢 **8 pretty as a picture** very pretty 非常漂亮的 **9 pretty pretty** *BrE* spoilt by too much pretty decoration【英】裝飾得過分的, 過分華麗的 —**prettily** *adv*: *Charlotte sang very prettily.* 夏洛特唱得很優美。—**prettiness** *n* [U]

pret·zel /ˋprɛtsḷ; ˈpretsəl/ *n* [C] a hard salty BISCUIT or CRACKER (1) baked in the shape of a stick or a loose knot 棒狀餅乾, 紐結狀鹹餅乾

pre·vail /prɪˋvel; prɪˈveɪl/ *v* [I] *formal*【正式】[not in progressive 不用進行式] **1** if a belief, custom etc prevails, it exists among a group of people〔信念、風俗等〕盛行, 流行: **[+in/among etc]** *Belief in magic still prevails in some rural parts of the country.* 這個國家的一些農村地區至今仍然相信魔法。**2** if someone or their ideas prevail, they win an argument or fight after a long time〔某人或其觀點〕獲勝; 佔優勢, 佔上風: **[+over]** *The military finally prevailed over the civilian resistance movement.* 軍隊最終戰勝了平民的反抗運動。| *Justice prevailed in the end.* 正義最終獲得了勝利。

prevail on/upon sb *phr v* [T] *formal* to persuade someone【正式】勸說, 說服〔某人〕: **prevail on sb to do sth** *David was prevailed upon to propose a vote of thanks.* 人們勸大衛提議公開致謝。

pre·vail·ing /prɪˋvelɪŋ; prɪˈveɪlɪŋ/ *adj* [only before noun 僅用於名詞前] **1** existing or accepted in a particular place or at a particular time; CURRENT¹ 流行的, 盛行的: *the prevailing state of education* 普遍的教育狀況 | *prevailing trends* 流行趨勢 **2 prevailing wind** a wind that blows over a particular area most of the time 盛行風

prev·a·lent /ˋprɛvələnt; ˈprevələnt/ *adj* common at a particular time or in a particular place〔在某時或某地〕普遍的, 盛行的, 流行的: **[+in/among etc]** *Solvent abuse is especially prevalent among younger teenagers.* 吸膠毒在青少年中特別普遍。| *prevalent attitudes* 普遍的態度 —**prevalence** *n* [U]

pre·var·i·cate /prɪˋværəˏket; prɪˈværɪkeɪt/ *v* [I] to try to hide the truth by not answering questions directly 支吾, 搪塞, 推諉, 含糊其辭 —**prevarication** /prɪˏværəˋkeʃən; prɪˌværɪˈkeɪʃən/ *n* [C,U]

pre·vent /prɪˋvɛnt; prɪˈvent/ *v* [T] to stop something from happening, or stop someone from doing something 阻止, 阻擋; 預防, 防止: *The rules are intended to prevent accidents.* 這些規定旨在防止事故發生。| **prevent sb/sth (from) doing sth** *Lacey has a back injury that may prevent him from playing in tomorrow's game.* 萊西背上受了傷, 這可能使他不能打明天的比賽。—**preventable** *adj* 2 1

pre·ven·ta·tive /prɪˋvɛntətɪv; prɪˈventətɪv/ *adj* another form of the word PREVENTIVE 預防(性)的, 防備的: *preventative measures* 預防措施

pre·ven·tion /prɪˋvɛnʃən; prɪˈvenʃən/ *n* [U] the act of preventing something, or the actions that you take in order to prevent something happening 預防; 防止; 阻止; 預防行動: **[+of]** *the prevention of war* 防止戰爭 | **crime/accident prevention** *Accident prevention is one of the main aims of the campaign.* 預防事故發生是這次活動的主要目標之一。

pre·ven·tive /prɪˋvɛntɪv; prɪˈventɪv/ also 又作 **preventative** *adj* [only before noun 僅用於名詞前] intended to prevent something you do not want to happen, such as illness, or crime 預防(性)的, 防備的: *preventive health programs* 預防性保健計劃 | **preventive actions/measures** (=actions intended to stop something happening or a situation getting worse) 預防行動/措施 *Simple preventive measures will reduce the risk of infection.* 簡單的預防措施將會減少感染的危險。—**preventively** *adv* —**preventatively** *adv*

preventive de·ten·tion /ˌ.. ˈ..ˌ../ *n* [U] *BrE law* a system in which people who are guilty of many crimes are kept in prison for a long time【英, 法律】〔對於慣犯的〕預防性拘留

preventive medi·cine /ˌ.. ˈ.../ *n* [U] medical treatment, advice, and health education that is designed to prevent disease happening rather than cure it 預防醫學

pre-verb·al /ˌ. ˈ..◂/ *adj* [only before noun 僅用於名詞前] happening before a child has learned to speak〔幼兒〕獲得語言能力前的: *the pre-verbal stages* 尚未獲得語言能力階段

pre·view /ˋpriˏvju; ˈpriːvjuː/ *n* [C] **1** an occasion when you can see a film, play etc before it is shown to the public〔戲劇、電影的〕預演, 預映: **sneak preview** *a sneak preview of his new play* 他的新劇的內部預演 **2** an advertisement for a film or television programme that often consists of short parts from it〔電影或電視節目的〕預告(片); TRAILER (3) *BrE*【英】

pre·vi·ous /ˋpriviəs; ˈpriːviəs/ *adj* **1** [only before noun 僅用於名詞前] happening or existing before the event, time, or thing that is being mentioned 以前的, 先前的, 前的: *a better result than we've had in previous years* 比我們前些年較好的結果 | *She has two children from a previous marriage.* 她前一次婚姻有兩個孩子。| **previous experience** *Do you have any previous experience* 

of this kind of work? 你以前有過做這種工作的經驗嗎? | **previous offences/convictions** (=things that a criminal has done, or been judged guilty of, before) 前科 **2 a bit previous** *BrE informal* done before the right or sensible time【英, 非正式】有點操之過急的; 有點過早的: *It's a bit previous to ask for the money before they've done the job.* 他們還沒做工作就要錢未免有點操之過急。 **3 previous to sth** before a particular time or event 在某事物以前: *There were almost no women MPs previous to 1945.* 1945年前幾乎沒有女性議員。

3 2 **pre·vi·ous·ly** /ˋpriviəslɪ; ˈpriːviəsli/ *adv* before the present time 以前, 先前: *The world record was previously held by a Spanish athlete.* 這個世界記錄以前是由一位西班牙運動員保持的。| **two days/three years etc previously** *The car was now worth twice what we'd paid for it six months previously.* 這部車現在的價錢比我們六個月前花的錢多一倍。

pre·vi·sion /prɪˋvɪʒən; ˌpriːˈvɪʒən/ *n* [C,U] *formal* something you see in your mind or knowledge you have of an event before it happens【正式】預知; 預感; 預見 —compare 比較 PREMONITION

pre-war /ˌ· ˈ·◂/ *adj, adv* happening or existing before a war, especially the First or Second World Wars 戰前(的)〔尤指第一次或第二次世界大戰之前〕: *conditions in pre-war Europe* 戰前歐洲的情況 —compare 比較 POST-WAR

prey[1] /pre; preɪ/ *n* **1** [U] an animal that is hunted and eaten by another animal or by a person 被〔其他動物或人〕捕食的動物, 獵物: *a tiger stalking its prey* 潛步跟蹤獵物的老虎 **2 bird/beast of prey** a bird or animal which lives by killing and eating other animals 食肉猛禽/猛獸: *falcons and other birds of prey* 獵鷹和其他食肉猛禽 **3 be/fall prey to sth** to be unable to avoid being affected by something unpleasant 為某事物所折磨: *During the long wait she was prey to all sorts of doubts and anxieties.* 在長時間的等待中, 她為各式各樣的疑惑和焦慮所折磨。 **4** [U] someone who can easily be deceived or influenced 容易受騙[受影響]的人: *Some salesmen consider young housewives easy prey.* 一些推銷員認為年輕的家庭主婦很容易被他們蒙騙。

prey[2] *v*

prey on sb/sth *phr v* [T] **1** if an animal or bird preys on another animal or bird it hunts and eats it 捕食: *Cats prey on birds and mice.* 貓捕食鳥和老鼠。 **2** to try to influence or deceive weaker people 試圖影響; 欺騙〔弱者〕: *religious cults that specialize in preying on young people* 專門欺騙年輕人的宗教派別 **3 prey on your mind** to make you worry continuously 使你持續苦惱, 折磨你: *The accident has been preying on my mind all week.* 那次事故使我整個星期惴惴不安。

prez·zie /ˋprɛzɪ; ˈprezi/ *n* [C] *BrE spoken* another spelling of PRESSIE【英口】pressie的另一種拼法

1 1 **price**[1] /praɪs; praɪs/ *n*

1 ►MONEY 錢◄ [C,U] the amount of money for which something is sold, bought, or offered 價格, 價錢: *Fuel prices are rising steadily.* 燃料價格正穩步上漲。| **[+of]** *Can you tell me what the price of a new window would be?* 你能告訴我一個新窗戶要多少錢嗎? | *They agreed on a price of £2,000 for the car.* 他們商定的這輛車的價錢為2,000英鎊。| **high/low price** *You can get cars in Europe at very low prices.* 在歐洲可以以很低的價錢買到汽車。| **price increase/rise** *Experts say that price rises will be gradual.* 專家說價格將逐漸上漲。| **right price** *We don't have to sell to the first buyer, we can wait for the right price.* 我們不必賣給第一個買主, 我們可以等待合適的價格。| **at a good/fair etc price** *You can get a three-course meal at a fairly reasonable price.* 你可以以相當公道的價格吃到一頓三道菜的飯菜。| **half/full price** *I bought these jeans half price in the sale.* 我在一次大減價中以半價買了這條牛仔褲。| **in price** *Videos vary in price depending on the make.* 錄影機根據牌子不同而價格不同。—see also 另見 ASKING PRICE, COST[1] (USAGE), COST PRICE, LIST PRICE, MARKET PRICE

2 at a price a) used to say that you can buy something, but only if you pay a lot of money 以很高的價錢: *You can get goat's cheese at the local delicatessen – at a price!* 你可以在當地的熟食店買到山羊乳酪 —— 不過價格很高! **b)** used to say that something can be achieved, but that it involves something unpleasant 以很高的代價: *She was finally made senior executive, but at what price!* 她最終當上了高級經理, 但那是以甚麼樣的代價呀!

3 at any price if you want to do something at any price you are determined to do it, even if it is very difficult 不惜任何代價, 無論如何: *She was determined to have a child at any price.* 她決心不惜任何代價要一個孩子。

4 not at any price used to say that you would never sell something, or do something, even for a lot of money 無論多高的價錢也不賣; 無論如何不: *Sorry, that painting's not for sale at any price.* 對不起, 那幅畫無論出多高的價錢也不賣。

5 put a price on sth a) to say how much something costs 給某物定價: *Could you put a price on the damage the storm caused?* 你能說出這次暴風雨造成的損失有多少錢嗎? **b)** to give something a financial value 定出某物的金錢價值: *You just can't put a price on their fighting spirit.* 他們的戰鬥精神是無法用金錢衡量的。

6 the price of success/freedom etc the unpleasant or unwelcome things that you must suffer in order to be successful, free etc 成功/自由等的代價: *Monroe paid the ultimate price of success, dying alone in her room.* 夢露為成功付出了最高的代價 —— 孤身死在她的房間裡。

7 What price fame/glory etc? *usually spoken* used to say that it is possible that it was not worth achieving something good, because too many bad things have happened as a result【一般口】名聲/榮耀等又有甚麼用?: *Homeless widows and orphans viewing tonight's carnage may well ask, what price political independence?* 無家可歸的寡婦和孤兒看了今晚的大屠殺很可能會問, 政治獨立有甚麼用?

8 ►AT HORSE RACE 在賽馬時◄ [C] the chance that a horse will win a race expressed in numbers; ODDS (4)〔賽馬中的〕投注賠率: *"What price are you offering on 'Lucky Shot'?" "Seven to four."* "你給'幸運射手'的賠率是多少?" "七賠四。"

9 be above/beyond/without etc price to be extremely valuable or important 極其珍貴的, 極其重要的; 無價的

10 a price on sb's head a reward for catching or killing someone 懸賞緝拿[殺死]某人的賞額: *running scared with a price on his head* 被懸賞緝拿而倉惶逃竄

11 everyone has their price used to say that you can persuade people to do anything if you give them what they want 人各有其價〔指人都是可以收買的〕—see also 另見 **cheap at the price** (CHEAP[1] (8)), **name your price** (NAME[2] (7)), **pay the price** (PAY[1] (6))

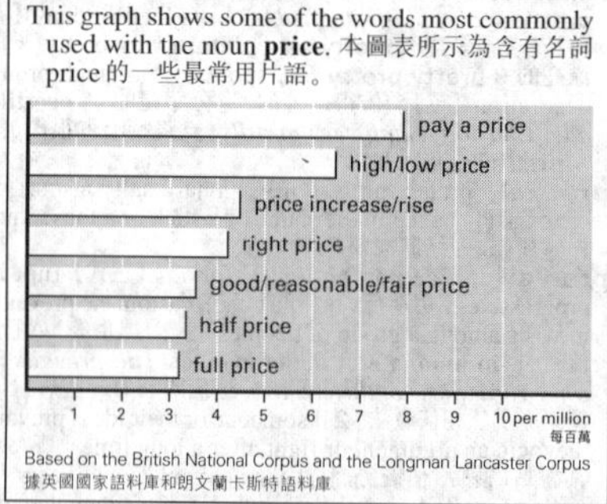

price[2] *v* [T] **1** [usually in passive 一般用被動態] to fix the price of something that is for sale 給…定價錢: a *mod-*

erately priced apartment 定價適中的公寓 | **be priced at** *The tennis rackets are priced at £75 each.* 這種網球拍的定價為每隻75英鎊。**2** to put the price on goods to show how much they cost 給…標價 **3** to compare the prices of things 比較…的價錢: *We spent Saturday morning pricing microwaves.* 我們花了星期六一上午的時間比較微波爐的價錢。**4 price yourself out of the market** to demand too much money for the services or goods that you are selling 漫天要價致使〔自己的服務或商品〕失去市場

price con·trol /'· ·,·/ *n* [U] a system in which the government sets the prices of things〔政府實行的〕價格管制, 物價控制

price fix·ing /'· ,··/ *n* [U] **1** a system in which the government sets the prices of things; PRICE CONTROL 價格管制, 物價控制 **2** an agreement between producers and sellers of a product to fix its price at a high level 價格壟斷, 操縱物價

price in·dex /'· ,··/ *n* [C] a system of numbers by which the prices of goods can be compared with what they were in the past 價格指數, 物價指數 —see also 另見 RETAIL PRICE INDEX

price·less /ˈpraɪslɪs; ˈpraɪsləs/ *adj* **1** so valuable that it is difficult to give a financial value 極其貴重的; 無價的: *priceless antiques* 極其貴重的古董 **2** a quality or skill that is priceless is extremely important or useful〔品質或技能〕極其重要的, 極其有用的: *The ability to motivate people is a priceless asset.* 能夠激發人們的積極性是難能可貴的優點。**3** *informal* extremely funny or silly【非正式】極其荒唐的, 極其可笑的: *The look on his face when I walked in was priceless.* 我走進來時他臉上的表情極為可笑。

price list /'· ·/ *n* [C] a list of prices for things being sold 價目表, 價格單

pric·es and in·comes pol·i·cy /,·· · '·· ,···/ *n* [C] government actions to prevent prices and incomes increasing, in order to stop or limit INFLATION 價格和收入政策〔政府為避免或限制通貨膨脹而阻止價格和收入增加的措施〕

price sup·port /'· ·,·/ *n* [U] a system in which the government keeps the price of a product at a fixed level by giving the producer money or buying the product itself〔政府以給製造商補貼或收購等形式給予的〕價格支持, 物價補貼

price tag /'· ·/ *n* [C] **1** a small ticket showing the price of something 價格標籤 **2** the amount that something costs 價格, 價值, 費用: *It's difficult to put a price tag on such a project.* 很難確定這樣的項目將耗資多少。

price war /'· ·/ *n* [C] a period when two or three companies reduce the prices of what they sell, all trying to get the most customers 價格戰

pric·ey, pricy /ˈpraɪsɪ; ˈpraɪsi/ *adj* **pricier, priciest** *informal* expensive【非正式】昂貴的, 價錢高的: *New books are pretty pricey nowadays.* 如今的新書相當貴。

prick (刺)破, 戳(穿), 扎(穿)

prick¹ /prɪk; prɪk/ *v* **1** [T] to make a small hole in something, using a sharp point 刺(破), 戳(穿), 扎(穿): *Prick the pastry lightly with a fork.* 用叉輕輕地在油酥麵團上扎孔。| **prick yourself/prick your finger** *Ouch! I've pricked my finger with the needle.* 哎喲! 我的手指被針扎了一下。**2** [I,T] to feel an unpleasant stinging feeling on your skin, or to make someone feel this (使)感到刺痛: **prick sth** *The coarse material was beginning to prick my whole body.* 這種粗糙的布料開始使我全身感到刺痛。—see also 另見 PRICKLE² (1) **3 prick sb's conscience** to make someone feel guilty or ashamed 使某人的良心受到譴責, 使某人的良心不安: *a documentary that should prick the consciences of the comfortable middle classes* 會使舒適的中產階級良心不安的記錄片 **4 prick (up) its ears** if an animal pricks up its ears it raises them and points them towards a sound〔動物〕豎起耳朵聽: *The rabbit stopped suddenly, pricking up its ears.* 那隻兔子突然停下來, 豎起耳朵聽。**5 prick (up) your ears** to listen carefully because you have heard something interesting〔人〕仔細傾聽: *Jay pricked up his ears when I mentioned vacation.* 我提到假期時, 傑伊豎起耳朵來仔細地聽。**6 prick the bubble (of sth)** to make someone see the uncomfortable truth of a situation 使〔對某事物的〕幻想破滅

prick sth **out** *phr v* [T] to place a young plant in a specially prepared hole 把〔幼苗〕移植到特別挖好的洞中

prick² *n* [C]

1 ►PAIN 疼痛◄ a slight pain you get when something sharp goes into your skin 刺痛: *Don't worry, it's just a little needle prick.* 別擔心, 只是有點刺痛感。

2 ►SMALL HOLE 小洞◄ a) a small hole made by a sharp point in your skin or the surface of something 刺孔; 刺痕; 刺點: *A sample of blood was drawn from a prick in the skin.* 從皮膚的刺孔採集了血樣。**b)** an act of pricking something 刺, 戳; 扎: *Give the sausages a prick.* 在那些香腸上扎孔。—see also 另見 PINPRICK

3 ►SEX ORGAN 性器官◄ *slang taboo* a PENIS【俚, 諱】陰莖

4 ►PERSON 人◄ *slang taboo* a stupid unpleasant man【俚, 諱】蠢材, 笨蛋; 討厭的傢伙

5 prick of conscience an uncomfortable feeling that you have done something wrong 良心的不安

6 a prick of light a small point or circle of light 小光點, 小光圈

prick·le¹ /ˈprɪkl; ˈprɪkəl/ *n* [C] **1** a long thin sharp point on the skin of some plants and animals〔動植物的〕皮刺; 刺, 棘 **2** a stinging feeling on your skin〔皮膚上的〕刺痛感: *prickles of perspiration* 汗水的刺痛感

prickle² *v* **1** [T] to give someone a stinging feeling on their skin 引起刺痛: *The bush prickled the back of his legs.* 這種灌木刺痛了他雙腿後部。**2** [I] if your skin prickles it begins to sting or feel cold because you are very frightened, angry etc〔由於非常害怕、生氣等皮膚〕感到刺痛, 感到發冷: *The skin on the back of her neck prickled as she heard the door creak open.* 她聽到門吱的一聲打開時, 後頸直起雞皮疙瘩。| **prickle with anger/excitement etc** (=to feel strong anger, excitement etc) 感到非常生氣/興奮等 *She spoke brusquely, prickling with an increasing dislike of Damien Flint.* 她說話粗魯, 對達米恩·弗林特感到越來越討厭。

prick·ly /ˈprɪklɪ; ˈprɪkli/ *adj* **1** covered with prickles 佈滿刺的, 多刺的: *Prickly brambles grew on either side of the path.* 那條小路兩邊長着多刺的灌木。**2** *informal* someone who is prickly gets annoyed or offended easily【非正式】〔人〕易生氣的, 易動怒的: *Fiona's in a very prickly mood this morning.* 菲安娜今天早上動不動就發火。**3** something prickly makes you feel a small stinging sensation on your skin 引起刺痛的: *a prickly woollen sweater* 使皮膚感到刺痛的毛線衣 | **a prickly feeling** *I've got a prickly feeling in my leg.* 我的一條腿感到發麻。**4** causing problems, disagreements, and difficulties 棘手的, 難處理的: *Nuclear power is still a prickly issue.* 核能仍然是一個棘手的問題。—**prickliness** *n* [U]

prickly heat /,·· '·/ *n* [U] a skin condition caused by

P

strong sunlight that consists of uncomfortable red spots on the skin〔皮膚上的〕痱子

prickly pear /ˌ·· ˈ·/ *n* [C,U] a kind of CACTUS with yellow flowers, or the fruit of this plant 仙人果（的果實）

pric·y /ˈpraɪsɪ; ˈpraɪsi/ *adj* another spelling of PRICEY pricey 的另一種拼法

S3 W3 **pride¹** /praɪd; praɪd/ *n* [U]

1 ▶FEELING OF PLEASURE 愉快的感覺◀ a feeling of satisfaction and pleasure in what you have done, or in what someone connected with you has done 自豪（感）；得意：**show/feel/take pride in (doing) sth** *The employees all show great pride in their company.* 所有的雇員都對公司感到非常自豪。| *She takes pride in doing a job well.* 她為能很好地完成一項工作而感到自豪。| **show/feel/take (a) pride in sth** *Scott takes a great pride in his appearance.* 史考特為自己的相貌深感自豪。| **a glow of pride** (=pride that is very clearly shown) 明顯的自豪 | **with pride** *They talked about their son with obvious pride.* 他們帶着明顯的自豪感談論他們的兒子。

2 ▶RESPECT 尊敬◀ a feeling that you like and respect yourself and that you deserve to be respected by other people 自尊（心）：**hurt sb's pride** *Don't offer her money, you'll hurt her pride.* 別提出給她錢，你會傷害她的自尊心的。| **give sb their pride back** *Getting a job gave Sam his pride back.* 找到一份工作使山姆重新獲得了自尊。

3 ▶TOO MUCH PRIDE 過分的自尊◀ a feeling that you are better than other people because you are cleverer, more important etc 驕傲，傲慢：*His pride would not allow him to ask for help.* 他自尊心作祟，不會向別人求助。

4 sb's pride and joy someone or something that someone is very proud of, and that is important to them 某人的快樂和驕傲：*The garden is my father's pride and joy.* 這個花園是我爸爸的快樂和驕傲。

5 the pride of a) the thing or person that the people in a particular place are most proud of ...引為自豪的人[事物]：*Wigan's rugby team was the pride of the town.* 威根的橄欖球隊是鎮裡的驕傲。**b)** the best thing in a group〔一組中〕最好的事物：*This Japanese sword is the pride of my collection.* 這把日本刀是我收藏品中的精品。

6 have/take pride of place to have the most important position in a group 佔據最重要的位置：*A huge birthday cake took pride of place on the table.* 桌子上最顯眼的位置放着一個巨大的生日蛋糕。

7 swallow your pride/put your pride in your pocket to forget your feelings of pride and do something that seems necessary, although you do not want to do it 放下你的架子：*Jerry swallowed his pride and apologised.* 傑里放下架子道了歉。

8 a group of lions 獅羣：*A young lion had strayed some distance from the pride.* 在與獅羣有一段距離的地方有一隻幼獅離了羣。

pride² *v* **pride yourself on sth** to be especially proud of something that you do well, or of a quality that you have 以某事物而自豪，對某事物感到得意：*The school prides itself on its academic record.* 這所學校為它的學術成就感到自豪。

W3 **priest** /prist; priːst/ *n* [C] **1** someone who is specially trained to perform religious duties and ceremonies in the Christian church〔基督教的〕牧師 **2** a man with religious duties and responsibilities in some non-Christian religions〔基督教之外一些宗教的〕神職人員

USAGE NOTE 用法說明：PRIEST

WORD CHOICE 詞語辨析：**priest, clergyman, clergy, minister, pastor, chaplain, padre**

A **priest** is someone in charge of the prayers, services etc for the people who attend a particular church, especially in the Roman Catholic Church. priest指為參加某個教會的人們主持祈禱、宗教儀式的人，尤在羅馬天主教教會中使用。

A priest in a Protestant church is often called a **minister**, and this is the most usual word in American English. A **vicar** is a priest who is in charge of a church in the Church of England. In the US **pastor** is also used for someone in charge of a particular church in the Protestant religion. 在新教教會中，priest 常稱作 minister，minister 在美國英語中是最常用的詞。vicar 指在英國國教中負責某個教會的牧師。在美國，pastor 也用來指負責某個新教教會的人。

More general words for priests include **the clergy, clergymen**, or a **clergyman**. 表示神職人員的較籠統的詞語包括 the clergy，clergymen，或 a clergyman：*talks between education chiefs and the clergy* 教育長官和牧師之間的對話 | *She married an impoverished clergyman.* 她嫁給了一個貧窮的牧師。

A priest who looks after the religious needs of an organization such as a university, hospital, or prison is a **chaplain**. A priest who looks after the religious needs of soldiers in the army, navy etc, is also called a **chaplain**, but can also be called a **padre**. 負責大學、醫院或監獄等機構中的宗教需要的神職人員稱為 chaplain。負責陸軍、海軍等士兵的宗教需要的神職人員也稱作 chaplain，但也可稱作 padre。

priest·ess /ˈpristɪs; ˈpriːstes/ *n* [C] a woman with religious duties and responsibilities in some non-Christian religions〔基督教之外一些宗教的〕女神職人員

priest·hood /ˈprist·hʊd; ˈpriːsthʊd/ *n* **1 the priesthood** the job or position of a priest 神職人員的工作，神職人員的職位：*He decided to enter the priesthood.* 他決定成為神父。**2** [C,U] all the priests of a particular religion or country〔某一宗教或國家的〕全體神職人員

priest·ly /ˈpristlɪ; ˈpriːstli/ *adj* connected with a priest 神職人員的，牧師的：*priestly garments* 牧師袍

prig /prɪg; prɪg/ *n* [C] someone who obeys moral rules very carefully, and shows in an annoying way that they think they are better than other people 一本正經的人，道學先生 —**priggish** *adj* —**priggishness** *n* [U]

prim /prɪm; prɪm/ *adj* **1** very formal and careful in the way you behave, and easily shocked by anything rude 一本正經的，拘謹的，古板的：*a prim and studious manner* 古板認真的樣子 | **prim and proper** *Andy's much too prim and proper to enjoy your jokes.* 安迪太古板了，不會喜歡你的玩笑。**2** small and neat 小而整潔的：*a prim apron* 整潔的圍裙 —**primly** *adv* —**primness** *n* [U]

pri·ma bal·le·ri·na /ˈprimə ˌbæləˈrinə; ˌpriːmə bæləˈriːnə/ *n* [C] the main woman dancer in a BALLET company 芭蕾舞團的主要[首席]女演員

pri·ma·cy /ˈpraɪməsɪ; ˈpraɪməsi/ *n* [U] *formal* the state of being the most important thing or person【正式】第一位，首位，首要：**[+over]** *the primacy of practical skill over theoretical knowledge* 實際技能重於理論知識

prima don·na /ˌprimə ˈdɑnə; ˌpriːmə ˈdɒnə/ *n* [C] **1** the most important woman singer in an OPERA company 歌劇團的主要[首席]女歌手 **2** someone who thinks that they are very good at what they do, and demands a lot of attention, admiration etc from other people 自以為了不起的人，妄自尊大的人：*In my view, football players are a bunch of over-paid pampered prima donnas.* 依我看，足球運動員是一幫收入過高、寵壞了的自大的傢伙。

pri·mae·val /praɪˈmivl; praɪˈmiːvəl/ *adj* a British spelling of PRIMEVAL primeval 的英式拼法

pri·ma fa·cie /ˌpraɪmə ˈfeʃɪ; ˌpraɪmə ˈfeɪʃi/ *adj Latin law* [only before noun 僅用於名詞前] based on what seems to be true, even though it may be disproved later【拉丁，法律】表面上的；貌似真實的，建立在表象基礎上的：*a prima facie case against him* 表面證據對他不利的案件 —**prima facie** *adv*

pri·mal /ˈpraɪml̩; ˈpraɪməl/ *adj* [only before noun 僅用於名詞前] *formal*【正式】**1** primal feelings seem to belong to a part of people's character that is ancient and animal-like 最初的, 原始的: *man's primal urge to explore the unknown* 人類探索未知世界的原始衝動 **2** basic 基本的, 根本的: *the primal truths of human existence* 人類生活的基本真理

3 **pri·ma·ri·ly** /praɪˌmɛrəlɪ; ˈpraɪmərəli/ *adv* mainly 主要地: *This research is concerned primarily with prevention of the disease.* 這項研究主要關注的是疾病的預防。

3 2 **pri·ma·ry[1]** /praɪˌmɛrɪ; ˈpraɪməri/ *adj* **1** most important; main 首要的, 主要的: *Our primary concern is to provide the refugees with food and health care.* 我們關注的首要問題是給難民提供食物和保健護理。| *a matter of primary importance* 至關重要的問題 **2 primary school/teacher/level etc** concerning the education of children between five and eleven years old 小學/小學教師/初級水平; ELEMENTARY (3) *AmE*【美】: *a primary teacher* 小學教師 | *at primary level* 初級水平 **3** happening or developing before other things 原始的; 最初的

primary[2] *n* [C] **1** *technical* one of the longest feathers on a bird's wing【術語】〔鳥的〕初級飛羽〔指鳥翼上最長的羽毛〕**2** a primary election 初選

primary col·our /ˌ··· ˈ··/ *n* [C] one of the three colours red, yellow, and blue, which you can mix together to make any of the other colours 原色, 基色〔指紅、黃、藍三色〕

primary e·lec·tion /ˌ··· ·ˈ··/ *n* [C] an election in the US at which members of a political party in one area vote to decide who will be their party's CANDIDATE for a political position〔美國推舉黨內候選人的〕初選

primary health care /ˌ··· ˈ· ·/ also 又作 **primary med·i·cal care** /ˌ··· ˈ··· ·/ *n* [U] the medical care that someone receives first when they become ill or have an accident 最初保健護理

primary school /ˈ··· ˌ·/ *n* [C] *BrE* a school for children between five and eleven years old in England and Wales【英】〔英格蘭和威爾斯五至十一歲兒童上的〕小學; ELEMENTARY SCHOOL *AmE*【美】

primary stress /ˌ··· ˈ·/ *n* [C,U] *technical* the strongest force given in speech to a part of a long word, like the force given to 'pri' in 'primary'. It is shown in this dictionary by the mark (ˈ).【術語】主重音, 第一重音

Pri·mate /ˈpraɪmɪt; ˈpraɪmə̩t/ *n* [C] the most important and powerful priest in a country or an area, especially in the Church of England; ARCHBISHOP〔尤指英國國教的〕大主教

pri·mate /ˈpraɪmet; ˈpraɪmeɪt/ *n* [C] a member of the group of MAMMALS that includes humans and monkeys 靈長目動物〔包括人、猴子等〕

prime[1] /praɪm; praɪm/ *adj* [only before noun 僅用於名詞前] **1** most important 最重要的, 首要的: *Smoking is the prime cause of heart disease.* 抽煙是引發心臟病的首要原因。| *Our prime concern is getting the economy back on its feet.* 我們關注的首要問題是恢復經濟。**2** of the very best quality or kind 質量最好的, 第一流的: *The hotel is in a prime location overlooking the valley.* 這個酒店俯瞰山谷, 位置極佳。| *prime cuts of beef* 上等牛肉切塊 **3 be a prime candidate/target etc** to be the person or thing that is most suitable or most likely to be chosen for a particular purpose 最適合的[最有可能被選中的]人[物]: *The railways are a prime candidate for privatization.* 鐵路最有可能私有化。**4 prime example** a very typical example of something 最好的例證, 非常典型的例子: *Sherlock Holmes is the prime example of the great detective.* 夏洛克·福爾摩斯是偉大偵探的傑出典型。

prime[2] *n* **1 be in your prime/be in the prime of life** to be at the time in your life when you are strongest and most active 正值盛年, 在壯年時期, 風華正茂: **past your prime** *Sadly I think the team are past their prime.* 很遺憾, 我認為這個隊的最佳時期已經過去。| **be cut off in your prime** (=die when you are in your prime) 英年早逝 **2** [C] a PRIME NUMBER 質數, 素數

prime[3] *v* [T] **1** [usually passive 一般用被動態] to prepare someone for a situation so that they know what to do 使〔某人〕準備好〔應付某個情況〕: *I felt fully primed by the day of the meeting.* 到了會面的那天, 我感到完全作好了準備。| **prime sb to do sth** *The witness had been primed to say nothing about the car.* 那名證人經人指點過, 要對有關汽車的事隻字不提。| **prime sb for sth** *primed for action* 準備戰鬥 **2** to prepare a gun or mine so that it can fire or explode 為〔槍〕裝填火藥; 為〔地雷〕裝雷管 **3** to put a special layer of paint on a surface, to prepare it for the next layer 在…上塗底漆[底色] **4 prime the pump** to encourage a business, industry, or activity to develop by putting money or effort into it 投入資金[精力]促使〔某企業、產業或活動〕得到發展

P

prime cost /ˌ· ˈ·/ *n* [C,U] the actual cost of producing something as opposed to money spent on selling it, renting factories etc 主要成本, 直接成本〔指生產商品的實際成本〕—compare 比較 OVERHEAD[2] (1)

prime fac·tor /ˌ· ˈ··/ *n* [C] a number that can be divided only by itself and the number one, and is a FACTOR of another number 質[素]因數, 質[素]因子: *7 is a prime factor of 21.* 7是21的質[素]因數。

Prime Me·rid·i·an /ˌ· ·ˈ···/ *n* the imaginary line drawn from north to south on the earth, from which east and west are measured in degrees on a map 本初子午線

Prime Min·is·ter /ˌ· ˈ···/ abbreviation 縮寫為 **PM** *n* [C] the chief minister and leader of the government in some countries with a parliamentary system of government 首相; 總理

prime mov·er /ˌ· ˈ··/ *n* [C] **1** someone who has great influence in the development of something important 對某重要事業的發展有很大影響的人; 倡導者, 推動者: *She's one of the prime movers in the Republican movement.* 她是共和運動的發起者之一。**2** *technical* a natural force, such as wind or water, that can be used to produce power【術語】原動力〈如風力或水力〉

prime num·ber /ˌ· ˈ··/ *n* [C] a number that can be divided only by itself and the number one 質數, 素數

prim·er[1] /ˈpraɪmɚ; ˈpraɪmə/ *n* **1** [C,U] paint that is spread over the bare surface of wood, metal etc before the main covering of paint is put on 塗底料, 底層塗料; 底漆 **2** [C] a tube containing explosive, used to fire a gun, explode a bomb etc 雷管; 火帽 **3** [C] *BrE old-fashioned* a beginner's book in a school subject【英, 過時】入門書, 初級讀本

pri·mer[2] /ˈprɪmɚ; ˈpraɪmə/ *n* [C] *AmE* a set of basic instructions【美】入門指南: *a primer of good management* 成功管理入門指南

prime rate /ˈ· ˌ·/ *n* [C] the lowest rate of interest at which money can be borrowed, which banks offer to their largest customers〔銀行給最大客戶提供的〕優惠貸款利率, 最低貸款利率 —compare 比較 BASE RATE

prime rib /ˌ· ˈ·/ *n* [singular, U] a piece of good quality BEEF that is cut from the chest of the animal 上等肋條牛肉

prime time /ˈ· ˌ·/ *n* [U] *especially AmE* the time in the evening when the greatest number of people are watching television【尤美】〔電視的〕黃金時間, 收視高峯時間

pri·me·val also 又作 **primaeval** *especially BrE*【尤英】/praɪˈmivl̩; praɪˈmiːvəl/ *adj* **1** belonging to the earliest period in the existence of the universe or the Earth 太古的, 太初的: *Primeval clouds of gas formed themselves into stars.* 太初的氣團發展成為星球。**2** very ancient 原始的, 遠古的: *primeval forests* 原始森林 **3** primeval emotions or attitudes are very strong, and seem to come from a part of people's character that is ancient and animal-like〔感情或態度〕出於人之原始天性的, 基於人類固有之本能的

prim·i·tive[1] /ˈprɪmətɪv; ˈprɪmə̩tɪv/ *adj* **1** belonging to a society that has a very simple way of life, without modern industries and machines 原始的, 遠古的: *primitive tools made from stones and animal bones* 用石頭和獸骨製成的原始工具 | *primitive art* 原始藝術 **2** belonging to an early stage of the development of humans, or of plants or animals〔人類或動植物〕原始的; 早期的: *primitive man* 原始人 | *a primitive fish* 原始魚 **3** very simple when compared to modern things 簡陋的, 粗糙的, 簡單的: *primitive machinery* 簡陋的機械 | *The house was primitive, with an earthen floor and mud walls.* 那所房子是泥土地面、泥牆, 很簡陋。**4** old-fashioned and uncomfortable 過時的, 老式的, 簡陋的, 不舒適的: *Conditions at a lot of our football stadiums are primitive.* 我們許多足球場的條件非常簡陋。—**primitively** *adv* —**primitiveness** *n* [U]

P

primitive² *n* **1** someone who comes from a simple society and is not used to modern machines and modern ways of life 原始人 **2** a painter who paints simple pictures like those of a child 原始派畫家 **3** a painter or SCULPTOR of the time before the Renaissance 文藝復興時期以前的畫家[雕塑家]

pri·mo·gen·i·ture /ˌpraɪməˋdʒɛnətʃɚ; ˌpraɪməʊˈdʒenɪ̩tʃə/ *n* [U] *technical* the system by which property owned by a man goes to his eldest son after his death【術語】長子繼承制[權]

pri·mor·di·al /praɪˋmɔrdɪəl; praɪˈmɔːdiəl/ *adj formal*【正式】**1** existing at the beginning of time or the beginning of the Earth 原始的, 原始時代存在的; 太古的, 太初的: *the primordial seas* 原始海洋 **2** in the simplest form 形式最簡單的, 基本的: *primordial passions* 最基本的情感 **3 primordial soup** the mixture of substances, gases etc thought to have existed before the beginning of life on Earth 原生漿液〔地球上生命開始之前存在的物質、氣體等混合物〕—**primordially** *adv*

primp /prɪmp; prɪmp/ *v* [I,T] to make yourself look attractive by arranging your hair, putting on MAKE-UP etc 梳妝打扮: *primping in front of the mirror* 在鏡子前梳妝打扮

prim·rose /ˋprɪmˌroz; ˈprɪmrəʊz/ *n* **1** [C] a small wild plant with light yellow flowers, or the flower from this plant 報春花 **2** [U] primrose yellow 報春花色, 淡黃色 **3 the primrose path** *literary* a way of life full of pleasure that harms the soul【文】貪圖享樂使人墮落的道路

primrose yel·low /ˌ‥ ˈ‥◂/ *n* [U] a light yellow colour 淡黃色 —**primrose yellow, primrose** *adj*

prim·u·la /ˋprɪmjulə; ˈprɪmjə̩lə/ *n* [C] a plant of the primrose family with brightly coloured flowers 報春花屬植物

Pri·mus /ˋpraɪməs; ˈpraɪməs/ also 又作 **primus stove** /ˈ‥ ·/ *n* [C] *trademark BrE* a small STOVE (=a piece of equipment for cooking) that burns oil and can be easily carried around【商標, 英】普賴默斯便攜式煤油爐

3 **prince** /prɪns; prɪns/ *n* [C] **1** the son of a king or queen, or one of their close male relatives 王子; 親王; 王孫; 國王或女王的男性近親: *Prince Albert* 艾伯特親王 **2** a male ruler of a small country or state〔小國的〕國君, 君主: *Prince Rainier of Monaco* 摩納哥國王雷尼爾 **3** the best man in a group〔一組中〕最好的男人: **the prince of/a prince among** *a prince among waiters* 男侍應中的佼佼者 **4 merchant prince** someone who has become very rich in business 商業巨頭, 商業鉅子

Prince Charm·ing /ˌ· ˈ‥/ *n* [C] *informal or humorous* a perfect man who a young girl might dream about meeting【非正式或幽默】〔少女理想中的〕完美男子, 白馬王子

prince con·sort /ˌ· ˈ‥/ *n* [C] a title sometimes given to the husband of a ruling queen 女王[女皇]的丈夫, 王夫

prince·dom /ˋprɪnsdəm; ˈprɪnsdəm/ *n* [C usually singular 一般用單數] *formal* a country ruled by a prince; PRINCIPALITY【正式】公國, 侯國; 封邑

prince·ly /ˋprɪnslɪ; ˈprɪnsli/ *adj* **1 princely sum** an expression meaning a large amount of money, often used jokingly to mean a very small amount of money 一大筆錢〔通常開玩笑地用來表示很少的錢〕: *My Dad offered me the princely sum of ten pence to wash his car!* 我爸爸給了我十便士的巨款讓我幫他洗車! **2** *formal* fine, splendid, or generous【正式】精美的; 壯觀的; 堂皇的; 慷慨的: *a princely gift* 精美的禮物 | *a princely man* 慷慨的男人 **3** belonging to or connected with a prince 王子的, 親王的; 屬於王子[親王]的: *the princely states* 由王公貴族統治的小國[公國, 侯國]

Prince of Wales /ˌprɪns əv ˋwelz; ˌprɪns əv ˈweɪlz/ *n* **the Prince of Wales** a title given to the first son of a British king or queen 威爾斯親王

prin·cess /ˋprɪnsɪs; ˌprɪnˈses◂/ *n* [C] **1** a close female relation of a king and queen, especially a daughter 公主; 國王或女王的女性近親: *Princess Anne* 安妮公主 **2** the wife of a prince 王妃; 親王夫人: *Princess Diana* 戴安娜王妃

prin·ci·pal¹ /ˋprɪnsəpḷ; ˈprɪnsə̩pəl/ *adj* [only before noun 僅用於名詞前] most important; main 最重要的, 首要的; 主要的: *My principal source of income is teaching.* 我主要的收入來源是教學。| *The principal character in the book is called Scarlett.* 這本書的主人公叫郝思嘉。—see also 另見 PRINCIPALLY 

principal² *n* **1** [singular] *technical* an amount of money lent to someone, put into a business etc, on which INTEREST is paid【術語】本金; 資本 **2** [C] *AmE* someone who is in charge of a school【美】〔中小學的〕校長; HEAD TEACHER *BrE*【英】**3** [C] *especially BrE* someone who is in charge of a university, college, or school【尤英】〔大學、學院或中小學的〕校長 **4** [C] the main performer in a play, group of musicians etc〔戲劇、音樂等演出的〕主角, 主要演員 **5** [C often plural 常用複數] a person for whom you are acting as a representative, especially in business〔代理關係中的〕委託人, 本人, 被代理人: *I will have to consult my principals before I can give you an answer on that.* 我得同我的委託人商量後才能就這個問題給你答覆。

principal boy /ˌ‥ ˈ·/ *n* [C] *BrE* the main male character in a PANTOMIME, usually played by a young woman【英】童話劇中的男主角〔通常由年輕女子扮演〕

prin·ci·pal·i·ty /ˌprɪnsəˋpælətɪ; ˌprɪnsə̩ˈpælə̩ti/ *n* [C] **1** a country ruled by a PRINCE 公國, 侯國; 封邑 **2 the Principality** *BrE* Wales【英】威爾斯

prin·ci·pally /ˋprɪnsəplɪ; ˈprɪnsə̩pli/ *adv* mainly 主要地: *The money is principally invested in government stock.* 這筆錢主要投資於政府公債上。

principal parts /ˌ‥ ˈ·/ *n* [plural] *technical* the parts of a verb from which other parts are formed in English; the INFINITIVE, past tense, present participle, past participle【術語】動詞的主要變化形式〔指英語動詞的不定式、過去式、現在分詞、過去分詞〕

prin·ci·ple /ˋprɪnsəpḷ; ˈprɪnsə̩pəl/ *n* 

1 ►MORAL RULE 道德準則◄ **a)** [C,U] a moral rule or set of ideas which makes you behave in a particular way 道德, 操守, 準則, 為人之道: *She resigned on a matter of principle.* 她因原則性問題而辭職了。| **the principle of the thing** *spoken*【口】*You shouldn't just take the car without asking, it's the principle of the thing.* 你不應該不說一聲就把車開走, 這是為人之道。| **on principle** (=because of a moral rule you follow) 由於道德準則 *I don't eat meat on principle.* 我出於道德準則而不吃肉。| **on the principle that** *We charge no fees on the principle that education should be available for all.* 我們不收取費用是出於每個人都應該受到教育的準則。**b)** strong ideas about what is morally right or wrong, that you try to follow in everything you do〔行為的〕準則, 規範: *He has no principles; he'll do anything, as long as it's profitable.* 他沒有絲毫的道德準則, 只要有利可圖, 他甚麼都會幹。| **against sb's principles** (=morally wrong to that person) 違背某人的行為準則

2 ►RULES OF A PROCESS 某個過程的規則◄ **a)** [C] a rule which explains the way something such as a machine works, or which explains a natural force in the universe 原理: *the principle of the internal combustion engine* 內燃機的原理 | *Archimedes' principle* 阿基米德原理 **b) principles** *plural* the general rules on which a skill, science etc is based 基本原理: *Einstein's theories form the basic principles of modern physics.* 愛因斯坦的理論構成了現代物理學的基本原理。| **first principles** (=the most important and basic rules) 基本原則〔原理〕

3 ▶BELIEF 信念◀ [C] a belief that is accepted as a reason for an action, way of thinking etc 原則; 信念: *the principle of free markets* 自由市場原則

4 man/woman of principle someone who has strong ideas about what is morally right or wrong 正直的男人/女人, 是非分明的人

5 in principle a) if something is possible in principle, there is no good reason why it should not happen, but it has not actually happened yet 按道理, 在理論上: *In principle you are entitled to a financial grant, but they're difficult to claim.* 按道理你有資格獲得經濟補助, 但是很難索取到。**b)** if you agree in principle, you agree about a general plan or idea without the details 原則上, 基本上, 大體上: *The scheme seems O.K. in principle, but I'd like to know more details.* 這項計劃大體上還可以, 但我想知道更多細節。

prin·ci·pled /ˈprɪnsəpḷd; ˈprɪnsɪ̣pəld/ *adj* **1** having a strong belief about what is morally right and wrong 原則性強的: *a principled woman* 原則性強的女人 **2** based on truths, beliefs or morals 原則性的; 依據行為準則的: *a principled distinction between physical and emotional injury* 身體傷害和感情傷害的原則性區別

S2 W3 **print¹** /prɪnt; prɪnt/ *v*

1 a) ▶WORDS BY MACHINE 機器印刷的文字◀ [I,T] to produce words, numbers, or pictures on paper, using a machine which puts ink onto the surface 印; 印刷: *That's what your letter's going to look like when it's printed.* 那就是你的信打印出來的樣子。| *Press this key to print a copy of the text.* 按這個鍵打印一份文本。| **print sth on/across** *the address printed on the form* 印在表格上的地址 | **print sth in** *The menu was printed in Japanese and English.* 這份菜單是用日語和英語印製的。| *The word 'scandal' was printed in bold type.* scandal 一詞是用粗體印刷的。| **be printed with** *cards printed with his name and address* 印着他的名字和地址的卡片 | **a printed card/acknowledgement/text etc** *You will receive a printed acknowledgement of your payment.* 你將收到一份打印的付款回執。| **the printed page/ word** (=language in printed form) 打印頁/打印文字 **b)** [I] to be printed by a computer〔電腦〕打印: *The document will print as it appears on the screen.* 該文件將如屏幕上顯示的那樣打印出來。

2 ▶BOOKS/NEWSPAPERS 書/報紙◀ [T] to produce many copies of a book, newspaper etc in printed form 印刷〔書、報紙等〕, 出版, 發行: *the first cookery book to be printed in America* 將在美國發行的第一本烹飪書

3 ▶IN A NEWSPAPER 在報紙上◀ [T] to print a letter, speech etc in a newspaper, magazine etc; PUBLISH〔在報章、雜誌等上〕刊登, 刊載: *The Telegraph has printed numerous articles criticising these sales techniques.*《郵報》已刊登了許多批評這些銷售技巧的文章。| *If you print that, I'll sue you.* 要是你把它刊登出來, 我就控告你。

4 ▶ON A SCREEN 在屏幕上◀ also 又作 **print sth out** [I,T] if a computer prints words and numbers on a screen it puts them there〔電腦屏幕上〕彈出〔文字、數字〕: *An error message is printed and the program ends.* 一條錯誤信息出現在屏幕上, 程式隨即關閉。

5 ▶PHOTOGRAPH 照片◀ [T] to produce a photograph from a photographic film 從底片印〔相片〕: *The pictures have to be developed and printed.* 這些照片必須沖印。

6 ▶CLOTH 布料◀ [T] to decorate cloth with a pattern put all over its surface by a machine 印圖案於: **printed with** *a new sari printed with brown and violet flowers* 印有棕色和紫色花的新莎麗

7 print money if a government prints money, it produces too many bank notes in order to pay for something〔政府為支付某物而〕大量印發鈔票

8 a licence to print money a way of making a lot of money easily 輕易賺大錢的門路: *This policy is a scandal – it's a licence to print money!* 這項政策是件醜聞——它是為某些人撈大錢而制定的。

9 ▶WRITE 寫◀ [I,T] to write words by hand without joining the letters 用印刷體書寫: *Please print your name.* 請用印刷體書寫你的姓名。| **print sth in** *a thin brown envelope with the address printed in capitals* 印有大寫字母地址的薄牛皮紙信封

10 ▶MARK 印記◀ [T] to make a mark on a surface or in a soft substance by pressing something on to it 印上〔印痕〕: *The mark of the man's shoe was clearly printed in the mud.* 那名男子的鞋印清楚地印在泥地上。

print sth ↔ **off/out** *phr v* [T] to produce a printed copy of a computer document〔電腦〕打印出: *Once you've designed your poster, you can print off as many copies as you like.* 一旦設計好宣傳海報, 你就可以喜歡打印多少份就打印多少份。

W3 **print²** *n*

1 ▶BOOKS/NEWSPAPERS 書/報紙◀ [U] writing that has been printed in books, newspapers etc 印刷品: *The information is available in many forms including print, microfilm, and CD-ROM.* 這些資料可以以多種形式獲得, 包括印刷品、縮微膠卷和唯讀光碟。| **in print** (=printed in a book, newspaper etc) 已印出來, 已發表出來 *He believed everything he saw in print.* 凡是印了出來的東西他都信以為真。| **see your name in print** *a politician who likes to see his name in print* 喜歡看見自己的名字出現在出版物中的政客 | **get into print** (=be printed) 付印, 發表 *It was the first of his stories to get into print.* 這是他發表的第一篇故事。| **get sth into print** (=have your work printed) 使某物發表 | **print unions/workers** (=those involved in printing newspapers, books etc) 印刷工人工會/印刷工人

2 be out of print if a book is out of print, it is no longer being printed and you cannot buy new copies〔書〕已絕版, 已停印: *This volume is now out of print.* 該卷現已絕版了。

3 be in print if a book is in print new copies of it are still being printed〔書〕仍可買到, 仍在印行: *Her book is still in print, a hundred years after its original publication.* 她的書在初版一百年之後仍在印刷。

4 ▶LETTERS 字母◀ [U] the letters in which something is printed 印出的字;〔印刷用的〕字體: *books with large print for elderly people* 用大號字體為老年人印的書 | *This printer can produce high quality print.* 這台打印機打印質量很高。

5 the small/fine print the details of a legal document, often in very small writing 法律文件的細節〔常常字體很小〕: *You should always read the small print before signing anything.* 在簽署任何東西之前, 務必讀一下用小號字印的細節。

6 ▶MARK 印記◀ [C] a mark made on a surface or in a soft substance by something that has been pressed onto it 印記, 印痕: *His feet left prints in the soft soil.* 他在鬆軟的泥土上留下了腳印。| *The children had decorated the walls with hand prints.* 孩子們用手印裝飾了牆壁。

7 prints [plural] the marks made by the pattern of lines on the ends of your fingers; FINGERPRINTS 指紋

8 ▶CLOTH 布料◀ [C,U] cloth, especially cotton, on which a coloured pattern has been printed 印花布〔尤指棉布〕: **a print dress/blouse** *She stood there in her print dress and white apron.* 她穿着印花布連衣裙戴着白圍裙站在那裡。

9 ▶PATTERN 圖案◀ [C] the pattern printed on a piece of cloth〔織品上的〕印花, 圖案: *The curtains were green with a print of sunflowers.* 窗簾是綠色的, 上面有向日葵印花。

10 ▶PHOTOGRAPH 照片◀ [C] a photograph in the form of a picture that has been produced from a film 〔印出的〕照片: *You get three sets of prints, plus a free film.* 你得到三套照片, 外加一個免費膠卷。
11 ▶PICTURE 圖片◀ [C] a picture that has been printed from a small sheet of metal or block of wood, or a copy of a painting produced by photography 印出的版畫, 印出的木刻書; 〔用攝影術製作的〕油畫複製品

prin·ta·ble /ˋprɪntəbl̩; ˈprɪntəbəl/ *adj* suitable to be printed and read by everyone 可以印刷出版的; 適合大眾閱讀的: *Her remarks were scarcely printable* (=were very rude). 她的話粗野得不適合刊出。—compare 比較 UNPRINTABLE

P

printed cir·cuit /ˌ·· ˈ··/ *n* [C] a set of connections between points in a piece of electrical equipment which uses a thin line of metal, not wire, to CONDUCT (=carry) the electricity 印刷電路

printed mat·ter /ˈ·· ˌ··/ *n* [U] printed articles, such as advertisements, that can be sent by post at a cheap rate 〔郵寄的〕印刷品

3 **print·er** /ˋprɪntɚ; ˈprɪntə/ *n* [C] **1** a machine which is connected to a computer and makes a printed record of computer information 〔與電腦連接的〕打印機 —compare 比較 PRINTING PRESS **2** someone employed in the trade of printing 印刷業從業人員, 印刷工人

printer's ink /ˈ··· ˌ·/ *n* [U] printing ink 油墨

print·ing /ˋprɪntɪŋ; ˈprɪntɪŋ/ *n* **1** [U] the act or process of making a book, magazine, etc by pressing or copying letters or photographs onto paper 印刷(術): *the invention of printing* 印刷術的發明 | *a printing error* 印刷[排印]錯誤 **2** [C] an act of printing a number of copies of a book 〔書的〕一次印刷: *the third printing* 第三次印刷

printing ink /ˈ··· ·/ *n* [U] a type of ink that dries very quickly and is used in printing books and newspapers etc 油墨

printing press /ˈ·· ·/ also 又作 **printing machine** /ˈ·· ·ˌ·/ *n* [C] a machine that prints newspapers, books etc; press 印刷機

print·out /ˋprɪntˌaut; ˈprɪntˌaʊt/ *n* [C,U] a sheet or length of paper with printed information on it, produced by a computer 〔電腦〕打印出來的資料

3 **pri·or¹** /ˋpraɪɚ; ˈpraɪə/ *adj* **1 prior to** *formal* before【正式】在…之前; 先於: *All the arrangements should be completed prior to your departure.* 所有安排都應在你離開之前完成。| *Guests can relax in the lounge prior to entering the theatre.* 客人在進入劇院前可在大堂休息一會兒。**2 prior warning/notice/discussion etc** a warning etc happening before something else happens 預先警告/通知/討論等: *The bomb exploded without any prior warning.* 炸彈沒有任何預先警報就爆炸了。**3 prior agreement/arrangement etc** an arrangement made before the present situation 事先協議/安排等: *Under a prior agreement the company will sell the land in ten years time.* 根據事先協議, 該公司將在十年後賣掉這塊土地。| **a prior engagement** *formal* (=something you have planned to do)【正式】預先的約會 *I won't be at the meeting as I have a prior engagement.* 由於我預先已有約會, 所以不能參加會議。

prior² *n* [C] **1** the man in charge of a PRIORY 小修道院院長 **2** the priest next in rank to the person in charge of an ABBEY 大修道院副院長

pri·or·ess /ˋpraɪərɪs; ˈpraɪərɪ̵s/ *n* [C] the woman in charge of a PRIORY 小修道院女院長

pri·o·ri·tize also 又作 **-ise** *BrE*【英】/praɪˋɔrəˌtaɪz; praɪˈɒrɪ̵taɪz/ *v* [T] **1** to put several things, problems etc in order of importance, so that you can deal with the most important ones first 按優先順序列出; 確定〔事項、問題等〕的優先順序: *Prioritize your tasks to ensure maximum efficiency.* 把你的工作按優先順序列出, 以確保最高的效率。**2** to deal with one thing first, because it is the most important 優先考慮; 給…優先權: *The public wants to see the fight against crime prioritized.* 公眾希望打擊犯罪能得到優先考慮。—**prioritization** /praɪˌɔrətəˋzeʃən; praɪˌɒrɪ̵taɪˈzeɪʃən/ *n* [U]

pri·or·i·ty /praɪˋɔrətɪ; praɪˈɒrɪ̵ti/ *n* **1** [C] the thing that you think is most important and that needs attention before anything else 優先考慮的事: *First let's decide what our priorities are.* 首先讓我們決定優先考慮的事項。| *Manufacturers are making safety a design priority.* 製造商以安全為產品設計中需要優先考慮的事項。| **top/high/low priority** (=important or unimportant thing) 應予以最優先考慮的事/非常重要的事/不重要的事 *Women's issues are often seen as a low priority.* 婦女問題常被看作不重要的事情。**2 have/take/get priority** also 又作 **be given priority** to be considered most important and dealt with before anything or anyone else 享有優先權: *If medical supplies are short, children will be given priorty.* 如果醫療供應品短缺的話, 兒童將得到優先考慮。| **[+over]** *Roosevelt decided that the war in Europe would take priority over the war in the Pacific.* 羅斯福認為當務之急是歐洲戰爭, 而不是太平洋戰爭。**3 get your priorities right** used to tell someone they should consider the most important things first 按照事情的輕重緩急行事: *Peter should get his priorities right and spend more time with his family.* 彼得應該按照輕重緩急, 花更多的時間與家人在一起。

pri·o·ry /ˋpraɪərɪ; ˈpraɪəri/ *n* a Christian religious house or group of MONKS or NUNS, (=men or women living a religious life) which is smaller and less important than an ABBEY 〔基督教的〕小修道院; 女小修道院

prise /praɪz; praɪz/ *v* [T] a British spelling of PRIZE³ (2) prize³ (2) 的英式拼法

pris·m /ˋprɪzəm; ˈprɪzəm/ *n* [C] **1** a transparent block of glass that breaks up white light into different colours 棱鏡 **2** *technical* a solid object with matching ends and several sides which are the same width all the way up【術語】棱柱(體)

pris·mat·ic /prɪzˋmætɪk; prɪzˈmætɪk/ *adj* **1** using or containing a PRISM 使用棱鏡的; 含棱柱體的: *a prismatic compass* 〔測量用〕棱鏡羅盤 **2** a prismatic colour is very clear and bright 〔顏色〕明亮的, 燦爛的

pris·on /ˋprɪzn̩; ˈprɪzən/ *n* **1** [C,U] a large building where people are kept as a punishment for a crime, or while waiting to go to court for their TRIAL¹ (1) 監獄; 看守所, 拘留所: *a maximum security prison* 防備措施最為嚴密的監獄 | *Forbes will be released from prison next week.* 弗比斯將在下星期從獄中獲釋。| **in prison** (=being kept in prison) 在獄中 *Bates was sentenced to three years in prison.* 貝茨被判三年監禁。| **prison cell** (=a room where prisoners are locked up) 牢房 | **prison sentence** (=the length of time someone has to stay in prison) 監禁期, 服刑期 | **send sb to prison** (=to officially order someone to be in prison) 將某人投入監獄 *Dow was sent to prison for six years for rape.* 道由於強姦罪被判入獄六年。| **put sb in prison** *He will be put in prison for a very long time.* 他將被判處長期監禁。**2** [U] the system of sending people to be kept in a prison 監禁, 關押: *I don't believe that prison deters criminals from offending.* 我認為監禁不能阻止罪犯犯罪。

prison camp /ˈ·· ·/ *n* [C] a special prison in which PRISONERS OF WAR are kept 戰俘營

pris·on·er /ˋprɪzn̩ɚ; ˈprɪzənə/ *n* [C] **1** someone who is kept in a prison as a punishment for a crime 犯人, 囚犯: *The prisoners are allowed an hour's exercise every day.* 囚犯獲許每天做一小時的運動。**2** someone who is taken by force and kept somewhere, for example during a war 被拘押的人; 俘虜; 戰俘: *enemy prisoners* 敵軍俘虜 | *political prisoners* 政治犯 | **hold/keep sb prisoner** *The guerillas kept her prisoner for three months.* 游擊隊員將她囚禁了三個月。| **take sb prisoner** *The captain was taken prisoner by enemy soldiers.* 那位上尉被敵軍士兵俘虜了。

prisoner of con·science /ˌ··· · ˈ··/ *n* [C] someone

who is put in prison because of their political ideas 政治犯

prisoner of war /ˌ··· · ˈ·/ *n* [C] a soldier, member of the navy etc who is caught by the enemy during a war and kept as a prisoner 戰俘

prison vis·i·tor /ˌ·· ˈ···/ *n* [C] someone who visits prisoners in Britain to help them〔英國探望囚犯以幫助他們的〕探監工作者

pris·sy /ˈprɪsɪ; ˈprɪsi/ *adj informal* behaving very correctly and easily shocked by anything rude【非正式】謹小慎微的; 一本正經的; 拘謹的, 刻板的: *"She's not a very nice girl," Jinny said in her prissy little voice.* "她不是很好的女孩。"吉妮用她一本正經的細嗓門說。—**prissily** *adv* —**prissiness** *n* [U]

pris·tine /ˈprɪstin; ˈprɪstiːn/ *adj* extremely fresh or clean 極其新鮮的, 潔淨的: *the pristine whiteness of newly fallen snow* 新降雪的潔白無瑕 | **in pristine condition** (=in the same condition as when it was made) 嶄新的; 完好無損的 *a '68 Volvo in pristine condition* 完好無損的 1968 年產的富豪汽車

prith·ee /ˈprɪðɪ; ˈprɪði/ *interjection old use* please【舊】請

priv·a·cy /ˈpraɪvəsɪ; ˈprɪvəsi/ *n* [U] **1** the state of being able to be alone, and not seen or heard by other people 隱居; 獨處; 清靜: *With seven people squashed in one house, you don't get much privacy.* 七個人擠在一間屋子裡, 想要獨處不大可能。**2** the state of being free from public attention 隱私: *each individual's right to privacy* 每個人的隱私權

1 1 **pri·vate¹** /ˈpraɪvɪt; ˈpraɪvɪ̈t/ *adj*

1 ►NOT FOR EVERYONE 不是供每個人的◄ only for use by one particular person or group, not for everyone 私人(用)的; 私有的, 個人的: *a private road* 私人道路 | *private property* 私人財產

2 ►SECRET 祕密的◄ **a)** private feelings, information, or opinions are personal or secret and not for other people to know about〔感情、消息、意見等〕個人的; 祕密的, 非公開的: *What I told you was private – I thought you would respect that.* 我告訴你的事不宜公開 — 我想你會遵守這一點。**b)** a private meeting, conversation etc involves only a small number of people, and is not for other people to know about〔會議、談話等〕祕密的, 私下的: *a peace deal hammered out in a series of private talks* 在一系列祕密會談中達成的和平協議

3 ►NOT GOVERNMENT 非政府的◄ [only before noun 僅用於名詞前] not connected with, owned by, or paid for by the government 私立的, 私營的, 民間的: *a private hospital* 私立醫院 | *private pension plans* 個人退休金計劃 | **go private** *BrE* (=pay for medical treatment instead of getting it free at a public hospital)【英】自付醫療費

4 ►NOT PART OF YOUR WORK 非工作的一部分◄ separate from and not connected with your work or your official position 與公事無關的, 與官職無關的, 私人的: *The president is paying a private visit to Europe.* 總統將對歐洲作私人訪問。| **private life** (=the parts of your life not connected with your job or your public life, especially your relationships) 私生活 *I never discuss my private life in interviews.* 我從不在採訪時談及我的私生活。

5 ►QUIET PLACE 安靜的地方◄ quiet and without lots of people 安靜的; 人不多的: *Is there a private corner where we can have a talk?* 有沒有一個僻靜的角落讓我們可以談一談?

6 ►PERSON 人◄ [only before noun 僅用於名詞前] a private person is one who likes being alone, and does not talk much about their thoughts or feelings〔人〕喜歡獨處的; 不喜歡談論自己的想法[感情]的: *Although he spends a lot of time in the public eye, he is really a very private man.* 儘管他經常在公開場合露面, 但是他其實性格很孤僻。

7 private joke a joke made between friends, family members etc that other people do not understand〔朋友、家庭成員等之間的〕私人玩笑 —see also 另見 PRIVATELY

private² *n* **1 in private** without other people being present 祕密地, 私下地: *I have something to tell you, but I'll speak to you about it in private.* 我有事情要告訴你, 但我要單獨跟你說。**2** [C] a soldier of the lowest rank 士兵, 列兵; 二等兵 —see table on page C6 參見 C6 頁附錄 **3 privates** [plural] *informal* PRIVATE PARTS【非正式】陰部, 私處

private de·tec·tive /ˌ·· ·ˈ··/ *n* [C] someone who can be employed to look for information or missing people, or to follow people and report on what they do 私人偵探, 私家偵探

private ed·u·ca·tion /ˌ·· ··ˈ··/ *n* [U] education provided for money, rather than free education provided by the government 私立教育

private en·ter·prise /ˌ·· ˈ···/ *n* **1** [U] the economic system in which private businesses are allowed to compete freely with each other, and the government does not control industry 私營企業制, 自由企業制 —see also 另見 PRIVATE SECTOR **2** [C] a business established by an individual person or group 私營企業

pri·va·teer /ˌpraɪvəˈtɪr; ˌpraɪvəˈtɪə/ *n* [C] **1** an armed ship in former times that was not in the navy but attacked and robbed enemy ships carrying goods〔舊時攻擊並搶奪敵人貨船的〕武裝民船; 私掠船 **2** someone who commanded or sailed on a ship of this kind 私掠船船長[船員]

private eye /ˌ·· ˈ·/ *n* [C] *informal* a PRIVATE DETECTIVE【非正式】私人偵探, 私家偵探

private in·come /ˌ·· ˈ··/ *n* [C] money that someone gets regularly, not from working but because they own part of a business or have money which earns INTEREST¹ (4)〔來自投資、利息等的非工資性〕私人收入

private in·ves·ti·gat·or /ˌ·· ·ˈ····/ *n* [C] a PRIVATE DETECTIVE 私人偵探, 私家偵探

private law /ˈ·· ˌ·/ *n* [U] *law* the part of the law concerned with ordinary people, private property, and relationships【法律】〔處理私人關係、私人財產的〕私法

pri·vate·ly /ˈpraɪvɪtlɪ; ˈpraɪvɪ̈tli/ *adv* **1** with no one else present 單獨, 私下: *Could I speak to you privately?* 我可以單獨跟你談談嗎? **2** if you feel or think something privately, you do not tell anyone about it [sentence adverb 句子副詞] 私下地; 沒有公開地: *Privately, Prue felt that the whole exercise was a waste of time.* 普魯私下認為整個練習就是浪費時間。**3** *especially BrE* using or involving private rather than government institutions【尤英】私立地, 私營地: *Both children are privately educated.* 兩個孩子接受的都是私立教育。| *a privately-owned company* 私有公司

private medi·cine /ˌ·· ˈ··/ *n* [U] *BrE* the system in which medical treatment and advice is not provided by the government but is paid for by the person who needs it, or by their insurance company【英】自費醫療〔醫療和醫療諮詢由個人或其保險公司支付而非政府提供的體制〕—compare 比較 NHS

private mem·ber /ˌ·· ˈ··/ *n BrE* [C] a member of parliament who is not a minister in the government【英】〔非內閣成員的〕下議院議員, 無公職議員

private member's bill /ˌ·· ˈ·· ˌ·/ *n* [C] a law introduced to the British parliament by a member of parliament who is not a minister in the government 非內閣成員的下議院議員提出的法案

private parts /ˌ·· ˈ·/ *n* [plural] an expression meaning 'sex organs', used when you want to avoid naming them directly 私處, 陰部, (外)生殖器

private pa·tient /ˌ·· ˈ··/ *n* [C] *BrE* someone who pays for medical treatment or advice, rather than receiving it free through the government's system【英】自費病人

private prac·tice /ˌ·· ˈ··/ *n* [U] **1** the business of a professional person that is independent of a bigger or government controlled organization 職業人士的私人企業[公司]: *Richard set up in private practice.* 理查德設立了私人事務所。**2** *AmE* the business of a professional person, especially a doctor, who works alone rather than with others【美】〔尤指醫生〕私人開業

private school /,·· '·/ *n* [C] a school not supported by government money, where education must be paid for by the parents of the children 私立學校

private sec·re·ta·ry /,·· '····/ *n* [C] a secretary who is employed to help one person, especially with CONFIDENTIAL business 私人祕書

private sec·tor /,·· '··◂/ *n* **the private sector** the industries and services in a country that are owned and run by private companies, and not by the state or government 私營企業: *pay increases in the private sector* 私營企業的工資增長 | *private sector employers* 私營企業的雇主 —compare 比較 PUBLIC SECTOR

private sol·dier /,·· '··/ *n* [C] *formal* a soldier of the lowest rank; PRIVATE² (2)【正式】士兵, 列兵; 二等兵

private view /,·· '·/ also 又作 **private view·ing** /,·· '···/ *n* [C] an occasion when a few people are invited to see a show of paintings before the rest of the public〔畫展在公開展出前只邀請少數人參觀的〕預展

pri·va·tion /praɪˋveʃən; praɪˈveɪʃən/ *n* [C,U] *formal* a lack or loss of the things that everyone needs, such as food, warmth, and shelter【正式】〔生活必需品的〕匱乏, 貧困: *Despite the privations of wartime she managed to keep the children healthy.* 儘管戰時生活必需品匱乏, 她仍設法使孩子的身體保持健康。

pri·vat·ise /ˋpraɪvɪtaɪz; ˈpraɪvɪ̈taɪz/ *v* a British spelling of PRIVATIZE privatize 的英式拼法

pri·vat·i·za·tion also 又作 **-isation** *BrE*【英】/ˌpraɪvətəˋzeʃən; ˌpraɪvətaɪˈzeɪʃən/ *n* [C, U] the act of privatizing something 私有化, 私營化

pri·vat·ize also 又作 **-ise** *BrE*【英】/ˋpraɪvətaɪz; ˈpraɪvətaɪz/ *v* [T] to sell an organization, industry, or service that was previously controlled and owned by a government 使私營化, 使歸私有 —compare 比較 NATIONALIZE

priv·et /ˋprɪvɪt; ˈprɪvɪ̈t/ *n* [U] a bush with leaves that stay green all year, often grown to form a HEDGE 女貞〔常作樹籬的常青灌木〕

3 **priv·i·lege** /ˋprɪvlɪdʒ; ˈprɪvɪ̈lɪdʒ/ *n* **1** [C] a special advantage that is given only to one person or group of people〔特定個人或羣體的〕特權: *Don't forget that using the car is a privilege, not a right!* 別忘了使用這輛汽車是特權, 而不是權利! | **the privilege of (doing) sth** *the privilege of having an office of my own* 擁有自己辦公室的特權 **2** [U] a situation in which people who are rich or of a high social class have many more advantages than other people〔某些有權有勢者的〕特權, 特別待遇: *an outdated system based on aristocratic privilege* 基於貴族特權的陳舊制度 **3** [singular] something that you are lucky to have the chance to do, and that you enjoy very much 榮幸: **the privilege of doing sth** *Ladies and gentlemen, I have the great privilege of introducing our speaker for tonight.* 女士們、先生們, 我非常榮幸地介紹我們今晚的演講者。| *It was a privilege to hear her play.* 能聽她演奏真是榮幸。**4** [C,U] the right to do or say something which might not normally be acceptable without being punished, especially in parliament 言行自由權, 〔尤指〕議員(言行不受懲罰)權: a **breach of privilege** (=a breaking of the rules about what a member of parliament can do or say) 侵犯議會言行自由權

priv·i·leged /ˋprɪvlɪdʒd; ˈprɪvɪ̈lɪdʒd/ *adj* **1** having a special advantage or a chance to do something that most people cannot do 有特權的; 榮幸的, 幸運的: **privileged to do sth** *Francis felt privileged to work for such a man.* 法蘭西斯對於為這樣的人工作感到很榮幸。| *Recently I was privileged to view his private collection.* 最近我很榮幸地看到了他的個人收藏。**2** having advantages because of your wealth, social position etc〔因為有錢有勢而〕有特權的: **the privileged few** *Only the privileged few were able to afford university then.* 那時, 只有享有特權的少數人才能上得起大學。**3** *law* privileged information does not have to be given even if a court of law asks for it【法律】無須公開的; 有權保守祕密的

priv·y¹ /ˋprɪvɪ; ˈprɪvi/ *adj* **1 privy to** sharing in the knowledge of facts that are secret 了解內情的, 私下知情的: *Colby was privy to the committee's decisions.* 科爾比知道委員會的祕密決定。**2** *old use* secret and private【舊】祕密的, 私下的 —**privily** *adv*

privy² *n* [C] *old use* a toilet, especially one outside a house【舊】〔尤指室外的〕廁所

Privy Coun·cil /,·· '··/ *n* **the Privy Council** a group of important people in Britain who advise the king or queen on political affairs〔英國的〕樞密院 —**Privy Councillor** *n* [C]

Privy Purse /,·· '·/ *n* **the privy purse** money given by the British government to the king or queen for their personal use〔英國政府撥給國王或女王的〕私用經費

prize¹ /praɪz; praɪz/ *n* [C] **1** something that is given to someone who is successful in a competition, race, game of chance etc〔給予獲勝者的〕獎品, 獎賞: *First prize was a weekend for two in Paris.* 頭獎是巴黎週末二人遊。| **[+for]** *Festival judges awarded 'Victims' the prize for the best feature film.* 電影節評委授予《受害者》最佳故事片獎。| **win a prize** *Hundreds of cash prizes to be won!* 可以贏得數以百計的現金獎! | **prize winner** *a list of prize winners* 獲獎者名單 | **award (sb) a prize** (=decide who will have a prize) 授予〔某人〕獎賞 **2** something that is very valuable to you or that it is very important to have 有價值的事物, 值得爭取的事物: *Toulouse was a rich prize, and the Count's army fought hard to keep it.* 圖盧茲是塊富饒的寶地, 伯爵的軍隊奮勇戰鬥守衛它。**3 (there are) no prizes for guessing sth** *spoken* used to say that it is very easy to guess something【口】某事一猜就知: *No prizes for guessing who told you that!* 是誰告訴你的, 一猜就能猜出來! **4** an enemy ship caught at sea in the past, or the goods it contained 捕獲的敵船(上的貨物)

prize² *adj* [only before noun 僅用於名詞前] **1** good enough to win a prize or to have won a prize 可獲獎的, 優等的; 已獲獎的: *a herd of prize cattle* 一羣優選的牛 —see also 另見 PRIZE-WINNING **2 prize money** money that is given to the person who wins a competition, race etc〔贏得比賽者所獲的〕獎金 **3 a prize idiot/fool** *informal* a complete IDIOT, fool etc【非正式】十足的白痴/傻瓜 **4** best, most important, or most useful 最好的; 最重要的; 最有用的: *The resource centre is one of our prize assets.* 那個資料中心是我們一個非常重要的資產。

prize³ *v* [T] **1** [often passive 常用被動態] to think that someone or something is very important or valuable 珍視; 高度重視: *a necklace which his mother had prized* 他母親珍愛的一條項鏈 **2** [T always+adv/prep] also 又作 **prise** *BrE* to move or lift something, by pushing it away from something else【英】撬; 撬開; PRY (2) *AmE*【美】: **prize sth off/up/apart etc** *Eventually we prized the lid off with a knife.* 最後我們用刀把蓋子撬開了。

prize sth **out** *phr v* [T] to get information from someone with difficulty or by using force〔從某人那裡〕挖出〔情報等〕, 強迫〔某人〕供出〔消息、情報〕: **prize sth out of sb** *It took an hour to prize the address out of him.* 花了一個小時才讓他供出那個地址。

prized /praɪzd; praɪzd/ *adj* extremely important or valuable to someone〔對某人〕非常重要的, 非常有價值的, 極其珍貴的: **prized possession** *Nathaniel's bicycle is his most prized possession.* 納撒尼爾的腳踏車是他最寶貴的財產。

prize day /'· ·/ *n* [C] *BrE* an occasion when prizes are given to pupils who have done well in particular subjects【英】〔學校的〕頒獎日

prize·fight /ˋpraɪzˌfaɪt; ˈpraɪzfaɪt/ *n* [C] **1** a public BOX-

ING match, in which two men fight each other with bare hands, in order to win money〔以贏錢為目的的〕公開徒手拳擊賽 **2** *AmE* a professional BOXING match【美】職業拳擊賽 —**prizefighter** *n* [C] —**prizefighting** *n* [U]

prize-win·ning /ˈ· ˌ··/ *adj* [only before noun 僅用於名詞前] a prize-winning film, book etc has won a prize〔電影、書籍等〕獲獎的: *a prize-winning science reporter* 獲獎的科學記者

PRO /ˌpi ɑr ˋo; ˌpiː ɑːr ˈəʊ/ *n* [C] a public relations officer; someone whose job is to supply information about an organization, so that people have a good opinion of it 公(共)關(係)人員 —see also 另見 PR (1)

pro- /pro; prəʊ/ *prefix* **1** in favour of or supporting something 贊成; 支持; 親: *pro-American* 親美的 | *the pro-abortion lobby* 贊成人工流產合法化的議院外活動集團 —compare 比較 ANTI- **2** *technical* doing a job instead of someone【術語】代: *the pro-vice-chancellor* 代理副大臣

pro¹ /pro; prəʊ/ *n* [C] **1** a PROFESSIONAL (=someone who earns money because they are good at a particular sport or skill) 專門職業者, 職業人員 **2** *informal* also 又作 **old pro** someone who has had a lot of experience with a particular type of situation【非正式】〔有經驗的〕老手: *Ben's an old pro at this type of thing – leave it to him.* 班恩是處理這種事情的老手, 交給他吧。**3 the pros and cons** the advantages and disadvantages of something〔某事物的〕利與弊: *the pros and cons of owning your own home* 擁有自己的家的利與弊 **4** *BrE informal* a PROSTITUTE【英, 非正式】妓女 —see also 另見 PRO FORMA, PRO RATA

pro² *prep* if you are pro an idea, plan, suggestion etc, you support it and hope that it will succeed 贊成的, 支持的: *As a party, they had always been pro nuclear power.* 作為一個政黨, 他們一直支持核能。

pro³ *adj informal* PROFESSIONAL【非正式】職業性的; 專業的: **turn/go pro** (=become pro) 成為職業人員 *Both skaters turned pro last year.* 兩名滑冰運動員去年都成為了職業選手。

pro-ac·tive /·ˈ··/ *adj* able to change events rather than react to them, and make things happen 積極的; 主動的, 預先採取行動的, 先發制人的: *a pro-active approach to staffing requirements* 人員需求問題的積極處理方法

pro-am /ˌpro ˋæm; ˌprəʊ ˈæm◂/ *n* [C] a competition, especially in GOLF, for PROFESSIONALs (=people who play for money) and AMATEURs (=people who play just for pleasure) 職業選手和業餘選手混合賽〔尤指高爾夫球賽〕 —**pro-am** *adj*

prob·a·bil·i·ty /ˌprɑbəˋbɪlətɪ; ˌprɒbəˈbɪləti/ *n* **1** [singular,U] how likely it is that something will happen, exist, or be true 可能性: **[+of]** *very little probability of finding it again* 再次找到它的可能性微乎其微 | **there is a strong probability that** *There is a very strong probability that she will make a full recovery.* 她很有可能完全康復。| **the probability is that** (=it is likely that) 可能… *If you can answer these questions, the probability is that you'd be good at the job.* 如果你能回答這些問題, 你就可能有能力做這份工作。**2 in all probability** an expression meaning very probably, used especially when you are making a judgment about something 很可能, 十有八九〔尤用於對某事物作出判斷時〕: *There will, in all probability, be parts that you do not understand.* 很有可能會有你不懂的部分。**3** [C] something that is likely to happen or exist 可能發生的事; 可能存在的事: *A peace agreement now seems a real probability.* 達成和平協定現在似乎成了完全可能的事。**4** the mathematically calculated chance that something will happen〔數學的〕概率, 或然率: *a probability of one in four* 四分之一的概率

prob·a·ble¹ /ˋprɑbəbl; ˈprɒbəbəl/ *adj* likely to exist, happen, or be true 可能存在的, 可能發生的, 很可能的, 大概的: *A victory doesn't seem very probable at this stage.* 在這個階段獲勝好像不大可能。| **it is probable that** *It seems highly probable that they'll have to move house.* 他們很有可能得搬家。| **probable result/outcome/effect etc** *The new building will go ahead at a probable cost of £2.5 million.* 新的大樓將要開工, 大概需花費250萬英鎊。—opposite 反義詞 IMPROBABLE

probable² *n* [C] someone who is likely to be chosen for a team, to win a race etc 很有可能入選的人; 很有可能獲勝的人

prob·a·bly /ˋprɑbəblɪ; ˈprɒbəbli/ *adv* [sentence adverb 句子副詞] used to say that something is likely to happen, likely to be true etc 很可能; 大概: *I probably still have my old army pictures.* 我大概還保留着我在部隊時的老照片。| *Probably the best way to learn Spanish is by actually going to live in Spain.* 學習西班牙語最好的方法大概是親身到西班牙生活。| *"Do you think you'll return to work after the baby?" "Yeah, probably."* "你認為生完孩子後你會再回來工作嗎?" "是的, 很可能會。" | **very/most probably** *She most probably thinks she's right when she says things like that.* 她極有可能認為自己是對的才會說出那種話。 S1 W1

pro·bate¹ /ˋprobet; ˈprəʊbeɪt/ *n* [U] *law* the legal process of deciding that someone's WILL² (2) has been properly made and can be carried out【法律】遺囑檢驗; 遺囑認證

probate² *v* [T] *AmE law* to prove that a WILL² (2) is legal【美, 法律】驗證〔遺囑〕的合法性

pro·ba·tion /proˋbeʃən; prəˈbeɪʃən/ *n* [U] **1** a system that allows some criminals not to go to prison, if they behave well and see a PROBATION OFFICER (=special adviser) regularly, for a fixed period of time 緩刑(制): *The court fined Kevin and gave him two years' probation.* 法庭對凱文處以罰款並判他緩刑兩年。| **(put sb) on probation** *Mike was put on probation for stealing a car.* 米克因偷一輛汽車而被判緩刑。**2** a period of time, during which someone who has just started a job is tested to see whether they are suitable for what they are doing 試用(期), 見習(期): *After six months' probation, Helen became a permanent member of staff.* 經過六個月的試用, 海倫成了一名固定職員。| **on probation** *I'm on probation for another month yet.* 我還有一個月的試用期。**3** *AmE* a fixed period of time in which you must improve your work or behave well so that you will not have to leave your job【美】〔留任〕察看期: **(put sb) on probation** *I'm afraid I have no choice but to put you on probation.* 恐怕我沒有別的選擇, 只能把你留下察看。—**probationary** *adj*: *a probationary period* 緩刑期; 試用期 | *probationary teachers* 試用中的老師

pro·ba·tion·er /proˋbeʃənɚ; prəˈbeɪʃənə/ *n* [C] **1** someone who has recently started a job, especially nursing or teaching, and who is being tested to see whether they are suitable for it 見習人員〔尤指見習護士或見習教師〕 **2** someone who has broken the law, and has been put on probation 緩刑犯 **3** someone who is being tested to see if they are suitable to be a member of a church or religious group 教會中的準會員

probation of·fi·cer /·ˈ·· ˌ···/ *n* [C] someone whose job is to watch, advise, and help people who have broken the law and are on probation 監視緩刑犯的官員, 緩刑監督官

probe¹ /prob; prəʊb/ *v* [I, T] **1** to ask questions in order to find things out, especially things that other people do not want you to know 調查; 打探, 探究: **[+into]** *I don't want to probe too deeply into your personal affairs.* 我不想太深入地打探你的私事。| **probe sth** *a report probing the official's involvement with drug dealing* 關於官員與販毒活動有牽連的調查報告 **2** to look for something or examine something, using a long thin instrument〔用細長的工具〕尋找, 探測, 探查: *Jules probed the mud gingerly with a stick.* 朱爾斯小心翼翼地用棍子探着泥地。—**probing** *adj*: *probing questions* 盤根究底的問題 —**probingly** *adv*

probe² *n* [C] **1** a long thin metal instrument that doctors and scientists use to examine parts of the body〔醫生和

科學家用的〕探針 **2** a SPACE PROBE 宇宙探測器, 太空探測器 **3** an expression meaning a very thorough INQUIRY into something, used by newspapers 深入調查, 徹底調查〔報紙用語〕: *a police corruption probe* 對警察貪污行為的徹底調查

pro·bi·ty /ˈprobətɪ; ˈprəʊbɨti/ *n* [U] *formal* complete honesty【正式】誠實, 正直: *I have always found Bentner to be a model of probity in our dealings.* 在我們的交往中, 我一直覺得班特納是誠實的典範。

prob·lem /ˈprɑbləm; ˈprɒbləm/ *n* [C]

1 ▶DIFFICULTY 困難◀ a situation that causes difficulties 問題; 難題, 困難: *There was rarely any problem in motivating the students to study.* 在激勵學生學習方面很少有甚麼問題。| **have a problem with** *I've been having a few problems with the car.* 這車子一直出毛病, 我解決不來。| **a drug/crime problem** *tough new measures to combat the drug problem* 打擊毒品問題的嚴厲的新措施 | **pose a problem** *The shortage of trained staff poses a serious problem.* 缺乏訓練有素的員工是個嚴重的問題。| **solve a problem** *a policy that will solve the unemployment problem* 將可解決失業問題的政策 —see 見 TROUBLE (USAGE)

2 no problem *spoken*【口】**a)** used to say that you are very willing to do something 沒問題〔用於表示很願意做某事〕: *"Could you make the booking in her name?" "Yes, no problem."* "你用她的名字預訂好嗎?""好的! 沒問題。" | *No problem! I'd love to show you around.* 沒問題! 我很願意帶你到處看看。**b)** used after someone has said thank you or said that they are sorry 沒甚麼〔用於回答對方的感謝或道歉〕: *"Thanks so much for all your help." "Oh, no problem!"* "非常感謝你所有的幫助。" "噢, 沒甚麼!"

3 that's your problem *spoken* used to tell someone to deal with their own problem or situation by themselves【口】那是你的問題〔用於告訴別人自己處理自己的問題〕: *If you can't get yourself there on time, that's your problem.* 如果你不能準時到達那裡, 那是你的問題。

4 it's/that's not my problem *spoken* used to say you do not care about a problem someone else has【口】那不是我的問題〔用來表示你不關心別人的問題〕: *"Your brother's under a lot of pressure." "That's not my problem."* "你的哥哥正在承受很大的壓力。" "那不是我的問題。"

5 What's your problem? *spoken* used to ask someone what is wrong, in a way that is not sympathetic, and shows that you think they are being unreasonable【口】你出甚麼問題了?〔這句問話並無同情意味, 而且表現出你認為對方不理智〕: *Look, what's your problem? I've never seen you act like this!* 喂, 你出甚麼毛病了? 我從未見過你這樣!

6 a problem child/family/drinker etc a child etc who behaves in a way that is difficult for other people to deal with 問題兒童/問題家庭/難對付的飲酒者

7 Do you have a problem with that? *spoken* used to ask someone why they oppose you or disagree with you, in a way that shows you think they are wrong【口】關於那一點你有問題嗎?〔用於詢問別人為甚麼反對你, 表現出你認為別人是錯的〕

8 ▶QUESTION 問題◀ a question, especially one connected with numbers or facts, that must be answered〔尤指與數字、事實相關的〕問題, 題: *The teacher gave them 20 mathematical problems.* 老師給他們出了 20 道數學題。

prob·lem·at·ic /ˌprɑbləˈmætɪk; ˌprɒbləˈmætɪk◂/ *adj* full of problems and difficult to deal with 有很多問題的, 難對付的, 成問題的: *The situation might become slightly problematic as more people are involved.* 隨着更多的人牽涉在內, 局勢可能變得有點難以對付。— **problematically** /-klɪ; -kli/ *adv*

problem page /ˈ·· ·/ *n* [C] a page in a magazine where letters about personal problems are printed, and answers are suggested 個人問題專頁〔指雜誌中刊登反映個人問題的來信和建議的解決辦法的專頁〕

problem-solv·ing /ˈ·· ˌ··/ *n* [U] finding ways of doing things, or finding answers to problems 解決問題的: *Involve the class in a problem-solving activity.* 使全班同學參與解決問題的活動中。

pro bo·no pub·li·co /pro ˌbono ˈpublɪko; prəʊ ˌbəʊnəʊ ˈpʊblɪkəʊ/ also 又作 **pro bono** *adj Latin* used to descibe work that someone, especially a lawyer, does without getting paid for it【拉丁】〔尤指律師〕免費工作的: *Some law firms will take on pro bono cases when possible.* 一些律師事務所在可能的情況下會承接免費服務的案子。

pro·bos·cis /proˈbɑsɪs; prəˈbɒsɨs/ *n* [C] *plural* **proboscises** /-sɪsiz; -sɨsiːz/ **1** a long thin tube that forms part of the mouth of some insects and worms〔某些昆蟲的〕針狀吻, 長嘴 **2** the long thin nose of certain animals, such as the elephant〔某些動物的〕長鼻;〔尤指〕象鼻

pro·ce·du·ral /prəˈsidʒərəl; prəˈsiːdʒərəl/ *adj formal* connected with a procedure, especially in a law court【正式】〔尤指法庭〕程序性的, 手續上的

pro·ce·dure /prəˈsidʒɚ; prəˈsiːdʒə/ *n* **1** [C] the correct or normal way of doing something〔正確的或通常的做事〕步驟, 手續: **[+for]** *What's the procedure for renewing your car tax?* 續交汽車稅的正確步驟是甚麼? | **correct/proper/standard procedure** *A lie-detector test is standard procedure.* 用測謊儀進行測試是標準的做法。**2** [U] the accepted method and order of doing things, especially in an official meeting, a law case etc〔尤指正式會議、法律訴訟等的〕程序: *Too much time was spent arguing about procedure.* 太多的時間花在了爭論程序問題上。

pro·ceed /prəˈsid; prəˈsiːd/ *v* [I] **1** to continue to do something that has already been started 繼續進行, 繼續做: *The work is proceeding according to plan.* 那項工作正按計劃進行。| **[+with]** *Travis paused to consult his notes, then proceeded with his questions.* 特拉維斯停下來看了看筆記, 然後繼續提問。| **[+to]** *We can now proceed to the main business of the meeting.* 我們現在可以進入會議的主要議程。**2 proceed to do sth** an expression meaning to do something next, used especially about something annoying or surprising 接着做某事〔尤指令人討厭或驚奇的事〕: **proceed to do sth** *Patrick said he liked my work, and then proceeded to tell me everything was wrong with it!* 柏特里克說他很欣賞我的作品, 接着又告訴我一切都不對! **3** [always+adv/prep] *formal* to move in a particular direction【正式】〔向某一方向〕前進, 移動: **[+in/to etc]** *Passengers for the Miami flight should proceed to gate 25.* 搭乘去邁阿密班機的旅客請前往 25 號門登機。—see also 另見 PROCEEDS

proceed against sb *phr v* [T] *law* to begin a legal case against someone【法律】起訴〔某人〕, 對〔某人〕提起訴訟

proceed from sth *phr v* [T not in passive 不用被動態] *formal* to happen or exist as a result of something【正式】源於某物, 出自: *diseases that proceed from poverty* 由貧困引起的疾病

pro·ceed·ings /prəˈsidɪŋz; prəˈsiːdɪŋz/ *n* [plural] **1** also 又作 **proceeding** [C] an event or series of actions, especially an unusual or annoying one〔尤指不尋常或令人討厭的〕事件,〔一連串的〕行為: *We watched the proceedings in the street from the window.* 我們通過窗戶注視着大街上的活動。**2** actions taken in a law court or in a legal case 訴訟: *Legal proceedings can be enormously expensive.* 法律訴訟可能會耗費非常大。**3** the official records of meetings 會議記錄: *the proceedings of the London Historical Society* 倫敦歷史學會會議記錄

pro·ceeds /ˈprosidz; ˈprəʊsiːdz/ *n* [plural] the money that has been gained from doing something or selling something〔做某事或出售某物所獲的〕收入, 收益: *We sold the business and bought a retirement condo with the proceeds.* 我們賣了公司, 並用所得的錢買了一套退休養老的公寓。

pro·cess¹ /ˈprɑsɛs; ˈprəʊses/ *n* [C] **1** a series of natural developments or events that produce gradual change 過程, 進程; 變化過程: *Coal was formed out of dead forests by a slow process of chemical change.* 煤是由埋在地底的森林經過長期而緩慢的化學變化形成的。| *the digestive process* 消化過程 **2** a series of actions that someone takes in order to achieve a particular result〔為取得某個結果而採取的〕步驟, 程序, 方法: *Teaching him to read was a slow process.* 教他認字是一個緩慢的過程。| *the electoral process* 選舉程序 | **by a process of elimination** (=by proving that no other possibility is true) 通過排除法 *The identity of the dead man was established by a process of elimination.* 死者的身分是通過排除法確認的。**3 be in the process of doing sth/be in process** to have started doing something and not yet be finished 在做某事的過程中, 在進行…中: *The company is in the process of moving to new offices.* 該公司正在搬往新的辦公室。| *New guidelines are in process.* 新的指引正在制訂中。**4** a system or a treatment of materials that is used to produce goods 製作法, 工序, 工藝流程: *an advanced industrial process* 先進的工業生產流程 **5 in the process** while you are doing something or something is happening 同時, 在…過程中: *Katie jumped out of the tree, spraining her ankle in the process.* 凱蒂從樹上跳下來時扭傷了腳踝。**6** *technical* a legal case, considered as a series of actions【術語】訴訟程序 —see also 另見 DUE PROCESS

process² *v* [T] **1** to treat food or some other substance by adding substances to give it colour, keep it fresh etc 加工〔食品或其他物質〕: *processed cheese* 經過加工的乳酪 **2** to print a picture from a photographic film 沖印〔照片〕**3** to deal with a document 處理〔文件〕: *Your application for a mortgage is being processed.* 你申請抵押貸款的事正在審理中。**4** to put information into a computer to be examined〔電腦〕處理〔數據〕—see also 另見 DATA PROCESSING, WORD PROCESSOR

pro·cess³ /proˈsɛs; prəˈses/ *v* [I always+adv/prep] to move in a procession, or to move very slowly and seriously 列隊行進; 緩慢而嚴肅地行進

processed food /ˌ·· ˈ·/ *n* [U] food that has been specially treated before it is sold, in order to make it look more attractive or last longer 加工食品

pro·ces·sion /prəˈsɛʃən; prəˈseʃən/ *n* [C] **1** a line of people or vehicles moving slowly as part of a ceremony〔人或車輛的〕行列, 遊行隊伍: *the funeral procession* 送葬行列 | *a carnival procession* 狂歡節[嘉年華會]的巡遊隊伍 | **in procession** *They marched in procession to the Capitol Building.* 他們排着隊向國會大廈行進。**2** several people or things of the same kind, appearing or happening one after the other 一(長)排; 一(長)串; 一連串: **[+of]** *a never-ending procession of unwelcome visitors* 源源不斷的不受歡迎的來訪者

pro·ces·sion·al /prəˈsɛʃənl; prəˈseʃənəl/ *adj* [only before noun 僅用於名詞前] connected with or used during a procession 列隊行進的; 列隊行進時用的: *Flags lined the processional route.* 隊伍行進路線的兩邊插滿了旗幟。

pro·ces·sor /ˈprɑsɛsɚ; ˈprəʊsesə/ *n* [C] the central part of a computer that does the calculations needed to deal with the information it is given; CENTRAL PROCESSING UNIT〔電腦的信息〕處理器[機] —see also 另見 FOOD PROCESSOR

pro-choice /ˌ· ˈ·/ *adj* someone who is pro-choice believes that women have a right to ABORTION, and uses this word to describe their views 主張女人有權人工流產的: *pro-choice activists* 主張人工流產為合法的積極分子

pro·claim /proˈklem; prəˈkleɪm/ *v* [T] *formal*【正式】**1** to say publicly that something important is true or exists 宣布, 聲明: *Their religion encouraged them to proclaim their faith.* 他們的宗教鼓勵他們公開表明信仰。| *A national holiday was proclaimed.* 宣布全國放假一天。| **proclaim sb sth** *His son was immediately proclaimed king.* 他的兒子立即被宣布為國王。**2** to show something clearly or be a sign of something 顯示, 表明: *The two gold stripes on Tanya's uniform proclaimed her seniority.* 坦妮亞制服上的兩條金條紋表明了她的高級別。

proc·la·ma·tion /ˌprɑkləˈmeʃən; ˌprɒkləˈmeɪʃən/ *n* **1** [C] an official public statement about something that is important 公告; 聲明(書), 宣言: *the country's proclamation of independence* 該國的獨立宣言 | *a royal proclamation* 王室公告 **2** [U] the act of stating something officially and publicly 宣布, 公布, 聲明

pro·cliv·i·ty /proˈklɪvətɪ; prəˈklɪvəti/ *n* [C+to/towards/for] *formal* a strong liking for something or natural tendency to do something, especially something bad【正式】〔尤指壞的〕嗜好, 癖性; 傾向: *The child shows no proclivity towards aggression as far as I can see.* 就我的觀察, 這孩子沒有表現出攻擊他人的傾向。

pro·con·sul /proˈkɑnsl̩; prəʊˈkɒnsəl/ *n* [C] someone who governed a part of the ancient Roman Empire〔古羅馬帝國的〕地方總督 —**proconsular** /-ˈkɑnsl̩ɚ; -ˈkɒnsjələ/ *adj*

pro·con·su·late /proˈkɑnsl̩ɪt; prəʊˈkɒnsjələt/ also 又作 **pro·con·sul·ship** /-ˈkɑnsl̩ˌʃɪp; -ˈkɒnsəlʃɪp/ *n* [C] the rank of a proconsul, or the time during which someone was a proconsul 古羅馬帝國地方總督的職位[任期]

pro·cras·ti·nate /proˈkræstəˌnet; prəˈkræstəneɪt/ *v* [I] *formal* to delay doing something that you ought to do, usually because you do not want to do it【正式】耽擱, 拖延: *Stop procrastinating – just go and tell her.* 別耽擱了 — 去告訴她吧。—**procrastination** /proˌkræstəˈneʃən; prəˌkræstəˈneɪʃən/ *n* [U]

pro·cre·ate /ˈprokrɪˌet; ˈprəʊkrieɪt/ *v* [I, T] *formal or technical* to produce children or baby animals【正式或術語】生育, 生殖 —**procreation** /ˌprokrɪˈeʃən; ˌprəʊkriˈeɪʃən/ *n* [U]

proc·tor¹ /ˈprɑktɚ; ˈprɒktə^r/ *n* [C] **1** a university officer, especially at Oxford or Cambridge, whose duties include making sure that students keep the rules〔尤指牛津或劍橋大學的〕校監, 學監〔負責監督學生的紀律〕**2** *AmE* someone who watches students in an exam to make sure that they do not cheat【美】監考人

proctor² *v* [T] *AmE* to watch students in an exam to make sure that they do not cheat【美】監〔考〕; INVIGILATE *BrE*【英】

pro·cu·ra·tor fis·cal /ˌ····ˈ··/ *n* [C] an official in Scotland who decides whether someone should be sent to court for a TRIAL¹ (1)〔蘇格蘭的〕(地方)檢察官

pro·cure /proˈkjur; prəˈkjʊə/ *v formal*【正式】**1** [T] to obtain something, especially something that is difficult to get 獲得, 取得〔尤指難以得到的事物〕: **procure sb sth/procure sth for sb** *Somehow he had procured us an invitation.* 他設法給我們弄到了一張請帖。**2** [I,T] *old-fashioned* to provide a PROSTITUTE for someone【過時】為〔某人〕介紹妓女, 給…拉皮條 —**procurable** *adj* —**procurement** *n* [U] —**procurer** *n* [C]

prod¹ /prɑd; prɒd/ *v* **prodded, prodding** [I,T] **1** to push or press something with your finger or a pointed object; POKE¹ (1)〔用手指或尖物〕刺, 戳, 捅: *She prodded me sharply in the ribs.* 她用力捅了捅我的肋骨。| **[+at]** *Theo prodded at the dead snake.* 西奧戳了戳那條死蛇。—see picture on page A21 參見A21頁圖 **2** to strongly encourage someone to do something 激勵; 促使, 督促: *She's not lazy, but she needs prodding.* 她並不懶, 但她需要人加以督促。| **prod sb into (doing) sth** *We just need something to prod them into action.* 我們只是需要點甚麼促使他們採取行動。

prod² *n* [C usually singular 一般用單數] **1** a sudden pressing or pushing movement, using your finger or a pointed object; POKE² (1) 刺, 戳, 捅: *Jerry gave me a sharp prod in the back.* 傑里在我背上猛戳了一下。**2 give sb a prod** to encourage or remind someone to do something 激勵[提醒]某人〔做某事〕: *You'll need to give him a prod to* *get him to clean his room.* 你得提醒他讓他打掃自己的房間。**3** an instrument used for prodding something 刺戳的工具, 刺針; 刺棒: *a cattle prod* 趕牛刺棒

prod·i·gal¹ /ˈprɑdɪgl̩; ˈprɒdɪgəl/ *adj* **1** tending to waste what you have, especially money 浪費的, 揮霍的; 奢侈的: *a prodigal lifestyle* 奢侈的生活方式 | **[+of/with]** *Don't be so prodigal of your time.* 別這樣浪費你的時間。**2** *formal* giving or producing large amounts of something; LAVISH¹ (1)【正式】慷慨的; 豐富的, 大量的: *a prodigal feast* 豐盛的宴會 | **[+of]** *The garden was filled with blossom and prodigal of scent.* 花園開滿了花, 香氣四溢。—**prodigally** *adv* —**prodigality** /ˌprɑdɪˈgælətɪ; ˌprɒdɪˈgæl̩ti/ *n* [U]

P

prodigal² *n humorous* someone who spends money carelessly and wastes their time【幽默】浪費〔時間與金錢〕者, 揮霍者; 浪子

pro·di·gious /prəˈdɪdʒəs; prəˈdɪdʒəs/ *adj* extremely or surprisingly large or powerful 巨大的, 龐大的, 大得驚人的: *a prodigious feat* 驚人的業績 —**prodigiously** *adv*

prod·i·gy /ˈprɑdədʒɪ; ˈprɒdɪdʒi/ *n* [C] **1** a young person who is extremely clever or good at doing something 奇才, 天才〔尤指神童〕: *a mathematical prodigy* 數學天才 | **a child/infant prodigy** *Mozart was a child prodigy.* 莫扎特是個神童。**2** something strange and wonderful 奇跡; 奇物; 奇觀: **[+of]** *prodigies of endurance* 忍耐力的奇跡

pro·duce¹ /prəˈdus; prəˈdjuːs/ *v*

1 ►NATURALLY 自然地◄ [T] to grow something or make it naturally〔自然地〕生產, 產生, 出產: *Canada produces high-quality wheat.* 加拿大出產優質小麥。| *The pancreas produces insulin in the body.* 胰腺在體內產生胰島素。| *More sun produces riper grapes.* 較多的陽光會結出較為成熟的葡萄。

2 ►RESULT 結果◄ [T] to make something happen or develop, or have a particular result or effect 引起; 造成; 產生: *New medicines are producing remarkable results in the treatment of cancer.* 新的藥物在治療癌症方面正產生着顯著的效果。| *a remark which produced howls of protest* 引起陣陣抗議吼聲的話 | *courses designed to produce better teachers* 為培養出更好的教師而設計的課程

3 ►SHOW 出示◄ [T] to show, bring out, or offer something so it can be seen or considered 出示; 拿出; 提出: *When challenged, he suddenly produced a gun.* 受到別人的挑戰, 他突然掏出一枝槍。| *She produced no evidence in support of her argument.* 她提供不出證據支持她的論點。

4 ►WITH SKILL 用技巧◄ [T] to make something using skill and imagination 製作, 創作: *In this play Eliot produces some of his most expressive poetry.* 在這部劇本中艾略特創作了他最具表現力的一些詩歌。| *Diane produced a fantastic meal.* 黛安做出了一頓美味的飯菜。

5 ►GOODS 貨物◄ [I,T] to make things to be sold 生產, 製造: *The factory produces an incredible 100 cars per hour.* 該廠每小時生產 100 輛汽車, 真不可思議。| *Gas can be produced from coal.* 煤氣可從煤中提製。—see also 另見 MASS-PRODUCED

6 ►PLAY/FILM 戲劇/電影◄ [T] to control the preparation of a play, film etc and then show it to the public 製作〔電影、戲劇等〕; 上演, 演出, 上映: *Jane's play was produced at a London theatre.* 簡的戲劇安排在倫敦劇院演出。—see also 另見 PRODUCER (2)

7 ►BABY 嬰兒◄ [T] to have a baby 生, 生育: *Anthea felt pressure from the family to produce a son.* 安西亞感受到家裡人想讓她生兒子的壓力。

8 ►MATHS 數學◄ [T] *technical* to lengthen or continue a line to a point, in GEOMETRY【術語】〔幾何中〕使〔線〕延長〔至某一點〕—see also 另見 PRODUCTION

prod·uce² /ˈprɑdjus; ˈprɒdjuːs/ *n* [U] something that has been produced, especially by growing or farming 產品,〔尤指〕農產品: *agricultural produce* 農產品 | *mangoes labelled 'produce of India'* 標有"印度產品"的芒果 —see 見 PRODUCTION (USAGE)

pro·duc·er /prəˈdusə; prəˈdjuːsə/ *n* [C] **1** a person, company, or country that makes or grows goods, foods, or materials 生產者, 製造者, 生產公司[國]: **[+of]** *England is a producer of high quality wool.* 英國是出產優質羊毛的國家。| **a coffee/wine/car etc producer** *one of the world's largest beef producers* 世界上最大的牛肉生產國之一 —compare 比較 CONSUMER **2** someone who has general control of the preparation of a play, film, or broadcast, but who does not direct the actors〔戲劇、電影、廣播的〕製作人, 製片人: *Ned's been the news producer at Channel 7 for some time now.* 內德現在在第七頻道做新聞節目製作人已經有一段時間了。—see 見 PRODUCTION (USAGE)

prod·uct /ˈprɑdʌkt; ˈprɒdʌkt/ *n* **1** [C,U] something useful that is made in a factory, grown, or taken from nature 產品; 製品; 物產: *A product with a strong brand name is very important for good sales.* 一種具有強大品牌的產品對於獲得好的銷量很重要。| *investing in product development* 投資於產品開發 | *Demand for products like coal and steel is declining.* 對於像煤和鋼這些產品的需求正在下降。| *I'm allergic to dairy products.* 我對奶製品過敏。—see 見 PRODUCTION (USAGE) **2 the product of a)** someone whose behavior, opinions etc can be explained by their experiences 產物, 結果: *Although he reacted violently against the society of his day, Nietsche's philosophy is a direct product of the Germany of that time.* 儘管尼采強烈反對他當時的社會, 但他的哲學是那時候德國的直接產物。**b)** something that is a result of someone's actions or of good or bad conditions 結果: *Today's housing problems are the product of years of neglect.* 今天的住屋問題是多年來忽視的結果。**3** [C] *technical* the number you get by multiplying two or more numbers in MATHEMATICS【術語】〔數學〕〔乘〕積: **[+of]** *The product of 3 times 5 is 15.* 3 乘 5 的積是 15。**4** [C] *technical* a new chemical compound produced by chemical action【術語】〔化學反應的〕生成物

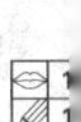

pro·duc·tion /prəˈdʌkʃən; prəˈdʌkʃən/ *n* **1** [U] the process of making or growing things to be sold as products, or the amount that is produced 生產; 產量: *The production of consumer goods has increased throughout the world.* 全世界消費品的產量都增加了。| *Smoking is banned in the factory's production areas.* 工廠的生產區禁止抽煙。| **production costs/manager/process etc** *Production costs for the plane were too high.* 飛機的生產成本太高了。| **go into (full) production** (=begin to be produced in large numbers) 開始〔大量〕生產, 投產 *The prototype engines never went into production.* 這種引擎機型從未投產。**2** [U] the act or process of making something new, or of bringing something into existence 產生, 生成: *The skin's natural production of oil slows down as we get older.* 隨着我們年齡的增長, 皮膚自然分泌油脂的速度逐漸減緩。**3** [C] something produced by skill or imagination, especially a play, film, or broadcast 藝術作品〔尤指戲劇、電影或廣播〕: *the new Shakespeare production at the Arts Theatre* 藝術劇院新排演的莎士比亞戲劇 **4** [U] the act of showing something 拿出, 出示: *Entrance is permitted only on production of a ticket.* 出示門票方可進入。**5 make a production (out) of sth** *informal* to do something in a way that takes more effort than is necessary【非正式】就…小題大作: *They only want a sandwich, Bella, don't make a production out of it!* 他們只想要一個三明治, 貝拉, 不要太麻煩!

USAGE NOTE 用法說明: PRODUCTION

WORD CHOICE 詞語辨析: **production, product, produce, producer**.

Production [U] is the process in which things are made, usually with the help of people, or in a factory. production 作不可數名詞時指生產過程, 通常是在人的幫助下或在工廠中進行: *We need to in-*

crease production (NOT 不用 *the production*). 我們需要擴大生產。| *mass production of computers* 電腦的大量生產

A **production** [C] is a play, film etc made for the theatre, television, or radio etc. production 作可數名詞時指供劇院、電視台或廣播電台上演、播放或播送的戲劇、電影等: *a new production of 'King Lear'* 新上演的《李爾王》

A **product** [C] is something that is made to be sold, often in a factory, or a natural substance like wood, coal etc that is taken from the ground or land to sell. product 作可數名詞時常指工廠製造的用來出售的產品, 或用來出售的自然產物如木材、煤等: *Glaxo produces a lot of pharmaceutical products.* 葛蘭索公司生產大量的藥品。| *food products such as cakes and ketchup* 如蛋糕和番茄醬之類的食品 | *The country's main products are timber, coal and sugar.* 該國的主要物產是木材、煤和蔗糖。**Product** can also be used to show where something is made, for example on a whiskey bottle you might see: *Product of Scotland.* product 也可用於表明某產品的產地, 如在威士忌酒瓶上可能會看到: 蘇格蘭出品。

In business, selling and advertising language, a wider range of things are beginning to be called products. For example a life insurance company might call the services it sells its products. 在商業、銷售和廣告用語中, 更廣泛的東西開始被稱為產品。如人壽保險公司可能會稱它們所售的服務為產品。

Produce [U] (which is pronounced differently from the verb) is a general word for food grown, especially on farms, and sold without being changed much. produce 作不可數名詞時〔其發音與動詞不同〕是農產品的一般用詞: *He works in the produce section at the local supermarket.* 他在當地超市的農產品部工作。

If a person, company or country produces something, they are a **producer** [C]. 生產產品的人、公司或國家稱為 producer〔可數名詞〕: *Brazil, the world's most important producer of coffee.* 巴西, 世界上最重要的咖啡生產國。

production line /ˈ·ˌ·· ·/ *n* [C] an arrangement of machines and workers in a factory where each worker or machine does one job in the making of a product and it is then passed on to the next worker or machine; ASSEMBLY LINE 生產線; 裝配線

production num·ber /ˈ·ˌ·· ˌ··/ *n* [C] a scene in a MUSICAL involving many people singing and dancing〔音樂劇中〕很多演員一起唱歌跳舞的場景

production plat·form /ˈ·ˌ·· ˌ··/ *n* [C] a large piece of equipment standing on very long legs, used for getting oil out of the ground under the sea; OIL RIG〔從海底開採石油的海上〕鑽井平台, 石油鑽塔

pro·duc·tive /prəˋdʌktɪv; prəˈdʌktɪv/ *adj* **1** producing or achieving a lot 多產的; 豐饒的; 富有成效的: *Most of us are more productive in the morning.* 我們大多數人在早上較有效率。| *productive land* 肥沃的土地 | *a productive meeting* (=having useful results) 富有成果的會議 —opposite 反義詞 UNPRODUCTIVE **2** producing goods, crops, or wealth 生產〔成品、莊稼或財富〕的; 生產性的: *Increased demand means developing more productive capacity in the factory.* 需求的增加意味着要加強工廠的生產能力。**3 productive of sth** *formal* causing or producing something【正式】造成...; 產生...: *Few ideas have been more productive of controversy than the redistribution of wealth.* 幾乎沒有甚麼觀點比財富的再分配更能引發爭議。—**productively** *adv* —**productiveness** *n* [U]

pro·duc·tiv·i·ty /ˌprɑdʌkˋtɪvətɪ; ˌprɒdʌkˈtɪvəti/ *n* [U] the rate at which goods are produced, and the amount produced, compared with the work, time, and money needed to produce them 生產力; 生產率, 生產效率: *Management is always seeking ways to increase worker productivity.* 管理層總是在尋求提高工人生產效率的方法。| *a productivity bonus* 生產效率獎金

prof /prɑf; prɒf/ *n* [C] **1** *informal* a PROFESSOR【非正式】教授 **2 Prof** the written abbreviation of 縮寫= PROFESSOR

pro·fane[1] /prəˋfen; prəˈfeɪn/ *adj* **1** showing disrespect for God or for holy things, using rude words, or religious words wrongly 瀆神的, 褻瀆上帝的; 不敬聖物的;〔語言〕褻瀆的, 下流的: *a profane action* 褻瀆行為 | *uttering profane curses* 說些下流的罵人話 **2** *formal* not religious or holy but dealing with human life【正式】世俗的, 非宗教的: *sacred and profane art* 宗教藝術和世俗藝術 —opposite 反義詞 SACRED —**profanely** *adv*

P

profane[2] *v* [T] *formal* to treat something holy in a disrespectful way【正式】褻瀆〔聖物〕—**profanation** /ˌprɑfəˋneʃən; ˌprɒfəˈneɪʃən/ *n* [C,U]

pro·fan·i·ty /prəˋfænətɪ; prəˈfænəti/ *n plural* **profanities** [C,U] **1** rude words, or religious words used wrongly 褻瀆的語言; 下流話 **2** an act of showing disrespect for God or for holy things 瀆神, 褻瀆聖物

pro·fess /prəˋfɛs; prəˈfes/ *v* [T] *formal*【正式】**1** [T] to make a claim about something, especially a false one 自稱; 偽稱, 妄稱: **profess to do sth** *Leon professes to love his son, but he shows precious little evidence of it.* 利昂聲稱愛他的兒子, 但他很少表現出這一點。| **profess to be sth** *Tusker professed to be an expert on Islamic art.* 塔斯克自稱是伊斯蘭藝術的專家。**2** to declare a personal feeling or belief openly and freely 聲稱, 公開表明〔個人感情或信仰〕: *Rodin always professed his admiration for Greek and Gothic sculpture.* 羅丹總是公開表示他對希臘和哥特式雕塑的讚賞。| **profess yourself (to be) sth** *The composer professed himself to be delighted with the way we played his work.* 這位作曲家表示喜歡我們演奏他的作品的方式。**3** [T] to have a religion or belief 信仰〔某宗教〕; 具有...信仰: *Matt professed no religion.* 馬特不信教。

pro·fessed /prəˋfɛst; prəˈfest/ *adj* [only before noun 僅用於名詞前] *formal*【正式】**1** clearly stating what you believe 公開表示的, 公開聲稱的: *a professed atheist* 公開聲稱為無神論者的人 **2** pretended, rather than real or sincere 假裝的: *Holly's professed uncertainty* 霍莉裝出來的猶豫 —**professedly** /prəˋfɛsɪdlɪ; prəˈfesədli/ *adv*

pro·fes·sion /prəˋfɛʃən; prəˈfeʃən/ *n* [C] **1** a job that needs special education and training〔需要專業教育和訓練的〕職業: *What made you choose law as a profession?* 是甚麼使你選擇法律作為職業的? —see 見 JOB (USAGE) **2 by profession** as your job 作為職業: *Castillo is a social worker by profession.* 卡斯蒂羅的職業是社會工作者。**3** all the people in a particular profession 某職業的全體人員; 同業, 同行: [also+plural verb *BrE* 英] *The medical profession are divided on the main causes of heart attacks.* 醫學界對於心臟病的主要病因意見不一。**4** a declaration of your belief, opinion, or feeling〔信念、觀點或感情的〕公開表示, 表白: *His speech was simply a profession of old-fashioned socialism.* 他的講話只是表白自己對老式社會主義的信仰。**5 the oldest profession** *humorous* the job of being a PROSTITUTE【幽默】賣淫 (S3 W3)

pro·fes·sion·al[1] /prəˋfɛʃənḷ; prəˈfeʃənəl/ *adj* (S2 W1)
1 ►**JOB** 工作◄ [only before noun 僅用於名詞前, no comparative 無比較級] connected with a job that needs special education and training 職業的, 專業的: *What professional qualifications does he have?* 他有哪些專業資格? | *on the basis of professional advice* 根據專業人士的指導

2 ►**WELL TRAINED** 受過良好訓練的◄ showing that someone has been well trained and is good at their work 專業的, 內行的: *This business plan looks very profes-*

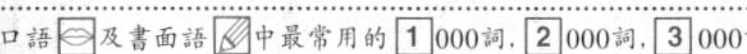

sional. 這個商業計劃看上去很有專業水平。| *a more professional approach to work* 更內行的工作方法

3 ▶PAID 有報酬的◀ [no comparative 無比較級] doing a job, sport or activity for money 職業性的; 專業的; 非業餘的: *a professional tennis player* 職業網球運動員 | *a professional army* 職業軍隊 | **turn professional** (=start to do something as a job) 開始以做某事為職業 —compare 比較 AMATEUR¹ (1)

4 ▶TEAM/EVENT 球隊/比賽項目◀ [no comparative 無比較級] done by or connected with people who are paid 由職業人員參加的; 職業性的: *Jim's the manager of a professional hockey team.* 吉姆是一支職業曲棍球隊的經理。| *The golf tournament is a professional event.* 這場高爾夫球錦標賽是職業球員參加的比賽。—compare 比較 AMATEUR¹ (1)

5 professional person/man/woman etc someone who works in a profession, or who has an important position in a company or business 專業人員; 專家: *We'd prefer to rent the house to a professional couple.* 我們更願意把房子租給一對專業人士夫婦。

6 a professional liar/complainer etc *humorous* someone who lies or complains too much【幽默】撒謊過多的人/抱怨過多的人等

7 professional foul *BrE* a FOUL (=a rule broken in a sport) done deliberately to gain some advantage【英】〔體育運動中的〕故意犯規

3 **professional²** *n* [C] **1** someone who earns money by doing a job, sport, or activity that many other people do just for enjoyment 把〔別人通常作為消遣的活動〕作為職業的人, 專門職業者; 職業選手: *Hurd signed as a professional in 1978.* 赫德於 1978 年簽約成為職業選手。—compare 比較 AMATEUR² **2** someone who works in a job that requires special education and training 專業人士, 專家: *the relationship between health professionals and patients* 健康專家和病人之間的關係 **3** someone who has a lot of experience and does something very skilfully 技術精湛經驗豐富的人, 內行: *You read that like a real professional.* 你讀起來像個行家。**4 tennis/golf/swimming etc professional** someone who is very good at a sport and is employed by a private club to teach its members〔私人俱樂部的〕網球/高爾夫球/游泳等教練

pro·fes·sion·al·is·m /prə`fɛʃənḷɪzəm; prəˈfeʃənəlɪzəm/ *n* [U] **1** the skill and high standards of behaviour expected of a professional person 專業技巧, 高超的水準; 專業道德: *The success of the orchestra is due to the professionalism of its members.* 該管弦樂隊的成功是由於樂隊成員高超的專業水平。**2** the practice of using professional players in sports〔在體育競賽中〕雇用職業選手的做法, 職業化

pro·fes·sion·al·ly /prə`fɛʃənḷɪ; prəˈfeʃənəli/ *adv* **1** as part of your work 作為工作的一部分: *Many foreign students will go on to use their English professionally.* 很多外國學生將繼續在工作中使用英語。**2** in a way that shows high standards and good training 專業地, 職業地: *Where did you learn to ski so professionally?* 你的滑雪水平這麼高, 是在哪裡學的? **3** as a paid job rather than just for enjoyment 作為職業, 職業性地: *a chance to play football professionally* 當職業足球員的機會

pro·fes·sor /prə`fɛsɚ; prəˈfesə/ *n* [C] **1** *especially BrE* a teacher of the highest rank in a university department【尤英】〔大學〕教授; FULL PROFESSOR *AmE*【美】: *Thank you, Professor Barclay, for your comments.* 謝謝您的評論, 巴克利教授。| *my science professor* 我的理科教授 | *a professor of history* 歷史學教授 **2** *AmE* a teacher at a university or college【美】大學教師: *Ted's a college professor.* 特德是一名大學教師。| *Professor, can I ask you a question?* 老師, 我能問你個問題嗎? —see also 另見 ASSISTANT PROFESSOR, ASSOCIATE PROFESSOR **3** a title taken by some people who teach various skills 師傅; 專家〔對傳授技藝者的稱呼〕: *Madame Clara, professor of dancing* 克拉拉女士, 舞蹈專家

USAGE NOTE 用法說明: PROFESSOR

BRITISH AND AMERICAN ENGLISH 英語和美語

In many countries all university teachers are called **professor**. In Britain **professor** is used only for members of the highest rank of university teachers. 在很多國家, 所有的大學教師都稱為 professor。在英國, professor 只用來稱呼等級最高的大學教師: *a research professor* 研究教授 | *Professor Leech is in charge of the department here.* 利奇教授是本系的負責人。Lower ranks in a university are **lecturer, senior lecturer,** and **reader**. 大學裡較低的等級有 lecturer〔講師〕, senior lecturer〔高級講師〕和 reader〔僅低於 professor 的教授〕。

In the US many more university teachers are called **professor**, which is used of any full member of the teaching staff of a university or college. There are three specific ranks: **associate professor, assistant professor**, and **full professor**. 在美國, 稱為 professor (教授) 的大學教師比較多, professor 可用來稱大學中所有的正式教師。它有三個特定的級別: associate professor (副教授), assistant professor (助理教授), 和 full professor (正教授)。

School teachers are never called professors in English. 在英語中, 中小學教師從不稱為 professor。

pro·fes·so·ri·al /ˌprɑfəˋsɔrɪəl; ˌprɒfəˈsɔːriəl◂/ *adj* connected with the job of a professor, or considered typical of a professor 教授的; 教授特有的: *His speech was clipped and precise – almost professorial.* 他的講話急促而精確——幾乎像教授講話一樣。—**professorially** *adv*

pro·fes·sor·ship /prə`fɛsɚˌʃɪp; prəˈfesəʃɪp/ *n* [C] the job or position of a university or college professor〔大學〕教授職位: *a professorship in Japanese* 日語教授職位

prof·fer /ˋprɑfɚ; ˈprɒfə/ *v* [T] *formal*【正式】**1** to offer something to someone, especially by holding it out in your hands〔給某人〕拿出; 遞給: *Sarah sipped from the glass proffered by the attendant.* 莎拉從服務員端過來的玻璃杯中小口啜飲。| **proffer sb sth** *Poirot proffered him a cigarette.* 普瓦羅遞給他一根煙。**2** to give someone advice, an explanation, etc 提出〔建議、解釋等〕: *the proffered invitation* 提出的邀請 —**proffer** *n* [C]

pro·fi·cien·cy /prə`fɪʃənsɪ; prəˈfɪʃənsi/ *n* [U] a high standard of ability and skill 熟練; 精通: **[+in]** *a high level of proficiency in grammar* 精通語法

pro·fi·cient /prə`fɪʃənt; prəˈfɪʃənt/ *adj* able to do something well or skilfully 熟練的, 精通的: **[+in/at]** *Martha's proficient in Swedish.* 瑪莎精通瑞典語。| *a proficient typist* 熟練的打字員 —**proficiently** *adv*

pro·file¹ /ˋprofaɪl; ˈprəʊfaɪl/ *n* [C] **1** a side view of someone's head〔人頭部的〕側面(像), 側影: *Dani has a lovely profile.* 丹尼的側面輪廓很可愛。| **in profile** *I only saw her face in profile.* 我只是從側面看到她的臉。**2** a short description that gives important details about a person, a group of people, or a place 人物簡介, 傳略; 〔某地方的〕概況: **[+of]** *The company has an employee profile of everyone working for them.* 該公司有每個雇員的簡介。| *We need a profile of the area: population, main roads, water supplies, etc.* 我們需要這一地區的概況: 人口、主要道路、供水系統等。**3 have a high profile/give sth a high profile** to be noticed by many people, or to make something get a lot of attention (使)引人注目: *Jack runs a department with a high public profile.* 傑克管理一個受到公眾注目的部門。**4 keep a low profile** to behave quietly and avoid doing things that will make people notice you 保持低姿態[低調] **5** an edge or shape of something seen against a background 外形, 輪廓: *the sharp profile of the western foothills against the sky* 在天空襯托下西面山麓小丘的清晰輪廓

profile² *v* [T] to write or give a short description of someone or something 寫…的傳略[概況]: *The new editor was profiled in the Sunday paper.* 星期天的報紙登載了這位新編輯的簡況。

pro·fil·ing /ˋprofaɪlɪŋ; ˈprəʊfaɪlɪŋ/ *n* **offender profiling** the process of studying a crime, especially a murder, and making judgments about the character of the person who did it 罪犯〔尤指謀殺犯〕特徵分析

1 1 **prof·it¹** /ˋprɑfɪt; ˈprɒfɪ̈t/ *n* **1** [C,U] money that you gain by selling things or doing business 利潤, 收益, 贏利: *They sold the business and bought a yacht with the profits.* 他們賣了公司並用所獲得的利潤買了一艘遊艇。| *The profit each day from the snack bar is usually around $500.* 這家小吃店每天所獲的利潤通常是 500 美元左右。| **make (a) profit** *The telephone companies are making handsome profits every day.* (=very large ones) 電話公司每天獲利豐厚。| **at a profit** *They sold their house at a huge profit.* 他們以高額利潤賣掉了房子。| **clear profit** *Suzanne made a clear profit of £200 on the car sale.* 蘇珊妮出售汽車獲得淨利潤 200 英鎊。| **net profit** (=after tax etc is paid) 淨利潤, 純利潤 | **gross profit** (=before tax etc is paid) 毛利 | **bring sth into profit** (=gain money from it) 從…中獲利 **2** [U] an advantage that you gain from doing something 益處, 好處: *reading for profit and pleasure* 為獲益和樂趣而閱讀 —see also 另見 NON-PROFITMAKING

profit² *v* [T] *formal* to be useful or helpful to someone【正式】有益於, 對〔某人〕有好處: *It will profit you nothing to follow his example.* 以他為榜樣對你沒甚麼好處。

profit by/from sth *phr v* [T] to learn from something that happens, or get something good from a situation 從…中獲益, 從…中得到教訓: *My wardrobe definitely profited from having a stylish older sister.* 我穿的衣服無疑得益於有一位時髦的姐姐。

prof·it·a·bil·i·ty /ˌprɑfətəˋbɪlətɪ; ˌprɒfɪ̈təˈbɪlɪ̈ti/ *n* [U] the state of producing a profit, or the degree to which a business or activity is profitable 獲利(能力), 盈利(能力): *a decline in company profitability* 公司盈利能力的下降

prof·i·ta·ble /ˋprɑfɪtəbl; ˈprɒfɪ̈təbəl/ *adj* producing a profit or a useful result 有利可圖的; 有益的, 有用的: *The advertising campaign proved very profitable.* 事實證明, 這次廣告宣傳活動很有用。| *a highly profitable business* 非常有利可圖的企業 | *a profitable afternoon* 有收穫的下午 —opposite 反義詞 UNPROFITABLE —**profitably** *adv*

profit and loss ac·count /ˌ‥ · ˋ· ·ˌ·/ *n* [C] a financial statement showing a company's income, spending, and profit over a particular period 損益賬〔反映公司某時期收支和利潤情況的報表〕

prof·i·teer /ˌprɑfəˋtɪr; ˌprɒfɪ̈ˈtɪə/ *n* [C] someone who makes unfairly large profits, especially by selling things at very high prices when they are difficult to get 投機商, 奸商, 牟取暴利者: *black market profiteers* 黑市上牟取暴利的商人 —**profiteer** *v* [I] —**profiteering** *n* [U]

pro·fit·e·role /prəˋfɪtərol; prəˈfɪtərəʊl/ *n* [C] *BrE* a small round PASTRY with a sweet filling and chocolate on the top【英】〔內有甜餡頂部有巧克力的〕小圓餅

prof·it·less /ˋprɑfɪtləs; ˈprɒfɪ̈tləs/ *adj* not making a profit, or not worth doing 無利的, 無利可圖的; 無益的, 不值得做的 —**profitlessly** *adv*

profit mar·gin /ˈ‥ ˌ‥/ *n* [C] the difference between the cost of producing something and the price you sell it at 利潤率, 盈利率

profit shar·ing /ˈ‥ ˌ‥/ *n* [U] a system by which all the people who work for a company share in its profits 分紅制〔公司人員分享利潤的制度〕

prof·li·gate¹ /ˋprɑfləgɪt; ˈprɒflɪ̈gɪ̈t/ *adj formal*【正式】**1** wasting money in a silly and careless way 恣意揮霍的; 極其浪費的: *profligate spending of the taxpayer's money* 恣意揮霍納稅人的錢 **2** behaving in an immoral way and not caring about it at all 放蕩的, 行為不檢點的 —**profligacy** *n* [U]

profligate² *n* [C] *formal* someone who is profligate【正式】恣意揮霍的人; 放蕩的人

pro for·ma /pro ˋfɔrmə; prəʊ ˈfɔːmə/ *adj adv Latin* if something is approved, accepted etc pro forma, this is part of the usual way of doing things, but does not involve any actual choice or decision【拉丁】形式上的[地]: *pro forma approval* 形式上的同意

pro forma in·voice /· ˌ‥ ˈ‥/ *n* [C] a bill sent to a customer to show what a price would be if he made an order; QUOTATION 形式發票, 估價單

pro·found /prəˋfaund; prəˈfaʊnd/ *adj* **1** showing strong, serious feelings〔感情〕強烈的; 深切的; 嚴肅的: *I owe you a profound apology.* 我應向你深深地道歉。**2** having a strong influence or effect〔影響〕深刻的, 極大的: *The mother's behavior has a profound impact on the developing child.* 母親的行為對於正在成長的孩子有極大的影響。**3** showing great knowledge and understanding 知識淵博的; 見解深刻的: *a profound remark* 精闢的話 | *Jenner is a profound thinker.* 詹納是學識淵博的思想家。**4** *literary* deep or far below the surface of something【文】深的; 深處的: *Her work engages something profound in the human psyche.* 她的作品涉及了人類心靈深處的某種東西。**5** *technical* complete【術語】完全的: *profound deafness* 全聾 —**profoundly** *adv*: *profoundly disturbing news* 令人極其不安的消息

pro·fun·di·ty /prəˋfʌndətɪ; prəˈfʌndɪ̈ti/ *n formal*【正式】**1** [U] the quality of knowing and understanding a lot, or having strong, serious feelings〔知識〕淵博;〔情感〕深刻: *a young woman of extraordinary profundity* 一個思想非常深刻的年輕女人 | *Fairy tales have a profundity absent in most children's literature.* 童話思想深刻、意味深長, 為大多數兒童文學所缺乏。**2** [C usually plural 一般用複數] something that someone says that shows this quality 淵博[深刻]的話: *The profundities of his speech were lost on the young audience.* 他深奧的講話對那些年輕的聽眾沒有影響力。

pro·fuse /prəˋfjus; prəˈfjuːs/ *adj* **1** given, flowing, or growing freely and in large quantities 大量〔給予、流出、生長〕的; 豐富的; 充沛的: *profuse tears* 淚如泉涌 **2** too eager or generous with your praise, thanks etc〔稱讚或感謝〕毫不吝惜的, 十分慷慨的; 過多的, 過濫的: **[+in]** *Stella was profuse in her thanks.* 斯特拉一再道謝。—**profusely** *adv*: *sweating profusely in the heat* 在高温下大汗淋漓 —**profuseness** *n* [U]

pro·fu·sion /prəˋfjuʒən; prəˈfjuːʒən/ *n* [singular,U] a supply or amount that is almost too large 大量; 豐富; 充沛: **[+of]** *The house was overflowing with a profusion of strange ornaments.* 這個房子裡擺滿了奇特的裝飾品。| **in profusion** *Corn marigolds grow in profusion in the fields.* 田裡長着茂盛的珍珠菊。

pro·gen·i·tor /proˋdʒɛnətɚ; prəʊˈdʒenɪ̈tə/ *n* [C] *technical*【術語】**1** a person or animal that lived a long time ago, to whom someone or something living now is related; ANCESTOR〔人或動物的〕祖先 **2** *formal* someone who first thought of an idea a long time ago; PRECURSOR【正式】創始人, 前輩, 先驅: **[+of]** *a progenitor of modern music* 現代音樂的創始人

prog·e·ny /ˋprɑdʒənɪ; ˈprɒdʒɪ̈ni/ *n* [U] **1** *technical or formal* the DESCENDANTS of a person, animal, or plant form, or the things that can develop from something else【術語或正式】〔人、動植物或事物的〕後代; 後裔: *The drug-resistant cells' progeny are also drug-resistant.* 抗藥細胞的後代同樣抗藥。**2** *old-fashioned or humorous* someone's children【過時或幽默】〔某人的〕兒女, 孩子: *Sarah with her numerous progeny* 莎拉和她的一大羣孩子

pro·ges·ter·one /proˋdʒɛstəˌron; prəʊˈdʒestərəʊn/ *n* [U] a female sex HORMONE that is produced by a woman when she is going to have a baby and is also used in CONTRACEPTIVE drugs 孕酮〔一種女性性激素〕, 黃體酮

prog·na·thous /ˋprɑgnəθəs; prɒgˈneɪθəs/ *adj technical* with a jaw that sticks out more than the rest of your face【術語】凸顎的, 下巴突出的

P

prog·no·sis /prɑgˋnosɪs; prɒgˈnəʊsɨs/ *n plural* **prognoses** [C] **1** *technical* a doctor's opinion of how an illness or disease will develop【術語】預後, 預斷〔醫生對於病情如何發展的預測〕: *The doctor's prognosis for Mum wasn't hopeful.* 醫生對媽媽病情的發展不樂觀。—compare 比較 DIAGNOSIS **2** *formal* a judgement about the future based on information or experience【正式】〔基於資料和經驗而作出的〕預測, 展望: **[+of]** *a hopeful prognosis of the country's future development* 對於該國未來發展的樂觀展望

prog·nos·ti·cate /prɑgˋnɑstɪˌket; prɒgˈnɒstɨkeɪt/ *v* [T] to say what will happen, or to be a sign of what will happen 預言; 預示; 是…的預兆 —**prognostication** /prɑgˌnɑstɪˋkeʃən; prɒgˌnɒstɨˈkeɪʃən/ *n* [C,U]

1 **pro·gram¹** /ˋprogræm; ˈprəʊgræm/ *n* [C] **1** a set of instructions given to a computer to make it perform an operation 〔電腦〕程序, 程式: *a new program for forecasting sales figures* 用於預測銷售數字的新程序 **2** the American spelling of PROGRAMME programme 的美式拼法

program² *v* **programmed, programming** [T] **1** to give a computer a set of instructions that it can use to perform a particular operation〔為電腦〕編製程序: **program sth to do sth** *Scientists are trying to program computers to think in the same way as humans.* 科學家正試圖為電腦設計一套能像人類那樣進行思維的程序。**2** the American spelling of PROGRAMME programme 的美式拼法 —see also 另見 PROGRAMMER

pro·gram·ma·ble /ˋprogræməbḷ; ˈprəʊgræməbəl/ *adj* able to be controlled by a computer or electronic program 可電腦控制的, 可程序控制的: *a programmable heating system* 程控供暖系統

1 1 **pro·gramme¹** *BrE*【英】, **program** *AmE*【美】/ˋprogræm; ˈprəʊgræm/ *n* [C] **1** an important plan, especially one organized by a government or large organization〔尤指政府或大型機構的〕重大計劃, 方案: *a United Nations programme to control the spread of AIDS* 聯合國控制愛滋病傳播的計劃 | *the US space program* 美國太空計劃 **2** a show or performance on television or radio, especially one that is played regularly〔電視或廣播的〕節目: *Northern Exposure is my favorite TV program.*《北國風雲》是我最喜歡的電視節目。| **[+about]** *There's a programme on about organic gardening.* 有一個關於使用有機肥進行園藝的節目正在播映。**3** a set of planned activities in education or training, with a specific purpose〔教育或訓練安排好的〕課程, 活動, 方案: *Stanford University's MBA program* 史丹福大學的工商管理碩士課程 | *Lucy's new fitness programme includes a 5 mile jog every morning.* 露西的新健身計劃包括每天早上五英里的慢跑。**4** a printed description of what will happen at a play, concert etc and of the people who will be performing〔戲劇、音樂會等的〕節目單 **5** the planned order of activities or events at a performance or meeting; SCHEDULE¹ (1)〔表演或會議的〕程序單, 計劃表, 活動安排, 進度表: *The next race on today's programme is the King George V Handicap.* 在今天的比賽程序單上, 下一場比賽是喬治五世讓步賽。**6** a series of actions done in a particular order by a machine such as a washing machine〔洗衣機等機器按固定步驟工作的〕工作程序: *The light goes off when it finishes its program.* 燈完成工作程序之後就會熄滅。—see also 另見 PROGRAM¹

programme² *BrE*【英】, **program** *AmE*【美】*v* [T] **1 be programmed** to be made to behave or think in a particular way because of the influence of a society, group, or situation〔由於社會、羣體或情況的影響〕使〔某人〕按某種方式行事[思考]: **[+to]** *Are girls programmed at an early age not to be interested in science subjects?* 女孩年幼時就受外界影響而對科學科目不感興趣嗎? **2** to set a machine to operate in a particular way 調好, 設置〔機器使之按某種方式運作〕: *I've programmed the video to come on at ten.* 我已經把這台錄像機設置好在十點鐘開機。—see also 另見 PROGRAM¹ **3** to arrange for something to happen as part of a series of planned events or activities 安排, 計劃: *What's programmed for this afternoon?* 今天下午有甚麼安排?

programmed course /ˌ‥ ˈ‥/ *n* [C] a course of study that is part of programmed learning 程序課程

programmed learn·ing /ˌ‥ ˈ‥/ *n* [U] a method of learning in which the subject to be learned is divided into small parts, and you have to get one part right before you can go on to the next 程序學習〔一種學習方法, 要學習的科目被分成小部分, 學習者必須把一部分掌握之後才能進入下一部分〕

programme mu·sic *BrE*【英】, **program music** *AmE*【美】/ˈ‥ ˌ‥/ *n* [U] descriptive music which uses sound to suggest a story, picture etc 標題音樂〔利用聲音描繪故事、畫面等的音樂〕

pro·gram·mer /ˋprogræmɚ; ˈprəʊgræmə/ *n* [C] someone whose job is to write computer PROGRAMS〔電腦的〕程序[式]編製員, 程序[式]設計員

pro·gram·ming /ˋprogræmɪŋ; ˈprəʊgræmɪŋ/ *n* [U] **1** the activity of writing PROGRAMS for computers〔電腦的〕程序編製, 程序設計: *programming languages* 程序設計語言 **2** television or radio programmes, or the activity of producing them〔電視或廣播〕節目; 電視[廣播]節目製作: *nearly 200 hours of sports programming* 將近 200 小時的體育節目

pro·gress¹ /ˋprɑgrɛs; ˈprəʊgres/ *n* **1** [U] the process of getting better at doing something, or getting closer to finishing or achieving something 進步; 進展: **[+of/on/towards]** *Nico had been candid with Stern about the progress of the investigation.* 尼科已把調查的進展情況向斯特恩坦言相告。| *tests designed to monitor the student's progress* 旨在檢查學生進步情況的測試  **2 make progress a)** to get better at doing something or come closer to finishing or achieving something 取得進步, 取得進展: *Nick has made good progress with his studies this year.* 今年尼克的學習有了很大進步。| *I'm afraid we're not making much progress.* 恐怕我們進步不大。**b)** to move towards a place〔向某地〕前進, 行進: *By nighttime we had still made very little progress.* 到了夜間我們仍然沒怎麼前行。**3** [U] change towards a better society because of developments in science or fairer methods of social organization〔社會的〕進步: *the great march of progress* 社會進步的巨大步伐 **4 in progress** *formal* happening now, and not yet finished【正式】進行中: *No Talking. Examination in Progress.* 不要講話, 考試正在進行。**5** [U] slow or difficult movement towards a place〔向某地的〕緩慢[艱難]行進: *We watched with apprehension their progress across the face of the cliff.* 我們提心吊膽地看着他們在崖面上緩慢前行。**6** [C] *old use* a journey, especially by a king or queen【舊】〔尤指國王或女王的〕巡行, 巡遊

progress² /prəˋgrɛs; prəˈgres/ *v* [I] **1** to develop over a period of time and become something better or more complete 進步; 進展: *Work on the ship progressed quickly.* 輪船的建造進展迅速。| *I asked the nurse how my son was progressing.* 我向護士詢問我兒子身體恢復得如何。| **[+to]** *Cindy has progressed to reading on her own.* 辛迪進步了, 開始自己閱讀了。**2** if an activity or situation progresses, it continues to happen or develop gradually〔活動等〕繼續進行; 逐步發展: *As the meeting progressed, Nina grew more and more bored.* 隨着會議的進行, 妮娜越來越感到無聊。**3** to move forward slowly 緩慢行進: *Our taxi seemed to be progressing with agonizing slowness.* 我們的出租車彷彿以令人難以忍受的緩慢速度向前行駛。**4** to move on from doing one thing to doing another〔從做一件事〕轉向〔做另一件事〕: **[+to]** *We started with a bottle of wine, and then progressed to whisky.* 我們先喝了一瓶葡萄酒, 之後便喝起了威士忌。—compare 比較 REGRESS

pro·gres·sion /prəˋgrɛʃən; prəˈgreʃən/ *n* **1** [U] a gradual process of change or development 進步, 進展: *They offer rapid career progression.* 他們提供迅速的職業晉升。| **progression from sth to sth** *The progression from* *infection to disease can take up to 7 years.* 從感染到發病可能長達七年。**2** [U] movement towards a goal or particular place〔向某一目標或地點的〕移動, 前行: *the river's stately progression towards the Gulf of Mexico* 這條河氣勢磅礴地奔流向墨西哥灣 **3** a number of things coming one after the other 接連, 連續, 一系列 —see also 另見 ARITHMETIC PROGRESSION, GEOMETRIC PROGRESSION

pro·gres·sive¹ /prəˋgrɛsɪv; prəˈgresɪv/ *adj* **1** supporting new or modern ideas and methods, especially in politics and education〔尤指在政治和教育方面〕進步的, 先進的: *a progressive administration* 進步的政府 | *progressive and forward-looking policies* 進步並有前瞻性的政策 **2** happening or developing gradually over a period of time 逐步發生的, 逐步發展的: *the progressive elimination of rural poverty* 農村貧困的逐步消除 | *Britain's progressive decline as a world power* 英國作為世界強國的逐步衰落 **3** the progressive form of a verb is used to show that an action or activity is continuing to happen, and is shown in English by the verb 'be', followed by a PRESENT PARTICIPLE, as in 'I was waiting for the bus'〔動詞形式〕進行式的 —**progressively** *adv*: *The situation became progressively worse.* 情況變得越來越糟。—**progressiveness** *n* [U]

progressive² *n* [C] someone with modern ideas who wants to change things 進步人士; 革新派人士

progressive tax /.,.. '../ *n* [singular] a tax that takes a larger PERCENTAGE of money from people with higher incomes than from people with lower incomes 累進稅 —compare 比較 REGRESSIVE TAX

progress re·port /'.. .,./ *n* [C] a statement about how something, especially work, is advancing or developing 工作進展報告

pro·hib·it /proˋhɪbɪt; prəˈhɪbɪ̀t/ *v* [T] **1** to officially stop an activity by making it illegal or against the rules〔以法令、規則等〕禁止: *Smoking is strictly prohibited inside the factory.* 該工廠內嚴禁抽煙。| **prohibit sb from doing sth** *Nuclear powers are prohibited from selling this technology.* 禁止核大國出售該項技術。**2** to make something impossible or prevent it from happening 使不可能, 阻止: *High costs had prohibited the building work from being completed.* 高額費用使這項建築工程無法完工。

pro·hi·bi·tion /ˌproəˋbɪʃən; ˌprəʊhɪ̀ˈbɪʃən/ *n* **1** [U] the act of officially stopping something by law〔以法律〕禁止: **[+of]** *prohibition of the sale of firearms* 禁止出售火器 **2** [C] an order stopping something 禁令, 禁律: **[+on/against]** *a prohibition on Sunday trading* 禁止星期天交易的法令 **3 Prohibition** the period from 1919 to 1933 in the US when the production and sale of alcoholic drinks was forbidden by law 禁酒時期〔1919-1933 年間美國以法律禁止生產和銷售酒的時期〕

pro·hi·bi·tion·ist /ˌproəˋbɪʃənɪst; ˌprəʊhɪ̀ˈbɪʃənɪ̀st/ *n* [C] someone who supported Prohibition 贊成禁酒者; 禁酒主義者 —**prohibitionism** *n* [U]

pro·hib·i·tive /proˋhɪbɪtɪv; prəˈhɪbɪ̀tɪv/ *adj* **1** prohibitive prices are so high that they prevent people from buying something〔價格〕高得負擔不起的, 貴得使人望而卻步的: *The cost of land in Tokyo is prohibitive.* 東京的地價高得離譜。**2** a prohibitive tax or rule prevents people from doing things〔稅收、規定〕禁止性的; 起阻止作用的: *a prohibitive tax on imports* 對進口物品徵收的寓禁稅 —**prohibitively** *adv*: *prohibitively expensive* 貴得使人負擔不起

pro·hib·i·to·ry /proˋhɪbəˌtorɪ; prəˈhɪbɪ̀təri/ *adj* intended to stop something 禁止的, 禁止性的

1 1 **proj·ect¹** /ˋprɑdʒɛkt; ˈprɒdʒekt/ *n* [C] **1** an important and carefully planned piece of work, that is intended to build or produce something new, or to deal with a problem 項目; 工程; 計劃; 規劃: *the Channel Tunnel project* 海峽隧道工程 | *a long-term project to help the homeless* 一項幫助無家可歸者的長期計劃 **2** a part of a school course that involves careful study of a particular subject over a period of time〔學校的〕課題, 研究項目: **[+on]** *We're doing a project on pollution.* 我們正在做一個有關污染的課題。**3** also 又作 **the projects** *AmE informal* a HOUSING PROJECT【美, 非正式】低收入人羣住宅區

pro·ject² /prəˋdʒɛkt; prəˈdʒekt/ *v*

1 ►CALCULATE 計算◄ [T] to calculate the size, amount, or rate of something as it will be in the future, using the information you have now 預計, 推斷: *The company projected an annual growth rate of 3%.* 該公司預計每年的增長率為 3%。| *projected sales forecasts* 預計的銷售數字

2 ►STICK OUT 突出◄ [I,T] to stick out beyond an edge or surface 凸出, 突出: **[+out/from/through etc]** *The huge guns projected outwards from the deck of the ship.* 巨砲從船甲板向外伸出。

3 ►FILM 電影◄ [T] to make the picture of a film, photograph etc appear in a larger form on a SCREEN¹ (2) or flat surface 放映; 投射

4 ►YOURSELF 你自己◄ [T] to make other people have a particular idea about you 使別人對自己有某種看法, 使〔自己的特點〕呈現, 表現〔自己〕: **project an image** *Regina always projects an image of quiet self-confidence.* 麗賈娜總是表現出安靜自信的樣子。| **project yourself** *You'll need to project yourself well in the interview.* 你必需在面試時好好表現自己。

5 ►FEELING 感情◄ [T] *technical* to avoid dealing with your own feelings by imagining that someone else is feeling them【術語】想像〔他人〕具有〔本人的思想感情〕; 把〔自己的感情〕投射給別人: **project sth on/onto sb** *You're projecting your insecurity onto me.* 你在把你的焦慮往我身上搬。

6 ►PLAN 計劃◄ **be projected** to be planned to happen in the future 計劃, 預定: *A visit by President Clinton is projected for March.* 克林頓總統擬於三月份出訪。

7 ►THROW 扔, 投◄ [T] *technical* to throw something up or forward with great force【術語】投擲, 發射

8 ►PICTURE 圖畫◄ *technical*【術語】**a)** to make a picture of a solid object on a flat surface 作〔立體物的〕投影圖 **b)** to make a map using this method 用投影法製作地圖

9 project yourself into the future/past etc to imagine that you are in the future, past etc 設想自己身處將來／過去等: *I kept trying to project myself back into a time when I thought those kind of parties were fun.* 我總是竭力想像自己回到從前, 當時我認為那種聚會很有趣。

10 project your voice to speak clearly and loudly so that you can be heard by everyone in a big hall or room 放開聲音〔使大廳或大房間的每個人都能聽見〕

pro·jec·tile /prəˋdʒɛktl̩; prəˈdʒektaɪl/ *n* [C] an object that is thrown or is fired from a weapon, such as a bullet, stone, or SHELL¹ (2,3) 投擲物; 拋射體; 發射物〈如子彈, 石頭或砲彈〉—**projectile** *adj*

pro·jec·tion /prəˋdʒɛkʃən; prəˈdʒekʃən/ *n* **1** [C] a calculation of the amount or rate of something as it will be 3
in the future, which is used for making official plans〔對於未來情況的〕預測, 估算: **[+of]** *projections of declining natural gas production* 對於下降的天然氣產量的預測 **2** [C] a statement about what will happen, based on information available now〔根據已知資料進行的〕推斷, 預測: *Early projections show a three point lead for the Socialists.* 早期預測顯示社會黨人領先百分之三。**3** [C] *formal* something that sticks out from a surface【正式】凸出物: *small projections of weathered rock on the hillside* 山坡上許多凸出的小塊風化岩石 **4** [U] the act of projecting a film or picture 投射〔電影等〕; 投影; 放映: *projection equipment* 投影器材 **5** [U] *technical* the act of imagining that someone else is feeling what you are in fact feeling【術語】投射〔想像別人與自己有同樣的感受〕**6** [C] *technical* an image of something that has been projected, especially an image of the world's surface on a map【術語】投影圖;〔尤指〕投影的地圖 —see also 另見 MERCATOR PROJECTION

P

pro·jec·tion·ist /prəˋdʒɛkʃənɪst; prəˈdʒekʃənɨst/ *n* [C] someone whose job is to operate the projector in a cinema 電影放映員

pro·jec·tor /prəˋdʒɛktɚ; prəˈdʒektə/ *n* [C] a piece of equipment that makes a film appear on a SCREEN[1] (2a) or a flat surface 電影放映機; 投影儀

pro·lapse /proˋlæps; ˈprəʊlæps/ *n* [C] *technical* the falling down or slipping of an inner part of your body, such as the WOMB, from its usual position【術語】〔身體內部器官的〕脫垂; 脫出; 下垂

prole /prol; prəʊl/ *n* [C] *BrE informal* an insulting word for a working class person【英, 非正式】無產者〔對工人的侮辱性說法〕

pro·le·tar·i·an /ˌproləˋtɛrɪən; ˌprəʊlɨˈteəriən◂/ *adj* concerning or involving the proletariat 無產階級的

pro·le·tar·i·at /ˌproləˋtɛrɪət; ˌprəʊlɨˈteəriət/ *n* **the proletariat** the class of workers who own no property and work for wages, especially in factories, building things etc 無產階級

pro-life /ˌ· ˈ·/ *adj* someone who is pro-life is opposed to ABORTION and uses this word to describe their views 反對墮胎的, 反對人工流產的

pro-lif·er /ˌ· ˈ··/ *n* [C] a member of a pro-life group 反對墮胎者, 反對人工流產者

pro·lif·e·rate /proˋlɪfəˌret; prəˈlɪfəreɪt/ *v* [I] if something proliferates it increases rapidly and spreads to many different places 激增, 擴散: *Self-help groups have proliferated all over London.* 自助小組迅速增加, 遍及整個倫敦。

pro·lif·e·ra·tion /proˌlɪfəˋreʃən; prəˌlɪfəˈreɪʃən/ *n* **1** [singular, U] a rapid increase in the amount or number of something〔數量〕激增; 擴散: **[+of]** *the proliferation of nuclear weapons* 核武器擴散 | *a proliferation of cafes and restaurants* 咖啡館和餐館的大量湧現 **2** [U] *technical* the very fast growth of new parts of a living thing, such as cells or BUDS【術語】增殖, 增生

pro·lif·ic /prəˋlɪfɪk; prəˈlɪfɪk/ *adj* **1** a prolific artist, writer etc produces many works of art, books etc〔藝術家、作家等〕多產的, 作品豐富的 **2** an animal or plant that is prolific produces many babies or many other plants〔動物或植物〕多產的, 多育的 **3** *literary* existing in large numbers【文】大量存在的: *the prolific bird life* 大量的鳥類 —**prolifically** /-klɪ; -kli/ *adv*

pro·lix /proˋlɪks; ˈprəʊlɪks/ *adj formal* a prolix piece of writing has too many words and is boring【正式】〔文章〕冗長乏味的, 囉唆的

PROLOG /ˈprolɔg; ˈprəʊlɒg/ *n* [U] *trademark* a computer language that is similar to human language【商標】PROLOG 語言, 邏輯式程序設計語言〔一種類似人類語言的電腦語言〕

pro·logue /ˋprolɔg; ˈprəʊlɒg/ *n* [C usually singular 一般用單數] **1** the introduction to a play, a long poem etc〔戲劇、長詩等的〕序幕; 開場白; 序詩; 序 **2** *literary* an act or event that leads to a much more important event【文】〔重大事件的〕開端, 序幕 —compare 比較 EPILOGUE

pro·long /prəˋlɔŋ; prəˈlɒŋ/ *v* [T] **1** to deliberately make something such as a feeling or activity last longer 延長〔感覺、活動等〕, 拉長, 拖長: *I was trying to think of some way to prolong the conversation.* 我正在努力想一些拖長交談時間的方法。**2 prolong the agony** *informal* to delay telling someone something that they very much want to know【非正式】延長痛苦〔拖延告訴某人他很想知道的事情〕: *There's no point in prolonging the agony. The situation won't get any better.* 讓痛苦延續下去沒有甚麼意義 —— 情況不會有甚麼好轉。

pro·lon·ga·tion /ˌprolɔŋˋgeʃən; ˌprəʊlɒŋˈgeɪʃən/ *n* **1** [U] the act of making something last longer 延長, 拉長; 拖延 **2** [C+of] something added to another thing which makes it longer 增加[延長]的部分

pro·longed /prəˋlɔŋd; prəˈlɒŋd/ *adj* continuing for a long time 持續很久的, 長期的: *a prolonged absence* 長時間的缺席

prom /prɑm; prɒm/ *n* [C] **1** *AmE* a formal dance party for HIGH SCHOOL students, often held at the end of a school year【美】〔常在學年末舉行的〕高中生的正式舞會 **2** *BrE informal* a PROMENADE (1)【英, 非正式】濱海步行道 **3** *BrE informal* a PROMENADE CONCERT【英, 非正式】漫步音樂會

prom·e·nade /ˌprɑməˋned; ˌprɒməˈnɑːd/ *n* [C] **1** *BrE* a wide road next to the beach where people can walk for pleasure【英】〔供人們散步的〕濱海散步道 **2** *old-fashioned* a walk for pleasure in a public place【過時】〔在公共場所〕散步

promenade con·cert /ˈ··ˌ· ˌ··/ *n* [C] *BrE* a concert at which many of the listeners stand rather than sit【英】逍遙音樂會, 漫步音樂會〔很多聽眾站着聽的音樂會〕

promenade deck /ˈ··ˌ· ·/ *n* [C] the upper level of a ship where people can walk for pleasure〔輪船的〕上層甲板, 散步甲板

prom·i·nence /ˋprɑmənəns; ˈprɒmɨnəns/ *n* **1** [U] the fact of being important and well-known 重要; 傑出; 著名: **come to/gain prominence** (=become important and well-known) 成名, 嶄露頭角 *Gandhi first came to prominence in South Africa in the 1920s.* 甘地最初於 20 世紀 20 年代在南非嶄露頭角。**2 give sth prominence/give prominence to sth** to put something in a position where it is easily noticed because you think it is important 把某事物置於顯著位置: *The topic didn't deserve the prominence it was given.* 這個主題本不應放在如此顯著位置。**3** *formal* a part or place that is higher or larger than what is around it【正式】突出部分; 突起; 凸地

prom·i·nent /ˋprɑmənənt; ˈprɒmɨnənt/ *adj* **1** [C] well-known and important 著名的; 卓越的, 傑出的; 重要的: *a prominent Russian scientist* 傑出的俄羅斯科學家 | **play a prominent role** *Mandela played a prominent role in the early years of the ANC.* 曼德拉在非洲人國民大會的最初幾年起着重要的作用。**2** something that is prominent is large and sticks out 突出的, 凸出的: *a prominent nose* 高鼻子 **3 a prominent place/position** somewhere that is easily seen and is usually used for things that are important 突出的[顯著的, 顯眼的]位置: *The Kaiser's photo displayed in a prominent position on the piano.* 德國皇帝的照片擺在鋼琴上一個顯眼的位置。

pro·mis·cu·ous /prəˋmɪskjuəs; prəˈmɪskjuəs/ *adj* **1** having sex with a lot of people 與多人發生性關係的, 淫亂的, 濫交的: *Single men were the most promiscuous group.* 單身男人是最不約束自己性行為的一夥人。**2** *old use* made of many different parts【舊】由很多不同部分組成的, 混雜的 **3** *old use* not choosing carefully; INDISCRIMINATE【舊】不加區別的, 隨便的 —**promiscuously** *adv* —**promiscuity** /ˌprɑmɪsˋkjuətɪ; ˌprɒmɨˈskjuːɨti/ *n* [U]

prom·ise[1] /ˋprɑmɪs; ˈprɒmɨs/ *v* **1** [I,T] to tell someone that you will definitely do something or that something will happen 保證, 答應: **promise (that)** *Hurry up, we promised that we wouldn't be late.* 快點, 我們保證過不會遲到。| **promise sb (that)** *You promised me the car would be ready on Monday.* 你答應過我這輛車星期一可以用。| **I/we promise** *"Promise me you won't do anything stupid." "I promise."* "答應我你不會做蠢事。" "我答應。" | **promise to do sth** *The children have promised to give us a hand with the packing.* 孩子們已答應幫我們打包。| **promise sb sth** (=promise to give someone something) 答應給某人某物 *The company promised us a bonus this year.* 公司答應今年給我們發獎金。| **Promise?** *spoken* (=used to ask if someone promises)【口】(你) 保證? *"I'll be back by 1.00." "Promise?" "Yes! Don't worry."* "我一點鐘前會回來。" "你能保證?" "是的! 別擔心。" | **promise sth to sb** *I can't give you the book – I've promised it to Ian.* 我不能把這本書給你 —— 我已經答應給伊恩了。| **as promised** (=at the time or place that is promised) 正如保證過的 *Here you are – one new watch as promised.* 給你 —— 一隻向你保證過的新手錶。| **I promise you** *spoken* (=I warn you)【口】

我警告你 *I promise you, the work won't be easy.* 我警告你, 這項工作可不容易。**2** [T] to make you expect that something will happen 有…的希望, 使…很有可能; 給人以…的指望: **promise to be** *Tonight's meeting promises to be a difficult one.* 今晚的會面有可能不容易對付。| *dark clouds promising showers later* 黑雲預示着稍後有陣雨 **3 promise sb the moon/the earth** to promise to give someone something that is impossible for you to give 向某人作無法兑現的承諾 **4 I can't promise anything** *spoken* used to tell someone that you will try to do what they want, but may not be able to 【口】我不能保證甚麼: *I'll try my best, but I can't promise anything.* 我會盡我所能, 但我不能保證甚麼。

3 3 **promise**[2] *n* **1** [C] a statement that you will definitely do something or that something will definitely happen 保證, 承諾, 諾言: *I'll never lie to you again. That's a promise.* 我再也不對你撒謊了, 我向你保證。| **[+of]** *a promise of help* 答應給予幫助的承諾 | **a promise to do sth** *They've given a promise to introduce equal pay for women.* 他們已許諾給婦女同等報酬。| **[+that]** *I kept thinking of my mother's promise that she'd read me the story if I was good.* 我老是想起我母親的承諾, 說如果我表現好, 她就給我讀故事。| **keep/break a promise** (=to do or fail to do something you promised) 信守/違背諾言 *Don't make promises you can't keep.* 不要作出你不能信守的諾言。| *You broke your promise to give up smoking.* 你違背了戒煙的諾言。**2** [U] signs that something or someone will be good or successful〔某事或某人有好結果或成功的〕跡象, 徵兆: *a young man full of promise* 一個大有前途的年輕人 | **[+of]** *the promise of future profits* 未來贏利的預兆 | **show promise** (=to be likely to become very good) 很有前途, 大有希望 *My son shows great promise as a chess player.* 我的兒子表現出成為棋手的巨大潛力。

Promised Land /ˌ·· ˈ·/ *n* [singular] **1** a situation or condition that you have wanted for a long time because it will bring you happiness and security 期盼中的樂土, 福地: *the promised land of full employment* 充分就業的希望之鄉 **2** the land of Canaan, which was promised to God by Abraham and his people in the Bible 迦南, 應許之地〔《聖經》中上帝賜給亞伯拉罕和他的族人的土地〕

prom·is·ing /ˈprɑmɪsɪŋ; ˈprɒmᵻsɪŋ/ *adj* showing signs of being successful in the future 大有希望的, 很有前途的: *a promising career in law* 很有前途的司法界職業 | *a promising young actor* 大有前途的年輕演員 —**promisingly** *adv*

prom·is·so·ry note /ˈprɑmɪsɔrɪ ˌnot; ˈprɒmᵻsəri ˌnəʊt/ *n* [C] a document promising to pay money before a particular date 期票; 本票

pro·mo /ˈpromo; ˈprəʊməʊ/ *plural* **promos** *n* [C] *informal* a short film that advertises an event or product 【非正式】廣告短片

prom·on·to·ry /ˈprɑmənˌtɔrɪ; ˈprɒməntəri/ *n* [C] a high long narrow piece of land which goes out into the sea 岬(角), 海角 —see picture on page A12 參見 A12 頁圖

3 2 **pro·mote** /prəˈmot; prəˈməʊt/ *v* [T] **1** to help something to develop and be successful 促進, 增進: *a meeting to promote trade between Taiwan and the U.K.* 促進台灣和英國之間貿易的會議 | *Fertilizer promotes leaf growth.* 肥料促進葉子的生長。**2** [usually passive 一般用被動態] to give someone a better, more responsible job in a company 擢升, 提升, 晉升〔某人〕: **promote sb to sth** *Helen was promoted to senior manager.* 海倫被提升為高級經理。—opposite 反義詞 DEMOTE **3** to make sure people know about a new product, film etc by offering it at a reduced price or advertising it on television 促銷, 推銷〔貨物〕; 推廣〔產品〕**4** to be responsible for arranging a large public event such as a concert or a sports game 負責籌辦, 主辦〔大型活動〕〈如音樂會或體育比賽〉**5** to try to persuade people to believe or support an idea or way of doing things 倡議; 提倡: *a passionate speech promoting equality* 宣揚平等的充滿激情的演講 **6 be promoted** if a sports team is promoted, they play in a different group of better teams the next year〔運動隊〕被升級 —opposite 反義詞 RELEGATE (2)

pro·mot·er /prəˈmotɚ; prəˈməʊtə/ *n* [C] **1** someone who arranges and advertises concerts or sports events〔音樂會或體育比賽的〕主辦者, 承辦者 **2** someone who tries to make people believe or support an idea or way of doing things 倡導者, 提倡者: *promoters of solar energy* 提倡太陽能的人

3 3 **pro·mo·tion** /prəˈmoʃən; prəˈməʊʃən/ *n* **1** [C,U] a move to a more important job or rank in a company or organization 擢升, 提升, 晉升: *I want a job with good promotion prospects.* 我想要一份有良好晉升機會的工作。| **[+to]** *Your promotion to Senior Editor is now official.* 現在你被正式提升為高級編輯。**2** [C,U] an activity intended to help sell a product, or the product that is being promoted〔產品的〕促銷, 推銷; 促銷[推銷]的產品: *a winter sales promotion* 冬季促銷活動 **3** [U] the activity of persuading people to support an idea or way of doing things 提倡, 倡導: *the promotion of equal opportunities* 提倡平等機會 **4** [U] the activity of helping something develop and succeed 促進, 增進: *the promotion of technology development centers* 促進技術開發中心的發展 **5** [U] a move by a sports team from playing in one group of teams to playing in a better group〔運動隊的〕升級 —opposite 反義詞 **relegation** (RELEGATE (2))

pro·mo·tion·al /prəˈmoʃənəl; prəˈməʊʃənəl/ *adj* promotional films, events etc are made or organized to advertise something〔電影、活動等〕旨在推銷[宣傳]〔某物〕的: *a series of interviews and promotional appearances* 一系列訪談和旨在宣傳的露面

prompt[1] /prɑmpt; prɒmpt/ *v* **1** [T] to make someone decide to do something, especially something that they had been thinking of doing 促使; 激勵: **prompt sb to do sth** *Her situation prompted me to do something about getting a new job.* 她的境況促使我設法找一份新工作。**2** to make people say or do something as a reaction 引起, 激起〔某人說或做某事〕: *What prompted that remark?* 那句話是由甚麼事引起的? **3** [T] to help a speaker who pauses, by suggesting how to continue 為〔說話者〕提示: *"I can't decide...." said Beatrice. "Decide what?" prompted Marlon.* "我不能決定…" 碧翠斯說。"決定甚麼?" 馬倫提示道。**4** [I,T] to remind an actor or actress of the next words in a speech 為〔演員〕提示台詞

prompt[2] *adj* **1** done quickly, immediately, or at the right time 迅速的; 立刻的; 及時的: *prompt delivery of your purchases* 你所購買物品的迅速送貨 **2** [not before noun 不用於名詞前] someone who is prompt arrives at the right time or does something on time 準時的: *Lunch is at two. Try to be prompt.* 兩點鐘吃午飯, 要盡量準時。| *Grandma is always prompt in answering letters.* 祖母總是及時回信。—**promptly** *adv*: *The performance begins promptly at nine o'clock.* 演出於九點鐘準時開始。—**promptness** *n* [U]

prompt[3] *adv informal* happening at the exact time 【非正式】準時: *We're meeting at 6.30 prompt, so don't be late.* 我們要六點半準時會面, 所以不要遲到。

prompt[4] *n* [C] **1** a word or words said to an actor in a play, to help them remember what to say〔給演員的〕提詞, 提白 **2** a sign on a computer screen which shows that the computer has finished one operation and is ready to begin the next〔電腦屏幕上的〕提示〔顯示電腦已完成某項操作, 準備進入下一項〕: *When you see the 'C' prompt type 'WP'.* 當看到提示符 C 時, 就鍵入 WP。

prompt·er /ˈprɑmptɚ; ˈprɒmptə/ *n* [C] someone who tells actors in a play what words to say when they forget 提詞員, 提白員

proms /prɑmz; prɒmz/ *n BrE informal* **the proms** a series of PROMENADE CONCERTS 【英, 非正式】系列漫步音樂會

prom·ul·gate /prəˈmʌlˌget; ˈprɒməlgeɪt/ *v* [T] **1** to spread an idea or belief to as many people as possible 傳播〔思想、信仰〕; 散佈 **2** to make a new law come into effect by announcing it officially 頒布〔並實施法律〕, 公布 —**promulgator** *n* [C] —**promulgation** /ˌprɑməlˈgeʃən; ˌprɒməlˈgeɪʃən/ *n* [U]

pron the written abbreviation of 縮寫= PRONOUN

prone /pron; prəʊn/ *adj* **1** likely to do something or suffer from something, especially something bad or harmful 易於發生某事〔尤指不好或有害的事〕的; 很可能…的; 有…傾向的: **[+to]** *Some plants are prone to a particular disease.* 有些植物容易生某種特定的疾病。| **prone to do sth** *Kids are all prone to eat junk food.* 孩子往往都喜歡吃垃圾食物。| **strike-prone/accident-prone etc** *I never saw a girl more accident-prone.* 我從未見過比她更容易出事故的女孩。**2** *formal* lying down with the front of your body facing down【正式】臉朝下臥倒的, 俯臥的: *Colley lay prone in his bunk.* 科利俯臥在鋪位上。—compare 比較 PROSTRATE[1] (1) —**proneness** *n* [U]

prong /prɔŋ; prɒŋ/ *n* [C] **1** a thin sharp point of something such as a fork that has several points〔叉子等的〕尖頭, 尖齒: *a pitchfork with three huge prongs* 有三個大叉頭的乾草叉 **2 two-pronged, three-pronged etc a)** having two, three etc prongs 兩齒的, 三齒的 **b)** a two-pronged or three-pronged attack is made on two or three parts of something at the same time〔進攻〕分兩路[三路]的, 從兩面[三面]的 **3** *AmE slang* a PENIS (=male sexual organ)【美俚】陰莖

pro·nom·i·nal /proˈnɑmənl; prəʊˈnɒmɪnəl/ *adj technical* related to or used like a PRONOUN【術語】代(名)詞的; 代(名)詞性的 —**pronominally** *adv*

pro·noun /ˈpronaʊn; ˈprəʊnaʊn/ *n* [C] a word that is used instead of a noun or noun phrase, such as 'he' instead of Peter or instead of 'the man' 代詞, 代名詞 —see also 另見 DEMONSTRATIVE PRONOUN, PERSONAL PRONOUN

pro·nounce /prəˈnaʊns; prəˈnaʊns/ *v* **1** [T] to make the sound of a letter, word etc, especially in the correct way〔尤指正確地〕發〔字母、詞等〕的音: *How do you pronounce your name?* 你的名字怎麼唸? **2** to officially state that something is true〔正式〕宣布, 宣告; 宣稱: **pronounce sb/sth (to be) sth** *The victim was pronounced dead on arrival.* 受害者送抵時被宣布已死亡。| *I now pronounce you man and wife.* 我現在宣布你們結為夫妻。**3** [I,T+on/against] *law* to give a legal judgment【法律】宣判 **4 pronounce on/upon sth** to state your opinion about a subject, especially when you do not really know much about it 對某事物〔尤指不甚了解的事物〕發表意見: *I don't want to listen to him pronounce on wine all night.* 我不想聽他整晚滔滔不絕地大談葡萄酒。**5 pronounce sentence** *law* if a judge pronounces sentence, he or she tells the court what kind of punishment a criminal will have【法律】宣布判決

pro·nounce·a·ble /prəˈnaʊnsəbl; prəˈnaʊnsəbəl/ *adj* a word, name etc that is pronounceable is easy to say〔詞、名字等〕容易唸的, 容易發音的 —opposite 反義詞 UNPRONOUNCEABLE

pro·nounced /prəˈnaʊnst; prəˈnaʊnst/ *adj* very strong or noticeable 明顯的; 明確的: *a pronounced Polish accent* 明顯的波蘭口音 | *a pronounced effect in reducing crime* 減少犯罪的明顯效果 —**pronouncedly** /prəˈnaʊnstlɪ; prəˈnaʊnsɪdli/ *adv*

pro·nounce·ment /prəˈnaʊnsmənt; prəˈnaʊnsmənt/ *n* [C] *formal* an official public statement【正式】公告, 聲明: *the Pope's latest pronouncement on birth control* 羅馬教皇關於控制生育的最新聲明

pron·to /ˈprɑnto; ˈprɒntəʊ/ *adv spoken* quickly or immediately【口】很快地; 馬上, 立刻: *Bring that hose over here, pronto!* 把那條軟管拿過來, 快點!

pro·nun·ci·a·tion /prəˌnʌnsɪˈeʃən; prəˌnʌnsiˈeɪʃən/ *n* **1** [C,U] the way in which a language or a particular word is pronounced 發音: *Make sure you give each word its correct pronunciation.* 要確保把每個詞唸正確。**2** [singular,U] a particular person's way of pronouncing a word or words〔某人的〕發音

-proof /pruf; pru:f/ *suffix* **1** [in adjectives 構成形容詞] treated or made so as not to be harmed by something, or to protect people against something 耐…的, 防…的, 抗…的: *a bulletproof car* 防彈汽車 | *an ovenproof dish* (=that cannot be harmed by heat) 耐熱盤 **2** [in verbs 構成動詞] to treat or make something so that it cannot be harmed by something, or gives protection against it 防, 抗, 使不受…影響: *to soundproof a room* (=so that sound cannot get into or out of it) 給房間隔音

proof[1] /pruf; pru:f/ *n* **1** [C,U] facts, information, documents etc that prove something is true 證明; 證據: **[+of]** *Bring a passport as proof of identity.* 帶上護照作為身分證明。| **[+(that)]** *Do you have any proof that this man stole your bag?* 你有甚麼證據證明這個人偷了你的包嗎? | **conclusive proof** (=that cannot be doubted) 確鑿的證據 | **proof positive** (=definite proof) 確切的證據 **2** [C] *technical* a printed copy of a piece of writing used to find and remove mistakes before the final printing is done【術語】校樣: *Can you check these proofs?* 你能核對一下這些校樣嗎? **3** [C] a photograph that is used as a test copy before an official copy is made 照片樣片 **4** [C] **a)** a test in MATHEMATICS of the correctness of a calculation〔數學〕驗算; 驗證 **b)** a list of reasons that shows a THEOREM (=statement) in GEOMETRY to be true〔幾何定理等〕證(明), 證法 **5 the proof of the pudding (is in the eating)** used to say that you can only know whether something is good or bad after you have tried it 布丁好不好, 吃了才知道〔評價事物的好壞只能憑實踐檢驗〕**6** [U] *technical* the standard strength of some kinds of alcoholic drink compared with that of PROOF SPIRIT【術語】〔酒類的〕標準酒精度: *This gin is 15% under proof.* 這種杜松子酒比標準酒精度低15%。**7 put sth to the proof** to test the quality or strength of something 檢驗[考驗]某事物〔的品質或力量〕

proof[2] *adj* **1 waterproof/bulletproof etc** something that is waterproof etc will not let water etc through it or into it 防水/防彈等: *a soundproof room* 隔音的房間 **2 child-proof/vandal-proof** not easily affected or damaged by someone or something 不易受到孩子/破壞者破壞的: *a child-proof latch on the cupboard* 櫥櫃上不易被孩子弄壞的門閂 **3 be proof against** to be too strong or good to be affected by something bad 能抵擋…的, 能耐…的, 可防…的: *a faith that is proof against temptation* 能抵擋誘惑的信念 **4 30° proof/40° proof etc** *BrE*【英】, also 又作 **30 proof/40 proof etc** *AmE*【美】whisky, bourbon etc that has a particular proof contains a specific amount of alcohol〔威士忌、波旁酒等〕30度/40度等

proof[3] *v* [T usually passive 一般用被動態] to treat a material with a substance in order to protect it against water, oil etc 把〔某材料〕作防水[油]處理: **[+against]** *climbing gear proofed against water* 作過防水處理的攀緣用具

proof·read /ˈprufˌrid; ˈpru:fˌri:d/ *past tense and past participle* **proofread** /-rɛd; -red/ *v* [I,T] to read through something written or printed in order to correct any errors in it 校對 —**proofreader** *n* [C]

proof spir·it /ˌ· ˈ··/ *n* [U] a standard mixture of alcohol and water with which the strength of some acoholic drinks is compared for the purposes of taxation 標準強度的酒〔用以測定一些酒的強度以定其稅率〕

prop[1] /prɑp; prɒp/ *v* **propped, propping** [T always+adv/prep] to support something by leaning it against something, or by putting something else under, next to, or behind it 把…靠在…上; 支住, 支撐: **prop sth against/on** *He propped his bike against a tree.* 他把自行車靠在一棵樹上。| **prop sth open** *Give me something to prop the door open.* 給我個東西頂住門, 不讓它關上。

prop sth ↔ **up** *phr v* [T] **1** to prevent something from falling by putting something against it or under it 支撐, 撐住〔某物〕: *The builders are trying to prop up the crum-*

bling walls of the church. 建築工人正試圖撐住傾頹的教堂牆壁。**2** if a government props up another government it helps it with financial or military support so that it can continue to exist〔在財政上或軍事上〕支持〔某政府〕; 維持 **3 prop yourself up** to stand or sit straight by leaning against something 靠着某物站直[坐直], 撐着站起[坐起]

prop² *n* [C] **1** an object placed under or against something to hold it in a position 支柱, 支撐物 —see also 另見 PIT PROP **2** a small object such as a book, weapon etc used by actors in a play or film〔戲劇或電影中的〕道具 **3** *informal* a short form of the word PROPELLER【非正式】螺旋槳; 推進器 **4** something or someone that helps you to feel strong, or that an idea or system needs in order to exist 支持者; 後盾; 靠山: *The big house and the car were all props to his ego.* 那座大房子和那輛汽車都是他自負的資本。

prop·a·gan·da /ˌprɑpəˋgændə; ˌprɒpəˈgændə/ *n* [U] false or partly false information used by a government or political party to make people agree with them〔政府或政黨為了影響民意的虛假、錯誤〕宣傳: *pure Fascist propaganda* 純粹的法西斯宣傳 | *a propaganda film* 宣傳影片 | **propaganda campaign** (=an organised plan to spread propaganda) 宣傳活動 —**propagandize** also 又作 **-ise** *BrE*【英】*v* [I,T] —**propagandist** *n* [C]

prop·a·gate /ˋprɑpəˌget; ˈprɒpəgeɪt/ *v formal*【正式】**1** [I,T] to grow and produce new plants or to make a plant do this〔植物〕繁殖; 使〔植物〕繁殖: *a species that propagates by spores* 靠孢子繁殖的物種 | *You can propagate these plants by root cuttings.* 你可以用根插的方法使這些植物繁殖。**2** [T] to spread an idea, belief etc to many people 傳播〔觀點、信仰等〕, 散播; 宣傳: *The group started a magazine to propagate its ideas.* 這羣人辦了一本雜誌來宣傳他們的主張。**3** [T] if an animal, insect, or CELL etc propagates itself or is propagated, it increases in number by reproducing; REPRODUCE (1)〔動物、昆蟲或細胞等〕繁衍, 繁殖 —**propagation** /ˌprɑpəˋgeʃən; ˌprɒpəˈgeɪʃən/ *n* [U]

prop·a·gat·or /ˋprɑpəˌgetə; ˈprɒpəgeɪtə/ *n* [C] **1** someone who spreads ideas, beliefs etc 傳播〔思想、信仰等〕的人, 宣傳者 **2** a covered box of soil in which seeds are planted to grow quickly〔供種子迅速生長的〕培育箱

pro·pane /ˋpropen; ˈprəʊpeɪn/ *n* [U] a colourless gas used for both cooking and heating 丙烷(氣)

pro·pel /prəˋpɛl; prəˈpel/ *v* **propelled, propelling** [T] to move, drive, or push something forward 推動; 推進; 驅動: *old ships propelled by steam* 由蒸汽推進的舊船隻 | *a rocket-propelled grenade* 用火箭砲發射的榴彈 —see also 另見 PROPULSION

pro·pel·lant, propellent /prəˋpɛlənt; prəˈpelənt/ *n* [C, U] **1** an explosive for firing a bullet or ROCKET¹ 發射火藥; 推進劑; 火箭燃料 **2** gas pressed into a small space in a container of liquid, which pushes out the liquid when the pressure is taken away〔置於噴霧容器中提供壓力的〕壓縮氣體 —**propellant** *adj*

pro·pel·ler /prəˋpɛlə; prəˈpelə/ *n* [C] a piece of equipment consisting of two or more blades that spin around, that makes an aircraft or ship move〔飛機或輪船的〕螺旋槳; 推進器

pro·pel·ling pen·cil /·ˌ·· ˈ··/ *n* [C] *BrE* a pencil made of plastic or metal, in which the stick of the LEAD can be pushed out as it is used up【英】活動鉛筆, 自動鉛筆; MECHANICAL PENCIL *AmE*【美】

pro·pen·si·ty /prəˋpɛnsətɪ; prəˈpensɨti/ *n* [C] *formal* a natural tendency to behave in a particular way【正式】傾向; 習性: **a propensity to do sth** *the male propensity to fight* 男性好鬥的傾向 | **a propensity for (doing) sth** *The child shows a propensity for disrupting class.* 這個孩子表現出喜歡擾亂課堂的傾向。

1 2 **prop·er¹** /ˋprɑpə; ˈprɒpə/ *adj* **1** [only before noun 僅用於名詞前, no comparative 無比較級] *especially BrE* right, suitable, or correct【尤英】正確的; 合適的, 適當的; 恰當的: *She needs proper medical attention.* 她需要妥善的治療。| *Put that back in its proper place.* 把那東西放回原處。| *I went through the proper process, I wrote to my MP.* 我遵循應有的步驟, 給我的下議院議員寫了信。**2** socially or legally correct and acceptable 合適的; 合理的; 合乎體統的; 正規的;〔法律上〕正確的, 可接受的: *I don't feel that it would be proper for me to give you that information.* 我覺得我把那資料給你不合適。| **be only (right and) proper** *It's only right and proper that Shari apologize for what she said!* 莎麗為她所說的話道歉是合情合理的。**3** [only before noun 僅用於名詞前] *BrE spoken* real【英口】真正的: *Can't you get a proper job?* 你就不能找一份真正的工作嗎? | *Try to eat proper meals instead of chips and baked beans.* 儘量好好吃飯而不要吃炸馬鈴薯條和烘豆。**4** [only after noun 僅用於名詞前] according to the real, most exact meaning of the word 嚴格意義上的: *Monkeys proper only began to evolve thirty five million years ago.* 真正意義上的猴子在三千五百萬年前才開始進化。**5 proper to sth a)** *formal* belonging to one particular type of thing【正式】…特有的, 為…專有的: *the reasoning abilities proper to our species* 我們這個物種所特有的推理能力 **b)** natural or normal in a particular place or situation 適宜的, 適合的: *dressed in a way that was proper to the occasion* 穿得適合這種場合 **6** [only before noun 僅用於名詞前] *BrE spoken* complete【英口】完全的, 徹底的: *He's made a proper fool of himself this time!* 這次他真是丟盡了醜! | *You're in a proper old mess.* 你真是狼狽不堪。**7** very polite, and careful to do what is socially correct 非常有禮貌的; 循規蹈矩的: *Andrew's behaviour was so proper that she couldn't help laughing.* 安德魯的行為如此循規蹈矩以至她忍不住笑起來。—see also 另見 PROPERLY

proper² *adv BrE spoken*【英口】**1** used by some people to mean PROPERLY, although most people think that this is incorrect 好好地, 適當地〔有些人把此詞當作 properly 用, 儘管大多數人認為這樣用不正確〕: *Why don't you talk proper?* 你為甚麼不好好說話? **2 good and proper** completely 完全地, 徹底地: *Tom drove the car into a wall and wrecked it good and proper.* 湯姆開車撞到了牆上, 把車完全撞毀了。

proper frac·tion /ˌ·· ˈ··/ *n* [C] a FRACTION such as ¾ in which the number above the line is smaller than the one below it〔數學〕真分數 —compare 比較 IMPROPER FRACTION

prop·er·ly /ˋprɑpəlɪ; ˈprɒpəli/ *adv* **1** correctly, or in a way that is considered right 正確地; 適當地: *Make sure the job is done properly.* 要確保把這項工作做好。| *He never explains anything properly.* 他從來不好好解釋任何事情。| *Granny will be there, so behave properly.* 祖母會在那裡, 所以要規矩點。**2** *especially BrE informal* completely; thoroughly【尤英, 非正式】完全地, 徹底地: *Is that cake properly defrosted?* 那蛋糕完全解凍了嗎? **3** really; in fact 真正地; 實際上: *Documents which properly belong to the family were taken away by the authorities.* 實際上屬於這個家庭的文件被當局拿走了。| **properly speaking** *especially BrE* (=really)【尤英】實際上 *He's not a policeman at all, properly speaking.* 其實他根本不是個警察。**4** used to say that someone was right to do something〔用於表示某人做某事是正確的〕: **quite/very/perfectly properly** *She told me, perfectly properly, that it was no business of mine.* 她告訴我這事與我無關, 她說得很對。 1 2

proper noun /ˌ·· ˈ·/ also 又作 **proper name** *n* [C] a noun such as 'James', 'New York', or 'China' that is the name of one particular thing and is spelt with a CAPITAL² (1) letter 專有名詞〈如 James, New York, China〉—see also 另見 NOUN

prop·er·tied /ˋprɑpətɪd; ˈprɒpətid/ *adj* [only before noun 僅用於名詞前] owning a lot of property or land 有很多財產的; 有大量地產的: *the propertied classes* 有產階級; 有房地產的階層

prop·er·ty /ˋprɑpətɪ; ˈprɒpəti/ *plural* **properties** *n* **1** [U] the thing or things that someone owns 所有物; 資產, 財產: *That's my personal property! Leave it alone!* 那是我的私人財產！別動它！| *Some of the stolen property was found in Mason's house.* 在梅森的房子裡找到了一些偷來的財物。**2** [U] land, buildings, or both together 房產; 地產; 房地產: *Property prices have shot up recently.* 最近房地產的價格暴漲。**3** [C] a word meaning a building, a piece of land, or both together, used especially by lawyers or ESTATE AGENTS〔尤指律師或房地產經紀人所指的〕房產, 建築, 房子; 地產, 房地產: *Several properties on this street are for sale.* 這條街上有幾處房地產要出售。**4** [C] a quality or power that belongs naturally to something 特性, 性質; 屬性: *a herb with healing properties* 具有治療功效的藥草 | *One of the most important properties of gold is its malleability.* 金的一個最重要特性是它的延展性。**5** [U] ownership of land, goods etc 所有權; 財產權: *a belief in the idea of communal property* 相信公有制的觀點 —see also 另見 LOST PROPERTY, REAL PROPERTY

property de·vel·op·er /ˈ···ˌ···/ *n* [C] someone who makes money by buying land and building on it 房地產開發商

property tax /ˈ···ˌ·/ *n* [C,U] a tax based on the value of someone's house 財產稅; 不動產稅

proph·e·cy also 又作 **prophesy** *AmE*【美】/ˋprɑfəsɪ; ˈprɒfɪ̈si/ *n plural* **prophecies 1** [C] a statement that something will happen in the future, especially one made by someone with religious or magic powers 預言: **[+that]** *The prophecy that David would become king was fulfilled.* 大衛將成為國王的預言果然應驗了。**2** [U] the making of statements about what will happen in the future〔尤指擁有宗教權力或魔力的人作出的〕預言 —see also 另見 **self-fulfilling prophecy** (SELF-FULFILLING)

proph·e·sy[1] /ˋprɑfəˌsaɪ; ˈprɒfɪ̈saɪ/ *v* **prophesies, prophesying, prophesied** [I,T] to use religious or magical knowledge to say what will happen in the future; FORETELL 預言: **[+that]** *The soothsayer prophesied that the war would be won.* 那個占卜者預言這場戰爭將會打贏。| **prophesy who/what/how etc** *He even prophesied how the crops would fail.* 他甚至預言農作物將如何歉收。

proph·e·sy[2] /ˋprɑfəsɪ; ˈprɒfəsi/ *n* [C] an American spelling of PROPHECY prophecy 的美式拼法

proph·et /ˋprɑfɪt; ˈprɒfɪ̈t/ *n* [C] **1** a man whom people in the Christian, Jewish, or Muslim religion believe has been sent by God to lead them and teach them their religion〔基督教、猶太教、伊斯蘭教的〕先知 **2 the Prophet** Muhammad, who formed the Muslim religion〔伊斯蘭教的創始人〕穆罕默德: *followers of the Prophet* 穆罕默德的追隨者 **3 the Prophets** the Jewish holy men whose writings form part of the OLD TESTAMENT, or the writings themselves 猶太教諸先知〔其著作構成《聖經·舊約》的一部分〕,《先知書》的作者們;《先知書》**4 prophet of doom/disaster** someone who believes that bad or unpleasant things will happen in the future 預言厄運／災難的人 **5** someone who introduces and teaches a new idea〔新觀念、新思想的〕提倡者, 首倡者, 倡導者: **[+of]** *Rontgen was regarded as the prophet of the new materialism.* 倫琴被認為是新唯物論的倡導者。

proph·et·ess /ˋprɑfɪtɪs; ˌprɒfɪ̈ˈtes/ *n* [C] a woman whom people believe has been sent by God to lead them 女先知

pro·phet·ic /prəˋfɛtɪk; prəˈfetɪk/ *adj* correctly saying what will happen in the future 預見正確的, 預言性的: *Nick's remark proved prophetic two months later.* 尼克的話在兩個月後被證明是正確的預言。—**prophetically** /-klɪ; -kli/ *adv*

pro·phet·i·cal /prəˋfɛtɪkl̩; prəˈfetɪkəl/ *adj* like a prophet, or related to the things a prophet says or does 似先知的; 預言的

pro·phy·lac·tic[1] /ˌprɑfəˋlæktɪk; ˌprɒfɪ̈ˈlæktɪk◂/ *adj technical* intended to prevent disease【術語】預防〔疾病〕(性) 的

prophylactic[2] *n* [C] *technical*【術語】**1** something used to prevent disease 預防疾病的東西 **2** *AmE often humorous* a CONDOM【美, 常幽默】避孕套

pro·phy·lax·is /ˌprɑfəˋlæksɪs; ˌprɒfɪ̈ˈlæksɪ̈s/ *n* [C,U] *technical* a treatment for preventing disease【術語】〔疾病〕預防 (法)

pro·pin·qui·ty /proˋpɪŋkwətɪ; prəˈpɪŋkwɪ̈ti/ *n* [U+**of**/**to**] *formal* the fact of being near someone or something, or of being related to someone【正式】〔空間上的〕接近; 鄰近;〔血統上的〕近親關係

pro·pi·ti·ate /prəˋpɪʃɪet; prəˈpɪʃieɪt/ *v* [T] *formal* to make someone who has been unfriendly or angry with you feel more friendly by doing something to please them【正式】撫慰; 勸解; 哄…息怒; 取悅 —**propitiation** /prəˌpɪʃɪˋeʃən; prəˌpɪʃiˈeɪʃən/ *n* [U]

pro·pi·ti·a·to·ry /prəˋpɪʃɪəˌtorɪ; prəˈpɪʃiətəri/ *adj formal* intended to please someone and make them feel less angry and more friendly【正式】撫慰的, 勸解的; 討好的; 哄人息怒的: *a propitiatory gift of flowers* 為討好某人而贈送的鮮花

pro·pi·tious /prəˋpɪʃəs; prəˈpɪʃəs/ *adj formal* good and likely to bring good results【正式】吉利的, 有利的, 吉祥的: *a propitious moment* 有利時機 | **[+for]** *Conditions after the 1905 revolution were propitious for stable development.* 1905 年革命之後的形勢有利於穩定發展。—**propitiously** *adv*

pro·po·nent /prəˋponənt; prəˈpəʊnənt/ *n* [C] someone who supports something or persuades people to do something; ADVOCATE[2] (1) 支持者; 擁護者; 鼓吹者: **[+of]** *Steinem has always been a strong proponent of women's rights.* 史坦能一向是女權的強烈支持者。—compare 比較 OPPONENT (2)

proportion 比例

The car is out of proportion to the man.
這輛汽車與這個人不成比例。

pro·por·tion[1] /prəˋporʃən; prəˈpɔːʃən/ *n*

2 2

1 ►AMOUNT 數量◄ [C] a part or share of a larger amount 部分: **[+of]** *Quite high proportions of their incomes are spent on fuel.* 他們收入的很大部分花在了燃料上。

2 ►NUMBER 數量◄ [C] a number of people or things, considered as a part or share of a larger number 部分: **[+of]** *Far higher proportions of part-time workers have no health insurance at all.* 較大部分的兼職工人根本沒有健康保險。| [also+plural verb *BrE* 英] *A large proportion of the people are illiterate.* 這些人中很大部分是文盲。

3 ►RELATIONSHIP 關係◄ [C,U] the relationship between the amounts, numbers, or sizes of different things that go together to form a whole 比例: *eating the right foods in the right proportions* 按比例吃適當的食物 | **proportion of sth to sth** *The proportion of men to women in the population has changed in recent years.* 人口中男性與女性的比例最近幾年有了改變。| **the proportion of** *Make salad dressing in the proportion of three parts oil to one part vinegar.* 按三份油、一份醋的比例製作色拉調味料。

4 ►ATTRACTIVENESS 吸引力◄ [U] **a)** the correct relationship between the size, shape and position of the different parts of something, which gives it an attractive appearance〔某物各組成部分的〕相稱; 協調; 均衡; 勻稱: *Builders must learn about scale and proportion.* 建築工必須學習比例和均衡。| **in proportion** *Reduce the drawing so that all the elements stay in proportion.* 縮小這幅畫以使所有組成部分比例協調。**b)** the correct relationship between the size or shape of something and the place where it is〔某物與所處地方的〕協調, 相稱: **out of proportion (to/with)** *They've built a house that's completely out of proportion with the size of the lot.* 他們建了一所與地皮面積完全不成比例的房子。

5 in proportion (to/with sth) according to a particular relationship in size, amount etc 與…成比例, 按某比例: *If you use a whole pineapple, increase the other ingredients in proportion.* 如果你用一整個菠蘿, 就要按比例增加其他配料。| *Tax is then calculated in proportion to what you earn.* 所得税則是根據你的收入額按比例計算的。

6 in proportion (to sth) when you compare sizes, amounts etc 與…相比: *Her feet are small in proportion to her height.* 她的腳相對於她的身高來説很小。

7 ►SIZE/IMPORTANCE 大小/重要性◄ proportions [plural] the size and shape of something, or the degree to which something is important 大小; 形狀; 重要性: *a building of classic proportions* 古典式的建築物 | *It may reduce the task to more manageable proportions.* 那可把工作縮小到大致可行的範圍。| **immense/huge/massive etc proportions** *an ecological tragedy of enormous proportions* 極其嚴重的生態悲劇 | **epic/heroic/mythic proportions** *For most of us, Scott was a hero of mythic proportions.* 對我們大多數人來説, 斯科特是一個神話般的英雄。| **crisis/epidemic etc proportions** *a fall in silk prices of catastrophic proportions* 絲綢價格災難性的下跌

8 keep things in proportion to react to a situation sensibly, and not think that it is worse or more serious than it really is 辦事情[看問題]恰如其分; 不把事情看得太糟[太嚴重]: *Try to keep things in proportion; you won't die if you don't get the job.* 要盡量恰如其分地看問題; 要是你得不到那份工作, 你也不會死掉。—see also 另見 PERSPECTIVE (2)

9 get/blow things (all) out of proportion to react to a situation as if it is worse or more serious than it really is 把某事物想得過糟[過於嚴重]

10 out of (all) proportion (to sth) a reaction, result, emotion etc that is out of proportion is too strong or great, compared to the situation in which it happens〔反應、結果、感情等〕(相對…來説) 過分; 與…不相稱: *The fear of violent crime has now risen out of all proportion to the actual risk.* 對於暴力犯罪的恐懼大大超出了其實際危險。

11 sense of proportion the ability to judge what is most important in a situation 區別輕重緩急的能力; 主次觀念: **keep/lose a sense of proportion** *You can protest by all means, but keep a sense of proportion.* 你自然可以抗議, 但是要分清主次。

12 ►MATHEMATICS 數學◄ [U] *technical* equality in the mathematical relationship between two sets of numbers, as in the statement '8 is to 6 as 32 is to 24'【術語】比例〈如 8:6 = 32:24〉

proportion² *v* [T usually passive 一般用被動態] *formal*【正式】**1 well/badly/beautifully etc proportioned** having a size and shape that is either pleasant or unpleasant to look at, or is either right or wrong for its use 勻稱的/比例不協調的/比例恰到好處的等: *a well proportioned room* 比例很協調的房間 | *long, beautifully proportioned legs* 修長而勻稱的雙腿 **2** to make something stay in a particular relationship with something else according to size, amount, position etc 使均衡; 使相稱; 使成比例: **proportion sth to sth** *Allowances for expenditure have been proportioned to your income.* 消費補助與你的收入成比例。

pro·por·tion·al /prəˋporʃənḷ; prəˈpɔːʃənəl/ *adj* something that is proportional to something else stays in a correct or suitable relationship to the other thing in size, amount, importance etc 成比例的; 相稱的: **[+to]** *Carlow will have to pay an amount of compensation proportional to the damage he did.* 卡羅必須根據他所造成的損失按比例支付賠償金。—**proportionally** *adv*

proportional rep·re·sen·ta·tion /ˌ... ...ˈ..../ *n* [U] PR; a system of voting in elections by which all political parties are represented in the government according to the number of votes they receive in the whole country 比例代表制〔各政黨按其在全國所得票數而獲得議席的一種選舉制度〕

pro·por·tion·ate /prəˋporʃənɪt; prəˈpɔːʃənət/ *adj* something that is proportionate to something else stays in a correct or suitable relationship to the other thing in size, amount, importance etc 成比例的; 相稱的: *The decline in production was offset by a proportionate increase in federal aid.* 產量的下降由相應增加的聯邦政府補助來彌補。—opposite 反義詞 DISPROPORTIONATE —**proportionately** *adv*

pro·pos·al /prəˋpozḷ; prəˈpəʊzəl/ *n* S3 W1 **1** [C,U] a plan or suggestion which is made formally to an official person or group, or the act of making it 計劃; 建議, 提議; 建議等的提出: *Clinton is facing a battle to get Congress to accept his budget proposals.* 克林頓為使國會接受他的預算方案正面臨着一場論戰。| **proposal to do sth** *The proposal to build a new bypass is meeting with stiff opposition.* 修建一條旁路的提議遭到強烈反對。| **proposal that** *The company had to put forward a proposal that layoffs be considered.* 該公司不得不提出考慮解雇工人的建議。—see 見 PROPOSE (USAGE) **2** [C] the act of asking someone to marry you 求婚

pro·pose /prəˋpoz; prəˈpəʊz/ *v* S3 W2

1 ►PLAN 計劃◄ [T] *formal* to suggest something as a plan or course of action【正式】提議, 建議: *Lyle proposed large cuts in the training budget.* 萊爾提出大量削減培訓經費。| **propose that** *Hansen has proposed that I become his business partner.* 漢森建議我成為他的生意夥伴。| *the proposed budget cuts* 所提議的預算削減

2 ►AT A MEETING 在會議上◄ [T] to formally suggest a course of action at a meeting and ask people to vote on it〔在會議上〕正式提議, 提付表決: *I propose the admission of Peter King as a new member.* 我提議接受彼得·金為新成員。| **propose a motion** (=formally suggest a plan at a meeting) 提出動議 | **propose sb** (=formally suggest someone for an official position) 提名[推舉]某人〔擔任某職位〕 *Mrs Banks has been proposed for the position of Treasurer.* 班克斯夫人已被提名擔任財務主管。

3 ►THEORY 理論◄ [T] to suggest an idea, method etc as an answer to a scientific question or as a better way of doing something 提出〔某觀點、方法等〕: *His theory proposes the existence of black holes in the universe.* 他的理論提出宇宙中存在黑洞。

4 ►MARRIAGE 結婚◄ a) [I] to ask someone to marry you, especially in a formal way〔尤指正式地向某人〕求婚: **[+to]** *Shaun proposed to me only six months after we met.* 肖恩在我們相識僅六個月後就向我求婚。**b) propose marriage** *formal* to ask someone to marry you【正式】求婚

5 propose a toast to sb also 又作 **propose sb's health** to formally ask a group of people at a social event to join you in wishing someone success, happiness, etc, while raising a glass of wine and then drinking from it 為某人[某人的健康]祝酒

6 ►INTEND 打算◄ [T] *formal* to intend to do something【正式】打算, 計劃: **propose to do sth** *How do you propose to explain your long absence?* 你打算如何解釋你的長時間缺席? | **propose doing sth** *Just how do you propose paying for all this?* 你究竟打算如何付清這一切? —**proposer** *n* [C]

USAGE NOTE 用法說明: PROPOSE

WORD CHOICE 詞語辨析: **propose, intend, suggest, proposal, suggestion, let's, why don't we**

Propose followed by the *to* form of a verb is a more formal way of saying you intend to do something. propose 後接不定式是表示打算做某事的較正式說法: *What are you proposing to do with that old car of yours?* 你打算如何處理你那輛舊車?

Propose followed by a noun means that you are formally suggesting something should be considered. propose 後接名詞表示正式地提議某事物應得到考慮: *propose a motion/solution/course of action etc* 提出動議/解決方案/做法等

Propose followed by a *that* clause has a similar meaning to **suggest**. propose 後接 that- 從句, 意思與 suggest 相同: *I propose/suggest that we buy a new car* (=I think that this is what we should do). 我建議我們買輛新車。

Propose followed by the *ing* form of a verb may have elther of the above senses. propose 後接動詞的 -ing 形式, 可能有以上兩個意思中的任意一個。

The difference between **suggest** and **propose** is that **propose** is more formal and often means that you have already thought about what you are proposing. But you may **suggest** an idea without a lot of careful thought. suggest 和 propose 的區別在於 propose 較正式, 而且常意味着你已經考慮過所建議的事情。但 suggest 可以表示未經太多仔細考慮: *At the meeting conservationists proposed a different route for the highway.* 在會上, 自然環境保護論者提出了一條不同的公路路線。| *As we came out of the theater, Jean suggested a Chinese meal.* 我們走出劇院時, 吉恩建議去吃中餐。

With similar differences you can also make a **proposal** or a **suggestion**. proposal 和 suggestion 的區別與其動詞形式相似: *the committee's proposal to raise local taxes* 委員會提出的提高地方稅收的建議 | *George's suggestion that we go skating tonight* 喬治建議我們今晚去滑冰

In spoken English people do not usually say **I suggest that** but rather **Let's** or **Why don't we?** 在英語口語中, 人們一般不說 I suggest that, 而用 Let's 或 Why don't we?: *Let's go for a Chinese meal.* 我們去吃中餐吧。| *Why don't we get a new car?* 我們為甚麼不買一輛新車呢?

GRAMMAR 語法

You **propose** or **suggest** something always **to** someone. 對某人建議某事可以用 propose/suggest something to someone 的結構: *He proposed a business deal to her* (NOT 不用 *He proposed her a business deal* or 或 *He proposed her to a business deal*). 他提出與她做一筆交易。Also you would say 你也可以說: *I suggested to her that we go to the disco* (NOT 不用 *I suggested her that we go to the disco*). 我向她提議我們去跳迪斯科。

Suggest is not used with the *to* form of the verb. suggest 後不接不定式: *He suggested leaving/that we leavse* (NOT 不用 *He suggested to leave*). 他提議我們離開。

3 **proposed** /prəˋpozd; prəˈpəʊzd/ *adj* a proposed charge, arrangement etc is one that has been formally suggested to an official person or group〔正式〕提議的, 建議的: *How will the proposed study be carried out?* 擬議中的研究將如何實施? | *The proposed site has several drawbacks.* 計劃的地點有幾個不利之處。

prop·o·si·tion¹ /ˌprɑpəˋzɪʃən; ˌprɒpəˈzɪʃən/ *n* [C] **1 ►JUDGMENT 判斷◄** a statement that consists of a carefully considered opinion or judgment 主張; 觀點, 見解: *Marx accepted several of the key propositions developed by Adam Smith.* 馬克思接受了亞當·史密斯闡發的幾個主要觀點。| **proposition that** *We were asked to discuss the proposition that women are satisfied with less money.* 我們被要求就婦女滿足於較少的金錢這一說法進行討論。

2 ►SUGGESTION 建議◄ an offer or suggestion, especially in business or politics〔尤指商業、政治上的〕提議, 建議: *I'll consider your proposition and let you know.* 我會考慮你的建議然後告訴你結果。| *We have a proposition to make.* 我們要提個建議。

3 an attractive/interesting/practical etc proposition something that is an attractive etc idea, especially in business or politics〔尤指商業、政治上的〕有吸引力的/有趣的/切實可行的提議: *The newest software makes computerized recruitment an attractive proposition.* 最新的軟件使電腦招聘成為一個很有吸引力的提議。

4 ►MATHEMATICS 數學◄ *technical* a word used in GEOMETRY meaning something that must be proved, or a question to which the answer must be found【術語】〔幾何〕命題

5 ►SEX 性◄ a statement that you would like to have sex with someone which avoids saying this to them directly〔男女間的〕求歡〔委婉向某人提出發生性關係的要求〕

6 ►LAW 法律◄ also 又作 **Proposition** a suggested change or addition to the law of a state of the US, which citizens vote on〔由公民表決的美國某個州提出的〕法律修正案 —**propositional** *adj*

proposition² *v* [T] to suggest to someone that they have sex with you 提出〔與某人〕發生性關係, 向〔某人〕求歡: *prostitutes propositioning the passers-by* 提出要與過路人上牀的妓女

pro·pound /prəˋpaund; prəˈpaʊnd/ *v* [T] *formal* to suggest an idea, explanation etc for other people to consider【正式】提出〔觀點、解釋等〕供考慮

pro·pri·e·ta·ry /prəˋpraɪəˌtɛrɪ; prəˈpraɪətəri/ *adj formal*【正式】**1** a proprietary medicine, cleaning liquid etc is one that is sold under a TRADE NAME〔藥物、清潔液等〕有商標的 **2** proprietary behaviour makes it seem that you think you own something or someone〔行為〕像所有者那樣的; 所有人(似)的: *Arnold wrapped his arm around his fiancée with a proprietary air.* 阿諾德用胳膊摟住他的未婚妻, 彷彿摟住自己的財產。**3 proprietary information** information about a company's products, methods etc which is known only to people who work for the company〔公司的〕專有信息〔只有內部人員才了解的有關公司產品、方法等的信息〕

pro·pri·e·tor /prəˋpraɪətɚ; prəˈpraɪətə/ *n* [C] *formal* an owner of a business【正式】所有人; 老闆: *Echenard was proprietor of the famous Hotel du Louvre.* 埃切納德是有名的羅浮宮酒店的老闆。—**proprietorial** /prəˌpraɪəˋtorɪəl; prəˌpraɪəˈtɔːriəl/ *adj* —**proprietorially** *adv*

pro·pri·e·tress /prəˋpraɪətrɪs; prəˈpraɪətrɨs/ *n* [C] *old-fashioned* a woman who owns a business【過時】女所有人; 女老闆

pro·pri·e·ty /prəˋpraɪətɪ; prəˈpraɪəti/ *n formal*【正式】**1** [singular, U] correctness of social or moral behaviour, especially between men and women or between people of different social ranks, age etc〔尤指男女之間或不同社會等級或年齡的人之間的〕禮貌; 規矩: *Jonathan behaved with the utmost propriety on our first date.* 喬納森在我們第一次約會時舉止極其得體。**2 the proprieties** the accepted rules of correct social behaviour 禮儀, 禮節: *strict in observing the proprieties* 嚴格遵守禮節 —see also 另見 IMPROPRIETY

pro·pul·sion /prəˋpʌlʃən; prəˈpʌlʃən/ *n* [U] *technical*【術語】**1** the force that drives a vehicle forward〔尤指車輛的〕推進力 **2 jet propulsion** the use of engines which push out hot gases to make an aircraft fly 噴氣推進 —**propulsive** /-sɪv; -sɪv/ *adj*: *propulsive force* 推(進)力

pro ra·ta /pro ˋretə; ˌprəʊ ˈrɑːtə/ *adj technical* a payment or share that is pro rata is calculated according to exactly how much of something is used, how much work is done, etc【術語】〔報酬或份額〕按比例計算的 —**pro rata** *adv*

pro·rate /pro'ret; prəʊ'reɪt/ *v* [T] *AmE* to calculate a charge, price, etc according to the actual amount of service received rather than by a standard sum【美】按實際接受的服務計算〔價錢等〕

pro·rogue /pro`rog; prəʊ'rəʊg/ *v* [T] *technical* to leave any unfinished business of a PARLIAMENT to be dealt with at the next meeting【術語】使〔議會〕休會 —**prorogation** *n* [U]

pros /proz; prəʊz/ *n* [plural] —see 見 **the pros and cons** (PRO[1] (3))

pro·sa·ic /pro`ze·ɪk; prəʊ'zeɪ-ɪk/ *adj* boring, ordinary, or lacking in imagination 乏味的, 平淡無奇的; 缺乏想像力的: *a prosaic writing style* 乏味的寫作風格 | *People said he'd been a pirate, but the truth was more prosaic.* 人們說他曾是一名海盜, 但事實卻沒那麼複雜。—**prosaically** /-klɪ; -kli/ *adv*

pro·sce·ni·um /pro`sinɪəm; prə'siːniəm/ *n* [C] **1** the part of a theatre stage which comes forward beyond the curtain〔劇院〕幕布前的舞台部分, 前舞台 **2 proscenium arch** the arch at the front of a theatre stage where a curtain can be lowered 舞台前台的拱架; 台口

pro·sciut·to /pro`ʃuto; prəʊ'ʃuːtəʊ/ *n* [U] uncooked, dried, Italian HAM (=salted meat) which is eaten in very thin pieces 意大利生火腿

pro·scribe /pro'skraɪb; prəʊ'skraɪb/ *v* [T] **1** *formal* to try to stop the existence of something such as a political organization【正式】禁止〔政治組織等〕**2** *old use* to state publicly that a citizen is no longer protected by the law【舊】宣布剝奪〔公民的〕法律保護權, 使失去法律保護 —**proscription** /-`skrɪpʃən; -'skrɪpʃən/ *n* [C,U]

prose /proz; prəʊz/ *n* **1** [U] written language in its usual form, as opposed to poetry 散文〔與韻文相對的文體〕: *Gilbert's clear, simple prose* 吉爾伯特簡潔而明快的散文 **2** [C] *BrE* a student's exercise in which you translate a piece of writing into a foreign language【英】〔學生的〕把原文譯成外文的練習

pros·e·cute /`prɑsɪˌkjut; 'prɒsɪkjuːt/ *v* **1** [I,T] to officially say that someone is guilty of a crime and must be judged by a court of law 起訴, 檢控: *Shoplifters will be prosecuted.* 在商店偷東西者將被起訴。| **prosecute sb for sth** *Buxton's being prosecuted for assault.* 巴克斯頓由於襲擊罪而被起訴。| *If payment is not received by 1 March we'll be forced to prosecute.* 如果3月1日之前還沒有收到付款, 我們將不得不提出訴訟。**2** [I,T] to represent someone in court as their lawyer, when they are bringing a criminal charge against someone else〔律師〕代表原告 —compare 比較 DEFEND (6) **3** [T] *formal* to continue doing something【正式】繼續: *We cannot prosecute the investigation further.* 我們不能繼續調查。

prosecuting at·tor·ney /'····· ·,··/ *n* [C usually singular 一般用單數] *AmE* a DISTRICT ATTORNEY【美】地方檢察官

3 **pros·e·cu·tion** /ˌprɑsɪ`kjuʃən; ˌprɒsɪ'kjuːʃən/ *n* **1** [C,U] the process or act of bringing a charge against someone for a crime, or of being judged for a crime in a court of law (被)起訴, (被)檢控: *The evidence is now sufficient to bring a prosecution against him.* 現有的證據足以對他提出訴訟。| *I want immunity from prosecution before I give you any names.* 在我向你提供任何名字前, 我想要求免於起訴。**2 the prosecution** the lawyers who represent the person bringing a criminal charge against someone in a court of law 檢控方, 控方: *the chief witness for the prosecution* 控方的主要證人 —compare 比較 DEFENCE (5) **3** [U] *formal* the doing of something that is your job【正式】執行〔職責〕, 進行: *the prosecution of her duties* 履行她的職責

pros·e·cu·tor /`prɑsɪˌkjutɚ; 'prɒsɪkjuːtə/ *n* [C] a lawyer who represents the person who is bringing a criminal charge against someone 代表起訴人的律師; 控方律師

pros·e·lyte /`prɑsḷˌaɪt; 'prɒsə̇laɪt/ *n* [C] *formal* someone who has recently been persuaded to join a religious group, political party etc; CONVERT[2]【正式】〔被說服〕新皈依某宗教者; 新加入政黨者

pros·e·lyt·ize also 又作 **-ise** *BrE*【英】/`prɑsəlɪtˌaɪz; 'prɒsələtaɪz/ *v* [I,T] *formal* to try to persuade someone to join a religious group, political party etc, especially in a way that people find offensive【正式】極力勸誘〔某人〕入教[加入政黨等]〔常含貶義〕—**proselytizer** *n* [C]

pros·o·dy /`prɑsədɪ; 'prɒsədi/ *n* [U] the rules for arranging the patterns of sounds and beats in poetry, or the study of these rules〔詩歌的〕韻律(學), 詩體(學) —**prosodic** /prə`sɑdɪk; prə'sɒdɪk/ *adj*

pro·spect¹ /`prɑspɛkt; 'prɒspekt/ *n* **1** [C,U] a possibility that something which you hope for will happen soon 2 2
〔成功的〕可能性; 機會: **[+of]** *There's little prospect of employment, I'm afraid.* 恐怕就業的可能性很小。| **[+for]** *There are good prospects for growth in the retail sector.* 零售行業有很好的發展前景。| **every prospect** (=a strong possibility) 很大的可能性 | *Peace talks start today with every prospect of success.* 和談今天開始, 成功的可能性很大。**2** [singular] something that is possible or is likely to happen in the future 可能的事情, 很可能發生的事情; 前景: **[+of]** *The prospect of marriage terrified Alice.* 想到要結婚艾麗斯就感到害怕。| *a depressing prospect* 令人沮喪的前景 **3 prospects** [plural] chances of future success 將來成功的機會, 前途, 前程: *You can't marry a man with no job and no prospects!* 你不能嫁給一個沒有工作也沒有前途的男人! **4** [C] a person, job, plan etc that has a good chance of success in the future 有前途的人[工作, 計劃]: *Reg was the brightest schoolboy rugby prospect in years.* 雷格是好幾年來最有希望的學生橄欖球隊員。**5** [C usually singular 一般用單數] *formal* a view of a wide area of land, especially from a high place【正式】〔尤指從高處看到的〕景象, 開闊的景觀, 景色: *a fine prospect across the valley* 山谷那邊的美好景色 **6 in prospect** *formal* likely to happen in the near future【正式】即將可能發生的

pro·spect² /`prɑspɛkt; prə'spekt/ *v* [I+for, T] to examine an area of land or water, in order to find gold, silver, oil etc 勘探, 勘察〔以尋找金、銀、石油等礦藏〕

pro·spec·tive /prə`spɛktɪv; prə'spektɪv/ *adj* [only before noun 僅用於名詞前] **1** likely to do a particular thing or achieve a particular position 預期的, 未來的, 可能的: **prospective employee/candidate/buyer etc** *I'm meeting a prospective buyer for the house today.* 今天我要見一位可能購買這所房子的人。**2** likely to happen 很可能發生的: **prospective costs/career/changes etc** *What are the prospective returns from an investment of $10,000 over five years?* 投資10,000美元五年有可能收益多少?

pro·spec·tor /`prɑspɛktɚ; prə'spektə/ *n* [C] someone who looks for gold, minerals, oil etc 勘探者, 探礦者

pro·spec·tus /prə`spɛktəs; prə'spektəs/ *n* [C] **1** a small book that advertises a college, university, new business etc〔學院、大學、新企業等的〕簡介, 廣告宣傳冊子 **2** a formal statement giving details of a future event in business, such as the sale of shares (SHARE[2] (5))〔商業企業等拓股之類的〕計劃書; 說明書

pros·per /`prɑspɚ; 'prɒspə/ *v* **1** [I] to be successful and become rich 成功; 興旺, 發達, 繁榮: *My father was no longer prospering in business.* 我父親生意不再興旺發達。**2** [I] to grow and develop in a healthy way; THRIVE 健康成長, 順利發展, 蓬勃發展: *The children seemed to prosper under their care.* 在他們的照管下, 孩子看來健康成長。**3** [T] *old use* to make something succeed【舊】使成功, 使繁榮

pro·sper·i·ty /prɑs`pɛrətɪ; prɒ'sperə̇ti/ *n* [U] a condition of having money and everything that is needed for a good life 興隆, 發達, 昌盛, 繁榮: *an era of unparalleled peace and prosperity* 空前和平與繁榮的時代

pros·per·ous /ˋprɑspərəs; ˈprɒspərəs/ *adj* successful and rich 成功的; 繁榮的, 興旺的, 發達的: *working for a strong, prosperous and united Europe* 為實現強大、繁榮、統一的歐洲而努力 —**prosperously** *adv*

pros·tate /ˋprɑstet; ˈprɒsteɪt/ also 又作 **prostate gland** *n* [C] the organ in the male body that produces a liquid in which SPERM (=seeds) are carried 前列腺

pros·the·sis /prɑsˋθisɪs; prɒsˈθiːsɪ̈s/ *plural* **prostheses** /-siz; -siːz/ *n* [C] *technical* an artificial leg, tooth, or other part of the body which takes the place of a missing part【術語】義肢, 假體〈如假肢、假牙等〉

P

pros·ti·tute¹ /ˋprɑstəˌtut; ˈprɒstɪ̈tjuːt/ *n* [C] **1** someone, especially a woman, who earns money by having sex with people who pay for it 娼妓, 妓女 **2 male prostitute** a man who earns money in this way 男妓

prostitute² *v* [T] **1** *formal* to use your skills, abilities etc in a way that does not show their true value, in order to earn money【正式】出賣〔才能〕, 為錢而濫用〔才能〕: *Olivier never prostituted his acting talent by appearing in TV commercials.* 奧利維爾從不做電視廣告折辱自己的表演才華。**2 prostitute yourself a)** to have sex in return for money 賣淫 **b)** to do unpleasant work just to get money 為掙錢而做難堪的工作

pros·ti·tu·tion /ˌprɑstəˋtuʃən; ˌprɒstɪ̈ˈtjuːʃən/ *n* [U] **1** the work of prostitutes 賣淫〔業〕: *an alarming rise in teenage prostitution* 少年賣淫的驚人增長 **2** *formal* the use of your skill, ability etc, in a way that does not show its true value【正式】濫用〔才能〕

pros·trate¹ /ˋprɑstret; ˈprɒstreɪt/ *adj* **1** lying on your front with your face towards the ground, for example because you are injured, or are praising God 俯臥的; 拜倒的, 匍伏的 —compare 比較 PRONE (2) **2** so shocked, upset etc that you can no longer do anything 非常震驚〔傷心〕而不能做任何事的: **[+with]** *Judy was prostrate with grief after her father's death.* 朱迪在她父親死後悲痛不已。

pro·strate² /ˋprɑstret; prəˈstreɪt/ *v* [T] **1 prostrate yourself** to lie on your front with your face towards the ground as an act of praise or a sign of obedience〔表示順從或崇拜〕拜倒, 匍伏 **2 be prostrated** *formal* to have lost all your strength, courage, or energy【正式】衰竭, 一蹶不振, 筋疲力盡: *prostrated by illness* 病倒 —**prostration** /prɑˋstreʃən; prɒˈstreɪʃən/ *n* [C,U]

pros·y /ˋprozɪ; ˈprəʊzi/ *adj* a prosy style of writing or speech is boring and shows no imagination〔文章或講話〕乏味的, 無想像力的 —**prosily** *adv* —**prosiness** *n* [U]

prot- /prot; prəʊt/ *prefix* another form of the prefix PROTO- 前綴 proto- 的另一種形式

pro·tag·o·nist /proˋtægənɪst; prəʊˈtægənɪ̈st/ *n* [C] **1** one of the main supporters of a new aim or policy, especially a social one〔新目標或政策的〕主要支持者, 主要擁護者: **[+of]** *Ogden was one of the earliest protagonists of educational reform.* 奧格登是教育改革的最早支持者之一。**2** *formal* the most important character in a play, film, or story【正式】〔戲劇、電影或故事的〕主要人物, 主角 **3** *formal* someone who is in a competition, battle, or struggle【正式】〔競賽、戰役、鬥爭的〕參加者, 參與者: *the protagonists in America's 'software wars'* 美國"軟件戰"的參與者 —compare 比較 ANTAGONIST

pro·te·an /ˋprotɪən; ˈprəʊtiən/ *adj literary* having the ability to change continually in appearance or behaviour【文】〔外表或行為〕多變的, 變化多端的

S2 W2 **pro·tect** /prəˋtɛkt; prəˈtekt/ *v* [T] **1** to keep someone or something safe from harm, damage, or illness 保護; 防護: **protect sb/sth from sth** *Try to protect your skin from the sun.* 盡量保護皮膚不受太陽曬。| *Kids should be protected from all that violence.* 應保護孩子免受那些暴力的侵害。| **protect sth** *laws protecting the rights of disabled people* 保護殘疾人權利的法律 | *I have to protect my reputation.* 我必須保護自己的聲譽。| **protect sb/sth against** *a natural camouflage that protects them against predators* 保護牠們免受食肉動物捕食的天然偽裝 | **[+against]** *locks to protect against burglars* 防盜鎖 **2** [usually passive 一般用被動態] to keep something such as an old building or a rare animal safe from harm or destruction, by means of special laws〔以特殊法律〕保護〔古老建築物或稀有動物〕**3** to help the industry and trade of your own country by taxing foreign goods〔通過徵收進口稅〕保護〔國內工商業〕—see also 另見 PROTECTIONISM, PROTECTIVE —**protected** *adj*: *Spotted owls are a protected species.* 斑點貓頭鷹是受保護的物種。

pro·tec·tion /prəˋtɛkʃən; prəˈtekʃən/ *n* **1** [U] the act of protecting or state of being protected 保護; 受保護: *You're guaranteed police protection if you testify in court.* 如果你在法庭上作證, 你一定會受到警方的保護。| **[+against]** *Take these vitamins daily for protection against minor infections.* 每天服用維生素片預防輕微感染。| **give/offer/provide protection** (=protect) 提供保護 *Helen's thin coat gave little protection against the cold.* 海倫單薄的外衣幾乎不能禦寒。**2** [U] the promise of payment from an insurance company if something bad happens〔保險〕保障: *Our Five-Star Policy offers complete protection in case of fire.* 我們的五星保險單在發生火災時提供完全的保障。**3** [singular] something that protects 防護物: **[+against]** *Wear a bullet-proof vest as a protection against snipers.* 穿一件防彈背心以防狙擊手。**4** [U] protection money 保護費 S2 W2

pro·tec·tion·is·m /prəˋtɛkʃənɪzm̩; prəˈtekʃənɪzəm/ *n* [U] the system of helping your country's trade, especially by taxing foreign goods 貿易保護主義 —**protectionist** *adj* —**protectionist** *n* [C]

protection mon·ey /.ˈ.. ˌ../ *n* [U] money paid to criminals to stop them from damaging your property〔付給不法分子的〕保護費

protection rack·et /.ˈ.. ˌ../ *n* [C] *informal* a system in which criminals demand money from you to stop them from damaging your property【非正式】〔不法分子〕勒索保護費的勾當

pro·tec·tive /prəˋtɛktɪv; prəˈtektɪv/ *adj* **1** [only before noun 僅用於名詞前] used or intended for protection 保護的, 防護的: *protective clothing* 防護服 | *protective legislation* 保護性法規 | *a protective layer of varnish* 一層保護性清漆 **2** wanting to protect someone from harm or danger, often in a way that unintentionally restricts their freedom〔對人〕關切保護的; 〔過於〕愛護的: **[+towards/of]** *I can't help feeling protective towards my kids.* 我忍不住想保護我的孩子。**3** intended to give an advantage to your own country's industry 旨在保護本國工業的, 保護性的: *a protective tariff on imports of foreign cars* 對進口外國汽車的保護性關稅 —**protectively** *adv* —**protectiveness** *n* [U]

protective cus·to·dy /.ˌ.. ˈ.../ *n* [U] a situation in which the police make you stay somewhere to protect you from other people 保護性拘留

pro·tec·tor /prəˋtɛktɚ; prəˈtektə/ *n* [C] something or someone that protects 保護者, 保護物: *He sees himself as her protector.* 他把自己看成是她的保護者。

pro·tec·tor·ate /prəˋtɛktərɪt; prəˈtektərɪ̈t/ *n* [C] a country that is protected and controlled by a more powerful country, especially in the areas of defence and foreign affairs〔由一個更強的國家保護並控制其國防和外交的〕保護國

prot·é·gé /ˋprotəˌʒe; ˈprɒtəʒeɪ/ *n* [C] a young person who is guided and helped by someone who has influence, power, or more experience 受有影響[有權勢, 有經驗]的人物指導[幫助]的年輕人, 門生, 門徒

prot·é·gée /ˋprotəˌʒe; ˈprɒtəʒeɪ/ *n* [C] a young woman who is guided and helped by someone who has influence, power, or more experience 受到有影響[有權勢, 有經驗]的人指導[幫助]的年輕女性, 女門生, 女門徒

pro·tein /ˋprotin; ˈprəʊtiːn/ *n* [C,U] one of the many substances that exist in food such as meat, eggs, and beans, which help your body to grow and keep it strong and healthy 蛋白質 

pro tem /ˌpro ˋtɛm; ˌprəʊ 'tem/ also 又作 **pro tem·po·re** /-ˋtɛmpəre; -'tempəreɪ/ *Latin*【拉丁】*adj, adv* happening now but only for a short time 暫時的[地], 臨時的[地]: *a pro tem committee of nine men* 臨時九人委員會

3 **pro·test¹** /ˋprotɛst; 'prəʊtest/ *n* **1** [C,U] a strong complaint that shows you disagree with, or are angry about something that you think is wrong or unfair 抗議, 反對: *a written protest alleging police brutality* 聲稱警察行為粗暴的書面抗議 | *I turned off the TV, despite loud protests from the kids.* 儘管孩子們大聲反對, 我還是關掉了電視機。| **[+against]** *American flags were burned as a protest against US intervention.* 作為對美國干涉的抗議, 美國國旗被燒了。| *a protest song* 抗議歌曲 | **in protest** (=as a way of making a protest) 作為抗議 *Seven prisoners are on hunger strike in protest against their treatment.* 七名囚犯在絕食以抗議他們所受的待遇。| *the protest movements of the 1960s* 20世紀60年代的抗議運動 | **a storm of protest/wave of protest** (=a lot of angry protest) 抗議風暴/抗議浪潮 *The price rises caused a storm of protest.* 價格上漲引起了抗議風暴。**2** [C] an occasion when people come together in public to express disapproval or opposition to something 抗議; 抗議活動: *Student protests swept across the nation's campuses.* 學生抗議活動席捲了全國的校園。**3 without protest** calmly and without complaining 平靜地, 毫無怨言地: *Ben accepted his punishment without protest.* 本毫無怨言地接受了懲罰。**4 under protest** unwillingly, and with the feeling that you have been unfairly treated 不情願地, 認為是不公正地: *I only signed the document under protest.* 我不情願地簽了這份文件。

pro·test² /prəˋtɛst; prə'test/ *v* **1** [I,T] to say or do something publicly to show that you disagree with, or are angry about something that you think is wrong or unfair 抗議, 反對: **[+against/at/about]** *Someone has to keep protesting against human rights violations.* 必須有人不斷抗議侵害人權的行為。| *I heard him protesting loudly as the medics took him away.* 醫生把他帶走時, 我聽到他在大聲抗議。| *"Let me go!" Sarah protested angrily.* "放開我!" 莎拉生氣地提出抗議。| **protest sth** *AmE*【美】*a large crowd protesting the war* 反對這場戰爭的一大羣人 **2** [T] to state very firmly that something is true, especially when other people do not believe you〔尤指當別人不相信你時〕堅持說, 力言; 聲言, 申明: **protest that** *Even if Mandy protests that she's not drunk, don't let her drive.* 即使曼迪力言她自己沒有醉, 也不要讓她開車。| **protest your innocence** (=keep saying that you are innocent) 堅持稱自己無罪

Prot·es·tant /ˋprɑtɪstənt; 'prɒtɪ̈stənt/ *n* [C] a member of a part of the Christian church that separated from the Roman Catholic church in the 16th century 新教徒〔16世紀脫離羅馬天主教的基督教教派成員〕—**Protestant** *adj* —**Protestantism** *n* [U]

prot·es·ta·tion /ˌprɑtəsˋteʃən; ˌprɒtɪ̈'steɪʃən/ *n formal*【正式】[C+of] a strong statement saying that something is true, especially when other people say it is not 宣言; 聲明; 斷言

pro·test·er /prəˋtɛstɚ; prə'testə/ *n* [C] someone who takes part in a public activity to show their opposition to something 抗議者

proto- /proto; prəʊtəʊ/ *prefix* also 又作 **prot-** *technical* first in time or order, before other things of the same kind are developed; original【術語】第一的, 最初的, 原始的: *the huge protogalaxy from which all the galaxies developed* 所有星系賴以形成的巨大原星系

pro·to·col /ˋprotəˌkɔl; 'prəʊtəkɒl/ *n* **1** [U] the system of rules on the correct and acceptable way to behave on official occasions 禮節, 禮儀: *a breach of diplomatic protocol* 違反外交禮節 **2** [C] *technical* a method for connecting computers so that they can exchange information【術語】電腦間為交換信息的連接方法, 協議

pro·ton /ˋprotɑn; 'prəʊtɒn/ *n* [C] a very small piece of matter that carries POSITIVE electricity and that together with a NEUTRON forms the NUCLEUS (=central part) of an atom 質子 —see also 另見 ELECTRON

pro·to·plas·m /ˋprotəˌplæzəm; 'prəʊtəplæzəm/ *n* [U] *technical* the colourless substance that forms the cells of plants and animals【術語】原生質, 原漿

pro·to·type /ˋprotəˌtaɪp; 'prəʊtətaɪp/ *n* [C] the first form that a new design of a car, machine etc has〔新型汽車、機器等的〕原型; 雛型: **[+of/for]** *a complete working prototype of the new model* 新樣式的完整工作樣機原型

pro·to·zo·a /ˌprotəˋzoə; ˌprəʊtə'zəʊə/ *n* [plural] very small living things that only have one cell 原生動物

pro·to·zo·an /ˌprotəˋzoən; ˌprəʊtə'zəʊən/ also 又作 **pro·to·zo·on** /-ˋzoɑn; -'zəʊɒn/ *n* [C] a single member of the protozoa〔單個的〕原生動物 —**protozoan** *adj*

pro·trac·ted /proˋtræktɪd; prə'træktɪ̈d/ *adj* lasting a long time, especially longer than usual, or necessary 長時間的; 延長的, 拖延的: *the likelihood of an ugly and protracted guerilla war* 發生一場可怕而持久的游擊戰的可能性 —**protract** *v* [T] —**protraction** /-ˋtrækʃən; -'trækʃən/ *n* [U]

pro·trac·tor /proˋtræktɚ; prə'træktə/ *n* [C] an instrument usually in the shape of a half-circle, used for measuring and drawing angles 量角器; 分度規

pro·trude /proˋtrud; prə'tru:d/ *v* [I] to stick out from somewhere 伸出, 突出: *protruding eyes* 突出的眼睛 | **[+from]** *A pair of shoes protruded from under the bed.* 從牀底下露出一雙鞋子。

pro·tru·sion /proˋtruʒən; prə'tru:ʒən/ *n* **1** [C] something that protrudes 伸出物, 突出物 **2** [U] the act of protruding 伸出, 突出

pro·tu·be·rance /proˋtubərəns; prə'tju:bərəns/ *n* [C] *formal* something that sticks out from the surface of something else【正式】隆起, 突出物

pro·tu·be·rant /proˋtubərənt; prə'tju:bərənt/ *adj* curving outwards from a surface 隆起的, 突出的 —**protuberantly** *adv*

proud /praud; praʊd/ *adj* 2 3

1 ►PLEASED 高興的◄ feeling pleased with your achievements, family, country etc because you think they are very good 自豪的, 得意的, 引以為榮的: *You should see them with the baby – they're so proud!* 你該看看他們與嬰兒在一起的樣子——他們多麼自豪! | **[+of]** *Jane's very proud of her new car.* 簡為她的新車頗感得意。| **proud (that)** *We are proud that a pupil from our school has won a prize.* 我們學校的一個學生得了獎, 我們感到很自豪。| **proud to do/be sth** *She was proud to be part of such a prestigious project.* 她為成為享有如此高聲譽項目的成員而感到自豪。—see also 另見 HOUSEPROUD

2 ►TOO PROUD 過分得意的◄ thinking that you are more important, skilful etc than you really are 驕傲的, 傲慢的, 自負的: *Proud and boastful, Jaggers was typical of the young brokers.* 賈格斯是典型的年輕經紀人, 傲慢且喜歡自吹自擂。

3 ►REFUSE HELP 拒絕幫助◄ having so much respect for yourself that you will not let other people help you when you are in a difficult situation 高傲的, 自尊心強的: *My grandfather's penniless, but he's too proud to ask for help.* 我祖父身無分文, 但他自尊心太強, 不願求助於人。

4 do sb proud a) *informal* to provide a lot of good food, drink etc when people are visiting you or celebrating something【非正式】盛情款待某人, 待某人以上賓之禮: *Clare did us proud last Christmas.* 去年聖誕節克萊爾盛情款待了我們。**b)** to make people feel proud of you by doing something well 使某人為你感到自豪: *Congratulations Bobby, you've done us proud!* 祝賀你, 博比, 你給我們爭了光!

5 as proud as a peacock feeling very pleased with yourself because you have done something well 驕傲如孔雀, 非常驕傲

6 ►IMPRESSIVE 給人以深刻印象的◄ *literary* tall and impressive【文】宏偉的, 壯觀的: *the proud cathedral*

spire 壯觀的教堂尖頂 —see also 另見 PRIDE[1] **—proudly** *adv*

2 **prove** /pruv; pruːv/ *v past tense* **proved** *past participle*
1 **proved** also 又作 **proven** /ˈpruvən; ˈpruːvən/ *especially AmE*【尤美】

1 ►SHOW THE TRUTH 展示真實情況◄ [T] to show that something is true by providing facts, information etc 證明, 證實: *Evidence has been found that proves his innocence.* 證明他無罪的證據已經找到。| **prove (that)** *It is impossible to prove that God exists.* 無法證明上帝存在。| **prove sb wrong/innocent etc** *It would give me great pleasure to prove Sam wrong.* 證明薩姆有錯我將感到非常高興。—see also 另見 DISPROVE

2 ►BE SOMETHING 是某事物◄ [linking verb 連繫動詞, T] if someone or something proves difficult, helpful etc, you find out that this is what they are like 證明是, 被發現是, 顯示出是: *Working from home proved a real advantage after my son was born.* 我兒子出生後, 我發現在家工作是非常便利的。| **prove to be sth** *Your computing experience should prove to be useful.* 你使用電腦的經驗會表明是有用的。

3 prove yourself to show how good you are at something by trying hard to do it well 證明自己的實力: *When I started the job, I felt I had to prove myself.* 當我開始幹這份工作時, 我覺得必須證明一下我自己。

4 ►BREAD 麵包◄ [I] if DOUGH (=unbaked bread mixture) proves, it rises and becomes light because of the YEAST in it〔麵團〕發酵

5 ►LAW 法律◄ [T] *law* to show that a WILL has been made properly【法律】檢驗, 認證〔遺囑〕**—provable** *adj* **—provably** *adv*

prov·en[1] /ˈpruvən; ˈpruːvən/ *adj* **1** [usually before noun 一般用於名詞前] tested and shown to be true 被證實的, 經驗證的: *a woman of proven ability* 已被證實確有才能的女人 **2 not proven** an expression used in Scottish law when a court cannot decide definitely that someone is guilty of a crime〔蘇格蘭法律用語〕證據不足的

proven[2] *especially AmE*【尤美】a past participle of PROVE

prov·e·nance /ˈprɑvənəns; ˈprɒvənəns/ *n* [U] *formal* the place where something originally came from【正式】起源(地); 出處: *a rug of Iranian provenance* 原產自伊朗的地毯

prov·en·der /ˈprɑvəndə; ˈprɒvɨndə/ *n* [U] *old-fashioned* dry food for horses and cattle【過時】〔牲畜的〕乾飼料, 糧秣

prov·erb /ˈprɑvɝb; ˈprɒvɜːb/ *n* [C] a short well-known statement that contains advice about life in general 諺語, 格言

pro·ver·bi·al /prəˈvɝbɪəl; prəˈvɜːbiəl/ *adj* **1 the proverbial** used when describing something using a well-known expression 俗話所說[常言中]的: *This was not the proverbial free lunch!* 這不是俗話所說的免費午餐! **2** well-known by a lot of people 眾所周知的: *It was a level of corruption which became proverbial.* 那是眾所周知的腐敗。**3** connected with a proverb 諺語的: *a proverbial saying* 諺語 **—proverbially** *adv*

1 **pro·vide** /prəˈvaɪd; prəˈvaɪd/ *v* [T] **1** to make sure that
1 someone gets what they need, especially by giving it to them 提供, 供應, 供給: **provide sth for sb** *The hotel provides a shoe-cleaning service for guests.* 該酒店為客人提供擦鞋服務。| **provide sb with sth** *a project designed to provide young people with work* 一項旨在為年輕人提供工作的計劃 | **provide sth** *I'll provide the food if you bring the wine.* 你帶酒我就提供吃的。**2** to produce a useful result, opportunity etc 產生有益的結果; 製造[提供]機會: *We are hoping the enquiry will provide an explanation for the accident.* 我們希望這次調查將為該事故提供一種解釋。| **provide sb with sth** *This has provided police with a vital clue.* 這為警方提供了一條重要的線索。**3 provide that** *formal* if a law or rule provides that something must happen, it states that it must happen【正式】〔法律、規章〕規定

provide against sth *phr v* [T] *formal* to make plans in order to deal with a bad situation that might happen【正式】預防, 防備, 防止

provide for sb/sth *phr v* [T] **1** to give someone the things they need, such as money, food etc 供養, 撫養: *Without work, how can I provide for my children?* 沒有工作, 我如何供養我的孩子? **2** *formal* to make plans in order to deal with something that might happen in the future【正式】為…作準備, 防備: *The policy provides for a 60% increase in traffic.* 這項政策旨在應付車輛增加60%的局面。**3** *formal* if a law or rule provides for something, it makes doing that thing possible【正式】〔法律、規章〕使〔某事〕可能, 准許

pro·vid·ed /prəˈvaɪdɪd; prəˈvaɪdɨd/ also 又作 **provided** 3
that *conjunction* used to say that something will only 2
be possible if something else happens or is done 只要; 如果…的話: *I don't mind Guy coming with us, provided he pays for his own meals.* 只要蓋伊自付餐費, 我不介意他和我們一起去。

Prov·i·dence, providence /ˈprɑvədəns; ˈprɒvɨdəns/ *n* [singular,U] a force that some people believe controls our lives, especially because it is what God wants 天意, 天命

prov·i·dent /ˈprɑvədənt; ˈprɒvɨdənt/ *adj formal* careful and sensible, especially by saving money for the future【正式】顧及未來的, 未雨綢繆的, 深謀遠慮的 —opposite 反義詞 IMPROVIDENT **—providently** *adv*

prov·i·den·tial /ˌprɑvəˈdɛnʃəl; ˌprɒvɨˈdenʃəl◄/ *adj formal* happening just when you need it; LUCKY【正式】幸運的, 湊巧的; 及時的: *To Robyn, it seemed a providential opportunity to make the break with Charles.* 對羅賓來說, 那好像是與查爾斯分手的大好機會。**—providentially** *adv*

pro·vid·er /prəˈvaɪdə; prəˈvaɪdə/ *n* [C] someone who provides something, especially someone who supports a family 供應者;〔尤指〕供養家庭的人

pro·vid·ing /prəˈvaɪdɪŋ; prəˈvaɪdɪŋ/ also 又作 **provid-** 2
ing that *conjunction* used to say that something will only be possible if something else happens or is done 只要; 如果…的話: *Sure you can borrow the car, providing you get it back to me before 10 o'clock.* 只要你在10點鐘之前還我, 你當然可以借車。

prov·ince /ˈprɑvɪns; ˈprɒvɨns/ *n* **1** also 又作 **Province** 3
[C] one of the large areas into which some countries are divided 省: *Sichuan is China's most populous province.* 四川是中國人口最多的省份。**2 the provinces** *especially BrE* the parts of a country that are not near to the capital city【尤英】外省〔指首都以外的地區〕, 外地 **3 sb's province** a subject that someone knows a lot about or something that they are responsible for〔知識、研究的〕範圍, 領域; 職責範圍: *Sales forecasts are outside my province – talk to the Sales Manager.* 銷售預測不屬我的職責範圍 — 去找銷售經理談吧。**4** an area that an ARCHBISHOP (=a priest of the highest rank) is responsible for 大主教轄區 —compare 比較 DIOCESE

pro·vin·cial[1] /prəˈvɪnʃəl; prəˈvɪnʃəl/ *adj* **1** connected with the parts of a country that are not near the capital city 外省的〔指首都以外的地區〕, 地方的: *a small provincial town* 一座地方小城鎮 **2** a provincial attitude shows that you are unwilling to accept new ideas or to think about things in new ways〔態度〕偏狹的, 守舊的 **—provincially** *adv*

provincial[2] *n* [C] someone who comes from the parts of a country that are not near the capital city (來自)首都以外的人; 地方居民

pro·vin·cial·is·m /prəˈvɪnʃəlɪzəm; prəˈvɪnʃəlɪzəm/ *n* [U] the attitude of not wanting to accept new ideas and not being interested in new things 偏狹守舊的態度

prov·ing ground /ˈ·· ·/ *n* [C] **1** a place or situation in which something new is tried out or tested〔新事物的〕

試驗場所[環境]: *High-crime areas make ideal proving grounds for new officers.* 犯罪高發地區是考驗新任警察的理想場所。**2** an area for scientific testing, especially of vehicles〔尤指車輛的〕檢驗場, 試驗場

S3 W1 **pro·vi·sion[1]** /prəˋvɪʒən; prəˈvɪʒən/ *n* **1** [C,U] the act of providing something that someone needs 供應, 供給, 提供: **[+of]** *Many women would welcome the provision of childcare facilities at work.* 很多婦女都會歡迎在工作地點提供托兒設施。| **[+for]** *provision for people with disabilities* 滿足殘疾人士的需要 **2 make provision for** to make plans for future needs 為…作好準備, 為…預先採取措施: *Ralph wanted to make proper provision for his children.* 拉爾夫想為他孩子的將來作好準備。**3 provisions** food supplies, especially for a journey〔尤指為旅行儲備的〕糧食, 食物 **4** [C] a condition in an agreement or law〔協議或法律中的〕規定, 條款, 條件: *Let me set out the main provisions of the contract.* 讓我闡明這份合同的主要條款。

provision[2] *v* [T] to provide someone or something with a lot of food and supplies, especially for a journey〔尤指為旅行〕提供大量的食品和其他供應品

pro·vi·sion·al /prəˋvɪʒənḷ; prəˈvɪʒənəl/ *adj* **1** intended to exist for only a short time and likely to be changed in the future 臨時的〔指短期存在〕, 暫時的, 暫定的: *a provisional government* 臨時政府 —compare 比較 TEMPORARY **2** provisional offers, arrangements etc are not yet definite but should become definite in the future 臨時的〔指尚待確定〕: *We accept provisional bookings by phone.* 我們接受電話臨時預約。—**provisionally** *adv*

provisional li·cence /·,··· ˈ··/ *n* [C] *BrE* an official document that you need when you are learning to drive【英】〔學習駕駛時需用的〕臨時駕駛執照; LEARNER'S PERMIT *AmE*【美】

pro·vi·so /prəˋvaɪzo; prəˈvaɪzəʊ/ *plural* **provisos** *n* [C] a condition that you ask for before you will agree to something〔同意某事的〕(前提) 條件, (附帶) 條件: *The only proviso is that your vacation has to be for a minimum of five nights.* 唯一的條件是你的假期必須至少有五個晚上。

prov·o·ca·tion /,prɑvəˋkeʃən; ,prɒvəˈkeɪʃən/ *n* [C,U] an action or event that makes someone angry or that is intended to do this 激怒; 挑釁; 挑釁性事件: *It was a vicious attack, with absolutely no provocation.* 那是在事先未發生任何挑釁情況下的惡意攻擊。

pro·voc·a·tive /prəˋvɑkətɪv; prəˈvɒkətɪv/ *adj* **1** provocative behaviour, remarks etc are intended to make people angry or to cause a lot of discussion〔行為、話語等〕使人生氣的; 挑釁的; 煽動的; 引起爭論的: *Some would say he wrote a deliberately provocative book.* 有人會說他寫了一本故意引起爭論的書。**2** provocative clothes, movements etc are intended to make someone sexually excited〔衣服、動作〕挑逗性的 —**provocatively** *adv*

pro·voke /prəˋvok; prəˈvəʊk/ *v* [T] **1** to cause a sudden reaction that is often very extreme or unpleasant 激起, 引起: *The decision to invade provoked storms of protest in the UN.* 侵略的決定激起聯合國的強烈抗議。| **provoke sb to do sth** *It's the first time an article has provoked me to write in to the newspaper.* 一篇文章激發我給這家報紙寫信發表意見, 這是第一次。**2** to try to make someone angry by doing or saying things that you know annoy them 激怒, 使惱火: **provoke sb into doing sth** *Don't let him provoke you into losing your temper!* 別讓他故意惹你發脾氣!

Prov·ost also 又作 **provost** /ˋprɑvəst; ˈprovəst/ *n* [C] **1** a person in charge of a college in a British university〔英國大學中學院的〕院長 **2** *AmE* an important university official【美】大學教務長 **3** the leader of a Scottish town council〔蘇格蘭的〕市長 —compare 比較 MAYOR **4** the main priest in a group of priests connected with a CATHEDRAL in Britain〔英國〕大教堂的教長

pro·vost court /ˈprovo kɔrt; prəˈvəʊ kɔːt/ *n* [C] a type of military court 軍事法庭

provost mar·shal /,provo ˋmɑrʃəl; prə,vəʊ ˈmɑːʃəl/ *n* [C] an officer who is in charge of military police 憲兵司令

prow /praʊ; praʊ/ *n* [C] *especially literary* the front part of a ship or boat【尤文】船頭, 船首

prow·ess /ˋpraʊɪs; ˈpraʊɪ̣s/ *n* [U] *formal* great skill at doing something【正式】〔做某事的〕高超技藝[技能, 技巧]: *Peregrines are known for their hunting prowess.* 遊隼以牠們高超的捕獵技巧而聞名。

prowl[1] /praʊl; praʊl/ *v* **1** [I,T] if an animal prowls, it moves around an area quietly, especially because it is hunting another animal〔尤指捕獵的動物在某處〕悄悄來回遊走 **2** [I,T] if someone prowls, they move around an area quietly, especially because they are involved in some criminal activity〔尤指參與某些犯罪活動的人在某處〕祕密[悄悄]來回遊走: *gangs prowling the streets* 在大街上鬼鬼祟祟四處遊蕩的匪幫 **3** [I always+adv/prep] to walk around a place because you do not have anything to do 徘徊, 閒蕩: **[+around/ about]** *Kim prowled restlessly around the room.* 金在房間裡不安地踱來踱去。

prowl[2] *n* [singular] **1 be on the prowl** to be moving around quietly looking for something or someone 悄悄地四處搜尋: *police cars on the prowl* 在巡邏的警車 **2** an act of prowling 四處覓食, 悄悄走動

prowl·er /ˋpraʊlɚ; ˈpraʊlə/ *n* [C] someone who follows people or waits near their home, especially at night, and frightens or harms them〔尤指晚上心懷不軌的〕盯梢的人, 潛伏的人: *If you think there is a prowler outside, don't go out to check – call the police.* 如果你覺得外面有潛伏的人, 不要出去查看 — 要叫警察。

prox·i·mate /ˋprɑksə,mɪt; ˈprɒksɪ̣mɪ̣t/ *adj formal*【正式】**1** nearest in time, order, or family relationship〔時間、順序、親屬關係〕最近的, 最接近的 **2** a proximate cause is a direct one〔原因〕直接的 —**proximately** *adv*

prox·im·i·ty /prɑkˋsɪmətɪ; prɒkˈsɪmɪ̣ti/ *n* [U] *formal* nearness in distance or time【正式】〔距離或時間的〕接近, 臨近; 鄰近: **[+to]** *Proximity to a good school is important.* 靠近一所好的學校很重要。| **in close proximity** (=very near) 非常靠近, 緊挨

prox·y /ˋprɑksɪ; ˈprɒksi/ *n* [C] **1** someone that you choose to represent you, especially to vote for you〔由個人委託的〕代理人, 代表〔尤指代人投票〕**2 by proxy** if you do something by proxy, you arrange for someone else to do it for you 由委託人代理

proxy vote /ˈ·· ,·/ *n* [C] a vote you make by officially sending someone else to vote for you 委託他人代投的選票

prude /prud; pruːd/ *n* [C] someone who is too easily shocked by anything connected with sex〔在性方面〕過分拘謹的人

pru·dence /ˋprudəns; ˈpruːdəns/ *n* [U] a sensible and careful attitude that makes you avoid unnecessary risks 小心謹慎, 慎重, 審慎

pru·dent /ˋprudṇt; ˈpruːdənt/ *adj* sensible and careful, especially by trying to avoid unnecessary risks 明智而謹慎的; 慎重的, 審慎的: *It might be prudent to get a virus detector for the network.* 為網絡裝上病毒檢測軟件可能是一種明智的做法。—opposite 反義詞 IMPRUDENT —**prudently** *adv*

pru·den·tial /pruˋdɛnʃəl; pruːˈdenʃəl/ *adj old-fashioned* PRUDENT【過時】謹慎的, 審慎的 —**prudentially** *adv*

prud·er·y /ˋprudərɪ; ˈpruːdəri/ *n* [U] prudish behaviour〔在性方面〕拘謹

prud·ish /ˋprudɪʃ; ˈpruːdɪʃ/ *adj* too easily shocked by things connected with sex〔在性方面〕過分拘謹的 —**prudishly** *adv* —**prudishness** *n* [U]

prune[1] /prun; pruːn/ *v* [T] **1** also 又作 **prune back** to cut some of the branches of a tree or bush to make it grow better 修剪〔樹枝〕: *I need to prune the roses this weekend.* 本週末我需要修剪這些玫瑰。**2** also 又作 **prune down** to get rid of the unnecessary parts of something 刪除, 刪節: *The essay's too long, you need to prune it down.* 這篇文章太長了, 你需要把它刪節一下。

prune² *n* [C] a dried PLUM, usually cooked before eating 西梅乾, (洋) 李脯

pruning hook /ˈ·· ·/ *n* [C] a knife that is shaped like a hook and is usually on a long pole, used for cutting branches off trees〔用於剪樹枝的〕修枝鉤刀

pru·ri·ent /ˈprurɪənt; ˈprʊəriənt/ *adj formal* too strongly interested in sex【正式】好色的, 荒淫的 —**pruriently** *adv* —**prurience** *n* [U]

Prus·sian blue /ˌprʌʃən ˈblu; ˌprʌʃən ˈbluː/ *n* [U] a deep blue colour 普魯士藍; 深藍色 —**Prussian blue** *adj*

prus·sic ac·id /ˌprʌsɪk ˈæsɪd; ˌprʌsɪk ˈæsɪ̈d/ *n* [U] a very poisonous acid 氫氰酸〔一種劇毒性酸〕

pry /praɪ; praɪ/ *v present participle* **prying** *past tense* **pried 1** [I] to try to find out details about someone else's private life in an impolite way 打聽, 探聽〔別人的私生活〕: *I don't wish to pry, but is it true that you're having problems at home?* 我並不想多管閒事, 但是你家出問題是真的嗎? **2** [T always+adv/prep] *especially AmE* to force something open, or force it away from something else; PRIZE³ (2)【尤美】撬開, 撬起: **pry sth open/away etc** *We finally managed to pry open the door with a screwdriver.* 我們最後設法用螺絲刀撬開了門。**3 away from prying eyes** in private, where people cannot see 私下, 避開窺視的目光: *I'd like to show you something, away from prying eyes.* 我想私下給你看樣東西。

PS /ˌpi ˈɛs; ˌpiː ˈes/ *n* [C] a note added at the end of a letter, giving more information〔信末的〕附言; 又及: *She added a PS asking me to send her some money.* 她在信末附言要我寄些錢去。| *Best wishes, Julie. PS If Thursday is not convenient, let me know.* 祝好, 朱莉。再者, 若星期四不便, 請告知。

psalm /sɑm; sɑːm/ *n* [C] a song or poem praising God 讚美詩; 聖歌

psalm·ist /ˈsɑmɪst; ˈsɑːmɪ̈st/ *n* [C] someone who has written a psalm 讚美詩作者, 聖歌作者

psal·ter /ˈsɔltɚ; ˈsɔːltə/ *n* [C] a book containing the psalms from the Bible, often with music, for use in a church〔《聖經》中的〕《詩篇》集〔禮拜時用的讚美詩集, 常配有音樂〕

psal·ter·y /ˈsɔltərɪ; ˈsɔːltəri/ *n* [C] an ancient musical instrument with strings stretched over a board 薩泰利琴〔古代的一種弦樂器〕

pse·phol·o·gy /siˈfɑlədʒɪ; seˈfɒlədʒi/ *n* [U] the study of how people vote in elections 選舉學 —**psephologist** *n* [C]

pseud /sud; sjuːd/ *n* [C] *BrE informal* someone who pretends to know a lot about art, literature etc【英, 非正式】假裝對藝術、文學等了解很多的人 —**pseudy** *adj*

pseudo- /sudo; sjuːdəʊ/ *prefix* not real; false 假, 偽: *pseudo-intellectuals* (=who pretend to be clever) 假知識分子 | *He says astrology's just a pseudoscience.* 他說占星術只是一種偽科學而已。

pseu·do·nym /ˈsudn̩ˌɪm; ˈsjuːdənɪm/ *n* [C] an invented name used by someone, especially a writer, instead of their real name〔尤指作家的〕筆名, 假名: *Charlotte Bronte wrote under the pseudonym of Currer Bell.* 夏洛蒂·勃朗特用柯勒·貝爾的筆名寫作。—**pseudonymy** /suˈdɑnəmɪ; sjuːˈdɒnəmi/ *n* [U]

pseu·don·y·mous /suˈdɑnəməs; sjuːˈdɒnɪ̈məs/ *adj* written or writing under a pseudonym 用筆名寫的, 署假名的: *the pseudonymous writer of the 'Insider' column* "局內人"專欄使用筆名的作者 —**pseudonymously** *adv*

pshaw /ʃɔ; pʃɔː/ *interjection old-fashioned* used to express annoyance, disapproval, or disagreement【過時】啐! 哼!〔表示厭惡、反對〕

pso·ri·a·sis /səˈraɪəsɪs; səˈraɪəsɪ̈s/ *n* [U] an illness which makes your skin dry, red, and FLAKY (=coming off in small bits) 牛皮癬

psst /ps; ps/ *interjection* used to attract someone's attention without other people noticing 噓〔一種暗中引起某人注意的聲音〕: *Psst! There's someone coming!* 噓! 有人來了!

PST /ˌpi ɛs ˈti; ˌpiː es ˈtiː/ the abbreviation of 縮寫= PACIFIC STANDARD TIME

psych /saɪk; saɪk/ *v*

psych sb/sth ↔ **out** *phr v* [T] *informal* to do or say things that will make your opponent in a game or competition feel nervous or confused, so that it is easier for you to win【非正式】〔在比賽、競賽中〕嚇住, 鎮住〔對手〕; 使〔對手〕心煩意亂: *Leonard stared hard at Duran before the fight, trying to psych him out.* 倫納德在開打前使勁瞪着杜蘭, 試圖鎮住他。

psych sb **up** *phr v* [T] *informal*【非正式】**1 psych yourself up** to prepare yourself mentally before doing something so that you feel confident 使自己心理上作好準備: **[+for]** *So George, tell us how the players psych themselves up for the big game.* 那麼喬治, 告訴我們選手是如何為這場大戰作心理準備的。**2 be psyched up** also 又作 **be psyched** *especially AmE* to be mentally prepared for an event and excited about it【尤美】〔為…〕作好心理準備, 鬥志昂揚

psych- /saɪk; saɪk/ *prefix* another form of the prefix PSYCHO- 前綴 psycho- 的另一種形式

psy·che /ˈsaɪkɪ; ˈsaɪki/ *n* [C usually singular 一般用單數] *technical or formal* someone's mind, or their basic nature, which controls their attitudes and behaviour【術語或正式】心靈; 靈魂, 精神: *The image of the independent pioneer lies at the heart of the American psyche.* 獨立的拓荒者形象深深植根於美國精神之中。

psy·che·del·ic /ˌsaɪkɪˈdɛlɪk; ˌsaɪkɪ̈ˈdelɪk◂/ *adj* **1** psychedelic drugs such as LSD make you HALLUCINATE (=see things that do not really exist)〔藥物、毒品〕引起幻覺的, 致幻的 **2** psychedelic art, clothing etc has complicated patterns of strong bright colours, shapes etc〔藝術、服裝等〕產生迷幻效果的 —**psychedelically** *adv*

psy·chi·at·ric /ˌsaɪkɪˈætrɪk; ˌsaɪkiˈætrɪk◂/ *adj* connected with the study and treatment of mental illness 精神病學的, 精神病治療的: *He'll have to undergo psychiatric treatment at the hospital.* 他必須在醫院進行精神治療。| *psychiatric unit* 精神病科 —**psychiatrically** /-klɪ; -kli/ *adv*

psychiatric hospital /ˌ··ˈ·· ˌ···/ *n* [C] a hospital where people with mental illnesses are treated 精神病醫院

psy·chi·a·trist /saɪˈkaɪətrɪst; saɪˈkaɪətrɪ̈st/ *n* [C] a doctor trained in the treatment of mental illness 精神科醫生 —compare 比較 PSYCHOLOGIST

psy·chi·a·try /saɪˈkaɪətrɪ; saɪˈkaɪətri/ *n* [U] the study and treatment of mental illnesses 精神病學, 精神病治療學

psy·chic¹ /ˈsaɪkɪk; ˈsaɪkɪk/ *adj* [no comparative 無比較級] **1** also 又作 **psychical** /ˈsaɪkɪkl̩; ˈsaɪkɪkəl/ connected with mysterious events involving the power of the human mind 通靈的, 對超自然力敏感的: *psychic phenomena* 通靈現象 | *psychic research* 通靈研究 **2** having the ability to know what other people are thinking or what will happen in the future 能洞察人心的; 能知未來的: *How did you know I was here? You must be psychic!* 你怎麼會知道我在這兒? 你一定能未卜先知! —compare 比較 CLAIRVOYANT **3** also 又作 **psychical** affecting the mind rather than the body 精神 (上) 的: *psychic disorders* 精神錯亂 —**psychically** /-klɪ; -kli/ *adv*

psychic² *n* [C] someone who has mysterious powers, especially the ability to receive messages from dead people 對超自然力敏感的人, 有神祕能力的人;〔尤指〕通靈的人

psy·cho /ˈsaɪko; ˈsaɪkəʊ/ *n* [C] *informal* someone who is likely to suddenly behave in a violent or crazy way【非正式】精神失常行為狂暴的人

psycho- /saɪko; saɪkəʊ/ *prefix* also 又作 **psych-** *technical* concerning the mind, as opposed to the body【術語】心理: *psychotherapy* (=treatment of the mind) 心理療法

psy·cho·a·nal·y·sis /ˌsaɪkoəˈnæləsɪs; ˌsaɪkəʊ-ə'nælǐsǐs/ *n* [U] a way of treating someone who is mentally ill by talking to them about their past life, feelings etc, in order to find out the hidden causes of their problems 精神分析(治療法); 心理分析(治療法) —**psychoanalytic** /ˌsaɪkoˌænl̩ˋɪtɪk; ˌsaɪkəʊ-ænə'lɪtɪk◂/ —**psychoanalytical** /-tɪkl̩; -tɪkəl/ *adj*: *psychoanalytic dream interpretation* 用精神分析法釋夢 —**psychoanalytically** /-kl̩ɪ; -kli/ *adv*

psy·cho·an·a·lyst /ˌsaɪkoˋænl̩ɪst; ˌsaɪkəʊ'ænəl-ǐst/ *n* [C] someone who is trained in psychoanalysis 精神分析專家

psy·cho·an·a·lyze *BrE*【英】also 又作 **-ise** /ˌsaɪkoˋænl̩ˌaɪz; ˌsaɪkəʊ'ænəlaɪz/ *v* [T] to treat someone by psychoanalysis 用精神分析法治療

psy·cho·bab·ble /ˋsaɪkoˌbæbl̩; 'saɪkəʊˌbæbəl/ *n* [U] *informal* the language that sounds scientific but is often annoying, that some people use when talking about their emotional problems【非正式】〔某些人用來談論感情問題時使用的〕聽起來具有科學性但常令人討厭的語言

psy·cho·bi·ol·o·gy /ˌsaɪkobaɪˋɑlədʒɪ; ˌsaɪkəʊbaɪ'ɒlədʒi/ *n* [U] the study of the body in relation to the mind 生物心理學, 精神生物學

psy·cho·drama /ˋsaɪkoˌdrɑmə; 'saɪkəʊˌdrɑːmə/ *n* [C] a way of treating mental illness in which people are asked to act in a situation together to help them understand their emotions 心理表演療法〔一種治療精神疾病的方法, 人們被要求在某場景中一起表演從而幫助他們了解自己的情感〕

psy·cho·ki·ne·sis /ˌsaɪkokɪˋnisɪs; ˌsaɪkəʊkaɪ'niːsǐs/ *n* [U] the moving of solid objects using only the power of the mind, which some people believe is possible 心靈致動, 意念移物 —**psychokinetic** /-kɪˋnɛtɪk; -kaɪ'netɪk◂/ *adj* —**psychokinetically** /-kl̩ɪ; -kli/ *adv*

3 **psy·cho·log·i·cal** /ˌsaɪkəˋlɑdʒɪkl̩; ˌsaɪkə'lɒdʒɪkəl◂/ *adj* **1** connected with the way that people's minds work and the way that this affects their behaviour 心理(上)的 **2** illness, fears etc that are psychological are in someone's mind and are not real〔疾病、恐懼等只存在於〕心理上的: *Max says he's got some sort of virus, but I'm sure it's psychological.* 麥克斯說他感染了某種病毒, 但我相信那是心理作用。 **3 psychological warfare** [U] behaviour intended to make your opponents less confident 心理戰 **4 the psychological moment** *informal* the exact time in a situation when you have the best chance to achieve what you want【非正式】〔做某事的〕最恰當的時機 —**psychologically** /-kl̩ɪ; -kli/ *adv*: *psychologically disturbed* 精神上受到困擾的 | *Psychologically* (=from a psychological point of view) *it's a good idea to praise a child for their efforts.* 從心理的角度講, 讚揚一個孩子所作的努力是個好主意。

psy·chol·o·gist /saɪˋkɑlədʒɪst; saɪ'kɒlədʒǐst/ *n* [C] someone who is trained in psychology 心理學家: *child psychologists* 兒童心理學家 —compare 比較 PSYCHIATRIST

3 **psy·chol·o·gy** /saɪˋkɑlədʒɪ; saɪ'kɒlədʒi/ *n* **1** [U] the study of the mind and how it works 心理學: *educational psychology* 教育心理學 **2** [C,U] the usual way in which a particular person or group thinks and reacts〔某個人或某羣體的〕心理: *the psychology of the mob* 暴民的心理 **3** [U] *informal* knowledge of the way that people think, that makes you able to control what they do【非正式】心機, 心計: *Use a bit of psychology. Tell them you think they'd do it better!* 用點心思, 告訴他們你認為他們會做得更好!

psy·cho·met·ric /ˌsaɪkoˋmɛtrɪk; ˌsaɪkəʊ'metrɪk◂/ *adj* for measuring mental abilities and qualities 心理測量的: *psychometric tests* 心理測量測試

psy·cho·path /ˋsaɪkəˌpæθ; 'saɪkəpæθ/ *n* [C] someone who has a serious and permanent mental illness that makes them behave in a violent or criminal way 精神嚴重失常行為狂暴的人; 精神變態的罪犯 —compare 比較 SOCIOPATH —**psychopathic** /ˌsaɪkəˋpæθɪk; ˌsaɪkə'pæθɪk◂/ *adj*: *a psychopathic personality* 精神變態人格 —**psychopathically** /-kl̩ɪ; -kli/ *adv*

psy·cho·sis /saɪˋkosɪs; saɪ'kəʊsǐs/ *n plural* **psychoses** /-siz; -siːz/ [C,U] a serious mental illness that can change your character and make you unable to behave in a normal way 精神病, 精神失常 —see also 另見 PSYCHOTIC

psy·cho·so·mat·ic /ˌsaɪkəsəˋmætɪk; ˌsaɪkəʊsə'mætɪk◂/ *adj* **1** a psychosomatic illness is caused by fear or anxiety rather than by any physical problem〔疾病〕心因性的, 由懼怕[焦慮]引起的 **2** concerned with the relationship between the mind and physical illness 身心的 —**psychosomatically** /-kl̩ɪ; -kli/ *adv*

psy·cho·ther·a·py /ˌsaɪkoˋθɛrəpɪ; ˌsaɪkəʊ'θerəpi/ *n* [U] the treatment of mental illness, for example DEPRESSION, by talking to someone and discussing their problems rather than using drugs or medicine 心理療法, 精神療法 —**psychotherapist** *n* [C]

psy·chot·ic /saɪˋkɑtɪk; saɪ'kɒtɪk/ *adj* suffering from psychosis 精神病的, 精神失常的: *psychotic behaviour* 精神病患者行為 —**psychotic** *n* [C] —**psychotically** /-kl̩ɪ; -kli/ *adv*

pt 1 the written abbreviation of 縮寫= PART: *Pt. II, Chapter 7, p. 157* 第二部分第七章第157頁 **2** the written abbreviation of 縮寫= PAYMENT **3** the written abbreviation of 縮寫= PINT: *Add 1 pt stock.* 加一品脫的原湯。 **4** the written abbreviation of 縮寫= POINT **5** often 常作 **Pt** the written abbreviation of 縮寫= PORT (1): *Pt Moresby* 莫爾斯比港

PT /ˌpi ˋti; ˌpiː 'tiː/ *n* [U] *especially BrE* physical training; organized games, physical exercises etc at school【尤英】體育鍛鍊: *a PT instructor* 體育教師 | *PT lessons at school* 學校的體育課 —compare 比較 GYM (2)

PTA /ˌpi ti ˋe; ˌpiː tiː 'eɪ/ *n* [C] Parent-Teacher Association; an organization of parents and teachers that tries to help and improve a particular school〔幫助改進學校工作的〕家長教師協會: *an active member of the PTA* 一位家長教師協會的活躍分子 —compare 比較 PTO[2]

Pte *BrE*【英】the written abbreviation of 縮寫= PRIVATE[2] (2): *Pte Larry Grossman* 二等兵拉里·格羅斯曼

pter·o·dac·tyl /ˌtɛrəˋdæktɪl; ˌterə'dæktɪl/ *n* [C] a type of large flying animal that lived many millions of years ago 翼手龍〔一種遠古動物〕

PTO[1] /ˌpi ti ˋo; ˌpiː tiː 'əʊ/ *BrE* please turn over; written at the bottom of a page to tell the reader to look at the next page【英】見下頁, 請翻至下頁〔注於頁末的字樣〕

PTO[2] *n* [C] *especially AmE* Parent-Teacher Organization; an organization of parents and teachers that tries to help and improve a particular school【尤美】〔幫助改進學校工作的〕家長教師組織

Ptol·e·ma·ic sys·tem /ˌtɑləˋme·ɪk ˌsɪstəm; ˌtɒlǐ'meɪ-ɪk ˌsɪstǐm/ *n* [singular] the old system of belief that the Earth was at the centre of the universe, with the sun, stars and PLANETS moving around it 托勒密體系〔舊時認為地球是宇宙的中心, 太陽、星辰繞地球旋轉的一種學說〕

pto·maine /ˋtomen; 'təʊmeɪn/ *n* [C,U] a poisonous substance formed by BACTERIA in decaying food 屍鹼, 屍毒

pty the written abbreviation of 縮寫= PROPRIETARY, used in Australia, New Zealand, and South Africa after the name of a business company〔用於澳大利亞、新西蘭和南非公司的名字後面〕: *Australian Wine Growers Pty* 澳大利亞酒業種植公司

pub /pʌb; pʌb/ *n* [C] a building in Britain where alcohol can be bought and drunk〔英國的〕酒館, 酒吧: *Do you* 3
fancy going to the pub? 你想去酒吧嗎? | *a pub lunch* 3 小酒館供應的午餐 —compare 比較 BAR[1] (1)

pub-crawl /ˋ· ˌ·/ *n* [C] *informal, especially BrE* a visit to several pubs, one after the other, during which you have a drink in each pub【非正式, 尤英】串遊酒吧〔從這家酒吧喝到另一家酒吧〕: *a Saturday night pub-crawl* 星期六晚上接連到好幾家酒館喝酒

pu·ber·ty /ˋpjubəˑtɪ; 'pjuːbəti/ *n* [U] the stage of physi-

P

cal development during which you change from a child to an adult able to have children 青春期

pu·bes·cent /pju`bɛsənt; pjuː'besənt/ *adj* a pubescent boy or girl is going through puberty〔男孩或女孩〕處於青春期的

pu·bic /`pjubɪk; 'pjuːbɪk/ *adj* [only before noun 僅用於名詞前] related to or near to the sexual organs〔靠近〕陰部的: *pubic hair* 陰毛

pub·lic¹ /`pʌblɪk; 'pʌblɪk/ *adj*

1 ▶ORDINARY PEOPLE 普通人◀ [no comparative 無比較級] connected with all the ordinary people in a country, who are not members of the government or do not have important jobs 公眾的, 大眾的: *The law was changed as a result of public pressure.* 這項法律由於公眾的壓力而作了修改。| **in the public interest** (=helpful or useful to ordinary people) 對公眾有益的 *Publishing this story was definitely in the public interest.* 發表這個故事肯定會對公眾有益。| **public outcry** (=strong objections from many people) 公眾的強烈抗議 *New taxes provoked a public outcry.* 新的稅收激起了公眾的強烈抗議。

2 ▶FOR ANYONE 為每個人◀ [no comparative 無比較級] available for anyone to use 公共的, 公用的: *a public telephone* 公用電話 | *a public beach* 公共沙灘 | *proposals to ban smoking in public places* 在公共場所禁止抽煙的建議

3 ▶GOVERNMENT 政府◀ [no comparative 無比較級] connected with the government and with the services it provides for people 公務的, 公眾事務的: **public money** *Simply pumping public money into the railways is not the answer.* 僅僅把公帑投入鐵路不是解決方法。| **public office** (=the job of being part of a government) 公職 *We do not believe he is fit for public office.* 我們認為他不適合擔任公職。—see also 另見 PUBLIC SERVICE

4 ▶KNOWN ABOUT 大家知道的◀ [no comparative 無比較級] known about by most people 公開的: **make sth public** (=tell everyone) 使某事公開 *The name of the victim has not been made public.* 受害人的姓名還未公開。| **be public knowledge** (=not secret) 眾所周知 *It's public knowledge that Ann has an alcohol problem.* 眾所周知安有酗酒的毛病。| **in the public eye/view** (=on television, radio etc a lot because you are famous)〔電視、廣播等上〕公眾熟悉的, 公眾常見的 | **public figure** (=famous person) 公眾人物, 名人

5 ▶NOT HIDDEN 非隱祕的◀ intended for anyone to know, see or hear 公開的: *Demands for a public investigation have been ignored.* 進行公開調查的要求沒有被理會。| **public display of grief/affection etc** (=showing your emotions so that everyone can see) 公開表現悲傷/愛慕等

6 ▶PLACE WITH A LOT OF PEOPLE 有很多人的地方◀ a public place usually has a lot of people in it〔地方〕公開的, 公共的: *Don't talk about it here; this place is too public.* 別在這裡談這件事, 這地方人太多。

7 public life work that you do, especially for the government, that makes you well-known to many people 公共事務: *Judge Carson retired from public life in 1944.* 卡森法官於1944年退出公共事務。

8 public image the character or attitudes that a famous person, organization etc is thought by most people to have 公眾形象: *Marilyn tried hard to protect her public image.* 瑪麗琳極力保護她的公眾形象。| *Violence doesn't help the game's public image.* 暴力對這項運動在公眾心目中的形象不利。

9 go public a) to tell everyone about something that was secret 公開, 公布於眾: *We have all the evidence, so now we can go public!* 我們有所有的證據, 所以現在我們可以公之於眾了! **b)** to become a PUBLIC COMPANY〔公司〕公開發售股票, 上市

10 public appearance a visit by a famous person in order to make a speech, advertise something etc〔某名人為演說、作宣傳等〕公開露面

11 public property a) something that is provided for anyone to use, and is usually owned by the government 公共財物: *Two demonstrators were charged with damaging public property.* 兩名示威者被控破壞公共財產。**b)** *informal* something that everyone has a right to know about【非正式】人人有權知道的事物: *When you're a TV star you're public property it seems!* 一旦你成為電視明星, 人人都好像有權知道你的一切!

12 public enemy number one the criminal, problem etc that is considered the most serious threat to people's safety 頭號公敵〔指被認為是對人民安全構成最嚴重威脅的罪犯、問題等〕: *Drugs have become public enemy number one.* 毒品已成為頭號人民公敵。—compare 比較 PRIVATE¹ —**publicly** *adv*: *publicly humiliated* 當眾受辱

public² *n* **1 the public** ordinary people who do not belong to the government or have any special position in society 公眾, 民眾, 大眾: *The castle is open to the public daily.* 這座城堡每天都向公眾開放。| [also+plural verb in *BrE* 英] *The public are not interested in this issue.* 公眾對這個問題不感興趣。| **the general public** *Our special offer is not available to the general public.* 一般公眾不能享受我們的特價。**2 in public** if you do something in public you do it where anyone can see 公開地, 當眾: *Her husband was always nice to her in public.* 她丈夫在公開場合總是對她很好。—opposite 反義詞 **in private** (PRIVATE² (1)), —see also 另見 **wash your dirty linen in public** (WASH¹ (6)) **3** [singular, U] the people who like listening to a particular singer, reading a particular writer etc〔喜歡聽某歌手的歌, 讀某作家作品等的〕大眾: *A star has to try to please her public.* 一個明星必須盡力取悅她的支持者。| [also+plural verb in *BrE* 英] *Today's theatre-going public are very demanding.* 當今喜歡看戲的人們要求很苛刻。

public ac·cess /,·· '··/ *n* [U] the right of ordinary people to go onto particular areas of land or read particular documents 公眾進入某區域[讀某些文獻]的權力: [+to] *public access to information* 公眾獲取信息的權力

public access chan·nel /,·· '·· ,··/ *n* [C] a television CHANNEL provided by CABLE¹ (3) television companies in the US on which anyone can broadcast 公共頻道〔美國有限電視公司提供的每個人都能使用的電視頻道〕

public-ad·dress sys·tem /,··· '·· ,··/ *n* [C] a PA (1) 有線廣播系統; 擴音系統

public af·fairs /,·· ·'·/ *n* [plural] events and questions, especially political ones, which have an effect on most people 公眾事務〔尤指影響大多數人的政治事件和問題〕: *a public affairs programme on TV* 電視上的公眾事務節目

pub·li·can /`pʌblɪkən; 'pʌblɪkən/ *n* [C] *formal, especially BrE* someone who is in charge of a PUB【正式, 尤英】酒館老闆

pub·li·ca·tion /,pʌblɪ`keʃən; ,pʌblɪ'keɪʃən/ *n* **1** [U] the action of making a book available for sale, or the time at which you do this 出版; 出版日期[時間]: *The book is ready for publication.* 這本書已經準備好出版了。**2** [C] a book, magazine etc 出版物, 書刊: *a monthly publication* 月刊 **3** [U] the act of making something known to the public 發表, 公布: *the publication of the election results* 選舉結果的公布

public bar /,·· '·/ *n* [C] *BrE* a room with plain furniture in a PUB, hotel etc where you can buy drinks【英】〔有簡單家具, 可從中買飲料的〕公眾酒吧

public com·pa·ny /,·· '···/ *n* [C] *BrE* a company that offers its SHARES for sale on the STOCK EXCHANGE【英】公開出售股份的公司, 股票上市公司; PUBLIC CORPORATION *AmE*【美】

public con·ve·ni·ence /,·· ·'···/ *n* [C] *BrE* a small building with toilets in it, provided for anyone to use【英】公廁

public cor·po·ra·tion /,·· ··'··/ *n* [C] **1** *AmE* a company that offers its SHARES for sale on the STOCK EXCHANGE【美】公開出售股份的公司, 股票上市公司; PUBLIC COM-

PANY *BrE*【英】**2** *BrE* a business that is run by a government【英】由政府經營的企業

public de·fend·er /ˌ·· ˈ··/ *n* [C] *AmE* a lawyer who is paid by the government to defend people in court, because they cannot pay for themselves【美】公設辯護律師〔由政府出錢為付不起律師費的人們辯護的律師〕—compare 比較 DISTRICT ATTORNEY

public do·main /ˌ·· ·ˈ·/ *n law* **in the public domain** a play, idea etc that is in the public domain is available for anyone to perform or use【法律】〔戲劇、觀點等〕不受版權[專利權]限制的

public ex·pen·di·ture /ˌ·· ·ˈ···/ *n* [U] the money that the government spends on public services 公共開支〔政府花在公共事業上的錢〕

public foot·path /ˌ·· ˈ··/ *n* [C] *BrE* a path that everyone has the right to use【英】公用人行小徑

public fund·ing /ˌ·· ˈ··/ also 又作 **public funds** /ˌ·· ˈ·/ *n* [U] money that the government gives to support organizations or events〔政府用來支持公共組織或活動的〕公共資金

public health /ˌ·· ˈ·/ *n* [U] **1** health care provided by the government, including medical care and public cleaning services〔由政府提供的〕公共衛生保健〔包括醫療保健和公共衛生服務〕**2** the health of all the people in an area 公眾健康: *a danger to public health* 對公眾健康的一個威脅

public hol·i·day /ˌ·· ˈ···/ *n* [C] a special day when people do not go to work and shops do not open 公眾假日

public house /ˌ·· ˈ·/ *n* [C] *BrE formal* a PUB【英, 正式】酒館, 酒吧

public hous·ing /ˌ·· ˈ··/ *n* [U] *AmE* houses or apartments built by the US government for poor people【美】政府為貧民所建的房子[公寓]—compare 比較 COUNCIL HOUSE

public in·quiry /ˌ·· ·ˈ··/ *n* [C] an official attempt to find out the cause of something, especially an accident 公開調查

pub·li·cist /ˈpʌblɪsɪst; ˈpʌbl$\frac{1}{2}$s$\frac{1}{2}$st/ *n* [C] someone whose job is to make sure that people find out about a new product, film, book etc or about what a famous person is doing 廣告員, 宣傳員

S2 W3 **pub·lic·i·ty** /pʌbˈlɪsətɪ; pʌˈblɪs$\frac{1}{2}$ti/ *n* [U] **1** the attention that someone or something gets from newspapers, television etc〔報紙、電視等對某人或某物的〕關注: *The case has received massive publicity.* 這個案子受到媒體的極大關注。| **bad/adverse publicity** (=publicity that makes you look bad) 不利的宣傳 | **publicity stunt** (=something that is only done to get publicity) 吸引公眾注意的花招[噱頭] **2** the business of making sure that people know about a new product, film etc or what a particular famous person is doing 宣傳, 推廣: *Who's going to do the show's publicity?* 誰來做這個節目的宣傳工作? | **publicity campaign** (=a series of activities intended to give something publicity) 宣傳運動

pub·li·cize also 又作 **-ise** *BrE*【英】/ˈpʌblɪˌsaɪz; ˈpʌbl$\frac{1}{2}$saɪz/ *v* [T] to give information about something to the public, so that they know about it 公布; 宣傳, 宣揚: *Schools need to publicize their exam results.* 學校需要公布考試結果。| **well-/widely/highly publicized** (=receiving a lot of attention) 廣受關注 *the well-publicized financial difficulties that Rochford has faced* 羅奇福德所面臨的被傳得沸沸揚揚的財政困難

public lend·ing right /ˌ·· ˈ·· ·/ *n* [C] a system in Britain by which writers are paid if their books are borrowed from public libraries〔英國的作者對公共圖書館出借其著作所享有的〕公共出借報酬權

public li·bra·ry /ˌ·· ˈ···/ *n* [C] a building where people can go to read or borrow books without having to pay 公共圖書館

public lim·it·ed com·pa·ny /ˌ·· ˌ··· ˈ···/ also 又作 **plc** *n* [C] a British company owned by at least two people and whose shares (SHARE[2] (5)) are available to everyone〔英國的〕公共有限公司〔至少為兩人所有、任何人可購其股份的公司〕

public nui·sance /ˌ·· ˈ··/ *n* [C] **1** *law* an action that is harmful to everyone【法律】妨害公眾利益的行為: *He committed a public nuisance by blocking the road.* 他堵塞道路, 妨害了公眾。**2** a person who does things that annoy a lot of people 妨害公眾者, 做事令大家討厭的人

public o·pin·ion /ˌ·· ·ˈ··/ *n* [U] the opinions or beliefs that ordinary people have about a particular subject 輿論, 民意: *The government is bowing to public opinion on this issue.* 在這個問題上, 政府正屈從於公眾的意見。

public own·er·ship /ˌ·· ˈ···/ *n* [U] businesses, property etc in public ownership are owned by the state〔企業、財產等〕國家所有(制), 公有(制): *The steel and coal industries were taken into public ownership.* 鋼鐵和煤炭工業被收歸國有。

public pros·e·cu·tor /ˌ·· ˈ····/ *n* [C] a British lawyer who works for the government, and tries to prove in a court of law that someone has done something illegal 檢察官, 檢控官, 公訴人 —compare 比較 DISTRICT ATTORNEY

public re·la·tions /ˌ·· ·ˈ··/ *n* **1** [U] PR; the work of explaining to the public what an organization does, so that they will understand it and approve of it 公關工作, 公共關係(工作): *a public relations officer in a big oil company* 一家大石油公司的公關人員 **2** [plural] the relationship between an organization and the public 組織[機構]與公眾的關係: *Helping the theatre would be good for public relations.* 幫助劇院會有利於公共關係。

public relations ex·er·cise /ˌ·· ·ˈ·· ˌ···/ *n* [C] something that an organization does just to make itself popular, rather than because it is the right thing to do 公關活動, 宣傳推廣活動: *The conference was largely a public relations exercise.* 這次大會很大程度上是一種公關活動。

public school /ˌ·· ˈ·/ *n* [C] **1** a private British school, paid for by parents, where children usually live as well as study〔英國私立的〕公學, 私立寄宿學校 **2** a free local school, especially in the US and Scotland, controlled and paid for by the government〔尤指美國和蘇格蘭免費的〕公立學校 —compare 比較 PRIVATE SCHOOL

public sec·tor /ˌ·· ˈ··/ *n* [singular] the industries and services in a country that are owned and run by the government 公營部門, 國營部門: *a job in the public sector* 公營部門的工作 | *public sector employees* 國營部門雇員 —compare 比較 PRIVATE SECTOR

public serv·ant /ˌ·· ˈ··/ *n* [C] someone who works for the government, especially someone who is elected 公務員

public serv·ice /ˌ·· ˈ··/ *n* **1** [C usually plural 一般用複數] a service or product that a government provides, such as electricity, TRANSPORT, etc 公用事業〈如供電、交通等〉: *What the people want is decent, local public services.* 人們需要的是良好的本地公共服務。**2** [C] a service provided to people because it will help them, and not for profit 公益服務: *This directory is provided as a public service to the community.* 這本名錄簿是作為公益服務提供給公眾的。**3** [singular,U] the government or its departments 政府; 政府部門: *a career in public service* 政府部門的職業

public service an·nounce·ment /ˌ·· ˈ·· ·ˌ·/ *n* [C] *especially AmE* a special message on television or radio, giving information about an important subject【尤美】〔電視或收音機上〕有關重要事情的通告

public speak·ing /ˌ·· ˈ··/ *n* [U] the activity of making speeches in public 公開演說: *a clear voice, used to public speaking* 慣於公開演說的清晰嗓音

public spend·ing /ˌ·· ˈ··/ *n* [U] the money that the government spends on public services〔政府花在公用事業上的〕公共開支: *We must cut public spending or impose higher taxes.* 我們必須削減公共開支或徵收更高的稅。

public-spir·it·ed /ˌ·· ˈ···◂/ *adj* willing to do what is helpful for everyone in society 熱心公益的: *decent, public-spirited people* 正派而熱心公益的人們

public tel·e·vi·sion /ˌ·· ˈ····/ *n* [U] a television service in the US which is paid for by the government, by large companies, and by the public〔美國由政府、大型公司和公眾出資的〕公眾電視

public trans·port /ˌ·· ˈ··/ *BrE*【英】, **public trans·por·ta·tion** /ˌ·· ··ˈ··/ *AmE*【美】*n* [U] bus services, train services etc, provided for everyone to use 公共交通

public works /ˌ·· ˈ·/ *n* [plural] buildings, roads, PORTS etc provided and built by the government 公共工程, 公共建設〈如公共建築物、公路、港口等〉

3 1 **pub·lish** /ˈpʌblɪʃ; ˈpʌblɪʃ/ *v* **1** [I,T] to arrange the writing, production and sale of a book, magazine etc 出版, 發行〔書刊等〕: *Her second novel was published in July.* 她的第二部小說於七月份出版了。| *We publish education books.* 我們出版教育書籍。**2** [T] if a book, magazine etc publishes a letter, article etc, it prints it for people to read〔書、雜誌等〕刊登; 登載; 發表: *We can't publish all the letters we receive.* 我們無法刊登收到的全部信件。**3** [T usually passive 一般用被動態] to make official information such as a report available for everyone to read 公布; 公開; 宣布: *The latest unemployment figures will be published tomorrow.* 最新的失業數字將於明天公布。**4** [I,T] if a writer or musician publishes their work, they arrange for it to be printed and sold〔作家或音樂家等〕發表〔自己的作品〕

3 **pub·lish·er** /ˈpʌblɪʃɚ; ˈpʌblɪʃə/ *n* [C] a person or company whose business is to arrange the writing, production and sale of books, newspapers etc〔書、報紙等的〕出版者; 出版商; 發行者; 出版社

pub·lish·ing /ˈpʌblɪʃɪŋ; ˈpʌblɪʃɪŋ/ *n* [U] the business of producing books and magazines 出版業: *Tony wants to get a job in publishing.* 托尼想在出版業找一份工作。| *a new publishing house* 一家新出版社 —see also 另見 **desktop publishing** (DESKTOP (2))

puce /pjus; pjuːs/ *adj* dark brownish purple 紫褐色的 —**puce** *n*

puck /pʌk; pʌk/ *n* [C] a hard flat circular piece of rubber that you hit with the stick in the game of ICE HOCKEY 冰球〔冰球運動中當球用的橡皮圓盤〕

puck·er /ˈpʌkɚ; ˈpʌkə/ also 又作 **pucker up** *v* [I,T] **1** if your mouth puckers or if you pucker it, the lips are pulled tightly together 撅起〔嘴〕: *Her mouth puckered up and she started to cry.* 她撅起嘴哭了起來。**2** [I] if cloth puckers, it gets lines or folds in it and is no longer flat〔布料〕起皺 —**pucker** *n* [C] —**puckered** *adj*

puck·ish /ˈpʌkɪʃ; ˈpʌkɪʃ/ *adj literary* showing that you are amused by other people, and like to make jokes about them【文】淘氣的, 頑皮的: *a puckish grin* 調皮的一笑 —**puckishly** *adv*

pud /pʊd; pʊd/ *n* [C,U] *BrE informal* a PUDDING【英, 非正式】布丁

3 **pud·ding** /ˈpʊdɪŋ; ˈpʊdɪŋ/ *n* **1** [C,U] a hot sweet dish, made from cake, rice, bread etc with fruit, milk or other sweet things added 布丁〔由蛋糕、大米、麵包等加水果、牛奶或其他甜味東西製成的熱甜食〕: *another helping of rice pudding* 再來一份大米布丁 | *bread and butter pudding* 麵包黃油布丁 **2** [C,U] a thick sweet creamy dish, usually made with milk, eggs, sugar, and a little flour, and served cold 布丁〔通常用牛奶、蛋、糖和少許麵粉製成的黏稠冷甜食〕: *chocolate pudding* 巧克力布丁 **3** [C,U] *BrE* any sweet dish served at the end of a meal【英】〔餐末食用的〕甜食; 甜點心: *There's ice-cream for pudding.* 有冰淇淋作為甜點。—see also 另見 DESSERT **4** [C,U] *BrE* a boiled dish that is not sweet, made of a mixture of flour, fat etc, with meat or vegetables inside【英】〔用油和麵粉混和、內包有肉餡或蔬菜餡的〕不加糖布丁: *steak and kidney pudding* 牛排加腰子布丁 **5** [C] *BrE informal* someone who is fat and stupid【英, 非正式】肥胖而蠢笨的人 —see also 另見 BLACK PUDDING, CHRISTMAS PUDDING, MILK PUDDING, PLUM PUDDING, YORKSHIRE PUDDING, **the proof of the pudding is in the eating** (PROOF[1] (5))

pudding ba·sin /ˈ·· ˌ··/ *n* [C] *BrE*【英】**1** a deep round dish in which puddings are cooked〔烹製布丁的圓而深的〕布丁盤 **2** a way of cutting someone's hair so that it is in the shape of an upside down bowl 碗狀髮型〔一種像倒置的碗狀的髮型〕

pud·dle /ˈpʌdl̩; ˈpʌdl/ *n* [C] a small pool of water, especially rainwater, on a path, road etc〔小徑、道路等上的〕水坑〔尤指雨水坑〕: *Children splashed through the puddles.* 孩子們濺潑着水走過一個個小水坑。

pu·den·dum /pjuˈdɛndəm; pjuːˈdendəm/ *n plural* **pudenda** /-də; -də/ [C] *old-fashioned* the sexual organs, especially of a woman【過時】〔尤指女性的〕陰部

pudg·y /ˈpʌdʒɪ; ˈpʌdʒi/ *adj* rather fat 肥胖的: *pudgy fingers* 胖嘟嘟的手指 —**pudginess** *n* [U]

pueb·lo /ˈpwɛblo; ˈpwebləʊ/ *n* [C] *Spanish* a small town, especially in the south west US【西班牙】〔尤指美國西南部的〕小城鎮

pu·er·ile /ˈpjuəˌrɪl; ˈpjʊəraɪl/ *adj formal* puerile jokes, remarks etc are silly and stupid; CHILDISH【正式】〔笑話、話等〕愚蠢的; 幼稚的: *He's got such a puerile sense of humour.* 他有如此幼稚的幽默感。—**puerility** /ˌpjuəˈrɪlətɪ; pjʊəˈrɪlə̥ti/ *n* [U]

pu·er·per·al /pjuˈɝpərəl; pjuːˈɜːpərəl/ *adj technical* happening while giving birth to a child or in the period after this【術語】分娩的; 產後的: *puerperal depression* 產後抑鬱症

puff¹ /pʌf; pʌf/ *v* **1** [I] to breathe quickly and with difficulty after running, carrying something heavy etc 喘粗氣: *Catherine was puffing loudly as she carried the box into the room.* 凱瑟琳喘着粗氣把那個箱子搬進房間。| [+up/along etc] *Duncan passed me, puffing up the hill.* 鄧肯從我旁邊經過, 氣喘吁吁地往那座小山上爬。—see also 另見 **huff and puff** (HUFF[1] (1)) **2** [I,T] to breathe in and out while smoking a cigarette, pipe etc〔抽煙等時〕吸[噴]〔煙〕: **puff at/on sth** *Dr Foulger paused to puff on his pipe before answering.* 福爾傑博士回答之前停下來抽了口煙斗。**3 a)** [T always+adv/prep] to blow smoke or steam out of something 使〔煙、氣〕噴出: *Don't puff smoke into my face.* 別把煙朝我臉上噴。**b)** [I] if smoke or steam puffs from somewhere, it comes out in little clouds〔煙或氣〕一陣陣噴出, 冒出: *Steam puffed out of the chimney.* 蒸汽從煙囪裡一股一股地噴出來。**4** [I always+adv/prep] if a steam train puffs along, it moves while sending out little clouds of steam〔蒸汽火車〕噴着氣前進: *By now we were puffing along at a good speed.* 至此, 我們的火車噴着一股股的煙, 正快速前進。

puff sth ↔ **out** *phr v* [T] **puff out your cheeks/chest** to make your cheeks etc bigger by filling them with air 鼓起雙頰/挺起胸膛: *George puffed out his chest proudly* 喬治驕傲地挺起胸膛。

puff up *phr v* **1** [I,T **puff** sth ↔ **up**] to become bigger by increasing the amount of air inside, or to make something bigger in this way〔使〕膨脹, 〔使〕鼓起: *Bake for 25-30 minutes until the souffle puffs up about 5cm.* 烘烤25-30分鐘直到蛋奶酥脹起五厘米。| *Birds puff up their feathers to keep warm.* 鳥膨起羽毛以保暖。**2** [I] if your eye, face etc puffs up, it swells painfully because of injury or infection〔眼睛、臉等〕腫脹: *My eye had puffed up because of a mosquito bite.* 我的一隻眼睛由於蚊子咬而腫了起來。**3** [T **puff** sb **up**] to make someone feel very pleased or proud 使〔某人〕感到高興[自豪]

puff² *n* [C] **1** the action of taking the smoke from a cigarette etc into your lungs 吸, 抽〔煙〕: [+at] *a puff at a cigarette* 吸一口香煙 | **have/take a puff** *"May I have just one puff?" "Sure, I thought you didn't smoke."* "我能就抽一口嗎?" "當然可以, 我以為你不抽煙呢。" **2** a sudden small movement of wind, air, or smoke〔風、空氣、煙霧的〕一陣, 一團, 一股: [+of] *puffs of smoke coming from the chimney* 從煙囪裡冒出的一股股的煙 | *The water was calm and there wasn't even a puff of wind.* 水

面平靜, 連一絲風也沒有。—see picture on page A7 參見A7頁圖 **3 cheese/cream/lemon puff** a piece of light PASTRY (2) with a soft mixture inside 乾酪/奶油/檸檬鬆餅 **4 get your puff back** *BrE informal* to be able to breathe normally again after doing something that made you breathe very hard【英, 非正式】喘過氣來 **5 out of puff** *BrE informal* breathing hard and very tired【英, 非正式】喘不過氣來: *He only has to climb the stairs and he's out of puff!* 他只要爬爬樓梯就累得喘不過氣來了!

puff·ball /ˋpʌfbɔl; ˈpʌfbɔːl/ *n* [C] a type of round FUNGUS that bursts to release its seeds 馬勃菌

puffed /pʌft; pʌft/ *adj* [not before noun 不用於名詞前] *BrE informal* breathing quickly because you have been using lots of energy【英, 非正式】氣喘吁吁的

puffed sleeve /ˌ· ˈ·/ *n* [C] a short sleeve that is wider in the middle than at each end 泡泡袖

puffed up /ˌ· ˈ·◂/ *adj* behaving in a way that shows you are too proud 得意洋洋的: *All these pompous, puffed up television pundits make me sick.* 所有這些傲慢自負的電視評論家使我感到厭惡。

puffed wheat /ˌ· ˈ·/ *n* [U] grains of wheat that have been cooked to make them very light and are eaten with milk〔與牛奶一起食用的〕膨化小麥

puf·fin /ˋpʌfɪn; ˈpʌfɪn/ *n* [C] a North Atlantic seabird with a black and white body and a large brightly coloured beak 海鸚〔一種北大西洋海鳥, 有黑白相間的身體和大而色彩鮮豔的喙〕

puff pas·try /ˌ· ˈ··/ *n* [U] a kind of very light PASTRY with a lot of air in it〔中間有很多空氣〕非常鬆軟的油酥點心

puff·y /ˋpʌfɪ; ˈpʌfi/ *adj* **puffier, puffiest** puffy eyes, faces, or cheeks are swollen〔眼睛、臉或臉頰〕腫的, 鼓起的 —**puffiness** *n* [U]

pug /pʌg; pʌg/ *n* [C] a small fat short-haired dog with a wide flat face and a short flat nose 哈巴狗

pu·gi·lis·m /ˋpjudʒəˌlɪzəm; ˈpjuːdʒəlɪzəm/ *n* [U] *formal* the sport of BOXING (=fighting with your hands)【正式】拳擊

pu·gi·list /ˋpjudʒəlɪst; ˈpjuːdʒəlɪst/ *n* [C] *formal* a BOXER (=a sportsman who fights with his hands)【正式】拳擊手, 拳師

pug·na·cious /pʌgˋneʃəs; pʌgˈneɪʃəs/ *adj formal* very eager to quarrel or fight with people【正式】愛爭吵的, 愛爭鬥的, 好鬥的 —**pugnaciously** *adv* —**pugnacity** /pʌgˋnæsətɪ; pʌgˈnæsəti/ *n* [U]

puke¹ /pjuk; pjuːk/ also 又作 **puke up** *v* [I,T] *informal*【非正式】**1** to bring food back up from your stomach through your mouth; VOMIT 嘔吐 **2 it makes me puke!** *informal* used to say that something makes you very angry or annoyed【非正式】真讓我噁心!: *It makes me puke when I hear rich people complaining about taxes!* 我聽到富人抱怨納稅時, 就感到噁心!

puke² *n* [U] *informal* food brought back up from your stomach through your mouth; VOMIT²【非正式】嘔吐物

puk·ey, puky /ˋpjukɪ; ˈpjuːki/ *adj slang* very unpleasant or unattractive【俚】令人不舒服的, 令人不愉快的, 令人討厭的

puk·ka also 又作 **pukha** /ˋpʌkə; ˈpʌkə/ *adj especially IndE, PakE*【尤印, 巴】**1** very good 很好的, 上等的 **2** real, or properly made 真正的; 品質優良的: *It can't compete with pukka racing cars.* 它比不過真正的賽車。**3** *humorous* too formal【幽默】太正式的

pul·chri·tude /ˋpʌlkrɪˌtjud; ˈpʌlkrətjuːd/ *n* [U] *formal* beauty, especially of a woman【正式】美麗〔尤指女性〕

S1 W1 **pull¹** /pul; pʊl/ *v*

1 ►MOVE STH TOWARDS YOU 把某物拉過來◄ [I,T] to use your hands to make something move towards you or in the direction that you are moving〔用手〕把〔某物〕拉過來; 拉: *Help me move the piano; you push and I'll pull.* 幫我搬動一下鋼琴, 你來推, 我來拉。| **pull sth** *I pulled the handle and it just snapped off!* 我拉了一下那把手, 它就啪一聲斷掉了。| **pull sth into/away from/over etc** *Pull the chair nearer to the fire.* 把那張椅子拉到火旁。| **pull sth open/shut** *Ally tried to pull the drawer open.* 阿莉試圖拉開抽屜。| **pull hard** *They pulled hard on the rope.* 他們用力拉那繩子。—see picture on page A3 參見A3頁圖

2 ►PUT ON/TAKE OFF 穿上/脫下◄ [T always+adv/prep] to put on or take off clothing, usually quickly〔常指迅速地〕穿上[脫下]〔衣服〕: *Ted pulled his socks on.* 特德穿上襪子。| *pulling off her hat and coat* 脫下她的帽子和外套

3 ►MOVE YOUR BODY 移動身體◄ [T always+adv/prep] **a)** to move your arm or your whole body away from someone or something that is holding it or touching it 掙脫, 移開, 抽出: **pull sth away/off/out of etc** *She pulled her arm out of his grasp.* 她抽出被他握着的胳膊。**b)** to hold onto something and use force to move your body〔抓住某物〕用力移動〔身體〕: **pull yourself up/through etc** *Harry pulled himself up onto the wall.* 哈里扒住牆爬了上去。

4 ►CARRIAGE/TRAIN 馬車/火車◄ [T usually passive 一般用被動態] if horses or a railway ENGINE pull a carriage etc, they make it move along behind them〔馬〕拉〔馬車〕;〔火車發動機〕牽引

5 ►USE A CONTROL 用控制裝置◄ [T] to move a control such as a SWITCH² (1) or TRIGGER towards you to make a piece of equipment work 拉〔開關〕; 扣〔扳機〕: *She raised the gun, and pulled the trigger.* 她舉起槍扣動扳機。

6 ►REMOVE 去掉◄ [T always+adv/prep] to use force to take something out of the place where it is fixed or held 拔: **pull sth out/up/away** *Gemma pulled the cork from the bottle.* 吉瑪拔出瓶塞。

7 ►SMOKE 煙◄ [T always+adv/prep] to take smoke from a cigarette, pipe etc into your lungs 吸[抽]〔煙、煙斗等〕: **pull on/at sth** *Todd sat thinking, pulling on his pipe.* 托德一邊抽着煙斗, 一邊坐着思考。

8 ►MUSCLE 肌肉◄ [T] to injure one of your muscles by stretching it too much during physical activity; STRAIN² (4) 拉傷, 扭傷〔肌肉〕: *Paul pulled a muscle trying to lift the freezer.* 保羅想把冰箱抬起來, 結果拉傷了肌肉。

9 ►CROWD/VOTES ETC 人羣/選票等◄ [T] if an event, performer etc pulls crowds or a politician pulls a lot of votes, a lot of people come to see them or vote for them 吸引〔觀眾〕, 獲得〔選票〕: *The big match pulled an enormous crowd.* 這場大賽吸引了大量觀眾。| *She's unlikely to pull many votes.* 她不大可能獲得很多選票。| **pull the punters** *informal* (=attract customers)【非正式】吸引顧客

10 ►SEXUALLY ATTRACT 勾引◄ [I,T] *BrE spoken* to attract someone in order to have sex with them【英口】勾引: *Ken's hoping to pull the girls with his flashy new car.* 肯希望用他俗麗的新車勾引那些女孩子。

11 ►GUN/KNIFE 槍/刀◄ [T] to take out a gun or knife ready to use it 掏出, 拔出〔槍、刀等〕: **pull sth on sb** *He suddenly pulled a gun on me.* 他突然拔出槍對準我。

12 ►BEER 啤酒◄ [T] *especially BrE* to get beer out of a BARREL by pulling a handle【尤英】拉酒桶把手放出〔啤酒〕: *to pull a pint* 從酒桶裡放出一品脫啤酒

13 ►CAR 汽車◄ [I] if a car pulls to the left or right as you are driving, it moves in that direction because of a mechanical problem〔汽車由於機械故障而〕側斜: *The car seems to be pulling to the left.* 那輛車好像在向左打斜。

14 pull sb's leg to tell someone something that is not true, as a joke 開某人的玩笑, 耍弄某人, 誆騙某人

15 pull the other one (it's got bells on) *spoken* used to tell someone that you think they are joking or not telling the truth【口】別逗了: *A racing driver? Pull the other one!* 賽車手? 別逗了!

16 pull a fast one *spoken* to deceive someone【口】欺騙[蒙騙]某人: *He was trying to pull a fast one when he told you he'd paid.* 他告訴你他已付過款時, 其實他在試圖欺騙你。

17 ►SUCCEED 成功◄ [T] *slang, especially AmE* to do something illegal or dishonest such as a crime or trick【俚，尤美】做〔壞事〕，犯罪: *The gang have pulled another bank robbery.* 那夥匪徒又搶劫了一家銀行。| *What are you trying to pull?* 你們想幹甚麼勾當?

18 pull the curtains/the blind to open or close curtains or a BLIND 拉開[拉上]窗簾/百葉窗: *Could you just pull the blind, please?* 請你把百葉窗拉開，好嗎?

19 ►HORSE 馬◄ [I] if a horse pulls it struggles and presses hard against the piece of metal in its mouth〔馬〕咬嚼子〔不聽指揮〕

20 pull sb's licence *informal* to take away someone's DRIVING LICENCE because they have done something wrong【非正式】吊銷某人的駕駛執照

21 pull a punch to deliberately hit someone with less force than you could do, so that it hurts less 故意不使出全力打某人〔以避免傷害〕—see also 另見 **not pull any punches** (PUNCH[2] (7))

22 ►CRICKET/GOLF 板球/高爾夫球◄ [I,T] *technical* to hit the ball in CRICKET or GOLF so that it does not go straight but moves to one side【術語】把〔板球、高爾夫球〕擊向左側[右側]

23 ►ROW A BOAT 划船◄ [I,T] to make a boat move by using OARS 划（船）—see also 另見 PUSH[1] —see also 另見 **make/pull a face** (FACE[1] (2)), **pull your finger out** (FINGER[1] (7)), **pull rank (on)** (RANK[1] (5)), **pull the rug (out) from under sb's feet** (RUG (3)), **pull your socks up** (SOCK[1] (3)), **pull strings** (STRING[1] (7)), **pull your weight** (WEIGHT[1] (13)), **pull the wool over sb's eyes** (WOOL (4))

pull ahead *phr v* [I] if one vehicle pulls ahead of another it gets in front of it by moving faster〔車輛〕加快速度趕到〔...的〕前面; 加速超越〔車〕

pull sb/sth **apart** *phr v* [T] **1** to separate people or animals when they are fighting 拉開〔打架的人或爭鬥的動物〕，分開 **2** to make someone feel very unhappy 使〔某人〕感到很不開心: *The constant rows were pulling her apart.* 沒完沒了的爭吵使她很不開心。

pull at sth *phr v* [T] **1** to take a hold of something and pull it several times 抓住並不斷拉扯: *The child pulled at his mother's coat.* 那孩子不斷拉扯他母親的外套。**2** to take smoke from a pipe or cigarette into your lungs 吸〔煙或煙斗〕: *He pulled at his pipe a couple of times.* 他抽了幾口煙斗。**3** *old-fashioned* to take a long drink from a bottle or glass【過時】從〔瓶子或玻璃杯〕中大口地喝

pull away *phr v* [I] **1 a)** to start to drive away from a place where you had stopped 開始駛離，開走: *Matt jumped onto the bus just as it was pulling away.* 公共汽車正要開走時，馬特跳了上去。**b)** to drive or run more quickly than another vehicle or person and leave them behind you 超越〔另一車輛或人〕，把...拋在後面: **pull away from sth/sb** *Nkoku is pulling away from the other runners.* 尼可庫把其他選手拋在後面。**2** to move backwards quickly when someone is trying to touch you or hold you 迅速後退避開〔觸摸等〕: *I tried to kiss her but she pulled away.* 我想吻她，但她避開了。

pull down *phr v* [T] **1 [pull** sth ↔ **down]** to destroy a building that is no longer used 拆毀，拆掉〔建築物〕: *The old chapel is dangerous and will have to be pulled down.* 那座舊的小教堂很危險，所以將不得不被拆除。**2 pull down a menu** to make a computer PROGRAM show you a list of the things it can do 拉下菜單〔使電腦程序顯示它可以做的事情〕**3 [pull** sb **down]** *AmE* to make someone less healthy or successful【美】使〔某人〕虛弱，使〔某人〕受挫: *Her problems over the last few months have really pulled her down.* 她幾個月以來的問題確實使她身體很虛弱。

pull in *phr v* **1** [I] if a train pulls in, it arrives at a station〔火車〕到站，進站 **2** [I] if a car or a driver pulls in they move to the side of the road and stop〔汽車或司機〕駛向路邊停下: *She pulled in to let the ambulance pass.* 她把車開到路邊停下讓救護車過去。—compare 比較 **pull over** (PULL[1]), —see also 另見 PULL-IN **3** [T **pull** sb ↔ **in]** if a police officer pulls someone in, they take them to a police station because they think they may have done something wrong〔警察〕把〔嫌疑犯〕帶回警察局，逮捕 **4** [T **pull** sth ↔ **in]** *informal* if you pull in a lot of money you earn it【非正式】掙〔錢〕，賺〔錢〕**5** [T **pull** sb/sth **in]** if an event, a show etc pulls in a lot of people they go to see it〔事件、演出等〕吸引〔觀眾〕: *'Les Miserables' has been pulling in huge crowds in New York.*《悲慘世界》一直吸引着紐約大批的觀眾。

pull off *phr v* [T] *informal*【非正式】**1** to succeed in doing something difficult 成功〔做困難的事〕: **pull sth ↔ off** *They gave you the money! How did you pull that off?* 他們給了你錢！你是如何得到的? **2** if a car pulls off a road it turns into a smaller road or entrance〔汽車〕駛離大路進入小路[入口]: **pull off sth** *We pulled off the road to get some food.* 我們駛離大路去找點食物。

pull out *phr v* **1** [I] if a train pulls out it leaves a station〔火車〕駛出車站，離站 —compare 比較 **pull away** (PULL[1]) **2** [I] **a)** to drive onto a road from another road, or after you have stopped at the side〔從另一條路或從路邊停靠的地方〕開到路上: *Don't pull out! There's something coming.* 別開出來！有車過來。**b)** to drive over to a different part of the road, especially where the traffic is moving faster, in order to OVERTAKE (1) 開出以超車: *That truck pulled straight out in front of me.* 那輛卡車直直地超車到我前面。—see picture on page A3 參見A3頁圖 **3** [I,T **pull** sb/sth ↔ **out]** to get out of a bad situation or dangerous place, or order someone else to do so（使）擺脱〔不好的局面〕，（使）撤離〔危險的地方〕: *Jim saw that the firm was going to be ruined, so he pulled out.* 吉姆看到公司即將垮台，於是就退了出來。| *Most of the troops have been pulled out.* 大部分軍隊已經撤離。—see also 另見 **pull out all the stops** (STOP[2] (6))

pull over *phr v* [I,T **pull** sth/sb **over]** to stop the vehicle you are driving at the side of the road, or order someone else to do so（使）〔車輛〕停靠在路邊: *The policeman signalled to him to pull over.* 警察示意他把車停靠在路邊。

pull through also 又作 **pull round** *phr v* [I,T **pull** sb **through]** **1** to stay alive after you have been very ill or badly injured, or help someone do this〔從重病或重傷中〕恢復健康; 幫助某人康復: *His injuries are severe but he's expected to pull through.* 他的傷勢很重，但有望康復。—compare 比較 **bring through** (BRING) **2** to succeed even though you have had a lot of difficulties, or help someone do this（幫助）克服困難，渡過難關: *Margaret had real problems, but the teacher pulled her through.* 瑪格麗特確實遇到了困難，但老師幫她渡過了難關。

pull together *phr v* **1** [I] if a group of people pull together, they all work hard to achieve something〔一羣人〕同心協力，通力合作: *If we all pull together, we'll finish on time.* 如果我們同心協力去做，就能按時完成。**2 pull yourself together** to force yourself to stop behaving in a nervous, frightened, or disorganized way 控制自己的感情: *Stop behaving like a baby! Pull yourself together.* 別像個孩子似的！要控制住自己的感情。**3** [T **pull** sth **together]** to improve something by organizing it more effectively 整頓，把...重新組織好: *We need an experienced manager to pull the department together.* 我們需要一位有經驗的經理來整頓這個部門。

pull up *phr v* **1** [I] to stop the vehicle that you are driving〔使車〕停住[停下]: *Don pulled up at the red light and we stopped behind him.* 唐在紅燈處停下車，而我們停在他後面。—see picture on page A3 參見A3頁圖 **2 pull up a chair/stool etc** to get a chair and sit down next to someone who is already sitting 拿把椅子/櫈子等〔坐在某人旁邊〕**3** [T **pull** sb **up]** to stop someone who is doing something wrong and tell them you do not approve 制止〔正在做錯事的人〕，責備，斥責: [+on] *I felt*

I had to pull her up on her lateness. 我覺得我必須制止她遲到。**4 pull sb up short/pull sb up with a jerk** if something pulls you up short it makes you stop and think about whether you are doing the right thing 使某人停下來思考〔自己是否做得對〕: *Jan's unexpected criticism pulled me up short.* 簡那出乎意料的批評使我停下來考慮自已是否做得對。

pull² *n*

1 ▶ACT OF PULLING 拉的動作◀ [C] an act of using force to move something towards you or in the same direction that you are moving 拉, 拔, 拖: *Give the rope a good pull.* 使勁拉一下繩子。—compare 比較 TUG[1]

2 ▶FORCE 力◀ [C usually singular 一般用單數] a strong force such as GRAVITY, that makes things move in a particular direction 拉力, 引力: *gravitational pull of the moon* 月球的引力

3 ▶EMOTIONAL 感情的◀ [C usually singular 一般用單數] a strong feeling that you want to go to a particular place or person〔想去某處或去見某人的〕強烈感情, 吸引(力): *The old sailor still felt the pull of the sea.* 老水手仍感到海上生活的吸引力。

4 ▶CLIMB 攀登◀ [singular] *BrE old-fashioned* a difficult climb up a steep road【英, 過時】費力攀登: *It was a long pull up that hill.* 登山的路又長又陡。

5 ▶INFLUENCE 影響◀ [singular, U] *informal* special influence that gives you an unfair advantage【非正式】〔特殊的〕影響力;〔不公正的〕照顧, 優待: *His family's name gives him a lot of pull in this town.* 他家族的名望使他在鎮上受到很多優待。

6 ▶SMOKE 煙◀ [C] an act of taking the smoke from a cigarette, pipe etc into your lungs 抽一口煙: *She took a long pull on her cigarette.* 她抽了一大口煙。

7 ▶DRINK 飲料◀ [C] an act of taking a long drink of something 喝一大口: *Brett took a good pull at his beer.* 布雷特喝了一大口啤酒。

8 ▶HANDLE 把手◀ [C] a rope or handle that you use to pull something〔用以拉動某物的〕拉繩; 把手: *a bell-pull* 拉鈴索

9 ▶CRICKET/GOLF 板球/高爾夫球◀ [C] a way of hitting the ball in CRICKET (2) or GOLF so that it does not go straight, but moves to one side 向左側[右側]的一擊

pul·let /ˈpulɪt; ˈpʊlɪ̵t/ *n* [C] a young chicken during its first year of laying eggs〔第一年下蛋的〕小母雞

pul·ley /ˈpulɪ; ˈpʊli/ *n* [C] a piece of equipment consisting of a wheel over which a rope or chain is pulled to lift heavy things〔用來提起重物的〕滑車, 滑輪

pull-in /ˈ· ·/ *n* [C] *BrE informal* a place by the side of a road where vehicles can stop and drivers can buy food and drinks【英, 非正式】〔供司機停車休息並供應飲食的〕路旁停車處

Pull·man /ˈpulmən; ˈpʊlmən/ *n* [C] a very comfortable train carriage, especially one that you can sleep in, or a train made up of these carriages〔設備特別舒適的〕普爾曼式火車車廂,〔尤指〕臥車車廂; 普爾曼式臥鋪列車

pull-on /ˈ· ·/ *adj* [only before noun 僅用於名詞前] a pull-on shirt, dress etc does not have any buttons, so you pull it on over your head〔無扣的襯衫、裙子等〕套穿的, 套頭的

pull-out /ˈ· ·/ *n* [C] **1** part of a book or magazine that can be removed and is like a separate small book〔書刊中可單獨取出的〕插頁, 活頁: *a 16-page pull-out on cake decorating* 有關蛋糕裝飾的16頁插頁 **2** the act of an army, business, etc leaving a particular place or area of activity〔軍隊、公司等的〕撤離, 撤出: *The pull-out of troops will begin after the treaty is signed.* 和約簽訂後軍隊即開始撤離。

pull·o·ver /ˈpulˌovɚ; ˈpʊlˌəʊvə/ *n* [C] a piece of WOOLLEN clothing without buttons that you wear on the top half of your body 套頭毛衣; SWEATER, JUMPER (1) *BrE*【英】

pull-up /ˈ· ·/ *n* [C] *AmE* an exercise in which you use your arms to pull yourself up towards a bar above your head【美】拉單槓(運動), 引體向上

pul·mo·na·ry /ˈpʌlməˌnɛrɪ; ˈpʊlmənəri/ *adj technical* connected with the lungs or having an effect on the lungs【術語】肺的; 對肺有影響的

pulp¹ /pʌlp; pʌlp/ *n* [U] **1** a very soft substance that is almost liquid 漿狀物: **boil/cook sth to a pulp** *First, boil the vegetables to a pulp.* 首先, 把蔬菜煮成糊狀。**2** the soft inside part of a fruit or vegetable 果肉; 菜心: *Halve the melon and scoop out the seeds and pulp.* 把瓜切成兩半, 挖出裡面的籽和瓤。**3** wood or other substances from plants that are used for making paper 紙漿 **4** books, magazines, films etc that are of poor quality or are badly written 劣質書刊, 低級書刊, 庸俗電影 **5 beat sb to a pulp** *informal* to hit someone until they are seriously injured【非正式】狠揍[痛打]某人 **6** part of the inside of a tooth 牙髓 —**pulpy** *adj*

pulp² *adj* [only before noun 僅用於名詞前] pulp magazines, stories etc are of poor quality and are often about sex and violence〔雜誌、故事等〕紙張和內容很差的; 庸俗的, 低級趣味的: *pulp novels* 色情、暴力小説 | *pulp fiction* 庸俗的小説

pulp³ *v* [T] **1** to beat or crush something until it becomes so soft that it is almost liquid 把…搗成[壓成]漿狀: *pulped apples* 製成漿狀的蘋果 **2** to make books or newspapers into paper 把〔書或報紙〕化成紙漿

pul·pit /ˈpulpɪt; ˈpʊlpɪt/ *n* [C] a raised, box-like structure at the front of a church, from which the priest speaks〔教堂中的〕講壇, 佈道壇

pulp·wood /ˈpʌlpwud; ˈpʌlpwʊd/ *n* [U] crushed wood that is used to make paper〔造紙用的〕木漿

pul·sar /ˈpʌlsɑr; ˈpʌlsɑː/ *n* [C] an object that is far away in space and like a star, that produces a regular radio signal 脈衝星〔發出週期性電波的星球〕

pul·sate /ˈpʌlset; pʌlˈseɪt/ *v* [I] **1** to make sounds or movements that are strong and regular like a heart beating 有規律地振動, 脈動: *The thumping, pulsating music shook the kitchen walls.* 砰砰的音樂聲振動着廚房的牆壁。**2** *literary* to be strongly affected by a powerful emotion or feeling【文】受震動; 激動: **[+with]** *The whole city seemed to be pulsating with excitement.* 整個城市好像都激動不已。

pul·sa·tion /pʌlˈseʃən; pʌlˈseɪʃən/ *n* **1** [C] *especially technical* a beat of the heart or any regular beat that can be measured【尤術語】〔心臟或其他有規律能測量的〕搏動; 跳動; 脈動 **2** [U] pulsating movement 有節奏的跳動, 搏動

pulse¹ /pʌls; pʌls/ *n* **1** [C usually singular 一般用單數] **a)** the regular beat that can be felt, for example at your wrist, as your heart pumps blood around your body 脈搏: *I checked his pulse – he was still alive.* 我檢查了他的脈搏——他還活着。**b)** also 又作 **pulse rate** the number of these beats per minute 脈率〔每分鐘的心跳數〕: **take/feel sb's pulse** (=to count how many times someone's heart beats in a minute, usually by feeling their wrist) 量某人的脈搏, 給某人把[診]脈 *The nurse took my pulse – it was faster than normal.* 護士給我量了脈搏——我的脈搏比正常的跳得快。| **your pulse quickens/races** (=it gets faster because you are excited, nervous etc) 脈搏加快 **2** [C] an amount of sound, light, or electricity that continues for a very short time〔聲波、光波、電流等的〕脈衝: *emitting pulses of sound at around 200 cycles per second* 發出每秒鐘大約200周波的聲波脈衝 **3 pulses** [plural] seeds such as beans, PEAS, and LENTILS that can be eaten 豆類植物的種子,〔豌豆、扁豆等可食用的〕豆子 **4** [C,U] a strong regular beat as in music, or on a drum〔音樂、鼓等的〕拍子; 節奏, 律動 —see also 另見 **have/keep your finger on the pulse** (FINGER[1] (12))

pulse² *v* [I] **1** to move or flow with a steady rapid beat or sound 以穩定、迅速的節拍[聲音]移動[流動]; 搏動; 跳動: *the blood pulsing through his veins* 在他的血管中奔湧的血液 | *coloured lights pulsing in time with the music* 隨着音樂閃動的彩燈 **2** if a feeling or emotion pulses through someone, they feel it very strongly〔感情等〕被

強烈地感覺到: *excitement pulsing through the crowd* 傳遍人羣的興奮情緒

pul·ver·ize also 又作 **-ise** *BrE*【英】/ˈpʌlvəˌraɪz; ˈpʌlvəraɪz/ *v* [T usually passive 一般用被動態] **1** to crush something into a powder 把…磨成粉 **2** *informal* to completely defeat someone【非正式】徹底打敗 —**pulverization** /ˌpʌlvərаɪˈzeʃən; ˌpʌlvəraɪˈzeɪʃən/ *n* [U]

pu·ma /ˈpjumə; ˈpjuːmə/ *n* [C] a COUGAR 美洲獅

pum·ice /ˈpʌmɪs; ˈpʌmɪ̣s/ also 又作 **pumice stone** /ˈ·· ·/ *n* **1** [U] very light silver-grey rock that has come from a VOLCANO, and is used as a powder for cleaning 浮石, 輕石〔用作清潔粉〕 **2** [C] a piece of this stone used for rubbing your skin to clean it or make it soft〔一塊〕浮石, 輕石〔用於清理皮膚或磨擦皮膚使其柔軟〕

pum·mel /ˈpʌml̩; ˈpʌməl/ **pummelled, pummelling** *BrE*【英】, **pummeled, pummeling** *AmE*【美】*v* [T] **1** to hit someone or something many times quickly with your FISTs (=closed hands) 用雙拳接連地捶打: *She flew at him and pummelled his chest.* 她衝向他並用拳頭捶打他的胸膛。**2** *informal* to completely defeat someone at a sport【非正式】〔在運動中〕徹底擊敗

3 **pump¹** /pʌmp; pʌmp/ *n* **1** [C] a machine for forcing liquid or gas into or out of something 泵; 唧筒; 抽水機; 打氣筒〔將氣體或液體注入或汲出某物的機器〕: **water/air/beer etc pump** (=for moving water/air etc) 抽水機／抽氣機／啤酒泵等 | **hand/foot pump** (=operated by your hand or foot) 手壓[搖]泵／腳踏泵 —see picture at 參見 BICYCLE[1] 圖 | **petrol pump/gas pump** (=for putting petrol or gas into cars) 汽油加油泵 —see also 另見 STOMACH PUMP —see picture at 參見 BICYCLE[1] 圖 **2** [C usually plural 一般用複數] *BrE* a flat light shoe for dancing, exercise etc【英】〔跳舞、鍛鍊等用的〕平底輕便鞋, 輕便舞鞋: *a pair of ballet pumps* 一雙芭蕾舞鞋 **3** [C usually plural 一般用複數] *especially AmE* a woman's plain shoe that does not fasten【尤美】無帶女便鞋 —see picture at 參見 SHOE[1] 圖 **4** [C usually plural 一般用複數] *BrE* a shoe made of CANVAS (=thick cloth) with rubber on the bottom, used for sports【英】〔橡膠底帆布面的〕運動鞋: *Don't forget your pumps for PE.* 別忘了體育課穿的運動鞋。**5** [C] an act of pumping 抽吸; 泵送; 抽運 **6 all hands to the pumps** used to say that everyone must work hard because a very difficult job has to be done〔為了完成困難的任務〕人人都要努力工作 —see also 另見 HEAT PUMP, **prime the pump** (PRIME[3] (4)), PARISH PUMP

pump² *v* **1** [T always+adv/prep] to make liquid or gas move in a particular direction with a pump〔用泵〕抽出, 注入〔液體、氣體等〕: **pump sth into/out of/through etc** *The fire department are still pumping floodwater out of the cellars.* 消防員仍在用泵抽吸地下室裡的洪水。| **pump gas** *AmE* (=put petrol into your car at a petrol station)【美】〔給汽車〕加油 **2** also 又作 **pump away** [I] to move very quickly in and out or up and down 快速地進進出出; 迅速地上下移動: *My heart was pumping fast.* 我的心臟跳得很快。**3** also 又作 **pump away** [I] to operate a pump 操作泵[唧筒]: *He pumped away furiously.* 他拚命地用泵抽吸。**4** [T] to bring a supply of water, oil etc to the surface from under the ground 從地下抽出〔水、油等〕 **5** [I always+adv/prep] when a liquid pumps from somewhere, it comes out in sudden small amounts〔液體〕間歇地噴出: **[+from/out of etc]** *The blood was pumping from the wound in his thigh.* 血從他大腿的傷口處噴出。**6** [T] *informal* to ask someone a lot of questions, in order to find out something【非正式】盤問, 套問: **pump sb for sth** *I tried to pump him for information about their other contacts.* 我想方設法從他嘴裡套出有關他們的其他聯繫人的情況。**7 pump sb full of sth** to put a lot of drugs into someone's body 把大量的〔藥物〕注入某人的身體: *athletes pumped full of steroids* 注射了大量類固醇的運動員 **8 pump iron** *informal* to do exercises by lifting heavy weights【非正式】舉重 **9 have your stomach pumped** to have the contents of your stomach removed by a pump, after swallowing something harmful〔吞食有害的東西後〕洗胃

pump sth into sb/sth *phr v* [T] **pump bullets into sb/sth** *informal* to shoot someone several times【非正式】將多發子彈射入某人身體[某物]

pump out *phr v* **1** [I,T] if something such as music, information, or a supply of products is pumped out or pumps out, a lot of it is produced〔音樂、信息、產品等〕大量提供, 大量供應; 連續播放: *There's a huge amount of propaganda pumped out by the food industry.* 食品工業進行了大張旗鼓的宣傳。| *Music pumped out from the loudspeakers overhead.* 音樂連續不斷地在頭頂的喇叭裡播放。**2** [T **pump sth ↔ out**] to remove liquid from something using a pump 用泵抽出〔某物中的液體〕: *You'll have to pump the boat out.* 你得用泵把船裡的水抽乾。

pump sth ↔ up *phr v* [T] **1** to fill a tyre, AIRBED etc with air until it is correctly filled; INFLATE (1) 給〔輪胎、充氣牀墊〕充滿氣 **2** to increase the value, amount etc of something 增加〔某物〕的價值、數量等: *The US was able to pump up exports.* 美國能夠增加出口量。**3 pump up the music/volume etc** *slang* to play music louder【俚】放大音量

pump sb ↔ up [T] to increase someone's excitement, interest etc 使興奮, 使更感興趣; 給〔某人〕打氣: *He was really pumped up before the game.* 比賽前他勁頭十足。

pump-ac·tion /ˈ· ˌ··/ *adj* **a pump-action shotgun/hairspray etc** a SHOTGUN etc that is operated by pulling or pressing part of it in or out 滑桿式獵槍／壓出式頭髮定型噴劑等

pum·per·nick·el /ˈpʌmpɚˌnɪkl̩; ˈpʌmpənɪkəl/ *n* [U] a heavy dark brown bread 粗製裸麥黑麵包

pump·kin /ˈpʌmpkɪn; ˈpʌmpkɪ̣n/ *n* **1** [C,U] a very large orange fruit that grows on the ground, or the inside of this fruit 南瓜: *pumpkin pie* 南瓜餅 —see picture on page A9 參見 A9 頁圖 **2** [singular] *AmE* a way of addressing someone you love【美】一種稱呼所愛的人的方式

pump room /ˈ· ·/ *n* [C] a room at a SPA where you can go to drink the water〔溫泉療養地的〕礦泉水飲用室

pun¹ /pʌn; pʌn/ *n* [C] an amusing use of a word or phrase that has two meanings, or of words with the same sound but different meanings, for example〔利用有兩重含義的詞或同音異義詞的〕雙關語, 語義雙關的俏皮話: *Seven days without water make one weak.* (=1 week) 七天沒水使人虛弱。〔weak 和 week 同音, 讀音也可理解為七天沒水為一週〕

pun² *v* **punned, punning** [I+on] to make a pun 使用雙關語

punch¹ /pʌntʃ; pʌntʃ/ *v* [T] **1** to hit someone or something hard with your FIST (=closed hand) 用拳猛擊〔某人或某物〕: **punch sb in/on sth** *Gallacher swung round and punched me hard in the stomach.* 加拉赫猛轉身朝我的腹部重擊一拳。| **punch sb/sth** *I punched the wall in anger.* 我生氣地用拳猛擊牆壁。| **punch the air** (=to make a movement like a punch, to show that you are very pleased about something) 朝空中打一拳〔表示非常高興〕 —see picture on page A20 參見 A20 頁圖 **2** to make a hole in something using a metal tool or other sharp object〔用金屬工具或其他利器〕在〔某物〕上打孔: **punch a ticket/card etc** *The guard punched my ticket.* 列車長在我的車票上打了孔。| **punch a hole in/through sth** *These bullets can punch a hole through 20mm steel plate.* 這些子彈可以穿透 20 毫米厚的鋼板。**3** [T] to push a button or key on a machine 按〔按鈕或鍵〕: *Sally punched the eighth floor button and the doors shut.* 莎莉按下八樓的按鈕, 門關上了。**4** *AmE* [T] to move cattle from one place to another【美】趕〔牲口〕 **5 punch holes in an argument/idea etc** *BrE* to disagree with someone's idea or plan and show what is wrong with it【英】不同意某人的觀點[計劃]並指出其毛病 **6 punch the clock** *AmE informal* to record the time that you start or finish work by putting a card into a special machine【美, 非正式】用特製機器打考勤卡記錄上下班時間, 打

卡上下班 **7 punch sb's lights out** *AmE informal* to hit someone hard in the face【美, 非正式】猛擊某人的臉

punch in *phr v* **1** [I] *AmE* to record the time that you arrive at work, by putting a card into a special machine; CLOCK IN【美】把卡插入特製機器中記錄上班時間, 打上班卡 **2** [T **punch** sth ↔ **in**] to put information into a computer by pressing buttons or keys〔按下按鈕或鍵〕往電腦裡輸入信息

punch out *phr v AmE*【美】**1** to record the time that you leave work, by putting a card into a special machine; CLOCK OUT 把卡插入特製機器中記錄下班時間, 打下班卡 **2** [T **punch** sb **out**] to hit someone so hard that they fall over 把某人打倒

punch² *n* **1** [C] a quick strong hit made with your FIST (=closed hand) 用拳打, 毆打: **punch in/on etc** *a punch in the kidneys* 打在腎上的一拳 | **throw a punch** (=aim a punch at someone) 用拳頭往某人身上打 **2** [U] a strong, effective quality in the way that you express things that makes people interested〔語言文字的〕力量, 感染力: *The speech was O.K. but it had no real punch.* 那演講還行, 但沒有真正的感染力。**3** [C] a metal tool for cutting holes or for pushing something into a small hole 打孔器, 把某物壓入小孔的金屬工具: *a hole punch* 打孔器 **4** [C,U] a drink made from fruit juice, sugar, water, and usually some alcohol〔用果汁、糖、水製成並常攙酒的〕賓治, 潘趣酒: *a bowl of rum punch* 一碗潘趣酒 **5 as pleased as Punch** very happy 非常快樂, 十分開心: *He's as pleased as Punch about the baby.* 寶寶使他感到十分開心。**6 beat sb/sth to the punch** *informal* to do or get something before someone else【非正式】先發制人, 搶先做某事[得到某物] **7 not pull any punches** *informal* to express your disapproval very clearly, without trying to hide what you feel【非正式】〔批評時〕毫不留情: *He wasn't pulling any punches! He said my work was 'pathetic'.* 他毫不留情地說我幹得"很差勁"。—see also 另見 **pack a (hard) punch** (PACK¹ (10))

Punch and Ju·dy show /ˈpʌntʃ ən ˋdʒudi ʃo; ˌpʌntʃ ən ˈdʒuːdi ʃəʊ/ *n* [C] a traditional type of entertainment for children, especially at British SEASIDE towns, that uses PUPPETS 潘趣和朱迪木偶戲〔一種傳統兒童娛樂形式, 尤指英國海濱城市供兒童看的木偶節目〕

punch·bag /ˋpʌntʃbæg; ˈpʌntʃbæg/ *BrE*【英】, **punching bag** *AmE*【美】/ˋ·· ·/ *n* [C] **1** a heavy leather bag hung from a rope, that is punched for exercise〔鍛鍊用的〕皮吊袋 **2 use sb as a punchbag** *BrE informal* to hit or punch someone【英, 非正式】打某人, 用拳猛打某人

punch ball /ˋ· ·/ *n* [C] a large leather ball that is fixed on a spring and is punched for exercise〔練習拳擊用的〕皮吊球

punch bowl /ˋ· ·/ *n* [C] a large bowl in which punch (=a mixed drink) is served 盛潘趣[賓治]酒的大碗

punch-drunk /ˋ· ·/ *adj* **1** *informal* very confused, especially because you have had continuous bad luck or have been treated badly【非正式】〔尤指因連遭不幸或受虐待而〕神志恍惚的 **2** a BOXER who is punch-drunk is suffering brain damage from being hit too much〔拳擊手〕被打得頭暈眼花的

punched card /ˌ· ˈ·/ also 又作 **punch card** /ˋ· ·/ *n* [C] a card with a pattern of holes in it that was used in the past for putting information into a computer〔過去用於往電腦中輸入信息的〕穿孔卡片

punch line /ˋ· ·/ *n* [C] the last few words of a joke or story, that make it funny or surprising〔笑話、故事中最後幾句點題或拋出笑料等的〕妙語, 畫龍點睛的結尾語

punch-up /ˋ· ·/ *n* [C] *BrE informal* a fight【英, 非正式】打鬥, 鬥毆: *Two people are to appear in court after a punch-up at their London home.* 兩個人在他們位於倫敦的家中打架之後將對簿公堂。

punch·y /ˋpʌntʃɪ; ˈpʌntʃi/ *adj* a punchy piece of writing or speech is very effective because it expresses ideas clearly in only a few words〔文章、演講〕簡短有力的; 簡潔的, 簡練的: *a punchy article* 一篇簡潔有力的文章 —**punchiness** *n* [U]

punc·til·i·ous /pʌŋkˋtɪlɪəs; pʌŋkˈtɪliəs/ *adj formal* being very careful to behave correctly and keep exactly to rules【正式】〔行為〕拘謹的, 一絲不苟的: *Jimmy was always most punctilious about repaying any loans.* 吉米總是小心謹慎地償還貸款。—**punctiliously** *adv* —**punctiliousness** *n* [U]

punc·tu·al /ˋpʌŋktʃuəl; ˈpʌŋktʃuəl/ *adj* arriving, happening etc at exactly the time that has been arranged 準時的, 守時的, 如期的: *She's always very punctual for appointments.* 她總是準時赴約。| *the punctual payment of invoices* 準時支付發票上的金額 —**punctually** *adv*: *The meeting began punctually at nine o'clock.* 會議於九點鐘準時開始。—**punctuality** /ˌpʌŋktʃuˋælətɪ; ˌpʌŋktʃuˈæləti/ *n* [U]

punc·tu·ate /ˋpʌŋktʃuˌet; ˈpʌŋktʃueɪt/ *v* **1** [T] to divide written work into sentences, phrases etc using COMMAS, FULL STOPS etc 在…中加標點 **2 be punctuated by/with sth** to be interrupted many times with something such as a noise 不時被某事物打斷: *silence occasionally punctuated by laughter* 有時被笑聲打破的寂靜

punc·tu·a·tion /ˌpʌŋktʃuˋeʃən; ˌpʌŋktʃuˈeɪʃən/ *n* [U] the marks used in dividing a piece of writing into sentences, phrases etc 標點符號〔總稱〕

punctuation mark /ˌ··ˋ·· ·/ *n* [C] a sign, such as a COMMA or QUESTION MARK, that is used in dividing a piece of writing into sentences, phrases etc 標點符號〈如逗號、問號〉

punctuation marks 標點符號

.	full stop *BrE*【英】/ period *AmE*【美】句號
,	comma 逗號
;	semi-colon 分號
:	colon 冒號
?	question mark 問號
!	exclamation mark *BrE*【英】/exclamation point *AmE*【美】感嘆號
( )	brackets 括號
" "	quotation marks 引號

punc·ture¹ /ˋpʌŋktʃɚ; ˈpʌŋktʃə/ *n* [C] **1** *BrE* a hole made accidentally in a tyre, so that air comes out of it【英】輪胎上的孔; FLAT² (2) *AmE*【美】: *I'm sorry I'm late; I had a puncture.* 對不起我來晚了, 我的車胎給扎了個洞。| *to mend a puncture* 修補車胎穿孔 **2** a small hole made by a sharp point〔尖物刺穿的〕小孔

puncture² *v* **1** [T] to make a small hole through the surface of something, especially in a tyre 刺破, 刺穿〔尤指輪胎〕: *A nail on the road punctured one of my tyres.* 路上的一根釘子把我的輪胎刺破了。| *Puncture some holes in the cover.* 在蓋子上刺幾個孔。**2** [I] if a ball, tyre etc punctures, it gets a small hole in it so that gas or air comes out〔球、輪胎等〕刺破, 戳破: *The ball punctured on the holly bush.* 那球落在冬青叢上刺破了。**3** [T] to suddenly destroy a feeling or belief, making someone feel unhappy, silly, or confused 突然破壞〔某人〕的感覺[信念], 突然使某人感到不快[愚蠢, 迷惑]: *The shocking news finally punctured his smug complacency.* 那個令人震驚的消息最終使他自滿的情緒受挫。

pun·dit /ˋpʌndɪt; ˈpʌndɪt/ *n* [C] someone who knows a lot about a particular subject, and is often asked for their opinions on it〔經常接受諮詢的〕權威, 專家: *political pundits* 政治(問題)專家

pun·gent /ˋpʌndʒənt; ˈpʌndʒənt/ *adj* **1** a pungent taste or smell is strong and sharp〔味道、氣味〕強烈的, 刺激性的, 刺鼻的: *the pungent aroma of garlic* 大蒜的刺鼻氣味 **2** pungent remarks or writing criticize something in a very direct and clever way〔話語、文章〕辛辣的, 尖銳的: *a few typically pungent remarks from Senator Moynihan* 參議員莫伊尼漢的幾句典型的辛辣評論 —**pungently** *adv* —**pungency** *n* [U]

pun·ish /ˋpʌnɪʃ; ˈpʌnɪʃ/ *v* [T] **1** to make someone suffer because they have done something wrong or broken the law 處罰, 懲罰〔做錯事或犯法的人〕: *Some people believe that smacking is not an acceptable way to punish a* *child.* 一些人認為動手打孩子不是一種值得接受的懲罰方法。| *In some countries women who have abortions can be punished by imprisonment.* 在有些國家, 墮胎的婦女會受到監禁的處罰。| **punish sb for (doing) sth** *Ewing was hauled before the Football Association to be punished for misconduct.* 尤因因行為不端而被傳到足協接受處罰。**2** if you punish a crime you punish anyone who is guilty of it 懲處〔犯罪行為〕: *Vandalism will be severely punished.* 蓄意破壞行為, 嚴懲不貸。**3 punish yourself (for sth/for doing sth)** to blame yourself for something 因為某事/做某事而責備自己: *The accident wasn't your fault; stop punishing yourself.* 這次事故不是你的錯, 別再怪罪自己了。

P

pun·ish·a·ble /ˈpʌnɪʃəbl; ˈpʌnɪʃəbəl/ *adj* a punishable act may be punished by law, especially in a particular way〔尤指以某種方式〕可依法懲處的: *a punishable offence* 應予懲罰的違例 | **[+by]** *Murder is punishable by death.* 犯謀殺罪可處以死刑。

pun·ish·ing¹ /ˈpʌnɪʃɪŋ; ˈpʌnɪʃɪŋ/ *adj* **punishing schedule/workload/journey etc** a SCHEDULE etc that is so long or difficult that it makes you tired and weak 累人的日程安排/繁重的工作負擔/使人疲憊不堪的旅行等: *a punishing regime of exercise and diet* 艱苦的鍛鍊與節食 **—punishingly** *adv*

punishing² *n* **take a punishing** *informal* to suffer rough or damaging treatment【非正式】遭到粗暴對待; 受到損壞: *The car took a real punishing on the journey.* 這輛汽車在旅行中飽受折騰。

3 **pun·ish·ment** /ˈpʌnɪʃmənt; ˈpʌnɪʃmənt/ *n* **1** [C] a way in which someone or something is punished 懲罰手段; 處罰: **[+for]** *I sent Alex to bed early as a punishment for breaking the window.* 因為亞歷克斯打破了窗玻璃, 我罰他早上牀睡覺。| *You know the punishment for treason, don't you?* 你知道叛國會受到甚麼樣的懲罰, 是吧? | **a harsh/severe punishment** (=one that makes someone suffer a lot) 嚴厲的懲罰 **2** [U] the act of punishing someone or the process of being punished 懲罰, 處罰; 受罰: *We are determined that the terrorists will not escape punishment.* 我們決心不讓那些恐怖分子逍遙法外。**3** [U] *informal* rough treatment; damage【非正式】粗暴對待; 損壞, 糟踏: *With five children in the house, the furniture has to take a lot of punishment.* 因家裡有五個孩子, 家具無法免於被糟蹋。—see also 另見 CAPITAL PUNISHMENT, CORPORAL PUNISHMENT

pu·ni·tive /ˈpjunətɪv; ˈpjuːnɪtɪv/ *adj* **1 punitive taxes/price increases etc** taxes etc that are so severe that people find it very difficult to pay 重稅/價格等的急劇上漲等: *The new Bill enables people to sue and win punitive damages for discrimination.* 新的法案使人們可以因受到歧視而提出訴訟並獲得高額補償金。**2 punitive actions/measures/damages etc** actions etc that are intended to punish someone 懲罰(性)行動/措施/賠償費等: *plans to take punitive action against terrorists* 對恐怖分子採取懲罰行動的計劃 **—punitively** *adv*

punk /pʌŋk; pʌŋk/ *n* **1** also 又作 **punk-rock** /ˌ· ˈ·/ [U] a type of loud violent music popular in the late 1970s and the 1980s 龐克搖滾樂〔一種20世紀70年代末期和80年代流行的音樂〕: *great punk bands like the Sex Pistols and X-Ray spex* 如"性手槍"和"透視器"之類偉大的龐克搖滾樂隊 **2** also 又作 **punk-rocker** [C] someone who dresses like people who follow punk rock, with brightly-coloured hair, chains and pins and torn clothing 龐克搖滾樂迷; 追隨龐克風格者〔模仿龐克搖滾樂師的衣着、將頭髮染成鮮豔的顏色、佩戴鏈子和飾針、穿襤褸衣衫〕: *Marilyn was a punk in '79.* 1979年, 瑪麗琳是個龐克搖滾樂迷。| *punk hairstyles* 龐克髮式 **3** [C] *AmE slang* a young man or a boy who fights and breaks the law【美俚】小流氓, 阿飛: *You little punk!* 你這個小流氓! **4** [U] *AmE* a substance that burns without a flame and is used to light FIREWORKS etc【美】〔用於點焰火的〕火絨

pun·kah /ˈpʌŋkə; ˈpʌŋkə/ *n* [C] *especially IndE, PakE* a FAN¹ (2) hung across a room and swung backwards and forwards by pulling a rope, especially in the past【尤印和巴】〔尤指舊時用繩索拉動的〕布(屏)風扇

pun·kin /ˈpʌŋkɪn; ˈpʌŋkɪn/ *n* [C] *AmE* another spelling of PUMPKIN (2)【美】pumpkin (2) 的另一種拼法

pun·net /ˈpʌnɪt; ˈpʌnɪt/ *n* [C] *BrE* a small square basket in which soft fruits such as strawberries (STRAWBERRY) are sold, or the amount contained in one of these【英】〔出售軟水果如草莓的〕小方籃[簍]; 一小籃[簍]之量

pun·ster /ˈpʌnstɚ; ˈpʌnstə/ *n* [C] someone who makes PUNS (=jokes involving two words that sound similar) 好用雙關語的人

punt¹ /pʌnt; pʌnt/ *n* **1** [C] a long narrow river-boat with a flat bottom and square ends, that is moved by pushing a long pole against the bottom of the river〔用篙撐行的〕方頭平底船 **2** [singular] the act of going out in a punt 撐方頭平底船: *Let's go for a punt.* 我們去撐船吧。**3** [C] in American football, a long kick that you make after dropping the ball from your hands〔美式足球中〕踢懸空球 **4** [C] *BrE informal* money that you risk on the result of something such as a race; a BET【英, 非正式】賭注 **5 take a punt** *informal* to make a guess when you do not have full enough information to make a proper decision【非正式】〔在沒有足夠的信息幫助作出正確決定時〕猜測

punt² *v* **1** [I,T] in American football, to drop the ball from your hands and kick it〔美式足球中〕踢(懸空球): *He punted the ball forty yards.* 他把球踢出四十碼。—see picture on page A22 參見A22頁圖 **2** [I,T] to go or take someone on a river by punt 乘方頭平底船; 用方頭平底船載運: *We were punting up the river.* 我們正用篙撐着方頭平底船溯河而上。

punt·er /ˈpʌntɚ; ˈpʌntə/ *n* [C] **1** *BrE informal* someone who makes a BET (=risks money) on the result of a horse race etc【英, 非正式】〔賽馬等〕賭徒: *a regular punter* 一位經常賭博的人 **2** *BrE informal* someone who uses a product or a service; customer【英, 非正式】顧客: *You've got to try to please the punters.* 我們必須盡量讓顧客滿意。**3** the player who punts the ball in American football〔美式足球中的〕踢懸空球的隊員

pu·ny /ˈpjunɪ; ˈpjuːni/ *adj* **1** small, thin, and weak 弱小的, 瘦小的: *a puny little guy* 瘦小的人 **2** unimpressive and ineffective 質量差的; 微薄的; 無效的: *my own puny attempts at humour* 我收效甚微的幽默 **—puniness** *n* [U]

pup¹ /pʌp; pʌp/ *n* [C] **1** a young dog; a PUPPY 小狗, 幼犬: *a spaniel pup* 西班牙獵犬幼崽 **2** a young SEAL¹ (1) or OTTER 小海豹; 小水獺: *seal pups* 小海豹 **3** *old-fashioned* an insulting word for a young man who is rude or too confident【過時】小崽子〔侮辱性詞語〕: *Don't you threaten me, you young pup!* 你別威脅我, 小兔崽子! **4 be sold a pup** *BrE old-fashioned* to be tricked into buying something that is worthless or useless【英, 過時】被欺騙購買了無價值[無用]的東西

pup² *v* [I] *technical* to give birth to pups【術語】〔狗等〕生幼崽

pu·pa /ˈpjupə; ˈpjuːpə/ *n plural* **pupas** or **pupae** /-pi; -piː/ [C] an insect in the middle stages of its development when it is protected inside a special cover〔昆蟲的〕蛹 **—pupal** *adj*: *in the pupal stage* 在蛹的階段

pu·pate /ˈpjupet; pjuːˈpeɪt/ *v* [I] *technical* to become a pupa【術語】化蛹, 變成蛹

pu·pil /ˈpjupl; ˈpjuːpəl/ *n* [C] **1** *especially BrE* someone 2
who is being taught, especially a child【尤英】學生,〔尤 1
指〕小學生: *This school has about 500 pupils.* 這所學校大約有500名學生。| *I teach private pupils on Wednesdays.* 我星期三去當家庭教師。**2** the small black round area in the middle of your eye 瞳孔 —see picture at 參見EYE¹圖

pup·pet /ˈpʌpɪt; ˈpʌpɪt/ *n* [C] **1** a model of a person or animal that you can move by pulling wires or strings, or by putting your hand inside it〔牽線〕木偶;〔套在手上操縱的〕布袋木偶, 手套式木偶: *a puppet show* 木偶戲 **2** a person or organization that has lost their independent position and allows someone else to control them 受他人操縱的人[組織], 傀儡: *She's just a puppet of the management.* 她只是資方的傀儡。| **puppet government/regime** (=a government controlled by a more powerful country or organization) 傀儡政府/政權

pup·pe·teer /ˌpʌpɪˋtɪr; ˌpʌpǝ̀ˈtɪǝ/ *n* [C] someone who performs with puppets 演木偶戲的人; 操縱木偶的人

S3 **pup·py** /ˋpʌpɪ; ˈpʌpi/ *n* [C] **1** a young dog 小狗, 幼犬 **2** *old-fashioned* a young man who is rude or too confident 【過時】無禮的年輕男人, 自負的年輕男子

puppy fat /ˋ·· ·/ *n* [U] *BrE informal* fat that children have on their bodies that they usually lose as they get older【英, 非正式】〔長大後通常消失的〕少年期的肥胖

puppy love /ˋ·· ·/ *n* [U] a young boy's or girl's love for someone, which people do not regard as serious〔少男、少女〕幼稚的迷戀, 不成熟的愛, 少年初戀: *It's only puppy love; he'll grow out of it.* 那只是少年初戀; 他長大後會清醒的。

pur·blind /ˋpɝˌblaɪnd; ˈpɜːblaɪnd/ *adj formal or literary* stupid or dull【正式或文】愚蠢的, 遲鈍的; 笨的

S3 W3 **pur·chase**[1] /ˋpɝtʃǝs; ˈpɜːtʃǝ̀s/ *v* [T] **1** *formal* to buy something, especially something big or expensive【正式】購買, 採購〔尤指大或貴的物品〕: *a loan to purchase a new car* 購買一輛新汽車的貸款 **2** *literary* to gain something but only by losing something else【文】〔以某種代價〕換得: *They purchased life at the expense of honour.* 他們以犧牲名譽為代價換得了生命。—**purchasable** *adj*

S3 W3 **purchase**[2] *n* **1** [C,U] *formal* the act of buying something【正式】購買, 採購: *Fill in the date of purchase.* 填上購買日期。| *The company spent a lot on expansion including the purchase of a large warehouse.* 這家公司為擴展花費了很多, 其中包括購買了一個大型倉庫。| **make a purchase** (=buy something) 購買 —see also 另見 HIRE PURCHASE —see graph at 參見 BUY[1] 圖表 **2** [C usually plural 一般用複數] *formal* something that has been bought【正式】購買的物品, 購得物: *Do you wish us to deliver your purchases?* 您買的東西要我們送貨嗎? **3 on special purchase** being sold at a cheaper price than usual 特價出售: *These boots are on special purchase.* 這些靴子特價出售。**4** [singular,U] *formal* a firm hold with your hands or feet【正式】〔手或腳的〕抓拿處, 搭腳處, 支點: *I tried to gain a purchase on the narrow ledge.* 我力圖在狹窄的邊緣處找到一個落腳點。

purchase price /ˋ·· ·/ *n* [singular] *formal* the price that has to be paid if you want to buy something【正式】購買價: *We need to borrow 80% of the purchase price.* 我們需要借貸購買價的八成。

pur·chas·er /ˋpɝtʃǝsɚ; ˈpɜːtʃǝ̀sǝ/ *n* [C] *formal* the person who buys something【正式】購買者, 買主

purchasing pow·er /ˋ··· ˌ··/ *n* [U] **1** the amount of money that a person or group has available to spend compared to other people 購買力: *Widespread wage rises result in increased purchasing power.* 工資的普遍上漲導致了購買力的增加。**2** the value of a unit of money considered in terms of how much you can buy with it 貨幣的購買力: *The purchasing power of the dollar has declined.* 美元的購買力下降了。

pur·dah /ˋpɝdǝ; ˈpɜːdǝ/ *n* [U] **1** the custom, especially among Muslim people, according to which women stay in their home or cover their faces so that they cannot be seen by men〔尤指穆斯林的〕深閨制度〔婦女閉門不出或以面紗蒙臉不讓男人窺見容貌〕**2 in purdah a)** women who are in purdah live according to this custom〔婦女〕按深閨制度生活的 **b)** staying away from other people 不與人交往的

S3 W3 **pure** /pjur; pjʊǝ/ *adj*

1 ►NOT MIXED 非混合的◄ not mixed with anything else 純的, 純淨的: *Is this sweater made of pure wool?* 這件毛線衫是純羊毛的嗎? | *The cocaine was 95% pure.* 這種可卡因的純度是 95%。| *The purest form of the southern accent can be heard in Tennessee.* 在田納西州可以聽到最純正的南方口音。

2 pure chance/greed/hell etc complete chance etc 純屬碰巧/十足的貪婪/簡直是地獄等: *By pure chance my boss was flying on the same plane as me.* 我老闆和我乘坐同一架飛機純屬碰巧。| *"How was the exam?" "Pure hell!"* "考試怎麼樣?" "糟糕透頂!" | *a work of pure genius* 完全是天才之作 | *the pure thrill of living* 生活激動人心的精粹之處

3 ►CLEAN 乾淨的◄ clean, without anything harmful or unhealthy 純淨的, 潔淨的, 無有害物質的: *The air by the sea is pure and healthy.* 海濱的空氣潔淨, 有益健康。| *pure drinking water* 純淨的飲用水

4 ►WITHOUT EVIL 純潔無邪的◄ having no evil ideas or plans, especially no sexual thoughts or experience; INNOCENT[1] (4) 純潔的, 貞潔的, 無邪的, 清白的: *a pure young girl* 純潔的少女 | *I'm sure he had the purest of motives.* 我相信他的動機非常單純。

5 ►COLOUR 顏色◄ clear and not mixed with other colours 純正的, 無雜色的: *a cloudless sky of the purest blue* 碧藍無雲的天空

6 ►SOUND 聲音◄ very clear and beautiful to hear 純正的, 清晰而優美的: *a pure note* 純音 | *a lovely pure soprano* 優美而純正的女高音

7 ►ART 藝術◄ a pure form of art is done exactly according to an accepted standard or pattern〔藝術〕精純的

8 as pure as the driven snow an expression meaning morally perfect, often used jokingly to describe someone who is not like this at all 像白雪一樣純潔,〔道德上〕完美無瑕〔常謔指與此根本不符的人〕

9 pure and simple *especially spoken* used to say that there is only one reason for something【尤口】完全是, 不折不扣的〔用來指某事只有唯一的原因〕: *The mistake was due to carelessness, pure and simple.* 這個錯誤完全是由於粗心造成的。

10 pure science/mathematics etc work done in science etc in order to increase our knowledge of it rather than to make practical use of it 純科學/理論數學等: *pure and applied research* 理論和應用研究 —compare 比較 APPLIED —see also 另見 IMPURE, PURELY, PURIFY, PURITY —**pureness** *n* [U]

pure·blood·ed /ˌpjurˋblʌdɪd; ˌpjʊǝˈblʌdǝ̀d◂/ *adj* with parents, grandparents etc from only one group or race of people, with no mixture of other groups 純血統的

pure·bred /ˋpjurˌbrɛd; ˈpjʊǝbred/ *adj* coming from only one breed of animal with no mixture of other breeds〔動物〕純種的: *purebred Irish wolfhounds* 純種愛爾蘭獵狼犬 —compare 比較 PEDIGREE[2], THOROUGHBRED (1) —**purebred** *n* [C]

pu·ree, purée /pjuˋre; ˈpjʊǝreɪ/ *n* [C,U] food that is boiled or crushed until it is a soft mass that is almost liquid〔經烹煮搗壓製成的〕醬, 泥, 糊: *apple puree* 蘋果醬[泥] | *tomato puree* 番茄醬 —**puree, purée** *v* [T]

S2 W3 **pure·ly** /ˋpjurlɪ; ˈpjʊǝli/ *adv* **1** completely and only, without anything else being involved 完全地, 純粹地, 僅僅: *a decision that was taken for purely political reasons* 純粹出於政治原因而作出的決定 | *I bumped into Sally purely by chance.* 我碰到莎莉純屬偶然。**2 purely and simply** used to emphasize that only one reason or purpose is involved in a situation or decision 完全是〔為了〕, 純粹是〔因為〕: *I can tell you now, I'm doing it purely and simply for the money.* 我現在可以告訴你, 我做這件事完全是為了錢。

pur·ga·tive /ˋpɝgǝtɪv; ˈpɜːgǝtɪv/ *n* [C] a medicine or food that makes your BOWELs empty themselves 瀉藥, 能通便的食物 —**purgative** *adj*: *Figs often have a purgative effect.* 無花果通常有通便的效用。

pur·ga·tory /ˋpɝgǝˌtorɪ; ˈpɜːgǝtǝri/ *n* [U] **1 Purgatory** a place where, according to Roman Catholic beliefs, the souls of dead people must suffer for the bad things they did, until they are pure enough to enter heaven〔羅馬天主教教義中的〕滌罪所, 煉獄 **2** *humorous* a place, situation, or time when you suffer a lot【幽默】受苦受難(的地方): *It's purgatory listening to Ben trying to play the violin!* 聽本練習拉小提琴簡直是活受罪! —**purgatorial** /ˌpɝɡəˈtɔriəl; ˌpɜːɡəˈtɔːriəl◂/ *adj*

purge¹ /pɝdʒ; pɜːdʒ/ *v* [T] **1** to force your opponents or people who disagree with you to leave an organization or place, often by using violence 清除〔對手或反對者〕, 清洗, 肅清: **purge sth of sb/sth** *an attempt to purge the region of ethnic minorities* 把少數民族清除出這一地區的企圖 | **purge sb/sth from sth** *purging dissidents from the party* 把不同政見者清除出黨 **2** *literary* to get rid of your bad feelings such as hatred【文】消除〔仇恨等不良情緒〕, 滌除: **purge sb/sth of sth** *It took her months to purge herself of her feelings of guilt.* 她花了好幾個月才消除自己的內疚感。| **purge sth from sth** *You must purge this hatred from your soul.* 你必須滌除靈魂中的這種仇恨。**3** *old-fashioned* to take a medicine to clear all the waste from your BOWELS【過時】〔服藥〕使〔腸〕瀉清, 使通便

purge² *n* [C] **1** an action to remove your opponents or people who disagree with you from an organization or place, often using violence〔通常使用暴力的〕清洗行動; 整肅: *The new president carried out a purge of disloyal army officers.* 新總統對不忠心的軍官進行了清洗。| *the Stalinist purges of the 1930s* 20 世紀 30 年代史太林的清黨行動 **2** *old-fashioned* a medicine that clears all the waste from your BOWELS【過時】瀉藥

pu·ri·fi·ca·tion /ˌpjurəfəˈkeʃən; ˌpjʊərɪfɪˈkeɪʃən/ *n* [U] **1** a process that removes the dirty or unwanted parts from something 淨化; 提純: *a water purification plant* 水淨化廠 **2** acts or ceremonies to remove evil from someone 滌罪 (儀式): *ritual purification* 滌罪儀式

pu·ri·fy /ˈpjurəˌfaɪ; ˈpjʊərɪfaɪ/ *v* **purified, purifying** [T] **1** to remove the dirty or unwanted parts from something 使純淨, 淨化: *The liquid is purified by passing it through charcoal.* 這種液體經由炭過濾後得到了淨化。**2** to get rid of evil from your soul 淨化〔靈魂〕—**purifier** *n* [C] *a water purifier* 水淨化器

pur·ist /ˈpjurɪst; ˈpjʊərɪst/ *n* [C] someone who has very strong ideas about what is correct, for example in matters of grammar, art, or music〔在語法、藝術、音樂上〕力求純正者, 純粹主義者: *The purists won't like it but opera on TV certainly brings in the audiences.* 純粹派不會喜歡這麼做, 但電視上播出歌劇的確吸引了觀眾。—**purism** *n* [U]

pu·ri·tan /ˈpjurətn; ˈpjʊərɪtən/ *n* [C] **1** someone who has very strict moral standards and thinks that pleasure is unnecessary or wrong 主張過清教徒式生活的人〔道德標準嚴格, 認為享樂沒有必要或是錯誤的〕**2 Puritan** a member of a Protestant religious group in the 16th and 17th centuries, who wanted to make religion simpler 清教徒〔16 世紀和 17 世紀基督教一教派成員, 主張簡化宗教儀式〕—**puritan** also 又作 **Puritan** *adj*: *a Puritan background* 清教徒出身 | *puritan beliefs* 清教徒式的信仰

pu·ri·tan·i·cal /ˌpjurəˈtænɪkl; ˌpjʊərɪˈtænɪkəl/ *adj* having extreme attitudes about religion and moral behaviour 對宗教和道德行為持極端態度的, 清教徒式的: *a puritanical father who wouldn't let his children watch television* 不讓孩子看電視的清教徒式的父親 —**puritanically** /-klɪ; -kli/ *adv*

pu·ri·tan·is·m /ˈpjurtənɪzəm; ˈpjʊərɪtənɪzəm/ *n* [U] **1** a way of living according to very strict rules, especially concerning religion and moral behaviour〔尤指在宗教或道德行為上〕非常拘謹的生活方式, 清教徒式的生活方式 **2 Puritanism** the beliefs and practices of the Puritans 清教徒的教義和行為; 清教主義

pu·ri·ty /ˈpjurətɪ; ˈpjʊərɪti/ *n* [U] the quality or state of being pure 純; 純潔; 潔淨; 純正; 純粹: *Strict controls are needed to ensure the purity of herbal drugs.* 需要嚴格的控制來保證草藥的純度。—opposite 反義詞 IMPURITY

purl¹ /pɝl; pɜːl/ *v* [I,T] to use the purl stitch when you KNIT (=make clothes from wool) 用反針編織

purl² *n* [U] one of the types of stitches that you use when you KNIT (=make clothes from wool)〔編織中的〕反針, 倒針

pur·lieus /ˈpɝluz; ˈpɜːljuːz/ *n* [plural] *literary* the area in and around a place【文】鄰近地區;〔某處的〕周圍

pur·loin /pɝˈlɔɪn; pɜːˈlɔɪn/ *v* [T] *formal or houmorous* to steal or borrow something without permission【正式或幽默】偷竊; 未經允許借〔某物〕: *Marek managed to purloin a copy of the house key.* 馬利克設法偷配了一把那房子的鑰匙。

pur·ple /ˈpɝpl; ˈpɜːpəl/ *n* [U] **1** a dark colour that is a mixture of red and blue 紫色 —see picture on page A5 參見 A5 頁圖 **2 purple with rage/purple in the face etc** very red in the face as a result of being angry or embarrassed 由於生氣[尷尬]而臉紅 **3 purple passage/prose/patch** a piece of writing that has a grander style 辭藻華麗的段落/風格華麗的散文/華而不實的章句 **4 born to the purple** *literary* born into a high social class or position【文】生於帝王之家, 生於顯貴之家 —**purple** *adj*

Purple Heart /ˌ.. ˈ./ *n* [C] a special MEDAL given to US soldiers who have been wounded in battle〔美國授予作戰中負傷者的〕紫心勳章

purple heart *n* [C] *informal* a PILL containing an illegal drug that gives you a feeling of energy and excitement【非正式】紫心丸〔一種興奮藥丸〕

pur·plish /ˈpɝplɪʃ; ˈpɜːplɪʃ/ *adj* slightly purple 略帶紫色的: *purplish blue* 略帶紫色的藍色

pur·port¹ /pɝˈport; pɜːˈpɔːt/ *v* [I,T] **purport to be/be purported to be** *formal* to claim to be something, and give the impression that it is true, even if it is not【正式】聲稱是..., 據稱是..., 像是...: *The letter is purported to be a secret agreement between the president and the general.* 這封信據稱是總統和將軍之間的祕密協議。

pur·port² /ˈpɝport; ˈpɜːpɔːt/ *n* [U] *formal* the general meaning of what someone says【正式】〔某人言論的〕大意, 主旨: [+of] *The purport of her remarks was clear.* 她的話意思很清楚。

pur·pose¹ /ˈpɝpəs; ˈpɜːpəs/ *n*

1 ►WHAT STH IS SUPPOSED TO DO 目的; 用途◄ [C] the thing that an event, process, or activity is supposed to achieve, or the job that something is supposed to do 目的; 用途 —see 見 REASON¹ (USAGE): [+of] *The purpose of this meeting is to elect a new committee.* 這次會議的目的是選舉新的委員會。| *What is the purpose of the little red button?* 這個小紅按鈕的用途是甚麼? | **the purpose of doing sth** *The sole purpose of conducting a business is to make money.* 做生意的唯一目的是賺錢。| **serve a purpose** (=have a particular purpose, or help you achieve a purpose) 起到某個作用; 幫助達到某個目的 *The discussion serves a twin purpose – instruction and feedback.* 這次討論有雙重的作用 —— 指導和反饋。| *No useful purpose will be served by re-opening the murder enquiry.* 對這次謀殺重新進行調查沒甚麼用處。

2 on purpose deliberately 故意(地), 有意(地): *Jack's been really annoying me and I think he's doing it on purpose.* 傑克一直讓我很煩, 我想他是故意那樣幹的。

3 ►PLAN 計劃◄ [C] *formal* an intention or a plan【正式】意圖, 目的; 計劃: *Tom went for a walk, with no definite purpose in mind.* 湯姆漫無目的地出去走走。| **purpose in doing sth** *My main purpose in setting up the experiment was to obtain fresh data.* 我設立該項實驗的主要目的是獲取新的數據。

4 ►AIM 目標◄ [U] the feeling of having an aim in life 生活目標: *I need to find meaning and purpose in my life.* 我需要找出我生活的意義和目的。

5 for all practical purposes also 又作 **for all intents and purposes** used to say that something may not exactly be true but it is true in general 實際上; 大體上: *She became for all practical purposes, a director of the*

company. 她實際上成了這個公司的董事。

6 for the purposes of used to say that someone or something will be considered in a particular way in a discussion, document etc 出於…目的, 為了…: *For tax purposes you will be treated as a married couple.* 報稅時你們將被當作夫妻對待。

7 serve its purpose if something serves its purpose, it does what you intended it to do 起到應有的作用: *Our holiday had served its purpose; we both felt thoroughly relaxed.* 我們的假期已起到了它應有的作用, 我們兩個都感到十分輕鬆自在。

8 to good purpose/to no purpose *formal* with good results or with no results【正式】大有效果/毫無效果: *Clara has used her musical talents to good purpose.* 克萊拉發揮了她的音樂天賦。

9 to the purpose *old-fashioned*【過時】useful or helpful 有用的, 有益的, 有幫助的 —see also 另見 **accidentally on purpose** (ACCIDENTALLY (2)), PURPOSELY, CROSS-PURPOSES

purpose² *v* [T] *old use* to intend to do something【舊】意欲, 打算: *Drake purposed to voyage around the globe.* 德雷克打算進行環球航行。

purpose-built /,·· '·◂/ *adj BrE* designed and made for a particular purpose【英】為某用途特製的, 特別為某一目的設計的: *purpose-built toilets for disabled people* 專為殘疾人設計的廁所

pur·pose·ful /ˈpɝpəsfəl; ˈpɜːpəsfəl/ *adj* having a clear aim or purpose; determined 有目的的, 有明確目標的; 堅決的, 果斷的: *a purposeful man who wouldn't worry about who he hurt* 一個志在必得的人, 不會因傷害了誰而煩憂的 —**purposefully** *adv* —**purposefulness** *n* [U]

pur·pose·less /ˈpɝpəslɪs; ˈpɜːpəsləs/ *adj* not having a clear aim or purpose 無目的的, 無目標的: *a purposeless existence on the streets of London* 在倫敦街頭毫無目標的生活 —**purposelessly** *adv* —**purposelessness** *n* [U]

pur·pose·ly /ˈpɝpəslɪ; ˈpɜːpəsli/ *adv formal* deliberately【正式】故意地: *a purposely provocative comment* 故意挑釁的評論

purr /pɝ; pɜː/ *v* **1** [I] if a cat purrs, it makes a soft, low sound in its throat to show that it is pleased〔貓愉快時〕發出嗚嗚聲: *A big grey tomcat sat in his lap purring contentedly.* 一隻灰色的大雄貓坐在他腿上, 滿足地嗚嗚叫着。**2** [I] if the engine of a vehicle or machine purrs, it works perfectly and makes a quiet smooth sound〔車輛或機器的發動機〕發出順利運作時的低沉聲音: *The big Bentley purred along the wide road.* 那輛大賓利車行駛在寬闊的公路上, 發出低沉的震顫聲。**3** [I,T] if someone purrs, they speak in a soft, low, and SEXY voice〔人〕以輕柔低沉的聲音說: *"Are you doing anything tonight?" she purred.* "你今晚有甚麼事嗎?" 她嬌聲說。—**purr** *n* [C]

purses 錢包

purse *BrE*【英】/ change purse *AmE*【美】錢包, 零錢包

purse *BrE*【英】/ wallet *AmE*【美】皮夾, 錢夾

wallet 皮夾, 錢夾

3 **purse¹** /pɝs; pɜːs/ *n* **1** [C] *BrE* a small container for keeping coins in, made of leather, cloth, plastic etc, used especially by women【英】〔裝零錢的〕錢包〔尤指女式錢包〕; CHANGE PURSE *AmE*【美】: *She took a pound coin out of her purse.* 她從錢包裡拿出一枚一英鎊的硬幣。| *Hayley snapped her purse shut.* 海利啪嗒一聲合上錢包。**2** [C] *BrE* a small flat leather container divided into parts for keeping paper money, cards, coins etc in, and used especially by women【英】〔裝鈔票、卡片、零錢等用的〕皮夾子, 錢夾〔尤指女式錢夾〕; WALLET *AmE*【美】: *Check my purse. I think I've only got a twenty pound note.* 查看一下我的錢夾, 我想我只有一張二十鎊的鈔票。**3** [C] *AmE* a bag, often made of leather, in which a woman carries her money and personal things【美】〔女用〕手提包, 手袋; HANDBAG *BrE*【英】: *She reached in her purse and took out a mirror.* 她把手伸進手提包內取出一面鏡子。—see picture at 參見 BAG¹ 圖 **4** [singular] *formal* the amount of money that a person, organization, or country has available to spend【正式】〔個人、組織或國家的〕備用金, 可以使用的資金, 財力: *It was an expense that my purse could not afford.* 我支付不起那項費用。| **the public purse** (=money controlled by a government) 國庫 *These defence commitments are a continuing drain on the public purse.* 這些防禦義務使國庫資金不斷流失。**5** [C] the amount of money given to someone who wins a BOXING match〔給予拳擊賽獲勝者的〕獎金 **6 hold/control the purse strings** to control the money in a family, company etc 控制〔家庭、公司等的〕開支, 掌管錢財: *Maureen definitely holds the purse strings.* 莫琳毫無疑問掌管着開支。

purse² *v* **purse your lips** to bring your lips together tightly into a small circle, especially to show disapproval or doubt 撅起〔嘴唇〕: *Mrs Biddell pursed her lips and stared.* 比德爾夫人撅起嘴瞪起眼。

purs·er /ˈpɝsɚ; ˈpɜːsə/ *n* [C] an officer who is responsible for the money on a ship and is also in charge of the passengers' rooms, comfort etc〔客輪上掌管賬目、管理旅客房間等的〕事務長

pur·su·ance /pɚˈsuəns; pəˈsjuːəns/ *n* **in pursuance of** *formal*【正式】**a)** with the aim of doing or achieving something 為了做…, 為了取得…: *Staff voted to take industrial action in pursuance of a better deal.* 全體職工投票決定採取勞工行動以期得到更好的待遇。**b)** during the process of doing or achieving something 在做某事的過程中, 在實行某事時

pur·sue /pɚˈsu; pəˈsjuː/ *v* [T] **1** to continue doing an activity or trying to achieve something over a long period of time 追求, 繼續進行: *Kristin pursued her acting career with great determination.* 克里斯汀意志堅定地追求她的表演事業。**2 pursue the matter/argument/question** to continue trying to ask about, find out about, or persuade someone about a particular subject 追究某件事/繼續爭論/追查某問題: *Janet did not dare pursue the matter too far.* 珍妮特不敢深入追查那件事。**3** to chase or follow someone or something, in order to catch them, attack them etc〔尤指為抓捕、襲擊等而〕緊隨…之後; 追捕, 追擊: *Briggs ran across the field with one officer pursuing him.* 布里格斯跑過田地, 一名警官正在追捕他。**4** to keep trying to persuade someone to have a relationship with you 追求〔某人〕 S3 W2

pur·su·er /pɚˈsuɚ; pəˈsjuːə/ *n* [C] someone or something that is chasing you 追趕者, 追捕者〔指人或物〕: *Luckily, Joey managed to outrun his pursuers.* 幸運的是, 喬伊比追趕他的人跑得快, 逃脫了。

pur·suit /pɚˈsut; pəˈsjuːt/ *n* **1** [singular] the act of trying to achieve something in a determined way 追求: **[+of]** *the right of all people to the pursuit of liberty and happiness* 所有人追求自由和幸福的權利 | **in pursuit of** (=while trying to get) 在追求…時 *I'm always amazed at the things people do in pursuit of love.* 我總是為人們在追求愛情時所做的事情感到驚訝。**2** [U] the act of chasing or following someone 追趕, 追蹤: **in pursuit** (=following behind) 追趕 *There were no fewer than four police cars in pursuit.* 至少有四輛警車在追趕。| **in hot pursuit** (=following close behind) 緊緊追趕, 窮追不捨 *The quarterback sprinted toward the end zone with*

Jansen in hot pursuit. 那名四分衛全速向球門區跑去，詹森窮追不捨。**3** [C usually plural 一般用複數] *formal* an activity such as a sport or HOBBY, which you spend a lot of time doing【正式】花很多時間做的事情; 工作; 嗜好, 消遣; 追求: *She immersed herself in academic pursuits.* 她投身於學術研究之中。

pu·ru·lent /ˈpjʊrələnt; ˈpjʊərələnt/ *adj technical* containing or producing PUS【術語】化膿的; 含膿的 —**purulence** *n* [U]

pur·vey /pɚˈve; pɜːˈveɪ/ *v* [T+**to**] *formal* to supply goods, services, or information to people【正式】提供, 供應〔貨物、服務或信息〕

pur·vey·or /pɚˈveɚ; pɜːˈveɪə/ *n* [C usually plural 一般用複數] *formal* someone who supplies information, goods, or services to people, especially as a business【正式】承辦商, 供應者, 提供者: *purveyors of farmyard fresh poultry* 農場鮮禽肉供應商

pur·view /ˈpɚvju; ˈpɜːvjuː/ *n* **within/outside the purview of** *formal* within or outside the limits of someone's job, activity, or knowledge【正式】〔工作、活動、知識等的〕範圍[權限]之內/之外: *This matter comes within the purview of the Department of Health.* 這件事屬於衛生部的管轄範圍。

pus /pʌs; pʌs/ *n* [U] a thick yellowish liquid produced in an infected part of your body 膿: *Pus was oozing out of the wound.* 膿正從傷口滲出。

push in 插隊

queue *BrE*【英】/ line *AmE*【美】隊

push¹ /pʊʃ; pʊʃ/ *v*

1 ▶MOVE 移動◀ [I,T] to make someone or something move by using your hands, arms, shoulders etc to put pressure on them 推; 推動: *It's still stuck – you'll have to push harder.* 那東西還卡着 —— 你得使勁推。| *When I give the signal, I want you all to push.* 我發出信號時, 你們就一起推。| **push sb/sth** *Johnson was penalised for pushing another player.* 約翰遜因推人犯規而被判罰。| **push sb/sth up/across/away etc** *They were trying to push me into the water.* 他們正試圖把我推入水中。| *He pushed away his plate when he had finished.* 他吃完後把盤子推開。| **push the door open/shut** *I slowly pushed the door open.* 我慢慢推開門。—see picture on page A21 參見A21頁圖

2 ▶BUTTON/SWITCH 按鈕/開關◀ [I,T] to press a button, SWITCH etc, especially in order to make a piece of equipment start working 按下〔按鈕、開關等〕: *You just push that button there, and the coffee comes out here.* 你只需按一下那邊的開關, 咖啡就會從這裡出來。

3 ▶TRY TO GET PAST SB 設法從某人旁邊經過◀ [I, T always+adv/prep] to use your hands, arms, shoulders etc to make someone move, especially so that you can get past them 擠, 推擠: *There's no need to push. There are enough tickets for everyone.* 沒有必要推擠 —— 有足夠的票給每個人。| **push past/through** *Jackson pushed past the journalists and escaped in his limousine.* 傑克遜從記者羣中擠出來, 坐上他的轎車逃走了。| **push your way towards/across etc** *She pushed her way to the front of the crowd.* 她擠到人羣的前面。

4 ▶ENCOURAGE/PERSUADE 鼓勵/勸説◀ [T] to encourage or persuade someone to do something that they do not want to do 鼓勵〔某人做其不想做的事〕, 力勸: **push sb to do sth** *Her husband keeps pushing her to accept the job.* 她丈夫一直勸她接受這份工作。| **push sb into doing sth** *My parents pushed me into going to college.* 我父母力勸我上大學。

5 ▶WORK HARD 努力工作◀ [T] to make someone work very hard 使〔某人〕努力工作: *The teachers don't seem to push these kids very hard.* 老師們好像對這些孩子督促不夠。| **push yourself** *He's been pushing himself too much.* 他一直在賣命工作。

6 ▶DRUGS 毒品◀ [T] *informal* to sell illegal drugs【非正式】販賣〔毒品〕—see also 另見 PUSHER

7 ▶ADVERTISE 做廣告◀ a) [T] *informal* to try to sell more of a product by advertising it a lot【非正式】〔通過大量廣告〕推銷〔商品〕

8 ▶IDEAS/OPINIONS 觀點/意見◀ [T] to try to make people accept your ideas or opinions, especially by talking about them a lot 竭力使別人接受〔自己的觀點或意見〕; 推銷, 兜售〔觀點或意見〕: *I wish you'd stop pushing all this political rubbish.* 我希望你不要再兜售這種政治垃圾了。

9 push the boat out *BrE informal* to spend a lot of money on something because you want to make sure that it is enjoyable, successful etc【英, 非正式】不惜費用地享樂[慶祝]

10 push your luck/push it *informal* to stupidly do something again, taking a risk that you will avoid problems because you have done it successfully before【非正式】〔因曾經成功而〕再次冒險; 得寸進尺; 想再交好運: *Look, just don't push it! I've had about enough of your criticism!* 哎, 別再得寸進尺了! 我已經受夠了你的批評!

11 push sth to the back of your mind to try to forget about an unpleasant feeling or situation 把某物拋在腦後, 忘記〔不愉快的感覺或情況〕: *I think you should push all these doubts to the back of your mind.* 我認為你應該把這些疑慮拋在腦後。

12 push the point *old-fashioned* to keep trying to make someone accept your opinion in a way that they find annoying【過時】〔令人討厭地〕拚命勸說某人接受自己的觀點 —see also 另見 PULL¹, PUSHED, PUSHING

push ahead *phr v* [I] to continue with a plan or activity, especially in a determined way〔尤指堅定地〕繼續進行〔計劃或活動〕, 大力推進: [+**with**] *After careful consideration they decided to push ahead with the deal.* 經過仔細考慮他們決定大力推動這項交易的實現。

push along *phr v* [I] *spoken* to leave a place【口】離開: *It's getting late, I think we should be pushing along.* 天晚了, 我們該走啦。—see also 另見 **push off** (PUSH¹)

push sb **around** also 又作 **push** sb **about** *BrE*【英】*phr v* [T] to give someone orders in a rude or threatening way 對〔某人〕發號施令; 擺佈〔某人〕: *Who do you think you're pushing around? Do it yourself.* 你以為你在對誰發號施令? 你自己做吧。

push sth ↔ **aside** *phr v* [T] to try to forget about something, especially something unpleasant, so that you can give your attention to what you are doing 忘掉〔尤指不愉快的事情〕: *You just have to try and push these negative thoughts aside.* 你必須盡量拋開這些消極的想法。

push (sb) **for** sth *phr v* [T] to keep asking for something or trying to persuade people to do something, because you believe it is important or necessary 一再地要求〔某事物〕, 力圖得到〔某物〕, 敦促〔某人〕做某事: *People living near the airport are pushing for new restrictions on night flights.* 住在機場附近的人們正強烈要求訂立限制夜航班機的新規定。| *I'll have to push you for a decision.* 我將不得不敦促你作出決定。

push forward *phr v* **1** [I] to continue moving towards a place, in spite of difficulties〔不顧困難〕繼續前進: *As* *the army pushed forward, the death toll mounted.* 隨着部隊的推進, 死亡人數在增加。**2 push yourself forward** to try to make other people notice you 使他人注意到自己; 出風頭: *If she's going to do well at school, she'll have to push herself forward more.* 要是她想在學校幹得好, 她就得盡量讓別人注意到自己。

push in *phr v* [I] **1** to give advice, join in a conversation etc when you are not really involved〔在不相干的情況下〕給人勸告; 插話; 干預: *No, it didn't seem like you were pushing in or anything, just trying to help.* 不, 看起來你不是在干預甚麼的, 只是試圖幫忙而已。**2** *BrE informal* to rudely and unfairly join a line of people, in front of other people who were already waiting【英, 非正式】插隊, 擠到等候的隊伍前面

push off *phr v* [I] **1** *spoken, especially BrE used to* tell someone rudely to go away【口, 尤英】走開〔用作不禮貌的命令語〕**2** *old-fashioned* to leave a place【過時】離開 —see also 另見 **push along** (PUSH[1]) **3** if a boat pushes off from the shore, it moves away from it〔船〕離岸

push on *phr v* [I] **1** to continue travelling somewhere, especially after you have had a rest〔尤指休息之後〕繼續前行: *It was getting dark but we decided to push on a little further.* 天越來越黑了, 但我們決定繼續往前走一段。**2** to continue doing an activity 繼續〔做某事〕: **[+with]** *I'd better push on with my homework.* 我最好繼續做我的作業。

push sb/sth ↔ **over** *phr v* [T] to make someone or something fall to the ground by pushing them 把〔某人或某物〕推倒: *Several people had been pushed over in the rush for bargains.* 在搶購便宜貨時有幾個人被推倒了。

push sth ↔ **through** *phr v* [T] to get a new law officially accepted 使〔新法律〕獲得通過: *The White House made every effort to push the policy through Congress.* 白宮盡力使這項政策獲得國會通過。

push sth ↔ **up** *phr v* [T] **1** to make the amount, number, or value of something increase 使〔某物的數量、價值〕增加, 使上漲: *The war has pushed up oil prices.* 戰爭使石油價格上漲。—compare 比較 **push down** (PUSH[1]) **2 be pushing up (the) daisies** *humorous* to be dead【幽默】死, 入土, 一命嗚呼

push² *n*

1 ►PUSHING MOVEMENT 推的動作◄ [C] the act of pushing or pressing something 推; 按: *With a gentle push, the car started moving down the slope.* 輕輕一推, 這輛車開始順坡而下。| **give sb/sth a push** *He gave her a push to see if she was awake.* 他推了她一下, 看她是否醒着。| *If the door's stuck, just give it a push.* 如果門卡住, 推一下就行了。| **at the push of a button** (=used to emphasize how easy a machine is to use) 按一下按鈕就行了〔用於強調機器容易操作〕*The liquidizer is marvellous, creating tasty soups at the push of a button.* 這種榨汁機非常棒, 只需按一下按鈕就能做出美味的湯來。

2 ►ENCOURAGEMENT 鼓勵◄ [singular] a small amount of encouragement, persuasion, or help from someone else〔少許〕激勵, 勸導, 幫助: *It looked like she would never go, but all she needed was a gentle push.* 她看起來好像決不會去, 其實只需稍稍一勸她也就去了。

3 ►ATTACK/ATTEMPT 進攻/攻勢◄ **a)** [C] a planned military attack into the area where the enemy is 有計劃的軍事攻擊, 推進: *The army has made another big push into enemy territory.* 大軍對敵佔區進行了又一次大規模進攻。**b)** [C] a determined and well-planned attempt to gain an advantage over your opponents in business, advertising etc〔生意、廣告等方面為贏得優勢而進行的〕努力: *The company has recently made a big push into the Japanese market.* 該公司最近大舉向日本市場推進。

4 give sb the push *BrE informal*【英, 非正式】**a)** to make someone leave their job, especially because they have done something wrong〔尤指因犯了錯誤而〕解雇 **b)** to tell someone that you no longer want to have a loving or sexual relationship with them 與情人分手, 斷絕關係

5 at a push *informal, especially BrE* if you can do something at a push, it will be difficult, but you will be able to do it【非正式, 尤英】真有必要時, 不得已時: *We have room for five people, maybe six at a push.* 我們有容納五個人的空間, 萬不得已的情況下或許可容納六個人。

6 it'll be a push *spoken* used to say that something will be difficult because you do not have enough time to do it【口】因為沒有足夠的時間做而覺得某事困難: *I'll do my best, but it'll be a bit of a push.* 我會盡我所能, 但時間會有點緊迫。

7 if it comes to the push also 又作 **when push comes to shove** *spoken* used to say what you can do if you are forced to make a decision or take action【口】一旦[當]情況緊急時; 當必須採取行動時; 當必須作出決定時: *When push comes to shove you can always borrow the extra money from the bank.* 如有急用, 你總能從銀行借到額外的錢。

push-bike /ˈ· ·/ *n* [C] *BrE informal* a BICYCLE【英, 非正式】腳踏車, 自行車, 單車

push-but·ton /ˈ· ,··/ *adj* [only before noun 僅用於名詞前] **1** operated by pressing a button with your finger 按鈕式的: *The old car had a push-button starter.* 這輛舊汽車有個按鈕式的起動裝置。**2** using computers or electronic equipment rather than traditional methods 使用電腦的, 使用電子設備的: *push-button warfare* 電子化戰爭 | *the push-button piloting of a ship* 輪船的電子化領航

push·cart /ˈpʊʃˌkɑrt; ˈpʊʃkɑːt/ *n* [C] a large flat container like a box with wheels, used especially by people who sell goods in the street〔尤指街頭小販使用的〕手推車

push·chair /ˈpʊʃˌtʃɛr; ˈpʊʃ-tʃeə/ *n* [C] *BrE* a small folding seat on wheels, in which a young child sits and is pushed along【英】(摺疊式) 輕便嬰兒手推車; STROLLER *AmE*【美】—compare 比較 BABY CARRIAGE —see picture at 參見 PRAM 圖

pushed /pʊʃt; pʊʃt/ *adj* [not before noun 不用於名詞前] *informal*【非正式】**1 be pushed for** to have difficulty finding enough time, money etc〔時間或金錢等〕不足, 拮据: *I'm always rather pushed for money at the end of the month.* 每當月底, 我總是手頭很緊。**2** too busy 太忙的: *I'd love to help, but I'm a bit pushed at the moment.* 我很願意幫忙, 但我現在有點忙。**3 be (hard) pushed to do sth** to have a lot of difficulty doing something 做某事有很多困難: *You'll be hard pushed to find someone to type your essay for you now.* 現在你很難找到人為你打論文。

push·er /ˈpʊʃə; ˈpʊʃə/ *n* [C] *informal* someone who sells illegal drugs【非正式】毒品販子 —compare 比較 PEDDLER (2) —see also 另見 PENPUSHER

push·ing /ˈpʊʃɪŋ; ˈpʊʃɪŋ/ *prep* **be pushing 18/30/60 etc** *usually spoken* to be nearly 18,30,60 years old etc【一般口】將近 18/30/60 歲等: *Sheila must be pushing 40 by now.* 希拉現在一定將近 40 歲了。

push·o·ver /ˈpʊʃˌovə; ˈpʊʃˌəʊvə/ *n informal*【非正式】**be a pushover a)** to be easy to persuade, influence, or defeat 易被勸服[影響, 擊敗]的: *Duncan will soon see that I'm no pushover.* 鄧肯將很快看到我不是容易對付的人。| **[+for]** *Mr Wasco is a pushover for blondes with green eyes.* 瓦斯科先生很容易被碧眼金髮的女人迷住。**b)** to be very easy to do or win 容易做的, 容易取勝的: *The exam was a pushover.* 這次考試很容易。

push-start /ˈ· ·/ *v* [T] to push a vehicle in order to make the engine start 推車發動 —**push-start** *n* [C]

push-up /ˈ· ·/ *n* [C] *AmE* an exercise in which you lie on the floor on your front and push yourself up with your arms【美】俯臥撐; PRESS-UP *BrE*【英】

push·y /ˈpʊʃɪ; ˈpʊʃi/ *adj* so determined to succeed and to get what you want that you behave in a way that seems rude 急於求成的, 咄咄逼人的: *a pushy salesman* 拚命勸別人買東西的推銷員 —**pushily** *adv* —**pushiness** *n* [U]

pu·sil·lan·i·mous /ˌpjusḷ`ænəməs; ˌpjuːsᶦ'lænᶦməs/ *adj formal* frightened of taking even small risks【正式】怯懦的, 膽小的 —**pusillanimously** *adv* —**pusillanimity** /pjusḷə`nɪmətɪ; ˌpjuːsᶦlə'nɪmᶦti/ *n* [U]

puss /pʊs; pʊs/ *n* [usually singular 一般用單數] **1** *informal* a name for a cat, or a way of calling a cat【非正式】貓咪〔貓的名字或喚貓語〕: *Come here, puss, puss, puss!* 過來, 貓咪! **2** *AmE slang* face【美俚】臉: *a smack in the puss* 打一個耳光

pus·sy /`pʊsɪ; 'pʊsi/ *n* [C] **1** also 又作 **pussy cat** /'·· ·/ an informal word for a cat, used especially by or to children 貓咪〔兒語〕 **2** *taboo* a woman's sex organs【諱】女性(外)生殖器 **3** *AmE informal* an insulting word for a man who is weak or not brave【美, 非正式】懦夫, 膿包〔對於怯懦男人的侮辱性說法〕

pus·sy·foot /`pʊsɪˌfʊt; 'pʊsifʊt/ also 又作 **pussyfoot around/about** *v* [I] *informal* to be too careful and frightened to do something, such as taking firm decisions or telling someone exactly what you think【非正式】縮手縮腳, 畏首畏尾; 優柔寡斷: *Stop pussyfooting around, and tell me what he said!* 別吞吞吐吐的, 告訴我他說了甚麼!

pussy wil·low /'·· ,··/ *n* [C,U] a tree with white flowers that are soft like fur 褪色柳

pus·tule /`pʌstʃul; 'pʌstjuːl/ *n* [C] *technical* a small raised spot on your skin containing PUS (=a thick yellow liquid)【術語】小膿疱

put /pʊt; pʊt/ *v past tense* put *present participle* putting

① MOVE STH 移動某物
② CHANGE SB'S SITUATION 改變某人的境況
③ SAY/EXPRESS 說/表達
④ ASK FOR AN ANSWER/DECISION 要求答覆/決定
⑤ ADD STH 加上某物
⑥ SEND SB SOMEWHERE 派某人到某處
⑦ PUT RIGHT/STRAIGHT 糾正/改正
⑧ STOP/END STH 停止/結束某事物
⑨ IN ORDER OF IMPORTANCE/QUALITY 按重要性/質量順序
⑩ OTHER MEANINGS 其他意思
⑪ WRITE 寫

① MOVE STH 移動某物

1 [T always+adv/prep] to move something from one place or position into another, especially using your hands 放; 放置: **put sth in/on/there etc** *Put those bags on the table.* 把那些包放在桌子上。| *You should put your hand over your mouth when you cough.* 你咳嗽時應用手捂住嘴。| *I can't remember where I put my keys.* 我記不起來把鑰匙放在哪裡。

② CHANGE SB'S SITUATION 改變某人的境況

2 [T always+adv/prep] to change someone's situation 改變〔某人〕的狀態[境地, 局面]: *This was the shot that put Sampras into the semifinal.* 這是使森柏斯進入半決賽的一次抽球。| **put sb in an awkward position** (=make someone's situation difficult or embarrassing) 使某人處境困難[尷尬] *Paul's resignation has put us in an awkward position.* 保羅的辭職使我們處境困難。| **put sb out of a job/out of work** (=make them lose their job) 使某人失業 *Pit closures have put thousands of miners out of a job.* 煤礦關閉使成千上萬的礦工失去了工作。| **put sb in a bad mood** (=make them feel annoyed) 使某人心情不好 *The long delay had put us all in a bad mood.* 長時間的延誤使我們大家心情都不好。

3 put sb in command/charge/control to give someone authority over a group, activity, organization etc 使某人主管[負責]…: *Tom Pendlebury has been put in charge of the project.* 湯姆·彭德爾伯里奉派負責這項計劃。

③ SAY/EXPRESS 說/表達

4 [T always+adv/prep] to express something using words in a particular way 說, 表達: **put sth well/cleverly/succinctly etc** *I thought her arguments were quite cleverly put.* 我認為她巧妙地表達了自己的論點。| *Well, since you put it like that, I can't really refuse.* 好, 既然你那麼說, 我確實無法拒絕。| **as sb puts it** (=used to repeat what someone else has said) 正如某人所說 *Long-term planning is a waste of time because – as Keynes puts it – in the long term we're all dead.* 長期規劃是浪費時間, 因為正如凱恩斯所說, 從長遠來看, 我們總有一死。| **put sth into words** (=express a feeling or idea) 用語言表達某感覺[思想]

5 to put it bluntly *spoken* used to tell someone that you are going to say exactly what you think【口】坦率地說: *To put it bluntly, Robert's just not good enough for the job.* 坦率地說, 羅伯特不能勝任這份工作。

6 to put it mildly *spoken* used to say that a situation is actually worse than the way you are describing it【口】往輕處說: *We are, to put it mildly, in a mess.* 說得輕點, 我們正身處困境。

7 how can I put it? *spoken* used when what you are going to say might sound unpleasant or impolite【口】我該怎麼說呢〔用於表示你要說的話可能聽起來令人不愉快或不禮貌〕: *Derek's – how shall I put it – not very attractive.* 德里克——我該怎麼說呢——不怎麼有吸引力。

8 to put it another way used when trying to explain something in a different way and make it clearer 用另一種方式說, 換句話說: *Money makes money. To put it another way, the greater the investment, the greater the profit.* 錢能生錢, 換句話說, 投資越大, 利潤越大。

④ ASK FOR AN ANSWER/DECISION 要求答覆/決定

9 [T] to ask a question, especially when you want to get someone's opinion about something 提出〔問題〕, 徵求某人意見: *After the break, you will be able to put your questions to the panel.* 短暫休息之後, 你們就可以向專題小組提問了。| **put it to sb** *I put it to you, Mr President, that these measures will not solve the problem of violent crime.* 總統先生請您考慮, 這些措施不能解決暴力犯罪問題。

10 put a proposition/proposal/case to to tell someone or a group of people about something and ask them to agree to it or make a decision about it 向…提出建議, 將提議交給…

⑤ ADD STH 加上某物

11 [T] to add something 加, 增加: *Put a little romance into your life.* 給你的生活增添一點浪漫。| *Just put a little more expression into it.* 對它再多投入些感情。

12 [T] to make money available to be used in a business, or add it to something such as a bank account 投資於; 投入; 加進; 存入〔銀行賬戶〕

⑥ SEND SB SOMEWHERE 派某人到某處

13 [T always+adv/prep] to arrange for or order some-

one to go to a place for a particular purpose 安排[命令]某人去某處: **put sb in/on etc** *Putting troops into Rwanda is not an option.* 派部隊進入盧旺達不是一種選擇。
14 put sb on a train/plane etc to take someone to a plane, train etc to start a journey 把某人帶上[送上]火車/飛機等

⑦ PUT RIGHT/STRAIGHT 糾正/改正
15 put sb straight/right to tell someone the true facts when they have made a mistake that annoys you 糾正[改正]某人的錯誤: *Let me put you straight on one thing, Andy's not a thief.* 讓我糾正你一個錯誤, 安迪不是賊子。
16 put sth straight to make something look clean and tidy 使某物看上去乾淨整潔, 把某物收拾[整理]好: *It took us all weekend to put the garden straight.* 我們花了一整個週末才收拾好花園。
17 put sth right to make a situation better, especially after someone has made a mistake or behaved badly 改正, 糾正: *I'll put it right at once.* 我立即改過來。

⑧ STOP/END STH 停止/結束某事物
18 put a stop to/put an end to to stop an activity that is harmful or unacceptable 結束, 終止〔有害或不能容忍的事物〕; 使…停止: *There's too much money being wasted, and it's time we put a stop to it.* 浪費太多錢了, 是我們結束這種活動的時候了。
19 put paid to *BrE* to spoil and end your hopes or plans completely【英】使〔希望或計劃〕成為泡影: *A car accident put paid to his chances of taking part in the race.* 一次汽車事故使他參加賽跑的機會成了泡影。

⑨ IN ORDER OF IMPORTANCE/QUALITY 按重要性/質量順序
20 [T always+adv/prep] to consider something as having a particular level of importance or quality 認為某事物具有某種重要性[品質], 將某物看作[列為]: **put sb as/among/in etc** *I'd put Porto amongst the top ten European teams.* 我把波圖隊看作是歐洲十大強隊之一。| **put sth first/before** *The job's important to him, but he puts his family first.* 這份工作對他來說很重要, 但他把自己的家庭放在首位。

⑩ OTHER MEANINGS 其他意思
21 put sth into action/effect/practice to start using a plan, idea, knowledge etc 把某事物付諸實踐, 實施, 實行計劃[想法等]: *James was keen to put some of the things he had learned into practice.* 詹姆斯渴望把他學到的一些東西運用到實踐中去。
22 put pressure on a) to make someone's situation difficult 使某人處境困難 **b)** to try to make someone do something 對某人施加〔做某事的〕壓力
23 put energy/work/enthusiasm etc into to use a lot of energy etc when you are doing an activity 投入[付出]精力/勞動/熱情等: *I hope the show's a success – they've put so much work into it.* 我希望這次演出成功 — 他們為之付出了很多心血。
24 put sth behind you to try to forget about an unpleasant event or experience and think about the future 忘掉〔不愉快的事情或經歷〕, 把某事物拋諸腦後: *The team must put Saturday's defeat behind them and concentrate on tonight's game.* 這個隊必須忘掉星期六的失敗而把心思集中在今晚的比賽上。
25 ►THROW 扔, 投◄ to throw a SHOT (=a heavy metal ball) in a sports competition 推〔鉛球〕
26 put it there *spoken* used to tell someone to put their hand in yours, either as a greeting or after making an agreement with them【口】請跟我握手〔用於問候或達成協議時〕: *$500? OK, it's a deal. Put it there!* 500美元? 好吧, 成交。握手吧!

⑪ WRITE 寫
27 [T] to write something or to make a mark with a pen or pencil 寫下; 標上〔記號〕: **put sth in/on/under** *Put your name at the top of each answer sheet.* 把你的名字寫在每張答題紙的上端。—see also 另見 **put your finger on** (FINGER[1] (4)), **put your foot down** (FOOT[1] (10)), **put your foot in it** (FOOT[1] (12)), **put sth to good use** (USE[2] (4)), **put your back into it** (BACK[2] (19))

put about *phr v* **1** [T **put** sth ↔ **about**] *BrE informal* to give other people news or information, especially when it is unpleasant or untrue【英, 非正式】散佈〔尤指令人不愉快或不真實的消息或信息〕: **put it about that** *Someone's been putting it about that she's splitting up with her husband.* 有人在散佈消息說她正和丈夫離婚。**2 put yourself about** *BrE informal* to have sexual relationships with a lot of different people【英, 非正式】與很多人有性關係 **3** [I,T] *technical* if a ship puts about or if you put it about, it changes direction【術語】〔船〕改變方向; 使〔船〕改變方向

put across *phr v* [T] **1** [**put** sth ↔ **across**] to explain your ideas, beliefs, policies etc in a way that people can understand 表達清楚〔自己的想法等〕, 解釋清楚: *The union representative put her argument across very effectively.* 工會代表非常清楚有力地表達了自己的論點。**2 put yourself across** to communicate effectively, so that people have a clear idea of your character, your ideas etc 有效地傳達自己的想法等; 清楚地表達自己的意思: *Sue's never been very good at putting herself across at interviews.* 蘇一向不善於在面試時把自己的意思講清楚。

put sth ↔ **aside** *phr v* [T] **1** to try to stop thinking about a problem, quarrel, or disagreement, because you want to achieve something 把〔某事物〕撇開不理, 不考慮: *The UN has called on the warring factions to put aside their differences.* 聯合國呼籲敵對各派拋開分歧。**2** to save money regularly, usually for a particular purpose 儲存〔錢〕備用: *We're trying to put aside a few hundred dollars every month toward our vacation.* 我們盡量每月存幾百美元供度假用。**3** to put down something you are reading or working with, in order to start doing something else 放下〔正在讀的東西或正在幹的活〕: *Charles put aside his newspaper and got up to answer the door.* 查爾斯放下他的報紙起身去開門。**4** to keep a period of time free in order to be able to do something 留出〔一段時間〕: *Try to put aside an hour each day for exercise.* 每天盡量騰出一個小時鍛鍊身體。

put sth **at** sth *phr v* [T] to calculate and state an amount, someone's age etc, without trying to be very exact 推測〔某物〕是…, 估計〔數量、年齡等〕是…: *Official estimates put the damage at over $10 million.* 官方估計損失大約為一千多萬美元。

put sb/sth **away** *phr v* [T] **1** [**put** sth ↔ **away**] to put something in the place where it is usually kept 把〔某物〕收拾起來〔放回原處〕: *Let me just put these files away.* 讓我把這些文件收拾好。**2** [**put** sb **away**] *informal* to put someone in a prison or in a mental hospital【非正式】把〔某人〕送入監獄[精神病院]: *He was put away for five years for armed robbery.* 他因持械搶劫而被關入監獄五年。**3** [**put** sth ↔ **away**] *informal* to eat or drink a lot【非正式】吃[喝]很多: *It's amazing the amount that child can put away.* 那孩子的食量真是驚人。**4** [**put** sth ↔ **away**] to save money 儲存〔錢〕: *My Grandfather had put away over £50,000.* 我祖父已存了50,000英鎊。

put back *phr v* **1** [T **put** sth ↔ **back**] to arrange for an event to start at a later time or date; POSTPONE 使〔某活動〕延期, 推遲: *The meeting has been put back to next Thursday.* 會議延期到下週四舉行。**2** [T **put** sth ↔ **back**] to delay a process or activity by a number of weeks, months etc 使〔某過程或活動〕延遲〔幾週、幾個月等〕: *This fire could put back the opening date by several weeks.* 這場火會使開業日期延遲幾個星期。**3 put a clock/a watch back** to make a clock or watch show an earlier time 把〔鐘、錶〕撥慢 —see also 另見 **put the**

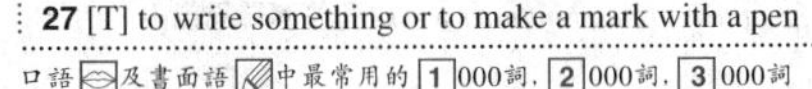

clock back (CLOCK[1] (2))

put sth ↔ **by** *phr v* [T] to save money regularly in order to use it later 儲存〔錢〕備用: *We're trying to put a little by each month for a new car.* 我們正盡量每月存一點錢以備買輛新汽車用。

put down *phr v*

1 ►CRITICIZE 批評◄ [T **put** sb ↔ **down**] to keep criticizing someone in front of other people 一再當眾批評某人: *I hate the way Dave puts me down the whole time.* 我很討厭戴夫老是當眾批評我。| **put yourself down** *"I don't stand a chance of getting the job." "Don't be silly, you mustn't put yourself down."* "我沒有機會得到那份工作。""別傻了, 你不應貶低自己。"

2 ►PAY 付款◄ [T **put** sth ↔ **down**] to pay part of the total cost of something, so that you can pay the rest later 付〔訂金〕: *How much could you afford to put down on a house?* 你付得起一所房子的多少訂金?

3 ►WRITE 寫◄ [T **put** sth ↔ **down**] *BrE* to write something, especially a name or number on a piece of paper or on a list【英】寫下, 記下: *I'll just put your phone number down in my book.* 我這就把你的電話號碼記在我的電話簿裡。

4 ►KILL 殺死◄ [T **put** sth ↔ **down**] to kill an animal without causing it pain, usually because it is old or ill 殺死〔老、病動物〕以免除其痛苦: *We had to have the dog put down.* 我們不得不讓人殺死這條狗。

5 put the phone down to put the RECEIVER back onto the telephone when you have finished speaking to someone 放下電話: **put the phone down on sb** (=to suddenly end a telephone conversation) 突然掛斷某人的電話

6 put down a revolution/revolt/rebellion etc to stop a REVOLUTION (2) etc by using force 鎮壓[平息]革命/反叛/叛亂等: *Military police were called in to put down the riot.* 憲兵被召來平定暴亂。

7 ►STOP A VEHICLE 使車輛停下◄ [T **put** sb **down**] *BrE* to stop a vehicle so that passengers can get off at a particular place【英】停車讓〔乘客〕下來: *Just put me down at the gate.* 在大門口停車讓我下來就行了。

8 ►AIRCRAFT 飛機◄ [I,T] if an aircraft puts down or if a pilot puts it down, it lands〔飛機〕着陸; 使〔飛機〕着陸: *The engine failed and the plane put down in the sea.* 發動機失靈, 飛機在海上降落了。

9 ►BABY 嬰兒◄ [T **put** sb **down**] to put a baby in its bed 把〔嬰兒〕放在他的牀上: *We try to put Amy down at six every evening.* 我們盡量每晚六點把艾米放在牀上讓她睡覺。

10 I couldn't put it down *spoken* used to say that you found a book, game etc extremely interesting【口】我不能放下它〔用於表示你認為某本書或遊戲極其有趣〕: *Once I'd started reading it I just couldn't put it down.* 我一開始讀就愛不釋手。

11 put down a motion/an amendment to suggest a subject, plan, change in the law etc for a parliament or committee to consider 提出一項動議/修正案〔供議會或委員會考慮〕

put sb **down as** sth *phr v* [T] to guess what someone is like or what they do, without having much information about them〔沒充分根據就〕認為〔某人〕是..., 把〔某人〕看作是...: *They'd already put me down as a good-for-nothing young artist.* 他們已把我當作一個無用的年輕藝術家。

put sb **down for** sth *phr v* [T] **1** to put someone's name on a list so that they can take part in an activity, join an organization etc 把〔某人的名字〕登記在參加者的名單上, 為〔某人〕報名參加某活動[加入某組織]: *We've put Simon's name down for nursery school.* 我們已給西蒙報名準備上幼兒園。**2 put sb down for £5/£20 etc** *especially BrE* to write someone's name on a list with an amount of money that they have promised to give【尤英】把〔某人的名字〕登記在認捐名單中並記錄五英鎊/二十英鎊等捐款數額

put sth **down to** sth *phr v* [T] **1** to explain the reason for something, especially when you are only guessing 把〔某事〕歸因於: *I put Jane's moodiness down to the stress she was under.* 我把簡的喜怒無常歸因於她所承受的壓力。**2 put it down to experience** used to tell someone not to feel too upset by failure, but to learn something useful from it 把它當作一次經驗教訓: *Everyone gets rejected from time to time; put it down to experience.* 每個人都偶爾會被拒絕, 把它當作一次經驗教訓吧。

put sth ↔ **forth** *phr v* [T] **put forth leaves/shoots/roots etc** *literary* if a tree or bush puts forth leaves etc it begins to grow them【文】〔樹或灌木〕長出葉子/新芽/根等

put sb/sth ↔ **forward** *phr v* [T] **1** to suggest a plan, proposal etc, especially in order to start discussions about something that needs to be decided 提出〔計劃、建議等〕: *The working party has put forward a good case for moving to a new site.* 特別工作組提出了一條很好的遷往新址的理由。| *the theories put forward by Dr. Kesner* 凱斯納博士提出的理論 **2** to arrange for an event to start at an earlier time or date 將...提前: *The men's final has been put forward to 1:30.* 男子決賽提前到一點半舉行。**3 put a clock/watch forward** to make a clock or watch show a later time 把〔鐘、錶〕撥快 **4 put yourself/sb's name forward** to suggest formally that you or someone else should be considered for a particular job, membership of an organization etc 提名〔推薦〕某人做某工作[成為某組織成員]: *We put Joe's name forward to serve on the local council.* 我們推舉喬為地方議會成員。

put in *phr v*

1 ►EQUIPMENT 設備◄ [T **put** sth ↔ **in**] to fix a piece of equipment into your home so that it is ready to be used 安裝〔設備〕: *We decided to have a new bathroom put in.* 我們決定安裝一套新的盥洗設備。

2 ►TIME/ENERGY 時間/能量◄ [T **put** sth ↔ **in**] to spend time or use energy working or practising something 花費〔時間或精力〕做某事[練習某事]: *You have to put in a lot of effort to learn a new language.* 要學一門新的語言需要付出很大的努力。

3 ►SAY STH 説某事◄ [T **put** sth ↔ **in**] to interrupt someone in order to say something 插話: *"I'm sure Daniel's the best man for the job." Mrs Weevers put in.* "我相信丹尼爾是這項工作最合適的人選。"威弗斯夫人插話説。

4 put in a claim/request to officially make a claim or request 提出要求/請求: *She put in a claim for damage to the photographs.* 她為照片的損壞提出索賠。

5 ►ELECT 選舉◄ [T **put** sb ↔ **in**] to elect a politician or political party 選舉〔政治家或政黨〕

6 put in an appearance to go to a social event, meeting etc for a short time〔在社交活動或會議上〕露面: *I don't really want to go to the party, but I'd better put in an appearance.* 我不大想去參加那個聚會, 但我最好露一下面。

7 ►SHIP 船◄ [I] if a ship puts in, it enters a port〔船〕進港

put in for sth *phr v* [T] to make a formal request for something 正式要求, 申請: *It's time you put in for a pay increase.* 是你申請加薪水的時候了。

put sb/sth ↔ **off** *phr v* [T] **1** to arrange to do something at a later time or date, especially because there is a problem, difficulty etc 推遲某事, 使某事延期: *The meeting's been put off till next week.* 會議已推遲到下星期了。| **put off doing sth** *We'll have to put off going on vacation until you're better.* 我們得把休假日期推遲, 直到你好些為止。**2** to delay meeting someone, paying someone etc because you do not want to do it until later 推遲〔與某人會面或付錢給某人〕, 搪塞〔某人〕, 敷衍〔某人〕: *I just don't have the money right now – I'll have to put him off for another week.* 我現在就是沒錢 —— 我得再拖一個星期還他。| *I managed to put Ron off with a promise to pay him next week.* 我答應羅恩説下星期付

給他錢, 應付過去了。**3** to delay doing something until later because you do not want to do it now 拖延: *You really ought to write to her. You can't just keep putting it off.* 你確實應該給她寫信, 你不能再拖了。**4** to make you dislike something or not want to do something 使不喜歡做某事, 使不想做某事: *The job sounded interesting but the idea of moving house again put me off.* 那份工作聽起來很有趣, 但是一想起要再次搬家, 我就不樂意了。| *Don't be put off by the title – it's a really good book.* 別對書名產生壞印象 — 它確實是一本好書。| **put sb off (doing) sth** *This lousy weather is enough to put anyone off camping.* 這種糟糕的天氣足以讓任何人打消野營的念頭。**5** to make it difficult for someone to do something, by preventing them from thinking clearly about what they are doing 影響某人做某事, 使分心: *The photographers put McEnroe off his game.* 那些攝影師影響了麥根萊比賽。| *Stop giggling! You're putting me off.* 別再咯咯笑啦! 你讓我分心了。**6** to let someone leave a vehicle at a particular place 讓〔某人〕下車: *I'll put you off at the bottom of the street.* 我會在這條街的盡頭停車讓你下來。

put sth ↔ **on** *phr v* [T]

1 ▶CLOTHES 衣服◀ [**put** sth ↔ **on**] to put a piece of clothing on your body 穿上, 戴上: *Put your coat on before you go outside.* 你出去之前把外套穿上。| *I'll have to put my glasses on; I can't read the sign from here.* 我得戴上我的眼鏡; 從這裡我看不清那個標誌。

2 ▶ON SKIN 在皮膚上◀ [**put** sth ↔ **on**] to put MAKE-UP, cream etc on your skin 在皮膚上塗[擦]〔化妝品、乳液等〕: *It takes Julie about half an hour to put her make-up on every morning.* 朱莉每天早上花大約半小時化妝。

3 ▶LIGHT/HEAT ETC 光/熱等◀ [**put** sth ↔ **on**] to make a light or a piece of electrical or gas equipment start working by pressing or turning a button 打開〔燈、電器或煤氣裝置〕: *Shall I put the kettle on?* 我要把水壺的開關打開嗎?

4 ▶MUSIC 音樂◀ to put a record, TAPE or CD into a machine and start playing it 播放〔唱片、磁帶或激光唱片〕

5 ▶PRETEND 假裝◀ [**put** sth ↔ **on**] to pretend to have a certain feeling, opinion, way of speaking etc especially in order to get attention 假裝有..., 裝出: *Sheila's not really that upset; she's just putting it on.* 希拉其實並沒有那麼難過, 她只是在裝腔。| *He always puts on that posh voice when he's on the phone.* 他打電話時總是裝出上流社會的腔調。

6 put on weight/12 lbs/4 kg etc to become fatter and heavier 增加體重/12磅/4公斤等: *Rosie's put on five kilos since she quit smoking.* 羅西戒煙以來體重已增加了五公斤。

7 ▶PLAY/SHOW ETC 戲劇/節目等◀ [**put** sth ↔ **on**] to arrange or perform a show, concert, play etc 上演〔戲劇等〕, 舉行〔音樂會等〕, 表演〔節目〕: *We're putting on a concert to raise money for famine victims.* 我們將舉行一場音樂會為飢民籌錢。

8 ▶COOK 烹調◀ [**put** sth ↔ **on**] to start cooking something 開始烹調...: *Robbie will be home in ten minutes; I'd better put the potatoes on.* 羅比十分鐘後到家, 我該開始做馬鈴薯了。

9 put on a bus/train/coach *BrE* to provide a bus or train in order to take people somewhere【英】提供公共汽車/火車/長途汽車: *British Rail will be putting on extra trains for football fans.* 英國鐵路公司將為足球迷加開火車。

10 you're putting me on! *spoken, especially AmE* used to tell someone that you think they are joking【口, 尤美】你在愚弄[欺騙]我!〔用於告訴某人你認為他們在開玩笑〕: *"They offered me a raise at work." "You're putting me on! How much?"* "他們提出給我加薪水。" "你在騙我! 多少?"

11 ▶ADD 增加◀ [**put** sth **on** sth] to add an amount of money or tax onto the cost of something 增加某物的價格, 對某事物徵稅: *The new tax could put another ten cents on the price of gas.* 新增的稅收會使汽油價格再上漲十美分。

12 ▶RISK MONEY 賭錢◀ [**put** sth **on** sth] to risk an amount of money on the result of a game, race etc 下賭注於〔比賽結果等〕: *We put £50 on Brazil to win the Cup.* 我們以50鎊賭巴西贏得世界杯。

13 put on a brake to make a vehicle stop or slow down by pressing a PEDAL or handle 煞車

put sb **onto** sb/sth *phr v* [T] *informal* to give someone information about something interesting or useful that they did not know about【非正式】向某人提供〔有趣或有用事物的〕信息, 向某人介紹某事: *Barbara put us onto this fantastic French restaurant in Baltimore.* 我們從芭芭拉那裡知道了這家位於巴爾的摩的極好的法國餐館。

put out 撲滅; 熄滅

Joan put the fire out. 瓊撲滅了火。

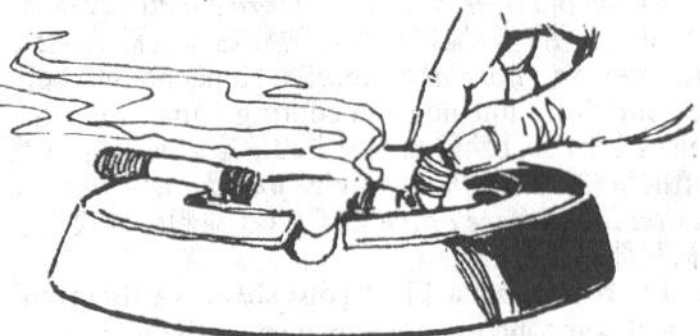

He put out his cigarette. 他熄滅了香煙。

put out *phr v*

1 put out a fire/cigarette etc to make a fire etc stop burning 撲滅火; 熄滅香煙 —see 見 FIRE[1] (USAGE)

2 put out a light/lamp to make a light stop working by pressing or turning a button 關燈

3 feel/be put out to feel upset or offended 感到煩亂[惱火]: *We were a little put out at not being invited to the wedding.* 我們為沒有被邀請參加婚禮感到有點惱火。

4 ▶MAKE WORK 麻煩◀ [T **put** sb ↔ **out**] to make extra work or cause problems for someone 給〔某人〕添麻煩: *Will it put you out if I bring another guest?* 我要是多帶一位客人來會不會給你添麻煩?

5 put yourself out to make an effort to do something that will help someone 努力做某事以幫助某人: *Fred rarely puts himself out on other people's behalf.* 弗瑞德很少費心幫助別人。

6 [T **put** sth ↔ **out**] to put something outside the house 將某物置於門外: *Remember to put the cat out before you go to bed.* 你睡覺前別忘了把貓趕出去。| **put the rubbish/garbage out** (=put dirty or unwanted things outside your house to be taken away) 把垃圾放在外面 | **put the washing out** (=put clothes outside to dry) 把衣服晾在外面

7 put your tongue out to push your tongue out of your mouth, especially as a rude sign to someone 伸出舌頭〔尤作為不禮貌的表示〕

8 put your back/knee/shoulder etc out to injure part of your body, especially by stretching it too much 扭傷背/膝關節脫臼/肩關節脫臼等: *I put my knee out playing tennis yesterday.* 我昨天打網球膝關節脫臼了。

9 put your hand/foot/arm out to stretch your hand etc forward 伸出手/腳/胳膊: *Jimmy put his foot out*

and tripped me up. 吉米伸出腳把我絆倒了。
10 ►MAKE UNCONSCIOUS 使失去知覺◄ [T **put** sb **out**] to make someone unconscious before a medical operation 使失去知覺, 對...實施麻醉
11 put out information/statistics/a statement etc to produce information etc for people to read or listen to 發布消息/公布統計數字/發表聲明等: *The police department has put out a statement apologizing for its officers' conduct.* 警察局發表了一項聲明為警員的行為道歉。
12 ►PRODUCE STH 製作某物◄ to produce radio signals, print magazines, broadcast programmes etc 發出〔無線電信號〕; 出版; 播出
13 put out feelers/antennae to try to discover information or opinions by listening to people or watching what is happening 伸出觸角; 通過傾聽[觀察]發現信息[了解觀點]: *It might be worth putting feelers out to see if there are any jobs going in Paul's school.* 或許值得打聽一下看保羅的學校有沒有甚麼工作可幹。
14 ►SHIP 船◄ [I] if a ship puts out, it starts to sail 〔船〕出航
15 ►HAVE SEX 發生性關係◄ [I] *AmE slang* if a woman puts out, she has sex with a man【美俚】〔女人〕與男人發生性關係
16 [T **put** sb **out**] to end a BATTER's innings in BASEBALL by, for example, catching the ball that they have hit 使〔棒球的擊球手〕出局

put sth ↔ **over** *phr v* [T] **1** to communicate an idea or feeling 傳達〔想法或感情〕: *The course is designed to help you put over your ideas more effectively.* 該課程是為幫助你更有效地傳達自己的觀點而設計的。**2 put one over on** *informal* to deceive someone into believing something untrue or accepting something that is useless【非正式】欺騙某人使之相信虛假的事情[接受無價值的事物]: *They think they've found a way to put one over on the welfare office.* 他們以為他們已經找到了欺騙福利部門的方法。

put through *phr v* [T] **1** [**put** sb/sth ↔ **through**] to connect someone to someone else on the telephone 為某人接通電話: *One moment please, I'm just trying to put you through.* 請等一下, 我這就給你接通電話。**2 put sb through school/college/university** to pay for someone to study at school or college 供某人上學/上大學: *Andrew's parents insisted on putting him through medical school.* 安德魯的父母堅持讓他上醫科大學。**3** [**put** sb **through** sth] to make someone do something unpleasant or difficult 使某人做〔不愉快或困難的事〕: *We put all new recruits through a rigorous week-long training programme.* 我們讓所有的新成員參加一套為期一個星期的嚴格的訓練課程。| **put sb through it** *They really put me through it at that job interview.* 在那次工作面試中, 他們確實使我經受了嚴格的考驗。**4** [**put** sth ↔ **through**] to do what is necessary in order to get a plan or suggestion accepted or approved 〔通過計劃或建議的準備等〕完成, 達成: *Production will start up again when these changes have been put through.* 這些改動順利完成後, 生產就將重新恢復。

put sth **to** sb *phr v* [T] **1** to ask someone a question or make a suggestion to them 向〔某人〕問〔問題〕, 向某人提〔建議〕: *Can I put a question to the speaker?* 我能向演講人提個問題嗎? **2** to offer a group of people something such as a proposal or plan which they can accept or reject 提出〔建議或計劃〕供考慮: *The latest offer will be put to the negotiating committee this afternoon.* 最新的出價將於今天下午提交談判委員會考慮。| **put sth to the vote** (=get people to vote on it) 投票表決某事 *Let's put the motion to the vote.* 讓我們投票表決這項動議。**3 put sb to trouble/inconvenience etc** [usually in questions and negatives 一般用於疑問句和否定句] to make someone do something that will cause them trouble or inconvenience 使某人為難/感到不便等 **4 put your name/signature to** to sign a letter, document etc saying that you agree with what is written in it 簽名表示同意

put sth ↔ **together** *phr v* [T] **1** to prepare or produce something by collecting pieces of information, ideas etc 〔通過收集資料、觀點等〕整理出, 拼湊, 湊成: *We're putting together an anthology of war poetry.* 我們正在編一本戰爭詩集。| *It took all morning to put the proposal together.* 湊成這個建議花了一整個早上。**2** to make a machine, model etc by joining all the different parts 裝配, 組裝〔機器、模型等〕: *I can't work out how to put this table together.* 我搞不清楚如何把這張桌子拼在一起。**3 more...than the rest put together** used when comparing two sets of people or things to say that one set contains more than the total of all the other sets ...比其他合在一起還多: *Italy scored more points than the rest of the group put together.* 意大利的得分比同組其他隊的得分加起來還多。

put up *phr v*
1 ►BUILD 建造◄ [T **put** sth ↔ **up**] to build a wall, fence, or tall building 建造〔牆、籬笆或高樓〕: *They're putting up several new office blocks in the centre of town.* 他們正在市中心建造幾幢新辦公樓。
2 ►ON A WALL 在牆上◄ [T **put** sth ↔ **up**] to put a picture, notice etc on a wall so that people can see it 〔在牆上〕張貼〔圖片、佈告等〕: *The exam results will be put up on Friday afternoon.* 這次考試結果將於星期五下午公佈。
3 ►INCREASE 增加◄ [T **put** sth ↔ **up**] to increase the cost or value of something 提高〔價錢等〕: *Our landlord keeps threatening to put the rent up.* 我們的房東老是威脅說要提高房租。
4 ►LET SB STAY 讓某人留下◄ [T **put** sb ↔ **up**] to let someone stay in your house and give them meals 為〔某人〕提供膳宿: *They agreed to put two foreign students up over the summer.* 他們同意夏季為兩個留學生提供膳宿。
5 ►STAY SOMEWHERE 在某處住宿◄ [I always+adv/prep] *especially BrE* to stay in a place for a short time 【尤英】短期住宿: [**+at/in/with**] *We can put up at a hotel for the night.* 我們可以在旅館住一夜。
6 put up a fight/struggle/resistance to show great determination to oppose something or get out of a difficult situation 奮勇戰鬥/鬥爭/抵抗: *Gina put up a real fight to overcome the disease.* 吉娜為戰勝疾病進行了頑強的鬥爭。
7 put up money/$3 million/£50 to give an amount of money for a particular purpose 捐款/捐300萬美元/捐50英鎊: *An anonymous donor put up $50,000 for the new science lab.* 一位不知名的捐贈者為新的科學實驗室捐了50,000美元。
8 ►ELECTIONS 選舉◄ [T **put** sb ↔ **up**] to suggest someone as a suitable person to be elected to a position 推舉, 提名〔某人擔任某職〕: *They're putting Tom Sackville up as a candidate in the next elections.* 他們要推舉湯姆·薩克維爾為下次選舉的候選人。
9 put up a proposal/argument/case etc to explain a suggestion or idea so that other people can think about it or discuss it 提出建議/論點/理由等: *If you can put up a good enough case, the board will provide the finance.* 如果你能提出足夠好的理由, 董事會將提供資金。

put sb **up to** sth *phr v* [T] to encourage someone to do something stupid or dangerous 唆使〔某人〕做〔愚蠢或危險的事〕: *It's not like Martha to play practical jokes; someone must have put her up to it.* 瑪莎不是玩惡作劇的人, 一定是有人唆使她這麼幹的。

put up with sb/sth *phr v* [T] to accept an unpleasant situation or person without complaining 忍受, 忍耐: *I don't know how you put up with their constant quarrelling.* 我不知道你是如何忍受他們無休止的爭吵的。| *You see what I have to put up with!* 你看到我不得不忍受些甚麼了吧!

pu·ta·tive /ˋpjutətɪv; ˈpjuːtətɪv/ *adj* [only before noun 僅用於名詞前] *formal* believed or accepted by most people【正式】公認的, 被普遍認為是的: *the putative father of her child* 被認為是她孩子的父親的那個人

put-down /ˋ· ·/ *n* [C usually singular 一般用單數] something you say that is intended to make someone feel stupid or unimportant; SNUB² 貶損的話, 奚落的話: *Some feminists see the put-downs girls experience as the means by which men control women.* 一些女權主義者認為女孩所經受的奚落是男人控制女人的手段。—see also 另見 **put down** (PUT)

put-on /ˋ· ·/ *n* [C usually singular 一般用單數] *AmE informal* something you say or do to try to make someone believe something that is not true【美, 非正式】欺騙, 愚弄的話

pu·tre·fac·tion /ˌpjutrəˋfækʃən; ˌpjuːtrɪ̯ˈfækʃən/ *n* [U] *formal* the process of decay in a dead animal or plant, especially when it smells very bad【正式】〔死去動物或植物的〕腐爛(作用)

pu·tre·fy /ˋpjutrəˌfaɪ; ˈpjuːtrɪ̯faɪ/ *v* [I,T] *formal* if a dead animal or plant putrefies, it decays and smells very bad【正式】〔死去動植物等〕腐爛

pu·tres·cent /pjuˋtrɛsn̩t; pjuːˈtresənt/ *adj formal* beginning to decay and smell very bad【正式】開始腐爛的, 腐臭的: *putrescent fish* 腐臭的魚 —**putrescence** *n* [U]

pu·trid /ˋpjutrɪd; ˈpjuːtrɪ̯d/ *adj* **1** dead animals, plants, or parts of the body that are putrid are decaying and smell very bad〔死去動物、植物或身體部位〕腐爛的, 腐臭的 **2** *informal* very unpleasant【非正式】令人非常不愉快的: *a putrid smell* 難聞的氣味

putsch /putʃ; pʊtʃ/ *n* [C] a secretly planned attempt to remove a government by force〔武裝〕政變, 武力顛覆政府的祕密企圖: *the communist putsch of 1948* 1948年共產黨的政變

putt /pʌt; pʌt/ *n* [C] a light hit intended to move a GOLF BALL a short distance along the ground towards the hole〔高爾夫球賽中向球洞〕輕擊球 —**putt** *v* [I,T] —see picture on page A23 參見A23頁圖

put·tee /pʌˋti; ˈpʌti/ *n* [C usually plural 一般用複數] a long piece of cloth that is wrapped arond the leg from the knee down, worn as part of an army uniform in the past〔舊時軍人的〕綁腿

put·ter¹ /ˋpʌtɚ; ˈpʌtə/ *n* a kind of GOLF CLUB (=stick) to hit the ball a short distance towards or into the hole〔高爾夫球的〕輕擊棒 —see picture on page A23 參見A23頁圖

putter² *v* [I always+adv/prep] **1** *AmE* to spend time doing things that are not very important in a relaxed way【美】放鬆地做〔不重要的事〕; POTTER² *BrE*【英】: *I puttered around for a while, tidying up the kitchen.* 我瞎忙了一會兒, 打掃了一下廚房。**2** *AmE* to walk or move slowly and without hurrying【美】閒逛; POTTER² *BrE*【英】 **3** *informal* to make the low repeating sound that a vehicle makes when it is moving slowly【非正式】〔車輛緩慢移動時〕發出重複低沉的聲音

put·ting /ˋpʌtɪŋ; ˈpʌtɪŋ/ *n* [U] a simple game of GOLF played on putting greens in Britain〔英國在高爾夫球輕擊區玩的〕簡易高爾夫球遊戲, 推桿遊戲

putting green /ˋ·· ·/ *n* [C] **1** one of the smaller smooth areas of grass on a GOLF COURSE where you hit the ball into the hole〔高爾夫球的〕輕擊區 **2** *BrE* a smooth area of grass with many holes in it for playing a simple type of GOLF【英】球洞草坪區〔用於玩簡易高爾夫球遊戲〕, 推桿草坪

put·ty /ˋpʌtɪ; ˈpʌti/ *n* [U] **1** a soft substance that dries hard and is used to fix glass into window frames 油灰, 腻子 **2 be putty in sb's hands** to be easily controlled or influenced by someone 易受某人擺佈的, 易受某人影響的

put-up job /ˋ· · ˌ·/ *n* [C usually singular 一般用單數] *informal* an attempt to trick someone by secretly arranging for something to happen【非正式】騙局, 奸計: *There were rumors that the kidnapping of Miletti was a put-up job.* 有謠傳說綁架米勒蒂是個騙局。

put-up·on /ˋ· ·ˌ·/ *adj* [not before noun 不用於名詞前] *informal* someone who feels put-upon thinks that other people are treating them unfairly by expecting them to do too much【非正式】被利用的, 被佔了便宜的

putz /pʌts; pʌts/ *n* [C] *AmE informal*【美, 非正式】**1** someone, especially a man, who is stupid, annoying, and unpleasant 愚蠢的人, 令人討厭的人〔尤指男人〕**2** *taboo* a PENIS【諱】陰莖

puz·zle¹ /ˋpʌzl̩; ˈpʌzəl/ *v* [T] **1** to confuse someone or make them feel slightly anxious because they do not understand something 使困惑, 使迷惑: *What puzzles me is how the burglar got into the house without setting off the alarm.* 這個竊賊如何進入房子而沒有使警報器響起來, 使我大惑不解。**2** [I,T] to think for a long time about something because you cannot understand or solve it (為...)絞盡腦汁, 苦思冥想: **[+over/about]** *I've been sitting here puzzling about what to do.* 我一直坐在這裡苦苦思索該怎麼辦。| **puzzle your head over** *I've been puzzling my head over this problem for weeks.* 好幾個星期我都在琢磨這個問題。

puzzle sth ↔ **out** *phr v* [T] to solve a confusing or difficult problem by thinking about it carefully 仔細考慮解決〔難題等〕, 設法想出: *I've been trying to puzzle out why she's so upset.* 我一直想試圖搞清楚她為甚麼如此煩惱。

puzzle² *n* [C] **1** [usually singular 一般用單數] something that is difficult to understand or explain 難題, 難解之事, 謎: *These computers are a puzzle to me.* 我搞不懂這些電腦。**2** a game or toy that has a lot of pieces that you have to fit together 拼圖遊戲, 拼圖玩具 —see also 另見 JIGSAW (1) **3** a game in which you have to think hard to solve a difficult question or problem〔需要動腦筋的〕益智遊戲: *a crossword puzzle* 填字遊戲 **4 a piece of the puzzle** a piece of information that helps you to understand part of a difficult question, mystery etc〔有助於理解難題、神祕事物等的〕信息, 線索

puz·zled /ˋpʌzl̩d; ˈpʌzəld/ *adj* confused and unable to understand something 困惑的, 無法理解的, 迷惑的: *I'm still slightly puzzled as to why she never called us.* 她為甚麼從不給我們打電話, 我還感到有點迷惑。| **puzzled look/expression** *Alice read the letter with a puzzled expression on her face.* 艾麗斯臉上帶着迷惑的表情讀了那封信。

puz·zle·ment /ˋpʌzl̩mənt; ˈpʌzəlmənt/ *n* [U] *formal* a feeling of being confused and unable to understand something【正式】迷惑, 困惑

puz·zler /ˋpʌzlɚ; ˈpʌzlə/ *n* [C] *informal* something that is difficult to understand or explain【非正式】難解的事, 難題

puz·zling /ˋpʌzlɪŋ; ˈpʌzlɪŋ/ *adj* confusing and difficult to understand or explain 令人迷惑的, 令人費解的: *The children showed a puzzling lack of curiosity about the new baby.* 孩子們對新生兒顯得缺乏好奇心, 這很令人費解。

PVC /ˌpi vi ˋsi; ˌpiː viː ˈsiː◂/ *n* [U] a type of plastic 聚氯乙烯

pvt *AmE* the written abbreviation of 縮寫= PRIVATE, the lowest military rank in the army【美】二等兵; PTE *BrE*【英】

pw the written abbreviation of 縮寫= per week: *Rent is £55 pw.* 租金為每週55鎊。

PWA /ˌpi dʌbl̩ju ˋe; ˌpiː dʌbəljuː ˈeɪ/ *n* [C] person with AIDS; someone who has the disease AIDS 愛滋病患者

PWR /ˌpi dʌbl̩ju ˋɑr; ˌpiː dʌbəljuː ˈɑː/ *n* [C] pressurized water reactor; a type of NUCLEAR REACTOR for producing electricity 壓水反應堆〔一種發電的核反應堆〕

PX /ˌpi ˋɛks; ˌpiː ˈeks/ *n* [C] a special shop for food and other supplies on a US military base〔美國的〕軍人消費合作社, 軍隊商店 —compare 比較 NAAFI

pyg·my, pigmy /ˈpɪgmɪ; ˈpɪgmi/ *n* [C] **1** also 又作 **Pygmy** a person belonging to a race of very small people, especially one of the tribes of central Africa 俾格米人〔身材非常矮小的一個種族, 尤指中非一些部族〕 **2 pygmy rabbit/hippo/elephant etc** a very small type of rabbit, HIPPO etc〔體形特別小的〕小兔/小河馬/小象等

py·ja·mas *especially BrE*【尤英】also 又作 **pajamas** *especially AmE*【尤美】/pəˋdʒæməz; pəˈdʒɑːməz/ *n* [plural] **1** a soft, loose pair of trousers and a top that you wear in bed〔一套〕睡衣褲: *a pair of striped pyjamas* 一套有條紋的睡衣褲 **2 pyjama party** a party where all the guests are asked to wear pyjamas 穿睡衣的聚會 **3** loose trousers that are tied around the waist, worn by Muslim men or women〔穆斯林男女穿的〕束腰寬鬆褲 **—pyjama** *adj*: *pyjama bottoms* 睡褲

py·lon /ˈpaɪlɑn; ˈpaɪlən/ *n* [C] **1** one of the tall metal structures that supports wires carrying electricity across the country 高壓電線架, 電纜塔 **2** *AmE* one of a set of plastic CONES placed on a road to control traffic and protect people working there【美】〔放置在公路上控制交通並保護路上工作人員的〕圓錐形塑料指示標 **3** a tall structure or post used to support something heavy or to help guide aircraft to land〔用於支撐重物的〕高架, 高柱;〔機場的〕標塔, 指示塔

PYO *BrE* the abbreviation of 縮寫= 'pick your own', used by farms that let people pick their own fruit and vegetables【英】水果[蔬菜]自摘

py·or·rho·ea *BrE*【英】also 又作 **pyorrhea** *especially AmE*【尤美】/ˌpaɪəˋriə; ˌpaɪəˈriːə/ *n* [U] a DISEASE of your GUMS that makes your teeth become loose 牙槽膿溢

pyr·a·mid /ˈpɪrəmɪd; ˈpɪrəmɪd/ *n* [C] **1** a large stone building with four TRIANGULAR (=3 sided) walls that slope in to a point at the top, especially in Egypt and Central America〔尤指埃及和中美的〕金字塔 **2** [usually singular 一般用單數] a system or organization in which a small number of people have power or influence over a much larger number of people 金字塔式組織[體系]: *different levels of the management pyramid* 金字塔式管理中的不同等級 **3** a pile of objects that have been put into the shape of a pyramid 擺成金字塔形的一堆東西: **[+of]** *a pyramid of oranges* 一堆擺成金字塔形的橙子 **4** a pyramid-shaped object 金字塔形物 **—pyramidal** /pɪˋræmɪdl; pɪˈræmɪdl/ *adj* —see picture at 參見 SHAPE¹ 圖

pyramid sel·ling /ˈ··· ˌ··/ *n* [U] a system of selling things in which someone buys the right to sell a particular kind of goods and then sells these goods to lots of other people, who sell them to others, especially in their houses 金字塔式銷售〔一種商品銷售體系, 某人先買下某商品的經銷權, 然後將這些商品再賣給許多其他人, 其他人再轉售〕, 層壓式推銷

pyre /paɪr; paɪə/ *n* [C] a high pile of wood on which a dead body is placed to be burned in a funeral ceremony 火葬柴堆

Py·rex /ˈpaɪrɛks; ˈpaɪreks/ *n* [U] *trademark* a special type of strong glass that does not break at high temperatures and is used for making cooking dishes【商標】派熱克斯玻璃, 耐熱玻璃〔用於製造炊具〕

py·ri·tes /pəˋraɪtiz; paɪˈraɪtiːz/ *n* [U] a compound of SULPHUR with a type of metal, usually iron, or iron and COPPER 硫化礦: *iron pyrites* 黃鐵礦 —see also 另見 FOOL'S GOLD

py·ro·ma·ni·a /ˌpaɪrəˋmenɪə; ˌpaɪrəʊˈmeɪniə/ *n* [U] *technical* a mental illness that gives you a strong desire to start fires【術語】縱火狂症

py·ro·ma·ni·ac /ˌpaɪrəˋmenɪˌæk; ˌpaɪrəʊˈmeɪniæk/ *n* [C] **1** *technical* someone who suffers from the mental illness of pyromania【術語】縱火狂症患者 **2** *informal humorous* someone who enjoys making and watching fires【非正式, 幽默】愛火者

py·ro·tech·nics /ˌpaɪrəˋtɛknɪks; ˌpaɪrəʊˈteknɪks/ *n* **1** [plural] *formal or technical* a public show of FIREWORKS【正式或術語】煙火[花]表演; 放煙火[花] **2** [U] *technical* the skill or business of making FIREWORKS【術語】煙火製造術; 煙火製造業 **3** [plural] an impressive show of someone's skill as a public speaker, musician etc〔演說家、音樂家等的〕高超技巧的展示 **—pyrotechnic** *adj*

Pyr·rhic vic·to·ry /ˌpɪrɪk ˋvɪktərɪ; ˌpɪrɪk ˈvɪktəri/ *n* [C] a victory in which the person who wins suffers so much that the victory was hardly worth winning 以極大代價換取的勝利, 得不償失的勝利

py·thon /ˈpaɪθɑn; ˈpaɪθən/ *n* [C] a large tropical snake that kills animals for food by winding itself around them and crushing them〔熱帶地區的〕大蟒

pyx /pɪks; pɪks/ *n* [C] a small container in which the holy bread used for the Christian ceremony of COMMUNION (2) is kept〔基督教聖餐儀式中的〕聖餅盒

Q,q

Q, q /kju; kjuː/ *plural* **Q's, q's** or **Qs, qs** *n* [C] the 17th letter of the English alphabet 英語字母表中的第十七個字母

q the written abbreviation of 縮寫= question

QC /ˌkju ˋsi; ˌkjuː ˈsiː/ *n* [C] Queen's Counsel; a BARRISTER (=type of lawyer) of high rank in the British legal system 王室法律顧問

QED /ˌkju i ˋdi; ˌkjuː iː ˈdiː/ the abbreviation of the Latin phrase quod erat demonstrandum, used to say that a fact, event etc proves that what you say is true 證畢, 證訖〔拉丁文 quod erat demonstrandum 的縮寫〕

qr the written abbreviation of 縮寫= QUARTER

qt the written abbreviation of 縮寫= QUART

q.t. /ˋkju ˋti; ˌkjuː ˈtiː/ *n* **on the q.t.** *informal* secret or secretly【非正式】祕密地, 悄悄地

Q-tip /ˋkju tɪp; ˈkjuː tɪp/ *n* [C] *AmE trademark* a COTTON BUD【美, 商標】Q 牌棉籤

qua /kwe; kweɪ/ *prep Latin formal* used to show you are talking about the main character or the general idea of something【拉丁, 正式】作為; 以…的資格[身分]: *Money, qua money, cannot provide happiness.* 錢本身不能給人帶來快樂。

quack¹ /kwæk; kwæk/ *v* [I] to make the sound that ducks make 作鴨叫聲, 發出〔鴨子般的〕嘎嘎聲

quack² *n* [C] *informal*【非正式】**1** someone who pretends to have medical knowledge or skills 冒牌醫生; 江湖醫生, 庸醫: *a quack doctor* 庸醫 **2** *BrE* a doctor【英】醫生: *You'd better go and see the quack with that burn.* 你最好去找醫生看看那處燒傷。**3** [C] a word used especially by or to children to mean the sound a duck makes 鴨叫聲, 嘎嘎聲〔尤兒語〕

quack·er·y /ˋkwækərɪ; ˈkwækəri/ *n* [U] the activities of someone who pretends to have medical knowledge or skills 庸醫的醫術; 江湖冒牌醫生的騙術

quad /kwɑd; kwɒd/ *n* [C] **1** a square open area with buildings all around it, especially in a school or college〔尤指中小學或大學中周圍有建築物的〕四方院子; 四方廣場 **2** a short form of 縮略式= QUADRUPLET

quadr- /kwɑdr; kwɒdr/ *prefix* another form of the prefix QUADRI- 前綴 quadri- 的另一種拼法

quad·ran·gle /ˋkwɑdræŋgl; ˈkwɒdræŋgəl/ *n* [C] **1** a square open area with buildings all around it〔周圍有建築物的〕四方院子, 四方廣場 **2** *technical* a flat shape that has four straight sides【術語】四邊形, 四角形

quad·rant /ˋkwɑdrənt; ˈkwɒdrənt/ *n* [C] **1** a quarter of a circle 四分之一圓(周); 九十度弧; 扇形體 —see picture at 參見 SHAPE¹ 圖 **2** an instrument for measuring angles, used when sailing or when looking at the stars〔航海或觀星時用的〕象限儀

quad·ra·phon·ic, quadrophonic /ˌkwɑdrəˋfɑnɪk; ˌkwɒdrəˈfɒnɪk◂/ *adj* using a system of sound recording, broadcasting etc in which sound comes from four different SPEAKERS at the same time 四聲道(立體聲)的 —compare 比較 MONO², STEREO²

quad·rat·ic e·qua·tion /kwɑdˋrætɪk ɪˋkweʒən; kwɒˌdrætɪk ɪˈkweɪʒən/ *n* [C] *technical* an EQUATION such as $ax^2+bx+c=y$, which includes numbers or quantities multiplied by themselves【術語】二次方程(式)

quadri- /kwɑdrɪ; kwɒdrɪ/ *prefix* also 又作 **quadru-** /kwɑdrə; kwɒdrʊ/, **quadr-** /kwɑdr; kwɒdr/ four; four times 四; 四倍: *quadrilateral* (=with four straight sides) 四邊的 | *a quadruped* (=an animal with four legs) 四足動物

quad·ri·lat·er·al /ˌkwɑdrəˋlætərəl; ˌkwɒdrɪˈlætərəl◂/ *n* [C] a flat shape with four straight sides 四邊形 —**quadrilateral** *adj*

qua·drille /kwəˋdrɪl; kwəˈdrɪl/ *n* [C] a dance, popular especially in the 19th century, in which the dancers form a square 夸德里爾舞〔一種由四對男女表演的方陣舞, 尤在 19 世紀流行〕

qua·dril·lion /kwadˋrɪljən; kwɒˈdrɪljən/ *number* **1** *BrE* the number one followed by 24 zeros【英】一百萬的四次冪 (10^{24})〔1 後有 24 個零〕**2** *AmE* the number one followed by 15 zeros【美】一千的五次冪, 千萬億 (10^{15})〔1 後有 15 個零〕

quad·ro·phon·ic /ˌkwɑdrəˋfɑnɪk; ˌkwɒdrəˈfɒnɪk◂/ *adj* another spelling of QUADRAPHONIC quadraphonic 的另一種拼法

quadru- /kwɑdrə; kwɒdrʊ/ *prefix* another form of the prefix QUADRI- 前綴 quadri- 的另一種拼法

quad·ru·ped /ˋkwɑdrəˌpɛd; ˈkwɒdrʊped/ *n* [C] *technical* an animal that has four legs【術語】四足動物 —compare 比較 BIPED

quad·ru·ple¹ /kwɑdˋrupḷ; ˈkwɒdrʊpəl/ *v* [I,T] to increase and become four times as big or as high or make something increase in this way (使) 成四倍, (使) 翻兩番: *Food prices quadrupled during the war.* 戰爭期間食品價格翻了兩番。| *The company has quadrupled its profits in just three years.* 該公司僅僅在三年時間裡就使其利潤增加至四倍。

quadruple² *adj, predeterminer* **1** four times as big or as many 四倍的: *The subjects were given quadruple the normal dosage of the drug.* 讓實驗對象服用了四倍於正常劑量的藥物。**2** having four parts 由四部分組成的 —**quadruple** *adj*

quad·ru·plet /kwɑdˋruplɪt; ˈkwɒdrʊplɪt/ *n* [C] one of four babies born at the same time to the same mother 四胞胎之一

quaff /kwæf; kwɒf/ *v* [T] *literary* to drink a lot of something quickly【文】痛飲, 狂飲: *wedding guests quaffing champagne* 婚禮上痛飲香檳酒的客人們

quag·mire /ˋkwægˌmaɪr; ˈkwægmaɪə/ *n* [C usually singular 一般用單數] **1** an area of soft wet muddy ground 沼澤地; 泥潭, 泥濘地: *In the rainy season the roads become a quagmire.* 在雨季, 道路變得一片泥濘。**2** a difficult or complicated situation 困難[複雜]的局勢, 困境: *Public housing regulations are a legislative quagmire.* 公共房屋管理條例是立法上的一大難題。

quail¹ /kwel; kweɪl/ *n* **1** [C] a small bird like a PARTRIDGE 鶉, 鵪鶉 **2** [U] the meat of a quail 鵪鶉肉

quail² *v* [I] *literary* to be afraid; TREMBLE【文】害怕; 發抖: **[+at]** *She quailed visibly at the sight of the grim prison walls.* 看到陰森森的監獄圍牆, 她害怕得直發抖。

quaint /kwent; kweɪnt/ *adj* unusual and attractive, especially in an old-fashioned way 奇特的; 老式而別緻的; 古色古香的: *one of those quaint British traditions* 那些奇特的英國傳統之一

quake¹ /kwek; kweɪk/ *v* [I] **1** to shake or tremble, usually because you are very frightened〔通常指因恐懼而〕顫抖, 哆嗦: **[+with]** *Quaking with fear, I reached for the phone to call the police.* 我伸手打電話報警, 害怕得抖個不停。**2 quake in your boots** *informal* to feel very afraid【非正式】怕得發抖 **3** if the earth, a building etc quakes, it shakes violently〔大地、建築物等〕劇烈顫動, 震動: *The explosion made the whole house quake.* 爆炸使整座房子都晃動起來。

quake² *n* [C] an EARTHQUAKE 地震

Quak·er /ˋkwekɚ; ˈkweɪkə/ *n* [C] a member of the Soci-

Q

ety of Friends, a Christian religious group that opposes all violence, has no priests or ceremonies, and holds its religious meetings in silence〔基督教〕貴格會教徒, 公誼會教徒, 教友會教徒 —**Quaker** *adj*

qual·i·fi·ca·tion /ˌkwɑləfəˋkeʃən; ˌkwɒlɪ̈fɪ̈ˈkeɪʃən/ *n* **1** [C usually plural 一般用複數] an examination that you have passed, especially at school or university 合格證明: *Eva had excellent academic qualifications, but no work experience.* 伊娃有不錯的學歷證明, 但沒有工作經驗。| *a teaching qualification* 教學資格證書 | **paper qualifications** (=official qualifications rather than experience or personal qualities) 書面資格證明 **2** [C] a skill, personal quality, or type of experience that makes you suitable for a particular job or position 資歷, 資格; 技能條件: [+for] *The status of barrister provides a qualification for various public appointments.* 大律師的地位為擔任各種公職提供了一個條件。| **qualification to do sth** *Isobel has all the right qualifications to become a good manager.* 伊澤貝爾具有成為一個好經理的所有條件。**3** [C,U] something that you add to a statement to limit its effect or meaning 限制; 限定性條件: *The committee expressed support for our plans but with certain qualifications.* 委員會表示支持我們的計劃, 但提出若干條件。**4** [U] the achievement of reaching the necessary standard to enter a sports competition, or passing examinations for a particular job 取得〔參賽或就業〕資格: *On qualification you can expect to find work abroad.* 在取得資格之後, 你就可以在國外找工作了。| *We need to beat Poland to ensure qualification for the World Cup finals.* 我們需要打敗波蘭隊以確保獲得參加世界盃決賽的資格。

qual·i·fied /ˈkwɑləˌfaɪd; ˈkwɒlɪ̈faɪd/ *adj* **1** having suitable knowledge, experience, or qualifications, especially for a particular job〔尤指對某項工作〕有資格的; 合格的, 勝任的: *a qualified accountant* 合格的會計師 | *highly qualified engineering staff* 非常勝任的工程人員 | **qualified to do sth** *He's qualified to teach in elementary school, but not in high school.* 他有資格教小學, 但還不夠教中學。| *It's a complex legal matter and I don't feel qualified to give an opinion.* 這是個複雜的法律問題, 我覺得沒資格提出看法。**2** qualified agreement, approval etc is limited in some way, because you do not completely agree or approve 有限制的, 有保留的: *The Gann Report received qualified approval from the colleges.* 甘恩報告得到了那些學院有保留的贊同。

qual·i·fi·er /ˈkwɑləˌfaɪɚ; ˈkwɒlɪ̈faɪə/ *n* [C] **1** someone who has reached the necessary standard for entering a competition 取得參賽資格的人; 合格者 **2** a game that you have to win in order to be able to take part in a competition 資格賽, 預選賽: *Rosenthal looks set to miss tomorrow's World Cup qualifier in Helsinki.* 看來羅森塔爾參加不了明天在赫爾辛基舉行的世界杯預選賽了。**3** *technical* a word or phrase that limits or adds to the meaning of another word or phrase【術語】〔語法中的〕限定語, 修飾語

qual·i·fy /ˈkwɑləˌfaɪ; ˈkwɒlɪ̈faɪ/ *v*
1 ►PASS EXAMS 通過考試◄ [I] to pass an examination or reach the standard of knowledge or skill that you need in order to do something 取得資格; 達到標準: [+as] *Olga recently qualified as a pilot.* 奧爾加最近取得了飛行員資格。| *After qualifying, doctors spend at least two years working in hospitals.* 在取得行醫資格後, 醫生至少要在醫院工作兩年。
2 ►HAVE A RIGHT 有權◄ [I] to have the right to claim something 有資格, 有權要求〔某物〕: [+for] *You may be able to qualify for unemployment benefit.* 你也許有資格獲得失業救濟金。
3 ►MAKE SB SUITABLE 使某人合適◄ [T] if your knowledge or ability qualifies you to do something, it makes you a suitable person to do it 使具有資格, 使合格: **qualify sb for sth** *Fluency in three languages qualifies her for work in the European Parliament.* 她能流利地說三種語言, 這使她能勝任在歐洲議會的工作。| **qualify sb to do sth** *Our four-week course will qualify you to teach English overseas.* 我們為期四週的課程將使你有資格在國外教英語。
4 ►HAVE THE RIGHT QUALITIES 具有符合要求的特徵◄ [I] to have all the necessary qualities to be considered to be a particular thing 可被認為是, 可算作: [+as] *I don't think that really qualifies as an answer.* 我認為那確實算不上一個答案。| *Does photography qualify as an art form?* 攝影算得上一種藝術形式嗎?
5 ►SPORT 體育◄ [I] to reach the necessary standard to enter or continue in a competition or sports event 取得參賽[下一輪比賽]的資格; 預賽及格: *If the French team wins, it will qualify for a place in the finals.* 如果法國隊獲勝, 它將取得參加決賽的資格。
6 ►ADD SOMETHING 增加某事物◄ [T] to add to something that has already been said, in order to limit its effect or meaning; MODIFY 限定, 限制, 修飾: *Could I just qualify that last statement?* 我可以修正一下最後那句話嗎?

qual·i·ta·tive /ˈkwɑləˌtetɪv; ˈkwɒlɪ̈tətɪv/ *adj* connected with the quality or nature of something 性質(上)的; 質量的, 定性的: *a qualitative study of educational services* 對教育服務的定性研究 —compare 比較 QUANTITATIVE

qual·i·ty¹ /ˈkwɑlətɪ; ˈkwɒlɪ̈ti/ *n* **1** [C] something such as courage, intelligence, or loyalty that people may have as part of their character 品德, 品性: *You need special personal qualities to work as a nurse.* 你需要具備一些特殊的個人品德才能當護士。| *Bravery was never a quality that I noticed in Gerald.* 我從未在傑拉爾德身上發現勇敢的品性。**2** [C] something such as size, colour, feel or weight that makes one thing different from other things 性質; 特性: *The analysis looks at the physical and chemical qualities of the sample.* 該分析測定樣品的物理和化學特性。**3** [C,U] the degree to which something is good or bad 質, 質量, 品質: *The higher the price the better the quality.* 價錢越高, 質量越好。| *The recent hot, humid weather is affecting air quality.* 近來炎熱、潮濕的天氣正影響着空氣的質量。| **high quality** (=very good) 高質量的, 優質的 *high quality ingredients* 優質配料 **4** [U] a high standard 優質: *Remember, it's quality we're aiming for, so don't rush the job.* 記住, 我們追求的是質量, 所以工作不要匆忙。| **of quality** *an actor of real quality* 非常優秀的演員 **5 quality of life** the satisfaction in your life that comes from having good health, comfort, good relationships etc, rather than from money 生活質量 **6 a man/lady of quality** *old-fashioned* a man or woman of high social rank【過時】上流社會的男士/女士

quality² *adj* [only before noun 僅用於名詞前] **1** *especially BrE* a word meaning very good, used especially by people who are trying to sell something【尤英】優質的, 非常好的〔尤為推銷某物的人所用〕: *We provide quality rented accommodation for professional people.* 我們為專業人士提供優質的租房。| *quality childcare at prices people can afford* 以人們能負擔的價錢提供的優質兒童照管服務 | *quality double glazing* 優質的雙層玻璃 **2 quality newspapers/press/journalism** *BrE* newspapers etc aimed at educated readers【英】內容嚴肅的報紙/新聞報道/新聞工作

quality as·sur·ance /ˈ··· ·,··/ *n* [U] management of the quality of goods or services so that they stay at a good standard 質量保證

quality con·trol /ˈ··· ·,·/ *n* [U] the practice of checking goods as they are produced to make sure that their quality is good enough 質量控制, 質量管理 —**quality controller** *n* [C]

quality time /ˈ··· ,·/ *n* [U] the time that you spend giving someone your full attention, especially time spent with your children after work〔用於全心照顧某人, 尤指下班後與孩子一起度過的〕寶貴時光

qualm /kwɑm; kwɑːm/ *n* [C usually plural 一般用複數]

a feeling of slight worry because you are not sure that what you are doing is right 疑慮, 不安, 擔憂: *Despite my qualms, I took the job.* 儘管有些疑慮, 我還是接受了那份工作。| **have no qualms about** (=not be worried) 對…沒有感到不安 *He seemed to have no qualms about breaking the speed limit.* 他對超速好像並沒有感到不安。

quan·da·ry /ˈkwɑndrɪ; ˈkwɒndəri/ *n* **be in a quandary (about/over)** to be unable to decide what to do about a difficult problem or situation 不知所措, 陷入窘境, 左右為難: *The city council is in a quandary over whether to raise taxes or not.* 市政會對是否提高稅收一事感到左右為難。

quan·go /ˈkwæŋgo; ˈkwæŋgəʊ/ *n plural* **quangos** [C] an independent organization in Britain, started by the government but with its own legal powers〔英國的〕準自治管理機構; 半官方機構

quan·ta /ˈkwɑntə; ˈkwɒntə/ the plural of QUANTUM

quan·ti·fi·er /ˈkwɑntəˌfaɪɚ; ˈkwɒntɪ̣faɪə/ *n* [C] *technical* a word or phrase such as 'much', 'few' or 'a lot of' that is used with a noun to show quantity【術語】數量詞

quan·ti·fy /ˈkwɑntəˌfaɪ; ˈkwɒntɪ̣faɪ/ *v* [T] to measure something and express it as a number, especially something that is difficult to measure 測定…的數量; 用數量表示, 量化: *Life has got worse for a lot of people, but in ways that are hard to quantify.* 對許多人來說, 生活已變得更糟糕了, 但其變化方式卻難以用數量表示。—**quantifiable** *adj*: *The damage caused by pollution is not easily quantifiable.* 污染造成的損害是難以估量的。—**quantification** /ˌkwɑntəfɪˈkeʃən; ˌkwɒntɪ̣fɪ̣ˈkeɪʃən/ *n* [U]

quan·ti·ta·tive /ˈkwɑntəˌtetɪv; ˈkwɒntɪ̣tətɪv/ *adj* connected with amounts rather than with the quality or nature of something (數) 量的; 與數量有關的; 定量的: *quantitative estimates* 數量估計 | *quantitative chemical analysis* 定量化學分析 —compare 比較 QUALITATIVE —**quantitatively** *adv*

3 2 **quan·ti·ty** /ˈkwɑntətɪ; ˈkwɒntɪ̣ti/ *n* **1** [C] also 又作 **quantities** [plural] an amount of something that can be counted or measured 若干數量: **[+of]** *microscopic quantities of heroin* 極少量的海洛因 **2** [U] amount 量, 數量: **[+in]** *Your work has improved in quantity and quality this term.* 這個學期你的工作在數量上和質量上都有了改善。**3** also 又作 **quantities** [plural] a large amount or number 大量, 許多: **[+of]** *Quantities of arms were discovered hidden in the trucks.* 卡車上發現藏有大量武器。| **in quantity** (=in large amounts) 大量地 *It's a lot cheaper if you buy it in quantity.* 大批量購買要便宜得多。—see also 另見 **be an unknown quantity** (UNKNOWN[1] (4))

quantity sur·vey·or /ˈ··· ·ˌ··/ *n* [C] someone whose job is to calculate the amount of materials that will be needed to build something, how long it will take to build and what it will cost〔估算建築材料的用量、所需工時、成本等的〕估算員, 建築工料測量師

quan·tum /ˈkwɑntəm; ˈkwɒntəm/ *n plural* **quanta** /-tə; -tə/ *technical* an amount of energy in NUCLEAR PHYSICS, which varies from the next possible smaller or larger amount by a specific degree【術語】量

quantum leap /ˌ·· ˈ·/ also 又作 **quantum jump** *AmE*【美】*n* [C] a very large and important improvement 長足的重大進展, 飛躍, 突飛猛進: *This discovery is a quantum leap for medical science.* 這一發現是醫學上的重大突破。

quantum me·chan·ics /ˌ·· ·ˈ··/ *n* [U] the study of the way that atoms and smaller pieces of MATTER[1] (30) behave 量子力學

quantum the·o·ry /ˈ·· ˌ··/ *n* [singular] the idea that energy, especially light, travels in separate pieces and not in a continuous form 量子論

quar·an·tine[1] /ˈkwɔrənˌtin; ˈkwɒrəntiːn/ *n* [U] a period of time when a person or animal is kept apart from others in case they are carrying a disease 檢疫隔離期: **in quarantine** (=being kept somewhere in a period of quarantine) 被隔離

quarantine[2] *v* **quarantined, quarantining** [T often passive 常用被動態] to put a person or animal in quarantine 對…進行檢疫隔離

quark /kwɑrk; kwɑːk/ *n* [C] **1** *technical* one of the smallest known amounts of MATTER[1] (30) that forms part of an atom【術語】夸克〔構成原子的最小粒子之一〕**2** [U] a type of German soft cheese 凝乳, 夸克乾酪〔一種德國乳酪〕

quar·rel[1] /ˈkwɔrəl; ˈkwɒrəl/ *n* [C] **1** an angry argument, often about something that is not important 爭吵, 吵架, 爭執: **[+with]** *She got into a silly quarrel with the other children.* 她傻乎乎地與其他孩子吵了起來。| **[+about/over]** *What was the quarrel all about?* 到底為了甚麼吵架? | **pick a quarrel (with)** (=deliberately start a quarrel) (向…) 尋釁, 故意找碴 *He seems to enjoy picking a quarrel with everyone he meets.* 他好像喜歡跟他遇到的每個人找碴吵架。**2** a reason or subject for disagreement 不同意的原因; 爭執的緣由: *Is there any quarrel between those two that I should know about?* 那兩個人之間的爭執有任何我該知道的原因嗎? **3 have no quarrel with** *formal* to have no reason to dislike someone or disagree with an idea, decision etc【正式】沒有理由厭惡〔某人〕; 沒有理由不同意〔某一想法、決定等〕: *We have no quarrel with the court's verdict.* 我們沒有理由不同意法庭的裁決。

quarrel[2] *v* **quarrelled, quarrelling** *BrE*【英】, **quarreled, quarreling** *AmE*【美】[I] to have an argument 爭吵, 吵架, 爭執: *I wish you two would stop quarreling.* 我希望你們兩個別再爭吵了。| **[+with]** *They're forever bickering and quarrelling with each other.* 他們總是爭吵不休。| **[+about]** *We're not going to quarrel about a few dollars.* 我們不想為了幾美元而吵架。

quarrel with sth *phr v* [T] to disagree with something or complain about something 不同意; 抱怨: *Few of us can quarrel with the idea of more choice and more competition.* 我們中幾乎沒人會反對更多選擇、更多競爭的想法。

quar·rel·some /ˈkwɔrəlsəm; ˈkwɒrəlsəm/ *adj* someone who is quarrelsome seems to like quarrelling 喜歡爭吵的; 好爭論的: *a quarrelsome tone in his voice* 他聲音中的火藥味 —**quarrelsomeness** *n* [U]

quar·ry[1] /ˈkwɔrɪ; ˈkwɒri/ *n* [C] **1** a place where large amounts of stone, sand etc are dug out of the ground 採石場: *a slate quarry* 板岩採石場 —compare 比較 MINE[2] (1) **2** [singular] the person or animal that you are hunting or chasing 獵取的目標; 獵物: *The police saw the empty room and knew their quarry had escaped.* 警察看到空蕩蕩的房間, 明白他們追蹤的疑犯已經逃走了。

quarry[2] *v* [T] to dig out stone, sand etc from a quarry〔在採石場〕採〔石〕; 挖〔沙〕: **[+from]** *It was built with stones quarried from Portland.* 這是用從波特蘭開採的石頭建成的。

quart /kwɔrt; kwɔːt/ *n* [C] **1** a unit used for measuring liquids and some dry goods 夸脫〔液體或固體的容積單位〕—see table on page C4 參見C4頁附錄 **2 put a quart into a pint pot** *BrE informal* to try to do more than you have time or space for【英, 非正式】以小容大; 做不可能做到的事

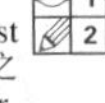

quar·ter[1] /ˈkwɔrtɚ; ˈkwɔːtə/ *n*

1 ►AMOUNT 數量◄ [C] one of four equal or almost equal parts into which something can be divided 四分之一: *Cut it into quarters.* 把它切成四份。| **[+of]** *a quarter of a mile* 四分之一英里 | *in the last quarter of the 19th century* 在19世紀最後二十五年裡 | *They're firing almost a quarter of the workforce.* 他們要解雇將近四分之一的勞動力。| *It's about a page and a quarter.* 約一又四分之一頁。

2 ►PART OF AN HOUR 一小時的一部分◄ [C] one of the four periods of 15 minutes into which each hour can be divided 一刻鐘, 十五分鐘: *I'll meet you in three-*

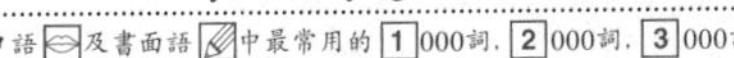

quarters of an hour. (=in 45 minutes) 我四十五分鐘後見你。| **quarter to** *BrE*【英】/**quarter of** *AmE*【美】(=15 minutes before the hour) 差一刻鐘到…點 *It's a quarter of two.* (=1:45) 現在差一刻鐘兩點。| **quarter past** *BrE*【英】/**quarter after** *AmE*【美】(=15 minutes after the hour) …點過一刻鐘 *a quarter past ten* (=10:15) 十點一刻

3 ▶MONEY 錢◀ [C] a coin in the US and Canada, worth 25 cents〔美國和加拿大〕二角五分的硬幣

4 ▶THREE MONTHS 三個月◀ [C] a period of three months, used especially in connection with bills, wages, and income 季度, 三個月: *The company's profits rose by 11% in the first quarter of the year.* 公司的利潤在那年的第一季度增長了11%。—see also 另見 QUARTERLY¹

5 ▶PART OF A CITY 城市的一部分◀ [C] an area of a town or city where a particular kind of people typically live or work 區, 地區: *the student quarter* 學生(居住)區 | *We took a rented house in the Creole quarter of New Orleans.* 我們在新奧爾良市的克里奧耳人居住區租了一幢房子。

6 ▶HOME 家◀ quarters [plural] a house or rooms where you can live, especially in the army〔尤指軍隊的〕營房; 住房, 宿舍: *staff quarters* 職工宿舍 | **married quarters** (=where soldiers with wives live) 已婚軍人宿舍

7 in/from ... quarters in or from different groups of people 在/來自…團體: *Offers of financial help came from the most unexpected quarters.* 財政援助是由那些最意想不到的團體提供的。| *There were doubts in many quarters about the country's ability to repay the debt.* 許多團體對那個國家償還債務的能力表示懷疑。

8 all quarters of the Earth/globe *literary* everywhere in the world【文】世界各地

9 give no quarter *old use* to show no pity towards someone, especially an enemy whom you have defeated【舊】不憐憫〔某人, 尤指被打敗的敵人〕: *It was a fight to the death, with no quarter given.* 那是一場殊死的搏鬥, 誰也不心慈手軟。

10 ▶WEIGHT 重量◀ [C] *BrE* a unit for measuring weight, equal to 28 pounds or about 13 kilos【英】夸特〔等於28磅, 約13公斤〕

11 ▶AT COLLEGE 在大學裡◀ [C] *AmE* a period of 10 to 12 weeks into which a teaching year is divided in some American colleges and universities【美】學季〔10至12週〕: *What classes are you taking this quarter?* 這個學季你要上甚麼課?

12 ▶SPORT 體育◀ [C] one of the four equal periods of time into which games of some sports are divided〔某些分四節進行的體育比賽的〕一節, 四分之一場

13 ▶MOON 月亮◀ [C] the period of time twice a month when you can see a quarter of the moon's surface 上弦; 下弦; 太陰月的四分之一

14 ▶MEAT 肉◀ [C] a large piece of meat from a large animal, including one of its legs〔從大型動物身上切下的〕包括整條腿的一大塊肉: *a quarter of beef* 包括整條腿的一大塊牛肉 —see also 另見 **at close quarters** (CLOSE² (2))

quarter² *v* [T] **1** to cut or divide something into four parts 把〔某物〕切成四部分, 把〔某物〕四等分: *Quarter the tomatoes and place them round the dish.* 把這些番茄一切四瓣, 排放在盤子裡。**2** *old use* to provide soldiers, workers etc with a place to sleep and eat【舊】為…提供食宿: *Our forces were quartered in tents on the edge of the woods.* 我們的部隊被安排住在樹林邊的帳篷裡。

quar·ter·back¹ /ˈkwɔrtɚˌbæk; ˈkwɔːtəbæk/ *n* [C] **1** the player in AMERICAN FOOTBALL who directs the team's attacking play and passes the ball to the other players at the start of each attacking move〔美式足球中組織進攻的〕樞紐前衛, 四分衛 **2 Monday morning quarterback** *AmE* someone who gives advice on something only after it has happened【美】放馬後炮的人, 事後孔明

quarterback² *v AmE*【美】**1** [I] to play in the position of quarterback in AMERICAN FOOTBALL〔在美式足球中〕擔任樞紐前衛[四分衛] **2** [T] *informal* to organize or direct an activity, event etc【非正式】組織, 指揮: *She quarterbacked the new sales campaign.* 她組織了那次新的促銷活動。

quarter day /ˈ·· ·/ *n* [C] *BrE* a day which officially begins a three-month period of the year, and on which payments are made, for example at the STOCK EXCHANGE【英】季度結賬日

quar·ter·deck /ˈkwɔrtɚˌdɛk; ˈkwɔːtədek/ *n* [C] the back part of the upper DECK (=floor level) of a ship, used mainly by officers〔主要供高級船員使用的〕上層後甲板區

quar·ter·fi·nal /ˌkwɔrtɚˈfaɪnḷ; ˌkwɔːtəˈfaɪnl/ *n* [C] one of the set of four games near the end of a competition, whose winners play in the two SEMIFINALS 四分之一決賽, 半準決賽

quarter horse /ˈ·· ˌ·/ *n* [C] a strong horse in the US, bred to run short races, usually of a quarter of a mile〔美國的〕夸特馬〔用於短距離比賽, 一般跑四分之一英里比賽〕

quar·ter·ly¹ /ˈkwɔrtɚlɪ; ˈkwɔːtəli/ *adj, adv* produced or happening four times a year 一年四次的[地], 每季度的[地]: *quarterly accounts* 季度賬 | *a quarterly newsletter* 按季度出版的新聞簡報

quarterly² *n* [C] a magazine that is produced four times a year 季刊

quar·ter·mas·ter /ˈkwɔrtɚˌmæstɚ; ˈkwɔːtəˌmɑːstə/ *n* [C] **1** a military officer in charge of providing food, uniforms etc 軍需官 **2** a ship's officer in charge of signals and guiding the ship on the right course 舵手

quarter note /ˈ·· ·/ *n* [C] *AmE* a musical note which continues for a quarter of the length of a WHOLE NOTE【美】四分音符; CROTCHET *BrE*【英】—see picture at 參見 MUSIC 圖

quarter ses·sions /ˈ·· ˌ··/ *n* [plural] an English law court in former times, which has been replaced by the Crown Court〔英國舊時的〕季審法院〔現已被刑事法庭取代〕

quar·ter·staff /ˈkwɔrtɚˌstæf; ˈkwɔːtəstɑːf/ *n* [C] a long wooden pole used as a weapon, especially in former times〔尤指舊時作武器用的〕鐵頭木棍

quar·tet /kwɔrˈtɛt; kwɔːˈtet/ *n* [C] **1** four singers or musicians who perform together 四重唱; 四重奏; 四重唱[奏]表演小組: *He's the trombonist in a jazz quartet.* 他是一個爵士樂四重奏小組中的長號手。**2** a piece of music written for four performers 四重唱曲; 四重奏曲 **3** four people or things of the same type 同類的四個[人/物]; 四人一組; 四個一套: *The same quartet of characters appears in another of her novels.* 同樣的四個人物出現在她的另一部小說中。—compare 比較 QUINTET, TRIO

quar·to /ˈkwɔrto; ˈkwɔːtəʊ/ *n* [C] *technical*【術語】**1** the size of paper, or the paper itself, produced by folding a large sheet of paper twice, to produce four sheets 四開; 四開的紙: *quarto sheets of paper* 一些四開的紙 **2** a book with pages of quarto size 四開本(的書)

quartz /kwɔrts; kwɔːts/ *n* [U] a hard mineral substance, used in making electronic watches and clocks 石英: *a quartz gold watch* 石英金錶

qua·sar /ˈkwezɑr; ˈkweɪzɑː/ *n* [C] *technical* a very bright, very distant object similar to a star【術語】類星體

quash /kwɑʃ; kwɒʃ/ *v* [T] *formal*【正式】**1** to officially state that a judgement or decision is no longer legal or correct 宣布〔判決、決定〕不再有效; 廢除, 撤銷: *The judge quashed the decision of the lower court.* 法官撤銷了下級法院的裁決。**2** to use force to end protests or disobedience 鎮壓, 以武力平息; 壓服: *quash a rebellion* 鎮壓叛亂

quasi- /kwezaɪ, kwɑzɪ; ˈkweɪzaɪ, kwɑːzi/ *prefix* **1** in some ways; partly 一定程度上; 部分地; 類似, 半, 準: *the chairman's quasi-judicial role* (=acting in some ways like a judge) 主席的準司法角色 **2** false or pretended 假

的; 假裝的: *quasi-scientific ideas* 偽科學思想

quat·er·cen·te·na·ry /ˌkwɑtɚˋsɛntəˌnɛrɪ; ˌkwætəsen-ˈtiːnəri/ *n* [C] the day or year exactly 400 years after a particular event 四百週年(紀念): *the quatercentenary of Shakespeare's birth* 莎士比亞誕生四百週年紀念

quat·rain /ˋkwɑtren; ˈkwɒtreɪn/ *n* [C] a group of four lines in a poem 四行詩; 四行的詩節

qua·ver¹ /ˋkwevɚ; ˈkweɪvə/ *v* [I,T] if your voice quavers, it shakes as you speak, especially because you are nervous 〔尤指因緊張令說話聲〕顫抖; 用顫抖的聲音說: *"Please help me," he quavered.* 他顫抖地說:"請幫幫我。" —**quavery** *adj*

quaver² *n* [C] **1** *BrE* a musical note which continues for an eighth of the length of a SEMIBREVE【英】〔音樂中的〕八分音符; EIGHTH NOTE *AmE*【美】— see picture at 參見 MUSIC 圖 **2** a shaking sound in your voice 顫音

quay /ki; kiː/ *n* [C] a place where boats can be tied up or can stop to load and UNLOAD 碼頭: *a quay lined with fishing boats* 泊有許多漁船的碼頭

quay·side /ˋkiˌsaɪd; ˈkiːsaɪd/ *n* [C] the area next to a quay 碼頭邊, 碼頭前沿地帶, 碼頭區: *people strolling along the quayside* 沿碼頭漫步的人們 | *a quayside restaurant* 碼頭邊上的餐廳

quea·sy /ˋkwizɪ; ˈkwiːzi/ *adj* feeling that you are going to VOMIT (感到) 噁心的, 想嘔吐的: *The sea got rougher, and I began to feel a little queasy.* 海上風浪更猛了, 我開始感到有點噁心想吐。—**queasiness** *n* [U]

S2 W2 **queen¹** /kwin; kwiːn/ *n* [C]

1 ▶RULER 統治者◀ also 又作 **Queen a)** the female ruler of a country 女王: *Elizabeth II became Queen of England in 1952.* 伊莉莎白二世於1952年成為英格蘭女王。 **b)** the wife of a king 王后

2 ▶CARD 紙牌◀ a playing card with a picture of a queen on it 王后, Q(牌): *the queen of hearts* 紅桃王后

3 ▶HOMOSEXUAL 同性戀◀ *informal* an insulting word for a male HOMOSEXUAL, especially one who behaves like a woman【非正式】〔侮辱性用語, 尤指舉止像女人的〕男同性戀者

4 queen bee a woman who behaves as if she is the most important person in a place 〔在某場合〕舉止宛若最重要人物的女子, 領導社交活動的婦女

5 the queen of a woman who is regarded as the best at a particular activity or in a particular field 〔指在某一活動或領域中〕最優秀的女子, 最出類拔萃的女子: *Tammy Wynette, the queen of country music* 鄉村音樂王后塔米·懷納特

6 ▶INSECT 昆蟲◀ a large female BEE, ANT etc, which lays the eggs for a whole group 〔蜂、蟻等的〕后

7 ▶CHESS 國際象棋◀ the most powerful piece in the game of CHESS 王后 —see also 另見 BEAUTY QUEEN, DRAG QUEEN, MAY QUEEN

queen² *v* [T] **1 queen it over** *informal* to behave in an annoying way as if you are more important than other people【非正式】大擺架子, 盛氣凌人 **2** *technical* to change a PAWN¹ (1) into a queen in the game of CHESS【術語】〔在棋戲中〕將卒子變為王后

queen·ly /ˋkwinlɪ; ˈkwiːnli/ *adj* suitable for or like a queen 適合女王的; 女王般的: *She gave a queenly wave as she rode past.* 她騎馬經過時像女王般地揮了揮手。

Queen Moth·er /ˌ· ˈ··/ *n* [singular] the mother of the ruling king or queen (王) 太后

Queen's Coun·sel /ˌ· ˈ··/ *n* a QC 王室法律顧問

Queen's En·glish /ˌ· ˈ··/ *n BrE*【英】**speak the Queen's English** to speak very correctly and in a way that is typical of people who belong to the highest social class 說標準英語 —see also 另見 KING'S ENGLISH

Queen's ev·i·dence /ˌ· ˈ···/ *n BrE*【英】**turn Queen's evidence** if a criminal turns Queen's evidence, they agree to help the police, law courts etc to catch other criminals by giving them information 提供對同案犯不利的證據, 〔罪犯〕作為污點證人指控同黨 —see also 另見 EVIDENCE¹, KING'S EVIDENCE, STATE'S EVIDENCE

queen-size /ˈ· ·/ *adj especially AmE* a queen-size bed, sheet etc is larger than the standard size for a bed for two people【尤美】〔牀、牀單等〕大號的, 大於標準尺寸的 —compare 比較 DOUBLE BED, KING-SIZE, SINGLE¹ (4)

queer¹ /kwɪr; kwɪə/ *adj* **1** *old-fashioned* strange or difficult to explain【過時】奇怪的; 難以解釋的: *This orange tastes queer.* 這個橘子吃起來有怪味。| *She gave a queer laugh.* 她古怪地笑了笑。**2** *informal* a word meaning HOMOSEXUAL, considered offensive when used by people who are not homosexual【非正式】同性戀的〔冒犯用語〕 **3** *BrE* ill or sick【英】不舒服的; 想嘔吐的: *I'm feeling a little queer – I think I'll go and lie down.* 我感覺有些不舒服——我想我要去躺一下。**4 queer in the head** *old-fashioned* talking or behaving strangely; crazy【過時】言談[舉止]古怪的; 精神不正常的 **5 be in queer street** *BrE old-fashioned* to owe people money【英, 過時】負債 —**queerly** *adv*: *queerly shaped* 形狀怪異的 —**queerness** *n* [U]

queer² *n* [C] *informal* an insulting word for a HOMOSEXUAL【非正式】同性戀者〔侮辱性用語〕

queer³ *v* **queer sb's pitch** *BrE informal* to spoil someone's plans or chance to do something【英, 非正式】破壞某人〔做某事〕的計劃[機會]

queer bash·ing /ˈ· ˌ··/ *n* [U] *informal* physical violence against people because they are HOMOSEXUAL【非正式】對同性戀者的暴力攻擊[無故毆打]

quell /kwɛl; kwel/ *v* [T] *formal*【正式】**1** to bring an end to a violent situation especially when people are protesting 平息, 鎮壓, 制止〔暴亂局面〕: **quell a riot/revolt/disturbance etc** *They needed more troops to quell the ever-rising tide of rioting.* 他們需要更多的軍隊以平息不斷上漲的暴亂潮。**2** to reduce unpleasant feelings, especially of doubt or worry 減輕, 消除〔疑慮〕: *I thought about the advantages of the deal, trying to quell a growing sense of unease.* 我考慮了一下那筆交易的好處, 設法消除內心越來越強烈的不安。

quench /kwɛntʃ; kwentʃ/ *v* [T] **1 quench your thirst** to stop yourself from feeling thirsty 止渴, 解渴: *Iced tea really quenches your thirst.* 冰茶真解渴。**2 quench a fire** to make a fire stop burning 滅火

quer·u·lous /ˋkwɛrələs; ˈkwerələs/ *adj formal* complaining all the time in an annoying way【正式】老是抱怨的, 好發牢騷的: *"But why can't I go?" he said in a querulous tone.* "但為甚麼我不能去?"他以抱怨的口氣問道。—**querulously** *adv* —**querulousness** *n* [U]

que·ry¹ /ˋkwɪrɪ; ˈkwɪəri/ *n* [C] a question you ask to get information, or to check that something is true or correct 問題; 疑問: *We will answer any queries by letter.* 我們將通過信函回答一切問題。

query² *v* [T] **1** to express doubt that something is true or correct 質疑, 對...表示疑問: **[+whether]** *I'd query whether these figures are reliable.* 我想問一下這些數字是否可靠。**2** [T] to ask a question 提〔問題〕: *"What time are we leaving?" queried Mrs Evans.* "我們甚麼時候離開?"埃文斯夫人問道。

quest /kwɛst; kwest/ *n* [C] *especially literary* a long search for something such as truth or knowledge【尤文】〔長期的〕尋求, 探求: **[+for]** *the quest for enlightenment* 對文明的追求 —**quest** *v* [I]: *to quest after the truth* 尋求真理

ques·tion¹ /ˋkwɛstʃən; ˈkwestʃən/ *n* [C] 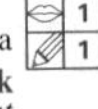

1 ▶ASKING FOR INFORMATION 要求得到信息◀ a sentence or phrase that asks for information 問題: **ask (sb) a question** *They asked me a lot of questions about my work experience.* 他們問了我許多有關我工作經驗的問題。| *May I ask a question?* 我可以問一個問題嗎? | **answer a question** *Answer three out of five questions on the exam paper.* 從試卷上五道問題中選答三道。| *Does anyone have any questions?* 誰有問題嗎? —see 見 ASK (USAGE)

2 ▶SUBJECT/PROBLEM 議題/難題◀ a subject or problem that needs to be settled, discussed, or dealt with;

ISSUE[1] (1) 需要解決[處理]的事; 問題: *Several questions had still not been resolved.* 好幾個問題仍然沒有得到解決。| *This brings us to the question of government funding.* 這給我們提出了政府資助的問題。| **the question is** *The question is, do I take the job in Japan, or stay here?* 問題是, 我是接受在日本的那份工作, 還是留在這兒呢?

3 ►DOUBT 疑問◄ a feeling of doubt about something 疑問, 不確定的事情: **raise questions about** *This incident raises further questions about the effectiveness of airport security.* 這起事故使人們對機場保安的有效性提出了進一步的疑問。| **there is no question** (=there is no doubt) 毫無疑問 *He's by far the best, there's no question about it.* 他是最好的, 這毫無疑問。| **open to question** (=likely or able to be doubted) 值得懷疑, 有待論證 *The wisdom of this policy is open to question.* 這一政策是否明智尚難定論。

4 without question a) without any doubt 毫無疑問: *Marilyn was, without question, a very beautiful woman.* 毫無疑問, 瑪麗琳是一個非常漂亮的女子。**b)** if you obey an order without question, you obey immediately and do not complain at all 毫無異議地〔服從命令〕

5 there's no question of used to say that there is no possibility of something happening …是不可能的: *There is no question of the government holding talks with terrorists.* 政府不可能與恐怖分子進行談判。

6 in question the things, people etc in question are the ones that are being discussed or talked about 正被討論的; 談論中的: *The goods in question had been stolen.* 所說的那些貨物已經被盜。

7 be a question of used when you are giving the most important fact, part, or feature or something 問題在於, 是一個…的問題: *Dance is a question of control and creative expression.* 舞蹈在於動作控制和創造性表現。| *I would love to come, but it's a question of time.* 我倒是想來, 但問題是要看有沒有時間。

8 out of the question not possible or not allowed 不可能的; 不允許的: *You can't go to the wedding in that old shirt – it's quite out of the question.* 你不能穿着那件舊襯衫去參加婚禮 —— 這是絕對不行的。

9 it's just a question of *spoken* used to say that something is easy or not complicated【口】只是個…的問題: *It's just a question of putting in a couple of screws.* 只要擰上兩顆螺絲釘問題就解決了。

10 pop the question *informal humorous* to ask someone to marry you【非正式, 幽默】求婚: *Simon finally plucked up the courage to pop the question.* 西蒙終於鼓起了勇氣求婚。

11 good question! *spoken* used to show that you do not know the answer to a question【口】好一個難題! 問得好!〔用以表示不知道某問題的答案〕: *"How can we afford this?" "Good question!"* "我們怎麼才能買得起這個呢?" "問得好!" —see also 另見 **leading question** (LEADING[1] (4)), **rhetorical question** (RHETORICAL (1)), **beg the question** (BEG (5)), **call into question** (CALL[1] (21))

2 3 **question²** *v* [T] **1** to ask someone questions to find out what they know about something, especially about a crime 詢問; 盤問; 審問: *We're taking them in for questioning.* 我們要把他們帶走審問。| **question sb about** *The police questioned him about the missing $10,000.* 警方就那丟失了的一萬美元盤問他。| **question sb closely** (=ask them a lot of difficult questions to find out exactly what they know) 仔細盤問某人 **2** to have doubts about something or tell someone about these doubts 懷疑, 對…提出質疑[異議]: *Are you questioning the truth of what I'm saying?* 你在懷疑我現在講的話的真實性嗎? | *It makes me question the whole basis of the research.* 這使我對該研究的整個基礎產生了疑問。

ques·tion·a·ble /ˈkwɛstʃənəbl̩; ˈkwestʃənəbəl/ *adj* **1** not definitely true or correct 不確定的; 有問題的: *The report's conclusions are questionable because the sample used was very small.* 那個報告的結論有問題, 因為取樣太少了。**2** behaviour or actions that are questionable seem likely to be dishonest or wrong〔行為〕不誠實的, 可疑的: *business deals of a rather questionable kind* 非常可疑的交易

ques·tion·er /ˈkwɛstʃənɚ; ˈkwestʃənə/ *n* [C] someone who is asking a question, for example in a public discussion 問問題的人, 提問者

ques·tion·ing /ˈkwɛstʃənɪŋ; ˈkwestʃənɪŋ/ *adj* a questioning look or expression shows that you have doubts about something or need some information 懷疑的; 詢問的: *the questioning eyes of a child* 孩子那探詢的目光 —**questioningly** *adv*

question mark /ˈ·· ·/ *n* [C] **1** the mark (?) that is used at the end of a sentence to show that it asks a question 問號 —see picture at 參見 PUNCTUATION MARK 圖 **2 a question mark over** if there is a question mark over something, there is a possibility that it will not be successful or will not continue to exist 不確定性: *A big question mark hangs over the company's future.* 這家公司的將來如何還是個大問號。

question mas·ter /ˈ·· ˌ··/ *n* [C] *BrE* the person who asks the questions in a QUIZ game【英】問答遊戲的主持人

ques·tion·naire /ˌkwɛstʃənˈɛr; ˌkwestʃəˈneə/ *n* [C] a written set of questions which you give to a large number of people in order to collect information〔收集信息用的〕問卷, 問題單, 調查表: **fill in/complete a questionnaire** (=answer all the questions in it) 填妥問卷

question tag /ˈ·· ·/ *n* [C] *technical* a phrase such as 'isn't it?', 'won't it?', or 'does she?' that you add to the end of a statement to make it a question or to check that someone agrees with you【術語】疑問尾句, 附加疑問句: *You're from Hamburg, aren't you?* 你來自漢堡, 對吧?

question time /ˈ·· ·/ *n* [U] the period of time in a parliament when ministers answer questions from members of the parliament〔議會中的〕質詢時間

queue¹ /kju; kjuː/ *n* [C] *BrE*【英】**1** a line of people waiting to enter a building, buy something etc, or a line of vehicles waiting to move〔人或車輛為等候而排的〕隊, 行列; LINE[1] (22) *AmE*【美】: *The queue for the cinema went right round the building.* 為看電影而排的隊拐過了那幢大樓。| *We were stuck in a queue for half an hour.* 我們在車流中被困了半個小時。| **jump a queue** (=go unfairly to the front of a queue instead of waiting) 插隊, 不按次序排隊, 加塞兒 —see picture at 參見 PUSH IN 圖 **2** *technical* a list of jobs that a computer has to do in a particular order【術語】隊列〔電腦必須按一定順序處理的一系列工作〕; ORDER[1] (26) *AmE*【美】: *the print queue* 打印隊列 —see also 另見 **the dole queue** (DOLE[1] (2))

queue² *v past tense and past participle* **queued** *present participle* **queuing** *or* **queueing** *also* 又作 **queue up** [I] 3
BrE to form or join a line of people or vehicles waiting to do something or go somewhere【英】排隊〔等候〕; **line up** (LINE²) *AmE*【美】: *The post office was really busy – we had to queue for ages to get served.* 郵局非常忙 —— 我們不得不排了好長時間的隊等候。| **[+for]** *people queuing for tickets* 排隊買票的人

queue-jump /ˈ· ·/ *v* [I] *BrE informal* to go unfairly to the front of a queue, instead of waiting【英, 非正式】插隊, 加塞兒

quib·ble¹ /ˈkwɪbl̩; ˈkwɪbəl/ *v* [I+over/about] to argue about small points or details that are completely unimportant〔為了細枝末節或瑣事而〕爭吵, 吹毛求疵: *Don't quibble about the money – just pay what she asks.* 別為錢爭執了 —— 她要多少就給她多少好了。

quibble² *n* [C] a small complaint or criticism about something very unimportant 小小的不滿[批評]; 吹毛求疵: *I have just one quibble – there's a spelling mistake here.* 我只有一點小意見 —— 這兒有一處拼寫錯誤。

quiche /kiʃ; kiːʃ/ *n* [C,U] a flat open piece of PASTRY (1) filled with a mixture of eggs, cheese, vegetables etc 什

錦烘餅，蛋奶火腿餡餅

quick[1] /kwɪk; kwɪk/ *adj*
1 ▶SHORT TIME 短時間◀ continuing or existing for only a short time 短時間的，短暫的；匆匆的：*I just have to make a quick phone call.* 我得打一個簡短的電話。| *John had a quick meal and then went out again.* 約翰匆匆地吃完了飯，然後又出去了。| *That was quick! I thought you'd be another hour.* 真是太快了！我原以為你還要一個小時呢。
2 ▶FAST 快的◀ moving or happening fast 快速的，迅速的：*She walked with short, quick steps.* 她邁着碎步急速走着。| *A series of quick changes take place as the chemicals bond.* 不同的化學品結合時會發生一連串快速的變化。
3 ▶SOON 不久◀ happening very soon, without any delay 馬上的，即刻的：*We've put the house on the market and we're hoping for a quick sale.* 我們已把房子投放到市場上，希望馬上就賣出去。
4 ▶CLEVER 聰明的◀ able to learn and understand things fast 聰敏的，敏銳的，腦子反應快的：*That child's a really quick learner.* 那個孩子確實學得快。| **a quick study** *AmE slang* (=a student who is clever and learns quickly)【美俚】聰明而學得快的學生
5 be quick to hurry 快點，抓緊時間：*If you want to come with me you'll have to be quick – I'm leaving in ten minutes.* 如果你想和我一塊去，你就得趕緊點——我十分鐘後走。| **be quick about it** *Just bring me that book, and be quick about it.* 請把那本書給我拿來，快一點。
6 be quick to do sth to react quickly to what someone says or does 性急地做某事：*You're always very quick to criticize my ideas – let's hear yours!* 你總是急不可耐地批評我的想法——讓我們聽聽你的！
7 be quick on the draw/uptake to quickly understand a situation or what someone tells you, so that you know what you have to do 理解力強，領悟快
8 a quick one/half/pint *especially BrE informal* a drink that you have in a hurry 【尤英，非正式】匆匆飲下的酒：*Let's stop for a quick one before the train comes.* 在火車到來之前，讓我們停下抓緊喝一杯。
9 have a quick temper to get angry very easily 易怒，性情急躁
10 a quick fix *informal* a repair to something or an answer to a problem that will work only for a short time 【非正式】應急解決辦法，權宜之計 —see also 另見 QUICKLY —**quickness** *n* [U]

quick[2] *interjection* used to tell someone to hurry or come quickly 快，快點：*Quick! We'll miss the bus!* 快點！我們趕不上公共汽車了！| *Come on! Quick!* 來吧！快點！

3 **quick**[3] *adv* quickly; fast 快速地，迅速地：*Come back quick – something terrible has happened!* 趕快回來——發生了可怕的事！| **quick as a flash** *informal* (=very quickly)【非正式】快如閃電 *Quick as a flash she replied "That's not what I've heard!"* 她迅速答道："我聽到的不是那樣！"

quick[4] *n* [U] **1 cut sb to the quick** if a remark or criticism cuts you to the quick, it makes you very upset〔用言語或批評〕刺痛某人，使某人很不痛快 **2 the quick** the sensitive flesh under your fingernails and toenails〔手指甲或腳趾甲下的〕活肉：*Her nails were bitten to the quick.* 她的指甲被咬到肉裡了。**3 the quick and the dead** *old use* all people, including those who are alive and those who are dead【舊】〔包括活人和死人的〕所有人

quick-change ar·tist /ˌ· ˈ· ˌ··/ *n* [C] an entertainer who can change their clothes or appearance very quickly 能迅速換服裝[扮相]的演員

quick·en /ˈkwɪkən; ˈkwɪkən/ *v* [I,T] **1** to become quicker or make something quicker (使) 變快，加快：*the quickening pace of technological change* 技術改革上加快的步伐 | **quicken your pace** (=walk faster) 加快步伐 *Ray glanced at his watch and quickened his pace.* 雷看了一眼手錶，加快了步伐。| **your heart/pulse quickens** (=your heart beats faster because you are afraid, excited etc)〔因害怕、激動等〕心臟/脈搏跳動加快 *Val caught sight of Rob and felt her heart quicken.* 瓦爾看見了羅伯，感覺到心跳加快了。**2** *formal* if a feeling quickens, or if something quickens it, it becomes stronger or more active【正式】(使)〔情緒〕變得更強烈[更活躍]：*This policy served only to quicken antigovernment feeling.* 這一政策只有加劇人們的反政府情緒。**3** *old use or literary* to come alive or make something come alive【舊或文】(使) 復活；(使) 有生氣

quick·en·ing /ˈkwɪkənɪŋ; ˈkwɪkənɪŋ/ *n* [U] the first movements of a baby that has not been born yet〔胎兒最初的〕蠕動

quick·fire /ˈkwɪkˌfaɪr; ˈkwɪkfaɪə/ *adj* quickfire conversation, speech etc is very fast and full of clever or amusing remarks〔談話、演說等〕像連珠炮似的；快速且睿智風趣的：*He's full of quickfire patter and smooth gestures.* 他妙語如珠，還有豐富的肢體語言。

quick·freeze /ˈkwɪkfriz; ˈkwɪkfriːz/ *v* [T] to freeze food very quickly so that it keeps all its taste 將〔食物〕速凍；FLASHFREEZE *AmE*【美】

quick·ie /ˈkwɪkɪ; ˈkwɪki/ *n* [C] *informal*【非正式】**1** something done or made quickly and easily 匆匆而做的事：*This recipe is a favourite quickie for when I'm in a hurry.* 這種做法是我趕時間時喜歡用的快捷烹飪法。**2** *humorous* a sexual act done in a hurry【幽默】匆匆完事的性交 —**quickie** *adj*: *a quickie divorce* 草率的離婚

quick·lime /ˈkwɪkˌlaɪm; ˈkwɪk-laɪm/ *n* [U] a white substance obtained by burning LIMESTONE 生石灰

quick·ly /ˈkwɪklɪ; ˈkwɪkli/ *adv* **1** fast 快速地：*She checked nothing was coming and walked quickly across the road.* 她確信沒有甚麼(車輛)過來，便快速地穿過馬路。| *Quickly, John, we don't have much time.* 快點，約翰，我們時間不多了。**2** after only a very short time 很快，馬上：*I realized fairly quickly that this wasn't going to be easy.* 我馬上就認識到這事沒那麼容易。**3** for a short time 短暫地，片刻地：*I'll just quickly nip into that shop.* 我只是去那家商店很快看一下。 1 1

quick march /ˌ· ˈ·/ *interjection* used as a command to tell a group of soldiers to march quickly〔口令〕齊步行進，快步走

quick·sand /ˈkwɪkˌsænd; ˈkwɪksænd/ also 又作 **quicksands** *plural n* [C,U] wet sand that is dangerous because it pulls you down into it if you try to walk on it 流沙

quick·sil·ver /ˈkwɪkˌsɪlvɚ; ˈkwɪkˌsɪlvə/ *n* [U] *old use* MERCURY (=a metal that is liquid at normal temperatures)【舊】水銀，汞

quick·step /ˈkwɪkˌstɛp; ˈkwɪkstep/ *n* [C] a dance with fast movements of the feet, or the music for this dance 快步舞；快步舞曲

quick-tem·pered /ˌ· ˈ··◂/ *adj* easily becoming angry 急躁的，易怒的：*Our young men were quick-tempered and likely to do rash things.* 我們的年輕小伙子性情急躁，有可能做出一些魯莽的事情。

quick-wit·ted /ˌ· ˈ··◂/ *adj* able to understand things quickly and give quick, clever replies 聰明的；機靈的；敏捷的 —**quickwittedness** *n* [U]

quid /kwɪd; kwɪd/ *n plural* **quid** [C] *BrE informal*【英，非正式】**1** one pound in money; £1 一英鎊：*She earns at least 600 quid a week.* 她每週至少掙 600 英鎊。**2 be quids in** to make a profit, especially a good profit 賺錢〔尤指賺大錢〕：*We'll be quids in if we get this contract.* 如果得到這份合同我們將賺大錢。 2

quid pro quo /ˈkwɪd pro ˈkwo; ˌkwɪd prəʊ ˈkwəʊ/ *n* [C] something that you give or do in exchange for something else, especially when this arrangement is not official 補償物；交換物：**[+for]** *The quid pro quo is that we pay them a very low rent.* 交換條件是我們支付他們很低的租金。

qui·es·cent /kwaɪˈɛsn̩t; kwiˈesənt/ *adj formal* not developing or doing anything, especially when this is only a temporary state【正式】靜止的，不活動的；休眠的 —

quiescently *adv* —**quiescence** *n* [U]

2 2 **qui·et¹** /ˋkwaɪət; ˈkwaɪət/ *adj*

1 ►NO NOISE 沒有聲音的◄ not making much noise 輕聲的; 安靜的: *We'll have to be quiet so as not to wake the baby.* 我們得保持安靜, 以免吵醒寶寶。| *The engine is 20% quieter than its nearest rival's.* 該發動機比性能最接近它的競爭對手噪音低 20%。| **(as) quiet as a mouse** (=very quiet) 悄無聲息; 非常安静

2 quiet!/be quiet! *spoken* used to tell someone, rather rudely, to stop talking or making noise【口】安靜! 別作聲!

3 ►PEACEFUL 平靜的◄ a quiet place or time is one where there is not much activity and there are not many people 平靜的, 寧靜的, 寂靜的: *I'd love to go on holiday somewhere where it's nice and quiet.* 我很想去一個既宜人又清靜的地方度假。| **quiet day/weekend** *a quiet weekend at home* 一個在家裡度過的清靜的週末

4 ►NOT SPEAKING 不說話的◄ a) not saying much or not saying anything 不大說話的, 沉默的: *You're very quiet, Mom – is anything the matter?* 媽, 你話很少——出甚麼事了嗎? **b)** someone who is quiet does not usually talk very much 話不多的, 沉默寡言的; 文靜的: *"What's she like?" "Oh, quiet – but friendly enough."* "她人怎麼樣?" "噢, 話不多——但對人很友好。"

5 ►NOT BUSY 不忙碌的◄ if business is quiet, there are not many customers〔生意〕清閒的, 清淡的: *August is a quiet time of year for the retail trade.* 八月是一年中零售買賣的淡季。

6 keep quiet to not say anything, because you do not know anything or because you do not want to tell a secret 保持沉默; 不聲張: *I didn't know anything about it so I just kept quiet.* 我對那事一無所知, 所以我一聲也沒有吭。

7 keep sth quiet/keep quiet about sth to keep information secret 對某事保密: *You're getting married? You kept that quiet!* 你要結婚了?這事你過去可一直沒說啊!

8 keep sb quiet to stop someone from talking, complaining, or causing trouble 使某人安靜: *I gave the children some candy to keep them quiet.* 我給了孩子們一些糖果, 讓他們安靜下來。

9 have a quiet word (with) *especially BrE* to talk to someone privately when you want to criticize them or tell them about something serious【尤英】(與…)私下談談: *I'll have a quiet word with Brian about his behaviour.* 我將就布萊恩的行為和他私下談談。—see also 另見 QUIETLY —**quietness** *n* [U]

quiet² *n* [U] **1** quietness; calmness 寧靜, 寂靜, 平靜: *the quiet of the churchyard* 教堂墓地的寧靜 | **peace and quiet** *I've had an awful day – now I just want some peace and quiet.* 我今天過得糟透了——現在只想清靜清靜。**2** silence 沉默, 安靜: *Can I have quiet please!* 請安靜! **3 on the quiet** *informal* without telling anyone; secretly【非正式】祕密地, 私下地: *We found out he'd been doing some freelance work on the quiet.* 我們發現他私下裡一直在做一些屬於自由職業的工作。

qui·et·en /ˋkwaɪətn̩; ˈkwaɪətn/ also 又作 **quiet** *AmE*【美】*v* **1** also 又作 **quieten down** [I,T] to become less noisy or less active, or to make someone or something do this (使)平靜; (使)安靜: *The chatter quietened briefly when she came into the room.* 她走進房間時, 喋喋不休的說話聲暫時平靜下來。| *Things tend to quieten down after the Christmas rush.* 聖誕節購物熱潮過去之後, 一切便會平靜下來。**2** [T] to make someone feel less frightened or worried 使〔某人〕減少〔恐懼或憂慮〕, 使緩解, 使減輕

qui·et·is·m /ˋkwaɪətɪzm̩; ˈkwaɪətɪzəm/ *n* [U] *formal* a calm state in which you accept situations and do not have any desire to change them【正式】淡泊; 清靜無為; 消極接受

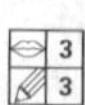

3 3 **qui·et·ly** /ˋkwaɪətlɪ; ˈkwaɪətli/ *adv* **1** without making much noise 輕聲地, 悄聲地; 靜靜地: *Peter spoke so quietly I could hardly hear him.* 彼得說得很輕, 我幾乎聽不見他的話。**2** in a way that does not attract attention 祕密地; 不張揚地: *They have quietly gathered enough support to challenge the leadership.* 他們已悄悄地爭取到足夠的支持來挑戰領導層。**3 quietly confident/optimistic** *especially BrE* fairly confident of success, but without talking proudly about it【尤英】〔對成功〕暗中有信心/持樂觀態度

qui·e·tude /ˋkwaɪə͵tjud; ˈkwaɪətjuːd/ *n* [U] *formal* calmness, peace, and quiet【正式】安靜; 平靜; 寂靜; 寧靜

qui·e·tus /kwaɪˋitəs; kwaɪˈiːtəs/ *n* [singular] *formal*【正式】**1** death 死亡 **2** the end of something 結束, 制止, 平息

quiff /kwɪf; kwɪf/ *n* [C] *BrE* a part of a man's hair style where the hair stands up at the front above his forehead【英】〔男子〕額前向上梳的一綹頭髮, 額髮

quill /kwɪl; kwɪl/ *n* [C] **1** a bird's feather, especially a large one, including the stiff, hard part at the base which joins to the bird's body 羽毛管, 翮 **2** also 又作 **quill pen** a pen made from a large bird's feather, used in past times 羽毛筆, 羽管筆, 翮筆 **3** a thing like a thin, sharp stick that grows on some animals such as a PORCUPINE, in order to protect them〔豪豬等的〕刺

quilt /kwɪlt; kwɪlt/ *n* [C] **1** a warm thick cover for a bed, made of cloth filled with something such as feathers 被子, 被褥 **2** *especially AmE* a thin cloth cover used on a bed to make it look attractive【尤美】牀罩

quilt·ed /ˋkwɪltɪd; ˈkwɪltɪ̆d/ *adj* quilted cloth or clothing has been made thicker and warmer by having a special layer of material stitched into it 絎有襯料的, 夾層的: *a quilted bath robe* 中間有襯裡的浴袍

quilt·ing /ˋkwɪltɪŋ; ˈkwɪltɪŋ/ *n* [U] the work of making a quilt, or the material and stitches that you use 被子絎縫; 被子料

quin /kwɪn; kwɪn/ *n* [C] *BrE informal* a QUINTUPLET【英, 非正式】五胞胎之一

quince /kwɪns; kwɪns/ *n* [C,U] a hard, yellowish fruit like a large apple, used for making JELLY 榲桲〔用以製作果凍〕—see picture on page A8 參見 A8 頁圖

quin·ine /ˋkwaɪnaɪn; ˈkwɪniːn/ *n* [U] a drug used for treating fevers, especially MALARIA 奎寧, 金雞納霜

quinine wa·ter /ˋ·· ͵··/ *n* [U] *AmE* a bitter-tasting drink often mixed with strong alcoholic drinks such as GIN【美】奎寧水

quint /kwɪnt; kwɪnt/ *n* [C] *AmE informal* a QUINTUPLET【美, 非正式】五胞胎之一

quin·tes·sence /kwɪnˋtɛsn̩s; kwɪnˈtesəns/ *n* **the quintessence of sth** *formal* a perfect type or example of something【正式】某事物的典範: *John is the quintessence of good manners.* 約翰是彬彬有禮的典範。

quin·tes·sen·tial /͵kwɪntəˋsɛnʃəl; ͵kwɪntɪ̆ˈsenʃəl◄/ *adj* being a perfect example of a particular type of person or thing 典型的; 典範的: *'Guys and Dolls' is the quintessential American musical.*《少男少女》是典型的美國音樂劇。—**quintessentially** *adv*: *a quintessentially English rural scene* 典型的英國鄉村景色

quin·tet /kwɪnˋtɛt; kwɪnˈtet/ *n* [C] **1** five singers or musicians who perform together 五重唱; 五重奏; 五重唱小組; 五重奏小組 **2** a piece of music written for five performers 五重唱曲; 五重奏曲 —compare 比較 QUARTET, SEXTET, TRIO

quin·tu·plet /kwɪnˋtuplɪt; ˈkwɪntjʊplɪ̆t/ *n* [C] one of five babies born to the same mother at the same time 五胞胎之一 —compare 比較 QUADRUPLET, SEXTUPLET

quip *v* [I] to say something short clever and amusing 說俏皮話, 說妙語: *"Practice makes perfect," quipped Peter when he saw Janet trying to ski.* "熟能生巧。" 彼得看見珍妮特在嘗試滑雪時風趣地說。—**quip** *n* [C]

quire /kwaɪr; kwaɪə/ *n* [C] *technical* 24 sheets of paper【術語】〔紙的〕一刀〔24張〕

quirk /kwɝk; kwɜːk/ *n* [C] **1** something strange that happens by chance〔偶然發生的〕奇事, 巧合: **quirk of**

fate/history etc (=something that happens by chance and influences later events) 命運/歷史等的巧合 *By a quirk of fate, he left just before the bomb exploded.* 由於命運的巧合，他在炸彈爆炸前一刹那離開了。**2** a strange habit or feature of someone's character 古怪；怪癖: *one of her many annoying little quirks* 她許多煩人的怪癖之一

quirk·y /ˈkwɜːkɪ; ˈkwɜːki/ *adj* strange and unusual, in an unexpected way 離奇的，古怪的；奇特的: *The music was a quirky mixture of jazz and classical violins.* 該樂曲是爵士樂和古典小提琴曲的奇妙組合。—**quirkily** *adv* —**quirkiness** *n* [U]

quis·ling /ˈkwɪzlɪŋ; ˈkwɪzlɪŋ/ *n* [C] someone who helps an army or enemy country that has taken control of his own country〔與佔領本國的敵人合作的〕賣國賊，內奸

quit /kwɪt; kwɪt/ *v past tense and past participle* **quit** also 又作 **quitted** *BrE*【英】*present participle* **quitting** **1** [I,T] *informal, especially AmE* to leave a job, school etc, especially because you are annoyed or unhappy【非正式，尤美】〔尤因煩惱或愉快而〕辭去〔工作〕；輟學: *I'm tired of being treated like this. I quit.* 我厭倦了別人這樣對待我。我不幹了。| *Her husband had to quit because of ill health.* 她丈夫由於身體不好，不得不辭去了工作。| **quit school/your job etc** *She quit school at 17 and left home.* 她17歲輟學後離開了家。**2** [T] *informal, especially AmE* to stop doing something bad or annoying【非正式，尤美】停止〔做壞事或令人厭煩的事〕: *Quit it Robby, or I'll tell mom!* 住手，羅比，否則我告訴媽媽！| **quit doing sth** *I wish you'd all quit complaining.* 我希望你們都別抱怨了。**3 be quit of** *formal* to be finished with something that was causing you problems【正式】了結，擺脫〔麻煩、難題等〕**4** [T] *old use* to leave a place【舊】離開〔某處〕

1 1 **quite** /kwaɪt; kwaɪt/ *predeterminer, adv* **1** [+adj/adv] *especially BrE* fairly【尤英】很，相當: **quite big/tall etc** *The restaurant does great food and the prices are quite reasonable.* 那家餐館烹製的食物味道很好，而且價錢相當合理。| *I got a letter from Sylvia quite recently.* 前不久我收到了西爾維亞的一封信。| **quite a big sth/a tall sth etc** *He's quite a good soccer player really.* 他確實是一個相當不錯的足球隊員。| **quite a lot/a few etc** *We managed to get quite a lot of information for the survey.* 我們設法收集到了大量的調查資料。—see 見 RATHER (USAGE) **2 quite good/funny etc** *AmE* very good, funny etc【美】非常好/有趣等: *The food was quite good!* 食物好極了！**3 quite a lot/bit/few** large number or amount 許多，大量: *She must have left here, oh, quite a few years ago.* 她一定是離開這兒了，噢，許多年以前就離開了。**4 not quite why/what/where etc** not exactly why, what, where etc 不完全是因為/是…那樣/是某地等: *I must admit, the play wasn't quite what we expected.* 我必須承認，那齣戲劇並不完全像我們所期望的那樣。**5 not quite** not completely 沒有完全地: *They weren't quite ready so we waited in the car.* 他們沒有完全準備好，所以我們在車裡等着。**6 quite a/quite some** used to describe something that is unusually good, long, interesting etc 不尋常的；出眾的；相當的〔用以表示某事物非常地好、長、有趣等〕: *That was quite a party you had last night.* 昨天晚上你們舉行的晚會很特別。| *That makes quite a noise, doesn't it?* 那會發出相當大的響聲，是嗎？| *He ran quite some distance before he found a public telephone.* 他跑了老遠的路才找到一部公共電話。**7** [+adj/adv] *BrE* very or completely【英】完全；非常，十分: *It's one thing driving a car but a lorry is quite different.* 開小汽車是一回事，開大卡車又完全是另外一回事。| *That's quite ridiculous!* 真荒唐！| **quite the best/the worst etc** *It was quite the most interesting museum I've ever visited.* 這絕對是我參觀過的最有趣的博物館。**8 I'm not quite sure** used to say that you are not certain about something 我不十分肯定，我拿不太準: *I'm not quite sure what her second name is.* 我說不太準她姓甚麼。

Frequencies of the adverb **quite** in spoken and written English 副詞quite在英語口語和書面語中的使用頻率

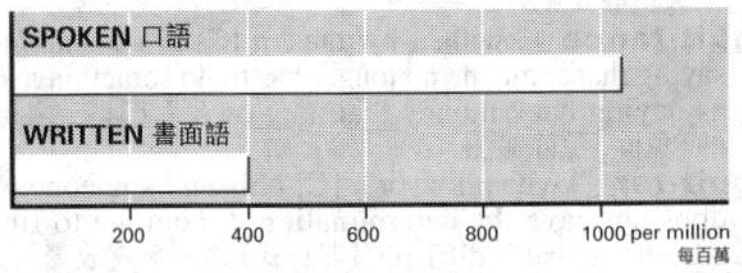

Based on the British National Corpus and the Longman Lancaster Corpus
據英國國家語料庫和朗文蘭卡斯特語料庫

This graph shows that the adverb **quite** is much more common in spoken English than in written English. This is because it is used a lot in spoken English to emphasize amounts, sizes etc or to emphasize how good, bad etc something is. It is also used in a lot of common spoken phrases. 本圖表顯示，副詞quite在英語口語中的使用頻率遠遠高於書面語，因為它經常用於口語中強調數量、大小、好壞等。口語中很多常用片語也是由quite構成的。

quite (*predeterminer, adv*) **SPOKEN PHRASES**
含quite的口語片語

9 quite right *BrE* used to show that you strongly agree with someone【英】完全正確: *"Why should they get paid more than us?" "Quite right, it's completely unfair."* "為甚麼他們的報酬就該比我們高呢？" "問的完全對，這完全不公平。" **10 quite like** *BrE* to like something, but not very much【英】有些喜歡，相當喜歡: *Well, I quite like maths, but I don't like the teacher.* 嗯，我相當喜歡數學，但我不喜歡數學老師。| *It's funny, but he quite likes it after all.* 雖然很可笑，但他畢竟還是相當喜歡它。**11 that's quite all right** used to reply to someone that you do not mind what they are doing 一點都沒關係: *"I hope I'm not disturbing you." "That's quite all right."* "我希望我沒有打擾你。" "一點都沒關係。" **12 I'm quite happy to do something** *BrE* used to say that you are very willing to do something【英】我很樂意做某事: *If they want to come in and discuss it, I'd be quite happy to meet them.* 如果他們想進來討論此事，我將很樂意見他們。**13 quite frankly/honestly** *BrE* used when you are giving a very direct or honest opinion【英】坦率地說/說老實話: *Well, quite frankly, I've never heard such rubbish in all my life!* 嗯，坦率地說，我這一輩子還從來沒聽說過這樣的胡話！**14 quite/quite so** *BrE formal* used to show that you agree with what someone is saying【英，正式】正是這樣，不錯，的確如此: *"They really should have thought of this before." "Yes, quite."* "他們以前確實該想到這一點。" "可不是嘛。" **15 quite enough** *especially BrE* used when you are annoyed with what someone is saying or doing and you want them to stop【尤英】夠了〔表示惱怒〕: *I've heard quite enough about your problems. What about mine?* 你的困難我已聽得夠多了。我的困難怎麼辦？**16 quite something** *especially BrE* used to say that someone or something is very impressive【尤英】令人難忘的人[事]；不尋常的人[事]: *You should have come to the Carnival, it was quite something, I can tell you.* 你真該去參加狂歡節，告訴你吧，真不錯呢。

quits /kwɪts; kwɪts/ *adj informal*【非正式】**1 be quits (with)** to be in an equal situation with someone again, especially because you have paid them what you owed (與…)兩相抵消；(與…)互不相欠: *You pay for the taxi, and that'll make us quits.* 你付計程車車費，我們就誰也不欠誰了。| *If I win the next game, we'll be quits.* 如果我贏了下一場比賽，我們就平了。**2 call it quits a)** to agree that a debt or argument is settled 彼此兩清；(同意)結束爭論: *Just give me $20 and we'll call it quits.*

給我 20 美元, 我們就兩清了。**b)** to agree to stop doing something (同意) 停止做某事: *Let's just paint this door then call it quits for the day.* 我們且把這扇門漆完, 然後今天就收工吧。

quit·tance /ˋkwɪtn̩s; ˈkwɪtəns/ *n* [C] *law* a statement saying that someone no longer has to do something such as paying back money that they owe【法律】〔債務等的〕免除; 免除證書

quit·ter /ˋkwɪtɚ; ˈkwɪtə/ *n* [C] *informal* someone who does not have the determination or courage to finish something that is difficult【非正式】遇困難就放棄的人, 半途而廢的人

quiv·er¹ /ˋkwɪvɚ; ˈkwɪvə/ *v* [I] to tremble slightly, especially because you feel angry, excited, or upset〔尤指因氣憤、激動或傷心而輕微地〕顫抖, 發抖: *Suddenly the child's mouth began to quiver, and he burst into tears.* 突然孩子的嘴巴微微發顫, 然後就放聲大哭。| **[+with]** *quivering with rage* 氣得直發抖

Q

quiver² *n* [C] **1** a slight trembling〔輕微的〕顫抖, 抖動: *I felt a quiver of excitement run through me.* 我全身感到了一陣興奮的顫抖。**2** a long case for carrying ARROWS 箭筒, 箭囊, 箭袋

qui vive /ˌki ˋviv; ˌkiː ˈviːv/ *n* **on the qui vive** taking special care to notice things; watching closely 警戒着, 警惕着

quix·ot·ic /kwɪksˋɑtɪk; kwɪkˈsɒtɪk/ *adj* having ideas that are not practical and plans based on unreasonable hopes of improving the world 唐吉訶德式的, 愚俠(式)的; 不切實際的, 空想的: *a silly quixotic proposal* 愚蠢的不切實際的建議

quiz¹ /kwɪz; kwɪz/ *n plural* **quizzes** [C] **1** a competition in which you have to answer questions 問答比賽, 智力競賽: **sports/news/general knowledge etc quiz** (=a quiz about sports, news etc) 體育知識/新聞知識/一般知識等問答比賽 *a quiz show on TV* 電視上的一個問答比賽節目 **2** a short test that a teacher gives to a class 小測驗, 小考: *a biology quiz* 生物測驗 —see also 另見 POP QUIZ

quiz² *v* **quizzed, quizzing** [T] to ask someone a lot of questions 查問, 盤問: *They kept quizzing me about my new boyfriend.* 他們不停地問我有關我新男友的問題。

quiz·mas·ter /ˈ·ˌ··/ *n* [C] *BrE* a QUESTION-MASTER【英】問答遊戲的主持人

quiz·zi·cal /ˋkwɪzɪkl̩; ˈkwɪzɪkəl/ *adj* **a quizzical look/smile/expression** a look, smile etc that seems to ask a question, often in an amused way 探詢[嘲弄]的目光/微笑/表情 —**quizzically** /-klɪ; -kli/ *adv*

quod /kwɑd; kwɒd/ *n* **in quod** *BrE old-fashioned* in prison【英, 過時】坐牢

quoit /kwɔɪt; kwɔɪt/ *n* **1 quoits** [U] a game in which you throw rings over a small upright post 套圈遊戲 **2** [C] a ring used in the game of quoits〔套圈用的〕環, 圈

quon·dam /ˋkwɑndəm; ˈkwɒndəm/ *adj formal* connected with an earlier time【正式】曾經的, 昔日的, 以前的: *my quondam tutor* 我過去的導師

Quon·set hut /ˋkwɑnsɛt ˋhʌt; ˈkwɒnset ˌhʌt/ *n* [C] *AmE trademark* a building that is shaped like half a tube and is made of iron sheets【美, 商標】匡西特活動房屋

quo·rate /ˋkwɔrət; ˈkwɔːrɪ̈t/ *adj technical* a meeting that is quorate has a quorum present【術語】〔會議〕有法定人數出席的 —opposite 反義詞 INQUORATE

Quorn /kwɔrn; kwɔːn/ *n* [U] *BrE trademark* a vegetable substance that can be used in cooking instead of meat【英, 商標】匡恩牌素肉[人造肉]

quo·rum /ˋkwɔrəm; ˈkwɔːrəm/ *n* [C usually singular 一般用單數] the smallest number of people who must be present at a meeting for official decisions to be made〔會議的〕法定人數

quo·ta /ˋkwotə; ˈkwəʊtə/ *n* [C] **1** the amount or share of something that you think is normal or that is officially expected 定額, 定量: *Salesmen selling over the quota receive a $1,000 bonus.* 超額完成銷售任務的推銷人員可獲得一千美元獎金。**2** a limit, especially an official limit, on the number or amount of something that is allowed in a particular period 限額; 配額: *Most countries have an immigration quota.* 大多數國家都有外來移民限額。| *a strict quota on imports* 嚴格的進口限額 | *I think I've had my quota of coffee for the day.* 我想我今天喝的咖啡已經夠多了。

quo·ta·ble /ˋkwotəbl̩; ˈkwəʊtəbəl/ *adj* a quotable remark or statement is interesting and noticeable, especially because it is clever or amusing 值得引用的

quo·ta·tion /kwoˋteʃən; kwəʊˈteɪʃən/ *n* **1** [C] a sentence or phrase, from a book, speech etc which you repeat in a speech or piece of writing because it is interesting, amusing etc 引語, 引文, 語錄: *a quotation from the Bible* 引自《聖經》的話 | *a dictionary of quotations* 引語詞典, 語錄匯編 **2** [C] a written statement of exactly how much money a piece of work will cost 報價; 行情: *Could you give us a quotation for fixing the roof?* 你能給我們一個修理屋頂的報價嗎? —compare 比較 ESTIMATE¹ (2) **3** [U] the act of quoting something that someone else has written or said 引用, 引述

quotation mark /ˈ·ˈ·· ˌ·/ *n* [C usually plural 一般用複數] one of a pair of marks (" ") or (' ') that show the beginning and end of reported speech or of a quoted word or phrase 引號; INVERTED COMMA *BrE*【英】—see picture at 參見 PUNCTUATION MARK 圖

quote¹ /kwot; kwəʊt/ *v* **1** [I,T] to repeat exactly what someone else has said or written 引用, 引述: **quote (sth) from sth** *She quoted from a newspaper article.* 她引用了報紙上一篇文章的內容。| **quote sb as saying sth** *The President himself was quoted as saying he would veto the bill.* 報道引述總統本人的話, 說他要否決那個法案。| **don't quote me (on this)** (=used to show that what you are saying is not an official statement)〔這話〕別說是我說的, 不要引用我的話 *Don't quote me on this, but the company is in deep trouble.* 這話別說是我說的, 這家公司已深陷困境。| **quote sb/sth** *To quote an old saying, every dog has his day.* 用句老話來說, 人人都有得意時。**2** [T] to mention an example of something to support what you are saying〔為支持論點〕舉例, 舉證, 引證 **3** [T] to tell a customer the price you will charge them for a service or product 報〔價〕, 開〔價〕: *They quoted us $800 for car repairs.* 他們向我們開出了 800 美元的汽車修理價。—compare 比較 ESTIMATE² **4 quote ... unquote** *spoken* used at the beginning and end of a quoted word or phrase to emphasize that it is exactly correct【口】引文開始…引文結束〔用於所引話語的前後〕

quote² *n* [C] *informal*【非正式】**1** a QUOTATION 引語, 引文; 引用 **2 in quotes** words that are in quotes are between a pair of QUOTATION MARKS 在引號中

quoth /kwoθ; kwəʊθ/ *v* [T] *old use*【舊】**quoth I/he/she etc** a way of saying 'I said', 'he said' etc 我/他/她等說過

quo·tid·i·an /kwoˋtɪdiən; kwəʊˈtɪdiən/ *adj old use* daily; ordinary【舊】每日的; 日常的; 平常的

quo·tient /ˋkwoʃənt; ˈkwəʊʃənt/ *n* [C] *technical* the number which is obtained when one number is divided by another【術語】商, 商數

Qu·r'an /kəˋræn; kɔːˈrɑːn/ *n* **the Qur'an** another spelling of KORAN (=the holy book of Islam)《古蘭經》,《可蘭經》〔Koran 的另一種拼法〕

q.v. *Latin* quod vide; used to tell readers to look in another place in the same book for a piece of information【拉丁】參見, 參照該條

qwert·y /ˋkwɝtɪ; ˈkwɜːti/ *adj BrE* a qwerty KEYBOARD on a computer or TYPEWRITER has the keys arranged in the usual way, with Q, W, E, R, T, and Y on the top row【英】〔電腦或打字機的鍵盤〕標準型的〔鍵盤的上行通常排列着 Q, W, E, R, T 和 Y 六個字母〕

R,r

R¹, r /ɑr; ɑː/ *plural* **R's, r's** the 18th letter of the English alphabet 英語字母表的第十八個字母 —see also 另見 **three** (THREE (2))

R² **1** *AmE* the written abbreviation of 縮寫= Republican Party【美】共和黨: *Steve Gunderson (R)* 史蒂夫·岡德森(共和黨) **2** the written abbreviation of 縮寫= REX or REGINA; the Latin words for king or queen〔拉丁文〕國王; 女王: *Elizabeth R* 伊莉莎白女王 **3** the written abbreviation of 縮寫= river, used especially on maps 河, 江〔尤用於地圖上〕 **4** *AmE* used to show that a film may not be watched by children under 17【美】R級電影〔17歲以下兒童不宜觀看〕

rab·bi /ˈræbaɪ; ˈræbaɪ/ *n* [C] a Jewish priest 拉比〔猶太教教士〕

rab·bin·i·cal /rəˈbɪnɪkḷ; rəˈbɪnɪkəl/ *adj* connected with the writings or teaching of rabbis 拉比(的著作或教義)的

rabbit 兔

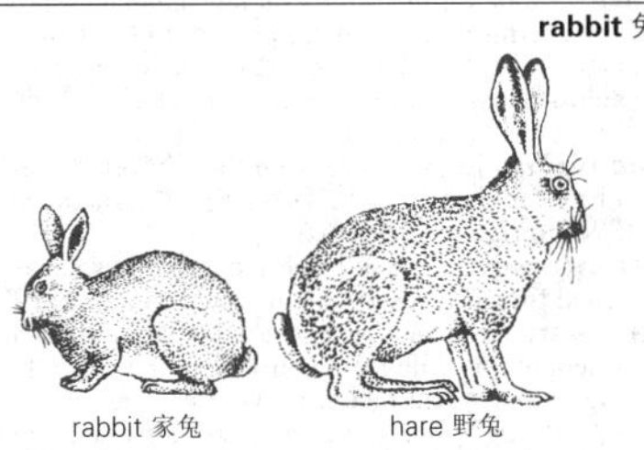

S 3 **rab·bit¹** /ˈræbɪt; ˈræbɨt/ *n* **1** [C] a common small animal with long ears and soft fur, that lives in a hole in the ground 兔 **2** [U] the fur or meat of a rabbit 兔子的毛皮; 兔肉

rabbit² *v* **rabbited, rabbiting 1 rabbit on** [I] *informal, especially BrE* to talk continuously, especially in an uninteresting or annoying way【非正式, 尤英】嘮叨, 喋喋不休 **2 go rabbiting** to hunt or shoot rabbits 獵兔, 打兔子

rabbit hutch /ˈ·· ·/ *n* [C] a wooden CAGE for pet rabbits 兔棚, 兔籠

rabbit punch /ˈ·· ·/ *n* [C] a quick hit on the back of the neck, made with the side of the hand〔用手的側面〕對着後頸項的一下猛擊

rabbit war·ren /ˈ·· ˌ··/ *n* [C] **1** an area under the ground where wild rabbits live in their holes 野兔羣居地, 野兔洞穴多的地方 **2** a building or place with a lot of narrow passages or streets where you can easily get lost 迷宮般的建築[地方]

rab·ble /ˈræbḷ; ˈræbəl/ *n* [singular] **1** a noisy crowd of people who are likely to cause trouble 烏合之眾; 暴民: *Their army was nothing more than an undisciplined rabble.* 他們的隊伍只不過是無紀律的烏合之眾。**2** used about a group of people that you do not respect 無賴, 一幫痞子: *How can you hang out with that rabble in the bar each night?* 你怎麼可以每天晚上都和那羣無賴在酒吧裡鬧混?

rabble-rous·er /ˈ·· ˌ··/ *n* [C] someone who tries to make a crowd of people angry and violent, especially in order to achieve political aims〔尤指抱有政治目的的〕煽動者, 蠱惑人心者 —**rabble-rousing** *adj*: *a rabble-rousing speech* 蠱惑人心的演說 —**rabble-rousing** *n* [U]

rab·id /ˈræbɪd; ˈræbɨd/ *adj* **1** having very extreme and unreasonable opinions, especially about politics; FANATICAL〔尤指在政治上〕過激的; 狂熱的: *rabid right-wingers* 極端右翼分子 **2** suffering from rabies 患狂犬病的: *a rabid dog* 瘋狗

ra·bies /ˈrebiz; ˈreɪbiːz/ *n* [U] a disease that kills animals and people, that you can catch if you are bitten by an infected dog etc 狂犬病

rac·coon, racoon /ræˈkun; rəˈkuːn/ *n* **1** [C] a small North American animal that lives in trees, and has a long tail with black and white rings on it 浣熊〔產於北美, 生活在樹上, 長尾上有黑白相間的環〕 **2** [U] the thick fur of a raccoon 浣熊的毛皮

race¹ /res; reɪs/ *n* S 2 W 2

1 ▶SPORT 運動◀ [C] a competition in which each competitor tries to run, drive etc fastest and finish first 賽跑; 賽車; 速度比賽: *She came fifth in the race.* 她在賽跑中獲第五名。| *a swimming race* 游泳比賽

2 ▶PEOPLE 民族◀ a) [C] one of the main groups that humans can be divided into according to the colour of their skin and other physical features 人種, 種族: *people of all races and creeds* 各種族和宗教的人 **b)** [U] the fact of belonging to one of these groups 種族區別: *The law forbids discrimination on the grounds of race or religion.* 法律禁止以種族或宗教為理由實行歧視。| *a person of mixed race* 混血兒 **c)** [C] a group of people with the same customs, history, language etc 民族: *the Nordic races* 北歐民族 —see also 另見 HUMAN RACE

3 ▶GET/DO STH FIRST 搶先得到/做某事◀ [C usually singular 一般用單數] a situation in which one group of people tries to obtain or achieve something before another group does 競賽, 爭奪, 搶先: **race to do sth** *the race to develop a nuclear bomb* 搶先發展核彈 | **[+for]** *an international race for power and prestige* 國際間權力與聲譽的爭奪 | **the race is on** (=people are competing to do something) 正在競爭 *The race is on to find a cure for AIDS.* 正在爭相尋找治療愛滋病的方法。

4 ▶HORSE RACE 賽馬◀ the races an occasion when horse races are held 賽馬的日子: *a day out at the races* 看賽馬的一天 | *Doncaster Races* 唐克斯特賽馬

5 a race against time an attempt to finish doing something very important fast 和時間賽跑, 爭分奪秒

6 ▶ANIMAL/PLANT 動/植物◀ [C] *technical* a type of animal or plant【術語】〔動植物的〕族, 小種 —see also 另見 ARMS RACE

USAGE NOTE 用法說明: RACE

WORD CHOICE 詞語辨析: **race, nation, people, state, tribe**

A **race** is a very large group of human beings of the same colour and/or physical type. race (種族) 指的是具有相同的膚色和/或體型的較大的人類集團: *different races and nationalities* 不同的種族和民族

A **nation** is a group of people who share the same history and usually a language, and often live in the same area or independent country. nation (民族) 指的是這樣一羣人, 他們具有共同的歷史, 一般也使用共同的語言, 通常居住在同一地區或獨立國家中: *the Indian nations of North America* 北美洲的諸印地安族 | *the Scottish nation* 蘇格蘭民族

A **race** or a **nation** may also be called a **people** [C]. This is sometimes considered to be a more acceptable word than race. race或nation也可叫作people。

這詞與race相比, 有時更能為人們接受: *the peoples of Asia* 亞洲各民族 | *the Jewish people* 猶太民族
A **state** is either a politically independent country, or one of the political parts that makes up a country. state指政治上獨立的國家, 或組成一個國家的邦或州: *the Polish state* 波蘭國家 | *the state of California* 加利福尼亞州 States can often contain people of different races or nations. 國家經常包括不同種族和民族的人。
A **tribe** is a social group, smaller than a nation, that shares the same customs and usually the same language, and often follows an ancient or traditional way of life. tribe (部落) 是比nation (民族) 小的集團, 有共同的風俗習慣, 一般使用相同的語言, 並通常遵循某種古老或傳統的生活方式: *the tribes living in the Amazon region* 居住在亞馬遜地區的部落

race² *v*
1 ►SPORT 運動◄ **a)** [I,T] to compete against someone or something in a race (和…) 比賽: **[+against]** *She'll be racing against some of the world's top athletes.* 她將與一些世界頂尖運動員進行比賽。| **race sb to/back/there** *I'll race you to the end of the road.* 我和你賽跑, 看誰先跑到路的盡頭。**b)** [T] to use an animal or a vehicle to compete in a race 使〔動物或車輛〕參加比賽: *Prouteau was racing a Ferrari in the Formula One championships.* 普魯托駕駛一輛法拉利跑車參加一級方程式錦標賽。| *young horses that had never been raced* 從未參加過比賽的馬駒
2 ►MOVE QUICKLY 迅速移動◄ [I always+adv/prep, T always+adv/prep] to move very quickly or make someone or something move very quickly (使) 快速移動, (使) 疾走[馳]: **[+out/home/into]** *I had to race back home for my umbrella.* 我不得不奔回家去取雨傘。| *I watched as her eyes raced over the page.* 我看着她很快地掃了那一頁。| **race sb to/back/there** *The sick woman was raced to the hospital.* 患病的婦人被迅速送往醫院。
3 ►TIME 時間◄ **race by/past** if time races by, it passes very quickly〔時間〕飛逝: *The seconds went racing past.* 幾秒鐘很快過去了。
4 ►HEART/MIND ETC 心臟/大腦等◄ [I] if your heart, PULSE¹ (1), or mind races, it works harder and faster than usual, especially because you are ill or anxious〔尤指因生病或焦慮而心臟〕狂跳;〔大腦〕快速轉動念頭: *My heart started racing at the sound of approaching footsteps.* 聽到越來越近的腳步聲, 我的心臟開始劇烈跳動。
5 ►ENGINE 發動機◄ [I] if an engine races, it runs too fast〔發動機〕轉動速度太高

race car /ˈ· ·/ *n* [C] *AmE* a RACING CAR【美】賽車, 跑車

race·card /ˈresˌkɑrd; ˈreɪskɑːd/ *n* [C] *BrE* a programme giving the races, times, and horses at a horse racing event【英】〔賽馬用的〕比賽程序單

race·course /ˈresˌkɔrs; ˈreɪs-kɔːs/ *n* [C] **1** *BrE* a track, usually covered with grass, around which horses race【英】賽馬跑道, 賽馬場; RACETRACK (2) *AmE*【美】**2** *AmE* a track around which runners, cars etc race【美】〔賽跑、賽車等用的〕跑道

race·go·er /ˈresˌgoɚ; ˈreɪsgəʊə/ *n* [C] someone who goes regularly to horse races 愛看賽馬的人

race·horse /ˈresˌhɔrs; ˈreɪshɔːs/ *n* [C] a horse specially bred and trained for racing〔專門培育的〕比賽用的馬

race meet·ing /ˈ· ˌ··/ *n* [C] *BrE* an occasion when horse races are held at a particular place【英】賽馬會

race re·la·tions /ˈ· ·ˌ··/ *n* [plural] the relationship that exists between people from different countries, religions etc who are living in the same place 種族關係: *The result of the trial could have a damaging effect on race relations in the city.* 審判結果可能對該市的種族關係產生不利的影響。

race ri·ot /ˈ· ˌ··/ *n* [C] violent behaviour, such as fighting and attacks on property, caused by hatred between people of different races 種族騷亂

race·track /ˈresˌtræk; ˈreɪs-træk/ *n* [C] **1** a track around which runners, cars etc race〔賽跑、賽車等用的〕跑道 **2** *AmE* a track, usually covered with grass, around which horses race【美】賽馬跑道; RACECOURSE (1) *BrE*【英】

ra·cial /ˈreʃəl; ˈreɪʃəl/ *adj* **1** [only before noun 僅用於名詞前] connected with the relationships between different races of people 種族(關係)的: *an appeal for racial and religious tolerance* 呼籲不同種族和宗教間的寬容 | *racial conflict* 種族衝突 | **racial discrimination** (=unfair treatment of people because of their race) 種族歧視 | **racial prejudice** (=the belief that other races are not as good or as intelligent as your own race) 種族偏見 | **racial harassment** (=insulting or annoying someone because of their race) 種族騷擾 **2** connected with the various races that humans can be divided into 種族的: *a broad range of racial and ethnic groups* 多種多樣的種族和民族羣體 | *people of different racial origin* 不同種族背景的人 —**racially** *adv*: *Police officers believe the attack was racially motivated.* 警察認定攻擊是出於種族原因。

ra·cial·is·m /ˈreʃəlˌɪzəm; ˈreɪʃəlɪzəm/ *n* [U] *BrE old-fashioned* RACISM【英, 過時】種族歧視; 種族暴力; 種族主義 —**racialist** *n, adj*

rac·ing¹ /ˈresɪŋ; ˈreɪsɪŋ/ *n* [U] **1** the sport of racing horses 賽馬: *watching the racing on television* 在電視上看賽馬 | **racing results/tips/paper etc** *today's racing results* 今天的賽馬結果 **2 car/bicycle/greyhound etc racing** the sport of racing cars etc 汽車/自行車/靈猩等比賽

racing² *adj* [only before noun 僅用於名詞前] designed or bred for racing 專為比賽設計[飼養]的: *racing pigeons* 賽鴿 | *a racing yacht* 賽艇

racing car /ˈ·· ·/ *n* [C] *BrE* a car that is specially designed for car races【英】賽車; RACE CAR *AmE*【美】

ra·cis·m /ˈresɪzəm; ˈreɪsɪzəm/ *n* [U] **1** unfair treatment of people, or violence against them, because they belong to a different race from your own 種族歧視; 種族暴力: *the ugly face of racism rearing its head again in Europe* 正在歐洲重新抬頭的種族歧視的醜惡嘴臉 **2** the belief that different races of people have different characters and abilities, and that the qualities of your own race are the best 種族主義

rac·ist /ˈresɪst; ˈreɪsɪst/ *n* [C] someone who believes that people of their own race are better than others, and who treats people from other races unfairly and sometimes violently 種族主義者: *white racists* 白人種族主義者 —**racist** *adj*: *racist attitudes* 種族主義態度

racks 擱物架

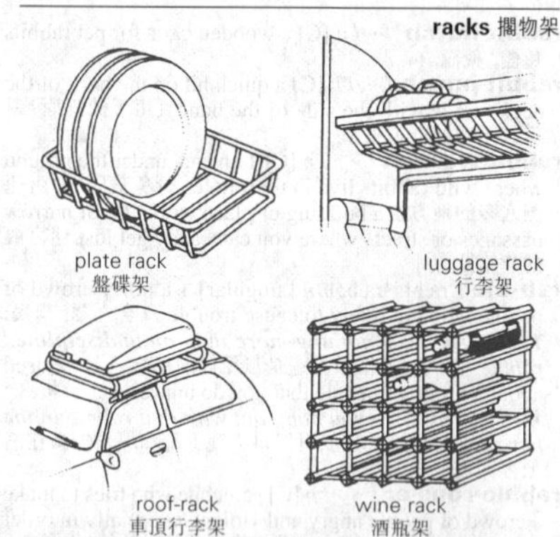

rack¹ /ræk; ræk/ *n* [C] **1** a frame or shelf, usually with bars or hooks, for holding things on〔通常帶有橫檔或

鈎子的〕架子, 擱物架: *The dishes are on the plate rack.* 盤子在盤子架上。| *a magazine rack* 雜誌架 —see also 另見 LUGGAGE RACK, ROOF-RACK **2 the rack** a piece of equipment used in the past to make people suffer severe pain by stretching their bodies 拉肢刑架〔舊時的一種酷刑刑具〕 **3 on the rack** suffering severe pain or anxiety 十分痛苦, 極度焦慮 **4 go to rack and ruin** to gradually get into a very bad condition as a result of not being looked after〔因缺乏照料所致的〕破損, 毀壞: *The old farmhouse had gone to rack and ruin.* 那間舊農舍已經破敗不堪了。**5** *AmE* a three-sided frame used for arranging the balls at the start of a game of SNOOKER[1] or POOL[1] (3)【美】〔用於枱球或撞球比賽開球時放置球的〕三角框 **6 a rack of lamb/pork** *BrE* a fairly large piece of meat from the side of an animal【英】羊/豬胸腹兩側較大塊的肉

rack² *v* **1** [T usually passive 一般用被動態] to make someone suffer great mental or physical pain 使受巨大〔精神或肉體〕痛苦: **be racked by/with** *She was racked by feelings of guilt.* 她深受負罪感的折磨。| *He lay on the ground racked with pain.* 他萬分痛苦地躺在地上。**2 rack your brain(s)** to think very hard or for a long time 絞盡腦汁: *I really had to rack my brains to remember his name.* 我真的得絞盡腦汁, 才能記起他的名字。

rack sth ↔ **up** *phr v* [T] *informal*【非正式】**1** *AmE* to gradually get points, votes etc, especially in a competition or election【美】〔尤指在競賽或競選中逐漸〕得〔分〕, 贏得〔選票〕: *The team racked up enough points to win the NFL title.* 該隊累積了足夠的得分獲得 (美國) 全國橄欖球聯盟冠軍。**2** *AmE* to damage or ruin something【美】破壞, 毀壞: *That motorcycle accident really racked up his leg.* 那場摩托車車禍確實毀了他的腿。**3** to make the value, amount, or level of something go up 使增值, 增加, 提高: *High interest rates have racked up the pound.* 高利率造成英鎊升值。

rack·et¹ /ˈrækɪt; ˈrækɨt/ *n* **1** [singular] *informal* a loud noise【非正式】吵鬧 (聲), 喧囂: *They're making a hell of a racket downstairs.* 他們正在樓下大吵大鬧。—see 見 NOISE[1] (USAGE) **2** [C] *informal* a dishonest way of obtaining money, such as by threatening people or selling them illegal goods【非正式】敲詐, 勒索; 非法勾當〔銷售違禁品〕: **drugs/gambling/smuggling etc racket** *He runs a numbers racket on the side.* 他私下經營非法彩票賭博。—see also 另見 PROTECTION RACKET **3** also 又作 **racquet** [C] a BAT[1] (2b) used for hitting the ball in games such as tennis 球拍: *a tennis racket* 網球拍 —see pictures at 參見 SQUASH and 和 TENNIS 圖 **4 rackets** also 又作 **racquets** [U] a fast ball game for two or four players, played with rackets and a hard ball on an indoor court 硬球壁球 (運動)

racket² *v* [I always+adv/prep] to make a lot of noise as you move around〔走動時〕發出大響聲: **[+around/about etc]** *racketing about upstairs* 在樓上弄出很大響聲

rack·e·teer /ˌrækɪˈtɪr; ˌrækɨˈtɪə/ *n* [C] someone who is involved in a dishonest method of obtaining money 敲詐[勒索]錢財者, 非法經營者

rack·e·teer·ing /ˌrækɪˈtɪrɪŋ; ˌrækɨˈtɪərɪŋ/ *n* [U] obtaining money dishonestly by means of a carefully planned system 敲詐, 勒索: *Keating is awaiting trial on fraud and racketeering charges.* 基廷因被指控欺詐和勒索正聽候審判。

rack·et·y /ˈrækɪtɪ; ˈrækɨti/ *adj informal* making a lot of noise【非正式】喧鬧的: *a rackety old typewriter* 咔咔作響的舊打字機

rac·on·teur /ˌrækɑnˈtɝ; ˌrækɒnˈtɜː/ *n* [C] someone who is good at telling stories in an interesting and amusing way 擅長講故事的人

ra·coon /ræˋkun; rəˈkuːn/ *n* [C] another spelling of RACCOON raccoon 的另一種拼法

rac·quet·ball /ˈrækɪtˌbɔl; ˈrækɨtbɔːl/ *n* [U] a game for two or four players, popular in the US, played in an enclosed court and following the rules of HANDBALL (1)〔流行於美國的〕短拍壁球 (運動)

rac·y /ˈresɪ; ˈreɪsi/ *adj* speech or writing that is racy is exciting and entertaining〔演講或文章〕有趣味的, 生動的: **racy jokes/humour/stories** (=connected with sex) 猥褻的笑話/幽默/故事 —**racily** *adv* —**raciness** *n* [U]

ra·dar /ˈredɑr; ˈreɪdɑː/ *n* [C,U] a method of finding the position of things such as planes or MISSILEs by sending out radio waves 雷達: *The missile was identified using radar.* 導彈已被雷達識別出來。| *a radar screen* 雷達屏幕

radar trap /ˈ·· ·/ *n* [C] a method or set of equipment that uses radar to catch drivers who are going faster than the legal speed〔捕獲超速行駛司機用的〕雷達監控法[器]

rad·dled /ˈrædḷd; ˈrædld/ *adj* **1** *BrE* looking old or tired【英】蒼老的; 疲憊的 **2** *AmE* confused or anxious【美】茫然的; 焦慮的

ra·di- /redɪ; reɪdi/ *prefix* another form of the prefix RADIO- 前綴 radio- 的另一種形式

ra·di·al¹ /ˈredɪəl; ˈreɪdiəl/ *adj* arranged in a circular shape with bars, lines etc coming from the centre 輻射狀的: *radial street patterns* 輻射狀的街道佈局

radial² *n* [C] *informal* a RADIAL TYRE【非正式】輻射狀[子午線]輪胎

radial tyre *BrE*【英】, **radial tire** *AmE*【美】/ˌ·· ˈ·/ *n* [C] a car tyre with wires inside the rubber that go completely around the wheel to make it stronger and safer 輻射狀[子午線]輪胎

ra·di·ance /ˈredɪəns; ˈreɪdiəns/ *n* [U] **1** great happiness, or energy that shows in the way someone looks〔人或其外表的〕喜氣洋洋, 容光煥發: *the unmistakeable radiance of youth* 顯而易見的青春朝氣 **2** a soft light that shines from or onto something 光彩

ra·di·ant /ˈredɪənt; ˈreɪdiənt/ *adj* **1** full of happiness and love, in a way that shows in your face, eyes etc 喜悦的, 容光煥發的, 光彩照人的: *a radiant smile* 粲然一笑 | **[+with]** *radiant with joy* 滿面春風 **2** [only before noun 僅用於名詞前] very bright 燦爛的, 明亮的: *a radiant blue sky* 湛藍的天空 **3** [only before noun 僅用於名詞前] *technical* radiant heat, energy etc is sent out by radiation【術語】〔熱、能等〕輻射的 —**radiantly** *adv*: *radiantly beautiful* 美得光彩照人

ra·di·ate /ˈredɪˌet; ˈreɪdieɪt/ *v* **radiated, radiating 1** [I always+adv/prep,T] if something radiates light or heat, or if light or heat radiates from something, it is sent out in all directions 輻射〔光或熱〕;〔向四面八方〕發射: *The log fire radiated a warm cosy glow.* 燃燒的圓木發出溫暖舒適的光。| **[+down/from/away etc]** *Warmth radiated down from the tin roof.* 暖流從白鐵屋頂發散下來。**2** [I,T] if someone radiates a feeling or quality, or if it radiates from them, they show it or feel it in a way that is easy to notice 流露, 顯示〔感情、態度等〕: *She radiated energy and self-confidence.* 她洋溢着活力與自信。| **[+from]** *Sexual magnetism radiated from him.* 他散發着性感。**3** to spread out from a central point 從中心散開: **[+from/to]** *A system of roads radiates from the town centre.* 一組公路從市中心向四面八方伸展出去。

ra·di·a·tion /ˌredɪˈeʃən; ˌreɪdiˈeɪʃən/ *n* [U] **1** a form of energy that comes especially from NUCLEAR reactions, which is very harmful to living things if present in large amounts (核) 輻射〔尤指核反應產生的能源形式, 如量大對生物非常危險〕: *an escape of low-level radiation from the nuclear power plant* 從核電廠泄漏的低強度輻射 | *lethal doses of radiation* 致命的輻射劑量 **2** energy in the form of heat or light sent out as beams that you cannot see〔熱或光的能量〕輻射: *electromagnetic radiation* 電磁輻射 | *sun cream that filters out harmful ultraviolet radiation* 能濾去有害紫外線輻射的防曬霜 **3** the radiating of heat, light etc 發熱; 發光

radiation sick·ness /ˌ··ˈ·· ˌ··/ *n* [U] an illness caused by your body receiving too much radiation 輻射病, 放射病

ra·di·a·tor /ˈredɪˌetɚ; ˈreɪdieɪtə/ *n* [C] **1** a thing used for heating a room, consisting of a flat hollow metal con-

R

tainer fixed to a wall, through which hot water passes〔指藉熱水循環供熱的〕暖氣裝置 **2** the part of a car or aircraft which stops the engine from getting too hot〔冷卻汽車、飛機發動機的〕散熱器 —see picture at 參見 ENGINE (1) 圖

3 **rad·i·cal¹** /ˈrædɪkl̩; ˈrædɪkəl/ *adj* **1** a radical change has a lot of important effects〔變革等〕重大的, 根本的: *radical alterations to the original script* 對原稿進行的重大修改 | *a radical reform of the tax system* 稅收制度的徹底改革 **2** radical opinions, ideas, leaders etc support thorough and complete social or political change〔人、觀點、領導人等〕激進的, 極端的: *the radical views of the left wing of the party* 黨內左翼的激進觀點 **3** related to the central or most important qualities of something; FUNDAMENTAL 根本的, 基本的: *a radical questioning of basic Communist tenets* 對共產主義基本信念提出的根本性懷疑 | *radical differences between the two groups* 兩派間的根本分歧 **4** *AmE slang* very good or enjoyable【美俚】頂呱呱的, 好玩的: *That was one radical party last night!* 昨晚的聚會太棒了! —**radically** /-kl̩ɪ; -kli/ *adv*

radical² *n* [C] someone who wants thorough and complete social and political change〔主張對社會和政治作徹底變革的〕激進分子 —**radicalism** *n* [U]

rad·i·i /ˈredɪˌaɪ; ˈreɪdiaɪ/ *n* the plural of RADIUS

ra·di·o- /redɪo; reɪdiəʊ/ *prefix* also 又作 **radi- 1** *technical*【術語】**a)** concerning waves of force, e.g. light, sound, or radio waves〔光、聲、無線電波〕輻射: *radiopaque* (=which waves will not pass through) 輻射穿不透的 **b)** using radio waves 使用無線電波的: *a radiotelephone* (=working without wires) 無線電話(機) | *radiopaging* (=calling people by radio) 無線電傳呼 **2** concerning RADIOACTIVITY 與放射有關的: *radiochemistry* (=the study of RADIOACTIVE chemicals) 放射化學

1 2 **ra·di·o¹** /ˈredɪˌo; ˈreɪdiəʊ/ *n* **1 a)** [C] a piece of electronic equipment which you use to listen to programmes that are broadcast, such as music and news 收音機: *turn on the radio* 打開收音機 | *listening to the radio in the car* 在汽車裡聽收音機 | **on the radio** (=broadcast on a radio) 廣播 *an interesting program on the radio this morning* 今晨廣播的一個有趣的節目 **b) the radio** programmes that are broadcast on the radio, considered in general〔泛指〕廣播節目: *I don't really listen to the radio much.* 我不怎麼聽廣播。 **c)** [U] the sending or receiving of programmes by radio 廣播: *Radio was a powerful medium during the war years, keeping up people's morale.* 戰爭年代裡, 廣播是一種很有力的媒介, 激勵着人們的士氣。 **2** [U] the activity of making and broadcasting programmes which can be heard on a radio (無線電) 廣播業: *David Jason worked in radio before TV.* 戴維·傑森到電視台工作前在電台工作過。| **local/national radio** (=programmes or companies broadcasting for a local area, or for the whole country) 地方/全國廣播節目[公司] | **radio programme/show/drama etc** *John Peel's late-night radio show* 約翰·皮爾的深夜廣播節目 **3 a)** [C] a piece of electronic equipment, for example on a plane or ship, which can send and receive spoken messages〔飛機、船上的〕無線電收發設備 **b)** [U] the sending or receiving of these messages 無線電通訊: *We've lost radio contact.* 我們失去了無線電聯繫。

radio² *v* [I,T] to send a message using a radio 用無線電發送(信息): *The ship radioed for help.* 這條船用無線電發出求救信號。| *Radio London for permission to land.* 用無線電請求倫敦准予降落。

ra·di·o·ac·tive /ˌredɪoˋæktɪv; ˌreɪdiəʊˈæktɪv◂/ *adj* containing RADIATION (=a form of energy that can harm living things) 具有放射性的: *a highly radioactive material* 高放射性物質 | *radioactive contamination* 放射性污染

radioactive dat·ing /ˌ····· ˈ··/ *n* [U] *AmE* a scientific method of calculating the age of a very old object by measuring the amount of a certain substance in it【美】放射性年代測定(法), 碳年代測定(法); CARBON DATING *BrE*【英】

radioactive waste /ˌ····· ˈ·/ *n* [U] harmful radioactive substances that remain after energy has been produced in a NUCLEAR REACTOR〔核反應堆產生的〕放射性廢料

ra·di·o·ac·tiv·i·ty /ˌredɪˌoækˋtɪvətɪ; ˌreɪdiəʊækˈtɪvəti/ *n* [U] **1** a quality that certain substances have which makes them send out RADIATION (=a form of energy that can harm living things) 放射(性) **2** the energy which is produced in this way 輻射能: *Workers were exposed to high levels of radioactivity.* 工人接觸到高強度輻射。

radio bea·con /ˈ··· ˌ··/ *n* [C] a tower that sends out radio signals to help aircraft stay on the correct course 無線電導航塔

ra·di·o·car·bon dat·ing /ˌredɪokɑrbən ˋdetɪŋ; ˌreɪdiəʊkɑːbən ˈdeɪtɪŋ/ *n* [U] *formal* CARBON DATING【正式】碳年代測定(法)

radio-cas·sette play·er /ˌ··· ·ˈ· ··/ *n* [C] a piece of electronic equipment that contains both a radio and a CASSETTE PLAYER 收音卡式機

radio-con·trolled /ˌ··· ·ˈ·◂/ *adj* **a radio-controlled aircraft/vehicle/vessel** controlled from far away using radio signals 無線電遙控飛機/車輛/船

ra·di·o·gram /ˈredɪəˌgræm; ˈreɪdiəʊgræm/ *n* [C] **1** *BrE* a piece of furniture, popular in the 1950s, which contained a radio and a record player【英】〔20世紀50年代流行的〕收音電唱兩用機 **2** a message sent by radio 無線電報

ra·di·og·ra·pher /ˌredɪˋɑgrəfɚ; ˌreɪdiˈɒgrəfə/ *n* [C] someone whose job is to take X-RAY photographs of the inside of someone's body, or who treats people for illnesses using an X-RAY machine X射線照相師; 放射科醫師

ra·di·og·ra·phy /ˌredɪˋɑgrəfɪ; ˌreɪdiˈɒgrəfi/ *n* [U] the taking of X-RAY photographs of the inside of someone's body for medical purposes〔醫用〕X射線照相術

ra·di·ol·o·gist /ˌredɪˋɑlədʒɪst; ˌreɪdiˈɒlədʒɪst/ *n* [C] a hospital doctor who is trained in the use of RADIATION to treat people 放射科醫師

ra·di·ol·o·gy /ˌredɪˋɑlədʒɪ; ˌreɪdiˈɒlədʒi/ *n* [U] the study and medical use of RADIATION〔醫用〕放射學

radio-tel·e·phone /ˌ··· ˈ···/ *n* [C] a telephone, used especially in cars, that works by sending and receiving radio signals〔尤指汽車的〕無線電話(機)

radio tel·e·scope /ˌ··· ˈ···/ *n* [C] a very large piece of equipment that collects the RADIO WAVES that come from stars and other objects in space 無線電望遠鏡

ra·di·o·ther·a·py /ˌredɪoˋθɛrəpɪ; ˌreɪdiəʊˈθerəpi/ *n* [U] the treatment of illnesses using RADIATION 放射治療 —**radiotherapist** *n* [C]

radio wave /ˈ··· ˌ·/ *n* [C usually plural 一般用複數] a form of electric energy that can move through air or space 無線電波

rad·ish /ˈrædɪʃ; ˈrædɪʃ/ *n* [C] a small vegetable whose red or white root is eaten raw and has a strong SPICY taste〔可生吃、有辣味的紅或白色的〕小蘿蔔 —see picture on page A9 參見A9頁圖

ra·di·um /ˈredɪəm; ˈreɪdiəm/ *n* [U] a rare metal that is RADIOACTIVE and is used in the treatment of diseases such as CANCER 鐳

ra·di·us /ˈredɪəs; ˈreɪdiəs/ *n plural* **radii** /-dɪˌaɪ; -diaɪ/ [C] **1** the distance from the centre to the edge of a circle〔圓的〕半徑: *The radius of the throwing circle should be 1.5 metres.* 投擲圈的半徑應為1.5米。**2 within a 10 mile/200 metre etc radius** within a distance of 10 miles, 200 metres in all directions from a particular place 在10英里/200米等的半徑範圍內: *All vegetation was destroyed within a 2km radius of the volcano.* 火山方圓2公里內所有的植被都毀了。**3** a line drawn straight out from the centre of a circle to its edge 半徑(線) —see picture at 參見 CIRCLE¹ 圖 **4** *technical* the outer bone of the lower part of your arm【術語】橈骨 —see picture at 參見 SKELETON 圖

ra·don /ˈredɑn; ˈreɪdɒn/ *n* [U] a RADIOACTIVE gas that can be dangerous in large amounts 氡

rad·waste /ˈrædˌwest; ˈrædweɪst/ *n* [U] *AmE* RADIOACTIVE WASTE【美】放射性廢料

RAF /ˌɑr e ˋɛf; ˌɑːr eɪ ˈef/ *n* the Royal Air Force; the British AIRFORCE〔英國〕皇家空軍

raf·fi·a /ˈræfɪə; ˈræfiə/ *n* [U] a soft substance like string that comes from the leaves of a PALM tree and is used for making baskets, hats, MATs etc〔編織籃子、帽子、蓆子等用的〕酒椰葉纖維

raf·fish /ˈræfɪʃ; ˈræfɪʃ/ *adj literary* behaving or dressing in a confident and cheerful way that shows no concern for what other people think but is still attractive【文】〔人的行為或裝束〕大膽脱俗的, 落拓不羈的: *a raffish air about him which some women found appealing* 他讓一些女人着迷的灑脱風度 —**raffishly** *adv* —**raffishness** *n* [U]

3 **raf·fle¹** /ˈræfḷ; ˈræfəl/ *n* [C] a kind of competition or game in which people buy numbered tickets and can win prizes 對獎售物(活動)

raffle² also 又作 **raffle off** *v* [T] to offer something as a prize in a raffle 在對獎售物活動中以…作獎品

raft¹ /ræft; rɑːft/ *n* [C] **1** a flat floating structure, usually made of pieces of wood tied together, used as a boat 木排, 木筏 **2** a flat floating structure that you can sit on, jump from etc when you are swimming〔游泳時可坐或跳水的〕浮台 **3 a (whole) raft of** *spoken, especially AmE* a large number of things or large amount of something【口, 尤美】許多, 大量: *He has a whole raft of camera equipment.* 他有一大堆照相器材。**4** a small flat rubber boat filled with air, used if a boat sinks or a plane crashes into the sea 充氣救生(橡皮)筏

raft² *v* [I,T] to travel by raft or carry things by raft 乘筏子; 用筏子運送

raf·ter /ˈræftɚ; ˈrɑːftə/ *n* [C usually plural 一般用複數] one of the large sloping pieces of wood that form the structure of a roof 椽

rag¹ /ræg; ræg/ *n*

1 ►CLOTH 布◄ [C,U] a small piece of old cloth, for example one used for cleaning things 一小塊舊布; 抹布: *Can I use this piece of rag for the car?* 我能用這塊布擦車嗎? | *an oily old rag* 沾滿油污的舊抹布

2 in rags wearing old torn clothes 衣衫襤褸: *an old beggar dressed in rags* 衣衫襤褸的老乞丐

3 go from rags to riches to become very rich after starting your life very poor 白手起家

4 ►NEWSPAPER 報紙◄ [C] *informal* a newspaper that you think is of low quality【非正式】粗製濫造的報紙: *The Evening News is just a provincial rag.*《晚報》不過是一份差勁的地方小報。

5 ►MUSIC 音樂◄ [C] a piece of RAGTIME music 雷格泰姆樂曲: *Georgia Rag* 喬治亞州雷格泰姆音樂

6 ►STUDENTS' EVENT 學生活動◄ [C] *BrE* an event organized by students every year in order to make money for people who are poor, sick etc【英】〔學生每年為窮人、病人等舉行的〕慈善募捐活動: *rag week* 慈善募捐週

7 ►TRICK 花招◄ [C] *BrE old-fashioned* a trick played on someone as a joke【英, 過時】戲弄, 惡作劇: *They did it as a rag.* 他們這樣做只是為了尋開心。—see also 另見 **glad rags** (GLAD (6)), **like a red rag to a bull** (RED¹ (6))

rag² *v* **ragged, ragging** [T] *BrE old-fashioned* to laugh at someone or play tricks on them【英, 過時】戲弄, 對…搞惡作劇

ra·ga /ˈrɑgə; ˈrɑːgə/ *n* [C] **1** a piece of Indian music based on an ancient pattern of notes 拉迦樂曲〔一種印度音樂〕**2** one of the ancient patterns of notes that are used in Indian music 拉迦曲調

rag·a·muf·fin /ˈrægəˌmʌfɪn; ˈrægəˌmʌfɪn/ *n* [C] *literary* a dirty young child wearing torn clothes【文】衣衫襤褸的髒孩子

rag-and-bone-man /ˌ· · ˈ· ·/ *n* [C] *BrE* a man who goes around the streets buying and collecting old clothes and other things that people no longer want【英】〔沿街收購舊衣物的〕流動舊貨商

rag·bag /ˈrægˌbæg; ˈrægbæg/ *n* **a ragbag of** a confused mixture of things that do not seem to go together or make sense ...雜亂無章的東西, ...的大雜燴: *a ragbag of ill-thought-out measures to help the homeless* 計劃不周的幫助無家可歸者的措施

rag doll /ˈ· ·/ *n* [C] a soft DOLL¹ (1) made of cloth 布娃娃

rage¹ /redʒ; reɪdʒ/ *n* [C,U] **1** a strong feeling of uncontrollable anger 盛怒, 狂怒: *His letter had filled her with rage and disappointment.* 他的信使她盛怒和失望。| **in a rage** *She stormed out of the room in a rage.* 她狂怒之下衝出房間。| **fly into a rage** (=suddenly become very angry) 勃然大怒 *Major Sanderson instantly flew into a terrible rage.* 山德森少校立即大發雷霆。| **shaking/trembling/quivering with rage** *Blake sprang to his feet, his face trembling with rage.* 布雷克一躍而起, 氣得臉直抽搐。**2 be (all) the rage** *informal* to be very popular and fashionable【非正式】流行, 時髦: *Platform shoes were all the rage then.* 厚底坡跟鞋當時風靡一時。**3 a rage for** *old-fashioned* a very popular fashion【過時】最時髦的東西, 時新式樣, 時尚: *There was a great rage for open sports cars at that time.* 當時敞篷跑車非常流行。

rage² *v* [I] **1** if something rages, such as a battle, a disagreement, or a storm, it continues with great violence or strong emotions〔戰鬥、爭論〕激烈進行,〔風暴〕狂吹: *Controversy over the scandal is still raging.* 有關醜聞的爭論仍然激烈。| *Outside a great storm was raging.* 屋外狂風大作。**2** [+at/about/against] to feel very angry about something and show this in the way you behave or speak 大怒, 發脾氣: *Margo raged against the unfairness of the situation.* 馬戈對不公正的情況勃然大怒。

rag·ga /ˈrægə; ˈrægə/ *n* [U] a form of popular music from the West Indies 拉加〔西印度羣島的一種流行音樂〕

rag·ged /ˈrægɪd; ˈrægḷd/ *adj*

1 ►CLOTHES 衣服◄ also 又作 **raggedy** *especially AmE* torn and in bad condition【尤美】破舊的: *A beggar was dozing on a pile of ragged blankets.* 一個乞丐正坐在一堆破毯子上打瞌睡。| *piles of ragged old books* 成堆的破舊書籍

2 ►PEOPLE 人◄ wearing clothes that are old and torn 衣衫襤褸的: *a group of ragged children* 一羣穿得破破爛爛的孩子

3 ►UNEVEN 不平的◄ also 又作 **raggedy** not straight or neat, but with rough uneven edges〔邊緣〕參差不齊的: *a ragged hedge* 參差不齊的樹籬

4 ►TIRED 疲倦的◄ *informal* tired after using a lot of effort【非正式】疲乏的: *The walkers looked pretty ragged by the end of the day.* 到這天結束時, 步行的人都顯得疲憊不堪。| **run sb ragged** (=make them do a lot of work) 使某人精疲力竭

5 ►PERFORMANCE 表演◄ a ragged performance, shout etc is one that people are not doing together or properly〔表演、呼喊聲等〕不協調的, 不齊的: *He gave a somewhat ragged performance, I thought.* 我覺得他的表演很差勁。| *a ragged cheer* 不整齊的歡呼聲

6 be on the ragged edge *AmE informal* to be feeling very tired or upset【美, 非正式】極度疲憊; 惴惴不安 —**raggedly** *adv*: *raggedly dressed* 衣衫襤褸的 —**raggedness** *n* [U]

rag·ing /ˈredʒɪŋ; ˈreɪdʒɪŋ/ *adj* **1** [only before noun 僅用於名詞前] raging feelings and emotions are extremely strong〔感情〕強烈的: *a raging thirst* 極度乾渴 | *raging jealousy* 強烈的嫉妒心 **2 a raging headache/toothache etc** a very bad pain in your head etc 劇烈的頭痛/牙痛等 **3 raging stream/torrent/waters** water that flows fast and violently 湍急的溪流/激流/河水

rag·lan /ˈræglən; ˈræglən/ *adj* **1 raglan coat/sweater etc** a coat etc which has arms that are joined in a side-

R

ways line from the arm to the neck〔袖縫由臂部直至領部的〕連肩袖大衣／毛衣等 **2 raglan sleeve** an arm of a coat etc joined in this way 連肩袖

ra·gout /ræˋgu; ræˈguː/ *n* [C,U] *French* a mixture of vegetables and meat boiled together; STEW[1] (1)【法】蔬菜燉肉

rag·tag /ˋræg,tæg; ˈrægtæg/ *adj* **1** *informal* looking untidy, poor, and dirty【非正式】邋遢的，骯髒的: *a ragtag bunch of kids* 一羣骯髒的小孩 **2 ragtag and bobtail** *old-fashioned* a crowd of untidy, poor people【過時】一羣邋遢的窮人

rag·time /ˋræg,taɪm; ˈrægtaɪm/ *n* [U] a type of music and dancing that has a strong beat and was popular in the US in the early part of the 20th century 雷格泰姆〔一種節奏強勁的音樂，20 世紀初流行於美國〕

rag trade /ˈ· ·/ *n* **the rag trade** *BrE* the business of making and selling clothes, especially women's clothes【英】〔尤指女裝的〕服裝業

rag·weed /ˋræg,wid; ˈrægwiːd/ *n* [U] a North American plant that produces a substance which causes HAY FEVER〔北美洲植物，可引起花粉病的〕豚草

rag·wort /ˋræg,wɝt; ˈrægwɜːt/ *n* [U] a common plant with yellow flowers, and leaves with uneven edges 千里光

raid[1] /red; reɪd/ *n* [C] **1** a short attack on a place by soldiers, planes, or ships, intended to cause damage but not take control 突襲，襲擊: **[+on]** *a bombing raid on the railway line* 對鐵路線進行的轟炸 | *cross border raids* 越境突襲 | **carry out/launch/make a raid** *Aircraft are carrying out raids on enemy ships.* 飛機正對敵艦進行空襲。**2** a sudden visit by the police searching for something illegal〔警察進行的〕突擊搜查: *Following this morning's raid, three people have been charged with possessing illegal drugs.* 在今天早上的突擊搜查之後，三個人被控持有違禁藥品。| **police raid** *a police raid on a club* 警方對一家俱樂部進行的突然搜查 | **dawn raid** (=carried out very early in the morning) 拂曉搜查 **3** an attack by criminals on a bank or similar place〔對銀行等處的〕搶劫，打劫: *a bank raid* 銀行劫案 | **[+on]** *raids on post offices in the area* 搶劫本區郵局 | **carry out a raid** *Armed robbers carried out a raid on the Gateway Bank last night.* 昨夜，持槍劫匪搶劫了蓋特威銀行。**4** *technical* an attempt by a company to buy enough SHARES in another company to take control of it【術語】〔某公司〕大量購買另一家公司的股票以獲得其控制權的企圖 —see also 另見 AIR RAID

raid[2] *v* [T] **1** if police raid a place, they go there suddenly to search for something illegal〔警察〕突然搜查: *Suspected drug dealers' homes were raided.* 販毒嫌疑分子的家被突然搜查。**2** to make a sudden armed attack on a place 武裝突襲: *Vikings raided settlements on the east coast.* 維京人襲擊了東海岸的村落。| **a raiding party** (=group taking part in an attack) 襲擊隊 **3** to take or steal a lot of things from a place 搶劫，洗劫: *She raided Jim's cash box.* 她洗劫了吉姆的錢箱。| *Animal-rights activists got in and raided the laboratories.* 動物權利積極分子洗劫了實驗室。| **raid the larder/refrigerator** *humorous* (=take food from your family's kitchen because you are hungry)【幽默】〔因飢餓而〕掃蕩食物櫥／冰箱 —see also 另見 RAM-RAIDING —**raider** *n* [C]

rail[1] /rel; reɪl/ *n* **1** [C] a bar that is fixed along or around something, especially to stop you from falling 欄杆，扶手: *Mrs Kellow held tightly onto the rail as she climbed the stairs.* 凱羅太太上樓梯時緊緊抓着欄杆。**2** [C] a bar that you use to hang things on〔掛東西用的〕横杆: *a clothes rail* 晾衣杆 | *a towel rail fixed to the bathroom door* 固定在浴室門上的毛巾杆 **3** [C] one of the two long metal tracks fixed to the ground that trains move along 鐵路路軌 **4** [U] travelling by train 乘火車旅行: *I prefer to go by rail.* 我喜歡乘火車去。| *rail travel* 乘火車旅行 **5 go off the rails** *informal* to start behaving in a strange or socially unacceptable way【非正式】〔行為〕越軌，不正常: *At 17 he suddenly went off the rails and started stealing.* 17 歲時，他突然走上歪路，開始偷竊。

rail[2] *v* **1** [T] to enclose or separate an area with rails 用欄杆把…圍起；把…隔開: **[+off/in]** *The police railed off the area where the accident happened.* 警察用圍欄把事發現場隔開。**2** [I] *formal* to complain angrily about something, especially something that you think is very unfair【正式】譴責，抱怨: **[+against/at]** *railing against injustice* 對不公正行為表示強烈不滿

rail·ing /ˋrelɪŋ; ˈreɪlɪŋ/ *n* [C usually plural 一般用複數] one of the metal bars in a fence that is made of a series of upright bars 欄杆: *Jimmy somehow got his head stuck in the railings.* 吉米不知怎的把頭卡在欄杆中間。

rail·le·ry /ˋrelərɪ; ˈreɪləri/ *n* [U] *formal* friendly joking about someone【正式】善意的嘲弄，逗弄: *affectionate raillery* 親熱的逗弄

rail·road[1] /ˋrel,rod; ˈreɪlrəʊd/ *n AmE*【美】**1** [C] a railway 鐵路: *The supplies were sent on the railroad.* 補給是由鐵路運送的。**2 the railroad** all the work, equipment etc connected with a train system 鐵路系統: *He had taken a job as a ticket agent on the railroad.* 他在鐵路部門任售票員。

railroad[2] *v* [T] to force or persuade someone do something without giving them enough time to think about it 迫使〔某人〕倉促行事: **railroad sb into doing sth** *The workers were railroaded into signing the agreement.* 工人們被迫草草地簽了這個協議。

rail·way /ˋrel,we; ˈreɪlweɪ/ *n BrE*【英】**1** [C] a method of travelling or moving things around by train 乘火車旅行，經鐵路運送; RAILROAD[1] (1) *AmE*【美】**2 the railway/the railways** all the work, equipment etc connected with a train system 鐵路系統; the RAILROAD[1] (2) *AmE*【美】: *working on the railways* 在鐵路系統工作

railway line /ˈ·· ·/ *n* [C] *BrE*【英】**1** one of the two metal tracks fixed to the ground that trains move along 鐵路路軌 **2** a part of the railway system that connects two places 鐵路線: *an old disused railway line* 廢棄的舊鐵路

railway sta·tion /ˈ·· ,··/ *n* [C] *BrE* the place where trains stop for passengers to get on and off【英】火車站; RAILROAD STATION *AmE*【美】

rai·ment /ˋremənt; ˈreɪmənt/ *n* [U] *literary* clothes【文】衣服，服装

rain[1] /ren; reɪn/ *n* **1** [U] water that falls in small drops from clouds in the sky 雨: *Rain is forecast for tomorrow.* 預報明天有雨。| *We've had 5 inches of rain in two days!* 兩天裡下了五英寸的雨！| *We got caught in the rain and I'm soaked through.* 我們給雨淋着，我渾身都濕透了。| **it looks like rain** *spoken* (=it is probably going to rain)【口】天好像要下雨 *It looks like rain, so let's go inside.* 天好像要下雨了，我們進屋去吧。| **heavy/light rain** (=a large or small amount) 大雨／小雨 *There will be heavy rain in most parts of the country.* 全國大部分地區將下大雨。| **pour with rain** *BrE* (=to rain very hard)【英】下大雨 *It was pouring with rain as we set off.* 我們動身的時候，正下着傾盆大雨。—see picture on page A13 參見 A13 頁圖 **2 the rains** a period in the year when there is a lot of rain in tropical countries; MONSOON〔熱帶國家的〕雨季: *The rains have started early this year.* 今年的雨季來得早。**3 be (as) right as rain** *spoken* to be healthy, especially after you have been ill or had a bad experience【口】健康；狀態良好〔尤指病後康復或經歷困難後〕**4 (come) rain or shine** *spoken* whatever happens or whatever the weather is like【口】在任何情況下；不論天氣好壞: *Don't worry. We'll be there – rain or shine.* 別擔心，不管情況如何，我們都會到那裡去的。**5 under a rain of arrows/blows etc** being hit by many arrows etc at the same time 箭如雨下／拳如雨下等 —see also 另見 ACID RAIN —**rainless** *adj*

rain[2] *v* **1** [I] if it rains, drops of water fall from clouds in the sky 下雨: *Oh no! It's raining again!* 糟糕！又下雨了！| *It was raining hard.* 正下着大雨。**2 be rained off**

BrE【英】/**be rained out** *AmE*【美】if an event or activity is rained off or rained out, it has to stop because there is too much rain〔活動〕因雨暫停: *We were supposed to go to a double header but it was rained out.* 我們本來要去看接連舉行的兩場比賽, 但因下雨取消了。**3 it never rains but it pours** *spoken* used to say that as soon as one thing goes wrong, a lot of other things go wrong as well【口】禍不單行 **4 it's raining cats and dogs** *spoken* it is raining very hard【口】下着傾盆大雨

rain down *phr v* [I,T] if something rains down, or is rained down, it falls in large quantities 雨點般落下, 傾盆而下: *Tears rained down her cheeks.* 淚水如雨般順着她的面頰流下。| *The falling chimney rained down dust and stones.* 灰塵和石塊從正在倒塌的煙囱上如雨點般落下。

rain·bow /ˈrenˌbo; ˈreɪnbəʊ/ *n* [C] a large curve of different colours that can appear in the sky when there is both sun and rain 彩虹, 虹

rain check /ˈ· ·/ *n* **1 take a rain check (on)** *informal, especially AmE* used to say that you will do something in the future but not now【非正式, 尤美】答應將來做(某事): *"Care for a drink?" "I'll take a rain check – I figure you'd like to be alone."* "想喝點甚麼嗎?" "改天吧, 我猜你想獨個兒靜一下。" **2** [C] *AmE* a ticket for an outdoor event, such as a sports game, that you can use again if it rains and the action stops【美】〔球賽等戶外活動因下雨而中止後〕可以再次使用的票根

rain·coat /ˈ· ·/ *n* [C] a coat that you wear when it is raining 雨衣 —see picture at 參見 COAT[1] 圖

rain drop /ˈ· ·/ *n* [C] a single drop of rain 雨點, 雨滴

rain·fall /ˈrenˌfɔl; ˈreɪnfɔːl/ *n* [C,U] the amount of rain that falls on an area in a particular period of time 雨量: *an area with very low rainfall* 雨量稀少的地區

rain for·est /ˈ· ˌ··/ *n* [C] a tropical forest with tall trees that are very close together, growing in an area where it rains a lot 熱帶雨林: *environmental groups campaigning against the destruction of the rain forest* 開展運動反對破壞熱帶雨林的環保團體

rain gauge /ˈ· ·/ *n* [C] an instrument that is used for measuring the amount of rain 雨量計, 雨量器

rain·proof /ˈrenˈpruf; ˈreɪnpruːf/ *adj* able to keep rain out 防雨的: *a rainproof jacket* 防雨短上衣

rain·storm /ˈrenˌstɔrm; ˈreɪnstɔːm/ *n* [C] a sudden heavy fall of rain 暴風雨

rain·wa·ter /ˈrenˌwɔtɚ; ˈreɪnwɔːtə/ *n* [U] water that has fallen as rain 雨水

rain·y /ˈrenɪ; ˈreɪni/ *adj* **1 rainy day/afternoon/weather etc** a day etc when it rains a lot 多雨的日子/下午/天氣等 **2 save it for a rainy day** to save something, especially money, for a time when you will need it 留着以備不時之需〔尤指錢〕; 未雨綢繆

S2 W1 **raise**[1] /rez; reɪz/ *v* [T]

1 ▶MOVE 移動◀ a) to move or lift something to a higher position, place, or level 舉起, 提起, 抬起; 使升高: *Can you raise your arm above you head?* 你能把胳膊舉過頭頂嗎? | *They're thinking of raising the ceiling in the kitchen.* 他們正在考慮升高廚房的天花板。| *The teacher raised his finger to his lips for silence.* 老師把手指舉到唇邊, 示意安靜。**b)** to move or lift something into an upright position 豎起, 扶起, 使直立: *The bridge can be raised in the middle to allow ships through.* 這橋的中央可以豎起來讓船隻通過。**c)** to move your eyes or face so that you are looking upwards 抬起〔眼睛〕; 仰起〔臉〕: *She raised her eyes from the newspaper when he came in.* 他進來的時候, 她把視線從報紙上抬起來。**d)** also 又作 **raise up** to lift the upper part of your body from a lying position 支起上半身: *She raised herself up on her arms and looked around sleepily.* 她用胳膊把上半身撐起來, 睡眼惺忪地環顧四周。

2 ▶INCREASE 增加◀ to increase an amount, number, or level 增加, 提高〔數量、數字或水平〕: *We have no plans to raise taxes at present.* 目前我們沒有提高稅收的計劃。| *The reaction is started by raising the temperature to 140°C.* 把溫度提高到攝氏140度, 反應便會開始。

3 ▶IMPROVE 改善◀ to improve the quality or standard of something 提高, 改善〔質量、標準〕: *Better training will raise the efficiency of the workforce.* 更好的培訓將提高勞動力的效率。

4 ▶CHILDREN 孩子◀ *especially AmE* to look after your children and help them grow【尤美】撫養, 養育; 撫養〔孩子〕成人; BRING UP *BrE*【英】: *Many women return to work after raising their families.* 許多婦女在子女長大後重新就業。| **raise sb (as) a Catholic/Muslim etc** *His parents raised him as a Protestant.* 他的父母以新教徒的標準培養他。| **born and raised** *She was born and raised a country girl.* 她是一個在農村出生和長大的姑娘。| **be raised on** *These kids are raised on a diet of junk food.* 這些孩子是吃高熱量劣等食品長大的。

5 ▶FARMING 飼養, 種植◀ to grow plants or keep cows, pigs etc so that they can be used as food 種植; 飼養: *raise wheat/pigs* 種小麥/養豬

6 raise hopes/consciousness/awareness etc to make people more hopeful etc 喚起希望/覺悟/認識等: *The peace talks have raised hopes for the hostages' release.* 和談增加了人質獲釋的希望。| *The conference is intended to raise people's awareness of AIDS.* 會議的目的是喚起人們對愛滋病的警覺。

7 ▶EMOTION/REACTION 情感/反應◀ a) to cause a particular emotion or reaction 引起, 激起〔某種情感或反應〕: *His long absence is beginning to raise fears for his safety.* 他很久未露面, 人們為他的安全擔心起來。| *His jokes barely raised a laugh.* 他的笑話幾乎沒有引起笑聲。**b)** to try to show a particular feeling or emotion although you do not really feel it 設法顯露出〔某種感覺、感情〕: *She felt so sad, she couldn't even raise a smile.* 她非常傷心, 根本笑不出來。

8 raise a question/objection/point etc to begin to talk or write about a question etc that you want to be considered 提出問題/反對/觀點等: *A number of objections were raised at the meeting.* 會上提出了許多反對意見。| *This raises important issues about security.* 此事提出了關於保安措施的重要問題。

9 ▶COLLECT MONEY/PEOPLE 籌款/徵集人員◀ a) to collect money, support etc so that you can use it to help people 籌集: *We are raising money to pay for a new hospital ward.* 我們正在籌集資金建一個新病房。**b)** *old-fashioned* to collect together a group of people, especially soldiers【過時】召集〔尤指士兵〕: *The king raised a vast army.* 國王召集起一支龐大的軍隊。

10 a) raise your eyebrows (at) to show surprise, doubt, disapproval etc by moving your EYEBROWS upwards (朝…)揚起眉毛〔表示吃驚、疑慮、反對等〕: *Chuck raised his eyebrows at her, not knowing what to say.* 查克朝她揚起眉毛, 不知道說甚麼好。**b) raise eyebrows** if something raises eyebrows it surprises people 使…吃驚: *The story raised a few eyebrows in the media world.* 這篇報道在大眾傳播媒界裡使一些人驚奇。

11 ▶VOICE 聲音◀ raise your voice to speak loudly or shout because you are angry〔因生氣而〕提高嗓門, 高聲說話: *Don't raise your voice to me, young man!* 別衝着我叫嚷, 年輕人! | **raised voices** *We could hear raised voices coming from the bar.* 我們聽到有人在酒吧高聲說話。

12 raise your glasses *spoken* used to tell a group of people to celebrate something by holding up their glasses and drinking from them【口】〔邀某人〕為…舉杯慶祝: *Ladies and gentlemen, will you raise your glasses to the bride and groom.* 各位女士、先生, 請大家舉杯, 祝賀新娘和新郎。

13 raise the spectre of sth *literary* to make you aware of something frightening【文】使人感到某事的恐怖: *The*

R

continuing violence has raised the spectre of civil war. 持續不斷的暴力事件使人擔心會爆發內戰。
14 ►DEAD PERSON 死者◄ *biblical* to make someone who has died live again【聖經】使…起死回生, 使…復活: *Jesus raised Lazarus from the grave.* 耶穌使拉撒路復活。
15 ►WAKE SB 喚醒某人◄ *literary* to wake someone who is difficult to wake【文】叫醒: *Try as he might he could not raise her.* 他想盡辦法, 卻仍然無法叫醒她。
16 raise the alarm to warn people about danger 發出警報: *A passerby raised the alarm before the fire got out of control.* 一位過路人趁火勢尚未失控時發出了警報。
17 raise a siege/embargo *formal* to allow goods to go in and out of a place again after they have been stopped by force or by a law【正式】解除包圍/禁運
18 ►CARD GAME 紙牌遊戲◄ to make a higher BID than an opponent in a card game 比〔對手〕多下賭注: *I'll raise you $100.* 我加你100美元。
19 ►SPEAK TO SB 對某人說話◄ to speak to someone on a piece of radio equipment 用無線電與…通話: *They finally managed to raise him at Miller's sheep farm.* 他們終於通過無線電在米勒的養羊場上與他取得了聯繫。
20 ►BUILD 建造◄ *formal* to build something such as a MONUMENT【正式】建造〔紀念碑等〕
21 raise hell/Cain a) *informal* to behave in an angry and threatening way【非正式】非常生氣/憤怒: *I'll raise hell with whoever is responsible for this mess.* 不管是誰惹的麻煩, 我都會跟他沒完。**b)** *especially AmE* to behave in a wild, noisy way that upsets other people【尤美】喧鬧: *The kids next door were raising hell last night.* 隔壁的孩子昨晚鬧翻了天。
22 raise the roof to make a very loud noise when singing, celebrating etc 高聲吵鬧〔唱歌、歡慶作樂時〕
23 raise your hand *especially AmE* to put your arm in the air to show that you want something【尤美】舉手: *Raise your hand if you know the answer.* 如果知道答案就請舉手。
24 raise 2/4/10 etc to the power of 2/3/4 etc *technical* to multiply a number by itself a particular number of times【術語】使2/4/10等自乘2/3/4等次: *2 raised to the power of 3 (=2^3) is 8.* 2的3次方是8。

USAGE NOTE 用法說明: RAISE
WORD CHOICE 詞語辨析: **raise, lift, increase, rise, bring up, rear, grow, improve**
People or other forces **raise** things to a higher position, though in informal language **lift** is usually used. 人或其他力量把東西提/抬/舉到高處時用 raise, 在非正式語言中通常用 lift: *The crane raised/lifted the whole house.* 起重機吊起了整座房子。In a court of law you may hear 在法庭上可以聽到: *Raise the book in your right hand.* 用右手把書舉起。
People, governments etc **raise** or **increase** the price, cost, or amount of something. 人或政府等提高某物的價格、費用或數量時用 raise 或 increase: *The government is raising the tax on cigarettes again.* 政府準備再次提高香煙稅。| *Heavy traffic is raising/increasing the level of pollution in the town.* 繁忙的交通正在加重城裡的污染程度。
When things or prices move upwards on their own, they **rise**. 東西或價格自己升高時用 rise: *The balloon rose slowly from the ground.* 氣球緩緩地從地面升起。| *the problem of rising inflation* 通貨膨脹加劇的問題 | *Industrial production looks set to rise in the new year.* 工業生產看來在新的一年裡很可能會增加。
You can also **raise** children, meaning you look after them as they grow up. This sense is more common in American English than in British English, where **bring up** is the more usual expression. 撫養孩子可用 raise。此義多用於美國英語, 英國英語更常用的表達方式是 bring up。
In both British and American English it is common either to **raise** or **bring up** a point, question etc in a discussion. 在英國英語和美國英語中, raise 或 bring up 均可表達在討論中提出觀點、問題等。
Again, especially in American English you may **raise** cattle or wheat on a farm. More generally, and in British English, you **rear** cattle and **grow** wheat, flowers or vegetables. 尤其在美國英語中, 可以用 raise 表示養牛, 種植麥子。在英國英語中, 則經常用 rear 表示養牛, 用 grow 表示種植麥子、花或蔬菜。
When you are talking about making something better, people often use either **raise** or **improve**. 表示"將某事做得更好"或"改進", 人們經常用 raise 或 improve: *I'm working hard to raise/improve my TOEFL score.* 我正在努力提高我的托福成績。| *Women still need to raise/improve their position in society* (NOT 不用 *raise up*). 婦女仍然需要提高她們的社會地位。
When something gets better on its own you can use **rise** or **improve**. 事物改善時可用 rise 或 improve: *Standards are rising/improving.* 水準正在提高。
The noun **raise** means a pay increase and is American English. In British English you say 名詞 raise 的意思在美國英語中是"加薪"。在英國英語中用: *He got a (pay) rise.* 他加了薪水。
Otherwise the noun is always **rise**. 在其他情況下 rise 總是名詞: *a rise in house prices/standards* 房屋價格/標準的提高 | *the rise of the Roman Empire* 羅馬帝國的興起
GRAMMAR 語法
The past tense of **rise** is **rose**, the perfect tense is **have risen** (NOT 不用 *raised*). rise 的過去式是 rose, 完成式是 have risen。

raise² *n* [C] *AmE* an increase in the money you earn【美】加薪; RISE² (2) *BrE*【英】
rai·sin /ˈrezn̩; ˈreɪzən/ *n* [C] a dried GRAPE (=the fruit that wine is made from) 葡萄乾
rai·son d'êt·re /ˈrezɔn ˈdɛt; ˌreɪzɒn ˈdetrə/ *n* [C] *French* the reason something exists, why someone does something etc【法】存在的理由; 做某事的目的: *Commerce was the main raison d'être of the town.* 商業是這個鎮存在的主要原因。
Raj /rɑdʒ; rɑːdʒ/ *n* [singular] **the (British) Raj** the rule of the British government in India before India became independent in 1947〔1947年印度獨立前〕英國在印度的統治(時期)
ra·jah, raja /ˈrɑdʒə; ˈrɑːdʒə/ *n* [C] the king or ruler of an Indian state〔印度的〕王公, 邦主 —see also 另見 RANEE
rake¹ /rek; reɪk/ *n* **1** [C] a gardening tool with a row of metal teeth at the end of a long handle, used for making soil level, gathering up dead leaves etc〔長柄〕耙子 **2** [C] *old-fashioned* a man who behaves in an unacceptable way, having many sexual relationships, drinking too much alcohol etc【過時】酒色之徒, 浪蕩子 **3** [C] a tool used by a CROUPIER for gathering in the money at a table where games are played for money〔賭枱上用的〕錢耙子 **4** [singular] the angle of a slope 坡度, 傾角: *the rake of the stage* 舞台的坡度
rake² *v* **1** [I,T] to move a rake across a surface in order to make the soil level, gather dead leaves etc〔用耙子〕耙, 耙平: **[+over/up]** *She raked over the soil to loosen the weeds.* 她用耙子翻地, 除掉雜草。**2** [I always+adv/prep] to search a place very carefully for something 仔細搜尋: **[+through/around/about]** *I've been raking through my drawers looking for those tickets.* 我一直在抽屜裡仔細翻找那些票。**3** [T] to point something such

as a gun, camera, or strong light, so that it covers a wide area, by slowly moving it from one side to another〔用槍、照相機或強光〕掃射: *The searchlight raked the open ground around the prison.* 探照燈在監獄周圍的空地上來回掃射。**4 rake a fire/ashes/coals** to push a stick backwards and forwards in a fire in order to remove ashes 撥弄火/灰/煤塊 **5 rake your fingers/nails** to pull your fingers or nails through something or across a surface〔用手指或指甲〕攏, 刮: *Ken raked his fingers through his hair.* 肯用手指攏頭髮。

rake sth ↔ **in** *phr v* [T] *informal* to earn a lot of money without trying very hard【非正式】輕易賺得〔許多錢〕: *Lou's been raking in the dollars since he opened his business.* 自從生意開張以來, 盧賺到了大把的美元。| **rake it in** *If someone opened a burger bar, they'd really rake it in.* 如果有人開一家漢堡包快餐店, 一定會發大財的。

rake sth ↔ **up** *phr v* [T] *informal*【非正式】**1** also 又作 **rake together** to collect things or people together for a purpose, but with difficulty 勉強拼湊: *Karen has had real problems raking up enough players for the volleyball game.* 卡倫遇上了麻煩, 她湊不夠參加排球比賽的隊員。| *Between them they could only rake together $300.* 他倆總共只湊到 300 美元。**2** to talk about something from the past that people would prefer you not to mention 重提〔別人不願提起的往事〕: *Don't rake up that old quarrel again!* 別再提那次吵架的舊賬了!

rake-off /'· ·/ *n* [C] *informal* a dishonest share of profits【非正式】〔非法取得的〕回扣: *The taxi driver gets a rake-off from the hotel.* 這個計程車司機從該旅館拿到回扣。

rak·ish /ˋrekɪʃ; 'reɪkɪʃ/ *adj* **1 at a rakish angle** if you wear a hat at a rakish angle, you do not wear it straight, and this makes you look relaxed and confident 瀟灑地〔歪戴帽子〕**2** *old-fashioned* a rakish man behaves in an unacceptable way, having many sexual relationships, wasting money, drinking too much alcohol etc【過時】放蕩的, 揮霍的, 縱情酒色的 —**rakishly** *adv* —**rakishness** *n* [U]

ral·ly¹ /ˋrælɪ; 'ræli/ *v* **rallied, rallying 1** [I,T] to come together or bring people together to support an idea, a political party etc〔為支持某種信念或政黨等而〕集合; 召集: *Margaret Thatcher's speech had the effect of rallying the party faithful.* 瑪格麗特·戴卓爾的講話起到了團結忠實黨員的作用。| [**+to**] *Fellow Republicans rallied to the President's defense.* 共和黨黨員都團結起來為總統辯護。| **rallying point** (=an idea, event etc that makes people come together to support something they believe in) 聚集點, 號召因素 *The demonstration was a rallying point for students fighting for lower rents.* 那次示威遊行使爭取降低房租的學生團結了起來。| **rallying cry** (=a word or phrase used to unite people in support of an idea) 使人們團結起來的口號 **2** [I] to become stronger again after a period of weakness or defeat〔在虛弱、受挫後〕振作, 恢復: *Towards the end of the race, Cram rallied and won in style.* 比賽接近尾聲時, 克蘭姆重新振作起來, 體面地獲勝。| *Stock prices rallied this afternoon after earlier falls.* 股票價格在較早時下跌之後, 今天下午回升。

rally round *phr v* [I,T] *informal* if a group of people rally round, they all try to help you in a difficult situation【非正式】〔一羣人〕扶持, 支持〔處於困境的人〕: *Her friends all rallied round when she was ill.* 在她患病期間, 她的朋友都來幫助她。

rally² *n* [C] **1** a large public meeting, especially one that is held outdoors to support a political idea, protest etc〔大型羣眾〕集會〔尤指為支持某政治觀點、抗議等在戶外舉行的集會〕: *a big anti-abortion rally* 反墮胎的大型羣眾集會 **2** a car race on public roads〔在公路上舉行的〕賽車, 汽車拉力賽: *the Monte Carlo Rally* 蒙特卡羅汽車拉力賽 **3** a series of hits of the ball between players in games like tennis〔網球等比賽中的〕持續對打, 拉鋸戰

RAM /ræm; ræm/ *n* [C,U] Random Access Memory; the memory in a computer system that is used as a temporary store for information, usually the software that organizes the DATA 隨機存取記憶器, 隨機存取存儲器〔電腦中短期存儲信息的部分〕

ram¹ /ræm; ræm/ *v* **rammed, ramming** [T] **1** to run or drive into something very hard 猛撞: *I was waiting at the traffic lights when a car rammed me from behind.* 我正在等綠燈的時候, 一輛汽車從後面撞了我。**2** [always+adv/prep] to push something into a position using great force 壓入, 硬塞, 壓實: **ram sth into/down** *First, you'll have to ram the posts into the ground.* 首先, 你必須把樁打進地裡。**3 ram sth down sb's throat** to try to make someone accept an idea or opinion by continually repeating it, especially when they are not interested 向某人反覆灌輸〔使其接受不感興趣的觀點或意見〕

ram sth ↔ **home** *phr v* [T] to make sure someone fully understands something by emphasizing it and by providing a lot of examples, proof etc〔通過強調和援引大量例證等〕使〔某事〕令人信服, 充分說明: *He rammed his points home with graphic pictures of neglect.* 他繪影繪聲地描述了種種玩忽職守的情況, 充分說明了自己的觀點。

ram² *n* [C] **1** an adult male sheep 公羊 —compare 比較 EWE **2** a BATTERING RAM 破城槌 **3** *technical* a machine that hits something again and again to force it into a position【術語】衝壓機, 撞錘

Ram·a·dan /ˌræməˋdɑn; 'ræmədæn/ *n* [U] the ninth month of the Muslim year, during which Muslims are not allowed to eat or drink during the day while it is light 齋月〔伊斯蘭曆的第九個月, 教徒白天禁飲食〕

ram·ble¹ /ˋræmbl̩; 'ræmbəl/ *v* [I] **1** [always+adv/prep] to go on a walk for pleasure 漫步, 閒逛: [**+through/along etc**] *We rambled through the woods.* 我們漫步穿過小樹林。**2** to talk in a very confused way so that other people find it hard to understand you 語無倫次地閒扯, 漫談; 說胡話: *The fever was getting worse and he was starting to ramble.* 他發燒越來越厲害, 開始說胡話。**3** a plant that rambles grows in all directions〔植物〕蔓生

ramble on *phr v* [I] to talk or write for a long time in a way that other people find boring 囉嗦地說[寫]: *He rambled on about his trip to Paris.* 他喋喋不休地談他的巴黎之行。

ramble² *n* [C] a long walk for pleasure 漫步, 閒逛: *We went on a ramble in the Peak District.* 我們在峯區裡漫步。

ram·bler /ˋræmblɚ; 'ræmblə/ *n* [C] **1** *BrE* someone who goes on rambles【英】喋喋不休的人 **2** a rose bush that rambles 蔓生薔薇

ram·bling /ˋræmblɪŋ; 'ræmblɪŋ/ *adj* **1** a building that is rambling has an irregular shape and covers a large area〔房子〕大而雜亂無章的: *a large rambling house on the hillside* 山坡上一座巨大而佈局零亂的房子 **2** speech or writing that is rambling is very long and does not seem to have any clear organization or purpose〔言語、文章〕雜亂無章的, 漫無邊際的: *a long and rambling letter* 東拉西扯的長信

ram·bunc·tious /ræmˋbʌŋkʃəs; ræm'bʌŋkʃəs/ *adj AmE humorous* full of energy, fun, and noise【美, 幽默】喧鬧的, 歡快的: *a weekend with three rambunctious kids* 與三個喧鬧的小孩共度的週末 —**rambunctiously** *adv* —**rambunctiousness** *n* [U]

ram·e·kin /ˋræməkɪn; 'ræmɨkɨn/ *n* [C] a small dish in which food for one person can be baked and served 一人用烤盤

ram·ie /ˋræmɪ; 'ræmi/ *n* [C,U] a plant from which cloth is made 苧蔴

ram·i·fi·ca·tion /ˌræməfəˋkeʃən; ˌræmɨfɨ'keɪʃən/ *n* [C usually plural 一般用複數] *formal*【正式】**1** an additional result of something you do, which may not have been clear when you first decided to do it 額外的後果, 派生

的影響: *The environmental ramifications of the road-building program had not been considered.* 沒有考慮築路工程對環境造成的影響。**2** a part of a system or structure that has many parts 分支

ram·i·fy /ˈræməˌfaɪ; ˈræmɪ̈faɪ/ *v* [I] *rare* to spread outwards and to form a system or network【罕】分支, 形成系統, 形成網絡

ramp /ræmp; ræmp/ *n* [C] **1** *AmE* a road for driving onto or off a large main road【美】支路, 岔道; SLIP ROAD *BrE*【英】: *Take the Lake Drive ramp at Charles Street.* 在查爾斯街雷克車道的支路。**2** a slope that has been built to connect two places that are at different levels〔連接高低不同的兩個點的〕人造斜坡; 坡道: *Ramps are needed at exits and entrances for wheelchair users.* 出入口處要有乘輪椅者使用的坡道。**3** *BrE* a change in the level between two parts of a road where repairs are being done【英】〔修路時〕路面高出部分 **4** a raised part on some roads, designed to make traffic drive more slowly; HUMP〔路上使車輛減速的〕小凸面

ram·page[1] /ræmˋpedʒ; ræmˈpeɪdʒ/ *v* [I] to rush about in groups wildly or violently 橫衝直撞: **[+about/through]** *football fans rampaging through the streets* 在街上橫衝直撞的足球迷

rampage[2] *n* **on the rampage** rushing about in a wild and violent way, often causing damage 橫衝直撞: *gangs of youths on the rampage* 成羣結隊橫衝直撞的年輕人

ram·pant /ˈræmpənt; ˈræmpənt/ *adj* **1** something bad that is rampant, such as crime or disease, is widespread and difficult to control〔犯罪、疾病〕猖獗的, 肆虐的, 失控的: *The country faces famine and rampant disease.* 這個國家面臨饑荒和肆虐的疾病。| *rampant inflation* 失控的通貨膨脹 **2** a plant that is rampant grows and spreads uncontrollably〔植物〕過於繁茂的, 蔓延的: *rampant garden weeds* 繁蕪的園中雜草 **3** *technical* an animal drawn in HERALDRY that is rampant is standing on its two back legs【術語】〔紋章上所繪的動物〕用後腿站立的 —**rampantly** *adv*

ram·part /ˈræmpɑrt; ˈræmpɑːt/ *n* [C usually plural 一般用複數] a wide pile of earth or a stone wall built to protect a castle or city in the past〔舊時城堡或城市周圍的〕護城牆, 土壘

ram-raid·ing /ˈ· ˌ··/ *n* [U] *BrE informal* the crime of driving a car into a shop window in order to steal goods from the shop【英, 非正式】飛車搶劫商店 —**ram-raider** *n* [C]

ram·rod /ˈræmˌrɑd; ˈræmrɒd/ *n* [C] **1 stiff/straight as a ramrod** sitting or standing with your back straight and your body stiff〔坐立時〕背部筆直的, 僵直的 **2** a stick for pushing GUNPOWDER into an old-fashioned gun, or for cleaning a small gun〔舊時槍的〕推彈桿,〔擦槍的〕通條

ram·shack·le /ˈræmʃækḷ; ˈræmʃækəl/ *adj* a ramshackle building or vehicle is in bad condition and in need of repair〔建築物、汽車等〕破舊的, 要散架似的, 需要維修的: *a ramshackle old farmhouse* 搖搖欲墜的舊農舍

ran /ræn; ræn/ the past tense of RUN

ranch /ræntʃ; rɑːntʃ/ *n* [C] **1** a very large farm in the western US and Canada where sheep, cattle, or horses are bred〔美國西部和加拿大的〕大牧場 **2** *AmE* a farm that produces a particular product【美】〔專門出產某種產品的〕農場: *a fruit ranch* 果園 **3** a RANCH HOUSE 平房; 農牧場主住宅

ranch·er /ˈræntʃɚ; ˈrɑːntʃə/ *n* [C] someone who owns or works on a ranch 牧場[農場]主; 牧場[農場]工人: *a cattle rancher* 養牛場場主[工人]

ranch house /ˈ· ·/ *n* [C] *AmE*【美】**1** a house built on one level, usually with a roof that does not slope much〔一般屋頂坡度不大的〕平房, 牧場式住宅 —see picture on page A4 參見 A4 頁圖 **2** a house on a ranch in which the rancher lives〔農牧場主居住的〕場內住宅

ranch·ing /ˈræntʃɪŋ; ˈrɑːntʃɪŋ/ *n* [U] work on a ranch (從事)農牧場工作

ran·cid /ˈrænsɪd; ˈrænsɪ̈d/ *adj* oily or fatty food that is rancid smells or tastes unpleasant because it is no longer fresh〔油脂食物的氣味、味道〕不新鮮的, 腐臭的, 酸臭的: *rancid butter* 變質黃油 —**rancidity** /rænˋsɪdətɪ; rænˈsɪdɪ̈ti/ *n* [U]

ran·cour *BrE*【英】, **rancor** *AmE*【美】/ˈræŋkɚ; ˈræŋkə/ *n* [U] *formal* a feeling of hatred, especially when you cannot forgive someone【正式】積怨, 深仇: *He spoke openly about the war without a trace of rancour.* 他不記前仇坦率地談論了這場戰爭。—**rancorous** *adj* —**rancorously** *adv*

rand /rænd; rænd/ *n plural* **rand** [C] the standard unit of money in South Africa 蘭特〔南非的貨幣單位〕

R and B /ˌɑr ən ˋbi; ˌɑːr ən ˈbiː/ *n* [U] rhythm and blues; a style of popular music that is a mixture of BLUES and JAZZ 節奏怨曲, 節奏勃魯斯〔一種勃魯斯與爵士樂結合的流行音樂〕

R and D /ˌɑr ən ˋdi; ˌɑːr ən ˈdiː/ *n* [U] research and development; the part of a business concerned with studying new ideas and planning new products 研究與開發(部)

ran·dom /ˈrændəm; ˈrændəm/ *adj* **1** happening or chosen without any definite plan, aim, or pattern 隨意的, 任意的, 隨機的: *a random sample* 隨機的抽樣 | *random drug testing of athletes* 對運動員進行的隨機藥物檢測 | *A few random shots were fired.* 胡亂放了幾槍。**2 at random** in a random way 任意地, 隨便地: *The killer appears to have selected his victims at random.* 兇手似乎是胡亂選擇被害人。—**randomly** *adv*: *7 randomly chosen numbers* 7個隨機選擇的數字 —**randomness** *n* [U]

random ac·cess mem·o·ry /ˌ·· ˈ·· ˌ···/ *n* [C,U] RAM 隨機存取記憶器

R and R /ˌɑr ənd ˋɑr; ˌɑːr ənd ˈɑː/ *n* [U] *AmE* rest and relaxation; a holiday given to people in the army, navy, etc after a long period of hard work or during a war【美】〔官兵長期執勤或戰時的〕休整假期

rand·y /ˈrændɪ; ˈrændi/ *adj BrE informal* full of sexual desire【英, 非正式】性慾衝動的: *She was feeling very randy.* 她感覺性慾強烈。—**randiness** *n* [U]

ra·nee, rani /ˈrɑnɪ; ˈrɑːni/ *n* [C] the queen or princess of an Indian state〔印度〕女邦主; 邦主妃 —see also 另見 RAJAH

rang /ræŋ; ræŋ/ the past tense of RING

range[1] /rendʒ; reɪndʒ/ *n*

1 ►GROUP 組◄ [singular] a number of things which are all different but of the same general type 批, 組, 類: **[+of]** *an interesting range of books and videos* 一批有趣的書籍和錄像帶 | *The drug is effective against a range of bacteria.* 這種藥品對一類細菌有效。| *We teach the full range of ballroom dances.* 我們教授全套交際舞。| **wide/broad/whole range of** *We have students from a wide range of backgrounds.* 我們的學生來自各種不同的背景。

2 ►LIMITS/AMOUNTS 範圍/數量◄ [singular] the limits within which amounts, quantities, ages etc can vary〔數、量、年齡等的〕範圍, 界限: **age/price etc range** *toys suitable for children in the pre-school age range* 適合學齡前兒童的玩具 | **in the range (of)** *I would expect a salary in the range of $25,000 to $30,000.* 我希望得到一份在兩萬五千到三萬美元之間的工資。| **beyond/out of sb's range** (=more than someone's limit on price, age etc) 超出某人〔關於價格、年齡等〕的範圍 *The price of the house is well beyond our range.* 這所房子的價格遠遠超出我們的預算。

3 ►POWER/RESPONSIBILITY ETC 權力/責任等◄ [singular] the area of power, responsibility, or activities that a person or organization has; SCOPE〔人或組織的權力、責任或活動的〕範圍: **the range of** *The range of his power was immense.* 他的權勢巨大。| **within/outside the range of** *These issues fall outside the range of the enquiry.* 這些問題不在調查範圍之內。

4 ►PRODUCTS 產品◄ [C] a set of similar products

made by a particular company or available in a particular shop〔某公司生產或某商店出售的〕成套產品；系列商品：*The coconut shampoo is the best in the range.* 椰子洗髮劑是此類產品中最好的。| [+of] *a new range of kitchenware* 一系列新的廚房用具 | **top of the range** (=best) 最好的 *a new top of the range racing bike* 新的頂尖比賽用自行車

5 ▶DISTANCE 距離◀ **a)** [singular,U] the distance within which something can be seen or heard〔視覺、聽覺的〕範圍：[+of] *The transmitter has a range of 10,000 miles.* 發報機的發射範圍是10,000英里。| **within range** (=near enough to reach, hear etc) 在〔可拿到、可聽到等的〕範圍內 *By now the ship was within range of enemy radar.* 該船現已進入敵人雷達的範圍。| **out of range** (=too far away to reach, hear etc) 在〔可拿到、可聽到等的〕範圍外 *He was relieved that the others were out of range of his mother's penetrating voice.* 其他人聽不到他媽媽刺耳的聲音，使他鬆了口氣。| **at close range** (=very near) 很近地 *You can see the animals at very close range.* 你可以在極近的距離看那些動物。**b)** [singular,U] the distance over which a particular weapon can hit things 射程：*the gun's range* 槍的射程 | [+of] *missiles with a range of 500 miles* 射程為500英里的導彈 | **within range** (=near enough to hit) 在射程內 | **out of range** (=too far away to hit) 在射程外 *I ducked down to get out of range of the gunshots.* 我低下頭避開槍彈。| **at close/short/point-blank range** (=from very close) 很近地 *Both men had been shot at point-blank range.* 兩個人都是在近距離被射殺的。| **long/short range missile** *The destroyer was equipped with short range missiles.* 這艘驅逐艦裝備了短程導彈。**c)** [C] the distance which a vehicle such as an aircraft can travel before it needs more petrol etc〔飛機等交通工具的〕續航距離：[+of] *The VR126 has a range of 2,000 miles.* VR126的續航距離達2,000英里。

6 ▶MUSIC 音樂◀ [C usually singular 一般用單數] all the musical notes that a particular singer or musical instrument can make 音域：*As the child grew older, his vocal range changed.* 隨着孩子年齡的增長，他的音域改變了。

7 ▶MOUNTAINS 山巒◀ [C] a group of mountains or hills, usually in a line 山脈：*a village in the foothills of the Karakoram range* 位於喀喇昆侖山脈丘陵地帶的村莊

8 ▶WEAPONS TESTING 武器試驗◀ [C] an area of land where you can test weapons or practise using them 射擊場，靶場：*a rifle range* 步槍射擊場 | *a missile testing range* 導彈試驗場

9 ▶GRASS LAND 草地◀ [C,U] *AmE* a large area of grass land used by cattle【美】牧場，牧區

10 ▶COOKING 烹調◀ [C,U] **a)** *especially AmE* a COOKER【尤美】灶具 **b)** *BrE* a place in a kitchen where there is a fire for cooking, used in the past【英】〔舊時用火烹飪的〕爐灶 —see also 另見 FREE-RANGE

3 **range²** *v*

1 ▶INCLUDE 包括◀ **a)** [I always+adv/prep] if prices, levels, temperatures etc range from one amount to another, they include both those amounts and anything in between〔價格、水平、温度等〕處於某範圍內〔包括這個範圍的上下限〕：**range from sth to sth** *There were 120 students whose ages ranged from 10 to 18.* 有120名學生，年齡在10至18歲之間。| **range between sth and sth** *The population of these cities ranges between 3 and 5 million inhabitants.* 這些城市的人口在三百萬到五百萬之間。| **range in age/size etc** (include many different ages, sizes etc) 年齡/大小的範圍在… *The shoes range in price from $25 to $100.* 這些鞋的價格在25美元至100美元不等。**b)** [I always+adv/prep] to include a range of different feelings, actions etc〔感情、行動等〕在某範圍內變化：**range from sth to sth** *Their reactions ranged from anger to humiliation.* 他們的反應不一，有的憤怒，有的感到丟臉。| *US intervention has taken many forms, ranging from supplying medicines to full-scale air strikes.* 美國以多種形式進行干預，從提供藥品到全面空襲。

2 ▶INCLUDE MANY SUBJECTS 包括許多話題◀ [I] to deal with a wide range of subjects or ideas in a book, speech, conversation etc〔在書籍、演講、交談等中〕涉及廣泛的內容：**range (widely) over** *His lectures ranged widely over a variety of topics.* 他的講座廣泛涉及了各種各樣的話題。—see also 另見 WIDE-RANGING

3 range yourself with/against to publicly state your agreement with, or opposition to, a particular group's beliefs and ideas 公開贊同/反對〔某種信念和思想〕：*Police rounded up any individuals who had ranged themselves against the authorities.* 警察拘捕了所有公開反對當局的人。

4 ▶ARRANGE 安排◀ [T always+adv/prep] to put things in a particular order or position 排列：**range sth on/along/against etc** *Cups and plates were neatly ranged on her shelves.* 杯子和盤子整齊地排列在她的架子上。

5 ▶MOVE AROUND 四處移動◀ [I always+adv/prep] to move around in an area of land; wander 漫遊，閒逛：[+over/through] *Cattle ranged over the pastures in search of food.* 牛在牧場上走來走去覓食。

range·find·er /ˈreɪndʒˌfaɪndə; ˈreɪndʒˌfaɪndə/ *n* [C] an instrument for finding the distance of an object when firing a weapon or taking photographs〔射擊或攝影用的〕測距儀

R

rang·er /ˈreɪndʒə; ˈreɪndʒə/ *n* [C] **1** someone whose job is to look after a forest or area of countryside 護林員：*a wildlife ranger* 野生動物管理員 **2** a police officer in North America in past times, who rode through country areas〔舊時北美的〕巡邏騎警 **3** a COMMANDO (=a specially trained soldier) 突擊隊員，特別行動隊隊員 **4** a girl who belongs to a part of the Guide Association in Britain, for girls between the ages of 14 and 19 英國高年級女童軍隊員〔14至19歲〕—compare 比較 GUIDE¹ (4)

ra·ni /ˈrɑːni; ˈrɑːni/ *n* a RANEE〔印度〕女邦主；邦主妃

rank¹ /ræŋk; ræŋk/ *n* 3

1 ▶POSITION IN ARMY/ORGANIZATION 軍隊/組織中的職位◀ [C,U] the position or level that someone holds in an organization, especially in the police or armed forces 等級；軍階，軍銜：*promotion to the rank of General* 晉升為將軍 | **high/senior/low/junior rank** *Bates is very young to hold such a senior rank.* 貝茨年紀很輕便擔任如此要職。

2 the ranks a) all the members of the armed forces who are not officers 普通士兵：**be reduced to the ranks** (=be punished by no longer being an officer) 降為士兵 | **rise from the ranks** (=become an officer after being an ordinary soldier) 從士兵升為軍官 **b)** the people who belong to an organization or to a group〔組織或團體的〕成員：*The pay freeze led to a lot of discontent in the ranks.* 工資凍結導致職員牢騷滿腹。| *The Christian Democrats now face opposition from within their own ranks.* 基督教民主黨目前面臨黨內的反對。| **join the ranks of** (=become a member of a group) 加入…的行列 *She was forced to join the ranks of the self-employed.* 她被迫加入了自由職業者的行列。

3 close ranks if the people in a group close ranks, they join together to support each other against other people〔一羣人〕團結一致〔以對付他人〕：*At the first hint of trouble their family closes ranks.* 剛有麻煩的跡象，他們全家便團結一致了。

4 break ranks a) to stop supporting a group that you are a member of 不再支持〔所屬團體〕**b)** if soldiers break ranks, they do not stay in line〔士兵〕打亂隊形：*The police broke ranks and used their batons indiscriminately.* 警察散開隊形，用警棍亂打。

5 pull rank (on) *informal* to use your authority over someone to make them do what you want, especially unfairly【非正式】〔尤指不公正地〕運用權勢：*You may just have to pull rank and tell them they have to do it.* 也

許你只需運用權勢, 告訴他們必須這樣做。
6 ▶LINE 行, 列◀ [C] **a)** a line of people or things〔人或物的〕行, 列: **rank after rank/rank upon rank** *On the shelves were rank after rank of liquor bottles.* 架子上是一排排的酒瓶。**b)** a line of soldiers, police officers etc, standing side by side〔士兵、警察等的〕隊列, 排
7 of the first rank of the highest quality 一流的: *Emily Dickinson is a poet of the first rank.* 埃米莉·迪金森是一流詩人。
8 ▶SOCIAL CLASS 社會階層◀ [C,U] someone's position in society 社會階層: *people of all ranks in society* 社會各階層的人
9 ▶TAXI 計程車◀ [C] a place where taxis wait in a line to be hired; TAXI RANK 計程車站

rank² *v* **1 a)** [I always+adv/prep, not in progressive 不用進行式] to have a particular position in a list of people or things that are put in order of quality or importance 具有...等級[地位]: **[+among/as/with]** *This recession ranks as one of the worst in recent times.* 近年來的經濟衰退, 此次為最嚴重之一。**b)** [T often passive 常用被動態] to decide the position of someone or something on a list based on quality or importance 確定...的地位[等級]: **be ranked fourth/number one etc** *Agassi was at that time ranked sixth in the world.* 阿加斯當時排名世界第六。| **rank sb/sth in order** *Rank them in order of ability.* 按能力把他們順序排列。**2** [T] *AmE* to have a higher rank than someone else; OUTRANK【美】級別高於: *A general ranks a captain.* 將軍的級別比上尉高。**3** [T often passive 常用被動態] to arrange things in a regular order 排列: *There were several pairs of riding boots ranked neatly in the hall.* 大廳裡整齊地排列着幾雙馬靴。

rank³ *adj* **1** having a very strong and unpleasant smell or taste 難聞的; 難吃的: *rank tobacco* 難聞的煙草 **2** [only before noun 僅用於名詞前] complete; total 完全的, 十足的: *a rank beginner at the job* 工作上十足的新手 | *rank disobedience* 根本的違抗 | **rank outsider** (=person or animal that is not expected to win) 不被看好的比賽者 *The Olympic champion was beaten by a rank outsider.* 奧運會冠軍敗給冷門選手。**3** a plant that is rank is too thick and has spread everywhere〔植物〕過於茂盛的, 蔓生的 —**rankly** *adv* —**rankness** *n* [U]

rank and file /,· · '·◂/ *n* **the rank and file** the ordinary members of an organization rather than the leaders〔組織中相對領袖而言的〕普通成員: *The rank and file of the party had lost confidence in the leadership.* 廣大黨員對領導人失去了信任。

rank·ing¹ /'ræŋkɪŋ; 'ræŋkɪŋ/ *n* [C] a position on a scale that shows how good someone or something is when compared with others 排行, 名次: *In the last two years, she has moved steadily up the world rankings.* 在過去兩年裡, 她的世界排名不斷上升。

ranking² *adj* [only before noun 僅用於名詞前] a ranking person has a high position in an organization or is one of the best at an activity 地位高的; 最出色的: *a ranking member of the department* 部門裡級別高的成員

ranking of·fi·cer /'·· ,···/ *n* [singular] the officer in a group who has the highest rank〔一組軍人中〕級別最高的軍官

ran·kle /'ræŋkḷ; 'ræŋkəl/ *v* [I] if something rankles, you still remember it angrily because it upset you or annoyed you a lot 令人懷恨: *a bitter dispute that still rankled months afterwards* 數月之後仍讓人耿耿於懷的激烈辯論

ran·sack /'rænsæk; 'rænsæk/ *v* [T] **1** to search a place very thoroughly 徹底搜索〔某地〕: *She's ransacking the desk drawers for old family photos.* 她把抽屜翻了個底朝天, 尋找家人的老照片。**2** to go through a place stealing things and causing damage 洗劫〔某處〕: *Houses were wrecked and ransacked by wandering gangs of soldiers.* 房屋遭到成羣結隊的散兵游勇的破壞和洗劫。

ran·som¹ /'rænsəm; 'rænsəm/ *n* [C] **1** an amount of money paid to free someone who is held as a prisoner〔為使被綁架者獲釋而支付的〕贖金: *The kidnappers were demanding a ransom of $25,000.* 綁匪索取25,000美元的贖金。**2 hold sb to ransom a)** to put someone in a situation where they are forced to agree to your demands 要挾某人: *The management will not allow the strikers to hold them to ransom.* 管理層不容許罷工者要挾他們。**b)** to keep someone prisoner until money is paid 劫持某人以索取贖金

ransom² *v* [T] to set someone free by paying a ransom〔付錢〕贖〔人〕

rant /rænt; rænt/ *v* [I] to talk or complain in a loud, excited, and rather confused way because you feel strongly about something 怒氣沖沖地叫嚷[抱怨]: *ranting on about the way his boss treats him* 怒氣沖沖地抱怨老闆對待他的方式 | **rant and rave** (=rant continuously) 大叫大嚷 *I see the tabloids are all ranting and raving about Fergie's skiing trip.* 我看到各家小報都在大叫大嚷, 批評弗吉的滑雪旅行。

rap¹ /ræp; ræp/ **rapped, rapping** *v*
1 ▶HIT 敲, 打◀ [I,T] to hit or knock something quickly and lightly 輕敲, 急拍: *She rapped the table with her pen and called for silence.* 她用筆輕敲桌子, 要求安靜。| **[+at/on]** *rapping loudly on the door* 大聲敲門
2 ▶SAY 說, 講◀ also 又作 **rap out** [T] to say something loudly, suddenly, and in a way that sounds angry 厲聲地說: *Captain Blake rapped out an order.* 布萊克上尉厲聲發出命令。
3 ▶CRITICIZE 批評◀ [T] a word meaning to criticize someone angrily used in newspapers〔在報紙上〕對...嚴厲指責: *a film rapped by critics for its excessive violence* 因過分渲染暴力而遭評論家嚴厲譴責的電影
4 ▶MUSIC 音樂◀ [I] to say the words of a RAP²(2) 表演說唱樂
5 ▶CONVERSATION 談話◀ [I] *old-fashioned* to talk in an informal way to friends; CHAT【過時】聊天, 閒談
6 rap sb over the knuckles to criticize someone, often officially, for something they have done wrong 譴責, 正式批評: *schools rapped over the knuckles for their failure to improve examination results* 因未能提高考試成績而受到正式批評的學校

rap² *n*
1 ▶KNOCK 敲◀ [C] a quick light hit or knock 輕敲: *We heard a sharp rap on the door.* 我們聽到急促的敲門聲。
2 ▶MUSIC 音樂◀ [C,U] a type of popular music in which the words of a song are not sung, but spoken in time to music with a steady beat 說唱樂〔歌詞按固定的音樂節奏唸出的流行音樂〕
3 ▶CRIME 犯罪◀ *AmE informal*【美, 非正式】**a)** a statement by the state that someone is responsible for a serious crime; CHARGE¹ (4) 指控: **murder rap/drunk driving rap** *He's in police custody facing a murder rap.* 他被警察拘留, 面臨謀殺指控。**b)** time spent in prison as punishment for a crime 服刑的時間: **beat the rap** (=escape punishment) 逃避懲罰
4 take the rap (for sth) to be blamed or punished for a mistake or crime, especially unfairly〔尤指不公正地〕(因某事) 受到責罰: *It didn't worry him that someone else would have to take the rap for his greed.* 其他人會因為他的貪婪而代他受過, 這並不使他擔心。
5 ▶CRITICISM 批評◀ **a rap on/over the knuckles** *informal* strong criticism for something you have done wrong【非正式】嚴厲的指責: *The New York Post received an official rap over the knuckles for the way it reported the story.*《紐約郵報》因報道該事件的方式而受到正式的嚴厲指責。
6 ▶NOT FAIR 不公正◀ **a bum rap** *AmE slang* unfair treatment or punishment【美俚】不公正的對待, 不公正的懲罰

ra·pa·cious /rə'peʃəs; rə'peɪʃəs/ *adj formal* taking everything that you can, especially by using violence【正式】掠奪的, 強取的: *a rapacious band of robbers* 一

夥窮兇極惡的強盜 —**rapaciously** *adv* —**rapaciousness** *n* [U] —**rapacity** /rəˋpæsətɪ; rəˈpæsɨti/ *n* [U]

rape¹ /rep; reɪp/ *v* [T] to force someone to have sex, especially by using violence 強姦: *Burgess will be in court today, accused of raping a fifteen-year old girl.* 伯吉斯今天出庭, 他被控強姦了一名十五歲的女孩。

rape² *n* **1** [C,U] the crime of forcing someone to have sex, especially by using violence 強姦(罪): *He was charged with the attempted rape of a female colleague.* 他被控企圖強姦一位女同事。| *a rape victim* 遭強姦者 —see also 另見 DATE RAPE, RAPIST **2** [singular] sudden unnecessary destruction, especially of the environment〔尤指對環境的〕突然、不必要的破壞: *The timber companies are carrying out a systematic rape of our forests.* 這些木材公司正在有組織地毀壞我們的森林。**3** [U] a European plant with yellow flowers, grown as animal food and for its oil 油菜

3 **rap·id** /ˋræpɪd; ˈræpɨd/ *adj* done or happening very quickly and in a very short time 快的, 迅速的: *The patient made a rapid recovery.* 病人迅速康復。| *a period of rapid population growth* 人口快速增長期 —**rapidly** *adv*: *the rapidly changing world of computer technology* 迅速變化的電腦技術領域 —**rapidity** /rəˋpɪdətɪ; rəˈpɪdɨti/ *n* [U]: *Their debts mounted with alarming rapidity.* 他們的債務以驚人的速度增加。

rapid-fire /ˋ‥ ·/ *adj* **1** rapid-fire questions, jokes etc are said quickly one after another〔問題、笑話等〕連珠砲地說出的 **2** a rapid-fire gun can fire shots quickly one after another〔槍〕速射的

rap·ids /ˋræpɪdz; ˈræpɨdz/ *n* [plural] part of a river where the water looks white because it is moving very fast over rocks 急流, 湍流; WHITEWATER *AmE*【美】

rapid tran·sit sys·tem /,‥ ˋ‥ ,‥/ also 又作 **rapid transit** *n* [C] *AmE* a system for moving people quickly around a city using trains; SUBWAY【美】城市高速鐵路系統; 地鐵

ra·pi·er /ˋrepɪɚ; ˈreɪpiə/ *n* [C] a long thin sword with two sharp edges 輕劍 —see picture at 參見 SWORD 圖

rap·ine /ˋræpɪn; ˈræpaɪn/ *n* [U] *literary* the taking away of property by force; PLUNDER² (2)【文】劫掠, 搶奪

rap·ist /ˋrepɪst; ˈreɪpɨst/ *n* [C] a man who has forced someone to have sex, especially by using violence 強姦犯

rap·pel /ræˋpɛl; ræˈpel/ *v* [I] *AmE* to ABSEIL【美】〔用繩索〕下陡坡 —**rappel** *n* [C]

rap·per /ˋræpɚ; ˈræpə/ *n* [C] someone who speaks the words of a RAP² (2) (=type of popular music) 說唱樂表演者: *world-famous rapper, Ice T* 世界著名說唱樂歌手艾斯·T

rap·port /ræˋpɔrt; ræˈpɔː/ *n* [singular,U] friendly agreement and understanding between people 融洽, 和睦的關係: **[+between/with]** *She's established a good rapport with her new colleagues.* 她與新同事們建立了良好的關係。

rap·proche·ment /,ræproʃˋmã; ræˈprɒʃmɒŋ/ *n* [singular,U] *formal* the establishment of a good relationship between two countries or groups of people, after a period of unfriendly relations【正式】友好關係的重建: *the signs of a rapprochement between the two countries* 兩國關係重新修好的跡象

rap·scal·lion /ræpˋskæljən; ræpˈskæljən/ *n* [C] *old use* someone who behaves badly, but whom you still like【舊】討人喜歡的無賴

rap sheet /ˋ· ·/ *n* [C] *AmE informal* a list kept by the police of someone's criminal activities【美, 非正式】〔警方保存的〕犯罪記錄

rapt /ræpt; ræpt/ *adj* **1** *AustrE informal* very pleased and happy【澳, 非正式】欣喜若狂的 **2** *literary* so interested in something that you do not notice anything else【文】全神貫注的, 出神的: *looks of rapt attention* 全神貫注的表情

rap·ture /ˋræptʃɚ; ˈræptʃə/ *n* [U] **1** great excitement and happiness 狂喜: *He stared with rapture at his baby son.* 他欣喜若狂地凝視着他的新生兒子。**2 go into raptures** to express great pleasure and happiness about something 因…欣喜若狂: **[+over/about/at]** *She went into raptures about the climate, the food, the spring flowers.* 她對天氣、飲食和春天的花朵着迷。

rap·tu·rous /ˋræptʃərəs; ˈræptʃərəs/ *adj formal* expressing great happiness or admiration【正式】狂喜的, 狂熱的: *The audience leapt to their feet in rapturous applause.* 觀眾一躍而起, 狂熱地鼓掌。| *A rapturous reception awaited the winning team.* 狂熱的歡迎等待着獲勝的球隊。—**rapturously** *adv*

rare /rɛr; reə/ *adj* **1** not seen or found very often, or not happening very often 稀有的, 罕見的, 不常發生的: *This species of plant is becoming increasingly rare.* 這種植物越來越罕見。| *We only went to the cinema on very rare occasions.* 我們難得去看電影。| **it is rare to do sth** *It is rare to find such an interesting group of people.* 難得發現這樣一羣有趣的人。| **it is rare for sb/sth to do sth** *It's very rare for her to miss a day at school.* 她很少有不上學的日子。**2** meat that is rare has only been cooked for a short time and is still red〔肉〕煮得半熟的: *I like my steak rare.* 我喜歡半熟的牛排。**3** [only before noun 僅用於名詞前] *BrE old-fashioned* unusually good or extreme【英, 過時】極好的; 極度的: *We had a rare old time at the party.* 我們在聚會中玩得高興極了。**4** air that is rare has less oxygen than usual because it is in a high place〔空氣〕稀薄的 —see also 另見 RARELY, RARITY —**rareness** *n* [U] 3 2

USAGE NOTE 用法說明: RARE

WORD CHOICE 詞語辨析: **rare, uncommon, scarce, infrequent, unusual, rarely, scarcely**

Things that do not exist in large numbers or amounts, are **uncommon**. uncommon 指罕見的、不尋常的東西: *an uncommon name/species of birds* 不尋常的名字/罕見的鳥類。**Rare** things are uncommon, and often valuable. rare 指罕見而多半珍貴的東西: *a rare hand-crafted book cover* 手工製作的珍貴書封面 | *He collects rare coins.* 他收藏珍稀的硬幣。

Things that you need and are difficult to find or get, though they may at other times be available, are **scarce**. scarce 指需要而又缺乏或不足的東西: *Food is scarce in the refugee camps.* 難民營裡食品短缺。| *Parking spaces are scarce on Saturdays.* 星期六停車位不夠用。

Events that do not happen often are **infrequent** or **rare**. infrequent 和 rare 指不經常(發生)的、難得的事件或情況: *Opportunities for promotion are rare/infrequent in this company.* 這家公司裡晉升的機會極少。| *the infrequent letters from her son* 她兒子偶爾來的信 | *the rare sight of a deer grazing* 鹿吃草的難得景象

It is unusual and rather formal to say 不常用且較正式的說法: *It is not rare to...* …並非偶然。People usually say **uncommon** or **unusual** or try to avoid using two negatives completely. For example, this sentence is perfectly acceptable. 人們常用 uncommon 或 unusual, 或完全避免使用兩個否定詞。如以下句子就是完全可以接受的: *It's not unusual to see tears at a wedding.* 婚禮上有人流淚並非不常見。But you could say instead 但也可以說: *You often see tears at a wedding.* 在婚禮上常會看到有人流淚。

Rarely means 'not often' but **scarcely** means 'hardly', or only 'just'. rarely 的意思是"不經常", scarcely 的意思是"幾乎不"或"僅僅": *I rarely visit Houston* (NOT 不用 *scarcely*, though you could say 但可以說 *'scarcely ever'*). 我很少去休斯頓。| *The train leaves in an hour – we've scarcely got time to pack.* 火車再過一小時就開 —— 我們幾乎沒有時間整理行裝。

R

rare earth /ˌ· ˈ·/ *n* [C] one of a group of rare metal substances 稀土元素

rar·e·fied /ˈrɛrəfaɪd; ˈreərɪ̵faɪd/ *adj* **1** *often humorous* rarefied ideas, opinions etc can only be understood by, or only involve, one small group of people【常幽默】〔想法、觀點等〕只限於小圈子內的: *the rarefied atmosphere of international diplomacy* 國際外交的玄妙氣氛 **2** rarefied air is the air in high places, which has less oxygen than usual〔空氣〕稀薄的, 缺氧的

2 **rare·ly** /ˈrɛrlɪ; ˈreəli/ *adv* not often 很少, 難得: *She very rarely complains.* 她極少抱怨。| *This method is rarely used in modern laboratories.* 現代實驗室裡很少使用這種方法。—see 見 RARE (USAGE) —see picture at 參見 FREQUENCY 圖

rar·ing /ˈrɛrɪŋ; ˈreərɪŋ/ *adj* **1 raring to go** very eager to start an activity 巴不得馬上開始: *They woke up early and were raring to go.* 他們很早就醒來, 急着開始幹。**2 raring to do sth** very eager to do something 急想[渴望]做某事: *The children were raring to get out into the snow.* 孩子們急着要到外面雪地裡去。

rar·i·ty /ˈrɛrətɪ; ˈreərɪ̵ti/ *n* **1 be a rarity** to not happen or exist very often 極為罕見: *The village was so remote that visitors were a rarity.* 那個村子非常偏僻, 來客很罕見。**2** [C] something that is valuable or interesting because it is rare〔因稀罕而〕珍貴的東西; 有趣的東西: *He had picked up all kinds of rarities on his travels.* 他在旅行中收集了各種各樣的珍奇物品。**3** [U] the quality of being rare 稀有, 罕見: *Such stamps are expensive because of their rarity.* 這種郵票由於罕見而價格昂貴。

ras·cal /ˈræskḷ; ˈrɑːskəl/ *n* [C] **1** *humorous* a child who behaves badly but whom you still like【幽默】小淘氣: *You little rascal! Where have you hidden my shoes?* 你這個小調皮鬼! 你把我的鞋子藏到哪裡去了? **2** *old-fashioned* a dishonest man【過時】惡棍, 無賴 —**rascally** *adj old use*【舊】: *a rascally trick* 卑鄙的伎倆

rash¹ /ræʃ; ræʃ/ *adj* doing something too quickly, without thinking carefully about whether it is sensible or not 急躁的, 魯莽的, 草率的: *Don't go making any rash decisions about your future!* 不要對你的未來作任何草率的决定! | *It was rather rash of you to lend them your car.* 你把汽車借給他們, 真是太輕率了。—**rashly** *adv*: *I rashly agreed to look after the children.* 我草率地答應照看那些孩子。—**rashness** *n* [U] *Strangely, it was his rashness which attracted me.* 奇怪的是, 正是他的魯莽吸引了我。

rash² *n* [C] **1** a lot of red spots on someone's skin, caused by an illness 皮疹: *She had a nasty rash on her arms.* 她的胳膊上起了嚴重的皮疹。| **come/break out in a rash** *My mother comes out in a rash if she eats seafood.* 我母親一吃海鮮就起疹子。| **heat rash/nettle rash/nappy rash etc** (=a rash caused by heat etc) 痱子/風疹/尿褲疹等 *The baby's got nappy rash again.* 寶寶又出尿褲疹了。**2 a rash of** *informal* a large number of unpleasant events, changes etc within a short time【非正式】大量的〔一下子出現的令人不快的事件、變化等〕: *a sudden rash of unofficial strikes* 突然出現的大量未經工會同意的罷工

rash·er /ˈræʃɚ; ˈræʃə/ *n* [C] *BrE* a thin piece of BACON or HAM¹ (1)【英】熏肉片; 火腿片: *a rasher of streaky bacon* 一片五花煙肉 —see picture on page A7 參見 A7 頁圖

rasp¹ /ræsp; rɑːsp/ *v* **1** [I,T] to make a rough unpleasant sound, like that of two surfaces rubbing together 發出刺耳的聲音: *metal rasping against stone* 磨擦石頭發出刺耳聲音的金屬 | *They could hear Peter's rasping breath as he fell to the ground.* 他們可以聽到彼得摔到地上時粗重的喘氣聲。**2** [T] to rub a surface with something rough〔粗糙地〕擦刮, 粗銼 —**raspingly** *adv*

rasp² *n* **1** [singular] an unpleasant noise, like the sound of two rough surfaces rubbing together 銼磨聲音, 刺耳聲: *With a rasp of steel, they drew their swords.* 他們錚的一聲拔出了劍。| *the rasp of a saw* 鋸子發出的刺耳聲音 **2** [C] a metal tool with a rough surface, like a FILE¹ (5), used for shaping wood or metal 銼, 粗銼刀

rasp·ber·ry /ˈræzbɛrɪ; ˈrɑːzbəri/ *n* [C] **1** a soft sweet red berry, or the bush that this berry grows on 懸鉤子, 覆盆子, 山莓: *raspberry jam* 山莓醬 —see picture on page A8 參見 A8 頁圖 **2** *informal* a rude sound made by putting your tongue out and blowing【非正式】〔吐舌爆氣發出無禮的〕呸呸聲: **blow a raspberry** *BrE*【英】**/give a raspberry** *AmE*【美】(=to make this sound) 發出呸呸聲

Ras·ta /ˈræstə; ˈræstə/ *n* [C] *informal* a Rastafarian【非正式】拉斯塔法里教派成員

Ras·ta·fa·ri·an /ˌræstəˈfɛrɪən; ˌræstəˈfeəriən◂/ *n* [C] someone who believes in a religion that is popular in Jamaica, which has Haile Selassie as its religious leader, and has the belief that black West Indians will return to Africa 拉斯塔法里教派成員〔牙買加一教派成員, 該教派尊崇海爾·薩拉西為其領袖, 相信西印度羣島的黑人將返回非洲〕—**Rastafarian** *adj* —**Rastafarianism** *n* [U]

Ras·ta·man /ˈræstəmæn; ˈræstəmæn/ *n* [C] *informal* a male Rastafarian【非正式】拉斯塔法里教派男性成員

rat¹ /ræt; ræt/ *n* [C] **1** an animal that looks like a large mouse with a long tail 大老鼠: *rat poison* 滅鼠藥 **2** *spoken* someone who has been disloyal to you or deceived you【口】卑鄙小人, 騙子: *But you promised to help us, you rat!* 可是你答應過幫助我們, 你這言而無信的小人! **3 look like a drowned rat** to look very wet and uncomfortable 看上去像隻落水老鼠 **4 like rats deserting the sinking ship** used to describe people who leave a company, organization etc when it is in trouble 就像老鼠逃離沉船一樣〔描寫人們在公司、組織等出現困難的時候紛紛離去〕—see also 另見 RAT RACE, RATS, RAT TRAP, **smell a rat** (SMELL² (7))

rat² *v* **ratted, ratting** [I] *informal* to be disloyal to someone, especially by telling someone in authority about something wrong that person has done【非正式】告密, 背信棄義: [+on] *They'll kill you if they find out you've ratted on them!* 假如他們發現是你告發他們, 他們會殺掉你的!

rat-arsed /ˈræt ˌɑrst; ˈræt ˌɑːst/ *adj BrE slang* extremely drunk【英俚】爛醉如泥的

rat-a-tat /ˌræt ə ˈtæt; ˌræt ə ˈtæt/ also 又作 **rat-a-tat-tat** /ˌ· · · ˈ·/ *n* [singular] the sound of knocking, especially on a door 敲擊聲;〔尤指敲門的〕砰砰聲

rat·bag /ˈrætˌbæg; ˈrætbæg/ *n* [C] *BrE, AustrE informal* an unpleasant person【英, 澳, 非正式】討厭的人

ratch·et /ˈrætʃɪt; ˈrætʃɪ̵t/ *n* [U] a machine part consisting of a wheel or bar with teeth on it, which allows movement in only one direction 棘輪, 單向齒輪

ratchet 棘輪

rate¹ /ret; reɪt/ *n* [C]

1 ►SPEED 速度◄ the speed at which something happens over a period of time 速率: *Our money was running out at an alarming rate.* 我們的錢正在以驚人的速度減少。| *Children learn at different rates.* 兒童學東西有快有慢。| [+of] *the rate of economic growth* 經濟增長的速度

2 ►AMOUNT 數量◄ the number of times something happens or the number of examples of something within a certain period 比率, 率: **birth/unemployment/divorce/crime rate** *The divorce rate rose from 20,000 in 1961 to 150,000 in 1985.* 離婚率從 1961 年的 2 萬例增加到 1985 年的 15 萬例。| **high/low rate of** *high rates of unemployment* 高失業率 | **success/failure rate** (=the number of times that something succeeds or fails) 成功/失敗率 *Penicillin has a high success rate in bacterial infections.* 青黴素治療細菌感染的成功率很高。

3 ►MONEY 錢◄ a charge or payment fixed according to a standard scale 費用; 價格: *The sports centre has*

reduced rates for students. 運動中心降低了對學生的收費。| *Nurses are demanding higher rates of pay.* 護士們正在要求提高工資。| **hourly/weekly rate** (=the amount paid per hour/week) 按小時/週付費 *What's the hourly rate for cleaning?* 打掃衛生每小時收費是多少? | **the going rate** (=the usual amount paid for work) 一般的收費 *I'm told $20 an hour is the going rate for private tuition.* 我聽説家教的一般收費是每小時20美元。

4 at this rate *spoken* used to say what will happen if things continue to happen in the same way as now【口】照這種情況繼續下去: *At this rate we won't even be able to afford a holiday.* 照這樣下去, 我們就連度假都負擔不起了。

5 at any rate *spoken* used when you are stating one definite fact in a situation that is uncertain or unsatisfactory【口】無論如何, 不管怎樣: *Well, at any rate, we won't starve!* 唉, 不管怎樣, 我們不會挨餓的! | *They've had technical problems – at any rate that's what they told me.* 他們遇到了技術問題 —— 反正他們是這麼跟我說的。

6 first-rate/second-rate/third-rate of good, bad, or very bad quality 一流/二流/三流的: *a cheap third-rate motel* 便宜的三流汽車旅館

7 at a rate of knots *BrE informal* very quickly【英, 非正式】飛快地: *Jack's getting through the ironing at a rate of knots!* 傑克熨衣服的活兒幹得飛快!

8 rates [plural] a local tax, paid before 1990 by owners of buildings in Britain〔英國1990年前向房產主徵收的〕房地產税 —see also 另見 BASE RATE, EXCHANGE RATE, INTEREST RATE

rate² *v*

1 ►JUDGE THE QUALITY 判斷質量◄ **a)** [T] to think that someone or something has a particular quality, value, or standard 對…作評估, 評價: **be rated (as) sth** *Lewis is currently rated the world's No. 1 athlete.* 劉易斯目前被認為是世界排名第一的田徑運動員。| *She is generally rated as one of the best modern poets.* 她被公認為最傑出的現代詩人之一。| **rate sb/sth highly** (=think they are very good or important) 對某人/某物評價高 *The company seems to rate him very highly.* 該公司似乎對他評價很高。**b)** [I] to be considered as having a particular quality, value, or standard 被認為, 被評價為: [+as] *Becker rates as one of the finest players of his generation.* 貝克爾被認為是他那一代人當中最優秀的球員之一。

2 ►THINK SB/STH IS GOOD 對某人/某物評價高◄ [T] *BrE informal* to think that someone or something is very good【英, 非正式】對…評價高: *I know they're your favourite team, but I just don't rate them.* 我知道他們是你喜歡的球隊, 可我卻認為他們不怎麼樣。

3 ►DESERVE 值得◄ [T] *informal, especially AmE* to deserve【非正式, 尤美】值得, 應得: *They rate a big thank-you for all their hard work.* 他們的辛勤工作值得好好感謝。| **rate a mention** (=be important enough to be in the news) 值得提及, 值得報道 *a local incident that didn't rate a mention in the national press* 不值得全國報紙報道的地方事件

4 ►FILMS 電影◄ **be rated G/U/PG/X** if a film is rated G, U etc it is officially judged to be suitable or unsuitable for children〔影片〕定為G/U/PG/X級〔即老少咸宜(美)/老少咸宜(英)/家長指導/只允許18歲以上者觀看級〕—see also 另見 X-RATED

5 ►ANGRY 生氣的◄ [I,T] *old use* to speak angrily to someone; BERATE【舊】責罵, 訓斥

rate·a·ble val·ue, ratable value /ˌretəbl ˈvælju; ˌreɪtəbəl ˈvæljuː/ *n* [C] a value given to buildings in Britain before 1990 in order to calculate how much local tax the owner should be charged〔英國1990年前對房地產的〕徵税估定價值

rate of ex·change /ˌ· · ·ˈ·/ *n* [C] the EXCHANGE RATE 外匯匯率, 兑換率

rate of re·turn /ˌ· · ·ˈ·/ *n* [singular] a company's profit for a year, expressed as a PERCENTAGE of the money that the company has spent during the year 收益率, 回報率

rate·pay·er /ˈretˌpeə; ˈreɪtpeɪə/ *n* [C] *BrE* someone who pays taxes that are used to provide local services【英】地方税納税人

rat fink /ˈ· ·/ *n* [C] *AmE informal* someone who you trusted who has given information to the police or done something else wrong【美, 非正式】告密者; 卑鄙小人

ra·ther /ˈræðə; ˈrɑːðə/ *predeterminer, adv* **1** [+adj/adv] quite; fairly 相當, 頗: *I was rather surprised to see him with his ex-wife.* 看到他與他的前妻在一起讓我相當吃驚。| *He was limping rather badly as he walked off the field.* 他走出運動場時, 腿跛得挺厲害。| *It's not too big for you at all. I rather like the way it fits you.* 這對你來説根本不太大, 看來很合身, 我挺喜歡。| **rather a big hat/a tall man etc** *Simon's always been rather a difficult person to get along with.* 西蒙一直是個相當難相處的人。| **rather too big/too tall etc** *They spoke rather too quietly to be heard at the back of the hall.* 他們講話的聲音太輕, 在大廳的後面聽不見。**2 would rather** if you would rather do or have something, you would prefer to do it or have it 寧願, 寧可: *I suppose I could lend it to them but I'd rather not.* 我想我是可以把它借給他們的, 但我還是不借的好。| *To be honest, I'd rather have a quiet night in front of the TV.* 老實説, 晚上我寧願靜靜地看看電視。| **would rather do sth than do sth** *I'd rather die than ask him for his autograph.* 我寧死也不會去求他簽名。| **would rather sb did sth** *We'd rather you didn't smoke in our home.* 我們希望你不要在我們家裡抽煙。**3 rather than a)** more than or to a greater degree than someone or something else 在更大程度上: *The parents should be blamed rather than the children.* 應該受到責備的是父母而不是孩子。| *I think you'd call it a lecture rather than a talk.* 我認為, 與其説這是演説, 不如説是講課。**b)** instead of someone or something else 而不是…: *Rather than squeezing your own oranges, have you tried buying packs of orange juice?* 你是否試過買包裝橙汁, 而不是自己榨橙汁? **4 or rather** used to correct something that you have said, or give more specific information 更確切地説: *You have to be sixteen for cheap tickets – or rather under sixteen.* 你必須是16歲才能買便宜票 —— 更確切地説是不滿16歲。**5 not...but rather...** used to say that someone does not do something but does something else instead 不是…而是…〔用以指某人不做某事, 而做另外的事〕: *The committee does not deal with individual correspondence, but rather discusses issues in its newsletter.* 該委員會不處理個人信件, 而是在定期通訊中討論問題。**6 Rather!** *spoken BrE old-fashioned* used to agree with someone【口, 英, 過時】當然! 的確!

USAGE NOTE 用法説明: RATHER

WORD CHOICE 詞語辨析: fairly, quite, pretty, rather

You use **fairly** or **quite** to describe something that is neither good nor bad. 表示某物既不好也不壞時用 fairly 或 quite: *The weather was fairly cold* (=more than a little cold, but not extremely cold). 天氣相當冷(有些冷, 但不十分冷)。| *The movie was quite good* (=more than a little good). 那部電影相當好。

Rather is fairly formal, and is especially used in British English. It often suggests that something is bad or unsuitable. rather 較正式, 尤用於英國英語, 常表示不好的或不恰當的性質: *It's rather cold* (=colder than I would like). 天挺冷的。| *I was driving rather fast* (=a little too fast). 當時我的車開得相當快。

British English speakers often use **rather** about things they like very much. 英國人用 rather 來表示他們非常喜歡的事物: *Yes I painted it myself – I'm rather pleased with it.* 對, 是我自己刷的漆, 我挺滿意的。

Pretty is the most usual way of saying 'fairly' or 'very' in American English, and is used in British English as well. It is more common in spoken English than in writing. 美國英語中一般用 pretty 來表示"相當"或"非常", 英國英語中也使用, 口語用得比書面多: *Charlie's Restaurant is pretty good, especially if you want somewhere cheap.* 查理餐廳非常好, 尤其是如果你想找個便宜的地方。| *You'd better wear a coat – it's pretty cold out.* 你最好穿件外衣吧, 外面很冷。

GRAMMAR 語法

Note that you say 注意, 可以說: *a rather/fairly/pretty long road* 一條相當長的路, but 但要說 *quite a long road* 一條相當長的路

Of these four words, only **rather** can be used with comparative forms. 上述四個詞中, 只有 rather 可以和比較級連用: *I'd prefer a rather shorter hairstyle.* 我想要理短一些的髮型。

Rather is not used before *than* when you are comparing people or things. 比較人或事物時, rather 不用在 than 之前: *Books are more interesting than TV* (NOT 不用 *Books are interesting rather than TV*). 書籍比電視更有意思。But it is used when you are using adjectives to compare. 但用形容詞進行比較時要用 rather: *TV is relaxing rather than interesting.* 電視使人放鬆, 而不是有意思。

Rather can only be used to mean **prefer** in the phrase **I/he would rather** followed by the base form of a verb or a clause. 在短語 I/he would rather 中, rather 只用於表示喜歡、寧願, 並後接動詞原形或從句: *They'd rather walk* (NOT 不用 *they rather to walk/walking/a walk*). 他們寧願步行。| *I'd rather not answer that question.* 我不想回答那個問題。

R

rat·i·fy /ˋrætəˏfaɪ; ˈrætɨfaɪ/ *v* [T] to make a written agreement official by signing it 批准, 正式簽署: *The government delayed ratifying the treaty.* 政府推遲簽署條約。—**ratification** /ˏrætəfəˋkeʃən; ˌrætɨfɨˈkeɪʃən/ *n* [U]: *an attempt to delay ratification of the treaty* 推遲批准條約的企圖

rat·ing /ˋretɪŋ; ˈreɪtɪŋ/ *n* **1** [C] a level on a scale that shows how good, important, popular etc someone or something is 等級, 程度: *The President's popularity rating is low according to recent opinion polls.* 根據最近的民意測驗, 總統的民眾支持率很低。**2 the ratings** a list that shows which films, television programmes etc are the most popular〔電影、電視節目等的〕排行榜: *The new comedy series shot up to the top of the ratings in the first week.* 這部新喜劇連續劇在第一週裡就躍居排行榜首位。**3** [singular] a letter that shows whether or not a film is suitable for children〔電影是否適合兒童的〕級別: *The Godfather had an X-rating when it was first shown in 1972.*《教父》在 1972 年首映時定為 X 級。**4** [C] a SAILOR in the British navy who is not an officer〔英國海軍〕水兵, 水手 **5** [C] the class in which a ship or machine is placed, according to its size〔船舶、機器依其大小所定的〕等級, 級別 —see also 另見 CREDIT RATING

3 **ra·ti·o** /ˋreʃo; ˈreɪʃiəʊ/ *n* [C] *plural* **ratios** a relationship
3 between two amounts that is represented by a pair of numbers showing how much greater one amount is than the other〔兩個數量之間的〕比, 比例, 比率: **the ratio of sth to sth** *The ratio of nursing staff to doctors is 2:1.* 護理人員與醫生的比例為二比一。—compare 比較 PROPORTION[1]

ra·tion[1] /ˋræʃən; ˈræʃən/ *n* **1** [C] a fixed amount of something such as food or petrol that you are allowed to have, when there is not much available〔食品或汽油等在短缺時的〕配給量, 定量配給: *the weekly meat ration* 肉類的每週配給量 **2 rations** [plural] the food that is given to a soldier or member of a group each day〔每日的〕口糧配給, 口糧定量: *The expedition had sufficient rations to last them another five days.* 探險隊有足夠的給養再維持五天。**3 have had your ration of** to have had as much of something as you would expect or consider to be fair 得到想要或應得的東西: *We've had more than our ration of bad luck this year.* 我們今年運氣不佳。

ration[2] *v* [T] **1** to control the supply of something such as food or petrol by allowing people to have only a fixed amount of it 對…實行配給, 定量供應: *Petrol was rationed during the war.* 戰爭期間, 汽油實行定量供應。**2** to allow someone to have only a small amount of something because there is not enough〔因不夠而〕實行定量供給, 配給: **ration sb to sth** *We were rationed to two eggs a week.* 每週配給我們兩個雞蛋。—**rationing** *n* [U]

ration sth ↔ **out** *phr v* [T] to give out supplies of something in small amounts 少量配給〔供應品〕: *They rationed out the remaining water as fairly as they could.* 他們儘可能公平地按量分配剩下的水。

ra·tion·al /ˋræʃənḷ; ˈræʃənəl/ *adj* **1** based on clear, practical or scientific reasons〔原因〕合理的, 基於理性的: *It can't have just disappeared! There must be a perfectly rational explanation.* 不可能就這麼消失了! 一定有某種非常合理的解釋。**2** sensible and able to make decisions based on intelligent thinking rather than on emotion 有理性的, 懂道理的: *rational behaviour* 合理的行為 | *We should be able to sort this out like rational human beings!* 我們應該像有理性的人那樣處理這件事! —**rationally** *adv*: *Scientific training makes you think rationally.* 科學的訓練能使人理性思考。—**rationality** /ˏræʃəˋnælətɪ; ˌræʃəˈnælɨti/ *n* [U] —opposite 反義詞 IRRATIONAL

ra·tio·nale /ˏræʃəˋnæl; ˌræʃəˈnɑːl/ *n* [C,U] *formal* the reasons and principles on which a decision, plan, belief etc is based【正式】〔決定、計劃、信念等的〕理據, 基本原因, 依據: *The rationale behind introducing this technique is that it will substantially speed up our work.* 引進這技術的依據是它將大大加快我們的工作。

ra·tion·al·ist /ˋræʃənḷɪst; ˈræʃənəlɨst/ *n* [C] someone who bases their opinions and actions on intelligent thinking, rather than on emotion or religious belief 理性主義者, 唯理論者 —**rationalism** *n* [U] —**rationalist, rationalistic** /ˏræʃənḷˋɪstɪk; ˌræʃənəˈlɪstɪk◂/ *adj*

ra·tion·al·ize also 又作 **-ise** *BrE*【英】/ˋræʃənḷˏaɪz; ˈræʃənəlaɪz/ *v* [I,T] **1** to find or invent a reasonable explanation for your behaviour or attitudes 合理地解釋, 為…找出辯解的理由: *Tony was still trying to rationalize his decision to leave his wife and children.* 托尼仍在試圖為他離開妻子兒女的決定辯解。**2** *especially BrE* to make a business system more effective by getting rid of unnecessary staff, equipment etc【尤英】對…進行合理化改革〔指裁減冗員、處理閒置設備等〕—**rationalization** /ˏræʃənələˋzeʃən; ˌræʃənəlaɪˈzeɪʃən/ *n* [C,U]: *Rationalization is a word management use when they are sacking people.* 管理層在解雇員工時總是用使機構合理化的說法。

rat race /ˋ· ·/ *n* [U] **the rat race** the unpleasant situation in business, politics etc in which people are continuously competing against each other for success〔商業、政治等中〕永無休止的競爭: *Paul went off to a Greek island to escape from the rat race.* 保羅跑到希臘的一個島上去躲避永無休止的競爭。

rats /ræts; ræts/ *spoken* used as an expression of annoyance【口】討厭〔用於表示惱怒〕: *Oh rats! I've left my purse at home.* 真討厭! 我把錢包留在家裡了。

rat·tan /ræˋtæn; rəˈtæn/ *n* [U] the plant from which wicker furniture is made 藤屬植物, 藤

rat-tat /ˏræt ˋtæt; ˌræt ˈtæt/ *n* [singular] RAT-A-TAT 敲擊聲〔尤指敲門聲〕

rat·ted *v* **get ratted** *BrE slang* to get extremely drunk【英俚】喝得爛醉

rat·tle[1] /ˋrætḷ; ˈrætl/ *v* **1** [I,T] to shake, or make something shake, with quick repeated knocking noises (使) 格格作響: *The windows rattled in the wind.* 窗戶被風吹

得格格作響。| *The beggar was rattling coins in an old mug.* 那個乞丐把舊杯子裡的硬幣搖得嘩嘩響。**2** [I] to move quickly, making a rattling noise 嘎拉嘎拉地快速移動: **[+along/past/over etc]** *The cart rattled along the stony road.* 那輛大車嘎拉嘎拉地沿着碎石路快速駛過。**3** [T] *informal* to make someone lose confidence or become nervous【非正式】使慌亂, 使緊張: *Keep calm – don't let yourself get rattled.* 沉住氣 —— 別緊張。| *It was an old trick of his – rattling people by getting their names wrong.* 這是他慣用的伎倆 —— 把人們的姓名搞錯使他們慌亂不安。**4 rattle sb's cage** *spoken humorous* to make someone feel angry or annoyed【口, 幽默】使某人生氣[惱怒]: *Who rattled your cage?* 是誰惹你了? —see also 另見 SABRE-RATTLING

rattle around *phr v* [I] *informal* to be in a house, office etc that is bigger than you need it to be【非正式】〔房子、辦公室等〕過大: *We rattle around a bit now that the children have all left.* 孩子們都離開了家, 屋子裡現在有點空蕩蕩的。

rattle sth ↔ **off** *phr v* [T] to say something quickly and easily, from memory 迅速地背誦: *He rattled off the poem.* 他一口氣背出了那首詩。

rattle on *phr v* [T] *informal* to talk quickly for a long time, about things that are not interesting【非正式】喋喋不休地說: *Nancy would rattle on for hours about her grandchildren.* 南茜能幾個小時喋喋不休地談論她的孫兒孫女們。

rattle through sth *phr v* [T] *informal* to do something very quickly because you want to finish it as soon as possible【非正式】迅速完成: *She rattled through her speech in five minutes.* 她匆匆忙忙在五分鐘內完成了演講。

rattle² *n* **1** [singular] the noise that you hear when the parts of something knock against each other〔碰撞而發出的〕格格聲, 嘎嘎聲: **[+of]** *the rattle of chains* 鐵鏈相互撞擊時發出的嘎嘎聲 **2** [C] a baby's toy that makes this noise 撥浪鼓〔一種幼兒玩具〕 **3** [C] a wooden instrument that makes a loud knocking noise, used by people watching football games〔觀眾在看足球比賽時使用的〕發出格格響聲的木器具 —see also 另見 DEATH RATTLE

rat·tler /ˈrætlɚ; ˈrætlə/ *n* [C] *informal* a rattlesnake【非正式】響尾蛇

rattle·snake /ˈrætl̩ˌsnek; ˈrætlsneɪk/ *n* [C] a poisonous American snake that makes a noise like a rattle with its tail 響尾蛇

rat·tling /ˈrætlɪŋ; ˈrætlɪŋ/ *adj, adv old-fashioned* **a rattling good yarn/story** a very good or interesting story【過時】非常好[有趣]的故事: *He tells a rattling good story.* 他講述一個非常有趣的故事。

rat trap /ˈ· ·/ *n* [C] *AmE informal* a dirty old building that is in very bad condition【美, 非正式】又髒又破的老房子

rat·ty /ˈrætɪ; ˈræti/ *adj* **1** *BrE informal* bad-tempered; IRRITABLE【英, 非正式】愛發脾氣的, 易怒的 **2** *AmE informal* in bad condition; SHABBY【美, 非正式】破舊的, 襤褸的: *a ratty old sofa* 一張破舊的沙發 **3** like a rat 像老鼠的

rau·cous /ˈrɔkəs; ˈrɔːkəs/ *adj* a raucous voice is unpleasantly loud 沙啞的, 粗嘎的: *raucous shouts from the street* 街上傳來的沙啞的叫喊聲 —**raucously** *adv*: *They laughed raucously.* 他們粗聲粗氣地笑。—**raucousness** *n* [U]

raunch·y /ˈrɔntʃɪ; ˈrɔːntʃi/ *adj informal* sexually exciting or intended to make you think about sex【非正式】色情的, 淫穢的: *a raunchy dance* 色情舞蹈 —**raunchily** *adv* —**raunchiness** *n* [U]

rav·age /ˈrævɪdʒ; ˈrævɪdʒ/ *v* [T often passive 常用被動態] to destroy, ruin, or damage something very badly; DEVASTATE (1) 嚴重破壞, 摧毀: **be ravaged by sth** *The population was ravaged by cholera.* 霍亂使許多人死去。

rav·ag·es /ˈrævɪdʒɪz; ˈrævɪdʒɪz/ *n* **the ravages of war/time/disease etc** the damage or destruction caused by something such as war, disease, storms etc 戰爭/時間/疾病等造成的破壞性後果: *The ravages of drink were clear in the dark rings under his eyes.* 他的黑眼圈證明了酗酒的惡果。

rave¹ /rev; reɪv/ *v* [I] **1** to talk in an angry, uncontrolled way 怒罵, 痛斥: **[+at]** *Dad raved at me for hours about how irresponsible I'd been.* 父親一連幾小時痛罵我不負責任。**2** to talk in a crazy way that is impossible to understand, especially because you are very ill〔尤指因病重〕胡言亂語 **3 rave about/over** to talk in a very excited way about something, saying how much you admire or enjoy it 極力讚美: *After the game people raved about Tommy Craig's performance.* 比賽後, 人們極力誇獎湯美·克雷格的表現。—see also 另見 **rant and rave** (RANT), RAVING

rave² *adj* **rave reviews/notices** newspaper articles that praise something a lot, for example a play or film〔報紙對某部戲劇或電影〕大加讚美的評論: *His last film got rave reviews in the British press.* 他的最後一部電影得到英國報刊的高度評價。

rave³ *n* [C] **1** a very large party held in an empty building in Britain, at which young people dance and sometimes take illegal drugs〔英國年輕人在無人居住的房子裡跳舞、吸毒的〕狂歡聚會: **rave scene/band/culture etc** (=a scene etc that is connected with raves) 狂歡的場面/狂歡聚會的樂隊/狂歡聚會的文化等 **2** *especially AmE* a piece of writing in a newspaper, magazine etc that praises a film, play, or performance very much【尤美】〔報紙、雜誌等上〕吹捧〔電影、戲劇、表演〕的文章 —see also 另見 RAVE-UP

rav·el /ˈrævl̩; ˈrævəl/ *v* **ravelled, ravelling** *BrE*【英】, **raveled, raveling** *AmE*【美】[I] **1** if something made from wool or cloth ravels, the threads in it become separated from one another〔織物〕開線, 散開 **2** if threads ravel, they become knotted and twisted〔線〕打結, 纏繞 —compare 比較 UNRAVEL

ra·ven¹ /ˈrevən; ˈreɪvən/ *n* [C] a large shiny black bird with a large black beak 渡鴉

raven² *adj* [only before noun 僅用於名詞前] raven hair is black and shiny〔頭髮〕烏黑發亮的

raven-haired /ˌ·· ˈ·◂/ *adj literary* having shiny black hair【文】長着一頭烏黑發亮的頭髮的

rav·e·ning /ˈrævənɪŋ; ˈrævənɪŋ/ *adj literary* ravening animals are extremely hungry【文】〔動物〕餓極了的: *a ravening beast* 極其飢餓的野獸

rav·e·nous /ˈrævənəs; ˈrævənəs/ *adj* extremely hungry 餓極了的: *Have a sandwich – you must be ravenous!* 吃塊三明治吧 —— 你一定餓極了! —**ravenously** *adv*

rav·er /ˈrevɚ; ˈreɪvə/ *n* [C] *BrE informal* someone who goes to a lot of parties and has many sexual partners【英, 非正式】〔經常參加聚會、有許多性夥伴的〕放蕩不羈的人

rave-up /ˈ· ·/ *n* [C] *BrE informal* a noisy party where people drink and dance a lot【英, 非正式】喧鬧的聚會

ra·vine /rəˈvin; rəˈviːn/ *n* [C] a deep narrow valley with steep sides 溝壑, 峽谷: *21 killed as bus swerves into ravine* 公共汽車突然轉向墜入深谷, 致使21人死亡

rav·ing /ˈrevɪŋ; ˈreɪvɪŋ/ *adj informal*【非正式】**1** talking or behaving in a crazy way 語無倫次的, 瘋瘋癲癲的: *a raving lunatic* 胡言亂語的瘋子 | **raving mad** *informal especially BrE* (=completely crazy)【非正式, 尤英】完全喪失理智的 **2 raving beauty/success** someone who is very beautiful or something that is very successful 絕色美人/巨大成功

rav·ings /ˈrevɪŋz; ˈreɪvɪŋz/ *n* [plural] things someone says that are crazy and have no meaning 胡言亂語, 瘋話: *Sometimes in his ravings he talks about a super-intelligent pig.* 有時候他會瘋言瘋語, 說是有一頭豬具有超級智能。

ra·vi·o·li /ˌrævɪˈolɪ; ˌræviˈəʊli/ *n* [U] small squares of PASTA filled with meat 小方形餃 —see picture at 參見 PASTA 圖

rav·ish /ˈrævɪʃ; ˈrævɪʃ/ *v* [T] *literary*【文】**1** to RAPE a

R

woman 強姦 **2 be ravished** to feel great pleasure when you look at or listen to something 狂喜, 陶醉, 銷魂: *I was ravished by her beauty.* 她的美貌使我傾倒。

rav·ish·ing /ˋrævɪʃɪŋ; ˈrævɪʃɪŋ/ *adj* very beautiful 非常美麗的, 十分標致的: *ravishing good looks* 令人傾倒的美貌 —**ravishingly** *adv*: *a ravishingly pretty young woman* 美豔絕倫的年輕女子

3 **raw**[1] /rɔ; rɔː/ *adj*
1 ▶FOOD 食品◀ not cooked 生的, 未燒煮的: *raw meat* 生肉 | *raw carrot* 生胡蘿蔔
2 ▶INFORMATION 信息◀ raw data/statistics etc information that has not been arranged, checked, or prepared for use 原始數據/統計數字等
3 ▶SKIN 皮膚◀ a part of your body that is raw is red and sore 又紅又痛的, 刺痛的: *My hands were raw with cold.* 我的手凍得發痛。
4 ▶MATERIALS 材料◀ raw cotton, sugar, wool etc are in their natural state and have not yet been prepared for use〔棉、糖、羊毛等〕天然狀態的, 未經過處理加工的 —see also 另見 RAW MATERIALS
5 ▶NOT EXPERIENCED 沒有經驗的◀ not experienced or not yet fully trained 沒有經驗的, 未經過充足訓練的: *Most of our soldiers were raw recruits.* 我們大多數的士兵都是新兵。
6 touch/hit a raw nerve to upset someone by something you say〔說話〕觸及某人痛處: *In mentioning his departure I knew I had touched a raw nerve.* 說到他的離去, 我知道我觸及了對方的傷心處。
7 get a raw deal to be unfairly treated 受到不公正的待遇: *Women tend to get a raw deal when it comes to pay.* 婦女常常在工資方面受到不公正的待遇。
8 ▶WEATHER 天氣◀ very cold and wet 濕冷的: *A raw wind chilled him to the bone.* 濕冷的風讓他感到寒氣刺骨。
9 ▶EMOTIONS/QUALITIES 情感/素質◀ raw emotions or qualities are strong and natural, but not completely developed or controlled 強烈的, 自然的〔但未經充分琢磨或約束的〕: *Katie was surprised by her own raw courage and endurance.* 凱蒂原始的勇氣和忍耐力使她自己吃了一驚。| *the singer's raw, husky voice* 那位歌手本色的、沙啞的嗓音
10 ▶LANGUAGE 語言◀ *AmE informal* containing a lot of sexual details【美, 非正式】下流的, 粗俗的
11 ▶DESCRIPTIONS 描述◀ giving the unpleasant facts, without trying to make them seem more acceptable 不加掩飾的: *a raw account of poverty in the cities* 對城市中的貧困狀況毫不掩飾的敘述 —**rawness** *n* [U]

raw[2] *n* **1 life/nature in the raw** the way humans or animals live in their natural state including all the violence and cruelty 未開化的生活/原始的自然狀態: *Her films portray nature in the raw.* 她的電影描繪了自然原來的狀態。**2 in the raw** *AmE informal* not wearing any clothes【美, 非正式】裸體的: *She sunbathes in the raw.* 她裸着身子沐日光浴。**3 catch/touch sb on the raw** *BrE* to say or do something that upsets someone【英】〔說話或做事〕觸及某人的痛處

raw·hide /ˋrɔˌhaɪd; ˈrɔːhaɪd/ *n* [U] natural leather that has not been specially treated 生皮

raw ma·te·ri·als /ˌ·ˈ···/ *n* [plural] materials such as coal, oil etc, in their natural state, before being treated in order to make things 原材料

ray /re; reɪ/ *n* [C] **1** [often plural 常用複數] a narrow beam of light from the sun or from something such as a lamp 光線, 光束: *the sun's rays* 太陽光 | **[+of]** *Rays of light filtered through the pine trees.* 一束束光線透過松樹。**2** *technical* a beam of heat, electricity, or other form of ENERGY (2)【術語】〔熱、電或其他能源的〕束: *a gun that fires invisible rays* 一支射出隱形射線的槍 —see also 另見 COSMIC RAY, GAMMA RAY, X-RAY **3 ray of hope/light/comfort etc** something that provides a small amount of hope or happiness in a difficult situation 一線希望/光亮/一絲安慰: *If only I could see some ray of hope for the future.* 但願我能看到未來的一線希望。**4 ray of sunshine** *informal* an expression meaning someone or something that makes a situation seem better【非正式】安慰, 希望: *Little Annie was an unexpected ray of sunshine in her life.* 小安妮是她生活中一線意外的陽光。**5** a large flat sea fish with a long pointed tail 魟; 鰩〔一種體大而扁的海魚, 尾長而尖〕

ray gun /ˈ· ·/ *n* [C] an imaginary gun in SCIENCE FICTION stories that fires rays which kill people〔科幻故事裡的〕光束槍, 射線槍, 激光槍

ray·on /ˋreɑn; ˈreɪɒn/ *n* [U] a smooth material used for making clothes 人造絲, 嫘縈

raze /rez; reɪz/ *v* [T] to completely destroy a town or building 把〔城鎮、建築物〕夷為平地: **raze sth to the ground** (=destroy it so that nothing is left) 夷為平地; 徹底破壞 *houses that had been razed to the ground in the war* 在戰爭中被夷為平地的房屋

razors 剃鬚刀

razor blade
剃鬚刀刀片

razor blade
安全剃刀刀片

safety razor
安全剃刀

cut-throat razor *BrE*【英】/
straight razor *AmE*【美】
(直柄) 剃刀

electric razor/
electric shaver
電動剃鬚刀

ra·zor /ˋrezɚ; ˈreɪzə/ *n* [C] **1** a sharp instrument used for removing hair, especially from a man's face 剃刀, 刮鬍刀: *an electric razor* 電動剃鬚刀 **2 be on a razor edge** to be in a dangerous position where a mistake could be very dangerous 處於險境: *Politically we are on a razor edge. Whatever judgment we make could have dire consequences.* 我們在政治上處於險境。無論我們作出甚麼樣的決定, 都有可能造成可怕的後果。

razor blade /ˈ·· ·/ *n* [C] a small flat blade with a very sharp cutting edge used in a SAFETY RAZOR〔安全剃刀上使用的〕刀片 —see picture at 參見 RAZOR 圖

ra·zor-sharp /ˌ·· ˈ·◂/ *adj* **1** very sharp 鋒利的, 銳利的: *a razor-sharp hunting knife* 一把非常鋒利的獵刀 **2** very intelligent 非常敏銳的: *his razor-sharp wit* 他非常敏銳的才智

razz /ræz; ræz/ *v* [T] *AmE spoken* to make a joke about someone that is insulting or makes them feel embarrassed; TEASE[1] (1)【美口】嘲笑, 譏諷: *The kids were razzing Tom about Jenny.* 孩子們戲弄湯姆說他和詹妮的事。

raz·zle /ˋræzḷ; ˈræzəl/ *n* **go on the razzle** *BrE slang* to go somewhere such as to a party to enjoy yourself【英俚】狂歡, 作樂

razzle-daz·zle /ˌ·· ˈ··/ *n* [U] *informal*【非正式】**1** a lot of activity that is intended to be impressive and excite people 起鬨, 歡鬧 **2** *AmE informal* a complicated series of actions intended to confuse your opponent, especially in American football【美, 非正式】〔尤指美式足球中〕障眼的假動作

razz·ma·tazz /ˌræzmə`tæz; ˌræzmə'tæz/ also 又作 **raz·za·ma·tazz** /ˌræzəmə`tæz; ˌræzəmə'tæz/ *n* [U] *informal* busy or noisy activity that is intended to attract people's attention【非正式】〔為了吸引人的〕令人眼花繚亂的活動: *all the razzmatazz surrounding presidential elections* 圍繞總統選舉的種種熱鬧喧囂

RC /ˌɑr `si; ˌɑː 'siː/ the abbreviation of 縮寫= Roman Catholic 羅馬天主教

RD /ˌɑr `di; ˌɑː 'diː/ *n* rural delivery; a postal service that delivers the mail in country areas in the US. The letters 'RD' are part of someone's address. 鄉村遞送〔美國鄉村地區遞送郵件的服務。RD是地址的一部分〕

Rd the written abbreviation of 縮寫= Road, used in addresses 路〔用於地址〕

-rd /rd; d/ *suffix* forms written ORDINAL numbers with 3 以3結尾的序數詞寫法: *the 3rd* (=third) *of June* 6月3日 | *his 53rd birthday* 他的53歲生日

RDA /ˌɑr di `e; ˌɑː diː 'eɪ/ *n* [singular] Recommended Daily Allowance; the amount of substances such as VITAMIN*s* or MINERAL*s* that you should have each day〔維生素、礦物質等的〕建議每日攝入量

're /ɚ; ə/ the short form of 縮略式= are: *We're ready to go but they're not.* 我們已經準備好出發了, 但他們還沒有。

RE /ˌɑr `i; ˌɑːr 'iː/ *n* [U] Religious Education; a school subject in Britain 宗教教育〔英國的學校課程〕

re- /ri; riː/ *prefix* **1** again 再, 重新: *They're rebroadcasting the play.* 他們正在重播這齣戲。**2** again in a new and better way 改進重來: *You'd better rewrite that letter.* 你最好重寫那封信。**3** back to a former state 回復原狀, 又(重): *After years of separation they were finally reunited.* 經過多年的離別, 他們終於團聚了。

re¹ /ri; riː/ *prep* used especially in business letters to introduce the subject that you are going to write 'about' 關於〔尤用於商業信函中〕: *re your enquiry of the 19th October* 關於你10月19日的詢問

re² /re; reɪ/ *n* [singular] the second note in a musical SCALE¹ (8) according to the SOL-FA system 全音階的第二音

1 **reach¹** /ritʃ; riːtʃ/ *v*

1 **1 ►ARRIVE 到達◄** [T] to arrive at a particular place, especially when it has taken a long time or a lot of effort to get there 到達, 抵達〔尤指經過長時間或花費大氣力以後〕: *It was a relief to reach the safety of our home at last.* 終於到家了, 這下安全了, 我們鬆了一口氣。| *Your letter reached me yesterday.* 我昨天收到了你的信。

2 ►WITH YOUR HAND 用手◄ a) [I always+adv/prep, T always+adv/prep] to move your hand or arm in order to touch, hold, or pick up something 伸出〔手、臂來碰、拿或撿起〕: **[+for/in/over etc]** *I saw Kelly reach for the gun.* 我看到凱利伸手去拿槍。| **reach out a hand** *One of the men suddenly reached out a hand and grabbed my arm.* 其中一個人突然伸手抓住我的胳膊。**b)** [I,T not in progressive 不用進行式] to succeed in touching something by stretching out your hand or arm, especially something that is above your head 伸手觸及〔尤指高於頭頂的東西〕: *Even when I stood on tiptoe I couldn't reach the top shelf.* 即使我踮起腳尖也夠不到架子最高一格。| *We picked all the fruit we could reach.* 我們摘了所有夠得着的果實。**c) ►TAKE STH/PICK STH UP 拿起/舉起某物◄** [T] to take or pick up something by stretching your arm, especially over your head 伸手去拿〔高處的東西〕: **reach sth down** *She reached down a can of peaches from the top shelf.* 她從架子頂格拿下一罐桃子。

3 ►LEVEL/STANDARD 水平/標準◄ [T] to increase, improve, or develop to a particular level or standard over a period of time 達到: *These plants take a long time to reach maturity.* 這些植物要過很長時間才成熟。| *wind speeds reaching over 100 mph* 風速達到每小時一百多英里

4 ►ACHIEVE AN AIM 實現目標◄ [T] to succeed in doing what you were trying to do 實現, 達到: **reach a decision/agreement/result etc** *After two years of negotiations, the warring parties have finally reached a settlement.* 經過兩年的談判, 交戰各方最終達成一項和解協議。

5 ►LENGTH/HEIGHT 長度/高度◄ [I always+adv/prep, T not in progressive 不用進行式] to be big enough, long enough, or high enough to get to a particular point or level 大得[長得, 高得]足以到達: *The flood waters reached the lower floor of the houses.* 洪水水位漲到房屋的下層。| **reach as far as/down to** *Her skirt reaches down to her ankles.* 她的裙子長及腳踝。

6 ►SPEAK TO SB 對某人說話◄ [T] to speak to someone or leave a message for them, especially by telephone; CONTACT² 〔尤指通過電話〕聯繫: *Here's my phone number, in case you need to reach me.* 如果你需要與我聯絡, 這是我的電話號碼。

7 ►BE SEEN/HEARD BY SB 被某人看到/聽到◄ [T] if a message, television programme etc reaches a lot of people, they hear it or see it 收聽, 收看〔信息、電視節目等〕: *The sales campaign reached a target audience of 12,000 women.* 促銷活動以(某些)女性為對象, 接觸了12,000人。

8 reach for the stars to aim for something that is very difficult to achieve 想摘天上的星星〔追求難以實現的東西〕

R

USAGE NOTE 用法說明: REACH

WORD CHOICE 詞語辨析: **reach, arrive, get to, achieve, catch**

To **arrive** somewhere is to come to it after travelling. arrive 指從一地到達另一地: *Sam usually arrives home from work at 5.15.* 薩姆通常在5點15分下班回到家。| *What time does the train arrive?* 這班火車何時到達?

Reach suggests more time or effort is involved. reach 指用了較多時間、付出較大努力後到達: *At last we reached the base camp.* 我們終於到達了大本營。

In spoken English people usually use **get to.** 口語中通常使用 get to: *You can easily get to the city centre from here.* 從這裡你可以方便地到達市中心。If a train, bus, plane etc arrives, you say **get in**. 火車、公共汽車、飛機等到達用 get in: *The bus gets in at four-thirty.* 這班公共汽車四點半到達。Note that you **get/arrive/reach etc home** (NOT 不用 **to home**). 請注意, 到家是 get/arrive/reach home。

You may **reach** a standard or level, especially through your own efforts, but **achieve** is often a better word. 達到某種標準或水平, 尤指通過自身努力時可用 reach, 但 achieve 往往更為恰當: *I want to reach/achieve a good level of English.* 我希望達到好的英語水平。| *He achieved his aim in life – to write a book* (NOT 不用 *reached*). 他實現了畢生的目標 —— 撰寫一本書。

If you get to a bus, train etc just in time, you **catch** it. catch 指趕上公共汽車、火車等: *You'd better hurry if you want to catch that bus.* 你要是想趕上那班公共汽車就最好快點。

GRAMMAR 語法

You **reach** a place (NOT 不用 **reach at** or **reach to** it) 到達某地用 reach: *He reached Tokyo at 5 am.* 他早上5點到達了東京。

You **arrive at** a particular place, town, or building. 到達某個具體地點、城鎮、房屋用 arrive at: *We arrived at the station at midnight.* 我們午夜時到達車站。| *What time will they arrive at his house?* 他們甚麼時候能到他家?

You **arrive in** a country or a big city. 到達某國家、大城市用 arrive in: *arrive in London/Tokyo/France* 到達倫敦/東京/法國

Sometimes you do not need a preposition at all. 有時不需要使用介詞: *When will they arrive there/here/home?* 他們甚麼時候到那裡/這裡/家?

reach² *n* **1** [singular,U] the distance that you can stretch out your arm to touch something 伸手可及的距離: *a boxer with a long reach* 一名有長臂的拳擊手 | **out of reach/beyond reach** *The cat jumped away, out of his reach.* 那隻貓跳開了, 他夠不着。| **within reach** *Adjust the car seat so that all the controls are within reach.* 把汽車座位調整一下, 以便所有的控制裝置伸手可及。**2** [singular, U] the limit to which someone or something can have a power or influence〔權力、影響〕能及的範圍: **beyond the reach of** *He lives in Paraguay, beyond the reach of the British authorities.* 他住在巴拉圭, 英國當局鞭長莫及。**3 within (easy) reach of** within a distance that you can easily travel 在…可(容易)到達的地方: *All the main tourist attractions are within easy reach of the hotel.* 這家旅館離所有的主要旅遊景點都很近。**4** [C] a straight part of a river between two bends〔兩個彎道之間的〕筆直河段

reach 伸手可及的距離

The oranges are out of Tim's reach/beyond Tim's reach.
這些橙子蒂姆夠不着。

 **re·act** /rɪˋækt; riˈækt/ *v* [I] **1** to behave in a particular way because of something that has happened or something that has been said to you 反應: **[+to]** *How did Wilson react to your idea?* 威爾遜對你的想法有甚麼反應? | *He reacted angrily to accusations of disloyalty.* 有人指責他不忠, 他非常氣憤。| **react by doing sth** *Ellie reacted by marching out of the room.* 埃利的反應是大步走出房間。—see also 另見 OVERREACT **2** *technical* if a chemical substance reacts, it changes when it is mixed with another chemical substance【術語】產生化學反應: **[+with/on]** *An acid reacts with a base to form a salt.* 酸與鹼產生化學反應形成鹽。**3** to become ill when you take a particular drug, eat a particular kind of food etc〔因服某種藥品、食用某種食物而〕產生不良反應: **[+to]** *The patient reacted badly to penicillin.* 病人對青黴素有不良反應。—compare 比較 RESPOND

react against sth *phr v* [T] to show that you dislike someone else's rules or way of doing something by deliberately doing the opposite 反抗: *Feminists reacted against the limitations of women's traditional roles.* 女權主義者反抗婦女傳統角色的局限。

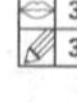 **re·ac·tion** /rɪˋækʃən; riˈækʃən/ *n*

1 ►TO A SITUATION/EVENT 對情形/事件◄ [C,U] something that you feel or do that is a result of something that has happened to you or been said to you 反應: *What was Jeff's reaction when you told him about the job?* 你把那份工作的情況告訴傑夫的時候, 他是甚麼反應? | **[+to]** *Her parents' reaction to the news was surprisingly calm.* 她父母對那消息的反應平靜得出乎意料。| **mixed reaction** (=people react in different ways) 各種不同的反應 *The pay offer brought a mixed reaction from union members.* 薪金建議引起工會會員不同的反應。| **gut reaction** (=what you immediately feel before you have time to think) 直覺反應 *My gut reaction to her story was disbelief!* 聽到她的故事, 我的直覺反應是不相信!

2 ►ABILITY 能力◄ **reactions** [plural] your ability to move quickly when something dangerous happens suddenly〔突發危險時的〕反應能力: **quick/slow reactions** *In motor racing the drivers need to have very quick reactions.* 賽車時, 車手需要具備非常迅速的反應能力。

3 ►TO FOOD/DRUGS 對食品/藥品◄ [C] a bad effect, such as illness, caused by food that you have eaten or a drug that you have taken 不良反應: *an allergic reaction* 過敏反應 | **[+to]** *Some people experience a mild reaction to the drug.* 有些人對這種藥會有輕微不良反應。

4 ►SCIENCE 科學◄ [C,U] **a)** a chemical change that happens when two or more chemical substances are mixed together; CHEMICAL REACTION 化學反應 **b)** a physical force that is the result of an equally strong physical force in the opposite direction 反作用力 —see also 另見 NUCLEAR REACTION

5 ►CHANGE 變化◄ [singular] a change in people's attitudes, behaviour, fashions etc that happens because they disapprove of what was done in the past〔態度、行為、時尚等的〕變化〔以示對過去的不滿〕: **[+against]** *The attitudes of this generation are a reaction against the selfish values of the 1980s.* 這一代人的態度是對20世紀80年代自私價值觀的不滿。

6 ►TIRED/SAD 疲憊/悲傷◄ [singular] a sudden feeling of weakness, tiredness, or unhappiness that you sometimes get after a lot of activity〔大量活動後引起的〕無力, 疲乏, 情緒低落: *Bridget seems depressed; I think she's suffering a reaction after all the excitement.* 布麗奇特似乎悶悶不樂; 我認為她是在極度興奮之後感到疲乏無力。

7 ►AGAINST CHANGE 反對變革◄ [U] *formal* strong and unreasonable opposition to all social and political changes【正式】反動: *The revolution was defeated by the forces of reaction.* 這場革命被反動勢力打敗了。—see also 另見 CHAIN REACTION

re·ac·tion·a·ry /rɪˋækʃən͵ɛrɪ; riˈækʃənəri/ *adj* strongly and unreasonably opposed to social or political change 反動的: *The new measures were opposed by reactionary elements within the party.* 新措施遭到黨內反動分子的反對。—**reactionary** *n* [C]

re·ac·tiv·ate /rɪˋæktɪ͵vet; riˈæktɪveɪt/ *v* [T] to make something start working again, or to start a process again 使重新開始工作; 使重新啟動程序

re·ac·tive /rɪˋæktɪv; riˈæktɪv/ *adj* **1** reacting to events or situations rather than starting something new 反應的〔而不是創新的〕: *Many businesses follow a reactive strategy rather than initiating new products.* 很多商家採取的是對市場環境作出反應的策略, 而不是研製新產品。**2** *technical* a reactive chemical substance changes when it is mixed with another chemical substance【術語】〔化學物質〕能起化學作用的

re·ac·tor /rɪˋæktɚ; riˈæktə/ *n* [C] a NUCLEAR REACTOR 核反應堆

read out 宣讀

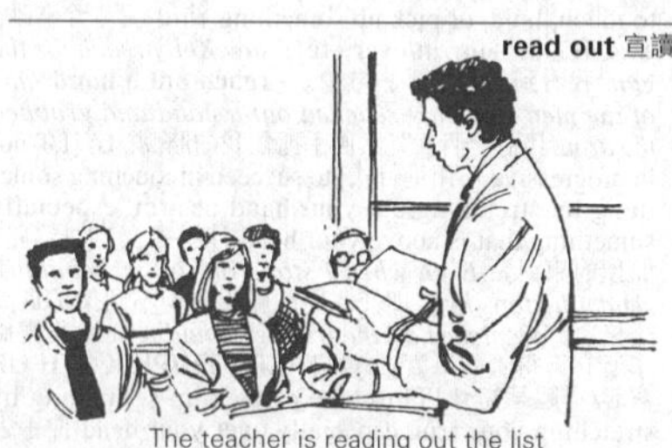

The teacher is reading out the list of successful students.
老師在宣讀優秀學生名單。

 **read¹** /rid; riːd/ *v past tense and past participle* **read** /rɛd; red/

1 ►WORDS/BOOKS 文字/書籍◄ [I;T] to look at written words and understand what they mean 閱讀, 看懂: *Tom could read by the time he was four.* 湯姆四歲時就能閱讀了。| **read sth** *Read the instructions carefully before you start.* 開始之前, 請仔細閱讀操作指南。| *I'm sorry, I can't read your handwriting.* 對不起, 我看不懂

你的字。| *I can read Spanish but I can't speak it very well.* 我能看懂西班牙文, 但說得不太好。| *I've read a lot of Agatha Christie.* 我讀過許多〔英國作家〕阿嘉莎·克里斯蒂的著作。| *reading the paper* 看報紙

2 ▶INFORMATION 信息◀ [I,T not in progressive 不用進行式] to find out information from books, newspapers etc〔從書籍、報紙等中〕找到: *You can't believe everything you read in the papers.* 你不能完全相信在報紙上看到的一切。| **[+about/of]** *Did you read about that terrible car crash?* 你在報上看到那起嚴重的撞車事件了嗎? | *I read of his death in the local newspaper.* 我在這份地方報紙上看到了他去世的消息。| **read (that)** *Simon was amazed when he read that Sally had won a literary prize.* 在報紙上看到莎利獲得一項文學獎, 西蒙感到吃驚。

3 ▶READ AND SPEAK 朗讀◀ [I,T] to say the written words in a book, newspaper etc so that people can hear them 讀出, 朗讀: **read sb sth** *Daddy, will you read me a story?* 爸爸, 給我唸個故事好嗎? | **read to sb** *Our mother reads to us every evening.* 媽媽每天晚上都給我們朗讀〔故事〕。| **read (sth) aloud** *He glanced at the letter and began to read it aloud.* 他看了一下信, 便開始大聲朗讀。

4 ▶MUSIC/MAPS/SIGNS ETC 樂譜/地圖/符號等◀ [T] to look at signs, pictures etc and understand what they mean 讀懂: *He plays the flute well but can't actually read music.* 他長笛吹得很好, 但其實他看不懂樂譜。| *map reading* 查閱地圖

5 ▶UNDERSTAND STH IN A PARTICULAR WAY 理解◀ [T] to choose to understand a situation, remark etc in one of several possible ways 理解, 洞察: **read sth as** *I read her reply as a refusal.* 我把她的答覆理解為拒絕。| *The poem can be read as a protest against war.* 這首詩可以理解為對戰爭的抗議。| **read sth well/accurately** (=understand something correctly) 正確理解〔某事〕*Reagan's speech showed that he had accurately read the mood of Congress.* 列根的講話表明他正確把握了國會的情緒。

6 ▶HAVE A PARTICULAR FORM/MEANING 具有某種形式/含義◀ [I not in progressive 不用進行式] if words read in a particular way, they have a particular form, or produce a particular effect when you read them 讀作: *The first sentence read: "If I should die before you receive this letter..."* 第一句的內容是:"假如我在你接到此信前離開人世..." | *The name should read 'Benson', not 'Fenton'.* 這個名字是 Benson, 而不是 Fenton。| **read well/awkwardly etc** (=be easy or difficult to read and understand) 易懂/難懂 *The report reads well, but it doesn't cover the most important points.* 報告雖然易懂, 但並未談到最重要的問題。

7 read sth as sth/for sth read sth used to tell someone to replace a wrong number or word with the correct one 換用, 改作〔用於訂正訛誤〕: *Please read £50 as £15.* 請把 50 英鎊改為 15 英鎊。| *For 'November'* (=instead of November) *on line 6, read 'September'.* 第六行的 November 應作 September。

8 ▶MEASURING 度量◀ [T] **a)** to look at the number or amount shown on a measuring instrument 讀〔度量儀器顯示的數字〕: *Read the meter and tell me how much electricity we've used.* 請查看一下電表, 然後告訴我, 我們用了多少電。**b)** if a measuring instrument reads a particular number, it shows that number〔度量儀器〕顯示, 指示: *The thermometer read 46 degrees.* 溫度計顯示 46 度。

9 ▶AT UNIVERSITY 上大學◀ [T] *BrE* to study a subject at a university【英】攻讀, 唸〔某課程〕: *I read history at Cambridge.* 我在劍橋大學攻讀歷史。

10 take it as read (that) a) *especially BrE* to feel certain that something is true without having proof; ASSUME【尤英】可以認為是正確的, 假定: *You can take it as read that the press will support our opponents.* 你可以假定新聞界會支持我們的對手。**b)** to accept a report, statement etc as correct and complete without reading or hearing it 沒看見[聽見]就視...為正確和全面的: *We'll have to take the secretary's report as read.* 我們得認為祕書的報告不會有錯。

11 read between the lines to guess someone's real feelings from something they say or write 看出字裡行間的意思; 聽出真實意思: *Reading between the lines, I'd say Robert's got a lot of problems.* 聽言外之意, 我看羅伯特遇上了許多麻煩。

12 read sb's mind/thoughts to guess what someone else is thinking 猜測某人的心思: *As if he had read her mind, he stood up and offered her his seat.* 他彷彿猜透了她的心思, 站起身來把座位讓給她。

13 read sb like a book to know someone so well that you immediately know what they are thinking or feeling 把某人琢磨透, 對某人瞭如指掌

14 read sb's palm to look carefully at someone's hand, in order to find out about their future 為...看手相: *Have you ever had your palm read?* 你請人看過手相嗎?

15 read sb's lips to understand what someone is saying by watching the way their lips move 唇讀, 觀唇辨意 —see also 另見 LIP-READ

16 ▶COMPUTER 電腦◀ [T] *technical* if the DISK DRIVE of a computer reads information from a disk, it takes the information and puts it into the computer's memory【術語】讀取〔軟盤中的信息並放入電腦的記憶器〕

17 do you read me? *spoken* used to ask someone whether they fully understand what you are saying【口】明白嗎?: *I do not want this to happen again! Do you read me?* 我不希望再發生這種事! 明白嗎?

18 well-read/widely-read having read a lot of books and gained a lot of knowledge 博覽羣書的, 博學的: *She is an intelligent, well-read human being.* 她是個聰明、博學的人。

19 widely-read/little-read etc read by a lot of people, few people etc 讀者眾多的/不多的: *Jon Naughton's widely-read column in the Observer* 喬恩·諾頓在《觀察家報》上讀者眾多的專欄 —see also 另見 READING, **read (sb) the riot act** (RIOT[1] (4))

read for sth *phr v* [T] **1** *BrE old-fashioned* to study a subject in order to get a university degree【英, 過時】攻讀〔學位〕: *She's reading for a degree in physics.* 她正在攻讀物理學學位。**2** to perform the part of a particular character from a play, as a test of your ability to act in the play; AUDITION[2] 試演

read sth **into** sth *phr v* [T] to think that a situation, action etc has a meaning or importance that it does not really have〔錯誤地〕認為〔某事〕含有某種意思: *It was only a casual remark. I think you're reading too much into it.* 那不過是隨便說說。我覺得你多心了。

read sth ↔ **out** *phr v* [T] to say the words that are written in a message, list etc, so that people can hear 朗讀, 宣讀: *He opened the envelope and read out the name of the winner.* 他打開信封, 宣讀獲勝者的姓名。

read sth ↔ **through/over** *phr v* [T] to read something carefully from beginning to end in order to check details or find mistakes 通讀, 從頭到尾細讀: *Read the contract over carefully before you sign it.* 仔細讀合同之後再簽字。

read sth ↔ **up** also 又作 **read up on** sth *phr v* [T] *informal* to read a lot about something because you will need to know about it【非正式】攻讀, 對...作大量閱讀: *I'll have to read up on the tax laws before the meeting tomorrow.* 在參加明天的會議之前, 我必須好好地研究一下稅法。

read² *n* [singular] **1** *BrE informal* an act of reading something, or time spent doing this【英, 非正式】閱讀; 閱讀時間: *have a nice quiet read* 安靜地看一會兒書 **2 a good read** something that you enjoy reading 喜歡的讀物: *It's not great literature, but it's a good read.* 這不是文學巨著, 但讀起來引人入勝。

rea·da·ble /ˈridəbḷ; ˈriːdəbəl/ *adj* **1** interesting or en-

R

joyable to read, and easy to understand 讀起來有趣的, 易懂的: *a very readable account of their research into genetics* 有關他們對遺傳學研究的非常有趣的敍述 **2** writing or print that is readable is clear and easy to read; LEGIBLE〔文章、印刷物〕清晰的, 易讀的 —**readibility** /ˌridəˋbɪlətɪ; ˌriːdəˈbɪlɪ̣ti/ *n* [U] —opposite 反義詞 UNREADABLE —see also 另見 MACHINE-READABLE

re·ad·dress /ˌriəˋdrɛs; ˌriːəˈdres/ *v* [T] *BrE* to FORWARD[3] (1)【英】轉寄

3 2 **read·er** /ˋridɚ; ˈriːdə/ *n* [C] **1** someone who reads a particular book, newspaper etc 讀者: *At this point in the novel, the reader still does not know the hero's true identity.* 小說讀到這裡, 讀者依然不知道主人公的真實身分。| *a Guardian reader*《衛報》的一名讀者 **2** someone who reads a lot, or reads in a particular way 讀書人; 以某種方式閱讀的人: *an avid reader* 廢寢忘食的讀者 | *Susan isn't much of a reader* (=does not read a lot). 蘇珊不太愛讀書。| **a fast/slow reader** *I'm not a very fast reader, but I do like novels.* 我閱讀的速度不快, 但我真的喜歡小說。**3** an easy book to help children learn to read, to help people learn a foreign language etc (初級)讀本, (初級)讀物 **4 Reader** a teacher in a British university who has the rank just below PROFESSOR〔英國大學的〕教授〔僅次於講座教授級〕*Reader in Sociology at Bristol* 布里斯托爾大學社會學教授 —see also 另見 MIND READER —see 見 PROFESSOR (USAGE)

R

read·er·ship /ˋridɚʃɪp; ˈriːdəʃɪp/ *n* [C,U] **1** the people who read a particular newspaper or magazine〔某報紙、雜誌的〕全體讀者: *The magazine has a readership of 60,000.* 這份雜誌擁有六萬名讀者。**2** the job that a Reader has in a British university〔英國大學的〕教授職位: *a readership in linguistics* 語言學教授職位

3 **read·i·ly** /ˋrɛdɪlɪ; ˈredɪ̣li/ *adv* **1** quickly and easily 迅速地, 容易地: *Computers make data readily available to users.* 電腦使用戶得以很容易地查到數據。**2** quickly, willingly, and without complaining 迅速地, 願意地, 心甘情願地: *He readily obeyed.* 他很樂意地服從了。

read·i·ness /ˋrɛdɪnɪs; ˈredinɪ̣s/ *n* **1** [U] a state of being prepared and ready for what is going to happen 準備就緒: **in readiness (for)** *They stacked the firewood in readiness for the evening campfire.* 他們堆起了木柴, 準備傍晚生營火。**2** [singular,U] willingness to do something 願意: **readiness to do sth** *the UN's readiness to intervene in the civil war* 聯合國願意干預這場內戰

2 **read·ing** /ˋridɪŋ; ˈriːdɪŋ/ *n*

1 ►THE ACTIVITY/SKILL 活動/技能◄ [U] the activity of understanding written words 讀, 閱讀: *Children are taught reading and writing in their first years at school.* 孩子們在上學的最初幾年裡學習閱讀和書寫。

2 ►UNDERSTANDING 理解◄ [C] your opinion of what a particular statement, situation, event etc means; INTERPRETATION 理解, 解釋: *What's your reading of this response?* 你怎麼看這樣的回應?

3 ►BOOKS 書籍◄ [U] the books, articles etc that you read 讀物: *Her main reading seems to be mystery novels.* 她主要閱讀的書似乎是懸疑小說。| **light reading** (=books that are easy and enjoyable) 輕鬆讀物

4 ►TO A GROUP 對一羣人◄ [C] **a)** an occasion when a piece of literature is read to a group of people 文學作品朗誦會: *a poetry reading* 詩歌朗誦會 **b)** a piece of literature or part of the Bible that is read to a group of people〔文學作品、《聖經》章節的〕朗讀內容: *The first reading is from Corinthians I, Chapter 3.* 朗讀的第一篇選自《聖經·新約·科林多書》前書第三章。

5 ►MEASUREMENT 度量◄ [C] a number or amount shown on a measuring instrument〔度量儀器上的〕讀數: **take a reading** *Thermometer readings were taken every two hours.* 每兩個小時記錄一遍溫度計的讀數。

6 ►THE ACT OF READING STH 閱讀◄ [singular] the act of reading something 讀, 閱讀: *Even a casual reading of the text gives you an idea of the theme.* 即使是隨意讀一下文本也會使你對主題有所了解。

7 ►IN PARLIAMENT 在議會中◄ [C] one of the three occasions in the British Parliament or the US Congress, when a BILL (=suggested new law) is read and discussed〔英國議會或美國國會〕宣讀議案, 一項議案三讀過程中的任何一讀: *the second reading of the Industrial Relations Bill*《勞資關係議案》的二讀

8 make good/interesting/boring etc reading to be enjoyable, interesting etc to read 讀起來有趣/乏味等: *Your report made fascinating reading.* 你的報告讀起來很吸引人。

re·ad·just /ˌriəˋdʒʌst; ˌriːəˈdʒʌst/ *v* **1** [I] to get used to a new situation, job or way of life 適應: **[+to]** *Soldiers struggled to readjust to life outside the army.* 士兵們努力適應部隊以外的生活。**2** [T] to make a small change to something or to its position 調整: *The unemployment figures need to be readjusted to allow for people on training programmes.* 失業數字需要調整, 以便把參加培訓項目的人考慮進去。—**readjustment** *n* [C,U]

read-only mem·o·ry /ˌ· ·· ˈ···/ *n* [C,U] ROM 只讀存儲器

read-out /ˈ· ·/ *n* [C] a record of information that has been produced by a computer, shown on a SCREEN or in print〔電腦屏幕上顯示或打印出的〕信息讀出: *This program gives you a read-out of all the areas where sales have increased.* 這種程序能使你得到銷售額增長地區的信息。—compare 比較 PRINTOUT

read·y[1] /ˋrɛdɪ; ˈredi/ *adj*

1 ►PREPARED 有準備的◄ [not before noun 不用於名詞前] prepared for what you are going to do 準備好的, 有準備的: *Come on. Aren't you ready yet?* 快來——你還沒準備好嗎? | **ready to do sth** *Everything's packed, and we're ready to leave.* 所有的東西都裝好了, 我們準備動身。| **[+for]** *I don't want to take the test yet; I'm not ready for it.* 我現在還不想考試, 我還沒有準備好。| **get ready** *I need about half an hour to get ready, so I'll see you at six.* 我需要大約半小時做準備, 那我就在6點見你吧。| **make ready** *formal* (=prepare to start doing something)【正式】做好準備 | **ready for anything** *I felt strong, fit, and ready for anything.* 我覺得精力充沛, 身體健康, 幹甚麼都行。| **ready and waiting** *When the right opportunity came, she was ready and waiting.* 當合適的機會到來時, 她已準備就緒。| **ready for (the) off** *spoken* (=ready to go somewhere)【口】準備動身: *Right, I'm ready for the off.* 對, 我馬上可以動身。| **when you're ready** *spoken* (=used to tell someone that you are ready for them to start doing something)【口】當你一切就緒的時候〔告訴對方已經準備好, 等他開始做某事〕| **ready when you are** *spoken* (=used to tell someone that you are ready to do what you have arranged to do together)【口】當你一切就緒的時候〔告訴對方自己隨時可以做安排了一起做的事〕| **ready to roll** *spoken* (=ready to start an activity, journey etc)【口】準備動手, 準備動身 —see graph at 參見 PREPARE 圖表

2 ►FOR IMMEDIATE USE 可立即使用◄ [not before noun 不用於名詞前] something that is ready can be used or eaten immediately 現成的;〔食物〕已做好的: *When will supper be ready?* 晚飯何時做好? | *The peaches are ripe and ready to eat.* 桃子熟了, 可以吃了。| **[+for]** *Is everything ready for the exhibition?* 展覽會一切就緒了嗎? | **get sth ready** *We must get the house ready for the new tenants.* 我們必須給新房客把房子準備好。| **have sth ready** *Next time, I had my answer ready.* 下一次, 我把我的答案準備好。| **ready cooked/mixed etc** (=already cooked or mixed, and ready to be eaten or used) 已做好/配好等

3 be ready for a drink/meal/holiday etc *spoken* to need or want a drink, meal etc as soon as possible【口】想喝飲料/吃飯/度假等: *You must be ready for a drink after all that hard work.* 幹了那麼費力的工作, 你一定想喝點甚麼。

4 be ready to cry/drop etc *informal* to be so upset or tired that you feel you will cry, fall down etc【非正式】

〔心煩意亂, 疲憊得〕想哭/快要癱倒等: *By the end of that walk, we were ready to drop.* 步行完時, 我們都累得要倒下來。

5 ▶WILLING 願意的◀ willing and quick to do or give something 願意〔做某事〕的; 樂意〔給某物〕的: **[+with]** *She's always ready with an excuse.* 她總能找到藉口。| **ready to do sth** *You're too ready to criticize.* 你太愛批評人了。| *They were wonderful neighbours – always ready to help in a crisis.* 他們真是好鄰居, 關鍵時刻總樂意幫忙。

6 ▶QUICK 快的◀ [only before noun 僅用於名詞前] quick or without delay 快的, 迅速的: *a ready answer* 脫口而出的回答 | *This system gives readier access to the data.* 這種系統能更迅速地提取數據。| **a ready wit** (=the ability to think quickly of clever, amusing things to say) 機智

7 ready money/cash money that can be spent at once in coins or notes 現金: *He was only willing to sell it for ready cash.* 他只收現錢才賣。

8 ready, steady, go! *BrE spoken* used to tell people to start a race【英口】各就各位, 預備, 跑!〔用於賽跑發令時〕—see also 另見 READILY, READINESS, **rough and ready** (ROUGH[1] (13))

ready[2] *n* **1 at the ready** *especially BrE* available to be used immediately【尤英】處於準備好的狀態, 可隨時使用: *The crowd stood around, cameras at the ready.* 人羣站在四周, 照相機隨時準備拍照。**2 the readies** *BrE slang* money that is available to be used immediately【英俚】現錢: *I'm trying to scrape together the readies to pay for a trip to Hong Kong.* 我正在努力攢現錢支付去香港旅行的費用。

ready[3] *v* [T] *formal* to make something ready【正式】預備, 準備

ready-made /ˌ·· ˈ··◂/ *adj* [only before noun 僅用於名詞前] **1** already prepared, and ready to be used immediately 現成的, 預先做好的: *ready-made bolognese sauce* 調製好的博洛尼亞調味汁 **2** convenient and immediately available for you to use 方便的, 現成的: *The rain gave us a ready-made excuse to stay at home.* 這場雨給了我們一個呆在家裡的現成藉口。**3** ready-made opinions or ideas have been copied from someone else〔觀點、思想〕老一套的, 照搬他人的 **4** READY-TO-WEAR〔衣服〕現成的

ready-to-wear /ˌ·· ·ˈ·◂/ *adj old-fashioned* ready-to-wear clothes are made in standard sizes, not made specially to fit one person【過時】〔衣服〕現成的, 預先做好的

re·af·firm /ˌriəˋfɝm; ˌriːəˈfɜːm/ *v* [T] to formally state an intention, belief etc again, especially as an answer to a question or doubt 重申, 再次肯定: *The conference overwhelmingly reaffirmed its commitment to nuclear disarmament.* 會議以壓倒多數重申它對裁減核武器所承擔的義務。| **[+that]** *The statement reaffirmed that the government would never make concessions to terrorists.* 該聲明重申, 政府決不向恐怖分子讓步。—**reaffirmation** /ˌriæfɚˋmeʃən; ˌriːæfəˈmeɪʃən/ *n* [C,U]

re·af·for·es·ta·tion /ˌriəfɔrəsˋteʃən; ˌriːəfɒrɪˈsteɪʃən/ *n* [U] *BrE technical* REFORESTATION【英, 術語】重新造林

re·a·gent /riˋedʒənt; riˈeɪdʒənt/ *n* [C] *technical* a substance that shows that another substance in a compound exists, by causing a chemical REACTION (4a)【術語】試劑, 試藥

1 1 **real**[1] /ˋriəl; rɪəl/ *adj*

1 ▶NOT ARTIFICIAL 非人造的◀ something that is real is actually what it seems to be and not false, artificial or pretended 真的, 真正的, 真實的: *Is that ring made of real gold?* 那枚戒指是真金的嗎? | *He calls himself Peter Jones, but it's not his real name.* 他說自己叫彼得·瓊斯, 但那不是他的真實姓名。| *He's never shown any real regret.* 他從未表示出真心的歉意。| **the real thing/the real McCoy** *I don't like reproductions. It has to be the real thing or nothing.* 我不喜歡複製品。要就要真貨。| *This is the real McCoy – genuine malt whisky.* 這是貨真價實的東西——純正的麥芽威士忌。

2 ▶NOT IMAGINARY 非幻想的◀ actually existing and not just imagined 實際存在的, 非想像的: *The children know that Santa Claus isn't a real person.* 孩子們知道聖誕老人不是真實的人物。| **very real danger/possibility/risk etc** *There is a very real danger of an explosion.* 確實存在着發生爆炸的危險。| **in real life** *That kind of thing only happens in films, not in real life.* 那種事只發生在電影裡, 而不是現實生活中。| **in the real world** (=in actual situations where people have to deal with practical problems) 在現實世界裡 *idealistic theories that don't work in the real world* 在現實世界裡行不通的理想主義理論

3 ▶TRUE 真的◀ actual and true, not what people think or say 真正的, 真實的: *John later told me the real reason for his absence.* 約翰後來告訴我他缺席的真正原因。

4 ▶PROPER 適當的◀ [only before noun 僅用於名詞前] having all the right qualities that you expect a particular kind of thing or person to have 真正的, 地道的: *Now he's what I'd call a real man.* 他就是我所說的真正的人。| *The next day we had our first real meeting.* 第二天我們開了第一次真正的會議。

5 a real idiot/beauty/disaster etc *spoken* used to emphasize how stupid, beautiful, terrible etc someone or something is【口】十足的傻瓜/絕色美女/巨大的災難等〔用於加強語氣〕: *You're a real idiot!* 你是個十足的傻瓜! | *Our marriage was a real disaster!* 我們的婚姻真是一場災難! | *Thanks – you've been a real help.* 謝謝, 你幫了我大忙。

6 no real chance/hope/reason etc if there is no real chance etc, there is almost no chance 幾乎沒有機會/希望/理由等: *There's no real hope of Rod passing this examination.* 羅德通過這次考試的希望渺茫。

7 ▶MOST IMPORTANT 最重要的◀ the real questions, problems etc are the most important ones 最重要的: *The government has failed to deal with the real issues.* 政府沒能解決最重要的問題。

8 real income/costs/value etc income etc that is calculated after including in the calculation the general decrease in the value of money〔已把貨幣貶值計算在內的〕實際收入/成本/價值等: *a 2% annual growth in real income* 實際收入年增長兩個百分點 | **in real terms** (=calculated in this way) 按照實際價值 *In real terms, the value of their wages has fallen.* 他們工資的實際價值減少了。

9 for real *spoken, especially AmE* seriously, not pretending【口, 尤美】真正地, 確實地, 認真地: *After two trial runs we did it for real.* 經過兩次試驗, 我們真正地幹了起來。

10 get real! *spoken, especially AmE* used to tell someone that they are being very silly or unreasonable【口, 尤美】別傻了! 別犯渾了!

11 are you for real? *AmE spoken* used when you are very surprised by or disapprove of what someone has done or said【美口】你是認真的?〔表示吃驚或不贊同〕

real[2] *adv AmE spoken* very【美口】非常: *I'm real sorry!* 我非常抱歉! | *He's real smart.* 他非常精明。

real es·tate /ˈ· ·ˌ·/ *n* [U] *especially AmE*【尤美】**1** property in the form of land or houses 房地產, 不動產 **2** the business of selling houses or land 房地產業

real estate a·gent /ˈ· ·· ˌ··/ *n* [C] *AmE* someone whose job is to sell houses or land for other people; ESTATE AGENT【美】房地產經紀人

re·a·lign /ˌriəˋlaɪn; ˌriːəˈlaɪn/ *v* [T] **1** to arrange something differently in relation to something else 重新排列: *You'll have to realign your text columns if you change the typeface.* 你如果要改動字體, 就必須重新排列正文各欄。**2** to change the aims and relationships that a political party or other organization has 重新組合, 調整〔政黨或其他組織的目標和關係等〕: *an attempt to realign the relationship between the state and private business* 調整國家與私營企業之間關係的嘗試

re·a·lign·ment /ˌriəˋlaɪnmənt; ˌriːəˈlaɪnmənt/ *n* [C,U] **1** a change in the way two or more things are organized, so that they have a different relationship to each other 重新組合: **[+of]** *a realignment of political parties* 政治黨派之間的重新組合 **2** the process of arranging parts of something so that they return to their correct positions in relation to each other 復位: *the realignment of broken bones* 斷骨的復位

re·al·is·m /ˈriəlˌɪzəm; ˈrɪəlɪzəm/ *n* [U] **1** the ability to accept and deal with situations in a practical way, without being influenced by feelings or false ideas 現實主義 **2** also 又作 **Realism** the style of art and literature in which everything is shown or described as it really is in life 現實主義, 寫實主義〔藝術、文學上的風格〕— **realist** *n* [C]

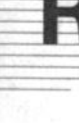 3 **re·al·is·tic** /ˌriəˈlɪstɪk; rɪəˈlɪstɪk/ *adj* **1** judging and dealing with situations in a practical way according to what is actually possible 現實的, 實際的: *It's just not realistic to expect a promotion so soon.* 這麼快就想升職根本不現實。| *a realistic estimate of the costs* 對費用的現實估計 | **be realistic** (=think in a sensible, practical way) 持現實的態度 *Come on, be realistic – you can't just afford it!* 得啦! 現實點, 你根本花費不起! —opposite 反義詞 UNREALISTIC **2** pictures, models, plays etc that are realistic show things as they are in real life〔圖畫、模型、戲劇等〕逼真的, 栩栩如生的: *Her drawings aren't very realistic.* 她的畫不太逼真。| *a realistic television drama* 一部寫實的電視劇

R

re·al·is·tic·al·ly /ˌriəˈlɪstɪklɪ; rɪəˈlɪstɪkli/ *adv* **1** in a practical way and according to what is actually possible 現實地, 實際地: *You have to look realistically at the options available.* 你必須現實地對待現有的選擇。| [sentence adverb 句子副詞] *Realistically, we can't expect things to improve before the end of next year.* 說實在的, 我們不能指望情況在明年年底之前有改善。**2** in a way that shows or describes things as they are in real life 逼真地, 栩栩如生地: *She told the ghost story so realistically that they were terrified.* 她把鬼故事講得活靈活現, 他們都感到害怕。

2 2 **re·al·i·ty** /rɪˈælətɪ; riˈæləti/ *n* **1** [U] things that actually happen or are true, not things that are imagined or thought about 真實, 現實: *She can't tell the difference between fantasy and reality.* 她無法區分幻想與現實。| *Books can be an escape from reality.* 讀書可以逃避現實。**2 in reality** used to say something is different from what people think 實際上: *Henry always seems so self-confident, but in reality he's extremely shy.* 亨利看來總是很自信, 實際上他極為腼腆。**3 become a reality** to actually happen 成為現實: *Marilyn's dream of being a film star became a reality.* 瑪麗蓮想當電影明星的夢想成為了現實。**4 the reality/realities of** what actually happens in a situation, rather than what you think might happen 實際情況: *They were unprepared for the reality of city life.* 他們對城市生活的現實情況毫無準備。| **harsh realities** *the harsh realities of unemployment* 失業的嚴酷現實 **5 the reality is that** used to say that the truth about a situation is very different from what people say 實際情況是…: *They keep saying we'll get the money, but the reality is that there's none left.* 他們再三說我們會得到錢的, 但實際情況是沒有錢剩下來。

re·a·liz·a·ble also 又作 **realisable** *BrE*【英】/ˈriəˌlaɪzəbl; ˈrɪəlaɪzəbəl/ *adj* **1** possible to achieve 可實現的: *realizable goals* 可實現的目標 **2** in a form that can be changed into money 可換為現款的: *realizable value* 可變現價值

re·a·li·za·tion also 又作 **realisation** *BrE*【英】/ˌriələˈzeʃən; ˌrɪəlaɪˈzeɪʃən/ *n* [singular,U] **1** the act of understanding something that you had not noticed before 認識, 領悟, 意識: **[+that]** *the realization that changes were needed in the organization* 對組織需要有改變的認識 **2** the act of achieving what you had planned, hoped, or aimed for〔計劃、希望、目標的〕實現: **[+of]** *the realization of happiness* 幸福的實現 **3 [+of]** the act of changing something into money by selling it 變賣, 變現

 **re·a·lize** also 又作 **-ise** *BrE*【英】/ˈriəˌlaɪz; ˈrɪəlaɪz/ *v* [T not usually in progressive 一般不用進行式]

1 ▶KNOW STH'S IMPORTANCE 知道某事物的重要性◀ to know and understand the importance of something 知道, 了解, 認識到〔某事物的重要性〕: **realize (that)** *Do you realize that you're an hour late?* 你知道你遲到了一小時嗎? | **realize who/what/how etc** *I realize how much she means to you.* 我知道她對你有多麼重要。| **realize sth** *None of us realized the danger we were in.* 我們當中誰也沒有意識到我們所處的險境。

2 ▶KNOW STH NEW 認識新事物◀ to start to know something that you had not noticed before 開始認識, 領悟, 意識到〔以前沒有注意的事物〕: **realize (that)** *I suddenly realized he was crying.* 我突然發現他在哭。| *Later, we realized that we'd met before in Paris.* 我們後來才想起我們曾在巴黎見過面。| **realize who/what/how etc** *I realized then how hungry I was.* 那時我才意識到我有多麼餓。| **realize sth** *Tim didn't realize his mistake until the next day.* 蒂姆直到第二天才知道他的錯誤。

3 realize an ambition/hope/goal etc *formal* to achieve something that you were hoping to achieve【正式】實現抱負/願望/目標等: *She has finally realized her ambition of becoming a teacher.* 她終於實現了當教師的抱負。

4 sb's worst fears were realized used to say that the thing that you were afraid of actually happened 某人最害怕的事情發生了: *My worst fears were realized when I saw the exam questions.* 我一看到考題, 就知道我最害怕的事情發生了。

5 ▶MONEY 金錢◀ a) to obtain an amount of money, especially by selling something〔通過出售而〕獲得: *The initial campaign has realized $5000 in cash and pledges.* 初次活動就籌到了5000美元, 包括現金和承諾捐款。| **realize a profit on sth** *We realized a profit on the house.* 我們賣房子賺了一筆錢。**b)** to change something that you own into money, especially by selling it 變賣: *We were obliged to realize most of our assets.* 我們不得不變賣我們的大部分資產。

 **real·ly** /ˈriəlɪ; ˈrɪəli/ *adv*

1 ▶THE REAL SITUATION 真實情形◀ used when you are saying what is actually the truth of a situation, rather than what people might wrongly think 真實地, 真正地: *What really happened?* 究竟發生了甚麼事? | *Oliver was not really her cousin.* 奧利弗其實不是她的表兄弟。| *You are pretending to be annoyed, but you're not really.* 你在裝出生氣的樣子, 其實你並不生氣。

2 ▶DEFINITELY 確實地◀ *especially spoken* used to emphasize something you are saying【尤口】確實地, 的確〔用於加強語氣〕: *You ought really to have asked me first.* 你真該事先問問我的。| *I really don't mind.* 我真的不介意。| *I'm absolutely fine, Dad – really.* 我絕對沒事, 爸爸, 真的。

3 ▶VERY MUCH 非常◀ very much; extremely 非常, 極其: *really nice* 非常好 | *His letter really irritated her.* 他的信着實激怒了她。| *It doesn't really matter, does it?* 這不太要緊, 對不對?

Frequencies of the adverb **really** in spoken and written English 副詞really在英語口語和書面語中的使用頻率

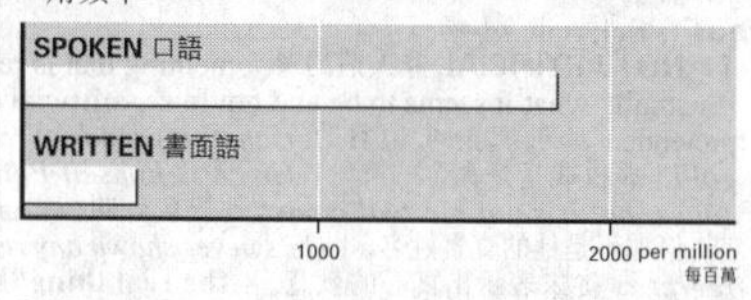

Based on the British National Corpus and the Longman Lancaster Corpus
據英國國家語料庫和朗文蘭卡斯特語料庫

This graph shows that the adverb **really** is much more common in spoken English than in written English.

This is because it is used a lot in spoken English to emphasize what you are saying. It also has some special uses as a reply in conversation and is used in some common spoken phrases. 本圖表顯示, 副詞really在英語口語中的使用頻率遠遠高於書面語, 因為口語中經常用它來強調所説的話。really 還有一些特殊的用法, 在對話中用於回答對方所説的話, 而且口語中一些常用片語是由really 構成的。

really (*adv*) SPOKEN PHRASES
含 really 的口語片語

4 really? a) used to show that you are surprised by what someone has said 是嗎? 真的?〔用於對某人的話表示吃驚〕: *"There are something like 87 McDonalds in Hong Kong." "Really?"* "香港有大約 87 家麥當勞快餐店。" "是嗎?" **b)** used in conversation to show that you are listening to or interested in what the other person is saying 真的?〔表示正在傾聽或對對方的話感興趣〕: *"I think we might go to the Grand Canyon in June." "Oh, really?"* "我看我們可以在六月份去大峽谷。" "噢, 真的嗎?" **c)** *AmE* used to express agreement【美】是啊〔表示贊同〕: *"It's a pain having to get here so early." "Yeah, really!"* "必須這麼早就到這裡可真讓人痛苦。" "可不是嗎!" **d)** *especially BrE* used to express disapproval【尤英】真是的〔表示不贊成〕: *Really, Larry, you might have told me!* 真的, 拉里, 你怎麼不早告訴我呀!
5 not really used to say 'no' or 'not completely' 不是; 不全是: *"Do you want to come along?" "Not really."* "你想一起去嗎?" "不太想。"
6 I don't really know used to say that you are not certain about something 我不太清楚〔表示沒有把握〕: *I don't really know what he's up to. I haven't heard from him for ages.* 我不太清楚他在幹甚麼。我已經好久沒聽到他的消息了。
7 I really don't know used to say that you definitely do not know something, especially when someone has asked you about it 我確實不知道: *I can't answer that, I really don't know.* 我無法回答這個問題, 我真的不知道。
8 really and truly used to emphasize a statement or opinion 真的〔用於加強語氣〕: *Really and truly, I think you should tell him.* 真的, 我認為你應該告訴他。

USAGE NOTE 用法説明: REALLY
UK-US DIFFERENCE 英國英語—美國英語的區別
Really with an adjective or adverb meaning 'very' is common in British English, and is the usual word in American English. 在英國英語中, 用 really 修飾形容詞或副詞, 意為 "非常" 是很普通的, 在美國英語中則是最常用的詞: *I'm really fed up with this job.* 我對這份工作厭倦透了。
In informal spoken American English **real** is often used. 在非正式美國口語中常用 real: *That's a real nice car.* 那是一輛很棒的汽車。
GRAMMAR 語法
Really meaning 'very' must go immediately before the adjective it strengthens. really 指 "非常" 時, 一定要緊接在所強調的形容詞前面: *He's a really nice man* (=a very nice man). 他是一個非常好的人。| *I think she's really stupid.* 我覺得她非常愚蠢。
Really in other positions usually emphasises that what you are saying is true even though it might not seem to fit. really 在其他位置時強調所説是事實, 儘管表面上不一定對: *He's really a nice man* (=he is nice, though you might not think so). 他的確是個好人。| *She uses lots of long words, but really she's pretty stupid.* 她愛用許多大字眼, 其實她非常愚蠢。
Really is usually used before a verb but not immediately after it (except after the verb **to be**). really 通常用在動詞前面而不是緊接其後 (除動詞 to be 外): *It's really cold in here.* 這裡面的確很冷。| *She doesn't really know what to do.* 她不清楚該做些甚麼。
SPELLING 拼法
Remember there are two 'l's in **really**. 記住 really 有兩個 l。

realm /rɛlm; relm/ *n* [C] **1** a general area of knowledge, interest, or thought〔知識、興趣、思想的〕領域, 範圍: *the spiritual realm* 精神領域 | [+of] *the realm of human history* 人類歷史範疇 **2 within the realms of possibility** possible 可能的: *Such a thing is not within the realms of possibility.* 這種事是不可能的。**3** *literary* a country ruled over by a king or queen【文】王國 **4 the Realm** *formal* the United Kingdom【正式】聯合王國: *the defence of the Realm* 聯合王國的防務
re·al·pol·i·tik /re`ɑl,polɪ,tik; reɪ'ɑːlpɒlɪtiːk/ *n* [U] politics based on practical situations and needs rather than on moral principles or ideas 現實政治〔基於現實情況和需要而不是道德原則或思想的政治〕
real prop·er·ty /,· '···/ *n* [U] *law* REAL ESTATE (1)【法律】房地產, 不動產
real-time /'· ·/ *adj* [only before noun 僅用於名詞前] *technical* a real-time computer system deals with information as fast as it receives it【術語】〔電腦〕即時處理的, 實時的 —**real time** *n* [U]: *Airline booking systems need to work in real time.* 航空公司的訂票系統需要實時工作。
real·tor /'rɪəltɚ; 'rɪəltə/ *n* [C] *AmE* a REAL ESTATE AGENT【美】房地產經紀人
ream[1] /rim; riːm/ *n* [C] **1 reams** [plural] *informal* a large amount of writing on paper【非正式】〔寫作的〕大量: [+of] *reams of notes* 大量的筆記 **2** *AmE* 500 pieces of paper【美】令〔紙張的計數單位, 在美國為 500 張〕**3** *BrE* 480 pieces of paper【英】令〔紙張的計數單位, 在英國為 480 張〕
ream[2] *v* [T] **1** *AmE informal* to treat someone badly, especially by cheating【美, 非正式】〔尤指通過欺騙而〕虧待; 欺詐 **2** *technical* to make a hole larger【術語】把〔孔〕擴大
re·an·i·mate /ri`ænə,met; riː'ænɪ̈meɪt/ *v* [T] *formal* to give someone or something new strength or the energy to start again【正式】重振, 使重新獲得力量
reap /rip; riːp/ *v* [I,T] **1** to cut and gather a crop of grain 收割 **2 reap the benefit/reward/profit (of)** to get something good as a result of what you have done 受益/得到回報/獲利: *Don't let others reap the benefits of your research.* 不要讓別人坐享你的研究成果。—**reaper** *n* [C] —compare 比較 HARVEST[2]
re·ap·pear /,riə`pɪr; ,riːə'pɪə/ *v* [I] to appear again after not being seen for some time 再現, 再出現: *They felt tense, knowing that he might reappear at any time.* 他們感到緊張, 因為知道他隨時可能再次出現。—**reappearance** *n* [C,U]
re·ap·praise /,riə`prez; ,riːə'preɪz/ *v* [T] to examine something again in order to consider whether you should change your opinion of it 重新估計, 重新評價: *The time had come to reappraise their economic strategy.* 應該重新評價他們的經濟策略了。—**reappraisal** *n* [C,U]
rear[1] /rɪr; rɪə/ *n* **1 the rear** the back part of an object, vehicle or building, or a position at the back of an object or area 後部, 後面, 背部: *a garden at the rear of the house* 屋後的花園 | *The engine is in the rear.* 發動機在後邊。—compare 比較 FRONT[1] (2) **2** [C] *informal* the part of your body which you sit on; BOTTOM[1] (7)【非正式】臀部 **3 bring up the rear** to be at the back of a line of people or in a race 殿後: *Bringing up the rear is the smallest yacht in the race.* 最後到終點的是本次比賽中最小的快艇。

R

rear² *v* **1** [T] to look after a person or animal until they are fully grown 養育, 撫養; 飼養: *She's reared a large family.* 她撫養一大羣孩子。| *cattle rearing* 養牛 —see 見 RAISE¹ (USAGE) **2** also 又作 **rear up** [I] if an animal rears, it rises upright on its back legs〔動物〕用後腿站起: *The horse reared and threw me off.* 那匹馬用後腿直立起來, 把我摔了下來。—compare 比較 BUCK² (1) **3 be reared on** to be given a particular kind of food, books, entertainment etc regularly while you are a child〔小時候〕總是吃〔某種食物〕; 看〔某類書〕; 玩〔某類遊戲〕: *reared on a diet of potatoes* 吃馬鈴薯長大的 **4 rear its ugly head** if a problem or difficult situation rears its ugly head, it appears and is impossible to ignore〔問題、困境〕冒頭, 出現: *Scandal rears its ugly head again.* 醜聞再次冒出來了。

rear³ *adj* [only before noun 僅用於名詞前] at or near the back of something 後部的, 後面的: *the rear door of the car* 汽車的後門 | *knock at the rear entrance* 敲後門

rear ad·mi·ral /ˌ· ˈ···◂/ *n* [C] a high rank in the navy 海軍少將 —see table on page C6 參見 C6 頁附錄

rear·guard /ˈrɪrˌgɑrd; ˈrɪəgɑːd/ *n* **fight a rearguard action a)** to make a determined effort to prevent a change that you think is bad, although it seems too late to stop it 竭盡全力〔防止…〕: *A rearguard action is being fought against the sale of the land for business development.* 正在竭盡全力地反對出售這塊地作商業開發。**b)** if an army fights a rearguard action, it defends itself at the back against an enemy that is chasing it 殿後作戰, 後衛戰鬥〔由後衛部隊阻擊追兵〕

re·arm /riˈɑrm; riːˈɑːm/ *v* [I,T] to obtain weapons again or provide someone else with new weapons 重新武裝: *If we're going to fight we must rearm.* 假如我們要打仗, 必須重新武裝。| **rearm sb with sth** *They rearmed their allies with modern missiles.* 他們用現代化導彈重新裝備了他們的盟國。—**rearmament** *n* [U]

rear·most /ˈrɪrˌmost; ˈrɪəməʊst/ *adj* [only before noun 僅用於名詞前] furthest back; last 最後(面)的: *the rearmost carriage of the train* 火車的最後一節車廂

re·ar·range /ˌriəˈrendʒ; ˌriːəˈreɪndʒ/ *v* [T] **1** to change the position or order of things 重新安排, 重新佈置: *Let's rearrange the furniture and have the desk by the window.* 我們來把家具重新佈置一下, 把書桌靠窗放。**2** to change the time of a meeting etc 重新安排〔會期等〕—**rearrangement** *n* [C,U]

rear·view mir·ror /ˌrɪrvju ˈmɪrɚ; ˌrɪəvjuː ˈmɪrə/ *n* [C] a mirror in a car etc that lets the driver see the area behind〔汽車〕後視鏡 —see picture on page A2 參見 A2 頁圖

rear·ward /ˈrɪrwɚd; ˈrɪəwəd/ *adj* in or towards the back of something 在後面的, 在後部的; 向後面的 —**rearwards** also 又作 **rearward** *adv*

S1 W1 **rea·son¹** /ˈrizn̩; ˈriːzən/ *n*

1 ►CAUSE 原因◄ [C] the cause or explanation for something that has happened or that someone has done 原因, 理由: *The reason I bought one was that it was so cheap.* 我買了一個的原因是價錢很便宜。| **reason (that)** *The only reason I went was that I wanted to meet your friends.* 我去的唯一理由是想見見你的朋友們。| **reason why** *We'd like to know the reason why she didn't accept the job.* 我們希望知道她不接受這份工作的理由是甚麼。| **[+for]** *I can see no reason for their behaviour.* 我不明白他們為何要這樣做。| **give a reason** (=explain) 解釋 *She just left without giving any reason.* 她沒作任何解釋就離開了。| **for personal/health etc reasons** *She wants to change her job for purely personal reasons.* 她想換工作純屬個人原因。| **for reasons of** *The main tower has been closed for reasons of safety.* 主塔由於安全原因已經關閉。| **by reason of** *formal*【正式】*He was found not guilty by reason of insanity.* 他因為精神失常而被判無罪。| **for some reason** *especially spoken* (=for a reason that you do not know or cannot understand)【尤口】由於某種原因 *They've decided to change all our job titles, for some reason.* 由於某種原因, 他們已決定更改我們所有人的職位名稱。| **have your reasons** *spoken* (=have a secret reason for doing something)【口】有自己的理由 *"Why did you tell him?" "Oh, I had my reasons."* "你為甚麼要告訴他?" "噢, 我有我的道理。" | **for reasons best known to yourself** (=for reasons that other people do not understand) 由於別人不知道的原因 *For reasons best known to herself, she's sold the house and left the country.* 她已經賣掉房子離開了這個國家, 沒有人知道原因。—see 見 EXCUSE² (USAGE)

2 ►GOOD OR FAIR REASON 好的或充分的理由◄ [U] a fact that makes it right or fair for someone to do something〔正確或充分的〕理由: **reason to do sth** *I have no reason to believe that Grant's death was not an accident.* 我沒有理由相信格蘭特的死不是意外事故。| *There is no reason to panic.* 沒有理由驚慌失措。| **have every reason to do sth** (=have very good reasons for doing something) 完全有理由做某事 *Under the circumstances we had every reason to be suspicious.* 在這種情況下, 我們有充分的理由表示懷疑。| **be no reason to do sth** *I know I'm late, but that's no reason to shout at me.* 我知道我遲到了, 但也沒理由對我大喊大叫。| **with (good) reason** (=not stupidly or unnecessarily) (完全) 合乎情理 *Natalie was alarmed by the news, and with reason.* 納塔利聽到消息很驚慌, 這是合乎情理的。

3 all the more reason to do sth *spoken* used to say that what has just been mentioned is an additional reason for doing what you have suggested【口】更有理由做某事: *"She's going on holiday soon." "All the more reason to ask her today."* "她就要去度假了。" "那更有理由今天去問她。"

4 ►GOOD JUDGMENT 好的判斷力◄ sensible judgment and understanding 道理: *There's reason in what he says.* 他說的話有道理。| **listen to reason** (=be persuaded by someone's sensible advice) 聽取意見 *We keep telling her why it won't work, but she just won't listen to reason.* 我們一再告訴她這樣做為甚麼不行, 可是她怎麼也不聽勸告。| **see reason** (=accept advice and make a sensible decision) 明白事理; 接受勸告 *They tried to make him see reason.* 他們試圖使他明白道理。

5 within reason within sensible limits 有道理, 合乎情理: *You can go anywhere you want, within reason.* 你可以想去哪裡就去哪裡, 不過要有分寸。

6 go/be beyond all reason to be more than is acceptable or reasonable 不合理: *Their demands go beyond all reason.* 他們的要求太不合理了。

7 ►ABILITY TO THINK 思考能力◄ [U] the ability to think, understand and form judgments that are based on facts 思考能力, 判斷力, 理智: *The power of reason separates us from other animals.* 理性使我們不同於其他的動物。| **lose your reason** *old-fashioned* (=become mentally ill)【過時】失去理智; 患精神病

8 no reason *spoken* used when someone asks you why you are doing something and you do not want to tell them【口】不為甚麼〔用於不想解釋自己為甚麼做某事〕: *"Why d'you want to go that way?" "Oh, no reason."* "你為甚麼想走那條路?" "噢, 不為甚麼。" —see also 另見 **without rhyme or reason** (RHYME¹ (4)), **it stands to reason** (STAND¹ (40))

USAGE NOTE 用法說明: REASON

WORD CHOICE 詞語辨析: **cause, reason, purpose**

A **cause** is anything that produces a result, often not a person. cause 指會產生結果的原因, 一般不用於人: *the causes of inflation* 通貨膨脹的原因 | *the cause of the accident* 事故的原因

A **reason** explains something, often after it has happened or been done. reason 是某件事情的解釋, 往往是它發生以後才提出的理由: *There was no reason for the attack.* 襲擊是沒有道理的。| *There are several reasons why the plan won't work.* 計劃

行不通有幾個理由。| *Give me one good reason.* 給我一個好的理由吧。

A **purpose** is what you hope to achieve by something you do, and is intentional. purpose 是指通過努力想要實現的目標, 是有意識的: *Their purpose is to attract attention to environmental issues.* 他們的目的是引起對環境問題的關注。

GRAMMAR 語法

Reason is often followed by **for**, **that**, or **why**. reason 後面常接 for, that, why: *What's the reason for all this noise?* (NOT 不用 the reason **of** or 或 **to**) 為甚麼這麼吵? | *the reason that/why he left* (NOT 不用 *the reason because/how he left...*) 他離開的原因 It is also possible to leave out **that**. that 也可省略: *the reason he left* 他離開的原因

The nature of a **reason** is usually described in a *that* clause. reason 後一般用 that 引導的從句説明原因: *The reason for the party was that it was Sue's birthday.* 這次聚會的理由是慶祝蘇的生日。In spoken English you may also hear *because* used, though this is considered to be incorrect by many speakers. 英語口語中也有人使用 because, 但不少人認為這種用法有誤: *The reason for the party is because it's Sue's birthday.* 這次聚會的原因是慶祝蘇的生日。

Purpose is often followed by **of** or **in**. purpose 常與 of 或 in 連用: *The purpose of the trip/of my coming is to see the President* (NOT 不用 *the purpose why I'm coming*). 此次旅行/我來的目的是見總統。| *My purpose in coming is to see the President* (NOT 不用 *of/for coming...*). 我來的目的是見總統。

People usually say 人們通常説 *For this reason/purpose...* (NOT 不用 *from/because of this reason..., in/on this purpose* or 或 *for this cause*) 為此原因/目的

reason² *v* **1** [T] to form a particular judgment about a situation after carefully considering the facts 論證, 推斷, 分析: **reason (that)** *We reasoned that the terrorists would not negotiate unless we made some concessions.* 我們推斷, 除非我們作出某些讓步, 否則恐怖分子是不會談判的。**2** [I] to think and make judgments 推理, 判斷, 思考: *the ability to reason* 推理的能力

reason sth **out** *phr v* [T] to find an explanation or solution to a problem, by thinking of all the possibilities〔通過推理〕解釋, 解決: *Let's reason this out instead of quarrelling.* 我們不要爭吵了, 還是想想其中的道理吧。

reason with sb *phr v* [T] to talk to someone in order to try to persuade them to be more sensible 與…講道理: *I tried to reason with her but she locked herself in the bathroom, crying.* 我想和她講講道理, 但她卻把自己鎖在浴室裡哭。

S1 W2 **rea·son·a·ble** /ˈrizn̩əbl̩; ˈriːzənəbəl/ *adj* **1** fair and sensible 講道理的, 合情理的: *Be reasonable – you can't expect her to do all the work on her own!* 要講道理, 你不能指望她一個人幹所有的工作! | *a reasonable request* 合情合理的要求 | **it is reasonable to do sth** *It's reasonable to suppose that prices will come down soon.* 認為價格很快會下降是有道理的。—opposite 反義詞 UNREASONABLE **2** fairly good, but not especially good 相當好的, 不錯的: *She has a reasonable chance of doing well in the exam.* 她考試考得好的可能性相當大。**3** a reasonable amount is not too much or too many 適度的: *They let a reasonable amount of time pass before visiting him again.* 他們在過了一段適當的時間之後才再次去看他。**4** prices that are reasonable seem fair because they are not too high〔價格〕公道的: *good quality furniture at reasonable prices* 價格公道的優質家具 —see 見 CHEAP¹ (USAGE) **5 beyond reasonable doubt** *law* if something is proved beyond reasonable doubt, it is shown to be almost certainly true【法律】無疑 —**reasonableness** *n* [U]

rea·son·a·bly /ˈrizn̩əblɪ; ˈriːzənəbli/ *adv* **1** [+adj/adv] to a satisfactory degree, although not completely 相當地: *The car is in reasonably good condition.* 這車的性能和車身都相當好。| *I was reasonably happy with the results.* 我對結果相當滿意。**2** in a way that is right or fair 合情理地, 公允地: *He can't reasonably be expected to have known that.* 按照情理, 他不應該知道情況。**3** in a sensible and reasonable way 理性地, 有理智地: *Despite her anger, she had behaved very reasonably.* 她雖然生氣, 但表現得很理智。 S2 W3

rea·soned /ˈrizn̩d; ˈriːzənd/ *adj* [only before noun 僅用於名詞前] based on careful thought, and therefore sensible 經過縝密思考的, 理智的: *a reasoned approach to the problem* 經過縝密思考的解決問題的辦法

rea·son·ing /ˈriznɪŋ; ˈriːzənɪŋ/ *n* [U] a process of thinking carefully about something in order to make a judgment 推理, 推論: *logical reasoning* 邏輯推理 | **the reasoning behind** *What is the reasoning behind this proposal?* 這項建議有甚麼道理?

re·as·sur·ance /ˌriəˈʃurəns; ˌriːəˈʃʊərəns/ *n* **1** [U] help or advice that makes you feel less worried or frightened about a problem 安慰, 慰藉: *Martin always looked to his sister for reassurance.* 馬丁總是指望他的姐姐來安慰他。**2** [C] a remark or statement that makes someone feel calmer about something that is worrying them 安慰, 寬慰 (的話): *The patient needed repeated reassurances.* 病人需要反覆的安慰。

re·as·sure /ˌriəˈʃur; ˌriːəˈʃʊə/ *v* [T] to make someone feel calmer and less worried or frightened about a problem or situation 使安心, 使放心, 安慰: *I was reassured by their offer of support.* 他們表示支持, 使我感到安慰。| **reassure sb (that)** *They apologized and reassured us that the matter would be dealt with immediately.* 他們表示歉意, 並向我們保證, 問題會立即得到處理。—see 見 INSURE (USAGE)

re·as·sur·ing /ˌriəˈʃurɪŋ; ˌriːəˈʃʊərɪŋ◂/ *adj* making you feel less worried or frightened 使人安心的, 使人放心的, 安慰的: *It's reassuring to know that there's always someone around to help.* 知道時刻會有人來幫忙會叫你感到放心。—**reassuringly** *adv*: *She smiled reassuringly at the newcomers.* 她微笑着讓新來的人放心。

re·bar·ba·tive /rɪˈbarbətɪv; rɪˈbɑːbətɪv/ *adj formal* very unattractive or offensive【正式】令人討厭的; 唐突的: *Karajan has been subject to rebarbative questioning and criticism.* 卡拉揚一直受到令人討厭的質詢和批評。

re·bate /ˈribet; ˈriːbeɪt/ *n* [C] an amount of money that is paid back to you when you have paid too much tax, rent etc〔稅、租金等的〕回扣; 部分退款: *In the end I managed to claim a tax rebate.* 最後我得到退回部分稅款。

reb·el¹ /ˈrɛbl̩; ˈrebəl/ *n* [C] **1** someone who opposes or fights against people in authority 造反者; 反叛者: *Anti-government rebels have seized the radio station.* 反政府的叛亂分子佔領了電台。| *rebel soldiers* 叛亂的士兵 **2** someone who refuses to do things in the normal way, or the way that other people want them to〔拒絕按常規辦事、我行我素的〕反叛者, 叛逆者: *Tom has always been the rebel of the family.* 湯姆始終是家庭的叛逆者。| *a teenage rebel* 叛逆少年

re·bel² /rɪˈbɛl; rɪˈbel/ *v* **rebelled, rebelling** [I] to oppose or fight against someone in a position of authority 造反; 反叛: **[+against]** *the story of a teenager who rebels against his father* 少年反抗父親的故事 | *those who had rebelled against the government* 那些反抗政府的人

re·bel·lion /rɪˈbɛljən; rɪˈbeljən/ *n* [C,U] **1** an organised attempt to change the government, or other authority, using violence 造反; 叛亂; 起義: *an armed rebellion* 武裝叛亂 | **[+against]** *a rebellion against the military regime* 反抗軍事政權的起義 | **put down/crush a rebellion** (=use violence to stop it) 鎮壓叛亂 **2** active opposition to someone in authority 反抗; 抗爭: *a rebellion by right-wing members of the party* 黨內右翼黨員的反抗 |

[+against] *a clear rebellion against parental control* 對家長控制的明確反抗 —compare 比較 REVOLUTION (2)

re·bel·lious /rɪˋbɛljəs; rɪˈbeljəs/ *adj* **1** deliberately disobeying 叛逆的; 反抗的: *rebellious teenagers* 叛逆的青少年 | *rebellious behaviour* 反叛行為 **2** fighting against the government of your country 造反的; 起義的: *rebellious warlords* 造反的軍閥 —**rebelliously** *adv* —**rebelliousness** *n* [U]

re·birth /riˋbɝθ; ˌriːˈbɜːθ/ *n* [singular] *formal* a change by which an important idea, feeling, or organization becomes active again【正式】〔思想、感情、組織的〕再生, 復興: *The 1980s saw a rebirth of conservative thinking.* 20世紀 80年代見證了保守主義思想的復興。| *spiritual rebirth* 精神上的再生

re·boot /riˋbut; ˌriːˈbuːt/ *v* [I,T] if you reboot a computer, or if it reboots, you start it up again after it has stopped working〔電腦死機後〕重新啟動: *Try rebooting the machine and see what happens.* 試試重新啟動電腦, 看會出現甚麼情況。

re·born /riˋbɔrn; ˌriːˈbɔːn/ *adj* [not before noun 不用於名詞前] *literary*【文】**1** having become active again after being inactive 再生的; 復興的: *Our hopes of success were reborn when we received thousands of letters of support.* 收到數以千計的支持信, 我們又有了成功的希望。**2 be reborn** to be born again, especially according to some beliefs, ancient stories etc〔信仰、傳說等中的〕再生, 轉世

R

re·bound¹ /rɪˋbaʊnd; rɪˈbaʊnd/ *v* **1** [I] if a ball or other moving object rebounds, it moves quickly back through the air, after hitting something〔球或其他運動物體〕彈回, 跳回: [+off] *The ball rebounded off the wall and I caught it.* 球從牆上反彈回來, 我把它接住了。**2** [I] if prices, values etc rebound, they increase again after decreasing〔價格、價值等下跌後的〕回升; 反彈: *Share prices rebounded today after last week's losses.* 股票價格在上週下跌之後今天反彈了。**3** [I,T] *technical* to catch a BASKETBALL after a player has tried unsuccessfully to get a point【術語】搶(籃板球)

rebound on/upon sb *phr v* [T not in passive 不用被動態] if a harmful action rebounds on someone, it has a bad effect on the person who did it 使自作自受

re·bound² /ˋriˌbaʊnd; ˈriːbaʊnd/ *n* **1 on the rebound a)** someone who is on the rebound is upset or confused because a romantic relationship they had has ended〔因失戀而〕處於情緒波動的狀態: *He married Victoria on the rebound, after Louise left him.* 露易絲離開他之後, 他在心灰意冷之餘, 與維多利亞結婚了。**b)** a ball that rebounds is moving back through the air after hitting something〔球〕在彈回時: *I caught the ball on the rebound.* 我接住了彈回的球。**2** [C] *technical* an act of catching a BASKETBALL after a player has tried unsuccessfully to get a point【術語】搶籃板球

re·buff /rɪˋbʌf; rɪˈbʌf/ *n* [C] *formal* an unkind or unfriendly answer to a friendly suggestion or offer of help; SNUB²【正式】回絕, 斷然拒絕: *Every attempt Yves made to befriend her met with a rebuff.* 伊維斯每次向她表示友好都碰了一鼻子灰。—**rebuff** *v* [T]: *Brady rebuffed all her suggestions.* 布雷迪斷然拒絕了她所有的建議。

re·build /riˋbɪld; ˌriːˈbɪld/ *past tense and past participle* **rebuilt** /-ˋbɪlt; -ˈbɪlt/ *v* [T] **1** to build something again, after it has been damaged or destroyed 重建: *Most of the houses you see were rebuilt after the Great Fire.* 你現在看到的房屋大多數都是倫敦大火之後重建的。**2** to make something strong and successful again 使復原, 恢復: *The first priority is to rebuild the area's manufacturing industry.* 當務之急是恢復該地區的製造業。

re·buke /rɪˋbjuk; rɪˈbjuːk/ *v* [T] *formal* to speak to someone severely, about something they have done wrong【正式】斥責, 指責: **rebuke sb for doing sth** *Father Cary rebuked her for using bad language.* 卡里神父指責她說粗言穢語。—**rebuke** *n* [C,U]: *a stern rebuke* 嚴厲的斥責

re·but /rɪˋbʌt; rɪˈbʌt/ *v* **rebutted, rebutting** [T] *formal* to prove that a statement or a charge made against you is false; REFUTE【正式】駁斥, 反駁 —**rebuttal** *n* [C]

re·cal·ci·trant /rɪˋkælsɪtrənt; rɪˈkælsɨtrənt/ *adj formal* refusing to do what you are told to do, even after you have been punished【正式】不順從的, 桀驁不馴的: *recalcitrant children* 難管束的孩子 —**recalcitrantly** *adv* —**recalcitrance** *n* [U]

re·call¹ /rɪˋkɔl; rɪˈkɔːl/ *v* [T]

1 ►REMEMBER STH 記起某事◄ [not in progressive 不用進行式] to deliberately remember a particular fact, event, or situation from the past, especially in order to tell someone about it 回憶, 回想: **recall that** *I seem to recall that Barry was with us at the time.* 我好像記得巴利當時是和我們在一起的。| **recall doing sth** *I don't recall ever meeting her.* 我想不起來曾經見過她。| **recall what/how/where etc** *Afterwards Olivia could not recall what they had talked about.* 之後, 奧莉維亞回想不起他們談了些甚麼。| **as I recall** *spoken* (=used when you are telling someone what you remember about a past situation)【口】據我回憶 *As I recall, it was you who suggested this idea in the first place.* 據我回憶, 是你首先提出這個想法的。

2 ►PERSON 人◄ to officially tell someone to come back from a place where they have been sent 召回: [+from] *The Ambassador was recalled from Washington.* 大使被從華盛頓召回。

3 ►PRODUCT 產品◄ if a company recalls one of its products, it asks you to return it because there may be something wrong with it 收回〔有問題的產品〕: *The B Series cars have been recalled to the manufacturers due to an engine fault.* 由於發動機有問題, B 系列汽車已被製造商收回。

4 ►ON A COMPUTER 在電腦上◄ to bring information back onto the screen of a computer〔在電腦屏幕上〕重新調出〔信息〕, 檢索

5 ►BE SIMILAR TO 相似◄ if something recalls something else, it makes you think of it because it is very similar〔由於酷似而〕使回憶起: *a style of film-making that recalls Alfred Hitchcock* 一種使人想起希治閣的電影攝製風格 —**recallable** *adj*

re·call² /ˋriˌkɔl; rɪˈkɔːl/ *n* **1** [U] the ability to remember something that you have learned or experienced 記憶力: **powers of recall** (=ability to remember) 記憶力 | **total recall** (=the ability to remember everything) 完整的記憶力 | **instant recall** (=the ability to remember a fact immediately) 瞬時記憶〔立刻記住一個事實的能力〕**2** [singular,U] a command telling someone to return from a place where they have been officially sent 召回: [+of] *the recall of all Allied seamen to their own countries* 將所有的盟軍水兵召回本國 **3 beyond/past recall** impossible to bring back or remember 無法回憶的, 記不起來的

re·cant /rɪˋkænt; rɪˈkænt/ *v* [I,T] *formal* to say publicly that you no longer have a political or religious belief that you had before【正式】公開宣布放棄〔以前的政治觀點或宗教信仰〕: *Galileo was forced to recant his belief in the Copernican theory.* 伽俐略被迫公開宣布放棄他對哥白尼理論的信仰。—**recantation** /ˌrikænˋteʃən; ˌriːkænˈteɪʃən/ *n* [C,U]

re·cap /ˋrikæp; ˈriːkæp/ *v* **recapped, recapping** [I,T] to repeat the main points of something that has just been said; short for RECAPITULATE 扼要重述, 摘要說明: *Let me just recap what's been said so far.* 讓我把已經談到的內容簡要複述一遍。—**recap** /ˋrikæp; ˈriːkæp/ *n* [C]

re·ca·pit·u·late /ˌrikəˋpɪtʃəˌlet; ˌriːkəˈpɪtʃʊleɪt/ *v* [I,T] *formal* to repeat the main points of something that has just been said【正式】扼要重述 —**recapitulation** /ˌrikəˌpɪtʃəˋleʃən; ˌriːkəpɪtʃʊˈleɪʃən/ *n* [C,U]

re·cap·ture /riˋkæptʃɚ; riːˈkæptʃə/ *v* [T] **1** to bring back the same feelings or qualities that you experienced in the past 使再現; 使再次經歷: *an attempt to recapture* *our childhood innocence* 重新體驗我們孩提時代天真無邪的嘗試 **2** to catch a prisoner or animal that has escaped 重新抓獲: *They travelled only at night, to avoid being recaptured by the enemy.* 為了避免被敵人重新抓獲, 他們只在夜間行走。**3** to take control of a piece of land again by fighting for it 收復〔失地〕—**recapture** *n* [U]

re·cast /ri`kæst; ˌriː'kɑːst/ *v past tense and past participle* **recast** [T] **1** to give something a new shape or a new form of organization 重鑄; 重塑; 重組: *an attempt to recast the statement in less formal language* 用不太正式的語言改寫聲明的嘗試 **2** to give parts in a play or film to different actors 更換〔戲劇、電影中〕的演員 —**recasting** *n* [C,U]

rec·ce /`rɛkɪ; 'reki/ *n* [C,U] *informal* RECONNAISSANCE【非正式】偵察

recd the written abbreviation of 縮寫= received (RECEIVE)

re·cede /rɪ`sid; rɪ'siːd/ *v* [I] **1** if something you can see or hear recedes, it gets further and further away until it disappears〔景物、聲音〕逐漸遠去以至消失: **[+into]** *footsteps receding into the distance* 漸漸遠去的腳步聲 **2** if a memory, feeling, or possibility recedes, it gradually goes away〔記憶〕變模糊;〔感情〕逐漸淡漠;〔可能性〕逐漸消失: *As the threat of attack receded, village life returned to normal.* 隨着襲擊的威脅漸漸消失, 村裡的生活恢復了正常。**3** if water recedes, it moves back from an area that it was covering〔水〕退, 退去: *Flood waters finally began to recede in November.* 洪水終於在十一月間開始退去。**4** if your hair recedes, you gradually lose the hair at the front of your head〔頭髮〕從前額開始向後脱落: **receding hairline** *Ian is getting self-conscious about his receding hairline.* 伊恩對自己不斷後移的髮際線感到越來越不自在。—see picture on page A6 參見A6頁圖 **5 receding chin** a chin that slopes backwards 向後收縮的下巴

2 **re·ceipt** /rɪ`sit; rɪ'siːt/ *n* **1** [C] a written statement that you give to someone, showing that you have received money or goods from them 收據, 收條: *Keep all your receipts for work-related expenses.* 保留你所有與工作相關的開支的收據。| **make out a receipt** (=write a receipt) 開收據 **2** [U] *formal* the act or fact of receiving something【正式】收到: **[+of]** *Receipt of benefits is permitted for up to 12 months.* 允許領取救濟金的時間最長為12個月。| **be in receipt of** *formal* (=to have received something)【正式】收訖 *We are now in receipt of your letter of the 17th.* 17日大函敬悉。| **on/upon receipt of** *formal* (=when you have received something)【正式】收到…後 *On receipt of your instructions, we will dispatch the goods.* 收到你的指示後, 我們將發貨。**3 receipts** [plural] *technical* the money that a business, bank, or government receives【術語】〔企業、銀行、政府的〕收款, 進款; 收入: *total revenue receipts of $18.4 million* 總收入1840萬美元

1 **re·ceive** /rɪ`siv; rɪ'siːv/ *v* [T]
1 **1 ▶BE GIVEN STH** 得到某物◀ to be officially given something 正式得到; 收到: *We have received numerous complaints about the airport noise.* 我們收到許多對機場噪音的投訴。| **receive sth from sb** *In 1962 she received an honorary doctorate from Harvard.* 1962年, 她獲得哈佛大學榮譽博士學位。| *You may be entitled to receive assistance from the state.* 你可能有資格領取國家的補助。—see 見 OBTAIN (USAGE)

2 ▶BE SENT STH 接到, 收到某物◀ *formal* to get a letter, message, telephone call etc【正式】接到〔信件、消息、電話等〕: *Yes, Anne received your letter Monday.* 對, 安妮星期一收到了你的信。| *By the time the police received the call it was too late.* 等警察接到電話, 已經太晚了。

3 ▶TREATMENT 待遇◀ *formal* if you receive a particular type of treatment, an injury etc, it is done to you or it happens to you【正式】受到〔某種待遇、傷害等〕; 接受〔治療〕: *The victim received injuries from which he has since died.* 受害者多處受傷, 並因此導致死亡。| *a cancer patient receiving radiation therapy* 一個接受放射治療的癌症患者

4 ▶IDEAS/INFORMATION 想法/信息◀ [usually passive 一般用被動態] to react in a particular way to a suggestion, idea, or piece of information 對〔建議、想法或消息〕作出反應; 回應: *Edith's plans were very well received by the board.* 董事會對伊迪絲的計劃反應很好。| *He did not receive the news very cheerfully.* 聽到這個消息他並不太開心。

5 be on the receiving end (of) to be the person who is most affected by someone else's actions, usually in an unpleasant way 遭受, 承受: *I'm the one who's always on the receiving end of his bad moods.* 他鬧情緒, 我總要受罪。

6 ▶PEOPLE 人◀ *formal* to officially accept someone as a guest or member of a group【正式】接待, 招待; 接受〔為成員〕: *She only receives guests on Sundays.* 她只在星期天會客。| **receive sb into sth** *Tessa was later received into the Church.* 特莎後來被這個教會接納為教友。

7 ▶BY RADIO 用無線電◀ **a)** if a radio or television receives radio waves or other signals, it makes them become sounds or pictures〔收音機、電視〕接收〔無線電或電視信號〕**b)** to be able to hear a radio message that someone is sending 收聽到〔無線電信號〕: *"Are you receiving me?" "Receiving you loud and clear!"* "你收到我的信號沒有?" "你的信號又響又清楚!"

Frequencies of the verbs **receive** and **get** in spoken and written English 動詞receive和get在英語口語和書面語中的使用頻率

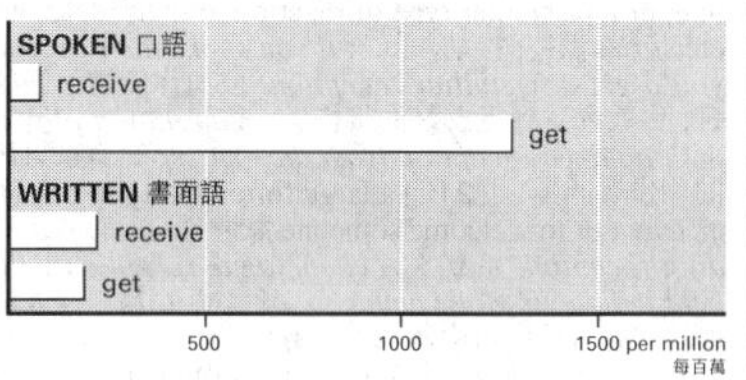

Based on the British National Corpus and the Longman Lancaster Corpus 據英國國家語料庫和朗文蘭卡斯特語料庫

This graph shows that it is much more usual in spoken English to use **get** rather than **receive**, which is more formal and is therefore more common in written English. 本圖表顯示, 英語口語中get的使用頻率遠遠高於receive, receive比較正式, 因而更多的是在書面語中使用。

re·ceived /rɪ`sivd; rɪ'siːvd/ *adj* [only before noun 僅用於名詞前] *formal* accepted or considered to be correct by most people【正式】被普遍接受的; 公認的: *Sonntag's articles challenged received notions about photography.* 桑塔格的這些文章對公認的攝影概念提出了異議。| **received wisdom** (=the opinions most people have about what is true) 多數人的看法 *The received wisdom in Washington is that the Defense Secretary will resign.* 華盛頓的普遍看法是國防部長將辭職。

Received Pro·nun·ci·a·tion /·,· ···'··/ *n* [U] RP 標準發音

re·ceiv·er /rɪ`sivɚ; rɪ'siːvə/ *n* [C]

1 ▶TELEPHONE 電話◀ the part of a telephone that you hold next to your mouth and ear〔電話〕聽筒: *Cory slammed down the receiver and stormed out of the room.* 科里砰的一聲摔下電話, 怒氣沖沖地走出房間。

2 ▶BUSINESS 公司◀ someone who is officially in charge of a business or company that is BANKRUPT (=has no money)〔破產企業、公司的〕管理人, 接管人: *The business is in the hands of the receivers.* 公司現在由破產管理人接管。

3 ▶STOLEN PROPERTY 贓物◀ someone who buys and sells stolen property 買賣贓物者

口語及書面語中最常用的 1 000詞, 2 000詞, 3 000詞

4 ►RADIO 無線電◄ *formal* a radio or television【正式】無線電接收機; 收音機; 電視機

5 ►AMERICAN FOOTBALL 美式足球◄ a player in American football who is in a position to catch the ball 接球手

re·ceiv·er·ship /rɪˋsivɚˌʃɪp; rɪˈsiːvəʃɪp/ *n* [U] **go into receivership** if a person or business goes into receivership, they are controlled by the official receiver (RECEIVER (2)) because they have no money〔破產者或公司〕由破產管理人看管

re·ceiv·ing /rɪˋsivɪŋ; rɪˈsiːvɪŋ/ *n* [U] the crime of buying and selling stolen goods 買賣贓物罪

2 1 **re·cent** /ˋrisn̩t; ˈriːsənt/ *adj* having happened or begun to exist only a short time ago 最近的, 不久前的, 近代的: *recent developments in medicine* 醫學領域的最新發展 | *my recent visit to China* 我最近去中國的旅行 | *In recent years, terrorism has become a greater threat.* 近年來, 恐怖主義已經成為更大的威脅。—**recentness** *n* [U]

1 1 **re·cent·ly** /ˋrisn̩tlɪ; ˈriːsəntli/ *adv* not long ago 最近, 不久前, 近來: *I've only recently started learning French.* 我只是最近才開始學法語的。| *Jerry lived in Cairo until quite recently.* 傑里住在開羅直至不久之前。| *a recently published biography* 一部最近出版的傳記

R

re·cep·ta·cle /rɪˋsɛptək̩l; rɪˈseptəkəl/ *n formal* a container for putting things in【正式】容器: *Please dispose of waste in the appropriate receptacle.* 請將廢物投進適當的容器。

3 **re·cep·tion** /rɪˋsɛpʃən; rɪˈsepʃən/ *n* **1** [C usually singular 一般用單數] a particular type of welcome for someone, or a particular type of reaction to their ideas, work etc 接待, 歡迎; 接納, 承認: *If you spoke their language you'd get a friendlier reception.* 假如你能講他們的語言, 你就會受到更友好的接待。| *Vaughan's play met with a mixed reception from the critics.* 評論家對沃恩的劇作褒貶不一。**2** [C] a large formal party to celebrate an event or to welcome someone 歡迎會, 招待會: *a wedding reception* 婚宴 | *A champagne reception will be held in honour of the ambassador's visit.* 為歡迎大使來訪將舉行香檳酒招待會。**3** [U] **a)** the desk or office where visitors arriving in a hotel or large organization go first〔旅店、大機構的〕接待處: *Please leave your key at the reception desk.* 請將你的鑰匙留在接待處。**b)** *BrE* the area around or in front of this desk or office; LOBBY[1] (1)【英】前廳: *I'll wait for you in reception.* 我在前廳等你。**4** [U] the quality of radio or television signals that you receive〔收音機、電視機的〕接收性能, 收聽[收視]質量: *listeners complaining about poor reception* 抱怨收聽質量太差的聽眾

re·cep·tion·ist /rɪˋsɛpʃənɪst; rɪˈsepʃənɪst/ *n* [C] someone whose job is to welcome and deal with people arriving in a hotel or office building, visiting a doctor etc 接待員

reception room /-ˈ·· ˌ/ *n* [C] *BrE* a word, used especially by people who sell houses, for a room, especially a LIVING-ROOM, in a private house that is not a kitchen, bedroom, or bathroom【英】客廳; 會客室〔尤為出售房屋者使用〕: *The house has three bedrooms, a large kitchen and two reception rooms.* 這所房子有三間臥室、一個大廚房和兩間客廳。

re·cep·tive /rɪˋsɛptɪv; rɪˈseptɪv/ *adj* willing to consider new ideas or listen to someone else's opinions〔對新思想、別人的意見等〕樂於接受的: *You might find them in a more receptive mood tomorrow.* 也許他們明天更樂於接受意見。| **[+to]** *receptive to new ideas and values* 善於接受新思想和新價值觀 —**receptively** *adv* —**receptiveness** also 又作 **receptivity** /ˌrisɛpˋtɪvətɪ; ˌriːsepˈtɪvɪti/ *n* [U]

re·cess¹ /ˋrisɛs; rɪˈses/ *n* **1** [C,U] a time for rest during the working day or year, especially in parliament, law courts etc 暫停; 休息; 休會; 休庭: *Parliament's summer recess* 議會的夏季休會期 | *After Slater's testimony, the judge called a recess.* 斯雷特作證後, 法官宣布休庭。**2** [U] *AmE* a short period of time between lessons at a school when children can go outdoors and play【美】課間休息; BREAK[2] (1c) *BrE*【英】: *The older kids were picking on Richie at recess.* 課間休息時, 大一點的孩子們欺負里奇。**3** [C] a space in the wall of a room for shelves, cupboards etc〔牆壁上裝架、櫃等的〕凹進處; 壁龕 **4 the recesses of** the inner hidden parts of something …的隱祕處, 幽深處: *the deep recesses of the cave* 洞穴的深處

re·cess² /ˋrisɛs; rɪˈses/ *v* [I] *especially AmE* to take a recess (RECESS[1] (1))【尤美】休假; 休會; 休庭

re·cessed /ˋrisɛst; rɪˈsest/ *adj* fitted into a part of a wall that is further back than the rest of the wall 裝入牆壁凹進處的: *a recessed bookshelf* 嵌進牆壁內的書架

re·ces·sion /rɪˋsɛʃən; rɪˈseʃən/ *n* [C] a period of time during which there is less trade, business activity, and wealth than usual〔經濟〕衰退期 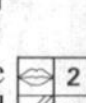

re·ces·sive /rɪˋsɛsɪv; rɪˈsesɪv/ *adj technical* a recessive physical feature is passed to children from their parents only if both parents have this feature in their GENES【術語】〔遺傳基因〕隱性的

re·charge /riˋtʃardʒ; ˌriːˈtʃɑːdʒ/ *v* [T] **1** to put a new supply of electricity into a BATTERY (1) 給〔電池〕重新充電 **2 recharge your batteries** to get back your strength and energy again 使自己恢復精力: *I'm going to spend a week in the mountains to recharge my batteries.* 我準備留在山裡一個星期, 以恢復精力。—**rechargeable** *adj* —**recharge** /ˋritʃardʒ; ˈriːtʃɑːdʒ/ *n* [C]

re·cher·ché /rəˋʃɛrʃe; rəˈʃeəʃeɪ/ *adj formal* a recherché subject, idea, word etc is uncommon and has been chosen to make people admire your knowledge【正式】〔主題、思想、字眼等〕罕見的〔選來炫耀知識〕

re·cid·i·vist /rɪˋsɪdəvɪst; rɪˈsɪdɪvɪst/ *n* [C] *technical* a criminal who keeps doing things that are illegal, even after they have been punished【術語】慣犯 —**recidivism** *n* [U]

re·ci·pe /ˋrɛsəpɪ; ˈresɪpi/ *n* [C] **1** a set of instructions for cooking a particular type of food 烹飪法; 食譜: **[+for]** *a recipe for tomato soup* 番茄湯的做法 | *a recipe book* 一本烹飪書 **2 be a recipe for** to be likely to cause a particular result 是…的祕訣[竅門]; 很可能是造成…的原因: *The fact that four different companies are writing the software sounds like a recipe for disaster to me.* 四家不同的公司在編寫這種軟件, 我覺得這很可能釀成災禍。 3

re·cip·i·ent /rɪˋsɪpɪənt; rɪˈsɪpiənt/ *n formal* someone who receives something【正式】接受者, 領受者: **[+of]** *the recipient of the Nobel Peace Prize* 諾貝爾和平獎得主

re·cip·ro·cal /rɪˋsɪprək̩l; rɪˈsɪprəkəl/ *adj formal* a reciprocal arrangement or relationship is one in which two people or groups do or give the same things to each other【正式】相互的; 交互的; 互惠的: *Such treaties provide reciprocal rights and obligations.* 這種協議提供了互惠的權利與義務。—compare 比較 MUTUAL —**reciprocally** /-k̩lɪ; -kli/ *adv*

re·cip·ro·cate /rɪˋsɪprəˌket; rɪˈsɪprəkeɪt/ *v* **1** [I,T] to do or give something, because something similar has been done or given to you 報答, 酬答; 互給: *I cannot accept his generosity – I am not in a position to reciprocate.* 我不能接受他的慷慨 —— 我無法回報他。**2** [T] to feel the same about someone as they feel about you 回報以〔相同的感情〕: *Kara had fallen in love with Dan, but her affection was not reciprocated.* 卡拉愛上了丹, 但她的愛沒有得到回報。—**reciprocation** /rɪˌsɪprəˋkeʃən; rɪˌsɪprəˈkeɪʃən/ *n* [U]

re·ci·pro·ci·ty /ˌrɛsəˋprɑsətɪ; ˌresɪˈprɒsɪti/ *n* [U] *formal* a situation in which two people, groups, or countries give each other similar kinds of help or special rights【正式】互惠

re·cit·al /rɪˋsaɪt̩l; rɪˈsaɪtl/ *n* [C] **1** a performance of music or poetry, usually given by one performer 演奏會; 演唱會; 朗誦會〔一般由一個人表演〕: *a piano recital* 鋼

琴獨奏會 | **[+of]** *a recital of operatic arias* 歌劇唱段演唱會 **2** *formal* a spoken description of a series of events【正式】〔一連串事件的〕敘述, 口頭描述: **[+of]** *Fred launched into a long recital of his adventures.* 弗雷德開始大談特談他的奇遇。

re·ci·ta·tion /ˌrɛsəˋteʃən; ˌresɪ̯ˈteɪʃən/ *n* [C,U] an act of saying a poem, piece of literature etc that you have learned, for people to listen to 背誦: *recitations from Shakespeare* 背誦莎士比亞的作品

re·ci·ta·tive /ˌrɛsətəˋtiv; ˌresɪ̯təˈtiːv/ *n* [C,U] *technical* a speech set to music sung by one person that continues the story of an OPERA (=musical play) between the songs【術語】〔歌劇中的〕宣敍部

re·cite /rɪˋsaɪt; rɪˈsaɪt/ *v* **1** [I,T] to say a poem, piece of literature etc that you have learned, for people to listen to 背誦: *a poem I had to recite at school* 我上學時必須背誦的一首詩 **2** [T] to tell someone a series or list of things 詳述; 列舉: *Don't encourage him, or he'll recite the whole family history!* 別鼓勵他, 不然他會把整部家族史從頭到尾講一遍。—**reciter** *n* [C]

reck·less /ˋrɛklɪs; ˈrekləs/ *adj* not caring or worrying about the possible bad or dangerous results of your actions 輕率的; 魯莽的; 不顧後果的: *reckless driving* 莽撞的駕駛 | *a reckless adventurer* 無所畏懼的冒險家 | *a reckless waste of money* 胡亂花錢 —**recklessly** *adv* —**recklessness** *n* [U]

reck·on /ˋrɛkən; ˈrekən/ *v* [T not in progressive 不用進行式] **1** *spoken especially BrE* to think that something is a fact, or have a particular opinion about something【口, 尤英】認為, 以為: **reckon (that)** *Wayne reckons we ought to call her.* 韋恩認為我們應該給她打個電話。| *Do you reckon they'll get married?* 你認為他們會結婚嗎? **2** to guess a number or amount, without calculating it exactly 估算, 估計: **reckon how much/how many etc** *How much do you reckon she earns?* 你估計她掙多少錢? | **reckon sth to be sth** *The likely cost of the system is reckoned to be about £10,000.* 估計這系統的成本可能在10,000英鎊左右。| **be reckoned in thousands/millions** *Her personal fortune is reckoned in millions.* 估計她的個人財產達數百萬。**3** *formal* to think that someone or something is a particular kind of person or thing【正式】認為〔某人或物〕是…: **be reckoned to be sth** *Julia is often reckoned to be the most beautiful woman in Hollywood.* 朱莉婭經常被認為是荷里活最漂亮的女性。| **reckon sb among/as** *I reckon him among my friends.* 我把他看作我的朋友。**4** *formal* to calculate an amount【正式】計算: *My pay is reckoned from the first of the month.* 我的工資從每月的第一天算起。

reckon sth ↔ **in** *phr v* [T] to include something when you are calculating 把…計算在內: *Have you reckoned in the cost of postage?* 你是否把郵費計算在內了?

reckon on sth *phr v* [T] to expect something to happen when you are making plans 指望: **reckon on doing sth** *We didn't reckon on spending so much on repairs.* 我們沒有想到維修要花這麼多錢。

reckon sth ↔ **up** *phr v* [T] *old-fashioned* to add up an amount, cost etc, in order to get a total【過時】把…加起來, 計算…的總數: *Can you reckon up the money we've made?* 你能不能把我們掙的錢加起來?

reckon with sb/sth *phr v* [T] **1 not reckon with** to not consider a possible problem when you are making plans 沒有考慮到: *We hadn't reckoned with the possibility that it might rain.* 我們沒有考慮到可能下雨。**2 sb/sth to be reckoned with** something or someone that is powerful and must be regarded seriously as a possible opponent, competitor, danger etc 必須認真考慮[對待]的某人/某事: *The principal was certainly a woman to be reckoned with.* 校長無疑是一個必須認真對付的女人。**3 have sb/sth to reckon with** to have to deal with someone or something powerful 必須對付某人/某事: *Any invader would have the military might of NATO to reckon with.* 任何入侵者都必須對付北約的軍事力量。

reckon without sb/sth *phr v* [T] *BrE* to not consider a possible problem when you are making plans【英】沒有考慮到; 對…不加考慮: *We had reckoned without the difficulty of selling the house.* 我們沒有考慮到出售房子的困難。

reck·on·ing /ˋrɛkənɪŋ; ˈrekənɪŋ/ *n* **1** [U] calculation that is based on a careful guess rather than on exact knowledge 估算, 估計: *By my reckoning it must be 60 km from here to the coast.* 據我估計, 從這裡到海邊應該有60公里。**2** [C] *old use* a bill【舊】賬單: *We paid our reckoning and left.* 我們付完賬便走了。**3 day of reckoning** the time when the results of your actions or behaviour become clear and start to affect you, especially in a bad way 報應來到的日子; 算總賬的日子 —see also 另見 DEAD RECKONING

re·claim /rɪˋklem; rɪˈkleɪm/ *v* [T] **1** to officially ask for something to be given back to you 要求收回; 要求恢復: *You may be entitled to reclaim some tax.* 你可以要求退回部分稅款。**2** to make an area of desert, MARSH (=wet land) etc suitable for farming or building 開墾, 開拓 **3** to obtain useful products from waste material 自廢料中回收〔有用材料〕: *metal reclaimed from old cars in junkyards* 從垃圾場的舊汽車上回收的金屬 —**reclamation** /ˌrɛkləˋmeʃən; ˌrekləˈmeɪʃən/ *n* [U] *land reclamation* 墾荒

re·cline /rɪˋklaɪn; rɪˈklaɪn/ *v* **1** [I] *formal* to lie or lean back in a relaxed way【正式】躺, 斜倚: **[+in/on]** *a girl reclining on a deck chair* 躺在帆布椅上的女孩 **2** [I,T] if you recline a seat or if it reclines, the back of the seat is lowered, so that you can lean back in it (使)〔椅背〕向後靠: *reclining seats* 躺椅

R

re·cluse /ˋrɛklus; rɪˈkluːs/ *n* [C] someone who chooses to live alone, and does not like seeing or talking to other people 隱居者, 隱士; 遁世者: *The guy was a recluse – a defrocked priest, so people said.* 那人是位隱士——一位被解除聖職的神父, 人們這麼說。—**reclusive** /rɪˋklusɪv; rɪˈkluːsɪv/ *adj*

rec·og·ni·tion /ˌrɛkəgˋnɪʃən; ˌrekəgˈnɪʃən/ *n* **1** [U] the act of knowing someone or something because you have known or learned about them in the past 認識, 認出; 識別: *Years later, she passed me in the street without even the smallest sign of recognition.* 若干年後, 她在街上從我身邊走過, 絲毫沒有認識我的跡象。| **beyond/out of all recognition** (=having become impossible to recognize) 認不出來 *His face was bruised and swollen almost beyond recognition.* 他的臉又青又腫, 幾乎認不出來了。**2** [singular,U] public admiration and thanks for someone's work or achievements 公開的讚揚, 表揚, 表彰: *Despite a life devoted to helping the poor, she never won any recognition before her death.* 儘管畢生致力於救助窮人, 但她在生前從未得到任何表揚。| **in recognition of** (=show public thanks and admiration for something) 表彰… *This medal is awarded in recognition of outstanding courage.* 授予這枚獎章以嘉獎非凡的勇氣。**3** [singular,U] the act of realizing and accepting that something is true or that something is important 意識到, 承認; 接受: **[+of]** *There is a growing recognition among doctors of the need for more preventative treatment.* 越來越多的醫生意識到需要更多的預防性治療。**4** [U] the act of officially accepting that an organization, government, document etc has legal or official authority 正式承認: **[+of]** *the recognition of Latvia as an independent state* 承認拉脫維亞為一個獨立國家 **5 speech/voice/image etc recognition** the ability of a computer to recognize voices, shapes etc 〔電腦的〕語音/圖像等識別能力

rec·og·nize also 又作 **-ise** *BrE*【英】/ˋrɛkəgˌnaɪz; ˈrekəgnaɪz/ *v* **1** [T not in progressive 不用進行式] to know who someone is or what something is, because you have seen, heard, experienced, or learned about them in the past 認出, 認識; 辨認出: *She was humming a tune I didn't recognize.* 她正在哼一首曲子, 可是我聽不出來是甚麼。| *Saleha came home so thin and weak her own children hardly recognized her.* 賽莉婭回家時又瘦又弱, 連她自己的孩子都幾乎認不出她來了。| *You shouldn't*

go yourself. You'll be recognized. 你不應該親自去，你會被人認出來的。| *It was malaria, but Dr Lee hadn't recognized the symptoms.* 患的是瘧疾，但李醫生沒有辨認出症狀。**2** [T] to officially accept that an organization, government, document etc has legal or official authority 正式承認，認可：*The management recognizes three main trade unions.* 資方承認三個主要的工會。| *British medical qualifications are recognized in Canada.* 英國的行醫資格在加拿大得到認可。| **recognize sth as** *The US has not recognized the Cuban government since 1961.* 自從1961年以來，美國一直不承認古巴政府。**3 be recognized as** to be thought of as being important or very good by a lot of people 得到承認，被公認為：*Lawrence's novel was eventually recognized as a work of genius.* 勞倫斯的小說最終被公認為天才之作。| **recognized expert/authority** *a recognized authority on the teaching of English* 公認的英語教學權威 **4** [T] to accept and admit, often unwillingly, that something is true〔往往勉強地〕接受，承認；明白：**recognize (that)** *We recognize that this is an unpleasant choice to have to make.* 我們承認這是不得已而作出的令人不快的決定。| **recognize what/how/who etc** *Do you think he recognized how foolish he looks?* 你覺得他明白自己顯得有多蠢嗎？**5** [T] to officially and publicly thank someone for something they have done, by giving them a special honour 表揚；表彰；嘉獎 —**recognizable** /ˋrɛkəg͵naɪzəbḷ; ˈrekəgnaɪzəbl/ *adj* —**recognizably** *adv*

re·coil¹ /rɪˋkɔɪl; rɪˈkɔɪl/ *v* [I] **1** to move back suddenly and quickly from something you dislike or are frightened of 退縮；畏縮：**[+from]** *She recoiled from his touch as if she had been slapped.* 他一碰她，她便往後縮，彷彿被打了一巴掌。**2** to feel such a strong dislike of a particular situation that you want to avoid it〔因厭惡某情形而〕拖拉，躊躇不前：**[+from]** *Rigby tends to recoil from making difficult decisions.* 里格比在難以作出決定時往往躊躇不前。**3** if a gun recoils, it suddenly moves backwards after it has been fired〔槍砲〕反衝；產生後坐力

re·coil² /ˋrikɔɪl; ˈriːkɔɪl/ *n* [singular,U] the sudden backward movement of a gun after being fired〔槍砲的〕反衝，後坐

rec·ol·lect /͵rɛkəˋlɛkt; ͵rekəˈlekt/ *v* [T] *old-fashioned* to be able to remember something, especially by deliberately trying to remember【過時】記起；想起：*As far as I recollect, I have never owned a black suit.* 就我的記憶所及，我從未有過一套黑色西服。| **recollect how/when/what etc** *Davenport tried to recollect when he had last used his car.* 達文波特努力回想他最後一次使用他的汽車是在甚麼時候。| **recollect that** *One witness recollected that the visitor had arrived by the side door.* 一位證人記得來客是從邊門進來的。| **recollect doing sth** *I recollect seeing Ryder some years ago in Bonn.* 我記得幾年前曾經在波恩見過賴德。

rec·ol·lec·tion /͵rɛkəˋlɛkʃən; ͵rekəˈlekʃən/ *n formal*【正式】**1** [U] an act of remembering something, especially something you try to remember 想起，記起：**have no recollection** (=not remember) 不記得 *I have no recollection of ever having received the money.* 我不記得收到過這筆錢。| **to the best of my recollection** (=used when you are unsure if you remember correctly) 如果我沒有記錯的話 *To the best of my recollection, she drives a Mercedes.* 如果我沒有記錯的話，她開的是一輛梅塞得斯牌汽車。**2** [C] something from the past that you remember 記憶中的往事：*His earliest recollection was a great branch of lilac hanging outside the window.* 他最早的記憶是窗外懸着的一根很大的丁香樹枝。

S3 W2 **rec·om·mend** /͵rɛkəˋmɛnd; ͵rekəˈmend/ *v* [T] **1** to advise someone to do something, especially because you have special knowledge of a situation or subject 勸告；建議：*The Senate Foreign Relations Committee recommended ratification of the treaty despite public opinion.* 儘管公眾輿論反對，參議院外交關係委員會建議批准這項條約。| **recommend that** *Doctors recommend that all children should be immunized against measles.* 醫生們建議所有兒童都應該接種麻疹疫苗。| **recommend doing sth** *The manufacturers recommend changing the oil after 500 km.* 製造廠商建議在行駛500公里之後更換機油。| **strongly recommend** *Graham's father strongly recommended sending the boy to school in England.* 格雷厄姆的父親極力建議把孩子送到英國上學。| **recommended limit/dosage/allowance etc** *It is dangerous to exceed the recommended dosage.* 超過建議的服用劑量是危險的。**2** to praise something or someone, or suggest them for a particular purpose or job 推薦，介紹：*I recommend the butter chicken – it's delicious.* 我推薦奶油雞，非常好吃。| *Can you recommend a good lawyer?* 你能不能介紹一位好律師？| **recommend sth to sb** *Oh, that book? Karen recommended it to me.* 噢，那本書嗎？是卡倫推薦給我的。| **recommend sth for** *My mother always recommends the market for fresh fruit and veg.* 我母親總是推薦去那個市場買新鮮水果和蔬菜。| **recommend sb for** *I would recommend Mr Bryant for the position of Assistant Manager.* 我想推薦布賴恩特先生擔任助理經理。| **highly/thoroughly recommend** *That new restaurant in town is highly recommended.* 人們極力推薦鎮上那家新餐館。**3 sth has much/little/nothing to recommend it** used to say that something has many, few, or no good qualities 某物有很多/少有/沒有可取之處：*As a tourist resort the place doesn't have anything to recommend it.* 這個地方遊客眾多，但沒有可取之處。

rec·om·men·da·tion /͵rɛkəmɛnˋdeʃən; ͵rekəmenˈdeɪʃən/ *n* **1** [C] official advice given to someone, especially about what to do 正式建議；意見：**make a recommendation** *The committee made a number of recommendations for improving safety standards.* 委員會提出了若干項提高安全標準的建議。**2** [U] the action of suggesting to someone that they should choose a particular thing or person that you think is very good 建議；推薦：**on sb's recommendation** *On Hawley's recommendation five officers were court martialled.* 根據霍利的建議，五名軍官被送上軍事法庭受審。**3** [C] *especially AmE* a formal letter or statement saying that someone would be a suitable person to do a job, take a course of study etc【尤美】推薦信 

rec·om·pense¹ /ˋrɛkəm͵pɛns; ˈrekəmpens/ *v* [T] *formal* to give someone a payment for trouble or losses that you have caused them, or a reward for their efforts to help you【正式】補償；賠償；酬謝：**recompense sb for sth** *We hope this payment will go some way to recompense you for any inconvenience we may have caused.* 我們可能已經給您造成不便，希望這筆款項可以作出些許補償。—compare 比較 COMPENSATE (2)

recompense² *n* [singular,U] *formal* something that you give to someone for trouble or losses that you have caused them, or as a reward for their help【正式】補償；賠償；報酬：**[+for]** *£1,000 isn't really much recompense for all they've been through.* 他們經歷了那麼多波折，1,000 英鎊其實算不了甚麼補償。—compare 比較 COMPENSATION (1)

rec·on·cile /ˋrɛkən͵saɪl; ˈrekənsaɪl/ *v* **1** [T] if you reconcile two ideas, situations, or facts you accept or show that they can exist together and are not directly opposed to each other 調和；調解：**reconcile sth with sth** *She could never reconcile his violent temper with his pacifist ideals.* 她無論如何也看不出他暴躁的脾氣同他的和平主義理想有甚麼相符的地方。| **reconcile accounts** (=to make two sets of figures add up to the same) 平賬 **2 be reconciled (with)** to have a good relationship again with someone after you have quarrelled with them（與…）和解，和好：*After 20 years of silence, he was finally reconciled with his family.* 經過20年的沉默後，他終於與家人言歸於好。

reconcile sb **to** sth *phr v* [T] to make someone able to accept a difficult or unpleasant situation 使接受〔困難

或不愉快的情況〕: **reconcile yourself to sth** *We watch the character as he tries to reconcile himself to the idea of his own death.* 我們看到這個人物設法坦然面對自己的死亡。

rec·on·cil·i·a·tion /ˌrɛkənˌsɪlɪˋeʃən; ˌrekənsɪliˈeɪʃən/ *n* [singular,U] a situation in which two people, countries etc become friendly with each other again after quarrelling 和解, 修好: *All our attempts at reconciliation have failed.* 我們為和解所作的一切努力都失敗了。| [+**between**] *There seemed little hope of reconciliation between the two superpowers.* 兩個超級大國之間幾乎沒有甚麼修好的希望。| **spirit of reconciliation** *a new spirit of reconciliation in the negotiations* 談判中表現出的新的和解精神

rec·on·dite /ˋrɛkənˌdaɪt; ˈrekəndaɪt/ *adj* [only before noun 僅用於名詞前] *formal* recondite information, knowledge etc is not known about or understood by many people【正式】〔信息、知識等〕玄妙的; 深奧的

re·con·di·tion /ˌrikənˋdɪʃən; ˌriːkənˈdɪʃən/ *v* [T] to repair something, especially an old machine, so that it works like a new one 修理, 修復, 修整〔尤指舊機器〕—**reconditioned** *adj*: *a reconditioned engine* 修復的發動機

re·con·nais·sance /rɪˋkɑnəsəns; rɪˈkɒnɪ̣səns/ *n* [C,U] the military activity of sending soldiers and aircraft to find out about the enemy's forces 偵察: *a reconnaissance mission* 偵察任務

re·con·noi·tre *BrE*【英】, **reconnoiter** *AmE*【美】/ˌrikəˋnɔɪtɚ; ˌrekəˈnɔɪtə/ *v* [I,T] to try to find out the position and size of your enemy's army, for example by flying planes over land where their soldiers are 偵察

re·con·sid·er /ˌrikənˋsɪdɚ; ˌriːkənˈsɪdə/ *v* [I,T] to think again about something you have decided, with the possibility that you might change your mind 重新考慮: *I have received your letter of resignation but I want you to reconsider your decision.* 我收到了你的辭職信, 但我希望你重新考慮你的決定。—**reconsideration** /ˌrikənˌsɪdəˋreʃən; ˌriːkənsɪdəˈreɪʃən/ *n* [U]

re·con·sti·tute /riˋkɑnstəˌtut; riːˈkɒnstɪ̣tjuːt/ *v* **1** [T] to bring something, especially an organization, back into existence in a different form 重組, 重建, 改編: **reconstitute sth as** *remnants of the old regiments reconstituted as the New Model Army* 把以前那幾個團的殘餘部隊重組為"新模範軍" **2 reconstituted milk/eggs etc** milk powder etc to which water has been added in order to change it back into the form it was in before it was dried 復水牛奶/雞蛋等 —**reconstitution** /riˌkɑnstəˋtuʃən; ˌriːkɒnstɪ̣ˈtjuːʃən/ *n* [U]

re·con·struct /ˌrikənˋstrʌkt; ˌriːkənˈstrʌkt/ *v* [T] **1** to produce a complete description or copy of something that happened by collecting together pieces of information〔由零碎的信息〕構想出…的全貌, 使〔完整的情景〕再現: *Police are trying to reconstruct the events of last Friday.* 警察在設法再現上星期五發生的那些事情。**2** to build something again after it has been destroyed or damaged 重建, 再建

re·con·struc·tion /ˌrikənˋstrʌkʃən; ˌriːkənˈstrʌkʃən/ *n* **1** [U] the work that is done after a war to repair the damage that was caused to a country's buildings, industry etc〔戰爭後的〕重建: *Reconstruction of the town began in 1948.* 該鎮的重建始於 1948 年。**2** [C usually singular 一般用單數] a copy of something that does not exist any more 復原物, 模型: [+**of**] *a reconstruction of a Native American village* 美洲印第安人村落的模型 **3** [C] a short film made using actors that tries to show how a real event happened 重現某真實事件的短片: *Police are broadcasting a reconstruction of the crime.* 警方正在播放一部再現犯罪經過的短片。

1 1 **rec·ord¹** /ˋrɛkɚd; ˈrekɔːd/ *n*

1 ▶INFORMATION 信息◀ [C] information about an event or series of events that is written down or stored on computer, film etc so that it can be looked at in the future 錄音; 錄像; 記錄: *medical records* 病歷 | [+**of**] *records of births, marriages, and deaths* 出生、婚姻和死亡記錄 | **keep a record** (=write down details of things as they happen) 做記錄 *Keep a record of any money you pay out.* 把你支出的每一筆錢都做個記錄。| **the biggest/lowest/highest etc on record** (=the biggest etc that has ever been recorded) 記載中最大/最低/最高的 *Today saw some of the hottest temperatures on record.* 今天出現了幾次有記載以來最高的溫度。| **place/put sth on record** (=include something in the official records) 把某事記錄在案 *I ask the court to place on record the fact that my client cooperated with the police.* 我要求法庭將我的當事人與警方合作這一事實記錄在案。

2 ▶HIGHEST/BEST EVER 最高/最好◀ [C] the fastest speed, longest distance, highest or lowest level etc that has ever been reached, especially in sport〔尤指體育運動的〕記錄: **break a record** (=do something faster, better etc than the previous record) 打破記錄 *Kenoco Oil's half-yearly profits broke all records.* 克諾科石油公司的半年度利潤打破了所有的記錄。| **hold a record** (=be the person who has achieved the fastest speed, the greatest distance etc) 保持一項記錄 | **set a record** (=achieve a new record) 創記錄 *The Americans set a new world record in the sprint relay.* 美國運動員在短跑接力賽中創造了一項新的世界記錄。| **record level/figure/sales etc** (=the highest level etc that has ever been reached) 創記錄的水平/數字/銷售額等 *a record level of unemployment* 創記錄的失業水平 | **an all-time record** (=the best that has ever been achieved) 有史以來最佳的記錄

3 ▶MUSIC 音樂◀ a round flat piece of plastic with a hole in the middle that music and sound is stored on 唱片: *the disc jockey who plays your favourite records* 播放你最喜歡的唱片的音樂節目主持人

4 ▶SB'S PAST BEHAVIOUR 某人過去的行為◀ [singular] the known facts about someone's past behaviour and how successful, good, or bad they have been 履歷, 經歷: *Laporte's service record in Indochina* 拉波特在印度支那服役的履歷 | **good/bad record** *The country has a fairly good record on human rights.* 該國有相當好的人權記錄。| **sb's record on** *Senator Donegan asked the President to justify his record on welfare.* 杜尼根參議員要求總統為他以往在福利方面的表現辯護。| **criminal record** (=a list made by the police of someone's crimes) 犯罪記錄 *He'll never get a job if they find out about his criminal record.* 假如他們發現他的犯罪記錄, 他永遠也別想找到工作。| **sb's track record** (=how successful someone has been up to now) 某人的成績記錄 *The company has a good track record in the export trade.* 該公司在出口貿易方面一直業績出色。

5 off the record if what you are telling someone is off the record, it is unofficial 私下說的, 不得引用的: *I'd like to emphasize that anything said here is strictly off the record.* 我想強調, 在這裡所說的任何話都嚴禁發表。

6 be/go on record as saying to be known to have said something publicly or officially 公開/正式說過: *She's on record as saying she thinks men and women should live separate lives.* 她公開說過, 她認為男人和女人應該有各自不同的生活。

7 for the record *spoken* used to mean that you want people to remember what you are now saying【口】為了記錄在案〔用於提起注意〕: *Let me just state for the record, that until yesterday my client had never seen Mr Rigati before.* 我必須鄭重聲明, 直到昨天之前, 我的當事人從未見過里加蒂先生。

8 put/set the record straight to tell people the truth about something, because you want to make it very clear that what they believe is not true 說明事實真相: *The director gave an interview to the newspapers to set the record straight.* 為澄清事實, 主管接受了報社記者的採訪。

re·cord² /rɪˋkɔrd; rɪˈkɔːd/ *v* **1** [T] to write information down or store it in a computer or on film so that it can be looked at in the future 記錄: *The expedition recorded* 

over 500 new species of plants. 探險隊記錄了五百多種新植物種類。| *Make sure you record the numbers of tickets you sell.* 一定要把你售出的票的號碼記錄下來。| **record that** *An official report records that at least half the nation's monuments are in need of repair.* 據一份官方報告記錄，這個國家至少一半的紀念碑需要維修。**2** [I, T] to store music, sound, television programmes etc on TAPE or DISCs so that people can listen to them or watch them again 錄(音)；錄(像)：*Are you going to record tonight's concert?* 今晚的音樂會你打算錄音嗎？| *The group has just recorded a new album.* 該組合剛錄製了一張新唱片。| *Is the machine still recording?* 機器還在錄音嗎？| *recording their conversation* 錄下他們的談話 **3** [T] if an instrument records the size, speed, temperature etc of something, it measures it and keeps that information〔儀器〕顯示，記錄：*Wind speeds of up to 100 kph have been recorded.* 已經記錄到高達每小時100公里的風速。

record-break·ing /ˈ·· ˌ··/ *adj* [only before noun 僅用於名詞前] higher, faster etc than anything similar ever achieved 破記錄的：*his record-breaking flight across the Atlantic* 他跨越大西洋的破記錄的飛行

re·cord·er /rɪˋkɔrdɚ; rɪˈkɔːdə/ *n* **1** [C] **cassette recorder/tape recorder/video recorder etc** a piece of electrical equipment that records music, films etc 卡式錄音機/磁帶錄音機/錄像機等 **2** [C] a simple musical instrument that you play by blowing straight down it 豎笛，直笛 **3** a judge in a city court, in some areas of Britain and the US〔英美某些地區市法院的〕法官

record-hold·er /ˈ·· ˌ··/ *n* [C] the person who has achieved the fastest speed, the longest distance etc in a sport 記錄保持者：*the current world record-holder for the discus throw* 擲鐵餅目前的世界記錄保持者

3 **re·cord·ing** /rɪˋkɔrdɪŋ; rɪˈkɔːdɪŋ/ *n* [C] **1** a piece of music or speech or a broadcast that has been recorded 錄製品；錄音；唱片：**[+of]** *Have you heard the new recording of Mozart's Requiem?* 你聽過莫扎特《安魂曲》的新唱片嗎？**2 recording studio/equipment etc** a studio etc used for recording music or sounds 錄音室/設備等

record li·bra·ry /ˈ·· ˌ···/ *n* [C] a place where lots of musical recordings are stored for people to borrow 唱片租借館

record play·er /ˈ·· ˌ··/ *n* [C] a piece of equipment for playing records or music 唱機 —compare 比較 STEREO[1]

re·count¹ /rɪˋkaunt; rɪˈkaʊnt/ *v* [T] *formal* to tell someone a story or describe a series of events【正式】敍述，描述

re·count² /ˋriˌkaunt; ˈriːkaʊnt/ *n* [C] a process of counting votes again 重新計算選票，重點選票：*I demand a recount!* 我要求重新計票！—**recount** /ˌriˋkaunt; riːˈkaʊnt/ *v* [T]

re·coup /rɪˋkup; rɪˈkuːp/ *v* [T] to get back an amount of money you have lost or spent 重新獲得〔失去或花掉的錢〕，收回：*Finance companies have managed to recoup some of the losses they made during the recession.* 金融公司挽回了經濟衰退期間蒙受的部分損失。| **recoup yourself** (=to get money for yourself after you have lost some) 為自己挽回損失 *Landlords recouped themselves by charging higher rents for their other properties.* 房東以提高其他房子的租金來補償自己的損失。

re·course /rɪˋkɔrs; rɪˈkɔːs/ *n formal* **have recourse to** to use something to help you when you are in a difficult situation【正式】求助於：**without recourse to** (=without having to use something) 無需 *We hope to solve this problem without recourse to further borrowing.* 我們希望不必依靠再借款來解決這個問題。

2 **re·cov·er¹** /rɪˋkʌvɚ; rɪˈkʌvə/ *v*

1 ►GET BETTER 好轉◄ [I] **a)** to get better after an illness, accident, shock etc 恢復健康：*After a few days of fever, he began to recover.* 發了幾天燒之後，他開始恢復健康。| **[+from]** *My boss is recovering from a heart attack.* 我的老闆心臟病發作，正在復原中。**b)** if something recovers after a period of trouble or difficulty, it returns to its normal condition 恢復(正常)：*After this war, the country will take a long time to recover.* 經過這場戰爭，這個國家將需要很長的時間才能恢復正常。

2 ►STH STOLEN/LOST ETC 被竊/丟失等的物品◄ [T] to get back something that was taken from you, lost, or almost destroyed 重新獲得；找回：*Police have so far failed to recover the stolen jewellery.* 警方尚未找回被盜的珠寶。| *A number of bodies were recovered from the wreckage.* 從殘骸中找出了若干具屍體。

3 ►MONEY 金錢◄ [T] to get back the same amount of money that you have spent or lost; RECOUP 重新獲得；收回：*The company hopes to recover the cost of developing their new product.* 公司希望能夠收回開發新產品的成本。

4 ►ABILITIES/SENSES 能力/知覺◄ [T] to get back an ability, a sense, or control over your feelings, movements etc 恢復〔能力、知覺、對情緒的控制、活動能力等〕：*It was some hours before she recovered consciousness.* 過了幾個小時她才恢復知覺。| **recover yourself** (=control yourself again after being upset, embarrassed etc) 使自己恢復到正常狀態 *It took Mom a few minutes to recover herself, but then she was back in control again.* 媽媽過了幾分鐘才鎮靜下來，然後又恢復了常態。| **recover your balance** (=stop yourself from falling) 恢復(身體)平衡 —**recoverable** *adj*

re·cov·er² /riˋkʌvɚ; ˌriːˈkʌvə/ *v* [T] to put a new cover on a piece of furniture 給〔家具〕換上新面子

re·cov·er·y /rɪˋkʌvərɪ; rɪˈkʌvəri/ *n* **1** [singular,U] a pro- 3
cess of getting better after an illness, injury etc 恢復健康，康復：**[+from]** *She made a quick recovery from the flu.* 流感後她很快恢復了健康。**2** [singular,U] the process of becoming stronger or more successful again after a difficult period 恢復，復蘇：*Hopes of economic recovery are fading.* 經濟復蘇的希望越來越渺茫。**3** [U] the act of getting something back 重新獲得；找回：**[+of]** *The recovery of the car from the lake took two hours.* 從湖裡打撈出汽車用了兩個小時。

recovery pro·gram /ˈ··· ˌ··/ *n* [C] *AmE* a course of treatment for people who are addicted (ADDICT (1)) to drugs or alcohol【美】〔戒毒、戒酒的〕康復計劃

recovery room /ˈ···· ·/ *n* [C] a room in a hospital where people first wake up after their operation〔手術後的〕護理病房，療養室

rec·re·ant /ˋrɛkrɪənt; ˈrekriənt/ *n* [C] *old use* someone who is disloyal and lacks courage【舊】怯懦的叛徒，變節者

re·cre·ate /ˌrikrɪˋet; ˌriːkriˈeɪt/ *v* [T] to make something from the past exist again or seem to exist again 使再現：*Scientists are trying to recreate these conditions.* 科學家們正在試圖重新創造這些條件。—**recreation** /ˌrikrɪˋeʃən; ˌriːkriˈeɪʃən/ *n* [C,U]

rec·re·a·tion /ˌrɛkrɪˋeʃən; ˌrekriˈeɪʃən/ *n* [C,U] an activity that you do for pleasure or amusement 娛樂，消遣：*His only recreations are drinking beer and watching football.* 他僅有的消遣就是喝啤酒和觀看足球比賽。| *a recreation center* 娛樂中心 —**recreational** *adj*: *recreational facilities* 娛樂設施

recreational ve·hi·cle /··ˌ··· ˈ···/ *n* [C] *AmE* an RV【美】活動房屋式旅遊車

recreation ground /··ˈ·· ·/ *n* [C] *BrE* an area of public land used for sports and games【英】公共遊樂場

recreation room /··ˈ·· ·/ *n* [C] **1** a public room, for example in a hospital, used for social activities or games〔醫院等處的〕娛樂活動室 **2** *AmE* a room in a private house, where you can relax, play games etc【美】〔家中的〕娛樂室

re·crim·i·na·tion /rɪˌkrɪməˋneʃən; rɪˌkrɪməˈneɪʃən/ *n* [C usually plural 一般用複數,U] a situation in which people blame each other, or what they say when they are blaming each other 互相指責：*Bitter accusations and recriminations followed the disaster.* 災難過後，嚴厲的指控和

相互歸咎隨之而來。

rec room /ˈrɛk rum; ˈrek ruːm/ *n* [C] *AmE informal* a RECREATION ROOM (2)【美, 非正式】〔家中的〕娛樂室

re·cru·des·cence /ˌrikruˈdɛsn̩s; ˌriːkruːˈdesəns/ *n* [usually singular 一般用單數] *formal* a sudden return or reappearance of something, especially something bad or unpleasant【正式】〔尤指壞事或令人不快之事的〕再次突然出現; 再發作: **[+of]** *a worrying recrudescence of urban violence* 都市暴力令人擔憂的再度爆發

re·cruit¹ /rɪˈkrut; rɪˈkruːt/ *v* **1** [I,T] to find new people to work in a company, join an organization, do a job etc 招聘, 吸收〔新成員〕: *We're having difficulty recruiting enough properly qualified staff.* 我們難以招聘到足夠的合格職員。**2 a)** [I,T] to get people to join the army or navy 招募〔新兵〕: *Most of the men in the village were recruited that day.* 村裡的大多數男子在那一天志願參軍。**b)** [T] to form a new army in this way〔通過招募〕組建〔新部隊〕**3** [T] *informal* to persuade someone to do something for you【非正式】勸說, 說服: **recruit sb to do sth** *I recruited three of my friends to help me move everything to the new apartment.* 我動員了三個朋友幫我把所有的東西搬入新公寓。—**recruitment** *n* [U]

recruit² *n* [C] **1** someone who has just joined the army, navy, or air force 新兵: **raw recruit** (=one who is completely untrained) 未經任何訓練的新兵 **2** someone who has recently joined an organization, group of people etc〔機構、團體的〕新成員: *The society was always trying to find ways of attracting new recruits.* 該社團總是在想方設法吸引新成員。

rec·tal /ˈrɛktl̩; ˈrektəl/ *adj technical* related to the RECTUM【術語】直腸的

rec·tan·gle /ˈrɛktæŋgl̩; ˈrektæŋgəl/ *n* [C] a shape that has four straight sides and four 90° angles at the corners. Usually two of the sides are longer than the other two. 長方形, 矩形 —compare 比較 SQUARE² (1) —see picture at 參見 SHAPE¹ 圖

rec·tan·gu·lar /rɛkˈtæŋgjələ; rekˈtæŋgjʊlə/ *adj* having the shape of a rectangle 長方形的, 矩形的

rec·ti·fi·er /ˈrɛktəˌfaɪə; ˈrektɪ̵faɪə/ *n* [C] *technical* an instrument that changes the flow of an electrical current in a wire【術語】整流器 —see also 另見 RECTIFY

rec·ti·fy /ˈrɛktəˌfaɪ; ˈrektɪ̵faɪ/ *v* **rectified, rectifying** [T] **1** *formal* to correct something that is wrong【正式】糾正, 矯正: *I did my best to rectify the situation, but the damage was already done.* 我竭盡全力整頓局面, 但損失已經造成。| *Please rectify the mistake at once.* 請立即糾正錯誤。**2** *technical* to make alcohol pure【術語】精餾〔酒精〕**3** *technical* to change an ALTERNATING CURRENT (=flow of electricity backwards and forwards along a wire) to a DIRECT CURRENT (=flow in only one direction)【術語】整流〔把電流由交流變成直流〕—**rectifiable** *adj* —**rectification** /ˌrɛktəfəˈkeʃən; ˌrektɪ̵fɪ̵ˈkeɪʃən/ *n* [C,U] —see also 另見 RECTIFIER

rec·ti·lin·e·ar /ˌrɛktəˈlɪnɪə; ˌrektɪ̵ˈlɪniə◂/ *adj technical* formed or moving in a straight line or consisting of straight lines【術語】成直線的; 直線運動的; 由直線組成的

rec·ti·tude /ˈrɛktəˌtud; ˈrektɪ̵tjuːd/ *n* [U] *formal* honesty and moral correctness【正式】誠實; 正直

rec·to /ˈrɛkto; ˈrektəʊ/ *n* [C] *technical* a page on the right-hand side of a book【術語】〔書的〕右頁 —**recto** *adj* —opposite 反義詞 VERSO

rec·tor /ˈrɛktə; ˈrektə/ *n* [C] **1** a priest in the Church of England or the Episcopal Church who is responsible for an area from which he receives his income directly〔英國國教會或美國新教聖公會的〕教區長 —compare 比較 VICAR **2** the person in charge of certain colleges and schools, especially in Scotland〔尤指蘇格蘭的〕學院院長, 學校校長

rec·to·ry /ˈrɛktərɪ; ˈrektəri/ *n* [C] a house where the rector of the local church lives, or used to live 教區長〔曾住過〕的住宅

rec·tum /ˈrɛktəm; ˈrektəm/ *n* [C] *technical* the lowest part of your BOWELS【術語】直腸 —see picture at 參見 DIGESTIVE SYSTEM 圖

re·cum·bent /rɪˈkʌmbənt; rɪˈkʌmbənt/ *adj formal* lying down on your back or side【正式】躺着的, 仰臥的; 側臥的: *a full-length portrait of the recumbent warrior* 一幅側臥武士的全身肖像

re·cu·pe·rate /rɪˈkjupəˌret; rɪˈkjuːpəreɪt/ *v* **1** [T] to get better again after an illness or injury 恢復, 復原: *The doctor sent her to the Sea View Rest Home to recuperate.* 醫生讓她去海景療養院休養。| **[+from]** *A good night's sleep was all I needed to recuperate from the stresses of the day.* 我只需好好睡上一晚, 就可從一天的緊張中恢復過來。**2** [T] to get back money that you have spent or lost in business 重新獲得; 彌補: *We've recuperated our losses.* 我們的損失已經得到補償 —**recuperation** /rɪˌkjupəˈreʃən; rɪˌkjuːpəˈreɪʃən/ *n* [U]

re·cu·pe·ra·tive /rɪˈkjupəˌretɪv; rɪˈkjuːpərətɪv/ *adj* helping you to get better again after an illness 有助康復的: *a recuperative vacation* 有助恢復健康的假日

re·cur /rɪˈkɝ; rɪˈkɜː/ *v* [I] **recurred, recurring 1** if something, especially something bad or unpleasant, recurs, it happens again〔尤指壞事或令人不快的事〕再次發生: *There is a danger that the disease may recur in later life.* 年紀大了之後這種病有復發的危險。| *a recurring nightmare* 一再出現的惡夢 **2** *technical* if a number or numbers after a DECIMAL POINT recur, they are repeated forever in the same order【術語】〔小數〕循環

R

re·cur·rence /rɪˈkɝəns; rɪˈkʌrəns/ *n* [C,U] *formal* an occasion when something that has happened before, happens again【正式】再發生, 再現: **[+of]** *Measures must be taken to stop a recurrence of last night's violence.* 必須採取措施防止昨晚的暴力事件再次發生。

re·cur·rent /rɪˈkɝənt; rɪˈkʌrənt/ *adj* happening or appearing repeatedly 一再發生的, 反覆出現的: *recurrent minor illnesses* 不斷反覆的小疾病 | *a recurrent theme in Eliot's poetry* 艾略特的詩歌中一再出現的主題 —**recurrently** *adv*

re·cy·cla·ble /riˈsaɪkləbl̩; ˌriːˈsaɪkləbəl/ *adj* used materials or substances that are recyclable can be recycled 可回收利用的 —**recyclable** *n* [usually plural 一般用複數] *AmE*【美】

re·cy·cle /riˈsaɪkl̩; ˌriːˈsaɪkəl/ *v* [I,T] to put used objects or materials through a special process, so that they can be used again 再利用, 回收利用: *We take all our bottles and newspapers to be recycled.* 我們把所有的瓶子和報紙都送去回收利用。—**recycled** *adj*: *recycled paper* 再生紙

re·cy·cling /riˈsaɪkl̩ɪŋ; ˌriːˈsaɪklɪŋ/ *n* [U] the process of treating things such as paper or steel so that they can be used again 回收利用: *Recycling is important to help protect our environment.* 回收利用對幫助保護我們的環境很重要。

red¹ /rɛd; red/ *adj* **redder, reddest** S1 W1

1 ►COLOUR 顏色◄ having the colour of blood or fire 紅色的: *We painted the door bright red.* 我們把門漆成鮮紅色。| *a beautiful red rose* 一朵美麗的紅玫瑰

2 ►HAIR 頭髮◄ hair that is red has an orange-brown colour 褐紅色的

3 ►SKIN 皮膚◄ skin that is red is a bright pink colour, usually only for a short time 粉紅色的: *Her cheeks were red with excitement.* 她興奮得面頰紅紅的。

4 ►POLITICS 政治◄ *informal* COMMUNIST or extremely LEFT-WING【非正式】共產主義的; 極左的

5 be as red as a beetroot *BrE*【英】**/beet** *AmE*【美】to have a very red face, usually because you are embarrassed〔因尷尬而〕滿臉通紅

6 like a red rag to a bull *BrE* very likely to make someone angry or upset【英】容易使人憤怒; 容易使人苦惱的: *Just mentioning his ex-wife's name was like a red rag to a bull.* 只要提到他前妻的名字他就會怒不可遏。

7 roll out the red carpet/give sb the red carpet

treatment to give special treatment to someone important who is visiting you 隆重歡迎: *He's our best customer, so make sure you give him the red carpet treatment.* 他是我們最好的客戶，你們務必要隆重接待他。
8 a red cent [usually in negatives 一般用否定式] *AmE informal* a very small amount of money【美，非正式】極少量的錢: *They'll never be able to pay that – they don't have a red cent!* 他們永遠也付不起這筆錢 —— 他們身無分文！| *not worth a red cent* 一文不值的 **—redness** *n* [U] —see also 另見 **paint the town red** (PAINT² (6))

red² *n* **1** [C,U] the colour of blood or fire 紅色: *Red is often used as a danger sign.* 紅色經常被用作危險的信號。| *the reds and yellows of the fall trees* 秋天樹木呈現的各種紅色和黃色 | *The corrections were marked in red.* (=in red ink) 修改的部分用紅筆標出。—see picture on page A5 參見 A5 頁圖 **2** [C,U] red wine 紅葡萄酒: *a nice bottle of red* 一瓶香醇的紅葡萄酒 **3** [C] *informal* a slightly insulting word for someone who has COMMUNIST or very LEFT-WING ideas or opinions【非正式】赤色分子；共產主義者；激進左翼分子〔帶有輕微侮辱意味〕**4 see red** to become very angry 發怒: *The way he treated that dog just made me see red.* 他對待那條狗的方式使我憤怒。**5 in the red** *informal* owing more money than you have【非正式】虧欠；有赤字: *These car payments are going to put me into the red again.* 這幾筆買車的付款讓我再次出現赤字。—compare 比較 **be in the black** (BLACK² (4))

red ad·mi·ral /ˌ· ˈ···/ *n* [C] a type of BUTTERFLY that has black wings with bright red marks on them 紅紋蝶

red a·lert /ˌ· ·ˈ·/ *n* [C usually singular 一般用單數] a warning of sudden very great danger 緊急警報: *Evacuate the building – this is a red alert!* 請撤離大樓，這是緊急警報！| **be on red alert** (=be ready to deal with a danger) 處於緊急待命狀態 *All the hospitals have been put on red alert.* 所有的醫院已處於緊急待命狀態。

red blood cell /ˌ· ˈ· ·/ also 又作 **red cor·pus·cle** /ˌ· ˈ···/ *n* [C] one of the cells in your blood that carry oxygen to every part of your body 紅細胞，紅血球 —compare 比較 WHITE BLOOD CELL

red-blood·ed /ˌ· ˈ··◂/ *adj* a red-blooded man is strong and full of sexual energy 強有力的；精力充沛的

red·breast /ˈrɛdˌbrɛst; ˈredbrest/ *n* [C] *poetic* a ROBIN【詩】(歐洲) 鴝，知更鳥

red·brick /ˈrɛdˌbrɪk; ˈredbrɪk/ *adj* a redbrick university is one of the British universities built in the late 19th or early 20th century〔19世紀末、20世紀初在英國建成的〕紅磚大學的 —compare 比較 OXBRIDGE

red card /ˌ· ˈ·/ *n* [C] a piece of red card held up by the REFEREE in a football match, to show that a player has done something against the rules and will not be allowed to play for the rest of the game〔足球〕紅牌 —see picture on page A23 參見 A23 頁圖

red·coat /ˈrɛdˌkot; ˈredkəʊt/ *n* [C] a British soldier during the 18th and 19th centuries〔18、19世紀的〕英國士兵

Red Cres·cent /ˌ· ˈ··/ *n* [singular] an organization in Muslim countries that helps people who are suffering as a result of war, floods, disease etc 紅新月會〔穆斯林國家中相當於紅十字會的組織〕

Red Cross /ˌ· ˈ·/ *n* [singular] an international organization that helps people who are suffering as a result of war, floods, disease etc 紅十字會

red·cur·rant /ˌrɛdˋkɝənt; ˌredˈkʌrənt◂/ *n* [C] a very small red fruit that grows on bushes in northern Europe〔北歐產的〕紅醋栗 —compare 比較 BLACKCURRANT

red·den /ˈrɛdn̩; ˈredn/ *v* [I,T] to become red, or make something red (使) 變紅: *Lynn's face reddened at this description of herself.* 聽到這樣對自己的描述，林恩漲紅了臉。

red·dish /ˈrɛdɪʃ; ˈredɪʃ/ *adj* slightly red 微紅的，淡紅的: *reddish-brown lipstick* 紅褐色的口紅

re·dec·o·rate /riˋdɛkəˌret; riːˈdekəreɪt/ *v* [I,T] *BrE* to put new paint or paper on the walls of a room【英】(給…) 重新粉刷牆壁；(給…) 重新貼上壁紙 **—redecoration** /riˌdɛkəˋreʃən; riːˌdekəˈreɪʃən/ *n* [U]

re·deem /rɪˋdim; rɪˈdiːm/ *v* [T] *formal*【正式】
1 ▶IMPROVE STH 改善某事物◀ to make something less bad 補救，補償: *Olivier's performance redeemed what was otherwise a second-rate play.* 要不是奧利弗的表演，這就是一齣二流的戲。| **redeeming feature** (=the one good thing about someone or something that is unpleasant) 起彌補作用的特點 *a brutal man, whose one redeeming feature was his honesty* 一個殘忍的人，他的唯一可取之處是誠實
2 ▶FREE SB 解放某人◀ to free someone from the power or evil, especially in the Christian religion〔尤指基督教中〕救贖，為…贖罪；解救: *Christ came to Earth to redeem us from our sins.* 基督來到人間為我們贖罪。—see also 另見 REDEEMER
3 redeem yourself to do something that will improve what other people think of you, after you have behaved badly or failed 使自己免受責難；挽回聲譽: *She was trying desperately to redeem herself after last week's embarrassing mistake.* 在犯了上星期那個令人難堪的錯誤之後，她拚命想挽回自己的聲譽。
4 redeem a promise/pledge/obligation etc *formal* to do what you promised to do【正式】履行諾言/承諾/義務等: *The government found itself unable to redeem its election pledges.* 政府無法履行在選舉中所作的承諾。
5 ▶GET MONEY FOR STH 以某物兑換錢◀ to exchange a piece of paper representing an amount of money for the money that it is worth 把…兑換成現金: *Redeem this coupon for 20p off your next jar of coffee.* 你再買一瓶咖啡時，用這張優惠券可省 20 便士。| *Bonus shares can be redeemed until 31st July.* 分紅的股份可以在 7 月 31 日之前兑換成現金。
6 ▶GET STH BACK 重新獲得某物◀ to buy something back which you had left with someone in order to borrow money from them 贖回: *I was finally able to redeem my watch from the pawnbrokers.* 我最終得以從當鋪裡贖回手錶。**—redeemable** *adj*

Re·deem·er /rɪˋdimɚ; rɪˈdiːmə/ *n* [singular] *literary* **the Redeemer** Jesus Christ【文】耶穌基督

re·demp·tion /rɪˋdɛmpʃən; rɪˈdempʃən/ *n* [U] **1** the state of being freed from the power of evil, believed by Christians to be made possible by Jesus Christ〔基督教指耶穌的〕救贖，贖罪 **2 past/beyond redemption** too bad to be saved, repaired, or improved 不可救藥的，無可挽回的 **3** *technical* the exchange of shares (SHARE² (5)), bonds (BOND¹ (1)) etc for money【術語】〔將股票、證券〕兑換現款 **—redemptive** /-tɪv; -tɪv/ *adj*

re·de·ploy /ˌridɪˋplɔɪ; ˌriːdɪˈplɔɪ/ *v* [T] to move someone or something to a different place or job 重新部署，調遣〔人員〕，調配〔物資〕: *Army tanks were redeployed elsewhere in the region.* 陸軍坦克被重新佈置在該地區的其他地方。**—redeployment** *n* [U]

re·de·vel·op /ˌridɪˋvɛləp; ˌriːdɪˈveləp/ *v* [T] to make an area more modern by putting in new buildings or changing the old ones 重建，重新開發，改建: *The old docks are being redeveloped as a business park.* 舊船塢正在被改建成商業園區。**—redevelopment** *n* [C,U]

red eye /ˈ· ·/ *n* [U] *AmE informal*【美，非正式】**1** a plane that makes a journey at night 夜間航班，紅眼航班: *I took the red eye to LA.* 我乘坐夜間航班去洛杉磯。**2** cheap WHISKY 廉價威士忌酒

red-faced /ˌ· ˈ·◂/ *adj* embarrassed or ashamed 尷尬的；羞愧的: *The election result left them rather red-faced.* 選舉結果使他們相當尷尬。

red gi·ant /ˌ· ˈ··/ *n* [singular] a star that is near the middle of its life, and is larger and less solid than the sun 紅巨星

red-hand·ed /ˌ· ˈ··◂/ *adj* **catch sb red-handed** to catch someone at the moment when they are doing something wrong 當場抓住某人: *Earl was caught red-handed taking money from the register.* 厄爾正從現金出納機中拿錢時被當場抓獲。

red·head /ˋrɛdˌhɛd; ˈredhed/ *n* [C] someone who has red hair 有紅頭髮的人

red her·ring /ˌ· ˈ··/ *n* [C] a fact or idea that is not important but is introduced to take your attention away from the points that are important 轉移注意力的事[想法]

red-hot /ˌ· ˈ·◂/ *adj* **1** metal that is red-hot is so hot that it shines red〔金屬〕赤熱的, 熱得通紅的: *The poker glowed red-hot in the fire.* 撥火棍在火裡閃着赤熱的光。**2** *informal* very hot【非正式】非常熱的, 燙的: *Be careful with those plates – they're red-hot.* 小心那些盤子, 燙極了。**3** *informal* extremely active or exciting【非正式】極富活力的; 令人十分激動的: *a red-hot news story* 令人興奮的新聞報道 | *red-hot enthusiasm* 高漲的熱情

re·dial /ˌriˋdaɪəl; ˌriːˈdaɪəl/ *v* [I,T] to DIAL a telephone number again 重撥〔電話號碼〕

Red In·di·an /ˌ· ˈ···/ *n* [C] a word for a Native American, that is now usually considered offensive 美洲土著居民, 印第安人〔這詞現在一般被認為是冒犯用語〕

re·di·rect, re-direct /ˌridəˋrɛkt; ˌriːdaɪˈrekt/ *v* [T] **1** to send something in a different direction, or use something for a different purpose 改向; 改用: *She was good at redirecting the children's energy into something useful.* 她善於把孩子們的精力轉移到做有用的事情上。| *redirecting funds to other departments* 將資金轉撥到其他部門 **2** *BrE* to send someone's letters to their new address from an address that they have left; FORWARD[3] (1)【英】改寄〔信件〕

re·dis·trib·ute /ˌridɪˋstrɪbjut; ˌriːdɪˈstrɪbjuːt/ *v* [T] to give something to each member of a group so that it is divided up in a different way than it was before 再分配, 再分發: *an attempt to redistribute the country's wealth more fairly* 更公平地重新分配國家財富的嘗試 —**redistribution** /ˌridɪstrɪˋbjuʃən; ˌriːdɪstrəˈbjuːʃən/ *n* [U]

red-let·ter day /ˌ· ˈ·· ·/ *n* [C] *informal* a day when something special happens that makes you very happy【非正式】喜慶的日子

red-light dis·trict /ˌ· ˈ· ˌ··/ *n* [C] the area of a town or city where there are many PROSTITUTEs (=women who have sex for money) 紅燈區

red meat /ˌ· ˈ·/ *n* [U] dark coloured meat such as BEEF or LAMB 紅色肉類〈如牛肉、羊肉〉—compare 比較 WHITE MEAT

red·neck /ˋrɛdˌnɛk; ˈrednek/ *n* [C] *AmE informal* a man who lives in a country area of the US, is uneducated, and may have strong unreasonable opinions【美, 非正式】〔尤指頑固的〕鄉巴佬 —**redneck** *adj*

re·do /riˋdu; riːˈduː/ *v* [T] *past tense* **redid** /-ˋdɪd; -ˈdɪd/ *past participle* **redone** /-ˋdʌn; -ˈdʌn/ to do something again 重做, 再做: *You'll have to redo this piece of work.* 你必須重新做這項工作。| *We're having the kitchen redone* (=decorated again) *professionally.* 我們正在請專業人員重新裝修廚房。

red·o·lent /ˋrɛdḷənt; ˈredəl-ənt/ *adj formal*【正式】**1** **redolent of** making you think of something 使人聯想起…的: *a style redolent of the sixties* 使人聯想起60年代的風格 **2** smelling strongly of something 散發出…強烈氣味的: *The air was redolent with roses.* 空氣中散發着玫瑰的芳香。—**redolence** *n* [U]

re·doub·le /riˋdʌbḷ; riːˈdʌbəl/ *v* [T] **redouble your efforts** to greatly increase your effort as you try to do something 加倍努力: *The musicians laughed and redoubled their efforts to keep up with the singer.* 樂師們笑了起來, 加倍努力跟上歌手的速度。

re·doub·ta·ble /rɪˋdautəbḷ; rɪˈdaʊtəbəl/ *adj literary* someone who is redoubtable is a person you respect or fear【文】令人敬畏的: *He was not looking forward to facing the redoubtable Mrs Macclesfield.* 他不希望面對令人敬畏的麥克萊斯菲爾德太太。

re·dound /rɪˋdaund; rɪˈdaʊnd/ *v* **redounded to sb's fame/credit/honour etc** *formal* to make someone more famous, more respected etc【正式】提高某人的聲譽/信譽/榮譽等: *glorious deeds that redound to the honour of our country* 提高我國聲譽的光榮事跡

red pep·per /ˌ· ˈ··/ *n* **1** [C] a red vegetable which you can eat raw or use in cooking; CAPSICUM 紅辣椒: *stuffed red peppers* 釀紅辣椒 **2** [U] a hot tasting red powder used in cooking; CAYENNE 辣椒粉

re·dress[1] /rɪˋdrɛs; rɪˈdres/ *v* [T] *formal*【正式】**1** to correct something that is wrong or unfair 修正, 改正; 矯正: *redressing the racial inequalities of society today* 糾正目前社會上種族不平等的現象 **2** **redress the balance** to make a situation fair or equal when it has been unfair or unequal 調整; 使重新平衡: *If one species breeds too much, the theory says a new epidemic will arise to redress the balance.* 該理論稱, 如果某一物種繁殖過多, 一種新的流行性傳染病就會出現以重新達到平衡。

re·dress[2] /ˋridrɛs; rɪˈdres/ *n* [U] *formal* money that someone pays you because they have caused you harm, or damaged your property; COMPENSATION (1)【正式】〔對傷害或財產損壞的〕賠償: *The only hope of redress is in a lawsuit.* 獲得賠償的唯一希望就是提出訴訟。

red·skin /ˋrɛdˌskɪn; ˈredˌskɪn/ *n* [C] *old use* a word for a Native American, that is now considered to be offensive【舊】美洲土著居民, 印第安人〔這詞現在一般被認為是冒犯用語〕

R

red tape /ˌ· ˈ·/ *n* [U] official rules that seem unnecessary and prevent things from being done quickly and easily 繁瑣費時的手續; 繁文縟節: *a procedure surrounded by bureaucracy and red tape* 充斥着官僚作風和繁文縟節的程序

re·duce /rɪˋdus; rɪˈdjuːs/ *v* **1** [T] to make something smaller or less in size, amount, or price 縮小; 減少; 降低: *We were hoping that they would reduce the rent a little.* 我們希望他們會把租金降低一點。| **reduce sth by half/ten percent etc** *The workforce has been reduced by half.* 勞動力已經減少一半。| **[+to]** *All the shirts were reduced to £10.* 所有襯衫都減價至十英鎊。—see also 另見 REDUCTION **2** [I] *especially AmE* to become thinner by losing weight【尤美】減肥 **3** [T] if you reduce a liquid or it reduces, you boil it or it boils until there is less of it〔煮沸液體以〕使濃縮 **4** **in reduced circumstances** *old-fashioned* poorer than you were before【過時】更貧窮, 更潦倒 **5** [T] *old use* to take control of a place by using military force【舊】〔用武力〕攻克, 攻佔

reduce sb/sth to sth *phr v* [T] **1** **reduce sb to tears/silence etc** to make someone cry, be silent etc 使某人流淚/沉默等: *David's extraordinary reply reduced me to silence.* 戴維不尋常的回答使我無言以對。**2** **reduce sb to doing sth** to force someone into a particular kind of behaviour or way of life 迫使某人做某事; 使不得不做某事: *Eventually Charlotte was reduced to begging on the streets.* 最後夏洛特被迫淪落到沿街乞討。**3** to change something into a shorter simpler form 縮短, 簡化: *The report can be reduced to three main points.* 報告可以歸納為三個要點。**4** **reduce sth to rubble/ashes etc** to destroy something, especially a building, completely 把某物〔尤指建築物〕夷為廢墟/化為灰燼等 **5** **reduce sb to the ranks** to make an army officer an ordinary soldier 把某人〔指軍官〕降級為士兵

re·duc·tion /rɪˋdʌkʃən; rɪˈdʌkʃən/ *n* **1** [C,U] the fact of something becoming or being made smaller 縮小; 減少: **[+in]** *a slight reduction in the price of oil* 油價略有下降 | *strategies for noise reduction* 減少噪音的對策 | **make a reduction** (=sell something more cheaply) 減價 *We can make a reduction if you buy in bulk.* 如果你大批購買, 我們可以降低價格。**2** [C] a smaller copy of a photograph, map, or picture〔照片、地圖或圖畫的〕縮版 —opposite 反義詞 ENLARGEMENT (1)

re·dun·dan·cy /rɪˋdʌndənsɪ; rɪˈdʌndənsi/ *n* **1** [C,U] *BrE* a situation in which someone has to leave their job, be- 

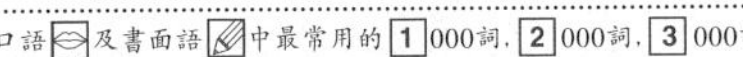

cause they are no longer needed【英】失業, 裁員, 解雇: *The closure of the export department resulted in over 100 redundancies.* 出口部的關閉導致一百多人被解雇。| *2,000 workers now face redundancy.* 2,000名工人目前面臨着失業。**2** [U] a situation in which something is not used because something similar or the same already exists 重複; 多餘; 累贅 **3** [C,U] *technical* the quality of containing additional parts that will make a system work if other parts fail【術語】〔部件的〕冗餘〔確保即使有部件失靈, 系統依然正常工作〕

redundancy pay /·'··· ,·/ *n* [U] *BrE* money you get from your employer when you are made redundant【英】解雇津貼, 遣散費; SEVERANCE PAY *AmE*【美】

re·dun·dant /rɪˋdʌndənt; rɪˈdʌndənt/ *adj* **1** *BrE* if you are redundant your employer no longer has a job for you【英】失業的, 被解雇的: **make sb redundant** *Seventy factory workers were made redundant in the resulting cuts.* 在繼而發生的裁員中七十名工人被解雇。**2** not necessary because something else does the same thing 多餘的, 累贅的: *The word gradually became redundant and dropped out of the language.* 這個詞逐漸變得累贅, 並從該語言中消失了。—**redundantly** *adv*

re·du·pli·cate /rɪˋdupləˌket; rɪˈdjuːplɪ̇keɪt/ *v* [T] *formal* to repeat a part of something, especially part of a word【正式】重複〔尤指詞的某部分〕—**reduplication** /rɪˌdupləˋkeʃən; rɪˌdjuːplɪ̇ˈkeɪʃən/ *n* [C,U]

R

red·wood /ˋrɛdˌwʊd; ˈredwʊd/ *n* [C,U] a very tall tree that grows in California, or the wood from this tree〔生長在美國加利福尼亞的〕紅杉 (木)

reed /rid; riːd/ *n* [C] **1** a type of tall plant like grass that grows in wet places 蘆葦: *Reeds grew in clumps all along the river bank.* 沿着河岸長着一叢叢蘆葦。**2** a thin piece of wood that is fixed into a musical instrument such as an OBOE or CLARINET, and produces a sound when you blow over it〔管樂器的〕簧片

re·ed·u·cate /riˋɛdʒəˌket; riːˈedjʊ̇keɪt/ *v* [T] to teach someone to think or behave in a different way 再教育, 重新教育: *Young criminals must above all be reeducated.* 最重要的是必須對青少年罪犯進行再教育。

reed·y /ˋridɪ; ˈriːdi/ *adj* **1** a voice that is reedy is high and unpleasant to listen to〔聲音〕尖的, 刺耳的 **2** a place that is reedy has a lot of reeds growing there 蘆葦叢生的

reef¹ /rif; riːf/ *n* [C] a line of sharp rocks, often made of CORAL, or a raised area of sand near the surface of the sea 礁; 礁脈: *The ship was wrecked on a reef.* 這條船觸礁失事了。| *the Great Barrier Reef*〔澳大利亞〕大堡礁

reef² also 又作 **reef in** *v* [T] *technical* to tie up part of a sail in order to make it smaller【術語】縮〔帆〕

ree·fer /ˋrifɚ; ˈriːfə/ *n* [C] *old-fashioned* a cigarette containing the drug MARIJUANA【過時】大麻香煙

reef knot /'· ·/ *n* [C] *especially BrE* a double knot that cannot come undone easily【尤英】縮帆結, 方結, 平結; SQUARE KNOT *AmE*【美】

reek¹ /rik; riːk/ *v* [I] **1** to smell strongly and unpleasantly of something 有臭味, 發出臭氣: *This room absolutely reeks.* 這個房間真的臭極了。| **[+of]** *His breath reeked of garlic.* 他的呼吸帶着蒜味。**2** to seem to be strongly connected with something bad or unpleasant 具有…的強烈氣息: **[+of]** *The whole business reeks of dishonesty.* 整個交易充滿欺詐的意味。

reek² *n* [singular] a strong unpleasant smell 濃烈的臭味, 惡臭: *a reek of tobacco and beer* 一股強烈的煙和啤酒的臭味

reel¹ /ril; riːl/ *n* [C] **1 a)** *BrE* a round object onto which thread, wire, fishing line, cinema film etc can be wound【英】卷軸, 卷筒; 卷盤; 繞線輪: *a cotton reel* 棉線團 —compare 比較 BOBBIN **b)** the amount that one of these objects will hold 一卷 (之量): *Have you got another reel of film?* 你是否還有一卷膠卷? **2** one of the parts of a cinema film that is contained on a reel〔一部影片的〕一盤: *a scene from the final reel of 'High Noon'* 電影《龍城殲霸戰》最後一盤中的一個場面 **3** a quick and cheerful Scottish or Irish dance, or the music for this 里爾舞〔一種輕快的蘇格蘭或愛爾蘭舞〕; 里爾舞曲

reel² *v* **1** also 又作 **reel back** [I] to step backwards suddenly and almost fall over, especially after being hit or getting a shock〔尤指遭受打擊或震驚而〕站立不穩: *Diane reeled back in amazement.* 黛安娜吃驚得朝後打了一個趔趄。| *A punch in his stomach sent him reeling.* 他的肚子上重重地挨了一拳, 使他直打趔趄。**2** [I] to feel very shocked or confused 震驚; 迷惑: *All these statistics make my head reel.* 所有這些數字搞得我頭昏腦脹。| **[+from]** *The party is still reeling from its recent election defeat.* 該黨由於最近選舉的失敗仍然驚魂未定。**3** [I] to seem to go around and around〔感覺〕暈眩, 天旋地轉: *The room reeled before my eyes and I fainted.* 房間在我眼前旋轉起來, 隨即我就失去了知覺。**4** [T always+adv/prep] to make something move on or off a reel by winding it 捲, 繞: *He reeled in his fishing line.* 他繞着收回魚線。**5** [I always+adv/prep] to walk in an unsteady way, moving from side to side as if you are drunk 蹣跚: *Captain Banks came reeling up the street.* 班克斯上校步履蹣跚地沿着街走來。

reel sth ↔ **off** *phr v* [T] *informal* to repeat a lot of information quickly and easily【非正式】滔滔不絕地重複: *Jack reeled off a list of names.* 傑克一口氣說出了一長串名字。

re-e·lect /ˌri əˋlɛkt; ˌriː ɪˈlekt/ *v* [T] to elect someone again 再次選, 重選 —**re-election** /-ˋlɛkʃən; -ˈlekʃən/ *n* [C,U] *Barnes is seeking re-election.* 巴恩斯正在尋求連任。

re·en·try /riˋɛntrɪ; riˈentri/ *n* [C,U] an act of entering a place again 再進入: *The shuttle made a successful reentry into the Earth's atmosphere.* 宇宙飛船成功地重返地球大氣層。

reeve /riv; riːv/ *n* [C] **1** the president of a modern Canadian town council〔加拿大的〕市鎮議會主席 **2** an English law officer in former times〔英國舊時的〕地方治安法官

ref¹ /rɛf; ref/ *n* [C] *BrE informal* a REFEREE【英, 非正式】裁判員

ref² the written abbreviation of 縮寫= REFERENCE 2

re·fec·to·ry /rɪˋfɛktərɪ; rɪˈfektəri/ *n* [C] *BrE* a large room in a school, college etc where meals are served and eaten【英】〔學校、學院等的〕食堂, 餐廳; CAFETERIA *AmE*【美】

re·fer /rɪˋfɝ; rɪˈfɜː/ *v* **referred, referring** 1

refer to *phr v* [T] **1** **[refer to** sb/sth] to mention or speak about someone or something 提到, 談到: *We agreed never to refer to the matter again.* 我們同意永遠不再提這件事。| *Although she didn't mention any names, everyone knew who she was referring to.* 儘管她沒有提到任何名字, 但大家都知道她指的是誰。| **refer to sth/sb as** *Johnson referred to the discovery as a major breakthrough in medical science.* 約翰遜稱這項發現是醫學領域裡的一個重大突破。**2** **[refer to** sth] to look at a book, map, piece of paper etc, for information 參考, 查看, 查閱: *Complete the exercise without referring to a dictionary.* 請不要查閱辭典完成這個練習。| *Let me just refer to my notes for the exact figures.* 讓我查看筆記, 找出確切的數字。**3** **[refer to** sth/sb] if a statement, number etc refers to someone or something, it is about that person or thing 涉及, 關於: *The figures in the left-hand column refer to our sales abroad.* 左欄裡的數字是關於我們的海外銷售額的。**4** **[refer** sb/sth **to** sb/sth] to send someone or something to another place or person for information, advice, or a decision 讓…去查詢; 提交…作決定: *My complaint was referred to the manufacturers.* 我的投訴已轉交給製造廠商。| *Professor Watson referred me to an article she had written on the subject.* 沃森教授要我去查閱她寫的關於這個題目的一篇文章。| *My doctor is referring me* (=is sending me for treatment) *to a dermatologist.* 我的醫生介紹我去看皮膚科醫生。—see also 另見 CROSS-REFER

re·fer·a·ble /rɪˋfɝəbl̩; rɪˈfɜːrəbəl/ *adj* **[+to]** *formal* something that is referable to something else can be related to it【正式】與…有關的

ref·er·ee¹ /ˌrɛfəˋri; ˌrefəˈriː/ *n* [C] **1** someone who is in charge of a game in sports such as football, BASKETBALL, or BOXING〔體育比賽的〕裁判員 —compare 比較 UMPIRE¹ —see picture on page A22 參見 A22 頁圖 **2** *BrE* someone who provides information about you when you are trying to get a job【英】證明人, 介紹人, 推薦人: *His headmaster agreed to act as his referee.* 他的校長同意做他的推薦人。**3** someone who is asked to settle a disagreement 仲裁者, 公斷者: *an independent referee* 一位獨立仲裁人

referee² *v* **refereed, refereeing** [I,T] to be the referee for a game 當裁判; 為…擔任裁判

3 1 **ref·er·ence** /ˋrɛfərəns; ˈrefərəns/ *n* **1** [C,U] something you say or write that mentions another person or thing 提及, 談到: **[+to]** *There is no direct reference to her own childhood in the novel.* 小說裡沒有直接提及她的童年。| **make reference to** *Winston made no reference to what had happened.* 溫斯頓沒有提及發生的事情。| **a passing reference (to)** (=a quick mention) 順便提及 *a speech about the economy without even a passing reference to the problem of unemployment* 有關經濟卻絲毫沒有提及失業問題的講話 **2** [C,U] the act of looking at something for information 查閱, 查看: *Use this dictionary for easy reference.* 為了查閱方便, 請使用這本辭典。| **for future reference** (=to have information in the future) 以供將來參考 *Keep their price list on file for future reference.* 請將他們的價目表存檔, 以供日後參考。**3 with reference to** *formal* used to say what you are writing or talking about, especially in business letters【正式】關於〔尤用於公函〕: *With reference to your recent advertisement, I am writing to request further details.* 關於貴方最近的廣告, 現特函查詢詳情。**4** [C] **a)** a letter written by someone who knows you well, usually to a new employer, giving information about you 推薦信, 介紹信: **take up references** (=get references) 得到推薦信 *We will need references from your former employers.* 我們需要你前雇主的推薦信。**b)** a person who provides information about your character and abilities 推薦人, 介紹人: *Ask your teacher to act as one of your references.* 請你的老師做你的推薦人之一。**5** [C] **a)** a note that tells you where the information that is used in a book, article etc comes from 出處; 參考書目: *a list of references at the end of the article* 文章結尾處的參考書目 **b)** a number that tells you where you can find the information you want in a book, on a map etc〔書籍或地圖等中的〕參照號, 參照符號: *map reference SG49* 地圖參照號 SG49 —see also 另見 CROSS-REFERENCE, FRAME OF REFERENCE, **terms of reference** (TERM¹ (18))

reference book /ˈ··· ·/ *n* [C] a book such as a dictionary or ENCYCLOPAEDIA that you look at to find information 工具書, 參考書

reference li·bra·ry /ˈ··· ˌ···/ *n* [C] a public place where books are stored, where you can use the books but cannot take them away 工具書閱覽室

ref·e·ren·dum /ˌrɛfəˋrɛndəm; ˌrefəˈrendəm/ *n* [C, U] *plural* **referenda** or **referendums** an occasion when everyone in a country votes in order to make a decision about a particular subject〔為表決某問題的〕全民投票: **hold a referendum** *A referendum was held on whether abortion should be made legal.* 就墮胎是否應該合法化進行了全民投票。

re·fer·ral /rɪˋfɝəl; rɪˈfɜːrəl/ *n* [C,U] *formal* an act of sending someone or something to another place for help, information, a decision etc【正式】提交; 介紹: *the referral of the case to the Court of Appeal* 把案件提交給上訴法庭

re·fill¹ /riˋfɪl; ˌriːˈfɪl/ *v* [T] to fill something again 再填充, 再注滿: *I'll just refill the coffee pot.* 我要把咖啡壺再灌滿。—**refillable** *adj*: *a refillable lighter* 可再充氣的打火機

re·fill² /ˋriˌfɪl; ˈriːfɪl/ *n* [C] **1** a container filled with something such as ink or petrol that you use to fill or replace the empty container in your pen, CIGARETTE LIGHTER etc〔筆、打火機等的〕添補物;〔筆芯等的〕替換物: *I must buy some refills for my pen.* 我必須給我的筆買些筆芯。**2** *spoken* another drink to refill your glass【口】再倒(一杯飲料): *Would you like a refill?* 你想再來一杯嗎?

re·fine /rɪˋfaɪn; rɪˈfaɪn/ *v* [T] **1** to improve a method, plan, system etc by gradually making slight changes to it〔慢慢地、微小地〕改進; 完善: *The current structure will be retained and refined.* 現有結構將予以保留並且不斷完善。**2** to make a substance pure using an industrial process 淨化; 提煉: *the petroleum refining industry* 煉油業

re·fined /rɪˋfaɪnd; rɪˈfaɪnd/ *adj* **1** [no comparative 無比較級] a substance that is refined has been made pure by an industrial process 精煉的; 精製的: *refined oil* 精煉油 | *refined white sugar* 精製白糖 **2** someone who is refined is polite and seems to be well-educated or to belong to a high social class 優雅的, 有教養的: *a refined way of speaking* 優雅的談吐 **3** a method or process that is refined has been improved to make it more effective 精妙的; 完善的 —opposite 反義詞 UNREFINED

re·fine·ment /rɪˋfaɪnmənt; rɪˈfaɪnmənt/ *n* **1** [C] an addition or improvement to an existing product, system etc 精巧的附加裝置; 改良品: *The new car has a number of refinements such as an air bag and a catalytic converter.* 這款新車有許多改良的設備, 如氣囊和催化轉化器。**2** [U] the quality of being polite and well-educated, in a way that is typical of someone from a high social class 優雅, 高雅, 有教養: *a woman of great refinement* 非常文雅的女士 **3** [U] the process of improving something 完善, 改進: **[+of]** *the continued refinement of existing systems* 現行體制的不斷完善 **4** [U+of] the process of making a substance pure 精煉; 提純

re·fin·e·ry /rɪˋfaɪnərɪ; rɪˈfaɪnəri/ *n* [C] a factory where something such as metal, sugar, or oil is refined〔金屬、糖或石油的〕提煉廠, 精煉廠: *an oil refinery* 煉油廠

re·fit /riˋfɪt; ˌriːˈfɪt/ *v* **refitted, refitting** [I,T] to make a ship ready to be used again, by doing repairs and putting in new machinery 整修; 重新裝備〔船隻〕: *We sailed into port to refit.* 我們駛入港口整修船隻。—**refit** /ˋriˌfɪt; ˈriːfɪt/ *n* [C,U]: *The yacht needs a refit.* 這艘遊艇需要重新裝修。

re·flate /riˋflet; riːˈfleɪt/ *v* [I,T] *technical* to increase the supply of money in a country or system, in order to encourage trade【術語】(使)通貨增加以鼓勵貿易: *measures to reflate the economy* 增加通貨使經濟復蘇的措施

re·fla·tion /riˋfleʃən; riːˈfleɪʃən/ *n* [U] *technical* the process of increasing the amount of money being used in a country in order to increase trade【術語】通貨再膨脹 —**reflationary** *adj* —compare 比較 DEFLATION, INFLATION (1)

re·flect /rɪˋflɛkt; rɪˈflekt/ *v* **1** [T] if a surface reflects light, heat, sound, or an image, it throws back the light etc that hits it 反射〔光、熱、聲或影像等〕: *White clothes are cooler because they reflect the heat.* 白色的衣服比較涼快, 因為它們能反射熱氣。| *The moon reflects the sun's rays.* 月亮反射太陽光。| **be reflected in** *She could see her face reflected in the water.* 她看見自己的臉倒映在水中。**2** [T not usually in progressive 一般不用進行式] to show or be a sign of a particular situation or feeling 顯示, 反映: *The low value of the dollar reflects growing concern about the US economy.* 美元幣值低反映出人們對美國經濟的憂慮日益增加。| **be reflected in** *The growing conflict has been reflected in the paper's editorial section.* 日益嚴重的衝突反映在該報的社論欄裡。| **reflect who/what/how etc** *Does this letter reflect how you really feel?* 這封信是否反映了你的真實感覺? **3** [I,T] to think carefully about something, or to express your thoughts 仔細思考; 表達意見: **[+on]** *Take some time to reflect on your future plans.* 抽點時間仔細考慮你未來的計劃。| **reflect that** *I reflected that there wasn't much point in continu-* 2 1

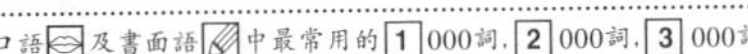

ing with my plans now that Al was gone. 我考慮過，既然阿爾走了，繼續我的計劃也就沒有多大意義了。

reflect on/upon *phr v* [T] to influence people's opinion of someone or something, especially in a bad way 給某人對…的評價造成〔尤指不利的〕影響: **reflect on sb/sth** *an economic record that reflects badly on government policy* 使政府政策引起非議的經濟記錄 | *If my children are rude, that reflects on me as a parent.* 假如我的孩子沒有禮貌，那會使我這個做家長的丟臉。

reflecting tel·e·scope /ˈ·· ˌ···/ *n* [C] an instrument for seeing distant objects that reflects an image in a mirror to make it bigger 反射（式）望遠鏡 —compare 比較 REFRACTING TELESCOPE

reflection 倒影

3 3 **re·flec·tion** /rɪˋflɛkʃən; rɪˈflekʃən/ *n* **1** [C] an image reflected in a mirror or similar surface〔鏡子或類似表面反射出來的〕影像: *We looked at our reflections in the lake.* 我們看着自己在湖中的倒影。**2** [C,U] careful thought, or an idea or opinion based on this 深思，考慮;〔經過仔細考慮形成的〕想法，見解: *A moment's reflection will show the stupidity of this argument.* 只需認真思考一會兒便可看出這種觀點多麼愚蠢。| **[+on]** *It was interesting to hear her reflections on the situation in the Far East.* 聽她發表對遠東局勢的看法十分有意思。| **on reflection** (=used to say that you have thought more about something, and changed your opinion) 經考慮之後〔改變看法〕 *At first I thought her ideas were crazy, but on reflection, I realized there was some truth in what she said.* 起初我覺得她的想法很荒唐，但經過一番考慮，我認識到她說的話有些道理。**3** [C] something that shows the effects of, or is a sign of, a particular situation 反映: **[+of]** *The rising crime rate is a reflection of an unstable society.* 犯罪率上升是社會不穩定的反映。| *His speech was an accurate reflection of the public mood.* 他的講話確切反映了公眾的情緒。**4 be a reflection on** to show someone's character, abilities, work etc in an unfavourable way 使人們對…產生惡劣的評價: *The students' bad grades are no reflection on the teachers, but they do say something about the tests.* 學生成績差並不說明老師不好，但的確反映出測驗的一些問題。**5** [U] the fact of light, heat, sound or an image being reflected〔光、熱、聲音或影像的〕反射

re·flec·tive /rɪˋflɛktɪv; rɪˈflektɪv/ *adj* **1** thinking quietly 沉思的: *in a reflective mood* 思潮起伏 **2** a reflective surface reflects (REFLECT (1)) the light〔表面〕反射的

re·flec·tor /rɪˋflɛktɚ; rɪˈflektə/ *n* [C] **1** a small piece of plastic that is fastened to a bicycle or piece of clothing, so that it can be seen more easily at night〔為夜間容易辨認而固定在自行車或衣服上的〕反光板；反射物 —see picture at 參見 BICYCLE 圖 **2** a surface that reflects light 反射器；反射鏡；反射物

re·flex /ˋriflɛks; ˈriːfleks/ *n* [C] **1** a sudden movement that your muscles make as a natural reaction to a physical effect〔生理〕反射（作用）: *The doctor checked my reflexes.* 醫生檢查了我的反射作用。**2 reflexes** [plural] the natural ability to react quickly and well to sudden situations 反應能力: *A tennis player needs to have good reflexes.* 網球運動員需要有良好的反應能力。**3** also 又作 **reflex action** something that you do when you react to a situation without thinking 反射動作，本能反應: *His hand went to his gun in a reflex action.* 他把手伸到槍上，那是本能的動作。

re·flex·ive /rɪˋflɛksɪv; rɪˈfleksɪv/ *adj technical* a reflexive verb or PRONOUN shows that the action in a sentence affects the person or thing that does the action【術語】〔動詞或代詞〕反身的 —**reflexive** *n* [C]

re·flex·ol·o·gy /ˌriflɛkˋsɑlədʒɪ; ˌriːflekˈsɒlədʒi/ *n* [U] a kind of ALTERNATIVE MEDICINE in which areas of the feet are touched or rubbed in order to cure a medical problem 反射療法〔按摩足部某些部位來治病的一種非傳統療法〕

re·for·est·a·tion /ˌrifɔrɪsˋteʃən; riːˌfɒrɪ̣ˈsteɪʃən/ *n* [U] the practice of planting trees in order to grow a forest for industrial use or to improve the environment 重新造林 —**reforest** /riˋfɔrɪst; riːˈfɒrɪ̣st/ *v* [I,T]

re-form /ˌriˋfɔrm; ˌriːˈfɔːm/ *v* [I,T] **1** to start to exist again or to make something start to exist again 重新組成；重建: *At the end of the year the company re-formed, and began trading again.* 在年底該公司重新組成，又開始經營。**2** to form into lines again, or to make soldiers do this（使）重新編隊: *The platoon re-formed, ready to attack.* 該排經過重新編隊，準備進攻。

re·form¹ /rɪˋfɔrm; rɪˈfɔːm/ *v* **1** [T] to change a system, law, organization etc so that it operates in a fairer or more effective way 改進，改革: *plans to reform the tax system* 改革稅收制度的計劃 **2** [I,T] to change your behaviour and become a better person, or to make someone do this 改過，改造: **be a reformed character** *Harry's a reformed character since he stopped taking drugs.* 戒毒以後，哈里已經改過自新。| **reformed criminal/sinner/alcoholic etc** (=someone who is no longer a criminal etc) 改過自新的犯人／罪人／酗酒者等

reform² *n* [C,U] a change made to a system or organization, in order to improve it, remove unfairness etc 改進，改革: *educational reform* 教育改革 | **[+of]** *a radical reform of the legal system* 法律制度的徹底改革 2

ref·or·ma·tion /ˌrɛfɚˋmeʃən; ˌrefəˈmeɪʃən/ *n* **1** [C,U] an improvement made by changing something a lot 改進；改善；改革 **2 the Reformation** the religious changes in Europe in the 16th century, that resulted in the Protestant churches being established〔歐洲16世紀的導致產生新教的〕宗教改革

re·for·ma·to·ry /rɪˋfɔrməˌtɔrɪ; rɪˈfɔːmətəri/ *n* [C] *AmE or old use* a special school where young people who have broken the law are sent【美或舊】少年管教所

re·form·er /rɪˋfɔrmɚ; rɪˈfɔːmə/ *n* [C] someone who tries to improve a system, law, or society 改革者，革新者，改良者: *a great social reformer* 偉大的社會改革者

re·form·ist /rɪˋfɔrmɪst; rɪˈfɔːmɪ̣st/ *adj* wanting to change systems or situations, especially in politics〔尤指政治上的〕改革主義的 —**reformist** *n* [C]

reform school /·ˈ· ·/ *n* [C] *AmE* a REFORMATORY【美】少年管教所

re·fract /rɪˋfrækt; rɪˈfrækt/ *v* [T] *technical* to make light change direction when passing through glass or water【術語】使〔光〕折射 —**refraction** /rɪˋfrækʃən; rɪˈfrækʃən/ *n* [U]

refracting tel·e·scope /·ˈ·· ˌ···/ *n* [C] an instrument for seeing distant objects that refracts images by passing them through a LENS (=a piece of glass) 折射望遠鏡

re·frac·to·ry /rɪˋfræktərɪ; rɪˈfræktəri/ *adj formal* disobedient and difficult to deal with or control【正式】難駕馭的，不服管教的

re·frain¹ /rɪˋfren; rɪˈfreɪn/ *v formal* to not do something that you want to do【正式】克制，節制，忍住: **[+from]** *Kindly refrain from smoking.* 請勿抽煙。

refrain² *n* [C] **1** part of a song that is repeated, especially at the end of each VERSE〔歌曲中, 尤指每小節末尾的〕反覆句, 疊句, 副歌 **2** *formal* a remark or idea that is often repeated【正式】經常重複的話[想法]: *Our proposal met with the constant refrain that the company could not afford it.* 我們的建議一再得到公司負擔不起費用的答覆。

re·fresh /rɪˋfrɛʃ; rɪˈfreʃ/ *v* **1** [T] to make someone feel less tired or less hot 使恢復精力, 提神; 使清涼: *He refreshed himself with a glass of beer.* 他喝了杯啤酒提提神。| *A shower will refresh you.* 洗個淋浴你就會精神一爽。**2 refresh sb's memory** to make someone remember something 使某人想起; 喚起某人的記憶: *I looked at the map to refresh my memory of the route.* 我看地圖以喚起自己對這條路線的記憶。**3 refresh sb's drink** *AmE spoken* to add more of an alcoholic drink to someone's glass【美口】給某人添酒精飲料: *Can I refresh your drink?* 我給你再加點酒好嗎? **4** [I,T] *technical* to provide computer OUTPUT again; UPDATE¹ (1)【術語】〔電腦輸出〕刷新, 更新: *This display will not refresh until you repeat the command.* 你要重複指令, 顯示的內容才會更新。—**refreshed** *adj*: *After a good sleep he awoke refreshed.* 好好睡了一覺後, 他醒來時恢復了精神。

re·fresh·er course /·ˈ··· ·/ *n* [C] a training course that teaches you about new developments in a particular subject or skill, especially one that you need for your job〔職業〕進修課程

re·fresh·ing /rɪˋfrɛʃɪŋ; rɪˈfreʃɪŋ/ *adj* **1** making you feel less tired or less hot 消除疲勞的, 提神的; 清涼的: *a long refreshing drink* 一大杯提神的飲料 | *The breeze was refreshing after the stuffy classroom.* 從悶熱的教室出來後, 微風使人感到涼爽。**2** pleasantly different from what is familiar and boring 令人耳目一新的: *It made a refreshing change to talk to someone new.* 換個人談話讓人感覺很新奇。—**refreshingly** *adv*

re·fresh·ment /rɪˋfrɛʃmənt; rɪˈfreʃmənt/ *n* **1 refreshments** [plural] small amounts of food and drink that are provided at a meeting, sports event etc 茶點; 點心和飲料: *Refreshments will be served after the meeting.* 會後有茶點招待。**2** [U] food and drink in general 食物和飲料: *We worked all day without refreshment.* 我們不吃不喝地工作了一整天。| **liquid refreshment** *humorous* (=alcoholic drink)【幽默】酒 **3** [U] the experience of being made to feel less tired or hot 恢復精力; 涼爽

re·fri·ge·rant /rɪˋfrɪdʒərənt; rɪˈfrɪdʒərənt/ *n* [C] *technical* a substance used in refrigeration systems【術語】致冷劑, 冷凍劑

re·fri·ge·rate /rɪˋfrɪdʒəˌret; rɪˈfrɪdʒəreɪt/ *v* [T] to make something such as food or liquid cold in order to preserve it 冷凍, 冷藏: *refrigerate the mixture overnight* 把混合物冷藏過夜 —**refrigeration** /rɪˌfrɪdʒəˋreʃən; rɪˌfrɪdʒəˈreɪʃən/ *n* [U]: *Meat must be kept under refrigeration.* 肉類必須冷藏。

re·fri·ge·ra·tor /rɪˋfrɪdʒəˌretə; rɪˈfrɪdʒəreɪtə/ *n* [C] *BrE formal or AmE* a special cupboard kept cold by electricity, in which you store food and drink; FRIDGE【英, 正式或美】冰箱 —see picture on page A10 參見 A10 頁圖

re·fuel /riˋfjuəl; ˌriːˈfjʊəl/ *v* **refuelled, refuelling** *BrE*【英】, **refueled, refueling** *AmE*【美】**1** [I,T] to fill a vehicle or plane with FUEL before continuing a journey (給) 加油, (給) 加燃料: *We stopped in Dubai to refuel.* 我們在迪拜停下來加油。**2** [T] to make feelings, emotions, or ideas stronger 使〔感情、情緒或想法〕更強烈: *The news has refuelled speculation about whether there might be something illegal going on.* 這消息增添了人們對是否存在非法勾當的揣測。

ref·uge /ˋrɛfjudʒ; ˈrefjuːdʒ/ *n* [C] a place that provides protection or shelter from danger 庇護所, 避難處: *a refuge for battered wives* 受虐待妻子的庇護所 | **[+from]** *a refuge from the storm* 躲避風暴的地方 | **take/seek refuge in sth** (=look for or find safety somewhere) 在…尋求庇護 *During the frequent air-raids people take refuge in their cellars.* 在頻繁的空襲中, 人們躲在地下室裡。

ref·u·gee /ˌrɛfjʊˋdʒi; ˌrefjʊˈdʒiː/ *n* [C] someone who has been forced to leave their country, especially during a war〔尤指戰爭中的〕難民, 避難者: *Refugees were streaming across the border.* 難民湧過邊界。| *a refugee camp* 難民營 W3

re·ful·gent /rɪˋfʌldʒənt; rɪˈfʌldʒənt/ *adj literary* very bright【文】光輝的, 燦爛的 —**refulgence** *n* [U]

re·fund¹ /ˋriˌfʌnd; ˈriːfʌnd/ *n* [C] a sum of money that is given back to you 退款: *You can apply for a refund of your travel costs.* 你可以申請退還旅費。

re·fund² /rɪˋfʌnd; rɪˈfʌnd/ *v* [T] to give someone their money back, especially because they are not satisfied with the goods or services they have paid for 退還; 償還〔尤指因對所購貨物或服務不滿意〕: *I took the radio back, and they refunded my money.* 我把收音機送回去, 他們給我退款。—compare 比較 REIMBURSE

re·fur·bish /riˋfɝbɪʃ; ˌriːˈfɜːbɪʃ/ *v* [T] **1** to thoroughly repair and improve a building by painting and cleaning it 翻修, 整修〔房子〕**2** to change and improve a plan, idea or skill 修改, 完善〔計劃、思想或技術〕—**refurbishment** *n* [C,U]

re·fus·al /rɪˋfjuzḷ; rɪˈfjuːzəl/ *n* [C,U] **1** an act of saying or showing that you will not do something that someone has asked you to do 拒絕: **refusal to do sth** *His refusal to pay the fine got him into trouble.* 他拒絕付罰款, 因而給自己惹了麻煩。| **point-blank refusal** (=an immediate direct refusal) 斷然拒絕 **2** an act of not accepting something that is being offered to you 拒絕接受, 謝絕: **[+of]** *They couldn't understand Raymond's refusal of a scholarship to Yale.* 他們無法理解雷蒙德為甚麼拒絕接受耶魯大學的獎學金。**3 give sb first refusal** to let someone decide whether they want to buy a house, car etc that you are selling before you offer it to other people 給某人優先權〔購房屋、汽車等〕

re·fuse¹ /rɪˋfjuz; rɪˈfjuːz/ *v* **1** [I] to say or show that you will not do something that someone has asked you to do 拒絕〔做某事〕: *I'm sure if you ask her to help you, she won't refuse.* 我肯定, 如果你向她求助, 她不會拒絕。| **refuse to do sth** *I refuse to take part in anything that's illegal.* 我拒絕參與任何違法的事情。| **flatly refuse/refuse point blank** (=refuse very firmly and directly) 斷然拒絕 *Mother flatly refused to go back into the hospital.* 母親斷然拒絕再進醫院。**2** [I,T] to say no to something that you have been offered; DECLINE² (4) 不接受, 謝絕〔別人給的東西〕: *Mrs Sutton refused a second piece of cake.* 薩頓太太謝絕了第二塊蛋糕。| *Their offer is too good to refuse.* 他們的開價好得無法抗拒。**3** [T] to not give or allow someone something that they want 拒絕把…給…: **refuse sb sth** *The US authorities refused him a visa.* 美國當局拒絕給他簽證。 S2 W1

USAGE NOTE 用法說明: REFUSE

WORD CHOICE 詞語辨析: **agree to, accept, refuse, reject, decline, turn down, deny**

Refuse, reject, decline, turn down all mean that you do not do something that someone has asked you to do (opposite: **agree to**), or do not take something that you are **offered** (opposite: **accept**). refuse, reject, decline, turn down 都表示拒絕, 指不去做別人要求你做的某事 (反義詞是 agree to) 或不接受別人提供的某物 (反義詞是 accept)。

You can **refuse** an invitation, application, offer, permission, or you can **refuse to** say or do something. 拒絕邀請、申請、建議、批准或拒絕講或做某事, 可用 refuse: *She refused to come with us.* 她拒絕和我們一道來。

More strongly, you **reject** an application, idea, proposal, offer, improvement, or plan. reject 語氣更堅決, 用於拒絕申請、想法、建議、提議、改進或計劃: *The Greens rejected the proposals for the new road.* 格林夫婦拒絕了修建新路的建議。| *Her first novel was rejected by over 30 publishers.* 她的第一部小說遭到三十多家出版商的拒絕。

You **decline** an invitation, offer, or to give permission by saying or writing something rather than doing something. This word is less strong but more formal and polite. 以口頭或書面方式拒絕邀請、建議或拒絕同意, 可用decline, 該詞語氣不太強, 但更正式和客氣: *The Senator has declined all our invitations to an open debate on the matter.* 我們多次邀請那位參議員公開辯論這個問題, 他全都拒絕了。

Less formally, you can **turn down** an invitation, application, suggestion, offer, or plan. turn down 的語氣不太正式, 用於謝絕邀請、申請、建議、提議或計劃等: *He turns down all offers of help.* 他拒絕了所有提出幫助的建議。

You can also **deny** someone permission, an opportunity, or their rights. But usually if you **deny** something especially something wrong that someone has said you have done, you say it is not true. 不予准許、拒絕給予機會或權利, 可用deny。但deny較常見的意思是"否認", 尤其是當deny的賓語是別人指責你做錯事的時候: The sentence 這句 *She denied working for the enemy,* means 意思是 *She said she was not working for the enemy.* 她否認在為敵人工作。(NOT 不用 *She refused to work for the enemy.* 她拒絕為敵人工作。)

ref·use² /ˋrɛfjus; ˈrefjuːs/ *n* [U] *formal* waste material; RUBBISH[1] (1)【正式】廢料, 廢物: *a refuse dump* 垃圾場 | *declining standards in housing maintenance, refuse collection and street lighting* 住房維修、垃圾收集和街道照明的水平下降

re·fute /rɪˋfjut; rɪˈfjuːt/ *v* [T] *formal*【正式】**1** to prove that a statement or idea is not correct 證明〔陳述或觀點〕不對, 反駁: *an attempt to refute Moore's theories* 企圖駁斥摩爾的理論 **2** to say that a statement is wrong or unfair 駁斥: *She refuted the allegations of malpractice.* 她駁斥了說她有失職行為的指控。—**refutable** *adj* —**refutation** /ˌrɛfjuˋteʃən; ˌrefjʊˈteɪʃən/ *n* [C,U]

reg. /rɛdʒ; redʒ/ an abbreviation of 縮寫= REGISTRATION: **L reg./M reg. etc** *BrE* (=to say what the age of a car is according to the year when it was registered)【英】〔表示註冊年數的汽車〕註冊類別

re·gain /rɪˋgen; rɪˈgeɪn/ *v* [T] **1** to get something back, especially an ability or quality that you have lost 收回, 復得, 恢復: *The family never quite regained its former influence.* 這個家族再也沒有恢復往昔的影響力。| **regain consciousness** (=wake up after being unconscious) 恢復知覺 | **regain control (of)** *Government forces have regained control of some areas.* 政府軍隊重新控制了一些地區。| **regain your balance** (=stop yourself from falling) 恢復平衡 **2** *literary* to reach a place again【文】再到〔某地〕, 重回

re·gal /ˋrigl; ˈriːgəl/ *adj formal* typical of a king or queen and therefore usually impressive【正式】帝王(般)的: *a regal manner* 王者風範 | *a ceremony of regal splendour* 富麗堂皇的儀式 —**regally** *adv*: *She held out her hand regally.* 她高貴地伸出手來。

re·gale /rɪˋgel; rɪˈgeɪl/ *v*

regale sb **with** sth *phr v* to entertain someone with something, especially stories 以…款待;〔尤指以故事〕使…愉悅: *Bailey regaled the customers with tales of our exploits.* 貝利給顧客講我們的事跡, 讓他們聽得津津有味。

re·ga·li·a /rɪˋgeliə; rɪˈgeɪliə/ *n* [U] traditional clothes and decorations, used at official ceremonies〔正式場合穿的〕盛裝, 華服: *the royal regalia* 皇家的禮服

re·gard¹ /rɪˋgɑrd; rɪˈgɑːd/ *n formal*【正式】 S3

1 ►RESPECT 尊敬◄ [U] respect for someone or something 尊敬: [+**for**] *She has so little regard for him, she is unlikely to follow his advice.* 她很不尊重他, 不太可能聽從他的勸告。| **hold sb/sth in high regard** (=admire and respect them very much) 對某人/某物懷有敬意 *a teacher who is held in high regard by his colleagues* 備受同事尊敬的老師

2 ►ATTENTION 關注◄ [U] *formal* attention or consideration that is shown towards someone or something【正式】關注, 關心: [+**for**] *He has no regard for her feelings.* 他無視她的感情。| [+**to**] *a report that pays scant regard to the facts of the case* 一份忽視案件事實的報告

3 as regards used to introduce the subject you are going to talk or write about 至於, 關於: *As regards environmental issues, the government will enforce existing regulations.* 關於環境問題, 政府將實施現行條例。

4 in this regard *formal* used to connect what you are going to say with something you have just mentioned【正式】關於此事〔用於承上啟下〕: *Progress is slow. In this regard, lack of funds is a factor.* 就進展緩慢而言, 缺乏資金是一個因素。

5 with/in regard to *formal* used to say what particular subject you are talking or writing about【正式】關於〔用於點題〕: *With regard to future oil supplies, the situation is uncertain.* 關於未來石油供應問題, 情況尚不確定。

6 ►GREETING 問候◄ **regards** [plural] good wishes 問候; 致意: *My husband sends his regards.* 我丈夫表示問候。| **with kind/best/warm regards** (=used to end a letter in a friendly but rather formal way) 謹致問候〔友善並相當正式的問候, 用於信的末尾〕

7 ►LOOK 看◄ [singular] *literary* a long look without moving your eyes【文】注視

regard² *v* [T] **1** [not in progressive 不用進行式] to think about someone or something in a particular way 認為, 看作: **regard sb/sth as sth** *Paul seems to regard sex as sinful and immoral.* 保羅好像把性看作是罪惡和不道德的。| *Edith wore strange clothes and was widely regarded as eccentric.* 伊迪絲穿着古怪, 被大家視為怪人。| **regard sb with admiration/fear/concern etc** *Sue regarded the others with fear and jealousy.* 蘇對其他人既害怕又嫉妒。| **regard sb well/badly etc** *a work of art that is highly regarded by the experts* 一件為專家們高度評價的藝術品 **2** *formal* to look at someone or something, especially in a particular way【正式】注視: *I stood back a little and regarded him coldly.* 我往後站了一點, 冷冷地注視着他。**3** *formal* to pay attention to something【正式】注意, 重視: *You must regard the safety regulations.* 你必須重視安全規則。 S2 W1

re·gard·ing /rɪˋgɑrdɪŋ; rɪˈgɑːdɪŋ/ *prep formal* a word used especially in business letters to introduce the subject you are writing about【正式】關於〔尤用於公函中〕: *Regarding your recent inquiry...* 關於你最近的詢問… S3

re·gard·less /rɪˋgɑrdlɪs; rɪˈgɑːdləs/ *adv* **1** if you continue doing something regardless, you do it in spite of difficulties or opposition 不管怎樣, 無論如何: *You get a lot of criticism but you just have to carry on regardless.* 你受到許多批評, 但無論如何你必須堅持下去。**2 regardless of** without being affected by different situations, problems etc 不管, 不顧: *equal treatment for all, regardless of race, religion, or sex* 不分種族、宗教或性別, 對所有人一視同仁 | *All our proposals were rejected regardless of their merits.* 我們所有的建議都遭到拒絕, 不管它們的可取之處。

re·gat·ta /rɪˋgætə; rɪˈgætə/ *n* [C] a sports event at which there are races for rowing boats or sailing boats〔划船或帆船比賽的〕賽船會

re·gen·cy /ˋridʒənsɪ; ˈriːdʒənsi/ *n* [C,U] a period of government by a REGENT (=person who governs instead of a king or queen) 攝政(期)

Regency *adj* Regency buildings, furniture etc are from or in the style of the period 1811-1820 in Britain 英國攝政時期〔1811–1820〕(風格)的

re·gen·e·rate /rɪˋdʒɛnəˏret; rɪˈdʒenəreɪt/ *v* [T] *formal* to make something develop and grow strong again【正式】使再生, 使恢復: *Given time the forest will regenerate itself.* 過一段時間後森林會自行再生。| *The Marshall Plan sought to regenerate the shattered Europe of 1947.* 馬歇爾計劃試圖重建1947年千瘡百孔的歐洲。—**regenerative** /-nəˏretɪv; -nərətɪv/ *adj*: *a regenerative process* 復興的過程 —**regeneration** /rɪˏdʒɛnəˋreʃən; rɪˌdʒenəˈreɪʃən/ *n* [U] *a new strategy for urban regeneration* 城市復興的新策略

re·gent /ˈridʒənt; ˈriːdʒənt/ *n* [C] someone who governs instead of a king or queen ruling who is ill, absent, or still a child 攝政者 —**regent** *adj* [only after noun 僅用於名詞後] *the Prince Regent* 攝政王

reg·gae /ˈrɛge; ˈregeɪ/ *n* [U] a kind of popular music from the West Indies with a strong regular beat 雷蓋〔西印度羣島的一種節奏強勁的流行音樂〕

re·gi·cide /ˈrɛdʒəˏsaɪd; ˈredʒɪsaɪd/ *n formal*【正式】**1** [U] the crime of killing a king or queen 弒君(罪) **2** [C] someone who does this 弒君者

2 **re·gime** /rɪˋʒim; reɪˈʒiːm/ *n* [C] **1** a government that has not been elected in fair elections〔未經公平選舉而掌權的〕政府, 政權: *The regime has liquidated all its opponents.* 該政權清除了所有的反對者。**2** a particular system of government or management, especially one you disapprove of 政體, 政權〔尤含貶義〕: **the old/new regime** (=the previous or present system of government) 舊/新政權 | **the Thatcher/Eisenhower/Faulkner etc regime** (=the government of Thatcher etc) 戴卓爾/艾森豪威爾/福克納等政府 **3** a regimen 養生之道, 攝生法

re·gi·men /ˈrɛdʒəˏmɛn; ˈredʒɪmɪn/ *n* [C] *formal* a special plan of food, exercise etc that is intended to improve your health【正式】養生之道, 攝生法

re·gi·ment¹ /ˈrɛdʒəmənt; ˈredʒɪmənt/ *n* [C] **1** a large military group usually consisting of several BATTALIONS〔軍隊的〕團: *the Royal Sussex Regiment* 皇家薩塞克斯團 **2** a large number of people, animals, or things〔人、動物、物的〕大羣, 大量: *a whole regiment of ants* 一大羣螞蟻

re·gi·ment² /ˈrɛdʒəˏmɛnt; ˈredʒɪment/ *v* [T usually passive 一般用被動態] to organize and control people firmly and usually too strictly 嚴格控制: *the regimented routine of boarding school* 寄宿學校嚴格的常規 —**regimentation** /ˌrɛdʒəmɛnˋteʃən; ˌredʒɪmenˈteɪʃən/ *n* [U]: *institutional regimentation* 大機構的嚴格管理

re·gi·ment·al /ˌrɛdʒəˋmɛntl; ˌredʒɪˈmentl◂/ *adj* connected with a regiment 團的: *the regimental band* 團的樂隊

Re·gi·na /rɪˋdʒaɪnə; rɪˈdʒaɪnə/ *n Latin*【拉丁】**1** used as a title in official writing after the name of the ruling British queen 女王〔公文中用於在位英國女王名字之後的稱謂〕: *Elizabeth Regina* 伊莉莎白女王 **2** used to mean the governing power of the state in the title of a British law case when a queen is ruling 王國政府〔女王在位時用於訟案的名稱中〕: *the case of Frankland v. Regina* (=Frankland against the government) 弗蘭克蘭德對王國政府訟案 —compare 比較 REX

1 1 **re·gion** /ˈridʒən; ˈriːdʒən/ *n* [C] **1** a fairly large area of a country or of the world, usually without exact limits〔無確定界限的〕地區, 區域: *oil fields in the Appalachian region of the US* 美國阿巴拉契亞地區的油田 | *The invaders occupied important coastal regions.* 入侵者佔領了重要的沿海地區。| *America's main ally in this region* 美國在這個地區的主要盟國 —see 見 AREA (USAGE) **2** a particular part of someone's body〔人體的〕部, 部位: *a pain in the lower back region* 後腰部疼痛 **3 (somewhere) in the region of** used to describe an amount of time, money, etc without being exact 大約, ...左右: *The school received a grant somewhere in the region of £2,500.* 學校收到一筆大約2,500英鎊的補助金。**4 the regions** the parts of a country that are away from the capital city〔首都以外的〕各地區: *Government policy is to relocate jobs from the capital to the regions.* 政府的政策是將就業機會從首都轉移到其他地區。

re·gion·al /ˈridʒənḷ; ˈriːdʒənəl/ *adj* connected with a particular region 地區的, 區域的: *regional cooking* 地方特色的烹飪 | *regional alliances such as NATO* 北約等區域性聯盟 1 2

re·gion·al·is·m /ˈridʒənḷˏɪzəm; ˈriːdʒənəlɪzəm/ *n* [U] loyalty to a particular region of a country and the desire for it to be more politically independent 地方主義

re·gis·ter¹ /ˈrɛdʒɪstə; ˈredʒɪstə/ *n* 3 3

1 ▶OFFICIAL LIST 正式名單◀ [C] an official list containing the names of all the people, organizations, or things of one particular type 名冊: *a civil register of births, deaths and marriages* 出生、死亡、婚姻的民政登記簿 | *children on the 'at risk' register* "危險"名冊上的兒童

2 ▶OFFICIAL BOOK 正式的簿/冊◀ [C] a book kept for a special purpose, such as in a church or REGISTRY OFFICE, which a man and woman sign after their marriage ceremony 登記簿: *the school attendance register* 學校點名冊

3 ▶MUSIC 音樂◀ [C] *technical* the range of musical notes that someone's voice or a musical instrument can reach【術語】〔人聲或樂器的〕音域

4 ▶LANGUAGE STYLE 語言風格◀ [C,U] *technical* the words, style, and grammar used by speakers and writers in a particular situation or in a particular type of writing【術語】語域: *the correct register for a formal social situation* 正式社交場合的正確語言風格

5 ▶BUSINESS MACHINE 商用機器◀ [C] a CASH REGISTER 現金出納機

6 ▶HEATING CONTROL 加熱控制裝置◀ [C] *AmE* a movable metal plate that controls the flow of air in a HEATING or COOLING system【美】〔加熱或冷卻系統中控制氣流的〕調風器, 節氣門

register² *v* 3

1 ▶ON A LIST 記入名單◀ **a)** [T] to record a name or details about someone or something in an official list 記錄, 登記: *We are registering the baby's birth this morning.* 我們今天上午要給剛出生的孩子登記。| *The tanker is registered in Rotterdam.* 這艘油輪是在鹿特丹註冊的。| **be registered (as) unemployed/disabled etc** (=be on an official list of a particular group) 登記的失業者/殘疾人等 **b)** [I] to put your name on an official list, for example when you arrive at a hotel, join a course of study etc〔旅館入住〕登記;〔課程〕註冊: **[+for]** *How many students have registered for English classes?* 有多少學生註冊了英語課?

2 ▶SHOW A FEELING 表示感情◀ [T] to show or express a feeling 流露[表達]感情: *Her face registered shock and anger.* 她臉上流露出震驚和憤怒。

3 ▶STATE YOUR OPINION 發表意見◀ [T] *formal* to officially state your opinion about something so that everyone knows what you think or feel【正式】正式表達, 說明: *The delegation registered their protests at the White House meeting.* 在白宮會議上, 代表團正式表達了他們的抗議。

4 ▶REALIZE 意識到◀ [I usually in negatives 一般用否定式, T] if something registers, or if you register it, you notice it or realize it and then remember it 受到注意; 注意到, 意識到: *She must have told me her name, but it just didn't register.* 她一定告訴過我她的名字, 不過我沒記住。| *I'd been standing there for several minutes before he registered my presence.* 我在那兒站了幾分鐘之後他才注意到我。

5 ▶MEASUREMENT 度量◀ [I,T] if an instrument registers an amount or if an amount registers on it, the instrument shows or records that amount〔儀器〕顯示, 記錄: *The thermometer registered 98.6°.* 溫度計顯示為98.6度。

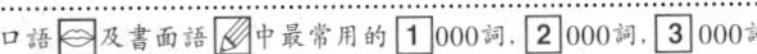

6 ▶MAIL 郵件◀ [T] to send a parcel, letter etc by REGISTERED POST 以掛號寄送: *Did you register the parcel?* 那包裹你是用掛號寄的嗎?

registered nurse /ˌ··· ˈ·/ also 又作 **RN** *n* [C] someone who has been trained and is officially allowed to work as a nurse 註冊護士

registered of·fice /ˌ··· ˈ··/ *n* [C] the office of a company in Britain, to which all letters and official documents must be sent〔英國公司接收信件和正式文件的〕註冊辦事處

registered post /ˌ··· ˈ·/ *n* [U] *BrE* a way of insuring something that you send by post in case it gets lost or damaged【英】掛號郵寄; REGISTERED MAIL *AmE*【美】

register of·fice /ˈ··· ˌ··/ *n* [C] a REGISTRY OFFICE〔英國〕戶籍登記處

re·gis·trar /ˈrɛdʒɪˌstrɑr; ˌredʒəˈstrɑː◂/ *n* [C] **1** someone who is in charge of official records, for example in a REGISTRY OFFICE or in a college〔登記處的〕註冊主管, 記錄員, 登記員;〔大學的〕註冊主任, 教務主任 **2** a British hospital doctor who has finished their training but is of a lower rank than a CONSULTANT (2)〔英國的〕專科住院醫生

3 **re·gis·tra·tion** /ˌrɛdʒɪˈstreʃən; ˌredʒəˈstreɪʃən/ *n* **1** [U] the act of recording names and details on an official list 登記, 註冊: *Student registration is the first week in September.* 學生註冊在九月的第一個星期。| **[+of]** *the registration of motor vehicles* 機動車的註冊 **2** [C] *AmE* an official piece of paper containing details about a motor vehicle and the name of its owner【美】〔汽車〕執照

registration doc·u·ment /··ˈ·· ˌ···/ *n* [C] *BrE* an official piece of paper containing details about a motor vehicle and its owner【英】〔汽車〕執照

registration num·ber /··ˈ·· ˌ··/ *n* [C] *BrE* the official set of numbers and letters shown on the front and back of a motor vehicle on the NUMBER PLATE【英】〔汽車的〕牌照號碼

registration plate /··ˈ·· ˌ·/ *n* [C] *AustrE, NZE* the metal plate on the front and back of a motor vehicle, which has a special number on it【澳, 新西蘭】〔汽車的〕號碼牌; NUMBER PLATE *BrE*【英】, LICENSE PLATE *AmE*【美】

re·gis·try /ˈrɛdʒɪstrɪ; ˈredʒəstri/ *n* [C] a place where all the information used by an organization is kept 檔案處, 檔案室

registry of·fice /ˈ··· ˌ··/ *n* [C] a local government building in Britain where you can get married, and where births, marriages, and deaths are officially recorded〔英國辦理出生、結婚、死亡登記的〕戶籍登記處

re·gress /rɪˈgrɛs; rɪˈgres/ *v* [I] *technical* to go back to an earlier and worse condition, or to a less developed way of behaving【術語】退步, 退化; 倒退: *The patient had regressed to a state of childish dependency.* 病人退回到像小孩一樣依賴他人的狀態。—**regression** /rɪˈgrɛʃən; rɪˈgreʃən/ *n* [U] —**regressive** *adj*

regressive tax /·ˈ·· ˌ·/ *n* [C] a tax that has less effect on the rich than on the poor 遞減稅

re·gret¹ /rɪˈgrɛt; rɪˈgret/ *v* [T] **1** to feel sorry about something you have done and wish you had not done it 懊悔, 悔恨; 遺憾, 惋惜: **regret doing sth** *She deeply regretted losing her temper.* 她為自己發了脾氣而深感後悔。| **[+that]** *He regrets that he never went to college.* 他遺憾自己從未上過大學。| **regret sth** *It's a great opportunity, Mr Jarvis – you'll never regret it.* 這是個非常好的機會, 賈維斯先生, 你絕不會後悔的。| **bitterly/deeply regret** (=regret something very much) 深感遺憾[懊悔] *It was a stupid decision and I bitterly regret it.* 這是個愚蠢的決定, 我非常遺憾。| **live to regret sth** (=regret something later) 日後為某事感到後悔 *I'm afraid this is a decision that he'll live to regret.* 恐怕這是一個他將來會感到後悔的決定。| **you'll regret it** *spoken* (=used when threatening someone)【口】你會後悔的〔表示威脅〕*You'd better not tell the police, or you'll regret it.* 你最好別報警, 否則你會後悔的。**2** [not in progressive 不用進行式] *formal* to be sorry and sad about a situation【正式】對…感到抱歉: *The management regrets any inconvenience caused to its customers.* 店主對給顧客造成的不便表示歉意。| **I regret that** *formal* (=used to politely say that you cannot do something)【正式】很遺憾〔委婉地表示你不能做某事〕*I regret that I will be unable to attend.* 很遺憾, 我不能參加。| **I regret to say/inform/tell** (=used when you are going to give someone bad news) 我遺憾地説/通知/告訴〔壞消息〕*I regret to inform you that your contract will not be renewed.* 我很遺憾地通知你, 你的合同不能續簽。

USAGE NOTE 用法説明: REGRET

GRAMMAR 語法

Regret is often followed by an *ing* form of a verb, not often by the *to* form unless it is related to something that is about to be said. regret 後面常用動詞 ing 形式, 只有在對將要談到的事情表示遺憾時用動詞不定式。So if you say 因此如果說: *I regret to tell you this, but I just crashed the car,* you mean 是指 *I'm sorry, but I crashed the car.* 我很遺憾, 我撞了車。Compare this with 比較: *I regret telling you I crashed the car.* This means 是指 *I'm sorry I told you I crashed the car.* 我後悔把撞車的事告訴了你。

You **regret** something (NOT 不用 **regret about/for something**). regret 後緊接感到抱歉的事。

regret² *n* [C,U] **1** sadness that you feel about something because you wish it had not happened or that you had not done it. 懊悔, 悔恨; 遺憾, 惋惜: **[+at]** *The company expressed deep regret at the accident.* 公司對事故深表遺憾。| *Jason detected a note of regret in her voice.* 賈森聽出她有懊悔的口氣。| **with (great/deep) regret** *With great regret they abandoned the idea of rebuilding the kitchen.* 他們非常遺憾地放棄了重修廚房的想法。| **have no/few regrets** (=not feel sorry about something that you have done) 不後悔, 沒有遺憾 *Hetty felt no regrets about her decision to leave home.* 對自己離開家的決定, 海蒂毫不後悔。**2 much to my regret** *formal* used to say that you are sorry about something【正式】非常遺憾: *Much to our regret, we will be unable to attend your wedding.* 非常遺憾, 我們不能參加你們的婚禮。**3 give/send your regrets** *formal* to say that you are unable to go to a meeting, accept an invitation etc【正式】〔因不能赴會、接受邀請等〕表示歉意: *My father was ill and had to send his regrets.* 家父因病缺席, 故此深表歉意!

re·gret·ful·ly /rɪˈgrɛtfəlɪ; rɪˈgretfəli/ *adv* **1** feeling sad because you do not want to do what you are doing 遺憾地; 惋惜地: *She looked at her watch and turned regretfully towards home.* 她看了看錶, 惋惜地轉身回家去了。**2** [sentence adverb 句子副詞] used to talk about a situation that you wish was different or that you are sorry about 懊悔地; 抱歉地: *Regretfully we cannot cater for small children or pets.* 對不起, 我們不能接待小孩或寵物。—**regretful** *adj*

re·gret·ta·ble /rɪˈgrɛtəbl; rɪˈgretəbəl/ *adj* something that is regrettable makes you feel sorry or sad because it has unpleasant results 令人遺憾的, 令人懊悔的: *Most workers regarded the strike as a regrettable necessity.* 大多數工人認為這次罷工雖然令人遺憾, 但十分必要。| *It is a regrettable fact that our hearing fails as we grow old.* 隨着年齡的增長, 我們的聽力會減退, 這是一個令人遺憾的事實。

re·gret·ta·bly /rɪˈgrɛtəblɪ; rɪˈgretəbli/ *adv* used when you consider the existing situation to be unsatisfactory [sentence adverb 句子副詞] 令人遺憾(地): *Regrettably, the patients weren't asked for their opinion.* 很遺憾, 沒有徵求病人的意見。| **[+adj/adv]** *Some of the students are regrettably ignorant of contraception.* 一些學生對避孕問題的無知, 令人嘆息。

re·group /ri`grup; ˌriː'gruːp/ *v* [I,T] to form new groups or form groups again, or to make people do this（使）重組: *The Russians retreated, needing to regroup their forces.* 俄國人需要重組軍隊, 於是撤退了。

reg·u·lar¹ /`rɛgjələ; 'regjʊlə/ *adj*
1 ▶EQUAL SPACES 均等的空間◀ a regular series of things has the same amount of time or space between each thing and the next 規則的, 有規律的: *His breathing was slow and regular.* 他的呼吸緩慢而有規律。| **at regular intervals** *Plant the seeds at regular intervals.* 在固定的間隔距離內播種。
2 ▶EVERY DAY/WEEK ETC 每天/週等◀ [usually before noun 一般用於名詞前] happening or doing something many times and often at the same times every day, month, year etc 定期的, 固定的: *I really miss the security of a regular pay cheque.* 我實在懷念定期領取工資支票的安全感。| **on a regular basis** *It has always been our policy to review staff productivity on a regular basis.* 我們的政策一貫是定期考核員工的生產效率。| **regular as clockwork** (=at exactly the same time every day, week etc) 準時（地）*He phones us every Sunday at six, regular as clockwork.* 他每星期天六點準時給我們打電話。
3 ▶OFTEN 經常◀ [only before noun 僅用於名詞前] happening or doing something very often 頻繁的, 經常的: **regular customer/visitor** *Old Joe is one of the bar's regular customers.* 老喬是這家酒吧的常客之一。
4 ▶USUAL 通常的◀ [only before noun 僅用於名詞前] normal or usual 平常的, 慣常的: *Driving the van was a change from his regular duties.* 駕駛小貨車不是他平時的工作。
5 ▶SHAPE 形狀◀ evenly shaped with parts or sides of equal size 等邊的, 勻稱的: *a regular hexagon* 正六邊形 | *He had strong, regular teeth.* 他的牙齒堅固整齊。| *regular features* (=an evenly shaped face) 端正的五官
6 ▶NORMAL 正常的◀ [only before noun 僅用於名詞前] *especially AmE* of a normal or standard size【尤美】通常的; 標準的: *a regular coke* 標準容量的可樂
7 ▶ORDINARY 平常的◀ *especially AmE* ordinary, without any special feature or qualities【尤美】普通的, 一般的: *Regular teachers just don't have the training to deal with problem children.* 一般的教師都沒有接受過應付問題兒童的訓練。
8 ▶FRIENDLY 友好的◀ *AmE* nice and friendly【美】可親的, 友好的: *a regular guy* 好人
9 be/keep regular *informal*【非正式】**a)** to get rid of waste from your BOWEL*s* often enough to be healthy 大便正常 **b)** a woman who is regular has her MENSTRUAL PERIOD at the same time each month〔婦女〕月經正常
10 ▶GRAMMAR 語法◀ *technical* a regular verb or noun changes its forms in the same way as most verbs or nouns; the verb 'dance' is regular but 'be' is not【術語】〔動詞、名詞的變化〕規則的〈如 dance 是規則動詞, 但 be 不是〉
11 ▶EMPHASIZING 強調◀ [only before noun 僅用於名詞前] *informal* used to emphasize what you think someone is like【非正式】十足的, 完全的: *The child's so bossy – a regular little dictator!* 這小孩這麼愛發號施令, 是個十足的小獨裁者!
12 regular soldier/army/troops etc having a permanent job in the army 正規兵/軍/部隊等 —**regularity** *n* [U]

regular² *n* **1** [C] *informal BrE* a customer who goes to the same shop, bar etc very often【非正式, 英】常客, 老主顧: *The barman knows all the regulars by name.* 這位酒吧男招待員叫得出所有常客的名字。**2** [C] a soldier whose permanent job is in the army 正規兵 **3** [U] *AmE* petrol that contains LEAD【美】含鉛汽油 —compare 比較 UNLEADED

reg·u·lar·ize also 又作 **-ise** *BrE*【英】/`rɛgjələˌraɪz; 'regjʊləraɪz/ *v* [T] to make a situation that has existed for some time legal or official 使合法化; 使正規化 —**regularization** /ˌrɛgjələrə`zeʃən; ˌregjʊləraɪ'zeɪʃən/ *n* [U]

reg·u·lar·ly /`rɛgjələlɪ; 'regjʊləli/ *adv* **1** at regular times, for example every day, week, or month 定期地: *The club meets regularly once a fortnight.* 俱樂部每兩星期開一次例會。**2** often 經常: *I am regularly invited to give talks about my time in Nepal.* 我經常被邀請去介紹我在尼泊爾時的情況。**3** evenly arranged or shaped 勻稱地, 整齊地: *a fence with regularly spaced vertical posts* 豎樁距離均等的圍欄

reg·u·late /`rɛgjəˌlet; 'regjʊleɪt/ *v* [T] **1** to control an activity or process, especially by rules〔尤指以規則〕控制, 管理: *There are strict rules regulating the use of chemicals in food.* 有嚴格的規定限制在食品中使用化學品。**2** to make a machine work at a particular speed, temperature etc; ADJUST 調撥, 校準, 調節: *You can regulate the thermostat by turning this little dial.* 轉動這個小控制盤就可以調節恒温器。

reg·u·la·tion¹ /ˌrɛgjə`leʃən; ˌregjʊ'leɪʃən/ *n* **1** [C] an official rule or order 規則; 條例; 法令: **building/planning/safety etc regulations** *The company is very strict on enforcing health and safety regulations.* 公司嚴格執行健康和安全規定。| **rules and regulations** *There are too many rules and regulations governing small businesses.* 約束小企業的規章制度太多。**2** [U] control over something, especially by rules 管制; 管理: *the regulation of public spending* 公共開支的管理

regulation² *adj* [only before noun 僅用於名詞前] used or worn because of a rule or custom 規定要求的, 正規的: *regulation uniforms* 標準的制服

reg·u·la·tor /`rɛgjəˌletə; 'regjʊleɪtə/ *n* [C] **1** an instrument for controlling the temperature, speed etc of something 調節器; 校準器 **2** someone who makes sure that, or makes it possible for, a system to operate properly or fairly 管理者, 調控者: *Oftel, the official telecommunications regulator*〔英國〕電信監督局, 官方的電訊業監管機構

reg·u·la·to·ry /`rɛgjələˌtorɪ; ˌregjʊ'leɪtəri/ *adj formal* having the purpose of controlling an activity or process, especially by rules【正式】調整的; 管理的, 控制的

re·gur·gi·tate /rɪ`gɝdʒəˌtet; rɪ'gɜːdʒɪteɪt/ *v formal*【正式】**1** [I,T] to bring food that you have already swallowed back into your mouth 回吐; 反芻: *Some birds and animals regurgitate food to feed their young.* 有些鳥類和動物回吐已吞下的食物來餵養自己的幼兒。**2** [T] to repeat facts, ideas etc that you have read or heard without thinking about them yourself〔不加思考地〕重複 —**regurgitation** /rɪˌgɝdʒə`teʃən; rɪˌgɜːdʒɪ'teɪʃən/ n [U]

re·hab /`rihæb; 'riːhæb/ *n* [U] *AmE* the process of curing someone who has an alcohol or drugs problem【美】〔酗酒、吸毒者的〕康復治療: *a rehab program* 康復治療計劃 | **in rehab** *She's been in rehab for a week.* 她接受康復治療一星期了。—**rehab** *v* [T]

re·ha·bil·i·tate /ˌrihə`bɪləˌtet; ˌriːhə'bɪlɪteɪt/ *v* [T] **1** to help someone to live a healthy, useful, or active life again after they have been seriously ill or in prison〔重病或坐牢後〕使恢復正常生活: *a special unit for rehabilitating stroke patients* 協助中風患者康復的特殊病房 **2** to improve a building or area so that it returns to the good condition it was in before 使恢復原狀, 修復〔建築或地區〕**3** to make people think that someone is good again after a period when they thought that person was bad 恢復…的名譽: *President Nixon seems to have been rehabilitated in the US.* 尼克遜總統似乎已經在美國恢復了名譽。—**rehabilitation** /ˌrihəˌbɪlə`teʃən; ˌriːhəbɪlɪ'teɪʃən/ *n* [U]

re·hash /ri`hæʃ; riː'hæʃ/ *n* [C] something such as a piece of writing or a film which is really a copy of an earlier one, although some things have been changed to make it seem new〔略加變動的〕改寫, 改編; 重拍; 改頭換面: *just a rehash of the original 1959 version* 只不過是1959年原作的翻版 —**rehash** /ri`hæʃ; riː'hæʃ/ *v* [T]: *He keeps rehashing the same old speech.* 他不斷用改頭換面的手法發表內容相同的演說。

re·hears·al /rɪˋhɝsl̩; rɪˈhɜːsəl/ *n* [C,U] a period or a particular occasion when all the people in a play, concert etc practise it before a public performance 排練, 排演 —see also 另見 DRESS REHEARSAL

re·hearse /rɪˋhɝs; rɪˈhɜːs/ *v* **1** [I,T] to practise or make people practise something such as a play or concert in order to prepare for a public performance (使) 排練〔戲劇或音樂會〕, 排演, 預演: *The musicians were rehearsing until 2 o'clock in the morning.* 樂師一直排練到凌晨兩點。**2** [T] to practise something that you plan to say to someone 練習, 演練: *Sandy rehearsed her resignation speech.* 桑迪演練她的辭職演說。**3** [T] *formal* to repeat an opinion that has often been expressed before【正式】反覆講〔過去經常有人表達的意見〕

re·heat /riˋhit; ˌriːˈhiːt/ *v* [T] to make a meal or drink hot again 重新加熱

re·house /riˋhaʊz; ˌriːˈhaʊz/ *v* [T] to put someone in a new or better home 為〔某人〕提供新住房: *All flood victims will be rehoused as soon as possible.* 將儘快為所有遭受水災的災民提供新住房。

Reich /raɪk; raɪk/ *n German* **the Third Reich** the German state between 1933 and 1945【德】第三帝國〔1933年至1945年間的德意志帝國〕

reign¹ /ren; reɪn/ *n* [C] **1** the period of time during which someone is king or queen 某君主的統治時期: *the reign of Queen Victoria* 維多利亞女王統治時期 **2** a period during which something is the most powerful or most important feature of a place 主宰期, 支配期, 極盛期: *the reign of Stalinism in Russia* 史太林主義在俄國佔統治地位時期 | **reign of terror** (=when a government kills many of its political opponents) 恐怖統治時期

reign² *v* [I] **1** to be the king or queen 為王, 為君: *George VI reigned from 1936 to 1952.* 喬治六世於1936至1952年在位。**2** *literary* to be the most important feature of a place at a particular time【文】支配, 盛行: *Anarchy reigned for many months.* 無政府狀態猖獗了好幾個月。**3 the reigning champion** the most recent winner of a competition 現任冠軍, 本屆冠軍: *the reigning Wimbledon champion* 本屆溫布頓網球賽冠軍

re·im·burse /ˌriɪmˋbɝs; ˌriːɪ̵mˈbɜːs/ *v* [T] *formal* to pay money back to someone who has had to spend the money because of their work【正式】償還, 付還: **reimburse sb for sth** *The company will reimburse you for any costs incurred on the course.* 你上課的全部費用可以向公司報銷。—**reimbursement** *n* [C,U]

rein¹ /ren; reɪn/ *n* [C] **1** also 又作 **reins** [plural] a long narrow band of leather that is fastened around a horse's head in order to control it 韁繩 —see picture at 參見 HORSE¹ 圖 **2 give (full/free) rein to** to allow an emotion or feeling to be expressed freely 放任, 對…不加約束: *He gave free rein to his imagination and produced a brilliant piece of writing.* 他充分發揮自己的想像力, 寫出了一篇極佳的作品。**3 give sb (a) free rein** to give someone complete freedom to do a job in whatever way they choose〔工作上〕給予某人絕對自由 **4 keep a tight rein on sb/sth** to control something strictly 對某人/某事嚴加控制: *The finance director keeps a tight rein on spending.* 財務主管對開銷嚴加控制。**5 take/hand over the reins** to take or give someone control over an organization or country 掌權; 交給〔某人〕掌管: *Who'll take over the reins while the boss is in hospital?* 老闆住院期間將由誰負責管理?

rein² *v*

rein sth ↔ **in** *phr v* [T] **1** to start to control a situation more strictly 開始嚴加控制: *The government is reining in public expenditure.* 政府正嚴格控制公共開支。**2** to make a horse go more slowly by pulling on the reins 用韁繩勒住馬

re·in·car·nate /ˌriɪnˋkarnet; ˌriːɪnˈkɑːneɪt/ *v* **be reincarnated** to be born again in another body after you have died〔靈魂〕被賦予新的肉體; 再生; 轉世

re·in·car·na·tion /ˌriɪnkarˋneʃən; ˌriːɪnkɑːˈneɪʃən/ *n* **1** [U] the belief that after someone dies their soul lives again 再生, 轉世: *Hindus believe in reincarnation.* 印度教徒相信人會轉世投胎。**2** [C] the person or animal that a reincarnated person has become 轉世化身: *She thinks she is a reincarnation of Cleopatra.* 她認為自己是〔古埃及女王〕克婁巴特拉轉世。

rein·deer /ˋrenˌdɪr; ˈreɪndɪə/ *n plural* **reindeer** [C] a large DEER with long wide horns 馴鹿: *Herds of reindeer graze on the tundra.* 成羣的馴鹿在凍原上吃草。

re·in·force /ˌriɪnˋfɔrs; ˌriːɪ̵nˈfɔːs/ *v* [T] **1** to give support to an opinion, idea, or feeling, and make it stronger 加強〔信心、信念、感覺等〕: *Conclusions from the report have been reinforced by more recent studies.* 更多的最新研究證實了報告的結論。**2** to make part of a building, structure, piece of clothing etc stronger 加強, 加固〔建築、結構、衣物等〕: *The sea wall is being reinforced with tons of cement.* 正在用成噸的水泥加固防波堤。**3** to make a group of people, especially an army, stronger by adding people, equipment etc 增援, 加強…的力量〔尤指軍隊〕

reinforced con·crete /ˌ… ˈ‥/ *n* [U] CONCRETE with metal RODS in it, used to make buildings stronger 鋼筋混凝土

re·in·force·ment /ˌriɪnˋfɔrsmənt; ˌriːɪnˈfɔːsmənt/ *n* **1** [U] the act of making something stronger 加強, 加固 **2 reinforcements** [plural] more soldiers who are sent to an army to make it stronger 援兵, 增援部隊: *The Spanish soon returned with reinforcements and firearms.* 西班牙人很快就帶着援兵和火器回來了。

re·in·state /ˌriɪnˋstet; ˌriːɪ̵nˈsteɪt/ *v* [T] to put someone back into a job or position of authority that they had before 使恢復原職: *The manager had been unfairly dismissed, and he was duly reinstated.* 經理被蒙冤解職, 後來還他清白, 予以復職。—**reinstatement** *n* [C,U]

re·in·sure /ˌriɪnˋʃʊr; ˌriːɪ̵nˈʃʊə/ *v* [T] *technical* to share the insurance of something between two or more companies, so that there is less risk for each【術語】分保, 給…再保險〔由至少兩家公司承保, 以分擔風險〕—**reinsurance** *n* [U]

re·invent /ˌriɪnˋvɛnt; ˌriːɪnˈvent/ *v* [T] **1** to produce an idea that is based on something that existed in the past 在已有事物的基礎上發明 **2 reinvent the wheel** *informal* to waste time trying to find a way of doing something when someone else has already discovered the best way to do it【非正式】徒勞, 白費功夫〔因為別人早已發現做此事的最好方法〕

re·is·sue /riˋɪʃu; ˌriːˈɪʃuː/ *v* [T] to produce a record, book etc again, after it has not been available for some time 再發行, 重印: *CBS reissued 'Lady in Satin'.* 哥倫比亞唱片公司重新發行了《身穿緞子服的女人》。—**reissue** *n* [C]

re·it·e·rate /riˋɪtəˌret; riːˈɪtəreɪt/ *v* [T] *formal* to repeat a statement or opinion in order to make your meaning as clear as possible【正式】反覆地說, 重申: **reiterate that** *Let me reiterate that we have absolutely no plans to increase taxation.* 我重申, 我們絕對沒有增加稅收的計劃。—**reiteration** /riˌɪtəˋreʃən; riːˌɪtəˈreɪʃən/ *n* [C,U]

re·ject¹ /rɪˋdʒɛkt; rɪˈdʒekt/ *v* [T]

1 ►OFFER/SUGGESTION 提議/建議◄ to refuse to accept an offer, suggestion, or request 拒絕 (接受): *Sarah rejected her brother's offer of help.* 莎拉拒絕了她弟弟的幫忙。—see 見 REFUSE¹ (USAGE)

2 ►NOT EMPLOY 不雇用◄ to refuse to accept someone for a job, course of study etc 拒絕〔雇用、錄取〕: *Ian was rejected by the army because of his bad eyesight.* 伊恩因為視力不好而被拒絕入伍。

3 ►PRODUCT 產品◄ to throw away something that has just been made, because its quality is not good enough〔因質量不好而〕廢棄: *We have very strict quality control, so anything that is imperfect is rejected.* 我們實行非常嚴格的質量檢查, 凡是有缺陷的一概剔除。

4 ►BELIEF 信念◄ to decide that you do not believe in something 摒棄: *The present generation has largely re-*

jected the beliefs of its parents. 現在這一代人在很大程度上摒棄了父母的觀念。
5 ▶ORGAN 器官◀ if your body rejects an organ, such as a heart, after a TRANSPLANT operation, it produces substances that attack that organ 排斥〔移植器官〕
6 ▶NOT LOVED 不受關愛的◀ to refuse to give someone any love or attention 冷落: *She was six months pregnant and feeling fat and rejected.* 她懷着六個月的身孕, 覺得自己又胖又遭嫌棄。—**rejection** /-ˋdʒɛkʃən; -ˈdʒekʃən/ *n* [C,U]: *Above all, Phillips feared rejection and loneliness.* 最重要的是, 菲利普斯懼怕受冷落和孤獨。| *China's rejection of the 1987 proposals* 中國對1987年建議的拒絕

re·ject² /ˋridʒɛkt; ˈriːdʒekt/ *n* [C] a product that has been rejected because there is something wrong with it 次品, 廢品

re·jig /riˋdʒɪg; riːˈdʒɪg/ *BrE*【英】, **re·jig·ger** /riˋdʒɪgɚ; riːˈdʒɪgə/ *AmE*【美】*v* **rejigged, rejigging** [T] *informal* to arrange or organize something in a different way, especially in order to make it better, more suitable, more useful etc【非正式】重新安排, 調整: *Many of his songs are rejigged versions of old Hooker numbers.* 他的許多歌都是由老胡克的樂曲改編的。—**rejig** /ˋridʒɪg; ˈriːdʒɪg/ *n* [singular]

re·joice /rɪˋdʒɔɪs; rɪˈdʒɔɪs/ *v* [I] *literary* to feel or show that you are very happy【文】喜悅: **[+at/over]** *His family rejoiced at the news.* 聽到這個消息他全家都很高興。

rejoice in sth *phr v* [T] **1** to be very happy about something 因…而高興: *We rejoiced in our good fortune.* 我們為自己的好運而感到高興。**2** *BrE humorous* to have a name or title that is silly or amusing【英, 幽默】擁有〔某個可笑的名字或稱號〕: *He rejoices in the name of Pigg.* 他有個有趣的姓氏, 叫 Pigg〔與 pig 諧音〕。

re·joic·ing /rɪˋdʒɔɪsɪŋ; rɪˈdʒɔɪsɪŋ/ also 又作 **rejoicings** [plural] *n* [U] *literary* a situation in which a lot of people behave in a very happy way because they have had good news【文】歡慶, 慶祝: **[+at/over]** *There was great rejoicing over the victory.* 人們熱烈慶祝勝利。

re·join¹ /ˌriˋdʒɔɪn; ˌriːˈdʒɔɪn/ *v* [T] **1** to go back to a group of people that you were with before 重返, 回到〔某一羣人身邊〕: *Crystal went to rejoin her friends in the lounge.* 克莉斯多爾回到休息室和她的朋友們在一起。**2** to join an organization again 重新加入: *In 1938 he rejoined the Socialists.* 1938年他重新加入社會黨。**3** to join two things together again 使再連接: *The cables need to be rejoined.* 電纜需要重新連接。

re·join² /rɪˋdʒɔɪn; rɪˈdʒɔɪn/ *v* [T] *formal* to say something in reply, especially rudely or angrily【正式】〔尤指粗魯或憤怒地〕回答

re·join·der /rɪˋdʒɔɪndɚ; rɪˈdʒɔɪndə/ *n* [C] *formal* a reply, especially a rude one【正式】〔尤指粗魯的〕回答: *A smart rejoinder only occurred to me later.* 我只是在後來才想到一個巧妙的回答。

re·ju·ve·nate /rɪˋdʒuvəˌnet; rɪˈdʒuːvəneɪt/ *v* [T] **1** to make an organization effective again, for example by bringing in new ideas 使〔組織〕恢復活力: *The Party was rejuvenated by an influx of younger members.* 由於大量吸收較年輕的黨員, 黨恢復了活力。**2** [usually passive 一般用被動態] to make someone look or feel young and strong again 使變得年輕, 使恢復活力 —**rejuvenation** /rɪˌdʒuvəˋneʃən; rɪˌdʒuːvəˈneɪʃən/ *n* [singular,U]

re·kin·dle /riˋkɪndl; riːˈkɪndl/ *v* [T] **1** to make someone have a particular feeling, thought etc again 重新激起, 重新引起: *a chance to rekindle an old friendship* 重修舊好的機會 **2** to light a fire or flame again 再點燃

re·laid /ˌriˋled; ˌriːˈleɪd/ past tense and past participle of RELAY[3]

re·lapse /rɪˋlæps; rɪˈlæps/ *v* [I] **1** to become ill again after you have seemed to improve〔舊病〕復發 **2** to start to behave badly again or become less active 故態復萌: **[+into]** *Clara relapsed into her usual sulky manner.* 克萊拉又像以前一樣悶悶不樂。—**relapse** /ˋrilæps; rɪˈlæps/ *n* [C,U]: *She's had an unexpected relapse.* 沒想到她舊病復發了。

re·late /rɪˋlet; rɪˈleɪt/ *v* **1** [I,T] to show or prove a connection between two or more things 把…聯繫起來, 證明…有關聯; 有關聯: *The police are still trying to relate the two pieces of evidence.* 警方還在試圖找出這兩個證據之間的聯繫。| **relate sth to** *The report seeks to relate the rise in crime to an increase in unemployment.* 報告想把犯罪率上升與失業率增加聯繫起來。**2** [T] *formal* to tell someone about events that have happened to you or to someone else【正式】講述: *Witnesses to the same crime related the events completely differently.* 目擊者對同一樁罪案經過的敘述完全不同。**3** [I] *AmE spoken* to feel that you understand someone's problem, situation etc【美口】認同, 理解〔別人的問題、處境等〕: *"I'm just swamped with work right now." "Yeah, I can relate."* "我現在工作應接不暇。" "是的, 我可以理解。" S2 W1

relate to sb/sth *phr v* [T] **1** to be concerned with or be about a particular subject 有關, 涉及: *This relates to something I mentioned earlier.* 這與我早先提到的某件事有關。**2** to be directly connected with and affected by something 與…直接相關: *The cost relates directly to the amount of time spent on the project.* 這個項目的成本與所費的時間有直接關係。**3** to be able to have a good relationship with people because you understand their feelings and behaviour 和睦相處; 認同: *Laurie finds it difficult to relate to children.* 勞麗發現很難和孩子相處得好。**4** *informal* to feel that you understand or sympathize with a particular idea or situation【非正式】認同, 產生共鳴: *I can really relate to that song.* 我完全能夠理解那首歌。

re·lat·ed /rɪˋletɪd; rɪˈleɪtɪd/ *adj* **1** connected in some way 有關係的: *drug abuse and other related issues* 吸毒及其他相關的問題 | **[+to]** *The heart attack could be related to his car crash last year.* 心臟病發作可能與他去年的車禍有關。| **drug/stress-related** *stress-related illness* 與壓力有關的疾病 **2** [not before noun 不用於名詞前] connected by a family relationship 與…有親戚關係的: *Catriona and I are related.* 卡特莉奥娜和我有親戚關係。| **[+to]** *I am related to Simon by marriage.* 西蒙是我的姻親。**3** animals, plants, languages etc that are related belong to the same group 同類的, 同族的, 同系的 —**relatedness** *n* [U] S2 W3

re·la·ting to /rɪˋletɪŋ tu; rɪˈleɪtɪŋ tuː/ *prep* about; relating 有關, 涉及: *documents relating to immigration laws* 與移民法相關的文件

re·la·tion /rɪˋleʃən; rɪˈleɪʃən/ *n* S2 W1
1 ▶FAMILY 家人◀ [C] a member of your family; relative 家人; 親戚: *We have relations in Canada and Scotland.* 我們在加拿大和蘇格蘭有親戚。| **close/distant relation** *Diane's a distant relation of mine – a third cousin, I think.* 黛安是我的遠親, 我想是隔三代的表姐。| **no relation** (=not a relative) 沒有親戚關係 *His name's Johnson too – no relation.* 他也姓約翰遜, 但與我沒有親戚關係。—see also 另見 BLOOD RELATION, **poor relation** (POOR (12)) —see 見 RELATIONSHIP (USAGE)
2 ▶BETWEEN PEOPLE/COUNTRIES 人民/國家之間◀ relations [plural] **a)** official connections between companies, countries etc (正式) 關係: *Canada and Italy established diplomatic relations in 1970.* 加拿大與意大利在1970年建立外交關係。**b)** the way in which people or groups of people behave towards each other (人際) 關係: **[+between]** *Relations between workers and management have improved recently.* 勞資關係最近有所改善。
3 in relation to used to talk about something that is connected with or compared with the thing you are talking about 關於; 與…相比: *Women's earnings are still very low in relation to men's.* 女性的收入相比於男性仍然很低。
4 ▶CONNECTION 聯繫◀ [C,U] a connection between two or more things〔事物間的〕聯繫: **bear no relation**

to (=have no connection with and be completely different from something) 與…無關; 與…完全不同 *The retail price bears no relation to the price the farmer receives.* 零售價格與農民得到的價格完全不相符。

5 have (sexual) relations (with) *old-fashioned* to have sex with someone【過時】(與…) 發生性關係

re·la·tion·al /rɪ`leʃənḷ; rɪˈleɪʃənəl/ *adj technical* a relational word is used as part of a sentence but without a meaning of its own, for example the word 'have' in 'I have gone'【術語】〔詞〕表示關係的〈如 I have gone 中的 have〉—compare 比較 NOTIONAL

relational da·ta·base /·,··· '···/ *n* [C] *technical* a computer DATABASE that allows a user to find and work with the same information in many different ways【術語】〔電腦〕關係數據庫

S1 W1 **re·la·tion·ship** /rɪ`leʃən,ʃɪp; rɪˈleɪʃənʃɪp/ *n* **1** [C] the way in which two people or two groups behave towards each other 關係: **[+between]** *an improved relationship between the police and local people* 警方與當地居民之間已改善的關係 | **[+with]** *We have a good working relationship with the managers.* 我們與管理人員有良好的工作關係。**2** [C,U] the way in which two or more things are connected and affect each other 聯繫, 關聯: **[+between]** *the relationship between poor housing and health problems* 惡劣的住房與健康問題之間的聯繫 **3** [C] a situation in which two people spend time together or live together, and have romantic or sexual feelings for each other 男女關係: *I just don't feel I'm ready for a relationship right now.* 我就是覺得現在不想談戀愛。**4** [U] the way in which you are related to someone in your family 親屬關係

> **USAGE NOTE 用法說明: RELATIONSHIP**
>
> WORD CHOICE 詞語辨析: **relationship, relations, relation, connection**
>
> A **relationship with** someone or something is usually close, and may involve strong feelings. relationship with 通常是指密切的關係, 可能涉及強烈的感情: *Jane's stormy relationship with her husband.* 簡與她丈夫之間一波三折的關係。| *What kind of relationship does she have with her mother?* 她與她母親之間的關係怎麼樣?
>
> **Relations** between people, groups, countries etc are often about working together or communicating. relations 用於人、團體、國家等時, 往往指共事或者交往的關係: *Relations between industrialists and environmentalists have improved recently.* 工業家與環境保護者之間的關係近來有所改善。Relations is a more official word. relations 這個詞更為正式: *friendly relations in the workplace/between East and West* 工作場所裡的友好關係/東西方之間的關係
>
> A **relation** or **relationship to** someone or something, like a **connection**, is usually about a simple fact. relation 或 relationship to, 如同 connection, 通常表示一個簡單的事實: *Jane's relationship to/connection with Jeff is that he is her uncle/boss.* 簡與傑夫的關係是他是她的叔叔/上司。| *What relation has temperature to humidity?* 溫度與濕度有甚麼聯繫?
>
> A **relationship between** people and other people or things may be either close and full of emotion, or simply a matter of fact. relationship between 既可以表示人們或事情之間關係非常親密或涉及強烈的情感, 也可以僅僅表示一個事實: *the relationship between bosses and workers* 老闆與工人的關係 | *What's the relationship between temperature and humidity?* 溫度與濕度有甚麼聯繫?

S3 W3 **rel·a·tive**[1] /`rɛlətɪv; ˈrelətɪv/ *n* [C] a member of your family; RELATION (1) 家人; 親屬, 親戚: *visit from friends and relatives at Christmas* 聖誕節時期朋友與家人的來訪

W2 **relative**[2] *adj* **1** having a particular quality when compared with something else 比較的, 相對的: **relative peace/comfort/safety etc** *an atmosphere of relative calm after the riots* 騷亂之後相對平靜的氣氛 | **relative merits/costs/values etc** (=the advantages, costs etc of two or more things that are compared with each other) 相對優點/成本/價值等 *discussing the relative merits of various sports cars* 討論各種跑車的相對優點 | **it's all relative** (=used to mean it cannot be judged on its own but must be compared with others) 一切都是相對的〔表示事情必須透過比較來評價〕*You think you're poor, but look at people in really poor countries – it's all relative.* 你以為你很窮, 可是你看看真正貧窮國家的人吧 —— 一切都是相對的。**2 relative to** connected with a particular subject 與…有關: *facts relative to this issue* 與這個問題有關的事實

relative clause /,··· '·/ *n* [C] *technical* a part of a sentence that has a verb in it, and is joined to the rest of the sentence by 'who', 'which', 'where' etc, for example, the phrase 'who lives next door', in the sentence 'The man who lives next door is a doctor'.【術語】關係從句〈如在 The man who lives next door is a doctor 一句中, who lives next door 是關係從句〉

rel·a·tive·ly /`rɛlətɪvlɪ; ˈrelətɪvli/ *adv* **1 relatively easy/few/cheap** fairly easy etc compared with other things 比較容易/少/便宜: *The drug has relatively few known side effects.* 這種藥已知的副作用比較少。**2 relatively speaking** used when comparing something with all similar things 相對來說: *Relatively speaking, it's not important.* 相對而言, 這並不重要。 S2 W2

relative pro·noun /,··· '··/ *n* [C] *technical* a PRONOUN such as 'who', 'which', or 'that' by which a relative clause is connected to the rest of the sentence【術語】關係代詞

rel·a·tiv·i·ty /,rɛlə`tɪvətɪ; ,reləˈtɪvəti/ *n* [U] the relationship in PHYSICS between time, space, and MOTION (=movement) according to Einstein's THEORY〔愛因斯坦理論中的〕相對性

re·launch /`rilɔntʃ; ˈriːlɔːntʃ/ *n* [C] a new effort to sell a product that is already on sale 再次促銷 —**relaunch** /ri`lɔntʃ; riːˈlɔːntʃ/ *v* [T]

re·lax /rɪ`læks; rɪˈlæks/ *v* 

1 ▶REST 休息◀ [I,T] to feel calm and comfortable and stop worrying, or to make someone do this (使) 放鬆, (使) 輕鬆: *After a hard day's work, relax in the swimming pool.* 在一天的辛勤工作後, 到游泳池裡去放鬆一下。| *Relax – I'm sure the kids will be back any minute.* 別緊張, 孩子們肯定馬上就會回來。| **relax sth/sb** *A nice hot bath should help to relax you.* 好好洗個熱水澡肯定會幫助你放鬆。

2 ▶LOOSEN 放鬆◀ [I,T] if you relax a part of your body or it relaxes, it becomes less stiff or less tight 使〔身體部位〕鬆弛, 放鬆: *Gentle exercise can relax stiff shoulder muscles.* 輕柔的運動可以放鬆僵硬的肩部肌肉。

3 relax your hold/grip a) to hold something less tightly than before 鬆開手: *Molassi relaxed his grip on my arm.* 莫萊西鬆開了抓着我胳膊的手。**b)** to become less strict in the way you control something 放寬: *It seemed unlikely that Britain would willingly relax her grip on the territories.* 看來英國不可能主動放鬆對領土的控制。

4 relax rules/controls/regulations etc to make rules etc less strict 放寬規定/控制/管制等: *Hughes believes that immigration controls should not be relaxed.* 休斯認為對移民的限制不能放寬。

5 relax your vigilance/concentration etc to reduce the amount of attention you give to something 放鬆警惕/使注意力鬆懈等

re·lax·a·tion /,rilæks`eʃən; ,riːlækˈseɪʃən/ *n* **1** [C,U] a way of resting and enjoying yourself 消遣, 娛樂: *I play the piano for relaxation.* 我彈鋼琴自娛。| *Playing golf is one of Bruce's favorite relaxations.* 打高爾夫球是布魯斯最喜歡的消遣之一。**2** [U] the process of making rules on the control of something less strict 放寬, 放鬆:

[+of] *a relaxation of government controls* 政府控制的放寬

re·laxed /rɪˋlækst; rɪˈlækst/ *adj* **1** feeling calm and comfortable and not worried 輕鬆的, 無拘無束的: *Gail was lying in the sun looking very relaxed and happy.* 蓋爾躺在陽光下, 看來十分輕鬆愉快。**2** a situation that is relaxed is comfortable and informal 舒適的, 隨便的, 輕鬆的: *a relaxed atmosphere* 輕鬆的氣氛

re·lax·ing /rɪˋlæksɪŋ; rɪˈlæksɪŋ/ *adj* making you feel relaxed 使人放鬆的, 使人懶洋洋的: *a relaxing afternoon in the garden* 在花園中度過一個懶洋洋的下午

re·lay¹ /ˋrile; ˈriːleɪ/ *n* **1 in relays** if people do something in relays, several small groups of them do it, one group after another, so that the activity is continuous 輪班, 輪換 **2** [C] a relay race 接力賽跑 **3** [C,U] a piece of electrical equipment that receives radio or television signals and sends them on 中繼設備, 轉播設備

re·lay² /ˋrile; ˈriːleɪ/ *v past tense and past participle* **relayed** [T] **1** to pass a message from one person or place to another 傳達, 傳遞: **relay sth to sb** *He quickly relayed this news to the other members of staff.* 他迅速地將消息傳達給其他工作人員。**2** to send out radio or television signals by relay 轉播: *The concert will be relayed at 9 pm.* 音樂會將於晚上九點轉播。

re·lay³ /ˌriˋle; ˌriːˈleɪ/ *v past tense and past participle* **relaid** /-ˋled; -ˈleɪd/ [T] to lay something such as a CARPET¹ (1) again 再鋪設〔地毯等〕

relay race /ˋ‥ ˌ·/ *n* [C] a running or swimming race between two or more teams in which each member of the team takes part one after another 接力賽

2 **re·lease¹** /rɪˋlis; rɪˈliːs/ *v* [T]
2 **1 ▶LET SB FREE** 釋放某人◀ to let someone go free 釋放, 放出: *The hostages were released in November 1988.* 人質於1988年11月獲釋。| **release sb from** *They decided to release the bird from its cage.* 他們決定把鳥從籠子裡放出來。

2 ▶STOP HOLDING 鬆手◀ to stop holding something that you have been holding tightly or carefully 鬆開, 放開〔某物〕: *The man finally released her arm.* 那個人最終鬆開了她的手臂。| **release your grasp/grip/hold (on)** *The noise made him release his grasp.* 嘈雜聲使他鬆開了緊握的手。

3 ▶MAKE PUBLIC 公佈◀ to let news or official information be known and printed 公開發表, 發佈: *The new trade figures have just been released.* 新的貿易數字剛剛公佈。

4 ▶MACHINERY 機器◀ to allow part of a piece of machinery or equipment to move from the position in which it is fixed 放開, 鬆開: *Don't forget to release the handbrake.* 別忘了鬆開手煞車。

5 ▶FEELINGS 感情◀ to express or get rid of feelings such as anger or worry 表達; 發泄: *Physical exercise is a good way of releasing tension.* 體育鍛鍊是釋放壓力的好方法。

6 ▶FILM/RECORD 電影/唱片◀ to make a record or film available for people to buy or see 發行; 上映

7 ▶CHEMICAL 化學品◀ to let a substance flow out 釋放: *Adrenalin is released in moments of danger.* 危險時腎上腺素會釋放出來。

8 ▶FROM A DUTY 從職務中◀ to allow someone not to do their duty or work 解除〔職務或工作〕; 解脫: **release sb from** *She was released from her teaching duties to attend the funeral.* 她獲准不教課而去參加葬禮。

9 ▶WEAPON 武器◀ to make a weapon fly or fall 發射, 投〔彈〕: *The missiles were released from a height of four thousand metres.* 導彈從四千米高空發射出去。

3 **release²** *n*
2 **1 ▶FROM PRISON** 從獄中◀ [singular,U] the act of allowing someone to go free or being allowed to go free 釋放: *She went to the Governor to beg for her son's release.* 她去懇求州長釋放她兒子。| **[+from]** *Simon has obtained early release from prison.* 西蒙獲准提早出獄。

2 ▶FEELINGS 感情◀ [U] **a)** freedom to show or express your feelings 流露, 表達: *Music has always provided me with a form of emotional release.* 音樂總給我某種形式的感情宣泄。**b)** a feeling that you are free from the worry or pain that you have been suffering 解脫, 擺脫: *that wonderful feeling of release when the examinations are over* 考完試之後那種如釋重負的美妙感覺

3 ▶RECORD/FILM 唱片/電影◀ [C] a new record or film 新唱片; 新電影: *the band's latest release* 該樂隊最新發行的唱片

4 on (general) release if a film, record etc is on release it has recently become possible to see or buy it 〔電影、唱片等〕已經上映[發行]

5 ▶OFFICIAL STATEMENT 正式聲明◀ [C] an official statement that is made available to be printed or broadcast 〔發布的〕正式聲明 —see also 另見 PRESS RELEASE

6 ▶CHEMICALS 化學品◀ [U] the act of letting a chemical, gas etc flow out of its usual container 釋放: *the slow release of toxic waste into the rivers* 有毒廢料向河流的緩慢排放

7 ▶MAKING STH AVAILABLE 供應某物◀ [U] the act of making something available 發布, 發行: *October 22nd is the date set for the report's release.* 定於10月22日發布該報告。

8 ▶ON A MACHINE 在機器上◀ [C] a handle, button etc that can be pressed to allow part of a machine to move 釋放裝置, 鬆脫裝置

rel·e·gate /ˋrɛləˌget; ˈreləgeɪt/ *v* [T] **1** *formal* to give someone or something a less important position than before【正式】將…置於次要地位; 貶低: *Academic excellence seems to have been relegated to a role of secondary importance.* 優異的學術成績似乎已經被置於次要地位。**2 be relegated (to)** *especially BrE* if a sports team is relegated, it is moved into a lower DIVISION【尤英】〔運動隊〕被降級(到…) —**relegation** /ˌrɛləˋgeʃən; ˌreləˈgeɪʃən/ *n* [U]

re·lent /rɪˋlɛnt; rɪˈlent/ *v* [I] to change your attitude and become less severe or cruel towards someone 變寬容, 變溫和: *She finally relented and let him borrow the car.* 最後她態度軟化下來, 讓他借用了車。

re·lent·less /rɪˋlɛntlɪs; rɪˈlentləs/ *adj* **1** someone who is relentless never stops being strict, cruel, or determined 嚴格的; 無情的; 堅決的: **[+in]** *a regime that was relentless in its persecution of dissidents* 一個殘酷鎮壓持不同政見者的政權 **2** something unpleasant that is relentless continues without ever stopping or getting less severe 〔不愉快的事物〕不間斷的: *the relentless fury of the waves* 滾滾惡浪 | *a relentless struggle for power* 永無休止的權力鬥爭 —**relentlessly** *adv*: *Kate listened to the rain beating relentlessly against the window.* 凱特聽着雨點不停地打在窗上的聲音。

rel·e·vant /ˋrɛləvənt; ˈreləvənt/ *adj* directly connected 2
with the subject or problem being discussed or considered 有關的, 切題的: *For further information see the relevant chapters in the users' manual.* 詳情請查閱使用說明中的相關章節。| **[+to]** *These issues are directly relevant to the needs of slow learners.* 這些問題與遲鈍的學習者的需要有直接關係。—opposite 反義詞 IRRELEVANT —**relevance** also 又作 **relevancy** *n* [U]: *What you say has no relevance to the subject.* 你所說的與主題無關。—**relevantly** *adv*

re·li·a·ble /rɪˋlaɪəbḷ; rɪˈlaɪəbəl/ *adj* someone or something that is reliable can be trusted or depended on 可信賴的, 可靠的: *She may forget – she's not very reliable.* 她可能會忘記——她不太靠得住。| *a reliable source of information* 可靠的信息來源 —opposite 反義詞 UNRELIABLE —**reliably** *adv*: *We are reliably informed that fighting has broken out between the two factions.* 我們獲得可靠情報, 兩派已經開戰。—**reliability** /rɪˌlaɪəˋbɪlətɪ; rɪˌlaɪəˈbɪləti/ *n* [U]

re·li·ance /rɪˋlaɪəns; rɪˈlaɪəns/ *n* **1** [singular,U] the state of being dependent on something 依賴, 依靠: **[+on]** *our country's reliance on imported oil* 我國對進口石油的依賴 **2 place reliance on** *formal* to trust someone or something【正式】信賴…

re·li·ant /rɪˋlaɪənt; rɪˈlaɪənt/ *adj* **be reliant on/upon** to depend on someone or something 依賴於…: *In my view she's far too reliant on her parents for financial support.* 我認為, 她過於依賴父母提供的經濟資助。—see also 另見 SELF-RELIANT

rel·ic /ˋrɛlɪk; ˈrelɪk/ *n* **1** [C] an old object or custom that reminds people of the past 遺跡; 遺物; 遺俗: *their crisp white uniforms, a relic of British colonial rule* 他們那挺括的白色制服, 是英國殖民統治的遺俗 | *She cleared up the glasses, the only relics of the previous night's party.* 她收拾了玻璃杯 —— 前一天晚上聚會唯一遺留下來的東西。**2** [C] a part of the body or clothing of a holy person which is kept after their death because it is thought to be holy 聖骨, 聖物: *the sacred relics of John the Baptist* 施洗者約翰的聖物 **3 relics** [plural] *old use* someone's dead body【舊】遺骸

re·lief /rɪˋlif; rɪˈliːf/ *n*

1 ►COMFORT 安慰◄ [singular,U] a feeling of comfort when something frightening, worrying, or painful has ended or has not happened〔因恐懼、憂慮或痛苦的解除而感到的〕安慰: *I felt a huge surge of relief and happiness.* 我如釋重負, 感到一陣欣慰。| **be a relief** *In a way it was a relief to know exactly what we were up against.* 確切了解我們面臨的局面在一定程度上使人寬慰。| **to your relief** (=making you feel relief) 令人感到寬慰 *To our great relief the children all arrived home safely.* 孩子都安全到家, 使我們大大鬆了一口氣。| **what a relief!** *"The boss didn't realize you were late." "What a relief!"* "老闆不知道你遲到了。" "謝天謝地!" | **a sigh of relief** *The men went away and she heaved a sigh of relief.* 男人都走了, 她如釋重負地鬆了一口氣。

2 ►REDUCTION OF PAIN 減少疼痛◄ [U] the reduction of pain or unhappy feelings〔疼痛或不快的〕減輕; 緩解: **pain relief** *the various methods of pain relief available to women in labor* 產婦分娩時減輕疼痛的各種方法 | **[+of]** *the relief of suffering* 減輕痛苦 | **[+from]** *Tranquillizers provide only temporary relief from depression.* 鎮靜劑只能暫時緩解抑鬱的情緒。

3 ►HELP 幫助◄ [U] money, food, clothes etc given to people who are poor or hungry 救濟品: *a relief fund for refugees* 難民救濟基金

4 ►MONEY 金錢◄ [U] *especially AmE* money given by the government to help people who are poor, old, unemployed etc【尤美】救濟金; BENEFIT[1] (2) *BrE*【英】

5 ►REPLACE SB 替換某人◄ [C] a person or group of people that replaces another one and does their duty after they have finished 接班[替班]的人: *the relief for the military guard* 接班的衛兵 | *a relief driver* 換班司機

6 the relief of the act of freeing a town when it has been surrounded by an enemy …的解圍, …的解救: *the relief of Mafeking*〔南非城市〕馬菲京的解圍

7 ►DECORATION 裝飾◄ [C] a shape or decoration that is raised above the surface it is on 浮雕, 浮雕品

8 ►STICKING OUT 凸出◄ in relief a shape or decoration that is in relief sticks out above the rest of the surface it is on 凸出: **in high/low relief** (=sticking out a lot or a little) 高/淺浮雕的

9 stand out in bold/stark/sharp relief to be very different from everything around and therefore very easy to notice 與周圍形成鮮明的反差; 非常突出: *The tree stood out in stark relief against the snow.* 樹在雪的襯托下顯得格外醒目。

10 light/comic relief a funny moment during a serious film, book, or situation〔嚴肅的電影、書或情景中作為調劑的〕輕鬆/滑稽場面: *There wasn't much in the way of light relief on the radio.* 廣播裡輕鬆的場面不多。

11 ►MAP 地圖◄ in relief if you show a part of the Earth's surface in relief, you show the differences in height between different parts of it 用地勢圖表示 —see also 另見 TAX RELIEF

relief map /ˈ·ˌ· ·/ *n* [C] a map with the mountains and high parts shown differently from the low parts, especially by being printed in a different colour〔用不同顏色表示地勢高低的〕地勢圖, 地形圖

re·lieve /rɪˋliv; rɪˈliːv/ *v* [T]

1 ►PAIN/PROBLEM 疼痛/問題◄ to make a pain, problem, unpleasant feeling less severe 減輕, 緩解〔疼痛、麻煩或憂慮〕: *Drugs helped to relieve the pain.* 藥物幫助舒緩疼痛。| *Volunteers were recruited to relieve the acute labour shortage.* 志願者被招募來緩解嚴重的勞動力短缺。| *Adults often swear in order to relieve their feelings.* 成年人經常說粗話以發泄情緒。—see graph at 參見 PAIN[1] 圖表

2 relieve the boredom/monotony etc to make something less dull and boring 排遣無聊/枯燥等: *I went for a walk to relieve the boredom of the day.* 一天下來無聊得很, 我去散步調劑一下。

3 relieve yourself a polite expression meaning to URINATE 小便〔禮貌的說法〕

4 ►REPLACE SB 替換某人◄ to replace someone when they have completed their duty or when they need a rest 換…的班, 替換: *The guard will be relieved at midnight.* 哨兵在午夜時換班。

5 ►A TOWN 城鎮◄ to free a town which an enemy has surrounded 給…解圍, 解救

relieve sb **of** sth *phr v* [T] **1** *formal* to help someone by taking something from them, especially a job they do not want to do or something heavy that they are carrying【正式】解除〔某人的〕負擔: *Jessie could relieve you of some of the chores.* 傑西可以幫你做一些日常雜活。| *A tall gentleman kindly offered to relieve her of her suitcase.* 一位高個子男士好心地表示幫她提箱子。**2 relieve sb of their post/duties/command etc** *formal* to take away someone's job because they have done something wrong【正式】免除某人的職務/職責/指揮權等: *After the defeat General Meyer was relieved of his command.* 戰敗之後, 邁耶將軍被免除了指揮權。**3** *humorous* to steal something from someone【幽默】偷竊: *A couple of guys I met in the bar relieved me of my wallet.* 我在酒吧遇到的兩個傢伙偷了我的錢包。

re·lieved /rɪˋlivd; rɪˈliːvd/ *adj* feeling happy because you are no longer worried about something 寬慰的, 不再憂慮的: *She looked immensely relieved when she heard this news.* 她聽說這個消息後, 流露出十分寬慰的神情。| **relieved to see/hear/know sth** *His mother was relieved to see him eating properly again.* 看到他吃飯又回復正常, 他媽媽放心了。| **[+that]** *I feel so relieved that I haven't got to take that wretched exam again.* 我不必再參加那個討厭的考試了, 感到很輕鬆。

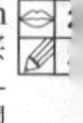

re·li·gion /rɪˋlɪdʒən; rɪˈlɪdʒən/ *n* **1** [U] people's belief in the life of the spirit and usually in one or more gods 宗教信仰: *The theme was the relationship between religion and literature.* 主題是宗教信仰與文學之間的關係。| **get religion** *informal* (=suddenly become interested in religion in a way that seems strange to other people)【非正式】〔突然〕皈依 *He got religion in a big way when he was at college.* 他在上大學時突然信教了。**2** [C] a particular system of this belief and all the ways of expressing your love for your god, ceremonies, and duties that are connected with it 宗教: *Islam and Buddhism are two of the great religions of the world.* 伊斯蘭教和佛教是世界上的兩大宗教。| *the Christian religion* 基督教 | **practise a religion** (=take part in the ceremonies and obey the rules of a religion) 信仰某種宗教〔參加儀式並遵守教規〕**3** [singular] an activity or area of interest which is extremely or unreasonably important in your life 狂熱的活動[愛好]: *Football was a religion in my family.* 足球是我們一家人狂熱的愛好。

re·li·gious /rɪˋlɪdʒəs; rɪˈlɪdʒəs/ *adj* **1** connected with religion in general or with a particular religion 宗教的: *I* *don't go along with her religious beliefs.* 我不贊同她的宗教信仰。| *a religious ceremony* 宗教儀式 **2** believing strongly in your religion and obeying its rules carefully 篤信宗教的; 虔誠的: *a deeply religious person* 非常虔誠的信徒

re·li·gious·ly /rɪˋlɪdʒəslɪ; rɪˈlɪdʒəsli/ *adv* **1** if you do something religiously, you are always very careful to do it 認真地, 嚴謹地: *I was religiously following all the instructions.* 我一絲不苟地遵循所有指示。**2** in a way that is connected with religion 與宗教信仰有關地

re·lin·quish /rɪˋlɪŋkwɪʃ; rɪˈlɪŋkwɪʃ/ *v* [T] *formal* to let someone else have your position, power, or rights, especially unwillingly【正式】〔尤指不情願地〕放棄, 交出〔權力、職位等〕: *The Duke was obliged to relinquish all rights and claims to the territory.* 公爵被迫放棄了對領地的所有權和其他權利。| **relinquish sth to sb** *He refused to relinquish sovereignty to his son.* 他拒絕把統治權交給他的兒子。| **relinquish your hold/grip on sth** *Richard stubbornly refused to relinquish his hold on the family business.* 理查德固執地拒絕交出管理家族生意的權力。

rel·i·qua·ry /ˋrɛlə͵kwɛrɪ; ˈrelɪkwəri/ *n* [C] a container for religious objects that are connected with holy people 聖骨盒; 聖物盒

rel·ish[1] /ˋrɛlɪʃ; ˈrelɪʃ/ *v* [T] to enjoy an experience or the thought of something that is going to happen 喜愛, 喜歡: *Peter didn't really relish the thought of spending Christmas at his in-laws.* 其實彼得並不喜歡在岳父母家過聖誕節。| *He spoke calmly, relishing the chance to infuriate his boss.* 他心平氣和地說話, 享受着激怒老闆的機會。

relish[2] *n* **1** [U] great enjoyment of something 享受: *There was a certain relish in his voice as he announced the news.* 他宣布該消息時語氣中有點得意。| **with (great) relish** *She looked forward with relish to the prospect of going abroad for the first time.* 她饒有興趣地期待着第一次出國。**2** [C,U] a SAUCE eaten with food which adds taste to it 佐料, 調味品: *tomato relish* 番茄調味汁

re·live /riˋlɪv; ˌriːˈlɪv/ *v* [T] to experience something again that happened in the past, or to remember or imagine it very clearly 重新體驗, 重温: *We often find ourselves reliving our schooldays when we meet up.* 我們聚會時經常重温我們的學生時代。

rel·lo /ˋrɛlo; ˈreləʊ/ *n* [C] *AustrE spoken* a relative【澳口】親戚, 親屬: *We're having the rellos over.* 有親戚要來我們這裡做客。

re·load /riˋlod; ˌriːˈləʊd/ *v* [I,T] to put another bullet into a gun, film into a camera, or PROGRAM into a computer 再裝填(槍或照相機); 再輸入(程序): *Reload the pistol, quick!* 給手槍裡再裝子彈, 快!

re·lo·cate /riˋloket; ˌriːləʊˈkeɪt/ *v* [I,T] if a group of people or a business relocates, or is relocated, they move to a different place 重新安置; 移遷; 搬遷: **[+to]** *A lot of firms are relocating to the North of England.* 許多公司正在遷往英格蘭北部。| **relocate sb/sth to** *The residents were relocated to temporary accommodation.* 居民被遷到臨時住處。—**relocation** /͵riloˋkeʃən; ˌriːləʊˈkeɪʃən/ *n* [U]

re·luc·tant /rɪˋlʌktənt; rɪˈlʌktənt/ *adj* slow and unwilling 勉強的, 不願的: *She gave a reluctant smile.* 她勉強笑了笑。| **reluctant to do sth** *She seemed reluctant to join in the discussion.* 她似乎不願意參加討論。—**reluctance** *n* [singular,U] *He answered these questions with a certain reluctance.* 他有些不情願地回答了這些問題。—**reluctantly** *adv*: *Reluctantly, he agreed.* 他答應了, 但是很勉強。

S2 W2 **re·ly** /rɪˋlaɪ; rɪˈlaɪ/ *v*

rely on/upon sb/sth *phr v* [T] **1** to trust someone or something to do what you need or expect them to do 信任, 信賴: **rely on sb/sth to do sth** *I think we can rely on Derek not to tell anyone.* 我認為我們可以信賴德里克, 他不會告訴任何人。| **rely on sb/sth doing sth** *You can't just rely on your parents lending you the money.* 你不能只指望父母借錢給你。| **rely on sb/sth for sth** *Tim always relies on his wife for advice on clothes.* 在穿着方面, 蒂姆一直靠他妻子指點。**2** to depend on something in order to continue to live or exist〔為生活或生存〕依賴: **rely on sth/sb for** *They have to rely on the river for their water.* 他們用水只能依靠這條河。

re·main /rɪˋmen; rɪˈmeɪn/ *v* **1** [I always+adv/prep, linking verb 連繫動詞] to continue to be in the same state or condition 繼續, 依然: *Would the audience please remain seated?* 請觀眾不要站起來! | *'La Strada' remains one of Fellini's best films.*《道路》依然是〔意大利導演〕費里尼最好的電影之一。| *The Government remained in power for twelve years.* 該政府執政了十二年。**2** [I] *formal* to stay in the same place without moving away【正式】停留, 留下: **[+at/in/with etc]** *She remained at home to look after the children.* 她留在家裡照顧孩子。**3** [I] to continue to exist, after others have gone or been destroyed 剩下, 留存: *Little of the original architecture remains.* 原來的建築留存下來的為數極少。| *What remains of the original art collection is now in the city museum.* 原來的藝術收藏品剩下來的現在都在市博物館裡。**4** [I] to be left after other things have been dealt with 留下, 剩餘: **remain to be done** *Several points remain to be settled.* 還剩幾個問題要解決。| **it only remains for me to say/thank etc** (=used to introduce the last remark in a speech or meeting) 最後我想說/要感謝等 *It only remains for me to thank our hosts.* 最後我要感謝我們的主人。| **the fact remains** (=used to say that a particular fact cannot be ignored) 不能忽略的是 *I know Benson has a PhD but the fact remains he has no practical experience.* 我知道本森有博士學位, 但不要忘記, 他沒有實踐經驗。**5 it remains to be seen** *spoken* used to say that it is still uncertain whether something will happen or is true【口】尚不確定, 說不準: *It remains to be seen whether or not the operation was successful.* 手術是否成功, 還有待觀察。—see also 另見 REMAINING S1 W1

Frequencies of the verbs **remain** and **stay** in spoken and written English 動詞 remain 和 stay 在英語口語和書面語中的使用頻率

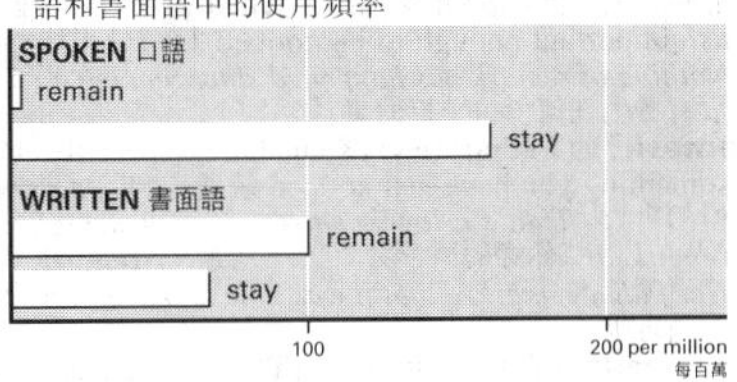

Based on the British National Corpus and the Longman Lancaster Corpus
據英國國家語料庫和朗文蘭卡斯特語料庫

This graph shows that it is much more usual in spoken English to use **stay** rather than **remain**, which is formal when used in this meaning and is therefore more common in written English. 本圖表顯示, 在英語口語中 stay 的使用頻率遠遠高於 remain, remain 表示這個意思時比較正式, 因而更多的是用於書面語中。

re·main·der /rɪˋmendɚ; rɪˈmeɪndə/ *n* **the remainder** the part of something that is left after everything else has gone or been dealt with 剩餘物, 剩餘部分: *Please pay half the money now and the remainder when you receive the goods.* 現在請付一半款, 餘款等你們收到貨後再付。| **[+of]** *The remainder of the class should use this time for study.* 班裡其餘的人必須用這段時間來學習。

re·main·ing /rɪˋmenɪŋ; rɪˈmeɪnɪŋ/ *adj* [only before noun 僅用於名詞前] the remaining people or things are those that are left when the others have gone, been used, or been dealt with 留下的; 剩餘的, 其餘的: *The few remaining guests were in the kitchen finishing off the wine.* 還 W2

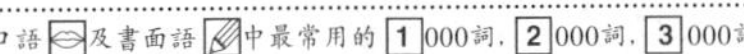

沒走的幾位客人在廚房裡把酒喝完。| *The only remaining question is whether we can raise the money.* 唯一剩下的問題是我們能否籌到這筆錢。

3 **re·mains** /rɪˋmenz; rɪˈmeɪnz/ *n* [plural] **1 the remains (of)** the parts of something that are left after the rest has been destroyed or has disappeared 剩下的東西[部分]; 遺跡: *He ate the remains of the casserole hungrily.* 他狼吞虎咽地吃掉剩下的燉菜。| *the extensive Roman remains* (=of ancient buildings) *at Arles* 在阿爾勒大片的古羅馬遺跡 **2** the body of someone who has died 遺體: *Her remains are buried in Westminster.* 她的遺體葬在威斯敏斯特。

re·make¹ /riˋmek; ˌriːˈmeɪk/ *v past tense and past participle* **remade** /-ˋmed; -ˈmeɪd/ [T] **1** to film a story or record a tune again 重新攝製; 重新錄製: *The band has just remade an old Frank Sinatra hit.* 樂隊剛剛重新錄製了法蘭仙納杜拉一首紅極一時的舊歌。**2** to build or make something again 再建; 再製

re·make² /ˋriˌmek; ˈriːmeɪk/ *n* [C] a record or film that has the same music or story as one that was made before 重新錄製的唱片; 重新攝製的電影

re·mand¹ /rɪˋmænd; rɪˈmɑːnd/ *v* [T usually passive 一般用被動態] *BrE* to send someone back from a court of law, to wait for their TRIAL¹ (1)【英】將…還押[保釋]候審: **be remanded in custody** (=be kept in prison until your TRIAL¹ (1)) 在押候審

remand² *n* [U] the period of time that someone spends in prison before their TRIAL¹ (1)〔審前〕在押期: *remand prisoners* 在押犯 | *a remand centre* 拘留中心 | **be on remand** (=in prison waiting for your TRIAL¹ (1)) 在押候審: *Evans committed suicide while on remand in Parkhurst prison.* 埃文斯在帕克赫斯特監獄在押候審期間自殺了。

remand home /ˈ· · ·/ also 又作 **remand cen·tre** /ˈ· · ˌ· ·/ *n* [C] *BrE* a place where young criminals are kept while waiting for a TRIAL¹ (1)【英】青少年犯拘留所

3
3 **re·mark¹** /rɪˋmɑrk; rɪˈmɑːk/ *n* **1** [C] something that you say when you express an opinion or say what you have noticed 意見, 評論: **make/pass a remark** *She could hear the other girls making rude remarks about her.* 她可以聽見其他女孩在說她的壞話。**2 (worthy) of remark** *old use* important enough to be noticed【舊】值得注意的: *Nothing of remark has happened since you left.* 你走後沒有發生任何值得一提的事。

remark² *v* [T+that] to say something, especially about something you have just noticed 談到, 說起〔尤指剛察覺的事〕: *"That's a lovely shirt you're wearing," she remarked.* "你穿的襯衫真漂亮。"她說。| **remark that** *Her father remarked that it was time to leave.* 她的父親說該走了。

remark on/upon sth *phr v* [T] to notice that something has happened and say something about it 談論, 評論: *Everyone remarked on his absence.* 大家對他的缺席議論紛紛。

3 **re·mar·ka·ble** /rɪˋmɑrkəbl̩; rɪˈmɑːkəbəl/ *adj* unusual or surprising and therefore deserving attention or praise 值得注意的; 不尋常的, 奇特的: *She has made remarkable progress.* 她取得了不起的進步。| *a remarkable coincidence* 奇特的巧合 | **[+about]** *There's nothing particularly remarkable about the landscape.* 這片景色沒有甚麼特別之處。| **[+for]** *Finland is remarkable for its large number of lakes.* 芬蘭以湖泊眾多而著稱。

re·mar·ka·bly /rɪˋmɑrkəblɪ; rɪˈmɑːkəbli/ *adv* unusually; noticeably 不尋常地; 突出地: **[+adj/adv]** *She plays the violin remarkably well for a child of her age.* 與同年齡的孩子比較, 她的小提琴拉得特別好。| [sentence adverb 句子副詞] *Remarkably, all of the passengers survived the crash.* 奇怪的是, 所有的乘客在事故中都活下來了。

re·mar·ry /riˋmærɪ; ˌriːˈmæri/ *v* [I,T] to marry again 再婚; 再娶; 再嫁: *Widowed in 1949, Mrs Hayes never remarried.* 1949年喪夫後, 海斯太太一直沒有再婚。—**remarriage** /riˋmærɪdʒ; riːˈmærɪdʒ/ *n* [C]

re·mas·ter /riˋmæstɚ; riːˈmɑːstə/ *v* [T] *technical* to use a computer to make a better musical recording from the original【術語】〔用電腦提高唱片原本音質〕翻錄: *digital remastering* 數碼翻錄

re·me·di·a·ble /rɪˋmidɪəbl̩; rɪˈmiːdiəbəl/ *adj formal* able to be put right or cured【正式】可糾正的; 可醫治的

re·me·di·al /rɪˋmidɪəl; rɪˈmiːdiəl/ *adj* **1** aimed at correcting a fault in something, or curing a problem with someone's health 補救的; 糾正的; 治療(上)的: *Some remedial work needs to be done on the foundations.* 需要對基礎部分做一些補救工作。| *remedial care for head injuries* 頭部受傷的治療護理 **2 remedial course/class/teacher etc** a special course etc that helps students who have more difficulty in learning than others 補習課程/班/老師等: *a remedial program for helping teenagers with basic communication skills* 幫助青少年培養基本溝通技巧的輔助計劃

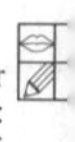

rem·e·dy¹ /ˋrɛmədɪ; ˈreməˌdi/ *n* [C] **1** a way of dealing with a problem or making an unsatisfactory situation better 補救(法): *Is Government intervention the appropriate remedy?* 政府干預是恰當的補救方法嗎? | **[+for]** *The law doesn't provide a remedy for this kind of injustice.* 現行法律糾正不了這種不公正現象。**2** a medicine to cure an illness or pain that is not very serious 藥物; 治療物: *an excellent remedy for period pains* 治療痛經的良藥 **3 beyond/past/without remedy** *formal* if a situation is beyond remedy nothing can be done to make it better【正式】不可救藥的; 無法挽回的: *She felt as if her marital problems were beyond remedy.* 她覺得她的婚姻問題已無法挽回。

remedy² *v* [T] to deal with a problem or improve a bad situation 補救; 糾正; 改善: *The company should act quickly to remedy these grievances.* 公司應該迅速採取行動消除這些不滿情緒。

re·mem·ber /rɪˋmɛmbɚ; rɪˈmembə/ *v*

1 ►THE PAST 過去◄ [I,T] to have a picture in your mind of people, events, places etc from the past 記得: **remember sb/sth** *Do you remember Rosa Davies?* 你記得羅莎·戴維斯嗎? | *Mr Wilson has lived on our street for as long as I can remember.* 威爾遜先生自我記事起一直住在我們這條街上。| **remember (that)** *I remember you two couldn't stand each other at first!* 我記得你們倆開始時互不相容! | **remember sb doing sth** *I remember my father bringing home a huge Christmas tree.* 我記得父親帶回家一棵巨大的聖誕樹。| **remember sb as sth** *I remember Clive as an irritable but tremendously creative man.* 我記得克萊夫是個容易激動但極富創造力的人。| **remember doing sth** *I remember meeting her at a party once.* 我記得曾在一次聚會上見過她。| **remember well/clearly** *"Do you remember a guy called Casey?" "Sure, I remember him well."* "你記得一個名叫卡西的人嗎?" "當然啦, 我清楚地記得他。" | **vaguely/dimly/scarcely remember** (=not remember well) 模糊地/隱約地/幾乎不記得 *I vaguely remember reading something about her husband in the paper.* 我隱約記得在報紙上看到過有關她丈夫的情況。| **remember correctly/rightly** *They had three children, if I remember rightly.* 如果我沒記錯, 他們有三個孩子。| **distinctly/vividly remember** *I distinctly remember telling you to be home by 10 o'clock.* 我清楚地記得告訴過你要在10點前回家。

2 ►INFORMATION/FACTS 信息/事實◄ [I,T] to bring information or facts that you know into your mind 想起; 回憶起: *What did I do with my car keys? Oh, I remember, I left them on the kitchen table.* 我把車鑰匙放在哪兒了? 噢, 想起來了, 我把它擱在廚房的桌子上。| *I can't remember her phone number.* 我想不起來她的電話號碼。| **[+that]** *I suddenly remembered that I'd left the stove on.* 我突然想起我沒有關爐子。| **remember what/how/why etc** *I'm trying to remember whether I said six or seven o'clock.* 我正在設法回憶我說的是六點還是七點。

3 ►TO DO/GET SOMETHING 要做/獲得某事物◄ [I,

T] to remember something that you must do, get, or bring 記住; 牢記: **remember to do sth** *Did you remember to get the bread?* 你記得要買麵包嗎? | *Remember to close the windows before you go out.* 出門之前別忘了關窗。| **remember sth** *I do hope he remembered the wine.* 我非常希望他沒忘記那些酒。| *The thing to remember is to keep stirring the sauce.* 需要記住的是不停地攪拌醬汁。
4 ▶KEEP STH IN MIND 記住某事◀ to keep a particular fact about a situation in your mind 記住; 牢記: **[+that]** *You must remember that we didn't have cars in those days.* 你要記住, 那時我們沒有汽車。
5 ▶HONOUR THE DEAD 紀念死者◀ to think about someone who has died with special respect, often in a ceremony 紀念; 悼念: *On this day we remember the dead of two world wars.* 我們在這一天紀念兩次世界大戰的死難者。
6 be remembered for sth/as sth to be famous for something important that you once did 因…而著名: *Bobby Moore will always be remembered as captain of the England squad in 1966.* 波比·摩亞因身為 1966 年英格蘭隊隊長而名垂後世。
7 ▶GIVE SB A PRESENT 給某人送禮物◀ [T] to give someone a present on a particular occasion 給〔某人〕送禮物: *She always remembers me at Christmas.* 每逢聖誕節她總送禮物給我。| **remember sb in your will** (=arrange for someone to have something of yours after you die) 在遺囑中把部分財產贈予某人
8 remember me to sb used to ask someone to give a greeting from you to someone else 代我向某人問好

This graph shows some of the words most commonly used with the verb **remember**. 本圖表所示為含有動詞 remember 的一些最常用詞組。

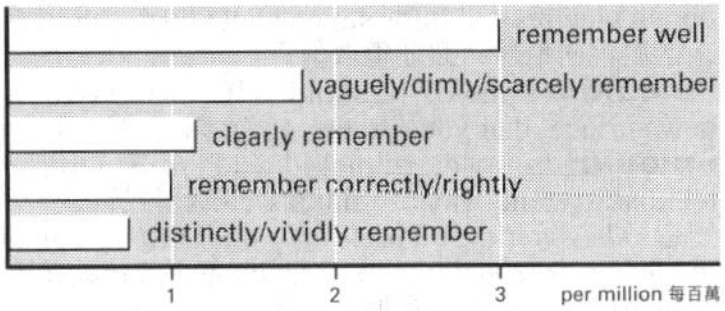

remember well
vaguely/dimly/scarcely remember
clearly remember
remember correctly/rightly
distinctly/vividly remember
1 2 3 per million 每百萬

Based on the British National Corpus and the Longman Lancaster Corpus
據英國國家語料庫和朗文蘭卡斯特語料庫

re·mem·brance /rɪˈmɛmbrəns; rɪˈmembrəns/ *n* **1 in remembrance of sb** in order to remember and give honour to someone who has died 為了悼念某人: *a service in remembrance of those killed in the war* 悼念戰爭死難者的儀式 **2** [C,U] *formal* a memory that you have of a person or event【正式】記憶; 回憶: *fond remembrances* 深情的回憶

Remembrance Day /·ˈ·· ·/ also 又作 **Remembrance Sunday** /·ˌ·· ˈ··/ *n* the Sunday nearest to November 11th, when a ceremony is held in Britain to remember people who were killed in the two world wars〔英國在最接近11月11日的星期日悼念兩次世界大戰中陣亡者的〕陣亡將士紀念日

[1] [2] **re·mind** /rɪˈmaɪnd; rɪˈmaɪnd/ *v* [T] **1** to make someone remember something that they must do 使想起; 提醒: *I must pay the gas bill. I'll put it here to remind me.* 我得付煤氣費了。我把賬單放在這裡提醒自己。| **remind sb about sth** *Will you remind me about that appointment?* 請你提醒我那個約會好嗎? | **remind sb to do sth** *"Remind me to buy stamps." "OK."* "請提醒我買郵票。" "好的。" | **remind sb (that)** *I'll just call Sylvia to remind her that we are meeting at 8.* 我要給西爾維婭打電話, 提醒她我們在8點見面。| **that reminds me** *spoken* (=used when something has just made you remember something you were going to say or do)【口】那使我想起〔用於某事剛使你想起要說或做的事情〕*Oh, that reminds me, I saw Jenny in town today.* 噢, 那讓我記起來, 我今天在城裡看見了詹妮。| **remind sb what/how/when etc** *Remind me what to do, I haven't used this machine for ages.* 請提醒我該怎麼做, 我已經很久沒用過這台機器了。| **remind yourself (to do sth)** *Find some way of reminding yourself to answer letters.* 想個辦法提醒你自己寫回信。**2** to make someone remember someone that they knew or something that happened in the past 使〔某人〕想起: **remind sb of sth** *Hearing that song always reminds me of a certain night in Santa Cruz.* 聽到那首歌總使我想起在聖克魯斯的某個夜晚。| **remind sb what/how etc** *The letter reminded me what a jerk Jim could be.* 這封信使我想起吉姆是個多麼愚蠢的人。**3 Don't remind me** *spoken* used in a joking way when someone has mentioned something that embarrasses or annoys you【口】別跟我提這事〔某人提到使你尷尬或不快的事情時詼諧的說法〕: *"We've got a test tomorrow." "Don't remind me!"* "我們明天有考試。" "別跟我提這事!" **4 let me remind you/may I remind you** *spoken formal* used to add force to a warning or criticism【口, 正式】讓我提醒你〔用於加強警告或批評的語氣〕: **[+that]** *Let me remind you that you are expected to arrive on time.* 讓我提醒你, 你要按時到達。

remind sb **of** sb/sth *phr v* [T not in progressive 不用進行式] to seem similar to someone or something else 使〔某人〕想起〔相似之人或物〕: *The view reminded her of Scotland.* 這景色使她想起了蘇格蘭。| *Corinne reminds me of myself when I was her age.* 科莉妮使我想起了我自己像她那麼大時的樣子。

re·mind·er /rɪˈmaɪndɚ; rɪˈmaɪndə/ *n* **1** [C] something that makes you notice something or understand it better 提醒物: **[+of]** *a reminder of the dangers of drinking and driving* 對酒後駕車的危險警告 | **[+about]** *Kids need constant reminders about crossing roads safely.* 小孩子需要不斷提醒他們要安全地過馬路。| **be a reminder that** *Occasional bursts of gunfire are a reminder that the battle isn't over yet.* 零星的砲聲提醒人們, 戰鬥尚未結束。| **serve as a reminder** (=be a reminder) 提醒 *The President's bodyguards serve as a reminder that he's no ordinary guy out for a walk.* 總統的保鏢提醒人們, 他不是一個出來散步的普通人。**2** [C] something that reminds you of something that happened or existed in the past 提醒人記憶之物: **[+of]** *Her disability remains as a perpetual reminder of the war years.* 她的殘疾使人永遠不會忘記戰爭的年代。**3** something, for example a letter, that reminds you to do something which you might have forgotten 起提醒作用的東西〈如信件〉

rem·i·nisce /ˌrɛməˈnɪs; ˌreməˈnɪs/ *v* [I] to talk or think about pleasant events in your past 追憶往事, 緬懷往事: **[+about]** *We walked on, reminiscing about the old days.* 我們向前走着, 追憶着過去的日子。

rem·i·nis·cence /ˌrɛməˈnɪsn̩s; ˌreməˈnɪsəns/ *n* [C,U often plural 常用複數] a spoken or written story about events that you remember 回憶往事的談話; 回憶錄: **[+of/about]** *reminiscences of the war* 戰爭回憶錄 —compare 比較 MEMOIR

rem·i·nis·cent /ˌrɛməˈnɪsn̩t; ˌreməˈnɪsənt/ *adj* **1 reminiscent of** reminding you of something 使人想起…的: *written in a style strongly reminiscent of Virginia Woolf's novels* 寫作風格酷似弗吉尼亞·吳爾芙的小說 **2** [only before noun 僅用於名詞前] thinking about the past 回憶往事的, 懷舊的: *"Those were the days," agreed Barrow with a reminiscent sigh.* "就是那些日子。" 巴羅嘆了口氣附和着, 流露出對往事的懷念。

re·miss /rɪˈmɪs; rɪˈmɪs/ *adj formal* [not before noun 不用於名詞前] careless about doing something that you ought to do【正式】玩忽職守的, 粗心的: **it is remiss of sb to do sth** *It was very remiss of me not to answer your letter.* 沒有給你回信是我的疏忽。—**remissness** *n* [U]

re·mis·sion /rɪˈmɪʃən; rɪˈmɪʃən/ *n* **1** [C,U] *BrE* a reduction of the time that someone has to spend in prison【英】縮短刑期: *He was given six months' remission for good behaviour.* 他因為行為好而減刑六個月。**2** [C,U] a period when an illness improves for a time〔疾病的〕減輕;

緩解(期): **go into remission** *The cancer has gone into remission.* 癌症已經有所好轉。**3** [U] *formal* the act of allowing someone to keep the money they owe you【正式】〔債務的〕免除 **4 the remission of sins** *formal* forgiveness from God for the bad things that you have done【正式】〔上帝〕饒恕罪惡

re·mit¹ /rɪˋmɪt; rɪˈmɪt/ *v formal*【正式】**1** [I,T] to send a payment by post 匯(款): *Please remit payment by cheque.* 請用支票匯出付款。**2** [T] to free someone from a debt or punishment 免除〔債務或處罰〕—compare 比較 UNREMITTING

remit sth **to** sb/sth *phr v* [T] *formal* to send a proposal, plan, or problem back to someone for them to make a decision about【正式】把〔建議、計劃或問題〕發回...〔以作出決定〕

re·mit² /ˈrimɪt; ˈriːmɪt/ *n* [singular,U] *BrE formal* the particular piece of work that someone has been officially asked to deal with【英, 正式】職權範圍: *It is not part of our remit to criticize government policy.* 批評政府的政策不在我們的職權範圍之內。

re·mit·tance /rɪˋmɪtṇs; rɪˈmɪtəns/ *n* **1** [C] *formal* an amount of money that you send by post to pay for something【正式】匯款額 **2** [U] the act of sending money by post 匯款: **on remittance of** (=when the money has been sent) 匯款收訖 *We will forward the goods on remittance of £10.* 十英鎊匯到後即行發貨。

re·mit·tent /rɪˋmɪtṇt; rɪˈmɪtənt/ *adj formal* a remittent fever or illness is severe for short periods but improves between those times【正式】〔發燒、疾病〕弛張的, 時重時輕的

rem·nant /ˈrɛmnənt; ˈremnənt/ *n* [C] **1** [usually plural 一般用複數] a small part of something that remains after the rest of it has been used, destroyed, or eaten 殘餘; 剩餘: *The remnants of a meal stood on the table.* 吃剩的飯菜擺在桌上。**2** a small piece of cloth left from a larger piece and sold cheap 零頭布料

re·mod·el /ˌriˋmɑdḷ; ˌriːˈmɒdl/ **remodelled, remodelling** *BrE*【英】**remodeled, remodeling** *AmE*【美】*v* [T] to change the shape or appearance of something 改變...的形狀[外觀]; 重新塑造: *He was in a terrible accident, and had to have his jaw remodelled.* 他遭遇了嚴重事故, 頜部必須接受整形。

re·mon·strance /rɪˋmɑnstrəns; rɪˈmɒnstrəns/ *n* [C,U] *formal* a complaint or protest【正式】抱怨; 抗議: *loud cries of remonstrance* 大聲的抗議

rem·on·strate /rɪˋmɑnstret; ˈremənstreɪt/ *v* [I] *formal* to tell someone that you strongly disapprove of something they have said or done【正式】抗議: **[+with/against]** *They only stopped teasing after Evans remonstrated with them.* 直到埃文斯提出抗議, 他們才停止捉弄他。—**remonstrative** /rɪˋmɑnstrətɪv; rɪˈmɒnstrətɪv/ *adj*

re·morse /rɪˋmɔrs; rɪˈmɔːs/ *n* [U] a strong feeling of being sorry that you have done something very bad 懊悔, 悔恨: *When he saw tears in her eyes, he was full of remorse for what he had said.* 看到她眼淚汪汪, 他對自己說的話悔恨不已。**remorseful** *adj* —**remorsefully** *adv*

re·morse·less /rɪˋmɔrslɪs; rɪˈmɔːsləs/ *adj* **1** something unpleasant or threatening that is remorseless continues to happen and seems impossible to stop〔令人不快或威脅人的事〕無休止的: *Their coats gave little protection against the remorseless Baltic winds.* 他們的外衣基本無法抵禦波羅的海持續不斷的大風。**2** cruel, and not caring how much other people are hurt 冷酷的, 無情的: *Within a few years, our country had been taken over by remorseless European settlers.* 在幾年裡, 我們國家被冷酷無情的歐洲移民接管了。—**remorselessly** *adv*: *Stray soldiers were remorselessly hunted down and shot.* 掉隊的士兵遭到無情的追捕和槍殺。—**remorselessness** *n* [U]

re·mort·gage /ˌriˋmɔrgɪdʒ; ˌriːˈmɔːgɪdʒ/ *v* [T] to borrow money by having a second MORTGAGE¹ (1) on your house, or increasing the one you have 再抵押, 轉抵押〔房子〕

 3 **re·mote¹** /rɪˋmot; rɪˈməʊt/ *adj* **1** far away in space or time 遙遠的: *remote stars* 遙遠的星星 | *something from the remote past, dimly remembered* 久遠的模糊記憶裡的事物 | **a remote ancestor** (=someone related to you, who lived a long time ago) 遠祖 **2** far from towns 偏僻的, 偏遠的: *As a westerner I was a strange sight in this remote spot.* 作為一個西方人, 我成了這個偏遠地方的奇觀。**3** very different from something 很不相同的: **[+from]** *It was so alien, so remote from anything he had ever known.* 這東西很古怪, 與他知道的所有東西都不一樣。**4 a remote chance/possibility** a very slight chance or possibility 渺茫的希望/微乎其微的可能性: **[+that]** *There's a remote chance that you will catch him before he leaves.* 你不大可能在他離開前抓住他。**5** unfriendly, and not interested in people 不友善的, 冷淡的: *She was quiet and remote, and had an annoying air of superiority.* 她話不多, 對人冷淡, 而且擺出高人一等的臭架子。**6 not have the remotest idea** used to emphasize the fact that you know nothing about something 一無所知: **[+what/where/who etc]** *Miranda hasn't the remotest idea where he's gone.* 米蘭達一點兒也不知道他去哪兒了。—**remoteness** *n* [U]

remote² *n* [C] *spoken* REMOTE CONTROL【口】遙控

remote con·trol /ˌ· ˌ·ˋ·/ *n* **1** [C] a thing you use for controlling a piece of electrical or electronic equipment without having to touch it, for example for turning a television on or off 遙控器 **2** [U] the process of controlling equipment from a distance, using radio or electronic signals〔用無線電或電子信號的〕遙控 —**remote-controlled** *adj*

re·mote·ly /rɪˋmotlɪ; rɪˈməʊtli/ *adv* **not remotely interested/similar/possible etc** not at all interested, similar etc 毫無興趣/毫不相似/毫無可能

remote sens·ing /ˌ· ˋ··/ *n* [U] the use of SATELLITE*s* to obtain pictures and information about the Earth 遙感〔用人造衛星向地球拍照並獲取信息〕

re·mould¹ /ˈriˌmold; ˈriːməʊld/ *n* [C] an old tyre with a new surface, that you can use again 翻新的輪胎

re·mould² /riˋmold; ˌriːˈməʊld/ *v* [T] *formal* to change an idea, system, way of thinking etc【正式】改造, 重新塑造: *They don't want to destroy the EC, but remould it in a more appropriate form.* 他們並不想毀掉歐共體, 而只是想以更合適的形式加以改造。

re·mount /ˌriˋmaunt; ˌriːˈmaʊnt/ *v* [I,T] to get onto a horse, bicycle etc again 再次騎上〔馬、自行車等〕

re·mov·a·ble /rɪˋmuvəbḷ; rɪˈmuːvəbəl/ *adj* easy to remove 可移動的; 可拆裝的: *The chair has a removable cover for easy cleaning.* 這椅子有可拆裝的椅套, 清洗很方便。

re·mov·al /rɪˋmuvḷ; rɪˈmuːvəl/ *n* [C,U] **1** the act of taking something away 移動, 搬動; 去掉: *We'll arrange for the removal of this rubbish as soon as possible.* 我們將儘快安排人把這堆垃圾運走。| *stain removal* 去污 **2** the process of taking furniture from your old house to your new one 搬遷: **removal company/man etc** *The removal men have been in and out all day.* 搬運工一整天都在進進出出。

removal van /-ˋ·· ˌ·/ *n* [C] *BrE* a large VAN used for moving furniture from one house to another【英】搬家車, 家具搬運車; MOVING VAN *AmE*【美】

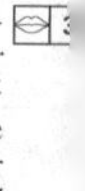

re·move /rɪˋmuv; rɪˈmuːv/ *v*

1 ►TAKE AWAY 移走◄ [T] to take something away from the place where it is 移動, 搬動, 拿開: *Do not remove this notice.* 別取下這個佈告。| **remove sth from** *Reference books may not be removed from the library.* 不得把參考書帶出圖書館。

2 ►CLOTHES 衣服◄ [T] to take off a piece of clothing 脫掉; 摘掉: *He removed his hat and gloves.* 他摘掉了帽子和手套。

3 ►GET RID OF 排除◄ [T] to get rid of something 清除; 除去: *an operation to remove a tumour* 切除腫瘤的手術 | *These reforms will not remove poverty and injustice.* 這些改革消除不了貧窮和不公正。

4 be far removed from to be very different from something 與…迥然不同: *Life in the army was far removed from the comfort of his parents' home.* 軍旅生活與在父母家的舒適相去甚遠。

5 removed from *old use* hidden from someone or something【舊】隱藏的

6 ▶FROM A JOB 免職◀ [T] to force someone out of an important position or dismiss them from a job 開除; 把…免職: [+from] *The governor was removed from office, pending an investigation.* 州長被免職, 等待調查。

7 ▶PLACE 地點◀ [I] *old use* to go to live or work in another place【舊】遷移, 移居: [+from/to] *Our office has removed from Boston to New York.* 我們的辦事處已經從波士頓遷至紐約。

8 cousin once/twice etc removed the child, GRANDCHILD etc of your COUSIN, or your cousin's father, grandfather etc 隔一代/兩代等的堂[表]親戚

re·mov·er /rɪˋmuvɚ; rɪˈmuːvə/ *n* [C,U] **paint/nail-varnish/stain etc remover** a substance that removes paint marks etc 脫漆劑/去光水/去污劑等

REM sleep /ˋrɛm ˌslip; ˈrem sliːp/ *n* [U] a period during sleep when there is rapid movement of the eyes, thought to be a sign that you are dreaming 快速眼動睡眠〔據信是做夢的跡象〕

re·mu·ne·rate /rɪˋmjunəˌret; rɪˈmjuːnəreɪt/ *v* [T] *formal* to pay someone for something they have done for you【正式】酬報 —**remuneration** /rɪˌmjunəˋreʃən; rɪˌmjuːnəˈreɪʃən/ *n* [C,U]: *Our company offers a competitive remuneration package, including a company car.* 本公司提供一套具有競爭力的報酬組合, 包括一輛汽車。

re·mu·ne·ra·tive /rɪˋmjunəˌretɪv; rɪˈmjuːnərətɪv/ *adj formal* making a lot of money【正式】賺錢多的; 報酬高的 —**remuneratively** *adv*

Re·nais·sance¹ /ˌrɛnəˋsɑns; rɪˈneɪsəns/ *n* **1 the Renaissance** the period of time in Europe between the 14th and 17th centuries when the art, literature, and ideas of ancient Greece were discovered again, examined, and developed〔歐洲14世紀至17世紀的〕文藝復興時期 **2 Renaissance art/furniture/architecture etc** art, furniture etc belonging to the Renaissance period 文藝復興時期的藝術/家具/建築等

renaissance² *n* [singular] a new interest in a particular form of art, music etc, that has not been fashionable〔藝術、音樂等某一領域的〕復興

re·nal /ˋrinl; ˈriːnl/ *adj* [only before noun 僅用於名詞前] *technical* concerning the kidneys (KIDNEY (1))【術語】腎(臟)的: *acute renal failure* 急性腎衰竭

re·name /riˋnem; riːˈneɪm/ *v* [T] [usually passive 一般用被動態] to give something a new name 給…重新命名: **rename sth sth** *Myddleton Way was renamed Allende Avenue.* 米德爾頓路已重新命名為阿連德大街。

re·nas·cent /rɪˋnæsn̩t; rɪˈnæsənt/ *adj* [only before noun 僅用於名詞前] *formal* becoming popular, strong, or important again【正式】復興的, 再生的: *Voters are flooding back to the renascent Labour Party.* 大批選民正重新支持東山再起的工黨。

rend /rɛnd; rend/ *past tense and past participle* **rent** /rɛnt; rent/ *v* [T] *literary* to tear or break something violently into pieces【文】猛力撕碎; 把…打碎

ren·der /ˋrɛndɚ; ˈrendə/ *v* **1 render sth useless/render sb harmless etc** to make someone or something useless etc 使某物變得無用/使某人變得無害: *New laws have rendered this kind of assistance virtually impossible.* 新法律使這類援助幾乎不可能。**2 render an apology/an explanation/a service etc** *formal* to say sorry to someone, give someone an explanation, etc【正式】道歉/解釋/提供服務: **for services rendered** (=in payment for something you have done) 支付所提供的服務 **3** [T] to express or present something in a particular way 表達; 表現: **render sth as sth** *Through her art, she attempts to render feelings as colors.* 通過她的藝術作品, 她試圖將情感描繪成不同的色彩。| **render sth in sth** *Children soon learn to render their thoughts in speech.* 兒童很快學會用語言表達自己的思想。**4 render sth into English/Russian/Chinese etc** *old use* to translate something into English, Russian etc【舊】將某物譯成英語/俄語/漢語等 **5** [T] *technical* to spread PLASTER¹ (1) or CEMENT on the surface of a wall【術語】往〔牆面〕抹灰泥[水泥]

render sth ↔ **down** *phr v* [T] to melt fat until it is pure 熬煉〔脂肪〕

render sth ↔ **up** *phr v* [T] *old use* to give something to someone, especially to a ruler or enemy【舊】給予〔尤指進貢〕

ren·der·ing /ˋrɛndərɪŋ; ˈrendərɪŋ/ *n* [U] **1** *BrE* the way a play or piece of music is performed; RENDITION (1)【英】表演; 演奏: *her passionate rendering of Elgar's cello concerto* 她充滿激情地演奏〔英國作曲家〕埃爾加的大提琴協奏曲 **2** a material made mainly of CEMENT and sand, used to protect the outside walls of buildings〔水泥和沙攪拌的外牆〕灰泥

ren·dez·vous¹ /ˋrɑndəˌvu; ˈrɒndɪvuː/ *n plural* **rendezvous 1** [C] an arrangement to meet at a particular time and place 約會, 會面: [+with] *a midnight rendezvous with Jose* 與喬斯的午夜約會 **2** [C usually singular 一般用單數] a place where two or more people have arranged to meet 約會地點: *We arrived early at the rendezvous.* 我們早早到達約會地點。**3** [C] a popular place for people to meet〔經常的〕聚會處: *The bar is a regular rendezvous for media people.* 這酒吧是傳媒界人士經常聚會的地點。

rendezvous² *v* [I+with] to meet someone as you have arranged〔與…〕會合; 聚會; 見面

ren·di·tion /rɛnˋdɪʃən; renˈdɪʃən/ *n* **1** [U] the way a play or piece of music is performed 表演, 演奏; RENDERING (1) *BrE*【英】**2** [C] a TRANSLATION of a piece of writing 翻譯, 譯文: *an English rendition of a Greek poem* 一首希臘詩歌的英譯

ren·e·gade /ˋrɛnɪˌged; ˈrenɪgeɪd/ *n especially literary* someone who joins an opposing side in a war, in politics etc【尤文】叛徒, 變節者: *a renegade, who had once been a leader of the Party* 曾經是該黨領袖的叛徒 | **renegade soldiers/troops etc** *At the meeting were several renegade Communists.* 有幾位變節的共產黨人出席了會議。

re·nege /rɪˋnɪg; rɪˈniːg/ *v* [I] *formal*【正式】**renege on an agreement/a deal etc** to not do something you have promised or agreed to do 違背諾言/協議等: *Why has the government reneged on its commitment to the welfare program?* 政府為何違背了自己對該福利計劃的承諾?

re·new /rɪˋnju; rɪˈnjuː/ *v* [T] **1** to arrange for a contract, membership of a club etc to continue 延長〔合同的期限或會員資格等〕, 使續期: *I must remember to renew the car insurance.* 我必須記得續辦汽車的保險。**2** to replace something that is old or broken with something new 更換; 更新: *The window frames will have to be renewed.* 窗框得換新的。**3** to begin to do something again, after a period of rest〔休止一段時間後〕重新開始: **renew an attack** *The naval attack was renewed the next morning.* 第二天早晨海軍再次發起進攻。| **renew a friendship/acquaintance etc** (=start a relationship again) 恢復友誼/交往等 **4 renew a book** to arrange to borrow a library book for a further period of time 續借圖書 —see also 另見 RENEWED

re·new·a·ble /rɪˋnuəbl̩; rɪˈnjuːəbəl/ *adj* **1** a renewable contract, ticket etc can be made to continue after the date on which it ends〔合同、票證等〕可延期的, 可續期的: *The permit is renewable after 12 months.* 許可證在12個月後可再續期。**2** something that is renewable can be replaced by natural processes or good management, so that it is never used up〔由於自然循環或管理有方〕可再生的: **renewable energy/resources** *Sun, wind and*

R

waves provide renewable sources of energy. 太陽、風和浪提供用之不竭的能源。

re·new·al /rɪˋnuəl; rɪˈnjuːəl/ *n* **1** [singular,U] an act of renewing something 更新; 恢復; 更換: [+of] *a renewal of interest in late Victorian culture* 對維多利亞時代後期文化恢復興趣 **2 inner city/urban renewal** the process of bringing new jobs, industry, homes etc to the poor areas of large towns 舊城區/市區重建

re·newed /rɪˋnud; rɪˈnjuːd/ *adj* **1 renewed interest/vigour/enthusiasm etc** interest etc that increases again after not being very strong 重新產生的興趣/活力/熱情等: *renewed concern about the effects of acid rain* 重新關注酸雨的影響 **2** [not before noun 不用於名詞前] feeling healthy and relaxed again, after feeling ill or tired 體力恢復的; 重新振作的

ren·net /ˋrɛnɪt; ˈrenɪ̈t/ *n* [U] a substance used for making milk thicker in order to make cheese 粗製凝乳酶〔用於製乾酪〕

re·nounce /rɪˋnaʊns; rɪˈnaʊns/ *v* **1** [T] to publicly say that you will no longer keep something, or stay in an important position, because you no longer have the right to it 宣布放棄〔職位等〕: *The only course left to Nixon was to renounce the presidency.* 尼克遜唯一能做的就是宣布辭去總統職位。| **renounce a claim** *James II renounced all claims to the English throne.* 詹姆斯二世宣布放棄繼承英國王位的全部權利。**2** [T] to publicly say that you no longer believe in or support something 宣布放棄〔信仰、支持〕: *Writers and artists were called upon to renounce all bourgeois values.* 號召作家和藝術家公開宣布放棄所有的資產階級價值觀。—see also 另見 RENUNCIATION

ren·o·vate /ˋrɛnəˌvet; ˈrenəveɪt/ *v* [T] to repair and paint a building so that it is in good condition again 修復; 裝修; 整修: *They are living in temporary accommodation while their apartment is being renovated.* 公寓修整期間他們臨時住在別處。—**renovation** /ˌrɛnəˋveʃən; ˌrenəˈveɪʃən/ *n* [U]

re·nown /rɪˋnaʊn; rɪˈnaʊn/ *n* [U] fame and admiration, that you get because of some special skill or something that you have done 名望, 聲譽: [+as] *At college, I'd acquired some renown as a football player.* 上大學的時候, 我因為足球踢得好而薄有名氣。| **win renown** *She eventually won international renown with her film 'Dispute'.* 她最終以她的電影《爭辯》而贏得國際聲譽。

re·nowned /rɪˋnaʊnd; rɪˈnaʊnd/ *adj* known and admired by a lot of people, especially for some special skill, achievement, or quality 有名望的, 著名的: **be renowned for** *The region is renowned for its fine Persian rugs.* 該地區以其精美的波斯地毯而著稱。| **be renowned as** *Goldman was renowned as a journalist and author.* 戈德曼是位著名的記者和作家。| **renowned footballer/statesman/architect etc** *The lecture will be delivered by renowned Marxist historian, Jeff Davies.* 講課的是著名馬克思主義歷史學家傑夫·戴維斯。—see 見 FAMOUS (USAGE)

S2 W3 **rent¹** /rɛnt; rent/ *v* **1** [I,T] to regularly pay money to live in a house or room that belongs to someone else, or to use something that belongs to someone else 租房; 租用, 租借: **rent sth from sb** *We rent our apartment from an old retired couple.* 我們的公寓是向一對退休老夫婦租的。| *Nick's been renting for five years now, and he can't afford to buy.* 尼克已經租了五年房, 他買不起。| *a rented video recorder* 租用的錄像機 —see 見 HIRE¹ (USAGE) **2** [T] also 又作 **rent ↔ out** to let someone live in a house, room etc that you own, in return for money 出租: *If you can't sell your house, why don't you think about renting it?* 如果你不能出售你的房子, 為何不考慮將它出租? | **rent sth out to sb** *She rents out her flat to students.* 她把公寓出租給學生。**3** [T] *especially AmE* to pay money for the use of something for a short period of time【尤美】租用; HIRE¹ (1) *BrE*【英】: *Why don't we rent a boat for the afternoon?* 我們下午為甚麼不租一條船呢? **4** [I+at/for] if a house rents at or rents for a particular amount of money, that is how much someone pays in order to use it 收取租金… **5 rent-a-crowd/mob etc** people who are willing to take part in a protest about something, even if they do not feel strongly about it〔花錢〕動員來的人羣

rent² *n* **1** [C,U] the money that someone pays for the use of a room, a house etc that belongs to someone else 租金: **high/low rent** *Office rents are extremely high in this part of London.* 倫敦這地區的辦公室租金非常昂貴。| **pay the rent** *I don't earn enough to pay the rent, let alone run a car.* 我的收入不夠交房租, 更不用說買汽車了。| **raise the rent/raise rents** (=make someone pay more rent) 提高租金 —see 見 COST¹ (USAGE) **2** [C,U] *especially AmE* an amount of money paid for the use of a car, boat etc that belongs to someone else【尤美】〔汽車、船等的〕租金 **3** [C] a large tear in cloth, or a hole shaped like a tear in something〔織物等的〕裂縫: *There were huge rents all down the side of the sofa.* 沙發側面從上到下有幾處大裂縫。

rent³ the past tense and past participle of REND

rent·al /ˋrɛntl; ˈrentl/ *n* **1** [C usually singular 一般用單數] the money that you pay to use a car, television, tools etc over a period of time〔汽車、電視、工具等的〕租金: *£20 of this telephone bill is for line rental.* 這份電話賬單上有20英鎊是線路租用費。**2** [C,U] an arrangement by which you rent something 租借, 租賃: *TV rentals* 電視租用 | *rental costs* 租金 | *a video rental shop* 錄像帶租借商店 **3** [C] *AmE* the act of renting something such as a car or house【美】〔汽車、房子等的〕租借: *Car rental is expensive in Ohio.* 在俄亥俄州租車非常貴。| **rental car** *We had a rental car when we were on vacation.* 我們度假時租了一輛車。| **rentals** (=houses for renting) 出租的房屋 *Are there any summer rentals in this area?* 這個地區有沒有在夏季出租的房屋?

rent book /ˈ· ·/ *n* [C] a small book used to record the amounts and dates of someone's rent payments 租金登記簿

rent boy /ˈ· ·/ *n* [C] *BrE* a young man who has sex with other men in return for money; a male PROSTITUTE【英】〔年輕的〕男妓

rent·ed /ˋrɛntɪd; ˈrentɪ̈d/ *adj* **rented accommodation/housing/apartment etc** houses etc that people pay rent for 租用的住房等: *financial aid for families living in rented accommodation* 為租房居住的家庭提供的經濟資助

rent-free /ˌ· ˈ·◂/ *adj, adv* without payment of rent 不付租金的[地]: *He lives there rent-free.* 他免費住在那裡。| *rent-free accommodation* 免收租金的住宿

rent re·bate /ˈ· ˌ··/ *n* [C] *BrE* money that some people get from local government to help them pay their rent【英】〔地方政府提供的〕房租補貼

rent strike /ˈ· ·/ *n* [C] a time when all the people living in a group of houses or apartments refuse to pay their rent, as a protest against something〔住戶〕集體抗租

re·nun·ci·a·tion /rɪˌnʌnsɪˋeʃən; rɪˌnʌnsiˈeɪʃən/ *n* [C,U] *formal* a decision not to keep a particular set of beliefs, way of life, power, or object【正式】〔對信仰、生活方式、權力或目標的〕放棄, 拋棄: [+of] *Eastern Europe's renunciation of communism* 東歐拋棄共產主義 | *The life of a monk is one of renunciation.* 僧侶過的是棄絕俗慾的生活。

re·o·pen /riˋopən; riːˈəʊpən/ *v* **1** [I,T] if a theatre, restaurant etc reopens or is reopened, it opens again after being closed (使)〔劇場、餐廳等〕重新開張 **2** [I,T] if you reopen a discussion or law case, or if it reopens, you begin it again after it has stopped 恢復〔談判〕; 續審: *A report from medical scientists has reopened the debate on tobacco advertising.* 醫學家的一份報告再次引發有關煙草廣告的辯論。**3** [T] if a government reopens the border of their country, they allow people to pass through it again after it has been closed 重新開放〔邊界〕

re·or·der /riˋɔrdə; riˈɔːdə/ *v* [I,T] **1** to order a product again 再訂購: *Stock levels are getting low – we need to* *reorder.* 庫存在減少, 我們需要再訂貨。**2** to change things or put them in a more suitable order 重新整理; 重新排列: *The whole system needs reordering.* 整個系統需要重新整理。

re·or·gan·ize also 又作 **-ise** *BrE*【英】/riˋɔrgə͵naɪz; riː-ˈɔːgənaɪz/ *v* [I,T] to arrange or organize something in a new way 改組; 改編: *I've reorganized my room so there's space for my new bookcase.* 我重新佈置房間, 這樣就有地方擺我的新書架了。—**reorganization** /͵riɔrgənəˋzeʃən; riː͵ɔːgənaɪˈzeɪʃən/ *n* [U]

rep /rɛp; rep/ *n* **1** [C] *informal* a SALES REPRESENTATIVE【非正式】推銷員 **2** [C] *informal* someone who speaks officially for a company or organization; REPRESENTATIVE² (1)【非正式】〔公司、組織的〕代表: *You need to speak to the union rep.* 你需要和工會代表談談。**3** [C] *informal* a REPERTORY theatre or company【非正式】〔輪演選定劇目的〕劇院, 劇團 **4** [U] *informal* REPERTORY【非正式】輪流演出選定的劇目 **5** [C] *AmE informal* a REPUTATION【美, 非正式】名聲, 名譽 **6 Rep a)** the written abbreviation of 縮寫= REPUBLICAN **b)** the written abbreviation of 縮寫= REPRESENTATIVE

re·paid /rɪˋped; rɪˈpeɪd/ *v* the past tense and past participle of REPAY

3 **re·pair¹** /rɪˋpɛr; rɪˈpeə/ *v* [T] **1** to fix something that is damaged, broken, or not working properly 修理, 修補: *I'll have to get the car repaired.* 我得把車修理一下。| *to repair a broken fence* 修補破柵欄 **2** *formal* to do something to remove the harm that your mistake or wrong action has caused【正式】糾正, 補救: *How can I repair the wrong I have done her?* 我冤枉了她, 怎樣才能補救呢? —see also 另見 IRREPARABLE

repair to sth *phr v* [T] *old-fashioned* to go to a place【過時】去, 赴: *Shall we repair to the drawing room?* 我們去客廳好嗎?

3 3 **repair²** *n* **1** [C,U] an act of repairing something 修理, 修補: *The garage is carrying out repairs on my car.* 汽車修理站正在修理我的車。| **be in need of repair** *The church roof was badly in need of repair.* 教堂的屋頂急需修理。| **under repair** (=being repaired) 在修理 *The road is under repair.* 這條路正在修補。| **beyond repair** (=so damaged that it cannot be mended) 無法修理 *My watch was crushed beyond repair.* 我的手錶被壓得沒法修理了。| **repair work** (=work to repair something) 修理(工作) **2 in good/bad/poor repair** in good or bad condition 維修良好/糟糕: *Many of our major roads are in bad repair.* 我們的許多主要道路都失修。**3** [C] place on something that has been repaired 修補處: *The repair on the table top can hardly be seen.* 桌面上修補的地方幾乎看不出來。—**repairer** *n* [C]

re·pair·a·ble /rɪˋpɛrəbl̩; rɪˈpeərəbəl/ *adj* able to be repaired 能修補的

rep·a·ra·ble /ˋrɛpərəbl̩; ˈrepərəbəl/ *adj formal* a reparable loss is one that you can get back in some way【正式】可補救的, 可挽回的 —opposite 反義詞 IRREPARABLE

rep·a·ra·tion /͵rɛpəˋreʃən; ͵repəˈreɪʃən/ *n* **1 reparations** [plural] money paid by a defeated country after a war, for all the deaths, injuries, and damage it has caused〔戰敗國償付的〕賠款 **2** [C,U] *formal* payment made to someone for damage, loss, or injury that you have caused them in the past【正式】賠償, 補償: **make reparation (to sb) for sth** *No reparation has been made to African countries for the damage of the slave trade.* 沒有向非洲國家賠償因販賣奴隸而造成的損害。

rep·ar·tee /͵rɛpɚˋti; ͵repɑːˈtiː/ *n* [U] conversation which is very fast and full of clever amusing remarks 機鋒迅捷、妙語連珠的談話

re·past /rɪˋpæst; rɪˈpɑːst/ *n* [C] *formal or humorous* a meal【正式或幽默】餐

re·pat·ri·ate /riˋpetrɪ͵et; riːˈpætrieɪt/ *v* [T] **1** to send someone back to their own country 遣送〔某人〕回國, 遣返: *At the end of the war, prisoners were repatriated.* 戰爭結束時, 俘虜被遣送回國。**2** to send profits or money you have earned back to your own country 把〔利潤、錢〕匯回國內

re·pay /rɪˋpe; rɪˈpeɪ/ *v* **repaid** /-ˋped; -ˈpeɪd/, **repaying** [T] **1** to pay back money that you have borrowed 付還, 償還: *The loan must be repaid with interest.* 貸款須與利息一起償還。| **repay sb sth** *Jenny repaid her parents the £1000 they lent her.* 珍妮還給父母借給她的1000英鎊。**2** to reward someone for helping you 報答, 回報: **repay sb for sth** *How can I ever repay you for what you've done?* 我怎麼才能報答你為我所做的一切? | **repay sb's kindness/generosity etc** *He wanted to repay their kindness, and took them out for a meal.* 他想報答他們的好意, 就請他們出去吃了一頓飯。**3 repay your effort** to seem worth the time you have spent 付出的努力值得

re·pay·a·ble /rɪˋpeəbl̩; rɪˈpeɪəbəl/ *adj* money that is repayable at a certain time has to be repaid by that time 應償還的: *Mortgages are usually repayable over 25 years.* 抵押借款的償還期通常為25年。

re·pay·ment /rɪˋpemənt; rɪˈpeɪmənt/ *n* **1** [U] the act of paying back money 付還, 償還: *The rate of repayment is based on your income.* 還款率根據你的收入而定。**2** [C] an amount of money that you pay back 還款(額): *mortgage repayments of about £330 per month* 每月約330英鎊的抵押還款

re·peal /rɪˋpil; rɪˈpiːl/ *v* [T] if a government repeals a law it officially ends that law 廢除〔法律〕: *It's high time this grossly unfair law was repealed.* 這項極不公正的法令該廢除了。—**repeal** *n* [U]: *the repeal of the prohibition laws* 禁酒法令的廢除

re·peat¹ /rɪˋpit; rɪˈpiːt/ *v* 2 2

1 ▶STATE AGAIN 再次陳述◀ [T] to say or write something again 重說; 重寫: *Can you repeat your question?* 你能重複一遍你的問題嗎? | **repeat that** *Steven repeated patiently that he was busy.* 史蒂文耐心地重複說他很忙。—see 見 SAY¹ (USAGE)

2 ▶DO AGAIN 再做◀ [T] to do something again 重做: *Repeat the treatment twice a day if necessary.* 如必要請每天重複兩次這項治療。| *Anyone who gets less than 45% will have to repeat the test.* 凡得分低於45分者須補考。

3 ▶ACHIEVE STH AGAIN 再次獲得某事物◀ [T] to achieve the same results or the same high level of performance 重獲, 再次達到: *Other scientists are trying to repeat these results.* 另一些科學家正在設法再次獲得這些結果。| *Can he repeat his success of 1993?* 他能否重複自己1993年的成功呢?

4 ▶LEARN 記住◀ [T] to say something you have learned 背誦: *Sandra repeated the poem hesitantly.* 桑德拉結結巴巴地背誦了那首詩。| **repeat after sb** *Repeat after me: amo, amas, amat...* 請跟我讀: amo, amas, amat...

5 ▶TELL STH YOU HEAR 講述所聽說的事物◀ [T] to say something that you have heard someone else saying 重複〔聽說的東西〕: *Don't repeat this to anyone but I think Derek's got a new girlfriend.* 別告訴任何人, 我覺得德里克有新的女朋友了。

6 repeat yourself to say something that you have already said without realizing that you have done it〔不自覺地〕重複自己說過的話: *Mrs Fardell repeats herself a bit, but she's very good for 85.* 法德爾太太說話有點重複, 但作為85歲的人她頭腦非常清楚。

7 ▶BROADCAST 播放◀ [T often passive 常用被動態] to broadcast a television or radio programme again 重播: *'Omnibus' will be repeated at 10 o'clock on Tuesday.* "薈萃"將於星期二10點鐘重播。

8 ▶FOOD 食物◀ [I+on] *informal* if food repeats on you, its taste keeps coming back into your mouth after you have eaten it【非正式】〔食物吃後〕在口中留有餘味

9 sth doesn't bear repeating used to say that you do not want to repeat what someone has said, especially because it is rude〔話〕粗魯得不堪重複: *Her comments about her ex-husband just don't bear repeating!* 她對前

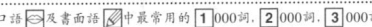

夫的評論真是不堪重複！

10 history repeats itself used to say that an event is like something that happened before 歷史重演

repeat² *n* [C] **1** a television or radio programme that has been broadcast before 重播(的節目): *There's nothing but repeats on the TV tonight.* 今晚電視上只有重播節目。**2** an event very like something that happened before〔事件的〕重演, 重現: **[+of]** *The England-Holland match was basically a repeat of last year's game at Wembley.* 英格蘭隊與荷蘭隊的比賽基本上是去年在溫布萊比賽的重演。| **repeat performance** (=something bad that happens again)〔壞事〕再度發生 *Last year's holiday was a disaster – we don't want a repeat performance this year.* 去年的假期搞得一塌糊塗, 我們不希望今年重蹈覆轍。**3 repeat order** a supply of the same products to a customer who has ordered them before 相同貨品的訂單 **4 repeat prescription** *BrE* an order for medicine that you have had before, which you can get without seeing your doctor【英】〔不用看醫生而取同樣藥物的〕相同處方 **5** *technical* the sign at the end of a line of written music that tells the performer to play the music again, or the act of playing the music again【術語】〔樂譜的〕反覆記號

re·peat·ed /rɪˋpitɪd; rɪˈpiːtɪ̈d/ *adj* [only before noun 僅用於名詞前] done or happening again and again 反覆的, 再三的: *repeated calls for change* 再三呼籲變革 | *repeated failure* 一再失敗

re·peat·ed·ly /rɪˋpitɪdlɪ; rɪˈpiːtɪ̈dli/ *adv* many times 一再; 多次: *Graham was repeatedly warned by the doctors to not work so hard.* 醫生一再告誡格雷厄姆工作不要這麼拚命。

re·peat·er /rɪˋpitɚ; rɪˈpiːtə/ *n* [C] *technical* a repeating gun or clock【術語】連發槍; 打簧錶[鐘]

re·peat·ing /rɪˋpitɪŋ; rɪˈpiːtɪŋ/ *adj* [C] **1** a repeating gun can be fired several times without being loaded again〔槍〕可連發的 **2** a repeating watch or clock can be made to repeat the last STRIKE (=sound made at an hour or quarter of an hour)〔鐘、錶〕自鳴的, 打簧的

re·pel /rɪˋpɛl; rɪˈpel/ *v* **repelled, repelling 1** [T] if something repels you, you want to avoid it because you do not like it 使厭惡, 使反感: *Her heavy make-up and cheap scent repelled him.* 她的濃妝和廉價香水使他厭惡。**2** [T] to fight a group or military force and make them stop attacking you 擊退: *repel invaders* 擊退入侵者 | *repel an attack* 擊退進攻 **3** [T] to keep something or someone away from you 驅除: *Fire repels wild animals.* 火能驅走野獸。**4** [I,T] *technical* if two things repel each other they push each other away with an electrical force【術語】排斥

re·pel·lent¹ /rɪˋpɛlənt; rɪˈpelənt/ *adj* **1** nasty or very unpleasant 令人厭惡的, 讓人反感的: *Stories about famous villains can be both repellent and fascinating.* 著名的惡棍的故事既令人不快又引人入勝。**2 water repellent** water repellent material does not let water pass through it〔材料〕不透水的

repellent², repellant *n* [C,U] a substance that keeps insects away 驅蟲劑: *mosquito repellent* 驅蚊劑

re·pent /rɪˋpɛnt; rɪˈpent/ *v* [I,T] **1** a word meaning to be sorry for something you have done, used especially in a religious context 懺悔〔尤用於宗教場合〕: **[+of]** *Repent of your sins and you will be forgiven.* 懺悔你的罪惡, 你將得到寬恕。**2** *formal* to be sorry for something and to wish you had not done it【正式】懊悔, 後悔: **repent doing sth** *I began to repent parting with you.* 我開始後悔與你分手。| **repent sth** *He repented his decision.* 他對自己的決定感到後悔。

re·pen·tance /rɪˋpɛntəns; rɪˈpentəns/ *n* [U] the state of being sorry for something you have done 懊悔, 後悔; 懺悔

re·pen·tant /rɪˋpɛntənt; rɪˈpentənt/ *adj formal* sorry for something wrong that you have done【正式】後悔的, 懊悔的; 懺悔的 —opposite 反義詞 UNREPENTANT —**repentantly** *adv*

re·per·cus·sion /ˌripəˋkʌʃən; ˌriːpəˈkʌʃən/ *n* **1 repercussions** [plural] the results of an action or event, especially a bad one, that continue to have an effect for some time, in complicated and unexpected ways〔尤指不好的行動或事件的〕持續影響;〔複雜而出乎意料的〕反響: *The break-up of the USSR has had world-wide repercussions.* 蘇聯的解體造成了世界性的影響。**2** [C] *technical* a sound or force coming back after it hits something【術語】回聲; 反衝; 反射

rep·er·toire /ˋrɛpɚˌtwɑr; ˈrepətwɑː/ *n* [C usually singular 一般用單數] **1** all of the plays, pieces of music etc, that a performer or group has learned and can perform〔演員、劇團的〕全部劇目, 常備節目 **2** the total number of things that someone or something is able to do 全部技能: *the behavioral repertoire of newborn infants* 新生兒的全部行為

rep·er·to·ry /ˋrɛpɚˌtorɪ; ˈrepətəri/ *n* **1** [U] a type of theatre work in which actors perform different plays on different days, instead of doing the same play for a long time 輪流演出選定的節目: *a repertory company* 輪流演出選定節目的劇團 **2** [C] a repertoire 保留劇目

rep·e·ti·tion /ˌrɛpɪˋtɪʃən; ˌrepɪ̈ˈtɪʃən/ *n* **1** [U] doing the same thing many times 重複: **[+of]** *his constant repetition of the same old jokes* 他不斷重複那些相同的老笑話 | *In my day, everything was learned by repetition.* 在我那個時代, 所有東西都是通過死背學會的。**2** [C] something that is done again 重複的事: **[+of]** *I don't want a repetition of this incident.* 我不希望這事重演。

rep·e·ti·tious /ˌrɛpɪˋtɪʃəs; ˌrepɪ̈ˈtɪʃəs◂/ *adj* saying the same thing several times〔說話〕重複的: *a boring, repetitious style* 乏味、疊牀架屋的風格

re·pet·i·tive /rɪˋpɛtɪtɪv; rɪˈpetɪ̈tɪv/ *adj* done many times in the same way〔做事〕重複的, 反覆的: *She hated the tedious, repetitive household tasks.* 她討厭那些枯燥乏味、日復一日的家務工作。—**repetitively** *adv*

repetitive strain in·ju·ry /·ˌ··· ˈ·,···/ *n* [U] *technical* RSI; pains in your hands, arms etc caused by doing the same hand movements very many times【術語】〔手掌、手臂等〕重複性勞損

re·phrase /riˋfrez; ˌriːˈfreɪz/ *v* [T] to express something in different words so that its meaning is clearer or more acceptable 重新措辭: *OK. Let me rephrase the question.* 好吧, 讓我換個說法來提這個問題。

re·place /rɪˋples; rɪˈpleɪs/ *v* [T] **1** to start doing something instead of another person, or being used instead of another thing 取代, 接替: *I'm replacing Sue on the team.* 我接替隊裡的蘇。| *These PCs replace the old system network.* 這些個人電腦替代了陳舊的系統網絡。**2** to remove someone from their job or something from its place, and put a different person or thing there 替換, 調換: *Well, if he can't manage he'll have to be replaced.* 如果他應付不了, 就得找人替換他。| **replace sth with sth** *They're replacing the old windows with double glazing.* 他們正在用雙層玻璃替換舊窗戶。**3** to get something new to put in the place of something that has been broken, stolen etc 更換: *I'll replace the vase I broke as soon as possible.* 我會儘快更換我打破的花瓶。**4** to put something back in its correct place 把…放回原處: *He replaced the book on the shelf.* 他把書放回架子上。—**replaceable** *adj*

re·place·ment /rɪˋplesmənt; rɪˈpleɪsmənt/ *n* [U] **1** the act of replacing something, often with something newer, better etc 更換: *Those tyres are badly in need of replacement.* 那些輪胎急需更換。**2** [C] someone or something that replaces another person or thing 替換的人[物]: **[+for]** *It will be difficult to find a replacement for Ted.* 很難找到接替泰德的人。| **replacement car/bulb/battery** *We'll need a replacement bulb for the hall light.* 我們需要給門廊裡的燈換一個燈泡。

re·play¹ /riˋple; ˌriːˈpleɪ/ *v* [T] **1** to play a game of sport again 重新舉行〔比賽〕: *The game ended in a draw and will be replayed on Wednesday.* 比賽結果不分勝負, 所

以星期三要再賽一次。**2** to play something again that has been recorded 重放〔錄音、錄像〕: *We replayed all the romantic bits of the video.* 我們重放了錄像中所有的浪漫片段。

re·play² /ˋriˌple; ˈriːpleɪ/ *n* [C] **1** a game of sport that is played again 重賽: *Milan won the semi-final replay 3-0.* 米蘭隊在半決賽的重賽中以三比零取勝。**2** a piece of action in a game of sport seen on television, that is immediately shown again〔電視中比賽鏡頭的〕重播, 回放: *You can see on the replay that the goalkeeper was clearly fouled.* 你可以在重播的鏡頭中看到, 明顯有人對守門員犯規。**3** *informal* something that is done exactly as it was before【非正式】重複: *a replay of the same mistakes* 重複相同的錯誤

re·plen·ish /rɪˋplɛnɪʃ; rɪˈplenɪʃ/ *v* [T+**with**] *formal* to fill something again or put new supplies into something【正式】再裝滿; 補充 —**replenishment** *n* [U]

re·plete /rɪˋplit; rɪˈpliːt/ *adj* [not before noun 不用於名詞前] **1** *formal* fully supplied with something【正式】充分供應的, 充足的: [**+with**] *a book replete with diagrams* 一本有許多圖解的書 **2** *old-fashioned* so full of food or drink that you want no more【過時】飽足的 —**repletion** /rɪˋpliʃən; rɪˈpliːʃən/ *n* [U]

rep·li·ca /ˋrɛplɪkə; ˈreplɪkə/ *n* [C] a very good copy, especially of a painting or other work of art〔尤指藝術〕複製品: [**+of**] *The model was an exact replica of the Taj Mahal.* 該模型是跟泰姬陵一模一樣的複製品。

rep·li·cate /ˋrɛplɪˌket; ˈreplɪ̈keɪt/ *v* [T] *formal* to do or make something again, so that you get the same result or make an exact copy【正式】重做, 重製 —**replication** /ˌrɛpləˋkeʃən; ˌreplɪ̈ˈkeɪʃən/ *n* [C,U]

3 2 **re·ply¹** /rɪˋplaɪ; rɪˈplaɪ/ *v* **1** [I,T] to answer someone by saying or writing something 回答, 答覆: *I asked Clive where he was going but he didn't reply.* 我問克萊夫他到哪兒去, 但他沒有回答。| [**+to**] *You must reply to Dennis's letter soon.* 你必須及早給丹尼斯回信。| **reply that** *I can only reply that I did not realise what was happening.* 我只能回覆, 我不知道發生了甚麼事。| *"That's what I expected," replied Mandy.* "那是我所期待的。"曼迪回答說。—see 見 ANSWER² (USAGE) **2** [I] to react to an action by doing something else 回應: [**+to/with**] *The terrorists replied to their threats with violence.* 恐怖分子以暴力回應他們的威脅。

2 3 **reply²** *n* [C] **1** something that is said, written, or done as a way of replying 回答, 答覆; 回應: [**+to**] *We've had 60 replies to our advertisement so far.* 到目前為止, 我們已經收到60份對我們廣告的回應。| **make no reply** (=not reply) 不回答 *I asked him if I could help, but he made no reply.* 我問他要不要幫忙, 但他沒有回答。| *The only reply was a burst of gunfire.* 唯一的回答是一陣槍聲。**2 in reply to** *formal* as a way of replying to something【正式】答覆: *I am writing in reply to your letter of 1st June.* 我寫此信回覆你6月1日的來信。**3 without reply** if a sports team gets a number of points or goals (GOAL (2)) without reply, their opponents get no points〔比賽〕己方得分[進球]但對方未得分[進球]

reply-paid /ˌ·ˌ· ˈ·◂/ *adj* a reply-paid envelope has had the cost of a stamp already paid by the person who sent it 回郵郵資已付的

re·po man /ˋripo mæn; ˈriːpəʊ mæn/ *n* [C] *informal* someone whose job is to REPOSSESS (=take away) cars that have not been paid for【非正式】〔未付款汽車的〕回收員

2 1 **re·port¹** /rɪˋport; rɪˈpɔːt/ *n* **1** [C] a written or spoken description of a situation or event, giving people the information they need 報告: *the chairman's report* 主席的報告 | [**+on/of**] *police reports of the accident* 警方關於事故的報告 **2** [C] a piece of writing in a newspaper about something that is happening, or part of a television or radio news programme 報道: *We're getting reports from the scene of the fighting.* 我們不斷得到發自交戰現場的報道。| *a weather report* 天氣預報 **3** [C] an official piece of writing that carefully considers a particular subject, and is often written by a group of people〔正式的〕研究報告: [**+on/of**] *a recent report on child abuse* 新近一份關於虐待兒童的報告 —see graph at 參見 NEWS 圖表 **4** [C,U] things people say that may or may not be true; RUMOUR 傳聞, 傳說: *According to reports he's not coming back.* 根據傳聞, 他不會回來了。**5** *BrE* [C] a written statement by teachers about a child's work at school, sent to their parents【英】(學生) 成績報告單; REPORT CARD *AmE*【美】: *Dad promised me a new bike if I got a good report.* 爸爸答應我, 如果成績報告單令人滿意就送我一輛新自行車。**6** [C] *formal* the noise of an explosion or shot【正式】爆炸聲; 槍聲: *a loud report* 巨響

report² *v* 3 1

1 ▶NEWS 新聞◀ [I,T] to give people information about recent events, especially in newspapers and on television and radio 報道: *This is Gavin Williams, reporting from the United Nations in New York.* 我是加文·威廉斯, 從紐約聯合國進行報道。| **report sth** *We aim to report the news as fairly as possible.* 我們的目標是盡量公正地報道新聞。| [**+on**] *The Post sent her to Bangladesh to report on the floods.*《郵報》派她去孟加拉報道水災的情況。| **report that** *The newspapers reported that he had died in a car accident.* 報紙報道說他死於車禍。| **report doing sth** *They reported having seen the remains of the body.* 他們報道說看到了屍體殘骸。| **be reported to be** *He is reported to have been driving whilst drunk.* 據報道, 他酒後開車。

2 ▶JOB/WORK 工作◀ [I,T] to tell someone about what has been happening, or what you are doing as part of your job 報告, 匯報: **report (to sb) on** *Come back next week to report on your progress.* 下星期回來報告你的進展情況。| *Anything to report, Sergeant?* 有甚麼要報告嗎, 中士?

3 ▶PUBLIC STATEMENT 公開聲明◀ [T] to officially give information to the public 公告: *Scientists are due to report the first step towards the development of an AIDS vaccine.* 科學家將公佈研製愛滋病疫苗的第一步情況。

4 ▶CRIME/ACCIDENT 犯罪/事故◀ [T] to tell the police or someone in authority that an accident or crime has happened 報告; 舉報: *I'd like to report a theft.* 我想舉報一樁偷竊案。| **report sth to sb** *All accidents must be reported to the safety officer.* 所有事故都必須向安全主任報告。| **report sb/sth missing** *The plane was reported missing in heavy fog.* 據報告, 那架飛機在大霧中失蹤了。

5 ▶COMPLAIN 投訴◀ [T] to complain about someone to people in authority 告發, 檢舉: *Robert reported Guy for smoking in school.* 羅伯特告發了蓋伊在學校裡抽煙。| **report sb to sb** *Kevin was eventually reported to the police.* 凱文最終被人向警方舉報了。

6 ▶ARRIVAL 到達◀ [I] to go somewhere and officially state that you have arrived 報到: [**+to**] *All visitors must report to the site office.* 所有來訪者必須向現場辦公室報到。

7 report sick to officially tell your employers that you cannot come to work because you are ill 請病假

report back *phr v* [I,T] to bring or send back an account of something 匯報: [**+to**] *Find out and report back to me quickly.* 搞清楚, 然後迅速向我匯報。| **report back that** *The soldiers reported back that enemy forces were moving towards the border.* 士兵匯報說, 敵軍正在向邊境移動。

report to sb *phr v* [T] to be responsible to someone at work and be managed by them 向…負責, 向…報告: *The accountants report to the Deputy Financial Director.* 會計們向財務副主任負責。

re·port·age /rɪˋportɪdʒ; rɪˈpɔːtɪdʒ/ *n* [U] **1** the particular style of reporting used in newspapers, radio or television 報告文學, 報道體裁 **2** the act of reporting news 報道 (新聞)

report card /ˋ· ·/ *n AmE* a written statement by teachers about a child's work at school, sent to their parents【美】(學生) 成績報告單; REPORT *BrE*【英】

re·port·ed·ly /rɪˋportɪdlɪ; rɪˈpɔːtɪ̱dli/ *adv* [sentence adverb 句子副詞] according to what people say 據報道, 據傳說: *He is reportedly not intending to return to this country.* 據說, 他不打算返回這個國家。

reported speech /·,·· ˈ·/ *n* [U] the style of speech or writing used to report what someone says without repeating their actual words; INDIRECT SPEECH 間接引語 —compare 比較 DIRECT SPEECH

3 **re·port·er** /rɪˋportɚ; rɪˈpɔːtə/ *n* [C] someone who writes about events for a newspaper, radio, or television 記者 —compare 比較 JOURNALIST —see also 另見 COURT REPORTER

re·pose¹ /rɪˋpoz; rɪˈpəʊz/ *n* [U] *formal* a state of calm or comfortable rest【正式】平靜; 憩息 —**reposeful** *adj*

repose² *v formal*【正式】**1** [I] if something reposes in a place it is put there 安置: [**+on**] *Two small glasses reposed on the tray.* 兩隻小玻璃杯安放在托盤上。**2** [I] if someone reposes somewhere they rest there 休息, 安息 **3 repose your trust/hope etc in sb** to trust someone to help you 信賴/寄希望於某人

re·pos·i·to·ry /rɪˋpɑzə,torɪ; rɪˈpɒzɪ̱təri/ *n* [C] **1** a place where things are stored in large quantities 貯藏室, 倉庫: *a furniture repository* 家具倉庫 **2** *formal or humorous* a person or book that gives a lot of information【正式或幽默】博學者; 包括大量信息的書: *Matthew is a repository of football statistics.* 馬修是各種足球統計數字的寶庫。

re·pos·sess /,ripəˋzɛs; ,riːpəˈzes/ *v* [T] to take back cars, furniture, or property from people who cannot pay for them as they had arranged 收回〔因購物者未能按計劃付款的貨物〕: *Eventually the bailiffs came to repossess the flat.* 最終, 查封官收回了那個公寓。—**repossession** /-ˋzɛʃən; -ˈzeʃən/ *n* [C,U]

rep·re·hend /,rɛprɪˋhɛnd; ,reprɪˈhend/ *v* [T] *formal* to express disapproval of a person or an action【正式】譴責, 申斥

rep·re·hen·si·ble /,rɛprɪˋhɛnsəbl; ,reprɪˈhensɪ̱bəl/ *adj formal* reprehensible behaviour is bad and deserves criticism【正式】〔行為〕應受斥責的: [**+of**] *It was really reprehensible of you to leave such young children alone.* 你把這麼小的孩子撇下不管, 的確應該受批評。

2 1 **rep·re·sent** /,rɛprɪˋzɛnt; ,reprɪˈzent/ *v*

1 ►SPEAK FOR SB 代表某人說話◄ [T] **a)** to speak officially for another person or group of people, giving their opinions and taking action for them 代表: *Mr Kobayashi was chosen to represent the company at the conference.* 小林先生被選為該公司出席會議的代表。| *He was represented in court by a famous criminal lawyer.* 在法庭上代表他的是一位著名的刑法律師。**b)** to say or do something that expresses the feelings, opinions etc of a group of people 表達〔某團體的情感、意見等〕: *The protesters represented only a small section of public opinion.* 抗議者僅陳述了一小部分民意。

2 be represented to have sent someone from your group to a meeting, ceremony etc〔某團體〕由〔某人〕代表出席: *All the local societies and clubs were represented in the parade.* 當地所有的社團和俱樂部都有代表參加遊行。

3 represent an improvement/an obstacle/a challenge etc *formal* used to say that something should be thought of as a particular thing【正式】應視為進步/障礙/挑戰等〔用於表示某事有某些特質〕: *This essay represents a considerable improvement on your recent work.* 這篇短論說明你最近的工作大有進步。

4 ►GOVERNMENT 政府◄ [T] to be the member of a parliament or other law making institution, such as the Congress, for a particular area 當〔某地區〕的議員[其他立法機構的成員]: *Does Kathryn Walker still represent Worcester?* 凱瑟琳·沃克還是代表伍斯特的議員嗎? | *He represents the 8th Congressional District of Illinois.* 他是代表伊利諾伊州第八國會選區的議員。

5 ►A SIGN 標誌◄ [T] to be a sign or mark that shows the position of a particular thing, especially on a map or plan; SYMBOLIZE〔尤指在地圖上或平面圖裡〕象徵, 表示: *The red lines on the map represent railways.* 地圖上的紅線表示鐵路。

6 ►SHOW STH 展現某物◄ [T] to be a picture or STATUE of something 用圖畫[雕塑]表示, 描繪, 雕出: *This painting represents the first settlers arriving in America.* 這幅畫描繪了首批移民到達美洲時的情景。

7 represent yourself as to say that you are something that you are not 佯稱自己是…: *They represented themselves as the party of low taxation.* 他們佯稱自己是主張低稅率的黨。

8 represent sb as to describe someone in a particular way, so that people have a particular opinion of them 把某人描寫為: *Shakespeare represents Richard III as a black-hearted villain.* 莎士比亞將理查三世描寫成一個心腸狠毒的反派角色。

re-pre·sent /,ri prɪˋzɛnt; ,riː prɪˈzent/ *v* [T] to give, offer, or send something again, especially an official document〔尤指正式文件〕再送給; 再提出; 再遞上: *The phone company re-presented the bill for payment.* 電話公司再度寄來賬單要求付款。

rep·re·sen·ta·tion /,rɛprɪzɛnˋteʃən; ,reprɪzenˈteɪʃən/ *n* **1** [U] the state of having representatives to speak, vote, or make decisions for you 代理, 代表; 代議權: *Minority groups need more effective parliamentary representation.* 少數派團體需要有更具實效的議會代表。| *Paul appeared in court without any representation.* 保羅出庭時沒有代理律師。—see also 另見 PROPORTIONAL REPRESENTATION **2** [U] the act of representing someone or something 代表, 代理 **3** [C] a painting, sign etc that shows or describes something else 描繪, 表現: *This painting is a representation of a storm at sea.* 這幅畫描繪的是海上的暴風雨。**4 representations** [plural] *especially BrE* official complaints made in a formal way【尤英】〔正式〕投訴; 抗議: **make representations about/to** *A group of students made representations to the college about bad accommodation.* 一羣學生就惡劣的住宿環境向校方提出抗議。

rep·re·sen·ta·tion·al /,rɛprɪzɛnˋteʃənḷ; ,reprɪzenˈteɪʃənəl/ *adj* a representational painting or style of art shows things as they actually appear in real life〔繪畫或藝術風格〕具象的; 寫實的 —compare 比較 ABSTRACT¹ (3)

Rep·re·sen·ta·tive /,rɛprɪˋzɛntətɪv; ,reprɪˈzentətɪv◄/ *n* [C] a member of the House of Representatives, the Lower House of Congress in the United States〔美國〕眾議院議員

representative¹ *adj* **1** like other members of the same group; typical 代表性的; 代表…的; 典型的: [**+of**] *Are your opinions representative of the views of all the students?* 你們的意見代表全體學生的觀點嗎? **2** a representative system of government allows everyone to express their opinions by voting for representatives〔政制〕代表制的, 代議制的: *Change is needed if we are to have a fully representative democracy.* 如果我們想擁有一種完全代議制的民主, 那就需要改革。

representative² *n* [C] **1** a person who has been chosen to speak, vote, or make decisions for someone else 代表, 代理人: [**+of**] *an elected representative of the people* 民選代表 **2 Representative** a member of the House of Representatives, the Lower House of Congress in the United States 美國眾議院議員 —see also 另見 SALES REPRESENTATIVE

re·press /rɪˋprɛs; rɪˈpres/ *v* [T] **1** to stop yourself expressing a feeling 壓抑, 抑制〔感情〕: *I could hardly repress my laughter.* 我忍不住笑起來。**2** to control a group of people by force 鎮壓 —compare 比較 SUPPRESS (1)

re·pressed /rɪˋprɛst; rɪˈprest/ *adj* having feelings or desires that you do not allow yourself to express 受約束

的; 被壓抑的: *a repressed child* 一個被管得太死的孩子 | *I was boiling over with repressed anger.* 壓抑着的憤怒在我心裡翻騰。

re·pres·sion /rɪˋprɛʃən; rɪˈpreʃən/ *n* **1** [U] very strong control of feelings or desires which you are ashamed of, until you no longer know that you have them〔對感到羞恥的感情或慾望的〕壓抑, 抑制: *years of sexual repression* 多年的性壓抑 **2** [U] cruel and severe control of a large group of people 鎮壓: *fleeing from repression* 逃避鎮壓 **3** [C] an act of repressing people, or a feeling that is repressed 鎮壓行為; 受壓抑的感情

re·pres·sive /rɪˋprɛsɪv; rɪˈpresɪv/ *adj* a repressive system of government or law is severe and cruel〔政制或法律〕殘酷的; 嚴苛的: *a repressive regime, which imprisoned thousands* 一個關押了數千人的殘酷政權 | *an old-fashioned and repressive education system* 一種壓抑人的守舊教育制度 **—repressively** *adv* **—repressiveness** *n* [U]

re·prieve¹ /rɪˋpriv; rɪˈpriːv/ *v* [T usually passive 一般用被動態] to officially stop a prisoner from being killed as a punishment 撤銷執行…的死刑

reprieve² *n* [C] an official order stopping the killing of a prisoner as a punishment 死刑撤銷令; 死刑暫緩令: *A last minute reprieve saved him.* 最後一分鐘的死刑撤銷令救了他的命。

rep·ri·mand /ˋrɛprəˌmænd; ˈreprɪmɑːnd/ *v* [T] to tell someone officially that something they have done is very wrong 訓斥, 譴責: *The military court reprimanded him for failing to do his duty.* 軍事法庭譴責他失職。**—reprimand** *n* [C]: *a severe reprimand* 嚴厲的斥責

re·print¹ /riˋprɪnt; ˌriːˈprɪnt/ *v* [I,T] if a book is reprinted or reprints, more copies are printed because the first ones have been sold 再版, 重印

re·print² /ˋriˌprɪnt; ˈriːprɪnt/ *n* [C] an act of printing a book again because all the copies of it have been sold 再版, 重印

re·pri·sal /rɪˋpraɪzḷ; rɪˈpraɪzəl/ *n* [C,U] also 又作 **reprisals** [plural] an act of violence or other strong reaction, to punish your enemies or opponents for something they have done 報復行為: *They didn't tell the police for fear of reprisal.* 由於害怕報復, 他們沒有報告警察。| **in reprisal (for)** *prisoners killed in reprisal for the raid* 為了對襲擊進行報復而被殺的囚犯

re·prise /rɪˋpriz; rɪˈpriːz/ *n* [C] the repeating of all or part of a piece of music, film etc〔樂章的〕重複, 再現;〔電影的〕重演, 重放

re·proach¹ /rɪˋprotʃ; rɪˈprəʊtʃ/ *n formal*【正式】**1** [U] blame or disapproval for the things you have done 責備, 指責, 責怪: *"Are you going already?" he cried, his voice full of reproach.* "你這就要走?"他喊道, 聲音中充滿責備。| **beyond/above reproach** *formal* (=impossible to criticize; perfect)【正式】無可非議; 十全十美 *His behaviour throughout this affair has been beyond reproach.* 他在整個事件中的行為無懈可擊。**2** [C] a remark that expresses criticism or disapproval 責備的話: *Her question was clearly a reproach.* 她的問題顯然是在責備。**3 a reproach to** something that makes a person, society etc feel bad or ashamed; DISGRACE¹ …的恥辱: *These derelict houses are a reproach to the city.* 這些棄置的破房是本市的恥辱。

reproach² *v* [T] **1** *formal* to blame or criticize someone in a way that shows you are disappointed, but not angry【正式】責備, 怪責〔表示失望但不含怒氣〕: **reproach sb for/with sth** *She reproached me for my lack of foresight.* 她責備我缺乏先見之明。| **reproach sb for doing sth** *Jake reproached her bitterly for abandoning him.* 傑克傷心地指責她拋棄了他。**2 reproach yourself** to feel guilty about something that you think you are responsible for 自責: *You've got nothing to reproach yourself for – it was his own decision.* 你沒有甚麼可自責的, 那是他自己的決定。

re·proach·ful /rɪˋprotʃfḷ; rɪˈprəʊtʃfəl/ *adj* a reproachful look, remark etc shows that you are criticizing someone or blaming them〔眼神、話語等〕責備的, 譴責的: *She shot me a reproachful glance.* 她向我投來責備的目光。**—reproachfully** *adv*

rep·ro·bate /ˋrɛprəˌbet; ˈreprəbeɪt/ *n* [C] *formal or humorous* someone who behaves in an immoral way【正式或幽默】墮落者, 放蕩者, 行為不檢者: *an old reprobate who spent all his money on gin* 一個把所有錢都花在杜松子酒上的老無賴

re·pro·cess /riˋprɑsɛs; riːˈprəʊses/ *v* [T] to treat a waste substance so that it can be used again 對〔廢棄物〕進行再加工, 再處理

re·pro·duce /ˌriprəˋdus; ˌriːprəˈdjuːs/ *v* **1** [I,T] if a plant or animal reproduces, or reproduces itself, it produces young plants or animals 生殖, 繁殖: *Fish reproduce by laying eggs.* 魚類產卵繁殖。**2** [T] to make a photograph or printed copy of something 複製; 翻印: *This edition reproduces the original text in full.* 這個版本全文刊登了原文。**3** [T] to make something that is just like something else, or make something happen again in the same way as it happened the first time 重演; 重現: *British scientists have so far been unable to reproduce these results.* 迄今為止, 英國科學家仍未能再次得出這些結果。| *They try to reproduce the exact sounds of early music.* 他們設法如實再現早期音樂的聲音。**—reproducible** *adj*

re·pro·duc·tion /ˌriprəˋdʌkʃən; ˌriːprəˈdʌkʃən◂/ *n* **1** [U] the act or process of producing young animals or plants 生殖, 繁殖: *Reproduction may not take place in poor conditions.* 在惡劣的條件下也許不能進行繁殖。**2** [U] the act of producing a copy of a book, picture, piece of music etc 複製; 再版; 翻印: *Unauthorized reproduction of this publication is strictly forbidden.* 未經許可嚴禁翻印本出版物。| *high quality sound reproduction* 高質量聲響複製 **3** [C] a copy of a work of art, piece of furniture etc〔藝術品、家具等的〕複製品: *a cheap reproduction of a famous painting* 一幅名畫的廉價複製品 | **reproduction furniture/chairs etc** *a reproduction Louis XIV table* 路易十四時期餐桌的複製品

re·pro·duc·tive /ˌriprəˋdʌktɪv; ˌriːprəˈdʌktɪv◂/ *adj* [only before noun 僅用於名詞前] **1** connected with the process of producing young animals or plants 生殖的, 繁殖的: *the human reproductive system* 人類生殖系統 **2** connected with the copying of books, pictures, music etc 翻印的, 複製的: *the reproductive quality of audio tape* 錄音磁帶的複製質量

re·proof /rɪˋpruf; rɪˈpruːf/ *n formal*【正式】**1** [U] blame or disapproval 責備, 斥責, 責怪: *She felt the reproof of her father's gaze.* 她感覺到父親的凝視裡帶着責備。**2** [C] a remark that blames or criticizes someone 責備之言: *a sharp reproof* 嚴厲的責備

re·prove /rɪˋpruv; rɪˈpruːv/ *v* [T] *formal* to criticize someone for something that they have done【正式】責備, 斥責: **reprove sb for doing sth** *I was reproved for wasting good paper.* 我因為浪費好紙而受到斥責。

re·prov·ing /rɪˋpruvɪŋ; rɪˈpruːvɪŋ/ *adj formal* expressing criticism of something that someone has done【正式】責備的, 責怪的: *There was a reproving tone in her voice.* 她的聲音裡帶着責備的語氣。**—reprovingly** *adv*

rep·tile /ˋrɛptḷ; ˈreptaɪl/ *n* [C] **1** a type of animal such as a snake or LIZARD whose blood changes according to the temperature around it, and that usually lays eggs 爬行動物 **2** *informal* someone who is unpleasant or cannot be trusted【非正式】可卑的人; 不可信賴的人: *That reptile must have told the police!* 那個卑鄙的傢伙肯定告訴了警察!

rep·til·i·an¹ /rɛpˋtɪlɪən; repˈtɪliən/ *adj* like a reptile or connected with reptiles 爬行動物(似)的

reptilian² *n* [C] *technical* a reptile【術語】爬行動物

re·pub·lic /rɪˋpʌblɪk; rɪˈpʌblɪk/ *n* [C] a country governed by elected representatives of the people, and led by a president, not a king or queen 共和國; 共和政體 —compare 比較 MONARCHY [W2]

R

re·pub·li·can¹ /rɪˋpʌblɪkən; rɪˈpʌblɪkən/ *adj* **1** connected with or supporting a system of government that is not led by a king or queen and is elected by the people 共和國的, 共和政體的 **2 Republican** connected with or supporting the Republican Party (=one of the two main political parties in the US)〔美國〕共和黨的; 支持共和黨的 **3 Republican** connected with or supporting political parties that want Northern Ireland to become part of the Republic of Ireland, not part of the United Kingdom〔北愛爾蘭〕共和派的〔主張北愛爾蘭脱離聯合王國而併入愛爾蘭共和國〕; 支持共和派的 —**republicanism, Republicanism** *n* [U]

republican² *n* [C] **1** someone who believes in government by elected representatives only, with no king or queen 共和主義者; 擁護共和政體者 **2 Republican** a member or supporter of the Republican Party in the US〔美國〕共和黨人; 共和黨的支持者 **3 Republican** someone from Northern Ireland who believes that Northern Ireland should become part of the Republic of Ireland, not the United Kingdom〔北愛爾蘭〕共和派人士;〔愛爾蘭〕共和軍支持者

re·pu·di·ate /rɪˋpjudɪˌet; rɪˈpjuːdieɪt/ *v* [T] *formal*【正式】**1** to refuse to accept something; REJECT¹ (1) 拒絕: *He repudiated all offers of friendship.* 他拒絕一切友好的表示。**2** to state formally that something is untrue or incorrect〔正式〕否認; 駁斥: *I repudiate emphatically any suggestion that I have acted dishonourably.* 有人指桑罵槐, 指我行徑可恥, 對此我鄭重否認。**3** *old-fashioned* to state that you no longer have any connection with someone, especially a relative; DISOWN【過時】聲明與…斷絕關係〔尤指親戚關係〕**4** to refuse to pay a debt 拒付債款 —**repudiation** /rɪˌpjudɪˋeʃən; rɪˌpjuːdiˈeɪʃən/ *n* [U]

re·pug·nance /rɪˋpʌgnəns; rɪˈpʌgnəns/ *n* [U] *formal* a strong feeling of dislike for something very unpleasant or morally wrong【正式】厭惡; 強烈的反感: *They shrank back from what they saw, with looks of repugnance etched on their faces.* 看到那個場面, 他們往後退了退, 極度的厭惡彷彿刻在臉上。

re·pug·nant /rɪˋpʌgnənt; rɪˈpʌgnənt/ *adj formal* very unpleasant and offensive【正式】令人厭惡的, 使人反感的: *I find his political beliefs completely repugnant.* 我認為他的政治信仰十分令人反感。

re·pulse¹ /rɪˋpʌls; rɪˈpʌls/ *v* [T] *formal*【正式】**1** to defeat a military attack 擊退〔進攻〕: *They attacked with cavalry but were repulsed.* 他們以騎兵進攻但被擊退。**2** if something or someone repulses you, you feel they are very unpleasant 使人厭惡, 使反感: *The very thought of his cold clammy hands repulsed me.* 一想到他那雙濕冷黏糊的手我就感到厭惡。—see also 另見 REPULSIVE (1) **3** to refuse an offer of friendship or help in a way that is rude〔無禮地〕拒絕

repulse² *n* [singular] **1** *formal* the act of rudely refusing when someone offers to help you or be your friend【正式】〔粗暴的〕拒絕 **2** *technical* the defeat of a military attack【術語】擊退

re·pul·sion /rɪˋpʌlʃən; rɪˈpʌlʃən/ *n* **1** [singular,U] a feeling that you want to avoid something or move away from it, because it is very unpleasant 厭惡, 反感 **2** [U] *technical* the electric or MAGNETIC force by which one object pushes another one away from it【術語】排斥力 —opposite 反義詞 ATTRACTION

re·pul·sive /rɪˋpʌlsɪv; rɪˈpʌlsɪv/ *adj* **1** very unpleasant 令人厭惡的, 使人反感的: *What a repulsive man!* 多麼討厭的人! **2** *technical* repulsive forces push objects away from each other【術語】排斥的; 相斥的 —**repulsively** *adv* —**repulsiveness** *n* [U]

rep·u·ta·ble /ˋrɛpjətəbl̩; ˈrepjʊtəbəl/ *adj* respected for being honest or for doing good work 聲譽好的, 有聲望的; 有信譽的: *a very reputable firm* 一家信譽卓著的公司 —**reputably** *adv*

 3 **rep·u·ta·tion** /ˌrɛpjəˋteʃən; ˌrepjʊˈteɪʃən/ *n* [C] **1** the opinion that people have about a particular person or thing because of what has happened in the past 名譽, 名望: **[+for]** *a reputation for honesty and efficiency* 以誠實和高效率著稱 | **[+as]** *She had already begun to establish a reputation as a writer.* 身為作家, 她已經小有名聲。| **a good/bad reputation** *This restaurant has a very good reputation.* 這家飯店名聲很好。| **win/earn/establish a reputation as** *His approach had won him a reputation as a tough manager.* 作為經理, 他的辦事方法使他以強硬著稱。**2 live up to your reputation** to behave in the way that people expect 名不虛傳, 不負盛名: *Martin lived up to his reputation and arrived late.* 馬丁果然名不虛傳, 姍姍來遲。**3 live up to its reputation** to be at least as bad or good as people had thought〔行為〕與名聲相符: *a mountain that lived up to its fearsome reputation* 與其令人生畏之名聲相符的山

re·pute /rɪˋpjut; rɪˈpjuːt/ *n* [U] *formal*【正式】**1** reputation 名譽, 名聲: **of good/evil/international etc repute** *a man of good repute* 名聲好的人 **2** a good reputation 好名聲: *a hotel of some repute* 一家名聲相當好的旅館

re·put·ed /rɪˋpjutɪd; rɪˈpjuːtɪ̈d/ *adj* [only before noun 僅用於名詞前] according to what most people say or think, but not definitely 據說的; 普遍認為的; 號稱的: *the reputed billionaire Pablo Escobar* 號稱億萬富翁的帕布羅·埃斯科巴爾 | **be reputed to be/do sth** *She is reputed to be extremely wealthy.* 據說她極為富有。

re·put·ed·ly /rɪˋpjutɪdlɪ; rɪˈpjuːtɪ̈dli/ *adv* [sentence adverb 句子副詞] according to what most people say or think 據說; 一般認為: *The committee had reputedly spent over $3000 on 'business entertainment'.* 據說, 委員會在"業務接待"上花了三千多美元。

re·quest¹ /rɪˋkwɛst; rɪˈkwest/ *n* **1** [C] a polite or formal demand for something 要求, 請求: **[+for]** *They have made an urgent request for international aid.* 他們緊急要求國際援助。| **request that** *He ignored the neighbours' requests that he should make less noise.* 他無視鄰居要他別那樣吵鬧的要求。| **at sb's request** (=because they asked you to) 應某人的要求 *I telephoned her in Paris, at Staunton's request.* 我應斯湯頓的要求, 在巴黎打了電話給她。| **on request** (=when you ask for it) 一經要求 *Further detail will be sent on request.* 詳情承索即寄。| **by request** (=because someone has especially asked for it) 應…的要求[請求] *There were no flowers at the funeral, by request.* 按照要求, 葬禮上沒有擺花。| **any requests?** *spoken* (=used to ask people if they want anything)【口】要甚麼東西嗎? *I'm going to the bar – any requests?* 我去酒吧——要甚麼嗎? **2** [C] a piece of music that is played on the radio because someone has asked for it 點播的樂曲

request² *v* [T] **1** *formal* to ask for something politely or formally【正式】要求, 請求: *I wrote them a letter, officially requesting permission to proceed.* 我寫信給他們, 正式請求允許我着手進行。| **request that** *The staff immediately requested that he reconsider his decision.* 員工立即要求他重新考慮他的決定。| **request sb to do sth** *All club members are requested to attend the annual meeting.* 請全體俱樂部會員出席年會。**2** to ask for a particular piece of music to be played on the radio 點播: *This song was requested by Mrs Simpson of Potters Bar.* 這首歌是波特斯吧的辛普森夫人點播的。

USAGE NOTE 用法説明: REQUEST

WORD CHOICE 詞語辨析: **ask (for), request, demand**

Ask is the usual word for speaking or writing to someone in order to get something done. 為了完成某事而口頭或書面向某人提出要求的最常用詞是 ask: *I asked one of my friends to help me.* 我請求我的一個朋友幫助我。You use **ask for** when you are trying to get something. ask for 則表示設法得到某物: *I asked for help.* 我請求幫助。

Request is more formal and official. Also if you **request** something, often you have the right to get what you are asking for. request 比較正式, 通常用於要求你有權得到的事物: *The letter politely requested that Miss Willis present herself for interview the next day.* 那封信很有禮貌地要求威利斯小姐第二天去參加面試。| *The government has requested a meeting with community leaders.* 政府已要求與社區領袖會面。
Demand is even stronger. If you **demand** something, you feel strongly that you have the right to it. demand 的語氣更強, 用於要求你強烈認為自己有權得到的事物: *I demand to see the manager!* 我要求見經理!
GRAMMAR 語法
You **request** something (NOT **request for** sth). But you do use **for** with the noun. 動詞 request 後不用 for, 但名詞 request 後需用 for: *requests for money* 要求金錢 (NOT 不用 *requests of money*)

req·ui·em /ˋrɛkwɪəm; ˈrekwiəm/ also 又作 **requiem mass** /ˌ··· ˈ·/ *n* [C] **1** a Christian religious ceremony of prayers for someone who has died 安魂彌撒 **2** a piece of music written for this ceremony 安魂曲

1 1 **re·quire** /rɪˋkwaɪr; rɪˈkwaɪə/ *v* [T not in progressive 不用進行式] **1** if a problem, or situation requires particular action it makes it necessary 需要〔某種行動〕: *It's a matter that requires very careful handling.* 這件事情需要謹慎處理。| *What's required is a complete reorganization of the system.* 需要徹底重組整個系統。**2** to need something 需要〔某物〕: *These plants require moist soil at all times.* 這些植物一直需要潮濕的土壤。**3** [usually passive 一般用被動態] to officially demand that people do something, because of a law or rule〔根據法規〕要求, 規定: **require sb to do sth** *You are required by law to wear seat belts.* 法律規定你要繫安全帶。| [+that] *Regulations require that students attend at least 90% of the lectures.* 規定要求學生的聽課率至少要達到90%。| **the required standard/level/period etc** *You have not yet reached the required standard to pass grade 3.* 你還沒有達到通過三年級考試要求的標準。**4** *formal* used to ask someone what they need【正式】需要〔用於詢問〕: *Is there anything further you require, sir?* 先生, 您還需要甚麼嗎?

Frequencies of the verbs **require** and **need** in spoken and written English 動詞 require 和 need 在英語口語和書面語中的使用頻率

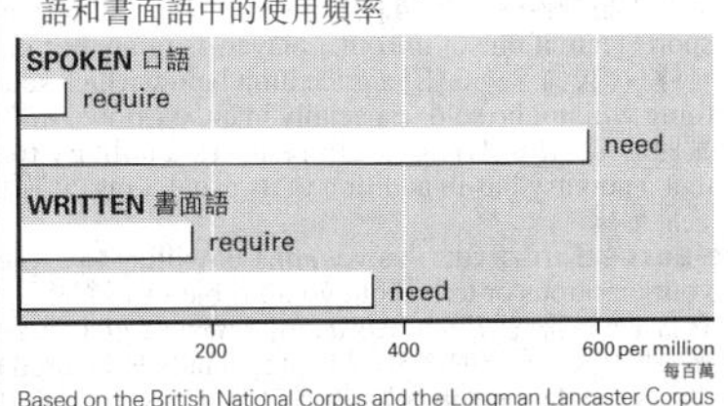

Based on the British National Corpus and the Longman Lancaster Corpus
據英國國家語料庫和朗文蘭卡斯特語料庫

This graph shows that **need** is much more common than **require** in both spoken and written English. **Require** is more formal than **need** and is therefore more common in written English than in spoken English. 本圖表顯示, 在英語口語和書面語中都是 need 比 require 常用得多。require 比 need 正式, 因而它在書面語中的使用頻率要高於口語。

2 2 **re·quire·ment** /rɪˋkwaɪrmənt; rɪˈkwaɪəmənt/ *n* [C] **1** something that is needed or asked for 必需品; 需要的事物: *The refugees' main requirements are food and shelter.* 難民的主要需求是食物和住所。| **meet a requirement** (=have what is necessary) 符合要求 *The new computer system will meet all our requirements.* 新電腦系統將滿足我們的全部要求。**2** something that a college, employer etc says you must have〔大學、雇主等的〕要求, 條件: *The minimum requirement was a degree in engineering.* 最低要求是具有工程學的學位。

req·ui·site /ˋrɛkwəzɪt; ˈrekwɨzɨt/ *adj formal* needed for a particular purpose【正式】需要的, 必要的: *He lacks the requisite qualifications.* 他不符合資格要求。

req·ui·sites /ˋrɛkwəzɪts; ˈrekwɨzɨts/ *n* [plural] *formal* a word meaning things that are needed for a particular purpose, used especially in shops【正式】必備品〔該詞尤在商店內使用〕: *The airport shop sells toilet requisites.* 機場商店出售梳洗必需品。

req·ui·si·tion[1] /ˌrɛkwəˋzɪʃən; ˌrekwɨˈzɪʃən/ *v* [T] to officially demand to have something, especially so that it can be used by an army〔尤指軍隊〕正式要求, 徵用: *Troops had requisitioned houses in the town.* 部隊徵用了鎮上的房屋。

requisition[2] *n* [C,U] an official demand to have something, usually made by an army or military authority〔軍隊的〕徵用令

re·quit·al /rɪˋkwaɪtḷ; rɪˈkwaɪtl/ *n* [U] *formal*【正式】**1** payment for something done or given 報酬 **2** something that you do to harm someone who has harmed you 報復

re·quite /rɪˋkwaɪt; rɪˈkwaɪt/ *v* [T] *formal* to give or do something in return for something done or given to you in the past【正式】報答; 回報

re·re·lease /ˌri rɪˋlis; ˌriː rɪˈliːs/ *v* [T] if a record or film is re-released, it is produced and sold for a second time, usually with small changes〔唱片或電影通常略加改動後〕再發行; 再上演 —**re-release** /ˋri rɪˌlis; ˈriː rɪliːs/ *n* [C]

re·route /ˌriˋrut; ˌriːˈruːt/ *v* [T] to send vehicles in a different direction from the normal one 使〔車輛〕改變路線

re·run[1] /ˋriˌrʌn; ˈriːrʌn/ *n* [C] **1** a film or old television programme that is being shown again 重映影片; 重播的電視節目 **2** something that happens in the same way as something that happened before〔舊事的〕重演: *The government wants to avoid a rerun of last year's currency crisis.* 政府希望避免去年貨幣危機的重演。**3** a race or competition that is held again 重賽

re·run[2] /riˋrʌn; riːˈrʌn/ *v* [T] **1** to show a film or recorded television programme again 重映, 重播 **2** to arrange for a race or competition to be held again 使重賽

re·sched·ule /riˋskɛdʒul; ˌriːˈʃedjuːl/ *v* [T] **1** to arrange for something to happen at a different time, because the time you had planned is no longer convenient 重新安排…的時間: *The press conference had to be rescheduled for March 19.* 記者招待會的時間不得不改在3月19日。**2** *technical* to arrange for a debt to be paid back later than was originally agreed【術語】重新安排債務償還時間

re·scind /rɪˋsɪnd; rɪˈsɪnd/ *v* [T] to officially end a law, decision, or agreement that has been made in the past〔正式〕廢除, 取消〔法規、決定、合同〕

rescue 救援

res·cue[1] /ˋrɛskju; ˈreskjuː/ *v* [T] to save someone or something from a situation of danger or harm 拯救, 解救; 救援: *Hundreds are still in the water, waiting to be* *rescued.* 數以百計的人仍在水中，等待着救援。| **rescue sb/sth from** *She died trying to rescue her children from the blaze.* 她在設法從大火中救出自己的孩子時身亡。| *a final attempt to rescue the company from ruin* 拯救公司使之免於破產的最後嘗試 —**rescuer** *n* [C]

rescue² *n* [C] an occasion when someone or something is rescued from danger 救援，營救：*a daring rescue at sea* 在海上英勇的營救工作 | **rescue team/attempt/bid etc** *A rescue team is trying to reach the trapped miners.* 營救隊正設法到達礦工被困的位置。| **come to the rescue** (=help someone in danger or difficulty) 救援 *His father came to his rescue and lent him the money.* 他的父親借錢給他，因而救了他。

S2 W1 **re·search¹** /ˈrisɝtʃ; rɪˈsɜːtʃ/ *n* [U] also 又作 **researches** [plural] **1** serious study of a subject, that is intended to discover new facts or test new ideas 研究；探討：**[+into/on]** *research into the causes of cancer* 癌症起因的研究 | **research project/student/grant etc** *Alison is a research student in our lab.* 阿莉森是我們實驗室的研究生。**2** the activity of finding information about something that you are interested in or need to know about 研究（工作）：**do research** *I'm doing some research for an article about student life.* 我正在為一篇關於學生生活的文章作一些研究。| *I've done some research – it looks as if the train will be fastest.* 我搜集了一些資料，看來火車將會是最快的。—see also 另見 MARKET RESEARCH, R AND D

re·search² /rɪˋsɝtʃ; rɪˈsɜːtʃ/ *v* [T] **1** to study a subject in detail, especially in order to discover new facts or test new ideas 研究，探索：*He's researching the effects of aerosols on the environment.* 他正在研究懸浮微粒對環境的影響。**2** to supply all the necessary facts and information for something 為…進行研究，搜集資料：*This book has been very well researched.* 這本書是經過大量的研究寫成的。—**researcher** *n* [C]

research and de·vel·op·ment /ˌ·ˌ· · ·ˋ···/ *n* [U] R AND D 研究與開發

re·sell /ˌriˋsɛl; ˌriːˈsel/ *v past tense and past participle* **resold** /-ˋsold; -ˈsəʊld/ [T] to sell something that you have bought 轉賣：*The retailer resells the goods at a higher price.* 零售商以高於進貨的價格轉賣商品。

re·sem·blance /rɪˋzɛmbləns; rɪˈzembləns/ *n* [C,U] a SIMILARITY between two things, especially in the way they look〔尤指樣子〕相似，類似：**[+between]** *You can see the resemblance between Susan and her sister.* 你可以看出蘇珊與她的妹妹很像。| **bear a resemblance to** (=look like) 像… *He bears a remarkable resemblance to Kurt Russell.* 他相貌酷似寇特·羅素。

re·sem·ble /rɪˋzɛmbl̩; rɪˈzembəl/ *v* [T not in progressive or passive 不用進行式或被動態] to look like, or be similar to, someone or something 像；與…類似，與…相似：**closely resemble** *Mick closely resembled his father.* 米克長得很像他的父親。

re·sent /rɪˋzɛnt; rɪˈzent/ *v* [T] to feel angry or upset about a situation or about something that someone has done, especially because you think that it is not fair〔因受委屈而〕對…感到憤恨，不滿；憎惡：**resent doing sth** *He resents having to get my permission first.* 他因為要先得到我的允許而忿忿不平。| **greatly/strongly/bitterly resent** *She greatly resented her brother's refusal to help.* 她對她哥哥拒絕幫助極為不滿。

re·sent·ful /rɪˋzɛntfl; rɪˈzentfəl/ *adj* feeling angry and upset about something that you think is unfair〔對不公平的事物〕感到憤怒的，不滿的，憎惡的：**[+of/at/about etc]** *His daughters became increasingly resentful of his authority.* 他的女兒們對被他支配越來越憎惡。—**resentfully** *adv*: *"You should have told me," said Marion resentfully.* "你應該告訴我的。"瑪麗昂不滿地說。—**resentfulness** *n* [U]

re·sent·ment /rɪˋzɛntmənt; rɪˈzentmənt/ *n* [U] a feeling of anger because something has happened that you think is unfair 憤恨，不滿，憎惡

S3 **res·er·va·tion** /ˌrɛzɚˋveʃən; ˌrezəˈveɪʃən/ *n* **1** [C] an arrangement made so that a place is kept for you in a hotel, restaurant, plane etc; BOOKING (1)〔房間、座位等的〕預訂：| **make a reservation** *Customers are advised to make seat reservations well in advance.* 建議顧客提前訂座。**2** [C,U] a feeling of doubt because you do not agree completely with a plan, idea, or suggestion 存疑；保留（意見）：**have/express reservations (about)** *I had serious reservations about his appointment as captain.* 我對任命他為船長鄭重地持保留態度。| **without reservation** (=completely) *We condemn their actions without reservation.* 我們毫無保留地譴責他們的行為。**3** [C] an area of land in the US kept separate for Native Americans to live on〔美國印第安人的〕居留地，保留地：*a Navajo reservation* 納瓦霍印第安人居留地 **4** [C] *especially AmE* an area of land where wild animals can live without being hunted; RESERVE【尤美】〔野生動物〕保護區：*a game reservation* 野生動物保護區，禁獵區 —see also 另見 CENTRAL RESERVATION

re·serve¹ /rɪˋzɝv; rɪˈzɜːv/ *v* [T] **1** to arrange for a place in a hotel, restaurant, plane etc to be kept for you 預訂：*Do you have to reserve tickets in advance?* 你需要預先訂票嗎？| *I'd like to reserve a table for two.* 我想預訂一張兩人的餐桌。**2** to keep something so that it can be used by a particular person or for a particular purpose 保留：**reserve sth for sb** *These seats are reserved for the elderly and disabled.* 這些座位是留給老人和殘疾人坐的。| *Reserve a little of the mixture to sprinkle over the top of the pie.* 留一些配好的作料灑在餡餅上。**3** to use or show something only in one particular situation 留作，用於〔特定場合〕：**reserve sth for** *a tone of voice she usually reserved for dealing with officials* 她通常在與官員打交道時才用的語氣 **4 reserve the right to do sth** *formal* an expression meaning that you will do something if you think it is necessary, used especially in notices or official documents【正式】保留做某事的權利〔尤用於通知或官方文件〕：*The management reserves the right to refuse admission.* 管理部保留拒絕進場的權利。 W3

reserve² *n* **1** [C] also 又作 **reserves** *plural* an amount of something kept for future use, especially for difficult or dangerous situations 貯藏（物）；儲備：**[+of]** *reserves of food* 食物的儲備 | *an inner reserve of strength* 體力蘊藏 **2 in reserve** ready to be used if needed unexpectedly 備用：*We always keep some money in reserve, just in case.* 我們總是存起一些錢以防萬一。**3** [U] a quality in someone's character that makes them not like expressing their emotions or talking about their problems 含蓄；寡言：*His characteristic detachment and reserve made it difficult to guess his thoughts.* 他一貫的超然和寡言使人難以猜測他的心思。**4** [C] someone who will play in a sports team if one of the other players is injured or ill 替補隊員，後備隊員 **5** [C] a price limit below which something will not be sold, especially in an AUCTION〔尤指拍賣時的〕底價 **6** [U] also 又作 **reserves** a military force that a country has in addition to its usual army 後備軍，後備部隊

re·served /rɪˋzɝvd; rɪˈzɜːvd/ *adj* **1** unwilling to express your emotions or talk about your problems 沉默寡言的；含蓄的；矜持的：*Ellen was a shy, reserved girl.* 艾倫是個靦腆、沉默寡言的姑娘。**2** kept specially to be used by one particular person 保留的，預訂的：*I'm sorry, but this seat's reserved.* 對不起，這個座位已經有人預訂了。| *reserved parking spaces* 專用停車處 | **[+for]** *The front row is reserved for the family of the bride.* 前排座位留給新娘的家人。**3 all rights reserved** used at the end of printed or recorded material to show that it is illegal to copy it without special permission 版權所有，不得翻版〔用於印刷品或音像製品的結尾部分〕—**reservedly** /rɪˋzɝvɪdlɪ; rɪˈzɜːvɪ̣dli/ *adv* —**reservedness** *n* [U] —see also 另見 UNRESERVED

reserve price /·ˈ· ·/ RESERVE² (5) 底價

re·serv·ist /rɪˋzɝvɪst; rɪˈzɜːvɪ̣st/ *n* [C] a soldier in the reserve (RESERVE² (6)), who is trained to fight and may join the professional army during a war 後備役軍人

res·er·voir /ˋrɛzə˞ˏvwɑr; ˈrezəvwɑː/ *n* [C] **1** a lake, especially an artificial one, where water is stored before it is supplied to people's houses 水庫, 蓄水池 **2** a large amount of something that has not yet been used 儲藏, 積蓄: *She found she had reservoirs of unexpected strength.* 她發現自己有意想不到的尚未使用的力量。**3** *technical* a place where something, such as liquid, is kept before it is used【術語】儲液器 —see picture at 參見 ENGINE 圖

re·set[1] /riˋsɛt; ˌriːˈset/ *v past tense and past participle* **reset** *present participle* **resetting** [T] **1** to change a clock, control etc so that it shows a different time or number 校正, 調整〔鐘錶、控制裝置等〕**2** to put a broken bone back into its correct place 重接〔斷骨〕; 正〔骨〕: *The doctor reset the fracture.* 醫生重接了骨折部位。**3** to load an OPERATING SYSTEM for a small computer from a DISK into the computer's memory; BOOT[2] (2) 重新啟動〔電腦〕**4** to put a jewel into a new piece of jewellery 重鑲〔寶石〕**5** to write a new set of questions for an examination 重出試題 **6** *technical* to make new pages from which to print a book【術語】給…重新排版: *The book had to be reset because there were so many mistakes in the first printing.* 這本書首次印刷時錯誤太多, 必須重排。—**reset** *n* [C,U]

re·set[2] /ˋriˌsɛt; ˈriːset/ *adj* a reset button is used to make a machine or instrument ready to work again〔按鈕、鍵〕復位的, 重新啟動的

re·set·tle /riˋsɛtl̩; riːˈsetl/ *v* **1** [I,T] to go to live in a new country or area, or help people to do this (協助人) 在新的國家[地區]定居: *Many Ugandan Asian families resettled in Canada.* 許多烏干達的亞裔家庭在加拿大定居。| *tribesmen who were forcibly resettled by the government* 被政府強迫搬遷的部落人 **2** [T] to start using an area again as a place to live 再〔在某地區〕定居: *The area was resettled in the latter half of the century.* 該世紀下半葉, 人們重新到這個地區定居。—**resettlement** *n* [U]

re·shuf·fle[1] /riˋʃʌfl̩; riːˈʃʌfəl/ *v* [T] *BrE* to change around the jobs of the people who work in an organization, especially in government【英】人事調整, 改組〔機構, 尤指政府〕: *The Prime Minister reshuffled his cabinet.* 首相改組了內閣。

re·shuf·fle[2] *n* [C] *BrE* the act of changing around the jobs of people who work in an organization, especially in a government【英】〔機構內的〕人事調整;〔尤指政府的〕改組: *a Cabinet reshuffle* 內閣改組

re·side /rɪˋzaɪd; rɪˈzaɪd/ *v* [I always+adv/prep] *formal* to live in a particular place【正式】居住

reside in sth/sb *phr v* [T not in passive 不用被動態] *formal*【正式】**1** to be present in something 存在於: *For Fellini, the poetry of cinema resides primarily in movement.*〔意大利導演〕費里尼認為, 電影的詩意首先存在於運動之中。**2** also 又作 **reside within** sth/sb if a power, right etc resides in something or someone, it belongs to them〔權力、權利等〕屬於

res·i·dence /ˋrɛzədəns; ˈrezɪdəns/ *n* **1** [C] *formal*【正式】**a)** a house, especially a large one 住宅, 住所, 公館 **b)** the place where an AMBASSADOR (=important representative from a foreign country) lives 大使官邸 **2** [U] **a)** the state of living in a place〔在某地〕居住〔的狀態〕**b)** permission to live somewhere permanently 永久居住許可 **3 in residence a)** *formal* living in a place or present there【正式】(住) 在某地的 **b)** a student who is in residence is at their university〔大學生〕住校的 **4 artist/poet/playwright etc in residence** an artist etc who has been officially chosen by a college or other institution to work there and to help the students〔大學等正式聘用工作和輔導學生的〕駐校藝術家/詩人/劇作家等 **5 take up residence** *formal* to start to live in a place【正式】開始居住: *He's taken up residence in an old castle.* 他在一座舊城堡裡住下來。—see also 另見 HALL of RESIDENCE

res·i·dent[1] /ˋrɛzədənt; ˈrezɪdənt/ *adj* **1** *formal* living in a place【正式】居住的, 居留的: [+in] *Many retired British people are now resident in Spain.* 許多退休的英國人現在住在西班牙。**2** [only before noun 僅用於名詞前] living or working in a particular place or institution〔在某處、某機構〕居住[工作]的: *a resident tutor* 住校輔導老師 **3** [only before noun 僅用於名詞前] *humorous* belonging to a particular group【幽默】屬於…的: *He's our resident expert on computer games.* 他是我們電腦遊戲的常駐專家。

resident[2] *n* [C] **1** someone who lives or stays in a place such as a house or hotel 居民; 住客: *Only residents can drink in the hotel bar.* 只有住客才能在旅館酒吧飲酒。**2** *AmE* a doctor working at a hospital where he is being trained【美】住院醫生; REGISTRAR (2) *BrE*【英】 S2 W3

res·i·den·tial /ˌrɛzəˋdɛnʃəl; ˌrezɪˈdenʃəl◂/ *adj* **1** a residential part of a town consists of private houses, with no offices or factories 住宅區的: *a quiet residential street* 一條安靜的住宅區街道 **2** living at a place while you are doing something, or in order to do something〔為做某事而〕在某處居住的: **a residential job/course/patient etc** *a residential school for the deaf* 聾人住宿學校 | *a weekend residential course* 週末住校課程 W3

residential care /ˌ····ˈ·/ *n* [U] a system of professional care for people who are too old or ill to look after themselves at home〔為不能自理的老人或病人提供的〕住院護理

residential treat·ment fa·cil·i·ty /ˌ····ˈ···ˌ···/ *n* [C] *AmE technical* an expression meaning a MENTAL HOSPITAL, used because you want to avoid saying this directly【美, 術語】精神病醫院〔委婉用語〕

resident phy·si·cian /ˌ···ˈ··/ *n AmE* a RESIDENT[2] (2)【美】住院醫生

residents' as·so·ci·a·tion /ˈ··· ···ˌ··/ *n* [C] an association of people who meet to discuss the problems and needs of the area where they live 居民協會

re·sid·u·al /rɪˋzɪdʒuəl; rɪˈzɪdʒuəl/ *adj* [only before noun 僅用於名詞前] *formal* remaining after a process, event etc is finished【正式】殘餘的, 剩餘的: *There was still some residual unrest after the rebellion had been crushed.* 叛亂被粉碎以後仍然餘波未平。| **residual income** (=the money left from what you earn after you have paid your taxes) 稅後收入

res·i·due /ˋrɛzəˌdu; ˈrezɪdjuː/ *n* [C] **1** *technical* a substance that is left after a chemical process【術語】〔化學過程的〕殘餘物, 渣滓: *a sticky residue in the bottom of the test tube* 試管底部黏稠的殘餘物 **2** the part of something that is left after the rest has gone or been taken away 剩餘, 殘餘: **[+of]** *The residue of his estate goes to his daughter.* 他的剩餘遺產歸其女兒所有。

re·sign /rɪˋzaɪn; rɪˈzaɪn/ *v* [I,T] **1** to officially and permanently leave your job or position because you want to 辭職, 放棄〔工作、職位〕: **[+from]** *She's just resigned from the committee.* 她剛辭去了委員會的職務。| **resign your post/position** *The manager was forced to resign his post after allegations of corruption.* 在涉嫌貪污後, 經理被迫辭職。**2 resign yourself to sth/to doing sth** to make yourself accept something that is unpleasant but cannot be changed 使自己安於某事/做某物〔無法避免的不愉快事〕, 聽任, 順從於…: *You must resign yourselves to waiting a bit longer.* 你們要耐心多等一會兒。—see also 另見 RESIGNED W3

res·ig·na·tion /ˌrɛzɪgˋneʃən; ˌrezɪgˈneɪʃən/ *n* **1** [C,U] the act of resigning, or a written statement to say you are doing this 辭職; 辭呈: *You have the choice between resignation and dismissal.* 辭職還是開除由你自己選擇。| **hand in your resignation/tender your resignation** (=resign) 遞交辭呈 *Guess what? Roy's handed in his resignation.* 你猜得着嗎? 羅伊遞交了辭職書。**2** [U] the act of calmly accepting a situation that cannot be changed though it is unpleasant 聽從, 順從: *She accepted her fate with resignation.* 她聽天由命。 W3

re·signed /rɪˋzaɪnd; rɪˈzaɪnd/ *adj* **1** a resigned look, sound etc shows that you are making yourself accept some-

R

thing that you do not like 屈從的, 順從的: *a resigned look on her face* 她臉上逆來順受的表情 | *He sounded resigned and dejected.* 他的語氣流露出無可奈何和沮喪的情緒。**2 be resigned to sth/to doing sth** to accept a situation that you do not like, but cannot change 安於某事/做某事: *Isabelle seems resigned to the fact that she's dying.* 伊莎貝拉似乎接受了她已來日無多的事實。—**resignedly** /rɪˋzaɪnədlɪ; rɪˈzaɪnɪ̥dli/ *adv*

re·sil·i·ence /rɪˋzɪlɪəns; rɪˈzɪliəns/ also 又作 **re·sil·i·en·cy** /-lɪənsɪ; -liənsi/ *n* [U] **1** the ability to return quickly to your usual health or state of mind after suffering an illness, difficulties etc 恢復力, 復原力: *resilience of character* 性格堅韌 **2** the ability of a substance to return to its former shape when pressure is removed; FLEXIBILITY 彈性

re·sil·i·ent /rɪˋzɪlɪənt; rɪˈzɪliənt/ *adj* **1** someone who is resilient quickly becomes healthy or happy again after an illness, difficulty, change etc 能恢復活力的; 堅韌的; 適應力強的: *I wouldn't worry – kids are very resilient.* 我不擔心, 孩子的適應力很強。**2** a resilient substance returns to its former shape when pressure is removed 〔物質〕有彈性的 —**resiliently** *adv*

res·in /ˋrɛzn̩; ˈrezɪ̥n/ *n* **1** [T] a thick sticky liquid that comes out of some trees 樹脂 **2** [C] an artificial plastic substance that is produced chemically and used in industry 合成樹脂, 人造樹脂 —**resinous** *adj*

3 **re·sist** /rɪˋzɪst; rɪˈzɪst/ *v* **1** [T] to try to prevent change or prevent yourself being forced to do something 抗拒, 對抗: *Demonstrators today violently resisted attempts to evict them from the building.* 示威者今天強烈地抗拒要他們離開大樓的企圖。| *I was in their power, and knew it was pointless to resist.* 我在他們股掌之中, 知道反抗毫無意義。**2** [I,T] to oppose or fight someone or something 反抗, 抵抗: *The city resisted the enemy onslaught for two weeks.* 這座城市抵禦敵人的猛攻達兩個星期之久。**3** [I,T usually in negatives 一般用於否定句] to stop yourself having something that you like very much or doing something that you want to do 忍住〔擁有某東西的慾望〕, 按捺: **cannot resist sth/doing sth** *I just can't resist chocolates.* 我無法拒絕巧克力的誘惑。| *I couldn't resist sneaking a look at her diary.* 我忍不住偷看了一眼她的日記。| **hard/impossible to resist** *It's hard to resist an invitation like that.* 難以拒絕那樣的邀請。| **resist the temptation/impulse etc** *She resisted the temptation to tell him what she really thought.* 她克制住自己, 沒有把真實想法告訴他。**4** [T] to not be changed or harmed by something 抵擋; 保持原狀; 不受…的損害: *A balanced diet will increase your ability to resist infection.* 飲食均衡會增強你抗感染的能力。**5 resist arrest** to try to prevent the police from taking you to the police station 拒捕 —**resistable** *adj*

2 3 **re·sist·ance** /rɪˋzɪstəns; rɪˈzɪstəns/ *n*

1 ▶AGAINST CHANGE 反對變化◀ [singular,U] a refusal to accept new ideas or changes 〔對新觀念或改變的〕反對, 抗拒: *When you introduced computerized billing, was there much resistance from consumers?* 你們採用電腦打印賬單時, 有顧客反對嗎? | **[+to]** *There has been a lot of resistance to this new law.* 對這項新法律有很大的反感。

2 ▶FIGHTING 戰鬥◀ [singular,U] fighting against someone or something that is attacking you 反抗, 抵抗: **put up/offer resistance** (=resist) 反抗, 抵抗 *The defenders put up strong resistance.* 守軍頑強抵抗。

3 ▶AGAINST INFECTION/ILLNESS 抗感染/疾病◀ [singular,U] the natural ability of an animal or plant to stop diseases from harming it 抗病能力: *Vitamins can build up your resistance to colds and flu.* 維生素可以增強抵抗感冒和流感的能力。

4 wind resistance/air resistance etc the degree to which a moving object, such as a car or plane, is made to move more slowly by the air it moves through 風的阻力/空氣阻力等

5 ▶ELECTRICITY 電◀ [U] the degree to which a substance can stop an electric current passing through 電阻

6 the resistance an organization that secretly fights against an enemy that now controls their country 抵抗組織: *Mitterand was in the French Resistance during the war.* 在戰爭期間, 密特朗是法國抵抗運動的成員。

7 take the line of least resistance to do the easiest thing in a difficult situation 〔在困境中〕採取最簡便的方法

8 ▶EQUIPMENT 設備◀ [C] a RESISTOR 電阻器 —see also 另見 PASSIVE RESISTANCE

re·sis·tant /rɪˋzɪstənt; rɪˈzɪstənt/ *adj* **1** not damaged or affected by something 有抵抗力的, 抵抗…的: **[+to]** *This type of flu is resistant to antibiotics.* 這種流感對抗生素有抗藥力。**2** opposed to something and wanting to prevent it happening 抵制的, 反抗的, 抗拒的: **[+to]** *The Club is resistant to any form of change.* 該俱樂部反對任何形式的變革。**3 heat-resistant/fire-resistant** something that is heat-resistant etc will not be damaged by heat etc 耐熱的/耐火的

re·sis·tor /rɪˋzɪstɚ; rɪˈzɪstə/ *n* [C] a piece of wire or other material used for increasing electrical resistance 電阻器

re·sit /ˌriˋsɪt; ˌriːˈsɪt/ *v past tense and past participle* **resat**, *present participle* **resitting** [T] *especially BrE* to take an examination again 【尤英】重新參加考試, 補考 —**resit** /ˋrisɪt; ˈriːsɪt/ *n* [C]

re·skill·ing /ˌri ˋskɪlɪŋ; ˌri ˈskɪlɪŋ/ *n* [U] *BrE* the teaching of new work skills, especially to unemployed people 【英】〔尤指對失業者的〕再培訓

res·o·lute /ˋrɛzəˌlut; ˈrezəluːt/ *adj* doing something in a very determined way because you have very strong beliefs, aims etc 堅決的, 堅定的 —opposite 反義詞 IRRESOLUTE —**resolutely** *adv*: *She resolutely resisted his amorous advances.* 她堅決拒絕了他的追求。—**resoluteness** *n*

res·o·lu·tion /ˌrɛzəˋluʃən; ˌrezəˈluːʃən/ *n* 3

1 ▶DECISION 決定◀ [C] a formal decision or statement agreed on by a group of people, especially after a vote 決議, 決定: *The resolution was passed by a two-thirds majority.* 該決議得到三分之二多數通過。

2 ▶SOLUTION 解決◀ [singular,U] the act of finding a way to deal with a difficulty 解決: *The lawyer's advice led to the resolution of this problem.* 律師的忠告使這個問題得以解決。

3 ▶DETERMINATION 決心◀ [U] *approving* the quality of having strong beliefs and determination 【褒】堅決, 堅定, 決心

4 ▶PROMISE 諾言◀ [C] a promise to yourself to do something 〔做事的〕決心: **make a resolution** *Carol made a resolution to work hard at school this year.* 卡羅爾下決心今年要用功學習。| **New Year's resolution** (=a resolution made on January 1st) 新年時下的決心 *a New Year's resolution to stop smoking* 新年時下決心戒煙 —compare 比較 RESOLVE[2]

5 ▶CLEARNESS 清晰◀ [C,U] the power of a television, camera, MICROSCOPE etc to give a clear picture of things, or a measure of this 〔電視、照相機、顯微鏡的〕清晰度, 分辨率: *a high resolution microscope* 高分辨率顯微鏡

re·solve[1] /rɪˋzɑlv; rɪˈzɒlv/ *v* **1** [T] to find a satisfactory 3
way of dealing with a problem or difficulty; settle 解決: *negotiations to resolve the dispute* 解決爭端的談判 | *There weren't enough beds, but the matter was resolved by George sleeping on the sofa.* 牀不夠用, 但喬治睡到沙發上問題就解決了。**2** [I,T] to make a definite decision to do something 下決心, 決定: **resolve to do sth** *After the divorce she resolved never to marry again.* 離婚以後, 她下決心永不再嫁。| **resolve that** *Mary resolved that she would try to work harder.* 瑪麗決心更加努力工作。**3** [I,T] to make a formal decision, especially by voting 〔尤指投票〕作出決議: **resolve to do sth** *The Senate resolved to accept the President's budget proposals by 70 votes to 30.* 參議院以70票對30票通過決

議, 同意總統的預算草案。**4** [T] to separate something into its different parts 分解, 使解體

resolve sth **into** sth *phr v* [T] **1** *technical* to separate or become separated into parts【術語】把…分解為…: *This mixture will resolve into two separate compounds.* 這個混合物將分解成兩種不同的化合物。**2 resolve itself into** to gradually change into something else; become 演變成: *The argument resolved itself into an uneasy truce.* 辯論停息了, 但很可能再爆發。

resolve[2] *n* [U] *formal* strong determination to succeed in doing something【正式】決心, 決意: *His encouragement and support strengthened our resolve.* 他的鼓勵和支持加強了我們的決心。

res·o·nance /ˋrɛzn̩əns; ˈrezənəns/ *n* **1** [U] the deep, loud, continuing quality of a sound 嘹亮; 洪亮: *the resonance of his voice* 他洪亮的嗓音 **2** [C,U] *formal* the special meaning that something has for you because it is connected with your own experiences【正式】〔親身經歷引起的〕共鳴 **3** [C,U] *technical* sound that is produced or increased in an object by sound waves from another object【術語】共鳴, 共振, 諧振

res·o·nant /ˋrɛzn̩ənt; ˈrezənənt/ *adj* **1** a resonant sound is deep, loud, clear, and continues for a long time〔聲音〕洪亮的, 回蕩的 **2 resonant with** filled with a particular sound 充滿…聲音的: *The air was resonant with the shouts of children.* 空中回響着孩子們的叫喊聲。**3** *technical* resonant materials increase any sound produced inside them【術語】共鳴的, 共振的 —**resonantly** *adv*

res·o·nate /ˋrɛzəˌnet; ˈrezəneɪt/ *v* [I] **1** to make a deep, loud, clear sound that continues for a long time 發出洪亮的聲音 **2** to make a sound that is produced as a reaction to another sound 產生共鳴, 共振

resonate with sth *phr v* [T] **1** *formal* to be full of a particular meaning or feeling【正式】充滿〔含義或感覺〕: *literature that resonates with biblical imagery* 充滿聖經意象的文學作品 **2** to be full of a sound 回響着: *a hall resonating with laughter* 笑聲蕩漾的大廳

res·o·na·tor /ˋrɛzəˌnetɚ; ˈrezəneɪtə/ *n* [C] a piece of equipment for making the sound louder in a musical instrument 共鳴器, 共振器

[W3] **re·sort[1]** /rɪˋzɔrt; rɪˈzɔːt/ *n* **1** [C] a place where people often go for holidays 度假勝地: **seaside/beach/mountain etc resort** *a seaside resort south of Tokyo* 東京以南的一個海濱度假勝地 | **resort hotel/beach/town** *Jan and Matt run a small resort hotel in Vermont.* 簡和馬特在佛蒙特州經營一家小型度假旅館。**2 as a last resort/in the last resort** used to say what you will do if everything else fails〔一切都失敗後〕作為最後的手段: *As a last resort we could borrow more money on the house.* 實在沒有別的辦法, 我們可以用房子抵押多借些錢。| **of last resort** (=used when everything else has failed) 最後一招 *a weapon of last resort* 最後使出的武器 **3 have resort to** *formal* to do something bad or extreme because you cannot think of any other solution【正式】〔不得已時〕訴諸〔壞的或極端的辦法〕: *It may be necessary to have resort to force.* 訴諸武力可能是必要的。**4** [C] *AmE* a hotel for people on holiday【美】度假旅館

resort[2] *v*

resort to sth *phr v* [T] to use something or do something that is bad, in order to succeed or deal with a problem 採取, 訴諸〔不好的事物〕: *When polite requests failed Paul resorted to threats.* 客氣的請求不起作用時, 保羅便採取威脅。| **resort to doing sth** *Sally resorted to stealing when her money ran out.* 莎利的錢用完了就去偷竊。

re·sound /rɪˋzaund; rɪˈzaʊnd/ *v* [I] **1** if a place resounds with a sound it is full of it; ECHO[1] (2)〔地方〕回蕩着聲音, 回響: **[+with/to]** *The hall resounded with laughter and cheering.* 大廳裡充滿了笑聲和歡呼聲。**2** if a sound such as a musical note resounds, it continues loudly and clearly for quite a long time〔聲音〕鳴響, 回蕩: **[+through/around etc]** *a horn resounding through the forest* 響徹森林的號角聲

re·sound·ing /rɪˋzaundɪŋ; rɪˈzaʊndɪŋ/ *adj* **1** [only before noun 僅用於名詞前] a resounding noise is so loud that it seems to continue for a few seconds 洪亮的, 回響的: *The vase fell to the floor with a resounding crash.* 花瓶掉到地板上, 鏗然一聲摔碎了。**2 resounding success/victory/defeat etc** a very great or complete success etc, that many people know about 巨大的成功/勝利/失敗等: *The show, Five Guys Named Moe, was a resounding success.*《五個名叫莫的人》這齣戲取得巨大成功。—**resoundingly** *adv*

re·source[1] /ˋrisɔrs; rɪˈzɔːs/ *n* [S2] [W1]

1 ►OIL/COAL ETC 石油/煤等◄ [C often plural 常用複數] something such as land, minerals, or natural energy that exists in a country and can be used to increase its wealth 資源: *Canada's vast mineral resources* 加拿大豐富的礦產資源 | **natural resources** *a country rich in natural resources* 自然資源豐富的國家

2 ►MONEY/PROPERTY ETC 錢/財產等◄ **resources** [plural] all the money, property, skills etc that you have available 物力, 財力; 資源: *We must make the best possible use of our limited financial resources.* 我們必須盡可能充分地利用有限的財力。| *resources for research and development* 研究與開發的資源 | **pool your resources** (=put together all the resources that each of you can provide) 集中所有資源

3 ►PERSONAL QUALITIES 個人素質◄ **resources** [plural] personal qualities, such as courage and a strong mind, that you need to deal with a difficult situation〔對付困境所需的〕個人素質: **inner resources** *Martin has inner resources that will see him through this crisis.* 馬丁是有內涵的人, 能渡過這次危機。—see also 另見 HUMAN RESOURCES

4 ►EDUCATIONAL 教育的◄ [C] something such as a book, film, or picture used by teachers or students to provide information 資料, 〔教學〕資源: *resources for learning* 學習資料 | *a valuable new computer resource* 有價值的新的電腦資料 | **resource room/centre etc** (=a room, building etc where resources are kept) 資料室/中心等

5 ►PRACTICAL ABILITY 實際能力◄ [U] *formal* ability in dealing with practical problems; RESOURCEFULNESS【正式】機智, 應變能力: *a man of great resource* 足智多謀的人

re·source[2] /riˋsɔrs; rɪˈzɔːs/ *v* [T] *technical* to provide money or other resources for something【術語】向…提供資源: *The program failed because it wasn't adequately resourced.* 由於資源不足, 計劃失敗了。

re·source·ful /rɪˋsɔrsfəl; rɪˈzɔːsfəl/ *adj approving* good at finding ways of dealing with practical problems【褒】足智多謀的, 機智的: *a resourceful woman who could cope in almost any circumstances* 幾乎任何局面都能夠應付的足智多謀的女人 —**resourcefully** *adv* —**resourcefulness** *n* [U]

re·spect[1] /rɪˋspɛkt; rɪˈspekt/ *n* [S1] [W1]

1 ►ADMIRATION 欽佩◄ [U] admiration for someone, especially because of their personal qualities, knowledge or skill 尊敬, 敬重: **[+for]** *I have the greatest respect for Jane's judgment.* 我非常欽佩簡的眼光。| **win/earn/gain the respect of** *With his decisive handling of the dispute, he had won the respect of everyone.* 由於果斷處理了糾紛, 他贏得了大家的尊敬。| **command the respect of** (=have and deserve someone's respect) 受到並值得尊敬 *Dr Weiss commands the respect of all who know him.* 所有認識威斯博士的人都對他非常尊敬。—opposite 反義詞 DISRESPECT

2 with (the greatest) respect/with (all) due respect *spoken formal* used to politely introduce an expression of disagreement【口, 正式】儘管我尊敬你〔用於禮貌地表示不同意見〕: *With respect, sir, I think you're quite wrong.* 先生, 我認為您完全錯了, 這樣說毫無不敬之意。

3 ►CONSIDERATION 考慮◄ [U] an attitude of regarding

R

something or someone as important so that you are careful not to harm them, treat them rudely etc 考慮; 顧及; 重視: [+**for**] *Out of respect for the wishes of her family, the affair was not reported in the newspapers.* 考慮到她家人的意願, 此事沒有在報上披露。| *children who show no respect for authority* 不尊重權威的孩子 | **treat sb/sth with respect** *Old people deserve to be treated with more respect.* 尊老敬老, 理所當然。

4 ►FOR DANGER 對於危險◄ [U] a careful attitude towards something or someone that is dangerous 謹慎, 小心: [+**for**] *Forbes has always shown a healthy respect for the treacherous currents of the Yangtze.* 福布斯一貫對長江變幻莫測的水流採取恰當的謹慎態度。

5 in one respect/in some respects/in every respect used to say that something is true in one way, in some ways, or in every way 在某個/某些/所有方面: *In many respects the new version is not so good as the old one.* 新版本在許多方面不如舊版本。| *Aunt Arabella is very stubborn. Kim takes after her in that respect.* 阿拉貝拉姨媽非常固執。基姆在這方面很像她。

6 ►GREETINGS 問候◄ **respects** [plural] *formal* polite greetings【正式】敬意; 問候: **give/send your respects** *Give my respects to your wife.* 請代我問候嫂夫人。| **pay your respects** (=make a polite visit) 拜訪 *I've come to pay my respects to the countess.* 我來向伯爵夫人請安。

7 pay your last respects (to) to go to someone's funeral 向〔死者〕告別, 參加...的喪禮

8 in respect of *formal*【正式】**a)** concerning or in relation to 關於, 有關: *This is especially true in respect of the United Kingdom.* 英國的情況尤其如此。**b)** an expression meaning in payment for, used in business letters 作為...的報酬〔尤用於商業信函中〕: *The builder will be paid £300 in respect of the work already done.* 將付給建築商300英鎊, 作為對已完成工程的報酬。

9 with respect to *formal* used to introduce a new subject, or to return to one that has already been mentioned【正式】關於, 談到〔用於另起一個話題或回到談過的話題〕: *With respect to your other proposals, I am not yet able to give you our decision.* 至於你的其他建議, 我現在還無法告訴你我們的決定。—see also 另見 SELF-RESPECT

respect² *v* [T] **1** [not in progressive 不用進行式] to admire someone because they have high standards and good personal qualities such as fairness and honesty 尊敬, 敬佩, 敬重: *He's not the most popular teacher, but the students respect him.* 他不是最受歡迎的老師, 但學生都尊敬他。| *John had always respected Matthew's opinion.* 約翰一向尊重馬休的意見。| **respect sb for** *Molly always told us exactly what she thought, and we respected her for that.* 莫莉總是與我們坦誠相見, 我們為此敬佩她。**2** to be careful not to do anything against someone's wishes, rights etc 尊重; 顧及〔某人的意願、權利等〕: *I promise to respect your wishes.* 我保證尊重你的意願。| *The President is expected to respect the constitution.* 人們期望總統尊重憲法。

re·spec·ta·bil·i·ty /rɪˌspɛktəˈbɪlətɪ; rɪˌspektəˈbɪlɨti/ *n* [U] the quality of being considered morally correct and socially acceptable 可敬的品格, 得體, 體面: *The couple exuded an air of quiet respectability.* 這對夫婦神態沉靜, 舉止優雅得體。

re·spec·ta·ble /rɪˈspɛktəbl̩; rɪˈspektəbəl/ *adj* **1** having standards of behaviour, appearance etc that are socially acceptable and approved of〔行為、外觀等〕體面的, 可敬的; 正派的: *a respectable married woman* 一位正經的已婚婦人 | *nice children from respectable homes* 來自正派家庭的好孩子 | *Let's make you look a bit more respectable before you go out.* 讓我們把你打扮得更體面些你再出去。**2** *informal* good or satisfactory【非正式】好的; 令人滿意的: *a respectable income* 不錯的收入 | *Her exam results were respectable, although not brilliant.* 她的考試成績不錯, 儘管不優秀。—**respectably** *adv* —**respectableness** *n* [U]

re·spect·ed /rɪˈspɛktɪd; rɪˈspektɨd/ *adj* admired by many people because of your work, achievements etc 受尊敬的, 受敬重的: *a highly respected journalist* 深受尊敬的記者

re·spect·er /rɪˈspɛktɚ; rɪˈspektə/ *n* [C] **be no respecter of persons** to be equally harmful towards all people whether they are rich or poor, important or ordinary 對所有人一樣有害: *Disease is no respecter of persons.* 疾病面前人人平等。

re·spect·ful /rɪˈspɛktfəl; rɪˈspektfəl/ *adj* feeling or showing respect 有禮貌的, 恭敬的: *The soldiers bowed their heads in respectful silence as the funeral procession went by.* 葬禮隊伍經過時, 士兵都低頭默哀。—opposite 反義詞 DISRESPECTFUL —**respectfully** *adv* —**respectfulness** *n* [U]

re·spec·tive /rɪˈspɛktɪv; rɪˈspektɪv/ *adj* [only before noun 僅用於名詞前] people's respective jobs, houses, families etc are the various ones that each of them has 各自的: *The two friends said goodbye and went their respective ways.* 兩個朋友互相道別後分道而去。

re·spec·tive·ly /rɪˈspɛktɪvlɪ; rɪˈspektɪvli/ *adv* each separately in the order mentioned 各自地, 依次地: *My two sons, Adam and Alexander, are five and nine respectively.* 我的兩個兒子亞當和亞歷山大, 分別是五歲和九歲。 3

res·pi·ra·tion /ˌrɛspəˈreʃən; ˌrespɨˈreɪʃən/ *n* [U] *technical* the process of breathing【術語】呼吸 —see also 另見 ARTIFICIAL RESPIRATION

res·pi·ra·tor /ˈrɛspəˌretɚ; ˈrespɨreɪtə/ *n* [C] a piece of equipment that you wear over your nose and mouth to help you breathe in a place where there is gas, smoke etc 口罩; 防毒面具; 呼吸器

the human respiratory system 人體呼吸系統

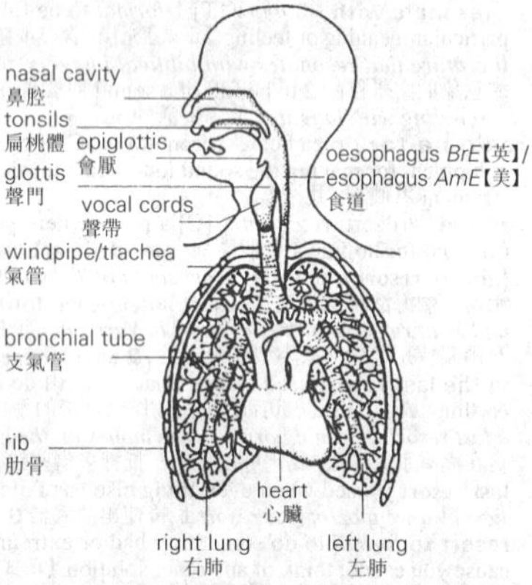

nasal cavity 鼻腔
tonsils 扁桃體
epiglottis 會厭
glottis 聲門
vocal cords 聲帶
windpipe/trachea 氣管
bronchial tube 支氣管
rib 肋骨
heart 心臟
right lung 右肺
left lung 左肺
oesophagus *BrE*【英】/ esophagus *AmE*【美】食道

re·spi·ra·to·ry /rɪˈspaɪrəˌtɔrɪ; rɪˈspɪrətəri/ *adj formal or technical* connected with breathing【正式或術語】與呼吸有關的; 呼吸道的: *respiratory diseases* 呼吸道疾病 | *the respiratory system* 呼吸系統

res·pite /ˈrɛspɪt; ˈrespɪt/ *n* [singular,U] **1** a short time when something unpleasant stops happening, so that the situation is temporarily better〔令人討厭的事情的〕暫息; 緩解: [+**from**] *a welcome respite from the constant pressure of work* 持續的工作壓力期間受歡迎的短暫休息 | **without respite** *The noise went on all night without even a moment's respite.* 吵鬧聲一刻不停地持續了一整夜。**2** a short period of delay before you have to do something that is unpleasant 暫緩: *We have a few days' respite before we need to pay the rent.* 我們還可以延遲幾天才交租金。

re·splen·dent /rɪˈsplɛndənt; rɪˈsplendənt/ *adj formal*

very beautiful, bright and shining in appearance【正式】華麗的; 輝煌的; 燦爛的: *the resplendent colours of the New England woods in the fall* 秋季新英格蘭樹林的瑰麗色彩 —**resplendence** *n* [U] —**resplendently** *adv*: *resplendently dressed in shimmering silk robes* 身着閃閃發光的華麗綢袍

re·spond /rɪˋspɑnd; rɪˈspɒnd/ *v* **1** [I] to react to something that has been said or done 反應, 回應: [+to] *Clive responded to my suggestion with a laugh.* 克利夫對我提的建議報以一笑。| **respond by doing sth** *The US responded by sending troops into Laos.* 美國的反應是派遣軍隊進入老撾。—see 見 ANSWER² (USAGE) **2** [I, T+that] to say or write something as a reply 答覆: *He responded that he would be pleased to attend.* 他回答說, 他很高興出席。| [+to] *No one has yet responded to our complaints.* 還沒有人對我們的投訴作出回覆。**3** [I] to improve as a result of a particular kind of treatment 有良好反應: [+to] *Her cancer failed to respond to treatment.* 治療對她的癌症沒起作用。| *Most children respond well to individual attention in class.* 在課堂上照顧到每個孩子對大多數兒童都有效。

re·spon·dent /rɪˋspɑndənt; rɪˈspɒndənt/ *n* [C] **1** *formal* someone who answers questions【正式】回答者, 答覆者 **2** *law* someone who has to defend their own case in a law court, especially in a DIVORCE case【法律】〔尤指離婚案的〕被告 —compare 比較 CO-RESPONDENT

re·sponse /rɪˋspɑns; rɪˈspɒns/ *n* **1** [C,U] something that is done as a reaction to something that has happened or been said 反應: *The attack provoked an angry response.* 攻擊引起憤怒的反應。| [+to] *a sympathetic response to our appeal for help* 對我們要求幫助的呼籲的反應積極 | **in response to** (=as a response to) 作為…的回應 *The law was passed in response to public pressure.* 在公眾壓力下該法規獲得通過。**2** [C] something that is said or written as a reply 回答: *His question failed to get a response from any of the students.* 沒有學生回答他提的問題。**3** [C] a part of a religious service that is spoken or sung by the people as an answer to a part that is spoken or sung by the priest〔宗教儀式上會眾同牧師〕輪流應答[吟唱]的祈禱文

re·spon·si·bil·i·ty /rɪˌspɑnsəˋbɪlətɪ; rɪˌspɒnsəˈbɪləti/ *n*
1 ►IN CHARGE 負責◄ [U] a duty to be in charge of or look after something, so that you make decisions and can be blamed if something bad happens 責任, 負責: *She was given promotion and more responsibility.* 她晉升了, 所負的責任也增加了。| **have responsibility for** *The Health Minister has overall responsibility for Britain's hospitals.* 衛生大臣全面負責英國的醫院。| **take responsibility for** (=agree to be in charge of something or someone) 對…負責 *My husband took full responsibility for organizing the trip.* 我丈夫全權負責組織這次旅行。| **assume responsibility for** (=agree to be in charge of) *formal*【正式】承擔…的責任 *Richard assumed responsibility for his brother's children.* 理查德承擔起照顧姪子姪女的責任。| **accept responsibility for** *The management accepts no responsibility for cars left in the car park.* 管理部門對留在停車場內的汽車不承擔責任。
2 ►DUTY 責任, 義務◄ [C] a duty that you have, especially because you are in charge of something 任務, 職責: *The head of a large company has many responsibilities.* 大公司的領導人負有很多責任。| **have a responsibility to do sth** *Every citizen has a responsibility to vote.* 每位公民都有投票的義務。| **it is sb's responsibility to do sth** *It is your responsibility to check that all doors and windows are locked.* 你的任務是查看所有的門窗是否都鎖好了。| **moral responsibility** (=a duty to do something because it is morally right) 道義責任
3 ►BLAME 責備◄ [U] blame for something bad that has happened〔對不良事件負的〕責任: **accept/take responsibility** *We refuse to accept responsibility for the breakdown of negotiations.* 我們拒絕承擔談判破裂的責任。
4 sense of responsibility an ability to behave sensibly so that you can be trusted to do the right thing 責任感: *Parents need to encourage a sense of responsibility in their children.* 家長必須培養孩子的責任感。
5 a responsibility to sb a duty to help or serve someone because of your work, position in society etc 對某人負有責任: *A doctor's first responsibility is to her patients.* 醫生首先要對病人負責。
6 do sth on your own responsibility to do something without being told to do it or officially allowed to do it 自行負責地做某事
7 claim responsibility (for) to officially state that you are the person or organization that did something, especially an act of TERRORISM (=violence in order to get political power) 聲稱對某事〔尤指恐怖行為〕負責

re·spon·si·ble /rɪˋspɑnsəbl̩; rɪˈspɒnsəbəl/ *adj*
1 ►GUILTY 有罪的◄ [not before noun 不用於名詞前] if someone is responsible for an accident, mistake, crime etc, it is their fault or they can be blamed〔對事故、錯誤、罪行等〕負有責任的, 應承擔責任的: [+for] *The police arrested those responsible for the burglaries.* 警察逮捕了那些盜竊犯。| *When he loses his temper, he isn't responsible for his actions.* 他發脾氣時不顧自己行為的後果。| *If any of the children got hurt, I should feel responsible.* 要是哪個孩子受了傷, 應該由我承擔責任。| **hold sb responsible (for)** (=blame someone for something) (因…) 怪罪某人 *I shall hold you personally responsible for anything that goes wrong.* 如果出甚麼差錯的話, 我將惟你是問。
2 ►IN CHARGE OF 負責◄ [not before noun 不用於名詞前] having a duty to be in charge of or to look after someone or something〔對某人、某事〕負責的: [+for] *Each commissioner is responsible for a department.* 每位委員負責一個部門。| *They're not my children, but I still feel responsible for them.* 他們不是我的孩子, 但我仍然覺得應對他們負責。
3 responsible job/position/post a job in which the ability to make good judgments and decisions is needed 要職
4 ►SENSIBLE 明智的◄ sensible and able to make good judgments so that you can be trusted 可信賴的, 可靠的: *You can leave the children with Stuart – he's very responsible.* 你可以把孩子留給斯圖爾特, 他非常可靠。—opposite 反義詞 IRRESPONSIBLE
5 be responsible to if you are responsible to someone, that person is in charge of your work and you must explain your actions to them 對〔某人〕負責: *In the US, cabinet members are directly responsible to the president.* 在美國, 內閣成員直接對總統負責。
6 ►CAUSE 起因◄ if something is responsible for a change, problem, event etc, it causes it 作為原由的: [+for] *Social changes are responsible for many of our modern problems.* 社會變革是引起我們許多現代問題的原因。

re·spon·si·bly /rɪˋspɑnsəblɪ; rɪˈspɒnsəbli/ *adv* in a sensible way which makes people trust you 負責地, 可靠地: *Can I rely on you to behave responsibly while I'm away?* 我外出時你要規規矩矩, 我可以信賴你嗎?

re·spon·sive /rɪˋspɑnsɪv; rɪˈspɒnsɪv/ *adj* **1** ready to react in a useful or helpful way 關心的; 積極的: [+to] *We try to be responsive to the needs of the customer.* 我們努力去滿足顧客的需求。**2** easily controlled, and reacting quickly in the way that you want 易操縱的; 反應快的; 靈敏的: *a car with very responsive steering* 方向盤操縱靈活的汽車 | *The disease is not proving responsive to treatment.* 這種病的療法都不奏效。**3** willing to give answers or show your feelings about something 積極回應的: *I tried to get him talking but he wasn't very responsive.* 我試圖讓他講話, 但他不太願意發表意見。—**responsively** *adv* —**responsiveness** *n* [U] —opposite 反義詞 UNRESPONSIVE

re·spray /ˌriˋspre; ˌriːˈspreɪ/ *v* [T] to change the colour of a car by putting new paint on it 給〔汽車〕重噴油漆 —**respray** /ˋrispre; ˈriːspreɪ/ *n* [C]

R

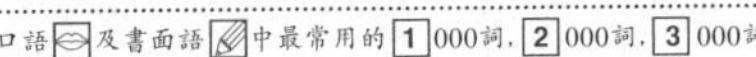

1 1 **rest¹** /rɛst; rest/ *n*

1 the rest what is left after everything else has been used, dealt with, killed etc 剩餘部分; 餘下的人[物]: *I got half way through reciting the poem and couldn't remember the rest.* 我背詩背到一半, 餘下的部分想不起來了。| *At least four of the enemy were killed and the rest fled.* 至少四個敵人被擊斃, 其餘的逃跑了。| **[+of]** *He'll be in a wheelchair for the rest of his life.* 他的餘生將在輪椅上度過。

2 ►RELAXING 放鬆◄ [C,U] a period of time when you are not doing anything tiring and you can relax or sleep 休息(時間): *The doctor says I need complete rest.* 醫生說我需要徹底休息。| *You'll feel much better after a good night's rest.* 好好睡上一晚後你會感覺好得多。| **have/take a rest** *You must be tired. Why don't you take a rest?* 你一定累了, 為甚麼不休息? | **well-earned rest** (=rest that you deserve because you have been working hard)〔辛勤勞動後〕應該享受的休息

3 put/set sb's mind at rest to make someone feel less anxious or worried 使某人放心: *I managed to set his mind at rest about my safety.* 我終於讓他不再為我的安全擔心。

4 come to rest a) to stop moving 停住: *The car braked sharply, coming to rest on the edge of the cliff.* 汽車猛地刹住, 停在懸崖邊上。**b)** if your eyes come to rest on something, you stop looking around and look at that one thing〔目光〕停留

5 give it a rest! *BrE spoken* used to tell someone to stop talking about something because they are annoying you【英口】安靜一下!〔用於因受到煩擾而叫對方停止說話〕: *Oh, give it a rest! I don't want to hear about your job!* 好啦, 別煩了! 我不想聽你談你的工作!

6 at rest a) *technical* not moving【術語】靜止的: *Measure the mass of an object at rest.* 測量物體在靜止時的質量。**b)** an expression meaning dead, used to avoid upsetting someone 安息〔委婉語〕: *He now lies at rest in the churchyard.* 他現在長眠在教堂墓地裡。

7 lay/put sth to rest to get rid of a false idea or belief by showing that it is not true 揭穿真相從而制止某事〔謬誤等〕: *At last these dangerous rumours have been put to rest.* 這些危險的謠傳終於被制止了。

8 and all the rest of it *BrE spoken* used at the end of a short list to mean other things of a similar type【英口】諸如此類, 不一而足: *They accused me of being unreliable, irresponsible, and all the rest of it.* 他們指責我不可靠、不負責任等等。

9 for the rest *BrE* used to introduce a short final remark at the end of a speech or piece of writing【英】至於其他, 至於其餘的(情況): *For the rest, we can only guess the effect of these changes.* 至於後事如何, 我們只能猜測這些變革產生的影響。

10 and the rest! *BrE spoken* used to emphasize in a humorous way that a number or amount is really much higher than someone thinks【英口】不止吧!: *"I'd say she's about 40." "Yeah, and the rest!"* "我說她40歲上下。" "噢, 不止吧!"

11 lay sb to rest an expression meaning to bury someone, used when you want to avoid saying this directly 安葬某人〔委婉語〕: *She was laid to rest in the graveyard behind the church.* 她被安葬在教堂後面的墓地中。

12 ►IN MUSIC 在音樂中◄ [C] **a)** a period of silence of a particular length in a piece of music〔音樂作品中的〕休止 **b)** a written sign that shows how long the period of silence should be 休止符

13 ►SUPPORT 支撐物◄ [C] a support that you can rest your arm, head etc on〔可供擱放胳膊、頭等的〕撐架, 托, 墊

3 3 **rest²** *v*

1 ►RELAX 放鬆◄ [I] to stop working or doing an activity for a time and sit down or lie down to relax 休息, 歇息: *If you're tired, we'll stop and rest for a while.* 如果你累了, 我們就停下來歇一會兒。

2 rest your feet/legs/eyes etc to stop using a part of your body because it is feeling sore or tired 歇歇腳/腿/眼睛等

3 ►GIVE SUPPORT 給予支撐◄ [T always+adv/prep] to support an object or part of your body by putting it on or against something 使依靠, 使得到支撐: **rest sth against/on etc** *Rest your head on my shoulder.* 把你的頭靠在我肩上。

4 ►LIE/LEAN ON 倚靠◄ [I always+adv/prep] to lie or lean on something for support 擱; 倚, 靠: **[+against/on etc]** *The ladder rested against the wall.* 梯子靠着牆。| *She sat with her elbows resting on the table.* 她坐着, 胳膊肘放在桌上。

5 let the matter rest also 又作 **let it rest** to stop discussing or dealing with something 不再討論[辦理]某事: *We could go on arguing but I think we'd better let the matter rest.* 我們可以爭論下去, 但我認為我們最好別再討論這個問題了。

6 rest assured (that) *formal* used to tell someone not to worry, because what you say about a situation is true【正式】請放心: *You can rest assured that I will never tell anyone.* 你儘管放心, 我絕不會告訴任何人。

7 will not rest until if you will not rest until something happens, you will not be satisfied until it happens 直到…才罷休: *We will not rest until the murderer is found.* 找不到兇手我們決不罷休。

8 ►LIE BURIED 安葬◄ [I always+adv/prep] a word meaning to lie buried, used when you do not want to say this directly 長眠〔委婉用語〕: *My mother rests beside my father in the family graveyard.* 我母親在家族墓地裡長眠在我父親身邊。| **last/final resting place** (=the place where someone is buried) 長眠之處 *He decided Rome, where he had been so happy, would be his final resting place.* 他選擇羅馬這個他曾經度過快樂時光的地方作為自己日後的長眠之地。| **rest in peace** (=often written on a grave) 安息〔常刻在墓碑上〕

9 rest on your laurels to be satisfied with what you have done, so that you do not make any further effort 滿足於既得的成就, 吃老本, 不再求進步

10 I rest my case *spoken*【口】**a)** *formal* used by a lawyer when they have finished trying to prove something in a court of law【正式】本人停止舉證; 本人對案情陳述完畢〔律師出庭用語〕**b)** *humorous* used when something happens or is said which proves that you were right【幽默】我講夠了; 還用我多說嗎〔表示發生的事或所說的話證明是正確的〕

rest on/upon sth *phr v* [T not in progressive 不用進行式] **1** *formal* to depend on or be based on something【正式】依賴; 以…為依據: *Success in management ultimately rests on good judgment.* 管理的成功最終依靠正確的判斷。**2** if your eyes rest on something, you look at it〔目光〕落在…上

rest with sb *phr v* [T not in progressive 不用進行式] if a decision rests with someone, they are responsible for it 由〔某人〕負責: *The final decision rests with the President.* 得由總統作最後的決定。

rest a·rea /ˈ· ,··/ *n* [C] *especially AmE* a place near a road where you can stop and rest, go to the toilet etc【尤美】〔公路旁的〕休息站

re·state /riˋstet; ˌriːˈsteɪt/ *v* [T] to say something again in a different way, so that it is clearer or more strongly expressed〔換一種方式〕重說: *He restated the question.* 他換個方式把問題重說了一遍。—**restatement** *n* [C,U]

res·tau·rant /ˋrɛstərənt; ˈrestərɒnt/ *n* [C] a place where you can buy and eat a meal 飯店, 餐館: *an expensive fish restaurant* 價格昂貴的魚餚餐館 3 2

restaurant car /ˈ··· ,·/ *n* [C] a carriage on a train where meals are served; DINING CAR〔火車的〕餐車

res·tau·ra·teur /ˌrɛstərəˋtɝ; ˌrestərəˈtɜː/ also 又作 **res·tau·ran·teur** /ˌrɛstərɑnˋtɝ; ˌrestərɒnˈtɜː/ *n* [C] someone who owns and manages a restaurant〔親自管理餐館的〕餐館老闆, 飯店主人

rest·ed /ˋrɛstɪd; ˈrestɪd/ *adj* [not before noun 不用於名

詞前] feeling healthier, stronger, or calmer because you have had time to relax〔休息之後感到〕精神的; 有精力的; 清醒的: *We came back feeling rested and ready for work.* 我們回來時感到精力充沛, 準備隨時投入工作。

rest·ful /ˋrɛstfəl; ˈrestfəl/ *adj* peaceful and quiet, making you feel relaxed 平靜的, 悠閒的: *restful music* 悠閒的音樂 —**restfully** *adv*

rest home /ˋ· ·/ *n* [C] a place where old or sick people can live and be looked after〔老人或病人的〕療養所

res·ti·tu·tion /ˌrɛstəˋtuʃən; ˌrestəˈtjuːʃən/ *n* [U] *formal* the act of giving back something that was lost or stolen to its owner, or of paying for damage【正式】歸還, 賠償: **make restitution** *The court ordered him to make full restitution to the family.* 法院命令他全數賠償給那家人。

res·tive /ˋrɛstɪv; ˈrestɪv/ *adj* unable to keep still, especially because you are impatient or bored 不安寧的, 焦躁不安的, 煩躁的: *The children were becoming restive from sitting at the dinner table so long.* 孩子們在飯桌邊坐得太久, 開始坐不住了。—**restively** *adv* —**restiveness** *n* [U]

rest·less /ˋrɛstlɪs; ˈrestləs/ *adj* **1** unable or unwilling to keep still, especially because you are nervous or bored〔尤指因緊張或沉悶〕煩躁的, 不耐煩的: *The children had been indoors all day and were getting restless.* 孩子們在屋內呆了一整天, 開始煩躁不安。**2** unwilling to stay in one place, and always wanting new experiences 呆不住的, 求變的: *After a few weeks in Marseille, I grew restless and decided to take a ship to Corsica.* 在馬賽呆了幾週後, 我開始呆不住了, 決定乘船去科西嘉。**3 restless night** a night during which you cannot sleep or rest 不眠之夜 —**restlessly** *adv* —**restlessness** *n* [U]

re·stock /riˋstɑk; ˌriːˈstɒk/ *v* [I,T+**with**] to bring in more supplies to replace those that have been used〔為…〕補充貨物; 備辦新貨

res·to·ra·tion /ˌrɛstəˋreʃən; ˌrestəˈreɪʃən/ *n* [C,U] **1** the act of thoroughly repairing something such as an old building or a piece of furniture so that it looks the same as it did when it was first made〔舊建築、家具的〕修復: *a fund for the restoration of historic buildings* 歷史建築的修復基金 **2** the act of bringing back a law, tax, or system of government〔法律、稅收、政體的〕重新採用, 恢復: [+**of**] *They're fighting for the restoration of democratic rights.* 他們正在為恢復民主權利而鬥爭。| *the restoration of the monarchy in Spain* 西班牙君主政體的復辟 **3 the Restoration** the return of Charles II to become King of England in 1660, and the period afterwards 王政復辟 (時期)〔1660年英王查理二世復辟及其後的一段時期〕: **Restoration comedy/drama** (=plays written during this time in England) 王政復辟時期的喜劇/戲劇 **4** the act of officially giving something back to its former owner (正式) 歸還: *an attempt to secure the restoration of their lands* 使他們的土地得以歸還的努力

re·sto·ra·tive¹ /rɪˋstɔrətɪv; rɪˈstɔːrətɪv/ *adj formal* making you feel healthier or stronger【正式】恢復健康[體力]的: *the restorative power of long walks* 長距離步行使人恢復健康的效力

restorative² *n* [C] *humorous* a drink, especially an alcoholic one, that makes you feel better【幽默】飲料〔尤指酒等令人舒暢的飲料〕

3 **re·store** /rɪˋstor; rɪˈstɔː/ *v* [T]

1 ▶FORMER SITUATION 以前的狀態◀ to make something return to its former level or condition 恢復: *So far all attempts to restore normal relations between the two countries have failed.* 迄今為止, 所有試圖恢復兩國正常關係的努力都失敗了。| **restore sth to sth** *The government promises to restore the economy to full strength.* 政府承諾使經濟完全恢復。

2 restore hope/confidence/calm etc to make a person or group feel hopeful, confident, calm etc again 恢復希望/信心/鎮靜等: *a victory that restored the team's confidence* 使球隊恢復了信心的一場勝利

3 restore order to make people stop fighting and breaking the law 恢復秩序: *Police were called in to restore order.* 警察被召來恢復秩序。

4 ▶REPAIR 修理◀ to repair an old building, piece of furniture, or painting etc so that it is in its original condition 修復: *The church was carefully restored after the war.* 戰後教堂得到精心修復。

5 ▶GIVE STH BACK 歸還某物◀ *formal* to give back to someone something that was lost or taken from them【正式】歸還: **restore sth to sb** *In 1972 a treaty restored Okinawa to Japan.* 1972年, 沖繩根據一份條約歸還給日本。

6 restore sb's sight/hearing etc to make someone able to see, hear etc again 恢復某人的視力/聽力等: *an operation to restore his hearing* 使他恢復聽力的手術

7 ▶BRING BACK A LAW 恢復法律◀ to bring back a law, tax, right etc 恢復, 重新採用〔法律、稅收、權利等〕: *a campaign to restore the death penalty* 鼓吹恢復死刑的運動

8 restore sb to power/the throne *formal* to give back power to a king, queen, or president【正式】使某人重新掌權/恢復王位

re·stored /rɪˋstord; rɪˈstɔːd/ *adj* [not before noun 不用於名詞前] feeling better and healthier 精神得到恢復的: *restored by the mountain freshness* 呼吸山間的清新空氣, 令人心曠神怡

re·strain /rɪˋstren; rɪˈstreɪn/ *v* [T] **1** to prevent someone from doing something harmful or stupid 阻止, 抑制〔某人做有害或愚蠢的事〕: **restrain sb from doing sth** *I had to restrain her from running out into the street after him.* 我不得不阻止她跑到街上去追他。| **restrain yourself (from)** *She could hardly restrain herself from hitting Walt.* 她幾乎克制不住自己, 要去揍沃爾特。**2** to control or limit something that is tending to increase 控制, 限制〔趨於增長的東西〕: *Price rises restrain consumer spending.* 價格上漲限制了消費開支。

re·strained /rɪˋstrend; rɪˈsteɪnd/ *adj* **1** behaviour that is restrained is calm and controlled and does not show your real feelings〔行為〕克制的, 有節制的: *a restrained and cool-headed response to their unfair criticisms* 對他們那些不公正的批評所作的克制而又冷靜的反應 **2** not too brightly coloured or decorated〔顏色或裝飾〕淡雅的, 樸素的: *The decor was subtle and restrained.* 佈置精巧而素雅。

re·straint /rɪˋstrent; rɪˈstreɪnt/ *n* **1** [U] the ability not to do something that you very much want to do, because you know it is more sensible not to do it 克制, 抑制〔指理智地抑制做某事的衝動〕: *The police were commended for their restraint in handling the disturbances.* 警方因為在處理騷亂事件中表現出的克制而受到嘉獎。| **show/exercise restraint** *I think he showed great restraint, considering how she treated him.* 考慮到她對待他的態度, 我認為他表現出極大的克制。**2** [C usually plural 一般用複數,U] a rule or principle that limits people's activity or behaviour 限制, 制約, 約束: [+**on**] *restraints on public spending* 對公共開支的限制 | *moral restraints on sexual behaviour* 對性行為的道德約束 | **impose restraints** (=make rules to control something) 加以限制 *The government imposed restraints on the export of military hardware.* 政府對軍事裝備出口實施限制。| **wage restraint** (=agreement not to demand or pay large wage increases) 工資增長限制 **3** [U] *formal* physical force used to stop someone from moving freely, especially because they are likely to be violent【正式】管制, 管束: *the proper use of physical restraint to control dangerous prisoners* 適當使用人身管制以控制危險囚犯 **4** [C] a SEAT BELT〔汽車座椅上的〕安全帶

re·strict /rɪˋstrɪkt; rɪˈstrɪkt/ *v* [T] 

1 ▶SIZE/AMOUNT/RANGE 體積/數量/範圍◀ to limit or control the size, amount, or range of something 限制; 控制: *The new law restricts the sale of hand guns.* 新法規限制了手槍的銷售。| **restrict sth to** *The speaker* *restricted her remarks to* (=only talked about) *the health care proposals.* 發言者只談了有關醫療保健的一些建議。

2 ►MOVEMENT/ACTIVITY 運動/活動◄ to limit someone's actions or movements 約束, 限制〔行動、活動〕: *The cramped living conditions severely restricted the children's opportunities for play.* 擁擠的居住條件嚴重限制了孩子遊戲的機會。

3 restrict yourself to to allow yourself to have only a particular amount of something, or do only a particular type of activity 限制自己…: *I'm restricting myself to two cigarettes a day.* 我限制自己每天只抽兩支煙。| *Journalists should restrict themselves to reporting the facts.* 記者應該只報道事實真相。

re·strict·ed /rɪˋstrɪktɪd; rɪˈstrɪktᵻd/ *adj* **1** small or limited in size, area, or amount 狹小的; 有限的: *It's difficult trying to work in such a restricted space.* 要在這麼狹窄的空間工作很困難。**2** limited or controlled, especially by laws or rules〔尤指在法律或規則上〕受限制的, 受約束的: *Press freedom is severely restricted.* 新聞自由受到嚴重限制。| **[+to]** *The sale of alcohol is restricted to* (=can only be sold to) *people over the age of 18.* 酒類僅限出售給18歲以上的人。| *restricted access for large vehicles* 大型車輛限制進入 **3** limited in what you can do, or in your movements〔活動、行動〕受限制的: *A stroke left her with restricted movement in her right leg.* 中風使她的右腿行動不便。| **restricted life** (=limited in your experiences) 生活範圍狹窄 *Many women lead very restricted lives, staying at home and bringing up children.* 許多婦女呆在家裡撫養子女, 生活圈子很小。**4** a restricted area or document can only be seen or used by a particular group of people because it is secret or dangerous〔地區或文件〕限某一類人使用[傳閱]的: *No Entry – restricted area for army personnel only.* 非軍事人員不得入內。**5 be restricted to** to only affect a limited area, group etc 僅限於…: *The damage is restricted to the left side of the brain.* 損傷僅限於大腦左側。

2 **re·stric·tion** /rɪˋstrɪkʃən; rɪˈstrɪkʃən/ *n* **1** [C often plu-
3 ral 常用複數] a rule or system that limits or controls what you can do or what is allowed to happen 限制, 約束: **[+on]** *restrictions on immigration from Mexico into the US* 對從墨西哥移居美國實施的限制 | **impose/place restrictions on sth** *The 1986 law imposed new financial restrictions on private companies.* 1986年的法律對私營公司規定了新的財務限制。| **raise/lift a restriction** (=remove a restriction) 解除限制 *Speed restrictions were lifted once the roadworks were completed.* 道路施工一竣工便取消了(行車)速度限制。**2** [U] the act of restricting the size, amount, or range of something 限制

re·stric·tive /rɪˋstrɪktɪv; rɪˈstrɪktɪv/ *adj* tending to restrict your activity too much 限制(性)的, 約束(性)的: *restrictive trade legislation* 限制性貿易立法 | *Rimbaud found life in Charleville too restrictive.* 蘭波認為在沙勒維爾生活受到太多限制。

restrictive clause /·,·· ˈ·/ also 又作 **restrictive rel·a·tive clause** /·,·· ,··· ˈ·/ *n* [C] *technical* a part of a sentence that says which person or thing is meant. For example in 'the man who came to dinner', the phrase 'who came to dinner' is a restrictive clause.【術語】限定性子句[從句]〔又稱限制性關係子句[從句]。例如在 the man who came to dinner 中, who came to dinner 是個限定性從句〕

restrictive prac·ti·ces /·,·· ˈ···/ *n* [plural] **1** unreasonable limits that one TRADE UNION puts on the kind of work that members of other trade unions are allowed to do〔工會實行的〕排他限制 **2** an unfair trade agreement between companies that limits the amount of competition there is〔公司之間不公平的〕限制競爭協議

rest room /ˈ· ·/ *n* [C] *AmE* a room with a toilet, in a place such as a restaurant or cinema【美】〔餐館、電影院等中的〕洗手間

re·struc·ture /ˌriˋstrʌktʃɚ; ˌriːˈstrʌktʃə/ *v* [T] to change the way in which something such as a government, business, or system is organized 重新組織, 調整, 改組: *The school curriculum has been restructured to include more science.* 學校課程進行了調整, 加進更多自然科學的內容。

re·sult¹ /rɪˋzʌlt; rɪˈzʌlt/ *n* 1
1 ►HAPPENING BECAUSE OF STH 因為某事而發生◄ 1
[C,U] something that happens or exists because of something that happened before 結果, 後果: **[+of]** *One result of the cold weather has been a sharp increase in our heating bill.* 寒冷天氣的結果之一是我們的暖氣費用大大增加了。| *Ken's illness is the result of an accident at work.* 肯的病是一次工傷事故造成的。| **as a result (of)** (=because of something that has happened) 作為…的結果; 由於 *As a result of the pilots' strike, all flights have had to be cancelled.* 由於飛行員罷工, 所有航班都取消了。| **with the result that** *Sara wasn't at school last week, with the result that she missed an important test.* 薩拉上星期沒上學, 結果錯過了一次重要考試。| **be a direct result (of)** (=caused by one thing only) 是…的直接結果 *High unemployment is a direct result of the recession.* 高失業率是經濟衰退的直接後果。| **end/final/net result** (=the result at the end of a long process) 最終結果 *The net result of all these changes is that people will pay more tax.* 所有這些變化的最後結果是人們將交更多的稅。—see 見 THUS (USAGE)

2 ►SPORTS/ELECTIONS 體育運動/選舉◄ [C] the final number of points, votes etc at the end of a competition, game, or election〔比賽〕成績, 比分;〔選舉的〕結果: *The election results were announced at midnight.* 選舉結果已於午夜宣布。| *the football results* 足球比賽的結果

3 ►SCIENTIFIC TESTS 科學測試◄ [C] the answers that are produced by a scientific study or test〔科學研究、測試的〕結果: *Results show that men are twice as likely to suffer from stress as women.* 結果顯示男性承受壓力的可能性比女性高出一倍。| *We should have the result of your blood test tomorrow.* 明天我們該有你驗血的結果了。

4 ►EXAMINATIONS 考試◄ [C] *BrE* the mark you get in an examination【英】成績: *When do we get our exam results?* 我們甚麼時候知道考試成績?

5 ►SUCCESS 成功◄ **results** [plural] things that happen successfully because of your efforts 成效: **get results** (=succeed in getting what you want) 取得成效 *If the program doesn't get results, it should be dropped.* 如果這計劃不見成效就應該放棄。

6 ►BUSINESS 生意◄ **results** [plural] a company's results are the accounts that show how successful it has been over a period of time, usually a year〔年度〕業績

7 get a result *BrE informal* to win a victory in a sports match【英, 非正式】〔在體育比賽中〕贏, 取勝: *We didn't play well but at least we got a result.* 我們打得不好, 但至少我們贏了。

result² *v* [I] to happen or exist as a result of something 3
〔因…〕產生, 發生;〔由…而〕造成: **[+from]** *problems resulting from past errors* 由於以往的過失而造成的問題

result in sth *phr v* [T not in passive 不用被動態] to make something happen; cause 導致, 造成: *an accident that resulted in the death of two passengers* 導致兩名乘客死亡的事故

re·sul·tant /rɪˋzʌltənt; rɪˈzʌltənt/ *adj* [only before noun 僅用於名詞前] *formal* happening or existing as a result of something【正式】作為…的後果而發生[存在]的: *a growing economy and its resultant benefits* 增長中的經濟以及由此帶來的效益

re·sume¹ /rɪˋzum; rɪˈzjuːm/ *v* **1** [I,T] *formal* to start doing something again after a pause or interruption【正式】〔中斷之後〕繼續: *They were silent, then Billy resumed his story.* 他們都靜下來, 然後比利繼續講故事。| *Let us resume where we left off.* 讓我們從中斷的地方繼續下去。**2** if an activity or process resumes, it starts again after a pause〔活動或過程〕重新開始: *Work resumed on the following day.* 工作在第二天重新開始。**3 resume**

your seat/place/position *formal* to go back to the seat, place, or position where you were before【正式】回到座位/原地/原職位: *Everyone resumed their seats for the second half of the performance.* 大家都回到座位上看下半場演出。

re·su·me², résumé /ˌrɛzuˋme; ˈrezjʊmeɪ/ *n* [C] **1** [+of] a short account of something such as an article or speech, that gives the main points but not details〔文章或講話等的〕梗概, 摘要 **2** *AmE* a short written account of your education and your previous jobs that you send to an employer when you are looking for a new job【美】個人簡歷; CV *BrE*【英】

re·sump·tion /rɪˋzʌmpʃən; rɪˈzʌmpʃən/ *n* [singular,U] *formal* the act of starting an activity again after a pause【正式】重新開始: [+of] *the resumption of underground nuclear testing* 地下核試驗的恢復

re·sur·face /riˋsɝfɪs; ˌriːˈsɜːfɪs/ *v* **1** [I] to appear again 重新出現: *Old rivalries began to resurface.* 昔日的競爭又重新開始了。**2** [I] to come back up to the surface of the water 重新露出水面 **3** [T] to put a new surface on a road 給…重鋪路面

re·sur·gence /rɪˋsɝdʒəns; rɪˈsɜːdʒəns/ *n* [singular,U] the appearance again and growth of a belief or activity, especially one that is harmful or undesirable〔尤指有害、不良的信仰或活動的〕復蘇, 再起: [+of] *a resurgence of racial violence* 種族暴力的再起 | [+in] *a resurgence in the popularity of 60s music* 20 世紀 60 年代音樂的再次流行 —**resurgent** *adj*

res·ur·rect /ˌrɛzəˋrɛkt; ˌrezəˈrekt/ *v* [T] to start an old practice, custom, belief etc again after it has not existed for a long time 使〔久已中斷的傳統、消亡的信仰等〕復活, 恢復: *Old theories about the origin of the universe have been resurrected.* 昔日關於宇宙起源的種種理論復活了。

res·ur·rec·tion /ˌrɛzəˋrɛkʃən; ˌrezəˈrekʃən/ *n* [U] **1** also 又作 **Resurrection** the return of Jesus Christ to life after his death after being crucified (CRUCIFY), which is one of the main beliefs of the Christian religion 耶穌復活 **2** also 又作 **Resurrection** the return of all dead people to life at the end of the world〔世界末日時所有死者的〕復活 **3** a situation in which an idea, custom, feeling etc is brought back into existence〔思想、傳統、感覺等的〕復活, 復興; 恢復: *a resurrection of old jealousies* 昔日嫉妒心的再次出現

re·sus·ci·tate /rɪˋsʌsəˌtet; rɪˈsʌsɪteɪt/ *v* [T] to make someone breathe again or become conscious after they have almost died 使恢復呼吸, 使蘇醒 —**resuscitation** /rɪˌsʌsəˋteʃən; rɪˌsʌsɪˈteɪʃən/ *n* [U] —see also 另見 CPR

re·tail¹ /ˋritel; ˈriːteɪl/ *n* [U] the sale of goods in shops to customers, for their own use and not for selling to anyone else 零售, 零賣: *goods for retail only* 僅供零售的商品 | **retail trade/business etc** *workers in the retail trade* 零售業工人 | **retail outlet** (=a shop) 零售店 —compare 比較 WHOLESALE¹

retail² /ˋritel; rɪˈteɪl/ *v* **1** [I,T] *technical* to sell goods in a shop【術語】零售, 零賣: *The product is retailed through a big chain of furniture stores.* 這產品通過一家大型連鎖家具商店零售。**2 retail at $5/£20 etc** *technical* to be sold at a particular price in shops【術語】以 5 美元/20 英鎊等的價格零售: *This wine retails at £6.95 a bottle.* 這種酒的零售價格是每瓶 6.95 英鎊。**3** [T] *formal* to tell people about something, especially about other people's private affairs【正式】散佈〔尤指關於別人私事的流言蜚語〕: *Who is responsible for retailing these rumours?* 是誰散佈這些流言蜚語?

retail³ *adv* from a shop 從商店裡: *We bought it retail.* 我們從商店裡買來的。

re·tail·er /ˋritelɚ; ˈriːteɪlə/ *n* [C] someone who sells things in a shop; SHOPKEEPER 零售商

re·tail·ing /ˋritelɪŋ; ˈriːteɪlɪŋ/ *n* [U] the business of selling goods to the public in shops 零售業: *People who work in retailing are often badly paid.* 從事零售業的人收入往往很低。| *retailing organizations* 零售業組織

retail park /ˈ·· ·/ *n* [C] *BrE* a special area outside a town with many large shops and space for cars to park【英】購物中心〔在鎮以外的地區, 有很多大型商店和停車位置〕

retail price in·dex /ˌ·· ˈ· ˌ··/ abbreviation 縮寫為 **RPI** *n* [singular] an official system of numbers that shows changes in the cost of living in Britain each month, based on the price of goods and services bought by an average person 零售價格指數 —see also 另見 CONSUMER PRICE INDEX

re·tain /rɪˋten; rɪˈteɪn/ *v* [T] *formal*【正式】**1** to keep something or continue to have something 保留, 保有: *A copy of the invoice should be retained by the Accounts Department.* 發票的副本須由財務部保留。| *It's important that the elderly should retain a sense of dignity.* 老年人保持尊嚴感很重要。| *a heavy soil that retains water* 能保持水分的黏質土 —see also 另見 RETENTION (1) **2** to keep facts in your memory 記住 **3** to make sure that you will have someone's help or services, by paying for them before you actually have them 付訂金聘請: *They decided to retain their lawyer at their own expense.* 他們決定自己花錢付訂金聘請律師。| **retaining fee** (=money paid to keep someone working for you) 聘金 S2 W2

re·tain·er /rɪˋtenɚ; rɪˈteɪnə/ *n* [C] **1** an amount of money paid to someone, especially a lawyer, for work that they are going to do〔尤指付給律師的〕律師費, 聘用訂金 **2** a reduced amount of rent that you pay for a room, flat etc when you are not there, so that it will still be available when you return〔外出期間為保留房間、公寓等支付的〕訂金 **3** *old use* a servant, especially one who has always worked for a particular person or family【舊】〔服務多年的〕僕人: *an old and trusted family retainer* 可靠的老家僕

re·take¹ /riˋtek; ˌriːˈteɪk/ *v* [T] **1** to get control of an area again in a war〔在戰爭中〕收復, 奪回〔失地〕: *Rebels have retaken the city.* 叛軍奪回了該城市。**2** to take an examination again because you have previously failed it〔由於不及格〕重新參加〔考試〕**3** to film or photograph something again 重拍, 重攝

re·take² /ˋriˌtek; ˈriːteɪk/ *n* [C] **1** an act of filming or photographing something again 重拍, 重攝: *They had to do several retakes before the director was satisfied.* 他們重拍了幾次導演才滿意。**2** *BrE* an examination or test that you take again because you failed it【英】補考

re·tal·i·ate /rɪˋtælɪˌet; rɪˈtælieɪt/ *v* [I] to do something bad to someone because they have done something bad to you 報復, 反擊: **retaliate by doing sth** *When the police started to arrest people, some of the demonstrators retaliated by throwing stones.* 當警察開始逮捕人時, 一些示威者投擲石塊以示報復。

re·tal·i·a·tion /rɪˌtælɪˋeʃən; rɪˌtæliˈeɪʃən/ *n* [U] action against someone who has done something bad to you 報復, 反擊: *the threat of retaliation* 要報復的威脅 | **in retaliation for** *Union leaders are threatening strike action in retaliation for the recent pay cuts.* 工會領袖威脅以罷工行動來報復最近的減薪。

re·tal·i·a·to·ry /rɪˋtælɪəˌtorɪ; rɪˈtæliətəri/ *adj formal* done against someone because they have harmed you【正式】報復(性)的: *retaliatory raids* 報復性襲擊

re·tard¹ /rɪˋtɑrd; rɪˈtɑːd/ *v* [T] *formal* to delay the development of something, or to make something happen more slowly than expected【正式】減緩, 阻礙: *Cold weather retards the growth of many plants.* 寒冷的天氣使許多植物生長緩慢。—**retardation** /ˌritɑrˋdeʃən; ˌriːtɑːˈdeɪʃən/ *n* [U]

re·tard² /ˋritɑrd; ˈriːtɑːd/ *n* [C] *slang* an offensive word meaning a stupid person【俚】笨蛋〔冒犯用語〕

re·tard·ed /rɪˋtɑrdɪd; rɪˈtɑːdɪd/ *adj* less intelligent than other people because of slower mental development 智力發育遲緩的, 弱智的: *a special programme for retarded children* 為弱智兒童制定的特殊計劃 | *mentally retarded* 智力遲鈍的

R

retch /rɛtʃ; retʃ/ *v* [I] to try to VOMIT, or feel as if you are going to vomit when you do not 噁心, 乾嘔: *Like someone drowning, she fought for air, gasping and retching.* 就像溺水的人一樣, 她拚命呼吸, 大口喘氣和乾嘔。

retd the written abbreviation for 縮寫= RETIRED; used after the name of a former military officer 退伍的〔用於退役軍官的姓名之後〕

re·tell /riˋtɛl; ˌriːˈtel/ *v* [T] *past tense and past participle* **retold** /-ˋtold; -ˈtəʊld/ to tell a story again, often in a different way or in a different language〔以不同的方式或語言〕重講, 複述

re·ten·tion /rɪˋtɛnʃən; rɪˈtenʃən/ *n* [U] **1** *formal* the act of keeping something【正式】保持, 保留: **[+of]** *Committee members voted for the retention of the existing voting system.* 委員會成員投票贊成保留現有的投票制度。 **2** *technical* the ability or tendency of something to hold liquid, heat etc within itself【術語】〔液體〕豬留;〔熱〕滯留 **3** the ability to keep something in your memory 記憶力: *powers of retention* 記憶力

re·ten·tive /rɪˋtɛntɪv; rɪˈtentɪv/ *adj* a retentive memory or mind is able to hold facts and remember them 記憶力強的 **—retentively** *adv* **—retentiveness** *n* [U]

re·think /riˋθɪŋk; ˌriːˈθɪŋk/ *v past tense and past participle* **rethought** /-ˋθɔt; -ˈθɔːt/ [I,T] to think about a plan or idea again in order to decide if any changes should be made 再思考, 重新考慮: *an opportunity to rethink our campaign strategy* 重新思考我們的競選戰略的機會 **—rethink** /ˋriˌθɪŋk; ˈriːθɪŋk/ *n* [singular]

ret·i·cent /ˋrɛtəsn̩t; ˈretɪ̈sənt/ *adj* unwilling to talk about what you feel or what you know 沉默的, 不願意談的: *She's naturally reticent, even with some of her closest friends.* 她素來沉默寡言, 即使和一些最親密的朋友在一起也是一樣。| **[+about]** *Mr Jamieson was very reticent about the reasons for his decision.* 賈米森先生對他所作決定的原因不肯多談。**—reticence** *n* [U] **—reticently** *adv*

re·tic·u·la·ted /rɪˋtɪkjəˌletɪd; rɪˈtɪkjʊ̈leɪtɪ̈d/ *adj technical* forming or covered with a pattern of squares and lines that looks like a net【術語】網狀的 **—reticulation** /rɪˌtɪkjəˋleʃən; rɪˌtɪkjʊ̈ˈleɪʃən/ *n* [C,U]

ret·i·na /ˋrɛtn̩ə; ˈretɪ̈nə/ *n* [C] the area at the back of your eye that receives light and sends an image of what you see to your brain 視網膜 —see picture at 參見 EYE[1] 圖

ret·i·nue /ˋrɛtn̩ju; ˈretɪnjuː/ *n* [C] a group of helpers or supporters who are travelling with an important person〔重要人物的〕隨從, 隨員: *visiting Congressmen and all their retinue* 來訪的國會議員及他們的全部隨員

re·tire /rɪˋtaɪr; rɪˈtaɪə/ *v* [2] [3]

1 ►FROM WORK 離開工作◄ **a)** [I] to stop work at the end of your working life 退休: *He retired when he was 65.* 他65歲時退休了。| **[+from]** *After retiring from the army it took William a long time to adjust to civilian life.* 從軍隊退役後, 威廉花了很長時間才適應平民的生活。| **retire early** (=retire before the usual age) 提前退休 **b)** [T usually passive 一般用被動態] to dismiss someone and pay them a PENSION, especially because of illness 使退職〔尤指因病〕: *The manager was retired on half salary.* 經理半薪退職了。

2 ►TO A QUIET PLACE 到僻靜處◄ [I] *formal* to go away to a quiet place【正式】去安靜的地方: *He often retires to his country home to work on his book.* 他經常躲到鄉間家中寫書。| *The jury has retired to consider its verdict.* 陪審團退庭去考慮其裁決。

3 ►FROM A GAME 從比賽中◄ [I] to stop competing in a game or race because you are losing or injured〔因失利或受傷〕退出比賽: *He was forced to retire from the competition due to a leg injury.* 因為腿部受傷, 他不得不退出比賽。

4 ►TO BED 上牀◄ [I] *literary* to go to bed【文】就寢

5 ►ARMY 部隊◄ [I] to move back from a battle after being defeated 撤退: *The army retired to regroup for a fresh attack.* 軍隊撤下來進行整編, 準備發起新的攻擊。 —compare 比較 RETREAT[1] (2)

re·tired /rɪˋtaɪrd; rɪˈtaɪəd/ *adj* having stopped working, usually because of your age 退休的: *a retired teacher* 退休教師 | *Both my parents are retired now.* 我父母現在都已退休。

re·tir·ee /rɪˌtaɪˋri; rɪˌtaɪəˈriː/ *n* [C] *AmE* someone who has stopped working, usually because of their age【美】退休者

re·tire·ment /rɪˋtaɪrmənt; rɪˈtaɪəmənt/ *n* **1** [C,U] the act of retiring from your job, or the time when you do this 退休: *June's colleagues arranged a surprise party for her retirement.* 瓊的同事為她的退休安排了一個令她驚喜的聚會。| **retirement present/party etc** (=a present, party etc for someone who is retiring) 退休禮物/聚會等 | **on retirement** (=from the time when you retire) 從退休起 *On retirement you will receive a small pension.* 退休後你將得到小額的退休金。| **take early retirement** (=retire at an earlier age than usual) 提前退休 | **retirement age** (=the age when people usually stop working) 退休年齡 **2** [singular,U] the period after you have retired 退休期間: *a long and happy retirement* 漫長而幸福的退休生活 | *a retirement pension* 退休金 [2] [3]

retirement plan /·ˈ·· ·/ *n* [C] *AmE* a system for saving money for your retirement, especially if you will not receive money from your employer【美】退休金計劃〔尤指雇主不付養老金, 而是本人為養老金儲蓄的制度〕— compare 比較 PENSION PLAN

re·tir·ing /rɪˋtaɪrɪŋ; rɪˈtaɪərɪŋ/ *adj* **1** not wanting to be with other people, especially people you do not know; SHY[1] (1) 離羣的; 害羞的: *As a child, Elizabeth was very retiring.* 小時候的伊莉莎白非常怯生。**2 the retiring president/manager/director etc** a president etc who is soon going to leave their job 即將卸任的總裁/經理/董事等

re·tool /riˋtul; ˌriːˈtuːl/ *v* **1** [T] *AmE informal* to organize something in a new way【美, 非正式】重新組織; 改組: *The College Board has retooled the admission exams.* 大學委員會重新組織了入學考試。**2** [I,T] to change or replace the machines or tools in a factory〔工廠〕更換機器[工具]

re·tort[1] /rɪˋtɔrt; rɪˈtɔːt/ *v* [T] to reply quickly, in an angry or humorous way〔立即憤怒或幽默地〕反駁, 回嘴: *"It's all your fault!" he retorted.* "那都是你的過錯!" 他反駁說。

retort[2] *n* [C] **1** a short and angry or humorous reply〔簡短的, 憤怒或幽默的〕反駁, 回嘴: *He was about to make a jovial retort, but stopped.* 他剛想友善地反駁, 但又止住了。**2** a bottle with a long narrow bent neck, used for heating chemicals 曲頸甑, 蒸餾甑, 蒸餾器

re·touch /riˋtʌtʃ; ˌriːˈtʌtʃ/ *v* [T] to improve a picture or photograph by painting over marks or making other small changes 修描, 潤色〔圖畫、照片〕: *postcards that have been retouched to cover the grey skies* 為遮蓋灰色天空而修描過的明信片

re·trace /rɪˋtres; rɪˈtreɪs/ *v* [T] **1** to go back the way you have come 順原路返回, 折返: **retrace your steps** *After about fifty paces, he turned around and began to retrace his steps.* 走了大約五十步之後, 他轉過身開始順着原路返回。**2** to repeat exactly the same journey that someone else has made 重走〔別人走過的路〕: *We shall be retracing the route taken by Marco Polo.* 我們將重走馬可孛羅走過的路。**3** to find out about a series of past actions or events 追查: *Detectives are hoping to retrace her movements.* 偵探們希望追查她的行蹤。

re·tract /rɪˋtrækt; rɪˈtrækt/ *v* **1** [T] to make an official statement saying that something which you said previously is not true; WITHDRAW (3) 正式收回〔聲明〕: *He confessed to the murder but later retracted his statement.* 他承認犯有謀殺罪但後來又翻供了。**2** [I,T] if part of a machine or an animal's body retracts or is retracted, it moves back into the main part (使) 縮回, (使) 縮入: *Cats can retract their claws.* 貓能把爪子縮進去。

re·tract·a·ble /rɪˋtræktəbḷ; rɪˈtræktəbəl/ *adj* **1** a retractable part of something can be pulled back into the main part 可收起的, 可縮回的: *a knife with a retractable blade* 刀片可收起的刀 **2** having a retractable part 有可縮回[收進]部分的: *a retractable ball-point pen* 可縮回式圓珠筆

re·trac·tion /rɪˋtrækʃən; rɪˈtrækʃən/ *n* **1** [C] an official statement saying that something which you said previously is not true 正式收回〔以前所說的不真實的話〕: *The newspaper was forced to publish a retraction of all its allegations.* 這家報紙被迫發表聲明收回它的所有指控。 **2** [U] the act of retracting something 收回, 撤回

re·train /riˋtren; ˌriːˈtreɪn/ *v* [I,T] to learn or to teach someone the skills that are needed to do a different job (對…)再訓練; 接受再培訓: *Staff are being retrained to use the new machinery.* 工作人員正在接受使用新機器的再培訓。—**retraining** *n* [U]: *a retraining programme for unemployed miners* 對失業礦工的再培訓計劃

re·tread[1] /ˋriˏtrɛd; ˈriːtred/ *n* [C] **1** a retreaded tyre 翻新的輪胎 **2** *AmE informal* something that is made or done again, with a few changes added【美, 非正式】〔只作少量變化的〕翻版: *retreads of old TV shows* 新瓶舊酒的電視節目 **3** *AmE informal* someone who has been trained to do work which is different from what they did before【美, 非正式】接受過再培訓的人員

re·tread[2] /riˋtrɛd; ˌriːˈtred/ *v* [T] to put a new rubber surface on an old tyre 給〔舊輪胎〕裝新胎面, 翻新〔輪胎〕

re·treat[1] /rɪˋtrit; rɪˈtriːt/ *v* [I]

1 ►MOVE BACK 後退◄ **a)** to walk back and away from someone or something because you are afraid or embarrassed〔因恐懼或尷尬而〕後退, 退卻: *He saw her and retreated, too shy to speak to her.* 他看見她便往後退, 不好意思跟她講話。| **[+to/from etc]** *Perry lit the fuse and retreated to a safe distance.* 佩里點燃導火線, 然後退至安全距離。**b)** if an area of water, snow or land retreats, it gradually gets smaller〔水、雪、土地〕範圍縮小: *The flood waters are slowly retreating.* 洪水正在慢慢退卻。

2 ►OF AN ARMY 軍隊◄ to move away from the enemy after being defeated in battle 撤退: *The rebels retreated, pursued by government troops.* 叛軍撤退了, 政府軍在後面追趕。

3 ►CHANGE YOUR MIND 改變主意◄ to change your mind about a promise you have publicly made or about a principle you have stated, because the situation has become too difficult〔承諾、立場等〕撤回: **[+from]** *Current economic problems have forced the government to retreat from its pledge to cut taxes.* 目前的經濟問題迫使政府撤回對削減稅收的承諾。

4 ►TO A QUIET PLACE 到僻靜處◄ to go away to a place that is quiet or safe 去寧靜、安全的地方: **[+from/into/to]** *After the noise of the city he was glad to retreat to his hotel room.* 經歷了城市的喧囂之後, 他很高興躲進自己的旅店房間。

5 retreat into yourself/your thoughts etc to ignore what is happening around you and give all your attention to your private thoughts 陷入沉思

retreat[2] *n*

1 ►MOVEMENT BACK 後退◄ [singular,U] a movement back and away from someone or something, because you are afraid, embarrassed etc 後退, 退卻, 躲避: **beat a retreat** (=walk away quickly) 匆匆離開 *Jim beat a hasty retreat when he saw his wife's mother at the door.* 吉姆看到岳母在門口便趕緊跑掉。

2 ►CHANGE OF INTENTION 改變意圖◄ [singular,U] an act of changing your mind about a promise you publicly made or a principle you stated, because the situation has become too difficult〔承諾的〕撤回,〔立場的〕改變, 放棄: *a retreat from hard-line policies* 放棄強硬政策

3 ►OF AN ARMY 軍隊◄ [C,U] a movement away from the enemy after a defeat in battle 撤退: *Napoleon's retreat from Moscow* 拿破侖從莫斯科撤退 —opposite 反義詞 ADVANCE[1] (3) | **be in full retreat** (=be retreating fast and continuously) 全線潰退 | **sound the retreat** (=give a loud signal for retreat) 吹號收兵, 鳴金收兵

4 ►PLACE 地方◄ [C] a place you can go to that is quiet or safe 靜養所, 靜居所: *von Mulne's retreat in the mountains* 馮·慕尼在山裡的靜居所

5 ►THOUGHT AND PRAYER 冥想與祈禱◄ [C,U] a period of time that you spend praying or studying religion in a quiet place〔宗教的〕靜修(期): *They go on retreat twice a year.* 他們每年靜修兩次。

re·trench /rɪˋtrɛntʃ; rɪˈtrentʃ/ *v* [I] if a government or organization retrenches, it spends less money〔開支〕緊縮 —**retrenchment** *n* [C,U]: *a government policy of retrenchment* 政府的緊縮政策

re·tri·al /riˋtraɪəl; ˌriːˈtraɪəl/ *n* [C] a process of judging a law case in court again 再審, 複審: *The jury was dismissed and the judge ordered a retrial.* 陪審團被解散, 法官下令對案件複審。

ret·ri·bu·tion /ˏrɛtrəˋbjuʃən; ˌretrɪˈbjuːʃən/ *n* [singular, U] severe punishment that is deserved 應得的懲罰: **[+for]** *retribution for terrorist attacks* 恐怖襲擊應得的嚴懲 | **divine retribution** (=punishment from God) 上帝的懲罰 | **mete out retribution** (=give retribution) 予以嚴懲 —**retributive** /rɪˋtrɪbjətɪv; rɪˈtrɪbjʊtɪv/ *adj*: *retributive justice* 報應

re·triev·al /rɪˋtrivḷ; rɪˈtriːvəl/ *n* [U] **1** *technical* the process of getting back information from a computer system【術語】〔電腦系統信息的〕檢索: *information retrieval* 信息檢索 | *a retrieval system* 檢索系統 **2** [U] the act of getting back something you have lost or left somewhere 找回, 取回 **3 be beyond/past retrieval** if a situation is beyond retrieval, it has become so bad that it cannot be made right again 無可挽回, 無可補救

re·trieve /rɪˋtriv; rɪˈtriːv/ *v* **1** [T] *formal* to find something and bring it back【正式】找回; 收回, 取回: **retrieve sth from** *I went back to the locker room to retrieve my jacket.* 我回更衣室取回我的上衣。| *The wreckage of the crashed plane was retrieved from the ocean.* 從海中打撈到了失事飛機的殘骸。**2 retrieve your losses** get back money equal to what you lost 抵償某人損失 **3** [T] *technical* to get back information that has been stored in the memory of a computer【術語】檢索〔儲存於電腦的信息〕**4 retrieve a situation** to make a situation satisfactory again after there has been a serious mistake or problem 挽回局面: *She tried to apologise but it was already too late to retrieve the situation.* 她企圖道歉, 想挽回局面, 但已經太遲。**5** [I,T] if a dog retrieves, it finds and brings back birds and small animals its owner has shot〔狗〕啣回〔主人擊中的獵物〕—**retrievable** *adj*

re·triev·er /rɪˋtrivɚ; rɪˈtriːvə/ *n* [C] a type of dog that can be trained to retrieve birds that its owner has shot 經訓練會啣回獵物的獵犬, 拾獚

retro- /rɛtro; retrəʊ/ *prefix* **1** back towards the past 追溯的: *retroactive legislation* (=which has an effect on things already done) 有追溯效力的立法 | *in retrospect* (=looking back at what has happened) 回顧, 回想 **2** back towards an earlier and worse state 倒退的: *a retrograde step* 倒退 | *to retrogress* 倒退, 退化 **3** backwards 向後: *a retrorocket* (=that fires backwards, opposite to the direction of travel) 反向火箭, 制動火箭, 減速火箭

ret·ro[1] /ˋrɛtro; ˈretrəʊ/ *adj* deliberately using styles of fashion or design from the recent past〔時裝、設計〕復舊的,〔早年式樣〕重新流行的: *retro clothing stores* 懷舊時裝店

retro[2] *n* [C] *AmE informal* a RETROSPECTIVE【美, 非正式】回顧展

ret·ro·ac·tive /ˏrɛtroˋæktɪv; ˌretrəʊˈæktɪv◂/ *adj formal* a law or decision that is retroactive is effective from a particular date in the past【正式】〔法律、決定〕有追溯效力的: *a retroactive pay increase* 應追溯補發的增薪 —see also 另見 RETROSPECTIVE[1] —**retroactively** *adv*

ret·ro·flex /ˋrɛtrəˏflɛks; ˈretrəfleks/ *adj technical* a retroflex speech sound is made with the end of your togue

R

pointing backwards and upwards【術語】捲舌（音）的

ret·ro·grade /ˈrɛtrəˌgred; ˈretrəgreɪd/ *adj formal* involving a return to an earlier and worse situation【正式】倒退的，後退的: **a retrograde step** *Privatisation is seen as a retrograde step.* 私營化被認為是倒退。

ret·ro·gress /ˈrɛtrəˌgrɛs; ˌretrəˈgres/ *v* [I+to] *formal* to go back to an earlier and worse state【正式】倒退，衰退，退化 —**retrogression** /-ˋgrɛʃən; -ˈgreʃən/ *n* [U]

ret·ro·gres·sive /ˌrɛtrəˋgrɛsɪv; ˌretrəˈgresɪv◂/ *adj formal* returning to an earlier and worse situation【正式】倒退的，衰退的，退化的: *a retrogressive idea* 倒退的想法 | *retrogressive change* 倒退的變化 —**retrogressively** *adv*

ret·ro·spect /ˈrɛtrəˌspɛkt; ˈretrəspekt/ *n* [U] **in retrospect** thinking back to a time in the past, especially with the advantage of knowing more now than you did then 回顧，回想: *In retrospect, it was the wrong time to set up a new company.* 回想起來，那時建立新公司的時機不對。| *My teenage years seem happier in retrospect than they were.* 我的青少年時代回憶起來似乎比實際情況更快樂。

ret·ro·spec·tion /ˌrɛtrəˋspɛkʃən; ˌretrəˈspekʃən/ *n* [U] *formal* thought about the past【正式】回顧，回想

ret·ro·spec·tive¹ /ˌrɛtrəˋspɛktɪv; ˌretrəˈspektɪv◂/ *adj* **1** a law or decision that is retrospective is effective from a particular date in the past; RETROACTIVE〔法律、決定〕有追溯效力的: *retrospective legislation* 有追溯效力的立法 **2** concerned with or thinking about the past 回顧的，追憶的: *in a retrospective mood* 沉浸在回憶之中

retrospective² *n* [C] a show of the work of an ARTIST, that includes all the kinds of work they have done〔一個藝術家各種作品的〕回顧展

re·try /riˋtraɪ; ˌriːˈtraɪ/ *v* [I] to judge a law case again in court 重審，複審

ret·si·na /rɛtˋsinə; retˈsiːnə/ *n* [U] a Greek wine that tastes of the RESIN (=juice) of certain trees 一種帶樹脂香味的希臘葡萄酒

2 1 **re·turn¹** /rɪˋtɝn; rɪˈtɜːn/ *v*

1 ►GO BACK 返回◄ [I] to go back to a place where you were before, or come back from a place where you have just been 返回，回來: **[+to]** *Conor did not return to Ireland until 1937.* 直到 1937 年康納才回到愛爾蘭。| **[+from]** *When Alice returned from university, she was a changed person.* 愛麗斯從大學回來時變成了一個人。| **return home** *We got lost, returning home well after midnight.* 我們迷了路，午夜後很久才回到家。| **never to return** *formal*【正式】*500 airmen flew from these airfields, never to return.* 500 名空軍士兵從這些機場起飛，一去不復返。

2 ►GIVE BACK 歸還◄ [T] to give something back to its owner, or put something back in its place 歸還，退還，放歸原處: *We lent them our lawnmower and they never returned it!* 我們把割草機借給他們，他們始終沒有還給我們！| **return sth to sb/sth** *I have to return some books to the library.* 我得去圖書館還一些書。

3 ►FEELING/PROBLEM 感覺/問題◄ [I] if a feeling, problem, quality etc returns, it starts to exist again or to have an effect again 重新出現: *If the pain returns, take two of the tablets every four hours.* 如果又出現疼痛的話，每四小時服兩片藥。| **[+to]** *Stability will only return to the region when the civil war ends.* 只有結束內戰，這個地區才能恢復穩定。

4 ►START AGAIN 重新開始◄ [I] to go back to an activity, job etc that you were doing before you stopped or were interrupted; RESUME¹ (1) 重新開始，繼續 **[+to]** *Nicholas looked up, grinned, then returned to his newspaper.* 尼古拉斯抬起頭，咧開嘴笑了笑，又接着看他的報紙。| **return to work** *Most mothers return to full-time work within twelve months.* 大多數母親在十二個月內重新開始全職工作。

5 ►DISCUSS AGAIN 再討論◄ [I] to start discussing or dealing with a subject that you have already mentioned, especially in a piece of writing〔某個主題〕再討論，重新處理: **[+to]** *I shall return to the subject of inflation in chapter five.* 我將在第五章再談通貨膨脹這個題目。| *Returning to sanctions, do you think they will really be effective?* 回到制裁問題，你認為制裁真的有效嗎？

6 ►REACT 作出反應◄ [T] to do something or give something to someone because they have given the same thing to you〔以相同的東西〕回報: *I smiled at her but she refused to return my smile.* 我朝她微笑，但她拒絕還以微笑。| *You never returned my call!* 你從沒給我回電話！| **return fire** (=shoot back at someone shooting at you) 還擊 *The enemy returned our fire.* 敵人向我們還擊。

7 ►BALL 球類◄ [T] to send the ball back to your opponent in a game such as tennis〔網球等〕回擊〔球〕

8 ►ELECT 選舉◄ [T usually passive 一般用被動態] *BrE* to elect someone to a political position, especially to represent you in parliament【英】選舉，選出〔尤指議會議員〕: *Durrant was returned with an increased majority.* 達蘭特當選了，得票比例比以往更大。

9 return a verdict if a jury return their VERDICT, they say whether someone is guilty or not〔陪審團〕宣布裁決

10 ►PROFIT 利潤◄ [T] if an INVESTMENT returns a particular amount of money, that is how much profit it produces 產生，獲得〔利潤〕: *Government bonds return around 10%.* 政府債券的利潤在 10% 左右。

11 ►TAX 稅收◄ [T] *formal* to give a particular amount as the answer to an official question concerning tax【正式】申報

Frequencies of **return, get/go/come back**, and **get/go/come home** in spoken and written English 英語口語和書面語中 return, get/go/come back 和 get/go/come home 的使用頻率

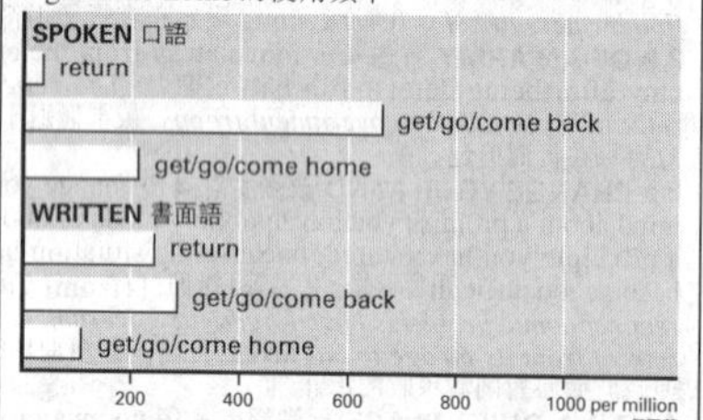

Based on the British National Corpus and the Longman Lancaster Corpus
據英國國家語料庫和朗文蘭卡斯特語料庫

This graph shows that it is much more usual in spoken English to use **get/go/come back** or **get/go/come home** rather than **return**. **Return** is much more common in written English than in spoken English. 本圖表顯示，在英語口語中 get/go/come back 和 get/go/come home 要比 return 常用得多。return 在書面語中的使用頻率遠遠高於口語。

return² *n* 2 2

1 ►GOING BACK 返回◄ [singular,U] the act of returning from somewhere, or your arrival back in the place where you started from 返回，回來: *We're all looking forward to your return!* 我們都盼着你回來！| **on/upon your return** (=when you return) 一回來（就…）*On his return from Germany he was promoted to Colonel.* 他從德國一回來就被晉升為上校。

2 ►OF A FEELING/PROBLEM 感覺/問題◄ [U] the fact of something such as a problem, feeling, or activity starting to happen or exist again 再發生，重新出現: **[+of]** *the return of nationalism to Eastern Europe* 民族主義在東歐的重新出現

3 ►GIVING BACK 歸還◄ [U] the act of giving, putting,

or sending something back 歸還, 送還, 放回: *The family are demanding the return of the dowry.* 這家人要求退還嫁妝。| *a return of prisoners* 遣返犯人

4 ▶TO AN ACTIVITY 回到某種活動◀ [singular] returning to an activity, job, or way of life〔某種活動、工作、生活方式的〕恢復: [**+to**] *the idea of a return to a simpler, more natural way of life* 回歸一種更簡樸、更自然的生活方式的想法 | **a return to work** (=after stopping work as a protest)〔罷工後〕復工 *an end to the strike and an immediate return to work* 結束罷工, 立即復工

5 ▶PROFIT 利潤◀ [U] also 又作 **returns** [plural] the amount of profit that you get from something 利潤(率), 收益: *The company returns over the last three years have been spectacular.* 過去三年公司的利潤可觀。| **return on investment/capital/sales** *£10,000! That's not a bad return on our investment, is it?* 10,000英鎊! 我們投資的回報不錯嘛, 對不對?

6 in return (for) in exchange for, or as payment for something 作為…的交換, 作為…的回報: *I'd like to buy you a meal in return for all your hospitality.* 我想請你吃飯來報答你的盛情好客。| *She gave us food and clothing and asked for nothing in return.* 她給了我們食物和衣服, 沒有要求任何回報。

7 ▶STATEMENT 聲明◀ [C] a statement giving information in reply to an official question 申報(書), 匯報: **tax return** *Have you sent in your tax return yet?* 你交了所得稅申報表嗎?

8 by return (of post) *BrE* if you reply to a letter by return, you send your reply almost immediately【英】〔接到信後〕立即回覆

9 ▶TICKET 票◀ [C] *BrE* a ticket for a trip from one place to another and back again【英】往返票, 來回票; ROUND TRIP *AmE*【美】—compare 比較 SINGLE[2] (4) —see also 另見 DAY RETURN

10 many happy returns *BrE* used to greet someone on their birthday【英】生日快樂〔生日賀詞〕

11 ▶COMPUTER 電腦◀ [U] the control that you press on a computer or TYPEWRITER after you have finished the line you are writing〔電腦、打字機的〕回車鍵: *Key in your file name and press return.* 請鍵入文檔名稱並按回車鍵。—see also 另見 **the point of no return** (POINT[1] (7))

return[3] *adj* **return ticket/fare** a ticket for, or the price charged for, a trip from one place to another and back again 來回票/票價; ROUND-TRIP *AmE*【美】—compare 比較 SINGLE[1] (6)

re·turn·a·ble /rɪˋtɝnəbl; rɪˈtɜːnəbəl/ *adj* **1** returnable bottles, containers etc can be given back to the shop, often to be used again〔瓶子、容器等〕可退還的 **2** *formal* something such as money or an official paper that is returnable must be given or sent back【正式】必須歸還的, 必須退回的: *a returnable deposit* 必須退還的押金

re·turn·er /rɪˋtɝnɚ; rɪˈtɜːnə/ *n* [C] *BrE* someone who goes back to work after a long time away, especially a woman who left work to look after her children【英】重返工作者〔尤指因照顧子女而離職的婦女〕

returning of·fi·cer /ˈ·ˈ·· ˌ···/ *n* [C] the official in each town or area of Britain who arranges an election to Parliament and announces the result〔英國市鎮、地區的〕議會議員選舉主持人

Reu·ben sand·wich /ˌrubin ˋsændwɪtʃ; ˌruːbɪn ˈsænwɪdʒ/ *n* [C] an American SANDWICH made with SALT BEEF, Swiss cheese and SAUERKRAUT 魯賓三明治〔用醃牛肉、瑞士乾酪和德國式泡菜製作的美式三明治〕

re·u·nify /riˋjunəˌfaɪ; riːˈjuːnɪfaɪ/ *v* [T] to join the parts of something together again, especially a country that was divided 使重新統一〔尤指曾分裂的國家〕—compare 比較 REUNITE —**reunification** /riˌjunəfəˋkeʃən; riːˌjuːnɪfɪˈkeɪʃən/ *n* [U]: *the reunification of Germany* 德國的重新統一

re·u·nion /riˋjunjən; riːˈjuːnjən/ *n* **1** [C] the state of being brought together again after a period of being separated 重聚: [**+with**] *Joseph's eventual reunion with his brother* 約瑟夫最終與他兄弟的重逢 **2** [C] a social meeting of people who have not met for a long time, especially people who were at school or college together〔尤指同學久別後的〕聚會, 聯誼活動: *our college reunion* 我們大學同學的聯誼聚會

re·u·nite /ˌrijuˋnaɪt; ˌriːjuːˈnaɪt/ *v* [I,T usually passive 一般用被動態] to come together again or bring people together again (使)再聯合, (使)重新結合; (使)重聚: **be reunited with** *reunited with his family* 與他的家人團聚

re·use /riˋjuz; ˌriːˈjuːz/ *v* [T] to use something again 再使用, 再利用: *Disposable syringes are not to be reused.* 用後即棄的注射器不得再次使用。—**reusable** *adj* —**reuse** /ˌriˋjus; ˌriːˈjuːs/ *n* [U]: *the reuse of derelict urban land* 城市棄荒地的再利用

Rev also 又作 **Revd** *BrE*【英】the written abbreviation of 縮寫= Reverend; a title used before the name of a minister of the Christian church〔基督教的〕牧師〔一種稱謂, 放在姓名前〕: *the Rev D Macleod* 麥克勞德牧師

rev[1] /rɛv; rev/ *n* [C] *informal* a complete turn of a wheel or engine part, used as a unit for measuring the speed of an engine; REVOLUTION (4)【非正式】〔輪子等的〕旋轉一周〔轉速單位〕

rev[2] also 又作 **rev up** *v* **revved, revving** [I,T] if you rev an engine, or if an engine revs, you make it work faster 加快(發動機)轉速: *the sound of a car revving up in the driveway* 汽車發動機在車道上加速的聲音

re·val·ue /riˋvælju; riːˈvæljuː/ *v* [T] **1** to examine something again in order to calculate its present value 對…再估價, 對…重新估價: *I'm having all my grandmother's jewelry revalued to see if I need to insure it.* 我正請人對我祖母的全部首飾重新估價, 看是否需要買保險。**2** to increase the value of a country's money in relation to that of other countries 使〔貨幣〕升值: *The dollar has just been revalued.* 美元剛剛升值。—compare 比較 DEVALUE —**revaluation** /ˌrivæljuˋeʃən; riːˌvæljuːˈeɪʃən/ *n* [C,U]

re·vamp /riˋvæmp; riːˈvæmp/ *v* [T] *informal* to arrange something in a new way so that it appears to be better although often there is no real improvement【非正式】修改, 翻新: *They've revamped the whole exam system.* 他們修改了整個考試制度。—**revamp** /ˋriˌvæmp; ˈriːvæmp/ *n* [C]: *an amazing revamp of her stage personality* 她的舞台個性的驚人變化

Revd *BrE* a British spelling of REV【英】Rev 的英式拼法

re·veal /rɪˋvil; rɪˈviːl/ *v* [T] **1** to show something that was previously hidden 展現, 顯露: *The curtains opened to reveal a darkened stage.* 大幕拉開, 露出一個漆黑的舞台。**2** to make known something that was previously secret or unknown 揭示, 揭露, 泄露: *The newspaper story revealed a cover-up of huge proportions.* 報紙的報道揭露了一件掩飾真相的事件, 此事牽連甚廣。| **reveal (that)** *He revealed that he had been in prison twice before.* 他透露自己以前曾兩次入獄。 S3 W1

re·veal·ing /rɪˋvilɪŋ; rɪˈviːlɪŋ/ *adj* **1** a remark or event that is revealing shows you something interesting or surprising about a situation or someone else's character 揭露性的, 揭示內情的: *Some of her comments during the interview were very revealing.* 她在採訪中作的一些評論揭示了許多鮮為人知的情況。**2** revealing clothes allow parts of your body to be seen which are usually kept covered〔衣服〕暴露的: *a very revealing dress* 非常暴露的連衣裙

re·veil·le /ˋrɛvlɪ; rɪˈvæli/ *n* [singular,U] a special tune played as a signal to wake soldiers in the morning, or the time at which it is played 起牀號; 吹起牀號的時間

rev·el /ˋrɛvl; ˈrevəl/ *v* **revelled, revelling** *BrE*【英】, **reveled, reveling** *AmE*【美】[I] *old use* to spend time dancing, eating, drinking etc, especially at a party【舊】狂歡, 縱酒, 作樂 —**revel** *n* [C usually plural 一般用複數]: *their drunken revels* 他們縱酒狂歡

revel in sth *phr v* [T] to enjoy something very much,

R

especially praise, popularity, or something that other people do not expect you to enjoy 陶醉於, 沉湎於: *He seems to be revelling in all the attention he's getting.* 他因自己引起別人注意而似乎飄飄然起來。| *revelling in their embarrassment* 對他們的尷尬幸災樂禍

rev·e·la·tion /ˌrɛvḷˋeʃən; ˌrevəˈleɪʃən/ *n* **1** [C] a surprising fact about someone or something that is made known and was previously secret 揭露/披露的(驚人)事實: *revelations in the papers about a government scandal* 報紙對一樁政府醜聞的揭露 **2 be a revelation** *informal* to be surprisingly good, enjoyable, or useful【非正式】出乎意外的〔樂趣、用處等〕: *Alice Walker's novel was a real revelation to me.* 愛麗斯·沃爾克的小說使我大開眼界。**3** [U] the act of suddenly making known a surprising fact that had previously been secret 揭露, 披露〔祕密的事〕**4** [C,U] an event, experience etc that is considered to be a message from God〔上帝的〕啟示

rev·ell·er *BrE*【英】, **reveler** *AmE*【美】/ˈrɛvlɚ; ˈrevələ/ *n* [C usually plural 一般用複數] someone who is having fun singing, dancing etc in a noisy way 狂歡者, 尋歡作樂者: *drunken revellers in Trafalgar Square on New Year's Eve* 除夕夜特拉法加廣場上醉醺醺的狂歡者

rev·el·ry /ˈrɛvḷrɪ; ˈrevəlri/ *n plural* **revelries** [U] wild noisy dancing, eating, drinking etc 狂歡, 歡宴作樂

re·venge¹ /rɪˋvɛndʒ; rɪˈvendʒ/ *n* [U] **1** something you do in order to punish someone who has harmed or offended you 報復, 報仇: **[+for]** *Hamlet was seeking revenge for his father's murder.* 哈姆雷特設法報殺父之仇。| **get/take revenge (on)** *He took revenge on his employers by setting fire to the factory.* 他對雇主進行報復, 放火燒了工廠。| **be out for revenge** (=be trying to get your revenge) 企圖報復 | **in revenge** (=to punish someone) 作為報復 *a bomb attack in revenge for the imprisonment of the terrorists* 為報復恐怖分子被抓而進行的炸彈襲擊 **2 get your revenge** to defeat someone who has previously defeated you in a sport 雪恥〔指在比賽中戰勝曾擊敗自己的對手〕—**revengeful** *adj*

revenge² *v* [T] **revenge yourself on/be revenged on** *formal* to punish someone who has harmed you【正式】向…報仇: *his unconscious desire to be revenged on her for her disloyalty* 因她不忠而在他潛意識中產生的復仇慾望

2 **rev·e·nue** /ˈrɛvəˌnu; ˈrevɪ̣njuː/ also 又作 **revenues** *plural n* [U] **1** money that a business or organization receives over a period of time, especially from selling goods or services 收益, 收入: *advertising revenue* 廣告收入 **2** money that the government receives from tax〔政府的〕稅收 —see also 另見 INLAND REVENUE, INTERNAL REVENUE SERVICE

re·ver·be·rate /rɪˋvɝbəˌret; rɪˈvɜːbəreɪt/ *v* [I] **1** if a loud sound reverberates, it is heard many times as it is sent back from different surfaces, so that the room or building where it is seems to shake〔聲音〕回蕩, 回響: **[+through/around/along etc]** *The sound of a train passing reverberated through the house.* 火車經過的聲音在整個房子裡回蕩。**2** if an event, action, or idea reverberates, it has a strong effect over a wide area〔事件、活動、思想的〕反響: *His death shocked the whole country and reverberated far beyond its boundaries.* 他的去世舉國震驚, 其反響遠遠超出了國界。

re·ver·be·ra·tion /rɪˌvɝbəˋreʃən; rɪˌvɜːbəˈreɪʃən/ *n* **1** [C usually plural 一般用複數] a severe effect that is caused by a particular event 反響, 巨大影響: *The reverberations of the energy crisis are felt especially by the car industry.* 能源危機的巨大影響在汽車業感受最強。**2** [C,U] a loud sound that hits a surface and is heard again and again 回蕩, 回響: *the deep reverberation of the bass drum* 低音鼓發出的深沉回響

re·vere /rɪˋvɪr; rɪˈvɪə/ *v* [T] *formal* to respect and admire someone or something very much【正式】尊敬, 崇敬: *a much revered teacher* 非常受尊敬的老師

rev·e·rence¹ /ˈrɛvərəns; ˈrevərəns/ *n* **1** [U] *formal* great respect and admiration for someone or something【正式】尊敬, 崇敬: **[+for]** *You should show proper reverence for the national flag.* 你對國旗必須表現出應有的崇敬。**2 your/his reverence** *old use* used when speaking to or about a priest【舊】尊敬的閣下〔對神職人員的尊稱〕: *The visitors have arrived, your reverence.* 來訪者已經到了, 牧師閣下。

reverence² *v* [T] *old use* to revere someone or something【舊】尊敬, 崇敬

Rev·e·rend¹ /ˈrɛvərənd; ˈrevərənd/ *n* a title of respect used before the name of a minister of the Christian church 牧師〔基督教教士的尊稱, 用於姓名前〕: *the Reverend John Graham* 約翰·格雷厄姆牧師

reverend² *adj* [only before noun 僅用於名詞前] *old use* deserving respect【舊】值得尊敬的

Reverend Moth·er /ˌ···ˈ··/ *n* [C] a title of respect for the woman in charge of a CONVENT; MOTHER SUPERIOR 女院長〔對女修道院主管的尊稱〕

rev·e·rent /ˈrɛvərənt; ˈrevərənt/ *adj formal* showing respect and admiration【正式】恭敬的, 虔誠的: *They sat in reverent silence.* 他們肅然坐着, 默默無聲。—**reverently** *adv*: *He kissed her hand reverently.* 他恭敬地吻了她的手。

rev·e·ren·tial /ˌrɛvəˋrɛnʃəl; ˌrevəˈrenʃəl◂/ *adj formal* showing respect【正式】恭敬的, 表示敬意的: *He spoke of the dead man in reverential tones.* 他以恭敬的口氣提及死者。—**reverentially** *adv*: *They treated him reverentially.* 他們對他畢恭畢敬。

rev·e·rie /ˈrɛvərɪ; ˈrevəri/ *n* [C,U] a state of imagining or thinking about pleasant things, that is like dreaming 幻想, 夢想: *She was startled out of her reverie by the door bell.* 門鈴聲將她從夢幻中驚醒。

re·vers·al /rɪˋvɝsḷ; rɪˈvɜːsəl/ *n* [C,U] **1** a change to an opposite arrangement, process or course of action 反向; 反轉; 倒轉: *There has been a dramatic reversal of government policy.* 政府政策發生了巨大轉變。**2** [C] a failure or other problem that prevents you from being able to do what you want 逆轉, 倒退〔指阻止人達到目標的失敗等〕: *In spite of setbacks and reversals, his business was at last making money.* 儘管遭遇挫折和失敗, 他的生意最後還是賺錢了。

re·verse¹ /rɪˋvɝs; rɪˈvɜːs/ *v*

1 ▶CHANGE STH 改變某事物◀ [T] to change something, such as a decision, judgment, or process so that it is the opposite of what it was before 推翻, 撤銷: *The court of appeal reversed the original verdict and set the prisoner free.* 上訴法院撤銷了原判, 釋放了那個犯人。| *What can we do to reverse the present trend of falling sales?* 我們能做些甚麼來扭轉目前銷售額下降的趨勢?

2 ▶CAR 汽車◀ [I,T] if a car or its driver reverses, they go backwards 倒車: **[+out/into etc]** *a car reversing out of a driveway* 正在倒退出車道的車 | *Before you reverse, make sure there are no pedestrians behind you.* 要確定後面沒有行人才倒車。| **reverse a car/bus etc** (=make it reverse) 倒車 —see picture on page A3 參見 A3 頁圖

3 ▶CHANGE THE ORDER 改變順序◀ [T] to change round the usual order of the parts of something 顛倒〔通常的次序〕: *They reversed the normal order for the ceremony and started with prayers.* 他們改變了儀式的常規順序, 以祈禱開始。

4 ▶TURN STH OVER 翻轉某物◀ [T] to turn something over, so as to show the back of it 翻轉: *Reverse the paper in the printer.* 請把打印機中的紙翻過來。

5 reverse the charges *BrE* to make a telephone call which is paid for by the person you are telephoning【英】〔電話〕由受話方付款; CALL COLLECT *AmE*【美】—**reversible** *adj*: *This coat is reversible, you can wear it inside out.* 這件上衣雙面式的, 裡子能朝外翻過來穿。—**reversibility** *n* [U]

reverse² *n*

1 ▶THE OPPOSITE 相反◀ the reverse the exact opposite of what has just been mentioned 正相反: *The economic situation is certainly improving, although recent trade figures suggest the reverse.* 經濟形勢無疑在好轉, 儘管最近的貿易數字説明的情況正相反。| **quite the reverse** (=completely the opposite) 完全相反 *I was not happy – quite the reverse, I was seething with anger.* 我並不高興, 恰恰相反, 我氣極了。

2 go into reverse if a trend or process goes into reverse, it starts to happen in the opposite way 逆轉: *a danger that the movement towards democracy will go into reverse* 民主運動發生逆轉的危險

3 ►IN A CAR 在汽車裡◄ [U] the control in a vehicle that makes it go backwards; REVERSE GEAR 倒車擋 | **into/in reverse** *Put the car into reverse.* 掛上倒擋倒車。

4 ►A DEFEAT 失敗◄ [C] *formal* a defeat or a problem that delays your plans; SETBACK【正式】失敗; 挫折: *Losing the Senate vote was a serious reverse for the President.* 被參議院投票否決對總統來説是個嚴重的挫折。

5 ►OTHER SIDE 另一面◄ [singular] the less important side or the back of an object that has two sides 背面: *Is there a pattern on the reverse of the cloth?* 布的背面有圖案嗎?

6 ►OF A COIN 硬幣◄ [singular] the side of a coin that does not show a person's head 背面: *The British ten-pence piece has a lion on the reverse.* 英國十便士硬幣反面的圖案是一頭獅子。

reverse[3] *adj* [only before noun 僅用於名詞前] **1 reverse order/procedure/process etc** the opposite order etc to what is usual or to what has just been stated 相反的順序/程序/過程等: **in reverse order** *Reassemble the parts in reverse order.* 按相反順序重新組裝零件。**2 the reverse side** the back of something 反面, 背面: *Sign the check on the reverse side.* 請在支票上背書。

reverse di·scrim·i·na·tion /ˌ.. ...ˈ../ *n* [U] the practice of giving unfair treatment to a group of people who usually have advantages, in order to be fair to the group of people who were unfairly treated in the past 逆向歧視〔以不公平的方式對待通常佔優勢的團體, 從而公平地對待過去受歧視的團體〕—compare 比較 POSITIVE DISCRIMINATION

reverse gear /ˌ. ˈ./ *n* [U] the control in a vehicle that makes it go backwards 倒車擋

reversing light /ˈ... ˌ./ *n* [C] a light on the back of a car which comes on when the car is going backwards 倒車燈 —see picture on page A2 參見 A2 頁圖

re·ver·sion /rɪˈvɝʒən; rɪˈvɜːʃən/ *n* [singular,U] *formal*【正式】**1** a return to a former, usually bad, condition or habit〔以前的情況或習慣, 一般是惡劣情況或不良習慣的〕恢復, 回復: [**+to**] *the danger of a reversion to tribal warfare in the region* 該地區再次爆發部族戰爭的危險 **2** *law* the return of property to a former owner【法律】〔財產的〕歸還

re·vert /rɪˈvɝt; rɪˈvɜːt/ *v*

revert to sb/sth *phr v* [T] **1** to go back to a former condition or habit, especially one that was bad 恢復, 回復〔尤指不好的情況或習慣〕: *As soon as they stopped farming, the land reverted to wilderness.* 他們一停止耕種, 土地又變成一片荒蕪。| *He had reverted to lazing in bed and coming in late to work.* 他故態復萌, 貪睡賴牀, 上班遲到。| **revert to type** (=return to your former type of behaviour) 故態復萌 **2** to return to an earlier subject of conversation 回到〔先前的話題〕: *I'd like to revert to the first point you made.* 我想回到你提出的第一點上。**3** *law* if land or a building reverts to someone, it becomes the property of its former owner again【法律】歸還〔地產、房屋等〕

re·vet·ment /rɪˈvɛtmənt; rɪˈvetmənt/ *n* [C] *technical* a surface of stone or other building material added for strength to a wall that holds back loose earth, water etc【術語】鋪面, 砌面; 護牆; 護坡, 護帶

3 2 **re·view**[1] /rɪˈvju; rɪˈvjuː/ *n* **1** [C,U] an act of carefully examining and considering a situation or process 回顧, 檢查, 檢討: *The Department of Agriculture ordered an urgent review of pesticide safety.* 農業部命令對殺蟲劑的安全性進行緊急審查。| *a review of progress in computer science over the last 20 years* 對過去20年電腦科學所取得的進步的回顧 | **under review** (=being examined and considered) 在審查中 *Nuclear weapons systems are currently under review.* 核武器系統目前正接受審查。| **come up for review** (=come to the time when there is supposed to be a review) 到提交審查的時間 *The ban on whaling came up for review in 1990.* 捕鯨的禁令在1990年應該進行審查。**2** [C] an article in a newspaper or magazine that gives an opinion about a new book, play, film etc〔報紙、雜誌上的〕評論(文章); 書評, 劇評, 影評: *Her latest novel got good reviews in the press.* 她的最新小説得到了報界的好評。**3** [U] the work of writing these 評論〔的寫作〕: *He sent her an offprint of the article for review.* 他寄給她該文章的印樣, 請她寫評論。| **review copy** (=a copy of a book etc sent to a magazine or newspaper for review) 書評用贈閱本 **4** [C] an official show of the army, navy etc in the presence of a king, president, or officer of high rank〔軍隊〕檢閱, 閱兵式: *a naval review* 海軍檢閱 **5** [C] a REVUE〔穿插歌舞和時事諷刺的〕表演劇

review[2] *v* **1** [T] to examine, consider and judge a situation or process carefully 仔細審度〔情況或程序〕; 詳查; 回顧, 檢討: *Government spending has been reviewed to try and reduce the budget deficit.* 對政府開支進行了審核, 以爭取減少預算赤字。**2** [I,T] to write an article judging a new book, play, film etc (為...)寫書評[影評等]: *Bernstein sometimes reviewed classical music in the 'Post'.* 伯恩斯坦有時在《郵報》上發表評論古典音樂的文章。| **be well reviewed** (=be praised by reviewers) 受到好評 **3** [T] to officially examine a group of soldiers, ships etc at a military show 檢閱〔軍隊〕: *The President will review the soldiers on parade.* 總統將在閱兵式中檢閱部隊。**4** [T] *AmE* to look again at something quickly, such as school work, notes of lessons, or a report etc【美】複習, 溫習〔功課、筆記、報告等〕—compare 比較 REVISE (2) 3

re·view·er /rɪˈvjuɚ; rɪˈvjuːə/ *n* [C] someone who writes about new books, plays etc in a newspaper or magazine〔評論新書、戲劇等的〕評論家

re·vile /rɪˈvaɪl; rɪˈvaɪl/ *v* [T] to express hatred of someone or something 謾罵, 辱罵: *The President was now reviled by the very Party he had helped to lead.* 總統目前受到了他曾協助領導的政黨的痛斥。—**reviler** *n* [C]

re·vise /rɪˈvaɪz; rɪˈvaɪz/ *v* **1** [T] to change your opinions, plans etc because of new information or ideas 改變〔意見、計劃等〕, 修正: *I've revised my opinion of Bill – he's much more intelligent than I thought.* 我改變了對比爾的看法, 他比我原來認為的要聰明得多。| *Our original forecast of this year's profits has now been revised upwards.* (=we think profits will be higher) 我們對本年度利潤的原先預測現在已經向上調整。| **revised estimate** (=a calculation that has been changed to make it more accurate) 修正的估計 *Are there any questions on the revised estimates of the budget?* 對財政預算的修訂估計還有甚麼問題嗎? **2** [I,T] *BrE* to study lessons or notes again, in order to learn them before an examination【英】複習: *She's still got a lot of revising to do before the exam.* 她在考試前還有許多東西要複習。**3** [T] to change a piece of writing by adding new information, making improvements, or correcting mistakes 審訂; 修訂, 校訂〔文稿〕: *Eliot revised his American lectures for publication.* 埃略特對他的美國講座文稿進行修正, 準備出版。| **revised edition** (=a new and improved form or copy of a book) 修訂版 *a revised edition of the encyclopedia* 百科全書的修訂版 —compare 比較 REVIEW[2] —**reviser** *n* [C]

re·vi·sion /rɪˈvɪʒən; rɪˈvɪʒən/ *n* **1** [C,U] the process of changing something, especially a piece of writing, in order to improve it by correcting it or including new information or ideas〔尤指文稿的〕修改, 修訂, 校訂: *His lecture needs a lot of revision.* 他的演講需要大加修改。| **be subject to revision** (=be considered for possible change) 可能需要修訂 *The department budget is subject to monthly revision.* 部門的預算須經每月審查修訂。**2** [C] a piece of writing that has been improved and corrected 修訂稿 **3** [U] *BrE* the work of studying lessons, notes etc again in order to learn them【英】複習, 温習: *I'll have to do some revision before my exam.* 考試前我得温習功課。

re·vi·sion·is·m /rɪˋvɪʒənɪzəm; rɪˈvɪʒənɪzəm/ *n* [U] ideas which are changing away from the main beliefs of a political system, especially a Marxist system 修正主義〔尤指對馬克思主義的修改〕**—revisionist** *adj* **—revisionist** *n* [C]: *revisionist writings* 修正主義的著作

re·vis·it /riˋvɪzɪt; ˌriːˈvɪzʒt/ *v* [T] **1** to return to a place you once knew well 重遊, 再訪: *They revisited the town where he grew up.* 他們重遊了那個鎮, 他是在那裡長大的。**2** to come back to in order to discuss again 回到〔某問題以重新討論〕: *OK, so we need to revisit this proposal as soon as the budget position is clearer.* 好, 預算的情況更明朗時, 我們就需要立即重新討論這項建議。**3** **revisited** an event, fashion etc revisited is something else very like it that reminds you of it〔事件、時尚的〕翻版: *a music festival that was essentially Woodstock revisited* 基本上是胡士托音樂節的翻版

re·vi·tal·ize also 又作 **-ise** *BrE*【英】/riˋvaɪtl̩ˌaɪz; riːˈvaɪtəlaɪz/ *v* [T] to put new strength or power into something 使恢復元氣, 注入新的活力: *They hope to revitalize the neighborhood by providing better housing.* 他們希望通過提供更好的住房條件使住宅區恢復活力。**—revitalization** /riˌvaɪtl̩əˋzeʃən; riːˌvaɪtəlaɪˈzeɪʃən/ *n* [U]

re·vi·val /rɪˋvaɪvl̩; rɪˈvaɪvəl/ *n* **1** [C,U] a process of something becoming active or strong again 復興, 復活: *The Roosevelt administration wanted to stimulate an economic revival.* 羅斯福政府希望刺激經濟復蘇。| **[+of]** *the revival of old fears and jealousies* 昔日的恐懼和嫉妒的復現 **2** [C,U] the fact of something becoming popular again 再流行: **[+of]** *the revival of Buddhism in China* 佛教在中國的復興 | *Opera is enjoying a revival.* 歌劇又流行起來。**3** [C] a new production of a play that has not been recently performed〔舊劇的〕重新上演: *a revival of 'West Side Story'*〔音樂劇〕《夢斷城西》的重新上演 **4** [C] a REVIVAL MEETING〔基督教的〕復興 (信仰) 布道會

re·vi·val·is·m /rɪˋvaɪvl̩ɪzəm; rɪˈvaɪvəlɪzəm/ *n* [U] an organized attempt to make a religion more popular 宗教復興運動 **—revivalist** *adj*

revival meet·ing /·ˈ·· ˌ··/ *n* [C] a public religious meeting with music, famous speakers etc, that is intended to make people interested in Christianity〔基督教的〕復興 (信仰) 布道會

re·vive /rɪˋvaɪv; rɪˈvaɪv/ *v* **1** [I,T] to become or make someone conscious, healthy, or strong again (使) 蘇醒, 復原: *The doctors revived her with injections of glucose.* 醫生給她注射葡萄糖使她蘇醒過來。| *The plant will revive if you water it.* 如果給那株植物澆水, 它就會再活過來。**2** [T] to come back or bring something back into existence or popularity 使再興起, 使再流行: *Helen's trip home has revived memories of her childhood.* 海倫的故鄉之旅喚起了她對童年的回憶。| *reviving old customs* 復興舊習俗

re·viv·i·fy /riˋvɪvəˌfaɪ; riːˈvɪvʒfaɪ/ *v* [T] *formal* to give new life and health to someone or something【正式】使恢復活力, 使恢復生氣: *The aim was to strengthen, revivify and revitalise the Labour Party.* 目的是加強、恢復和振興工黨。

rev·o·ca·tion /ˌrɛvəˋkeʃən; ˌrevəˈkeɪʃən/ *n* [C,U] the act of revoking a law, decision etc〔法律、決定等的〕廢除, 撤銷, 取消

re·voke /rɪˋvok; rɪˈvəʊk/ *v* [T] to officially state that a law, decision, contract etc is no longer effective; CANCEL〔正式〕廢除, 取消〔法律、決定、合同等〕: *Their work permits have been revoked.* 他們的工作許可證被吊銷了。

re·volt[1] /rɪˋvolt; rɪˈvəʊlt/ *v* **1** [I] if a group of people revolt, they take strong and often violent action against the government, usually with the aim of taking power away from them; REBEL[2] 造反, 起義; 反叛: *George III's repressive measures forced the Colonies to revolt.* 喬治三世的高壓手段迫使各殖民地起義。**2** [I] to refuse to accept someone's authority or obey rules, laws etc〔對權威、規章、法律等〕反抗, 拒絕服從: **[+against]** *Public opinion will revolt against any further increase in taxes.* 公眾輿論將反對進一步增加稅收。**3** [T] if something revolts you, it is so unpleasant that it makes you feel sick and shocked 使作嘔, 使反感, 使憎惡; 使震驚: **be revolted by/at** *We were revolted by their cruelty.* 我們對他們的殘忍感到震驚。—see also 另見 REVULSION

revolt[2] *n* **1** a refusal to accept someone's authority or obey rules, laws etc 反抗, 反對: *The President faces a Senate revolt.* 總統面臨參議院的反對。| *a child's revolt against rigid, oppressive parents* 孩子對固執、霸道的父母的反抗 **2** strong and often violent action by a lot of people against their ruler or government 造反, 起義; 反叛: **[+against]** *an armed revolt against a tyrannical regime* 反對暴政的武裝起義 | **in revolt** *The peasants rose up in armed revolt.* 農民發動了武裝起義。**3** a feeling of being sick and very shocked at something unpleasant 作嘔, 反感: *a sense of revolt at the bloody scenes* 看到血腥場面後想吐的感覺

re·volt·ing /rɪˋvoltɪŋ; rɪˈvəʊltɪŋ/ *adj* extremely unpleasant; DISGUSTING 使人厭惡的, 令人作嘔的: *the revolting taste of sour milk* 變酸的牛奶極難聞的味道 | *His leering glances were revolting to her.* 他色迷迷的目光令她反感。**—revoltingly** *adv*: *Your socks are revoltingly dirty.* 你的襪子髒得叫人噁心。

rev·o·lu·tion /ˌrɛvəˋluʃən; ˌrevəˈluːʃən/ *n* **1** [C] a complete change in ways of thinking, methods of working etc〔思想、工作方式等的〕徹底變革: *Computer technology has caused a revolution in business practices.* 電腦技術引起了商務活動的巨大改變。—see also 另見 INDUSTRIAL REVOLUTION **2** [C,U] a time of great, usually sudden, social and political change, especially the changing of a ruler or political system by force 革命: *the French Revolution* 法國大革命 | *social inequalities that led to revolution* 導致革命的社會不平等 —see also 另見 COUNTER-REVOLUTION **3** [C,U] one complete circular movement, or continued circular movement, around a fixed point 旋轉一周; 循環 (運動): **[+round/around]** *The Earth makes one revolution round the sun each year.* 地球每年繞太陽公轉一圈。**4** one complete circular spinning movement, made by something such as a wheel fixed on a central point 旋轉一周: *a speed of 100 revolutions per minute* 每分鐘100轉的轉速 —see also 另見 REVOLVE

rev·o·lu·tion·a·ry[1] /ˌrɛvəˋluʃənˌɛrɪ; ˌrevəˈluːʃənəri◂/ *n* [C] someone who joins in or supports a political or social revolution 革命者, 革命家: *socialist revolutionaries* 社會主義革命者

revolutionary[2] *adj* **1** completely new and different, especially in a way that leads to great improvements 革命性的, 創新的: *The new cancer drug is a revolutionary breakthrough.* 這種新抗癌藥是革命性的突破。**2** [only before noun 僅用於名詞前] connected with a political or social revolution 革命的: *a revolutionary leader* 革命領袖

rev·o·lu·tion·ize also 又作 **-ise** *BrE*【英】/ˌrɛvəˋluʃənˌaɪz; ˌrevəˈluːʃənaɪz/ *v* [T] to completely change the way people think or do things, especially because of a new idea or invention 使徹底變革: *New metal alloys have revolutionized car manufacture.* 新金屬合金使汽車製造業發生了根本變革。

re·volve /rɪˋvalv; rɪˈvɒlv/ *v* [I,T] to spin around or make something spin around, on a central point; ROTATE (1) (使) 旋轉: *The metal disc revolves at high speed.* 那個

金屬盤以高速旋轉。| **revolve sth** *Revolve the drum to get all the clothes out of the dryer.* 轉動滾筒把所有衣服從烘乾機中取出。

revolve around sth *phr v* [T not in passive 不用被動態] **1** [not in progressive 不用進行式] to have something as a main subject or purpose 以…為主題[目的], 圍繞: *The story revolves around a young girl who runs away from home.* 故事圍繞着一個離家出走的年輕姑娘展開。| *Her life seems to revolve around her career.* 她的生活似乎以她的事業為中心。| **think the world revolves around you** *informal* (=think that you are more important than anyone or anything else)【非正式】認為自己比誰都重要 **2** to move in circles around something 圍繞…旋轉: *The moon revolves around the Earth.* 月球圍繞地球旋轉。

re·volv·er /rɪˋvɑlvɚ; rɪˈvɒlvə/ *n* [C] a small gun which has a revolving container for bullets, so that several shots can be fired without having to put more bullets in 左輪手槍

re·volv·ing /rɪˋvɑlvɪŋ; rɪˈvɒlvɪŋ/ *adj* a revolving object is designed so that it turns with a circular movement 旋轉的: *a revolving stage in the theatre* 旋轉舞台

revolving door /ˌ·ˌ·· ˈ·/ *n* [C] a type of door in the entrance of a large building, that goes round and round as people go through it 旋轉門

re·vue /rɪˋvju; rɪˈvjuː/ *n* [C] a show in a theatre, that includes songs, dances, and jokes about recent events〔穿插歌舞和時事諷刺的〕表演劇

re·vul·sion /rɪˋvʌlʃən; rɪˈvʌlʃən/ *n* [U] a strong feeling of shock and very strong dislike 厭惡, 憎惡, 強烈的反感: *News of the atrocities produced a wave of anger and revulsion.* 暴行的消息激起一陣憤怒和反感。

3 **re·ward¹** /rɪˋwɔrd; rɪˈwɔːd/ *n* **1** [C,U] something that you receive because you have done something good or helpful 報答, 報償, 酬謝, 獎賞: **[+for]** *She received a crystal decanter as a reward for her services.* 作為對她服務的酬謝, 她得到一隻水晶盛酒瓶。| *$100 was a poor reward for all my work!* 100美元對於我做的所有工作來說太少了! **2** [C] an amount of money that is offered to someone who finds something that was lost or gives the police information 賞金: *A reward was offered for the return of the jewels.* 為找回珠寶而懸賞。**3 be its own reward** if something that you do is its own reward, it makes you feel happy and satisfied 本身就是獎賞: *Working for a good cause can be its own reward.* 為有意義的事業工作本身就是獎賞。

reward² *v* [T] to give something to someone because they have done something good or helpful 酬謝, 報答, 獎賞: *How can I reward your kindness?* 對你的好意, 我怎麼來報答呢? | **reward sb with sth** *Larry complimented her and was rewarded with a smile.* 拉里恭維她, 她報以微笑。| **reward sb for sth** *She was generously rewarded for her work.* 她的工作得到了慷慨的報酬。

re·ward·ing /rɪˋwɔrdɪŋ; rɪˈwɔːdɪŋ/ *adj* making you feel happy and satisfied because you feel you are doing something useful or important, even if you do not earn much money 值得做的, 有益的, 有意義的: *Teaching can be a very rewarding career.* 教書可以是一種很有意義的職業。

re·wind /riˋwaɪnd; riːˈwaɪnd/ *v* to make a CASSETTE TAPE or VIDEO go backwards so as to see or hear it again 倒回〔錄音帶或錄像帶〕

re·wire /riˋwaɪr; ˌriːˈwaɪə/ *v* [T] to put new electric wires in a building, machine, light etc 更換…的電線

re·word /riˋwɝd; ˌriːˈwɜːd/ *v* [T] to say or write something again in different words, in order to make it easier to understand or more suitable 重述, 改寫, 改變…的措辭: *Let me reword my question.* 讓我換個說法來提問。

re·work /riˋwɝk; ˌriːˈwɜːk/ *v* [T] to make changes in music or a piece of writing, in order to use it again 改編〔樂曲、作品〕

re·write /riˋraɪt; ˌriːˈraɪt/ *v past tense* **rewrote** /-ˋrot; -ˈrəʊt/ *past participle* **rewritten** /-ˋrɪtn̩; -ˈrɪtn/ [T] to change something that has been written, especially in order to improve it, or because new information is available〔尤指為改進或有新資料〕重寫, 改寫: *Rewrite the passage in your own words.* 用你自己的話改寫這段。— **rewrite** /ˈriˌraɪt; ˈriːraɪt/ *n* [C]: *Software packages may need complete rewrites to match new hardware.* 套裝軟件可能需要全部改寫以便與新的硬件相配。

Rex /rɛks; reks/ *n Latin*【拉丁】**1** a title used in official writing after the name of a king, when the king's name has been written in Latin 王, 君王, 國王〔公文中用於以拉丁文寫成的君王名字之後的稱謂〕: *Henricus Rex* 亨利國王 **2** *law* a word meaning the state, used in the names of law cases in Britain when a king is ruling【法律】王國政府〔英國國王在位時用於訟案的名稱中, 代表國家〕: *Rex v Jones* 王國政府對瓊斯訟案

rhap·so·dize also 又作 **-ise** *BrE*【英】/ˋræpsəˌdaɪz; ˈræpsədaɪz/ *v* [I] to talk about something in an eager, excited, and approving way 熱烈地讚美, 稱頌: **[+about/over]** *rhapsodizing about the aroma of the mountain forests* 讚美山林的芳香

rhap·so·dy /ˋræpsədɪ; ˈræpsədi/ *n* [C] **1** a piece of music that is written to express emotion, and does not have a regular form 狂想曲 **2** an expression of eager and excited approval 讚美之辭, 熱情讚頌: *listening to Miss Duval's rhapsodies about Venice* 聽杜瓦爾小姐對威尼斯的讚美之辭

rhe·o·stat /ˋriəˌstæt; ˈriːəstæt/ *n* [C] a piece of equipment that controls the loudness of a radio or the brightness of an electric light, by limiting the flow of electric current 變阻器

Rhe·sus fac·tor /ˋrisəs ˌfæktɚ; ˈriːsəs ˌfæktə/ *n* [singular] *technical* a substance whose PRESENCE (RHESUS POSITIVE) or absence (RHESUS NEGATIVE) in the red blood cells may have dangerous effects for some babies or when a person receives blood from another person【術語】獼因子, Rh 因子〔紅血球中含有此種物質 (即 Rh 陽性), 或缺乏此種物質 (即 Rh 陰性) 都有可能對某些嬰兒或接受輸血的人造成危險的後果〕

rhesus mon·key /ˋrisəs ˌmʌŋkɪ; ˈriːsəs ˌmʌŋki/ *n* [C] a small monkey from northern India that is often used in medical tests〔產於印度北部的〕恆河猴

rhet·o·ric /ˋrɛtərɪk; ˈretərɪk/ *n* [U] **1** language used to persuade or influence people, especially by politicians〔尤指政治家使用的〕雄辯言辭, 煽動性語言: *the rhetoric of their political rallies* 他們在政治集會上使用的煽動性語言 **2** speech or writing that sounds impressive, but is not actually sincere or very useful 巧辯, 浮誇之詞: *Positive action is better than rhetoric.* 積極的行動勝過浮華的詞藻。**3** the art of speaking or writing to persuade or influence people 修辭學

rhe·tor·i·cal /rɪˋtɔrɪkl̩; rɪˈtɒrɪkəl/ *adj* **1 rhetorical question** a question that you ask as a way of making a statement, without expecting an answer, such as 'Who knows what might happen?' 修辭性疑問句 **2** using speech or writing in special ways in order to persuade people or to produce an impressive effect 修辭的, 與修辭有關的: *impassioned rhetorical phrases* 慷慨激昂的巧辯華辭 — **rhetorically** /-kl̩ɪ; -kli/ *adv*

rhet·o·ri·cian /ˌrɛtəˋrɪʃən; ˌretəˈrɪʃən/ *n* [C] *formal* someone who is trained or skilful in the art of persuading or influencing people through speech or writing【正式】修辭學家

rheu·mat·ic /ruˋmætɪk; ruːˈmætɪk/ *adj* **1** connected with rheumatism 風濕病的, 風濕性的: *a rheumatic condition of the joints* 關節風濕 **2** suffering from rheumatism 患風濕病的

rheumatic fe·ver /ˌ·ˌ·· ˈ··/ *n* [U] a serious infectious disease that causes fever, swelling in your joints, and sometimes damage to your heart 風濕熱

rheu·mat·ick·y /ruˋmætəkɪ; ruːˈmætɪki/ *adj informal* rheumatic【非正式】風濕病的, 風濕性的

rheu·mat·ics /ru`mætɪks; ruː'mætɪks/ *n* [plural] *informal especially BrE* rheumatism【非正式, 尤英】風濕病

rheu·ma·tis·m /`rumə͵tɪzəm; 'ruːmətɪzəm/ *n* [U] a disease that makes your joints or muscles painful and stiff 風濕病

rheu·ma·toid ar·thri·tis /͵rumətɔɪd ɑr`θraɪtɪs; ͵ruːmətɔɪd ɑː'θraɪtɪs/ *n* [U] a disease that continues for many years, and makes your joints painful and stiff, and often makes them lose their proper shape 類風濕性關節炎

RH fac·tor /͵ɑr `etʃ ͵fæktɚ; ͵ɑːr 'eɪtʃ ͵fæktə/ *n* [C] the RHESUS FACTOR 獼因子, Rh因子

rhine·stone /`raɪn͵ston; 'raɪnstəʊn/ *n* [C,U] a jewel made from glass or a transparent rock that is intended to look like a diamond 萊茵(水晶)石

rhi·no /`raɪno; 'raɪnəʊ/ *n plural* **rhinos** [C] *informal* a rhinoceros【非正式】犀牛

rhi·no·ce·ros /raɪ`nɑsərəs; raɪ'nɒsərəs/ *n* [C] a large heavy African or Asian animal with thick skin and either one or two horns on its nose 犀牛

rhi·no·plas·ty /`raɪnə͵plæstɪ; 'raɪnəʊ͵plæsti/ *n* [U] PLASTIC SURGERY on your nose 鼻整形手術 —**rhinoplastic** /͵raɪnə`plæstɪk; ͵raɪnəʊ'plæstɪk◂/ *adj*

R

rhi·zome /`raɪzom; 'raɪzəʊm/ *n* [C] *technical* the thick stem of some plants such as the IRIS, which lies flat along the ground with roots and leaves growing from it【術語】根莖, 根狀莖

rho·do·den·dron /͵rodə`dɛndrən; ͵rəʊdə'dendrən/ *n* [C] a bush with bright flowers which keeps its leaves in winter 杜鵑花屬植物

rhom·boid[1] /`rɑmbɔɪd; 'rɒmbɔɪd/ *n* [C] *technical* a shape with four sides whose opposite sides are equal; PARALLELOGRAM【術語】長菱形, 長斜方形, 平行四邊形 —see picture at 參見 SHAPE[1] 圖

rhomboid[2] also 又作 **rhom·boid·al** /rɑm`bɔɪdḷ; rɒm'bɔɪdl/ *adj technical* shaped like a rhombus【術語】菱形的

rhom·bus /`rɑmbəs; 'rɒmbəs/ *n* [C] *technical* a shape with four equal straight sides, especially one that is not a square【術語】菱形 —see picture at 參見 SHAPE[1] 圖

rhu·barb /`rubɑrb; 'ruːbɑːb/ *n* **1** [U] a plant with broad leaves and a thick red stem that can be eaten (食用)大黃 **2** [U] *spoken* a word used by actors to make a sound like many people talking【口】演員模仿人聲嘈雜時使用的詞 **3** [C] *AmE old-fashioned* a noisy argument【美, 過時】激烈的爭吵

rhyme[1] /raɪm; raɪm/ *n* **1** [C] a short poem or song, especially for children, using words that rhyme 押韻詩;(押韻的)兒歌 —see also 另見 NURSERY RHYME **2** [C] a word that rhymes with another word, for example 'fold' and 'cold' 同韻詞: **[+for]** *I can't find a rhyme for 'orange'.* 我找不到和 orange 同韻的詞。**3** [U] the use of words that rhyme in poetry, especially at the ends of lines 在詩中同韻詞的使用, 押韻: *Shakespeare sometimes wrote in rhyme.* 莎士比亞有時寫韻文。**4 without rhyme or reason** in a way that cannot be reasonably explained 無緣無故, 毫無道理: *Joe's moods change without rhyme or reason.* 喬的情緒會無緣無故地變化。

rhyme[2] *v* [not in progressive 不用進行式] **1** [I] if two words or lines of poetry rhyme, they end with the same sounds, including a vowel 押韻, 成韻: **[+with]** *'House' rhymes with 'mouse'.* house 和 mouse 押韻。| **rhyming couplet** (=two lines of poetry that end in words that rhyme) 押韻的兩行詩 **2** [T] to put two or more words together to make them rhyme 用...押韻, 使成韻: **[+with]** *You can't rhyme 'box' with 'backs'.* box 和 backs 不押韻。

rhyming slang /͵·· '·/ *n* [U] a way of talking, used especially by COCKNEYS (=people from east London), in which you use words or phrases that rhyme with the words you mean, instead of using the normal words. For example, 'plates of meat' is rhyming slang for 'feet' 同韻俚語〔尤在倫敦東區方言中常用, 如 plates of meat 表示 feet〕

rhyth·m /`rɪðəm; 'rɪðəm/ *n* [C,U] **1** a regular repeated pattern of sounds or movements 節律, 節奏; 律動: *the exciting rhythms of African drum beats* 非洲鼓聲那激動人心的節拍 | *the rhythm of your heartbeat* 你的心跳節律 **2** a regular pattern of changes 規則變化(模式): *the rhythm of the seasons* 四季的交替

rhythm and blues /͵·· · '·/ *n* [U] R AND B (=a type of music) 節奏怨曲

rhyth·mic /`rɪðmɪk; 'rɪðmɪk/ also 又作 **rhyth·mic·al** /-ɪkḷ; -ɪkəl/ *adj* having rhythm 有節奏的: *the rhythmic thud of the bass drum* 低音鼓有節奏的重擊聲 —**rhythmically** /-kḷɪ; -kli/ *adv*: *tapping rhythmically on the table* 有節奏地敲擊桌子

rhythm meth·od /'·· ͵··/ *n* [singular] a method of BIRTH CONTROL which depends on having sex only at a time when the woman is not likely to become PREGNANT 安全期避孕法

rhythm sec·tion /'·· ͵··/ *n* [C] the part of a band that provides a strong RHYTHM with drums and other similar instruments〔樂團的〕節奏樂器組

ri·al /rɪ`ɑl; ri'ɑːl/ *n* [C] a RIYAL 里亞爾〔沙特阿拉伯及其他許多阿拉伯國家的貨幣單位〕

rib[1] /rɪb; rɪb/ *n* [C] **1** one of the 12 pairs of curved bones that surround your chest 肋骨: *He broke a rib in the accident.* 他在事故中折斷了一根肋骨。—see picture at 參見 RESPIRATORY 圖 **2** a piece of meat that includes an animal's rib 肋條(肉): *barbecued ribs* 烤肋條 **3** a curved piece of wood, metal etc that is used as part of the structure of something such as a boat or building〔木製或金屬的〕肋條, 肋材 —see also 另見 PRIME RIB, SPARERIBS, **dig sb in the ribs** (DIG[1] (5))

rib[2] *v* **ribbed, ribbing** [T] *informal* to make jokes and laugh at someone so that you embarrass them, but in a friendly way【非正式】〔友善地〕開...的玩笑, 取笑: *Tony's always ribbing me about my accent.* 托尼總是取笑我的口音。

rib·ald /`rɪbḷd; 'rɪbəld/ *adj* ribald songs, remarks, riddles, or jokes are humorous, rude and usually about sex〔歌曲、玩笑等〕粗俗的, 下流的

rib·ald·ry /`rɪbḷdrɪ; 'rɪbəldri/ *n* [U] ribald songs, remarks, or jokes 粗俗下流的歌曲; 猥褻的笑話

ribbed /rɪbd; rɪbd/ *adj* having a pattern of raised lines 有稜線的, 有凸起條紋的, 有羅紋的: *ribbed stockings* 羅紋長襪

rib·bing /`rɪbɪŋ; 'rɪbɪŋ/ *n* [U] **1** friendly jokes and laughter about someone that embarrasses them〔友善的〕開玩笑, 取笑, 戲弄: *Jake always took some ribbing about his lack of hair.* 傑克總是因為頭髮少而被取笑。**2** a pattern of raised lines in knitting (KNIT (1))〔編織中的〕稜線, 羅紋, 凸條

rib·bon /`rɪbən; 'rɪbən/ *n*

1 ►SILK 絲綢◄ [C,U] a long narrow piece of cloth used to tie things or as a decoration 絲帶, 緞帶: *a red ribbon in her hair* 她頭髮上繫的紅緞帶

2 ►STH NARROW 窄的東西◄ [singular] something that is long and narrow 狹長的東西, 條, 帶: *a ribbon of shining water* 一條波光粼粼的狹長水道

3 be cut/torn to ribbons to be very badly damaged by being cut or torn in many places 割爛/撕爛: *Her feet were cut to ribbons on the rocks.* 她的腳在岩石上磨爛了。| **be in ribbons** (=be badly torn in many places) 多處撕裂 *His coat was in ribbons.* 他的外衣破爛不堪。

4 ►PRIZE 獎品◄ [C] *AmE* a small arrangement of coloured ribbon in the form of a flat flower, that is given as a prize in a competition; ROSETTE【美】〔作為比賽獎品的〕綬帶: **blue ribbon** (=the first prize) 藍色綬帶〔一等獎〕

5 ►MILITARY HONOUR 軍隊的榮譽◄ [C] a piece of ribbon with a special pattern or colours on it, worn to show that you have received a military honour〔軍功的〕勳章, 勳帶

6 ▶INK 墨汁◀ a long narrow piece of cloth or plastic with ink on it that is used in a TYPEWRITER〔打字機用的〕色帶

ribbon de·vel·op·ment /ˈ‥ ˌ‥ˈ‥/ *n* [U] *BrE* long lines of houses along the side of the main roads leading out of a city, or the practice of arranging houses in this way【英】〔城市沿着幹道兩側向郊外建房的〕帶狀發展

rib cage /ˈ· ·/ *n* [C] the structure of RIBs around your lungs, heart, and other organs 胸廓, 胸腔

ri·bo·fla·vin /ˌraɪbəˈflevɪn; ˌraɪbəʊˈfleɪvɪn/ *n* [U] *technical* VITAMIN B2, a substance that exists in meat, milk, and some vegetables, and that is important for your health【術語】核黃素, 維生素 B2

rice /raɪs; raɪs/ *n* [U] **1** a food that consists of small white or brown grains that you boil in water until they become soft enough to eat 米; 米飯: *a tasty sauce served with rice or pasta* 與米飯或麵食一起上的美味醬汁 **2** the plant that produces this grain (水)稻

rice pad·dy /ˈ· ˌ‥/ *n* [C] a field in which rice is grown 稻田

rice pa·per /ˈ· ˌ‥/ *n* [U] **1** a thin paper made especially in China and used by painters there〔中國的〕宣紙 **2** a similar type of thin paper that can be eaten, which is used in cooking〔用於烹飪、可以吃的〕米紙

rice pud·ding /ˌ· ˈ‥/ *n* [U] a sweet dish made of rice, milk, and sugar cooked together 大米布丁〔用大米、牛奶、糖一起做成的甜食〕

2 2 **rich** /rɪtʃ; rɪtʃ/ *adj*

1 ▶WEALTHY 富的◀ **a)** having a lot of money or valuable possessions 有錢的, 富有的: *one of the richest women in America* 美國最富有的女性之一 | *He got rich by making money on the stock market.* 他在股票市場上賺錢致富。| *a rich and powerful nation* 富有的強國 **b) the rich** people who have a lot of money and possessions 富人: *tax laws that benefit the rich* 使富人受益的稅法

2 ▶LARGE AMOUNT 大量◀ having or containing a lot of something 富含…的: **[+in]** *Citrus fruits are rich in vitamin C.* 柑橘類水果富含維生素 C。| **oxygen-rich/nutrient-rich/protein-rich etc** (=containing a lot of oxygen etc) 富含氧氣/營養/蛋白質等的 *Pregnant women should eat protein-rich foods.* 孕婦應該吃富含蛋白質的食物。

3 ▶FULL OF INTEREST 非常有趣的◀ full of interesting or important events, ideas etc 豐富的: *the rich literary tradition of England* 英格蘭豐富的文學傳統 | **[+in]** *a story that was rich in detail* 充滿細節描述的故事

4 ▶SMELL 氣味◀ having a strong pleasant smell〔氣味〕濃郁的: *The rich scent of the pine trees was heavy in the air.* 空氣中散發着松樹的濃郁芳香。

5 ▶COLOUR 顏色◀ having a beautiful strong colour〔色彩〕濃豔的: *stained glass dyed a rich blue* 染成鮮豔的藍色的彩色玻璃

6 ▶FOOD 食物◀ containing foods such as butter, cream, and eggs, which make you feel full very quickly〔含黃油、奶油、雞蛋等〕容易讓人感到飽的; 油膩的: *a rich fruit cake* 脂肪含量高的水果蛋糕

7 ▶MUSIC/SOUNDS 音樂/聲音◀ having a pleasant low sound〔聲音〕低沉渾厚的: *the rich tone of a cello* 大提琴低沉渾厚的音色

8 ▶SOIL/LAND 土壤/土地◀ good for growing plants in; FERTILE (1) 肥沃的, 富饒的: *Cotton grew well in the rich, black soil.* 棉花在肥沃的黑土地裡生長得很好。

9 ▶CLOTH/JEWELLERY ETC 衣物/珠寶等◀ expensive and beautiful 昂貴的, 華麗的: *She stroked the rich velvet of the dress enviously.* 她羨慕地撫摸着連衣裙華貴的天鵝絨。

10 that's rich (coming from him/you etc) used to say that what someone has said is unreasonable and that they are criticizing you for doing something that they do themselves (他/你等說的話) 不合情理[真荒謬]: *Ron told me I was disloyal. That's pretty rich coming from a married man.* 羅恩說我不忠誠。這話出自一個有婦之夫實在可笑。

11 ▶PETROL 汽油◀ having too much petrol mixed with the air, so that a car's engine does not operate smoothly〔汽車的內燃機裡汽油與空氣的混合物中〕汽油成分過高的

rich·es /ˈrɪtʃɪz; ˈrɪtʃɪz/ *n* [plural] *especially literary* expensive or beautiful possessions and large amounts of money【尤文】財富, 財寶: *the riches he had brought back from his travels* 他出門旅行帶回來的財寶

rich·ly /ˈrɪtʃlɪ; ˈrɪtʃli/ *adv* **1 richly decorated/embroidered etc** beautifully and expensively decorated etc 裝飾華麗的/刺繡精美的等: *a cloak richly embroidered with gold thread* 用金線刺繡的華麗披風 **2 richly coloured** having beautiful strong colours 色彩濃豔的: *the richly coloured mosaic* 色彩濃豔的鑲嵌工藝品 **3 richly deserve** to completely deserve something such as success or punishment 完全應該得到〔成功或懲罰〕: *They got the punishment they so richly deserved.* 他們真是罪有應得。**4** in large amounts 大量(地): *He was richly rewarded for his services.* 他的服務得到了豐厚的報酬。

rick[1] /rɪk; rɪk/ *n* [C] a large pile of STRAW or grass that is kept in a field until it is needed 禾堆; 乾草堆[垛]

rick[2] *v* [T] *BrE* to twist and slightly injure your back, neck, ANKLE etc【英】扭傷: *He whirled around so quickly he ricked his neck.* 他轉身太快, 扭傷了脖子。

rick·ets /ˈrɪkɪts; ˈrɪkɪts/ *n* [U] a disease that children get in which their bones become soft and bent, caused by a lack of VITAMIN D〔兒童由於缺乏維生素 D 而患的〕佝僂病

rick·et·y /ˈrɪkətɪ; ˈrɪkɪti/ *adj* a rickety piece of furniture or part of a building is in such bad condition that it looks as if it will break if you use it 快要散架的, 搖搖晃晃的: *an old rickety wooden chair* 一把快要散架的舊木椅 — see picture on page A18 參見 A18 頁圖

rick·shaw /ˈrɪkʃɔ; ˈrɪkʃɔː/ *n* [C] a small vehicle used in South East Asia for carrying one or two passengers, that is pulled by someone walking or riding a bicycle 人力車, 黃包車

ric·o·chet[1] /ˈrɪkʃe; ˈrɪkəʃeɪ/ *v* [I] if a moving object, such as a bullet or stone, ricochets, it changes direction when it hits a surface at an angle〔子彈、石塊等運動物體〕回跳, 反彈: **[+off]** *Bullets ricocheted off the boulders around him.* 子彈從他周圍的巨石上彈飛了。

ricochet[2] *n* [C] **1** something such as a bullet or a stone that has ricocheted 彈飛的物體 **2** an act of ricocheting 彈飛, 反彈

rid[1] /rɪd; rɪd/ *adj* **1 get rid of a)** to throw away some- 1
thing you do not want or use any more 丟棄, 扔掉: *It's time we got rid of all these old toys.* 該是我們把這些舊玩具全部丟掉的時候了。**b)** to take action so that you no longer have something unpleasant that you do not want 擺脫, 除去: *I can't get rid of this cough.* 我咳嗽老是不好。| *He opened the windows to get rid of the smell of stale tobacco.* 他打開窗戶想排除污濁的煙草味。**c)** to make someone leave because you do not like them or because they are causing problems 趕走〔某人〕: *I had to get rid of my assistant because he was habitually late.* 我不得不把我的助手開除, 因為他總是遲到。**2 be rid of** to have got rid of something or someone so that they are not there to worry or annoy you 擺脫, 除掉, 除去: *The clerical part of his job was tedious, and he was glad to be rid of it.* 他的那部分文書工作枯燥乏味, 擺脫了之後他很高興。| **be well rid of** *especially spoken* (=be lucky to be rid of)【尤口】有幸擺脫了… *You're well rid of her, she's nothing but trouble.* 你幸虧擺脫了她, 她只會給人添麻煩。

rid[2] *v past tense* **rid** or **ridded** *past participle* **rid** *present participle* **ridding**

rid sb/sth of sth *v* [T] **1** to remove something or someone that is bad or harmful from a place, organization etc 使擺脫, 使除掉〔不好或有害的人或東西〕: *A huge vaccination program rid the world of smallpox.* 龐大的疫苗接種計劃使天花在世界上絕跡。**2 rid yourself of sth** to take action so that you do not have a feeling, thought, or problem that was causing you trouble any more 使自己擺脫某事物: *She's trying to rid herself of a dependence on drugs.* 她正在努力戒除毒癮。

rid·dance /ˈrɪdṇs; ˈrɪdns/ *n* [U] **good riddance** *spoken* a rude way of saying you are glad someone has left【口】總算擺脫了〔慶幸某人走後說的不禮貌的話〕: *"Jim's left." "Well, good riddance," said Faye. "I never liked him."* "吉姆走了。" "哦, 謝天謝地," 費伊說, "我壓根就不喜歡他。"

-ridden /rɪdṇ; rɪdn/ *suffix* [in adjectives 構成形容詞] **1** feeling too much of a strong emotion 為…所苦的: *her guilt-ridden dreams* 她那充滿內疚感的夢 **2** too full of something 充斥…的, 全是…的: *mosquito-ridden swamps* 蚊蟲為患的沼澤

rid·dle¹ /ˈrɪdḷ; ˈrɪdl/ *n* [C] **1** a question that is deliberately very confusing and usually has a humorous or clever answer 謎, 謎語: *Solve this riddle – What is black and white and red all over? Answer – An embarrassed zebra.* 猜猜這個謎語: 甚麼東西黑白相間卻全身通紅? 謎底是: 一匹難為情的斑馬。**2** a mysterious action, event, or situation that you do not understand and cannot explain 奧祕, 費解之事: *The origins of the Basque language remain a riddle.* 巴斯克語的起源仍是個謎。| *the riddle of the universe* 宇宙的奧祕 **3** a large wire container with holes in it used to separate earth from stones 〔篩分土石的〕粗篩

riddle² *v* [T] **1** to shake the coal etc in a fire or push it about with a stick, in order to remove ashes 搖動〔爐柵〕, 用〔撥火棍〕使灰落下 **2** to make a lot of small holes in something 在…上弄許多小洞

rid·dled /ˈrɪdḷd; ˈrɪdld/ *adj* **1 riddled with** very full of something, especially something bad or unpleasant 充斥, 佈滿: *awful concrete apartment blocks, riddled with damp* 令人討厭的、潮濕的混凝土公寓住宅區 | *an isolated village community, riddled with prejudice* 一個與世隔絕、充滿偏見的村落 **2 riddled with holes** full of small holes 到處是小洞的: *The wall of the fort was riddled with bullet holes.* 城堡的牆壁上到處是子彈洞。| *streets riddled with potholes* 到處坑坑窪窪的街道

ride¹ /raɪd; raɪd/ *v past tense* **rode** /rod; rəʊd/ *past participle* **ridden** /ˈrɪdṇ; ˈrɪdn/

1 ►ANIMAL 動物◄ [I,T] to sit on an animal, especially a horse, and make it move along 騎〔馬等〕: *She learnt to ride when she was seven.* 她七歲時學會了騎馬。| **ride away/across/back etc** *He rode away across the marshes.* 他騎馬穿過沼澤離去。| **ride sth** *I've never ridden a horse.* 我從未騎過馬。| **ride on sth** *She arrived riding on a white horse.* 她騎着一匹白馬到來。| **go riding** *I go riding every Saturday.* 我每個星期六都去騎馬。| **ride a race** *I rode a good number of races last season.* 上個賽季我參加了許多次賽馬。| **ride a winner** (=ride a horse that wins a race) 賽馬獲勝 *I rode my first winner last year.* 去年我第一次在賽馬中獲勝。| **ride the countryside/range** *AmE* (=to travel on a horse across the countryside)【美】騎馬穿過鄉間 *They rode the countryside in search of her.* 他們騎馬穿過鄉間尋找她。

2 ►BICYCLE/MOTORBIKE 自行車/摩托車◄ [I always+adv/prep,T] to travel on a bicycle or MOTORBIKE 騎〔自行車或摩托車〕**ride away/down/to etc** *They mounted their bikes and rode off.* 他們騎上自行車離開了。| **ride sth** *She rode her bicycle to school every day.* 她每天騎自行車上學。| **ride on sth** *Can I ride on your bike?* 我能騎你的自行車嗎?

3 ►VEHICLE 車輛◄ [I always+adv/prep,T] *especially AmE* to travel in a bus, car, or other vehicle【尤美】乘坐〔車輛〕: **ride in/on sth** *It was the first time they had ridden in a train.* 這是他們第一次坐火車。| *I ride in cabs whenever I can.* 只要可能我總是坐計程車。| **ride to/into/back etc** *We got onto the bus and rode into San Francisco.* 我們上了公共汽車, 到三藩市去。| **ride a bus** *AmE*【美】: *Ann rode a bus for the rest of the distance.* 剩下的路程安乘了公共汽車。

4 ride on sb's shoulders/back if a child rides on someone's shoulders or back, they are carried in that way〔小孩〕騎在某人肩上/揹在某人背上: *He was tired so he rode on his father's shoulders.* 他累了, 於是騎在父親的肩上。

5 ►IN A LIFT 在電梯裡◄ [I always+adv/prep,T] *especially AmE* to travel up or down in a lift【尤美】乘坐〔電梯〕: **ride up/down** *I walked to the elevator and rode back down.* 我走過去乘電梯回到樓下。| **ride sth** *When the elevator arrived he rode it down to his floor.* 電梯來了, 他乘電梯下到他那層。

6 ►IN WATER 在水裡◄ a) [I always+adv/prep] to move or float on the water 航行; 漂浮: *The smaller boat was lighter and rode higher in the water.* 那條較小的船比較輕, 在水裡浮得比較高。| **ride at anchor** *There was a large ship riding at anchor in the bay.* 一艘大船拋錨停泊在海灣。**b) ride a wave** to float on a wave and move forward with it 隨浪漂浮〔前進〕: *The sea was full of surfboarders riding the waves.* 海裡到處是踏浪而行的衝浪者。

7 be riding high to feel very happy and confident 春風得意, 揚揚自得: *They were riding high on their election victory.* 他們因在選舉中獲勝而春風得意。

8 let sth ride *spoken* to take no action about something that is wrong or unpleasant【口】聽之任之, 放任自流: *He made a derogatory remark, but I let it ride.* 他說了無禮的話, 不過我並沒有計較。

9 ride roughshod over to ignore someone else's feelings or ideas because you have the power or authority to do this 忽視〔別人的感受或意見〕: *He was accused of riding roughshod over his colleagues' proposals.* 他被指責無視同事的建議。

10 ►ANNOY SB 惹惱某人◄ [T] *AmE spoken* to annoy someone by repeatedly criticizing them or asking them to do things【美口】數落, 纏住: *Stop riding her – she's doing her best.* 不要纏着她不放, 她正在盡全力。

11 ride a punch/blow to move back slightly when someone hits you, so that you are not hit with so much force〔稍微後退以〕躲閃拳擊/重擊: *He managed to ride the punch.* 他往後一閃, 雖然中了一拳, 但力量減輕了。

12 be riding for a fall *informal* to be doing something unwise which could result in failure【非正式】〔不顧後果地〕蠻幹, 魯莽行事: *I had a feeling he was riding for a fall, and tried to tell him so.* 我感覺他在蠻幹, 於是設法告訴他這一點。

ride sb ↔ **down** *phr v* [T] to knock someone down when you are riding on a horse 騎馬撞倒〔某人〕: *They were almost ridden down by the cavalry.* 他們差一點兒被騎兵撞倒。

ride on sth *phr v* [T] if someone's success or the respect that they get is riding on something, it depends on it〔成功、名譽等〕取決於: *He knew he had to win – his reputation was riding on it.* 他知道自己必須取勝, 他的名聲都繫於此。

ride sth ↔ **out** *phr v* **1** [T] if a ship rides out a storm, it manages to keep floating until the storm has ended〔船隻〕平安度過〔風暴〕**2** [T] if you ride out a difficult situation, you are not badly harmed by it 安然渡過〔難關〕: *The company was deeply involved in the scandal, but managed to ride it out successfully.* 該公司深陷醜聞中, 但還是成功地渡過了難關。

ride up *phr v* [I] if a skirt rides up, it moves upwards so that it is no longer covering your body properly〔衣服等〕向上拱, 往上縮

ride² *n* [C] 

1 ►JOURNEY 旅行◄ a journey on a horse or bicycle, or in a vehicle〔騎馬、騎自行車或乘車的〕旅行, 旅程: *It* *was a lovely morning for a ride.* 那天早上天氣很好, 適合出去兜風。| **[+in/on]** *a ride in the director's personal car* 乘坐主任的私人汽車 | **go for a ride** *Let's go for a ride in the countryside.* 讓我們乘車到郊外去兜一圈吧。| **have a ride** *Can I have a ride on your motorbike?* 我能不能搭你的摩托車? | **take sb for a ride** *Shall I take you for a ride in my car?* 我帶你坐我的車去兜一圈好嗎? | **give sb a ride** *A man gave me a ride back to Harrisburg.* 一位男士讓我搭車回到哈里斯堡。| **a car/lorry/train etc ride** *He was exhausted after the coach ride from Manchester.* 他從曼徹斯特乘長途汽車來, 非常疲勞。| **get a (free) ride** *I managed to get a free ride down to the station.* 我設法免費搭車到了車站。| **hitch a ride** *She hitched a ride into town.* 她搭便車進了城。

2 give sb a rough ride *informal* to make a situation difficult or unpleasant for someone in authority【非正式】使某人難受, 給某人出難題: *The journalists gave the Prime Minister a pretty rough ride.* 記者們讓首相下不了台。

3 take sb for a ride *spoken* to trick someone, especially in order to get money from them【口】欺騙某人〔尤指騙錢〕: *I'd just begun to realise he was taking me for a ride.* 我才開始意識到他在騙我。

4 come/go along for the ride *spoken* to join what other people are doing just for pleasure, not because you are seriously interested in it【口】湊熱鬧: *I had nothing better to do, so I thought I'd go along for the ride.* 我沒有甚麼事可做, 因此想去湊湊熱鬧。

5 have/be in for a bumpy ride *informal* to have or be likely to have difficulties or problems【非正式】會有麻煩

6 ►MACHINE 機器◄ a large machine that people ride on for pleasure at a FAIR〔遊樂場中〕供人乘坐娛樂的裝置: *The rides are exciting, but very expensive.* 乘坐那些玩意兒令人興奮, 可是很貴。

7 ►PATH 小路◄ a path that is suitable for horses but not for cars〔供馬走的〕小道: *a grassy ride* 長滿草的小道

rid·er /ˈraɪdə; ˈraɪdə/ *n* [C] **1** someone who rides a horse, bicycle etc 騎師; 騎車者 **2** a statement that is added, especially to an official decision or judgment〔尤指正式決議或裁決的〕附文, 附件; 附加條款: *The rider stated that paragraph 27 applied only to foreign imports.* 附件説第27段僅適用於外國進口貨物。

ridge¹ /rɪdʒ; rɪdʒ/ *n* [C] **1** a long area of high land, especially at the top of a mountain 山脊: *a windswept ridge* 當風的山脊 —see picture on page A12 參見 A12 頁圖 **2 a)** a line of something that rises above a surface 一列隆起物: *a ridge of boulders* 一列隆起的巨石 | *a sandy ridge* 沙脊 **b)** a long narrow raised part of a surface 狹長的隆起部分: *The ridges on the soles give the shoes a better grip.* 鞋底上隆起的棱可以更好地防滑。**3 a ridge of high pressure** *technical* a long area of high ATMOSPHERIC pressure【術語】高壓脊

ridge² *v* [T] to make a ridge or ridges in something 使成脊狀, 使隆起

ridged /rɪdʒd; rɪdʒd/ *adj* something that is ridged has ridges on its surface 隆起的, 皺起的: *gnarled, ridged bark* 扭曲起皺的樹皮

rid·i·cule¹ /ˈrɪdɪkjul; ˈrɪdʒkjuːl/ *n* [U] unkind laughter or remarks intended to make someone or something seem stupid 嘲笑, 奚落: **be held up to ridicule** (=be publicly made to look stupid) 成為笑話 | **an object of ridicule** (=a person or thing that everyone laughs at and regards as stupid) 被取笑[嘲笑]的對象 *In 'The Lord of the Flies', Piggy had become an object of ridicule, ignored by the other boys.* 在《蒼蠅王》中, 皮吉成了眾人取笑的對象, 其他男孩都不把他放在眼裡。

ridicule² *v* [T] to laugh at a person, idea, institution etc 嘲笑, 嘲弄, 奚落: *My ideas were ridiculed by the rest of the team.* 我的想法受到其他隊員的嘲笑。| *He used his acute brain and mischievous wit to ridicule Tory MPs.* 他用自己敏鋭的頭腦和頑皮的機智來嘲笑保守黨的議員。

ri·dic·u·lous /rɪˈdɪkjələs; rɪˈdɪkjələs/ *adj* silly or unreasonable 愚蠢的; 荒唐的, 可笑的: *She looked absolutely ridiculous in those trousers.* 她穿着那條褲子顯得非常可笑。| *"I'm too scared to go on my own." "Oh, don't be ridiculous!"* "我很害怕, 不敢自己一個人去。" "噢, 別傻啦!" | **it is ridiculous that** *It's ridiculous that we have to wait six weeks.* 我們得等六個星期, 這太荒唐了。—**ridiculously** *adv* —**ridiculousness** *n* [U] 2

rid·ing /ˈraɪdɪŋ; ˈraɪdɪŋ/ *n* [U] the sport or activity of riding horses 騎馬(運動)

rife /raɪf; raɪf/ *adj* **1** [not before noun 不用於名詞前] if something bad or unpleasant is rife, it is very common〔壞事或討厭的事〕普遍存在的, 流行的: *Violent crime is rife in our inner cities.* 暴力犯罪在我們的貧民區非常普遍。—see also 另見 **run rife** (RUN¹ (37)) **2 rife with** full of something bad or unpleasant 充斥着...: *The streets were rife with rumors of the President's resignation.* 大街小巷都充斥着總統辭職的謠傳。

riff /rɪf; rɪf/ *n* [C] a repeated series of notes in popular or JAZZ music〔流行音樂或爵士樂中的〕重複樂段: *whistling a Scott Joplin riff* 用口哨吹奏〔美國作曲家〕斯科特·喬普林一首樂曲的重複樂段

rif·fle /ˈrɪfl; ˈrɪfəl/ also 又作 **riffle through** *v* [T] *informal* to quickly turn over the pages of a book, magazine etc【非正式】快速翻閱〔書、雜誌等〕

riff-raff /ˈrɪf ˌræf; ˈrɪf ræf/ *n* [U] an insulting word for people who are noisy, badly-behaved, or of low social class 地痞流氓; 烏合之眾〔含侮辱之意〕: *She seemed to have invited most of the local riff-raff.* 她似乎邀請了當地大部分不三不四的人。

ri·fle¹ /ˈraɪfl; ˈraɪfəl/ *n* [C] a gun with a long BARREL (=tubeshaped part) which you hold up to your shoulder 來復槍, 步槍

rifle² *v* [T] **1** also 又作 **rifle through** to search quickly through a cupboard, drawer etc 迅速翻遍〔櫃子、抽屜等〕: *He rifled through his pockets for a coin.* 他為找一枚硬幣翻遍了口袋。**2** to steal things from a place 偷竊: *The warehouse's entire stock was rifled.* 倉庫的全部存貨都被偷走了。

rifle range /ˈ·· ·/ *n* [C] a place where people practise shooting with rifles 步槍射擊場

rift /rɪft; rɪft/ *n* [C] **1** a situation in which two people or groups have begun to dislike or distrust each other, usually caused by a serious disagreement 分裂, 不和: *The government has been weakened by internal rifts.* 內部不和把政府削弱了。**2** a crack or narrow opening in a large mass of rock, cloud etc〔岩石、雲等的〕裂縫, 裂口

rift val·ley /ˈ· ˌ··/ *n* [C] a valley with very steep sides, formed by the cracking and moving of the Earth's surface 裂谷

rig¹ /rɪg; rɪg/ *v* **rigged, rigging** [T] **1** to arrange or influence an election, competition etc in a dishonest way so that you get the result that you want〔以不正當手段〕操縱〔選舉、比賽等〕; 在〔選舉、比賽等〕中做手腳: *She claimed the election was rigged.* 她聲稱這次選舉被人操縱。**2** [usually passive 一般用被動態] to provide a ship with ropes, sails etc 給〔船〕配備索具、帆具等: *a fully-rigged vessel* 一艘配備齊全的船

rig sb ↔ **out** *phr v* [T] *informal* to dress someone in special or unusual clothes【非正式】給〔某人〕穿上特別[奇異]的衣服: *They had rigged the little boy out in a sailor suit.* 他們給那個小男孩穿上了水手服。

rig sth ↔ **up** *phr v* [T] *informal* to make equipment, furniture etc quickly from objects that you find around you【非正式】倉促拼湊: *We rigged up a simple shower at the back of the cabin.* 我們在小木屋的後面匆匆裝了一個簡單的淋浴器。

rig² *n* [C] **1** a large structure in the sea used for getting oil from the ground under the sea〔油田的〕海上鑽台 **2** the way in which a ship's sails and MASTS are arranged 帆桅的裝配(方式) **3** *informal* a large TRUCK【非正式】

R

大型卡車: *driving the rig down to Baltimore* 將大型卡車開到巴爾的摩 **4** *AmE informal* a set of equipment for a special purpose【美, 非正式】成套設備: *the photographer's camera and all the rest of his rig* 攝影師的照相機和他其餘的設備 **5** *old-fashioned* a set of clothes【過時】套裝

rig·a·ma·role /ˈrɪgəmərol; ˈrɪgəmərəʊl/ *n* [C] an American spelling of RIGMAROLE rigmarole 的美式拼法

rig·a·to·ni /ˌrɪgəˋtonɪ; ˌrɪgəˈtəʊni/ *n* [U] a type of PASTA in the shape of short tubes 波紋管狀通心粉 —see picture at 參見 PASTA 圖

rig·ging /ˋrɪgɪŋ; ˈrɪgɪŋ/ *n* [U] all the ropes, chains etc that hold up a ship's sails 船上的全部帆纜, 索具 —see picture at 參見 YACHT 圖

S1 W1 **right¹** /raɪt; raɪt/ *adj*

1 ►TRUE/CORRECT 真實的/正確的◄ based on true facts; correct 如實的; 正確的: *Is that the right time?* 那時間對嗎? | *Yes. $6.47 is the right answer.* 對, 6.47美元是正確答案。| *New research has proved their theories right.* 新的研究證明他們的理論是正確的。| **be right about** *You were right about the party – it was awful.* 聚會的事你說對了 —— 非常糟糕。| **half right** (=partly but not completely right) 對了一半 *Well, you're half right – he's not actually an actor, but he does work in the theatre.* 啊, 你說對了一半 —— 他其實不是演員, 但確實在劇院工作。

R

2 ►CORRECT/NORMAL 正確的/正常的◄ in the position, order or state which is correct or where something works best 正確的; 正常的: *This diagram's not right!* 這張圖表不對! | **put sth right** (=change something so that it is correct or works properly) 糾正某事 *You'll have to call a plumber to put the machine right.* 你得請管子工來把機器修理好。

3 that's right *spoken*【口】**a)** used to agree with what someone says or to answer 'yes' to a question 沒錯; 對: *"Is this Piccadilly Circus?" "That's right, mate."* "這裡是皮卡迪利廣場嗎?" "是的, 老兄。" | *"...and before you know it, it's too late." "That's right, that's right."* "...再等就太晚了。" "是的, 是的。" **b)** used when you are telling someone that you are angry about what they are doing 行啦; 夠啦〔用於對別人所做的事感到憤怒時〕: *That's right! Just go out and leave me to do the dishes as usual!* 行啦! 你出去算了, 還是跟平時一樣讓我來洗碗吧!

4 ►SIDE 側面◄ [only before noun 僅用於名詞前] **a)** concerning or belonging to the right side of your body, which has the hand that most people write with 右邊的, 右側的: *Raise your right arm.* 請舉起右手。| *My right shoe pinches.* 我右腳的鞋夾腳。—opposite 反義詞 LEFT¹ (1) **b)** on the same side of something as your right side 右方的, 靠右的: *Take the next right turn.* 在下一個路口往右拐。| *the right bank of the river* 河的右岸 —opposite 反義詞 LEFT¹ (2)

5 ►SUITABLE 合適的◄ most suitable for a particular occasion or purpose 恰當的: *This is definitely the right decision for the company.* 這對於公司來說肯定是正確的決定。| **be right for/be the right person for** *Floella is the right person for that job.* 佛羅埃拉是那份工作的恰當人選。| **be right for sb/be the right person for sb** (=to be a suitable partner for someone) 對某人是合適的/是合適的搭檔 *Elaine and Stu are so right for each other!* 伊萊恩和斯圖如此般配!

6 ►MORALLY 道義上◄ an action that is right is morally correct 符合道德的, 正當的: **right to do sth** *Do you think I was right to report them to the police?* 你覺得我向警方檢舉他們做得對嗎? | *It can't be right to keep lying to your husband.* 老是欺騙你的丈夫是不對的。| **it's only right** (=anything else would not be right) 唯一正確的 *It's only right that the children get an equal share.* 只有平均分給孩子們才是正確的。| **it is right that** *I think it's right that the people who work hardest should earn the most.* 我認為工作最努力的人報酬最高是合理的。—opposite 反義詞 WRONG¹ (4)

7 ►TOTAL 完全的◄ [only before noun 僅用於名詞前] *BrE spoken* used to emphasize how bad someone or something is【英口】完全的, 地道的〔強調某人或某事壞的程度〕: *He sounds like a right idiot!* 他聽起來像個十足的白痴! | *Don't go in there, it's a right rip-off.* 別進去, 那簡直是敲竹槓。| **right royal** (=extremely special in a way that is suitable for a king, queen etc) 皇家氣派的 *a right royal welcome* 非常隆重的歡迎

8 things are not right used to say that there are problems connected with a relationship or situation〔關係或情況〕不對頭, 有問題: *Things haven't been right between Carl and me for a while now.* 卡爾和我之間的關係不好已經有段時間了。

9 be in the right place at the right time to seem to always be in the place where something useful becomes available or is being offered 在恰當的時間出現在恰當的地方: *Being a news photographer is all about being in the right place at the right time.* 當新聞攝影師, 就是要在恰當的時間出現在恰當的地點。

10 ►HEALTHY 健康的◄ *spoken* healthy【口】健康的: *I haven't been feeling right all day.* 我一整天都覺得不舒服。| **put sb right** (=make someone feel healthy again) 讓某人恢復健康 *A week's rest will put you right again.* 休息一個星期, 你就沒事了。—see also 另見 **put sb straight/right** (PUT (15))

11 not right in the head/not in your right mind *usually humorous* crazy【通常幽默】瘋了: *If he thinks he can get to the Olympics, he's not in his right mind!* 他如果以為自己可以參加奧運會, 那真是瘋了!

12 (as) right as rain *informal* completely healthy, especially after an illness【非正式】〔尤指病後〕完全健康: *The doctor says I'll be as right as rain in a couple of days.* 醫生說我過兩天就會完全恢復正常。

13 ►SOCIALLY 社交上◄ *BrE* the right people, places, schools etc are considered to be the best or most important【英】〔人、地方、學校等〕最優秀的, 地位最高的: *Sonia's always careful to be seen with the right people.* 索尼婭交朋友很謹慎, 總是讓人看見她和有社會地位的人在一起。

14 right you are/righto/righty ho *BrE spoken* used to agree with what someone is saying or telling you to do【英口】沒錯; 好的: *"Shut the door, will you?" "Righto."* "把門關上好嗎?" "好的。"

15 am I right in thinking (that) *spoken* used when you think that something is true, but you are not completely sure【口】我認為...對嗎: *Am I right in thinking that you come from Australia?* 我覺得你是澳大利亞人, 對不對?

Frequencies of the word **right** in spoken and written English 單詞 right 在英語口語和書面語中的使用頻率

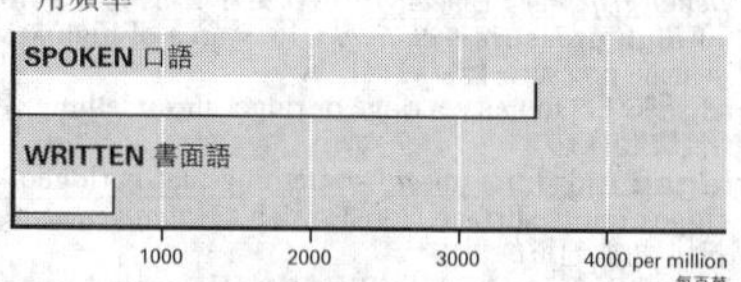

Based on the British National Corpus and the Longman Lancaster Corpus
據英國國家語料庫和朗文蘭卡斯特語料庫

This graph shows that the word **right** is much more common in spoken English than in written English. This is because it has several uses as an interjection in conversations. 本圖表顯示, 單詞 right 在英語口語中的使用頻率遠遠高於書面語, 因為它有些用法是在對話中用作感嘆語。

right (*adj*) **SPOKEN USES**
right 的口語用法

16 *BrE* used to get someone's attention so that you

can tell them something【英】好〔用來引起注意〕: *Right! Open your books on page 16.* 好！將書翻到第16頁。
17 *BrE* used to say you are ready to do something【英】好〔表示準備就緒〕: *Right, let's go!* 好，我們走吧！
18 *especially BrE* used to say 'yes' to a suggestion or order【尤英】是的，好的〔用於對建議或命令的回答〕: *"Come over tomorrow." "Right, OK, see you then."* "請明天過來。" "好的，好，明天見。"
19 used to agree with what someone says 對，是〔表示同意〕: *"I mean, why shouldn't she go out with him if she wants to?" "Yeah, right."* "我的意思是，如果她願意，為甚麼不跟他談戀愛?" "對，就是。"
20 used as a question to ask if what you have said is correct 對不對〔詢問自己所說的是否正確〕: *We're leaving at 10.30, right?* 我們10點30分走，對不對?
21 used to check that someone is understanding what you are saying 對不對〔問對方明不明白你說的話〕: *So I went into the bar, right, and I saw the manager, right, and I said...* 於是我走進酒吧，對不對，我看見了經理，對不對，我說…

1 1 **right[2]** *adv*
1 right at/behind/in front of exactly in a particular position or place 就在…/…後面/…前面: *She was standing right in the middle of the room.* 她就站在屋子的正中間。| *There's the house, right in front of you.* 就是那所房子，就在你面前。
2 ►IMMEDIATELY 立刻◄ immediately and without any delay 立刻，立即: **right now/away/after** *I'll find the address for you right away.* 我馬上就給你找到地址。| *It's on right after the 6:30 news.* 6點30分的新聞之後馬上播出。| **right off the bat** *AmE* (=without much thought)【美】立即，不假思索 *Kay wrote the answers down right off the bat.* 凱立刻就寫下了答案。
3 ►CORRECTLY 正確地◄ correctly 正確地: *We guessed right – they'd already gone.* 我們猜對了——他們已經走了。
4 ►DIRECTION/SIDE 方向/側面◄ towards the direction or side that is on the right 向右，朝右: *Turn right at the crossroads.* 在十字路口向右拐。—opposite 反義詞 LEFT[2]
5 right along/through/into/around etc all the way along, through etc 一直沿着/穿過/進入/圍繞等: *Go right to the end of the road.* 一直走到路的盡頭。| *I haven't read the book right through yet.* 我還沒看完這本書。
6 be right behind sb *spoken* to completely support someone in their ideas or in what they are trying to achieve【口】完全支持某人
7 I'll be right with you/right there *spoken* used to ask someone to wait because you are coming very soon【口】我馬上就來/到: *"Lunch is ready!" "I'll be right there."* "吃午飯啦!" "我馬上就到。"
8 be right up there (with) *informal* to be as good or as important as the very best【非正式】(與…) 不相上下; (與…) 同等重要: *As far as I'm concerned he's right up there with Bob Dylan.* 依我看，他與巴布迪倫不相上下。
9 right, left and centre *BrE*【英】, **right and left** *AmE*【美】everywhere or in every way 到處，處處: *We're losing money right, left and centre.* 我們處處都在虧本。

2 1 **right[3]** *n*
1 ►ALLOWED 允許的◄ [C usually singular 一般用單數] if you have the right to do something you are morally, legally, or officially allowed to do it 權利: **right to do sth** *We have a constitutional right to defend ourselves.* 憲法賦予我們自衛的權利。| *Everyone should have the right to live in peace.* 每個人都應該擁有和平生活的權利。| **be within your rights (to do sth)** (=be morally or legally allowed to do something)〔在道德或法律上做某事〕是正當的 *You'd be well within your rights to take him to court.* 你完全有權控告他。| **as of right** *formal* (=because it is their right)【正式】有權 *Every shareholder will receive an invitation as of right.* 每一位股東都將接到邀請，這是他們的權利。
2 have a right to be annoyed/upset/angry to have a good or understandable reason for being annoyed, upset etc 感到煩惱/不快/生氣是有道理的: *You had every right to be angry with them.* 你有充分理由生他們的氣。
3 have no right to do sth used to say that someone's actions are completely unreasonable or unfair 沒有權利做某事: *You have no right to treat us like this – we are innocent.* 你沒有權利這樣對待我們，我們是無辜的。
4 the right a) the side of your body that has the hand that most people write with, or this side of anything else 右邊，右方，右側: *Take the first turning on the right.* 在右邊第一個路口轉彎。| *On your right, you can see the Houses of Parliament.* 在你的右側你可以看到議會大廈。| *Take two steps to the right.* 向右走兩步。**b)** also 又作 **the Right** [singular] political parties or groups such as the CONSERVATIVES in Britain or the REPUBLICANS in the US, which strongly support the CAPITALIST economic system 右翼政黨〈如英國的保守黨、美國的共和黨等〉
5 rights [plural] the freedom and advantages that everyone should be allowed to have〔人人應有的〕權利，權益: *We must stand up and fight for our rights!* 我們必須起來為我們的權利而鬥爭！| *a denial of basic human rights* 剝奪基本人權 | **women's/workers' rights etc** *New legislation is gradually taking away workers' rights.* 新的立法正在逐漸削減工人的權利。| **equal rights** (=the same rights for everyone, whatever their sex, race, or social position) 平等的權利 —see also 另見 CIVIL RIGHTS, HUMAN RIGHTS
6 ►CORRECT BEHAVIOUR 恰當的行為◄ [U] behaviour that is generally agreed to be morally correct〔道德上〕正確，對: *You're old enough to know what's right.* 你已經長大了，該知道甚麼是對的。| *Some of these kids don't seem to know the difference between right and wrong.* 這些孩子當中有的似乎不能分辨是非。
7 be in the right to have the best reasons, arguments etc in a disagreement with someone else〔在與別人的爭論中〕有理: *Both sides are convinced that they are in the right.* 雙方都相信自己有理。
8 by rights *spoken* used to describe what should happen if things are done fairly or correctly【口】按理 (說): *By rights Jenkins should have had a promotion by now.* 按理說，詹金斯現在應該提升了。
9 in your own right without depending on anyone or anything else 依靠自己的能力，根據自己的權利〔而不依賴於其他因素〕: *Elizabeth II is Queen in her own right.* 伊麗莎白二世是名正言順地繼承王位的。
10 put sth/sb to rights to make a place, person, or situation return to normal again 使某事/某人恢復正常，糾正某事/某人: *This medicine will soon put you to rights.* 這藥會很快使你痊癒的。| *It took ages to put the room to rights again.* 把房間收拾好花了很長時間。
11 the rights and wrongs of all the different reasons for and against something …的是非曲直: *I'm not interested in the rights and wrongs of the system, I just want my money back!* 我對這個制度的是與非不感興趣，我只是想取回我的錢！
12 do right by *old-fashioned* to do what is morally correct for someone【過時】公正對待 (某人): *I mean to do right by her.* 我打算公正待她。
13 ►HIT 擊打◄ [C] a hit using your right hand 右手打出的一擊，右手拳: *He got me with a right on the jaw.* 他一個右拳打在我的下巴上。—**rightness** *n* [U] —see also 另見 **two wrongs don't make a right** (WRONG[3] (5))

right[4] *v* [T] **1 right a wrong** to do something to prevent an unjust situation from continuing 矯枉; 平反 **2** to put something back into the state or situation that it should

R

be in 矯正, 糾正: *We must try to right the balance between taxation and government spending.* 我們必須設法矯正稅收與政府開支之間的平衡。**3** to put something, especially a boat, back into its correct upright position 把〔尤指小船〕扶正, 擺正; 扭轉: *I finally managed to right the canoe.* 我終於把獨木舟翻過來了。

right an·gle /ˈ· ˌ··/ *n* [C] **1** an angle of 90°, like the angles at the corners of a square 直角 —see picture at 參見 ANGLE[1] 圖 **2 be at right angles (to sth)** if two things are at right angles, they make a 90° angle where they touch (與某物) 成直角 —**right-angled** *adj*: *a right-angled triangle* 直角三角形

right·eous /ˈraɪtʃəs; ˈraɪtʃəs/ *adj* **1 righteous indignation/anger etc** strong feelings of anger when you think a situation is not morally right or fair 義憤: *"You should have asked me first," said Corrine, full of righteous indignation.* "你應該先問問我的。"科林義憤填膺地說。**2** *formal* morally good and fair【正式】正派的, 正直的: *a righteous and loving God* 正義、慈愛的上帝 —see also 另見 SELF-RIGHTEOUS —**righteously** *adv* —**righteousness** *n* [U]

right field /ˈ· ·/ *n* **1** [C] one of the main areas of the playing field in BASEBALL〔棒球〕右外場 —opposite 反義詞 LEFT FIELD **2** [U] the position of someone who plays in this area 右外場手

right·ful /ˈraɪtfəl; ˈraɪtfəl/ *adj* [only before noun 僅用於名詞前] *formal* according to what is legally and morally correct【正式】合法的; 正義的, 公正的: *Every effort was made to return the purse to its rightful owner.* 盡了一切努力把錢包還給它的合法主人。| *the rightful heir to the throne* 王位的合法繼承人 —**rightfully** *adv*: *the lands that are rightfully yours* 理應屬於你的土地 —**rightfulness** *n* [U]

right-hand /ˈ· ·/ *adj* [only before noun 僅用於名詞前] on the right side of something 右邊的, 右側的: *Get into the right-hand lane.* 進右邊的車道。| *It's on the right-hand side.* 在右邊。—opposite 反義詞 LEFT-HAND

right-hand drive /ˌ· ·ˈ·/ *adj* [only before noun 僅用於名詞前] a right-hand drive vehicle is one in which the driver sits on the right〔交通工具〕右御的, 司機坐在右邊駕駛的 —opposite 反義詞 LEFT-HAND DRIVE

right-hand·ed /ˌ· ˈ··◂/ *adj* **1** a right-handed person uses their right hand for writing, throwing etc〔寫字、投擲等〕慣用右手的 **2** a right-handed tool is designed for right-handed people〔工具〕為慣用右手的人設計的: *right-handed scissors* 供右手用的剪子 —opposite 反義詞 LEFT-HANDED —**right-handed** *adv*

right-hand·er /ˌ· ˈ··/ *n* [C] **1** someone who uses their right hand for writing, throwing etc 慣用右手的人 **2** a hit with your right hand 右手打出的一擊, 右手拳 —opposite 反義詞 LEFT-HANDER

right-hand man /ˌ· · ˈ·/ *n* [singular] the person who supports and helps you the most, especially in your job〔尤指工作中的〕得力助手

Right Hon the written abbreviation of 縮寫= Right Honourable

Right Hon·our·a·ble /ˈ· ˌ····/ *adj* used when formally announcing or talking about lords or important government ministers in Britain 閣下〔對英國貴族或政府大臣的尊稱〕: *the Right Honourable Giles Williams MP* 賈爾斯·威廉斯議員閣下

right·ist /ˈraɪtɪst; ˈraɪtɪst/ *adj* supporting RIGHT-WING ideas or groups 右派的, 右傾的 —opposite 反義詞 LEFTIST —**rightist** *n* [C] —**rightism** *n* [U]

right·ly /ˈraɪtlɪ; ˈraɪtli/ *adv* **1** for a good or sensible reason 有道理地, 有充分理由地: *The audience was rightly outraged at this suggestion.* 聽眾對這個建議感到憤慨是有道理的。| **quite rightly** *BrE*【英】*She insisted, quite rightly, that we all put our seat belts on.* 她堅持要我們全都繫好安全帶, 這很有道理。**2** correctly 正確地: *As she rightly pointed out, this will do nothing to solve the problem.* 如她正確指出的那樣, 這絲毫無助於解決問題。| **if I remember rightly** *spoken*【口】*If I remember rightly, Ray's parents emigrated shortly after the war.* 如果我沒記錯, 雷的父母戰後不久就移居國外了。**3 rightly or wrongly** used to say that whatever you think of someone's action, this is what they did 不管怎樣, 不問對不對: *Rightly or wrongly, the Italians decided to withdraw from the competition.* 無論如何, 意大利隊決定退出比賽。**4 and rightly so** *spoken* used to say that a decision or action you have just described is fair and morally right【口】應該的〔指決定或行動公正且合乎道德〕: *Bryan was punished, and rightly so.* 布賴恩受到了懲罰, 這是罪有應得。**5 I can't rightly say/don't rightly know** *spoken* used to say that you are not sure whether something is correct or not【口】我無法肯定

right-mind·ed /ˌ· ˈ··◂/ *adj* a right-minded person has opinions, principles, or standards of behaviour that you approve of 有正義感的, 正直的: *All right-minded people will support us.* 所有有正義感的人都會支持我們。—**right-mindedness** *n* [U]

right of ap·peal /ˌ· · ·ˈ·/ *n plural* **rights of appeal** [C] *law* the legal right to ask for a court's decision to be changed【法律】上訴權

right-of-cen·tre /ˌ· · ˈ··◂/ *adj* supporting ideas and aims that are between the centre and the right in politics〔政治上〕中間偏右的 —opposite 反義詞 LEFT-OF-CENTRE

right of way /ˌ· · ˈ·/ *n* **1** [U] the right to drive into or across a road before other vehicles〔車輛的〕先行權: *I never know who has right of way at this junction.* 我從來搞不清這個交叉路口誰有先行權。**2** [C] *plural* **rights of way a)** the right to walk across someone else's land〔穿過他人土地的〕穿行權: *We have a right of way across his field to our house.* 我們有穿過他的田地回家的穿行權。**b)** a path that people have the right to use 有權通行的小路: *Private property – no right of way.* 私人土地——禁止穿行。

right on /ˌ· ˈ·◂/ *adj* **1** *BrE* someone who is right on or has right on opinions, supports social justice, equal rights etc【英】伸張正義的; 主張平等的: *It's one of those annoyingly right on magazines about the environment.* 這是那些對環境問題主持公道得讓人厭煩的雜誌之一。**2** *AmE* someone is right on when they say something that is correct or that you completely agree with【美】〔某人〕完全正確的: *Jodie was right on with that remark.* 喬迪那樣說是完全正確的。

rights is·sue /ˈ· ˌ··/ *n* [C] *technical* an offer of company SHARES (=part of the company you can own) at a cheaper price than usual, to people who own some already【術語】股權股發行, 權利股發行〔公司以優惠價向原股東出售新股〕

right-think·ing /ˌ· ˈ··◂/ *adj* a right-thinking person has opinions, principles or standards of behaviour that you approve of 有正義感的, 正直的: *Any right-thinking woman would agree.* 任何有正義感的女人都會贊同。

right·ward /ˈraɪtwəd; ˈraɪtwəd/ *adj* on or towards the right 在右的; 向右的: *a rightward glance* 向右一瞥 —opposite 反義詞 LEFTWARD

right·wards /ˈraɪtwədz; ˈraɪtwədz/ *especially BrE*【尤英】, usually 一般作 **rightward** *AmE*【美】*adv* on or towards the right 在右側; 向右 —opposite 反義詞 LEFTWARDS

right wing /ˌ· ˈ·◂/ *n* **the right wing** political groups that believe very strongly in the CAPITALIST economic system〔政治上的〕右翼, 右派: *The party is dominated by its right wing.* 該黨受到右翼控制。—**right-wing** *adj*: *right-wing views* 右翼觀點 —**right-winger** *n* [C]: *a prominent right-winger in the party* 黨內著名的右翼人士 —opposite 反義詞 LEFT WING

ri·gid /ˈrɪdʒɪd; ˈrɪdʒɪd/ *adj* **1** rigid methods, systems etc are very strict and difficult to change〔方法、體制等〕嚴格的, 不易改變的: *Betty's finding it hard to keep to the school's rigid rules.* 貝蒂認為很難遵守學校各項嚴格的規定。| *the rigid discipline of army life* 軍旅生活嚴格

的紀律 **2** someone who is rigid is very unwilling to change their ideas〔人〕不願改變的, 頑固的: *He's very rigid and old fashioned.* 他非常頑固, 而且老派。| *rigid attitudes* 固執的態度 **3** stiff and not moving or bending 僵硬的; 不動的; 不能彎曲的: *a tent supported on a rigid framework* 由堅固的骨架支撐的帳篷 | *The rabbit stopped, rigid with fear.* 那隻兔子停下來, 嚇得一動不動。**4 bore sb rigid** to make someone very bored 使某人感到極度厭煩 —**rigidly** *adv*: *rigidly opposed to all new ideas* 頑固地反對一切新思想 —**rigidity** /rɪˋdʒɪdətɪ; rɪˈdʒɪdɪ̣ti/ *n* [U] —**rigidify** /rɪˋdʒɪdəˌfaɪ; rɪˈdʒɪdɪ̣faɪ/ *AmE*【美】*v* [I,T]

rig·ma·role /ˋrɪgməˌrol; ˈrɪgmərəʊl/ also 又作 **rigamarole** *AmE*【美】*n* **1** [singular,U] a long confusing process or description 漫長紛亂的過程; 冗長雜亂的話: *Omar went into this rigmarole about how he lost his passport.* 奧馬爾拉拉雜雜講了半天, 説他如何丢失了護照。**2** [U] a long confusing series of actions that seems silly 一長串混亂而愚蠢的舉動: *I had to go through the whole rigmarole of kissing the Bible and swearing to tell the truth.* 我不得不完成吻《聖經》和宣誓保證講實話這一長串煩瑣的程序。

rig·or /ˋrɪgɚ; ˈrɪgə/ *n* [U] the American spelling of RIGOUR rigour 的美式拼法

rig·or mor·tis /ˌrɪgɚˋmɔrtɪs; ˌrɪgə ˈmɔːtɪ̣s/ *n* [U] *Latin* the condition in which someone's body becomes stiff after they die【拉丁】屍僵, 死後強直

rig·or·ous /ˋrɪgərəs; ˈrɪgərəs/ *adj* **1** careful, thorough, and exact 嚴密的, 縝密的; 精確的: *rigorous safety checks* 仔細徹底的安全檢查 **2** very severe or strict 嚴酷的, 嚴厲的: *rigorous army training* 嚴苛的軍訓 —**rigorously** *adv*

rig·our *BrE*【英】, **rigor** *AmE*【美】/ˋrɪgɚ; ˈrɪgə/ *n* [U] **1 the rigours of** the problems and unpleasant conditions of a difficult situation〔環境的〕嚴酷[艱苦]: *all the rigours of a Canadian winter* 加拿大冬天的嚴寒 **2** *BrE formal* strictness or severity of a punishment【英, 正式】〔懲罰的〕嚴厲, 嚴格: *He deserves to be punished with the full rigour of the law.* 他應該受到法律最嚴厲的懲罰。**3** great care and thoroughness in making sure that something is correct 嚴密, 縝密, 嚴謹: *Their research seems to me to be lacking in rigour.* 他們的研究在我看來不夠嚴謹。

rig-out /ˋ· ·/ *n* [C] *BrE informal* a set of clothes【英, 非正式】一套衣服: *You can't go out in that rig-out!* 你不能穿着那身衣服出去! —see also 另見 **rig out** (RIG¹)

rile /raɪl; raɪl/ *v* [T] *informal* to make someone extremely angry【非正式】激怒, 使非常生氣: *It really riled her to think that Henry was lying.* 想到亨利在説謊, 她非常生氣。

Ri·ley /ˋraɪlɪ; ˈraɪli/ *n* **lead the life of Riley** *BrE informal* to have enough money to do what you like【英, 非正式】過着無憂無慮的生活: *Barbara's been leading the life of Riley since that lottery win.* 中彩之後芭芭拉一直過着無憂無慮的生活。

rim¹ /rɪm; rɪm/ *n* [C] **1** the outside edge of something circular〔圓形物的〕外緣, 邊緣, 邊: *the rim of a glass* 玻璃杯口 | *Fit the tyre round the rim of the wheel.* 把輪胎安在輞圈上。**2 gold-rimmed/red-rimmed etc** with a gold, red etc rim 金框/紅框的等: *gold-rimmed spectacles* 金邊眼鏡 —**rimless** *adj*: *Annie wore rimless glasses.* 安妮戴着無邊眼鏡。

rim² **rimmed, rimming** *v* [T] *literary* to be around the edge of something【文】環繞〔邊緣〕: *Trees rimmed the lake.* 湖周圍樹木環繞。

rime /raɪm; raɪm/ *n* [U] *literary* FROST (=powdery ice)【文】(白)霜

rind /raɪnd; raɪnd/ *n* [C,U] **1** the thick outer skin of some types of fruit, such as oranges〔某些果實的〕外皮: *grated lemon rind* 磨碎了的檸檬皮 —compare 比較 PEEL² **2** the thick outer skin of some foods, such as BACON or cheese〔熏豬肉、乾酪等的〕外皮

ring¹ /rɪŋ; rɪŋ/ *n* [S1] [W2]

1 ►JEWELLERY 首飾◄ [C] a piece of jewellery that you wear on your finger 戒指, 指環: *a diamond ring* (=decorated with diamonds) 鑽戒 —see also 另見 ENGAGEMENT RING, WEDDING RING —see picture at 參見 JEWELLERY 圖

2 ►CIRCLE 環狀物◄ [C] **a)** a circular line or mark 環狀線; 環形記號: *Martha had dark rings round her eyes from too many sleepless nights.* 瑪莎好多夜沒睡, 眼睛周圍都有黑圈了。**b)** an object in the shape of a circle 環, 圓圈: *curtain rings* 簾子圈 | *piston rings* 活塞環 | *Slice the onions into rings.* 把洋葱切成薄圈。**c)** a group of people or things arranged in a circle〔人或物的〕環形排列: *A ring of armed troops surrounded the building.* 一圈武裝士兵包圍了該建築。

3 ►BELLS 鐘; 鈴◄ [C] the sound made by a bell or the act of making this sound 鐘[鈴]聲; 敲鐘; 按鈴: *He gave several loud rings at the door.* 他在門口使勁搖了幾下鈴。—see picture on page A19 參見 A19 頁圖

4 give sb a ring *BrE informal* to make a telephone call to someone【英, 非正式】給某人打電話: *I'll give you a ring later in the week.* 我會在本週晚些時候給你打電話。

5 ►CRIMINALS 罪犯◄ [C] a group of people who illegally control a business or criminal activity〔非法交易或犯罪的〕團夥, 幫派: **drugs/spy ring** *Police suspect a drug ring may be operating in the area.* 警察懷疑有一個販毒團夥在該地區活動。| *revelations of a massive spy ring* 一個龐大間諜團夥的揭露

6 have a ring of truth to seem likely to be true 看來是真的: *Mrs Datchet's story had a ring of truth about it.* 達切特夫人所講的情況似乎是真實的。

7 have a familiar ring if something has a familiar ring, you feel that you have heard it before 聽起來耳熟: *Jerry's excuse had a strangely familiar ring.* 傑里的藉口聽起來有點耳熟。

8 run rings around *informal* to be able to do something much better than someone else can【非正式】大大勝過: *My five-year-old can run rings around me on the computer.* 我五歲的孩子用電腦比我強得多。

9 ►COOKING 烹調◄ [C] *especially BrE* one of the circular areas on top of a COOKER that is heated by gas or electricity【尤英】環形灶盤 —see picture on page A10 參見 A10 頁圖

10 ►SPORT/ENTERTAINMENT 體育/娛樂◄ **a)** a small square area surrounded by ropes, where people BOX or WRESTLE〔用繩子圍起來的〕拳擊台; 摔跤台 **b)** a large circular area surrounded by seats at a CIRCUS〔馬戲團的〕圓形表演場 **c) the ring** the sport of BOXING 拳擊運動: *He retired from the ring at 34.* 他 34 歲結束了拳擊生涯。

ring² *v past tense* **rang** /ræŋ; ræŋ/ *past participle* **rung** /rʌŋ; rʌŋ/ [S1] [W2]

1 ►BELL 鐘; 鈴◄ **a)** [T] to make a bell make a sound 使鳴響〔鐘、鈴〕: *I rang the doorbell but no one came.* 我按了門鈴, 但沒有人來。**b)** [I] if a bell rings, it makes a noise〔鐘、鈴〕鳴響: *At that moment, the bell rang for lunch.* 就在那時, 午餐鈴響了。**c)** [I] to ring a bell to call someone to serve you 搖[按]鈴呼喚: **[+for]** *Ring for service.* 請按鈴叫人。

2 ►SOUNDS 聲音◄ [I] **a)** to make a high continuous sound 發出連續的嗡嗡聲: *Tap the glass gently, and you'll hear it ring.* 輕輕地敲玻璃杯, 就會聽到嗡嗡的聲音。**b)** your ears ring after you have been somewhere very noisy or heard a loud sound〔耳〕鳴: *The explosion made our ears ring.* 爆炸聲使我們耳鳴。**c)** *literary* if a place rings with a sound it is full of that sound【文】回響, 響徹: *The courtyard rang with the sound of horses' hooves.* 院子裡回響着馬蹄聲。

3 ►TELEPHONE 電話◄ **a)** [I,T] *BrE* to make a telephone call to someone【英】(給...)打電話; CALL¹ (7) *especially AmE*【尤美】: *I rang you yesterday but you weren't in.* 我昨天給你打了電話, 但是你不在。| *Ring 192 for information.* 查詢請撥打 192。| **[+for]** *Sally rang* *for a taxi.* 莎莉打電話叫計程車。—see 見 TELEPHONE (USAGE) **b)** [I] if a telephone rings, it makes a sound to show that someone is phoning you〔電話鈴〕鳴響: *The phone hasn't stopped ringing all day.* 電話鈴整天響個不停。

4 ring a bell *informal* if something rings a bell, you think you have heard it before【非正式】聽起來耳熟: *Her name rings a bell but I can't remember her face.* 她的名字好像很熟, 但是我記不起她的面孔。

5 not ring true if something does not ring true, you do not believe it, even though you are not sure why 聽起來不真實: *It was a clever excuse but it didn't really ring true.* 這是個巧妙的託辭, 但是聽起來不真實。

6 ring the changes to make changes to something, not because it needs changing but just in order to make it more interesting, more attractive etc〔為了裝飾或增加趣味而〕推出新花樣, 作出不同的安排: *It's easy to ring the changes in your living room with some new cushion covers.* 用一些新的座墊套就很容易給你的客廳畫龍點睛。

7 ring hollow if words ring hollow, you do not feel that they are true or sincere 聽起來不真實[無誠意]: *Their expressions of sympathy rang hollow.* 他們的同情顯得很虛偽。

8 ring in your ears if a sound or remark rings in your ears, you seem to continue to hear it after it has finished 在耳際回響: *She went out, his cruel laughter ringing in her ears.* 她走了出去, 他那冷酷的笑聲在她耳際回響。

ring back *phr v* [I,T **ring** sb **back**] *BrE* to telephone someone again, for example because you were not available when they telephoned you【英】回 (…的) 電話: *John rang, and he wants you to ring him back.* 約翰給你打過電話, 他要你給他回電話。

ring in *phr v* **1** [I] *BrE* to telephone the place where you work【英】給辦公室打電話: *Jane's rung in to say she'll be late.* 簡來電話說她要晚到一會兒。**2 ring in the New Year** to celebrate the beginning of the New Year by ringing church bells 教堂鳴鐘迎接新年

ring off *phr v* [I] *BrE* to end a telephone call【英】掛斷電話: *He rang off without giving his name.* 他沒留下姓名就掛了電話。

ring out *phr v* **1** [U] a voice, bell etc that rings out is loud and clear〔嗓音、鐘聲等〕響亮: *The sound of a shot rang out.* 傳來一聲響亮的槍聲。**2 ring out the Old Year** to celebrate the end of the year by ringing church bells 教堂鳴鐘辭別舊歲

ring round *phr v* [I,T] *BrE* to make telephone calls to a group of people, in order to organize something, find out information etc【英】(給…) 遍打電話: *I'll ring round to see whether anyone's interested in coming with us.* 我會給朋友打電話, 看誰有興趣和我們一起來。

ring sth/sb ↔ **up** *phr v* **1** [I,T **ring** sb ↔ **up**] *BrE* to telephone someone【英】(給…) 打電話: *I'll ring the manager up tomorrow.* 明天我會給經理打電話。**2** [T **ring** sth ↔ **up**] to press buttons on a CASH REGISTER to record how much money is being put inside 把〔收進的錢〕記入現金記錄機: *The cashier rang up $300 by mistake.* 出納員在現金收入記錄機上誤記了收進 300 美元。

ring³ *v past tense and past participle* **ringed** [T] **1** to surround something 包圍, 環繞: *Police marksmen ringed the office block.* 警察狙擊手包圍了辦公大樓。| **ring sth with** *Her fair hair was ringed with light.* 她的金髮光閃閃的。**2** to draw a circular mark around something 把…圈起來: *Ring the mistakes in red.* 用紅筆把錯誤圈出來。**3** to put a metal ring around a bird's leg 給〔鳥腿〕繫環

ring·er /ˈrɪŋɚ; ˈrɪŋə/ *n* [C] someone who rings church bells or hand bells〔教堂的〕打鐘人; 搖手鈴的人 —see also 另見 **dead ringer** (DEAD¹ (28))

ring-fence /ˈrɪŋˌfɛns; ˈrɪŋfens/ *v* [T] to decide officially that something, especially money, can only be used for a particular purpose〔尤指錢〕指定用於…: *Ok, so this £20,000 is ringfenced as the training budget.* 好吧, 這 20,000 英鎊指定作為培訓預算。

ring fin·ger /ˈ· ˌ··/ *n* [C] the finger that you traditionally wear your WEDDING RING on 無名指

ring·ing /ˈrɪŋɪŋ; ˈrɪŋɪŋ/ *adj* a ringing sound or voice is loud and clear 洪亮的, 響亮的; 清脆的: *"Come here!" he commanded, in ringing tones.* "過來!" 他聲音洪亮地命令道。

ring·lead·er /ˈrɪŋˌlidɚ; ˈrɪŋˌliːdə/ *n* [C] someone who leads a group that is doing something illegal or wrong〔匪徒的〕頭目, 首惡, 魁首: *Police arrested the ringleaders but let the others go free.* 警察逮捕了那些頭目, 但把其他人都放了。

ring·let /ˈrɪŋlɪt; ˈrɪŋlɪ̆t/ *n* [C] a long curl of hair that hangs down〔下垂的〕長鬈髮

ring-pull /ˈ· ·/ *n* [C] the ring on the top of a can of drink that you pull to open it〔易拉罐上的〕拉環

ring road /ˈ· ·/ *n* [C] *BrE* a road that goes around a large town to keep the traffic away from the centre【英】環城公路; BELTWAY *AmE*【美】

ring·side /ˈrɪŋˌsaɪd; ˈrɪŋsaɪd/ *n* [singular] **1** the area nearest to the performance in a CIRCUS, BOXING match etc〔馬戲團表演、拳擊比賽等的〕台邊區 **2 ringside seat** a seat very near to the performers in a CIRCUS, BOXING match etc 台邊區前排座位

ring span·ner /ˈ· ˌ··/ *n* [C] *BrE* a tool with a circular end that fits over a NUT to make it tighter or looser【英】套筒扳手, 梅花扳手; BOX END WRENCH *AmE*【美】—see picture at 參見 TOOL¹ 圖

ring·worm /ˈrɪŋˌwɝm; ˈrɪŋwɜːm/ *n* [U] a skin infection that causes red rings, especially on your head〔尤指頭上的〕癬

rink /rɪŋk; rɪŋk/ *n* [C] **1** a specially prepared area of ice for skating (SKATE²) 溜冰場 **2** a special area with a smooth surface where you can go around on ROLLER SKATES 旱冰場

rink·y-dink /ˈrɪŋkɪ ˌdɪŋk; ˈrɪŋki dɪŋk/ *adj AmE informal* cheap and of bad quality【美, 非正式】廉價的, 劣質的

rinse¹ /rɪns; rɪns/ *v* [T] **1** to wash clothes, dishes etc quickly with water, especially running water, and without soap 沖洗,〔用流動的水〕清洗: *Let me just rinse my hands.* 讓我把手沖洗一下。| *Rinse the vegetables under a cold tap.* 在冷水龍頭下面沖洗這些蔬菜。**2** to wash something in clean water in order to remove soap from it〔用乾淨的水〕把〔肥皂〕從…上沖洗掉: *Rinse your hair thoroughly to get all the shampoo out.* 把你頭髮上的洗髮劑徹底沖乾淨。**3** to remove soap, dirt etc from something by washing it quickly with water 把〔肥皂、污垢等〕沖洗掉: **rinse sth out/away/off etc** *I tried to rinse the mud off under the tap.* 我努力在水龍頭下面把泥巴沖掉。**4** to put colour into your hair 染髮

rinse sth ↔ **out** *phr v* [T] to wash something in clean water, especially to remove soap from it〔用清水〕漂洗〔尤指沖掉肥皂〕: *Don't forget to rinse out your swimsuit.* 別忘記用清水漂洗乾淨你的游泳衣。

rinse² *n* **1 give sth a rinse** to rinse something 漂洗[沖洗]某物: *I'll just give this shirt a quick rinse.* 我要把這件襯衣很快地漂洗一下。**2** [C,U] a product you use to change the colour of your hair or to make it more shiny 染髮液: *a blue rinse for grey hair* 染灰白頭髮用的藍色染髮液

ri·ot¹ /ˈraɪət; ˈraɪət/ *n* **1** [C] a situation in which a large crowd of people are behaving in a violent and uncontrolled way especially when they are protesting about something 騷亂, 暴亂, 暴動: *The army were called in to put down the riot.* 軍隊奉命前來平息暴亂。| **race riot** (=between people of different races) 種族騷亂 *Ethnic tensions led to a massive race riot.* 種族之間的緊張關係導致了大規模的種族騷亂。**2 a riot of colour** something with many different bright colours 五顏六色, 色彩繽紛: *The garden is a riot of colour in May.* 在五月,

花園色彩繽紛，美不勝收。**3 run riot a)** if people run riot, they behave in a violent, noisy, and uncontrolled way 狂暴，無法無天：*Demonstrators are running riot through the town.* 示威者發瘋似地在城裡到處鬧事。**b)** if your imagination, thoughts etc run riot, you cannot control them〔想像、思緒等〕無法控制 **c)** if a plant runs riot, it grows very quickly〔植物〕瘋長 **4 read (sb) the riot act** *often humorous* to give someone a strong warning that they must stop causing trouble【常幽默】嚴厲警告（某人）必須停止鬧事：*If the kids don't settle down soon, I'll go up and read them the riot act.* 如果孩子不馬上安靜下來，我就上去嚴厲警告他們。**5** [singular] *old-fashioned* someone or something that is very funny or enjoyable【過時】有趣的人[事]：*Sally's a riot when she's had a few drinks!* 幾杯酒下肚，莎莉就變得非常有趣！| **have a riot** (=have a lot of fun) 有趣，好玩 *"How was the party?" "Oh, we had a riot!"* "聚會怎麼樣？" "噢，我們玩得很痛快！"

riot² *v* [I] if a crowd of people riot, they behave in a violent and uncontrolled way, for example by fighting the police and damaging cars or buildings 騷亂，鬧事：*Students were rioting in the streets.* 學生們在街上鬧事。—**rioting** *n* [U] —**rioter** *n* [C]

ri·ot·ous /ˋraɪətəs; ˈraɪətəs/ *adj* **1** wild, exciting, and uncontrolled 狂暴的，興奮的，無法控制的：*riotous drinking and singing* 狂飲高歌 **2** uncontrolled, noisy, and perhaps dangerous 放縱的，喧鬧的：**riotous behaviour** *BrE*【英】*Steve was arrested for riotous behaviour the night before his wedding.* 史蒂夫在婚禮前一天晚上因行為放縱而被捕。—**riotously** *adv* —**riotousness** *n* [U]

riot po·lice /ˈ‥ ·ˌ·/ *n* [U] police whose job is to stop riots 防暴警察：*The riot police used tear gas to control the mob.* 防暴警察使用了催淚彈來控制暴徒。

RIP /ˌɑr aɪ ˋpi; ˌɑːr aɪ ˈpiː/ the written abbreviation of 縮寫= Rest in Peace (=words written on a stone over a grave) 願其靈魂安息〔墓碑上的銘文〕

rip¹ /rɪp; rɪp/ **ripped, ripping** *v* **1** [I,T] to tear something or be torn quickly and violently 撕，扯，撕裂，扯開：*I've ripped my skirt on a nail.* 我的裙子被釘子劃破了。| *The sails ripped under the force of the wind.* 強勁的風把帆扯破了。| **rip sth open** (=open something by tearing it) 把某物撕開 *Impatiently, Sue ripped the letter open.* 蘇急不可待地撕開信封。—see picture on page A18 參見 A18 頁圖 **2** [T always+adv/prep] to remove something quickly and violently, using your hands〔迅速而粗暴地用手〕移去某物：**rip sth out/off/away/down** *We've had to rip down all the old wallpaper.* 我們得把所有的舊牆紙都扯下來。**3 rip sth/sb to shreds a)** to destroy something or damage it badly by tearing it in many pieces 扯碎；撕碎：*Jill's kitten is ripping her sofa to shreds.* 吉爾的小貓把她的沙發扯得稀爛。**b)** to strongly criticize someone, or their opinions, remarks, behaviour etc 嚴厲批評，抨擊：*My argument was ripped to shreds at once.* 我的論點立即被批駁得體無完膚。**4 let rip** *informal* to speak or behave violently or emotionally【非正式】説話[行為]激烈的，強烈的：**[+at/about]** *Mom really let rip about the state of my room.* 媽媽果真對我房間的狀況大發雷霆。**5 let sth rip** *informal* to make a car, boat etc go as fast as it can【非正式】讓〔車、船等〕全速前進：*Put your foot on the gas and let her rip!* 踩着油門，讓車子飛馳吧！

rip off *phr v* [T] *spoken*【口】**1** [**rip** sb ↔ **off**] to charge someone too much money for something 對〔某人〕索價過高[敲竹槓]：*They really ripped us off at that hotel!* 那家旅館着實敲了我們一下竹槓！**2** [**rip off** sth] to steal something 偷竊：*Somebody's ripped off my bike!* 有人偷了我的自行車！—see also 另見 RIP-OFF

rip through sth *phr v* [T] to move through a place quickly and with violent force 迅猛地衝過：*A huge explosion ripped through the courthouse.* 猛烈的爆炸嚴重損毀了法院。

rip sth ↔ **up** *phr v* [T] to tear something into several pieces 把…撕成碎片：*Pru ripped his photo up into tiny bits.* 普魯把他的相片撕得粉碎。

rip² *n* [C] a long tear or cut 長的裂口[裂縫]：*There was a rip in the tire caused by a sharp stone.* 輪胎上有一長條被尖石劃破的口子。

rip·cord /ˋrɪpkɔrd; ˈrɪpkɔːd/ *n* [C] **1** the string that you pull to open a PARACHUTE〔降落傘的〕開傘索 **2** the string that you pull to let gas out of a BALLOON〔氣球放氣用的〕拉索

ripe /raɪp; raɪp/ *adj* **1** ripe fruit or crops are fully grown and ready to eat〔水果、莊稼〕成熟的：*Those apples aren't ripe yet.* 那些蘋果還沒熟。—opposite 反義詞 UNRIPE **2 be ripe for** to be in a suitable condition for something, especially for some kind of change 適宜…，〔尤指變革等〕條件成熟：*The land was ripe for industrial development.* 這個國家已經具備了發展工業的條件。**3 the time is ripe (for)** used to say it is a very suitable time for something to happen（…的）時機已經成熟：*The time was ripe for a challenge to the government.* 向政府挑戰的時機已經成熟。**4 ripe old age** if you live to a ripe old age, you are very old when you die 很大年紀：*Grandad lived to the ripe old age of 94.* 爺爺活到 94 歲高齡。**5** ripe cheese has developed a strong taste and is ready to eat〔乾酪〕熟透的 **6** a ripe smell is strong and unpleasant〔氣味〕濃烈難聞的：*The office was so hot that we all smelled rather ripe by the end of the day.* 辦公室非常熱，下班時我們個個身上都散發着難聞的氣味。**7** *BrE informal* rude but amusing【英，非正式】〔語言〕粗俗有趣的：*I thought his language was a bit ripe.* 我認為他的語言有些粗俗，但不乏幽默。—**ripeness** *n* [U]

rip·en /ˋraɪpən; ˈraɪpən/ *v* [I,T] to become ripe or to make something ripe（使）成熟：*The tomatoes quickly ripened in the hot weather.* 天氣炎熱，番茄很快就熟了。

rip-off /ˈ‥ ·/ *n* [C] *informal* something that is unreasonably expensive【非正式】〔某物〕價格太高，要價不合理：*Five pounds for a coffee? What a rip-off!* 一杯咖啡就要五英鎊？真是敲竹槓啊！—see also 另見 **rip off** (RIP¹)

ri·poste¹ /rɪˋpost; rɪˈpɒst/ *n* [C] **1** *formal* a quick, clever, and amusing reply【正式】迅速而巧妙的回答：*a suitably witty riposte* 恰如其分的機敏的答覆 **2** *technical* a quick return stroke with a sword in FENCING (=the sport of fighting with swords)【術語】〔擊劍〕敏捷的還擊

riposte² *v* **1** [I,T] *formal* to reply quickly and cleverly【正式】機敏地答覆[反駁] **2** [I] *technical* to make a riposte in FENCING【術語】〔擊劍〕敏捷地還擊

rip·ple¹ /ˋrɪpl̩; ˈrɪpəl/ *v* **1** [I,T] to move in small waves, or to make something move in this way（使）起漣漪，（使）起細浪：*Arnie's muscles rippled as he carried the huge crates.* 阿尼搬大板條箱時，肌肉一起一伏。| *Look how the breeze is rippling the long grass.* 看微風吹拂着長長的草，泛起陣陣細浪。**2** [I always+adv/prep] to pass from one person to another like a wave〔在人羣中〕傳開：**ripple around/through etc** *Excitement rippled around the courtroom.* 法庭裡人人心潮澎湃。| *A thrill of pleasure rippled through me.* 一陣快感傳遍我全身。**3** [I] to make a noise like water that is flowing gently 發出潺潺聲：*The water rippled over the stones.* 石頭上流水潺潺。| *a rippling brook* 潺潺的小溪

ripple² *n* **1** [C] a small low wave on the surface of a liquid 細浪，漣漪：*The wind made ripples on the surface of the pond.* 風吹皺池水。—see picture at 參見 REFLECTION 圖 **2 a ripple of applause/laughter etc** a sound that gets gradually louder and softer 此起彼伏的掌聲／笑聲等：*A ripple of laughter ran through the audience.* 聽眾發出陣陣笑聲。**3 a ripple of shock/unease/nervousness etc** a feeling that spreads through a person or a group because of something that has happened 一陣震驚／不安／緊張等：*A ripple of shock ran around the meeting.* 與會者都感到震驚。**4** [C] a shape or pattern that looks like a wave 波痕，波紋：*ripples on the sand* 沙上的波痕 **5 raspberry ripple/chocolate ripple etc** a type of ICE CREAM that has different coloured bands of

R

fruit, chocolate etc in it 山莓/巧克力等彩條冰淇淋 **6 ripple effect** a situation in which one action causes another, which then causes a third, etc 漣漪作用, 連鎖反應

rip-roar·ing /ˌ· ˈ··◂/ *adj informal*【非正式】**1 rip-roaring success** a very big success 巨大成功: *The new musical looks set to become a rip-roaring success.* 那部新音樂劇看來注定會非常賣座。**2** noisy, exciting, and uncontrolled 喧鬧的; 歡騰的: *Micky had a rip-roaring time spending his first wage packet.* 米琪第一次拿到工資, 痛快地玩了個夠。| **rip-roaring drunk** (=very drunk) 爛醉如泥

rip·snort·er /ˌrɪpˋsnɔrtɚ; ˌrɪpˈsnɔːtə/ *n* [C] *old-fashioned* something very exciting【過時】非常刺激的事物: *The roller coasters there are real ripsnorters.* 那裡的過山車真夠刺激的。

2 1 **rise**[1] /raɪz; raɪz/ *v past tense* **rose** /roz; rəʊz/ *past participle* **risen** /ˋrɪzn̩; ˈrɪzən/ [I]

1 ►INCREASE 增加◄ to increase in number, amount or value〔數、量或價值的〕增加, 增長: *House prices are likely to rise towards the end of this year.* 今年年底房價可能會上漲。| **rise by 10%/$3/a large amount etc** *Sales rose by 20% over the Christmas period.* 聖誕節期間銷售量增加了20%。| **rise dramatically/sharply** (=increase greatly) 急劇增長 *The number of people seeking asylum in the United Kingdom has risen sharply from five thousand a year in 1988 to over thirty thousand in 1990.* 在英國尋求政治庇護的人數從1988年的每年五千人, 猛增到1990年的三萬多人。| **rise steadily** (=increase slowly but continuously) 持續增長 *The divorce rate has risen steadily since the 1950s.* 20世紀50年代以來, 離婚率不斷上升。| **rising prices/unemployment etc** *Rising crime has driven many families out of down-town areas.* 上升的犯罪率迫使許多家庭離開了市中心。| **rise and fall** *Populations rise and fall in response to the availability of food.* 人口數目隨糧食的供應量而增減。| **...and rising** *The unemployment level is twelve percent and rising.* 失業水平是百分之十二並且在上升。—see 見 RAISE[1] (USAGE)

2 ►GO UPWARDS 上升◄ to go upwards 升高, 上升: *The polar ice caps will melt and the sea level will rise.* 極地的冰蓋將融化, 海平面將升高。| *Smoke rose from the chimney.* 煙從煙囱中冉冉升起。| *The road rises steeply from the village.* 公路從那個村子起突然變得陡峭。

3 ►STAND 站立◄ *especially written* to stand up【尤書面】站起; 起立: *Mick McGrath rose and shouted, "Right, lads! Five minutes to finish your beer and then let's go."* 米克·麥格拉斯站起來喊道: "好吧, 小伙子們! 給你們五分鐘喝完啤酒, 然後我們就走。" | **rise from the table/your chair etc** *Charlotte rose from the table and went over to the window.* 夏洛特從桌旁站起身走到了窗邊。| **rise to your feet** *He rose to his feet and tapped on the table as if he was going to speak.* 他站起身輕輕敲打桌子, 彷彿要發言似的。

4 ►BECOME SUCCESSFUL 取得成就◄ to become important, powerful, successful or rich 地位提高; 發跡: **[+from]** *Damascus had risen from a provincial centre of commerce to the capital of the world's greatest empire.* 大馬士革從一個地方貿易中心變成世界上最大帝國的首都。| **[+to]** *He had entered the army as a boy and risen to the rank of colonel by 1914.* 他參軍時還是個少年, 到1914年已經升到上校。| **rise to the top** *The people who rise to the top in politics are usually the most ruthless.* 政壇巨頭通常都是最無情的。| **rise to fame** *The Beatles rose to fame in the early 60s.* 披頭四樂隊在60年代初聲名大噪。| **rise to power** *Mussolini rose to power in Italy in 1922.* 1922年墨索里尼在意大利奪取政權。

5 ►VOICE/SOUND 嗓音/聲音◄ a) to be heard〔聲音〕發出: **[+from]** *The sound of children playing rose from the street.* 孩子玩耍的聲音從街上傳來。| **rise above sth** (=be louder than something) 比…響亮 *He could hear the rhythm of chanting voices rising above the sound of the traffic.* 他聽到有節奏的呼喊聲蓋過了來往車輛的聲音。**b)** to become louder or higher〔聲音〕變響, 提高: *Her voice rose with anger and emotion: "I trusted you!"* 她怒氣沖沖, 提高嗓門叫道: "我居然相信了你!"

6 ►SUN/MOON/STAR 太陽/月亮/星星◄ to appear in the sky 升起, 在天空出現: *The sun rose and the sea turned gold.* 太陽升起來, 大海變成了金色。

7 ►EMOTION 感情◄ if a feeling or emotion rises, you feel it more and more strongly〔感情或情緒〕變得強烈: *I felt panic rising, and my heart banged loudly in my chest.* 我感到越來越恐慌, 我的心在胸膛裡怦怦地跳。| *rising excitement* 越來越激動 | **sb's spirits rise** (=they become much happier) 某人的情緒高漲 *Our spirits rose when we heard of the ship's safe return.* 我們聽説船安全返航, 精神大振。

8 ►BE TALL 高◄ to be very tall 聳立, 矗立: *Snow-capped mountains rose in the distance.* 白雪覆蓋的山峯聳立在遠方。| **rise above** (=be much taller than) 大大高於 *The tower rose above the surrounding trees.* 那座塔高高凌駕於周圍的樹木之上。

9 rise from if something tall rises from a place, its base is in that place 從…升起: *Spiro was pointing at a gentle curve of hillside that rose from the glittering sea.* 斯皮羅正指着從波光粼粼的大海中升起的緩緩山坡。

10 ►BREAD/CAKES ETC 麵包/蛋糕等◄ if bread, cakes etc rise they become bigger because they contain YEAST or as they are baked〔麵包、蛋糕等〕因發酵[被烘烤]而脹大, 膨鬆

11 ►BED 牀◄ *literary* to get out of bed in the morning【文】起牀

12 ►AGAINST A GOVERNMENT/ARMY 反抗政府/軍隊◄ also 又作 **rise up** if a large group of people in a country rise, they try to defeat the government or army that is controlling them 反抗, 造反: *The Russian people rose in rebellion in 1917.* 俄國人民於1917年起義。

13 rise to the occasion/challenge to deal successfully with a difficult situation or problem 成功應付困難局面/挑戰

14 rise to sth if you rise to a remark, you reply to it rather than ignoring it, especially because it has made you angry 對某事〔尤指令人氣憤的評論〕反應強烈: *She refused to rise to his sexist remarks.* 她把他的性別歧視的話置之不理。

15 rise from the dead/grave to come alive after having died 復活: *On the third day Jesus rose from the dead.* 耶穌在第三天復活。

16 rise through the ranks to start working for an organization in a low-paid job, and to gradually improve your position, until you get a very important, well-paid job〔在一家機構中工作〕由低職位開始晉升高位: *She had risen through the ranks, having joined the company as a secretary after she graduated from high school.* 高中畢業後她到這家公司當祕書, 一步步升到了重要的職位。

17 rise from the ranks to become an officer in the army after having been an ordinary soldier〔軍官〕士兵出身

18 rise out of sth to be caused by sth or begin with sth 起因於…, 由…引起: *The quarrel had risen out of a misunderstanding.* 這場爭吵是由誤會引起的。| *All this fuss and extravagance rose out of a sudden whim to please his small, first-born son.* 所有的小題大作和鋪張浪費都是因為他突發奇想要取悦他年幼的長子。

19 ►COURT/PARLIAMENT 法庭/議會◄ if court etc rises, that particular meeting is formally finished 休庭; 休會

20 all rise *spoken formal* used to tell people to stand up at the beginning of a meeting of a court of law【口, 正式】全體起立〔用於法庭開庭前〕

21 rise and shine *spoken humorous* used to tell someone to wake up and get out of bed【口，幽默】快起牀〔用於叫醒某人〕

22 ►RIVER 河流◄ if a river rises somewhere, it begins there〔河流〕發源: *The River Rhine rises in Switzerland.* 萊茵河發源於瑞士。

23 ►WIND 風◄ if the wind rises, it becomes stronger〔風力〕增強: *battling against the rising gale* 與越來越強的大風搏鬥

rise above *phr v* [T] **1** to deal with an insult or unpleasant situation without letting yourself become upset by it 超脱，不計較: *Her name was splashed across the newspapers every day, but somehow she managed to rise above it.* 她的名字每天都出現在報紙的顯著位置，但她總能泰然處之。**2** to be morally good or wise enough to be able to avoid something that you should not do 克服，擺脱: *We must rise above the desire for power, personal advancement and material gain.* 我們必須擺脱對權力、個人升遷和物質利益的慾望。**3** to be of a higher standard than other things that are similar〔水平〕超過〔相似的東西〕；優於: *The novel is spirited and witty, but rarely rises above the level of pulp fiction.* 這部小説充滿生氣和情趣，但總的來説沒有超出庸俗小説的水平。**4** to have the knowledge and wisdom to understand and realize things that other people do not notice〔知識和智慧〕超越〔他人〕: *A true historian seeks the truth: he rises above his own race and writes for mankind.* 真正的歷史學家追求的是真理：他超越自己的種族，為人類撰寫歷史。**5** to improve your situation by becoming more successful, rich or important〔通過成功、致富或勢力〕改善〔境遇〕: *I was ambitious and wanted to rise above such a life.* 我雄心勃勃，不安於這種生活。

rise against *phr v* [T] **1** if a group of people rise against the government, king etc they try to defeat them so that they can control the country 起義；反抗: *Rebels rose in discontent against the government and began killing people indiscriminately.* 叛亂分子因不滿而起來反抗政府，並濫殺無辜。**2** *literary* to be very angry and upset by something【文】對…反感: *His whole heart rose against this.* 他對此深惡痛絕。

2 **rise²** *n*

1 ►INCREASE 增加◄ [C] an increase in number, amount or value〔數、量、值的〕增加: *We have sold 120,000 cars this year, a 20% rise on 1988.* 今年我們已售出 12 萬輛汽車，比 1988 年增加了 20%。| [+in] *In the last ten years we have seen a three percent rise in serious and fatal accidents on our roads.* 過去十年裡，公路上的嚴重致命事故增加了百分之三。| **rise in costs/prices/taxes etc** *A rise in taxes will be necessary if we are to improve our education system.* 我們要改善教育制度，就需要增加税收。| **rent/price rise** *Tenants face a 20% rent rise.* 房客們面臨房租上漲 20% 的局面。| **rise and fall** *the rise and fall of the temperature during the day* 一天當中溫度的升降

2 ►WAGES 工資◄ [C] *BrE* an increase in wages【英】加薪; RAISE² *AmE*【美】: *After you've worked here for one year you get a rise.* 你在這裡工作一年後就會加薪。| **pay rise** *The railworkers were offered a 3% pay rise.* 鐵路工人獲得了 3% 的加薪。

3 ►SUCCESS/POWER 成功/權力◄ [singular] the achievement of importance, success or power 升遷；成功，興起: [+of] *The fifteenth century saw the rise of a new social class – the merchant class.* 15 世紀見證了一個新的社會階級 —— 商人階級的興起。| *the rise of fascism in Italy* 法西斯主義在意大利的興起 | **rise to power** *Thatcher's rise to power in the late 1970s* 戴卓爾夫人在 20 世紀 70 年代末掌權 | **rise to fame** *The band's sudden rise to fame took everyone by surprise.* 這樂隊突然走紅讓所有人都感到意外。| **rise and fall** *the rise and fall of the Roman Empire* 羅馬帝國的興亡

4 give rise to sth *especially written* to be the reason why something, especially something bad or unpleasant happens【尤書面】引起[導致]某事〔尤指壞事〕: *Two phenomena are giving rise to world-wide concern – mass unemployment and mass migration into cities.* 有兩個現象 —— 大規模失業和向城市大規模移民 —— 正引起全球關注。| *The President's absence has given rise to speculation about his health.* 總統的缺席引發了對他健康狀況的猜測。

5 ►SLOPE 坡◄ [C] an upward slope 斜坡: *There's a slight rise in the road just before our house.* 就在我們房子前的路有一個小斜坡。

6 get a rise out of sb to make someone become annoyed or embarrassed by making a joke about them〔開玩笑〕激怒某人；使某人尷尬: *You can always get a rise out of Peter by teasing him about his age.* 拿彼得的年齡開玩笑，準能把他惹惱。—see also 另見 HIGH RISE

ris·er /ˈraɪzə; ˈraɪzə/ *n* [C] **1 early/late riser** someone who usually gets out of bed very early or very late 早起/晚起的人 **2** *technical* the upright part of a step on a set of stairs【術語】〔樓梯的〕豎板

ris·i·ble /ˈrɪzəbl̩; ˈrɪzɨbəl/ *adj formal* something that is risible is so stupid that it deserves to be laughed at【正式】令人發笑的，滑稽的: *a risible suggestion* 可笑的建議 —**risibility** /ˌrɪzəˈbɪlətɪ; ˌrɪzɨˈbɪlɨti/ *n* [U]

ris·ing¹ /ˈraɪzɪŋ; ˈraɪzɪŋ/ *n* [C] a sudden attempt by a large group of people to violently remove a government or ruler 造反，起義

rising² *adj* **1** [only before noun 僅用於名詞前] becoming more important or famous〔重要性或名望〕上升的，興起的: *a rising young actor* 嶄露頭角的年輕演員 **2 rising five/six etc** nearly five, six etc years old 將近五/六歲等 **3 the rising generation** young people who will soon be old enough to vote, have jobs etc 即將成年的一代

rising damp /ˌ·· ˈ·/ *n* [U] *BrE* a condition where water comes up from the ground and gets into the walls of a building【英】〔由地面滲入牆壁的〕上升潮氣

risk¹ /rɪsk; rɪsk/ *n* 2 1

1 ►POSSIBILITY OF BAD RESULT 不良後果的可能性◄ [C,U] the possibility that something bad, unpleasant, or dangerous may happen 危險性，風險: *If you're considering starting a business, think carefully about the risks involved.* 如果你在考慮創辦公司，要認真地想想所涉及的各種風險。| [+of] *the risk of serious injury* 嚴重受傷的危險 | **reduce/increase the risk of** *Wear rubber gloves to reduce the risk of infection.* 戴上橡皮手套以減少感染的危險。| [+that] *There was some risk that fire would break out again.* 大火有死灰復燃的危險。| **a calculated risk** (=a risk you think will have a good result) 利大於弊的風險 *It was a calculated risk to appoint a man without management experience to such a senior post.* 委任一個沒有管理經驗的人擔任這樣高的職位得冒風險，但應該利大於弊。| **an element of risk** (=some risk, but not much) 略有風險 *There's an element of risk in any kind of investment.* 任何種類的投資都存在一定的風險。| **it's worth the risk** *I never walk home alone at night – it's not worth the risk.* 我從不在夜裡獨自步行回家 —— 不值得冒這個險。

2 take a risk to decide to do something even though you know it may have bad results 冒險: *The fuel tank could blow up, but that's a risk we'll have to take.* 燃料罐有可能爆炸，但我們必須冒這個險。

3 at risk be in a situation where you may be harmed 處境危險: *We must stop these rumours; the firm's reputation is at risk.* 我們必須制止這些謠傳；公司的名譽有受損的危險。| **be at risk of** *People with fair skins are more at risk of skin cancer.* 皮膚白的人患皮膚癌的危險較大。| **put sb/sth at risk** *I've no respect for a man who would put his children at risk like that.* 我鄙視一個像那樣使自己的孩子遭受危險的人。

4 run a risk to be in a situation where there is a risk of something bad happening to you 冒險: *Anyone travelling without a passport runs the risk of being arrested.* 任何不帶護照旅行的人都有被逮捕的危險。

5 at the risk of doing sth used when you think that what you are going to say or do may have a bad result, may offend or annoy people etc 冒着...的危險: *At the risk of sounding stupid, can I ask a simple question?* 恕在下愚昧, 我能否問一個簡單的問題?

6 at your own risk if you do something at your own risk, you do it even though you understand the possible dangers and have been warned about them 自擔風險, 責任自負: *You leave valuables in the classroom at your own risk.* 將貴重物品留在教室裡, 一旦丢失, 責任自負。

7 ►CAUSE OF DANGER 危險的起因◄ [C] something or someone that is likely to cause harm or danger 可能造成傷害[危險]的事[人]: **[+to]** *Polluted water supplies are a risk to public health.* 受到污染的供水會危害公眾健康。| **health risk** (=something likely to harm people's health) 對健康的威脅 *Meat from the infected animals is regarded as a serious health risk.* 受感染動物的肉被視為對健康的嚴重威脅。| **fire risk** (=something that could cause a dangerous fire) 火災隱患 *The tyre dump is a major fire risk.* 那堆車胎是一個嚴重的火災隱患。| **security risk** (=someone who may tell important secrets to an enemy country) 危險分子〔有可能向敵對國家提供重要機密的人〕

8 ►INSURANCE/BUSINESS 保險/商業◄ [C] a person or business judged according to the danger involved in giving them insurance or lending them money〔按其風險評估的〕保險對象; 貸款對象: **a good/bad/poor risk** *a good credit risk* 信譽好的貸款對象 | *Drivers under 21 are regarded as poor risks by insurance companies.* 21歲以下的駕車者被保險公司看成是風險較高的保險對象。

This graph shows some of the words most commonly used with the noun **risk**. 本圖表所示為含有名詞 risk 的一些最常用詞組。

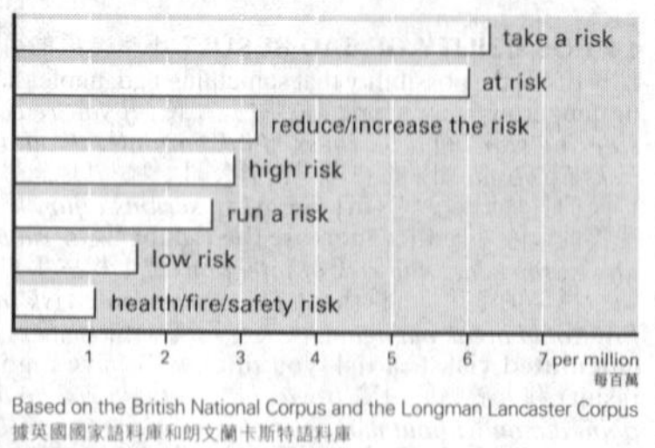

Based on the British National Corpus and the Longman Lancaster Corpus
據英國國家語料庫和朗文蘭卡斯特語料庫

risk² *v* [T] **1** to put something in a situation in which it could be lost, destroyed, or harmed 使遭受〔失去、毀壞或傷害〕的危險: *When children start smoking, they don't realize that they're risking their health.* 兒童開始抽煙時, 並沒有意識到是拿自己的健康去冒險。| **risk sth on sth** *You'd be crazy to risk your money on an investment like that!* 把錢冒險用於那樣的投資, 你簡直瘋了! | **risk your life** *Martina risked her life to save her dog from the fire.* 瑪蒂娜冒着生命危險從火場中救出她的狗。| **risk your neck** *informal* (=do something very dangerous in order to help someone)【非正式】冒極大的危險〔幫助別人〕*I'm not going to risk my neck just to save a common criminal.* 我不會拚了命去救一個普通的犯人。| **risk life and limb** (=do something very dangerous) 冒極大的危險 *Why risk life and limb jumping out of a plane without a parachute on your back?* 為甚麼要冒着巨大的危險不揹降落傘跳出飛機? **2** to get into a situation where something unpleasant may happen to you 擔...風險, 冒...的危險: **risk defeat/death/dismissal etc** *The government risks an embarrassing defeat if it calls an election now.* 政府如果現在進行選舉, 就有遭受令人尷尬的失敗的危險。| **risk being defeated/killed/dismissed etc** *Workers who broke the strike risked being attacked when they left the factory.* 破壞罷工的工人在離開工廠時有遭受攻擊的危險。**3** to do something that you know may have dangerous or unpleasant results 冒險做〔某事, 其結果是危險或令人討厭的〕: **risk doing sth** *Are you prepared to risk traveling without an armed guard?* 你準備冒險不帶武裝警衛出行嗎? | **risk it** *spoken*【口】*You could slip out of school between classes, but I wouldn't risk it.* 你可以在課間溜出學校, 但我不會冒險這樣幹。

risk man·age·ment /ˈ· ˌ···/ *n* [U] a system to prevent or reduce dangerous accidents or mistakes 風險管理

risk-tak·ing /ˈ· ˌ··/ *n* [U] the practice of doing things that involve risks in order to achieve something 冒險 —**risk-taker** *n* [C]

risk·y /ˈrɪski; ˈrɪski/ *adj* involving a risk that something bad will happen; rather dangerous 冒險的; 非常危險的: *It's risky to go out so soon after being ill.* 病後這麼快就外出, 太危險啦。| *a risky investment* 有風險的投資 | **a risky business** (=a dangerous action or situation) 危險的事 *Buying a secondhand car is a risky business.* 買二手汽車是有風險的事。—**riskily** *adv* —**riskiness** *n* [U]

ri·sot·to /rɪˈsɔto; rɪˈzɒtəʊ/ *n plural* **risottos** [C,U] a hot meal made from rice mixed with cheese, vegetables, or pieces of meat〔用乾酪、蔬菜或肉等烹製的〕煨飯

ris·qué /rɪsˈke; ˈrɪskeɪ/ *adj* a joke, remark etc that is risqué is slightly shocking, especially because it is about sex〔笑話、評論等〕粗野的, 近乎淫穢的

ris·sole /ˈrɪsol; ˈrɪsəʊl/ *n* [C] cooked meat cut into very small pieces mixed with potato or bread, and cooked in hot fat〔加進馬鈴薯或麵包的〕炸肉餅, 炸肉丸

rite /raɪt; raɪt/ *n* [C] **1** a ceremony that is always performed in the same way, usually for religious purposes〔常指宗教〕儀式, 典禮: *funeral rites* 葬禮 | *satanic rites* 撒旦崇拜儀式 | **perform a rite** *a traditional rite that was performed at harvest time* 收穫期舉行的傳統儀式 **2 rite of passage** a special ceremony or action that is a sign of a new stage in someone's life, especially when a boy starts to become a man "人生新階段"儀式〔標誌着人生進入新階段, 尤其是男孩成年的特殊儀式〕, 成人儀式 **3 last rites** final prayers or religious ceremonies for someone who is dying 臨終聖禮: *A priest came to give him the last rites.* 一位神父來為他舉行臨終聖禮。

rit·u·al¹ /ˈrɪtʃuəl; ˈrɪtʃuəl/ *n* [C,U] **1** a ceremony that is always performed in the same way, in order to mark an important religious or social occasion〔為紀念重要宗教或社會事件舉行的〕儀式, 典禮: *the ritual of communion in the Christian Church* 基督教教會的聖餐儀式 | **perform a ritual** *The shaman performed the ritual on the young boy.* 那位薩滿教巫師為小男孩舉行了儀式。**2** something that you do regularly and in the same way each time 慣例, 老規矩, 例行公事: *The children performed the bedtime ritual of washing and brushing their teeth.* 孩子按照慣例在睡覺前洗臉刷牙。

ritual² *adj* [only before noun 僅用於名詞前] **1** done as part of a rite or ritual 作為儀式一部分的: *ritual dances* 儀式中的舞蹈 **2** done in a fixed and expected way, but without real meaning or sincerity 例行的: *The police issued the usual ritual apology.* 警方發表了官樣文章式的道歉。—**ritually** *adv*

rit·u·al·is·tic /ˌrɪtʃuəlˈɪstɪk; ˌrɪtʃuəˈlɪstɪk◄/ *adj* ritualistic words, types of behaviour etc always follow the same pattern, especially because they form part of a ritual〔話語、行為等〕慣常的, 例行的; (遵守) 儀式的: *ritualistic incantations* 舉行儀式時說的咒語 | *I got tired with the boring, almost ritualistic weekly meeting.* 我厭倦了無聊的、幾乎是例行公事的週會。—**ritualistically** /-klɪ; -kli/ *adv*

ritz·y /ˈrɪtsɪ; ˈrɪtsi/ *adj informal* fashionable and expensive【非正式】時髦而豪華的: *a ritzy restaurant* 時髦而豪華的飯店

ri·val¹ /ˈraɪvl̩; ˈraɪvəl/ *n* [C] **1** a person, group, or organization that you compete with in sport, business, a fight etc 對手, 競爭者: *He left the government to become her most formidable rival.* 他離開政府, 成了她最難以應付的對手。| **[+for]** *The two girls were rivals for Jack's attention.* 這兩個女孩為獲得傑克的青睞而爭風吃醋。| **rival company/nation/team etc** *Sheena left her job and went to work for a rival company.* 希娜辭了職, 轉到一家對頭公司工作。| **arch-rival** (=main rival) 最主要的對手 *Hanover High School was our arch-rival in football.* 漢諾威中學隊是我們最主要的足球對手。**2** something that is equally as good or important as something else 匹敵者, 可相比的東西: **rival claim/explanation/argument etc** *The court listened to the rival explanations in turn.* 法庭逐一聆聽控辯雙方針鋒相對的辯解。| **have no/few rivals** (=be better than all others or most others) 沒有/鮮有敵手

rival² *v* **rivalled, rivalling** *BrE*【英】, **rivaled, rivaling** *AmE*【美】[T] to be as good or important as someone or something else 與…匹敵[媲美]: *The college's facilities rival those of Harvard and Yale.* 這所學院的設施可以同哈佛和耶魯的媲美。—see also 另見 UNRIVALLED

ri·val·ry /ˈraɪvl̩rɪ; ˈraɪvəlri/ *n* [C,U] continuous competition 不斷的競爭: *a fierce rivalry between the two basketball teams* 這兩支籃球隊之間的激烈競爭

riv·en /ˈrɪvən; ˈrɪvən/ *adj formal* split violently apart【正式】撕裂的, 分裂的: *a community riven by religious differences* 因宗教分歧而分裂的社區

2 2 **riv·er** /ˈrɪvɚ; ˈrɪvə/ *n* [C] **1** a natural and continuous flow of water in a long line across a country into the sea 江, 河: *the Mississippi River* 密西西比河 | *We swam to a large rock in the middle of the river.* 我們游到河心的一塊大石頭那裡。| **river bank** (=the land at the side of a river) 河岸 *We ate our lunch on the river bank.* 我們在河邊吃了午餐。| **mouth of the river** (=where a river joins the sea) 河口 | **up river** (=in the opposite direction from the way the river is flowing) 向上游, 逆流 *a ship sailing up river* 逆流而上的船 | **down river** (=in the same direction as the way the river is flowing) 向下游, 順流 **2** a large amount of moving liquid 巨流; 大量流動液體: **[+of]** *a river of hot lava flowing from the volcano* 從火山湧出的熾熱熔岩流 —see also 另見 **sell sb down the river** (SELL¹ (12))

river ba·sin /ˈ·· ˌ··/ *n* [C] an area from which all the water flows into the same river〔江、河的〕流域, 河流盆地

river bed /ˈ·· ·/ *n* [C] the ground over which a river flows 河牀

riv·er·side /ˈrɪvɚˌsaɪd; ˈrɪvəsaɪd/ *n* [singular] the land on the banks of a river 河邊, 河畔: *We had a picnic by the riverside.* 我們在河邊野餐。| **riverside path/cottage etc** *a riverside inn* 河畔小旅館

riv·et¹ /ˈrɪvɪt; ˈrɪvɪ̣t/ *v* **1 be riveted on/to** if your attention is riveted on something, you are so frightened or so interested that you keep looking at it 目不轉睛, 緊盯在…上: *Barnes watched in terror, his eyes riveted on the huge tiger.* 巴恩斯恐懼地注視着, 眼睛緊盯着那隻大老虎。**2 be riveted to the spot** to be so shocked or frightened that you cannot move〔驚嚇得〕動彈不得 **3** [T] to fasten something with rivets〔用鉚釘〕固定, 鉚接

rivet² *n* [C] a metal pin used to fasten pieces of metal together 鉚釘

riv·et·ing /ˈrɪvɪtɪŋ; ˈrɪvɪ̣tɪŋ/ *adj* **1** something that is riveting is so interesting or exciting that you cannot stop watching it or listening to it 令人着迷的; 非常精彩的; 引人入勝的: *a riveting performance* 非常精彩的演出 **2** *humorous* used when you do not really think something is interesting at all【幽默】有趣的〔反話〕: *What a riveting conversation!* 多麼有趣的談話!

ri·vi·e·ra /ˌrɪvɪˋɛrə; ˌrɪviˈeərə/ *n* **the Riviera** a warm coast that is popular with people who are on holiday, especially the Mediterranean coast of France 氣候溫暖的海濱度假勝地〔尤指法國的地中海沿岸地區里維埃拉〕

riv·u·let /ˈrɪvjəlɪt; ˈrɪvjʊ̣lɪ̣t/ *n* [C] a very small stream of liquid, especially water 小溪, 小河: *Rivulets of sweat ran down his face.* 津津汗水順着他的臉流淌下來。

ri·yal, rial /rɪˋɔl; riˈɑːl/ *n* [C] the standard unit of money in Saudi Arabia and other Arab countries 里亞爾〔沙特阿拉伯及其他阿拉伯國家的貨幣單位〕

RN /ˌɑr ˋɛn; ˌɑːr ˈen/ **1** Royal Navy; the British navy 英國皇家海軍: *Captain Anstruther, RN* 皇家海軍安斯特拉瑟上校 **2** REGISTERED NURSE 註冊護士

RNA /ˌɑr ɛn ˋe; ˌɑːr en ˈeɪ/ *n* [U] an important chemical that exists in all living cells 核糖核酸

roach /rotʃ; rəʊtʃ/ *n* **1** *AmE informal* a COCKROACH【美, 非正式】蟑螂 **2** a European fish similar to a CARP 擬鯉, 斜齒鯿〔歐洲產的魚, 類似鯉魚〕**3** *slang* the part of a MARIJUANA cigarette that you suck smoke through【俚】大麻煙卷的煙蒂

road /rod; rəʊd/ *n* **1** [C,U] a specially prepared hard surface for cars, buses, bicycles etc to travel on 路, 道路, 公路: *a busy road* 交通繁忙的馬路 | *at the end of the road* 在路的盡頭 | **up/down/along the road** (=further along the road) 沿着路 *We live just down the road.* 我們就住在這條路上不遠處。| **by road** (=driving) 開車 *It takes three hours by road.* 開車去要花三個小時。| **main road** *Take the main road out of town and turn left at the first light.* 走幹道出城, 在第一個有交通燈的路口向左拐。| **side road** (=a small road that is not used much) 支路, 小路 | **dirt road** *especially AmE* (=a road without a hard surface)【尤美】未鋪平的土路 | **road accident/repairs/user etc** *He was killed in a road accident.* 他死於道路交通事故。| **road sense** (=knowledge about how to behave sensibly near traffic) 開車[走路]時注意安全的意識 *Kids of that age have no road sense.* 那個年齡的孩子走路時沒有注意安全的意識。| **road safety** (=how to be safe when driving or walking on roads) 道路交通安全 *a road safety campaign* 道路交通安全運動 —see 見 STREET (USAGE) **2 Road** written abbreviation 縮寫為 **Rd** used in addresses after the names of roads 路〔用在地址中街道名稱之後〕: *65 Maple Road* 楓樹路65號 **3 on the road a)** travelling in a car, especially for long distances〔尤指長途〕乘車[開車]旅行: *I've been on the road since 5.00 a.m. this morning.* 我從今早5點起就一直在路上行駛。**b)** if a group of actors or musicians is on the road they are travelling from place to place giving performances 巡迴演出 **c)** if your car is on the road, you have paid for the repairs, tax etc necessary for you to legally drive it〔汽車〕可以合法行駛〔指維修好、已交稅等〕: *It costs a lot of money to keep these old cars on the road.* 開這些舊汽車很費錢。**4 on the road to success/recovery/peace etc** developing in a way that will result in success etc 向成功/復原/和平等邁進: *It was this deal that set him on the road to his first million.* 正是這筆交易使他賺到頭一筆一百萬元。**5 go down a road** *informal* to follow a particular course of action【非正式】按某方法做事: *You could move your pension to a private scheme, but I wouldn't advise going down that road.* 你可以把你的養老金轉到私人計劃中, 不過我建議你不要這樣做。**6 one for the road** *spoken* a last alcoholic drink before you leave a party, PUB etc【口】〔離開聚會、酒吧等前喝的〕最後一杯酒 **7 get out of the road!** *BrE spoken* a rude way of telling someone to move【英口】〔無禮地叫人〕走開! —see also 另見 **the end of the road** (END¹ (18)), **hit the road** (HIT¹ (16))

road·block /ˈrodˌblɑk; ˈrəʊdblɒk/ *n* [C] **1** a place where the police are stopping traffic〔警察設置的〕路障: *Roadblocks were set up after two prisoners escaped from the county jail.* 兩名犯人從縣監獄越獄後, 路障已經設置起來。**2** *AmE* something that stops the progress of a plan【美】障礙: *mental roadblocks that get in the way of success* 妨礙成功的心理障礙

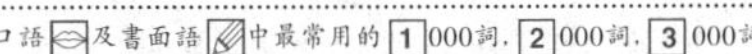
口語及書面語中最常用的 1 000詞, 2 000詞, 3 000詞

road hog /ˈ· ·/ *n* [C] *informal* someone who drives too fast without thinking about other people's safety【非正式】〔開快車而不顧他人安全的〕莽撞駕車者

road·house /ˈrodˌhaus; ˈrəʊdhaʊs/ *n* [C] *AmE* a restaurant or bar on a main road outside a city【美】〔城外公路邊的〕路旁餐館, 路旁酒吧

road·ie /ˈrodɪ; ˈrəʊdi/ *n* [C] *informal* someone whose job is moving equipment for musicians【非正式】為〔巡迴演出的〕樂師搬運設備的人

road man·a·ger /ˈ· ˌ···/ *n* [C] someone who makes arrangements for entertainers when they are travelling 巡迴演出表演者的經紀人

road rage /ˈ· ·/ *n* [U] violence and angry behaviour by car drivers towards other car drivers 當路暴怒〔指路上的駕駛者對其他駕駛者所表現的暴力和憤怒行為〕: *a road rage attack* 因當路暴怒引發的攻擊行為

road·run·ner /ˈrodˌrʌnɚ; ˈrəʊdrʌnə/ *n* [C] a small bird that runs very fast 走鵑

road·show /ˈrodˌʃo; ˈrəʊdʃəʊ/ *n* [C] *BrE* a group that travels around the country giving performances for entertainment or advertising【英】巡迴演出隊

road·side /ˈrodˌsaɪd; ˈrəʊdsaɪd/ *n* [singular] the edge of the road 路邊, 路旁: **roadside cafe/pub etc** (=next to a road) 路邊小餐館/酒吧等

road·sign /ˈrodˌsaɪn; ˈrəʊdsaɪn/ *n* [C] a sign next to a road, that gives information to drivers 路標

road tax /ˈ· ·/ *n* [C,U] a tax in Britain that the owner of a vehicle must pay in order to drive it on the roads〔在英國對車主徵收的〕道路稅, 通行稅

road test /ˈ· ·/ *n* [C] a test to check that a vehicle is in good condition and safe to drive〔檢查車輛性能的〕道路試車 —**roadtest** *v* [T]

road·way /ˈrodˌwe; ˈrəʊdweɪ/ *n* [singular] the part of the road used by vehicles 車行道

road·work /ˈrodˌwɝk; ˈrəʊdwɜːk/ *n* **roadworks** [plural] *BrE* repairs that are being done to a road【英】道路施工

road·wor·thy /ˈrodˌwɝðɪ; ˈrəʊdˌwɜːði/ *adj* a vehicle that is roadworthy is in good condition and safe enough to drive〔車輛〕適於行駛的 —**roadworthiness** *n* [U]

roam /rom; rəʊm/ *v* **1** [I,T] to walk or travel, usually for a long time, with no clear purpose or direction 閒逛, 漫步; 漫遊: **[+over/around/about etc]** *herds of wild deer roaming freely over the hills* 在小山上自由漫步的野鹿羣 | **roam the streets/hills etc** *You shouldn't let your children roam the streets.* 你不應該讓孩子在街上遊蕩。**2** [I+over] if your eyes roam over something, you look slowly at all parts of it〔目光緩慢地〕端詳: *His eyes roamed over the bookshelves.* 他仔細端詳書架上一排排的書, 從一個書架看到另一個書架。

roan /ron; rəʊn/ *n* [C] a horse of a particular colour, especially light brown〔尤指〕栗色馬 —**roan** *adj*

roar[1] /rɔr; rɔː/ *v* **1** [I] to make a deep, very loud noise 吼叫, 呼嘯: *We heard a lion roar.* 我們聽到一聲獅吼。**2** [T] to say or shout something in a deep, powerful voice 咆哮, 大聲喊叫: *"Get out of my house!" he roared.* "滾出我的房子!" 他大聲吼道。**3** [I] also 又作 **roar with laughter** *especially BrE* to laugh loudly and continuously【尤英】哄笑, 大笑, 狂笑: *When Charlie's trousers fell down, the audience roared.* 查理的褲子掉下來時, 觀眾哄堂大笑。**4** [I always+adv/prep] if a vehicle roars somewhere, it moves very quickly and noisily〔車輛〕轟鳴着疾駛: **[+past/down etc]** *There was a cloud of dust as a truck roared past.* 一輛卡車轟鳴着疾駛而過, 揚起一大團灰塵。

roar[2] *n* [C] **1** a deep, loud noise made by an animal such as a LION, or by someone's voice 吼叫聲, 咆哮聲: *A roar of approval came from the crowd.* 人羣大聲叫喊表示同意。**2** a continuous loud noise, especially made by a machine or a strong wind〔機器〕轟鳴聲;〔風〕呼嘯聲: *the roar of the traffic* 來往車輛的轟鳴聲

roar·ing /ˈrɔrɪŋ; ˈrɔːrɪŋ/ *adj* **1** [only before noun 僅用於名詞前] making a deep, very loud, continuous noise 發出吼聲的, 咆哮的, 呼嘯的: *the roaring wind and waves* 咆哮的風浪 **2 roaring fire** a roaring fire burns with a lot of flames and heat 熊熊烈火 **3 do a roaring trade (in)** *BrE informal* to sell a lot of something very quickly【英, 非正式】生意興隆 **4 be a roaring success** *BrE* to be extremely successful【英】獲得極大成功: *The new musical has been a roaring success.* 這部新音樂劇非常賣座。**5 roaring drunk** *BrE* very drunk and noisy【英】酩酊大醉

roast[1] /rost; rəʊst/ *v* **1** [I,T] to cook something, such as meat, in an OVEN or over a fire 烤〔肉等〕—see picture on page A10 參見 A10 頁圖 **2** [I,T] to heat nuts, coffee, beans etc quickly in order to dry them and give them a particular taste 烘, 焙〔堅果、咖啡、豆類等〕: *dry-roasted peanuts* 乾烘的花生 **3** [T] *informal* to strongly criticize or make insulting remarks about someone or something【非正式】嚴厲地批評; 嘲諷: *Her first play got roasted by the critics.* 她的第一部劇被評論家批評得一無是處。

roast[2] *n* [C] **1** a large piece of roasted meat 大塊烤肉 —see also 另見 POT ROAST **2** *AmE* an occasion at which people celebrate a special event in someone's life by telling funny stories or giving speeches about them【美】慶祝聚會: *We're going to have a roast for Jack when he retires.* 傑克退休時, 我們要為他舉行一個慶祝會。**3 hot dog roast/oyster roast etc** *AmE* an outdoor party at which food is cooked on an open fire【美】戶外燒烤熱狗/牡蠣等野餐會

roast[3] *adj* [only before noun 僅用於名詞前] roasted 烤好的, 烤製的: *roast chicken* 烤雞

roast·ing[1] /ˈrostɪŋ; ˈrəʊstɪŋ/ also 又作 **roasting hot** /ˌ·· ˈ·◂/ *adj informal* very hot, especially so that you feel uncomfortable【非正式】灼熱的〔尤指令人感到不舒服〕: *a roasting hot day* 酷熱的一天 | *I'm absolutely roasting in this suit.* 穿着這套衣服, 我着實熱死了。

roasting[2] *n* **give sb a roasting** *informal especially BrE* to talk angrily to someone in order to tell them that you disapprove of their behaviour【非正式, 尤英】申斥, 非難

rob /rɑb; rɒb/ *v* **robbed, robbing** [T] **1** to steal money or property from a person, bank etc 搶劫, 搶奪, 打劫: *The gang tried to rob a bank using a sawn-off shotgun.* 那夥罪犯企圖用一支截短的獵槍搶劫一家銀行。| **rob sb of sth** *Mrs Clegg was severely beaten and robbed of all her possessions.* 克萊格太太遭到毒打, 並被搶去全部財物。| *The company director robbed pensioners of millions.* 這名公司董事侵吞了養老金領取者數以百萬計的錢。—see 見 STEAL[1] (USAGE) —see picture at 參見 STEAL[1] 圖 **2 rob sb/sth of sth** to take away an important quality, ability etc from someone or something 使…喪失…: *Being bullied has robbed Duane of his self-confidence.* 杜安尼受到欺侮, 使他喪失了自信。**3 rob Peter to pay Paul** to take money away from someone or something that needs it in order to pay someone else or use it for something else 拆東牆補西牆; 剜肉補瘡 **4 I was robbed!** *spoken* used when you think that you were beaten unfairly in a sport【口】我輸得很冤枉!〔用於體育比賽中〕**5 rob the cradle** *AmE humorous* to have a sexual relationship with someone who is a lot younger than you【美, 幽默】與比自己年齡小很多的人發生性關係; CRADLE-SNATCH *BrE*【英】

rob·ber /ˈrɑbɚ; ˈrɒbə/ *n* [C] someone who steals money or property 強盜, 盜賊, 搶劫者: *a bank robber* 搶劫銀行的強盜

robber bar·on /ˌ·· ˈ··/ *n* [C] a powerful man who used force to get money, land etc, for example a businessman in US in the 19th century who made a lot of money in a dishonest way 強盜貴族〈如19世紀靠不正當手段發財的美國商人〉

rob·ber·y /ˈrɑbərɪ; ˈrɒbəri/ *n* [C,U] the crime of stealing things from a bank, shop etc, especially using violence 搶劫, 劫奪: *Police are investigating a series of bank robberies in South Wales.* 警方正在調查南威爾斯

發生的一連串銀行搶劫案。| **armed robbery** (=robbery using a gun) 持槍搶劫 *a 10 year prison sentence for armed robbery* 因持槍搶劫被判十年監禁 —see also 另見 **daylight robbery** (DAYLIGHT (2))

robe¹ /rob; rəʊb/ *n* [C] **1** also 又作 **robes** a long loose piece of clothing, especially one worn for official ceremonies〔尤指正式典禮時穿的〕長袍, 禮服: *a priest's robes* 牧師的長袍 **2** *especially AmE* a long loose piece of clothing that you wear over your night clothes or after a bath【尤美】睡袍; 浴衣; DRESSING GOWN *especially BrE*【尤英】—see also 另見 BATHROBE

robe² *v formal*【正式】**1 be robed in** to be dressed in a particular way 穿着…: *The hostess looked very glamorous, robed in emerald velvet.* 女主人身穿翠綠色天鵝絨衣服, 看上去非常迷人。**2 robe yourself** *literary* to put on your clothes【文】穿上衣服

rob·in /ˈrɑbɪn; ˈrɒbɪ̣n/ *n* [C] **1** a common small European bird with a red breast and brown back〔歐洲〕鴝, 知更鳥 **2** a North American bird like a European robin, but larger〔北美〕鶇

ro·bot /ˈrobət; ˈrəʊbɒt/ *n* [C] **1** a machine that can move and do some of the work of a person, and is usually controlled by a computer 機器人: *cars built by robots* 機器人製造的汽車 **2** someone who works or behaves like a machine, without having thoughts or feelings 機器一般的人 —**robotic** /roˋbɑtɪk; rəʊˈbɒtɪk/ *adj*

ro·bo·tics /roˋbɑtɪks; rəʊˈbɒtɪks/ *n* [U] the study of how robots are made and used 機器人(製造或應用)學

ro·bust /roˋbʌst; rəˈbʌst/ *adj* **1** a robust person is strong and healthy 強健的, 健壯的: *a robust 85-year-old* 一位健壯的85歲老人 **2** a robust object is strong and not likely to break〔東西〕結實的, 堅固的: *a six-foot giant who seemed likely to flatten even the most robust of deckchairs* 一個看來可能會把最結實的帆布躺椅坐塌的六英尺高的大漢 **3** a robust system, organization etc is strong and not likely to have problems〔系統、組織等〕健全的, 穩固的: *The US economy is now much more robust.* 美國經濟目前穩固多了。**4** behaving or speaking in a strong and determined way〔行為或說話〕強硬的, 堅定的: *a typically robust performance by the former Prime Minister* 前首相一如既往的堅定表現 —**robustly** *adj* —**robustness** *n* [U]

S2 W2 **rock¹** /rɑk; rɒk/ *n*

1 ▶STONE 石頭◀ a) [U] stone, or a type of stone that forms part of the Earth's surface 岩石: *To build the tunnel, they had to cut through 500 feet of solid rock.* 為了建造這條隧道, 他們必須鑿穿500英尺的堅硬岩石。| **rock formation** (=a shape made naturally from rock) 岩層, 岩石 *the rock formations of the Arizona desert* 亞利桑那沙漠的岩層 **b)** [C] a piece of stone, especially a large one 岩塊, 石塊: *Kim sat down on a rock.* 吉姆坐在一塊大石頭上。**c) rocks** [plural] a line of rock under or next to the sea 礁石: *A ship had been driven onto the rocks during the storm.* 一條船在暴風雨中觸礁。

2 ▶MUSIC 音樂◀ [U] also 又作 **rock music** a type of popular modern music with a strong loud beat, played using GUITARS and drums 搖滾樂: *a rock concert* 搖滾樂音樂會 | *rock veteran, Eric Clapton* 搖滾樂老牌歌星埃里克·克萊普頓

3 as solid/steady as a rock a) very strongly built or well supported and not likely to break or fall 堅如磐石/穩如磐石的 **b)** someone who is as solid or steady as a rock is very strong and calm in difficult situations and you can depend on them〔指人面對困難時〕堅定的, 鎮定的, 可靠的 —see also 另見 ROCK-SOLID

4 be on the rocks *informal* a relationship or business that is on the rocks is having a lot of problems and is likely to fail soon【非正式】困難重重, 瀕臨失敗: *Tim's marriage is on the rocks.* 蒂莫的婚姻瀕臨破裂。

5 scotch/vodka etc on the rocks an alcoholic drink that is served with ice but no water 加冰塊的蘇格蘭威士忌/伏特加酒等

6 ▶SWEET FOOD 甜食◀ [U] *BrE* a hard sweet food made in long round pieces【英】棒形硬糖: *a stick of Blackpool rock* 一條布萊克浦硬棒糖

7 ▶JEWEL 首飾◀ [C usually plural 一般用複數] *informal* a DIAMOND or other jewel【非正式】鑽石; 寶石

8 be (stuck) between a rock and a hard place to have a choice between two things, both of which are unpleasant 左右為難, 進退維谷

9 get your rocks off *slang* if a man gets his rocks off, he has sex【俚】〔男人〕發生性行為

rock² *v* **1** [I,T] to move gently backwards and forwards or from side to side, or to make something do this (使)來回擺動, (使)搖擺: *Paul sat gently rocking the child in his arms.* 保羅坐着, 把孩子抱在懷裡輕輕搖晃。| *The waves made the boat rock from side to side.* 波浪使那條船搖來搖去。| **rock with laughter** *Jim rocked with laughter when he heard what had happened.* 吉姆聽了發生的事情後笑得前仰後合。**2** [T] to make the people in a place or organization feel very shocked or surprised 使震驚, 使震動: *In 1970, the city of Newark was rocked by a major scandal.* 1970年, 一宗重大的醜聞震撼了紐瓦克市。**3 rock the boat** *informal* to cause problems for other members of a group by criticizing something or trying to change the way something is done【非正式】提出批評; 改變做事的方式〔從而給別人惹麻煩〕: *A lot of people didn't really agree with the policy, but they didn't want to rock the boat.* 許多人事實上都不贊成這項政策, 但他們不想惹事生非。**4** [T] if an explosion, or EARTHQUAKE (=violent movement of the earth) rocks an area, it makes it shake〔爆炸或地震〕使劇烈震動

rock and roll /ˌ· · ˈ·/ *n* [U] ROCK 'N' ROLL 搖滾樂

rock bot·tom /ˌ· ˈ··◂/ *n* **hit/reach rock bottom** *informal* to become as unhappy or unpleasant as it is possible to be【非正式】極不愉快: *My personal life had hit rock bottom.* 我的私生活糟透了。

rock-bottom *adj* a rock-bottom price is as low as it can possibly be〔價格〕最低的, 不能再低的: *bargain holidays at rock-bottom prices* 特價旅行團, 折扣價無可再低

rock cake /ˈ· ·/ also 又作 **rock bun** *n* [C] *BrE* a small hard cake with a rough surface that has dried fruit in it【英】岩皮餅〔一種表面粗硬有乾果的小甜餅〕

rock climb·ing /ˈ· ˌ··/ *n* [U] the sport of climbing up very steep rock surfaces such as the sides of mountains 攀岩(運動) —**rock climber** *n* [C]

rock-crys·tal /ˈ· ˌ··/ *n* [U] pure natural QUARTZ (=a very hard mineral) that is transparent 水晶

rock·er /ˈrɑkɚ; ˈrɒkə/ *n* [C] **1** one of the curved pieces of wood fixed to the bottom of a ROCKING CHAIR, that allows it to move backwards and forwards if you push it〔搖椅底部的〕弧形搖板 **2 be off your rocker** *spoken* to be crazy【口】發瘋 **3** a member of a group of young people in Britain in the 1960s who wore leather JACKETS, rode MOTORCYCLES, and listened to ROCK 'N' ROLL music 搖滾青年〔20世紀60年代英國穿皮短上衣、騎摩托車、聽搖滾樂的年輕人〕—compare 比較 MOD **4** a ROCKING CHAIR 搖椅

rock·e·ry /ˈrɑkərɪ; ˈrɒkəri/ *n* [C] part of a garden where there are rocks with small plants growing between them 岩石庭園〔園林中陳設岩石、有花草生長的部分〕; 假山

rock·et¹ /ˈrɑkɪt; ˈrɒkɪ̣t/ *n* [C] **1** a vehicle used for travelling or carrying things into space, which is shaped like a big tube 火箭 **2** a similar object used as a weapon, especially one that carries a bomb 火箭式投射器, 火箭彈: *anti-tank rockets* 反坦克火箭 **3** a small tube fixed to a stick, that contains explosive powder and is used as a FIREWORK 流星煙火, 火箭式煙火 **4 give sb a rocket** *BrE informal* to criticize someone angrily because they have done something wrong【英, 非正式】斥責某人

rocket² *v* [I] **1** also 又作 **rocket up** if a price or amount rockets, it increases quickly and suddenly〔價格、數量〕迅速上升, 猛漲: *Interest rates rocketed.* 利率急速上升。

2 [always+adv/prep] to move somewhere very fast 急速移動: **[+through/along etc]** *The train rocketed through the tunnel.* 火車高速駛過隧道。**3** [always+adv/prep] to achieve a successful position very quickly 迅速取得成功地位; 一躍成名: **[+to]** *Their new album rocketed to number one in the charts.* 他們的新唱片迅速攀升到排行榜榜首。

rocket launch·er /ˈ·· ˌ··/ *n* [C] a weapon like a tube used for firing military rockets into the air 火箭發射裝置, 火箭發射筒

rock·fall /ˈrɑkˌfɔl; ˈrɒkˌfɔːl/ *n* [C] a pile of rocks that are falling or have fallen 岩崩; 塌方

rock gar·den /ˈ· ˌ··/ *n* [C] a ROCKERY 岩石庭院; 假山

rock-hard /ˌ· ˈ·◂/ *adj* **1** extremely hard 非常堅硬的: *The bread was stale and rock-hard.* 這個麵包既不新鮮又很硬。**2** *BrE humorous* strong and not afraid of anyone【英, 幽默】堅強的; 誰也不怕的

rock·ing chair /ˈ·· ·/ *n* [C] a chair that has two curved pieces of wood fixed under it, so that it moves backwards and forwards 搖椅 —see picture at 參見 CHAIR[1] 圖

rocking horse /ˈ·· ·/ *n* [C] a wooden horse for children that moves backwards and forwards when you sit on it〔小孩騎的〕搖動木馬

R

rock mu·sic /ˈ· ˌ··/ *n* [U] a type of popular modern music with a strong loud beat, played using GUITARs and drums 搖滾樂

rock 'n' roll /ˌrɑk ən ˈrol; ˌrɒk ən ˈrəʊl/ *n* [U] a style of music that was very popular in the 1950s, and has a strong loud beat〔流行於 20 世紀 50 年代的〕搖滾樂: *Elvis, the king of rock 'n' roll* 搖滾樂之王皮禮士利

rock pool /ˈ· ·/ *n* [C] *BrE* a small pool of water between rocks by the sea【英】〔海邊岩石間的〕小水潭; TIDE POOL *AmE*【美】

rock salt /ˈ· ·/ *n* [U] a kind of salt which is obtained from under the ground 岩鹽

rock-sol·id /ˌ· ˈ··◂/ *adj* **1** very strong so that you can depend on it 穩健的, 可靠的 **2** very hard and not likely to break 堅硬的; 結實的, 牢固的

rock-stead·y /ˌ· ˈ··◂/ *adj* very strong or very calm 堅如磐石的; 極鎮定的: *rock-steady nerves* 極堅強的神經

rock·y /ˈrɑkɪ; ˈrɒki/ *adj* **1** covered with rocks or made of rock 多岩石的; 由岩石形成的: *the rocky hills of New England* 新英格蘭滿是岩石的丘陵 **2** *informal* a relationship or situation that is rocky is difficult and may not continue or be successful【非正式】〔關係或環境〕難以維持的, 可能失敗的: *The company faces a rocky road ahead.* 公司面臨着一條坎坷的道路。—**rockiness** *n* [U]

ro·co·co /rəˈkoko; rəˈkəʊkəʊ/ *adj* rococo buildings and furniture have a lot of curly decoration and were fashionable in Europe in the 18th century〔建築、家具〕洛可可式的〔18 世紀流行於歐洲, 多用彎曲形裝飾的風格〕

rod /rɑd; rɒd/ *n* [C] **1** a long thin pole or bar 竿, 棒: *The walls are reinforced with steel rods.* 這些牆是用鋼筋加固的。**2** a long thin pole used with a line and hook for catching fish 釣竿: *a fishing rod* 釣魚竿 **3 make a rod for your own back** to do something that will cause trouble for you in the future 自討苦吃, 自找麻煩 —see also 另見 HOT ROD, **rule sb/sth with a rod of iron** (RULE[2] (6))

rode /rod; rəʊd/ the past tense of RIDE[1]

ro·dent /ˈrodn̩t; ˈrəʊdənt/ *n* [C] one of a group or small animals with long sharp front teeth, such as rats or rabbits 齧齒動物〈如大老鼠、兔子〉

ro·de·o /ˈrodɪˌo; ˈrəʊdiəʊ/ *n plural* **rodeos** [C] a type of entertainment in which COWBOYs ride wild horses, and catch cattle with ropes 牛仔競技表演〔馴服烈馬、用繩圈套牛〕

roe /ro; rəʊ/ *n* [C,U] fish eggs eaten as a food〔供食用的〕魚子

roe deer /ˈ· ·/ *n* [C] a small European and Asian DEER that lives in forests 狍〔產於歐亞森林的小鹿〕

roent·gen, röntgen /ˈrɛntgən; ˈrɒntgən/ *n technical* the international measure for X-RAYS【術語】倫琴〔X 光的國際放射量單位〕

ro·ger[1] /ˈrɑdʒɚ; ˈrɒdʒə/ *interjection* used in radio conversations to say that a message has been understood 已收到, 明白〔無線電對話用語〕

roger[2] *v* [T] *BrE slang taboo* to have sex with someone【英俚, 諱】與...性交

rogue[1] /rog; rəʊg/ *n* [C] **1** *often humorous* a man or boy who behaves badly or causes trouble, but who you like in spite of this【常幽默】壞蛋, 淘氣鬼〔指男人或男孩〕: *What's the little rogue done now, I wonder?* 不知道那個小淘氣鬼幹甚麼啦? | *a lovable rogue* 可愛的搗蛋鬼 **2** *old-fashioned* a man who is dishonest and has a bad character【過時】無賴, 流氓: **rogues' gallery** (=a group of bad people) 一羣無賴 —**roguery** *n* [U]

rogue[2] *adj* [only before noun 僅用於名詞前] **1** a rogue person or organization does not follow the usual rules or methods and often causes trouble 不循常規的; 常製造麻煩的 **2** a rogue wild animal lives apart from the main group and is often dangerous〔野獸〕離羣而危險的

rogu·ish /ˈrogɪʃ; ˈrəʊgɪʃ/ *adj* someone with a roguish expression or smile looks amused, especially because they have done something slightly dishonest or wrong〔表情或笑容〕淘氣的, 調皮的 —**roguishly** *adv* —**roguishness** *n* [U]

rois·ter /ˈrɔɪstɚ; ˈrɔɪstə/ *v* [I] *old-fashioned* to behave in a cheerful, rough, noisy way【過時】喧鬧作樂 —**roisterer** *n* [C]

role /rol; rəʊl/ *n* [C] **1** the way in which someone or something is involved in an activity or situation, and how much influence they have on it 作用: **play a leading/major/key role** (=be important in making changes happen) 起最重要/主要/關鍵作用 *Mandela played a leading role in ending apartheid in South Africa.* 曼德拉在結束南非種族隔離的運動中起了主要作用。| *China's growing role in Hong Kong's economy* 中國大陸在香港經濟中所起的越來越重要的作用 | *the role of diet in the prevention of diseases such as cancer* 飲食對預防癌症等疾病的作用 **2** the character played by an actor in a play or film〔戲劇、電影中的〕角色: **play a role** (=act a role) 擔任一個角色 *Matthews plays the role of a young doctor suspected of murder.* 馬修斯扮演一位涉嫌謀殺的年輕醫生。| **the lead/leading role** (=the most important role) 主角 | **minor role** (=an unimportant role) 配角 **3** the position that someone has in society, in an organization etc, or the way they are expected to behave in a relationship with someone else〔社會、組織等中的〕地位, 職責;〔關係中的〕角色: *Women are often forced into a supportive role.* 婦女往往被迫在社會中處於從屬地位。| **role reversal** (=a situation in which two people, especially a man and a woman, take each other's roles)〔尤指男、女角色〕反串, 角色倒轉

role mod·el /ˈ· ˌ··/ *n* [C] someone whose behaviour, attitudes etc people try to copy because they admire them 模範, 榜樣

role-play /ˈ· ·/ *n* [C,U] an exercise in which you behave in the way that someone else would behave in a particular situation, especially to help you learn something〔尤指協助學習某事物的〕角色扮演: *the use of role-play in the classroom* 在教室裡使用角色扮演的方法 —**role-play** *v* [I,T]

roll[1] /rol; rəʊl/ *v*

1 ►ROUND OBJECT 圓形物件◄ [I always+adv/prep, T] if something that is round rolls or if you roll it, it moves along a surface by turning over and over (使) 滾動: *The ball rolled into the street.* 球滾到了街上。| **roll sth** *Maybe we can roll the log to the middle of the campsite.* 也許我們可以把這根原木滾到營地中央。

2 ►PERSON/ANIMAL 人/動物◄ [I always+adv/prep] to turn your body over one or more times while lying down 打滾, 翻身: *The dog had been rolling in mud puddles.* 那條狗一直在泥坑裡打滾。| *Ralph rolled onto* *his stomach.* 拉爾夫翻身趴下。

3 ▶STH WITH WHEELS 有輪子的東西◀ [I always+adv/prep, T always+adv/prep] to move on wheels, or make something that has wheels move 開動, 行駛: **[+into/forwards/past etc]** *We watched as the bus rolled slowly backwards down the hill.* 我們望着那輛公共汽車緩緩地倒着下山。| **roll sth to/around/by etc** *The waitress rolled the dessert cart over to our table.* 女服務員把甜點車推到我們桌子跟前。

4 ▶PAPER/STRING ETC 紙/繩等◀ [T] also 又作 **roll up** to bend or wind something such as paper, string etc into the shape of a tube or ball 捲, 繞, 把〔紙、繩等〕捲成筒[球狀]: *Harry rolled the newspaper and put a rubber band around it.* 哈利把報紙捲起來, 再套上一根橡皮圈。| *Roll the yarn into a ball.* 把線繞成團。

5 ▶DROP OF LIQUID 液滴◀ [I always+adv/prep] to move over a surface smoothly without stopping〔平穩地〕滾動: **[+down/onto]** *Tears rolled down her cheeks.* 眼淚順着她的面頰滾滾流下。

6 ▶WAVES/CLOUDS 浪/雲◀ [I always+adv/prep] to move in a particular direction〔朝着特定方向〕滾動, 飄移: **[+into/towards etc]** *Mist rolled in from the sea.* 霧從海上滾滾而來。| *waves rolling onto the beach* 海浪湧上沙灘

7 roll your eyes to move your eyes round and upwards, especially in order to show that you are annoyed 骨碌碌地轉動眼睛, 翻白眼〔尤表示不快〕: *Marta rolled her eyes as Will started to tell another stupid joke.* 威爾開始講另一個愚蠢的笑話時, 瑪爾塔翻了個白眼。

8 ▶GAME 遊戲◀ [I,T] if you roll DICE, you throw them as part of a game 擲〔骰子〕

9 ▶SHIP/PLANE 船/飛機◀ [I] if a ship or plane rolls, it leans one way and then another with the motion of the water or air〔隨着水流或氣流〕左右搖晃, 搖擺

10 ▶MAKE STH FLAT 弄平某物◀ [T] to make something flat by moving something heavy over it 把…碾平: *Roll the pie crust flat with a rolling pin.* 用擀麵杖把餡餅的油酥皮擀平。

11 ▶WALK 行走◀ [I always+adv/prep] to walk in a rather uncontrolled way, moving your body from side to side, usually because you are drunk 搖搖晃晃地走〔一般指喝醉酒〕: *We rolled out of the bar at about 3.00 that morning.* 那天清晨大約 3 點鐘我們搖搖晃晃地走出酒吧。

12 ▶SOUND 聲音◀ [I] if drums or THUNDER[1] (1) roll, they make a long low series of sounds〔鼓或雷〕隆隆作響

13 ▶MACHINE/CAMERA 機器/照相機◀ [I] if a machine such as a film camera or a PRINTING PRESS rolls, it operates 啟動: *Quiet! The cameras are rolling!* 肅靜! 拍攝開始了!

14 (all) rolled into one if something is several different things rolled into one, it includes qualities of all those things 合為一體: *Mum was cook, chauffeur, nurse, and entertainer all rolled into one.* 媽媽集廚師、司機、護士和演員於一身。

15 get rolling if a plan, business etc gets rolling, it starts operating〔計劃、企業等〕開始實施; 開始運作: *When the business gets rolling, we'll have more time to think about other things.* 企業開始運作後, 我們將有更多時間思考其他事情。

16 roll a cigarette to make your own cigarette, using loose tobacco and special paper 捲煙: **roll your own** (=make your own cigarettes) 自己捲煙 *It's cheaper to roll your own.* 自己動手捲煙比較便宜。

17 roll out of bed *informal* to get out of bed【非正式】起牀: *I finally rolled out of bed about noon.* 中午前後我終於起牀了。

18 be rolling in the aisles if people in a theatre, cinema etc are rolling in the aisles, they are laughing a lot〔劇院、戲院觀眾〕笑得東倒西歪

19 be ready to roll *spoken especially AmE* used to say you are ready to do something【口, 尤美】準備就緒: *OK, everything's in the car. Is everybody ready to roll?* 好, 所有東西都裝進了汽車。大家準備好了嗎?

20 roll on *BrE* used to say that you wish a time or event would come quickly【英】但願…早日來到: *Roll on the weekend!* 但願週末早點來到!

21 ▶ATTACK 攻擊◀ [T] *AmE* to rob someone, especially when they are drunk and asleep【美】〔趁人醉酒和睡着時〕搶劫: *punks on the streets rolling drunks for small change* 搶劫醉漢零錢的街頭小流氓

22 roll your r's to pronounce the sound /r/ using your tongue in a way that makes the sound very long 用舌尖顫音發 r 音

23 a rolling stone gathers no moss used to say that someone who often changes jobs, etc does not have any real relationships or responsibilities 滾石不生苔〔形容經常轉換工作等的人沒有實在的關係或責任〕—see also 另見 **set/start the ball rolling** (BALL[1] (9)), **heads will roll** (HEAD[1] (52)), **be rolling in it** (ROLLING (3))

roll around/round *phr v* [I] if something that happens regularly rolls around, it happens again 周而復始, 循環: *By the time autumn rolled around, we still hadn't finished painting the house.* 當秋天又來臨時, 我們還沒有粉刷完房子。

roll away *phr v* [I always+adv/prep] if countryside rolls away, it is full of small hills as far as you can see 延綿起伏: *green pastures rolling away into the distance* 綠油油的牧場延綿起伏, 伸向遠方

roll sth ↔ **back** *phr v* [T] **1** to force your opponents in a war to move back from their position 使〔敵方〕退卻, 擊退 **2** to reduce the influence or power of a system, government etc, especially because it has too much power 降低〔影響或權力〕, 削減: *Dulles saw communism as something evil to be rolled back, not just contained.* 〔美國艾森豪政府的國務卿〕杜勒斯認為共產主義是邪惡的, 應該加以削弱而不僅僅是抵制。**3** *AmE* to reduce the price of something【美】降低〔價格〕: *the administration's promise to roll back taxes* 政府關於減税的承諾

roll sth ↔ **down** *phr v* [T] **roll a window down** to open a car window 搖下車窗

roll in *phr v* [I] **1** to happen or arrive in large numbers or quantities 大量發生[湧來]: *Pleas for help were made to the public, and the money came rolling in.* 呼籲公眾提供幫助後, 錢源源不斷地湧來。**2** to arrive later than usual or expected without seeming to be worried〔心安理得地〕遲到: *Chris finally rolled in at about 4.00 am.* 克里斯終於若無其事地在凌晨 4 點左右回來了。**3** if clouds, mist etc roll in, they begin to cover an area of the sky or land〔雲、霧等〕滾滾而來: *Fog rolled in from the sea.* 霧從海上滾滾而來。

roll sth ↔ **out** *phr v* [T] **1** to make something flat and thin by pushing a special tube shaped object over it 把…碾平, 把…擀薄: *Roll out the pastry.* 把麵團擀薄。—see picture on page A11 參見 A11 頁圖 **2** to make something flat and straight on the ground, after it has been rolled into a tube shape 把…鋪開: *Roll out your sleeping bag inside the tent.* 在帳篷裡把你的睡袋鋪開。**3 roll out the red carpet** to make special preparations for an important visitor 鋪開紅地毯〔隆重歡迎〕

roll over *phr v* **1** [I] to turn your body round once so that you are lying in a different position 翻身: *Ben rolled over and kissed her.* 本翻過身來吻了吻她。**2** [T] **roll sb/sth over** to turn someone's body over on the ground 把某人/某物翻身: **roll sb onto** *The guards rolled him over onto his front.* 衛兵們把他翻過身來臉衝下。

roll up *phr v* **1 roll your sleeves/trousers up** to turn the ends of your sleeves etc over several times so that they are shorter 捲起衣袖/褲腿 **2 roll your sleeves up** to start doing a job even though it is difficult or unpleasant 捲起袖子〔準備苦幹〕: *We're just going to have to roll our sleeves up and get on with it.* 我們正準備動手繼續幹呢。**3 roll a window up** to close the window of

R

a car 搖上車窗 **4** [I] to arrive somewhere, especially late or unexpectedly 姍姍來遲; 意外到來: *Brad and Debbie rolled up in their new convertible at about 9.00.* 布拉德和黛比大約9點才開着新敞篷車姍姍而來。**5 roll up!** *BrE spoken* used to call people to come and watch or buy things at a CIRCUS (1), FAIR³ (2) etc【英口】快來呀! 快來看!〔尤用於招呼人們進去看馬戲或在集市上購物〕

roll² *n*

1 ▶PAPER/FILM/MONEY ETC 紙/膠片/錢等◀ [C] a piece of paper, film, money that has been rolled into the shape of a tube〔紙、膠片、錢的〕一卷: **[+of]** *a roll of film* 膠卷 | *8 rolls of toilet paper for $1.99* 1.99 美元八卷衛生紙 | *Dusty pulled a huge roll of $100 bills from his pocket.* 達斯蒂從口袋裡抽出一大卷100美元的鈔票。

2 ▶BREAD 麵包◀ [C] a small round LOAF of bread for one person 麵包卷, 小圓麵包: *Put the rolls on the table.* 把麵包卷放在桌上。| **ham/cheese etc roll** *BrE* (=one that is filled with ham, cheese etc)【英】火腿/乾酪等麵包卷

3 ▶PHYSICAL MOVEMENT 身體動作◀ [C] **a)** the action of moving by rolling your body 滾動: *a young horse having a roll in the field* 在田野裡打滾的小馬 **b)** a movement done, often as part of a sport, by rolling on the ground in a controlled way with your body curled 打滾, 翻筋斗: *tumblers doing rolls and handstands at the circus* 在馬戲團裡翻筋斗和倒立的雜技演員

4 ▶SHIP/PLANE 船/飛機◀ [C] the movement of a ship or plane when it leans from side to side with the motion of the water or air 搖晃

5 ▶SKIN/FAT 皮膚/脂肪◀ [C+of] a thick layer of skin or fat, usually just below your waist〔通常指腰部以下的〕贅皮; 肥肉

6 roll of drums/guns/thunder a long low fairly loud sound made by drums etc 隆隆的鼓/砲/雷聲

7 be on a roll *informal* to be having a lot of success with what you are trying to do【非正式】取得接二連三的巨大成就

8 ▶GAME 遊戲◀ [C] the action of throwing DICE as part of a game 擲骰子: *It's your roll, Rob.* 該你擲了, 羅布。

9 ▶LIST OF NAMES 名單◀ an official list of names, especially of people at a meeting, in a class etc〔尤指參加會議、上課等的〕名單, 名冊: **call/take the roll** (=say the list of names to check that everyone on it is there) 點名

10 roll in the hay *informal* an act of having sex with someone【非正式】做愛

roll bar /ˈ· ·/ *n* [C] a strong metal bar over the top of a car, intended to protect the people inside if the car turns over〔汽車頂蓋上的〕翻車保護杆

roll-call /ˈ· ·/ *n* [C,U] the act of reading out an official list of names to check who is there 點名

rolled gold /ˌ· ˈ·/ *n* [U] a thin layer of gold on the surface of another metal 金箔, 包金; FILLED GOLD *AmE*【美】

rolled oats /ˌ· ˈ·/ *n* [plural] *especially BrE* a kind of oats (OATS (1)), used for making PORRIDGE【尤英】燕麥片

roll·er /ˈrolɚ; ˈrəʊlə/ *n* [C] **1** a tube-shaped piece of wood, metal etc that can be rolled over and over, used in a machine for crushing, printing etc〔用於輾壓、印刷等的〕軋輥, 滾筒, 滾軸 **2** a large tube-shaped piece of stone, metal etc that you roll over the surface of grass or roads to make them smooth 碾壓機, 壓路機: *a garden roller* 碾草坪機 **3** a long, powerful wave 巨浪: *great Atlantic rollers* 大西洋的巨浪 **4** a tube-shaped piece of metal or wood, used for moving heavy things that have no wheels〔用於移動無輪重物的〕滾棒, 滾杆, 滾柱 **5** a small tube-shaped piece of metal or plastic that you wrap your hair around to make it curl 捲髮夾 **6** a ROLLS-ROYCE 勞斯萊斯汽車

Rollerblade /ˈ· · ·/ *n trademark* special boots with a single row of wheels fixed under it【商標】一字輪旱冰鞋 —compare 比較 ROLLER SKATE

roller blind /ˈ· · ·/ *n* [C] *BrE* a piece of cloth or other material that can be rolled up and down to cover a window【英】〔窗戶的〕捲簾 —see picture at 參見 BLIND³ 圖

roller coaster 過山車

roller coast·er /ˈ·· ˌ··/ *n* [C] **1** a track with sudden steep slopes and curves, which people ride on for excitement in special small carriages 過山車, 雲霄飛車 **2** a situation that is impossible to control, because it keeps changing very quickly〔因為情況一直在快速變化而〕無法控制的局面, 急轉突變: *Their relationship was a continual emotional roller coaster.* 他們的感情時好時壞。

roller skate /ˈ·· ·/ *n* [C] a special boot with four wheels fixed under it 四輪旱冰鞋 —**roller-skate** *v* [I] —**roller skating** *n* [U]

roller tow·el /ˈ·· ˌ··/ *n* [C] a cloth you use for drying your hands, which is joined together at the ends and wound around a bar of wood or metal〔兩頭縫結、套在木製或金屬棒上的〕環狀擦手毛巾

rol·lick·ing¹ /ˈrɑlɪkɪŋ; ˈrɒlɪkɪŋ/ *adj* [only before noun 僅用於名詞前] *old-fashioned* noisy and cheerful【過時】喧鬧的, 歡鬧的: *a rollicking song* 歡樂喧鬧的歌

rollicking² *n* **give sb a rollicking** *BrE informal* to criticize someone angrily for something they have done【英, 非正式】斥責某人

roll·ing /ˈrolɪŋ; ˈrəʊlɪŋ/ *adj* **1** [only before noun 僅用於名詞前] rolling hills have many long gentle slopes 綿延起伏的 **2** if you have a rolling walk, you move from side to side as you walk〔走路的樣子〕搖晃的, 搖擺的 **3 be rolling in it** *informal* to be extremely rich【非正式】非常有錢, 十分富有: *If James can afford that car, he must be rolling in it!* 如果詹姆斯能買得起那輛車, 他必定非常有錢!

rolling mill /ˈ·· ·/ *n* [C] a factory or machine in which metal is rolled into large, flat, thin pieces 軋鋼廠; 軋鋼機

rolling pin /ˈ·· ·/ *n* [C] a long tube-shaped piece of wood used for making PASTRY flat and thin before you cook it 擀麵杖

rolling stock /ˈ·· ·/ *n* [U] all the trains, carriages etc that are used on a railway 鐵路上使用的所有車輛〈如火車、客車車廂等〉

roll·mop /ˈrolˌmɑp; ˈrɒlmɒp/ *n* [C] a HERRING that has been rolled up and preserved in VINEGAR 醋醃鯡魚卷

roll of hon·our /ˌ· · ˈ··/ *n* [C] *BrE* a list of the names of people who are officially praised, especially because they were brave in battle【英】榮譽名冊〔尤用於表揚在戰爭中表現英勇者〕; HONOR ROLL *AmE*【美】

roll-on /ˈ· ·/ *n* [C] **1** also 又作 **roll-on de·o·dor·ant** /ˌ· · ˈ··· ·/ a bottle which contains liquid that you rub under your arms in order to stop your SWEAT² (1) from smelling unpleasant 滾抹除臭劑 **2** a woman's GIRDLE (=type of underwear) that you pull on in one piece, worn in the past〔舊時女子穿的〕束腹

roll-on roll-off /ˌ· · ˌ· ˈ·/ *adj* [only before noun 僅用於名詞前] *BrE* a roll-on roll-off ship is one that vehicles can drive straight on and off【英】〔船〕車輛可開上開下的: *a roll-on roll-off car ferry* 汽車渡輪

Rolls-Royce /ˌrolz ˈrɔɪs; ˌrəʊlz ˈrɔɪs◂/ *n* [C] **1** *trademark* a very expensive and comfortable car made by a British company【商標】勞斯萊斯, 羅爾斯一羅伊斯汽車〔英國生產的一種極昂貴和舒適的汽車〕**2** *BrE informal*

something that is regarded as the highest quality example of a particular type of product【英, 非正式】〔同類中〕最優良的產品; CADILLAC *AmE*【美】: *the Rolls-Royce of video recorders* 攝錄機中的極品

roll-top desk /,· ·'·/ *n* [C] a desk that has a cover that you roll back when you open it 捲蓋式書桌

roll-up /'· ·/ *n* [C] *BrE* a cigarette that you make yourself【英】自捲香煙

ro·ly-po·ly¹ /ˈrolɪ ˌpolɪ; ˌrəʊli ˈpəʊli◂/ *adj* a roly-poly person is round and fat〔人〕圓圓胖胖的

roly-poly² *n* [C,U] a British sweet food made of JAM¹ (1) that is rolled up inside PASTRY〔英國的〕果醬布丁卷

ROM /rɑm; rɒm/ *n* [U] read-only memory; the part of a computer where permanent instructions and information are stored 只讀存儲器, 唯讀記憶體 —compare 比較 RAM

Ro·man /ˈromən; ˈrəʊmən/ *adj* **1** connected with ancient Rome or the Roman Empire 古羅馬的, 羅馬帝國的 **2** connected with the city of Rome 羅馬城的 —**Roman** *n* [C]

roman *n* [U] *technical* the ordinary style of printing that uses small upright letters, like the style used for printing these words【術語】羅馬字體, 正體字 —compare 比較 ITALICS

Roman al·pha·bet /,·· '···/ *n* [singular] the alphabet used in English and many other European languages, which begins with the letters A, B, C 羅馬字母表〔以A, B, C等字母開始, 用於英語和許多其他歐洲語言中〕

Roman Cath·o·lic /,·· '···◂/ *adj* belonging to or connected with the part of the Christian religion whose leader is the Pope 羅馬天主教的 —**Roman Catholic** *n* [C] —**Roman Catholicism** /,·· ·'····/ *n* [U]

ro·mance¹ /roˈmæns; rəʊˈmæns/ *n* **1** [C] an exciting and often short relationship between two people who love each other 羅曼史, 豔事: **a whirlwind romance** (=one that happens very suddenly and quickly) 閃電式的風流韻事 **2** [U] love, or a feeling of being in love 浪漫, 愛情: *The romance had gone out of their relationship.* 他們的關係已經失去了浪漫。**3** [U] the feeling of excitement and adventure that is connected with a particular place, activity etc 傳奇色彩, 浪漫色彩: *the romance of life in the Wild West* 西大荒生活的浪漫色彩 **4** [C] a story about the love between two people 愛情故事 **5** [C] a story that has brave characters and exciting events 傳奇故事: *a Medieval romance* 中世紀的傳奇故事

romance² *v* [I] to describe things that have happened in a way that makes them seem better or more important than they really were 誇張, 渲染: **[+about]** *an old man romancing about the past* 一位誇張地大談往事的老人

Romance lan·guage /'·· ··/ *n* [C] a language that comes from Latin, for example French or Spanish〔由拉丁語演變而成的〕羅曼語〈如法語或西班牙語〉

Ro·man·esque /ˌromənˈɛsk; ˌrəʊməˈnesk◂/ *adj* in the style of building that was popular in Western Europe in the 11th and 12th centuries, and had many round ARCH*es* and thick PILLAR*s* 羅馬式的〔多用圓拱頂和粗圓柱的建築風格, 流行於 11 和 12 世紀的西歐〕

Roman law /,·· '·/ *n* [U] *law* CIVIL LAW【法律】民法, 民事法

Roman nose /,·· '·/ *n* [C] a nose that curves out near the top 高鼻梁, 鷹鉤鼻 —see picture on page A6 參見 A6 頁圖

roman nu·mer·al /,·· '···/ *n* [C] a number in a system first used in ancient Rome that uses the combinations of the letters I, V, X, L, C, D, and M 羅馬數字

Romano- /ramano; rəmɑːnəʊ/ *prefix* **1** connected with ancient Rome; Roman 古羅馬的; 羅馬的 **2** ancient Roman and 古羅馬和…的: *Romano-British art* 古羅馬—不列顛藝術

ro·man·tic¹ /roˈmæntɪk; rəʊˈmæntɪk/ *adj*

1 ►SHOWING LOVE 表現感情的◄ showing strong feelings of love 多情的: *"Tom always sends me red roses on my birthday." "How romantic!"* "我過生日時湯姆總給我送紅玫瑰。" "真是多情啊!"

2 ►CONNECTED WITH LOVE 與愛情有關的◄ connected with feelings of love or with a loving relationship 浪漫的, 風流的: *It's not a romantic relationship – they're just business partners.* 這不是甚麼浪漫關係——他們只是生意上的夥伴。

3 ►BEAUTIFUL 美麗的◄ beautiful in a way that affects your emotions and makes you think of love or adventure 富於浪漫色彩的; 充滿傳奇色彩的: *a romantic village nestling at the foot of the mountains* 一個坐落在山腳下富有浪漫氣息的村莊

4 ►NOT PRACTICAL 不實際的◄ not practical, and basing your actions too much on an imagined idea of the world 不切實際的, 耽於幻想的, 空想的: *romantic notions about becoming a famous actress* 希望成為著名女演員的幻想

5 ►STORY/FILM 故事/電影◄ a romantic story or film is about love 關於愛情的, 浪漫的: *a romantic comedy* 愛情喜劇

6 Romantic art/literature etc art or literature that is based on the ideas of romanticism 浪漫主義的藝術/文學等 —**romantically** /-klɪ; -kli/ *adv*

romantic² *n* [C] **1** someone who shows strong feelings of love and likes doing things that are connected with love such as buying flowers, presents etc 富於浪漫氣息的人: *Oh, Andy, you're such a romantic!* 噢, 安迪, 你是如此浪漫的人! **2** someone who is not practical, and bases their ideas too much on an imagined idea of the world 愛幻想的人, 浪漫主義者: *an incurable romantic* 不可救藥的幻想家 **3** also 又作 **Romantic** a writer, painter etc, whose work is based on romanticism 浪漫主義作家[畫家等]

ro·man·ti·cis·m, Romanticism /roˈmæntəˌsɪzəm; rəʊˈmæntɪ̣sɪzəm/ *n* [U] a way of writing or painting that was popular in the late 18th and early 19th century, in which feelings and wild natural beauty were considered more important than anything else 浪漫主義〔18 世紀末至 19 世紀初流行的寫作或繪畫風格〕

ro·man·ti·cize also 又作 **-ise** *BrE*【英】/roˈmæntəˌsaɪz; rəʊˈmæntɪ̣saɪz/ *v* [T] to talk or think about things in a way that makes them seem more romantic or attractive than they really are 使浪漫化, 使具有浪漫色彩: *a rather romanticized picture of life in the war* 對戰時生活浪漫的描繪

Ro·ma·ny /ˈrɑmənɪ; ˈrəʊməni/ *n* **1** [C] a GIPSY 吉卜賽人 **2** [U] the language of the GIPSY people 吉卜賽語

ro·me·o, Romeo /ˈromɪˌo; ˈrəʊmiəʊ/ *n* [C] *often humorous* a man who tries to attract all the women he meets in a ROMANTIC¹ (1) or sexual way【常幽默】羅密歐式的男人〔浪漫多情的男子〕: *the office Romeo* 辦公室的羅密歐

romp¹ /rɑmp; rɒmp/ *v* [I] **1** [always+adv/prep] to play in a noisy way, especially by running, jumping etc〔尤指又跑又跳地〕嬉鬧: **[+around/about]** *They could hear the children romping around upstairs.* 他們聽得到孩子們在樓上蹦跳打鬧的聲音。**2 romp home** if someone or something, especially a horse in a race, romps home, they win the race or competition easily〔尤指賽馬〕輕鬆取勝

romp through sth *phr v* [T] *BrE informal* to succeed in doing or finishing something quickly and easily【英, 非正式】輕易獲得成功, 輕易完成

romp² *n* [C] **1** *informal* a piece of amusing entertainment which has a lot of exciting scenes【非正式】打鬧逗笑的表演節目: *Branagh's new film is an enjoyable romp.* 布拉納的新片子是一部有趣的鬧劇。**2** *BrE humorous* a word for sexual activity, used especially by newspapers【英, 幽默】調情〔尤用於報紙上〕**3** an occasion when people play noisily and roughly 嬉鬧

romp·ers /ˈrɑmpəz; ˈrɒmpəz/ *n* [plural] a piece of clothing for babies, made like a top and trousers joined together〔嬰兒穿的〕連衫褲

ron·do /ˈrɑndo; ˈrɒndəʊ/ *n plural* **rondos** [C] a piece of music in which the main tune is repeated several times 迴旋曲

R

rönt·gen /ˈrɛntgən; ˈrɒntgen/ *n* [C] another spelling of ROENTGEN roentgen的另一種拼法

rood /rud; ruːd/ *n* [C] *old use or technical* a Christian cross, usually in a church【舊或術語】〔常指基督教教堂中的〕耶穌受難像十字架

rood screen /ˈ· ·/ *n* [C] a decorated wooden or stone wall in a Christian church, that divides the part where the CHOIR (=singers) sit from the part where other people sit〔基督教教堂中把唱詩班與會眾隔開的〕聖壇隔屏

3 2 **roof**[1] /ruf; ruːf/ *n* [C]

1 ►OF A BUILDING 建築的◄ the outside surface or structure on top of a building, vehicle, tent etc 屋頂; 車頂; 帳篷頂: *Our roof used to leak whenever it rained.* 以前, 只要下雨我們的屋頂就會漏水。| *We can probably strap the cases to the roof of her car.* 我們也許可以把箱子捆在她的車頂上。—see picture on page A4 參見 A4 頁圖

2 ►OF A PASSAGE 通道的◄ the top of passage under the ground; CEILING (1)〔地下通道的〕頂部; 天花板: *Soon, the whole tunnel roof was collapsing on top of the miners.* 很快, 整個坑道頂部開始塌陷, 落到礦工們身上。

3 a roof over your head somewhere to live 住處: *I may not have a job, but at least I've got a roof over my head.* 我可能沒有工作, 但我至少有家可回。

4 go through the roof *informal*【非正式】**a)** also 又作 **hit the roof** to suddenly become very angry〔突然〕暴跳如雷, 火冒三丈: *Put that back before Dad sees you and hits the roof!* 趁早放回去, 省得爸爸看見時大發雷霆! **b)** if a price, cost etc goes through the roof, it increases to a very high level〔價格〕飛漲

5 ►OF YOUR MOUTH 嘴的◄ the hard upper part of the inside of your mouth 上顎

6 under the same roof/under one roof in the same building or home 在同一個屋簷下: *We enjoy each other's company, but we can't live under the same roof or we argue all the time.* 我們在一起非常愉快, 但不能住在一起, 否則會吵個不停。

7 under my/her etc roof in your home 在我/她等的家裡: *As long as you live under this roof, young man, you'll do as your mother says.* 只要你住在這個家裡, 年輕人, 你就必須照你媽媽說的辦。

8 the roof falls in/caves in *AmE informal* if the roof falls in or caves in, something bad suddenly happens to you when you do not expect it【美, 非正式】飛來橫禍; 突遭不幸

9 red-roofed/slate-roofed etc having a roof that is red, made of SLATE[1] (2) etc 紅頂/石板瓦頂等的 —see also 另見 **raise the roof** (RAISE[1] (22)), SUNROOF

roof[2] *v* [T usually passive 一般用被動態] to put a roof on a building 給〔建築物〕蓋屋頂: **be roofed with** *a cottage, roofed with the local slate* 用當地的石板瓦做房頂的小屋

roof sth ↔ **in/over** *phr v* [T] to cover an open space by putting a roof over it 在〔空地上〕加蓋頂: *We're going to roof in the yard to make a garage.* 我們打算給院子加上頂蓋做個車庫。

roof·ing /ˈrufɪŋ; ˈruːfɪŋ/ *n* [U] stones, tiles (TILE[1] (2)) etc for making or covering roofs〔石、瓦等〕蓋屋頂的材料

roof-rack /ˈ· ·/ *n* [C] *BrE* a metal frame fixed on top of a car and used for carrying bags, cases etc【英】〔汽車〕車頂行李架; LUGGAGE RACK *AmE*【美】—see picture at 參見 RACK[1] 圖

roof·top /ˈrufˌtɑp; ˈruːftɒp/ *n* [C] the upper surface of a roof 屋頂: *the view across the rooftops* 屋頂上看到的景色 —see also 另見 **shout sth from the rooftops** (SHOUT[1] (3))

rook[1] /rʊk; rʊk/ *n* [C] **1** a large black European bird like a CROW[1] (1) 禿鼻烏鴉, 白嘴鴉 **2** one of the pieces in a game of CHESS; CASTLE〔國際象棋中的〕車

rook[2] *v* [T] *old-fashioned* to cheat someone, especially to get their money【過時】詐騙〔尤指金錢〕

rook·e·ry /ˈrʊkərɪ; ˈrʊkəri/ *n* [C] a group of NESTs made by rooks 連成一片的禿鼻烏鴉巢

rook·ie /ˈrʊkɪ; ˈrʊki/ *n* [C] **1** *especially AmE* someone who has just started doing a job and has little experience【尤美】新手: *rookie cops* 警察新手 **2** *AmE* someone who is in their first year of playing a professional sport【美】〔第一年參加某項職業體育比賽的〕新隊員: *a rookie out of Georgia Tech* 來自佐治亞理工大學的新隊員

room[1] /rum; ruːm/ *n* 

1 ►IN A BUILDING 在建築物裡◄ [C] a part of the inside of a building that has its own walls, floor and ceiling 房間, 室: **bathroom/dining room/meeting room etc** (=a room used for washing, eating etc) 浴室/飯廳/會議室等 *The meeting room's upstairs on your right.* 會議室在樓上右側。| *We could hear someone laughing in the next room.* 我們聽得見隔壁有人在笑。| *It's bedtime – you'd better go up to your room.* 該睡覺了——你最好到樓上自己房間去。| *I'm staying at the Arosa Hotel – Room 348.* 我住在阿羅沙酒店 348 號房間。| **single/double room** (=a room in a hotel for one person or for two) 單人/雙人房間 —see 見 PLACE[1] (USAGE)

2 ►SPACE 空間◄ [U] enough space for a particular purpose〔足夠的〕空間, 空地: **there's room in** *I'd like to bring the children if there's room in the car.* 如果車子坐得下, 我想帶孩子去。| **there's room for** *There's not enough room in the fridge for all this food.* 冰箱裡裝不下所有這些食物。| **there's room to do sth** *There wasn't really room to lie down comfortably.* 地方實在太小, 無法舒服地躺下。| **have room (for sth)** *Do you have room for another book in your bag?* 你的包裡能再裝下一本書嗎? | *Have you got room for some dessert?* (=can you eat some?) 你還吃得下甜點嗎? | **make room (for sth)** *I'll just clear out the cupboard to make room for your stuff.* 我就把櫥櫃清理一下給你騰出地方放東西。| **leave room (for sth)** (=make sure there is enough room for something)〔為某物〕留出〔足夠〕地方 *Leave room for people to get past.* 留出地方給人們通過。| **take up room** (=use a lot of space) 佔地方 *That old wardrobe takes up too much room.* 那個舊衣櫃太佔地方。| **leg-room/head-room** (=space for your legs or head in a vehicle)〔交通工具內〕腿/頭可以活動的空間 *You have more leg-room if you travel first class.* 如果你坐頭等艙, 腿的活動空間就較多。| **there's not enough room to swing a cat** *informal* (=used to say that there is very little space in a room)【非正式】〔房間裡〕空間狹窄得無法轉身 —see also 另見 ELBOW-ROOM

3 ►OPPORTUNITY 機會◄ [U] the chance to do the things that you want to do or need to do 機會; 餘地: **[+for]** *There's little room for innovation.* 沒有多少創新的空間。| **room to do sth** *Children need to have room to develop their natural creativity.* 兒童需要發揮他們天生創造力的機會。| **room for manoeuvre** (=freedom to change your plans or decisions) 迴旋餘地 *The strict export regulations left us no room for manoeuvre.* 嚴格的出口規定使我們沒有迴旋餘地。

4 ►POSSIBILITY 可能性◄ [U] the possibility that something may exist or will happen〔某事物存在或發生的〕可能性: **room for doubt** *The evidence left no room for doubt – Brooks was guilty.* 證據確鑿——布魯克斯有罪。

5 there's room for improvement used to say that someone's work or performance is not perfect and needs to be improved 有改進的餘地

6 one-roomed/two-roomed etc having one room, two rooms etc 有一個/兩個等房間的

7 ►APARTMENT 公寓◄ rooms [plural] *old-fashioned especially BrE* two or more rooms that you rent in a building, or stay in at a college【過時, 尤英】一套房間; 寓所 —see also 另見 FRONT ROOM, LIVING ROOM, SITTING ROOM

room[2] *v* [I] *AmE*【美】**1 room with sb** to share a room with someone at college〔大學〕與某人同住一室 **2 [+in]** to rent and live in a room somewhere 租住〔一個房間〕

room and board /ˌ· ·ˈ·/ *n* [U] *AmE* a room to sleep in and food【美】食宿: *I pay $1200 a quarter for room and board.* 我一個季度交1,200美元食宿費。

room·er /ˈrumɚ; ˈruːmə/ *n* [C] *AmE* someone who pays rent to live in a house with its owner【美】房客, 寄宿者; LODGER *BrE*【英】

room·ful /ˈrumful; ˈruːmfʊl/ *n* [C] a large number of things or people that are all together in one room 一屋子的物[人]: **[+of]** *It's too intimidating to read my poetry to a roomful of strangers.* 向一屋子陌生人朗讀我的詩太令人恐懼了。

rooming house /ˈ·· ·/ *n* [C] *AmE* a house where you can rent a room to live in【美】〔出租房間的〕公寓; LODGING HOUSE *BrE*【英】

room·mate /ˈrumˌmet; ˈruːmˌmeɪt/ *n* [C] **1** someone who you share a room with, especially at college〔尤指大學的〕室友, 住在同室的人: *Ben and I were roommates at university.* 本和我是大學的室友。**2** *AmE* someone you share a room, apartment, or house with【美】同住一室[一套公寓, 一所房子]的人; FLATMATE *BrE*【英】: *I hate the way my roommate never does the dishes.* 我討厭我的室友從不洗碗。

room ser·vice /ˈ· ˌ··/ *n* [U] a service provided by a hotel, by which food, drink etc can be sent to a guest's room〔旅館提供的〕客房用餐服務

room tem·pe·ra·ture /ˈ· ˌ····/ *n* [U] the normal temperature inside a house 室温, 常温

room·y /ˈrumɪ; ˈruːmi/ *adj* a house, car etc that is roomy is large and has a lot of space inside it〔房子、汽車等裡面〕寬敞的 —**roominess** *n* [U]

roost¹ /rust; ruːst/ *n* [C] a place where birds rest and sleep〔鳥的〕棲息處 —see also 另見 **rule the roost** (RULE² (5))

roost² *v* [I] **1** if a bird roosts, it rests or sleeps somewhere〔鳥類〕棲息 **2 sb's chickens come home to roost** used to say that someone's past mistakes are causing problems for them now 惡有惡報

roost·er /ˈrustɚ; ˈruːstə/ *n* [C] *especially AmE* a male chicken【尤美】公雞; COCK¹ (1) *BrE*【英】

3 **root**¹ /rut; ruːt/ *n* [C]

2 **1 ▶PLANT 植物◀** the part of a plant or tree that grows under the ground and gets water from the soil 根: *Be careful not to damage the roots when repotting.* 換盆時小心別傷了根。| *tree roots* 樹根 —see picture at 參見 GERMINATE 圖

2 ▶CAUSE OF A PROBLEM 問題的起因◀ the main cause of a problem〔問題的〕根源, 起因: *Money is the root of all evil.* 金錢是萬惡之源。| **be/lie at the root of** (=be the cause of a problem) 是…的根本原因 *Often allergies are at the root of a lot of the problems.* 過敏往往是許多問題的根源。| **get to the root of** (=find out the cause of a problem) 探本溯源 | **root cause** (=the main reason for a problem) 根本原因

3 ▶OF A CUSTOM/TRADITION 風俗/傳統的◀ roots the origins of a custom or TRADITION that has continued for a long time 根源, 起源: **has its roots in** *Jazz has its roots in the folk songs of the southern states of the US.* 爵士樂起源於美國南部諸州的民歌。

4 ▶OF AN IDEA/BELIEF 思想/信仰的◀ the main part of an idea or belief which all the other parts come from 根本, 基礎: **has its roots in** *The revival of the Gaelic language has its roots in 19th century nationalism.* 蓋爾語復興的基礎是19世紀的民族主義。

5 ▶FAMILY CONNECTION 家族聯繫◀ sb's roots your connection with a place because you were born there, or your family used to live there 某人的出生地, 老家: *Naita has come to Ghana in search of her roots.* 內塔來到加納尋找她的根。

6 put down roots if you put down roots somewhere, you start to feel that this place is your home and to have relationships with the people there 扎根〔某地〕

7 ▶TOOTH/HAIR ETC 牙齒/頭髮等◀ the part of a tooth, hair etc that fixes it to the rest of your body 根部

8 take root a) if an idea takes root, people begin to accept or believe it〔思想〕深入人心: *The concepts of democracy and free trade are finally beginning to take root.* 民主和自由貿易的概念終於開始深入人心。**b)** if a plant takes root, it starts to grow where you have planted it〔植物〕生根

9 have a (good) root round *informal especially BrE* to search for something by moving other things around【非正式, 尤英】翻找

10 root and branch if you destroy something root and branch, you get rid of it completely and permanently because it is bad 徹底地, 永久地〔把壞事物消除〕

11 ▶LANGUAGE 語言◀ *technical* the basic part of a word which shows its main meaning, to which other parts can be added【術語】詞根: *The suffix 'ness' can be added to the root 'cold' to form the word 'coldness'.* 後綴ness可以加在詞根cold上構成coldness一詞。—compare 比較 STEM¹ (4)

12 ▶MATHEMATICS 數學◀ *technical* a number that when multiplied by itself a certain number of times, equals the number that you have【術語】根: *2 is the fourth root of 16.* 2是16的4次方根。—see also 另見 CUBE ROOT, SQUARE ROOT, GRASS ROOTS

root² *v*

1 ▶SEARCH 尋找◀ [I always+adv/prep] to search for something by moving things around 翻找: **[+through/in/around]** *"Hang on a second," said Leila, rooting through her handbag for a pen.* "請稍等。"莉拉說着, 一邊在手提包裡翻找鋼筆。| **[+for]** *pigs rooting for food* 拱土尋覓食物的豬

2 ▶PLANT 植物◀ a) [I] to grow roots 生根: *New shrubs will root easily in summer.* 新灌木在夏季容易生根。**b)** [T usually passive 一般用被動態] to fix a plant firmly by its roots 使〔植物〕牢牢扎根: *The bush was too firmly rooted in the hard earth to dig up easily.* 這灌木在堅實的土壤裡牢牢扎根, 不容易挖出來。| **root itself** *Clumps of thyme had rooted themselves between the rocks.* 一叢叢百里香在岩石中間扎了根。—see also 另見 **deeply rooted** (DEEPLY (5))

3 be rooted in to have developed from something and be strongly influenced by it 起源於: *policies that are rooted in Marxist economic theory* 源於馬克思主義經濟學理論的政策

4 be rooted to the spot to be so shocked, surprised, or frightened that you cannot move〔震驚、驚訝或害怕得〕呆若木雞

root for sb *phr v* [T] *informal*【非正式】**1** to give support and encouragement to someone in a competition, test or difficult situation, because you want them to succeed 給〔參賽者、應試者或面對困難的人〕支持, 鼓勵, 聲援: *Good luck – we'll all be rooting for you!* 祝你好運, 我們都支持你! **2** *especially AmE* to support a sports team or player by shouting and cheering【尤美】為〔參賽隊或運動員〕歡呼, 喝采, 加油: *We'll all be rooting for the Dallas Cowboys in the Superbowl.* 在超級盃賽中我們都為達拉斯牛仔隊歡呼。

root sth ↔ **out** *phr v* [T] **1** to find out where a particular kind of problem exists and get rid of it 把〔問題〕根除, 杜絕: *Racism cannot be rooted out without strong government action.* 如果政府不採取有力行動, 種族主義是無法根除的。**2** *informal* to find something by searching for it【非正式】搜尋: *I'll try and root out something suitable for you to wear.* 我會設法找出一些合適的衣服給你穿。

root sth ↔ **up** *phr v* [T] to dig or pull a plant up with its roots 將〔植物〕連根拔起

root beer /ˈ· ·/ *n* [C,U] a sweet, non-alcoholic drink made from the roots of some plants, drunk especially in the US 根啤, 根汁汽水〔尤在美國飲用一種由某些植物根製成的不含酒精的飲料〕

R

root·bound /ˋrut͵baund; ˈruːtbaʊnd/ *adj AmE* a plant that is rootbound cannot grow any more because its roots have filled the pot it is growing in【美】〔植物〕根長滿盆後不能再生長的, 盆縛的; POTBOUND *BrE*【英】

root crop /ˋ· ·/ *n* [C] a vegetable or plant that is grown so that its root parts can be used 根用植物

root·le /ˋrutl̩; ˈruːtl/ also 又作 **rootle around/about** *v* [I] *BrE informal* to search for something by moving many other things around【英, 非正式】翻找, 搜尋

root·less /ˋrutlɪs; ˈruːtləs/ *adj* having nowhere that you feel is really your home 無家可歸的, 無歸屬的: *a rootless existence on the street* 流浪街頭, 無家可歸 —**rootlessness** *n* [U]

root veg·e·ta·ble /ˋ· ͵···/ *n* [C] a vegetable such as a potato or CARROT that grows under the ground〔可食用的〕塊根植物 —see picture on page A9 參見 A9 頁圖

rope¹ /rop; rəʊp/ *n* **1** [C,U] very strong, thick string, made by twisting together many threads of NYLON or other material 粗繩, 繩索, 纜: *They tied up the prisoner with rope.* 他們用繩子把犯人捆起來。| *a bell rope* 鐘繩 **2 know the ropes** to know how to do all the parts of a job, deal with a system etc, because you have a lot of experience of it 精通, 在行 **3 show sb the ropes** to teach someone how to do a job or deal with a system 教某人〔做某項工作的〕方法, 給某人指點竅門: *This is Shirley's first day, so will you show her the ropes?* 這是雪莉第一天上班, 你能教教她這裡的規矩嗎? **4 be on the ropes** *informal* to be in a very bad situation, in which you are likely to be defeated【非正式】處境十分困難〔可能被擊敗〕 **5 give sb plenty of rope** to give someone a lot of freedom to do something in the way they want to do it 給某人許多自由 **6 give sb enough rope to hang themselves** to give someone freedom to do what they want to do, because you think they will cause problems for themselves 任由某人自作自受, 聽任某人自取滅亡 **7 be at the end of your rope** *especially AmE* to have no more PATIENCE or strength left to deal with a problem or a difficult situation【尤美】忍無可忍, 計窮力竭〔無法解決困難〕 **8 the rope** *old-fashioned* HANGING as a punishment【過時】絞刑 **9 the ropes** the rope fence that surrounds an area used for BOXING or WRESTLING〔拳擊、摔跤場地的〕欄索 **10 a rope of pearls** PEARLS on a string, worn around your neck as jewellery〔用作項鏈的〕一串珍珠 —see also 另見 JUMP ROPE, **money for old rope** (MONEY (16))

rope² *v* **1** [T always+adv/prep] to tie things together using rope〔用繩索〕捆, 綁: **rope sth to sth** *Harvey roped his horse to a nearby tree.* 哈維把馬拴在附近的一棵樹上。| **rope sb/sth together** *Two firemen roped themselves together and plunged into the lake.* 兩名消防員用繩索把自己繫在一起, 跳入湖中。**2** [T] *AmE* to catch an animal using a circle of rope【美】用繩套捕捉〔動物〕

rope sb ↔ **in** *phr v* [T] *informal* to persuade someone to help you in a job, or to join in an activity, especially when they do not want to【非正式】勸說〔尤指不願意者〕幫忙[參加]: **rope sb in to do sth** *I've roped Dad in to help with the entertainment.* 我把爸爸拉來幫忙招待。| **rope sb into doing sth** *Have you been roped into selling tickets?* 你是被拉來幫忙賣票的嗎?

rope sth ↔ **off** *phr v* [T] to surround an area with ropes, especially in order to separate it from another area 用繩把〔某一區域〕圍起來, 用繩分隔: *Last night police roped off the area of the find.* 昨晚警察用繩把發現的現場隔開了。

rope lad·der /ˋ· ͵··/ *n* [C] a LADDER made of two long ropes connected by wooden pieces that you stand on 繩梯

rop·ey, ropy /ˋropɪ; ˈrəʊpi/ *adj BrE informal*【英, 非正式】**1** in bad condition or of bad quality 破舊的; 劣質的: *We stayed in a really ropey hotel.* 我們住在一家非常蹩腳的旅館裡。**2** slightly ill 輕微不舒服的: *I'm feeling a bit ropey this morning.* 今天早上我覺得有些不舒服。

ro-ro /ˋro ͵ro; ˈrəʊ rəʊ/ *n* [C] *BrE informal* a ROLL-ON ROLL-OFF ship【英, 非正式】容許車輛開上開下的船

Ror·schach test /ˋrɔrʃɑk tɛst; ˈrɔːʃɑːk test/ *n* [C] a method of testing someone's character, by making them say what spots of ink with various shapes look like 羅爾沙赫測驗〔讓測試對象解釋不同的墨跡圖形, 以判斷其性格的一種測試方法〕

ro·sa·ry /ˋrozərɪ; ˈrəʊzəri/ *n* **1** [C] a string of BEADS used by Roman Catholics for counting prayers〔羅馬天主教徒用的〕念珠 **2 the Rosary** the set of prayers that are said by Roman Catholics while counting rosary BEADS〔羅馬天主教的〕玫瑰經

ro·sé /roˋze; ˈrəʊzeɪ/ *n* [U] pink wine 玫瑰葡萄酒

rose¹ /roz; rəʊz/ *n*

1 ►FLOWER 花◄ [C] a flower that has a pleasant smell, and is usually red, pink, white, or yellow, or the bush that this grows on 玫瑰; 薔薇

2 ►COLOUR 顏色◄ [U] a pink colour 玫瑰〔紅〕色 —see picture on page A5 參見 A5 頁圖

3 not all roses also 又作 **not a bed of roses** *informal* if a job or situation is not all roses, it is not always pleasant and there are often difficult things to deal with【非正式】不盡如人意, 並非事事順利

4 put the roses back in sb's cheeks *informal* to make someone look healthy again【非正式】使某人恢復健康的容貌

5 be coming up roses *informal* be happening or developing in the best possible way【非正式】一帆風順

6 not come out of sth smelling of roses *informal* to have been involved in a situation that makes you seem dishonest, so that people stop trusting you【非正式】顯得不誠實〔因而失去人們的信任〕

7 ►FOR WATER 供水◄ [C] a circular piece of metal with holes in it, that is fitted to the end of a pipe or WATERING CAN so that liquid comes out in several thin streams〔水管或灑水壺上的〕蓮蓬式噴嘴

8 ►LIGHT 燈◄ [C] *technical* the circular object from which an electric CEILING light hangs【術語】〔天花板上的〕燈線盒

rose² *adj* having a pink colour 玫瑰色的, 粉紅色的

rose³ the past tense of RISE¹

ro·se·ate /ˋrozɪ·ɪt; ˈrəʊzi-ət/ *adj poetic* pink【詩】玫瑰色的, 粉紅色的

rose·bud /ˋroz͵bʌd; ˈrəʊzbʌd/ *n* [C] the flower of a rose before it opens 玫瑰花苞

rose bush /ˋ· ·/ *n* [C] the plant that roses grow on 薔薇叢, 玫瑰叢

rose-col·oured *BrE*【英】, **rose-colored** *AmE*【美】/ˋ· ͵··/ *adj* **1** having a pink colour 玫瑰色的, 粉紅色的 **2** a rose-coloured idea of what something is like shows that you think something is more pleasant than it really is, because you do not notice anything unpleasant〔對事物的看法〕過於樂觀的, 想得比實際更美好的: **see sth through rose-coloured/rose-tinted spectacles** (=never notice bad things) 盲目樂觀的看法

rose hip /ˋ· ·/ *n* [C] the small red fruit of some kinds of rose bush, used in medicines and juices 玫瑰果: *rose hip syrup* 玫瑰果糖漿

rose·ma·ry /ˋroz͵mɛrɪ; ˈrəʊzməri/ *n* [U] leaves that have a strong, pleasant smell and are used in cooking, or the bush that these come from 迷迭香葉〔可用作調味料〕; 迷迭香

rose-tint·ed /ˋ· ͵··/ *adj especially BrE* ROSE-COLOURED【尤英】玫瑰色的; 〔過分〕樂觀的

ro·sette /roˋzɛt; rəʊˈzet/ *n* [C] **1** a circular BADGE made of coloured RIBBON that is given to the winner of a competition or that people in Britain wear to show support for a particular football team or political party 玫瑰花結〔授予比賽的勝利者; 英國人佩戴以示對某足球隊或政黨的支持〕 **2** a shape like a round flat flower that has been made in stone or wood 玫瑰花形石[木]雕

rose·wa·ter /ˋroz͵wɔtɚ; ˈrəʊz͵wɔːtə/ *n* [U] a liquid made from roses, used for its pleasant smell 玫瑰香水

rose·wood /ˈrozˌwud; ˈrəʊzwʊd/ *n* [U] a hard dark red wood, used for making expensive furniture 紅木, 花梨木, 黃檀木

ros·in /ˈrɑzɪn; ˈrɒzɪn/ *n* [U] a solid, slightly sticky substance that you rub on the BOW of a VIOLIN etc, to keep it moving correctly on the strings 松香 —**rosin** *v* [T]

ros·ter[1] /ˈrɑstɚ; ˈrɒstə/ *n* [C] a list of people's names showing the jobs they must do and the times when they must do them 值勤表, 勤務表: *a duty roster* 值勤表

roster[2] *v* [T] to put someone's name on a roster 把〔某人的名字〕列入值勤表

ros·trum /ˈrɑstrəm; ˈrɒstrəm/ *n* [C] a small PLATFORM (=raised area) that you stand on when you are making a speech or conducting (CONDUCT[1] (2)) musicians 講壇; 〔樂隊指揮站的〕指揮台

ros·y /ˈrozɪ; ˈrəʊzi/ *adj* **1** pink 粉紅色的: *rosy cheeks* 紅潤的面頰 **2** seeming to offer hope of success or happiness 充滿成功希望的, 美好的: *The future is beginning to look much rosier.* 未來開始顯得有希望多了。| *rosy optimism* 充滿希望的樂觀主義 | **paint a rosy picture of** (=describe a situation in a way that makes it seem much better than it really is) 對…作不切實際的樂觀描繪 —**rosiness** *n* [U]

rot[1] /rɑt; rɒt/ *v* **1** [I,T] to decay by a gradual natural process, or to make something do this (使) 腐敗, 腐爛: *Sugar rots your teeth.* 糖會蛀蝕牙齒。| *the stench of rotting eggs* 壞雞蛋的臭氣 **2 rot in jail/prison etc** to get into a bad mental or physical condition because you have been forced to stay in a place such as a prison 在監獄等處逐漸憔悴[衰弱]: *As far as they're concerned we can rot in jail.* 我們會在監獄中慢慢死去, 他們才不管呢。

rot away *phr v* [I,T] to decay completely and disappear or break into small pieces, or to make something do this (使) 徹底腐爛: *In places the timbers have rotted away.* 有些木材腐朽了。

rot[2] *n* [U] **1 stop the rot** *informal* to stop a bad situation from getting worse and worse【非正式】使壞情況不再惡化: *If Leeds don't stop the rot soon they can say goodbye to a top eight team ranking.* 如果利兹隊無法阻止這種走下坡的勢頭, 他們將與八強排名無緣。**2 the rot set in** *informal* used to say that a situation starts to get worse, and nothing could stop this process【非正式】〔情況〕開始惡化並無可挽回 **3** the natural process of decaying or the part of something that has decayed 腐敗, 腐爛; 腐爛物 **4** *BrE old-fashioned* nonsense【英, 過時】廢話, 愚蠢的話: *You do talk rot!* 你盡說蠢話! —see also 另見 DRY ROT

ro·ta /ˈrotə; ˈrəʊtə/ *n* [C] *BrE* a list that shows when each person in a group must do a particular job【英】勤務輪值表: *a cleaning rota* 打掃值勤表

ro·ta·ry[1] /ˈrotərɪ; ˈrəʊtəri/ *adj* **1** turning in a circle around a fixed point, like a wheel 旋轉的, 轉動的: *the rotary movement of the helicopter blades* 直升機槳葉的旋轉運動 **2** having a main part that does this〔機器〕有旋轉部件的: *a rotary engine* 旋轉式發動機

rotary[2] *n* [C] *AmE* a ROUNDABOUT【美】環島

Rotary Club /ˈ··· ˌ·/ *n* **the Rotary Club** an organization of business people in a town who work together to raise money for people who are poor or sick 扶輪社〔城市工商界人士為貧困者和病人籌款的組織〕

ro·tate /ˈrotet; rəʊˈteɪt/ *v* **1** [I,T] to turn around a fixed point, or to make something do this (使) 旋轉, 轉動: *a rotating blade* 旋轉的葉片 **2** [I,T] if a job rotates, or if people rotate jobs, they each do the jobs for a fixed period of time, one after the other (使) 輪流做…, 輪換: *The chairmanship of the committee rotates annually.* 委員會主席的職位每年輪換一次。| *We usually rotate the worst jobs, so that no one gets stuck with them.* 我們通常輪流做最難堪的工作, 這樣誰都不至於老幹那種活。**3** [T] *technical* to regularly change the crops grown on a piece of land, in order to preserve the quality of the soil【術語】輪種, 輪作

ro·ta·tion /roˈteʃən; rəʊˈteɪʃən/ *n* **1** [U] the action of turning around a fixed point 旋轉: **[+about/around/on]** *the rotation of the Earth on its axis* 地球的自轉 **2** [C] one complete turn around a fixed point 旋轉一周: *The blades spin at 100 rotations per minute.* 葉片每分鐘旋轉100圈。**3 in rotation a)** if a group of people do something in rotation they do it one after the other in a regular order〔按一定順序〕循環, 輪換: *The four were Area Board chairmen, serving in rotation.* 這四個人輪流擔任地區董事會主席。**b)** if a group of things are used in rotation they are used one after the other in a regular order〔按一定順序〕交替使用: *It's good practice to use three balls in rotation in cold weather.* 在寒冷的天氣裡, 輪流使用三個球是個好辦法。**4** [U] the practice of changing regularly from one thing to another, or regularly changing the person who does a particular job 輪換, 交替 **5 crop rotation** *technical* the practice of regularly changing the crops that are grown on a piece of land, in order to preserve the quality of the soil【術語】輪作制 —**rotational** *adj*

rote /rot; rəʊt/ *n* [U] *formal* a method of learning that involves repeating something until you remember it, without having to understand it【正式】死記硬背: **learn (sth) by rote** *old-fashioned grammar teaching and learning by rote* 舊式的語法講授和死記硬背的學習方法

rot·gut /ˈrɑtˌgʌt; ˈrɒtgʌt/ *n* [U] *informal* strong cheap low-quality alcohol【非正式】廉價的劣質烈酒

ro·tis·ser·ie /roˈtɪsərɪ; rəʊˈtɪsəri/ *n* [C] a piece of equipment for cooking meat by turning it around and around on a metal rod 旋轉式烤肉架

ro·tor /ˈrotɚ; ˈrəʊtə/ *n* [C] *technical*【術語】**1** a part of a machine that turns around on a fixed point〔機器的〕旋轉部分, 轉子 **2** also 又作 **rotor blade** the long flat part on top of a HELICOPTER that turns around and around〔直升機的〕(水平) 旋翼

rot·ten[1] /ˈrɑtn̩; ˈrɒtn/ *adj* **1** badly decayed 腐爛的, 變質的: *rotten fruit* 腐爛的水果 | *the smell of rotten eggs* 變質雞蛋的氣味 | *The wood was completely rotten.* 這木頭完全腐朽了。**2** *informal* very nasty or unpleasant【非正式】非常糟糕的, 非常討厭的: *What rotten weather!* 多麼糟糕的天氣! | *It's a rotten thing to do.* 幹這件事非常討厭。**3** *informal* a word meaning very bad at doing something, or very badly done, used especially when you feel annoyed about this【非正式】極差的, 糟糕透了〔尤用於表示惱怒〕: *He's a rotten driver.* 他是個糟糕的司機。**4 feel rotten a)** to feel ill 感到不舒服 **b)** to feel unhappy and guilty about something 感到不高興, 感到內疚的: **[+about]** *I felt rotten about having to fire him.* 不得不解雇他我感到很遺憾。**5 a rotten apple** one bad person who has a bad effect on all the others in a group 害羣之馬 —**rottenly** *adv* —**rottenness** *n* [U]

rotten[2] *adv informal*【非正式】**1 spoil sb rotten** to treat someone too well or too kindly, especially a child 溺愛, 寵壞某人〔尤指小孩〕: *Melanie's beautiful, wilful, and she's been spoiled rotten all her life.* 梅蘭妮漂亮、任性, 她一生被寵壞了。**2 fancy sb rotten** *BrE humorous* to be extremely attracted to someone in a sexual way【英, 幽默】對某人神魂顛倒[極為迷戀]

rot·ter /ˈrɑtɚ; ˈrɒtə/ *n* [C] *BrE old-fashioned* an unpleasant person who treats other people badly【英, 過時】無賴, 惡棍

rott·wei·ler /ˈrɑtˌwaɪlɚ; ˈrɒtwaɪlə/ *n* [C] **1** a type of strong and dangerous dog, often used as a guard dog 洛威拿狗, 羅特韋爾狗〔一種強壯兇猛的看門狗〕**2 rottweiler politics/tendencies etc** *humorous* politics etc in which politicians attack each other in a very determined way【幽默】政客相互猛烈攻擊的政治手腕/傾向等

ro·tund /roˈtʌnd; rəʊˈtʌnd/ *adj humorous* having a fat round body【幽默】〔身體〕圓胖的 —**rotundity** *n* [U]

ro·tun·da /roˈtʌndə; rəʊˈtʌndə/ *n* [C] a round building or hall, especially one with a DOME (=a round bowl-shaped roof)〔尤指有圓頂的〕圓形建築; 圓形大廳

R

rou·ble, ruble /ˈrubļ; ˈruːbəl/ *n* [C] the standard unit of money in Russia and Belarus 盧布〔俄羅斯和白俄羅斯的貨幣單位〕

rouge /ruʒ; ruːʒ/ *n old-fashioned* [U] pink or red powder or cream that women put on their cheeks【過時】胭脂 —**rouge** *v* [T]

rough¹ /rʌf; rʌf/ *adj*

1 ►NOT SMOOTH 不平的◄ having an uneven surface〔表面〕粗糙的, 不平的: *Her hands were rough from hard work.* 她的雙手因幹重活而變得粗糙。| *A rough track led to the farm.* 一條崎嶇的小路通向那個農場。| *rough grass* 高矮不齊的草 —opposite 反義詞 SMOOTH¹ (1)

2 ►NOT EXACT 不精確的◄ not exact or not containing many details; APPROXIMATE 粗略的, 大致的: *This is just a rough sketch but it gives you the idea.* 這只是個草圖, 但能給你一個大概意思。| *a rough translation* 粗略的翻譯 | **a rough idea** *Could you give me a rough idea what time you'll be home?* 你能告訴我你大概甚麼時候回家嗎? | **at a rough guess** *spoken* (=without being at all certain or exact)【口】粗略地猜測 *At a rough guess, I'd say he was about 45.* 大致猜猜, 我看他在45歲上下。| **a rough estimate** *I can only give you a rough estimate of the cost at this stage.* 目前我只能給你粗略估計一下費用。—see graph at 參見 IDEA 圖表

3 ►NOT GENTLE 不溫柔的◄ using force or violence 粗野的, 粗暴的: *Rugby is a very rough game.* (英式) 橄欖球是一項非常粗野的運動。| *A stroller should be easy to fold and capable of withstanding rough treatment.* 輕便嬰兒手推車應該容易摺疊, 並且堅固耐用。

4 ►TOWN/AREA ETC 城鎮/地區等◄ a rough area is a place where there is a lot of violence or crime〔地方〕多暴力的, 犯罪率高的: *a rough part of town* 城市裡犯罪率高的地區

5 ►HAVING A LOT OF PROBLEMS/DIFFICULTIES 有許多問題/困難◄ [usually before noun 一般用於名詞前] a rough period is one in which you have a lot of problems or difficulties 艱難的〔時期〕: *Don't be too angry with her – she's had a very rough time of it lately.* 不要太生她的氣, 最近她的日子很艱難。| *I've had a really rough day.* 今天我很不走運。| **go through a rough patch** (=experience problems or difficulties) 歷經磨難, 日子不好過 | **give sb/sth a rough ride** (=a very difficult time) 使某人/某事遇到麻煩 *The bill may have gotten through the House but it's in for a rough ride in the Senate.* 提案獲得了眾議院通過, 但在參議院會有麻煩。

6 ►UNFAIR/UNLUCKY 不公平的/不幸的◄ unfair or unlucky 不公平的; 倒霉的: **it's rough on sb** *It's rough on him, losing his job like that.* 他就那樣丟掉了工作, 真倒霉。| *Two burglaries in one week? That's a bit rough!* 一週遭受兩次入室盜竊? 太倒霉了!

7 ►WEATHER/SEA 天氣/海◄ with strong wind or storms 狂暴的: *In the evening we were sick, it was a very rough crossing.* 晚上我們暈船了, (因為) 渡海時碰上了暴風雨。

8 ►NOT COMFORTABLE 不舒服的◄ uncomfortable, with difficult conditions 不舒服的, 條件艱苦的: *a rough, pioneering way of life* 艱苦的、拓荒者的生活方式

9 ►VOICE/SOUND 嗓音/聲音◄ **a)** not sounding soft or gentle, and often rather unpleasant or angry〔聲音〕不悅耳的, 粗聲粗氣的: *the rough voices of the workmen* 工匠們沙啞的說話聲 **b)** having an unpleasant sound, especially because there is something wrong with a machine〔尤指機器出故障時發出的聲音〕刺耳的, 難聽的: *The clutch sounds rough, better get it checked.* 離合器的聲音聽起來不對頭, 最好請人檢查一下。

10 ►SIMPLE/NOT WELL MADE 簡單的/做得不好的◄ simple and often not very well made 簡單的, 粗糙的: *We constructed a rough shelter using whatever materials we could find.* 我們用能找到的材料搭了一個簡陋的棚子。

11 feel rough *informal* to feel ill【非正式】感覺生病: *I think I'd better go to bed – I'm feeling pretty rough.* 我想我最好去睡覺, 我很不舒服。

12 look rough *informal* to look untidy, dirty, or unhealthy【非正式】看上去不整潔[髒亂, 不健康]: *We had been travelling for two days, and must have looked pretty rough.* 我們已經旅行了兩天, 看上去肯定很邋遢。

13 rough and ready simple, but just good enough for a particular purpose 簡單[不講究]但實用的

14 rough justice punishment that is severe or unfair 嚴厲[不公平]的懲罰

15 a rough night a night when you did not sleep well 不眠之夜, 輾轉反側的一夜

16 rough stuff *spoken* violent behaviour【口】粗野的行為

17 a bit of rough *BrE humorous* someone from a lower social class than you, with whom you have a sexual relationship【英, 幽默】〔社會地位低於自己的〕性夥伴

18 give sb the rough side of your tongue *BrE old-fashioned* to speak angrily to someone【英, 過時】嚴斥某人 —**roughness** *n* [U] —see also 另見 ROUGH DIAMOND, ROUGH PAPER, ROUGHLY

rough² *n* **1 take the rough with the smooth** to accept the bad things in life as well as the good ones 既能享樂也能吃苦; 好壞都能接受 **2** [C] a picture drawn very quickly, not showing all the details 草圖, 略圖 **3 the rough** uneven ground with long grass on a GOLF course〔高爾夫球場〕生有長草的起伏地面, 深草區 —see picture on page A23 參見A23頁圖 **4 in rough** *BrE* if you write or draw something in rough, you do it without paying attention to details or tidiness【英】粗略地, 馬虎地: *It's best to work in rough first, and then write it out neatly.* 最好先打一個草稿, 然後再工整地謄寫出來。—see also 另見 DIAMOND IN THE ROUGH

rough³ *v* **rough it** *informal* to live for a short time in conditions that are not very comfortable【非正式】〔短時期〕過不很舒適的生活: *Let's just take the tent – I don't mind roughing it for a bit.* 我們只帶帳篷就行, 我不在乎過點兒簡陋的生活。

rough sth ↔ **in** *phr v* [T] to add something to a picture, without showing all the exact details 勾勒, 畫…的輪廓: *If you look here you can see another angle for the arm roughed in.* 如果你從這兒看, 可以從另一個角度看到畫上去的胳膊輪廓。

rough sth ↔ **out** *phr v* [T] to draw or write something, without showing all the exact details 草擬〔某事物〕; 畫…的草圖: *Iain was peering at a diagram the engineer had roughed out on his notepad.* 伊恩凝視着工程師在便箋簿上畫的一幅草圖。

rough sb ↔ **up** *phr v* [T] *informal* to attack someone and hurt them by hitting them【非正式】揍, 向〔某人〕動粗

rough⁴ *adv* **1 sleep rough** *BrE* to sleep outside with nothing to protect you from the weather【英】露宿: *sleeping rough on the street* 露宿街頭 **2 play rough** to play in a fairly violent way 玩得粗野 —see also 另見 **cut up rough** (CUT¹)

rough·age /ˈrʌfɪdʒ; ˈrʌfɪdʒ/ *n* [U] a substance contained in some foods that helps your BOWELS to work; DIETARY FIBRE 食物中的粗纖維: *Wholemeal bread is a valuable source of roughage.* 全麥麵包含有豐富的粗纖維。

rough-and-tum·ble /ˌ· · ˈ·· / *n* **1** [singular,U] noisy rough behaviour when playing or fighting, especially by children〔尤指孩子的〕喧鬧, 打鬧, 粗野的舉止 **2** [U] the usual busy, noisy, or rough way in which a particular activity takes place〔某事發生時的〕喧鬧, 混亂, 鬥爭: *the rough-and-tumble of politics* 政治的眾聲喧譁, 爭強好勝

rough·cast /ˈrʌfˌkæst; ˈrʌfkɑːst/ *n* [U] a rough surface on the outside of a building, made of PLASTER¹ (1) mixed with little stones or broken shells〔建築物外牆用石灰混合石子或碎貝殼打的〕底子, 粗灰泥 —**roughcast** *adj*

rough di·a·mond /ˌ· ˈ··· / *n* [C] *informal* someone who seems rude, rough, or unfriendly, but is actually kind and generous【非正式】外粗內秀的人; DIAMOND IN THE ROUGH *AmE*【美】

rough·en /ˈrʌfən; ˈrʌfən/ *v* [I,T] to become rough, or to make something rough（使）變得粗糙,（使）變得不平

rough-hewn /ˌ· ˈ·◂/ *adj* rough-hewn wood or stone has been roughly cut and its surface is not yet smooth〔木材或石頭〕粗砍成的, 粗鑿成的, 不光滑的

rough-house¹ /ˈ· ·/ *n* [singular] *BrE old-fashioned* a noisy fight, usually without weapons【英, 過時】〔一般指徒手〕打鬥, 毆鬥

rough·house² *v* [I] *AmE* to play roughly or fight; WRESTLE (1)【美】打鬧; 扭打: *Either stop roughhousing or play outside!* 要麼停止打鬧, 要麼到外面去玩!

2 **rough·ly** /ˈrʌflɪ; ˈrʌfli/ *adv* **1** not exactly; about 粗略地, 大致上: *There were roughly 200 people there.* 那兒大約有200人。| *How much have you got, roughly?* 你大約有多少錢? | *Azaleas flower at roughly the same time each year.* 杜鵑花每年大致在相同的時間開放。| **roughly speaking** (=used when saying something without giving exact details or information) 粗略地說 *Roughly speaking, I'd say we need about $500.* 粗略地說, 我認為我們大約需要500美元。—see graph at 參見 APPROXIMATELY 圖表 **2** not gently or carefully 粗暴地, 粗野地, 粗魯地: *Alan dropped the cat roughly to the floor.* 阿倫粗暴地把貓摔到地上。

rough·neck /ˈrʌfˌnɛk; ˈrʌfnek/ *n* [C] **1** a member of a team of people who make or operate an OIL-WELL 油井工人 **2** *informal especially AmE* someone who usually behaves in a rough, rude, or angry way【非正式, 尤美】粗暴的人, 脾氣暴躁的人

rough pa·per /ˌ· ˈ··/ *n* [U] *BrE* paper that is used for writing or drawing things that will later be changed or copied more neatly【英】草稿紙

rough·shod /ˈrʌfˈʃɑd; ˈrʌfʃɒd/ *adj* **ride roughshod over** to behave in a way that ignores other people's feelings or opinions 輕蔑地對待, 對…橫行霸道

rou·lette /ruˈlɛt; ruːˈlet/ *n* [U] a game in which a small ball is spun around on a moving wheel, and people try to win money by guessing which hole it will fall into 輪盤賭 —see also 另見 RUSSIAN ROULETTE

1 2 **round¹** /raund; raʊnd/ *adj* **1** shaped like a circle 圓(形)的: *a round table* 圓桌 | *Jamie's eyes grew round with delight.* 傑米高興得眼睛睜得滾圓。**2** shaped like a ball 球形的: *a plant with small round berries* 長着小圓漿果的植物 **3** fat and curved 滾圓的, 豐滿的: *Charlie had a chubby face and round cheeks.* 查理的臉很豐滿, 雙頰圓滾滾的。**4** a round number is a whole number, often ending in 0 整數的〔常指10的倍數〕: *Let's make it a round £50 I owe you.* 我就欠你整50英鎊吧。| **a round hundred/dozen etc** (=a complete hundred etc) 整一百/一打等 **5 in round figures** not expressed as an exact number but as the nearest 10, 100, 1000 etc 以約整數表示〈如10, 100, 1000等〉: *In round figures, the expected profit is about £600 million.* 以整數計, 預期利潤約為六億英鎊。—see also 另見 ROUNDLY, **a square peg in a round hole** (SQUARE¹ (11)) —**roundness** *n* [U]

2 2 **round²** *adv* [only after verb 僅用於動詞後] *especially BrE*【尤英】**1** if something moves round, it moves in a circular movement 繞圈子, 圍繞地: *It is water moving through the mechanism which pushes the wheel round.* 水流過機械裝置推動輪子轉動。| **round and round** *He stared at the washing machine, just watching the clothes go round and round.* 他盯着洗衣機, 看着衣物一圈圈地轉。**2** if something such as a group of people or things are round something, they surround that thing 在周圍: *If you'll all gather round we'll begin the experiment.* 請大家圍成一圈, 我們將開始實驗。| **all round** *The garden had a fence all round to keep out dogs.* 花園四周圍着籬笆防止狗進入。**3** to many people or in many parts of a place, a room etc 挨個地, 逐一地; 到處: *Please, come in, let me show you round.* 請進, 讓我帶你到處看看。| *Would someone hand the drinks round please.* 請哪位把飲料遞給所有在場的人好嗎? | **all round** *It was a beautiful room, with cushions scattered all round.* 這是個漂亮的房間, 到處擺着靠墊。| **enough to go round** (=enough for everyone) 足夠分配 *Do you think there are enough seats to go round?* 你看座位夠不夠? **4** in the opposite direction 朝相反方向, 轉過來: *When he turned round I recognised him immediately.* 他轉過身來, 我立即認出了他。**5** if you go round, you do not go the most direct way to get somewhere 繞道地, 迂迴地: *I don't mind driving round by the market on my way to the station.* 我不介意在開車去車站的路上繞道去市場。**6 the wrong/the other/the opposite etc way round a)** facing the wrong, other, opposite etc direction 方向相反: *You're wearing your T-shirt the wrong way round.* 你把T恤衫穿反了。**b)** in the wrong, other, opposite etc order 順序顛倒: *You got it the wrong way round. She left him, he didn't walk out on her!* 你搞錯了。是她離開了他, 而不是他扔下了她! **7 round about** about a particular time or amount 大約: *It's a coincidence that all his grandparents died round about the same time.* 他的祖父母和外祖父母差不多同時去世, 這是個巧合。**8 change/switch etc round** to change the position that things are in so that they are in each other's places 交換位置: *The dartboard was at the back, but they've changed things round.* 飛鏢的圓靶原來在後面, 但他們把東西的位置調換了。**9** *informal* to or in someone's house【非正式】去[在]〔某人〕家: *I'm inviting the neighbours round for a drink.* 我打算請鄰居到我家來喝酒。| *Sally left a note saying she'd be round at her cousin's house.* 莎莉留下便條, 說她去了她表姐家。**10 (just) round the corner** not very far away at all 在附近,（就）在拐角上: *She could walk, it's only round the corner.* 她可以步行去, 就在附近。**11 go round the shops/pub etc** to go to the shops etc 到商店/酒吧等去: *I could go round the village and see if something's still open.* 我可以去村裡轉轉, 看還有甚麼地方開門。**12 go round (and round) in circles** to not make progress at something such as trying to solve a problem〔解決問題等〕原地打轉, 沒有進展 **13 2 metres/12 feet etc round** having a CIRCUMFERENCE of 2 metres, 12 feet etc 周長2米/12英尺等 **14 the first/second etc time round** the first, second etc time that you do something 第一次/第二次等〔做某事〕: *Who says marriage is better the second time round?* 誰說第二次婚姻較美滿? —see also 另見 ALL-ROUND —compare 比較 AROUND

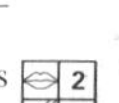

2 2 **round³** *prep especially BrE*【尤英】**1** if something moves round something, it moves around it in a circular movement 圍繞, 環繞: *The earth goes round the sun.* 地球圍繞着太陽旋轉。| *The lions slowly circled round the gazelle, waiting to pounce.* 那些獅子圍着瞪羚慢慢轉, 等待着猛撲上去。—see picture on page A1 參見A1頁圖 **2** surrounding or covering something 圍着〔某物〕; 覆蓋着〔某物〕: *sitting round the table* 圍着桌子坐 | *Why have you got a bandage round your wrist?* 你的手腕上為甚麼纏着繃帶? **3** if you go round something you do not go the most direct way to get somewhere 繞過: *You'll have to go right round the roadworks to get there.* 你必須繞過道路施工處才能到那裡去。**4** at or to the other side of something 在[向]…另一側: *Suddenly the thief disappeared round the corner.* 突然, 小偷在拐角處消失了。| *There must be another entrance round the back of the house.* 房子背後肯定還有一個入口。**5** to or in all parts of a place 到處, 在各處: *Let me show you round the castle.* 我帶你到城堡裡四下看看。| *travelling round Europe* 遊歷歐洲各國 **6** a way round a difficult situation or problem is a way to solve it or avoid it 解決〔問題〕; 繞過〔問題〕: *We'll have to leave earlier – there's no other way round it!* 我們得早點走, 沒有別的辦法! **7 round here** in the place, area of a town etc where you are now 在此地, 在附近: *Do you live round here?* 你在附近住嗎? | *There must be a pen round here somewhere.* 這裡的甚麼地方肯定有枝鋼筆。**8** at about a particular time〔時間〕大約: *It must have been round midnight when I heard the scream.* 我聽到尖叫聲時一定是午夜

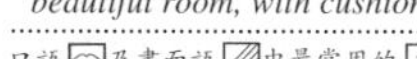

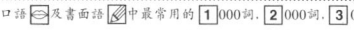

前後。—compare 比較 AROUND —see also 另見 **round the clock** (CLOCK[1] (6))

USAGE NOTE 用法說明: ROUND

WORD CHOICE 詞語辨析: **round, around, about**

In many contexts, **round** and **around** have the same meaning in British English, though American speakers do not use **round** in this way. 在許多語境中, round 和 around 在英國英語中意義相同, 但講美國英語的人則不會這樣使用 round: *The price was somewhere round three thousand* (*BrE* 英). 價格在三千左右。| *The price was somewhere around three thousand.* 價格在三千左右。

In British English, you can use **round** for describing a circular movement. 在英國英語裡, 可以用 round 來描述"旋轉": *The satellite travelled right round the Earth.* 衞星圍繞着地球運轉。Americans would always use **around** in this meaning. 美國人總是用 around 表達這個意思: *The satellite traveled right around the Earth.* 衞星圍繞着地球運轉。The same is true when you use **around** and **round** to mean moving to different places. 用 around 和 round 表示"到各處"時也是如此: *He's travelling round the world for a few years* (*BrE* 英). 幾年來他周遊世界各地。| *He's traveling around the world for a few years.* 幾年來他周遊世界各地。Both **round** and **around** are correct in British English, although **round** is slightly less formal. 在英國英語裡, round 和 around 都正確, 不過 round 稍微不那麼正式。

British English speakers often use **about** instead of **around** in some meanings. 在表達某些意義時, 講英國英語的人經常使用 about 而不用 around: *Stop fooling about, you two.* 別再瞎混了, 你們倆。| *"Where's my bag?" "It must be about somewhere."* "我的包呢?" "肯定就在附近某個地方。"

Both British and American speakers use **about** to mean 'approximately'. 講英國英語和美國英語的人都用 about 來表示"大約": *He's about six feet tall.* 他大約六英尺高。

round⁴ *n* [C]

1 ►SERIES 系列◄ a number or set of events that are connected 一連串相關的事件: **[+of]** *For Jodie, life was a continual round of parties.* 對於喬迪來說, 生活是一連串的宴會, 玩樂不斷。| *the next round of arms talks* 下一輪軍備談判

2 ►FOOD/NEWSPAPERS/LETTERS ETC 食品/報紙/信件等◄ a regular visit to a number of houses, offices etc to deliver or sell things 例行路線〔有規律地到住宅、辦公室等遞送或售賣東西〕: **paper/milk round etc** (=a job in which you deliver newspapers, milk etc to people's houses) 按固定路線送報紙/牛奶等

3 ►VISITS 探訪◄ rounds the usual visits that someone, especially a doctor, regularly makes as part of their job 巡訪, 〔尤指醫生的〕定期巡診: **be (out) on your rounds** *I'm sorry; the doctor is out on her rounds till 3 o'clock.* 對不起, 醫生出去巡診, 3 點以後才回來。

4 do the rounds of to go around from one place to another, often looking for work 在…到處轉〔常指尋找工作〕: *Daniela's doing the rounds of the theatrical agents.* 達妮埃拉正在到一個個劇院經紀人那兒找工作。

5 do the rounds *informal* 【非正式】 also 又作 **go the rounds** *BrE* 【英】 if an illness or piece of news does the rounds, it is passed on from one person to another 〔疾病、新聞〕傳播: *There's a nasty kind of flu doing the rounds this winter.* 今年冬天一種非常厲害的流感正在蔓延。

6 ►ALCOHOL 酒◄ if you buy a round of drinks in a bar, you buy drinks for all the people in your group 〔在酒吧為同伴買的〕每人一份〔飲料〕: **it's my/your etc round** (=used to say that you or another person should buy drinks for all the other people in your group) 我/你等請客 *What are you having? It's my round.* 你們想喝甚麼? 我請客。

7 round of applause a period when people are clapping (CLAP[1] (1)) to show that they enjoyed a performance 一陣掌聲

8 round of sandwiches *especially BrE* SANDWICHes made from two whole pieces of bread 【尤英】〔用兩整片麵包做成的〕三明治

9 round of toast *especially BrE* one whole piece of bread that has been toasted (TOAST[2] (2)) 【尤英】一整片烤麵包

10 ►GOLF 高爾夫球◄ a complete game of GOLF 一場〔指打完球場中所有的洞〕

11 ►BOXING 拳擊◄ one of the periods of fighting in a boxing (BOX[2] (1)) or wrestling (WRESTLE (1)) match that are separated by short rests 拳擊[摔跤]比賽的一個回合: *Bruno was knocked out in the second round.* 布魯諾在第二個回合中被擊倒。

12 ►COMPETITION 比賽◄ one of the stages in a sports competition, especially in tennis or football 〔尤指網球或足球比賽的〕輪, 階段: *Did Sampras get through to the third round?* 森柏斯進入第三輪比賽了嗎?

13 ►GUN SHOT 槍彈發射◄ a single shot from a gun, or a bullet for one shot 一發, 一槍: *I've only got ten rounds of ammunition left.* 我就剩十發子彈了。

14 ►CIRCLE 圓◄ something that has a circular shape 圓形物: *Slice the potatoes into rounds.* 把馬鈴薯切成圓形薄片。

15 ►SONG 歌曲◄ a song for three or four singers, in which each one sings the same tune, starting at different times 輪唱(曲)

16 the daily round the things that you have to do every day 每天的例行工作: *the daily round of cooking and cleaning* 每日的做飯和打掃工作

17 in the round a play that is performed in the round is performed on a central stage surrounded by the people watching it 舞台設在中央〔觀眾圍繞着舞台四周〕

round⁵ *v* [T] **1** to go round something such as a bend or the corner of a building 環繞…而行, 拐〔彎〕: *The Ferrari rounded the bend at top speed.* 那輛法拉利車全速拐過彎道。**2** to make something into a round shape 使成圓形: *Jenny rounded her lips and blew him a kiss.* 珍妮撮起嘴唇給了他一個飛吻。

round sth ↔ **down** *phr v* [T] to reduce an exact figure to the nearest whole number 把數下捨入〔取僅比某數小的整數為其近似值〕—compare 比較 **round up**

round sth ↔ **off** *phr v* [I,T] **1** to do something as a way of ending an event, performance etc in a suitable or satisfactory way (使)〔活動、表演等〕圓滿完成: **round sth ↔ off with** *Fresh strawberries would round the meal off nicely.* 最後來些新鮮草莓, 這頓飯就吃得心滿意足了。**2** [T] to take the sharp edges off something 去掉〔某物〕的鋒利邊緣: *Round off the corners with a pair of scissors.* 用剪刀把角剪圓。**3** to change an exact figure to the nearest whole number 四捨五入成整數

round on sb/sth *phr v* [T] to suddenly turn and attack someone when they do not expect it, physically or with words 突然攻擊, 突然責罵: *Then, for no reason at all, she rounded on me and started screaming.* 這時她毫無理由地突然衝着我尖聲大叫大嚷起來。

round out *phr v* [T] to make an experience more thorough or complete 徹底完成: **round sth ↔ out** *Denise decided to round out her education with a year in Paris.* 丹尼斯決定在巴黎花一年時間完成學業。

round sb/sth ↔ **up** *phr v* [T] **1** to find a particular group of people and force them to go to prison 逮捕, 肅清: *The government's opponents are being rounded up and thrown in jail.* 反對政府的人遭到逮捕, 被投入監獄。**2** to find and gather together a group of people or things 集攏〔人或物〕: *See if you can round up a few friends to help you!* 看你能否找幾個朋友幫你忙! —see also 另見

ROUND-UP (1) **3** to increase an exact figure to the next highest whole number 把數上捨入〔取僅比某數大的整數為其近似值〕—compare 比較 **round down** **4** to finish a meeting or other event by doing something 以…結束〔會議或其他活動〕: *Frances likes to round up a speech with a joke.* 弗朗西斯喜歡以笑話來結束演講。

round·a·bout¹ /ˈraʊndəˌbaʊt; ˈraʊndəbaʊt/ *n* [C] *BrE*【英】**1** a raised circular area which cars drive around, used where three or more roads join 環島, 環形交叉路口; TRAFFIC CIRCLE *AmE*【美】**2** round structure which children sit on while people push it around and around〔兒童坐的〕旋轉椅; MERRY-GO-ROUND *AmE*【美】**3** a MERRY-GO-ROUND (1)〔遊樂場裡的〕旋轉木馬 —see also 另見 **swings and roundabouts** (SWING² (8))

roundabout² *adj* not done in the shortest, most direct way possible 繞彎子的; 不直截了當的, 轉彎抹角的: *a roundabout route to avoid the worst of the traffic* 繞道避開交通最擁擠的地段 | *It was a roundabout way of telling us to leave.* 這是在轉彎抹角地要我們離開。

round·ed /ˈraʊndɪd; ˈraʊndɪd/ *adj* having a round shape; curved 圓形的; 彎曲的 —see also 另見 WELL-ROUNDED

roun·ders /ˈraʊndəz; ˈraʊndəz/ *n* [singular] a British ball game, similar to BASEBALL, in which players hit the ball and then run around the edge of an area 圓場棒球

Round·head /ˈraʊndˌhɛd; ˈraʊndhed/ *n* [C] someone who supported Parliament against the King in the English Civil War in the 17th century〔17世紀英國內戰時支持議會反對國王的〕圓顱黨人 —compare 比較 CAVALIER

round·ly /ˈraʊndlɪ; ˈraʊndli/ *adj* **roundly condemn/criticize etc** (=criticize someone strongly and severely) 強烈譴責/嚴厲批評等 *All the major parties roundly condemned the attack.* 所有主要政黨都強烈譴責這次襲擊。

round rob·in /ˌ· ˈ··/ *n* [C] **1** a competition in which every player or team plays against each of the other players or teams 循環賽 **2** a letter expressing opinions or complaints, signed by many people and sent as a form of protest〔由很多人簽名的〕圓形簽名請願[抗議]書

round-shoul·dered /ˌ· ˈ··◂/ *adj* having shoulders that are bent forwards or slope downwards 圓肩的, 拱背曲肩的

round-ta·ble /ˌ· ˈ··◂/ *adj* [only before noun 僅用於名詞前] a roundtable discussion or meeting is one in which everyone can talk about things in an equal way 圓桌的〔討論或會議, 指與會者不分主次參與討論〕

round-the-clock /ˌ· · ˈ·◂/ *adj* [only before noun 僅用於名詞前] all the time, both day and night 二十四小時不間斷的, 不分晝夜的: *He'll need round-the-clock hospital care.* 他需要不分晝夜的住院照顧。—see also 另見 **round the clock** (CLOCK¹ (6))

round trip /ˌ· ˈ·/ *n* [C] a journey to a place and back again 往返旅程: *The round trip took just over an hour.* 往返旅程需要一個小時多一點。

round-trip /ˌ· ˈ·◂/ *adj AmE* a round-trip ticket includes the journey to a place and back again【美】〔票〕往返的; RETURN² (9) *BrE*【英】

round-up /ˈ· ·/ *n* [C] **1** an occasion when people, or animals, of a particular type are all brought together, often using force〔把某類人或動物強行〕集攏, 聚集: *a round-up of suspected drug-dealers* 搜捕涉嫌毒品販子 **2** a short description of the main parts of the news, on the radio or on televison〔廣播或電視裡的〕新聞簡報 —see also 另見 **round up** (ROUND⁵)

rouse /raʊz; raʊz/ *v* **1 rouse sb (from their sleep/slumbers)** to wake someone up with difficulty because they are sleeping deeply〔艱難地把某人從熟睡中〕喚醒 **2** [T] to make someone start doing something, especially when they have been too tired or unwilling to do it 激勵〔某人做某事, 尤其在他很疲倦或不願意做時〕, 使振奮: **rouse sb into action** *The commander tried to rouse them all into action.* 指揮員設法激勵他們都行動起來。| **rouse yourself** *When Alice finally roused herself, she realized Harold was already home.* 等到愛麗斯終於振作起來的時候, 她才知道哈羅德已經到家了。**3** [T] to make someone feel a particular emotion, such as hope or fear 激起〔希望、恐懼等〕—compare 比較 AROUSE

roused /raʊzd; raʊzd/ *adj* [not before noun 不用於名詞前] angry 發怒的: **when roused** *When roused, he could be quite violent.* 一旦被激怒, 他會變得相當粗暴。

rous·ing /ˈraʊzɪŋ; ˈraʊzɪŋ/ *adj* a rousing song, speech etc makes people feel excited and eager to do something〔歌曲、講演等〕激動人心的, 鼓勵人(行動)的

roust /raʊst; raʊst/ *v* [T] *AmE* to make someone move from a place【美】攆出, 驅逐: *Go roust the kids, it's time we went.* 去把孩子趕出來, 我們該走了。

rous·ta·bout /ˈraʊstəˌbaʊt; ˈraʊstəbaʊt/ *n* [C] *especially AmE* a man who does work for which he needs to be strong but not skilled, especially in a port, an OILFIELD, or a CIRCUS (1)【尤美】〔尤指在港口、油田或馬戲團幹重活的〕非熟練工, 普通工; 場地工

rout¹ /raʊt; raʊt/ *v* [T] to defeat someone completely in a battle, competition, or election〔在戰鬥、競賽或選舉中〕擊潰, 徹底擊敗

rout² *n* [singular] a complete defeat in a battle, competition or election〔在戰鬥、競賽或選舉中〕潰敗, 徹底失敗: **put sb to rout** *literary* (=defeat them completely in a battle)【文】徹底擊敗某人

route¹ /rut; ruːt/ *n* [C] **1** the way from one place to another, especially a way that is regularly used and can be shown on a map〔尤指經常使用, 可在地圖上顯示的〕路線: **[+to/from]** *What's the best route to Cambridge?* 到劍橋的最佳路線怎麼走? | **take/follow a route** (=use a route) 沿某路線走 *We weren't sure about which route we should take.* 我們拿不準應該走哪條路線。**2** a road, railway, or imaginary line along which vehicles often travel〔交通工具常用的〕路線: *The London-New York route is the busiest.* 倫敦至紐約的航線是最繁忙的。| *Is your office on a bus route?* 你的辦公室在公共汽車路線上嗎? **3** a way of doing something or achieving a particular result〔做事或達到特定結果的〕途徑, 方法: *the surest route to disaster* 必定會招致災難的途徑 | *his route to fame and fortune* 他的成名發財之路 **4 Route 66, 54 etc** used to show the number of a main road in the US〔美國〕66[54]號等公路: *Take Route 95 through Connecticut.* 走95號公路穿過康涅狄格州。—see also 另見 EN ROUTE, SNOW ROUTE, TRADE ROUTE W2

route² *v* [T] to send something or someone using a particular route 按特定路線發送〔東西或人〕: **[+through/by]** *They had to route the goods through Germany.* 他們必須經由德國運送貨物。—see also 另見 RE-ROUTE

route march /ˈ· ·/ *n* [C] a long march done by soldiers when they are training〔士兵在訓練中作的〕長途行軍

rou·tine¹ /ruˈtin; ruːˈtiːn/ *n* **1** [C,U] the usual or normal way in which you do things 慣例, 常規: *John's departure had upset their daily routine.* 約翰的離去打亂了他們每日的常規。| *Mark longed to escape from the same old familiar routine.* 馬克渴望擺脫千篇一律的老套。| **a break in the routine** (=a change from what you normally do) 打破常規 **2** [C] a set of steps learned and practised by a dancer for a public performance〔表演的〕一套固定舞步, 舞蹈動作 **3** [C] *technical* a set of instructions given to a computer so that it will do a particular operation【術語】〔輸入電腦的〕程序 —**routinize** /ruˈtinaɪz, ruːˈtiːnaɪz/ *v* [T] *AmE*【美】 W3

rou·tine² /ruˈtin; ˌruːˈtiːn◂/ *adj* **1 routine questions/examination/visit etc** (=usual questions etc that are not concerned with any kind of serious problem) 例行問題/檢查/訪問等 *It's just a routine medical examination, nothing to get worried about.* 這只是例行的體格檢查, 沒有甚麼好擔心的。| *a routine visit to the dentist* 例行看牙醫 **2** ordinary and boring 一般的, 平淡的, 乏味的: **routine jobs/tasks** *What's more, routine jobs make people less motivated.* 此外, 枯燥乏味的工作會減少人們的動力。

rou·tine·ly /ruˈtinlɪ; ruːˈtiːnli/ *adv* if something is routinely done, it is usually done as part of the normal process of working, doing a job etc 慣常地, 例行地

roux /ru; ruː/ *plural* **roux** /ruz; ruːz/ *n* [C,U] a mixture of flour, butter, and milk that is used for making SAUCE*s* 〔做調味汁用的〕黃油牛奶麵粉糊

rove /rov; rəʊv/ *v* [I] **1** to travel from one place to another 漫遊, 流浪: **roving reporter** (=someone who works for a newspaper or television company, and moves from place to place) 流動記者 **2** if someone's eyes rove, they look continuously from one part of something to another 掃視: [+**around/over**] *Benedict's eyes roved boldly over her sleeping body.* 本尼迪的眼睛放肆地掃視着熟睡中的她的身軀。**3 have a roving eye** *old-fashioned* to be always looking for a chance to have romantic relationships【過時】好色

rov·er /ˈrovɚ; ˈrəʊvə/ *n* [C] *literary* someone who travels around from place to place【文】流浪者, 漂泊者

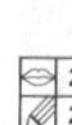

row¹ /ro; rəʊ/ *n* [C] **1** a line of things or people next to each other 一排, 一行, 一列: [+**of**] *a row of houses* 一排房子 | *rows of trees* 成排的樹 | *Plant the seedlings in parallel rows.* 把這些秧苗插成平行的幾行。| **in a row** (=next to each other) 成一行 *On a long table, place the containers in a row.* 在長桌上把這些容器擺成一排。| *The children were asked to stand in a row.* 孩子們被要求站成一排。| **row upon row** (=many rows) 一排又一排 *row upon row of shelves stacked with books* 一排排堆滿書的架子 **2** a line of seats in a theatre or cinema 〔劇院或電影院裡的〕一排座位: *We sat in the front row.* 我們坐在前排。**3 three/four etc times in a row** happening a number of times in exactly the same way or with the same result 連續三/四次等: *She won four times in a row.* 她連續四次獲勝。**4 go for a row** to take a short journey in a ROWING BOAT 去划船

row² /raʊ; raʊ/ *n BrE*【英】**1** [C] an angry argument that lasts a short time, especially between people who know each other well 〔尤指互相熟悉的人之間的〕爭吵, 吵架: *The news caused a terrible family row.* 這消息使全家人激烈爭吵。| **have a row (with sb)** *Those two are always having rows.* 那兩個人老是吵架。**2** [C] a situation in which people disagree strongly about important public matters; CONTROVERSY 爭辯, 爭論: [+**about/over**] *The Prime Minister is at the centre of a new row over government secrecy.* 在有關政府機密的新爭論中, 首相成了中心人物。**3** [singular] a loud unpleasant noise that continues for a long time 〔持續時間長的〕喧鬧聲, 吵嚷聲: *Stop that row – I'm trying to get to sleep!* 別吵啦, 我要睡覺了!

row³ /ro; rəʊ/ *v* **1** [I,T] to make a boat move across water using OAR*s* (=long poles that are flat at the end) 划 (船): [+**away/towards/across**] *She rowed across the lake.* 她划船到湖對岸。**2** [I] to be able to make a boat move in this way, or to do this as a sport 划船; 參加划船比賽: *Jenny used to row at college.* 珍妮以前在大學裡經常參加划船比賽。

row⁴ /raʊ; raʊ/ *v* [I+**about**] *BrE* to argue in an angry way【英】爭吵, 吵架

row·an /ˈroən; ˈrəʊən/ *n* [C] a small tree that has bright red berries 花楸樹

row·boat /ˈroˌbot; ˈrəʊbəʊt/ *n* [C] *AmE* a small boat that you move through the water with OAR*s* (=long poles that are flat at the end)【美】划艇, 用槳划的小船; ROWING BOAT *BrE*【英】

row·dy¹ /ˈraʊdɪ; ˈraʊdi/ *adj* behaving in a noisy, rough way that is likely to cause arguments and fighting 吵鬧的, 粗暴的: *a rowdy group of soccer fans* 一羣粗野的足球迷 —**rowdily** *adv* —**rowdiness** *n* [U]

rowdy² *n* [C, usually plural 一般用複數] *old-fashioned* someone who behaves in a rough noisy way【過時】吵鬧的人, 粗野的人

row house /ˈro haʊs; ˈrəʊ haʊs/ *n* [C] *AmE* a house that is part of a line of houses that are joined to each other【美】排屋〔互相連接的一排房屋之一幢〕; TERRACED HOUSE *BrE*【英】—see picture on page A4 參見 A4 頁圖

row·ing /ˈroɪŋ; ˈrəʊɪŋ/ *n* [U] the sport or activity of making a boat move through water with OAR*s* 划船運動

rowing boat /ˈroɪŋ bot; ˈrəʊɪŋ bəʊt/ *n* [C] *BrE* a small boat that you move through the water with OAR*s* (=long poles that are flat at the end)【英】划艇, 用槳划的小船; ROWBOAT *AmE*【美】

row·lock /ˈroˌlɑk; ˈrɒlək; *technical* 術語 ˈroˌlɑk; ˈrəʊlɒk/ *n* [C] *BrE* one of the U-shaped pieces of metal that holds the oars of a rowing boat【英】槳架; OARLOCK *AmE*【美】

roy·al¹ /ˈrɔɪəl; ˈrɔɪəl/ *adj* [only before noun 僅用於名詞前] **1** connected with or belonging to a king or queen 國王的, 女王的, 王室的: *the royal chapel at Versailles* 凡爾賽王宮的教堂 —compare 比較 REGAL **2** very impressive, as if done for a king or queen 盛大的, 隆重的: *a royal welcome* 隆重的歡迎 —see also 另見 **right royal** (RIGHT¹ (7)) **3** *informal* used to emphasize how bad something or someone is【非正式】極度的〔用以強調某物或某人的壞處〕: *She's a royal pain in the neck!* 她是個極其討厭的人! **4 the royal 'we'** *BrE* the use of the word 'we' instead of 'I', by the Queen or King【英】御用"我們"〔女王或國王自稱時使用 we 而不用 I〕—**royally** *adv* 3 1

royal² *n* [C] *informal* a member of a royal family【非正式】王室成員

royal as·sent /ˌ·· ·ˈ·/ *n* [U] the signing of a law by the British king or queen after it has been decided by Parliament, so that it officially becomes law 御准〔英國國王或女王簽署議會通過的法令〕

royal blue /ˌ·· ˈ·◂/ *n* [U] a strong, bright blue colour 品藍色, 紅光藍色 —**royal blue** *adj* —see picture on page A5 參見 A5 頁圖

royal com·mis·sion /ˌ·· ·ˈ··/ *n* [C] a group of people who make suggestions about a subject that the British government thinks may need new laws 皇家專門調查委員會〔負責就英國政府認為可能需要制定新法律的事項提出建議〕

royal flush /ˌ·· ˈ·/ *n* [C usually singular 一般用單數] a set of cards that someone has in a card game, which are the five most important cards in a SUIT (=one of the four different types of card) 〔紙牌遊戲中的〕同花大順

Royal High·ness /ˌ·· ˈ··/ *n* [C] **your/his/her royal Highness** used when speaking about or to a royal person, especially a prince or princess 殿下〔用於間接提及或當面稱呼王室成員, 尤指王子或公主〕

roy·al·ist /ˈrɔɪəlɪst; ˈrɔɪəlɪst/ *n* [C] someone who supports a king or queen, or believes that a country should be ruled by kings or queens 君主主義者, 保皇主義者 —**royalist** *adj*

royal pre·rog·a·tive /ˌ·· ·ˈ···/ *n* [singular,U] the special rights that a king or queen has 國王[女王]的特權

roy·al·ty /ˈrɔɪəltɪ; ˈrɔɪəlti/ *n* **1** [U] members of a royal family 王室[皇族]成員 **2 royalties** [plural] payments made to the writer of a book or piece of music 〔付給作家、作曲家的〕版税

RP /ˌɑr ˈpi; ˌɑː ˈpiː/ *n* [U] Received Pronunciation; the form of British pronunciation that many educated people in Britain use, and that is thought of as the standard form 英語標準發音〔在英國, 很多接受過教育的人使用的英語發音形式, 被視為發音的標準〕

rpm /ˌɑr pi ˈɛm; ˌɑː piː ˈem/ revolutions per minute; a measurement of the speed at which an engine or RECORD PLAYER turns 〔發動機或唱機的〕每分鐘轉數, 轉/分

RR /ˌɑr ˈɑr; ˌɑːr ˈɑː/ rural route; used in addresses in country areas of the US, to show which mail delivery area a letter should go to 鄉村投遞路線〔美國鄉村地區的通信地址中使用〕

RSI /ˌɑr ɛs ˈaɪ; ˌɑːr es ˈaɪ/ *n* [U] repetitive strain injury; pain in your hands, arms etc caused by doing the same movements very many times, especially when typing (TYPE² (2)) 重複性緊張勞損〔手掌、手臂等重複做相同動作, 尤其是打字, 而引致的疼痛〕

RSVP /ˌɑr ɛs vi ˈpi; ˌɑːr es viː ˈpiː/ *French* used on invitations to ask someone to reply【法】敬請賜覆〔請柬用語〕

Rt Hon the written abbreviation of 縮寫= RIGHT HONOURABLE

3 **rub**[1] /rʌb; rʌb/ **rubbed, rubbing** *v* **1** [I,T] to move your hand, a cloth etc over a surface while pressing against it 擦, 磨擦: *Kolchinsky nodded and then rubbed his eyes wearily.* 科爾琴斯基點了點頭, 然後疲倦地揉了揉眼睛。| *She began rubbing her hair with a towel.* 她開始用毛巾擦頭髮。| *You'll have to rub harder if you want to get it clean.* 如果想使它乾淨, 你就要更用勁地擦。—see picture on page A20 參見 A20 頁圖 **2** [T] to make something press against something else and move it around 使…相互磨擦, 揉搓: **rub sth against/on** *Celia's cat purred loudly, rubbing against her legs.* 西莉婭的貓咕嚕咕嚕地大聲叫着, 在她的腿上蹭來蹭去。| **rub sth together** *We tried to make a fire by rubbing two pieces of wood together.* 我們嘗試用兩塊木頭相互磨擦來生火。**3** [I] to move around while pressing against another surface, often causing pain, damage etc〔在另一表面上〕磨擦引致疼痛, 磨損: **[+against/on]** *These shoes are too tight – they keep rubbing on my heels.* 這雙鞋子太緊, 老是磨我的腳跟。**4** [T always+adv/prep] to put a substance into or onto the surface of something by pressing it and moving it about with your hand, a cloth etc 把…塗擦在表面,〔揉搓〕使滲入, 搽: **rub sth on/into/over/etc** *Can you rub some sun cream on my back for me, please?* 請給我的背上塗些防曬霜好嗎? **5 rub it in** *informal* to remind someone about something they want to forget, especially because they are embarrassed about it【非正式】提起某人的痛處: *Look, I know I should have been more careful, but there's no need to keep rubbing it in.* 聽我說, 我知道我本應該更小心一點兒, 但也沒有必要老提那件事。**6 rub shoulders with** *informal* to spend time with rich or famous people【非正式】與〔富人、名人〕交往: *As a reporter he gets to rub shoulders with all the big names in politics and the media.* 作為記者, 他有機會與政界和媒體的大人物打交道。**7 rub salt into the wound** *informal* to make a bad situation even worse for someone【非正式】加深傷害[痛楚] **8 rub sb's nose in it/in the dirt** *informal* to keep reminding someone about something they did wrong or failed to do, especially in order to punish them【非正式】不斷提起某人以前的過失, 揭某人的瘡疤〔尤指為懲罰某人〕**9 rub sb up the wrong way** *informal* to annoy someone by the way you behave towards them【非正式】惹惱某人, 觸犯某人: *I don't know what it is about Paula, but she really rubs me up the wrong way.* 我不清楚葆拉是怎麼回事, 但她的確惹得我很不高興。**10 be rubbing your hands** *informal* to be pleased because something has happened which gives you an advantage, especially because something bad has happened to someone else【非正式】〔某事發生帶給你好處而〕高興得兩手搓來搓去〔尤因壞事發生在他人身上〕**11 not have two pennies/halfpennies to rub together** *BrE humorous* to not have any money【英, 幽默】身無分文

rub along *phr v* [I+**with/together**] *BrE* to have a friendly relationship with someone【英】與…保持友好關係

rub down *phr v* [T] **1** [**rub** sth ↔ **down**] to make a surface dry or smooth by rubbing it with a cloth or SANDPAPER〔用布〕把〔表面〕擦乾;〔用砂紙〕把〔表面〕擦平滑 **2** [**rub** sb **down**] **a)** to MASSAGE (=rub their muscles) someone, especially after hard exercise 按摩〔尤在劇烈運動後〕**b)** [**rub** sb/sth **down**] to dry a person or animal by rubbing them with a cloth, TOWEL etc〔用布、毛巾等〕擦乾〔人或動物〕全身 —see also 另見 RUBDOWN

rub off *phr v* [**rub** (sth ↔) **off**] **1** [I,T] to remove something from a surface by rubbing it, or to come off a surface because of being rubbed 擦掉, 磨去: *Be careful not to rub off the paint.* 小心, 別把油漆擦掉。**2** [I] if a feeling, quality, or habit rubs off on someone, they start to have it because they are with another person who has it〔感情、特質、習慣等〕影響〔某人〕: **[+on]** *His enthusiasm shines through and seems to rub off on everyone else.* 他熱情洋溢, 似乎感染了每一個人。

rub sb/sth **out** *phr v* [T] **1** *BrE* to remove writing, a picture etc from a surface by rubbing it with a piece of rubber, a cloth etc【英】〔用橡皮、布等〕把〔字跡、圖等〕擦掉; ERASE (2) *especially AmE*【尤美】: *You might as well rub the whole thing out and start over.* 你不妨把所有東西都擦掉重新開始。**2** *AmE old-fashioned* to murder someone【美, 過時】殺掉〔某人〕

rub[2] *n* **1 give sb/sth a rub** to rub something or MASSAGE[2] (1) someone for a short time〔短時間〕擦某個東西; 給某人按摩: *Give the table a good rub with a damp cloth.* 用濕布好好擦一擦桌子。**2 there's/here's the rub** used when saying that a particular problem is the reason why a situation is so difficult 困難就在那兒/這兒

rub·ber /ˈrʌbɚ; ˈrʌbə/ *n*

1 ►MATERIAL 材料◄ [U] a substance used to make tyres, gloves, boots etc, which is made from the juice of a tropical tree or artificially 橡膠; 合成橡膠: *a rubber ball* 橡皮球

2 ►FOR REMOVING MARKS 用於擦去痕跡◄ *BrE*【英】**a)** a thing you use for removing pencil marks; ERASER 橡皮 **b)** a thing you use for cleaning marks from a BLACKBOARD; ERASER 黑板擦

3 ►SEX 性◄ [C] *AmE informal* a CONDOM【美, 非正式】避孕套

4 ►SHOE 鞋◄ [C usually plural 一般用複數] *AmE old-fashioned* a rubber shoe that you wear over an ordinary shoe when it rains or snows【美, 過時】雨[雪]天用的橡膠鞋套; GALOSH *BrE*【英】

5 ►SERIES OF GAMES 連續的比賽◄ [C] a series of games of BRIDGE (=a card game) or CRICKET (2)〔橋牌或板球的〕一盤〔規定先勝多少局才贏得一盤〕

6 ►FOR STANDING ON/IN 供站立用◄ [C] the piece of white rubber where the PITCHER (=person who throws the ball) stands in a BASEBALL game〔棒球比賽中的〕投手板, 本壘板

rubber band /ˌ·· ˈ·/ *n* [C] a thin circular piece of rubber used for fastening things together 橡皮筋, 橡皮圈; ELASTIC BAND *BrE*【英】

rubber boot /ˈ·· ·/ *n* [C] a tall boot made of rubber that keeps your feet and the lower part of your legs dry 防水橡膠靴, 長統橡膠雨靴; WELLINGTON *BrE*【英】—see picture at 參見 BOOT[1] 圖

rubber bul·let /ˌ·· ˈ··/ *n* [C] a bullet made of rubber that is not intended to seriously hurt or kill people, but is used to control violent crowds 橡膠子彈

rubber check /ˌ·· ˈ·/ *n* [C] *AmE informal* a cheque that the bank refuses to accept because the person who wrote it does not have enough money【美, 非正式】空頭支票

rubber din·ghy /ˌ·· ˈ··/ *n* [C] a small rubber boat that is filled with air 橡皮艇, 橡皮船

rub·ber·neck /ˈrʌbɚˌnɛk; ˈrʌbənek/ *v* [I] *informal especially AmE* to look around at something, especially something such as an accident while you are driving past【非正式, 尤美】〔尤指開車經過發生意外事故等地方時〕回頭看熱鬧: *tourists rubbernecking at the White House* 在白宮東張西望的遊客 —**rubbernecker** *n* [C]

rubber plant /ˈ·· ·/ *n* [C] a plant with large, shiny, dark green leaves that is often grown indoors 橡膠植物〔一種室內生長的植物, 葉子大、深綠而有光澤〕

rubber stamp /ˌ·· ˈ·/ *n* [C] a small piece of rubber with a handle, used for printing dates or names on paper 橡皮圖章

rubber-stamp /ˌ·· ˈ·/ *v* [T] to give official approval to something without really thinking about it 不加思考就照例批准: *Democrats in Congress refused to rubber-stamp the Reagan program.* 國會的民主黨議員拒絕例行公事式地批准列根的計劃。

rub·ber·y /ˈrʌbəri; ˈrʌbəri/ *adj* **1** looking or feeling like rubber 橡皮似的: *The meat was rather rubbery.* 肉太老了。**2** if your legs or knees are rubbery, they feel weak or unsteady〔腿或膝〕軟[不穩]的

rub·bing /ˈrʌbɪŋ; ˈrʌbɪŋ/ *n* [C] a copy of a shape or pattern made by rubbing wax, CHALK etc onto a piece of paper laid over it〔用蠟、粉筆等〕拓印: *a brass rubbing* 銅像拓印

rubbing al·co·hol /ˈ·· ˌ···/ *n* [U] *AmE* a type of alcohol used for cleaning wounds or skin【美】消毒用酒精; SURGICAL SPIRIT *BrE*【英】

3 **rub·bish[1]** /ˈrʌbɪʃ; ˈrʌbɪʃ/ *n* [U] *especially BrE*【尤英】**1** food, paper etc that is no longer needed and has been thrown away 垃圾, 廢棄物; GARBAGE (1) *AmE*【美】: *The dustmen collect the rubbish on Thursdays.* 垃圾工每星期四收垃圾。**2** *informal* objects, papers etc that you no longer use and should throw away【非正式】沒用的東西, 該扔掉的東西: *I must clear some of the rubbish from my desk.* 我必須把桌上一些沒用的東西清理掉。**3** *informal* an idea, statement etc that is rubbish is silly or wrong and does not deserve serious attention; nonsense【非正式】胡說八道, 廢話: *Oh, don't talk such rubbish!* 噢, 別說這種廢話! | **a load of (old) rubbish** *I reckon all this stuff about reincarnation is a load of rubbish.* 我認為關於轉世投胎的種種說法都是無稽之談。| **rubbish!** *spoken* (=used to tell someone that what they have just said is completely wrong)【口】胡說八道!〔指對方說的話完全錯誤〕**4** *informal* a film, book etc that is rubbish is very bad【非正式】水平低劣的/粗製濫造的電影[書等]: *the usual Hollywood rubbish* 荷里活慣常的低劣電影

Frequencies of the nouns **rubbish**, **garbage** and **trash** in British and American English 名詞rubbish, garbage 和 trash 在英國英語和美國英語中的使用頻率

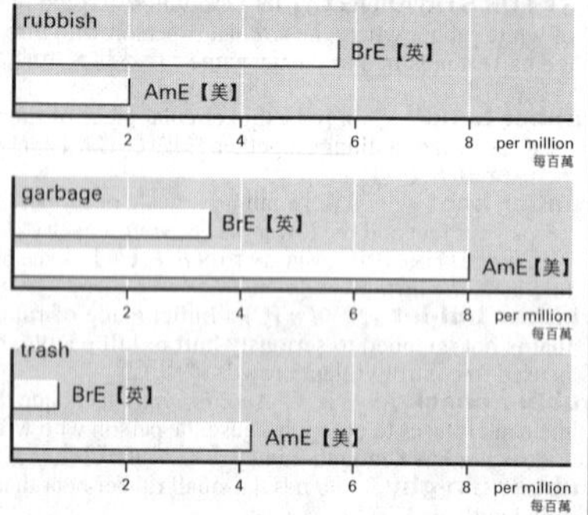

Based on the British National Corpus and the Longman Lancaster Corpus
據英國國家語料庫和朗文蘭卡斯特語料庫

In British English **rubbish** is commonly used to mean something that is no longer needed and has been thrown away, or something that is very bad in quality or does not deserve serious attention. In American English **garbage** and **trash** are commonly used for these meanings. **Trash** is only used in British English to mean something, especially a book, film etc that is of very bad quality. 在英國英語中, rubbish 經常用來指不再需要而被扔掉的垃圾, 或品質極差、無須重視的東西。在美國英語中則常用 garbage 和 trash 來表示這些意思。英國英語中的 trash 只用來指品質很差的東西, 尤指書、電影等。

rubbish[2] *v* [T] *BrE* to say something is bad or useless【英】把〔某物〕說得一無是處

rubbish[3] *adj BrE informal* not skilful at a particular activity【英, 非正式】技術差勁的: *They're a rubbish football team.* 他們是一支末流的足球隊。

rub·bish·y /ˈrʌbɪʃɪ; ˈrʌbɪʃi/ *adj BrE informal* silly or of a very low quality; TRASHY【英, 非正式】愚蠢的, 低劣的, 毫無價值的: *rubbishy magazines* 垃圾雜誌

rub·ble /ˈrʌbḷ; ˈrʌbəl/ *n* [U] broken stones or bricks from a building or wall that has been destroyed〔被毀的建築物或牆壁的〕碎石, 碎磚, 瓦礫

rub·down /ˈrʌbˌdaun; ˈrʌbdaʊn/ *n* [C] **1** *especially AmE* if you give someone a rubdown, you rub their body to make them relaxed, especially after exercise; MASSAGE[1]【尤美】〔尤指運動後的〕按摩 **2** if you give a surface a rubdown, you rub it to make it smooth or clean〔把表面〕磨平滑; 擦乾淨 —see also 另見 **rub down** (RUB[1])

rube /rub; ruːb/ *n* [C] *AmE slang* someone, usually from the country, who has no experience of other places and thinks in a simple way【美俚】鄉巴佬, 土包子

Rube Gold·berg /ˌrub ˋgoldbɝg; ˌruːb ˈgəʊldbɜːg/ *adj AmE* a Rube Goldberg machine etc is very complicated and impractical, in an amusing way【美】〔機器等〕複雜卻可笑而不實用的; HEATH ROBINSON *BrE*【英】

ru·bel·la /ruˈbɛlə; ruːˈbelə/ *n* [U] *technical* an infectious disease that causes red spots on your body, and can damage an unborn child; GERMAN MEASLES【術語】風疹; 德國麻疹

Ru·bi·con /ˈrubɪˌkɑn; ˈruːbɪkən/ *n* **cross the Rubicon** to do something that will have extremely important effects in the future and that you cannot change 破釜沉舟; 採取斷然行動

ru·bi·cund /ˈrubəˌkʌnd; ˈruːbɪkənd/ *adj literary* someone who is rubicund is fat and has a red face【文】〔人〕肥胖而面色紅潤的

ru·ble /ˈrubḷ; ˈruːbəl/ *n* [C] another spelling of ROUBLE rouble 的另一種拼法

ru·bric /ˈrubrɪk; ˈruːbrɪk/ *n* [C] *formal* a set of instructions or an explanation in a book, examination paper etc【正式】〔書、考卷等中的〕指示, 說明

ru·by /ˈrubɪ; ˈruːbi/ *n* **1** [C] a red jewel 紅寶石 **2** [U] the colour of this jewel 紅寶石色, 深紅色

ruck[1] /rʌk; rʌk/ *n* [C] **1 the ruck** ordinary events or people, which seem rather boring compared to the lives of rich or famous people 普通的事件[人]〔與富人或名人比較〕: *She dreamed of getting out of the ruck and becoming a famous singer.* 她夢想出人頭地, 成為著名的歌星。**2** a group of RUGBY players trying to get the ball when it is lying on the ground〔橄欖球賽中〕逼攻爭球的一羣球員

ruck[2] *v*

ruck (sth) ↔ **up** *phr v* [I,T] if a piece of cloth rucks up, or if you ruck it up, it forms folds in an untidy way〔布〕起皺, 起褶: *Your coat's all rucked up at the back.* 你的外套後背全起皺了。

ruck·sack /ˈrʌkˌsæk; ˈrʌksæk/ *n* [C] *especially BrE* a bag used for carrying things on your back, especially by people on long walks; BACKPACK[1]【尤英】〔尤指長途步行用的〕背包, 背囊

ruck·us /ˈrʌkəs; ˈrʌkəs/ *n* [singular] *informal especially AmE* a noisy argument or confused situation; RUMPUS【非正式, 尤美】高聲爭吵, 喧鬧, 騷亂: *drunken fraternity boys raising a ruckus at 3 in the morning* 喝醉酒的大學生聯誼會的小夥子在凌晨3點大吵大鬧

ruc·tions /ˈrʌkʃənz; ˈrʌkʃənz/ *n* [plural] *informal especially BrE* complaints and comments because many people are annoyed about a situation【非正式, 尤英】大吵大鬧

rud·der /ˈrʌdɚ; ˈrʌdə/ *n* [C] a flat part at the back of a ship or aircraft that can be turned in order to control the direction in which it moves〔船或飛機的〕方向舵 —see picture at 參見 YACHT 圖

rud·der·less /ˈrʌdɚlɪs; ˈrʌdələs/ *adj* without a leader who can make decisions 無人領導的: *a company left rudderless by the resignation of its CEO* 因行政總裁辭

職而處於無人領導狀態的公司

rud·dy /ˈrʌdɪ; ˈrʌdi/ *adj* **1** a ruddy face looks pink and healthy〔臉色〕紅潤的, 健康的: *ruddy cheeks* 紅潤的面頰 **2** a word used instead of BLOODY when saying strongly that you are annoyed with someone or something 可惡的, 討厭的, 該死的, 十足的〔用於代替 bloody, 加強語氣, 表示憤怒〕: *I wish that ruddy dog would stop barking!* 我希望那隻該死的狗不要再吠了！**3** *literary* red【文】紅色的: *The fire cast a ruddy glow over the room.* 火把房間映得通紅。—**ruddiness** *n* [U] —**ruddy** *adv*

rude /rud; ruːd/ *adj* **1** speaking or behaving in a way that is not polite and is likely to offend or annoy people〔說話或行為〕不禮貌的, 粗魯的, 討厭的: *Don't be so rude to your father!* 不要對你爸爸這麼沒禮貌！| *a rude remark* 粗魯的話 | *I didn't mean to be rude, but I had to leave early.* 我並不想不講禮貌, 但我必須早走。| **it is rude to do sth** *It's rude to stare.* 盯着人看是不禮貌的。**2** rude jokes, words, songs etc are about sex〔玩笑、話語、歌曲等〕粗俗的, 下流的 **3 a rude awakening** a situation in which you suddenly realize something unpleasant 突然察覺〔不愉快的事〕**4 in rude health** *BrE* very healthy【英】十分健壯的 **5** *literary* made in a simple, basic way【文】簡單的, 粗製的: *a rude wooden hut* 簡陋的小木屋 —**rudely** *adv* —**rudeness** *n* [U]

ru·di·men·ta·ry /ˌrudəˈmɛntərɪ; ˌruːdʒˈmentəri◂/ *adj* **1** a rudimentary knowledge or understanding of a subject is very simple and basic〔對某學科的知識或理解〕基本的, 初步的, 粗淺的: *a rudimentary knowledge of Japanese* 略通日語 **2** rudimentary equipment, methods, systems etc are very basic and not advanced〔設備、方法、系統等〕簡陋的, 不先進的: *The classroom equipment is pretty rudimentary.* 教室裡的設備相當簡陋。**3 a rudimentary tail/wing/eye** a part of an animal that has only developed into a very simple form 雛形的尾巴／翅膀／眼睛

ru·di·ments /ˈrudəmənts; ˈruːdʒmənts/ *n* [plural] *formal* the most basic parts of a subject, which you learn first【正式】〔某學科的〕基礎（部分）, 入門: **[+of]** *the rudiments of tennis* 網球入門

rue /ru; ruː/ *v* [T] *literary* to wish that you had not done something; REGRET¹ (1)【文】後悔, 遺憾: **rue the day (that)** *She learned to rue the day she had met Henri.* 不快的經歷使她後悔認識亨利。

rue·ful /ˈrufəl; ˈruːfəl/ *adj* feeling or showing that you wish you had not done something 後悔的, 悔恨的: *a rueful smile* 悔恨的苦笑 —**ruefully** *adv*

ruff /rʌf; rʌf/ *n* [C] **1** a stiff circular white collar, worn in Europe in the 16th century〔16 世紀歐洲人服飾的〕白色輪狀硬領 **2** a circle of feathers or fur around the neck of an animal or bird〔野獸的〕頸毛;〔鳥的〕頸羽

ruf·fi·an /ˈrʌfɪən; ˈrʌfiən/ *n* [C] *old-fashioned* a violent man, involved in crime【過時】流氓, 暴徒: *a gang of ruffians* 一夥流氓 —**ruffianly** *adj*

ruf·fle¹ /ˈrʌfl; ˈrʌfəl/ *v* [T] **1** also 又作 **ruffle up** to make a smooth surface uneven 把〔平整的表面〕弄亂, 弄皺, 使起伏不平: *Birds ruffle up their feathers for warmth.* 鳥把羽毛豎起來保暖。**2** to offend or upset someone slightly 使稍微生氣, 使有點不快: **ruffle sb's feelings/pride etc** *Louise's sharp comments had ruffled his pride.* 路易斯的尖鋭評論打擊了他的自尊心。| **get ruffled** *Some of the audience were shouting, and the speaker began to get ruffled.* 一些觀眾在大喊大叫, 演講者開始有點生氣了。| **ruffle sb's feathers** (=upset or annoy someone slightly) 使某人稍微不高興, 惹惱

ruffle² *n* [C] a band of thin cloth sewn in folds as a decoration around the edge of something such as a collar〔衣領等的〕褶邊, 飾邊; 褶飾

rug /rʌg; rʌg/ *n* [C] **1** a piece of thick cloth or wool that is smaller than a CARPET and is put on the floor as decoration 小地毯 —compare 比較 MAT¹ **2** *BrE* a large piece of material that you can wrap around yourself, especially when you are travelling【英】〔尤指旅行用的〕大毛毯 **3 pull the rug (out) from under sb's feet** *informal* to suddenly take away something that someone was depending on to achieve what they wanted【非正式】突然停止對某人的支持 **4** *humorous especially AmE* a TOUPÉE【幽默, 尤美】（男用）假髮

rugby (英式)橄欖球

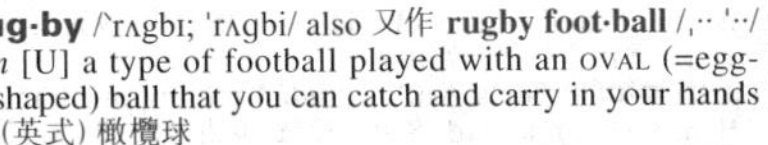

rug·by /ˈrʌgbɪ; ˈrʌgbi/ also 又作 **rugby foot·ball** /ˌ·· ˈ··/ *n* [U] a type of football played with an OVAL (=egg-shaped) ball that you can catch and carry in your hands（英式）橄欖球 [S3] [W3]

Rugby League /ˌ·· ˈ·/ *n* [U] a type of rugby played by teams of players who are usually paid for playing 橄欖球聯合會運動

Rugby U·nion /ˌ·· ˈ··/ *n* [U] a type of rugby played by teams of 15 players 橄欖球聯盟運動

rug·ged /ˈrʌgɪd; ˈrʌgʒd/ *adj* **1** land that is rugged is rough and uneven 不平的, 崎嶇的, 起伏的: *rugged terrain* 起伏的地形 | *a rugged coastline* 崎嶇不平的海岸線 **2** a rugged car or piece of equipment etc is strongly built and not likely to break easily; STURDY〔汽車、設備等〕堅固的, 結實的 **3** a man who is rugged is good-looking and has strong features which are often not perfect〔人〕相貌粗獷的: *Ann admired his rugged good looks.* 安喜歡他粗獷而英俊的容貌。**4** rugged behaviour is confident and determined but not always polite〔行為舉止〕自信而堅決的〔但有時有點粗魯的〕—**ruggedly** *adv* —**ruggedness** *n* [U]

rug·ger /ˈrʌgɚ; ˈrʌgə/ *n* [U] *BrE informal* Rugby Union【英, 非正式】橄欖球聯盟運動

ru·in¹ /ˈruɪn; ˈruːʒn/ *v* [T] **1** to spoil or destroy something completely〔完全地〕毀壞, 毀掉: *The rain ruined our holiday.* 這場雨把我們的假期毀了。| *My new white dress was totally ruined!* 我那件白色的新裙子全給毀了！—see 見 DESTROY (USAGE) **2** to make someone lose all their money 使破產: *Jefferson was ruined by the law suit.* 傑弗遜因那場官司而傾家蕩產。—**ruined** *adj* [only before noun 僅用於名詞前]: *ruined houses* 頹垣敗瓦的房屋 

ruin² *n* **1** [U] a situation in which you have lost all your money, your social position, or the good opinion that people had about you 破產; 垮台; 身敗名裂: **lead to sb's ruin** *Joe's rashness led ultimately to his ruin.* 喬的魯莽輕率最終葬送了自己。| **be on the road to ruin** (=be doing something that will make you lose your money, position etc) 正在走向毀滅〔做某事將會使自己破產、垮台等〕| **be on the brink of ruin** (=be about to lose all your money or your position) 瀕臨破產[垮台] *With the collapse of grain prices, small farmers are on the brink of financial ruin.* 穀物價格的暴跌使小農場主們陷於破產的邊緣。**2 be the ruin of** *humorous* to make someone lose all their money, their good health, the good opinion that other people have about them etc【幽默】使…破產[身體垮掉, 名譽掃地等]: *Drinking was the ruin of him.* 酗酒毀了他。**3** [C] also 又作 **ruins** [plural] the part of a building that is left after the rest has been destroyed 倒塌的建築物, 廢墟: *an interesting old ruin* 很有意思的古老廢墟 | *the ruins of a bombed-out office block* 被炸毀的辦公樓的廢墟 **4 the ruins of** the parts of something such as an organization, system, or set of ideas that remain after the rest have been destroyed〔組織、體制或思想〕的殘餘部分: *the ruins of the Welfare State in post Thatcher Britain* 英國後戴卓爾時期福利國家殘存的制度 **5 be/lie in ruins a)** if a building is in ruins it has fallen down or been badly damaged〔建築物〕傾塌了的, 破敗不堪的: *The castle now lies in ruins.* 那座城堡現在已成一片廢墟了。**b)** if someone's life, hopes, plans, or an organization is in ruins, they are having great problems and cannot continue〔人的生命、希望、計劃或組織有嚴重困難, 無法繼續而〕垮掉: *After the war the Japanese economy lay in ruins.* 戰後日本的經濟完全崩潰。**6 go to ruin** also 又作 **fall into ruin** if something goes to ruin it becomes damaged or destroyed because no one is taking care of it〔某物因缺乏照料而〕衰落, 敗落: *His brother had let the farm go to ruin.* 他的弟弟使農場走向破敗。—see also 另見 MOTHER'S RUIN, **go to rack and ruin** (RACK[1] (4))

ru·in·a·tion /ˌruɪˋeʃən; ˌru:ɪˈneɪʃən/ *n* [U] *old-fashioned or humorous* a situation in which someone or something is ruined, or the cause of this【過時或幽默】毀滅; 毀壞; 崩潰; 毀滅之原因, 禍根

ru·in·ous /ˈruɪnəs; ˈru:ɪnəs/ *adj* **1** costing much more than you can afford 導致破產的, 極昂貴的 **2** causing great destruction 招致極大破壞的: *ruinous civil war* 毀滅性的內戰 —**ruinously** *adv*: *ruinously expensive* 極其昂貴的

2 2 **rule¹** /rul; ru:l/ *n*

1 ▶INSTRUCTION 指示◀ [C] an official instruction that says how things must be done or what is allowed, especially in a game, organization, or job〔正式的〕規則; 章程; 條例〔尤用於遊戲、團體或工作〕: *the school rules* 校規 | **against the rules** *You can't come in if you're not a member – it's against the rules.* 非會員不得入內——這樣做違反規定。| **break the rules** (=disobey) 犯規 *There's a penalty if you break the rules.* 違反規則的話, 就要受到懲罰。| **stick to the rules** (=obey) 遵守規則 *I'm not going to play if you won't stick to the rules!* 如果你不遵守規則我就不玩了! | **bend/stretch the rules** (=say that on this occasion someone does not have to obey a particular rule) 變通執行規則, 通融 *We might be able to bend the rules just this one time.* 我們或許可以通融這一次。| **the rules that govern sth** (=the rules that say how something should be done) 行事規則 *changes to the rules governing international athletics* 國際田徑運動規則的變更 | **rules and regulations** *I'm sick of all their petty rules and regulations.* 我討厭他們那些瑣碎的規章制度。| **hard and fast rule** (=clear and definite rule) 清楚嚴格的規定 *There are no hard and fast rules about what to wear to classes.* 對於上課時的穿着沒有清楚嚴格的規定。| **unwritten rule** (=something that people usually expect you to do) 不成文規定 *an unwritten rule concerning being late for work* 關於上班遲到的不成文規定 | **rules are rules** *spoken* (=used to tell someone that rules must be obeyed)【口】規定就是規定〔告訴某人要遵守規則〕

2 ▶BEHAVIOUR 行為◀ [C] the way of behaving that is accepted as right by most people 習慣, 慣例: *the rules of etiquette* 禮儀習慣

3 ▶OF GRAMMAR/OF A SYSTEM 語法/系統的◀ [C] a statement about what is usually allowed in the grammar of a language, or according to a particular system 語法規則: *English grammar has very few rules that cannot be broken.* 英語語法很少有不能打破的規則。

4 ▶GOVERNMENT 政府◀ [U] the government of a country by a particular group of people or using a particular system 統治: *an end to over 200 years of French rule* 結束二百多年的法國統治 | *rule by a social elite* 社會精英的統治 | **under sb's rule** (=when someone is the leader of a country) 在…的統治下 *Britain prospered under Elizabeth's rule.* 英國在伊莉莎白女王的統治下繁榮昌盛。| **foreign rule** (=government by foreigners) 外國人的統治 | **majority rule** (=government by the political party that most people have voted for) 多數黨執政 *majority rule in South Africa* 南非的多數黨統治 | **the rule of law** (=a situation in which the people in a country obey the laws) 法治 *The rule of law had broken down and the army was sent in to restore order.* 法治崩潰後, 軍隊奉命恢復秩序。

5 ▶CONTROL 控制◀ [U] a system for controlling a group of people〔支配一羣人的〕體系: **[+by]** *rule by the gun* 軍人統治

6 as a (general) rule used to say that something usually happens or is usually true 通常, 一般來說: *As a rule most students finish their coursework by the end of May.* 一般來說, 大多數學生在五月底結束課程。

7 be the rule used to say that something is the usual situation 普遍情況: *It tends to be the rule that boys are more interested in cars than girls.* 普遍情況是, 男孩比女孩對汽車更有興趣。

8 sth is the exception, not the rule used to say that something is unusual 某事是例外, 不是常見的: *You do get some women in managerial positions, but it's the exception rather than the rule.* 的確有一些婦女擔任管理職務, 但這是例外, 不是常見的。

9 rule of thumb a rough method of calculation, based on practical experience〔根據實際經驗的〕粗略的計算方法: *As a rule of thumb, you'll pay £10 a month for each £100 you borrow.* 據經驗估計, 你所借的每100英鎊每月要償還10英鎊。

10 the rule is *spoken* used when advising someone what to do in a particular situation【口】慣例是…〔用於對人提出忠告〕: *The rule is: if you feel any pain you should stop exercising immediately.* 一般來説, 如果你感到疼痛, 就應立即停止鍛鍊。

11 make it a rule (to do sth) to try to make sure that you always do something 有做〔某事〕的習慣: *I generally make it a rule to be up by 7.* 我通常7點前起牀。

12 ▶FOR MEASURING 供度量用◀ [C] *old-fashioned* RULER (2)【過時】尺子, 直尺 —see also 另見 GOLDEN RULE, GROUND RULES, HOME RULE, SLIDE RULE, **work to rule** (WORK[1] (29))

rule² *v*

1 ▶GOVERNMENT 政府◀ [I,T] to have the official power to control a country and the people who live there 統治, 治理: *Queen Victoria ruled England for 64 years.* 維多利亞女王統治英國64年。| **[+over]** *Alexander the Great ruled over a large empire.* 亞歷山大大帝統治着一個龐大的帝國。

2 ▶CONTROL/INFLUENCE 控制/影響◀ [T] if a feeling or desire rules someone it has a powerful and controlling influence on their actions〔情感或慾望〕控制, 支配: *the passion for power and success which rules her life* 對權力和成功的慾望控制着她的一生

3 ▶COURT/LAW 法庭/法律◀ [I always+adv/prep,T] to make an official decision about something, especially a legal problem〔尤指對法律問題〕判定, 裁定: **rule that** *The judge ruled that she should have custody.* 法官判定她有監護權。| **[+on]** *The Supreme Court has yet to rule on the case.* 最高法院尚未裁定此案。| **rule in favour of** *The tribunal ruled in her favour.* 審理委員會作出了有利於她的裁決。—see also 另見 RULING[1]

4 let your heart rule your head to make decisions based on what you feel not what you think 感情用事

5 rule the roost *informal* to be the most powerful person in a group【非正式】當家作主, 支配一切: *It's his wife who*

rules the roost in their house. 他們家裡他妻子說了算。

6 rule sb with a rod of iron to control a group of people in a very severe way 實行嚴酷的高壓統治

7 sb rules an expression, often written on walls, used to say that the team, GANG etc mentioned is better than anyone else ...必勝〔寫在牆上的標語, 表示某隊等比其他優秀〕: *Arsenal rules OK.* 阿仙奴隊必勝。| *Midland High rules!* 米德蘭高中必勝!

8 ▶DRAW A LINE 劃線◀ [T] to draw a line using a ruler or other straight edge〔用尺子等〕劃線: *Rule a line under each answer.* 請在每一個答案下面劃一條線。

9 be ruled by sb *old-fashioned* to do what someone else tells you to do【過時】聽人擺佈 —see also 另見 OVERRULE

rule sth/sb ↔ **out** *phr v* [T] **1** to decide that something is not possible or suitable 排除, 拒絕考慮: *The police have ruled out suicide.* 警方已經排除了自殺的可能。**2** to make it impossible for something to happen 使〔某事〕不可能發生: *The mountainous terrain rules out most forms of agriculture.* 多山的地形使大多數形式的農業耕作無法進行。

rule·book /ˈrulˌbuk; ˈruːlbʊk/ *n* **1 go by the rulebook** *informal* to obey exactly the rules about how something should be done【非正式】按規則行事: *If we went by the rulebook I'd have to report this conversation.* 如果我們按照規則行事, 我就必須匯報這次談話。**2** [C] a book of rules, especially one that is given to workers in a job〔尤指給工人的〕規則手冊

ruled /ruld; ruːld/ *adj* ruled paper has parallel lines printed across it〔紙張〕有平行線條的

rul·er /ˈrulɚ; ˈruːlə/ *n* [C] **1** someone such as a King or Queen who has official power over a country or area 統治者 **2** a flat narrow piece of plastic, metal etc with straight edges, that you use for measuring things or drawing straight lines 尺子, 直尺: *a 12-inch ruler* 12英寸長的尺子

rul·ing¹ /ˈrulɪŋ; ˈruːlɪŋ/ *n* [C+**on**] an official decision, especially one made by a court〔尤指法庭的〕裁決, 裁定

ruling² *adj* [only before noun 僅用於名詞前] **1** the ruling group in a country or organization is the group that controls it〔在國家中〕執政的;〔在組織中〕起領導作用的 **2 sb's ruling passion** the thing that interests someone more than anything else 某人的最大樂趣: *The martial arts are Sandy's ruling passion.* 武術是桑迪最大的愛好。

rum¹ /rʌm; rʌm/ *n* [C,U] a strong alcoholic drink made from sugar, or a glass of this drink 朗姆酒〔一種由糖製成的酒精濃度高的酒〕; 一杯朗姆酒

rum² *adj old-fashioned* unusual or strange【過時】古怪的, 離奇的

rum·ba /ˈrʌmbə; ˈrʌmbə/ *n* [C,U] a popular dance from Cuba, or the music for this dance〔源於古巴的〕倫巴舞(曲)

rum·ble¹ /ˈrʌmbl̩; ˈrʌmbəl/ *v* **1** [I] to make a series of long low sounds, especially a long distance away from you 發出隆隆聲〔尤指來自遠處〕: *We could hear thunder rumbling in the distance.* 我們聽得見遠處雷聲轟鳴。**2** [I always+adv/prep] to move slowly while making this sound 緩慢而隆隆地行進: [**+along/past etc**] *A tank rumbled past.* 一輛坦克隆隆駛過。**3** if your stomach rumbles, it makes a noise, especially because you are hungry〔肚子因飢餓〕發出轆轆聲 **4** [T] *informal especially BrE* to find out what someone is secretly intending to do【非正式, 尤英】發現〔某人祕密的企圖〕: *We've been rumbled; someone must have told the police.* 我們已經被發現了, 一定是有人告訴了警察。

rumble² *n* [singular] a series of long low sounds 隆隆聲, 轟轟聲: *the rumble of distant gunfire* 遠處隆隆的砲聲

rum·bling /ˈrʌmblɪŋ; ˈrʌmblɪŋ/ *n* **1 rumblings** comments that show that people are starting to become annoyed, or that a difficult situation is developing 不滿的言論, 抱怨: *rumblings of discontent* 怨聲載道 **2** [C usually singular 一般用單數] a rumbling noise 隆隆聲, 轟轟聲

ru·mi·nant /ˈrumənənt; ˈruːmɪnənt/ *n* [C] *technical* an animal such as a cow that has several stomachs and eats grass【術語】反芻動物〈例如牛〉

ru·mi·nate /ˈruməˌnet; ˈruːmɪneɪt/ *v* [I] **1** *formal* to think for a long time about something【正式】沉思, 反覆思考: [**+about/on etc**] *He sat ruminating on the answer he'd been given.* 他坐在那裡, 反覆思考得到的答案。**2** *technical* if animals such as cows ruminate, they bring food back into their mouths from their stomachs and CHEW it again【術語】〔動物〕反芻 —**rumination** /ˌruməˈneʃən; ˌruːmɪˈneɪʃən/ *n* [C,U]

rum·mage¹ /ˈrʌmɪdʒ; ˈrʌmɪdʒ/ *v* [I always+adv/prep] also 又作 **rummage around** to search for something by moving things around in a careless way 翻找, 亂翻: [**+in/through etc**] *Looks like someone's been rummaging around in my desk.* 看來有人翻過我的書桌。

rummage² *n* **1 have a rummage** *informal* to rummage【非正式】翻找, 亂翻 **2** [U] *especially AmE* old clothes, toys etc that you no longer want【尤美】〔舊衣物、舊玩具等〕無用的東西; JUMBLE¹ (2) *BrE*【英】

rummage sale /ˈ.. ˌ./ *n* [C] *AmE* an event at which old clothes, toys etc are sold as a way of getting money, for example to help a school or church【美】舊雜物的義賣〔如為資助學校或教堂〕; JUMBLE SALE *BrE*【英】

rum·my /ˈrʌmɪ; ˈrʌmi/ *n* [U] a simple card game 拉米紙牌遊戲

ru·mour *BrE*【英】, **rumor** *AmE*【美】/ˈrumɚ; ˈruːmə/ *n* [U] information that is passed from one person to another and which may or may not be true, especially about someone's personal life or about an official decision 流言, 謠言, 謠傳: [**+about/of**] *I've heard all sorts of rumors about him and his secretary.* 我聽說了有關他和他的祕書的各種傳聞。| [**+that**] *There's a rumour going around that Eddie's bankrupt.* 埃迪破產的謠言正四處流傳。| **rumour has it (that)** (=there is a rumour that) 據謠傳 *Rumour has it that Jean's getting married again.* 傳說瓊又要結婚了。

ru·moured *BrE*【英】, **rumored** *AmE*【美】/ˈrumɚd; ˈruːməd/ *adj* if something is rumoured to be true, people are saying secretly or unofficially that it may be true 傳聞的, 謠傳的: **it is rumoured that** *It was rumoured that Johnson had been poisoned.* 謠傳約翰遜被毒死了。| **be rumoured to be sth** *She was rumoured to be a millionaire.* 據說她家財百萬。| **widely rumoured** *a young man widely rumoured to be her lover* 盛傳是她情人的小伙子

ru·mour·mon·ger *BrE*【英】, **rumormonger** *AmE*【美】/ˈrumɚˌmʌŋgɚ; ˈruːməˌmʌŋgə/ *n* [C] someone who tells other people rumours 散佈謠言的人, 造謠的人

rump /rʌmp; rʌmp/ *n* **1** [C] the part of an animal's back that is just above its legs〔動物的〕臀部 **2 rump steak** meat that comes from this part of a cow 後腿肉牛排 **3** [C] *humorous* the part of your body that you sit on; BOTTOM¹ (7)【幽默】〔人的〕臀部 **4** *BrE* [singular] the part of a group or government that remains after most of the other members have left【英】殘餘分子, 餘黨

rum·ple /ˈrʌmpl̩; ˈrʌmpəl/ *v* [T] to make hair, clothes etc less tidy 把〔頭髮、衣服等〕弄亂, 弄皺 —**rumpled** *adj*: *rumpled sheets* 皺了的牀單

rum·pus /ˈrʌmpəs; ˈrʌmpəs/ *n* [singular] *informal* a lot of noise, especially made by people quarrelling【非正式】爭吵, 喧鬧: *There's a real rumpus going on upstairs.* 樓上正吵得不可開交。

rumpus room /ˈ.. ˌ./ *n* [C] *AmE* a room in a house that is used by the family for games, parties etc【美】〔家庭的〕聚會室, 遊藝室, 娛樂室

rump·y pump·y /ˌrʌmpɪ ˈpʌmpɪ; ˌrʌmpi ˈpʌmpi/ *n* [U] *BrE humorous* sexual activity【英, 幽默】性行為

R

run¹ /rʌn; rʌn/ *v past tense* **ran** /ræn; ræn/ *past participle* **run** *present participle* **running**

① MOVE QUICKLY ON FOOT 奔跑
② CONTROL/BE IN CHARGE OF 控制/掌管
③ MACHINES/SYSTEMS 機器/系統
④ CARS/TRAINS/BOATS ETC 汽車/火車/船等
⑤ WATER/LIQUIDS 水/液體
⑥ CONTINUE 繼續
⑦ HAPPEN/TAKE PLACE 發生
⑧ TOUCH/RUB A SURFACE 接觸/磨擦表面
⑨ THOUGHTS/FEELINGS 思想/感情
⑩ ROADS/FENCES ETC 道路/籬笆等
⑪ COLOUR/PAINT 顏色/油漆
⑫ NOT ENOUGH/NONE LEFT 不足/沒有剩餘
⑬ BECOME UNCONTROLLED 失去控制
⑭ DO/ARRANGE STH 做/安排某事
⑮ OTHER MEANINGS 其他意思

① MOVE QUICKLY ON FOOT 奔跑

1 [I] to move quickly on foot by moving your legs more quickly than when you are walking 跑, 奔跑: *I had to run to catch the bus.* 我不得不跑着去趕那輛公共汽車。| *Two youths were killed when running to help people injured in the bomb blast.* 兩個年輕人跑過去救助被炸彈炸傷的人時喪生。| [+adv/prep] *Each morning we ran down to the harbour to see the previous night's catch.* 每天早晨我們都跑去港口觀看前一天夜裡的魚穫。| **run for cover** (=run in order to find shelter or protection) 跑着找掩蔽物 *Suddenly shots rang out, and we had to run for cover.* 突然響起了槍聲, 我們不得不跑着尋找躲避之處。| **run for your life** (=in order to avoid being killed) 逃命 *Hundreds ran for their lives from the burning building.* 數以百計的人從着火的大樓裡跑出來逃命。

2 ►IN A RACE 賽跑中◄ **a)** [I,T] to take part in a running race 參加(賽跑): *I'd never run a marathon before.* 我以前從未參加過馬拉松比賽。| **[+in]** *Are you running in the 100 metres?* 你參加100米賽跑嗎? **b)** [T] to hold a race 舉行〔比賽〕: *The Derby will be run at 3 o'clock.* 打比馬賽將於3點鐘舉行。

3 run for it *spoken* to run as quickly as possible in order to escape【口】趕快逃跑: *Police – quick, run for it!* 警察——快跑!

4 run and fetch/get/do sth *spoken* used to ask a child to get or do something quickly for you【口】快去取/拿/幹某事〔用於要求孩子給你做事〕: *Run and tell your father supper's ready.* 快去告訴你爸爸晚飯好啦。

5 run along *spoken* used to tell a child to go away【口】走開〔用於要求孩子〕: *Run along now, all of you, I'm busy.* 你們都走開, 我忙着呢。

② CONTROL/BE IN CHARGE OF 控制/掌管

6 [T] to control or be in charge of a company, an organization, or system 控制〔一個公司、機構或系統〕, 支配, 管理, 經營: *For a while, she ran a restaurant in Boston.* 她在波士頓開了一段時間餐館。| *Many people belong to a pension scheme run by their employers.* 許多人參加了由雇主管理的養老金計劃。| **well/badly run** (=organized efficiently/inefficiently) 經營良好/不好 *A well-run company should not have problems of this kind.* 一家經營良好的公司不應該有這種問題。| **state-run** (=controlled and paid for by the state) 國營的 *a state-run airline* 國營航空公司 —see 見 CONTROL² (USAGE)

7 run sb's life *informal* to keep telling someone what they should do all the time, in a way that they find annoying【非正式】不斷指使某人〔令對方討厭〕: *Don't try to run my life!* 不要試圖主宰我的生活!

③ MACHINES/SYSTEMS 機器/系統

8 ►MACHINES 機器◄ [I] if a machine runs, it operates 運轉, 開動: *Don't touch the engine while it's running.* 發動機運轉的時候不要去碰它。| **run on electricity/gas/unleaded petrol etc** (=get its power from electricity etc) 以電/汽油/無鉛汽油等為動力 | **run smoothly** (=operate with all its parts working exactly as they should) 運轉正常 *My car's not running too smoothly at the moment.* 我的汽車現在開起來有點不順暢。

9 ►COMPUTERS 電腦◄ [I,T] to operate a computer PROGRAM¹ (1) (使)〔電腦程序〕運行: *The RS8 system runs both Unix and MPX-32.* RS8系統運行Unix和MPX-32。

10 up and running working fully and correctly 全面而正確地展開工作: *The new system won't be up and running until next week.* 新的系統要到下週才能完全投入使用。

④ CARS/TRAINS/BOATS ETC 汽車/火車/船等

11 ►PUBLIC TRANSPORT 公共交通◄ **a)** [I] if a bus, train etc service runs, it takes people from one place to another at fixed times of the day〔公共汽車、火車等〕定時行駛: *The buses don't run on Sundays.* 公共汽車星期天停駛。**b)** [T] if someone runs a bus, train etc service, they make it operate 經營〔公共汽車、火車等〕: *They're running special trains to and from the exhibition.* 他們經營去展覽會的往返火車專線。

12 ►FAST/OUT OF CONTROL 快速/失控◄ [I always+adv/prep] to move too fast or in an uncontrolled way 過於快速移動, 失控: **[+into/down/through etc]** *The truck ran downhill at a frightening speed.* 卡車以驚人的速度向山下衝去。| *Her car ran into a tree.* 她的汽車撞到了樹上。

13 run aground/ashore if a ship runs aground, it cannot move because the water is not deep enough〔船隻〕擱淺: *An oil tanker has run aground near the Valdez oil terminal.* 一艘油輪在瓦爾迪茲石油集散碼頭附近擱淺。

14 run a car to pay for all the things that are needed to keep a car working 養車〔指為保持一輛汽車處於工作狀態而支付所有必要費用〕: *I can't really afford to run a car.* 我的確養不起車。

15 run sb home/to the station etc *informal* to take someone somewhere in your car【非正式】用汽車把某人送到家/車站等: *Shall I run you home?* 要我開車送你回家嗎?

⑤ WATER/LIQUIDS 水/液體

16 [I always+adv/prep] to flow in a particular direction or place〔向特定方向或地方〕流動: **[+down/along etc]** *Big tears ran down Stephanie's face.* 大顆的眼淚順着斯蒂芬尼的臉頰往下流。| *A stream ran through the* garden. 一條小溪流過花園。

17 ▶TAP 龍頭◀ [I] if a TAP (=thing for controlling the supply of water) is running, there is water coming out of it〔水從龍頭〕流出: *Did you leave the kitchen faucet running?* 你是不是忘了關廚房的水龍頭?

18 run a bath to fill a bath with water 把〔浴缸〕放滿水: **run sb a bath** *Could you run me a nice hot bath while I finish my meal?* 你能不能在我吃飯時給我放上一浴缸熱水?

19 ▶SB'S NOSE 某人的鼻子◀ [I] if someone's nose is running, liquid is flowing out of it 流鼻涕

⑥ CONTINUE 繼續

20 ▶OFFICIAL PAPERS 官方文件◀ [I] to continue to be officially able to be used for a particular period of time 有效, 可以合法使用: *The contract runs for a year.* 合同有效期為一年。| *My car insurance only has another month to run.* 我的汽車保險期只剩一個月了。

21 ▶PLAY/FILM 戲劇/電影◀ [I] to continue being performed regularly in one place〔在某處〕定期上演: *The play ran for two years.* 那個劇連續演了兩年。

22 ▶STORY/ACCOUNT ETC 故事/敍述等◀ [I] to continue in a particular way〔以特有的方式〕繼續: *I forget now how the story runs.* 我現在不記得故事怎麼發展的了。

23 run its course to continue in the expected way until finished 聽其自然發展〔直至結束〕: *Wait until the illness has run its course.* 等到病自己好吧。

24 this one will run and run *BrE humorous* used to say that you think a problem, joke etc will continue for a long time【英, 幽默】〔問題、玩笑等〕將持續很長時間

⑦ HAPPEN/TAKE PLACE 發生

25 [I] to happen or take place, especially in the way that was intended〔尤指按照預想計劃〕發生: **run according to plan** (=happen in the way that you had planned) 按計劃進行 *So far, it had all run exactly according to plan.* 到目前為止, 一切都完全按照計劃進行。| **run smoothly** (=happen with no unexpected problems) 運作順利 *Her job is to ensure university catering runs smoothly.* 她的職責是確保辦好大學的伙食供應服務。

⑧ TOUCH/RUB A SURFACE 接觸/磨擦表面

26 [T always+adv/prep] to move or rub something lightly along a surface〔在表面〕輕輕移動, 輕擦: **run sth down/through/along** *Charles ran his fingers through her hair.* 查爾斯用手指攏了攏她的頭髮。

⑨ THOUGHTS/FEELINGS 思想/感情

27 [I always+adv/prep] if thoughts or feelings run through you, you experience them suddenly 突然而來, 掠過: **[+through/down etc]** *The same thought kept running through his mind.* 同一想法一直在他腦海裡縈迴。| *I felt a sharp pain run down my leg.* 我感到一陣劇痛傳遍我的腿。

28 be running high if feelings are running high, people are becoming angry or upset about something〔情緒〕激動, 不安: *Feelings at the game were running high.* 比賽場上情緒激動。

⑩ ROADS/FENCES ETC 道路/籬笆等

29 [I always+adv/prep] to exist in a particular place or continue in a particular direction 存在於某處; 朝某方向延伸: **[+along/through etc]** *The road runs along a valley.* 這條路沿着山谷延伸。

⑪ COLOUR/PAINT 顏色/油漆

30 [I] if colour runs, it spreads from one area of cloth to another, when the cloth is wet〔濕織物上的顏色〕褪色: *The colour ran when I washed your red shirt, and now all your socks are pink!* 你的紅襯衣洗的時候掉色了, 現在你的襪子全都成了粉紅色!

31 [I] if paint runs, it moves onto an area where you did not intend it to go〔油漆〕流到別處, 擴散

⑫ NOT ENOUGH/NONE LEFT 不足/沒有剩餘

32 be running short (of sth) to have very little of something left〔某物〕沒剩多少,〔某物〕快用完: *I'm running short of cash – do you think you could lend me some?* 我的現金快用完了——你能否借給我一些?

33 time is running short used to say that there is little time left 時間不多了: *Time was already running short.* 剩下的時間已經不多了。

34 be running low (on sth) to have very little left of something that you normally keep a supply of〔正常的供應〕快用完, 不足: *We're running low on fuel again.* 我們的燃料又快用完了。

35 run dry if a river or WELL (=hole in the ground for getting water) runs dry, there is no water left in it〔河流或水井〕乾涸: *The drought was so severe that even the well ran dry.* 乾旱十分嚴重, 連井都乾涸了。

⑬ BECOME UNCONTROLLED 失去控制

36 run wild to behave in an uncontrolled way 放肆, 撒野: *Since their mother left, those children have been running wild.* 媽媽出門後, 那些孩子一直在撒野。

37 run rife to spread quickly in an uncontrolled way 迅速蔓延: *Disease is running rife in the shanty towns.* 疾病在貧民區迅速蔓延。

38 run riot a) if people run riot, they start to behave in a violent or uncontrolled way 粗暴, 不受控制: *Angry demonstrators ran riot through the town.* 憤怒的示威者發瘋似地在市區到處鬧事。**b)** if feelings run riot, they increase quickly in a way that you cannot control〔感情〕約束不住: *Let your imagination run riot.* 讓你的想像力自由馳騁吧。

⑭ DO/ARRANGE STH 做/安排某事

39 run a check/test on to arrange for something or someone to be checked or tested 安排對…的檢查/測試: *A check had to be run on all participants, for security reasons.* 出於安全理由, 需要對所有參與者進行檢查。| *We'd better run a test on all the equipment before we begin.* 開始前我們最好測試一下所有設備。

40 run an errand a) to go to a shop, office etc in order to buy, do, or get something for someone else〔給某人〕跑腿: *a boy running errands for his mother* 一個給媽媽跑腿的男孩 **b)** *AmE* to go to a shop, office etc to buy or get something that you need【美】〔去商店、辦公室等〕採購, 辦事: *I have a few errands to run downtown.* 我在城裡有幾件事要辦。

⑮ OTHER MEANINGS 其他意思

41 ▶IN AN ELECTION 選舉中◀ [I] to try to be elected in an election; STAND¹ (41) 競選: **[+for]** *Bob Dole's running for President.* 鮑伯·多爾在競選總統。| **[+against]** *The Democrats chose Mondale to run against Reagan.* 民主黨人選派蒙代爾與列根競選。

42 ▶HOLE IN CLOTHES 衣物上的洞◀ [I] if a hole in TIGHTS, STOCKINGS etc runs, it gets bigger in a straight line〔褲襪、長統襪等〕脱線, 抽絲

43 run drugs/guns to bring drugs or guns into a country illegally in order to sell them 走私毒品/槍支 —see also 另見 DRUG RUNNER, GUN-RUNNING

44 run a story/feature/article to print a story etc in a newspaper or magazine〔在報紙或雜誌上〕刊登消息/特寫/文章: *The editor decided at the last minute not to run the story.* 在最後一刻編輯決定不登這則消息。

45 run in the family if something such as a quality, disease, or skill runs in the family, many people in that family have it 家族遺傳, 具有家族特徵: *Karen's very good at music too – it runs in the family.* 卡琳也非常擅

長音樂, 這是家族遺傳。

46 run a temperature/fever to have a body temperature that is higher than normal, because you are ill 發燒: *She's running a temperature of a 102°.* 她發燒102華氏度。

47 run a mile *informal* to try very hard to avoid a situation, person, or place, because you find them frightening or embarrassing【非正式】〔對令人驚慌或尷尬的情況、人或地方〕盡量避而遠之: *She's so shy that if a man ever spoke to her I think she'd run a mile!* 她很害羞, 如果有男人和她說話, 我看她一定會躲得遠遠的!

48 be running late to be doing everything later than planned or expected 比計劃[預期]的晚: *They were running late, so I didn't get interviewed until nearly 4 o'clock.* 他們晚了, 所以我差不多4點才面試。

49 be running scared to have become worried about the power of an enemy or opponent 擔心〔敵人或對手的力量〕, 煩惱: *Their new software has the competition running scared.* 他們的新軟件使競爭對手坐立不安。

50 come running a) *informal* to respond in a very eager way when someone asks or tells you to do something【非正式】熱心〔做別人要自己做的事〕: *He thinks he's only got to crook his finger and I'll come running.* 他以為他只要彎彎手指, 我就會迫不及待地給他幹。**b)** *especially spoken* to ask someone for help, advice, or sympathy when you have a problem【尤口】請求幫助[指點, 同情]: **[+to]** *Well I warned you, so don't come running to me when it all goes wrong!* 我警告過你的, 所以出了問題別來求我!

51 run your eyes over *informal* to look quickly at something【非正式】掃視, 瀏覽: *Could you run your eyes over my report before I turn it in?* 我把報告交上去之前, 你能看一下嗎?

52 run that by me again *spoken* used to ask someone to explain something again, because you did not completely understand【口】請再解釋一下 —see also 另見 RUNNING, **run amok** (AMOK), **make your blood run cold** (BLOOD¹ (5)), **run counter to** (COUNTER³), **cut and run** (CUT¹ (30)), **run deep** (DEEP¹ (5)), **run sb/sth to earth** (EARTH¹ (13)), **run to fat** (FAT² (6)), **run the gauntlet** (GAUNTLET (5)), **run sb to ground** (GROUND¹ (22)), **run rings around** (RING¹ (8)), **run to seed** (SEED¹ (3))

run across sb/sth *phr v* [T] to meet or find someone or something by chance 與…不期而遇, 偶然碰見: *I ran across an old friend last week.* 上星期我偶然碰見了一個老朋友。

run after sb/sth *phr v* [T] **1** to chase someone or something 追逐, 追趕: *Her dog was running after a rabbit.* 她的狗在追趕一隻兔子。**2** *informal* to try to get someone's attention, especially because you are sexually attracted to them【非正式】〔因愛慕而〕追求 **3** *spoken* to do many small jobs for someone, like a servant【口】伺候, 服侍: *I can't keep running after you all day!* 我不能整天跟着伺候你!

run around *phr v* [I] **1** to run in an area, without a definite direction or purpose 到處跑: *The children were running around in the garden.* 孩子們在花園裡跑來跑去。**2 run around with sb** to spend a lot of time with someone, especially in a way that other people disapprove of 常與某人混在一起, 廝混: *Is it true that she's been running around with an older man?* 她和一個歲數較大的男人混在一起, 這是真的嗎? **3** *informal* to be very busy doing many small jobs【非正式】忙於瑣事: *At fifty, I didn't want to be running around making bottles and changing diapers.* 五十歲時, 我不想再忙忙碌碌地沖牛奶和換尿布了。—see also 另見 RUNAROUND

run away *phr v* [I] **1** to leave a place, especially secretly, in order to escape from someone or something 〔祕密地〕逃跑: **[+from]** *Toby ran away from home at the age of 14.* 托比14歲時離家出走。| *They ran away together to get married.* 他們私奔結了婚。—see also 另見 RUNAWAY **2** to try to avoid a problem or difficult situation because it is unpleasant or embarrassing 逃避問題[困局]: *You've got to stop running away, and learn to face your problems.* 你不能再逃避了, 要學會面對問題。

run away with sb/sth *phr v* [T] **1 run away with you** if your feelings, ideas etc run away with you, they start to control how you behave because you can no longer think in a sensible way〔感情、思想等〕控制住〔某人〕, 使按捺不住: *Don't let your imagination run away with you!* 不要想入非非! **2** to leave a place secretly or illegally with someone else 帶着〔某人〕潛逃; 和〔某人〕私奔: *He ran away with the boss's wife.* 他和老闆的妻子私奔了。**3 run away with the idea/impression that** *spoken* to think that something is true when it is not【口】誤有…想法/印象: *Don't run away with the idea that this is going to be easy!* 別以為這會是輕而易舉的事。**4** *informal* to win a competition or sports game very easily【非正式】輕易贏得〔比賽〕: *The Reds ran away with the championship.* 紅隊輕易地奪得冠軍。**5** to steal something 偷竊: *They found that the treasurer had run away with the proceeds.* 他們發現財務主管捲款逃走了。

run down *phr v* **1** [T **run** sb/sth ↔ **down**] to drive into a person or animal and kill or injure them〔開車〕撞死[撞傷]: *Their daughter was run down by a car just outside their house.* 他們的女兒就在他們的房子外面被車撞倒。**2** [T **run** sb/sth ↔ **down**] *informal* to say things that are rude, unpleasant, or unfair about someone or something【非正式】指責, 非難: *Paula's jealous of you – that's why she keeps running you down.* 葆拉妒忌你, 所以她老派你的不是。| *Don't run yourself down!* 不要自咎! **3** [I] if a clock, machine, BATTERY etc runs down, it has no more power and stops working〔鐘、機器因缺乏動力〕停了;〔電池〕用完了 **4** [T **run** sth ↔ **down**] to let a company, organization etc gradually become smaller or stop working 使〔公司、機構等的規模〕逐漸縮減, 使逐漸停辦: *The coal industry is being slowly run down.* 煤炭工業在慢慢衰退。**5** [T **run** sb/sth ↔ **down**] to find someone or something after searching for a long time〔經過長時間尋找而〕發現; 找到: *I finally ran him down at his new office in Glendale.* 最後我是在格蘭代爾他的新辦公室裡找到他的。—see also 另見 RUNDOWN, RUN-DOWN

run sb/sth ↔ **in** *phr v* [T] **1** *old-fashioned* if the police run a criminal in, they catch them; ARREST¹ (1)【過時】〔警察〕抓獲〔罪犯〕, 逮捕 **2** if you run in a new car, you drive it slowly and carefully at first〔小心慢慢地〕試開新車

run into sb/sth *phr v* [T] **1** to hit someone or something with a car or other vehicle〔汽車〕撞上: *His car skidded and ran into a lamp-post.* 他的車打滑, 撞到一根路燈柱上。**2** *informal* to meet someone by chance【非正式】偶然遇見: *Guess who I ran into in town today!* 猜猜今天我在城裡碰見了誰! **3 run into difficulties/problems/debt etc** to start to experience difficulties 遇到困難/問題; 負債等: *After a promising start, the company ran into trouble.* 公司起初很有生氣, 但之後便陷入了困境。**4 run into hundreds/thousands etc** to reach an amount of several hundred, several thousand etc 累計達到數百/數千等: *By now they had debts running into thousands of pounds.* 目前他們的債務達到了幾千英鎊。**5** if something such as a word, colour etc runs into another word, colour etc, it joins it or mixes with it so that it is difficult to separate them〔詞、顏色等〕混合在一起〔難以分辨〕**6 run sth into the ground a)** to use something so much that you destroy it〔因使用太多〕把某物用壞: *We ran that Chevrolet right into the ground.* 我們把那輛雪佛萊汽

R

車一直用到報廢。**b)** to talk about a subject so much that there is nothing more left to say 把〔某個話題的〕話都談盡

run off *phr v* **1** [I] to leave a place or person in a way that people disapprove of 逃跑, 離棄: *Amy's husband had run off and left her with two children to bring up.* 愛米的丈夫棄家而去, 留下她撫養兩個孩子。**2** [T **run** sth ↔ **off**] to quickly print several copies of something 快速印出: *Shall I run off some more of those notices for you on the photocopier?* 要不要我用複印機給你再複印幾份通知? **3** [T **run** sth **off**] to write a speech, poem, piece of music etc quickly and easily 迅速地寫出〔演講稿、詩、樂譜等〕: *He could run off a comedy monologue in half an hour.* 他可以在半小時內很快寫出一篇喜劇獨白。**4 be run off your feet** to be so busy that you do not have time to stop or rest 忙得腳不沾地, 疲於奔命 **5 run off at the mouth** *AmE informal* to talk too much【美, 非正式】話多, 喋喋不休 **6** [T **run** sth ↔ **off**] to get rid of weight by running 通過跑步減輕〔體重〕: *I'm trying to run off some of my excess fat!* 我正努力跑步減肥!

run off with sth/sb *phr v* [T] *informal*【非正式】**1** to go away somewhere with someone, because you are having a sexual relationship that people do not approve of 與…私奔: *Liz shocked us all by running off with a married man.* 莉茲與一個有婦之夫私奔了, 使我們都感到震驚。**2** to take something without permission 偷走, 拐走: *Then I found that he had run off with all my savings.* 這時我才發現, 他已帶着我的全部積蓄逃走了。

run on *phr v* [I] to continue happening for longer than expected or planned 持續〔超出預定的時間〕: *The lecture ran on until 11 o'clock.* 講座一直持續到11點。

run out *phr v* **1** [I] to use all of something and not have any of it left 用完, 耗盡〔某東西〕: [**+of**] *The truck's run out of gas again.* 卡車的汽油又用完了。**2** [I] if food, money etc runs out, there is none left 〔食物、金錢等〕用完, 沒有了: *Our supplies soon ran out.* 我們的補給很快就用盡了。| *My patience was running out.* 我有點忍無可忍了。**3** [I] if an agreement, official document etc runs out, it reaches the end of the period when it is officially allowed to continue; EXPIRE (1)〔協議、正式文件等〕期滿, 到期: *My contract runs out in September.* 我的合同九月份期滿。**4 run out on** to leave someone, when you should not 離開〔某人〕, 遺棄: *He ran out on his second wife two years later.* 兩年以後他遺棄了他第二任妻子。**5 run out of steam** *informal*【非正式】also 又作 **run out of gas** *AmE*【美】to have no energy or eagerness left for something that you are trying to do 泄氣, 對…提不起勁[失去熱情]: *The whole team seemed to have run out of gas.* 全隊似乎都失去了熱情。**6 run**

run out 用完

sb out of town *old-fashioned* to force someone to leave a place, because they have done something wrong【過時】〔把做錯事的人〕趕走, 逐出 **7** [T **run** sb ↔ **out**] to end a player's INNINGS in CRICKET (2) by hitting the stumps (STUMP¹ (4)) with the ball while they are running〔板球比賽中以球觸三門柱〕使〔正在奔跑的擊球手〕出局

run over *phr v* **1** [T **run** sb/sth ↔ **over**] to hit someone or something with a car or other vehicle, and drive over them〔開車〕輾過, 壓過: *He was run over by a bus and killed.* 他被公共汽車輾死了。**2** [T **run over** sth] to explain or practise something again 反覆解釋, 練習, 排練: *Could we just run over the section on verbs again?* 我們把有關動詞的部分再練習一遍好嗎? **3** [T **run over** sth] to think about a series of events, possibilities etc 思考〔一連串事件、可能等〕: *I ran over the options in my mind.* 我把各種選擇一一作了考慮。**4** [I] also 又作 **run over time** to continue past the arranged time 超過時間: *The meeting ran over, and I was late for lunch.* 會議散得晚, 我吃午飯遲了。**5** [I] if a container runs over, there is so much liquid inside that some flows out; OVERFLOW〔容器〕滿溢,〔液體〕溢出

run through *phr v* [T] **1** [**run through** sth] to repeat something so that you remember it or get better at it 複習; 反覆練習, 排練: *Let's run through the first scene again.* 讓我們再排練一遍第一場。**2** [**run through** sth] to read, look at, or explain something quickly 匆匆閱讀[瀏覽, 解釋]: *I'll just run through the figures with you.* 我們很快地把這些數字看一遍。**3** [**run through** sth] to be present in many parts of something or continue through it, for example in an artist's work or in a society 貫穿於…之中: *This theme runs through the whole book.* 該主題貫穿全書。| *a fundamental problem running right through our society* 我們社會普遍存在的根本問題 **4** [**run** sb **through**] *literary* to push a sword completely through someone【文】〔用劍〕把〔某人〕刺穿 —see also 另見 RUN-THROUGH

run to sth *phr v* [T] **1** to reach a particular amount 達到〔一定數量〕: *The damages awarded by the court could easily run to one billion pounds.* 法院判付的賠償費不難達到十億英鎊。**2** *BrE* to be enough money to pay for something, or have enough money for it【英】〔錢〕足夠做某事: *My wages won't run to a new car.* 我的工資買不起一輛新車。

run sth ↔ **up** *phr v* [T] **1 run up a bill/expenses/debts** to use a lot of something or borrow a lot of money, so that you will have to pay a lot of money 積欠大量賬款/花費/債務: *She ran up an enormous phone bill.* 她積欠下很多電話費。**2** to make something, especially clothes, very quickly 趕製〔尤指衣服〕: *I ran this dress up in a single evening.* 我用了一個晚上趕做出這件衣服。**3** to raise a flag on a pole 升旗

run up against sth/sb *phr v* [T] to have to deal with unexpected problems or a difficult opponent 碰到〔突如其來的問題或難應付的對手〕: *We ran up against some unexpected opposition.* 我們遭到了意想不到的反對。

2
2
run² *n*

1 ►ON FOOT 跑, 跑步◄ [C] a period of time spent running, or a distance that you run 跑步的時間[距離]: *a 5-mile run* 五英里賽跑 | **go for a run** (=for exercise or pleasure) 跑步 *She usually goes for a run before breakfast.* 她通常在早飯前跑步。| **break into a run** (=start running) 開始跑 *He was still following me, and in a panic I broke into a run.* 他仍然尾隨着我, 慌亂中我拔腿就跑。| **at a run** (=running) 跑着 *Sarah left the house at a run.* 莎拉跑着離開了房子。

2 be on the run a) to be trying to escape or hide, especially from the police〔尤指為逃避警察而〕逃跑, 躲藏: *A dangerous criminal is on the run in the bay area of the city.* 一名危險的罪犯潛逃在該市的海灣區。**b)** if an army or an opponent is on the run, they may soon be defeated〔軍隊或對手〕行將失敗

3 make a run for it to suddenly start running, in order to escape 突然逃跑: *One of the prisoners made a run for it.* 一名囚犯突然逃跑。

4 in the long run later in the future, not immediately 從長遠來看, 終究: *The less you rely on painkillers now, the better it will be for your health in the long run.* 從長遠來看, 你現在越少依賴止痛片, 對你的健康越有益。

5 in the short run in the near future 從短期來看, 不久: *Economies like these save money in the short run, but in the end you'll be no better off.* 像這樣節省從短期來看

能省錢, 但到頭來你不會更富有。

6 a run of good/bad luck several lucky or unlucky things happening quickly after each other 一連串的好運/倒霉事: *Losing my job was the start of a run of bad luck that year.* 那一年, 失業是我碰到的一連串倒霉事的開始。

7 a run of failures/wins/strikes etc a series of failures, wins etc 一連串的失敗/勝利/打擊等: *The company has had a run of spectacularly successful years.* 這家公司一連幾年業績輝煌。

8 a run on a situation in which lots of people suddenly buy a particular product 搶購: *There's been a big run on ice-cream during this hot weather.* 天氣炎熱, 冰淇淋銷量激增。

9 have the run of to be allowed to use a place when and how you want 可以隨意使用〔某地方〕: *I had the run of the house for the afternoon.* 下午我可以隨意使用那所房子。

10 in the normal run of events used when saying what usually happens 按照一般情況, 通常: *In the normal run of events, I would never have gone there.* 按照一般情況, 我是決不會去那裡的。

11 have a (good) run for your money *informal* if you have a good run for your money, you have succeeded in doing something for an unusually long time or you have been unusually successful【非正式】該滿足了〔用於表示某人的成功比一般長久或巨大〕: *He lived to be 92, so I think he had a good run for his money.* 他活到92歲, 我想他應該滿足了。

12 give sb a good run for their money to play well in a competition or sports game, so that your opponent has to use all their skill and effort to defeat you 讓對手竭盡全力才獲勝: *They beat us, but we certainly gave them a good run for their money.* 他們打敗了我們, 不過是費盡九牛二虎之力才贏的。

13 ►ILLNESS 疾病◄ **the runs** *informal* DIARRHOEA (=an illness that makes you need to go to the toilet often)【非正式】腹瀉, 拉肚子

14 ►PLAY/FILM 戲劇/電影◄ [C] a continuous series of performances of a play, film etc in the same place〔在相同地方〕連續演出: *His first play had a three-month run in the West End.* 他的第一部戲在倫敦西區連續上演了三個月。

15 ►JOURNEY 旅程◄ [singular] **a)** a journey by train, ship, TRUCK etc, made regularly between two places〔火車、船、卡車等的〕固定行程[航程]: *It's only a 55-minute run from London to Brighton.* 從倫敦到布賴頓只是55分鐘的車程。 **b)** *informal* a short journey in a car, for pleasure【非正式】〔乘車〕兜風: *Let's take the car out for a run.* 我們開車兜兜風去。

16 ►FOR ANIMALS 動物使用的◄ [C] an enclosed area where animals such as chickens or rabbits are kept〔雞、兔子等的〕飼養場

17 ►SPORT 體育◄ [C] a point won in CRICKET or BASEBALL〔板球或棒球比賽中的〕一分

18 ►SKIING 滑雪◄ [C] a sloping area of land that you can SKI down 滑雪斜坡: *They don't let beginners go on the higher runs.* 他們不允許初學者使用高坡滑道。

19 ►IN CLOTHES 在衣物上◄ *AmE* [C] a line of torn stitches in TIGHTS, STOCKINGS etc【美】〔褲襪、長統襪等的〕脫線, 抽絲; LADDER[1] (3) *BrE*【英】

20 ►BANK 銀行◄ [singular] an occasion when lots of people all take their money out of a bank at the same time 擠提存款, 擠兑

21 run on the dollar/pound etc a situation in which a lot of people sell dollars etc and the value goes down〔很多人〕拋售美元/英鎊等

22 ►MUSIC 音樂◄ [C] a set of notes played or sung quickly up or down a SCALE in a piece of music〔按音階順序的〕速奏; 速唱

23 ►CARD GAMES 紙牌遊戲◄ [C] a set of cards with numbers in a series, held by one player 順子 —see also 另見 DRY RUN, DUMMY RUN, FUN RUN, MILK RUN, TRIAL RUN

run·a·bout /ˈrʌnəˌbaut; ˈrʌnəbaʊt/ *n* [C] *informal* a small car used for short journeys【非正式】輕便小汽車

run-a·round /ˈ· ·ˌ·/ *n* **give sb the run-around** *informal* to deliberately avoid giving someone a definite answer, especially when they are asking you to do something【非正式】〔尤指別人要你做事時〕搪塞, 顧左右而言他: *Every time we ask the landlord about fixing the roof, he gives us the run-around.* 每次我們要求房主修理屋頂時, 他總是搪塞。—see also 另見 **run around** (RUN[1])

run·a·way[1] /ˈrʌnəˌwe; ˈrʌnəweɪ/ *adj* [only before noun 僅用於名詞前] **1** a runaway vehicle or animal has gone out of control〔車輛或動物〕失控的 **2 runaway success/inflation etc** success, INFLATION etc that happens quickly or uncontrollably 迅速的成功; 失控的通貨膨脹: *The film was a runaway success.* 這部電影一砲打響。**3** a runaway person has left the place where they are supposed to be 逃跑的: *a runaway child* 一個離家出走的孩子

runaway[2] *n* [C] someone, especially a child, who has left home without telling anyone and does not intend to come back 離家出走者〔尤指小孩〕—see also 另見 **run away** (RUN[1])

run·down /ˈrʌnˋdaun; ˈrʌndaʊn/ *n* [C usually singular 一般用單數] **1** a quick report or explanation of an idea, situation etc〔關於某構想、情況等的〕簡要報告, 扼要說明, 梗概: **give sb a rundown on** *Someone give Charlie a quick rundown on what we've done so far.* 請誰給查理簡要報告一下到目前為止我們所做的工作。**2** [singular] the process of making a business or industry smaller and less important〔公司、工業等的規模或重要性的〕縮減

run-down /ˌ· ˈ·◂/ *adj* **1** a building or area that is run-down is in very bad condition〔建築物或地區〕破舊的, 失修的: *a run-down inner-city area* 破敗的舊城區 **2** [not before noun 不用於名詞前] someone who is run-down is tired and not healthy〔人〕精疲力竭的, 衰弱的: *You look a bit run-down – maybe you need a rest.* 你看來有點兒累, 也許你需要休息。

rune /run; ruːn/ *n* [C] *technical*【術語】**1** one of the letters of the alphabet used in the past by people in Northern Europe 如尼字母〔古代北歐的一種字母〕 **2** a magic song or written sign 神祕的歌; 神祕的符號 —**runic** *adj*

rung[1] /rʌŋ; rʌŋ/ the past tense of RING[2]

rung[2] *n* [C] **1** one of the bars that form the steps of a ladder 梯子的橫檔, 梯級 **2** *informal* a particular level or position in an organization or system【非正式】〔組織或體制中的〕等級, 地位: *on the highest rung of the salary scale* 薪金級別最高的一級 **3** a bar between two legs of a chair〔椅子腿間的〕橫檔

run-in /ˈ· ·/ *n* [C] an argument or disagreement, especially with someone in an official position〔尤指與公務人員〕爭吵, 爭執: **have a run-in with** *Michael got drunk and had a run-in with the police.* 邁克爾喝醉了, 跟警察發生了爭執。

run·ner /ˈrʌnɚ; ˈrʌnə/ *n* [C] **1** someone who runs as a sport 參加賽跑的人: *a long-distance runner* 長跑運動員 **2** someone who walks or runs from place to place carrying messages, especially in former times〔尤指舊時的〕送信者 **3 do a runner** *BrE* to leave somewhere quickly in order to avoid paying for something or having to meet someone【英】〔為避免付款或逃避某人而〕迅速逃離, 溜掉: *By the time the police got there, the boys had done a runner.* 警察到達那裡的時候, 那些男孩子已經溜掉了。**4** one of the two thin pieces of metal that a SLEDGE has, or the single piece of metal under a SKATE[1] (1)〔雪橇的〕滑板,〔冰鞋的〕冰刀 **5** the bar of wood or metal that a drawer or curtain slides along〔抽屜或簾子的〕滑槽, 滑道 **6** *technical* a stem with which a plant such as a STRAWBERRY spreads itself along the ground【術語】長匐莖, 匍匐莖 **7** a long narrow piece of cloth or CARPET 狹長的布[地毯] —see also 另見 DRUG RUNNER, FRONT-RUNNER

runner-bean /ˌ·· ˈ·/ *n* [C] *BrE* a vegetable that grows as a long green POD (=seed container) on a climbing plant【英】紅花菜豆 —see picture on page A9 參見A9頁圖

runner-up /ˌ·· ˈ·/ *n plural* **runners-up** [C] the person or team that comes second in a race or competition〔比賽中的〕第二名，亞軍

run·ning¹ /ˈrʌnɪŋ; ˈrʌnɪŋ/ *n* [U] **1** the act or sport of running 跑步，賽跑: **running shoes/track etc** *new facilities including a pool and a running track* 包括一個游泳池和一條跑道的新設施 **2 the running of** the way in which a business, home, organization etc is managed or organized 管理，經營: *Brian took over the running of the company while his father was away.* 父親不在期間，布賴恩接手公司管理。**3 be in the running/out of the running** to have some hope or no hope of winning a race or competition〔在比賽中〕有/沒有希望取勝: *Bruno is still in the running for the world title.* 布魯諾仍有希望獲得世界冠軍。**4 make (all) the running** *BrE informal*【英，非正式】**a)** to be the person who makes most of the suggestions in a relationship, plan, activity etc〔在關係、計劃、活動等中〕主動；帶頭 **b)** to be the leader in a competition, race, election etc〔在比賽、競選等中〕領先

running² *adj* [only before noun 僅用於名詞前] **1 running water a)** water that comes from a TAP¹ (1) 自來水: *Disease spreads fast in villages where there is no running water.* 疾病在沒有自來水的村莊裡迅速傳播。**b)** water that is flowing or moving 流動的水: *Many fish prefer running water.* 許多魚喜歡流動的水。**2 running repairs** small repairs that you do to a machine to keep it working〔維持機器繼續運作的〕小修理 **3 running total** a total that is continually increased as new costs, amounts etc are added 不斷增加的總數: *Keep a running total of your expenses as you go along.* 你一面幹，一面記下開支的總數。**4 running commentary** a spoken description of an event, especially a race or game, made while the event is happening〔比賽或體育運動的〕現場實況報道: *a running commentary on the basketball game* 籃球比賽的現場實況報道 **5 running battle/argument** an argument that continues or is repeated over a long period of time 爭執不下，持續的爭論 **6 running sore** a sore area on your skin, that has liquid coming out of it 流膿的創口 **7 in running order** a machine that is in running order is working correctly〔機器〕運轉正常的 **8 the running order** the order in which the different parts of an event have been arranged to take place 日程表，安排: *changes in the running order for the teachers' conference* 教師大會日程表的變更

running³ *adv* **three years/five times etc running** for three years etc without a change or interruption 連續三年/五次等: *Sylvie has won the poetry prize for the fourth year running.* 西爾維已經連續四年獲得詩歌獎。

running costs /ˈ·· ·/ *n* [plural] the amount of money that is needed to operate an organization, system etc〔組織等的〕經營成本

running jump /ˌ·· ˈ·/ *n* [C] **1** a jump made by running up to the point at which you leave the ground 跑跳，跑步跳遠 **2 take a running jump** *spoken* used to tell someone to go away and stop annoying you【口】走開〔用於斥退討厭的人〕: *If he hassles you again tell him to take a running jump!* 如果他再打攪你，就叫他滾開！

running mate /ˈ·· ·/ *n* [C usually singular 一般用單數] the person who someone who is trying to become president, leader etc chooses to help them in an election〔總統候選人等的〕競選夥伴: *Al Gore was Bill Clinton's running mate in the 1992 election.* 在1992年的選舉中，阿爾·戈爾是比爾·克林頓的競選夥伴。

run·ny /ˈrʌnɪ; ˈrʌni/ *adj informal*【非正式】**1** something, especially a food, that is runny is not solid or thick enough〔尤指食物〕稀的，黏軟的: **go runny** (=become runny) 融化 *The butter had gone runny in the heat.* 黃油遇熱融化了。**2** a runny nose, runny eyes etc have liquid coming out of them, usually because you have a cold〔尤指因感冒而〕流鼻涕的；流淚的

run-off /ˈ· ·/ *n* **1** [C] a second competition or election that is arranged to decide the winner when two competitors get an equal number of points or votes the first time〔比賽打平手後的〕重賽，〔得票相同者之間的〕決勝選舉 —compare 比較 PLAY-OFF —see also 另見 **run off** (RUN¹) **2** [U] *technical* rain or other liquid that flows off the land into rivers【術語】徑流，溢流〔指流入河流中的雨水或其他液體〕: *nitrogen-rich run-off from agricultural land* 從農田流出的高含氮量溢流

run-of-the-mill /ˌ· · · ˈ·◂/ *adj* not special or interesting in any way; ordinary 普通的，一般的，不突出的: *a run-of-the-mill performance* 平平的表現

run-on sen·tence /ˈ· · ˌ·· / *n* [C] *especially AmE* a sentence that has two main CLAUSES without connecting words or correct PUNCTUATION【尤美】連寫句〔含有兩個主句，但沒有連接詞或正確的標點符號〕

runt /rʌnt; rʌnt/ *n* [C] **1** the smallest and least developed baby animal of a group born at the same time〔一胎中〕最小且發育不全的小動物: *the runt of the litter* 一窩中最小的一個 **2** *informal* a small, unpleasant or unimportant person【非正式】矮小[討厭，無足輕重]的人

run-through /ˈ· ·/ *n* [C] a short practice before a performance, test etc〔時間短的〕排練，預演；預習: *a final run-through of the play* 這場戲的最後一次排練

run-up /ˈ· ·/ *n* **1 the run-up to** the period of time just before an important event〔重要事件的〕前奏期，預備期間: *the run-up to the 1992 election* 1992年選舉的競選階段 **2** [C] the act of running, or the distance that you run, before you kick a ball, jump over a pole etc〔踢球、跳高等之前的〕助跑；助跑距離

run·way /ˈrʌnˌwe; ˈrʌnweɪ/ *n* [C] **1** a long specially prepared hard surface like a road on which aircraft land and take off〔機場的〕跑道 **2** *AmE* a long narrow part of a stage that stretches out into the area where the AUDIENCE sits【美】伸入觀眾席的延伸舞台

ru·pee /ruˋpi; ruːˈpiː/ *n* [C] the standard unit of money in India, Pakistan, and some other countries 盧比〔印度、巴基斯坦等國家的貨幣單位〕

rup·ture¹ /ˈrʌptʃɚ; ˈrʌptʃə/ *n* **1** [C,U] an occasion when something suddenly breaks apart or bursts〔突然的〕破裂，裂開: *the rupture of a blood vessel* 血管的突然破裂 **2** [C] a situation in which two countries or groups of people suddenly disagree and often end their relationship with each other〔兩個國家或團體之間關係的〕突然決裂，斷絕: *the rupture between the two religious communities* 兩個宗教團體之間關係的突然決裂 **3** [C,U] a medical condition in which an organ of the body sticks out through the wall of muscle that normally surrounds it; HERNIA 疝

rupture² *v* **1** [I,T] to break or burst, or make something break or burst (使) 破裂，爆裂: *A pipeline carrying crude oil has ruptured.* 一條輸送原油的管道破裂了。**2 rupture yourself** to cause a RUPTURE¹ (3) in your body 使〔自己〕發疝氣

ru·ral /ˈrurəl; ˈrʊərəl/ *adj* **1** happening in or connected with the countryside, not the city 農村的，鄉村的，田園的: *a peaceful rural setting* 平靜的鄉村景象 | *rural bus routes* 農村的公共汽車路線 **2** like the countryside or reminding you of the countryside 像農村的；使人想起農村的: *It's very rural round here, isn't it?* 這周圍很像農村，對不對？—opposite 反義詞 URBAN 2

rural de·liv·er·y /ˌ·· ·ˈ···/ *n* RD 鄉村遞送

rural route /ˈ·· ·/ *n* RR 鄉村投遞路線

ruse /ruz; ruːz/ *n* [C] a clever trick used to deceive someone 詭計，計策: *It dawned on me that this was only a ruse, done to gain time.* 我猛然醒悟，這不過是緩兵之計。

rush¹ /rʌʃ; rʌʃ/ *v* 2 3

1 ▶MOVE QUICKLY 快速移動◀ [I always+adv/prep]

to move very quickly, especially because you need to be somewhere very soon〔尤因為要很快到某處而〕急速行進, 猛衝: **[+out/past/through/along etc]** *We rushed home to find out what had happened to Julie.* 我們急速趕回家去看朱莉出了甚麼事。| *One of the pipes burst and water came rushing out.* 有一條管道破裂了, 水不斷湧出來。

2 ▶DO STH QUICKLY 急速做某事◀ [I,T] to do something too quickly, especially so that you do not have time to do it carefully or well 倉促行事, 倉促完成: *There's plenty of time – we don't need to rush.* 時間有的是, 我們不必匆忙。| **rush sth** *You shouldn't rush this sort of work.* 這種工作你不應匆匆忙忙地做。

3 rush to do sth to do something eagerly and without delay 搶着做, 趕緊做: *Fans rushed to buy tickets as soon as they went on sale.* 一開始售票, 支持者就搶着去買。

4 ▶TAKE/SEND URGENTLY 急忙地送◀ [T always+adv/prep] to take or send something somewhere very quickly, especially because of an unexpected problem〔尤指因意外事件而〕急送〔某物到某地〕: *The Red Cross rushed medical supplies to the war zone.* 紅十字會火速將醫療供應品送往作戰地區。| **rush sb somewhere** *Dan was rushed to the hospital with serious head injuries.* 丹因頭部受重傷被迅速送往醫院。

5 ▶MAKE SB HURRY 催促某人◀ [T] to try to make someone do something more quickly than they want to 催促〔某人做某事〕: *I'm sorry to rush you, but we need a decision by Friday.* 很抱歉催你, 不過我們在星期五之前需要作出決定。| **rush sb into doing sth** *Don't let them rush you into signing the contract.* 別讓他們催你簽合同。

6 ▶ATTACK 攻擊◀ [T] to attack someone suddenly and in a group〔一夥人〕突然襲擊: *They rushed the guard and stole his keys.* 他們突然襲擊守衛, 偷了他的鑰匙。

7 ▶AMERICAN UNIVERSITIES 美國大學◀ *AmE*【美】 **a)** [T] to give parties for students, have meetings etc, in order to decide whether to let them join a FRATERNITY or SORORITY (=type of club) 招待〔大學生聯誼會用舞會、聚會等來吸收新會員〕 **b)** [I,T] to go through the process of trying to be accepted into these clubs 爭取加入〔大學生聯誼會〕

8 ▶AMERICAN FOOTBALL 美式足球◀ [I,T] to carry the ball forward 帶(球)跑動 —see also 另見 RUSHED

rush about/around *phr v* [I] to try to do a lot of things in a short period of time 匆匆忙忙: *I was rushing around all morning trying to get everything ready for the trip.* 整個上午我都在忙忙碌碌地為旅行做準備。

rush into sth *phr v* [T] to get involved in something without taking enough time to think carefully about it 倉促做, 急忙做: **rush into things** *spoken*【口】: *He's asked me to marry him, but I don't want to rush into things.* 他要我嫁給他, 但是我不想太倉促。

rush sth ↔ **out** *phr v* [T] to make a new product, book etc available for sale very quickly 趕製〔新產品〕; 趕印〔書〕

rush sth ↔ **through** *phr v* [T] to deal with official or government business, more quickly than usual 加急處理〔公務〕: *The legislation was rushed through Parliament.* 議會倉促通過了法律。

rush² *n*

1 ▶FAST MOVEMENT 急速行動◀ [singular] a sudden fast movement of things or people 衝, 奔: *Someone shouted 'fire!', and there was a rush towards the door.* 有人大聲叫喊"失火啦!", 人們都朝門口湧去。| **in a rush** *Her words came out in a rush.* 她急急忙忙地說。| *a sudden rush of wind* 突然颳起的風

2 ▶HURRY 趕緊◀ [singular,U] a situation in which you need to hurry 匆忙, 趕緊: *There's always such a rush to get things done.* 做事總是這麼匆忙。| **there's no rush** *spoken* (=there is no need to hurry)【口】不必着急 *There's no rush. We don't have to leave till 10.30.* 不必着急, 我們到10時30分才走。| **do sth in a rush** (=do something quickly, especially so that it is not done well) 匆忙做某事〔尤指事情因而做得不好〕 *It all seems to have been decided in such a rush.* 決定似乎非常倉促。| **be in a rush** *I'm sorry, I can't talk now – I'm in kind of a rush.* 對不起, 我現在不能聊, 我得趕時間。

3 ▶BUSY PERIOD 繁忙時期◀ **the rush** the time in the day, month, year etc when a place or group of people are particularly busy〔一天、一月、一年中, 某地或某些人〕特別忙碌的時期: *The café is quiet until the lunchtime rush begins.* 在最忙碌的午飯時間前, 小餐館很寧靜。| *the Christmas rush* 聖誕節購物熱潮 —see also 另見 RUSH HOUR

4 ▶PEOPLE WANTING STH 人們需要某物◀ [singular] a situation in which a lot of people suddenly try to do or get something〔很多人〕爭做, 急需: **[+on]** *a rush on swimsuits in the hot weather* 天氣炎熱, 泳衣的需求激增 | **rush to do sth** *There was a big rush to get tickets for the football game.* 人們搶購那場足球賽的門票。—see also 另見 GOLD RUSH

5 ▶PLANT 植物◀ [C] a type of tall grass that grows in water, often used for making baskets, mats etc 燈心草〔常用來編筐、墊等〕

6 ▶FEELING 感覺 **a)** [C] *informal* a strong, usually pleasant feeling that you get from taking a drug or from doing something exciting【非正式】〔服用藥物或做了令人興奮的事而得到〕快感: *Playing in front of a packed house was a real rush.* 在滿座的劇場表演真帶勁。**b) rush of excitement/panic etc** a sudden very strong feeling of excitement etc 一陣激動/慌亂等: *I felt a rush of excitement as she walked through the door.* 她走進門時我感到一陣激動。

7 ▶FILM 電影◀ **rushes** [plural] the first prints of a film before it has been edited (EDIT (1)) 拍攝後未經剪輯的影片; DAILY³ (3) *AmE*【美】

8 ▶AMERICAN STUDENTS 美國學生◀ [singular] *AmE* the time when students in American universities who want to join a FRATERNITY or SORORITY (=type of club) go to a lot of parties【美】〔大學生聯誼會為吸收新會員而舉辦的〕一連串活動期間: *rush week* 大學生聯誼會吸收新會員活動週 | *a rush party* 大學生聯誼會吸收新會員舉行的聚會

rushed /rʌʃt; rʌʃt/ *adj* **1** done very quickly or too quickly, because there was not enough time 匆忙的, 倉促的: *a rather rushed meeting* 非常匆忙的會議 **2 be rushed off your feet** *especially BrE* to be so busy that you do not have time to stop or rest【尤英】忙得不可開交

rush hour /'· ·/ *n* [C,U] the time of day when the roads, buses, trains etc are most crowded, because people are travelling to or from work〔上下班的〕高峯時間, 交通擁擠時間: *heavy rush hour traffic* 高峯時間擁擠的交通

rusk /rʌsk; rʌsk/ *n* [C] *especially BrE* a hard sweet dry bread for babies to eat【尤英】〔嬰兒食用的〕甜麵包乾, 脆餅乾

rus·set /ˈrʌsɪt; ˈrʌsɪt/ *n* [U] *especially literary* a reddish-brown colour【尤文】赤褐色 —**russet** *adj* —see picture on page A5 參見A5頁圖

Rus·sian¹ /ˈrʌʃən; ˈrʌʃən/ *n* **1** [U] the language of Russia 俄語 **2** [C] someone from Russia 俄羅斯人; 俄國人

Russian² *adj* from or connected with Russia 俄國的, 俄羅斯的

Russian rou·lette /,·· ·'·/ *n* [U] a game in which you risk killing yourself by shooting at your head with a gun that has a bullet in only one of six CHAMBERS 俄羅斯輪盤賭〔一種玩命的遊戲。在有六個彈位的左輪手槍內僅裝一顆子彈, 然後旋轉彈膛, 舉槍對準自己的頭部扣動扳機〕

rust¹ /rʌst; rʌst/ *n* [U] **1** the reddish-brown substance that forms on iron and steel when they get wet 鏽, 鐵鏽: *There were large patches of rust on the car.* 汽車上有大塊的鏽斑。**2** a plant disease that causes reddish-brown spots〔植物的〕鏽病 —see also 另見 RUSTPROOF, RUSTY

rust² *v* [I,T] to become covered with rust or make something become covered in rust (使)生鏽: *a rusted old* *basketball hoop* 一個生鏽的舊籃圈

rust away *phr v* [I] to be gradually destroyed by rust 因生鏽而慢慢爛掉

rus·tic[1] /ˋrʌstɪk; ˈrʌstɪk/ *adj* **1** simple, old-fashioned, and not spoiled by modern developments, in a way that is typical of the countryside 質樸的, 鄉村的, 農村風味的: *The village had a certain rustic charm.* 這個村莊有一種迷人的田園風情。**2** [only before noun 僅用於名詞前] roughly made from wood 用木頭粗製的: *a rustic chair* 一把用木頭粗製而成的椅子 **—rusticity** [U]

rustic[2] *n* [C] *literary or humorous* someone from the country, especially a farm worker【文或幽默】鄉下人, 莊稼人, 鄉巴佬

rus·tle[1] /ˋrʌsl; ˈrʌsəl/ *v* **1** [I,T] if leaves, papers, clothes etc rustle, or if you rustle them, they make a noise as they rub against each other（使）〔樹葉、紙、衣物等〕沙沙作響: *Stop rustling that newspaper!* 別把報紙弄得沙沙響! **2** [T] to steal farm animals such as cattle, horses, or sheep 偷〔牧場的牲畜, 如牛、馬、羊〕

rustle sth ↔ **up** *phr v* [T] *informal* to find or make something quickly, especially food or a meal【非正式】迅速弄到, 倉促拼湊〔尤指食物或一頓飯〕: *I'll rustle up a couple of steaks on the barbecue.* 我要在烤肉架上趕緊烤兩塊牛排。

rustle[2] *n* [singular] the noise made when something rustles 沙沙聲, 窸窣聲: *a rustle of leaves* 樹葉的沙沙聲 —see picture on page A19 參見 A19 頁圖

rus·tler /ˋrʌslɚ; ˈrʌslə/ *n* [C] someone who steals farm animals such as cattle, horses, or sheep 偷牲畜的賊

rust·proof /ˋrʌstˌpruf; ˈrʌstpruːf/ *adj* metal that is rustproof will not RUST〔金屬〕防鏽的, 抗鏽的

rust·y /ˋrʌstɪ; ˈrʌsti/ *adj* **1** metal that is rusty is covered in RUST[1] (1) 生鏽的: *a rusty nail* 生鏽的鐵釘 —see picture on page A18 參見 A18 頁圖 **2** if someone's skill in a particular activity or subject is rusty, it is not as good as it used to be, because they have not practised it for a long time〔技術等〕荒疏的, 荒廢的: *My French is very rusty these days.* 近來我的法語相當生疏了。**—rustiness** *n* [U]

rut /rʌt; rʌt/ *n* **1** [C] a deep narrow track left in soft ground by a wheel 車轍 **2 in a rut** living or working in a situation that never changes , so that you feel bored〔生活或工作〕固定又乏味, 一成不變: **be stuck in a rut** *I was stuck in a rut, and decided to look for a new job.* 我幹的都是老一套, 所以決定找一份新工作。**3 the rut** *technical* the period of the year when some male animals, especially DEER, are sexually active【術語】〔雄性動物, 尤指鹿的〕發情期

ru·ta·ba·ga /ˌrutəˋbegə; ˌruːtəˈbeɪgə/ *n* [C] *AmE* a large round yellow vegetable【美】蕪菁甘藍〔一種圓形黃色的蔬菜〕; SWEDE *BrE*【英】—see picture on page A9 參見 A9 頁圖

ruth·less /ˋruθlɪs; ˈruːθləs/ *adj* **1** so determined to get what you want that you do not care if you have to hurt other people in order to do it 無情的, 冷酷的, 殘忍的: *a ruthless dictator* 殘忍的獨裁者 | *a ruthless disregard for basic human rights* 對基本人權無情的蔑視 **2** determined and firm when taking unpleasant decision〔作出令人不快的決定時〕堅決的: *We'll have to be ruthless if we want to eliminate this kind of time-wasting.* 如果我們想杜絕這種對時間的浪費就必須堅決果斷。**—ruthlessly** *adv* **—ruthlessness** *n* [U]

rut·ted /ˋrʌtɪd; ˈrʌtɨd/ *adj* a surface that is rutted has deep narrow tracks in it left by the wheels of vehicles 留有車轍的: *a rutted dirt road* 留有車轍的土路

RV /ˌɑr ˋvi; ˌɑː ˈviː/ *n* [C] *AmE* recreational vehicle; a large vehicle, usually with cooking equipment and beds in it, that a family can use for travelling or camping【美】活動房屋式旅遊車〔通常有炊具和牀, 供家庭旅行、露營時使用〕

Rx. *AmE*【美】the written abbreviation of 縮寫= PRESCRIPTION (1)

rye /raɪ; raɪ/ *n* [U] **1** a type of grain that is used for making bread and WHISKY 黑麥, 裸麥: *rye bread* 黑麥麵包 **2** also 又作 **rye whis·key** /ˌ· ˈ··/ *AmE* a type of American WHISKY made from rye【美】黑麥威士忌酒: *rye and Coke* 黑麥威士忌酒加可口可樂

rye·grass /ˋraɪˌgræs; ˈraɪgrɑːs/ *n* [U] a type of grass that is grown as food for animals 黑麥草〔一種作動物飼料的草〕

R

S,s

S, s /ɛs; es/ *plural* **S's, s's** *n* [C] **1** the 19th letter of the English alphabet 英語字母表的第十九個字母 **2** the written abbreviation of 縮寫= south or southern

-s /z, s; z, s/ *suffix* **1** forms the plural of nouns〔構成名詞的複數〕: *a cat and two dogs* 一隻貓和兩條狗 **2** forms the third person singular of the present tense of most verbs〔構成大多數動詞的第三人稱單數現在式〕: *he plays* 他玩 | *she sits* 她坐 **3** *especially AmE* forms adverbs meaning during a particular time【尤美】〔構成副詞表示"在某一段特定時間"〕: *Do you work Sundays?* (=regularly each Sunday) 你星期天工作嗎? | *Summers we go to the seaside.* 我們每年夏天都去海濱。

-s' /z, s; z, s/ *suffix* forms the possessive case of plural nouns〔構成複數名詞的所有格〕: *the girls' dresses* (=the dresses belong to the girls) 姑娘們的連衣裙

-'s¹ /z, s; z, s/ **1** the short form of 縮略式= 'is': *John's here.* 約翰在這兒。| *What't that?* 那是甚麼? | *She's writing a letter.* 她在寫信。**2** the short form of 縮略式= 'has': *Polly's gone out.* 波莉出去了。| *A spider's got eight legs.* 蜘蛛有八條腿。**3** a short form of 縮略式= 'does' used in questions after who, what etc and that many people think is incorrect〔用於疑問句中的 who, what 等詞後, 但許多人認為這種用法不正確〕: *How's he plan to do it?* 他計劃怎樣去做這件事? —compare 比較 -'D **4** a short form of 縮略式= 'us' used only in 'let's'〔只用於 let's 一詞〕

-'s² *suffix* **1** forms the possessive case of singular nouns, and of plural nouns that do not end in -s〔構成單數名詞和非 -s 結尾的複數名詞的所有格〕: *my sister's husband* 我的妹[姐]夫 | *Mary's generosity* 瑪麗的慷慨 | *yesterday's lesson* 昨天的功課 | *the children's bedroom* 孩子們的臥室 | *the man in the corner's coat* (=the coat belonging to the man in the corner) 角落裡那個男子的上衣 **2** *BrE* the shop or home of someone【英】〔某人的〕店, 家: *I bought it at the baker's.* (=at the baker's shop) 這是我在麵包店買的。| *I met him at Mary's.* (=at Mary's house) 我是在瑪麗家遇見他的。

S & L /ˌɛs ənd ˋɛl; ˌes ənd ˈel/ *n* [C] *informal* SAVINGS AND LOAN ASSOCIATION【非正式】購房互助協會

sab·ba·tar·i·an /ˌsæbəˋtɛrɪən; ˌsæbəˈteəriən◂/ *n* [C] someone who strongly believes that the Sabbath should be a holy day on which people do not work 嚴守安息日的人 —**sabbatarian** *adj*

Sab·bath /ˋsæbəθ; ˈsæbəθ/ *n* **1 the Sabbath a)** Sunday, considered as a day of rest and prayer by most Christian churches 安息日〔星期日, 大多數基督徒認為應當休息和祈禱的日子〕 **b)** Saturday, considered as a day of rest and prayer in the Jewish religion 安息日〔星期六, 猶太教認為應當休息和祈禱的日子〕 **2 keep/break the Sabbath** to obey or not obey the religious rules of this day 守/不守安息日

sab·bat·i·cal /səˋbætɪkḷ; səˈbætɪkəl/ *n* [C,U] a period when someone, especially someone in a university job, stops doing their usual work in order to study or travel 休假〔尤指大學教師暫停平時的工作去進行研究或旅行的假期〕: **be on sabbatical** *Dr Watson's not here at the moment, she's on sabbatical.* 沃森博士目前不在這裡, 她正在休假。—**sabbatical** *adj*: *a sabbatical year* 休假年

sa·ber /ˋsebɚ; ˈseɪbə/ *n* [C] the usual American spelling of SABRE sabre 的一般美式拼法

sa·ble¹ /ˋsebḷ; ˈseɪbəl/ *n* [C,U] an expensive fur used to make coats etc, or the small animal that this fur comes from 貂皮; 貂

sable² *adj poetic* black or very dark【詩】黑色的; 深色的

sab·o·tage¹ /ˋsæbəˌtɑʒ; ˈsæbətɑːʒ/ *v* [T] **1** to secretly damage or destroy equipment, vehicles etc that belong to an enemy or opponent, so that they cannot be used 暗中破壞〔敵人或對手的設備、車輛等〕: *Every single fighter plane had been sabotaged.* 每架戰鬥機都遭到了破壞。**2** to deliberately spoil someone's plans because you do not want them to succeed 故意破壞〔某人的計劃〕: *Her father sabotaged her acting ambitions by refusing to pay for her to go to drama school.* 她父親有意挫傷她學演藝的抱負, 拒絕供她上戲劇學校。

sabotage² *n* [U] damage that has been done deliberately to equipment, vehicles etc in order to prevent an enemy or opponent from using them〔對敵人或對手的設備、車輛等的〕蓄意破壞: *This is no accident – it's a deliberate act of sabotage.* 這不是甚麼事故 — 這是一次蓄意破壞行為。

sab·o·teur /ˌsæbəˋtɝ; ˌsæbəˈtɜː/ *n* [C] someone who deliberately damages, destroys, or spoils someone else's property or activities, in order to prevent them from doing something 蓄意破壞者 —see also 另見 HUNT SABOTEUR

sa·bre *BrE*【英】, **saber** *AmE*【美】/ˋsebɚ; ˈseɪbə/ *n* [C] **1** a light pointed sword with one sharp edge used in FENCING〔擊劍用的〕佩劍 **2** a heavy sword with a curved blade, used in more former times 軍刀, 馬刀 —see picture at 參見 SWORD 圖

sabre-rat·tling /ˋ‥ ˌ‥/ *n* [U] threats to use military force, especially when you do not think they are very frightening or serious 炫耀武力, 武力恫嚇

sac /sæk; sæk/ *n* [C] *technical* a part inside a plant or animal that is shaped like a bag and contains liquid or air【術語】〔動物、植物的〕囊; 液囊

sac·cha·rin /ˋsækərɪn; ˈsækərɨn/ *n* [U] a chemical substance that tastes sweet and is used instead of sugar in drinks 糖精

sac·cha·rine /ˋsækəˌrin; ˈsækəriːn/ *adj formal* too romantic in a way that seems silly and insincere【正式】故作多情的; 過分甜蜜的: *a saccharine love story* 過於纏綿的愛情故事

sac·er·do·tal /ˌsæsɚˋdotḷ; ˌsæsəˈdəʊtl◂/ *adj technical* connected with or belonging to a priest【術語】牧師的, 神甫的

sach·et /sæˋʃe; ˈsæʃeɪ/ *n* [C] a small plastic or paper package containing a liquid or powder〔裝有液體或粉末的〕小袋: *a sachet of shampoo* 一小袋洗髮劑 —see picture at 參見 CONTAINER 圖

sack¹ /sæk; sæk/ *n* **1** [C] **a)** a large bag made of strong rough cloth or strong paper, used for storing or carrying flour, coal, vegetables etc〔裝麵粉、煤、蔬菜等用的〕麻袋; 粗布袋; 厚紙袋; 大口袋: *a sack of potatoes* 一大袋馬鈴薯 **b)** also 又作 **sackful** the amount that a sack can contain 一(大)袋 **2 get the sack/give sb the sack** *BrE informal* to be dismissed from your job or to dismiss someone from their job【英, 非正式】被解雇/開除某人: *He got the sack for stealing.* 他因偷東西而被解雇。| *They've never actually given anyone the sack.* 他們實際上從未辭退過任何人。**3 hit the sack** *spoken* to go to bed【口】上牀睡覺: *It's one o'clock – time to hit the sack I think.* 一點鐘了 — 我想該上牀睡覺了。**4 in the sack** *informal* in bed【非正式】(躺)在牀上

sack² *v* [T] **1** *BrE informal* to dismiss someone from their job【英, 非正式】解雇〔某人〕; FIRE² (2) *especially AmE*【尤美】: *She was sacked for organizing a union.* 她因組織工會而被解雇。**2** to knock down the QUARTER-

BACK[1] (1) in American football〔在美式足球中〕擒抱〔四分衛〕**3** if an army sacks a place they go through it destroying or stealing things, and attacking people〔軍隊〕劫掠, 洗劫〔所到之處〕

sack out *phr v* [I] *AmE informal* to go to sleep【美, 非正式】上牀睡覺: *He sacked out on the sofa.* 他在沙發上睡覺。

sack·cloth /ˋsækˏklɔθ; 'sæk-klɒθ/ also 又作 **sacking** /ˋsækɪŋ; 'sækɪŋ/ *n* [U] **1** rough cloth for making sacks 麻袋布, 粗麻布 **2 wear sackcloth and ashes** to behave in a way that shows everyone you are sorry about something you have done wrong 表示懊悔, 悔恨

sack race /'· ·/ *n* [C] a race in which the competitors, usually children, have to jump forwards with both legs inside a SACK[1] (1a) 套袋賽跑〔通常為兒童玩的、雙腳套上袋子的跳躍式賽跑〕

sac·ra·ment /ˋsækrəmənt; 'sækrəmənt/ *n* [C] **1 the Sacrament** the bread and wine that is eaten at Christian ceremonies〔基督教的〕聖餐 **2** one of the important Christian ceremonies, such as marriage or COMMUNION (2) 聖事, 聖禮〈如婚禮、聖餐等〉—**sacramental** /ˌsækrəˋmɛntl; ˌsækrə'mentl◂/ *adj*

sa·cred /ˋsekrɪd; 'seɪkrɪ̵d/ *adj* **1** connected with a god or religion 神的, 宗教(性)的: *sacred painting* 聖畫 | *a sacred vow* 莊嚴的誓言 **2** greatly respected, or believed to be holy 受崇敬的, 神聖的: *Cows are sacred to Hindus.* 對印度教徒來說, 牛是神聖的。| *Human life is sacred.* 人的生命是神聖的。**3** extremely important to you, especially in a way that other people think is silly or annoying 極重要的〔尤指在他人看來有點愚蠢〕: *He thinks his parking space is sacred.* 他認為他的停車位不容侵犯。**4 is nothing sacred?** *spoken* used to express shock when something you think is valuable or important is being changed or harmed【口】怎麼能這樣呢?〔表示在貴重物品或重要事物受到損害時的驚訝〕: *They're putting a tax on books – is nothing sacred?* 他們要對圖書徵稅 —— 怎麼能這樣為所欲為? —**sacredly** *adv* —**sacredness** *n* [U]

sacred cow /ˌ·· '·/ *n* [C] a belief that is so important to some people that they will not let anyone criticize it 不容置疑的信念

sac·ri·fice[1] /ˋsækrəˏfaɪs; 'sækrɪ̵faɪs/ *n* **1** [C,U] something valuable that you decide not to have, in order to get something that is more important 犧牲: *the need for economic sacrifice* 在經濟上作出犧牲的必要性 | **make sacrifices** *My parents were forever reminding me of the sacrifices they made to give me an education.* 我父母不斷提醒我他們為了供我受教育所作出的犧牲。**2** [C,U] the act of offering something to a god, especially in former times by killing an animal or a person in a religious ceremony 獻祭〔尤指從前在宗教儀式中把動物或人殺死作祭品〕: **make a sacrifice** *It was common to make sacrifices to the gods to ensure a good harvest.* 為了保豐收而祭神是很普通的事。**3** [C] an object or animal that is offered to a god in a ceremony of sacrifice 祭品, 供品: **human sacrifice** (=a person killed as a sacrifice) 殺死後用作祭品的人 **4** *literary* **the final/supreme sacrifice** the act of dying while you are fighting for a principle【文】犧牲自己的生命, 捐軀

sacrifice[2] *v* **1** [T] to willingly stop having something you want or doing something you like in order to get something more important 犧牲, 獻出: **sacrifice sth for** *It's not worth sacrificing your health for your career.* 你為事業而犧牲健康是不值得的。| **sacrifice sth to do sth** *He sacrificed a promising career to look after his handicapped daughter.* 他為了照顧殘疾女兒犧牲了有前途的事業。**2** [I,T] to offer something or someone to a god as a sacrifice 獻祭; 以…作祭品

sac·ri·fi·cial /ˌsækrəˋfɪʃəl; ˌsækrɪ̵'fɪʃəl◂/ *adj* connected with or offered as a sacrifice (用於)獻祭的; (作為)犧牲的: *a sacrificial gift* 供品, 祭品 —**sacrificially** *adv*

sac·ri·lege /ˋsækrəlɪdʒ; 'sækrɪ̵lɪdʒ/ *n* [C,U] **1** the act of treating something holy in a way that does not show respect 瀆聖行為 **2** *spoken* the act of treating something badly when someone else thinks it is very important【口】不敬: *You recorded over his Jimi Hendrix tapes? That's sacrilege!* 你拿他的吉米·亨德里克斯的磁帶來錄音? 真是太不敬了! —**sacrilegious** /ˌsækrɪˋlɪdʒəs; ˌsækrɪ̵'lɪdʒəs◂/ *adj* —**sacrilegiously** *adv*

sac·ris·tan /ˋsækrɪstən; 'sækrɪ̵stən/ *n* [C] *technical* someone whose job is to take care of the holy objects in a church【術語】〔教堂的〕聖器保管員, 司事

sac·ris·ty /ˋsækrɪstɪ; 'sækrɪ̵sti/ *n* [C] *technical* a small room in a church where holy cups and plates are kept, and where priests put on their ceremonial clothes; VESTRY【術語】〔教堂的〕聖器室

sac·ro·sanct /ˋsækroˏsæŋkt; 'sækrəʊsæŋkt/ *adj* something that is sacrosanct is considered to be so important that no one is allowed to criticize or change it 神聖不可侵犯的: *Weekends are sacrosanct in our family so I never take any work home.* 我們家的週末時間是神聖不可侵犯的, 所以我從來不把工作帶回家裡去做。

sad /sæd; sæd/ *adj* 2 3

1 ▶UNHAPPY 不愉快的◀ unhappy, but especially because something unpleasant has happened to you or someone else 不愉快的, 傷心的, 難過的: *What's the matter with him? He looks so sad.* 他怎麼啦? 看上去愁容滿面的樣子。| **be sad to do sth** *I was sad to see them go in the end.* 看到他們終於要走, 我心裡很難過。| **[+about]** *I was glad to be going home, but sad about the friends I was leaving behind.* 快要回家讓我高興, 但要離開朋友卻又使我難過。| **sad smile/face/ expression etc** *There was such a sad look in her eyes.* 她的眼神很是憂傷。—opposite 反義詞 HAPPY (1)

2 ▶STH THAT MAKES YOU SAD 傷心的事◀ a sad event, situation etc makes you feel unhappy 令人傷心的, 使人難過的: *A special meeting was called to announce the sad news of his death.* 召開了特別會議宣布他去世的噩耗。| **sad book/song/film etc** *What a sad movie! I cried all the way through.* 多麼令人悲傷的電影! 我從頭到尾都在哭。| **it is sad that** *It's sad that James can't be with us.* 詹姆斯不能和我們在一起, 真令人難過。| **it is sad to see/hear etc** *It was sad to see all that food going to waste.* 看到要浪費那麼多食物真讓人痛心。| **sad time/day/moment etc** *This is a sad day for all of us.* 這是使我們大家都感到傷心的一個日子。

3 ▶NOT SATISFACTORY 不能令人滿意的◀ [only before noun 僅用於名詞前] a sad situation is very bad or unacceptable〔狀況〕糟糕的, 不能令人接受的: **sad state of affairs** (=bad situation) 糟糕的狀況 *It's a sad state of affairs when you can't go out at night for fear of being attacked.* 晚上怕被襲擊而不敢出門, 這種狀況真糟糕。| **the sad fact is (that)** *spoken*【口】: *The sad fact is that prejudice and discrimination still exist.* 可悲的是, 偏見和歧視依然存在。| **sad to say** *spoken*【口】: *Sad to say, we never found them.* 很遺憾, 我們從未找到他們。

4 ▶LONELY 孤獨的◀ a sad person or someone who has a sad life seems lonely and unhappy and you feel sorry for them 寂寞的, 可憐的: *She's a sad character – I don't think she has any friends at all.* 她是個孤獨的人 —— 我認為她沒有甚麼朋友。| **sad case** (=someone you feel sorry for) 可憐的人

5 ▶BORING 令人厭煩的◀ *spoken slang* used to say that someone or something is boring and unfashionable【口, 俚】乏味的, 不流行的, 不受歡迎的: *I think Carole's a bit of a sad name. Oh, sorry, is your mum called Carole?* 我覺得"卡羅爾"是個有點乏味的名字。啊, 對不起, 你媽媽是叫"卡羅爾"嗎? | **sad bastard** *Get a life, you sad bastard.* 別再煩人了, 你這個討厭鬼。

6 sadder but wiser having learned something from an unpleasant experience 因吃過苦頭而變得聰明: *He came out of the relationship sadder but wiser.* 他擺脫了那種關係, 吃了苦頭也學了乖。—**sadness** *n* [singular,U] —see also 另見 SADLY

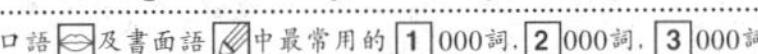

sad·den /ˈsædn̩; ˈsædn/ *v* [T often passive 常用被動態] *formal* to make someone feel sad or disappointed【正式】使傷心, 使難過: *Dorothea was saddened by his sudden change of heart.* 他突然變心, 這使多蘿西婭很難過。| **it saddens sb** *It saddened him to think that the others no longer trusted him.* 一想起大家不再信任他了, 他就很傷心。

sad·dle¹ /ˈsædl̩; ˈsædl/ *n* **1** [C] a seat made of leather that is put on a horse's back so that someone can ride it (馬) 鞍 —see picture at 參見 HORSE¹ 圖 **2** [C] a seat on a bicycle or a MOTORCYCLE〔腳踏車、摩托車等的〕車座 —see picture at 參見 BICYCLE¹ 圖 **3 be in the saddle** *informal*【非正式】**a)** to be in a position in which you have power or authority 在位, 掌權: *He's been in the saddle for 30 years now, and it's time he retired.* 他已經在位 30 年, 也該退休了。**b)** to be riding a horse 騎着馬: *They were weary after many hours in the saddle.* 他們騎了幾個小時的馬之後都很疲倦。

saddle² *v* [T] to put a saddle on a horse 給〔馬〕裝上鞍

saddle up *phr v* [I,T] to put a saddle on a horse 給 (馬) 裝上鞍: *We saddled up and rode quickly back to the farm.* 我們裝上馬鞍, 騎馬迅速回到農場。

saddle sb **with** sth *phr v* [T] to give someone a difficult or boring job 使〔某人〕承擔〔苦差事〕: *It's his party, but I've been saddled with organizing the whole thing!* 這是他要舉行的聚會, 但一切都要我來張羅!

saddle bag /ˈ·· ·/ *n* [C] a bag for carrying things that is fixed to the saddle on a horse or bicycle 鞍囊, 馬褡褳; 〔腳踏車車座後的〕掛包

sad·dler /ˈsædlɚ; ˈsædlə/ *n* [C] someone who makes saddles and other leather products, or a shop where these are sold 鞍匠, 馬具工; 馬具店

sad·dler·y /ˈsædlərɪ; ˈsædləri/ *n* [U] **1** goods made by a saddler 鞍具, 馬具 **2** the art of making saddles and other leather goods 鞍具製造 (術)

saddle shoe /ˈ·· ·/ *n* [C] *AmE* a shoe that has a toe and heel of one colour, with a different colour in the middle【美】鞍脊鞋〔一種鞋面中部與鞋頭、鞋跟顏色不同的鞋〕

saddle-sore /ˈ·· ·/ *adj* [not before noun 不用於名詞前] feeling stiff and sore after riding a horse or bicycle〔騎馬或騎腳踏車後〕疼痛並發僵的, 感到坐鞍痛的

sa·dhu /ˈsɑdu; ˈsɑːduː/ *n* [C] a Hindu holy man who lives a very simple life〔印度教的〕聖人, 苦行高僧

sa·dis·m /ˈsedɪzəm; ˈseɪdɪzəm/ *n* [U] **1** the practice of getting pleasure from being cruel to someone 施虐狂: *New recruits were treated with ruthless sadism.* 新兵受到施虐狂般的殘酷對待。**2** the practice of getting sexual pleasure from hurting someone 性虐待狂

sa·dist /ˈsedɪst; ˈseɪdɪst/ *n* [C] someone who enjoys being cruel to other people 施虐狂者

sa·dis·tic /səˈdɪstɪk; səˈdɪstɪk/ *adj* cruel and enjoying making other people suffer 施虐狂的: *He took a sadistic delight in humiliating her.* 他通過羞辱她獲取施虐的快感。—**sadistically** /-kl̩ɪ; -kli/ *adv*

sad·ly /ˈsædlɪ; ˈsædli/ *adv* **1** in a way that shows that you are sad 傷心地, 悲傷地: *Peter shook his head sadly and turned away.* 彼得難過地搖搖頭走開了。**2** [sentence adverb 句子副詞] unfortunately 不幸地; 說來遺憾: *Sadly, they just can't be trusted.* 遺憾的是, 他們就是不可信任。**3** in a way that makes you sad 令人傷心地: *He was a popular man and will be sadly missed.* 他的人緣很好, 大家都會憂傷地懷念他。| *We were sadly disappointed.* 我們萬分失望。**4 sadly lacking/neglected etc** in a way that seems bad or wrong 嚴重地缺乏/受忽視等: *The garden was beautiful once, but it has been sadly neglected.* 這個花園曾經很漂亮, 但現在已經完全荒蕪了。**5 be sadly mistaken** to be completely wrong about something 完全弄錯: *If you think you'll get any money from him, you're sadly mistaken.* 如果你以為可以從他那兒弄到錢, 那你就完全搞錯了。

sa·do·mas·o·chis·m /ˌsedoˈmæsəkɪzm̩; ˌseɪdəʊˈmæsəkɪzəm/ *n* [U] the practice of getting sexual pleasure from hurting someone or being hurt (性) 施虐狂; 受虐狂 —**sadomasochist** *n* [C] —**sadomasochistic** /ˌsedomæsəˈkɪstɪk; ˌseɪdəʊmæsəˈkɪstɪk◂/ *adj*

sae /ˌɛs e ˈi; ˌes eɪ ˈiː/ *BrE*【英】**1** stamped addressed envelope; an envelope that you put your name, address, and a stamp on, so that someone else can send you something〔貼足郵票並寫有自己姓名地址的〕回郵信封 **2** self-addressed envelope; an envelope that you put your own name and address on 寫有自己姓名地址的信封 —see also 另見 SASE

sa·fa·ri¹ /səˈfɑrɪ; səˈfɑːri/ *n* [C] a trip through countryside in Africa, that you go on to watch wild animals〔在非洲的〕野外觀獸旅行: **go/be on safari** *They spent their vacation on safari in Kenya.* 他們假期在肯尼亞進行野外觀獸旅行。

safari² *adj* **safari suit/jacket** a suit or JACKET (1) that is made of light-coloured material, usually with a belt and two pockets on the chest 輕便獵裝/獵裝夾克〔用淺色衣料做成, 通常有腰帶和兩個胸袋〕

safari park /ˈ·· ·/ *n* [C] an enclosed area of land where wild animals are kept, so that people can drive round and look at them〔可以駕車遊覽的〕野生動物園

safe¹ /sef; seɪf/ *adj* S2 W2

1 ▶**NOT CAUSING HARM** 不會引起傷害◀ not likely to cause any physical injury or harm 安全的: *Flying is one of the safest forms of travel.* 乘飛機是最安全的旅行方式之一。| *the safe disposal of radioactive waste* 放射性廢物的安全處理 | *Don't go too near the edge – it isn't safe.* 不要太靠近邊緣 —— 那樣不安全。| **it is safe to do sth** *Is it safe to swim here?* 在這兒游泳安全嗎? | **[+for]** *Parents want play-areas that are safe for their children.* 家長希望自己的孩子有安全的遊戲場地。

2 ▶**NOT IN DANGER** 沒有危險◀ [not before noun 不用於名詞前] not in danger of being lost, harmed, or stolen 安全的, 保險的: *Will you feel safe in the house on your own?* 你一個人待在房子裡感到安全嗎? | **[+from]** *We were safe from attack in the shelter.* 我們在掩蔽所裡很安全, 不會受到襲擊)。| **keep sth safe** *I'm trusting you with these documents – so make sure you keep them safe.* 我把這些文件託付給你 —— 你一定要保管好。| **safe and sound** (=unharmed, especially after being in danger) 平安無恙 *The missing children were found safe and sound.* 失蹤的孩子們都安然無恙。

3 ▶**PLACE** 地方◀ a safe place is one where something is not likely to be stolen or lost 保險的, 安全的: *Keep the receipt in a safe place.* 把收據放在安全的地方。

4 safe journey/arrival/return etc a journey etc that ends safely 平安的旅行/到達/歸來等: *They prayed for their father's safe return.* 他們祈求父親平安歸來。| **safe journey** *spoken* (=what you say to someone when they start a long journey)【口】一路平安

5 ▶**NO RISK** 沒有風險◀ not involving any risk and very likely to succeed 沒有風險的: *a safe investment* 沒有風險的投資 | *a safe method of contraception* 安全的避孕方法 | **(as) safe as houses** (=completely safe) 絕對安全

6 ▶**SUBJECT** 話題◀ a subject of conversation that is safe is not likely to upset anyone or make people argue 不會令人不快的, 不會引起爭議的: *I kept to safe subjects, like the weather.* 我只談一些無關痛癢的話題, 例如天氣。

7 better (to be) safe than sorry *spoken* used to say that it is better to be careful now, even if this takes time, effort etc, so that nothing bad will happen later【口】寧願穩妥免致後悔: *I've checked all the safety harnesses – better safe than sorry!* 我檢查過所有的安全帶了 —— 但求穩妥以免後悔呀!

8 to be on the safe side *spoken* to do something especially carefully in order to avoid an unpleasant situation【口】為安全起見, 為了穩妥: *I'd take an umbrella, just to be on the safe side.* 為穩妥起見, 我還是帶把傘好。

9 be in safe hands to be with someone who will look after you very well 受到妥善照顧: *I've needed to know*

my kids were in safe hands. 我必須知道我的孩子都得到妥善的照顧。

10 a safe pair of hands someone you can trust to do a difficult job without making mistakes 信得過的人 —**safely** *adv*: *Drive safely!* 安全駕駛! | *I think we can safely assume that she will pass the exam.* 我想我們可以有把握地假定她會通過考試。—see also 另見 **play (it) safe** (PLAY[1] (11)), **a safe bet/a sure bet that** (BET[2] (6)), **a safe seat** (SEAT[1] (5))

safe[2] *n* [C] a strong metal box or cupboard with special locks where you keep money and valuable things 保險櫃, 保險箱

safe con·duct /,· '·/ *n* [C,U] official protection for someone when they are passing through a dangerous area 安全通行(權): *This letter should guarantee you safe conduct through the war zone.* 這封信應能保證你安全通過戰區。

safe-de·pos·it box /'· ·,·· ,·/ *n* [C] a SAFETY-DEPOSIT BOX 貴重物品存放箱

safe·guard[1] /ˋsef,gard; ˈseɪfgɑːd/ *v* [T] to protect something from harm or damage 保護, 保衛〔某物〕: *New regulations were introduced to safeguard the environment.* 制定了新條例以保護環境。| **safeguard sth against** *a program for safeguarding the computer system against viruses* 電腦防病毒程序

safeguard[2] *n* [C] a rule, agreement etc that is intended to protect someone or something from possible dangers or problems 保障條款; 保護措施: *The law contains important safeguards to protect housebuyers.* 該法律包含了保護購房者利益的重要條款。| **[+against]** *safeguards against the exploitation of children* 避免兒童受剝削的保護措施

safe ha·ven /,· '··/ *n* [C] a place where someone can go to in order to escape from possible danger or attack 庇護所, 避難所

safe house /,· '·/ *n* [C] a house where someone can hide when their enemies are looking for them〔躲避敵人搜尋的〕安全房, 安全藏身處

safe·keep·ing /ˋsefˋkipɪŋ; ˌseɪfˈkiːpɪŋ/ *n* [U] **1 for safekeeping** if you put something somewhere for safekeeping, you put it in a place where it will not get damaged, lost, or stolen 為了安全保管 **2 be in sb's safekeeping** to be in a position or situation where someone is looking after you 受到某人的妥善照顧

safe sex /,· '·/ *n* [U] ways of having sex that reduce the risk of the spread of AIDS and other sexual diseases, especially by using a CONDOM〔尤指使用避孕套的〕安全性交

S3 W2 **safe·ty** /ˋseftɪ; ˈseɪfti/ *n*

1 ▶NOT IN DANGER 沒有危險◀ [U] the state of being safe from danger or harm 安全: *The company seemed totally unconcerned about the safety of its workers.* 這家公司好像完全不關心自己員工的安全。| **in safety** (=without any danger) 毫無危險 *Spectators could watch the launch in complete safety.* 觀眾可以絕對安全地觀看發射。| **for safety's sake** (=in order to be safe) 為了安全起見 *We travelled in pairs, for safety's sake.* 為了安全起見, 我們兩人一組結伴旅行。

2 sb's safety how safe someone is in a particular situation 某人的安全(問題): *The boy has now been missing for 5 days and there are fears for his safety.* 男孩失蹤已經五天了, 大家都擔心他會遇到不測。| **for sb's own safety** *For your own safety please do not smoke inside the plane.* 為了您自身的安全, 請勿在飛機內抽煙。

3 ▶NOT DANGEROUS 不危險◀ [U] the state of not being dangerous or likely to cause harm or injury 安全, 無害: *Some scientists expressed concern over the safety of the test.* 一些科學家對這次試驗是否安全表示擔心。| **safety measures/precautions/checks** (=things that are done in order to make sure that something is safe) 安全措施/防範措施/安全檢查 *The accident would never have happened if the correct safety procedures had been followed.* 如果正確的安全程序得以遵循的話, 這次事故根本不會發生。| **road safety** (=safety of people using the roads) 交通安全 *Police are visiting schools as part of their latest road safety campaign.* 作為他們最近開展的交通安全運動的一部分, 警察正在巡視各個學校。

4 ▶SAFE PLACE 安全的地方◀ [U] a place where you are safe from danger 沒有危險的地方: **the safety of** *When the shelling began people fled to the safety of the city.* 砲轟開始時, 人們逃往城裡安全的地方。| **lead/take sb to safety** *Fire fighters led the children to safety.* 消防人員把孩子們帶到安全的地方。| **reach safety** *We were relieved to reach dry land and safety.* 我們到了岸上安全的地方後, 全都鬆了一口氣。

5 safety in numbers *spoken* used to say that a dangerous or unpleasant situation is better if there are a lot of people with you【口】人多勢眾, 人多保險

6 ▶SPORT 體育運動◀ [C] *technical* a way of getting two points in American football by making the other team put the ball down in its own GOAL (3)【術語】安全得分〔美式足球中迫使對方在自己球門區內將球放下的得分方式〕

safety belt /'·· ·/ *n* [C] a SEAT BELT 安全帶

safety catch /'·· ·/ *n* [C] a lock on a gun that stops it from being fired accidentally〔槍枝的〕保險機, 保險栓

safety cur·tain /'·· ,··/ *n* [C] a thick curtain at the front of a theatre stage that prevents fire from spreading〔舞台上的〕防火幕, 安全幕

safety-de·pos·it box /'·· ·,·· '·/ *n* [C] a small box used for storing valuable objects, usually kept in a special room in a bank〔銀行裡的〕貴重物品存放箱, 出租保險箱

safety glass /'·· ·/ *n* [U] strong glass that breaks into very small pieces that are not sharp, used for example in car windows〔用於車窗等的〕安全玻璃

safety is·land /'·· ,··/ *n* [C] *AmE* a TRAFFIC ISLAND【美】安全島

safety lamp /'·· ·/ *n* [C] a special lamp used by MINERs, that has a flame which will not make underground gases explode〔礦工用的〕安全燈

safety match /'·· ·/ *n* [C] a match that can only be lit by rubbing it along a special surface on the side of its box 安全火柴〔只有在火柴盒側面特定的地方才能刮着〕

safety net /'·· ·/ *n* [C] **1** a large net used to catch someone who is performing high above the ground if they fall〔高空雜技表演等用的〕安全網 **2** a system or arrangement that exists to help you if you have serious problems or get into a difficult situation〔一種幫助遇到嚴重問題或陷入困境者的〕安全保障措施[系統]: *a safety net of welfare payments for the poor* 窮人福利金支付安全系統

safety pin /'·· ·/ *n* [C] a wire pin with a cover that its point fits into so that it cannot hurt you 安全別針 —see picture at 參見 PIN[1] 圖

safety ra·zor /'·· ,··/ *n* [C] a RAZOR that has a cover over part of the blade to protect your skin〔刀片上有蓋的〕安全剃刀 —see picture at 參見 RAZOR 圖

safety valve /'·· ·/ *n* [C] **1** something you do that allows you to express strong feelings such as anger without doing any harm〔無害的〕用以發泄情緒的途徑: *Exercise provided him with a good safety valve from pressure at work.* 運動成了他消除工作壓力的一種良好方式。**2** a part of a machine that allows gas, steam etc to be let out when the pressure becomes too great〔機器的〕安全閥

saf·fron /ˋsæfrən; ˈsæfrən/ *n* [U] **1** bright orange powder that is used in cooking to give food a special taste and colour 番紅花粉〔用於調味〕: *saffron rice* 番紅花米飯 **2** a bright orange-yellow colour 番紅花色, 橘黃色

sag[1] /sæg; sæg/ **sagged, sagging** *v* [I] **1** to sink or bend downwards and away from the usual position 下垂; 下陷; 下彎: *The branch sagged under the weight of the apples.* 樹枝因蘋果的重壓彎下來了。| *His shoulders sagged dejectedly.* 他沮喪地垂着肩。**2** to become weaker

S

or less valuable 下降; 蕭條: *attempts to revive the sagging economy* 為了使衰退中的經濟復蘇所作的努力 | *My morale sagged still further.* 我越發意志消沉了。

sag² *n* [singular,U] a downward bending or sinking movement or position 下垂; 下陷: *a sag in a mattress* 褥墊陷下的部位

sa·ga /ˋsɑgə; ˈsɑːgə/ *n* [C] **1** a long story, especially one that continues over a period of many years 長篇故事, 家世小說: *an absorbing family saga* 吸引人的家世小說 **2** *informal* a long and complicated series of events or a description of this【非正式】一長串的事件; 長篇的描述: *I had to listen to a great long saga about her medical problems.* 我不得不聽關於她的醫療問題的一番冗長不堪的敍述。**3** one of the stories written about the Vikings of Norway and Iceland 薩迦〔關於挪威和冰島地區海盜的傳說〕

sa·ga·cious /səˋgeʃəs; səˈgeɪʃəs/ *adj formal* able to understand and judge things very well; WISE¹ (2)【正式】聰慧的, 明智的 —**sagaciously** *adv*

sa·gac·i·ty /səˋgæsətɪ; səˈgæsɪ̈ti/ *n* [U] *formal* good judgment and understanding; WISDOM【正式】聰慧, 明智

sage¹ /sedʒ; seɪdʒ/ *n* **1** [U] a plant with grey-green leaves that are used in cooking 鼠尾草, 洋蘇草〔其灰綠色葉子可用於烹調〕**2** [C] *literary* someone, especially an old man, who is very wise【文】聖人, 哲人

sage² *adj literary* very wise, especially as a result of a lot of experience【文】睿智的, 賢明的: *sage advice* 明智的忠告 —**sagely** *adv*

sage·brush /ˋsedʒˌbrʌʃ; ˈseɪdʒbrʌʃ/ *n* [U] a small plant that is very common in the western US〔美國西部常見的〕灌木蒿

sag·gy /ˋsægɪ; ˈsægi/ *adj informal* having a shape that sinks or drops downwards【非正式】下垂的; 下陷的: *The mattress was rather saggy in the middle.* 牀墊中間下陷得相當深。

Sag·it·tar·i·us /ˌsædʒɪˋtɛrɪəs; ˌsædʒɪ̈ˈteəriəs/ *n* **1** [singular] the ninth sign of the ZODIAC, represented by an animal that is half-horse and half-human, and believed to affect the character and life of people born between November 22 and December 21 人馬宮[座]〔黃道十二宮的第九宮〕**2** [C] someone who was born between November 22 and December 21 出生於人馬宮時段〔即11月22日至12月21日〕的人

sa·go /ˋsego; ˈseɪgəʊ/ *n* [U] a white food substance used to make sweet dishes with milk 西穀米, 西米

sahib /ˋsɑ·ɪb; sɑːb/ *n* [C] *IndE & PakE* used as a title of respect for a man in India, especially in former times【印和巴】先生, 老爺〔過去印度對男子的一種尊稱〕: *Good morning, sahib!* 早上好, 先生!

said¹ /sɛd; sed/ the past tense and past participle of SAY¹

said² *adj* [only before noun 僅用於名詞前] *law or humorous* used when giving more information about someone or something that has just been mentioned【法律或幽默】該…, 上述的: *The said weapon was later found in the defendant's home.* 該武器後來在被告家中發現。

3 **sail¹** /sel; seɪl/ *v* **1** [I always+adv/prep] to travel across an area of water in a boat or ship (乘船) 航行: *the first Europeans to sail across the Atlantic* 乘船橫渡大西洋的首批歐洲人 | *Three tall ships sailed past.* 三艘大船駛了過去。**2** [I,T] to direct or control the movement of a boat or ship 駕駛 (船隻): *The captain sailed his ship safely through the narrow passage.* 船長駕船安全通過狹窄的航道。| *My father taught me to sail when I was 14.* 我 14 歲時父親就教我駕船。**3** [I] to start a journey by boat or ship 啟航: *We sail at dawn.* 我們在黎明時啟航。| **[+for]** *They're sailing for Antigua next week.* 他們下星期要啟航前往安提瓜島。**4** [I always+adv/prep] to move quickly and smoothly through the air 飄過; 飛過: *At that moment a ball came sailing over the fence and landed in my lap.* 就在那時, 一個球飛過籬笆, 落在我的膝上。**5** [I always+adv/prep] to move forwards gracefully and confidently 優雅而自信地走: *Penelope sailed into the room, her dress billowing behind her.* 佩妮洛普婀娜地步入房間, 裙子在身後飄起。**6 sail close to the wind** to do or say something that is nearly wrong, illegal, or dishonest 接近非法, 幾乎逾規, 近乎說謊: *You're sailing a bit close to the wind with that remark.* 你那樣說未免有點冒失。—see also 另見 **sail/fly under false colours** (FALSE (10))

sail through *phr v* [I,T] to succeed very easily in a test, examination etc 順利通過 (考試等)

sail² *n* [C] **1** a large piece of strong cloth fixed onto a boat, so that the wind will push the boat along 帆: *a yacht with white sails* 揚着白帆的小艇 | **hoist/lower the sails** (=put the sails up or down) 揚/下帆 **2 set sail** to begin a journey by boat or ship 啟航: *The following week the 'Queen Elizabeth' set sail for Jamaica.* "伊莉莎白女王號" 於下星期啟航前往牙買加。**3 under sail** *literary* moving along on a ship or boat that has sails【文】揚帆航行

sail·board /ˋselbɔrd; ˈseɪlbɔːd/ *n* [C] a flat board with a sail, that you stand on in the sport of WIND-SURFING〔風帆滑浪用的〕帆板

sail·boat /ˋselˌbot; ˈseɪlbəʊt/ *n* [C] *AmE* a small boat with one or more sails【美】小帆船

sail·ing /ˋselɪŋ; ˈseɪlɪŋ/ *n* **1** [U] the sport or activity of travelling in or directing a small boat with sails 帆船運動: *Sylvia had always enjoyed sailing.* 西維亞向來喜歡帆船運動。**2** [C] a time when a ship leaves a port 啟航時間;〔船的〕航班: *Luckily, there was another sailing at 2 o'clock.* 幸好兩點鐘還有一班船。—see also 另見 PLAIN SAILING

sailing boat /ˈ·· ·/ *n* [C] *BrE* a small boat with one or more sails【英】小帆船

sailing ship /ˈ·· ·/ *n* [C] a large ship with sails 大帆船

sail·or /ˋselɚ; ˈseɪlə/ *n* [C] **1** someone who works on a ship 水手, 海員 **2** someone who travels in a boat 乘船者: **bad/good sailor** (=someone who does or does not feel sick when they are in a boat) 暈船的/不暈船的人

sailor suit /ˈ·· ·/ *n* [C] a blue and white suit that looks like an old-fashioned sailor's uniform, worn by children〔兒童穿的〕水手裝

saint /sent; seɪnt/ *n* [C] **1** someone who is given a special honour by the Christian church after they have died, because they were very good or holy〔死後由基督教會追封的〕聖徒, 聖人: *Saint Patrick* 聖帕特里克〔愛爾蘭守護聖人〕**2** *informal* someone who is extremely good, kind, or patient【非正式】道德高尚的人; 極為慈愛的人; 極有耐心的人: *His wife must have been a saint to put up with him for all those years.* 他妻子容忍了他那麼多年, 一定是個極有耐心的人了。**3 the patience of a saint** a very large amount of patience 極大的耐心: *You need the patience of a saint for this job.* 做這份工作你要有極大的耐心。

saint·ed /ˋsentɪd; ˈseɪntɪ̈d/ *adj* **1** having been made a saint by the Christian church 被 (基督教會) 追封為聖徒的 **2** *old-fashioned* used when talking about a dead person【過時】已進天國的, 已升天的 **3 my sainted aunt!** *old-fashioned spoken* used to express surprise or shock【過時, 口】我的媽呀!〔用於表示驚訝或震驚〕

saint·hood /ˋsentˌhʊd; ˈseɪnthʊd/ *n* [U] the state of being a saint 聖徒的身分

saint·ly /ˋsentlɪ; ˈseɪntli/ *adj* seeming to be completely good and honest, with no faults 聖賢似的; 聖潔的: *a doctor who had led a saintly and blameless life* 生平道德高尚無可指摘的醫生 —**saintliness** *n* [U]

saint's day /ˈ· ·/ *n* [C] the day of the year when the Christian church remembers a particular saint〔基督教紀念某一聖徒的〕聖徒節

saith /sɛθ; seθ/ *biblical* says【聖經】說

sake¹ /sek; seɪk/ *n* [U] **1 for the sake of** in order to help, improve, or please someone or something 由於, 為了〔…的緣故〕: *He moved to the seaside for the sake of his health.* 他為了健康而遷居海濱。| *I only went for*

Kay's sake. 我只是為了凱才去的。| **for sb's own sake** (=because it will be good for them) 為了自己的利益 *I hope he's told her the truth for his own sake.* 為了他自己好，我希望他已經把真相告訴了她。**2 for the sake of it** if you do something for the sake of it, you do it because you want to and not for any particular reason 只想那樣做〔沒有特殊的原因〕: *I'm sure she agrees with you really – she just likes arguing for the sake of it.* 我肯定她其實是同意你的 — 她只是為爭論而爭論罷了。**3 for the sake of argument** *spoken* if you say something for the sake of argument, what you say may not be true but it will help you to have a discussion【口】為了便於討論: *Let's say, just for the sake of argument, that you've got £200 to invest.* 為了便於討論，比方説吧，你有 200 英鎊，打算進行投資。**4 for God's/Christ's/goodness'/Heaven's etc sake** *spoken*【口】**a)** used when you are telling someone how important it is to do something or not to do something 看在上帝的份上，行行好吧〔表示某事很重要〕: *For goodness' sake, don't tell him that!* 行行好，千萬別把這事告訴他！**b)** used to show that you are angry or annoyed 天哪〔表示生氣或厭煩〕: *What's the matter now, for God's sake?* 天哪，到底出了甚麼事？—see 見 GOD (USAGE)

sa·ke² /ˋsɑkɪ; ˈsɑːki/ *n* [U] a Japanese alcoholic drink made from rice, served in small cups, usually warm 日本清酒〔一種米酒〕

sa·laam /səˋlɑm; səˈlɑːm/ *v* [I] to bend forwards and put your hand against your forehead, as a polite greeting in some Eastern countries 行額手禮〔右手掌置額前，深彎腰；某些東方國家的行禮方式〕—**salaam** *n* [C]

sal·a·ble /ˋseləbḷ; ˈseɪləbəl/ *adj* another spelling of SALEABLE saleable 的另一種拼法

sa·la·cious /səˋleʃəs; səˈleɪʃəs/ *adj formal* expressing too much unpleasant sexual detail【正式】淫穢的，誨淫的: *salacious jokes* 黃色笑話 —**salaciously** *adv* —**salaciousness** *n* [U]

sal·ad /ˋsæləd; ˈsæləd/ *n* [C,U] **1** a mixture of raw vegetables, especially LETTUCE, CUCUMBER, and TOMATO 色拉，沙拉，沙律〔用生菜、黃瓜、番茄等生的蔬菜作原料的涼拌菜〕: *a cheese salad* 乳酪沙拉 | *Would you like some salad with your pasta?* 你的通心粉要放些沙拉嗎？| *a salad bowl* 沙拉碗 | **toss a salad** (=mix it all together, usually with a DRESSING) 拌沙拉 **2** raw or cooked food cut into small pieces and served cold〔用生或熟的食物切成小塊做的〕涼拌菜: *potato salad* 馬鈴薯沙拉

salad cream /ˈ‥ ˌ/ *n* [U] *BrE* a thick light-coloured liquid, similar to MAYONNAISE, that you put on salad【英】〔奶油狀的〕沙拉醬

salad days /ˈ‥ ˌ/ *n* [plural] *old-fashioned* the time of your life when you are young and not very experienced【過時】經驗不足的青年時代，初出茅廬的時期

salad dress·ing /ˈ‥ ˌ‥/ *n* [C,U] a liquid mixture made from oil and VINEGAR, for putting on salads 沙拉調味料

sal·a·man·der /ˋsæləˌmændɚ; ˈsæləmændə/ *n* [C] a small animal similar to a LIZARD 蠑螈〔一種形似蜥蜴的小動物〕

sa·la·mi /səˋlɑmɪ; səˈlɑːmi/ *n* [C,U] a large SAUSAGE with a strong taste, that is eaten cold 薩拉米香腸

sal·a·ried /ˋsælərɪd; ˈsælərid/ *adj* receiving money every month for the work you do, rather than for every week or every hour (按月) 領薪水的: *salaried workers* 領薪水的員工

3 **sal·a·ry** /ˋsælərɪ; ˈsæləri/ *n* [C,U] money that you receive as payment from the organization you work for, usually paid to you every month〔通常按月發的〕薪水: **be on a salary of** (=be earning a particular amount) 薪水為… *She's on a salary of £16,000.* 她的薪水為 16,000 英鎊。—compare 比較 WAGE¹ (1) —see 見 PAY² (USAGE)

2 1 **sale** /sel; seɪl/ *n*

1 ►ACT OF SELLING 賣◄ [C,U] the act of giving property, food, or other goods to someone in exchange for money 出售，販賣: [+of] *The use and sale of marijuana remains illegal.* 吸食和販賣大麻仍然是非法的。| *The house sale was completed in two weeks.* 那棟房子的出售是在兩週內完成的。| **make a sale** (=sell something) 賣出，做成一筆買賣 *Every time Harvey makes a sale he gets $50 commission.* 哈維每做成一筆生意，都得到 50 美元的佣金。| **lose a sale** (=not sell something that you were going to sell) 未賣成，做不成某筆生意 *Rather than lose a sale, car salesmen will often bring down the price.* 汽車推銷員往往寧願降價也不想讓一筆生意落空。

2 for sale available to be bought 待售: *Excuse me, are these for sale?* 請問，這些要出售嗎？| *There was a "for sale" sign in the yard.* 院子裡有一塊寫着"待售"字樣的牌子。| **put sth up for sale** (=to make something, especially a house, available to be bought) 將〔房子等〕出售 *Reluctantly, they put the family home up for sale.* 他們很不情願地着手賣掉自己的家庭住宅。

3 ►LOWER PRICES 降價◄ a period of time when shops sell their goods at lower prices than usual 大減價，賤賣: *Marsdon's department store is having a sale this week.* 馬斯頓百貨店本週大減價。| **the sales** *BrE* (=when all the shops have a sale)【英】〔各商店的〕大減價期間 | **the January/summer/autumn etc sales** *I picked up some real bargains in the January sales this year.* 我在今年 1 月份大減價時買了一些真正的便宜貨。

4 ►EVENT 事件◄ [C] an event at which things are sold to the person who offers the highest price; AUCTION¹ 拍賣: *a sale of 17th century paintings* 17 世紀繪畫拍賣會

5 sales a) [plural] the total number of products that a company sells during a particular period of time 總銷售量: *We grossed more than $500,000 in sales last year.* 我們去年的銷售總額超過五十萬美元。| **sales figures/targets etc** *We've already reached our sales targets for this year.* 我們已經達到了今年的銷售指標。**b)** [U] the part of a company that deals with selling products 銷售部，營業部: *She found a job in sales.* 她找到了一份銷售部的工作。| *a sales manager* 銷售部經理

6 sales drive/campaign an effort made by a company to try to increase the number of products it sells 促銷行動/推銷運動

7 sales pitch/talk the things that someone says when they are trying to persuade you to buy something 推銷游説/宣傳

8 on sale a) available to be bought in a shop 上市，出售: *Stephen King's new novel will go on sale next week.* 斯蒂芬·金的新小説將於下星期出售。**b)** *especially AmE* available to be bought at a lower price than usual【尤美】廉價出售: *I could only afford to buy the CD player because it was on sale.* 只是因為大減價我才買得起這台激光唱機。

9 (on) sale or return if a shop buys something on sale or return, it can return the goods that it is unable to sell 剩貨包退〔零售商可以把賣不完的貨物退還給批發商〕—see also 另見 BILL OF SALE, JUMBLE SALE, POINT OF SALE

sale·a·ble, salable /ˋseləbḷ; ˈseɪləbəl/ *adj* something that is saleable can be sold, or is easy to sell 可出售的；易於銷售的: *a saleable commodity* 有銷路的商品 —**saleability** /ˌseləˋbɪlətɪ; ˌseɪləˈbɪləti/ *n* [U]

sale of work /ˌ· · ˈ·/ *n* [C] *BrE* an event at which people sell things they have made, especially in order to get money for a good purpose【英】自製品售賣，〔尤指〕義賣

sale·room /ˋselˌrum; ˈseɪlrʊm/ *n* [C] *BrE* a room where things are sold by AUCTION¹【英】拍賣廳，拍賣行

sales·clerk /ˋselzˌklɝk; ˈseɪlzklɑːk/ *n* [C] *AmE* someone who sells things in a shop【美】售貨員，店員，營業員; SHOP ASSISTANT *BrE*【英】

sales·girl /ˋselzˌgɝl; ˈseɪlzgɜːl/ *n* [C] *old-fashioned* a young woman who sells things in a shop【過時】女售貨員，女店員，女營業員

sales·man /ˋselzmən; ˈseɪlzmən/ *n plural* **salesmen** /-mən; -mən/ [C] a man whose job is to persuade people

S

to buy his company's products 男推銷員

sales·per·son /ˈselzˌpɝsn; ˈseɪlzpɜːsən/ *n* [C] someone whose job is selling things 售貨員

sales rep·re·sen·ta·tive /ˈ· ·‥ˌ‥/ also 又作 **sales rep** /ˈ· ·/ *n* [C] someone who travels around, usually within a particular area, selling their company's products〔公司的〕銷售代表

sales slip /ˈ· ·/ *n* [C] *AmE* a small piece of paper that you are given in a shop when you buy something; RECEIPT (1)【美】售貨單據, 售貨收據

sales tax /ˈ· ·/ *n* [C,U] *AmE* a tax that you have to pay in addition to the cost of something you are buying【美】〔顧客購物時付的〕銷售稅 —compare 比較 VAT

sales·wom·an /ˈselzˌwʊmən; ˈseɪlzˌwʊmən/ *n plural* **saleswomen** /-ˌwɪmɪn; -ˌwɪmɪn/ [C] a woman whose job is selling things 女售貨員

sa·li·ent /ˈselɪənt; ˈseɪliənt/ *adj formal* the salient points or features of something are the most important or most noticeable parts of it【正式】顯著的, 突出的: *The salient features of his plan are summarized in this report.* 他那個計劃的顯著特點已經概括在這份報告中了。—**salience** *n* [U]

sa·line[1] /ˈselaɪn; ˈseɪlaɪn/ *adj* containing or consisting of salt (含) 鹽的: *saline solution* 鹽溶液 —**salinity** /səˈlɪnətɪ; səˈlɪnɜti/ *n* [U]

saline[2] *n* [U] a special mixture of water and salt 生理鹽水

sa·li·va /səˈlaɪvə; səˈlaɪvə/ *n* [U] the liquid that is produced naturally in your mouth 涎, 唾液

salivary gland /ˈ·ˈ‥ ˌ·/ *n* [C] a part of your mouth that produces saliva 唾液腺

S

sal·i·vate /ˈsæləˌvet; ˈsælɜveɪt/ *v* [I] to produce more saliva in your mouth than usual, especially because you see or smell food〔因見到或聞到食物而〕流口水, 分泌唾液 —**salivation** /ˌsæləˈveʃən; ˌsælɜˈveɪʃən/ *n* [U]

sal·low /ˈsælo; ˈsæləʊ/ *adj* sallow skin looks slightly yellow and unhealthy〔皮膚〕灰黃色的, 土色的: *a sallow complexion* 灰黃的臉色 —**sallowness** *n* [U]

sal·ly[1] /ˈsælɪ; ˈsæli/ *n* [C] **1** an amusing clever remark 俏皮話, 妙語 **2** a sudden quick attack and return to a position of defence 突擊

sally[2] *v*

sally forth *phr v* [I] *old-fashioned* to leave somewhere that is safe in order to do something that you expect to be difficult or dangerous【過時】出發; 出來〔指從安全處出來面對困難或危險〕: *Each morning they sallied forth in search of jobs.* 他們每天早上外出找工作。

salm·on /ˈsæmən; ˈsæmən/ *n* **1** [C] *plural* **salmon** a large fish with silver skin and pink flesh that lives in the sea but swims up rivers to lay its eggs 鮭魚, 三文魚, 大麻哈魚 **2** [U] this fish eaten as food〔食用〕鮭肉

sal·mo·nel·la /ˌsælməˈnɛlə; ˌsælməˈnelə/ *n* [U] a kind of BACTERIA in food that makes you ill 沙門氏菌屬

sal·on /səˈlɑn; ˈsælɒn/ *n* [C] **1** a shop where you can get your hair cut etc〔提供理髮等服務的〕廳, 院, 廊: *a beauty salon* 美容院 **2** a shop where fashionable and expensive clothes are sold 高級服裝店; 時裝店 **3** a room in a very large house where people can meet and talk〔大宅中的〕客廳 **4** a regular meeting of famous people at which they talk about art, literature, or music, popular in 18th century France 沙龍〔18 世紀法國名流定期談論文藝的社交集會〕

sa·loon /səˈlun; səˈluːn/ *n* [C] **1** a public place where alcoholic drinks were sold and drunk in the western US in the 19th century〔19 世紀美國西部的〕酒館 **2** *BrE* a car that has a separate enclosed space for your bags etc【英】〔可裝行李的〕箱式小客車; 大轎車; SEDAN *AmE*【美】**3** a large comfortable room where passengers on a ship can sit and relax〔客輪上的〕交誼廳

saloon bar /ˈ·ˈ· ·/ *n* [C] *BrE* a comfortable room in a PUB【英】〔酒館中的〕雅座酒吧

sal·sa /ˈsælsə; ˈsælsə/ *n* [U] **1** a type of Latin American dance music〔拉丁美洲的〕薩爾薩舞曲 **2** a SAUCE (1) made from onions, tomatoes (TOMATO) and chillies (CHILLI (2)) that you put on Spanish or Mexican food 辣醬〔一種用洋蔥、番茄和辣椒做的西班牙或墨西哥調味辣汁〕

salt[1] /sɔlt; sɔːlt/ *n* **1** [U] a natural white mineral that is added to food to make it taste better or to preserve it; SODIUM CHLORIDE *technical* 鹽, 食鹽;【術語】氯化鈉: *Try to reduce the amount of salt you use.* 你要盡量少吃些鹽。| *a pinch of salt* 一撮鹽 | **table salt** (=very small grains of salt you use in cooking) 精製食鹽, 佐餐鹽 | **sea salt** (=large grains of salt made by drying sea water)〔粗粒〕海鹽, 粗鹽 | **rock salt** (=salt in a solid form rather than in grains)〔塊狀〕岩鹽 **2 the salt of the earth** someone who is ordinary, but good and honest 普通但誠實的好人 **3 take sth with a pinch/grain of salt** *informal* to not completely believe what someone tells you because you know that they do not always tell the truth【非正式】〔因某人老是不説實話而〕對某事半信半疑 **4** [C] *technical* a type of chemical substance【術語】鹽類〔一種化學物質〕—see also 另見 BATH SALTS, EPSOM SALTS, SMELLING SALTS, OLD SALT, **rub salt into the wound** (RUB[1] (7)), **worth his/her salt** (WORTH[1] (10))

salt[2] *v* [T] **1** to add salt to food to make it taste better 給食物放鹽〔調味〕**2** also 又作 **salt down** to add salt to food to preserve it 用鹽醃製〔食物〕**3** to put salt on the roads to prevent them from becoming icy〔為融化冰雪〕撒鹽於〔道路〕上

salt sth ↔ **away** *phr v* [T] to save money for the future, especially dishonestly by hiding it 儲蓄〔尤指把錢私存起來〕

salt[3] *adj* [only before noun 僅用於名詞前] **1** preserved by salt 用鹽醃製的: *salt pork* 醃豬肉 **2 salt water** water that contains salt, especially naturally in the sea 海水, 鹹水; 鹽水 **3** consisting of salt water 鹹水的, 由鹹水形成的: *a salt lake* 鹽湖

salt cel·lar /ˈ· ˌ‥/ *n* [C] *BrE* a small container for salt【英】小鹽瓶; SALT SHAKER *AmE*【美】

salt·pe·tre *BrE*【英】, **saltpeter** *AmE*【美】/ˈsɔltˈpitɚ; ˌsɔːltˈpiːtə/ *n* [U] a substance used in making GUNPOWDER (=powder that causes explosions) and matches 硝石, 硝酸鉀

salt shak·er /ˈ· ˌ‥/ *n* [C] *AmE* a small container for salt【美】小鹽瓶

salt truck /ˈ· ·/ *n* [C] *AmE* a large vehicle that puts salt or sand on the roads in winter to make them less icy【美】撒鹽車; 撒沙車〔冬季在路面撒鹽或沙以融化冰雪的卡車〕; GRITTER *BrE*【英】

salt·wa·ter /ˈsɔltˈwɔtɚ; ˈsɔːltˌwɔːtə/ *adj* [only before noun 僅用於名詞前] living in salty water or in the sea 海生的, 生活於鹹水的: *saltwater fish* 海產魚

salt·y /ˈsɔltɪ; ˈsɔːlti/ *adj* **1** tasting of or containing salt 含鹽的, 鹹的 **2** *old-fashioned* a story, joke, or conversation that is salty is amusing and often about sex【過時】〔故事、玩笑或談話〕不正經的; 下流的

sa·lu·bri·ous /səˈlubrɪəs; səˈluːbriəs/ *adj formal* a place that is salubrious is pleasant and healthy to be in【正式】〔場所〕有益於健康的: *They've moved to a more salubrious part of town.* 他們已經搬到城裡更清潔宜人的地方去了。

sal·u·ta·ry /ˈsæljəˌtɛrɪ; ˈsæljɜtəri/ *adj* a salutary experience is unpleasant but teaches you something〔不愉快但〕有教益的

sal·u·ta·tion /ˌsæljəˈteʃən; ˌsæljɜˈteɪʃən/ *n formal*【正式】**1** [C] a word or phrase used at the beginning of a letter or speech, such as "Dear Mr. Smith"〔書信、演講等開頭的〕稱呼語 **2** [C,U] something you say or do when greeting someone 問候, 致意

sa·lute[1] /səˈlut; səˈluːt/ *v* **1** [I,T] to move your right hand to your head in order to show respect to an officer in the army, navy etc (向…) 行軍禮, (向…) 致敬 **2** [T] *formal* to praise someone for the things they have achieved, especially publicly【正式】〔尤指公開地〕讚揚, 頌揚:

salute sb as *James Joyce was saluted as the greatest writer of the 20th century.* 詹姆斯·喬伊斯被頌揚為20世紀最偉大的作家。**3** [T] *old-fashioned* to greet someone in a polite way, especially by moving your hand or body【過時】〔以揮手等〕向〔某人〕打招呼, 致意

salute[2] *n* **1** [C] an act of raising your right hand to your head as a sign of respect, usually done by a soldier to an officer〔通常指士兵向軍官的〕敬禮, 致敬 **2** [C] an occasion when guns are fired into the air in order to show respect for someone important〔向要人致敬的〕鳴禮砲(儀式): *a 21-gun salute* 鳴禮砲21響 **3** [C,U] *formal* a movement made to greet someone with your hand or head【正式】〔以揮手、點頭等動作表示的〕打招呼, 致意

sal·vage[1] /ˋsælvɪdʒ; ˈsælvɪdʒ/ *v* [T] **1** to save something from a situation in which other things have already been damaged, destroyed, or lost〔在火災、洪水等災難中〕搶救出〔某物〕: **salvage sth from** *We managed to salvage a few photo albums from the fire.* 我們設法從大火中搶救出幾本相冊。**2** to do something to make sure that you do not fail completely or lose something completely 挽救, 挽回〔某物〕: *They brought on Christiansen in a last-minute attempt to salvage the game.* 他們在最後一分鐘換克里斯蒂安森上場, 試圖挽回敗局。| *Is there still a chance of salvaging their marriage?* 他們的婚姻還有望挽救嗎? | **salvage your reputation** (=do something so that you do not lose people's respect) 挽回聲譽

salvage[2] *n* [U] **1** the act of saving things from a situation in which other things have already been damaged, destroyed, or lost 搶救, 救援: *a salvage operation* 搶救行動 **2** things that have been saved in this way 搶救出的財物

S3 **sal·va·tion** /sælˋveʃən; sælˈveɪʃən/ *n* [U] **1** the state of being saved from evil or death in the Christian religion〔基督教中〕對靈魂的拯救, 救贖 **2** something that prevents danger, loss, or failure 解救物; 救星, 救助者: **be the salvation of** *The recent rain will be the salvation of this year's wheat crop.* 最近這場雨會成為今年小麥作物的救星。

Salvation Ar·my /·ˌ·· ˈ··/ *n* **the Salvation Army** a Christian organization that tries to help poor people 救世軍〔基督教慈善組織〕

salve[1] /sæv; sælv/ *n* [C,U] a substance that you put on sore skin to make it less painful〔緩解疼痛的〕藥膏, 軟膏

salve[2] *v* [T] *formal*【正式】**salve your conscience** if you do something to salve your conscience, you do it to make yourself feel less guilty 使良心得到寬慰: *Buying his wife flowers helped to salve his conscience.* 他給妻子買花, 以使自己的良心得到寬慰。

sal·ver /ˋsælvɚ; ˈsælvə/ *n* [C] a large metal plate used for serving food or drink at a formal meal〔端飯菜或飲料用的〕金屬托盤: *a silver salver* 銀托盤

sal·vo /ˋsælvo; ˈsælvəʊ/ *n* [C usually singular 一般用單數] *formal*【正式】**1** [+of] the firing of several guns during a battle or as part of a ceremony〔火砲的〕齊放;〔禮砲的〕齊鳴 **2 opening salvo** the first in a series of questions, statements etc that you use to try to win an argument〔在爭論中提出的〕第一個問題, 頭一砲: *In his opening salvo against the education practices of the 1960s, Stein mentioned several important studies.* 在向20世紀60年代教育實踐開第一砲時, 斯坦提到幾項重要的研究。**3** sudden laughter, APPLAUSE etc from many people at the same time〔突如其來的〕一陣, 一片〔笑聲、掌聲等〕

Sa·mar·i·tan /səˋmærətn̩; səˈmærɪtən/ also 又作 **good samaritan** *n* [C] someone who helps you when you have problems 助人為樂者

sam·ba /ˋsæmbə; ˈsæmbə/ *n* [C,U] a fast dance from Brazil, or the type of music played for this dance〔巴西的〕桑巴舞; 桑巴舞曲

S1 W1 **same[1]** /sem; seɪm/ *adj* [only before a noun 僅用於名詞前] **1 the same person/place/thing etc a)** one particular person, thing etc and not a different one 同一人/地方/物品等: *He is in the same chair every evening.* 他每晚都坐在同一張椅子上。| *I'll never make the same mistake again.* 我再也不會犯同樣的錯誤了。| **[+as]** *It's hard to believe she's the same age as Brian.* 真難相信她和布賴恩同齡。| **this same person/that same thing etc** *It is those same people who voted for the Democrats who now complain about their policies.* 正是那些投了民主黨票的人, 現在卻抱怨起民主黨的政策。**b)** used to say two or more people, things etc are exactly like each other; IDENTICAL 同樣的人/地方/物品等: *It was so embarrassing! Both women were wearing the same dress.* 真尷尬, 兩位女士穿着一模一樣的連衣裙。| *It's the same kind of work, just a different department.* 還是同樣的工作, 只是換了個部門。| **[+as]** *He gets the same pay as me but he gets his own office.* 他和我拿同樣的工資, 但他有自己專用的辦公室。| **just/exactly the same** *If you can ride a pushbike then riding a motorbike is exactly the same thing. It's a question of balance.* 如果你會騎自行車, 那麼騎摩托車也完全一樣。只要保持平衡就行。| **much the same** (=almost the same) 大致相同 *The furniture is made in much the same way as it was over 200 years ago.* 這家具的製造工藝和二百多年前的大致一樣。**2** used to say that a particular person or thing does not change 沒有變化的, 一成不變的: *Her perfume has always had the same effect on me.* 她身上的香水味一直對我起着同樣的作用。| *He's the same old Peter, moody and irritable.* 他還是以前那個老樣子的彼得——喜怒無常, 動不動就發火。**3 at the same time** if two things happen at the same time they both happen together 同時: *Kate and I both went to live in Spain at the same time.* 我和凱特在同時移居西班牙。**4 the very same/the self same** used when you are surprised that someone or something is the same person or thing and not a different one 正是這一個/就是原來那個〔用於表示驚奇〕: *It is hard to believe it was in the very same house that Shakespeare wrote his plays.* 真難相信, 莎士比亞正是在這所房子裡寫出了他的劇作。**5 amount/come to the same thing** to have the same result or effect 結果[效果]都一樣: *It doesn't matter whether she was happy to leave or not – it amounts to the same thing. We need a new secretary.* 她是否樂意走並沒有甚麼關係, 反正我們需要換個祕書。**6 the same old story/excuse etc** *informal* something that you have heard many times before【非正式】老一套/老藉口〔指聽過多次的話〕: *It's the same old story – his wife didn't really love him.* 還是那一套——他老婆並不真正愛他。**7 same difference** *spoken especially AmE* used to say that different actions, behaviour etc have the same result or effect【口, 尤美】都一樣, 反正一個樣〔用於表示行為或表現等不同但效果一樣〕: *"I could mail the letter tomorrow morning or send a fax." "Same difference, it'll still not get there on time."* "我可以在明天上午發封信或發個傳真。" "都一樣, 反正都來不及。" **8 by the same token** in the same way, or for the same reasons 同樣地; 由於同樣的原因: *I realise that he hasn't come up with any new ideas, but by the same token we haven't needed any.* 我知道他沒有提出甚麼新的想法, 不過我們也並不需要。**9 be in the same boat** to be in the same difficult situation that someone else is in 處於同樣的困境

USAGE NOTE 用法說明: SAME

GRAMMAR 語法

Remember that **same** almost always has *the* or *this/that* etc before it. 切記, same 幾乎總用在 the, this, that 等詞之後: *They wear the same clothes every day* (NOT 不用 *They wear same clothes*). 他們每天都穿同樣的衣服。| *People are the same all over the world.* 全世界的人都一樣。| *That very same day, Trisha phoned him.* 就在同一天, 特里莎給他打了個電話。

In informal spoken English you will hear **same** used with *the* left out, but this is not considered correct

S

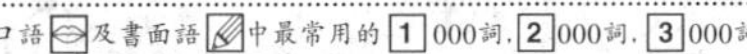

in writing. 在非正式口語中有時與 same 連用的 the 被省略, 但在書面語中則認為是不正確的: *"I thought the game was really good." "Same here."* "我認為這場比賽打得很精彩。" "我也有同感。" | *"What would you like?" "Same again please."* "你想要些甚麼?" "請再來一杯同樣的。"

When you are comparing, you always say that one things is **the same as** another. 進行比較時, the same as 表示一物與另一物相同: *Bob dresses just the same as his father did.* 鮑勃的衣着跟他父親當年的完全一樣。| *I go to the same college as you* (NOT 不用 *...to the same college with*). 我和你上的是同一所大學。

1 1 **same²** *pron* **1 the same a)** used to say that two or more people or things are exactly like each other 同樣的〔人或事物〕: *The coins may look the same but one's a forgery.* 這些硬幣看起來也許一樣, 但其中有一個是假的。| *Thanks for your help – I'll do the same for you one day.* 謝謝你的幫助 — 有一天我會報答你的。**b)** used to say that a particular person or thing does not change 沒有變化: *"How's your wife?" "About the same, thanks."* "你太太好嗎?" "還是老樣子, 謝謝。" | *Now that Sam's retired, things just won't be the same.* 既然薩姆已經退休, 情況就會不一樣了。**2 (and the) same to you!** *spoken* used as a reply to a greeting or as an angry reply to a rude remark【口】你也一樣!〔用於對問候語或粗魯話的回答〕: *"Happy Christmas!" "And the same to you, Ben."* "聖誕快樂!" "也祝你聖誕快樂, 本。" **3 just/all the same** in spite of a particular situation, opinion etc 仍然, 還是, 照樣: *I realise she can be very annoying, but I think you should apologise all the same.* 我知道她可能很討厭, 但我認為你還是應當向她道歉。**4 same here** *spoken* used to say that you feel the same way as someone else【口】我也一樣〔用於表示與別人有同感〕: *"I'm absolutely exhausted." "Same here!"* "真累死我了。" "我也一樣。" **5 (the) same again** used to ask for another drink of the same kind 再來一杯〔用於吩咐要同樣的飲料〕 **6 more of the same** used to mean a person, thing etc like the one just mentioned 也是一樣[相同]的〔用於指人或事物與剛才提及的那個一樣〕: *He has produced a string of thrillers, and this movie is just more of the same.* 他製作了一連串的驚慄片, 這部電影又屬這一類。—see also 另見 **it's all the same to me** (ALL² (10)), **one and the same** (ONE³ (7))

1 1 **same³** *adv* **1 the same (as)** in the same way 相同地, 一樣地: *"Rain" and "reign" are pronounced the same even though they are spelt differently.* rain 和 reign 發音相同, 儘管拼法不一樣。| *Everyone had to dress the same as a well known historical figure.* 每個人都必須裝扮成一位歷史名人。**2 same as sb** *spoken* just like someone else【口】和某人一樣: *I have my pride, same as anyone else.* 和別人一樣, 我有自尊心。

same·ness /ˋsemnɪs; ˈseɪmnɪ̵s/ *n* [U] a boring lack of variety, or the quality of being very similar to something else 千篇一律, 單調; 相同性, 共同之處

same·y /ˋsemɪ; ˈseɪmi/ *adj informal* boring and having very little variety【非正式】單調的, 無變化的: *His novels tend to be very samey.* 他的小説往往單調乏味。

sa·mo·sa /səˋmosə; səˈməʊsə/ *n* [C] a type of Indian food made from meat or vegetables covered in thin PASTRY (1) and cooked in hot oil 油炸三角餃〔印度的一種肉餡或菜餡餃〕

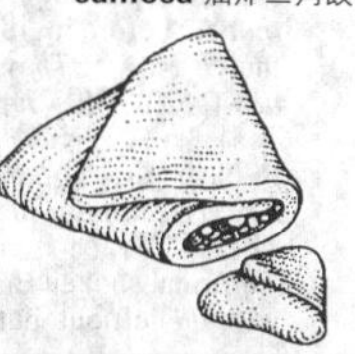
samosa 油炸三角餃

sam·o·var /ˋsæməˌvɑr; ˈsæməvɑː/ *n* [C] a large metal container used in Russia to boil water for making tea 俄式茶炊

sam·pan /ˋsæmpæn; ˈsæmpæn/ *n* [C] a small boat used in China and Southeast Asia〔中國和東南亞用的〕舢舨

3 2 **sam·ple¹** /ˋsæmpḷ; ˈsɑːmpəl/ *n* [C] **1** a small part or amount of something that is examined in order to find out something about the whole 樣品, 標本, 試樣: *They took a blood sample to test for hepatitis.* 他們取了血樣以檢查有無肝炎。| **[+of]** *I'd like to see some samples of your work.* 我想看看你作品的一些樣品。**2** a small amount of a product that people can try in order to find out what it is like 試用產品, 貨樣: **[+of]** *samples of a new shampoo* 新型洗髮劑的貨樣 **3** a group of people who have been chosen to give information or answers to questions〔抽樣調查時〕被抽選的一組人: *The sample consisted of 344 elementary and secondary school teachers.* 這次調查的抽樣包括 344 位中小學教師。| **random sample** (=one in which you choose people without knowing anything about them) 隨機抽樣 *Out of a random sample of drivers, 21% had been involved in an accident in the previous year.* 在隨機抽樣調查的駕駛員中, 有 21% 曾在上一年發生過事故。| **representative sample** (=one that is planned to include several different types of people) 代表性抽樣 *a nationally representative sample of over 4,500 elderly persons* 抽選四千五百餘位老人的全國代表性抽樣

sample² *v* [T] **1** to taste food or drink in order to see what it is like 品嘗, 嘗試〔食品、飲料等〕—see 見 TASTE² (USAGE) **2** [often passive 常用被動態] to choose some people from a larger group in order to ask them questions or get information from them 對〔人羣〕作抽樣調查: *18% of the adults sampled admitted having had problems with alcohol abuse.* 在接受抽樣調查的成年人中有 18% 承認有酗酒問題。**3** to try an activity, go to a place etc in order to see what it is like 體驗: *Here's your chance to sample the delights of country life.* 你去體驗鄉村生活樂趣的機會來了。

sam·pler /ˋsæmplɚ; ˈsɑːmplə/ *n* [C] a piece of cloth with different stitches on it, made to show how good someone is at sewing 刺繡樣品

sam·u·rai /ˋsæmʊˌraɪ; ˈsæmʊraɪ/ *n* [C] *plural* **samurai** a member of a powerful military class in Japan in former times〔日本從前的〕武士 —**samurai** *adj*: *a samurai sword* 武士刀

san·a·to·ri·um /ˌsænəˋtorɪəm; ˌsænəˈtɔːriəm/ *n* [C] a kind of hospital for sick people who are getting better but still need rest and a lot of care 療養院

sanc·ti·fy /ˋsæŋktəˌfaɪ; ˈsæŋktɪ̵faɪ/ *v* [T] **1** to make something socially or religiously acceptable or to give something official approval 正式認可, 批准, 使成為可接受的: *sexual roles that are sanctified by marriage* 為婚姻所認可的兩性角色 **2** to make something holy 使神聖化, 使聖潔化 —**sanctification** /ˌsæŋktəfəˋkeʃən; ˌsæŋktɪ̵fɪ̵ˈkeɪʃən/ *n* [U]

sanc·ti·mo·ni·ous /ˌsæŋktəˋmonɪəs; ˌsæŋktɪ̵ˈməʊniəs◂/ *adj formal* behaving as if you are morally better than other people, in a way that is annoying【正式】假裝聖潔的, 偽善的, 自認為道德高尚的: *sanctimonious politicians preaching to everyone about family values* 逢人便大談家庭價值觀的虛偽政客 —**sanctimoniously** *adv* —**sanctimoniousness** *n* [U]

sanc·tion¹ /ˋsæŋkʃən; ˈsæŋkʃən/ *n* **1 sanctions** [plural] official orders or laws stopping trade, communication etc with another country, as a way of forcing its leaders to make political changes〔對某國的〕制裁: **[+against]** *US sanctions against Cuba* 美國對古巴的制裁 | **impose sanctions on** (=start using sanctions) 實施制裁 | **lift sanctions** (=stop using sanctions) 解除制裁 **2** [U] official permission, approval, or acceptance 正式許可, 批准, 接受: *It emerged that the aide had acted without White House sanction.* 真相暴露, 原來該助理的行動並未經過白宮批准。**3** [C] a form of punishment that can be used if someone disobeys a rule or law 處罰, 懲罰

sanction² *v* [T] *formal*【正式】**1** to officially accept or allow something 批准, 准許: *The church refused to sanction the king's second marriage.* 教會拒絕批准國王的第二次婚姻。**2 be sanctioned by** to be made acceptable by something 為…所認可: *a barbaric custom, but one sanctioned by long usage* 一種野蠻但由來已久的風俗

sanc·ti·ty /ˋsæŋktətɪ; ˈsæŋktɨti/ *n* [U] **1 the sanctity of life/marriage etc** the quality that makes life, marriage etc so important that it must be respected and preserved 生命/婚姻等的神聖: *the sanctity of the Constitution* 憲法的無上尊嚴 **2** *formal* the holy or religious character of a person or place【正式】神聖, 聖潔: *an aura of sanctity* 神聖的氣氛

sanc·tu·a·ry /ˋsæŋktʃʊˌɛrɪ; ˈsæŋktʃuəri/ *n* **1** [C,U] a peaceful place that is safe and provides protection, especially for people who are in danger 庇護所, 避難所: **find/seek sanctuary** *Refugees fleeing from the advancing army found sanctuary in Geneva.* 大軍逼近, 難民們逃到日內瓦避難。**2** [C] an area for birds or animals where they are protected and cannot be hunted 禁獵區, 鳥獸保護區: **bird/wildlife etc sanctuary** *The park is the largest wildlife sanctuary in the US.* 這個公園是美國最大的野生動物保護區。**3** [U] the right that people had under Christian law, especially in former times, to be protected from police, soldiers etc by staying in a church〔從前教堂的〕庇護權〔指根據基督教教規, 在教堂的人有權不受警察或軍人的逮捕〕**4** [C] the part of a religious building that is considered to be the most holy〔教堂內的〕聖壇 **5** [C] *AmE* the room where religious services take place【美】〔進行宗教活動的〕殿堂, 聖所

sanc·tum /ˋsæŋktəm; ˈsæŋktəm/ *n* [C] **1 inner sanctum** *often humorous* a place or room that only a few important people are allowed to enter【常幽默】〔只允許少數要人入內的〕私室, 密室 **2** a holy place inside a temple〔廟宇中的〕聖所, 內殿

3 **sand¹** /sænd; sænd/ *n* [U] **1 a)** a substance consisting of very small pieces of rocks and minerals, that forms beaches and deserts 沙, 沙子: *footprints in the sand* 沙子上的腳印 **b)** this substance when it is found in soil, used in building etc〔建築用的〕砂; 沙子: *a mixture of sand and cement* 砂和水泥的混合物 **2 sands** [plural] *BrE* an area of beach【英】沙灘: *miles of golden sands* 綿延幾英里的金黃色沙灘 **3 the sands of time** *literary* moments of time that pass quickly【文】光陰, 時光

sand² *v* **1** [I,T] also 又作 **sand down** to make a surface smooth by rubbing it with SANDPAPER or using a special piece of equipment〔用砂紙等〕把…磨光, 擦淨 **2** [T] to put sand on a frozen road to make it safer〔為防滑〕撒沙於〔結冰的路面〕

san·dal /ˋsændḷ; ˈsændl/ *n* [C] a light shoe that is fastened onto your foot by leather bands and worn in warm weather 涼鞋 —see picture at 參見 SHOE¹ 圖

san·dal·wood /ˋsændḷˌwʊd; ˈsændlwʊd/ *n* [U] pleasant-smelling wood from a Southern Asian tree, or the oil from this wood 檀香木; 檀香油

sand·bag /ˋsændˌbæg; ˈsændbæg/ *n* [C] a bag filled with sand used for protection against floods, explosions etc〔用於防洪、防爆炸等的〕沙包, 沙袋

sand·bank /ˋsændˌbæŋk; ˈsændbæŋk/ *n* [C] a raised area of sand in a river, ocean etc〔河川、海洋中的〕沙壩

sand bar /ˈ· ·/ *n* [C] a long pile of sand in a river or the ocean formed by the movement of the water 河口沙洲〔河流或海洋中由水流形成的長條形沙洲〕

sand·blast /ˋsændˌblæst; ˈsændblɑːst/ *v* [T] to clean or polish metal, stone, glass etc with a machine that sends out a powerful stream of sand 對…噴砂〔以清洗或研磨金屬、石頭、玻璃等〕

sand·box /ˋsændˌbɑks; ˈsændbɒks/ *n* [C] *especially AmE* a special area of sand for children to play in【尤美】〔供兒童玩的〕沙池; SANDPIT *BrE*【英】

sand·cas·tle /ˋsændˌkæsḷ; ˈsændˌkɑːsəl/ *n* [C] a small model of a castle made out of sand by children playing on a beach〔兒童在海灘堆成的〕沙堡

sand dune /ˈ· ·/ *n* [C] a hill formed of sand in a desert or near the sea〔沙漠或海邊的〕沙丘 —see picture on page A12 參見 A12 頁圖

sand·er /ˋsændɚ; ˈsændə/ also 又作 **sanding ma·chine** /ˈ·· ·ˌ·/ *n* [C] an electric tool with a rough surface that moves very quickly, used for making surfaces smooth 打磨機

sand fly /ˈ· ·/ *n* [C] a small fly that bites people and lives on beaches 白蛉

sand·man /ˋsændmæn; ˈsændmæn/ *n* [singular] an imaginary man who is supposed to make children go to sleep〔童話中能使兒童入睡的〕睡魔

sand·pa·per¹ /ˋsændˌpepɚ; ˈsændˌpeɪpə/ *n* [U] strong paper covered on one side with sand or a similar substance, used for rubbing wood in order to make the surface smooth 砂紙

sandpaper² *v* [T] to rub something with sandpaper 用砂紙擦[磨]

sand·pip·er /ˋsændˌpaɪpɚ; ˈsændˌpaɪpə/ *n* [C] a small bird with long legs and a long beak that lives around muddy or sandy shores 鷸〔一種生活在泥岸或沙灘的腿和喙較長的小鳥〕

sand·pit /ˋsændˌpɪt; ˈsændˌpɪt/ *n* [C] *BrE* a special area of sand for children to play in【英】〔供兒童玩的〕沙池; SANDBOX *AmE*【美】

sand·stone /ˋsændˌston; ˈsændstəʊn/ *n* [U] a type of soft yellow or red rock often used in buildings 砂岩

sand·storm /ˋsændˌstɔrm; ˈsændstɔːm/ *n* [C] a storm in the desert in which sand is blown around by strong winds 沙暴

sand·trap /ˋsændˌtræp; ˈsændtræp/ *n* [C] *AmE* a hollow place on a GOLF course, filled with sand, from which it is difficult to hit the ball【美】〔高爾夫球場作為障礙的〕沙坑; BUNKER (3) *BrE*【英】—see picture on page A23 參見 A23 頁圖

sand·wich¹ /ˋsændwɪtʃ; ˈsænwɪdʒ/ *n* **1** [C] two pieces of bread with cheese, meat, egg etc between them 夾心麵包片, 三明治: *I've brought sandwiches for lunch today.* 我今天帶了三明治作午餐。| *a ham sandwich* 火腿三明治 **2** [C] *BrE* a cake consisting of two layers with JAM¹ (1) and cream between them【英】果醬奶油夾心蛋糕 —see also 另見 CLUB SANDWICH, OPEN SANDWICH 2

sandwich² *v* [T] **be sandwiched between** to be in a very small space between two other things 被夾在…中間: *The car was sandwiched between two big trucks.* 小汽車被夾在兩輛大貨車中間。

sandwich board /ˈ·· ·/ *n* [C] two boards with advertisements on them that hang in front and behind someone who is paid to walk around in public〔在公共場所到處走動做廣告者胸前和背後所掛的〕人身懸掛夾板廣告牌, 三明治廣告牌

sandwich course /ˈ·· ·/ *n* [C] *BrE* a course of study at a college or university that includes periods spent working in industry or business【英】〔學院或大學的〕工讀交替制課程

sand·y /ˋsændɪ; ˈsændi/ *adj* **1** covered with sand 被沙覆蓋的: *My towel's all sandy!* 我的毛巾上全是沙子! | **sandy beach** *BrE* (=one that is made of sand not stones)【英】沙灘 **2** hair that is sandy is a yellowish-brown〔頭髮等〕沙色的, 淺黃灰色的, 淺黃棕色的 —**sandiness** *n* [U] —see picture on page A12 參見 A12 頁圖

sane /sen; seɪn/ *adj* **1** able to think in a normal and reasonable way 心智健全的, 神智正常的 —opposite 反義詞 INSANE **2** reasonable and based on sensible thinking 明智的, 清醒的: *a sane solution to a delicate problem* 解決微妙問題的明智方法 **3 keep sb sane** to stop someone from thinking about their problems and becoming upset 不讓某人擔憂 —**sanely** *adv* —see also 另見 SANITY

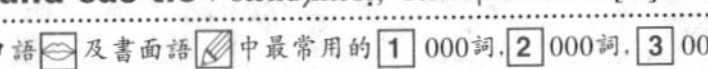

sang /sæŋ; sæŋ/ the past tense of SING

sang-froid /sɑŋ `frwɑ; ˌsɒŋ 'frwɑː/ *n* [U] courage and the ability to keep calm in dangerous or difficult situations 鎮定, 沉着, 冷靜: *The British, once renowned for their stiff upper lip and sang-froid, were now regarded as a nation of hooligans.* 曾經以沉着冷靜著稱的英國人, 後來卻被看成是一個無賴民族。

san·gri·a /sæŋ`griə; sæŋ'griːə/ *n* [U] a Spanish drink made from red wine, fruit, and fruit juice 桑格利亞汽酒〔一種由紅葡萄酒、水果和果汁配成的西班牙飲料〕

san·gui·na·ry /`sæŋgwɪnˌɛrɪ; 'sæŋgwɪ̈nəri/ *adj formal* involving violence and killing【正式】血腥的, 殘暴的: *a bitter and sanguinary war* 慘烈的血戰

san·guine /`sæŋgwɪn; 'sæŋgwɪ̈n/ *adj formal*【正式】**1** cheerful and hopeful about the future; CONFIDENT 樂觀的; 充滿自信的: *We are less sanguine about the prospects for peace since the row at the UN.* 自從在聯合國發生那場爭吵以後, 我們對和平的前景就不那麼樂觀了。**2** red and healthy looking 有血色的, 紅潤的: *a sanguine complexion* 紅潤的膚色 —**sanguinely** *adv*

san·i·tar·i·um /ˌsænə`tɛrɪəm; ˌsænɪ̈'teəriəm/ *n* [C] an American spelling of SANATORIUM sanatorium 的美式拼法

san·i·ta·ry /`sænəˌtɛrɪ; 'sænɪ̈təri/ *adj* **1** [only before noun 僅用於名詞前] connected with health, especially with the removal of dirt, infection, or human waste 有關衛生的, 與健康有關的: *After examining the sanitary arrangements, they ordered the whole place to be disinfected*. 檢查過公共衛生的安排之後, 他們下令整個地方都要消毒。**2** clean and not involving any danger to your health 清潔的; 於健康無害的 —opposite 反義詞 INSANITARY

S

sanitary pad /'···· ˌ·/ also 又作 **sanitary tow·el** /'····ˌ··/ *BrE*【英】, also 又作 **sanitary napkin** *AmE*【美】*n* [C] a piece of soft material that a woman wears between her legs during her PERIOD[1] (4) 衛生巾, 月經帶

san·i·ta·tion /ˌsænə`teʃən; ˌsænɪ̈'teɪʃən/ *n* [U] the protection of public health by removing and treating waste, dirty water etc 公共衛生, 環境衛生

sanitation work·er /ˌ··'··ˌ··/ *n* [C] *AmE formal* someone who removes waste material that people put outside their houses【美, 正式】垃圾工, 清潔工〔挨家挨戶收垃圾的工人〕

san·i·tize also 又作 **-ise** *BrE*【英】/`sænəˌtaɪz; 'sænɪ̈taɪz/ *v* [T] **1** to make news, literature etc less offensive by taking out anything unpleasant, with the result that it is not complete or interesting 刪除…的令人不快內容, 淨化〔以減少冒犯性, 因而使作品不完整或乏味〕: *The film is a highly sanitized version of his life, making no mention of his many affairs.* 這部傳記影片經過了大量刪節, 沒有提到他的許多風流韻事。**2** to clean something thoroughly, removing dirt and BACTERIA 對…作衛生處理, 使…衛生, 給…消毒

san·i·ty /`sænətɪ; 'sænɪ̈ti/ *n* [U] **1** the ability to think in a normal and sensible way 神智清楚, 心智健全: *I took a vacation by myself to try to regain my sanity.* 我獨自去休假, 想讓自己清醒一下。**2** the condition of being mentally healthy 明智, 清醒: *The man's story became stranger and stranger, and I began to doubt his sanity.* 那個人的話越說越離奇, 我開始懷疑他是否神智正常。—opposite 反義詞 INSANITY

sank /sæŋk; sæŋk/ the past tense of SINK

San·skrit /`sænskrɪt; 'sænskrɪt/ *n* [U] an ancient language of India 梵文, 梵語〔印度古代的語言〕

sans ser·if /sæn `sɛrɪf; ˌsæn 'serɪ̈f/ *n* [U] *technical* a style of printing in which letters have no SERIF【術語】〔印刷中的〕無襯線字體

San·ta Claus /`sæntɪ ˌklɔz; 'sæntə klɔːz/ also 又作 **Santa** *n* [singular] an imaginary old man with red clothes and a long white BEARD who, children believe, brings them presents at Christmas 聖誕老人; FATHER CHRISTMAS *BrE*【英】

sap[1] /sæp; sæp/ *n* **1** [U] the watery substance that carries food through a plant〔植物的〕液, 汁 **2** [C] *AmE informal* a stupid person who is easy to deceive or treat badly【美, 非正式】傻瓜, 容易上當的人 **3 feel the sap rising** *humorous* to begin to feel full of energy, especially in a sexual way【幽默】覺得精力〔尤指性慾〕旺盛起來, 覺得元氣旺盛

sap[2] *v* **sapped, sapping** [T] to gradually weaken or destroy something〔逐漸〕削弱;〔逐漸〕破壞: **sap sb's courage/energy/strength** *Her long illness was gradually sapping Charlotte's strength.* 長期生病正逐漸消耗着夏洛特的元氣。

sa·pi·ent /`sepɪənt; 'seɪpiənt/ *adj literary* very wise【文】睿智的, 賢明的 —**sapiently** *adv* —**sapience** *n* [U]

sap·ling /`sæplɪŋ; 'sæplɪŋ/ *n* [C] a young tree 幼樹, 樹苗

sap·per /`sæpɚ; 'sæpə/ *n* [C] *BrE* a soldier whose job involves digging and building【英】工兵, 工程兵

sap·phic /`sæfɪk; 'sæfɪk/ *adj literary* LESBIAN【文】女性同性戀的

sap·phire /`sæfaɪr; 'sæfaɪə/ *n* [C,U] a transparent bright blue jewel 藍寶石

sap·py /`sæpɪ; 'sæpi/ *adj* **1** *AmE* expressing love and emotions in a way that seems silly【美】多情得傻乎乎的; SOPPY (1) *BrE*【英】: *a sappy song* 傷感的歌曲 **2** full of SAP (=liquid in a plant)〔植物〕多汁液的

sap·ro·phyte /`sæproˌfaɪt; 'sæprəfaɪt/ *n* [C] a kind of plant that eats substances that were once living 腐生植物 —**saprophytic** /ˌsæpro`fɪtɪk; ˌsæprə'fɪtɪk/ *adj*

sap·wood /`sæpˌwʊd; 'sæpwʊd/ *n* [U] the younger outer wood in a tree, that is paler and softer than the wood in the middle〔樹皮和心材之間較輕軟的〕邊材

sar·a·band /`særəˌbænd; 'særəbænd/ *n* [C] a slow piece of music based on a type of 17th century dance 薩拉班德舞曲〔源自 17 世紀的一種緩慢的舞曲〕

Sar·a·cen /`særəsn̩; 'særəsən/ *n* [C] *old use* a word for a Muslim, used in the Middle Ages【舊】薩拉森人〔中世紀時對穆斯林的稱呼〕

Sa·ran Wrap /sə`ræn ræp; sə'ræn ræp/ *n* [U] *AmE trademark* thin transparent plastic used for wrapping food【美, 商標】塞綸(食物)保鮮膜; CLINGFILM *BrE*【英】

sar·cas·m /`sɑrkæzəm; 'sɑːkæzəm/ *n* [U] a way of speaking or writing that involves saying the opposite of what you really mean in order to make an unkind joke or to show that you are annoyed 諷刺, 挖苦: **heavy sarcasm** (=very clear sarcasm) 尖刻的諷刺 *She was an hour late. "Good of you to arrive on time," George said, with heavy sarcasm.* 她遲到一個鐘頭。"你準時到達, 真難得," 喬治以尖刻的諷刺口吻說。

sar·cas·tic /sɑr`kæstɪk; sɑː'kæstɪk/ *adj* saying things that are the opposite of what you mean in order to make an unkind joke or to show that you are annoyed 挖苦的, 嘲諷的: *a sarcastic remark* 諷刺的話 —**sarcastically** /-klɪ; -kli/ *adv*

sar·coph·a·gus /sɑr`kɑfəgəs; sɑː'kɒfəgəs/ *n* [C] a decorated stone box for a dead body, used in ancient times〔古代有裝飾的〕石棺

sar·dine /sɑr`din; ˌsɑː'diːn◂/ *n* **1** [C] a small young fish that is often packed in flat metal boxes〔罐頭〕沙丁魚 **2 be packed like sardines** to be crowded tightly together in a small space 擠得像沙丁魚一樣, 擁擠不堪: *commuters packed like sardines on the evening train* 晚班火車上擠得像沙丁魚一樣的下班乘客

sar·don·ic /sɑr`dɑnɪk; sɑː'dɒnɪk/ *adj* speaking or smiling in an unpleasant way, that shows you do not have a good opinion of someone or something 嘲諷的, 譏諷的: *Brett raised a sardonic eyebrow.* 布雷特嘲諷地揚起一道眉毛。—**sardonically** /-klɪ; -kli/ *adv*

sa·ree /`sɑri; 'sɑːri/ *n* [C] another spelling of SARI sari 的另一種拼法

sarge /sɑrdʒ; sɑːdʒ/ *n* [singular] *spoken* SERGEANT【口】中士; 巡佐

sa·ri /ˋsɑri; ˈsɑːri/ *n* [C]a long piece of cloth that you wrap around your body, worn especially by women from India〔印度婦女用以裹身的〕莎麗（服）

sari 莎麗（服）

sar·ky /ˋsɑrkɪ; ˈsɑːki/ *adj BrE informal* SARCASTIC【英，非正式】嘲諷的

sar·nie /ˋsɑrnɪ; ˈsɑːni/ *n* [C] *BrE informal* a SANDWICH【英，非正式】三明治

sa·rong /səˋrɔŋ; səˈrɒŋ/ *n* [C] a loose skirt consisting of a long piece of cloth wrapped around your waist 紗籠〔裹在腰部的一種寬鬆服裝〕

sarsa·pa·ril·la /ˌsæspəˋrɪlə; ˌsɑːspəˈrɪlə/ *n* [U] a sweet non-alcoholic drink made from the root of the SASSAFRAS plant 菝葜汽水

sar·to·ri·al /sɑrˋtorɪəl; sɑːˈtɔːriəl/ *adj formal* connected with men's clothes or how they are made【正式】男裝的；關於男裝縫製的：**sartorial elegance** *a man of great sartorial elegance* 着裝極其講究的男子 —**sartorially** *adv*

SAS /ˌɛs e ˋɛs ˌes eɪ ˈes/ *n* [singular] Special Air Service; a British military force that is specially trained to do secret and dangerous work 特種航空隊〔英國一支經特殊訓練、執行祕密危險任務的特種部隊〕

SASE /ˌɛs e ɛs ˋi; ˌes eɪ es ˈiː/ *n* [C] *AmE* self-addressed stamped envelope; an envelope that you put your name, address, and a stamp on, so that someone else can send you something【美】〔寫有自己姓名地址並貼足郵票的〕回信信封

sash /sæʃ; sæʃ/ *n* [C] **1** a long piece of cloth that you wear around your waist like a belt 腰帶：*a party dress with a blue sash* 有藍色腰帶的晚禮服 **2** a long piece of cloth that you wear over one shoulder and across your chest as a sign of a special honour〔斜掛在肩上標誌榮譽的〕綬帶，肩帶：*a sash with the words Miss USA* 寫着"美國小姐"字樣的綬帶 **3** a wooden frame that has a sheet of glass fixed into it to form part of a window 窗框，窗扇

sa·shay /sæˋʃe; sæˈʃeɪ/ *v* [I always+adv/prep] *informal* to walk in a confident way moving your body from side to side, especially so that people look at you【非正式】大搖大擺地走；輕快自信地走：*Olivia sashayed down the catwalk.* 奧利維亞輕快自如地走在T形台上。

sash win·dow /ˋ· ˌ··/ *n* [C] a window consisting of two frames that you open by sliding one up or down, behind or in front of the other 上下拉窗，框格窗

sass /sæs; sæs/ *v* [T] *AmE informal* to talk in a rude way to someone you should respect【美，非正式】對…粗魯無禮，與…頂嘴：*Don't you sass me young lady!* 你可別頂撞我，小姑奶奶！

sas·sa·fras /ˋsæsəˌfræs; ˈsæsəfræs/ *n* [C,U] a small Asian or North American tree, or the pleasant-smelling roots of this tree used in food and drink 檫樹〔產於亞洲或北美的小喬木〕；檫樹根〔用作食品和飲料的香料〕

Sas·se·nach /ˋsæsn̩ˌæk; ˈsæsənæk/ *n* [C] *ScotE* a word meaning an English person, used as a joke or to show disapproval【蘇格蘭】英格蘭人〔戲謔或貶稱用語〕

sas·sy /ˋsæsɪ; ˈsæsi/ *adj AmE*【美】**1** a child who is sassy is rude to someone they should respect〔小孩〕粗魯的，無禮的 **2** a woman who is sassy behaves in a way that is intended to be attractive to men〔女人〕活潑的，輕佻的

Sat a written abbreviation 縮寫= SATURDAY

sat /sæt; sæt/ the past tense and past participle of SIT

Sa·tan /ˋsetn̩; ˈseɪtn/ *n* [singular] the Devil, considered to be the main evil power and God's opponent 撒旦，魔鬼，惡魔

sa·tan·ic /seˋtænɪk; səˈtænɪk/ *adj* **1** connected with practices that treat the Devil like a god 崇拜惡魔的：*satanic rites* 撒旦崇拜儀式 **2** extremely cruel or evil 窮兇極惡的，極其邪惡的：*satanic laughter* 猙獰的笑 —**satanically** /-klɪ; -kli/ *adv*

sat·an·is·m /ˋsetn̩ˌɪzəm; ˈseɪtənɪzəm/ *n* [U] the practice of respecting the Devil as if he were a god 撒旦崇拜，對惡魔的崇拜 —**satanist** *n* [C] —**satanist** *adj*

sat·ay sauce /ˌsate ˋsɔs; ˌsæteɪ ˈsɔːs/ *n* [U] a thick liquid made with PEANUTS and used to give a special taste to meat〔烹調用的〕花生醬，沙爹醬

satch·el /ˋsætʃəl; ˈsætʃəl/ *n* [C] a leather bag that you carry over your shoulder, used especially in the past by children for carrying books to school〔皮製〕書包，小背包 —see picture at 參見 BAG¹ 圖

sate /set; seɪt/ *v* [T] *literary* **be sated (with)** to have had enough or more than enough of something to satisfy you【文】充分滿足於（…）；（對…）感到膩煩

sat·el·lite /ˋsætl̩ˌaɪt; ˈsætəlaɪt/ *n* [C] **1** a machine that has been sent into space and goes around the Earth, moon etc, used for radio, television, and other electronic communication 人造衛星：*the launch of a communications and weather satellite* 氣象通訊衛星的發射 | **by satellite** (=using a satellite) 通過人造衛星 *This broadcast comes live by satellite from New York.* 本節目是通過人造衛星從紐約現場直播的。**2** a moon that moves around a PLANET 衛星：*The moon is a satellite of the Earth.* 月亮是地球的衛星。**3 a)** a country, town, or organization that is controlled by or is dependent on another larger one 衛星國；衛星城；附屬機構：**satellite country/town/suburb** (=one that has developed next to a large city) 衛星國/衛星城/郊區

satellite dish /ˈ··· ˌ·/ *n* [C] a large circular piece of metal that receives special television signals so that you can watch satellite television 碟形衛星天線

satellite dish 碟形衛星天線

satellite tel·e·vi·sion /ˌ··· ˈ····/ also 又作 **satellite TV** /ˌ··· ··ˈ·/ *n* [U] television programmes that are broadcast using satellites in space 衛星電視

sa·ti·ate /ˋseʃɪˌet; ˈseɪʃieɪt/ *v* [T usually passive 一般用被動態] *literary* to satisfy a desire or need for something such as food or sex, especially so that you feel you have had too much【文】使充分滿足，使過飽 —**satiated** *adj*: *Zeke lay on the couch, satiated after his meal.* 齊克吃飽飯後，在長沙發上躺着。—**satiety** /səˋtaɪətɪ; səˈtaɪəti/ *n* [U]

sat·in¹ /ˋsætɪn; ˈsætən/ *n* [U] a type of cloth that is very smooth and shiny 緞子

satin² *adj* having a smooth shiny surface 緞子般光滑的

sat·in·wood /ˋsætn̩ˌwʊd; ˈsætənwʊd/ *n* [C,U] an East Indian tree, or the hard smooth wood that comes from this tree〔產於印度東部的〕緞木；〔堅硬平滑的〕緞木木材

sat·in·y /ˋsætɪnɪ; ˈsætəni/ *adj* smooth, shiny, and soft 光滑的，柔軟的，緞子似的

sat·ire /ˋsætaɪr; ˈsætaɪə/ *n* **1** [U] a way of talking or writing about something, for example politics and politicians, in which you deliberately make them seem funny so that people will see their faults 諷刺，譏諷：*the characteristic use of satire in Jonson's work* 瓊生作品中諷刺手法的典型運用 **2** [C] a play, book, story etc written in this way〔戲劇、書、故事等的〕諷刺作品：*a political satire* 政治諷刺作品 —**satirical** /səˋtɪrɪkl̩; səˈtɪrɪkəl/ *adj* —**satiric** *adj* —**satirically** /-klɪ; -kli/ *adv*

sat·i·rist /ˋsætərɪst; ˈsætərɪst/ *n* [C] someone who writes satire 諷刺作家，諷刺作品創作者

sat·ir·ize also 又作 **-ise** *BrE*【英】/ˋsætəˌraɪz; ˈsætəraɪz/ *v* [T] to use satire to make people see someone or something's faults 諷刺: *a play satirizing the fashion industry* 一部諷刺時裝業的戲劇

3 3 **sat·is·fac·tion** /ˌsætɪs`fækʃən; ˌsætɪ̵s'fækʃən/ *n* **1** [C, U] a feeling of happiness or pleasure because you have achieved something or got what you wanted 滿足, 滿意; 稱心: *She got great satisfaction from helping people learn.* 她從幫助人們學習中得到很大的滿足。| *a sigh of deep satisfaction* 深感滿足地舒一口氣 | **job satisfaction** (=enjoyment of your job) 從工作中得到的滿足感 —opposite 反義詞 DISSATISFACTION **2** [U] fulfilment of a need, demand, claim, desire etc〔需要、願望等的〕滿足, 實現: *the satisfaction of public demand* 對公眾要求的滿足 | *sexual satisfaction* 性慾的滿足 **3** [U] *formal* a reply to a complaint that you have made【正式】〔對投訴的〕回應: **get satisfaction** *I got no satisfaction from the customer complaints department.* 我沒有得到顧客投訴部的圓滿答覆。**4 have/get the satisfaction of doing sth** to get a small amount of pleasure from a situation that is unsatisfactory in other ways 得到做某事的補償: *Well, at least you'll get the satisfaction of knowing you were right.* 哎, 你至少可以知道自己沒有錯並感到欣慰吧。**5 to sb's/sth's satisfaction a)** if something is explained, proved etc to someone's satisfaction, they now accept and believe it 讓…相信和接受 **b)** if a situation, arrangement etc is to someone's satisfaction, they are pleased with it 使…感到滿意: *Finally we got the furniture arranged to her satisfaction.* 我們終於把家具佈置得令她滿意。

sat·is·fac·to·ry /ˌsætɪs`fæktərɪ; ˌsætɪ̵s'fæktəri◂/ *adj* **1** good enough for a particular situation or purpose 合適的, 滿足要求的: *Reicher could not provide a satisfactory excuse for his absence.* 理查對自己的缺席提不出一個言之成理的解釋。| *None of the solutions was entirely satisfactory.* 這些解決辦法沒有一個是完美的。**2** making you feel pleased and happy 令人滿意的, 令人高興的: *a satisfactory conclusion* 令人滿意的結論 —**satisfactorily** *adv* —opposite 反義詞 UNSATISFACTORY

3 **sat·is·fied** /`sætɪsˌfaɪd; 'sætɪ̵sfaɪd/ *adj* **1** pleased because something has happened in the way that you want, or because you have achieved something 滿意的, 滿足的: *a satisfied smile* 滿意的微笑 | **[+with]** *I'm not really satisfied with the way he cut my hair.* 我對他給我理的髮型不太滿意。—opposite 反義詞 DISSATISFIED **2** feeling sure that something is right or true 確信的: **[+that]** *The police weren't satisfied that Boyet was telling the truth.* 警方不相信博伊特講的是真話。**3 satisfied?** *spoken* used to show that someone has annoyed you by asking too many questions or making too many demands【口】該滿意了吧?〔對提出過多的問題或要求表示不耐煩〕: *Okay, okay, I'll go over there and ask him this afternoon. Satisfied?* 好吧, 好吧, 我今天下午就過去問他。該滿意了吧? —see also 另見 SELF-SATISFIED

2 2 **sat·is·fy** /`sætɪsˌfaɪ; 'sætɪ̵sfaɪ/ *v* [T] **1** to please someone by providing enough of what they want 使〔某人〕滿意: *Nick felt that nothing he did would satisfy his boss.* 尼克覺得他做的工作沒有一件能使老闆滿意。**2 satisfy a request/desire/need etc** to provide what someone has asked for, what they need etc 滿足要求/慾望/需要等: *Just to satisfy my curiosity, how much did it cost?* 我只是出於好奇心, 這花了多少錢? | *The salad just didn't satisfy her hunger.* 那份沙拉她根本吃不飽。**3** *formal* to make someone feel sure that something is right or true; CONVINCE【正式】使〔某人〕確信[信服]: **satisfy sb of sth** *Jackson tried to satisfy me of his innocence.* 傑克遜盡量讓我相信他的清白無辜。**4** *formal* to be good enough for a particular purpose, standard etc【正式】符合〔要求、標準等〕: *You have not yet satisfied all the conditions for admission.* 你尚未符合所有的錄取條件。**5** *formal* to FULFIL an EQUATION (1) in mathematics, etc【正式】滿足〔方程〕

sat·is·fy·ing /`sætɪsˌfaɪ·ɪŋ; 'sætɪ̵sfaɪ-ɪŋ/ *adj* **1** making you feel pleased and happy, especially because you have got what you wanted 令人高興的, 令人滿意的: **it is satisfying to do sth** *After all he'd put me through, it was very satisfying to see him begging for once.* 吃了他那麼多苦頭之後, 我終於看到他有一次向人求乞, 這真是大快人心。**2** food that is satisfying makes you feel that you have eaten enough〔飯菜〕豐足的: *a satisfying meal* 豐盛的一餐 —**satisfyingly** *adv*

sat·su·ma /sæt`sumə; sæt'suːmə/ *n* [C] a fruit that looks like a small orange, and has no seeds 無籽小蜜橘

sat·u·rate /`sætʃəˌret; 'sætʃəreɪt/ *v* [T] **1** *formal* to make something very wet; SOAK[1] (2)【正式】浸濕, 使濕透: *Water poured through the hole, saturating the carpet.* 水從洞裡流出來, 浸濕了地毯。**2** to put a large number of people or things into a particular place, especially so that you could not add any more 使充滿, 使充斥: *The area was saturated with police to prevent further trouble.* 那個地區到處都部署了警察, 以防進一步的騷亂。**3 saturate the market** to offer so much of a product for sale that there is more than people want to buy 使市場飽和 **4** *technical* to mix as much of a solid into a chemical mixture as possible【術語】使〔化學溶液〕飽和

sat·u·rat·ed /`sætʃəˌretɪd; 'sætʃəreɪtɪ̵d/ *adj* **1** extremely wet 濕透的, 浸透的: *By the time I arrived home, I was completely saturated.* 回到家時, 我全身都濕透了。| **[+with]** *saturated with sweat* 被汗水濕透的 **2** *technical* if a chemical mixture is saturated, it has had as much of a solid mixed into it as possible【術語】飽和的

saturated fat /ˌ···· '·/ *n* [C,U] a kind of fat from meat and milk products that is thought to be less healthy than other kinds of fat from vegetables or fish 飽和脂肪

sat·u·ra·tion /ˌsætʃə`reʃən; ˌsætʃə'reɪʃən/ *n* [U] **1** the act or result of making something completely wet 浸透, 濕透 **2 saturation bombing** a military attack in which a whole area is bombed 飽和轟炸 **3 saturation coverage** a situation in which a particular event is given so much attention by newspapers, television etc that everyone has heard about it 飽和報道: *The trial was given saturation coverage by the press.* 新聞界對這次審訊進行了飽和報道。**4** *technical* the state of a chemical mixture that has reached its SATURATION POINT (2)【術語】飽和(狀態)

saturation point /··'·· ·/ *n* [C usually singular 一般用單數] **1** a situation in which no more people or things can be added because there are already too many 飽和點; 極限: *The number of summer tourists in the area has now reached saturation point.* 來這一地區避暑的旅遊者人數已趨飽和。**2** *technical* the state that a chemical mixture reaches when it has had as much of a solid substance mixed into it as possible【術語】〔化學溶液的〕飽和點

Sat·ur·day /`sætɚdɪ; 'sætədi/ *n* [C,U] the day between Friday and Sunday. In Britain, Saturday is considered the sixth day of the week, and in the US it is considered the seventh day of the week 星期六〔在英國, 星期六被看作是一週中的第六天, 而在美國, 它是一週中的第七天〕: **on Saturday** *We went for a picnic on Saturday.* 我們星期六去野餐。| *Deats always goes home on Saturdays.* 迪茨每個星期六都回家。| **last/next Saturday** *I saw Sally last Saturday at the Mall.* 我上星期六在購物中心見到了莎莉。| **on a Saturday** *My birthday is on a Saturday this year.* 我今年的生日是個星期六。

Sat·urn /`sætɚn; 'sætən/ *n* [singular] the PLANET that is sixth in order from the sun and is surrounded by large rings 土星 —see picture at 參見 SOLAR SYSTEM 圖

sat·ur·na·li·a /ˌsætɚ`nelɪə; ˌsætə'neɪliə/ *n* [C] *literary* an occasion when people enjoy themselves in a very wild and uncontrolled way【文】縱情歡樂, 狂歡

sat·ur·nine /`sætɚˌnaɪn; 'sætənaɪn/ *adj literary* looking sad and serious, especially in a threatening way【文】憂鬱的, 陰沉的: *Goebbel's lean saturnine face had the hypnotic power of a swaying cobra.* 戈培爾那副瘦削陰鬱的臉孔具有眼鏡蛇昂首擺動時的催眠力。

sat·yr /ˋsætɚ; ˈsætə/ *n* [C] a god in ancient Greek literature, represented as half human and half goat 薩梯〔古希臘神話中半人半羊的神〕

sauce /sɔs; sɔːs/ *n* **1** [C,U] a thick cooked liquid that is served with food to give it a particular taste 沙司，(濃)調味汁，醬汁: **tomato/chocolate etc sauce** *pasta with tomato sauce* 澆了番茄醬的意大利麵條 **2** [U] *BrE old-fashioned* rude remarks made to someone that you should respect【英，過時】無禮的話，頂撞的話: *Less of your sauce, my girl!* 不得無禮，女孩子！

sauce boat /ˈ· ·/ *n* [C] a container that has a handle and is shaped like a boat, used for serving sauce with a meal〔有柄的〕船形調味汁碟[碗]

sauce·pan /ˋsɔsˌpæn; ˈsɔːspæn/ *n* [C] a deep round metal container with a handle that is used for cooking〔有柄的〕深平底鍋 —see picture at 參見 PAN¹ 圖

sau·cer /ˋsɔsɚ; ˈsɔːsə/ *n* [C] a small round plate that curves up at the edges that you put a cup on 茶托 —see also 另見 FLYING SAUCER

sauc·y /ˋsɔsɪ; ˈsɔːsi/ *adj* **1** *especially BrE* saucy pictures, jokes etc are about sex in a way that is amusing but not shocking【尤英】講無傷大雅的性笑話的: *saucy postcards* 印有性笑話圖畫的明信片 **2** slightly rude, in a way that is amusing 戲謔的，沒大沒小的: *a saucy remark* 莽撞的話語 —**saucily** *adv* —**sauciness** *n* [U] —see also 另見 SAUCE (2)

sau·er·kraut /ˋsaurˌkraut; ˈsaʊəkraʊt/ *n* [U] a German food made from CABBAGE (=a round green vegetable) that has been left in salt so that it tastes sour (德國式)泡菜

sau·na /ˋsaunə; ˈsaʊnə/ *n* [C] **1** a room that is heated to a very high temperature by hot air, where people sit because it is considered healthy 蒸氣浴室，桑拿浴室 **2** a period of time when you sit or lie in a room like this 蒸氣浴，桑拿浴: **have/take a sauna** *I have a sauna and massage every week.* 我每星期洗一次桑拿浴並做一次按摩。

saun·ter /ˋsɔntɚ; ˈsɔːntə/ *v* [I always+adv/prep] to walk in a slow unhurried way, that makes you look confident or proud〔自信或傲慢地〕漫步: *Will came sauntering down the road with his hands in his pockets.* 威爾兩手插在衣袋裡大搖大擺地沿路漫步。—**saunter** *n* [singular]

3 **saus·age** /ˋsɔsɪdʒ; ˈsɒsɪdʒ/ *n* [C,U] **1** [C] a small tube of skin filled with a mixture of meat, SPICEs etc, eaten hot or cold 香腸: *pork sausages* 豬肉香腸 **2 not a sausage!** *BrE old-fashioned, informal* nothing at all【英，過時，非正式】一點也沒有！: *"Have you heard from Tom yet?" "No, not a sausage!"* "你有沒有湯姆的消息?" "沒有，毫無音訊!"

sausage dog /ˈ·· ·/ *n* [C] *BrE informal* a DACHSHUND【英，非正式】臘腸狗〔即達克斯獵狗〕

sausage meat /ˈ·· ·/ *n* [U] the soft meat mixture that is used to make sausages 灌香腸用的碎肉，香腸肉餡

sausage roll /ˌ·· ˈ·/ *n* [C] *BrE* a piece of sausage meat inside a tube of PASTRY【英】〔外包麵皮的〕香腸肉卷

sau·té /soˋte; ˈsəʊteɪ/ *v* [T] to cook something quickly in a little hot oil or fat〔用少量油〕快炸；快煎；快炒: *Sauté the potatoes for 5 minutes.* 把馬鈴薯炸上五分鐘。

sav·age¹ /ˋsævɪdʒ; ˈsævɪdʒ/ *adj* **1** very cruel and violent 兇猛的，殘暴的: *a savage dog* 惡狗 | *The punishment seemed too savage.* 這種懲罰似乎太兇殘了。**2** criticizing someone or something very severely〔批評〕猛烈的，惡狠狠的: **savage attack/criticism etc** *an unexpectedly savage attack on the President's record* 對總統政績出其不意的猛烈抨擊 **3** very severe and harmful 極嚴重的；有害的: *savage pay cuts* 大幅度減薪 **4** [only before noun 僅用於名詞前] *old-fashioned* an insulting way of describing a person or group from a country where the way of living seems very simple and undeveloped; PRIMITIVE¹ (1)【過時】未開化的，原始的，野蠻的〔侮辱性說法〕—**savagely** *adv* —**savageness** *n* [U]

savage² *n* [C] *old-fashioned* an insulting word for someone from a country where the way of living seems very simple and undeveloped【過時】未開化的人，野蠻人〔侮辱性用詞〕: *This culture flourished while Europeans were still savages living in caves.* 當歐洲人還是穴居的野蠻人時，這個地方的文化早已十分發達了。

savage³ *v* [T] **1** if an animal savages someone, it attacks and bites them, causing serious injuries〔動物〕亂咬，兇猛地攻擊: *savaged by a mad dog* 被瘋狗咬了 **2** to criticize someone or something very severely 激烈地批評: *The play was savaged by the critics.* 這齣戲受到評論家的猛烈批評。

sav·ag·e·ry /ˋsævɪdʒrɪ; ˈsævɪdʒəri/ *n* [C,U] extremely cruel and violent behaviour 野蠻，殘暴(行為): *He used to beat the boy with great savagery.* 他過去常常極其殘暴地毆打那個男孩。

sa·van·na, savannah /səˋvænə; səˈvænə/ *n* [C,U] a large flat area of grassy land in a warm part of the world〔熱帶或亞熱帶的〕稀樹草原

sav·ant /səˋvɑnt; ˈsævənt/ *n* [C] *literary* someone who knows a lot about a particular subject【文】博學之士，專家，學者

save¹ /sev; seɪv/ *v* 1 1

1 ►FROM HARM/DANGER 免除傷害/危險◄ [T] to make someone or something safe from danger, harm, or destruction 救，拯救，挽救: *Thousands of lives have been saved by this drug.* 這種藥挽救了成千上萬人的生命。| **save sb/sth from** *He saved his friend from drowning.* 他救起了他那位溺水的朋友。| *The sudden fall in interest rates saved the company from bankruptcy.* 利率的突然下降救了這家公司，使其免於破產。

2 ►MONEY IN A BANK 銀行存款◄ also 又作 **save up** [I,T] to keep money so that you can use it later, especially when you gradually add more money over a period of time 儲蓄，積攢: **[+for]** *I'm saving up for a new car.* 我正在攢錢準備買輛新車。| *So far, I've saved about £500.* 到目前為止，我已儲蓄了大約500英鎊。—see also 另見 SAVER

3 ►NOT WASTE 不浪費◄ [T] to use less money, time, energy etc so that you do not waste any 節省，節約，避免〔金錢、時間、精力等的〕浪費: *We'll save a lot of time if we go by car.* 我們要是乘汽車去可以節省很多時間。| *modern energy-saving devices* 現代化的節能裝置 | **save sb sth** *Reserving a seat in advance could save you $10.* 提前訂座可以讓你節省十美元。

4 ►TO USE LATER 以備後用◄ [T] to keep something so that you can use or enjoy it in the future 保留，保存: *Let's save the rest of the cake for later.* 我們把剩下的蛋糕留着以後吃吧。| *He saved his strength for the end of the race.* 他保存體力準備在賽跑的最後關頭衝刺。

5 ►COLLECT 收集◄ also 又作 **save** sth ÷ **up** [T] to keep all the objects of a particular kind that you can find, so that they can be used for a special purpose 收集〔以備後用〕，積存: *She always saved foreign stamps for her grandson's album.* 她經常為孫子的集郵簿收集外國郵票。| *I'm saving up tokens for a free set of wine glasses.* 我正在積存禮品券，以便免費換取一套酒具。

6 ►HELP TO AVOID 使避免◄ [T] to help someone by making it unnecessary for them to do something unpleasant or inconvenient 使…免除〔不愉快或不方便的事情〕: **save sb sth** *If you could lend me £5, it would save me a trip to the bank.* 如果你能借我五英鎊，我就省得去一趟銀行了。| **save sb doing sth** *A brush with a long handle will save you having to bend down.* 用長柄刷子，你就不必彎腰了。| **save sb the trouble/bother (of doing sth)** *I'll wash up and save you the trouble of doing it later.* 我來洗碗吧，省得你待一會兒還得洗。

7 ►KEEP FOR SB 替某人保留◄ [T] to stop people from using something so that it is available for someone else〔為某人〕保留: **save sb sth** *Will you save me a seat on the bus?* 請在公共汽車上給我留個座位好嗎？| **save sth for sb** *We'll save some dinner for you if you're late.* 你要是回來晚了，我們會給你留飯的。

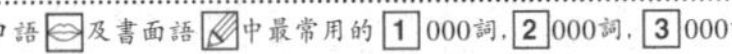

8 save sb's life to prevent someone from dying 救某人的命: *Surgeons operated in an attempt to save her life.* 外科醫生給她動了手術，試圖挽救她的生命。

9 you saved my life *spoken* used to thank someone who has got you out of a difficult situation or solved a problem for you【口】你幫了我的大忙: *Thanks again for the loan – you really saved my life.* 再一次謝謝你那筆貸款，你真是幫了我大忙了。

10 save sb's skin/neck/bacon etc *informal* to make it possible for someone to escape from an extremely difficult or dangerous situation【非正式】逃脫危險；免遭傷害: *He lied in court to save his skin.* 他為了保命在法庭上撒了謊。

11 save the day to make a situation end successfully when it seemed likely to end badly 扭轉局面；挽回敗局；解圍: *Frank saved the day by offering to drive us all there.* 弗蘭克提出要開車送我們大家去，使問題迎刃而解。

12 save face to do something that will stop you looking stupid or feeling embarrassed 保全面子 —see also 另見 FACE-SAVING

13 saving grace the one good thing that makes someone or something acceptable〔彌補不足的〕可取之處: *Beautiful photography was the saving grace of an otherwise awful film.* 這部電影拍得很糟糕，但優美的攝影彌補了它的不足。

14 not be able to do sth to save your life *informal* to be completely unable to do something【非正式】完全不會做某事: *He couldn't paint to save his life!* 他無論如何也不會畫畫！

15 save your breath *spoken* used to tell someone that it is not worth saying anything, because nothing they say will make any difference to the situation【口】用不着白費唇舌，說也沒有用

16 save sb from themselves to prevent someone from doing something that is likely to harm them in the end 阻止某人做某事以免自嘗苦果

17 ►SPORT 體育運動◄ [T] to stop the other side from getting a GOAL (2) in a sport such as football, HOCKEY etc〔足球、曲棍球等〕阻礙對方得分，救〔球〕—see picture on page A23 參見 A23 頁圖

18 ►COMPUTER 電腦◄ [I,T] to make a computer keep the work that you have done on it 儲存〔輸入的資料〕: *Don't forget to save before you close the file.* 在關閉文件之前，不要忘記儲存。

19 ►RELIGION 宗教◄ [I,T] in the Christian church, to free someone from the power of evil and SIN〔基督教〕拯救（某人）；使擺脫罪孽: *Jesus came to save sinners.* 基督降世以拯救罪人。

save on sth *phr v* [T] to avoid wasting something by using as little as possible of it 節省，避免浪費: *We use a wood stove to save on electricity.* 我們使用燒柴的爐子以節省電力。

save² *n* [C] an action by the GOALKEEPER in football, HOCKEY etc that prevents the other team from getting a GOAL (2)〔足球、曲棍球等守門員的〕救球，阻礙對方得分

save³ also 又作 **saving** *prep formal* except for【正式】除…（之）外: *She answered all the questions save one.* 除了一個問題以外，她回答了所有問題。| [+that] *I agree with you, save that you've got one or two details wrong.* 除了你有一兩處細節弄錯以外，我同意你的看法。

sav·er /ˈsevɚ; ˈseɪvə/ *n* [C] *especially BrE* someone who saves money in a bank or BUILDING SOCIETY【尤英】〔存款於銀行或購房互助會等的〕儲蓄者: **regular saver** (=someone who usually saves money with a particular bank etc) 固定儲戶，老儲戶 *Regular savers can benefit from a 3% annual bonus.* 固定儲戶每年可獲得3%的紅利。

3 **sav·ing** /ˈsevɪŋ; ˈseɪvɪŋ/ *n* **1 savings** [plural] all the money that you have saved, especially in a bank 銀行存款，儲蓄金，積蓄 **2** [C usually singular 一般用單數] an amount of something that you have not used or spent 未使用[消耗]的量: *This amount represents a considerable saving over last year's expenditure.* 這個數額表示去年的開支有相當大的節餘。**3** [U] the act of keeping money so that you can use it later 存錢〔以備後用〕—see also 另見 SAVE¹ (2)

savings ac·count /ˈ‥ ‥ˌ‥/ *n* [C] a bank account that pays INTEREST¹ (4) on the money you have in it〔可獲利息的〕儲蓄賬戶

savings and loan as·so·ci·a·tion /ˌ‥ ‥ ‥ˈ‥ ‥ˌ‥/ *n* [C] *AmE* a business that lends money, usually so that you can buy a house, and into which you pay money to be saved【美】購房互助協會，儲蓄貸款協會〔貸款給會員作購房用，會員也可在其中儲蓄的商業機構〕; BUILDING SOCIETY *BrE*【英】

savings bank /ˈ‥ ‥/ *n* [C] a bank that encourages people to save small amounts of money〔鼓勵小額存款的〕儲蓄銀行

savings bond /ˈ‥ ‥/ *n* [C] *technical* a BOND¹ (1) sold by the US government that cannot be sold from one person to another【術語】〔美國政府發行的不能轉賣給他人的〕儲蓄公債

sa·viour *BrE*【英】, **savior** *AmE*【美】/ˈsevjɚ; ˈseɪvjə/ *n* **1** [C usually singular 一般用單數] someone or something that saves you from a difficult or dangerous situation 救助者，挽救者，救星 **2** [singular] in the Christian religion, a word for Jesus Christ〔基督教的〕耶穌基督，救世主

sav·oir-faire /ˌsævwɑr ˈfɛr; ˌsævwɑː ˈfeə/ *n* [U] the ability to do or say the right things, especially in social situations 機敏處事的才幹，隨機應變的能力: *famous in diplomatic circles for his savoir-faire* 在外交界以他靈活應變的能力而聞名

sa·vo·ry /ˈsevərɪ; ˈseɪvəri/ *n* **1** [U] a plant used in cooking to add taste to meat, beans etc〔烹調用的〕香薄荷 **2** [C] the American spelling of SAVOURY savoury 的美式拼法

sa·vour¹ *BrE*【英】, **savor** *AmE*【美】/ˈsevɚ; ˈseɪvə/ *v* [T] to make an activity or experience last as long as you can, because you are enjoying every moment of it 品嘗；欣賞: *She sipped her wine, savouring every drop.* 她慢慢地啜着酒，細細品嘗每一滴的滋味。—see 見 TASTE (USAGE)

savour of sth *phr v* [T] *formal* to seem to have a small amount of a quality that people do not like【正式】具有〔少量人們討厭〕的性質，帶有…的意味: *radical ideas savouring of revolution* 帶有革命意味的激進思想

savour² *BrE*【英】, **savor** *AmE*【美】*n* [singular,U] *formal*【正式】**1** a taste or smell, especially one that is pleasant 滋味，氣味，〔尤指令人愉快的〕味道 **2** interest and enjoyment 趣味，樂趣，吸引力: *Life seemed to have lost its savour for him.* 對他來說，生活似乎已經失去了樂趣。

sa·vour·y¹ *BrE*【英】, **savory** *AmE*【美】/ˈsevərɪ; ˈseɪvəri/ *adj* **1** *BrE* having a taste that is not sweet【英】鹹味的；辛辣的 **2** having a pleasant and attractive smell or taste 味道可口的，美味的: *A savoury smell of stew came from the kitchen.* 從廚房飄出一陣燉肉的香味。**3 not very savoury/none too savoury etc** something that is not savoury seems unpleasant or morally unacceptable 令人不快的，名聲不好的: *This hotel doesn't have a very savoury reputation.* 這家旅館的名聲可不大好。

savoury² *BrE*【英】, **savory** *AmE*【美】*n* [C] a small amount of salty food, sometimes served at the end of a formal meal〔最後上的〕鹹味小菜

sa·voy /səˈvɔɪ; səˈvɔɪ/ *n* [C] a type of CABBAGE (=round green vegetable) with curled leaves 皺葉甘藍，皺葉卷心菜

sav·vy /ˈsævɪ; ˈsævi/ *n* [U] *informal* practical knowledge and ability【非正式】實際知識和能力 —**savvy** *adj AmE*【美】: *I just wasn't savvy enough in high school to keep up.* 我讀高中時水平不夠，總是跟不上。

saw¹ /sɔ; sɔː/ the past tense of SEE

saw² *n* [C] **1** a tool that has a flat blade with a row of V-shaped metal pieces, used for cutting wood 鋸 —see picture at 參見 TOOL¹ 圖 **2** *old use* a well-known wise statement; PROVERB【舊】格言, 諺語

saw³ *v past tense* **sawed** *past participle* **sawn** /sɔn; sɔːn/ *especially BrE*【尤英】, **sawed** *especially AmE*【尤美】[I,T] to cut something using a saw〔用鋸子〕鋸, 鋸開: *We had to saw the board in half.* 我們不得不把那塊板鋸成兩半。| **[+through]** *He sawed through a power cable by mistake.* 他誤把電纜給鋸斷了。

saw at sth *phr v* [T] to cut something with a repeated backwards and forwards movement 拉鋸似地來回切: *He sawed at the loaf with a blunt knife.* 他用鈍刀拉鋸似地切那條麵包。

saw sth ÷ **off** *phr v* [T] to remove something by cutting it off with a saw 鋸掉〔某物〕: *One branch was dead and needed to be sawn off.* 有根樹枝枯死了, 需要鋸掉。

saw sth ÷ **up** *phr v* [T] to cut something into many pieces, using a saw 把〔某物〕鋸成小塊: *I sawed up the tree for firewood.* 我把那棵樹鋸成一段段作木柴用。

saw·bones /ˋsɔˌbonz; ˈsɔːbəʊnz/ *n* [C] *AmE informal* a doctor or SURGEON【美, 非正式】醫生; 外科醫生

saw·buck /ˋsɔˌbʌk; ˈsɔːbʌk/ *n* [C] *AmE old-fashioned* a $10 note【美, 過時】面額十元的鈔票

saw·dust /ˋsɔˌdʌst; ˈsɔːdʌst/ *n* [U] very small pieces of wood that are left when you cut wood with a SAW² (1) 鋸末, 鋸(木)屑

saw·mill /ˋsɔˌmɪl; ˈsɔːmɪl/ *n* [C] a factory where logs are cut into boards using a machine〔把木材鋸成木板的〕鋸木廠

sawn-off shot·gun /ˌ· · ˈ··/ *BrE*【英】, **sawed-off shotgun** *AmE*【美】*n* [C] a SHOTGUN that has had its BARREL (=long thin part) cut short 槍管鋸短的獵槍

sawyer /ˋsɔjɚ; ˈsɔːjə/ *n* [C] *old use* someone whose job is sawing wood【舊】鋸工, 鋸材手, 操鋸手

Sax·on /ˋsæksn̩; ˈsæksən/ *n* [C] a member of the German race that came to live in England in the 5th century 撒克遜人〔在5世紀定居於英格蘭的日耳曼人〕—**Saxon** *adj*

sax·o·phone /ˋsæksəˌfon; ˈsæksəfəʊn/ *n* [C] also 又作 **sax** /sæks; sæks/ *informal*【非正式】a metal musical instrument with a single REED (2), used mostly in JAZZ and dance music 薩克斯管〔一種銅管樂器〕

sax·oph·o·nist /ˋsæksəˌfonɪst; sækˈsɒfənɪst/ *n* [C] someone who plays the saxophone 薩克斯管吹奏者

S 1 W 1

say¹ /se; seɪ/ *v past tense and past participle* **said** /sɛd; sed/ *3rd person singular present tense* **says** /sɛz; sez/

S

① USE WORDS 運用詞語
② WRITING/NUMBERS 文字/數字
③ MEAN/SHOW 表示/表明
④ GENERAL OPINION 普遍觀點
⑤ SUGGEST/SUPPOSE 認為/假定
⑥ SPOKEN PHRASES 口語片語
⑦ OTHER MEANINGS 其他意思

① USE WORDS 運用詞語

1 ▶WORD/SOUND 詞/聲音◀ [T] to pronounce a word or sound 說, 講: *"What did you say?"* "你說甚麼?" | *"I'm so tired," she said.* "我很累," 她說。| **say hello/goodbye etc** *She left without even saying goodbye.* 她連一聲再見也沒說就走了。—see 見 SPEAK (USAGE)

2 ▶THOUGHT/OPINION 思想/意見◀ [I only in questions and negatives 僅用於疑問句和否定句,T] to express a thought, opinion, explanation etc in words〔用言語〕表達〔思想、意見等〕: *Don't believe anything he says.* 他說的你都不要相信。| *"Why did she leave?" "I don't know – she didn't say."* "她為甚麼走了?" "我不知道 —— 她沒有說。" | **thing to say** *What a ridiculous thing to say!* 說這樣的話真荒唐! | **say (that)** *Adam says he's thirsty.* 亞當說他口渴。| *I always said that you'd do okay in the end, didn't I?* 我總是說你一定會有好結局的, 我沒這樣說嗎? | **say how/why/who etc** *Did she say what happened?* 她有沒有說發生了甚麼事? | *The doctor couldn't say how long it would take.* 醫生沒有說清楚這需要多長時間。| **say yes/no (to)** (=agree or refuse) 同意/拒絕 *Can I go, Mum? Oh please say yes!* 媽, 我可以去嗎? 求求你讓我去吧! | **say so/not** *"Do you think they're happy?" "I wouldn't say so."* "你認為他們快樂嗎?" "我可不這麼說。" | **sth to say** *Does anyone else have anything to say?* 還有誰要說甚麼嗎? | *I couldn't think of anything to say to him.* 我想不出有甚麼話要對他說。| **say (you're) sorry** *Look, I've said I'm sorry – what more do you want?* 哎, 我都已經道歉了 —— 你還想怎麼樣? | **say a few words** (=make a short speech) 說幾句話, 作簡短的發言 *I'd just like to say a few words about the schedule.* 我只想簡單談談關於時間安排的問題。| **say your piece** (=say what you want to say) 暢所欲言, 說自己想說的話 *OK, you've said your piece – now shut up.* 行了, 你要說的話都說了 —— 現在該閉嘴了。

3 say to yourself to think something 心裡想, 自忖, 暗自思量: *So I said to myself "It's time I left."* 於是我心裡想, "我該走了。"

4 ▶TELL SB TO DO STH 吩咐某人做某事◀ [T not in progressive 不用進行式] to tell someone to do something 叫某人去做某事: **say to do sth** *Nina said to meet her at 4.30.* 妮娜吩咐4點30分去接她。

5 ▶RULES 規則◀ [T] to state what people are allowed to do 規定, 要求: **say (that)** *The law says you can't sell alcohol on a Sunday afternoon.* 法律規定星期日下午不能出售酒類。| *Mom says we're not allowed to talk to strangers.* 媽媽吩咐我們不要和陌生人說話。

6 say your prayers/say grace etc [T] to speak the fixed set of words that form a prayer etc 祈禱: *Have you said your prayers?* 你祈禱了嗎?

7 say sth to sb's face *informal* to make an unpleasant or criticizing remark to the person that the remark is about【非正式】當着某人的面直說[直接批評]: *If you're going to make comments about my work, at least have the courage to say them to my face!* 你如果要對我的工作評頭品足, 至少要有勇氣當着我的面說!

8 say sth you shouldn't *informal* to say something that is embarrassing or secret【非正式】說不該說的話: *Oh dear, have I said something I shouldn't again?* 噢, 親愛的, 我又說了甚麼不該說的話了嗎? —see also 另見 **say a mouthful** (MOUTHFUL (4))

② WRITING/NUMBERS 文字/數字

9 [T not in passive 不用被動態] to give information in written words, numbers, or pictures〔用文字、數字、圖畫等〕表示〔信息〕, 說明: *The clock in the hall said it was 7.30.* 大廳的鐘是7點30分。| *What does this word say?* 這個詞是甚麼意思? | *Well that's what Sue said in her letter.* 唔, 那就是蘇在她信中所說的意思了。| **say (that)** *It said in the paper that there were no survivors.* 報上說沒有生還者。| **say to do sth** *The label says to take one before meals.* 標籤上說要在飯前服一片。| **say who/what/how etc** *Does it say in the instructions how* *much you should use?* 說明書上有沒有說明該用多少？

③ **MEAN/SHOW 表示/表明**

10 ▶NOT DIRECTLY 非直接地◀ [T] to suggest what you mean in an indirect way 間接表示，表達: *What do you think the writer is saying in this passage?* 你認為作者在這一段要表達甚麼意思？| *So what you're saying is, there's none left.* 那麼你的意思是說，一個都沒剩下？| **say (that)** *Are you saying I'm fat?* 你的意思是說我胖嗎？

11 ▶SHOW CHARACTER/QUALITIES 表明特性/性質◀ [T] to show what someone or something's real character or qualities are 表明〔某人的性格或某物的特質〕是…: **say a lot about** (=show something very clearly) 清楚地表明 *The fact that he returned the money says a lot about his character.* 他退還那筆錢這件事清楚地表明了他的品格。| **say a lot for** (=show that someone or something has a lot of good qualities) 表明〔某人或某物〕有許多優點 *It says a lot for Jayne that she had the sense not to tell them.* 傑恩懂得不該告訴他們，這表明她品德很好。| **not say much for** (=show that something is not of a high standard or quality) 表明〔某事物〕質量不高 *These results don't say much for the quality of the teaching.* 這些成績表明教學的質量不高。

12 ▶HAVE MEANING 有意義◀ [T] to have or show a meaning that someone can understand 表達〔某種意義〕: *Most modern art doesn't say much to me.* 大部分現代藝術在我看來沒有多大意思。

S

④ **GENERAL OPINION 普遍觀點**

13 [T] to express an opinion that a lot of people have 多數人認為: *Well, you know what they say – blood's thicker than water.* 噢，你知道，常言說: 血濃於水。| **they say (that)** (=people think that) 人們認為 *They say he's been all round the world.* 大家都說他周遊過全世界。| **(be) said to do sth** *She's said to be the richest woman in the world.* 據說她是世界上最富有的女人。| **it is said (that)** *It is said that he was a spy during the war.* 據說在戰爭時期他是個間諜。

⑤ **SUGGEST/SUPPOSE 認為/假定**

14 [T usually in imperative 一般用於祈使句] to suggest or suppose that something might happen or might be true 認為; 假定，比方說: *I say we should forget the whole thing.* 我認為我們應該把整件事情都忘掉。| **let's/just say (that)** *Let's say your plan fails, then what?* 假定你的計劃失敗了，那時候怎麼辦？| *Just say you won the lottery – what would you do?* 假定你的彩票中了獎——你將會做甚麼？

Frequencies of the verb **say** in spoken and written English 動詞 say 在英語口語和書面語中的使用頻率

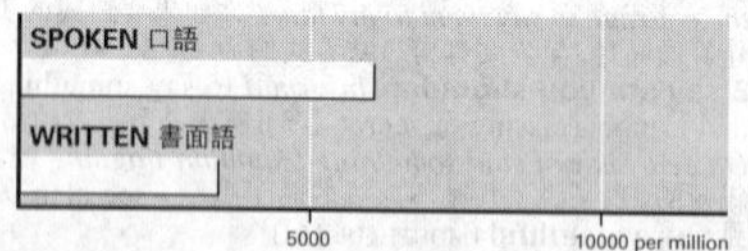

Based on the British National Corpus and the Longman Lancaster Corpus 據英國國家語料庫和朗文蘭卡斯特語料庫

This graph shows that the verb **say** is much more common in spoken English than in written English. This is because it is used in a lot of common spoken phrases. 本圖表顯示，動詞 say 在英語口語中的使用頻率遠遠高於書面語，因為口語中很多常用片語是由 say 構成的。

⑥ **SPOKEN PHRASES 口語片語**

15 I must say used when you want to emphasize what you are saying 我得說〔用以表示強調〕: *Well, that's clever, I must say!* 這個，我得說那可真聰明！| *I must say it made me jump.* 我跟你說，它嚇了我一跳。

16 I can't say (that) used to say that you definitely do not think or feel something 我絕不認為: *I can't say I envy her being married to him!* 我絕對不會羨慕她能嫁給他！

17 having said that used before saying something that makes the opinion you have just given seem less strong 儘管如此，話雖如此: *Hannah didn't do a very good job, but having said that, I don't think I could have done any better.* 漢娜幹得不太好，但儘管如此，我想我也不見得會幹得更好。

18 say no more used to show that you understand what someone means, although it has not been said directly 不用再說了〔用以表示明白了某人的意思〕: *"I saw him leaving her flat at 6.30 this morning." "Say no more!"* "我看見他今天早晨6點30分離開她的住處。" "不用再說了！"

19 enough said used to say that something is clear, and does not need to be explained any further 無須再作解釋〔用以表示某事已經清楚〕

20 I'd rather not say used when you do not want to tell someone something 我最好還是不說〔表示不想把某事告訴某人〕: *"So what are your plans now?" "I'd rather not say at the moment."* "你現在有甚麼打算？" "眼下我最好不去談它。"

21 you can say that again! used to say that you completely agree with someone 你說得真對〔用以表示完全同意某人的意見〕: *"Gosh, it's hot today." "You can say that again!"* "哎呀，今天真熱。" "你說得真對！"

22 say when used to ask someone to tell you when to stop doing something, especially pouring them a drink 夠了就請說一聲〔尤用於斟酒時〕

23 who says? used to say that you do not agree with a statement, opinion etc 誰說的？〔用以表示不同意別人的說法〕: *Who says I have to retire at 60?* 誰說我 60 歲一定要退休？

24 who can say? used to say that nobody knows the answer to a question 誰能說得準？〔用以表示沒有人知道問題的答案〕: *Who can say whether they'll ever find a cure?* 誰也不能肯定他們能否找到一種治療的辦法。

25 who's to say? used to say that your judgment of a situation might not be correct, because you can never be sure what will happen in the future 誰能斷定？〔用以表示對將來發生的事沒有把握〕: *But who's to say that she won't do better than him in the end?* 誰能斷定她最終不會幹得比他好？

26 what do you say? used to ask someone if they agree with a suggestion 你覺得怎樣？你看行嗎？〔用以詢問某人是否同意所提的建議〕: *We could go into partnership; what do you say?* 我們可以合夥做生意，你覺得怎樣？| **what do you say we do sth?** *What do you say we all go to a movie?* 我們大家一起去看電影，你看怎麼樣？| **what do/would you say to (doing) sth?** *What would you say to a meal out?* 我們出去吃飯，你說好嗎？

27 you don't say! used to show that you are not at all surprised by what someone has just told you 你用不着說！〔用以表示對某人告訴你的事一點也不覺得驚訝〕

28 say the word used to tell someone they have only to ask and you will do what they want 只要你說一聲〔用以表示願意做某人要求的事〕: *Just say the word and I'll get rid of her.* 只要你開口，我就叫她走人。

29 I'll say this for him/her etc used when you want to mention something good about someone, especially when you have been criticizing them 我也要為他/她等說句(公道)話〔尤用在批評過某人之後〕: *I will say this for Tom – at least he's consistent.* 我要為湯姆說句公道話——他至少能始終如一。

30 say what you like *especially BrE* used when giving an opinion that you are sure is correct, even if the person you are talking to might disagree with you【尤英】即使你不同意，不管你怎麼認為〔用以強調自己的看法沒錯〕: *Say what you like, she's a very good mother.*

不管你怎麼認為，她就是個好母親。

31 whatever you say used to tell someone that you agree to do what they want, accept their opinion etc, especially because you do not want an argument 不管你怎麼說我都同意〔尤用於不想爭論時〕

32 can't say fairer than that *BrE* used to say that you have given the best offer that you can【英】不能給更優厚的條件了，不能出更高的價格了：*I'll give you £25 for it; I can't say fairer than that.* 我給你 25 英鎊買它，不能出更高的價了。

33 you said it! a) used when someone says something that you agree with, although you would not have actually said it yourself 正是如此！〔表示同意對方的話，但自己不會那麼說〕：*"I was always stubborn as a kid." "You said it!"* "我小時候總是很固執。""這話你可說對了。" **b)** *AmE* used to say that you agree with someone【美】我同意！你說得對！：*"Let's go home." "You said it! I'm tired."* "我們回家去吧。""同意！我也累了。"

34 what have you got to say for yourself? used to ask someone for an explanation when they have done something wrong 你還有甚麼理由可說？：*Late again? What have you got to say for yourself?* 又遲到了吧？這回你怎麼解釋？

35 that's not saying much used to emphasize that something is not very strange or unusual 沒甚麼奇怪的，沒甚麼不尋常的〔用以強調〕：*She's taller than me, but I'm only 5 foot 2, so that isn't saying much.* 她比我高，不過我才五英尺二英寸，所以那也沒甚麼奇怪的。

36 when all's said and done used to remind someone about an important point that they should remember 說到底，畢竟〔用以提醒某人記住某個重要情況〕：*When all is said and done, he's only nine years old – don't expect too much.* 他畢竟才九歲——不能對他期望過高。

37 I wouldn't say no (to) used to say that you would like something, and would accept if you were offered it 我想（要）...：*I wouldn't say no to a cup of coffee.* 我不反對喝杯咖啡。

38 I say *old-fashioned*【過時】**a)** *BrE* used to get someone's attention【英】喂；我說呀〔用以引起他人的注意〕：*I say, could you pass me that book?* 喂，請把那本書遞給我好嗎？ **b)** used to show you are slightly interested, angry etc 啊，嘿〔用以表示略感興趣或生氣等〕：*"My husband's ill today." "I say! I'm sorry to hear that."* "我丈夫今天病了。""啊！聽到這事我很難過。"

⑦ OTHER MEANINGS 其他意思

39 go without saying used to say that something is so clear that it does not really need to be stated 顯然；不言而喻：*It goes without saying that I'll return the money afterwards.* 用不着說，我以後會把錢歸還的。

40 to say the least used to say that you could have described something, criticized someone etc a lot more severely than you have 至少可以說：*Jane could have been more considerate, to say the least.* 簡本來應當考慮得更周到一點，至少可以這麼說。

41 that is to say used before describing what you mean in more detail 那就是說；換句話說；更具體地說：*Let's do as he suggested, that is to say, you fly down and I'll bring the car.* 我們就按他的建議做吧，也就是說，你乘飛機去，我則開汽車過去。

42 that's not to say used to make it clear that something is not true, when you think someone might think that it is 那並不是說，那並不表示：*That's not to say that I agree with what you're doing, of course.* 當然，這並不是說我贊同你在做的事。

43 not to say *especially BrE* used to show that you could have used a stronger word to describe something【尤英】近乎，甚至可以說：*It would be silly, not to say mad, to sell your car.* 你要是把汽車賣掉那就太蠢了，簡直是瘋了。

44 say £45/100 years/Tuesday etc used to suggest a possible example, amount etc when discussing something 比方說 45 英鎊／100 年／星期二等〔用於在商討時提出一個可能的例子、數量等〕：*They must owe say $2,000 in rent.* 他們一定欠了比方說 2,000 美元的租金。| *Can you come to dinner? Say, 7.30?* 你能來吃晚飯嗎？7 點 30 分怎麼樣？

45 there's no saying how/what/when etc used to say that it is impossible to know something 說不準怎樣／甚麼／甚麼時候等：*There's no saying what he'll do next.* 不可能知道他下一步要做甚麼。

46 nothing/something/not much etc to be said for used to say that there are a lot of, not many etc good reasons for doing something〔某種做法〕沒有／有些／沒有多少道理：*There's a lot to be said for taking a few days off now and then.* 偶爾休假幾天是大有好處的。| *It was a strange plan, with very little to be said for it.* 那是一份很奇怪的計劃，看不出它有甚麼道理。

47 to say nothing of used to say that you have described only some of the bad points about something 更不用說；何況〔用以表示對某事物的壞處只提及了其中的幾點〕：*It was a complete waste of time, to say nothing of all the stress and bother!* 這完全是浪費時間，緊張和麻煩就更不用說了！

48 have something to say about to be angry about something 為...不高興，對...生氣：*If you don't do your homework your father will have something to say about it!* 你要是不做作業，你父親就會生氣了！

49 have a lot to say for yourself someone who has a lot to say for themselves talks all the time 有許多話要說，說個沒完

50 what sb says goes used to emphasize who is in control in a situation 某人說了算；照某人說的辦〔用於強調〕：*My wife wants to go to Italy this year, and what she says goes!* 我妻子想今年去意大利，而去哪裡是她說了算！ —see also 另見 **wouldn't say boo to a goose** (BOO[2] (3)), **easier said than done** (EASY[2] (6)), **no sooner said than done** (SOON (4))

USAGE NOTE 用法說明: SAY

WORD CHOICE 詞語辨析: **say, tell, repeat, give, tell sb about/of, talk about/of, speak about/of**

In general, you **say** words **to** someone, but what you **tell** someone is facts, information etc. 一般地說，say ... to 是對別人說話，而 tell 表示把事實、信息等告訴別人：*I said hello/sorry/thanks/a few words to her* (NOT 不用 *told her 'Hello'*). 我向她問好／道歉／道謝／說了幾句話。| *I told her the reason/the truth/a lie/a story/a joke* (NOT 不用 *said*). 我告訴她原因／告訴她真相／對她撒謊／給她講了個故事／給她講了個笑話。

You usually only use **say** with the actual words that are spoken. 在表達某人所說的原話時通常只能用 say: *He said, "Open the door."* "開門。"他說。Only **tell** can be used to report commands. 而引述命令時只能用 tell: *He told me to open the door.* 他叫我開門。

There are special verbs for **say**ing certain things. 說某些事要用某些特殊動詞：*I asked "Where is it?"* (less often 較少用 *I said...*). 我問道："在甚麼地方？" | *I'd like to welcome you* (NOT usually 一般不用 *say welcome*). 我歡迎你。| *He congratulated her* (=said 'Congratulations!'). 他向她表示祝賀。| *She explained why she had done it* (=said why she had done it). 她說明她為甚麼要那樣做。If you **say** something **again**, you **repeat** it. 如果你把某事再說 (say) 一遍，你就用 repeat（重複）。

With some kinds of information **give** is more usual than **tell**. 表示"提供"某些信息時，較常用動詞

give, 而少用 tell: *He gave (us) his opinion/some advice/the details/a lot of information/an order/a message.* 他(向我們)談了他的意見/提了一些忠告/談了具體的細節/提供了許多信息/發佈了一道命令/傳達了一條信息。

You usually **tell** someone **about**, **talk about** or **speak about** (formal) people, things etc that are not themselves information. 表示"向某人談及某人某事"或"談及某人、某事"時, 通常用 tell someone about, talk about 或 speak about〔正式〕, 這裡所傳達的信息不是某人、某事本身(而是與其有關的情況): *He told us about Harvey/the accident* (NOT 不用 *said the accident to us*). 他向我們談及哈威/那起事故的情況。| *I'm here to talk about the school/the school fair on Friday* (NOT 不用 *tell you the fair*). 我來這裡是想談談學校/星期五學校義賣會的情況。

Of can be used instead of **about** with these verbs, but this can sound old-fashioned or literary. 上面的幾個動詞也可以不與 about 連用, 而和 of 連用, 但這樣就會顯得過時或文雅了: *a story that tells of a frog* (you would usually just say 通常只說 *a story about a frog*) 關於一隻青蛙的故事。

GRAMMAR 語法

Say cannot have a person as its object. The person you are speaking to can be mentioned as well, but only after *to*. 動詞 say 不能以人作受詞, 除非在人的前面加介詞 to: *She said goodbye to her parents.* (NOT 不用 *She said her parents goodbye.*) 她向父母說再見。| *I said to them 'What do you need?'* 我對他們說:"你們需要些甚麼?" | *Celia once said to me that her husband tended to be violent.* 西莉亞有一次對我說, 她丈夫有暴力傾向。

However, where the object is a *that* clause, and you want to mention the person you are talking to as well, people often use **tell**, which can have a person as object. 但是, 當受詞是以 that 引導的子句, 而又要表達這是對誰說的, 那就常用動詞 tell〔因為它可以用人作受詞〕: *You used to tell me that he was a nice person.* 你過去常對我說他是個好人。With a *wh-* clause in indirect speech **tell** is far more common. 在帶有 wh- 子句的間接引語中, tell 要常用得多: *Tell me what you need* (NOT 不用 *Say to me what you need*). 告訴我你需要甚麼。

Where the object is a clause and you do not want to mention the person you are talking to it is usual to use **say**. 當受詞是個子句, 又不希望提到是對誰說的時, 則動詞常用 say: *Call us to say when you'll arrive* (NOT 不用 *to tell when*). 給我們打電話說你將在甚麼時候到達。

In spoken English *that* is often left out of the *that* clause. 在英語口語中, 引導子句的 that 常被省略: *Tell me it's not true!* 告訴我那不是真的! | *I said I was sorry.* 我說我很抱歉。

Tell (but not **say**) can be followed by *to* forms of verbs. tell (而不是 say) 後面可以接帶 to 的動詞不定詞: *He told us to do it* (NOT 不用 *said to us to do it*). 他叫我們去做。However, there must be an object noun as well (NOT 不用 *He told to do it*). 不過, 在 tell 之後必須有個受詞。

Tell (unlike **say**) is not usually followed immediately by *to* and a noun. tell (不同於 say) 後面通常不能直接帶介詞 to 加名詞: *I'll tell my parents the truth/tell the truth to my parents* (NOT 不用 *...tell to my parents the truth*). 我會把真相告訴我父母。

Say and **tell** can both be used with **about**, but usually you use it with an object as well. say 和 tell 都可以和 about 連用, 但通常也要有受詞: *Let me say something about my family.* 讓我談談我的家庭情況吧! | *Sally was telling us all about the party.* 莎莉在給我們講晚會的情況。In informal spoken English you will quite often hear things like 在非正式口語中, 經常可以聽到下面這類說法: *I've already said about that!* 這個問題我已經說過了! | *You were saying about Harvey?* 你是在談哈威的情況嗎? But some people would consider these to be incorrect. More often people use other verbs here. 不過, 有些人認為這類說法不正確。在這種句子中, 人們常用其他動詞: *I've already talked about my family.* 我已經談過我的家庭情況了。

say² *n* [singular,U] **1** the right to take part in deciding something (參與)決定權; 發言權: [+in] *The workers had no say in how the factory was run.* 工人們在工廠管理方面沒有發言權。| *Don't I have any say in the matter?* 難道我對這件事情沒有發言權了嗎? **2 have/say your say** *informal* to have the opportunity to give your opinion about something【非正式】有發表意見的機會: *Mark always has to have his say, even if he knows nothing about the subject.* 馬克即使對該問題一無所知, 也總是非發表自己的意見不可。

say³ *interjection AmE informal* used to express surprise, or to introduce an idea you have just had【美, 非正式】哎呀〔用於表示驚訝、突然想到的主意等〕: *Say, haven't I seen you before somewhere?* 哎呀, 我以前是不是在甚麼地方見過你?

say·ing *n* [C] **1** a well-known short statement that expresses an idea most people believe is true and wise 格言, 諺語, 警句 —compare 比較 PROVERB **2 as the saying goes** used to introduce a particular phrase that people often say 常言道, 正如俗話所說: *One thing led to another as the saying goes.* 常言道: 一不離二。 3

say-so *n* [singular] *informal*【非正式】**1** someone's permission 允許, 許可: *Without his say-so, you can't leave the hospital.* 沒有他的許可, 你不能離開醫院。**2 on sb's say-so** based on someone's personal statement without any proof 根據某人的個人意見〔而不是真憑實據〕: *Why should I believe it on your say-so?* 為甚麼你隨便說說我就要相信它?

S-bend /ˈɛs ˌbɛnd; ˈes bend/ *n* [C] *BrE*【英】**1** a bend in a road in the shape of an 'S' that can be dangerous to drivers〔道路的〕S 形險彎; S-CURVE *AmE*【美】**2** part of a waste pipe in the shape of an 'S' that keeps bad smells out of a building〔建築為防止臭氣溢出的〕S 型曲管

scab /skæb; skæb/ *n* [C] **1** a hard layer of dried blood that forms over a cut or wound while it is getting better〔傷口上結的〕痂 **2** an insulting word for someone who works while the other people in the same factory, office etc are on STRIKE² (1) 拒不參加罷工的人; 破壞罷工者, 工賊〔侮辱性用詞〕—**scab** *v* [I]

scab·bard /ˈskæbɚd; ˈskæbəd/ *n* [C] a metal or leather cover for the blade of a knife or sword; SHEATH (1)〔刀、劍的〕鞘

scab·by /ˈskæbɪ; ˈskæbi/ *adj* **1** scabby skin is covered with scabs 結(滿)痂的: *scabby knees* 結滿痂的膝蓋 **2** *BrE* a word meaning nasty or unpleasant, used especially by children【英】卑鄙的, 討厭的〔尤為兒語〕

sca·bies /ˈskebiˌiz; ˈskeɪbiz/ *n* [U] a skin disease caused by very small insects 疥瘡, 疥蟎病

sca·brous /ˈskebrəs; ˈskeɪbrəs/ *adj literary* rude or shocking, especially in a sexual way【文】猥褻的, 淫猥的; 粗俗的: *The film is a joy – hilariously funny and unremittingly scabrous.* 看這部電影是樂事——它滑稽逗笑、葷鏡頭源源不絕。

scads /skædz; skædz/ *n* [plural] *informal* large numbers or quantities of something【非正式】大量, 大批: *scads of money* 大批的錢

scaf·fold /ˈskæfḷd; ˈskæfəld/ *n* [C] **1** a structure built next to a building or high wall, for workmen to stand on while they build, repair, or paint the building〔建築工人用的〕腳手架 **2** a structure with a raised stage used for killing criminals by hanging them or cutting off their heads 絞刑架;〔行斬首刑的〕刑台 **3** *AmE* a structure that can be moved up and down to help people work on high buildings【美】〔建築工人用的〕升降吊架, 吊籃; CRADLE[1] (5) *BrE*【英】

scaf·fold·ing /ˈskæfḷdɪŋ; ˈskæfəldɪŋ/ *n* [U] poles and boards that are built into a structure for workmen to stand on when they are working next to a high wall on the outside of a building 搭腳手架(的材料)

scal·a·wag /ˈskæləˌwæg; ˈskæləwæg/ *n* [C] the usual American spelling of SCALLYWAG scallywag 的一般美式拼法

scald[1] /skɔld; skɔːld/ *v* [T] to burn your skin with hot liquid or steam〔沸騰的液體或蒸汽等〕燙傷〔皮膚〕: *Mind you don't scald yourself with that kettle!* 小心別讓水壺燙着你!

scald[2] *n* [C] a burn caused by hot liquid or steam〔沸騰的液體或蒸汽造成的〕燙傷

scald·ing /ˈskɔldɪŋ; ˈskɔːldɪŋ/ *adj* **1** extremely hot 滾燙的; 灼熱的: *a cup of scalding tea* 一杯滾燙的茶 **2** scalding criticism is very severe〔批評〕嚴厲的, 尖銳的

S3 W2 **scale[1]** /skel; skeɪl/ *n*

1 ►SIZE/LEVEL 大小/程度◄ [singular,U] the size or level of something, or the amount that something is happening or being done 規模, 範圍, 程度: **[+of]** *The scale of the pollution problem was much worse than scientists had predicted.* 污染問題的程度比科學家所預言的還嚴重。| **large/small etc scale** *There has been development on a massive scale since 1980.* 自 1980 年以來一直在大規模地發展。| *a large-scale research project* 大規模的研究項目

2 ►RANGE 範圍◄ [C usually singular 一般用單數] the whole range of different types of people, things, ideas etc, from the lowest level to the highest 等級, 級別: *At the other end of the scale are the super-rich.* 在這個等級範圍的另一端是那些超級富翁。| *Fish are lower down the evolutionary scale.* 魚類在進化等級中屬於較低的。

3 ►MEASURING INSTRUMENT 計量器具◄ **scales** [plural] also 又作 **scale** *AmE*【美】**a)** a machine for weighing people or objects 磅秤: *the bathroom scales* 浴室磅秤 —see picture on page A10 參見 A10 頁圖 **b)** a piece of equipment with two dishes used especially in the past for weighing things by comparing them to a known weight 天平 —see also 另見 **tip the balance/scales** (TIP[2] (8))

4 ►MEASURING SYSTEM 計量制◄ [C] a system for measuring the force, speed, amount etc of something〔用於計量強度、速度、數量等的〕標準, 級別: *Earthquakes are measured on the Richter scale.* 地震強度是按黎克特震級測定的。| *the company pay scale* 公司的工資級別

5 on a scale of 1 to 10 *spoken* used when you are asking someone to say how good they think something is【口】按照 1 到 10 的等級〔用於徵詢別人對某事物的評價〕: *On a scale of 1 to 10, how do you rate his performance?* 按照 1 到 10 的等級, 你怎樣評價他的表現?

6 ►MEASURING MARKS 計量標度◄ [C] a set of marks with regular spaces between them on a tool or instrument used for measuring 刻度, 標度: *a ruler with a metric scale* 有公制刻度的尺子 | *the scale on a thermometer* 溫度計上的刻度

7 ►MAP/MODEL 地圖/模型◄ [C,U] the relationship between the size of a map, drawing, or model and the actual size of the place or thing that it represents〔實物與圖表、模型之間的〕比例(尺), 比率: *a scale of 1:250,000* 1:250,000 的比例尺 | *What's the scale of this map?* 這張地圖的比例尺是多少?

8 ►MUSIC 音樂◄ [C] a series of musical notes moving upwards or downwards in PITCH[1] (3) with fixed distances between each note 音階

9 ►FISH 魚類◄ [C usually plural 一般用複數] one of the small flat pieces of skin that cover the bodies of fish, snakes etc〔魚、蛇等的〕鱗 —see picture at 參見 FISH 圖

10 ►TEETH 牙齒◄ [U] a white substance that forms on your teeth 牙垢

11 ►WATER PIPES 水管◄ [U] a white substance that forms around the inside of hot water pipes or containers in which water is boiled〔熱水管、容器內的〕水垢, 水鏽

12 the scales fell from my eyes *literary* used to say that you suddenly realized what had been clear to other people【文】恍然大悟, 突然看清真相 —see also 另見 FULL-SCALE

scale[2] *v* [T] **1** to climb to the top of something that is high and difficult to climb 攀登: *Rescuers had to scale a 300m cliff to reach the injured climber.* 救援人員要登上 300 公尺的懸崖才能到達受傷的登山者身旁。**2** to remove the SCALES (=skin) from a fish 刮去〔魚鱗〕—compare 比較 DESCALE

scale sth ÷ **down** *phr v* [T] *BrE*【英】, **scale** sth ÷ **back** *AmE*【美】to reduce the size of an organization, plan etc so that it operates at a lower level【美】縮減, 縮小〔組織、計劃等的規模〕: *Both companies have announced plans to scale back auto production next year.* 兩家公司都宣布了明年縮減汽車生產的計劃。

sca·lene tri·an·gle /ˌskelin ˈtraɪæŋgḷ; ˌskeɪliːn ˈtraɪæŋgəl/ *n* [C] a flat shape with three angles and three sides of unequal length 不等邊三角形 —see picture at 參見 SHAPE[1] 圖

scal·lion /ˈskæljən; ˈskæljən/ *n* [C] *AmE* a young onion with a small round end and a long green stem【美】大葱; SPRING ONION *BrE*【英】

scal·lop[1] /ˈskɑləp; ˈskɒləp/ *n* [C] **1** a small sea creature that has a hard flat shell made of two parts that fit together 扇貝〔一種貝殼類海產動物〕**2** [usually plural 一般用複數] one of a row of small curves decorating the edge of clothes, curtains etc 扇形飾邊

scallop[2] also 又作 **scollop** *v* [T] **1** to decorate something by making the edge into a row of small curves 在〔邊緣〕裝飾扇形飾邊 **2** to bake something in a cream or cheese SAUCE (1)〔澆上奶油或乾酪等調味汁〕烤製, 烘焙: *scalloped potatoes* 烤馬鈴薯

scal·ly·wag /ˈskælɪˌwæg; ˈskæliwæg/ *especially BrE*【尤英】, also 又作 **scalawag** *AmE*【美】*n* [C] *humorous* someone, especially a child, who causes trouble but not in a serious way【幽默】調皮鬼, 小壞蛋〔尤指小孩〕

scalp[1] /skælp; skælp/ *n* [C] **1** the skin on your head 頭皮 **2** *informal* a clear sign that you have completely defeated someone else【非正式】〔表明擊敗他人的〕標誌, 戰利品: *The public were calling for his scalp.* 公眾要置他於死地而後快。

scalp[2] *v* [T] **1** *AmE informal* to buy tickets for an event and sell them again at a much higher price【美, 非正式】倒賣, 炒賣〔戲票、球票等〕**2** to cut off a dead enemy's scalp as a sign of victory 割下〔敵人〕的頭皮作為戰利品

scal·pel /ˈskælpəl; ˈskælpəl/ *n* [C] a small very sharp knife used by doctors in operations 手術刀, 解剖刀 —see picture at 參見 KNIFE[1] 圖

scal·per /ˈskælpɚ; ˈskælpə/ *n* [C] *AmE* a person who makes money by buying tickets for an event and selling them again at a very high price【美】〔戲票、球票等的〕倒賣者; TOUT[2] (1) *BrE*【英】

scal·y /ˈskelɪ; ˈskeɪli/ *adj* **1** an animal, such as a fish, that is scaly is covered with small flat pieces of hard skin 有鱗的 **2** scaly skin is dry and rough〔皮膚〕乾澀粗糙的 —**scaliness** *n* [U]

scam /skæm; skæm/ *n* [C] *slang* a clever but dishonest plan, usually to get money【俚】騙局, 詭計, 欺詐

scamp /skæmp; skæmp/ *n* [C] *old-fashioned* a child who has fun by tricking people【過時】小淘氣, 調皮鬼: *Come back here with my hat, you young scamp!* 快把我的帽子拿回來, 你這個小淘氣。

scam·per /ˈskæmpɚ; ˈskæmpə/ *v* [I always+adv/prep] to run with quick short steps, like a child or small animal 跳跳蹦蹦地跑: **[+in/out/off etc]** *Giggling, the chil-*

dren scampered back to the house. 孩子們咯咯地笑着，蹦蹦跳跳地跑回屋裡。

scam·pi /ˋskæmpɪ; ˈskæmpi/ *n BrE*【英】**1** [plural] large PRAWNS (=sea creature that can be eaten)〔海裡的〕大蝦 **2** [U] PRAWNS covered in BATTER and cooked in oil〔外裹麵糊的〕油炸大蝦: *scampi and chips* 炸大蝦和馬鈴薯條

scan¹ /skæn; skæn/ *v* **scanned, scanning 1** [T] to examine an area carefully, because you are looking for a particular person or thing 細看，審視，查找: *He scanned the horizon ahead, but there was no sign of the convoy.* 他仔細瞭望前面的地平線，但看不見車隊的蹤影。| [+for] *The police scanned the whole area but found no trace of her body.* 警察仔細搜查了這個地區，但沒有找到她屍體的蹤跡。**2** also 又作 **scan through** [I,T] to read something quickly in order to understand its main meaning or to find some particular information 粗略地看，瀏覽，快讀: *I scanned the page quickly for her name.* 我迅速瀏覽那一頁找她的名字。**3** [T] if a machine scans an object or a part of your body, it passes an ELECTRICAL BEAM¹ (1) over it to produce a picture of what is inside〔用電磁波等〕掃描: *All luggage has to be scanned at the airport.* 所有行李在機場都得接受掃描檢查。—see also 另見 SCANNER (1) **4** [T] if a machine or instrument scans an area it searches it with RADAR or SONAR〔用雷達或聲納〕搜索，尋找，探測: *The ship scanned the area ahead for enemy submarines.* 那艘船探測前面海域，尋找敵軍潛艇。**5** *technical*【術語】**a)** [I] poetry that scans has a correct regular pattern of beats〔詩〕符合格律 **b)** [T] to find or show a regular pattern of beats in a poem or line of poetry 找出[標出]〔詩或詩句的〕格律 —see also 另見 SCANSION

S

scan² *n* [C] **1** the act of scanning something 細查，審視 **2** a test done by a SCANNER (=special machine for producing a picture) 掃描(檢查): *a brain scan* 腦部掃描檢查 **3** an image of an unborn baby, produced by a SCANNER〔胎兒的〕掃描影像: *The scan showed the baby was normal.* 掃描影像顯示胎兒正常。

scan·dal /ˋskændḷ; ˈskændl/ *n* **1** [C,U] behaviour or events, often involving famous people, that are considered to be immoral or shocking〔常牽涉知名人士的〕醜聞，醜事: *a sex scandal involving several government officials* 涉及幾個政府官員的性醜聞 | *Some newspapers thrive on spreading gossip and scandal.* 一些報紙因傳播流言蜚語和醜聞而銷量大增。| **a scandal breaks** (=becomes known to everyone) 醜聞廣為傳播 *They had already left the country when the scandal broke.* 醜聞傳開時，他們已經離境了。**2 be a scandal** *spoken* to be very shocking or unacceptable【口】令人震驚；不能接受: *The price of beef these days is an absolute scandal!* 近日的牛肉價格高得簡直讓人不能接受!

scan·dal·ize also 又作 **-ise** *BrE*【英】/ˋskændḷˌaɪz; ˈskændəl-aɪz/ *v* [T usually passive 一般用被動態] to do something that shocks people very much 使震驚，使憤慨: *The entire village was scandalized by the affair.* 全村都為這起事件感到震驚。

scan·dal·mon·ger /ˋskændḷˌmʌŋgɚ; ˈskændəlˌmʌŋgə/ *n* [C] someone who tells people untrue and shocking things about someone else 散布流言蜚語者，搬弄是非者，誹謗他人者 —**scandalmongering** *n* [U]

scan·dal·ous /ˋskændḷəs; ˈskændələs/ *adj* completely unfair and wrong 極不公正的，令人反感的: *a scandalous waste of public money* 駭人聽聞的公款浪費 | *It's scandalous that you still haven't been paid!* 你到現在還領不到錢，這太不像話了! —**scandalously** *adv*

Scan·di·na·vi·an /ˌskændəˋnevɪən; ˌskændḷˈneɪviən◂/ *n* [C] someone from the area of Northern Europe that consists of Norway, Sweden, Denmark, and usually Finland and Iceland 斯堪的納維亞人〔指北歐的挪威、瑞典、丹麥、芬蘭和冰島諸國的人〕—**Scandinavian** *adj*: *Scandinavian languages* 斯堪的納維亞諸語言

scan·ner /ˋskænɚ; ˈskænə/ *n* [C] **1** a machine that passes an ELECTRICAL BEAM¹ (1) over something in order to produce a picture of what is inside 掃描器，掃描檢測儀: *An electronic scanner was passed over the package.* 電子掃描器掃描了這個包裹。—see picture on page A14 參見 A14 頁圖 **2** a piece of computer equipment that copies an image from paper onto a computer〔可把頁面上的文字、圖像等複製到電腦中的〕掃描裝置，掃描儀

scan·sion /ˋskænʃən; ˈskænʃən/ *n* [U] the pattern of regular beats in poetry, or the marks you write to represent this〔詩的〕韻律；韻律分析〔劃分音步、標出重音等〕

scant /skænt; skænt/ *adj* [only before noun 僅用於名詞前] not enough 不足的，缺乏的: **scant attention/regard/consideration** *I paid scant attention to all my father's warnings.* 我沒怎麼注意聽父親對我的種種告誡。

scant·y /ˋskæntɪ; ˈskænti/ *adj* not big enough for a particular purpose〔大小或數量〕不夠的，不足的: *a scanty bikini* 衣不蔽體的比基尼泳裝 —**scantily** *adv*: *scantily clad models* 幾乎全裸的模特兒

-scape /skep; skeɪp/ *suffix* (in nouns 構成名詞) a wide view of a particular area, especially in a picture 景色，圖景: *the impressive cityscape of New York* 令人難忘的紐約市區景色 | *some old Dutch seascapes* (=pictures of the sea) 幾幅古老的荷蘭海景畫

scape·goat /ˋskepˌgot; ˈskeɪpgəʊt/ *n* [C] someone who is blamed for something bad that happens, even if it is not their fault 代人受過的人，替罪羊: *He claimed he had been made a scapegoat for the administration's failures.* 他聲稱自己成了行政失當的替罪羊。—**scapegoat** *v* [T]

scap·u·la /ˋskæpjələ; ˈskæpjələ/ *n* [C] *technical* one of the two flat bones on each side of your upper back; SHOULDER-BLADE【術語】肩胛骨 —see picture at 參見 SKELETON 圖

scar¹ /skɑr; skɑː/ *n* [C] **1** a permanent mark that is left after you have had a cut or wound (傷) 疤 —see picture on page A6 參見 A6 頁圖 **2** a permanent emotional or mental effect caused by an upleasant experience〔精神上的〕創傷: **leave scars** *The trauma of her mother's death had left deep scars.* 母親的死給她留下了很深的精神創傷。**3** an ugly permanent mark on something 疤痕，傷痕: *The old mines are a scar on the rural landscape.* 這些廢礦井成了這一帶鄉村風景的醜陋疤痕。**4** *BrE* a cliff on the side of a mountain【英】懸崖，峭壁，陡岩坡

scar² *v* **1 be scarred** to have a permanent mark on your skin because of a cut or wound 留下傷痕[疤痕]: *His hands were badly scarred by the fire.* 他的雙手滿是那次失火中嚴重燒傷的疤痕。**2** [T] if an unpleasant experience scars you, it has a permanent effect on your character or feelings 使〔精神上〕受創傷: **be scarred for life** (=never completely recover from an unpleasant experience) 留下終身的精神創傷 *She's likely to be scarred for life by the attack.* 她很可能因那次遭襲擊而留下終身的精神創傷。**3** [I] also 又作 **scar over** if a wound scars, it becomes healthy but leaves a permanent mark on your skin 留下傷疤

scar·ab /ˋskærəb; ˈskærəb/ also 又作 **scarab bee·tle** /ˈ·· ˌ··/ *n* [C] a large black BEETLE (=insect with a hard shell) or a representation of this 聖甲蟲；聖甲蟲形護符[飾物]

scarce¹ /skɛrs; skeəs/ *adj* **1** if food, clothing, water etc is scarce, there is not enough of it available 不足的，缺乏的: *Fruit was always scarce in winter, and cost a lot.* 冬天水果總是稀少，而且價格昂貴。—see 見 RARE (USAGE) **2 make yourself scarce** *informal* to leave a place, especially in order to avoid an unpleasant situation【非正式】〔為避免麻煩等〕離開；溜走

scarce² *adv literary* scarcely【文】幾乎不[沒有]；僅僅

scarce·ly /ˋskɛrslɪ; ˈskeəsli/ *adv* **1** almost not or almost none at all 幾乎不，幾乎沒有: *Parts of the city had scarcely changed since we were last there.* 自從我們上次來過這個城市之後，有些地方至今幾乎沒有甚麼改變。| **scarcely any/ever** *There's scarcely any coffee left.*

咖啡幾乎沒剩下多少了。| **can/could scarcely** *It was getting dark and she could scarcely see in front of her.* 天越來越黑, 她幾乎看不見前面的東西。| **scarcely a word/moment/day etc** *Scarcely a day goes by when I don't think of him.* 我幾乎沒有一天不想起他。—see 見 RARE (USAGE) **2** only just 僅僅, 剛剛: **have scarcely done sth when** *Scarcely had I opened the door when the dog came running in.* 我一開門那條狗就跑進來了。—see 見 ALMOST (USAGE) **3** definitely not or almost certainly not 決不, 一定不: *This is scarcely the place to talk about your personal problems.* 這決不是談你個人問題的地方。

scar·ci·ty /ˈskɛrsətɪ; ˈskeəsɪ̇ti/ *n* [singular,U+of] a situation in which there is not enough of something 不足, 短缺: *the present scarcity of labour* 當前勞工的短缺

scare[1] /skɛr; skeə/ *v* **1** [T] to make someone feel frightened 使〔某人〕驚恐, 嚇唬: *Ignore him, he's just trying to scare us.* 不要理他, 他只是想嚇唬我們罷了。| **scare the hell/life/shit out of sb** (=scare someone very much) 把某人嚇得魂不附體 / 要命 / 屁滾尿流 *You scared the hell out of me jumping out like that!* 你這樣跳出來, 嚇死我了。**2** [I] to become frightened 受驚嚇, 感到害怕: *I don't scare easily you know!* 你知道我不是那麼容易給嚇倒的！

scare sb ↔ **into** *phr v* [T] to make someone do something by frightening them or threatening them 恐嚇〔某人去做某事〕: **scare sb into doing sth** *Some parents try to scare their children into behaving well.* 有些父母試圖用嚇唬的法子使孩子守規矩。

scare sb/sth ↔ **off/away** *phr v* [T] **1** to make someone or something go away by frightening them 把…嚇跑: *We lit fires to scare away the wolves.* 我們點起火堆來把狼羣嚇跑。**2** to make someone uncertain or worried so that they do not do something they were going to do 把…嚇得不敢…: *Rising prices are scaring off many potential customers.* 漲價把很多潛在的顧客都嚇跑了。

scare up sth *phr v* [T] *AmE informal* to make something although you have very few things to make it from 【美, 非正式】〔在東西不夠用時〕湊合做成: *Let me see if I can scare up something for you to eat.* 讓我看看能不能湊合着做點東西給你吃。

scare[2] *n* **1** [singular] a sudden feeling of fear 驚恐, 驚嚇: **give sb a scare** *That car only just missed me – it gave me a real scare!* 那輛車差一點就撞着我 — 真把我嚇了一大跳！**2** [C] a situation in which a lot of people become frightened about something 〔社會上的〕大恐慌: *a bomb scare* 炸彈恐嚇 | *An escape of radioactive gas caused a major scare.* 一次放射性氣體的泄漏造成了社會上的大恐慌。

scare·crow /ˈskɛrˌkro; ˈskeəkrəʊ/ *n* [C] an object made to look like a person that a farmer puts in a field to frighten birds 〔放在田裡嚇鳥用的〕稻草人

S3 **scared** /skɛrd; skeəd/ *adj* frightened of or nervous about something 害怕…的; 對…感到驚慌[恐懼]的: **[+of]** *I've always been scared of dogs.* 我一向都怕狗。| *Don't be scared of asking if you need any help.* 你要是需要甚麼幫助, 不要怕開口。| **scared (that)** *I was scared that they might tell the police.* 我害怕他們可能向警方告發。| **scared to do sth** *Janice lay on the floor trembling, too scared to move.* 賈妮絲躺在地板上直發抖, 嚇得動都不敢動。| **scared stiff/scared to death/scared out of your wits** (=extremely frightened) 被嚇呆了 / 被嚇得要死 / 被嚇傻了 *I was scared stiff at the thought of having to make a speech.* 我一想到要去演講就嚇得發呆。

scare·dy-cat /ˈskɛrdɪkæt; ˈskeədikæt/ *n* [C] *informal* an insulting word for someone who is easily frightened, used especially by children 【非正式】膽小鬼〔尤為兒語〕

scare·mon·ger·ing /ˈskɛrˌmʌŋgərɪŋ; ˈskeəˌmʌŋgərɪŋ/ *n* [U] the practice of deliberately making people worried or nervous, especially in order to get a political or other advantage 〔為取得政治或其他優勢而〕散播引起憂慮或恐慌的消息, 危言聳聽: *Jackson publicly accused the anti-nuclear lobby of scaremongering.* 傑克遜公開譴責反核團體在危言聳聽。—**scaremonger** *n* [C]

scare sto·ry /ˈ· ˌ··/ *n* [C] a report, especially in a newspaper, that makes a situation seem more serious or worrying than it really is 〔尤指報紙上的〕誇大報道

scare tac·tics /ˈ· ˌ··/ *n* [plural] methods of persuading people to do something by frightening them 恐嚇戰術: *Employers had used scare tactics to force a return to work.* 雇主們已使用恐嚇戰術迫使雇員復工。

scare·y /ˈskɛrɪ; ˈskeəri/ *adj* another spelling of SCARY scary 的另一種拼法

scarves 圍巾

scarf[1] /skɑrf; skɑːf/ *n* [C] *plural* **scarfs** *or* **scarves** /skɑrvz; skɑːvz/ **1** a long narrow piece of material that you wear around your neck to keep it warm 〔長的〕圍巾 **2** a square piece of material that a woman wears over her head or around her neck 〔女用的方形〕頭巾; 領巾

scarf[2] also 又作 **scarf down/up** *v* [I,T] *AmE slang* to eat something very quickly and noisily 【美俚】狼吞虎嚥地吃; SCOFF (2) *BrE* 【英】

scar·i·fy /ˈskɛrəˌfaɪ; ˈskeərɪ̇faɪ/ *v* [T] **1** to break and make loose the surface of a road or field using a pointed tool 〔用尖鋭的工具〕挖開, 翻鬆〔路面等〕 **2** *technical* to make small cuts on an area of skin using a sharp knife 【術語】〔用利刃〕在皮膚上切〔小口〕 **3** *literary* to criticize someone very severely 【文】嚴厲地批評

scar·let /ˈskɑrlɪt; ˈskɑːlɪ̇t/ *adj* bright red 緋紅色的, 猩紅色的, 鮮紅色的 —**scarlet** *n* [U] —see picture on page A5 參見 A5 頁圖

scarlet fe·ver /ˌ·· ˈ··/ also 又作 **scar·la·ti·na** /ˌskɑrləˈtinə; ˌskɑːləˈtiːnə/ *n* [U] a serious infectious illness that causes a sore throat and red spots on your skin 猩紅熱

scarlet pim·per·nel /ˌ·· ˈ···/ *n* [C] a small wild plant with bright red flowers 〔開鮮紅色花的〕海綠, 海絲

scarlet wom·an /ˌ·· ˈ··/ *n* [C] *old-fashioned* a woman who has sexual relationships with many different people 【過時】淫婦, 蕩婦

scarp /skɑrp; skɑːp/ *n* [C] *technical* a line of natural cliffs 【術語】斷線崖

scar·per /ˈskɑrpɚ; ˈskɑːpə/ *v* [I] *BrE informal* to run away 【英, 非正式】逃跑, 溜走: *Those kids scarpered without paying their bill!* 那些孩子不付錢就溜走了！

scarves /skɑrvz; skɑːvz/ the plural of SCARF[1]

scar·y, scarey /ˈskɛrɪ; ˈskeəri/ *adj informal* frightening 【非正式】可怕的, 駭人的, 恐怖的: *a scary movie* 恐怖電影

scat[1] /skæt; skæt/ *interjection* used to tell a child or an animal to go away 〔用於叫小孩或動物〕走開！: *Go on, scat! And don't come back!* 快點, 走開！不要回來！

scat[2] *n* [U] a style of JAZZ[1] (1) singing, in which the voice is made to sound like a musical instrument 〔爵士音樂中模仿樂器聲的〕擬聲唱法

scath·ing /ˈskeðɪŋ; ˈskeɪðɪŋ/ *adj* scathing remarks, comments etc criticize someone or something very severely 〔批評等〕嚴厲的, 尖刻的: *The newspapers were extremely scathing about him.* 報紙對他的批評極其嚴厲。| *scath-*

ing criticism 尖刻的批評 —**scathingly** *adv*

scat·o·lo·gic·al /ˌskætəˋlɑdʒɪk]; ˌskætəˈlɒdʒɪkəl◂/ *adj formal* too interested in or connected with human waste, in a way that is unpleasant【正式】對糞便過分感興趣的; 關於糞便的: *scatological humor* 髒笑話 —**scatology** /skæˋtɑlədʒɪ; skæˈtɒlədʒi/ *n* [U]

scat·ter /ˋskætɚ; ˈskætə/ *v* **1** [T] to throw or drop a lot of things over a wide area in an irregular way 撒: **scatter sth over/on/around** *Books lay scattered all over the floor.* 地板上到處散放着書。| **scatter sth with sth** *The sky was scattered with stars.* 天上繁星點點。**2** [I,T] if a group of people scatter, or if something scatters them, everyone suddenly moves in different directions, especially to escape danger (使) 分散, 驅散, (使) 散開〔尤指為逃離危險〕: *There was a sudden crack of gunfire and the crowd scattered in all directions.* 突然一聲槍響, 人羣向四處逃散。**3 be scattered to the four winds** *literary* to be broken up or separated and lost【文】東零西散 —see also 另見 SCATTERED, SCATTERING

scat·ter·brain /ˋskætɚˌbren; ˈskætəbreɪn/ *n* [C] someone who often forgets or loses things because they do not think in a practical way 疏忽健忘的人, 心不在焉的人, 精神不集中的人: *Don't tell me you've lost your glasses again, you scatterbrain!* 不要跟我說你又把眼鏡丟了, 你這個丟三落四的傢伙! —**scatterbrained** *adj*

scat·tered /ˋskætɚd; ˈskætəd/ *adj* spread over a wide area or over a long period of time 分散的, 稀疏的: *houses scattered across the hillside* 稀稀落落地散佈在小山坡上的房子 | **scattered showers** (=used in weather reports to say there will be some short periods of rain) 零星陣雨〔用於天氣預報〕

S

scat·ter·ing /ˋskætərɪŋ; ˈskætərɪŋ/ *n* [C] a small number of things or people spread out over a large area 少量分散的人或物: **[+of]** *a largely Catholic country with a scattering of Protestant communities* 以天主教徒為主但亦有少量新教徒社區分佈的國家

scat·ty /ˋskætɪ; ˈskæti/ *adj BrE informal* someone who is scatty often forgets or loses things because they are not sensible or practical【英, 非正式】心不在焉的, 丟三落四的, 沒有頭腦的 —**scattiness** *n* [U]

scav·enge /ˋskævɪndʒ; ˈskævɪ̥ndʒ/ *v* [I,T] **1** if an animal scavenges, it eats anything that it can find〔動物〕以〔垃圾、腐肉等〕為食: *dogs scavenging from the dustbins* 在垃圾桶裡覓食的狗 **2** if someone scavenges, they search through things that other people do not want for food or useful objects〔人〕在廢棄物中尋找〔可食或可用的東西〕: **[+for]** *a man scavenging for food in piles of garbage* 在垃圾堆裡翻找食物的男人 —**scavenger** *n* [C]

sce·na·ri·o /sɪˋnærɪˌo; sɪ̥ˈnɑːriəʊ/ *n plural* **scenarios** [C] **1** a situation that could possibly happen but has not happened yet 可能發生的事, 可能出現的情況: *Try to imagine a scenario where only 20% of people have a job.* 設想一下這個情況: 只有20%的人有工作。| **worst-case/nightmare scenario** (=the worst possible situation) 可能出現的最壞/噩夢般的情況 *the nightmare scenario of a radiation leak* 可能出現的放射物泄漏的可怕情況 **2** a written description of the characters, place, and things that will happen in a film, play etc〔電影、戲劇的〕劇情概要

2 2 **scene** /sin; siːn/ *n*

1 ►PLAY/FILM 戲劇/電影◄ [C] **a)** part of a play during which there is no change in time or place〔戲劇中的〕一場: *Hamlet, Act 5 Scene 2*《哈姆雷特》第五幕, 第二場 **b)** a single piece of action that happens in one place in a film, book etc〔電影、書等中的〕場景, 場面: *Some of the more violent scenes are very disturbing.* 一些暴力較多的場面着實令人不安。| *a love scene* 戀愛場面

2 ►VIEW/PICTURE 風景/圖畫◄ [C] a view of a place as you see it, or as it appears in a picture〔某地方或圖畫中的〕景色: *a peaceful country scene* 寧靜的鄉村景色 | *a painter of street scenes* 畫街景的畫家

3 ►ACCIDENT/CRIME 事故/罪行◄ [singular] the place where an accident, crime etc happened〔事故或罪行的〕發生地點, 現場: **[+of]** *the scene of the crime* 犯罪現場 | **on/at the scene** *Investigators are now at the scene, searching for clues to the cause of the explosion.* 調查人員正在出事現場, 尋找爆炸案的線索。| *Journalists were on the scene within minutes of the crash.* 新聞記者在發生撞車事故幾分鐘後就到達了出事現場。

4 the gay/fashion/political etc scene a particular set of activities and the people who are involved in them 同性戀者天地/時裝界/政治領域: *Keith is heavily involved in the London theatre scene.* 基思與倫敦的戲劇界關係甚為密切。| *the drugs scene* 毒品圈子

5 ►ARGUMENT 爭辯◄ [C] a loud angry argument, especially in a public place〔在公開場合的〕爭吵, 吵嘴: *a terrible scene that ended with Rachel running out of the restaurant in tears* 一場最後以蕾切爾哭着跑出餐館而結束的激烈爭吵 | *There were angry scenes in parliament today.* 議會今天出現了憤怒的爭吵場面。| **make a scene** *If you don't sit down and stop making a scene, I'm leaving!* 你要是再不坐下來, 還繼續大吵大鬧, 那我就走了!

6 ►SITUATION 情景◄ [C] all the things that are happening in a place, and the effect or situation that they cause 情景, 景象: **[+of]** *The burning building was a scene of panic as everyone ran to get out.* 人們從起火的大樓逃出來時, 真是一片慌亂的景象。| *a scene of perfect peace and harmony* 一片理想的寧靜和諧的景象

7 bad scene *AmE informal* a difficult or unpleasant situation【美, 非正式】困境: *We realized by the looks on their faces that we had walked into a bad scene.* 根據他們臉上的表情, 我們知道已經陷入了困境。

8 not your scene *informal* not the type of thing you like【非正式】並非某人喜愛的事物, 不合口味的東西: *Loud discos aren't really my scene.* 喧鬧的的士高並不合我的口味。

9 behind the scenes secretly, while other things are happening publicly 祕密地, 在幕後: *Most important political decisions are made behind the scenes.* 大多數的重要政治決定都是祕密作出的。

10 set the scene a) to provide the conditions in which an event can happen〔為...〕提供條件: *The government seems unaware that these policies are setting the scene for social unrest.* 政府似乎沒有意識到這些政策為社會動亂提供了條件。**b)** to describe the situation before you begin to tell a story〔在講故事前〕敍述背景

11 be/come on the scene to be or become involved in a situation, activity etc 出現, 到來; 參與, 捲進: *By then, there was a boyfriend on the scene.* 那時, 她已經有一位男朋友了。—see also 另見 **change of scenery/air etc** (CHANGE[2] (3)), **steal the show/limelight/scene** (STEAL[1] (3))

sce·ne·ry /ˋsinərɪ; ˈsiːnəri/ *n* [U] **1** the natural features of a particular part of a country, such as mountains, forests, deserts etc 風景, 景色: *The best part of the trip was the scenery. It was fantastic.* 這次旅行最精彩的部分就是自然景色, 那真是美極了。**2** the painted background, furniture etc used on a theatre stage 舞台佈景

sce·nic /ˋsinɪk; ˈsiːnɪk/ *adj* surrounded by views of beautiful countryside 景色優美的: *Let's take the scenic route home.* 我們走這條風景優美的路回家吧。—**scenically** /-klɪ; -kli/ *adv*

scent¹ /sɛnt; sent/ *n* **1** [C] a pleasant smell that something has 香味: *the scent of roses* 玫瑰的芳香 **2** [C] the smell of a particular animal or person that some other animals, for example dogs, can follow〔動物或人的〕臭氣, 臭跡: **on the scent** (=following this smell) 循着線索[氣味] *The hounds were soon on the stag's scent.* 那羣獵犬馬上循着臭氣追蹤公鹿。**3 throw/put sb off the scent** to give someone false information to prevent them from catching you or discovering something〔給某人錯誤信息〕使某人失去線索: *The gang changed car to throw* *the police off the scent.* 歹徒們換車以擺脱追捕他們的警察。**4** [C,U] *especially BrE* a liquid that you put on your skin to make it smell nice; PERFUME[1] (1)【尤英】香水

scent[2] *v* **1** [T] if an animal scents another animal or a person, it knows that they are near because it can smell them〔動物〕嗅出…的氣味: *The deer scented our presence and ran back into the forest.* 那頭鹿嗅出我們在那裡, 便跑回樹林裡去了。**2 scent fear/danger/victory etc** *literary* to feel sure that something is going to happen【文】覺察到恐怖/危險/勝利等的氣息: *We scented danger and decided to leave.* 我們覺察到有危險, 便決定離開。

scent·ed /ˋsɛntɪd; ˈsentɪ̠d/ *adj* having a particular smell, especially a pleasant one【文】芬芳的, 有香氣的: **[+with]** *an air freshener scented with spring flowers* 一種散發春天花香的空氣清新劑

scent·less /ˋsɛntləs; ˈsentləs/ *adj* without a smell 無氣味的, 無香味的

scep·ter /ˋsɛptɚ; ˈseptə/ *n* [C] the American spelling of SCEPTRE sceptre 的美式拼法

scep·tic *BrE*【英】, **skeptic** *AmE*【美】/ˋskɛptɪk; ˈskeptɪk/ *n* [C] someone who does not believe things unless they have definite proof 持懷疑態度的人: *A lot of my friends believe in astrology, but I'm a sceptic myself.* 我的許多朋友都相信占星術, 但我自己卻持懷疑態度。

scep·ti·cal *BrE*【英】, **skeptical** *AmE*【美】/ˋskɛptɪkḷ; ˈskeptɪkəl/ *adj* tending to doubt or not believe what other people tell you 持懷疑態度的, 不相信的: **[+about]** *Many scientists remain skeptical about the value of this research program.* 很多科學家對這個研究方案的價值仍持懷疑態度。—**sceptically** /-klɪ; -kli/ *adv*

scep·ti·cis·m *BrE*【英】, **skepticism** *AmE*【美】/ˋskɛptəˏsɪzəm; ˈskeptɪ̠sɪzəm/ *n* [U] a sceptical attitude 懷疑態度; 懷疑論: *The government's claim that the country is now coming out of recession is being treated with deep scepticism.* 政府聲稱國家正在擺脱經濟衰退, 但這種說法受到極大的懷疑。

scep·tre *BrE*【英】, **scepter** *AmE*【美】/ˋsɛptɚ; ˈseptə/ *n* [C] a short decorated stick carried by kings or queens at ceremonies〔國王或女王在儀式中手持的表示權力的〕權杖

3 3 **sched·ule**[1] /ˋskɛdʒul; ˈʃedjuːl/ *n* [C] **1** a plan of what someone is going to do and when they are going to do it 計劃表, 進度表, 日程表: **full schedule** (=busy schedule) 排得很滿的日程表 *I've got a very full schedule today.* 我今天的日程表排得滿滿的。| **tight schedule** (=including a lot of things that must be done in a short time) 時間很緊的日程表 *Our production schedule is so tight that we may have to take on extra staff.* 我們的生產進度排得這樣緊, 大概只能雇用臨時工了。| **ahead of/on/behind schedule** (=before, at, after the planned time) 先於/按照/遲於預定時間 *We finished the project three weeks ahead of schedule.* 我們提前三個星期完成了這項工程。**2** *AmE* a list that shows the times that buses, trains etc leave or arrive at a particular place【美】〔公共汽車、火車等的〕時間表, 時刻表; TIMETABLE[1] (1) *BrE*【英】**3** a formal list of something, for example prices 一覽表, 清單, 明細表: *a schedule of postal charges* 郵費價目表

schedule[2] *v* [T] [usually passive 一般用被動態] to plan that something will happen at a particular time 排定, 把…安排在, 預定: **[+for]** *The meeting has been scheduled for this afternoon.* 會議已定於今天下午舉行。| **be scheduled to do sth** *The new airport is scheduled to open just before Christmas.* 新機場定於聖誕節前開始使用。| **scheduled flight** (=a plane service that flies at the same time every day or every week) 定期航班

sche·ma /ˋskimə; ˈskiːmə/ also 又作 **sche·ma·ta** /ˋskimətə; ˈskiːmətə/ *n* [C] *technical* a plan showing only the important parts of something; DIAGRAM【術語】綱要, 概要; 圖解, 圖表

sche·mat·ic /skiˋmætɪk; skiːˈmætɪk/ *adj* in the form of a basic plan or arrangement 概要的, 計劃的; 圖解的: *a schematic outline* 計劃綱要 | *a schematic diagram of DNA* 脱氧核糖核酸結構簡圖

sche·ma·tize also 又作 **-ise** *BrE*【英】/ˋskiməˏtaɪz; ˈskiːmətaɪz/ *v* [T] to arrange something in a system 對…作系統性組合

scheme[1] /skim; skiːm/ *n* [C] **1** *BrE* an official plan that is intended to help people in some way, for example by providing education or training【英】計劃, 規劃, 方案〔指正式計劃, 如教育、培訓等〕: *a government training scheme for the unemployed* 政府對失業者的培訓計劃 | *a pension scheme* 養老金方案 **2** a clever plan, especially to do something bad or illegal 陰謀, 詭計: *another one of his dumb schemes for making money* 他的又一個愚蠢的掙錢詭計 **3** a system that you use to organize information, ideas etc〔用於組織資料等的〕系統, 體系, 組合: *classification scheme* 分類系統 | **colour scheme** (=the way the colours have been organized in a room) 色彩佈局 **4 be in the scheme of things** to be part of the way things generally happen, or are organized 按事物的一般規律, 在一般格局中: *It was seen as a medium-sized company in the general scheme of things.* 在芸芸企業中, 它被視為一家中等規模的公司。 1

scheme[2] *v* [I] to secretly make clever and dishonest plans to get or achieve something 搞陰謀, 密謀, 策劃: **scheme to do sth** *He spent the next two years bitterly scheming to get his revenge.* 他在隨後的兩年中苦苦策劃如何報仇。| **scheme against sb** *She became convinced that her family was scheming against her.* 她已經確信她的全家都在處心積慮地反對她。—**schemer** *n* [C]

scher·zo /ˋskɛrtso; ˈskeətsəʊ/ *n* [C] a cheerful piece of music played quickly and happily 詼諧曲, 諧謔曲 —**scherzo** *adj, adv*

schis·m /ˋsɪzəm; ˈsɪzəm/ *n* [C,U] the separation of a group into two groups, caused by a disagreement about its aims and beliefs, especially in the Christian church〔由於信仰、目標等分歧引起的〕分裂; 〔尤指基督教的〕教會分裂

schis·mat·ic /sɪzˋmætɪk; sɪzˈmætɪk/ *adj* related to or connected with schism 分裂的, 引起分裂的, 分裂教會的

schist /ʃɪst; ʃɪst/ *n* [U] *technical* a type of rock that naturally breaks apart into thin flat pieces【術語】片岩, 頁岩

schiz·o /ˋskɪtso; ˈskɪtsəʊ/ *n* [C] *slang* a SCHIZOPHRENIC【俚】精神分裂症患者

schiz·oid /ˋskɪtsɔɪd; ˈskɪtsɔɪd/ *adj* **1** *technical* typical of schizophrenia【術語】精神分裂症的 **2** *informal* quickly changing between opposite opinions or attitudes【非正式】〔意見、態度等〕反覆無常的, 自相矛盾的

schiz·o·phre·ni·a /ˏskɪzəˋfrinɪə; ˌskɪtsəʊˈfriːniə/ *n* [U] a serious mental illness in which someone's thoughts and feelings become separated from what is really happening around them 精神分裂症

schiz·o·phren·ic[1] /ˏskɪzəˋfrɛnɪk; ˌskɪtsəʊˈfrenɪk◂/ *adj* **1** *technical* typical of or connected with schizophrenia【術語】(患)精神分裂症的 **2** *informal* quickly changing from one opinion, attitude etc to another【非正式】〔意見、態度等〕反覆無常的, 朝秦暮楚的

schizophrenic[2] *n* [C] someone who has schizophrenia 精神分裂症患者

schlep /ʃlɛp; ʃlep/ *v* [T] *AmE informal* to carry or pull something heavy【美, 非正式】攜帶〔重物〕; 拖拽: **[+down/out/along etc]** *I schlepped his bag all the way to the airport and he didn't even thank me.* 我把他的行李一直送到飛機場, 他竟然連謝謝也不説一聲。

schlep around *phr v* [I] to spend your time lazily doing nothing useful 遊手好閒, 無所事事

schmaltz·y /ˋʃmɔltsɪ; ˈʃmɔːltsi/ *adj informal especially AmE* a schmaltzy piece of music, book etc deals with emotions such as love and sadness in a way that seems silly and insincere【非正式, 尤美】〔音樂、書等〕煽情的, 情感淺薄的: *a schmaltzy love song* 造作的情歌 —**schmaltz, schmalz** *n* [U]

S

schmooze /ʃmuz; ʃmuːz/ *v* [I] *AmE informal* to talk about unimportant things【美, 非正式】閒聊, 閒扯: *drinking and schmoozing after filming was done* 拍完電影後喝酒閒聊

schmuck /ʃmʌk; ʃmʌk/ *n* [C] *AmE informal* a stupid person【美, 非正式】蠢貨, 笨蛋

schnapps /ʃnæps; ʃnæps/ *n* [U] a strong alcoholic drink 荷蘭烈酒; 荷蘭杜松子酒

schnit·zel /ˋʃnɪtsəl; ˈʃnɪtsəl/ *n* [C,U] a small piece of VEAL covered with small pieces of bread and cooked in oil〔裹麵包屑的〕炸小牛肉片

schnook /ʃnuk; ʃnʊk/ *n* [C] *AmE informal* a stupid person【美, 非正式】蠢傢伙, 笨蛋

schnoz·zle /ˋʃnɑzəl; ˈʃnɒzəl/ *n* [C] *AmE humorous* a nose【美, 幽默】鼻子

schol·ar /ˋskɑlɚ; ˈskɒlə/ *n* [C] **1** someone who knows a lot about a particular subject, especially one that is not a science subject 學者〔尤指精於一門文科學問的人〕: *a Latin scholar* 研究拉丁語的學者 **2** *informal* a clever and well-educated person【非正式】聰明且受過良好教育的人, 有學問的人: *I'm afraid I'm not much of a scholar.* 我恐怕是算不上有學問的人。**3** someone who has been given a SCHOLARSHIP (=money) to study at a school or college 大學獎學金獲得者: *a Rhodes scholar* 羅兹獎學金獲得者 **4** *literary or BrE old use* a child who is at school【文或英, 舊】小學生

schol·ar·ly /ˋskɑlɚlɪ; ˈskɒləli/ *adj* **1** concerned with serious study of a particular subject 學術性的: *a scholarly journal* 學術刊物 **2** someone who is scholarly spends a lot of time studying, and knows a lot about a particular subject 好學並〔對某一學科〕具有淵博學識的

schol·ar·ship /ˋskɑlɚˌʃɪp; ˈskɒləʃɪp/ *n* **1** [C] an amount of money that is given to someone by an educational organization to help pay for their education 獎學金 **2** [U] the knowledge, work, or methods involved in serious studying 學問, 學識; 學術研究: *Her latest publication is a fine piece of scholarship.* 她最新出版的書是一部優秀的學術著作。

scho·las·tic /skəˋlæstɪk; skəˈlæstɪk/ *adj* [only before noun 僅用於名詞前] *formal*【正式】**1** connected with schools or teaching 學校的, 教學的: *scholastic books* 教學用書 **2** connected with scholasticism 經院哲學的, 煩瑣哲學的

scho·las·ti·cis·m /skəˋlæstəˌsɪzəm; skəˈlæstɪsɪzəm/ *n* [U] a way of studying thought, especially religious thought, based on things written in ancient times〔古代的〕經院哲學, 煩瑣哲學

1 1 **school**[1] /skul; skuːl/ *n*

1 ►WHERE CHILDREN LEARN 供孩子學習的地方◄ [C] a place where children are taught 學校: *Which school do you go to?* 你上哪所學校? | *There are several good schools in the area.* 這個地區有幾所好學校。| **school bus/building etc** *the school hall* 學校禮堂 | **to/from school** *Mum takes us to school every morning.* 媽媽每天早晨送我們上學。

2 ►TIME AT SCHOOL 在學校的時間◄ [U] **a)** a day's work at school〔在學校的〕上課, 一天的課程: *School begins at 8.30.* 8點30分開始上課。| **before/after school** *I'll see you after school.* 下課後我來看你。**b)** the time during your life when you go to a school 受學校教育的時間, 上學期間: *After two years of school, he still couldn't read.* 他上了兩年學仍然不會閱讀。| **start/leave school** *She started school when she was four.* 她四歲開始上學。| *I left school two years ago.* 我兩年前就畢業離校了。

3 ►UNIVERSITY 大學◄ **a)** [C,U] *AmE* a university, or the time when you study there【美】大學; 在大學學習期間: *Where did you go to school?* 你在哪兒上大學? | **law/medical/graduate etc school** *After two years of medical school, I thought I knew everything.* 在醫學院學習兩年後, 我以為自己甚麼都懂了。**b)** [C] a department that teaches a particular subject at a university〔大學的〕學院: **[+of]** *the School of Oriental Languages* 東方語言學院

4 ►ONE SUBJECT 一門課程◄ [C] a place where a particular subject or skill is taught 專科學校: *a language school in Brighton* 布賴頓的一所語言學校 | *the Pastern Riding School* 帕斯頓騎術學校 | **[+of]** *Amwell School of Motoring* 阿姆威爾汽車駕駛學校

5 at school a) in the school building 在學校裡: *I can get some work done while the kids are at school.* 孩子上學以後我可以做一些工作。**b)** *BrE* attending a school, rather than being at college or university or having a job【英】在求學, 在上學〔指中、小學〕: *We've got two children at school, and one at university.* 我們有兩個孩子在讀中學, 一個在讀大學。

6 in school a) in the school building 在學校裡: *Sandra's not in school today – she's not well.* 桑德拉今天沒上學 —— 她身體不舒服。**b)** *AmE* attending a school or university as opposed to having a job【美】在求學: *Are your boys still in school?* 你們的孩子還在學校念書嗎?

7 ►ART 藝術◄ [C] a number of people who are considered as a group because of their style of work 學派, 流派: *the Impressionist school* 印象派

8 school of thought an opinion or way of thinking about something that is shared by a group of people 學派, 流派; 有類似觀點的一批人: *There are two schools of thought on drinking red wine with fish.* 關於紅葡萄酒配魚的問題, 有兩派不同的看法。

9 of the old school having old-fashioned values or qualities, especially good ones 老派的, 老式的, 具有傳統觀念的〔尤指好的傳統〕: *an officer of the old school* 老派軍官

10 ►SEA ANIMALS 海裡的動物◄ [C] a large group of fish, WHALES[1] (1), DOLPHINS etc that are swimming together〔魚、鯨、海豚等的〕羣: **[+of]** *a school of whales* 一羣鯨魚

11 the school of hard knocks *old-fashioned* the difficult or unpleasant experiences you have in life【過時】艱難困苦的磨鍊, 不愉快的經歷

school[2] *v* [T] *old-fashioned* to train or teach someone【過時】訓練; 教育: **be schooled in sth** *a young lady schooled in all the usual accomplishments* 受過各種普通技藝訓練的年輕女子

school board /ˌ· ˈ·/ *n* [C] a group of people, including some parents, who are elected to govern a school or group of schools in the US〔美國的〕校董會, 學校教育委員會

school·boy /ˋskulˌbɔɪ; ˈskuːlbɔɪ/ *n* [C] *especially BrE*【尤英】**1** a boy attending school〔中、小學的〕男生 **2** **schoolboy humour** jokes that are silly and rude but not offensive 幼稚的玩笑, 小惡作劇

school·child /ˋskulˌtʃaɪld; ˈskuːltʃaɪld/ *n plural* **schoolchildren** /ˋskulˌtʃɪldrən; ˈskuːltʃɪldrən/ [C] a child attending school 學童, 中小學生

school·day /ˋskulˌde; ˈskuːldeɪ/ *n* [C] **1** a day of the week when children are usually at school 學校上課日 **2** **schooldays** the time of your life when you go to school 學生時代

school dis·trict /ˈ· ˌ··/ *n* [C] an area in one state of the US that includes a number of schools which are governed together〔美國的〕學區

school friend /ˈ· ·/ *n* [C] *especially BrE* a friend who goes to the same school as you【尤英】校友; 同學

school·girl /ˋskulˌgɝl; ˈskuːlgɜːl/ *n* [C] *especially BrE* a girl attending school【尤英】〔中、小學的〕女生

school gov·ern·or /ˌ· ˈ···/ *n* [C] a member of a group of people in Britain who are elected to make decisions about how a school should be managed〔英國的〕學校管理委員會委員

school·house /ˋskulˌhaus; ˈskuːlhaʊs/ *n* [C] a school building, especially for a small village school〔尤指鄉村學校的〕校舍

school·ing /ˋskulɪŋ; ˈskuːlɪŋ/ *n* [U] school education 學校教育

school·kid /ˋskulkɪd; ˈskuːlkɪd/ *n* [C] *informal* a child attending school【非正式】學童

school-leav·er /ˈ· ˌ··/ *n* [C] *BrE* someone who leaves school, especially when they are looking for a job rather than going to college, university etc【英】〔中學的〕輟學學生; 離校生: *a shortage of jobs for school-leavers* 中學離校生就業機會的不足

school·marm /ˋskulˌmɑrm; ˈskuːlmɑːm/ *n* [C] a woman who is considered to be old-fashioned, strict, and easily shocked 古板嚴厲、大驚小怪的女人 —**schoolmarmish** *adj*

school·mas·ter /ˋskulˌmæstɚ; ˈskuːlˌmɑːstə/ *n* [C] *especially BrE* a male teacher, especially in a PRIVATE SCHOOL (=one that parents pay to send their children to)【尤英】〔尤指私立中、小學的〕男教師

school·mate /ˋskulˌmet; ˈskuːlmeɪt/ *n* [C] someone who goes or went to the same school as you 同學

school mis·tress /ˈ· ˌ··/ *n* [C] *especially BrE* a female teacher, especially in a PRIVATE SCHOOL (=one that parents pay to send their children to)【尤英】〔尤指私立中、小學的〕女教師

school·room /ˋskulˌrum; ˈskuːlruːm/ *n* [C] a room used for teaching in a small school 教室

school·teach·er /ˋskulˌtitʃɚ; ˈskuːlˌtiːtʃə/ *n* [C] a TEACHER〔中、小學的〕教師

school tie /ˌ· ˈ·/ *n* [C] **1** a special tie with a particular colour or pattern that children wear at some schools in Britain〔英國某些中、小學的〕校服上的領帶 **2 the old school tie** *BrE informal* the unofficial system by which people who went to the same school, especially an expensive one, help each other to gain important positions later in their lives【英, 非正式】〔校友離校後相互扶持的〕校友關係網

school·work /ˋskulˌwɝk; ˈskuːlwɜːk/ *n* [U] work done for or during school classes 功課, 〔課堂〕作業

schoo·ner /ˋskunɚ; ˈskuːnə/ *n* [C] **1** a fast sailing ship with two sails (斯庫納) 雙桅縱帆船 **2** a large tall glass for SHERRY or beer 大玻璃酒杯〔尤指盛雪利酒或啤酒的杯子〕

schwa /ʃwɑ; ʃwɑː/ *n* [C] *technical* a vowel typically heard in parts of a word that are spoken without STRESS¹ (4), such as the "a" in "about"【術語】非重讀音節中的輕讀元音〈如 about 中的 a〉

sci·at·ic /saɪˋætɪk; saɪˈætɪk/ *adj technical* connected with the hips (HIP¹(1))【術語】坐骨的

sci·at·i·ca /saɪˋætɪkə; saɪˈætɪkə/ *n* [U] pain in the lower back, hips (HIP¹ (1)) and legs 坐骨神經痛

1 1 **sci·ence** /ˋsaɪəns; ˈsaɪəns/ *n* **1** [U] knowledge about the world, especially based on examination and testing, and on facts that can be proved 科學: *Science has taught us how atoms are made up.* 科學使我們明白原子是怎樣構成的。| *The computer is one of the marvels of modern science.* 電腦是現代科學的奇跡之一。| *developments in science and technology* 科學技術的發展 **2** [U] the study of science 理科: *a degree in science* 理科學位 **3** [C] a particular part of science, for example BIOLOGY, CHEMISTRY, or PHYSICS 理科的一門學科〈如生物、化學、物理〉: *the physical sciences* 自然科學 —see also 另見 NATURAL SCIENCE, SOCIAL SCIENCE, **blind sb with science** (BLIND² (4))

science fic·tion /ˌ·· ˈ··/ *n* [U] a kind of writing in which imaginary future developments in science and their effect on life are described 科幻小說

science park /ˈ·· ·/ *n* [C] an area where there are a lot of companies or organizations that do scientific work 科學園區, 新技術 (研究) 開發區

3 2 **sci·en·tif·ic** /ˌsaɪənˋtɪfɪk; ˌsaɪənˈtɪfɪk◂/ *adj* **1** [no comparative 無比較級] about or connected with science, or using its methods 科學 (上) 的: *scientific discoveries* 科學發現 | *scientific proof* 科學證明 **2** *informal* done very carefully, using an organized system【非正式】精細的; 有系統的, 有條理的: *We do keep accounts for the business, but we're not very scientific about it.* 我們做生意確是有賬目的, 但我們做得不夠精細有條理。—**scientifically** /-kḷɪ; -kli/ *adv*

sci·en·tist /ˋsaɪəntɪst; ˈsaɪəntɪ̣st/ *n* [C] someone who works or is trained in science 科學家 3 2

sci·en·tol·ogy /ˌsaɪənˋtɑlədʒɪ; ˌsaɪənˈtɒlədʒi/ *n* [U] a religion which says that Christ was only one of several important teachers 科學論 (教) 派〔該教派宣稱耶穌基督只是幾位重要的導師之一〕

sci-fi /ˌsaɪ ˋfaɪ; ˌsaɪ ˈfaɪ◂/ *n* [U] *informal* SCIENCE FICTION【非正式】科幻小說

scim·i·tar /ˋsɪmətɚ; ˈsɪmɪ̣tə/ *n* [C] a sword with a curved blade 彎刀 —see picture at 參見 SWORD 圖

scin·til·la /sɪnˋtɪlə; sɪnˈtɪlə/ *n* [singular] **not a scintilla of truth/evidence etc** not even the smallest amount of truth etc 毫無真實性/證據等: *There isn't a scintilla of evidence to prove it.* 沒有絲毫的證據可以證明它。

scin·til·late /ˋsɪntḷˌet; ˈsɪntɪ̣leɪt/ *v* [I] *literary* to shine with small quick flashes of light; SPARKLE¹ (1)【文】閃爍, 閃閃發光 —**scintillation** /ˌsɪntəˋleʃən; ˌsɪntɪ̣ˈleɪʃən/ *n* [U]

scin·til·lat·ing /ˋsɪtḷˌetɪŋ; ˈsɪntɪ̣leɪtɪŋ/ *adj* interesting, clever, and amusing 有趣的; 聰明靈巧的: *scintillating conversation* 妙趣橫生的談話

sci·on /ˋsaɪən; ˈsaɪən/ *n* [C] **1** *technical* a living part of a plant that is cut off, especially for fixing onto another plant【術語】〔尤指為接枝而剪下的〕幼枝, 接穗 **2** *literary* a young member of a famous or important family【文】〔名門貴族的〕子孫, 後裔: *scions of wealthy East coast families* 東海岸的富家子弟

scissors 剪刀

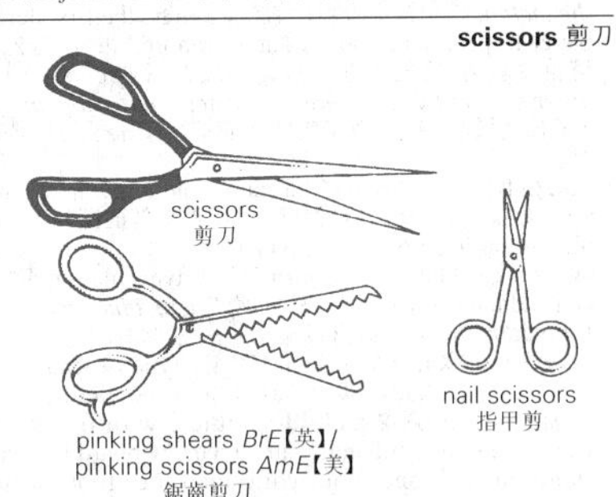

scis·sors /ˋsɪzɚz; ˈsɪzəz/ *n* [plural] a tool for cutting paper, made of two sharp blades and a handle with two holes for your fingers 剪刀: *a pair of scissors* 一把剪刀

scle·ro·sis /sklɪˋrosɪs; sklɪ̣ˈrəʊsɪ̣s/ *n* [C,U] *technical* a disease that causes an organ or soft part of your body to become hard【術語】硬化 (症) —**sclerotic** /sklɪˋrɑtɪk; sklɪ̣ˈrɒtɪk/ *adj* —see also 另見 MULTIPLE SCLEROSIS

scoff /skɔf; skɒf/ *v* **1** [I] to laugh at a person or idea, and talk about them in a way that shows you think they are stupid 嘲笑, 譏笑, 嘲弄: [+at] *They scoffed at the idea that anything could be changed.* 他們嘲笑那種認為任何事情都可以改變的想法。**2** [T] *BrE informal* to eat something very quickly【英, 非正式】狼吞虎嚥地吃: *Who's scoffed all the cake?* 是誰把蛋糕都吃光了?

scold¹ /skold; skəʊld/ *v* [T] to angrily criticize someone, especially a child, about something they have done 責罵, 斥責〔某人, 尤指小孩〕: *As kids we were always getting scolded by the local farmer.* 我們小時候經常被當地的農場主責罵。—**scolding** *n* [C,U]

scold² *n* [C] *old use* a woman who often complains or criticizes【舊】愛埋怨指責的婦人

scol·lop /ˋskɑləp; ˈskɒləp/ *n* [C] another spelling of SCALLOP scallop 的另一種拼法

sconce /skɑns; skɒns/ *n* [C] an object that is fixed to a wall and holds CANDLES or electric lights 壁式燭台[燈台]

scone /skon; skɒn/ *n* [C] a small round, soft cake sometimes containing dried fruit 司康, (圓形) 烤餅: *scones and cream* 烤餅塗奶油

scoop¹ /skup; skuːp/ *n* [C] **1** a round deep spoon for holding or serving food such as corn, flour, or ICE CREAM 勺, 球形勺: *an icecream scoop* 冰淇淋勺 **2** also 又作 **scoopful** an amount of food removed with this kind of spoon 一勺之量: **[+of]** *three scoops of ice cream* 三勺冰淇淋 **3** an important or exciting news story that is printed in one newspaper before any of the others know about it〔搶先登出的〕獨家新聞: *Royal Diary Scoop!* 王室日記的獨家報道! **4** a very big profit that a company makes〔公司賺到的〕巨額利潤 **5 what's the scoop?** *spoken especially AmE* used to ask someone for information or news about something【口, 尤美】有甚麼消息嗎?〔用以詢問某人關於某事的情況〕

scoop² *v* [T] **1** to pick something up with a scoop, a spoon, or with your curved hand〔用勺或勺狀物〕舀出, 取出, 鏟出: **[+up/out/off etc]** *She scooped up a handful of sand.* 她舀起一把沙子。| *Scoop out the seeds from the melon.* 用勺挖出香瓜裡的籽。**2** to be the first newspaper to print an important news report〔報紙〕首先報道重要新聞, 搶先報道: *The Daily News scooped the other papers by revealing the prince's marriage plans.*《每日新聞報》搶在別家報紙前面披露了王子的結婚計劃。

scoop neck /ˌ· ˈ·◂/ *n* [C] a round, quite low neck on a woman's TOP〔女服的〕湯匙領, 開得較低的圓領 —see picture on page A17 參見 A17 頁圖

scoot /skut; skuːt/ *v* [I] *informal* to leave a place quickly and suddenly【非正式】突然跑開: *There's the bus now – I'd better scoot!* 公共汽車來了 — 我得快跑!

scoot·er /ˈskutə; ˈskuːtə/ *n* [C] **1** a type of small less powerful MOTORBIKE 低座小摩托車 —see picture at 參見 MOTORBIKE 圖 **2** a child's vehicle with two small wheels, an upright handle, and a narrow board that you stand on with one foot, while the other foot pushes against the ground〔兒童的〕踏板車〔以一腳站在踏板上, 另一腳蹬地前行〕

3 **scope¹** /skop; skəʊp/ *n* [U] **1** the range of things that a subject, activity, book etc deals with〔學科、活動、書籍等的〕範圍: *a repertoire of extraordinary scope* 範圍特別大的常備劇目 | **beyond/within the scope of** *The politics of the country is really beyond the scope of a tourist book like this.* 一國的政情確實超出了這樣一本旅遊手冊涉及的範圍。| **widen/broaden the scope of** (=include more things) 擴大…的範圍 *an attempt to broaden the scope of the inquiry* 擴大調查範圍的嘗試 **2** the opportunity to do or develop something〔發揮能力的〕機會, 施展餘地: **[+for]** *Is there much scope for initiative in this job?* 這份工作有沒有機會讓人施展才華?

scope² *v* [T]

scope sth/sb out *phr v* [T] *AmE old-fashioned* to look at something or someone to see what they are like【美, 過時】了解, 查清, 探明: *Let's scope out that new club tonight.* 讓我們今晚去看看那個新俱樂部是甚麼樣的。

scorch¹ /skɔrtʃ; skɔːtʃ/ *v* **1** [I,T] if you scorch something, or if it scorches, its surface burns slightly and changes colour (使) 燒焦, (使) 烤焦: *The walls had been blackened and scorched by the fire.* 這些牆被大火燒黑了。| *I scorched my new shirt with the iron.* 我用熨斗把新襯衫給燙焦了。**2** [T] if strong heat scorches plants, it dries them and kills them〔炙熱把植物〕灼傷, 使枯萎: *All the grass had been scorched brown.* 所有的草都被曬得一片枯黃。**3** [T] if strong heat scorches you, it burns you 燙, 燙傷: *The hot sand scorched our feet.* 炙熱的沙子燙着我們的腳。**4** [I always+adv/prep] *BrE informal* to travel extremely fast【英, 非正式】飛馳, 高速行駛: **[+along/down/across etc]** *A car came scorching down the fast lane at 110 miles an hour.* 一輛汽車以每小時 110 英里的速度在快車道上疾馳。

scorch² *n* **1** [C] a mark made on something where its surface has been burnt 焦痕, 燒焦或烤焦處 **2** [U] brown colouring on plants caused by some plant diseases〔植物因病害出現的〕枯萎

scorched earth pol·i·cy /ˌ· ˈ· ˌ···/ *n* [C] the destruction by an army of everything useful in an area, especially crops, so that the land cannot be used by an enemy 焦土政策〔軍隊放棄某地區前實行的燒毀農作物等的徹底破壞行動〕

scorch·er /ˈskɔrtʃə; ˈskɔːtʃə/ *n* [C usually singular 一般用單數] *informal* an extremely hot day【非正式】大熱天: *Phew, what a scorcher!* 啊, 天氣真熱!

scorch·ing /ˈskɔrtʃɪŋ; ˈskɔːtʃɪŋ/ *adj* extremely hot 極熱的, 灼熱的: *scorching sun* 烈日 | **scorching hot** *a scorching hot day* 極熱的一天

score¹ /skɔr; skɔː/ *n* [C] 3 2

1 ►IN A GAME 在比賽中◄ [C] the number of points that each team or player has won in a game or competition〔遊戲、競賽中得的〕分數, 比分: **the score** *What's the score?* 比分是多少? | **keep (the) score** (=make a record of the score) 記分 *Is anybody keeping score?* 有沒有人負責記分? | **final score** *The final score was Everton 2, Spurs 4.* 最後的比分是二比四, 愛華頓隊敗給熱刺隊。

2 ►MUSIC 音樂◄ [C] a written or printed copy of a piece of music, especially for a large group of performers 樂譜: *a vocal score* 聲部樂譜 | *Who wrote the score for the movie?* 這部電影的配樂是誰譜寫的?

3 ►IN A TEST 考試◄ [C] *AmE* the number of points a student has earned for correct answers in a test【美】〔學生考試的〕分數

4 on that score *spoken* concerning the particular thing you have just mentioned【口】關於那一點, 關於那個問題: *As for the cost, you don't need to worry on that score.* 至於費用, 你不需要為這個問題操心。

5 know the score *informal* to know the real facts of a situation, including any unpleasant ones【非正式】知道事情真相, 了解實情: *John won't do anything risky – he knows the score.* 約翰不會去做任何冒險的事 — 他心中有數。

6 settle a score to do something to harm or hurt someone who has harmed or hurt you in the past 報宿怨, 算舊賬: *Jack came back after five years to settle some old scores.* 傑克在五年之後回來報仇雪恥。

7 ►MARK 記號◄ a mark that has been cut onto a surface with a sharp tool〔利器造成的〕刻痕, 劃痕: *deep scores in the wood* 木頭上一道道很深的劃痕

score² *v* 2

1 ►WIN POINTS 得分◄ [I,T] to win a point in a sport, game, or competition〔在運動、遊戲、比賽中〕得 (分): *Arsenal scored in the final minute of the game.* 阿仙奴隊在比賽的最後一分鐘進了球。| **score a goal/point/run** *Which player has scored the most runs this season?* 這個賽季哪個球員得分最多?

2 ►RECORD POINTS 記分◄ [I] to record the number of points someone has in a game or competition as it is played〔在比賽中〕記分: *Will you score for us?* 你來給我們記分好嗎?

3 ►GIVE POINTS 評分◄ [T] **a)** to give someone a particular number of points in a game or competition〔在遊戲、競賽等中〕給〔某人〕評分, 打分: **score sb 6/8 etc** *The Canadian judge scored her 15.* 加拿大裁判給

她打了 15 分。**b)** to be worth a particular number of points in a game or competition〔在遊戲、競賽等中〕得分: *A bull's-eye scores 50 points.* 擊中靶心可得 50 分。

4 score points also 又作 **score off sb** to argue with someone in order to prove that you are better than they are〔在辯論中〕駁倒對方

5 ►SUCCEED 成功◄ [I,T] *informal* to be very successful in something you do【非正式】成就輝煌: *Atwood has scored again with another popular book.* 阿特伍德的另一部暢銷書又獲得很大成功。| **score a success** *The Green party scored some successes in the north west.* 綠黨在西北部獲得了幾次成功。

6 ►HAVE SEX 做愛◄ [I] *slang* to have sex with someone you have just met【俚】〔與新認識的人〕發生性關係: *Did you score, then?* 那麼你們有沒有做愛?

7 ►PAPER 紙張◄ [T] to mark a line on a piece of paper, using a sharp instrument〔用利器〕在〔紙上〕刻痕, 劃線: *Scoring the paper first makes it easier to fold.* 先在上面劃一道痕, 紙就比較容易摺了。

8 ►MUSIC 音樂◄ [usually passive 一般用被動態] to arrange a piece of music for a group of instruments or voices〔為一組樂器演奏或聲部〕配樂, 譜曲

9 ►GET DRUGS 弄到毒品◄ [I,T] *slang* to manage to buy or get illegal drugs【俚】非法買到[弄到]毒品

score sth ↔ **out/through** *phr v* [T] to draw a line through something that has been written 劃掉, 刪去〔文字〕

score[3] *number* **1** *old use* twenty【舊】二十 **2 scores of** a lot of 很多, 大量: *scores of people in line for food* 很多人在排隊等候食物

score·board /ˋskor͵bord; ˈskɔːbɔːd/ *n* [C] a board on which the points won in a game are recorded〔比賽中的〕記分牌

score·card /ˋskor͵kard; ˈskɔːkɑːd/ *n* [C] a printed card used by someone watching a sports match or race to record what happens〔觀賽者持的〕比賽成績記錄卡

scor·er /ˋskorɚ; ˈskɔːrə/ *n* [C] **1** also 又作 **scorekeeper** someone who keeps an official record of the points won in a sports game〔體育比賽的〕記分員 **2** a player who wins a point or GOAL (2) 得分[進球]的運動員 **3 high/low scorer** someone who gets a large or small number of points in a test 高/低分者〔在考試中獲得高分或低分者〕

scorn[1] /skɔrn; skɔːn/ *n* [U] the feeling that someone or something is stupid, old-fashioned, or not as good as other people or things; CONTEMPT 鄙視, 蔑視, 輕視: **[+for]** *They had nothing but scorn for their working-class parents.* 他們對自己勞動階級的父母完全看不起。| **pour scorn on** *Davis poured scorn on the proposal.* 戴維斯對那個提議嗤之以鼻。

scorn[2] *v* [T] to refuse to accept ideas, suggestions etc because you think they are stupid, old-fashioned, or unreasonable〔認為愚蠢、過時或不合理而〕拒絕接受〔思想、建議等〕; 鄙視: *Most young people today scorn the idea that virginity is important.* 當今大部分年輕人都對認為童貞很重要的看法不屑一顧。| **scorn to do sth** (=refuse to do something, because you think it is not good enough) 不屑做某事 *She scorned to hide away like a coward.* 她不屑像懦夫一樣躲起來。

scorn·ful /ˋskɔrnfəl; ˈskɔːnfəl/ *adj* feeling or showing scorn 輕蔑的, 鄙視的: *a scornful look* 輕蔑的表情 | **[+of]** *They remained scornful of all our attempts to find a solution.* 他們對我們尋找解決辦法的一切努力都持鄙視態度。—**scornfully** *adv*

Scor·pi·o /ˋskɔrpɪ͵o; ˈskɔːpiəʊ/ *n* **1** [singular] the eighth sign of the ZODIAC, represented by a SCORPION, and believed to affect the character and life of people born between October 23 and November 21 天蝎宮[座]〔黃道第八宮〕 **2** [C] someone who was born between October 23 and November 21 出生於天蝎宮時段〔10月23日至11月21日〕的人

scor·pi·on /ˋskɔrpɪən; ˈskɔːpiən/ *n* [C] a tropical animal like an insect with a curving tail and a poisonous sting 蝎子

scorpion 蝎子

Scot /skɑt; skɒt/ *n* [C] someone from Scotland 蘇格蘭人

scotch /skɑtʃ; skɒtʃ/ *v* [T] to stop something happening by firmly doing something to prevent it 遏止, 制止, 阻止: *British delegates soon scotched any idea of a deal.* 英國代表們很快就把任何想達成協議的意見壓了下去。| **scotch a rumour** (=stop people saying something untrue) 制止謠言

Scotch[1] *n* [C,U] a strong alcoholic drink made in Scotland, or a glass of this (一杯) 蘇格蘭威士忌 (酒)

Scotch[2] *adj* SCOTTISH 蘇格蘭的

Scotch broth /͵· ˈ·/ *n* [U] thick soup made from vegetables, meat and BARLEY (=type of grain)〔用蔬菜、肉類、大麥等熬煮的〕蘇格蘭濃湯

Scotch egg /͵· ˈ·/ *n* [C] a cooked egg covered with meat and small pieces of bread〔外裹肉和麵包屑的〕蘇格蘭式煮蛋

Scotch mist /͵· ˈ·/ *n* [C,U] thick mist with light rain 蘇格蘭霧〔一種帶毛毛雨的濃霧〕

Scotch pan·cake /͵· ˈ··/ *n* [C] a small round flat cake 蘇格蘭烙餅〔一種小圓烙餅〕

Scotch tape /͵· ˈ·/ *n* [U] *AmE trademark* sticky thin transparent material used for sticking light things together【美, 商標】思高透明黏膠帶; SELLOTAPE *BrE trademark*【英, 商標】

scotch tape *v* [T] *AmE* to stick things together with Scotch tape【美】用透明膠帶黏貼; SELLOTAPE *BrE*【英】

scot-free /͵skɑt ˋfri; ͵skɒt ˈfriː/ *adv* **get away/off scot-free** *informal* to avoid being punished although you deserve to be【非正式】逃脱懲罰

Scot·land Yard /͵skɑtlənd ˋjɑrd; ͵skɒtlənd ˈjɑːd/ *n* [singular] *BrE* the part of the London police that deals with serious crimes, or their main office【英】蘇格蘭場〔倫敦警察廳的刑事偵緝部或總部〕

Scots /skɑts; skɒts/ *adj* Scottish 蘇格蘭的; 蘇格蘭人的; 蘇格蘭英語的

Scots·man /ˋskɑtsmən; ˈskɒtsmən/ *n* [C] a man who comes from Scotland 蘇格蘭男人

Scots·wom·an /ˋskɑts͵wʊmən; ˈskɒts͵wʊmən/ *n* [C] a woman who comes from Scotland 蘇格蘭女人

Scot·tish /ˋskɑtɪʃ; ˈskɒtɪʃ/ *adj* from or belonging to Scotland 蘇格蘭的; 蘇格蘭人的; 蘇格蘭英語的

scoun·drel /ˋskaʊndrəl; ˈskaʊndrəl/ *n* [C] *old-fashioned* a bad or dishonest man【過時】惡棍, 無賴: *a charming scoundrel, without morals* 一個有魅力而無道德的無賴

scour /skaʊr; skaʊə/ *v* [T] **1** to search very carefully and thoroughly through an area, a document, etc〔徹底地〕搜查〔某地或某物〕: *A team of detectives is scouring the countryside.* 一隊偵探正在搜查整個鄉村地區。 **2** also 又作 **scour out** to clean something very thoroughly by rubbing it with a rough material 擦淨, 擦亮: *The pans really needed to be scoured.* 這些鍋真需要好好擦一擦了。—see picture at 參見 CLEAN[2] 圖 **3** also 又作 **scour out** to form a hole by continuous movement over a long period〔長期不斷地〕沖刷成〔洞〕: *Over the years, the stream had scoured out a round pool in the rock.* 溪水長年累月地在岩石上沖出了一個圓形水坑。—**scour** *n* [singular]

scour·er /ˋskaʊrɚ; ˈskaʊərə/ *n* [C] a small ball of wire or rough plastic for cleaning cooking pots and pans 刷洗鍋盤用的金屬[塑料]團

scourge[1] /skɝdʒ; skɜːdʒ/ *n* [C] **1** something that causes a lot of harm or suffering 禍根, 禍害: **[+of]** *The scourge of apartheid has finally ended.* 種族隔離的禍害終於結

束了。**2** a WHIP used to punish people in former times〔舊時用作刑具的〕鞭子

scourge² *v* [T] **1** to cause a lot of harm or suffering to a place or group of people 使遭受苦難, 蹂躪: *a country scourged by disease and war* 飽受疾病和戰火蹂躪的國家 **2** to hit someone with a whip as punishment in former times 鞭打〔舊時的一種刑罰〕

scouring pad /ˈ·· ·/ *n* [C] a scourer 刷鍋盤用的金屬[塑料]團

Scouse /skaus; skaʊs/ *n* [U] *BrE*【英】**1** the way of speaking that is typical of people from Liverpool 利物浦地區的方言 **2** a thick soup with meat, potatoes, and vegetables〔用肉、馬鈴薯、蔬菜等做的〕利物浦濃湯 — Scouse *adj*

Scous·er /ˈskausə; ˈskaʊsə/ *n* [C] someone from Liverpool 利物浦人

scout¹ /skaut; skaʊt/ *n* [C] **1 a) the scouts** an organization for young boys that teaches them practical skills 童子軍〔組織〕 **b)** also 又作 **boy scout** a boy who is a member of this organization 男童子軍〔成員〕 **2** *AmE* also 又作 **girl scout** a girl who is a member of an organization for girls that teaches them practical skills【美】女童子軍; GUIDE *BrE*【英】**3** a soldier, plane etc that is sent to search the area in front of an army, get information about the enemy 偵察兵; 偵察機; 偵察艇: *He sent three scouts ahead to take a look at the bridge.* 他派遣三名偵察兵到前頭偵察大橋的情況。**4** someone whose job is to look for good sports players, musicians etc in order to employ them 物色新秀者, 人才發掘者〔尤指發掘運動員、音樂人才等〕, 星探: *He was spotted by a scout at the age of 13.* 他在13歲時被星探發現。—see also 另見 TALENT SCOUT **5 a scout round/around** *BrE informal* a quick search of an area【英, 非正式】搜索, 到處尋找: *I'll have a scout round to see if I can find it.* 我要去四處找一下, 看能否把它找出來。

S

scout² *v* **1** also 又作 **scout round/around** [I] to look for something in a particular area〔在某地區〕尋找: **[+for]** *I want you all to scout round for any wood you can find.* 我想要你們大家去盡量找點木柴回來。**2** also 又作 **scout out** [T] to examine a place or area in order to get information about it, especially in a military situation〔尤指軍事上〕對〔某地〕進行偵察: *A group was sent off to scout out the area ahead.* 一隊人被派去偵察前面的地區。**3** [T] *AmE* to find out about the abilities of sports players, musicians etc【美】弄清〔運動員、音樂人才等〕的才能

scout·ing /ˈskautɪŋ; ˈskaʊtɪŋ/ *n* [U] the activities that scouts take part in 偵察活動; 童子軍活動

scout·mas·ter /ˈskautˌmæstə; ˈskaʊtˌmɑːstə/ *n* [C] a man who is the leader of a group of scouts (SCOUT¹ (1a)) 童子軍領隊[小隊長]

scowl¹ /skaul; skaʊl/ *v* [I+at] to look at someone in an angry way 怒視〔某人〕

scowl 怒視

scowl² *n* [C] an angry or disapproving expression on someone's face 怒容; 不悅之色

Scrab·ble /ˈskræbl; ˈskræbəl/ *n* [U] *trademark* a game in which players try to make words from the separate letters they have【商標】〔用得到的若干字母組詞的〕縱橫拼字遊戲

scrab·ble *v* [I always+adv+prep] to try to find something by feeling with your fingers, especially quickly among a lot of other things〔用手指〕扒找〔尤指在一堆物品中快速翻找〕: **[+around/about etc]** *She was scrabbling through her pockets for a cigarette.* 她用手在衣袋裡摸索着找香煙。

scrag end /ˌ· ˈ·/ also 又作 **scrag** *n* [U] *BrE* the bony part of a sheep's neck, that is sometimes boiled for soup【英】〔有時用於熬湯的〕羊頸肉

scrag·gly /ˈskræglɪ; ˈskrægəli/ *adj AmE informal* growing in a way that looks uneven and in bad condition【美, 非正式】〔長得〕參差不齊的; 散亂的: *his scraggly unwashed hair* 他的又髒又亂的頭髮

scrag·gy /ˈskrægɪ; ˈskrægi/ *adj* too thin and bony 骨瘦如柴的, 皮包骨的: *scraggy wrists* 皮包骨的手腕

scram /skræm; skræm/ *v* [I usually in imperative 一般用於祈使句] *informal* to leave a place very quickly, especially so that you do not get caught【非正式】〔尤指為避免被抓住而〕迅速離開, 跑開: *Scram, you two!* 快走開, 你們兩個!

scram·ble¹ /ˈskræmbl; ˈskræmbəl/ *v*

1 ►CLIMB 攀爬◄ [I always+adv/prep] to climb up or over something with difficulty, using your hands to help you 爬, 攀登: **[+up/down/back etc]** *We scrambled up a rocky slope.* 我們爬上一個岩石陡坡。

2 scramble to your feet to stand up quickly and awkwardly 狼狽地趕快爬起來: *He scrambled to his feet, blushing furiously.* 他狼狽地趕快站了起來, 羞得滿臉通紅。

3 ►COMPETE 競爭◄ [I] to struggle or compete with other people to get or reach something 爭奪, 搶奪: **[+for]** *People were scrambling madly for shelter.* 人們發瘋似地搶着奔向隱蔽所。

4 ►INFORMATION/MESSAGE 情報/消息◄ [T] *technical* to use special equipment to mix messages, radio signals etc into a different form, so that they cannot be understood by other people, especially an enemy【術語】加擾, 擾亂〔用儀器把信息、無線電等加密使別人無法理解〕: *A magnetic field will scramble the information on a computer disk.* 磁場會擾亂儲存在電腦磁盤上的信息。

5 scramble an egg to cook an egg by mixing the white and yellow parts together and heating it 炒蛋〔把蛋白和蛋黃攪和了炒〕

6 scramble sb's brains *informal* to make someone unable to think clearly or reasonably【非正式】使某人頭腦糊塗, 使某人思維混亂: *This girl has taken enough drugs to completely scramble her brains.* 這個女孩吸了大量毒品, 足以使她頭腦一片混亂。

7 ►AIRCRAFT 飛機◄ [I] *technical* if a military plane scrambles, it goes up into the air very quickly in order to escape or to attack an enemy【術語】〔軍用飛機為逃跑或進攻敵人而〕緊急起飛

scramble² *n* **1** [singular] a difficult climb in which you have to use your hands to help you 攀爬, 爬行: *a rough scramble over boulders* 在巨石上艱難的攀爬 **2** [singular] a situation in which people compete with and push each other in order to get what they want〔互相推撞的〕爭奪, 爭搶: **[+for]** *a scramble for the best seats* 爭搶最好的座位 | **a scramble to do sth** *a scramble to pick up the scattered coins* 爭着去拾散落的硬幣 **3** [singular] a situation in which something has to be done very quickly, with a lot of rushing around〔因趕任務出現的〕忙亂, 亂作一團: **mad scramble** *It was a mad scramble trying to get things ready in time.* 為了及時把東西準備好, 結果亂成了一團。**4** [C] a MOTORCYCLE race over rough ground 摩托車越野賽

scrambled egg /ˌ·· ˈ·/ *n* [C,U] egg cooked in a pan after the white and yellow parts have been mixed together〔蛋黃和蛋白攪和後的〕炒蛋

scram·bler /ˈskræmblə; ˈskræmblə/ *n* [C] a machine that mixes up a radio or telephone message so that it cannot be understood without special equipment 加擾器〔擾亂無線電、電話等信號, 使無特殊儀器者無法接收〕

scrap¹ /skræp; skræp/ *n*

1 ►PAPER/CLOTH 紙/布◄ [C] a small piece of paper, cloth etc 小片, 小塊; 碎屑: **[+of]** *He wrote his address on a scrap of paper and gave it to me.* 他把住址寫在小紙片上交給了我。| *a quilt made out of scraps of old*

fabric 用各種舊布片綴成的被子 —see picture on page A7 參見A7頁圖
2 ▶OLD OBJECTS 舊物◀ [U] materials or objects that are no longer used for the purpose they were made for, but can be used again in another way 廢品, 廢棄材料: *The car was eventually sold for scrap.* 那輛汽車最後當作廢鐵賣掉了。| **scrap metal** (=metal from old cars, machines etc that is melted and used again) 廢舊金屬
3 ▶FOOD 食物◀ **scraps** [plural] pieces of food that are left after you have finished eating 吃剩的東西, 殘羹剩飯: *They fed the dog on scraps.* 他們用吃剩的飯菜餵狗。
4 ▶INFORMATION 信息◀ [C] a small piece of information, truth etc〔消息、事實等的〕一點點, 點滴: [+of] *There wasn't a single scrap of evidence to connect him with the murder.* 沒有絲毫證據説明他與這宗謀殺案有關。| *scraps of news* 零星的消息
5 not make a scrap of difference *informal* to not change a situation at all【非正式】〔對情況〕沒有影響, 毫無作用: *Nothing I said made a scrap of difference.* 我説的話絲毫不起作用。
6 ▶FIGHT 打架◀ [C] *informal* a short fight or argument【非正式】爭吵, 吵架; 打架: *The girls have scraps over their toys sometimes, but nothing serious.* 女孩子們有時會為了玩具爭吵, 但不嚴重。

scrap² *v* **scrapped, scrapping 1** [T] to decide not to use a plan or system because it is not practical〔因不切實際而〕放棄, 拋棄〔計劃、體系等〕: *We've decided to scrap the whole idea of renting a car.* 我們決定放棄租車的想法。**2** [T] to get rid of an old machine, vehicle etc, and use its parts in some other way 把〔舊機器、舊汽車等〕當作廢料處理, 報廢: *The navy's biggest aircraft carrier is being scrapped this year.* 海軍最大的一艘航空母艦今年就要被當作廢鋼鐵處理了。**3** [I] *informal* to have a short fight or argument【非正式】打架; 吵架

scrap·book /ˈskræpˌbuk; ˈskræpbʊk/ *n* [C] a book with empty pages where you can stick pictures, newspaper articles, or other things you want to keep〔黏貼圖片、剪報等的〕剪貼簿

scrape¹ /skrep; skreɪp/ *v* **1** [T] to remove something from a surface, using the edge of a knife, stick etc〔用小刀等〕刮除: *Scrape the carrots and slice them thinly.* 把這些胡蘿蔔刮皮並切成薄片。| **scrape sth away/off etc** *I tried to scrape some of the mud off my boots.* 我設法把靴子上的泥刮掉一些。| *We scraped away several layers of old varnish.* 我們把幾層舊漆刮掉了。| **scrape sth clean** *The plates had all been scraped clean.* 這些盤子都已經擦乾淨了。**2** [I always+adv/prep,T] to rub against a rough surface in a way that causes slight damage or injury, or to make something do this (使) 摩擦, 擦傷; 刮壞: [+on/against etc] *The car exhaust was hanging down and scraping the ground.* 汽車的排氣管垂了下來, 擦着了地面。| **scrape sth on/against etc** *I scraped my knee painfully on the concrete.* 我的膝蓋在水泥地上擦得很痛。**3** [I,T] to make an unpleasant noise by rubbing roughly against a surface (使) 亂擦發出刺耳聲: *Chairs scraped loudly as they stood up.* 他們站起來時椅子發出刺耳的響聲。| **scrape (sth) on/down/against etc** *Her fingernails scraped down the blackboard.* 她的指甲在黑板上刮出了聲音。**4 scrape home** *especially BrE* to win a race, election, or competition by a very small amount【尤英】〔在賽跑、選舉、競賽中〕險勝: *Johnson scraped home just milliseconds ahead of Lewis.* 約翰遜僅以千分之幾秒領先劉易斯而獲勝。**5 scrape a hole** to make a hole or hollow place in the ground by rubbing the surface〔在地上〕挖出窟窿, 刨成一個洞 **6 scrape (the bottom of) the barrel** *informal* to have to use something even though it is not very good because there is nothing better available【非正式】〔因為沒有更好的選擇而〕勉強使用某物; 把標準降到最低 —see also 另見 **bow and scrape** (BOW[1] (4)), **pinch and scrape** (PINCH[1] (5)), **scrape/scratch a living** (LIVING[2] (1))

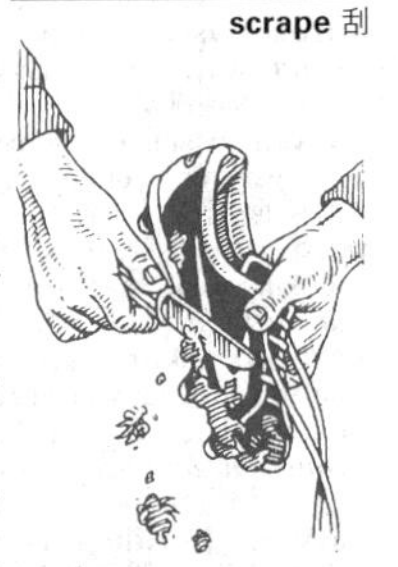
scrape 刮

scrape by *phr v* [I] **1** to have just enough money to live 收入僅夠維持生活, 勉強糊口: *They just managed to scrape by on Fred's tiny salary.* 他們僅靠弗雷德的微薄工資勉強度日。**2** *especially AmE* to only just succeed in passing an examination or dealing with a difficult situation【尤美】勉強通過 (考試); 勉強克服 (困難)

scrape in/into *phr v* [I,T] to only just succeed in getting a job, place at university, position in government etc 勉強通過 (考試); 勉強獲得 (一份工作或政府職位): *He just scraped into college.* 他勉強進了大學。| *Labour scraped in by a small majority.* 工黨以微弱的優勢上台執政。

scrape through *phr v* [I,T] to only just succeed in passing an examination or dealing with a difficult situation 勉強通過 (考試); 勉強克服 (困難): *Dani just scraped through her exams.* 丹妮勉強通過了考試。

scrape sth ↔ together/up *phr v* [T] to get enough money for a particular purpose, when this is difficult〔為某目的〕勉強籌集; 湊足〔款項〕: *She scraped together the last of her savings to buy the cottage.* 她動用了全部積蓄才湊夠錢買那所小屋。

scrape² *n* **1** [singular] the unpleasant noise made when one surface rubs roughly against another 刮擦聲: *We heard the scrape of a chair downstairs and then footsteps.* 我們聽到樓下拖動椅子的聲音, 接着是腳步聲。**2** [C] a situation that is difficult or slightly dangerous 困境, 窘境; 麻煩: *He got himself into all sorts of scrapes as a boy.* 他在童年時惹出過各種麻煩事。**3** [C] a mark or slight injury caused by rubbing against a rough surface 擦傷, 擦痕: *We came away from the accident with only a few cuts and scrapes.* 我們在事故中安全脱險, 只是有幾處劃破和擦傷。

scrap·er /ˈskrepɚ; ˈskreɪpə/ *n* [C] a tool used to remove something from a surface by rubbing 刮削用具〈如刮刀、刮板等〉: *a paint scraper* 刮漆刀

scrap·heap /ˈskræpˌhip; ˈskræphiːp/ *n* **1 throw sb/sth on the scrapheap** *informal* to get rid of someone or something because you no longer think they are useful, in a way that seems unfair【非正式】把某人/某物扔到廢物堆裡, 拋棄某人/某物: *Twenty years of loyal service and they're throwing him on the scrapheap!* 他忠心耿耿地服務了二十年, 而他們準備把他一腳踢開! **2** [C] a pile of unwanted things, especially pieces of metal 廢料堆〔尤指廢金屬堆〕

scra·pie /ˈskrepɪ; ˈskreɪpi/ *n* [U] a serious disease that sheep get 癢病〔綿羊患的一種嚴重疾病〕

scrap·ings /ˈskrepɪŋz; ˈskreɪpɪŋz/ *n* [plural] small pieces that have been scraped from a surface 刮屑, 削片, 刮下的碎屑

scrap pa·per /ˈ· ˌ··/ *n* [U] *BrE* paper, often paper that has already been used on one side, that you use for making notes, lists etc【英】作便紙〔常指一面已用過, 另一面可用於記瑣事的廢紙〕; SCRATCH PAPER *AmE*【美】

scrap·ple /ˈskræpl; ˈskræpl/ *n* [U] *AmE* food made from pieces of meat mixed together with CORNMEAL【美】碎肉玉米餅

scrap·py /ˈskræpɪ; ˈskræpi/ *adj* **1** untidy or badly organized 不整潔的; 散亂的, 無條理的: *a scrappy, badly written report* 一篇雜亂無章、寫得很差的報告 | *a scrappy bit of paper* 一些零碎的廢紙 **2** *AmE informal* always wanting to argue or fight【美, 非正式】好爭鬥的; 愛吵架的

S

scratch¹ /skrætʃ; skrætʃ/ *v*

1 ▶RUB YOUR SKIN 撓皮膚◀ [I,T] to rub your skin with your nails, especially because it itches (ITCH¹ (1))〔用指甲〕撓，搔，輕抓: *Try not to scratch those mosquito bites.* 盡量別撓那些蚊子叮起的包。

2 ▶MAKE A MARK 劃痕◀ [T] to rub something sharp or rough against a hard surface so that it makes a thin mark〔用尖利或粗糙的東西〕刮出〔痕跡〕，劃傷: *Mind you don't scratch the table with those scissors!* 小心別用剪刀劃壞桌面！

scratch 刮擦

3 ▶MAKE A CUT 割破◀ [I,T] to make a small cut by pulling something sharp against someone's skin〔利器把皮膚〕劃傷，割破: *I scratched my hand on a blackberry bush.* 我的手被黑莓樹叢劃破了。| *Be careful. That cat scratches.* 小心，那隻貓會抓傷人的。

4 ▶MAKE A NOISE 發出聲音◀ [I always+adv/prep] to make a noise by rubbing something with a sharp or pointed object〔用尖利物〕刮擦出聲音: *The dog kept scratching at the door to be let in.* 狗在不斷地抓門想進屋。

5 ▶REMOVE STH 除去某物◀ [T always+adv/prep] to remove something from a surface by rubbing it with something sharp 刮掉，劃掉: **scratch sth off/away etc** *I scratched away a little of the paint with my fingernail.* 我用指甲把一點油漆刮掉了。

6 ▶STOP PLANNING 停止計劃◀ [T] to stop planning to do something because it is no longer possible or practical〔因不可能或不切實際而〕取消〔計劃等〕: *I guess we can scratch that idea.* 我想我們可以打消那個念頭。

7 scratch the surface to deal with only a very small part of a subject 僅觸及問題的表面: *In this essay I can only hope to scratch the surface of the topic.* 在這篇文章裡，我只希望能對這個問題作個粗淺的探討。

8 scratch your head *informal* to think hard about a difficult question or problem【非正式】動腦筋，〔對難題〕苦思冥想: *The last question really had us scratching our heads.* 最後那個問題真讓我們傷腦筋。

9 ▶REMOVE FROM RACE 取消比賽資格◀ [I,T] to remove someone from a race or competition before it begins（令…）退出比賽

10 you scratch my back, I'll scratch yours *spoken* used to say that you will help someone if they agree to help you【口】你幫我，我也幫你 —see also 另見 **scrape/scratch a living** (LIVING² (1))

scratch sth ↔ **out** *phr v* [T] to draw a line through a word, in order to remove it 劃掉〔文字〕，刪掉: *Philippa's name had been scratched out.* 菲莉帕的名字被去掉了。

scratch² *n*

1 ▶MARK OR CUT 痕跡或破痕◀ [C] a thin mark or cut on the surface of something or on someone's skin〔物件或皮膚上的〕劃痕，刮痕，劃傷: *a scratch on the car door* 車門上的刮痕

2 from scratch if you do or start something from scratch, you begin it without using anything that existed or was prepared before 從零開始，從頭開始，白手起家: *It was years since I'd learnt any German, and I really had to start again from scratch.* 多年前我學過一點德語，現在只得再從頭學起。

3 not come/be up to scratch to not be good enough for a particular standard 達不到標準: *His schoolwork really hasn't been up to scratch lately.* 他近來的功課確實達不到標準。

4 ▶SOUND 聲音◀ [C] a sound made by something sharp or rough being rubbed on a hard surface〔利器在硬物上刮的〕刮擦聲: *I could hear the scratch of the dog's claws on the floor.* 我能聽到狗爪子抓地板的聲音。

5 have a scratch to rub part of your body with your nails〔用指甲在身上〕抓撓

6 it's only/just a scratch *spoken* used to say that you are not seriously hurt or injured【口】只是擦破一點皮罷了〔用以表示傷勢不重〕

7 without a scratch if you escape from a dangerous situation without a scratch, you are not injured at all 安然無恙，安然脱險

8 ▶MUSIC 音樂◀ [U] a type of popular music produced by stopping a record while it is playing and moving it with your hands to make a sound 刮擦樂〔一種流行音樂，在唱片播放時用手中斷唱片並轉動它使其發出聲音〕

scratch³ *adj* [no comparative 無比較級] **1** a scratch team, game, side etc is put together in a hurry, using anyone that is available〔球隊等〕倉促拼湊的，匆匆組成的 **2** a scratch player in a sport does not have a HANDICAP (=officially arranged disadvantage)〔體育比賽〕無讓步優待的，平等的

scratch·ings /ˈskrætʃɪŋz; ˈskrætʃɪŋz/ *n* [plural] *BrE* small pieces of pig's skin that have been cooked in hot fat and are eaten cold【英】炸豬皮片; PORK RINDS *AmE*【美】

scratch·pad /ˈskrætʃˌpæd; ˈskrætʃpæd/ *n* [C] *especially AmE* several sheets of cheap paper joined together at the top or side, used for writing notes or lists【尤美】拍紙簿

scratch pa·per /ˈ· ˌ··/ *n* [U] *AmE* paper, often paper that has already been used on one side, that you use for making notes, lists etc【美】便條紙〔常指一面已用過、另一面可用於記瑣事的廢紙〕; SCRAP PAPER *BrE*【英】

scratch test /ˈ· ·/ *n* [C] a medical test that involves cutting someone's skin slightly and putting a substance on it to see how their body reacts 劃痕試驗〔指在皮膚上劃破一點後施用某種物質以觀察身體的反應〕

scratch·y /ˈskrætʃɪ; ˈskrætʃi/ *adj* **1** scratchy clothes or materials feel rough and uncomfortable〔衣物等〕粗糙的，扎人的，使皮膚發癢的 **2** a scratchy record makes a lot of unpleasant noises because it is old or damaged〔舊唱片、錄音帶等〕發沙沙聲的 —**scratchiness** *n* [U]

scrawl¹ /skrɔl; skrɔːl/ *v* [T] to write in a careless and untidy way, so that your words are not easy to read 潦草地寫，亂塗亂畫

scrawl² *n* [singular] something written in an untidy careless way, or an untidy careless way of writing 潦草寫成的東西; 潦草的筆跡

scraw·ny /ˈskrɔnɪ; ˈskrɔːni/ *adj* thin, unattractive, and looking weak 瘦弱的，皮包骨的: *a scrawny kid in jeans and a T-shirt* 穿着牛仔褲和T恤衫的瘦弱孩子

scream¹ /skrim; skriːm/ *v* **1** [I] to make a loud high noise with your voice because you are hurt, frightened, excited etc〔因疼痛、驚恐、興奮等〕尖聲大叫: *Shots rang out, and people started screaming.* 突然響起槍聲，人們尖聲大叫起來。| *a screaming baby* 尖聲哭叫的嬰兒 | **[+with/in]** *The woman lay there, screaming with pain.* 那個女人躺在那兒，痛得直尖叫。| **scream with laughter** (=laugh very loudly in a high voice) 尖聲大笑 **2** also 又作 **scream out** [I,T] to shout something in a very loud high voice because you are angry or frightened〔因憤怒或恐懼而〕高聲喊叫: *"Get out!" she screamed.* "出去！"她高聲叫道。| **[+for]** *I screamed for help.* 我高聲呼救。| **[+at]** *Calm down and stop screaming at me!* 冷靜點，不要對我大聲嚷嚷！| **scream insults/abuse etc** *Lola screamed insults at him as he left.* 在他離開時洛拉大聲辱罵他。**3** [I] to make a very loud high noise 發出尖鋭的叫聲: *The police car approached, its siren screaming.* 警車駛近，警報器尖聲呼嘯着。

scream (out) at sb *phr v* [I] *informal* if something such as a very bright colour or a mistake screams at you, it is very noticeable and annoying【非正式】〔顏色〕刺

眼;〔錯誤〕觸目驚心

scream² *n* [C] **1** a loud high sound made with your voice because you are very frightened, angry, hurt, or excited〔因恐懼、痛苦或興奮而發出的〕尖叫聲: *Her screams could be heard all down the block.* 整個街區都能聽到她的尖叫聲。| **scream of laughter/terror etc** *There were screams of excitement when he finally walked on stage.* 當他終於登台時, 觀眾報以激動的尖叫聲。| **let out a scream** *He let out a scream of terror.* 他發出驚恐的尖叫聲。**2** a very loud high sound 大而尖的聲音, 尖銳刺耳的聲音: *The scream of the jet taking off drowned Ryan's response.* 噴氣式飛機起飛時的呼嘯聲淹沒了瑞安的回答。**3 be a scream** *informal* used to describe someone or something that is very funny【非正式】是非常滑稽的人[事物]: *We went to the party dressed as twins. It was a scream!* 我們打扮成雙胞胎去參加聚會, 真是滑稽!

scream·ing·ly /ˈskrimɪŋlɪ; ˈskriːmɪŋli/ *adv* **screamingly funny** extremely funny 極其滑稽可笑地

scree /skri; skriː/ *n* [C] an area of small loose broken rocks on the side of a mountain 山坡上的碎石地帶, 岩屑堆: *a scree slope* 碎石斜坡 —see picture on page A12 參見A12頁圖

screech /skritʃ; skriːtʃ/ *v* **1** [I,T] to make a very unpleasant, high noise with your voice, especially because you are angry〔因生氣等〕尖叫, 尖聲喊叫: [+at] *She screeched at me to take off my muddy shoes.* 她尖聲地叫我脱掉黏滿泥污的鞋子。**2** [I] if a vehicle or its wheels screech, they make a high loud unpleasant noise〔車輛或輪子〕發出尖銳刺耳聲: *The train's wheels screeched and clattered as it drew out of the station.* 火車開出車站時, 輪子發出尖銳刺耳的聲音。**3 screech to a halt/stop/standstill** if a vehicle screeches to a halt, it stops very suddenly, so that the wheels make a loud unpleasant noise〔車輛〕嘎的一聲突然停住 —**screech** *n* [singular]: *a screech of tires* 輪胎發出的刺耳聲音

2 2 **screen¹** /skrin; skriːn/ *n*

1 ▶TELEVISION/COMPUTER 電視機/電腦◀ [C] the flat glass part of a television or computer 屏幕, 螢光屏: *This popular show will be back on your screens in the autumn.* 這個受歡迎的節目將在秋天再次和大家見面。| **on screen** (=on a computer screen) 在電腦屏幕上 *It's easy to change the text on screen before printing it.* 打印前在屏幕上作文字修改是很容易的。

2 ▶CINEMA 電影◀ **a)** [C] the large white surface that pictures are shown on in a cinema 銀幕, 屏幕 **b)** [singular, U] films in general 電影〔總稱〕: *The play was adapted for the screen.* 這部戲劇被改編成電影了。

3 ▶MOVABLE WALL 活動的牆◀ [C] a kind of wall that can be moved around, used to divide one part of a room from another 屏風: *The nurse put a screen around my bed.* 護士圍着我的牀豎起一道屏風。

4 ▶HIDE OR PROTECT 隱藏或保護◀ [C usually singular 一般用單數] something or someone that protects or hides someone or something else 掩蔽物, 屏障: *We planted these bushes as a screen, as the shed is so ugly.* 我們種這些灌木叢作屏障, 因為工具房太難看了。| *It turned out that the used car business was just a screen for his drug-dealing activities.* 原來他做舊車買賣只是為了掩護他的販毒活動。

5 ▶DOOR/WINDOW 門/窗◀ [C] a wire net put in front of a window or door that allows air into the house but keeps insects out〔防蚊蟲進入的〕紗門, 紗窗

6 ▶CHURCH 教堂◀ [C] a decorative wall in some churches 裝飾性圍屏

7 ▶SPORTS 體育運動◀ [C] *AmE* a player or group of players in a game who protect the player who has the ball【美】掩護(動作) —see also 另見 SMOKESCREEN, SUNSCREEN

screen² *v* [T]

1 ▶TEST FOR ILLNESS 檢查疾病◀ to do tests on a lot of people to find out whether they have a particular illness 給〔很多人〕作檢查〔以確定是否患有某種疾病〕: *Because of the higher risks, we try to screen all women over 50.* 50歲以上的婦女由於發病率較高, 我們盡量對她們進行普查。| **screen sb for** *We were all screened for hepatitis.* 我們都接受檢查以確定是否患有肝炎。

2 ▶HIDE STH 隱藏某物◀ to hide or protect something by putting something in front of it〔在前面放置某物以〕隱藏, 遮蔽, 隱蔽: [+off] *A large hat screened her face.* 一頂大帽子遮住了她的臉。| *Part of the room was screened off as a reception area.* 房間的一部分被隔開作接待室用。| **screen sth (off) from** *The house is screened from the road by a row of trees.* 一排樹木把那所房子和大路分隔開來。

3 ▶TEST EMPLOYEES 考查雇員◀ to examine or test people to make sure that they will be loyal to your company, organization etc〔為確保雇員的忠誠而進行〕審查, 甄別: *All applicants are screened for security.* 對所有申請人都要審查以確保安全。

4 ▶PROTECT SB 庇護某人◀ to protect someone who is involved in dishonest or illegal activities 包庇, 掩護, 袒護〔違法者〕: *He had been screening his business partner during the fraud investigation.* 在那宗詐騙案的調查中, 他一直在包庇他的生意合夥人。

5 ▶TELEVISION 電視◀ to show a film or television programme 放映〔影片〕; 播放〔電視節目〕

screen sth ↔ **out** *phr v* [T] **1** to prevent something harmful from entering or passing through 把〔有害東西〕擋住, 把…隔開: *Sun lotions screen out damaging ultraviolet light.* 防曬油把有害的紫外線擋住。**2** to decide that someone or something is not suitable for a job, position etc 剔除, 清除〔不符合條件者〕

screen door /ˈ· ˌ·/ *n* [C] *AmE* a door outside the main door, that will let air in but keep insects out【美】〔防止蚊蟲等進入的〕紗門

screen·ing /ˈskrinɪŋ; ˈskriːnɪŋ/ *n* **1** [C,U] the showing of a film or television programme 放映電影, 播放電視節目: *a screening of Spielberg's new movie* 放映史匹堡的新影片 **2** [U] tests done to make sure that someone does not have a particular disease 檢查〔以確定未患某種病〕: *screening for breast cancer* 檢查是否患乳腺癌 **3** [U] tests or checks done to make sure that someone or something is suitable for a particular purpose 甄別, 審查〔是否符合要求〕

screen·play /ˈskrinˌple; ˈskriːnpleɪ/ *n* [C] a story written for film or television 電影[電視]劇本: *her first screenplay, an adaptation of Austen's 'Sense and Sensibility'* 她的第一個電影劇本改編自奧斯汀的《理智與情感》

screen print·ing /ˈ· ˌ··/ *n* [U] a way of printing pictures by pushing paint or ink through a specially prepared cloth onto paper〔圖畫的〕絲網印刷法

screen test /ˈ· ˌ·/ *n* [C] an occasion when someone is filmed while performing, in order to see if they are suitable to act in a film 試鏡頭〔以挑選電影演員〕

screen·writ·er /ˈskrinˌraɪtɚ; ˈskriːnˌraɪtə/ *n* [C] someone who writes plays for film or television 影視劇本作家

screws 帶螺紋的物體

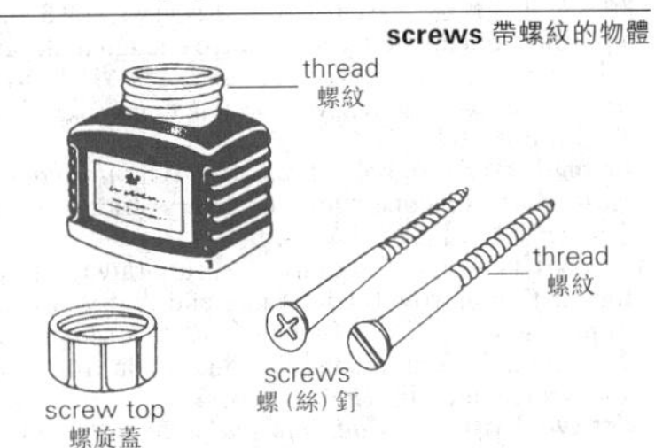

screw¹ /skru; skruː/ *n* **1** [C] a thin pointed piece of metal that you push and turn in order to fasten pieces of metal or wood together 螺絲, 螺 (絲) 釘: *Tighten the screws on the plug.* 把插座上的螺絲擰緊。**2** [C] *slang taboo* an act of having sex【俚, 諱】性交 **3 have a screw loose** *informal often humorous* to be slightly crazy【非正式, 幽默】有點瘋瘋癲癲, 頭腦有些不正常 **4 put/tighten the screws on sb** *informal* to force someone to do something by threatening them【非正式】威逼某人做某事 **5** [C] *BrE slang* a word for a prison officer, used especially by prisoners【英俚】監獄看守人〔尤為囚犯用語〕**6 a screw of tobacco/tea etc** *BrE old-fashioned* a small amount of tobacco, tea etc in a twisted paper packet【英, 過時】一小包煙草/茶葉等

screw² *v* **1** [T always+adv/prep] to fasten one object to another using a screw〔用螺絲〕將…固定: **screw sth into/onto/to sth** *Screw the socket into the wall.* 用螺絲把插座安在牆上。| *The bar stools were screwed to the floor.* 酒吧的櫈子是被螺釘固定在地板上的。**2** [T always+adv/prep] to fasten or close something by turning it until it cannot be turned anymore 擰緊, 旋緊: **screw sth on/together etc** *Don't forget to screw the cap back onto the toothpaste.* 不要忘記擰好牙膏的蓋子。**3** [I,T] *taboo* to have sex with someone【諱】與 (某人) 發生性關係 **4 screw you/him/that etc** *spoken taboo* used to show that you are very angry with someone【口, 諱】讓你/他/那等見鬼去〔對某人表示憤怒〕: *"Screw you!" he yelled.* "去你的!" 他吼道。**5** [T always+adv/prep] to twist paper or cloth into a small round shape 把〔紙或布〕擰成小卷: **screw sth (up) into sth** *She screwed the letter up into a ball and threw it in the bin.* 她把信揉成一團扔進垃圾桶裡。**6** [T often passive 常用被動態] *informal* to cheat someone or treat them in a dishonest way, especially to get money from them【非正式】欺騙〔尤指騙錢〕: *They really screwed you in that nightclub, charging £10 for a drink.* 他們的那個夜總會一杯飲料要收費十英鎊, 這完全是詐騙。| **screw sb for** *They screwed us for $60 in the end.* 他們最後敲詐了我們 60 美元。—see also 另見 **have your head screwed on (straight)** (HEAD¹ (28))

screw around *phr v* [I] *taboo* to have sex with a lot of different people【諱】到處亂搞男女關係, 亂交

screw up *phr v* **1 screw your eyes/face up** to move the muscles in your face in a way that makes your eyes seem narrow 眯緊眼睛/扭歪臉: *He screwed up his eyes against the bright light.* 他對着強光眯起眼睛。**2** [I] *informal* to make a bad mistake or do something very stupid【非正式】犯大錯, 做蠢事: *I really screwed up, didn't I?* 我的確做了蠢事, 不是嗎? **3** [T **screw** sth ↔ **up**] *informal* to spoil something such as a plan, by doing something stupid【非正式】把〔計劃等〕搞糟, 弄糟: *Breaking my ankle really screwed up our holiday plans!* 我摔斷了腳踝, 完全打亂了我們的度假計劃! **4** [T **screw** sb ↔ **up**] *informal* to make someone feel very unhappy, confused, or anxious, especially for a long time【非正式】〔尤指長時間〕使〔某人〕很不愉快[為難, 焦慮]: *It really screwed her up when her mother died.* 她母親去世時, 她真是非常難過。—see also 另見 SCREWED UP **5 screw up your courage** to try to be brave enough to do something you are very nervous about 鼓起勇氣: *I screwed up my courage and went over to talk to her.* 我鼓起勇氣走過去對她說話。

screw·ball /ˈskru͵bɔl; ˈskruːbɔːl/ *n* [C] *informal especially AmE* someone who seems very strange or crazy【非正式, 尤美】古怪的人; 瘋子

screw·driv·er /ˈskru͵draɪvɚ; ˈskruː͵draɪvə/ *n* [C] **1** a tool with a narrow blade at one end that you use for turning screws 螺絲刀, 螺絲起子, 改錐 —see picture at 參見 TOOL¹ 圖 **2** an alcoholic drink made from VODKA and orange juice 伏特加橙汁雞尾酒

screwed up /͵· ˈ·◂/ *adj informal* unhappy or anxious because you have had bad experiences in the past【非正式】不愉快的, 焦慮不安的, 神經質的: *sexually and emotionally screwed up* 在性和情感方面受到困擾

screw top /͵· ˈ·◂/ *n* [C] a cover that you twist onto the top of a bottle or other container〔容器的〕螺旋蓋, 螺旋塞 —**screw-top** *adj*

screw·y /ˈskruɪ; ˈskruːi/ *adj informal* an idea, plan, etc that is screwy seems strange or crazy【非正式】〔意見、計劃等〕古怪的, 荒謬的: *The whole thing sounds pretty screwy to me!* 我覺得整個事情相當古怪!

scrib·ble¹ /ˈskrɪbl; ˈskrɪbəl/ *v* **1** [T] to write something quickly and untidily 潦草地寫: *I scribbled his phone number in my address book.* 我在地址簿上潦草地寫下他的電話號碼。**2** [I] to draw marks that have no meaning 亂塗, 亂畫, 亂寫: *Don't scribble on the desk like that!* 不要這樣在桌子上亂寫亂畫!

scribble² *n* **1** [U] also 又作 **scribbles** meaningless marks or pictures, especially done by children〔尤指小孩的〕亂塗的無意義的東西, 塗鴉 **2** [singular,U] untidy writing that is difficult to read 潦草的字

scrib·bler /ˈskrɪblɚ; ˈskrɪbələ/ *n* [C] *informal* a writer, especially an unimportant one【非正式】作家〔尤指無足輕重者〕

scribe /skraɪb; skraɪb/ *n* [C] someone employed to copy things in writing, especially before printing was invented〔尤指在印刷術發明之前的〕抄寫員

scrim·mage /ˈskrɪmɪdʒ; ˈskrɪmɪdʒ/ *n* **1** [C] *informal* a fight【非正式】扭打, 打架 **2** [U] a practice game of football, BASKETBALL etc〔足球、籃球等的〕練習比賽, 隊內分組比賽

scrimp /skrɪmp; skrɪmp/ *v* [I] to try to save as much money as you can even though you have very little 盡力攢錢, 盡量節省: **scrimp and save** *We had to scrimp and save to pay for the holiday.* 我們得拚命節省才能攢下度假的錢。

scrip /skrɪp; skrɪp/ *n* [U] an official piece of paper, especially a SHARE that is instead of money or a DIVIDEND 代股息的股份; 臨時憑證: *scrip dividend* 股息憑證 | *scrip issue* 紅股發行

script /skrɪpt; skrɪpt/ *n* **1** [C] the written form of a speech, play, film etc〔演講的〕原稿, 講稿; 戲劇[電影]劇本: *Galton and Simpson wrote some excellent comedy scripts.* 高爾頓和辛普森寫了一些精彩的喜劇腳本。**2** [C,U] the set of letters used in writing a language; ALPHABET〔一種語言的〕全套字母, 字母表: *Arabic script* 阿拉伯語字母表 **3** [C] *BrE* a piece of work written by a student in an examination【英】〔考生的〕筆試答卷, 考卷 **4** [singular,U] *formal* writing done by hand, especially with the letters of the words joined【正式】筆跡, 手跡; 〔尤指〕英語中字母連寫的手寫體

script·ed /ˈskrɪptɪd; ˈskrɪptɪ̈d/ *adj* a speech or broadcast that is scripted has been written down before it is read〔演講、廣播〕照原稿宣讀[廣播]的

scrip·tur·al /ˈskrɪptʃərəl; ˈskrɪptʃərəl/ *adj* connected with or based on the Bible 根據[源出]《聖經》的

scrip·ture /ˈskrɪptʃɚ; ˈskrɪptʃə/ *n* **1** also 又作 **the (Holy) Scriptures** [U] the Bible《聖經》**2** [C,U] the holy books of a particular religion〔某一宗教的〕經文, 經籍, 聖書: *Buddhist scriptures* 佛經 **3** [U] *old-fashioned* the study of the Bible, taught as a school subject【過時】〔學校課程中的〕《聖經》課

script·writ·er /ˈskrɪpt͵raɪtɚ; ˈskrɪpt͵raɪtə/ *n* [C] someone who writes SCRIPTS for films, television etc〔電影、電視等〕劇本作者, 劇作家

scrof·u·la /ˈskrɑfjələ; ˈskrɒfjɪ̈lə/ *n* [U] a disease that makes the organs in your neck swell up 頸淋巴結結核, 瘰癧 —**scrofulous** *adj*

scroll¹ /skrol; skrəʊl/ *n* [C] **1** a long piece of paper that can be rolled up, and is used as an official document〔用於寫正式文件的〕紙卷, 卷軸 **2** a decoration shaped like a roll of paper 渦卷形裝飾

scroll² *v* [I,T] to move information on a computer screen up or down so that you can read it〔在電腦屏幕上〕將信息上下移動〔以便閱讀〕: **[+up/down]** *Could you scroll down a few lines?* 請你往下移幾行好嗎?

scroll·work /ˋskrol͵wɝk; ˈskrəʊlwɜːk/ *n* [U] *technical* decoration in the shape of scrolls【術語】渦卷形裝飾

scrooge /skrudʒ; skruːdʒ/ *n* [C] *informal* someone who hates spending money【非正式】吝嗇鬼, 守財奴: *My landlord's a real scrooge.* 我的房東是個十足的吝嗇鬼。

scro·tum /ˋskrotəm; ˈskrəʊtəm/ *n plural* **scrota** /-tə; -tə/ *or* **scrotums** [C] the bag of flesh that contains the TESTICLES of men and male animals 陰囊

scrounge[1] /skraundʒ; skraʊndʒ/ *v* [I,T] *informal* to get money or something you want by asking other people for it rather than by paying for it yourself【非正式】乞討, 索取: **scrounge (sth) off/from sb** *I managed to scrounge some money off my dad.* 我設法從爸爸那兒要到了一點錢。—**scrounger** *n* [C]

scrounge[2] *n* **be on the scrounge** *BrE informal* to be trying to get money or things you want by asking other people for them【英, 非正式】向人伸手索要錢[物], 在索取錢物

scrub[1] /skrʌb; skrʌb/ *v* **1** [I,T] to rub something hard, especially with a stiff brush in order to clean it〔尤指用硬刷子〕擦洗, 擦淨: *She was down on her hands and knees scrubbing the floor.* 她在趴着擦地板。| **[+at]** *Tom scrubbed at the stain but it wouldn't come out.* 湯姆擦洗污跡, 但是擦不掉。—see picture at 參見 CLEAN[2] 圖 **2** [T] *informal* to decide not to do something that you had planned【非正式】取消〔計劃等〕: *We had to scrub our plans for a party.* 我們不得不取消開晚會的計劃。

scrub sth ↔ **out** *phr v* [T] to clean the inside of a place or object thoroughly 徹底擦洗〔某物內部〕: *Prisoners must scrub their cells out once a week.* 囚犯們每星期必須把牢房徹底擦洗一次。

scrub up *phr v* [I] to wash your hands and arms before doing a medical operation〔醫生〕在手術前刷洗雙手和手臂

scrub[2] *n* **1** [U] low bushes and trees that grow in very dry soil 矮樹叢, 灌木叢 **2 give sth a scrub** *especially BrE* to clean something by rubbing it hard【尤英】把某物好好擦洗一番

scrub·ber /ˋskrʌbɚ; ˈskrʌbə/ *n* [C] **1** *BrE* an offensive word for PROSTITUTE (=a woman who has sex for money)【英】妓女, 賣淫婦〔冒犯用詞〕**2** a plastic or metal object you use to clean pans〔塑料或金屬製的〕刷子

scrubbing brush /ˋ·· ·/ *especially BrE*【尤英】, **scrub brush** /ˋ· ·/ *AmE*【美】—*n* [C] a stiff brush that you use for cleaning things 硬毛刷, 板刷 —see picture at 參見 BRUSH[1] 圖

scrub·by /ˋskrʌbɪ; ˈskrʌbi/ *adj* **1** covered by low bushes 長滿矮樹叢的: *scrubby terrain* 灌木叢生的地帶 **2** *informal* looking dirty and untidy【非正式】不整潔的, 髒亂的: *a scrubby schoolboy* 邋遢的小男生

scrub·land /ˋskrʌblənd; ˈskrʌblənd/ *n* [U] land that is covered with low bushes 灌木叢林地

scruff /skrʌf; skrʌf/ *n* **1 by the scruff of the neck** if you hold a person or animal by the scruff of their neck, you hold the flesh, fur, or clothes at the back of the neck 抓住〔動物的〕頸背; 抓住〔人的〕衣領 **2** [C] *BrE informal* someone who looks untidy or dirty【英, 非正式】不整潔的人, 骯髒的人

scruf·fy /ˋskrʌfɪ; ˈskrʌfi/ *adj* dirty and untidy 邋遢的, 不整潔的: *a scruffy old pair of jeans* 一條骯髒的舊牛仔褲 —**scruffily** *adv* —**scruffiness** *n* [U]

scrum[1] /skrʌm; skrʌm/ *n* **1** [C] a particular arrangement of players in the game of RUGBY 並列爭球〔橄欖球賽中球員的一種隊形排列〕**2** [singular] *BrE informal* a crowd of people who are all pushing each other to try and get something【英, 非正式】互相推擠着爭奪某物的人羣: *There was the usual scrum for tickets when the box office opened.* 售票處一開門, 照例出現了互相推擠搶先購票的混亂場面。

scrum[2] *v*

scrum down *phr v* [I] to form a scrum during a game of RUGBY〔橄欖球賽的〕並列爭球, 混戰

scrum-half /͵skrʌmˋhæf; ͵skrʌmˈhɑːf/ *n* [C] a player in RUGBY who has to put the ball into the SCRUM[1] (1)〔橄欖球賽中的〕爭球前衛

scrum·mage /ˋskrʌmɪdʒ; ˈskrʌmɪdʒ/ *n* [C] a SCRUM[1] (1) 並列爭球〔橄欖球賽中球員的一種隊形排列〕

scrump /skrʌmp; skrʌmp/ *v* [T] *BrE old-fashioned* to steal fruit, especially apples, from trees【英, 過時】偷摘〔水果, 尤指蘋果〕

scrump·tious /ˋskrʌmpʃəs; ˈskrʌmpʃəs/ *adj informal* food that is scrumptious tastes very good【非正式】〔食物〕美味的, 可口的, 頂刮刮的: *a scrumptious chocolate dessert* 美味可口的巧克力甜食

scrum·py /ˋskrʌmpɪ; ˈskrʌmpi/ *n* [U] *BrE* a strong alcoholic drink made from apples【英】烈性蘋果酒

scrunch /skrʌntʃ; skrʌntʃ/ *v* [I] *informal* if stones or other objects scrunch under your feet, they make a noisy sound when you walk on them【非正式】〔腳踩碎石等時〕發出咯吱聲: *The pebbles scrunched as we walked along the beach.* 我們在海灘漫步時, 腳下的礫石咯吱咯吱地直響。

scrunch sth ↔ **up** *phr v* [T] to crush and twist something into a small round shape 把…揉成一團: *I scrunched up the letter and threw it in the bin.* 我把信揉成一團扔進垃圾桶。

scru·ple[1] /ˋskrupḷ; ˈskruːpəl/ *n* [C usually plural 一般用複數] a belief about right and wrong that prevents you from doing something bad 顧忌, 顧慮: *Atkins was a ruthless man with few moral scruples.* 阿特金斯這個人殘酷無情, 對甚麼道德良心滿不在乎。| **without scruple** (=without caring about the effects your actions may have on other people) 毫無顧忌 *They made thousands of families homeless without scruple.* 他們肆無忌憚地使成千上萬個家庭流離失所。

scruple[2] *v* **not scruple to do sth** *literary* to be willing to do something even though it may have harmful or unpleasant effects【文】毫無顧忌地做某事: *I did not scruple to tell him what I thought.* 我毫無顧忌地把我的想法告訴了他。

scru·pu·lous /ˋskrupjələs; ˈskruːpjʊ̈ləs/ *adj* **1** careful to be honest and fair 力求誠實公平的, 正直的: *Mr Samuel has always been most scrupulous in his dealings with us.* 塞繆爾先生和我們進行交易向來是很誠實公平的。—opposite 反義詞 UNSCRUPULOUS **2** done very carefully so that every detail is correct 極仔細認真的, 一絲不苟的: *scrupulous attention to detail* 對細節的一絲不苟 —**scrupulously** *adv*: *scrupulously clean* 極其清潔的 —**scrupulousness** *n* [U]

scru·ti·neer /͵skrutəˋnɪr; ͵skruːtɪ̈ˈnɪə/ *n* [C] *BrE* an official who examines or counts votes in an election【英】〔選舉中的〕監票人, 點票員

scru·ti·nize also 又作 **-ise** *BrE*【英】/ˋskrutn̩͵aɪz; ˈskruːtɪ̈naɪz/ *v* [T] to examine someone or something very thoroughly and carefully 仔細徹底地檢查, 詳審: *James scrutinized the painting closely.* 詹姆斯認真審視那幅畫。

scru·ti·ny /ˋskrutn̩ɪ; ˈskruːtɪ̈ni/ *n* [U] careful and thorough examination of someone or something 仔細的審視; 徹底的檢查: **careful/close scrutiny** *Close scrutiny of the document showed it to be a forgery.* 經過仔細檢查證明這份文件是偽造的。| **under scrutiny** *Diana resented her private life being under such public scrutiny.* 戴安娜對自己的私生活受到這樣的公開監視非常反感。

scu·ba div·ing /ˋskubə ͵daɪvɪŋ; ˈskuːbə ͵daɪvɪŋ/ *n* [U] the sport of swimming under water while breathing through a tube connected to a container of air on your back 斯庫巴潛泳, 水肺式潛泳〔戴自攜式潛水呼吸器潛泳〕

scud /skʌd; skʌd/ *v* [I always+adv/prep] *literary* if clouds scud past, they move quickly across the sky【文】〔雲〕飄過, 掠過

scuff /skʌf; skʌf/ *v* **1** [T often passive 常用被動態] to make a mark on a smooth surface by rubbing it against something rough 使磨損: *scuffed brown shoes* 磨損了

S

的褐色皮鞋 **2 scuff your feet/heels** to walk in a slow lazy way, dragging your feet along the ground〔懶洋洋地〕拖着腳走路

scuf·fle¹ /ˈskʌfḷ; ˈskʌfəl/ *n* [C] a short fight between a few people that is not very violent 扭打〔不太猛烈的短時打鬥〕: *a brief scuffle in a corner of the bar* 酒吧一角的短暫鬥毆

scuffle² *v* [I] **1** to have a short fight with someone, in a way that is not very serious or violent〔與某人〕扭打，廝打 **2** [always+adv/prep] to walk or move quickly in a way that makes a noise〔發出聲響地〕匆匆急走: *a mouse scuffling in the leaves* 在樹葉間匆匆地爬過的老鼠

scuff·mark /ˈskʌfˌmɑrk; ˈskʌfmɑːk/ *n* [C] a mark made on something by scuffing 磨痕，擦痕

scull¹ /skʌl; skʌl/ *n* [C] **1** a small light boat for only one person〔單人〕輕便小船 **2** one of the OARs that you use when you are sculling a boat 槳

scull² *v* [I,T] to ROW³ (1) a small light boat, especially a boat that is only for one person〔用槳〕划〔尤指單人輕便小船〕

scul·le·ry /ˈskʌlərɪ; ˈskʌləri/ *n* [C] a room next to the kitchen, especially in a large old house, where cleaning jobs are done〔尤指古老大宅中緊挨廚房的〕洗滌室

scul·lion /ˈskʌljən; ˈskʌljən/ *n* [C] *old use* a boy employed to work in a kitchen【舊】幹粗活的男廚工，廚師幫工

sculpt /skʌlpt; skʌlpt/ *v* [T often passive 常用被動態] **1** to make a solid object that represents someone or something, by shaping stone, wood, clay etc 雕刻，雕塑 **2** to make something into a particular shape as a result of a natural process, for example the movement of a river〔自然進程如河水流動等〕刻蝕，侵蝕

sculp·tor /ˈskʌlptə; ˈskʌlptə/ *n* [C] someone who makes sculptures 雕刻家，雕塑家

sculp·ture /ˈskʌlptʃə; ˈskʌlptʃə/ *n* **1** [U] the art of making solid objects representing people or animals out of stone, wood, clay etc 雕刻[雕塑]藝術: *a talent for sculpture* 雕刻天才 **2** [C,U] the objects produced in this form of art 雕刻[雕塑]作品: *an interesting abstract sculpture* 有趣的抽象派雕塑作品

sculp·tured /ˈskʌlptʃəd; ˈskʌlptʃəd/ *adj* **1 sculptured features/beauty/muscles etc** features etc that have a clear shape as if they had been made by an artist 似雕塑成的面貌/美貌/肌肉等 **2** [only before noun 僅用於名詞前] decorated with sculptures 有雕刻裝飾的: *a sculptured pedestal* 有雕刻裝飾的柱基

scum /skʌm; skʌm/ *n* **1** [singular,U] an unpleasant substance that forms on the surface of a liquid〔液體表面的〕浮渣，浮垢: *The pond was covered with green scum.* 池塘水面蓋滿了綠色的浮藻。**2** [C] *plural* **scum** *spoken* an unpleasant nasty person【口】社會渣滓，人渣: *Don't you ever dare say that again you scum!* 你還敢再說那樣的話就有你好看的，你這個人渣！| **scum of the earth** (=the worst people you can imagine) 世上的人渣，敗類 —**scummy** *adj*

scum·bag /ˈskʌmˌbæg; ˈskʌmbæg/ *n* [C] *spoken* an unpleasant person【口】卑鄙的人

scup·per¹ /ˈskʌpə; ˈskʌpə/ *v* [T] *BrE*【英】**1** [usually passive 一般用被動態] *informal* to ruin someone's plans or chances of success【非正式】破壞〔計劃、機會等〕: *The recent terrorist attacks have scuppered any chance of a peace settlement.* 最近的恐怖分子襲擊事件已經毀了和平解決的任何機會。**2** to deliberately sink your own ship 故意使〔自己的船〕沉沒

scupper² *n* [C] *technical* a hole in the side of a ship that allows water to flow back into the sea【術語】〔船舷上的〕排水孔

scur·ri·lous /ˈskɝələs; ˈskʌrələs/ *adj formal* scurrilous remarks, articles etc contain damaging and untrue statements about someone【正式】〔話語、文章等〕辱罵(性)的，傷人的 —**scurrilously** *adv* —**scurrilousness** *n* [U]

scur·ry /ˈskɝɪ; ˈskʌri/ *v* [I always+adv/prep] to move quickly with short steps〔用小步〕急跑，急走，急趕: [**+along/past/across**] *A beetle scurried across the path.* 一隻甲蟲匆匆爬過小路。—**scurry** *n* [singular,U]

S-curve /ˈɛs ˌkɝv; ˈes kɜːv/ *n* [C] *AmE* a bend in the road in the shape of an 'S', that can be dangerous to drivers【美】S 形險彎; S-BEND *BrE*【英】

scur·vy /ˈskɝvɪ; ˈskɜːvi/ *n* [U] a disease caused by not eating foods such as fruit and vegetables that contain VITAMIN C 壞血病〔因缺乏維生素 C 所致〕

scut·tle¹ /ˈskʌtḷ; ˈskʌtl/ *v* **1** [I always+adv/prep] to move quickly with short steps 小步急跑，疾走: [**+along/past/down**] *I caught sight of Miss Rawlings scuttling down the corridor.* 我瞥見羅林絲小姐沿着走廊快步走過。**2** [T] to sink a ship by making holes in the bottom, especially in order to prevent it being used by an enemy 鑿沉〔船隻，尤指不讓敵人使用〕

scuttle² *n* [C] a container for carrying coal 煤斗，煤筐

scut·tle·butt /ˈskʌtḷˌbʌt; ˈskʌtlbʌt/ *n* [U] *AmE informal* stories about other people's personal lives, especially containing things that are unkind and untrue about them【美，非正式】〔對別人私生活的〕流言蜚語

scuz·zy /ˈskʌzɪ; ˈskʌzi/ *adj informal* unpleasant and dirty【非正式】髒得令人難受[討厭]的

scythe /saɪð; saɪð/ *n* [C] a farming tool that has a long curved blade fixed to a long wooden handle, and is used to cut grain or long grass 長柄大鐮刀

SE the written abbreviation of 縮寫= SOUTHEAST or SOUTHEASTERN

sea /si; siː/ *n* **1** [singular] *especially BrE* the large area of salty water that covers much of the earth's surface; OCEAN【尤英】海，海洋: *You don't often get the chance to swim in the sea in England – it's too cold!* 在英格蘭你不常有機會在海裡游泳 — 因為太冷了！| **rough/calm sea** (=with or without large waves) 波濤洶湧/風平浪靜 *The sea was calm and there was no breeze.* 海不揚波，沒有一絲風。| **by sea** (=on a ship) 坐船，經由海路 *I sent my luggage ahead of me by sea.* 我先把行李經海路託運。| **by the sea** (=on the coast) 在海濱，在海邊 *She lives in a little cottage by the sea.* 她住在海邊的一間小屋裡。| **at sea** *Life at sea was never easy and he was always pleased to be back home.* 海上生活從來都不輕鬆，他回到家裡總是非常高興。| **put to sea** (=start a journey on the sea) 出海，出航 | **the open sea** (=far away from land) 外海，外洋；公海 | **lost at sea** (=drowned) 在海裡淹死[溺死] **2** [C] a large area of salty water that is mostly enclosed by land 內海: *the Mediterranean Sea* 地中海 **3 a sea of** a large number of something 大量，一大片: *A sea of faces stared up at me from the audience.* 數不清的觀眾仰起臉注視着我。**4 be (all) at sea** to be confused or not sure what to do 困惑，茫然不知所措: *I'm all at sea with this maths homework.* 我完全不知道這些數學作業怎麼做。**5 the seas** *literary* the sea, used especially when you are not talking about a particular ocean【文】海，大海〔尤用於談論非特定海洋時〕: **across the seas** (=far away) 遙遠，遠隔重洋 *She was born in a northern land far, far across the seas.* 她出生在一個遙遠的北方國家。**6** [C] one of the broad plains on the moon and Mars 海〔指月球或火星表面的一片廣闊平原〕

sea a·nem·o·ne /ˈ·,·,···/ *n* [C] a brightly-coloured sea animal that sticks onto rocks and looks like a flower 海葵〔色澤鮮豔的海生動物〕

sea bed /ˈ· ·/ *n* [singular] the land at the bottom of the sea 海床，海底

sea·bird /ˈsiˌbɝd; ˈsiːbɜːd/ *n* [C] a bird that lives near the sea and finds food in it 海鳥

sea·board /ˈsiˌbɔrd; ˈsiːbɔːd/ *n* [C] the part of a country that is near the sea 海岸，海濱，沿海地區: *the eastern seaboard of the US* 美國的東海岸

sea·borne /ˈsiˌbɔrn; ˈsiːbɔːn/ *adj* carried on or arriving in ships 海運的，經由[來自]海上的: *the threat of a seaborne invasion* 從海上入侵的威脅

sea breeze /ˈ· ·/ *n* [C] a light wind that blows from the

sea onto the land 吹向陸地的微風, 海風
sea cap·tain /ˈ· ˌ··/ *n* [C] the CAPTAIN of a ship 船長
sea change /ˈ· ·/ *n* [singular] a very big change in something 巨變: *a sea change in public opinion* 公眾輿論的巨大變化
sea dog /ˈ· ·/ *n* [C] *literary or humorous* someone with a lot of experience of ships and sailing【文或幽默】有經驗的水手, 老海員
sea·far·ing /ˈsiˌfɛrɪŋ; ˈsiːˌfeərɪŋ/ *adj* [only before noun 僅用於名詞前] **1** connected with the life and activities of a sailor 航海的, 水手生活的: *a story from my seafaring days* 我的航海歲月中的一件事 **2** having strong connections with ships and the sea, especially because of international trade 和航海有密切關係的, 以航海為業的: **seafaring nation/country** *The Danes are an ancient seafaring nation.* 丹麥人是一個古老的航海民族。—**seafarer** *n* [C]
sea·food /ˈsiˌfud; ˈsiːfuːd/ *n* [U] animals from the sea that you can eat, especially SHELLFISH 海產食品, 海味〔尤指貝類等〕
sea·front /ˈsiˌfrʌnt; ˈsiːfrʌnt/ *n* [C usually singular 一般用單數] *especially BrE* the part of a town where the shops, houses etc are next to the beach【尤英】〔城鎮的〕濱海區: *a hotel right on the seafront* 濱海區旅館
sea·go·ing /ˈsiˌgo·ɪŋ; ˈsiːˌgəʊɪŋ/ *adj* [only before noun 僅用於名詞前] built to travel on the sea〔船〕適於航海的: *a seagoing yacht* 航海帆船
sea·gull /ˈsiˌgʌl; ˈsiːgʌl/ *n* [C] a common grey and white bird that lives near the sea 海鷗
sea·horse /ˈsiˌhɔrs; ˈsiːhɔːs/ *n* [C] a small sea fish with a head and neck that look like those of a horse 海馬〔海生小型魚類〕

3 **seal¹** /sil; siːl/ *n* [C]

seal 海豹

1 ►ANIMAL 動物◄ a large sea animal that eats fish and lives around coasts or on floating pieces of ice 海豹
2 ►OFFICIAL MARK 正式印記◄ a mark that has a special design and shows the legal or official authority of a person or organization 印章, 圖章, 印鑑: *a black book stamped with the Presidential Seal* 蓋着總統印章的黑皮書
3 ►ON CONTAINERS/PIPES 在容器/管子上◄ a) a piece of rubber or plastic that keeps air, water, dirt etc out of something〔防止空氣、水等滲入的〕密封條, 密封紙: *Do not use this product if the inner seal is broken.* 如內部密封紙破損, 請勿用此產品。**b)** a piece of WAX¹ (1), paper, wire etc that you have to break in order to open something 封蠟, 封條, 火漆
4 seal of approval if you give something your seal of approval, you say that you approve of it, especially officially（正式）認可[批准]: *All we need now is the chairman's seal of approval.* 我們現在所需要的就是主席的正式批准。
5 set the seal on to make something definite or complete 使確定, 使成定局: *A last-minute goal set the seal on Tottenham's victory.* 最後一分鐘的一個進球使托定咸隊的勝利成為定局。
6 seal of friendship/success/victory etc something that makes your friendship stronger, your success more certain etc 友誼的締造/成功的保證/勝利的保證等
seal² *v* **1** also 又作 **seal up** [T] to close an entrance or a container with something that stops air, water etc from coming in or out of it〔為防止空氣、水、污物滲入或滲出〕把…封住, 封閉: *The windows have been sealed up for years.* 這些窗戶已經封閉多年了。**2** [T] to close an envelope, pack etc by using something sticky to hold its edges in place 黏住〔信封等〕, 封住: *Don't seal the envelope yet.* 先不要把這個信封封上。**3 my lips are sealed** *spoken* used to say that you are not going to tell someone something【口】我一定會守口如瓶〔表示決不把某事說出來〕**4 seal sb's fate** to make something, especially something bad, sure to happen 決定某人的命運〔尤指厄運〕: *He was about to say the words that would seal my fate for ever.* 他即將說出決定我今後命運的那些話。**5 seal a friendship/promise/agreement etc** to do something that makes a friendship, promise etc more formal or definite 締交/鄭重承諾/正式達成協議等
seal sth ↔ **in** *phr v* [T] to stop what something contains from getting out 密藏〔某物〕, 將〔某物〕封住: *Fry the meat quickly to seal in the flavor.* 把肉快速煎好以保持原味。
seal sth ↔ **off** *phr v* [T] to stop people entering an area or building, because it is dangerous 封閉, 〔因有危險而〕封鎖〔某地區或某幢建築〕: *Following a bomb warning, police have sealed off the whole area.* 接到有炸彈的警報後, 警方封鎖了整個地區。
sea lane /ˈ· ·/ *n* [C] a fixed path across the sea that ships regularly use 海上航線[航路]
seal·ant /ˈsilənt; ˈsiːlənt/ *n* [C,U] a layer of paint, polish etc that is put on the surface of something to protect it from air, water etc 密封膠, 密封劑, 防滲漏劑
sealed /sild; siːld/ *adj* shut with something that prevents air, water etc from getting in or out 密封的, 封閉的: *Keep all dressings in a sealed sterile pack.* 把各種包紮用品保存在一個消毒的密封袋裡。
sea legs /ˈ· ·/ *n* [plural] **find/get your sea legs** to begin to be able to walk normally, not feel ill etc when you are travelling on a ship 開始能在顛簸的航船甲板上平穩走動, 開始不暈船
seal·er /ˈsilɚ; ˈsiːlə/ *n* **1** [C,U] a layer of paint, polish etc put on the surface of something to protect it from air, water etc 密封劑, 密封材料 **2** [C] a person or ship that hunts seals (SEAL¹ (1)) 捕獵海豹的人[船]
sea lev·el /ˈ· ˌ··/ *n* [U] the average height of the sea, used as a standard for measuring other heights and depths, such as the height of a mountain 海平面: **above/below sea level** *1,000m above sea level* 海拔1,000米
seal·ing /ˈsilɪŋ; ˈsiːlɪŋ/ *n* [U] the hunting or catching of seals (SEAL¹ (1)) 捕獵海豹
sealing wax /ˈ·· ·/ *n* [U] a red substance that melts and becomes hard again quickly, used for sealing (SEAL² (2)) letters, documents etc 封蠟, 火漆
sea li·on /ˈ· ˌ··/ *n* [C] a large type of SEAL¹ (1) 海獅〔大型海豹的一種〕
seal·skin /ˈsilˌskɪn; ˈsiːlˌskɪn/ *n* [U] the skin or fur of some types of SEAL¹ (1), used for making leather or clothes 海豹皮〔用於製作皮革或衣服〕
seam /sim; siːm/ *n* [C] **1** a line where two pieces of cloth, leather etc have been stitched together〔兩塊布、皮革等連接處的〕縫, 線縫: *a split in the seam of his jeans* 他的牛仔褲綻開的線縫 —see picture on page A17 參見A17頁圖 **2** a layer of a mineral, especially coal, under the ground 礦層〔尤指煤層〕: **a rich seam** (=one that contains a lot of high quality coal) 優質的富煤層 **3** a line where two pieces of metal, wood etc have been joined together〔兩塊金屬、木板等的〕接合處, 接縫 **4 be coming/falling apart at the seams a)** if a plan, organization etc is coming or falling apart at the seams, so many things are going wrong with it that it will probably fail〔計劃〕失敗; 〔組織〕分崩離析: *Her whole life was threatening to come apart at the seams.* 她的整個生活面臨着崩潰的危險。**b)** if a piece of clothing etc is coming or falling apart at the seams, the stitches on it are coming unfastened〔衣服等的〕線縫裂開; 縫口破裂 **5 be bursting at the seams** if a room or building is bursting at the seams, it is so full of people that hardly anyone else can fit into it〔房間等〕擠滿, 過於擁擠
sea·man /ˈsimən; ˈsiːmən/ *plural* **seamen** /-mən; -mən/ *n* [C] **1** a sailor on a ship or in the navy who is not an officer 水手, 海員; 水兵: *a merchant seaman* 商船船員

—see table on page C6 參見C6頁附錄 **2** someone who has a lot of experience of ships and the sea 航海老手

sea·man·ship /ˈsimənˌʃɪp; ˈsiːmənʃɪp/ *n* [U] the skills and knowledge that an experienced sailor has 航海術，航海技能，船舶駕駛術

seamed /simd; siːmd/ *adj* [only before noun 僅用於名詞前] **1** having a seam 有縫的，縫合的：*seamed stockings* 有接縫的長襪 **2** a seamed surface has many deep lines on it 有皺紋的：*A gentle smile spread over her old, seamed face.* 慈祥的微笑展現在她那蒼老的、有皺紋的臉上。

sea mile /ˈ· ·/ *n* [C] a unit for measuring distance at sea that is slightly longer than a land mile, and equals 1,853 metres; NAUTICAL MILE 海里〔較陸上英里略長的長度單位，等於1,853米〕

sea mist /ˈ· ·/ *n* [U] a mist on land that comes in from the sea 海霧〔從海上漂到陸上的霧〕

seam·less /ˈsimləs; ˈsiːmləs/ *adj* **1** not having any seams (SEAM (1)) 無縫的：*seamless stockings* 無縫長統襪 **2** something seamless is done or happens so smoothly that you cannot tell where one thing stops and another begins 平滑的，渾然一體的：*I see the piece very much as a flowing, seamless whole.* 我覺得這件作品流暢自然，渾然一體。

seam·stress /ˈsimstrɪs; ˈsiːmstr̩s/ *n* [C] *old-fashioned* a woman whose job is SEWING and making clothes【過時】女縫紉工，女裁縫

seam·y /ˈsimɪ; ˈsiːmi/ *adj* involving unpleasant things such as crime, violence, poverty, or immorality〔犯罪、暴力、貧困、不道德行為等〕令人不快的，醜惡的：**seamy side (of sth)** *the seamy side of the film industry* 電影業的陰暗面

se·ance /ˈseɑns; ˈseɪɑːns/ *n* [C] a meeting where people try to talk to or receive messages from the spirits of dead people 降神會〔試圖與亡靈對話的集會〕

sea·plane /ˈsiˌplen; ˈsiːpleɪn/ *n* [C] a plane that can take off from and land on the surface of the sea 水上飛機

sea·port /ˈsiˌpɔrt; ˈsiːpɔːt/ *n* [C] a large town on or near a coast with a HARBOUR[1] that big ships can use 海港，海港市鎮

sea pow·er /ˈ· ˌ··/ *n* **1** [U] the size and strength of a country's navy〔一國的〕海軍力量，海上實力 **2** [C] a country with a powerful navy 海軍強國

sear[1] /sɪr; sɪə/ *v* **1** [I always+adv/prep,T] to burn something with a sudden powerful heat 烙，燒灼：*The choking fumes seared their lungs.* 那些令人窒息的濃煙灼傷了他們的肺部。**2** [T] to cook the outside of a piece of meat, quickly at a high temperature, in order to keep its juices in 用快速高溫燒烤〔肉的表層以保存其汁液〕**3** [I always+adv/prep] to have a very strong sudden and unpleasant effect on you〔在思想上〕留下烙印，銘刻：**[+into/onto/on]** *The scene will be forever seared onto my memory.* 那景象將永遠銘刻在我的記憶裡。

sear[2] *adj literary* another spelling of SERE【文】sere的另一種拼法

3 2 **search**[1] /sɝtʃ; sɜːtʃ/ *n* **1** [C usually singular 一般用單數] an attempt to find someone or something 尋找，查找；搜尋，搜查：**[+for]** *Bad weather is hampering the search for survivors.* 惡劣的天氣妨礙了對倖存者的搜尋。| **in search of** (=looking for) *Mario went off in search of some matches.* 馬里奧出去找火柴。| **call off a search** (=stop looking for someone or something) 終止尋找〔某人或某物〕，停止搜索 | **carry out a search** *Security guards will be carrying out a search of the premises.* 保安人員即將搜查這幢建築物及其周圍地帶。| **house-to-house search** (=one that involves searching every house or building in an area) 挨家挨戶的搜查 | **strip search** (=an official search in which you must take off all of your clothes)〔官方對疑犯的〕裸身搜查 **2** [singular] an attempt to find a solution to a problem or an explanation for something 探索，尋求：*the search for the meaning of life* 對生命意義的探索 **3 search and rescue** the process of searching for someone who is lost and who may need medical help, for example in the mountains or at sea〔在山中或海上對失蹤者或遇險者的〕搜尋和營救

search[2] *v* 3

1 ►LOOK FOR 找尋◄ [I,T] to spend time looking for someone or something 查找，搜查，搜尋：*Rescue workers searched all night in the hope of finding more survivors.* 營救人員徹夜搜尋，希望找到更多的倖存者。| **[+for]** *a mother bird searching for food* 覓食的母鳥 | **search sth for sth** *Detectives are out searching the yard for clues* 偵探們出動在院子尋找線索。| **search through sth** (=look for something among papers in a drawer etc) 翻遍〔抽屜內的文件等〕以尋找某物 | **search in/under/around etc** *"Two beers, please," Patricia ordered, searching in her purse.* "兩杯啤酒。"帕特里夏邊吩咐邊在錢包裡摸索。

2 ►PERSON 人◄ [T] to look in someone's pockets, clothes etc in order to find something, especially drugs or weapons 搜查〔口袋、衣服等看是否藏有毒品、武器等〕：*Visitors to the prison are thoroughly searched before they are allowed in.* 探監者要經徹底檢查後才獲准入內。

3 ►SOLUTION/EXPLANATION ETC 解答/解釋等◄ [I] to try to find a solution to a problem, an explanation for something etc 探索，尋找解決辦法：**[+for]** *Scientists are still searching for a cure for the disease.* 科學家仍在尋求治療這種疾病的方法。

4 Search me! *spoken* used to tell someone that you do not know the answer to a question【口】我不知道！：*"So where's she gone tonight then?" "Search me!"* "她今晚上哪兒去了？""我不知道！"

5 ►EXAMINE 檢查◄ [T] to examine something very carefully in order to find something out 細察，細查：*Anya searched his face anxiously.* 安妮亞焦慮不安地察看他臉上的表情。

search sth ↔ **out** *phr v* [T] to find or discover something by searching 找到，找出，查出，搜尋出：*We were too tired to search out extra blankets.* 我們太累了，不想再找出更多的毯子了。

Frequencies of **search, look for** and **try to find** in spoken and written English 英語口語和書面語中 search, look for 和 try to find 的使用頻率

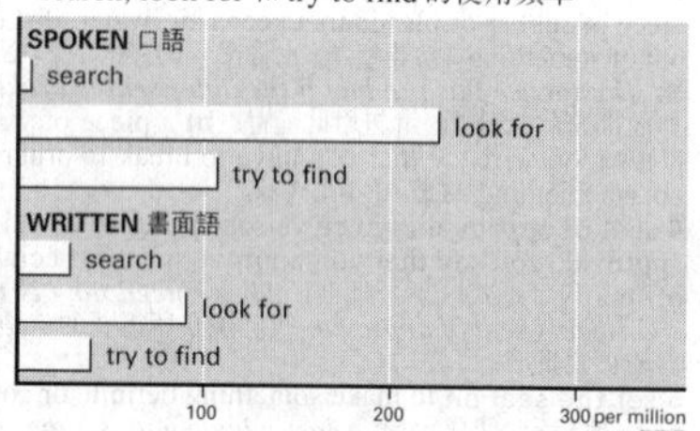

Based on the British National Corpus and the Longman Lancaster Corpus
據英國國家語料庫和朗文蘭卡斯特語料庫

This graph shows that the expressions **look for** and **try to find** are much more common in both spoken and written English than the verb **search**. **Look for** and **try to find** are used in a very general way. **Search** is used when someone, often a group of people, spends time looking for something or someone in a careful, organized way. It is more common in written English than in spoken English. 本圖表顯示，片語 look for 和 try to find 在英語口語和書面語中的使用頻率遠遠高於動詞 search。look for 和 try to find 用於一般性的說法，而 search 則用於表示某人〔通常是一組人〕細緻而有序地去搜尋某物或某人，它在書面語中的使用頻率高於口語。

search·ing /ˈsɝtʃɪŋ; ˈsɜːtʃɪŋ/ *adj* [only before noun 僅用於名詞前] **1 searching look/glance** a look from someone who is trying to find out as much as possible about someone's thoughts and feelings 探究的目光 **2 searching examination/investigation/analysis** an examination etc that looks thoroughly at all the facts 徹底的檢查/調查/分析 —**searchingly** *adv*

search·light /ˈsɝtʃˌlaɪt; ˈsɜːtʃlaɪt/ *n* [C] a powerful light that can be turned in any direction, used for finding people, vehicles etc in the dark 探照燈

search par·ty /ˈ· ˌ··/ *n* [C] a group of people organized to look for someone who is missing or lost 搜索隊, 救援隊

search war·rant /ˈ· ˌ··/ *n* [C] a legal document that gives the police official permission to search a building, for example in order to look for stolen goods 搜查令, 搜查證

sear·ing /ˈsɪrɪŋ; ˈsɪərɪŋ/ *adj* **1** searing heat is extremely hot 熾熱的, 灼熱的 **2** searing pain is severe and feels like a burn 灼痛的, 劇痛的: *a searing pain behind the eyes* 眼底的灼痛 **3** searing words or attitudes are very severe and critical〔言語、態度〕嚴厲的, 苛刻的: *an expression of deep, searing contempt* 極其嚴厲而鄙屑的表情

sea·scape /ˈsiˌskep; ˈsiːskeɪp/ *n* [C] a picture or painting of the sea 海景畫

sea ser·pent /ˈ· ˌ··/ *n* [C] an imaginary large snake-like animal that people used to think lived in the sea〔傳說中的〕海蛇怪

sea·shell /ˈsiˌʃɛl; ˈsiːʃel/ *n* [C] the shell of some types of sea animal 海貝殼

sea·shore /ˈsiˌʃɔr; ˈsiːʃɔː/ *n* **the seashore** the land along the edge of the sea, usually consisting of sand and rocks 海濱, 海岸, 海灘 —compare 比較 BEACH, SEASIDE

sea·sick /ˈsiˌsɪk; ˈsiːˌsɪk/ *adj* feeling very ill because of the movement of a boat or ship 暈船的 —**seasickness** *n* [U]

sea·side /ˈsiˌsaɪd; ˈsiːsaɪd/ *n* **the seaside** *especially BrE* an area or town along the edge of the sea, especially a place you go to have a holiday or to enjoy yourself【尤英】〔尤指作為度假地的〕海濱; 海濱城鎮: **seaside resort** (=where a lot of people go for their holidays) 海濱度假勝地 —see 見 SHORE¹ (USAGE)

3 1 **sea·son¹** /ˈsizn; ˈsiːzən/ *n*

1 ▶IN A YEAR 一年之中◀ [C] one of the four main periods in a year; spring, summer, autumn, or winter〔春、夏、秋、冬的〕季(節)

2 ▶USUAL TIME FOR STH 通常會發生某事的時期◀ [singular] a period of time in a year when something happens most often or when something is usually done〔每年某事發生最頻繁的〕季節: **rainy/dry/wet etc season** (=when there is a lot of rain etc) 雨季/旱季/潮濕季節等 | **growing/raspberry/asparagus etc season** (=when particular plants are growing) 種植/懸鉤子生長/蘆筍生長季節 | **hunting/shooting/fishing etc season** (=when you can do that sport) 狩獵/射獵/釣魚等季節 | **mating/breeding season** (=when animals breed)〔動物的〕交配/繁殖季節 | **football/basketball etc season** (=when a sport is officially played) 足球/籃球等賽季 | **tourist season** *AmE*【美】, **holiday season** *BrE*【英】(=the time of year when people come to a particular place for a holiday) 度假旺季 | **high/peak season** (=the time of year when a place is most busy, especially a holiday place) 旺季, 極盛時期 | **low/off/slack season** (=the time of year when a place or company is not busy) 淡季 | **the holiday season** *AmE* (=Thanksgiving, Christmas, and New Year's)【美】〔感恩節、聖誕節、新年的〕節期

3 be in season a) if vegetables or fruit are in season, it is the time of year when they are ready to eat〔蔬菜、水果〕當令(的), 應時(的) **b)** if a female animal is in season, she is ready to MATE² (1)〔雌性動物〕在發情期

4 out of season a) if vegetables or fruit are out of season, it is not the time of year when they would normally become ready to eat〔蔬菜、水果〕不當令(的), 反季(的) **b)** if you travel or stay somewhere out of season, you do it at the time of year when most people do not〔旅遊或度假的〕淡季

5 ▶FASHION 時裝◀ [C] a time during which particular designs of clothes are produced and sold and are considered to be fashionable〔特殊設計的時髦服裝展出和銷售的〕時裝季節: *The Paris season began in May.* 巴黎時裝季節5月份開始。

6 ▶FILMS ETC 電影等◀ [singular] a time during which a series of films, television programmes etc is shown, especially ones made by the same person or about the same subject 電影節, 電影週〔尤指放映一系列同一製作者或同一主題的片子〕: *a new season of comedy on BBC1* 在英國廣播公司電視一台播出的新喜劇系列

7 season's greetings used especially on greetings cards to say that you hope someone has a happy Christmas 聖誕快樂, 恭賀聖誕〔聖誕賀卡上的祝詞〕

8 the season of good will the time around Christmas 聖誕節節期 —see also 另見 CLOSE SEASON, OPEN SEASON, SILLY SEASON

season² *v* [T] **1** to add salt, pepper etc to something you are cooking to make it taste better〔加鹽、胡椒粉等〕給〔食品〕調味 **2** to make wood hard and ready to use by gradually drying it 使〔木材〕風乾

sea·so·na·ble /ˈsizn̩əbl; ˈsiːzənəbəl/ *adj formal*【正式】**1** suitable for the time of year 合時令的 **2** coming or happening at a suitable time 及時的, 正合時宜的 —**seasonably** *adv*

sea·son·al /ˈsizn̩əl; ˈsiːzənəl/ *adj* **1** usually happening or available during a particular season 季節的, 時令的, 當令的: *a pie made with seasonal fruits* 用時令水果做的餡餅 | **seasonal norm** *BrE* (=the average weather conditions for a particular season)【英】某一季節的平均天氣狀況 **2** happening or needed only at a particular time of year 季節性的, 隨季節而變化的: **seasonal workers/labour/employment etc** *seasonal jobs in the tourist industry* 旅遊業的季節性工作

sea·son·ally /ˈsizn̩əlɪ; ˈsiːzənəli/ *adv* according to what is usual for a particular season 季節性地, 隨季節地: **seasonally adjusted figures** *BrE* (=figures, especially about the number of unemployed people, that are changed according to what usually happens at a particular time of year)【英】隨季節調整的數字〔尤指失業率〕

sea·soned /ˈsiznd; ˈsiːzənd/ *adj* **1 seasoned traveller/campaigner/veteran etc** a very experienced traveller etc 經驗豐富的旅行者/競選者/老兵等 **2** seasoned food has salt, pepper etc added 已調味的, 調過味的: **well seasoned/highly-seasoned** (=with a strong taste) 調味得恰到好處的/佐料味濃的

sea·son·ing /ˈsizn̩ɪŋ; ˈsiːzənɪŋ/ *n* [C,U] salt, pepper, spices (SPICE¹ (1)) etc that add a more interesting taste to food 調味品, 佐料

season tick·et /ˈ·· ˌ··/ *n* [C] a ticket for several journeys, performances, games etc that costs less than you would pay altogether if you paid for each journey etc separately〔價格優惠的〕季票, 定期車票;〔觀看表演、比賽的〕長期入場券: **season ticket holder** (=someone who owns a season ticket) 季票持有者

seat¹ /sit; siːt/ *n* 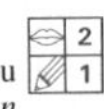

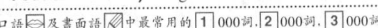

1 ▶PLACE TO SIT 坐的地方◀ [C] a place where you can sit, for example a chair 座, 座位: *Excuse me, can you tell us where our seats are?* 勞駕, 你能告訴我們座位在哪裡嗎? | *a 150-seat airliner* 有150個座位的客機 | **have/take a seat** *spoken* (=used to politely invite someone to sit down)【口】請坐 *If you'd like to take a seat, the doctor will see you shortly.* 你稍坐一會兒, 醫生很快就會給你看的。| **back/front seat** (=the seats in the back or front of a car etc)〔汽車的〕後座/前座 | **passenger seat** (=the seat next to the driver in a car)〔汽車司機旁邊的〕乘客座位 | **take your seat** (=sit down in your seat) 就座 *The judge hurried in and took his seat.* 法官匆匆進來並就座。| **reserve a seat** (=pay for a theatre seat before you go) 預定座位, 訂座 —see picture at 參見 THEATRE 圖

2 ►PART OF A CHAIR 椅子的一部分◄ [C usually singular 一般用單數] the flat part of a chair etc that you sit on〔椅子等的〕座部: *Don't put your feet on the seat!* 不要把腳放在椅座上!

3 seat of your trousers/pants the part of your trousers that you sit on 褲子的臀部

4 two-seater/three-seater etc a vehicle or piece of furniture with two seats, three seats etc 兩座位/三座位〔的車輛或家具〕等

5 ►OFFICIAL POSITION 正式職位◄ [C] a position as a member of a government or a group that makes official decisions 職位, 席位, 成員資格: *a seat on the board of directors* 董事會的一個席位 | **win/lose a seat** *The Tories won 419 seats in the last election.* 保守黨在上屆選舉中獲得 419 個席位。| **a safe seat** (=a position held by a political party that is not likely to be lost in an election)〔某政黨在選舉中〕能穩保的席位

6 seat of learning/government etc *formal* a place, usually a city, where a university or government is based【正式】學府/政府等所在地

7 take a back seat to let someone else make the important decisions 退居次要位置, 讓別人去作重要決定

8 be on the edge of your seat to be waiting excitedly to see what happens next 心情緊張地等待, 興奮地等待〔某事〕

9 do sth by the seat of your pants to do something by using only your own skill and experience, without any help from anyone or anything else 僅憑本人的技能和經驗做某事

10 be in the driving seat *BrE*【英】also 又作 **be in the driver's seat** *especially AmE*【尤美】to control everything that happens in an organization, relationship, or situation 處於控制地位

11 be in the hot seat to be in a position in which you have to make important decisions or answer a lot of difficult questions 處於〔必須作出重大決定、回答很多難題的〕困難地位

12 ►ON A HORSE 騎馬◄ [singular] *technical* the way someone sits on a horse【術語】〔騎馬的〕坐姿, 騎姿: *Sally's got a good seat.* 莎莉的騎姿很優美。

13 ►HOUSE 房子◄ [C] a home of a rich, important family in the countryside〔富人、要員在鄉間的〕別墅, 宅邸: **family/country seat** 家庭/鄉間宅第 —see also 另見 **back seat driver** (BACK SEAT (2)), LOVESEAT, WINDOW SEAT

seat² *v* [T]

1 be seated a) to be sitting down 坐下: *Paul was seated at the head of the table with his wife next to him.* 保羅坐在飯桌的上首, 他的妻子在旁邊坐着。**b)** *spoken formal* used to politely invite people to sit down【口, 正式】請(就)座〔禮貌用語〕: *Please be seated so we can begin the meeting.* 請坐下, 我們的會議可以開始了。

2 remain/stay seated to stay in your seat 繼續坐着: *Remain seated until the aircraft has come to a complete stop.* 請繼續坐着, 等飛機完全停下。

3 seat yourself beside/in/on etc *formal* to sit down somewhere【正式】坐在…旁邊/裡面/上面等

4 ►ARRANGE WHERE PEOPLE SIT 給人們安排座位◄ [always+adv/prep] to arrange for someone to sit somewhere 安排某人坐在…: **seat sb beside/on/near etc** *Whatever you do, make sure you don't seat Alan and Pat next to each other.* 不管你怎麼做, 千萬不要把阿倫和帕特安排在相鄰的座位。—see 見 SIT (USAGE) —see picture on page A15 參見 A15 頁圖

5 ►HOLD A NUMBER OF PEOPLE 容納若干人◄ [not in progressive 不用進行式] if a room, vehicle, table etc seats a certain number of people, it has enough seats for that number〔房間、車輛、桌子等〕坐得下…人, 能供給…座位: *The new stadium seats 60,000.* 新體育場能容納 60,000 人。

6 ►FIT STH SOMEWHERE 將某物固定於某處◄ *technical* to fit something, tightly into a space that is specially made for it【術語】使牢牢地固定於〔某處〕

seat belt /ˈ· ·/ *n* [C] a strong belt fastened to the seat of a car or plane which you fasten around yourself to prevent yourself being thrown out of your seat in an accident〔汽車或飛機上的〕安全帶 —see picture on page A2 參見 A2 頁圖

seat·ing /ˈsitɪŋ; ˈsiːtɪŋ/ *n* [U] **1** all the seats in a theatre, cinema etc〔劇院、電影院等內的〕全部座位: **seating capacity** (=the number of people that can fit in a theatre, cinema etc) 座位數, 可容納人數 **2** a way of arranging seats, or a plan of who will sit in them〔某人坐某位置的〕座位安排, 座位設置: **seating plan/arrangements etc** *Do you have a seating plan for the dinner guests?* 你有沒有宴會賓客的座位示意圖?

sea ur·chin /ˈ· ˌ··/ *n* [C] a small round sea animal that has a hard shell, sometimes with sharp points 海膽

sea·wall /ˈsiˌwɔl; ˌsiːˈwɔːl/ *n* [C] a wall built along the edge of the sea to stop the water from flowing over an area of land 海堤, 防波堤

sea·ward /ˈsiwɚd; ˈsiːwəd/ *adj* facing or directed towards the sea 向海的, 朝海的: *the seaward side of the town* 城鎮的朝海一邊 | **seaward wind/breeze** (=going towards the sea) 吹向大海的風/微風

sea·wards /ˈsiwɚdz; ˈsiːwədz/ also 又作 **seaward** *adv* towards the sea 向海, 朝海

sea·way /ˈsiˌwe; ˈsiːweɪ/ *n* [C] **1** a line of travel regularly used by ships on the sea 海上航道 **2** a river or CANAL (1) used by ships to go from the sea to places that are not on the coast〔供輪船從海上進入內陸港的〕內河航道[運河]

sea·weed /ˈsiˌwid; ˈsiːwiːd/ *n* [U] a common plant that grows in the sea 海藻, 海草

sea·wor·thy /ˈsiˌwɝðɪ; ˈsiːwɜːði/ *adj* a ship that is seaworthy is safe and in good condition〔船〕能安全行駛的, 狀況良好的, 適於航行的 —**seaworthiness** *n* [U]

se·ba·ceous /səˈbeʃəs; səˈbeɪʃəs/ *adj technical* related to a part of the body which produces special oils【術語】分泌油脂的: *sebaceous glands* 皮脂腺

sec /sɛk; sek/ *n* [C] *spoken*【口】**1** a very short time 一小會兒, 片刻: **hang on a sec/hold on a sec/just a sec etc** (=used to ask someone to wait a short time) 稍等一會兒 *"Is Clive there, please?" "Hold on a sec, I'll go and see."* "請問克萊夫在嗎?" "請等一會兒, 我去看看。" | **in a sec** (=very soon) 不久, 很快 *I'll be with you in a sec.* 我一會兒就回來。**2** the written abbreviation of 縮寫= SECRETARY

sec·a·teurs /ˌsɛkəˈtɝz; ˈsekətɜːz/ *n* [plural] *BrE* large, very strong sharp scissors that you use for cutting plant stems【英】修枝剪, 整枝剪; CLIPPERS (1) *AmE*【美】

se·cede /sɪˈsid; sɪˈsiːd/ *v* [I] *formal* to formally leave an organization, especially because there has been a disagreement about its aims etc【正式】〔尤因意見分歧而〕退出〔團體、組織〕, 脱離: **[+from]** *By 1861, 11 states had seceded from the Union.* 到 1861 年, 已有 11 個州從聯邦退出。—**secession** *n* [singular,U]

se·clude /sɪˈklud; sɪˈkluːd/ *v* [T] *formal* to keep yourself or someone else away from other people【正式】使〔自己或某人與其他人〕隔離

se·clud·ed /sɪˈkludɪd; sɪˈkluːdɨd/ *adj* **1** a secluded place is private and quiet because it is a long way from other places and people 僻靜的, 偏僻的: *We eventually came to a secluded farmhouse.* 最後我們到了一間僻靜的農舍。**2 a secluded life/existence** a way of living that is quiet and private because you do not see many people 隱居生活, 離羣索居

se·clu·sion /sɪˈkluʒən; sɪˈkluːʒən/ *n* **1** [U] the state of being private and away from other people 與世隔絕, 隱居: **live/dwell/rest etc in seclusion** *The Emperor lived* *in utter seclusion behind the walls of the Forbidden City.* 皇帝生活在紫禁城的高牆之內完全與世隔絕。| **the seclusion of** *Writers are attracted to the peace and seclusion of the area.* 作家們被這個地方的安寧和僻靜所吸引前來居住。**2** [singular,U] an act of keeping yourself or someone else alone and away from other people 深居簡出; 隔離: **keep sb in seclusion** *In some societies, women are still kept in seclusion.* 在某些社會裡, 婦女仍處於被隔離狀態, 不許與人接觸。| **be in seclusion** (=be in a situation where you will not or cannot see or speak to other people) 處於被隔離狀態

1 1 **sec·ond¹** /ˈsɛkənd; ˈsekənd/ *number* **1** 2nd; the person, thing, event etc after the first one 第二的: *His second goal was from a penalty.* 他的第二次進球是罰球得分。| *a second year student at University* 大學二年級學生 | *In the second of a series of programmes we look at the role of women in industry.* 在系列節目中的第二集, 我們可以看到婦女在工業中的作用。| **the second largest/biggest etc** (=the one after the largest, the biggest etc) 第二大的, 僅次於最大的 *Dalton is the second tallest boy in the class.* 多爾頓在班裡是第二高的男孩。| **come/finish second** (=be the one after the winner of a race or competition) 〔在比賽中〕獲第二名 **2 second home/car etc** another home, car etc besides the one you use most of the time 〔除了常用的第一個之外的〕另一個住所/另一輛汽車等 **3 be/come a poor second** to not be as good, interesting etc as something else 與第一名相差甚遠的第二名: *Once you've tasted real vanilla, the artificial stuff is a poor second.* 一旦你嚐過真正的香子蘭精之後, 就知道人造香草精差多了。**4 every second year/person/thing etc** the second, then the fourth year etc 每隔一年/一人/一事等: *Only water the plants every second day.* 只要隔天給這些植物澆水就行了。**5 be second only to sth** to be the most important thing, the best thing etc, apart from one other particular thing 僅次於某物: *Colin's career was second only to his family.* 柯林看重事業僅次於他的家庭。**6 be second to none** to be the best 不亞於任何人[事物], 首屈一指: *As a singer, Ella Fitzgerald was second to none.* 作為歌唱家, 艾拉·菲茨傑拉德是首屈一指的。

1 2 **second²** *n* **1** [C] a unit for measuring time that is equal to 1/60 of a minute 秒〔時間單位, 等於 1/60 分〕: **for 5/20/30 etc seconds** *Hold your breath for four seconds.* 請你屏氣四秒鐘。| **take 5/20/30 etc seconds** *The whole operation takes about twenty seconds.* 整個工作大概需要二十秒鐘。**2** [C] *especially spoken* a very short period of time【尤口】一會兒, 片刻, 瞬間: **a few seconds** *Just wait there for a few seconds.* 請在那裡稍等一會兒。| **within seconds** (=after a few seconds) 立刻, 馬上 *Within seconds Cassie called me back.* 卡西立刻給我回了電話。| **just a second** *spoken* (=wait a moment)【口】稍等一會 *Just a second and I'll come and help.* 稍等一會, 我就過來幫忙。| **in a matter of seconds** (=in a very short time) 片刻間 —see also 另見 SPLIT SECOND **3 seconds** [plural] **a)** *informal* another serving of the same food after you have eaten your first serving【非正式】添加的飯菜, 添菜: *Does anyone want seconds?* 有誰想添菜嗎? **b)** clothes or other goods that are sold cheaply in shops because they are not perfect 〔衣物等削價出售的〕次貨, 次品 —compare 比較 SECOND-HAND **4** [C] someone who helped and supported someone who was fighting in a DUEL¹ (1) or other organized fight in former times 〔舊時決鬥者等的〕副手, 助手

second³ *adv* [sentence adverb 句子副詞] used to add another piece of information to what you have already said or written; SECONDLY 第二, 其次: *Firstly the church is a place of worship and second, is somewhere the community can congregate.* 教堂首先是做禮拜的地方, 其次是社區大眾的聚集地。

second⁴ *v* [T] to formally support a suggestion or plan made by another person in a meeting 〔在會議上〕附議〔動議或計劃〕: **second a motion/proposal/amendment etc** *Who'll second the motion?* 這項動議有誰附議?

second⁵ /sɪˈkɑnd; sɪˈkɒnd/ *v* [T] *BrE* to send someone to do someone else's job for a short time【英】臨時調派, 借調...: **second sb to** *Jill's been seconded to the marketing department while David's away.* 戴維不在的時候, 吉爾被臨時調到市場部工作。—see also 另見 SECONDMENT

sec·ond·a·ry /ˈsɛkənˌdɛrɪ; ˈsekəndəri/ *adj* **1 secondary education/schooling/teaching etc** the education, teaching etc of children between the ages of 11 and 16 中等教育/教學〔指對 11 歲至 16 歲孩子的教育〕 **2** not as important or urgent as something else 第二的, 次要的: *a secondary role* 次要角色 | **be of secondary importance/be a secondary consideration** *Getting there's the main thing – how we get there is a secondary consideration.* 要去那裡是主要的 —— 至於怎樣去, 那是第二位的考慮。| **be secondary to** *Social skills shouldn't necessarily be seen as secondary to academic achievement.* 社交技巧的重要性不應被看成一定遜於學術成就。**3** coming after or developing from something else of the same type 從屬的, 繼發(性)的: *The danger isn't from the disease itself, but from secondary infections that might occur.* 危險不在於這種病本身, 而在於可能發生的繼發感染。—**secondarily** *adv* 2

secondary mod·ern /ˌ.... ˈ../ *n* [C] a type of school that existed in Britain until the 1960s, where children who were thought not to be the most intelligent were sent 中等學校〔英國 20 世紀 60 年代以前專為智力一般的兒童開設的學校〕—compare 比較 COMPREHENSIVE SCHOOL, GRAMMAR SCHOOL

secondary school /ˈ.... ˌ./ *n* [C] a school for children between the ages of 11 and 16 or 18 〔為年齡在 11 至 16 或 18 歲之間的兒童開辦的〕中等學校, 中學 —compare 比較 ELEMENTARY SCHOOL, PRIMARY SCHOOL

secondary stress /ˌ.... ˈ./ *n* [C,U] *technical* the second strongest STRESS¹ (4) given in speech to part of a word or sentence, and shown in this dictionary by the mark ˌ【術語】次重音

second base /ˌ.. ˈ./ *n* [singular] the second place you have to run to in games such as BASEBALL 〔棒球〕二壘

second best¹ /ˌ.. ˈ.◂/ *adj* not quite as good as the best thing of the same type 僅次於最好的, 居於第二位的: *Allie was the second best shooter on the team.* 阿莉是隊裡的二號射手。

second best² *n* [U] something that is not as good as the best 居第二位者, 次於最好的事物: *I've never been able to accept second best.* 我從來不接受第二好的東西。

second child·hood /ˌ.. ˈ../ *n* [U] **be in your second childhood** a polite expression meaning that an old person is behaving and thinking like a small child because their mental abilities are not as good as they used to be 處於老年昏聵期〔禮貌說法〕

second class /ˌ.. ˈ./ *n* **1** [U] a way of delivering mail in Britain that is cheaper and slower than sending things by FIRST CLASS (2) mail 二類郵件〔在英國指比一類郵件收費便宜但速度較慢的郵件〕: **send sth second class** *If you send it second class, it won't get there till the end of the week.* 假如你把它作為二類郵件寄出, 要在週末才能收到。**2** [U] the system in the US for delivering newspapers, magazines, advertisements etc 二類郵件〔在美國指寄遞報紙、雜誌、廣告等〕 **3** [U] a way of travelling, especially on a train, that is cheaper but not as comfortable as FIRST CLASS (1) travel 〔尤指火車的〕二等(車): **travel second class** *Are you travelling first or second class?* 你此行準備坐頭等車還是坐二等車? **4** [singular] a level of a university degree in Britain that is below the top level 二級榮譽學位〔英國大學的學士學位, 僅次於優等的一級〕

second-class /ˌ.. ˈ.◂/ *adj* **1** [only before noun 僅用於名詞前] considered to be less important than other people or things 二等的, 次等的, 較差的: **second-class citizen**

S

(=someone who is not as important as other people in society) 二等公民 *Why should children be treated like second-class citizens?* 為甚麼小孩就該受到二等公民的待遇? **2 second-class carriage/compartment/ticket etc** connected with cheaper and less comfortable travel on a train 二等車廂/(車廂)隔間/車票等: *Two second-class tickets, please.* 請給兩張二等票。**3 second-class mail/post/stamp etc** connected with posting things more cheaply and slowly 二類郵件/郵票等 —compare 比較 FIRST CLASS

second cous·in /ˌ.. ˈ../ *n* [C] a child of a COUSIN (1) of one of your parents 父母的堂[表]兄弟姐妹的子女

second-de·gree /ˌ.. .ˈ.◂/ *adj* **second-degree burn/burns** *technical* the second most serious form of burn 【術語】二度燒傷

second-guess /ˌ.. ˈ./ *v* [T] **1** to try to say what will happen or what someone will do before they do it 猜測, 預測, 預言 **2** *AmE* to criticize something after it has already happened 【美】事後批評, 放馬後砲

second hand /ˈ.. ˌ./ *n* [C] the pointer that shows seconds on a clock or watch 〔鐘錶的〕秒針

second-hand /ˌ.. ˈ./ *adj* not new, and used by someone else before you 舊的, 用過的, 第二手的: *When I was a kid I hated wearing second-hand clothes.* 我小時候最不喜歡穿別人穿過的衣服。| **get/buy sth second-hand** *They get all their furniture second-hand.* 他們全部家具都是二手貨。

second-hand shop /ˌ.. ˈ. ./ *n* [C] a shop where you can buy cheap second-hand goods, especially clothes 〔尤指經營舊衣服的〕舊貨店

second-in-com·mand /ˌ.. . .ˈ./ *n* [C] the person who has the next highest rank to the person who has the highest rank, especially in a military organization 〔尤指軍隊的〕副司令員, 第二把手

second lan·guage /ˌ.. ˈ../ *n* [C usually singular 一般用單數] a language that you speak in addition to the language you learned as a child 第二語言〔母語以外所講的另一種語言〕

second lieu·ten·ant /ˌ.. .ˈ../ *n* [C] a middle rank in several of the US and British military forces, or someone who has this rank 少尉〔美、英軍隊的軍階〕—see table on page C6 參見C6頁附錄

3 **sec·ond·ly** /ˈsɛkəndlɪ; ˈsekəndli/ *adv* [sentence adverb 句子副詞] used to introduce the second fact, reason, subject etc that you want to talk about 第二, 其次: *First we must establish exactly what happened. Secondly, we must try to find out why.* 首先我們必須確切查明出了甚麼事, 其次我們要盡力找出原因。

se·cond·ment /sɪˈkɑndmənt; sɪˈkɒndmənt/ *n* [singular, U] *especially BrE* a period of time that you spend away from your usual job, either doing another job or studying 【尤英】臨時調任, 暫調, 借調: **be on secondment from** *He's not at the university permanently – he's on secondment.* 他不是固定在這所大學工作 —— 他只是臨時借調來的。

second na·ture /ˌ.. ˈ../ *n* [U] **be second nature (to sb)** something that is second nature to you is something you have done so often that you do it almost without thinking 是(某人的)第二天性, 成為習性: *Wearing a seatbelt is second nature to most drivers.* 對大多數駕駛員來說, 繫安全帶已經習以為常了。

second per·son /ˌ.. ˈ../ *n technical* a form of a verb or PRONOUN that is used to show the person you are speaking to. For example, 'you' is a second person PRONOUN, and 'you are' is the second person singular and plural of the verb 'to be' 【術語】〔動詞或代名詞的〕第二人稱〈例如you是第二人稱代名詞, 而you are是動詞to be的第二人稱單數和複數〉—compare 比較 FIRST PERSON, THIRD PERSON

second-rate /ˌ.. ˈ.◂/ *adj* [usually before noun 一般用於名詞前] not very good 二流的, 較差的, 次等的: *second-rate artists* 二流藝術家

second sight /ˌ.. ˈ./ *n* [U] the ability to know what will happen in the future, or to know about things that are happening somewhere else 預見力, 洞察力; 神異的視力

second-string /ˌ.. ˈ.◂/ *adj* [only before noun 僅用於名詞前] *AmE* not regularly part of a team, group etc, but sometimes taking someone else's place in it 【美】〔隊、組等成員〕替補的, 二線的

second thought /ˌ.. ˈ./ *n* **1 on second thoughts** *BrE* 【英】, **on second thought** *AmE* 【美】 *spoken* used to say that you have changed your mind about something 【口】〔經過重新考慮之後〕改變主意: *I'll have a coffee please. Oh no, on second thought, make it a beer.* 請來杯咖啡。啊, 不, 想想還是換成啤酒吧。**2 have second thoughts** to change your mind, or start having doubts about something 改變主意; 開始懷疑: *You're not having second thoughts, are you?* 你不會改變主意吧, 是嗎?

second wind /ˌsɛkənd ˈwɪnd; ˌsekənd ˈwɪnd/ *n* [singular] a new feeling of energy that you get when you have been working or exercising very hard and had thought you were too tired to continue 〔感到筋疲力盡以後的〕恢復精力, 重振精神: **get your second wind** *OK, let's go – you should have got your second wind by now.* 好吧, 我們走吧 —— 你現在應該已經恢復精力了。

se·cre·cy /ˈsikrəsɪ; ˈsiːkrəsi/ *n* [U] **1** the process of keeping something secret, or the state of being kept a secret 保密, 祕密狀態: *I must stress the need for absolute secrecy about the project.* 我必須強調對這項計劃絕對保密的必要。**2 be sworn to secrecy** if you have been sworn to secrecy by someone, you have promised them that you will not repeat what they have told you 發過誓要保密: *I really can't tell you, I've been sworn to secrecy.* 我真的不能告訴你, 我發過誓要保密的。

se·cret¹ /ˈsikrɪt; ˈsiːkrɪ̥t/ *adj* **1** known about by only a few people and kept hidden from others 祕密的, 隱祕的: **secret passage/hideout/hiding place etc** *Rosie took them to a secret hideout in the woods.* 羅齊把他們帶到樹林裡一個祕密的藏匿處。| **secret diplomacy/negotiations/meetings etc** *She's had secret meetings with him behind your back.* 她背着你和他祕密會面。| **keep sth secret** *They kept their marriage secret until last year.* 他們結了婚卻祕而不宣, 直到去年才公開。—see also 另見 TOP-SECRET **2** [only before a noun 僅用於名詞前] secret feelings or actions are ones that you do not want other people to know about 〔感情、行動〕不公開的, 暗自的: *I still have my secret fears about his intentions.* 我內心裡依然對他的意圖感到害怕。| **a secret admirer** *Did you know you had a secret admirer?* 你知道有人在暗戀你嗎? | **a secret drinker/smoker** *the watery eyes of a secret drinker* 祕密酗酒者一雙濕潤的眼睛 **3 secret about sth** liking to keep things secret; SECRETIVE 對某事嚴守祕密 —**secretly** *adv*: *They were secretly married last week.* 他們上週祕密結婚。 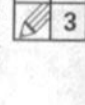

secret² *n* **1** something kept hidden or known about by only a few people 祕密: *Our plans must remain a secret.* 我們的計劃必須保密。| **keep a secret** (=not tell a secret to anyone) 保守祕密 *Can you keep a secret?* 你能保守祕密嗎? | **let sb in on the secret** (=tell someone a secret) 讓某人知道某個祕密 | **closely-guarded secret** (=one that is carefully kept) 嚴守的祕密 **2 the secret of** a particular way of achieving a good result, that is the best or only way …的祕訣, …的訣竅: *the secret to making good bread* 製作上乘麵包的祕訣 | **the secret of success** *What do you think is the secret of her success?* 你認為她成功的訣竅是甚麼? **3 in secret** in a private way or place that other people do not know about 祕密地, 暗地裡: *Lilian cried in secret, afraid to tell anyone.* 莉蓮偷偷地哭, 不敢告訴任何人。**4 make no secret of** to make your opinions about something clear 不隱瞞〔意見〕: *Howard made no secret of his disappointment.* 霍華德毫不掩飾他的失望。**5 the secrets of nature/the universe etc** the things no one yet knows about nature etc 大自然/宇宙等的奧祕 

secret a·gent /ˌ.. ˈ../ *n* [C] someone whose job is to find out and report on the military and political secrets of other countries 特工人員, 特務〔收集他國軍事和政治祕密的人〕

sec·re·tar·i·al /ˌsɛkrəˋtɛrɪəl; ˌsekrɜ̆ˈteəriəl/ *adj* connected with the work of a secretary（有關）祕書工作的: *a secretarial course* 祕書課程

sec·re·tar·i·at /ˌsɛkrəˋtɛrɪət; ˌsekrɜ̆ˈteəriət/ *n* [C] a government office or the office of an international organization with a SECRETARY (2) or SECRETARY GENERAL who is in charge 祕書處, 書記處: *the United Nations Secretariat in New York* 設在紐約的聯合國祕書處

3 1 **sec·re·ta·ry** /ˋsɛkrəˌtɛrɪ; ˈsekrɜ̆təri/ *n* [C] **1** someone who works in an office typing (TYPE[2] (1)) letters, keeping records, arranging meetings etc 祕書: *Julie works as a secretary in a lawyer's office.* 朱莉在一個律師事務所當祕書。| *You can ring my secretary to make an appointment.* 你可以打電話給我的祕書預約時間。**2 a)** a British government official, such as a minister or someone who has a high rank in a department〔英國的〕大臣, 高級官員: *the Foreign Secretary* 外交大臣 | **Secretary of State** *the Secretary of State for Home Affairs* 內政大臣 | **Permanent Secretary** (=someone in charge of a government department) 政府部門主管 **b)** an official who is chosen by the president of the US, who is in charge of a large government department〔美國政府的〕部長: *the Secretary of the Treasury* 財政部長 | **Secretary of State** (=the person who deals with American relations with other countries) 國務卿 **c)** a British government representative, below the rank of AMBASSADOR〔英國的〕大使館秘書: *the First Secretary at the British Embassy* 英國大使館的一等祕書 **3** an official of an organization who keeps records, writes official letters etc〔一個組織的〕書記員, 幹事: *secretary of the Wilton Tennis Club* 威爾頓網球俱樂部幹事

secretary gen·e·ral /ˌ···· ˈ···/ *n* [C] the most important official in charge of a large organization, especially an international organization〔主管大機構, 尤其是國際組織的〕祕書長, 書記長, 總幹事: *the UN Secretary General* 聯合國祕書長

se·crete /sɪˋkrit; sɪˈkriːt/ *v* [T] *technical*【術語】**1** if a part of an animal or plant secretes a substance, it produces it〔動物或植物的某一部分〕分泌〔某物質〕: *Hormones are secreted by various glands.* 激素是由各種腺體分泌的。—see also 另見 EXCRETE **2** *formal* to hide something【正式】隱藏, 藏匿〔某物〕: *McCready secreted the package inside his donkey-jacket.* 麥克里迪把包裹藏在他的厚外衣裡面。

se·cre·tion /sɪˋkriʃən; sɪˈkriːʃən/ *n* **1 a)** [C,U] *technical* a substance, usually liquid, produced by part of a plant or animal【術語】〔動物或植物某一部分的〕分泌物 **b)** [U] the production of this material 分泌: *the secretion of enzymes* 酶的分泌 **2** [U] *formal* the act of hiding something【正式】藏匿

se·cre·tive /ˋsikrətɪv; ˈsiːkrɜ̆tɪv/ *adj* someone who is secretive likes to keep their thoughts, intentions or actions hidden from others〔某人〕守口如瓶的, 遮遮掩掩的: *Everyone was very secretive about their earnings.* 每個人都閉口不談自己的薪酬。—**secretively** *adv* —**secretiveness** *n* [U]

secret po·lice /ˌ·· ˈ··/ *n* **the secret police** a police force controlled by a government, that secretly tries to defeat the political enemies of that government〔政府用以打擊政敵的〕祕密警察

secret ser·vice /ˌ·· ˈ··/ *n* [singular] **1** a British government organization that uses SECRET AGENTs to obtain secret information about other countries〔英國的〕特工部門, 特務機關 **2** a US government department dealing with special kinds of police work, especially protecting the President〔尤指保護美國總統的〕特工處

sect /sɛkt; sekt/ *n* [C] a group of people with their own particular set of beliefs and practices, especially within or separated from a larger religious group 派別, 宗派; 〔尤指宗教的〕教派: *an early, ascetic Christian sect* 一個早期的基督教禁慾教派

sec·tar·i·an /sɛkˋtɛrɪən; sekˈteəriən/ *adj* **1 sectarian violence/conflict/murder etc** violence etc that is connected with the strong feelings between people of different religious groups 教派之間的暴力/衝突/謀殺等 **2** *especially AmE* supporting a particular religious group and its beliefs【尤美】宗派的, 教派的: *a sectarian journal* 教派的期刊 —**sectarianism** *n* [U]

sec·tion[1] /ˋsɛkʃən; ˈsekʃən/ *n* 1 1

1 ▶PLACE/OBJECT 地方/物品◀ [C] one of the parts that something, such as an object or place is divided into 部分: [+of] *The spoons go in the front section of the drawer.* 匙子放在抽屜內靠前的地方。| *one of the older sections of Philadelphia* 費城舊城區的一部分 | *Decorate the torte with orange sections.* 用一瓣瓣的橙子裝飾這個大蛋糕。| *the back section of the plane* 飛機的後部

2 ▶GROUP OF PEOPLE 人羣◀ [C] a separate group within a larger group of people〔大集體中的〕小團體, 小集團: [+of] *a large section of the American public* 美國公眾的一大部分 | **all sections of the community** (=everyone in a particular place) 社區內的每一個人

3 ▶ORGANIZATION/INSTITUTION 組織/機構◀ [C] one of the parts of an organization, institution, department etc 部門; 處, 科, 組: *all the salespeople in my section* 我這個部門的全體銷售人員 | *the reference section of the library* 圖書館的參考書閱覽室 | **brass/woodwind etc section** (=the part of an orchestra that plays those instruments)〔交響樂隊中的〕銅管/木管樂組

4 ▶FITTING TOGETHER 裝配◀ [C] one of the parts of something that you fit together 部件, 零件: *You buy the bookcase in sections and assemble it.* 你買書櫥的部件, 然後自己把它組裝起來。

5 ▶BOOK/NEWSPAPER/REPORT 書/報紙/報道◀ [C] a separate part of something that is written, such as a book or newspaper〔書、報等的〕節; 欄; 版: *Who has the sports section?* 誰拿走了報紙的體育版? | *in the final section of this chapter* 在這一章的最後一節

6 ▶SIDE/TOP VIEW 側視/頂視圖◀ [C,U] a picture that shows what a building, part of the body etc would look like if it were cut from top to bottom or side to side 縱剖面, 縱切面; 橫切面, 斷面: **in section** *Here's the outside view, and here are the floors in section.* 這是外視圖, 而這是各樓層的剖面圖。

7 ▶MEDICAL/SCIENTIFIC 醫學的/科學的◀ *technical*【術語】**a)** [C,U] a medical operation that involves cutting〔醫療手術的〕切開, 開刀 **b)** [C] a very thin flat piece that is cut from skin, a plant etc to be looked at under a microscope〔放在顯微鏡下觀察的皮膚、植物等的〕切片

8 ▶PART OF A TOWN 城鎮的一部分◀ [C] *AmE* a part of a town in the western US that is one mile square【美】〔美國西部城鎮〕一英里見方的面積

9 ▶MATHEMATICS 數學◀ [C] *technical* the shape that is made when a solid figure is cut by a flat surface in mathematics【術語】〔數學中的〕截面: *conic sections* 圓錐截面 —see also 另見 CROSS-SECTION

section[2] *v* [T] *technical*【術語】**1** to cut a SECTION from skin, a plant, or a shape in mathematics etc 做〔皮膚或植物〕的切片; 顯示[做]〔數學圖形〕的截面 **2** to draw a SECTION[1] (6) of something such as a house 畫〔房子等的〕剖面圖 **3** to cut a part of the body in a medical operation〔在醫療手術中〕把〔身體的某部分〕切開, 開刀

section sth ↔ **off** *phr v* [T] to divide an area into parts, by making a dividing line between them 將〔某物〕分成部分: *The vegetable plots were sectioned off by a low wall.* 菜地被矮牆分成一塊一塊的。

sec·tion·al /ˋsɛkʃənl̩; ˈsekʃənəl/ *adj* **1** made up of sections that can be put together or taken apart 拼合而成的, 可拆卸的: *a six-foot sectional sofa* 一張六英尺長的組合沙發 **2** limited to one particular group or area within a larger group 某一羣體的, 局部的: *different sectional interests each seeking to represent working women* 尋求代表職業婦女的各個不同利益集團 **3** connected with a SECTION[1] (6) 斷面的, 截面的: *a sectional view of the new building* 新大樓的斷面圖

sec·tion·al·is·m /ˈsɛkʃənḷˌɪzəm; ˈsekʃənəlɪzəm/ *n* [U] too much loyalty towards your own political or social group 宗派主義; 地方主義; 本位主義

1 **sec·tor** /ˈsɛktɚ; ˈsektə/ *n* [C] **1** a part of an area of activity, especially of business, trade etc〔尤指商業、貿易等的〕部門; 行業: **[+of]** *the agricultural sector of the economy* (國民) 經濟中的農業部門 | *understaffing in all sectors of the educational system* 教育系統各部門的人員不足問題 | **public/private sector** (=business controlled by the government or by private companies)〔商業的〕國營/私營部門 **2** one of the parts into which an area is divided for a purpose, especially for military reasons〔為某種目的設立的〕地區;〔尤指軍事的〕防區, 戰區: *Planes searched a broad sector of the Indian Ocean.* 飛機搜索了印度洋的一大片海域。**3** *technical* an area in a circle enclosed by two straight lines drawn from the centre to the edge【術語】扇形 —see picture at 參見 SHAPE[1] 圖

sec·u·lar /ˈsɛkjəlɚ; ˈsekjʊlə/ *adj* **1** not connected with or controlled by a church or other religious authority 不與教會聯繫的, 不受教會管轄的: *secular education* 世俗教育 | *our modern secular society* 我們現代的世俗化社會 **2** a secular priest lives among ordinary people, rather than with other priests in a MONASTERY〔教士〕住在俗人之中的, 不住在修道院內的

sec·u·lar·is·m /ˈsɛkjələrˌɪzəm; ˈsekjʊlərɪzəm/ *n* [U] a system of social organization that keeps out all forms of religion 現世主義, 世俗化〔指拒絕一切宗教教義或活動的社會組織體系〕—**secularist** *n* [C]

sec·u·lar·ize also 又作 **-ise** *BrE*【英】/ˈsɛkjələrˌaɪz; ˈsekjʊləraɪz/ *v* [T] to remove the control or influence of religious groups from a society or an institution 使世俗化, 使脫離宗教影響 —**secularization** /ˌsɛkjələrəˈzeʃən; ˌsekjʊləraɪˈzeɪʃən/ *n* [U]

2 **se·cure**[1] /sɪˈkjʊr; sɪˈkjʊə/ *v* [T] **1** to get or achieve something that will be permanent, especially after a lot of effort〔尤指經過努力而〕獲得, 永久得到〔某物〕: *UN negotiators are still trying to secure the release of the hostages.* 聯合國的談判人員仍在努力爭取人質獲釋。| *a deal to secure the company's future* 為保障公司前途的交易 **2** to make something safe from being attacked, harmed, or lost 使安全, 保護...〔免受攻擊、傷害或損失〕: **[+against]** *Extra men will be needed to secure the camp against attack.* 需要增加兵員以保護兵營免遭攻擊。**3** to fasten or tie something firmly in a particular position 縛牢, 繫緊, 將〔某物〕固定: *a tent secured with heavy wooden pegs* 用粗大木樁牢牢固定的帳篷 | **secure sth to sth** *John secured the boat firmly to the jetty.* 約翰把小船牢牢地繫在碼頭上。**4** to legally promise that if you cannot pay back money you have borrowed, you will give the lender goods or property of the same value instead 向〔債權人〕提供保證〔償還債務〕, 為〔借款〕作保: *a secured loan* 有擔保的貸款

3 **secure**[2] *adj*

1 ►PERMANENT/CERTAIN 永久的/確定的◄ a situation that is secure is one that you can depend on because it is not likely to change 穩固的, 可靠的, 穩定的: *There is no such thing as a secure job these days.* 近來已沒有穩定的工作這種事情了。| *a secure source of funds* 可靠的資金來源 | **on secure ground** (=when you know exactly what to do or say) 有把握

2 ►SAFE PLACE 安全的地方◄ **a)** locked or guarded so that people cannot get in or out, or steal anything 鎖牢的; 關緊的: *Make sure the doors and windows are secure before you leave.* 出門之前一定要把門窗關好。**b)** safe from and protected against attacks 安全的, 受保護的: **[+from]** *The southern border is secure from enemy shelling.* 南部邊境不會遭受敵人的砲轟。

3 ►SAFE FEELING 安全感◄ feeling safe and protected from danger 安心的, 無恐懼的, 感到安全的: *I'll feel more secure with a burglar alarm.* 裝了防盜警報器, 我就更加安心了。

4 ►CONFIDENT 有信心的◄ **a)** feeling confident about yourself and your abilities〔對自己和自己的能力〕有自信的: *a secure and happy child* 自信而快樂的小孩 —opposite 反義詞 INSECURE (1) **b)** feeling confident and certain about a situation and not worried that it might change 有保障的, 沒有顧慮的: *We're waiting to have kids until we're financially secure.* 我們要等到經濟上有保障時才生養孩子。| **secure in the knowledge that** *Myles relaxed, secure in the knowledge that they wouldn't find him.* 邁爾斯知道他們不會發現他, 因而放下心來。

5 ►FIRMLY FIXED 牢固的◄ firmly fixed, tied, or fastened 固定住的, 繫牢的, 縛緊的: *Are you sure that shelf is secure?* 你肯定那個架子牢固嗎?

se·cure·ly /sɪˈkjʊrlɪ; sɪˈkjʊəli/ *adv* tied, fastened etc tightly, especially in order to make something safe 牢靠地: **securely locked/fastened/tied etc** *Make sure the saddle is securely buckled so it doesn't come loose.* 一定要把馬鞍牢牢扣緊, 以免鬆開。

se·cu·ri·ty /sɪˈkjʊrətɪ; sɪˈkjʊərəti/ *n*

1 ►PUBLIC/GOVERNMENT SAFETY 公眾/政府的安全(保障)◄ [U] things that are done in order to keep someone or something safe 保安, 保安措施: *For reasons of security, all luggage must be searched.* 出於安全考慮, 所有行李必須接受檢查。| **security measures/checks/procedures etc** *Strict security measures were in force during the President's visit.* 總統訪問期間實行了嚴密的保安措施。| **national/state security** (=protection of a country from attack or harm) 國家的安全 | **tight security** (=careful protection using a lot of soldiers, police etc) 嚴密的保安(措施) | **security man/guard** (=someone employed to protect a person or building) 保安人員 | **security forces/operations etc** (=those whose job is to protect a country, sometimes used to avoid saying military) 保安部隊/行動 *the UN Security Forces* 聯合國維和部隊 | **security firm** (=a company that provides protection for other people's property, money etc)〔向別人提供對財產、金錢等保護的〕保安公司 | **maximum security prison** (=for very dangerous prisoners, from which it is very difficult to escape) 採取最嚴密警戒措施的監獄 | **high security** (=carefully protected or made safe) 嚴密保護

2 ►PROTECTION FROM BAD SITUATIONS 對不良環境的抵禦◄ [U] **a)** the state of being protected from the bad things that could happen to you 保障, 保護: **job security** (=not being in danger of losing your job) 工作保障 | **financial security** (=knowing you have enough money to pay for the things you need) 經濟保障 *This plan can offer your family financial security in the event of your death.* 這個方案能在你意外死亡時給你的家庭提供經濟保障。**b)** something that protects you from the bad things that could happen to you 提供保障的東西, 防禦物: **[+against]** *Does your insurance provide enough security against illness?* 你的保險對疾病的治療能提供足夠的保障嗎? | **[+of]** *the security of a loving family* 相親相愛的家庭所帶來的安全感

3 ►GUARDS 保安◄ [U] the department of a company which deals with the protection of its buildings and equipment〔公司的〕保安部門: *I'll have to report this to Security.* 我將不得不把此事報告保安部門。

4 ►BORROWING MONEY 借錢◄ [U] something such as property that you promise to give someone if you cannot pay back money you have borrowed from them 抵押品: **put sth up as security** *She had to put up her house as security on the loan.* 她不得不以自己的房子作為那筆貸款的抵押品。

5 ►SAFETY FROM HARM 不受損害◄ [U] how safe something is from being lost, stolen, or damaged 安全: *If you're worried about their security, put your jewels in the hotel safe.* 要是你擔心珠寶的安全, 那就存放在旅館的保險櫃裡吧。

6 securities [plural] stocks (STOCK[1] (3)) or shares (SHARE[2] (5)) 證券

security blank·et /ˈ·ˈ··· ˌ··/ *n* [C] a BLANKET[1] (1), soft toy etc that a child likes to hold and touch to comfort themselves 安樂毯〔小孩喜歡抱着和撫摸而產生舒適感的小絨毯〕

security clear·ance /ˈ·ˈ··· ˌ···/ *n* [C,U] official permission for someone to see secret documents etc, or to enter a building, after a strict checking process 安全審查〔經嚴格審查後正式准予閱讀機密文件或進入某處〕

security guard /ˈ·ˈ··· ˌ·/ *n* [C] someone whose job is to guard a building or a vehicle carrying money 保安人員〈如門衛或押解運鈔車者〉

security light /ˈ·ˈ··· ˌ·/ *n* [C] a light that turns on when someone tries to enter a dark building or area 智控安全燈〔當有人進入黑暗建築物或地區時能自動啟亮的燈〕—see picture on page A4 參見A4頁圖

security risk /ˈ·ˈ··· ˌ·/ *n* [C] someone who cannot be trusted by a government and who therefore is not allowed to do particular jobs〔不能擔任涉及國家安全職務的〕不可靠分子, 政府不信任的人

security ser·vice /ˈ·ˈ··· ˌ··/ *n* [C] a government organization that protects a country's secrets against enemy countries or protects the government against attempts to take away its power〔政府的〕保安部門, 安全機構

se·dan /sɪˋdæn; sɪˈdæn/ *n* [C] *AmE and AustrE* a large car that has a separate enclosed space for your bags etc【美和澳】大轎車, 廂式轎車; SALOON (2) *BrE*【英】

sedan chair /ˌ·ˌ· ˈ·/ *n* [C] a seat on two poles with a cover around it on which an important person was carried in former times〔舊時的〕轎子

se·date[1] /sɪˋdet; sɪˈdeɪt/ *adj* **1** moving in a slow and rather formal way〔行進〕緩慢而莊重的: *a sedate procession* 緩慢而莊重的隊伍 **2** peaceful, ordinary, and not very exciting 安靜的, 安詳的: *a sedate seaside town on the South Coast* 南部海岸寧靜的海邊小鎮 —**sedately** *adv* —**sedateness** *n* [U]

sedate[2] *v* [T often passive 常用被動態] to make someone sleepy or calm by giving them drugs 給〔某人〕服鎮靜劑

se·da·tion /sɪˋdeʃən; sɪˈdeɪʃən/ *n* [U] the use of drugs to make someone sleepy or calm〔服鎮靜劑後的〕鎮靜〔狀態〕: **under (heavy) sedation** *I couldn't speak to her as she was still under sedation.* 我不能同她說話, 因為她仍處於服藥後的鎮靜狀態。

sed·a·tive /ˋsɛdətɪv; ˈsedətɪv/ *n* [C] a drug used to make someone sleepy or calm 鎮靜藥, 鎮靜劑

sed·en·ta·ry /ˋsɛdn̩ˌtɛrɪ; ˈsedəntəri/ *adj formal*【正式】**1** a sedentary job is done while sitting down, and without moving around very much〔工作〕坐着做的, 案頭的 **2** a sedentary group of people tend always to live in the same place; SETTLED〔人羣〕固定不遷移的, 定居的: *a sedentary population* 定居人口

sedge /sɛdʒ; sedʒ/ *n* [U] a plant like grass that grows in groups on low wet ground〔生長於低窪地的〕苔草

sed·i·ment /ˋsɛdəmənt; ˈsedɪ̥mənt/ *n* [singular,U] solid matter that settles at the bottom of a liquid 沉澱物, 沉積物: *a brownish sediment at the bottom of the tank* 罐底的褐色沉澱物 —see picture on page A12 參見A12頁圖

sed·i·men·ta·ry /ˌsɛdəˋmɛntərɪ; ˌsedɪ̥ˈmentəri◂/ *adj* made of the solid matter that settles at the bottom of the sea, rivers, lakes etc〔在海、河、湖等的底部〕沉積的, 由沉澱物形成的: *sedimentary rock* 沉積岩 | *sedimentary deposits* 沉積礦牀

sed·i·men·ta·tion /ˌsɛdəmɛnˋteʃən; ˌsedɪ̥menˈteɪʃən/ *n* [U] the natural process by which small pieces of rock, earth etc settle at the bottom of the sea etc and form a solid layer〔地質上的〕沉積〔作用〕

se·di·tion /sɪˋdɪʃən; sɪˈdɪʃən/ *n* [U] *formal* speech, writing, or actions intended to encourage people to disobey a government【正式】煽動反政府的言論[行動]: *Leading activists of their party were charged with sedition.* 他們黨的主要活動分子被指控犯有煽動反政府罪。

se·di·tious /sɪˋdɪʃəs; sɪˈdɪʃəs/ *adj formal* intended to illegally encourage people to disobey the government【正式】〔非法〕煽動性的, 煽動反政府的: *a seditious speech* 煽動性的演說 —**seditiously** *adv*

se·duce /sɪˋdjus; sɪˈdjuːs/ *v* [T often passive 常用被動態] **1** to persuade someone to have sex with you, especially someone who is younger than you or in a weaker position than you〔尤指對比自己年輕或處於弱勢的人的〕誘姦, 勾引: *The head lecturer here was sacked for seducing female students.* 這兒的首席講師因誘姦女學生而被解雇。**2** to make someone want to do something by making it seem very attractive or interesting to them 引誘, 誘使: **seduce sb into doing sth** *Jim was seduced into leaving the company by the offer of higher pay.* 吉姆受了更優厚薪酬的誘惑而離開公司。—**seducer** *n* [C]

se·duc·tion /sɪˋdʌkʃən; sɪˈdʌkʃən/ *n* **1** [C,U] an act of persuading someone to have sex with you for the first time 引誘, 勾引: *the seduction scene in Act 2 of the Opera* 歌劇第二幕的誘姦戲 **2** [C usually plural 一般用複數] something that strongly attracts people, but often has a bad effect on their lives〔常指對人產生不良後果的〕誘惑物, 有魅力的東西: *the seduction of money* 金錢的誘惑

se·duc·tive /sɪˋdʌktɪv; sɪˈdʌktɪv/ *adj* **1** someone who is seductive is sexually attractive〔人〕性感的, 勾引人的: *She had a low, seductive voice.* 她有一種低沉而富有誘惑力的嗓音。**2** something that is seductive is very interesting or attractive to you, in a way that persuades you to do something you would not usually do〔某物〕有吸引力的, 有誘惑力的: *the seductive power of advertising* 廣告的誘惑力 —**seductively** *adv*: *She smiled seductively at him across the table.* 她坐在桌子的對面向他展現誘人的微笑。—**seductiveness** *n* [U]

sed·u·lous /ˋsɛdʒələs; ˈsedjɪ̥ləs/ *adj formal* hard working and determined【正式】勤奮的, 孜孜不倦的: *a sedulous worker* 勤奮的工人 —**sedulously** *adv*

see 看(見)

Karen was blindfolded so she couldn't see anything.
卡倫被蒙住了眼睛, 甚麼也看不見。

They looked at the paintings.
他們看着畫。

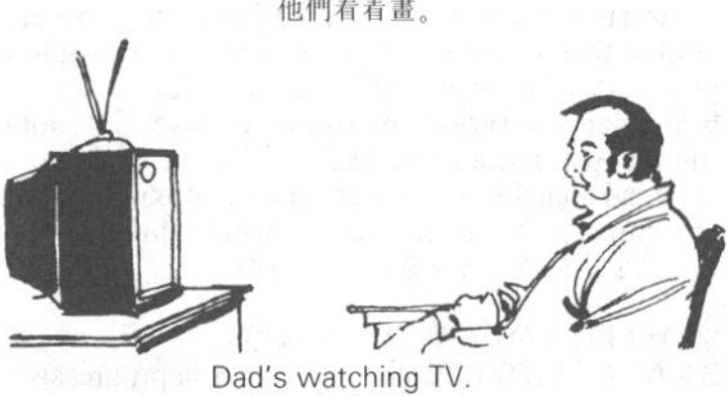

Dad's watching TV.
爸爸在看電視。

S

see¹ /si; siː/ *v past tense* **saw** /sɔ; sɔː/ *past participle* **seen** /sin; siːn/

① UNDERSTAND/REALIZE 理解/意識
② WITH YOUR EYES 用眼睛
③ FIND OUT 發現
④ GOODBYE 道別
⑤ VISIT/MEET 探訪/見面
⑥ CONSIDER 考慮
⑦ FUTURE 將來
⑧ IMAGINE 想像
⑨ MAKE SURE 確保
⑩ EXPERIENCE 經驗
⑪ GO WITH SB 陪同某人
⑫ OTHER MEANINGS 其他意思

① UNDERSTAND/REALIZE 理解/意識

1 [I,T] to understand or realize something 明白, 理解, 認識到: *I can see that you're not very happy with the situation.* 我能理解你對這種狀況不太愉快。| *Seeing his distress, Louise put her arm around him.* 看到他苦惱, 路易絲伸出手臂摟住他。| **[+why/what/who etc]** *"Ann's really fed up." "I can see why!"* "安確實厭煩了。" "我知道為了甚麼!" | **see what sb means** *usually spoken* (=understand what someone is saying)【一般口】明白某人的意思 *Do you see what I mean?* 你明白我的意思嗎? | **see the point** (=understand the reason for something) 認識〔某事的〕意義 *I can't see the point of learning Latin when you're never going to use it.* 既然你永遠用不上拉丁文, 我就不明白你學習它有甚麼意義。| **see both sides** (=understand both opinions in a discussion or argument) 〔在討論或爭辯中〕了解雙方的觀點 | **not see that it matters** (=not think something is important) 認為它無關緊要 *The recipe says to use fresh cream, but I can't see that it matters.* 食譜說要用新鮮奶油, 但我認為這無關緊要。| **not see the joke** (=not understand why something is funny) 聽不懂那有甚麼好笑 *Ian laughed politely even though he couldn't see the joke.* 伊恩儘管聽不懂那個笑話, 但還是禮貌地笑了笑。| **not see reason/sense** (=realize you are being silly or unreasonable) 不明白道理 *I've tried to explain that we can't afford it, but he just won't see reason.* 我已盡力解釋過我們買不起, 但他就是不明白這個道理。

2 I see *spoken* used to show that you are listening to what someone is telling you and that you understand it【口】我明白了〔用於表示聽懂別人所說的話〕: *"You turn this dial to control the central heating." "Oh, I see."* "你轉動這個標度盤來控制中央暖氣的溫度。" "噢, 我明白了。"

3 you see *spoken* used when you are explaining something to someone【口】你瞧, 你知道〔用於對別人解釋某事〕: *The shop's open till 8 you see, so I can pick some stuff up after work.* 你知道, 這商店一直要開到 8 點, 所以我可以在下班後買點東西。| *You see the thing is I'm really busy right now.* 你瞧, 事實上我此刻的確很忙。

4 see *spoken* used to check that someone is listening and understands what you are explaining to them【口】明白了吧〔用於弄清對方是否在聽並理解所作的解釋〕: *You mix the flour and eggs like this, see.* 你把麵粉和雞蛋這樣混在一起, 明白了嗎?

5 see sth for what it is/see sb for what they are to realize that someone or something is not as good or pleasant as they seem 看透某事/識破某人

6 not see the wood for the trees also 又作 **not see the forest for the trees** *AmE*【美】to be unable to understand something because you are looking too much at small details rather than the whole thing 見木不見林, 見小不見大, 只見細節不見全面

② WITH YOUR EYES 用眼睛

7 ►ABILITY TO SEE 視力◄ [I,T not in progressive 不用進行式] to be able to use your eyes to look at things and know what they are 看, 看見, 看到: *I can't see a thing without my glasses!* 我不戴眼鏡甚麼也看不見! | **not see to do sth** *It's so dark I can hardly see to do my work.* 天太黑了, 我幾乎看不見, 沒法做我的工作。

8 ►NOTICE/EXAMINE 注意/察看◄ [T not in progressive 不用進行式] to notice, examine, or recognize someone or something by looking 看出, 留意 (到), 察看, 認出: *Can I see your ticket, please?* 我可以查看一下你的票嗎? | *You see a lot of men with long hair these days.* 如今你可以看到很多男人留着長頭髮。| **[+where/what/who]** *Can you see where I put my pen?* 你看到我把筆放在哪兒了嗎? | **see (that)** *They could see that he had been crying.* 他們能看出他一直在哭。| **see sb/sth doing sth** *I see the neighbours are having a barbecue again.* 我看鄰居們又在燒烤了。| *The suspect was seen entering the building at 15.00 hours.* 有人看到疑犯在下午 3 點鐘進入那幢大樓。| **see sb/sth do sth** *Pat thought he saw her drive off about an hour later.* 帕特認為自己看到她大約在一小時後駕車離去。| **[+if/whether]** *Nick went out to see if the pond had frozen over.* 尼克出去看看水塘是否結了冰。| **see sb around** (=notice someone regularly in places you go to without knowing them) 經常見到某人〔但並不認識〕 *I don't know his name but I've seen him around.* 我不知道他的姓名, 但我常常在那兒見到他。

9 see a film/movie/play to watch a film etc 看電影/看戲: *I saw a really good movie last night.* 昨晚我看了一部很精彩的電影。

10 ►TELEVISION 電視◄ [T not in progressive 不用進行式] to watch a particular programme on television 看〔電視節目〕: *Did you see the game last night?* 你昨晚看了球賽沒有?

11 ►FIND INFORMATION 發現信息◄ [T only in imperative 僅用於祈使句] used to tell you where you can find information 參閱, 見: *See p.58.* 參閱第 58 頁。| *See press for details.* 詳情請閱報紙。| **see above/below** *The results are shown in Table 7a (see below).* 結果如表 7a 所示 (見下文)。

12 be seen to look at or be noticed by people who are important in society 〔重要人物〕露面; 受〔重要人物〕注意: *Royal Ascot is the place to be seen.* 皇家阿斯科特賽馬會是要人露面的場所。

13 be seen to be doing sth to make sure that other people notice you working hard or doing something good 讓他人注意到自己在努力做某事: *The government must be seen to be doing something about the rise in violent crime.* 政府必須向大家證明確實採取行動對付暴力犯罪的增加。

③ FIND OUT 發現

14 [T] to find out information or a fact 查看, 發現〔信息或事實〕: **[+what/when/who/how etc]** *Can you see who's at the door?* 你去看看門外是誰來了, 好嗎? | **[+if/whether]** *Sharon! See if there's any beer in the fridge!* 莎倫! 看看冰箱裡還有沒有啤酒! | *an experiment to see whether the new material melts at high temperatures* 觀察這種新材料在高溫下是否熔化的實驗 | **see for yourself** (=used to tell someone to look at something so that they can find out if it is true) 親眼看看 *If you don't believe me, see for yourself.* 你要是不相信我，那就親自去看看吧。

15 see what sb/sth can do *spoken*【口】**a)** to find out if you can deal with a situation or problem 弄清楚某人/某物能做甚麼: **[+about]** *I'll see what I can do about speeding up the process.* 我會看看我能否做些甚麼來加快這個進程。**b)** to find out how good someone or something is at what they are supposed to be able to do 弄清某人/某物是否真能…: *Let's take the Porsche out to the racetrack and see what it can do!* 我們把這輛保時捷開到跑道上去，看看它到底能跑多快！

④ GOODBYE 道別

16 see you! *spoken* used to say goodbye when you know you will see someone again【口】再見: **see you tomorrow/at 3/Sunday etc** *See you Friday – your place at 8:30.* 星期五見——8點30分在你家。| **see you in a bit** *BrE* (=see you soon)【英】待會兒見 | **see you in a while** (=see you soon) *AmE*【美】待會兒見 | **(I'll) be seeing you!** (=see you soon) 再見！待會兒再見！

17 see you around *spoken* used to say goodbye to someone when you have not made a definite arrangement to meet again【口】再見〔用於在分別時沒有約定再見面的具體時間〕

18 see you later *spoken* used to say goodbye to someone when you are going to see them again soon or later in the same day【口】回頭見〔用於在當天晚些時候或不久後還要再見面〕

⑤ VISIT/MEET 探訪/見面

19 ►VISIT/MEET SB 探訪/會見某人◄ [T] to visit or meet someone 探訪，會見: *We're going to see Lucy after work.* 我們下班後去探望露西。| **see you** (=I will meet you) 再見 *See you at 8 at Bear's Place.* 8點在貝厄餐館見。

20 ►HAVE A MEETING 會見◄ [T] to have an arranged meeting with someone 約見，接待: *Mr Thomas is seeing a client at 2:30.* 托馬斯先生兩點半要接待一位客戶。| **see sb about sth** (=see someone to discuss something) 會見某人討論某事 *I have to see my teacher about my grades.* 我得去見老師談我的分數問題。

21 ►BY CHANCE 偶然地◄ [T, not in progressive 不用進行式] to meet someone by chance 偶遇，碰見: *I saw Penny in town today.* 今天我在城裡遇見了彭妮。

22 ►SPEND TIME WITH SB 與某人在一起◄ [T] to spend time with someone 與…來往，與…見面: *Do you still see any of your old college friends?* 你還和昔日的大學同學保持來往嗎？| **see a lot of sb** (=see someone often) 常與某人見面 *She's been seeing a lot of John recently.* 她近來與約翰經常見面。| **see more/less of sb** (=see someone more or less often) 較多/較少見到某人 *They've seen much more of each other since Dan moved to London.* 自從丹搬到倫敦之後，他們彼此見面的機會就多得多了。

23 ►HAVE A VISIT 接待來訪◄ [T] to have a visit from someone 接待〔某人〕的造訪，來訪: *She's too sick to see anyone at the moment.* 她目前病得很重，不能見任何人。

24 be seeing sb to be having a romantic relationship with someone 與某人談戀愛: *Is she seeing anyone at the moment?* 她這陣子是否正在和甚麼人談戀愛？

⑥ CONSIDER 考慮

25 see sb/sth as sth to consider something to be a particular thing or to have a particular quality 把某人/某物看作…: *Jake saw any man who spoke to his wife as a potential threat.* 傑克認為任何一個與他妻子說話的男人都是一個潛在的威脅。| **be seen as sth** *America is seen as the land of opportunity.* 美國被認為是充滿機遇的國家。

26 ►CONSIDER STH IN A PARTICULAR WAY 以特定方式考慮某事◄ [T always+adv/prep] to regard or consider something in a particular way〔以特定方式〕考慮，看待〔問題〕: *He sees things differently now that he's in management.* 他既已進了管理層，看問題就不同了。| **as sb sees it** (=according to someone's opinion of a situation) 依某人的觀點 *As they see it, I'm the one to blame.* 他們認為，我是難辭其咎的人。| **the way I see it** *spoken*【口】*Well, the way I see it, nothing's really going to change around here.* 嗯，依我看，這兒不會有甚麼真正的改變。| **see fit (to do sth)** (=consider an action to be right and sensible) 認為〔某種做法〕妥當[合適] *You must do whatever you see fit.* 你必須做你認為合情合理的事情。

27 seeing that considering that 考慮到: *She writes very well seeing that English isn't her first language.* 考慮到英語不是她的第一語言，她寫得算是夠棒的了。

28 (be) seen against sth to be considered together with something else 與某事擺在一起來考慮: *The unemployment data must be seen against the backdrop of world recession.* 失業數字一定要放在全球經濟不景氣的背景下來考慮。

⑦ FUTURE 將來

29 [I,T] to find out about something in the future〔將來〕見到: **[+if/whether]** *It will be interesting to see whether Glenn gets the job.* 看格倫能否得到這份工作將會是很有意思的。| **[+how/what/when etc]** *I might come – I'll see how I feel tomorrow.* 我也許會來——我要等明天看看身體如何。| **we'll see** *spoken* (=used when you do not want to make a decision immediately)【口】看看再說 *"Can we go to the zoo, Dad?" "We'll see."* "爸爸，我們可以去動物園嗎？" "看看再說吧。" | **I'll/we'll have to see** (=used when you cannot make a decision immediately) 我/我們得看看再說 *I don't know if I can lend you that much – I'll have to see.* 我不知道能否借給你那麼多錢——我得看看再說。| **wait and see** *spoken*【口】*We'll just have to wait and see.* 我們還得等着瞧。| **see how it goes/see how things go** *usually spoken* (=used when you are going to do something and will deal with problems as they appear)【一般口】看看情況怎樣發展 | **you'll see** *spoken* (=used to tell someone that something will happen in the way you have described it)【口】將來你就知道 *I'll do better than any of them, you'll see.* 我會做得比他們任何人都好，你等着瞧吧。

30 see sth coming to realize that there is going to be a problem before it actually happens 預見會出現某事[問題]: *We should really have seen this mess coming.* 我們早該預料到會有這種麻煩的。

⑧ IMAGINE 想像

31 [T not in progressive 不用進行式] to form a picture of something or someone in your mind; IMAGINE (1) 想像，設想: *He could see a great future for her in music.* 他能看出她在音樂方面前途遠大。| **can't see sth** (=think that something is unlikely to happen or be true) 無法想像某事 *Stuart thinks the car will go, but I can't see it myself.* 斯圖爾特認為這輛車能走，但我自己認為這不可能。| **see sb as sth** (=be able to imagine someone being something) 能夠想像某人就是… *I just can't see her as a ballet dancer.* 我簡直無法想像她竟然是一位芭蕾舞演員。

32 be seeing things to imagine that you see something which is not really there 產生幻覺，見神見鬼: *There's no one there – you must have been seeing things.* 那裡沒有人——你大概是見鬼了。

⑨ MAKE SURE 確保

33 [T not in progressive 不用進行式] to make sure or check that something is done correctly 確保，查明: **see that** *It's up to you to see that the job's done properly.* 由你負責確保該項工作做得妥妥當當。| **see to it** (=make sure that something is done) 確保辦妥某事 *Don't worry – I'll see to it.* 不用擔心——我一定會辦好的。

S

34 ►WARNING 警告◄ [T, only in imperative 僅用於祈使句] used as a warning that something is important and must be done 務必注意, 一定要做到〔用於提醒某事重要, 必須辦妥〕: **see (that)** *Please see that the room is straightened up before you leave.* 你離開之前務必要把房間整理好。

⑩ EXPERIENCE 經驗

35 ►PERSON 人◄ [T not in progressive 不用進行式] to have experience of something 有…的經驗; 經歷: *We've seen some good times together, Dave and I.* 戴夫和我, 我們共同度過了一些美好的時光。| **have seen it all (before)** (=to have experienced something before, especially so that there is nothing else for you to learn about it) (這一切) 早已經歷過了 —see also 另見 **(been there), seen that, done that** (BEEN (3))

36 ►TIME/PLACE 時間/地方◄ [T] if a time or place has seen a particular event or situation, it happened or existed in that time or place〔事件或情況在某時或某地〕發生, 存在: *This year has seen a big increase in road accidents.* 今年道路交通事故大增。

⑪ GO WITH SB 陪同某人

37 see sb across the road to help someone to cross a road safely 陪伴[攙扶]某人過馬路

38 see sb home to go with someone when they go home to make sure that they are safe 送某人回家: *Wait a minute! I'll get Nick to see you home.* 等一會兒! 我叫尼克送你回家。

39 see sb to the door to go to the door with someone when they leave your house, to say goodbye to them 送某人到門口

⑫ OTHER MEANINGS 其他意思

40 let me see/let's see *spoken* used to show that you are trying to remember something【口】讓我/我們想想: *Let me see…where did I put that letter?* 讓我想想…我把信放在哪兒了?

41 seeing as/how/that *spoken* an expression meaning because, used especially when a situation makes you decide or suggest something that you had not intended【口】由於…, 既然…〔尤用於表示臨時的想法〕: *Seeing as you're going into town, can you get a few things for me?* 既然你要進城, 能不能替我捎點東西回來? | **seeing (as) it's you** *humorous* (=used to say that you are treating someone especially well because you like them)【幽默】只因為是你〔表示因喜歡某人, 所以對其特別好〕

42 I don't see why not *spoken* used to say yes in answer to a request【口】我認為沒有甚麼不可以的, 有何不可〔用於表示答應某人的請求〕: *"Can we go to the park?" "I don't see why not."* "我們可以去公園嗎?" "我看沒甚麼不可以的。"

43 have seen better days *informal* to be in a bad condition【非正式】已經破敗, 已經破舊: *This coat has seen better days.* 這件外套已經破舊了。

44 see the back of sb *spoken* used to say that you will be happy when someone leaves because you do not like them【口】擺脱某人〔因不喜歡與其打交道〕: *I can't wait to see the back of him.* 我巴不得他離開。

45 see the last of sb/sth to not see someone or something again because they have gone or are finished〔因某人已離開或某事已完成〕不再與某人/某事打交道: *By Friday we should be seeing the last of the rain for a while.* 到星期五雨就會停一段時間。

46 see the light a) to realize that something is true 明白, 領悟 **b)** to have a special experience that makes you believe in a religion〔宗教上〕省悟, 皈依 **c)** also 又作 **see the light of day** to exist or first appear 問世, 首次出現: *The book that she had planned to write never saw the light of day.* 她計劃寫的書始終沒有面世。

47 I'll see what I can do *spoken* used to say that you will try to help someone【口】我會盡量幫忙的: *Leave the ones you haven't done with me, and I'll see what I can do.* 把你還沒有做完的留給我吧, 我會盡力幫你忙的。

48 see your way (clear) to *spoken* to be able and willing to help someone【口】能夠並願意幫助人: *I think I could see my way to lending you a little.* 我想我能借點錢給你。

49 see sb coming (a mile off) *spoken* to recognize that someone will be easy to trick or deceive【口】看出某人容易上當受騙: *You paid £500 for that! They must have seen you coming!* 你花 500 英鎊買這東西! 他們肯定看出你會上當的!

50 not see beyond the end of your nose to be so concerned with yourself and what you are doing that you do not realize what is happening to other people around you 眼睛只能看到鼻子尖, 目光短淺, 沒有遠見

51 see sb right *BrE spoken* to make sure that someone is properly rewarded【英口】確保某人得到適當報酬: *Just do this for me and I'll see you right.* 你就替我做這個, 我一定不會虧待你的。

52 ►GAME OF CARDS 紙牌遊戲◄ to risk the same amount of money as your opponent in a CARD[1] (7) game 與〔對方〕下同樣的賭注

see about sth *phr v* [T] **1** to make arrangements or deal with something 安排, 着手處理: *I'd better see about dinner.* 我還是去料理晚飯吧。| **see about doing sth** *Claire's gone to see about getting tickets for that concert.* 克萊爾已經去打點買音樂會門票的事了。**2 we'll have to see about that** *spoken* used to say that you do not know if something will be possible【口】我們還得看看行不行: *"The school trip's really cheap and Dad says I can go." "We'll have to see about that!"* "學校組織的旅行真便宜, 爸爸説我可以去。" "我們還得再看看!" **3 we'll soon see about that** *spoken* used to say that you intend to stop someone doing something they are planning to do【口】我們等着瞧吧〔用於阻止某人計劃要做的事〕

see around also 又作 **see round** *BrE*【英】*phr v* [T] to visit a place and walk around looking at it 四處[到處]看看: *Would you like to see around the old castle?* 你想看看那座古城堡嗎?

see in *phr v* **1** [T **see** sth ↔ **in** sb/sth] to notice a particular quality in someone or something that makes you like them 注意到〔某人或某物有某種讓人喜歡的特點〕: *He saw a gentleness in Susan.* 他覺得蘇珊有一種溫柔的氣質。| **not know what sb sees in sb** *spoken* (=not know why someone likes someone)【口】不知道某人為何喜歡某人 *I really don't know what she sees in him!* 我真不知道她看中他甚麼! **2** [T **see sb in**] to show a visitor the way when they arrive at a building 帶領〔某人〕進入: *Will you see the guests in when they arrive?* 客人到達後, 你把他們領進來好嗎? **3** [I] to be able to see into someone's house 看到〔某人的〕室內: *Close the curtains so that no one can see in while I dress.* 把窗簾拉上, 以免我穿衣服時讓外面的人看見。**4 see in the new year** to celebrate the beginning of a new year 迎接新年的開始[來臨]

see sb/sth **off** *phr v* [T] **1** to go to an airport, train station etc to say goodbye to someone〔到機場、火車站等〕給〔某人〕送行: *I think they've gone to the airport to see their daughter off.* 我想他們是去機場給女兒送行了。**2** to chase someone away, or make someone leave an area 趕走, 逐出; 使離開: *Security guards saw him off the premises.* 保安人員把他趕出門外。**3** to defend yourself successfully in a fight or battle, or beat an opponent in a game〔在戰鬥中〕抵擋住;〔在比賽中〕擊敗〔對手〕: **see off the competition** *They saw off the competition to become the nation's number one bestseller.* 它們在競爭中勝出, 成為全國的第一暢銷商品。**4** *BrE slang* to kill someone【英俚】殺死〔某人〕

see sb/sth **out** *phr v* [T] **1** to go to the door with someone to say goodbye to them when they leave 將〔某人〕

送到門口: **I'll see myself out** *spoken* (=used to tell someone they do not have to come to the door with you)【口】我自己出去, 不用送了 **2** to continue to do something until it finishes, even if you do not like doing it 堅持到〔某事〕結束, 堅持把〔某事〕做完: *I don't enjoy the course but I'll see it out.* 我不喜歡這門課, 但我會堅持上完它。

see over sth *phr v* [T] *BrE* to examine something large such as a house, especially when you are considering buying it【英】察看〔房屋等, 尤指在考慮購買它時〕

see through *phr v* [T] **1 [see through** sth] to recognize the truth about something that is intended to deceive you 看穿, 識破〔騙局等〕: *I could see through his lies.* 我能識破他的謊言。**2 [see through** sb] to know what someone is really like, especially what their bad qualities are 看透〔某人, 尤指其惡劣品質〕 **3 [see** sth **through]** to continue doing something, especially something difficult or unpleasant, until it is finished 把〔某事〕進行到底〔尤指某種困難或惹人討厭的工作〕: *Martin felt sick with nerves, but was determined to see the thing through.* 馬丁因神經緊張而感到不適, 但還是决心把事情做完。**4 [see** sb **through** sth] to give help and support to someone during a difficult time 幫助〔某人〕渡過〔難關〕: *I've given him a sedative; that should see him through the night.* 我已經給了他一服鎮靜劑; 那應該能使他安度這一夜了。

see to sb/sth *phr v* [T] to deal with something or do something for someone 處理〔某事〕; 照料, 關照〔某人〕: *We'll have to see to that window – the wood's rotten.* 我們得修理那窗戶了——木頭已經朽了。| **have/get sth seen to** *You should get that tooth seen to by a dentist.* 你應該找牙醫看看你那顆牙了。| **see to it that** *Will you see to it that this letter gets mailed today?* 請你務必今天把這封信寄出去, 好嗎? —see also 另見 **not see sb for dust** (DUST[1] (6)), **it remains to be seen** (REMAIN (5)), **see red** (RED[2] (4)), **see the colour of sb's money** (COLOUR[1] (12)), **I wouldn't be seen dead** (DEAD[1] (17))

Frequencies of the verb **see** in spoken and written English 動詞 see 在英語口語和書面語中的使用頻率

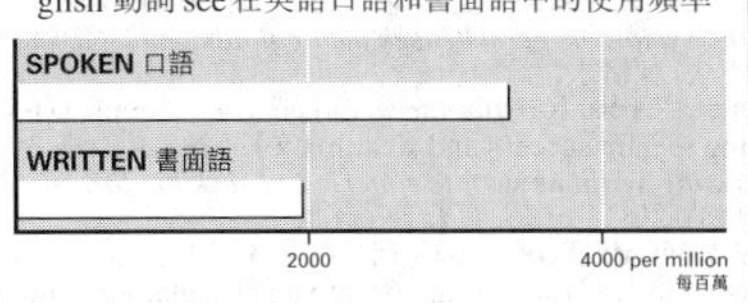

Based on the British National Corpus and the Longman Lancaster Corpus 據英國國家語料庫和朗文蘭卡斯特語料庫

This graph shows that the verb **see** is much more common in spoken English than in written English. This is because it is used in a lot of common spoken phrases. 本圖表顯示, 動詞 see 在英語口語中的使用頻率遠遠高於書面語, 因為口語中很多常用片語是由 see 構成的。

see² *n* [C] *technical* an area governed by a BISHOP (1)【術語】主教教區

S3 W3 **seed¹** /sid; siːd/ *n plural* **seeds** or 或 **seed** **1 a)** [C,U] a small, hard object produced by plants, from which a new plant of the same kind grows 種子: *sunflower seeds* 葵花籽 | **plant/sow seeds** (=put them into the ground) 播種 *Plant the seeds in sandy soil, about 10 cm apart.* 把種子種在沙土裡, 每粒相隔約 10 厘米。| **grow sth from seed** (=grow a plant from a seed, rather than planting it when it is already partly grown) 用種子種〔某物〕 **b)** [U] a quantity of seeds〔若干〕種子, 籽: *grass seed* 草籽 **2** *AmE* [C] one of the small hard objects in a fruit such as an apple or orange, from which new fruit trees grow【美】〔蘋果、橙子等水果的〕果核; PIP[1] (1) *BrE*【英】**3 go/run to seed a)** if a plant or vegetable goes or runs to seed, it starts producing flowers and seeds as well as leaves〔植物或蔬菜〕開花結子 **b)** if a person goes or runs to seed, they become unattractive, fat, or unhealthy especially because of getting old or lazy〔人, 尤指因漸老或懶惰而〕衰頹, 頹廢 **4 the seeds of sth** something that makes a new situation start to grow and develop 某物的起因[根源]: *the seeds of victory* 勝利的種子 | **sow (the) seeds of doubt/destruction/rebellion etc** (=do or say something which makes a bad feeling or situation develop and become a much more serious problem) 播下懷疑/毀滅/叛亂等的種子 *Sectarian agitators did much to sow the seeds of discontent among the people.* 宗派主義鼓動者在人民中間大力播下不滿的種子。**5 number one/number three etc seed** [C] a tennis player who is given a particular position according to how likely they are to win a competition 頭號/三號種子選手等〔在比賽中實力較強的網球選手, 按其獲勝的可能排序〕: *He's been top seed for the past two years.* 他在過去兩年中一直是頭號種子選手。**6** *biblical or humorous* SEMEN or SPERM【聖經或幽默】精液, 精子 **7** [U] *biblical* the group of people who have a particular person as their father, grandfather etc, especially when they form a particular race【聖經】子孫, 後裔

seed² *v* **1** [T] to remove seeds from fruit 給〔果實〕去籽[去核]: *seeded raisins* 無籽葡萄乾 **2** [T usually passive 一般用被動態] to give a tennis player a particular position, according to how likely they are to win a competition〔根據網球運動員在比賽中獲勝的可能〕挑選〔某人〕為種子選手: *seeded fourth at Wimbledon* 被定為温布頓網球賽四號種子 **3** [T often passive 常用被動態] to plant seeds in the ground 在〔地裡〕播種 **4** [I] to produce seeds 結籽

seed·bed /ˈsidˌbɛd; ˈsiːdbed/ *n* [C] **1** an area of ground where young plants are grown from seeds before they are planted somewhere else 苗牀 **2** a place or condition that encourages something, especially a bad situation, to develop〔尤指容易滋生壞事的〕温牀: **[+of]** *The city's slums were a seedbed of rebellion.* 這個城市的貧民窟是叛亂的温牀。—see also 另見 HOTBED

seed cap·i·tal /ˈ· ˌ···/ *n* [U] the money you have to start a new business with 本錢, 原始資本

seed·ling /ˈsidlɪŋ; ˈsiːdlɪŋ/ *n* [C] a young plant grown from seed 籽苗, 種苗, 幼苗

seed pearl /ˈ· ·/ *n* [C] a very small and often imperfect PEARL〔常有點瑕疵的〕小粒珍珠

seed·y /ˈsidɪ; ˈsiːdi/ *adj informal*【非正式】**1** a seedy person or place looks dirty or poor, and is often involved in or connected with illegal, immoral, or dishonest activities〔人或地方〕骯髒的; 破舊的: *a bunch of seedy characters* 一羣衣衫襤褸的人 **2** *old-fashioned informal* feeling slightly ill【過時, 非正式】有點不舒服的, 有小病的 —**seediness** *n* [U]

see·ing /ˈsiɪŋ; ˈsiːɪŋ/ *conjunction spoken* because a particular fact or situation is true【口】鑑於, 由於: **seeing (that)** *We could have a joint party, seeing that your birthday is the same day as mine.* 既然你和我的生日是在同一天, 我們可以一起開個生日派對。| **seeing as** *I won't stay long, seeing as you're busy.* 我不會待太久, 因為你很忙。 S3

seeing eye dog /ˌ·· ˈ· ˌ·/ *n* [C] *AmE* a dog trained to guide blind people; GUIDE DOG【美】〔經過特殊訓練能為盲人引路的〕領路犬, 導盲犬

seek /sik; siːk/ *v past tense and past participle* **sought** /sɔt; sɔːt/ W1

1 ►LOOK FOR 尋找◄ [I,T] **a)** a word meaning to look for something that you need such as a job or friendship, used especially in newspapers and advertisements 尋求, 尋找: *Virgo woman seeks Scorpio man.* 室女座女士尋找天蝎座男士。| *new graduates seeking employment* 正在求職的新畢業生 **b)** *formal* to look for the answer to a question or problem【正式】尋覓〔答案〕, 探索

2 ▶TRY TO GET 設法得到◀ [T] *formal* to try to achieve or get something【正式】設法獲得, 尋求: *Do you think the President will seek reelection?* 你認為總統會競選連任嗎? | *We only seek justice, not revenge.* 我們只是尋求公正, 不是報復。| **seek to do sth** *We are always seeking to improve productivity.* 我們一直在設法提高生產力。| **attention-seeking/publicity-seeking** (=trying to attract people's attention) 追求別人注意/知名度的 *a publicity-seeking stunt* 為了出名的花招
3 ▶ASK FOR 請求◀ seek (sb's) advice/help/assistance etc *formal* to ask someone for advice or help【正式】徵求(某人的)意見/請求(某人的)幫助/援助等: *If the symptoms persist, seek medical advice.* 如症狀持續下去, 便需求醫診治。
4 seek your fortune *literary* to go to another place hoping to gain success and wealth【文】尋找成功致富之路: *Young William went to America to seek his fortune.* 年輕的威廉到美國去闖天下。
5 ▶MOVE TOWARDS 向…移動◀ [T] to move naturally towards something or into a particular position 自然地向…移動: *Water seeks its own level.* 水會自動地流成水平面。—see also 另見 HEAT-SEEKING, HIDE-AND-SEEK, SELF-SEEKING, SOUGHT-AFTER

seek sb/sth ↔ **out** *phr v* [T] to look very hard for someone or something, especially someone who is avoiding you or hiding from you 找出[找到]〔某人或某物〕: *Our mission is to seek out the enemy and destroy them.* 我們的任務是要找到敵人並把他們消滅。

seek·er /ˈsikɚ; ˈsiːkə/ *n* [C] someone who is trying to find or get something 找尋者, 追求者: **job-seeker/asylum-seeker** *a brilliant politician and a ruthless power-seeker* 一位傑出的政治家和一個冷酷無情的權力追求者

seem /sim; siːm/ *v* [linking verb 連繫動詞, not in progressive 不用進行式] **1** to appear to be a particular thing or to have a particular quality, feeling, or attitude 看來, 似乎, 好像: *Dinah didn't seem very sure.* 黛娜似乎不是很有把握。| **seem to sb** *Larry seemed pretty angry to me.* 我覺得拉里好像很生氣。| *"How did she seem to you?" "Kind of upset."* "你覺得她怎麼了?" "有點不高興。" | **seem like** *Well, it seemed like a good idea at the time.* 這個嘛, 在當時似乎是個好主意。| **sb/sth seems a** *That seems a risky thing to try.* 那件事似乎做起來有風險。| **not be what he/she/it etc seems** *Things aren't always what they seem.* 事物並不總是與表象一致的。**2** to appear to exist or be true 似乎存在, 好像真實: **seem to** *I seem to have lost my car keys.* 我好像把汽車鑰匙給丟了。| **it seems to sb (that)** *It seems to me you don't have much choice.* 在我看來你沒有多少選擇的餘地。| **It seems (that)/it would seem (that)** *It would seem that someone left the building unlocked.* 似乎有人沒鎖大門就出去了。| **it seems like** *It seems like only yesterday that Tommy was born.* 湯米出生彷彿才是昨天的事。| **it seems as if/as though** *It seemed as though she didn't have a friend in the world.* 看起來她在這個世界上沒有一個朋友。| **so it seems** (=it appears to be true) 好像是這樣, 看起來是這樣 *"So Bill's leaving her?" "So it seems."* "那麼說, 比爾要離開她?" "好像是這樣。" **3** to appear to be happening or to be doing something 好像正在發生, 似乎正在〔做某事〕: **seem to do sth** *The rainbow seemed to end on the hillside.* 彩虹好像一直延續到山坡為止。| **seem like** *It seemed like the whole town had come to the show.* 好像全鎮的人都出來看演出。**4 can't/couldn't seem to do sth** used to say that you have tried to do something but cannot do it 似乎無法做某事〔用於表示某事已經試過但做不了〕: *I just can't seem to get it into his head that he has to plan things better.* 我好像根本沒法使他明白他做事必須加強計劃性。

seem·ing /ˈsimɪŋ; ˈsiːmɪŋ/ *adj* [only before noun 僅用於名詞前] *formal* appearing to be something, especially when this is not actually true; APPARENTLY【正式】似是而非的, 表面上的: *It was a seeming piece of good luck which later led to all kinds of trouble.* 那件事看上去是個好運, 而後來卻招致了各種各樣的麻煩。

seem·ing·ly /ˈsimɪŋlɪ; ˈsiːmɪŋli/ *adv* **1** appearing to be something when this is not actually true; APPARENT 看上去, 表面上, 外觀上: *The road was dusty and seemingly endless.* 路上塵土飛揚, 似乎沒有盡頭。**2** [sentence adverb 句子副詞] according to the facts as you know them 從已知事實來看, 看樣子: *There is seemingly nothing we can do to stop the plans going ahead.* 看樣子我們無法阻止這些計劃的實施。

seem·ly /ˈsimlɪ; ˈsiːmli/ *adj old-fashioned* suitable for a particular situation or social occasion, according to accepted standards of behaviour【過時】適宜的, 得體的, 合乎行為規範的: *It would be more seemly to keep quiet about it in front of the guests.* 在賓客面前對此事保持沉默會顯得更加得體。—opposite 反義詞 UNSEEMLY —**seemliness** *n* [U]

seen /sin; siːn/ the past participle of SEE

seep /sip; siːp/ *v* [I always+adv/prep] to flow slowly through small holes or spaces 滲漏: [**+in/into/through etc**] *Whenever it rained water started seeping in.* 每逢下雨, 水就滲漏進來。

seep·age /ˈsipɪdʒ; ˈsiːpɪdʒ/ *n* [singular,U] a gradual flow of liquid through small spaces or holes〔液體的〕滲漏: *Looks like a seepage problem in your basement.* 看來你的地下室有滲漏問題。

seer /sɪr; sɪə/ *n* [C] *especially literary* someone who can see into the future and say what will happen【尤文】預言者, 先知

seer·suck·er /ˈsɪrˌsʌkɚ; ˈsɪəˌsʌkə/ *n* [U] a light cotton cloth with an uneven surface and a pattern of lines 縐面薄織物, 泡泡紗

see·saw¹ /ˈsiˌsɔ; ˈsiːsɔː/ *n* [C] a piece of equipment that children play on, made of a board that is balanced in the middle, so that when one end goes up the other goes down 蹺蹺板

seesaw² *v* [I] to move repeatedly from one state or condition to another and back again 交替重複: *seesawing emotions* 時起時伏的情感

seethe /sið; siːð/ *v* [I] if a place is seething with people, insects etc there are a lot of them all moving quickly in different directions〔某地方〕充滿〔人羣、昆蟲等〕,〔人、昆蟲等〕密集(於): *seething with ants* 到處是亂爬的螞蟻 | *a seething mass of people* 密密麻麻走向四面八方的人羣

seeth·ing /ˈsiðɪŋ; ˈsiːðɪŋ/ *adj* extremely angry, but unable or unwilling to show it 內心極度憤怒的: *By the time we got home, David was seething.* 我們回到家時, 戴維氣極了。

see-through /ˈ··/ *adj* a see-through piece of clothing is made of cloth that you can see through〔衣服〕透明的: *This dress is completely see-through when it's wet!* 這件連衣裙濕了以後完全是透明的。—compare 比較 TRANSPARENT (1)

seg·ment /ˈsɛgmənt; ˈsegmənt/ *n* [C] **1** a part of something that is in some way different from or affected differently from the whole 部分: *A large segment of the public is against the new tax.* 公眾中一大部分人反對徵收新稅。**2** a part of a fruit, flower or insect that naturally divides into parts〔水果、花或自然形成的〕片, 塊, 瓣;〔昆蟲的〕節: *the segments of an orange* 橙子的瓣 —see picture on page A7 參見A7頁圖 **3** *technical* a part of a circle separated from the rest of the circle by a straight line across it【術語】弓形, 弦 —see picture at 參見 SHAPE¹ 圖 **4** *technical* the part of a line between two points【術語】〔線的〕段

seg·men·ta·tion /ˌsɛgmɛnˈteʃən; ˌsegmenˈteɪʃən/ *n* [U] the act of dividing something or to be divided into smaller parts 分割(成部分)

seg·ment·ed /sɛgˈmɛntɪd; segˈmentɪd/ *adj* made up of separate parts that are connected to each other 分割的, 分段的

seg·re·gate /ˋsɛgrɪˏget; ˈsegrɪgeɪt/ *v* [T often passive 常用被動態] to separate one group of people from others, especially because they are of a different race, sex or religion〔尤指因種族、性別、宗教不同而〕使分開, 分離, 隔離: *Blacks were segregated from whites in churches, schools and colleges.* 在教堂、學校和大學裡, 黑人都與白人隔離開。

seg·re·gat·ed /ˋsɛgrəˏgetɪd; ˈsegrɪgeɪtɪ̣d/ *adj* a segregated school or other institution can only be attended by members of one sex, race etc〔男女〕分開的;〔種族〕隔離的: *a segregated audience* 清一色是女性[男性、某種族等]的聽眾 —compare 比較 INTEGRATED

seg·re·ga·tion /ˏsɛgrɪˋgeʃən; ˌsegrɪˈgeɪʃən/ *n* [U] the practice of keeping people of different races or religions apart and making them live, work, or study separately〔不同種族、宗教的〕分開, 隔離: *The US Supreme Court ruled in 1954 that segregation in schools was unconstitutional.* 美國最高法院於 1954 年裁定, 學校實行種族隔離是違反憲法的。—compare 比較 INTEGRATION

sei·gneur /sinˋjɝ; seˈnjɜː/ *n* [C] someone who owned land in a FEUDAL system〔封建社會的〕領主, 莊園主

seis·mic /ˋsaɪzmɪk; ˈsaɪzmɪk/ *adj technical* connected with or caused by EARTHQUAKE*s* or powerful explosions【術語】地震[強烈爆炸]的, 地震[強烈爆炸]引起的: *an increase in seismic activity* 地震活動的增加

seis·mo·graph /ˋsaɪzməˏgræf; ˈsaɪzməgrɑːf/ *n* [C] an instrument that measures and records the movement of the earth during an EARTHQUAKE 地震儀

seis·mol·o·gy /saɪzˋmɑlədʒɪ; saɪzˈmɒlədʒi/ *n* [U] the scientific study of EARTHQUAKE*s* 地震學 —**seismologist** *n* [C]

3 **seize** /siz; siːz/ *v* **1** [T] to take hold of something suddenly and violently〔突然猛烈地〕抓取, 攫取: *He seized my hand and dragged me away from the window.* 他抓住我的手, 把我從窗戶旁拉開。| **seize sth from sb** *Maggie seized the letter from her and began to read out loud.* 瑪吉從她手上把信搶過去並開始大聲朗讀。**2** [T] to take control of a place suddenly and quickly, using military force〔用武力〕奪取, 佔領, 搶去: **seize power/seize control (of)** *The rebels have seized power in a violent coup.* 叛亂分子已在暴力政變中奪取了政權。**3** [T] if the police or government officers seize something, they take away illegal goods such as drugs or guns 沒收〔毒品、武器等非法物品〕, 收繳〔物品〕 **4 seize a chance/opportunity (with both hands)** to quickly and eagerly do something when you have the chance to 抓住機會/機遇 **5 be seized with terror/desire etc** to suddenly be affected by an extremely strong feeling 突然感到恐懼/受到慾望支配等: *I was seized with a sudden desire to laugh out loud.* 我突然想要放聲大笑。**6** [T] to suddenly catch someone and make sure they cannot get away 抓獲, 捕獲: *The gunmen were seized in a military style operation.* 那些持槍歹徒在一場軍事式的行動中被抓獲。

seize on/upon sth *phr v* [T] to suddenly become very interested in an idea, excuse, what someone says etc 抓住, 利用〔藉口等〕: *Margot seized on the excuse to get out of choir practice.* 瑪戈利用那個藉口逃避合唱隊的練習。

seize up *phr v* [I] **a)** if an engine or part of a machine seizes up, its moving parts stop working and can no longer move, for example because of lack of oil〔發動機或機器部件在運轉中因缺油等〕卡住, 停止運轉 **b)** if a part of your body, such as your back, seizes up you suddenly cannot move it and it is very painful〔背等身體部位〕突然僵痛

sei·zure /ˋsiʒɚ; ˈsiːʒə/ *n* **1** [U] the act of suddenly taking control or possession of something 奪取; 沒收: *the Fascist seizure of power in 1922* 1922 年法西斯的奪取政權 **2** [C] a sudden attack of an illness, for example a HEART ATTACK〔心臟病等疾病的〕突然發作: *an epileptic seizure* 癲癇發作

sel·dom /ˋsɛldəm; ˈseldəm/ *adv* very rarely 很少, 罕見, 不常: *She seldom reads newspapers.* 她很少讀報。—see picture at 參見 FREQUENCY 圖

se·lect¹ /səˋlɛkt; sɪ̣ˈlekt/ *v* [T] to choose something by carefully thinking about which is the best, most suitable etc〔經過認真思考〕挑選, 選擇, 選拔: *I selected four postcards and handed them to the cashier.* 我挑選了四張明信片, 然後交給收銀員。| **select sb to do sth** *Simon's been selected to represent us at the conference in Rio.* 西蒙已被推選出來代表我們出席里約熱內盧的會議。 2 2

select² *adj formal*【正式】**1** a select group of people or things is a small special group that has been carefully chosen 挑選出的, 精選的: *The information was only given to a select group of reporters.* 這條消息只提供給一組經過挑選的記者。| *select cuts of beef* 幾塊精選的牛肉 **2** only lived in, visited, or used by a small number of rich people; EXCLUSIVE¹ (1) 僅限於少數富人居住[參觀, 使用]的, 專用的, 高級的, 奢華的: *a select apartment block* 高檔的公寓大樓

select com·mit·tee /·ˌ· ·ˋ··/ *n* [C] a small group of politicians and advisers from various parties that has been chosen to examine a particular subject〔從各黨派選拔出來負責審查某一特殊問題的〕特別委員會

se·lec·tion /səˋlɛkʃən; sɪ̣ˈlekʃən/ *n* **1** [U] the careful choice of a particular person or thing from among a group of similar people or things 挑選, 選擇, 選拔: *the process of jury selection* 陪審團(成員)的挑選過程 | **make a selection** *Please make your selections and move along.* 請作出選擇並向前移動。**2** [C] something that has been chosen from among a group of things 挑選出來的東西: **[+from]** *a program of selections from Gilbert and Sullivan* 演奏吉爾伯特和沙利文的歌曲選的節目 **3** [C usually singular 一般用單數] a collection of things of a particular type, especially of things that are for sale; range 供選購的同類物品: **[+of]** *a fine selection of perfumes* 可供選購的各種精選香水 —see also 另見 NATURAL SELECTION 2 2

se·lec·tive /səˋlɛktɪv; sɪ̣ˈlektɪv/ *adj* **1** careful about what you choose to do, buy, allow etc〔做事、購物等〕認真選擇[挑揀]的: **[+about]** *We're very selective about what we let the children watch on TV.* 我們對於讓孩子們看哪些電視節目是經過慎重選擇的。**2** affecting or concerning the best or most suitable people or things from a larger group 有選擇的, 選擇性的, 擇優的: *the selective breeding of horses* 選擇性的馬種培育 —**selectively** *adv* —**selectivity** /səˏlɛkˋtɪvətɪ; sɪ̣ˌlekˈtɪvɪ̣ti/ *n* [U]

se·lec·tor /səˋlɛktɚ; sɪ̣ˈlektə/ *n* [C] **1** *BrE* a member of a committee that chooses the best people for something such as a sports team【英】〔運動隊〕選拔委員會委員 **2** *technical* a piece of equipment that helps you find the right thing, for example the correct GEAR¹ (1) in a car【術語】選擇器〔例如汽車的換擋器〕

se·le·ni·um /səˋlinɪəm; sɪ̣ˈliːniəm/ *n* [U] a poisonous ELEMENT (1) that is not a metal and is used in some electrical instruments to make them sensitive to light 硒〔一種非金屬有毒元素, 用於一些電子器材使其感光〕

self /sɛlf; self/ *n plural* **selves** /sɛlvz; selvz/ **1** [usually singular 一般用單數] the type of person you are, your character, your typical behaviour etc 自身, 本身, 自己, 自我: **sb's usual/normal self** *Sid was not his usual smiling self.* 西德不像往常那樣笑容滿面了。| **be/look/feel (like) your old self** (=be the way you usually are again, especially after having been ill, unhappy etc)〔尤指生病或不愉快等之後〕恢復老樣子 *Howard was beginning to feel like his old self again.* 霍華德又開始感到自己和以前一樣了。| **sb's true self** (=what someone is really like, rather than what they pretend to be like) 某人的真面目 **2** [U] **sb's sense of self** someone's consciousness of being a separate person, different from other people 某人的自我意識 **3 be a shadow/ghost of your former self** to not be at all like the cheerful, healthy, strong etc person that you used to be 判若兩人〔已不再像從前那樣開朗、健康、強壯了〕**4** [U] *spoken* your 2 3 own desires and satisfaction rather than anyone else's【口】私利, 私心, 自私: *It's always self, self, self! You never think of anyone else!* 你總是自己, 自己, 自己！從不考慮一下別人！**5** [U] a word written in business letters, on cheques etc meaning yourself 本人〔用於商業函件、支票等〕

3 **self-** /sɛlf; self/ *prefix* **1** by yourself or by itself 由[靠]自己的: *He's self-taught.* (=he taught himself) 他是自學成材。| *self-propelled* 自行驅動的 **2** of, to, with, for, or in yourself or itself (對)自身的; 為自己的; 獨自的: *a self-addressed envelope* (=which you address to yourself) 寫給自己收的信封 | *a self-portrait* (=a picture that you have drawn or painted of yourself) 自畫像 | *self-restraint* 自我克制

self-ab·ne·ga·tion /ˌ· ··ˈ··/ *n* [U] *formal* a lack of interest in your own needs and desires; ABNEGATION【正式】忘我, 克己

self-ab·sorbed /ˌ· ·ˈ·◂/ *adj* concerned only with yourself and the things that affect you 只顧自己的, 自我專注的: *I wouldn't worry – teenagers always seem totally self-absorbed.* 我不會擔心 —— 青少年總是顯得完全只顧自己。—**self-absorption** *n* [U]

self-ad·dressed /ˌ· ·ˈ·◂/ *adj* a self-addressed envelope has the sender's address on it so that it can be sent back to them〔信封〕寫上發信人自己地址的 —see also 另見 SAE, SASE

self-ad·he·sive /ˌ· ·ˈ··◂/ *adj* a self-adhesive envelope, BANDAGE etc has a sticky surface and does not need liquid or glue to make it stay closed〔信封等〕自粘的

self-ap·point·ed /ˌ· ·ˈ··◂/ *adj* thinking that you are the best person to lead other people or represent their wishes and opinions, especially when you are not 自命的, 自封的: *a self-appointed guardian of morality* 一個自封的道德衛士

self-as·sem·bly /ˌ· ·ˈ··◂/ *adj* sold as separate parts that you put together yourself at home〔由顧客〕自行組裝的

self-as·ser·tive /ˌ· ·ˈ··◂/ *adj* very confident and not shy about saying what you think or want 極自信的, 勇於説出自己的想法或要求的 —**self-assertiveness** *n* [U] —**self-assertion** *n* [U]

self-as·sur·ance /ˌ· ·ˈ··/ *n* [U] confidence and the belief that you are able to deal with people and problems easily 自信

self-as·sured /ˌ· ·ˈ·◂/ *adj* calm and confident about what you are doing 自信的: *His air of self-assured confidence made him a born leader.* 他那種充滿自信的氣派使他成為一個天生的領袖。—**self-assurance** *n* [U]

self-a·ware·ness /ˌ· ·ˈ··/ *n* [U] knowledge and understanding of yourself 自知, 自我了解, 自我意識: *Personal doubts often serve to focus self-awareness.* 自我懷疑往往能有助於自我了解。

self-ca·ter·ing /ˌ· ˈ···/ *adj BrE* a self-catering holiday is one where you stay in a place where you can cook your own food【英】〔在度假住宿處〕自己做飯的, 自辦伙食的 —**self-catering** *n* [U]

self-cen·tred *BrE*【英】, **self-centered** *AmE*【美】/ˌ· ˈ··◂/ *adj* paying so much attention to yourself that you do not notice what is happening to other people; SELFISH 自我中心的, 只顧自己的, 自私的 —**self-centredness**

self-con·fessed /ˌ· ·ˈ·◂/ *adj* [only before noun 僅用於名詞前] admitting that you have a particular quality, especially one that is bad 自己承認的, 自動坦白的〔尤指壞事〕: *a self-confessed television addict* 自認的電視迷

self-con·fi·dent /ˌ· ˈ···/ *adj* sure that you can do things well, that people like you, that you are attractive etc, and not shy or nervous in social situations 自信的, 對自己信心十足的 —**self-confidently** *adv* —**self-confidence** *n* [U]

self-con·gra·tu·la·tion /ˌ· ····ˈ··/ *n* [U] behaviour that shows in an annoying way that you think you have done very well at something 沾沾自喜, 洋洋自得 —**self-congratulatory** /ˌ· ···ˈ···/ *adj*: *a smug, self-congratulatory smile* 沾沾自喜的笑容

self-con·scious /ˌ· ˈ··/ *adj* **1** worried and embarrassed about what you look like or what other people think of you〔因顧慮他人看法而〕忸怩(作態)的, 害羞的, 不自然的: *I hate wearing glasses – they make me feel self-conscious.* 我討厭戴眼鏡 —— 它讓我感到很不自然。| [+about] *Jerry's pretty self-conscious about his weight.* 傑里對自己的體重頗為敏感。**2** self-conscious art, writing etc shows that the artist etc is too aware of how the public will react to them〔藝術作品等〕過於重視公眾反應的, 強調社會效果的: *self-conscious art-house movies* 太重視觀眾反應的藝術影片 —**self-consciously** *adv* —**self-consciousness** *n* [U]

self-con·tained /ˌ· ·ˈ·◂/ *adj* **1** something that is self-contained is complete in itself, and does not need other things or help from somewhere else to make it work 配套齊全的, 自成體系的: *a self-contained database package* 配套齊全的數據庫軟件包 **2** someone who is self-contained tends not to be friendly or show their feelings〔人〕不友善的, 感情不外露的 **3** *BrE* a self-contained FLAT² (1) has its own kitchen and bathroom【英】〔公寓〕有獨立廚房和浴室的

self-con·tra·dic·to·ry /ˌ· ··ˈ···/ *adj* containing two opposite statements or ideas that cannot both be true 自相矛盾的

self-con·trol /ˌ· ·ˈ·/ *n* [U] the ability to behave calmly and sensibly even when you feel very excited, angry etc 自制力, 控制情感的能力: *Greater self-control is the simple answer to most people's eating problems.* 更好的自我克制就是解決大多數人飲食問題的簡單答案。—**self-controlled** *adj*

self-de·cep·tion /ˌ· ·ˈ··/ *n* [U] the act of making yourself believe something is true when it is not 自欺: *He was unwilling to admit that the visionary idea was sheer self-deception.* 他不願意承認那種不切實際的想法純粹是自欺。—**self-deceptive** *adj*

self-de·feat·ing /ˌ· ·ˈ··◂/ *adj* causing exactly the same problems and difficulties that you are trying to prevent or deal with 適得其反的, 弄巧成拙的

self-de·fence *BrE*【英】, **self-defense** *AmE*【美】/ˌ· ·ˈ·/ *n* [U] **1** something you do to protect yourself or your property 自衛, 防身: **in self-defence** (=to protect yourself) 出於自衛 *I swear, I shot him in self-defense.* 我發誓, 我開槍打死他是出於自衛。**2** skills that you learn to protect yourself if you are attacked 自衛術, 防身本領: *a self-defence class for women* 婦女自衛訓練班

self-de·ni·al /ˌ· ·ˈ··/ *n* [U] the practice of not doing or having the things you enjoy, either because you cannot afford it, or for moral or religious reasons〔由於經濟、道德原因〕克己;〔宗教的〕苦行 —**self-denying** *adj*

self-dep·re·cat·ing /ˌ· ˈ····/ *adj* trying to make your own abilities or achievements seem unimportant 自我貶低的, 謙遜的: *self-deprecating humour* 自貶身價的幽默

self-des·truct /ˌsɛlf dɪˈstrʌkt; ˌself dɪˈstrʌkt◂/ *v* [I] if something such as a bomb self-destructs, it destroys itself, usually by exploding〔炸彈等〕自爆, 自毀 —**self-destruct** *adj*: *a self-destruct mechanism* 自爆裝置

self-des·truc·tion /ˌ· ·ˈ··/ *n* [U] the practice of deliberately doing things that are likely to seriously damage or kill you 自殘; 自毀: **be bent on self-destruction** (=be determined to damage or destroy yourself) 一心要傷害[毀滅]自己 —**self-destructive** *adj*: *self-destructive behaviour* 自毀行為

self-de·ter·min·a·tion /ˌ· ···ˈ··/ *n* [U] the right of the people of a particular country to govern themselves and to choose the type of government they will have〔民族〕自決權, 自決

self-dis·ci·pline /ˌ· ˈ···/ *n* [U] the ability to make yourself do the things you know you ought to do, without someone making you do them 自我約束, 自律: *I just* *wonder if I've got enough self-discipline to finish the course.* 我只是懷疑自己是否有足夠的自我約束能力去完成這個課程。—**self-disciplined** *adj*

self-doubt /ˌ· ˈ·/ *n* [U] the feeling that you and your abilities are not good enough 自我懷疑, 缺乏自信心

self-drive /ˌ· ˈ·◂/ *adj* [only before noun 僅用於名詞前] *BrE* a self-drive car is one that you have hired (=paid for) to drive yourself【英】〔汽車〕租來自己駕駛的

self-ed·u·cat·ed /ˌ· ˈ····◂/ *adj* having taught yourself by reading books etc, rather than learning things in school 自學〔而非由學校教育〕的, 自修的

self-ef·fac·ing /ˌ· ·ˈ··◂/ *adj* not wanting to attract attention to yourself or your achievements, especially because you are not socially confident 避免引人注目的, 不愛拋頭露面的: *He was loved for his skill and also his self-effacing modesty.* 他受到愛戴是由於他有技術, 還有他的謙遜。—**self-effacement** *n* [U]

self-em·ployed /ˌ· ·ˈ·◂/ *adj* working for yourself and not employed by a company 自己經營而不受雇於人的, 自雇的, 個體戶的: **go self-employed** (=become self-employed) 做個體戶 | **the self-employed** (=people who are self-employed) 自雇者, 個體戶 *pension plans for the self-employed* 為自雇者安排的養老金計劃 —**self-employment** *n* [U]

self-es·teem /ˌ· ·ˈ·/ *n* [U] the feeling that you are someone who deserves to be liked, respected, and admired 自尊(心): *Teachers need to help build up their students' sense of self-esteem.* 教師需要幫助學生建立起自尊心。| **low self-esteem** (=not much self-esteem) 不強的自尊心

self-ev·i·dent /ˌ· ˈ···◂/ *adj* clearly true and needing no more proof; OBVIOUS (1) 不證自明的, 顯而易見的: *self-evident truths* 不證自明的真理

self-ex·am·in·a·tion /ˌ· ···ˈ··/ *n* [U] **1** careful thought about whether your actions and your reasons for them are right or wrong 自省, 〔對自己行為等的〕反省 **2** the practice of checking parts of your body for early signs of some illnesses 自我檢查(身體)

self-ex·plan·a·to·ry /ˌ· ·ˈ····/ *adj* clear and easy to understand without needing further explanation 無須解釋的, 不解自明的: *Messages displayed as a result of user error are self-explanatory.* 使用者操作有誤時顯示出的信息一看即明。

self-ex·pres·sion /ˌ· ·ˈ··/ *n* [U] the expression of your feelings, thoughts, ideas etc, especially through activities such as painting, writing, or acting etc〔尤指通過繪畫、寫作、演戲等的〕自我表現: *The curriculum needs room for creative self-expression.* 這套課程需要給創造性的自我表現留有餘地。—**self-expressive** *adj*

self-ful·fil·ling /ˌ· ·ˈ··◂/ *adj* **self-fulfilling prophecy** a statement about what is likely to happen in the future that becomes true because you expected it to happen and therefore changed your behaviour 自我完成的預言〔指作出預言的人改變自己的行為因而使預言實現〕

self-gov·ern·ing /ˌ· ˈ···/ *adj* a country or organization that is self-governing is controlled by its own members rather than by someone from another country or organization〔國家、組織〕自治的, 自己管理的: *a self-governing trust* 自己管理的信託機構

self-gov·ern·ment /ˌ· ˈ···/ *n* [U] the government of a country by its own citizens, without people from other countries having any control or influence 自治, 獨立自主

self-help /ˌ· ˈ·/ *n* [U] the use of your own efforts to deal with your problems instead of depending on other people 自助, 自救: **self-help group** (=a group of people with a particular illness or problem who help each other)〔患同一種病或有相同問題者的〕自助小組

self-hood /ˈsɛlfhʊd; ˈselfhʊd/ *n* [U] *technical* the knowledge of yourself as an independent person separate from others【術語】自我意識; 個性

self-im·age /ˌ· ˈ··/ *n* [C] the idea you have of your own abilities, physical appearance, and character 自我形象〔指對自己的能力、外表、性格的自我感覺〕: *Bullies often have a poor self-image.* 恃強凌弱者往往自我形象不佳。

self-im·port·ance /ˌ· ·ˈ··/ *n* [U] the attitude that shows you think you are more important than other people 妄自尊大, 自負, 高傲

self-im·por·tant /ˌ· ·ˈ··◂/ *adj* behaving in a way that shows you think you are more important than other people 妄自尊大的, 自負的, 高傲的: *a self-important, pompous little man* 妄自尊大、自命不凡的小人物 —**self-importantly** *adv*

self-im·posed /ˌ· ·ˈ·◂/ *adj* a self-imposed rule, condition, responsibility etc is one that you have made yourself accept, and which no one has asked you to accept〔法規、條件等〕自願遵守的, 〔責任〕自己主動承擔的: *five years of self-imposed exile in Bolivia* 在波利維亞自我流放的五年

self-in·dul·gence /ˌ· ·ˈ··/ *n* [singular,U] the act of allowing yourself to have or do something that you enjoy but do not need 自我放縱, 放任自己: *My one self-indulgence is expensive coffee.* 我對自己的一個放縱就是喝昂貴的咖啡。

self-in·dul·gent /ˌ· ·ˈ··◂/ *adj* allowing yourself to have or do things you enjoy but do not need, especially if you do this too much 放縱自己的, 放任自己的 —**self-indulgently** *adv*

self-in·flict·ed /ˌ· ·ˈ··◂/ *adj* self-inflicted pain, problems, illnesses etc are those you have caused yourself〔痛苦、問題、疾病等〕自己造成的, 自己施加的: *It cannot be a self-inflicted blow, so it must be murder.* 這不可能是自己打的, 因此必然是謀殺。

self-in·terest /ˌ· ˈ··/ *n* [U] consideration only of what is best for you rather than other people 自私自利, 利己之心: *His offer was motivated solely by self-interest.* 他的提議僅僅是出於私利。—**self-interested** *adj*

self·ish /ˈsɛlfɪʃ; ˈselfɪʃ/ *adj* caring only about yourself and not about other people 自私的, 自私自利的: *How can you be so selfish?* 你怎能這樣自私? | *selfish motives* 自私的動機 —**selfishly** *adv* —**selfishness** *n* [U]

self-knowl·edge /ˌ· ˈ··/ *n* [U] an understanding of your own character, your reasons for doing things etc 自我認識, 自知(之明)

self·less /ˈsɛlflɪs; ˈselfləs/ *adj* caring about other people more than about yourself 忘我的, 無私的: *selfless devotion to their work* 他們對工作的無私奉獻 —**selflessly** *adv* —**selflessness** *n* [U]

self-made /ˌ· ˈ·◂/ *adj* a self-made man or woman has become successful and rich by their own efforts, and did not have advantages like money or a high social position when they started 靠個人奮鬥而成功的, 白手起家的: *a self-made millionaire* 白手起家的百萬富翁

self-o·pin·ion·at·ed /ˌ· ·ˈ····◂/ *adj* always believing that your own opinions and ideas are always right and that everyone else should always agree with you 自以為是的, 固執己見的

self-pit·y /ˌ· ˈ··/ *n* [U] the feeling of being sorry for yourself because you have been unlucky or you think people have treated you badly 自憐: *Stop wallowing in your own self-pity and do something about it!* 不要再自嘆自憐了, 做點實事吧! —**self-pitying** *adj*

self-por·trait /ˌ· ˈ··/ *n* [C] a drawing, painting, or description that you do of yourself 自畫像; 自我描述

self-pos·sessed /ˌ· ·ˈ·◂/ *adj* calm, confident, and in control of your feelings, even in difficult or unexpected situations〔在困難或意外情況下〕鎮定的, 沉着的, 泰然自若的 —**self-possession** *n* [U]

self-pres·er·va·tion /ˌ· ··ˈ··/ *n* [U] protection of yourself in a threatening or dangerous situation 自我保存, 自我保護: *the instinct for self-preservation* 自我保護的本能

self-pro·claimed /ˌ· ·ˈ·◂/ *adj* having given yourself a position or title without the approval of other people 自

S

稱的, 自封的: *a self-proclaimed champion of the working class* 自封的工人階級鬥士

self-rais·ing flour /ˌ· ·· ˈ·/ *n* [U] *BrE* a type of flour that contains BAKING POWDER【英】〔摻有發酵粉的〕自發麵粉; SELF-RISING FLOUR *AmE*【美】

self-reg·u·la·to·ry /ˌ· ˈ····/ also 又作 **self-regulating** /ˌ·ˈ····/ *adj* a self-regulatory system, industry, or organization is one that controls itself, rather than having an independent organization or laws to make sure that rules are obeyed〔系統、工業或組織〕自我調節的, 自動控制的 —**self-regulation** /ˌ· ··ˈ··/ *n* [U]

self-re·li·ant /ˌ· ·ˈ··◂/ *adj* able to decide what to do by yourself, without depending on the help or advice of other people 依靠自己的, 自力更生的: *In his famous essay, Emerson called on the US to be self-reliant.* 埃默生在他那篇著名的文章中號召美國(人)要自力更生。—**self-reliance** *n* [U]

self-re·spect /ˌ· ·ˈ·/ *n* [U] a feeling of being happy about what you are, what you do, and what you believe in 自尊, 自重: *It's difficult to keep your self-respect when you have been unemployed for a long time.* 你在長時間失業之後, 就很難保持自尊了。

self-re·spect·ing /ˌ· ·ˈ··◂/ *adj* [only before noun 僅用於名詞前] having respect for yourself and your abilities and beliefs 自尊的, 自重的, 有自尊心的: **no self-respecting ... would do sth** *No self-respecting actor would appear in a porn movie.* 自重的演員是不演色情電影的。

self-re·straint /ˌ· ·ˈ·/ *n* [U] the ability not to do or say something you very much want to, because you know this is more sensible 自我克制, 自我約束: **exercise self-restraint** *Police officers must learn to exercise self-restraint.* 警察必須學會自我克制。

self-right·eous /ˌ· ˈ··◂/ *adj* proudly sure that your beliefs, attitudes, and morals are good and right, in a way that annoys other people 自以為正直善良的; 自以為是的: *That's the most unfair, self-righteous statement I've ever heard!* 那是我聽過最不公正、最自以為是的聲明。—**self-righteously** *adv* —**self-righteousness** *n* [U]

self-ris·ing flour /ˌ· ·· ˈ·/ *n* [U] *AmE* a type of flour that contains BAKING POWDER【美】〔摻有發酵粉的〕自發麵粉; SELF-RAISING FLOUR *BrE*【英】

self-rule /ˌ· ˈ·/ *n* [U] the government of a country or part of a country by its own citizens 自治

self-sac·ri·fice /ˌ· ˈ···/ *n* [U] the act of doing without things you want, need, or care about in order to help someone else 自我犧牲, 獻身 —**self-sacrificing** *adj*

self-same /ˈ· ·/ *adj* [only before noun 僅用於名詞前] *literary* exactly the same【文】完全相同的, 同一的: *two great victories on the self-same day* 同一天內的兩大勝利

self-sat·is·fied /ˌ· ˈ···/ *adj* too pleased with yourself and what you have done 沾沾自喜的, 自鳴得意的: *He seemed as smug and self-satisfied as his father.* 他看來和他父親一樣自鳴得意。—**self-satisfaction** /ˌ· ··ˈ··/ *n* [U]

self-seek·ing /ˌ· ˈ··◂/ *adj* doing things only because they will give you an advantage that other people do not have 追逐私利的, 為自己打算的: *a self-seeking politician* 追求私利的政客

self-serv·ice /ˌ· ˈ··◂/ *adj* a self-service restaurant, shop etc is one in which you get things for yourself and then pay for them 自助(式)的 —**self-service** *n* [U]

self-start·er /ˌ· ˈ··/ *n* [C] someone who is able to work successfully on their own without needing other people's help or a lot of instructions 有獨立工作能力的人, 工作主動積極的人

self-styled /ˈ· ·/ *adj* [only before noun 僅用於名詞前] having given yourself a title or position without having a right to it 自封的, 自稱的: *a self-styled professor* 自封的教授

self-suf·fi·cient /ˌ· ·ˈ··◂/ *adj* providing all the things you need without help from outside 自給自足的: *In those days the farm was largely self-sufficient.* 在那些日子裡, 這個農場基本上能自給自足。—**self-sufficiency** *n* [U]

self-sup·port·ing /ˌ· ·ˈ··◂/ *adj* able to earn enough money to support yourself 自食其力的, 自立的: *The business will soon become self-supporting.* 這家公司很快就能自力經營了。

self-taught /ˌ· ˈ·◂/ *adj* having learned a skill or subject by yourself, rather than in a school 自學而成的, 自學成材的: *a self-taught accountant* 自學成材的會計

self-willed /ˌ· ˈ·◂/ *adj* very determined to do what you want, even when this is unreasonable 任性的, 固執的, 執拗的: *a wild and self-willed child* 野蠻任性的小孩 —**self-will** *n* [U]

self-wind·ing /ˌsɛlf ˈwaɪndɪŋ; ˌself ˈwaɪndɪŋ◂/ *adj* a self-winding watch is one that you do not have to WIND[2] (2) to make it work〔手錶〕自動上發條的

sell[1] /sɛl; sel/ *v past tense and past participle* **sold** /sold; səʊld/ 1 1

1 ►GIVE STH FOR MONEY 把某物賣錢◄ [I,T] to give something to someone in exchange for money 賣, 銷售, 把…賣給…: *If you offer them another thousand, I think they'll sell.* 如果你再給他們一千元錢, 我想他們會賣的。| **sell sth for £100/$50/30p etc** *Toni's selling her car for £700.* 冬妮準備以 700 英鎊賣掉她的汽車。| **sell sb sth/sell sth to sb** *I'm not selling you my shares!* 我是不會把我的股份賣給你的! | *The vase was sold to an American buyer.* 那個花瓶賣給了一位美國買主。| **sell sth** *Now he regrets selling all his old records.* 他現在後悔賣掉了所有的舊唱片。| **sell sth at a profit/loss** (=making or losing money on a sale) 出售某物賺錢/以虧損出售 —opposite 反義詞 BUY

2 ►MAKE STH AVAILABLE 有現貨出售◄ [T] to offer something for people to buy 有…出售[賣]: *Do you sell cigarettes?* 你們有香煙賣嗎? | *a job selling advertising space* 推銷廣告版面的工作

3 sell at/for £100/$50/30p to be offered for sale at a particular price 以 100 英鎊/50 美元/30 便士出售: *Smoke alarms sell for as little as five pounds.* 煙霧警報器最低價僅五英鎊。

4 ►MAKE STH ATTRACTIVE 使某物吸引人◄ [T] to make people want to buy something 使〔某物〕吸引顧客, 使〔某物〕暢銷: *Scandal sells newspapers.* 醜聞可使報紙暢銷。| **sell sb sth/sell sth to sb** (=persuade someone that they want to buy something) 向某人推銷某物 *You have to go out and really sell the stuff, Leo.* 你得走出去真正推銷這東西才行, 利奧!

5 ►SELL A LOT 銷量大◄ [I] to be bought by people in large numbers 有銷路, 大量售出: *Tickets for the concert just aren't selling.* 這場音樂會的門票沒有銷路。| **sell well/badly** *Anti-age creams always sell well.* 抗衰老霜總是暢銷的。

6 sell like hot cakes to sell quickly and in large amounts 非常暢銷, 搶手

7 ►IDEA/PLAN 主意/計劃◄ [I,T] to try to make someone accept a new idea or plan, or to become accepted〔意見或計劃〕使(人)接受, 被接受: *It's all right for Washington, but will it sell in small-town America?* 這在華盛頓沒有問題, 但在美國小城鎮能被接受嗎? | **sell sb sth/sell sth to sb** *Just try selling taxes to the voters.* 試試去說服選民接受稅收政策吧。| **be sold on (doing) sth/be sold on the idea** (=think an idea or plan is very good) 認為(做)某事極好/認為主意不錯 *Joe's completely sold on the concept – he thinks it's brilliant.* 喬完全接受了這個思想, 認為它非常棒。

8 sell yourself a) to be able to make yourself seem impressive to other people 自我宣傳, 自薦: *If you want a promotion, you've got to sell yourself better.* 你如果想晉升, 就得更好地推銷自己。**b)** to do something that is against your principles in exchange for money or some other advantage 出賣自己(的原則)

9 sell sb/sth short to not give someone or something the praise, attention, or reward that they deserve 對某人/某事評價太低: *You're selling yourself short – tell*

them about all your qualifications. 你委屈自己了——把你所有的資歷都告訴他們。

10 sell your body to have sex with someone for money 賣淫, 出賣肉體

11 sell your soul (to the devil) to do something bad in exchange for money, power etc 出賣靈魂〔以換取金錢、權力等〕

12 sell sb down the river to do something that harms a group of people who trusted you to help them, in order to gain money or power for yourself〔為個人利益或權力〕出賣[背叛]某一羣人

13 sell your support/vote *AmE* to give your support or vote to the person who will give you the biggest financial advantage【美】誰給錢多就支持誰/投誰的票

sell off *phr v* [T] **1 sell** sth ↔ **off** to try to get rid of things that no one seems to want to buy by selling them cheaply 廉價處理掉, 削價賣掉〔某物〕: *Looks like they're trying to sell off a bunch of junk.* 看來他們好像在設法廉價處理掉一批廢舊雜物。**2** to sell something because you need the money〔因需要錢而〕把…賣掉: *After the war we were forced to sell off part of the farm.* 戰爭結束後, 我們被迫賣掉農場的一部分。**3** to sell all or part of an industry or company 賣掉〔部分或整個企業或公司〕

sell out *phr v* **1 be/have sold out** if a shop sells out of something, it has no more of that particular thing left to sell〔貨物〕已賣完: *Sorry, we're sold out.* 對不起, 全賣完了。| **have sold out of sth** *We've completely sold out of those shirts in your size, sir.* 先生, 您那個尺碼的襯衫已經全部賣完了。**2** [I] if a product, tickets, places at a concert etc sell out, they are all sold and there are none left〔產品、入場券等〕賣光, 售完: *Wow! Those scarves sold out fast.* 哇! 那些圍巾很快就銷售一空。| **be sold out** *Tonight's performance is completely sold out.* 今晚的演出門票全賣光了。**3** [I,T] to not keep to your beliefs or principles in order to get more money, a comfortable life, or a political advantage〔為了錢財或政治利益〕出賣原則, 放棄信仰: *ex-hippies who've sold out and become respectable businessmen* 放棄了原有宗旨而成了體面商人的前嬉皮士 **4** [I+to] to sell your business or your share in a business 賣掉生意, 出售股份: *Wyman says he'll sell out if business doesn't pick up.* 懷曼說如果生意沒有起色, 他就要把商店賣掉。

sell up [I,T] *especially BrE* to sell most of what you own, especially your house or your business【尤英】賣掉(絕大部分財產)〔尤指住房或企業〕: *Liz decided to sell up and move abroad.* 莉茲決定賣掉房子移居外國。

sell² *n* [singular] *BrE informal* something you have been tricked into buying or doing that disappoints you【英, 非正式】受騙所購之物; 受騙所做之事: *What a sell! It's only plastic that looks like wood.* 真是騙人! 這只是一件看似木製的塑料品。—see also 另見 HARD SELL, SOFT SELL

sell-by date /ˈ· · ˌ·/ *n* [C] *BrE*【英】**1** the date stamped on a food product, after which it should not be sold〔印在食品包裝上的〕銷售期限, 售出的截止日期; EXPIRATION DATE *AmE*【美】**2 be past its sell-by date** *informal* if an idea, method, system etc is past its sell-by date it has become no longer useful or interesting【非正式】〔思想、方法、體系等〕過時, 無用; 不再受關注

sell·er /ˋsɛlɚ; ˈselə/ *n* [C] **1** someone who sells something 賣方, 賣者 —opposite 反義詞 BUYER **2 good/bad etc seller** a product that sells well, badly etc 暢銷/滯銷品等 —see also 另見 BEST-SELLER

seller's mar·ket /ˌ·· ˈ··/ *n* [singular] a situation in which there is not much of a particular product available for sale, so prices tend to be high 賣方市場〔某種商品因供不應求而價格偏高, 因而對賣方有利的市場狀況〕—opposite 反義詞 BUYER'S MARKET

sell·ing /ˋsɛlɪŋ; ˈselɪŋ/ *n* [U] the job and skill of persuading people to buy things; sales (SALE (5b)) 推銷(術): *a career in selling* 推銷工作

selling point /ˈ·· ·/ *n* [C] something about a product that will make people want to buy it〔吸引顧客的〕商品特色, 銷售特色, 賣點: *The computer's two main selling points are that it's cheap and portable.* 這種電腦的兩大賣點是價格便宜和便於攜帶。

selling price /ˈ·· ·/ *n* [C] the price at which something is actually sold〔實際的〕售價 —compare 比較 **asking price** (ASK (8))

sell-off /ˈ· ·/ *n* [C] *BrE* the act of selling an industry, especially one that the government owns, to private buyers【英】〔尤指政府所有的〕工業企業向私人的出售, 私有化: *fears that services will be cut after the sell-off* 對私有化之後公共服務將會削減的擔心

Sel·lo·tape /ˋsɛləˌtep; ˈseləteɪp/ *n* [U] *BrE trademark* sticky thin clear material in a long narrow length that is used for sticking things together【英, 商標】〔用於黏貼東西的〕透明膠帶; SCOTCH TAPE *AmE*【美】: *a roll of sellotape* 一卷透明膠帶 —**sellotape** *v* [T]

sell-out /ˈ· ·/ *n* [singular] **1** a performance, sports game etc, for which all the tickets have been sold〔演出、體育比賽等〕爆滿, 滿座 **2** *informal* a situation in which someone has not done what they promised to do or were expected to do by the people who trusted them【非正式】違背諾言; 出賣, 背叛: *a political sell-out* 政治背叛

sel·vage, selvedge /ˋsɛlvɪdʒ; ˈselvɪdʒ/ *n* [C] the edge of a piece of cloth, made strong in such a way that the threads will not come out〔用於防脫線的布的〕織邊

selves /sɛlvz; selvz/ the plural of SELF

se·man·tic /səˋmæntɪk; sɪˈmæntɪk/ *adj* connected with the meanings of words 語義的 —**semantically** /-klɪ; -kli/ *adv*: *"Purchase" and "buy" are semantically the same.* (=they mean the same thing) purchase 和 buy 語義相同。

se·man·tics /səˋmæntɪks; sɪˈmæntɪks/ *n* [U] **1** the study of the meaning of words and other parts of language 語義學 **2 the semantics of** *technical* the meaning of a word or piece of writing【術語】〔詞或文章〕的語義

sem·a·phore /ˋsɛməˌfor; ˈseməfɔː/ *n* [U] a system of sending messages using two flags, that you hold in different positions to represent letters and numbers 旗語

sem·blance /ˋsɛmbləns; ˈsembləns/ *n* **1 semblance of** a condition or quality that is similar to another one〔情況或性質的〕相似, 類似: *The herbs slow the heart and give the body a semblance of death.* 這些草藥降低心率, 使身體處於某種假死狀態。**2** a condition or quality that is at least slightly like another one 稍微相似, 有點類似: **some semblance of** *The troops were called in to bring some semblance of order to the riot-torn city.* 這些部隊被調來維持這個騷亂城市的起碼秩序。

se·men /ˋsimən; ˈsiːmən/ *n* [U] the liquid produced by the male sex organs in humans and animals that contains SPERM 精液

se·mes·ter /səˋmɛstɚ; sɪˈmestə/ *n* [C] one of the two periods into which a year at high schools and universities is divided, especially in the US〔尤指美國中學和大學的〕一學期, 半學年 —compare 比較 TERM¹ (9)

sem·i /ˋsɛmɪ; ˈsemi/ *plural* **semis** *n* [C] **1** *BrE informal* a house that is joined to the one next to it to form a pair【英, 非正式】〔一側與他屋相連的〕聯式房屋, 半獨立式住宅; DUPLEX (1) *AmE*【美】: *a two-bedroomed semi* 一所兩臥室的聯式住宅 **2** *informal* a SEMIFINAL【非正式】半決賽 **3** *AmE* a very large heavy vehicle consisting of two connected parts, that carries goods over long distances【美】〔長途運輸的〕鉸接式重型卡車; JUGGERNAUT (1) *BrE*【英】

semi- /sɛmɪ; semi/ *prefix* **1** exactly half (一)半: *a semicircle* 半圓 **2** partly but not completely 部分(地): *in the semidarkness* 在半明半暗之中 | *a semi-invalid* 半病弱者 | *semi-literate people* 半文盲 **3** happening, appearing etc twice in a particular period〔在一段時間內〕出現兩次的: *a semi-weekly visit* 一週兩次的訪問 | *a semi-annual publication* 半年一期的出版物 —compare 比較 BI-

S

semi·au·to·mat·ic /ˌ·· ··ˈ··◂/ *adj* a semi-automatic weapon moves each new bullet into position ready for you to fire, so that you can fire the next shot very quickly〔武器〕半自動的 —**semi-automatic** *n* [C]

sem·i·breve /ˋsɛməˌbriv; ˈsemibriːv/ *n* [C] *BrE* a musical note which continues as long as two MINIMS【英】全音符; WHOLE NOTE *AmE*【美】—see picture at 參見 MUSIC 圖

sem·i·cir·cle /ˋsɛməˌsɝk]; ˈsemiˌsɜːkəl/ *n* [C] **1** half a circle 半圓 —see picture at 參見 SHAPE[1] 圖 **2** a group arranged in a curved line, as if on the edge of half a circle 半圓形排列: *Get the kids to sit in a semicircle.* 叫孩子們圍成半圓形坐。—**semicircular** /ˌsɛməˋsɝkjələ; ˌsemiˈsɜːkjɜlə◂/ *adj*

sem·i·co·lon /ˋsɛməˌkolən; ˌsemiˈkəʊlən/ *n* [C] a PUNCTUATION MARK (;) used to separate independent parts of a sentence or list 分號〔;〕—see picture at 參見 PUNCTUATION MARK 圖

sem·i·con·duc·tor /ˌsɛməkənˋdʌktə; ˌsemikənˈdʌktə/ *n* [C] a substance, such as SILICON, that allows some electric currents to pass through it and is used in electronic equipment for this purpose 半導體 —compare 比較 CONDUCTOR (3)

sem·i·de·tached /ˌsɛmədɪˋtætʃt; ˌsemidɪˈtætʃt◂/ *adj BrE* a semi-detached house is joined to another house by one shared wall【英】〔房屋〕一側與他屋相連的, 半獨立式的 —compare 比較 DETACHED (2), TERRACED HOUSE —see picture on page A4 參見 A4 頁圖

sem·i·fi·nal /ˌsɛməˋfaɪnl; ˌsemiˈfaɪnl◂/ *n* [C] one of a pair of sports games, whose winners then compete against each other to decide who wins the whole competition 半決賽: *the world chess championship semifinal at Linares, Spain* 在西班牙利納雷斯舉行的世界國際象棋錦標賽半決賽

sem·i·fi·nal·ist /ˌsɛməˋfaɪnəlɪst; ˌsemiˈfaɪnəl-ɜst/ *n* [C] a person or team that competes in a semifinal 參加半決賽的選手[隊]

sem·i·nal /ˋsɛmən]; ˈsemɜnəl/ *adj* **1** *formal* a seminal book, piece of music etc is new and important, and influences the way in which literature, music etc develops in the future【正式】〔書、樂曲等〕開創性的, 有重大影響的: *Barry Commoner's seminal 1970s book on ecology* 巴里·康芒納 20 世紀 70 年代關於生態學的開創性著作 **2** [only before noun 僅用於名詞前] *technical* producing or containing SEMEN【術語】(產生或含有) 精液的: *seminal fluid* 精液

sem·i·nar /ˋsɛməˌnɑr; ˈsemɜnɑː/ *n* [C] a class in which a small group of students meet to study or talk about a particular subject〔學生分組對專題進行討論的〕研討班: *a Shakespeare seminar* 莎士比亞研討班

sem·i·na·ry /ˋsɛməˌnɛrɪ; ˈsemɜnəri/ *n* [C] **1** a college for training priests or ministers〔培養神父、牧師的〕神學院 **2** *old-fashioned* a school【過時】學校

sem·i·ot·ics /ˌsɛmɪˋɑtɪks; ˌsemiˈɒtɪks/ also 又作 **sem·i·ol·o·gy** /ˌsɛmɪˋɑlədʒɪ; ˌsemiˈɒlədʒi/ *n* [U] *technical* the way in which people communicate through signs and images, or the study of this【術語】符號學 —**semiotician** /ˌsɛmɪəˋtɪʃən; ˌsemiəˈtɪʃən/, **semiologist** /ˌsɛmɪˋɑlədʒɪst; ˌsemiˈɒlədʒɜst/ *n* [C] —**semiotic** *adj*

sem·i·pre·cious /ˌsɛməˋprɛʃəs; ˌsemiˈpreʃəs◂/ *adj* a semiprecious jewel or stone is valuable, but not as valuable as a DIAMOND, RUBY etc〔寶石〕次貴重的,〔僅次於鑽石或紅寶石等的〕半寶石的

semi-pro·fes·sion·al /ˌ·· ·ˈ···◂/ *adj* **semi-professional player/footballer/musician etc** someone who is paid for doing a sport etc, but does not do it as their main job 半職業的球員/足球員/音樂家等

sem·i·qua·ver /ˋsɛməˌkwevə; ˈsemiˌkweɪvə/ *n* [C] *BrE* a musical note which continues for a sixteenth of the length of a SEMIBREVE【英】十六分音符; SIXTEENTH NOTE *AmE*【美】—see picture at 參見 MUSIC 圖

semi-skilled /ˌ·· ˈ·◂/ *adj* **a)** a semi-skilled worker is not highly skilled or professional, but needs some skills for the job they are doing〔工人〕半熟練的 **b)** a semi-skilled job is one that you need some skills to do, but you do not have to be highly skilled〔工作〕需半熟練工人做的

semi-skimmed /ˌ·· ˈ·◂/ *n* [U] *BrE* milk that has had about half the fat removed【英】〔牛奶〕半脱脂的; TWO PERCENT MILK *AmE*【美】

Se·mite /ˋsɛmaɪt; ˈsiːmaɪt/ *n* [C] someone who belongs to the race of people that includes Jews, Arabs and, in ancient times, Babylonians, Assyrians etc 閃米特人〔包括猶太人、阿拉伯人、古巴比倫人和古亞述人等〕—see also 另見 ANTI-SEMITISM

Se·mit·ic /səˋmɪtɪk; sɜˈmɪtɪk/ *adj* **1 a)** belonging to the race of people that includes Jews, Arabs and, in ancient times, Babylonians, Assyrians etc 閃米特人的〔包括猶太人、阿拉伯人、古巴比倫人和古亞述人等〕 **b)** belonging to or connected with any of the languages of these people 閃米特語的 **2** another word for JEWISH 猶太人的

sem·i·tone /ˋsɛməˌton; ˈsemitəʊn/ *n* [C] *BrE* the difference in PITCH[1] (3) between any two notes that are next to each other on a piano【英】半音; HALF STEP *AmE*【美】

sem·i·trop·i·cal /ˌsɛməˋtrɑpɪk]; ˌsemiˈtrɒpɪkəl◂/ *adj* SUBTROPICAL 副熱帶的, 亞熱帶的

semi-vo·wel /ˈ·· ˌ·/ *n* [C] *technical* a sound made in speech that sounds like a vowel, but is in fact a consonant, like /w/【術語】半元音〈如 /w/〉

sem·i·week·ly /ˌsɛməˋwiklɪ; ˌsemiˈwiːkli◂/ *adj, adv* appearing or happening twice a week 每週兩次的[地]: *a semiweekly paper* 每週出版兩次的報紙

sem·o·li·na /ˌsɛməˋlinə; ˌseməˈliːnə/ *n* [U] **1** grains of crushed wheat, used especially in making sweet dishes and PASTA〔尤指用於做甜食和意大利麵食的〕粗粒麵粉 **2** a sweet dish made with these grains and milk 用粗粒麵粉和牛奶做的甜食

Sem·tex /ˋsɛmtɛks; ˈsemteks/ *n* [U] *trademark* a powerful explosive often used illegally to make bombs【商標】森泰克斯塑膠炸藥〔一種烈性炸藥〕

sen·ate, Senate /ˋsɛnɪt; ˈsenɜt/ *n* **1** [singular] one of the two parts of the government that has the power to make laws, in countries such as the US, Australia, and France, which is smaller than the other part but has a higher rank〔美國、澳大利亞、法國等國家的〕參議院: *The Senate may veto this year's spending bill.* 參議院可能否決今年的開支議案。**2** [singular] the highest level of government in ancient Rome〔古羅馬政府最高級別的〕元老院 **3** [C] the governing council at some universities〔某些大學的〕理事會, 評議會

sen·a·tor, Senator /ˋsɛnətə; ˈsenətə/ *n* [C] a member of a senate 參議員: *Senator Kennedy* 甘迺迪參議員 —**senatorial** /ˌsɛnəˋtɔrɪəl; ˌsenəˈtɔːriəl◂/ *adj*: *senatorial duties* 參議員的職責

send /sɛnd; send/ *v past tense and past participle* **sent** /sɛnt; sent/ 

1 ►BY POST/RADIO ETC 通過郵政/無線電等◄ [T] to arrange for something to go or be taken to another place, especially by post 送出, 發出,〔尤指用郵政〕寄出: **send sb a letter/message/card** *Honestly, I get tired of sending Christmas cards.* 老實說, 我對寄聖誕賀卡已經厭倦了。| **send sth to** *Send your bill to the above address.* 把你的賬單寄到上述地址。| **send sth by post/sea/air etc** *It will get there quicker if you send it by airmail.* 如果你寄航空, 它將較快到達。| **send a letter/message/card** *I sent her a message to say that I'd be late.* 我給她捎了口信說我會遲到。| **send a signal** *Radio signals were sent into deep space.* 無線電信號被發送到遙遠的太空。| **send sth back/up/over etc** *I've ordered some coffee to be sent up here.* 我已經叫了一些咖啡並要他們送到這裡來。

2 ►SEND SB TO DO STH 派某人做某事◄ [T] to tell someone to go somewhere, usually so that they can do something for you there 派〔某人〕往〔某處〕, 派遣: *Who* sent you? 誰派你來的? | Richard couldn't come so he sent his sister instead. 理查德不能來, 所以派了妹妹來代替他。| **send sb to** The United Nations will send troops to the region. 聯合國將派遣部隊到該地區。| **send sb around/over/home etc** At noon the principal sent everyone home. 中午校長把大家都打發回家了。| **send sb to do sth** I sent Jean to go get some more butter. 我叫吉恩去再買些黃油來。

3 ►SEND SB TO STAY SOMEWHERE 派送某人到某地停留◄ [T always+adv/prep] to arrange for someone to go somewhere and spend some time there 安排〔某人〕到〔某地〕, 將〔某人〕送往〔某地〕: **send sb to** *I'd never send my kids to boarding school.* 我永遠也不會把孩子送去上寄宿學校。| *People get sent to jail for doing stuff like that!* 幹那種勾當的人是要坐牢的! | **send sb on sth** *We want to send you on a short management course.* 我們想送你去參加短期管理課程。

4 send your love/regards/best wishes etc to ask someone to give your greetings, good wishes etc to someone else 請某人代為致意/問候/致良好祝願等: *Mother sends her love.* 母親向你問好。

5 ►AFFECT SOMEONE 影響某人◄ [T] to affect someone's feelings or condition 影響〔某人的感情或狀態〕: **send sb to/into** *His boring speeches always send me to sleep.* 他那枯燥乏味的講話總是使我昏昏入睡。| **send sb** (=make them feel extremely happy) 使人感到非常快樂 *Oh, doesn't his music just send you?* 啊, 他的音樂不是令你心曠神怡嗎?

6 send sb/sth flying/sprawling/reeling etc to make someone or something move quickly through the air 使某人/某物亂飛/趴倒在地/搖晃等: *The explosion sent glass flying everywhere.* 爆炸使玻璃到處亂飛。

7 send out/up/forth etc to make something come out of itself 〔從自身〕發出等: *The fire was sending up thick clouds of smoke.* 大火中升起一股股濃煙。

8 send word to tell someone something by sending them a letter or message 捎信, 傳話: **send word (to sb) that** *Somebody should send word that Rhoda's ill.* 應該找人將羅達生病的消息讓大家知道。| **send word through sb** *Send word through Davies that we need more supplies.* 讓戴維斯捎信説我們需要更多補給。

9 send sb packing also 又作 **send sb about their business** *informal*【非正式】to tell someone who is not wanted that they must leave at once 叫某人立即離開, 攆走某人

send away *phr v* **1** [T **send** sb ↔ **away**] to send someone to another place 把〔某人〕送往〔某處〕, 送走: *I was sent away to school at the age of seven.* 我七歲時就被送往別處上學。**2 send away for sth** to order something to be sent to you by post 郵購某物, 函索某物: *Send away for your free poster.* 請來信索取免費招貼畫。

send sth ↔ **back** *phr v* to return something to where it came from 送回, 退還; 發送回來: *The steak was completely raw so I sent it straight back.* 牛排完全是生的, 所以我立刻把它退了回去。

send down *phr v* **1** [T **send** sth ↔ **down**] to make something lose value 使〔價格〕下降: *Reports of the company's bad trading figures sent its share prices down.* 關於該公司營業額差的報道使它的股票價格下跌了。**2** [T **send** sb **down**] *BrE informal* to send someone to prison【英, 非正式】送〔某人〕進監獄: *Do you think he'll be sent down for it?* 你認為他會因為這件事坐牢嗎? **3 be sent down** *BrE* to be told to leave a university because of bad behaviour【英】〔大學生因行為不檢而〕被開除, 被勒令退學

send for sb/sth *phr v* [T] **1** to ask or order someone to come to you by sending them a message 派人去叫[請]〔某人〕來: *Should I send for a doctor?* 要我派人去請醫生嗎? | **send for help** *Quick – go send for help.* 快——去請人來幫幫忙。**2** to ask or order that something be brought or sent to you 索取: *We'll have to send for the spare parts.* 我們必須派人把備用零件送來。

send sth ↔ **in** *phr v* [T] **1** to send something, usually by post, to a place where it can be dealt with 寄去,〔郵寄〕遞交: *I sent in a couple of job applications last week.* 上星期我寄出了幾封求職信。**2** to send soldiers, police etc somewhere to deal with a very difficult or dangerous situation 派遣〔軍隊、警察等〕: *It's time to send in the troops.* 是應當出動軍隊的時候了。

send off *phr v* **1** [T **send** sth ↔ **off**] to send something somewhere by post 郵寄出〔某物〕, 發送: *I sent off the check this morning.* 我今天早上把支票寄出去了。**2 send off for sth** to order something to be sent to you by post 函購某物; 函索某物: *I'd better send off for an application form.* 我還是寄信去要份申請表吧。**3** [T **send** sb ↔ **off**] to send someone to another place 把〔某人〕送往〔另一地方〕: *We sent the kids off to their grandparents this morning.* 我們今天上午把孩子送到他們的 (外) 祖父母那裡去了。**4** [T **send** sb ↔ **off**] *BrE* to order a sports player to leave the field because they have broken the rules【英】罰〔犯規的運動員〕出場 —see picture on page A23 參見A23 頁圖

send sth ↔ **on** *phr v* [T] **1** *especially BrE* to send someone's letters or possessions to their new address from their old address【尤英】〔從舊地址〕把〔信件等〕轉寄到新地址; FORWARD[3] (1) *AmE*【美】: *My flatmate said she'd send on all my post.* 曾和我合租公寓的朋友説她會把我的全部郵件轉寄給我。**2** to send something that has been received to another place so that it can be dealt with 把〔收到的東西〕轉送〔到另一處〕: *The data is then sent on to the Census Bureau.* 那些數據資料接着被轉送到統計局。

send out *phr v* **1** [T **send** sth/sb ↔ **out**] to send something from a central point to various other places 發出〔某物〕; 送出〔某人〕: *Make sure you send out the invitations in good time.* 你務必及時把邀請信發出去。| *Search parties were sent out to look for survivors.* 搜索隊被派出去尋找倖存者。**2** [**send** sth ↔ **out**] to broadcast or produce a signal, light, sound etc 廣播[發射]〔信號等〕: *The ship is sending out an SOS signal.* 那艘船正在發出呼救信號。**3 send out for sth** to ask a restaurant or food shop to deliver food to you at home or at work 要餐館[食品店]送食物上門: *Halfway through the meeting we sent out for sandwiches.* 會議開到一半時我們叫餐館送三明治來。

send up *phr v* [T **send** sth/sb ↔ **up**] **1** to make something increase in value 使〔價格〕上升: *The shortage is bound to send prices up.* 供應短缺必將導致價格上漲。**2** *BrE informal* to show how silly something is by copying it in a very funny way【英, 非正式】〔通過滑稽模仿〕使顯得可笑, 取笑, 嘲弄: *The film sends up all those Hollywood disaster movies.* 這部電影嘲笑荷里活所有那些災難片。

send·er /ˈsɛndɚ; ˈsendə/ *n* [C] the person who sent a particular letter, package, message etc 〔信件、包裹、信息等的〕發送者, 寄件人: **Return to Sender** (=stamped on a parcel when it could not reach the person it was sent to) 退回寄件人〔印在無法投遞的郵件上〕

send-off /ˈ· ·/ *n* [C] *informal* a party or other occasion when people gather together to say goodbye to someone who is leaving【非正式】歡送會, 送別: **give sb a good send-off** *We gave her a really good send-off.* 我們非常熱情地歡送她。

send-up /ˈ· ·/ *n* [C] *BrE informal* the act of copying someone or something in a way that makes them look funny or silly【英, 非正式】嘲弄性模仿: **[+of]** *a brilliant send-up of Clint Eastwood* 對奇連依士活唯妙唯肖的諷刺性模仿

se·nes·cent /səˈnɛsn̩t; sɪˈnesənt/ *adj technical* becoming old and showing the effects of getting older【術語】變老的, 衰老的: *a senescent industry* 衰落的行業 —**senescence** *n* [U]

se·nile /ˈsinaɪl; ˈsiːnaɪl/ *adj not technical* mentally confused or behaving strangely, because of old age【非術

語】因年老而糊塗的，老邁的：*The poor old lady's getting senile: she hardly recognizes me now.* 那位可憐的老太太開始老糊塗了：她現在幾乎不認識我了。—**senility** /sə`nɪlətɪ; sɪ'nɪləti/ *n* [U]

senile de·men·tia /,·· ·'··/ *n* [U] a medical condition that can affect the minds of old people 老年性痴呆（症）

Se·ni·or /`sinjɚ; 'siːniə/ written abbreviation 縮寫為 **Sr.** *AmE*【美】, **Snr** *BrE*【英】*adj* [only after noun 僅用於名詞後] *especially AmE* used after a man's name to show that he is the older of two men who have the same name and come from the same family【尤美】年紀較大的，年長的〔用於一個家庭裡同名的兩個男人中〕：*John J. Wallace, Sr.* 老約翰·J·華萊士

2 **senior[1]** *adj* **1** [only before noun 僅用於名詞前] older 年長的：*Senior pupils have certain privileges.* 年紀較大的學生有一定的特權。**2** having a higher position or rank〔地位或級別〕較高的：*a very senior officer* 級別很高的軍官 | **[+to]** *Only one manager is senior to me now.* 現在只有一位經理比我地位高。| **senior partner** (=the more important person in a business partnership)〔商行等合股公司的〕主要合夥人 —compare 比較 JUNIOR[1]

senior[2] *n* [C] **1 be two/five/ten etc years sb's senior** to be two, five, ten etc years older than someone 比某人大二歲/五歲/十歲：*Her husband was nine years her senior.* 她丈夫比她大九歲。—opposite 反義詞 JUNIOR[2] (1) **2** *AmE* a student in their last year of HIGH SCHOOL or university【美】〔中學或大學〕最高年級的學生，畢業班學生：*Jen will be a senior this year.* 詹今年是畢業班學生了。—compare 比較 FRESHMAN, JUNIOR[2] (4), SOPHOMORE **3** *CanE* a SENIOR CITIZEN【加】老年人

S

senior cit·i·zen /,··· '···/ *n* [C] an old person, especially someone who is over 60, or who is RETIRED 老年人〔尤指60歲以上或已退休者〕—see 見 OLD (USAGE)

senior high school /,··· '· ·/ also 又作 **senior high** /,··· '·/ *n* [C] *AmE* a school in the US for students between 14 and 18【美】高級中學〔學生年齡為14歲至18歲〕—compare 比較 JUNIOR HIGH SCHOOL

se·ni·or·i·ty /sin`jɔrətɪ; ,siːni'ɒrəti/ *n* [U] **1** the situation of being older or higher in rank than someone else 年長；職位[級別]高：*Her seniority finally earned her some respect.* 她的老資格終於使她贏得了人們的幾分尊敬。**2** official advantage that you have because of the length of time you have worked in a company or organization 年資，資歷：*Workers with less than 5 years' seniority may be laid off.* 資歷不足五年的工人可能被解雇。

sen·na /`sɛnə; 'senə/ *n* [U] a tropical plant with a fruit that is often used to make a medicine to help your bowels (BOWEL (1)) work 番瀉樹〔一種熱帶植物，其果實常用作瀉藥〕

sen·sa·tion /sɛn`seʃən; sen'seɪʃən/ *n* **1** [U] the ability to feel, especially through your sense of touch〔感官的〕感覺能力〔尤指觸覺〕：*Jerry realized with alarm that he had no sensation in his legs.* 傑里吃驚地意識到他的雙腿已經沒有感覺了。**2** [C,U] a feeling that you get from one of your five senses, especially the sense of touch〔由感官得到的〕感覺〔尤指觸覺〕：*a tingling sensation in the skin* 皮膚的刺痛感 | **[+of]** *a strange sensation of weightlessness* 一種失重的奇特感覺 **3** [C] a feeling that is hard to describe, caused by a particular event, experience, or memory〔由某一事件、經歷或記憶引起的難以描述的〕感受：**sensation (that)** *The fog gave me the strange sensation that I was alone in the world.* 大霧使我產生一種世界上只有我孤零零一個人的奇異感覺。**4 a sensation** extreme excitement or interest, or someone or something that causes this 轟動，激動；引起轟動的人[事]：*News of their engagement created a great sensation.* 他們訂婚的消息引起很大的轟動。

sen·sa·tion·al /sɛn`seʃənḷ; sen'seɪʃənəl/ *adj* **1** very interesting and exciting 令人極度興奮的，轟動的：*The effect of the discovery was sensational.* 這個發現有轟動的效果。| *a sensational result* 令人興奮不已的結果 **2** intended to interest, excite, or shock people, in a way that you disapprove of or find unpleasant 為了引起轟動的；聳人聽聞的：*sensational press coverage of the divorce* 新聞界對這起離婚大事渲染的報道 **3** *informal* very good or impressive【非正式】極好的，令人難忘的：*You look sensational in that dress!* 你穿那件連衣裙漂亮極了。—**sensationally** *adv*

sen·sa·tion·al·is·m /sɛn`seʃənḷ,ɪzəm; sen'seɪʃənəlɪzəm/ *n* [U] a way of reporting events or stories that makes them seem as strange, exciting, or shocking as possible, and in a way that people disapprove of〔新聞報道、文藝作品中的〕追求轟動效應；聳人聽聞的手法 —**sensationalist** *adj*: *a sensationalist magazine article on teenage sex* 雜誌上一篇採用聳人聽聞的手法描寫青少年性問題的文章

sen·sa·tion·al·ize also 又作 **-ise** *BrE*【英】/sɛn`seʃənə,laɪz; sen'seɪʃənəlaɪz/ *v* [T] to deliberately make something seem as strange, exciting, or shocking as possible, in a way that people disapprove of 用追求轟動效應[聳人聽聞]的手法處理〔某事〕：*a sensationalized account of the trial* 對這場審判聳人聽聞的報道

1
1

sense[1] /sɛns; sens/ *n*

① JUDGMENT/UNDERSTANDING 判斷/理解（力）
② A FEELING 感覺
③ MAKE SENSE 有意義
④ SEE/SMELL/TOUCH ETC 看見/嗅到/觸摸等
⑤ SKILL/ABILITY 技能/能力
⑥ MEANING 意思
⑦ CRAZY/SILLY 瘋狂的/愚蠢的
⑧ OTHER MEANINGS 其他意思

① JUDGMENT/UNDERSTANDING 判斷/理解（力）

1 [U] good understanding and judgment, especially about practical things〔尤指對某具體事物的〕判斷力，辨別力：**have the sense to do sth** *You should have had the sense to turn off the electricity before touching the wires.* 你本該懂得在觸摸電線之前先把電源切斷。—see also 另見 COMMON SENSE

2 there is no sense in (doing) sth *spoken* used to say that it is not sensible to do something【口】（做）某事是沒意義的：*There's no sense in getting upset about it now.* 現在為這件事苦惱是沒有意義的。

3 talk sense *spoken* to say things that are reasonable or sensible【口】說話有道理：**talk sense!** (=used when you are annoyed with someone for saying something silly) 說話要頭腦清楚！〔用於表示對某人的蠢話感到厭煩〕*Oh talk sense, Stuart, we couldn't possibly go without the car.* 斯圖爾特，說話得講道理！沒有車我們根本走不了。

4 talk/knock some sense into sb to try to persuade someone to stop behaving in a way that you think is silly 說服某人改變愚蠢行為：*He says he's dropping out of school – will you try and talk some sense into him?* 他說他要退學 —— 你去試試說服他不要這麼犯傻好嗎？

5 see sense to realize that you are being silly and unreasonable 明白事理，意識到自己犯傻：*I hope Jack sees*

sense before it's too late. 我希望傑克盡快明白過來, 免得後悔莫及。

6 bring sb to their senses to make someone think or behave in a reasonable and sensible way 使某人醒悟, 使某人恢復理智: *I hope she fails. That'll bring her to her senses.* 我巴不得她失敗, 那樣才會讓她醒悟過來。

7 come to your senses to realize that what you are doing is not sensible 恢復理智, 醒悟過來: *One day he'll come to his senses and see what a fool he's been.* 總有一天他會醒悟過來, 認識到自己是多麼愚蠢。

② A FEELING 感覺

8 [C] a feeling about something〔對某物的〕感覺: **[+of]** *The whole affair left me with a sense of complete helplessness.* 整個事情讓我產生一種完全無助的感覺。| *A new sense of urgency had entered into their negotiations.* 在他們的談判中出現了一種新的緊迫感。| **have the sense that** *I don't know why, but I had the sense that he was lying.* 我不知道為甚麼, 但我覺得他是在撒謊。

③ MAKE SENSE 有意義

9 make sense a) to have a clear meaning that is easy to understand 有〔明確而容易理解的〕意義: *Read this and tell me if it makes sense.* 讀讀這篇東西, 告訴我它的意思是否明確。**b)** to have a good reason or explanation 有道理, 合乎情理: *It just doesn't make sense – why would she do a thing like that?* 這真是無法解釋 —— 她為甚麼會做出這樣的事情? **c)** to be a sensible thing to do 是明智的做法: *It makes sense to save money while you can.* 能省錢時就節省, 這是明智的。

10 make sense of sth to understand something, especially something difficult or complicated 了解某事的意義, 理解〔尤指困難或複雜的〕某事物: *Can you make any sense of this article at all?* 你究竟能不能理解這篇文章的意思?

④ SEE/SMELL/TOUCH ETC 看見/嗅到/觸摸等

11 [C] one of the five natural powers of sight, hearing, feeling, taste, and smell, that give us information about the things around us 感覺官能; 視覺; 聽覺; 觸覺; 味覺; 嗅覺: **sense of smell/taste/touch etc** *a poor sense of smell* 嗅覺遲鈍 | **the five senses** (=all of the senses) 五種官能 | **the senses** (=several or all of the five senses) 五種感覺官能〔或其中的幾種〕*combinations of flavors, textures, and color to delight the senses* 使感官愉悅的風味、質地和顏色的組合 —see also 另見 SIXTH SENSE

⑤ SKILL/ABILITY 技能/能力

12 [singular] a natural ability to judge something 判斷力, 辨別力: **sense of direction/rhythm/timing etc** *I'll probably get lost – I haven't got a very good sense of direction.* 我可能會迷路 —— 我的方向感不太好。| **dress/clothes sense** *He has no dress sense at all.* (=does not know what clothes look good) 他對服裝毫無鑑賞力。

⑥ MEANING 意思

13 [C] the meaning of a word, phrase, sentence etc〔單詞、短語、句子等的〕意義, 意思: *I'm using the word 'family' in its broadest sense.* 我是在最廣義上用 family (家庭) 這個詞。| *In this dictionary the different senses of a word are marked by numbers.* 本辭典中每個詞的不同義項用數碼標明。| **in every sense of the word** (=using all possible meanings of this word) 從這個詞的各種意義上說 *He's a gentleman in every sense of the word.* 從各方面來講, 他都是個紳士。

14 the sense of sth the basic meaning of something 某事物的基本意義

⑦ CRAZY/SILLY 瘋狂的/愚蠢的

15 take leave of your senses to start to behave in an unreasonable or silly way 發瘋: *You're challenging him to a fight? Have you taken leave of your senses?* 你提出要和他打架? 你瘋了嗎?

16 be out of your senses to behave in a way that other people think is unreasonable and possibly risky 不明智, 愚蠢

⑧ OTHER MEANINGS 其他意思

17 sense of humour *BrE*【英】, **sense of humor** *AmE*【美】the ability to understand or enjoy things that are funny, or to make people laugh 幽默感: *I like Michelle – she's got a really good sense of humour.* 我喜歡米雪兒 —— 她很有幽默感。

18 in no sense used to emphasize that something is definitely not true 決不〔用於強調〕: *In no sense does this excuse their actions.* 這決不能成為他們行為的託辭。

19 in a very real sense used to emphasize the fact that something is definitely true 確實地, 毫無疑問地〔用於強調〕: *In a very real sense, we can say that education is the most vital of all resources.* 毫無疑問, 我們可以說在所有資源中教育是最重要的。

20 sense of occasion a feeling or understanding that an event or occasion is very serious or important 對某重要事件或時刻的感覺或理解

21 in a sense/in one sense/in some senses etc in one particular way, but without considering all the other facts or possibilities 在某種意義上等: *In some senses this may be true, but it's not really relevant.* 從某些意義上說, 這也許是真實的, 但它並非真正至關重要。| *In a sense, I think he likes being responsible for everything.* 從某種意義上說, 我認為他喜歡包攬一切。

22 regain your senses *old-fashioned* to stop feeling FAINT[1] (3) or unwell【過時】恢復清醒的頭腦, 恢復精神: *Out in the fresh air, she quickly regained her senses.* 她在室外呼吸點新鮮空氣, 很快就恢復精神了。

sense² *v* [T] **1** if you sense something, you feel that it exists or is true, without being told or having proof 感覺到, 意識到: *The horse sensed danger and stopped.* 那匹馬感到有危險, 於是停了下來。| *I could sense her growing irritation.* 我察覺到她越來越不耐煩。| **sense (that)** *I sensed that there was someone in the room with me.* 我感覺到有人和我一起在房間裡。| **sense what/how/who etc** *Hugo had already sensed how unhappy she was.* 雨果已經察覺到她是多麼的不開心。**2** if a machine senses something, it discovers and records it〔機器〕檢測: *an electronic device used for sensing intruders* 自動檢測闖入者的電子裝置

sense·less /ˋsɛnslɪs; ˈsensləs/ *adj* **1** happening or done for no good reason or with no purpose 無道理的, 無目的的, 無意義的: *the senseless death of a young girl* 一個少女毫無意義的死 | *senseless violence* 毫無意義的暴力行為 **2** unconscious 失去知覺的: *They beat him senseless, and left him for dead.* 他們把他打得失去知覺, 以為死了便丟下不管。—**senselessly** *adv* **senselessness** *n* [U]

sense or·gan /ˈ· ˌ··/ *n* [C] a part of your body through which you see, smell, hear, taste, or feel something〔用以看、嗅、聽、品嘗或觸摸的〕感覺器官

sen·si·bil·i·ty /ˌsɛnsəˋbɪlətɪ; ˌsensɪ̈ˈbɪlɪ̈ti/ *n plural* **sensibilities 1 wound/offend sb's sensibilities** to offend someone by being rude or unpleasant etc 傷害/觸犯某人的感情: *It wounded her delicate sensibilities to be addressed in such a vulgar manner.* 用這樣粗俗的態度對她說話, 傷害了她脆弱的感情。**2** [U] the ability to understand feelings, especially those expressed in literature or art〔尤指對文學、藝術的〕感受力, 鑑賞力: *Basil was above all a person of sensibility and perception.* 巴兹爾尤其是一個有鑑賞力和洞察力的人。

sen·si·ble /ˋsɛnsəbḷ; ˈsensɪ̈bəl/ *adj* **1** *especially BrE* reasonable, practical, and able to judge things well【尤英】明智的, 合理的, 實際的: *I think that's a very sensible* [S3] [W3] *suggestion.* 我看這是一個非常合理的建議。| *Surely it would be sensible to get a second opinion.* 多聽取一種意見肯定是明智的。| *Come now, be sensible.* 嗨, 明智點! **2 sensible clothes/shoes** *especially BrE* clothes or shoes that are practical, comfortable, and strong rather than attractive or fashionable【尤英】實用的衣服/鞋子 **3 sensible of sth** *old-fashioned* knowing or recognizing something【過時】感知某事, 察覺到某事: *He was sensible of the trouble he had caused.* 他意識到自己造成的麻煩。**4** *formal* noticeable【正式】可感覺到的, 明顯的: *a sensible increase in temperature* 溫度的明顯上升 —**sensibly** *adv*: *Sensibly, Barbara had brought an umbrella.* 巴巴拉明智地帶了一把雨傘。

3 3 **sen·si·tive** /ˋsɛnsətɪv; ˈsensɪ̈tɪv/ *adj*
1 ►UNDERSTANDING PEOPLE 理解別人◄ able to understand other people's feelings and problems 能理解〔別人的感情和問題〕的: *Underneath all that macho stuff, he's really a sensitive guy.* 在所有那些大男子氣概下面, 他實際上是個體貼的人。| **[+to]** *We must be sensitive to the community's needs.* 我們必須善於體察大眾的需要。—opposite 反義詞 INSENSITIVE
2 ►EASILY OFFENDED 容易生氣的◄ easily hurt, upset, or offended by things that people say〔感情〕易受傷害的, 神經過敏的: *Don't be so sensitive – I wasn't criticizing you!* 別那麼神經過敏——我不是在批評你! | **[+about]** *Lara's very sensitive about her figure.* 拉臘對她自己的體形非常敏感。| **sensitive soul** (=someone who is easily upset by small or unimportant things) 過度敏感的人 —see also 另見 HYPERSENSITIVE
3 ►COLD/PAIN ETC 冷/疼痛等◄ able to feel physical sensations, especially pain, more than usual〔尤對疼痛〕易感受的, 敏感的: *Make sure you protect sensitive areas of your skin with a good suncream.* 一定要用好的防曬霜保護你皮膚的敏感部分。| **be sensitive to sth** *Ruth is very sensitive to cold.* 露思對寒冷很敏感。
4 ►ART/MUSIC ETC 藝術/音樂等◄ able to understand or express yourself through art, music, literature etc〔對文學藝術〕感受力強的, 有表現能力的: *a sensitive musician* 表現力強的音樂家 | *a very sensitive performance* 非常細膩的演出
5 ►SITUATIONS/SUBJECTS 情況/問題◄ a situation or subject that is sensitive needs to be dealt with very carefully because it may offend people or make them angry〔情況、問題等〕需小心處理的, 敏感的, 可能觸怒人的: *Sorry I didn't realize it was such a sensitive issue.* 對不起, 我沒有認識到這是個如此敏感的問題。
6 ►HEAT/LIGHT ETC 熱/光等◄ able to measure or react to very small changes in heat, light etc〔對光、熱等的變化〕能準確計量的, 靈敏度高的: *We need a more sensitive thermometer for this.* 我們需要一個靈敏度高些的溫度計來對此測量。| **highly sensitive** (=very sensitive) 高度敏感的 *a highly sensitive electronic camera* 高敏感度的電子攝像機 | **[+to]** *film that is sensitive to ultraviolet light* 對紫外光敏感的膠卷 | **light-sensitive/heat-sensitive etc** *light-sensitive photographic paper* 感光相紙 —**sensitively** *adv* —**sensitivity** /ˌsɛnsəˋtɪvətɪ; ˌsensɪ̈ˈtɪvɪ̈ti/ also 又作 **sensitiveness** /ˋsɛnsətɪvnəs; ˈsensɪ̈tɪvnɪ̈s/ *n* [U]

sen·si·tiv·i·ties /ˌsɛnsəˋtɪvətɪz; ˌsensɪ̈ˈtɪvɪ̈tiz/ *n* [plural] someone's feelings and the fact that they could be upset or offended〔感情上的〕敏感性, 易受傷害的特性: *The sensitivities of the black community were largely ignored.* 黑人社會心理上的敏感性在很大程度上被忽視了。

sen·si·tize also 又作 **-ise** *BrE*【英】/ˋsɛnsəˌtaɪz; ˈsensɪ̈taɪz/ *v* **1** [T usually passive 一般用被動態] to give someone some experience of a particular problem or situation so that they can notice it and understand it easily 使〔某人對某問題或情況〕敏感: **sensitize sb to sth** *Her upbringing had sensitized her to discrimination.* 她所受的教養使她對歧視很敏感。**2** [T] *technical* to treat a material or a piece of equipment so that it will react to physical or chemical changes【術語】使對物理[化學]變化有反應: *sensitized photographic paper* 感光相紙 —**sensitization** /ˌsɛnsətəˋzeʃən; ˌsensɪ̈taɪˈzeɪʃən/ *n* [U]

sen·sor /ˋsɛnsɚ; ˈsensə/ *n* [C] *technical* a piece of equipment used for discovering the presence of light, heat, sound etc, especially in small amounts【術語】〔探測光、熱、聲等的〕傳感器, 感應裝置

sen·so·ry /ˋsɛnsərɪ; ˈsensəri/ *adj* connected with or using your senses of sight, hearing, smell, taste or touch 感官的; 感覺上的: *sensory stimuli* 感官刺激 | *sensory deprivation* 感覺剝奪 —see also 另見 ESP (1)

sen·su·al /ˋsɛnʃuəl; ˈsenʃuəl/ *adj* **1** connected with the feelings of your body rather than your mind 肉體上的, 官能的: *purely sensual pleasures* 純粹肉體上的快樂 **2** interested in or making you think of physical pleasure, especially sexual pleasure 肉慾的; 刺激性慾的; 性感的: *sensual lips* 性感的嘴唇 | *a sensual woman* 性感的女人 —**sensuality** /ˌsɛnʃuˋælətɪ; ˌsenʃuˈælɪ̈ti/ *n* [U] —**sensually** *adv*

sen·su·al·ist /ˋsɛnʃuəlɪst; ˈsenʃuəlɪ̈st/ *n* [C] someone who is only interested in physical pleasure 追求感官享受的人, 耽於酒色的人

sen·su·ous /ˋsɛnʃuəs; ˈsenʃuəs/ *adj* **1** pleasing to your senses 給感官以快樂的, 給人以快感的: *the sensuous feeling of silk on her skin* 絲綢給她皮膚帶來的美妙感受 **2** full of powerful images or sounds that suggest physical pleasure 使人賞心悅目的, 使人愉悅的: *sensuous music* 動聽悅耳的音樂 —**sensuously** *adv* —**sensuousness** *n* [U]

sent /sɛnt; sent/ the past tense and past participle of SEND

sen·tence[1] /ˋsɛntəns; ˈsentəns/ *n* [C] **1** a group of words that usually contains a subject and a verb, expresses a complete idea or asks a question, and that, when written in English, begins with a capital letter and ends with a FULL STOP[1] (1) 句子, 句 **2** a punishment that a judge gives to someone that has been declared guilty of a crime 判決, 判刑: *a six year prison sentence* 六年徒刑 | **heavy/light sentence** (=long or short time in prison) 重判/輕判 | **life sentence** (=very long time in prison) 無期徒刑 *a life sentence for murder* 因謀殺罪被判無期徒刑 | **death sentence** (=punishment by death) 死刑 | **serve a sentence** (=spend time in prison as a punishment) 服刑 **3 pass/pronounce sentence** to officially state what a punishment will be 宣布判決, 宣判 

sentence[2] *v* [T often passive 常用被動態] if a judge sentences someone found guilty of a crime, they officially and legally give them a punishment〔法官〕判決, 宣判: **[+to]** *Sanchez was sentenced to three years in prison for his part in the crime.* 桑切茲因參與犯罪被判處三年徒刑。

sentence ad·verb /ˈ.. ˌ../ *n* [C] an adverb that expresses an opinion about the whole sentence that contains it 句子副詞

sen·ten·tious /sɛnˋtɛnʃəs; senˈtenʃəs/ *adj formal* saying clever things about morality or the way people should behave【正式】說教的, 勸誡的: *sententious remarks* 說教式的言語 —**sententiously** *adv*

sen·tient /ˋsɛnʃənt; ˈsenʃənt/ *adj formal or technical* having feelings and knowing that you exist【正式或術語】有感知力的: *Man is a sentient being.* 人是有感知的生物。

sen·ti·ment /ˋsɛntəmənt; ˈsentɪ̈mənt/ *n* **1** [C,U] *formal* an opinion or feeling you have about something【正式】意見, 觀點, 感想: *It is my sentiment that we should vote against the motion.* 我的意見是我們應該對這個動議投反對票。| **popular sentiment** (=what most people think) 民意 | **my/your sentiments** *I share your sentiments entirely.* 我和你的看法完全相同。**2** [U] feelings of pity, love, sadness etc that are often considered to be too strong or not suitable for a particular situation 多愁善感: *There's no place for sentiment in business!* 做生意容不得感情用事。

sen·ti·ment·al /ˌsɛntəˋmɛntḷ; ˌsentɪ̵ˈmentl◂/ *adj* **1** someone who is sentimental is too easily affected by emotions such as love, sympathy, sadness etc 多愁善感的, 感情用事的: *There's nothing wrong with being a little sentimental!* 有點多愁善感沒甚麼不對! **2** based on or connected with your feelings rather than on practical reasons 感情上的, 情緒上的, 非理性的: **for sentimental reasons/purposes** *I only keep these old photos for sentimental reasons.* 我只是因感情上的原因才保存這些舊照片。**3 sentimental value** if something has sentimental value, it is not worth much money, but it is important to you because it reminds you of someone you love or a happy time in the past 感情價值: *The stolen rings were of great sentimental value to the owner.* 那些被盜的戒指對失主是有很大感情價值的。**4** a story, film, book etc that is sentimental deals with emotions such as love and sadness in a way that seems silly and insincere〔故事、電影、書等〕感傷的; 感情輕浮虛偽的: *I enjoyed the movie but the ending was too sentimental.* 我喜歡這部電影, 但它的結局太傷感了。—**sentimentally** *adv*

sen·ti·men·tal·ist /ˌsɛntəˋmɛntḷɪst; ˌsentɪ̵ˈmentl-ɪ̵st/ *n* [C] someone who behaves or writes in a sentimental way 多愁善感的人, 傷感主義者 —**sentimentalism** *n* [U]

sen·ti·men·tal·i·ty /ˌsɛntəmɛnˋtæləti; ˌsentɪ̵menˈtælɪ̵ti/ *n* [U] the quality of being sentimental 多愁善感, 感情用事

sen·ti·ment·al·ize also 又作 **-ise** *BrE*【英】/ˌsɛntəˋmɛntḷˌaɪz; ˌsentɪ̵ˈmentl-aɪz/ *v* [I,T] to speak, write or think about something in a way that mentions only the good or happy things about something, but not the bad things 只談[思考]某事美好的一面: *a sentimentalized account of life during the war* 對戰爭時期生活的美化 | **[+about/over]** *Listen to Albert sentimentalizing about his childhood again.* 你再聽聽艾伯特把他的童年說成多麼浪漫美好吧。

sen·ti·nel /ˋsɛntənḷ; ˈsentɪnəl/ *n* [C] *old-fashioned* a sentry【過時】哨兵, 衛兵, 崗哨

sen·try /ˋsɛntrɪ; ˈsentri/ *n* [C] a soldier standing outside a building as a guard〔守衛於建築物外面的〕哨兵, 衛兵, 崗哨

sentry box /ˈ·· ·/ *n* [C] a tall narrow shelter with an open front where a soldier can stand while guarding a building 崗亭

se·pal /ˋsɛpḷ; ˈsepəl/ *n* [C] *technical* one of the small leaves directly under a flower【術語】〔花的〕萼片

sep·a·ra·ble /ˋsɛpərəbḷ; ˈsepərəbəl/ *adj* two things that are separable can be separated or considered separately 可分開[分隔, 分離]的: *Supply and demand are not easily separable.* 供給和需求不易分開。—opposite 反義詞 INSEPARABLE —**separably** *adv* —**separability** /ˌsɛpərəˋbɪlətɪ; ˌsepərəˈbɪlɪ̵ti/ *n* [U]

S2 W2 **sep·a·rate¹** /ˋsɛpərɪt; ˈsepərɪ̵t/ *adj* **1** things, places, buildings etc that are separate are not joined to each other or touching each other〔事物、地方、建築物等〕分開的; 不相連的; 獨立的: *separate bedrooms* 不相連[獨立]的臥室 | *The poor travelled in a separate carriage.* 過去窮人外出時乘坐分開的車廂。| **[+from]** *Keep the fish separate from the other food.* 把魚和其他食物分開存放。**2** ideas, information, activities etc that are separate are not connected or do not affect each other in any way〔主意、信息、活動等〕互不相關的, 各自的: *two separate problems* 兩個互不相關的問題 | **[+from]** *He tries to keep his professional life completely separate from his private life.* 他盡量把他的職業生活和私人生活完全分開。**3** different 不同的, 不一樣的: *This word has 3 separate meanings.* 這個詞有三個不同的意思。| *She's been warned on three separate occasions that her work is not good enough.* 她已受到三次警告, 被指出工作不夠好。**4 go your separate ways a)** to finish a relationship with someone, especially a romantic relationship 結束(與某人的)關係〔尤指戀愛關係〕; 不再交往 **b)** to start travelling in a different direction from someone you have been travelling with 分手, 分道而行 —**separately** *adv*: *They did arrive together, but I think they left separately.* 他們確實是一起到達的, 但我想他們是各自離開的。

sep·a·rate² /ˋsɛpəˌret; ˈsepəreɪt/ *v* S2 W2

1 ▶BE BETWEEN 在…之間◀ [T often passive 常用被動態] if something separates two places or two things, it is between them so that they are not touching each other or connected with each other 把…隔開: *The two towns are separated by a river.* 這兩個城鎮被一條河隔開。| *Seventeen years had separated them.* 他們離別已有十七年了。

2 ▶DIVIDE 分開◀ [I,T] to divide or split into different parts, or layers, or to make something do this (把…)分成不同部分; (使)分離: *Here's a trick to keep your salad dressing from separating.* 這裡有個能使色拉調味汁不沉澱的訣竅。| **[+from]** *At this point the satellite separates from its launcher.* 在這個時候, 衛星就脫離發射器。| **separate sth into** *It would help if we separated this stuff into three different piles.* 要是我們把這東西分開成三堆, 也許會有幫助。| **separate eggs** (=divide the white part from the yellow part) 把蛋白和蛋黃分開

3 ▶STOP LIVING TOGETHER 停止同居◀ [I] to start to live apart from your husband, wife or sexual partner〔夫妻〕分居;〔性伴侶〕分手: *It's the children who suffer when their parents separate.* 父母分居時受罪的是子女。

4 ▶RECOGNIZE DIFFERENCE 識別差異◀ [T] to recognize that one idea is different from another, and to deal with each idea alone 識別〔思想的〕差別; 分別處理: **[+from]** *It's not always easy to separate cause from effect.* 因果關係並不總是容易區分的。

5 ▶MOVE APART 分開◀ [I,T] to move apart, or make people move apart (使)分開, 把〔人〕隔開: **[+from]** *We had to separate Philip and Jason because they were talking all the time.* 我們不得不把菲利普和賈森分開, 因為他們老在講話。

6 ▶MAKE SB/STH DIFFERENT 使某人/某事物不同◀ [T+from] to be the thing that makes someone or something different from other similar people or things 使區別於, 使與眾不同: *What is it that you think separates her from the other applicants?* 你認為是甚麼使她不同於其他申請人?

7 separate the men from the boys *informal* to do something that makes it clear which people are brave or strong and which are not【非正式】區分強者與弱者; 識別勇敢者與懦弱者: *The climb through the mountains will definitely separate the men from the boys.* 這次登山肯定會把強者和弱者區分開來。

8 separate the sheep from the goats also 又作 **separate the wheat from the chaff** to separate the good things from the bad things 區分好的和壞的; 區別優劣

separate sth ↔ **out** *phr v* [I,T] if part of something separates out or is separated out, it becomes separate from the other parts (使)分離, 析出

sep·a·rat·ed /ˋsɛpəˌretɪd; ˈsepəreɪtɪ̵d/ *adj* not living with your husband, wife or sexual partner any more〔夫妻〕分居的;〔性伴侶〕不再同居的: *David and I have been separated for six months but we're not divorced yet.* 我和大衛已經分居六個月了, 但還沒有離婚。

sep·a·rates /ˋsɛpərɪts; ˈsepərɪ̵ts/ *n* [plural] women's clothing, such as skirts, shirts, and trousers, that can be worn in different combinations 可以任意配套穿的女服〈如裙子、襯衫、褲子等〉

sep·a·ra·tion /ˌsɛpəˋreʃən; ˌsepəˈreɪʃən/ *n* **1** [C,U] a period of time that two or more people spend apart from each other 分開的時期: *Their separation lasted over 20 years.* 他們分離已逾 20 年。**2** [C] a situation in which a husband and wife agree to live apart even though they are still married 夫婦分居 —compare 比較 DIVORCE¹ (1) **3** [U] the act of separating or the state of being separate 分開, 分離; 分居

S

sep·a·ra·tist /ˋsɛpəˏretɪst; ˈsepərətɪst/ *n* [C] a member of a group in a country that wants to establish a new separate country with its own government〔企圖另組獨立國家的〕分離主義者 —**separatism** *n* [U]

sep·a·ra·tor /ˋsɛpəˏretɚ; ˈsepəreɪtə/ *n* [C] a machine for separating liquids from solids, or cream from milk 分離器, 離析器; 脫脂器

se·pi·a /ˋsipɪə; ˈsiːpiə/ *n* [U] **1** a dark reddish brown colour 深褐色 **2 sepia photograph/print** a photograph, picture etc, especially an old one, that is this colour〔尤指舊的〕深褐色照片/圖畫 **3** an ink used for drawing which has this colour 深褐色墨汁

sep·sis /ˋsɛpsɪs; ˈsepsɪs/ *n* [U] *technical* an infection in part of the body, in which PUS is produced【術語】膿毒病[症]

Sep·tem·ber /sɛpˋtɛmbɚ; sepˈtembə/ written abbreviation 縮寫為 **Sept** *n* [C,U] the ninth month of the year, between August and October 九月: **in September (1998/2000 etc)** *The project is due to finish in September.* 工程預定在 9 月完成。| **last/next September** *We haven't seen each other since last September.* 我們自從(去年) 9 月就沒有見過面了。| **on September 6th** (also 又作 **on 6th September** *BrE* 英): *The meeting will be on September 6th.* 會議將於 9 月 6 日舉行。(spoken as 讀作: *on the sixth of September* or 或 on *September the sixth* or 或 (*AmE* 美) *on September sixth*)

sep·tet /sɛpˋtɛt; sepˈtet/ *n* [C] **1** a group of seven singers or musicians who perform together 七重唱; 七重奏 **2** a piece of music written for seven performers 七重唱[奏]曲

sep·tic /ˋsɛptɪk; ˈseptɪk/ *adj especially BrE* a wound or part of your body that is septic is infected with BACTERIA【尤英】〔傷口等〕膿毒性的, 受感染的: *a septic finger* 感染化膿的手指

sep·ti·cae·mi·a *BrE*【英】, **septicemia** *AmE*【美】/ˏsɛptəˋsimɪə; ˏseptɪˈsiːmiə/ *n* [U] *technical* a serious condition in which infection spreads from a small area of your body through your blood; BLOOD POISONING【術語】敗血症

septic tank /ˈ·· ˏ·/ *n* [C] a large container kept under ground used for putting human body waste into 化糞池

sep·tu·a·ge·nar·i·an /ˏsɛptʃuədʒəˋnɛrɪən; ˏseptʃuədʒɪˈneəriən/ *n* [C] someone who is between 70 and 79 years old 70 至 79 歲的人

se·pul·chral /səˋpʌlkrəl; sɪˈpʌlkrəl/ *adj* **1** *literary* sad, serious and slightly frightening【文】憂傷的, 陰沉的, 陰森森的: *a sepulchral voice* 低沉憂鬱的嗓音 **2** *technical* related to burying dead people【術語】埋葬死人的, 喪葬的

sep·ul·chre *BrE*【英】, **sepulcher** *AmE*【美】/ˋsɛplkɚ; ˈsepəlkə/ *n* [C] *old use* a small room or building in which the bodies of dead people were put【舊】墓室, 塚

se·quel /ˋsikwəl; ˈsiːkwəl/ *n* **1** [C] a book, film, play etc that continues the story of an earlier one, usually written or made by the same person〔書、電影、戲劇等的〕續集, 續篇 **2** [C usually singular 一般用單數] an event that happens as a result of something that happened before 隨之而來的事; 後果; 後續; 餘波

2 **se·quence** /ˋsikwəns; ˈsiːkwəns/ *n* [C,U] **1** a series of related events, actions etc which have a fixed order and usually lead to a particular result〔通常導致某種結果的〕一連串相關事件[行動]: **sequence of events** *the sequence of events leading up to the war* 導致那次戰爭的一連串事件 **2** [C,U] the order that events or actions happen in, or are supposed to happen in〔事件或行動發生的〕順序, 次序: **in/out of sequence** (=in or out of order) 按順序/不按順序 *Please check that the page numbers are in sequence.* 請檢查這些頁碼是否按順序排列。**3** [C] one part of a story, film etc that deals with a single subject or action〔電影中描述同一主題或動作的〕連續鏡頭; 一段情節; 〔故事的〕片段: *the dream sequence at the beginning of Ryder's film* 賴德影片開始時的連續夢境鏡頭

se·quenc·ing /ˋsikwənsɪŋ; ˈsiːkwənsɪŋ/ *n* [U] *formal* the arrangement of things into an order, especially events or actions【正式】〔尤指事件或動作的〕先後安排; 編排順序

se·quen·tial /sɪˋkwɛnʃəl; sɪˈkwenʃəl/ *adj formal* connected with or happening in a sequence【正式】連續的; 相繼的; 順序的; 序列的 —**sequentially** *adv*

se·ques·ter /sɪˋkwɛstɚ; sɪˈkwestə/ *v* [T] **1** to force a group of people, such as a JURY, to stay away from other people 使〔陪審團等〕與他人隔離; 使隔絕 **2** to sequestrate 扣押〔債務人的財產〕

se·ques·tered /sɪˋkwɛstɚd; sɪˈkwestəd/ *adj literary* a sequestered place is quiet and far away from people【文】〔地方〕僻靜的, 與世隔絕的

se·ques·trate /sɪˋkwɛstret; sɪˈkwestreɪt/ *v* [T usually passive 一般用被動態] to take property away from the person it belongs to because they have not paid their debts 扣押〔債務人的財產〕—**sequestration** /ˏsikwɛsˋtreʃən; ˏsiːkwɪˈstreɪʃən/ *n* [C,U]

se·quin /ˋsikwɪn; ˈsiːkwɪn/ *n* [C] a small shiny round flat piece of metal that you SEW onto clothing for decoration〔裝飾衣服用的〕閃光金屬裝飾圓片 —**sequined, sequinned** *adj*

se·quoi·a /sɪˋkwɔɪə; sɪˈkwɔɪə/ *n* [C] a tree from the western US that can grow to be 100 metres in height 紅杉〔產於美國西部, 樹高可達 100 米〕

se·ra·glio /sɪˋrɑljo; sɪˈrɑːljəʊ/ *n* [C] a HAREM〔伊斯蘭教徒的〕女眷居住的內室

ser·aph /ˋsɛrəf; ˈserəf/ *plural* **seraphs** also 又作 **seraphim** /-rəfɪm; -rəfɪm/ *n* [C] one of the ANGELS that protects the seat of God, according to the Bible 撒拉弗〔《聖經》中守護上帝寶座的天使〕

se·raph·ic /səˋræfɪk; sɪˈræfɪk/ *adj literary* extremely beautiful or pure, like an ANGEL【文】天使般的, 美麗純潔的

sere /sɪr; sɪə/ *adj literary* very dry【文】極乾的, 乾枯的

ser·e·nade[1] /ˏsɛrəˋned; ˏserɪˈneɪd/ *n* [C] **1** a song that a man performs for the woman he loves, especially standing below her window at night〔尤指男子晚上站在其意中人窗外唱或奏的〕小夜曲 **2** a piece of gentle music 柔和的樂曲

serenade[2] *v* [T] if you serenade someone, you sing or play music to them to show them that you love them〔為表愛慕之情而〕對…唱[奏]樂曲

ser·en·dip·i·ty /ˏsɛrənˋdɪpətɪ; ˏserənˈdɪpɪti/ *n* [U] *literary* the natural ability to make interesting or valuable discoveries by accident【文】善於無意中發現有趣或珍奇事物的天賦

se·rene /səˋrin; sɪˈriːn/ *adj* **1** someone who is serene is very calm and relaxed 安詳的, 寧靜的: *Mother sat in the evening sunlight, serene and beautiful.* 母親坐在夕陽下, 安詳而美麗。**2** a place or situation that is serene is very peaceful〔地方或環境〕寧靜的, 安寧的, 平靜的: *a serene summer night* 寧靜的夏夜 —**serenely** *adv* —**serenity** /səˋrɛnətɪ; sɪˈrenɪti/ *n* [U]

serf /sɝf; sɜːf/ *n* [C] someone in former times who lived and worked on land that they did not own and who had to obey the owner of this land〔舊時的〕農奴 —compare 比較 SLAVE[1] (1)

serf·dom /ˋsɝfdəm; ˈsɜːfdəm/ *n* [U] the state of being a serf 農奴身分; 農奴制

serge /sɝdʒ; sɜːdʒ/ *n* [U] strong, usually WOOLLEN cloth 嗶嘰〔衣料〕

ser·geant /ˋsɑrdʒənt; ˈsɑːdʒənt/ *n* [C] a low rank in the army, air force, police etc, or someone who has this rank 軍士〔一種低級軍階〕; 中士; 〔警察的〕巡佐, 警佐 —see table on page C6 參見 C6 頁附錄

sergeant-at-arms /ˏ··ˈ·/ *n* [C] a SERJEANT-AT-ARMS〔在英國法庭、議會等維持秩序的〕警衛官

sergeant ma·jor /ˏ·· ˈ··◂/ *n* [C] a military rank 軍士長

—see table on page C6 參見C6頁附錄

se·ri·al[1] /ˈsɪrɪəl; ˈsɪəriəl/ *n* [C] a story that is broadcast or printed in several separate parts on television, in a newspaper etc〔報紙上的〕連載小說; 電視連續劇: *a six-part serial* 六集連續劇[連載故事]

serial[2] *adj* [only before noun 僅用於名詞前] **1** arranged or happening one after the other in the correct order 順序排列的, 連續的; 一連串[系列]的: *placed in serial order* 按順序放置的 | *serial processing on a computer* 電腦上的串行處理 **2 serial killings/murders** killings or murders that are done in the same way one after the other〔手法相同的〕連環殺人/謀殺(案) —**serially** *adv*

se·ri·al·ize also 又作 **-ise** *BrE*【英】/ˈsɪrɪəlˌaɪz; ˈsɪəriəlaɪz/ *v* [T often passive 常用被動態] to print or broadcast a story in several separate parts〔小說等〕連載; 連播: *His book was first serialized in The New Yorker.* 他的書首先是在《紐約人》雜誌上連載的。—**serialization** /ˌsɪrɪələˈzeʃən; ˌsɪəriəlaɪˈzeɪʃən/ *n* [U]

serial kill·er /ˈ··· ˌ··/ *n* [C] someone who has killed several people, one after the other and in the same way 連環殺手

serial num·ber /ˈ··· ˌ··/ *n* [C] a number put on things that are produced in large quantities so that each one is slightly different〔同類物的〕連續編號, 順序號碼: *serial numbers on dollar bills* 美鈔上的順序號碼

S2 W1 **se·ries** /ˈsɪriz; ˈsɪəriːz/ *n plural* **series** [C] **1** [singular] several events or actions of the same kind that happen one after the other but that are not connected 連續發生的同類事件; 系列: **[+of]** *There's been a whole series of accidents on this stretch of road recently.* 近來在這一路段發生了一連串事故。**2** a group of events that are connected and have a particular result〔相互聯繫並有特定結果的〕系列(事件): *a strange series of events that led to his death* 導致他死亡的一連串怪事 **3** a set of television or radio programmes in which each one tells the next part of a story or deals with the same kind of subject〔電視、廣播等的〕系列片; 系列節目: *a new comedy series* 新的喜劇系列片 **4** a group of events or actions of the same kind that are planned to happen one after another in order to achieve something〔有計劃的〕系列活動: *It'll have to undergo a series of tests.* 這必須經過一系列的試驗。| *a series of lectures on the subject of biotechnology* 以生物工藝學為主題的系列講座 **5 in series** *technical* being connected so that electricity passes through the parts of something electrical in the correct order【術語】〔電器的〕串聯

ser·if /ˈsɛrɪf; ˈserɪ̣f/ *n* [C] a short flat line at the top or bottom of some printed letters 襯線〔某些印刷體字母頂部或底部的短線〕—see also 另見 SANS SERIF

S1 W1 **se·ri·ous** /ˈsɪrɪəs; ˈsɪəriəs/ *adj*

1 ►SITUATION/PROBLEM 情況/問題◄ a serious situation, problem, accident etc is extremely bad or dangerous〔情況、問題等〕嚴重的, 危險的: *a serious illness* 重病 | *How serious do you think the situation is?* 你認為情況有多嚴重? | **serious crime** *The number of serious crimes has increased dramatically in the last year.* 重大罪案數字在去年急劇上升。

2 be serious a) if someone is serious about something, they say what they really mean and are not joking or pretending 認真的, 並非開玩笑的; 非假裝的: **[+about]** *I stopped laughing when I realized Jen was serious about it.* 當我意識到詹並非開玩笑時, 我就不再笑了。| **I'm serious!** *spoken* (=used to emphasize that something is important)【口】我是當真的!〔用於強調某事很重要〕*I'm serious, Kerry. You'd better listen!* 我是認真的, 克里。你最好聽着! | **deadly serious** (=extremely serious) 極為認真的 **b)** *spoken* used to tell someone that what they have just said is silly or impossible【口】你別開玩笑了〔用於告訴對方他所說的是蠢話或辦不到的〕: *"We could make it from here to Florida if we drove all night." "Be serious! It's a three day drive."* "我們要是通宵開車, 可以從這裡到達佛羅里達州。" "別瞎扯了! 那是要開三天車才行的。" | **you can't be serious!** *"I thought I'd try to fix the car myself." "You can't be serious!"* "我想過要設法自己修理這輛汽車。" "你真會開玩笑!"

3 ►CAREFUL 仔細的◄ careful and thorough 細心縝密的, 細緻的: *I think this matter needs serious consideration.* 我想這件事需要深思熟慮。| *a serious article* 發人深省的文章

4 ►ROMANTIC RELATIONSHIP 浪漫關係◄ a serious romantic relationship is intended to continue for a long time 嚴肅認真的, 真誠的: *Oo, sounds like it's serious!* 啊, 聽起來像是認真的! | **[+about]** *Are you really serious about her then?* 那你對她是真心實意的嗎? | **serious boyfriend/girlfriend** *Don't even think about Peter. He has a serious girlfriend.* 不用考慮彼得了, 他已經有了一個真心相愛的女朋友。

5 ►PERSON 人◄ someone who is serious is always very sensible and quiet 明智的; 嚴肅的; 莊重的: *He's a nice guy, but very serious.* 他是個好人, 但很嚴肅。

6 ►IMPORTANT 重要的◄ important 重要的, 重大的: *They agreed to have lunch before starting on the serious business.* 他們同意先吃午飯, 然後開始辦正事。

7 serious money/exercise etc *informal* a large amount of money etc【非正式】大量的錢/運動: *I'll have to do some serious exercise before I can fit into that dress.* 我得做相當多的運動才能穿上那套連衣裙。

8 ►VERY GOOD 非常好的◄ [only before noun 僅用於名詞前] *informal* very good and often expensive【非正式】很好的, 質優價高的: *He's got some serious stereo equipment!* 他有些高檔的立體聲音響設備!

9 ►SPORT/ACTIVITY 體育運動/活動◄ [only before noun 僅用於名詞前] someone very interested in something, and spending a lot of time doing it 極感興趣的, 熱衷的: *a serious golfer* 熱衷於打高爾夫球者 | *Any serious student of psychology should read this article.* 凡是對心理學真正感興趣的學生都應該讀讀這篇文章。

10 ►WORRIED/UNHAPPY 憂慮的/不愉快的◄ seeming slightly worried or unhappy 擔心的, 不愉快的: *You look serious. What's wrong?* 你顯得心事重重, 出了甚麼事? —**seriousness** *n* [U]

se·ri·ous·ly /ˈsɪrɪəslɪ; ˈsɪəriəsli/ *adv* **1** in a serious way 認真地; 嚴肅地; 嚴重地: *I think it's about time we talked seriously about our relationship.* 我想現在該是認真嚴肅地談談我們之間關係的時候了。| *Is she seriously ill?* 她病得很重嗎? | *I'm seriously concerned about Ben.* 我對本真的很擔心。**2 take sb/sth seriously** to believe that someone or something is worth paying attention to or should be respected 認真對待某人/某事: *No-one's likely to take Laurie seriously.* 恐怕沒有人會把勞麗當回事的。| *Don't joke with Linda, she takes everything far too seriously.* 不要和琳達開玩笑, 她對待每件事都過於認真。| **never take anything seriously** *It's infuriating that he never takes anything seriously.* 他對任何事從來都不認真, 很讓人惱火。**3 seriously?** *spoken* used to ask someone if they really mean what they have just said【口】真的?〔用於弄清對方的話是否當真〕: *Quit your job? Seriously?* 你要辭職, 真的嗎? **4 seriously** *spoken* [sentence adverb 句子副詞] used to show that what you say next is not a joke【口】說正經的〔用於表示將要說的話並非開玩笑〕: *Seriously though, I really think Toby likes you!* 說正經的, 我真的認為托比喜歡你。 S2 W2

ser·jeant-at-arms, sergeant-at-arms /ˌsɑrdʒənt ət ˈɑrmz; ˌsɑːdʒənt ət ˈɑːmz/ *n* [C] an officer of a British law court or parliament whose job is to keep meetings quiet enough to be useful〔英國法庭、議會等維持秩序的〕警衛官

ser·mon /ˈsɝmən; ˈsɜːmən/ *n* [C] **1** a religious talk given as part of a Christian church service, usually based on a part of the Bible〔基督教的〕佈道, 講道: **preach a sermon** *Pastor Grisson preached a sermon on evangelism.* 格里森牧師以傳福音為題進行講道。**2** *informal* a talk in which someone tries to give you unwanted moral advice;

LECTURE[1] (2)【非正式】說教, 訓誡

ser·mon·ize also 又作 **-ise** *BrE*【英】/ˈsɝmən,aɪz; ˈsɜːmənaɪz/ *v* [I] to give a lot of unwanted moral advice in a serious way〔喋喋不休地〕訓誡,〔不中聽地〕說教

ser·pent /ˈsɝpənt; ˈsɜːpənt/ *n* [C] **1** *literary* a snake, especially a large one【文】蛇〔尤指大蛇〕**2 the Serpent** the evil snake in the Garden of Eden according to the Bible〔《聖經》所載〕伊甸園中邪惡的蛇

ser·pen·tine /ˈsɝpən,tin; ˈsɜːpəntaɪn/ *adj* twisting or winding like a snake 曲折的, 蜿蜒的: *the serpentine course of the river* 彎彎曲曲的河道

ser·rat·ed /ˈsɛretɪd; sə̇ˈreɪtə̇d/ *adj* **serrated knife/edge** with a sharp edge made of a row of connected V shapes like teeth 鋸齒狀刀子/邊緣 —**serration** /-ˈreʃən; -ˈreɪʃən/ *n* [C,U]

ser·ried /ˈsɛrɪd; ˈserid/ *adj* [no comparative 無比較級] *literary* pressed closely together; CROWDED【文】排緊的, 靠攏的, 密集的

se·rum /ˈsɪrəm; ˈsɪərəm/ *n* [C,U] **1** a liquid containing substances that fight infection, that is put into a sick person's blood〔用於治療的〕免疫血清 —compare 比較 VACCINE **2** *technical* the watery part of blood or the liquid from a plant【術語】血清;〔植物的〕漿液, 樹液 —**serous** *adj*

W2 **ser·vant** /ˈsɝvənt; ˈsɜːvənt/ *n* [C] **1** someone who is paid to clean someone's house, cook for them, answer the door etc 僕人, 傭人 **2 servant of sth/sb** someone who is controlled by someone or something 受某人/某物支配的人: *Are we the masters or the servants of computers?* 我們是電腦的主人還是奴僕? —see also 另見 CIVIL SERVANT

S1 W1 **serve[1]** /sɝv; sɜːv/

1 ►FOOD/DRINK 食物/飲料◄ [I,T] to give someone food or drink as part of a meal 送上〔食物或飲料〕, 端上〔飯菜等〕; 侍候〔某人進餐〕: *What kind of wine should we serve?* 請問要上甚麼酒? | **serve sth with sth** *Serve the dish with rice and a green salad.* 用米飯和蔬菜沙拉配這道菜。| **serve sb** *Why aren't you out there serving the guests?* 你為甚麼不出去侍候客人? | **serve sth hot/cold etc** *delicious served hot or cold* 冷熱均可, 味美可口 | **serve breakfast/lunch/dinner** *Breakfast is served between 7 and 9 a.m.* 早上7點至9點供應早餐。| **serving spoon/dish** (=one used to serve food) 分菜餚用的大匙/上菜用的盤子 —see picture on page A15 參見A15頁圖

2 serve two/three/four etc if food serves two, three etc people, there is enough for that number of people〔食品〕足夠供二人/三人/四人吃: *One large fish should serve two to three people.* 一條大魚應夠兩個至三個人吃。

3 ►BE USEFUL/HELPFUL 有用/有幫助◄ [I,T] to be useful or helpful for a particular purpose or reason 適合作…用: **serve as sth** *The old couch had to serve as a guest bed.* 這張舊的長沙發只好用作客人的牀了。| **serve sb well** *Her talent for selling will serve her well in the future.* 她的推銷本領將來對她會很有用。| **serve sb's needs** *We don't get enough aid to serve our needs.* 我們得不到足夠的援助來滿足我們的需要。| **serve a purpose** *If you haven't got a crate, a large cardboard box will serve the purpose.* 要是你沒有板條箱, 一隻大的硬紙箱也行。| *Sure, you could phone her, but what purpose would that serve?* 當然, 你可以給她打電話, 但這又管甚麼用?

4 ►DO A HELPFUL JOB 做有益的工作◄ [I,T] to spend a period of time doing a job, especially one that helps the organization 為…工作; 供職; 服役: *The school board members serve a two-year term.* 學校董事會的董事任期兩年。| **[+in]** *He returned to Greece to serve in the army.* 他回到希臘服役。| **[+on]** *Annette serves on various local committees.* 安內特擔任當地多個委員會的委員。| **[+as]** *Martin served as ambassador to Burma in the '60s.* 馬丁在60年代擔任駐緬甸大使。| **serve sb/sth** *And let's not forget the women who served their country in the war.* 讓我們不要忘記那些在戰爭中為國盡職的婦女。

5 ►HAVE AN EFFECT 產生效果◄ [I,T] to have a particular effect or result 起作用, 產生效果: **serve to do sth** *Let that serve to demonstrate what happens if you don't pay attention.* 讓這件事向你證明, 如果你粗心大意會出甚麼樣的問題。| **serve (sb) as sth** *The pictures only served as a reminder of happier times.* 這些照片只能令人憶及過去的美好時光。

6 ►SHOP/RESTAURANT 商店/餐館◄ [I,T] to help the customers in a shop, restaurant etc, especially by bringing them the things that they want 接待(顧客)〔尤指為他們取來所需之物〕, 為(顧客)服務: *The waitress doesn't seem to want to serve us.* 那個女服務員似乎不想接待我們。| *Are you being served?* 有人接待您了嗎?

7 ►PROVIDE STH 供應某物◄ [T] to provide a group of people with something that is necessary or useful 向〔某羣體〕供應必須[有用]的東西, 供給: *water mains to serve the new homes in the area* 給這個地區新建住宅供水的總水管

8 ►PRISON 監獄◄ [T] to spend a particular period of time in prison 服刑, 坐牢: **serve a sentence** *Fox had served an eighteen-month sentence for burglary.* 福克斯因入屋盜竊罪坐了十八個月的牢。| **serve time** (=spend time in prison) 服刑, 坐牢

9 it serves sb right *spoken* used to say that you think someone deserves it if something unpleasant happens to them, because they have been stupid or unkind【口】〔某人〕活該! 這是某人應得的懲罰: *"Ouch! She pinched me!" "Serves you right, teasing her like that."* "哎唷! 她掐我!" "活該! 誰叫你那樣取笑她。"

10 ►SPORT 體育運動◄ [I,T] to start playing in a game such as tennis or VOLLEYBALL by throwing the ball up in the air and hitting it to your opponent〔網球、排球等〕發球, 開球 —see picture on page A23 參見A23頁圖

11 serve an apprenticeship to learn a job or skill by working for a fixed period of time for someone who has a lot of experience 當學徒

12 serve a summons/writ etc to officially send or give someone a written order to appear in a court of law 發傳票〔傳某人出庭〕

13 ►CHURCH 教堂◄ [I] to help a priest during the EUCHARIST〔做彌撒時〕充當助祭 —see also 另見 **if my memory serves me (well/correctly)** (MEMORY (4))

serve sth ↔ **out** *phr v* [T] **1** to continue doing something until the end of a fixed period of time 繼續做到期滿: *Dillon's served out nearly all his sentence.* 狄龍服刑快要期滿了。**2** *BrE* to put food onto plates【英】把食物盛到各人盤子裡: *Serve out the rice, will you?* 你來給大家盛飯, 好嗎?

serve sth ↔ **up** *phr v* [T] to put food onto plates so that people can eat it 把〔食物〕分到大家的盤子裡

serve[2] *n* [C] the action in a game such as tennis or VOLLEYBALL in which you throw the ball in the air and hit it to your opponent〔網球、排球等的〕發球

serv·er /ˈsɝvɚ; ˈsɜːvə/ *n* [C] **1** a special spoon or tool for putting a particular kind of food onto a plate 分菜餚用具〈如匙、叉、勺等〉: *salad servers* 盛取沙拉用的叉匙 **2** a player who hits a ball to begin a game in tennis, VOLLEYBALL etc〔網球、排球等的〕發球者 **3 a)** the main computer on a NETWORK[1] (4), that controls all the others〔電腦網絡的〕主機 **b)** one of the computers on a network that provides a special service〔電腦網絡中的〕服務器: **file/print/mail server** *All important data is stored on a central file server.* 所有的重要數據資料都儲存在中央檔案服務器內。**4** someone who helps a priest during the EUCHARIST〔做彌撒時的〕助祭(者)

ser·ve·ry /ˈsɝvərɪ; ˈsɜːvəri/ *n* [C] *BrE* the part of a restaurant where people get food to take back to their tables【英】〔餐廳裡擺放做好的食物供客人自己選取的〕供餐處, 取餐處

1 1

ser·vice¹ /ˈsɝvɪs; ˈsɜːvɪ̵s/ *n*

① FOR THE PUBLIC 為公眾
② HELP 幫助
③ WORK DONE FOR SB 為某人做的工作
④ ARMY/NAVY ETC 陸軍/海軍等
⑤ OTHER MEANINGS 其他意思

① FOR THE PUBLIC 為公眾

1 public services [C often plural 常用複數] things such as education, hospitals, banks etc that are provided for the public to use〔教育、醫院、銀行等的〕公共服務: *the decline in public services in recent times* 近期公共服務的減少 | **the welfare/medical/social etc service** (=services provided especially by the government)〔尤指政府提供的〕福利/醫療/社會等服務 | **police/fire/ambulance etc service** *He joined the police service at the age of 18.* 他18歲就參加警察工作。

2 jury/military/community etc service something that ordinary people can be asked to do for the public as a public duty or as a punishment 陪審團工作/兵役/社區服務: *You're lucky you were only sentenced to community service.* 你算走運的了, 只判你社區服務。

② HELP 幫助

3 [singular,U] help that you give to someone〔對別人的〕幫助, 效勞: **be of service** (=help someone) 有用, 能幫忙 *Don't thank me – I'm glad to be of service.* 不用謝——我很高興能幫點忙。| **do sb a service** (=do something to help someone) 幫某人的忙 *Oh, thanks, it'll be doing me a service.* 噢, 謝謝, 這就幫了我的忙了。| **provide a service** (=provide help for someone) 提供幫助, 給予幫忙 | **for services rendered** *formal* (=for help that you have given)【正式】為了所給予的幫助

4 ►SHOP/HOTEL ETC 商店/旅館等◄ [U] the help that people who work in a shop, restaurant, bar etc give you 服務, 接待, 侍候: *What was the service in that new restaurant like?* 那家新飯館的服務如何? | **customer service** *For refunds, please go to the customer service counter.* 退貨請到顧客服務櫃台。

5 ►ORGANIZATION 機構◄ [C] an organization that provides advice and help, for example with legal or personal problems〔提供諮詢、幫助等的〕服務機構: *a careers information service* 職業信息服務機構

6 be at your service *formal or humorous* if someone or something is at your service, they are available to help you in some way if you need them【正式或幽默】願為您效勞, 聽候您的吩咐: *My secretary and library are at your service.* 我的祕書和藏書都隨時為您效勞。

7 press sb/sth into service to persuade someone to help you, or use something to help you do something 說服某人幫忙/使用某物協助做某事: *We pressed Georgie's old bike into service.* 我們臨時拿喬吉的舊自行車來用。

③ WORK DONE FOR SB 為某人做的工作

8 ►EMPLOYMENT 雇用◄ [plural,U] the work you do for a person or organization 為某人[某機構]做的工作: **20/30 years etc of service** *Brian's retiring after 25 years of loyal service to the company.* 布賴恩為公司忠心耿耿地效力25年後就要退休了。| **services to sb** (=work, especially successful work, you have done for someone) 為某人做的工作〔尤指成功的工作〕 *an award for services to the printing industry* 因對印刷業所作貢獻而獲得的獎賞 | **public service** (=work done for the public or the government) 公益服務

9 ►SERVANT 傭人◄ [U] the job of working as a servant in someone's house, especially in former times〔尤指舊時的〕幫傭的工作: **be in service** (=be working as a servant in someone's house) 當傭人 | **domestic service** (=the job of working for someone in their house) 家庭幫傭的工作

10 ►BUSINESS 商業◄ [C] a business that provides help or does jobs for people rather than producing things 服務性行業, 非生產性行業: *the export of both manufactured goods and services* 成品和勞務的輸出 | **a baby-sitting/press-cutting/ironing etc service** *She's set up a dog-walking service in her local area.* 她在本地區開了一家遛狗服務中心。—see also 另見 SERVICE INDUSTRY

11 ►GOVERNMENT 政府◄ [C usually singular 一般用單數] an organization that works directly for a government 政府機構, 政府部門: *the diplomatic service* 外交部門 | *the foreign service* 外交機構

④ ARMY/NAVY ETC 陸軍/海軍等

12 the services a country's military forces, especially considered as a job 各軍種〔尤用於把參軍作為職業時〕: *I'm not sure what I'll do, maybe join the services.* 我還說不定要幹甚麼, 也許去參軍。

13 (be on) active service to be actually fighting in a battle or war while you are in the army, navy etc 正在參戰

⑤ OTHER MEANINGS 其他意思

14 ►RELIGION 宗教◄ [C] a formal religious ceremony, for example in church 正式的宗教儀式, 禮拜: **hold/conduct a service** (=be the person in charge of a service) 主持宗教儀式 *The Reverend James Wilkins will conduct the service.* 詹姆士·威爾金斯牧師將主持禮拜儀式。| **marriage/funeral/christening etc service** *memorial service for the disaster victims* 為罹難者舉行的追悼儀式

15 ►SPORT 體育運動◄ [C] an act of hitting a ball through the air in order to start a game, for example in tennis〔網球等的〕發球: *It's your service.* 該你發球了。

16 services *BrE* a place near a MOTORWAY where you can stop and have a meal or drink, or buy food, petrol etc【英】路邊服務站〔高速公路上的服務設施, 有餐飲、加油站等〕: *How far is it to the next services?* 這裡距下一個服務站有多遠? —see also 另見 SERVICE STATION

17 ►CAR/MACHINE 汽車/機器◄ [C] an examination and repair of a machine or car to keep it working properly 檢修, 保養: *I'm getting the bus home – my car's in for a service.* 我要坐公共汽車回家——我的汽車送去檢修了。

18 ►PLATES ETC 盤子等◄ **dinner/tea service** a set of matching plates, bowls, cups etc 餐具/茶具

19 ►BUS/TRAIN 公共汽車/火車◄ [C usually singular 一般用單數] a regular journey made by a bus, train, boat etc to a particular place or at a particular time〔車、船等的〕交通服務, 班次: *the 8:15 service to Cambridge* 8點15分開往劍橋的班次 —see also 另見 LIP SERVICE

service² *v* [T] **1** to examine a machine or vehicle and fix it if necessary 檢修, 維修〔機器或車輛〕: *I'm having the car serviced next week.* 我的汽車下星期檢修。**2** to provide people with something they need or want 為…提供服務: *city departments that service the local communities* 向地方社區提供服務的市政部門 **3** *technical* to pay the INTEREST¹ (4) on a debt【術語】支付〔借款〕利息

service³ *adj* **service stairs/elevator etc** stairs etc that are only for the use of people working in a place, rather than the public〔員工的〕專用樓梯/電梯等

ser·vice·a·ble /ˈsɝvɪsəbl; ˈsɜːvɪ̈səbəl/ *adj* ready or suitable to be used for a particular purpose 可供使用的, 宜用的: *serviceable shoes* 適穿的鞋子 —**serviceability** /ˌsɝvɪsəˈbɪlətɪ; ˌsɜːvɪ̈səˈbɪlɪ̈ti/ *n* [U]

service a·re·a /ˈ·· ˌ···/ *n* [C] *BrE* a place where you can stop on a MOTORWAY that has petrol, food, toilets etc【英】〔高速公路旁的〕路邊服務區〔有餐館、加油站、廁所等〕

service charge /ˈ·· ˌ·/ *n* [C] **1** *BrE* an amount of money that is added to a bill in a restaurant and given to the waiters【英】〔加在餐館賬單上的〕服務費, 小費 **2** an amount of money paid to the owner of a block of FLATs for services such as cleaning the stairs〔付給公寓房東的〕清潔衛生等服務費

service club /ˈ·· ˌ·/ *n* [C] *AmE* a usually national organization made of smaller local groups in which members do things to help their COMMUNITY【美】〔由全國各地方團體組成的〕服務社〔成員為社區做好事或謀福利〕

service in·dus·try /ˈ·· ˌ···/ *n* [C,U] an industry that provides a service such as insurance, bank accounts, or advertising rather than a product 服務性行業, 服務業〈如保險、銀行、廣告等〉

ser·vice·man /ˈsɝvɪsˌmæn; ˈsɜːvɪ̈smən/ *n plural* **servicemen** /-ˌmɛn; -mən/ [C] a man who is a member of the military 軍人

service sta·tion /ˈ·· ˌ··/ *n* [C] a place that sells petrol, food, etc〔有餐飲等出售的〕汽車加油站

ser·vice·wom·an /ˈsɝvɪsˌwʊmən; ˈsɜːvɪ̈sˌwʊmən/ *n plural* **servicewomen** /-ˌwɪmɪn; -ˌwɪmɪn/ [C] a woman who is a member of the military 女軍人

ser·vi·ette /ˌsɝvɪˈɛt; ˌsɜːviˈet/ *n* [C] *BrE & CanE* a NAPKIN【英和加】餐巾 —see picture on page A15 參見 A15 頁圖

ser·vile /ˈsɝvl; ˈsɜːvaɪl/ *adj* **1** too eager to obey someone without questioning them 過分屈從的, 卑躬屈膝的: *a servile attitude* 卑躬屈膝的態度 **2** connected with SLAVEs or with being a slave 奴隸的; 有關奴隸的 —**servilely** *adv* —**servility** /sɝˈvɪlətɪ; sɜːˈvɪlɪ̈ti/ *n* [U]

serv·ing /ˈsɝvɪŋ; ˈsɜːvɪŋ/ *n* [C] an amount of food that is enough for one person; HELPING〔供一人食用的〕一份食物: *How many servings does the recipe make?* 這個食譜的量夠多少人吃?

ser·vi·tor /ˈsɝvətɚ; ˈsɜːvɪ̈tə/ *n* [C] *old use* a male servant【舊】男僕, 男侍從

ser·vi·tude /ˈsɝvəˌtud; ˈsɜːvɪ̈tjuːd/ *n* [U] the condition of being a SLAVE or being forced to obey someone else 奴役; 苦役, 勞役: *The legislation of 1781 abolished penal servitude in Bohemia.* 1781 年的立法廢除了波希米亞的勞役監禁。—see also 另見 **penal servitude** (PENAL (1))

ses·a·me /ˈsɛsəmɪ; ˈsesəmi/ *n* [U] a tropical plant grown for its seeds and oil and used in cooking 芝麻 —see also 另見 OPEN SESAME

ses·sion /ˈsɛʃən; ˈseʃən/ *n* [C] **1** a meeting or period of time used for a particular purpose, especially by a group of people 會期;〔某團體從事某項活動的〕集會〔時間〕: *a drinking session* 飲酒聚會 | *question-and-answer sessions* 問答時間 | *a jazz session* 爵士樂演奏會 **2** a formal meeting or group of meetings of an organisation, especially a court or parliament 正式會議;〔法院的〕(一次) 開庭;〔議會的〕一次會議: **in session** *the noise of Parliament in session* 英國議會開會時的喧鬧聲 **3 sessions a)** petty sessions 簡易法庭 **b)** QUARTER SESSIONS 季審法庭

set¹ /sɛt; set/ *v past tense and past participle* **set**

① PUT DOWN 放下
② START STH HAPPENING 引發某事
③ DECIDE/ESTABLISH 決定/確立
④ JOB/STH TO DO 工作/要做的事
⑤ MAKE READY 作好準備
⑥ MUSIC/BOOKS 音樂/書籍
⑦ WANT/NOT WANT 想要/不想要
⑧ OTHER MEANINGS 其他意思

① PUT DOWN 放下

1 ►PUT 放◄ [T always+adv/prep] to carefully put something down somewhere, especially something that is difficult to carry 放置, 放下〔尤指不便攜帶的物件〕: **set sth down/on etc** *She set the tray down on a table next to his bed.* 她把盤子放在他牀邊的桌子上。

② START STH HAPPENING 引發某事

2 set sth on fire/alight/ablaze to make something start burning 點燃某物; 放火燒某物; 把某物付之一炬: *Crowds of youths started overturning cars and setting them on fire.* 一羣羣年輕人開始把汽車推翻並放火將其點燃。

3 set the pattern/tone/trend to happen or do something in a particular way that is then repeated many times or which continues for a long time 定模式/定調子/領潮流: *Gabriel's style set the trend for the scores of rock videos that followed.* 加布里埃爾的風格為後來的許多搖滾樂錄像開了先河。

4 set in motion/progress/train to make something start happening, especially by means of an official order 使開始運作[產生影響]〔尤指用正式命令〕: *The government is to set in motion a wide-ranging review of defence spending.* 政府要着手進行一次對國防開支的大範圍檢查。

③ DECIDE/ESTABLISH 決定/確立

5 set a time/date/price etc to decide that something should happen at a particular time, cost a particular amount of money etc 確定時間/日期/價格等: *Have you set a date for the wedding?* 你們確定了婚禮的日期沒有?

6 set guidelines/standards/conditions/limits etc to officially establish rules, standards etc for doing something 制定方針/標準/條件/界限等: *standards of hygiene set by the Health Department* 衛生部制定的衛生標準

7 set a precedent if an event or action sets a precedent, it shows people a way of doing something which they can use or copy 開創先例: *If her claim against her employers is successful, it could set a legal precedent.* 她向雇主提出的索賠如果得到滿足, 這將開創一個法律上的先例。

④ JOB/STH TO DO 工作/要做的事

8 set sb a task/challenge/goal etc to decide that someone should try and achieve something, especially something that needs a lot of effort 向某人提出任務/挑戰/目標等: *Wilkins then set himself the task of tagging all the birds on the island.* 威爾金斯於是給自己定下任務, 要給島上所有的鳥帶上標籤。| **set yourself to do sth** *She had set herself to write a novel.* 她已下了決心去寫一部長篇小說。

9 ►GIVE SB A PIECE OF WORK 給某人規定任務◄

[T] *BrE* to give someone a piece of work to do, especially a student in your class or someone who works for you【英】〔給學生〕佈置作業;〔給下屬〕指派任務: **set sb sth** *Mr. Phipps set us an essay on the origins of the French Revolution.* 菲普斯老師給我們佈置了作業, 要寫一篇關於法國大革命起因的論文。
10 ►EXAMINATION 考試◄ [T] *BrE* to invent questions for students to answer, especially in an examination【英】出〔題目〕〔尤指出考題〕: *Whoever set the questions obviously didn't know much about physics.* 出考題的人顯然對物理學懂得不多。
11 set to work to start doing something in a determined way, especially something that is difficult and needs a lot of effort 堅決地着手做某事〔尤指困難的需要努力去做的工作〕: **set to work to do sth** *They set to work to paint the outside of the building.* 他們着手給大樓的外牆刷油漆。| **[+on]** *Davies is about to set work on a second book.* 戴維斯即將開始寫第二本書了。
12 set sb to work to make someone start doing a particular kind of work for you 使某人着手幹活: **set sb to work doing sth** *Before dawn Harry had set them to work collecting firewood for breakfast.* 天亮之前哈里已佈置他們去拾柴火做早餐。
13 set sb/sth doing sth to make someone start doing something or make something start happening 使某人開始做某事/某事開始發生: *Her last remark had set me thinking.* 她最後的話引起了我的思考。| *The wind set the trees rustling.* 風吹得樹木沙沙作響。

⑤ MAKE READY 作好準備

14 ►MOVE PART OF A MACHINE/CLOCK ETC 調整儀器/撥準鐘錶◄ [T] to move part of a machine, clock etc so that it is in a particular position and is ready to be used 調整〔儀器〕至所需位置; 撥正〔鐘錶〕; 撥〔鬧鐘〕至指定時間: *Have you set the alarm?* 你撥好鬧鐘了嗎? | **set sth to/at** *Just set the dial to 'hot wash' and press the 'on' button.* 把刻度盤調到"熱洗"位置, 再按"開始"按鈕。
15 set the table to arrange plates, knives, cups etc on a table so that it is ready for a meal 擺好餐桌[準備開飯]
16 set a trap a) to make a trap ready to catch an animal 設陷阱〔以捕捉動物〕 **b)** to invent a plan to show that someone is doing something wrong 佈下圈套〔以誘人自我暴露〕: *The FBI set a trap for the Congressmen it believed were taking bribes.* 聯邦調查局對那些被認為受賄的國會議員佈下了圈套。

⑥ MUSIC/BOOKS 音樂/書籍

17 ►FILM/PLAY/STORY 電影/戲劇/故事◄ [T usually passive 一般用被動態] if a film, play, story etc is set in a place or period, it happens there or at that time 為〔電影、戲劇、小說等〕設定發生的地點和時間; 設置〔電影、戲劇、小說等的〕背景: *The novel is set in France in the early 19th century.* 這部小說以 19 世紀初的法國為背景。
18 ►PRINTING 印刷◄ to make the words and letters of a book, newspaper etc ready to be printed 為〔書、報等〕排字, 排版: *In those days books had to be set by hand.* 在那時, 書籍得用手工排版。
19 set sth to music to write music for a story or a poem, so that it can be sung 為〔故事或詩歌等〕譜曲

⑦ WANT/NOT WANT 想要/不想要

20 set your mind/sights/heart on sth to be determined to achieve something or decide that you definitely want to have it 一心想達成某目標[得到某物]: *Once Sharon sets her mind on something, she usually gets what she wants.* 莎倫一旦決心想得到某樣東西, 她通常都會如願以償。
21 set yourself against to be determined that you do not want something to happen or you do not want to take part in something 堅決反對; 堅決不參加: *Angie seems to have set herself against the idea completely.* 安吉似乎完全反對這個主意。

⑧ OTHER MEANINGS 其他意思

22 set a record to run a race in a faster time than anyone else, jump further than anyone else, win a competition more times than anyone else etc〔在體育競賽中〕創造紀錄: *The Kenyan runner set a new Olympic Record in the 3000 metres.* 肯尼亞的跑步選手創下了 3000 米賽跑的奧林匹克新記錄。
23 ►SUN 太陽◄ [I] if the sun sets, it moves close to the horizon and then goes below it〔日〕落,〔太陽〕下山
24 set an example to behave in a way that shows other people how to behave 樹立榜樣: *Teachers should set an example for their students.* 教師應該給學生樹立榜樣。
25 set sb straight/right to tell someone the right way to do something or the true facts about something 糾正某人的做法[想法]: **[+on]** *I set him right on one or two points of procedure.* 我幫助他糾正了一兩處程序上的問題。—see also 另見 **set the record straight** (STRAIGHT² (7))
26 set sth right to deal with any problems, mistakes etc 解決問題, 改正錯誤: *I wish you'd been here – you could easily have set things right.* 我真希望你當時在這裡 —— 那樣很容易就可以把問題解決了。
27 set sb free/loose to allow someone to be free, or to allow a dangerous person to escape 釋放某人; 把〔危險人物〕放走: *Brian Keenan and the other hostages were finally set free.* 布賴恩·基南和其他人質終於獲釋。
28 set great store by/set a high value on to consider something to be very important 認為〔某物〕非常重要: *At my old school they set great store by athletic achievements.* 我以前那所學校極其重視體育成績。
29 ►LIQUID/GLUE/CEMENT ETC 液體/膠水/水泥等◄ [I] to become hard and solid 凝結, 凝固: *How long does it take for the glue to set?* 這種膠需要多長時間才能凝固?
30 ►BONE 骨頭◄ **a)** [T] if you set a broken bone, you move the broken ends so that they are in the right place to grow together again 將〔斷骨〕復位〔以便癒合〕 **b)** [I] if a broken bone sets, it joins together again〔斷骨〕癒合
31 ►HAIR 頭髮◄ [T] to arrange someone's hair while it is wet so that it has a particular style when it dries〔趁頭髮潮濕時〕把〔某人的頭髮〕梳理成某種髮型, 做〔頭髮〕
32 be set into to be fixed into the surface of something 被嵌入: *a large brick fireplace which was set into the wall* 嵌建在牆裡的寬大磚砌壁爐
33 be set with gems etc to be decorated with jewels 鑲嵌着寶石的: *a gold bracelet set with rubies* 鑲有紅寶石的金手鐲

set about *phr v* [T] **1** to start doing something, especially something that needs a lot of time and effort 開始[着手]做某事〔尤指費時費勁的事〕: **set about doing sth** *She set about clearing up after the party.* 聚會之後, 她開始收拾東西打掃衛生。**2** to deal with something in a particular way 處理: *I think you're setting about the problem in the wrong way.* 我認為你處理這個問題的方法錯了。**3** *especially literary* to attack someone by hitting and kicking them【尤文】攻擊; 對…拳打腳踢: *They set about him with their fists.* 他們揮拳打他。

set against *phr v* [T] **1** [**set** sb **against** sb] to make someone start to fight or quarrel with another person, especially a person who they had friendly relations with before 使與〔某人〕對立, 敵對; 使與〔朋友等〕打[吵]架: *The bitter civil war has set brother against brother.* 激烈的內戰使兄弟反目成仇。**2** [**set** sth **off against** sth] to consider something in relation to another thing, espe-

S

cially when that other thing is very important 將…與…聯繫起來考慮: *The recent improvement in output has to be set against increased labour costs.* 最近的產量提高必須與人工成本的增加聯繫起來考慮。**3 set sth (off) against tax** to make an official record of the money you have spent on something connected with your job, in order to reduce the amount of tax you have to pay 將與工作相關的開支列入以減少應納稅款

set apart *phr v* [T] **1** [**set** sb/sth **apart**] to make someone or something different and often better than other people or things 使〔某人或某物〕與眾不同, 使優於〔他人或他物〕: *It is man's ability to think which sets him apart from other animals.* 是人類的思維能力使其有別於其他動物。**2** [**set sth apart**] to keep something for a special purpose and only use it for that purpose 留出…〔作某種用途〕, 撥出: *Regular times should be set apart for seeing patients.* 應該留出查看病人的固定時間。

set sth ↔ **aside** *phr v* [T] **1** to keep something, especially money or time, for a special purpose and only use it for that purpose〔為某種目的〕留出, 撥出〔金錢或時間等〕: [+for] *Try to set aside at least an hour each day for learning new vocabulary.* 爭取每天至少抽出一個小時學習新詞彙。| *a room that had been set aside for visitors* 留給客人用的房間 **2** to decide that you will not be influenced by a particular feeling, belief, or principle, because something else is more important 不受〔某種感情、信仰、原則等的〕影響, 不顧; 把…置之不理: *Congress ought to set aside its political differences to pass a health care bill.* 國會應當拋開政治分歧, 通過一項關於衛生保健的議案。**3** to declare that a previous legal decision or agreement no longer has any effect 宣布〔以前的法律決定或協議〕無效, 撤銷, 駁回: *The judge set aside the verdict of the lower court.* 法官宣布下級法院的判決無效。

set back *phr v* [T] **1** [**set** sb/sth ↔ **back**] to delay the progress or development of something, or delay someone from finishing something 延緩〔某事的進展〕; 阻礙〔某人完成某事〕; 拖…後腿: *The Cultural Revolution set back the modernization of China by many years.* 文化大革命使中國的現代化延緩了許多年。**2** [**set sb back**] *informal* to cost someone a lot of money【非正式】使〔某人〕花費大筆錢: *The new laptop from Toshiba will set you back a cool $2000.* 這台東芝牌手提電腦得花你整整2000美元。

set down *phr v* [T] **1** [**set** sth ↔ **down**] to write about something so that you have a record of it 寫下, 記下: *I wanted to set my feelings down on paper.* 我想把我的感想寫下來。**2** [**set** sth ↔ **down**] to establish how something should be done in an official set of rules or an official document〔在正式文件中〕制定, 規定: *The club rules are set down in its constitution.* 俱樂部的規則都寫在其章程裡。**3** [**set** sb ↔ **down**] *BrE* to stop a car, bus etc and allow someone to get out【英】將〔汽車、公共汽車等〕停下讓〔乘客〕下車: *The driver set her down at the station.* 司機在車站停下車讓她下去。

set forth *phr v* **1** [T **set** sth ↔ **forth**] *formal* to write or talk about an idea, argument, or set of figures【正式】〔書面或口頭〕陳述〔觀點等〕, 闡明: *Rousseau set forth his theories on education in his book "Emile".* 盧梭在他的小說《愛彌爾》中闡述了他的教育理論。**2** [I] *literary* to begin a journey【文】出發, 啟程: *They were about to set forth on a voyage into the unknown.* 他們即將啟航前往一個未知的世界。

set in *phr v* [I] if something sets in, especially something unpleasant, it begins and seems likely to continue for a long time〔尤指不愉快的事情〕開始, 來臨: *Winter seems to be setting in early this year.* 今年的冬天似乎來得早。| *A period of further economic decline set in during the 1930s.* 20世紀30年代出現了一段經濟進一步衰退的時期。

set off 出發; 觸發

She set off early in the morning.
她一大早就出發了。

The burglar set the alarm off.
小偷觸動了警報器。

set off *phr v* **1** [I] to start to to go somewhere 出發, 啟程, 動身: *I wanted to set off early in order to avoid the traffic.* 我想早點出發以避開交通擁堵。| *The old man set off down the path towards the river.* 老人開始沿着小路向河邊走去。**2** [T **set** sth ↔ **off**] to make something start happening or make people suddenly start doing something, especially when you do not intend to do so 引起, 激發〔尤指意外事件〕: *The incident set off a chain of events which resulted in the outbreak of World War I.* 這一事件引起了連鎖事件, 從而導致第一次世界大戰的爆發。| *News of the deal set off a flurry of activity on Wall Street.* 那宗交易的消息引起了華爾街一陣騷動。**3** [T **set** sth ↔ **off**] to make something such as an alarm system start operating, especially when you do not intend to do so〔尤指無意中〕引起某事〈如觸響警報系統〉; 觸發: *The high winds set off a lot of car alarms.* 強風使很多汽車的報警器響了起來。**4** [T **set** sth ↔ **off**] to make a bomb explode, or cause an explosion 使〔炸彈等〕爆炸; 引發〔爆炸〕: *The slightest movement would have set off the device and blown us all sky high.* 最輕微的動作都會使這個炸彈爆炸, 把我們炸得血肉橫飛。**5** [T **set** sth ↔ **off**] if a piece of clothing, colour, decoration etc sets something off, it makes it look attractive〔衣服、顏色、裝飾等〕將〔某物〕襯托得很漂亮; 使更具吸引力: *a stylish beige dress, set off by a blue jacket and scarf* 用藍色外套和圍巾襯托的一套時髦的米色連衣裙 **6** [T **set** sb **off**] to make someone start laughing, crying, or talking about something 激起〔某人的某種情感〕; 引起〔某人笑、哭、談論某事等〕: *Don't mention anything about weddings – you'll only set her off again.* 不要提及任何有關婚禮的事——否則你又會使她喋喋不休了。

set on *phr v* [T] [**set** sb **on/onto** sb] to make people or animals attack someone 使〔人或動物〕攻擊〔某人〕: *The farmer threatened to set his dogs on them if they didn't get off his land.* 農場主威嚇說, 他們如果不離開他的土地, 他就要放狗咬他們。| **be set on/upon by sb** (=be suddenly attacked by people or animals) 突然遇襲, 突然被〔某人或動物〕襲擊 *He was set on by a gang of hooligans as he was leaving the bar.* 他離開酒吧時突然遭到一夥流氓的襲擊。

set out *phr v* **1** [I] to start a journey, especially a long journey 動身踏上〔漫長的旅途〕: *Columbus and his crew set out from Europe in 1492.* 哥倫布和他的船員

在 1492 年從歐洲啟航。| [+for] *We packed our rucksacks and set out for the hills.* 我們收拾好背包向羣山進發。**2 set out to do sth** to start doing something or making plans to do something in order to achieve a particular result〔為達到某個結果而〕開始做某事, 着手進行: *She deliberately set out to poison her husband.* 她蓄意着手毒殺她的丈夫。| **set out with the intention of doing sth** *They set out with the intention of becoming the number one team in the league.* 他們決意爭取成為球賽聯合會中最強的球隊。**3** [T **set** sth ↔ **out**] to write or talk about something such as a group of facts, ideas, or reasons, especially in a clearly organized way〔清楚而系統地用書面或口頭〕陳述, 闡明: *He set out the reasons for his decision in his report.* 他在報告中陳述了他作出這個決定的理由。| *The guidelines are set out in paragraph two.* 第二段闡述了指導原則。**4** [T **set** sth ↔ **out**] to put a group of things down and arrange them in order 擺放, 安排, 陳列: *Auntie Lou set out the dinner on the table.* 盧阿姨在桌上擺好了晚餐。**5 set out on a career/course of action** to start a particular kind of job or start doing something in a particular way 開始從事某種職業/開始採取某種行動: *My nephew is just setting out on a career in journalism.* 我的姪兒剛開始從事新聞工作。

set to *phr v* [I] *BrE* to start doing something eagerly and with a lot of effort and determination【英】開始積極做某事, 決心努力做某事: *If we all set to, we can finish the cleaning in half an hour.* 如果我們大家都努力幹, 半個小時內就可以完成打掃工作。

set up *phr v*

1 ►COMPANY/ORGANIZATION ETC 公司/機構等◄ [I,T] to start a company, organization, committee etc; ESTABLISH 建立, 設立, 創立〔公司、機構等〕: **set sth ↔ up** *The Race Relations Board was originally set up in 1965.* 種族關係委員會最初建立於 1965 年。| *They want to set up their own import-export business.* 他們想創辦自己的進出口公司。| **set up as** (=start your own business as) 當上…, 開業做… *John used his inheritance to set up as a graphic designer.* 約翰用他獲得的遺產開業, 當了個平面造型設計師。| **set up shop/set up in business** (=begin operating a business) 開業, 開始經營〔生意〕 *We mortgaged our house and set up shop with the money from that.* 我們用自己的房子抵押貸款並用這筆錢來創業。

2 ►ARRANGE/ORGANIZE 安排/組織◄ [T **set** sth ↔ **up**] to make the necessary arrangements so that something can happen, such as a meeting, an event, or a system for doing something 安排〔會議等〕; 建立〔制度等〕: *I'll get my secretary to set up a working lunch for us.* 我去吩咐祕書給大家安排工作午餐。| *There was a lot of work involved in setting up the festival.* 安排好這個節日活動需要做很多工作。| *We need to set up emergency procedures to deal with this sort of problem.* 我們需要建立應急程序來處理這類問題。

3 ►EQUIPMENT 設備◄ [I,T] to prepare the equipment that will be needed for an activity so that it is ready to be used 安裝; 架設: *The next band was already setting up on the other stage.* 下一支樂隊已經開始在另一個舞台架設裝備了。| **set** sth ↔ **up** *Does anyone know how to set up this generator?* 有誰懂得怎樣安裝這台發電機嗎? | *Why don't you set up the Monopoly game while I finish washing the dishes?* 你為甚麼不趁我洗盤子的時候先擺好"大富翁"遊戲棋呢?

4 ►BUILD/PUT UP 建立/豎立◄ [T **set** sth ↔ **up**] to place or build something such as a sign or STATUE somewhere 建起, 豎起〔標誌牌、塑像等〕: *The army has set up road blocks round the city.* 軍隊已在城市四周設置了路障。

5 set up home/house to start living in your own home, especially with someone else, instead of living with your parents〔尤指離開父母〕成家, 過獨立生活: *Lucy and Paul are thinking of setting up house together.* 露西和保羅正在考慮成家的事。

6 set up camp a) to put up a tent or group of tents in a place so that you can stay there 搭帳篷: *We set up camp near the shore of the lake.* 我們在湖濱搭起了帳篷。**b)** *informal* to move all your things to a place so that you can start to live or work there【非正式】搬遷到某地〔工作或生活〕: *She's set up camp in my office.* 她已經搬到我的辦公室工作了。

7 ►MAKE SB SEEM GUILTY 使某人似乎有罪◄ [T **set** sb ↔ **up**] *informal* to deliberately make other people think that someone has done something wrong, or illegal【非正式】誣陷, 陷害〔某人〕: *The four terrorists claimed they had been set up by the police.* 那四名恐怖分子聲稱他們是被警察誣陷的。

8 ►HEALTHY/FULL OF ENERGY 健康/精力充沛◄ [T **set** sb **up**] to make you feel healthy and full of energy 使〔某人〕覺得健康, 使〔某人〕精力旺盛: **set sb up for the day** *A good breakfast will set you up for the day.* 一頓豐盛的早餐可以使你整天都精力充沛。

9 set sb up for life *informal* if something sets you up for life, it provides you with enough money for the rest of your life【非正式】使某人一生有足夠的錢: *In a few more years you should be set up for life.* 再過幾年, 你就該擁有終生夠用的錢了。

10 ►START HAPPENING 引發◄ [T **set up** sth] *especially technical* to make a condition or a process start happening【尤術語】使〔某種情況〕產生; 引起, 造成: *If one reactor has a meltdown, it could set up a chain reaction.* 假如一個核反應堆的堆芯熔毀, 那就會引發連鎖反應。| *Stimulation of the sensory receptors sets up neural activity.* 對感官感受器的刺激會引起神經的活動。

11 ►NOISE 噪聲◄ **set up a commotion/din/racket etc** to stark making a loud, unpleasant noise 發出喧鬧聲/嘈雜聲/吵鬧聲: *At this, the two babies set up a tremendous howling.* 那兩個嬰兒隨即都哇哇大哭起來。

S

set² *n* [S1] [W1]

1 ►GROUP OF THINGS 一組事物◄ [C] a group of things that form a whole〔物品的〕一套, 一副, 一組: *a chess set* 一副棋 | [+of] *a set of tools* 一套工具 | *We are now facing a whole new set of problems.* 我們現在面臨着一大堆新問題。

2 ►TELEVISION/RADIO 電視/無線電◄ [C] a television, or a piece of equipment for receiving radio signals 電視機, 收音機: *a colour television set* 彩色電視機 —see also 另見 CRYSTAL SET

3 ►STAGE 舞台◄ [C] the scenery, furniture etc that is put on a stage to represent where the action of the play is taking place〔舞台的〕佈景, 場景〈如自然景色、家具佈置等〉: *The play wasn't that good but the set was impressive.* 這齣戲並不怎麼好, 但佈景倒是給人印象很深。

4 ►FILM 影片◄ [C] a place where a film or television programme is acted and filmed〔拍攝電影或電視節目的〕拍攝場地, 攝影場: *Everyone must be on the set to start filming at eight o'clock.* 大家都必須準時到達拍攝現場, 8 點鐘開拍。

5 ►SPORT 體育運動◄ [C] one part of a game such as tennis or VOLLEYBALL〔網球或排球等的〕一盤: *Agassi won the second set 6–4.* 阿加斯以 6 比 4 贏了第二盤。

6 ►MUSIC 音樂◄ [C] a series of songs performed by one band or singer as part of a concert〔音樂會中由某個樂隊或歌手演出的〕一組樂曲[歌曲]

7 ►HAIR 頭髮◄ [singular] an act of arranging your hair in a particular style when it is wet 做髮型, 做頭髮: a **shampoo and set** (=washing the hair and arranging it in a style) 洗頭和做髮型

8 ►PEOPLE 人羣◄ [singular] a group of people with similar interests〔趣味相投的〕一羣人: *Joanna got in*

with a rather wild set at college. 喬安娜在大學時和一夥相當放蕩的人厮混。—see also 另見 JET SET

9 ►FIRMNESS 結實◄ [singular] the state of becoming firm or solid 凝結, 凝固: *You'll get a better set if you use gelatine.* 如果你用明膠, 就會凝結得好些。

10 ►PART OF BODY 身體某個部分◄ [C] the way in which you are sitting, standing etc, especially when you look stiff〔坐或站的〕姿態, 姿勢: **[+of]** *From the set of her shoulders it was obvious that Sue was exhausted.* 從她肩膀的姿態來看, 蘇顯然是精疲力竭了。

11 ►STUDENTS 學生◄ [C] *BrE* a group of children who have the same level of ability in a subject at school【英】〔在某個科目上能力相似的〕一組學生, 一班學生: *Adam's in the top set for maths.* 亞當在數學成績最好的一組學生中。

12 ►MATHS 數學◄ [C] *technical* a collection of numbers etc in MATHEMATICS【術語】〔數學中的〕集: *The set (x, y) has two members.* (x, y)這個集有兩個項。

13 ►ONION 洋葱◄ [C] a small brown root planted in order to grow onions〔種植用的〕球莖: *onion sets* 洋葱球莖

set³ *adj*

1 ►PLACED 位於某處的◄ being in the position that is mentioned 在…位置的, 位於…的: *a town set on a hill* 山丘上的市鎮 | *Diane had very deep-set eyes.* 黛安娜的眼窩很深。| *a house set back from the road* 離公路有一段距離的房子

S

2 ►WAGE/TIME 工資/時間◄ a set time, amount etc is fixed and cannot be changed〔時間、數目等〕固定的, 不變的: *We pay a set amount each week.* 我們每星期支付一筆固定的錢。

3 a set book/text etc *BrE* a book that must be studied for an examination【英】考試必讀的書/課本等 —see also 另見 SET¹ (10)

4 a set menu/meal *BrE* a set meal has a fixed price and includes a combination of foods that the restaurant suggests【英】〔固定價格和菜式的〕套菜/套餐

5 be set on/upon/against to be very determined about something 決心要…/堅決反對…: *Nina's very set on going to this party.* 尼娜決心要去參加這個聚會。| **be dead set on/upon/against** *The government's dead set against the plan.* 政府堅決反對這項計劃。

6 have your heart set on sth to be determined to do something 決心做某事: *She's got her heart set on going to France this summer.* 她下了決心要在今年夏天去法國。

7 ►READY 準備好的◄ [only after noun 僅用於名詞後] *informal* someone who is set for something is prepared for it【非正式】準備就緒的: **set for sth** *Are you all set for the journey?* 你們都為旅行作好準備了嗎? | **set to do sth** *I was all set to leave when the phone rang.* 我正準備要離開時, 電話鈴響了。| **get set** (=get ready) 預備, 作好準備 *"On your marks – get set – go!" said the starter.* "各就各位 — 預備 — 跑!"發號員喊道。| **all set** *Okay, I'm all set, let's get going.* 好了, 我一切都準備停當了, 咱們走吧。

8 set smile/teeth/jaw a set smile etc shows that you are not happy about something or are determined to do something 假笑/咬緊牙關〔表示不悦或堅決〕: *Gloria greeted her guests with a set smile.* 格洛麗亞面帶假笑迎接客人。

9 set opinions/beliefs etc set opinions or beliefs are ones you are not likely to change 執着的主張/信念等

10 be set in your ways to be used to doing the same things every day 積習難改, 習慣根深蒂固: *Uncle's 80 now and very set in his ways.* 叔叔80歲了, 種種習慣都根深蒂固。

11 set to (do sth) likely to do something 很可能(做某事): *The temperature is set to drop very low tonight.* 今晚的氣溫很可能會降得很低。| *This issue is set to cause the government serious embarrassment.* 這個問題很可能給政府造成非常尷尬的局面。

set·back /ˋsɛtˏbæk; ˈsetbæk/ *n* [C] something that delays or prevents progress, or makes things worse than they were 阻礙發展的事物; 挫折: *The recent crime figures are a major setback for the law and order reforms.* 最近的犯罪率使治安改革嚴重受挫。—see also 另見 **set back** (SET¹)

set piece /ˌ· ˈ·◄/ *n* [C] part of a play, piece of music, painting etc that follows a well-known formal pattern or style, and is often very impressive〔戲劇、音樂、繪畫等遵循著名的固定模式或風格的〕精彩部分: *The trial scene at the end of the play is a classic set piece.* 這齣戲結尾的一場審判是經典的場景。

set·square /ˋsɛtˋskwɛr; ˈsetskweə/ *n* [C] a flat piece of plastic or metal with three sides and one right angle, used for drawing or testing angles; TRIANGLE (4)〔繪圖和測量直角用的〕三角板

set·tee /sɛˋti; seˈtiː/ *n* [C] a long seat with a back and usually with arms, for more than one person to sit on; SOFA 長沙發, 長靠椅

set·ter /ˋsɛtɚ; ˈsetə/ *n* [C] **1** a long-haired dog often trained to find where animals or birds are so they can be shot 塞特種獵犬, 蹲伏獵狗〔一種長毛狗, 被訓練去發現獵物位置以助獵〕 **2** someone who does a particular job, or who does things that other people copy 制定者; 倡導者: **exam setter/trap setter/fashion setter etc** (=someone who gives exams, puts out traps etc) 考試命題者/陷阱設置者/時尚倡導者 —see also 另見 **set the pattern/tone/trend** (SET¹ (3)), TRENDSETTER

set·ting /ˋsɛtɪŋ; ˈsetɪŋ/ *n* [C usually singular 一般用單數]  **1 a)** all the things that surround someone or something at a particular time, including the events that happen, their environment, or the people they are with 背景, 環境〔指周圍的一切事物與人〕: *an old farm house in a beautiful setting* 環境優美的古老農舍 | *children brought up in a privileged setting* 在優越環境中長大的小孩 **2** the place or time that the action of a book, film etc happens〔書、影片等中情節發生的〕地點[時間]: *Canberra is the setting for his latest novel.* 他的最新小說以堪培拉為背景。**3** [C] the position in which you fix the controls on a machine or instrument〔機器、儀器等調控裝置的〕設定位置: *The freezer's already on its highest setting.* 冷凍室已經調到最高一擋了。**4** [C] the metal that holds a stone in a piece of jewellery, or the way the stone is fixed〔寶石的〕鑲嵌底座[式樣]: *a diamond ring in a gold setting* 黃金鑽戒 **5** [C] music that is written to go with a poem, prayer etc〔為詩、禱文等譜寫的〕樂曲

6 the setting of the sun *literary* the time when the sun goes down【文】日落 —see also 另見 PLACE SETTING

set·tle¹ /ˋsɛtl; ˈsetl/ *v*

1 ►MAKE COMFORTABLE/SAFE 使舒適/安全◄ **a)** [I always+adv/prep, T always+adv/prep] to put yourself or someone else in a comfortable position (使)處於舒適的位置: **[+back/into/down]** *Mel settled back in his chair and closed his eyes.* 梅爾舒舒服服地坐在椅子上閉上眼睛。| **settle yourself** *Kari had already settled herself in a corner where she could watch.* 卡里早已在一個方便觀察的小角落裡舒服地坐下來了。**b)** to put something carefully in a particular place so that it stays there 放置, 安放〔某物〕: *Lee settled the cup on the saucer.* 李把杯子放在茶碟上。

2 ►MOVE DOWN/STAY 落下/停留◄ [I] **a)** if dust, snow etc settles it comes down and stays in one place〔灰塵、雪等〕降落; 落下; 沉降: **[+on/in]** *snow settling on the roofs* 房頂上的積雪 | *The sediment will settle in the bottle after a few days.* 沉澱物過幾天就會沉積到瓶底。**b)** if a bird, insect etc settles it flies down and rests on something〔鳥、昆蟲等〕停下, 落下, 棲息於: **[+on]** *A fly settled on the plate of cookies.* 一隻蒼蠅落在那盤小甜餅上。

3 ►END AN ARGUMENT 結束爭辯◄ [I,T] to end an argument by agreeing on something〔通過取得一致意

見面〕結束〔爭論〕: **[+with]** *It looks like they're finally going to settle with the railroad.* 看來他們最終要和鐵路部門結束爭端了。| **settle a quarrel/argument/dispute etc** *There's only one way to settle the dispute, and they know it.* 要解決爭端只有一種方法, 他們是知道的。| **settle out of court** (=come to an agreement to avoid going to a court of law) 庭外和解 | **settle your differences** (=agree to stop arguing with someone) 解決分歧

4 ▶DECIDE 決定◀ [T] to decide on something, especially so that you can make definite arrangements 確定, 決定: **settled (that)** *It was settled that Jim would visit us on the weekend.* 已經確定, 吉姆週末將來探訪我們。| **It is settled** (=it is now decided) 現在決定 *It's settled then. I'll go back to the States in June.* 那麼現在就定下來, 我六月份回美國。| **That settles it!** (=this is enough information for a decision to be made) 那就解決了!; 那就可以決定了! *Carol's only 15? That settles it. We are not taking her with us.* 卡羅爾只有 15 歲? 那就定了, 我們不帶她一起去。

5 ▶PAY MONEY 付錢◀ [T] to pay money that is owed 支付〔欠債、賬目〕, 結算: **settle a bill/account/claim** *We expect you to settle your account in full each month.* 我們要求你每月結清全部賬目。| *These insurance companies take forever to settle a claim.* 這些保險公司要拖很久才支付賠償金。

6 ▶TAKE CARE OF DETAILS 處理細節◀ [T] to put all the details of a piece of business into order and deal with them, for example before you travel or because you may die soon〔在旅行前或臨終前〕安排好某事的細節: **settle the details** (=deal with the details of a plan, agreement etc) 安排細節 | **settle your affairs** (=put your personal business in order) 安排好自己的事 | **settle an estate** (=deal with the way someone's property is divided after they die) 辦理遺產分配

7 ▶QUIET/CALM 平靜/安定◀ [I,T] to become quiet or calm, or to make someone or something quiet or calm (使) 平靜, (使) 安定: *When the children had settled, Miss Brown gave out the new reading books.* 孩子們靜下來後, 布朗小姐分發新的讀本。| **settle your nerves/stomach** (=stop your nerves or stomach from being upset) 使神經鎮靜; 緩解胃部不適 *A little soda should settle your tummy.* 喝點蘇打水, 你的肚子就不會難受了。

8 ▶LIVE IN A PLACE 住在某地◀ **a)** [I] to go to live in a new place, and stay there〔到新的地方〕定居: *After returning from abroad they settled in Chicago.* 從國外回來以後他們就在芝加哥定居。**b)** [T] to go to a new place where there are few people and start to live there〔到人口稀少的地方〕定居: *Jamestown was already settled when the Pilgrims came to America.* 當英國的清教徒來到美洲時, 詹姆斯敦已經有人定居了。

9 ▶A FEELING/QUALITY 感覺/特質◀ [I always+adv/prep] if a quality or feeling settles over a place or on someone it has a strong effect 圍繞; 充滿; 強烈影響着: **[+over/on]** *Despair seemed to settle on him and he could hardly work.* 絕望情緒好像老在困擾着他, 使他無法工作。| *A velvety silence settled over the room.* 房間裡一片寧靜。

10 settle a score/account to do something to hurt or cause trouble for someone because they have harmed or offended you 清算積怨, 報宿仇: *She's got a few old scores to settle with him.* 她有幾筆舊賬要跟他算。

11 ▶SINK 沉降◀ [I] if something such as a building or the ground settles it sinks slowly to a lower level 下陷, 下沉: *The crack in the wall is caused by the ground settling.* 牆壁的裂縫是地面沉降造成的。

12 ▶LOOK 看◀[I] if your eyes settle on someone or something you look at them carefully for a period of time〔目光〕停留, 凝視: **[+on]** *The teacher's steely eyes settled on Bobby.* 老師冷峻的目光注視着博比。

13 ▶EXPRESSION 表情◀ [I] if a particular expression settles on your face, it stays there〔某種表情在臉上〕固定下來: *His face settled into a severe frown.* 他雙眉緊鎖, 神色凝重。

14 ▶FOOD 食物◀ [I] if something you eat settles, it is digested (DIGEST[1] (1)) well〔食物〕被消化: *Give your lunch a chance to settle.* 吃午飯後要讓它消化一下。

settle down *phr v* **1** [I,T **settle** sb **down**] to stop talking or behaving in an excited way, or to make someone do this (使) 安靜下來, (使) 停止講話: *Everybody settle down so we can hear the story.* 大家安靜下來, 好讓我們聽故事。| *Sheila seems to have settled down more since school started.* 自開學以來, 希拉似乎已經安定多了。**2** [I] to start living in a place with the intention of staying there, especially after you have travelled a lot〔尤指四處奔波之後〕安頓下來, 定居: *They'd like to see her daughter settle down, get married, and have kids.* 他們想看到女兒安頓下來, 結婚生子。**3** [I,T] to start giving all of your attention to a job, activity etc 開始專心於〔工作、活動等〕, 着手認真做〔某事〕: **[+to]** *They settled down to a serious discussion over coffee.* 他們喝着咖啡, 開始認真討論問題。| **settle yourself down** *Sally sighed, and settled herself down to listen.* 莎莉嘆了口氣, 靜下心來聽。

settle for sth *phr v* [T not in passive 不用被動態] to accept or agree to something, especially something that is less than what you want〔勉強〕接受, 〔將就着〕同意: *We've no TV and have had to settle for hearing the news on the radio.* 我們沒有電視機, 只好用收音機收聽新聞。| *They want $3000 for their car and won't settle for anything less.* 他們的汽車要賣 3000 美元, 少於此數就不行。| *You'll have to settle for a cheaper car.* 你只好買輛便宜些的車算了。

settle in/into *phr v* **1** [I,T **settle** sb **in**] to become used to a new home, job, surroundings etc or to help someone do this (使) 適應〔新的家、工作、環境等〕: *Are you settling in OK?* 你已經逐漸適應了嗎? | *It takes a few months to settle into life at college.* 要經過幾個月才能習慣大學生活。**2** [I] to make yourself comfortable and prepare to stay somewhere for a period of time 安定下來, 安心下來: **[+for]** *They settled in for a long wait in the airport lounge.* 他們在機場大廳安下心來, 準備長時間等候。

settle on/upon *phr v* [T] **1** [**settle on** sth/sb] to decide or agree on something 決定, 同意〔某事〕: *They haven't settled yet on a name for the baby.* 他們還沒有決定給嬰兒取甚麼名字。**2** [**settle** sth **on** sb] *BrE formal* to make a formal arrangement to give money or property to someone【英, 正式】〔正式〕授予, 贈與〔金錢或財產〕: *She settled a small yearly sum on each of her children.* 她辦了手續, 確定每年給每個孩子一小筆錢。

settle up *phr v* **1** [I] to pay what you owe on an account or bill 付清欠賬, 結清賬單: **[+with]** *I'll settle up with the bartender and we can leave.* 我先和酒吧侍者結賬, 然後我們就可以走了。**2** [I] if two or more people settle up, they agree on a final arrangement for paying money, dividing property etc 協議清賬; 還清債務; 分清財產: *It's time we settled up. What do I owe you?* 我們現在該清清賬了, 我欠你多少錢?

settle[2] *n* [C] a long wooden seat with a high back that usually has a hollow place for storing things under the seat 高背木製長椅〔座位下有空櫃放東西〕

set·tled /ˈsɛtld; ˈsetld/ *adj* **1** unlikely to change; fixed 不大可能改變的, 固定的: *They lead a settled life.* 他們過着穩定的生活。| *The community has firm and settled ideas on this question.* 公眾對這個問題有固定不變的看法。**2 feel/be settled** to feel comfortable about living or working in a particular place〔對某地的生活或工作〕感到舒適愜意: *I'd work better if I felt more settled in my job.* 如果我對自己那份工作感到愜意, 就會工作得更好。

set·tle·ment /ˈsɛtl̩mənt; ˈsetlmənt/ *n* 2

1 ▶OFFICIAL AGREEMENT 正式協議◀ [C,U] an offi-

S

cial agreement or decision that ends an argument between two sides〔解決雙方爭端的〕正式協議, 和解: **reach/achieve a settlement** *failure to reach a settlement in the trade war* 在貿易戰中未能達成協議 | **negotiated/political/peaceful etc settlement** (=made after discussions are held, political decisions taken etc) 談判/政治/和平等協定 | **divorce/peace/financial etc settlement** (=the agreement about what the two sides will do after a divorce, after fighting stops etc) 離婚/和平/經濟等協議 *Martin lost the house in their divorce settlement.* 馬丁在他們的離婚協議中失去了房子。| **out-of-court settlement** (=money you pay or things you agree to do to prevent someone going to court) 庭外和解〔指用付錢等辦法使對方不向法院起訴〕

2 ▶GROUP OF HOUSES 住宅羣◀ [C] a group of houses and buildings where people live, in an area where no group lived before〔人口稀少地區的〕拓居羣, 小村落: *a Bronze Age settlement* 青銅器時代的村落 | *Wrangell is Alaska's second oldest settlement.* 蘭格爾是阿拉斯加第二古老的拓居地。

3 ▶NEW AREA/PLACES 新的地區/地方◀ [U] the movement of a new population into a place to live there 殖民, 移民, 拓居: **[+of]** *the settlement of the American West* 向美國西部的移民

4 ▶PAYMENT 支付◀ [C,U] the payment of money that you owe someone〔欠款的〕清償: **in settlement** *a $1,000 check in settlement* 用以清償賬目的 1,000 美元支票

5 ▶GIFT 禮物◀ [C,U] a formal gift of money or property〔金錢或財產的〕正式授予, 贈與: **on/upon** *He made a handsome settlement on his daughter when she married.* 他女兒結婚時, 他贈與她一筆可觀的財產。

6 ▶SINKING 下沉◀ [U] the slow sinking of a building, the ground under it etc; SUBSIDENCE〔建築物、地基等的〕沉降, 下陷

set·tler /ˈsɛtlɚ; ˈsetlə/ *n* [C] someone who goes to live in a new place where there are few people〔到人口稀少的新地區定居的〕移民, 殖民者: *early settlers in Australia* 澳大利亞的早期移民

set-to /ˈ· ·/ *n* [C usually singular 一般用單數+**with**] *informal* a short fight or quarrel【非正式】〔短時間的〕打鬥[爭吵] —see also 另見 **set to** (SET[1])

set-up /ˈ· ·/ *n* [usually singular 一般用單數] **1** a way of organizing or arranging something 組織機構;〔事物的〕安排, 佈局: *a less traditional classroom setup* 不太傳統的教室座位安排 | *He has a nice little set-up, with a studio at the back and gallery space at the front.* 他的安排相當精巧, 工作室在後面, 藝術品陳列在前面。**2** all the parts that work together in a system, for example in a computer system〔電腦等的〕裝配; 調試 **3** *informal* a dishonest plan that tricks you【非正式】圈套, 騙局, 詭計: *How do I know this isn't a set-up?* 我怎麼才知道這不是個騙局? —see also 另見 **set up** (SET[1])

sev·en /ˈsɛvən; ˈsevən/ *number* **1** 7 七 **2 the seven year itch** *humorous* the idea that after seven years of being married, people feel less satisfied with their relationship【幽默】七年之癢〔指結婚七年後對婚姻關係感到不夠滿意〕—**seventh** *number* —see also 另見 **at sixes and sevens** (SIX (3))

sev·en·teen /ˌsɛvənˈtin; ˌsevənˈtiːn◂/ *number* 17 十七

sev·enth /ˈsɛvənθ; ˈsevənθ/ *n* **1** [C] one of seven equal parts of something 七分之一 (1/7) **2 be in seventh heaven** *informal* to be extremely happy【非正式】感到非常快活, 非常幸福: *He's in seventh heaven when he's watching football.* 他一看足球比賽就快活似神仙。

sev·en·ty /ˈsɛvəntɪ; ˈsevənti/ *number* **1** 70 七十 **2 the seventies** the years from 1970 to 1979 70年代〔從 1970 年至 1979 年〕**3 in your seventies** aged between 70 and 79 從 70 歲至 79 歲: **in your early/late seventies** (=below or above 75) 70 (歲) 開外〔不到75〕/ 年將 80〔75 歲以上〕**4 in the seventies** if the temperature is in the seventies, it is between 70° and 79° FAHRENHEIT〔溫度〕在 70 至 79 華氏度之間 —**seventieth** *adj*

seventy-eight /ˌ··ˈ·/ *n* [C] an old-fashioned record that is played by being turned 78 times a minute 每分鐘 78 轉的舊式唱片

sev·er /ˈsɛvɚ; ˈsevə/ *v formal*【正式】**1** [I,T] to cut through something, separating it into two parts, or to become severed in this way 切斷, 割斷: *Martin's hand was severed in the accident.* 馬丁的一隻手在事故中被切斷了。| *a severed rope* 切斷的繩子 **2** to end a relationship with someone, or a connection with something 與...斷絕(關係): *severing family ties* 斷絕家庭關係 —see also 另見 SEVERANCE PAY —**severance** *n* [U]

sev·er·al[1] /ˈsɛvərəl; ˈsevərəl/ *quantifier* a number of people or things that is more than a few, but not a lot 幾個, 數個, 一些: *I visited him in Kansas several times.* 我曾幾次去堪薩斯拜會他。| *several million dollars* 數百萬美元 | *Several people have volunteered to go.* 有幾個人自願前往。| **[+of]** *Several of us think it's a bad idea.* 我們當中好幾個人認為這是個壞主意。 1 1

several[2] *adj* [only before noun 僅用於名詞前, no comparative 無比較級] *formal or literary* different and separate; RESPECTIVE【正式或文】不同的, 各自的, 各別的: *They shook hands and went their several ways.* 他們握手後便各自走了。—**severally** *adv*: *These issues can be considered severally, or as a whole.* 這些問題可以分開考慮, 也可以作為一個整體來考慮。

sev·er·ance pay /ˈ··· ·/ *n* [U] money you get when you leave a company because your employer no longer has a job for you 遣散費; 解雇費; 離職金

se·vere /səˈvɪr; səˈvɪə/ *adj*

1 ▶VERY BAD 非常糟◀ very bad, or serious enough for you to worry about 嚴重的, 劇烈的: *severe injuries to the head and neck* 頭部和頸部的重傷 | *severe depression* 嚴重抑鬱 | *a severe setback to hopes of peace* 對和平希望的嚴重挫折 —see graph at 參見 PAIN[1] 圖表

2 ▶WEATHER 天氣◀ severe weather conditions are extremely hot, cold, dry etc and are unpleasant or dangerous 嚴酷的; 惡劣的; 極熱[冷, 乾]的: *the severest winter since 1948* 自 1948 年以來最寒冷的冬天 | *severe flooding* 嚴重的水災

3 ▶STRICT 嚴格的◀ someone who is severe is very strict and demands that rules of behaviour are obeyed or standards are followed〔人〕嚴格的, 嚴厲的, 苛刻的: *Don't be so severe with the children.* 對小孩不要這麼嚴厲。

4 ▶EXTREME 極度的◀ criticism or punishment that is severe is extreme, and intended to prevent more crimes or bad behaviour〔批評、懲罰等〕極其嚴厲的: *Drug smuggling continues to flourish despite the severe sentences of the courts.* 儘管法院的判決極為嚴厲, 毒品走私仍然十分猖獗。| *a report containing severe criticism of the company's actions* 包含對這家公司的行為尖銳批評的報告

5 ▶UNFRIENDLY 不友好的◀ disapproving or unfriendly 不贊成的; 不友好的: *a severe expression* 嚴厲的表情

6 ▶PLAIN 樸素的◀ plain and simple in style with little or no decoration; AUSTERE 樸素的; 簡潔的; 不加裝飾的: *The town hall of Bruges is less severe but equally imposing.* 布魯日的市政大廳不那麼簡樸, 但同樣顯得莊嚴。—**severity** *n* [C,U]: *We didn't realize the severity of her illness.* 我們沒有意識到她病得如此嚴重。| *"You can't leave now," he said with some severity.* "你現在不能走。" 他用略帶嚴厲的口吻說。

se·vere·ly /səˈvɪrlɪ; səˈvɪəli/ *adv* **1** very badly or to a great degree 嚴重地: *a severely damaged building* 嚴重毀壞的建築物 | *severely disabled* 有嚴重殘疾的 | *His movements are severely restricted.* 他的活動被嚴加限制。**2** in a strict way 嚴厲地, 嚴格地: *Parents don't punish their children so severely these days.* 如今父母不再那麼嚴厲地懲罰孩子了。**3** in a way that shows you disapprove greatly 嚴肅地〔表示很不贊成〕: *"Stop behaving like a fool!" she said severely.* "別再像個傻瓜一樣!" 她嚴肅地說。**4** in a plain simple style with little or no decoration 樸素地, 樸實無華地: *severely dressed* 穿着樸素的

sew /so; səʊ/ *v past tense* **sewed** *past participle* **sewn** /son; səʊn/ also 又作 **sewed** *AmE*【美】[I,T] to use a needle and thread to join pieces of cloth together to make or repair clothes or fasten something such as a button to them 縫, 縫紉; 縫製; 縫補: *I learned to sew at school.* 我在學校學過縫紉。| **sew sth on sth** *Can you sew a patch on my jeans?* 你能幫我這條牛仔褲縫塊補丁嗎?

sew sth ↔ **up** *phr v* [T] **1** to close or repair something by sewing it 縫合; 縫補: *Could you sew up this hole in my trousers?* 你能補好我褲子上這個洞嗎? **2** [usually passive 一般用被動態] *informal* to finish a business agreement or plan and get the result you want【非正式】順利完成〔協議或計劃〕; 解決; 決定: *Bob reckons the deal should be sewn up in a week.* 鮑勃估計那宗交易一週之內應可談妥。**3** [usually passive 一般用被動態] to gain control over a situation so that you are sure to win or gain something 控制〔局勢〕; 確保〔勝利、利益等〕: *It seems like the Democrats have the election all sewn up.* 看來民主黨人這次選舉穩操勝券了。

sew·age /ˋsuɪdʒ; ˈsjuːɪdʒ/ *n* [U] the mixture of waste from the human body and used water that is carried away from houses by sewers 下水道的污水, 污物: *Chlorine is used in sewage treatment.* 氯被用於污水處理。

sewage farm /ˈ‥ ·/ *BrE*【英】, **sewage plant** *AmE*【美】*n* [C] a place where sewage is treated to stop it being harmful 污水處理場

sew·er /ˋsuɚ; ˈsjuːə/ *n* [C] a pipe or passage under the ground that carries away waste material and used water from houses and factories 下水道; 陰溝; 污水管

sew·er·age /ˋsuərɪdʒ; ˈsjuːərɪdʒ/ *n* [U] the system by which waste material and water is carried away in sewers and then treated to stop it being harmful 污水處理系統; 下水道系統

sew·ing /ˋsoɪŋ; ˈsəʊɪŋ/ *n* [U] **1** the activity or skill of making or repairing clothes or decorating cloth with a needle and thread〔用針線的〕縫紉〔技巧〕 **2** something you have sewn or are going to sew〔縫好或未縫好的〕縫製品: *Imogen sighed and picked up her sewing.* 伊莫金嘆了口氣, 拿起了她的針線活。

sewing ma·chine /ˈ‥ ·,·/ *n* [C] a machine for stitching cloth or clothes together 縫紉機

1 2 **sex¹** /sɛks; seks/ *n* **1** the activity in which a male and female join their sexual organs in order to create babies, or for pleasure 性活動, 性行為: *All you see on TV is sex and violence these days.* 這些日子在電視上看到的盡是性行為和暴力的鏡頭。**2 have sex** when two people have sex they take part in an activity that involves contact between their sexual organs 做愛, 性交: *Would you have sex with someone on your first date?* 你會和初次約會的人做愛嗎? **3** the male or female nature of a person, animal, or plant〔人、動物、植物的〕性別: *Please put your name, age, and sex at the top of the form.* 請在表格上方填上你的姓名、年齡和性別。| *You can now tell the sex of a baby before it is born.* 現在在嬰兒出生之前就能知道他的性別了。**4** the two sexes are the two groups of male and female people, animals etc 男性或女性; 雌性或雄性: **the opposite sex** (=the group that you are not in) 異性 *He's terrified of the opposite sex.* 他對異性怕得要命。| **sex discrimination** (=unfair treatment because of which sex you are) 性別歧視 *She's prosecuting the company for sex discrimination.* 她因性別歧視在起訴該公司。**5 single-sex school/college etc** *BrE* a school etc for either males or females, but not for both together【英】單一性別的學校/學院等

sex² *v* [T] *technical* to find out whether an animal is male or female【術語】鑑別〔動物的〕性別

sex·a·ge·na·ri·an /ˌsɛksədʒəˋnɛrɪən; ˌseksədʒəˈneəriən/ *n* [C] *formal* someone who is between 60 and 69 years old【正式】60到69歲之間的人 —**sexaganarian** *adj*

sex ap·peal /ˈ· ·,·/ *n* [U] the quality of being sexually attractive 性感, 性魅力: *He's a nice guy – but he's got no sex appeal!* 他這人挺不錯 —— 就是沒有性魅力!

sex change /ˈ· ·/ *n* [C usually singular 一般用單數] a medical operation or treatment which changes someone's body so that they look like someone of the other sex〔通過外科手術等手段達到的〕性別改變, 變性

sex drive /ˈ· ·/ *n* [C usually singular 一般用單數] someone's ability or need to have sex regularly 性慾

sex ed·u·ca·tion /ˈ· ‥,‥/ *n* [U] education in schools about the physical processes and emotions involved in sex〔學校中的〕性教育

sex·is·m /ˋsɛksɪzəm; ˈseksɪzəm/ *n* [U] the belief that women are weaker, less intelligent, and less important than men〔對女性的〕性別偏見[歧視]: *The book gives a range of examples of sexism in education.* 這本書列舉了一系列在教育領域歧視女性的事例。

sex·ist /ˋsɛksɪst; ˈseksɪst/ *adj* **1** believing that women are weaker, less intelligent, and less important than men 歧視婦女的, 性別歧視的 **2** resulting from or connected with this belief 由於性別歧視的; 與性別歧視有關的: *sexist attitudes* 性別歧視的態度 —**sexist** *n* [C]

sex·less /ˋsɛkslɪs; ˈsekslәs/ *adj* **1** not sexually attractive; not SEXY 缺乏性魅力的, 不性感的 **2** neither male nor female; NEUTER¹ (1) 無性(別)的, 無雌雄特徵的; 中性的

sex life /ˈ· ·/ *n* [C] someone's sexual activities 性生活: *Jim's too busy to have much of a sex life.* 吉姆太忙, 沒有多少性生活。

sex-linked /ˈ· ·/ *adj technical* an illness or medical condition that is sex-linked is caused by the GENEs of only one sex and so is passed to children by parents of that sex【術語】性連鎖的, 伴性(遺傳)的

sex ma·ni·ac /ˈ· ,‥·/ *n* [C] someone who always wants to have sex, thinks about it all the time, and is unable to control these feelings 性慾狂者

sex ob·ject /ˈ· ,‥/ *n* [C] someone you consider only as a means of satisfying your sexual desire rather than as a whole person 發泄性慾的對象, 性玩物

sex of·fend·er /ˈ· ·,‥/ *n* [C] someone who is guilty of a crime related to sex 性侵犯者, 性犯罪者

sex·ol·o·gy /sɛksˋɑlədʒɪ; sekˈsɒlədʒi/ *n* [U] the study of sexual behaviour, especially among humans〔尤指人類的〕性(行為)學 —**sexologist** *n* [C]

sex or·gan /ˈ· ,‥/ *n* [C] a part of the body concerned with the production of children, such as the PENIS or VAGINA 性器官, 生殖器官

sex·ploi·ta·tion /ˌsɛksplɔɪˋteʃən; ˌseksplɔɪˈteɪʃən/ *n* [U] *informal* a word meaning the use of sex in films and magazines in order to make money, used by people who think this is wrong【非正式】〔在電影、雜誌中為賺錢的〕色情利用

sex·pot /ˋsɛkspɑt; ˈsekspɒt/ *n* [C] *informal* a word meaning a sexually attractive woman, that many women think is offensive【非正式】性感的女人〔被多數女性視為是冒犯語〕

sex shop /ˈ· ·/ *n* [C] *BrE* a shop selling goods, magazines etc related to sex and sexual activities【英】〔出售色情雜誌、性用具等的〕性用品商店

sex sym·bol /ˈ· ,‥/ *n* [C] someone who represents society's idea of what is sexually attractive 性感偶像: *sex symbols such as Madonna and Tom Cruise* 像麥當娜和湯告魯斯那樣的性感偶像

sex·tant /ˋsɛkstənt; ˈsekstənt/ *n* [C] a tool for measuring angles between stars in order to calculate the position of your ship or aircraft 六分儀〔用於測量星與星之間的角度以計算船或飛機的位置〕

sex·tet /sɛksˋtɛt; seksˈtet/ *n* [C] **1** a group of six singers or musicians performing together 六重唱; 六重奏 **2** a piece of music for six performers: *Brahms' sextet in B flat* 勃拉姆斯的降 B 調六重奏曲

sex·ton /ˋsɛkstən; ˈsekstən/ *n* [C] someone who takes care of a church building, and sometimes rings the bells

S

and digs graves 教堂司事〔負責管理教堂房屋、敲鐘、挖掘墓穴等工作〕

sex·tu·plet /sɛk`stʌplɪt; sek'stju:plɨt/ *n* [C] one of six people who are born at the same time and have the same mother 六胞胎之一

2 2 **sex·u·al** /`sɛkʃuəl; 'sekʃuəl/ *adj* **1** connected with sex 性的; 與性（生活）有關的: *a disease passed on by sexual contact* 由性接觸傳染的疾病 | *sexual relationships* 性關係 | *sexual desire* 性慾 **2** connected with the social relationships between men and women 性別的, 兩性社會關係的: *sexual politics* 性別政治 **3** connected with the way people or animals have babies 生殖的: *sexual reproduction* 有性繁殖 —**sexually** *adv*: *sexually experienced* 性經驗豐富的 | *sexually attractive* 具有性吸引力的

sexual har·ass·ment /···'··/ *n* [U] unwelcome touching or remarks about sex from someone, especially if you are expected to accept this to make progress in your job〔尤指利用工作之便的〕性騷擾

sexual in·ter·course /,···'···/ *n* [U] *formal* the act of two people having sex with each other【正式】性交

sex·u·al·i·ty /,sɛkʃu`ælətɪ; ,sekʃu'ælɨti/ *n* [U] the things people do and feel that are connected with their desire or ability to have sex 性慾; 性能力; 性行為: *Sexuality was never discussed.* 性的問題從未討論過。| **male/female sexuality** *a study of male sexuality* 對男性性行為的研究

sex·u·al·ly trans·mit·ted dis·ease /,···· ·,·· ·'·/ *n* [C,U] STD; a disease that is passed on through sexual intercourse, such as AIDS, HERPES etc 性傳播疾病〈如愛滋病、疱疹等〉

sex·y /`sɛksɪ; 'seksi/ *adj* **sexier, sexiest 1** sexually exciting or attractive 引起情慾的, 性感的: *Oh, don't you think he's sexy?* 啊, 難道你不認為他性感嗎? | *a sexy picture* 性感的圖片 **2** *informal* exciting to think about or use【非正式】吸引人的; 令人興奮的: *Constitutional change is not a sexy issue.* 憲法的修改不是一個令人興奮的問題。| *sexy computer software* 誘人的電腦軟件 —**sexily** *adv* —**sexiness** *n* [U] —see 見 BEAUTIFUL (USAGE)

SF /,ɛs `ɛf; ,es 'ef/ *adj* the abbreviation of 縮寫 = SCIENCE FICTION

Sgt the written abbreviation of 縮寫 = SERGEANT

3 **sh** /ʃ; ʃ/ *interjection* used to tell someone to be quiet 噓! 別作聲!〔用於要求某人安靜〕: *Sh! I'm trying to sleep.* 噓, 安靜點! 我想要睡覺了。

shab·by /`ʃæbɪ; 'ʃæbi/ *adj* **1** untidy and in a bad condition from being used for a long time 骯髒破舊的: *a shabby suit* 又髒又舊的套服 | *shabby hotel rooms* 破舊的旅館房間 **2** wearing clothes that are old and worn 衣衫襤褸的, 衣着寒酸的: *a shabby tramp* 衣衫襤褸的流浪漢 **3** unfair and unkind 不公平的; 不仁慈的: *That's a shabby way to treat someone.* 這樣待人是不公正的。| *a shabby trick* 卑鄙的花招 —**shabbily** *adv* —**shabbiness** *n* [U]

shack¹ /ʃæk; ʃæk/ *n* [C] a small building that has not been built very well 簡陋的小屋, 棚屋: *a tin shack* 鐵皮棚屋

shack² *v*

shack up *phr v* [I] *informal* to start living with someone who you have sex with but are not married to【非正式】〔未婚者〕同居: **shack up together/with** *Last I heard, they were shacked up together in Croydon.* 最近一次我聽說, 他們在克羅伊登同居。

shack·le¹ /`ʃækḷ; 'ʃækəl/ *n* [C] **1 the shackles of slavery/convention etc** *literary* the limits put on your freedom and happiness by SLAVERY etc【文】奴隸制/傳統等的枷鎖 **2** one of a pair of metal rings joined by a chain that are used for fastening together a prisoner's hands or feet 鐐銬; 手鐐; 腳鐐

shackle² *v* [T] **1** to put many limits on what someone can do 束縛, 羈絆: *Industrial progress is being shackled by a mass of regulations.* 工業的進步正受到諸多規定的束縛。**2** to put shackles on someone 給〔某人〕戴上鐐銬

shad /ʃæd; ʃæd/ *n* [C,U] a north Atlantic fish used for food 西鯡〔產於北大西洋的食用魚〕

shade 蔭

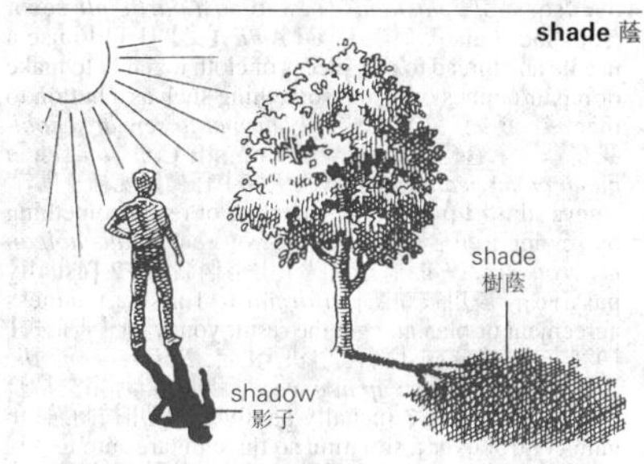

shade¹ /ʃed; ʃeɪd/ *n*

1 ▶SLIGHT DARKNESS 陰暗◀ [U] slight darkness or shelter from the direct light of the sun made by something blocking it 蔭, 背陰處: *a plant that likes a lot of shade* 特別喜歡陰涼的植物 | **in the shade** *Let's find a table in the shade.* 我們在陰涼處找張桌子吧。| *It's 35°C in the shade.* 背陰處的氣溫為 35°C。| **in the shade of a tree/wall etc** *sitting in the shade of a large oak tree* 坐在一棵大橡樹的樹陰下 —compare 比較 SHADOW¹ (1)

2 ▶FOR BLOCKING LIGHT 用於遮光◀ [C] **a)** something you use to reduce or block light 遮光物: **lampshade/eyeshade** (=over a lamp, or above your eyes) 燈罩/遮光帽簷[眼罩] **b)** *AmE* a BLIND³ (1)【美】〔能上下捲疊的〕窗簾, 百葉窗

3 shades [plural] *informal* SUNGLASSES【非正式】太陽鏡, 墨鏡

4 ▶IN A PICTURE 在圖畫中◀ [U] the dark places in a picture〔圖畫等中的〕陰影, 陰暗部分: **light and shade** *using light and shade to mould figures* 用明暗來勾畫圖形

5 ▶COLOUR 顏色◀ [C] a particular kind of red, green, blue etc〔某一色彩的〕濃淡, 深淺, 色度: **[+of]** *a wonderful shade of pink* 一種濃淡恰到好處的粉紅色

6 shade of meaning/opinion/feeling etc a meaning etc that is slightly different from other ones; NUANCE 有細微差別的含義/意見/情感等: *various shades of opinion in the party* 政黨內各種不同的意見

7 a shade *formal* very slightly【正式】有點, 略為: *Ken was just a shade too honest about his feelings.* 肯對自己感情的表白未免有點太老實了。

8 shades of used to say that something reminds you of someone or something else, especially when you would rather forget 使人聯想起〔尤指寧願忘卻的人或事〕: *Huh. Shades of my poorer days.* 嘿, 這又使我想起那些窮日子。

9 put sth in the shade to be so good or impressive that other similar things or people seem much less important or interesting 使某事物遜色: *Well Arthur, your choir puts our little town chorus in the shade.* 噢, 阿瑟, 你們的合唱隊使我們這個小鎮的歌詠隊黯然失色了。

10 *literary* the spirit of a dead person; GHOST¹ (1)【文】幽靈, 鬼魂

11 have it made in the shade *AmE informal* to be extremely rich【美, 非正式】極其富有

shade² *v* [T] **1** to protect something from direct light 為…遮陽[擋光], 遮蔽〔光線〕: *See, the yucca plant's being shaded by that tree.* 看, 這株絲蘭被那棵樹擋住陽光了。| **shade your eyes/face etc** *Shading her eyes, Anita scanned the horizon.* 阿妮塔用手擋住陽光, 仔細瞭望着地平線。**2** also 又作 **shade in** to make part of a picture or drawing darker 將〔圖畫某部分的〕顏色加深; 畫陰影於〔圖畫的某部分〕: *You still need to shade in that bit there.* 你還要把那裡的一小塊畫得暗些。

shade into sth *phr v* [T] if one thing shades into another, it is impossible to tell where one stops and another starts 漸漸與…分辨不清, 逐漸融合於: *Sea shades into sky at the horizon.* 在地平線上, 海天融為一體。| *Right and wrong often shade into each other.* 正確和錯誤之間常常劃不清界限。

shad·ing /ˈʃedɪŋ; ˈʃeɪdɪŋ/ *n* **1** [U] the areas of a drawing or painting that have been made to look darker〔圖畫中〕較暗的部分 **2 shadings** [plural] slight differences between things, situations, or ideas〔事物、情況、意見等的〕細微差別

2 **shad·ow¹** /ˈʃædo; ˈʃædəʊ/ *n*

1 ►DARKNESS 黑暗◄ [U] also 又作 **shadows** *plural* darkness caused by something preventing light from entering a place 陰影, 暗影, 陰暗區: **in shadow** *The room was half in shadow.* 這房間有一半是暗的。| **in the shadows** *a thief lurking in the shadows* 潛伏在陰暗處的小偷

2 ►DARK SHAPE 黑影◄ [C] a dark shape that someone or something makes on a surface when they are between that surface and the light 影子: *Look how long our shadows are!* 瞧, 我們的影子有多長啊! | **in the shadow of** (=under something, where its shadow will sometimes fall) 在…的蔭蔽之下 *We buried Mama in the shadow of the old elm.* 我們把母親埋葬在一棵老榆樹的樹陰下面。—see picture at 參見 SHADE¹ 圖

3 cast a shadow over/on *literary*【文】**a)** to make a dark shape appear on a surface by being between that surface and the light 影子映在…, 投影於…上: *The house cast long shadows on the lawn.* 這房子在草坪上投下長長的影子。**b)** to make something seem less attractive or impressive 使蒙上陰影; 使遜色: *After that, a shadow was cast over his reputation.* 從此以後, 他的聲譽便蒙上了陰影。

4 without/beyond a shadow of a doubt without any doubt at all 毫無疑問: *Without a shadow of a doubt he's the most talented player we've ever had.* 毫無疑問, 他是我們遇到的天賦最高的選手。

5 be in sb's shadow to be less happy and successful than you could be because someone else gets noticed much more 在某人的盛名之下〔顯得遜色〕: *Kate grew up in the shadow of her film star sister.* 凱特在她那位影星姐姐的盛名之下長大, 無法讓世人注意到自己。

6 be a shadow of your former self to be so unhappy that you seem like a different person 因很不愉快而前後判若兩人

7 shadows under sb's eyes small dark areas under someone's eyes that show they are tired 眼睛下面的黑圈〔表示疲勞〕

8 sb's shadow someone who follows someone else everywhere they go 形影不離的人; 某人的跟隨者 —see also 另見 **afraid of your own shadow** (AFRAID (4)), FIVE O'CLOCK SHADOW

shadow² *v* [T] **1** to follow someone closely in order to watch what they are doing 跟蹤, 尾隨, 釘…的梢: *Detectives shadowed them for weeks, collecting evidence.* 偵探跟蹤他們好幾個星期收集證據。**2** [usually passive 一般用被動態] *literary* to cover something with a shadow, or make it dark【文】投陰影於; 遮蔽: *a shadowed alley* 陰暗的小巷

shadow³ *adj* **1 shadow chancellor/foreign secretary etc** the politician in the main opposition party in the British parliament who would become CHANCELLOR (1) etc if their party was in government, and who is responsible for speaking on the same subjects 影子財政大臣/外交大臣〔指英國議會中, 主要反對黨若執政時成為財政大臣等的人〕**2 shadow cabinet** the group of politicians in the British parliament who would become ministers if their party was in government 影子內閣〔指英國議會中, 若其政黨執政則會成為部長的一羣政治家〕

shadow box·ing /ˈ·· ˌ··/ *n* [U] fighting with an imaginary opponent, especially as training for BOXING〔尤指拳擊訓練時〕與假想對手的拳擊, 假想拳

shadow pup·pet /ˈ·· ˌ··/ *n* [C] a flat PUPPET that makes special shapes on a wall when you shine a light behind it 影偶

shad·ow·y /ˈʃædəwɪ; ˈʃædəʊi/ *adj* **1** mysterious and difficult to know anything about 神祕的, 難以捉摸的: **shadowy figure** *Anastasia Romanov is a shadowy figure.* 阿納斯塔西婭·羅曼諾夫是個難以捉摸的人物。**2** full of shadows, or difficult to see because of shadows 多陰影的; 幽暗的; 模糊的: *a shadowy room* 幽暗的房間

shad·y /ˈʃedɪ; ˈʃeɪdi/ *adj* **1** protected from the sun or producing shade 遮陽的; 背陰的, 成蔭的: *the shady side of the street* 街道背陰的一邊 | *shady trees* 多蔭的樹木 **2** probably dishonest or illegal 可能不誠實的, 可疑的; 不正當的: *a shady character* 可疑的人物 | *She's been involved in some shady deals.* 她捲進了一些不正當的交易。

shaft¹ /ʃæft; ʃɑːft/ *n* 3

1 ►HANDLE 柄◄ [C] a long handle on a tool, SPEAR etc〔工具的〕長柄; 矛桿 —see picture on page A23 參見 A23頁圖

2 ►PASSAGE 通道◄ [C] a passage which goes up through a building or down into the ground, so that someone or something can get in or out 豎井: **mine/elevator/ventilation shaft** *a 300-foot elevator shaft* 一個300英尺的電梯井

3 shaft of light/sunlight [C] a narrow beam of light 一道光線/陽光

4 ►ENGINE PART 引擎部件◄ [C] a thin long piece of metal in an engine or machine that turns and passes on power or movement to another part of the machine〔機器的〕軸; 傳動軸

5 ►FOR A HORSE 馬用的◄ [C usually plural 一般用複數] one of a pair of poles between which a horse is tied to pull a vehicle〔馬車的〕轅

6 shaft of wit [C] *literary* a clever amusing remark, especially an unkind one【文】機智風趣的話〔尤指挖苦話〕

7 ►ARROW 箭◄ [C] *literary* an ARROW (1)【文】(一枝) 箭

8 give sb the shaft *AmE slang* to treat someone unfairly, for example by dismissing them from their job without a good reason【美俚】不公正地對待某人, 虧待某人〈如無理辭退〉

shaft² *v* [T] *slang* to treat someone unfairly, especially by dishonestly getting money from them【俚】不公正地對待〔尤指騙錢〕: *We really got shafted in that computer deal.* 我們在那宗電腦交易中的確吃了虧。

shag¹ /ʃæg; ʃæg/ *adj* **shag carpet/rug** a CARPET¹ (1) or RUG (1) with a rough surface made from long threads of wool 長絨地毯

shag² *n* **1** [C] *BrE taboo* an act of having sex with someone【英諱】性交 **2** [C] a large black sea bird 長鼻鸕鷀 **3** [U] strong-tasting TOBACCO with thick leaves cut into small thin pieces 濃味煙絲

shag³ *v* [I,T] *BrE taboo* to have sex with someone【英諱】(與某人) 性交

shagged /ʃægd; ʃægd/ also 又作 **shagged out** /ˌ· ˈ·/ *adj BrE slang taboo* very tired【英俚, 諱】疲憊不堪的, 精疲力竭的: *I'm not going – I'm too shagged!* 我不去了——我太累了!

shag·gy /ˈʃægɪ; ˈʃægi/ *adj* **1** shaggy hair or fur is long and untidy〔頭髮、毛等〕又長又亂的, 蓬亂的: *a shaggy black beard* 蓬亂的黑鬍子 **2** having shaggy hair 有亂蓬蓬毛髮的: *a shaggy sheepskin coat* 表面粗糙的羊皮外套 —**shagginess** *n* [U]

shaggy dog sto·ry /ˌ·· ˈ· ˌ··/ *n* [C] a long joke that often ends in a silly or disappointing way 冗長的笑話〔其結尾通常很無聊, 令人失望〕

Shah /ʃɑ; ʃɑː/ *n* [C] the title of the kings of Iran, used in the past 沙〔舊時伊朗國王的稱號〕

shake¹ /ʃek; ʃeɪk/ *past tense* **shook** /ʃuk; ʃʊk/ *past participle* **shaken** /ˈʃekən; ˈʃeɪkən/ *v*

1 ►MOVEMENT 動作◄ [I] to move up and down or from side to side with quick repeated movements〔上下或左右〕搖動, 搖撼; 顫抖: *His hand shook as he signed the paper.* 他在文件上簽名時手在發顫。| *The ground was shaking beneath their feet.* 大地在他們腳下顫動。| **shake with anger/fear/laughter etc** (=be so angry, frightened etc that you cannot stop shaking) 氣得/怕得/笑得渾身發抖 | **shake like a leaf** (=shake a lot, especially because you are very nervous or frightened)〔因緊張、害怕而〕全身發抖 *What's the matter? You're shaking like a leaf.* 怎麼回事? 你渾身在發抖。

shake 搖動

2 ►SHAKE STH 搖動某物◄ [T] to make something or someone move up and down or from side to side with quick repeated movements 抖; 使搖動; 使顫抖: *The blast shook windows five miles away.* 爆炸使五英里以外的窗戶都顫動了。| **shake sth onto/out/over etc** *Shake the sand out of your shoes.* 把你鞋裡的沙子抖掉。

3 ►SHAKE SB 搖晃某人◄ [T] to hold someone by their shoulders and push and pull them backwards and forwards roughly, especially because you are angry with them〔尤指生氣時抓住某人的肩膀〕搖晃, 猛搖: *She was being such a brat, I felt like shaking her.* 她那樣淘氣, 我真想揪住她晃幾下。

4 shake your head to move your head from side to side as a way of saying no 搖頭〔表示"不"〕: *He didn't reply, but just shook his head.* 他不回答, 只是搖頭。

5 shake hands (with) also 又作 **shake sb's hand/shake sb by the hand** to move someone's hand up and down with your own hand as a greeting or as a sign you have agreed something (與某人) 握手: *Wilkinson shook my hand warmly.* 威爾金森熱情地和我握手。

6 shake on it *spoken* to agree on a decision or business agreement by shaking hands【口】握手為定: *Let's shake on it.* 讓我們握手為定吧。

7 be shaken to feel very shocked and upset 感到震驚; 受到驚嚇; 被弄得心煩意亂: *Kerrie was so shaken by the attack that she still won't go out alone.* 凱利被那次襲擊嚇壞了, 現在還不願意單獨外出。

8 shake sb's confidence/faith/belief to make someone feel less confident, less sure about their beliefs etc 動搖某人的信心/信仰/信念

9 shake your fist to show that you are angry by holding up and shaking your tightly closed hand 揮動拳頭〔表示憤怒〕

10 ►VOICE 聲音◄ [I] if your voice shakes it sounds nervous or uncertain〔因精神緊張等而〕聲音發顫: *Reg's voice shook with rage.* 雷吉氣得聲音發顫。

11 shake a leg *spoken* used to tell someone to start doing something now【口】趕忙, 趕緊, 快點兒〔用以催促別人開始做某事〕: *C'mon you guys, shake a leg! We haven't got all day.* 喂, 你們這些傢伙, 快點啦! 我們沒有多少時間了。

12 shake in your shoes/boots *informal* to be very nervous【非正式】非常緊張: *I was shaking in my shoes – I thought he'd give me the sack.* 我緊張得要命 —— 我想他要解雇我了。

shake down *phr v* **1** [I] *BrE informal* to get used to a new situation that you are working or living in【英, 非正式】適應新環境, 安頓下來 **2** [T **shake** sb **down**] *AmE informal* to get money from someone by using threats【美, 非正式】敲詐, 勒索〔某人〕 **3** [T **shake** sb/sth ↔ **down**] *AmE informal* to search a person or place thoroughly【美, 非正式】徹底搜查 **4** [T **shake** sth ↔ **down**] *BrE* to test a ship or plane under real conditions【英】對〔船或飛機〕進行試航 —see 見 SHAKEDOWN **5** [I+in/on etc] *BrE informal* to sleep on the floor, on a seat etc, instead of in a proper bed【英, 非正式】在沒有牀的地方湊合着睡〈如睡地板、椅子等〉

shake sb/sth ↔ **off** *phr v* **1** [T **shake** sth ↔ **off**] to get rid of an illness, problem etc 治好〔疾病〕; 擺脫〔問題〕: *I can't seem to shake off this cold.* 我好像就是沒法治好這感冒。**2** [T] to escape from someone who is chasing you 甩掉〔跟蹤者〕, 擺脫〔追趕者〕

shake sth ↔ **out** [T] to shake a cloth, a bag, a sheet etc so that any small pieces of dirt, dust etc come off 把…抖落乾淨: *Shake the crumbs out of the tablecloth.* 把桌布上的麵包屑抖乾淨。

shake sb/sth ↔ **up** *phr v* [T] **1** [T **shake** sb ↔ **up**] to give someone a very unpleasant shock, so that they feel very upset and frightened 使震驚; 使震動; 使不安: *Seeing that accident really shook me up.* 目睹那次事故, 我真的被嚇壞了。—see also 另見 SHAKEN **2** [T] to make changes to an organization in order to make it more effective 改組〔機構〕, 整頓 —see also 另見 SHAKEUP

shake² *n* **1** [C] an act of shaking 搖動, 搖晃: **give sth a shake** *Give the bottle a good shake before you pour.* 倒出前先把瓶子好好搖一搖。| **shake of the head** (=a movement of the head from side to side to say no) 搖頭 *She just refuses with a smile and a shake of the head.* 她搖搖頭微笑着拒絕。**2 the shakes** *not technical* a nervous shaking of your body caused by illness, fear, too much alcohol etc【非術語】〔因生病、恐懼、喝酒過多等而〕哆嗦: **get the shakes** *As soon as they left I started getting the shakes.* 他們一走, 我就開始打哆嗦。**3 in a couple of shakes/two shakes** *informal* very soon【非正式】一剎那, 立刻, 馬上: *We'll be back in a couple of shakes.* 我們馬上就回來。**4 no great shakes** *spoken* not very skilful【口】技術並不高明的, 不大出色的: *He's no great shakes, but he's better than the last chef they had.* 他算不上廚藝高超, 但比他們上次雇的那位廚師長要強些。**5** [C] *AmE* a cold drink made from milk that tastes of fruit, chocolate etc; MILK SHAKE【美】泡沫牛奶, 奶昔〔牛奶與水果、巧克力等攪打而成的飲料〕 **6 fair shake** *AmE informal* fair treatment【美, 非正式】公正的對待, 公平的待遇: *Dave didn't get his fair shake – everyone else had the chance of an interview.* 戴夫沒有得到公平的待遇 —— 其他人個個都有一次面試的機會。

shake·down /ˈʃekˌdaun; ˈʃeɪkdaʊn/ *n* **1** [C] *AmE informal* the act of getting money from someone by using threats【美, 非正式】敲詐, 勒索 **2** [C] *AmE informal* a thorough search of a place or a person【美, 非正式】徹底搜查 **3** [C] a final test of a boat, plane etc before it is put into general use〔船、飛機等的〕最後測試, 試航: *a shakedown flight* 試飛 **4** [singular] *BrE informal* a place prepared as a bed on the floor, on a seat etc【英, 非正式】〔地板、椅子等上的〕臨時牀鋪

shak·en /ˈʃekən; ˈʃeɪkən/ also 又作 **shaken up** *adj* [not usually before noun 一般不用於名詞前] upset, shocked, or frightened 心煩的; 震驚的; 受驚的: *"How's Jacob?" "Pretty shaken up, but nothing's broken."* "雅各布怎麼樣?" "幾乎嚇壞了, 不過有驚無險。"

shake·out /ˈʃekˌaut; ˈʃeɪkaʊt/ *n* **1** [C usually singular 一般用單數] a situation in which several companies fail because they cannot compete with stronger companies in difficult economic conditions〔在困難的經濟條件下〕某些公司無法與大公司競爭而被淘汰 **2** [C] a SHAKEUP 改組, 重新組合

shak·er /ˈʃekɚ; ˈʃeɪkə/ *n* [C] **1** a container with holes in the lid, used to shake sugar etc onto food〔蓋上有小孔的〕佐料瓶: *a salt shaker* 鹽瓶 **2** also 又作 **cocktail shaker** a container in which drinks are mixed 雞尾酒調酒器 **3** a small container for shaking DICE¹ (1) 骰子搖盒 —see also 另見 **movers and shakers** (MOVER (4))

Shakes·pea·re·an /ʃekˈspɪrɪən; ʃeɪkˈspɪəriən/ *adj* [only before noun 僅用於名詞前] **1** in the style of Shakespeare 莎士比亞風格的: *an almost Shakespearean richness of* *language* 近乎莎士比亞那樣豐富多彩的語言 **2** connected with the work of Shakespeare (涉及) 莎士比亞作品的: *a famous Shakespearean actor* 莎士比亞戲劇的著名演員

shake·up /ˈʃekˌʌp; ˈʃeɪkʌp/ *n* [C] a process by which an organization makes a lot of big changes in a short time to improve its effectiveness 改組, 重新組合: *a huge shakeup of the education system* 教育體制的大改組

shak·y /ˈʃekɪ; ˈʃeɪki/ *adj* **1** weak and unsteady because of old age, illness or shock〔因年邁、疾病、驚嚇而〕搖晃的; 顫抖的; 衰弱的: *shaky voice* 顫抖的聲音 | **be shaky on your feet** (=not able to walk very well) 步履不穩 *Grandad was a little shaky on his feet after the accident.* 爺爺在那次事故之後走路有點不穩。**2** not thorough, complete, or certain 不全面的; 不完整的; 沒有把握的: *My knowledge of history is a little shaky.* 我的歷史知識不夠全面。| *shaky evidence* 不可靠的證據 **3** not firm or steady 不牢的, 不穩固的: *shaky foundations* 不牢固的基礎 —**shakily** *adv* —**shakiness** *n* [U]

shale /ʃel; ʃeɪl/ *n* [U] a smooth soft rock which breaks easily into thin flat pieces 頁岩

3 1 **shall** /ʃəl; ʃəl *strong* 強讀 ʃæl; ʃæl/ *modal verb negative short form* 否定縮略式= **shan't 1 I/we shall** used to express what you will do in the future 我/我們將要〔用於表示未來要做的事〕: *We shall be away next week.* 我們下週不在這裡。| *I shall have finished it by Friday.* 到星期五我就會把它完成了。**2 shall I/we?** *BrE* used to make a suggestion, or ask a question that you want the other person to decide about【英】…好嗎? 要不要…?〔用於提建議或要求他人作決定的問句中〕: *Shall I open the window?* 我要開窗嗎? | *What shall I get for dinner?* 我弄些甚麼來作晚餐? | *Shall we say 6 o'clock, then?* 那麼, 我們就定在6點鐘好嗎? **3 you/he/she/they shall** *formal or old-fashioned* used to describe what will happen to someone, especially when you are saying that it is very definite【正式或過時】你(們)/他/她/他們一定會[一定要]〔用於表示必然性和必要性〕: *They shall be judged only by God.* 他們一定只會受到上帝的審判。| *I said you could go, and so you shall.* 我說過你能去, 所以你一定要去。**4 we shall see** *spoken* used when you do not know what will happen in the future, or when you do not want to give someone a definite answer【口】我們看看再說〔用於不清楚將會發生何事或不想給某人明確答覆之時〕**5** *formal* used in official documents to show a law, command, promise etc【正式】應該, 必須〔用於正式文件中, 表示法律、命令、允諾等〕: *All payments shall be made by the end of the month.* 所有款項必須在月底前付清。

shal·lot /ʃəˈlɑt; ʃəˈlɒt/ *n* [C] a vegetable like a small onion 青葱

shal·low¹ /ˈʃælo; ˈʃæləʊ/ *adj* **1** something that is shallow has only a short distance from the bottom to the surface 淺的, 不深的: *a shallow river* 淺河 | *the shallow end of the swimming pool* 游泳池的淺水區 | *a shallow grave* 埋得淺的墳墓 —see picture at 參見 LOW¹ 圖 **2** not interested in or showing any understanding of important or serious matters〔對問題的理解等〕膚淺的, 淺薄的: *a shallow argument* 膚淺的論點 | *If he's only interested in your looks, that just shows how shallow he is.* 如果他只是對你的外貌感興趣, 那正好說明他多麼淺薄。**3 shallow breathing** breathing that only takes in small amounts of air 淺呼吸〔吸入少量空氣〕—**shallowly** *adv* —**shallowness** *n* [U]

shallow² *v* [I] to become shallow 變淺

shal·lows /ˈʃæloz; ˈʃæləʊz/ *n* **the shallows** an area of shallow water 淺水區, 淺灘: *We could see fish darting about in the shallows.* 我們可以看見魚兒在淺水區游來游去。

Sha·lom /ʃæˈlom; ʃæˈlɒm/ *interjection* a Jewish word used to say hello or goodbye 喂, 你好; 再見〔猶太人打招呼或告別用語〕

shalt /ʃəlt; ʃəlt; *strong* 強讀 ʃælt; ʃælt/ *v* **thou shalt** *old use*【舊】= you shall

sham¹ /ʃæm; ʃæm/ *n* **1** [singular] an attempt to deceive people by pretending something is true or good, especially when it is easy to see that it is not 虛偽, 偽善; 假象: *These so-called democratic reforms are a complete sham.* 這些所謂的民主改革全是假象。**2** [singular] someone who pretends to be something they are not, especially to gain an advantage or sympathy〔尤指要得到好處或同情的〕假冒者, 假裝者: *He was bogus, a sham, an imposter!* 他是偽裝的, 一個假冒者, 一個騙子! **3** [U] behaviour or actions intended to deceive people by pretending that something is true or good 虛假行為; 假冒; 假裝

sham² *adj* [only before noun 僅用於名詞前] made to appear real in order to deceive people; false 假的; 仿製的; 偽造的; 冒充的: *sham jewellery* 假珠寶

sham³ *v* [I,T] to pretend to be upset, ill etc to gain sympathy or an advantage 假裝, 佯裝〔苦惱、生病等〕: *She's not ill, she's only shamming.* 她沒有病, 只不過是裝病罷了。

sha·man /ˈʃɑmən; ˈʃɑːmən/ *n* [C] someone with religious authority in some tribes, who is believed to be able to talk to spirits, cure illnesses etc 薩滿 (教巫師) —**shamanism** *n* [U]

sham·ble /ˈʃæmbḷ; ˈʃæmbəl/ *v* [I always+adv/prep] to walk slowly and awkwardly, dragging your feet in a tired, weak, or lazy way〔疲倦地或懶洋洋地〕拖着腳走; 蹣跚而行: **[+along/past/out etc]** *The old man shambled out of the room muttering to himself.* 那個老人蹣跚地走出房間, 口中喃喃自語。| **shambling gait** (=a shambling way of walking) 步履蹣跚

sham·bles /ˈʃæmblz; ˈʃæmbəlz/ *n informal*【非正式】**a shambles a)** an event or situation that is a complete failure because it has not been organized or planned properly〔因缺乏組織或計劃而造成事情的〕失敗; 一團糟; 混亂場面: **be (in) a shambles** *By 1985 the economy was in a shambles.* 到1985年, 經濟已經變得一團糟。| **make a shambles of sth** *Potts, you made a complete shambles of that speech.* 波茨, 你的演講雜亂無章。**b)** a place where there is a lot of damage, destruction, and confusion 遭嚴重破壞的地方; 淩亂的景象: *This kitchen is a shambles!* 這個廚房淩亂不堪!

S

sham·bol·ic /ʃæmˈbɑlɪk; ʃæmˈbɒlɪk/ *adj informal* lacking organization or planning【非正式】混亂的, 淩亂的: *The way they run this place is totally shambolic.* 他們對這個地方的管理完全雜亂無章。

shame¹ /ʃem; ʃeɪm/ *n* **1 it's a shame (that)/what a shame!** 2 *spoken* used to say that a situation is disappointing, and you wish things had happened differently【口】…真遺憾! 多可惜啊!: *It's a shame you have to leave so soon.* 真遺憾, 你們那麼快就要走了。| *Oh it's raining. What a shame!* 啊, 下雨了, 真糟糕! **2** [U] the uncomfortable feeling of being guilty and embarrassed that you have when you have done something wrong〔因做錯事感到的〕羞愧, 羞恥, 慚愧: *a deep sense of shame* 深深的羞愧感 | **to your shame** (=making you feel ashamed) 使你感到慚愧 *She realized to her shame that she had forgotten Nina's birthday.* 她感到不好意思的是居然忘了尼娜的生日。| **hang/bow your head in shame** (=look downwards and avoid looking at other people because you feel ashamed) 慚愧地低下頭來 **3 Shame on you!** *spoken* used to tell someone that they should feel shame because of something they have done【口】你應該感到羞恥! **4** [U only in questions and negatives 僅用於疑問句和否定句] the ability to feel shame 羞愧感, 羞恥之心: *How could you do such a thing? Have you no shame?* 你怎麼能做出這種事? 你難道就不知道羞恥嗎? **5 put sb/sth to shame** *informal* to be so much better than someone or something else that it makes the other thing seem very bad or ordinary【非正式】使某人/某物黯然失色, 使某人/某物相形見絀: *His cooking puts mine to shame.* 與他的烹飪技術相比, 我的大為遜色。**6** [U] loss of honour and respect 恥辱, 丟臉: **there is no shame in sth** (=it should not make you feel ashamed) 某事並非恥辱 *There's no shame in being poor.* 貧窮並不是恥辱。| **bring shame on sb** *You've brought shame on this family.* 你已經使這個家庭蒙羞了。

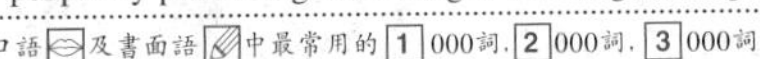

USAGE NOTE 用法說明: SHAME

WORD CHOICE 詞語辨析: **shame, embarrassment, ashamed, feel silly, embarrassed**

Shame is an uncomfortable feeling you have when you have done something wrong, and you feel that people will no longer respect you. If you make a mistake this may cause **embarrassment**, but not usually **shame** because **shame** is much stronger. shame（羞恥, 羞愧）指做了錯事擔心自己不再受人尊重, 因而產生的一種不自在的感覺。如果犯了一般性錯誤或有失誤, 那就可能感到 embarrassment（不好意思）, 但通常不用 shame, 因為它的意思要強得多。

Ashamed (adj) is not quite so strong, but still not usually used about unimportant or accidental things. 形容詞 ashamed（慚愧的）的意思不那麼強, 但也不用於小事或偶然的失誤上: *I couldn't think of anything to say and felt silly/embarrassed* (NOT 不用 *ashamed*). 我想不出該說些甚麼, 覺得有點不好意思。However, someone might be **ashamed** if they are caught cheating in test, for example, because they have done something morally wrong. 不過, 做了有損道德的錯事, 例如在考試中作弊被抓住, 那就可能感到 ashamed（羞愧）了。

shame² *v* **1** [T] **shame sb** to make someone feel ashamed 使某人感到羞恥: *It shames me to say it, but I lied.* 說出來令我羞愧, 但我是撒了謊。**2 shame sb into doing sth** to force someone to do something by making them feel ashamed 使某人因羞愧而不得不做某事: *His wife shamed him into handing the money back.* 他的妻子使他羞愧得只好把錢交回去。**3** to be so much better than someone else that you make them seem bad or feel embarrassed 使黯然失色, 使相形見絀: *They have a training record that would shame most other companies.* 他們的培訓記錄很好, 足以使其他大多數公司相形見絀。**4** make someone feel that they have lost honour and respect 使蒙羞, 玷辱: **shame sb** *Your cowardice has shamed us all.* 你的懦弱行為使我們大家蒙羞。

shame·faced /ˋʃemˏfest; ˌʃeɪmˈfeɪst◂/ *adj* looking ashamed or embarrassed about having behaved badly 羞怯的, 慚愧的: *"You really blew it, Ian." He nodded, shamefaced.* "你確實把事情搞糟了, 伊恩。"他點了點頭, 面帶愧色。—**shamefacedly** /-ˏfesɪdlɪ; -ˈfeɪsɪ̣dli/ *adv*

shame·ful /ˋʃemfəl; ˈʃeɪmfəl/ *adj* shameful behaviour is so bad that people think you should be ashamed of it〔行為〕可恥的, 丟臉的: *It's shameful the way some people treat their pets.* 有些人如此對待他們的寵物, 真是可恥。| *a shameful family secret* 家醜 —**shamefully** *adv* —**shamefulness** *n* [U]

shame·less /ˋʃemlɪs; ˈʃeɪmləs/ *adj* not seeming to be ashamed of your bad behaviour 無恥的, 不知羞恥的, 不要臉的: *a shameless liar* 無恥的說謊者 —**shamelessly** *adv* —**shamelessness** *n* [U]

sham·my /ˋʃæmɪ; ˈʃæmi/ *n* [C] a piece of soft leather used for cleaning and polishing glass or metal; CHAMOIS (2) 羚羊皮軟革〔用於擦拭玻璃、金屬等〕

sham·poo¹ /ʃæmˋpu; ʃæmˈpuː/ *n* **1** [C,U] a liquid soap for washing your hair 洗髮劑, 香波 **2** [C,U] a liquid used for cleaning carpets (CARPET¹ (1))〔清潔地毯用的〕洗滌劑 **3** [C] an act of shampooing or having your hair shampooed 洗頭, 洗髮: *$21 for a shampoo, cut, and blow-dry* 洗頭、理髮、吹乾共 21 美元

shampoo² *v* [T] to wash something with shampoo 用洗髮劑洗; 用洗滌劑洗

sham·rock /ˋʃæmrɑk; ˈʃæmrɒk/ *n* [C] a small plant with three green leaves on each stem that is the national EMBLEM of Ireland 三葉草, 白花酢漿草〔愛爾蘭的國花〕

shan·dy /ˋʃændɪ; ˈʃændi/ *n* [C,U] a drink made of beer mixed with LEMONADE (2), or a glass of this drink（一杯）香迪酒〔啤酒與檸檬水混合的飲料〕

shang·hai /ʃæŋˋhaɪ; ʃæŋˈhaɪ/ *v* [T+into] to trick or force someone into doing something unwillingly 誘騙; 強迫〔某人做某事〕: *I got shanghaied into organizing the kids' party.* 我被騙去組織孩子們的聚會。

shank /ʃæŋk; ʃæŋk/ *n* **1** [C] a straight narrow part of a tool or object that connects the two ends〔工具或物件的〕柄, 桿: *the shank of a key* 鑰匙柄 **2** [C,U] a piece of meat cut from the leg of an animal〔動物的〕一塊腿肉 **3** [C usually plural 一般用複數] *old use* the part of a person's or animal's leg between the knee and ANKLE【舊】〔人或動物的〕脛〔膝蓋至腳踝的部分〕—see picture at 參見 HORSE¹ 圖

shan't /ʃænt; ʃɑːnt/ *especially BrE*【尤英】the short form of 縮略式= shall not: *I shan't see you again.* 我不會再見到你了。

shan·ty /ˋʃæntɪ; ˈʃænti/ *n* [C] **1** a small, roughly built hut made from thin sheets of wood, TIN¹ (1), plastic etc that very poor people live in〔窮人居住的〕簡陋小木屋, 鐵皮[塑料板]棚屋 **2 sea shanty** a song sung by sailors in former times, as they did their work〔昔日水手工作時唱的〕號子, 船夫號子, 船歌

shan·ty·town /ˋʃæntɪˏtaʊn; ˈʃæntiˌtaʊn/ *n* [C] an area in or near a town where people live in shanties〔城鎮或其附近的〕貧民區, 棚戶區

shapes 形狀

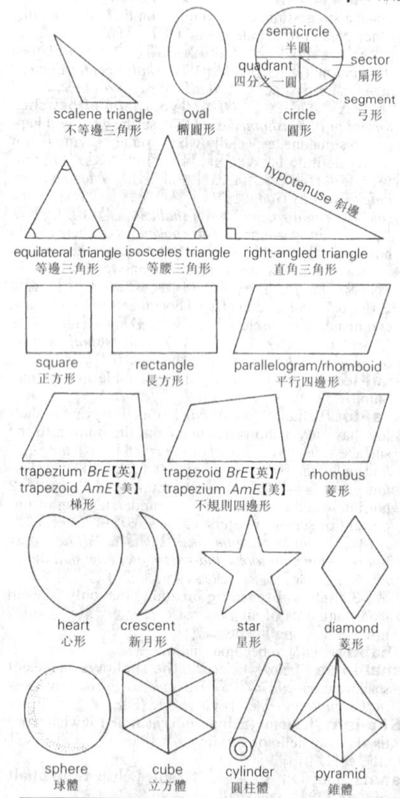

shape¹ /ʃep; ʃeɪp/ *n*

1 ►OUTER FORM 外形◄ **a)** [C,U] the outer form of

something, that you see or feel 形, 形狀, 外形: *What shape is the table – round or oval?* 那張桌子是甚麼形狀的 ── 圓形還是橢圓形? | *You can recognize a tree by the shape of its leaves.* 你可以根據樹葉的形狀辨認出是甚麼樹。| **round/square etc in shape** *The eyeball is almost spherical in shape.* 眼球幾乎是球形的。| **lose its shape** (=become the wrong shape) 變形 *His battered old hat had completely lost its shape.* 他那頂破舊不堪的帽子完全變形了。| **out of shape** (having become the wrong shape) 變形, 走樣 *Meryl's sweater had stretched completely out of shape.* 梅里爾的毛衣撐得完全走樣了。| **in the shape of** (=having the same shape as something) 某種形狀的 *She was wearing a pin in the shape of a bird.* 她佩戴着一枚鳥狀的飾針。**b)** [C] a particular shape, or thing that is that shape 某種形狀; 某形狀之物: *OK Katie, which of these shapes are triangles?* 好, 凱蒂, 你看這些形狀中哪幾個是三角形?

2 ►THING NOT SEEN CLEARLY 看不清楚的東西◄ [C] a thing or person that you cannot see clearly enough to recognize〔物或人〕朦朧的形狀, 看不清的東西: *A large shape loomed up out of the mist.* 霧中隱約出現一個很大的影像。

3 ►CHARACTER OF STH 某物的特色◄ [singular] a particular combination of qualities and features that something has 形態; 形式; 方式: **the shape of** *the shape of British politics today* 今日英國的政治形態 | *Dr Singh was responsible for the final shape of the report.* 辛格博士負責這份報告的定稿。| **in any shape or form** (=of any kind) 任何形式的 *We will not tolerate racism in any shape or form.* 我們不會容忍任何形式的種族主義。| **the shape of things to come** (=an example of the way things will develop in the future) 未來事物的發展狀態[方向]

4 in the shape of used to explain what something consists of 以…的形式〔用以解釋某物的組成〕: **sth comes in the shape of** *Help came in the shape of a $10,000 loan from his parents.* 幫助來了, 他從父母那裡得到10,000美元的貸款。

5 in good/bad/poor shape a) in a good or bad condition 情況良好/不好; 處於良好/不佳狀態: *Considering how old the car is, it's not in bad shape.* 這麼老的汽車, 狀況就算不錯了。**b)** in a good or bad state of health or physical FITNESS (1) 健康狀況良好/不好: *After three months without any exercise or training the champion's in poor shape.* 那位冠軍三個月根本不運動也不訓練, 身體狀況很差。

6 in shape/out of shape in a good or bad state of health or physical FITNESS (1) 健康[身體]狀況良好/不好: **get (yourself) into shape** *I've got to get into shape before summer.* 我必須在夏天之前把身體鍛煉好。

7 knock/lick sb into shape *informal* to make someone better so that they reach the necessary standard【非正式】把某人訓練好, 使達到標準, 使趨於完善: *Some of them lack experience, but we'll soon knock them into shape.* 他們有些人還缺乏經驗, 但我們很快就會把他們訓練好的。

8 take shape to develop into a clear and definite form 形成, 使成形: *An idea was beginning to take shape in his mind.* 一個主意開始在他腦子裡形成。

9 in/of all shapes and sizes of many different types 各種各樣的: **come in all shapes and sizes** *Domestic pets come in all shapes and sizes.* 家庭寵物五花八門, 甚麼都有。

S3 **shape²** *v* **1** [T] to influence something such as a belief, opinion etc and make it develop in a particular way 形成〔某種信仰、看法等〕, 決定〔某事物的發展方向等〕: *People's political beliefs are often shaped by what they read in the newspapers.* 人們的政治信仰常常是在他們所讀報紙內容的影響下形成的。**2** to make something have a particular shape, especially by pressing it〔尤指通過擠、壓等〕使成為某種形狀, 使成形: **shape sth into sth** *Shape the dough into small balls.* 把麵團搓成小圓球。

shape up *phr v* [I] *informal*【非正式】**1** to make progress and improve in the way you want 進展;〔按要求〕發展: *The new recruits are shaping up nicely.* 新兵進步很快。**2** to improve your behaviour or work 改進〔行為、工作〕: *If you don't shape up, I'll have to contact your parents.* 假如你不改進的話, 我只好和你父母聯繫了。**3 shape up or ship out** *AmE spoken* used to tell someone that if they do not improve they will be made to leave a place or their job【美口】不改進就走人

shaped /ʃept; ʃeɪpt/ *adj* having a particular shape 具有某種形狀的: **egg-shaped/V-shaped etc** *an L-shaped living room* 一間呈 L 形的起居室 | **be shaped like** *The building was shaped like a giant pyramid.* 這幢大樓的形狀像座巨型金字塔。

shape·less /ˈʃeplɪs; ˈʃeɪpləs/ *adj* **1** not having a clear or definite shape 無[不成]形狀的: *Why should fat women have to wear baggy, shapeless dresses?* 為甚麼肥胖的女人就得穿寬鬆、不成形的衣服? **2** something such as a book or a plan that is shapeless does not seem to have a clear structure〔書、計劃等〕沒有條理的, 結構凌亂的 —**shapelessly** *adv* —**shapelessness** *n* [U]

shape·ly /ˈʃeplɪ; ˈʃeɪpli/ *adj* having a body that has an attractive shape 身材好的, 勻稱的: *shapely curved legs* 線條優美的腿 —**shapeliness** *n* [U]

shard /ʃɑrd; ʃɑːd/ also 又作 **sherd** *n* [C] a sharp piece of broken glass, metal etc〔玻璃、金屬等的〕鋒利碎片

share¹ /ʃɛr; ʃeə/ *v* S1 W1

1 ►USE EQUALLY 共同使用◄ [I,T] to have or use something that other people also have or use at the same time〔與他人〕共有〔某物〕, 共享; 共用: *We don't have enough books for everyone, so you'll have to share.* 我們的書不夠每人一本, 所以大家要合着用。| **share sth** *The last bus had gone, so the three of us shared a taxi.* 最後一班公共汽車已經開走, 所以我們三人合乘一輛計程車。| **share sth with sb** *I shared a room with her at college.* 我上大學時和她共住一個房間。| **shared house/flat** *BrE* (=with people not related to each other living in it)【英】共住的房子/公寓 —see 見 BETWEEN (USAGE)

2 ►LET SB USE STH 讓某人用某物◄ [T] to let someone have or use something that belongs to you 讓別人分享〔自己的東西〕: *Even as a kid he'd never share his toys.* 即使在小時候他也從不讓別的孩子玩他的玩具。| **share sth with** *I shared my lunch with a few hungry pigeons.* 我和幾隻飢餓的鴿子分享我的午餐。

3 ►DIVIDE 劃分◄ also 又作 **share** sth ↔ **out** [T] to divide something between two or more people〔在若干人之間〕分配: **share sth between/among sb** *At his death, his property was shared out between his children.* 他死後財產分給了子女們。

4 ►SAME INTEREST/OPINION ETC 相同的興趣/看法等◄ [T] to have the same opinion, experience, feeling etc as someone else 與某人有共同的〔看法、經歷、感受等〕: *I share your concern about this.* 我和你一樣為這件事擔心。| **share in sth** *His daughters did not share in his happiness.* 他的女兒們沒有分享過他的快樂。| **share sth with sb** *Stubbornness was a characteristic he shared with his mother.* 固執是他和他母親共有的一個特徵。| **share an interest** (=have the same interest in something as someone else) 興趣相同

5 ►RESPONSIBILITY 責任◄ [T] to be equally responsible for doing something, paying for something etc 分擔〔責任〕, 分攤〔費用〕: *I own the house, but we share the bills.* 我擁有這所房子, 但我們分擔各項開支。| *We all share some blame for the mess-up.* 弄得這樣糟, 我們大家都有一定責任。

6 ►TELL SB STH 將某事告訴某人◄ [I,T] to tell other people about an idea, secret, problem etc 把〔想法、祕密、問題等〕向別人訴說: *It's always better to share your*

worries. 向別人傾訴你的憂慮總比憋在心裡要好。| **share sth with sb** *Are you going to share the joke with us?* 你要把笑話講給我們聽嗎? | **share** *especially AmE* 【尤美】: *If you feel the need to share we're all listening.* 你如果覺得有必要講出來, 我們都將洗耳恭聽。

7 share and share alike *spoken* used to say that you should share things fairly and equally between everyone 【口】應均分[平均分擔; 平均分享]

share² *n*

1 ▶PART OF STH 某事物的一部分◀ [singular] the part of something that belongs to you, or that should be paid for or done by you〔某人應得或應負擔的〕一份: **[+of/in]** *I gave them my share of the bill and left.* 我把賬單上我該付的那份錢交給他們就走了。| *a share in the profits* 一份利潤 | **do your share** (=do your part of a job, duty etc that you share with other people) 做你那一份〔分擔的工作、義務等〕*I do my share of the housework.* 我做我那份家務活。

2 flat/house share *BrE* a situation in which people who are not related to each other live together 【英】公寓/房子共用

3 your (fair) share a) as much or more of something as you could reasonably expect to have 應得的一份: *She's had more than her fair share of bad luck this year.* 她今年倒霉事特別多。| *You've sure had your share of problems, haven't you?* 你肯定也有過你自己的問題, 是嗎? **b)** as much as everyone else 和每個人一樣多的一份: *Don't worry – you'll get your fair share.* 不用擔心── 你會得到同樣多的一份。| *I've made my share of mistakes.* 我自己也犯了不少錯誤。

S

4 share in your part in an activity, event etc〔活動、事件等的〕參與: *Employees are always given a share in decision-making.* 雇員始終有參與決策的權利。

5 ▶FINANCIAL 經濟的◀ [C] one of the equal parts into which the ownership of a company is divided 股, 股份: **[+in]** *He decided to sell his shares in Allied Chemicals.* 他決定出售他在聯合化工公司的股份。| **share offer/issue** (=a time when shares in a company are sold or begin to be sold) 股票發行 —compare 比較 STOCK¹ (3)

6 ▶FARM TOOL 農具◀ [C] *old-fashioned* a PLOUGHSHARE 【過時】犁鏵 —see also 另見 **the lion's share** (LION (3)), TIMESHARE —**sharing** *n* [U]

share·crop·per /ˈ· ˌ··/ *n* [C] *especially AmE* a farmer who uses someone else's land, and gives the owner half the crop in return 【尤美】收益分成的佃農〔耕種他人的土地, 收穫各分一半〕

share·hold·er /ˈʃɛrˌholdɚ; ˈʃeəˌhəʊldə/ *n* [C] *especially BrE* someone who owns shares in a business 【尤英】股東, 股票持有者; STOCKHOLDER *especially AmE* 【尤美】: *Shareholders have been told to expect an even lower result for 1995.* 股東們被告知, 1995 年業績預計會更差。

share in·dex /ˈ· ˌ··/ *n* [C] *technical* an official and public list of SHARE² (5) prices 【術語】股票指數

share·ware /ˈʃɛrˌwɛr; ˈʃeəweə/ *n* [U] free or cheap computer SOFTWARE that is produced by small companies 共享軟件〔小公司生產的免費或廉價電腦軟件〕

sha·ri·a, sheria /ʃəˈriə; ʃəˈriːə/ *n* [U] a system of religious laws followed by Muslims 伊斯蘭法

shark /ʃɑrk; ʃɑːk/ *n* [C] **1** *plural* **shark** or **sharks** a large fish with several rows of very sharp teeth that is sometimes considered to be dangerous to humans 鯊(魚) **2** *informal* someone who cheats other people out of money 【非正式】詐騙(錢財)者 —see also 另見 LOAN SHARK

sharp¹ /ʃɑrp; ʃɑːp/ *adj*

1 ▶ABLE TO CUT 能切割的◀ having a very thin edge or point that can cut things easily 鋒利的, 銳利的, 尖的: *Peel the apples using a sharp knife.* 用鋒利的刀子削蘋果。| *The metal was jagged with lots of sharp edges.* 這塊金屬表面粗糙, 有很多鋒利的邊緣。| **razor sharp** (=very sharp) 非常鋒利的 —opposite 反義詞 BLUNT¹ (1)

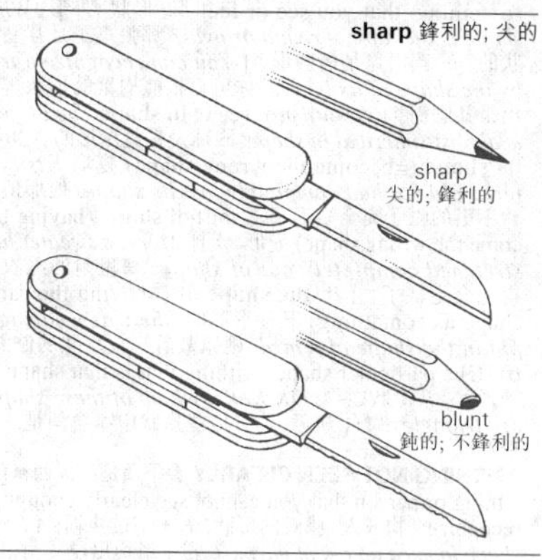

2 ▶SOUNDS 聲音◀ loud, short, and sudden 刺耳的, 短促的, 突如其來的: *The branch broke with a sharp crack.* 樹枝折斷, 發出刺耳的劈啪一聲。| *a sharp cry of pain* 痛苦的尖叫聲

3 ▶TASTE 味道◀ having a slightly bitter taste 辛辣的: *Add mustard to give the dressing a sharper taste.* 加些芥末使調料帶點辛辣味。

4 ▶DIRECTION 方向◀ a sudden extreme change of direction 急轉彎的, 方向突變的: **sharp bend/turn** *We came to a sharp bend in the road.* 我們到了公路的一個急轉彎處。| **sharp left/right** *Take a sharp left after the church.* 過了教堂之後, 向左急轉彎。

5 ▶PAIN 疼痛◀ sudden and severe 急劇的, 劇烈的: *I felt a sharp pain in my back.* 我感到背部一陣劇痛。—see graph at 參見 PAIN¹ 圖表

6 ▶REMARK 話語◀ severe, angry, and criticizing 尖銳的, 嚴厲的, 憤怒的, 責備的: *a sharp rebuke* 嚴厲的斥責 | *John's tone was sharp.* 約翰語氣尖刻。| **be sharp with sb** *The boss can be very sharp with people when she's busy.* 老闆忙起來會訓斥人。

7 have a sharp tongue to often talk to people in an angry, unkind, or criticizing way 說話尖酸刻薄

8 ▶PEOPLE 人◀ able to think and understand things very quickly, and not easily deceived 敏銳的, 機靈的: *a journalist with an extremely sharp mind* 頭腦極其敏銳的新聞記者

9 ▶EYES 眼睛◀ able to see and notice details very well 靈敏的, 銳利的: **a sharp eye for detail** (=the ability to notice and deal with details) 觀察入微的眼力

10 keep a sharp eye on sb to watch someone very carefully, especially because you do not trust them 密切注意某人〔尤指因對其不信任〕: *Keep a sharp eye on the kids at all times!* 任何時候都要睜大眼睛盯住這些孩子!

11 ▶PENCIL 鉛筆◀ having a very thin point, that can draw an exact line〔筆心〕很尖的 —opposite 反義詞 BLUNT¹ (1)

12 ▶SHAPE 形狀◀ not rounded or curved; ANGULAR 尖突的, 有突邊的, 線條分明的: *Janice had the same sharp features as her mother.* 賈妮絲像她母親, 五官輪廓也很分明。

13 ▶CHANGE 變化◀ a sharp increase, rise etc is very sudden and very big〔增長、上升等〕急劇的, 猛烈的: *a sharp increase in prices* 價格的急劇上漲

14 ▶DIFFERENCE 差別◀ clear and definite, so that there is no doubt 明顯的, 清楚的: *The distinction between public and private services is much less sharp here.* 公共服務和私人服務的差別在這裡遠沒有那樣明顯。| **in sharp contrast** (=very different from someone or something else) 形成鮮明的對照 *Keele wore a smart suit, in sharp contrast to everyone's else's casual attire.* 基爾

穿着一套帥氣的西裝, 與其他人的便裝形成鮮明對照。
15 ►PICTURE/IMAGES 圖畫/影像◄ having a shape that is clear and detailed 輪廓清晰的, 線條分明的: *The outlines of the cypress trees were sharp and clear.* 那些柏樹輪廓清晰, 枝條挺拔。
16 a) F sharp/D sharp/C sharp etc a musical note that is sharp has been raised by one SEMITONE from the note F, D, C etc 升 F (調) /D (調) /C (調)〔指音符升半音〕—see picture at 參見 MUSIC 圖 **b)** if music or singing is sharp, it is played or sung at a slightly higher PITCH[1] (3) than it should be〔比準確音調〕略偏高的
17 ►MOVEMENT 動作◄ quick and sudden 急促的, 突然的: *The wind blew across the lake in sharp gusts.* 一陣陣急風颳過湖面。| *a sharp intake of breath* 猛吸一口氣
18 ►FEELINGS 感情◄ very strong and unexpected 非常強烈的, 意料不到的: *I was left with a sharp sense of disappointment.* 我落下了一種強烈的失望感。
19 sharp practice behaviour, especially in business, that is dishonest but not illegal〔尤指商業中合法但〕不誠實的交易手段
20 a sharp frost a very cold severe FROST[1] (1) 刺骨的寒霜
21 be on the sharp end of sth to experience the worst effects of something 經歷某事的最壞情況: *We were always on the sharp end of clients' complaints.* 處理顧客投訴的壓力總是由我們來承受。
22 sb looks sharp *AmE* if someone looks sharp, they are dressed well and attractively【美】〔人〕衣着時髦的, 漂亮的, 吸引人的; SMART[1] (2) *especially BrE*【尤英】: *Tod looked really sharp in his tux.* 托德穿着晚禮服看上去挺帥。—**sharpness** *n* [U] —see also 另見 SHARPLY

sharp² *adv* **1 at ten-thirty/2 o'clock etc sharp** at exactly 10.30, 2.00 etc 在十時三十分/二時正: *We're meeting at 10 o'clock sharp.* 我們將在十時正會面。**2 sharp left/right** if you turn sharp left or right, you make a sudden change of direction to the left or right 向左轉/向右急轉彎: *You turn sharp right at the crossroads.* 在十字路口向右急轉彎。**3 look sharp** *spoken*【口】**a)** *BrE* used to tell someone to do something quickly【英】〔用於叫別人〕趕快, 趕緊: *If you look sharp you might catch him before he leaves for London.* 你如果趕緊去, 也許能在他出發去倫敦前見到他。**b)** *especially AmE* used to warn someone about something【尤美】留神, 注意〔用於提醒別人〕: *Look sharp, the boss is coming!* 留心, 老闆來了! **4** played or sung at a slightly higher PITCH[1] (3) than is correct〔演奏或演唱得比正確的音調〕略為偏高

sharp³ *n* [C] **1** a musical note that has been raised one SEMITONE above the note written〔音符的〕升半音 **2** the sign *(#)* in a line of written music used to show this 升號〔#, 表示升半音〕—see picture at 參見 MUSIC 圖

sharp-eared /,· '·◄/ *adj* able to hear very well 聽覺靈敏的, 耳靈的

sharp·en /ˈʃɑrpən; ˈʃɑːpən/ *v* **1** [I,T] to become sharper or make something sharper (使) 變鋒利[尖銳, 清晰]: *Sharpen all your pencils before the test.* 考試前把你所有的鉛筆削尖。| *The light grew brighter and the shadows sharpened.* 燈光變得更加明亮, 陰影也更清晰。**2** [T] to make a feeling stronger and more urgent 使〔某種感覺〕增強, 使感到迫切: *These latest moves have sharpened fears of a military conflict.* 最近的這些行動增加了人們對發生軍事衝突的擔心。
sharpen sth ↔ up *phr v* [T] to improve something so that it is up to the necessary standard, quality etc 使達到標準; 使符合質量要求: *We need more rehearsals to sharpen up the dance routine.* 我們需要更多的排練使舞步更加完美。

sharp·en·er /ˈʃɑrpənɚ; ˈʃɑːpənə/ *n* [C] a tool or machine for sharpening pencils, knives etc 磨削的工具〈如鉛筆刀、磨刀器等〉

sharp·er /ˈʃɑrpɚ; ˈʃɑːpə/ *n* [C] *old-fashioned* someone who cheats or is dishonest【過時】騙子, 詐騙者

sharp-eyed /,· '·◄/ *adj* able to see very well and notice small details 目光敏銳的: *My sharp-eyed mother had already spotted him.* 我那目光敏銳的母親已經認出他了。

sharp·ish /ˈʃɑrpɪʃ; ˈʃɑːpɪʃ/ *adv BrE spoken* quickly【英口】迅速地: *We'd better leave pretty sharpish if we want to catch that bus.* 如果我們想趕上那趟公共汽車, 那就最好快點動身。

sharp·ly /ˈʃɑrplɪ; ˈʃɑːpli/ *adv* [W3]
1 ►SPEAK/LOOK 說/看◄ in a severe and disapproving way 嚴厲地, 毫不客氣地: *"What do you mean by that?" Paul asked sharply.* "你那樣說是甚麼意思?" 保羅厲聲問道。| *I glanced at her sharply, but said nothing.* 我嚴厲地看了她一眼, 但沒有說話。| **sharply critical** (=very critical and disapproving) 非常苛刻[挑剔]的
2 ►CHANGE 變化◄ if something rises, falls etc sharply, it rises or falls quickly and suddenly 急劇地; 急〔升〕, 驟〔降〕, 暴〔跌〕: *Prices have risen sharply over the last few months.* 過去幾個月裡價格一直在急劇上漲。
3 ►MOVE 移動◄ quickly and suddenly 迅速地, 突然地: *She heard a noise behind her and turned around sharply.* 她聽到背後有聲音, 便迅速地轉過身來。
4 ►SHOW DIFFERENCES 出現分歧◄ clearly and definitely 明顯地, 確切地: *Opinion is sharply divided.* 意見分歧明顯。
5 sharply contrasted/contrasting very different 呈鮮明的對照, 截然不同: *His aggressive behaviour contrasted sharply with the mild manners of his brother.* 他那種咄咄逼人的行為跟他兄弟的溫和舉止形成鮮明的對照。

sharp-wit·ted /,· '··◄/ *adj* able to think and react very quickly〔思維和反應〕敏捷的, 敏銳的, 機智的

shat /ʃæt; ʃæt/ the past tense and past participle of SHIT²

shat·ter /ˈʃætɚ; ˈʃætə/ *v* **1** [I,T] to break suddenly into very small pieces, or to make something break in this way (使) 粉碎, (使) 破碎: **[+into]** *The plate hit the floor, and shattered into tiny bits.* 盤子砸在地板上, 摔得粉碎。| **shatter sth** *A stone shattered the window.* 一塊石頭把窗戶玻璃打碎了。**2** [T] to make someone feel disappointed by showing or proving that someone's hopes or beliefs are impossible or wrong 使〔希望、信念〕破滅, 粉碎: *Hopes of a peace agreement were shattered today when talks broke down again.* 今天談判再次失敗, 達成和平協議的希望破滅了。| **shatter sb's illusions** *A few weeks in a tiny damp room soon shattered his illusions about university life.* 在狹小潮濕的房間裡住了幾個星期後, 他對大學生活的幻想破滅了。

shat·tered /ˈʃætɚd; ˈʃætəd/ *adj* [not before noun 不用於名詞前] **1** very shocked and upset 感到震驚的; 難過的; 心煩意亂的: *I wasn't just disappointed, I was absolutely shattered.* 我不僅是失望, 我簡直是十分難過。**2** *BrE informal* very tired; EXHAUSTED (1)【英, 非正式】精疲力竭的, 極度疲勞的: *By the time we got home we were both shattered.* 回到家時, 我們兩人都精疲力竭了。

shat·ter·ing /ˈʃætərɪŋ; ˈʃætərɪŋ/ *adj* **1** very shocking and upsetting 令人震驚的; 使人心煩意亂的: *shattering news from home* 從家鄉傳來的令人震驚的消息 **2** *BrE informal* making you very tired【英, 非正式】使人疲倦的, 使人精疲力竭的

shat·ter·proof /ˈʃætɚ,pruf; ˈʃætəpruːf/ *adj* glass that is shatterproof is specially designed so that it will not form sharp dangerous pieces if it is broken〔玻璃〕防碎的〔經特殊設計的一種玻璃, 即使打破也不會形成鋒利的碎片〕

shave¹ /ʃev; ʃeɪv/ *v* **1** [I,T] to cut off hair very close to the skin, especially from the face 刮 (鬍子); 刮 (臉), 剃 (鬚): *I washed and shaved, then hurried out of the house.* 我洗臉, 刮鬍子, 然後匆匆出了門。| *His hands shake so badly his wife has to shave him.* 他的手顫抖得很厲害, 他妻子只好給他刮鬍子。| **shave your head/legs/armpits etc** *Once Jenni shaved her head for a bet.* 詹妮有一次為打賭剃了光頭。**2** [T] to touch something slightly [S3] as you pass it; SCRAPE[1] (2) 輕輕擦過: *The car just shaved the wall as we went round the corner.* 我們轉彎時汽車輕輕擦撞到牆壁。

shave sth ↔ **off** *phr v* [T] **1** to remove hair by shaving 剃掉〔毛髮〕: *They made me shave off my beard when I joined the army.* 我參軍時，他們要我把鬍子刮掉。**2** to remove very thin pieces from the surface of something, using a knife or other cutting tool〔用刀或刨等〕刮去〔表層〕，把…刨去〔一層〕: *I had to shave a few millimetres off the bottom of the door to make it shut.* 我不得不把門的底部刨掉幾毫米使它能夠關上。**3** to reduce an amount or number very slightly 略減，削減: *She's shaved half a second off the world record.* 她把世界紀錄縮短了半秒。

shave² *n* [C usually singular 一般用單數] **1** an act of shaving your face 刮臉，刮鬍子: *He looked as if he needed a shave.* 他看上去似乎需要刮刮鬍子。| **have a shave** *I'll just have a shave before we go.* 我們走之前我要去刮刮鬍子。**2 a close shave a)** a situation in which you only just avoid an accident or something 倖免，僥倖脫險 **b)** a shave that cuts the hair very close to your face 把鬍子剃得乾淨

shav·en /ˈʃevən; ˈʃeɪvən/ *adj* with all the hair shaved off 剃光毛髮的: *his shaven head* 他那剃光了的頭 —see also 另見 CLEAN-SHAVEN, UNSHAVEN

shav·er /ˈʃevɚ; ˈʃeɪvə/ *n* [C] a tool used for shaving, especially a small electric machine 剃刀〔尤指電動剃刀〕—compare 比較 RAZOR

shav·ing bag /ˈ·· ·/ *n* [C] *AmE* a TOILET BAG【美】化妝包 —see picture at 參見 BAG[1] 圖

shaving brush /ˈ·· ·/ *n* [C] a brush used for spreading soap or shaving cream over your face when you shave〔刮鬍前用以塗抹皂液的〕修面刷

shaving cream /ˈ·· ·/ *n* [U] a mixture made of soap, used for putting on your face when you shave 修面霜，剃鬚膏

shaving foam /ˈ·· ·/ *n* [U] a special cream that you put on your face when you shave 泡沫剃鬚膏

shav·ings /ˈʃevɪŋz; ˈʃeɪvɪŋz/ *n* [plural] very thin pieces, especially of wood, cut from a surface with a sharp blade〔尤指木頭的〕刨片，削片: *a pile of wood shavings on the floor* 地上的一堆（木）刨花

shawl /ʃɔl; ʃɔːl/ *n* [C] a piece of soft cloth, in a square or TRIANGULAR shape, that is worn around the shoulders or head, especially by women〔尤指女用的〕披巾，披肩大圍巾: *an embroidered shawl* 刺繡披肩

she- /ʃi; ʃiː/ *prefix* female 雌（性），女（性）: *a she-goat* 母山羊 | *a she-devil* (=evil woman) 女魔

1 **she¹** /ʃɪ; ʃi *strong* 強讀 ʃi; ʃiː/ *pron* [used as the subject
1 of a verb 用作動詞的主詞] **1 a)** a woman or girl who has been mentioned already, or who the person you are talking to already knows about 她〔指人〕: *What did she say when you told her?* 你告訴她之後，她說了些甚麼？| *Why don't you ask Beth – she's got plenty of money.* 你為甚麼不問貝思 —— 她有很多錢。| *I saw you talking to that girl. Who is she?* 我看見你和那個女孩子說話。她是誰？**b)** a female animal who has been mentioned already 她〔指提及過的雌性動物〕**2 a)** used to talk about a boat or ship 她〔指船舶〕: *The QE2 docked at Portsmouth Harbour where she will spend the next few months being refurbished.* "伊莉莎白女王二世號"郵輪停靠在樸次茅斯港，她將要在那裡花幾個月重新整修。**b)** used to talk about a country 她〔指一個國家〕**c)** used to talk about a vehicle or machine that you are very fond of 她〔指非常喜愛的車輛、機器〕

she² /ʃi; ʃiː/ *n* [singular] *informal* a female【非正式】女性，雌性: *What a beautiful child! Is it a he or a she?* 多漂亮的孩子！是男孩還是女孩？

sheaf /ʃif; ʃiːf/ *plural* **sheaves** /ʃivz; ʃiːvz/ *n* [C+of] **1** a bunch of wheat, corn etc tied together after it has been cut〔穀物等收割後捆成的〕束，捆 **2** several pieces of paper held or tied together〔紙張等的〕紮，疊，捆

shear /ʃɪr; ʃɪə/ *v past tense* **sheared** *past participle* **sheared** *or* **shorn** /ʃɔrn; ʃɔːn/ **1** [T] to cut the wool off a sheep 給〔羊〕剪羊毛 **2 be shorn of** to have something valuable or important taken away from you 被剝奪，被除去: *Shorn of all real power by the new laws, the deputy soon resigned.* 實權被新法律剝奪淨盡，議員不久就辭職了。**3** also 又作 **shear off, shear away** [I,T] *technical* to break apart because of a sideways or twisting force【術語】折斷，扭斷；剪斷 **4** [T] *literary* to cut off someone's hair【文】給〔某人〕剪〔頭髮〕

shear·er /ˈʃɪrɚ; ˈʃɪərə/ also 又作 **sheep shearer** *n* [C] someone who cuts the wool off sheep 剪羊毛的人

shears /ʃɪrz; ʃɪəz/ *n* [plural] a heavy tool for cutting, like a big pair of scissors 大剪刀: **a pair of shears** *Sam was trimming the hedge with a pair of garden shears.* 薩姆在用園藝剪刀修剪樹籬。

sheath /ʃiθ; ʃiːθ/ *plural* **sheaths** /ʃiðz; ʃiːðz/ *n* [C] **1** a cover for the blade of a knife or sword〔刀、劍的〕套，鞘 **2** *BrE* CONDOM【英】避孕套；保險套 **3** a close-fitting part of a plant or animal that acts as a protective covering〔植物或動物包覆的起保護作用的〕鞘狀物

sheathe /ʃið; ʃiːð/ *v* **1** [T] to put a knife or sword into a sheath 將〔刀、劍〕插入鞘中: *He sheathed his sword.* 他把劍插入鞘內。**2** to be enclosed in a protective outer cover〔用鞘、護套等〕包覆: **be sheathed in/with** *The nuclear reactor is sheathed with lead.* 核反應堆是用鉛包封住的。

sheath·ing /ˈʃiðɪŋ; ˈʃiːðɪŋ/ *n* [C usually singular 一般用單數] a protective outer cover, for example for a building or a ship〔建築物的〕保護性外層，包覆材料；〔船的〕船底包板

sheath knife /ˈ· ·/ *n* [C] a knife with a fixed blade that does not fold, that is carried in a sheath 鞘刀〔刀身固定且有刀鞘的非摺合式刀〕

sheaves /ʃivz; ʃiːvz/ the plural of SHEAF

she·bang /ʃəˈbæŋ; ʃɪˈbæŋ/ *n* **the whole shebang** *informal, especially AmE* the whole thing【非正式，尤美】全部事情: *It's a big project, and she's in charge of the whole shebang.* 這是項大工程，而她負責全部事務。

she·been /ʃɪˈbin; ʃɪˈbiːn/ *n* [C] *informal, especially IrishE* a place where alcoholic drinks are sold illegally【非正式，尤愛爾蘭】非法經營的酒館

she'd /ʃɪd; ʃid *strong* 強讀 ʃid; ʃiːd/ **1** the short form of 縮略式= she had: *She'd already gone when we got there.* 我們到達那裡時她已經走了。**2** the short form of 縮略式= she would: *She'd like to come with us.* 她想和我們一起來。

shed¹ /ʃɛd; ʃed/ *n* [C] **1** a small building, often made of wood, used especially for storing things 棚屋，小屋，小庫房〔通常為簡陋小木房，尤用於存放雜物〕: *We had a tool shed in our back yard.* 我們後院有一間工具房。| *a cattle shed* 牲口棚 | *a garden shed* 園子裡的棚屋 **2** a large industrial building where work is done, large vehicles are kept or machinery is stored etc〔用作車間、停放大型車輛或存放機器等的〕棚式建築物 3

shed² *v* [T] *past tense and past participle* **shed** *present participle* **shedding**

1 ►LIGHT 光線◄ if something sheds light, it lights the area around it〔燈〕發出〔光線〕；照亮，照射: *The lamp shed a yellow glow onto the desk.* 燈的黃色光線照射在書桌上。

2 ►DROP/FALL OFF 落下◄ **a)** to drop something or allow it to fall 落下，使〔某物〕脫落: *He strode across the bathroom, shedding wet clothes as he went.* 他大步走過浴室，邊走邊把濕衣服脫下來。**b)** if an animal sheds skin or hair or a plant sheds leaves etc, they fall off as part of a natural process〔動物或植物〕使〔外皮、毛髮、葉子等〕蛻下，脫落，剝落: *Deciduous trees shed their leaves in autumn.* 落葉樹在秋天落葉。| *As it grows, a snake will regularly shed its skin.* 蛇在成長時每到一定時候就會蛻皮。

3 ►GET RID OF 去掉◄ to get rid of something that you

no longer need or want 去掉〔不需要或不想要的東西〕: *The company is planning to shed about a quarter of its workforce.* 這家公司正在計劃削減四分之一的人手。| *I shed my inhibitions and joined the dancing.* 我丟開思想顧慮, 和大家一起跳舞。| **shed pounds/stones** (=get thinner by losing several pounds etc) 減輕體重 *I'd like to shed a few pounds.* 我希望減掉幾磅體重。
4 shed light on to make something easier to understand, by providing new or better information 〔通過提供新信息等〕使〔某事物〕清楚些[易於理解]: *We're hoping his letter will shed some light on the mystery.* 我們希望他的信將有助於解開這個疑團。
5 ►WATER 水◄ if something sheds water, the water flows off its surface, instead of sinking into it 〔表面〕排掉, 不沾〔水〕
6 shed blood to kill or injure people, especially during a war or a fight 流血〔尤指戰爭或打鬥中的殺戮或傷害〕: *Too much blood has already been shed in this conflict.* 這次衝突已造成太多的流血犧牲了。—see also 另見 BLOODSHED
7 shed tears *especially literary* to cry【尤文】流淚: *She had not shed a single tear during the funeral.* 在葬禮上她一滴淚也沒有流。
8 shed its load *BrE* if a vehicle sheds its load, the goods it is carrying accidentally fall off【英】〔車輛不經意〕掉落〔所載貨物〕

sheen /ʃin; ʃiːn/ *n* [singular,U] a soft smooth shiny appearance; LUSTRE (1) 〔外表的〕光澤, 光彩: *Her hair had a lovely coppery sheen.* 她的頭髮有一種美麗的紫銅色光澤。

sheep /ʃip; ʃiːp/ *n* [C] *plural* **sheep 1** a grass-eating farm animal that is kept for its wool and its meat 羊, 綿羊: *Sheep were grazing on the hillside.* 羊羣在山坡上吃草。| *a sheep farmer* 養羊者 | **a flock of sheep** (=a group of sheep) 一羣羊 —see also 另見 LAMB **2** [often plural 常用複數] someone who does not think independently, but follows what everyone else does or thinks 沒有主見的人, 任人擺佈的人, 隨大流的人 **3 separate the sheep from the goats** to find out which people are intelligent, skilful, successful etc, and which are not 分出優劣, 辨明好壞: *This test should really separate the sheep from the goats.* 這次考試應能真正分出考生的優劣。**4 make sheep's eyes at** *old-fashioned* to look at someone in a way that shows you love them【過時】用充滿愛意的眼神看某人, 向某人送秋波 —see also 另見 **black sheep, count sheep** (COUNT[1] (2)), **a wolf in sheep's clothing** (WOLF[1] (2))

sheep-dip /ˈ· ·/ *n* [C,U] a chemical used to kill insects that live in sheep's wool, or a special bath in which this chemical is used 浴羊藥液〔一種用以殺死羊毛中的昆蟲的消毒液〕;〔使用該藥液的〕羊隻滅蟲浴

sheep dog /ˈ· ·/ *n* [C] **1** a dog that is trained to control sheep 牧羊犬 **2** *informal* a dog of a type that is often used for this, usually a COLLIE【非正式】一種常用作牧羊犬的狗〔通常為柯利犬〕—see also 另見 OLD ENGLISH SHEEPDOG

sheep·fold /ˈʃipˌfold; ˈʃiːpfəʊld/ *n* [C] an area of land with a fence or wall around it, used for keeping sheep in 羊欄, 羊圈, 羊舍

sheep·ish /ˈʃipɪʃ; ˈʃiːpɪʃ/ *adj* uncomfortable or embarrassed because you know that you have done something silly or wrong 侷促不安的, 靦腆的, 困窘的: *Richard was looking sheepish.* 理查德看上去有點侷促不安。—**sheepishly** *adv*: *She grinned sheepishly.* 她靦腆地笑了一笑。—**sheepishness** *n* [U]

sheep-pen /ˈ· ·/ *n* [C] a small area of ground with a fence around it, used for keeping sheep together for a short time 羊欄, 羊圈, 羊舍

sheep·skin /ˈʃipˌskɪn; ˈʃiːpˌskɪn/ *n* [C,U] the skin of a sheep with the wool still on it 帶毛的羊皮: *a sheepskin coat* 羊皮大衣

sheer[1] /ʃɪr; ʃɪə/ *adj* **1 sheer luck/happiness/stupidity etc** luck, happiness etc with no other feeling or quality mixed with it 十足的運氣/快樂/愚蠢等: *It was sheer bliss not having to get up.* 不用起牀真幸福。| *sheer hypocrisy* 十足的虛偽 **2 the sheer weight/size etc of** used to emphasize how heavy, big etc something is 〔某物〕之重/之大等〔用於強調〕: *The sheer size of the country makes communications difficult.* 該國幅員遼闊, 造成了通訊的困難。**3** a sheer drop, cliff, slope etc is very steep and almost VERTICAL[1] (1) 〔懸崖、斜坡等〕垂直的, 陡峭的: *There was a sheer drop to the sea 200 feet below.* 懸崖直下 200 英尺, 下面就是海。**4** sheer NYLON, silk etc is very thin and fine, so that it is almost transparent 〔尼龍、絲綢等〕很薄的, 幾乎透明的: *sheer stockings* 透明的長統襪

sheer[2] *adv* straight up or down in an almost VERTICAL[1] (1) line 陡峭地, 垂直地: *The mountains rise sheer from the sea.* 羣山從海面峭拔而起。

sheer[3] *v* [I] **sheer off/away** to change direction suddenly, especially in order to avoid something 突然轉向〔尤指為了避開某物〕: *The boat sheered away and headed out to sea again.* 這艘船突然調頭, 又駛向大海。

sheet /ʃit; ʃiːt/ *n* [C] **1** a large piece of thin cotton or NYLON cloth that you put on a bed to lie on or lie under 牀單, 被單: **change the sheets** (=put clean sheets on a bed) 換上乾淨的牀單 **2** a thin flat piece of something such as paper, glass, or metal, that usually has four sides 〔紙、玻璃、金屬等的〕片, 塊, 張: **[+of]** *I picked up a clean sheet of paper and began to write.* 我拿起一張空白紙寫了起來。| *a sheet of glass* 一塊玻璃 —see picture on page A7 參見 A7 頁圖 **3** a large flat area of something such as ice or water spread over a surface 〔冰、水等的〕一大片: *A sheet of ice covered the lake.* 湖面上覆蓋着一大片冰。**4** a sheet of rain or fire is a very large moving mass of it 〔大雨、火的〕一團, 一片, 一層: *The rain was coming down in sheets.* 大雨傾盆而下。**5** *technical* a rope or chain that controls the angle between a sail and the wind on a ship【術語】〔帆船的〕帆腳索 —see also 另見 BAKING SHEET, BALANCE SHEET, **white as a sheet** (WHITE[1] (2)), **a clean sheet** (CLEAN[1] (10))

sheet an·chor /ˈ· ˌ··/ *n* [C] **1** a ship's largest ANCHOR[1] (1), used only in times of danger 備用大錨〔船上最大的錨, 只在危險時用〕**2** someone or something that you depend on very much in a difficult or dangerous situation 在困難[危險]時主要依靠的人[物]

sheet·ing /ˈʃitɪŋ; ˈʃiːtɪŋ/ *n* [U] cloth or other material that is made into sheets, or used in the form of a sheet 〔用作牀單、被單等的〕布料; 薄板材料: *The roof was covered in plastic sheeting.* 房頂是用塑料薄板蓋的。| *cotton sheeting* 棉質牀單布料

sheet light·ning /ˌ· ˈ··/ *n* [U] a type of LIGHTNING that appears as a sudden flash of brightness covering a large area of sky 片狀閃電 —compare 比較 FORKED LIGHTNING

sheet met·al /ˈ· ˌ··/ *n* [U] metal in the form of thin sheets 金屬薄板

sheet mu·sic /ˈ· ˌ··/ *n* [U] music that is printed on single sheets and not fastened together inside a cover 活頁樂譜, 印在散頁上的樂譜

sheikh, sheik /ʃik; ʃeɪk/ *n* [C] **1** an Arab chief or prince 〔阿拉伯的〕酋長, 族長, 首領; 王子 **2** a Muslim religious leader or teacher 伊斯蘭教的領袖, 教士, 教長

sheikh·dom, sheikdom /ˈʃikdəm; ˈʃeɪkdəm/ *n* [C] a place that is governed by an Arab chief or prince 〔阿拉伯〕酋長統治的領土, 酋長國

shei·la /ˈʃilə; ˈʃiːlə/ *n* [C] *AustrE or NZE slang* a young woman【澳或紐西蘭, 俚】少婦, 少女, 女郎

shek·el /ˈʃɛkl; ˈʃekəl/ *n* [C] **1** the standard unit of money in Israel 錫克爾〔以色列的貨幣單位〕**2 shekels** [plural] *humorous* money【幽默】錢

shelf /ʃɛlf; ʃelf/ *n plural* **shelves** /ʃɛlvz; ʃelvz/ **1** [C] a long flat narrow board fixed onto a wall or in a frame or cupboard, used for putting things on or storing things on 〔靠牆架設可存放東西的〕架子;〔書櫥、櫃子的〕擱板: *Put it back on the top shelf.* 把它放回到頂層的擱板上。|

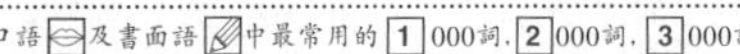

shelves of books 幾架子書 | *supermarket shelves* 超級市場的貨架 **2** [C] a narrow surface of rock shaped like a shelf, especially underwater 擱板狀岩石;〔尤指海底的〕暗礁, 大陸架 **3 off the shelf** available to be bought immediately without having to be specially designed or ordered 現貨供應: *off-the-shelf computer software packages* 現貨供應的電腦軟件組件 —compare 比較 OFF-THE-PEG **4 be (left) on the shelf a)** *old-fashioned* considered to be too old to get married【過時】因年齡太大而找不到結婚對象 **b)** if a plan, idea etc is left on the shelf it is not used or considered〔計劃、主意等〕不被考慮, 擱置不用 —see also 另見 SHELVE

shelf life /ˈ· ·/ *n* [singular] the length of time that food, chemicals etc can be kept in a shop before they become too old to sell〔食品、藥品等的〕保存期限, 在商店的存貨期限: *Chocolate has a shelf life of 9 months.* 巧克力的保存期限為九個月。

she'll /ʃɪl; ʃil *strong* 強讀 ʃil; ʃiːl/ the short form of 縮略式= she will: *She'll be back in a minute.* 她過一會就會回來。

shells 貝殼

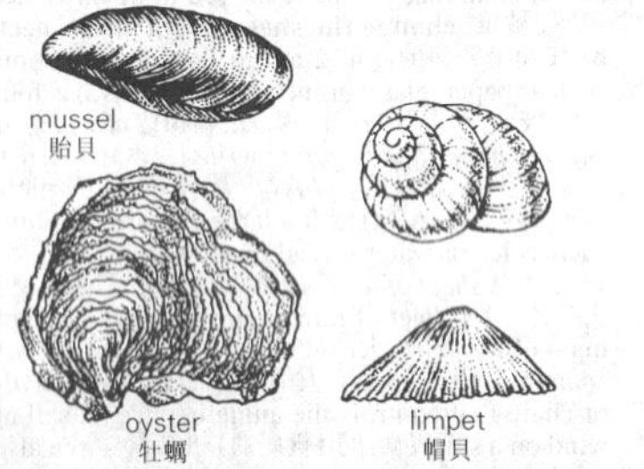

mussel 貽貝

oyster 牡蠣

limpet 帽貝

3 **shell**[1] /ʃɛl; ʃel/ *n* **1** [C] **a)** a hard outer part that covers or protects a nut, egg, or seed and some types of animal〔堅果、禽蛋、種子或某些動物的〕殼: *a snail shell* 蝸牛殼 **b)** the shell of a small sea animal such as a COCKLE or MUSSEL especially one that is lying on a beach〔鳥蛤、貽貝等的〕殼;〔尤指海灘上的〕貝殼 **2** [C] a metal container, like a large bullet, which is full of an explosive substance and is fired from a large gun 砲彈: *We ran for cover as shells dropped all around us.* 砲彈落在我們周圍, 我們都跑着找地方掩蔽。**3** [C] *especially AmE* a metal tube containing a bullet and an explosive substance used in a gun; CARTRIDGE (1)【尤美】子彈; 彈藥筒 **4** [C] the outside structure of something, especially the part of a building that remains when the rest of it has been destroyed〔尤指建築物等遭破壞後剩下的〕框架, 骨架 **5 come out of your shell** to become less shy and more confident and willing to talk to people 不再羞怯, 願意與人攀談, 開始活躍起來: *She's really come out of her shell since she went to college.* 她自從上了大學後, 的確變得大方活躍了。

shell[2] *v* [T] **1** to fire shells at something 砲轟: *Opposition forces have been shelling the town since yesterday.* 反政府部隊從昨天起一直在砲轟該城鎮。**2** to remove something such as beans or nuts from a shell or a POD[1] (1) 剝去〔豆莢或堅果等〕的殼: *Josie was shelling peas on the verandah.* 喬西在走廊裡剝豌豆莢。

shell out *phr v* [T] *informal* to pay a lot of money for something, especially unwillingly【非正式】〔尤指不情願地〕花大筆錢, 付款: *If you want the repairs done right, you'll have to shell out at least $800.* 假如你想修得妥當, 你至少得花 800 美元。

shel·lac /ʃəˈlæk; ʃəˈlæk/ *n* [U] a kind of transparent paint for protecting or hardening surfaces〔用於保護表面或使表面堅硬的〕蟲膠(清漆)

shel·lack·ing /ʃəˈlækɪŋ; ʃəˈlækɪŋ/ *n* [singular] *AmE informal* a situation in which you are severely defeated or criticized【美, 非正式】徹底失敗, 慘敗; 受到嚴厲批評: *The Chargers got a shellacking in the Superbowl.* 電光隊在超級盃賽中慘敗。

shell·fire /ˈʃɛlˌfaɪə; ˈʃelfaɪə/ also 又作 **shell·ing** /ˈʃɛlɪŋ; ˈʃelɪŋ/ *n* [U] the firing of large guns at a place 砲轟: **come under shellfire** (=have these guns fired at you) 遭到砲轟 *The city came under heavy shellfire.* 這城市遭到猛烈的砲轟。

shell·fish /ˈʃɛlˌfɪʃ; ˈʃelˌfɪʃ/ *plural* **shellfish** *n* **1** [C,U] a sea or water animal that does not have a BACKBONE, but has a shell〔無脊但有殼的〕水生貝類動物: *Lobsters and oysters are shellfish.* 龍蝦和牡蠣都是水生貝類動物。**2** [U] such animals as a type of food 可食的水生貝類動物: *Do you like shellfish?* 你喜歡吃水生貝類動物嗎?

shell shock /ˈ· ·/ *n* [U] *old-fashioned* a type of mental illness caused by the shock of fighting in a war or battle【過時】砲彈休克〔因曾參加戰爭而產生的一種精神異常〕

shell shocked /ˈ· ·/ *adj* **1** *informal* feeling tired, confused or anxious because of a recent difficult experience【非正式】疲勞的; 慌亂的, 焦慮的: *I think she's a bit shell-shocked after her exams.* 我想她考完試後有點頭昏腦脹。**2** mentally ill because of the terrible experiences of war〔因戰爭的可怕經歷而精神異常的〕患砲彈休克的

shell suit /ˈ· ·/ *n* [C] *BrE* a light brightly-coloured piece of clothing consisting of trousers and a JACKET (1), that fit tightly at the wrists and at the bottom of the legs【英】緊身便裝〔包括夾克和長褲, 其袖口和褲腿束緊〕

shel·ter[1] /ˈʃɛltɚ; ˈʃeltə/ *n* **1** [U] a place to live, considered as one of the basic needs of life 棲身之地, 住處: *They are in desperate need of food, clothing and shelter.* 他們急需食物、衣服和住處。**2** [U] protection, from danger or from wind, rain, hot sun etc 庇護; 掩蔽, 遮蔽: **the shelter of** *We eventually reached the shelter of the caves.* 我們終於到了可供掩蔽的山洞裡。| *They grow well in the shelter of big oak trees.* 它們在大橡樹的遮蔽下生長得很好。| **take shelter** *The men took shelter in a bombed-out farmhouse.* 那些男人躲在一間被炸毀的農舍裡。| **run for shelter** *All around me, people were running for shelter.* 我周圍的人都在急忙找地方躲避。| **give sb shelter** (=protect them, especially from the weather or from danger) 庇護某人〔尤指使之避開惡劣天氣或危險〕—see also 另見 TAX SHELTER **3** [C] a building or an area with a roof over it that protects you from the weather or from danger 庇護所; 避難所; 遮蔽物: *a shelter for the homeless* 無家可歸者的收容所 | *We tried to fix up a shelter from the rain.* 我們設法搭起一個遮雨的地方。| **air-raid shelter** (=to protect people from bombs dropped by planes) 防空洞 | **bus shelter** (=a small structure with a roof where you wait for a bus) 公共汽車站的候車亭

shelter[2] *v* **1** [T] to provide a place where someone or something is protected, especially from the weather or from danger 為…提供庇護處〔使之避開惡劣天氣或危險〕; 收容: *Collins was arrested for sheltering enemy soldiers.* 科林斯因窩藏敵兵而被逮捕。| **shelter sb/sth from** *Plant herbs next to a wall to shelter them from the wind.* 把藥草種在牆邊以免風吹。**2** [I] to stay in or under a place where you are protected from the weather or from danger 躲避; 避難: **[+from]** *We sat in the shade, sheltering from the sun.* 我們坐在樹陰下免受太陽暴曬。

shel·tered /ˈʃɛltɚd; ˈʃeltəd/ *adj* **1 a sheltered life/childhood/existence etc** a life etc in which someone has been too protected from difficult or unpleasant experience 受到庇護的生活/童年/生存等: *Marian's sheltered upbringing had left her unprepared for such extreme poverty.* 瑪麗安在優越的環境中長大, 這使她對如此極度的貧困毫無準備。**2** a place that is sheltered is protected from extreme weather conditions〔地方〕受掩護的, 免遭惡劣天氣影響的: *a sheltered valley* 不受暴風雨侵襲的山谷 **3 sheltered accommodation/housing** *BrE* a place for people to live who cannot fully look after themselves where help is provided if they need it【英】收容所; 救濟院: *sheltered accommodation for the elderly* 老人收容所

shelve /ʃɛlv; ʃelv/ *v* **1** [T] to decide not to continue with a plan, idea etc, although you might continue with it at a later time 將〔計劃、意見等〕擱置: *We had to shelve the new building plans due to lack of funding.* 由於缺乏資金, 我們不得不把建新樓的計劃擱置起來。**2** [I always+adv/prep] land that shelves is at a slight angle〔地面〕輕微傾斜: **[+up/down/towards etc]** *The garden shelves gently towards the sea.* 這個花園稍微向海面傾斜。**3** [T] to put something on a shelf, especially books 將〔書等〕放在架子上, 上架

shelves /ʃɛlvz; ʃelvz/ the plural of SHELF

shelv·ing /ˈʃɛlvɪŋ; ˈʃelvɪŋ/ *n* **1** [U] wood, metal etc used for shelves 擱板材料〈如木頭、金屬等〉**2** a set of shelves fixed to a wall〔安在牆上的〕架子; 一組擱板

she·nan·i·gans /ʃəˈnænəgənz; ʃəˈnænɪgənz/ *n* [plural] *informal*【非正式】**1** bad behaviour that is not very serious; MISCHIEF 惡作劇, 胡鬧, 淘氣 **2** slightly dishonest activities 詭計, 欺騙行為

shep·herd¹ /ˈʃɛpɚd; ˈʃepəd/ *n* [C] someone whose job is to take care of sheep 牧羊人, 羊倌

shepherd² *v* [T always+adv/prep] to lead or guide a group of people somewhere, making sure that they go where you want them to go 帶領〔一羣人〕, 引導〔人羣〕: **shepherd sb into/out/towards etc** *I don't enjoy those tours where you're always being shepherded around some old ruins.* 我不喜歡那些老是被人帶去看古老廢墟的旅遊。

shep·herd·ess /ˈʃɛpɚdɪs; ˈʃepədes/ *n* [C] a woman or girl whose job is to take care of sheep 牧羊女

shepherd's pie /,·· ˈ·/ *n* [U] a baked dish made of small pieces of cooked meat covered with cooked potato 肉餡馬鈴薯餅

sher·bet /ˈʃɝbɪt; ˈʃɜːbət/ *n* **1** [C] *AmE* a frozen sweet made with water, fruit, milk and the white part of an egg【美】果汁冰糕〔一種用水、水果、牛奶、蛋白等製成的冷凍甜食〕**2** [U] *BrE* a powder that is eaten as a sweet【英】甜味果味粉〔一種甜食〕

sherd /ʃɝd; ʃɜːd/ *n* [C] another spelling of SHARD shard 的另一種拼法

sher·iff /ˈʃɛrɪf; ˈʃerɪf/ *n* [C] **1** an elected law officer of a COUNTY in the US〔美國的〕縣治安官〔由選舉產生的縣級司法長官〕**2** also 又作 **High Sheriff** the chief officer of the King or Queen in a COUNTY of England and Wales, who has mostly ceremonial duties〔英格蘭和威爾斯的〕郡長〔一種禮儀性職務〕**3** the chief judge in a DISTRICT (2) or COUNTY in Scotland〔蘇格蘭的〕區[郡]法官

sheriff's court /ˈ·· ,·/ *n* [C] the lower court of law in Scotland, dealing with CIVIL (3) and criminal cases〔蘇格蘭的〕郡法院, 初等法院〔兼管民事和刑事案件〕

Sher·pa /ˈʃɝpə; ˈʃɜːpə/ *n* [C] a Himalayan person who is often employed to guide people through mountains 夏爾巴人〔喜馬拉雅人, 常受雇當登山者向導〕

sher·ry /ˈʃɛrɪ; ˈʃeri/ *n* [C, U] a pale or dark brown strong wine, originally from Spain 雪利酒〔原產於西班牙的一種白色或深褐色烈性酒〕

she's /ʃɪz; ʃiz *strong* 強讀 ʃiz; ʃiːz/ **1** the short form of 'she is' 縮略式= she is **2** the short form of 'she has' 縮略式= she has

Shet·land po·ny /,ʃɛtlənd ˈponɪ; ,ʃetlənd ˈpəʊni/ *n* [C] a small strong horse with long rough hair 設得蘭矮種馬〔一種體小毛粗但強壯耐勞的馬〕

shew /ʃo; ʃəʊ/ *v* [I,T] an old spelling of SHOW show 的舊式拼法

shh /ʃ; ʃ/ *interjection* used to tell people to be quiet 噓, 別作聲〔用以叫別人安靜下來〕: *Shh! I can't hear what he's saying.* 噓! 我聽不見他在說甚麼了。

Shi·a, Shiah /ʃiə; ˈʃiːə/ *n* **1 the Shiah** the Shiite branch of the Muslim religion 什葉派〔伊斯蘭教的一派〕**2** [C] a Shiite 什葉派教徒

shi·a·tsu /ʃɪˈɑtsu; ʃiˈɑːtsuː/ *n* [U] a Japanese form of MASSAGE (=pressing and rubbing someone's body) used to prevent or treat physical or emotional problems 日式按摩, 指壓按摩

shib·bo·leth /ˈʃɪbəlɪθ; ˈʃɪbəleθ/ *n* [C] *formal* an old idea, custom or principle you think is no longer important or suitable for modern times【正式】〔認為已不重要或已過時的〕陳舊思想, 陳規陋習

shields 盾牌

shield 盾牌

riot shield 防暴盾牌

shield¹ /ʃild; ʃiːld/ *n* [C] **1 a)** a thing that soldiers used consisting of a broad piece of metal or leather 盾, 盾牌 **b)** also 又作 **riot shield** a piece of equipment made of strong plastic, used by the police to protect themselves against angry crowds〔警察用來保護自己的〕防暴盾牌 **2** something in the shape of a shield, wide at the top and curving to a point at the bottom, that is used for a COAT OF ARMS, a prize in sport etc 盾形紋[徽]章, 〔體育比賽中的〕盾形獎牌 **3** something that protects a person or thing against harm or damage 護蓋, 護罩; 保護[防禦]物: *the ozone layer, the shield that protects the Earth from the Sun's harmful rays* 臭氧層, 使地球免受太陽有害射線輻射的保護層

shield² *v* [T] to protect someone or something from being harmed, or damaged 保護, 保衛: *Women will often lie to shield even the most abusive partner.* 婦女常會撒謊以保護哪怕是對她最粗暴的伴侶。| **shield sb/sth from sth** *He held up his hands, shielding his eyes from the sun.* 他舉起雙手, 遮住眼睛免受陽光照射。| *import tariffs that shield firms from foreign competition* 保護企業免受外國競爭的進口關稅

shift¹ /ʃɪft; ʃɪft/ *v* 3

1 ►MOVE 移動◄ a) [I,T] to move from one place or position to another, or make something do this (使) 移動〔地點、位置〕, (使) 轉移: *Jonas stood and listened, shifting uncomfortably from one foot to another.* 喬納斯站着聽, 不自在地把重心從一隻腳轉移到另一隻腳。| *The sun had shifted around to the west.* 太陽已經轉到西邊了。| *She shifted her gaze from me to Bobby with a look of suspicion.* 她用懷疑的目光凝視着我, 然後又轉向博比。**b)** [T] *informal* to move something, especially by picking it up and carrying it【非正式】移動; 搬動〔尤指提起來搬〕: *Give me a hand to shift these chairs.* 請幫我挪一挪這幾把椅子。

2 shift attention/emphasis/focus to change a situation, discussion etc by giving special attention to one idea or subject instead of to a previous one 轉移注意力/重點/中心: *The president is shifting the focus of the debate to foreign policy issues.* 總統正在把辯論的焦點轉移到外交政策問題上。| **attention/emphasis/focus shifts** *Under these new arrangements, the emphasis has shifted from state provision to personal responsibility.* 在這些新的安排下, 重點已經從國家供應轉移到個人責任上來。

3 ►COSTS/SPENDING 費用/開支◄ [T always+adv/prep] to change the way that money is paid or spent 轉嫁, 轉給: *This simply shifts the cost of medical insur-*

ance from employer to employee. 這不過是把醫療保險費從雇主轉嫁給雇員了。| *the need to shift more resources towards the alleviation of poverty* 把更多財力物力轉向緩解貧困的需要

4 ▶OPINIONS 意見◀ [I,T] to change your opinions or beliefs, especially about political matters 改變〔意見、信仰, 尤指政治方面〕: *Opinion in the country was beginning to shift to the right.* 國內輿論開始向右轉變。| *shifting attitudes towards marriage* 改變對待婚姻的態度 | **shift your ground** (=change your opinion) 改變立場[看法]*The government shifted its ground, and gradually lent its support to African nationalism.* 政府改變了立場, 對非洲民族主義逐漸採取支持的態度。

5 shift the blame/responsibility to make someone else responsible for something, especially for something bad that has happened 推卸責任: *It was a blatant attempt to shift the responsibility for the crime on to the victim.* 這是個無恥的企圖, 想把犯罪的責任轉嫁給受害者。

6 ▶DIRT/MARKS 污垢/痕跡◀ [T] *BrE* to remove dirt or marks from a surface or piece of clothing【英】除去〔表面或衣服上的污跡〕: *a new washing powder that will shift any stain* 一種能洗掉任何污跡的新洗衣粉

7 ▶IN A CAR 在汽車中◀ [I,T] *especially AmE* to change the gears (GEAR[1] (1)) when you are driving【尤美】換擋, 調擋: *I shifted into second gear.* 我把車速調到第二擋。

shift² *n* [C] **1** a change in the way people think about something, in the way something is done etc〔想法、做法等的〕改變: **[+from/to]** *a major shift from manufacturing to service industries* 從製造業到服務業的重大改變 | **[+in]** *a shift in emphasis from defense spending to civilian spending* 從國防開支到民用開支的重心轉移 | **a marked shift** (=a very noticeable change) 明顯的改變 *There has been a marked shift in attitudes towards homosexuality.* 人們對同性戀的態度有了明顯的改變。**2 a)** one of the periods during each day and night when workers in a factory, hospital etc are at work〔工作人員在工廠、醫院等輪值工作的〕當班時間: **do/work a shift** *I usually work the night shift, which is from 10 at night till 6 in the morning.* 我通常上夜班, 從晚上 10 點到早上 6 點。| *Do you do shift work?* 你們是不是輪班工作? **b)** the workers who work during one of these periods 輪班工人 **3 a)** a simple straight loose-fitting woman's dress 寬鬆直筒式家常女服 **b)** *old use* a similar piece of clothing worn as underwear【舊】裙式女內衣 **4** the KEY² (3) on a computer or TYPEWRITER that you press to print a capital letter〔電腦、打字機上的〕大寫字母轉換鍵: *To run the spellchecker, press SHIFT and F7.* 要使用拼寫檢查程序, 按轉換鍵和 F7。**5** *old use* a clever trick or method【舊】手段, 計謀

shift key /'· ·/ *n* [C] the KEY² (3) on a KEYBOARD that you press to make a capital letter〔鍵盤上的〕大寫字母轉換鍵

shift·less /ˈʃɪftlɪs; ˈʃɪftləs/ *adj* lazy and seeming to have no interest in working hard or trying to succeed 懶惰的, 不求上進的, 得過且過的: *my shiftless nephew, who was never any good* 我那個不求上進、一無是處的姪兒 —**shiftlessly** *adv* —**shiftlessness** *n*

shift·y /ˈʃɪftɪ; ˈʃɪfti/ *adj informal* looking dishonest and slightly nervous【非正式】狡詐的, 躲躲閃閃的, 鬼鬼祟祟的: *a shifty-looking little man* 模樣詭詐的矮小男子 | *shifty eyes* 一雙賊眼 —**shiftily** *adv* —**shiftiness** *n* [U]

Shi·ite /ˈʃiaɪt; ˈʃiː-aɪt/ *n* a member of one of the two main branches of the Muslim religion〔伊斯蘭教兩大分支之一的〕什葉派教徒 —compare 比較 SUNNI —**Shiite** *adj*

shil·ling /ˈʃɪlɪŋ; ˈʃɪlɪŋ/ *n* [C]**1** a coin used in Britain until 1971, worth 12 old pence and $^1/_{20}$ of £1 先令〔1971 年之前英國的貨幣單位, 等於 12 舊便士或 $^1/_{20}$ 英鎊〕**2** a unit of money used in Austria, Kenya, Uganda, and Somalia 先令〔奧地利、肯尼亞、烏干達和索馬里的貨幣單位〕

shil·ly-shal·ly /ˈʃɪlɪˌʃælɪ; ˈʃɪli ˌʃæli/ *v* [I] *informal* to waste time or take too long to make a decision【非正式】〔作決定時〕猶豫不決, 躊躇

shim·mer /ˈʃɪmə; ˈʃɪmə/ *v* [I] to shine with a soft light that looks as if it shakes slightly 發微光, 閃閃發亮: *The lake shimmered in the moonlight.* 湖水在月色下閃閃發光。—**shimmer** *n* [U]: *the shimmer of the desert air in the midday heat* 中午酷熱時分沙漠熱氣中發出的閃光

shin¹ /ʃɪn; ʃɪn/ *n* [C] the front part of your leg between your knee and your foot (外) 脛, 脛部 —see picture at 參見 BODY 圖

shin² *v* [I] **shin up/shin down** to climb up or down a tree, pole etc by using your hands and legs, especially quickly 爬上/爬下〔尤指快速地用手和腿爬樹或杆等〕; SHINNY *AmE*【美】: *to shin up the drainpipe* 沿着排水管往上爬

shin·bone /'· ·/ *n* [C] the front bone in your leg below your knee; TIBIA 脛骨 —see picture at 參見 SKELETON 圖

shin·dig /ˈʃɪndɪg; ˈʃɪndɪg/ *n* [C] *old-fashioned* a noisy party【過時】喧鬧的聚會

shine¹ /ʃaɪn; ʃaɪn/ *v past tense and past participle* **shone** /ʃɒn; ʃɒn/ **1** [I] to produce light 發光, 發亮: *At last the sun was shining after weeks of rain.* 下了幾個星期的雨, 太陽終於出來了。| **[+in/on]** *That lamp's shining in my eyes.* 那盞燈的光直刺我的眼。**2** [I] to look bright and shiny〔看上去〕光亮, 閃光, 發亮: *a big basket of shining fish of every shape and size* 一大筐各種各樣閃閃發亮的魚 | *I want you to clean this kitchen until it shines.* 我要你把廚房收拾得乾乾淨淨。**3** [T] to hold or point a lamp, light etc so that the light from it goes in a particular direction 使〔燈光等〕向…照射: **shine sth into/across/onto etc** *Shine the flashlight over here so that I can see what I'm doing.* 把手電筒照到這邊, 好讓我看清我幹的活。**4** [I] if your eyes shine, or your face shines, you have an expression of happiness〔眼睛、臉上〕流露出快樂的表情: *"I passed!" exclaimed Rufus, his eyes shining.* "我及格了!" 魯弗斯喊道, 高興得兩眼放光。**5** [I not in progressive 不用進行式] to be very good at something 表現突出, 出眾: **[+in/at]** *He really shines in history.* 他在歷史方面確有特長。

shine through *phr v* [I] if a quality that someone has shines through, you can easily see that they have it〔某種特質〕顯而易見, 表現明顯: *What shines through in all her work is her enthusiasm for life.* 她的所有作品都顯示出她對生活的熱情。

shine² *past tense and past participle* **shined** *v* [T] to make something bright by rubbing it; polish 擦亮, 磨光

shine³ *n* **1** [singular,U] the brightness that something has when light shines on it 光澤; 光亮: *The old table has a beautiful shine.* 這張舊桌子閃着漂亮的光澤。**2** [singular] an act of making something bright by polishing it 擦亮: **give sth a shine** *Give your shoes a good shine before you go.* 你走之前要把鞋子好好地擦擦。**3 take a shine to** *informal* to like someone very much when you have only just met them【非正式】一眼就喜歡上〔某人〕—see also 另見 **(come) rain or shine** (RAIN¹ (4))

shin·gle /ˈʃɪŋgl; ˈʃɪŋgəl/ *n* **1** [C,U] one of many small thin pieces of building material, especially wood, used to cover a roof or wall〔蓋房頂或牆用的〕木瓦; 屋面板, 牆面板 **2** [U] small round pieces of stone on a beach〔海灘上的〕小圓石: *shingle glistening with broken shells* 夾雜着碎貝殼的閃閃發光的小圓石 —see picture on page A12 參見 A12 頁圖 **3 hang out your shingle** *AmE* to start your own business, especially as a doctor or lawyer【美】〔尤指醫生或律師〕掛牌開業

shin·gles /ˈʃɪŋglz; ˈʃɪŋgəlz/ *n* [U] a disease caused by an infection of the nerve endings, which produces painful red spots 帶狀疱疹

shin·ing /ˈʃaɪnɪŋ; ˈʃaɪnɪŋ/ *adj* [only before noun 僅用於名詞前] excellent in a way that is easy to see 傑出的, 出眾的: **a shining example of** *O'Reilly was a shining example of courage on the battlefield.* 奧賴利在戰場上是英勇的光輝典範。

shin·ny /ˈʃɪnɪ; ˈʃɪni/ *v* [I] *AmE*【美】**shinny up/down** to SHIN² 爬上/爬下

Shin·to /ˈʃɪnto; ˈʃɪntəʊ/ also 又作 **Shin·to·is·m** /ˈʃɪntoɪzm̩; ˈʃɪntəʊɪzəm/ *n* [U] the ancient religion of Japan that has gods who represent various parts of nature, and gives great importance to people who died in the past〔日本的〕神道教

shin·ty /ˈʃɪntɪ; ˈʃɪnti/ *n* [U] a game played in Scotland, similar to HOCKEY (1) 簡化曲棍球戲〔一種蘇格蘭人玩的類似曲棍球的運動〕

shin·y /ˈʃaɪnɪ; ˈʃaɪni/ *adj* smooth and bright 光滑發亮的, 閃光的: *a shiny polished table* 擦得閃閃發亮的桌子 | *shiny hair* 發亮的頭髮 | *a big shiny limousine* 閃閃發亮的豪華大轎車 —**shininess** *n* [U] —see picture at 參見 SLIP¹ 圖

-ship /ʃɪp; ʃɪp/ *suffix* (in nouns 構成名詞) **1 a)** the state of having a particular position or job 身分, 地位, 資格: *Full membership* (=being a full member) *of the club costs $35.* 該俱樂部的正式會員需交會費 35 美元。| *professorship* (=the job of PROFESSOR) 教授職位 **b)** the time during which this lasts (…期間的) 狀況: *their long friendship* 他們的長久友誼 | *during his premiership* 在他擔任總理期間 **2** the art or skill of a particular person〔某人的〕技能, 技巧: *her peerless musicianship* 她無與倫比的音樂才華 | *a work of great scholarship* 一部學術巨著 —see also 另見 -MANSHIP **3** the whole group of a particular group 某羣體的全部: *a magazine with a readership of 9000* (=with 9000 readers) 擁有 9,000 名讀者的雜誌 **4** forms part of certain title 構成某種頭銜或身分: *your ladyship* 夫人

S2 W2 **ship¹** /ʃɪp; ʃɪp/ *n* [C] **1** a large boat used for carrying people or goods across the sea 大船; 海輪, 艦: *a cruise ship* 海上遊船 | *a merchant ship* 商船 | **by ship** *Most of the island's supplies are brought in by ship.* 這個海島的大部分給養都是由船隻運來的。**2** a large SPACECRAFT or aircraft 宇宙飛船, 太空船; 飛船 **3 ships that pass in the night** people who meet for a short time and then never meet again 萍水相逢的人〔以後不再相遇〕**4 when your ship comes in** used when you are wishing that something will suddenly happen to make you rich 有朝一日發大財[發跡]的時候: *When my ship comes in, I'll quit work and travel around the world.* 等我發了財, 我就辭掉工作並周遊世界。

ship² *past tense* **shipped** *present participle* **shipping** *v* [T] **1** to send or carry something by ship 用船運送: **ship sth out/to etc** *I'm flying over to the States and having my car shipped out later.* 我坐飛機前往美國, 會安排我的汽車稍後經海運送去。**2** to deliver goods or make them available for people to buy 發貨; 供貨; 使〔商品〕上市: *The new Windows software was announced in April and they're planning to ship it in October.* 這種新視窗軟件在四月宣布推出, 並計劃於十月供貨。**3** to order someone to go somewhere 遣送〔某人〕, 將〔某人〕送往…: **ship sb off/out etc** *As soon as the doctor saw her, he shipped her straight off to the hospital.* 醫生給她檢查以後, 立即把她送往醫院。| *I was in Heidelberg at the time, about to be shipped out to Vietnam.* 我當時在海德堡, 即將被送往越南。**4 ship water** if a boat ships water, water comes into it over its sides〔船〕在舷側進水 **5 ship oars** to stop rowing and to bring the OARs into the boat〔停止划槳〕把槳收進船內 —see also 另見 **shape up or ship out** (SHAPE UP (3))

ship·board /ˈʃɪpˌbord; ˈʃɪpbɔːd/ *n* [U] **on shipboard** on a ship 在船上

ship·build·er /ˈʃɪpˌbɪldɚ; ˈʃɪpˌbɪldə/ *n* [C] a company that makes ships 造船公司 —**shipbuilding** *n* [U]: *an old shipbuilding town* 古老的造船業城鎮

ship·load /ˈʃɪpˌlod; ˈʃɪpləʊd/ *n* [C] the amount of goods or people a ship can carry 一艘船的裝貨量; 載人量: **[+of]** *A shipload of new cars has just arrived.* 一船新汽車剛剛運到。

ship·mate /ˈʃɪpˌmet; ˈʃɪpmeɪt/ *n* [C] a SAILOR's shipmate is another sailor who is working on the same ship 同船的水手[船員]

ship·ment /ˈʃɪpmənt; ˈʃɪpmənt/ *n* [C,U] a load of goods sent by sea, road, or air, or the act of sending them〔經海路、陸路或航空運送的〕貨物;〔貨物的〕裝運, 運送: **[+of]** *The goods are now ready for shipment.* 這批貨物現已準備好, 可以裝運了。| *a large shipment of grain* 一大批裝運的穀物

ship·per /ˈʃɪpɚ; ˈʃɪpə/ *n* [C] a company that sends goods to places by ship 承辦貨運的輪船公司, 航運商

ship·ping /ˈʃɪpɪŋ; ˈʃɪpɪŋ/ *n* [U] **1** ships considered as a group 船舶〔總稱〕: *The port is closed to all shipping.* 這個港口已封港。**2** all the ships belonging to a particular country〔一國的〕船舶總數: *Israeli shipping was excluded from the Straits of Tiran.* 以色列船隻不得進入蒂朗海峽。**3** the delivery of goods, especially by ship〔貨物的〕運輸〔尤指船運〕

shipping fore·cast /ˈ·· ˌ··/ *n* [C] *BrE* a radio broadcast that says what the weather will be like at sea【英】海洋天氣預報

shipping lane /ˈ·· ˌ·/ *n* [C] an officially approved path of travel that ships must follow〔官方規定的〕海上航道, 商船航線

ship's chand·ler /ˌ· ˈ··/ *n* [C] someone who sells equipment for ships 船具供應商

ship·shape /ˈʃɪpˌʃep; ˈʃɪpʃeɪp/ *adj* [not before noun 不用於名詞前] neat and clean 整齊清潔的, 井井有條的: *Let's get this house shipshape.* 讓我們把這所房子收拾乾淨。

ship-to-shore /ˌ· · ˈ·◂/ *adj* providing communication between a ship and people on land〔通訊〕船與岸之間的: *ship-to-shore radio* 船與岸之間的無線電

ship·wreck¹ /ˈʃɪpˌrɛk; ˈʃɪp-rek/ *n* [U] the destruction of a ship in an accident 海難, 船隻失事: *The survivors of the shipwreck were flown to land by helicopter.* 海難的生還者被直升機送上了岸。

shipwreck² *v* **be shipwrecked** to have been sailing in a ship that has had a serious accident and can no longer sail 遭遇海難: *Beatty was shipwrecked off the coast of Africa.* 比蒂在非洲海岸附近遭遇了海難。

ship·wright /ˈʃɪpˌraɪt; ˈʃɪp-raɪt/ *n* [C] someone who builds or repairs ships 造船者; 修船工

ship·yard /ˈʃɪpˌjɑrd; ˈʃɪp-jɑːd/ *n* [C] a place where ships are built or repaired 造[修]船廠, 船塢

shire /ʃaɪr; ʃaɪə/ *n* [C] **1 the shires** the country areas in the central part of England 英格蘭中部的農村地區 **2** *BrE old use* a COUNTY【英舊】郡

shire horse /ˈ· ·/ *n* [C] a type of large powerful horse used for pulling large loads〔一種高大強壯的〕拉車馬, 重挽馬

shirk /ʃɝk; ʃɜːk/ *v* [I,T] to deliberately avoid doing something you should do, because you are lazy〔因懶惰而〕逃避〔工作、責任等〕: *a salesman who was fired for shirking* 由於逃避工作而被解雇的推銷員 | **shirk your responsibilities/duties/obligations** *Are you accusing me of shirking my responsibilities?* 你是在指責我逃避責任嗎? —**shirker** *n* [C]

shirt /ʃɝt; ʃɜːt/ *n* [C] **1** a piece of clothing that covers the upper part of your body and your arms, usually has a collar, and is fastened at the front by buttons 襯衫, 恤衫: *I have to wear a shirt and tie to work.* 我上班要穿襯衫, 繫領帶。—see picture on page A17 參見 A17 頁圖 **2 keep your shirt on** *spoken* used to tell someone who is becoming angry that they should stay calm【口】請保持冷靜, 請不要發火〔用以勸告正在發火的人〕**3 have the shirt off someone's back** *informal* to take everything that someone owes you, without showing any sympathy【非正式】拿走某人所欠的一切東西, 冷酷無情地討債 **4 put your shirt on sth** *BrE* to risk all your money on something【英】對…孤注一擲, 把所有錢財押在…上 —see also 另見 STUFFED SHIRT S2 W3

shirt·front /ˈʃɝtˌfrʌnt; ˈʃɜːtfrʌnt/ *n* [C] the part of a shirt

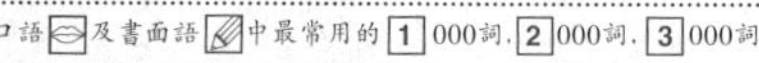

that covers your chest 襯衫的前胸

shirt·sleeves /ˈʃɝtˌslivz; ˈʃɜːtsliːvz/ *n* **in (your) shirt-sleeves** wearing a shirt but no JACKET (1) 只穿襯衣〔不穿外套〕: *It was 90° and the men were in their shirtsleeves.* 氣温達到90華氏度, 男士都只穿襯衣, 不穿外套。

shirt tail /ˈ· ·/ *n* [C] the part of a shirt that is below your waist and is usually inside your trousers 襯衫的下擺

shirt·waist·er /ˈʃɝtˌwestɚ; ˈʃɜːtˌweɪstə/ *BrE*【英】, **shirtwaist** /ˈʃɝtˌwest; ˈʃɜːtweɪst/ *AmE*【美】*n* [C] a woman's dress in the style of a long shirt 襯衫式連衣裙

shirt·y /ˈʃɝtɪ; ˈʃɜːti/ *adj BrE informal* bad-tempered, angry, and rude【英, 非正式】脾氣壞的, 動輒發怒的, 粗暴的: *Phil got a bit shirty when I tried to tell him he was wrong.* 我向菲爾指出他不對時, 他有點生氣。

shish ke·bab /ˈʃɪʃ kɪˌbɑb; ˈʃɪʃ kəˌbæb/ *n* [C] small pieces of meat that are put on a long thin metal stick and cooked 烤肉串

2 **shit¹** /ʃɪt; ʃɪt/ *n taboo, especially spoken*【諱, 尤口】

1 shit!/oh shit! used to express anger, fear, or disappointment 呸! 放屁!〔表示憤怒、恐懼或失望〕: *Shit! I've left my purse at home.* 媽的! 我把錢包忘在家裡了。

2 ►BODY WASTE 身體排泄物◄ [U] solid waste that comes out of your body from your BOWELS 糞, 大便: *Mind that dog shit!* 當心那些狗屎!

3 have/get the shits to have or get DIARRHOEA 腹瀉, 瀉肚

4 ►STH UNPLEASANT/BAD QUALITY 討厭/劣質的東西◄ [U] something that is useless or very bad quality 無用之物, 劣質品: *Their apartment is full of cheap modern shit.* 他們公寓裡盡是些廉價劣質的時髦貨。| *What's that shit you're reading?* 你在讀甚麼屁東西?

5 ►STUPID/UNTRUE TALK 蠢話/假話◄ [U] something that you think is stupid or untrue 胡說八道, 謊言: *You expect me to believe that shit?* 你以為我會相信那種屁話? | **full of shit** (=saying things that are stupid or not true) 全是胡說八道, 胡扯 *You're full of shit, Rudy. All this stuff about money and cars is just to impress the girls.* 魯迪, 你盡胡扯。所有這些關於錢財名車的謊話都是說來哄女孩子的。

6 ►PERSON 人◄ [C] someone who is very unpleasant and treats other people badly 討厭的人, 卑鄙的人: *You don't want to get involved with Colin – he's a complete shit.* 你別和科林打交道 —— 他是個十足的混蛋。

7 in deep shit also 又作 **in the shit** *BrE*【英】in a lot of trouble 遇到大麻煩, 陷入困境: *Pete's in deep shit because his wife's found out that he lied to her.* 皮特這回可遇上大麻煩了, 他老婆發現他對她撒了謊。

8 not give/care a shit to not care at all about something 毫不在乎, 毫不關心: *I don't give a shit what you think!* 我才不在乎你是怎麼想的!

9 feel like shit to feel very ill 感到很不舒服: *I woke up with a hangover, and felt like shit for the rest of the day.* 我醒來後宿酒未消, 一整天都覺得很難受。

10 beat/kick the shit out of to beat or kick someone very violently 把〔某人〕打得屁滾尿流: *I'll beat the shit out of you!* 我要狠狠地揍你!

11 give sb shit to insult someone or criticize them 侮辱某人; 批評某人: *She's always giving me shit about my clothes and stuff.* 她總是把我的衣服等等都說得一錢不值。

12 the shit will hit the fan used to say that there will be a lot of trouble when someone finds out about something 大麻煩到來, 災難臨頭: *He'll be back this afternoon, and that's when the shit will really hit the fan.* 他今天下午就回來, 到那時可就麻煩了。—see also 另見 **scare the shit out of** (SCARE¹ (1)), **tough shit** (TOUGH¹ (7))

shit² *v past tense and past participle* **shit** or **shat** /ʃæt; ʃæt/ *taboo, especially spoken*【諱, 尤口】**1** [I] to pass solid waste out of your body from your BOWELS 拉屎, 排便 **2 shit yourself** to feel very worried or frightened 極其擔憂[害怕]: *I'm absolutely shitting myself about the test next week.* 我對下星期的考試真是怕得要命。**3** [T] *AmE* to tell someone something that is untrue【美】撒謊, 胡說: *Are you shitting me?* 你在對我撒謊?

shit³ *adj taboo, spoken*【諱, 口】**1** *especially BrE* very bad【尤英】極壞的, 極差的: *Jim is shit at football.* 吉姆足球踢得蹩腳透了。| *It's a really shit job.* 這種工作真是糟透了。**2 be up shit creek** to be in a very difficult or dangerous situation 處境十分困難[危險]

shite /ʃaɪt; ʃaɪt/ *n BrE, spoken* another word for SHIT¹ (1)【英口】呸, 放屁〔shit¹ 的另一說法〕

shit-faced /ˈ· ·/ *adj taboo, spoken* very drunk【諱, 口】大醉的, 爛醉如泥的

shit-for-brains /ˌ· · ˈ·/ *n* [C] *taboo* someone who is very stupid【諱】笨蛋, 白痴

shit hole /ˈ· ·/ *n* [C] *taboo, spoken* a place that is very dirty and unpleasant【諱, 口】極骯髒的地方; 令人極不愉快的地方: *They live in a total shit hole.* 他們住在一個骯髒透頂的地方。

shit-hot /ˌ· ˈ·◄/ *adj taboo, spoken* extremely good【諱, 口】極好的

shit·less /ˈʃɪtlɪs; ˈʃɪtləs/ *adj* **scare sb shitless** *taboo, spoken* to make someone feel very frightened【諱, 口】嚇得某人魂不附體

shit stir·rer /ˈ· ˌ··/ *n taboo, especially BrE*【諱, 尤英】[C] someone who deliberately makes trouble for other people 故意搗亂者, 製造麻煩者

shit·ty /ˈʃɪtɪ; ˈʃɪti/ *adj taboo, spoken* very bad, unpleasant, or nasty【諱, 口】令人不愉快的; 極壞的: *Dave's been in a shitty mood all morning.* 戴夫整個上午情緒都很不好。

shiv·er¹ /ˈʃɪvɚ; ˈʃɪvə/ *v* [I] to shake slightly because you are cold or frightened〔因寒冷或害怕而〕顫抖, 哆嗦, 發抖: *The children stood outside shivering.* 孩子們站在外面直發抖。| **[+with]** *Juanita was shivering with cold.* 朱厄妮塔凍得直發抖。

shiver 發抖

shiver² *n* [C] **1** a slight shaking movement of your body caused by cold or fear〔因寒冷或恐懼引起身體的〕顫抖, 發抖: *A shiver ran through her at the thought of Worrel's ugly face.* 她想起沃雷爾那張醜陋的臉就毛骨悚然。**2 give you the shivers** *informal* to make you feel afraid【非正式】使人打寒顫[害怕]: *Snakes give me the shivers.* 蛇令我顫慄。**3 send shivers (up and) down your spine** *informal* to make you feel very frightened or excited【非正式】使人脊骨發涼, 令人毛骨悚然; 令人興奮: *A sudden scream from outside sent shivers down his spine.* 外邊突然傳來一聲尖叫, 令他毛骨悚然。**4 shivers** [plural] *literary* one of the very small pieces into which something breaks when it is hit or dropped【文】碎片, 破片

shiv·er·y /ˈʃɪvərɪ; ˈʃɪvəri/ *adj* trembling or shaking because of cold, fear, or illness〔因寒冷、恐懼或疾病〕顫抖的, 發抖的: *He felt shivery and nauseous.* 他感到顫抖和噁心。

shoal /ʃol; ʃəʊl/ *n* [C] **1** a large group of fish swimming together 魚羣, 一大羣游魚 **2** a small hill of sand just below the surface of water that makes it dangerous for boats 淺灘, 沙洲

shock¹ /ʃɑk; ʃɒk/ *n*

1 ►SHOCKING EVENT/SITUATION 令人震驚的事件/情況◄ [C *usually singular* 一般用單數] an unexpected and unpleasant event, situation, or piece of news that surprises and upsets you 令人震驚的事件[情況, 消息]: *It was a real shock to hear that the factory would have to close.* 聽到工廠將不得不倒閉的消息, 真是令人

震驚。| **come as a shock** (=be a shock) 令人震驚 *We knew Rob had cancer, but it still came as a shock when he died.* 我們早知道羅布患了癌症，但他的死仍然令人震驚。

2 ▶UNEXPECTED UNPLEASANT FEELING 意外的不愉快感覺◀ [singular U] the feeling of surprise and disbelief you have when something very unpleasant happens unexpectedly 吃驚，震驚，驚愕: *I was numb with shock when I found out Graham was having an affair.* 我發現格雷厄姆和別人私通時真是驚呆了。| **get a shock** *They'll get a shock when they get this bill.* 他們收到這份賬單時必定會大吃一驚。| **in a state of shock** (=extremely shocked by something and unable to think or react normally) 大為震驚 *Several hours after we had heard that Cobain was dead, we were still in a state of shock.* 我們聽到科貝恩去世的噩耗後，好幾小時後都還是震驚得不知所措。

3 ▶MEDICAL 醫學的◀ [U] a medical condition in which someone looks pale and their hearts and lungs are not working correctly, usually after a sudden very unpleasant experience 休克: **suffer from shock** *Several witnesses were taken to hospital suffering from shock.* 好幾位目擊者因休克被送進醫院。| **in (a state of) shock** *Paul's in shock, but otherwise his injuries are not serious.* 保羅處於休克狀態，但他的傷勢不算嚴重。

4 ▶ELECTRICITY 電◀ also 又作 **electric shock** [C] a sharp, painful feeling caused by a dangerous flow of electricity passing through your body 電震，電擊: **get a shock** *I got a shock off the toaster this morning.* 今天早上我在碰到多士爐時被電擊了一下。

5 ▶SHAKING 震動◀ [C,U] violent shaking caused for example by an explosion or EARTHQUAKE etc〔爆炸、地震等引起的〕劇烈震動: *The shock of the explosion was felt miles away.* 爆炸引起的震動在好幾英里以外都能感覺到。—see also 另見 SHOCK WAVE

6 a shock of hair a very thick mass of hair 一頭濃密的頭髮 —see also 另見 SHOCKED, SHELL SHOCK, TOXIC SHOCK SYNDROME

USAGE NOTE 用法說明: SHOCK

WORD CHOICE 詞語辨析: **shock, surprise, shocking**

Shock and **shocking** are both fairly strong words and you may have to think whether they are the words you really need to express your meaning. shock和shocking的含義都相當強，因此在使用時必須考慮它們是否恰當地表達自己的意思。

If something **is, comes as**, or **gives you a shock** it is unexpected and often very bad. 如果某事is, comes as, 或 gives you a shock, 即表示其來得突然，而且常指不好的事情: *It came as a great shock to hear she was leaving home.* 她要離家的消息聽了令人大吃一驚。| *He'll be OK once he gets over the shock.* 等他從震驚中恢復過來就沒事了。

A **surprise** is something that is unexpected, but is not necessarily bad. surprise也表示意外的事，但不一定是不好的: *What a nice surprise! I didn't even think you were in the country!* 多令人驚喜呀！我壓根沒想到你在國內。| *It was quite a surprise to know I was actually good at drawing.* 我發現我自己原來很會畫畫，真叫人大感意外。

Something that is **shocking** is extremely bad, often in an offensive or immoral way. 說某事shocking, 則表示此事極其不好，而且常指令人反感，在道德上不好: *shocking violence* 令人震驚的暴力。So you would not use **shocking** to describe, for example, your first day at school, or something that was simply an unpleasant surprise. 因此，如果是第一天上學，或僅是一件不太愉快的意外之事，就不該用shocking去形容。

shock[2] *v* **1** [T] to make someone feel very surprised and upset, and unable to believe what has happened 使震驚，使驚愕，使難以置信: *The murder of such a young child deeply shocked the whole community.* 殺害這樣年幼的孩子使整個社區極度震驚。| **it shocks sb to do sth** *It shocked me to think how close we had come to being killed.* 想到我們差一點喪命，我就非常害怕。**2** [I,T] to make someone feel very offended, by talking or behaving in an immoral or socially unacceptable way〔言語或行為〕(使) 憤慨，(使) 生氣，(使) 不快: *He seems to enjoy shocking people.* 他好像喜歡得罪人。| *Just ignore all their bad language – they only do it to shock.* 不要管他們的污言穢語 — 他們只是想使人生氣罷了。**3** [T] to give an electric shock to someone 使受電擊，使觸電

shock[3] *adj* [only before noun 僅用於名詞前] a word meaning very surprising, used especially in newspapers 令人吃驚的，令人大感意外的〔尤用於報紙〕: *England's shock defeat by Luxembourg in last night's game* 昨晚英格蘭隊對盧森堡隊的意外敗北

shock ab·sorb·er /'· ·,··/ *n* [C] a piece of equipment connected to each wheel of a vehicle to make travelling more comfortable〔車輛的〕減震器，緩衝裝置

shocked /ʃɑkt; ʃɒkt/ *adj* **1** feeling surprised and upset by something very unexpected and unpleasant 驚愕的，受震驚的: [+at] *We were shocked at their terrible working conditions.* 我們看到他們如此惡劣的工作條件感到大為吃驚。| **shocked to see/hear/learn etc** *I was very shocked to hear of Brian's death.* 聽到布賴恩去世的噩耗我感到非常震驚。**2 a shocked silence** a situation in which no one speaks because they are all very shocked 驚愕得一片沉默: *A shocked silence greeted Helen's announcement that she was pregnant.* 海倫宣布她懷孕後，大家驚愕得一片沉默。 S3

shock·er /ˈʃɑkɚ; ˈʃɒkə/ *n* [C] *informal* a film, news story etc that shocks you【非正式】〔影片、新聞等〕引起震驚的東西: *TV star in drugs shocker!* 電視明星吸毒的驚人大新聞！

shock·ing /ˈʃɑkɪŋ; ˈʃɒkɪŋ/ *adj* **1** very offensive or upsetting 令人討厭的；令人惱怒的: *The book was originally thought to be too shocking to publish.* 這本書原先被認為過於離譜，不能出版。**2** *BrE informal* very bad【英，非正式】極壞的，很糟的: *It's shocking, the way he treats his wife.* 他那樣對待自己的妻子，真是太糟糕了。—**shockingly** *adv* S3

shocking pink /,·· '·◂/ *n* [U] a very bright pink colour 鮮豔的粉紅色 —**shocking pink** *adj*

shock·proof /ˈʃɑk,pruf; ˈʃɒkpruːf/ *adj* a watch, machine etc that is shockproof is designed so that it is not easily damaged if it is dropped or hit〔手錶、機器等〕防震的

shock tac·tics /'· ,··/ *n* [plural] methods of achieving what you want by deliberately shocking someone〔為達到某個目的而採取的〕驚人舉動

shock treat·ment /'· ,··/ also 又作 **shock ther·a·py** /'· ,···/ *n* [U] treatment of mental illness using powerful electric shocks〔治療精神病的〕休克療法

shock wave /'· ·/ [plural] *n* **1 shock waves** strong feelings of shock that people feel when something bad happens unexpectedly〔對發生意外壞事的〕激烈反應: *The stock market crash sent shock waves through the financial community.* 股市暴跌在金融界引起強烈反應。**2** [C,U] a very strong wave of air pressure or heat from an explosion, EARTHQUAKE etc〔爆炸、地震等引起的〕衝擊波

shod /ʃɑd; ʃɒd/ the past tense and past participle of SHOE[2]

shod·dy /ˈʃɑdɪ; ˈʃɒdi/ *adj* **1** made or done cheaply or carelessly 劣質的，粗製濫造的: *shoddy workmanship* 低劣的工藝 **2** unfair and dishonest 不正當的，卑鄙的: *a shoddy trick* 卑鄙的伎倆 —**shoddily** *adv* —**shoddiness** *n* [U]

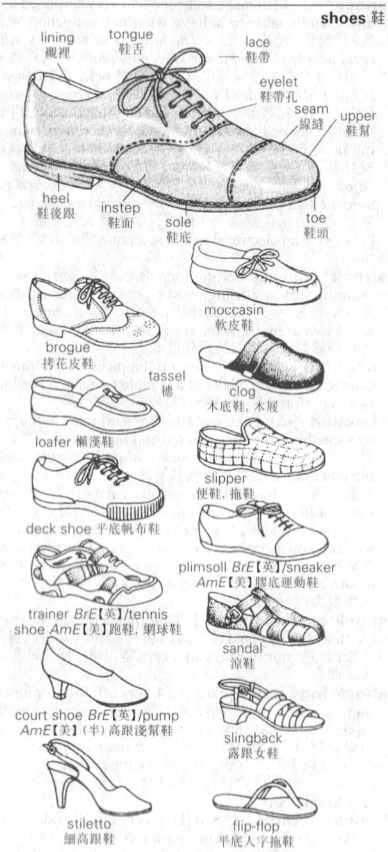

shoes 鞋

lining 襯裡
tongue 鞋舌
lace 鞋帶
eyelet 鞋帶孔
seam 線縫
upper 鞋幫
heel 鞋後跟
instep 鞋面
sole 鞋底
toe 鞋頭
moccasin 軟皮鞋
brogue 拷花皮鞋
tassel 穗
clog 木底鞋, 木屐
loafer 懶漢鞋
slipper 便鞋, 拖鞋
deck shoe 平底帆布鞋
plimsoll *BrE*【英】/sneaker *AmE*【美】膠底運動鞋
trainer *BrE*【英】/tennis shoe *AmE*【美】跑鞋, 網球鞋
sandal 涼鞋
court shoe *BrE*【英】/pump *AmE*【美】(半) 高跟淺幫鞋
slingback 露跟女鞋
stiletto 細高跟鞋
flip-flop 平底人字拖鞋

2 3 **shoe¹** /ʃu; ʃuː/ *n* [C] **1** something that you wear to cover your feet, made of leather or some other strong material 鞋: *Children grow out of shoes very quickly.* 小孩長得快, 鞋子很快就會小了。| *high-heeled shoes* 高跟鞋 | *a pair of tennis shoes* 一雙網球鞋 —compare 比較 BOOT¹ (1), SANDAL, SLIPPER **2** a curved piece of iron that is nailed onto a horse's foot; HORSESHOE〔馬的〕蹄鐵, 馬掌 **3 be in sb's shoes** to be in someone else's situation, especially a bad one 處於某人的境地〔尤指惡劣處境〕: *I'm glad I'm not in his shoes with all those debts to pay off.* 我很慶幸自己不是處在他那種境況, 有那麼多的債要還。| *If I were in your shoes, I'd tell Jan to get lost!* 我要是處在你的位置, 我會叫簡滾開的! **4 step into/fill sb's shoes** to do a job that someone else used to do, and do it as well as they did 接替某人的工作[職位]: *It'll be hard to find someone to fill Pete's shoes.* 很難找到合適的人接替皮特的工作。**5 if the shoe fits (, wear it)** *AmE spoken* used to say that if a remark that has been made about you is true, then you should accept it【美口】如果批評得對〔那就應當接受〕: *"Are you saying I'm a fool?" "If the shoe fits..."* "你在說我是個笨蛋?" "如果說得對..."

shoe² *v* [T] *past tense* **shod** /ʃɑd; ʃɒd/ *present participle* **shoeing 1 well/badly/elegantly etc shod** *especially literary* wearing good, bad etc shoes【尤文】穿着很好/破舊/漂亮的鞋子 **2** to put a shoe on a horse 給〔馬〕釘蹄鐵

shoe·horn, shoe-horn /ˈʃuˌhɔrn; ˈʃuːhɔːn/ *n* [C] a curved piece of metal or plastic that you can put inside the back of a shoe when you put it on, to help your heel go in easily 鞋拔

shoe·lace /ˈʃuˌles; ˈʃuːleɪs/ *n* [C] a thin piece of material, like string, that goes through holes in the front of your shoes and is used to fasten them 鞋帶: *Tie your shoelaces or you'll trip.* 把鞋帶繫好, 不然你會絆倒的。

shoe·mak·er /ˈʃuˌmekɚ; ˈʃuːmeɪkə/ *n* [C] someone who makes shoes and boots; COBBLER (2) 製鞋匠

shoe·shine stand /ˈ·· ˌ·/ *n AmE* a place, often in the street, where you pay to have your shoes polished【美】擦鞋亭, 擦鞋攤位

shoe·string /ˈʃuˌstrɪŋ; ˈʃuːˌstrɪŋ/ *n* **1 on a shoestring** *informal* if you do something on a shoestring, you do it without spending much money【非正式】以極少的錢: *The program was run on a shoestring for years until they found a sponsor.* 這個計劃靠極少的資金支撐了幾年之後才找到了贊助者。| *a movie that was made on a shoestring budget* 一部以很小的預算拍攝的電影 **2** *AmE* a shoelace【美】鞋帶

shoe·tree /ˈʃuˌtri; ˈʃuːtriː/ *n* [C] an object shaped like a shoe that you put inside a shoe so that it keeps its shape 鞋楦

sho·gun /ˈʃoˌgun; ˈʃəʊgʌn/ *n* [C] a military leader in Japan until the middle of the 19th century 幕府將軍〔19世紀中葉前統治日本的軍事領袖〕

shone /ʃon; ʃɒn/ the past tense and past participle of SHINE

shoo¹ /ʃu; ʃuː/ *interjection* used to tell a child or an animal to go away 噓!〔用以叫小孩走開或將動物趕走〕

shoo² *v* [T always+adv/prep] to make a child or animal go away, especially because they are annoying you〔尤因受到小孩或動物煩擾時〕發噓聲把...趕走: **shoo sb out/away etc** *He shooed the kids out of the kitchen.* 他發出噓聲把孩子們趕出廚房。

shoo-in /ˈ· ·/ *n* [C] *AmE informal* someone who is expected to win a race, election etc easily【美, 非正式】〔比賽、選舉中〕預期會輕易取勝的人, 穩操勝券者

shook /ʃuk; ʃʊk/ the past tense of SHAKE

2 2 **shoot¹** /ʃut; ʃuːt/ *v past tense and past participle* **shot** /ʃɑt; ʃɒt/

① **GUNS/WEAPONS** 槍砲/武器
② **SPORT** 體育運動
③ **SPEAK/TALK/ASK** 說話/交談/詢問
④ **QUICK/SUDDEN** 迅速/突然
⑤ **OTHER MEANINGS** 其他意思

① **GUNS/WEAPONS** 槍砲/武器

1 ►KILL/INJURE 殺死/傷害◄ [T] to deliberately kill or injure someone using a gun〔用槍〕擊斃, 擊傷; 射死, 射傷: *Lincoln was shot while watching a play in Ford's Theater.* 林肯在福特大戲院看戲時遭到槍殺。| **shoot sb in the leg/head etc** *He had been shot in the back while trying to escape.* 他試圖逃跑時背部中槍。| **shoot sb dead** *They were shot dead in their home by armed robbers.* 他們在家中被武裝劫匪開槍打死。| **shoot (sb) on sight** (=shoot as soon as you see someone)

一看到(某人)就開槍 *The guards have orders to shoot intruders on sight.* 警衛們奉命一見闖入者就立即開槍。

2 ▶FIRE A GUN 開槍◀ [I,T] to fire a weapon at someone, or make a weapon fire 開(槍); 放(砲), 發射(武器): *I'm coming out with my hands up, don't shoot.* 我現在就舉起手出來, 不要開槍。| **shoot at** (=try to shoot someone) 向…開槍 *We spent the afternoon shooting at pigeons on the roof.* 我們整個下午都在射殺房頂上的鴿子。| **shoot bullets/arrows etc** *It's only a toy – it doesn't shoot real bullets.* 那只是玩具槍——不能打真的子彈。| **shoot a gun/rifle etc** *I learned to shoot a revolver when I was a child.* 我小時候就學會了打左輪手槍。| **shoot to kill** (=shoot at someone with the intention of killing them, because they are considered very dangerous) 開槍把人打死〔因為認為某人非常危險〕 *The police were told to shoot to kill.* 警察奉命可以開槍把人打死。

3 ▶BIRDS/ANIMALS 鳥/獸類◀ [I,T] to shoot and kill animals or birds as a sport 獵殺〔動物或鳥〕, 打獵: *They spent the weekend in Scotland shooting grouse.* 他們週末在蘇格蘭打松雞。

② SPORT 體育運動

4 [I,T] to kick or throw a ball in a sport such as football or BASKETBALL towards the place where you can get a point 射(門); 投(籃): *Magic turned and shot the ball, making a 3 pointer in the final second.* 魔術手〔莊遜〕轉身投籃, 在最後一秒鐘投進一個三分球。| **[+at]** *The striker shot at goal but missed.* 前鋒射門但沒有射中。—see picture on page A23 參見A23頁圖

5 shoot pool/billiards etc *AmE informal* to play a game such as POOL¹ (3) or BILLIARDS【美, 非正式】打撞球/桁球

③ SPEAK/TALK/ASK 說話/交談/詢問

6 shoot questions at to ask someone a lot of questions very quickly〔連珠砲似地〕急促提問: *The lawyer shot a series of rapid questions at Hendrickson.* 律師連珠砲似地向亨得里克森提了一連串問題。

7 shoot your mouth off *informal* to talk about something that you should not talk about or that you know nothing about【非正式】信口開河, 瞎說一通: *Don't go shooting your mouth off, now.* 行了, 不懂就不要瞎說了。

8 shoot the bull/shoot the breeze *AmE informal* to have an informal conversation about unimportant things【美, 非正式】談天, 閒聊, 閒扯: *Cal and I were sitting on the porch shooting the breeze.* 卡爾和我坐在門廊裡閒聊。

9 ▶SHOOT! 說吧!◀ *AmE spoken* used to tell someone to start speaking【美口】開始講: *"Shoot, Ward," Richards said, "ask anything you want."* "沃德, 說吧," 理查茲說, "隨便問吧。"

④ QUICK/SUDDEN 迅速/突然

10 ▶MOVE QUICKLY 迅速移動◀ [I always+adv/prep, T always+adv/prep] to move quickly in a particular direction, or to make something move in this way (使)疾馳: **[+past/along etc]** *She shot past me and ran into the house.* 她從我身邊飛奔過去, 跑進屋裡。| *Flames were shooting skyward.* 火焰直衝高空。| **shoot sth up/in/along etc** *The fountains shoot water at the walls of the pool.* 噴泉把水噴到池壁上。

11 shoot to fame/stardom etc to suddenly become very successful 一舉成名/躍為明星: *Their new album shot straight to the top of the album charts.* 他們的新專輯迅速躍居唱片排行榜的榜首。

12 ▶PAIN 疼痛◀ [I always+adv/prep] if pain shoots through your body, you feel it going quickly through it 刺痛, 劇痛: **[+through/along]** *A spasm of pain suddenly shot along his arm.* 他的手臂突然感到一陣劇痛。| **shooting pains** (=continuous short pains passing through your body) 一陣陣的劇痛 *shooting pains in your back* 你背部的陣陣劇痛

13 shoot a look/glance (at) to look at someone quickly, especially so that other people do not see, to show them how you feel 迅速地向…看一眼: *Jack shot an anxious look at his mother.* 傑克焦急地看了母親一眼。

⑤ OTHER MEANINGS 其他意思

14 ▶PHOTOGRAPH 照片◀ [I,T] to take photographs or make a film of something 拍攝(照片); 拍(電影): *When one of the actors died, they had to shoot the final scene again.* 一名演員死了, 他們只好重拍最後的鏡頭。

15 ▶PLANTS 植物◀ [I] if a plant shoots, a new part of it starts to grow, especially a new stem and leaves 發芽, 長出新枝[新葉]

16 ▶LOCK ON A DOOR 門閂◀ to move the BOLT on a door so that it is in the locked or unlocked position 拉上, 打開〔門閂〕

17 shoot! *AmE spoken* used to show that you are annoyed or disappointed about something【美口】呸! 甚麼!〔表示不耐煩、失望等〕: *Shoot! I knew this would happen.* 呸! 我早知道這種事一定會發生。

18 shoot yourself in the foot to say or do something stupid that will cause you a lot of trouble〔因說錯話或做錯事而〕自找麻煩, 自尋煩惱: *Glen really shot himself in the foot shouting at his boss like that.* 格倫對老闆這樣大吵大嚷, 真是自找麻煩。

19 shoot the lights *BrE informal* to keep driving even though the traffic lights say you should stop【英, 非正式】〔開車〕闖紅燈

20 shoot your bolt *BrE*【英】also 又作 **shoot your wad** *AmE*【美】*informal* to have used all of your money, power, energy etc【非正式】竭盡全力; 用盡了財力[能力, 精力等] —see also 另見 SHOT¹, **blame/shoot the messenger** (MESSENGER (2))

shoot down 擊落

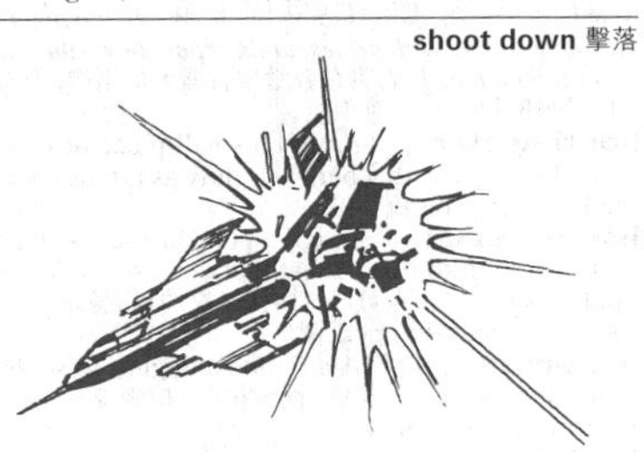

shoot sb/sth ↔ **down** *phr v* [T] **1** to destroy an enemy plane while it is flying 擊落〔敵機〕, 擊毀: *Rhodes's plane was shot down over France.* 羅茲的飛機是在法國上空被擊落的。**2** to kill someone with a gun, especially someone who cannot defend themselves 擊斃〔尤指無法自衛者〕: *They are accused of shooting down unarmed demonstrators.* 他們因開槍打死手無寸鐵的示威者而受到指控。**3 shoot sb/sth down (in flames)** *informal* to tell someone that what they are saying or suggesting is wrong or stupid【非正式】否決, 駁倒: *Another of my great ideas shot down in flames!* 我的又一個好主意被否定了。

shoot for/at sth *phr v* [T] *informal, especially AmE* to try to achieve a particular aim, especially one that is very difficult【非正式, 尤美】試圖達到〔尤指困難的目標〕, 為…而努力: *Management is shooting for a 50% increase in sales in the next financial year.* 管理層正在爭取下一財政年度的銷售額增加50%。

shoot off *phr v* [I] *BrE informal* to leave quickly or suddenly【英, 非正式】迅速走開, 突然離開: *Sorry, but I'll have to shoot off before the end of the meeting.* 對不起, 我得在會議結束前先走了。

shoot through *phr v* [I] *informal especially AustrE*【非正式, 尤澳】**1** to leave a place, especially very quickly〔尤指迅速地〕離開 **2** to die 死去

shoot up *phr v* **1** [I] to quickly increase in number or amount〔數字或數量〕猛增: *Prices have certainly shot up recently.* 最近價格確實在猛漲。| *Supermarkets are shooting up all over the area.* 這個地區超級市場的數量正在猛增。**2** [I] to grow taller very quickly 迅速長高: *Your son's really shot up since we last saw him.* 我們上次見過你兒子後, 他真是長高了許多。**3** [T **shoot** sb/sth ↔ **up**] to injure or damage someone or something by shooting them with bullets 開槍擊傷〔某人〕, 擊壞〔某物〕: *The building was so badly shot up it was unrecognizable.* 這幢大樓遭到嚴重槍擊, 已經面目全非了。**4** [I,T] *slang* to take illegal drugs by using a needle【俚】注射毒品

shoot² *n* [C] **1** the part of a plant that comes up above the ground when it is just beginning to grow〔植物的〕芽, 苗, 嫩枝 —see picture at 參見 GERMINATE 圖 **2** an occasion when someone takes photographs or makes a film〔照片、電影的〕拍攝: *One of the models is on a shoot for that new perfume Passion.* 一位模特兒正在為"激情"牌新香水拍廣告。**3** an occasion when people shoot birds or animals for sport, or the area of land where they do this 打獵, 狩獵; 狩獵區

shoot·er /ˈʃutɚ; ˈʃuːtə/ *n* [C] *informal* a word meaning a gun, used especially in films about COWBOYS or criminals【非正式】槍〔尤用於有關牛仔或罪犯的電影裡〕

shoot·ing /ˈʃutɪŋ; ˈʃuːtɪŋ/ *n* **1** [C] a situation in which someone is injured or killed by a gun 槍擊; 槍殺: *politically-motivated shootings* 有政治動機的槍殺事件 **2** [U] the sport of shooting animals and birds 打獵, 射獵: *the shooting season* 狩獵季節

shooting gal·le·ry /ˈ·· ˌ···/ *n* [C] **1** a place where people shoot guns at objects to win prizes 打靶場, 射擊場 **2** *AmE slang* a large empty building in a city, where people buy drugs and INJECT (1) them【美俚】〔城市中〕人們購買及注射毒品的荒廢的大樓

shooting match /ˈ·· ·/ *n* **the whole shooting match** *spoken* the whole of a situation, or an event that is the best or most complete of its kind【口】全部的人[事物], 有關的全部東西; 最好[最完備]的事: *We're having a big church wedding with bridesmaids, a pageboy – the whole shooting match.* 我們將在教堂舉行盛大的婚禮, 有女儐相, 男小儐相 —— 一應俱全。

shooting star /ˌ·· ˈ·/ *n* [C] a small piece of rock or metal from space, that burns brightly as it falls towards the Earth; METEOR 流星

shooting stick /ˈ·· ·/ *n* [C] a pointed stick with a top that opens out to form a seat that you use when doing outdoor sports〔頂端可以打開作坐櫈的〕摺疊座手杖 —see picture at 參見 STICK² 圖

shoot-out /ˈ· ·/ *n* [C] **1** a fight using guns to settle an argument〔為解決爭執的〕開槍格鬥, 槍戰 **2** a PENALTY SHOOT-OUT 點球決勝賽

S 1 W 1 **shop¹** /ʃɑp; ʃɒp/ *n*

1 ▶PLACE WHERE YOU BUY THINGS 購物處所◀ [C] **a)** *BrE* a building or part of a building where things are sold to the public【英】商店; STORE *AmE*【美】: *The shops in town close at 5:30.* 城裡的商店五點三十分關門。| **toy shop/pet shop etc** *Have you seen that new shoe shop?* 你去過那家新開的鞋店沒有? **b)** a small shop that sells one particular type of thing 專賣〔某種商品的〕店, 專櫃: *a candle shop* 蠟燭店 —see also 另見 BUCKET SHOP, CORNER SHOP, COFFEE SHOP

2 ▶MAKING/REPAIRING THINGS 製造/修理物件◀ [C] a place where things are made or repaired 製造廠, 修配店: *After assembly, the cars go to the paint shop to be painted.* 這些汽車裝配後就送到噴漆車間去噴漆。| *a repair shop* 修配廠 —see also 另見 SHOP FLOOR, SHOP STEWARD

3 ▶SCHOOL SUBJECT 學校科目◀ [U] *AmE* a subject taught in schools that shows students how to use tools and machinery to make things out of wood and metal【美】〔學校開設的教學生使用工具和機器做木製品或金屬製品的〕手藝課

4 set up shop *informal* to start a business【非正式】開業

5 shut up shop *informal* to close a shop or business, either temporarily or permanently【非正式】〔暫時或永久性地〕停止營業, 關店

6 talk shop *informal* to talk about things that are connected to your work, especially in a way that other people find boring【非正式】談與業務有關的事, 談公事, 談工作: *I'm fed up with you two talking shop.* 你們兩人老談業務, 我都聽膩了。

7 all over the shop *BrE spoken*【英口】**a)** scattered around untidily 凌亂放置, 到處散置: *There were bits of paper all over the shop.* 小紙片撒得到處都是。**b)** confused and disorganized 混亂的, 雜亂無章的: *I'm all over the shop this morning.* 我今天早上真是亂得一團糟。

8 ▶GO SHOPPING 去購物◀ [singular] *BrE spoken* an occasion when you go shopping, especially for food and other things you need regularly【英口】去買東西〔尤指買食品或日常必需品〕: *doing the weekly shop* 進行每週的購物

Frequencies of the nouns **shop** and **store** in British and American English 名詞 shop 和 store 在英國英語和美國英語中的使用頻率

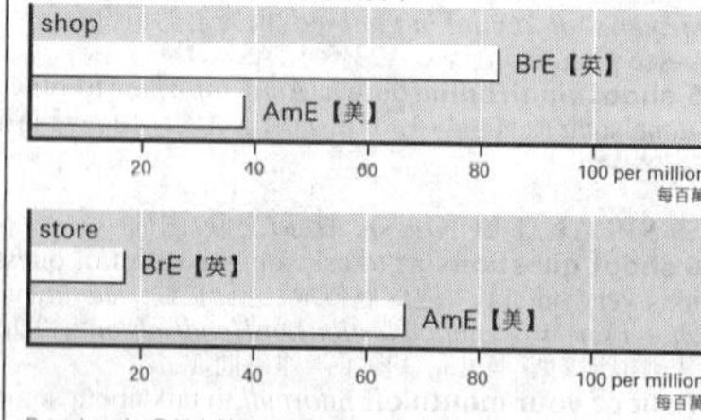

Based on the British National Corpus and the Longman Lancaster Corpus
據英國國家語料庫和朗文蘭卡斯特語料庫

This graph shows that when talking about a building where things are sold, **shop** is the usual word in British English and **store** is the usual word in American English. Americans use **shop** to mean a small shop where one particular type of thing is sold. In British English **store** is used to mean a very large shop that sells many different types of things, and is usually used in the expression **department store**. 本圖表顯示, 指商店時英國英語常用 shop, 而美國英語常用 store。美國人用 shop 指專賣某種商品的小店, 而英國英語的 store 指售賣各種商品的大商店, 而且通常用於 department store〔百貨商店〕這一說法中。

shop² *v* **shopped, shopping** **1** [I] to go to one or more shops to buy things 去買東西, 購物: [**+for**] *I was shopping for a new dress, but couldn't find anything I liked.* 我要買件新衣服, 但沒有找到一件我喜歡的。**2 go shopping a)** *BrE* to go to one or more shops to buy things, often for enjoyment【英】逛街, 購物 **b)** *especially AmE* to go to shops to buy clothes【尤美】去商店買衣服 **3** [T] *BrE informal* to tell the police about someone who has done something illegal【英, 非正式】向〔警方〕告發, 告密: *He was shopped by his ex-wife.* 他被前妻告發。—**shopper** *n* [C] S 2

shop around *phr v* [I] to compare the price and quality of different things before you decide which to buy〔買前〕比較各種商品價格與質量, 逐店比較地選購: *Shop around before you decide which insurance policy to take out.* 你在決定買保險之前, 要把各家保險公司作個比較。

shop as·sis·tant /ˈ· ·ˌ··/ *BrE n* [C] someone whose job is to help customers in a shop【英】售貨員, 店員;

SALESCLERK *AmE*【美】

shop·fit·ting /ˈʃɑpˌfɪtɪŋ; ˈʃɒpˌfɪtɪŋ/ *n* [U] *BrE* the business of putting equipment in shops such as shelves, containers etc【英】商店的內部裝修或安裝〔業務〕 —**shopfitter** *n* [C]

shop floor /ˌ· ˈ·◂/ *n* **the shop floor** *BrE*【英】**1** the area in a factory where the ordinary workers do their work 工廠的生產區, 工作車間: *The chairwoman started her working life on the shop floor.* 這位主席是從生產車間開始她的工作生涯的。**2** the ordinary workers in a factory, not the managers〔工廠的〕普通工人,〔與資方相對的〕勞方

shop front /ˈ· ·/ *n* [C] the outside part of a shop that faces the street〔向街的〕店面, 鋪面; STOREFRONT *AmE*【美】

shop·keep·er /ˈʃɑpˌkipɚ; ˈʃɒpˌkiːpə/ *n* [C] *especially BrE* someone who owns or is in charge of a small shop【尤英】〔小店的〕店主, 店老闆; STOREKEEPER *AmE*【美】

shop·lift /ˈʃɑpˌlɪft; ˈʃɒpˌlɪft/ *v* [I] to take something from a shop without paying for it 在商店內偷竊商品, 在商店順手牽羊 —**shoplifter** *n* [C]: *Shoplifters will be prosecuted.* 順手牽羊者必究。

shop·lift·ing /ˈʃɑpˌlɪftɪŋ; ˈʃɒpˌlɪftɪŋ/ *n* [U] the crime of stealing things from shops, for example by hiding them in your bag, or under your clothes 商品偷竊

shop·per /ˈʃɑpɚ; ˈʃɒpə/ *n* [C] someone who buys things in shops〔商店的〕顧客, 購物者: *The streets were crowded with shoppers.* 街上擠滿了購物者。

2 3 **shop·ping** /ˈʃɑpɪŋ; ˈʃɒpɪŋ/ *n* [U] **1** the activity of going to shops to buy things 買東西, 購物: *Shopping is now a major leisure industry.* 購物現在是一種重要的休閒產業。—see also 另見 WINDOW-SHOPPING **2 do the shopping** *BrE* to go shopping to buy food and other things you need regularly【英】買食品和日常必需品: *We always do our shopping on Fridays.* 我們總是在星期五去買日常需要的東西。**3** *BrE* the things that you have just bought from a shop【英】剛買的東西: *Do you need some help carrying your shopping?* 要不要幫你提這些剛買的東西?

shopping cen·tre *BrE*【英】, **shopping center** *AmE*【美】/ˈ·· ˌ··/ *n* [C] a group of shops built together in one area, often under one roof 購物中心

shopping mall /ˈ·· ·/ *n* [C] *AmE* a large, specially built covered area where there are a lot of shops; MALL【美】〔有頂蓋的〕大型購物商場

shopping pre·cinct /ˈ·· ˌ··/ *n* [C] *BrE* an area in a town where there are a lot of shops and where cars are not allowed【英】〔城內禁止車輛通行的〕購物區, 商業步行街

shop-soiled /ˈ· ·/ *adj BrE*【英】**1** something that is shop-soiled is slightly damaged or dirty because it has been in a shop for a long time〔商品在商店陳列過久而〕殘舊的, 弄髒了的; SHOPWORN *AmE*【美】**2** an idea that is shop-soiled is no longer interesting because it has been discussed many times before〔主意因談論過多次〕不再令人感興趣的, 陳舊的: *the same old shop-soiled arguments* 還是那老一套陳詞濫調

shop stew·ard /ˌ· ˈ··/ *n* [C] a worker who is elected by members of a TRADE UNION in a factory or other business to represent them in dealing with managers〔由工會會員選出與資方打交道的〕工會代表

shop·walk·er /ˈʃɑpˌwɔkɚ; ˈʃɒpwɔːkə/ *n* [C] *especially BrE* someone who is employed in a large shop to help the customers and watch the other workers to make sure they are working properly【尤英】〔大商店中協助顧客、監督店員的〕店[鋪]面巡視員

shop·worn /ˈʃɑpˌwɔrn; ˈʃɒpwɔːn/ *adj AmE*【美】= SHOP-SOILED

shore[1] /ʃɔr; ʃɔː/ *n* **1** [C,U] the land along the edge of a large area of water, such as an ocean or lake〔海、湖等大水域的〕岸, 濱: *We could see a boat about a mile from shore.* 我們能看見離岸約一英里處有一艘船。| *the shores of the Mediterranean* 地中海海岸 | **on shore** (=away from a ship) 在岸上 *We had a couple of hours on shore.* 我們有幾個小時可以上岸。**2 these shores/British shores/our shores etc** *especially literary* a particular country that has a border on the sea【尤文】這個國家/英國/我們的國家〔指沿海的國家〕: *Millions of immigrants flocked to these shores in the 19th century.* 數百萬移民在 19 世紀蜂擁到這個國家。—see also 另見 ASHORE, OFFSHORE, ONSHORE

USAGE NOTE 用法說明: SHORE

WORD CHOICE 詞語辨析: **shore, bank, coast, seaside, beach**

The usual word for the land at the edge of a sea or lake is **shore**. 表示海或湖的岸邊通常用 shore: *At night he would stand on the shore and gaze out to sea.* 晚上, 他常會站在岸邊凝視遠處的海面。| *There was a little cabin on the opposite shore.* 對岸有間小屋。

The edges of a river are its **banks**. 河流的兩岸則稱 banks。

When you are talking about a country, or a large area of a country, you call the land next to the sea the **coast**. 一個國家或其一大片土地的沿海陸地稱為 coast: *the Atlantic coast of Spain* 西班牙的大西洋海岸 | *I could tell from his clothes that he was from the West Coast.* 我從他穿的衣服可以斷定他來自西海岸。

In British English the **seaside** is the area by the sea considered as a place of enjoyment. 在英國英語中, seaside (海濱) 是指可供遊樂的場所: *a holiday at the seaside* 在海濱度假。In American English you are more likely to use **beach**. 但在美國英語中, 人們更多使用 beach (海灘) : *In summer, my mother used to take me to the beach.* 以前在夏天, 我母親經常帶我去海灘玩。But you can also use **beach** in both British and American English for the flat land right at the edge of the sea, that is covered by water some of the time. 不過, 在英國英語和美國英語中都可以用 beach 表示海灘: *They walked hand in hand along the beach.* 他們手挽手地沿着海灘走。

shore[2] *v*

shore sth ↔ **up** *phr v* [T] **1** to support a wall with large pieces of wood, metal etc to stop it from falling down〔用木頭、金屬等支柱〕支撐〔牆〕: *The roof had been shored up with old timbers.* 這房頂一直用舊木柱支撐着。**2** to help or support something that is likely to fail or is not working well 幫助, 支持〔可能失敗或運轉失常的事〕: *attempts to shore up the struggling economy* 為支撐搖搖欲墜的經濟而作的努力

shorn /ʃɔrn; ʃɔːn/ *v* the past participle of SHEAR

short[1] /ʃɔrt; ʃɔːt/ *adj*

① LENGTH/HEIGHT/DISTANCE 長度/高度/距離
② TIME 時間
③ NOT ENOUGH 不足
④ AMOUNT 數量
⑤ BOOK/SPEECH ETC 書/演說等
⑥ SHORT FORM OF ...的縮略形式
⑦ PRONUNCIATION 發音
⑧ OTHER MEANINGS 其他意思

① **LENGTH/HEIGHT/DISTANCE 長度/高度/距離**

1 measuring a small amount in distance or length〔距離或長度〕短的: *a short corridor with two rooms on each side* 每邊兩個房間的短過道 | *a short skirt* 一條短裙 | *It's a short drive from the airport.* 從飛機場到這裡的車程不長。| *Anita had her hair cut short.* 阿妮塔把頭髮剪短了。—see picture on page A6 參見A6頁圖
2 ►PERSON 人◄ someone who is short is of less than average height 矮的: *a short plump woman* 一個又矮又胖的女人
3 be 3 feet/10 miles/2 metres short of to have not quite reached a place you are trying to get to 距離…還差三英尺/十英里/二米: *Our car broke down two miles short of the town.* 我們的汽車在離城鎮兩英里處拋錨了。

② **TIME 時間**

4 happening or continuing for only a little time or for less time than usual 短(暫)的: *a short meeting* 一個短會 | *I'm afraid there will be a short delay.* 怕是要耽擱一會兒。| *Morris gave a short laugh.* 莫里斯笑了一聲。| *I've only been living in Brisbane a short time.* 我在布里斯班才住了很短的一段時間。| *Some people have short memories, don't they?* 有些人記憶力很差，是嗎? | **a short space of time** *Both her parents died within a short space of time.* 她的雙親在很短時間內相繼去世。
5 at short notice *BrE*【英】also 又作 **on short notice** *AmE*【美】with very little warning that something is going to happen 沒有提前多少時間的通知，很遲才通知: *The party was arranged at very short notice.* 聚會是匆忙接到通知後籌備的。| *I can't make it Friday. It's a bit short notice I'm afraid.* 我無法在星期五去，通知得恐怕有點太遲了。
6 in the short term during the period of time that is not very far into the future 在短期內: *Interest rates are unlikely to fall in the short term.* 利率在短期內不會下降。—see also 另見 SHORT-TERM
7 in short order in a short time and without delay 迅速地，在短時間內; 毫不拖延地: *All the tents were put up in short order.* 所有的帳篷很快就搭起來了。
8 make short work of *informal* to finish something quickly and easily, especially a meal or a job【非正式】迅速完成，輕易解決〔尤指一頓飯或一項工作〕: *The kids made short work of the sandwiches.* 孩子們很快就把三明治都吃光了。
9 short and sweet *spoken* not taking a long time and less boring or unpleasant than you expected【口】簡短扼要: *They won't listen to a long lecture, so just keep it short and sweet.* 他們不願聽冗長的演講，所以要講得簡短扼要。

③ **NOT ENOUGH 不足**

10 a) not having enough of something you need 短缺的，不足的: **be short of** *I'm a little short of money at the moment.* 目前我的錢不大夠。| *Your little girl's not short of confidence, is she?* 你的小女兒不缺乏自信，是嗎? | **be 5p/$10 etc short** *Have you all paid me? I'm still about $9 short.* 你們全都付錢給我了嗎? 我這裡大約還差九美元。**b) be short** if time, money etc is short, there is not as much of it as you need〔時間、金錢等〕不夠的，不足的: *Money was short in those days. We had to get by on $30 a week.* 那些日子錢不夠用。我們只能靠每週30美元度日。| *It'll be difficult – time and resources are short.* 會有困難的 — 時間和資源短缺。
11 be in short supply if something is in short supply, there is not enough of it available 供應不足: *Gasoline was in short supply just after the war.* 戰爭剛結束時汽油供應不足。
12 be (a bit/rather) short *BrE* to not have much money【英】缺錢，錢不夠: *Could you lend me £5? I'm a bit short tonight.* 你能借給我五英鎊嗎? 今晚我的錢有點不大夠。
13 be short on *informal* to have less of something than you should have【非正式】欠缺: *Sometimes I think he's a little short on common sense.* 有時候我覺得他多少有點缺乏常識。
14 give sb short measure to give someone less than the correct amount of something, especially in a shop〔尤指商店售貨〕少給分量，分量不足，短斤缺兩

④ **AMOUNT 數量**

15 just short of/a little short of etc not quite as much as; a little less than 差不多達到/只差一點就達到〔某數目〕: *The total cost will be just short of $17 million.* 全部費用差不多達到1700萬美元。| *Her time was only 2 seconds short of the world record.* 她的成績比世界記錄只差兩秒鐘。

⑤ **BOOK/SPEECH ETC 書/演說等**

16 a book, letter, speech etc that is short does not have many words or pages〔書、信、演說等〕簡短的: *a short article on energy conservation* 一篇關於節省能量的短文 —see also 另見 SHORT STORY

⑥ **SHORT FORM OF ...的縮略形式**

17 be short for to be a shorter way of saying a name 簡稱: *Her name is Alex, short for Alexandra.* 她名叫Alex(亞力克斯)，是Alexandra(亞力山德拉)的簡稱。
18 for short as a shorter way of saying a name 簡略為; 縮寫; 簡稱: *the Reformed Electoral System (or the RES for short)* 新的選舉制度(簡稱RES)

⑦ **PRONUNCIATION 發音**

19 *technical* a short vowel is pronounced quickly and without being emphasized【術語】〔母音〕發短音的: /æ/, *as in 'cat', is a short vowel.* 如在cat一詞中的/æ/音是個短母音。

⑧ **OTHER MEANINGS 其他意思**

20 be short with to speak to someone using very few words, in a way that seems rude or unfriendly〔對人說話〕簡短得像無禮的; 簡慢的: *Sorry I was short with you on the phone this morning – I was being hassled by the kids.* 對不起，我今天上午和你通話時對你簡慢無禮 — 我被孩子們弄煩了。
21 give sb/sth short shrift to not give much attention or sympathy to someone 對某人/某事怠慢[冷淡]: *Her suggestions were given short shrift by the chairman.* 她的建議受到主席的冷落。| **get short shrift** *My warnings, as usual, got short shrift.* 我的告誡照例無人理睬。
22 have a short temper to get angry very easily 脾氣暴躁
23 nothing/little short of used to emphasize that something is very good, very surprising etc 毫不遜於: *Brigitte's recovery seemed nothing short of a miracle.* 布麗吉特的康復簡直是個奇跡。
24 draw/get the short straw to be given something difficult or unpleasant to do, especially when other people have been given something better 得個苦差事; 比別人吃虧
25 life's too short *spoken* used to say that something is too unimportant to worry about or spend time on【口】人生太短暫〔表示沒必要為瑣事浪費時間〕—**shortness** *n* [U]

short² *adv* **1 be running short** if you are running short of something, or if something is running short, it is being used up and there will soon not be enough left 使用殆盡，幾乎用完: *We're running short of coffee again.* 我們的咖啡又差不多沒有了。| *Our supplies of beer were running short.* 我們的啤酒存貨不多了。| *Let's go –*

time's running short. 我們走吧 — 時間不多了。**2 stop short** to suddenly stop speaking or stop what you are doing, for example because something has surprised you or you have just thought of something〔在說話或工作時〕突然停下 **3 stop short of doing sth** to almost do something but decide against actually doing it 將要做某事時突然罷手, 險些做某事: *Paula stopped just short of accusing me of lying.* 葆拉差點兒要說我撒謊。**4 pull/bring sb up short** to make someone suddenly stop moving or stop what they are doing 使某人突然停止移動或做某事: *The sight of the gun in her hand pulled me up short.* 我一看見她手裡拿着槍就愣住了。**5 cut sb short** to stop someone before they have finished speaking, by interrupting them 打斷某人的話: *I was halfway through my explanation when Walter cut me short.* 我才解釋了一半, 沃爾特就打斷了我的話。**6 cut sth short** to suddenly bring something to an end before it has properly finished 突然中斷某事: *His death at the age of 38 cut short a brilliant career.* 他 38 歲英年早逝, 使其輝煌事業未竟全功。**7 fall short of** to be less than the result, level, or standard that you expect or to fail to achieve something you are hoping for 達不到〔目的、水平、標準〕: *The appeal for money has fallen well short of its target.* 籌集的資金遠未達到目標。| *I'm afraid the results fell short of our expectations.* 這些結果怕是達不到我們的預期目的。**8 go short (of)** to have less food, money etc than you need〔食品、錢等〕不夠, 欠缺: *She made sure that her children never went short.* 她保證自己的孩子甚麼都不缺。**9 short of (doing) sth** without actually doing something 除非; 除了〔某種做法〕外: *Short of locking her in her room, he couldn't really stop her from seeing Jack.* 除非把她鎖在房間裡, 他無法真正制止她和傑克會面。**10 be taken short/be caught short** *BrE informal* to have a sudden strong need to go to the toilet【英, 非正式】突然要上廁所

short[3] *n* **1 in short** used when you want to say, in just a few words, what is the most important point about a situation 總而言之, 簡單地說: *In short, he is a liar.* 總而言之, 他是個騙子。**2 shorts** [plural] **a)** short trousers ending at or above the knees 短褲: *a pair of tennis shorts* 一條網球短褲 **b)** *especially AmE* men's UNDERPANTS【尤美】男短內褲 **3** [C] *BrE informal* a strong alcoholic drink, drunk in a small glass【英, 非正式】〔用小酒杯喝的〕烈性酒 **4** [C] *informal* a short film shown before the main film at a cinema【非正式】〔在電影正片前放映的〕短片 **5** [C] *informal* a SHORT CIRCUIT【非正式】短路: *a short in the system* 系統短路

short[4] *v* [I,T] *informal* to SHORT-CIRCUIT, or make something do this【非正式】(使) 短路: *Maybe the battery has shorted.* 可能電池短路了。

short·age /ˈʃɔrtɪdʒ; ˈʃɔːtɪdʒ/ *n* [C,U] a situation in which there is not enough of something that people need 短缺, 不足, 缺乏: **[+of]** *a shortage of skilled labour* 缺乏熟練工 | **water/gasoline/bread etc shortage** *water shortages in the summer* 夏季供水不足

short back and sides /ˌ· · · ˈ·/ *n* [singular] *BrE* a way of cutting a man's hair so that it is very short at the back and sides of his head and slightly longer on top【英】男子蓋式髮型〔後面和兩邊剪得很短, 頂部略長〕

short·bread /ˈʃɔrtˌbrɛd; ˈʃɔːtbred/ *n* [U] a hard, sweet BISCUIT made with a lot of butter 牛油甜酥餅乾

short·cake /ˈʃɔrtˌkek; ˈʃɔːtkeɪk/ *n* [U] **1** *BrE* thick SHORTBREAD【英】〔較厚的〕牛油甜酥餅 **2** *AmE* cake over which a sweet fruit mixture is poured【美】〔上面覆有水果混合物的〕蛋糕

short-change /ˌ· ˈ·/ *v* [T often passive 常用被動態] **1** to treat someone unfairly by not giving them what they deserve 欺詐, 欺騙, 少給〔某人〕應得的東西: *When the band only played for 15 minutes the fans felt they had been short-changed.* 樂隊只演奏了 15 分鐘, 歌迷們覺得受了欺騙。**2** to give back too little money to someone who has paid for something by giving more than the exact price 少找錢給〔顧客〕

short cir·cuit /ˌ· ˈ··/ *n* [C] the failure of an electrical system caused by bad wires or a fault in a connection in the wires 短路

short-circuit *v* **1** [I, T] to have a short circuit or cause a short circuit in something (使) 短路 **2** [T] to get something done without going through the usual long methods 使〔某事〕簡化; 繞過; 避開: *I short-circuited the whole process by a simple telephone call.* 我把整個程序給簡化了, 只打了個簡單的電話。

short·com·ing /ˈʃɔrtˌkʌmɪŋ; ˈʃɔːtˌkʌmɪŋ/ *n* [C usually plural 一般用複數] a fault in someone's character or abilities, or in a product, system etc, that makes something less successful or effective than it should be〔性格、能力、產品、制度等的〕缺點, 短處: *In spite of all her shortcomings, she's still the best teacher the school has.* 她儘管有些缺點, 但仍然是該校最好的教師。| *The present system, whatever its shortcomings, has worked well for several years.* 目前的制度儘管有缺點, 幾年來還一直運行得很好。| **[+in]** *The inspection revealed some serious shortcomings in our safety procedures.* 這次檢查暴露出我們在安全程序上的一些嚴重缺陷。

short·crust pas·try /ˌʃɔrtkrʌst ˈpestrɪ; ˌʃɔːtkrʌst ˈpeɪstri/ *n* [U] a kind of PASTRY (1) made with half as much fat as flour 起酥餅, 酥 (皮) 點心

short cut /ˌ· ˈ·/ *n* [C] **1** a quicker, more direct way of going somewhere than the usual one 捷徑, 近路: *We were late for the game, but found a short cut through the fields.* 我們看球賽出發遲了, 但找到了一條穿過田野的近路。| **take a short cut** *Carlos decided to take a short cut home.* 卡洛斯決定抄近路回家。**2** a quicker way of doing something〔做事情的〕快捷辦法, 捷徑: **[+to]** *There aren't really any short cuts to learning English.* 學英語實在沒有捷徑可走。

short·en /ˈʃɔrtn̩; ˈʃɔːtn/ *v* [I,T] to become shorter or make something shorter (使) 變短, 縮短: *The days are shortening now.* 現在白天變得越來越短了。| **shorten sth** *They're talking about shortening the working week.* 他們在談論有關縮短工作週的問題。—opposite 反義詞 LENGTHEN

short·en·ing /ˈʃɔrtn̩ɪŋ; ˈʃɔːtnɪŋ/ *n* [U] fat made from vegetable oil that you mix with flour when making PASTRY (1)〔用植物油做的〕起酥油〔用於和麵做糕點〕

short·fall /ˈʃɔrtˌfɔl; ˈʃɔːtfɔːl/ *n* [C] the difference between the amount you have and the amount you need or expect 不足之數, 差額: *severe crop shortfalls* 嚴重的農作物歉收 | **[+in/of]** *a shortfall in staffing levels* 人員配備不足 | *a shortfall of about £1 million* 約一百萬英鎊的差額

short·hand /ˈʃɔrtˌhænd; ˈʃɔːthænd/ *n* [U] **1** a fast method of writing using special signs or shorter forms to represent letters, words, and phrases 速記(法): **in shorthand** *The reporter took notes in shorthand.* 記者用速記作記錄。—compare 比較 LONGHAND **2 be shorthand for** to be a shorter but less clear way of saying something 簡短而意思隱晦的說法: *He's been 'relocated', which is shorthand for 'given a worse job a long way away'.* 他已經被"調職", 這個說法的實際意義是"被派到很遠的地方做一份更差的工作"。

short·hand·ed /ˈʃɔrtˈhændɪd; ˌʃɔːtˈhændɪd◂/ *adj* having fewer helpers or workers than you need 人手不夠的: *We'll be shorthanded next month as five of my staff will be on holiday.* 我們下個月將會人手不足, 因為我的員工中有五人要休假。

shorthand typ·ist /ˌ·· ˈ··/ *n* [C] *BrE* someone whose job is to use shorthand to write down what someone else says and then TYPE[2] (1) a copy of it【英】速記 (打字) 員〔其工作是速記後用打字機打出來〕; STENOGRAPHER *especially AmE*【尤美】

short-haul /ˈʃɔrtˈhɔl; ˈʃɔːthɔːl/ *adj* a shorthaul aircraft or flight travels a fairly short distance〔飛機航程〕短距離的, 短途的

S

short·ie /ˈʃɔrtɪ; ˈʃɔːti/ *adj* [only before noun 僅用於名詞前] *informal* a shortie coat or JACKET (1) etc is one that is shorter than the usual size【非正式】〔外套、夾克等〕較通常尺碼短的 —see also 另見 SHORTY

short list[1] /ˈ· ·/ *n* [C] *BrE* a list of the most suitable people for a job, chosen from all the people who were first considered【英】〔從初選名單篩選出的〕決選名單

short-list[2] *v* [T usually passive 一般用被動態] *BrE* to put someone on a short list for a job【英】把〔某人〕列入決選名單: **short-list sb for** *She's been shortlisted for the sales director's job.* 她已被列入銷售經理職務的決選名單。

short-lived /ˈʃɔrt ˈlaɪvd; ˌʃɔːt ˈlɪvd◂/ *adj* lasting only a short time 短暫的: *Our happiness was short-lived.* 我們的快樂是短暫的。

3 **short·ly** /ˈʃɔrtlɪ; ˈʃɔːtli/ *adv* **1** soon 不久, 很快, 立刻: *Ms Jones will be back shortly.* 瓊斯小姐很快就會回來。| **shortly before/after** *The accident happened shortly before midday.* 事故是在正午前不久發生的。**2** speaking impatiently〔說話〕不耐煩地: *"I've explained that already," Rod said shortly.* "那個問題我已經解釋過了。" 羅德不耐煩地說。

short-or·der cook /ˌ· ·· ˈ·/ *n* [C] *AmE* someone in a restaurant kitchen who makes the food that can be prepared easily or quickly【美】快餐廚師

short·range /ˌ·ˈ·◂/ *adj* **1** designed to travel or operate only within a short distance 短程的: *a shortrange missile* 短程導彈 **2 shortrange plan/goal/forecast etc** concerned only with the period that is not very far into the future 短期計劃/目標/預測等: *shortrange plans* 短期計劃

short-sheet /ˈ· ·/ *v* [T] *AmE* to fold the top sheet on a bed so that no one can get into it, as a trick; APPLE PIE BED【美】把…的牀單疊短〔為了捉弄別人, 把牀單摺疊成兩層, 使牀單看似已經鋪好, 但人鑽進被窩時雙腿卻不能伸直〕

short-sight·ed /ˌ· ˈ··◂/ *adj* **1** *especially BrE* unable to see objects clearly unless they are very close【尤英】近視的; NEARSIGHTED *especially AmE*【尤美】—opposite 反義詞 LONGSIGHTED **2** not considering the possible effects of something that seems to save time, money, or effort at the moment 目光短淺的, 無遠見的: *a short-sighted policy of stopping investment in training* 一項停止在培訓上投入資金的目光短淺的政策 —opposite 反義詞 FAR-SIGHTED —**short-sightedly** *adv* —**short-sightedness** *n* [U]

short-staffed /ˌ· ˈ·◂/ *adj* having fewer than the usual or necessary number of workers 人員不足的: *We'll try to get the order through by Monday, but we're very short-staffed at the moment.* 我們將設法在星期一前交貨, 但目前我們人手非常不足。

short·stop /ˈʃɔrtˌstɑp; ˈʃɔːtstɒp/ *n* [C] a player in BASEBALL who tries to stop any balls that are hit between second and third BASE[2] (8)〔棒球第二壘與第三壘之間的〕游擊手

short sto·ry /ˌ· ˈ··/ *n* [C] a short written story about imaginary situations, usually containing only a few characters 短篇小說

short-tem·pered /ˌ· ˈ··◂/ *adj* **1** easily becoming angry or impatient 脾氣暴躁的, 易怒的: *Roger's back pain is making him pretty short-tempered these days.* 羅傑這幾天背疼, 弄得他脾氣相當暴躁。**2** angry and impatient 氣沖沖的, 不耐煩的: *a short-tempered reply* 不耐煩的回答

short-term /ˌ· ˈ·◂/ *adj* [usually before noun 一般用於名詞前] continuing for only a short time, or concerned only with the period that is not very far into the future 短期的: *The treatment may bring short-term benefits to Aids sufferers.* 這種療法對愛滋病患者會有短期的好處。| *Most of the staff are on short-term contracts.* 大部分職員都是訂短期合同的。—opposite 反義詞 LONG-TERM —**short-term** *adv*

short-term·is·m /ˌ· ˈ···/ *n* [U] a way of planning or thinking that is concerned only with what gives you advantage now, rather than what might happen in the future 短期效益主義〔只考慮目前利益的做法〕: *short-termism in the banking world* 銀行界的短期效益主義 —**short-termist** *adj*

short time /ˌ· ˈ·◂/ *n* **be on short time** *BrE* a factory or office that is on short time is operating for less than the usual number of hours or days【英】〔工廠、辦公室的〕縮短工作時間, 實行短工時: *Workers were put on short time because raw materials were scarce.* 由於原料短缺, 工人的工時都減少了。

short wave /ˌ· ˈ·◂/ *n* [U] radio broadcasting on waves of less than 60 metres in length, which can be sent around the world 短波〔波長在60公尺以下, 可在全球範圍內傳送的無線電波〕—see also 另見 LONG WAVE, MEDIUM WAVE

short·y /ˈʃɔrtɪ; ˈʃɔːti/ *n* [C] an insulting name for someone who is not very tall 矮子, 矬子〔侮辱性稱謂〕

shot[1] /ʃɑt; ʃɒt/

① GUNS/SHOOTING 槍/射擊
② SPORT 體育運動
③ FILM/PHOTOGRAPHS 電影/照片
④ ATTEMPT/GUESS 嘗試/猜測
⑤ OTHER MEANINGS 其他意思

① GUNS/SHOOTING 槍/射擊

1 fire a shot to fire a gun 開槍: *He pulled out his rifle and fired three shots.* 他掏出來復槍開了三槍。

2 take a shot at to try to kill or injure someone by firing a gun at them 向…開槍: *Someone took a shot at him as he was getting out of his car.* 他下車時有人向他開槍。

3 ►SOUND 聲音◄ [C] the sound of a gun being fired 槍聲: *Where were you when you heard the shot?* 聽到槍聲時你在甚麼地方?

4 ►BULLETS 子彈◄ [U] **a)** small metal balls for shooting from a SHOTGUN〔獵槍用的〕彈丸 **b)** *old use* large metal balls for shooting from a CANNON[1]【舊】砲彈

5 a good shot/bad shot someone who can shoot a gun well, badly etc 優秀的/差勁的射手: *Sergeant Cooper is an excellent shot.* 庫珀中士是一位優秀的槍手。

② SPORT 體育運動

6 [C] an attempt to throw, kick, or hit the ball towards the place where you can get a point〔為得分的〕投球, 射球, 擊球: *Shaw made the shot and turned to run down the court.* 肖投籃得分後轉身跑向球場的另一頭。| *Good shot!* 好球!

7 [C] a heavy metal ball that competitors try to throw as far as possible in the sport of SHOT PUT〔推鉛球用的〕鉛球

8 a 10 to 1 shot/50 to 1 shot etc a horse, dog etc in a race, whose chances of winning are expressed as numbers that show the ODDS〔賽馬、賽狗等的〕10比1/50比1的獲勝機會

③ FILM/PHOTOGRAPHS 電影/照片

9 [C] a photograph 一張照片: *I managed to get some good shots of the carnival.* 我總算拍到幾張狂歡節的精彩照片。

10 [C] the view of something in a film, television programme, or photograph that is produced by having the camera in a particular position〔電影、電視節目或照片的〕鏡頭: *In the opening shot we see Garfield at his desk reading.* 在開始的鏡頭中, 我們看到加菲爾德坐在書桌旁看書。

④ **ATTEMPT/GUESS 嘗試/猜測**

11 [C] *informal* an attempt to do something or achieve something【非正式】嘗試, 試圖, 設法: **[+at]** *This will be his second shot at the championship.* 這將是他第二次嘗試奪取冠軍。| **have a shot (at sth)** *I decided to have a shot at decorating the house myself.* 我決定試試自己動手裝修房子。

12 a long shot an attempt or guess at something that is not very likely to be successful, but is still worth trying〔成功希望不大但值得作的〕嘗試[猜測]: *It's a long shot, but if we hurry we might still find her.* 看來希望不大, 但我們如果趕緊行動, 也許還能找到她。

13 a shot in the dark an attempt to guess something without having any facts or definite ideas 瞎猜, 亂猜: *My answer to the last question was a complete shot in the dark.* 我最後一道題的答案完全是瞎猜的。

⑤ **OTHER MEANINGS 其他意思**

14 ►DRINK 飲料◄ [C] a small amount of a strong alcoholic drink〔烈酒的〕少量, 一小口: **[+of]** *He poured himself another shot of whiskey.* 他又給自己斟了一點威士忌。

15 ►DRUG 藥物◄ [C] *AmE* an INJECTION of a drug (when it is put into the body with a needle)【美】一次注射, 一針: *Have you had your typhoid and cholera shots?* 你打過傷寒和霍亂的預防針了嗎?

16 ►REMARK 話語◄ [C] an angry remark 憤怒的話, 尖銳的話: **a parting shot** (=something you say as you are leaving) 分手時說的氣話, 臨別惡語 *Carl turned for one parting shot: "You marry him, then!"* 卡爾在分手時轉身說了句氣話: "那你就嫁給他好了。" | **a cheap shot** (=an unnecessarily rude remark) 多餘的粗話, 不必要的氣話

17 big shot an important or powerful person, especially in business〔尤指商界的〕要人, 權勢人物: *a big shot in the record business* 唱片業的大腕

18 like a shot if you do something like a shot, you do it very quickly and eagerly〔做事〕飛快地, 毫不遲疑地, 立刻: *If he asked me to go to Africa with him, I'd go like a shot!* 如果他叫我和他一起去非洲, 我會毫不遲疑地去!

19 a shot in the arm something that makes you more confident or more successful 令人增強信心的事物, 令人鼓舞的事物: *The latest opinion poll has given the Socialists a much needed shot in the arm.* 最近的民意調查給社會黨人打了一劑他們急需的興奮劑。

20 a shot across the bows *especially BrE* something you say or do to warn someone about what might happen if they fail to do what you want them to do【尤英】警告〔表示如不服從將有嚴重後果〕—see also 另見 **call the tune shots** (CALL[1] (25)), MUGSHOT, **not by a long chalk/shot** (LONG[1] (16)

shot² *adj* [not before noun 不用於名詞前] **1 be shot** to be in bad condition because of being used too much or treated badly 用壞的; 耗盡的; 破舊的: *My back tires are shot. I'll have to get new ones before we go.* 我車子的後胎已經磨壞了, 我得換上新的才能動身。| **shot to pieces** *After a long day of exams, my nerves were shot to pieces.* 考試了一整天, 我已經筋疲力盡了。**2 be/get shot of** *informal* to get rid of someone or something【非正式】擺脫…, 把…處理掉: *I don't care how nice the house is any more. I just want to be shot of it.* 我已不在乎房子有多漂亮了, 我只想把它處理掉。**3 be shot through with** *formal*【正式】**a)** if a piece of cloth is shot through with a colour, it has very small threads of that colour woven into it〔布料等〕閃色的, 顏色閃變的〔因織入了這種顏色的細線〕: *a fine silk shot through with gold threads* 一塊閃着金色條紋的精美絲綢 **b)** to have a lot of a particular quality or feeling 充滿〔某種特質或情感〕的: *a charming collection of stories, shot through with a gentle humour* 一本妙趣橫生引人入勝的小説集

shot³ *v* the past tense and past participle of SHOOT

shot·gun /ˈʃɑtˌɡʌn; ˈʃɒtɡʌn/ *n* [C] a long gun fired from the shoulder, especially one used for killing birds or animals 獵槍

shotgun wed·ding /ˌ·· ˈ··/ *n* [C] a wedding that has to take place immediately because the woman is going to have a baby〔因女方已懷孕〕不得不立即舉行的婚禮

shot put /ˈ· ·/ *n* [singular] a sporting competition in which you throw a heavy metal ball as far as you can 推鉛球 —**shot putter** *n* [C]: *an Olympic shot putter* 奧林匹克鉛球選手

S1 W1 **should** /ʃəd; ʃəd *strong* 強讀 ʃud; ʃʊd/ *modal verb* [negative short form 否定縮略式= **shouldn't**] **1** used to show that something is the best thing to do because it is morally right, fair, honest etc 應當, 應該〔表示這樣做是最好的, 因為體現道德、公正、誠實等〕: *He should learn to be more polite.* 他應該學會更有禮貌。| *What you should have done is call the police.* 你本該叫警察來。| *I have no sympathy for him. He shouldn't accept bribes.* 我一點也不同情他, 他不應該接受賄賂。| *"I don't care what people think." "Well, you should."* "我才不在乎人們怎麼想。" "啊, 你應該注意的。" **2** used to show that something is the best thing to do because it helps you, is good for you etc 應當, 應該〔表示這樣做是最好的, 因為對自己有好處〕: *The leaflet tells you what you should do if the power fails.* 這份傳單告訴你萬一停電應該怎樣做。| *Why shouldn't I smoke if I want to?* 如果我想吸煙, 為甚麼不? | *I think he should have tried to get some more qualifications before applying for the job.* 我認為他在申請這份工作之前應努力取得更多的資歷。**3** used to show what the correct or expected amount, situation etc is, especially when it is not correct or not what is expected 應當, 應該〔表示某數量或事應當是怎樣的, 尤用於表示原來並非如此〕: *Eat noodles the way they should be eaten, with chopsticks.* 該怎麼吃麵條就怎麼吃 —— 用筷子。| *What do you mean there are only ten tickets? There should be twelve.* 只有十張票, 你這是甚麼意思? 應該有十二張才對。**4** used to say that something will probably be good, bad, interesting etc 應, 應當〔表示推測〕: *It should be a good movie – its reviews were very good.* 這應當是一部好電影 —— 各種評論都很肯定。| *With her talent and experience, she should do well for herself.* 憑着她的才能和經驗, 她自己應能做得很好。**5** used after 'that' in some expressions showing an opinion or feeling〔用在 that 之後, 表示某種意見或感情〕: *It's odd that he should react in this way.* 很奇怪, 他竟然作出這樣的反應。| *The residents demanded that there should be an official inquiry.* 居民要求進行一次正式調查。**6 should it rain/should there be a problem etc** if it rains, if there is a problem etc 要是下雨/有問題的話: *Should anyone phone, tell them I'm in conference.* 要是有人來電話, 告訴他我在開會。**7** *formal, especially BrE*【正式, 尤英】used after 'I' or 'WE' in conditional sentences〔用於條件句中, 置於 I 或 we 之後〕: *I should stay in bed if I were you.* 我要是你就臥牀休息。| *I should be surprised if he came.* 他要是來, 我會感到意外。**8** *formal especially BrE* used after IF, to emphasize that something might or might not happen【正式, 尤英】〔用在 "if" 之後, 強調某事有可能發生〕: *If the wound should become inflamed do not hesitate to call me.* 萬一傷口發炎, 請隨時打電話給我。**9** used in reported speech to mean SHALL 將會〔用於間接引語中, 表示 shall〕: *I promised I should be back by midnight.* 我保證會在午夜之前回來。**10 what should happen but/who should appear but etc** *especially humorous* used to

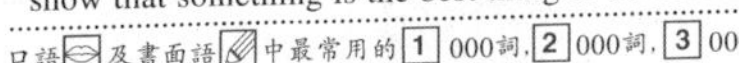

show that you were surprised when something happened, a particular person appeared etc【尤幽默】〔用以表示驚訝〕你猜發生了甚麼, 你猜誰來了: *Just at that moment who should walk in but old Jim himself.* 就在那時, 你猜是誰進來了? 是老吉姆親自來了。**11 I should worry/he should care etc** *humorous* used to mean the opposite of what you seem to be saying【幽默】〔表示相反的意思〕我用不着擔心/他不會計較的: *With all his money, he should worry about giving the waiter a tip!* 他有那麼多錢, 還會計較給服務員那點小費嗎! **12 I should have thought** *spoken especially BrE* used as a polite or joking way of showing that you disagree with what someone has said【口, 尤英】我想〔用於禮貌地或開玩笑地表示不同意對方的話〕: *"Why isn't it working?" "I should have thought that was obvious."* "為甚麼它不在運轉?" "我想那是明顯不過的了。" **13 I should like** *formal, especially BrE* used to say politely that you want something【正式, 尤英】我想要…〔用於禮貌地表示想要某物〕: *"Will you require anything else?" "Yes, I should like a dry martini."* "您還需要其他甚麼嗎?" "是的, 我想要一杯乾馬丁尼酒。" **14 I should think** used to say what you believe or expect to be true 我相信, 我估計: *I shouldn't think there'll be a problem parking at that time of night.* 我想晚上這個時間停車不會成問題的。**15 I should think so/not** *spoken* used to strongly agree with what someone has said【口】〔表示強調〕當然! 當然不!: *"I'm not going out tonight." "I should think not, with so much work to do!"* "我今晚不準備外出了。" "當然不出去啦, 還有那麼多工作要做!"

shoul·der¹ /ˈʃoldɚ; ˈʃəʊldə/ *n* [C]

1 ►BODY PART 身體的一部分◄ one of the two parts of the body at each side of the neck where the arm is connected 肩膀: *Put a shawl around your shoulders in case you get cold.* 如果你覺得冷就披一條披肩。| **shrug your shoulders** (=raise them to show that you do not know something or do not care) 聳聳肩〔表示不知道或不在乎〕 *Keith just shrugged his shoulders and said it wasn't his problem.* 基思只是聳聳肩, 並説這不是他的問題。—see pictures at 參見 BODY, HORSE¹ 圖

2 ►CLOTHES 衣服◄ the part of a piece of clothing that covers your shoulders 衣服的肩部, 衣肩: *a jacket with padded shoulders* 一件有墊肩的夾克 (衫)

3 ►MEAT 肉類◄ the upper part of the front leg of an animal that is used for meat〔動物前腿上半部的〕肩肘肉, 前腿肉: *a shoulder of pork* 豬肘子

4 a shoulder to cry on someone who gives you sympathy 給予同情[安慰]的人: *Ben is always there when I need a shoulder to cry on.* 我需要人安慰時, 本總是在我身邊。

5 shoulder to shoulder working together to achieve the same thing 肩並肩地: *We worked shoulder to shoulder for five years in that hell-hole.* 我們在那個地獄般的地方肩並肩地工作了五年。

6 stand shoulder to shoulder with to completely share someone's opinions about something and support them in what they are doing 和〔某人〕肩並肩地站在一起, 完全同意並支持〔某人〕

7 on sb's shoulders if a difficult or unpleasant responsibility is on someone's shoulders, they are the person that has that responsibility〔任務〕落在某人肩上,〔責任〕由某人承擔: *The duty of informing the children's parents fell on the shoulders of Sergeant Flynn.* 通知小孩家長的責任落在弗林警佐的肩上。| *The blame rests squarely on Jim's shoulders.* 過失的責任無疑該由吉姆承擔。

8 put your shoulder to the wheel to start to work with great effort and determination 開始奮力工作

9 ►ROAD-SIDE 路邊◄ *AmE* an area of ground beside a road where drivers can stop their cars if they are having trouble【美】路肩,〔公路兩旁的〕緊急停車道 —see also 另見 HARD SHOULDER, SOFT SHOULDER —see picture on page A3 參見 A3 頁圖

10 ►MOUNTAIN 山◄ a rounded part of a mountain just below the top 山肩〔山頂以下的圓形部分〕—see also 另見 **cry on sb's shoulder** (CRY¹ (4)), **give sb the cold shoulder** (COLD¹ (8)), **have a chip on your shoulder** (CHIP¹ (5)), **rub shoulders with** (RUB¹ (6)), **head and shoulders above the rest** (HEAD¹ (50)), **straight from the shoulder** (STRAIGHT¹ (9))

shoulder² *v* **1** [T] **shoulder a responsibility/duty/cost etc** to accept a difficult or unpleasant responsibility, duty etc 承擔責任/職責/費用等: *The residents are being asked to shoulder the costs of the repairs.* 居民們被要求承擔這筆修理費用。**2** [T] to lift something onto your shoulder to carry it〔用肩〕挑, 扛, 掮: *They shouldered the boat and took it down to the river.* 他們把船扛在肩上抬到河裡。**3 shoulder your way through/into etc** to move through a large crowd of people by pushing with your shoulder 用肩膀擠着過去/進去: *She shouldered her way through the onlookers.* 她用肩膀擠着穿過圍觀的人羣。**4 shoulder arms** an order given to a soldier telling him to hold his weapon against his shoulder〔命令士兵〕槍上肩

shoulder bag /ˈ‥ ˌ/ *n* [C] a bag that hangs from your shoulder〔有肩帶的〕背包式手提包

shoulder blade /ˈ‥ ˌ/ *n* [C] one of the two flat bones on each side of your back SCAPULA 肩胛骨 —see picture at 參見 SKELETON 圖

shoulder-high /ˌ‥ ˈ◂/ *adj, adv* as high as your shoulder 齊肩高的[地]: *shoulder-high grass* 齊肩高的草

shoulder-length /ˈ‥ ˌ/ *adj* shoulder-length hair hangs down to your shoulders〔頭髮〕長至肩部的 —see picture on page A6 參見 A6 頁圖

shoulder pad /ˈ‥ ˌ/ *n* [C] a thick flat piece of material that is fixed under the shoulders of a piece of clothing to make your shoulders look bigger〔縫在衣肩內的〕墊肩

shoulder strap /ˈ‥ ˌ/ *n* [C] **1** a long narrow piece of material on a piece of women's clothing that goes over the shoulder 女服的肩帶 **2** a long narrow piece of material fixed to a bag etc so that you can carry it over your shoulder 手提包的肩帶

should·n't /ˈʃʊdn̩t; ˈʃʊdnt/ *v* the short form of 'should not' 縮略式= should not

shouldst /ˈʃədst; ʃədst *strong* 強讀 ʃʊdst; ʃʊdst/ *v old use* the second person singular form of the verb SHOULD【舊】動詞 should 的第二人稱單數形式

shout¹ /ʃaut; ʃaʊt/ *v* **1** [I, T] to say something very loudly 大聲說, 喊叫, 呼喊: *There's no need to shout, I'm not deaf!* 用不着這樣大聲喊叫, 我又不是聾子! | *We could hear them shouting for help.* 我們能聽到他們在大聲呼救。| *"Watch out!" she shouted, as the car started to move.* "小心!" 汽車開動時她大聲喊道。| **shout at sb** *I wish you'd stop shouting at the children.* 我希望你別再對孩子們大喊大叫。| **shout sth at sb** *He was shouting insults at the lorry driver.* 他對那個貨車司機破口大罵。| **shout yourself hoarse** (=make your voice rough and weak by shouting a lot) 喊得嗓子沙啞 **2** to call out loudly, for example because you are angry or in pain〔因憤怒或疼痛等〕大叫: *My brother shouted in pain as the ball hit him.* 我兄弟被球擊中時痛得大叫了起來。**3 shout sth from the rooftops** to tell everyone about something because you want everyone to know about it 使盡人皆知, 使某事家喻戶曉: *But she was in love, and she wanted to shout the fact from the rooftops.* 她在談戀愛, 而且希望所有的人都知道這件事。**4 be all over bar the shouting** *BrE spoken* used to say that something is almost finished and there is no doubt what the result will be【英口】〔事情快要結束而且〕大局已定: *The kids were arrested and pleaded guilty. It was all over bar the shouting.* 孩子們被逮捕並承認犯了罪, 一切已成定局。

shout sb ↔ **down** *phr v* [T] to shout in order to prevent someone from being heard 用喊叫壓倒某人[淹沒某人的聲音]: *Unpopular speakers were shouted down* *by the crowd.* 聽眾向不受歡迎的演講者大喝倒采。

shout out *phr v* [I **shout** sth ↔ **out**] to say something suddenly in a loud voice 突然大聲地說: *Don't shout out the answer in class, put up your hand.* 上課時不要大聲喊着回答問題，先要舉手。

shout[2] *n* **1** [C] a loud call expressing anger, pain, excitement etc〔表示生氣、疼痛、興奮等的〕喊叫（聲），呼叫（聲）: *a warning shout* 表示警告的呼喊聲 | *shouts of delight from the football crowd* 足球觀眾的歡呼聲 | **give a shout** *Tom gave a shout of triumph as he realized he'd won.* 湯姆知道自己獲勝時發出了勝利的歡呼。**2 give sb a shout** *spoken* to go and find someone and tell them something【口】去告訴某人某事: *Give me a shout when you're ready to go.* 你準備好動身時告訴我一聲。**3 sb's shout** *AustrE or BrE informal* someone's turn to buy drinks【澳或英，非正式】輪到某人請喝飲料: *It's my shout. Same again?* 輪到我負責買飲料了，還要上次那種嗎？

3 **shove**[1] /ʃʌv; ʃʌv/ *v* **1** [I,T] to push someone or something, in a rough or careless way, using your hands or shoulders〔用手或肩〕推，推擠，推撞: **shove sb aside/into etc** *Secret Service men shoved people aside to make way for the President.* 特工人員把人羣推到一旁為總統開路。| **shove sb/sth** *Stop shoving me or I'll tell the teacher!* 不要再推我，否則我要告訴老師了。| **pushing and shoving** (=pushing with your body, especially in a crowd)〔尤指在人羣中〕推推搡搡 *There was no trouble at the rally apart from a little pushing and shoving.* 在羣眾集會上除了有點推推搡搡之外，沒有出現麻煩事。—see picture on page A21 參見 A21 頁圖 **2** [T always+adv/prep] to put something somewhere carelessly or without thinking much 隨意地放〔東西〕，漫不經心地亂放: **shove sth into/under etc** *Let's shove everything into the closet just for now.* 我們暫時把所有東西都放進壁櫥裡吧。**3 shove up/over** *spoken, especially BrE* to move along on a seat to make space for someone else【口，尤英】移動身子〔騰出位置〕: *Shove up mate, there's no room to sit down here.* 老兄，挪過去一點，這裡沒地方坐了。—see also 另見 **when push comes to shove** (PUSH[2] (7))

shove off *phr v* [I] **1** *spoken* used to tell someone rudely or angrily to go away【口】〔粗暴地或生氣地叫人〕走開，離開: *Shove off! I'm busy.* 走開！我忙得很。**2** to push a boat away from the land, usually with a pole〔用篙〕把船撐離岸

shove[2] *n* [C] a strong push 猛推: **give sth a shove** *We gave the door one good shove and it came open.* 我們用力一推，門就開了。

shov·el[1] /ˈʃʌvl̩; ˈʃʌvəl/ *n* [C] **1** a tool with a rounded blade and a long handle used for moving earth, stones etc 鏟子，鐵鍬 —compare 比較 SPADE (1) **2** a part of a large vehicle or machine used for moving or digging earth 推土機[挖土機]前面的鏟形部分

shovel[2] *v* **shovelled, shovelling** *BrE*【英】, **shoveled, shoveling** *AmE*【美】[I,T] **1** to lift and move earth, stones etc with a shovel〔用鏟子〕鏟起: *The workmen shovelled loads of gravel onto the road.* 工人們把大量的碎石鏟到路面上。| **shovel the driveway/sidewalk etc** *AmE* (=shovel snow from a road or path)【美】鏟去車道／人行道上的積雪 *Chris, I asked you two days ago to shovel the front path.* 克里斯，兩天前我就叫你把門前路上的積雪鏟掉。**2 shovel sth into/onto etc** to put something into a place quickly 迅速將某物放進／放上…: *He was shovelling spaghetti into his mouth.* 他大口大口地吃意大利麵條。

shov·el·ful /ˈʃʌvl̩fʊl; ˈʃʌvəlfʊl/ *n* [C] the amount of coal, snow, earth etc that you can carry on a shovel〔煤、雪、泥等〕一滿鏟的量

1 1 **show**[1] /ʃo; ʃəʊ/ *v past tense* **showed** *past participle* **shown** /ʃon; ʃəʊn/

1 ►PROVE 證明◄ [T] to provide facts or information that make it clear that something is true or that something exists〔提供事實、信息〕證明，證實: **show (that)** *The latest poll clearly shows that most voters are unaware of this.* 最新的民意調查清楚地說明，大部分選民都不知道這件事。| *As her record plainly shows, Wyler is one of the world's all-time great players.* 懷勒的記錄清楚表明，她是世界上空前卓越的一位球員。| **show how/what** *Her experience shows how easily young women can get into trouble abroad.* 她的經歷證明，年輕女子在國外是多麼容易遇到麻煩。| **show sth** *Recent events in Somalia show the futility of war.* 最近在索馬里發生的事件證明戰爭無濟於事。| *Statistics show a marked rise in nitrogen levels at this point.* 統計數字說明氮的濃度在此刻顯著升高。| **show sb/sth to be** *formal*【正式】: *He later showed himself to be an excellent chess player.* 他後來證明自己是一名優秀的棋手。| **it just shows/it just goes to show** *spoken* (=when a bad experience you have been talking about proves something)【口】〔某經驗教訓〕恰恰證明 *And he took everything she had. It just goes to show, you should never trust a stranger.* 他竟然席捲了她所有的東西逃走，這恰恰證明你絕對不可以相信一個陌生人。—see graph at 參見 INDICATE 圖表

2 ►SHOW YOUR FEELINGS ETC 流露感情等◄ [T] to let your feelings, attitudes, or personal qualities be clearly seen in the way you behave, the way you look etc 表現出，流露出〔感情、態度、個人品質〕: *She's never shown much interest in my work.* 她從不對我的工作表示多大的興趣。| *I think it shows great determination on her part.* 我認為這表現出她的巨大決心。| *He showed his agreement by a slight nod.* 他輕輕地點了一下頭表示同意。| **show how/what etc** *I was determined not to show how upset I was.* 我決心不流露出我是多麼地難過。

3 ►INFORMATION/MEASUREMENTS ETC 信息／計量等◄ [T not usually in progressive 一般不用進行式] **a)** if a picture, map etc shows something, you can see it on the picture, map etc〔圖片、地圖等〕標示，標明: *This diagram shows the correct position of the gear lever.* 此圖標出了變速桿的正確位置。| *a useful chart showing all the flights coming into and out of Paris* 一張很有用的，標明進出巴黎的所有航班的一覽表 **b)** if a clock or other measuring instrument shows a time, a number etc, you can see that time etc on it〔時鐘〕指示〔時間〕；〔計量儀等〕指示數目: *The victim's watch showed five minutes past two.* 遇難者的手錶指針指着兩點零五分。

4 ►LET SB SEE 向某人出示◄ [T] to let someone see something, for example by holding it out so that they can look at it 把…指給別人看，出示: **show sb sth** *Jackie showed the official her passport.* 傑姬向那位官員出示了護照。| **show sth to sb** *Show your ticket to the man at the entrance.* 向入口處的那個人出示你的門票。| **show sth** *All passes must be shown on entering the building.* 進入這幢大樓必須出示通行證。

5 ►TELL/EXPLAIN STH 說／解釋某事◄ [T] **a)** to tell someone how to do something, by explaining it to them, often by doing it yourself so that they can see you〔通過示範〕解釋，說明: **show sb how to do sth** *I showed him how to work the coffee machine.* 我給他示範如何使用這台咖啡機。| **show sb sth** *Show her the right way to do it.* 請向她解釋做這件事的正確方法。**b)** to tell someone where a place or thing is, for example by pointing to it 向…指出…在何處: **show sb sth** *I'll show you the exact spot where it happened.* 我會告訴你事情發生的確切地點。| **show sb where** *Could you show me where I can put my coat?* 告訴我我的大衣該放在哪兒好嗎？

6 ►GUIDE SB 指引某人◄ [T always+adv/prep] to go with someone and guide them to a place 帶領，指引: **show sb to/in/out/around** *Goodbye, Mrs Davies. My secretary will show you out.* (=out of the office or building) 再見，戴維斯太太，我的祕書會送你出去的。| **show sb sth** *Come on out, and I'll show you the garden.* 出來，我帶你去看看花園。—see also 另見 **show sb ↔ around, show sb over sth** —see 見 LEAD[1] (USAGE)

7 ►CAN BE SEEN 可被看見◄ a) [I] if something shows it is easy to see 看得見, 顯露: *His happiness showed in his face.* 他喜形於色。| *Don't worry about that tiny stain; it won't show.* 不用擔心那點小小的污跡, 看不出來的。**b)** [T] if material shows dirt or a mark, it is easy to see the dirt or mark on it〔材料容易〕顯露〔污跡或痕跡〕: *That light jacket will show the slightest crease.* 那件淺色夾克稍有一點摺痕都會看得出來。

8 ►FILM 電影◄ a) [I] if a film is showing at a cinema, you can see it there〔電影〕放映 **b)** [T] if a cinema shows a film, it makes it available for people to see〔電影院〕上映〔影片〕: *The local movie theater is showing Tom Cruise's latest picture.* 當地的電影院正在上映湯告魯斯的最新影片。—see also 另見 SHOWING

9 have something/nothing etc to show for if you have something to show for your efforts, hard work etc, you have achieved something as a result of them 在…方面的努力有成績/沒有成績: *Is that all you've got to show for a whole week's work?* 這就是你整整一週工作所取得的全部成績嗎?

10 show a profit/loss if a company shows a profit or loss, it makes a financial profit or loss〔公司〕盈利/虧本

11 show your hand to make your true power or intentions clear, especially after you have been keeping them secret〔尤指保密一段時間後〕顯露實力; 表明意圖和打算: *She needed to be cautious, and not show her hand too soon.* 她需要謹慎行事, 不急於表明意圖。

12 show your face if you will not show your face somewhere, you will not go there because you have a good reason to feel ashamed or embarrassed about being there 露面, 出現: *He wouldn't dare show his face here after the way he behaved last week!* 他經過上星期那番表現之後不敢再在這兒露面了!

13 ►ART/PICTURES 藝術/圖畫◄ [T often passive 常用被動態] to put a collection of paintings or other works of art in one place so that people can come and see them 展覽, 展出: *Her recent sculptures are being shown at the Hayward Gallery.* 她最近的雕塑作品正在海沃德畫廊展出。

14 ►ANIMAL 動物◄ [T] to put an animal into a competition with other animals 參賽展示〔動物〕

15 ►ARRIVE 抵達◄ [I] *informal, especially AmE* to arrive at the place where someone is waiting for you; show up【非正式, 尤美】到場, 出席, 露面: *I came to meet Hank, but he never showed.* 我來見漢克, 但他始終沒有露面。

16 ... and it shows *spoken* used to say that something, especially something bad, is very clear to see【口】〔尤指不好的東西〕顯而易見, 完全看得出來: *"I did the whole report in only two days!" "And it shows!"* "我寫整份報告只花了兩天時間。" "這看得出來!"

17 I'll show him/them etc *spoken* used to say that you will prove to someone that you are better, more effective etc than they think you are【口】我要讓他/他們看看〔證明自己比別人想的更好, 更高效等〕: *They're convinced I'm going to fail, but I'll show them!* 他們相信我會失敗, 但我要幹給他們看看。

18 show sb in a good/bad etc light if an action shows you in a good or bad light, it makes people have a good or bad opinion about you 提高/降低人們對某人的評價: *a decision which does not show Roosevelt in a particularly favourable light* 一項並不顯示羅斯福有多高明的決策

19 show sb the door to make it clear that someone is not welcome and should leave 攆某人出去, 對某人下逐客令

20 show sb who's boss *informal* to prove to someone who is threatening your authority that you are more powerful than they are【非正式】讓某人明白該聽誰的, 要某人服從指揮: *Don't let your horse pull his head down – show him who's boss.* 不要讓馬弃拉着頭 —— 要讓牠聽你的。

21 show the way if you show the way for other people, you do something new that others then try to copy 指出路子, 做出榜樣: *In the 70s Panderm showed the way with its revolutionary new techniques.* (20世紀) 70年代, 潘德姆公司以其創新的技術闖出條新路子。

22 show a leg! *BrE spoken* used to tell someone to get out of bed【英口】〔用於叫某人〕起牀

23 show a clean pair of heels *BrE old-fashioned informal* to run away very fast【英, 過時, 非正式】迅速逃脫, 逃之夭夭

show sb ↔ around (sth) *phr v* [T] to go around a place with someone when they first arrive there, to show them what is interesting, useful etc 為新到的客人作嚮導, 帶某人參觀: *Pat will show you around the building so you can meet everyone.* 帕特會帶你到樓裡各處看看, 讓你和大家見個面。| *We were shown around by an elderly guide.* 我們由一位年長的嚮導帶着四處參觀。

show off *phr v* **1** [I] to try to impress people and make them admire your abilities, achievements, or possessions〔自我〕炫耀, 賣弄[表現]自己: *Pay no attention to Susan – she's just showing off.* 不要理蘇珊 —— 她只是在賣弄自己。**2** [T **show** sth ↔ **off**] to show something to a lot of people because you are very proud of it 誇耀〔引以自豪的東西〕, 炫耀〔某物〕: *Peter was keen to show off his new car.* 彼得很喜歡炫耀他的新汽車。**3** [T **show** sth ↔ **off**] if one thing shows off something else, it makes the other thing look especially attractive 使〔某物〕更具吸引力, 使奪目: *The white dress showed off her dark skin beautifully.* 白色的裙子把她那黝黑的皮膚襯托得很漂亮。

show sb **over** sth *phr v* [T] *especially BrE* to guide someone through an interesting building or a house that is for sale【尤英】帶領某人參觀〔有趣的建築物或待售的房子〕: *Our company chairman showed the Prime Minister over the new plant.* 我們公司的董事長陪同首相參觀新工廠。

show sb ↔ **round** (sth) *phr v BrE* to SHOW AROUND【英】帶某人參觀

show up *phr v* **1** [I] *informal* to arrive, especially at the place where someone is waiting for you【非正式】到達〔尤指有人在等候之處〕: *I was almost asleep when Chris finally showed up.* 克里斯最終來到時, 我幾乎睡着了。**2** [T **show** sth ↔ **up**] to make it possible to see or notice something that was not clear before 使〔某物〕顯現出來: *The sunlight showed up the cracks in the wall.* 陽光使牆上的裂縫顯現出來。| *These riots show up the deficiencies in police training.* 這些騷亂暴露出警察訓練不足。**3** [I] to be easy to see or notice 顯露, 顯現出來: *The subtitles won't show up against such a light background.* 這些字幕在這樣淺色的背景太不顯眼。| *A lot of bugs showed up when I ran the program.* 我在運行這個程序時, 出現了許多故障。**4** [T **show** sb ↔ **up**] to make someone feel embarrassed by behaving in a stupid or unacceptable way when you are with them〔因舉止失當〕使某人羞於與之為伍, 使別人難堪: *Why must you always show me up at these occasions?* 你為甚麼總是在這些場合令我難堪呢?

show² *n*

1 ►PERFORMANCE 表演◄ [C] an entertaining performance, especially one that includes singing, dancing, or jokes〔尤指包括唱歌、舞蹈、笑話的〕娛樂表演, 演出: *She is appearing in a show on Broadway.* 她正在百老匯參加演出。| *Cowan's one-man show opens on April 16th.* 考恩的個人表演從4月16日開始。—see also 另見 FLOOR SHOW

2 ►TV/RADIO 電視/無線電◄ a programme on television or on the radio〔電視或無線電廣播的〕節目: *She's been in a lot of popular TV shows.* 她出演過很多流行電視節目。| *comedy shows* 喜劇節目 | **chat/talk show** (=a show on which well-known people talk about their lives, work etc) 談話[漫談]節目; 〔由知名人士談他們的生活、工作等〕脱口秀 | **game show** (=a show in which people play games for prizes) 遊戲節目〔一種有獎遊戲〕|

quiz show (=a show in which people compete to answer questions) 問答遊戲節目〔要參賽者回答問題的競賽節目〕

3 ►A COLLECTION OF THINGS 收集物◄ [C] an occasion when a lot of similar things are brought together in one place so that people can come and look at them, or so that they can compete against each other; EXHIBITION〔供參觀或進行評比的〕展覽會, 展評(會): **flower/dog etc show** *The annual pet show takes place in August.* 一年一度的寵物展覽在八月份舉行。| *Are you entering your pony in the show?* 你準備為你的小馬報名參展嗎? | **fashion/air etc show** *We have a stand at the 1996 travel show.* 我們在1996年旅遊展覽會上設有一個攤位。| *exhibits at the Motor Show* 汽車展覽會上的展品 | **hold/put on/stage a show** *The gallery is holding a major show of her work next month.* 該畫廊將在下月舉辦一個她的作品的大型展覽會。

4 be on show to be shown to the public 在陳列, 在展出: *The painting will be on show until the end of the month.* 這幅畫將展出到這個月底。| *Frink's works will go on show next week.* 弗林克的作品將在下星期開始展出。

5 ►FEELINGS/QUALITIES 感情/質量◄ **a show of** [C] something that shows what something is like, how someone feels etc; DISPLAY OF 顯示, 表示: *a little show of bad temper* 發點小脾氣 | **a show of strength/force** *Their army staged a big military parade as a show of strength.* 他們的軍隊舉行盛大軍事檢閱以顯示其軍力。

6 [singular,U] something you do to pretend to other people that something is true; PRETENCE 假裝, 假象: **[+of]** *"Oh, no. I don't mind," she said, with a show of cheerfulness.* "啊, 不, 我不介意。"她裝出高興的樣子說。| **make a show of/put on a show of** *I made a show of interest, but I didn't really care what happened.* 我表面上裝作感興趣, 其實對發生了甚麼我並不在乎。| **for show** *We went through a marriage ceremony, but it was all for show, to convince the authorities.* 我們舉行了婚禮, 但這只是做給別人看的, 以便取得當局的信任。

7 ►EVENT/SITUATION 事件/情況◄ *informal singular* a place or situation where something is being done or organized【非正式】事情, 活動: **run the show** (=be in charge of something) 負責某事, 主管 *Who's running this show, you or me?* 誰負責這次活動, 是你還是我?

8 put up a good/poor etc show *informal* to perform, play etc well or badly【非正式】表現得好/差: *Our team put up a pretty good show, but we lost in the end.* 我們隊發揮得相當好, 但最後還是輸了。

9 let's get this show on the road *spoken* used to tell people it is time to start working or start a journey【口】咱們幹起來吧; 咱們出發吧

10 (jolly) good show *BrE old-fashioned spoken* used to express your approval of something【英, 過時, 口】幹得好! 真棒! 真不錯!〔用以表示讚賞〕—see also 另見 **steal the show** (STEAL[1] (3))

show³ *adj* **show-house/-flat** *BrE* a house or apartment that has been built and filled with furniture to show buyers what similar new houses or apartments look like【英】〔配有家具向顧客展示的〕樣板房; 樣板公寓, 示範單位

show and tell /,· · '·/ *n* [U] an activity for school children in which they bring an object to school and tell the other children about it "展示和講述"課〔小學教學的一種課堂練習形式, 學生帶一件實物到班上向同學展示並講述與該物有關的事〕: *Ramona brought in a fossil for show and tell.* 拉蒙娜帶了一塊化石去上"展示和講述"課。

show·biz /ˈʃo,bɪz; ˈʃəʊbɪz/ *n* [U] *informal* SHOW BUSINESS【非正式】演藝界

show busi·ness /'· ,··/ also 又作 **showbiz** *informal*【非正式】*n* [U] the entertainment industry, for example television, films, popular theatre etc 娛樂界, 演藝界, 娛樂性行業〈如電視、電影等〉: *Some of the biggest names in show business will be at the gala.* 娛樂界的一些名人將出席這次盛會。

show·case /ˈʃo,kes; ˈʃəʊkeɪs/ *n* [C] **1** an event or situation that is designed to show the good qualities of a person, organization, product etc 顯示優點的地方[機會]: **[+for]** *The new musical is a good showcase for her talents.* 這齣新的音樂劇是她展示才華的好機會。**2** a glass box containing objects for people to look at in a shop, at an art show etc 玻璃陳列櫃, 櫥窗 —**showcase** *v* [T]

show·down /ˈʃo,daun; ˈʃəʊdaʊn/ *n* [C usually singular 一般用單數] a meeting, argument, fight etc that will settle a disagreement or competition that has continued for a long time 攤牌, 決一雌雄: *Sunday's game will be a showdown between the two leading teams.* 星期天的比賽將是這兩支積分領先球隊決一雌雄的一戰。| **[+with]** *a showdown with the striking auto workers* 與罷工的汽車工人攤牌

show·er¹ /ˈʃauɚ; ˈʃaʊə/ *n* [C] 2

1 ►FOR WASHING IN 洗澡用◄ a thing that you stand under to wash your whole body 淋浴用的噴頭, 淋浴器: *Why does the phone always ring when I'm in the shower?* 為甚麼在我淋浴時電話鈴總要響起來?

2 ►ACT OF WASHING 洗澡◄ an act of washing your body while standing under a shower 淋浴: *I need a shower.* 我需要洗個淋浴。| **take a shower** *especially AmE*【尤美】**have a shower** *especially BrE*【尤英】: *Nick rolled out of bed, took a shower and got dressed.* 尼克翻身起牀, 洗個淋浴, 然後穿上衣服。

3 ►RAIN 雨◄ a short period of rain or snow〔短時間的〕降雨, 陣雨; 降雪: *Heavy showers are forecast in the hills tomorrow.* 預報明天山區有強陣雨。| *a snow shower* 短時間的降雪

4 ►THINGS IN THE AIR 空中的東西◄ a lot of small, light things falling or appearing together〔許多細小而輕的東西〕大量灑落或出現: **[+of]** *Peter kicked the fire and sent up a shower of sparks.* 彼得抬腳去踢那堆火, 揚起了很多火星。

5 ►PARTY 聚會◄ *especially AmE* a party at which presents are given to a woman who is going to get married or have a baby【尤美】〔為將要結婚或分娩的女子舉行的〕送禮會: *We're having a shower for Sherri on Friday.* 我們星期五要為謝麗舉行送禮會。| *a baby shower* 分娩送禮會

6 ►PEOPLE 人◄ *BrE informal* a group of stupid or lazy people【英, 非正式】一羣笨[懶]人

shower² *v* **1** [I] to wash your whole body while standing under a shower 洗淋浴 **2** [I always+adv/prep, T] to scatter a lot of small light things onto a person or place, or to be scattered in this way (使)〔大量細而輕的東西〕灑落: **[+down/over/upon]** *Volcanic dust showered down on the onlookers.* 火山灰灑落在觀看者身上。| **shower sb/sth with** *The branches of the trees showered me with snow.* 樹枝上的雪花灑落在我身上。| **shower sth down/over/on** *Thousands of leaflets were showered over occupied France.* 成千上萬張傳單撒在被佔的法國領土上。**3** to generously give someone a lot of things 給〔某人〕大量東西: **shower sb with sth** *They were set on by a mob that showered them with stones.* 他們遭到一羣暴徒石頭的襲擊。| **shower sth on/upon sb** *Childless herself, she'd shower my kids with toys.* 她自己沒有子女, 常送很多玩具給我的孩子。

shower cap /'·· ·/ *n* [C] a plastic hat that keeps your hair dry in a shower〔防止頭髮被淋濕的〕浴帽

shower gel /'·· ·/ *n* [U] *BrE* a type of liquid soap that you use to wash yourself in a shower【英】浴液

show·er·proof /ˈʃauɚ,pruf; ˈʃaʊəpru:f/ *adj* showerproof clothes keep you dry in light rain but not in heavy rain〔只能防小雨的〕防雨服

show·er·y /ˈʃauərɪ; ˈʃaʊəri/ *adj* raining frequently for short periods 多陣雨的: *a showery day* 陣雨頻繁的一天

show·girl /ˈʃogɝl; ˈʃəʊgɜ:l/ *n* [C] one of a group of women who sing or dance in a musical show〔音樂劇中的〕歌舞女演員

show·ing /ˈʃoɪŋ; ˈʃəʊɪŋ/ *n* **1** [C] an occasion when a film, art show etc can be seen or looked at, especially a special occasion that people are invited to〔電影的〕放映;〔藝術品的〕展覽, 陳列: *a private showing of the film 'King Kong'* 電影《金剛》的私人專場放映 **2** [singular] something that shows how well or how badly you are doing 成績, 表現: **a good/poor showing** *Their poor showing in the mid-term elections is being blamed on the President.* 他們在中期選舉中的欠佳表現被歸咎於總統。| **on sb's present/current showing** (=judging by the way they are performing now) 根據某人目前的表現 *On our present showing, we're unlikely to get into the finals.* 根據我們目前的表現, 我們不大可能進入決賽。

show jump·ing /ˈ· ˌ··/ *n* [U] a sport in which horses with riders have to jump a series of fences as quickly and skilfully as possible 騎馬跳越障礙運動 —**show jumper** *n* [C]

show·man /ˈʃomən; ˈʃəʊmən/ *n plural* **showmen** /-mən; -mən/ [C] someone who is good at entertaining people and getting a lot of public attention 善於賣弄並引起公眾注意的人物, 愛出風頭的人物: *In politics it helps to be a bit of a showman.* 喜歡出點風頭在政治上不失為一種有用的手段。

show·man·ship /ˈʃomənˌʃɪp; ˈʃəʊmənʃɪp/ *n* [U] skill at entertaining people and getting public attention 引起公眾注意的技巧

shown /ʃon; ʃəʊn/ the past participle of SHOW

show-off /ˈ· ·/ *n* [C] *informal* someone who always tries to show how clever or skilled they are so that other people will admire them【非正式】喜歡賣弄的人, 愛炫耀自己的人: *Don't be such a show-off!* 不要這樣炫耀自己!

show of hands /ˌ· · ˈ·/ *n* [singular] a vote taken by counting the raised hands of the people at a meeting〔會議上的〕舉手表決: *The dispute was settled with a show of hands.* 這次爭論以舉手表決的方式解決。

show·piece /ˈʃoˌpis; ˈʃəʊpiːs/ *n* [C usually singular 一般用單數] something that an organization, government etc wants people to see, because it is a very good or successful example 成功的典範, 樣板: *The modern languages department is the showpiece of the university.* 現代語言系是這所大學的模範系。| *a showpiece factory* 模範工廠

show·place /ˈʃoˌples; ˈʃəʊpleɪs/ *n* [C] a place which is open to the public because of its beauty, historical interest etc 供參觀的地方, 遊覽勝地

show·room /ˈʃoˌrum; ˈʃəʊrʊm/ *n* [C] a large room where you can look at things that are for sale such as cars or electrical goods〔商品的〕陳列室: *a car showroom* 汽車展廳

show-stop·ping /ˈ· ˌ··/ *adj* a show-stopping performance is extremely good or impressive〔表演〕極精彩的, 令人難忘的: *his show-stopping performance as Stanley Kowalski* 他扮演斯坦利·考威爾斯基的精彩表演 —**showstopper** *n* [C]

show tri·al /ˈ· ˌ··/ *n* [C] an unfair TRIAL[1] (1) that is organized by a government for political reasons, not in order to find out whether someone is guilty〔政府為政治宣傳而舉行的〕儆戒式公審: *inadequacies of the Soviet system that made such show trials necessary* 蘇維埃制度的缺陷使得有必要實施這種儆戒式公審

show·y /ˈʃoɪ; ˈʃəʊi/ *adj* something that is showy is very colourful, big, expensive etc, especially in a way that attracts people's attention 花哨的, 華麗的; 引人注目的: *a showy car* 引人矚目的汽車 —**showily** *adv* —**showiness** *n* [U]

shrank /ʃræŋk; ʃræŋk/ the past tense of SHRINK

shrap·nel /ˈʃræpnəl; ˈʃræpnəl/ *n* [U] small pieces of metal from a bomb, bullet etc that are scattered when it explodes〔炸彈、子彈等炸開後的〕彈片, 榴霰彈 (彈片): *Robert suffers from an old shrapnel wound.* 羅伯特經常感到舊彈傷的疼痛。

shred[1] /ʃrɛd; ʃred/ *n* **1** [C] a small thin piece that is torn or cut roughly from something〔撕下或切下的〕細條, 碎片, 薄片: **[+of]** *a shred of cloth* 碎布條 | *shreds of dried coconut* 乾椰絲 | **tear/rip/cut sth to shreds** *Jackie was so mad with Tom she tore all his letters to shreds.* 傑姬對湯姆非常惱火, 把他所有的信都撕得粉碎。—see picture on page A7 參見A7頁圖 **2 in shreds a)** torn in many places 撕破多處的, 破成碎片的: *My scarf was in shreds after the dog had played with it.* 我的圍巾被狗扯得破爛不堪。**b)** completely ruined 徹底毀掉: *Simon went home with his career in shreds.* 西蒙回家去了, 他的事業一敗塗地。**3** [singular] a very small amount 少量, 些微: **not a shred of proof/evidence/doubt** (=not at all) 沒有絲毫證明/證據/懷疑 | *There's not a shred of evidence to convict him.* 沒有絲毫證據給他定罪。

shred[2] *v* **shredded, shredding** [T] **1** to cut or tear something into small thin pieces 把…切成碎片, 把…撕成細條: *Coleslaw is made with shredded cabbage.* 涼拌卷心菜絲是用切成細絲的卷心菜做的。**2** to put a document into a shredder 把〔文件〕放進碎紙機切碎: *By the time the police got there the files had all been shredded.* 警察到達那裡時, 檔案已被碎紙機切碎了。

shred·der /ˈʃrɛdɚ; ˈʃredə/ *n* [C] a machine that cuts documents into small pieces so that no one can read them 碎紙機

shrew /ʃru; ʃruː/ *n* [C] **1** a very small animal like a mouse with a long pointed nose 鼩鼱〔鼻子長而尖的鼠狀動物〕 **2** *old use* an unpleasant woman who always argues and disagrees with people【舊】潑婦, 悍婦

shrewd /ʃrud; ʃruːd/ *adj* **1** good at judging what people or situations are really like, especially in a way that makes you successful in business, politics etc〔尤指在生意、政治等方面〕善於判斷的, 精明的, 敏銳的: *Martin's a shrewd judge of character.* 馬丁能敏銳地判斷人的性格。| *a shrewd businesswoman* 精明的女商人 **2** well judged and likely to be right 判斷準確的, 有把握的: *At a shrewd guess, I'd say Henry is going to leave his job.* 我猜亨利十有八九要辭去他的工作。| **have a shrewd idea** (=have an opinion about something that is probably correct) 持有高見 —**shrewdly** *adv*: *"Were you jealous of her?" asked Sara shrewdly.* "你忌妒她嗎?"薩拉尖銳地問道。—**shrewdness** *n* [U]

shrew·ish /ˈʃruɪʃ; ˈʃruːɪʃ/ *adj old use* a shrewish woman is one who always argues and disagrees with people【舊】潑婦般的, 愛罵街的

shriek[1] /ʃrik; ʃriːk/ *v* [I] **1** to make a very high, loud sound 尖叫, 尖聲喊叫: *Judith suddenly shrieked and looked to see what had bitten her.* 朱迪思突然尖叫起來, 看看是甚麼東西咬了她。| **shriek with joy/pain/fright etc** *Everyone was shrieking with laughter in the bar.* 酒吧裡每個人都在開懷大笑。**2** [T] to say something in a high, loud voice because you are excited, afraid, or angry〔由於激動、害怕或憤怒〕大叫大嚷: *Anne stood in the doorway shrieking abuse at him.* 安妮站在門口對他高聲謾罵。

shriek[2] *n* [C] a loud high sound made because you are frightened, excited, angry etc〔由於受驚、興奮、憤怒等的〕尖叫聲: **[+of]** *a shriek of terror* 一聲恐懼的尖叫 | **with a shriek** *Miss Lavish, with a shriek of dismay, dragged her backwards.* 拉維施小姐驚慌地尖叫了一聲, 忙把她往後拖。

shrill[1] /ʃrɪl; ʃrɪl/ *adj* **1** a shrill sound is very high and unpleasant; PIERCING (1)〔聲音〕尖銳的, 刺耳的: *He heard the shrill voice of a woman in the next room.* 他聽到隔壁房間一個女人刺耳的聲音。| *a shrill whistle* 刺耳的汽笛聲 **2** shrill words express repeated, often unreasonable complaints or criticism〔話語等〕反反覆覆而不講道理的; 不斷埋怨的: *We use quiet persuasion rather than shrill denunciation.* 我們採取平心靜氣的說服而不是尖刻粗暴的譴責。—**shrillness** *n* [U] —**shrilly** /ˈʃrɪl-lɪ; ˈʃrɪl-li/ *adv*

shrill[2] *v* **1** *especially literary* [I] to produce a very high and unpleasant sound【尤文】發出尖銳刺耳的聲音: *The telephone shrilled twice.* 刺耳的電話鈴響了兩下。**2** [T] to say something in a very high voice 尖聲說: *"Shame!" she shrilled.* "真可恥!"她尖聲叫道。

shrimp /ʃrɪmp; ʃrɪmp/ *n* [C] **1 a)** *BrE* a small pink sea creature that you can eat, with ten legs and with a soft shell【英】(小) 蝦 **b)** *AmE* a creature like this, but bigger【美】蝦, 大蝦; PRAWN *BrE*【英】**2** *humorous* someone who is very small【幽默】小個子, 矮子

shrimp cock·tail /ˌ· ˈ··/ *n* [C,U] *AmE* shrimps without their shells in a red sauce, eaten before the main part of a meal【美】大蝦冷盤〔一道開胃菜〕; PRAWN COCKTAIL *BrE*【英】

shrimp·ing /ˈʃrɪmpɪŋ; ˈʃrɪmpɪŋ/ *n* [U] the activity of fishing for shrimps 捕 (小) 蝦

shrine /ʃraɪn; ʃraɪn/ *n* [C] **1** a place that is connected with a holy event or holy person, and that people visit to pray 聖壇, 神殿 **2** a place that people visit and respect because it is connected with a famous person or event 聖地: *Elvis's home has become a shrine for his fans.* 皮禮士利的故居成了他的歌迷的聖地。

shrink¹ /ʃrɪŋk; ʃrɪŋk/ *v past tense* **shrank** /ʃræŋk; ʃræŋk/ *past participle* **shrunk** /ʃrʌŋk; ʃrʌŋk/ **1** [I,T] to become smaller or to make something smaller through the effects of heat or water (使) 縮小, (使) 收縮: *Hot water shrinks woollen clothes.* 熱水會使羊毛衣服縮水。| *Will it shrink if I wash it?* 它會縮水嗎? —see also 另見 PRE-SHRUNK, SHRUNKEN **2** [I,T] to become smaller in amount, size or value〔數量、體積或價值〕變小, 減少, 縮小: *The number of students has shrunk from 120 to 70.* 學生人數已從120人減至70人。| *The shrinking pound damages the tourist trade.* 日益貶值的英鎊使旅遊業遭受損失。**3** [I always+adv/prep] *especially literary* to move back and away from something, especially because you are frightened【尤文】〔因恐懼而〕退縮, 畏縮: **[+back/away/from]** *Jenny shrank back against the wall in horror.* 詹妮害怕地後退, 背靠着牆。

shrink from sth *phr v* [T] to avoid doing something difficult or unpleasant 避免做, 不願做〔困難或不愉快的事〕: *I will not shrink from my duties.* 我不會逃避責任。| **shrink from doing sth** *The Prime Minister is unlikely to shrink from making tough decisions.* 首相不大可能優柔寡斷。

shrink² *n* [C] *informal humorous* a PSYCHOANALYST or PSYCHIATRIST【非正式, 幽默】精神分析學家; 精神科醫生

shrink·age /ˈʃrɪŋkɪdʒ; ˈʃrɪŋkɪdʒ/ *n* [C] the act of shrinking, or the amount that something shrinks 縮小; 減少 (量); 收縮 (程度): *a further shrinkage in the size of the workforce* 勞工人數的進一步減少

shrink·ing vi·o·let /ˌ·· ˈ···/ *n* [C] *humorous* someone who is very shy【幽默】羞怯的人

shrink-wrapped /ˌ· ˈ·◂/ *adj* goods that are shrink-wrapped are wrapped tightly in plastic〔用塑料薄膜〕收縮包裝的 —**shrink-wrap** *n* [U]

shriv·el /ˈʃrɪvl; ˈʃrɪvəl/ also 又作 **shrivel up** *v* **shrivelled, shrivelling** *BrE*【英】, **shriveled, shriveling** *AmE*【美】[I,T] if something shrivels or is shrivelled, it becomes smaller and its surface is covered in lines because it is very dry or old (使) 皺縮; (使) 乾枯; (使) 乾癟: *The grapes are left out in the sun to shrivel up and become raisins.* 葡萄被放在太陽下曬成葡萄乾。—**shrivelled** *adj*: *Mrs Carey was a tiny, shrivelled old lady.* 凱里太太是一位矮小乾癟的老太太。

shroud¹ /ʃraud; ʃraʊd/ *n* [C] **1** a cloth that is wrapped around a dead person's body before it is buried 壽衣, 裹屍布 **2** something that hides or covers something 覆蓋物, 遮蔽物: *The fog rolled in, and a grey shroud covered the city.* 大霧滾滾而來, 一張灰色的天幕籠罩着這個城市。| **[+of]** *A shroud of silence surrounded the general's death.* 將軍之死籠罩在一片靜默中。

shroud² *v* **1 be shrouded in mist/smoke etc** to be covered and hidden by mist, smoke etc 被霧/煙等籠罩着: *The black streets were shrouded in fog.* 大霧籠罩着黑沉沉的街道。**2 be shrouded in mystery/secrecy etc** to be mysterious, secret etc 籠罩在神祕/祕密之中: *The origins of this ritual are shrouded in mystery.* 這種儀式的起源被蒙上了神祕的色彩。

Shrove Tues·day /ˌʃrov ˈtjuzdɪ; ˌʃrəʊv ˈtjuːzdi/ *n* [C,U] the day before the first day of the Christian period of Lent, when people traditionally eat PANCAKES〔基督教的〕懺悔星期二,〔基督教〕大齋首日的前一天

shrub /ʃrʌb; ʃrʌb/ *n* [C] a small bush with several woody stems 灌木 (叢)

shrub·be·ry /ˈʃrʌbərɪ; ˈʃrʌbəri/ *n* [C,U] shrubs planted close together in a group, or a part of a garden where shrubs grow 灌木叢;〔花園裡的〕灌木栽植地

shrug¹ /ʃrʌg; ʃrʌg/ *v* [I,T] to raise and then lower your shoulders in order to show that you do not know something or do not care about something 聳 (肩)〔表示不知道或不感興趣〕

shrug 聳肩 3

shrug ↔ sth **off** *phr v* [T] to treat something as unimportant and not worry about it〔認為不重要而〕不予理會, 對…不屑一顧: *We can't just shrug these objections off.* 我們不能不理會這些反對意見呀。

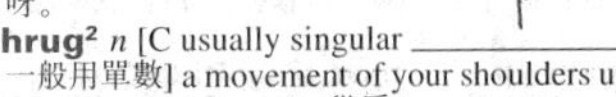

shrug² *n* [C usually singular 一般用單數] a movement of your shoulders upwards and then downwards again 聳肩

shrunk /ʃrʌŋk; ʃrʌŋk/ the past tense and past participle of SHRINK

shrunk·en /ˈʃrʌŋkən; ˈʃrʌŋkən/ *adj* [usually before noun 一般用於名詞前] having become smaller or been made smaller 萎縮的, 收縮的, 乾癟的: *a shrunken old woman* 乾癟的老太太

shtick, schtick /ʃtɪk; ʃtɪk/ *n* [U] *AmE* the style of humour that a particular actor or COMEDIAN typically uses【美】滑稽逗笑風格

shuck /ʃʌk; ʃʌk/ *v* [T] *AmE* to remove the outer cover of a vegetable such as corn or PEAS, or the shell of OYSTERS or CLAMS【美】剝去〔穀物、豆類的〕外殼, 去莢; 剝去〔牡蠣或蛤蜊〕殼

shuck off *phr v* [T] *AmE informal* to take off a piece of clothing【美, 非正式】脫掉〔一件衣服〕: *She shucked off her jacket and ran upstairs.* 她脫掉夾克, 跑上樓去。

shucks /ʃʌks; ʃʌks/ *interjection AmE old-fashioned* used to show you are a little disappointed about something【美, 過時】唉! 糟了!〔表示有點失望〕

shud·der¹ /ˈʃʌdə; ˈʃʌdə/ *v* [I] **1** to shake uncontrollably for a short time because you are frightened, or cold, or because you think something is very unpleasant〔因恐懼、寒冷等而短暫地〕打顫, 顫抖: **[+at]** *He touched Ralph's bare shoulder and Ralph shuddered at the human contact.* 他摸摸拉爾夫赤裸的肩膀, 拉爾夫嚇得顫了一下。**2** if a vehicle or machine shudders, it shakes violently〔車輛或機器〕劇烈震動, 顫動: *The train shuddered to a halt.* 火車劇烈震動了一下便停住了。**3 I shudder to think** used to say that you do not want to think about something because it is too unpleasant 一想到…就顫抖〔用於表示想到不願想的某種不愉快之事〕: *I shudder to think what they'll say when they see the mess the house is in.* 一想到他們看見房子這樣髒亂會說些甚麼, 我就心裡打顫。

shudder at *phr v* [T] to think that something is very bad or unpleasant 對…感到恐懼: *Modern doctors shudder at treatments such as bleeding people with leeches.* 現代醫生對用水蛭給病人放血之類的療法感到恐懼。

shudder² *n* [C usually singular 一般用單數] a shaking movement 戰慄, 發抖: *The building gave a sudden* *shudder.* 這幢大樓突然顫動了一下。

shuf·fle[1] /ˈʃʌfḷ; ˈʃʌfəl/ *v* **1** [I always+adv/prep] to walk very slowly and noisily, without lifting your feet off the ground 拖着腳步走, 緩慢地走: **[+along/towards/down etc]** *The old man shuffled along the sidewalk.* 那位老人拖着步子在人行道上慢慢地走。| *The class came shuffling in from the playground.* 全班學生從操場慢吞吞地走了進來。—see picture on page A24 參見A24頁圖 **2** [T] to move something such as papers into a different order or into different positions 把〔文件等〕移來移去, 反覆改變...的順序[位置]: *Jack sat nervously shuffling the papers around on his desk.* 傑克緊張地坐在那裡, 不停地亂翻桌子上的文件。**3** [I,T] to mix PLAYING CARDS around into a different order before playing a game with them 洗〔牌〕: *Is it my turn to shuffle?* 輪到我洗牌了嗎? **4 shuffle your feet** to move your feet slightly, especially because you are bored or embarrassed〔尤指因厭煩或尷尬而〕移動雙足: *Malcolm shuffled his feet and apologized again.* 馬爾科姆尷尬地來回移動着雙腳, 再一次表示歉意。—**shuffler** *n* [C] —see also 另見 RESHUFFLE[1]

shuffle[2] *n* **1** [singular] a slow walk in which you do not lift your feet off the ground 拖着腳步走 **2** [C] the act of mixing cards into a different order before playing a game 洗牌

shuf·fle·board /ˈʃʌfḷˌbɔrd; ˈʃʌfəlbɔːd/ *n* [U] a game played in the US in which you use a long stick to push a flat round object towards an area with numbers on it〔美國的〕推移板遊戲〔用長的推桿把圓盤推入標有號碼的得分區〕

shuf·ti /ˈʃuftɪ; ˈʃʊfti/ *n* **have a shufti** *BrE spoken* to have a quick look at something【英口】瞥上一眼, 瞥視

shun /ʃʌn; ʃʌn/ *v* [T] to avoid someone or something deliberately〔故意〕避開〔某人或某物〕, 躲開: *a shy woman who shunned publicity* 避免惹人注意的羞怯女子 | *Victims of the disease found themselves shunned by society.* 這種病的受害者發現社會上的人都躲着他們。

shunt[1] /ʃʌnt; ʃʌnt/ *v* [T] **1** to move a train or railway carriage onto a different track 使〔火車〕轉軌 **2** to move someone or something to another place, especially in a way that seems unfair 將〔某人或某物〕轉移至另一地方〔尤指帶有不公正的意味〕: **shunt sb off/around/aside etc** *Smith was shunted off to one of the company's smaller offices.* 史密斯被調到公司屬下一個較小的辦事處。

shunt[2] *n* [C] an act of moving a train or railway carriage to a different track 調軌, 轉軌

shush /ʃʌʃ; ʃʊʃ/ *v* **1 shush!** *spoken* used to tell someone, especially a child, to be quiet【口】噓! 安靜!〔尤指叫小孩安靜〕: *"Shush!" said Jerry, "Not so loud."* "噓!" 傑里說, "別這麼大聲。" **2** [T] to tell someone to be very quiet, especially by putting your fingers against your lips or by saying 'shush' 使安靜, 使肅靜〔尤指以手指抵住雙唇或發"噓"聲表示〕: *He started to cry and Francesca shushed him.* 他哭了起來, 弗朗西斯卡發出"噓"聲要他安靜。

shut[1] /ʃʌt; ʃʌt/ *v past tense and past participle* **shut** *present participle* **shutting** **1** [I,T] to close something, or to become closed (使) 關[合]上, (使) 關閉: *The door shut with a bang.* 門砰的一聲關上了。| *She lay down on her bed and shut her eyes.* 她在牀上躺下, 閉上眼睛。| *Laruelle put the jewels back and shut the lid of the box.* 拉呂埃勒把珠寶放回盒子裡, 合上蓋子。—see 見 OPEN[2] (USAGE) **2 shut sth in the door/drawer etc** to shut a door etc against something so that it gets trapped there 把...夾在門縫裡/抽屜縫裡: *Watch out! You're going to get the cat's tail shut in the door.* 小心! 你要把貓尾巴夾在門縫裡了。**3 shut your mouth/trap/face!** *spoken* used to rudely and angrily tell someone to stop talking【口】閉嘴! 住嘴!〔用於粗暴、生氣地制止別人講話〕 **4 shut it!** *BrE spoken* used to tell someone rudely and angrily to stop talking【英口】住嘴〔用於粗暴地、生氣地制止別人講話〕 **5** [I,T] *especially BrE* to stop being open to the public for a short time or permanently; CLOSE[1] (3)【尤英】(使)〔暫時或永久地〕關門, 停止營業: *The post office shuts at 5 o'clock.* 郵局五點鐘關門。| *He lost his job when they shut the factory.* 他們把工廠關閉以後, 他就失業了。**6 shut your eyes/ears to** to refuse deliberately to notice or pay attention to something〔故意地〕閉眼不看; 不願考慮; 拒不理會: *You simply can't shut your eyes to the truth of the matter.* 你不能對真相置之不理呀。**7 shut your ears to** to deliberately not listen to something 故意不聽某事, 拒不聽某事: *He could not shut his ears to the cries and groans coming from inside the room.* 對房裡傳出的喊聲和呻吟聲, 他無法置若罔聞。

shut sb/sth ↔ **away** *phr v* [T] **a)** to put someone or something in a place away from other people where they cannot be seen 把...關起來, 把...藏起來, 使...與人隔開 **b) shut yourself away** to stay at home or go somewhere quiet, so that you can be alone 把自己關起來, 使自己與別人隔開: *She shut herself away in her room to work on her novel.* 她把自己關在房間裡寫小說。

shut down *phr v* **1** [I,T] if a company, factory, large machine etc shuts down or is shut down, it stops operating (使)〔公司、工廠等〕關閉; (使)〔機器〕停止運轉: *There's a rumor going around that the plant is shutting down next year.* 有傳聞說這個工廠明年要關閉。| *The printing press had been shut down for servicing.* 這台印刷機已被關掉進行維修。**2** [T **shut** sb ↔ **down**] *AmE informal* to prevent an opposing team or player from playing well or getting points【美, 非正式】〔在比賽中〕阻止對方得分[正常發揮]: *We all knew that if we wanted to win we'd have to shut down Bobby Mitchell.* 我們都知道, 如果要贏, 就一定不能讓博比·米切爾得分。

shut sb **in** *phr v* [T] to put or keep someone in a room and stop them from getting out 將〔某人〕關在房內: *The children would be shut in the dormitory at night.* 孩子們晚上都會被關在宿舍裡面不得外出。

shut off *phr v* **1** [I,T] if a machine, tool etc shuts off or if you shut it off, it stops operating (把)〔機器〕關掉: *The machine shuts off automatically if it gets too hot.* 這台機器在溫度過高時會自動關掉。| **shut sth ↔ off** *I let the engine run for a minute and then shut it off.* 我讓發動機運轉一分鐘, 然後把它關掉。**2** [T **shut** sth ↔ **off**] to prevent goods or supplies from being available or being delivered 切斷〔商品、物資等的〕供應: *a strike that closed the mines and shut off coal supplies* 一次使礦井關閉和煤供應中斷的罷工 **3 shut yourself off** to avoid meeting and talking to other people 使自己與...隔絕: **[+from]** *After her last movie, Garbo shut herself off from the world.* 拍完她最後一部電影, 嘉寶便退隱了。**4 be shut off from** to be separated from other people or things, especially so that you are not influenced by them〔尤指為了不受別人影響而〕與...隔絕: *The valley is completely shut off from the modern world by a range of high mountains.* 高山使這個山谷與現代世界完全隔絕。

shut sb/sth **out** *phr v* [T] **1** [**shut** sb ↔ **out**] to deliberately not let someone join you in an activity or share your thoughts and feelings〔故意〕把某人排斥在外: *I felt I was being shut out from all the family's affairs.* 我覺得我正被排斥在一切家庭事務之外。| *How can I help you if you just keep shutting me out all the time?* 如果你總是把我排除在外, 我又怎麼能幫你? **2** [**shut** sb/sth ↔ **out**] to prevent someone or something from entering a place 不讓...進入, 擋住: *Paula packed the bottom of the doors with blankets to shut out the draught.* 波拉用毛毯塞住門底的空隙, 把風堵在門外。| *heavy curtains that shut out the sunlight* 擋住陽光的厚窗簾 **3** [**shut** sth ↔ **out**] to stop yourself from thinking about or noticing something, so that you are not affected by it 不去想〔某事〕, 排除〔干擾〕, 使自己不受...影響: *When she's reading, she seems to be able to shut out the rest of the world.* 她在讀書時似乎能夠完全不受外界的干擾。**4** [**shut out**

sb] *AmE* to defeat an opposing team and prevent them from getting any points【美】〔在比賽中〕獲勝並使〔對方〕不能得分: *The Chicago Bears shut out the Broncos.* 野馬隊連一分都得不到, 被芝加哥熊隊打得一敗塗地。

shut up *phr v* **1 shut up!** *spoken* used to tell someone rudely to stop talking【口】閉嘴! 住嘴! 別說了!: *Oh, shut up! I don't want to hear your excuses.* 噢, 別說了! 我不想聽你的藉口。| **[+about]** *We know you won, but just shut up about it, okay!* 我們知道你贏了, 不要再講了, 行不行! **2 [T shut** sb **up]** to make someone stop talking or be quiet 使〔某人〕停止講話, 堵住〔某人〕的嘴: *The only way to shut Philippa up was to give her something to eat.* 要菲莉帕不講話, 唯一的辦法就是拿甚麼吃的堵上她的嘴。**3 [T shut up** sb**]** to keep someone in a place away from other people, and prevent them from leaving 把〔某人〕隔離: *I've had a terrible cold and been shut up in my room for a week.* 我患了重感冒, 只好在房間裡關了一個星期。**4 [T shut** sth **↔ up]** to close a shop, room etc so that people cannot get into it 關閉〔商店、房間等〕: *Bernadette cleaned the attic and then shut it up for another year.* 伯納黛特把閣樓打掃乾淨, 然後又把它關了一年。**5 shut up shop** *informal BrE* to close a business or stop working, at the end of the day or permanently【非正式, 英】〔商店在一天營業結束後〕關門, 打烊;〔永久地〕停業;〔工作暫時或永久〕停止

shut² *adj* [not usually before noun 一般不用於名詞前] **1** not open; closed 關閉的, 關上的: *Is the door shut properly?* 門關好了嗎? | *He sat with his eyes shut.* 他閉上眼睛坐着。| **blow/slam/bang shut** *The door slammed shut behind him.* 那扇門在他身後砰的一聲關上。| **pull/kick/slide etc sth shut** *Jenny pulled the window shut.* 珍妮把窗戶拉上。**2** *BrE* not open for business【英】〔商店〕停止營業的, 關門的; closed *AmE*【美】: *It's 6.30 pm and the banks are shut.* 現在是下午六點半, 銀行已經關門了。| **[+for]** *The first four hotels we tried were shut for the winter.* 我們最早聯繫過的四家旅館冬季都停止營業。

shut·down /ˈʃʌtˌdaun; ˈʃʌtdaʊn/ *n* [C] the closing of a factory, business, or piece of machinery〔工廠、生意的〕停止, 停業, 關閉;〔機器的〕停止運轉: *the shutdown of several power stations* 幾家電廠的關閉

shut-eye /ˈ· ·/ *n* [U] *informal* sleep【非正式】睡覺: *I've got to get some shut-eye.* 我得去睡一會兒。

shut-in /ˈ· ·/ *n* [C] *AmE* someone who is ill or DISABLED and cannot leave their house very easily【美】〔因病、殘而〕不能隨意外出的人: *visiting the sick and shut-ins* 探訪臥病在家和不方便出門的人

shut-out /ˈ· ·/ *n* [C] *AmE* a game in which one team is prevented by the other from getting any points【美】不讓對方得分的比賽

shut·ter /ˈʃʌtɚ; ˈʃʌtə/ *n* [C] **1** [usually plural 一般用複數] one of a pair of wooden or metal covers on the outside of a window that can be closed to keep light out or prevent thieves from coming in 百葉窗; 窗板 —see picture on page A4 參見 A4 頁圖 **2** a part of a camera that opens for a very short time to let light onto the film〔照相機的〕快門, 遮光器 **3 put up the shutters** *BrE informal* to close a business at the end of the day or permanently【英, 非正式】〔暫時或永久性地〕停止營業; 打烊; 關門

shut·ter·bug /ˈʃʌtɚˌbʌg; ˈʃʌtəbʌg/ *n* [C] *AmE informal* someone who likes to take a lot of photographs【美, 非正式】攝影愛好者, 攝影迷

shut·tered /ˈʃʌtɚd; ˈʃʌtəd/ *adj* with closed shutters, or having shutters 關上百葉窗的; 裝有百葉窗的: *A gust of wind shook the shuttered windows.* 一陣狂風吹得百葉窗搖搖晃晃。

shut·tle¹ /ˈʃʌtl; ˈʃʌtl/ *n* [C] **1** a plane, bus, or train that makes regular short journeys between two places〔飛機、公共汽車或火車的〕短程穿梭運行: *He took the Washington-New York shuttle.* 他乘坐華盛頓—紐約的穿梭客機。**2** a SPACECRAFT that can fly into space and return to Earth, and can be used more than once; SPACE SHUTTLE〔可以多次使用的〕航天飛機, 太空穿梭機 **3 shuttle service** a plane, bus, or train service that goes regularly between two places that are fairly near each other〔飛機、公共汽車、火車的〕短程穿梭服務, 往返運輸業務: *There's a shuttle service from the city center to the airport.* 市中心和飛機場之間有往返的班車。**4** a pointed tool used in weaving, to pass a thread over and under the threads that form the cloth〔織布機的〕梭子 **5 shuttle diplomacy** international talks, for example to make a peace agreement, carried out by someone who travels between countries and talks to members of the governments 穿梭外交(活動)

shuttle² *v* **1** [I always+adv/prep] to travel frequently between two places 穿梭往返(兩地): **[+between/back and forth]** *Susan shuttles between Rotterdam and London for her job.* 蘇珊因為工作穿梭來往於鹿特丹和倫敦兩地。**2** [T] to move people from one place to another place that is fairly near 短程穿梭運送〔人〕: *The passengers were shuttled to the hotel by bus.* 旅客由班車送到酒店。

shut·tle·cock /ˈʃʌtḷˌkɑk; ˈʃʌtlkɒk/ *n* [C] a small light object that you hit over the net in the game of BADMINTON 羽毛球; BIRDIE¹ (3) *AmE*【美】—see picture on page A23 參見 A23 頁圖

shy¹ /ʃaɪ; ʃaɪ/ *adj* **1** nervous and embarrassed about talking to other people, especially people you do not know〔尤指在陌生人面前〕羞怯的, 靦腆的: *Billy's very shy with adults, but he's fine with other children.* 比利在大人面前很害羞, 但和其他孩子在一起時就不這樣。| *a shy smile* 靦腆的微笑 | **painfully shy** (=extremely shy) 極其羞怯的 *At 15, I was painfully shy.* 我在 15 歲時靦腆得很。| **be too shy to do sth** *I needed a ride home but was too shy to ask anyone.* 我想搭便車回家, 但不好意思向別人提出來。| **go all shy** *spoken* (=suddenly become very shy)【口】突然變得很害羞 *Look, she's gone all shy – stop teasing her!* 你看, 她已經很難為情了, 不要再拿她開玩笑了! **2** unwilling to do something or get involved in something 不願意的: **[+about/of]** *Men are often shy about sharing their problems.* 男人常常不願意把自己的問題告訴別人。| *Madonna is certainly not shy of publicity.* 麥當娜絕對不怕出名。**3** [not before noun 不用於名詞前] *especially AmE* less than the amount needed【尤美】不足的, 未達到所需數量的: **[+of]** *He was only 30 votes shy of the number he needed for the nomination.* 他只差 30 票就達到被提名所需的票數。**4 fight shy of (doing) sth** to avoid doing something or getting involved in something 避免做某事, 避免介入某事: *He fought shy of an open quarrel.* 他避免公開爭吵。**5** shy animals get frightened easily and are unwilling to come near people〔動物〕易受驚的, 不願近人的, 膽怯的 —see also 另見 **once bitten twice shy** (BITE¹ (13)), CAMERA-SHY —**shyly** *adv*: *"I have a question," she said, shyly stroking Ralph's arm.* "我有個問題。" 她說, 羞怯地撫着拉爾夫的手臂。—**shyness** *n* [U]

shy² *v* **1** if a horse shies, it makes a sudden movement away from something because it is frightened〔馬〕驚退, 驚跳 **2** [T] *old-fashioned* to throw a ball or other object at something【過時】向…投, 擲, 扔〔球等〕

shy away from sth *phr v* [T] to avoid doing something because you are not confident enough or you are worried or nervous about it〔因缺乏信心, 擔心或緊張而〕迴避, 避開: *They criticized the leadership, but shied away from a direct challenge.* 他們批評領導層, 但避免進行正面質疑。

shys·ter /ˈʃaɪstɚ; ˈʃaɪstə/ *n* [C] *AmE informal* a dishonest person, especially a lawyer or politician【美, 非正式】奸詐的人〔尤指律師或政客〕

Si·a·mese cat /ˌsaɪəmiz ˈkæt; ˌsaɪəmiːz ˈkæt/ *n* [C] a type of cat that has blue eyes, short grey or brown fur, and a dark face 暹羅貓

Siamese twin /ˌ··· ˈ·/ *n* [C usually plural 一般用複數]

one of two people who are born joined to each other 連體雙胞胎, 暹羅孿生子

sib·i·lant¹ /ˈsɪbḷənt; ˈsɪbḷənt/ *adj formal* making or being an "s" or "sh" sound【正式】發出嘶嘶的: *a sibilant, fluttering voice* 顫動的嘶嘶聲

sibilant² *n* [C] *technical* a sibilant sound such as /ʃ/ in English【術語】英語中的嘶音〔如/ʃ/〕

sib·ling /ˈsɪblɪŋ; ˈsɪblɪŋ/ *n* [C] **1** *formal* a brother or sister【正式】兄弟或姊妹 **2 sibling rivalry** competition between brothers and sisters for their parents' attention or love 同胞競爭, 手足相爭〔指兄弟姐妹為得到父母的關注或愛的競爭〕

sib·yl /ˈsɪbḷ; ˈsɪbɪl/ *n* [C] one of a group of women in the ancient world who were thought to know the future〔古代的〕女預言家, 女先知

sic¹ /sɪk; sɪk/ *adv Latin* used after a word that you have copied in order to show that you know it was not spelled or used correctly【拉丁】原文如此〔置於所引用文字之後, 表示雖知該詞有錯誤, 卻是原文〕: *We had seen several signs that said 'ORANGE'S (sic) FOR SALE'.* 我們看到幾個牌子寫着 ORANGE'S〔原文如此〕FOR SALE。

sic² *v* [T] *AmE informal*【美, 非正式】**1** to tell a dog to attack someone 嗾使〔狗〕去攻擊: *He sicced his dog on me.* 他嗾使他的狗來攻擊我。**2 sic 'em!** *spoken* used to tell a dog to attack someone【口】咬他! 追他!〔嗾使狗攻擊某人〕

S1 W3 **sick¹** /sɪk; sɪk/ *adj*

1 ▶ILL 生病的◀ suffering from a disease or illness 有病的, 患病的: *Where's Sheila – is she sick?* 希拉在哪兒 — 她病了嗎? | *a sick child* 病孩 | **get sick** *AmE* (=become ill)【美】生病, 患病 *At the last minute I got sick and couldn't go.* 我在最後一刻病倒, 結果不能去。| **sick as a dog** (=very sick) 病得很重 *Pete's at home in bed, sick as a dog.* 皮特在家臥牀不起, 病得很重。| **be off sick** (=be away from work or school because you are ill) 因病缺勤[缺課] *I was off sick for four days with the flu.* 我因患流感休了四天病假。| **call in sick** (=telephone to say you are not coming to work because you are ill) 打電話請假 *You have to call in sick before 9.30.* 必須在9點30分之前打電話請病假。| **take sick** *old-fashioned* (=become ill)【過時】生病 *He took sick and died a week later.* 他得了病, 一個星期後死了。— see graph at 參見 ILL¹ 圖表

2 be sick to bring food up from your stomach through your mouth; VOMIT 嘔吐: *The cat's been sick on the carpet.* 貓吐在地毯上了。| *You'll be sick if you eat any more of that chocolate!* 你如果再多吃一口那種巧克力, 你就要吐了。| **violently sick** (=suddenly and severely sick) 突然嘔吐得厲害 *I was violently sick the last time I ate prawns.* 我上次吃了大蝦以後, 吐得很厲害。

3 feel sick also 又作 **be/feel sick to your stomach** to feel as if you are going to VOMIT 反胃的, 噁心的, 作嘔的: *As soon as the ship started moving I began to feel sick.* 輪船一開動, 我就開始覺得想吐了。—see also 另見 CARSICK, SEASICK, TRAVEL-SICK

4 be sick (and tired) of also 又作 **be sick to death of** to be angry and bored with something that has been happening for a long time 對...感到厭煩的, 膩煩的, 厭倦的: *I'm really sick of housework!* 我對家務活厭倦透了。| *We're getting sick and tired of listening to them argue all the time.* 一天到晚聽着他們爭論, 我們都感到膩煩得很。

5 be worried sick/be sick with worry to be extremely worried 極為擔心: *Why didn't you tell me you were coming home late? I've been worried sick!* 你為甚麼不早說你要晚歸? 我都擔心死了!

6 make me/you sick *spoken*【口】**a)** to make you feel very angry 令我/你非常氣憤: *People like you make me sick!* 像你這樣的人真叫我生氣。**b)** *spoken humorous* to make someone feel jealous【口, 幽默】令人眼紅: *You make me sick with your 'expenses paid' holidays!* 你享受"一切費用由公司支付"的度假待遇, 真叫我眼紅。

7 ▶STRANGE/CRUEL 反常的/殘酷的◀ a) someone who is sick does things that are strange and cruel, and seems mentally ill 變態的,〔心理〕不正常的, 精神有病的: *I keep getting obscene phone calls from some sick pervert.* 我不斷收到一個性變態者打來的下流電話。| *a sick mind* 病態的心理 **b)** sick stories, jokes etc deal with death and suffering in a cruel or unpleasant way〔故事、笑話等〕殘忍的, 殘酷的, 可怖的: *Did you see that film 'Brain Dead'? Sick, isn't it ?* 你看過那部叫《新空房禁地》的電影沒有? 真恐怖, 是嗎? | *Has he told you his sick joke about the undertaker?* 他給你講過他那個關於殯儀工人的恐怖笑話沒有?

8 sick as a parrot *BrE spoken humorous* extremely disappointed【英口, 幽默】極為失望的: *"How did you feel when you missed that penalty?" "Sick as a parrot."* "你那次罰球不中有甚麼感覺?" "失望極了。"

9 sick at heart *literary* very unhappy, upset, or disappointed about something【文】很不愉快, 很失望: *I was sick at heart to think that I would never see the place again.* 我想到再也看不到這個地方時, 心裡非常難過。

USAGE NOTE 用法說明: SICK

WOLD CHOICE 詞語辨析: **sick, vomit, throw up, ill, not well, unwell, something wrong with**

In spoken British English to **be sick** is more often used to mean 'to throw up the contents of the stomach through the mouth' than 'to be generally ill'. 在英國英語口語中, be sick 較多用於表示"嘔吐", 而較少用於表示"生病": *If you eat too many sweets you'll be sick.* 如果你吃太多的糖果, 你會嘔吐的。The more formal word in British and American English is **vomit**, and a less formal word is **throw up**. 在英國英語和美國英語中表示"嘔吐"時, 動詞 vomit 的用法比較正式, 而 throw up 則比較口語化。

If you are talking about general illness, especially when you do not say exactly what illness it is, you would usually use **ill** in British English, and **sick** in American English. 表示"生病"但不必具體說明甚麼病時, 英國英語通常用 ill, 而美國英語用 sick: *She's been ill for several days now.* 她生病已有好幾天了。| *You'll end up getting sick if you don't get more rest.* 如果你不多休息, 你最終會生病的。In British and American English you can also use **not well**. 在英國英語和美國英語中都可以用 not well: *Diana hasn't been feeling very well lately.* 戴安娜近來身體一直不大好。

Ill usually has a stronger meaning than **not well**. You may be **not well** because of a bad cold but **ill** with cancer. **Unwell** is a more formal word for **not well** or **ill**. ill 的含義通常要比 not well 強。得了重感冒時可以說是 not well, 但患了癌症則使用 ill。與 not well 或 ill 相比, unwell 是比較正式的用法。

Before a noun **sick** always means 'generally not well' (**ill** and **unwell** are not usually used before a noun). 用於名詞前時, sick 表示"生病的"〔但 ill 和 unwell 通常不用於名詞之前〕: *He's gone to visit his sick mother.* 他已去探望他生病的母親了。

When you want to talk about a particular part of the body that is hurt or has a disease you can say there is **something wrong with...**. 要表示身體某部分受了傷或有病時, 可以用 there is something wrong with...: *Tommy can't play today – there's something wrong with his knee.* (NOT 不用 *He has a sick knee* | *he is sick with his knee*). 湯米今天不能打球了 — 他膝部有點不適。

SPELLING 拼寫

Note that **homesick** is written as one word. 注意 homesick 需拼作一個單詞。

sick² *n* **1 the sick** people who are ill 病人, 生病的人: *The sick and wounded were allowed to go free.* 傷病員獲得釋放。**2** [U] *BrE informal* VOMIT【英, 非正式】嘔吐物

sick³ *v*

sick sth ↔ **up** *phr v* [T] *BrE informal* to bring up food from your stomach; VOMIT¹【英, 非正式】嘔吐

sick·bay /ˈsɪkˌbe; ˈsɪkbeɪ/ *n* [C] a room on a ship, in a school etc where there are beds for people who are sick〔船上、學校等的〕醫務室

sick·bed /ˈsɪkˌbɛd; ˈsɪkbed/ *n* [C usually singular 一般用單數] the bed where a sick person is lying 病牀: *The president carried on working from his sickbed.* 總裁臥病在牀還繼續工作。

sick·en /ˈsɪkən; ˈsɪkən/ *v* **1** [T] to make you feel shocked and angry, especially because you strongly disapprove of something 使厭惡; 使氣憤: *The idea of organized dog fights sickens me.* 組織鬥狗的主意使我噁心。| *All decent people should be sickened by such a pointless waste of lives.* 一切正直的人都應對這種毫無意義的浪費生命感到憤慨。**2 be sickening for something** *spoken especially BrE* to start to have an illness and show signs of having it【口, 尤英】開始生病, 有生病的症狀: *I think Tommy must be sickening for something, the way he's been moping around.* 看他那副無精打采到處轉悠的樣子, 我想湯米可能得甚麼病了。**3** [I] *old-fashioned* to gradually become very ill【過時】病情逐漸加重: *The older people just sickened and died as food supplies ran low.* 食品供應減少時, 老人的病情加重, 相繼死亡。

sicken of sth *phr v* [T] to lose your desire for something or your interest in it 對…感到厭煩, 對…失去興趣: *He finally sickened of the endless round of parties and idle conversation.* 他終於對那一連串無休止的聚會和閒聊感到厭煩了。

sick·en·ing /ˈsɪkənɪŋ; ˈsɪkənɪŋ/ *adj* **1** very shocking, annoying, or upsetting; DISGUSTING 令人震驚的, 令人厭惡的, 令人作嘔的: *Local police said it was one of the most sickening attacks they had come across.* 當地警方說這是他們所遇到過的最令人震驚的襲擊之一。| *their sickening hypocrisy* 他們那令人噁心的虛偽嘴臉 **2 a sickening thud/crash** an unpleasant sound that makes you think someone has been injured or something has been broken 可怕的重擊聲/碰撞聲: *His head hit the floor with a sickening thud.* 他的頭砰的一聲撞在地板上。**3** *BrE spoken* making you feel jealous【英口】令人羨慕的; 令人妒忌的: *"Helen's just bought herself a new BMW." "God, how sickening!"* "海倫剛剛買了一輛新寶馬汽車。" "啊, 真叫人羨慕!" —**sickeningly** *adv*

sick·ie /ˈsɪkɪ; ˈsɪki/ *n* [C] *AustrE & BrE informal* a day when you say that you are ill and do not go to work, even though you are not really ill【澳和英, 非正式】託病休息的一天

sick·le /ˈsɪkḷ; ˈsɪkəl/ *n* [C] a tool with a blade in the shape of a hook, used for cutting wheat or long grass 鐮刀

sickle-cell a·nae·mi·a *BrE*【英】, **sickle-cell anemia** *AmE*【美】/ˌ·· ·ˈ···/ *n* [U] a serious illness that mainly affects black people, in which the blood cells change shape, causing weakness and fever 鐮狀細胞貧血〔患此病者多為黑人〕

sick·ly /ˈsɪklɪ; ˈsɪkli/ *adj* **1** weak, unhealthy, and often ill 虛弱的, 不健康的, 常生病的: *a sickly child* 體質差的孩子 | *a sickly pallor to his face* 他臉色病態的蒼白 **2** a sickly smell, taste etc is unpleasant and makes you feel sick〔氣味等〕令人噁心的: *the sickly odor of rotting garbage* 令人噁心的腐爛垃圾味

sick·ness /ˈsɪknɪs; ˈsɪknəs/ *n* **1** [U] the state of being ill; ILLNESS 患病: *an insurance policy against long-term sickness and injury* 對長期患病和受傷的保險 | *working days lost due to sickness* 因病損失的工作日 **2** [U] the feeling that you are about to bring up food from your stomach; NAUSEA 嘔吐, 噁心: *A wave of sickness came over him.* 他感到一陣噁心。| **morning sickness** (=sickness that some women get when they are going to have a baby)〔孕婦〕晨吐 | **travel/car/sea/air sickness** (=sickness that some people get while travelling) 旅行眩暈/暈車/暈船/暈機 **3** [C] a particular illness〔某種〕疾病: *They died within a few days of each other, probably from a sickness like the plague.* 他倆在幾天內相繼死去, 也許是死於鼠疫那樣的疾病。**4** [U] the serious problems and weaknesses of a social, political, or economic system〔社會、政治、經濟制度的〕弊病, 不健全狀態: *He said the idea of 'success' was part of the sickness of Western cultures.* 他說, 對"成功"的理解是西方文化弊端的一部分。

sickness ben·e·fit /ˈ·· ˌ···/ *n* [U]*BrE* money paid by the government to someone who is too sick to work【英】〔政府發給因病不能工作的人的〕疾病補助金

sick note /ˈ· ·/ *n* [C] *BrE* a note written by your doctor or your parents saying that you were too sick to go to work or school【英】〔醫生開的〕病假單, 〔父母為子女寫的〕因病請假便條; EXCUSE² (5) *AmE*【美】

sick·o /ˈsɪko; ˈsɪkəʊ/ *n* [C] *slang especially AmE* someone who gets pleasure from things that most people find unpleasant or upsetting【俚, 尤美】有精神病的人, 心理變態的人: *There's plenty of twisted sickos out there who are into kiddie porn.* 有很多心理變態的人沉迷於兒童色情。

sick-out /ˈ· ·/ *n* [C] *AmE* a STRIKE (=protest about pay or working conditions) in which all the workers at a company say they are sick and stay home on the same day【美】集體託病罷工

sick pay /ˈ· ·/ *n* [U] money paid by an employer to a worker who cannot work because of illness 病假工資

sick·room /ˈsɪkˌrum; ˈsɪk-rʊm/ *n* [C] a room where someone who is sick can go to lie down 病房

S1 W1

side¹ /saɪd; saɪd/ *n* [C]

① **PLACE/AREA/POSITION** 地方/區域/位置
② **DIRECTION** 方向
③ **SUBJECT/SITUATION** 主題/形勢
④ **IN A QUARREL/WAR/SPORT** 在吵架/戰爭/體育運動中
⑤ **PEOPLE** 人們
⑥ **SUPPORT** 支持
⑦ **OTHER MEANINGS** 其他意思

① **PLACE/AREA/POSITION** 地方/區域/位置

1 ►PART OF AN AREA 區域的一部分◄ one of the two areas that are on either the left or the right of an imaginary line, or on either the left or the right of a border, wall, river etc〔在想像中的分界線的左或右的〕部分, 地帶, 半; 〔邊界、牆、河等的左或右的〕邊, 面, 側: *Drive on the left-hand side of the road.* 車輛靠道路左側行駛。| *a scar on the right side of his face* 他右邊臉上的傷疤 | *Fuel is cheaper on the French side of the border.* 燃料在法國境內便宜些。| *The south side of town is pretty run-down.* 這個城鎮的南邊相當破舊。| **the far/other side** (=the area furthest from you or opposite you) 另一邊[頭], 那一邊[頭] *I could just see Rita on the far side of the square.* 我勉強能看見在廣場那一邊的麗塔。| **to one side (of)** *Off to one side was a small wooden shed.* 在那邊有間小木屋。

2 ►NEXT TO 在旁邊, 挨着◄ [usually singular 一般用單數] the place or area directly next to someone or something, on the right or the left 身邊, 身旁, 旁邊: *Put the table on the left side of the couch.* 把桌子放在長沙發的左側。| *Stand on this side of me so Dad can get a photo.* 站在我這一側, 好讓爸爸給照張相。| **by/at sb's side** (=beside them) 在某人身旁 *Tyler's daughter walked at his side.* 泰勒的女兒走在他身旁。| **side by side** (=next to each other) 並排地, 肩並肩地 *Two bottles stood side by side on the shelf.* 兩個瓶子並排地放在架子上。| *We walked along the beach, side by side.* 我們並肩沿着海濱走。| **on either side** (=on the left side and the right) 在兩邊, 在兩旁 *On either side of the front gates stood a tall tree.* 前門兩旁各有一棵大樹。

3 ►EDGE 邊緣◄ the part of an object or area that is furthest from the middle, at or near the edge〔物體或範圍的〕邊, 邊緣: *a little store by the side of the highway* 公路邊上的小店 | *a triangle with unequal sides* 不等邊三角形 | *Jack sat down heavily on the side of the bed.* 傑克在牀邊重重地坐了下來。| **roadside/lakeside etc** *a charming hotel on the riverside* 河邊漂亮的旅店 —see also 另見 SEASIDE

4 ►OF A BUILDING/OBJECT/VEHICLE ETC 屬於建築物/物體/車輛等的◄ a surface of something that is not its front, back, top, or bottom 側面, 旁邊: *There's an entrance at the side of the building.* 大樓旁邊有個入口。| *The lifeboat was lowered over the ship's side.* 救生艇從船舷放下。| *Someone ran into the side of my car.* 有人撞到我汽車的側面。| *Scrape the batter from the sides of the bowl.* 把碗邊上的麵糊刮掉。

5 ►MOUNTAIN/VALLEY ETC 大山/山谷等◄ one of the sloping areas of a hill, mountain etc 山坡: *an old cave in the side of the valley* 山坡上的古老洞穴 | **hillside/mountainside etc** *sheep grazing on the steep hillside* 在陡峭的山坡上吃草的羊羣

6 ►FLAT SURFACE 平面◄ one of the flat surfaces of something〔物體的〕(一個) 平面: *Which side of the box do you put the label on?* 你把標籤貼在箱子的哪一面? | *A cube has six sides.* 立方體有六個面。

7 ►OF A THIN OBJECT 薄物體的◄ one of the two surfaces of a thin flat object 扁平物體兩面中的任何一面: *Write only on one side of the paper.* 請只在紙的一面上寫。| *I'll paint the other side of the fence tomorrow.* 我將在明天油漆籬笆的另一面。| *Try playing side A of the tape.* 試試放磁帶的 A 面。

8 three-sided/four-sided etc with three sides, four sides etc 三/四邊的: *a five-sided shape* 五邊形 —see also 另見 ONE-SIDED

9 steep-sided/bare-sided etc with a particular type of side 山坡陡峭的/邊上光禿禿的〔用於表示某種類型的坡、邊、面等〕: *a sheer-sided gorge* 兩邊都是懸崖峭壁的峽谷 | *a huge flat-sided rock* 表面平整的巨石

10 ►PAGE 頁◄ *BrE* a page of writing on one side of a piece of paper【英】〔寫上文字的〕一頁; 〔紙張的〕一面: *How many sides have we got to write?* 我們要寫多少頁?

② DIRECTION 方向

11 from side to side moving continuously, first in one direction then in the other 從一邊到另一邊: *The rope bridge swung from side to side in a terrifying manner.* 索橋左右搖晃, 十分嚇人。

12 from all sides from every direction 從各個方向, 從四面八方: *Planes were attacking us from all sides.* 飛機從四面八方向我們發起攻擊。

13 on all sides/on every side in every direction 在各方面, 到處: *We were surrounded on all sides by a wall of flames.* 我們四面八方都被一堵火牆包圍了。| *Gunfire erupted on every side.* 四面八方響起了砲火的轟鳴聲。

③ SUBJECT/SITUATION 主題/形勢

14 one part or feature of a subject, problem, or situation, especially when compared with another part〔主題、問題、形勢的〕一個方面〔尤指與其他方面相比時〕: *Tell me your side of the story.* 請把你對情況的看法告訴我。| *We expect you to keep your side of the bargain.* 我們期望你方信守在這項交易中所作的承諾。| **all/both sides** *Try to look at all sides of the issue.* 要從各個方面考慮這個問題。| **technical/financial/social etc side** *She takes care of the financial side of the business.* 她負責公司財務方面的工作。| **serious/funny etc side** *Can't you see the funny side of all this?* 難道你看不出這件事滑稽的一面嗎?

④ IN A QUARREL/WAR/SPORT 在吵架/戰爭/體育運動中

15 one of the people, groups, or countries opposing each other in a quarrel, war etc〔吵架、交戰等雙方的〕一方: *fighting on the Bosnian side in the civil war* 在內戰中為波斯尼亞一方而戰 | *My sympathy lay on the side of the rebels.* 我同情叛亂者一方。| **take sides** (=choose to support a particular person or opinion) 支持一方, 偏袒一方 *I'm sorry, but I'm not taking sides on this one.* 很抱歉, 但在這個問題上我不能支持一方。| **be on sb's side** (=agree with someone and support them) 站在某人一邊 *Thank God at least you're on my side.* 謝天謝地, 至少你是站在我一邊的。| **whose side are you on?** *spoken* (=used when someone is arguing against you when they should be supporting you)【口】你究竟站在哪一邊?〔用於表示某人本應支持你但卻發表了反對你的意見〕

16 ►IN SPORT 在體育運動方面◄ [also+plural verb *BrE*] *BrE* a sports team【英】運動隊, 球隊: *He plays for the Welsh side.* 他是威爾斯隊球員。

⑤ PEOPLE 人們

17 ►PART OF SB'S CHARACTER 某人性格的一部分◄ [usually singular 一般用單數] one part of someone's character, especially when compared with another part〔某人性格的〕一面〔尤指相對於另一面而言〕: *One side of me is cautious, and another side says go ahead and do it!* 我性格的一面是謹慎, 但另一面卻說"幹吧, 動手幹!" | *It was a side of Shari I hadn't seen before.* 我以前從沒見過莎麗性格的這一面。| **emotional/romantic/funny etc side** *Jeff does have his romantic side, honestly!* 一點不假, 傑夫確有他浪漫的一面。

18 ►PART OF YOUR BODY 身體的一部分◄ the part of your body from your shoulder to the top of your leg〔肩膀以下至大腿上端的〕身體的側邊: *He had a scar running right the way down his side.* 他肋部有一條從上到下的大傷疤。

19 ►OF A FAMILY 家庭的◄ the parents, grandparents etc of your mother or your father 血統, 家系, 父[母]系: *Ken is Scottish on his mother's side.* 肯的母系是蘇格蘭血統。

⑥ SUPPORT 支持

20 not leave sb's side to always be with someone and look after them 永遠照顧某人: *Promise me you'll never leave her side.* 答應我你會永遠照顧她。

21 side by side closely together with each other and helping each other 並排地, 肩並肩地: *We've worked side by side for years.* 我們肩並肩地一道工作好多年了。

⑦ OTHER MEANINGS 其他意思

22 on the high side/the heavy side etc *spoken* a little too high, too heavy etc【口】偏高/偏重等: *Ooh, the price is a bit on the high side, isn't it?* 噢, 這個價錢有點偏高, 不是嗎? | *The sheets are still a little on the damp side.* 這些被單還是有點潮。

23 on the side: a) in addition to your regular job 作為副業, 作為兼職: *Freelancing can help you make a little money on the side.* 當自由撰稿人可以幫助你業餘掙點小錢。—see also 另見 SIDELINE¹ (1) **b)** dishonestly or

S

illegally 暗地裡, 非法地: *Simms didn't seem the type to have a lover on the side.* 西姆斯不像是暗中有情婦的那種人。—see also 另見 **a bit on the side** (BIT[1] (21)) **c)** food that is served on the side is ordered with the main dish in a restaurant, but is not usually part of that dish〔與主菜同時點的〕配菜: *Could I have waffles with an egg on the side?* 我可以要一份華夫餅加雞蛋作配菜嗎?
24 have sth on your side to have an advantage that increases your chances of success 有…方面的優勢, …對某人有利: *Greg has youth on his side, he'll recover.* 格雷格年輕, 他會恢復健康的。| *We've got the law on our side.* 我們有法律的支持。
25 get on the right/wrong side of sb *informal* to make someone very pleased with you or very angry with you【非正式】使某人很高興/生氣: *Be careful not to get on the wrong side of her.* 你要小心別惹她生氣。
26 let the side down *BrE informal* to behave in a way that makes things difficult for your family, team etc, or makes them embarrassed【英, 非正式】使自己的家人或隊友等難堪, 辱沒自己一方: *I'm disappointed in you, Alex, you've really let the side down.* 我對你太失望了, 亞歷克斯, 你真叫大家難堪。
27 ►TV STATION 電視台◄ [usually singular 一般用單數] *BrE informal* a television station; CHANNEL[1] (1)【英, 非正式】電視頻道: *What's on the other side?* 其他頻道有甚麼節目?
28 a side of beef/bacon one half of an animal's body, cut along the BACKBONE and bought for food 牛肋肉/醃熏豬肋肉〔沿脊骨切開供食用的動物的半邊軀體或肋肉〕
29 put/leave/set sth to one side to save something to be dealt with or used later 將…留到以後再用/處理: *Let's leave that question to one side for now.* 咱們暫時把那個問題放在一邊吧。| *Put a little money to one side each week.* 你要每星期都存一點錢。
30 on the right/wrong side of 30, 40 etc *spoken* younger or older than 30, 40 etc【口】不到/已過30歲、40歲等
31 take etc sb to one side to take someone away from other people for a short time for a private talk 把某人拉到一旁〔私下交談〕: *Maybe you can quietly take Pam to one side and ask about Henry.* 也許你可以把帕姆悄悄地拉到一旁, 問他關於亨利的事。
32 on the wrong/right side of the law *informal* breaking/not breaking the law【非正式】犯法/不犯法: *OK, do it, but keep on the right side of the law!* 好, 幹吧, 可別犯法!
33 this side of without going as far as 不去…那麼遠: *It's the best Chinese food this side of Peking.* 除非跑到北京, 否則這就是最好的中國菜了。
34 criticize/scold/curse sb up one side and down the other *AmE spoken* criticize someone, treat them unkindly etc without worrying about how they feel【美口】狠狠地批評/責罵/詛咒某人 —see also 另見 FLIP SIDE, **to be on the safe side** (SAFE[1] (8)), **split your sides** (SPLIT[1] (9)), **two sides of the same coin** (COIN[1] (4)), **the other side of the coin** (COIN[1] (3)), **get out of bed (on) the wrong side** (BED[1] (9)), **err on the side of caution** (ERR (1))

S

side² *adj* [only before noun 僅用於名詞前] **1** in or on the side of something 旁邊的, 側面的: **a side door/panel etc** *Hannah slipped out through a side exit.* 漢納從側門溜了出去。**2** from the side of something 從一側的, 從側面來的: *Can you get a side view?* 你能看到側景嗎? **3 side street/road etc** a street, road etc that is smaller than a main street but is often connected to it〔與大街相連的〕小街, 小巷;〔與幹線相連的〕支路, 岔路, 小路: *He'd found a nice quiet side street off San Vincente.* 他在聖文森特大街旁找到一條安靜的小街。

side³ *v* [I] to support or argue against a person or group in a quarrel, fight etc 站在…一邊, 偏袒…: **[+with/against]** *Frank sided with David against their mother.* 弗蘭克站在大衛一邊反對媽媽。

side·arm /ˈsaɪd,ɑrm; ˈsaɪd-ɑːm/ *n* [C often plural 常用複數] a weapon carried or worn at someone's side, for example a gun or sword〔佩帶在腰間的〕隨身武器〈如手槍或佩劍〉

side·board /ˈsaɪd,bɔrd; ˈsaɪdbɔːd/ *n* **1** [C] a long low piece of furniture usually in a DINING ROOM, used for storing plates, glasses etc〔餐廳裡的〕餐具櫃 **2 sideboards** *BrE* sideburns【英】〔男子的〕鬢角

side·burns /ˈsaɪd,bɜnz; ˈsaɪdbɜːnz/ *n* [plural] hair grown down the sides of a man's face in front of his ears〔男子的〕鬢角 —see picture on page A6 參見A6頁圖

side·car /ˈsaɪd,kɑr; ˈsaɪdkɑː/ *n* [C] a seat, often enclosed, that is joined to the side of a MOTORCYCLE and has a separate wheel〔附在摩托車旁的〕邊車, 跨斗

side dish /ˈ· ·/ *n* [C] a small amount of food such as a SALAD that you eat with a main meal〔正菜以外的〕小菜, 配菜〈如沙拉〉

side ef·fect /ˈ· ·,·/ *n* [C] **1** an effect that a drug has on your body in addition to curing pain or illness〔藥物的〕副作用: *a natural remedy with no harmful side effects* 一種沒有副作用的天然藥物 **2** an unexpected or unplanned result of a situation or event〔事態發展等的〕意外後果; 意想不到的效果: *These policy changes could have beneficial side effects for the whole economy.* 政策的這些改變可能對整個經濟產生良好的效果。

side is·sue /ˈ· ,··/ *n* [C] *especially BrE* a subject or problem that is not as important as the main one, and may take people's attention away from the main subject【尤英】〔可能分散注意力的〕次要問題: *We mustn't let the meeting get bogged down in side issues.* 我們絕對不要在會上就次要問題糾纏不清。

side·kick /ˈsaɪd,kɪk; ˈsaɪd,kɪk/ *n* [C] *informal* someone who spends time with or helps another person, especially when that person is more important than they are【非正式】助手,〔次要的〕夥伴: *He starred as Sherlock Holmes' bumbling sidekick Watson.* 他在影片中扮演夏洛克·福爾摩斯笨手笨腳的助手華生。

side·light /ˈsaɪd,laɪt; ˈsaɪdlaɪt/ *n* [C] *BrE* one of the two small lights next to the main front lights on a car【英】〔汽車的〕側燈〔前燈旁的小燈〕; PARKING LIGHT *AmE*【美】—see picture on page A2 參見A2頁圖

side·line¹ /ˈsaɪd,laɪn; ˈsaɪdlaɪn/ *n* **1** [C] an activity that you do as well as your main job or business in order to earn more money 副業, 兼職: *Zoe does a bit of freelance photography as a sideline.* 佐伊搞一點自由攝影作為副業。**2 on the sidelines** not taking part in an activity even though you want to or should do 旁觀, 不直接參與: *A severe knee injury put him on the sidelines for the rest of the season.* 膝部嚴重受傷使他不能參加本賽季其餘的比賽了。| *You can't stay on the sidelines for ever; it's time you got involved.* 你總不能永遠旁觀呀, 這是你親身體驗的時候了。**3 sidelines** [plural] the area just outside the lines that form the edge of a sports field〔球場等的〕界外地區, 場外: *Beckenbauer stood on the sidelines shouting instructions to his team.* 碧根鮑華站在場邊向他的隊員們高喊着指令。**4** [C] a line at the side of a sports field, which shows where the players are allowed to play〔球場的〕邊線—see picture at 參見 TENNIS 圖

sideline² *v* **be sidelined** to be unable to play in a game because you are injured, or unable to take part in something because you are not as good as someone else〔因傷病或水平不夠而〕不讓〔運動員〕參加比賽; 使不能參加〔活動〕, 使靠邊: *Baggio was once again sidelined through injury.* 巴治奧又一次因傷成為替補隊員。

side·long /ˈsaɪd,lɔŋ; ˈsaɪdlɒŋ/ *adj* **1 a sidelong look/glance** a way of looking at someone by moving your eyes to the side, especially so that it seems secret, dishonest, or disapproving〔看人時眼睛〕斜向的, 橫向的〔表示有祕密、不誠實或不以為然等〕: *He stole a side-*

long glance at the woman sitting next to him. 他斜着眼瞥了一下坐在身旁的女子。**2 a sidelong look at** an unusual and often humorous way of considering a subject 以不平常[幽默]的眼光看待: *The book takes a sidelong look at life in Hollywood.* 這本書以與眾不同的眼光來看荷里活生活。—**sidelong** *adv*

side-on /,· '·◂/ *adj* coming from one side rather than from in front or behind 從側面的, 從一側的: *a side-on collision* 從側面的碰撞 —**side-on** *adv*

side or·der /'· ,··/ *n* [C] a small amount of food ordered in a restaurant to be eaten with a main meal but served on a separate dish〔餐館中〕主菜之外另點的小菜: *a side order of onion rings* 另點的洋葱圈

si·der·e·al /saɪˋdɪrɪəl; saɪˈdɪəriəl/ *adj technical* related to or calculated using the stars【術語】恒星的, 以恒星為計算標準的: *the sidereal day* 恒星日

side-sad·dle /'· ,··/ *adv* **ride/sit side-saddle** to ride or sit on a horse with both legs on the same side of the horse 坐在女鞍上, 偏坐在馬鞍上〔雙腿在同側〕

side·show /ˋsaɪd,ʃo; ˈsaɪdʃəʊ/ *n* [C] **1** a separate small part of a FAIR[3] (1) or CIRCUS (1), where you pay to play games or watch a performance〔遊樂場或馬戲中的〕雜耍, 主場以外的遊樂節目 **2** an event that is much less important or serious than another one 次要的事件, 附帶的活動: *The initial conflict was a mere sideshow compared with the World War that followed.* 起初的衝突同隨後發生的世界大戰相比, 只是一個次要的事件。

side·split·ting /ˋsaɪd,splɪtɪŋ; ˈsaɪd,splɪtɪŋ/ *adj* extremely funny 令人捧腹大笑的, 極其滑稽的: *He told some sidesplitting jokes.* 他講了一些令人笑破肚皮的笑話。

side·step /ˋsaɪd,stɛp; ˈsaɪdstep/ *v* **1 sidestep a problem/issue/question** to avoid doing something that will cause you difficulty or inconvenience, such as dealing with a difficult problem 迴避問題: *The report simply sidesteps the environmental issues.* 報告乾脆迴避了環境問題。**2** [I,T] to step quickly sideways to avoid being hit or walking into someone 橫跨一步以避免〔被打擊或撞到人〕—**sidestep** *n* [C]

side·swipe[1] /ˋsaɪd,swaɪp; ˈsaɪdswaɪp/ *n* **take a sideswipe at** to criticize someone or something while you are talking about something different 旁敲側擊, 指桑罵槐, 附帶批評: *At the end of the speech he couldn't resist taking a sideswipe at his former boss.* 講話結束時, 他忍不住對他的前任老闆指桑罵槐地説上幾句。

sideswipe[2] *v* [T] *AmE* to hit the side of a car with another car so that the two sides touch quickly【美】〔駕車時〕擦邊撞擊〔另一車〕: *She was going too fast and sideswiped a parked car.* 她車開得太快, 擦邊撞到一輛停着的汽車。

side·track[1] /ˋsaɪd,træk; ˈsaɪdtræk/ *v* [T usually passive 一般用被動態] to make someone stop doing what they should be doing, or stop talking about what they started talking about, by making them interested in something else 岔開…的思路, 使離題, 使轉移目標: **get sidetracked** *Don't get too sidetracked by the audience's questions.* 不要因觀眾的提問而離題太遠了。

sidetrack[2] *n* [C] *AmE* a short railway track connected to a main track【美】〔鐵路的〕側線

side·walk /ˋsaɪd,wɔk; ˈsaɪdwɔːk/ *n* [C] *AmE* a hard surface or path at the side of a street for people to walk on【美】人行道; PAVEMENT *BrE*【英】—see graph at 參見 PAVEMENT 圖表 —see picture on page A4 參見A4頁圖

sidewalk art·ist /'·· ,··/ *n* [C] *AmE* someone who draws pictures on a sidewalk, hoping that people will give them money【美】街頭畫家〔在人行道上畫畫, 以此向行人討錢的人〕; PAVEMENT ARTIST *BrE*【英】

side·ways /ˋsaɪd,wez; ˈsaɪdweɪz/ *adv* **1** to or towards one side 向一邊地, 橫着地: *A strong gust of wind blew the car sideways into the ditch.* 一陣狂風把汽車橫着颳進了溝裡。**2** with the side, rather than the front or back, facing forwards 側面朝前地: *They brought the piano sideways through the front door.* 他們把鋼琴側面朝前地抬着通過前門。—**sideways** *adj*: *a furtive sideways glance* 偷偷側目一瞥

side-wheel·er /ˋsaɪd,hwiləˑ; ˈsaɪd ,wiːlə/ *n* [C] *AmE* an old-fashioned type of ship which is pushed forward by a pair of large wheels at the sides【美】明輪船〔兩舷有輪子推動船前進的舊式船舶〕; PADDLE STEAMER *BrE*【英】

sid·ing /ˋsaɪdɪŋ; ˈsaɪdɪŋ/ *n* [C] a short railway track connected to a main track, where trains are kept when they are not being used〔鐵路的〕側線, 旁軌

si·dle /ˋsaɪdl; ˈsaɪdl/ *v* [I always+adv/prep] to walk towards something or someone slowly and quietly, as if you do not want to be noticed 悄悄地慢慢走近, 鬼鬼祟祟地走向某人[某物]: **[+up/towards/along]** *A woman in dark glasses sidled up to us and asked if we wanted to buy a watch.* 一個戴墨鏡的女人鬼鬼祟祟地走近我們, 問我們要不要買手錶。

siege /sidʒ; siːdʒ/ *n* [C,U] **1** a military operation during which an army surrounds a place and tries to gain control of it by stopping supplies of food, weapons etc from reaching it〔軍隊的〕包圍, 圍困, 圍攻: *The siege lasted almost four months.* 這次圍困歷時近四個月。| **lay siege to** (=start a siege) 實施包圍 *In June 1176 King Richard laid siege to Limoges.* 理查一世國王於1176年6月對利摩日實施包圍。| **raise a siege** (=end it) 解除包圍, 解圍 **2** a situation in which the police surround a building to try and force the people inside to come out〔警察對建築物的〕包圍: **lay siege to** *When the scandal broke, dozens of journalists laid seige to Mellor's apartment.* 爆出醜聞後, 數十名記者包圍了梅勒的公寓。**3 be under siege a)** to be surrounded by an army in a seige 被軍隊包圍 **b)** to be continually criticized, or attacked by questions, problems, threats etc 不斷受到批評[質問, 威脅等], 受到圍攻: *The TV station has been under siege from irate viewers phoning in to complain.* 電視台受到憤怒觀眾的圍攻, 他們不斷打電話來投訴。**4 siege mentality** the feeling among a group of people that they are surrounded by enemies and must do everything they can to protect themselves 受圍心態, 被圍困時必須奮力自衛的心態

si·en·na /sɪˋɛnə; siˈenə/ *n* [U] a type of earth that is dark yellow, used to make paint〔用作顏料的〕濃黃土, 赭石

si·er·ra /sɪˋɛrə; siˈerə/ *n* [C] a row or area of sharply pointed mountains 鋸齒山脊, 峯巒起伏的山脈

si·es·ta /sɪˋɛstə; siˈestə/ *n* [C] a short sleep in the afternoon, especially in warm countries〔尤指炎熱國家的〕午後小睡, 午睡: **take/have a siesta** *The stores all close after lunch when everyone takes a siesta.* 午飯後所有商店都關門, 這段時間人人都在睡午覺。

sieve[1] /sɪv; sɪv/ *n* [C] **1 a)** a round wire kitchen tool with a lot of small holes, used for separating solid food from liquid or small pieces of food from large pieces〔廚具中的〕漏勺 **b)** a round wire tool for separating small objects from large objects 篩子, 細篩 **2 have a memory like a sieve** *informal* to forget things easily【非正式】記性很差

sieve[2] *v* [T] to put flour or other food through a sieve 篩; 濾

sieve sth ↔ **out** *phr v* [T] to separate solid objects from liquid or smaller objects from larger ones by using a sieve 篩出; 濾出: *sieve out the seeds from the raspberry jam* 把籽從山莓果醬中濾出來 —see picture on page A11 參見A11頁圖

sift /sɪft; sɪft/ *v* [T] **1** to put flour, sugar etc through a sieve or similar container in order to remove large pieces 篩〔麵粉、白糖等〕**2** also 又作 **sift through** to examine information, documents etc carefully in order to find something out or decide what is important and what is not 細查, 詳查, 嚴密檢查〔信息、文件等〕: *Police are sifting through the evidence in the hope of finding more clues.* 警方正在對證據作詳細審查, 希望能找

出更多的線索。

sift sth ↔ **out** *phr v* [T] to separate something from other things 挑選出, 篩選: **[+from]** *It's hard to sift out the truth from the lies in this case.* 在這個案件中, 不容易把事實和謊言區分出來。

sift·er /ˈsɪftə; ˈsɪftə/ *n* [C] a container with a lot of small holes in the top used for shaking flour, sugar etc onto things〔蓋上有小孔、用於篩撒麵粉、白糖等的〕撒粉瓶

sigh¹ /saɪ; saɪ/ *v* [I] **1** to breathe in and out making a long sound, especially because you are bored, disappointed, tired etc〔尤指因厭煩、失望、疲倦等〕嘆氣, 嘆息: *"Well, there's nothing we can do about it now," she sighed.* "唉, 我們現在已經無能為力了。"她嘆口氣說。| **sigh heavily/deeply** *Frankie stared out of the window and sighed deeply.* 弗蘭基凝望着窗外, 深深地嘆了口氣。| **[+with]** *He sighed with despair at the thought of all the opportunities he had missed.* 他想到自己失去的許多機會, 絕望地嘆着氣。**2** if the wind sighs, it makes a long sound like someone sighing〔風〕呼嘯, 嗚咽: *The wind sighed in the trees.* 風在樹叢中呼嘯。**3 sigh for sth** to be sad because you are thinking about a pleasant time in the past 思念, 惋惜: *Emilia sighed for her lost youth.* 埃米莉亞惋惜逝去的青春。

sigh² *n* [C] an act or sound of sighing 嘆氣[嘆息]: **[+of]** *She settled down in her chair with a long sigh of relief.* 她坐在扶手椅上, 長長地舒了一口氣。| **breathe/give/heave/let out a sigh of relief** *We all heaved a sigh of relief when we heard they were safe.* 我們聽到他們平安無事時, 大家都鬆了一口氣。

S2 W2 **sight¹** /saɪt; saɪt/ *n*

1 ►ABILITY TO SEE 視力◄ [U] the physical ability to see 視力, 視覺: *Anne's sight is very good for someone of her age.* 在安妮這種年齡, 她的視力算是很好的了。| *He has no sight in his right eye, but his left eye is fine.* 他的右眼已經沒有視力了, 但左眼還很好。| **lose your sight** (=become blind) 失明 *She had lost her sight in a riding accident.* 她在一次騎馬事故中失明了。

2 ►ACT OF SEEING 看見◄ [singular,U] the act of seeing something 看, 看到, 看見: *The crowd was waiting for a sight of the Queen.* 人羣在等着一睹女王的風采。| **at the sight of** *I always faint at the sight of blood.* 我一看見血就要犯暈。| **catch sight of** (=suddenly see or notice something) 突然看到[瞥見, 注意到] *Sheila caught sight of her own face in one of the shop windows.* 希拉在一扇櫥窗裡瞥見了自己的臉。| **be hidden from sight** *The house is hidden from sight behind trees.* 這座房子隱藏在樹叢後面, 人們看不見。| **on sight** (=as soon as you see someone) 一看見就… *soldiers trained to shoot on sight* 受過訓練一看到目標就能立即開槍的士兵 | *Jo disliked him on sight.* 喬一見到他就討厭。| **at first sight** (=the first time you see someone) 初見; 乍看 *We fell in love with the cottage at first sight.* 我們一見到那個小屋就愛上它了。

3 ►THING YOU SEE 所見之物◄ [C] **a)** something you can see, especially something unusual, beautiful etc 景物, 景象: *Tourists are a familiar sight in this part of the city.* 在城裡這一帶地方, 遊客是人們熟悉的景象了。| *the rare sight of a fox* 難得一見的狐狸 | *all the sounds and sights of the forest* 森林中的種種聲音和景象 | **a sorry sight** *often humorous* (=something you see that makes you feel sad or sympathetic)【常幽默】一副可憐相 *Fiona was a sorry sight in her wet clothes.* 菲奧娜渾身濕透, 一副可憐兮兮的樣子。**b) the sights** [plural] famous or interesting places that tourists visit 名勝, 風景, 奇觀: *In the afternoon, you'll have a chance to relax or to go and see the sights.* 大家下午可以休息, 也可以去參觀風景名勝。—see also 另見 SIGHTSEEING

4 in/within sight a) inside the area that you can see 在視野內, 看得見: *When we got to the beach, there wasn't a soul in sight.* 我們到達海灘時一個人也見不到。| *If you don't lock up the food, they'll eat everything in sight.* 如果你不把食物鎖起來, 他們看見就會吃光的。**b)** likely to happen soon 可能即將發生: *Six months from the start of the strike, there is still no end in sight.* 罷工開始至今六個月了, 眼下還看不出結束的跡象。| *Peace is now in sight.* 和平在望了。

5 out of sight a) outside the area that you can see 在視野外, 看不見: *Karen waved until the car was out of sight.* 卡倫不斷揮手, 直到汽車看不見為止。**b)** *old-fashioned slang* extremely good【過時, 俚】極好的: *The skiing there is out of sight!* 那裡滑雪棒極了!

6 be within sight of a) to be in the area where you can see something 在…視野內, 看得見…: *We camped within sight of the lake.* 我們在看得見湖的地方露營。**b)** to be in a position where you will soon be able to get something or achieve something 眼看就能得到[成功]: *Dan was now within sight of the championship.* 丹現在眼看就要拿到錦標賽冠軍了。

7 lose sight of a) to forget to think about or deal with something important 忘記考慮[處理]某要事: *It's easy to lose sight of the real issue.* 真正的問題倒是容易忘掉的。| *Never lose sight of the fact that you have a lot of talent.* 永遠不要忘記其實你很有才能。**b)** to stop being able to see something or someone 不再看得見…: *I lost sight of him in the crowd.* 在人羣中, 我再也看不到他了。

8 come into sight/disappear from sight etc to appear or disappear 出現/消失: *Soon the train came into sight.* 很快就看見火車了。

9 not let sb out of your sight to make sure that someone stays near you 讓某人留在自己眼皮下: *Since the accident, Donna hasn't let the children out of her sight.* 出過事以後, 唐娜從未讓孩子離開過自己半步。

10 be sick of/hate/can't stand the sight of to dislike someone or something very much 非常不喜歡…: *Alan and Sam can't stand the sight of each other.* 阿倫和薩姆都非常討厭對方。

11 a sight for sore eyes *spoken*【口】**a)** someone or something that you feel very happy to see 使人看着高興的人; 賞心悅目的東西 **b)** *BrE* someone or something that is very unattractive or very funny to look at【英】難看的[樣子滑稽的]人[物]

12 set your sights on to decide that you want something and will make a determined effort to achieve it 決心要做到: *I was still young then, and my sights were set on an acting career.* 我當時還年輕, 就決心要從事演藝事業。

13 come in sight of to arrive at a position from which you can see a particular place, building etc 來到看得見…的地方: *At last they came in sight of the city.* 他們終於看見那座城市了。

14 at first sight when you first start considering something 乍看起來, 開始考慮時: *The results of the tests were, at first sight, surprising.* 乍看起來, 測試的結果是驚人的。

15 a sight more/a sight better etc *spoken* a lot more etc【口】多得多/好得多: *You'd earn a damn sight more if you got a proper qualification.* 如果你有張合適的資格證書, 你掙的錢就會多得多。

16 be a sight/look a sight to look very funny or stupid, or very untidy or unpleasant 樣子滑稽[愚蠢、髒亂、難看]: *We'd had an all-night party, and the place looked a bit of a sight.* 我們開了個通宵晚會, 那地方看起來有點不像樣子了。

17 ►GUN 槍◄ [C often plural 常用複數] the part of a gun or other weapon that guides your eye when you are aiming at something〔步槍等武器的〕瞄準器, 準星 —see picture at 參見 GUN¹ 圖

18 out of sight, out of mind used to say that you will soon forget someone if you do not see them for a while 眼不見, 心不想: *I pestered him continuously: I wasn't going to allow myself to become a case of out of sight, out of mind.* 我不斷去纏着他, 我可不想讓自己成為"眼不見, 心不想"的實例。—see also 另見 **know sb by sight** (KNOW¹ (16))

S

sight² *v* [T] to see something from a long distance away, or see something you have been looking for〔從很遠處或經過一番尋找後〕看見, 發現: *The sailors gave a shout of joy when they sighted land.* 水手們看到陸地時高聲地歡呼了起來。| *Several rare birds have been sighted in the area.* 這個地區已經發現了好幾種珍稀的鳥。

sight·ed /ˋsaɪtɪd; ˈsaɪtɨd/ *adj* someone who is sighted can see, and is not blind〔人〕看得見的, 有視力的, 不盲的: **partially sighted** (=having limited ability to see) 視力受限制的 —see also 另見 CLEAR-SIGHTED, FAR-SIGHTED, LONGSIGHTED, SHORT-SIGHTED

sight·ing /ˋsaɪtɪŋ; ˈsaɪtɪŋ/ *n* [C] an occasion on which something is seen, especially something rare or something that people are hoping to see 看見, 發現〔尤指見到少見的或希望見到的事物〕: *Several people in the area have reported sightings of UFOs.* 這個地區有好幾個人都曾報告發現過不明飛行物。

sight·less /ˋsaɪtlɪs; ˈsaɪtləs/ *adj literary* blind【文】看不見的, 失明的, 盲的

sight-read /ˋsaɪt ˌrid; ˈsaɪt riːd/ *v past tense and past participle* **sightread** /-ˌrɛd; -red/ [I,T] to play or sing written music when you look at it for the first time, without practising it first〔不經準備〕隨看〔樂譜〕隨奏, 看譜即唱 —**sight-reader** *n* [C] —**sight-reading** *n* [U]

sight·see·ing /ˋsaɪtˌsiɪŋ; ˈsaɪtˌsiːɪŋ/ *n* [U] the act of visiting famous or interesting places, especially as tourists〔尤指旅客的〕觀光, 遊覽: **go sightseeing** *We bought souvenirs and then went sightseeing.* 我們買了紀念品, 然後就去參觀遊覽。

sight·se·er /ˋsaɪtˌsiɚ; ˈsaɪtˌsiːə/ *n* [C] someone, especially a tourist, who is visiting a famous or interesting place 觀光者, 遊覽者

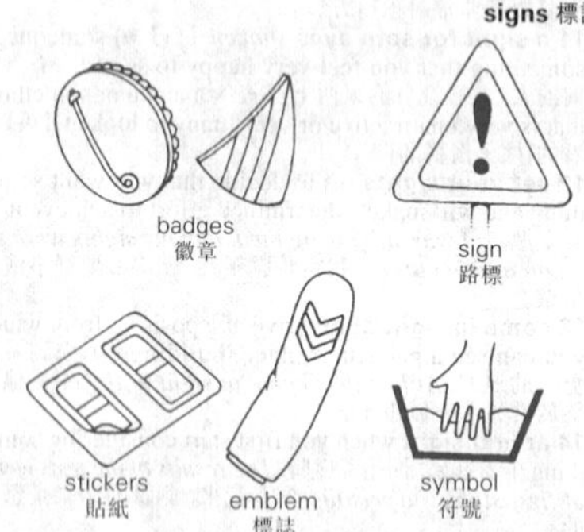

sign¹ /saɪn; saɪn/ *n*

1 ▶STH THAT PROVES STH 證明◀ [C] an event, fact etc that shows that something is happening or that something is true; INDICATION 跡象, 痕跡, 徵兆: **sign of** *The tests can detect early signs of disease.* 這些檢查可以發現疾病的早期徵兆。| **sign that** *Exports have risen by 20%, a sign that the economy is improving.* 出口增長了 20%, 這是經濟正在好轉的跡象。| **a sure sign** (=clear proof) 明顯的證據 *You know Eric, if he won't eat, it's a sure sign that he's in love again!* 你是了解埃里克的, 如果他不想吃飯, 那就表明他一定又在談戀愛了! | **telltale sign** (=a sign that is easy to recognize, usually of something bad)〔常為壞事的〕明顯跡象 *telltale signs of drug abuse* 濫用毒品的明顯跡象 | **show signs of** *For the first time she was beginning to show signs of her age.* 她頭一次開始顯露青春不再的痕跡。| **every sign of** (=clear signs of) …的明顯跡象 *They showed every sign of being willing to cooperate.* 他們表現出願意合作的種種跡象。—see graph at 參見 INDICATE 圖表

2 there's no sign of a) if there is no sign of something, you cannot see anything which shows that it exists or has happened 沒有…的跡象: *The police looked all around the house, but there was no sign of a struggle.* 警察搜查了整幢房子, 但沒有發現打鬥過的跡象。**b)** if there is no sign of someone, you cannot see them anywhere, or they have not arrived when you expected them to 不見〔某人的〕蹤影, 蹤影全無: *Jerry kept looking out of the window, but there was still no sign of her.* 傑里不斷往窗外看, 但還是不見她的蹤影。

3 ▶MOVEMENT OR SOUND 動作或聲音◀ [C] a movement, sound etc that you make in order to tell someone to do something or give them information; GESTURE¹ (1) 手勢, 姿勢, 信號: **give/make a sign** *Nobody move until I give the sign.* 在我發出信號之前, 誰也不許動。| **[+that]** *Bruce made a sign that he was ready to leave.* 布魯斯作了一個姿勢, 表示他準備走了。| **sign for sb to do sth** *Three short blasts on the whistle was the sign for us to begin.* 三下短哨聲就是我們開始的信號。

4 ▶GIVES INFORMATION 傳達信息◀ [C] a piece of paper, metal etc in a public place, with words or drawings on it that give people information, warn them not to do something etc 標記, 指示牌, 標牌: *road signs* 路標 | *a no smoking sign* 不准抽煙的告示牌

5 ▶PICTURE/SYMBOL 圖畫/符號◀ [C] a picture, shape etc that has a particular meaning; SYMBOL 圖形, 符號, 記號: *For some reason the computer can't display the dollar sign.* 由於某種原因, 這台電腦不能顯示元的符號。

6 ▶STAR SIGN 星座◀ [C] also 又作 **star sign** a group of stars, representing one of 12 parts of the year, that some people believe influences your behaviour and your life 宮〔黃道十二宮之一〕, 星座: *I'm a Scorpio – what sign are you?* 我是天蠍座的 — 你是甚麼星座?

7 ▶LANGUAGE 語言◀ [U] a language that uses hand movements instead of spoken words, used by people who cannot hear; SIGN LANGUAGE〔聾啞人的〕手語

8 sign of life a movement that shows that someone is alive, or something that shows that there are people in a particular place〔人〕活着的跡象; 有人的跡象: *We entered the building with caution but strangely there was no sign of life.* 我們小心翼翼地進入那棟樓房, 但是很奇怪, 裡面見不到有人待過的跡象。

9 sign of the times something that shows how bad society has become〔壞的〕時尚, 潮流, 時代特徵: *So many houses have burglar alarms nowadays. It's a sign of the times I suppose.* 如今那麼多家庭都安裝了防盜報警器, 我想這就是世風日下的特徵吧。

10 the sign of the Cross the hand movement that some Christians make in the shape of a cross, to show respect for God or to protect themselves from evil〔基督徒在祝福等時在胸前〕畫十字的手勢

sign² *v* **1** [I,T] to write your SIGNATURE on a letter or document to show that you wrote it, agree with it 簽(名), 署(名); 〔在文件等上〕簽字: *Sign here please.* 請在這裡簽字。| **sign sth** *You forgot to sign the check!* 你忘了在支票上簽字! | *Over a hundred people have signed the petition.* 已有一百多人在請願書上簽了名。| *a signed photo of Paul McCartney* 一張保羅·麥卡尼的簽名照片 | **sign your name** *The artist had signed his name in the corner of the painting.* 畫家在畫的角上署了名。

2 sign an agreement/treaty etc to show formally that you agree to do something, by signing a legal document 簽署協議書/條約等: *Both presidents signed*

the treaty as part of the new peace plan. 兩位總統簽署了那個條約作為新和平計劃的一部分。| **sign sth with sb** *France has just signed a new trade deal with Japan.* 法國和日本剛剛簽訂了一項貿易協定。**3** [T] if an organization such as a football team or music company signs someone, that person signs a contract agreeing to work for it 簽約聘請, 簽約雇用: *CBS Records had signed her back in 1988 on a three-album contract.* 哥倫比亞唱片公司早在1988年就和她簽訂了發行三套唱片集的合同。**4** [I] to try to tell someone something or ask them to do something by using signs and movements 做手勢〔示意〕: **sign to sb to do sth** *He was desperately signing to me to not mention anything about Jack.* 他拚命地向我打手勢, 叫我不要提起傑克的任何事。| **sign for sb to do sth** *She signed for us to go inside.* 她打手勢讓我們進去。**5 all signed and sealed** with all the necessary legal documents agreed and signed 手續完備: *It'll all be signed and sealed by Friday, you can move in then.* 星期五之前所有手續都會辦完, 你也就可以搬進來了。**6** [I,T] to use SIGN LANGUAGE 用手語表達, 把...譯成手語: *The whole performance was signed* (=translated into sign language) *by a local interpreter.* 整場演出都由一位本地譯員譯成手語。—**signer** *n* [C]

sign sth ↔ **away** *phr v* [T] to sign a document that gives your property or legal right to someone else 簽字放棄[讓與]〔財產或法定權利〕: *She had signed away all claims to the house.* 她已簽字放棄對該房子的一切權利。

sign for sth *phr v* [T] **1** to sign a document to prove that you have received something 簽收: *This is a registered letter, someone will have to sign for it.* 這是一封掛號信, 必須有人簽收才行。**2 sign for Liverpool/Arsenal etc** *BrE* to sign a contract agreeing to play for a particular football team【英】簽約於利物浦足球隊/阿仙奴足球隊

sign in *phr v* **1** [I] to write your name on a form, in a book etc when you enter a place such as a hotel, office or club 簽到: *Remember to sign in at reception.* 記住要在接待室簽到。**2** [T **sign** sb ↔ **in**] to write someone else's name in a book so that they are allowed to enter a club that you are a member of〔會員〕為〔某人〕登記使其得以進入俱樂部[會所等]

sign off *phr v* [I] **1** *informal* to end a radio or television programme by saying goodbye【非正式】〔以告別〕結束廣播[電視節目] **2** to finish an informal letter by writing your name at the end of it〔寫非正式信件時以簽名〕結束寫信: *It's getting late so I'll sign off now. Love, John.* 時間不早了, 我就此擱筆。愛你的約翰。

sign on *phr v* **1** [I,T] to sign a document agreeing to work for someone, especially as a soldier, sailor etc, or to persuade someone to do this (使) 簽約受雇〔尤指當兵、當水手等〕, 受聘: *He signed on as a soldier in the US army.* 他報名參加美國軍隊當士兵。| **sign sb ↔ on** *I went to the local recruiting office and was signed on for three years.* 我到當地新兵徵募辦事處去, 簽約當兵三年。**2** [I] *BrE* to state officially that you are unemployed by signing a form, so that you can get money from the government【英】登記失業〔以便領取政府的救濟款〕

sign out *phr v* **1** [I] to write your name in a book when you leave a place such as a hotel, office or club〔在離開旅館、辦公室、俱樂部等時〕簽名登記離開 **2** [T **sign** sth ↔ **out**] to write your name on a form or in a book to show that you have taken or borrowed something 登記拿走[借走]: *Bernstein signed out a company car and drove to the meeting.* 伯恩斯坦登記借用公司的一輛汽車去參加會議。

sign sth ↔ **over** *phr v* [T] to sign an official document that gives your property or rights to someone else 簽字將〔財產、權利等〕轉讓[給與]〔某人〕: **[+to]** *When he became ill, he signed his property in France over to his son.* 他生病後便簽字把在法國的財產給了他兒子。

sign up *phr v* **1** [T usually passive 一般用被動態] if someone is signed up by an organization, they sign a contract agreeing to work for that organization 使簽約受雇, 簽約雇用: *Several well-established researchers have been signed up for the project.* 好幾名很有聲望的研究人員都已簽約參加這個項目了。**2** [I] to arrange to take part in a course of study 經報名參加〔課程學習〕: **[+for]** *I'm thinking of signing up for the philosophy course this term.* 我在考慮報名參加這個學期的哲學課。| **sign up to do sth** *Over half the people who signed up to do engineering were women.* 報名讀工程的人過半都是女子。

sign with sth *phr v* [T] **1** *AmE* to sign a contract agreeing to play for a particular sports team【美】簽約受雇參加〔某球隊〕 **2** to sign a contract agreeing that a particular company has the right to record and sell your music 與〔唱片公司〕簽約

sig·nal¹ /ˈsɪgnl; ˈsɪgnəl/ *n* [C] **1** a sound or action that you make in order to give information to someone or tell them to do something 信號, 暗號: **signal (for sb) to do sth** *A bell began to ring, the 8 o'clock signal to start work.* 鈴聲響起, 這是 8 點鐘開工的信號。| *When he closes his book, it's a signal for everyone to stand up.* 當他把書合上時, 這就表示該全體起立了。| **give a signal** *Don't start yet – wait for me to give the signal.* 先別開始 — 等我發信號。| **at a signal (from sb)** *At a signal from their leader the worshippers knelt to pray.* 禮拜者依照領頭人的示意下跪禱告。| **danger signal/warning signal etc** *A red flag is often used as a danger signal.* 紅色的旗子常被用作危險的信號。—see also 另見 SMOKE SIGNAL **2** an event or action that shows what someone feels or what is likely to happen 暗示, 預示: **signal that** *Gorbachev's speech was a signal that major changes were on the way.* 戈爾巴喬夫的演說暗示即將發生重大的變化。| **a clear signal** *The opinion poll is a clear signal that voters do not support the President's foreign policy.* 民意測驗清楚地表明選民不支持總統的對外政策。| **danger signal/warning signal** *Rapid breathing is a danger signal and you should call your doctor.* 呼吸急促是個危險的徵兆, 該去請醫生了。| **send/give a signal** *This will send the wrong signal to potential investors.* 這會給潛在的投資者發出錯誤的信號。**3** a series of light waves, sound waves etc that carry an image, sound, or message, such as is used in radio or television〔無線電或電視的〕訊號, 訊息, 圖像: **send out/transmit a signal (to)** *The signal was sent out to our troops immediately.* 訊號被馬上發送到我們的部隊。| **receive/pick up a signal** *Astronomers have been picking up faint signals that may be from a distant planet.* 天文學家一直在接收可能來自遙遠行星的微弱訊號。**4** a piece of equipment with coloured lights, used on a railway to tell train drivers whether they can continue or must stop 鐵路信號: **signal failure** (=when these lights do not work) 信號燈故障 *The report confirmed that signal failure had been the cause of the accident.* 報告確定信號燈失靈是這次事故的原因。

signal² *v* **signalled, signalling** *BrE*【英】, **signaled, signaling** *AmE*【美】 **1** [I,T] to give a signal in order to give information or tell someone to do something 發信號, 打信號: **[+at]** *Mary was signalling wildly at us, but we didn't even notice.* 瑪麗拚命向我們打信號, 但我們根本沒有注意。| **[+to]** *The judge signaled to a police officer and the man was led away.* 法官向一位警察示意, 帶走了那個人。| **[+for]** *He pushed his plate away and signaled for coffee.* 他把盤子推開, 並示意要杯咖啡。| **signal (to) sb to do sth** *She was signalling to the children to stay outside.* 她在向孩子們打手勢, 要他們留在外面。—see picture on page A3 參見A3頁圖 **2** [T] to make something clear by what you say or do〔用語言或行動〕表明, 表示: *Both sides have signaled their willingness to start negotiations.* 雙方都表明了他們談判的意願。**3** [T] to be a sign or proof of something 標誌, 證明: *the lengthening days that signal the end of winter* 白

天變長標誌着冬天的結束

signal³ *adj* [only before noun 僅用於名詞前] *formal* important【正式】重要的: **signal achievement/success/failure etc** *Getting the health care bill passed was a signal personal triumph for the President.* 使保健醫療法案得以通過是總統一次重大的個人勝利。

signal box /ˈ‥ ˌ/ *n* [C] *BrE* a small building near a railway from which the signals and tracks are controlled【英】〔鐵路旁的〕信號房, 信號塔; SIGNAL TOWER *AmE*【美】

sig·nal·ize also 又作 **-ise** *BrE*【英】/ˋsɪgnəˌlaɪz; ˈsɪgnəlaɪz/ *v* [T usually passive 一般用被動態] *formal* to be a clear sign of something【正式】使成為…的明確標誌, 標誌着: *a quaint tradition that signalizes our attainment of learning* 代表我們學問造詣的古雅傳統

sig·nal·ly /ˋsɪgnl̩ɪ; ˈsɪgnəli/ *adv formal* very noticeably【正式】顯著地: *These principles are signally lacking in modern society.* 這些準則在現代社會是明顯地欠缺了。

sig·nal·man /ˋsɪgnl̩ˌmæn; ˈsɪgnəlmən/ *n plural* **signalmen** /-ˌmən; -mən/ [C] **1** *especially BrE* someone whose job is to control railway signals【尤英】〔鐵路的〕信號員 **2** a member of the army or navy who is trained in signalling〔陸軍或海軍的〕信號手, 信號兵

signal tow·er /ˈ‥ ˌ‥/ *n* [C] *AmE* a building next to a railway track from which signals and tracks are controlled; SIGNAL BOX【美】信號塔, 信號房

sig·na·to·ry /ˋsɪgnəˌtorɪ; ˈsɪgnətəri/ *n* [C] one of the people or countries that sign an official agreement, especially an international one〔尤指國際條約的〕簽署者; 簽約國: **[+to/of]** *Most Western countries are signatories of this treaty.* 大多數西方國家都是這個條約的簽約國。

sig·na·ture /ˋsɪgnətʃə; ˈsɪgnətʃə/ *n* [C] your name written in the way you usually write it, for example at the end of a letter or contract or on a cheque〔書信、合同、支票等結尾處的〕簽字, 簽名: *I couldn't read his signature.* 我認不出他的簽字。| *a petition with four thousand signatures* 一份有四千人簽名的請願書 | **put your signature to/on** (=sign something to show that you agree with it) 在…上簽字〔表示同意〕 —see picture at 參見 SIGN² 圖

signature tune /ˈ‥‥ ˌ/ *n* [C] a short piece of music used at the beginning and end of a television or radio programme〔一項電視或廣播節目開始和結束時的〕信號曲, 主題曲

sig·net /ˋsɪgnɪt; ˈsɪgnɨt/ *n* [C] a metal object used for printing a small pattern in WAX¹ (1) as an official SEAL 圖章, 私章

signet ring /ˈ‥ ˌ/ *n* [C] a ring that has a signet on it 圖章戒指

2 **sig·nif·i·cance** /sɪgˋnɪfəkəns; sɪgˈnɪfɪkəns/ *n* [singular, U] **1** the meaning of a word, sign, action etc, especially when this is not immediately clear〔尤指尚未清楚的〕意義, 含義: **[+of]** *Could you explain the significance of this part of the contract?* 請你解釋一下合同這一部分的意思好嗎? | **the full/real/true significance** *It was only later that we realized the true significance of his remark.* 後來我們才領會到他那些話的真正意義。**2** the importance of an event, action etc, especially because of the effects or influence it will have in the future〔事件、行動等的〕重要性, 重大意義: **[+of]** *It is impossible to overestimate the significance of this major discovery.* 對這次重大發現的意義怎樣高估都不過分。| **[+for]** *a judgment that has long-term significance for the rights of disabled people* 對殘疾人權益有長遠重大意義的判決 | **be of great/major/little significance** *So far, research has not produced anything of very great significance.* 迄今為止, 研究尚未產生任何具有重大意義的結果。

3 1 **sig·nif·i·cant** /sɪgˋnɪfəkənt; sɪgˈnɪfɪkənt/ *adj* **1** having an important effect or influence, especially on what will happen in the future 重要的, 重大的, 影響深遠的: *His most significant political achievement was the abolition of the death penalty.* 他最重大的政治成就是廢除了死刑。| *Please inform us if there are any significant changes in your plans.* 如果你們的計劃有甚麼重大改變, 請通知我們。| **highly significant** (=very significant) 非常重要的 *a highly significant discovery that might eventually lead to a vaccine* 一項可能最終導致一種新疫苗研製成功的重大發現 | **[+for]** *The result is highly significant for the future of the province.* 這一結果對該省的未來極為重要。| **it is significant that** *Police believed it was significant that he had recently opened a bank account abroad.* 警方認為, 他最近在國外銀行開賬戶的事很重要。**2** large enough to be noticeable or have noticeable effects 相當數量的, 影響明顯的: *A significant number of drivers fail to keep to speed limits.* 有相當多的司機不遵守車速限制。| *A background in computing will give you a significant advantage.* 電腦專業的背景將是你的一大優越條件。**3** a significant look, smile etc has a special meaning that is not known to everyone〔眼神、微笑等〕表示某種意義的, 有特殊含義的: *They exchanged significant glances.* 他們彼此交換了意味深長的目光。

sig·nif·i·cant·ly /sɪgˋnɪfəkəntlɪ; sɪgˈnɪfɪkəntli/ *adv* **1** in an important way or to an important degree 重大地, 可觀地: *Health problems can be significantly reduced by careful diet.* 通過注意飲食可以大大減少健康方面的問題。| **[+from]** *Methods used by younger teachers differ significantly from those used by older ones.* 年輕教師所用的方法與老教師的方法相比有重大差別。| **significantly better/greater/worse etc** *Delia's work has been significantly better since her training course.* 自從參加培訓班之後, 迪莉婭的工作好得多了。| [sentence adverb 句子副詞] *Significantly, no newspaper has dared to print this shocking story.* 值得注意的是, 沒有一份報紙敢發表這個駭人聽聞的消息。**2** in a way that seems to have a special meaning 意味深長地, 含義深遠地: *Tom nodded significantly at the suggestion, but did not comment.* 聽了這個建議以後, 湯姆意味深長地點了點頭, 但是沒有發表意見。 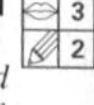

sig·nif·i·ca·tion /ˌsɪgˌnɪfəˋkeʃən; ˌsɪgnɪfɨˈkeɪʃən/ *n* [C] *formal* the intended meaning of a word【正式】〔詞的〕含義, 意義

sig·ni·fy /ˋsɪgnəˌfaɪ; ˈsɪgnɨfaɪ/ *v* [not in progressive 不用進行式] **1** [T] to represent, mean, or be a sign of something 代表, 表示, 象徵, 意味着: *Some tribes use special facial markings to signify status.* 有些部落的人用特殊的面部符號代表他們的地位。| **signify that** *Recent changes in climate may signify that global warming is starting to have an effect.* 最近的氣候變化可能表示全球變暖正在開始產生影響。**2** [T] *formal* to make a wish, feeling, or opinion known by doing something【正式】〔用動作〕表示〔願望、感覺或意見〕: **signify that** *With a gesture Mr Bosch signified that the three representatives could depart.* 博世先生做了個手勢, 表示三位代表可以走了。| **signify sth (to sb)** *He turned away from her slightly to signify his indifference.* 他稍稍背過臉以表示對她的冷淡。**3** [I] to be important enough to have an effect on something 要緊, 有關係, 有重要性: *These figures don't really signify in the overall results.* 這些數字對於總體結果沒有實際重要意義。

sign·ing /ˋsaɪnɪŋ; ˈsaɪnɪŋ/ *n* **1** [U] the act of signing something such as an agreement or contract〔協議或合約的〕簽字, 簽署: *The club was excited about the signing of these two Argentinian football stars.* 俱樂部全體成員對這兩位阿根廷足球明星的簽約感到興奮。**2** [C] *BrE* someone who has just signed a contract to join a sports team【英】已簽約參加球隊的運動員: *United's latest signing will make his debut for the club on Saturday.* 聯隊的最新簽約球員將於星期六代表俱樂部首次出場。

sign lan·guage /ˈ· ˌ‥/ *n* [C,U] a language that uses hand movements instead of spoken words, used by people who cannot hear〔聾人的〕手語, 手勢語

sign·post¹ /ˋsaɪnˌpost; ˈsaɪnpəʊst/ *n* [C] a sign on a road showing directions and distances 路標: *The signpost said*

'Bedford 3 miles'. 路標上寫着"距貝德福德三英里"。| [+to] *Just follow the signposts to Padua.* 只要按往博杜瓦的路標指示走就行了。

signpost² *v* [T] *BrE*【英】**1 be well/badly signposted** to be clearly or unclearly marked by signposts 給/未給…設置明顯的路標: *The village isn't very well signposted so it's quite hard to find.* 這個村子沒有設置明顯的路標, 所以很難找。**2** to show something clearly so that everyone will notice and understand it 清楚地表明: *They have signposted their conclusions in the report.* 他們已在報告中清楚地表明了自己的結論。

Sikh /sik; siːk/ *n* [C] a member of an Indian religious group that developed from Hinduism in the 16th century 錫克教教徒〔16 世紀從印度教分出的宗教的信徒〕—**Sikh** *adj*

Sikh·is·m /ˈsikɪzm; ˈsiːkɪzəm/ *n* [U] the religion of the Sikhs 錫克教

si·lage /ˈsaɪlɪdʒ; ˈsaɪlɪdʒ/ *n* [U] grass or other plants cut and stored so that they can be used as winter food for cattle 青貯飼料

2 **si·lence¹** /ˈsaɪləns; ˈsaɪləns/ *n*

1 ▶NO NOISE 沒有響聲◀ [U] complete absence of sound or noise 無聲, 寂靜: *In the silence he heard a faint clicking noise.* 寂靜中他聽到一聲微弱的咔噠聲。| **[+of]** *Nothing disturbed the silence of the night.* 沒有甚麼打破這夜晚的寂靜。| **silence falls (on/upon)** (=it begins to be completely quiet) 變得完全寂靜 *After the explosion, an eerie silence fell upon the scene.* 爆炸之後, 現場陷入一片可怕的寂靜。| **break/shatter the silence** *The silence was suddenly broken by a loud scream.* 一聲刺耳的尖叫突然打破了沉寂。| **absolute/complete/dead silence** *the complete silence of the forest at night* 夜間森林的絕對寂靜

2 ▶NO TALKING 不說話◀ a) [C,U] complete quiet because no one is talking, or a period of complete quiet 靜默, 緘默, 默不作聲: *There was a long silence before anyone answered.* 長時間的靜默以後才有人回答。| *She raised her hand and waited for silence.* 她舉起手, 等待大家靜下來。| *"Silence!" thundered the judge.* "安靜!"法官大聲叫道。| **in silence** (=not saying anything) 甚麼話也不說 *We walked back to the house in silence.* 我們默不作聲地走回房子去。| **embarrassed/awkward/stunned etc silence** *There was a moment's embarrassed silence.* 有一陣子大家都尷尬地默不作聲。| **stony silence** (=when someone has said something very shocking or unreasonable)〔當有人說了一些非常令人震驚或不合理的話時〕無任何反應 *Their suggestion was met with a stony silence.* 他們的建議沒有引起任何反應。**b)** [U] failure or refusal to discuss something or answer questions about something 隻字不提, 保持沉默: **[+on]** *The government's silence on such an important issue seems very strange.* 政府對如此重大的問題保持沉默, 顯得非常奇怪。| **take sb's silence for/as** (=think that someone's silence has a particular meaning) 認為某人的沉默有特殊的含義 *She took his silence as an agreement.* 她把他的沉默視作同意。

3 ▶NO COMMUNICATION 沒有交流◀ [C,U] failure to write a letter to someone, telephone them etc 無音信, 失去聯繫: *After two years of silence he suddenly got in touch with us again.* 兩年杳無音信之後, 他突然又跟我們取得了聯繫。

4 reduce sb to silence to speak to someone so angrily, rudely etc that they are too shocked or upset to reply〔因說話粗暴等〕使某人不能回答[作聲]: *This stinging criticism reduced me to silence for the rest of the meeting.* 這種尖刻的批評使我噤若寒蟬直到會議結束。

5 a one-minute silence/two-minute silence etc a period of time in which everyone stops talking as a sign of honour and respect towards someone who has died 靜默一分鐘/兩分鐘〔對死者表示敬意〕

silence² *v* [T] **1** to make someone stop talking, or stop something making a noise 使安靜, 使緘默: *"Just a minute," she snapped, silencing him with a look of hatred.* "你等一等。"她厲聲地說, 用帶着仇恨的眼神使他靜了下來。**2** to make someone stop expressing opposition or criticisms 壓制〔反對意見或批評〕: *Opponents of the regime were silenced by threats of violence.* 政權的反對者因受到暴力威脅而不敢發表意見。| *a brilliant new book that silenced her critics* 她的一部使批評家無話可說的出色新書

si·lenc·er /ˈsaɪlənsə; ˈsaɪlənsə/ *n* [C] **1** a thing that is put on the end of a gun so that it makes less noise when it is fired〔手槍末端的〕消聲器 **2** *BrE* a piece of equipment that is connected to the EXHAUST² (1) of a vehicle to make its engine quieter【英】〔與車輛內燃機排氣管裝置相連的〕消聲器; MUFFLER (2) *AmE*【美】

si·lent /ˈsaɪlənt; ˈsaɪlənt/ *adj* 3

1 ▶NOT SPEAKING 不說話◀ a) not saying anything 不語的, 緘默的, 默默的: *Phil was silent for a moment as he thought about his reply.* 菲爾在回答前沉默了一會兒。| **fall silent** (=become quiet) 安靜下來 *The crowd fell silent when the President appeared.* 總統出現時, 人羣安靜了下來。**b)** not talking much to other people 沉默寡言的: *Nate was in his late teens, a silent and self-contained boy.* 內特將近二十歲, 是個沉默寡言、性格內向的男孩。| **the strong silent type** (=a man who looks strong and does not talk very much) 堅強而沉默寡言的人

2 ▶NOT COMMUNICATING 不交流◀ failing or refusing to talk about something or express an opinion 不表態的, 隻字不提的: **[+on/about]** *The company is suspiciously silent about its plans for cutting costs.* 公司對於削減開支的計劃隻字不提, 令人疑惑。| **remain silent** *The prisoner remained silent when questioned.* 犯人被訊問時保持緘默。

3 ▶QUIET 安靜的◀ without any sound, or not making any sound 無聲的, 寂靜的: *In the early morning the village was completely silent.* 村子在清晨一片寂靜。| *At last the guns were silent.* 槍聲終於沉寂下來了。

4 ▶FILMS 影片◀ a silent film is a cinema film with no sound, of the type made before about 1927〔約在 1927 年前攝製的電影〕無聲的: *silent movies* 無聲電影

5 ▶LETTER 字母◀ a silent letter in a word is not pronounced and does not have a sound 不發音的: *The 'w' in 'wreck' is silent.* 單詞 wreck 中的字母 w 是不發音的。

6 silent as the grave completely silent, often in a way that seems mysterious 寂靜無聲的, 像墳墓一樣寂靜的 —**silently** *adv*

silent ma·jor·i·ty /,·· ·ˈ···/ *n* **the silent majority** all the people in a country who are not politically active, whose opinions are believed to represent the ideas that most ordinary people have 沉默的大多數〔指一國中在政治上不積極的人們, 其意見被認為代表了大多數普通人的觀點〕

silent part·ner /,·· ˈ··/ *n* [C] *AmE* someone who owns part of a business but is not actively involved in the way it operates【美】不參與經營的合夥人; SLEEPING PARTNER *BrE*【英】

sil·hou·ette /ˌsɪluˈɛt; ˌsɪluˈet/ *n* [C] a dark image, shadow, or shape, seen against a light background 側面影像, 黑色輪廓像, 剪影: *The silhouette of the cathedral could be seen against the dawn sky.* 在黎明的天空映襯下可以看見大教堂的輪廓。—**silhouetted** *adj*: *tall chimney stacks silhouetted against the orange flames* 在橙色火焰映襯下高大煙囪的輪廓

sil·i·ca /ˈsɪlɪkə; ˈsɪlɪkə/ *n* [U] a chemical compound that exists naturally as sand, QUARTZ, and FLINT, used in making glass 硅石, 二氧化硅〔製造玻璃的原料〕

sil·i·cate /ˈsɪlɪˌket; ˈsɪlɪkeɪt/ *n* [C,U] *technical* one of a group of common solid mineral substances【術語】硅酸鹽

sil·i·con /ˈsɪlɪkən; ˈsɪlɪkən/ *n* [U] *technical* a simple substance that is not a metal, and exists naturally in large quantities combined with other metals, minerals

S

etc【術語】硅

silicon chip /ˌ··· ˈ·/ *n* [C] a CHIP[1] (4) (=in a computer)〔用於電腦的〕硅片

sil·i·cone /ˈsɪləˌkon; ˈsɪlɨkəʊn/ *n* [U] one of a group of chemicals that are not changed by heat or cold and are used in making types of rubber, oil, and RESIN (2) 硅酮〔一種不因冷熱而變化的化學物質, 用於製造各種橡膠、石油、樹脂等產品〕

silicone im·plant /ˌ··· ˈ··/ *n* [C] a piece of silicone that is put into the body, especially into a woman's breasts to make them larger〔尤指女子隆胸用的〕硅酮植入物

sil·i·co·sis /ˌsɪlɪˈkosɪs; ˌsɪlɨˈkəʊsɨs/ *n* [U] an illness of the lungs caused by breathing SILICA, common among people who work in mines etc 石末沉着病, 硅肺〔常見於礦工〕

silk /sɪlk; sɪlk/ *n* **1** [U] a thin, smooth, soft cloth made from very thin thread which is produced by a silkworm 絲綢: *a silk shirt* 絲綢襯衣 | *a dress made of the finest silk* 用最好的絲綢做的連衣裙 **2** [C] *BrE law* a KC or QC (=type of important lawyer)【英, 法律】英國王室法律顧問, 御用大律師 | **take silk** (=become a KC or QC) 成為御用大律師 **3 silks** *technical* the coloured shirts worn by JOCKEYS (=people who ride horses in races)【術語】〔騎士在賽馬時穿的〕彩色絲綢賽馬服

silk·en /ˈsɪlkən; ˈsɪlkən/ *adj literary*【文】**1** soft, smooth, and shiny like silk〔絲綢般〕柔軟、光滑並有光澤的: *her silken hair* 她那柔軟光滑的頭髮 **2** made of silk 絲綢製的: *a silken handkerchief* 絲綢手絹

silk screen /ˈ· ·/ also 又作 **silk screen print·ing** /ˌ· ·ˈ··/ *n* [U] a way of printing by forcing paint or ink onto a surface through a stretched piece of cloth 絲網印刷(術)

silk·worm /ˈsɪlkˌwɝm; ˈsɪlkwɜːm/ *n* [C] a type of MOTH whose young produces silk thread 蠶

silk·y /ˈsɪlkɪ; ˈsɪlki/ *adj* **1** soft, smooth and shiny, like silk〔絲綢般〕柔滑並有光澤的: *silky fur* 柔滑的皮毛 **2** a silky voice is gentle, and is used especially when someone is trying to persuade you to do something〔聲音〕柔和的〔尤指在試圖説服別人做某事時的話音〕—**silkily** *adv* —**silkiness** *n* [U]

sill /sɪl; sɪl/ *n* [C] **1** the narrow shelf at the base of a window frame 窗台 **2** the part of a car frame at the bottom of the doors 底梁〔指汽車的框架在車門以下的部分〕: *You've got a lot of rust on your sills.* 你汽車的底梁已經銹得很厲害了。

sil·la·bub /ˈsɪləˌbʌb; ˈsɪləbʌb/ *n* [C,U] SYLLABUB 乳酒凍

3 **sil·ly**[1] /ˈsɪlɪ; ˈsɪli/ *adj* **1** not sensible, showing bad judgment 蠢的, 愚昧的: *This may sound like a silly question, but what is the point of this exercise?* 也許我問得很傻, 可是, 這種運動有甚麼意思? | **a silly thing to do/say** *I left my keys at home, which was a pretty silly thing to do.* 我把鑰匙落在家裡了, 幹了件沒腦子的事。—see 見 SHAME[1] (USAGE) **2** stupid in a childish or embarrassing way 傻的, 可笑的: *I wish you kids would stop being so silly.* 我希望你們這些小傢伙不要這麼傻了。| *a silly hat* 一頂可笑的帽子 | *I hate their parties – we always end up playing silly games.* 我討厭他們的聚會 —— 最後總是玩一些愚蠢的遊戲。**3** *spoken* not serious or practical【口】隨便的; 不切實際的; 不實用的: *They served us coffee in these silly little cups.* 他們竟然用這種不實用的小杯子給我們上咖啡。| *Try making a silly offer – they might just accept it.* 隨便開個價 —— 他們也許就會接受的。**4 bore sb silly** *informal* to make someone extremely bored【非正式】令某人極為厭煩 **5 drink yourself silly** *informal* to get very drunk【非正式】喝得爛醉 —**silliness** *n* [U]

silly[2] *n* [singular] *spoken* used to tell someone that you think they are being stupid【口】傻瓜, 笨蛋: *No, silly, I didn't mean that!* 不, 傻瓜, 我不是那個意思!

silly bil·ly /ˈ·· ˌ··/ *n* [C] *spoken* used to tell someone, especially a child, that they are behaving in a silly way【口】〔尤指小孩〕笨蛋, 小傻瓜

silly sea·son /ˈ·· ˌ··/ *n* **the silly season** *BrE informal* a period in the summer when newspapers print stories that are not very serious because there is not much political news【英, 非正式】新聞淡季,〔新聞界的〕無聊季節〔在夏季, 報上因政治新聞不多而登載一些不很嚴肅的內容〕

si·lo /ˈsaɪlo; ˈsaɪləʊ/ *n* [C] **1** a tall structure like a tower that is used for storing grain, winter food for farm animals etc〔貯藏牲畜冬季用飼料等的〕青貯塔 **2** a large structure under the ground from which a large MISSILE can be fired 導彈地下發射井

silt[1] /sɪlt; sɪlt/ *n* [U] moving sand, mud, soil etc that is carried in water and then settles at a bend in a river, an entrance to a port etc 淤泥,〔沉積的〕泥沙

silt[2] *v*

silt up *phr v* [I,T] to fill or become filled with silt (使)淤塞; (被)淤塞: *The old harbour silted up years ago.* 這個老港灣在許多年前就淤塞了。

sil·van /ˈsɪlvən; ˈsɪlvən/ *adj* SYLVAN (在)森林和鄉村中的

sil·ver[1] /ˈsɪlvɚ; ˈsɪlvə/ *n* **1** [U] a shiny, whitish, valuable metal that is used to make jewellery, knives, coins etc, 3
and is a chemical ELEMENT 銀 **2** [U] spoons, forks, dishes etc that are made of silver or a similar metal 銀餐具〈如湯匙、叉子、碟子等〉: *As kitchen-maid, it was my job to polish the silver.* 作為幫廚女傭, 我的工作是擦亮銀餐具。**3** [U] the colour of silver 銀(白)色 **4** [C] *informal* a SILVER MEDAL【非正式】銀獎牌 **5** [U] *BrE old-fashioned* coins that are made partly or completely of silver【英, 過時】銀幣 —see also 另見 **be born with a silver spoon in your mouth** (BORN[2] (11)), **every cloud has a silver lining** (CLOUD[1] (7))

silver[2] *adj* **1** made of silver 銀製的, 銀質的: *a silver teapot* 銀茶壺 **2** coloured silver 銀(白)色的: *a silver Mercedes* 銀白色的平治汽車

silver[3] *v* [T] *technical* to cover a surface with a thin shiny silver coloured surface in order to make a mirror【術語】給...包銀, 在...上鍍銀〔或銀色物質以製作鏡子〕

silver an·ni·ver·sa·ry /ˌ·· ··ˈ···/ *n* [C] SILVER WEDDING ANNIVERSARY 銀婚

silver birch /ˌ·· ˈ·/ *n* [C,U] a type of BIRCH tree that has a silvery-white TRUNK and branches 紙皮樺, 銀樺(樹)

silver dol·lar /ˌ·· ˈ··/ *n* [C] a former US one dollar coin, that is now very valuable〔美國過去的〕銀元, 一元銀幣〔現已很珍貴〕

sil·ver·fish /ˈsɪlvɚˌfɪʃ; ˈsɪlvəfɪʃ/ *n plural* **silverfish** or **silverfishes** [C] a small silver-coloured insect that is found in houses and sometimes damages paper or cloth 蠹魚〔一種蛀蝕紙和布的銀色小昆蟲〕

silver foil /ˌ·· ˈ·/ *n* [U] *BrE* FOIL (=very thin sheets of metal)【英】箔; 金屬薄片

silver ju·bi·lee /ˌ·· ˈ···/ *n* [C] *especially BrE* the date that is exactly 25 years after the date of an important public event, especially a CORONATION【尤英】25週年紀念〔尤指加冕紀念〕: *the Queen's Silver Jubilee* 女王加冕25週年紀念

silver med·al /ˌ·· ˈ··/ *n* [C] a MEDAL made of silver that is given to the person who finishes second in a race or competition〔獎給亞軍的〕銀獎牌

silver pa·per /ˌ·· ˈ··◂/ *n* [U] *BrE* paper that is shiny like metal on one side, used especially for wrapping food【英】錫紙, 銀箔紙〔尤用於包裝食物〕

silver plate /ˌ·· ˈ·◂/ *n* [U] metal with a thin covering of silver 外層鍍銀的金屬 —**silver-plated** *adj*: *a silver-plated candlestick* 鍍銀的燭台

silver screen /ˌ·· ˈ·/ *n* **the silver screen** *old-fashioned* the film industry, especially of Hollywood【過時】電影業〔尤指荷里活〕: *stars of the silver screen* 電影明星

sil·ver·smith /ˈsɪlvɚˌsmɪθ; ˈsɪlvəˌsmɪθ/ *n* [C] someone who makes things out of silver 銀(器)匠

silver-tongued /ˌ·· ˈ·◂/ *adj especially literary* good at talking to people and persuading them【尤文】講話有説

服力的, 雄辯的

sil·ver·ware /ˈsɪlvɚˌwɛr; ˈsɪlvəweə/ *n* [U] **1** objects made of silver, especially knives, spoons, dishes etc 銀器; 銀餐具 **2** *AmE* knives, spoons and forks made of any metal【美】金屬餐具〔刀子、湯匙、叉子等〕—see picture on page A15 參見A15頁圖

silver wed·ding an·ni·ver·sa·ry /ˌ.. ˈ.. ..ˌ.../ *n* [C] the date that is exactly 25 years after the date of a wedding 銀婚〔結婚25週年紀念日〕

sil·ver·y /ˈsɪlvərɪ; ˈsɪlvəri/ *adj* **1** shiny and silver in colour 光亮如銀的, 銀白色的: *the silvery light of the moon* 銀色的月光 **2** *especially literary* having a pleasant, light, musical sound【尤文】〔聲音〕銀鈴般的, 清脆悦耳的: *peals of silvery laughter* 一陣陣銀鈴般的笑聲

sim·i·an /ˈsɪmɪən; ˈsɪmiən/ *adj technical* connected with or similar to a monkey or APE[1] (1)【術語】(像) 猿[猴]的 —**simian** *n* [C]

1 1 **sim·i·lar** /ˈsɪmələ˞; ˈsɪmələ/ *adj* **1** almost the same but not exactly the same 相似的, 近似的, 類似的: *We have similar tastes in music.* 我們對音樂的品味相近。| *students of roughly similar abilities* 能力相當的學生 | *These two signatures are so similar it's very difficult to tell them apart.* 這兩個簽名非常相似, 很難區別。| *I saw something similar in yesterday's 'Times'.* 我在昨天的《泰晤士報》上看到類似的內容。| [+to] *My opinions on the matter are similar to Kay's.* 我對這件事的見解和凱差不多。**2** [no comparative 無比較級] *technical* exactly the same in shape but not size【術語】相似的〔形狀相同但大小有異的〕: *Similar triangles have equal angles.* 相似三角形的諸角都相等。—see also 另見 SIMILARLY

2 **sim·i·lar·i·ty** /ˌsɪməˈlærətɪ; ˌsɪmɪ̣ˈlærɪ̣ti/ *n* **1** [U] the fact of being similar to something else, or the degree to which two or more things are similar to each other; RESEMBLANCE 類似, 相似: **[+between]** *a striking similarity between the two designs* 這兩項設計之間驚人的相似 | [+to] *What I like about his poetry is its similarity to Wordsworth's.* 我喜歡他的詩是它跟華茲華斯的很相似。| *The stories show some similarity to parts of the Old Testament.* 這些故事與《舊約全書》的若干部分有些近似。**2** [C] a way in which things or people are similar 類似之點, 相似之處: *The police say there are some similarities between the two attacks.* 警方説這兩次襲擊之間有些相似之處。| [+in] *When studying children and other young animals we can see similarities in their behaviour.* 在研究小孩和其他動物幼兒時, 我們可以看到兩者在行為上的一些類似之處。

sim·i·lar·ly /ˈsɪmələ˞lɪ; ˈsɪmɪ̣ləli/ *adv* in a similar way 差不多, 相似地; 同樣地, 相同地: **similarly situated/expressed/inclined etc** *This idea is similarly expressed in his most recent book.* 這一觀點在他最近出版的新書中也有類似的表達。| [sentence adverb 句子副詞] *Men must wear a jacket and tie. Similarly, women must wear a skirt or dress and not trousers.* 男士必須穿外套並打領帶。同樣, 女士必須穿裙子或連衣裙, 不能穿褲子。

sim·i·le /ˈsɪməlɪ; ˈsɪmɪ̣li/ *n* **1** [C] an expression that describes something by comparing it with something else, using the words 'as' or 'like', for example 'as white as snow' 明喻〔用as或like將兩件事物作比較, 如"像雪一樣白"〕 **2** [U] the use of expressions like this 明喻的用法

sim·mer[1] /ˈsɪmɚ; ˈsɪmə/ *v* **1** [I,T] to cook something slowly in water that is gently boiling 〔用文火〕慢慢地煮, 煨, 燉: *A pot was simmering on the stove.* 一隻鍋在爐子上煨着。**2** [I] if you are simmering or your emotions are simmering, you feel anger, hate, love etc very strongly, and can only just prevent yourself from expressing it 內心充滿某種強烈的感情〈如怒火、仇恨、愛等〉;〔怒火、仇恨、愛等〕即將爆發: *Passions were simmering underneath the surface.* 激情正在內心湧動。| [+with] *The crowd was simmering with rage by the time the defendant arrived in court.* 當被告到達法庭時, 人羣怒火中燒。**3 simmer down!** *spoken* used to tell someone to be less excited, angry etc【口】冷靜下來! 請息怒!: *Simmer down, Holly – it won't help to lose your temper.* 冷靜點, 霍莉——發脾氣是無濟於事的。

simmer[2] *n* [singular] the condition of simmering 慢慢沸騰的狀態, 將沸未沸狀態, 小沸: *Bring the vegetables to a simmer.* 用文火煮這些菜。

sim·nel cake /ˈsɪmnəl ˌkek; ˈsɪmnəl ˌkeɪk/ *n* [C] *BrE* a cake made with dried fruit, that is traditionally eaten at Easter【英】水果蛋糕〔復活節傳統食品〕

sim·pat·i·co /sɪmˈpætɪko; sɪmˈpætɪkəʊ/ *adj AmE informal*【美, 非正式】**1** someone who is simpatico is easy to like 可愛的, 討人喜歡的 **2** in agreement 一致的, 和諧的: *He and I are simpatico about a lot of things.* 我和他對許多問題的看法都很一致。

sim·per /ˈsɪmpɚ; ˈsɪmpə/ *v* [I] to smile in a silly, annoying way 傻笑, 假笑: *Betsy simpered coyly at him as she spoke.* 貝特西説話時對他靦腆地傻笑。—**simper** *n* [C] —**simperingly** *adv*

sim·ple /ˈsɪmpl; ˈsɪmpəl/ *adj* 1 1

1 ▶PLAIN 樸素◀ without a lot of decoration or unnecessary things added 無裝飾的, 簡樸的, 樸素的: *a simple dress* 樸素的連衣裙 | *simple but delicious food* 簡單美味的食物 | *a building constructed in a simple, classic style* 建築風格樸實無華的傳統式樓房

2 ▶EASY 容易◀ not difficult or complicated 簡單的, 簡易的, 容易的: *I'm sure there's a perfectly simple explanation.* 我肯定有一個十分簡單的解釋。| *a simple but effective solution to the problem* 對這個問題簡單而有效的解決辦法 | **it's not as simple as that** *spoken* (=used to say that something is not as easy as someone thinks it is)【口】沒有〔某人〕所想的那麼容易 *I wish we could offer you more money but I'm afraid it's not as simple as that.* 我希望我們能多給你一點錢, 但事情並沒有那麼簡單。

3 ▶ONLY 僅僅◀ [only before noun 僅用於名詞前] not complicated or involving anything else 單純的, 純粹的; 不複雜的: *Completing the race is not just a simple matter of physical fitness.* 要跑畢全程不僅是具備強健體格的問題。| *We can't do it, for the simple reason that we don't have enough time.* 我們做不了, 這純粹是因為我們沒有足夠的時間。| **the simple truth/fact is** (=used to emphasize the truth about something) 事實就是〔用於強調事實〕*The simple truth is, he isn't good enough for the job.* 坦白地説, 他不能勝任這份工作。| **pure and simple** (=without any other reason or feature) 僅僅如此, 沒有其他原因 *Their motive was greed, pure and simple.* 他們的動機就是貪婪, 就是這樣。

4 ▶NOT HAVING MANY PARTS 沒有許多部分◀ consisting of only a few necessary parts 結構簡單的: *Bacteria are simple forms of life.* 細菌是結構簡單的生命形式。| *A knife is a simple tool.* 刀子是一種簡單的工具。

5 ▶ORDINARY 普通◀ honest and ordinary and not special in any way 誠實的, 樸實的, 普通的: *Joe was just a simple farmer.* 喬只是一個普普通通的農民。

6 the simple life *informal* life without all the problems of the modern world, especially life in the countryside, without too many possessions, or modern machines【非正式】簡樸的生活〔尤指鄉村生活〕

7 ▶UNINTELLIGENT 不聰明◀ [not before noun 不用於名詞前] not intelligent 頭腦簡單的, 愚蠢的: *I'm afraid old Luke's a bit simple.* 我覺得老盧克似乎有點傻。

simple frac·ture /ˌ.. ˈ../ *n* [C] *technical* a broken or cracked bone that does not cut through the flesh that surrounds it【術語】單純骨折 —compare 比較 COMPOUND FRACTURE

simple in·terest /ˌ.. ˈ.../ *n* [U] INTEREST[1] (4) that is calculated on the sum of money that you first invested (INVEST (1)), and does not include the interest it has already earned 單利 —compare 比較 COMPOUND INTEREST

simple-mind·ed /ˌ.. ˈ..◂/ *adj* unable to understand complicated things, and not showing much understanding of the world 頭腦簡單的, 愚鈍的, 不懂事的: *a simple-*

S

minded desire for a return to the past 一種想要回到過去的愚蠢的想法

sim·ple·ton /ˋsɪmpl̩tən; ˈsɪmpəltən/ *n* [C] *old-fashioned* someone who has a very low level of intelligence【過時】智能低下的人, 傻子, 蠢人

sim·pli·ci·ty /sɪmˋplɪsətɪ; sɪmˈplɪsɪ̈ti/ *n* [U] the quality of being simple, especially when this is attractive or useful 樸素, 簡樸, 簡單: *Mona wrote with a beautiful simplicity of style.* 莫娜的文筆優美而質樸。| *For the sake of simplicity, the tax form is divided into three sections.* 為簡單明瞭起見, 稅務表格分成三個部分。| **be simplicity itself** (=be very simple) 十分簡單 *The plan was simplicity itself – how could she have misunderstood?* 這個計劃簡單得很 —— 她怎麼可能誤解了?

sim·pli·fy /ˋsɪmpləˌfaɪ; ˈsɪmplɪ̈faɪ/ *past tense and past participle* **simplified** *v* [T] to make something easier or less complicated 使簡易, 使簡明, 簡化: *an attempt to simplify the tax laws* 簡化稅收法的嘗試 | *Try to simplify your explanation for the children.* 設法解釋得簡明一些, 好讓孩子們聽懂。—see also 另見 OVERSIMPLIFY —**simplified** *adj*: *a simplified version of Chinese script* 簡化漢字 —**simplification** /ˌsɪmpləfəˋkeʃən; ˌsɪmplɪ̈fɪ̈ˈkeɪʃən/ *n* [C,U]

sim·plis·tic /sɪmˋplɪstɪk; sɪmˈplɪstɪk/ *adj* treating difficult subjects in a way that is too simple 過分簡單化的: *a naive and simplistic approach to economic policy* 對經濟政策問題幼稚而簡單化的處理方法 —**simplistically** /-klɪ; -kli/ *adv*

1 1 **sim·ply** /ˋsɪmplɪ; ˈsɪmpli/ *adv* **1** only 僅僅, 只不過: *Some students lose marks simply because they don't read the question properly.* 有些學生失分只是因為沒有把題目看清楚。| *Simply fill in the coupon and take it to your local store.* 只要把這張優惠券填好交給當地的商店就行。| *It isn't simply a question of money.* 這不僅僅是錢的問題。**2** in a way that is easy to understand 簡易地, 簡單明瞭地; 清楚地: *Try to express yourself more simply.* 試把你的意思表達得更簡單明瞭。| **to put it simply** (=to explain things in a simple way) 簡單地說 *To put it simply, the tax cuts mean the average worker will be about 3% better off.* 簡單地說, 減稅意味着每個普通工人的工資大約增加3%。**3** used to emphasize what you are saying 簡直, 完全, 實在〔用以強調所說的話〕: *What a simply wonderful idea!* 一個多麼精彩的想法啊! | *This piece of work simply isn't good enough.* 這項工作做得實在不夠好。| **quite simply** *It is, quite simply, the most ridiculous idea I've ever heard.* 這簡直是我所聽到過的最荒謬的想法。**4** in a plain and ordinary way, without spending much money 樸素地, 簡樸地: *We had to live very simply on my father's small salary.* 我們只能依靠父親微薄的工資簡樸地過活。

sim·u·la·crum /ˌsɪmjəˋlekrəm; ˌsɪmjʊ̈ˈleɪkrəm/ *n* [C+of] *formal* an image of something【正式】像, 影像

sim·u·late /ˋsɪmjuˌlet; ˈsɪmjʊ̈leɪt/ *v* [T] **1** to make or produce something that is not real but has the appearance of being real 模仿, 模擬: *a machine that simulates conditions in space* 一台模擬太空狀況的機器 | *A sheet of metal can be shaken to simulate thunder.* 抖動金屬片可以模仿雷聲。**2** *formal* to pretend to have a feeling; FEIGN【正式】假裝, 偽裝: *We tried to simulate surprise.* 我們假裝吃驚。

sim·u·lat·ed /ˋsɪmjəˌletɪd; ˈsɪmjʊ̈leɪtɪ̈d/ *adj* not real, but made to look, feel etc like a real thing, situation, or feeling 模仿的, 模擬的, 仿製的; 假裝的: *simulated leather* 仿皮革 | *a simulated nuclear explosion* 模擬的核爆炸

sim·u·la·tion /ˌsɪmjəˋleʃən; ˌsɪmjʊ̈ˈleɪʃən/ *n* **1** [C,U] an activity or situation that produces conditions which are not real, but have the appearance of being real, used especially for testing something〔用於試驗的〕模擬操作; 模擬研究: *a computer simulation used to train airline pilots* 用於訓練飛行員的電腦模擬程序 | **[+of]** *an audio-visual simulation of the beginning of the universe* 對宇宙誕生情景的一次視聽模擬試驗 **2** [U] the act or process of simulating something 模擬, 模仿

sim·u·la·tor /ˋsɪmjəˌletɚ; ˈsɪmjʊ̈leɪtə/ *n* [C] a piece of equipment used for training people by letting them feel what real conditions are like, for example in an aircraft〔用於人員訓練的〕模擬裝置, 模擬器: *a flight simulator* 飛行模擬裝置

sim·ul·cast /ˋsɪməlˌkæst; ˈsɪməlkɑːst/ *v* [T usually passive 一般用被動態] *AmE* to broadcast a programme on television and radio at the same time【美】〔無線電和電視〕聯播〔節目〕—**simulcast** *n* [C]

sim·ul·ta·ne·ous /ˌsaɪml̩ˋtenɪəs; ˌsɪməlˈteɪniəs◂/ *adj* happening or done at exactly the same time 同時〔發生或做出〕的: *a simultaneous broadcast of the concert on TV and radio* 電視和電台對音樂會的聯播 | **simultaneous translation** (=immediate translation of what someone is saying as they are speaking) 同聲翻譯 —**simultaneously** *adv*: *two pictures taken simultaneously from different camera angles* 同時從兩個不同攝影角度拍下的兩張照片 —**simultaneity** /ˌsaɪml̩təˋniətɪ; ˌsɪməltəˈniːɪ̈ti/ *n* [U]

sin¹ /sɪn; sɪn/ *n* **1** [C,U] disobedience to God, or an offence against God or religious laws〔冒犯上帝或宗教法規的〕罪, 罪惡, 罪孽: *The Bible says adultery is a sin.* 《聖經》說通姦是一種罪。| *the sin of pride* 傲慢之罪 | *the Christian concept of sin* 基督教對罪的概念 | **commit a sin** (=do something that breaks a religious law) 造孽 **2** [singular] *informal* something that you strongly disapprove of【非正式】過錯, 罪過: *It's a sin the way they waste all this money.* 他們浪費那麼多錢, 真是罪過。| **commit a sin** *I had committed the unforgivable sin of forgetting her birthday.* 我忘記了她的生日, 犯了不可饒恕的過錯。| **it's a sin to do sth** *It'd be a sin to evict them just because they haven't paid their rent.* 僅僅因為沒有交房租就把他們趕出去, 這是很不對的。**3 live in sin** *old-fashioned* if two people live in sin they live together in a sexual relationship without being married【過時】〔未婚男女〕同居, 姘居 **4 as miserable/ugly/guilty as sin** *spoken* very unhappy, ugly, guilty etc【口】非常不愉快/難看/內疚 **5 for my sins** *spoken especially BrE* an expression used to suggest jokingly that something is like a punishment【口, 尤英】自作自受, 活該, 該死: *I'm the local party organizer, for my sins.* 我是當地聚會的組織者, 真是自討苦吃。—see also 另見 SINFUL, **cover/hide a multitude of sins** (MULTITUDE (3)), ORIGINAL SIN —**sinless** *adj* 2

sin² *v* **sinned, sinning** [I] **1** to break God's laws 違反上帝的戒律, 違犯教規: **[+against]** *He has sinned against God.* 他得罪了上帝 **2 be more sinned against than sinning** *old-fashioned* used to say that someone should not be blamed for what they have done wrong, because they have been badly treated by other people【過時】人負我甚於我負人; 受到超過應得的懲罰

sin³ *technical*【術語】the written abbreviation of 縮寫= SINE

since¹ /sɪns; sɪns/ *conjunction* [used with the present perfect and the past perfect tenses 與現在完成式及過去完成式連用] **1** at a time after a particular time or event in the past 自從…以來, 自從…以後: *In the 12 months since I last wrote to you a lot has happened to me.* 自從上次我給你寫信以後的12個月裡, 我經歷了許多事。| *I can't have seen him since 1983.* 自1983年以來, 我不可能見過他。| *It's been years since I enjoyed myself so much.* 我已有很多年沒有那樣痛快過了。**2** during the period of time after a particular time or event in the past 從…以後〔的一段時間裡〕, 自從…以來就一直…: *Since he started that diet he's lost over 20 lbs in weight.* 自從開始節食以來, 他體重已減了二十多磅。| **ever since** *We've been friends ever since we met at school.* 我們自從在學校認識以來一直是朋友。**3** used to give the reason for something 因為, 既然: *I'll be forty next month, since you ask.* 既然你問起, 我下個月就滿四十歲了。| *Since you are unable to answer perhaps we should ask someone else.* 既 1 1

然你不能回答，我們也許該問問別人。

[口語 2] [書面語 2] **since²** *prep* [used with the present perfect and the past perfect tenses 與現在完成式及過去完成式連用] **1** at a time in the past after a particular time or event 自從…以來，自從…之後: *They haven't met since the wedding last year.* 自從去年那個婚禮之後，他們就再沒有見過面了。| *Since the end of the war over a dozen hostages have been released.* 自從戰爭結束以來，已有超過十二名人質獲釋了。—compare 比較 FOR¹ (8) **2** for the whole of a long period of time after a particular time or event in the past 自從…以後(的整段時間裡)，從…以後一直…: *Since the day we met I have known he was not to be trusted.* 從我們認識那天起，我就知道他不可靠。| **ever since** *Ever since the war she's been able to feed a whole family with a few potatoes and eggs.* 自從戰爭以來，她只能一直用幾個馬鈴薯和雞蛋養活全家。**3 since when?** *spoken* used in questions to show surprise, anger etc【口】自從甚麼時候起…?〔用於問句表示驚訝、氣憤等〕: *Have you checked this bill? Since when does £42 plus £5 service charge come to £48?* 你檢查過這張賬單沒有? 甚麼時候起42英鎊加5英鎊服務費等於48英鎊?

[口語 3] **since³** *adv* [used with the present perfect and the past perfect tenses 與現在完成式及過去完成式連用] **1** at a time in the past after a particular time or event 從那時以來，後來: *Her husband died over ten years ago but she has since remarried.* 她丈夫於十多年前去世，但她後來又結婚了。| *I've since forgotten what our argument was about.* 我後來就忘掉我們為甚麼爭吵了。| *He walked out of that door last Tuesday and no one's seen him since.* 他上星期二從那個門口走了出去，以後就再沒有人見過他了。**2** for the whole of a long period of time after a particular time or event in the past 從那時至今〔的整段時間裡〕，從那時起一直…: *The accident happened four years ago and she has hardly spoken since.* 四年前發生了事故，從那以後她幾乎一直沒有說過話。| **ever since** *We came to the UK in 1974 and have lived here ever since.* 我們於1974年來英國，自此便一直住在這裡。**3 long since** if something has long since happened, it happened a long time ago 很久以前，早已…: *I've long since forgiven her for what she did.* 我早已原諒她的所作所為了。

USAGE NOTE 用法說明: SINCE

WORD CHOICE 詞語辨析: **since (prep/conj), from, after, from..to/till/until, for**

Since is mainly used where you want to talk about a state or activity that started at some time in the past and has continued to the time when you are speaking. since 主要用於表示在過去某個時間發生並持續至說話時的情況或活動: *I've been here since ten o'clock this morning.* 我今天上午十點以後一直都在這裡。| *The place had completely changed since I went there three years ago* (NOT 不用 *It has changed since three years/three years before*). 自從我三年前去過那裡以後，那個地方已經完全變樣了。

From or **after** may be used to show the starting points of periods of time where you do not use **since**. 表示某段時間的起點用 from 或 after 而不用 since。For example 例如: *I hope they'll be friends from now on* (NOT 不用 *since now on*)（我希望他們從現在起成為朋友）means I hope they will be friends from now and into the future. 這表示我希望他們從現在到將來都是朋友。*She was very unhappy for a while after leaving home* (NOT 不用 *since*)（她離家以後有一段時間很不愉快）means that she was unhappy from a period of time in the past until a later time in the past. 這表示她這一段不愉快的時間是從過去某個時間開始，到後來某個時間結束。

From...to/until/till is used where you want to give both ends of a period of time during which some state existed or some activity was being done. This construction can go with most tenses of the verb. from...to/until/till 用於表示某種狀態或活動所持續時段的起止，並可與大多數時態連用: *I was here from ten till two.* 我從十點到兩點都在這裡。| *From 1990 to the present he's had no regular job* (NOT 不用 *since 1990 to the present*). 從1990年到現在，他一直沒有固定的工作。| *She works from sunrise until sunset.* 她從日出工作到日落。

For is used where you want to give the length of a period of time, but do not need to say exactly when it started or finished. It goes with all tenses of verbs. for 用於表示時段的長度，但不必準確說明起止的時間。它可與動詞各種時態連用: *We lived there for a long time.* 我們在那裡住了很長時間。| *She's only staying for a week.* 她只準備逗留一個星期。When you use **for** with the present perfect tense, it gives a period of time that ends at the time of speaking. 當 for 與現在完成式連用時，所指時段在說話之時結束: *I've been waiting for two hours* (NOT 不用 *since two hours*). 我已等了兩小時了。

In spoken English the **for** is often left out 在英語口語中 for 常被省略: *I've been here two hours.* 我在這裡已有兩小時了。| *She's only staying a week.* 她只準備逗留一星期。

GRAMMAR 語法

The point of time with **since** may be shown by a clause, which may contain a verb in the simple past. since 所指的時間起點可以用從句表示，從句中的時態可以用一般過去式: *He's been ill ever since he arrived.* 他自從到達後就一直在生病。

The point of time with **since** may also be shown less exactly, by mentioning a period of time that ended in the past. since 所指的時間起點也可以不甚明確，而只用一個在過去結束的時段來表示: *He's been working here since last week/the 60s* (=he started at some time during the 60s). 他自從上個星期以來/從60年代以來一直在這裡工作。| *Since I was a kid I've always wanted to visit Disney World.* 從我的孩提時代起，我就一直想去迪士尼樂園。

A **since** clause may also itself cover the whole period from a point in the past to the time of speaking. since 所引導的從句本身也可以覆蓋從過去的時間起點直至說話之時的整個時段: *Since she's been living here she's made a lot of friends.* 自從她住在這裡以來，她已結交了許多朋友。

However, as in all the above examples, the main verb in any clause with **since** usually has to be in one of the perfect tenses. 但是，正如以上各例所示，凡用 since 的句子，其主動詞通常得用其中一種完成時態。Compare also 還請比較: *Yesterday Bobby told me he hadn't eaten since Tuesday.* (=between Tuesday and yesterday he did not eat anything) 昨天博比告訴我，他從星期二起就沒吃甚麼東西了。

Non-perfect tenses are used only in particular situations, for example where you are talking about the length of time itself. 非完成時態只用於特殊情況，例如談的是時段本身的長度: *It's two weeks since I've seen you* (NOT 不用 *...since I haven't seen you*). 從我上次見你到現在已有兩星期了。| *It seems like months since you last paid me.* 從你上次給我發工資到現在，好像有幾個月了。Note also 另請注意: *Since the car accident she can't walk properly.* (=she hasn't been able to walk properly) 自從出了車禍以後，她一直不能正常走路。

sin·cere /sɪn`sɪr; sɪn'sɪə/ *adj* **1** a feeling, belief, statement etc that is sincere is honest and true, and based on what you really feel and believe; GENUINE (1)〔感情等〕由衷的，真誠的，真心實意的: *sincere admiration* 由衷的

欽佩 | *a sincere desire to find out the truth* 弄清真相的真誠願望 **2** someone who is sincere is honest and says what they really feel or believe〔人〕誠實的, 不虛偽的, 誠懇的: *He was gentle and sincere by nature.* 他本性温和正直。| **[+in]** *They were completely sincere in their beliefs.* 他們對自己的信仰是完全真誠的。—opposite 反義詞 INSINCERE

sin·cere·ly /sɪnˋsɪrlɪ; sɪnˈsɪəli/ *adv* **1** in a sincere way 由衷地, 真誠地; 真摯地: *I sincerely hope I'll see her again.* 我衷心希望再見到她。| *a sincerely held belief* 虔誠的信仰 **2 sincerely/yours sincerely** an expression used to end a formal letter that you have begun by addressing someone by name 謹上, 敬上, 謹啟〔寫在正式信件末尾的客套話〕

sin·cer·i·ty /sɪnˋsɛrətɪ; sɪnˈserɪ̣ti/ *n* [U] **1** the quality of honestly believing something or really meaning what you say 真誠, 真摯, 誠實: *I don't doubt her sincerity, but I think she's got her facts wrong.* 我不懷疑她的誠意, 但我認為她沒弄清楚事實。**2 in all sincerity** *formal* very sincerely【正式】十分真誠地: *May I say in all sincerity that your support has been most valuable.* 請讓我由衷地說, 你的支持極為寶貴。

sine /saɪn; saɪn/ *n* [C] *technical* the FRACTION (2) calculated for an angle by dividing the length of the side opposite it in a TRIANGLE with a RIGHT ANGLE by the length of the side opposite the RIGHT ANGLE【術語】〔數學上的〕正弦 —compare 比較 COSINE, TANGENT (3)

si·ne·cure /ˋsaɪnɪˌkjʊr; ˈsaɪnɪkjʊə/ *n* [C] a job which you get paid for even though you do not have to do very much〔有薪酬而工作不多的〕閒職, 掛名職務, 領乾薪的職位

si·ne qua non /ˋsaɪnɪ kwe ˋnɑn; ˌsɪni kwɑː ˈnəʊn/ *n* [singular] *Latin formal* something that you must have, or which must exist, for something else to be possible【拉丁, 正式】必要的條件, 必需的東西, 必具的資格: **[+for/of]** *The control of inflation is a sine qua non for economic stability.* 控制通貨膨脹是經濟穩定的必要條件。

sin·ew /ˋsɪnju; ˈsɪnjuː/ *n* [C,U] **1** *not technical* a long strong piece of TISSUE (3) in your body that connects a muscle to a bone【非術語】腱〔連接骨與肌肉的索狀組織〕**2** [usually plural 一般用複數] *literary* a means of strength or support【文】力量的源泉, 支柱: *the sinews of our national defense* 我國國防的中流砥柱

sin·ew·y /ˋsɪnjəwɪ; ˈsɪnjuːi/ *adj* having strong muscles 肌肉發達的, 強壯的: *a big man with long, sinewy arms* 胳膊又長又壯的高個男子

sin·ful /ˋsɪnfʊl; ˈsɪnfəl/ *adj* **1** *literary or biblical* morally wrong or guilty of doing something morally wrong【文或聖經】有罪過的: *a sinful man* 罪孽深重的男子 | *Even within marriage they believed it was sinful to seek pleasure in sex.* 他們認為, 即使在婚姻生活中追求性愉悅也是罪過。**2** very wrong or bad 有嚴重過錯的, 極不應該的: *a sinful waste of taxpayers' money* 對納稅人錢款極不應該的浪費 —**sinfully** *adv*

1 2 **sing** /sɪŋ; sɪŋ/ *v past tense* **sang** /sæŋ; sæŋ/ *past participle* **sung** /sʌŋ; sʌŋ/ **1** [I,T] to produce musical sounds, songs etc with your voice 唱, 歌唱: *Sophie's been singing in the church choir for years.* 索菲參加教會合唱團唱歌已經多年了。| **sing a song/tune etc** *We all enjoy singing carols at Christmas.* 我們都喜歡在聖誕節唱頌歌。| **sing sb a song/tune etc** *Come on, sing us a song!* 來吧, 給我們唱支歌! | **sing to sb** *She walked along, singing to herself.* 她邊走邊唱。**2 sing sb to sleep** to sing to a baby or child until they go to sleep 唱歌哄〔嬰兒或小孩〕入睡 **3** [I] if birds sing, they produce high musical sounds〔鳥〕啼, 囀: *I awoke to hear the birds singing outside my window.* 我醒來聽到鳥兒在窗外啼囀。**4** [I always+adv/prep] to make a high, continuous, ringing sound 嗚嗚作響, 發嗡嗡[嗖嗖]聲: **[+on]** *A kettle was singing on the stove.* 爐上的水壺在嗚嗚作響。| **[+past/by etc]** *An enemy bullet sang past my ear.* 敵人的一顆子彈從我耳邊嗖的一聲飛過。**5 sing sb's praise(s)** to praise someone very much 高度讚揚某人: *Diane really admires you – she's always singing your praises.* 黛安娜的確很佩服你 —— 她總是高度讚揚你。**6** [I] *slang* to tell someone or the police everything you know about a crime, especially a crime you were involved in yourself【俚】招供, 交待罪行: *We'll soon make him sing.* 我們很快就會讓他老實交待了。**7** [I+of,T] *literary* to praise someone in poetry【文】用詩歌讚美,〔用詩〕歌頌, 吟詠

sing along *phr v* [I] to sing with someone else who is already singing 跟着〔某人〕一起唱: *Sing along if you know the words.* 如果你們知道歌詞, 就跟着一起唱吧。

sing out *phr v* [I,T] *informal* to sing or shout out clearly and loudly【非正式】大聲唱; 高聲叫喊: *If you see anything that looks interesting, sing out.* 如果你們看到甚麼有趣的東西就喊出來。

sing up *phr v* [I] to sing more loudly 放聲[大聲]唱: *Sing up, boys, I can't hear you!* 唱大聲些, 孩子們, 我聽不見呢!

sing·a·long /ˋsɪŋəˌlɔŋ; ˈsɪŋəlɒŋ/ *n* [C] *AmE* an informal occasion when people sing songs together【美】〔非正式的大家一起唱的〕唱歌聚會; SINGSONG *BrE*【英】

singe¹ /sɪndʒ; sɪndʒ/ *v* [I,T] to burn something slightly on its surface or edge, or to be burned in this way (把)〔表面或邊上〕略微燒焦: *If the iron's too hot it'll singe your shirt.* 如果熨斗太熱, 它會把你的襯衣燙焦。

singe² *n* [C] a mark made by burning something slightly 輕微燒焦的痕跡

sing·er /ˋsɪŋɚ; ˈsɪŋə/ *n* [C] someone who sings, especially as a profession〔尤指職業的〕歌手, 歌唱家: *an opera singer* 歌劇演唱家 | *a pop singer* 流行歌手 3

singer-song·writ·er /ˌ.. ˋ..../ *n* [C] someone who writes songs and sings them 創作型歌手, 歌手兼歌曲作者

sing·ha·lese /sɪŋgəˋliz; ˌsɪŋgəˈliːz◂/ *n, adj* SINHALESE 僧伽羅人; 僧伽羅語

sin·gle¹ /ˋsɪŋgl; ˈsɪŋgəl/ *adj* 2 1

1 ▶ONE 一(個)◀ [only before noun 僅用於名詞前] only one 單一的, 唯一的, 僅一個的: *A single tree gave shade from the sun.* 僅有的一棵樹擋住了太陽, 給我們提供了陰涼處。| *They won the game by a single point.* 他們僅以一分贏了這場比賽。| *Write your answer on a single sheet of paper.* 只用一張紙寫上你的答案。| **not a single** (=not even one) 一個也沒有 *We didn't get a single reply to our advertisement.* 我們的廣告連一個回應也沒有。

2 ▶SEPARATE 分別的◀ [only before noun 僅用於名詞前] considered on its own 個別的, 單獨的: *the highest price ever paid for a single work of art* 為單件藝術品所支付的最高價格 | **the single most/biggest/greatest etc** *Cigarette smoking is the single most important cause of lung cancer.* 吸煙是導致肺癌的一個最重要的原因。| *The single biggest problem we face is apathy.* 我們面臨的一個最大的問題就是冷漠。| **every single word/day etc** *There's no need to write down every single word I say.* 沒有必要把我說的每一個字都記下來。

3 ▶PEOPLE 人們◀ **a)** not married 未婚的, 單身的: *changes in the tax rate for single people* 適用於單身人士的稅率調整 **b)** not involved in a romantic relationship 沒有男[女]朋友的, 沒有情侶關係的: *I never meet any attractive single men!* 我從來沒有遇見過沒有女朋友的英俊男子! —see also 另見 SINGLE PARENT

4 single bed/room etc meant for or used by one person only 單人牀/房間等: *You have to pay extra for a single room.* 你要住單人房就得額外付費。—compare 比較 DOUBLE¹ (4) —see picture at 參見 BED¹ 圖

5 ▶NOT DOUBLE 不是雙重的◀ having only one part, quality etc, as opposed to having two or more 單一的, 單個的, 非雙重或多重的: *Use double, not single, thread to reinforce the seams.* 要用雙線而不是單線加固縫口。| *A single flower has only one set of petals.* 單瓣花只有一層花瓣。| *a single-sex school* (=either for boys or for girls, but not both) 單性別學校〔指男校或女校〕

6 ►TICKET 票◄ *BrE* a single ticket etc is for a trip from one place to another but not back again; ONE-WAY【英】〔車票等〕單程的 —compare 比較 RETURN[3] —see also 另見 SINGLY

single² *n* [C] **1** a musical record that has only one short song on each side 每面只有一首歌曲的唱片, 單曲唱片: *Have you heard their latest single?* 你聽過他們最新的單曲唱片沒有? **2 a)** a single RUN² (17) in CRICKET (2)〔板球中擊球後完成一次交換位置的跑動而得的〕一分 **b)** a hit that allows the person who is hitting the ball to reach first BASE¹ (8) in BASEBALL〔棒球的〕一壘打, 安全打〔使擊球手能上第一壘的擊球〕**3 singles** a game, especially in tennis, played by one person against another〔尤指網球的〕單打比賽: *I prefer singles – you get more exercise.* 我更喜歡單打——這樣運動量比較大。| *Who won the women's singles?* 女子單打誰贏了? —compare 比較 **doubles** (DOUBLE² (5)) | **singles bar/club/night** (=a bar, club etc intended for people who are not married or involved in a romantic relationship) 獨身者酒吧/俱樂部/晚會 **4** *BrE* a ticket for a trip from one place to another but not back again【英】單程票: *A single to Oxford, please.* 請給我一張到牛津的單程票。—compare 比較 RETURN² (9) **5** *AmE* a one dollar BILL¹ (3)【美】一美元紙幣: *Anybody have five singles?* 誰有五張一元鈔票?

single³ *v*

single sb/sth ↔ **out** *phr v* [T] to choose someone or something from among a group of similar people or things, especially in order to praise them or criticize them 挑出, 選出〔人或物以進行表揚或批評〕: *His article starts by singling out the five key goals of US foreign policy.* 他的文章一開頭就突出了美國對外政策的五個重要目標。| **single sb out for praise/blame etc** *The report singles out Mr Clarke and Mr Heseltine for special criticism.* 這份報告挑出克拉克先生和赫塞爾坦先生給予特別的批評。

single-breast·ed /ˌ·· ˈ··◂/ *adj* a single-breasted suit has a JACKET with only one set of buttons at the front〔上衣〕單排〔鈕〕扣的, 單襟的 —compare 比較 DOUBLE-BREASTED —see picture on page A17 參見A17頁圖

single cream /ˌ·· ˈ·/ *n* [U] thin cream that can be poured〔可以倒出的〕稀奶油 —compare 比較 DOUBLE CREAM *BrE*【英】; HEAVY CREAM *AmE*【美】

single cur·ren·cy /ˌ·· ˈ···/ *n* [C] a unit of money that is shared by several different countries 統一[單一]貨幣〔幾國共用的貨幣單位〕: *paving the way for monetary union and a single currency in Europe* 為歐洲的幣制聯合和單一貨幣鋪平道路

Single Eu·ro·pe·an Mar·ket /ˌ·· ˌ···· ˈ··/ *n* [singular] the unrestricted movement of goods and services between the countries of the European Union 歐洲單一市場〔指歐盟國家之間貨物和服務性工作的自由流動〕

single fig·ures /ˌ·· ˈ··/ *n* **in single figures** any number below 10 單位數, 個位數字: *Interest rates have stayed in single figures for over a year now.* 利率保持在個位數字已有一年多了。

single file /ˌ·· ˈ·/ *n* [U] moving in a line, with one behind another (成) 一路縱隊, (成) 單行: *We walked in single file across the narrow bridge.* 我們排成一行走過狹窄的橋。—**single file** *adv*: *kids shuffling single file down the hall* 成單行沿着走廊慢慢走去的孩子

single-hand·ed /ˌ·· ˈ··◂/ *adj* [only before noun 僅用於名詞前] done by one person without help from anyone else 單人完成的, 獨力的: *a single-handed voyage across the Atlantic* 橫渡大西洋的單人航行 —**single-handed, single-handedly** *adv*: *She rebuilt the house single-handed.* 她獨自一人重建了這所房子。

single hon·ours /ˌ·· ˈ··/ *n* [U] a university degree course in Britain in which only one main subject is studied〔英國只修一門主課的〕單科學位課程 —compare 比較 JOINT HONOURS

single lane road /ˌ·· · ˈ·/ *n* [C] *AmE* a road that is only wide enough for one car to go along it【美】單行車道

single mar·ket /ˌ·· ˈ··/ *n* [singular] the SINGLE EUROPEAN MARKET 歐洲單一市場

single-mind·ed /ˌ·· ˈ··◂/ *adj* someone who is single-minded has one clear aim and works very hard to achieve it 目的專一的, 一心一意的, 專心致志的: *Molly worked with single-minded determination, letting nothing distract her.* 莫莉對工作專心致志, 不受任何東西干擾。—**single-mindedly** *adv* —**single-mindedness** *n* [U]

sin·gle·ness /ˈsɪŋɡlnɪs; ˈsɪŋɡəlnɪs/ *n* [U] *formal* **singleness of purpose** great determination when you are working to achieve something【正式】專一, 堅定不移

single par·ent /ˌ·· ˈ··/ *n* [C] a mother or father who looks after their children on their own, without a partner 單親

sin·glet /ˈsɪŋɡlɪt; ˈsɪŋɡlɪt/ *n* [C] *BrE* a piece of clothing without SLEEVES that is worn as underwear or as a light shirt when playing some sports【英】無袖汗衫, 運動背心

single track road /ˌ·· · ˈ·/ *n* [C] *BrE* a road that is only wide enough for one car to go along it【英】單行車道

sin·gly /ˈsɪŋɡlɪ; ˈsɪŋɡli/ *adv* one at a time; separately 一個一個地, 各自地, 單獨地: *The children walked along the beach singly or in groups of two or three.* 孩子們各自或三兩成羣地沿着海灘走。

sing·song /ˈsɪŋˌsɔŋ; ˈsɪŋsɒŋ/ *n* **1** [C] *BrE* an informal occasion when people sing songs together【英】〔非正式的〕唱歌聚會, "大家唱"; SINGALONG *AmE*【美】: *There was a bit of a singsong at the pub.* 有些人在酒館裡唱歌自娛。**2** [singular] a way of speaking in which your voice repeatedly rises and falls 說話時聲音的抑揚頓挫: *She talked in a strange singsong.* 她說話時怪聲怪調的。—**singsong** *adj*: *a singsong voice* 有起伏節奏的聲音

sin·gu·lar¹ /ˈsɪŋɡjələ; ˈsɪŋɡjələ/ *adj* **1** a singular noun, verb, form etc is used when writing or speaking about one person or thing〔名詞、動詞等〕單數的: *If the subject is singular, use a singular verb.* 如果主語是單數, 就用動詞的單數式。**2** *formal* very great or very noticeable【正式】極大的, 突出的; 非凡的: *a woman of singular beauty* 美貌超羣的女子 | *He showed a singular lack of tact in the way he handled the situation.* 他處理這件事情的方式顯得極不機敏。**3** *literary* very unusual or strange【文】異常的, 奇異的: *a singular novel by an eccentric writer* 一位特立獨行的作家寫的怪異小說

singular² *n* [C] the form of a word used when writing or speaking about one person or thing〔詞的〕單數形式

sin·gu·lar·i·ty /ˌsɪŋɡjəˈlærətɪ; ˌsɪŋɡjəˈlærəti/ *n* **1** [C] *technical*【術語】**a)** another word for a BLACK HOLE black hole 的另一種說法 **b)** a set of events that do not obey the usual laws of nature, especially the events that happened at the BIG BANG (=beginning of the universe)〔宇宙開端時的〕奇點〔指不遵循已知自然規律而發生的事件〕**2** [U] *old-fashioned* strangeness【過時】異常, 奇怪, 奇特

sin·gu·lar·ly /ˈsɪŋɡjələlɪ; ˈsɪŋɡjələli/ *adv formal*【正式】**1** very noticeably 突出地, 異常地: *a singularly beautiful woman* 非常漂亮的女子 | *a singularly unsuccessful attempt to gain publicity* 一次為博得名聲的極不成功的嘗試 **2** *old-fashioned* in an unusual way; strangely【過時】奇異地, 奇特地

Sin·ha·lese /ˌsɪnhəˈliz; ˌsɪnhəˈliːz◂/ *n* [C] **1** a person from one of the groups of people who live in Sri Lanka〔斯里蘭卡的〕僧伽羅人 **2** one of the languages of Sri Lanka 僧伽羅語 —**Sinhalese** *adj*

sin·is·ter /ˈsɪnɪstə; ˈsɪnɪstə/ *adj* making you feel that something evil, wrong, or illegal is happening or will happen 不祥的, 凶兆的; 陰險的, 邪惡的: *a sinister figure lurking in the shadows* 埋伏在陰影中的邪惡身影 | *a sinister looking mask* 樣子兇惡的面具 | *Was it all a cover-up for more sinister activities?* 那是不是為了掩蓋更加險惡的陰謀活動?

S

3 **sink¹** /sɪŋk; sɪŋk/ *v past tense* **sank** /sæŋk; sæŋk/ or **sunk** /sʌŋk; sʌŋk/ *past participle* **sunk**

1 ►IN WATER 在水裡◄ **a)** [I] to go down below the surface of water, mud etc 沉, 下沉, 沉沒: *The Titanic sank after hitting an iceberg.* 鐵達尼號撞到冰山後沉沒。| *If you put it in water, will it float or sink?* 如果你把它放在水中, 它會浮起來還是沉下去? | *The heavy guns sank up to their barrels in the mud.* 這些沉重的槍支在泥裡直陷到槍管。**b)** [T] to damage a ship so badly that it sinks 使〔船〕沉沒: *Three ships were sunk that night by enemy torpedoes.* 那天夜裡有三艘船被敵人的魚雷擊沉。

2 ►MOVE LOWER 降低◄ [I] **a)** to move downwards to a lower level 下降〔至某一高度〕, 降低: *It was several days before the flood waters sank and life returned to normal.* 幾天之後洪水才退去, 生活於是恢復了正常。| *Her head sank onto her chest as she dozed off in her chair.* 她在椅子上打瞌睡, 腦袋垂到胸前。**b)** to fall down or sit down heavily, especially because you are very tired and weak〔尤指因疲倦或無力〕倒下, 頹然坐下: **[+into/on/down etc]** *Sinking down on the bed, she tried to collect her thoughts.* 她倒在牀上, 努力集中思緒。| **sink to your knees** (=fall into a kneeling position) 下跪 *The prisoner sank to his knees, begging for mercy.* 那個囚犯跪下乞求寬恕。

3 ►SUN/MOON 太陽/月亮◄ [I] to move downwards in the sky, and disappear from sight 落下, 下沉: *The sun was sinking behind the coconut palms.* 太陽在椰子樹後漸漸落下。

4 ►CHANGE/GET WORSE 改變/變壞◄ [I always+adv/prep] to gradually pass into a different state, especially one that is worse 衰退, 惡化: **sink into crisis/despair/decay etc** *The Soviet economy was sinking deeper and deeper into crisis.* 蘇聯經濟漸漸陷入危機。| *neglected buildings sinking into decay* 無人管理的樓房日漸衰敗 | **be sinking fast** (=getting weaker and about to die) 越來越虛弱, 瀕臨死亡 *By this time, she was sinking fast and there was little we could do for her.* 到這時, 她的病情急劇惡化, 我們也回天乏術。

5 ►LOWER AMOUNT/VALUE 數量減少/價值降低◄ [I] to go down in amount or value〔數量、價值等〕減少, 降低: *The population had sunk to a few dozen families.* 那裡的人口已經減到幾十戶了。| *efforts by the central banks to prop up the sinking dollar* 各中央銀行為支撐正在貶值的美元所作的努力

6 ►QUIET 安靜◄ [I] if your voice sinks you start talking more quietly〔聲音〕降低: *Holmes's voice sank as he revealed the truth about the murders.* 福爾摩斯在揭開那些謀殺案的真相時聲音放得很低。| **sink into silence** *moaning and crying out in pain, and finally sinking into silence* 痛苦地呻吟和喊叫, 後來終於陷入寂靜

7 your heart sinks/your spirits sink to lose hope or confidence, especially when you feel unable to do everything that you have to do 心情沉重/情緒低落〔失去信心或希望〕: *The journey seemed never-ending, and her spirits sank lower.* 旅程好像沒完沒了, 她的情緒更加低落了。| *I realized, with a sinking heart, that I had forgotten to post that vital letter.* 我發現我竟忘了寄出那封重要的信件, 我的心直往下沉。

8 that sinking feeling *informal* the unpleasant feeling that you get when you suddenly realize that something bad is going to happen【非正式】不安的感覺: *I had that sinking feeling you get when you know you've made a huge mistake.* 我當時心亂如麻, 那就是當一個人意識到自己犯了大錯時的感覺。

9 be sunk a) *informal* to be in a situation when you are certain to fail or have a lot of problems【非正式】陷入麻煩: *If we can't find a taxi we'll really be sunk.* 如果我們找不到計程車, 那就麻煩了。**b) be sunk in gloom/misery/apathy etc** to be so unhappy, tired etc that you feel completely unable to improve your situation 陷於憂愁/痛苦/麻木不仁: *He wandered around aimlessly all day, then returned home sunk in gloom.* 他整天漫無目的地到處閒逛, 然後心情一片灰暗地回到家裡。

10 sink without trace a) if a ship sinks without trace, it sinks and no one knows where it has sunk〔船〕沉沒後無影無蹤 **b)** if someone sinks without trace, they disappear mysteriously and you never hear about them again〔人〕神祕地消失, 銷聲匿跡: *Actors who quarrelled with their studios just seemed to sink without trace.* 一些影星跟製片公司爭吵後好像就消失得無影無蹤了。

11 sink so low/sink to doing sth to be dishonest enough or selfish enough to do something very bad or unfair 不老實[自私]到這種地步/幹出這種事來: *Cheating his own sister – how could he have sunk so low?* 騙他自己的妹妹 —— 他怎能幹出這種事來?

12 sink your teeth/claws/knife etc into sth to put your teeth or something sharp into someone's flesh, into food etc 用牙咬/用爪子抓/用刀子捅: *The dog sank its teeth into my arm.* 那條狗狠狠地咬了我的手臂。

13 sink a well/hole/mine etc to dig a deep hole in the ground 挖井/挖洞/開礦等

14 ►MONEY 錢◄ [T] to lend or spend a lot of money on a business, in the hope of making more money in the future; INVEST 投入, 投下〔資金〕: **sink sth in/into** *They had sunk most of their savings into a property venture.* 他們把大部分積蓄投資於房地產生意。

15 ►BALL 球類◄ [T] to hit a ball into a hole in games such as GOLF or SNOOKER〔高爾夫球、桌球等〕將〔球〕擊入洞中[袋中]

16 sink your differences to agree to stop arguing and forget about your disagreements, especially in order to unite and oppose someone else 摒棄分歧, 摒除歧見〔尤指為了聯合對付別人〕

17 sink or swim to suceed or fail without help from anyone else 沉浮全憑自己, 無論成功或失敗也無人援手: *They don't give you a lot of guidance – you're just left to sink or swim, really.* 他們不會給你很多指導 —— 你失敗或成功只能靠你自己, 真的。

18 ►DRINK 喝酒◄ [T] *BrE informal* to drink alcohol, especially in large quantities【英, 非正式】喝〔酒, 尤指痛飲〕: *We sank a few pints at the pub first.* 我們先在酒館裡痛飲了幾品脫的酒。

sink in *phr v* [I] if information, facts etc sink in, you gradually understand them or realize their full meaning 逐漸被充分理解: *For a moment her words didn't sink in.* 有一會兒, 她的話不能被人們完全理解。| *The stupidity of what I had done began to sink in with an awful finality.* 等我開始意識到了自己所做的蠢事之後, 壞事已成定局。

sink² *n* [C] **1** *BrE* a large open container, especially in a kitchen, that you fill with water and use for washing dishes etc【英】〔尤指廚房的〕洗滌槽: *Dirty plates were piled high in the sink.* 髒盤子在洗滌槽裡堆得很高。—see picture on page A10 參見A10頁圖 **2** *AmE* an open container in a kitchen or bathroom that you can fill with water and use for washing yourself, washing dishes etc【美】〔廚房的〕洗滌槽; 〔浴室的〕洗臉盆 —see also 另見 **everything but the kitchen sink** (EVERYTHING (6))

sinker —see 見 **hook, line and sinker** (HOOK¹ (7))

sinking fund /'.. ,./ *n* [C] *technical* money saved regularly by a business to pay for something in the future【術語】〔公司儲備的〕償債基金

sin·ner /ˈsɪnɚ; ˈsɪnə/ *n* [C] *especially biblical* someone who has sinned (SIN) by not obeying God's laws【尤聖經】〔違犯上帝律法的〕罪人, 有罪過者

Sinn Fein /ˌʃɪn ˋfen; ʃɪn ˈfeɪn/ *n* [singular] an Irish political organization that wants Ireland to become a united republic〔希望愛爾蘭成為一個統一共和國的〕新芬黨

Sino- /saɪno; saɪnəʊ/ *prefix* **1** of China; Chinese 中國的; 中國人的 **2** Chinese and 中國與…的: *Sino-Japanese trade* 中日貿易

S

si·nol·o·gy /saɪˋnɑlədʒɪ; saɪˈnɒlədʒi/ *n* [U] *technical* the study of Chinese language, history, literature etc【術語】漢學〔對中國的語言、歷史、文學等的研究〕

sin·u·ous /ˋsɪnjuəs; ˈsɪnjuəs/ *adj* smoothly curving and twisting, like the movements of a snake 蜿蜒的, 彎彎曲曲的, 迂迴的: *a dance with sinuous movements* 婀娜多姿的舞蹈 | *the river's sinuous course* 河流的迂迴

si·nus /ˋsaɪnəs; ˈsaɪnəs/ *n* [C] one of the hollow spaces filled with air in the bones of your face that have an opening in your nose 竇〔顱骨中與鼻孔相通的空穴〕

sip¹ /sɪp; sɪp/ *v* [I,T] to drink something slowly, taking very small mouthfuls 小口地喝, 〔慢慢地〕飲, 啜, 呷: *She was sitting at the bar sipping a Martini.* 她坐在吧台旁啜着馬丁尼酒。| **[+at]** *Kruger sipped at his whisky thoughtfully.* 克魯格若有所思地啜着威士忌酒。

sip² *n* [C] a very small amount of a drink 一小口〔飲料〕, 一啜之量: **take a sip (of)** *George took another sip of coffee.* 喬治又啜了一口咖啡。

si·phon¹, syphon /ˋsaɪfən; ˈsaɪfən/ *n* [C] **1** a bent tube used for getting liquid out of a container, by holding the other end of the tube at a lower level than the container 虹吸管 **2** also 又作 **soda siphon** *BrE* a kind of bottle for holding SODA WATER that is forced out of the bottle using gas pressure【英】〔以氣體壓力壓出蘇打水的〕蘇打水瓶

siphon², syphon *v* [T always+adv/prep] **1** to remove liquid from a container by using a siphon 用虹吸管吸出: **siphon sth off/out/into etc** *I siphoned some gasoline out of the tank.* 我用虹吸管從油箱中吸出一些汽油。**2** to dishonestly take money from a business, account etc to use it for a purpose for which it was not intended〔非法地〕抽調〔資金等〕, 挪用: **siphon sth off/from etc** *Corrupt officials had been siphoning off public funds for private business ventures.* 貪官污吏一直在挪用公款進行私人商業投資。| *I later found she had siphoned thousands of dollars from our bank account.* 我後來發現她私自從我們的銀行賬戶調走了數千美元。

3 **sir** /sə; sə *strong* 強讀 sɜ; sɜː/ *n* **1** *spoken* a way of addressing a man, for example a male customer in a shop or a military officer that shows respect【口】先生, 閣下; 長官〔對男子的敬稱, 例如店員對顧客, 士兵對長官等〕: *"Report back to me in an hour, sergeant." "Yes, sir."* "一小時後向我報告, 中士。" "是, 長官。" | *Can I help you, sir?* 我能為你效勞嗎, 先生? —compare 比較 MADAM (1) *BrE*【英】; MA'AM *AmE*【美】**2** *AmE spoken* used to get the attention of a man whose name you do not know【美口】先生〔用於引起一個不知其名的男子的注意〕: *Sir! You dropped your wallet!* 先生！你的錢包掉了！—compare 比較 MA'AM **3 Dear Sir** used at the beginning of a formal letter to a man 敬啟者〔對男子的稱呼, 用於正式信函的開頭〕**4 Sir** a title used before the first name of a KNIGHT or BARONET 爵士〔冠於爵士或準男爵名字之前的尊稱〕: *Sir James Wilson* 詹姆斯·威爾遜爵士 | *Sir Jasper* 賈斯珀爵士 **5** *BrE spoken* used by children at school as a way of addressing or talking about a male teacher【英口】老師〔中小學生對男教師的直接或間接稱呼〕: *Sir, I've forgotten my homework.* 老師, 我忘了做家庭作業。| *Look out – sir's coming back!* 當心 —— 老師回來了! —compare 比較 MISS² (2) **6 no sir!** also 又作 **no siree!** *AmE old-fashioned spoken* used to emphasize that you do not want something, will not accept something etc【美, 過時, 口】絕不接受, 絕不: *I will not have that man in my home, no sir!* 我不要那個人待在我家裡, 絕對不行!

sire¹ /saɪr; saɪə/ *n* **1** *old use* a way of addressing a king【舊】陛下〔對國王的尊稱〕: *The people await you, sire.* 臣民在恭候你, 陛下。**2** [C usually singular 一般用單數] *technical* the father of a four-legged animal, especially a horse【術語】〔馬等四足動物的〕雄性種獸, 種馬

sire² *v* [T] **1** to be the father of an animal, especially a horse〔尤指雄馬〕生殖, 繁殖: *a stallion that has sired several race winners* 繁殖了好幾匹賽馬冠軍的雄種馬 **2** *old-fashioned or humorous* to be the father of a person【過時或幽默】為〔人〕之父

si·ren /ˋsaɪrən; ˈsaɪərən/ *n* [C] **1** a piece of equipment that makes very loud warning sounds, used on police cars, fire engines etc〔警車、消防車等的〕汽笛, 警報器: *police sirens wailing in the distance* 警車的警報器在遠處嗚嗚地響 **2 siren voices/call/song** *literary* encouragement to do something that sounds very attractive, but will have bad results【文】誘人犯錯的聲音/號召/歌聲: *The government must ignore the siren voices calling for a cut in interest rates.* 政府絕不能聽信那些要求降低利率的讒言。**3** a word used especially in newspapers meaning a woman who is very attractive but also dangerous to men 妖豔而危險的女人, 妖婦〔尤用於報刊〕: *Hollywood sirens like Marilyn Monroe* 像瑪麗蓮·夢露一樣的荷里活性感女星 **4 the Sirens** a group of women in ancient Greek stories, whose beautiful singing made sailors sail towards them into dangerous water 塞壬〔古希臘故事中用美妙歌聲引誘水手進入危險水域的一羣女妖〕

sir·loin /ˋsɝlɔɪn; ˈsɜːlɔɪn/ also 又作 **sirloin steak** /,·· ˈ·/ *n* [C,U] expensive meat cut from a cow's lower back〔一塊〕上好的牛腰肉, 牛裡脊肉, 西冷牛扒

si·roc·co /səˋrɑko; sɪˈrɒkəʊ/ *n* [C] a hot wind blowing from the desert of North Africa across to southern Europe 西洛哥風〔由北非沙漠吹向南歐的一種熱風〕

sir·rah /ˋsɪrə; ˈsɪrə/ *n old use* an angry and disrespectful way of addressing a man【舊】小子, 傢伙〔對男子表示生氣或輕蔑的稱呼〕

sis /sɪs; sɪs/ *n spoken especially AmE* used when speaking to your sister【口, 尤美】姐姐; 妹妹〔用於稱呼自己的姊妹〕

S

sis·sy, cissy /ˋsɪsɪ; ˈsɪsi/ *n* [C] *informal* a boy that other boys dislike because he prefers doing things that girls enjoy【非正式】女孩子氣的男孩〔為其他男孩所看不起〕: *David played with dolls and used to get called a sissy by the other kids.* 戴維喜歡玩洋娃娃, 所以曾被其他小孩叫做娘娘腔的男孩。—**sissy** *adj*

sis·ter /ˋsɪstə; ˈsɪstə/ *n* [C] **1** a girl or woman who has the same parents as you 姊妹; 姐姐; 妹妹: *Janet and Abigail are sisters.* 詹妮特和阿比蓋爾是兩姐妹。| *He has three sisters and two brothers.* 他有三個姊妹和兩個兄弟。—see picture at 參見 FAMILY 圖 **2** also 又作 **Sister** *BrE* a nurse in charge of a hospital WARD¹ (1)【英】護士長: *I'm feeling a bit better today, Sister.* 我今天覺得好些了, 護士長。| *the night sister* 夜班護士 **3** also 又作 **Sister** a NUN 修女: *Good morning, Sister Mary.* 早上好, 瑪麗修女。**4 sister company/organization/ship etc** a company etc that belongs to the same group or organization 姊妹公司/組織/船等: *the Daily Express and its sister paper the Daily Star*《每日快報》及其姊妹報《每日星報》**5** *AmE spoken* a way of addressing a woman, used especially by African Americans【美口】〔尤指美國黑人對女子的稱呼〕大姐, 小妹, 小姐 **6** a word used by women to talk about other women and to show that they have feelings of friendship and support towards them 姊妹, 大姐, 妹妹〔婦女對其他婦女表示友好和支持時的用語〕: *We have to support our sisters in southern Africa.* 我們一定要支持我們在南非的姊妹們。 1 1

sis·ter·hood /ˋsɪstəhud; ˈsɪstəhʊd/ *n* **1** [U] a special, loyal relationship among women who share the same ideas and aims, especially among FEMINISTS〔尤指女權主義者之間的〕姊妹關係[情誼] **2** [C] a group of women who live a religious life together 修女會, 女修道會

sister-in-law /ˈ·· · ,·/ *plural* **sisters-in-law** or **sister-in-laws** *n* [C] **1** the sister of your husband or wife 夫或妻的姊妹; 姑子, 姨子 **2** your brother's wife 兄或弟的妻子; 嫂子, 弟媳 **3** the wife of the brother of your husband or wife 配偶的兄弟之妻; 妯娌 —see picture at 參見 FAMILY 圖

sis·ter·ly /ˋsɪstəlɪ; ˈsɪstəli/ *adj* typical of a loving sister 姊妹的, 親如姊妹的: *sisterly affection* 姊妹般的愛 —**sisterliness** *n* [U]

sitting on a chair 坐在椅子上 sitting at a desk 坐在書桌旁 sitting in an armchair 坐在扶手椅裡

sit /sɪt; sɪt/ *v past tense and past participle* **sat** /sæt; sæt/ *present participle* **sitting**

1 ►IN A CHAIR ETC 在椅子上等◄ **a)** [I] to be on a chair or seat, or on the ground, with the top half of your body upright and your weight resting on your BUTTOCK*s* 坐: **[+on/in/by etc]** *sitting in a comfortable armchair* 坐在一張舒適的扶手椅裡 | *We all sat around the campfire and sang songs.* 我們大家圍坐在營火邊唱歌。| *She's the girl that sits next to me in my math class.* 她是在數學課上坐我旁邊的女同學。| **sit at a desk/table etc** (=sit facing it) 面向桌子坐 *Harry sat at his desk and stared out of the window.* 哈里坐在書桌前, 凝望着窗外。| **sit doing sth** *We sat watching TV for a while.* 我們坐着看了一會兒電視。| **sit still** *I wish you children would sit still for 5 minutes.* 我希望你們這些孩子能安靜地坐五分鐘。**b)** [I always+adv/prep] to get to a sitting position after you have been standing up 坐下: *Jim walked over and sat beside her.* 吉姆走過來, 在她身旁坐下。**c)** [T always+adv/prep] to make someone sit down or help them to sit down 使坐下, 使就座: **sit sb down/on/in etc** *I sat him down in the armchair by his bed.* 我讓他坐在牀邊的扶手椅裡。

2 ►OBJECTS/BUILDINGS ETC 物件/樓房等◄ [I always+adv/prep] to lie or be placed in a particular position 在某位置, 位於, 坐落在: **[+on/in etc]** *"Where's my coat?" "It was sitting on the bottom of the stairs last time I saw it."* "我的上衣在哪裡?" "我上次見到它是在樓梯腳上。" | *a village sitting on the side of a hill* 坐落在山腰處的村莊 | *When I got to work I found a huge bunch of flowers sitting on my desk.* 我上班時發現一大束花擺在我的桌子上。

3 ►DO NOTHING 不幹事◄ [I always+adv/prep] to stay in one place for a long time, especially sitting down, doing nothing useful or helpful 閒(坐)着: *I spent half the morning sitting in a traffic jam.* 我遇上塞車, 在車裡待了半個上午。| *Well, I can't sit here chatting all day.* 好了, 我可不能整天坐在這兒閒扯。| *She just sits there complaining all day.* 她就會整天坐在那裡發牢騷。

4 ►COMMITTEE/PARLIAMENT ETC 委員會/議會等◄ [I] **a)** to be a member of a committee, parliament, or other official group 佔議席, 當委員, 擔任職務: **[+in/on]** *She sits on several government committees.* 她擔任政府裡好幾個委員會的委員。| *Their father sits in the National Assembly.* 他們的父親在國民議會任職。**b)** to have a meeting in order to carry out official business 〔官方機構〕開會; 開庭: *The council only sits once a month.* 該委員會每月只開一次會。| *The court will sit until all the evidence has been heard.* 法院將一直開庭到所有證詞都陳述完畢為止。

5 sit tight a) to stay where you are and not move 留在原處, (穩坐)不動: *If your car breaks down, just sit tight and wait for the police.* 如果你的汽車拋錨, 你就留在原地等待警察到來。**b)** to stay in the same situation, and not change your mind and do anything new 堅持立場, 不改變主意: *We're advising all our investors to sit tight till the market improves.* 我們奉勸所有投資者不要動搖, 等待市場復蘇。

6 be sitting pretty to be in a very good or favourable position 處於有利地位: *With profits up by over 80%, the company is sitting pretty.* 這家公司利潤增長超過80%, 生意很好。

7 sit in judgment on/over to give your opinion about whether someone has done something wrong, especially when you have no right to do this 對...進行評論〔尤指妄加評論〕, 指手畫腳

8 sit on sb's tail to drive very close behind a car, especially because you are waiting for a chance to pass it 緊跟在一輛汽車後面〔尤指因等待機會超車〕

9 ►ANIMAL/BIRD 獸類/鳥類◄ [I always+adv/prep] **a)** to be in, or get into, a resting position, with the tail end of the body resting on a surface 〔獸或鳥〕尾巴着地而坐, 棲息: *The cat likes to sit on the wall outside the kitchen.* 這隻貓喜歡坐在廚房外的牆頭上。**b)** if a bird sits on its eggs, it covers them with its body to make the eggs HATCH 〔鳥類〕孵蛋

10 ►PICTURE/PHOTO 畫像/照片◄ **[I+for]** to sit somewhere so that you can be painted or photographed 坐着讓人畫像[照相]

11 ►LOOK AFTER 照看◄ **[I+for]** to look after a baby or child while its parents are out; BABYSIT 代人臨時照看孩子

12 ►EXAMS 考試◄ **[I+for,T]** *BrE* to take an examination【英】參加〔考試〕, 參加...的考試: *Tracy's sitting her GCSEs this year.* 特蕾西準備參加今年的普通中學教育證書考試。

sit around/about *phr v* [I] to spend a lot of time sitting and doing nothing very useful 閒坐, 無所事事: *We used to just sit around for hours talking about the meaning of life.* 我們過去常常一坐幾個小時, 討論生活的意義。

sit back *phr v* [I] **1** to settle yourself in a comfortable chair and relax 輕鬆地坐在椅子上: *You sit back and watch TV – I'll wash up.* 你去輕輕鬆鬆地坐下看電視 —— 我來洗碗。**2** to relax and make no effort to get involved in something or influence what happens 不採取行動, 袖手旁觀: *Don't just sit back and wait for new business to come to you.* 你可不能只是悠閒地等待新業務來找你呀。| *All we have to do now is sit back and watch the checks roll in.* 我們現在只要舒舒服服地坐看支票滾滾而來就行了。

sit down *phr v* [I] **1** to be in a sitting position or get into a sitting position 坐着; 坐下: *Come over here and sit down!* 到這邊來坐下! | *If you work sitting down, you need to take plenty of exercise.* 如果你都是坐着工作, 你就需要大量的體育鍛鍊。| **sit yourself down** *spoken*【口】*Come in Sally, sit yourself down.* 進來, 莎莉, 坐吧。**2 sit down and ...** to try to solve a problem or deal with something that needs to be done, by giving it all your attention 坐下來〔專心解決或認真研究〕: *I think we need to sit down and analyse these figures properly.* 我想我們有必要坐下來好好分析分析這些數字。| *Maybe if you sat down and talked it through you could reach an agreement.* 要是你們坐下來好好談談, 也許就能達成一致的意見。

sit in *phr v* [I] **1** to be present at a meeting but not take an active part in it 列席, 旁聽: **[+on]** *Do you mind if I sit in on some of the interviews?* 如果我來旁聽幾場面試, 你介意嗎? **2** to do a job, go to a meeting etc instead of the person who usually does it 代理〔某人的〕工作; 代表〔某人〕出席會議: **[+for]** *This is Alan James sitting in for Suzy Williams on the mid-morning show.* 我是阿倫·詹姆斯, 代替蘇茲·威廉斯主持今天上午十點鐘的節目。**3** to take part in a SIT-IN (=kind of protest) 參加靜坐示威

sit on sth *phr v* [T] *informal* to delay dealing with something【非正式】拖延不辦, 擱置: *I sent my application about six weeks ago and they've just been sitting on it.* 我大約六週前就把申請寄去了, 可他們就是一直壓着不辦。

sit sth ↔ **out** *phr v* [T] to stay where you are until something finishes, especially something boring or unpleasant 坐到〔不快之事等〕結束, 一直等到…過去: *We forced ourselves to sit the play out.* 我們逼着自己坐在那裡, 直到那齣戲演完。| *rich businessmen who had sat the war out comfortably in South Africa* 舒適地住在南非等着戰爭結束的富商們

sit through sth *phr v* [T] to attend a meeting, performance etc, and stay until the end, even if it is very long and boring 一直坐到〔會議、演出等〕結束: *As a councillor, you have to sit through endless planning meetings.* 作為政務委員, 你就非得待到那些沒完沒了的計劃會議結束不可。

sit up *phr v* **1** [I] to be in a sitting position or get into a sitting position after you have been lying down 坐起來: *By the time I got there he was sitting up in bed and reading a book.* 我到那裡時, 他已經在牀上坐着看書了。| *At this, Faye sat up and flung aside the bed covers.* 一聽這話, 費伊從牀上坐了起來, 把被子掀到一邊。**2** [T **sit** sb **up**] to help someone to sit after they have been lying down 幫助〔某人〕坐起來 **3** [I] to sit in a chair with your back up straight 坐直, 端坐: *Just sit up straight and stop slouching.* 坐直身子, 別無精打采的了。**4** [I] to stay up very late 熬夜: *Sometimes we just sit up and watch videos all night.* 有時我們通宵熬夜看錄像。**5 make sb sit up (and take notice)** to do something surprising or impressive that makes someone pay attention to you 使某人驚訝, 引起某人的注意: *a fantastic performance that made all the critics sit up and take notice* 使所有評論家都大感興趣的精彩表演

USAGE NOTE 用法說明: SIT

WORD CHOICE 詞語辨析: **sit, sit at/in front of/on/in, sit down, seat, be seated**

You **sit at** a table, piano, or desk (unless you choose to **sit on** them!), and also **at** a computer or the controls of a car or plane. However, you sit **in front of** the television or the fire (though you can also sit *by* or *around* a fire). 如果要說"坐在桌子、鋼琴或書桌前"就用 sit at ... (真的要說"坐在...上面", 那就用 sit on ...)。要說"坐在電腦前或汽車、飛機等的操縱器之前", 也用 sit at ...。但"坐在電視機或火爐前"要用 sit in front of ...。表示"坐在火爐前"或"圍爐而坐"還可以用 sit by ... 或 sit around...。

You **sit on** something that has a flat, level surface such as the floor, the grass, a simple chair or seat, a bench, or a bed. 表示坐在表面平坦的東西〈如地板、草地、椅子、長橈或牀〉上面, 用 sit on ...。

You **sit in** a tree, long grass, a car, a room, a corner, an armchair, the driving seat of a car. 表示"坐在樹上, 坐在長的草叢中, 坐在汽車、房間、角落、扶手椅裡"或"坐在汽車駕駛座位上", 用 sit in ...。

When you are talking about the action of moving from standing to sitting, it is more common to use **sit down** rather than **sit** on its own. 如果談的是從站姿到坐姿的動作變化, 比較普通的用語是 sit down 而不只是 sit: *They quietly sat down again.* (NOT usually 一般不用 *sat again*). 他們又安靜地坐了下來。*Please sit down!* 請坐(下來)! You usually only say *Sit!* to a dog. Sit! 通常只在對狗發命令時說。

Note that **seat** as a verb is only transitive, is a little formal, and is used in these ways 注意 seat 作為動詞只有及物的用法, 文體也比較正式, 其用法見下面例句: *This hall will seat 100 people* (=has seats for 100 people). 這個大廳可以容納 100 人。| *They seated us at the front* (=put us in seats at the front). 他們請我們在前排就座。

Be seated is a formal expression for **sit down**. be seated 是 sit down 的正式表達法。At a formal dinner for example, you might hear 例如在正式晚宴上會聽到: *Please be seated* (=please sit down). 請就座。

sit·com /ˈsɪtkɑm; ˈsɪtkɒm/ *n* [C,U] a popular type of television or radio entertainment consisting of a series of amusing stories about the same set of characters 情境喜劇, 連續單元喜劇〔一種以固定人物為中心, 故事相對獨立的流行電視或廣播喜劇〕

sit-down /ˈ· ·/ *adj* **1 sit-down meal/dinner/lunch etc** a meal served to people sitting at a table〔由服務員端上〕坐在飯桌邊吃的一頓飯/晚餐/午餐等: *a sit-down meal for 20 people* 供 20 人吃的一頓飯 **2 sit-down strike/protest** a protest in which people sit down, especially to block a road or other public place, until their demands are listened to〔尤指在道路等公共場所舉行的〕靜坐罷工/靜坐抗議

site¹ /saɪt; saɪt/ *n* [C] **1** a place where something important or interesting happened〔重要事件發生的〕場所; 遺址; 地方: *an archaeological site* 考古現場 | **[+of]** *the site of the Battle of Waterloo* 滑鐵盧戰役遺址 **2** an area of ground where something is being built or will be built〔建築的〕工地, 用地: *a construction site* 建築工地 | **[+of]** *the site of a proposed missile base* 計劃中的導彈基地 **3 camp/camping/caravan site** *especially BrE* a piece of ground where you can camp【尤英】露營場所/拖車式活動房屋停泊場地 W2

site² *v* **be sited** be placed or built in a particular place 坐落於, 建於〔選定地點〕: **[+in/near etc]** *The new factory is to be sited in Fort Collins.* 按計劃新工廠將建於柯林斯堡。

sit-in /ˈ· ·/ *n* [C] a type of protest in which people refuse to leave the place where they work or study until their demands are agreed to 靜坐示威: **hold/stage a sit-in** *Students staged a sit-in to protest about experimentation on animals.* 學生們舉行靜坐示威, 抗議用動物進行實驗。

sit·ter /ˈsɪtɚ; ˈsɪtə/ *n* [C] **1** someone who sits or stands somewhere so that someone else can paint them or take photographs of them 坐着供人畫像[拍照]的人,〔供畫家或攝影師畫像或拍照的〕模特兒 **2** *especially AmE* a BABYSITTER【尤美】代人臨時照看小孩的人

sit·ting /ˈsɪtɪŋ; ˈsɪtɪŋ/ *n* [C] **1** one of the times when a meal is served in a place where there is not enough space for everyone to eat at the same time〔分批接待用餐的其中〕一批: *The first sitting is at 12:30, and the second is at 1:30.* 第一輪的開飯時間為 12:30, 第二輪為 1:30。**2** an occasion when you have yourself painted or photographed (一次) 坐着供人畫像或照相 (的時間) **3** a meeting of a law court or parliament〔法庭〕開庭;〔議會〕開會 **4 at/in one sitting** during one continuous period when you are sitting in a chair 持續坐着: *I sat down and read the whole book in one sitting.* 我坐下來, 一口氣看完了這本書。

sitting duck /ˌ·· ˈ·/ *n* [C] someone who is easy to attack or easy to cheat 易被擊中的目標, 易被攻擊者; 易上鈎者: *Out in the open, the soldiers were sitting ducks for enemy fire.* 在毫無掩蔽的地方, 士兵容易被敵人的砲火擊中。

sitting mem·ber /ˌ·· ˈ··/ *n* [C] *BrE* someone who is a member of a parliament at the present time【英】現任議員: *the sitting member for Newbury* 紐伯里的現任議員

sitting room /ˈ·· ·/ *n* [C] *especially BrE* the room in a house where you sit, relax, watch television etc; LIVING ROOM【尤英】起居室, 客廳

sitting ten·ant /ˌ·· ˈ··/ *n* [C] *BrE* someone who lives in a rented house or flat, especially when this gives them legal rights to stay there【英】〔房屋或公寓的〕承租人, 現住房客, 現任租戶

sit·u·ate /ˋsɪtʃʊˏet; ˈsɪtʃueɪt/ *v* [T] *formal* to describe or consider something as being part of something else or connected with something else【正式】認定…為…的部分; 說明[認為]…與…有聯繫; 將…置於某環境中: **situate sth in** *Freud situates the origins of these anxieties in the subconscious.* 弗洛伊德認為這些焦慮起源於潛意識。

sit·u·at·ed /ˋsɪtʃʊˏetɪd; ˈsɪtʃueɪtɪ̥d/ *adj* **1 be situated** to be in a particular place or position 位於…的, 坐落在…的: *a small town situated just south of Cleveland* 地處克利夫蘭以南的小鎮 | **beautifully/conveniently/pleasantly situated** *All the apartments are beautifully situated overlooking the beach.* 所有的公寓都環境優美, 俯瞰海濱。**2 be well/badly situated** to be in a particular situation 境況良好/處境困難: *Microsoft is well situated to exploit this new market.* 微軟具備良好的條件開拓這個新市場。

sit·u·a·tion /ˏsɪtʃʊˋeʃən; ˌsɪtʃuˈeɪʃən/ *n* [C] **1** a combination of all the things that are happening and all the conditions that exist at a particular time in a particular place 形勢, 情況, 狀況: *In the present situation, I wouldn't advise you to sell your house.* 在目前情況下, 我不建議你把房子賣掉。| *You're putting me in a very awkward situation.* 你使我陷於非常尷尬的境地。| *I'd better go and see the boss and explain the situation.* 我最好去見老闆, 把情況向他解釋一下。| *With no rain for three months and food supplies running out, the situation here is getting desperate.* 三個月無雨, 食品供應也將消耗殆盡, 這裡的情況越來越危急了。| **the economic/political/financial situation** *In view of the company's financial situation, there will be no salary increases this year.* 鑑於公司的財務狀況, 今年將不會加薪。| **fire situation/crisis situation etc** *especially spoken*【尤口】*We are unlikely to have a full-employment situation this year.* 今年不大可能出現全體就業的情況。| **no-win situation** (=a situation which will end badly, whichever choice you make) 必敗的局面 **2** a word meaning the kind of area where a building is situated, used especially by people who sell or advertise buildings 環境, 位置〔尤用於房地產廣告〕: *The house is in a charming situation, on a wooded hillside.* 樓房位於林木茂密的山坡上, 環境優美迷人。**3** *old-fashioned* a job【過時】工作, 職位: *She managed to get a situation as a parlour maid.* 她設法找到了一份做女僕的工作。

situation com·e·dy /ˏ····ˈ···/ *n* [C,U] *formal* a SITCOM【正式】情境喜劇, 連續單元喜劇

Situations Va·cant /ˏ····ˈ··/ *n* [singular] *BrE* the title of the part of a newspaper where jobs are advertised【英】〔報刊的〕招聘廣告欄, 招聘啟事

sit-up /ˈ··/ *n* [C] an exercise in which you sit up from a lying position, while keeping your feet on the floor 仰臥起坐

six /sɪks; sɪks/ *number* **1** 6〔數字〕六 **2 it's six of one and half a dozen of the other** *spoken* used to say there is not much difference between two possible choices, situations etc【口】半斤八兩, 不相上下 **3 at sixes and sevens** *BrE informal* disorganized and confused【英, 非正式】亂七八糟; 七上八下; 雜亂無章: *When the visitors arrived we were still at sixes and sevens.* 客人到來時我們這兒還是亂七八糟的。**4** a hit in the game of CRICKET, worth six runs (RUN² (17)), in which the ball goes beyond the edge of the playing area before touching the ground〔板球〕得六分的擊球[安打]〔球落地前飛出球場〕—**sixth** *number*: *our sixth child* 我們的第六個孩子

six·fold /ˋsɪksˏfold; ˈsɪksfəʊld/ *adv* by six times as much or as many 六倍: *Burglaries have increased sixfold.* 入屋盜竊案已經增加了六倍。—**sixfold** *adj*: *a sixfold increase in teenage pregnancies* 青少年懷孕數字的六倍增加

six-foot·er /ˏ·ˈ··/ *n* [C] *informal* someone who is at least six feet (1.83 metres) tall【非正式】身高六英尺〔1.83 米〕以上的人

six-pack /ˈ··/ *n* [C] six CANs or bottles of a drink, especially beer, sold together as a set〔尤指啤酒等飲料的〕六罐[瓶]包裝, 半打裝: *There's a six-pack in the fridge.* 冰箱裡還有一盒半打裝的。

six·pence /ˋsɪkspəns; ˈsɪkspəns/ *n* [C,U] a small silver-coloured coin worth six old pennies (PENNY), used in Britain until 1971, or this amount of money〔1971 年以前英國的〕六便士 (硬幣)

six-shoot·er /ˈ·ˏ··/ *n* [C] *old-fashioned, especially AmE* a small gun holding six bullets【過時, 尤美】六發手槍, 六響手槍

six·teen /sɪksˋtin; ˌsɪkˈstiːn◂/ *number* 16〔數字〕十六 —**sixteenth** *number*

six·teenth /sɪkˋstinθ; ˌsɪkˈstiːnθ◂/ *n* [C] one of sixteen equal parts of something 十六分之一

sixteenth note /ˈ··ˏ·/ *n* [C] *AmE* a musical note which continues for a sixteenth of the length of a WHOLE NOTE【美】〔音樂的〕十六分音符; SEMIQUAVER *BrE*【英】—see picture at 參見 MUSIC 圖

sixth /sɪksθ; sɪksθ/ *n* [C] one of six equal parts of something 六分之一: *About one sixth of the children admitted to taking drugs.* 大約六分之一的兒童承認吸毒。

sixth form /ˈ··/ *n* [C] the highest level in the British school system, for students, usually aged between 16 and 18, who are preparing to take A LEVEL*s* (=the highest level of exams) 六年級, 中六〔英國中學的最高年級〕—**sixth former** *n* [C]

sixth form col·lege /ˈ··ˏ··/ *n* [C] a type of school in Britain for students over the age of 16 六年級學校, 預科學校〔英國為16歲以上學生開設的學校〕

sixth sense /ˏ·ˈ·/ *n* [singular] a special feeling or ability to know things without using any of your five ordinary senses such as your hearing or sight 第六感官, 第六感, 直覺: *A sixth sense told me that I was in danger.* 我憑直覺感到自己有危險。

six·ties /ˋsɪkstɪz; ˈsɪkstiz/ *n* [plural] **1 the sixties** also 又作 **the '60s** the years from 1960 to 1969 1960 年至 1969 年期間, 六十年代 **2 in your sixties** aged from 60 to 69 60 歲至 69 歲之間, 六十多歲: **early/late sixties** *I'd say she was in her late sixties.* 我說她已經年近 70 了。**3** the numbers from 60 to 69, especially when used to measure temperature〔尤指氣溫〕60 度至 69 度之間, 六十多度: **the low sixties/the upper sixties** *a fine spring day with the temperature in the upper sixties* (=about 68 or 69 degrees) 氣溫將近 70 度的一個晴朗春日

six·ty /ˋsɪkstɪ; ˈsɪksti/ *number* 60〔數字〕六十 —**sixtieth** *number*

sixty-four-thou·sand-dol·lar ques·tion /ˏ···ˏ···ˈ··/ *n* [singular] *informal* the most important question, which you do not know the answer to【非正式】最重要的問題, 關鍵問題: *But will they accept the offer? That's the sixty-four-thousand-dollar question.* 但是他們會接受這個建議嗎? 這可是關鍵問題。

siz·a·ble /ˋsaɪzəbḷ; ˈsaɪzəbəl/ *adj* another spelling of SIZEABLE sizeable 的另一種拼法

size¹ /saɪz; saɪz/ *n*

1 ▶HOW BIG 有多大◀ [C,U] how big or small something is 大小, 尺寸, 規模: *The American states vary enormously in size and population.* 美國各州的面積大小和人口數量懸殊很大。| *The firm underestimated the size of the market for their new product.* 公司低估了他們的新產品的市場。| **be the size of** (=be the same size as) 和…同樣大小 *There were rats the size of cats.* 有些老鼠和貓一樣大。| *He's a small boy, about John's size.* 他是個小個子男孩, 個頭和約翰差不多。| *Their apartment is half the size of ours.* 他們的公寓有我們的一半大。| **that size/this size** (=as big as that/this) 和那個/這個一樣大 *In a class this size, there are bound to be a few trouble-makers.* 在一個這樣大的班裡, 難免會有幾個調皮搗蛋的學生。| **in all/different/various shapes and sizes** *They make these replacement windows in all shapes and sizes.* 他們所生產的這類替換窗備有各種形狀和尺寸。| **full size** (=the biggest size that something usually is) 通常的最大尺寸 *He's quite a big dog, but he's still not full size yet.* 牠是一隻體形很大的狗, 但牠還沒有完全長大。| **be a good/fair/nice size** (=be fairly big) 相當大的 *The garden's a pretty good size.* 這花園相當大。| *It's a nice size bedroom.* 這間臥室相當大。

2 ▶VERY BIG 很大的◀ [U] the fact of being very big 大, 巨大: *You should have seen the size of their car!* 你該看看他們的汽車有多大! | **sheer size** *What offends people is the sheer size of these pay increases.* 觸怒人們的是這些巨額的工資增長。

3 ▶CLOTHES/GOODS 衣服/商品◀ [C] one of a set of standard measures according to which clothes and other goods are produced and sold 尺碼, 型, 號: *These shoes are one size too big.* 這雙鞋子大了一碼。| *The shirts come in three sizes, small, medium, and large.* 這些襯衣分三種尺碼: 小號, 中號, 大號。| **size 8/16 etc** *I take size 10 shoes.* 我穿十號鞋。

4 large-sized/medium-sized etc large in size etc 大號/中號的: *a medium-sized car* 中型汽車 | **bite-sized** (=small enough to be eaten easily) 一口一個的 *Cut the meat into bite-sized chunks.* 把肉切成一口一個的小塊。

5 try sth for size to try something, especially clothing, to see if it is the right size for you〔尤指對衣物〕試穿以確定尺寸是否合適, 試穿, 試用

6 to size if you cut, make, or prepare something to size, you make it the right size for a particular use 成為合適的尺寸: *Cut the tile to size and fix it to the wall with adhesive.* 把瓷磚切成合適的尺寸, 用黏合劑黏到牆上。

7 that's about the size of it *spoken* used to agree that what someone has said about a situation is a good or correct way of describing it【口】(大體) 就是這麼一回事, 實際情況 (大致) 就是這樣

8 ▶GLUE 膠◀ [U] a thick sticky liquid used for giving stiffness and a shiny surface to paper, cloth etc 膠料, 漿料〔用於使紙張、布料等挺直而有光澤〕—see also 另見 **cut sb down to size** (CUT[1])

size² *v* [T] **1** to sort things according to their size 按大小把…分類: *Shrimp are sized for canning into large, medium and small.* 蝦被分成大、中、小三類來做罐頭。**2** to cover or treat something with SIZE[1] (8) 給…上漿[上膠]

size sth/sb ↔ **up** *phr v* [T] to look at or consider a person or situation and make a judgment about them 估計, 估量, 判斷: *It only took a few seconds for her to size up the situation.* 她只花了幾秒鐘就對情況作出判斷。

size·a·ble, sizable /ˋsaɪzəbl̩; ˈsaɪzəbəl/ *adj* fairly large 相當大的: *a sizeable cash payment* 數目龐大的現金支付

siz·zle /ˋsɪzl̩; ˈsɪzəl/ *v* [I] to make a sound like water falling on hot metal〔像水落在燒熱的金屬上〕發嘶嘶聲: *The steak was sizzling on the barbecue.* 肉排在烤架上嘶嘶作響。—**sizzle** *n* [singular] —see picture on page A19 參見A19頁圖

siz·zler /ˋsɪzlɚ; ˈsɪzələ/ *n* [C] *informal* a very hot day【非正式】大熱天: *Yesterday was a real sizzler!* 昨天真是個大熱天!

siz·zling /ˋsɪzlɪŋ; ˈsɪzəlɪŋ/ *adj especially AmE* very hot【尤美】很熱的: *It's sizzling in the sun.* 太陽底下非常熱。

SJ a written abbreviation used after a priest's name, to show that he is a JESUIT 耶穌會〔用於神職人員的名字後, 表示他是耶穌會會士〕

ska /skɑ; skɑː/ *n* [U] a kind of popular music from the West Indies with a fast regular beat, similar to REGGAE 斯卡音樂〔一種源於西印度羣島的節奏明快的音樂, 與"雷蓋"樂相似〕

skag, scag /skæg; skæg/ *n* [U] *slang* HEROIN【俚】海洛因

skate¹ /sket; skeɪt/ *n* **1** [C] one of a pair of boots with metal blades on the bottom, for moving quickly on ice; ICE-SKATE[2] (溜) 冰鞋 **2** [C] one of a pair of boots or frames with small wheels on the bottom, for moving quickly on flat smooth surfaces; ROLLER SKATE 四輪旱冰鞋 **3** [C,U] *plural* **skate** *or* **skates** a large flat sea fish that can be eaten 鰩〔一種可食用的扁平大海魚〕**4 get/put your skates on** *BrE spoken* used to tell someone to hurry【英口】〔用於催促別人〕趕快, 趕緊: *Put your skates on, or you'll be late for school.* 動作快點, 不然你上學要遲到了。

skate² *v* [I] **1** to move on skates 滑冰, 溜冰: *The children skated on the frozen pond.* 孩子們在結冰的池塘上滑冰。**2 be skating on thin ice** *informal* to be doing something that may get you into trouble【非正式】做冒險的事 —**skater** *n* [C]

skate over/around sth *phr v* [T] to avoid mentioning a problem or subject, or not give it enough attention 避免提起〔某問題等〕, 把〔問題等〕輕輕帶過, 迴避: *The President was accused of skating over the issue of the homeless.* 總統因在無家可歸者的問題上輕描淡寫而受到指責。

skate·board /ˋsketˌbɔrd; ˈskeɪtbɔːd/ *n* [C] a short board with two small wheels at each end, which you can stand on and ride as a sport 滑板 —**skateboarding** *n* [U]

skat·ing /ˋsketɪŋ; ˈskeɪtɪŋ/ *n* [U] the activity or sport of moving on skates 滑冰, 溜冰: **go skating** *Zelda's going skating in the afternoon.* 澤爾達準備下午去溜冰。

skating rink /ˈ‥ ˌ·/ *n* [C] a place or building where you can SKATE[2] (1) 滑冰場, 溜冰場

ske·dad·dle /skɪˋdædl̩; skɪˈdædl/ *v* [I] *spoken humorous* to leave a place quickly, especially because you do not want to be caught【口, 幽默】逃跑, 倉惶逃竄

skeet shoot·ing /ˋskit ˌʃutɪŋ; ˈskiːt ˌʃuːtɪŋ/ *n* [U] *AmE* the sport of shooting at clay objects that have been thrown into the air【美】飛靶射擊, 打飛靶; CLAY PIGEON SHOOTING *BrE*【英】

skein /sken; skeɪn/ *n* [C] a long loosely wound piece of thread, wool, or YARN (1)〔線、紗等的〕一束, 一綹

skel·e·tal /ˋskɛlətəl; ˈskelɪ̣təl/ *adj* like a skeleton or connected with a skeleton 骨骼的, 像骨骼的: *the skeletal bodies of the starving people* 飢民們骨瘦如柴的身軀

skeleton 骨骼

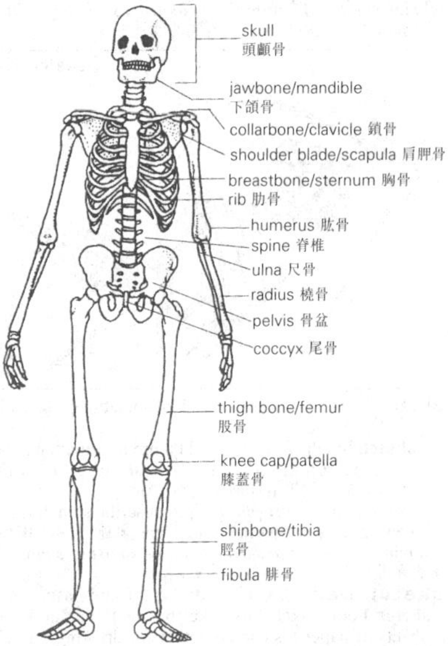

skull 頭顱骨
jawbone/mandible 下頜骨
collarbone/clavicle 鎖骨
shoulder blade/scapula 肩胛骨
breastbone/sternum 胸骨
rib 肋骨
humerus 肱骨
spine 脊椎
ulna 尺骨
radius 橈骨
pelvis 骨盆
coccyx 尾骨
thigh bone/femur 股骨
knee cap/patella 膝蓋骨
shinbone/tibia 脛骨
fibula 腓骨

skel·e·ton /ˋskɛlətn̩; ˈskelɪ̣tən/ *n* [C]

1 ▶BONES 骨◀ **a)** the structure consisting of all the bones in a human or animal body〔人體或動物的〕全副

骨骼: *the human skeleton* 人體骨骼 **b)** a set of these bones or a model of them, fixed in their usual positions, used for example by medical students〔醫學研究用的〕骷髏, 骨架; 骨架模型

2 ▶MAIN PART 主要部分◀ the most important parts of something, to which more detail can be added later 骨架, 框架; 梗概, 綱要: **[+of]** *It is just a skeleton of the report, showing the three basic points.* 這只是報告的梗概, 提出了三個要點。

3 ▶THIN 瘦的◀ *informal* an extremely thin person or animal【非正式】骨瘦如柴的人[動物]: *The prisoners were just skeletons.* 這些囚犯真是骨瘦如柴。

4 a skeleton in the cupboard/closet *informal* an embarrassing or unpleasant secret about something that happened to you in the past【非正式】不可外揚的家醜, 隱私, 祕密

5 skeleton staff/service only enough to keep an operation or organization running 最基本的人員/服務: *British Rail is operating a skeleton service on Christmas Day.* 英國鐵路公司在聖誕節只提供最基本的服務。

skeleton key /ˈ··· ·/ *n* [C] a key made to open a number of different locks 萬能鑰匙

skep·tic /ˈskɛptɪk; ˈskeptɪk/ *n* [C] the American spelling of SCEPTIC sceptic 的美式拼法

skep·ti·cal /ˈskɛptɪkəl; ˈskeptɪkəl/ *adj* the American spelling of SCEPTICAL sceptical 的美式拼法

skep·ti·ci·sm /ˈskɛptəˌsɪzəm; ˈskeptɪsɪzəm/ *n* [C,U] the American spelling of SCEPTICISM scepticism 的美式拼法

S

sketch¹ /skɛtʃ; sketʃ/ *n* [C] **1** a simple, quickly-made drawing that does not show much detail 素描, 速寫; 草圖: *First she makes a sketch of a scene and then she paints it.* 她先畫一幅風景素描, 然後上顏料。**2** a short humorous scene on stage, television etc that is part of a larger show〔舞台、電視等上的〕滑稽短劇: *Her TV programme is made up of a series of comic sketches.* 她的電視節目是由一系列滑稽短劇組成的。**3** a short written or spoken description 短篇描寫, 隨筆; 簡介, 梗概: *a brief sketch of the main weaknesses of the British economy* 對英國經濟主要弱點的簡述

sketch 素描

sketch² *v* [I,T] to draw a sketch of something (給…) 寫生, (給…) 畫素描

sketch in sth *phr v* [T] to add more information about something 補充〔內容〕: *I'd like to sketch in a few details for you.* 我想給你補充幾點細節。

sketch sth ↔ **out** *phr v* [T] to describe something in a general way giving the basic ideas 概述; 草擬: *We're having a meeting to sketch out a new business plan.* 我們在開會草擬一份新的業務計劃。

sketch·pad /ˈskɛtʃˌpæd; ˈsketʃpæd/ also 又作 **sketch·book** /ˈskɛtʃˌbʊk; ˈsketʃbʊk/ *n* [C] a number of sheets of paper fastened together for drawing on 寫生簿, 素描簿

sketch·y /ˈskɛtʃɪ; ˈsketʃi/ *adj* not thorough or complete, and not having enough details to be useful 不完全的, 粗略的, 簡略的: *We were only able to provide the police with sketchy details.* 我們只能向警方提供粗略的細節。—**sketchily** *adv*

skew¹ /skju; skjuː/ *v* [T] to affect a test or an attempt to get information in a way that makes the results incorrect 使偏頗; 歪曲, 曲解: *All the people we questioned lived in the same area, which had the effect of skewing the figures.* 我們查詢的所有人都住在同一地區, 這就影響了數字的準確性。

skew² *adj* not straight (歪) 斜的

skew·bald /ˈskjuˌbɔld; ˈskjuːbɔːld/ *n* [C] a horse with large white and brown shapes on it 有大片白色和棕色斑點的馬, 雜色馬, 花斑馬 —**skewbald** *adj*

skewed /skjud; skjuːd/ *adj* **1** an opinion, piece of information, result etc that is skewed is incorrect, especially because you do not know all the facts〔看法等〕偏頗的, 不正確的〔尤因對事實掌握不全〕: *The results of a telephone poll will always be skewed since those who do not have phones are obviously excluded.* 電話民意調查的結果總會有偏頗, 因為沒有電話的人明顯地被排除在外。**2** something that is skewed is not straight and is higher on one side than the other 歪 (斜) 的, 傾斜的: *The picture on the wall was slightly skewed.* 牆上的畫稍微有點歪。

skew·er¹ /ˈskjuɚ; ˈskjuːə/ *n* [C] a long metal or wooden stick for putting through pieces of meat while cooking them〔金屬或木做的〕串肉扦, 烤肉叉

skewer² *v* [T] to make a hole through a piece of food, an object etc with a skewer or with something similar〔用烤肉叉或類似東西〕把…串起來: *Grant skewered bits of meat and put them on the barbecue.* 格蘭特用烤肉叉把肉片串好放到烤架上。—see picture on page A11 參見A11頁圖

skew-whiff /ˌ· ˈ·◂/ *adj BrE informal* not straight【英, 非正式】不正的, 歪斜的: *The top of the bookcase is skew-whiff.* 書櫥頂是歪的。

ski¹ /ski; skiː/ *n plural* **skis** [C] **1** one of a pair of long thin narrow pieces of wood or plastic that you fasten to your boots and use for moving on snow 滑雪板 **2** a piece of strong material shaped like a ski under a small vehicle so that it can travel on the snow〔滑雪車等的〕滑橇

ski 滑雪

skiing 滑雪

snowboarding 踏板滑雪

ski² *v past tense and past participle* **skied** *present participle* **skiing** [I] to move on skis for sport or in order to travel on snow 滑雪: *I'm learning to ski.* 我在學滑雪。| **go skiing** *We went skiing in Colorado last winter.* 去年冬天我們去科羅拉多州滑雪了。—see also 另見 SKIER

ski·bob /ˈskiˌbɑb; ˈskiːbɒb/ *n* [C] a vehicle like a bicycle with skis instead of wheels〔形狀像腳踏車的〕滑雪車, 雪車

ski boot /ˈ· ·/ *n* [C] a specially made boot that fastens onto a ski 滑雪鞋[靴]

skid¹ /skɪd; skɪd/ *v* **skidded, skidding** [I] if a vehicle or wheel skids, it suddenly slides sideways and you cannot control it〔車輛或車輪〕打滑, 失控滑向一側: *The wheels of the truck skidded on the wet snow.* 貨車的輪子在濕雪地上打滑。

skid² *n* **1** [C] a sudden uncontrollable sliding movement of a vehicle〔車輛的〕打滑: *She could hear the skid of the car as it went around the corner.* 她可以聽到車子拐彎時打滑的聲音。| **go into a skid** (=start skidding) 開始打滑 *He slammed on the brakes and we went into a long skid.* 他使勁煞車後我們的車子向前滑了很久。| **skid marks** *The only sign of the crash were the skid marks on the road.* 撞車事故的唯一痕跡是路面上車輪的打滑印跡。**2 on the skids** *informal* being in a situation that is bad and getting worse【非正式】處境越來越壞的: *He's been on the skids since losing his job.* 他丟了工作以後境況越來越糟。**3 put the skids under** *informal* to make it likely or certain that something will fail【非正式】使…失敗: *The recession put the skids under his plans for starting a new business.* 經濟衰退使他難以實現開新店的計劃。**4** [C] a part that is underneath some aircraft used in addition to wheels for landing on〔某種飛機的〕起落橇, 滑橇: *helicopter skids* 直升機起落橇 **5** [usually plural 一般用複數] a piece of wood that is put under a heavy object to lift or move it〔支承重物的〕墊木;〔使重物易於滑動的〕滑動墊木

skid·pan /ˈskɪdˌpæn; ˈskɪdpæn/ *n* [C] *BrE* a special slippery surface where drivers can practise controlling skidding cars【英】滑面試車場〔供駕駛者練習控制打滑車輛的特製路面〕

skid row /ˌskɪd ˈro; ˌskɪd ˈrəʊ/ *n* [U] **be on skid row** *informal* if someone is on skid row, they drink too much and have no job, nowhere to live etc【非正式】〔失業酒徒〕無家可歸, 流落街頭

ski·er /ˈskiə; ˈskiːə/ *n* [C] someone who skis (SKI²) 滑雪者

skies /skaɪz; skaɪz/ *n* the plural form of SKY

skiff /skɪf; skɪf/ *n* [C] a small light boat for one person〔單人划或駕駛的〕小艇, 輕舟

skif·fle /ˈskɪfəl; ˈskɪfəl/ *n* [U] *especially BrE* a type of popular music played in the 1950s and often using instruments made by the players themselves【尤英】即興演奏的爵士樂〔20世紀50年代的一種流行音樂, 其樂器常由演奏者自製〕

ski·ing /ˈskiɪŋ; ˈskiːɪŋ/ *n* [U] the sport of moving down hills or across the countryside in the snow, wearing SKIS〔在山坡上或野地裡的〕滑雪運動

ski jump /ˈ· ·/ *n* [C] **1** a competition in which people wearing SKIS jump off a cliff at the bottom of a slope to see how far they can go through the air 跳台滑雪比賽 **2** a steep slope ending in a cliff, used for ski jump competitions 跳台滑雪助滑道

skil·ful *BrE*【英】, usually 一般作 **skillful** *AmE*【美】 /ˈskɪlfəl; ˈskɪlfəl/ *adj* **1** good at doing something, especially something that needs special ability or training 有技術的, 熟練的, 靈巧的: *a skillful team player* 技巧嫻熟的隊員 **2** made or done very well and cleverly 顯示技巧的; 製作精良的: *her skilful handling of a difficult problem* 她處理難題的熟練技巧 | *the skilful use of sound effects* 音響效果的巧妙運用 —**skilfully** *adv*

ski lift /ˈ· ·/ *n* [C] a piece of equipment that carries SKIERS up to the top of a slope〔運送滑雪者上坡的〕上山吊椅

S3 W1 **skill** /skɪl; skɪl/ *n* [C,U] an ability to do something well, especially because you have learned and practised it〔尤指經學習和實踐而得到的〕技能, 技巧, 技藝: *Reading and writing are two different skills.* 閱讀和寫作是兩種不同的技能。| *You need computing skills for that job.* 你必須掌握電腦技能以勝任那份工作。| **[+at/in]** *I admired his skill at driving.* 我佩服他的駕駛技術。| **with great skill/with a lot of skill** *The whole team played with great skill and determination.* 整支球隊都表現出純熟的技巧和爭勝的決心。

skilled /skɪld; skɪld/ *adj* **1** someone who is skilled has the training and experience that is needed to do something well 有技巧的, 熟練的: *Skilled craftsmen, such as carpenters, bricklayers, etc are in great demand.* 熟練工匠如木工、磚瓦匠等都很需要。| **highly skilled** *a highly skilled negotiator* 老練的談判手 | **[+at/in]** *She's very skilled at dealing with members of the public.* 她和公眾打交道很有一套。**2** work that is skilled needs special abilities or training in order to do it〔工作〕需要技能的, 要有熟練能力的: *Bricklaying is very skilled work.* 砌磚是一項需要高度技能的工作。—opposite 反義詞 UNSKILLED

skil·let /ˈskɪlɪt; ˈskɪlɪt/ *n* [C] a flat heavy cooking pan with a long handle 長柄平底煎鍋 —see picture at 參見 PAN¹ 圖

skill·ful /ˈskɪlfəl; ˈskɪlfəl/ *adj* an American spelling of SKILFUL skilful 的美式拼法

skim /skɪm; skɪm/ *v* **skimmed, skimming 1** [T] to remove floating fat or solids from the surface of a liquid 從液體表面撇去〔漂浮的油脂或固體物質〕: **skim sth off/from** *After simmering the meat and vegetables skim the fat from the surface.* 把那些肉和蔬菜燉好後, 再撇去表面的油脂。**2** [I,T] to read something quickly to find the main facts or ideas in it〔為掌握大意的〕略讀, 瀏覽: *She skimmed the sports page to find out who had won the game.* 她瀏覽體育新聞版, 想知道誰贏了那場比賽。| **skim through sth** *Just skim through the second section to save time.* 只略讀第二部分以節省時間。**3** [T] to move along quickly, nearly touching a surface 飛快掠過, 擦過: *seagulls skimming the waves* 掠過浪尖的海鷗 **4 skim stones/pebbles etc** *BrE* to throw smooth, flat stones into a lake, river etc in a way that makes them jump across the surface【英】〔用扁石在水面〕打水漂 —compare 比較 SKIP¹ (8) **5** [T] *AmE* to take money illegally, especially by not saying that you have made profits so that you do not have to pay tax【美】〔為逃稅而〕瞞報〔收入〕; 非法撈到〔錢〕

skim sb ↔ **off** *phr v* [T] to take and keep for yourself the best people, the most money etc 挖走〔最優秀的人〕; 選取〔精華〕;〔通過瞞報而〕撈走〔大部分的錢〕: *Professional sport skims off all the best players.* 職業體育運動界總要把最優秀的選手都挖走。

skimmed milk /ˌ· ˈ·/ *n* [U] milk that does not contain much fat because the cream has been removed from it 脫脂(牛)奶

skim·mer /ˈskɪmɚ; ˈskɪmə/ *n* [C] **1** a kitchen tool with holes in it, used for removing solids from the surface of a liquid 撇沫器, 漏勺 **2** a sea bird that flies low over the sea 掠水鷗, 剪嘴鷗〔在海面上低飛的海鳥〕

skimp /skɪmp; skɪmp/ *v* [I,T] to not spend enough money or time on something, or not use enough of something, so that what you do is unsuccessful or of bad quality 捨不得花〔足夠的錢、時間等〕, 克扣, 少給: **[+on]** *It's vital not to skimp on staff training.* 對員工培訓不能吝嗇, 這點十分重要。

skimp·y /ˈskɪmpɪ; ˈskɪmpi/ *adj* **1** a skimpy dress or skirt etc is very short and does not cover very much of your body〔衣、裙等〕太短[小]的; 過分暴露的 **2** not providing enough of something 不足的; 吝嗇的, 過分節省的: *a skimpy meal* 不夠吃的一頓飯 —**skimpily** *adv* —**skimpiness** *n* [U]

skin¹ /skɪn; skɪn/ *n*

1 ►BODY 身體◄ [C,U] **a)** the natural outer layer of a human or animal body〔人或動物的〕皮, 皮膚: *Babies have beautifully soft skin.* 嬰兒皮膚細嫩。| *amphibians with their smooth, moist skins* 皮膚光滑濕潤的兩棲動物 | *a skin disease* 皮膚病 | **fair/dark skin** *Madhur was beautiful with her thick black hair and smooth dark skin.* 瑪德赫有一頭濃密的黑髮, 皮膚光滑呈深色, 非常漂亮。**b)** the skin on your face 臉部的皮膚: *Some soaps* *just seem to dry my skin up.* 有幾種香皂好像會使我臉上的皮膚變得乾燥。| **bad skin** (=unhealthy-looking skin) 看起來不健康的皮膚 —see also 另見 SKINCARE

2 dark-skinned/fair-skinned/smooth-skinned etc having dark skin, smooth skin etc 皮膚黑的/白皙的/光滑的: *If you are very fair-skinned you should avoid going in the sun too much.* 如果你膚色很白, 就不應過多地去曬太陽。—see also 另見 **have a thick skin** (THICK[1] (11))

3 ►ANIMAL SKIN 獸皮◄ [C,U] the skin of an animal, used as leather, fur etc 皮革, 毛皮, 獸皮: *a tiger skin* 一張虎皮 | *a sheepskin jacket* 羊皮夾克

4 ►FOOD 食物◄ [C,U] **a)** the natural outer cover of some fruits and vegetables〔某些水果和蔬菜的〕皮, 外皮: *banana skins* 香蕉皮 | *onion skin* 洋葱皮 **b)** the outer cover of a SAUSAGE〔香腸的〕腸衣 **c)** a thin solid layer that forms on the top of a liquid when it gets cold or is left uncovered〔液體冷卻後或置於空氣中時形成的〕薄層: *Cover the soup to stop a skin from forming.* 把湯蓋上以免結一層皮。

5 by the skin of your teeth *informal* if you do something by the skin of your teeth, you only just succeed in doing it【非正式】好不容易才..., 差點就沒..., 勉強: *We woke up late and caught the plane by the skin of our teeth.* 我們起牀遲了, 差點沒趕上班機。

6 get under sb's skin *informal* if someone gets under your skin, they annoy you, especially by the way they behave【非正式】激怒某人: *What really gets under my skin is people who push straight to the front of the line.* 那些插隊的人真叫我惱火。

7 be skin and bone *informal* to be extremely thin in a way that is unattractive and unhealthy【非正式】瘦得皮包骨: *Tania was all skin and bone when she got back from her world tour.* 塔尼婭周遊世界回來時瘦得皮包骨。

8 it's no skin off my nose *spoken* used to say that you do not care what someone else thinks or does because it does not affect you【口】我根本不在乎, 我才不管呢: *Well, I offered to help out, but if she doesn't want me to it's no skin off my nose!* 我已經提出要幫助她, 但是她如果不想我幫助, 我才不在乎呢! —see also 另見 **save sb's skin** (SAVE[1] (10)), **jump out of your skin** (JUMP[1] (4))

skin² *v* **skinned, skinning** [T] **1** to remove the skin from an animal, fruit, or vegetable 剝去...的皮: *Add the tomatoes, skinned and sliced.* 把去了皮和切成片的番茄加進去。**2** to hurt yourself by rubbing off some skin 擦破...皮, 擦傷...的皮: *She skinned her knee when she fell off her bike.* 她從腳踏車上摔下來時擦破了膝蓋。**3 skin sb alive** *humorous* to punish someone very severely【幽默】嚴厲懲罰某人, 活剝某人的皮: *I'll skin him alive if I get hold of him!* 如果我抓住他就活剝了他的皮! **4** *AmE informal* to completely defeat someone【美, 非正式】徹底擊敗: *The football team really skinned Watertown last year.* 該足球隊去年徹底擊敗了水城隊。

skin up *phr v* [I] *BrE slang* to make a cigarette with MARIJUANA in it【英俚】製香煙時摻進大麻

skin·care /ˈskɪnˌkɛr; ˈskɪnkeə/ *adj* skincare products are intended to improve the condition of your skin, especially the skin on your face〔尤指對臉部皮膚〕護膚的, 潤膚的 —**skincare** *n* [U]

skin-deep /ˌ· ˈ·◄/ *adj* [not before noun 不用於名詞前] something that is skin-deep seems to be important or real, but in fact it is not because it only affects the way things appear 膚淺的, 表面的: *Beauty is only skin deep.* 美貌只是表面的。

skin-div·ing /ˈ· ˌ··/ *n* [U] the sport of swimming under water with light breathing equipment but without a protective suit〔不穿潛水衣的〕潛水[泳], 裸潛 —**skin-diver** *n* [C]

skin·flint /ˈskɪnˌflɪnt; ˈskɪnˌflɪnt/ *n* [C] *informal* someone who hates spending money or giving it away; MISER【非正式】吝嗇鬼, 小氣鬼

skin·ful /ˈskɪnˌful; ˈskɪnfʊl/ *n* **have a skinful** *BrE spoken* to drink a lot of alcohol and become drunk【英口】醉酒

skin·graft /ˈskɪnˌgræft; ˈskɪngrɑːft/ *n* [C] a medical operation in which healthy skin is removed from one part of your body and used on another to replace burned or damaged skin 表皮移植(術), 植皮(術)

skin·head /ˈskɪnˌhɛd; ˈskɪnhed/ *n* [C] a young man who has hair that is cut very short, especially one who behaves violently 短髮青年, 光頭暴徒: *a gang of noisy skinheads* 一幫吵吵嚷嚷的光頭青年

skin·ny /ˈskɪnɪ; ˈskɪni/ *adj informal* very thin, especially in a way that is unattractive【非正式】瘦削的, 皮包骨的: *Some supermodels are far too skinny.* 有些超級模特兒過於瘦骨嶙峋了。—see 見 THIN (USAGE) 3

skinny-dip·ping /ˈ·· ˌ··/ *n* [U] *informal* swimming with no clothes on【非正式】裸(體游)泳

skint /skɪnt; skɪnt/ *adj* [not before noun 不用於名詞前] *BrE informal* having no money, especially for a short time【英, 非正式】〔暫時〕不名一文的: *I'm skint at the moment.* 我現在身無分文。

skin-tight /ˈ· ˌ·◄/ *adj* clothes that are skin-tight fit tightly against your body〔衣服〕緊身的: *skin-tight jeans* 緊身牛仔褲

skip¹ /skɪp; skɪp/ *v*

1 ►MOVEMENT 移動◄ [I] to move forwards with quick steps and jumps 蹦跳着走: **[+across/along etc]** *Maria skipped along at her mother's side.* 瑪麗亞在她媽媽身旁蹦蹦跳跳地向前走。

2 ►NOT DO STH 不做某事◄ [T] *informal* to not do something that you usually do or that you should do【非正式】不做〔本來常做或應做的事〕: *Children who skip breakfast often don't concentrate as well as others.* 不吃早飯的小孩常常沒有其他小孩那樣注意力集中。| *He skipped chemistry class three times last month.* 他上個月三次沒上化學課。

3 ►NOT DEAL WITH 不處理◄ [I,T] to leave something out, or not do something that would normally be the next thing you deal with 略過, 跳過, 遺漏: *I decided to skip the first two chapters.* 我決定跳過開頭兩章。| **[+to]** *Let's skip to the last item on the agenda.* 讓我們跳到議程上的最後一項吧。| **[+over]** *I suggest we skip over the details and get to the main point.* 我建議我們略過細節, 就談要點。

4 ►CHANGE SUBJECTS 換主題◄ [I always+adv/prep] to go from one subject to another in no fixed order 不按次序地改變話題, 隨意跳動: **[+about/around/to etc]** *It was a badly organized talk – he just kept skipping around from one idea to another.* 那次演講條理很差 —— 他不斷地隨意變換話題。

5 also 又作 **skip rope** *AmE*【美】[I] to jump over a rope as you pass it over your head and under your feet as a game 跳繩

6 skip town/skip the country to leave a place suddenly and secretly, especially to avoid being punished or paying debts 逃出城/國境: *Martin skipped the country with £5,000.* 馬丁帶着5,000英鎊潛逃國外。

7 skip it! *spoken* used to say angrily that you do not want to talk about something【口】〔生氣地說〕別再提這件事了!: *"Sorry, what were you saying?" "Oh, skip it!"* "對不起, 你說甚麼?" "噢, 別再提了!"

8 skip rocks/stones *AmE* to throw smooth, flat stones into a lake, river etc in a way that makes them jump across the surface【美】〔用扁平小石〕打水漂 —compare 比較 SKIM (4)

9 skip a year/grade to start a new school year in a class that is one year ahead of the class you would normally enter〔在學校〕跳級

10 sb's heart skips a beat used to say that someone is very excited, surprised, or frightened 心跳停一下〔用於表示非常興奮、驚訝或害怕〕: *His heart skipped a beat when he realized Mattie was there.* 當他發現瑪蒂在那裡時, 他嚇得心跳都停了一下。

skip out also 又作 **skip off** *phr v* [I] to leave suddenly and secretly, especially in order to avoid being punished or paying money 偷偷離開, 祕密逃走: *Martha skipped out without paying her bill.* 瑪莎沒有付賬就偷偷溜走了。| **skip out on** *AmE* (=leave someone when they need you) 【美】拋棄〔某人〕 *Joel skipped out on his wife when she was 8 months pregnant.* 喬爾在妻子懷孕八個月時拋棄了她。

skip[2] *n* [C] **1** a quick light stepping and jumping movement 輕跳, 蹦跳 **2** *BrE* a large container for bricks, wood and similar heavy waste 【英】〔用來清理磚、木等沉重廢料的〕廢料桶; DUMPSTER *AmE* 【美】

ski pants /ˈ· ·/ *n* [plural] tight trousers with a band of cloth that goes under your foot, worn by women 滑雪褲; 女子緊身褲

ski plane /ˈ· ·/ *n* [C] an aircraft that has skis (SKI[1] (2)) for landing on snow, instead of wheels〔裝有滑橇的〕雪上飛機

ski pole /ˈ· ·/ *n* [C] one of two pointed short poles used for balancing and for pushing against the snow when skiing (SKI[2]) 滑雪杖

skip·per[1] /ˈskɪpɚ; ˈskɪpə/ *n* [C] *informal* 【非正式】 **1** the person in charge of a ship 船長 **2** the leader of a sports team〔運動隊的〕隊長

skipper[2] *v* [T] *informal* to be in charge of a ship, sports team etc 【非正式】當船長; 當〔運動隊等的〕隊長

skipping rope /ˈ·· ˌ·/ *n* [C] *BrE* a long piece of rope with handles that children use for jumping over 【英】〔帶手柄的〕跳繩用的繩子, 跳繩; JUMP ROPE *AmE* 【美】

skirl /skɝl; skɜːl/ *v* [I] to make a high sharp sound 發出尖（叫）聲: *A seagull skirled overhead.* 一隻海鷗在頭上鳴叫。—**skirl** *n* [singular]

skir·mish[1] /ˈskɝmɪʃ; ˈskɜːmɪʃ/ *n* [C] **1** a fight between small groups of soldiers, ships etc, especially one that happens away from the main part of a battle 小規模戰鬥, 小衝突 **2** a short argument, especially between political opponents〔尤指政治對手間的〕小爭論, 小衝突, 口角: *Bates was sent off after a skirmish with the referee.* 貝茨和裁判衝突後被罰下場。

skirmish[2] *v* [I+with] to be involved in a short fight or argument 進行小規模戰鬥; 捲入小爭論 —**skirmisher** *n* [C]

skirt[1] /skɝt; skɜːt/ *n* [C] **1** a piece of outer clothing worn by women and girls, which hangs down from the waist like the bottom part of a dress 裙子: *She wore a white blouse and a plain black skirt.* 她穿着白襯衣和樸素的黑裙子。—compare 比較 DRESS[1] (1) —see picture on page A17 參見 A17 頁圖 **2** also 又作 **skirts** [plural] the part of a dress or coat that hangs down from the waist〔連衣裙或大衣的〕下擺 **3 the skirts of a forest/hill/village etc** the outside edge of a forest etc 森林的邊緣; 小山/村子的周圍 **4 a bit of skirt** *BrE informal* an offensive expression meaning an attractive woman 【英, 非正式】有吸引力的女人〔冒犯說法〕

skirt[2] also 又作 **skirt around** *v* [T] **1** to go around the outside edge of a place or area 沿着…邊緣走, 圍繞着…: *The old footpath skirts around the village.* 那條古老的小路圍繞着村莊。**2** to avoid talking about an important subject, especially because it is difficult or embarrassing 繞過, 避開〔重要話題〕: *a disappointing speech that skirted around all the main issues* 迴避了所有主要問題的令人失望的演說

skirting board /ˈ·· ·/ *n* [C,U] *BrE* a long narrow piece of wood that is fixed along the bottom of the walls in a room 【英】〔牆壁與地板相接處的〕壁腳板, 踢腳板; BASEBOARD *AmE* 【美】—see picture on page A4 參見 A4 頁圖

ski run /ˈ· ·/ *n* [C] a marked track on a slope for skiing (SKI[2]) 滑雪坡, 滑雪道

skit /skɪt; skɪt/ *n* [C] a short humorous performance or piece of writing that shows how silly something is by copying it〔通過模仿進行諷刺的〕滑稽短劇; 諷刺短文: [+on] *They did a skit on beauty contests.* 他們演了一齣諷刺選美的滑稽短劇。

skit·ter /ˈskɪtɚ; ˈskɪtə/ *v* [I] to run very quickly and lightly, like a small animal〔像小動物那樣〕輕快地跑

skit·tish /ˈskɪtɪʃ; ˈskɪtɪʃ/ *adj* **1** a horse or other animal that is skittish easily gets excited or frightened〔馬等動物〕易受驚的, 易激動的 **2** a person who is skittish is not very serious, and their feelings, behaviour, and opinions keep changing〔人〕輕浮的, 輕佻的; 善變的 —**skittishly** *adv* —**skittishness** *n* [U]

skit·tle /ˈskɪtl; ˈskɪtl/ *n* **1 skittles** [U] a British game in which a player tries to knock down objects shaped like bottles by rolling a ball at them〔英國的〕撞柱戲, 九柱戲〔沿球道以球擊倒數根瓶狀木柱的遊戲〕 **2** [C] one of the objects you roll the ball at in the game of skittles〔撞柱戲用的〕瓶狀小木柱 —see also 另見 **not all beer and skittles** (BEER (3))

skive /skaɪv; skaɪv/ also 又作 **skive off** *v* [I] *BrE informal* to avoid work or school by staying away or leaving without permission 【英, 非正式】逃避工作, 曠工; 逃學, 曠課 —**skiver** *n* [C]

skiv·vies /ˈskɪvɪz; ˈskɪviz/ *n* [plural] *AmE* a man's underwear 【美】男用內衣

skiv·vy[1] /ˈskɪvɪ; ˈskɪvi/ *n* [C] *BrE humorous* a servant who does only the dirty unpleasant jobs in a house 【英, 幽默】〔專幹髒活的〕傭人, 僕人: *You iron your shirt – I'm not your skivvy.* 你自己熨襯衣吧 —— 我不是你的傭人。

skivvy[2] *v* [I] *BrE* to do all the dirty unpleasant jobs in a house, as if you were a servant 【英】〔像傭人似地〕幹髒[雜]活

skul·dug·ge·ry /skʌlˋdʌgərɪ; ˌskʌlˈdʌgəri/ *n* [U] *often humorous* secretly dishonest or illegal activity 【常幽默】弄虛作假, 詭計, 花招; 非法活動: *Some skulduggery no doubt went on during the election.* 肯定有人在選舉過程中做了手腳。

skulk /skʌlk; skʌlk/ *v* [I always+adv/prep] to hide or move about secretly, trying not to be noticed, especially when you are intending to do something bad〔為了不良企圖而〕躲藏; 鬼鬼祟祟地走動: **[+about/around/in etc]** *He was still skulking around outside when they left the building.* 他們離開大樓時他還在外面躲着。

skull /skʌl; skʌl/ *n* [C] **1** the bones of a person's or animal's head〔人或動物的〕頭顱骨, 頭骨 —see picture at 參見 SKELETON 圖 **2 sb can't get it into their (thick) skull** *spoken* to be unable to understand something very simple 【口】笨腦袋無法明白: *He can't seem to get it into his skull that I'm just not interested in him.* 他這個笨蛋好像無法明白我根本對他不感興趣。

skull and cross·bones /ˌ· · ˈ··/ *n* [singular] **1** a picture of a human skull with two bones crossed below it, used in former times on the flags of PIRATE[1] (3) ships〔從前海盜船上的〕骷髏旗 **2** a picture of a human skull with two bones crossed below it, used on containers to show that what is inside is very dangerous〔畫在裝毒藥的瓶子上表示危險的〕骷髏圖標誌

skull cap /ˈ· ·/ *n* [C] a simple close-fitting cap for the top of the head, worn sometimes by priests or Jewish men〔牧師或猶太男子有時戴的〕無檐便帽

skunk[1] /skʌŋk; skʌŋk/ *n* [C] a small black and white North American animal that produces a strong unpleasant smell if it is attacked 臭鼬〔一種北美產的黑白色動物, 受襲擊時會放出惡臭自衛〕

skunk[2] *v* [T] *AmE informal* to defeat a player or team very easily 【美, 非正式】輕易地擊敗對手[對方球隊]

skunk cab·bage /ˈ· ˌ··/ *n* [C,U] a large North American plant similar to a CABBAGE, with an unpleasant smell〔北美產的〕臭鼬草, 臭菘

sky /skaɪ; skaɪ/ *n* [singular,U] **1** the space above the earth where clouds and the sun and stars appear 天, 天空: *The rocket shot up into the sky.* 火箭升上了天空。| *The sky turned dark just before the storm.* 暴風雨將至, 天色轉暗。| **a patch/strip etc of sky** *There's a patch of blue*

S

sky between the clouds. 烏雲之間漏出小片藍天。| **a blue/cloudy etc sky** (=used to describe how the sky looks at a particular time) 藍色的/多雲的天空 *The sun blazed down from a clear blue sky.* 太陽在晴朗的藍天發出耀眼的光芒。**2 skies** a word meaning sky, used especially when describing the weather 天空〔尤用於描寫天氣〕: *a land of blue skies and warm sunshine* 擁有蔚藍色天空和温暖陽光的土地 | **the skies** *The skies were filled with scudding clouds.* 滿天都是飛掠而過的雲彩。| *the crowded skies above our major airports* 我國各大機場上往來航班繁忙的天空 **3 the sky's the limit** *spoken* used to say that there is no limit to what someone can achieve, spend, win etc【口】〔指對花錢、取得成績等〕毫無限制, 沒有上限 —see also 另見 **pie in the sky** (PIE (4)), **praise sb/sth to the skies** (PRAISE[1] (1))

sky-blue /ˌ· ˈ·◂/ *n* [U] the bright blue colour of a clear sky 天藍色 —**sky-blue** *adj* —see picture on page A5 參見 A5 頁圖

sky·cap /ˈskaɪˌkæp; ˈskaɪkæp/ *n* [C] *AmE* someone who carries passengers' cases at an airport【美】機場行李搬運工

sky·div·ing /ˈskaɪˌdaɪvɪŋ; ˈskaɪˌdaɪvɪŋ/ *n* [U] the sport of jumping from an aircraft and falling through the sky before opening a PARACHUTE〔延緩張傘的〕跳傘運動 —**sky-diver** *n* [U]

sky-high /ˌ· ˈ·◂/ *adj informal* extremely high【非正式】極高的, 高入雲霄的: *If this thing explodes we'll be blown sky-high.* 這個東西如果發生爆炸, 我們就要給拋到半空中。—**sky-high** *adv* —see also 另見 **blow sth sky-high** (BLOW[1] (19))

S

sky·lark /ˈskaɪˌlɑrk; ˈskaɪlɑːk/ *n* [C] a small bird that sings while flying high in the sky 雲雀

sky·light /ˈskaɪˌlaɪt; ˈskaɪlaɪt/ *n* [C] a window in the roof of a building〔屋頂的〕天窗

sky·line /ˈskaɪˌlaɪn; ˈskaɪlaɪn/ *n* [C] the shape made by hills or buildings against the sky〔山或建築物在天空映襯下的〕輪廓(線)

sky·rock·et /ˈskaɪˌrɑkɪt; ˈskaɪˌrɒkɪt/ *v* [I] *informal* to increase suddenly and greatly【非正式】急升, 猛升, 劇增, 劇漲: *The trade deficit has skyrocketed.* 貿易逆差已經急劇增長。

sky·scrap·er /ˈskaɪˌskrepɚ; ˈskaɪˌskreɪpə/ *n* [C] a very tall modern city building 摩天大樓

sky·wards /ˈskaɪwɚdz; ˈskaɪwədz/ *adv* up into the sky or towards the sky 向着天空; 朝向天空: *The bird soared skywards.* 鳥兒向高空翱翔。

slab /slæb; slæb/ *n* [C] **1** a thick flat four-sided piece of a hard material such as stone〔石頭等四邊形硬質材料的〕平板, 厚板: *The patio was made of stone slabs.* 露台是用石板鋪砌的。—see picture on page A7 參見 A7 頁圖 **2 a slab of cake/chocolate etc** a large flat piece of cake etc 一大塊蛋糕/巧克力等 **3 on the slab** *slang* lying dead in a hospital or MORTUARY【俚】停屍在醫院[太平間]

slack¹ /slæk; slæk/ *adj* **1** not taking enough care or making enough effort to do things right 懶散的, 懈怠的, 馬虎的: *Tollitt blundered with a slack header towards the goalkeeper.* 托利特向守門員頂出一記有氣無力的頭球, 犯了大錯。| *The report criticized airport security as 'disgracefully slack'.* 那份報告批評機場的保安工作"鬆懈得令人顏面盡失"。**2** with less business activity than usual〔生意〕蕭條的, 清淡的: *Business is slack just now.* 目前生意清淡。**3** hanging loosely, or not pulled tight〔繩子等〕不(拉)緊的, 鬆弛的: *The fan belt is a little slack.* 〔引擎上的〕風扇皮帶有點鬆了。| *a slack mouth* 沒合攏的嘴 | *Keep the rope slack till I say 'pull'.* 讓繩子鬆着, 等到我喊"拉"。—**slackly** *adv* —**slackness** *n* [U]

slack² *n* **1** [C] money, space, or people that an organization has, but does not need 閒置的資源〈如不需要的資金、場地、人力等〉: *There is very little slack in the training budget for this year.* 在今年的培訓預算中沒有多少閒置資金了。**2 take up the slack a)** to make a rope tighter 把繩子拉緊 **b)** to do something that needs to be done because someone else is no longer doing it 接替別人停下的工作: *We're relying on Walters to take up the slack while Gonzalez is gone.* 我們靠沃爾特斯來接替岡薩雷斯離開期間的工作。**3** [U] looseness in the way that something such as a rope hangs or is fastened〔繩子、繩結等的〕鬆弛, 不緊 **4 slacks** [plural] *old-fashioned* trousers【過時】寬鬆長褲, 便褲 **5** [U] coal in very small pieces 煤屑

slack³ also 又作 **slack off** *v* [I] to make less of an effort than usual or be lazy in your work 放鬆, 鬆勁, 懈怠

slack·en /ˈslækən; ˈslækən/ also 又作 **slacken off** *v* [I, T] **1** to gradually become slower, weaker, less active etc, or to make something do this (使)減慢, (使)放緩, (使)減弱: *The heavy rain showed no signs of slackening off.* 大雨沒有減弱的跡象。| **slacken your pace/speed** (=go or walk more slowly) 放慢腳步/速度 *Once outside the gates, I slackened my pace.* 一出大門, 我就放慢了腳步。**2** to make something looser or to become looser (使)鬆弛, (使)變鬆: *Just slacken the screws a little.* 把螺絲擰鬆一點。—opposite 反義詞 TIGHTEN

slack·er /ˈslækɚ; ˈslækə/ *n* [C] someone who is lazy and does not do all the work they should 懶惰的人, 偷懶者

slag¹ /slæg; slæg/ *n* **1** [U] light waste material rather like glass, which is left when metal is obtained from rock 礦渣, 熔渣, 爐渣 **2** [C] *BrE slang* an insulting word for a woman, used to suggest that she has had a lot of sexual partners【英俚】淫婦, 蕩婦〔此詞具侮辱性〕—**slaggy** *adj*

slag²

slag sb ↔ **off** *phr v* [T] *BrE informal* to talk about someone in a very critical way, especially when they are not there【英, 非正式】〔尤指在背後〕詆毀; 責難; 批評: *He's always slagging her off behind her back.* 他老是在背後說她的壞話。

slag heap /ˈ· ·/ *n* [C] *especially BrE* a pile of waste material at a mine or factory【尤英】礦渣堆, 熔渣堆

slain /slen; sleɪn/ *v* the past participle of SLAY

slake /slek; sleɪk/ *v* [T] *literary*【文】**1 slake your thirst** to drink so that you are not THIRSTY any more 解渴 **2** to satisfy a desire 滿足〔慾望〕

sla·lom /ˈslɑləm; ˈslɑːləm/ *n* [U] a race for people on SKIS or in CANOES down a winding course marked by flags〔穿過插有旗杆的蜿蜒賽道進行的〕回轉滑雪賽; 小划子[獨木舟]回旋賽

slam¹ /slæm; slæm/ *v*

1 ►DOOR/GATE 門/大門◄ [I,T] if a door, gate etc slams, or if someone slams it, it shuts with a loud noise (使)砰地關上, 使勁關閉: *Please don't slam the door.* 請不要使勁關門。| *We could hear people shouting and doors slamming in the house next door.* 我們可以聽到隔壁人家大聲喊叫和用力關門的聲音。| **slam shut** *A door slammed shut in the distance.* 遠處有一扇門砰地關上了。

2 ►PUT STH SOMEWHERE 放東西◄ [T always+adv/prep] to put something on or against a surface with a fast violent movement 砰地放下, 使勁放下: **slam sth on/down etc** *Henry slammed the phone down and walked angrily out of the room.* 亨利摔下電話筒, 怒氣沖沖地走出了房間。

3 slam on the brakes to make a car stop very suddenly 猛踩煞車

4 ►CRITICIZE STH 批評某事◄ [T] a word used especially in newspapers, meaning to criticize something strongly 猛烈抨擊〔報刊用語〕: *The government's amnesty for tax-dodgers was slammed today by opposition leaders.* 政府對逃稅者的赦免今天遭到反對黨領袖的猛烈抨擊。| **slam sb for sth** *The television company was slammed by the media for its portrayal of a gang rape.* 這家電視台因為播出一段輪姦片段而受到媒體的猛烈抨擊。

5 slam the door in sb's face a) to shut a door hard

when someone is trying to come in 用力關門不讓某人進入, 讓某人吃閉門羹 **b)** to rudely refuse to meet someone or talk to them〔粗魯地〕拒絕會見某人; 拒絕與某人談話

slam into sth *phr v* [T] to drive or move very fast towards something and hit it〔駕駛等因速度太快而〕撞到…: *The car slammed into a lamp-post.* 那輛汽車撞上了燈柱。

slam² *n* [C usually singular 一般用單數] the noise or action of a door or gate slamming 砰的關門;〔門〕砰的關上 —see also 另見 GRAND SLAM

slam dunk /ˈ· ·/ *v* [I, T] to put a ball through the net in BASKETBALL using a lot of force〔籃球運動中〕扣籃, 塞籃, 塞投 —**slam dunk** *n* [C]

slam·mer /ˈslæmɚ; ˈslæmə/ *n* **in the slammer** *slang* in prison【俚】坐牢: *He was thrown in the slammer.* 他被投進監獄。

slan·der¹ /ˈslændɚ; ˈslɑːndə/ *n* **1** [C] a false spoken statement about someone that is intended to damage the good opinion that people have 誹謗, 詆毀 **2** [U] the legal offence of making a statement of this kind〔法律上的〕誹謗罪: *The doctor was awarded record damages against her partners for slander.* 這位醫生因合作夥伴對她犯了誹謗罪而獲得創紀錄的損害賠償金。—compare 比較 LIBEL¹ —**slanderer** *n* [C]

slander² *v* [T] to say untrue things about someone in order to damage other people's good opinion of them 誹謗, 詆毀, 造謠中傷

slan·der·ous /ˈslændərəs; ˈslɑːndərəs/ *adj* a slanderous statement about someone is untrue, and is intended to damage other people's good opinion of them 誹謗的, 詆毀的, 造謠中傷的: *slanderous allegations* 誹謗性的提法

slang /slæŋ; slæŋ/ *n* [U] very informal language that includes new and sometimes rude words, especially words used only by particular groups of people such as criminals, schoolchildren, or people who take drugs 俚語: *schoolboy slang* 學生俚語 | **a slang word/expression/term** *'Screw' is a slang word used by prisoners to mean prison officer.* screw 是囚犯用以指監獄看守的俚語詞。—**slangy** *adj*: *slangy expressions* 俚語表達法

slanging match /ˈ·· ˌ·/ *n* [C] *BrE informal* an angry argument in which people insult each other【英, 非正式】互相謾罵, 對罵, 辱罵: *They got into a bit of a slanging match in the pub.* 他們在酒館裡對罵了一陣子。

slant¹ /slænt; slɑːnt/ *v* [I] *especially literary* to slope or move in a sloping line【尤文】傾斜, 歪斜; 斜穿: *slanting handwriting* 傾斜的字跡 | *The sun's rays slanted through the trees.* 陽光斜射進樹林。—**slantingly** *adv*

slant² *n* **1** a sloping position or angle 斜面; 斜線; 斜角: *a steep slant* 陡峭的斜面 | **at/on a slant** *Set the pole at a slant.* 把柱子斜着豎起來。**2** a way of writing about or thinking about a subject that shows strong support for a particular opinion or set of ideas〔有傾向性的〕觀點, 看法, 意見; 偏見: *The editorial had an anti-union slant.* 這篇社論帶有一種反工會的偏見。| *The report provides a new slant on important environmental issues.* 這份報告對重要的環境問題提出了一種新的見解。

slant·ed /ˈslæntɪd; ˈslɑːntɪ̈d/ *adj* **1** providing facts or information in a way that unfairly favours one opinion, one side of an argument etc; BIASED 有偏見的: **[+towards]** *The survey was heavily slanted towards the ruling party.* 這篇調查報告嚴重地偏向執政黨。**2** sloping to one side 傾斜的, 歪斜的

2 **slap¹** /slæp; slæp/ *v* **slapped, slapping 1** [T] to hit someone quickly with the flat part of your hand 用巴掌打, 摑; 拍: *Do you think it's OK to slap children if they're really rude?* 孩子要是真的粗魯無禮, 你認為打他們耳光妥當嗎? | **slap sb on the back** (=hit them on the back in a friendly way)〔友好地〕拍某人的肩膀 —see picture on page A20 參見 A20 頁圖 **2** [T always+adv/prep] to put something down noisily on a surface, especially when you are angry〔尤指生氣時〕啪的一聲放下, 擲下, 扔下: **slap sth on/down** *I slapped the report down on his desk and told him to do it again.* 我把那份報告扔在他桌上, 叫他重寫。**3** [I] to hit a surface, making a sound like someone being slapped noisily 啪啪地撞擊, 拍擊: **[+against]** *Small waves slapped against the jetty.* 細浪拍擊着防波堤。

slap sb **down** *phr v* [T] to unfairly and unkindly criticize someone so that they lose confidence 粗暴地批評, 壓制

slap sth ↔ **on** *phr v* [T] *informal*【非正式】**1** to put or spread something quickly or carelessly onto a surface 匆匆地塗, 草草地抹: *She rushed upstairs and slapped on some make-up.* 她衝上樓, 匆匆上了點妝。**2** to suddenly announce a new charge, tax etc, especially unfairly or without warning〔尤指突然或強行地〕增加〔費用、税款等〕: *Many tour operators slap on supplements for single people.* 許多旅遊公司對散客強行增收額外的費用。

slap² *n* [C] **1** a quick hit with the flat part of your hand 一巴掌; 一拍: **give sb a slap** *Julia gave Roy a friendly slap on the cheek.* 朱莉婭友好地拍了拍羅伊的臉頰。**2 a slap in the face** an action that seems to be deliberately intended to offend or upset someone, especially someone who has tried very hard to do something 侮辱, 打擊: *When I wasn't promoted it felt like such a terrible slap in the face.* 我沒得到晉升時, 覺得好像受了極大的打擊。**3 a slap on the wrist** *informal* a punishment that is not very severe【非正式】輕微的處罰

slap³ /slæp; slæp/ also 又作 **slap-bang** /ˌ· ˈ·/ *adv informal* hitting something very hard, especially when you are running, driving etc【非正式】〔尤指在跑着或開車時〕猛烈地, 重重地〔撞到某物〕: **[+into]** *I ran slap-bang into a lamp-post.* 我猛然撞在燈柱上。

slap·dash /ˈslæpˌdæʃ; ˈslæpdæʃ/ *adj* careless and done too quickly 粗心的, 草率的, 倉促的: *a very slapdash piece of work* 非常倉促完成的工作

slap·hap·py /ˈslæpˌhæpɪ; ˈslæpˌhæpi/ *adj* cheerfully careless and likely to make mistakes 大大咧咧的, 滿不在乎的; 粗心大意的

slap·per /ˈslæpɚ; ˈslæpə/ *n* [C] *BrE slang* a sexually immoral woman, or a woman who remains strong and cheerful in spite of a difficult life【英俚】淫蕩的女人;〔在困境中仍〕堅強開朗的婦女

slap·stick /ˈslæpˌstɪk; ˈslæpˌstɪk/ *n* [U] humorous acting in which the performers fall over, throw things at each other etc 滑稽表演, 打鬧劇

slap-up /ˈ· ·/ *adj* **slap-up meal/dinner etc** *BrE informal* a very large enjoyable meal【英, 非正式】美餐/精美大餐等

slash¹ /slæʃ; slæʃ/ *v* **1** [I always+adv/prep,T] to violently cut or try to cut something with a knife, sword etc〔用刀、劍、棒等〕猛削, 猛砍, 亂打: *Most of the seats on the train had been slashed by vandals.* 火車上大多數的座位都被破壞公物者劃破了。| **[+at/through]** *Alan was slashing at the snake with a huge stick.* 阿倫用大棒猛打那條蛇。| **slash your way through** (=make a path through something by slashing) 從…中劈出一條路 *They had to slash their way through thick undergrowth.* 他們得在茂密的灌木叢中劈出一條路。| **slash your wrists** (=deliberately cut your wrists with the intention of killing yourself) 割腕〔自殺〕**2** [T often passive 常用被動態] a word used especially in newspapers and advertising meaning to greatly reduce an amount, price etc 大幅度削減〔數量、價格等, 尤用於報刊及廣告中〕: *Over the last year the workforce has been slashed by 50%.* 去年勞動力已削減了 50%。

slash² *n* [C] **1** a quick movement that you make with a sword, knife etc in order to cut someone or something〔用刀、劍等〕砍, 劈, 削 **2** also 又作 **slash mark** a line (/) used in writing to separate words, numbers, or letters 斜線符號〔用以分隔單詞、數字或字母〕**3** a long narrow wound or a long narrow cut in a piece of material〔長條的〕傷痕, 砍痕;〔長條的〕切口, 裂口: *He staggered into hospital with slashes across his face.* 他搖搖晃晃地走進醫院, 臉上傷痕累累。**4 have/take a slash** *BrE spoken* an impolite expression meaning to URINATE【英口】撒尿〔不雅的說法〕

slat /slæt; slæt/ *n* [C] a thin flat piece of wood, plastic etc used especially in furniture〔家具的〕細長板條 —**slatted** *adj*: *a slatted bench* 板條長椅

slate¹ /slet; sleɪt/ *n*

1 ►ROCK 岩石◄ [U] a dark grey rock that can easily be split into flat thin pieces 板岩, 板石: *a slate mine* 板石礦

2 ►ON A ROOF 房頂上◄ [C] one of the small pieces of slate or similar material used for covering roofs 石板瓦: *There were several slates missing from the roof.* 房頂有幾塊石板瓦掉了。

3 slate blue/grey a dark grey or blue colour 深灰色; 藍灰色

4 ►POLITICS 政治◄ [C] *especially AmE* a list of people that voters can choose in an election or that are being considered for an important job【尤美】候選人名單

5 put sth on the slate *BrE old-fashioned* to arrange to pay for something later, especially food or drink【英, 過時】〔尤指對食物和飲料〕賒賬, 掛賬: *Two whiskies, and could you put them on the slate!* 來兩杯威士忌, 請給掛賬。

6 ►FOR WRITING ON 寫字用的◄ [C] a small board in a wooden frame used for writing on in schools in former times〔從前學校裡寫字用的〕石板 —see also 另見 **a clean slate** (CLEAN¹ (10)), **wipe the slate clean** (WIPE¹ (6))

slate² *v* [T] **1** *BrE informal* to criticize a book, film etc severely, especially in a newspaper【英, 非正式】〔尤指在報紙上〕嚴厲批評〔書、電影等〕: *Donkin's most recent novel has been slated by the critics.* 唐金的最新小說受到評論家的嚴厲批評。**2 be slated** *especially AmE*【尤美】**a)** to be expected to succeed in getting a particular position or job 可望擔任某職: **be slated to be/do sth** *Rogers is slated to be the Democratic candidate.* 羅傑斯被提名為民主黨候選人。**b)** to be expected or planned to happen at a time in the future 預定〔舉行〕, 定於: **be slated for** *The office buildings are slated for demolition next June.* 這些辦公大樓定於明年六月拆毀。—**slated** *adj*

slath·er /ˈslæθɚ; ˈslæθə/ *v* [T] *AmE* to cover something with a thick layer of a soft substance【美】給…厚厚地塗抹〔醬狀物〕: *toast slathered with butter* 塗着厚厚一層黃油的烤麵包

slat·tern /ˈslætɚn; ˈslætən/ *n* [C] *old-fashioned* a dirty untidy woman【過時】邋遢女人, 懶婆娘 —**slatternly** *adj*

slaugh·ter¹ /ˈslɔtɚ; ˈslɔːtə/ *v* [T] **1** to kill large numbers of people in a cruel or violent way 屠殺, 殺戮, 殘殺: *Hundreds of innocent civilians were slaughtered.* 數以百計的無辜平民遭到殺戮。—see 見 KILL¹ (USAGE) **2** to kill an animal for food 屠宰〔動物〕**3** *informal* to defeat an opponent by a large number of points【非正式】〔在體育比賽中〕使慘敗: *We got slaughtered 110–54.* 我們以 54 比 110 慘敗。

slaughter² *n* [U] **1** the act of killing large numbers of people in a cruel or violent way 屠殺, 殺戮, 殘殺 **2** the act of killing animals for food〔對動物的〕屠宰, 宰殺

slaugh·ter·house /ˈslɔtɚˌhaus; ˈslɔːtəhaʊs/ *n* [C] a building where animals are killed 屠宰場

slave¹ /slev; sleɪv/ *n* [C] **1** someone who is legally owned by another person and works for them for no money 奴隸: *accusing her mother of treating her like a slave* 控告她母親把她當奴隸看待 **2 be a slave to/of** to be completely influenced by something so that you cannot make your own decisions 完全受某物的控制: *A lot of kids nowadays are slaves of fashion.* 如今許多孩子都成為了時尚的奴隸。**3 slave driver** *informal* someone who makes people work extremely hard【非正式】逼迫他人拚命幹活的人, 苛刻的工頭: *She knew the girls called her a slave driver behind her back.* 她知道姑娘們在背後把她叫做無情的工頭。

slave² *v* [I always+adv/prep] to work very hard with little time to rest 拚命幹, 苦幹: [**+away/over/for**] *I've been slaving away for hours to get this report finished.* 為了完成這份報告, 我已經苦幹好幾個鐘頭了。| **slaving away over a hot stove** (=a humorous way of saying you are cooking) 在火熱的灶頭拚命幹〔下廚做飯的幽默說法〕

slave la·bour *BrE*【英】, **slave labor** *AmE*【美】/ˌ· ˈ··/ *n* [U] **1** *informal* work for which you are paid an unreasonably small amount of money【非正式】奴隸勞動, 報酬極低的工作: *£2 an hour! That's slave labour!* 每小時兩英鎊！這是廉價勞動！**2** work done by SLAVES or the people who do this work 奴隸做的苦工; 做苦工的奴隸: *The Pyramids were largely built by slave labour.* 金字塔大部分是由做苦工的奴隸建成的。

slav·er¹ /ˈslævɚ; ˈslævə/ *v* [I] to let SALIVA (=liquid produced inside your mouth) come out of your mouth, especially because you are hungry 垂涎, 淌口水: *The dog started slavering at the sight of the bone.* 那條狗看見骨頭就流口水。

slaver over sth *phr v* [T] *informal* to be very excited about something, especially in an unpleasant or stupid way【非正式】渴望, 對…垂涎: *slavering over the parked Ferrari out front* 對停在面前的法拉利轎車垂涎三尺

slav·er² /ˈslevɚ; ˈsleɪvə/ *n* [C] *old use*【舊】**1** someone who sells slaves 奴隸販子 **2** a ship for slaves 奴隸販運船

sla·ve·ry /ˈslevərɪ; ˈsleɪvəri/ *n* [U] **1** the system of having slaves 奴隸制度: *the abolition of slavery* 奴隸制的廢除 **2** the condition of being a slave 奴隸身分: **sell sb into slavery** (=to sell someone as a SLAVE) 把某人賣去當奴隸

slave trade /ˈ· ·/ *n* [singular] the buying and selling of slaves, especially Africans who were taken to America 奴隸買賣〔尤指過去對被抓到美洲的非洲人進行的買賣〕

slav·ish /ˈslevɪʃ; ˈsleɪvɪʃ/ *adj* **slavish imitation/devotion etc** behaviour or actions that show that you cannot make your own decisions about what you should do 一味的模仿／奴性的忠誠: *a slavish devotion to duty* 奴性地忠於職守 —**slavishly** *adv* —**slavishness** *n* [U]

slaw /slɔ; slɔː/ *n* [U] *AmE* a cold dish made with CABBAGE, CARROTS, and onions; COLESLAW【美】〔用捲心菜、胡蘿蔔和洋蔥做的〕生拌涼菜, 涼拌捲心菜絲

slay /sle; sleɪ/ *v past tense* **slew** /slu; sluː/ *past participle* **slain** /slen; sleɪn/ [T] **1** *literary* a word meaning to kill someone, often used in newspaper reports; MURDER² (1)【文】殺害, 殘殺, 謀殺〔常用於新聞報道〕: *Thousands were slain in the battle.* 數以千計的人在這場戰役中被殺害。**2** *AmE informal* to amuse someone a lot【美, 非正式】逗…樂[笑], 使笑倒: *That guy really slays me!* 那個人真把我逗樂了。—**slayer** *n* [C]

sleaze /sliz; sliːz/ *n* **1** [U] immoral behaviour, especially involving sex or dishonesty 不道德; 不誠實; 卑劣〔尤涉及性或虛偽〕: *the sleaze factor in US politics* 美國政治中的不道德因素 **2** also 又作 **sleazebag** *slang especially AmE* someone who is immoral or cannot be trusted【俚, 尤美】卑劣的人, 卑鄙小人

slea·zy /ˈslizɪ; ˈsliːzi/ *adj* **1 sleazy hotel/bar etc** a hotel etc that looks dirty and cheap 骯髒的廉價旅館／酒吧等 **2** someone who is sleazy is immoral or unpleasant〔人〕卑劣的, 討厭的: *sleazy business associates* 卑劣的生意合夥人 —**sleaziness** *n* [U]

sledge¹ /slɛdʒ; sledʒ/ *BrE*【英】, **sled** /slɛd; sled/ *AmE*【美】—*n* [C] a vehicle for travelling over snow with two long narrow pieces of wood or metal fixed under it 雪橇

sledge² *BrE*【英】, **sled** *AmE*【美】—*v* [I] to travel or ride on a sledge 乘雪橇

sledge·ham·mer /ˈslɛdʒˌhæmɚ; ˈsledʒˌhæmə/ *n* [C] a

large heavy hammer 大錘

sleek¹ /slik; sliːk/ *adj* **1** sleek hair or fur is straight, shiny, and healthy-looking〔頭髮、皮毛〕平直光滑的, 有光澤的, 健康的: *The cat had sleek black fur.* 這隻貓有着光滑的黑毛。**2** a vehicle or other object that is sleek has a smooth attractive shape〔汽車等〕光潔漂亮的, 造型優美的: *the sleek lines of the new Mercedes* 新平治汽車的優美外型 **3** someone who is sleek looks rich, but you feel that you cannot trust them〔人〕裝扮得時髦闊氣的: *sleek executive types in their expensive suits* 身穿華服的時髦的行政人員 —**sleekly** *adv* —**sleekness** *n* [U]

sleek² *v* [T always+adv/prep] to make hair or fur smooth and shiny by putting water or oil on it〔在頭髮或皮毛上抹水或油〕使平滑光亮: **sleek sth back/down etc** *His hair was sleeked back with oil.* 他的頭髮用油向後梳理得平滑光亮。

S1 W2 **sleep¹** /slip; sliːp/ *v past tense and past participle* **slept** /slɛpt; slept/

1 ►REST 休息◄ [I] to rest your mind and body by being asleep 睡, 睡覺, 睡着: *I normally sleep on my back.* 我通常都仰臥着睡覺。| *You're welcome to stay if you don't mind sleeping on the floor.* 你如果不介意睡地板的話, 那就歡迎你住下來。| **sleep well/soundly** *Did you sleep well?* 你睡得好嗎? | **sleep like a log/top** *informal* (=sleep very well)【非正式】睡得很熟/很死 | **sleep late** (=sleep until late in the morning) 睡到很晚才起牀 *We usually sleep late on Sundays.* 我們通常在星期天早上睡懶覺。| **not sleep a wink** (=not sleep at all)〔整夜〕沒有合眼, 完全沒有睡着 *I didn't sleep a wink all night.* 我整夜都沒合過眼。| **sleep the night** *BrE* (=sleep at someone else's house for the night)【英】在別人家裡過夜 *We talked till late and then Bob ended up sleeping the night.* 我們談到很晚, 結果鮑勃留下過夜。

2 sleep rough *BrE* to sleep outdoors in uncomfortable conditions, especially because you have no money【英】〔尤因沒有錢而〕在戶外隨便找個地方睡覺, 露宿

3 sleep on it *informal* to not make a decision about something important until the next day【非正式】把某事留待第二天決定: *Why don't you sleep on it and give me your final reply tomorrow?* 你為甚麼不多考慮一個晚上, 明天才把你的最後決定告訴我?

4 sleep tight *spoken* used especially to children before they go to bed to say that you hope they sleep well【口】睡個好覺〔尤對睡覺前的小孩子說〕: *Good night, sweetheart. Sleep tight!* 晚安, 親愛的。睡個好覺!

5 ►NUMBER OF PEOPLE 人數◄ [T] to have enough beds for a particular number of people〔有牀〕可供〔若干人〕睡: **sleep two/four/six etc** *The villa will sleep four easily.* 這間別墅足可以供四人住宿。

6 let sleeping dogs lie to deliberately avoid mentioning a problem or argument that you had in the past, so that you do not cause any problems 別惹是生非; 別自尋煩惱: *She decided to let sleeping dogs lie and not to ask her son about the missing money.* 她決定不去自尋煩惱, 不去問兒子關於丟錢的事。

7 ►BE QUIET AT NIGHT 夜裡靜悄悄◄ [I] *literary* if a village, house etc sleeps it is night time and very quiet【文】〔入夜後的房子、村莊等〕靜寂, 保持安靜: *While the house slept, he crept downstairs and out of the front door.* 等全家人進入夢鄉之後, 他躡手躡腳地下了樓, 從前門溜了出去。

sleep around *phr v* [I] *informal* to be too willing to have sex with a lot of different people【非正式】到處和別人睡覺, 亂搞男女關係

sleep in *phr v* [I] to sleep later than usual in the morning〔早上〕睡懶覺: *They like to sleep in on Saturdays.* 他們喜歡在星期六早上睡懶覺。—compare 比較 OVERSLEEP

sleep sth ↔ **off** *phr v* [T] to sleep until you do not feel ill any more, especially after drinking too much alcohol〔尤指在醉酒後〕用睡眠解除〔不適〕: *sleeping off the effects of last night's party* 用睡覺解除昨天晚會後的醉意

sleep over *phr v* [I] to sleep at someone's house for a night 在別人家裡過夜, 借宿: *If you don't want to drive, you're welcome to sleep over.* 如果你不想開車, 歡迎你在我家過夜。

sleep through *phr v* **1** [T **sleep through** sth] to sleep while something is happening and not be woken by it 在...發生時未醒來: *How did you manage to sleep through that thunderstorm?* 雷雨那麼大你怎麼能睡得着? **2** [I] to sleep continuously for a long time 一直睡到...: *I slept right through till lunchtime.* 我一覺睡到吃午飯的時候。

sleep together *phr v* [I] *informal* to have sex【非正式】性交: *I'm sure those two are sleeping together.* 我肯定那兩個人是睡在一起了。

sleep with sb *phr v* [T] *informal* to have sex with someone, especially someone you are not married to【非正式】與某人〔尤指非配偶〕發生性關係: *It's common knowledge that he's sleeping with his secretary.* 大家都知道他和祕書有染。

sleep² *n* S2 W3

1 ►AT NIGHT 在晚上◄ [U] the natural state of being asleep 睡眠, 睡覺: *I didn't get much sleep last night.* 我昨天晚上睡得不多。| *Try and get some sleep before the journey.* 去旅行之前盡量多睡點覺。| **get to sleep** (=succeed in sleeping) 入睡 *I had terrible trouble getting to sleep last night.* 我昨晚怎麼也睡不着。| **in your sleep** (=while you are sleeping) 在(你)睡着時 *She sometimes talks in her sleep.* 她有時睡覺說夢話。| **send sb to sleep** (=make someone sleep) 使某人入睡 *The combination of warmth and music sent him to sleep.* 暖意和音樂伴他進入夢鄉。| **sing/rock sb to sleep** (=sing to a baby until it sleeps or gently move it) 唱歌哄嬰兒入睡/輕輕地搖嬰兒入睡

2 ►PERIOD OF SLEEPING 睡眠時間◄ [singular] a period of sleeping (一段) 睡眠時間: *I usually have a sleep after lunch.* 我通常在午飯後睡一會兒。| **a light/deep sleep** *She was woken from a deep sleep by a ring at the door.* 她在酣睡中被門鈴聲吵醒。| **a good night's sleep** (=a night when you sleep well and after which you feel healthy and active) 一夜的酣睡

3 go to sleep a) to start sleeping 入睡: *I went to sleep at 9 o'clock and woke up at 6.* 我九點鐘入睡, 六點鐘醒來。**b)** *informal* if a part of your body goes to sleep, you cannot feel it for a short time because it has not been getting enough blood【非正式】〔身體某部位〕麻木, 發麻〔因供血不足所致〕

4 don't lose sleep over it *spoken* used to tell someone not to worry about something【口】〔勸人〕不要為擔心某事而失眠

5 put sb/sth to sleep a) to give drugs to a sick animal so that it dies without too much pain 使〔動物〕長眠; 人道毀滅〔動物〕〔指用藥使有病痛的動物無痛苦地死去〕**b)** *informal* to make someone unconscious before an operation by giving them drugs【非正式】〔手術前用麻醉藥〕使〔某人〕失去知覺

6 can do sth in your sleep *informal* to be able to do something very easily, especially because you have done it many times before【非正式】〔尤指因已做過多次而能〕輕而易舉地做; 閉上眼睛都能做

7 ►IN YOUR EYES 在眼睛內◄ [U] *informal* a substance that forms in the corners of your eyes while you are sleeping【非正式】眵, 眼眵, 眼屎

sleep·er /ˈslipɚ; ˈsliːpə/ *n* [C] **1 a) a heavy sleeper** someone who does not wake easily 睡得很死的人, 不易醒的人 **b) a light sleeper** someone who wakes easily 睡得不熟的人, 易醒的人 **2** someone who is asleep 睡着的人 **3** a train with carriages that have beds for passengers to sleep in, or a bed on this kind of train〔火車的〕臥鋪車廂;〔火車上的〕臥鋪 **4** *especially BrE* a heavy piece of wood or CONCRETE supporting a railway track【尤英】〔鐵路的〕枕木; TIE² (7) *AmE*【美】**5** *BrE* a small ring worn in your ear【英】小耳環, 耳環圈 —see picture at 參見 JEWELLERY 圖 **6** *AmE* a film, book etc which is successful but not immediately【美】〔長期遭忽視後〕突然獲得成功的影片[書籍]

sleeping bag /'·· ·/ *n* [C] a large warm bag for sleeping in, especially when camping〔尤指露營用的〕睡袋

sleeping bag 睡袋

sleeping car /'·· ·/ *n* [C] a part of a train with beds for passengers〔火車的〕臥鋪車廂, 臥車

sleeping draught /'·· ·/ *n* [C] *old use* a special drink which makes you sleep【舊】安眠藥水

sleeping part·ner /,·· '··/ *n* [C] *BrE* someone who owns part of a business but is not actively involved in operating it【英】不參與經營的合夥人; SILENT PARTNER *AmE*【美】

sleeping pill /'·· ·/ *n* [C] a PILL which helps you to sleep 安眠藥(片)

sleeping po·lice·man /,·· ·'··/ *n* [C] *BrE* a narrow raised part in a road which makes traffic go slowly; SPEED BUMP【英】交通減速板, 減速路埂〔為防止車速過快而橫設於路面的隆起物〕

sleeping sick·ness /'·· ,··/ *n* [U] a serious African disease that causes extreme tiredness, fever and makes you lose weight 昏睡病〔非洲一種使人極度疲倦、發燒和消瘦的嚴重疾病〕

sleep·less /'sliplɪs; 'sli:pləs/ *adj* unable to sleep 失眠的, 不眠的: **sleepless night** *David spent a sleepless night wondering what to do.* 戴維一夜未眠, 想着該怎麼辦。—**sleeplessly** *adv* —**sleeplessness** *n* [U]

sleep·o·ver /'slip,ovə; 'sli:pəʊvə/ *n* [C] *AmE* a party for children in which they stay the night at someone's house【美】不在自己家過夜的兒童晚會, 睡衣晚會

sleep·walk·er /'slip,wɔkə; 'sli:p,wɔ:kə/ *n* [C] someone who walks while they are sleeping 夢遊者 —**sleepwalk** *v* [I] —**sleep-walking** *n* [U]

sleep·y /'slipɪ; 'sli:pi/ *adj* **1** tired 困乏的, 想睡的: *The warmth from the fire made her feel sleepy.* 爐旁的溫暖使她昏昏欲睡。**2** a sleepy town or village is very quiet and not much happens there〔城鎮、鄉村〕寂靜的; 冷清的; 死氣沉沉的 —**sleepily** *adv* —**sleepiness** *n* [U]

sleep·y·head /'slipɪ,hɛd; 'sli:pihed/ *n* [C] *spoken* someone, especially a child, who looks as if they want to go to sleep【口】〔尤指孩子〕想睡的人, 貪睡的人, 懶蟲: *Come on sleepyhead, wake up!* 好了, 小懶蟲, 快醒醒!

sleet /slit; sli:t/ *n* [U] snow and rain which falls when it is very cold 凍雨, 雨夾雪 —**sleet** *v* [I] —**sleety** *adj* —see picture on page A13 參見 A13 頁圖

sleeve /sliv; sli:v/ *n* [C] **1** the part of a piece of clothing which covers your arm or part of your arm 袖子: *a dress with long sleeves* 長袖連衣裙 —see picture on page A17 參見 A17 頁圖 **2 long-sleeved/short-sleeved etc** having sleeves that are long or short 長袖/短袖的 **3 have something up your sleeve** *informal* to have a secret plan or idea that you are going to use later【非正式】暗中已有應急的打算[計劃]; 有錦囊妙計: *Come on, what have you got up your sleeve?* 你說, 你有甚麼錦囊妙計? **4** *especially BrE* a stiff envelope for keeping a record in【尤英】唱片套; JACKET (3) *AmE*【美】**5** *technical* a tube that surrounds a machine part【術語】〔機器部件的〕套筒, 套管 —see also 另見 **laugh up your sleeve** (LAUGH[1] (13))

sleeve·less /'slivlɪs; 'sli:vləs/ *adj* a sleeveless jacket, dress etc has no sleeves 無袖的

sleigh /sle; sleɪ/ *n* [C] a large vehicle pulled by animals, used for travelling over snow〔動物拉的〕雪橇, 雪車

sleight of hand /,slaɪt əv 'hænd; ,slaɪt əv 'hænd/ *n* [U] **1** the use of clever tricks and dishonesty to achieve something〔為達到某目的的〕手腕, 花招 **2** quick skilful movement with your hands, especially when performing magic tricks〔尤指變戲法中的〕巧妙手法

slen·der /'slɛndə; 'slendə/ *adj* **1** thin and graceful 細長而優美的, 修長的; 苗條的; 纖細的: *She had a long slender neck.* 她的脖子細長好看。| *a row of slender columns* 一排細長優美的柱子 —see 見 THIN (USAGE) **2** not enough to be useful, helpful, or effective 微少的, 微薄的, 不足的: **slender chance/hope** *The company now only has a slender hope of survival.* 這家公司現在很難維持下去了。| **by/with a slender majority** *The Republicans won by a slender majority.* 共和黨人以微弱多數獲勝。—**slenderness** *n* [U]

slept /slɛpt; slept/ the past tense and past participle of SLEEP

sleuth /sluθ; slu:θ/ *n* [C] *old-fashioned* someone who tries to find out information about a crime; DETECTIVE【過時】偵探

slew[1] /slu; slu:/ *v* [I,T always+adv/prep] to turn or swing suddenly and violently, or to make something do this (使) 急轉, (使) 突然側滑: **[+around/sideways]** *I lost control of the car and it slewed sideways into the ditch.* 我的車子突然失去控制, 側滑掉進了溝裡。

slew[2] the past tense of SLAY

slew[3] *n* **a slew of** *informal* a large number of【非正式】大量, 許多: *We've got a whole slew of difficulties.* 我們有一大堆的困難。

slice[1] /slaɪs; slaɪs/ *n* **1** [C] a flat piece of bread, meat etc cut from a larger piece 片, 薄片, 切片: *a slice of bread and butter* 一片 (抹上) 黃油 (的) 麵包 | *Cut the pork into thin slices.* 把豬肉切成薄片。—see picture on page A7 參見 A7 頁圖 **2** [C] a part or share of something good〔指好東西的〕份兒, 部分: *Everyone wanted a slice of the profits.* 這利潤每個人都想佔一份。**3** [C] a kitchen tool used for lifting and serving pieces of food〔用於分菜或鏟起食物的〕小鏟子, 鍋鏟 —see also 另見 FISH SLICE **4 a)** [U] a spinning movement of the ball in sports such as tennis and golf, which makes it move to one side rather than straight ahead〔網球、高爾夫球等的〕削球, 斜切球, 側旋球 **b)** [C] a way of hitting the ball which makes it do this 削球打法, 斜切球打法 **5 a slice of life** a description or image in a film, play, or book which shows life as it really is〔電影、書等中〕如實地反映生活的一個側面, 現實生活的片段 —see also 另見 **a slice of the cake** (CAKE[1] (7))

slice[2] *v* **1** also 又作 **slice up** [T] to cut meat, bread etc into thin flat pieces 把…切成薄片: *Could you slice the joint for me?* 你能替我把這一大塊肉切成薄片嗎? —see picture on page A11 參見 A11 頁圖 **2** [I always+adv/prep,T] to cut something easily with one long movement of a sharp knife or edge〔乾淨利落地〕切, 割, 切開, 割破: **[+into/through]** *The blade's so sharp it could easily slice through your finger.* 這刀片鋒利得很, 一下就能割破你的手指。| **slice sth in two/in half etc** 把…切成兩半 **3** [I always+adv/prep,T] to move quickly and easily through something such as water or air, or to make something do this (使) 輕鬆迅速地劃過〔水面等〕; (使) 輕快地穿過〔空中等〕: **[+through/into]** *The speedboat sliced through the waters of the lake.* 快艇輕快地在湖水中前進。**4** [T] to hit the ball in sports such as tennis or golf so that it spins sideways instead of moving straight forward〔打網球、高爾夫球等時〕削〔球〕, 斜切〔球〕, 打〔側旋球〕**5 any way you slice it** *AmE spoken* whatever way you choose to consider the problem【美口】無論你怎樣考慮這個問題

slice sth ↔ **off** *phr v* [T] to cut something with one long movement of a sharp knife etc so that it becomes separate〔一刀〕切下,〔一刀〕割去: *With one blow of his sword, Igor sliced off the man's head.* 伊格爾把劍一揮, 砍下了那個人的頭。

sliced bread /,· '·/ *n* [U] **1** bread that is sold already cut into slices〔出售時已切好的〕切片麵包 **2 the best thing since sliced bread** *informal* to be new and very helpful, useful etc【非正式】新且非常有用的東西: *He reckons his new word processor is the best thing since* *sliced bread.* 他認為他那台新的文字處理機是最近面世的最好的東西。

slick¹ /slɪk; slɪk/ *adj* **1** using clever talk to persuade people but in a way that does not seem sincere or honest 圓滑的, 花言巧語的: *a slick salesman* 圓滑的推銷員 **2** a slick film, programme etc is cleverly made and attractive but contains no important or interesting ideas〔電影等〕製作精巧而內容膚淺的; 華而不實的: *the usual slick Hollywood stuff* 那種技巧高明而內容膚淺的荷里活常見貨色 **3** *informal* working or moving very smoothly, skilfully and effectively【非正式】熟練的, 靈巧的: *a slick operation* 技巧純熟的手術 | *He got round the defender using some slick footwork.* 他用靈巧的步伐突破了後衞的防守。**4** smooth and slippery 光滑的, 滑溜的: **[+with]** *He felt his hands grow slick with sweat.* 他覺得自己雙手在出汗變滑。**5** *AmE old-fashioned* very good or attractive【美, 過時】很好的, 吸引人的 **—slickly** *adv* **—slickness** *n* [U]

slick² *n* [C] **1** an area of oil on the surface of water or on a road; OIL SLICK〔水面或路面的〕浮油, 油層, 油膜 **2** *AmE* a magazine printed on good quality paper with a shiny surface, usually with a lot of colour pictures【美】用優質有光紙印刷並帶有大量彩色圖片的雜誌; glossy magazine (GLOSSY²(1)) *especially BrE*【尤英】**3** a smooth car tyre used for racing〔賽車的〕磨光輪胎

slick³ *v*

slick sth ↔ **down/back** *phr v* [T] to make hair or fur smooth and shiny by using oil, water etc〔用油、水等〕使〔頭髮〕光滑發亮: *His hair was slicked back, as was the fashion then.* 他的頭髮用油向後梳理得光溜溜的, 那是當時的時尚。

slick·er /ˈslɪkɚ; ˈslɪkə/ *n* [C] *AmE* a coat made to keep out the rain【美】油布雨衣, 防水衣 —see also 另見 **city slicker**

3 **slide¹** /slaɪd; slaɪd/ *v past tense and past participle* **slid** /slɪd; slɪd/ **1** [I,T] to move smoothly over a surface while continuing to touch it, or to make something move in this way (使) 滑動: **[+along/across/down etc]** *The kids were sliding on the ice.* 孩子們在冰上滑行。| **slide sth across/along etc** *Peter slid his glass across the table.* 彼得推動玻璃杯使它滑到桌子對面。**2** [I,T always+adv/prep] to move somewhere quietly without being noticed, or to move something in this way (使) 悄悄移動, 偷偷溜走: **[+into/out of etc]** *Daniel slid out of the room when no one was looking.* 丹尼爾趁沒人看見, 偷偷溜出了房間。| **slide sth into/out of etc** *She slid a gun into her pocket.* 她悄悄地把手槍放進口袋。**3** [I] if prices etc slide, they become lower〔價格等〕下滑, 降低: *When will the government take action to support the sliding pound?* 政府甚麼時候才會採取行動支持正在下跌的英鎊? **4 let sth slide** to let a situation get gradually worse, without trying to stop it〔對某事〕聽其自然, 任其惡化, 放任不管: *Simon had really let things slide and the house was a mess.* 西蒙真的是不聞不問, 任由房子變得一團糟。

slide² *n*

1 ►FOR CHILDREN 兒童用的◄ [C] a large structure for children to slide down at a PLAYGROUND〔兒童遊戲用的〕滑梯

2 ►FOR HAIR 用於頭髮◄ [C] a small metal or plastic object that holds your hair in place 小髮夾

3 ►MOVEMENT 移動◄ [singular] a sliding movement across a surface 滑動, 打滑: *The car went into a slide on the surface.* 汽車在地面上打滑。

4 ►PICTURE 圖片◄ [C] a small piece of film in a frame that shows a picture on a SCREEN¹ (2a) when you shine light through it 幻燈片: *Don't you want to see my slides of Korea?* 你不想看看我那介紹韓國的幻燈片嗎?

5 ►PRICE/AMOUNT 價格/數量◄ [singular] a fall in prices, amounts etc 滑落, 跌落, 下降: *a slide in living standards* 生活水平的下降

6 ►IN SCIENCE 在科學上◄ [C] a small piece of thin glass used for holding something when you look at it under a MICROSCOPE〔顯微鏡用的〕載(物)玻(璃)片 —see picture at 參見 LABORATORY 圖

7 ►MUSIC 音樂◄ [C] a part of a machine or musical instrument, such as the U-shaped tube of a TROMBONE〔機器或樂器的〕滑動部件〈如長號的U字形伸縮管〉

8 ►EARTH/SNOW 土/雪◄ [C] *AmE* a sudden fall of earth, stones, snow etc down a slope【美】〔土、石、雪等的〕崩落, 崩塌 —see also 另見 LANDSLIDE

slide rule /ˈ· ·/ *n* [C] an old-fashioned instrument that looks like a ruler with a middle part that slides, used for calculating 計算尺, 滑尺〔一種舊式計算工具〕

sliding door /ˌ·· ˈ·/ *n* [C] a door that slides open rather than swinging from one side 拉門, 滑門

sliding scale /ˌ·· ˈ·/ *n* [C] a system for paying tax, wages etc in which the rates that you pay VARY according to changing conditions〔工資、稅額等隨情況的變化而調整的〕滑動折算制, 浮動計算法, 比例相應增減制

slight¹ /slaɪt; slaɪt/ *adj* **1** not serious or not important 輕微的, 微小的, 少量的: *a slight headache* 輕微的頭痛 | *a slight improvement* 些許改善 | *There's been a slight change of plan.* 計劃略有變動。| **not the slightest chance/doubt/difference etc** (=no chance, doubt etc at all) 沒有一點機會/懷疑/差別等 *It doesn't make the slightest difference whether we discuss it today or tomorrow.* 我們今天還是明天討論, 沒有任何不同。| *"What were they talking about?" "I haven't the slightest idea."* "他們當時在談甚麼?" "我一點也不知道。" **2** thin and delicate 纖細的, 瘦小的; 纖弱的; 脆弱的: *a slight figure in a red dress* 一個穿着紅色連衣裙的纖弱身影 2 3

slight² *v* [T] to offend someone by treating them rudely or without respect 輕視, 怠慢, 冷落: *Denver felt slighted when no one called him back.* 沒人給丹弗回電話, 他覺得自己受了冷落。**—slighting** *adj*: *slighting remarks* 輕蔑的話

slight³ *n* [C] *formal* a remark or action that offends someone【正式】輕蔑, 怠慢, 冷落: **[+on/to]** *Jane took your comment as a slight on her work.* 簡把你的評論看作是對她工作的輕視。

slight·ly /ˈslaɪtlɪ; ˈslaɪtli/ *adv* **1 slightly different/older/worried etc** a little bit different, older etc 略為不同/年長了些/有點擔心: *a slightly different attitude* 略為不同的態度 | *Alison is slightly older than the others.* 阿莉森比其他人略為年長。| *"Are you worried about him?" "Just slightly."* "你為他擔心嗎?" "稍微有一點。" **2 slightly-built** having a thin and delicate body 身材瘦小的 1 2

slim¹ /slɪm; slɪm/ *comparative* 比較級 **slimmer** *superlative* 最高級 **slimmest** *adj* **1** someone who is slim is attractively thin 苗條的, 修長的: *a slim waist* 苗條的腰身 —see 見 THIN (USAGE) **2 slim chance/hopes etc** very little chance etc of getting what you want〔機會、希望等〕微小的, 渺茫的: *There's a slim chance someone may have survived.* 有人倖存下來的可能性不大。**3** thinner than usual or less than usual 非常薄[少]的: *a slim volume of poetry* 薄薄的一冊詩歌集 | *the slimmest of majorities* 極微弱的多數 3

slim² *v* **slimmed, slimming 1** [I] to make yourself thinner by eating less, taking a lot of exercise etc〔通過節食、加強運動等〕減肥: *I'm going to start slimming after Christmas.* 我準備過了聖誕節就開始減肥。**2** [I,T] also 又作 **slim down** to reduce the size or number of something (使) 減少, 縮小; 裁減: *It was decided to slim down the workforce.* 已經決定要裁減人員。**—slimmer** *n* [C]

slime /slaɪm; slaɪm/ *n* [U] **1** a thick slippery substance that looks or smells unpleasant〔令人不愉快的〕黏質物 **2** a slippery substance that comes from the bodies of SNAILs and slugs (SLUG¹ (1))〔蝸牛、鼻涕蟲等的〕黏液

slim·line /ˈslɪmˌlaɪn; ˈslɪmlaɪn/ *adj* **1** a slimline drink has fewer CALORIEs than the normal type〔飲料〕低卡路里的, 低熱量的, 適於減肥的 **2** a slimline piece of equipment is smaller or thinner than others of the same type〔設備〕體型較小的, 小巧型的: *a slimline dishwasher* 小

型洗碗機

slim·ming /ˈslɪmɪŋ; ˈslɪmɪŋ/ *n* [U] the activity of trying to make yourself thinner by eating less, taking exercise etc〔通過節食、運動等〕減輕體重, 減肥: **slimming club/magazine/foods etc** *I've found a good slimming plan.* 我發現了一個很好的減肥方案。

slim·y /ˈslaɪmɪ; ˈslaɪmi/ *adj* **1** covered with slime 有黏液的, 黏糊糊的: *slimy mud* 黏糊糊的泥巴 **2** *informal* unpleasantly friendly in order to get something for yourself【非正式】諂媚的, 討好的: *a slimy manner* 諂媚的態度 **—sliminess** *n* [U]

sling¹ /slɪŋ; slɪŋ/ *v past tense and past participle* **slung** /slʌŋ; slʌŋ/ [T always+adv/prep] **1** to throw something roughly or with a lot of force 用力投, 擲, 拋〔某物〕: *Sling me the keys, will you?* 把鑰匙拋給我, 好嗎? | **sling sth across/into etc** *Fiona slung her bag across the room.* 費奧娜把手提包扔到房子那邊。**2** to throw or put something somewhere so that it can hang 懸起, 使吊起, 使落在...上: **sling sth on/over etc** *He slung his coat over his shoulder.* 他把外衣搭在肩上。| *A line of flags was slung between the trees.* 一行旗幟掛在兩棵樹之間。**3** *informal* to make someone leave or go to a place【非正式】把〔某人〕趕出..., 開除; 把〔某人〕投進...: **sling sb into/out of etc** *Sam was slung into jail for punching a cop.* 山姆因出拳毆打警察而被投進監獄。| *Watch it, or you'll be slung out of school.* 當心點, 不然你會被學校開除的。**4** **sling your hook** *BrE slang* to go away【英俚】走開, 離開 —see also 另見 MUDSLINGING

sling² *n* [C] **1** a piece of cloth tied around your neck to support your injured arm or hand〔用以固定斷臂或斷手的〕懸帶, 吊帶: *She had her arm in a sling for months.* 她的胳膊吊了幾個月的懸帶。**2** a set of ropes or strong pieces of cloth that hold heavy objects to be lifted or carried〔用以提起或懸掛重物的〕吊索, 吊鏈 **3** a special cloth seat that fastens over your shoulders for carrying a baby〔揹小孩的〕背帶 **4** a cloth band on a weapon for carrying it〔槍的〕肩帶, 背帶 **5** a long, thin piece of rope with a piece of leather in the middle, used in the past as a weapon for throwing stones〔從前的〕投石器; 彈弓

sling·back /ˈslɪŋˌbæk; ˈslɪŋbæk/ *n* [C] a kind of woman's shoe that is open at the back and has a band going round the heel〔鞋後幫為一條帶的〕露跟女鞋 —see picture at 參見 SHOE¹ 圖

sling·shot /ˈslɪŋˌʃɑt; ˈslɪŋʃɒt/ *n* [C] *AmE* a small stick in the shape of a Y with a thin band of rubber, used by children to throw stones【美】〔兒童用以發射石子的〕彈弓; CATAPULT¹ (2) *BrE*【英】

slink /slɪŋk; slɪŋk/ *past tense and past participle* **slunk** /slʌŋk; slʌŋk/ *v* [I always+adv/prep] to move somewhere quietly and secretly, especially because you are afraid or ashamed 鬼鬼祟祟地走, 偷偷溜走: **[+away/off/back etc]** *I saw you slinking off early!* 我看見你一早就偷偷溜走!

slink·y /ˈslɪŋkɪ; ˈslɪŋki/ *adj* a slinky dress etc is smooth and tight and shows the shape of your body〔衣服等〕緊身的, 顯出體形線條的: *a slinky black dress* 緊身的黑色連衣裙

slip 滑倒

slip¹ /slɪp; slɪp/ *v* **slipped, slipping**

1 ►SLIDE 滑◄ [I] to accidentally slide a short distance quickly or to fall by sliding 滑; 滑倒, 失足: *Suddenly, Frank slipped and fell over the edge.* 弗蘭克突然滑倒, 從邊上掉了下去。| *My foot slipped and I nearly fell.* 我的腳一滑, 差點摔倒。—see also 另見 SLIPPERY

2 ►MOVE QUICKLY 快速移動◄ [I always+adv/prep] to move quickly, smoothly, or secretly 溜走, 悄悄地走: **slip out/through/by etc** *Nobody saw her slip silently out.* 沒有人看到她悄悄地溜了出去。| *The weeks slipped slowly by.* 這幾個星期在不知不覺中慢慢流逝了。| *The terrorists had slipped through the airport's security net.* 恐怖分子混過了機場的安全檢查。

3 ►PUT STH SOMEWHERE 把某物置於某處◄ [T] to put something somewhere or give someone something quietly, secretly, or smoothly 把...悄悄放在[遞給]..., 偷偷塞進[給]; 利落地放置: **slip sth around/into/through etc** *I slipped a note into his hand under the table.* 我偷偷從桌子底下塞給他一張條子。| *I slipped the Mercedes into gear.* 我利落地把平治車掛上擋。| **slip sb sth** *Jerry slipped the waiter £5 to get them a good table.* 傑里悄悄塞給侍者五英鎊, 以便給他們安排個好桌位。

4 ►LOSE YOUR HOLD 鬆手◄ [I always+adv/prep] if something that you are holding slips, it falls because it is difficult to hold or was not held firmly 滑落, 滑掉, 滑跌: *The soap slipped out of my hand.* 肥皂從我手中滑落。| *The knife slipped and cut my finger.* 刀子一滑, 劃破了我的手指。

5 ►GET WORSE 變壞◄ [I] to become worse or lower than before 變壞; 下降, 下跌: *Profits have slipped slightly this year.* 今年利潤略有下降。| *You must be slipping – you never used to miss a shot like that.* 你肯定退步了 — 你過去打槍從沒有這樣失過手。

6 slip your mind/memory if something slips your mind you forget to do something 被忽略/被遺忘: *I'm sorry I missed your birthday; it completely slipped my mind.* 我很抱歉錯過了你的生日; 我完全忘了。

7 let sth slip (through your fingers) to not take an opportunity, offer etc 錯過〔機會等〕: *You're not going to let a chance like that slip through your fingers, are you?* 你不會錯過那樣的好機會吧, 是嗎?

8 slip a disc to suffer an injury when one of the connecting parts between the bones in your back moves out of place 椎間盤滑出[滑脫]

9 ►GET FREE 獲得自由◄ [T] to get free from something that was holding you 掙脫, 擺脫: *The dog slipped his collar and ran away.* 那條狗掙脫項圈跑掉了。

10 let (it) slip (that) to say something without meaning to, when you had wanted it to be a secret 無意中說出〔秘密〕: *Leila let slip that she's thinking about leaving the company.* 莉拉無意中說出她打算離開公司。

11 slip through the net if someone or something slips through the net, they are not caught or dealt with by the system that is supposed to catch them or deal with them 漏網; 未受到有關部門的抓捕[處理]: *homeless people slipping through the social security net* 社會福利制度未照顧到的無家可歸者

slip into sth *phr v* [T] **1** to put clothes on quickly 迅速穿上〔衣服〕: *I'll just slip into something more comfortable.* 我要穿件舒服一點的衣服。**2 slip into sleep/unconsciousness etc** to gradually fall asleep, become unconscious etc 慢慢入睡/逐漸失去知覺: *Granny slipped into a coma and died peacefully that night.* 奶奶那天晚上逐漸陷入昏迷, 安詳辭世。

slip sth ↔ **off** *phr v* [T] to take clothes off quickly 迅速脫去〔衣服〕: *Slip off your shirt and I'll take your blood pressure.* 把襯衣脫掉, 我來給你量血壓。

slip sth ↔ **on** *phr v* [T] to put clothes on quickly 迅速穿上〔衣服〕: *Amanda slipped her robe on.* 阿曼達匆忙地穿上了長袍。

slip out *phr v* [I] if something slips out, you say it

without really intending to 被無意說出: *I'm sorry I spoilt your surprise. It just slipped out.* 很抱歉我泄露了你要給人的驚喜, 我不小心說漏了嘴。

slip out of sth *phr v* [T] to take clothes off quickly 迅速脫下〔衣服〕: *Keith slipped out of his jacket.* 基思迅速脫下夾克。

slip sth **over on** sb *phr v* [T] *informal, especially AmE* to play a clever trick on someone【非正式, 尤美】巧妙地捉弄某人, 欺騙某人

slip up *phr v* [I] to make a mistake 犯錯誤, 疏忽: *The office slipped up and the letter was never sent.* 辦公室出了點差錯, 根本沒有發出那封信。—see also 另見 SLIP-UP

slip² *n*

1 ▶PAPER 紙◀ [C] a small or narrow piece of paper 小紙片, 紙條: **[+of]** *Rosie marked her place with a slip of paper.* 羅齊用紙條作記號, 標出她(看書)看到了甚麼地方。

2 ▶MISTAKE 錯誤◀ [C] a small mistake 小錯誤: *If you make a slip, rub it out neatly.* 如果你寫錯了, 那就擦乾淨。

3 a slip of the tongue/pen something that you say when you meant to say something else 口誤/筆誤: *"Jim" was a slip of the tongue; I meant to say 'John'.* Jim(吉姆)是口誤, 我是想說 John(約翰)。—see also 另見 FREUDIAN SLIP

4 give sb the slip *informal* to manage to escape from someone who is chasing you【非正式】擺脫某人的追逐, 甩掉某人: *Bates gave the police the slip.* 貝茨擺脫了警察的追捕。

5 ▶SLIDE 滑◀ [C] an act of sliding a short distance or of falling by sliding 滑動; 滑倒

6 ▶WOMAN'S CLOTHES 女服◀ [C] a piece of clothing that a woman wears under her clothes, and which hangs from her shoulders or her waist〔背帶式〕襯裙;〔半截式〕襯裙

7 a slip of a girl/boy etc *old-fashioned* a small thin young person【過時】瘦小的女孩/男孩等: *He was only a slip of a lad.* 他只是一個瘦小的男孩。

8 ▶CRICKET 板球◀ [C usually plural 一般用複數] a part of the field where players stand, trying to catch the ball in CRICKET〔板球運動中擊球員右後方的〕防守位置

9 ▶CLAY 黏土◀ [U] clay that is almost liquid and is used for making pots〔製陶器用的〕泥漿, 泥釉

slip case /ˈ· ·/ *n* [C] a hard cover for putting a book in〔厚紙做的〕書套

slip co·ver /ˈ· ˌ··/ *n* [C] *AmE*【美】**1** a paper cover for a book; DUST JACKET〔書的〕封套, 書套 **2** a loose cloth cover for furniture 家具套

slip·knot /ˈslɪpˌnɑt; ˈslɪpnɒt/ *n* [C] a knot that you can make tighter or looser by pulling one of its ends 活結, 滑結

slip-on /ˈ· ·/ *n* [plural] shoes without a fastening that you can slide onto your feet 無帶扣的鞋子, 便鞋 **—slip-on** *adj*: *slip-on shoes* 無帶扣的便鞋

slip·page /ˈslɪpɪdʒ; ˈslɪpɪdʒ/ *n* [C,U] the amount by which something slips, or the act of slipping 滑動(量); 下降, 下跌

slipped disc /ˌ· ˈ·/ *n* [C usually singular 一般用單數] a painful injury caused when one of the connecting parts between the bones in your back moves out of place 椎間盤滑脫

slip·per /ˈslɪpɚ; ˈslɪpə/ *n* [C] a light soft shoe that you wear at home 室內便鞋, 拖鞋 —see picture at 參見 SHOE¹ 圖

slip·per·y /ˈslɪpərɪ; ˈslɪpəri/ *adj* **1** something that is slippery is difficult to hold, walk on etc because it is wet or GREASY〔因濕或有油脂〕滑的, 滑溜的: *Be careful! The floor's very slippery.* 小心! 地板很滑。**2** *informal* someone who is slippery cannot be trusted and usually manages to avoid being punished【非正式】滑頭的, 不可信賴的: **slippery customer** (=someone you cannot trust) 狡猾的傢伙 *I wouldn't lend him any money, he's a real slippery customer.* 我一點錢也不會借給他, 他是個不折不扣的老滑頭。**3 be on the slippery slope** *BrE informal* to have begun a process or habit which is hard to stop and which will develop into something extremely bad【英, 非正式】〔惡習等〕無法克制以至後果嚴重: *Once you start taking soft drugs you're on the slippery slope to becoming an addict.* 一旦開始吸食軟性毒品, 你就會無法克制, 一定會變成個癮君子。**—slipperiness** *n* [U]

slip·py /ˈslɪpɪ; ˈslɪpi/ *adj informal* a slippy surface or object is difficult to hold, walk on etc because it is wet or GREASY【非正式】〔因濕或有油脂〕滑的, 滑溜的

slip road /ˈ· ·/ *n* [C] *BrE* a road for driving onto or off a MOTORWAY【英】高速公路的支路, 叉道; RAMP (1) *AmE*【美】—see picture on page A3 參見 A3 頁圖

slip·shod /ˈslɪpˌʃɑd; ˈslɪpʃɒd/ *adj* done too quickly and carelessly 馬虎的, 隨便的, 草率的: *a slipshod piece of work* 馬虎完成的工作

slip·stream /ˈslɪpˌstrim; ˈslɪpstriːm/ *n* [singular] the area of low air pressure just behind a fast-moving vehicle〔飛馳的賽車後面形成的〕低壓氣穴

slip-up /ˈ· ·/ *n* [C] a careless mistake that spoils a process or plan〔影響進程或計劃的〕失誤, 疏忽: *We should have informed you, I'm sorry for the slip-up.* 我們本該通知你們的, 對這一失誤我表示歉意。

slip·way /ˈslɪpˌwe; ˈslɪpweɪ/ *n* [C] a sloping track that is used for moving boats into or out of the water〔船的〕下水滑道, 滑台, 船台

slit¹ *v* /slɪt; slɪt/ *past tense and past participle* **slit** *present participle* **slitting** [T] to make a straight narrow cut in cloth, paper, skin etc 切開; 裁開; 撕開: **slit sth open** (=open it by slitting it) 撕開[裁開]某物 *Guy slit open the envelope.* 蓋伊拆開信封。| **slit sb's throat** (=kill someone with a knife) 割開某人的喉嚨

slit² *n* [C] a long straight narrow cut or hole 狹長的切口; 裂縫: *light shining through a slit in the door* 透過門縫照進來的光線 | *a skirt with a slit up the side* 側邊開叉的裙子

slith·er /ˈslɪðɚ; ˈslɪðə/ *v* [I always+adv/prep] to slide smoothly across a surface, twisting or moving from side to side 蜿蜒地滑動; 搖晃地滑行: **[+through/across etc]** *snakes slithering through the grass* 蜿蜒爬過草叢的蛇 | *He slithered down the muddy bank into the water.* 他搖搖晃晃地走下泥濘的堤岸踩入水裡。

slith·er·y /ˈslɪðərɪ; ˈslɪðəri/ *adj* unpleasantly slippery〔令人不快地〕滑溜溜的

sliv·er /ˈslɪvɚ; ˈslɪvə/ *n* [C] a very small thin pointed piece of something that has been cut or broken off something〔切下或裂開的〕碎片, 裂片: *a sliver of glass* 一塊玻璃碎片 | *a sliver of cake* 一小塊蛋糕 —see picture on page A7 參見 A7 頁圖

sliv·o·vitz /ˈslɪvəvɪts; ˈslɪvəvɪts/ *n* [U] a strong alcoholic drink made in SE Europe from PLUMS 梅子白蘭地〔產於東南歐的一種烈性酒〕

slob /slɑb; slɒb/ *n* [C] *informal* someone who is lazy, dirty, untidy, or rude【非正式】懶蟲; 髒鬼; 粗魯漢: *Come on, get up and do something you big slob!* 來吧, 起來幹點活, 你這條大懶蟲!

slob around *phr v* [I] *BrE slang* to spend time doing nothing and being lazy【英俚】游手好閒, 無所事事

slob·ber /ˈslɑbɚ; ˈslɒbə/ *v* [I] to let SALIVA (=the liquid produced by your mouth) come out of your mouth and run down 流涎, 淌口水: *I hate dogs that slobber everywhere.* 我討厭到處淌口水的狗。

slobber over sth/sb *phr v* [T] to keep saying how much you love someone in a way that embarrasses or annoys other people〔使他人難為情地〕對…表達愛慕, 肉麻地示愛: *They keep slobbering over each other.* 他倆老是肉麻地示愛。

slob·ber·y /ˈslɑbərɪ; ˈslɒbəri/ *adj* a slobbery kiss or mouth is unpleasantly wet〔嘴巴〕口水多的, 濕得討厭的

sloe /slo; sləʊ/ *n* [C] a small bitter fruit like a PLUM 黑刺李

sloe gin /,· ˈ·/ *n* [U] an alcoholic drink made with SLOES, GIN, and sugar 黑刺李杜松子酒

slog¹ /slɑg; slɒg/ *v informal*【非正式】**1 slog (away) at** *especially BrE*【尤英】also 又作 **slog through** to work hard at something without stopping, especially when the work is boring or difficult 不停地賣力苦幹: *I've been slogging away at this essay for days.* 為了這篇文章我已經埋頭苦幹了好幾天了。| *all those books we had to slog through at school* 我們必須在學校啃完的那些書 | **slog your guts out** *informal* (=work extremely hard)【非正式】拚命幹 *slogging their guts out to get it finished on time* 拚命幹爭取按時完成 **2** [I always+adv/prep] to make a long hard journey somewhere, especially on foot〔徒步〕長時間艱苦地行進: [**+down/up/through etc**] *We slogged up the hill with the wind blowing against us.* 我們頑強地頂着風爬上了山。**3 slog it out** *BrE* to fight or argue about something until one side wins【英】鬥個勝負, 爭出個高低

slog² *n* [singular] **1** *BrE informal* a piece of work that takes a lot of time and effort and is usually boring【英, 非正式】艱苦乏味的工作: *It was a bit of a slog addressing all those envelopes.* 給這麼多信封寫上姓名地址, 真是一件乏味的苦差事。**2** a long period of tiring walking 長途跋涉: *a long hard slog uphill* 長時間的艱苦爬山

slo·gan /ˈslogən; ˈsləʊgən/ *n* [C] a short easily-remembered phrase used by an advertiser, politician etc 口號, 標語: *demonstrators chanting anti-racist slogans* 齊聲高呼着反種族歧視口號的示威者 | *We need an advertising slogan for the new campaign.* 我們這次新的促銷活動需要一條廣告標語。

sloop /slup; sluːp/ *n* [C] a small sailing ship with one central MAST (=pole for sails) 單桅小帆船

slop¹ /slɑp; slɒp/ *v* **slopped, slopping 1** [I always+adv/prep] if liquid in a container slops, it moves around or over the edge in an uncontrolled way〔液體〕晃蕩; 濺出, 溢出: [**+around/about/over**] *The water slopped around in the bucket.* 水在桶裡晃蕩。**2** [T] to make liquid do this 使〔液體〕晃蕩; 使濺出, 使溢出: **slop sth over/into etc** *He slopped his beer all over her skirt.* 他把啤酒濺了她一裙子。**3** [T] *AmE* to feed slop to pigs【美】用食物殘渣餵〔豬〕

slop about *phr v* [I] *BrE informal*【英, 非正式】**1** to spend time being lazy 懶散地消磨時間: *We spent the day slopping about the house.* 我們在家裡懶懶散散地過了一天。**2** to play or move around in mud, dirty water etc 在泥漿[髒水等]中玩耍[走動]

slop out *phr v* [I] when prisoners slop out, they empty their toilet buckets〔囚犯〕倒便桶 —**slopping-out** *n* [U]

slop² also 又作 **slops** *plural n* [U] **1** food waste that is used to feed animals〔餵動物的〕食物殘渣, 殘湯剩菜 **2** *BrE* liquid waste from food or drinks【英】〔食物或飲料的〕剩汁, 殘汁, 泔水: *Empty all your slops into the bucket over there.* 請把你們的剩飯全部倒進那邊的桶裡。**3** *BrE* dirty water or URINE【英】髒水; 糞尿 **4** food that is too soft and tastes bad 稀軟味差的流質食物: *They served up some kind of slop I just couldn't eat.* 他們端上一些我簡直無法下嚥的湯湯水水。

3 **slope¹** /slop; sləʊp/ *n* **1** [C] a piece of ground or a surface that slopes 斜坡, 斜面: *walking slowly up a steep slope* 慢慢爬上陡峭的斜坡 | **a gentle slope** (=a slope that is not steep) 平緩的斜坡 **2** [singular] the angle at which something slopes in relation to a flat surface 斜度, 坡度: *a slope of 30 degrees* 30°的斜坡

slope² *v* [I] if the ground or a surface slopes, it is higher at one end than the other 傾斜, 成斜坡: [**+up/down/away etc**] *The land slopes down to the sea.* 地面向海傾斜。

slope off *phr v* [I] *BrE informal* to leave somewhere quietly and secretly, especially when you are avoiding work【英, 非正式】〔尤指為了逃避工作〕悄悄走開, 溜掉: *Mike's always sloping off when it's time to do the dishes.* 到了洗碗的時候邁克總要溜掉。

slop·py /ˈslɑpɪ; ˈslɒpi/ *adj* **1** not done carefully or thoroughly 馬虎的, 隨便的, 草率的: *This piece of work is very sloppy.* 這件工作做得非常馬虎。| *sloppy writing* 草率的寫作 **2** sloppy clothes are loose-fitting, untidy, or dirty〔衣服〕太寬的, 不整潔的, 邋遢的: *a sloppy old sweater* 一件又髒又舊的毛衣 **3** expressing your feelings of love too strongly and in a silly way 痴情得可笑的, 庸俗地多情善感的: *He keeps sending me sloppy letters.* 他不斷給我寄痴情可笑的求愛信。**4** not solid enough 太稀的, 不結實的: *sloppy jelly* 稀果凍 —**sloppily** *adv* —**sloppiness** *n* [U]

sloppy joe /ˌslɑpɪ ˈdʒo; ˌslɒpi ˈdʒəʊ/ *n* [C] **1** *AmE* a kind of food, made from BEEF with SPICES added and served on a BUN (2)【美】〔塗麵包用的〕炒牛肉醬 **2** *BrE* a big loose-fitting SWEATER【英】寬鬆套衫, 運動衣

slosh /slɑʃ; slɒʃ/ *v* **1** [I always+adv/prep] if a liquid in a container sloshes around, it moves against the sides of its container in an uncontrolled way〔容器中的液體〕搖動, 晃蕩: [**+around/about**] *Water sloshed about in the bottom of the boat.* 水在船底嘩啦嘩啦地晃蕩。**2** [T always + adv/prep] to make a liquid do this 搖動〔液體〕, 使晃蕩: **slosh sth around/about** *Joe sloshed the whisky around in his glass.* 喬搖動着他杯子裡的威士忌酒。**3** [I always+adv/prep] to walk through water or mud noisily 嘩嘩地涉水而行, 在泥濘中走: [**+through/about**] *sloshing through the mud* 在泥濘中跋涉 **4** [T] *BrE slang* to hit someone; PUNCH¹ (1)【英俚】打, 猛擊〔某人〕

sloshed /slɑʃt; slɒʃt/ *adj* [not before noun 不用於名詞前] *informal* drunk【非正式】喝醉的: *He was already well sloshed when we got there.* 我們到那裡時, 他已經喝得爛醉了。

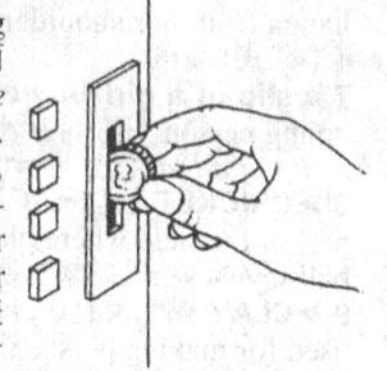

slot¹ /slɑt; slɒt/ *n* [C] **1** a long narrow hole made in a surface, especially for putting something into〔可放進東西的〕狹孔, 狹縫; 投幣口: *Place your coins in the slot slowly.* 把你的硬幣慢慢放進投幣口。**2** a short period of time allowed for one particular event on a programme or timetable〔節目單或時間表上為某節目或事項排定的〕一段時間: *a regular ten-minute slot on the breakfast show* 早餐節目中定時的十分鐘廣播時間 | *landing slots at Heathrow Airport* 希斯路機場的規定飛機降落時間

slot² *v* **slotted, slotting** [I,T always+adv/prep] to go into a slot, or to make something do this (把...) 插進窄孔, 插入狹縫: [**+in**] *The disc slots in at the front.* 磁盤是從前面插進去的。| **slot sth together** (=fit together) *You buy the bookshelf in pieces and then slot them together yourself.* 這種書櫥你買的是組件, 然後自己把組件組裝起來。

slot in *phr v* [I,T] *informal* to find a time or a place for someone or something in a plan, organization etc【非正式】(給) 定時間; (給) 定位置: **slot sb/sth ↔ in** *We should be able to slot the meeting in before lunch.* 我們應該可以把會議安排在午飯之前。

sloth /sloθ; sləʊθ/ *n* **1** [C] an animal of Central and South America that moves very slowly, has grey fur, and lives in trees 樹獺〔產於中、南美洲, 有灰色的皮毛, 在樹上生活, 動作遲緩〕**2** [U] *formal* laziness【正式】懶惰, 懶散: *combination of sloth and boredom* 懶惰加上厭倦

sloth·ful /ˈsloθfəl; ˈsləʊθfəl/ *adj formal* lazy or not active【正式】懶惰的, 懶散的, 不活躍的 —**slothfully** *adv* —**slothfulness** *n* [U]

slot ma·chine /ˈ· ·,·/ *n* [C] **1** a machine used for playing a game that starts when you put money into it 吃角子老虎機, 投幣式自動賭博機 **2** *BrE* a machine that you buy cigarettes, food, or drink from; VENDING MACHINE【英】〔投幣式〕自動售貨機

slotted spat·u·la /,·· ˈ···/ *n AmE* a FISH SLICE【美】

煎魚鏟, (長柄) 鍋鏟

slotted spoon /ˌ·· ˈ·/ *n* [C] a large spoon with holes in it 有孔的大勺

slouch¹ /slaʊtʃ; slaʊtʃ/ *v* [I] to stand, sit, or walk with a slouch 低頭垂肩地站[坐、走], 無精打采地站[坐、走]: *Stop slouching, it's not good for your back.* 不要低着頭, 這樣對你的背不好。| *I slouched in my chair.* 我無精打采地靠在椅子上。—**slouchingly** *adv*

slouch² *n* **1** [singular] a way of standing, sitting, or walking with your shoulders bent forward that makes you look tired or lazy〔站、坐、走路時表現出來的〕無精打采, 萎靡不振 **2 be no slouch (at)** *informal* to be very good or skilful at something【非正式】善於做〔某事〕: *She's certainly no slouch where organization is concerned.* 在組織工作方面她的確是個能手。

slough¹ /slʌf; slʌf/ *v*

slough sth ↔ **off** *phr v* [T] **1** *technical* to get rid of a dead outer layer of skin【術語】蛻〔皮〕, 脱〔皮〕 **2** *literary* to get rid of a feeling, belief etc【文】拋棄, 消除〔感覺、信念等〕: *He was unable to slough off the stigmatizing label of criminal.* 他無法消除那個恥辱的犯罪標籤。

slough² /slaʊ; slaʊ/ *n* **1** [C] an area of land covered in deep dirty water or mud 泥沼, 沼澤地, 泥坑 **2 a slough of despair/troubles etc** *literary* a bad situation or condition that you cannot get out of easily【文】絕望的境地/煩惱的深淵: *He soon became the forgotten man and was able to return to his slough of despondency.* 他很快就成為被遺忘的人, 又回到他絕望的深淵。

slov·en·ly /ˈslʌvənlɪ; ˈslʌvənli/ *adj* lazy and untidy and not caring about your appearance 不整潔的, 邋遢的, 不修邊幅的: *The landlady was fat and slovenly.* 女房東又胖又不修邊幅。—**slovenliness** *n* [U]: *a man with shabby clothes and a general air of slovenliness* 衣着襤褸、一身邋遢相的男子

S2 W2 **slow¹** /slo; sləʊ/ *adj*

1 ►MOVE ETC 移動等◄ not moving, being done, or happening quickly 慢的, 緩慢的: *a slow train* 緩慢的火車 | *a slow, smoochy dance at the end of the evening* 晚會快結束時摟抱着跳的慢舞 | *The computer's just so slow today, isn't it?* 電腦今天速度真慢, 是吧?

2 ►LONG TIME 長時間◄ a) taking a long time or a longer time than usual〔比平常〕緩慢的, 費時長的, 耗費時日的: *With the fog and ice, our journey was very slow.* 又有霧又結冰, 我們的旅程非常緩慢。| *It's quite a slow process.* 進程相當慢。**b)** taking too long, especially because of someone being unwilling〔尤指因不願意而〕慢吞吞的, 不利索的, 磨磨蹭蹭的: *a slow response to our requests for help* 對我們的求助反應遲緩 | **slow to recognize/see/follow etc** *Our companies have been very slow to react to foreign competition.* 我們各公司對外國競爭的反應一直都很遲緩。

3 ►CLOCK 時鐘◄ [not before noun 不用於名詞前] if a clock is slow it is showing a time earlier than the correct time〔走得〕慢了的, 慢了…的: **ten minutes/five minutes etc slow** *The station clock was five minutes slow.* 火車站的鐘慢了五分鐘。

4 ►LARGE ROAD 大馬路◄ [only before noun 僅用於名詞前] the slow lane on a large road is not intended for fast-moving vehicles〔慢車道〕不容許快速行駛的

5 ►BUSINESS 生意◄ if business or trade is slow, there are not many customers or not much is sold 停滯的, 清淡的

6 ►STUPID 愚蠢的◄ not good or quick at understanding things 遲鈍的, 愚笨的: *Sometimes he can be rather slow.* 有時他會相當遲鈍。| *helping the slower pupils* 幫助學得比較慢的學生 | **slow off the mark/slow on the uptake** (=not good at understanding things) 理解能力不好 —**slowly** *adv*: *The time passed slowly.* 時間過得很慢。| *slowly gathering speed as we rolled downhill* 我們的車子下坡時漸漸加快的速度

S2 W2 **slow²** *v* [I,T] also 又作 **slow up** to become slower or make something slower (使) 放慢, (使) 減速: *The train slowed as it went around the bend.* 火車在拐彎時減速。| *Business slows up at this time of year.* 每年在這個時候生意漸趨清淡。—see picture on page A3 參見 A3 頁圖

slow down *phr v* **1** [I,T **slow** sth ↔ **down**] to become slower or make something slower (使) 慢下來, (使) 減速: *Motorists should slow down and take extra care in foggy conditions.* 司機在霧天應減速行駛並特別小心。| *My aching knee was beginning to slow me down.* 膝蓋的疼痛開始影響到我走路的速度。**2** [I] to become less active or busy than you usually are 減少活動[工作]: *You're sixty, it's time you slowed down a bit.* 你六十歲了, 到了該放鬆一點的時候了。

slow³ *adv* slowly 慢慢地, 緩慢地 —see also 另見 GO-SLOW

slow burn /ˌ· ˈ·/ *n* **do a slow burn** *AmE informal* to slowly get angry【美, 非正式】逐漸發火: *Tony fumbled the ball and I could see the coach do a slow burn.* 托尼漏接了球, 我能看出教練的火氣在漸漸上升。

slow·coach /ˈsloˌkotʃ; ˈsləʊkəʊtʃ/ *n* [C] *BrE informal* someone who moves or does things too slowly【英, 非正式】慢性子的人, 遲鈍的人, 行動緩慢的人; SLOWPOKE *AmE*【美】: *Come on slowcoach, hurry up!* 嘿, 磨磨蹭蹭的傢伙, 快點!

slow·down /ˈsloˌdaʊn; ˈsləʊdaʊn/ *n* **1** [C usually singular 一般用單數] a reduction in activity or speed 減速;〔活動的〕減少, 減慢; 減退: *a slowdown in the US economy* 美國經濟發展的放緩 **2** [C] *AmE* a period when people deliberately work slowly in order to protest about something【美】〔工人表示抗議的〕怠工

slow mo·tion /ˌ· ˈ··/ *n* [U] movement on film shown at a slower speed than it really happened〔影片中的〕慢動作: **in slow motion** *Let's show that goal again in slow motion.* 讓我們用慢動作重放這次進球得分的情況。

slow pitch /ˈ· ·/ *n* [U] *AmE* a game like SOFTBALL, played by mixed teams of men and women【美】慢投壘球〔一種男女混合對打的壘球〕

slow·poke /ˈsloˌpok; ˈsləʊpəʊk/ *n* [C] *AmE informal* SLOWCOACH【美, 非正式】慢性子的人, 遲鈍的人

slow-wit·ted /ˌ· ˈ··◂/ *adj* not good at understanding things 頭腦遲鈍的, 笨的: *He was a big, slow-witted man who would hurt no-one.* 他這個人身材高大但頭腦遲鈍, 不會傷害任何人。

slow-worm /ˈ· ·/ *n* [C] a small European LIZARD with no legs, which looks like a small snake〔歐洲產的〕無足蛇蜥

sludge /slʌdʒ; slʌdʒ/ *n* [U] **1** soft thick mud, especially at the bottom of a liquid〔沉澱於液體下面的〕軟泥, 爛泥 **2** the solid substance that is left when SEWAGE (=the liquid waste from houses, factories etc) has been cleaned〔從下水道清理出的〕淤泥, 污泥, 污物 **3** thick dirty oil in an engine〔引擎中的〕油垢, 油污, 油泥 —**sludgy** *adj*

slug¹ /slʌg; slʌg/ *n* [C] **1** a small slow-moving creature with a soft body like a SNAIL but without a shell 鼻涕蟲, 蛞蝓 **2** *AmE informal* a bullet【美, 非正式】子彈 **3** *informal* a small amount of a strong alcoholic drink【非正式】少量烈酒: *a slug of brandy* 一口白蘭地 **4** *AmE informal* a piece of metal shaped like a coin used to illegally get a drink, ticket etc from a machine【美, 非正式】〔用以開動自動售貨機獲取飲料、票等的〕硬幣狀金屬塊, 假硬幣

slug² *v* [T] **1** *informal* to hit someone hard with your closed hand【非正式】用拳猛擊: *I stood up and he slugged me again.* 我站了起來, 他又用拳對我猛擊。**2** to hit a ball hard〔對球〕重擊, 強打 **3 slug it out** if two people slug it out, they fight by hitting each other hard 狠鬥, 決一雌雄

slug·ger /ˈslʌgɚ; ˈslʌgə/ *n* [C] *informal AmE* a BASEBALL player who hits the ball very hard【非正式, 美】〔棒球運動的〕強擊手

slug·gish /ˈslʌgɪʃ; ˈslʌgɪʃ/ *adj* moving or reacting more slowly than normal 行動緩慢的, 反應遲緩的: *I always feel sluggish first thing in the morning.* 我早上剛起牀時

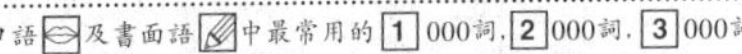
口語 及書面語 中最常用的 1 000詞, 2 000詞, 3 000詞

S

總覺得提不起精神來。| *the company's sluggish sales performance* 公司的滯銷狀況 **—sluggishly** *adv*: *The stream flows sluggishly through the fields.* 小溪緩緩地流過田野。**—sluggishness** *n* [U]

sluice¹ /slus; sluːs/ *n* [C] a passage for water to flow through, with a special gate which can be opened or closed to control it 水閘, 水門

sluice² *v* **1** [T] to wash something with a lot of water〔用大量的水〕沖洗: **sluice sth out/down** *Can you sluice out the cow shed?* 你把牛棚沖洗一下好嗎? | **sluice sth over/into etc** *I sluiced water over the wound.* 我用水沖洗傷口。**2** [I+out/over] if water sluices somewhere, a large amount of it suddenly flows there〔水〕奔流, 奔泄, 奔瀉

slum¹ /slʌm; slʌm/ *n* **1** [C] a house or an area of a city that is in very bad condition, where very poor people live〔城市中的〕貧民窟, 貧民區: **the slums** (=a slum area) 貧民區 *He grew up in the East London slums.* 他是在倫敦東部的貧民區長大的。**2** [singular] *informal* a very untidy place【非正式】非常髒亂的地方

slum² *v* **slum it/be slumming** *informal often humorous* to spend time in conditions that are much worse than you are used to【非正式, 常幽默】過簡陋的生活: *If we're going to travel for 6 months we'll have to slum it most of the time.* 如果我們準備出去旅行六個月, 大部分時間就得勒緊褲腰帶了。

slum·ber¹ /ˈslʌmbɚ; ˈslʌmbə/ *v* [I] *literary* to sleep【文】睡眠, 安睡

slumber² *n* also 又作 **slumbers** [singular,U] *literary* sleep【文】睡眠: *He passed into a deep slumber.* 他酣然入夢。

S

slumber par·ty /ˈ·· ˌ··/ *n* [C] *AmE* a children's party when a group of children sleep at one child's house【美】睡衣晚會〔兒童的聚會, 當晚都在一個孩子家裡過夜〕

slum·lord /ˈslʌmlɔrd; ˈslʌmlɔːd/ *n* [C] *AmE* someone who owns houses in a very poor area and charges high rents for buildings that are in bad condition【美】〔出租簡陋房屋收取高額租金的〕貧民區房東

slum·my /ˈslʌmɪ; ˈslʌmi/ *adj* a slummy area is one where very poor people live and the buildings are in bad condition 貧民區的,〔地方〕貧困的: *a little junk shop in the slummy quarter of the town* 城裡貧民區的一家小舊貨店

slump¹ /slʌmp; slʌmp/ *v* **1** [I] to suddenly go down in price, value, or number〔物價、價值等〕暴跌, 劇降: *Sales slumped by 20% last year.* 去年的銷售額暴跌了20%。**2 be slumped** to be sitting with your body leaning completely backwards or forwards, because you are tired or unconscious〔由於疲倦或失去知覺而〕倒伏的, 後仰頹坐的: **[+in/against]** *a drunk slumped against the wall* 頹然靠牆倒伏的醉鬼 **3** [I] to suddenly fall down or sit down because you feel weak or become unconscious〔因乏力或失去知覺而〕頹然倒下, 突然跌坐: **[+back/over/on]** *His head slumped on his chest.* 他的頭無力地垂在胸前。| *Father slumped back in his chair.* 父親頹然跌坐到椅子上。

slump² *n* [C usually singular 一般用單數] **1** a sudden fall in prices, sales, profits etc〔物價、銷售額、利潤等〕突然下跌: **[+in]** *a slump in agricultural prices* 農產品價格的突然下降 **2** a period when there is a big reduction in trade so that many companies have to close and many people lose their jobs 貿易銳減, 衰退, 蕭條(時期): *the slump in the late 80s* 80年代後期的經濟蕭條 **3** *especially AmE* a period when a player or team does not play well【尤美】〔運動員或運動隊〕競技狀態不佳的時期: *The Dodgers have been in a slump for the last three weeks.* 道奇隊在過去三週競技狀態一直不佳。

slung /slʌŋ; slʌŋ/ *v* the past tense and past participle of SLING

slunk /slʌŋk; slʌŋk/ *v* the past tense and past participle of SLINK

slur¹ /slɝ; slɜː/ *v* **1** [I,T] to speak unclearly without separating your words or sounds correctly 含糊地說(話): **slur your words/speech** *He was obviously drunk and slurring his words.* 他顯然喝醉了, 說話含糊不清。**2** [T] to criticize someone or something unfairly 誹謗, 詆毀 **3** [T] to play a group of musical notes smoothly together〔圓渾地〕連奏 **—slurred** *adj*: *slurred speech* 含糊不清的話

slur² *n* **1** [C] an unfair criticism that is intended to make people dislike someone or something 詆毀, 誹謗: **[+on]** *a slur on my reputation* 對我名譽的中傷 **2** [singular] an unclear way of speaking in which the words are not separated 含糊不清的說話: *the slur in his voice* 他說話聲音含糊不清 **3** [C] a curved line written over musical notes to show they must be played together smoothly 標於樂譜音符上的連(接)線

slurp /slɝp; slɜːp/ *v* [I,T] to drink a liquid while making a noisy sucking sound 出聲地喝〔水等〕, 咕嘟咕嘟地喝: *Don't slurp your soup!* 喝湯不要咕嘟咕嘟地出聲。**—slurp** *n* [C usually singular 一般用單數]: *He drank his coffee with a slurp.* 他咕嘟咕嘟地喝咖啡。

slur·ry /ˈslɝɪ; ˈslʌri/ *n* [U] a mixture of water and mud, coal, or animal waste 泥漿, 淤漿〔水和泥土、煤或牲畜糞的混合物〕

slush /slʌʃ; slʌʃ/ *n* **1** [U] partly melted snow 半融雪 **2** [U] *informal* feelings or stories that seem silly because they are too concerned with love and romantic subjects【非正式】庸俗的浪漫情調; 無聊的愛情故事: *And don't give us that slush about your children just to make us feel sorry for you!* 不要光為了博得我們的同情而大講你兒女無聊的羅曼史! **3** [C,U] *especially AmE* a drink made with crushed ice and a sweet liquid【尤美】加碎冰的甜飲料, 果冰: *cherry slush* 櫻桃冷飲**—slushy** *adj*: *a slushy movie* 無聊的愛情片

slush fund /ˈ· ·/ *n* [C] a sum of money kept for dishonest purposes, especially by a politician〔尤指政客的〕行賄基金, 祕密收藏起來作不正當用途的基金

slut /slʌt; slʌt/ *n* [C] **1** an offensive word for a woman who has had many sexual partners 淫婦, 蕩婦: *Get out of here you slut!* 滾出去, 你這個婊子! **2** an offensive word for a lazy untidy woman 懶婆娘, 邋遢女人〔冒犯用語〕**—sluttish** *adj*: *a dress that was nasty and sluttish* 又髒又臭的連衣裙 **—sluttishness** *n* [U]

sly /slaɪ; slaɪ/ *adj* **1** very clever in the way that you use tricks and dishonesty to get what you want 狡猾的, 狡詐的: *The way he did it was really sly.* 他的做法真夠狡猾的。**2 sly smile/glance/wink etc** a smile, look etc shows that you are hiding something you know from other people 詭祕的微笑/一瞥/眼色等: *She gave me a sly look.* 她詭祕地看了我一眼。**3 on the sly** *informal* secretly, especially when you are doing something that you should not do【非正式】祕密地, 偷偷地, 暗地裡: *They'd been seeing each other on the sly for months.* 他們偷偷約會已有幾個月了。**—slyly** *adv* **—slyness** *n* [U]

smack¹ /smæk; smæk/ *v* [T] **1** to hit a child with your hand in order to punish them〔用手掌〕打, 摑, 拍〔小孩, 以示懲罰〕: *To bed now, or I'll smack your bottom!* 現在就上牀睡覺, 不然我要打你的屁股! —see picture on page A20 參見A20頁圖 **2** to hit something against something else so that it makes a short loud noise〔用某物〕啪啪地打: **smack sth against/into etc** *He smacked his fist against his palm.* 他用拳頭啪啪地擊打掌心。**3 smack your lips** to make a short loud noise with your lips because you are hungry〔由於肚子餓〕出聲地咂嘴唇 **4** *BrE informal* to hit someone hard with your closed hand; PUNCH¹ (1)【英, 非正式】用拳猛揍: *Say that again and I'll smack you!* 你再說一遍我就狠狠地揍你!

smack of sth *phr v* [T] if something smacks of dishonesty, desperation etc it seems to contain some of that quality 有…的含義, 含有…的意味: *I don't want to say anything that smacks of disloyalty.* 我不想說甚麼顯得我不夠忠誠的話。

smack² *n* **1** [C] **a)** a hit made with your hand held flat, especially to punish a child 打一巴掌〔尤指給小孩的懲罰〕: *Quiet, or I'll give you a smack!* 安靜，不然我就給你一巴掌！ **b)** *BrE informal* a hard hit with your closed hand; PUNCH[2] (1)【英，非正式】猛擊一拳 **2** [C] a short loud noise caused especially when something hits something else 啪的一聲〔尤指一物打着另一物的響聲〕 **3 give sb a smack on the lips/cheek** *informal* to kiss someone【非正式】給某人的嘴唇/臉頰一個響吻 **4 have a smack at** *BrE informal* to try to do something【英，非正式】嘗試做 **5** [U] *slang* HEROIN (=a dangerous illegal drug)【俚】海洛因〔一種危險的毒品〕 **6** [C] a small fishing boat 小漁船

smack[3] *adv informal*【非正式】**1** exactly or directly in the middle or in front of something 恰好，準確地，不偏不倚地: **smack in the middle/in front of etc** *There was a hole smack in the middle of the floor.* 正好在地板的中央有一個洞。| **smack-bang** *BrE*【英】/**smack-dab** *AmE*【美】*The plane was stuck there, smack-dab in the middle of the lake!* 飛機就倒插在那兒，正好在湖的中央！ **2** if something moves smack into or against something, it hits it with a lot of force, making a loud noise 猛烈地，砰地一聲: *The car ran smack into the side of the bus.* 小轎車猛地撞在公共汽車的側面。

smack·er /ˈsmækɚ; ˈsmækə/ *n* [C] *slang*【俚】**1** a pound or a dollar 一英鎊；一美元: *It cost me fifty smackers.* 這花了我五十英鎊[美元]。 **2** also 又作 **smack·er·oo** /ˌsmækəˈru; ˌsmækəˈruː/ a loud kiss 響吻

small[1] /smɔl; smɔːl/ *adj* (S1 W1)

1 ►SIZE 尺寸◄ not large in size or amount〔體積、尺寸、數量等〕小的；少的: *He's a small man, only five feet tall.* 他是個矮小的男子，只有五英尺高。| *Luxembourg is one of the smallest countries in Europe.* 盧森堡是歐洲最小的國家之一。| *No, not that one – the small one with the red handle!* 不，不是那個 —— 是那個紅柄的小的！| *a smaller increase in the inflation rate than last year* 增幅小於去年的通脹率 —see 見 LITTLE[1] (USAGE)

2 ►UNIMPORTANT 不重要的◄ a small problem, job, mistake etc is unimportant or easy to deal with〔問題、錯誤、工作等〕小的，瑣細的，微不足道的，容易對付的: *Your work is good, but I found a number of small mistakes.* 你的工作做得不錯，不過我也發現了一些小的差錯。| *It's a small matter but worth mentioning.* 這是件小事，不過值得一提。

3 ►YOUNG CHILD 年幼小孩◄ a small child is young 幼小的，年幼的: *She's married with three small children.* 她已經結婚，有三個年幼的孩子。

4 small farmer/dealer/business a farmer, business etc that does not involve large amounts of money 小農/小生意人/小本生意: *Most of the land in this region belongs to small farmers.* 這個地區的大部分土地都歸小農場主所有。

5 ►LETTER 字母◄ small letters are the smaller of the two forms that we use, for example 'b' rather than 'B' 小寫體的，小寫的

6 a conservative with a small 'c'/a pacifist with a small 'p' etc *informal* someone who believes in the principles you have mentioned, but not very strongly【非正式】温和的保守派/和平主義者

7 small fortune a lot of money 一大筆錢: *That dress must have cost you a small fortune.* 那件連衣裙一定花了你不少錢。

8 make sb feel small to do something to make someone feel stupid, unimportant, or ashamed 令人自覺渺小，使人自慚形穢: *She was always laughing at me and making me feel small.* 她老是嘲笑我，使我感到自卑。

9 in a/some small way if something helps, affects, influences etc in a small way it has an effect but not an important one 小規模地，有點: *It was good to feel we had helped in some small way.* 知道我們能幫上一點小忙，我們已覺得不錯了。

10 ►VOICE 聲音◄ a small voice is quiet and soft 低的，細弱的，柔和的: *"I don't want to stay here," she said in a small voice.* "我不想呆在這兒。" 她低聲地說。

11 small beer *BrE*【英】/**small potatoes** *AmE*【美】someone or something that is not at all important 微不足道的人[東西]: *Parking fines? Pretty small beer compared with some of the things he's done in the past.* 違規停車罰款？和他過去做過的一些事情相比算是小事一樁。

12 small fry *informal*【非正式】**a)** unimportant people or things 小人物；小事情: *Of course no one bothers about small fry like us.* 當然，誰也不會為我們這樣的小人物操心。 **b)** *AmE* children【美】小孩子們: *I've sent the small fry out to play in the yard.* 我已經把孩子們打發到外面院子裡去玩了。—**small** *adv*: *He writes so small I can't read it.* 他寫的字太小，我沒法看。—**smallness** *n* [U]

small[2] *n* **1 the small of your back** the lower part of your back where it curves 腰背部 **2 smalls** [plural] *BrE old-fashioned informal* underwear【英，過時，非正式】內衣褲

small ad /ˈ· ·/ *n* [C] *BrE* an advertisement put in a newspaper by someone who wants to buy or sell something【英】小廣告，分類廣告〔出售或求購物品的短廣告〕; WANT AD *AmE*【美】

small arms /ˈ· ·/ *n* [plural] guns that are held in one or both hands for firing 輕武器〔可用一隻手或雙手拿着射擊的武器〕

small change /ˌ· ˈ·/ *n* [U] money in coins of low value 小額硬幣，零錢: *Do you have any small change?* 你有零錢嗎？

small claims court /ˌ· ˈ· ˈ·/ *n* [C] a court where people can try to get back small amounts of money from other people or from companies when they think it has been taken unfairly 小額錢債（賠償）法庭

smallest room /ˌ·· ˈ·/ *n* [singular] *BrE* the room where the toilet is, used to avoid the word toilet【英】廁所，洗手間〔委婉的說法〕

small·hold·ing /ˈsmɔlˌholdɪŋ; ˈsmɔːlˌhəʊldɪŋ/ *n* [C] *BrE* a piece of land used for farming that is smaller than an ordinary farm【英】〔比普通農場小的〕小塊農田 —**small-holder** *n* [C]

small hours /ˈ· ·/ *n* [plural] **the small hours** the early morning hours, between about one and four o'clock 凌晨時分〔約從一時至四時〕: *We stayed up talking into the small hours.* 我們沒去睡覺，而是一直談到凌晨。

small in·tes·tine /ˌ· ·ˈ··/ *n* [singular] the long tube that food goes through after it has gone through your stomach 小腸 —see picture at 參見 DIGESTIVE SYSTEM 圖

small·ish /ˈsmɔlɪʃ; ˈsmɔːlɪʃ/ *adj especially BrE* fairly small【尤英】略小的，較小的: *a smallish town* 小鎮 | *She's smallish with red hair.* 她個子略小，一頭紅髮。

small-mind·ed /ˌsmɔlˈmaɪndɪd; ˌsmɔːlˈmaɪndɪd◂/ *adj* too concerned with the small problems and details of your life, so that you do not think about what is really important; PETTY (1) 小氣的，心胸狹窄的，目光短淺的: *a greedy, bigoted and small-minded man* 貪婪、固執、心胸狹窄的男人 —**small-mindedness** *n* [U] —compare 比較 NARROW-MINDED

small·pox /ˈsmɔlˌpɑks; ˈsmɔːlpɒks/ *n* [U] a serious disease that causes spots which leave marks on your skin 天花

small print /ˈ· ˌ·/ *n* [U] all the details in a contract or agreement which contain many rules and restrictions〔合約中的〕限制性附屬細則: *Always read the small print before you sign anything.* 在簽約前，一定要閱讀附屬細則。

small-scale /ˌ· ˈ·◂/ *adj* small in size 小規模的: *a small-scale study* 小規模的研究

small screen /ˈ· ˌ·/ *n* [singular] television 電視: *a film made for the small screen* 為電視拍攝的影片

small talk /ˈ· ·/ *n* [U] polite friendly conversation about unimportant subjects 閒談，聊天: *small talk about the weather* 關於天氣情況的閒聊

small-time /ˌ· ˈ·◂/ *adj* **small-time crook/gangster etc** a criminal who is not very successful 輕罪犯/小流氓 —**small-timer** *n* [C]

small-town /ˈ· ·/ *adj* [only before noun 僅用於名詞前] **1** connected with a small town 小鎮的, 鄉鎮的: *a small-town lawyer* 鄉鎮律師 **2** *especially AmE* not very interested in anything new or different【尤美】偏狹的, 對新事物不感興趣的: *small-town attitudes* 狹隘的觀點

smarm·y /ˈsmɑrmɪ; ˈsmɑːmi/ *adj* polite in an insincere way that you think is unpleasant 奉承的, 討好的, 假殷勤的: *He fooled us with his soft smarmy ways.* 他用甜言蜜語騙了我們。

S3 W2 **smart¹** /smɑrt; smɑːt/ *adj*

1 ▶CLEVER 聰明的◀ *especially AmE*【尤美】**a)** intelligent 聰穎的, 精明的, 機靈的: *The smart kids get good grades and go off to college.* 聰明的孩子成績好, 可直升大學。| *Some smart lawyer got him out of jail.* 有個精明的律師幫他出了獄。**b)** trying to seem clever in a disrespectful way 自命不凡的, 不恭的: *Don't get smart with me, young man.* 不要跟我耍小聰明, 年輕人。

2 ▶WELL-DRESSED 穿着考究的◀ *BrE* wearing neat attractive clothes and having a generally tidy appearance【英】衣着整潔漂亮的, 帥氣的: *Chris was looking very smart in his new grey suit.* 克里斯穿着一身灰色的新西服, 看上去非常帥氣。

3 ▶FASHIONABLE 時髦的◀ *BrE* fashionable or used by fashionable people【英】時髦的, 時髦人士用的: *one of Bonn's smartest restaurants* 波恩其中一家最時髦的餐館

4 ▶QUICK 迅速的◀ a smart movement is done quickly and with force〔動作〕迅猛的, 厲害的: *a smart blow on the head* 在頭上猛力的一擊 | **at a smart pace** (=fairly fast) 輕快地 *The horse set off at a smart pace.* 馬兒輕快地跑了起來。

5 ▶EXCELLENT 優秀的◀ *BrE old-fashioned* excellent【英, 過時】極好的, 傑出的 —**smartly** *adv*: *smartly dressed women* 穿着時髦的婦女 | *He turned smartly and walked away.* 他輕快地轉身走開了。—**smartness** *n* [U]

smart² *v* [I] **1** to be upset because someone has hurt your feelings or offended you 感到痛苦[傷心]: **be smarting from** *She was still smarting from the insult.* 她還在為那次受辱而感到傷心。**2** if a part of your body smarts, it hurts with a stinging pain 感到刺痛, 感到劇痛: *My eyes were smarting from the smoke.* 我的眼睛被煙熏得刺痛。

smart³ *n* [singular] **1** a feeling that you have when you are upset and offended by something 傷心, 痛苦, 難受 **2** a stinging pain 刺痛 **3 smarts** [U] *AmE informal* intelligence【美, 非正式】聰明, 智慧: *If she had any smarts, she'd get rid of the guy.* 她如果有一點頭腦, 就該把那個傢伙甩掉。

smart al·eck /ˌsmɑrt ˈælɪk; ˈsmɑːt ˌælɪk/ *n* [C] *informal* someone who always says clever things or always has the right answer in a way that is annoying【非正式】自作聰明的人, 自以為是的人

smart arse /ˈ· ·/ *BrE*【英】, also 又作 **smart ass** *AmE*【美】—*n* an impolite word for a smart aleck 自作聰明的人, 自以為是的人: *He got in trouble with the teacher for being such a smart ass in class.* 他因在班上過分自以為是而受到老師的批評。—**smart-arse** also 又作 **smart-ass** *adj*: *smart-arse remarks* 自以為是的話

smart bomb /ˈ· ·/ *n* [C] a bomb that is fired from an aircraft and guided by a computer〔飛機發射並由電腦制導的〕聰明炸彈[導彈]

smart card /ˈ· ·/ *n* [C] a small plastic card with an electronic part that records and remembers information 智能卡

smart·en /ˈsmɑrtn̩; ˈsmɑːtn/ *v*

smarten up *phr v especially BrE*【尤英】**1** also 又作 **smarten yourself up** [I] to make yourself look neat and tidy 打扮得乾淨整齊: *You'd better smarten yourself up a bit before the interview.* 你參加面試前最好打扮得乾淨整齊一點。**2** [T] **smarten** sth ↔ **up** to make something look neater 使〔某物〕整潔: *a coat of paint to smarten the room up* 塗一層油漆使房間煥然一新

smart·y·pants /ˈsmɑrtɪˌpænts; ˈsmɑːtipænts/ *n* [C] *humorous* someone who always says clever things or always has the right answer, in a slightly annoying way【幽默】自以為是的人, 自以為樣樣都懂的人

smash¹ /smæʃ; smæʃ/ *v* **1** [I,T] to break into many small pieces violently or noisily, or to make something do this by dropping, throwing, or hitting it 打破, 打碎, (使) 粉碎: *I dropped the plate and it smashed.* 我失手把盤子掉在地上, 摔得粉碎。| *He used a chair to smash the window.* 他用椅子把窗玻璃砸碎。**2** [I always+adv/prep, T always+adv/prep] to hit an object or surface violently, or to make something do this (使) 猛撞, 猛擊, 猛擲: **smash sth against/down/into** *Larry smashed his fist down on the table.* 拉里用拳頭猛擊桌子。**3** [T] to destroy something such as a political system or criminal organization 擊潰, 擊毀; 消滅: *The French police claim to have smashed a massive drugs racket.* 法國警方宣稱已破獲一大宗販毒交易。**4** [T] to hit a high ball in tennis etc with a strong downward action〔在網球等運動中〕殺〔球〕, 猛扣〔球〕—see picture on page A23 參見 A23 頁圖

smash sth ↔ **down** *phr v* [T] to hit a door, wall etc violently so that it falls to the ground 擊倒〔門、牆等〕

smash sth ↔ **in** *phr v* [T] to hit something so violently that you break it and make a hole in it 將〔某物〕撞出窟窿: **smash sb's face/head in** *informal* (=hit someone hard in the face or head)【非正式】狠擊某人的臉/頭 *He had threatened to smash Jo's head in if he ever went there again.* 他曾威脅說, 如果喬再去那兒他就砸碎他的腦袋。

smash sth ↔ **up** *phr v* [T] to deliberately damage or destroy something〔故意〕撞毀, 打碎: *A gang of thugs came into the bar and smashed the place up.* 一幫暴徒闖進酒吧, 把東西砸得粉碎。—see also 另見 SMASH-UP

smash² *n* **1** [singular] the loud sound of something breaking 撞碎聲, 破碎聲: **[+of]** *We heard the smash of plates breaking in the kitchen.* 我們聽到廚房裡盤子的碎裂聲。**2** [C] a hard downward shot in tennis or similar games〔網球等的〕殺球, 扣球 **3** [C] *BrE* a serious road or railway accident【英】嚴重的交通事故, 車禍

smash-and-grab /ˌ· · ˈ·/ *adj* **smash-and-grab raid** the act of robbing a shop by breaking the window and stealing valuable goods 砸破櫥窗劫掠貴重商品的暴行 —**smash and grab** *n* [C]

smashed /smæʃt; smæʃt/ *adj* [not before noun 不用於名詞前] *informal* very drunk or affected by a drug【非正式】喝醉酒的; 吸毒後神魂恍惚的: *She's smashed out of her mind.* 她醉得神志不清。

smash·er /ˈsmæʃɚ; ˈsmæʃə/ *n* [C] *BrE old-fashioned* someone that you think is very attractive, or something that is very good【英, 過時】非常漂亮的人; 極好的東西: *It's a beautiful boat – a real smasher!* 非常漂亮的船——真是漂亮極了!

smash hit /ˌ· ˈ·/ *n* [C] a very successful new play, book, film etc 非常成功的新戲[新書、新影片等]: *This film is going to be a smash hit.* 這部電影將會大受歡迎。

smash·ing /ˈsmæʃɪŋ; ˈsmæʃɪŋ/ *adj BrE old-fashioned* very good【英, 過時】非常好的, 極佳的: *We had a smashing holiday.* 我們過了一個非常痛快的假日。

smash-up /ˈ· ·/ *n* [C] a serious road or railway accident〔公路或鐵路上〕嚴重的撞車事故

smat·ter·ing /ˈsmætərɪŋ; ˈsmætərɪŋ/ *n* [C+of] **1** a small number or amount of something 少數, 少量: *a smattering of rain* 一點點的雨 **2 have a smattering of** [not in progressive 不用進行式] to have a small amount of knowledge about a subject, especially a foreign language 略知, 懂得一點點〔某門學科, 尤指外語〕

smear¹ /smɪr; smɪə/ *n* [C] **1** a dirty or oily mark on something 污斑, 油漬: *There were smears of chocolate on Charlie's shirt.* 查理的襯衣上有些巧克力污跡。**2** a SMEAR TEST 子宮頸抹片檢查, 塗片試驗 **3** an attempt to harm someone by spreading untrue stories about them 污蔑, 誹謗 —**smeary** *adj*

smear[2] *v*

1 ▶SPREAD 塗抹◀ [T always+adv/prep] to spread a liquid or soft substance over a surface, especially carelessly or untidily〔尤指胡亂地〕塗, 抹〔液體或醬狀物〕: **smear sth with** *The tablecloth was smeared with jam, crayon and berry juice.* 桌布上塗滿了果醬、蠟筆顏料和漿果汁。| **smear sth on/over etc** *Elaine smeared sun tan lotion liberally on her body.* 伊莱恩往身上抹了很多防曬霜。

2 ▶DIRTY 髒的◀ [T] to make something dirty or oily; SMUDGE 弄髒: *Careful! You'll smear my shirt!* 小心! 你會弄髒我的襯衣!

3 ▶UNCLEAR 不清楚的◀ [I,T] to become unclear or make something unclear by rubbing it (使)〔因擦拭而〕變模糊: *Several words were smeared and I couldn't read them.* 有幾個字給擦得很模糊, 我看不清。

4 ▶TELL LIES 說謊◀ [T] to spread an untrue story about someone in order to harm them 污蔑, 誹謗: *an attempt to smear the party leadership* 企圖污蔑黨的領導

5 ▶PAINT 油漆◀ [I] if a substance such as paint smears when something touches it, it spreads over parts of a surface where it should not be〔油漆等〕沾染, 塗污: *Don't lean on the wall or the paint will smear.* 不要靠在牆上, 不然塗料會沾你一身。

smear cam·paign /'· ·,·/ *n* [C] a deliberate plan to tell untrue stories about someone, especially a politician etc in order to harm them 有預謀的誹謗活動〔尤指針對政客〕

smear test /'· ·/ *n* [C] a medical test in which cells from the entrance to a woman's WOMB (=the place where a baby grows) are examined under a microscope; CERVICAL SMEAR 子宮頸抹片檢查, 塗片試驗〔一種探查子宮頸癌變的方法〕

2 3 **smell**[1] /smɛl; smel/ *n* **1** [C] the quality that people and animals recognize by using their nose 氣味: *Some flowers have a stronger smell than others.* 有些花的氣味比別的花強烈。| *The wine has a light, lemony smell.* 這種酒有一種淡淡的檸檬香味。| **[+of]** *I opened the window to get rid of the smell of beer and cigarettes.* 我打開窗戶把啤酒和香煙的味道放出去。—compare 比較 AROMA, FRAGRANCE **2** [C] an unpleasant smell 難聞的氣味, 臭味: *Pooh! What a smell!* 呸! 多難聞的氣味啊! —compare 比較 ODOUR, STINK[2] (1) **3** [U] the ability to notice or recognize smells 嗅覺: *A mole finds its food by smell alone.* 鼴鼠覓食全憑嗅覺。| **sense of smell** *Blind people often have an excellent sense of smell.* 盲人的嗅覺大多特別靈敏。**4** [C usually singular 一般用單數] an act of smelling something 聞, 嗅: *Have a smell of this cheese; does it seem all right?* 你聞一聞這些乳酪, 有問題嗎?

2 3 **smell**[2] *v past tense and past participle* **smelled** *especially AmE*【尤美】, **smelt** /smɛlt; smelt/ *BrE*【英】

1 ▶A PARTICULAR SMELL 某種味道◀ [I always+adv/prep; linking verb+adj] to have a particular smell 有…氣味, 發出…氣味: **smell nice/good/spicy etc** *That soup smells delicious!* 那湯聞起來真香! | *a sweet-smelling flower* 氣味芬芳的花 | **[+of]** *The car smelled of leather and wood.* 這輛汽車發出皮革和木頭的氣味。| **smell like** *It smells like a hospital in here – has anyone been using disinfectant?* 這裡聞起來好像醫院似的 —— 有誰用了消毒劑嗎?

2 ▶UNPLEASANT 難聞的◀ [I] to have an unpleasant smell 發出臭氣, 氣味難聞: *His breath smells.* 他有口臭。| *We must clean out the bird-cage – it's starting to smell.* 我們必須清洗鳥籠了 —— 它開始發臭了。

3 ▶RECOGNIZE A SMELL 聞到味道◀ [T] to notice or recognize a particular smell 聞到, 嗅到: *I think I smell gas!* 我覺得聞到了煤氣味! | **smell that** *I could smell that the milk wasn't fresh.* 我聞得出這牛奶不新鮮。

4 ▶PUT YOUR NOSE NEAR STH 把鼻子靠近某物◀ [T] to put your nose near something to discover what kind of smell it has; SNIFF[1] (2) 聞一聞〔看有甚麼氣味〕: *Diane smelled his breath to see if he'd been drinking.* 黛安聞了聞他呼出的氣味, 看他有沒有喝過酒。

5 ▶ABILITY TO SMELL 聞到氣味的能力◀ [I] to have the ability to notice and recognize smells 有嗅覺: *I've got a cold and I can't smell.* 我得了感冒, 聞不出味道。

6 smell trouble/danger etc to feel that something bad is going to happen 感到有麻煩/有危險: *He smelt trouble and got up to leave.* 他覺得會有麻煩, 便站起來走了。

7 smell a rat *informal* to guess that something wrong or dishonest is happening【非正式】懷疑某事不對頭, 懷疑其中有詐: *They know we hate them and will smell a rat if we try to be nice to them.* 他們知道我們恨他們, 所以如果我們試圖對他們好, 他們倒會產生懷疑了。

8 smell fishy if a story, excuse etc smells fishy, you think it is likely to be untrue〔說法、理由等〕可疑的, 似乎是假的: *Max can't be working late again! It smells very fishy to me.* 馬克斯不可能又工作到這麼晚! 我覺得非常可疑。

9 ▶SEEM 似乎◀ [linking verb 連繫動詞] *informal* to seem【非正式】好像, 似乎: **smell wrong/odd/worrying etc** *Sarah's description of events didn't smell right to me.* 我覺得莎拉對事情的描述好像不大對頭。

smell sb/sth ↔ **out** *phr v* [T] **1** to find something by smelling 聞出, 嗅出: *The hounds smelt out a fox.* 獵犬嗅出有狐狸。**2** *informal* to find something such as trouble or violence because you have a natural ability to do this【非正式】感覺到, 覺察到〔麻煩事等〕: *Wherever the fighting is, Sergeant Cooper can smell it out.* 無論哪裡有毆鬥, 庫珀警官都能覺察出來。**3** to make a place smell unpleasant 使〔某處〕充滿難聞的氣味: *That fish is smelling the kitchen out.* 那條魚使廚房臭氣熏天。

smelling salts /'·· ·/ *n* [plural] a strong-smelling chemical that you hold under someone's nose to make them conscious again 嗅鹽〔一種蘇醒劑〕

smell·y /ˈsmɛlɪ; 'smeli/ *adj* **smellier, smelliest** having an unpleasant smell 有臭味的: *smelly socks* 臭襪子 —**smelliness** *n* [U]

smelt[1] /smɛlt; smelt/ *BrE*【英】a form of the past tense and past participle of SMELL

smelt[2] *v* [T] to melt a rock that contains metal in order to remove the metal 熔煉, 提煉, 煉取〔礦石〕

smelt[3] *n* [C] a small fish 銀白魚〔胡瓜魚科海魚〕

smid·gin, smidgen /ˈsmɪdʒɪn; 'smɪdʒ₃n/ *n* [singular] *informal* a small amount of something, especially food【非正式】〔尤指食物〕少量, 一點點: *"More cheese?" "Just a smidgin, please."* "再來點乳酪好嗎?" "那就再來一點兒吧。"

3 1 **smile**[1] /smaɪl; smaɪl/ *v*

1 [I] to have or make a smile on your face 微笑: **smile at sb** *Joanna was smiling at us in a friendly way.* 喬安娜在友好地向我們微笑。| *Neil smiled to himself, thinking about how he had tricked them.* 尼爾在偷笑着, 心裡在想他是怎樣捉弄了他們。

2 smile at sth to be amused by something, often without showing it 覺得某事好笑; 嘲笑: *Graham smiled at his colleague's suggestion.* 格雷厄姆覺得他同事的建議很可笑。

3 [T] to say or express something with a smile 微笑着說; 以微笑表示: *"So this is your secret weapon." he smiled.* "原來這就是你的祕密武器。" 他笑道。| *She smiled a welcome.* 她微笑着表示歡迎。—compare 比較 GRIN[1] (1)

4 smile to think/see/remember etc to be amused when you think about something, see something etc 想起來/看見/回憶起來等就覺得好笑: *When I look back at my youth I smile to think how naive I was.* 我在回顧青年時代時, 一想到自己有多麼幼稚就覺得好笑。

5 ▶LUCK/FORTUNE 運氣/幸運◀ [T] *especially literary* if luck or FORTUNE smiles on you, you have very good luck【尤文】〔幸運之神〕向…微笑, 對…有利 —**smilingly** *adv*: *Melissa smilingly reached for a cigarette.* 梅莉莎微笑着伸手拿煙。

smile² *n* [C] an expression on your face in which your mouth curves upwards to show that you are happy, amused, friendly, etc 微笑, 笑容: *George had a big smile on his face.* 喬治笑容滿面。| *"Hello," he said with a smile.* "你好。"他笑着說。| **give sb a smile** *Tracy gave the girl a warm smile.* 特蕾西對那女孩熱情地一笑。| **be all smiles** (=to look very happy and to behave in a friendly way) 滿面笑容, 顯得非常愉快

smirk /smɝk; smɜːk/ *v* [I+**at**] to smile in an unpleasant way that shows that you are pleased by someone else's bad luck 得意地笑, 幸災樂禍地笑: *They smirked knowingly at each other across the table.* 他們隔着桌子彼此會意地壞笑。—**smirk** *n* [C]: *Wipe that smirk off your face – there's nothing funny about it!* 收起你臉上的傻笑 —— 沒有甚麼好笑的!

smite /smaɪt; smaɪt/ *v past tense* **smote** /smot; sməʊt/ *past participle* **smitten** /ˈsmɪtn̩; ˈsmɪtn/ [T+**down**] **1** *old use* to hit something hard【舊】猛打, 重擊 **2** *biblical* to destroy, attack, or punish someone【聖經】摧毀; 襲擊; 懲罰

smith /smɪθ; smɪθ/ *n* [C] **1** someone who makes and repairs things made of iron; BLACKSMITH 鐵匠, 鍛工 **2** **goldsmith/silversmith etc** someone who makes things from gold, silver etc 金匠/銀匠等

-smith /smɪθ; smɪθ/ *suffix* [in nouns 構成名詞] a maker of something 工匠; 製作者: *a gunsmith* (=someone who makes guns) 槍砲工匠 | *a wordsmith* (=someone who works with words, for example a JOURNALIST) 耍筆桿子的人〈如新聞記者〉—see also 另見 -SMITH

S

smith·e·reens /ˌsmɪðəˈrinz; ˌsmɪðəˈriːnz/ *n* [plural] **smash sth to smithereens** *informal* to completely destroy something by breaking it into very small pieces【非正式】把某物撞成碎片

smith·y /ˈsmɪθɪ; ˈsmɪði/ *n plural* **smithies** [C] a place where iron objects such as HORSESHOES were made and repaired in the past〔從前的〕鐵匠鋪

smit·ten /ˈsmɪtn̩; ˈsmɪtn/ *v* **1** the past participle of SMITE **2** **be smitten (with sb/sth)** to suddenly feel that you love someone or like something very much〔一見鍾情地〕愛上…的;〔突然〕迷上…的: *The young man was smitten with Miranda and her charms.* 那位年輕人對米蘭達一見鍾情, 為她的魅力傾倒。| **be smitten with a desire to do sth** (=want to do it very much) 極想做某事 *She was smitten with a sudden desire to be rich like them.* 她突然產生一種要和他們一樣富有的強烈慾望。

smock /smɑk; smɒk/ *n* [C] **1** a piece of clothing like a long, loose shirt, worn especially by women who are PREGNANT (=going to have a baby) 寬鬆上衣, 孕婦服 **2** a piece of clothing like a coat, worn by artists, hospital workers etc〔畫家、醫生等穿的〕罩衣, 工作服

smock·ing /ˈsmɑkɪŋ; ˈsmɒkɪŋ/ *n* [U] a type of decoration made on cloth by pulling the cloth into small regular folds held tightly with stitches〔衣服的〕褶子, 褶飾

smog /smɑg; smɒg/ *n* [U] brown unhealthy air caused by smoke from cars and factories in cities〔由汽車和工廠廢氣所造成的褐色〕煙霧

smoke¹ /smok; sməʊk/ *n* **1** [U] grey gas that is produced by something burning〔燃燒所產生的〕煙: *Clouds of black smoke belched from the building.* 一團團黑煙從大樓噴出。| *cigarette smoke* 香煙的煙霧 **2** [C usually singular 一般用單數] an act of smoking a cigarette etc 抽(一支)煙: *a cup of coffee and a smoke* 喝杯咖啡抽支煙 **3** [C] *slang* a cigarette or drugs that are smoked【俚】〔抽的〕香煙;〔吸的〕毒品 **4** **the Smoke** *BrE, AustrE* London or any large town or city【英, 澳】倫敦;〔類似的〕大城市[城鎮] **5** **go up in smoke** *informal* if your plans go up in smoke, you cannot do what you intended to do【非正式】〔計劃等〕化為泡影, 化為烏有 **6** **there's no smoke without fire** *spoken* used to say that if something bad is being said about someone, it is probably partly true【口】無火不冒煙; 無風不起浪; 事出有因 —**smokeless** *adj*

smoke² *v* **1** [I,T] to suck or breathe in smoke from a cigarette, pipe etc 抽〔香煙或煙斗等〕, 吸煙: *I haven't smoked for over two years.* 我已有兩年多不抽煙了。**2** [T] to breathe in smoke from burning an illegal drug 吸〔毒品〕, 抽〔麻醉品〕: *smoking dope* 吸毒 **3** [I] if something smokes it has smoke coming out of it 冒煙: *a smoking chimney* 冒煙的煙囱 **4** [I] if a fire smokes it lets too much smoke into a room〔室內的火爐〕冒濃煙 **5** [T] to give fish and meat a special taste by hanging it in smoke〔用煙〕熏製〔魚、肉等〕

smoke sb/sth ↔ **out** *phr v* [T] **1** to fill a place with smoke to force someone or something to come out〔用煙〕把〔人、動物等〕熏出 **2** to discover who is causing a particular problem and force them to make themselves known 揭露, 查出〔鬧事者〕: *an attempt to smoke out and defeat the subversive forces in government* 揭露和挫敗政府中顛覆勢力的一次嘗試

smoke a·larm /ˈ· ·ˌ·/ also 又作 **smoke detector** /ˈ· ·ˌ··/ *n* [C] a piece of electronic equipment which warns you when there is smoke or fire in a building 煙霧警報器 —see picture at 參見 ALARM¹ 圖

smoke bomb /ˈ· ·/ *n* [C] something that you throw that lets out clouds of smoke, used by police to control crowds〔警察為驅散人羣用的〕煙霧彈

smoked /smokt; sməʊkt/ *adj* **smoked salmon/bacon/sausage etc** fish, meat etc that has been left in smoke to give it a special taste 熏三文魚/熏鹹肉/熏香腸等

smoked glass /ˌ· ˈ·/ *n* [U] glass that is a dark grey colour 煙色玻璃

smoke-free /ˌ· ˈ·◂/ *adj* **smoke-free area/zone etc** a place where you are not allowed to smoke 禁煙區/地帶

smok·er /ˈsmokɚ; ˈsməʊkə/ *n* [C] **1** someone who smokes cigarettes, CIGARS etc 吸煙者: **heavy smoker** (=someone who smokes a lot) 煙癮很大的人, 抽煙很多的人 **2** a railway carriage in which smoking is allowed〔火車上的〕吸煙車廂

smoke·screen /ˈsmokˌskrin; ˈsməʊkskriːn/ *n* [C] **1** something that you do or say to hide your real plans or actions 偽裝, 障眼法,〔用以掩蓋真相的〕煙幕: *All that stuff about being a businessman was just a smokescreen to hide his criminal activities.* 甚麼商人身分, 這些都是用以掩飾他犯罪活動的煙幕。**2** a cloud of smoke produced so that it hides soldiers, ships etc during a battle〔戰役中用以掩蔽士兵、船隻等的〕煙幕

smoke sig·nal /ˈ· ˌ··/ *n* [C] a message sent out to people who are far away, using the smoke from a fire 煙霧信號

smoke·stack /ˈsmokˌstæk; ˈsməʊkstæk/ *n* [C] a tall CHIMNEY at a factory or on a ship〔工廠或輪船的〕大煙囱

smokestack in·dus·try /ˈ·· ˌ···/ *n* [C usually plural 一般用複數] *especially AmE* a big traditional industry such as car-making or coal-mining【尤美】〔傳統的〕重型製造業, 有大煙囱的工業〈如汽車製造業、採煤業等〉

smok·ing /ˈsmokɪŋ; ˈsməʊkɪŋ/ *n* [U] the habit or activity of breathing in tobacco smoke from a cigarette, pipe etc 吸煙, 抽煙: *The sign says 'No Smoking'.* 牌上寫着"不准吸煙"。| **give up smoking** (=stop) 戒煙, 不再吸煙 *I gave up smoking nearly ten years ago.* 我差不多十年之前就戒煙了。—see also 另見 PASSIVE SMOKING

smoking jack·et /ˈ·· ˌ··/ *n* [C] a type of man's JACKET (1) 吸煙服〔男子在家穿的一種外衣〕

smoking room /ˈ·· ·/ *n* [C] a room where smoking is allowed in a building such as a hotel or factory〔旅館、工廠等的〕吸煙室

smok·y /ˈsmokɪ; ˈsməʊki/ *adj* **1** filled with smoke 多煙的, 煙霧瀰漫的: *a smoky room* 煙霧瀰漫的房間 **2** producing too much smoke 冒煙的: *a smoky old diesel engine* 冒煙的舊柴油機 **3** having the taste, smell, or appearance of smoke 有煙熏味的; 似煙的: *his smoky green eyes* 他那煙青色的眼睛 —**smokiness** *n* [U]

smol·der /ˈsmoldɚ; ˈsməʊldə/ *v* [I] the American spelling of SMOULDER smoulder 的美式拼法

smooch /smutʃ; smuːtʃ/ *v* [I+with] *informal* if two people smooch, they kiss and hold each other in a romantic way【非正式】擁抱接吻

smooch·y /ˈsmutʃɪ; ˈsmuːtʃi/ *adj BrE informal* a smoochy song is slow and romantic【英, 非正式】〔歌曲〕節奏緩慢而浪漫的

3 **smooth**[1] /smuð; smuːð/ *adj*

1 ►FLAT 平的◄ a smooth surface is completely flat and even 平滑的; 平坦的; 平整的: *The stone steps had been worn smooth by centuries of visitors.* 這些石級已被幾個世紀的參觀者踩得很平滑了。—opposite 反義詞 ROUGH[1] (1)

2 ►SOFT 柔軟的◄ skin or fur that is smooth is soft and pleasant to touch, and your hand moves easily over it 柔軟的, 光滑的: *Sheila stroked the cat's silky smooth fur.* 希拉撫摸着貓兒像絲一樣柔軟光滑的毛。| *as smooth as a baby's bottom* 像嬰兒屁股一樣光滑

3 ►LIQUID 液體◄ a liquid mixture that is smooth is thick but with no big pieces in it〔液體混合物〕無結塊的, 均勻的, 調勻的: *Beat the eggs and flour until they are smooth.* 把雞蛋和麵粉一直攪拌至均勻為止。—opposite 反義詞 LUMPY

4 ►GRACEFUL 優美的◄ [only before noun 僅用於名詞前] a smooth movement, style, way of doing something etc is graceful and has no sudden awkward changes〔動作、風格等〕平穩的; 流暢的; 優美的: *Swing the tennis racquet in one smooth motion.* 用流暢優美的動作揮動網球拍。—opposite 反義詞 JERKY[1]

5 ►WITHOUT PROBLEMS 沒有問題的◄ a system, operation, or process that is smooth operates well and without problems 順利的, 無困難的, 無問題的: *contributing to the smooth running of the company* 有助於公司的順利經營 —see also 另見 **go smoothly** (SMOOTHLY (2))

6 ►PLEASANT TASTE 美味的◄ a drink such as WHISKY or beer that is smooth is not bitter but tastes pleasant and is easy to swallow〔酒〕不苦的, 味美的, 醇和的

7 ►POLITE 客氣的◄ someone who is smooth is polite, confident, and relaxed, but does not seem sincere 圓滑的, 八面玲瓏的, 迎合討好的: *I never trust these smooth salesmen.* 我從不相信這些油腔滑調的推銷員。

8 ►COMFORTABLE 舒適的◄ a journey that is smooth is comfortable because the plane does not shake, or the sea is not rough〔旅途等〕平穩的, 平靜的, 無顛簸的, 順暢的: *We had a smooth crossing on the boat.* 我們坐船平穩地渡了過去。| *a smooth flight* 平穩的飛行 —opposite 反義詞 BUMPY —see also 另見 SMOOTHLY, SMOOTH-TALKING —**smoothness** *n* [U]

smooth[2] *v* [T] **1** also 又作 **smooth out** to make something such as paper or cloth flat by moving your hands across it〔用手〕弄平, 撫平, 使平滑: *They smoothed out the map on the table and planned their route.* 他們把地圖在桌上鋪平, 定出要走的路線。**2** also 又作 **smooth down** to make something that is raised flat by moving your hands across it〔用手把凸起的東西〕抹平, 捋平: *Angela smoothed her hair down neatly.* 安琪拉把頭髮捋得平順整齊。**3** also 又作 **smooth down** to take away the roughness from the surface of wood, clay etc〔把粗糙表面等〕磨光, 擦平: *You have to smooth it before you varnish it.* 在上清漆前先要把它打磨光滑。**4** [always+adv/prep] to rub a liquid, cream, etc gently over a surface or into a surface 輕輕地塗擦〔液體、面霜等〕: **smooth sth into/over** *She smoothed suntan lotion over her legs.* 她輕輕地給雙腿抹上防曬霜。**5 smooth the way** to make it easier for something to happen, by dealing with any problems first〔為…〕鋪平道路: *an agreement smoothing the way to an eventual merger* 為最終合併鋪平道路的協議

smooth sth ↔ **away** *phr v* [T] to get rid of problems or difficulties easily〔順利地〕擺脱〔困境〕, 排除〔困難〕: *A few objections have to be smoothed away before we can start the project.* 我們在開展這個項目之前, 先得排除幾種反對意見。

smooth sth ↔ **over** *phr v* [T] to make problems or difficulties seem less important 緩和〔困難等〕, 減輕; 紓解: *Sally managed to smooth over the bad feelings between them.* 莎莉設法緩和了他們之間的對立情緒。

smooth·ie, smoothy /ˈsmuðɪ; ˈsmuːði/ *n* [C] *informal* someone who is good at persuading people, but does not seem to be sincere【非正式】圓滑的人: *Yuk! What a smoothie!* 呸! 多圓滑的傢伙!

smooth·ly /ˈsmuðlɪ; ˈsmuːðli/ *adv* **1** in a smooth way 平穩地, 順暢地, 順利地 **2 go smoothly** if a planned event, piece of work etc goes smoothly, there are no problems to spoil it 順利進行: *It'll take about three hours, if everything goes smoothly.* 如果一切順利的話, 大約需要三小時。

smooth talk·ing /ˈ· ˌ··/ *adj* a smooth-talking person is good at persuading people and saying nice things but you do not trust them 油嘴滑舌的, 花言巧語的: *a smooth-talking salesman* 花言巧語的推銷員

smor·gas·bord /ˈsmɔrgəsˌbɔrd; ˈsmɔːgəsbɔːd/ *n* [C,U] a meal in which people serve themselves from a large number of different dishes〔有大量的各式精美食物的〕自助餐

smote /smot; sməʊt/ the past tense of SMITE

smoth·er /ˈsmʌðɚ; ˈsmʌðə/ *v* **1** [T always+adv/prep] **smother sth with/in** to cover the whole surface of something with something else 完全覆蓋; 籠罩: **smother sth with/in** *a delicious sponge cake smothered in chocolate* 裹着一層巧克力的美味鬆蛋糕 | *He smothered her with kisses.* 他吻得她透不過氣來。**2 smother your anger/irritation** to hide your feelings 抑制憤怒/忍住怒氣: *struggling to smother her jealousy* 拚命想掩蓋她的妒忌心 **3 smother sb with love/kindness etc** to express your feelings for someone too strongly, so that your relationship with them cannot develop normally 愛得/體貼得過分使人受不了 **4** [T] to kill someone by putting something over their face to stop them breathing 使〔某人〕窒息, 把〔某人〕悶死: *One night she took a pillow and smothered him.* 一天夜裡, 她用枕頭把他悶死。**5** [T] to make a fire stop burning by preventing air from reaching it 把〔火〕悶熄 **6** [T] to get rid of anyone who opposes you 清除, 壓制〔對手〕: *They ruthlessly smother all opposition.* 他們無情地壓制一切反對的聲音。

smoul·der *BrE*【英】, **smolder** *AmE*【美】/ˈsmoldɚ; ˈsməʊldə/ *v* [I] **1** if something such as wood smoulders, it burns slowly without a flame 無火焰地慢慢燒, 悶燃: *a smouldering log* 一塊悶燒着的木頭 **2** if someone smoulders or if their feelings smoulder, they have strong feelings that they do not express〔強烈的情緒〕悶在心裡, 鬱積: *He sensed a smouldering hostility towards him.* 他覺察到別人壓抑着對他的敵對情緒。| **smoulder with passion/anger** *The workforce were smouldering with discontent.* 勞工們壓抑着不滿的情緒。

smudge[1] /smʌdʒ; smʌdʒ/ *n* [C] a dirty mark 污跡, 污斑, 污痕: *There's a smudge of grease on your chin.* 你下巴上沾了一點油。—**smudgy** *adj*

smudge 弄髒

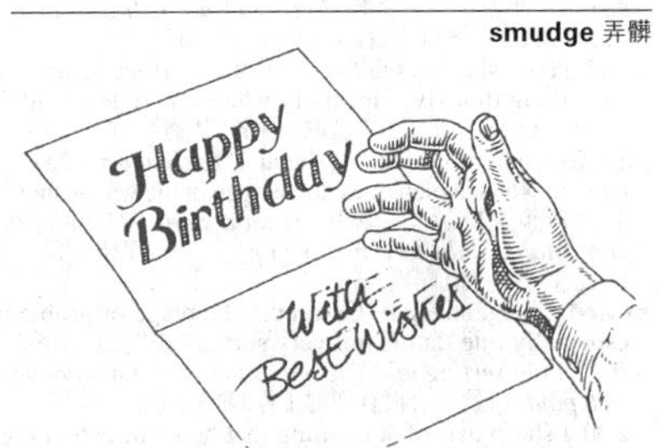

smudge[2] *v* **1** [T] to make writing, painting etc become unclear by touching or rubbing it 把〔字、畫等〕弄髒, 使

S

變髒: *Don't touch it! You'll smudge the ink.* 別碰它！你會把墨抹花的。**2** [I] if ink, writing etc smudges, its edges become unclear because it has been touched or rubbed〔墨跡、字跡等〕被抹髒, 被碰髒; 被擦模糊 **3** [T] to make a dirty mark on a surface 在…上留下污跡: *Someone had smudged the paper with their greasy hands.* 有人用油膩的手把這張紙弄髒了。

smug /smʌg; smʌg/ *adj* **smugger, smuggest** showing too much satisfaction with your own cleverness or success 自滿的, 自鳴得意的, 沾沾自喜的: *"I knew I'd win," she said with a smug smile.* "我早知道我會贏的。" 她自鳴得意地笑着說。| *What are you looking so smug about?* 你為甚麼這樣洋洋得意? —**smugly** *adv*: *Simon sat back smugly as Gould left the room.* 古爾德離開房間時, 西蒙得意地坐了回去。—**smugness** *n* [U]: *his unbearable smugness* 他那令人難以容忍的得意神氣

smug·gle /ˈsmʌgḷ; ˈsmʌgəl/ *v* [T] **1** to take something or someone illegally from one country to another 走私, 偷運: **smuggle sth into/out of** *They caught her trying to smuggle drugs into France.* 他們發現她企圖把毒品偷運進法國。| **smuggle sth through customs** (=to illegally take something past the officials who check what is being brought into the country) 走私某物混過海關 **2** *informal* to take something or someone secretly to a place where they are not allowed to be【非正式】偷偷攜帶, 夾帶: *He managed to smuggle his notes into the examination.* 他設法把筆記偷偷帶進了考場。

smug·gler /ˈsmʌglɚ; ˈsmʌglə/ *n* [C] someone who takes something illegally from one country to another 走私者: *a drug smuggler* 毒品走私者

smug·gling /ˈsmʌglɪŋ; ˈsmʌgəlɪŋ/ *n* [U] the crime of taking things illegally from one country to another 走私: *a diamond-smuggling operation* 鑽石走私活動

smut /smʌt; smʌt/ *n* **1** [U] books, stories, talk etc that offend some people slightly because they are about sex 淫穢圖書[故事], 淫詞穢語: *I won't have smut like that in my house!* 我不准家裡有那種淫穢東西! **2** [C,U] dirt or SOOT (=black powder produced by burning), or a piece of this (一小塊) 污垢, 煤煙 (灰)

smut·ty /ˈsmʌtɪ; ˈsmʌti/ *adj* **smuttier, smuttiest 1** books, stories etc that are smutty offend some people slightly because they are about sex〔圖書、作品等〕淫穢的, 黃色的: *smutty jokes* 黃色笑話 **2** marked with small pieces of dirt or SOOT 煤灰弄黑的, 弄髒的 —**smuttiness** *n* [U] —**smuttily** *adv*

snack /snæk; snæk/ *n* **1** [C] a small amount of food that is eaten between main meals or instead of a meal〔正餐以外的〕小吃, 點心: *I only had time to grab a quick snack.* 我只能匆匆地抓點零食吃。| **snack food** (=food, such as PEANUTS or POPCORN that is intended to be eaten as a snack) 小食, 零食〈如花生、爆玉米花等〉**2 snacks** [plural] small things to eat that are provided at a party, meeting etc〔開會、開晚會時的〕點心, 小食品

snack bar /ˈ· ·/ *n* [C] a place where you can buy snacks 點心店, 小吃店, 快餐部: *Let's get a chilli dog at the snack bar.* 我們到快餐部買個辣味熱狗吧。

snaf·fle /ˈsnæfl; ˈsnæfəl/ *v* [T] *BrE informal* to take something quickly, especially when it is rude or unfair to do this【英, 非正式】扒取, 偷竊〔某物〕

sna·fu /snæˋfu; snæˈfuː/ *n* [singular] *AmE informal* a situation in which a plan does not happen in the way it should【美, 非正式】混亂, 一團糟: *What a snafu! Three of the contestants didn't even show up!* 真是一團糟! 有三名參賽者竟然沒有露面!

snag¹ /snæg; snæg/ *n* [C] **1** a disadvantage or problem, especially one that is not very serious 小問題, 小障礙: *It's an interesting job. The only snag is that it's not very well paid.* 這是一份很有趣的工作, 唯一缺憾是工資不高。**2 a)** a sharp part of something that holds or cuts things that touch it〔會鉤住或鉤破東西的〕尖銳突出物 **b)** a tear in something made by getting it stuck on a snag〔衣物等的〕被鉤破處, 被刮破的裂口

snag² *v* **snagged, snagging** [T] **1** to damage something such as a piece of clothing by getting it stuck on something 鉤住; 撕破: *Oh damn! I've snagged my stockings.* 噢, 該死! 我把長筒襪鉤破了。**2** *AmE informal* to try to get someone to notice you, especially when you want help【美, 非正式】〔尤指在需要幫助時〕引起〔某人的〕注意; 抓住: *I'll try to snag the waiter next time he comes by.* 下次服務員走過時我會叫住他的。

snail /snel; sneɪl/ *n* [C] **1** a small soft creature that moves very slowly and has a hard shell on its back 蝸牛 **2 at a snail's pace** extremely slowly 極慢地, 慢吞吞地

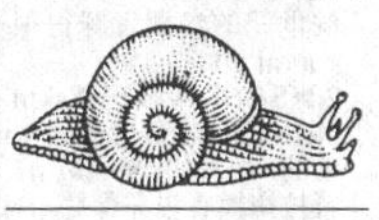
snail 蝸牛

snail mail /ˈ· ·/ *n* [U] *humorous* an expression meaning letters that are sent by post, used especially by people who send computer messages【幽默】蝸牛郵件, 普通郵件〔尤為使用電子郵件者用語〕

snake¹ /snek; sneɪk/ *n* [C] **1** an animal with a long thin body and no legs, that often has a poisonous bite 蛇 **2** an insulting word meaning someone who cannot be trusted 奸險的人, 狡猾的人 **3 snake in the grass** *informal* someone who pretends to be your friend but does something to harm you【非正式】偽裝成朋友的陰險小人 3

snake² *v* [I always+adv/prep] if a river, road, train, or line snakes somewhere, it moves in long, twisting curves 彎彎曲曲地移動, 蜿蜒前進: **[+along/past/down etc]** *The road snaked along the valley far below.* 大路沿着谷底彎彎曲曲伸向遠方。| **snake its way through/into etc** *The train was snaking its way through the mountains.* 火車在山區蜿蜒地向前行駛。

snake·bite /ˈsnekˌbaɪt; ˈsneɪkbaɪt/ *n* **1** [C,U] the bite of a poisonous snake 毒蛇咬傷 **2** [C] *BrE* an alcoholic drink that is half LAGER and half CIDER【英】淡啤酒和蘋果酒各半的混合酒

snake charm·er /ˈ· ˌ··/ *n* [C] someone who entertains people by controlling snakes by playing music to them〔用音樂聲使蛇起舞的〕玩蛇者, 弄蛇人

snakes and lad·ders /ˌ· · ˈ··/ *n* [U] *BrE* a children's game played on a board in which you can move forwards and upwards along pictures of LADDERS or go downwards and backwards along pictures of snakes【英】蛇梯棋〔一種兒童棋類遊戲, 棋子沿梯形圖前進, 沿蛇形圖後退〕; CHUTES AND LADDERS *AmE*【美】

snake·skin /ˈsnekˌskɪn; ˈsneɪkˌskɪn/ *n* [U] the skin of a snake used to make shoes, bags etc 蛇皮 (革): *snakeskin shoes* 蛇皮鞋

snak·y /ˈsnekɪ; ˈsneɪki/ *adj* moving or lying in twisting curves 像蛇一樣彎曲的, 彎曲地移動的: *a snaky road* 蜿蜒曲折的道路

snap¹ /snæp; snæp/ *v* 3

1 ►BREAK 折斷◄ [I,T] if something snaps, or if you snap it, it breaks with a sudden sharp noise (使) 啪的一聲折斷, 斷開: *Pablo felt the second blow on his collar bone and heard it snap.* 帕伯羅覺得鎖骨受到第二次擊打, 並聽到它啪的一聲斷了。| *The impact must have snapped the cable.* 這次衝擊一定把纜繩弄斷了。| **snap sth off** *Patricia snapped a twig off.* 帕特里夏啪地折下一根小樹枝。| **snap sth in two/in half etc** (=break it into two pieces) 折成兩半 *The teacher snapped the chalk in two and gave me a piece.* 老師把粉筆折成兩段, 給了我一段。

2 ►MOVE (STH) SUDDENLY 突然移動◄ [I always+adv/prep, T always+adv/prep] to move into a particular position suddenly, making a short sharp noise, or to make something move like this (使) 突然啪地移動〔至某位置〕: **snap together/back etc** *The pieces just snap together like this.* 這兩個部件就像這樣啪的一聲合在一起。| *The sails would be flat one minute, then snap and billow out with the wind the next.* 風帆一會兒是平的, 一會兒又啪地迎風揚起。| **snap open/shut** *She snapped*

her briefcase shut. 她啪的一聲合上了公文包。
3 ▶SAY STH ANGRILY 怒氣沖沖地說◀ [I,T] to say something quickly in an angry or annoyed way 急速地說; 厲聲說: *He laughed. "What's so funny?" I snapped.* 他哈哈大笑。"有甚麼好笑的?"我厲聲說。| **[+at]** *He was jumpy and aggressive, and snapped at Walter for no reason.* 他神經過敏又咄咄逼人, 無緣無故喝斥沃爾特。| **snap sb's head off** *BrE* (=say something in a very angry way)【英】呵叱某人, 怒氣沖沖地頂撞某人 *I told her I was going to be late and she nearly snapped my head off!* 我告訴她我會遲到一會兒, 她便火冒三丈地呵叱我!
4 ▶ANIMAL 動物◀ [I] if an animal such as a dog snaps, it tries to bite you〔狗等〕咬, 噬: **[+at]** *Boxer was snapping at his ankles.* 拳師狗正要咬他的腳踝。
5 ▶PHOTOGRAPH 攝影◀ [T] to take a photograph 給…拍快照, 拍攝〔照片〕: *wandering around Paris, snapping all the landmarks* 在巴黎到處逛, 拍攝所有的名勝古跡
6 snap your fingers to make a short, sharp noise by moving one of your fingers quickly against your thumb, for example in order to get someone's attention 打響指
7 ▶BECOME ANGRY/ANXIOUS ETC 變得生氣/焦慮等◀ [I] to suddenly stop being able to control your anger, anxiety, or other feelings in a difficult situation〔精神等〕崩潰: *I was handling the stress OK but then suddenly I just snapped.* 正當我把壓力調節得不錯的時候, 突然間就垮了。
8 ▶MIND 神志◀ *old-fashioned* if your mind snaps, you become mentally ill【過時】患上精神病
9 snap to it also 又作 **snap it up** *AmE spoken* used to tell someone to hurry and do something immediately【美口】趕快, 快幹: *Come on, snap to it, get that room cleaned up!* 來吧, 趕快, 把那個房間打掃乾淨!
10 snap to attention if soldiers snap to attention, they suddenly stand very straight〔士兵們〕猛地立正 —see also 另見 SNAP-ON

snap sth ↔ **on/off** *phr v* [T] to turn a light on or off 開/關〔燈〕

snap out of sth *phr v* [T not in passive 不用被動態] **snap out of it** to stop being sad or upset and make yourself feel better 克服悲傷或煩亂情緒, 打起精神, 振作起來: *Chantal's been depressed for days. I wish she'd snap out of it.* 珊塔爾情緒低落已經好幾天了, 我希望她能振作起來。

snap sb/sth ↔ **up** *phr v* [T] **1** to buy something immediately, especially because it is very cheap 把…趕快弄到手, 搶購: *If you see one for under $100, you should snap it up.* 如果你看到一件東西售價在100美元以下, 你就應當馬上買下來。**2** to eagerly take an opportunity to have someone as part of your company, team etc 急於聘請〔某人〕: *They needed a good quarterback and would have snapped him up if they'd had a chance.* 他們需要一名優秀的四分衛, 一旦有機會, 就會把他搶到手。

snap² *n*
1 ▶SOUND 聲音◀ [singular] a sudden loud sound, especially made by something breaking or closing 突然折斷[閉上]的聲音, 啪的一聲: *I shut the book with a snap, and put it away.* 我啪地把書合上, 放到一旁 —see picture on page A19 參見A19頁圖
2 ▶PHOTOGRAPH 攝影◀ [C] *informal especially BrE* a photograph taken by someone who is not a professional photographer【非正式, 尤英】〔由非專業攝影師拍的〕快照, 快相: *holiday snaps* 假日留影
3 be a snap *AmE informal* to be very easy to do【美, 非正式】輕而易舉: *The test was a snap.* 這次測驗容易得很。
4 a snap of your fingers a sudden sound made by quickly moving one of your fingers against your thumb 打響指的噼啪聲
5 ▶GAME 遊戲◀ [U] a card game in which players put down one card after another and try to be the first to shout 'snap' when there are two cards that are the same 呼"同"牌戲〔玩牌者將手中的牌一張張地發到桌上, 搶先認出兩張相同者即呼"同"〕
6 ▶CLOTHES FASTENER 衣服扣子◀ [C] *AmE* a small metal fastener on clothes that works by pressing two parts together【美】〔金屬的〕揿扣, 摁扣, 子母扣 —see also 另見 BRANDY SNAP, COLD SNAP —see picture at 參見 FASTENER 圖

snap³ *adj* **snap judgment/decision** a judgment or decision made quickly and without enough thought or preparation 倉促的判斷/匆忙的決定: *I hate making snap decisions.* 我不喜歡匆忙作出決定。

snap⁴ *interjection* **1** *BrE spoken* used when you see two things that are exactly the same【英口】真巧啊! 一模一樣!〔發現兩件相同的物品時的驚嘆語〕: *Hey, snap! I've got a dress just like that!* 嘿, 真巧! 我有一件和那件一模一樣的連衣裙! **2** *spoken* said in the game of snap when two cards that are the same are put down【口】"同!"〔在呼"同"牌戲中發現兩張相同的牌一起擺出時的呼喊〕

snap·drag·on /ˈsnæpˌdræɡən; ˈsnæpˌdræɡən/ *n* [C] a garden plant with white, red, or yellow flowers 金魚草, 龍嘴花〔一種開白色、紅色或黃色花朵的庭園花卉〕

snap-on /ˈ· ·/ *adj* [only before noun 僅用於名詞前] a snap-on part of a toy or tool can be fastened on and removed easily〔玩具或工具部件〕容易拆下[裝上]的, 可吧嗒一聲合上的

snap·per /ˈsnæpɚ; ˈsnæpə/ *n* [C] a type of fish that lives in warm seas, often used as food 嘯魚〔產於熱帶海域的食用魚〕

snap·pish /ˈsnæpɪʃ; ˈsnæpɪʃ/ *adj* bad-tempered 急躁的, 脾氣暴躁的: *Children are often spiteful and snappish.* 小孩子常常故意刁難人而且急躁。—**snappishly** *adv* —**snappishness** *n* [U]

snap·py /ˈsnæpɪ; ˈsnæpi/ *adj* **1** quick to react in an angry way 反應快的, 易怒的 **2** a snappy title or phrase is easy to remember〔標題、詞語等〕短小精悍的, 易記的 **3 make it snappy** also 又作 **look snappy** *informal* used to tell someone to hurry【非正式】快點! 趕快!: *Get me a drink and make it snappy.* 給我一杯飲料, 快一點。**4** *BrE informal* snappy clothes are attractive and fashionable【英, 非正式】〔衣服〕漂亮的, 時髦的: *a snappy suit* 一套時髦的西服 | **a snappy dresser** (=someone who wears fashionable clothes) 穿着入時的人 —**snappily** *adv* —**snappiness** *n* [U]

snap·shot /ˈsnæpˌʃɑt; ˈsnæpʃɒt/ *n* [C] **1** an informal photograph 快照, 快相: *holiday snapshots* 假日快照 **2** a piece of information that quickly gives you an idea of what the situation is like at a particular time 簡訊, 簡況: *The US balance sheet provides a snapshot of what Americans own and owe.* 這份美國資產負債表提供了美國人擁有的財富和負債的概況。

snare¹ /snɛr; sneə/ *n* [C] **1** a trap for catching an animal, especially one that uses a wire or rope to catch the animal by its foot 羅網, 套索, 陷阱〔尤指用繩索絆住獸類足部的捕獸器〕**2** *literary* something that is intended to trick someone and get them into a difficult situation【文】〔誘人上當的〕圈套, 騙局, 陷阱

snare² *v* [T] **1** to catch an animal by using a snare〔用陷阱等〕捕捉, 誘捕〔獸類〕**2** to deceive someone so that they cannot escape from a difficult situation 誘使〔某人〕上當, 設計陷害〔某人〕

snare drum /ˈ· ·/ *n* [C] a small flat drum that makes a hard continuous sound when you hit it〔扁形〕小鼓

snarl /snɑrl; snɑːl/ *v* **1** [I] if an animal snarls it makes a low angry sound and shows its teeth〔動物張牙露齒低聲地〕咆哮, 吼: **[+at]** *The alsatian snarls at strangers.* 這隻德國種狼狗對陌生人總是呲牙咧嘴地低聲咆哮。**2** [I,T] to speak or say something in a nasty angry way 咆哮着說, 怒吼: *"Shut up," he snarled.* "住口。"他怒吼道。**3** also 又作 **snarl up** [T usually passive 一般用被動態] to prevent traffic from moving 使〔交通〕堵塞: *The traffic was snarled up on both sides of the road.* 馬路兩邊

的交通都被堵塞了。—**snarl** *n* [C]

snarl-up /ˈ· ·/ *n* [C] **1** a confused situation that prevents work from continuing 混亂, 糾纏 **2** a situation in which traffic is prevented from moving 交通堵塞: *There was a big snarl-up on the M1.* 在一號高速公路上交通嚴重堵塞。

snatch¹ /snætʃ; snætʃ/ *v* [T] **1** to take something away from someone with a quick violent movement; GRAB¹ (1) 搶, 強奪, 攫取: *The thief snatched her purse and ran.* 小偷搶過她的錢包後拔腿便跑。**2** to quickly take the opportunity to do something for an hour etc because you do not have much time 抓住〔機會〕, 抓緊〔時間〕: *I managed to snatch an hour's sleep on the train.* 我在火車上抓緊時間睡了一小時。**3** to take someone or something away from a place by force 抓走, 搶去, 奪走: *Vargas was snatched from his home by two armed men.* 瓦格斯被兩名持槍男子從家中抓走。

snatch at sth *phr v* [T] to quickly put out your hand to try to take or hold something 伸手試圖抓住[攫取]: *Jessie snatched at the bag but I pulled it away.* 傑西伸手想抓袋子, 但我把它拉了過來。

snatch² *n* [C] **1 a snatch of conversation/music/song etc** a short and incomplete part of a conversation, song etc that you hear 談話/音樂/歌曲等的片段 **2 in snatches** for short periods 斷斷續續地: *I only slept in snatches during the night.* 我夜裡睡覺不時會醒。**3** [+with] a quick movement with your hand in order to take or hold something or someone 抓, 搶, 奪

snatch squad /ˈ· ˌ·/ *n* [C] a group of policemen who go quickly into a crowd to ARREST¹ (1) people〔在人羣中抓人的〕特別搜捕隊

snaz·zy /ˈsnæzɪ; ˈsnæzi/ *adj informal* clothes that are snazzy are bright, fashionable, and attractive【非正式】〔衣服〕華麗的, 時髦的, 鮮豔奪目的: *a snazzy red jacket* 鮮豔的紅外套 —**snazzily** *adv*

sneak¹ /snik; sniːk/ *v past tense and past participle* **sneaked** /snikt; sniːkt/ **snuck** /snʌk; snʌk/ *AmE*【美】**1** [I always+adv/prep] to go somewhere secretly and quietly in order to avoid being seen or heard 鬼鬼祟祟地行動, 偷偷地走, 潛行: **[+in/past/around etc]** *They managed to sneak past the guard on the gate.* 他們總算躡手躡腳躲着門衛溜了過去。**2** [T always+adv/prep] to hide something and take it somewhere secretly 偷偷攜帶: **sneak sth through/by/past etc** *I'm going to try and sneak these bottles of wine through Customs.* 我準備偷偷帶這幾瓶酒過海關。**3 sneak a look/glance at** to look at something quickly and secretly, especially something that you are not supposed to see 偷看一眼〔尤指不該看的東西〕 **4** [T] *informal* to quickly and secretly steal something unimportant or of little value【非正式】偷竊〔不貴重的小東西〕: **sneak sth from** *We used to sneak cigarettes from Dad to smoke in the garden.* 我們過去常常偷爸爸的香煙到花園裡抽。

sneak on sb *phr v* [T] *informal* to tell someone such as a parent or teacher about something that another person has done wrong, because you want to cause trouble for that person【非正式】〔向老師或同學的家長〕告密, 打小報告: *Adrian's not popular because he's always sneaking on other kids.* 大家都不喜歡艾德里安, 因為他總是給其他孩子打小報告。

sneak up *phr v* [I] to come near someone very quietly, so that they do not see you until you reach them 偷偷地走近, 躡手躡腳地靠近: **[+on/behind etc]** *Don't sneak up on me like that! You gave me quite a shock.* 不要那樣悄悄地走近我! 你嚇了我一跳。—see also 另見 **sneak preview** (PREVIEW (1))

sneak² *n* [C] *BrE informal* a child who is disliked because they tell adults about bad things that other children have done wrong【英, 非正式】向大人告密的孩子

sneak·er /ˈsnikɚ; ˈsniːkə/ *n* [C] *especially AmE* a type of light soft shoe with a rubber SOLE (=bottom) used for sports【尤美】膠底運動鞋 —see picture at 參見 SHOE¹ 圖

sneak·ing /ˈsnikɪŋ; ˈsniːkɪŋ/ *adj* **1 have a sneaking admiration/affection etc for** to have a secret feeling of admiration etc for someone 暗地欽佩/愛慕等 **2 have a sneaking suspicion/feeling (that)** to have a slight feeling that someone has done something wrong without being sure 暗自有點懷疑/隱隱覺得: *I have a sneaking suspicion he throws away my letters without even reading them.* 我心裡有一種感覺, 我的信他連看也不看就扔掉了。

sneak·y /ˈsnikɪ; ˈsniːki/ *adj* doing things in a secret and dishonest or unfair way 偷偷摸摸的, 鬼鬼祟祟的: *That was really sneaky, hiding his wallet!* 那樣太不老實了, 竟然把他的錢包藏了起來! —**sneakily** *adv*

sneer¹ /snɪr; snɪə/ *v* [I,T] to smile or speak in a very unkind way that shows you have no respect for someone or something 冷笑; 譏笑, 嘲笑: **[+at]** *Bob always sneers at my taste in clothes.* 鮑勃總是嘲笑我的衣着品味。—**sneering** *adj*: *a sneering letter* 冷言冷語的信 —**sneeringly** *adv*

sneer² *n* [C] an unkind smile or remark that shows you have no respect for something or someone 冷笑; 譏笑, 嘲笑; 鄙視

sneeze¹ /sniz; sniːz/ *v* [I] **1** to have sudden uncontrolled burst of air out of your nose, for example when you have a cold 打噴嚏: *The baby keeps sneezing – she must be getting a cold.* 寶寶不停地打噴嚏 —— 她一定是着涼了。
2 not to be sneezed at *spoken* good enough to be considered carefully【口】不可輕視, 值得認真考慮: *An offer of £900 is not to be sneezed at.* 900英鎊的出價可是值得認真考慮的。

sneeze² *n* [C] an act or sound of sneezing 噴嚏(聲)

snick /snɪk; snɪk/ *v* [T] *BrE* to make a small cut or mark on something; NICK² (1)【英】刻細痕於, 留刻痕於 —**snick** *n* [C]

snick·er /ˈsnɪkɚ; ˈsnɪkə/ *v* [I] *AmE* to laugh quietly, and often unkindly, at something which is not supposed to be funny【美】暗笑, 竊笑; SNIGGER *BrE*【英】—**snicker** *n* [C]

snide /snaɪd; snaɪd/ *adj informal* making unkind criticisms, often in a clever, indirect way【非正式】挖苦的, 諷刺的: **snide remarks/comments** *She's always making snide remarks about Marco's pronunciation.* 她老是針對馬可的發音說些挖苦的話。—**snidely** *adv*

sniff¹ /snɪf; snɪf/ *v*

1 ▶**BREATHE NOISILY** 有聲地吸氣◀ [I] to breathe air into your nose noisily, especially in short breaths〔短促有聲地〕以鼻吸氣: *Stop sniffing – why can't you blow your nose?* 別再哧哧地抽鼻子了 —— 你為甚麼不能擤擤鼻涕?

2 ▶**SMELL** 聞◀ [I,T] to breathe air in through your nose in order to smell something〔出聲地〕聞, 嗅: *He opened the milk and sniffed it.* 他打開牛奶罐聞了一聞。| **[+at]** *The dog was sniffing at the dead bird.* 狗在嗅着那隻死鳥。

3 [T] to say something in a proud complaining way 嗤之以鼻地說, 輕蔑地說: *"I expected something much better," she sniffed.* "我還以為是甚麼好東西呢。" 她不屑地說。

4 not to be sniffed at *spoken* good enough to be considered carefully【口】不可嗤之以鼻, 值得認真考慮: *An 8% salary increase is not to be sniffed at.* 對8%的工資增長不該嗤之以鼻了。

5 [T] to take a harmful drug through your nose 用鼻子吸入〔有害藥物〕: *sniffing cocaine* 吸可卡因 —see also 另見 GLUE SNIFFING

sniff out sth *phr v* [T] **1** to discover or find something by its smell 靠嗅覺發現, 嗅出: *They've got dogs at the customs for sniffing out drugs.* 海關人員用狗嗅查毒品。**2** *informal* to find out something【非正式】找出, 發現, 察覺: *Vic's been asking questions, trying to sniff out where you went last night.* 維克一直在問這問那, 想探出昨晚你去了甚麼地方。

sniff² *n* [C] an act or sound of sniffing 以鼻吸氣(聲)

sniffer dog /'‥ ·/ *n* [C] a dog that has been trained to find drugs or explosives by using its sense of smell〔用於探查毒品和炸藥的〕嗅探犬, 嗅探警犬

snif·fle¹ /ˈsnɪfl; ˈsnɪfəl/ *v* [I] to sniff repeatedly to stop liquid from running out of your nose, especially when you are crying or you have a cold 反覆抽鼻子〔尤指在哭或感冒時為了不讓鼻涕流出〕: *For goodness sake, stop sniffling!* 看在老天爺面上, 別再抽鼻子了!

sniffle² *n* an act or sound of sniffling 抽鼻子; 抽鼻子聲: **have the sniffles** (=keep sniffing) 不停地抽鼻子

sniff·y /ˈsnɪfɪ; ˈsnɪfi/ *adj BrE informal* having a disapproving attitude towards something or someone especially because you think they are not good enough for you【英, 非正式】瞧不起人的, 傲慢的: *Don't get sniffy, he's a friend of mine!* 別瞧不起人, 他可是我的朋友啊!

snif·ter /ˈsnɪftɚ; ˈsnɪftə/ *n* [C] **1** *AmE* a special glass for drinking BRANDY【美】〔喝白蘭地用的〕小口短腳酒杯 —see picture at 參見 GLASS¹ 圖 **2** *BrE old-fashioned* a small amount of an alcoholic drink【英, 過時】少量的酒, 一口酒

snig·ger /ˈsnɪgɚ; ˈsnɪgə/ *v* [I] *BrE* to laugh quietly, and often unkindly, at something which is not supposed to be funny【英】暗笑, 竊笑; SNICKER *AmE*【美】: [+at] *What are you sniggering at? This is a serious poem.* 你偷笑甚麼? 這是一首嚴肅的詩。—**snigger** *n* [C]

snip¹ /snɪp; snɪp/ *n* [C] **1** a quick small cut with scissors〔剪刀的〕一剪, 剪口 **2 be a snip** *BrE informal* to be surprisingly cheap【英, 非正式】極其廉價的: *At £20 for a dozen, they're a snip.* 20英鎊一打, 真便宜。—see 見 CHEAP (USAGE)

snip² *v* [I,T] to cut something by making quick cuts with scissors 用剪刀迅速地剪: *I hurriedly snipped the string and untied the parcel.* 我匆忙地把繩子剪斷, 將包裹解開。| **snip sth off** (=remove it by snipping) 剪掉某物 *Snip the ends of the beans off before you cook them.* 先把菜豆兩頭剪掉然後才煮。—see picture on page A11 參見 A11 頁圖

snipe¹ /snaɪp; snaɪp/ *v* [I] **1** to shoot from a hidden position at unprotected people 伏擊, 狙擊, 打冷槍 **2** to criticize someone in a nasty way 誹謗, 中傷: [+at] *I wish you two would stop sniping at each other.* 我希望你們兩個別再互相誹謗。—**sniping** *n* [U]

snipe² *n* [C] **1** a bird with a very long thin beak that lives in wet areas, and is often shot for sport 沙錐〔嘴細長、居於濕地的一種鳥〕**2** *AmE* someone who is strongly disliked【美】極討厭的人

snip·er /ˈsnaɪpɚ; ˈsnaɪpə/ *n* [C] someone who shoots at unprotected people from a hidden position 狙擊手: *Edwards was shot and killed by snipers.* 愛德華茲被幾名狙擊手槍殺。

snip·pet /ˈsnɪpɪt; ˈsnɪpɨt/ *n* [C] **snippet of information/news etc** a small piece of information etc 簡短的消息/新聞等: *We'd welcome any odd snippets of information you might pick up.* 你能打聽到的任何零星消息我們都要。

snip·py /ˈsnɪpɪ; ˈsnɪpi/ *adj AmE informal* quick to show that you are angry or offended, or that you will not obey someone【美, 非正式】脾氣急躁的; 目中無人的

snit /snɪt; snɪt/ *n* **be in a snit** *AmE informal* to be unreasonably annoyed about something【美, 非正式】不合理地生氣: *Martha's in a snit because I used her omelet pan.* 瑪莎因我用過她的炒蛋鍋而生氣。

snitch¹ /snɪtʃ; snɪtʃ/ *v informal*【非正式】**1** [I+on] to tell someone such as a parent or teacher about something that another person has done wrong because you want to cause trouble for that person〔向家長或老師〕告密, 告發 **2** [T] to quickly steal something unimportant or of little value 偷, 扒竊〔不太值錢的東西〕

snitch² *n* [C] **1** *informal* someone who is disliked because he or she tells a parent or teacher about something wrong that another person has done【非正式】〔向家長或老師告密的〕告密者 **2** *BrE humorous* a nose【英, 幽默】鼻子

sniv·el /ˈsnɪvl; ˈsnɪvəl/ *v* **snivelled, snivelling** *BrE*【英】, **sniveled, sniveling** *AmE*【美】[I] to behave or speak in a weak complaining way, especially when you are crying 啜泣, 抽泣; 哭訴: *I warned you – so don't come snivelling back to me when it all goes wrong!* 我早已警告過你 —— 所以現在出問題, 你就不要哭哭啼啼回來找我! | *a snivelling coward* 哭哭啼啼的膽小鬼

snob /snɑb; snɒb/ *n* [C] **1** someone who thinks they are better than people from a lower social class and dislikes being with them or doing the things they do 勢利的人; 自命不凡者: *John wouldn't go to a football match, he's too much of a snob.* 約翰不會去看足球賽, 他這個人太自命高雅了。**2 intellectual snob** someone who thinks they are too intelligent to enjoy ordinary forms of entertainment 自以為學識超羣蔑視流行娛樂方式的人 **3 music/wine etc snob** someone who knows a lot about music, wine etc and thinks their opinions are better than other people's 自以為很懂音樂/很會品酒的人 **4 snob value/appeal** something that has snob value is liked by people who think they are better than other people〔商品〕在勢利者眼中的價值/對勢利者的吸引力: *A Rolls-Royce has snob appeal.* 勞斯萊斯汽車對愛慕虛榮者頗具吸引力。

snob·be·ry /ˈsnɑbərɪ; ˈsnɒbəri/ *n* [U] **1** the feelings and behaviour of snobs 勢利(行為), 諂上欺下 **2 inverted snobbery** a type of snobbery in which people of a low social class think they are better than people of a higher social class 反面勢利(行為)〔社會地位低的人認為自己比社會地位高的人優秀〕

snob·bish /ˈsnɑbɪʃ; ˈsnɒbɪʃ/ also 又作 **snob·by** /ˈsnɑbɪ; ˈsnɒbi/ *adj* having attitudes, behaviour etc that are typical of a snob 勢利眼的; 諂上欺下的 —**snobbishly** *adv* —**snobbishness** *n* [U]

snog /snɑg; snɒg/ *v* **snogged, snogging** [I,T] *BrE informal* if two young people snog, they kiss each other, especially for a long time【英, 非正式】〔長時間〕接吻 —**snog** *n* [C usually singular 一般用單數]

snook /snuk; snuːk/ *n* —see 見 **cock a snook** (COCK² (5))

snoo·ker¹ /ˈsnukɚ; ˈsnuːkə/ *n* [U] a game played on a special table covered in green cloth, in which two people hit coloured balls into holes at the sides and corners of the table with CUEs (=long sticks) 彩色桌球, 落袋枱球

snooker² *v* [T, often passive 常用被動態] *BrE informal* to make it impossible for someone to do what they want to do【英, 非正式】使陷於困境: *If the council refuses our planning application, we're snookered.* 如果政務委員會不批准我們的規劃申請, 我們就一籌莫展了。

snoop /snup; snuːp/ *v* [I] to try to find out about someone's private affairs by secretly looking in their house, examining their possessions etc 探聽, 窺探, 窺視: [+around/about] *I caught him snooping around in my office.* 我發現他在我辦公室裡到處窺探。—**snoop** *n* [singular] **snooper** *n* [C]

snoot /snut; snuːt/ *n* [C] *AmE informal* your nose【美, 非正式】鼻子

snoot·y /ˈsnutɪ; ˈsnuːti/ *adj informal* rude and unfriendly, because you think you are better than other people【非正式】傲慢的, 目中無人的, 妄自尊大的: *snooty neighbours* 傲慢的鄰居 —**snootily** *adv* —**snootiness** *n* [U]

snooze /snuz; snuːz/ *v* [I] *informal* to have a short, light sleep【非正式】小睡, 打盹: *Dad was snoozing in a deckchair.* 爸爸在躺椅上打盹。—**snooze** *n* [C]

snore¹ /snor; snɔː/ *v* [I] to breathe noisily through your mouth and nose while you are asleep 打鼾, 打呼嚕: *Bill's snoring is driving me nuts.* 比爾的呼嚕真把我氣壞了。

snore² *n* [C] the noise you make when you snore 打鼾聲

snor·kel¹ /ˈsnɔrkl; ˈsnɔːkəl/ *n* [C] **1** a tube that allows a swimmer to breathe air under water〔潛水者的〕呼吸管 **2** a piece of equipment that allows a SUBMARINE to take in air when it is under water〔潛水艇的〕通氣管

snorkel² *v* [I] to swim under water using a snorkel 使用呼吸管潛泳 —**snorkelling** *BrE*【英】, **snorkeling** *AmE*【美】—*n* [U]

snort¹ /snɔrt; snɔːt/ *v* **1** [I,T] to express anger, impatience, or amusement by breathing air noisily through your nose 發哼聲; 哼着鼻子〔表示生氣、不耐煩、被逗樂〕: *"Certainly not," he snorted.* "肯定不是。"他哼了一聲說。| [+with] *She snorted with contempt at the suggestion.* 她哼了一聲表示對這個建議的輕蔑。**2** [I] to make a loud noise by forcing air out through your nose 從鼻子呼氣作聲, 噴鼻息: *The horse snorted and stamped its hoof impatiently.* 這匹馬呼哧呼哧地噴着氣, 不耐煩地跺着蹄。**3** [T] *slang* to take drugs by breathing them in through your nose【俚】用鼻吸入〔毒品〕: *snorting cocaine* 用鼻吸可卡因

snort² *n* [C] **1** a loud sound made by breathing through your nose, especially to show anger, impatience, or amusement 哼聲, 噴鼻息聲: *a snort of laughter* 撲哧一笑 **2** a small amount of a drug that is breathed in through the nose〔用鼻吸入的〕少量毒品: *a snort of cocaine* 用鼻吸入的一點可卡因

snot /snɑt; snɒt/ *n informal*【非正式】**1** [U] an impolite word for the thick MUCUS (=liquid) produced in your nose 鼻涕〔非禮貌用詞〕**2** [C] someone who is SNOTTY (1) 高傲的人

snot-nosed /'· ·/ *adj AmE informal* an impolite word used to describe children who are not very clean【美, 非正式】〔小孩〕髒兮兮的〔非禮貌用詞〕: *that snot-nosed kid next door* 隔壁那個髒兮兮的孩子

S

snot·ty /'snɑtɪ; 'snɒti/ *adj informal*【非正式】**1** thinking that you are more important than other people 高傲的, 妄自尊大的: *I won't be told what to do by some snotty little clerk!* 我不許一個妄自尊大的小職員來告訴我該幹甚麼! **2** wet and dirty with MUCUS 被鼻涕弄得髒濕的

snotty-nosed /'·· ·/ *adj BrE informal* SNOTTY (2)【英, 非正式】被鼻涕弄得髒濕的

snout /snaut; snaʊt/ *n* [C] **1** the long nose of some kinds of animals, such as pigs〔豬等動物的〕口鼻部, 長鼻子 **2** *BrE informal* a criminal who gives information about other criminals to the police【英, 非正式】向警方告發其同夥的罪犯

snow¹ /sno; snəʊ/ *n* **1** [U] water frozen into soft white FLAKES (=pieces) that fall from the sky in cold weather and cover the ground 雪: *mountain peak covered with snow* 白雪覆蓋的山峯 | *roads blocked by deep snow* 為厚厚的積雪所阻塞的道路 | *melting snow* 在融化的積雪 —see picture on page A13 參見 A13 頁圖 **2** [C] a period of time in which snow falls 降雪; 降雪期, 下雪天: *one of the heaviest snows this winter* 今年冬天最大的降雪之一 **3** [U] *slang* COCAINE【俚】可卡因

snow² *v* **1** [I] **it snows** if it snows, snow falls from the sky 下雪: *It snowed all night.* 下了一整夜雪。| *Look! It's snowing!* 瞧! 下雪了! **2** [T] *AmE informal* to persuade someone to believe or support something, especially by lying to them【美, 非正式】〔尤指靠說謊〕說服〔某人〕, 贏得〔某人的〕信任[支持]: *I was completely snowed by his Southern charm.* 我完全被他那種南方人的魅力蒙騙了。**3 be snowed in/up** to be unable to travel from a place because so much snow has fallen there〔人〕被雪困住/〔地方〕被雪封住: *We were snowed in for three days last winter.* 去年冬天我們被大雪困了三天。**4 be snowed under (with sth)** to have more work than you can deal with 被…壓得透不過氣來, 〔工作多得〕忙不過來, 窮於應付

snow·ball¹ /'sno,bɔl; 'snəʊbɔːl/ *n* [C] **1** a ball of snow that children make and throw at each other 雪球: *a snowball fight* 打雪球仗 **2 not have a snowball's chance in hell** *informal* to have no chance at all【非正式】毫無機會, 機會渺茫

snowball² *v* [I] if a plan, problem, business etc snowballs it grows bigger at a faster and faster rate〔計劃、問題、生意等〕滾雪球似地迅速增大: *Once the contest became popular, it quickly snowballed into an all-day event with TV coverage.* 這種比賽一流行起來, 就迅速發展成為電視的全天播放節目。

snow·bird /'sno,bɝd; 'snəʊbɜːd/ *n* [C] *AmE informal* someone, especially an old person, who moves to a warmer place every winter【美, 非正式】每年遷往温暖地方過冬的人〔尤指老人〕

snow blind·ness /'· ,··/ *n* [U] eye pain and difficulty in seeing things, caused by looking at snow in bright sunlight 雪盲(症)〔由於雪地陽光反射刺激而引起的眼睛痛和暫時失明〕—**snow blind** *adj*

snow·blow·er /'· ,··/ *n* [C] *especially AmE* a machine which clears snow from roads by blowing it away【尤美】〔清除路面積雪的〕吹雪機

snow·board /'sno,bord; 'snəʊbɔːd/ *n* [C] a long wide board made of plastic, which people use to travel over snow for sport〔運動用的〕滑雪板 —**snowboarder** *n* [C] —**snowboarding** *n* [U] —see picture at 參見 SKI² 圖

snow·bound /'sno,baund; 'snəʊbaʊnd/ *adj* blocked or prevented from leaving a place by large amounts of snow 被雪困住[封閉]的: *snowbound traffic* 被雪封閉的交通

snow-capped /'· ·/ *adj literary* snow-capped mountains are covered in snow at the top【文】〔山的〕頂部被雪覆蓋的

snow chains /'· ·/ *n* [plural] a set of chains that are fixed around the wheels of a car so that it can drive over snow without slipping〔汽車輪胎上的〕防滑鏈

snow·drift /'sno,drɪft; 'snəʊ,drɪft/ *n* [C] a deep mass of snow piled up by the wind〔風吹成的〕雪堆

snow·drop /'sno,drɑp; 'snəʊdrɒp/ *n* [C] a European plant with a small white flower which appears in early spring〔歐洲產的〕雪花蓮

snow·fall /'sno,fɔl; 'snəʊfɔːl/ *n* [C,U] the amount of snow that falls, or the amount that falls in a particular period of time 降雪; 〔某一時期的〕降雪量: *an average snowfall of eight centimetres a year* 每年平均的八厘米降雪量 | *Heavy snowfalls are forecast.* 天氣預報說將有幾次大雪。

snow·field /'sno,fild; 'snəʊfiːld/ *n* [C] a wide area of land that is always covered in snow〔終年積雪的〕雪原, 雪野

snow·flake /'sno,flek; 'snəʊfleɪk/ *n* [C] a small soft flat piece of frozen water that falls as snow 雪片, 雪花

snow job /'· ·/ *n* [singular] *AmE informal* an act of persuading someone to believe or support something, especially by lying to them【美, 非正式】花言巧語的勸說

snow line /'sno,laɪn; 'snəʊlaɪn/ *n* **the snow line** the level above which snow on a mountain never melts 雪線〔高山上終年積雪的最低界線〕—see picture on page A12 參見 A12 頁圖

snow·man /'sno,mæn; 'snəʊmæn/ *n* [C] a figure of a person made of snow, made especially by children〔尤指兒童用雪堆成的〕雪人

snow·mo·bile /'snomo,bil; 'snəʊməbiːl/ *n* [C] a small vehicle with a motor that moves over snow or ice easily 雪地機動車, 摩托雪橇

snow pea /'· ·/ *n* [C] *AmE* a kind of PEA whose POD (=cover) and seeds you can eat【美】糖莢豌豆; MANGETOUT *BrE*【英】

snow plough *BrE*【英】, **snow plow** *AmE*【美】/'· ·/ *n* [C] a vehicle or piece of equipment for pushing snow off roads, railways etc 雪犁, 掃雪機

snow route /'· ·/ *n* [C] *AmE* an important road in a city that cars must be removed from when it snows, so that it can be cleared of snow【美】雪道〔在下雪天不准停放車輛以便掃雪的交通要道〕

snow·shoe /'sno,ʃu; 'snəʊʃuː/ *n* [C] one of a pair of wide flat frames which you attach to your shoes, so that you can walk on snow without sinking〔裝在鞋底, 用於在雪地上行走的〕雪鞋

snow·storm /'sno,stɔrm; 'snəʊstɔːm/ *n* [C] a storm with strong winds and a lot of snow 雪暴, 暴風雪

snow·suit /ˈsno͵sut; ˈsnəʊsuːt/ *n* [C] a warm piece of clothing that covers the whole of a child's body 兒童風雪服

snow tire /ˈ· ·/ *n* [C] *AmE* a special car tyre used when driving on snow or ice【美】〔用於雪地、冰上的〕防滑輪胎

snow-white /͵· ˈ·◂/ *adj* pure white 雪白的, 純白的

snow·y /ˈsnoɪ; ˈsnəʊi/ *adj* **1** full of snow or snowing 多雪的, 積雪的; 下雪的: *Today it will be snowy in many areas.* 今天許多地區將下雪。**2** *literary* pure white【文】雪白的, 純白的: *snowy hair* 雪白的頭髮 —**snowiness** *n* [U]

Snr the written abbreviation of 縮寫= SENIOR, used after someone's name 年紀較大的, 老〔用於名字之後〕: *James Taylor, Snr* 老詹姆斯·泰勒

snub¹ /snʌb; snʌb/ *v* **snubbed, snubbing** [T] to treat someone rudely, especially by intentionally ignoring them when you meet 冷落, 怠慢, 對…不予理睬: *Mayor Koch snubbed the Giants and refused to offer them a victory parade.* 科克市長對巨人隊不予理睬, 拒絕給他們舉行慶祝勝利的遊行。

snub² *n* [C] an act of snubbing someone 冷落, 怠慢, 不理睬: *Still smarting from the snub, he stalked from the room.* 他受冷落後傷心不已, 大步走出了房間。

snub³ *adj* a snub nose is short and flat and points slightly upwards〔鼻子〕短扁微上翹的

snub-nosed /͵· ˈ·◂/ *adj* having a snub nose that points slightly upwards 翹鼻子的, 獅子鼻的

snuck /snʌk; snʌk/ *AmE*【美】past tense and past participle of SNEAK

snuff¹ /snʌf; snʌf/ *v* **1** also 又作 **snuff out** [T] to put out a CANDLE flame by pressing the burning part with your fingers or covering it with a snuffer 掐滅, 熄滅〔蠟燭〕 **2** [I,T] if an animal snuffs, it breathes air into its nose noisily in order to smell something; SNIFF¹ (2)〔動物〕出聲地吸氣, 聞〔味〕 **3 snuff it** *BrE informal* to die【英, 非正式】斷氣, 死

snuff sth **out** *phr v* [T] to suddenly end something, especially someone's life〔突然地〕結束〔生命〕, 扼殺: *a young life snuffed out* 突然結束的年輕生命

snuff² *n* [U] a type of tobacco in powder form, which people suck in through their noses 鼻煙: *a pinch of snuff* 一撮鼻煙

snuff·er /ˈsnʌfɚ; ˈsnʌfə/ *n* [C] a tool with a small bell-shaped end on a handle for putting out CANDLEs 燭剪

snuf·fle /ˈsnʌfl; ˈsnʌfəl/ *v* [I] to breathe noisily through your nose making low sounds 呼哧呼哧地呼吸, 抽鼻子: *pigs snuffling round* 到處嗅來嗅去的豬

snug¹ /snʌg; snʌg/ *adj* **snugger, snuggest 1** a room or space that is snug is small, warm, and comfortable and makes you feel protected〔房間或空間〕小而溫暖舒適的, 安適的: *a snug little sitting-room with a log fire burning* 一間生着火、溫暖舒適的小客廳 **2** someone who is snug feels comfortable, happy, and warm〔人〕舒服的, 快樂的, 溫暖的: *The kids were soon tucked up snug in their beds.* 孩子們馬上鑽進被窩, 舒服地睡到牀上。**3** clothes that are snug fit closely〔衣服〕貼身的, 緊身的 —**snugly** *adv* —**snugness** *n* [U]

snug² *n* [C] *BrE* a small comfortable room in a PUB【英】〔酒館的〕舒適小房間

snug·gle /ˈsnʌgl̩; ˈsnʌgəl/ *v* [I always+adv/prep] *informal* to settle into a warm comfortable position【非正式】依偎, 〔舒服地〕蜷縮: [**+up/down/into etc**] *Let's snuggle up together and watch TV.* 我們靠在一起看電視吧。

S1 W1 **so¹** /so; səʊ/ *adv* **1 a) so big/tall etc** [+adj/adv] used to describe how big, tall etc something is, especially when it is very big or very tall 這麼大/高等〔用於形容大或高等的程度〕: *Why does life have to be so complicated?* 為甚麼生活非得這樣複雜不可? | *It was so embarrassing – everyone was standing there looking at us!* 多麼尷尬——人人都站在那兒望着我們! | *I've never seen so many people attend this church before.* 我以前從未見過有這麼多人來這個教堂做禮拜。| **so tall a man/so high a mountain etc** *formal*【正式】*I've never seen so beautiful a baby before.* 我以前從未見過這麼漂亮的小寶寶。**b) worry/talk etc so** *formal* to worry, talk etc a great deal【正式】非常擔心/說得很多: *I wish he wouldn't fuss so – it makes me feel nervous.* 我希望他不要那麼大驚小怪——這樣會使我感到精神緊張。**2 so tall/big etc (that)** used when you mean that because someone or something is very tall, big etc, something happens or someone does something 這麼高/大等(以致…): *He was so fat he couldn't get through the door.* 他胖得無法通過這門。| *You couldn't hear yourself think, the music was so loud.* 甚麼也聽不清——那音樂太響了。| **so tall etc as to be sth** *The statement was so ambiguous as to be totally meaningless.* 那句話這麼含糊不清, 根本不知所云。**3** used to talk about an idea, suggestion, situation etc that has been mentioned before 如此, 如是〔用於提及已經提到過的想法、建議、情況等〕: *"Will I need my umbrella?" "I don't think so."* "我需要帶雨傘嗎?" "我認為不需要。" | *He seemed to be very understanding, more so than I expected.* 他好像非常理解, 超過了我的期望。**4 so would John/so do I/so is he etc** used to add a positive statement to one that has just been mentioned 約翰也會這樣/我也這樣/他也這樣: *If you're going to take the day off then so will I.* 如果你想那天休息, 那麼我也一樣。| *Frank adores dogs and so does his wife.* 弗蘭克非常愛狗, 他妻子也一樣。**5 not so tall/big etc as...** not as tall, big etc as something else 沒有…那麼高/大等, 不像…那樣高/大等: *You know, Harry's not so clever as I first thought.* 你知道, 哈里不像我原先想的那麼聰明。—see also 另見 **as far as** (FAR¹ (3)), **as/so long as** (LONG² (6)) **6 so as to do sth** in order to do something 以便做某事: *Credit has been arranged so as to spread the payments over a 10 month period.* 貸款已經安排好, 在 10 個月內分期償還。| *So as not to cause offence many of the mourners stood at the back of the church.* 為了避免引起反感, 許多送葬者都站到教堂的後部。**7 so many/much a)** a particular amount, number, level, degree etc 這麼多, 那麼多〔指特定的數量、數目、程度等〕: *There's only so much you can do with hair this fine.* 頭髮這麼細, 只能做到這個程度了。**b)** used to say that something is the same as something else that is worse 等於, 簡直是〔用於指某物與另一物一樣糟〕: *Teenage magazines are just so much wasted paper.* 青少年雜誌完全就是浪費紙張。**8 (just) as...so...** used to compare two people or things, when they are the same 正如…, …也一樣〔用於比較兩個相同的人或東西〕: *Just as the French love their wine, so the English love their beer.* 正如法國人喜歡喝葡萄酒, 英國人則愛喝啤酒。**9** used when you are being polite to mean 'very' 很, 十分〔用於表示禮貌〕: *I'm so pleased to meet you at last.* 我非常高興終於見到你了。| **ever so** *BrE*【英】*The children are ever so excited. It's the first time they've been to Disneyland.* 孩子們非常興奮, 這是他們第一次來迪士尼樂園。**10** *formal* therefore【正式】因此: *The passport was found to have passed its expiry date and so to be void.* 護照已經過期, 因而無效。—see 見 THUS (USAGE) —see also 另見 **and so forth** (FORTH), **even so** (EVEN¹ (4)), **so far** (FAR¹ (24)), **so far as possible** (FAR¹ (25)), **so much for** (MUCH² (12)), **just so** (JUST¹ (29))

Frequencies of the word **so** in spoken and written English 單詞 so 在英語口語和書面語中的使用頻率

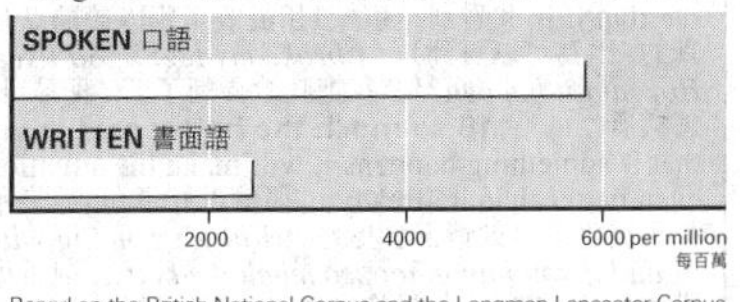

Based on the British National Corpus and the Longman Lancaster Corpus 據英國國家語料庫和朗文蘭卡斯特語料庫

S

This graph shows that the word **so** is much more common in spoken English than in written English. This is because it has special uses in spoken English and is used in some common spoken phrases. 本圖表顯示, 單詞so在英語口語中的使用頻率遠遠高於書面語, 因為它在英語口語中有特殊的用法, 而且口語中一些常用片語是由so構成的。

SO (*adv*) **SPOKEN USES AND PHRASES**
含so的口語用法和片語

11 so a) used to get someone's attention, especially in order to ask them a question 那麼〔尤在提問題前用於引起別人的注意〕: *So, how long do you think you'll be staying in England?* 那麼, 你將在英國逗留多久? **b)** used to check that you have understood something 這麼說〔用於核對自己已清楚某事〕: *So let me get this straight. You two aren't actually married then?* 這麼說, 讓我來弄清楚這一點吧。你們實際上並沒有結婚? **c)** used to show that you do not think something is important 那又怎麼樣〔用於表示某事並不重要〕: *So, I lied. They can't put me in prison for that!* 我撒了謊, 那又怎麼樣, 他們總不能因此把我送進監獄去吧! **d)** used to show that you have found something out about someone 哦〔用於表示發現了某人的某事〕: *So! You've got a new girlfriend, huh?* 哦! 你有新的女朋友了, 嗯? **e)** used with a movement of your hand to show how big, high etc something or someone is 這麼, 這樣〔用於配合手勢表示有多高、多大等〕: *Oh, he must be about so tall.* 哦, 他一定有這麼高。**f)** also 又作 **like so** used when you are showing someone how to do something using your hands, feet etc 像這樣〔用於以手、腳等演示某事該如何做〕: *Fold the material, so, and push the needle through.* 把材料摺起來, 像這樣, 然後把針穿過去。**g)** used when asking a question about what has just been said 那麼〔用於對某人剛說過的話發問〕: *"I've decided to leave." "So what are you going to do?"* "我決定要離開。" "那麼, 你打算幹甚麼?" **12 so she is/so they are etc** used to agree with something that has just been mentioned and that you had not noticed or had forgotten 她/他們是…的〔用於表示同意某人剛提到的事, 而自己未曾注意或已忘記了此事〕: *"Don't forget your brother is coming round for dinner." "So he is. I'd better get some food in."* "別忘記你弟弟會來吃晚飯。" "對了, 他要來的。我還是去買點吃的回來。" **13 so what?** used to show that you do not think that something that has been mentioned is important 那有甚麼關係?〔用於表示某事並不重要〕: *Yeah, I do smoke. So what?* 是啊, 我是抽煙的。那又怎麼樣? **14 so long!** *AmE* used to say goodbye【美】再見! **15 so be it** used to show that you do not agree with someone's decision but you will accept it anyway 就那樣吧, 只好如此〔用於表示勉強同意某人的決定〕: *If you're sure you want to sell your car, then so be it!* 如果你確定要把汽車賣掉, 那就隨便吧。**16 I do so/it is so etc** *AmE* used especially by children to say that something is true, can be done etc when someone else says that it is not, cannot etc【美】我會的/它是真的等〔尤為小孩用於否定別人的陳述〕: *"You can't swim." "I can so."* "你不會游泳。" "我會的。" **17 so I see** used to say that you know that what someone is telling you is true because you can see that it is 我看到是這樣〔用於表示別人說的話是真的, 因為可以看到〕: *"I broke my leg." "So I see. How did it happen?"* "我把腿給弄斷了。" "我看到。怎樣發生的?" **18 so much the better** used to say that if something happens it will make the situation even better than it already is 那就更好了〔用於表示如果發生某事則情況會更好〕: *Katie's coming with us and if you join in too, so much the better.* 凱蒂準備和我們一起去。如果你也參加, 那就更好了。**19 so help me** used to say that you are determined to do something bad to someone, even though you know it is wrong 我發誓; 上天作證〔用於表示明知故犯地傷害某人〕: *One more word and so help me I'll kill you!* 你再說一句, 我發誓我會殺了你!

so² *conjunction* **1** used to give the reason why something happens, why someone does something etc 因此, 所以: *I heard a noise so I got out of bed and turned the light on.* 我聽到喧鬧聲, 所以起牀開燈。| *There was no food in the house so we rang out for a pizza.* 家裡沒有吃的東西, 所以我們打電話叫了一個意大利薄餅。**2 so (that) a)** in order to make something happen, something possible etc 為了, 以便〔表示目的〕: *So that everyone can see, will the taller children stand at the back.* 為了讓大家都看得見, 請個子高的孩子站到後面去。| *The vase had been put on top of the cupboard so it wouldn't get broken.* 花瓶放了在櫥櫃頂, 以免打破。**b)** used to say that something happens as a result of something else 結果; 以致: *Many contestants later failed drug tests, so that the race had to be rerun.* 許多參賽者後來都沒有通過藥物測試, 比賽只得重新進行。

so³ *adj* [not before noun 不用於名詞前] **1 be so** *especially spoken* to be true or correct【尤口】是這樣的, 真的, 對的: *The newspapers claim she killed him in self defence but that just isn't so.* 報紙宣稱她出於自衛殺死了他, 但那根本不是真的。| *"Bill says that you appeared in court last week." "Is that so? Well let me tell you one or two things about Bill."* "比爾說, 你上星期去法庭了。" "真的嗎? 好吧, 讓我告訴你比爾的一兩件事吧。" **2 more so/less so/too much so** phrases in which 'so' is used instead of repeating an adjective that you have mentioned before 更…/沒那麼…/太…〔用於避免重複剛才用的形容詞〕: *Bill is very popular and Ted is even more so.* 比爾非常受歡迎, 而特德更受歡迎。| *Jerry is very honest, maybe too much so.* 傑里很誠實, 也許太誠實了。**3 be just/exactly so** to be arranged tidily, with everything in the right place 安排妥貼, 井井有條: *With Tim, if everything isn't just so he can't relax.* 對於蒂姆, 如果每件事不是都安排得妥妥貼貼, 他是不能放心的。— see also 另見 so-so

so⁴ *n* [singular] the fifth note in a musical SCALE¹ (8) according to the SOL-FA system 全音階的第五音

soak¹ /sok; səʊk/ *v* **1** [I,T] if you soak something or let it soak, you keep it covered with a liquid for a period of time, especially in order to make it softer or easier to clean 浸, 泡: *Soak the beans overnight.* 把豆子浸泡過夜。| **leave sth to soak** *Just leave the dishes to soak; I'll wash them later.* 盤子就放到水裡泡着吧; 我晚些再洗。| **soak sth off/out** (=remove it by soaking) 浸掉, 浸除 *Soak the label off the jar.* 把罐子上的標籤浸掉。**2** [I always+adv/prep,T] to make something completely wet, or to become completely wet 把〔某物〕浸透; 滲透, 濕透: **[+through/into etc]** *If the ink soaks through the paper, it'll stain the table underneath.* 墨水如果滲透這張紙, 就會把下面的桌子弄髒。| **soak sth** *The rain came suddenly and soaked all the washing.* 突然下雨, 把所有曬的衣服都淋濕了。**3** [I] to spend a long time taking a bath 長時間泡浴 **4** [T] *informal* to make someone pay too much money in prices or taxes【非正式】向…敲竹槓[徵重稅]: *the new President's supposed plans to soak the rich to give to the poor* 新總統的那些被信以為真的損富濟貧計劃 3

soak sth ↔ **up** *phr v* [T] **1** if something soaks up a liquid, it takes the liquid into itself 吸收〔液體〕, 吸乾: *He used a towel to soak up the blood.* 他用毛巾把血吸掉。**2** to learn something quickly and easily 很快學會〔某事物〕: *That child just soaks up information.* 那個小孩吸收知識很快。**3 soak up the sun** to sit outside for a long time enjoying the sun 曬太陽, 沐日光浴

soak² *n* [C] **1** a long and enjoyable time spent in the bath〔在浴缸裡〕長時間泡浴: *a good long soak after shopping all day* 購物一整天後在浴缸裡好好地泡一泡

2 an act of soaking something 浸泡: **give sth a soak** *Give the towels a good soak, they're very dirty.* 把毛巾好好泡一泡，太髒了。**3 an old soak** *BrE humorous* someone who is often drunk【英，幽默】酒鬼，經常喝醉的人

soaked /sokt; səʊkt/ *adj* [not before noun 不用於名詞前] **1** very wet or wearing very wet clothes 很濕的；穿濕衣服的: *The rain's coming on heavier – we're going to get soaked.* 雨越下越大，我們快濕透了。| **soaked through** (=completely wet) 全濕的，濕透的 *Get those clothes off; they're soaked right through!* 把衣服脱掉，都濕透了。| **soaked to the skin** (=wearing clothes that are completely wet) 衣服濕透 **2 be soaked in** to be full of a particular quality 充滿〔某種特質〕的: *a city soaked in history* 歷史悠久的城市

soak·ing¹ /ˋsokɪŋ; ˈsəʊkɪŋ/ also 又作 **soaking wet** /ˌ·· ˈ·◂/ *adj* very wet 很濕的，濕透的: *You're soaking! Come in and dry off.* 你渾身都濕透了！快進來弄乾。

soaking² *n* [C] a SOAK² (2) 浸泡

soaking sol·u·tion /ˈ·· ·ˌ··/ *n* [C,U] a liquid that you keep CONTACT LENSes in when you are not wearing them 隱形眼鏡護理液

so-and-so /ˈ· · ·ˌ·/ *n plural* **so-and-sos** **1** [U] an expression meaning a particular person or thing, used when you do not give their name 某某人；某某事: *They're always gossiping about so-and-so having an affair with so-and-so.* 他們老是説某男與某女關係曖昧的閒話。—compare 比較 SUCH AND SUCH **2** [C] a word meaning a very unpleasant or unreasonable person, used to avoid saying a stronger word, such as BASTARD 討厭[無理]的人〔用以代替"狗雜種"一類強烈的字眼〕: *Peter can be a real so-and-so at times.* 彼得有時候討厭得很。

3 **soap¹** /sop; səʊp/ *n* **1** [U] the substance that you use to wash your body 肥皂: *Wash thoroughly with soap and water.* 用肥皂和水徹底洗一洗。| *a bar of soap* 一條肥皂 —compare 比較 DETERGENT **2** [C] *informal* a television or radio story about the daily lives of the same group of people, which is broadcast regularly; SOAP OPERA【非正式】肥皂劇〔一種以同一羣人的日常生活為題材的電視或廣播連續劇〕

soap² *v* [T] to rub soap on or over someone or something 給…擦肥皂: *Will you soap my back for me?* 你給我背上擦點肥皂好嗎?

soap·box /ˋsopˌbɑks; ˈsəʊpbɒks/ *n* **get on your soapbox** *informal* to tell people your own strong opinions about something loudly and forcefully【非正式】大發議論，高談闊論: *Don't mention politics, or Burt will be back on his soapbox again.* 不要提政治，否則伯特又要大發議論一番。

soap·flakes /ˋsopˌfleks; ˈsəʊpfleɪks/ *n* [plural] small thin pieces of soap used for washing delicate clothes 〔洗精緻衣服用的〕皂片

soap op·e·ra /ˈ· ˌ···/ *n* [C] a SOAP¹ (2) 肥皂劇

soap pow·der /ˈ· ˌ··/ *n* [U] *BrE* a powder that is made from soap and other chemicals, used for washing clothes【英】〔洗滌用的〕皂粉

soap·stone /ˋsopˌston; ˈsəʊpstəʊn/ *n* [U] a soft stone that feels like soap 皂石〔一種軟岩石〕

soap·suds /ˋsopˌsʌdz; ˈsəʊpsʌdz/ *n* [plural] the mass of small BUBBLEs formed on top of soapy water 肥皂泡沫

soap·y /ˋsopɪ; ˈsəʊpi/ *adj* **1** containing soap 含有肥皂的: *warm soapy water* 温暖的肥皂水 **2** like soap 像肥皂的: *This cheese is kind of soapy-tasting.* 這種乾酪味道有點像肥皂。**3** *BrE informal* so pleasant that it seems false【英，非正式】油腔滑調的，討好的: *Joan reads those awful soapy romances.* 瓊經常看那些討厭的媚俗的浪漫故事。—**soapiness** *n* [U]

soar /sɔr; sɔː/ *v* [I]

1 ▶AMOUNTS/PRICES ETC 數量/價格等◀ to increase quickly to a high level 猛增，驟升: *The temperature soared to 90 degrees.* 温度驟升至90度。| *Health care costs continue to soar.* 保健費用在繼續猛增。

2 ▶IN THE SKY 在天上◀ **a)** to fly, especially very high up in the sky, floating on air currents 高飛，翱翔 **b)** to go quickly upwards to a great height 急速升高: *The rocket soared into orbit.* 火箭升空進入軌道。

3 ▶SPIRITS/HOPES 情緒/希望◀ if your spirits or hopes soar, you begin to feel very happy or hopeful 高漲，騰飛: *Adam's smile sent her spirits soaring.* 亞當的微笑使她神采飛揚。

4 ▶LOOK TALL 顯得很高◀ [not in progressive 不用進行式] if buildings, trees, towers etc soar they look very tall and impressive 聳立，屹立: *Here the cliffs soar 500 feet above the sea.* 這裡懸崖聳立，高出海面500英尺。—**soaring** *adj*: *a soaring skyscraper* 高聳入雲的摩天大廈 | *soaring crime figures* 猛升的犯罪數字

sob /sɑb; sɒb/ *v* **sobbed, sobbing** **1** [I] to cry noisily while breathing in short, sudden bursts 啜泣，嗚咽，抽噎: *Josie flung herself on the bed, sobbing.* 喬西抽抽搭搭地撲倒在牀上。**2** also 又作 **sob out** [T] to say something or tell someone something while you are sobbing 哭訴，嗚咽地説: *Joshua sobbed out the whole sad story.* 喬舒亞嗚咽着訴説那個悲慘的故事。—**sob** *n* [C]: *loud sobs* 大聲的啜泣 —**sobbingly** *adv*

so·ber¹ /ˋsobɚ; ˈsəʊbə/ *adj* **1** not drunk 未喝醉的，清醒的: *I've never seen him sober.* 我從未見他有過不醉的時候。| **as sober as a judge** (=completely sober) 一點不醉的，完全清醒的 **2** having a serious attitude to life 認真的，嚴肅的: *a sober and intelligent young man* 認真而有才智的年輕人 **3** plain and not at all brightly coloured 素淡的，樸素的: *a sober grey suit* 一套樸素的灰色衣服 —**soberly** *adv*

sober² *v* also 又作 **sober down** [I,T] to become or make someone become more serious in behaviour or attitude (使)變得嚴肅[謹慎；持重]: *Diane sobered down a lot as she got older.* 隨着年齡的增長，黛安變得持重多了。

sober sb ↔ **up** *phr v* [I,T] to gradually become or make someone become less drunk (使)酒醉後清醒過來，(使)醒酒: *A cup of black coffee might sober you up.* 喝一杯黑咖啡也許可以使你醒酒。

so·ber·ing /ˋsobərɪŋ; ˈsəʊbərɪŋ/ *adj* making you feel very serious 使覺得嚴肅的；使認真的: *a sobering thought* 嚴肅的思想 | *The news had a sobering effect.* 這消息是發人深省的。

so·bri·e·ty /səˋbraɪətɪ; səˈbraɪəti/ *n* [U] *formal* behaviour that shows a serious attitude to life【正式】嚴肅，莊重

so·bri·quet /ˋsobrɪˌke; ˈsəʊbrɪkeɪ/ also 又作 **soubriquet** *n* [C] *literary* an unofficial title or name; NICKNAME【文】綽號，諢名

sob sto·ry /ˈ· ˌ··/ *n* [C] *informal* a story, especially one that is untrue, that someone tells you in order to make you feel sorry for them【非正式】〔尤指不真實的〕為了博取同情的故事，傷感故事: *She had some sob story about her cat getting run over.* 她有個她的貓被汽車輾死的所謂傷感故事。

Soc. the written abbreviation of 縮寫= SOCIETY (3)

so-called /ˌ· ˈ·◂/ *adj* [only before noun 僅用於名詞前] 3 a word used to describe someone or something that has been given a name that you think is wrong 所謂的: *The so-called expert on international affairs turned out to be a research student.* 這個所謂的國際事務專家原來是個研究生。

soc·cer /ˋsɑkɚ; ˈsɒkə/ *n* [U] a word for the game of FOOTBALL (1) used so that it is not confused with AMERICAN FOOTBALL or RUGBY *BrE* 足球 —see picture on page A23 參見A23頁圖

so·cia·ble¹ /ˋsoʃəbḷ; ˈsəʊʃəbəl/ *adj* someone who is sociable enjoys being with other people 好交際的，喜歡與人交往的: *a pleasant, sociable couple* 一對和善、喜歡與人交往的夫婦 —opposite 反義詞 UNSOCIABLE —**sociably** *adv* —**sociability** /ˌsoʃəˋbɪlətɪ; ˌsəʊʃəˈbɪləti/ *n* [U]

sociable² *n* [C] *AmE old-fashioned* a SOCIAL²【美，過時】社交聚會

2 1 **so·cial¹** /ˈsoʃəl; ˈsəʊʃəl/ *adj*
1 ►SOCIETY 社會◄ concerning human society and its organization, or the quality of people's lives 社會的, 有關社會的: *Various social issues, such as unemployment and education, were discussed.* 討論了各種社會問題, 如失業和教育等。| *social trends* 社會趨勢 | *demands for social change* 對社會變革的要求
2 ►RANK 地位◄ related to the position in society that you have, according to your job, family, wealth etc 社會地位[階層]的: *social status* 社會地位 | *a wide circle of friends from different social backgrounds* 廣泛的社會背景各異的朋友圈子 | **social class** (=a group of people who have the same social position) 社會階層 *every social class, from manual workers to aristocrats* 從勞工到貴族的各個社會階層 | **social mobility** (=ability to move into a higher social class) 社會流動能力
3 ►MEETING PEOPLE 與人交往◄ related to the way you meet people and form relationships 社交的, 交際的: **social skills** (=ability to meet people easily and deal well with them) 社交技能 *College gives you an opportunity to develop your social skills.* 大學給你提供一個發展社交技能的機會。| **social contacts** (=people you meet outside work) 〔工作以外的〕社交關係 | **social graces** (=attractive manners, behaviour etc when you meet people) 社交風度
4 ►WITH FRIENDS 和朋友在一起◄ related to the time you spend with your friends for enjoyment 交誼的, 聯誼的: **social life** (=activities with your friends) 社交生活 *You sure seem to have a busy social life these days!* 你近來的社交生活好像的確很忙碌! | **social club/evening/gathering etc** (=a club or occasion at which people can enjoy being together) 聯誼俱樂部/晚會/聚會等 | **social drinking** (=drinking alcohol with your friends) 與朋友相聚歡飲
5 ►ANIMALS 動物◄ forming groups or living together in their natural state 羣居的, 合羣的: *Elephants are social animals.* 大象是羣居動物。—see also 另見 ANTISOCIAL, SOCIABLE, UNSOCIAL —**socially** *adv*: *socially acceptable behaviour* 在社會上可以接受的行為 | *Do you and your colleagues ever meet socially?* 你和同事們有社交聚會嗎?

social² *n* [C] *old-fashioned* a planned informal party for the members of a group, club or church 【過時】社交聚會; 聯誼會; 教友聯誼會

social climb·er /ˌ·· ˈ··/ *n* [C] someone who tries to get accepted into a higher social class by becoming friendly with people who belong to that class 結交權貴向上爬的人, 設法擠進上流社會的人

social de·moc·ra·cy /ˌ·· ·ˈ···/ *n* **1** [U] a political and economic system based on socialism combined with DEMOCRATIC principles, such as personal freedom and government by elected representatives 社會民主主義 **2** [C] a country with a government based on this system 社會民主主義國家 —**social democrat** /ˌ·· ˈ···/ *n* [C]

social di·sease /ˈ·· ·ˌ·/ *n* [C] an expression meaning VENEREAL DISEASE, used to avoid saying this directly 社交病〔性病的一種委婉說法〕

social en·gi·neer·ing /ˌ·· ··ˈ··/ *n* [U] the practice of making changes in the law in order to change society according to a political idea 社會工程〔指根據一種政治思想來改革法律從而變革社會的做法〕

so·cial·is·m /ˈsoʃəlˌɪzəm; ˈsəʊʃəl-ɪzəm/ *n* [U] a system of political beliefs and principles whose main aims are that everyone should have an equal opportunity to share wealth and that industries should be owned by the government 社會主義 —compare 比較 CAPITALISM, COMMUNISM

so·cial·ist¹ /ˈsoʃəlɪst; ˈsəʊʃəl-ɪst/ *adj* **1** based on socialism or connected with a political party that supports socialism 社會主義的; 社會黨的: *socialist principles* 社會主義原則 | *the socialist manifesto* 社會黨宣言 **2** a socialist country or government has a political system based on socialism 社會主義的〔國家或政府〕

socialist² *n* [C] someone who believes in socialism 社會主義者

so·cia·lite /ˈsoʃəˌlaɪt; ˈsəʊʃəl-aɪt/ *n* [C] someone who is well known for going to many fashionable parties 社交界名人, 社會名流: *He's married to some rich Miami socialite.* 他娶了邁阿密某位富有的社交名媛。

so·cial·i·za·tion /ˌsoʃələˈzeʃən; ˌsəʊʃəl-aɪˈzeɪʃən/ *n* [U] the process by which people, especially children, are made to behave in a way that is acceptable in their society 適合過社會生活, 〔尤指兒童的〕合羣: *the socialization of young offenders* 青年罪犯回歸社會的問題

so·cial·ize also 又作 **-ise** *BrE* 【英】 /ˈsoʃəˌlaɪz; ˈsəʊʃəl-aɪz/ *v* **1** [I] to spend time with other people in a friendly way 交友, 交誼: [+**with**] *I enjoy socializing with my students after class.* 我喜歡在課後和學生交往。**2** [T] *technical* to train someone to behave in a way that is acceptable in the society they are living in 【術語】使適合過社會生活, 使合羣

socialized medi·cine /ˌ··· ˈ···/ *n* [U] *AmE* medical care provided by a government and paid for through taxes 【美】〔由政府提供、靠稅收支付的〕公費醫療

social sci·ence /ˌ·· ˈ··/ *n* **1** [U] the study of people in society, which includes history, politics, ECONOMICS, SOCIOLOGY and ANTHROPOLOGY 社會科學〔包括歷史、政治、經濟、社會學和人類學〕 **2** [C] one of these subjects 一門社會科學 —compare 比較 NATURAL SCIENCE —**social scientist** *n* [C]

social se·cu·ri·ty /ˌ·· ·ˈ···/ *n* [U] **1** *BrE* government money that is paid to people who are unemployed, old, ill etc 【英】〔政府發給失業者、老人、病人等的〕救濟金; WELFARE (3) *AmE* 【美】: **be on social security** (=be receiving money from the government) 領取社會福利金 **2 Social Security** a system of insurance run by the American government, into which workers make regular payments, and which provides money when they are unable to work, especially because they are old 社會保障(制度)〔美國的社會保險制度, 工人定期交納保險金, 退休後領取退休金〕 —compare 比較 NATIONAL INSURANCE

social serv·ice /ˌ·· ˈ··/ *n* **1** [C] a service that is necessary for society to work properly and is provided by the government or supported by government money 〔由政府提供或資助的〕社會服務: *Should the railways make a profit or should they be run as a social service?* 鐵路應當營利, 還是應當作為社會服務來管理? **2 social services** [plural] *especially BrE* the special services provided by a government or local council to help people who have particular problems 【尤英】〔向有特殊問題者提供幫助的〕社會福利事業, 公益事業: *Cuts in social services have been widespread.* 削減公益事業的做法已經很普遍了。

social stud·ies /ˈ·· ˌ··/ *n* [plural] the study of people in society; SOCIAL SCIENCE 社會科學

social work /ˈ·· ·/ *n* [U] work done by government or private organizations to improve bad social conditions and help people with particular social problems 社會福利工作〔由政府或私人機構進行, 旨在改善社會環境和幫助有特殊社會問題的人〕

social work·er /ˈ·· ˌ··/ *n* [C] someone who is employed in SOCIAL WORK 社會福利工作者

so·ci·e·tal /səˈsaɪətḷ; səˈsaɪətl/ *adj technical* related to a particular society 【術語】社會的: *societal attitudes* 社會態度

so·ci·e·ty /səˈsaɪətɪ; səˈsaɪəti/ *n* 1 1
1 ►PEOPLE IN GENERAL 整個社會◄ [U] people in general, considered in relation to the structure of laws, organizations etc that makes it possible for them to live together 社會, 羣體: *Society has a right to expect people to obey the law.* 社會有權要求人們遵守法律。| **a danger to society** *He should be locked up; he's a danger to society!* 他應當被關起來; 他對社會是個禍害!

2 ▶A PARTICULAR GROUP 某一羣體◀ [C,U] a particular large group of people who share laws, organizations, customs etc〔有共同的法律、組織、習俗等的〕某類社會: *Britain is a multi-racial society.* 英國是個多種族社會。| *Drug abuse is one of the problems confronting modern Western society.* 濫用藥物是現代西方社會面臨的問題之一。| **the consumer society** *Is greed a product of the consumer society?* 貪婪是不是消費型社會的一種產物? | **the affluent society** *Shopaholics are a new problem, born of the affluent society.* 購物成癮是富足型社會所產生的一個新問題。| **polite society** (=people who think they have the highest standards of behaviour) 上流社會〔自認為有最高言行標準的人羣〕

3 ▶CLUB 社團◀ [C] an organization or a club with members who share similar interests, aims etc 社團, 協會: *the university film society* 大學的電影協會 | *the Law Society* 法律協會

4 ▶UPPER CLASS 上等階層◀ [U] the fashionable group of people who are rich and belong to the upper class 上層社會, 社交界: *a society wedding* 上層社會的婚禮 | **high society** (=the richest, most fashionable etc people) 上流社會 | **be introduced into society** (=to begin to attend the fashionable events organized by this group) 被介紹進入上流社會

5 ▶COMPANY 交誼◀ [U] *formal* the companionship of other people【正式】交誼, 交際, 交往: *Jacob shunned the society of others, preferring to be alone.* 雅各布避免與人交往, 寧願獨個兒生活。—see also 另見 BUILDING SOCIETY, FRIENDLY SOCIETY

socio- /ˈsosɪo; səʊsiəʊ/ *prefix technical*【術語】**1** concerning society; social (關於) 社會的: *sociology* (=study of society) 社會學 **2** social and 社會以及...的: *sociopolitical* 社會政治的

so·ci·o·e·co·nom·ic /ˌsosɪoˌɛkəˈnɑmɪk; ˌsəʊsiəʊekəˈnɒmɪk/ *adj* based on a combination of social and economic conditions 社會經濟的 —**socioeconomically** /-klɪ; -kli/ *adv*

so·ci·ol·o·gy /ˌsosɪˈɑlədʒɪ; ˌsəʊsiˈɒlədʒi/ *n* [U] the scientific study of societies and the behaviour of people in groups 社會學 —compare 比較 ANTHROPOLOGY, ETHNOLOGY, SOCIAL SCIENCE —**sociologist** *n* [C] —**sociological** /ˌsosɪəˈlɑdʒɪkḷ; ˌsəʊsiəˈlɒdʒɪkəl/ *adj*: *a sociological study of the working class* 對工人階級的社會學研究 —**sociologically** /-klɪ; -kli/ *adv*

so·ci·o·path /ˈsosɪəˌpæθ; ˈsəʊsiəˌpæθ/ *n* [C] *technical* someone whose behaviour towards other people is considered unacceptable, strange, and possibly dangerous【術語】〔在行為上〕反社會者 —**sociopathic** /ˌsosɪəˈpæθɪk; ˌsəʊsiəˈpæθɪk◂/ *adj*

3 **sock¹** /sɑk; sɒk/ *n* [C] **1** a piece of clothing made of soft material that you wear on your foot inside your shoe 短襪: *a pair of cotton socks* 一雙棉線短襪 **2 give sb/sth a sock** *informal* to hit someone or something very hard, especially with your hand closed【非正式】狠擊某人/某物一拳 **3 pull your socks up** *BrE informal* to make an effort to improve your behaviour or your work【英, 非正式】努力, 用功: *If you don't pull your socks up, you'll fail the exam.* 如果你不用功, 你考試會不及格的。**4 put a sock in it** *BrE informal* used to tell someone in a joking way to stop talking【英, 非正式】〔以玩笑的方式要某人〕閉嘴, 住口 **5 knock sb's socks off** *AmE informal* to surprise someone very much【美, 非正式】使某人大吃一驚: *When I saw all the people there, it knocked my socks off!* 看到所有人在那兒, 我大吃一驚!

sock² *v* [T] **1** *informal* to hit someone very hard【非正式】猛擊, 狠打: *He socked the intruder on the jaw.* 他猛擊闖入者的下巴。**2 sock it to sb** *old-fashioned* to tell someone something in a direct and forceful way【過時】直截了當地對某人說: *Go on, sock it to him!* 去吧, 直截了當地跟他說清楚!

sock in *phr v* [T] *AmE* **be socked in** if an airport, road, or area is socked in, it is very difficult to see far because of bad fog, snow, or rain【美】〔機場、道路或地方因大霧、大雪、大雨〕能見度很低, 看不清

sock·e·roo /ˌsɑkəˈru; ˌsɒkəˈruː/ *n* [singular] *AmE informal* something that is very successful and impressive【美, 非正式】非常成功的事物, 印象深刻的東西: *That was one sockeroo of a firework show!* 那次的煙火節目精彩極了!

sock·et /ˈsɑkɪt; ˈsɒkḷt/ *n* [C] **1** a piece of plastic with holes in it, which is fixed into a wall and which you can connect electrical equipment to (電源) 插座: *Don't let the baby stick her fingers in the socket.* 別讓嬰兒把她的手指伸進插座。**2** a hollow part of a structure into which something fits 窩, 臼, 槽, 穴: *Kendrick grabbed my arm, nearly pulling it out of its socket.* 肯德里克抓住我的胳膊, 差點把它拉脫了臼。

sock·ing /ˈsɑkɪŋ; ˈsɒkɪŋ/ *adv* **socking great** *BrE spoken* extremely big【英口】極大的: *a socking great hole in the floor* 地板上的大洞

sock·o /ˈsɑko; ˈsɒkəʊ/ *adj AmE informal* very impressive or strong【美, 非正式】給人以強烈印象的; 強壯的

sod¹ /sɑd; sɒd/ *n* **1** [C] *BrE informal* an impolite word meaning a stupid or annoying person, especially a man【英, 非正式】笨蛋, 討厭鬼〔尤指男人, 非禮貌用語〕: *Get up, you lazy sod!* 起來, 你這個懶鬼! **2 be a sod** *BrE informal* an impolite expression meaning to be very difficult【英, 非正式】難對付的, 棘手的〔非禮貌說法〕: *That door's a sod to open.* 那扇討厭的門真難開。**3 poor sod** *BrE spoken* an impolite expression meaning someone you feel sorry for, or have no respect for【英口】可憐的傢伙〔非禮貌說法〕: *The poor sod's wife left him.* 那個可憐的傢伙被老婆甩了。**4** [C,U] a piece of earth or the layer of earth with grass and roots growing in it 草皮; 草地

sod² *v* [T only in imperative or infinitive 僅用於祈使句或不定式] *BrE spoken*【英口】**1 sod it/that** used to rudely express anger or great annoyance at something or someone 該死, 真糟糕〔用於粗魯地對某人或某事表示生氣〕: *Sod it, I've missed the train.* 真糟糕, 我誤了火車。| *"He thinks you should apologize." "Well, sod that!"* "他認為你應當道歉。""嘿, 見鬼去吧!" **2** used to say rudely that something is not important 去你的〔用於粗魯地表示某事並不重要〕: *Sod the job, I'm going home.* 去你的工作, 我要回家啦。**3 sod off** used to tell someone rudely to go away 走開, 滾蛋〔非禮貌說法〕: *Just tell him to sod off.* 叫他給我滾蛋。

so·da /ˈsodə; ˈsəʊdə/ *n* **1** [C,U] water containing bubbles (BUBBLE¹ (1)) of gas that is added to alcoholic drinks 蘇打水: *Do you want soda in your Scotch?* 你的蘇格蘭威士忌要加蘇打水嗎? **2** [U] a sweet drink filled with gas 汽水: *a bottle of orange soda* 一瓶橘子汽水 **3** [C] *AmE* an ICE-CREAM SODA【美】冰淇淋蘇打 **4** [U] a compound of SODIUM in powder form that is used for cooking or cleaning〔烹飪或清潔用的〕蘇打; 碳酸鈉: *baking soda* 小蘇打

soda foun·tain /ˈ·· ˌ··/ *n* [C] *AmE old-fashioned* a place in a shop at which drinks, ice cream etc are served【美, 過時】〔商店中的〕冷飲櫃台; 冷飲部

sod all /· ˈ·/ *n* [U] *BrE informal* an impolite expression meaning nothing at all【英, 非正式】甚麼也沒有〔非禮貌說法〕: *I got sod all from the deal.* 這筆交易我甚麼也得不到。

soda si·phon /ˈ·· ˌ··/ *n* [C] a special type of bottle from which SODA WATER is forced out in a fast stream by gas pressure 蘇打水瓶, 汽水瓶

soda wa·ter /ˈ·· ˌ··/ *n* [U] water with bubbles (BUBBLE¹ (1)) of gas in it that is added to alcoholic drinks〔加進酒精飲料的〕蘇打水

sod·den /ˈsɑdṇ; ˈsɒdn/ *adj* very wet and heavy 非常濕和重的, 濕透的, 濕淋淋的: *the sodden ground* 濕透的地面 | *sodden clothing* 濕淋淋的衣物

sod·ding /ˈsɑdɪŋ; ˈsɒdɪŋ/ *adj BrE informal* an impolite word used to emphasize that you are angry【英, 非正式】

倒霉的, 他媽的〔用於強調憤怒, 非禮貌用詞〕: *This sodding computer's crashed again!* 這台倒霉的電腦又壞了!

so·di·um /ˈsodɪəm; ˈsəʊdiəm/ *n* [U] a silver-white metal that is an ELEMENT (=simple substance) and only exists naturally in combination with other substances 鈉

sodium bi·car·bo·nate /,··· ·ˈ··· / *n* [U] a white powder used in baking to make cakes etc lighter 碳酸氫鈉, 小蘇打

sodium chlo·ride /,··· ˈ··/ *n* [U] *techincal* salt【術語】氯化鈉, 食鹽

sod·o·mite /ˈsɑdəm,aɪt; ˈsɒdəmaɪt/ *n* [C] *old use* a word meaning someone who practices sodomy【舊】雞姦者

sod·o·my /ˈsɑdəmɪ; ˈsɒdəmi/ *n* [U] *old use or law* a sexual act in which a man puts his sex organ into someone's ANUS, especially that of another man【舊或法律】〔尤指男性間的〕雞姦

Sod's law /,· ˈ·/ *n* [U] *BrE humorous* the natural tendency for things to go wrong whenever possible【英, 幽默】墨菲定律〔一種認為凡有可能出差錯的事終將出差錯的論斷〕: *It's Sod's law that the car breaks down when you need it most.* 在你最需要汽車的時候汽車就會壞掉——這就是墨菲定律。

so·fa /ˈsofə; ˈsəʊfə/ *n* [C] a comfortable seat with raised arms and a back, wide enough for two or three people; SETTEE〔兩或三人坐的〕長沙發

sofa bed /ˈ·· ·/ *n* [C] a sofa which can be changed into a bed (坐臥) 兩用沙發, 沙發牀

S2 W2 **soft** /sɔft; sɒft/ *adj*

1 ►NOT HARD 不硬◄ **a)** not hard or firm, but easy to press (柔) 軟的, 鬆軟的: *a soft pillow* 軟枕頭 | *My feet sank into the soft ground.* 我的雙腳陷進了鬆軟的地裡。| **get/go soft** *Cook the onions until they go soft.* 把洋蔥煮到變軟為止。**b)** less hard than average 中等硬度以下的, 硬度低的: *a soft lead pencil* 軟鉛筆 | *a soft cheese* 軟乾酪

2 ►NOT ROUGH 不粗糙的◄ having a surface that is smooth and pleasant to touch 柔滑的, 細嫩的: *a baby's soft skin* 嬰兒細嫩的皮膚 | *The fur was soft to the touch.* 這皮毛摸起來很柔滑。

3 ►NOT LOUD 不響亮的◄ a soft sound, voice, or music is quiet and pleasant to listen to 輕柔的, 低聲的: *a whisper so soft that I could hardly hear it* 聲音輕得我幾乎聽不見的耳語 | *a soft accent* 輕柔的音調

4 ►NOT BRIGHT 不鮮豔的◄ [only before noun 僅用於名詞前] soft colours or lights are pleasant and relaxing because they are not too bright〔顏色、燈光〕柔和的, 不刺眼的: *Soft lighting creates a romantic atmosphere.* 柔和的燈光營造出一種浪漫的氣氛。| *The room was a soft peach colour.* 這個房間用淡淡的桃紅色。

5 ►GENTLE 溫和的◄ gentle and without much force 輕輕的, 溫和的: *a soft breeze* 和風

6 ►TOO EASY 過於容易的◄ *informal* a soft job, life etc is too easy and does not involve much work or hard physical work【非正式】〔工作、生活等〕輕鬆的, 容易的: *Mike's landed himself a soft job in the stores.* 邁克在商店裡謀到一份輕鬆的工作。| **soft option** (=a choice that allows you to avoid difficulties or hard work) 省事的選擇[捨難求易] *The computer course isn't a soft option – it's pretty tough.* 電腦課程並不輕鬆——是相當繁重的。| *If you agree, you're taking the soft option.* 如果你同意, 你就是在挑輕鬆的工作。

7 ►NOT STRICT 不嚴厲的◄ someone who is soft seems weak because they are not strict enough with other people 軟弱的, 過於溫和的: *If you give way, the kids'll think you're soft.* 你如果讓步的話, 孩子們就會以為你軟弱可欺了。| **be soft on** *No politician wants to seem soft on crime.* 政治家都不想對犯罪行為顯得心慈手軟。| **take a soft line** (=not be strict enough) 態度溫和, 不夠嚴厲 *Courts have been taking too soft a line with young offenders.* 法庭對年輕罪犯過於寬容了。—opposite 反義詞 TOUGH

8 ►WATER 水◄ not containing much LIME[1] (3) so that it forms bubbles (BUBBLE[1] (1)) from soap easily 不含石灰的, 軟性的〔肥皂容易起泡沫〕

9 ►PHYSICAL CONDITION 體質◄ *informal* having a body that is not in a strong physical condition, because you do not do enough exercise【非正式】〔由於運動不夠而〕健康欠佳的, 虛弱的: *He'd got soft after all those years in a desk job.* 他幹了那麼多年辦公室工作之後, 身體變得虛弱了。

10 have a soft spot for to be fond of someone even when they do not behave well 偏愛, 對...有好感: *She's always had a soft spot for Grant.* 她一向對格蘭特有好感。

11 a soft touch *informal* someone from whom you can easily get money, because they are kind or easy to deceive【非正式】輕易借錢給他人的人; 寬厚[容易受騙]的人: *The children regard their aunt as a bit of a soft touch.* 孩子們把姑母當作有點容易上當受騙的人。

12 ►STUPID 愚蠢的◄ *BrE* stupid or silly【英】笨的; 傻的: *You must be soft if you think I'll give you fifty quid!* 你如果以為我會給你五十英鎊, 那你一定是傻了。

13 soft in the head *old-fashioned* very stupid or crazy【過時】很蠢的; 瘋的

14 be soft on *old-fashioned* to be sexually attracted to someone【過時】受異性吸引 —**softly** *adv*: *She stroked his head softly.* 她輕輕地撫摸着他的頭。| *Music played softly in the background.* 背景音樂輕柔地演奏着。—**softness** *n* [U]

soft·ball /ˈsɔft,bɔl; ˈsɒftbɔːl/ *n* **1** [U] a game similar to BASEBALL but played on a smaller field with a slightly larger and softer ball 壘球 (運動) **2** [C] a special ball used to play this game 壘球

soft-boiled /,· ˈ·◂/ *adj* an egg that is soft-boiled is boiled long enough for the white part to become solid, but not the yellow part in the centre〔蛋〕煮得半熟的, 溏心的 —compare 比較 HARD-BOILED

soft cop·y /ˈ· ,··/ *n* [U] *technical* information stored in a computer's memory or shown on a SCREEN[1] (1) rather than printed on paper【術語】〔電腦的〕軟拷貝〔指儲存於電腦中或顯示在螢屏上而不是以紙張打印出的資料〕—compare 比較 HARD COPY

soft cur·ren·cy /,· ˈ···/ *n* [C,U] money of a particular country that may fall in value and is difficult to exchange for the money of a country that is economically stronger 軟通貨, 軟貨幣〔指幣值不夠穩定、難以與經濟實力較強國家的貨幣相兑換的通貨〕

soft drink /ˈ· ·/ *n* [C] a cold drink that does not contain alcohol 軟飲料〔指不含酒精的飲料〕

soft drug /,· ˈ·/ *n* [C] an illegal drug such MARIJUANA that is not considered to be harmful 軟性毒品〔指大麻等被認為無害的毒品〕

soft·en /ˈsɔfən; ˈsɒfən/ *v* [I,T] **1** to become softer or make something softer (使) 變軟, (使) 變柔滑, (使) 變輕柔: *Choose a good moisturizer to soften and protect your skin.* 選用一種好的潤膚霜以保護你的皮膚, 並使它變得柔滑。| *Cook until the onion has softened.* 把洋蔥煮到變軟為止。**2** if your attitude softens, or if something softens it, it becomes less strict and more sympathetic (使)〔態度等〕軟化, (使) 變溫和: *The British position on textile imports is softening.* 英國對紡織品進口問題的立場正在軟化。| *Local police have softened their attitude towards young people who live on the streets.* 地方警察對待流浪街頭的年輕人的態度已經變溫和了。**3 soften the blow/impact etc** to make the effect of something less severe 緩和打擊/衝擊等: *The minister may try to soften the blow of pay freezes by announcing a cut in interest rates.* 部長以宣布降低利率來企圖緩和凍結工資的打擊。**4** if your expression, or voice softens or if something softens it, you look or sound kinder and more gentle (使)〔表情、聲音〕變輕柔, (使) 變柔和: *His voice softened when he spoke to her.* 他對她說話時聲音變輕柔了。—opposite 反義詞 HARDEN (2)

soften sb/sth ↔ **up** *phr v* [T] **1** *informal* to be nice to someone before you ask them to do something so that they will be ready to help you【非正式】使…心軟, 打動: *You'll have to soften Alison up before you ask to borrow her car.* 在向阿莉森借汽車之前, 你必須先打動她。**2** to make an enemy's defences weaker so that they will be easier to attack, especially by bombing them〔尤指通過轟炸〕削弱〔敵人的防禦設施以便進攻〕

sof·ten·er /ˈsɔfənɚ; ˈsɒfənə/ *n* [C] a substance that you add to water to make clothes feel soft after washing〔衣物〕柔軟劑, 軟化劑: *a fabric softener* 織物柔軟劑 —see also 另見 WATER SOFTENER

soft fo·cus /ˌ· ˈ··◂/ *n* [U] the arrangement of a photographic LENS (2) in a camera so that the edge of the object that is being photographed is not clear〔攝影的〕軟聚焦, 模糊焦點〔使影像周邊模糊不清的聚焦〕

soft fruit /ˌ· ˈ·/ *n* [C,U] *especially BrE* small fruit that you can eat that has no hard skin【尤英】〔無硬皮的〕無核小果: *Strawberries and raspberries are soft fruit.* 草莓和山莓都是無核小果。

soft fur·nish·ings /ˌ· ˈ···/ *n* [plural] *BrE* things such as curtains, chair covers etc that are made of cloth and are used in decorating a room【英】〔窗簾、椅子套等用布料做的〕室內陳設品

soft·heart·ed /ˈsɔftˌhɑrtɪd; ˌsɒftˈhɑːtɪ̥d◂/ *adj* easily affected by feelings of pity or sympathy for other people 心腸軟的, 好心的, 仁慈的: *Paul's really kind and softhearted.* 保羅確實很仁慈, 富於同情心。

soft·ie /ˈsɔftɪ; ˈsɒfti/ *n* [C] another spelling of SOFTY softy 的另一種拼法

soft land·ing /ˌ· ˈ··/ *n* [C] a situation in which a SPACECRAFT comes down onto the ground gently and without any damage〔宇宙飛船的〕軟着陸

softly-softly /ˌ·· ˈ··/ *adj BrE* **softly-softly approach** a way of dealing with something or somone which involves being very patient and careful【英】耐心謹慎的方法: *I think we need to adopt a softly-softly approach with Mike.* 我認為我們對待邁克需要採取耐心謹慎的方法。

softly-spok·en /ˌ·· ˈ··/ *adj* another form of the word SOFT-SPOKEN soft-spoken 的另一種形式

soft pal·ate /ˌ· ˈ··/ *n* [C] the soft part of the back of the top of your mouth〔口中的〕軟顎

soft ped·al /ˌ· ˈ··/ *v* [T] *informal* to make something seem less important or less urgent than it really is【非正式】使…顯得不那麼重要[緊迫], 淡化

soft porn /ˌ· ˈ·/ *n* [U] magazines, pictures etc that show sexual acts and images in a way that is intended to be sexually exciting, but which are not of the most offensive type 軟性色情作品〔雜誌、圖片等, 不太露骨的〕—compare 比較 HARD PORN

soft sell /ˌ· ˈ·◂/ *n* [singular] a way of advertising or selling things that involves gently persuading people to buy something in a friendly and indirect way 軟推銷〔指用友好誘導的方法進行的廣告宣傳或推銷〕—compare 比較 HARD SELL

soft shoul·der /ˌ· ˈ··/ *n* [C] ground at the edge of a road that is too soft to drive on〔不適宜車輛行駛的〕軟質路肩 —compare 比較 HARD SHOULDER

soft-soap /ˈ· ·/ *v* [T] *informal* to say nice things to someone in order to persuade them to do something, change their mind etc【非正式】用甜言蜜語説服: *Don't think you can soft-soap me!* 別以為你能用好話來説服我! —**soft soap** *n* [U]

soft-spok·en /ˌ· ˈ··◂/ *adj* having a pleasant gentle voice 聲音柔和悦耳的

soft toy /ˌ· ˈ·/ *n* [C] *BrE* a toy for young children made of cloth and filled with soft material【英】軟玩具〔用布和軟填塞物做成〕; STUFFED ANIMAL *AmE*【美】

W2 **soft·ware** /ˈsɔftˌwɛr; ˈsɒftweə/ *n* [U] the sets of PROGRAMS (=instructions) that you put into a computer when you want it to do particular jobs〔電腦〕軟件: *She loaded the new software.* 她給電腦裝上新的軟件。| *word processing software* 文字處理軟件 —compare 比較 HARDWARE (1)

soft·wood /ˈsɔftˌwud; ˈsɒftwʊd/ *n* [C,U] wood from trees such as PINE[1] (1) and FIR that is cheap and easy to cut, or a tree with this type of wood 軟(木)材, 針葉樹材〔如松木、冷杉木等價格低、易切割的木材〕; 針葉樹 —compare 比較 HARDWOOD

soft·y, softie /ˈsɔftɪ; ˈsɒfti/ *n* [C] *informal* someone who is too easily affected by feelings of pity or sympathy, or who is too easily persuaded【非正式】心腸軟的人; 極易被説服的人: *He's a big softy.* 他是個過分心軟的人。

sog·gy /ˈsɑgɪ; ˈsɒgi/ *adj* unpleasantly wet and soft 濕透的, 濕軟的: *The ground was soggy from the rain.* 雨後地面濕透了。| *The bottom of the pie has gone all soggy.* 餡餅底部全都濕乎乎的。—**soggily** *adv* —**sogginess** *n* [U]

soh /so; səʊ/ *n* [singular,U] another spelling of SO[4] so[4] 的另一種拼法

So·Ho /ˈsoˌho; ˈsəʊˌhəʊ/ *n* Small Office; Home Office; an expression referring to electronic office systems, including especially E-MAIL 小型辦公室; 家庭辦公室〔是指包含電子郵件的電子辦公室系統〕: *SoHo accounting software* 供家庭辦公室使用的會計軟件

soi·gné, soignée *fem*【陰性】/swɑˋnje; ˈswɑːnjeɪ/ *adj formal* dressed or arranged fashionably and with care【正式】衣着講究的, 時髦的: *a soignée divorcee in her forties* 一個四十多歲穿着入時的離婚女人

soil[1] /sɔɪl; sɔɪl/ *n* **1** [C,U] the top layer of the earth in which plants grow 土壤, 土地, 泥土: *an area of rich soil* 一片肥沃的土地 | *The bush grows well in a sandy soil.* 這種灌木在沙質土地裡生長良好。—see 見 LAND[1] (USAGE) **2 the soil** *literary* farming as a job or way of life【文】務農, 種地為生: *They make their living from the soil.* 他們以務農為生。**3 on British soil/French soil etc** *formal* in Britain, in France etc【正式】在英國/法國等(國土上): *The crime was committed on American soil.* 這樁罪案是在美國犯下的。**4 sb's native soil** *literary* your own country【文】某人的故土[故鄉, 故國] —see also 另見 NIGHT SOIL W2

soil[2] *v* [T] **1** *formal* to make something dirty, especially with waste from your body【正式】〔尤指用人的排泄物〕弄髒, 弄污 **2 not soil your hands** to not do something because you consider it too dirty, unpleasant, or dishonest 不玷污雙手〔指不做卑污的事〕: *I wouldn't soil my hands with such a devious scheme.* 我不會讓這個骯髒的計劃玷污我的雙手。—**soiled** *adj*: *soiled diapers* 髒尿布

soi·ree, soirée /swɑˋre; ˈswɑːreɪ/ *n* [C] *old-fashioned* a formal evening party, often including a performance of music【過時】晚會〔常指有音樂表演的正式晚會〕

soj·ourn /ˈsodʒɝn; ˈsɒdʒɜːn/ *n* [C] *literary* a short period of time that you stay in a place that is not your home【文】逗留, 暫住: *a brief sojourn in Europe* 在歐洲的小住 —**sojourn** *v* [I]

sol /sɑl; sɒl/ *n* [singular,U] SO[4] 全音階的第五音

sol·ace[1] /ˈsɑlɪs; ˈsɒlɪ̥s/ *n* **1** [U] *formal* a feeling of emotional comfort at a time of great sadness or disappointment【正式】安慰, 慰藉: **seek/find solace in** *After the death of her son, Val found solace in the church.* 在兒子死後, 瓦爾在教會找到了慰藉。**2 be a solace to** to bring a feeling of comfort and calmness to someone, when they are sad or disappointed 是…的安慰[慰藉]: *Mary was a great solace to me after Arthur died.* 阿瑟死後瑪麗就是我最大的安慰。

solace[2] *v* [T] *literary* to give emotional comfort to someone; CONSOLE[1]【文】安慰, 撫慰

so·lar /ˈsolɚ; ˈsəʊlə/ *adj* **1** connected with the sun 太陽的, 和太陽有關的 **2** using the power of the sun's light and heat 利用太陽光[能]的: *solar energy* 太陽能

solar cell /ˌ·· ˈ·/ *n* [C] a piece of equipment for producing electric power from sunlight 太陽能電池

so·lar·i·um /soˋlɛrɪəm; səʊˈleəriəm/ *n* [C] **1** a place with SUNBEDS (=beds with special lamps) where you can get an artificial SUNTAN 日光浴室〔設有日光浴牀, 讓人把皮

solar system 太陽系

膚曬黑〕: *The hotel has a solarium and sauna.* 這家旅店有日光浴室和蒸汽浴室。**2** a room, usually enclosed by glass, where you can sit in bright sunlight〔通常用玻璃建的〕日光室

solar pan·el /ˌ·· ˈ··/ *n* [C] a piece of equipment, usually on a roof, that uses the heat of the sun to heat water or to make electricity〔通常放在房頂的〕太陽能電池板

solar plex·us /ˌsolɚ ˈplɛksəs; ˌsəʊlə ˈpleksəs/ *n* [singular] *not technical* the front part of your body below your chest【非術語】心窩, 心口〔胸部靠下的部位〕

solar sys·tem /ˈ·· ˌ··/ *n* **1 the solar system** the sun and the PLANETS that go around it 太陽系〔太陽和繞太陽運行的所有行星〕 **2** [C] this kind of system around another star 繞其他星球運行的太陽系

solar year /ˌ·· ˈ·/ *n* [C] the period of time which the Earth travels around the Sun, equal to just over 365 days 太陽年〔地球繞太陽運行一周的時間, 稍稍超過365天〕

sold /sold; səʊld/ the past tense and past participle of SELL

sol·der¹ /ˈsɑldɚ; ˈsɒldə/ *n* [U] a soft metal, usually a mixture of lead and tin, which can be melted and used to join two metal sufaces, wires etc 焊料, 焊錫〔通常為鉛與錫的合金〕

solder² *v* [T] to join or repair metal surfaces with solder 焊接, 焊合

soldering i·ron /ˈ··· ˌ··/ *n* [C] a tool which is heated, usually by electricity, for melting and putting on solder〔焊接用的〕烙鐵

2 2 **sol·dier¹** /ˈsoldʒɚ; ˈsəʊldʒə/ *n* [C] a member of the army of a country, especially someone who is not an officer 士兵, 軍人〔尤指不是軍官的軍隊成員〕

soldier² *v*

soldier on *phr v* [I] *especially BrE* to continue working in spite of difficulties【尤英】〔不畏困難地〕繼續幹下去, 堅持幹下去: *He doesn't like the job, but he'll soldier on until they can find a replacement.* 他不喜歡這份工作, 但他會堅持幹下去, 直到他們找到接替他的人為止。

sol·dier·ing /ˈsoldʒərɪŋ; ˈsəʊldʒərɪŋ/ *n* [U] the life or job of a soldier 軍人的生活[工作]

sol·dier·ly /ˈsoldʒɚlɪ; ˈsəʊldʒəli/ *adj* typical of a good soldier 像軍人的, 有軍人風度的

soldier of for·tune /ˌ··· ˈ··/ *n* [C] *literary* someone who works as a soldier for anyone who will pay him; MERCENARY【文】雇傭兵

sol·dier·y /ˈsoldʒərɪ; ˈsəʊldʒəri/ *n* [singular,U] *literary* a group of soldiers of a particular, usually bad, kind【文】〔通常指壞的〕軍人, 軍隊

sold-out /ˌ· ˈ·◂/ *adj* a concert, performance etc that is sold-out has no more tickets left〔音樂會、表演等〕門票已全部售完的, 滿座的

3 **sole¹** /sol; səʊl/ *adj* [only before noun 僅用於名詞前] **1** the sole person, thing etc is the only one 唯一的, 僅有的: *the sole American in the room* 房間裡唯一的一位美國人 **2** a sole duty, right, responsibility etc is one that is not shared with anyone else 專有的, 獨佔的, 唯一的: *Derek has sole responsibility for sales in Eire.* 德里克獨自負責在愛爾蘭的銷售業務。

sole² *n* **1** [C] the bottom surface of your foot, especially the part you walk or stand on 腳掌, 腳底(板): *The soles of his feet were caked in mud.* 他的兩隻腳掌黏滿泥巴。 —see picture at 參見 FOOT¹ 圖 **2** [C] flat bottom part of a shoe, not including the heel 鞋底〔不包括鞋跟〕—see picture at 參見 SHOE¹ 圖 **3 thick-soled/leather-soled etc** having soles that are thick, made of leather etc〔鞋〕厚底/皮底的 **4** [C,U] a flat fish that is often used for food 鰨(魚) —see also 另見 LEMON SOLE

sole³ *v* [T usually passive 一般用被動態] to put a new sole on a shoe 給〔鞋〕配新底, 給〔鞋〕換底

so·le·cis·m /ˈsɑləˌsɪzəm; ˈsɒlɪsɪzəm/ *n* [C] *formal*【正式】**1** something that is different from what is considered polite behaviour 失禮, 出格: *a social solecism* 社交上的失禮 **2** a mistake in grammar 語法錯誤

sole·ly /ˈsol·lɪ; ˈsəʊl-li/ *adv* not involving anything or anyone else; only 唯一地, 僅僅, 獨一無二地: *Scholarships are given solely on the basis of financial need.* 獎學金完全是根據經濟需要發放的。| *I shall hold you solely responsible for anything that goes wrong.* 出現任何問題我都要讓你全權負責。

sol·emn /ˈsɑləm; ˈsɒləm/ *adj* **1** very serious in behaviour or style 嚴肅的, 莊重的: *a solemn expression* 嚴肅的表情 | *solemn music* 嚴肅音樂 **2 solemn promise/pledge/word etc** a promise that is made very seriously and with no intention of breaking it 鄭重的諾言/誓言/話語等: *I'll never be unfaithful again. I give you my solemn word.* 我再也不會對你不忠了, 我鄭重向你保證。**3** a solemn ceremony is performed in a very serious way〔儀式〕莊嚴的, 隆重的 —**solemnly** *adv* —**solemness** *n* [U]

so·lem·ni·ty /səˈlɛmnətɪ; səˈlemnɪ̇ti/ *n* **1** [U] the quality of being serious in behaviour or manner 莊嚴, 隆重; 莊重, 嚴肅: *the solemnity of a great religious occasion* 重大宗教場合的莊嚴肅穆 **2 solemnities** [plural] the ceremonies of an important and serious occasion 隆重的儀式: *He was buried with all the solemnities befitting a monarch.* 他以君主應有的隆重儀式安葬。

sol·em·nize also 又作 **-ise** *BrE*【英】/ˈsɑləmˌnaɪz; ˈsɒləmnaɪz/ *v* **solemnize a marriage** *formal* to perform a wedding ceremony in a church【正式】在教堂舉行婚禮 —**solemnization** /ˌsɑləmnəˈzeʃən; ˌsɒləmnaɪˈzeɪʃən/ *n* [U]

sol-fa /sol ˈfɑ; ˌsɒl ˈfɑː/ *n* [U] the system in which the notes of the musical SCALE¹ (8) are represented by seven short words DO, RE, MI etc, used especially in singing〔尤指聲樂中的〕階名唱法

so·li·cit /səˈlɪsɪt; səˈlɪsɪ̇t/ *v* **1** [I] to offer to have sex with someone in exchange for money〔賣淫者〕拉(客): *She was arrested for soliciting.* 她因拉客而被逮捕。**2** [I,T] *formal* to ask someone for money, help, or information【正式】請求; 懇求; 乞求: **solicit sth from sb** *The governor sent two officials to Mexico City to so-*

licit aid from the President. 州長派出兩名官員去墨西哥城向總統求助。**3** [T] *AmE* to sell something by taking orders for a product or service, usually by going to people's houses or businesses【美】〔上門〕招攬〔生意〕, 兜銷 —**solicitation** /səˌlɪsɪˋteʃən; səˌlɪsǀˈteɪʃən/ *n* [C, U]

3 2 **so·lic·i·tor** /səˋlɪsətə; səˈlɪsǀtə/ *n* [C] a type of lawyer in Britain who gives advice, does the necessary work when property is bought and sold, and defends people, especially in the lower courts of law 事務律師〔英國的一種律師, 其職責為提供諮詢、辦理房地產買賣手續、在下級法庭出庭替人辯護等〕—compare 比較 ADVOCATE[2] (2), BARRISTER —see 見 LAWYER (USAGE)

so·lic·i·tor gen·e·ral /·ˌ··· ˈ···/ *n* [C] the government law officer next in rank below the ATTORNEY GENERAL〔英國的〕副檢察長

so·lic·i·tous /səˋlɪsɪtəs; səˈlɪsǀtəs/ *adj formal* anxiously caring about someone's safety, health, or comfort【正式】關懷的, 關切的, 操心的: **[+of/for/about]** *Mary was always solicitous of my health.* 瑪麗總是為我的健康操心。—**solicitously** *adv* —**solicitousness** *n* [U]

so·lic·i·tude /səˋlɪsəˌtud; səˈlɪsǀtjuːd/ *n* [U+**for**] *formal* anxious and eager care for someone's health, safety etc【正式】關懷, 關切, 牽掛

3 3 **sol·id**[1] /ˋsɑlɪd; ˈsɒlǀd/ *adj*

1 ▶FIRM/HARD 堅實/堅硬的◀ having a firm shape, and usually hard 固體的; 堅硬的: *Even the milk was frozen solid.* 連牛奶也凍結了。| *After wading through the marshes we were glad to be on solid ground.* 我們跋涉過了沼澤之後, 很高興又踏上堅實的地面。| **solid food(s)** *The baby isn't old enough to eat solid foods yet.* 這個嬰兒還太小, 不能吃固體食物。

2 ▶STRONGLY MADE 做得堅固的◀ strong and well made 結實的, 牢固的: *good, solid furniture* 結實的優質家具 | **as solid as a rock** (=very solid) 堅如磐石, 非常堅固 *The frame looks quite flimsy, but in fact it's as solid as a rock.* 這個框架看起來不怎麼結實, 但其實非常堅固。

3 ▶VALUABLE WORK 有價值的工作◀ well done and of real practical value 出色的; 紮實的: *five years of solid achievement* 五年的出色成績 | *a good solid education* 良好紮實的教育

4 ▶DEFINITE FACTS 明確的事實◀ [only before noun 僅用於名詞前] based on real facts; definite 實在的; 明確的: *We need some solid evidence to prove our case.* 我們需要一些可靠的證據來證明我們的案例。

5 solid basis/foundation a strong principle on which something is based 堅實的基礎: *Our relationship is built on a solid foundation of mutual trust.* 我們的關係建立在互相信任的堅實基礎上。

6 ▶HONEST AND RESPECTED 誠實而受尊敬的◀ respected because you are honest and people can depend on you to behave well 有信譽的, 可靠的: *a respectable solid citizen* 體面可敬的市民 | *a firm with a solid reputation* 有良好聲譽的公司

7 solid gold/silver/oak etc consisting completely of gold 純金/銀/橡木等: *a solid gold cup* 純金獎盃

8 ▶NOT HOLLOW 非空心的◀ having no holes or spaces inside 無孔的; 實心的: *a solid rubber ball* 實心皮球 | *a shrine carved out of the solid rock* 用整塊岩石鑿成的神龕 —see picture at 參見 HOLLOW[1] 圖

9 ▶LOYAL 忠誠的◀ giving loyal support that you can depend on 忠實可靠的: *a solid supporter of the Clinton administration* 克林頓政府的忠實支持者

10 ▶CONTINUOUS 連續不斷的◀ *informal* without any pauses【非正式】不斷的: *The lecture lasted two solid hours.* 那講座持續了整整兩個小時。| **five hours/two weeks solid** *On Saturday I went to bed and slept fourteen hours solid.* 我從星期六開始睡覺, 連續睡了整整十四個鐘頭。

11 ▶CLOSE TOGETHER 密集在一起的◀ very close together without any spaces in between 密密麻麻的, 沒有空隙的: *The road was blocked by a solid mass of protesters.* 公路被密密麻麻的抗議者堵塞了。| *a solid line of traffic stretching away into the distance* 一輛接一輛的汽車延伸到很遠的地方

12 ▶GEOMETRY 幾何圖形◀ *technical* having length, width, and height; THREE-DIMENSIONAL【術語】立體的; 三維的: *A sphere is a solid figure.* 球體是立體形狀。

13 ▶IN AGREEMENT 一致◀ **be solid** *BrE* to be in complete agreement【英】全體一致: *The workers are 100% solid on this issue.* 工人們在這個問題上是百分之百地一致。| **[+for/against]** *The members were solid against the idea.* 全體成員一致反對這個意見。—**solidly** *adv*: *solidly built* 體格結實的 —**solidness** *n* [U]

solid[2] *n* **1** [C] a firm object or substance that has a fixed shape, unlike a gas or liquid 固體: *Water changes from a liquid to a solid when it freezes.* 水結冰時從液體變成固體。**2 solids a)** [plural] food that is not liquid 固體食物, 非流質食物: *He's still too ill to eat solids.* 他仍病得很重, 不能吃固體食物。**b)** [C] *technical* the part of a liquid which has the qualities of a solid when it is separated from the SOLVENT[2]【術語】〔液體中的〕固形物: *milk solids* 牛奶中的固體物質 **3** *technical* a shape which has length, width, and height【術語】立體

sol·i·dar·i·ty /ˌsɑləˋdærətɪ; ˌsɒlǀˈdærǀti/ *n* [U] loyalty and general agreement between all the people in a group, or between different groups because they all have a shared aim 團結, 一致: *an appeal for workers' solidarity* 呼籲工人們團結一致 | **[+with]** *The rail workers will strike to show their solidarity with the miners.* 鐵路工人將舉行罷工以顯示與礦工間的團結一致。

solid fu·el /ˌ·· ˈ··/ *n* [C] a solid substance such as coal that is burnt to produce heat or power 固體燃料〈如煤〉

so·lid·i·fy /səˋlɪdəˌfaɪ; səˈlɪdǀfaɪ/ *v* **1** [I,T] to become solid or make something solid (使)變成固體: *The volcanic lava solidifies as it cools.* 火山熔岩一冷卻就變成固體。**2** [T] to make an agreement, plan, attitude etc firmer and less likely to change 使鞏固; 使堅固: *The two countries signed a treaty to solidify their alliance.* 這兩個國家簽訂條約以鞏固雙方的聯盟。—**solidification** /səˌlɪdəfəˋkeʃən; səˌlɪdǀfǀˈkeɪʃən/ *n* [U]

so·lid·i·ty /səˋlɪdətɪ; səˈlɪdǀti/ *n* [U] **1** the strength or hardness of something 堅固, 堅硬: *the solidity of the stone walls* 石牆的堅固性 **2** the quality of something that is permanent and can be depended on 穩固, 可靠(性): *the solidity and respectability of bourgeois institutions* 資產階級制度的穩固與體面

solid-state /ˌ·· ˈ·◂/ *adj* **1** a solid-state electrical system uses TRANSISTORS〔電子裝置〕固態的, 全晶體管的 **2** solid-state PHYSICS is concerned with the qualities of solid substances, especially the way in which they CONDUCT[1] (3) electricity〔物理學〕固態的〔固態物理學研究固態物質的性質, 尤指其導電方式〕

sol·i·dus /ˋsɑlɪdəs; ˈsɒlǀdəs/ *n plural* **solidi** /-daɪ; -daɪ/ [C] an OBLIQUE[2] 斜線符號

so·lil·o·quy /səˋlɪləkwɪ; səˈlɪləkwi/ *n* [C,U] a speech in a play in which a character talks to himself or herself so that the audience knows their thoughts〔戲劇中的〕獨白 —compare 比較 MONOLOGUE —**soliloquize** /-ˌkwaɪz; -kwaɪz/ *v* [I]

sol·ip·sis·m /ˋsɑlɪpsɪzṃ; ˈsɒlǀpsɪzəm/ *n* [U] the idea that only the SELF exists or can be known 唯我論〔認為只有自我存在或可知的思想〕

sol·i·taire /ˌsɑləˋtɛr; ˌsɒlǀˈteə/ *n* **1** [C] a single jewel or a piece of jewellery with a single jewel in it, especially a large diamond 獨粒寶石〔尤指大粒的鑽石〕; 鑲有獨粒寶石的飾物 **2** [U] a game played by one person with small wooden or plastic pieces on a board 單人跳棋 **3** [U] *AmE* a game of cards for one person【美】單人紙牌戲; PATIENCE (4) *BrE*【英】

sol·i·ta·ry[1] /ˋsɑləˌtɛrɪ; ˈsɒlǀtəri/ *adj* **1** [only before noun 僅用於名詞前] a solitary person or thing is the only one

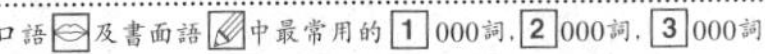

you can see in a place 單個的, 唯一的: *a solitary tree in the middle of the field* 田野中孤零零的一棵樹 **2** spending a lot of time alone, usually because they like being alone 喜歡獨處的, 不喜與人接觸的: *a solitary man who never spoke to anyone* 一個喜歡獨處、從不與人講話的男子 —see 見 ALONE¹ (USAGE) **3** done or experienced without anyone else around 單獨的, 無伴的: *a long, solitary walk across the moors* 獨自長途跋涉通過荒野 **4 not a solitary word/thing etc** if there is not a solitary thing or person, there is not even one 一言不發/空無一物: *He followed her round without a solitary word.* 他跟着她到處走, 一句話也不說。—**solitarily** *adv* —**solitariness** *n* [U]

solitary² *n* **1** [U] *informal* solitary confinement【非正式】單獨監禁 **2** [C] someone who lives completely alone; HERMIT 隱士, 隱居者

solitary con·fine·ment /ˌ···· ·'··/ *n* [U] an additional punishment for a prisoner in which they are kept alone and are not allowed to see anyone else 單獨監禁〔作為對囚犯的加重懲罰〕

sol·i·tude /ˈsɑləˌtud; ˈsɒlɪ̈tjuːd/ *n* [U] the state of being alone especially when this is what you enjoy 孤獨, 孤單, 獨居: *She wished for the solitude of her house on the lake.* 她嚮往她在湖邊那所房子的獨居生活。

so·lo¹ /ˈsolo; ˈsəʊləʊ/ *adj* **1** done alone without anyone else helping you 獨自的, 單獨的: *Ridgeway's solo voyage across the Atlantic* 里奇韋橫跨大西洋的單獨航行 | **go solo** (=start doing something on your own) 獨自幹 **2** related to or played as a musical solo 獨奏的; 獨唱的: *a solo passage for viola* 中提琴獨奏的段落 —**solo** *adv*: *When did you first fly solo?* 你第一次單獨飛行是甚麼時候?

solo² *n plural* **solos** [C] **1** a piece of music for one performer 獨奏曲; 獨唱曲 —compare 比較 DUET **2** a job or performance that is done alone, especially an aircraft flight 單獨表演〔尤指單人飛行〕

so·lo·ist /ˈsoˌlo-ɪst; ˈsəʊləʊɪ̈st/ *n* [C] a musician who performs a solo 獨奏者; 獨唱者

sol·stice /ˈsɑlstɪs; ˈsɒlstɪ̈s/ *n* [C] the time of either the longest or the shortest day of the year 至, 至日〔一年中最長或最短的一天〕—compare 比較 EQUINOX

sol·u·ble /ˈsɑljəbl̩; ˈsɒljʊ̈bəl/ *adj* **1** a soluble substance can be dissolved (DISSOLVE (1)) in a liquid 可溶的, 易溶解的: *soluble aspirin* 可溶性阿斯匹林 **2** *formal* a problem that is soluble, can be solved【正式】〔問題〕可解決的; 可解答的 —opposite 反義詞 INSOLUBLE —**solubility** /ˌsɑljəˈbɪlətɪ; ˌsɒljʊ̈ˈbɪlɪ̈ti/ *n* [U]

2 1 **so·lu·tion** /səˈluʃən; səˈluːʃən/ *n* **1** [C] a way of solving a problem or dealing with a difficult situation〔對問題、困難局面的〕解決, 解決方法: *The best solution would be for them to separate.* 最好的解決方法是他們分開。| **[+to/for]** *There are no simple solutions to the problem of overpopulation.* 對人口過多的問題沒有簡單的解決方法。| **find a solution** *Both sides are trying to find a peaceful solution.* 雙方都在努力尋求和平的解決方案。**2** [C] the correct answer to a problem in an exercise or competition〔練習或比賽的〕解答, 答案: **[+to]** *The solution to last week's puzzle is on page 12.* 上星期字謎的謎底在第12頁。**3** [C,U] a liquid mixed with a solid or gas, usually without a chemical change 溶液〔液體與固體或氣體的混合物, 通常不產生化學反應〕: *a weak sugar solution* 稀淡的糖溶液

2 3 **solve** /sɑlv; sɒlv/ *v* [T] **1** to find or provide a way of dealing with a problem 解決〔問題〕: *Charlie thinks money will solve all his problems.* 查理認為金錢會解決他所有的問題。**2** to find the correct answer to a problem or the explanation for something that is difficult to understand 解答, 解釋〔難題〕: *solving a mathematical equation* 解一個數學方程式 | **solve a crime/mystery/case** *The police haven't been able to solve the murder yet.* 警方至今未能偵破這宗謀殺案。—**solvable** *adj*

sol·vent¹ /ˈsɑlvənt; ˈsɒlvənt/ *adj* having enough money to pay your debts 有還債[償付]能力的: *I have to wait until my paycheck arrives before I'm solvent again.* 我要等拿到薪金支票才有錢還債。—opposite 反義詞 INSOLVENT —**solvency** *n* [U]

solvent² *n* [C,U] a liquid that is able to turn a solid substance into liquid 溶劑

solvent a·buse /'·· ·,·/ *formal n* [U] the habit of breathing in gases from glues or similar substances in order to get a pleasant feeling; GLUE-SNIFFING【正式】吸膠毒〔可得到快感〕

som·bre *BrE*【英】, **somber** *AmE*【美】/ˈsɑmbɚ; ˈsɒmbə/ *adj* **1** sad and serious; GRAVE² (1) 憂鬱的; 嚴峻的: *They sat in sombre silence.* 他們默默地坐着, 神情嚴肅。| *a sombre expression* 憂鬱的表情 | *on the sombre occasion of his mother's funeral* 在他母親葬禮的憂傷場合 **2** dark and without any bright colours 昏暗的, 陰沉的, 暗淡的: *a suit of sombre grey* 一套暗灰色的衣服 —**sombrely** *adv* —**sombreness** *n* [U]

som·bre·ro /sɑmˈbrɛro; sɒmˈbreərəʊ/ *n plural* **sombreros** [C] a Mexican hat for men that is tall with a wide, round BRIM¹ (1) turned up at the edges〔墨西哥男子戴的〕闊邊帽 —see picture at 參見 HAT 圖

some¹ /səm; səm *strong* 強讀 sʌm; sʌm/ *determiner* **1** a number of people or things or an amount of something, when the exact number or amount is not stated 一些, 若干: *I need some apples for this recipe.* 我需要一些蘋果來做這道菜。| *My mother has inherited some land in western Australia.* 我母親繼承了一些在澳大利亞西部的土地。| *They're looking for someone with some experience.* 他們在找有些經驗的人。| *The doctor gave her some medicine for her cough.* 醫生給了她一些治咳嗽的藥。**2** a number of people or things or an amount of something but not all 有些, 一部分: *Some people believe in life after death.* 有些人相信有來世。| *She's been so depressed that some days she can't get out of bed in the morning.* 她一直很消沉, 有幾天早上都無法起牀。**3** used to mean a person or thing, when you do not know or say exactly which 有個, 某個〔未知或不確指的人或物〕: *There must be some reason for her behaviour.* 她的行為一定有某種理由的。| *Some woman came up to me and told me we'd been to school together.* 有個婦女走到我跟前來告訴我, 我們曾經一起上學。| *Can you give me some idea of the cost?* 你能告訴我這大約要花多少錢嗎? **4** a fairly large number of people or things or a fairly large amount of something 相當多(的), 不少(的): *Some days later I read that he had died.* 許多天以後我才獲悉他已經去世。| *It was some time before they managed to turn the alarm off.* 過了好長時間他們才關掉警報器。| *The donation went some way towards paying for the damage.* 這筆捐款支付了相當大的一部分損壞賠償。**5 some friend/help! etc** *especially spoken* used, especially when you are annoyed, to mean someone has not been friendly, helpful etc【尤口】這算甚麼朋友/毫無幫助!〔尤用於生氣之時〕: *"Surely you can have a day off soon?" "Some hope with this new boss!"* "你肯定很快就可以休假一天了吧?" "在這個新老闆手下, 根本沒有希望!" **6** used to say that something was very good or very impressive 出色的, 了不起的: *That was some party last night!* 昨晚的聚會好極了! | *Some speech you made last night Tom!* 湯姆, 你昨晚做了一次精彩的演講! **7 some...or other/another** *informal* used to show that you are not certain exactly which person, thing or place and do not think it matters【非正式】某個, 某一; 某幾個, 某些〔用於表示不確指何人、何物、何地等〕: *Just give him some excuse or other.* 就給他說個理由吧。| *I think he's staying with some friends or another in Wales.* 我想他正住在威爾斯的某些朋友家裡。 1 1

some² /sʌm; sʌm/ *pron* **1** a number of people or things or an amount of something, when the exact number or amount is not stated 一些, 若干: *I've made a pot of coffee. Would you like some?* 我沖了一壺咖啡, 你想喝點嗎? |

"Do you know where the screws are?" "Yes, there are some in the garage." "你知道螺絲釘在哪兒嗎?" "知道, 車庫裡有一些。" | *People gave plenty of suggestions and we used some in the new show.* 人們提了許多建議, 我們在新的演出中採用了一些。**2** a number of people or things or an amount of something but not all 有些, 一部分: *Some say it was an accident but I don't believe it.* 有些人說那是一次事故, 但我不相信。| *Many of the exhibits were damaged in the fire and some were totally destroyed.* 許多展品在那場大火中損壞了, 一部分則被完全焚毀了。| [+of] *Some of his jokes were very rude indeed.* 他講的笑話有一些真的很粗魯。**3 and then some** *informal especially AmE* and more【非正式, 尤美】更多, 還不止這麼多: *"They say he earns $40,000." "Yes, and then some!."* "他們說他一年掙四萬美元。" "是的, 還不止這些呢!"

some³ *adv* **1 some 10 people/50%/£100 etc** an expression meaning about 10 people, 50%, £100 etc 大約50人/50%/100英鎊等: *She gained some 25 pounds in weight during pregnancy.* 她在懷孕期間體重增加了大約25磅。**2** *AmE* a fairly or a little【美】有幾分, 稍微, 有點: *"Are you feeling better today?" "Some, I guess."* "你今天覺得好些了嗎?" "我想稍微好些吧。" **3 some little/some few** a fairly large number or amount of something 相當多: *We travelled some little way before noticing that Bradley wasn't with us.* 我們走了相當長的路程才注意到, 布拉德利沒跟我們在一起。**4 some more** an additional number or amount of something 再要一點: *Would you like some more cake?* 你再要一點蛋糕嗎?

-some¹ /səm; səm/ *suffix* [in adjectives 構成形容詞] **1** causing or producing something 引起[產生]…的: *a troublesome boy* (=who causes trouble) 煩人的孩子 **2** liking to do something 喜歡…的: *a quarrelsome woman* (=who likes to quarrel) 愛吵架的女人 | *frolicsome* 愛嬉戲的 **3** describes someone or something that can be treated in a particular way, or that you would like to treat in that way 可用某種方式〔對待〕的, 想要…的: *a cuddle-some baby* (=that you would like to hold in your arms) 逗人喜愛的嬰孩

-some² *suffix* [in nouns 構成名詞] a group of a particular number, especially in a game〔尤指在體育活動中〕…人一組: *a golf foursome* (=four people playing GOLF together) 打高爾夫球的四個人

some·bod·y¹ /ˈsʌmˌbɑdɪ; ˈsʌmbɒdi/ *pron* used to mean a person, when you do not know, or do not say who the person is 某人, 有人: *There's somebody waiting to see you.* 有人在等着要見你。| *Somebody's car alarm kept me awake all night.* 不知誰的汽車警報器吵得我整晚都無法入睡。| **somebody new/different etc** *We need somebody neutral to sort this out.* 我們需要個中立的人來處理這件事。| **somebody else** (=a different person) 另一個人 *If you can't make it, we can always invite somebody else.* 如果你做不到, 我們完全可以另請他人。| **or somebody** (=or someone similar) 諸如此類的人 *"Who was at the door?" "It was a priest or somebody wanting to talk about religion."* "誰在門外?" "是個牧師之類的人, 想談談宗教方面的問題。"

somebody² *n* **be somebody** to be or feel important 很重要; 感覺很重要: *She was the first teacher who'd made Paul feel like he was somebody.* 她是第一位使保羅覺得自己還有所作為的老師。

some·day /ˈsəmˌde; ˈsʌmdeɪ/ *adv* at an unknown time in the future especially a long time in the future 將來會有一天, 有朝一日: *Maybe someday I'll be rich!* 也許有朝一日我會富起來的!

some·how /ˈsʌmˌhau; ˈsʌmhaʊ/ *adv* **1** in some way, or by some means, although you do not know how 用某種方法; 不知怎麼地: *Don't worry, we'll get the money back somehow.* 別擔心, 我們總會把那些錢拿回來的。| **somehow or other** *Maybe we could glue it together somehow or other.* 說不定我們總會有辦法把它給黏起來。**2** for some reason that is not clear 由於某種不明原因, 不知為甚麼: *Somehow, I just don't think it'll work.* 不知為甚麼, 我就是覺得行不通。

some·one¹ /ˈsʌmˌwʌn; ˈsʌmwʌn/ *pron* used to mean a person, when you do not know, or do not say, who the person is 某人, 有人: *What would you do if someone tried to rob you in the street?* 要是有人在街上搶劫你, 你怎麼辦? | *Will someone please explain what's going on.* 誰來解釋一下正在發生的事。| **someone new/different etc** *We'll make an appointment as soon as we find someone suitable.* 我們一找到合適的人, 就會加以任命。| **someone else** (=a different person) 另一個人 *They noticed someone else in the water.* 他們注意到水中還有另外一個人。| **or someone** (=or someone similar) 諸如此類的人 *You have to get a doctor or someone to sign as a witness.* 你必須找一位醫生之類的人簽字作證。

someone² *n* **be someone** to be or feel important 很重要; 感覺很重要

some·place /ˈsʌmples; ˈsʌmpleɪs/ *adv especially AmE* somewhere【尤美】某個地方, 某處: *I must have left my jacket someplace.* 我一定是把外套遺忘在甚麼地方了。

som·er·sault /ˈsʌmɚˌsɔlt; ˈsʌməsɔːlt/ *n* [C] a movement in which someone rolls or jumps forwards or backwards so that their feet go over their head before they stand up again 跟頭, 觔斗;〔向前或向後的〕滾翻: **do/turn a somersault** *Lana turned a somersault in midair.* 拉娜在半空中翻了個觔斗。—**somersault** *v* [I]: *The car somersaulted twice before coming to a stop.* 那輛車翻滾了兩下才停下來。

some·thing /ˈsʌmθɪŋ; ˈsʌmθɪŋ/ *pron* [not usually in questions or negatives 一般不用於疑問句或否定句] **1** used to mean a particular thing when you do not know its name, do not know exactly what it is etc 某物, 某事, 某種東西: *There's something in my eye.* 我眼睛裡有東西。| *Sarah said something about coming over later.* 莎拉說她等一會要來甚麼的。| **something new/old etc** *It's a good little car but I'm looking for something faster.* 這輛小車不錯, 不過我想找一輛跑得更快的。| **something else** (=something different) 另外的東西, 別的東西 *The house was too small so they decided to look for something else.* 那棟房子太小, 所以他們決定另外找一棟。**2 there is something about** used to say that a person, situation etc has a quality or feature that you recognize but you cannot say exactly what it is 具有某種難以言傳的特點: *There's something about America that I find really exciting.* 美國有某種我覺得真正令人興奮的東西。| **there is something unusual/strange etc about** *There was always something a little sad about her.* 她總是帶着一點憂傷(的樣子)。**3 do something** to do something in order to deal with a problem or difficult situation 動手去解決問題, 做點甚麼: *Don't just stand there – do something!* 不要只是袖手旁觀 —— 要動動手! | **do something about sth** *Can't you do something about that smell!* 難道你不能設法去除掉那味道! **4 it's (quite/really) something** used to say that something should be admired because it is impressive 真了不起, 真精彩: *Running your own company at age 21 is really something!* 你21歲就經營自己的公司, 真了不起。**5 something like 100/two thousand etc** approximately 100, two thousand etc 100/二千等左右: *Something like 80% of the population has no running water.* 大約80%的人口沒有自來水用。**6 something of a** used like 'rather' to emphasize the effect of something, the seriousness of something etc 多少有點, 頗有幾分〔用於強調某事的效果、嚴重性等〕: *He has made something of a name for himself in the world of tennis.* 他在網球界可以說是頗有名氣。**7 be something of a gardener/an expert etc** to know a lot about something or to be very good at something 算得上是園藝家/專家等: *Charlie's always been something of an expert on architecture.* 查理一直可以算得上是建築方面的專家。**8 have some-**

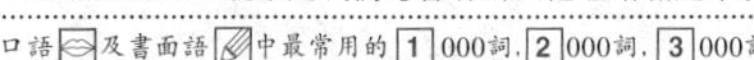

thing of to have a few of the same features or qualities that someone else has 有〔某人〕的某些特點: *It was clear that Jenkins had inherited something of his father's brilliance.* 很明顯, 詹金斯繼承了他父親的某些聰明才智。**9 there's something in** used to admit that someone's words are true or their ideas are successful etc〔某人的話、主意等〕有道理: *They had to concede that there was something in his teaching methods.* 他們不得不承認他的教學方法有道理。**10 have/be something to do with** to be connected with or related to a particular person or thing, but you are not sure in what way 與…有聯繫, 和…有關係: *I don't know much about his work, but I know it's something to do with animals.* 我不太了解他的工作, 但我知道和動物有關。**11 thirty-something/forty-something etc** *especially humorous* used to say that someone is aged between 30 and 39, between 40 and 49 etc when you do not know exactly【尤幽默】三十多歲/四十多歲等 **12 a little something** a small or cheap gift 一件小[廉價]禮物: *I got you a little something from my holiday.* 我度假時給你買了一件小禮物。

Frequencies of the word **something** in spoken and written English 單詞something在英語口語和書面語中的使用頻率

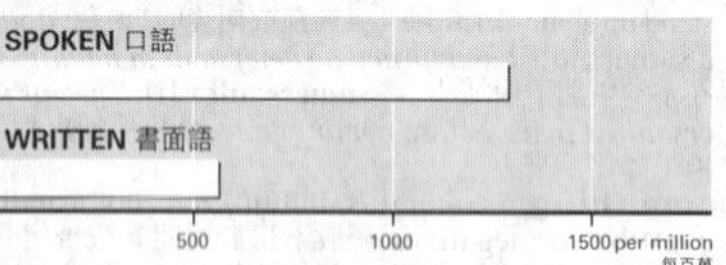

Based on the British National Corpus and the Longman Lancaster Corpus
據英國國家語料庫和朗文蘭卡斯特語料庫

This graph shows that the word **something** is much more common in spoken English than in written English. This is because it is used in a lot of common spoken phrases. 本圖表顯示, something在英語口語中的使用頻率遠遠高於書面語, 因為口語中很多常用片語是由something構成的。

something (*pron*) **SPOKEN PHRASES**
含something的口語片語

13 or something used when you cannot remember or do not want to give another example of something you are mentioning 或者甚麼的, 諸如此類: *Here's some money. Get yourself a sandwich or something.* 這裡有一點錢, 你給自己去買三明治之類的東西吃吧。| *Her name was Judith, or Julie or something.* 她的名字叫朱迪斯, 或者朱莉甚麼的。**14 something like that** used when you cannot remember or do not want to say something exactly 大致是那樣: *She works in sales or promotion, something like that.* 她從事銷售或推銷, 大致是這一類工作。**15 there's something wrong with** used to say that something is not working properly …出了問題[故障]: *There's something wrong with my car so I had to get the bus.* 我的汽車壞了, 所以我不得不去坐公共汽車。**16 something to eat/drink** some food or a drink 吃的/喝的東西: *Would you like something to drink?* 你想喝點甚麼嗎? | *We had something to eat after the show.* 表演結束後我們吃了一點東西。**17 something to do** an activity or task 活動; 任務: *If you're looking for something to do, why not clean up the kitchen?* 你如果想找點事情幹, 為甚麼不把廚房打掃乾淨? **18 sixty something/John something etc** used when you cannot remember the rest of a number or name 六十多/約翰甚麼的〔表示記不清尾數或某人的全名等〕: *It cost over a hundred pounds. A hundred and twenty something it was.* 這花了一百多英鎊, 大概有一百二十多英鎊。**19 that's something** used to say that there is one thing that you should be glad about 那還算不錯〔表示某事可以聊以自慰〕: *At least we have some money left. That's something, isn't it?* 至少我們還剩一點錢。還算不錯, 是不是?

some·time¹ /ˋsʌmˏtaɪm; ˈsʌmtaɪm/ *adv* at a time in the future or in the past, although you do not know exactly when 在〔將來或過去的〕某個時候: *We'll take a vacation sometime in September.* 我們將在9月的某個時候休假。| *Our house was built sometime around 1900.* 我們的房子建於1900年左右。

sometime² *adj* [only before noun 僅用於名詞前] *formal* former【正式】曾經的, 以前的: *Sir Richard Marsh, the sometime chairman of British Rail* 理查德·馬什爵士, 前英國鐵路公司董事長

some·times /ˋsʌmˏtaɪmz; ˈsʌmtaɪmz/ *adv* on some occasions but not all 有時, 不時, 間或: *Sometimes I stay late in the library after class.* 我有時課後在圖書館待到很晚。—see picture at 參見 FREQUENCY 圖 S1 W1

some·way /ˋsʌmˏwe; ˈsʌmweɪ/ *adv AmE informal* SOMEHOW (1)【美, 非正式】用某種方法; 不知怎地

some·what /ˋsʌmˏhwɑt; ˈsʌmwɒt/ *adv* **1** more than a little but not very 有點兒, 有幾分: *The price is somewhat higher than I expected.* 這價格比我預料的高了一點。**2 more than somewhat** *BrE formal* very much【英, 正式】非常, 極其: *His behaviour displeased me more than somewhat.* 他的行為讓我非常不快。 S2 W2

some·where /ˋsʌmˏhwɛr; ˈsʌmweə/ *adv* [not usually in questions or negatives 一般不用於疑問句或否定句] **1** in or to a place, but you do not say or know exactly where 在某處; 到某處: *My car keys are around here somewhere.* 我的汽車鑰匙就在這周圍甚麼地方。| **somewhere to live/to sleep etc** *There must be somewhere to eat cheaply in this town.* 這個鎮裡一定有個吃飯便宜的地方。| **somewhere safe/different etc** *Is there somewhere safe where I can leave my bike?* 這裡有我可以放自行車的安全地方嗎? | **somewhere else** *Go and play somewhere else – I'm trying to work.* 到別的地方去玩——我正想工作。| **or somewhere** (=or a similar place) 或類似的地方 *We could hold the meal at Giorgio's or somewhere.* 我們可以在喬治家或別的甚麼地方吃飯。—see 見 PLACE¹ (USAGE) **2 somewhere around/between etc** a little more or a little less than a particular number or amount; APPROXIMATELY〔數字或數量〕大約在…左右/在…之間: *We now have somewhere in the region of 500 firefighters in this area alone.* 光在這個地區, 我們現在大約有消防隊員500名左右。**3 be getting somewhere** to be making progress 有進步, 有進展: *Well, that's a problem solved! At last I feel we're getting somewhere.* 好, 這就解決問題了! 我終於覺得我們有進展了。 S1 W2

som·nam·bu·list /sɑmˋnæmbjəˏlɪst; sɒmˈnæmbjʊlɪst/ *n* [C] *formal* someone who walks while they are asleep【正式】夢遊者 —**somnambulism** /sɑmˋnæmbjəˏlɪzəm; sɒmˈnæmbjʊlɪzəm/ *n* [U]

som·no·lent /ˋsɑmnələnt; ˈsɒmnələnt/ *adj literary*【文】**1** almost starting to sleep 想睡的, 瞌睡的 **2** making you want to sleep 催眠的: *a somnolent summer's afternoon* 催人欲睡的夏日午後 —**somnolence** *n* [U]

son /sʌn; sʌn/ *n* **1** [C] someone's male child 兒子: *Her son Sean was born in 1983.* 她的兒子肖恩出生於1983年。| *They have three sons and a daughter.* 他們有三個兒子和一個女兒。—see also 另見 **like father like son** (FATHER¹ (7)) —see picture at 參見 FAMILY 圖 **2** [singular] used by an older person as a friendly way to address a boy or young man 孩子〔長者對男孩或年輕男子的友好稱呼〕: *What's your name, son?* 孩子, 你叫甚麼名字? **3 the Son** Jesus Christ; the second member of the group that includes God the Father and the HOLY SPIRIT 聖子, 耶穌基督〔聖父、聖子、聖靈三位一體中的第二位〕**4 my son** used by a priest to address a man or boy 孩子〔神父 S1 W1

對男子或男孩的稱呼〕 **5** [C usually plural 一般用複數] *literary* a man from a particular place or country, or a man who has a particular job【文】〔來自特定地方或國家的, 或有特定職業的〕男子: *sons of Britain who fell in battle* 陣亡的英國男兒 —see also 另見 **favourite son** (FAVOURITE[1] (2))

so·nar /ˈsonɑr; ˈsəʊnɑː/ *n* [U] equipment on a ship or SUBMARINE that uses sound waves to find out the position of objects under the water 聲納(設備)〔船上或潛艇上利用聲波探測水下目標位置的儀器〕

so·na·ta /səˈnɑtə; səˈnɑːtə/ *n* [C] a piece of music with three or four parts that is written for a piano, or for a piano and another instrument 奏鳴曲

son et lu·mi·ère /ˌsɑn e lumˈjɛr; ˌsɒn eɪ ˈluːmieə/ *n* [singular,U] *especially BrE* a performance that tells the story of a historical place or event using lights and recorded sound【尤英】〔配以聲光效果的〕實地歷史劇; 聲光表演

S2 W2 **song** /sɔŋ; sɒŋ/ *n*

1 ▶MUSIC WITH WORDS 歌曲◀ **a)** [C] a short piece of music with words for singing 歌曲: *The students played guitars and sang folk songs.* 學生們一邊彈結他一邊唱民歌。| *a pop song on the radio* 收音機裡播放的流行歌曲 **b)** [U] songs in general 歌曲〔統稱〕: *He's doing research into popular song.* 他正在研究流行歌曲。| **burst/break into song** (=suddenly start singing) 突然唱起歌來 *Patty must be in love – she keeps bursting into song!* 帕蒂一定是在談戀愛了 —— 她常常會突然唱起歌來!

2 ▶BIRDS 鳥類◀ [C,U] the musical sounds made by birds 鳴唱, 鳥囀: *the song of the lark* 雲雀的鳴唱

3 for a song very cheaply 極便宜地, 以賤價: *He bought the house for a song five years ago.* 他在五年前以極低的價格買下那棟房子。

4 a song and dance about a) *BrE* if you make a song and dance about something you complain too much about it in a way that seems unnecessary【英】太多的嘮叨, 不停的抱怨: *There's no need to make such a song and dance about a little scratch on the car.* 沒必要為汽車上的一點刮痕而嘮叨個沒完。**b)** *AmE* a very complicated explanation or excuse for something you have done【美】諸多解釋, 藉口: *She gave us a long song and dance about why she hadn't sent the order on time.* 她向我們長篇大論地解釋, 想說明為甚麼沒有按時送貨。

song·bird /ˈsɔŋˌbɝd; ˈsɒŋbɜːd/ *n* [C] a bird that can make musical sounds 鳴禽

song·book /ˈsɔŋˌbʊk; ˈsɒŋbʊk/ *n* [C] a book with the words and music of many songs 歌本, 歌曲集

song·ster /ˈsɔŋstɚ; ˈsɒŋstə/ *n* [C] *literary*【文】**1** someone who sings and sometimes writes songs 歌手〔有時會創作歌曲〕**2** a songbird 鳴禽

song·writ·er /ˈsɔŋˌraɪtɚ; ˈsɒŋˌraɪtə/ *n* [C] someone who writes the words and usually the music of a song 歌詞作家, 詞曲作家

son·ic /ˈsɑnɪk; ˈsɒnɪk/ *adj technical* connected with sound, SOUND WAVES, or the speed of sound【術語】聲音的; 聲波的; 聲速的

sonic boom /ˌ·· ˈ·/ also 又作 **sonic bang** *BrE*【英】*n* [C] the loud sound like an explosion, that an aircraft makes when it starts to travel faster than the speed of sound 音爆, 聲震〔飛機開始以超音速飛行時所發出的像爆炸般的巨響〕

son-in-law /ˈ· · ˌ·/ *n* [C] the husband of your daughter 女婿 —compare 比較 DAUGHTER-IN-LAW —see picture at 參見 FAMILY 圖

son·net /ˈsɑnɪt; ˈsɒnɪt/ *n* [C] a poem with fourteen lines which RHYME with each other in a fixed pattern 十四行詩: *Shakespeare's sonnets* 莎士比亞的十四行詩

son·ny /ˈsʌnɪ; ˈsʌni/ *n* [singular] *old-fashioned spoken* used when speaking to a boy or young man who is much younger than you【過時, 口】乖孩子, 小伙子〔用於稱呼男孩或比自己年輕得多的男子〕: *Now you just listen to me, sonny.* 現在你聽我說, 乖孩子。

Sonny Jim /ˌsʌnɪ ˈdʒɪm; ˌsʌni ˈdʒɪm/ *n BrE old-fashioned or humorous* used as a friendly way of speaking to someone, especially a man【英, 過時或幽默】老兄, 好小子, 傢伙〔尤用於對男子的友好稱呼〕

son of a bitch, sonofabitch /ˌsʌn əv ə ˈbɪtʃ; ˌsʌn əv ə ˈbɪtʃ/ *n spoken especially AmE*【口, 尤美】**1** [C] an impolite expression meaning a man or object that you are very angry or annoyed with 雜種, 狗娘養的〔對人或物很生氣時的非禮貌用語〕: *That son of a bitch isn't going to get away with this!* 那個狗娘養的別想這樣脫身! **2 son of a bitch!** an impolite expression of annoyance 他媽的! 真見鬼!〔表示生氣的非禮貌用語〕: *Son of a bitch! The car won't start!* 他媽的! 汽車發動不起來! **3 be a son of a bitch** to be very difficult 是極難的事: *Getting the new tire on was a real son of a bitch.* 裝上新輪胎真是吃力得要命。

son of a gun /ˌ· · · ˈ·/ *n* [C] *AmE old-fashioned spoken*【美, 過時, 口】**1** a man that you are annoyed with 流氓, 惡棍, 壞傢伙〔表示生氣〕: *That son of a gun didn't show up to fix the washer again today.* 那個修洗衣機的傢伙今天又沒來。**2** *humorous* a man you like or admire【幽默】老兄, 傢伙, 好小子〔表示親昵〕: *John, you old son of a gun, where have you been?* 約翰, 你這個老傢伙, 上哪兒去了? **3** *humorous* an object that is difficult to deal with【幽默】難對付的東西, 鬼東西: *The sofa was huge, and we couldn't get the son of a gun to fit through the door!* 那張沙發大得很, 我們沒法把那個鬼東西搬進門! **4 son of a gun!** used to express surprise 他媽的! 真見鬼!〔表示驚訝〕

Son of God /ˌ· · ˈ·/ *n* [singular] used by Christians to mean Jesus Christ 聖子〔基督徒對耶穌基督的稱呼〕

so·nor·ous /səˈnɔrəs; ˈsɒnərəs/ *adj* having a pleasantly deep loud sound 聲音洪亮的: *a sonorous voice* 洪亮的聲音 —**sonorously** *adv* —**sonorousness** *n* [U]

soon /sun; suːn/ *adv* **1** in a short time from now, or a short time after something else happens 不久, 即刻, 很快: *It will be dark soon.* 很快就要天黑了。| *David arrived back from Paris sooner than I expected.* 戴維從巴黎回來得比我預料的快。| *They wanted to climb to the top, but they soon abandoned this idea.* 他們想要爬上頂部, 但很快就放棄了這個念頭。| **[+after]** *Paula was pregnant soon after their honeymoon.* 葆拉度完蜜月不久就懷孕了。| **how soon** (=how quickly) 多快, 多久 *How soon can you finish the report?* 你最快幾時能完成這份報告? | **as soon as possible** (=as quickly as possible) 儘快 *Try and get the car fixed as soon as possible.* 設法儘快把這輛車修好。| **as soon as you can** *I'll come over to your place as soon as I can.* 我會儘快到你這裡來。| **all too soon** (=much sooner than you would like) 太快 *Children grow up all too soon.* 小孩子長得太快了。| **the sooner the better** (=used to say that it is important that something should happen very soon) 越快越好 *The sooner you answer Jack's letter the better.* 你給傑克回信越快越好。| **the sooner ... the sooner** (=used to say that if something happens soon, then something that you want will happen soon afterwards) ...越快...也會越快 *The sooner I get this work done, the sooner I can go home.* 我越快做完這件工作, 就可以越早回家。**2 as soon as** immediately after something has happened 一...就...: *I came as soon as I heard the news.* 我一聽到消息馬上就來了。**3 no sooner had ... than** used to say that something happened almost immediately after something else 一...就..., 剛...就...: *No sooner had he sat down than the phone rang.* 他剛坐下, 電話鈴就響了。**4 no sooner said than done** used to say that you will do something immediately 說了就立即做, 說到做到 **5 sooner or later** used to say that something is certain to happen at some time in the future, though you cannot be sure exactly when 遲早, 總有一天: *She's bound to find out sooner or later.* 她遲早總會發現的。**6 not a moment too soon/none too soon** almost too late, and S1 W1

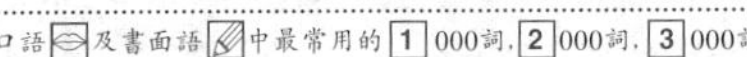
口語及書面語中最常用的 1 000詞, 2 000詞, 3 000詞

S

when you thought that something was not going to happen in time 未免太遲, 幾乎太晚: *"The doctor's here!" "And not a moment too soon!"* "醫生來了!" "未免(來得)太遲了!" **7 would sooner do sth** if you would sooner do something, you would much prefer to do it, especially instead of something that seems unpleasant 寧願做某事(也不...): *I'd sooner die than marry you!* 我寧死也不和你結婚! **8 would (just) as soon** used to say that you would prefer to do something or would prefer something to happen 寧願, 寧可: *I'd just as soon you didn't drive the car while I'm gone.* 我倒是希望我不在時你不要開車。

soot /sʊt; sʊt/ *n* [U] black powder that is produced when something is burnt 炱, 煤煙(灰): *There was a lot of soot up the chimney.* 煙囱裡煤灰很多。—**sooty** *adj*

soothe /suð; suːð/ *v* [T] **1** to make someone feel calmer and less anxious, upset, or angry 撫慰, 安慰, 使平息: *Rocking often soothes a crying baby.* 輕輕的搖動常常使哭泣的嬰兒安靜下來。**2** to make a pain less severe 減輕, 緩和(疼痛): *I bought some lozenges to soothe my sore throat.* 我買了一些潤喉片來減輕喉嚨痛。—**soothing** *adj*: *gentle, soothing music* 柔和而舒緩的音樂 —**soothingly** *adv*

sooth·say·er /ˈsuθˌseɚ; ˈsuːθˌseɪə/ *n* [C] *old use* someone who is believed to be able to say what will happen in the future【舊】占卜者, 預言者

sop¹ /sɑp; sɒp/ *n* [C usually singular 一般用單數] something not very important or valuable that you offer to someone to prevent them from complaining or getting angry about something〔為息事寧人而給予價值不大的〕撫慰的東西: **[+to]** *The company agreed to inspect the river regularly, as a sop to the environmental lobby.* 這家公司同意定期對那條河進行檢測, 以敷衍環保遊說團。

sop² *v* **sopped, sopping**

sop sth ↔ **up** *phr v* [T] to remove liquid from a surface by using a piece of cloth that takes the liquid into itself〔用布〕抹乾, 吸乾: *Jesse sopped up the spilled drink with a towel.* 傑西用毛巾抹乾灑出的飲料。

so·phis·ti·cate /səˈfɪstɪˌket; səˈfɪstɪkeɪt/ *n* [C] someone who is sophisticated 老於世故的人

3 **so·phis·ti·cat·ed** /səˈfɪstɪˌketɪd; səˈfɪstɪkeɪtɪd/ *adj* **1** having a lot of experience of life, good judgment about socially important things such as art, fashion etc 老於世故的; 有判斷力的; 有鑑賞力的: *a play that will only appeal to a sophisticated audience* 只會吸引有鑑賞力的觀眾的戲劇 | *a suave, sophisticated Frenchman* 一位彬彬有禮、談吐得體的法國人 **2** a sophisticated machine, system, method etc is very cleverly designed and very advanced and often works in a complicated way〔機器、系統、方法等〕複雜的, 精密的, 尖端的: **highly sophisticated** *highly sophisticated weapons systems* 高度複雜的武器系統 **3** having a lot of knowledge and experience of difficult or complicated subjects and therefore able to understand them well 富有經驗的, 老練的; 精通的: *British voters today are much more sophisticated than they were in the 60's.* 今天的英國選民比60年代的要成熟多了。—**sophistication** /səˌfɪstɪˈkeʃən; səˌfɪstɪˈkeɪʃən/ *n* [U]: *social institutions that show a high level of sophistication* 表現出高度成熟的社會制度

soph·ist·ry /ˈsɑfɪstrɪ; ˈsɒfɪstri/ *n formal*【正式】**1** [U] the clever use of reasons or explanations that seem correct but are really false, in order to deceive people 詭辯術 **2** [C] a reason or explanation used like this 詭辯

soph·o·more /ˈsɑfmˌɔr; ˈsɒfəmɔː/ *n* [C] *AmE* someone who is in their second year of study at a college or HIGH SCHOOL【美】〔大學或高中的〕二年級學生

soph·o·mor·ic /ˌsɑfəˈmɔrɪk; ˌsɒfəˈmɒrɪk◂/ *adj AmE formal* childish and not very sensible【美, 正式】幼稚的, 不明智的, 不切實際的

sop·o·rif·ic /ˌsɑpəˈrɪfɪk; ˌsɒpəˈrɪfɪk/ *adj formal* making you feel ready to sleep【正式】使人昏昏欲睡的, 催眠的: *His voice had an almost soporific effect.* 他的聲音幾乎有催眠作用。—**soporifically** /-klɪ; -kli/ *adv*

sopped /sɑpt; sɒpt/ *adj AmE* very wet【美】很濕的, 濕透的

sop·ping /ˈsɑpɪŋ; ˈsɒpɪŋ/ also 又作 **sopping wet** /ˌ.. ˈ.◂/ *adj* very wet 很濕的, 濕透的: *My shoes were sopping.* 我的鞋子濕透了。

sop·py /ˈsɑpɪ; ˈsɒpi/ *adj BrE informal*【英, 非正式】**1** expressing romantic feelings of love or sadness in a way that seems silly or weak 多情得傻乎乎的, 多愁善感的; SAPPY (1) *AmE*【美】: *a soppy film* 傷感的電影 **2 be soppy about** to be very fond of someone or something, in a way that seems silly to other people 非常喜愛...的, 對...很痴迷〔在旁人看來是愚蠢〕: *She's soppy about dogs.* 她非常喜歡狗。

so·pra·no /səˈpræno; səˈprɑːnəʊ/ *n* [C] **1** a woman, girl, or young boy whose singing voice is very high 女高音歌手; 男童聲最高音歌手: *the famous soprano Kiri Te Kanawa* 著名女高音歌唱家基莉·特·卡納瓦 **2** a type of SAXOPHONE that can produce very high notes 高音薩克斯管〔一種銅管樂器〕—**soprano** *adj, adv*: *She sings soprano.* 她唱女高音。

sor·bet /ˈsɔrbɪt; ˈsɔːbeɪ/ *n* [C,U] a frozen sweet food made of fruit juice, sugar, and water〔用果汁、糖和水調製的〕雪芭, 冰糕; WATER ICE, SHERBET *AmE*【美】

sor·cer·er /ˈsɔrsərɚ; ˈsɔːsərə/ *n* [C] a man who uses magic and receives help from evil spirits, especially in stories〔尤指故事中的〕男巫師, 術士, 魔法師

sor·cer·ess /ˈsɔrsərɪs; ˈsɔːsərɪs/ *n* [C] a woman who uses magic and receives help from evil spirits, especially in stories〔尤指故事中的〕女巫, 女術士, 女魔法師

sor·cer·y /ˈsɔrsərɪ; ˈsɔːsəri/ *n* [U] magic that uses the power of evil spirits 魔法, 妖術: *a cult practicing sorcery and witchcraft* 施魔法行妖術的迷信活動

sor·did /ˈsɔrdɪd; ˈsɔːdɪd/ *adj* **1** involving immoral or dishonest behaviour 猥褻的; 卑鄙的, 齷齪的: *sordid political motives* 卑鄙的政治動機 | **sordid details** *She revealed all the sordid details of her affair with Pascal.* 她透露了她和帕斯卡之間曖昧關係的全部見不得人的細節。**2** very dirty and unpleasant; SQUALID (1) 骯髒的, 污穢的: *a sordid little room at the top of the house* 房子頂層一個骯髒的小房間

sore¹ /sɔr; sɔː/ *adj* **1** a part of your body that is sore is 3
painful and often red because of a wound or infection or because you have used a muscle too much 疼痛的;〔肌肉〕痠痛的: *My legs were really sore after aerobics last week.* 我上星期做了有氧健身運動之後, 雙腿痠痛得很。| *a sore finger* 手指痛 | **a sore throat** *Val woke up with a sore throat and a temperature of 102°.* 瓦爾醒來時覺得喉嚨痛, 還有102度的熱度。**2** [not before noun 不用於名詞前] *informal, especially AmE* upset, angry, and annoyed, especially because you have not been treated fairly【非正式, 尤美】〔尤指因受到不公平對待而〕惱火的, 氣憤的: *He was still sore because I didn't call him back on Friday night.* 他還在生氣, 因為我星期五晚上沒有給他回電話。| **[+at/about]** *Don't be sore at me. I was going to tell you, I just forgot.* 別生我的氣, 我本來是想告訴你的, 可是忘了。**3 a sore point/spot** something that is likely to make someone upset or angry when you talk about it 容易惹人煩惱[生氣]的話題: *His lack of education has always been a sore point with him.* 他受教育少, 這向來是他的傷心事。**4** [only before noun 僅用於名詞前] used to emphasize how serious, difficult etc something is 極度的, 劇烈的: *Inner city schools are in sore need of extra funds.* 市中心貧民區的學校極需增加經費。—see also 另見 **be like a bear with a sore head** (BEAR² (4)), **a sight for sore eyes** (SIGHT¹ (11)), **stick out like a sore thumb** (STICK OUT (4))

sore² *n* [C] a painful, often red, place on your body caused by a wound or infection〔因受傷或感染而致的〕痛處, 瘡: *They were starving and covered with sores.* 他們在挨餓, 身上長滿了瘡。—see also 另見 COLD SORE, BEDSORE

sore·head /ˈsɔrˌhɛd; ˈsɔːhed/ *n* [C] *AmE informal* someone who is unpleasant or angry in an unreasonable way【美, 非正式】隨便發火的人

sore·ly /ˈsɔrlɪ; ˈsɔːli/ *adv* very much or very seriously 非常地; 極嚴重地: **sorely tempted** (=extremely tempted) 極想, 恨不得 *I was sorely tempted to just walk away from him after his rudeness.* 他那樣無禮, 我真恨不得走開不去理他。

sor·ghum /ˈsɔrgəm; ˈsɔːgəm/ *n* [U] a type of grain that is grown in tropical areas 高粱

so·ror·i·ty /səˈrɔrətɪ; səˈrɒrɪti/ *n* [C] a club for women students at an American university〔美國大學的〕女生聯誼會

sor·rel /ˈsɔrəl; ˈsɒrəl/ *n* [U] a plant with leaves that taste sour that is used in cooking 酸模〔一種葉子味酸, 可用於烹調的植物〕

sor·row¹ /ˈsɑro; ˈsɒrəʊ/ *n* **1** [U] a feeling of great sadness, usually because someone has died or because something terrible has happened to you 悲傷, 悲痛: *He expressed his sorrow at my father's death.* 他對我父親的去世表示悲痛。**2** [C] an event or situation that makes you feel great sadness 引起悲傷的事, 不幸: *the family's joys and sorrows* 家庭的悲歡 **3 more in sorrow than in anger** in a way that shows you are sad or disappointed rather than angry about a particular situation〔對某事〕悲哀多於憤怒 —see also 另見 **drown your sorrows** (DROWN (4))

sorrow² *v* [I] *formal* to feel or express sorrow【正式】感到[表示]悲傷

sor·row·ful /ˈsɑrofəl; ˈsɒrəʊfəl/ *adj literary* very sad【文】傷心的, 悲傷的: *an old woman with a sorrowful expression* 表情悲傷的老太太 —**sorrowfully** *adv* —**sorrowfulness** *n* [U]

S1 W2 **sor·ry** /ˈsɔrɪ; ˈsɒri/ *adj*

1 ▶ASHAMED 慚愧的◀ [not before noun 不用於名詞前] feeling ashamed or unhappy about something bad you have done〔因做了壞事而感到〕抱歉的, 遺憾的; 難過的: **be sorry about** *We're sorry about all the mess, Mom.* 對不起, 媽媽, 我們把事情搞得一場糊塗。| **be sorry (that)** *Casey was sorry he'd gotten so angry at the kids over nothing.* 凱西因無故對孩子們大發脾氣而感到內疚。| **say (you are) sorry** *Go say you are sorry to your sister for hitting her, Larry.* 拉里, 你打了妹妹, 去向她說聲對不起。| **sorry for** *Tell Barbara you're sorry for pulling her hair.* 告訴芭芭拉你為扯了她的頭髮而感到抱歉。| **say sorry** *especially BrE*【尤英】*Say sorry to your mother, Andrew.* 給你媽媽道歉, 安德魯。

2 be/feel sorry for to feel pity or sympathy for someone because something bad has happened to them 為〔某人〕難過, 替〔某人〕感到惋惜: **feel/be sorry for** *Tina was sorry for Pat; she seemed so lonely.* 蒂娜很同情帕特, 她看來多麼寂寞。| *I've got no sympathy for him, but I feel sorry for his wife.* 我並不同情他, 但我可憐他的妻子。| **feel sorry for yourself** (=feel unhappy and pity yourself) 情緒低落, 覺得自己倒霉 *It's no good feeling sorry for yourself. It's all your own fault.* 你垂頭喪氣是沒有用處的。這都是你自己的過錯。

3 ▶DISAPPOINTED 失望的◀ [not before noun 不用於名詞前] feeling sad about a situation or about something you have done, and wishing you had not done it or the situation was different 後悔的, 懊悔的: *You'll be sorry if your father catches you!* 如果讓你爸爸抓住你就會後悔了! | **be sorry (that)** *Brigid was always sorry she hadn't kept up her piano lessons.* 布里吉德總是後悔沒有堅持上鋼琴課。| *I'm sorry you didn't enjoy the meal.* 可惜你不喜歡這頓飯菜。| **be sorry to do sth** *We were sorry to miss your concert.* 我們很後悔沒有去聽你的音樂會。| *I won't be sorry to leave this place.* 我不會為離開這個地方而(感到)後悔。| **be sorry to hear/learn/see** *I was sorry to hear about your accident.* 我聽到你出了事感到很難過。

4 ▶VERY BAD 很糟的◀ [only before noun 僅用於名詞前] very bad, especially in a way that makes you feel pity or disapproval 很糟的; 可憐的, 可悲的: **sorry sight** *Milly was a sorry sight, dirty and dishevelled, by the time she got home.* 米莉回到家時, 衣冠不整又邋遢, 一副可憐相。| **sorry state of affairs** *It's a sorry state of affairs when a sick old lady has to wait three hours to see a doctor.* 一位生病的老太太看醫生要等上三個鐘頭, 那真是太糟糕了。

Frequencies of the word **sorry** in spoken and written English 單詞 sorry 在英語口語和書面語中的使用頻率

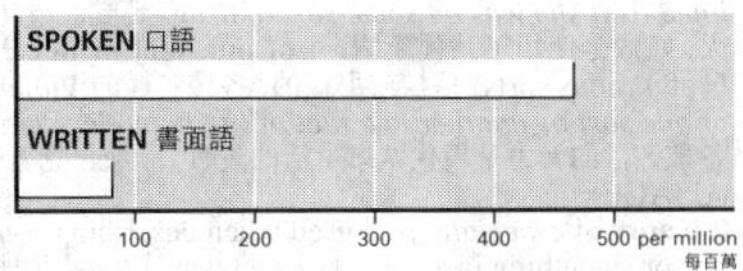

Based on the British National Corpus and the Longman Lancaster Corpus 據英國國家語料庫和朗文蘭卡斯特語料庫

This graph shows that the word **sorry** is much more common in spoken English than in written English. This is because it has special uses in spoken English and is used in some common spoken phrases. 本圖表顯示, sorry 在英語口語中的使用頻率遠遠高於書面語, 因為它在口語中有特殊用法, 而且口語中一些常用片語是由 sorry 構成的。

sorry (*adj*) **SPOKEN USES AND PHRASES**
含 sorry 的口語用法和片語

5 sorry/I'm sorry a) used to tell someone that you feel ashamed and unhappy about something bad you have done to them 對不起〔用於對人表示歉意〕: *I'm sorry. I didn't mean to hurt you. Please forgive me.* 對不起, 我不是故意傷害你的。請原諒。| **[+about]** *Sorry about that. I'll buy you a new one.* 這事我真抱歉, 我會給你買回一個新的。| **I'm sorry (that)** *I'm so sorry that I missed your birthday. I just completely forgot.* 我很抱歉錯過了你的生日。我完全忘記了。**b)** used as a polite way of excusing yourself in a social situation 對不起〔用於在社交場合中禮貌地要求得到原諒〕: *I'm sorry, did I step on your foot?* 對不起, 我是不是踩到你的腳? | *It's about ten miles, sorry, kilometres from here.* 距離這裡大約十英里, 對不起, 是十公里。| **sorry (that)** *Sorry we're a bit late – we got lost.* 對不起, 我們來晚了點 —— 我們迷路了。| **sorry to do sth** *I'm sorry to bother you, but Ms. Duggan is on the line.* 對不起打擾一下, 達根女士請你接電話。—see 見 EXCUSE¹ (USAGE) **c)** used to politely disagree with someone 對不起〔用於禮貌地表示不同意〕: *I'm sorry, Alex, but you've got your figures wrong.* 對不起, 亞歷克斯, 你把數字搞錯了。

6 sorry? *especially BrE* used to ask someone to repeat something that you have not heard properly; PARDON¹ (1)【尤英】請重複一遍, 請再說一遍〔因沒有聽清楚〕: *Sorry? What was that again?* 對不起, 請再說一遍, 那是甚麼? | *"Like a drink?" "Sorry?" "I said, would you like a drink?"* "想喝一杯嗎?" "請原諒, 你說甚麼?" "我說, 你想喝一杯嗎?"

7 you'll be sorry used to tell someone they will regret what they have done 你會後悔的: *You'll be sorry when I tell your Dad about this.* 等我把這件事告訴你爸爸時你就要後悔了。| **you'll be sorry (that)** *One day you'll be sorry that you didn't study harder at school.* 總有一天你會後悔在學校學習時不夠努力。

8 I'm sorry to say used to say that you are disappointed that something has happened 很遺憾, 真叫人失望: *I wrote to them several times but they never replied, I'm sorry to say.* 我給他們寫了好幾封信, 可是他們從不答覆, 真叫人失望。

sort[1] /sɔrt; sɔːt/ *n*

1 ►TYPE 類型◄ [C] *especially BrE* a group or class of people, things etc that have similar qualities or features; type【尤英】〔人或物的〕種, 類; 類型: **[+of]** *What sort of shampoo do you use?* 你用的是哪一種洗髮劑? | **all sorts of** (=a lot of different types of things) 各種各樣的 *soup flavoured with all sorts of herbs* 用了各種香草調味的湯 | **of this/that sort** *On expeditions of this sort you have to be prepared for trouble.* 從事這種探險時, 你得有遇上麻煩的準備。| **of some sort/some sort of** (=of an unknown type) 某種/某類 *Her pupils were dilated as if she was on some sort of drug.* 她雙眼瞳孔放大, 好像是使用了某種藥物。| **of one sort or another** (=of various sorts) 這樣或那樣的, 各種各樣的 *Violence of one sort or another is a fact of life in modern cities.* 各種各樣的暴力是現代城市生活的現實。—see 見 KIND[1] (USAGE)

2 a sort of *especially BrE* used when describing someone or something in a not very exact way【尤英】某種的〔表示不確切〕: *The walls are a sort of greeny-blue colour.* 四周的牆壁是某種藍綠的顏色。

3 of sorts/of a sort used when something is of a particular type but is not a very good example of it 勉強稱得上的, 一般的: *I taught myself to type and got a job of sorts.* 我自學打字, 找到了一份勉強過得去的工作。

4 ►PERSON 人◄ [singular] *BrE* someone who has a particular type of character, and is therefore likely to behave in a particular way【英】某一種人, 某種性格的人: *Iain's never even looked at another woman. He's not the sort.* 伊恩從來對別的女人連看也不看一眼。他不是那種人。| **a good/bad sort** *old-fashioned*【過時】 *Jane's not a bad sort, she's just a bit careless.* 簡不是壞人, 只是有點兒粗心大意罷了。

5 out of sorts feeling a little ill or upset 身體不適; 心緒煩亂: *Louise went back to work feeling rather out of sorts after their row.* 路易絲吵架後回去上班, 心裡很不痛快。

6 ►COMPUTER 電腦◄ [singular] if a computer does a sort, it puts things in a particular order〔電腦操作的〕分類, 排序 —compare 比較 KIND[1]

Frequencies of the noun **sort** in spoken and written English 名詞 sort 在英語口語和書面語中的使用頻率

SPOKEN 口語

WRITTEN 書面語

500 1000 per million 每百萬

Based on the British National Corpus and the Longman Lancaster Corpus 據英國國家語料庫和朗文蘭卡斯特語料庫

This graph shows that the noun **sort** is much more common in spoken English than in written English. This is because it is used in a lot of common spoken phrases. 本圖表顯示, 名詞sort在英語口語中的使用頻率遠遠高於書面語, 因為口語中很多常用片語是由sort構成的。

sort (*n*) **SPOKEN PHRASES**
含 sort 的口語片語

7 sort of a) used to say that something is partly true but does not describe the exact situation 有幾分, 有點: *I sort of like him, but I don't know why.* 我有點兒喜歡他, 但不知道為甚麼。| *"Were you disappointed?" "Well, yes, sort of. But it didn't matter really."* "你感到失望是嗎?" "嗯, 是的, 有一點。不過沒有甚麼關係。" **b)** *especially BrE* used when you are not sure you are using the best word to describe something【尤英】有點像, 好像〔表示不肯定自己是不是用了最恰當的詞語〕: *Then they started sort of chanting, you know, like singing and shouting at the same time.* 然後他們開始吟唱起來, 你知道吧, 好像同時又唱又叫那樣。 **c) sort of price/time/speed etc** *especially BrE* a price etc that is within a certain range【尤英】大概的價格/時間/速度等: *What sort of time were you thinking of starting?* 你考慮大概甚麼時候出發? | *That's the sort of price I was looking for.* 我想找的就是那樣上下的價格。

8 sort of thing *especially BrE* used when you are not giving an exact description or list of something【尤英】某一類的東西: *Just keep away from drink, drugs, that sort of thing.* 千萬不要沾染酒、毒品那一類東西。| *We could just stay here and pass the time, sort of thing.* 我們可以就待在這裡打發時間或甚麼的。

9 sort of like *especially BrE* used when you are trying to describe something but cannot think of the exact words【尤英】有點像, 好像〔用於想不出確切詞語來描述的時候〕: *It was sort of like really strange and mysterious, walking round this empty building.* 在這棟空樓房裡走動, 好像真有點怪怪的和神祕的感覺。

10 all sorts *especially BrE* a lot of different types of things【尤英】各種各樣的事物: *They play pop, rock, jazz, soul, all sorts in there.* 他們在那裡面演奏流行樂、搖滾樂、爵士樂、靈樂等各種各樣的樂曲。| **[+of]** *I like all sorts of food, I'm not fussy.* 我對各種食物都喜歡, 一點也不挑剔。

11 it takes all sorts (to make a world) *BrE* used to say that you think someone is behaving in a strange or crazy way【英】世上的人形形色色, 世界上無奇不有〔用於表示認為某人行為古怪或瘋狂〕: *He goes climbing up cliffs without ropes or anything? Oh well, it takes all sorts.* 他不帶繩子或甚麼的就去爬懸崖? 噢, 真是甚麼奇人都有。

12 what sort of...? *especially BrE* used when you are angry about what someone has said or done【尤英】那叫甚麼...?〔對某人的說話或行為表示生氣〕: *What sort of time do you call this to come in?* 都甚麼時候了, 你才來?

13 nothing of the sort *especially BrE* used to say angrily that something is not true or that someone should not do something【尤英】根本不是; 絕對不行〔用於氣憤地否認某事或不讓某人做某事〕: *"I'm going to watch TV." "You'll do nothing of the sort."* "我要看電視。" "不可以。"

sort[2] *v* **1** [T] to put things in a particular order or arrange them in groups according to size, rank, type etc 將...分類, 整理: *The eggs are sorted according to size.* 這些雞蛋是按大小分類的。| **sort sth into** *The teacher sorted the children into teams.* 老師把孩子們分成幾隊。**2 be sorted** *BrE spoken* if something such as a problem is sorted, you have dealt with it in a satisfactory way【英口】〔問題等〕得以解決, 處理好: **get sth sorted** (=repaired) 修理好 *We need to get the washing machine sorted.* 我們需要找人來修理洗衣機。| **get yourself sorted** (=deal with all your problems) 解決自己所有的問題

sort sb/sth **out** *phr v* [T] **1** to organize something that is mixed up or untidy 整理, 使整齊: *I must sort out my clothes for tomorrow.* 我一定要把明天穿的衣服整理好。 **2** to separate something from a group〔從一羣中〕揀出: *I've sorted out the papers that can be thrown away.* 我已經把可以扔掉的文件揀出來了。**3 sort itself out** if something sorts itself out, it stops being a problem without you having to do anything〔問題〕自行解決: *Our financial problems should sort themselves out in a week or two.* 我們的財政問題過一兩個星期就會自行解決。**4** *especially BrE* to deal with problems【尤英】解決, 處理〔問題〕: *There's been a mistake. I'll try to sort things out and call you back.* 有一個錯誤。我會處理的, 然後給你回個電話。| **get sth sorted out** *I want to get everything sorted out before we leave.* 我想在我們離開之前

把所有事情都處理好。| **sort yourself out** (=deal with all your problems and difficulties) 處理自己所有的問題和困難 *I'm staying with a friend until I manage to sort myself out.* 我暫住朋友家, 直到我把所有問題都解決了為止。**5** *BrE* to make someone stop doing something annoying or unpleasant, especially by punishing them【英】收拾, 整治〔某人〕: *If he bothers you again I'll soon sort him out.* 如果他再來煩你, 我會馬上去收拾他。

sort through sth *phr v* [T] to look for something among a lot of similar things, especially when you arrange these things into an order 查看並整理〔某堆相似的東西〕: *Vicky swiftly sorted through a pile of papers.* 維基迅速地查看並整理了一堆文件。

sor·tie[1] /ˋsɔrti; ˈsɔːti/ *n* [C] **1** an attack in which an army leaves its position for a short time to attack the enemy〔軍隊離開陣地所作的〕出擊 **2** a short flight made by a plane over enemy land, in order to bomb a city, military defences etc〔軍機的〕出動: *flying sorties into the Pacific war zone* 進入太平洋戰區的飛行任務 **3** a short trip, especially to an unfamiliar place〔尤指到陌生地方的〕短程旅行: *We made a sortie from our hotel to the open-air market.* 我們從旅館到露天市場走了一趟。**4** an attempt at doing something〔做某事的〕嘗試: *The article marked my first sortie into print.* 這篇文章是我第一次嘗試發表作品。

sortie[2] *v* [I] to make a short attack on an enemy's position or a flight over enemy land 出擊;〔飛機〕出動

sorting of·fice /ˈ·· ˌ··/ *n* [C] a place where letters and packages are put into groups according to where they have to be delivered 郵件分揀處

sort-out /ˈ· ·/ *n* [singular] *BrE informal* an act of tidying a room, desk etc and getting rid of the things you do not need【英, 非正式】〔對房間、桌子等的〕整理, 清理: *These cupboards need a good sort-out.* 這些櫥櫃需要好好清理一下。

SOS /ˌɛs ˌo ˋɛs; ˌes əʊ ˈes/ *n* [singular] **1** used as a signal calling for help by a ship or a plane that is in danger〔遇險船隻或飛機發出的〕緊急求救信號 **2** an urgent message that someone is in trouble and needs help 緊急求助的表示: *This is an SOS for a Mr. Tucker, whose mother is seriously ill.* 緊急尋找塔克先生, 他的母親病重。—compare 比較 MAYDAY

so-so /ˈ· ·/ *adj, adv spoken* neither very good nor very bad; average【口】不太好也不太壞; 一般: *"How was the party?" "Oh, so-so."* "聚會開得怎麼樣?" "噢, 還可以。"

sot /sɑt; sɒt/ *n* [C] *old-fashioned* someone who is drunk all the time【過時】酒鬼, 酒徒

sot·tish /ˋsɑtɪʃ; ˈsɒtɪʃ/ *adj old-fashioned* stupid and often drunk【過時】愚蠢的, 常醉酒的 —**sottishness** *n* [U]

sot·to vo·ce /ˌsɑtoˋvotʃɪ; ˌsɒtəʊ ˈvəʊtʃi/ *adv formal* in a very quiet voice, so that other people cannot easily hear【正式】低聲地, 輕聲地: *"No, it was Daniel," she continued, sotto voce.* "不, 那是丹尼爾。"她接着低聲說道。

sou /su; suː/ *n* [singular] *BrE old-fashioned* a very small amount of money【英, 過時】極少量的錢: *He didn't have a sou.* 他一個子兒也沒有。

sou·bri·quet /ˋsubrɪˌke; ˈsuːbrɪkeɪ/ *n* [C] another spelling of SOBRIQUET sobriquet 的另一種拼法

souf·flé /suˋfle; ˈsuːfleɪ/ *n* [C,U] a baked dish that is very light and is made with egg whites and often cheese or fruit 蛋奶酥

sough /sʌf; sʌf/ *v* [I] *literary* if the wind soughs, it makes a soft sound when passing through trees【文】〔風吹過樹時〕發出颯颯[沙沙]聲 —**sough** *n* [U]

sought /sɔt; sɔːt/ the past tense and past participle of SEEK

sought-af·ter /ˈ· ˌ··/ *adj* wanted by a lot of people but rare or difficult to get 廣受歡迎的, 吃香的〔但罕有或難得到〕: **much/highly sought-after** *Bryce became a much sought-after defense lawyer.* 布賴斯成了大為吃香的辯護律師。

souk /suk; suːk/ *n* [C] a market in an Arab country〔阿拉伯國家的〕露天市場

soul /sol; səʊl/ *n* S3 W3

1 ▶SPIRIT 靈魂◀ [C] the SPIRITUAL part of a person that is believed to continue to exist after they die 靈魂: *A prayer was said for the souls of those who had died in the accident.* 為在事故中喪生者的靈魂作了禱告。

2 ▶INNER CHARACTER 內心深處◀ [singular] the part of a person that contains their true character, where their deepest thoughts and feelings come from 心靈: *Deep down in her soul she knew she could never marry him.* 她在心靈深處知道自己絕對不會和他結婚。

3 ▶PERSON 人◀ [C] a person (一個) 人: *Betty's a happy soul with a ready smile.* 貝蒂是個快樂的人, 臉上常帶着笑容。| **not a (living) soul** (=no one) 沒有人 *I won't tell a living soul.* 我不會告訴任何人的。| **not a soul to be seen** *There wasn't a soul to be seen in the park.* 公園裡一個人也沒有。| **poor old soul** *The poor old soul had fallen and broken her hip.* 這位可憐的老太太跌了一跤, 摔壞了髖部。

4 ▶POPULATION 人口◀ souls [plural] *literary* people, considered as the population of a place【文】〔某地的〕人們, 人口: *a village with a population of 300 souls* 有300人的一個村子

5 ▶SENSE OF BEAUTY 審美觀◀ [U] **a)** the ability to be emotionally affected by great art, music, or literature〔對藝術、音樂、文學等的〕審美能力: *My brother doesn't appreciate poetry – he has no soul.* 我的兄弟不會欣賞詩歌, 他缺乏審美能力。**b)** the quality of sincere human feelings that makes a painting, piece of music, performance etc attractive 真情實感, 熱誠, 內涵: *Her performance was technically perfect, but it lacked soul.* 她的表演在技巧上無懈可擊, 但缺乏內涵。

6 ▶SPECIAL QUALITY 特質◀ [U] the special quality or part that gives something its true character 精神, 精髓: **[+of]** *Basho's poems capture the true soul of old Japan.* 松尾芭蕉的詩歌抓住了古代日本的真正精神。

7 be the soul of discretion etc to always be extremely careful to keep secrets 是謹慎等的化身: *You can trust Leon, he's the very soul of discretion.* 你可以相信利昂, 他是個極能嚴守祕密的人。

8 ▶MUSIC 音樂◀ [U] SOUL MUSIC 靈樂

9 bless my soul/upon my soul *old-fashioned spoken* used to express surprise【過時, 口】天哪/哎呀〔用於表示驚訝〕

10 be good for the soul *humorous* if something is good for the soul, it is good for you and you should do it, even though it may seem unpleasant【幽默】對人有好處[有益]: *They say that hardship is good for the soul.* 人們說艱難困苦對人有好處。

11 God rest his/her soul used when you mention the name of someone who is dead 願上帝保佑他/她的靈魂安息〔在提到已故者的名字時說的話〕: *Your Uncle Edward, God rest his soul, loved cricket.* 你的伯父愛德華——願上帝保佑他的靈魂安息——喜歡打板球。—see also 另見 **bare your soul** (BARE[2] (2)), **be the life and soul of the party** (LIFE (32)), **keep body and soul together** (BODY (14)), **heart and soul** (HEART (2)), **sell your soul (to the devil)** (SELL[1] (11)), SOUL MUSIC

soul broth·er /ˈ· ˌ··/ *n* [C] *AmE informal* an expression meaning a black man, used especially by young black people in the 1960s and 1970s【美, 非正式】黑人兄弟〔尤為20世紀60、70年代黑人青年用語〕

soul-des·troy·ing /ˈ· ·ˌ··/ *adj* something soul-destroying is extremely boring or makes you feel unhappy 極枯燥乏味的; 令人厭煩的: *the soul-destroying monotony of routine jobs* 單調乏味、消磨精神的日常事務

soul food /ˈ· ·/ *n* [U] *AmE* food that is typically cooked and eaten by black people in the Southern US【美】美國南方黑人常吃的食物

soul·ful /ˋsolfəl; ˈsəʊlfəl/ *adj* expressing deep, usually sad emotions 深情的,〔常指〕傷感的: *a soulful look* 傷感的表情 —**soulfully** *adv* —**soulfulness** *n* [U]

soul·less /ˈsol·lɪs; ˈsəʊl-ləs/ *adj* lacking attractive qualities that make human beings happy 沒有靈魂的, 沒有生氣的, 無情的: *a soulless city of grey concrete and steel* 一座毫無生氣的灰色鋼筋水泥城市 —**soullessly** *adv* —**soullessness** *n* [U]

soul mate /ˈ· ·/ *n* [C] someone you have a close relationship with because you share the same emotions and interests 知己, 摯友

soul mu·sic /ˈ· ˌ··/ *n* [U] a type of popular music that often expresses deep emotions, usually performed by black singers and musicians; SOUL (8) 靈樂〔一種通常由黑人演唱和演奏、表達強烈情感的通俗樂曲〕

soul-search·ing /ˈ· ˌ··/ *n* [U] careful examination of your thoughts and feelings because you are very worried about whether or not it is normally right to do something 深刻反省, 自省: *After much soul-searching, I decided to resign.* 經過一番自我反省之後, 我決定辭職。

soul sis·ter /ˈ· ˌ··/ *n* [C] *AmE informal* an expression meaning a black woman, used especially by young black people in the 1960s and 1970s【美, 非正式】黑人姊妹〔尤為20世紀60、70年代黑人青年用語〕

S

1 1 **sound**[1] /saund; saʊnd/ *n*

1 ▶SENSATION 感覺◀ [U] something that you hear, or what can be heard 聲, 聲音: *strange sounds coming from the next room* 從隔壁房間傳來的奇怪聲音 | **[+of]** *the sound of voices* 談話的聲音 | **not make a sound** (=keep quiet) 別出聲 *Don't make a sound, any of you!* 你們誰也別出聲! | *Light travels faster than sound.* 光比聲音傳得快。| *a vowel sound* 母音 —see 見 NOISE[1] (USAGE)

2 ▶TV/RADIO 電視/無線電◀ [U] **a)** the sound produced by a television or radio broadcast, a film etc〔電視、廣播、電影等的〕聲音; 播音: *We apologize for the loss of sound during that report.* 對於剛才的報道節目聲音中斷我們很抱歉。| *a sound engineer* 一位音響工程師 **b)** the loudness of a television, radio, film etc〔電視、廣播、電影等的〕音量: *Turn the sound down will you?* 請把音量調低一點好嗎?

3 by the sound of it/things judging from what you have heard or read about something 聽起來; 看來: *By the sound of it, her problems are worse than we thought.* 聽起來, 她的問題比我們原來想的要嚴重。

4 not like the sound of to feel worried by something that you have heard or read 感覺〔某事〕不妙: *I don't like the sound of this. How long has she been missing?* 我感覺這事不妙。她失蹤有多久了?

5 sounds [plural] *BrE spoken* music, especially on a record, CASSETTE etc【英口】〔尤指唱片、錄音帶中的〕音樂: *Have you got any sounds?* 你有甚麼盒帶嗎?

1 2 **sound**[2] *v*

1 ▶SEEM 好像◀ [linking verb 連繫動詞] if something or someone sounds good, bad, strange etc, that is how they seem to you when you hear or read about them 聽起來, 看起來, 好像: **sound like** *Serge's idea sounds like fun.* 瑟奇的想法聽起來很有趣。| **sound good/bad/awful etc** *Istanbul sounds really exciting.* 伊斯坦布爾聽起來真夠刺激的。| *Sue sounds a strange person.* 蘇這個人好像很怪。| *£50 sounds about right.* 50英鎊好像差不多是對的。| **it sounds as if/as though** *It sounds to me as if he needs professional help.* 我覺得他似乎需要專業幫助。

2 ▶VOICE 話音◀ [linking verb 連繫動詞] to seem to show a particular quality with your voice 聽起來: **sound tired/cheerful/awful etc** *Josie didn't sound very keen when I spoke to her.* 我跟喬西講話時, 她顯得興趣不大。| **sound as if/as though** *You sound as if you've got a cold.* 你聽起來好像感冒了。

3 ▶MAKE A NOISE 發出響聲◀ [I,T] if something sounds or if you sound it, it makes a noise 鳴響, (使) 發出響聲: *The bell sounded for dinner.* 吃晚飯的鈴聲響了。| **sound sth** *Sound your horn to warn other drivers.* 按喇叭以提醒其他的司機。

4 sound the alarm to warn people of danger 按響警鈴, 拉響警報〔以示有危險〕

5 ▶PRONOUNCE 發音◀ [T usually passive 一般用被動態] *technical* to make the sound of a letter in a word【術語】發音: *The 's' in 'island' is not sounded.* island 中的字母 s 是不發音的。

6 ▶MEASURE DEPTH 測量深度◀ [T] *technical* to measure the depth of the sea, a lake etc【術語】測量〔海、湖等的〕水深 —see also 另見 SOUNDINGS (2)

sound off *phr v* [I] **1** *informal* to express strong opinions about something especially when you are complaining angrily【非正式】大發議論〔表示強烈的不滿〕: **sound off about** *Philip's always sounding off about the environment.* 菲利普總是對環境問題大發議論。**2** *AmE* if soldiers sound off they shout out their names to show that they are present【美】報數;〔士兵〕大聲報出姓名〔表示已到〕

sound sb/sth ↔ **out** *phr v* [T] to talk to someone in order to find out what they think about a plan or idea 試探...的意見, 探聽...的意圖, 探詢: *I think I ought to sound him out about it before doing anything.* 我想, 在做任何事之前我都應當聽聽他的意見。| *We'd like to sound out your ideas on the new project.* 我們希望聽聽你對這項新計劃的想法。

sound[3] *adj* 3

1 ▶WELL-JUDGED 判斷正確的◀ sensible and likely to produce the right results 明智的, 合理的, 正確的: **sound advice/judgement/reasons** *Ted'll always give you sound advice.* 特德總會給你提出明智的忠告。| *an environmentally sound policy* 有利於環境保護的政策 | *a sound investment* 合理的投資 —opposite 反義詞 UNSOUND

2 ▶PERSON 人◀ someone who is sound can be depended on to make good decisions and give good advice 有判斷力的, 見地高的: *a sound person to have on a committee* 委員會裡需要的一位有見地的委員 | **[+on]** *Brown is not altogether sound on matters of finance.* 布朗在財務問題上並不總是判斷正確。—opposite 反義詞 UNSOUND

3 ▶THOROUGH 徹底的◀ complete and thorough 完全的, 徹底的: *a sound knowledge of the European market* 對歐洲市場的全面了解

4 ▶IN GOOD CONDITION 狀況良好的◀ in good condition and not damaged in any way 完好的, 無損的: *The bodywork's sound but the engine needs replacing.* 汽車車身完好, 但引擎需要更換了。| **sound as a bell** (=in perfect condition) 完美無缺 (的)

5 ▶HEALTHY 健康的◀ physically or mentally healthy〔生理或心理上〕健康的: **sound as a bell** (=in perfect health) 十分健康的 | **of sound mind** *law* (=not mentally ill)【法律】心智健全的 *Dorothy contested the will, saying that Mr. Palmer had not been of sound mind when it was drawn up.* 多蘿西對這份遺囑提出質疑, 說在立遺囑時帕爾默先生已經神智不健全了。

6 ▶SLEEP 睡覺◀ sound sleep is deep and peaceful 酣的, 深沉的, 平靜的: **sound sleeper** (=someone who always sleeps well) 睡得香甜的人, 睡得酣暢的人

7 ▶PUNISHMENT 懲罰◀ severe and thorough 嚴厲的, 沉重的: *a sound beating* 一頓痛打 —**soundness** *n* [U]

sound[4] *adv* **sound asleep** deeply asleep 熟睡

sound bar·ri·er /ˈ· ˌ···/ *n* **the sound barrier** the sudden increase in the pressure of air against an aircraft when it reaches the speed of sound 聲障: **break the sound barrier** (=go faster than the speed of sound) 突破聲障〔以超音速飛行〕*Chuck Yeager flew the first jet to break the sound barrier.* 查克·耶格爾駕駛第一架噴氣式飛機突破聲障。

sound bite /ˈ· ·/ *n* [C] a very short part of a speech or statement, especially one made by a politician, that is broadcast on radio or television〔尤指廣播或電視中政

治人物的〕演説[聲明]片斷

sound check /ˈ· ·/ *n* [C] the process of checking that all the equipment needed for broadcasting or recording is working properly〔廣播或錄音前對音響設備的〕效果檢查, 校音

sound ef·fects /ˈ· ·,·/ *n* [plural] sounds produced artificially for a radio or television broadcast, a film etc〔廣播、電視、電影等的〕音響效果

sounding board /ˈ·· ·/ *n* **1** [C] someone you discuss your ideas with in order to try them out 被徵詢意見的人: **[+for]** *Ivan uses his secretary as a sounding board.* 伊凡把祕書當作自己觀點的諮詢人。**2** [C] a board that is placed behind someone who is speaking to a large group of people so that they can be heard more easily〔置於演講者後方以增加音響效果的〕增音板, 響板

sound·ings /ˈsaʊndɪŋz; ˈsaʊndɪŋz/ *n* [plural] **1** careful or secret questions that you ask someone to find out what they think about something〔小心或祕密的〕試探, 調查: **take soundings** *We're taking soundings to find out how people feel about the changes.* 我們正在調查, 以找出人們怎樣看待這些變化。**2** measurements you make to find out how deep water is 為量度水深而作的探測

sound·less /ˈsaʊndlɪs; ˈsaʊndləs/ *adj* without any sound 無聲的, 寂靜的 —**soundlessly** *adv*: *Theo crept soundlessly into the room.* 西奧躡手躡腳地走進房間。—**soundlessness** *n* [U]

soundly /ˈsaʊndlɪ; ˈsaʊndli/ *adv* **1** if you sleep soundly, you sleep deeply and peacefully〔睡覺〕酣暢地, 沉沉地: *The baby slept soundly all night.* 寶寶整晚睡得很香甜。**2 soundly beaten/whipped/defeated** completely defeated or severely punished 受到痛打/被徹底擊敗: *The Green candidate was soundly beaten.* 那位綠黨候選人被徹底擊敗。

sound·proof¹ /ˈsaʊnd,pruf; ˈsaʊndpruːf/ *adj* a soundproof wall, room etc is one that sound cannot pass through or into 隔音的

soundproof² *v* [T] to make something soundproof 使隔音

sound sys·tem /ˈ· ,··/ *n* [C] a very large STEREO system, especially one that includes the equipment a band needs to control its sound at a performance 音響系統〔尤指樂隊演出用的大型立體聲音響設備〕

sound·track /ˈsaʊnd,træk; ˈsaʊndtræk/ *n* [C] **1** the recorded music from a film 電影配樂 **2** the band near the edge of a piece of film where the sound is recorded〔電影膠片邊上的〕聲帶, 聲跡

sound wave /ˈ· ·/ *n* [C] the form that sound takes when it travels 聲波

S3 **soup¹** /sup; suːp/ *n* **1** liquid cooked food often containing small pieces of meat, fish, or vegetables 湯: *chicken noodle soup* 雞湯麵條 **2 be in the soup** *informal* to be in trouble【非正式】陷入困境: *If Dad catches you you'll be in the soup.* 要是被爸爸抓住, 你就麻煩大了。

soup² *v*

soup sth ↔ **up** *phr v* [T] *informal* to improve something by making it bigger, more attractive, or more exciting【非正式】〔使增大、更有吸引力、更刺激〕以改善〔某物〕: *software programs to soup up the office E-mail* 能改進辦公室電子郵件（系統）的軟件程式

soup·çon /supˈsɑn; ˈsuːpsɒn/ *n* [singular] *French, formal or humorous* a small amount of something【法, 正式或幽默】少量, 一點點: *It needs a soupçon more salt.* 需要再加一點點鹽。

souped-up /,· ˈ·◂/ *adj* a souped-up car has been made more powerful, especially by adding special parts to the engine〔指汽車尤因引擎增加了特殊零件〕增大了馬力的: *a souped-up Mustang* 加大了馬力的野馬牌汽車

soup kitch·en /ˈ· ,··/ *n* [C] a place where people with no money and no homes can get free food〔救濟窮人的〕施粥所, 施食處

soup spoon /ˈ· ·/ *n* [C] a round spoon that is used for eating soup 湯匙 —see picture at 參見 SPOON¹ 圖

sour¹ /saʊr; saʊə/ *adj* **1** having a sharp acid taste that stings your tongue, like the taste of a LEMON 酸的, 酸味的: *sour, tangy apples* 味道濃烈的酸蘋果 | *Sprinkle a little sugar over the strawberries if they are sour.* 草莓如果酸, 就撒上一點糖吧。—compare 比較 BITTER¹ (4), SWEET¹ (1) **2** milk or other food that is sour is not fresh and has an unpleasant taste because it has fermented (FERMENT¹) 餿(味)的, 酸臭的〔牛奶等發酵後的味道〕: **turn/go sour** (=become sour) 變酸 *In warm weather, milk can go sour in just a few hours.* 在熱天, 牛奶只要幾小時就變酸了。**3** unfriendly or looking bad-tempered 不友善的, 脾氣壞的: *Rob gave me a sour look.* 羅布狠狠地瞪了我一眼。| **sour-faced** *a sour-faced old man* 繃着臉的老人 **4 sour grapes** the attitude of someone who pretends to dislike something that they really want, because they cannot have it 酸葡萄〔指某人其實想要某物, 但因得不到而裝作不喜歡聊以自慰的心態〕**5 turn/go sour** *informal* if a relationship or plan turns or goes sour, it becomes less enjoyable, pleasant, or satisfactory【非正式】〔關係、計劃等〕變壞, 變得令人不快[不滿意]: *As time went by their marriage turned sour.* 隨着時間的推移, 他們的婚姻關係變壞了。—**sourly** *adv* —**sourness** *n* [U]

sour² *v* [I,T] **1** if a relationship or someone's attitude sours, or if something sours it, it becomes unfriendly or unfavourable（使）〔關係、態度等〕變壞, 變得不友善: *An unhappy childhood has soured her view of life.* 不幸的童年扭曲了她的人生觀。**2** if milk sours or something sours it, it begins to have an unpleasant sharp taste（使）〔牛奶〕變酸, 變餿

source¹ /sɔrs; sɔːs/ *n* [C] **1** a thing, place, activity etc that you get something from 來源, 出處: *They get their money from various sources.* 他們從各種來源得到錢。| **[+of]** *Milk is a very good source of calcium.* 牛奶含有豐富的鈣。| *For me, music is a great source of enjoyment.* 對我來說, 音樂是樂趣的重大源泉。| **at source** *Is your pension taxed at source?* (=before it is paid to you) 你的養老金是不是在領取時就扣除了稅金? **2** the cause of something, especially a problem, or the place where it starts〔問題等的〕原因, 根源: **[+of]** *We've found the source of the trouble – a faulty connection.* 我們已找出故障的原因 —— 接觸不好。| *Two players have the same name, which has been the source of some confusion.* 兩位球員名字相同, 這就是為甚麼有時會搞錯。**3** a person, book, or document that supplies you with information 提供消息者; 資料來源: *List all your sources at the end of the essay.* 請在文章末尾列出你所有資料的來源。| **reliable sources** *I've heard from reliable sources that the company is in trouble.* 我從可靠消息來源那裡獲悉, 那家公司遇上了麻煩。**4** the place where a stream or river starts 溪流的發源地, 水源 S2 W1

source² *v* [T] to find out where something can be obtained from 找出…的來源; 找…的貨源

source code /ˈ· ·/ *n* [U] *technical* a computer PROGRAM¹ that can be read by someone who knows the language it is written in【術語】〔電腦的〕源（代）碼 —compare 比較 MACHINE CODE

sour cream /,· ˈ·/ also 又作 **soured cream** *BrE*【英】*n* [U] cream which has been made sour by adding a kind of BACTERIA〔加細菌發酵致酸的〕酸奶油

sour·dough /ˈsaʊr,do; ˈsaʊədəʊ/ *n* [U] *AmE* uncooked DOUGH (=bread mixture) that is left to FERMENT¹ before being used to make bread【美】麵肥, 酵頭: *sourdough bread* 用麵肥發的麵包

sour·puss /ˈsaʊr,pʊs; ˈsaʊəpʊs/ *n* [C] *humorous* a BAD-TEMPERED person, who always complains and is never satisfied【幽默】脾氣壞的人, 滿腹牢騷的人

sou·sa·phone /ˈsuzə,fon; ˈsuːzəfəʊn/ *n* [C] a very large musical instrument made of metal, which you blow into, used especially in marching bands〔遊行樂隊用的〕大號, 低音大喇叭

souse /saʊs; saʊs/ *v* [T] to put something in water or pour water over something, making it completely wet 把…浸入水中; 倒水於…上; 使濕透

soused /saʊst; saʊst/ *adj* **1** soused fish has been preserved in water, salt, and VINEGAR〔魚〕醃漬的: *soused herrings* 醃鯡魚 **2** *informal* drunk【非正式】喝醉酒的: *He was so soused he couldn't even write his name.* 他喝得爛醉, 連自己的名字也寫不了。

south¹, South /saʊθ; saʊθ/ written abbreviation 縮寫為 S *n* [singular,U] **1** the direction that is at the bottom of a map of the world, below the EQUATOR, and is on the right of someone facing the rising sun 南, 南方, 南面: *I'm lost; which direction is South?* 我迷失方向了, 哪個方向是南? | **from/towards the south** *winds blowing from the south* 從南面吹來的風 | **to the south (of)** *Gatwick airport is a few miles to the south of London.* 蓋特威克機場在倫敦以南數英里處。| **in the south** *A strange star appeared in the south.* 一顆奇怪的星星出現在南方。**2 the south** the southern part of a country〔一國的〕南部: *There'll be showers in the south tomorrow.* 明天南部將有陣雨。| *the South of France* 法國南部 **3 the South** the southern states of the US 美國南部各州: *the cotton fields of the South* 美國南部各州的棉田

south² *adj* [only before noun 僅用於名詞前] **1** in the south or facing the south 在南方的; 向南的: *The south side of the building gets a lot of sun.* 建築物向南的那面陽光充足。| *South America* 南美洲 **2** a south wind comes from the south〔風〕來自南方的

south³ *adv* **1** towards the south 向南: *The swallows fly south in the winter.* 冬季燕子向南飛。| *The garden faces south so it gets a lot of sun.* 花園朝南, 所以陽光充足。**2 down south** *BrE informal* in or to the southern part of England【英, 非正式】在〔英格蘭的〕南部, 向〔英格蘭的〕南部: *We moved down south about five years ago.* 我們大約五年前遷居英格蘭南部。**3 go south** *AmE informal* if a situation, organization, or set of standards goes south, it becomes very bad although it was once very good【美, 非正式】變壞; 下跌, 下降: *Seems like all our moral standards have just gone south.* 我們的道德準則好像都已下降。

south·bound /ˋsaʊθˌbaund; ˈsaʊθbaʊnd/ *adj* travelling or leading towards the south 向南行的: *southbound traffic* 南行的車輛

south·east¹ /ˌsaʊθˋist; ˌsaʊθˈiːst◂/ *n* [U] **1** the direction that is exactly between south and east 東南, 東南方 **2 the southeast** the southeastern part of a country〔一國的〕東南部 —**southeast** *adv*: *The road runs southeast.* 這條路通往東南方向。

southeast² *adj* [only before noun 僅用於名詞前] **1** a southeast wind comes from the southeast〔風〕來自東南方的 **2** in the southeast of a place〔一地區的〕東南部的: *the southeast quarter of the city* 該市的東南部分

south·east·er /ˌsaʊθˋistɚ; ˌsaʊθˈiːstə/ *n* [C] a strong wind or storm coming from the southeast 東南強風[風暴]

south·east·er·ly /ˌsaʊθˋistɚlɪ; ˌsaʊθˈiːstəli/ *adj* **1** towards or in the southeast 向東南的; 在東南的: *Snow will spread to southeasterly regions tonight.* 今晚降雪將蔓延到東南地區。**2** a southeasterly wind comes from the southeast〔風〕來自東南方的

south·east·ern /ˌsaʊθˋistɚn; ˌsaʊθˈiːstən/ *adj* in or from the southeast part of a country 位於[來自]〔一國〕東南部的

south·east·ward /ˌsaʊθˋistwɚd; ˌsaʊθˈiːstwəd/ *adj* going towards the southeast 向東南方行進的: *in a southeastward direction* 朝東南的方向 —**southeastwards, southeastward** *adv*

south·er·ly /ˋsʌðɚlɪ; ˈsʌðəli/ *adj* **1** in the south or towards the south 在南方的; 向南的: *Tara walked in a southerly direction.* 塔拉朝南走去。**2** a southerly wind comes from the south〔風〕來自南方的

south·ern /ˋsʌðɚn; ˈsʌðən/ *adj* in or from the south part of the world or of a country 位於[來自]〔世界或一國之〕南方的: *southern Italy* 意大利南部 | *the southern hemisphere* 南半球 | *a strong southern accent* 濃重的南方口音

South·ern·er /ˋsʌðɚnɚ; ˈsʌðənə/ *n* [C] someone who lives in or comes from the southern part of a country〔一國的〕居住在南方的人, 南方人

Southern Lights /ˌ‥ ˈ‧/ *n* [plural] bands of coloured light in the night sky, seen in the most southern parts of the world 南極光

south·ern·most /ˋsʌðɚnˌmost; ˈsʌðənməʊst/ *adj* furthest south 極南的, 最南端的: *the southernmost tip of the island* 海島的最南端

south·paw /ˋsaʊθˌpɔ; ˈsaʊθpɔː/ *n* [C] someone who uses their left hand more than their right hand, especially a PITCHER (3) in BASEBALL or a BOXER 左撇子; 左撇子棒球投手[拳擊手]

South Pole /ˌ‧ ˈ‧/ *n* **the South Pole** the most southern point on the Earth's surface, and the land around it 南極(地帶) —see also 另見 MAGNETIC POLE, NORTH POLE —see picture at 參見 EARTH¹ 圖

south·ward /ˋsaʊθwɚd; ˈsaʊθwəd/ *adj* going towards the south 往南行的: *the southward journey* 去南方的旅程

south·wards /ˋsaʊθwɚdz; ˈsaʊθwədz/ also 又作 **southward** *adv* towards the south 向南方: *The ship sailed southwards.* 這艘船向南航行。

south·west¹ /ˌsaʊθˋwɛst; ˌsaʊθˈwest◂/ *n* [U] **1** the direction that is exactly between south and west 西南, 西南方 **2 the southwest** the southwestern part of a country〔一國的〕西南部 —**southwest** *adv*: *We headed southwest.* 我們向西南進發。

southwest² *adj* [only before noun 僅用於名詞前] **1** a southwest wind comes from the southwest〔風〕來自西南方的 **2** in the southwest of a place〔一地的〕西南部: *down in the southwest corner of France* 在法國西南隅

south·west·er /ˌsaʊθˋwɛstɚ; ˌsaʊθˈwestə/ also 又作 **sou'wester** *n* [C] a strong wind or storm from the southwest 西南強風[風暴]

south·west·er·ly /ˌsaʊθˋwɛstɚlɪ; ˌsaʊθˈwestəli/ *adj* **1** towards or in the southwest 向西南的, 在西南方向的 **2** a southwesterly wind comes from the southwest〔風〕來自西南方的

south·west·ern /ˌsaʊθˋwɛstɚn; ˌsaʊθˈwestən/ *adj* in or from the southwest part of a country 位在[來自]〔一國〕西南部的

south·west·ward /ˌsaʊθˋwɛstwɚd; ˌsaʊθˈwestwəd/ *adj* going towards the southwest 往西南行進的: *in a southwestward direction* 朝西南方向 —**southwestwards, southwestward** *adv*

sou·ve·nir /ˌsuvəˋnɪr; ˌsuːvəˈnɪə/ *n* [C] an object that you keep to remind yourself of a special occasion or a place you have visited 紀念品, 紀念物: **[+of]** *I bought a model of the Eiffel Tower as a souvenir of Paris.* 我買了一個埃菲爾鐵塔模型作為去過巴黎的紀念品。| *a souvenir shop* 紀念品商店 | *a souvenir programme from the Gala Concert* 慶典音樂會的紀念節目單

sou'west·er /ˌsaʊˋwɛstɚ; saʊˈwestə/ *n* [C] **1** a hat made of shiny material that keeps the rain off, with a wide piece at the back that covers your neck〔後沿寬至頸後的〕防水帽 **2** a SOUTHWESTER 西南強風[風暴]

sove·reign¹ /ˋsɑvrɪn; ˈsɒvrɪn/ *n* [C] **1** *formal* a king or queen【正式】國王; 女王; 君主 **2** a former British gold coin worth £1 從前英國的一英鎊金幣

sovereign² *adj* **1** having the highest power in a country〔國家內〕權力至高無上的: *Most European monarchs no longer have sovereign control.* 大多數歐洲君主不再擁有至高無上的控制權了。**2** a sovereign country or state is independent and governs itself〔國家〕獨立自主的, 具有獨立主權的: *The UN was designed as an association of sovereign states.* 聯合國是作為主權國家的聯盟

而成立的。**3 sovereign remedy** *old-fashioned* an excellent way of curing all kinds of illnesses and problems【過時】萬能藥, 靈丹妙藥

sove·reign·ty /ˈsɑvrɪntɪ; ˈsɒvr̩nti/ *n* [U] **1** complete freedom and power to govern 至高無上的權威: *the sovereignty of Parliament* 議會至高無上的權威 **2** the power that an independent country has to govern itself 國家的主權, 國家的獨立自主

So·vi·et /ˈsovɪət; ˈsəʊviət/ *adj* from or connected with the former USSR (Soviet Union) or its people 前蘇聯的; 前蘇聯人民的

soviet *n* [C] an elected council in a Communist country 蘇維埃〔共產黨國家中通過選舉產生的委員會〕

sow¹ /so; səʊ/ *past tense* **sowed** *past participle* **sown** /son; səʊn/ *or* **sowed** *v* **1** [I,T] to plant or scatter seeds on a piece of ground 播(種): *Sow the seeds in late March.* 三月底播這些種子。| **sow sth with sth** *We're sowing the field with grass.* 我們正在這塊地裡種草。**2 sow the seeds of** to do something that will cause a bad situation in the future 播下〔引致壞情況的〕種子, 造成〔問題〕的根源: *repressive policies that are sowing the seeds of future conflicts* 正在播下未來衝突的種子的高壓政策 —**sower** *n* [C]

sow² /sau; saʊ/ *n* [C] a fully grown female pig〔已成熟的〕母豬, 牝豬 —opposite 反義詞 BOAR

sown /son; səʊn/ the past participle of sow

sox /sɑks; sɒks/ *n* [plural] an American spelling of socks, used especially in advertising 襪子〔socks 的美式拼法, 尤用於廣告中〕

soy /sɔɪ; sɔɪ/ also 又作 **soy·a** /ˈsɔɪə; ˈsɔɪə/ *n* [U] soy beans 大豆

soy bean /ˈ· ·/ also 又作 **soya bean** /ˈ·· ·/ *n* [C] the bean of an Asian plant from which oil and food containing a lot of PROTEIN is produced 大豆

soy sauce /ˌ· ˈ·/ *n* [U] a dark brown liquid that is used especially in Japanese and Chinese cooking〔尤指日本和中國烹飪用的〕醬油

soz·zled /ˈsɑzəld; ˈsɒzəld/ *adj BrE humorous* drunk【英, 幽默】喝醉酒的

spa /spɑ; spɑː/ *n* [C] **1** a place that has a spring of mineral water that people believe makes you healthy 礦泉療養地: *the spas of Germany* 德國的礦泉療養地 **2** *AmE* a bath or pool that sends currents of hot water around you; JACUZZI【美】熱水漩水式浴缸[浴池]

S1 W1 **space¹** /spes; speɪs/ *n*

1 ▶AMOUNT OF SPACE 空間大小◀ [U] the amount of an area, room, container etc that is empty or available to be used 空間, 空地方: *There's space for a table and two chairs.* 有空間放得下一張桌子和兩把椅子。| *How much space is there on each disk?* 每張磁盤有多大容量? | **make space** *I'm trying to make space for all Tom's canoeing gear.* 我正在設法給湯姆的划船工具騰出地方。| **leave space** *Leave enough space for the suitcases.* 留出足夠的地方放衣箱。| **closet/cupboard/office space** *There's plenty of closet space in our new apartment.* 我們的新公寓有足夠的壁櫥空間。| **sense/feeling of space** (=the feeling that a room has plenty of space) 空間寬大的感覺 *Mirrors give a sense of space.* 鏡子給人空間寬大的感覺。—see 見 PLACE¹ (USAGE)

2 ▶PIECE OF SPACE 空間範圍◀ [C,U] an area, especially one used for a particular purpose〔有特定目的的〕空位, 處所: *a parking space* 停車處 | *There was just an empty space where the book had been.* 原來放書的地方正好有個空位。| **clear a space** *Lucy cleared a space on her desk for her new computer.* 露西在她的書桌上清理出一塊空地方放新電腦。

3 ▶BETWEEN EARTH AND STARS 地球與各個星體之間◀ [U] the area outside the Earth's air where the stars and PLANETs are 太空: *space travel* 太空旅行, 宇宙飛行 | **outer space** (=far away in space) 外太空 *creatures from outer space* 來自外太空的生物

4 ▶ALL AROUND EVERYTHING 萬物周圍◀ [U] all of the space in which everything exists, and in which everything has a position or direction 空間, 空中: *the exact point in space where two lines meet* 兩線在空間中的確切交點 | *beyond the dimensions of space and time* 在空間與時間兩維之外

5 ▶BETWEEN THINGS 在物體之間◀ [C] an empty space between two things, or between two parts of something; GAP (1)〔兩物或某物兩部分之間的〕空間, 距離; 空隙: *The children hid in the space between the wall and the shed.* 孩子們躲在牆和棚屋之間的空隙裡。

6 ▶TIME 時間◀ **a) in/during the space of** within a particular period of time 在一段...的時間裡, 在...期間: *Mandy had four children in the space of four years.* 曼迪在四年裡生了四個孩子。**b) a short space of time** a short period of time during which a lot of things happen 短短的一段時間〔指期間有許多事情發生〕: *It's amazing how well we knew each other after such a short space of time.* 令人驚奇的是我們在短短的一段時間裡彼此就這麼了解。

7 ▶EMPTY LAND 空地◀ [C,U] land, or an area of land that has not been built on〔尚無建築物的〕空地: **open space** *a pleasant town centre with plenty of open space* 開闊宜人的城市中心區 | **wide open spaces** *the wide open spaces of the prairies* 遼闊的大草原

8 ▶IN WRITING 在書寫方面◀ [C] **a)** an empty space between written or printed words, lines etc〔字或行之間的〕間隔, 距離 **b)** the width of a typed letter of the alphabet 打出一個字母所佔的寬度: *The word 'the' takes up three spaces.* the 這個詞佔三格。**c)** a place provided for you to write your name or other information on a document, piece of paper etc〔紙上預留的〕空白處: *Please write any comments in the space provided.* 請把意見寫在預留的空白處。

9 ▶IN A NEWSPAPER 在報紙上◀ [U] the amount of space in a newspaper, magazine or book that is used for a particular subject〔報紙、書刊對某題目的〕篇幅: *Endless space has been devoted to Princess Di.* 對戴妃的報道已經用去無數篇幅了。

10 ▶FREEDOM 自由◀ [U] the freedom to do what you want or do things on your own, especially in a relationship with someone else〔個人的〕生活空間,〔不受別人牽制的〕個人自由: *I've split up with Phil because I need more space.* 我和菲爾分手了, 因為我需要更多個人空間。

11 look/stare into space to look straight in front of you without looking at anything in particular, usually because you are thinking〔常因為思考〕凝視前方, 茫然直視: *What's wrong with Jenny? She's just been staring into space all day.* 珍妮怎麼了? 她整天只是瞪着眼睛發呆。—see also 另見 BREATHING SPACE

space² *v* also 又作 **space out 1** [T always+adv/prep] to arrange objects or events so that they have equal spaces or periods of time between them 將...均勻地隔開: **space sth ÷ out/along etc** *Try to space out your classes and study in between.* 設法將上課時間分開, 當中進行溫習。| *Space the desks one metre apart.* 把這些書桌隔開一米排列。| **be evenly spaced** (=with equal spaces) 均勻相隔 **2** also 又作 **space out** [I] *AmE informal* to stop paying attention and just look in front of you without thinking, especially because you are bored or because you have taken drugs【美, 非正式】〔尤指因無聊或吸毒後〕變得昏昏沉沉, 瞪着眼發呆: *I was so tired I just spaced out, completely unable to concentrate.* 我累得很, 只知道愣着發呆, 根本不能集中思想。—see also 另見 SPACED OUT

space-age /ˈ· ·/ *adj informal* very modern【非正式】太空時代的, 非常現代化的: *This space-age device can remember up to 100 phone numbers.* 這個非常現代化的裝置能存儲多達一百個電話號碼。

space bar /ˈ· ·/ *n* [C] the part at the bottom of a TYPEWRITER that you press to make a space〔打字機的〕間隔檔, 空格桿[鍵]

space ca·det /ˈ· ·ˌ·/ *n* [C] *informal* someone who forgets things, does not pay attention, and often behaves strangely【非正式】健忘、散漫的人，行為怪異者：*I like her, but she's kind of a space cadet.* 我喜歡她，不過她這個人有點怪怪的。

space cap·sule /ˈ· ˌ··/ *n* [C] the part of a space vehicle that carries people into space to obtain information and then comes back to Earth 太空艙，航天艙

space·craft /ˈspesˌkræft; ˈspeɪs-krɑːft/ *n* [C] a vehicle that is able to travel in space 航天器，太空船，宇宙飛船

spaced out /ˌ· ˈ·◂/ *adj informal* not fully conscious of what is happening around you, for example because you are extremely tired or because you have taken drugs【非正式】〔因極度疲倦或吸毒後〕頭腦不清醒的，迷迷糊糊的：*JD looked spaced out, face flushed, hair in disarray.* JD 看上去頭腦不清，臉色發紅，頭髮蓬亂。—see also 另見 **space** (SPACE[2] (2))

space heat·er /ˈ· ˌ··/ *n* [C] a small machine for heating a room 小型供暖器

space·man /ˈspesˌmæn; ˈspeɪsmæn/ *n plural* **spacemen** /-ˌmɛn; -men/ [C] **1** *informal* a man who travels into space; ASTRONAUT【非正式】宇航員，航天員，太空人 **2** someone in stories who visits the Earth from another world〔小說中的〕外星人：*little green spacemen from Mars* 來自火星的小個綠色外星人

space probe /ˈ· ·/ *n* [C] a SPACECRAFT without people in it, that is sent into space to collect information about the conditions there and send it back to Earth 宇宙探測器，太空探測船：*a space probe investigating Jupiter* 探測木星的宇宙探測器

S

space·ship /ˈspesˌʃɪp; ˈspeɪsˌʃɪp/ *n* [C] a vehicle for carrying people through space, especially in stories〔尤指小說中的〕宇宙飛船，太空船

space shut·tle /ˈ· ˌ··/ *n* [C] a vehicle that is designed to go into space and back to Earth several times to do experiments and carry people 航天飛機，太空穿梭機

space sta·tion /ˈ· ˌ··/ *n* [C] a large SPACECRAFT that stays above the Earth and is a base for people travelling in space or for scientific tests 航天站，宇航站，太空站：*Mir, the Soviet space station orbiting earth* 圍繞地球運行的前蘇聯太空站和平號

space·suit /ˈspesˌsut; ˈspeɪs-suːt/ *n* [C] a special suit for wearing in space, that covers and protects your whole body and provides an air supply 航天服，太空服

space-time con·tin·u·um /ˌ· ˈ· ·ˈ···/ *n* [U] *technical* the universe considered as having four measurements: length, width, depth, and time【術語】時空連續體〔指有長度、寬度、深度與時間四種量度的宇宙〕

space·walk /ˈspesˌwɔk; ˈspeɪswɔːk/ *n* [C] the act of moving around outside a spacecraft while in space, or the time spent outside it 太空行走〔指離開航天器外出活動〕；太空行走的時間

space·wom·an /ˈspesˌwʊmən; ˈspeɪsˌwʊmən/ *n plural* **spacewomen** /-ˌwɪmɪn; -ˌwɪmɪn/ [C] *informal* a woman who travels into space; ASTRONAUT【非正式】女宇航員，女航天員，女太空人

spac·y /ˈspesɪ; ˈspeɪsi/ *adj informal* behaving as though you are not fully conscious of what is happening around you【非正式】頭腦不清醒的，迷迷糊糊的：*June is pretty spacey; I'd never let her take care of the kids.* 瓊相當糊塗，我絕不會讓她帶孩子。—**spacey** *adv*: *Dan acts kind of spacey.* 丹的舉動有點兒糊裡糊塗。

spac·ing /ˈspesɪŋ; ˈspeɪsɪŋ/ *n* [U] the amount of space between each printed letter, word, or line on a page〔印刷的字母與字母、單詞與單詞或行與行之間的〕間隔，空白：**single spacing** (=lines with no empty lines between them) 單行行距〔行與行之間不留空行〕| **double spacing** (=lines with one empty line between each one) 雙行行距〔行與行之間留一行間隔〕

spa·cious /ˈspeʃəs; ˈspeɪʃəs/ *adj* a spacious house, room etc is large and has plenty of space to move around in 寬敞的，廣闊的；廣大的：*a spacious, comfortably furnished living room* 一間寬敞的、陳設舒適的起居室 —**spaciously** *adv* —**spaciousness** *n* [U]

spack·le /ˈspækl; ˈspækl/ *n* [U] *AmE* a substance used to fill holes in walls, that becomes very hard when it dries【美】〔填牆洞用的〕填泥料

spade /sped; speɪd/ *n* [C] **1** a tool for digging that has a long handle and a broad metal blade you push into the ground 鏟，鐵鍬 **2** [C] a PLAYING CARD belonging to the set of cards that have one or more black shapes that look like pointed leaves printed on them 印有黑桃的紙牌：*the queen of spades* 黑桃王后 **3 call a spade a spade** to say exactly what you think is true, without trying to be polite 有一說一，照直說，直言不諱 **4 in spades** *informal especially AmE* to a much greater degree, or in a much greater amount, than you expected【非正式，尤美】非常，極其：*It may have been tough, but Ginny's effort was repaid in spades.* 這事也許艱苦，但吉尼的努力得到了非常豐厚的回報。**5** [C] *old-fashioned* a very offensive word for a black person【過時】黑鬼〔極具冒犯性的用語〕

spade·work /ˈspedˌwɜk; ˈspeɪd-wɜːk/ *n* [U] hard work that has to be done in preparation before something can happen 艱苦的準備工作：*Credit must go to the researchers, who did a lot of the spadework.* 功勞應當歸於研究人員，他們做了大量艱苦的準備工作。

spa·ghet·ti /spəˈgɛtɪ; spəˈgeti/ *n* [U] a type of PASTA in very long thin pieces, that is cooked in boiling water 意大利粉，意大利麵條 —compare 比較 MACARONI, TAGLIATELLE, VERMICELLI —see picture at 參見 PASTA 圖

spaghetti west·ern /ˌ·ˌ·· ˈ··/ *n* [C] a film about American COWBOYs in the Wild West, especially one made in Europe by an Italian director〔尤指意大利導演在歐洲攝製的〕美國西部牛仔影片

spake /spek; speɪk/ *biblical or poetic*【聖經或詩】a past tense of SPEAK

Spam /spæm; spæm/ *n* [U] *trademark* a type of inexpensive CANNED meat made mainly of PORK【商標】好味寶午餐肉

spam *v* [I,T] *technical* to send copies of the same information to many different groups on the INTERNET【術語】在網上廣發垃圾郵件：*spamming the newsgroups* 向各新聞組發送垃圾郵件

span[1] /spæn; spæn/ a past tense of SPIN

span[2] *n* [C] **1** the length of time over which someone's attention, life etc continues〔注意力、生命等持續的〕時間：*A four-year-old's concentration span is usually about 10 minutes.* 一個四歲孩子的注意力持續時間通常為十分鐘左右。**2** a period of time between two dates or events〔兩個日期或兩件事之間的〕時距，期間：*Over a span of ten years, the company has made great strides.* 十年間，這家公司有了很大的發展。**3** the part of a bridge, ARCH[1] (1) etc that goes across from one support to another〔橋梁、拱門等的〕跨距；墩距 **4** the distance from one side of something to the other〔從一端到另一端的〕全長：*a bird with a large wing span* 一隻翼展寬大的鳥

span[3] *v* **spanned, spanning** [T] **1** to include all of a period of time〔時間〕持續，延伸：*a career spanning four decades* 長達四十年的職業生涯 **2** to include all of a particular space or area〔空間、地域〕跨越，包括：*The Mongol Empire spanned much of Central Asia.* 蒙古帝國包括了中亞的許多地區。**3** if a bridge spans an area of water it goes from one side to the other〔橋梁〕跨越〔水面〕，橫跨

span·gle[1] /ˈspæŋgl; ˈspæŋgəl/ *v* [T] to cover something with shiny spots 用閃亮的斑點覆蓋，使閃閃發亮：**be spangled with** *His mackintosh was spangled with drops of rain.* 他的雨衣上佈滿了閃閃發亮的雨珠。—**spangled** also 又作 **spangly** *adj*: *acrobats in spangled tights* 穿着閃亮緊身衣的雜技演員

spangle[2] *n* [C] a small piece of shiny metal or plastic sewn on to clothes to give them a shining effect; SEQUIN〔衣服上用作裝飾的〕閃亮的金屬[塑料]片，閃光飾片

Spang·lish /ˈspæŋglɪʃ; ˈspæŋglɪʃ/ *n* [U] *especially AmE* a mixture of the Spanish and English languages【尤美】西英混合語〔西班牙語和英語的混合語〕

Span·iard /ˈspænjəd; ˈspænjəd/ *n* [C] a Spanish person 西班牙人

Span·iel /ˈspænjəl; ˈspænjəl/ *n* [C] a type of dog with long ears that hang down 西班牙獵犬〔一種長毛垂耳狗〕—see picture at 參見 DOG[1] 圖

Span·ish[1] /ˈspænɪʃ; ˈspænɪʃ/ *adj* from or connected with Spain 西班牙的

Spanish[2] *n* [U] the language of Spain and parts of South America 西班牙語

Spanish fly /ˌ·· ˈ·/ *n* [U] a substance made from dried insects, that is supposed to be an APHRODISIAC (=drug causing sexual excitement) 斑蝥劑〔一種用風乾昆蟲製成的藥, 據説可以引起性慾〕

Spanish ome·lette /ˌ·· ˈ··/ *n* [C] a thick OMELETTE made with cooked vegetables〔拌以蔬菜的〕西班牙煎蛋卷

spank /spæŋk; spæŋk/ *v* [T] to hit a child, on their bottom with your open hand〔用手掌〕打〔小孩的〕屁股 —compare 比較 SMACK[1] —**spanking, spank** *n* [C,U]: *If you don't stop that noise, you'll get a spanking.* 如果你繼續吵鬧的話, 那就要打屁股了。

spank·ing[1] /ˈspæŋkɪŋ; ˈspæŋkɪŋ/ *adj old-fashioned*【過時】**at a spanking pace/rate** very fast 快速地: *They started walking at a spanking rate.* 他們開始以很快的速度走。

spanking[2] *adv old-fashioned*【過時】**spanking new/clean etc** very new, clean etc 非常新/乾淨等: *a spanking new car* 嶄新的汽車

span·ner /ˈspænə; ˈspænə/ *n* [C] **1** *BrE* a metal tool that fits over a nut (NUT[1] (2)) and is used for turning it to make it tight or to undo it【英】扳手, 扳子; WRENCH[2] (3) *AmE*【美】—see also 另見 RING SPANNER —see picture at 參見 TOOL[1] 圖 **2 put/throw a spanner in the works** *BrE informal* to unexpectedly do something that prevents a plan or process from continuing or succeeding【英, 非正式】打亂〔計劃〕, 破壞〔過程〕: *He won't lend us the money? Well, that really puts a spanner in the works.* 他不肯借錢給我們? 哦, 那可真要壞事了。

spar[1] /spɑr; spɑː/ *v* **sparred, sparring** [I] **1** to practise BOXING with someone〔與某人〕練拳: *He once sparred with Mike Tyson.* 他曾與邁克·泰臣練拳。**2** to argue with someone but not in an unpleasant way〔友好地〕爭論, 爭辯: *gentle sparring between the generations* 兩代人之間並不激烈的爭論

spar[2] *n* [C] a thick pole, especially one used on a ship to support sails or ropes 圓材〔尤用作船舶的桅杆、帆桁等〕—compare 比較 MAST (1)

S2 **spare**[1] /spɛr; speə/ *adj*

1 ▶ADDITIONAL 附加的◀ **spare key/bulb/battery etc** a key etc that you have in addition to the ones you normally use, so that it is available if another is needed 備用鑰匙/燈泡/電池等

2 ▶AVAILABLE 可用的◀ not being used by anyone and available to be used 多餘的, 現成的: *Have you got any spare boxes?* 你有沒有多餘的盒子?

3 spare time time when you are not working 空閒時間: *What do you do in your spare time?* 你閒下來時幹甚麼?

4 spare change coins of little value that you do not need and can give to other people 多餘的零錢: *Do you have any spare change for the phone?* 你有打電話用的零錢嗎?

5 be going spare *spoken* if something is going spare it is available for you to have or use【口】可以使用; 可以擁有: *I'll have some of that cake if it's going spare.* 如果那蛋糕沒有人要, 我就吃一點。

6 ▶THIN 瘦的◀ *literary* tall and thin【文】瘦削的, 又高又瘦的: *an old man with a spare wiry frame* 一位精瘦結實的老人

7 go spare *BrE informal* to become very angry or worried【英, 非正式】非常生氣, 氣急敗壞: *Dad would go spare if he knew I'd stayed out all night.* 爸爸如果知道我整夜不歸, 他會氣壞的。

spare[2] *v* [T] S3

1 ▶GIVE 給予◀ if you can spare something, you can give it to someone because you are not using it or do not need it〔把不用的或多餘的東西〕撥出, 抽出, 騰出, 讓給: *I can't spare the time.* 我抽不出時間。| *We're too busy to spare anyone to help you right now.* 我們目前太忙, 騰不出人來幫助你。| **spare sb sth** *Could you spare me £5?* 你能給我五英鎊嗎?

2 money/time to spare if you have time, money etc to spare, there is some left in addition to what you have used or need 餘錢/餘暇: *We had an hour to spare so we looked round the shops.* 我們有一小時的空餘時間, 於是就去逛商店。| *They got there with seconds to spare.* 他們到那裡時只剩幾秒鐘了。

3 spare sb trouble/difficulty/pain etc to prevent someone from having to experience something difficult or unpleasant 免除某人的麻煩/困難/痛苦等: *They did what they could to spare him any pain.* 他們盡了一切努力使他免受任何痛苦。

4 spare a thought for to think about another person who is in a worse situation than they are 想一想〔某人〕: *Spare a thought for Nick, who's doing his exams while we lie in the sun.* 想一想尼克吧, 他正在考試, 而我們在躺着曬太陽。

5 spare no expense to spend as much money as necessary to make something really good and not worry about the cost 不惜工本: *Janet's parents spared no expense on her wedding.* 珍妮特的父母不惜工本, 給她辦婚禮。

6 spare sb the details to not tell someone all the details about something, because it is unpleasant or boring 不對某人談...的細節〔以免使人不快或厭煩〕

7 ▶NOT DAMAGE OR HARM 不損壞或傷害◀ to not damage or harm someone or something even though other people or things are being damaged, killed or destroyed 使免受〔損壞、傷亡〕, 倖免: *Only the children were spared.* 只有孩子們得以倖免。

8 spare sb's feelings to avoid doing something that would upset someone 免使某人難過: *We carefully avoided mentioning Cathy's break-up to spare her feelings.* 我們小心地避免提起凱西離婚的事, 以免讓她難過。

9 spare sb's blushes *BrE* to avoid doing something that would embarrass someone【英】不使某人難為情

spare[3] *n* **1** [C] an additional thing of a particular kind that you keep so that it is available 備用品: *If the fuse has gone, the spares are kept in the garage.* 保險絲如果斷了, 車庫裡有備用的。**2** [C] a SPARE TYRE (1) 備用輪胎 **3 spares** [plural] *BrE* new parts for vehicles or machines【英】〔車輛或機器的〕零件, 備件

spare part /ˌ· ˈ·/ *n* [C] a new part for a vehicle or machine, that is used to replace a part that is damaged or broken〔車輛或機器的〕備用零件, 備件

spare-part sur·ge·ry /ˌ· · ˈ···/ *n* [U] *informal* an operation to put an artificial organ, or an organ from a dead person, into the body of a living person【非正式】器官移植手術

spare·ribs /ˈspɛrˌrɪbz; ˈspeəˌrɪbz/ *n* [plural] the ribs (RIB[1] (2)) of a pig and the meat on them served as a food〔食用的〕帶肉豬排骨

spare room /ˌ· ˈ·/ *n* [C] a bedroom in your house, that is kept for guests to use when they come to stay〔家中的〕備用臥室, 客房

spare tyre *BrE*【英】, **spare tire** *AmE*【美】/ˌ· ˈ·/ *n* [C] **1** an additional wheel with a tyre on it, that you keep in a car for use if another tyre gets damaged 備用輪胎 **2** *humorous* a large ring of fat around someone's waist【幽默】肥胖的腰腹部

spar·ing /ˈspɛrɪŋ; ˈspeərɪŋ/ *adj* using or giving only a little of something; FRUGAL 省着用的, 節約的, 節儉的: [+with] *There's not much shampoo left, so be sparing with it.* 剩下的洗髮劑不多了, 所以要省着點用。| [+in] *The critics were sparing in their praise.* 那些批評家很少讚揚別人。—**sparingly** *adv*: *Apply the glue sparingly.* 少塗點膠水。

spark[1] /spɑrk; spɑːk/ *n*
1 ►FIRE 火◄ [C] a very small bit of brightly burning material produced by a fire or by hitting or rubbing together two hard objects 火花, 火星: *In a gas leak, any small spark will cause an explosion.* 煤氣泄漏時, 任何一個小火花都會引起爆炸。| *a shower of sparks from the fire* 從火中飛出的一陣火花
2 ►ELECTRICITY 電◄ [C] a flash of light caused by electricity passing across a space 電火花
3 spark of interest/excitement/anger etc a small amount of a feeling or quality, that can be noticed in someone's expression or behaviour 一點點興趣/激動/怒氣等: *Meg's eyes lacked their usual spark of humour.* 梅格的眼睛裡缺少了常有的幽默的火花。
4 ►INTELLIGENCE/ENERGY 智慧/精力◄ [U] a quality of intelligence or energy that makes someone successful or fun to be with 生氣, 活力, 〔才智的〕煥發: *Ali has plenty of spark and wit.* 阿里充滿了活力和智慧。
5 ►CAUSE 原因◄ [C] a small action or event that quickly causes trouble or violence 〔麻煩、暴力等的〕起因, 禍根: *Hani's murder was the spark that started the riot.* 哈尼被殺是引起這次暴亂的根源。
6 sparks fly if sparks fly between two people, they argue angrily 激烈爭吵: *Sparks were flying at the Conroy's last night!* 昨晚在康羅伊家發生了激烈的爭吵!

S

spark[2] *v* **1** also 又作 **spark off** [T] to be the cause of trouble or violence 引起, 導致〔麻煩、暴力等〕: *a minor incident that sparked off the conflict* 引發了這場衝突的一件小事 **2** [T] to start someone's interest in something 激發〔興趣〕, 激勵, 鼓舞: *Going to an exhibition sparked Chris's interest in photography.* 參觀一次展覽會激發了克里斯對攝影的興趣。**3** [I] to produce sparks of fire or electricity 發出火花[電火花] **4** [I] *AmE old-fashioned* to pay special attention to someone you are sexually attracted to 【美, 過時】受到異性吸引, 為異性傾倒

sparking plug /'‥ ·/ *n* [C] *BrE* a SPARK PLUG 【英】火花塞

spar·kle[1] /'spɑrkl; 'spɑːkəl/ *v* [I] **1** to shine in small bright flashes 閃閃發光, 閃耀, 閃爍: *The diamond ring sparkled in the sunlight.* 鑽石戒指在陽光下閃閃發光。**2** if someone's eyes sparkle, they shine brightly, especially because the person is happy or excited 〔眼睛〕發亮, 閃耀〔尤因快樂或興奮〕: [+with] *Ron's eyes sparkled with excitement.* 羅恩的眼睛閃爍着興奮的神情。—see also 另見 SPARKLING

sparkle[2] *n* [C,U] **1** a bright shiny appearance, with tiny points of flashing light 閃耀, 閃光 **2** a quality that makes something seem interesting and full of life 生氣, 活力: *The dialogue doesn't have much sparkle.* 這對話不是很生動。

spar·kler /'spɑrklɚ; 'spɑːklə/ *n* [C] **1** a FIREWORK in the shape of a thin stick, that gives off sparks of fire as you hold it in your hand 〔燃燒時發出火花的手持〕煙花棒 **2 sparklers** [plural] *informal* diamonds 【非正式】鑽石

spark·ling /'spɑrklɪŋ; 'spɑːklɪŋ/ *adj* **1** shining brightly with points of flashing light 閃亮的, 閃光的: *a sparkling lake* 湖光瀲灩 **2** a sparkling drink has bubbles (BUBBLE[1] (1)) of gas in it 〔飲料〕起泡沫的: *a sparkling wine* 氣泡葡萄酒 **3** full of life and intelligence 充滿生氣的, 才智煥發的: *sparkling wit* 才華橫溢

spark plug /'· ·/ *n* [C] *technical* a part in a car engine that produces an electric SPARK[1] (2) to make the petrol mixture start burning 【術語】〔汽車引擎的〕火花塞

spark·y /'spɑrkɪ; 'spɑːki/ *adj* full of life and energy 活潑的, 充滿活力的: *a sparky debating partner* 一位充滿活力的辯論夥伴

sparring match /'‥ ·/ *n* [C] a friendly argument that is not serious 友好的爭論

sparring part·ner /'‥ ,‥/ *n* [C] **1** someone you practise BOXING with 練拳的對手 **2** someone you regularly have friendly arguments with 〔經常地〕友好爭論的對手

spar·row /'spæro; 'spærəʊ/ *n* [C] a small brown bird, very common in many parts of the world 麻雀

sparse /spɑrs; spɑːs/ *adj* existing only in small amounts 稀少的, 稀疏的: *sparse vegetation* 稀疏的植被 | *Data on fatal accidents are sparse and difficult to obtain.* 關於死亡事故的資料很少, 也很難獲得。—**sparsely** *adv*: *a sparsely populated area* 人煙稀少的地區 —**sparseness** *n* [U]

spar·tan /'spɑrtn; 'spɑːtn/ *adj* spartan conditions or ways of living are simple and without any comfort 〔生活條件或方式〕簡樸而艱苦的: *spartan accommodation* 簡樸的住處 | *adjusting to the spartan life of boarding school* 適應寄宿學校的清苦生活

spas·m /'spæzəm; 'spæzəm/ *n* [C] **1** a sharp pain when your muscles suddenly become tighter in an uncontrolled way 痙攣, 抽搐 **2 a spasm of grief/laughter/coughing** a sudden strong feeling or reaction that lasts for a short period 一陣悲傷/歡笑/咳嗽

spas·mod·ic /spæz'mɑdɪk; spæz'mɒdɪk/ *adj* **1** happening for short irregular periods, not continuously 間歇的, 不規則的, 斷斷續續的: *spasmodic bursts of energy* 一陣陣的精力迸發 **2** like or connected with a muscle spasm 痙攣性的, 抽搐的 —**spasmodically** /-klɪ; -kli/ *adv*

spas·tic /'spæstɪk; 'spæstɪk/ *adj* **1** *slang* an offensive word meaning stupid or lacking in skill, used especially by children 【俚】愚笨的, 拙劣的〔冒犯語, 尤用於兒語〕**2** *old-fashioned* having CEREBRAL PALSY, a disease that prevents control of the muscles 【過時】患大腦性麻痺的 —**spastic** *n* [C]

spat[1] /spæt; spæt/ the past tense and past participle of SPIT

spat[2] *n* **1** [C] *informal* a short unimportant quarrel 【非正式】口角, 小爭吵: *It's just your normal, average sibling spat.* 那只是你們兄弟間正常的小吵吵而已。**2** [plural] special pieces of cloth worn in former times by men above their shoes and fastened with buttons 〔舊時男子穿的〕鞋罩, 鞋套

spate /spet; speɪt/ *n* **1 a spate of** a large number of similar unpleasant things that happen in a short period of time 大量, 大批, 許多〔短時間內發生類似的不愉快事件〕: *a spate of burglaries* 接連發生的多宗入室盜竊案 **2 in spate** a river, stream etc that is in spate, is very full and flowing very fast 〔河水等〕猛漲, 泛濫

spa·tial /'speʃəl; 'speɪʃəl/ *adj technical* concerning the position, size, shape etc of things 【術語】空間的, 關於空間的 —**spatially** *adv*

spat·ter /'spætɚ; 'spætə/ *v* **1** [T] to scatter or throw small amounts of mud, dirt etc all over a surface 濺, 灑: **spatter sb/sth with** *a passing car spattered with mud* 一輛駛過的車身濺滿污泥的汽車 | **spatter sth on/over etc** *Grey flicked his brush spattering paint over my shirt.* 格雷甩了甩刷子, 把油漆濺到了我的襯衣上。**2** [I] if liquid spatters on a surface, drops of it fall or are thrown on it 〔液體〕灑落, 滴下: [+on] *The first drops of rain spattered on the stones.* 開始落下的雨滴灑落在石頭上。—**spatter** *n* [C]

spat·u·la /'spætʃələ; 'spætjʊlə/ *n* [C] **1** a kitchen tool with a wide flat blade used for spreading, mixing, or lifting soft substances 〔廚房裡煎炒東西用的〕鏟 **2** *BrE* a small instrument with a flat surface, used by doctors to hold your tongue down so that they can examine your throat 【英】〔醫生用的〕壓舌板

spawn[1] /spɔn; spɔːn/ *v* **1** [I,T] if a fish or FROG spawns it produces eggs in large quantities together 〔魚、蛙等〕大

量產（卵） **2** [T] to make a series of things happen or start to exist 使大量出現，使大量產生；釀成：*the massive bureaucracy spawned by these programs* 這些計劃所引起的官僚主義泛濫

spawn² *n* [U] the eggs of a fish, FROG etc laid together in a soft mass〔魚、蛙等產的〕成團的卵，卵塊

spay /spe; speɪ/ *v* [T] to remove part of the sex organs of a female animal so that it is not able to have babies 切除〔雌性動物的〕卵巢，閹割〔雌性動物〕

S1 W1 **speak** /spik; spiːk/ *v past* **spoke** /spok; spəʊk/ *past participle* **spoken** /ˈspokən; ˈspəʊkən/

1 ►IN CONVERSATION 在會話中◄ [I always+adv/prep] to talk to someone about something or have a conversation 談話，交談：**speak to sb about sth** *I intend to speak to the manager about the way I have been treated.* 我想對經理談談我所受到的那種待遇。| *I know her by sight but not to speak to* (=not well enough to talk to her). 我只認得她的模樣，但沒跟她說過話。| **speak with** *especially AmE*【尤美】*Sally would like to speak with you for a minute.* 莎莉想和你談一會兒。| **speak of** *formal*【正式】*It was the first time she had ever spoken of marriage.* 那是她頭一次談及婚姻問題。—see 見 SAY[1] (USAGE)

2 ►SAY WORDS 說話◄ [I] to use your voice to produce words 說話，講話：*I was so shocked I couldn't speak.* 我震驚得說不出話來。| **[+to]** *John! Speak to me! Are you alright?* 約翰！跟我說話呀！你沒事吧？

3 ►A LANGUAGE 一種語言◄ [T not in progressive 不用進行式] to be able to speak a particular language 會說，會講〔某種語言〕：*Do you speak English?* 你會說英語嗎？| **not speak a word of** (=not speak it at all) 一個字也不會說／完全不會說 *He doesn't speak a word of French.* 他一句法語也不會說。| **French-speaking/Italian-speaking etc** *a German-speaking secretary* 會說德語的秘書

4 ►FORMAL SPEECH 正式演講◄ [I] to make a formal speech 演說，演講；發言：*Diana's been invited to speak at the annual conference.* 戴安娜被邀請在年會上作演講。| **speak in favour of/against** (=support or oppose) 發言支持／反對 *Only one MP spoke against the bill.* 只有一位議會議員發言反對那項提案。—see also 另見 SPEAKER

5 be not speaking/not be on speaking terms if two people are not speaking they will not be polite or talk to each other, especially because they have quarrelled 彼此不說話／互不理睬〔尤因為吵架了〕

6 ►EXPRESS IDEAS/OPINIONS 表達想法/意見◄ [T] to say something that expresses your ideas or opinions 表達，表明〔觀點、意見〕：*Not a word was spoken about the whole affair.* 對於整個事件沒有人表達過半點意見。| **speaking as a parent/teacher/democrat etc** *Speaking as a parent, I would like to see more discipline in schools.* 作為一位家長來說，我希望看到學校能加強紀律。| **speak well/badly/ill of** (=say good or bad things about someone) 說某人的好話／壞話 *It's wrong to speak ill of the dead.* 說死者的壞話是不對的。| **speak highly of** (=praise someone) 讚揚〔某人〕*I'm so pleased to meet you – my wife has always spoken very highly of you.* 見到你真高興——我太太經常稱讚你。| **speak your mind** (=tell people exactly what you think, even if it offends them) 坦率地說出自己的想法，直言不諱 *She's very direct, the kind of person who believes in speaking their mind.* 她這個人非常坦率，是那種認為說話應當直言不諱的人。

7 generally/personally/technically speaking used when you are expressing a general, personal etc opinion 一般來說／就個人來說／從技術上說〔用於表示從某個角度發表意見〕：*Generally speaking, rural schools provide a better environment for the students.* 一般來說，鄉村學校能給學生提供更好的環境。

8 speak out of turn to say something when you do not have the right or authority to say it 說話魯莽，講話不合身分：*I hope I haven't spoken out of turn – I didn't know it was supposed to be a secret.* 希望我沒有說了冒失的話——我不知道這是應當保密的。

9 none/nothing to speak of not large or important enough to mention 不值一提：*There's been no rain to speak of – only a few drops.* 沒有下過像樣的雨，只是下過幾滴。

10 so to speak used when you are saying something in words that do not have their usual meaning 可以說〔在使用不平常表達方法時說的話〕：*We all learned this theory, so to speak, at our mother's knee.* 可以說，還在媽媽膝頭的時候，我們大家就都知道了這種說法。

11 speak volumes to express something very clearly, without using words〔不用說話〕有力地說明，充分地證明：*Mary could not express the high hopes she had for her daughter, but her actions spoke volumes.* 瑪麗不能表達她對女兒的深厚期望，但她的行動充分說明了這一點。

speak for sb/sth *phr v* [T] **1** to express the feelings, thoughts, or beliefs of a person or group of people 代表…講話，充當…的代言人：*I think I speak for everyone here when I say we wish you all the best.* 祝你一切順利，我想我的話代表了大家的心意。**2 speak for yourself** *spoken* used to tell someone that you do not have the same opinion as they do【口】你只代表你自己說話〔用於表示不同意對方的意見〕：*"We were all bored in that lecture." "Speak for yourself! I liked it."* "那次講座我們都聽得很厭煩。" "你只是說你自己吧！我是喜歡那次講座的。" **3 be spoken for** if something or someone is spoken for, it has already been promised to someone else 已被預訂，已被訂購：*The first 300 cars off the production line have already been spoken for.* 第一批300輛汽車剛剛離開生產線便已被訂購一空。**4 speak for itself/themselves** to show something so clearly that no explanation is necessary 不言而喻，不辯自明：*1994 has been a very good year for us – the figures speak for themselves.* 1994年對我們是很好的一年——一看數字便知道。—see also 另見 **actions speak louder than words** (ACTION (15)), **in a manner of speaking** (MANNER (4))

speak of sth *phr v* [T] *literary* to show clearly that something happened or that it exists【文】表明…：*The lush vegetation spoke of a richer, damper climate.* 茂盛的草木表明氣候濕潤，適宜植物生長。

speak out *phr v* [I] to publicly speak in protest about something, especially when protesting could be dangerous 公開地說出來〔尤指冒險表示抗議〕：**[+about/against]** *Five students who had spoken out against the regime were arrested.* 五名公開地抗議政府的學生均遭逮捕。

speak to sb *phr v* [T] *informal* to talk to someone who has done something wrong, to tell them not to do it again【非正式】當面提醒，責備，告誡：*Joe was late again today, you'll have to speak to him.* 喬今天又遲到了，你得說說他。

speak up *phr v* [I] **1** used to ask someone to speak louder 大聲地說，提高嗓門說〔用於要求別人〕：*Speak up, please, I can't hear you.* 請說大聲一點，我聽不見你說的話。**2** to express your opinion freely and clearly 自由地、清楚地表達意見：*"Is that wise?" Isidore spoke up, gathering courage.* "那樣明智嗎？"伊西多鼓起勇氣，直截了當地問道。**3 speak up for** to speak in support of someone 替…說話，支持：*It's about time someone spoke up for single mothers.* 該是有人替單身母親說話的時候了。

USAGE NOTE 用法說明: SPEAK

WORD CHOICE 詞語辨析: **speak, talk, discuss, describe, say**

Speak is a little formal and often gives the idea that one person is saying more than any others in a conversation. speak 這個詞略為正式，並常表示在

S

談話中一個人說得比其他人多: *He won't listen to me – will you speak to him?* 他不肯聽我的 —— 你去跟他說說好嗎? | *Could you speak a little louder please?* 請你講大聲一點好嗎?

Talk is over twice as frequent in spoken English and usually suggests that two or more people are having a conversation. talk在口語中的使用頻率要高一倍多, 並通常表示兩人或更多的人在進行談話: *We stayed up all night talking.* 我們整個晚上都在談話, 沒有睡覺。| *Are you two talking about me?* 你們兩個是不是在談論我?

If you **talk about** something with someone, for example, in order to reach a decision, you **discuss** it. talk about 表示討論某事以便作出決定時, 也就是說在 discuss: *The boss wants to discuss next year's budget at the meeting.* 老闆想在會議上討論明年的預算問題。You can **discuss** or **describe** something either in speech or in writing. discuss 或 describe 既可以表示口頭上的討論或描述, 也可以表示書面的討論或描述。

In British English **speak with** and **talk with** often mean a longer more formal talk than **speak to** or **talk to**, but in American English they are used more generally. 在英國英語中, speak with 和 talk with 常用於比 speak to 和 talk to 更長、更為正式的談話, 但在美國英語中一般無此區別。

Compare **speak** a language and **speak in** a language. 比較 speak 和 speak in 在表示說某種語言時的用法: *Catherine may speak Greek* means either 'she may know Greek' or 'she knows Greek and may use it on this occasion'; *'Catherine may speak in Greek'* means only the second of these. Catherine may speak Greek 這個句子可以表示"她可能會說希臘語"或"她懂希臘語, 而且她這次可能用希臘語發言"這兩種意思。但 Catherine may speak in Greek 只表示上述第二種意思。

GRAMMAR 語法

When **speak** is transitive, its object is usually a language. 當 speak 用作及物動詞時, 其受詞通常為某種語言: *What's she speaking* (=what language)*?* 她講的是甚麼語言? | *I don't speak a word of Thai* (NOT 不用 *talk*). 我一句泰語也不會講。You **say** other things 說其他事情則用 say: *What's she saying?* (=what words?) 她在說些甚麼? Note that you say 注意, 我們可以說: *I didn't say it/anything/those things* (NOT 不用 *speak it* etc). 我沒說過這件事/任何事/那些事。| *I gave my opinion* (NOT 不用 *spoke* my opinion). 我提出我的意見。But you would sometimes say 但我們有時候會說: *She spoke the truth* (=told the truth). 她說了真話。

In writing **talk** is rarely transitive and can take only a few objects. 在書面語中, talk 很少用作及物動詞, 只有一些單詞可用作它的受詞: *He's talking nonsense/business.* 他在胡說八道/談正經事。Otherwise you need to say **talk about** 一般則必須說 talk about: *She talked about her childhood for a long time.* 她談自己的童年談了很久。In informal spoken English, however, you will hear things like 不過, 在非正式口語中, 有時也可以聽到這些用法: *We're talking big bucks!* (=there is a lot of money involved in this situation) 我們在談大筆錢的事! or 或 *They're talking cars again* (=they are talking about cars). 他們又在談汽車了。

When it is transitive neither **talk** nor **speak** can have a person as its object. 在用作及物動詞時, talk 和 speak 都不能用人作受詞: *I spoke to him yesterday* (NOT 不用 *spoke him*). 我昨天跟他說過了。| *They should talk to each other more* (NOT 不用 *talk each other*). 他們應當多互相交談。

See also 另見 **say** (WORD CHOICE).

S

-speak /spik; spiːk/ *suffix* [in nouns 構成名詞] the special language, especially slang words or words that are difficult to understand, used in a particular business or activity 行話, 術語, 語言: *computerspeak* 電腦語言

speak·eas·y /ˈspikˌizi; ˈspiːkˌiːzi/ *n* [C] a place in the US in the 1920's and 1930's where you could buy alcohol illegally〔20世紀20、30年代美國的〕非法經營的售酒處

speak·er /ˈspikɚ; ˈspiːkə/ *n* [C] **1** someone who makes a speech, usually at a meeting 演講者: *Our speaker tonight is Mr Pearson.* 我們今晚的演講者是皮爾遜先生。| **after-dinner speaker** (=someone who makes a speech after a formal meal) 宴會後的演講者 **2 French speaker/English speaker etc** someone who speaks French etc 講法語/講英語等的人 **3** the part of a radio or record player where the sound comes out〔收音機或唱機的〕揚聲器 **4 the Speaker** an official who controls discussions in a parliament〔議會的〕議長 S2 W2

speaking tube /ˈ·· ·/ *n* [C] a pipe through which people in different rooms can talk to each other〔各個房間之間的〕通話管

spear¹ /spɪr; spɪə/ *n* [C] **1** a pole with a sharp pointed blade at one end, used as a weapon in the past 矛, 標槍 **2** a thin pointed stem of a plant, shaped like a spear 嫩芽, 嫩枝, 嫩莖: *asparagus spears* 蘆筍嫩莖

spear² *v* [T] **1** to push or throw a spear into something, especially in order to kill it 用矛刺: *The huntsmen were spearing fish from the river.* 獵人正從河中叉魚。**2** to push a pointed object, usually a fork, into something, so that you can pick it up 用叉叉起, 用尖物叉起

spear·head¹ /ˈspɪrˌhɛd; ˈspɪəhed/ *v* [T] to lead an attack or organized action 當…的先鋒, 帶頭〔做某事〕: *Ross spearheaded a campaign to improve sales.* 羅斯帶頭發起一場促銷活動。

spearhead² *n* [C usually singular 一般用單數] a person or group of people who lead an attack or organized action 先鋒, 前導, 先頭部隊: *The group became the spearhead of the labor union movement.* 這個團體成了工會運動的先鋒。

spear·mint /ˈspɪrˌmɪnt; ˈspɪəˌmɪnt/ *n* [U] **1** a fresh MINT¹ (1) taste, often used in sweets 留蘭香 (味): *spearmint chewing gum* 留蘭香味口香糖 **2** the MINT¹ (2) plant that this taste comes from 留蘭香 (植物)

spec /spɛk; spek/ *n BrE informal*【英, 非正式】**1 on spec** if you do something on spec, you do it without being sure that you will get what you are hoping for 碰運氣: *I sent in an application on spec.* 我寄去一份申請書碰碰運氣。**2 specs** [plural] glasses (GLASS¹ (3)) to help you see 眼鏡

spe·cial¹ /ˈspɛʃəl; ˈspeʃəl/ *adj* **1** not ordinary or usual but different in some way and often better or more important 特殊的, 特別的: *a special case, deserving special treatment* 一種應加以特殊處理的特殊情況 | *diabetics on a special diet* 實行特殊飲食的糖尿病患者 | **special occasion** (=an important social event) 特殊場合 *I keep this suit for special occasions.* 我把這套西服留在特殊場合穿。| **anything special** *spoken*【口】*Are you doing anything special for Christmas?* 你過聖誕節有甚麼特別活動嗎? | **special edition** (=a special type of car, watch etc produced only for a short time)〔只在一段短時間內生產的汽車、手錶等的〕特別版本 **2 special offer** a low price charged for a product for a short time 特價出售: *There's a special offer on this shampoo – two for the price of one.* 這種洗髮劑特價出售 —— 買一瓶送一瓶。**3** particularly important to someone and deserving attention, love etc 特別親密的, 特別受喜愛的: *Rob's a special friend of mine.* 羅布是我一位特別親密的朋友。| *a wonderful teacher who made every child feel special* 能使每個孩子都感到自己受重視的優秀教師 **4** unusually good 特別好的: *I'd like you to try some of this whisky. It's rather special.* 我想請你嚐一嚐這種威士忌酒。這是一種不同尋常的好酒。| **nothing special** (=not particu- S1 W1 larly good) 並非特別好的, 一般的 *"What was the food like?" "Nothing special."* "飯菜怎麼樣?" "只是一般。" **5** more than usual 格外的, 特别的: *Take special care on the roads tonight – it's icy.* 今晚在路上要格外小心 —— 結冰了。—see 見 ESPECIALLY (USAGE)

special² *n* [C usually singular 一般用單數] **1** something that is not usual or ordinary, and is made or done for a special purpose 特別的東西, 特殊的事物: *a two-hour television special on famine in Africa* 長達兩小時的關於非洲饑荒的電視特別節目 **2** *informal, especially AmE* a lower price than usual for a particular product for a short period of time【非正式, 尤美】特價: *The supermarket has a special on chicken.* 超級市場有特價雞出售。| **on special** *Breyer's ice cream is on special this week.* 布賴亞店的冰淇淋本週特價。**3** *ScotE* a type of beer【蘇格蘭】一種啤酒

special a·gent /,·· '··/ *n* [C] *AmE* someone who works for the FBI【美】〔聯邦調查局的〕特工, 特別調查員

Special Branch /'·· ,·/ *n* [U] a department of the British police force that deals with political crimes or crimes affecting the safety of the government, for example TERRORISM〔英國警察部門的〕政治保安處

special con·sta·ble /,·· '···/ *n* [C] someone in Britain who has an ordinary job, but is sometimes employed as a police officer when the police need more help〔英國在警力不足時協助維持社會治安的〕特種警察

special de·liv·e·ry /,·· ·'···/ *n* [C,U] a service that delivers a letter or package very quickly〔郵件〕快遞, 限時專送

special ed·u·ca·tion /,·· ··'··/ *n* [U] the education of children who have particular physical problems or learning problems〔向身體或智力有缺陷的學生提供的〕特殊教育

special ef·fect /,·· ·'·/ *n* [C] an unusual image or sound in a film or television programme that has been produced artificially〔電影、電視等的〕特技效果: *the amazing special effects in 'Jurassic Park'* 《侏羅紀公園》中驚人的特技效果

special forc·es /,·· '··/ *n* [plural] soldiers who have been specially trained to fight against GUERRILLA or TERRORIST groups〔從事反游擊戰和反恐怖主義的〕特種部隊

special in·terest group /,·· '·· ,·/ *n* [C] a group of people who all share the same aims 特殊利益集團

spe·ci·al·is·m /ˈspɛʃəlˌɪzəm; ˈspeʃəlɪzəm/ *n* **1** [U] the practice of limiting your interests or activities to particular subjects 專門研究, 專修 **2** [C] an activity or subject that you know a lot about 特長, 專長, 專門學科

S3 W3 **spe·cial·ist** /ˈspɛʃəlɪst; ˈspeʃələ̇st/ *n* [C] **1** someone who knows a lot about a particular subject, or is very skilled at it 專家: [+in] *a specialist in African history* 非洲史專家 **2** a doctor who knows more about one particular type of illness or treatment than other doctors 專科醫生: *a heart specialist* 心臟專科醫生

spe·ci·al·i·ty /ˌspɛʃɪˈælətɪ; ˌspeʃiˈælə̇ti/ *n plural* **specialities** [C] *BrE*【英】**1** a kind of food that is always very good in a particular restaurant or area〔一家飯館或某地方的〕特色菜, 名菜; SPECIALTY (1) *AmE*【美】: *Try the mushroom paté – it's our speciality.* 試試肉醬蘑菇吧 —— 這是我們的特色菜。**2** a subject or skill that you know a lot about or have a lot of experience of 專業, 專門研究; 專長; SPECIALTY (2) *AmE*【美】: *Preston's speciality was night photography.* 普雷斯頓的專長是夜間攝影。

S3 **spe·cial·ize** also 又作 **-ise** *BrE*【英】/ˈspɛʃəlˌaɪz; ˈspeʃəlaɪz/ *v* [I] to limit all or most of your study, business etc to a particular subject or activity 專門研究, 專門從事, 專攻: [+in] *After qualifying, Zelda decided to specialize in contract law.* 取得資格後, 澤爾達決定專門從事合同法業務。—**specialization** /ˌspɛʃələˈzeʃən; ˌspeʃəlaɪˈzeɪʃən/ *n* [C,U]

spe·cial·ized also 又作 **-ised** *BrE*【英】/ˈspɛʃəlˌaɪzd; ˈspeʃəlaɪzd/ *adj* trained, designed, or developed for a particular purpose or type of work 專門的; 專用的: *Don't try repairing it yourself – it requires specialized knowledge.* 不要試着自己去修理 —— 這需要具有專業知識。| **highly specialized** (=very specialized) 高度專業化的 *a highly specialized field of study* 高度專門化的研究領域

special li·cence /,·· '··/ *n* [C,U] special permission given by the Church of England for a marriage to take place at a time or place not usually allowed 結婚特許證〔英國教會發出的, 允許在通常不准結婚的時間或地點結婚〕

spe·cial·ly /ˈspɛʃəlɪ; ˈspeʃəli/ *adv* **1** for one particular purpose, and only for that purpose 為了特殊目的, 特意地, 專門地: *I had this dress made specially for the wedding.* 我特地為那次婚禮做了這件連衣裙。**2** *especially spoken* much more than usual, or much more than other people or things; ESPECIALLY【尤口】特別, 尤其: *We specially wanted to visit Disneyland.* 我們特別想去參觀迪士尼樂園。—see 見 ESPECIALLY (USAGE)

special needs /,·· '·/ *n* [plural] needs that someone has because they have mental or physical problems〔智力或身體有缺陷的人的〕特殊需要: *children with special needs* 有特殊需要的兒童

special school /'·· ,·/ *n* [C] a school for children with physical problems or problems with learning〔專為智力或身體有缺陷的孩子開辦的〕特殊學校

spe·cial·ty /ˈspɛʃəltɪ; ˈspeʃəlti/ *n* [C] *especially AmE*【尤美】**1** a kind of food that is always very good in a particular area or restaurant〔一地或一家飯館的〕特色菜, 拿手菜; SPECIALITY (1) *BrE*【英】: *Our specialty is clam chowder.* 我們的特色菜是蛤肉湯。**2** a subject or job that you know a lot about or have a lot of experience of 專業, 專門研究; 專長; SPECIALITY (2) *BrE*【英】 *Johnson's specialty is Medieval European history.* 約翰遜的專業是中世紀歐洲史。

S

spe·cies /ˈspiʃiz; ˈspiːʃiːz/ *n plural* **species** [C] a group of animals or plants which are all similar and can breed together to produce young animals or plants of the same kind as them〔動植物的〕物種, 種: **endangered species** (=one that may soon no longer exist) 瀕危物種 *This type of rattlesnake has been declared an endangered species.* 這類響尾蛇已被宣布為瀕危物種了。 W3

spe·cif·ic¹ /spɪˈsɪfɪk; spə̇ˈsɪfɪk/ *adj* **1** [only before noun 僅用於名詞前] a specific thing, person, or group is one particular thing etc 具體的, 特定的, 特有的: *Is this game meant for a specific age-group?* 這種遊戲是專為特定年齡組的人安排的嗎? **2** detailed and exact 詳細的, 明確的, 確切的: *Una gave us very specific instructions.* 尤娜給了我們非常詳盡的指示。| *You said you live in the West Country, could you be a bit more specific?* 你說你住在英格蘭西南部, 你能說得更確切一點嗎? **3 specific to** *formal* limited to, or affecting only one particular thing【正式】僅限於...的, 只對...有影響的: *a disease specific to horses* 只有馬才會得的病

specific² *n* **1 specifics** [plural] particular details that must be decided exactly 細節, 詳情: **get down to/go into specifics** *I can't go into specifics at this time, but I can tell you that we have an agreement.* 我現在不能詳談具體情況, 但我可以告訴你我們已經有一項協議。**2** [C] *technical* a drug that has an effect only on one particular DISEASE【術語】特效藥

spe·cif·ic·ally /spɪˈsɪfɪklɪ; spə̇ˈsɪfɪkli/ *adv* **1** concerning or intended for one particular type of person or thing only 特定地, 具體地, 專門地: *a video specifically aimed at teenagers* 專門以青少年為對象的錄像片 **2** in a detailed or exact way 明確地: *I specifically asked you not to do that!* 我明確地要求你不要那樣做! **3** [sentence adverb 句子副詞] used when you are adding more exact information 說明確些, (說具體些) 就是: *Tom's hoping to move to Spain, or more specifically, Barcelona.* 湯姆希望遷往西班牙, 說具體些就是巴塞羅那。

spe·ci·fi·ca·tion /ˌspɛsəfəˈkeʃən; ˌspesə̇fə̇ˈkeɪʃən/ *n* **1** [C usually plural 一般用複數] a detailed instruction about how something should be designed or made 規格說明, 明細規範: *a car manufactured according to exact speci-*

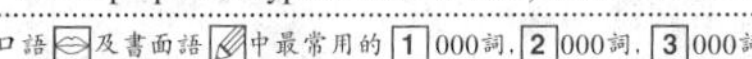

fications 按照嚴格的規格製造的汽車 | **job specification** (=detailed description of what a job involves) 工作職責說明 **2** [C] a clear statement of what is needed or wanted 具體[明確]說明: *Any student can apply for a loan, the only specification being that you must be in full-time education.* 任何學生均可申請貸款, 唯一要求是申請人必須是全日制學生。

specific grav·i·ty /·,··'···/ *n* [U] *technical* the weight of a substance divided by the weight of the amount of water that would fill the same space【術語】比重

3 **spe·ci·fy** /ˋspɛsə,faɪ; 'spesɪ̈faɪ/ *v* **specified, specifying** [T] to state something in an exact and detailed way 具體指明, 明確規定, 詳述: *Names and numbers were not specified.* 名字和號碼都沒有具體指明。| **specify who/what/how etc** *Did you specify where the new work station has to go?* 你有沒有指明新的工作站必須設在甚麼地方? | **specify that** *The rules clearly specify that competitors must not accept payment.* 規則清楚地說明參賽者不得接受報酬。

spe·ci·men /ˋspɛsəmən; 'spesɪ̈mɪ̈n/ *n* [C] **1** a small amount or piece of something that is taken from a plant or animal, so that it can be tested or examined 樣品, 樣本, 標本: *a zoological specimen* 動物標本 | **[+of]** *The doctor will need a specimen of your blood.* 醫生需要你的血樣。**2** a single example of something 實例, 範例: *a very fine specimen of 12th century glass* 12世紀玻璃的極好的樣品 **3** *humorous* a person you are describing in a particular way, usually in an unpleasant way【幽默】某種類型的人, 傢伙: *Who's that revolting specimen your daughter's going out with?* 那個和你女兒出雙入對的討厭傢伙是誰?

spe·cious /ˋspiʃəs; 'spi:ʃəs/ *adj formal* seeming to be true or correct, but actually false【正式】似是而非的, 貌似正確的: *a specious argument* 貌似有理的論據 —**speciously** *adv* —**speciousness** *n* [U]

speck /spɛk; spek/ *n* [C] a very small mark, spot, or piece of something 小斑點; 小片: *The boat was soon just a speck on the horizon.* 那艘船很快就變成了地平線上的一個小點。—see picture on page A7 參見A7頁圖

speck·le /ˋspɛkl̩; 'spekəl/ *n* [plural] small marks or spots covering a background of a different colour〔許多〕小斑點

speck·led /ˋspɛkl̩d; 'spekəld/ *adj* covered with many small marks or spots 帶有許多小斑點的, 佈滿小斑點的: *speckled eggs* 蛋殼上佈滿小斑點的雞蛋 —see picture on page A16 參見A16頁圖

spec·ta·cle /ˋspɛktəkl̩; 'spektəkəl/ *n* [C] **1** a very impressive show or scene 奇觀, 壯觀的場面[景象]: *The military parade was a magnificent spectacle.* 這次軍事檢閱場面非常壯觀。**2** [usually singular 一般用單數] an unusual thing or situation to be seen or noticed 不同尋常的事[現象]: **[+of]** *the curious spectacle of a cat actually chasing a dog* 一隻貓竟然在追逐一隻狗的稀奇事 **3 make a spectacle of yourself** to behave in a way that is likely to make other people notice you and laugh at you 出洋相 **4 spectacles** [plural] *formal* two pieces of round glass in a frame, worn in front of your eyes to help you to see clearly; glasses (GLASS[1] (3))【正式】眼鏡 —see also 另見 **see sth through rose-coloured spectacles** (ROSE-COLOURED (2))

spec·tac·u·lar[1] /spɛkˋtækjələ˞; spek'tækjɪ̈lə/ *adj* **1** very impressive and exciting 壯觀的, 精彩的, 引人注目的: *a spectacular fireworks display* 壯觀的煙火表演 **2** unusually great or large 巨大的, 輝煌的: *His new show is a spectacular success.* 他的新演出取得巨大的成功。—**spectacularly** *adv*

spectacular[2] *n* [C] an event or performance that is very large and impressive 壯觀的場面; 盛大的演出: *a television spectacular* 場面浩大的電視節目

spec·tate /ˋspɛktet; spek'teɪt/ *v* [I] to watch a sports event 觀看體育比賽

spec·ta·tor /ˋspɛkteta˞; spek'teɪtə/ *n* [C] someone who is watching an event or game〔體育運動或比賽的〕觀看者, 觀眾: *The match attracted over 40,000 spectators.* 這場比賽吸引了四萬多名觀眾。

spectator sport /·'·· ,·/ *n* [C] a sport that people go and watch 觀眾眾多的體育運動

spec·ter /ˋspɛktə˞; 'spektə/ *n* [C] the American spelling of SPECTRE spectre的美式拼法

spec·tra /ˋspɛktrə; 'spektrə/ the plural of SPECTRUM

spec·tral /ˋspɛktrəl; 'spektrəl/ *adj* **1** *literary* connected with or like a spectre【文】鬼魂的; 幽靈般的: *a spectral apparition* 幽靈 **2** *technical* connected with or made by a SPECTRUM【術語】光譜的, 由光譜所作的

spec·tre *BrE*【英】, **specter** *AmE*【美】/ˋspɛktə˞; 'spektə/ *n* **1 the spectre of** something that people are afraid of because it may affect them soon 引起恐懼的事物: *the spectre of unemployment* 失業的恐懼 **2** [C] *literary* a GHOST【文】鬼魂, 幽靈

spec·tro·scope /ˋspɛktrə,skop; 'spektrəskəʊp/ *n* [C] an instrument used for forming and looking at spectra (SPECTRUM (2)) 分光鏡 —**spectroscopy** /spɛkˋtrɑskəpɪ; spek'trɒskəpi/ *n* [U] —**spectroscopic** /,spɛktrəˋskɑpɪk; ,spektrə'skɒpɪk◂/ *adj*

spec·trum /ˋspɛktrəm; 'spektrəm/ *n plural* **spectra** /-trə; -trə/ [C] **1** a complete range of opinions, ideas, situations etc, going from one extreme to its opposite〔觀點、思想、情況等的〕範圍, 幅度: *Our speakers tonight come from both ends of the political spectrum.* 我們今晚的演講人來自政壇的兩個極端。| **[+of]** *a wide spectrum of opinion* 眾說紛紜 **2** the set of bands of coloured light into which a beam of light may be separated by passing it through a PRISM 光譜 **3** a complete range of radio, sound etc waves 頻譜: *the electromagnetic spectrum* 電磁(波)譜

spec·u·late /ˋspɛkjə,let; 'spekjɪ̈leɪt/ *v* **1** [I,T] to think or talk about the possible causes or effects of something without knowing all the facts or details 猜測, 推測: **[+on/about]** *We can only speculate about why he did it.* 我們只能猜測他為甚麼那樣做。| **speculate that** *George began to speculate that the two events might be linked.* 約翰開始猜測那兩件事可能有聯繫。**2** [I] to buy goods, property, shares (SHARE[2] (5)) in a company etc hoping that you will make a large profit when you sell them 投機, 做投機買賣: **[+in]** *Ned had speculated in gold and lost heavily.* 內德曾作黃金投機買賣, 損失慘重。—**speculator** *n* [C]: *property speculators* 房地產投機者[炒家]

spec·u·la·tion /,spɛkjəˋleʃən; ,spekjɪ̈'leɪʃən/ *n* [C,U] **1** the act of guessing without knowing all the facts about something, or the guesses that you make 猜測, 推測: **[+about]** *increased speculation about the possibility of tax cuts* 關於減稅可能性的諸多猜測 | **speculation that** *There is some speculation that the president was aware of the situation.* 有人猜測總統是了解情況的。| **pure speculation** (=speculation that is not based on any facts) 純屬猜測 *The jury should disregard the witness's last statement as pure speculation.* 陪審團應當認為證人的最後陳述毫無事實根據而不予考慮。| **wild/idle speculation** (=speculation that is unlikely to be true) 胡亂猜測 **2** the act of trying to make a profit by speculating (SPECULATE (2)) 投機買賣, 投機生意: *property speculation* 房地產投機買賣

spec·u·la·tive /ˋspɛkjə,letɪv; 'spekjɪ̈lətɪv/ *adj* **1** based on guessing, not on information or facts 猜測的, 猜想的: *These figures are, at best, speculative.* 這些數字頂多也是個猜測。**2** bought or done in the hope of making a profit later 投機的: *speculative investments* 投機性的投資 —**speculatively** *adv*

sped /spɛd; sped/ the past tense and past participle of SPEED

speech /spitʃ; spi:tʃ/ *n* **1** [C] a talk, especially a formal one about a particular subject, given to a group of people 演說, 演講: *an election speech* 競選演說 | **give/make/**

deliver a speech *Dr Ozu made a brilliant speech about the need for change.* 奧祖博士發表了關於必須進行改革的精彩演說。**2** [U] the ability to speak 說話的能力: *Only humans are capable of speech.* 只有人類才具備說話能力。| **power of speech** (=the ability to speak) 說話能力 *brain damage resulting in the loss of the power of speech* 導致說話能力喪失的腦部損傷 | **speech impediment** (=a physical or nervous problem that affects your speech) 言語障礙 **3** [U] spoken language rather than written language 口語: *In speech we use a smaller vocabulary than in writing.* 在口語中我們用的詞彙比在書面語中用的少。| **freedom of speech** (=the right to say whatever you want) 言論自由 **4** [U] the particular way in which someone speaks〔某人的〕說話方式: *Bob's speech was slurred, and he sounded drunk.* 鮑勃說話含糊不清, 聽起來像是喝醉了酒。**5** [C] a set of lines that an actor must say in a play〔演員的〕台詞: *Hamlet's longest speech* 哈姆雷特最長的那段台詞 —see also 另見 DIRECT SPEECH, FIGURE OF SPEECH, INDIRECT SPEECH, PART OF SPEECH, REPORTED SPEECH, **speech bubble** (BUBBLE[1] (3))

speech day /ˈ· ·/ *n* [C] an occasion held once a year in some British schools, when prizes are given to children〔英國的一些學校一年一度的〕畢業典禮日

spee·chi·fy /ˈspitʃəˌfaɪ; ˈspiːtʃɪfaɪ/ *v* [I] *informal* to make speeches in order to seem important【非正式】〔高談闊論地〕發表演說: *speechifying about the dishonesty of politicians* 高談闊論地大談政客的不誠實問題

speech·less /ˈspitʃlɪs; ˈspiːtʃləs/ *adj* unable to speak because you feel very angry, upset etc〔因憤怒、難過等而〕說不出話的, 啞口無言的: **[+with]** *speechless with rage* 氣得說不出話來 —**speechlessly** *adv* —**speechlessness** *n* [U]

speech marks /ˈ· ·/ *n* [plural] the marks (" ") or (' ') that show when someone starts speaking and when they stop 引號〔表示說話開始和結束的符號" "或' '〕

speech syn·the·siz·er /ˈ· ˌ····/ *n* [C] a computer system that produces sounds like human speech 言語合成器〔能產生類似人聲的電腦系統〕

speech ther·a·py /ˌ· ˈ···/ *n* [U] treatment that helps people who have difficulty in speaking properly 言語障礙矯治(法), 言語治療 —**speech therapist** *n* [C]

S1 W2 **speed[1]** /spid; spiːd/ *n*

1 ▶OF MOVEMENT 運動的◀ [C,U] how fast something moves or travels 速度, 速率: *What speed are we doing?* 我們的速度如何? | *Police are advising motorists to reduce speed.* 警方勸告駕車者減速。| **pick up/gather speed** (=gradually start to travel faster) 逐漸加快速度 *Once outside the station, the train began to pick up speed.* 一出車站, 火車就開始加速。| **a speed of 60 mph/80 kph etc** *a truck traveling at a speed of 50 mph* 以每小時50英里的速度行駛的卡車 | **at top/full speed** (=as fast as possible) 以最高速度, 全速 *Forster was bundled into a waiting car and driven away at top speed.* 福斯特被匆匆塞進一輛正在等候的汽車, 然後以最高速度被帶走了。| **at high/low speed** (=very fast or very slow) 以高速/慢速 *a metal disc revolving at high speed* 高速轉動着的金屬盤 | **at breakneck speed** (=dangerously fast) 以極危險的高速 | **at speed** *formal* (=fast)【正式】快速 *The bus was already travelling at speed.* 這輛公共汽車已經在疾馳了。

2 ▶OF ACTION 行動的◀ [U] the rate at which something happens or is done〔事物發生或進行的〕速度; 快速: *Everyone was surprised by the speed of events.* 每個人都為這些事件發生得如此之快而感到吃驚。| **with speed** *formal* (=quickly)【正式】迅速地 *The government acted with speed and efficiency.* 政府的行動迅速而有效。| **reading/operating speed** (=the speed at which a person reads or a machine operates) 閱讀速度/〔機器〕運行速度

3 ▶PHOTOGRAPHY 攝影◀ [C] **a)** the degree to which photographic film is sensitive to light〔攝影膠片的〕感光速度 **b)** the time it takes for a camera SHUTTER (2) to open and close 快門速度: *a shutter speed of 1/250 second* 1/250秒的快門速度

4 ▶DRUG 毒品◀ [U] *slang* an illegal drug that makes you very active; AMPHETAMINE【俚】安非他明, 苯丙胺〔一種興奮劑〕

5 five-speed/ten-speed etc having five etc gears (GEAR[1] (1)) 五擋的/十擋的等: *a five-speed gearbox* 有五擋的變速箱

speed[2] *v past* **sped** /spɛd; sped/ also 又作 **speeded** S3 **1** [I always+adv/prep] to go quickly 快行, 急走: **[+along/by/off etc]** *The robbers sped off in their getaway car.* 劫匪們開着逃跑用的汽車疾馳而去。**2** [T always+adv/prep] take someone or something somewhere very quickly 挾[帶]着…快走: **speed sb to/away/back etc** *Security guards sped her to a waiting helicopter.* 保安員把她迅速帶往一架正在等候的直升機。**3 be speeding** to be driving faster than the legal limit 超速駕駛: *I got caught speeding on Route 40 yesterday.* 我昨天在40號公路上超速駕駛被抓住了。

speed by *phr v* [I] if time speeds by, it seems to pass very quickly〔時間〕很快地過去, 飛逝: *The weeks sped by and soon it was time to go back to school.* 幾個星期轉眼就過去了, 很快又到了開學的時候。

speed up *phr v* [I,T] to move or happen faster or make something move or happen faster (使) 加快速度: *We'd better speed up if we want to be on time.* 我們如果想要準時趕到, 最好還是加快速度。| **speed sth ÷ up** *The new system will speed up the registration process.* 這個新制度將加快註冊過程。

speed·boat /ˈspidˌbot; ˈspiːdbəʊt/ *n* [C] a small boat with a powerful engine designed to go fast 快艇

speed bump /ˈ· ·/ *n* [C] a narrow raised part across a road that forces traffic to go slowly〔橫在路面上的〕交通減速板

speed·ing /ˈspidɪŋ; ˈspiːdɪŋ/ *n* [U] the offence of driving faster than the legal limit 超速駕駛: *Liz was found guilty of speeding and fined £50.* 莉茲被判犯有超速駕駛罪, 罰款50英鎊。

speed lim·it /ˈ· ˌ··/ *n* [C] the fastest speed allowed by law on a particular piece of road〔為特定路段設定的〕最高速度限制, 速度極限: *a 30 mph speed limit* 每小時30英里的速度限制

speed·om·e·ter /spiˈdɑmətɚ; spɪˈdɒmɪ̣tə/ *n* [C] an instrument in a vehicle that shows how fast it is going〔車輛上的〕速度計 —see picture on page A2 參見A2頁圖

speed read·ing /ˈ· ˌ··/ *n* [U] the skill of reading very quickly 快速閱讀

speed skat·ing /ˈ· ˌ··/ *n* [U] the sport of racing on ice wearing ICE SKATEs 速度滑冰

speed trap /ˈ· ·/ *n* [C] a place on a road where police wait to catch drivers who are going too fast 車速監視區[路段]

speed·way /ˈspidˌwe; ˈspiːdweɪ/ *n* [U] **1** the sport of racing MOTORCYCLEs or cars on a special track 摩托車賽; 汽車比賽 **2** [C] a special track for this sport 賽車跑道

speed·well /ˈspidwɛl; ˈspiːdwel/ *n* [U] a small European wild plant with light blue or white flowers 婆婆納〔一種小型歐洲野生植物, 開淺藍色或白色花〕

speed·y /ˈspidɪ; ˈspiːdi/ *adj* **1** happening or done quickly or without delay 迅速的, 很快的; 及時的: *We hope you make a speedy recovery.* 我們希望你迅速康復。| *The accusations brought a speedy denial.* 那些指責迅即遭到否認。**2** a speedy car goes fast〔汽車〕快速的 —**speedily** *adv* —**speediness** *n* [U]

spe·le·ol·o·gy /ˌspilɪˈɑlədʒɪ; ˌspiːliˈɒlədʒi/ *n* [U] *technical*【術語】**1** the sport of walking and climbing in CAVEs 洞穴攀行運動 **2** the scientific study of CAVEs 洞穴學 —**speleologist** *n* [C] —**speleological** /ˌspilɪəˈlɑdʒɪkl; ˌspiːliəˈlɒdʒɪkəl◂/ *adj*

spell[1] /spɛl; spel/ *v past tense and past participle* **spelt** S2

S

/spɛlt; spelt/ *especially BrE*【尤英】, **spelled** *especially AmE*【尤美】**1** [I,T] to form a word by writing or naming the letters in the correct order〔用字母〕拼寫, 拼出: *"How do you spell your name?" "S-M-Y-T-H."* "你的名字怎樣拼寫?" "是 S-M-Y-T-H。" | **can spell** (=be good at spelling words correctly) 拼寫能力強 *I used to fail exams because I couldn't spell.* 我過去考試總是不及格, 因為我的拼寫能力很差。| **spell sth wrong/wrongly** *You've spelled my name wrong.* 你把我的名字拼錯了。**2** [T not in passive 不用被動態] if letters spell a word, they form it〔字母〕拼成〔某詞〕: *B-O-O-K spells 'book'.* B-O-O-K 拼成 book (書)。**3 spell trouble/disaster/danger etc** if a situation or action spells trouble etc, it makes you expect trouble etc 招致[帶來]麻煩/災難/危險等: *Such a scandal could spell disaster for the government.* 這樣的醜聞可能給政府帶來災難。**4** [T] *AmE & AustrE* to do someone else's work for them for a short period so that they can rest【美和澳】暫時代替〔某人的工作〕: *Can I spell you at the wheel?* 我替你開會兒車好嗎?

spell sth ↔ **out** *phr v* [T] **1** to show how a word is spelled by writing or saying the letters separately in the right order 逐個字母寫[讀]出〔某個單詞〕: *"Could you spell that out for me?" "F-A-H-E-R-T-Y."* "你能給我逐個字母拼出那個詞嗎?" "F-A-H-E-R-T-Y。" **2** to explain something clearly and in detail 清楚地說明; 詳細地解釋: **spell out how/what etc** *Will the Minister spell out exactly how he intends to finance these tax cuts?* 部長會具體地詳細解釋他打算怎樣填補減稅所造成的財政缺口嗎? **3** to write a word in its complete form instead of using an ABBREVIATION 寫出〔某詞的〕全部字母〔而不是其縮略式〕: *If you are using initials for the title of a group, be sure to spell them out at least once in your article.* 如果你要用首字母代表一個團體的名稱, 在文章中至少要有一次把它的全名拼寫出來。

spell² *n* [C] **1** a piece of magic that someone does or the special words or ceremonies used in doing it 魔法; 符咒, 咒語: **put a spell on/cast a spell over** (=do a piece of magic to change something) 用符咒鎮住 *The wizard had put a spell on the city to send all its people to sleep.* 巫師對那個城市施了咒語, 讓所有人都進入夢鄉。| **break the spell** (=stop the spell from working) 破除符咒 | **under a spell** *The frog was really a handsome young prince under a spell.* 那隻青蛙其實是一位中了妖術的年輕英俊的王子。**2** a period of a particular kind of activity, weather etc, usually a short period〔某種活動、天氣等的〕一段時間, 一陣子: *After a brief spell in the army I returned to teaching.* 我在軍隊幹了很短一段時間之後, 又回到了教學崗位。| **[+of]** *a spell of bad luck* 倒霉的日子 | **a cold/wet/dry spell** *Do you remember that foggy spell we had in April?* 你還記得我們四月份那段大霧時期嗎? **3** a power that attracts and influences you so strongly that it completely controls your feelings 吸引力, 魅力; 迷惑力: **be/fall under sb's spell** *Maya fell under his spell within minutes of meeting him.* 梅耶認識他幾分鐘後就被他的魅力迷住了。**4** a very short period of feeling ill〔疾病的〕一陣發作: *a dizzy spell* 一陣頭暈

spell·bind·ing /ˈspɛlˌbaɪndɪŋ; ˈspelbaɪndɪŋ/ *adj* extremely interesting and holding your attention completely 極有趣的, 使人入迷的: *a spellbinding tale* 引人入勝的故事 —**spellbinder** *n* [C]

spell·bound /ˈspɛlˌbaund; ˈspelbaʊnd/ *adj* extremely interested in something you are listening to 聽得入迷的: **hold sb spellbound** *The storyteller held his audience spellbound.* 那個講故事的人使聽眾聽得入迷。

spell-check·er /ˈ· ˌ··/ *n* [C] a computer PROGRAM that checks what you have written and makes your spelling correct〔電腦的〕拼寫檢查程序 —**spell-check** *v* [I,T]

spel·ler /ˈspɛlɚ; ˈspelə/ *n* [C] **1 good/bad/poor speller** someone who is good or bad at spelling words correctly 拼寫能力好/不好的人 **2** *AmE* a book for teaching spelling【美】單詞拼寫課本

spell·ing /ˈspɛlɪŋ; ˈspelɪŋ/ *n* **1** [U] the act of spelling words correctly or the ability to do this 拼寫能力; 拼字: *Her spelling has improved.* 她的拼寫能力有進步。**2** [C] the way in which a word is spelled〔單詞的〕拼(寫)法: *What's the American spelling of 'colour'?* colour 這個詞的美式拼法是甚麼? 2

spelling bee /ˈ·· ·/ *n* [C] *AmE* a competition in which the winner is the one who spells the most words correctly【美】單詞拼寫比賽

spelt /spɛlt; spelt/ *especially BrE*【尤英】the past tense and past participle of SPELL

spe·lunk·ing /spɪˈlʌŋkɪŋ; spɪˈlʌŋkɪŋ/ *n* [U] *AmE* the sport of walking and climbing in CAVES【美】洞穴攀爬運動 —**spelunker** *n* [C]

spend /spɛnd; spend/ *past tense and past participle* **spent** /spɛnt; spent/ *v* 1 1

1 ▶MONEY 錢◀ [I,T] to use your money to buy or pay for things 用(錢), 花費: **spend money/£5/$10/a lot** *I spent so much money this weekend!* 我這個週末花錢太多! | **spend money etc on sth** *More money should be spent on health and education.* 應該把更多的錢花在醫療保健和教育上。| **spend money etc on sb** (=buy things for someone) 花錢買東西給某人 *Cecilia spends far too much money on those spoilt kids of hers.* 塞西莉亞在她那些慣壞了的孩子身上花的錢太多了。| **money well spent** (=a sensible way of spending money) 值得花的錢 *The repairs cost a lot, but it's money well spent.* 維修費用很高, 但這些錢是值得花的。

2 ▶TIME 時間◀ [T] to pass or use time 度過, 消磨: **spend time in/with etc** *We'll have to spend the night in a hotel.* 我們將不得不住旅館過夜。| *I want to spend more time with my family.* 我想花更多的時間和家人在一起。| **spend time doing sth** *Much of my time is spent studying financial reports.* 研究財政報告花去我很多時間。

3 spend the night with to stay for the night and have sex with someone 同...一起過夜並發生性關係

4 ▶FORCE/EFFORT 力量/努力◀ [T] *literary* to use all of something【文】用盡, 耗盡: *The storm had spent its force.* 暴風雨已經停了下來。

5 spend a penny *BrE spoken* an expression meaning to URINATE, used when you want to avoid saying this directly【英口】小便〔委婉說法〕: *I need to spend a penny – where are the loos?* 我要方便一下 —— 請問洗手間在哪兒?

spend·er /ˈspɛndɚ; ˈspendə/ *n* [C] someone who spends money 花錢者, 用錢的人: **big spender** (=someone who regularly spends very large amounts of money) 花錢大手大腳的人

spend·ing /ˈspɛndɪŋ; ˈspendɪŋ/ *n* [U] the amount of money spent, especially by a government or organization〔尤指政府或組織的〕開銷, 花費: **government/public/defence spending** *a reduction in government spending on defense* 政府的國防開支下降

spending mon·ey /ˈ·· ˌ··/ *n* [U] money that you have available to spend on your own personal pleasures 零用錢, 零花錢: *$25 a week in spending money* 每星期 25 美元的零花錢

spend·thrift /ˈspɛndˌθrɪft; ˈspendˌθrɪft/ *n* [C] someone who spends money carelessly, even when they do not have a lot of it 揮霍者, 浪費金錢的人

spent¹ /spɛnt; spent/ the past tense and past participle of SPEND

spent² *adj* **1** already used, and now empty or useless 用過的; 失效的: *spent cartridges* 空彈殼 **2 be a spent force** if a political idea or organization is a spent force, it no longer has any power or influence〔政治思想〕已喪失影響; 〔政治組織〕已經失去權力: *They had written Wilson off as a spent force in British politics.* 他們已經認定威爾遜在英國政治中不再具有影響力了。**3** *literary* extremely tired【文】精疲力竭的

sperm /spɝm; spɜːm/ *n* **1** *plural* **sperm** *or* **sperms** [C] a cell produced by the sex organs of a male animal, which is able to join with the female egg to produce a new life 精子 **2** [U] the liquid from the male sex organs that these cells swim in; SEMEN 精液

sper·ma·cet·i /ˌspɝməˈsɛtɪ; ˌspɜːməˈseti/ *n* [U] a solid oily substance found in the head of the SPERM WHALE and used in making skin creams, CANDLE*s* etc 鯨蠟, 鯨腦油

sper·ma·to·zo·on /ˌspɝmətəˈzoən; ˌspɜːmətəˈzəʊɒn/ *n plural* **spermatozoa** /-ˈzoə; -ˈzəʊə/ [C] *technical* a sperm【術語】精子

sperm bank /ˈ· ·/ *n* [C] a place where SEMEN is kept to be used in medical operations to help women to become PREGNANT〔供人工授精用的〕精子庫

sper·mi·cide /ˈspɝməˌsaɪd; ˈspɜːmɪ̣saɪd/ *n* [C,U] a cream or liquid that kills SPERM*s*, used while having sex to prevent the woman from becoming PREGNANT〔用於避孕的〕殺精子劑 —**spermicidal** /ˌspɝməˈsaɪdəl; ˌspɜːmɪ̣ˈsaɪdl◂/ *adj*: *spermicidal jelly* 殺精膏

sperm whale /ˈ· ·/ *n* [C] a large WHALE, hunted for its oil, fat and SPERMACETI 抹香鯨

spew /spju; spjuː/ *v* **1** also 又作 **spew out/forth** [I always+adv/prep,T] to flow out of something in large quantities, or to make something flow out in this way (使) 噴出, (使) 湧出: **[+from/into/over]** *Lava spewed from the volcano.* 熔岩從火山口噴出。| **spew sth (out)** *The burst pipe was spewing out dirty water.* 污水正從破裂的管子中湧出來。**2** also 又作 **spew up** [I,T] *BrE informal* to VOMIT【英, 非正式】嘔吐

SPF /ˌɛs pi ˈɛf; ˌes piː ˈef/ Sun Protection Factor; a number on a bottle of SUNTAN cream that tells you how much protection it gives you from the sun〔防曬霜的〕防曬係數: *SPF 25* 防曬係數 25

sphag·num /ˈsfægnəm; ˈsfægnəm/ *n* [C,U] *technical* a type of MOSS【術語】泥炭蘚〔一種苔蘚〕

sphere /sfɪr; sfɪə/ *n* [C] **1** a ball shape 球, 球形, 球體: *The Earth is not a perfect sphere.* 地球並不是一個完全的球體。—see picture at 參見 SHAPE[1] 圖 **2** a particular area of activity, work, knowledge etc〔活動、工作、知識等的〕範圍, 領域: *His reputation lies in the scientific sphere.* 他在科學領域中頗有聲譽。**3 sphere of influence** a person or country's sphere of influence is the area where they have power to change things 勢力範圍, 影響所及的範圍

-sphere /sfɪr; sfɪə/ *suffix technical* [in nouns 構成名詞] the air surrounding the Earth at a particular height【術語】距離地球表面某一高度的氣體外層: *the stratosphere* 平流層

spher·i·cal /ˈsfɛrəkl; ˈsferɪkəl/ *adj* having the shape of a sphere 球形的, 球狀的

sphe·roid /ˈsfɪrɔɪd; ˈsfɪərɔɪd/ *n* [C] *technical* a shape that is similar to a ball, but not a perfect sphere【術語】扁球體, 橢球體

sphinc·ter /ˈsfɪŋktɚ; ˈsfɪŋktə/ *n* [C] *technical* a muscle that surrounds a passage in your body, and can tighten in order to close it【術語】括約肌: *the anal sphincter* 肛門括約肌

sphinx /sfɪŋks; sfɪŋks/ *n* [C] an ancient Egyptian image of a lion with a human head lying down〔古埃及的〕獅身人面像, 斯芬克斯 (像)

spic, spik /spɪk; spɪk/ *n* [C] *AmE* a very offensive word meaning a Spanish-speaking American【美】講西班牙語的美國佬〔極具冒犯性的用語〕

spice[1] /spaɪs; spaɪs/ *n* **1** [C,U] one of the various types of powder or seed, taken from plants, that you put into food you are cooking to give it a special taste〔從植物中提取, 烹調用的〕香料; 調味品: *Indian spices such as cumin and saffron* 小茴香、番紅花之類的印度香料 **2** [singular,U] interest or excitement that is added to something〔為某事增添〕趣味, 情趣, 風味: *They need gossip to add a bit of spice to their dull lives.* 他們需要流言蜚語來給枯燥乏味的生活增添一點趣味。—see also 另見 **variety is the spice of life** (VARIETY (5))

spice[2] *v* [T] **1** also 又作 **spice up** to add interest or excitement to something 使增添趣味: *an essay that needs spicing up* 需要增添趣味的小品文 **2** to add spice to food 給〔食物〕加香料: **[+with]** *baked apples spiced with cinnamon and nutmeg* 加進肉桂和肉豆蔻的烤蘋果

spick-and-span /ˌspɪk ən ˈspæn; ˌspɪk ən ˈspæn/ *adj* a room, house etc that is spick-and-span is completely clean and tidy〔房間、房子等〕乾乾淨淨的, 整潔的

spic·y /ˈspaɪsɪ; ˈspaɪsi/ *adj* **1** food that is spicy has a pleasantly strong taste, and gives you a pleasant burning feeling in your mouth〔食物〕加有香料的, 辛辣的: *pasta with a spicy tomato sauce* 加上辣番茄醬的麵條 **2** a story that is spicy is slightly shocking or rude〔故事〕下流的, 粗俗的: *a spicy rumour* 猥褻的傳聞 —**spicily** *adv* —**spiciness** *n* [U]

spi·der /ˈspaɪdɚ; ˈspaɪdə/ *n* [C] a small creature with eight legs which makes networks of thread for catching insects 蜘蛛

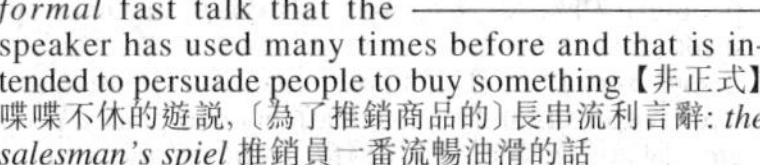

spi·der·web /ˈspaɪdɚˌwɛb; ˈspaɪdəweb/ *n* [C] *AmE* a very fine network of sticky threads made by a spider to catch insects【美】蜘蛛網; COBWEB *BrE*【英】

spi·der·y /ˈspaɪdərɪ; ˈspaɪdəri/ *adj* writing that is spidery is untidy with long thin lines〔字跡〕細長而不整齊的

spiel /spil; ʃpiːl/ *n* [C,U] *informal* fast talk that the speaker has used many times before and that is intended to persuade people to buy something【非正式】喋喋不休的遊說,〔為了推銷商品的〕長串流利言辭: *the salesman's spiel* 推銷員一番流暢油滑的話

spif·fing /ˈspɪfɪŋ; ˈspɪfɪŋ/ *adj BrE old-fashioned* excellent【英, 過時】極好的, 出色的, 一流的

spif·fy /ˈspɪfɪ; ˈspɪfi/ *adj informal especially AmE* very neat and fashionable【非正式, 尤美】非常整潔而時髦的: *a spiffy little red car* 一輛漂亮時髦的紅色小汽車

spig·ot /ˈspɪgət; ˈspɪgət/ *n* [C] **1** a TAP[1] (1,2) in a large container that controls the flow of liquid from it〔大容器的〕塞子, 栓 **2** *especially AmE* an outdoor TAP[1] (1)【尤美】室外水龍頭

spik /spɪk; spɪk/ *n* [C] another spelling of SPIC spic 的另一種拼法

spike[1] /spaɪk; spaɪk/ *n* [C] **1** something long and thin with a sharp point, especially a pointed piece of metal 尖狀物; 金屬釘狀物: *spikes along the top of a fence* 柵欄頂上的尖頭 **2 spikes** [plural] metal points on the bottom of a shoe used for running, or the shoe itself〔跑鞋鞋底上的〕鞋釘; 釘鞋 —see picture at 參見 STUD[1] 圖 **3** *technical* a sharp point on a GRAPH【術語】〔圖表〕曲線上的陡升線 **4** *technical* the head of a plant that produces grain such as corn or wheat【術語】〔玉米、麥子等的〕穗

spike[2] *v* [T] **1** to push a sharp point into something〔把尖物〕刺進, 刺穿: *a guy spiking litter and putting it in a garbage bag* 用尖頭棍子戳起廢紙放進垃圾袋的人 **2** to add a strong alcoholic drink to a weak or non-alcoholic one 加烈酒於〔淡酒或不含酒精的飲料中〕: **[+with]** *Bill's drink had been spiked with vodka.* 比爾的飲料攙了伏特加酒。**3** to prevent someone from saying something or printing something in a newspaper 阻止〔某人〕在報紙上發表〔言論〕: *a clumsy attempt to spike rumours of a cabinet split* 企圖阻止在報刊上發表內閣分裂傳聞的笨拙做法 **4 spike sb's guns** *BrE* to spoil an opponent's plans【英】打亂[破壞]某人的計劃

spik·y /ˈspaɪkɪ; ˈspaɪki/ *adj* **1** having long sharp points

帶(尖)刺的, 有刺的: *a spiky cactus* 帶刺的仙人掌 **2** hair that is spiky is stiff and stands up on top of your head〔頭髮〕挺直的, 豎起的 —see picture on page A6 參見A6頁圖 **3** *BrE informal* easily offended or annoyed【英, 非正式】暴躁的, 易怒的 —**spikiness** *n* [U]

3 **spill¹** /spɪl; spɪl/ *past tense and past participle* **spilt** /spɪlt; spɪlt/ *especially BrE*【尤英】, **spilled** *especially AmE*【尤美】*v* **1** [I,T] if you spill a liquid or if it spills, it accidentally flows over the edge of a container (使)溢出, (使)潑出, (使)灑落: **spill sth down/on/over** *Oh no! I've spilt coffee all down my shirt!* 糟糕, 我把咖啡灑在襯衫上了! | **[+on/over]** *He slipped and the wine spilled all over the carpet.* 他滑倒, 酒灑了一地毯。**2** [I always+adv/prep] if people spill out of somewhere, they move out in large groups〔人羣〕湧出: **[+out/into/onto etc]** *Crowds from the theatre were spilling onto the street.* 人羣從戲院湧到了街上。**3 spill the beans** *informal* to tell something that someone else wanted you to keep a secret【非正式】泄露祕密, 走漏風聲 **4 spill your guts** *AmE* to tell someone everything you know about something, especially because you are upset【美】〔尤指因心情不好〕把自己知道的一切和盤托出: *some drunk spilling his guts to me at the bar* 在酒吧裡把心事向我和盤托出的一個醉漢 **5 spill blood** *literary* to kill or wound people【文】殺人; 傷人 —see also 另見 **cry over spilt milk** (CRY¹ (5))

spill 灑落

spill over *phr v* [I] if a problem or bad situation spills over, it spreads and begins to affect other places, people etc〔問題或壞情況〕蔓延, 擴散: **[+into]** *There is a danger that the conflict will spill over into neighbouring towns.* 這場衝突有蔓延到鄰近城鎮的危險。

spill² *n* **1** [C,U] an act of spilling something or an amount of something that is spilled 灑出, 溢出; 灑出量, 溢出量: **oil spill** *The oil spill in Alaska threatens ecological catastrophe.* 阿拉斯加的溢油將給生態環境帶來災難。**2** [C] a piece of wood or twisted paper for lighting lamps, fires etc〔用於點燈、生火等的〕木片; 紙捻 **3** [C] *old-fashioned* a fall from a horse, bicycle etc【過時】〔從馬、自行車等上的〕摔下

spil·lage /ˈspɪlɪdʒ; ˈspɪlɪdʒ/ *n* [C,U] a SPILL² (1) 灑出(量), 溢出(量)

spill·way /ˈspɪlˌwe; ˈspɪlweɪ/ *n* [C] a passage for water to flow over or around a DAM (=wall for holding back water)〔水壩的〕溢洪道

spilt /spɪlt; spɪlt/ *especially BrE*【尤英】the past tense and past participle of SPILL

3 **spin¹** /spɪn; spɪn/ *past tense and past participle* **spun** /spʌn; spʌn/ *v*

1 ►TURN AROUND 旋轉◄ [I,T] to turn around and around very quickly, or to make something do this (使)快速旋轉: *The ice skater was spinning faster and faster.* 滑冰者轉得越來越快。| *spin the roulette wheel* 轉動輪盤賭的轉輪 | **spin (sth/sb) around** *Liz spun around on her heel to face me.* 莉茲猛地轉過身來面對着我。

spin 快速旋轉

2 ►WOOL/COTTON 羊毛/棉花◄ [I,T] to make cotton, wool etc into thread by twisting it 將〔棉花、羊毛等〕紡成〔紗、線〕, 紡〔紗、線〕: *The wool is spun into thread and then woven.* 先將羊毛紡成線, 然後再織。

3 ►WET CLOTHES 濕衣服◄ [T] to get water out of clothes using a machine after you have washed them〔用機器〕使〔洗過的衣物〕脱水, 旋乾

4 ►INSECT 昆蟲◄ [T] if a SPIDER or insect spins a WEB (1) or COCOON, it produces thread to make it〔蜘蛛〕吐絲結網;〔昆蟲〕吐絲作繭

5 sb's head spins if your head spins, you feel as if you might FAINT because you are shocked, excited, or drunk〔因震驚、興奮、醉酒等〕某人頭都暈了: *My head was spinning with all this new information.* 所有這些新資料把我頭都弄暈了。

6 spin a story/yarn/line [T] to tell someone a story that is not true in order to deceive them〔為了騙人〕編造故事: *beggars spinning hard-luck stories* 編造倒霉故事騙人的乞丐

7 ►DRIVE 駕駛◄ [I always+adv/prep] to drive or travel quickly 開車疾馳: **[+past/along etc]** *Barbara waved as she spun past in her new sportscar.* 芭芭拉一邊招手一邊開着她那輛新跑車飛馳而過。

spin sth ↔ **off** *phr v* [T] **1** to produce a new television programme using characters from another programme〔根據另一個電視節目〕編出〔新的節目〕: *'The Rifleman' spun off another new series, 'Wanted Dead or Alive.'*《步槍手》又派生出一部新的電視系列劇《通緝令》。**2** to form a separate and partly independent company from parts of an existing company〔從現存公司中〕組成〔一個部分獨立的子公司〕: *The company spun off its financial services division in 1988.* 這家公司於1988年組成了它的金融服務子公司。

spin sth ↔ **out** *phr v* [T] **1** to make something continue for longer than is necessary 拖長, 拖延: *I'm paid by the hour, so I spin the work out as long as I can.* 我拿計時工資, 所以我盡量把工作拖長。**2** to use money, food etc as carefully and slowly as possible because you do not have very much of it 盡可能延長使用〔錢、食物等〕: **[+over]** *I've only got £10 left, so we'll have to spin it out over the whole week.* 我只剩10英鎊, 所以我們必須省着用, 使它能維持整個星期。

spin² *n*

1 ►TURNING 旋轉◄ [C] an act of turning around quickly 快速旋轉: *the spin of a top* 陀螺的快速旋轉 | *The dance ended with a dramatic spin.* 這場舞蹈以一陣激動人心的快速旋轉結束。

2 ►CAR 汽車◄ [C] *informal* a short trip in a car for pleasure【非正式】〔乘車〕兜風: *Let's go for a spin in the country.* 我們開車到鄉下去兜兜風吧。

3 ►BALL 球◄ [U] if you put spin on a ball in a game such as tennis or CRICKET (2), you deliberately make the ball turn very quickly so that it is difficult for your opponent to hit〔網球、板球等的〕旋轉(球)

4 fall/go into a (flat) spin a) to become very confused and anxious 陷入恐慌, 變得驚慌失措: *The sudden fall on the stock-market sent brokers into a spin.* 股市暴跌使經紀人驚慌失措。**b)** if an aircraft goes into a spin it falls suddenly, turning around and around〔飛機的〕螺旋下降, 旋衝

5 ►WET CLOTHES 濕衣服◄ **give sth a spin** *BrE* to turn clothes around very fast in a machine to remove water from them【英】〔用機器〕給〔濕衣服〕脱水

6 ►INFORMATION 消息◄ [singular] *informal especially AmE* a way of providing information that makes it seem to be favourable for a particular person or political party【非正式, 尤美】〔對某人或政黨有利的〕傾向性的報道[看法]: *trying to put a positive spin on the economic figures* 試圖對經濟數字作傾向性的樂觀報道 —see also 另見 SPIN DOCTOR

7 ►SCIENCE 科學◄ [singular] a quality of an ELEMENTARY PARTICLE that influences its behaviour with other particles〔基本粒子的〕自旋

spi·na bif·i·da /ˌspaɪnə ˈbɪfɪdə; ˌspaɪnə ˈbɪfɪ̈də/ *n* [U] a serious condition in which a person's SPINE is split down the middle from birth, leaving their SPINAL CORD unprotected 脊柱裂

spin·ach /ˈspɪnɪtʃ; ˈspɪnɪdʒ/ *n* [U] a vegetable with large dark green leaves 菠菜 —see picture on page A9 參見A9頁圖

spin·al /ˈspaɪnl; ˈspaɪnl/ *adj* belonging to or affecting your SPINE (1) 脊柱的; 脊椎的: *spinal injuries* 脊柱受傷

spinal col·umn /ˌ·· ˌ··/ *n* [C] *technical* your SPINE (1)【術語】脊柱

spinal cord /ˌ·· ˈ·/ *n* [C] the thick string of nerves enclosed in your SPINE (1) by which messages are sent to and from your brain 脊髓

spin·dle /ˈspɪndl; ˈspɪndl/ *n* [C] **1** a part of a machine shaped like a stick, around which something turns〔機器的〕軸; 心軸 **2** a round pointed stick used for twisting the thread when you are spinning wool 紡錘; 紗錠

spin·dly /ˈspɪndlɪ; ˈspɪndli/ *adj* long and thin in a way that looks weak 細長的, 纖弱的: *spindly legs* 細長的雙腿

spin doc·tor /ˈ· ˌ··/ *n* [C] *informal* someone whose job is to give information to the public in a way that gives the best possible advantage to a politician or organization【非正式】輿論導向專家: *The White House spin doctors are hard at work explaining the President's about-face on taxes.* 白宮的輿論導向專家正在努力為總統在稅收問題上的徹底改變作出解釋。

spin-dry·er /ˌ· ˈ··/ *n* [C] *especially BrE* a machine that removes most of the water from washed clothes by spinning them around and around very fast【尤英】旋轉式脱水機 —**spin-dry** *v* [T]

spine /spaɪn; spaɪn/ *n* [C] **1** the row of bones down the centre of your back that supports your body and protects your SPINAL CORD 脊柱, 脊椎 —see picture at 參見 SKELETON 圖 **2** a stiff sharp point on an animal or plant〔動植物的〕刺, 刺毛: *cactus spines* 仙人掌的刺 **3** the part of a book that the pages are fastened onto 書脊

spine-chil·ling /ˈ· ˌ··/ *adj* a spine-chilling story or film is very frightening in a way that people enjoy〔故事、電影〕令人毛骨悚然的 —**spine-chiller** /ˈspaɪn ˌtʃɪlə; ˈspaɪn ˌtʃɪlə/ *n* [C]

spine·less /ˈspaɪnlɪs; ˈspaɪnləs/ *adj* **1** lacking courage and determination 沒有骨氣的, 懦弱的: *a bunch of spineless do-gooders* 一羣懦弱的空想的社會改良家 **2** without a spine 無脊柱的: *spineless creatures such as jellyfish* 水母一類的無脊椎動物 —**spinelessly** *adv* —**spinelessness** *n* [U]

spi·net /ˈspɪnɪt; spɪˈnet/ *n* [C] a musical instrument of the 16th and 17th centuries, which is played like a piano 斯皮內琴〔16、17世紀類似鋼琴的一種鍵琴〕

spin·na·ker /ˈspɪnəkə; ˈspɪnəkə/ *n* [C] a sail with three points at the front of a boat, used when the wind is directly behind〔賽艇的〕大三角帆 —see picture at 參見 YACHT 圖

spin·ner /ˈspɪnə; ˈspɪnə/ *n* [C] **1** someone whose job is to make thread by twisting cotton, wool etc 紡紗工 **2** a BOWLER in a game of CRICKET (2) who throws the ball with a spinning action〔板球的〕旋轉球投手 **3** a thing used for catching fish that moves around and around when pulled through the water〔釣魚用的〕旋式誘餌 —see also 另見 MONEY-SPINNER

spin·ney /ˈspɪnɪ; ˈspɪni/ *n* [C] *BrE* a small area of trees and bushes【英】小樹林, 灌木叢

spinning jen·ny /ˈspɪnɪŋ ˌdʒenɪ; ˈspɪnɪŋ ˌdʒeni/ *n* [C] an industrial machine used in the past for making cotton, wool etc into thread〔舊時的〕詹妮紡紗機

spinning wheel /ˈ·· ·/ *n* [C] a simple machine consisting of a wheel on a frame that people used in their homes in the past for making cotton, wool etc into thread〔從前家用的〕紡車

spin-off /ˈ· ·/ *n* [C] **1** an unexpected but useful result of something, that happens in addition to the intended result 副產品, 派生產品; 附帶的結果: *Laser research has had important spin-offs for eye surgery.* 激光研究產生了一些適用於眼科手術的重要附帶成果。—see also 另見 **spin off** (SPIN¹) **2** a television programme involving characters that were previously in another programme or film〔利用其他節目或電影中人物編成的〕派生電視節目: *'Maude' was a spin-off from 'All in the Family'.*《莫德》是《一家人》的派生電視劇。

spin·ster /ˈspɪnstə; ˈspɪnstə/ *n* [C] *old-fashioned* an unmarried woman, usually one who is no longer young and seems unlikely to marry【過時】〔年齡不小的〕未婚女人, 老處女 —**spinsterhood** *n* [U]

spin the bot·tle /ˌ· · ˈ··/ *n* [U] a game in which people sitting in a circle spin a bottle in the middle and when the bottle stops spinning and points to someone, that person must do something, such as kissing another person 轉瓶遊戲〔玩時大家圍成一圈, 轉動放在中間的瓶子, 瓶停下來時瓶口所指的人得做一事, 如親吻一人〕

spin·y /ˈspaɪnɪ; ˈspaɪni/ *adj* having a lot of spines (SPINE (2)) 多刺的: *a spiny gorse bush* 多刺的荊豆叢

spi·ral¹ /ˈspaɪrəl; ˈspaɪərəl/ *adj* in the form of a continuous line or curve that winds around a central point, moving further away from it all the time 螺旋形的, 螺線形的: *a spiral watch spring* 螺旋形的手錶發條 —**spirally** *adv*

spiral² *n* [C] **1** a spiral curve 螺線 **2** a process, usually a harmful one, in which something gradually but continuously rises, falls, gets worse etc 螺旋式過程〔持續上升或下降、惡化等, 通常指有害的變化〕: *Shipbuilding entered a spiral of decline.* 造船業陷入了持續衰退之中。| **upward/downward spiral** *a vicious downward spiral of debt* 債務的惡性持續增加 **3 inflationary spiral** a situation where wages and prices rise continuously because the level of INFLATION (1) is high 惡性通貨膨脹

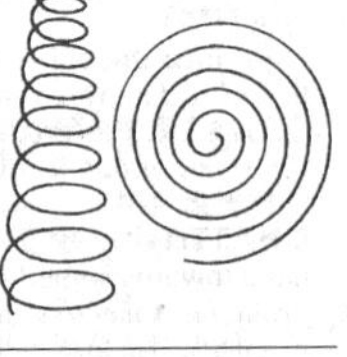

spiral³ *v* **spiralled, spiralling** *BrE*【英】, **spiraled, spiraling** *AmE*【美】[I] **1** [always+adv/prep] to move in a continuous curve that gets nearer to or further from its central point as it goes round 螺旋形地上升[下降]: [**+to/around etc**] *The damaged plane spiralled to the ground.* 損壞了的飛機盤旋墮地。**2** if debt or the cost of something spirals, it increases quickly and uncontrollably〔債務、物價〕急劇而失控地上升: *the spiraling cost of legal services* 法律服務費的急劇上漲

spiral stair·case /ˌ·· ˈ··/ *n* [C] a set of stairs arranged in a circular pattern so that they go around a central point as they get higher 螺旋狀樓梯

spire /spaɪr; spaɪə/ *n* [C] a roof that rises steeply to a point on top of a tower, especially on a church〔教堂等的〕塔尖, 尖頂

spir·it¹ /ˈspɪrɪt; ˈspɪrɨt/ *n* S3 W2

1 ►INNER PART 內部◄ [singular,U] an inner part of someone that includes their thoughts and feelings, and is thought of as making them what they are 精神, 心靈〔指人的內部世界, 包括思想、感情〕: *His spirit was untameable.* 他的精神不可馴服。| *strong in spirit* 內心堅強的 | **independent/proud/free etc spirit** (=a person with a particular type of character) 獨立/驕傲/自由等的人 *a toddler already showing an independent spirit* 已經表現出獨立性格的學步的小孩

2 ►SOUL 靈魂◄ [C] the part of someone that is believed to continue to live after they have died 靈魂: *Although Laurie is dead, I can feel his spirit with me.* 勞里雖然已經死了, 但我還能感覺到他的靈魂和我在一起。—compare 比較 SOUL (1)

3 ►DEAD PERSON 死人◄ [C] a dead person who is believed to have returned to this world and has strange or magical powers; GHOST¹ (1) 鬼, 鬼魂: *Some people believe that evil spirits can be removed by exorcism.* 有

些人相信驅邪術可驅除惡鬼。
4 ►HAPPY/SAD 快樂的/悲傷的◄ **spirits** [plural] the way someone feels at a particular time, for example if they are cheerful or sad 心境, 情緒, 興致: **be in good/low spirits** (=be happy or sad) 心情好/不好 | **be in high spirits** (=be excited) 情緒高漲 *We started our journey in high spirits.* 我們興高采烈地踏上旅途。| **keep sb's spirits up** (=make sure someone does not become less cheerful) 使某人保持心情開朗 | **raise/lift sb's spirits** (=make someone feel happier and more hopeful) 鼓舞/振奮某人的情緒 *long, hot summer days that lift the spirits* 令人精神煥發的炎熱長夏 | **sb's spirits lift/sink** (=become more or less cheerful) 某人高興起來/不起來 *My spirits sank when I saw the mess they'd left.* 我看見他們弄得那樣亂七八糟就高興不起來。
5 in spirit you say you will be somewhere in spirit or with someone in spirit, when you cannot be with them but are thinking about them 在內心裡, 在精神上: *I can't come to your wedding but I'll be there in spirit.* 我不能參加你們的婚禮, 但到時候我的心會和你們在一起的。
6 ►DRINK 酒◄ [C usually plural 一般用複數] **a)** *especially BrE* a strong alcoholic drink such as WHISKY or BRANDY【尤英】烈(性)酒〈如威士忌或白蘭地〉**b)** *BrE* liquid such as alcohol, used for cleaning【英】〔用於清潔的〕酒精
7 get into the spirit/enter into the spirit *BrE* to start to feel as happy, excited etc as the people around you【英】融入歡樂的氣氛中: *Judith couldn't really enter into the spirit of the occasion.* 朱迪思不能真正投入那場合的歡樂氣氛中。
8 ►ATTITUDE 態度◄ [singular] the attitude that you have towards something 心態, 態度: *You've got to approach this meeting in the right spirit.* 你一定要以正確的心態來對待這個會議。| *a true spirit of friendship* 友誼的真正態度
9 ►DETERMINATION 決心◄ [U] *approving* courage, energy, and determination【褒】勇氣; 活力; 決心: *Our team played with great spirit.* 我們隊打[踢]得勁頭十足。| **fighting spirit** (=brave determination) 鬥志 | **break sb's spirit** (=make someone lose their courage and determination) 挫某人的銳氣 *slaves whose spirits had been broken* 銳氣已經受挫的奴隸
10 that's the spirit *spoken* used to express approval of someone's behaviour or attitude【口】這就對了, 這種精神才對〔用於認可某人的行為或態度〕
11 team/community/public etc spirit a strong feeling of belonging to a particular group and wanting to help them 團隊/團體/公益等精神
12 the spirit of the age/times the set of ideas, beliefs, and aims that are typical of a particular period in history 時代精神
13 when/as the spirit moves you when you feel that you want to do something 當你有心要做的時候

spirit² *v* [T] **spirit sb/sth away/off** to remove someone or something in a secret or mysterious way 祕密[神祕地]把某人/某物帶[弄]走: *At the end of the press conference Jackson was spirited away through a back door.* 記者招待會結束時, 傑克遜被偷偷地從後門送走了。

spir·it·ed /ˋspɪrɪtɪd; ˈspɪrɨtɨd/ *adj approving* having energy and determination【褒】精神飽滿的, 生氣勃勃的; 有決心的: *Raphael is so young and spirited.* 拉斐爾非常年輕, 生氣勃勃。| **a spirited defence/debate** *a spirited defence of her decisions* 對她的決定所作的有力辯護 —see also 另見 HIGH-SPIRITED, LOW-SPIRITED, MEAN-SPIRITED, PUBLIC-SPIRITED

spirit lamp /ˈ·· ·/ *n* [C] *BrE* a small lamp that burns METHYLATED SPIRITS【英】酒精燈

spir·it·less /ˋspɪrɪtlɪs; ˈspɪrɨtləs/ *adj* **1** having no energy or determination 沒精打采的, 無朝氣的; 沒有決心的 **2** not cheerful 情緒低落的, 垂頭喪氣的 —**spiritlessness** *n* [U]

spirit lev·el /ˈ·· ,··/ *n* [C] a tool for testing whether a surface is level 水準儀; LEVEL¹ (11) *AmE*【美】

spir·i·tu·al¹ /ˋspɪrɪtʃuəl; ˈspɪrɨtʃuəl/ *adj* **1** connected with your spirit rather than with your body or mind 精神(上)的, 心靈的: *As a priest I'm responsible for your spiritual welfare.* 作為一個神父, 我對你精神上的幸福負責。| *spiritual values* 精神價值 **2** connected with religion 宗教(上)的: *the spiritual authority of the church* 教會的宗教權威 **3 spiritual home** a place where you feel you belong because you share the ideas and attitudes of that society 精神家園, 精神歸宿〔指一個自己能認同其思想和態度的地方〕—**spiritually** *adv*

spiritual² *n* [C] a religious song of the type sung originally by the black people of the US 靈歌〔一種原為美國黑人唱的宗教歌曲〕

spir·i·tu·al·is·m /ˋspɪrɪtʃuəl,ɪzəm; ˈspɪrɨtʃʊlɪzəm/ *n* [U] the belief that dead people may send messages to living people, usually through a MEDIUM (=someone with special powers) 招魂說, 降靈說〔認為死人可以通過靈媒把信息傳給活人〕—**spiritualist** *n* [C] —**spiritualistic** /,spɪrɪtʃuəˋlɪstɪk; ,spɪrɨtʃʊˈlɪstɪk◄/ *adj*

spir·i·tu·al·i·ty /,spɪrɪtʃuˋælətɪ; ,spɪrɨtʃuˈælɨti/ *n* [U] the quality of being interested in religion or religious matters 靈性, 對宗教[宗教事物]的熱衷

spir·i·tu·ous /ˋspɪrɪtʃuəs; ˈspɪrɨtʃuəs/ *adj* [only before noun 僅用於名詞前] *technical* containing alcohol【術語】含酒精的

spit¹ /spɪt; spɪt/ *past tense and past participle* **spat** /spæt; spæt/ also 又作 **spit** *AmE*【美】; *present participle* **spitting** *v*
1 ►LIQUID FROM YOUR MOUTH 口水◄ [I] to blow a small amount of SALIVA (=the liquid in your mouth) out of your mouth 吐口水, 吐唾沫: **[+at/on]** *Mom, Judy spit at me!* 媽媽, 朱迪向我吐口水! | *Kevin cleared his throat and spat on the path.* 凱文清了清喉嚨, 往路上啐了一口。| *Don't get too close to the camels – they spit!* 不要太靠近那些駱駝——牠們會吐唾沫的!
2 ►FOOD ETC 食物等◄ [T] to force something out of your mouth 吐: *spit blood* 吐血 | **spit sth out** *Ian was chewing on some gristle but was too polite to spit it out.* 伊恩嚼到一些軟骨頭, 但他很講禮貌, 沒有把它吐出來。
3 ►RAIN 雨◄ **be spitting** to rain very lightly 下小雨: *You don't need an umbrella, it's only spitting.* 你不用帶雨傘, 只飄着一點小雨。
4 ►SAY STH 說話◄ [T] also 又作 **spit out** to say something quickly in a very angry way 急促憤怒地說: *"Don't even think of taking it!" she spat.* "你甚至連想也別想拿它!" 她憤怒地說。
5 spit it out *spoken* used to ask someone to tell you something that they seem too frightened or embarrassed to say【口】爽快地說出來〔用於讓人說其不敢或不願說的話〕: *Come on Jean, spit it out!* 說吧, 吉恩, 爽爽快快地說出來吧!
6 ►SMALL PIECES 小片片◄ [I] to send out small bits of something, for example fire or hot oil, into the air〔火花、滾燙的油花等〕迸濺, 發出噼啪[畢剝]聲: *sausages spitting in a pan* 在鍋裡噼啪作響的香腸 | *The van drove off, gravel spitting from under the wheels.* 小貨車開走了, 碎石從輪子下噼噼啪啪地彈出。
7 ►CAT 貓◄ [I] if a cat spits it makes short, angry sounds〔貓在憤怒時〕發出咕嚕咕嚕聲
8 be within spitting distance *spoken* to be very close to where you are【口】在很近處
9 I could just spit *spoken* used to say that you are very angry or annoyed【口】我簡直氣壞了

spit² *n* **1** [U] the watery liquid that is produced in your mouth; SALIVA 唾液, 唾沫, 口水 **2** [C] a long thin stick that you put through meat to turn it and cook it over a fire 烤肉扦子, 炙扦子 **3** [C] a long narrow piece of land that sticks out into the sea, a river etc 沙嘴〔伸入水域中的狹長條陸地〕—see picture on page A12 參見 A12 頁圖 **4 be the (dead) spit of** *BrE spoken* to look exactly like someone else【英口】一模一樣: *Sam is the dead spit of his dad.* 山姆長得和他爸爸一模一樣。**5 spit and polish** *informal* thorough cleaning and polishing【非正式】徹底的打掃擦洗 **6 spit and sawdust** *BrE spoken* a spit and sawdust PUB is rough, dirty and simple in style【英口】〔酒館〕破舊的, 骯髒的, 簡陋的

spit·ball /ˋspɪtˏbɔl; ˈspɪtbɔːl/ *n* [C] *AmE* a small piece of paper that children put in their mouth and then throw at each other【美】小孩放進嘴裡弄濕後投向別人的小紙團

3 **spite**[1] /spaɪt; spaɪt/ *n* **1 in spite of** without being prevented by something; DESPITE 雖然; 不顧; 儘管...（仍...）: *We went out in spite of the rain.* 儘管下着雨, 我們還是出去了。| **in spite of the fact that** *Kelly loved her husband in spite of the fact that he drank too much.* 雖然她丈夫喝酒很兇, 凱莉仍然愛着他。**2** [U] a feeling of wanting to hurt or upset people, for example because you are JEALOUS or think you have been unfairly treated 惡意, 怨恨, 壞心眼: **out of spite** (=because of spite) 出於惡意 *She broke it just out of spite.* 她就是出於惡意把它打破的。| **pure/sheer spite** (=spite and nothing else) 純屬惡意 **3 in spite of yourself** if you do something in spite of yourself, you do it although you did not expect or intend to do it 不由自主地, 身不由己地

spite[2] *v* [T only in infinitive 僅用於不定式] to deliberately annoy or upset someone 故意與〔某人〕作對, 惡意對待: *The neighbours throw things over the garden wall just to spite us.* 鄰居把東西扔過花園圍牆, 故意和我們作對。—see also 另見 **cut off your nose to spite your face** (CUT OFF (9))

spite·ful /ˋspaɪtful; ˈspaɪtfəl/ *adj* deliberately nasty to someone in order to hurt or upset them 有惡意的, 懷恨在心的: *What I can't forgive is that it was such a spiteful thing to do.* 我不能原諒的是, 竟然幹出那樣可惡的事。—**spitefully** *adv* —**spitefulness** *n* [U]

spit·fire /ˋspɪtˏfaɪr; ˈspɪtfaɪə/ *n* [C] someone, especially a woman, who becomes angry very easily 烈性子的人〔尤指女人〕

spitting im·age /ˌ·· ˈ··/ *n* **be the spitting image of sb** to look exactly like someone else 長相與某人一模一樣

spit·tle /ˋspɪtl̩; ˈspɪtl/ *n* [U] *old-fashioned* the liquid in your mouth; SPIT[2] (1)【過時】唾沫, 口水

spit·toon /spɪˋtun; spɪˈtuːn/ *n* [C] a container used to SPIT[1] (1) into 痰盂

spiv /spɪv; spɪv/ *n* [C] *BrE old-fashioned* a man who gets money from small dishonest business deals【英, 過時】不務正業、專靠欺詐謀生的人

splash[1] /splæʃ; splæʃ/ *v* **1** [I] if a liquid splashes, it hits or falls on something noisily or it moves noisily〔液體〕濺潑, 飛濺, 濺落: **[+against/on/over]** *Great drops of rain splashed on the window.* 大滴大滴的雨點劈裡啪啦地打在窗戶上。**2** [T always+adv/prep] to make someone or something wet with a lot of small drops of water or other liquid 潑濺〔液體〕於: **splash sth on/over/with etc sth** *Shivering, he splashed cold water on his face and washed his hands.* 他一邊發抖, 一邊用冷水潑臉、洗手。**3** also 又作 **splash about/around** [I] to make water fly up in the air with a loud noise by hitting it or by moving around in it 嘩啦嘩啦地濺水, 蹚水: *Maggie watched the children splashing about in the pool.* 瑪吉看着孩子們在游泳池裡嘩啦嘩啦地玩水。**4** [T] *informal* if a newspaper splashes a story or picture over its pages, it makes it very large and easy to notice【非正式】以大篇幅報道, 以顯著版面刊載

splash down *phr v* [I] if a SPACECRAFT splashes down it deliberately lands in the sea〔宇宙飛船在海面上〕濺落 —see also 另見 SPLASHDOWN

splash out on sth *phr v* [T] *informal* to spend a lot of money on something【非正式】在...上花很多錢: *We splashed out on a new kitchen.* 我們花了一大筆錢重新裝備廚房。

splash[2] *n* **1** [C] the sound of a liquid hitting something or being moved around quickly〔液體〕濺潑聲, 飛濺聲: *Rachel fell into the river with a loud splash.* 雷切爾撲通一聲掉進河裡。—see picture on page A19 參見 A19 頁圖 **2** [C] a mark made by a liquid splashing onto something else 灑濺的斑點: *There were splashes of paint all over my clothes.* 我衣服上濺滿了油漆斑點。**3 a splash of colour** small area of bright colour 一片鮮豔的顏色 **4 make a splash** *informal* to do something that gets a lot of public attention【非正式】惹人注目, 引起轟動: *Russell's new show made a big splash in New York.* 拉塞爾的新演出在紐約引起很大的轟動。**5** [singular] *especially BrE* a small amount of liquid added to a drink【尤英】〔加入飲料中的〕少量液體: *Just a splash of milk in my coffee, please.* 請給我的咖啡加點牛奶。

splash[3] *adv informal* with a splash【非正式】撲通一聲地: *You should have seen Rex – he jumped splash into the lake!* 可惜你沒有親眼看見雷克斯——他撲通一聲跳進湖裡!

splash·back /ˋsplæʃˏbæk; ˈsplæʃbæk/ *BrE*【英】, **splashboard** /ˋsplæʃˏbɔrd; ˈsplæʃbɔːd/ *AmE*【美】*n* [C] the area of a bathroom or kitchen wall that is behind TAPS and covered in tiles (TILE[1] (1))〔浴室或廚房水龍頭後面貼有瓷磚的〕擋濺板

splash·down /ˋsplæʃˏdaun; ˈsplæʃdaʊn/ *n* [C,U] a landing by a SPACECRAFT in the sea〔宇宙飛船在海上的〕濺落

splash guard /ˈ· ·/ *n* [C] *AmE* a flat piece of rubber hanging behind the wheel of a vehicle to prevent mud being thrown up【美】〔汽車車輪後的〕擋泥板; MUDFLAP *BrE*【英】

splash·y /ˋsplæʃɪ; ˈsplæʃi/ *adj AmE* big, bright and very easy to notice; FLASHY【美】顯眼的, 惹人注意的

splat[1] /splæt; splæt/ *n* [singular] *informal* a noise like something wet hitting a surface hard【非正式】〔濕物擊打表面時發出的〕啪噠聲

splat[2] *v* **splatted, splatting** [I,T] to make a noise like something wet hitting a surface, or to make something make this noise（使）發啪噠聲: **[+against]** *Big raindrops splatted against the windscreen.* 很大的雨點啪噠啪噠地打在擋風玻璃上。

splat·ter /ˋsplætɚ; ˈsplætə/ *v* [I,T] to cover something with small drops of liquid 飛濺（在）, 濺潑（於）: *Mud splattered the hem of her kimono.* 污泥濺在她的和服下襬上。

splay /sple; spleɪ/ also 又作 **splay out** *v* [I,T] if fingers or legs splay or are splayed, they spread further apart, often in a way that looks strange（使）〔手指、雙腿〕張開: *He sat sturdily on the floor, legs splayed apart.* 他張開雙腿, 紮紮實實地坐在地板上。

splay foot·ed /ˌ· ˈ··◂/ *adj* having very flat wide feet 八字腳的, 外翻足的

spleen /splin; spliːn/ *n* **1** [C] an organ near your stomach that controls the quality of your blood 脾臟 —see picture at 參見 DIGESTIVE 圖 **2** [U] *formal* anger【正式】怒氣: **vent your spleen on sb** (=get angry with someone) 向某人大發脾氣, 拿某人出氣

splen·did /ˋsplɛndɪd; ˈsplendɪ̈d/ *adj formal*【正式】**1** excellent or very fine 極好的, 優秀的, 傑出的: *a splendid person* 傑出的人物 | *a splendid suggestion* 極好的建議 **2** beautiful and impressive 壯麗的, 華麗的, 輝煌的, 燦爛的: *There are some splendid villas near Rome.* 羅馬附近有一些豪華別墅。| *a splendid view of the port* 港口的壯麗景象 —**splendidly** *adv*: *Joe and my father are getting along splendidly.* 喬和我父親相處得極好。

splen·dif·e·rous /splɛnˋdɪfərəs; splenˈdɪfərəs/ *adj BrE informal humorous* splendid【英, 非正式, 幽默】極好的, 華麗的, 壯麗的

splen·dour *BrE*【英】, **splendor** *AmE*【美】/ˋsplɛndɚ; ˈsplendə/ *n* **1** [U] impressive beauty and richness, usually in a large building or large place 壯麗, 華麗, 壯觀: *the gothic splendor of the cathedral* 大教堂歌特式的壯麗 **2 splendours** [plural] impressive, beautiful, rich fea-

S

tures, especially of a large building or place〔尤指大建築物或地方的〕雄偉[華麗]的特質: *the splendours of Versailles* 凡爾賽宮的雄偉之處

sple·net·ic /splɪˋnɛtɪk; splɪ̆ˈnetɪk/ *adj literary* bad-tempered and often angry【文】脾氣壞的, 易怒的

splice¹ /splaɪs; splaɪs/ *v* [T] **1** to join the ends of two pieces of rope, film etc so that they form one continuous piece 將〔兩條繩子、膠片等的頭〕連接[捻接, 黏接] **2 get spliced** *BrE informal* to get married【英, 非正式】結婚

splice² *n* [C] the act of joining the ends of two things together, or the place where this join has been made 連接, 接合; 連接處, 接合點

splic·er /ˋsplaɪsɚ; ˈsplaɪsə/ *n* [C] a machine for joining pieces of film or recording TAPE¹ (1a) neatly together〔膠片或磁帶的〕連接器

splint /splɪnt; splɪnt/ *n* [C] a flat piece of wood, metal etc, used for keeping a broken bone in position while it mends〔用以固定斷骨的〕夾板

splin·ter¹ /ˋsplɪntɚ; ˈsplɪntə/ *n* [C] a small sharp piece of wood, glass, or metal, that has broken off a larger piece〔木頭、玻璃或金屬的〕碎片, 尖片: *I've got a splinter in my finger.* 我的手指扎了一根刺。| **[+of]** *splinters of glass* 玻璃碎屑 —**splintery** *adj*: *splintery plywood* 容易碎裂的膠合板 —see picture on page A7 參見 A7 頁圖

splinter² *v* [I,T] if something such as wood splinters, or you splinter it, it breaks into thin sharp pieces (使) 裂成碎片: *Soft wood splinters easily.* 軟木容易碎裂。

splinter group /ˈ·· ˌ·/ also 又作 **splinter or·ga·niz·a·tion** /ˈ·· ···ˌ··/ *n* [C] a group of people that has separated from a political or religious organization because they have different ideas etc〔因意見分歧而從政治、宗教等團體〕分裂出來的小團體[小派別]: *Green Realignment, a splinter group of the British Green Party* 綠色新聯盟 —— 從英國綠黨分裂出來的小派別

split¹ /splɪt; splɪt/ *v past tense and past participle* **split** *present participle* **splitting**

1 ►INTO GROUPS 成為幾個團體◄ also 又作 **split up** [I,T] if a group of people splits or is split, it divides into two or more groups, because one group strongly disagrees with the other〔由於意見嚴重分歧而〕分裂: *The issue of women's ordination is splitting the church.* 關於給婦女授神職的問題正使教會陷於分裂。| **[+over/on]** *The party split over segregation.* 這個黨在種族隔離問題上分歧嚴重。| **be split on/over** *The National Defense Committee is split over the use of military force.* 國防委員會在如何使用軍事力量的問題上意見分歧。

2 ►INTO PARTS 成為幾部分◄ also 又作 **split up** [I,T] to divide or separate something into different parts, or to be divided into different parts 分割, 把…分開〔成幾部分〕: **[+into]** *Each district was split up into a number of sub-divisions.* 每個區被分成若干個分區。| *At the end of the bridge the expressway split into two roads.* 這條高速公路在橋的盡頭分成兩條路。

3 ►BREAK OR TEAR 裂開或撕開◄ [I,T] if something splits or if you split it, it tears or breaks along a straight line (使) 裂開, 撕開: *Harry split his trousers climbing over the fence.* 哈里在爬過圍欄時撕破了褲子。| **[+open]** *One of the pumpkins had split open.* 有一個南瓜裂開了。| **split (sth) in two/half** *The board had split in two.* 這塊板裂成了兩塊。| **split (sth) down/across/along etc** *He split the stone down the middle.* 他把石頭從中間破成兩半。

4 ►SHARE 分攤◄ [T] to divide something into separate parts so that two or more people each get a part 均分, 分配: **split sth between** *Profits will be split between three major charities.* 利潤將在三個主要慈善機構之間分配。| **split sth three/four etc ways** (=into three, four, or more equal parts) 將某物平均分成三份/四份等 *I think we should split what's left three ways.* 我認為我們應當把剩下的均分成三份。| **split the bill/cost** *It's only fair to split the cost of the bills.* 分攤這些賬單的費用才是公平的。

5 ►INJURE 損傷◄ also 又作 **split open** [T] to cut someone's head or lip, by hitting them 碰破〔頭或嘴唇〕, 把…碰得裂開: *The poor guy had his head split right open.* 那個可憐傢伙把頭撞破了。

6 ►LEAVE 離開◄ [I] *slang* to leave quickly【俚】迅速離去: *They grabbed her purse and split.* 他們搶了她的錢包後逃之夭夭。

7 split hairs to argue that there is a difference between two things, when the difference is really too small to be important 在瑣細的問題上爭辯: *Let's stop splitting hairs and get back to the main issue.* 我們別再在瑣細問題上爭辯了, 還是回到主要的問題上來吧。

8 split the difference to agree on an amount that is exactly between two amounts that have been mentioned〔在數額上〕互相讓步, 折衷, 妥協: *You want $20, I'm offering $10. Why don't we split the difference?* 你要 20 美元, 我出 10 美元, 我們為甚麼不互相讓步, 折衷一下呢?

9 split your sides to laugh very hard 捧腹大笑

split off *phr v* **1** [I] to completely separate from a group〔從羣體中〕分離出來: **[+from]** *The ancestors of this animal split off from the rest and established themselves as an independent species.* 這種動物的祖先從原種分離出來後自己成為一個獨立的物種。**2** [I,T] to break something away from something so that it is completely separate, or to break off in this way (使) 分離 (出來): *Huge boulders had split off and rolled down the mountainside.* 巨石崩裂開來, 滾下山坡。

split on sb *phr v* [T] *informal especially BrE* to tell someone in authority about something wrong that someone else has done【非正式, 尤英】告發: *You wouldn't split on a pal would you?* 你不會告發老朋友吧?

split up *phr v* **1** [I] to end a marriage or relationship 離婚; 決裂, 絕交: *Steve's parents split up when he was four.* 史蒂夫四歲時父母離了婚。| **[+with]** *Jackie's splitting up with her boyfriend.* 傑姬要和男友分手。**2** [I,T] to divide into groups 分組: *Please don't split up when we get to the museum.* 到達博物館後請大家不要散開。| **split sth ↔ up** *The teacher split up the class into three groups.* 老師把全班分成三組。**3** [T **split** sth **↔ up**] to divide or separate something into different parts 把…分成若干部分: *The article is easier to read if you split it up into sections.* 這篇文章如果分成幾部分就更容易讀了。

split² *n* [C] **1** a long straight hole caused when something breaks or tears 裂口, 裂縫: *a split in the seat of his trousers* 他褲子臀部上的裂縫 **2** a serious disagreement that divides an organization or group of people into smaller groups〔團體內部的〕分裂, 分離: *Arguments over admitting women to the club may lead to a split.* 接受婦女參加俱樂部的爭論可能導致俱樂部的分裂。**3** the part of something you receive when something, especially money, is shared〔尤指錢的〕一份, 份額: **a three-way/four-way etc split** (=a share of something that is divided equally between three, four etc people) 三人/四人等均分的一份 **4** *informal* a difference between two things, ideas etc【非正式】〔兩者之間的〕差別, 差異: *the split between ideals and reality* 理想和現實之間的差別 **5 do the splits** to spread your legs wide apart so that your legs touch the floor along their whole length 劈叉, 劈一字腿 —see also 另見 BANANA SPLIT

split ends /ˌ· ˈ·/ *n* [plural] a condition of someone's hair in which the ends have split into several parts 開叉的髮梢

split in·fin·i·tive /ˌ· ·ˈ···/ *n* [C] a phrase in which you put an adverb or other word between 'to' and an INFINITIVE, as in 'to easily win'. Some people think this is incorrect English. 分裂不定式〔副詞或其他詞插在 to 和動詞原形之間, 如 to easily win。有些人認為這是不正

確的英語〕

split-lev·el /ˌ· ˈ··◂/ *adj* a split-level house, room or building has floors at different heights in different parts〔房子、房間或建築物〕錯層式的

split pea /ˌ· ˈ·◂/ *n* [C] a dried PEA split into its two halves 乾豌豆瓣

split per·son·al·i·ty /ˌ· ··ˈ···/ *n* [C] *not technical* a condition in which someone has two very different ways of behaving; SCHIZOPHRENIA【非術語】分裂人格, 雙重人格

split ring /ˌ· ˈ·/ *n* [U] a metal ring, used for keeping keys on, that can be opened to allow the keys to be put on or taken off 開口[疊口]鑰匙圈

split screen /ˌ· ˈ·◂/ *n* [C] a method used in films and on television screen (SCREEN[1] (1,2)) to show different scenes or pieces of information at the same time〔電影或電視的〕分畫面: *a split-screen movie* 分畫面電影

split sec·ond /ˌ· ˈ··◂/ *n* **a split second** an extremely short period of time 一剎那, 頃刻: *I just turned round for a split second and she vanished!* 我轉過身去就那麼一轉眼的時間, 她就沒了人影兒! —**split-second** *adj*: *a split-second decision* 剎那間作出的決定

split shift /ˌ· ˈ·/ *n* [C] a period of work that is divided into two or more parts on the same day 間隔班〔一天的上班時間分成兩段或幾段的輪班〕: *Chefs work a split shift.* 廚師上間隔班。

split tick·et /ˌ· ˈ··/ *n* [C] a vote in US elections in which the voter has voted for some CANDIDATES of one party and some of the other party〔美國選舉的〕分裂票〔一個選民同時選兩黨候選人的選票〕—**split-ticket** *adj*: *split-ticket voting* 分裂票選舉

split·ting /ˈsplɪtɪŋ; ˈsplɪtɪŋ/ *adj* a splitting HEADACHE is very bad〔頭痛〕劇烈的

splodge /splɑdʒ; splɒdʒ/ *n* [C] *informal* a large mark of mud, paint etc with an irregular shape【非正式】〔污泥、油漆等的〕斑塊, 污漬: *a splodge of ketchup on his shirt* 他襯衣上的大片番茄醬污漬 —**splodgy** *adj*

splosh /splɑʃ; splɒʃ/ *v* [I always+adv/prep] *BrE informal* to make a noise by falling into or moving through water; SPLASH[1]【英, 非正式】啪啦啪啦地濺水, 潑水 —**splosh** *n* [C]: *a discreet splosh as the eel-fisherman cast off* 捕鰻者在解纜開船時盡量小的聲音

splotch /splɑtʃ; splɒtʃ/ *n* [C] a SPLODGE 斑塊, 污跡

splurge /splɝdʒ; splɜːdʒ/ *v* [I] *informal* to spend more money than you can usually afford【非正式】亂花錢, 揮霍金錢: *Let's splurge and take a cab.* 我們奢侈一回, 叫計程車吧。—**splurge** *n* [C]

splut·ter /ˈsplʌtɚ; ˈsplʌtə/ *v* [I] **1** to talk quickly in short confused phrases, especially because you are angry or surprised 急促而慌亂地說話〔尤因生氣或吃驚〕: *"But…But…I can't believe…how could you?" she spluttered.* "可…可是…我不能相信…你怎麼能?" 她語無倫次地說。| **[+with]** *Katie was spluttering with rage.* 凱蒂氣得說話結結巴巴。**2** to make short sharp noises, like someone spitting (SPIT[1] (1)) 發出噼啪[畢剝]聲: *Bill was coughing and spluttering.* 比爾在咳嗽, 唾沫星子四濺。| *The boat's engine spluttered and stopped.* 小船的發動機噼噼啪啪響了幾下就停了。—**splutter** *n* [C]

spoil /spɔɪl; spɔɪl/ *past tense and past participle* **spoiled** *or* **spoilt** /spɔɪlt; spɔɪlt/ *BrE*【英】*v*

1 ▶RUIN STH 毀掉某物◀ [T] to have a bad effect on something so that it is no longer attractive, enjoyable, useful etc 損壞, 糟蹋, 破壞: *The countryside has been spoiled by the new freeway.* 郊區被新修的高速公路破壞了。| *Don't spoil your sister's birthday by crying at her party.* 不要在你妹妹的聚會上哭, 使她的生日掃興。| **spoil everything** (=completely ruin someone's plan) 完全打亂某人的計劃 *Mom arrived home just then, which spoiled everything.* 媽媽就在這時回家了, 完全打亂了我們的計劃。—see also 另見 **spoil/ruin your appetite** (APPETITE (1)) —see 見 DESTROY (USAGE)

2 ▶FOOD 食物◀ [I] to start to decay〔開始〕變壞, 變質; 腐敗: *Food will spoil if the temperature in your freezer rises above 8°C.* 冷藏箱裡的溫度如果高於攝氏8度, 食物就會變壞。

3 ▶CHILD 小孩◀ [T] to give a child whatever they want, or let them do what they want, with the result that they behave badly 寵壞, 慣壞, 溺愛〔小孩〕: **spoil sb with sth** *Jimmy's grandmother spoils him with toys and candy.* 吉米的祖母用玩具和糖果把他慣壞了。

4 ▶TREAT KINDLY 體貼地對待◀ [T] to look after someone in a way that is kind or too kind 無微不至地關心; 過分地照顧, 縱容: *You know you're spoiling me with all this good cooking.* 你用這麼多美味佳餚招待我, 太讓我受寵若驚了。| **spoil yourself** *Go on, spoil yourself. Have another piece of cake.* 來吧, 縱容自己一下, 再來一塊蛋糕。

5 ▶VOTING PAPER 選票◀ [T] to mark a BALLOT PAPER wrongly so that your vote is not included〔因劃票不符規定〕使〔選票〕成廢票

6 be spoiling for a fight/argument to be very eager to fight or argue with someone 一心想打架/吵架 —see also 另見 SPOILS, SPOILER

spoil·age /ˈspɔɪlɪdʒ; ˈspɔɪlɪdʒ/ *n* [U] *technical* waste resulting from something being spoiled【術語】變壞, 變質, 腐敗; 〔因變壞造成的〕浪費

spoiled /spɔɪld; spɔɪld/ *usually* 一般作 **spoilt** *BrE*【英】*adj* **1** someone, especially a child, who is spoiled is rude and behaves badly because their parents have always given them what they want and allowed them to do what they want〔小孩〕慣壞的, 寵壞的: **spoiled brat** (=spoiled, annoying child) 寵壞的孩子 | **spoiled rotten** (=very spoiled) 極度慣壞的 **2 be spoilt for choice** *BrE* to have so many good things to choose from that you cannot decide which one to choose【英】可供選擇的好東西太多〔以至無從下手〕

spoil·er /ˈspɔɪlɚ; ˈspɔɪlə/ *n* [C] **1** a piece of an aircraft wing that can be lifted up to slow the plane down〔機翼上用以降低飛行速度的〕擾流器 **2** a raised part on a racing car that stops the car lifting off the road at high speeds〔賽車上〕氣流偏導器 **3** a book, article etc that is produced to take attention away from another similar book and spoil its success 搗亂作品〔指為分散讀者對某作品的注意並破壞其成功而同時出版的類似的書或文章等〕**4** *AmE* a person or team that spoils another's winning record【美】〔個人或團隊〕妨礙他人取勝者, 拆台者

spoils /spɔɪlz; spɔɪlz/ *n* [plural] *formal or literary*【正式或文】**a)** things taken by an army from a defeated enemy, or things taken by thieves 戰利品, 掠奪物; 贓物: *the spoils of war* 戰利品 | *dividing up the spoils* 分贓 **b)** profits gained through political power 通過政治權力獲得的利益

spoil·sport /ˈspɔɪlˌspɔrt; ˈspɔɪlspɔːt/ *n* [C] *informal* someone who spoils other people's fun【非正式】掃興者, 破壞別人興致的人: *Don't be a spoilsport, Richard. We can't play without you.* 不要掃興, 理查德, 你不參加我們就玩不成了。

spoilt /spɔɪlt; spɔɪlt/ *adj* another form of the word SPOILED spoiled 的另一種形式

spoke[1] /spok; spəʊk/ the past tense of SPEAK

spoke[2] *n* [C] **1** one of the thin metal bars which connect the outer ring of a wheel to the centre, especially on a bicycle〔尤指自行車輪子上的〕輪輻, 輻條 —see picture at 參見 BICYCLE[1] 圖 **2 put a spoke in sb's wheel** to prevent someone from doing something they have planned 破壞某人的計劃: *I feel like telling the press everything. That'd put spoke in their wheel.* 我很想向報紙公開一切。那樣他們的計劃就行不通了。

-spoken /spokən; spəʊkən/ *suffix* [in adjectives 構成形容詞] speaking in a particular way 以…方式說話的: *a softly-spoken girl* (=who speaks quietly) 說話柔聲細氣的姑娘

S

spok·en¹ /ˋspokən; ˈspəʊkən/ the past participle of SPEAK

spoken² *adj* **1 spoken English/language** the form of language that you speak rather than write 英語口語/口語 **2 quietly/softly/well-spoken** speaking in a quiet, educated etc way 說話輕輕的/柔柔的/有教養的 **3 be spoken for** *informal*【非正式】**a)** if something is spoken for, you cannot buy it because it is being kept for someone else〔東西〕為某人保留 **b)** if someone is spoken for, they are married or already have a serious relationship with someone 已結婚; 已與別人有正式關係

2 **spokes·man** /ˋspoksmən; ˈspəʊksmən/ *n plural* **spokesmen** /-mən; -mən/ [C] someone who has been chosen to speak officially for a group, organization or government 發言人, 代言人: *a White House spokesman* 白宮發言人 | [+for] *a spokesman for victims' families* 受害者家屬代言人

spokes·per·son /ˋspoksˌpɝsn̩; ˈspəʊksˌpɜːsən/ *n plural* **spokespeople** /-ˌpipl̩; -ˌpiːpəl/ [C] a word meaning spokesman or spokeswoman which some people use because they think that 'spokesman' should not be used for both sexes 發言人, 代言人

spokes·wom·an /ˋspoksˌwʊmən; ˈspəʊksˌwʊmən/ *n plural* **spokeswomen** /-ˌwɪmɪn; -ˌwɪmɪn/ [C] a woman who has been chosen to speak officially for a group, organization, or government 女發言人, 女代言人

spo·li·a·tion /ˌspolɪˋeʃən; ˌspəʊliˈeɪʃən/ *n* [U] *formal* the violent or deliberate destruction or spoiling of something【正式】〔粗暴或故意的〕破壞, 毀壞: *the spoliation of the environment* 自然環境的破壞

sponge¹ /spʌndʒ; spʌndʒ/ *n* **1** [C,U] a piece of a soft natural or artificial substance full of small holes, which can suck up liquid and is used for washing（一塊）海綿; 海綿狀物: *The physio ran onto the field with a wet sponge.* 物理治療師拿着一塊濕海綿跑到賽場上去。**2** [C] a simple sea creature from which natural sponge is produced 海綿〔一種可以產生天然海綿的海洋生物〕 **3** [singular] *especially BrE* an act of washing something with a sponge【尤英】用海綿擦拭: *Give my back a quick sponge, would you?* 你用海綿替我擦幾下背, 好嗎? **4** [C] a SPONGER 寄生者 **5** [C,U] *BrE* SPONGE CAKE【英】海綿蛋糕

sponge² *v* **1** also 又作 **sponge down** [T] to wash something with a wet cloth or sponge 用濕布[海綿]擦洗: *Sponge down the walls before you paint them.* 先用海綿洗牆, 再上塗料。**2** [T always+adv/prep] to remove liquid or a mark with a wet cloth or sponge 用濕布[海綿]吸掉〔液體〕, 揩掉〔斑點〕: **sponge sth off/out/up** *Wendy tried to sponge the wine off her dress.* 溫迪試圖用海綿吸乾灑在她連衣裙上的酒。**3** [I] to get money, free meals etc from other people, without doing anything for them 依賴他人生活, 寄生: *Right-wing politicians accuse the poor of sponging.* 右翼政客指責窮人過着寄生生活。| **sponge off sb** *Carl's been sponging off his family ever since he left college.* 卡爾大學畢業後, 一直依賴家庭生活。

sponge bag /ˈ· ·/ *n* [C] *BrE* a small bag for carrying the things that you need to wash with【英】盥洗用具袋

sponge bath /ˈ· ·/ *n* [C] an act of washing your whole body with a wet cloth when you cannot use a BATHTUB or SHOWER¹ (1)〔不入水的〕海綿擦浴

sponge cake /ˈ· ·/ *n* [C,U] a light cake made from eggs, sugar, and flour but usually no fat 海綿蛋糕

sponge pud·ding /ˌ· ˈ··/ *n* [C] *BrE* a food made of eggs, butter, flour and sugar which is eaten hot【英】海綿布丁

spon·ger /ˋspʌndʒɚ; ˈspʌndʒə/ *n* [C] someone who gets money, free meals etc, from other people and does nothing for them 依賴他人生活者, 寄生者

spong·y /ˋspʌndʒɪ; ˈspʌndʒi/ *adj* soft and full of holes that contain air or liquid like a SPONGE¹ (1) 鬆軟多孔的, 海綿似的: *The earth was soft and spongy underfoot.* 腳下的地像海綿一樣鬆軟。—**sponginess** *n* [U]

spon·sor¹ /ˋspɑnsɚ; ˈspɒnsə/ *n* [C] **1** a person or company that pays for a show, broadcast, sports event etc in exchange for the right to advertise at that event〔出資舉辦表演、廣播、體育比賽等以在其中做廣告的〕贊助者, 贊助商: *the Championship's sponsor, Martell Cognac* 錦標賽的贊助商馬爹利白蘭地公司 **2** someone who agrees to give someone else money for a CHARITY (2) if they walk, run, swim etc a particular distance 慈善募捐活動的贊助者 **3** someone who officially agrees to help someone else, or to be responsible for what they do 擔保人, 保證人: *You need a sponsor to get a working visa.* 你必須有擔保人才能獲得工作簽證。**4** someone who officially introduces or supports a proposal for a new law 提案人; 發起者, 倡議者 **5** a GODPARENT 教父; 教母

sponsor² *v* [T] **1** to give money to a sports event, theatre etc 贊助, 資助〔體育比賽、演出等〕: *The bank is sponsoring a sports day for children in the area.* 銀行在贊助為本區兒童舉辦的運動日。**2** to agree to give someone money for CHARITY if they walk, run etc a particular distance 贊助〔某人的慈善募捐活動〕: *I've sponsored Alison $1 for every mile in the walkathon.* 艾莉森在步行馬拉松中每走一英里我贊助一美元。**3** to officially support a proposal for a new law 倡議〔法案〕; 支持〔法案〕

spon·sored /ˋspɑnsɚd; ˈspɒnsəd/ *adj* **sponsored walk/swim etc** *BrE* an event in which many people walk, swim etc a particular distance in order to collect money for a CHARITY (2)【英】慈善步行/游泳等〔一種募捐活動〕

spon·sor·ship /ˋspɑnsɚˌʃɪp; ˈspɒnsəʃɪp/ *n* [U] support, usually financial support for an activity or event 贊助, 資助: *The expedition is looking for sponsorship from one of the major banks.* 探險隊正在向一家大銀行尋求贊助。

spon·ta·ne·ous /spɑnˋtenɪəs; spɒnˈteɪniəs/ *adj* happening or done without being planned or organized, but because you suddenly feel you would like to do it 自發的, 自動的; 一時衝動的: *The crowd gave a spontaneous cheer when the result was announced.* 宣布結果時人羣即時爆發出一陣歡呼聲。—**spontaneously** *adv* —**spontaneousness, spontaneity** /ˌspɑntəˋniətɪ; ˌspɒntəˈniːəti/ *n* [U]

spontaneous com·bus·tion /·ˌ··· ·ˈ··/ *n* [U] burning caused by chemical changes inside something rather than by heat from outside 自發燃燒, 自燃

spoof /spuf; spuːf/ *n* [C] a funny book, play, film etc that copies a serious or important one and makes it seem silly 嘲諷性的模仿作品: [+of/on] *'A Five Minute Hamlet' is an amusing spoof of Shakespeare's most famous play.*《五分鐘哈姆雷特》是一齣模仿莎士比亞最著名的戲劇的滑稽劇。—**spoof** *v* [T]

spook¹ /spuk; spuːk/ *n* [C] *informal*【非正式】**1** a GHOST¹ (1) 鬼 **2** *slang* a SPY¹【俚】密探, 間諜: *Yup. He was a real live CIA spook.* 是的。他是個真正的中央情報局間諜。

spook² *v* [T] *informal especially AmE* to frighten someone【非正式, 尤美】使驚慌, 驚嚇: *You've really spooked me with that story about plane crashes.* 你講的那個飛機墜毀故事讓我聽了很害怕。

spook·y /ˋspukɪ; ˈspuːki/ *adj informal* strange or frightening in a way that makes you think of ghosts (GHOST¹ (1))【非正式】陰森恐怖的, 使人毛骨悚然的: *a spooky old house with creaking stairs* 陰森恐怖的樓梯嘎吱作響的老房子

spool /spul; spuːl/ *n* [C] **1** an object shaped like a wheel that you wind electric wire, recording TAPE¹ (1a), photographic film etc around〔電線、錄音帶、膠卷等的〕卷軸; 線軸 **2** *AmE* a REEL¹ (1a)【美】〔電線、棉紗等的〕一卷;〔膠片、磁帶等的〕一盤;〔電影的〕一本: *Don't forget to rewind the spool.* 別忘記倒帶子。

spoons 匙

tablespoon *BrE*【英】/ serving spoon *AmE*【美】 大湯匙

dessertspoon *BrE*【英】/ tablespoon *AmE*【美】 點心匙

soup spoon 湯匙

teaspoon 茶匙

ladle 杓

wooden spoon 木匙

spoon¹ /spun; spuːn/ *n* [C] **1** a thing used for eating, cooking, or serving food, consisting of a small bowl-shaped part and a long handle 匙子, 杓 **2** a SPOONFUL 一匙之量, 一滿匙 —see also 另見 **be born with a silver spoon in your mouth** (BORN² (11)), DESSERTSPOON, GREASY SPOON, SOUP SPOON, WOODEN SPOON

spoon² *v* [T] to pick up or move food with a spoon 用匙舀: **[+into/on]** *Spoon the mixture into glasses.* 用匙把混合物舀進玻璃杯裡。

spoo·ner·is·m /ˈspunəˌrɪzəm; ˈspuːnərɪzəm/ *n* [C] a phrase in which the speaker makes the mistake of exchanging the first sounds of two words, with a funny result, for example 'sew you to a sheet' for 'show you to a seat'〔兩個詞的〕首音誤置〔如把 show you to a seat 説成 sew you to a sheet, 因而產生可笑的效果〕

spoon-feed /ˈ· ·/ *v past tense and past participle* **spoon-fed** [T] **1** to give too much information and help to someone 填鴨式地給…灌輸〔信息等〕: *Spoon-feeding students does not help them remember things.* 對學生進行填鴨式灌輸並不能幫助他們記住東西。**2** to feed someone, especially a baby, with a spoon 用匙餵〔尤指嬰兒〕

spoon·ful /ˈspunˌful; ˈspuːnfʊl/ *n* [C] the amount that a SPOON will hold 一匙之量, 一滿匙: **[+of]** *Two spoonfuls of sugar, please.* 請放兩匙糖。

spoor /spʊr; spɔː/ *n* [C] the track of foot marks or FAECES (=solid waste) left by a wild animal〔野生動物留下的〕腳印, 足跡; 臭跡

spo·rad·ic /spəˈrædɪk; spəˈrædɪk/ *adj* happening often but not regularly; INTERMITTENT 偶爾發生的, 零星的, 分散的: *sporadic fighting in the west of the city* 城西的零星戰鬥 —**sporadically** /-kḷɪ; -kli/ *adv*

spore /spɔr; spɔː/ *n* [C] a cell like a seed, produced by some plants such as MUSHROOM*s*, and by some very simple animals, which is able to develop into a new plant or animal 孢子; 芽孢

spor·ran /ˈspɑrən; ˈspɒrən/ *n* [C] a special bag made of leather or fur, worn in front of a KILT by a Scotsman〔蘇格蘭男子佩於短裙前面的〕毛皮袋

S2 W2 **sport¹** /sport; spɔːt/ *n*

1 ►GAMES 運動◄ **a)** [C] a physical activity in which people compete against each other 運動, 體育運動; 體育比賽: *My favourite sports are tennis and swimming.* 我最喜愛的運動是網球和游泳。| *I was never any good at sports when I was young.* 我年輕時一點也不擅長運動。| **spectator sport** (=one which is watched by large groups of people) 人們喜歡觀看的運動 *Football is one of the most popular spectator sports.* 足球是最受觀眾喜愛的體育運動之一。**b)** [U] *BrE* sports in general【英】體育運動〔總稱〕: *Here's news about today's sport.* 現在是今天的體育新聞。| *Why is there so much sport on TV?* 為甚麼電視上的體育節目這麼多?

2 ►HUNTING 打獵◄ [C] a country outdoor activity such as hunting or fishing 野外運動〈如打獵、釣魚等〉: **blood sports** (=sports that involve killing animals) 以獵殺〔鳥獸〕為樂的運動

3 sports [plural] *BrE* an occasion when people compete in running, jumping, throwing etc【英】運動會: **school/county sports** *The school sports are usually held in July.* 學校運動會通常在7月份舉行。

4 ►HELPFUL PERSON 熱心人◄ also 又作 **good sport** *old-fashioned* a helpful cheerful person who lets you enjoy yourself and never complains when there is trouble【過時】熱心、開朗、大度的人: *His Mum will let us have a party. She's a good sport.* 他媽媽會讓我們開聚會的。她是個慷慨大度的人。| **be a sport** (=used when asking someone to help you) 大方一點〔用於向人求助時〕 *Be a sport and lend me your bike.* 慷慨一點, 把自行車借我用一下。

5 ►MAN/BOY 男子/男孩◄ *spoken*【口】**a)** *AustrE* a friendly way of addressing someone, especially a man【澳】老兄, 朋友〔用作友好的稱呼, 尤用於男子〕**b)** *AmE old-fashioned* a friendly way of addressing a young boy【美, 過時】小伙子, 小朋友, 哥兒〔用作對小男孩的友好稱呼〕

6 ►FUN 玩笑◄ [U] *old use* fun or amusement【舊】玩笑, 戲謔

7 make sport of *old use* to joke about someone in a way that makes them seem stupid【舊】開…的玩笑, 嘲笑〔某人〕

8 ►PLANT/ANIMAL 植物/動物◄ [C] *technical* a plant or animal that is different in an important way from its usual type【術語】變態的動[植]物, 變種

9 the sport of kings horse racing 賽馬 —see also 另見 FIELD SPORTS, WINTER SPORTS, WATER SPORTS

sport² *v* **1 be sporting sth** to be wearing or showing something publicly, especially in a proud way 炫耀某物, 賣弄某物: *Eric was sporting a new camel-hair coat.* 埃里克炫耀地穿着一件駱駝毛外衣。**2** [I] *literary* to play together happily【文】嬉戲, 玩耍: *dolphins sporting amidst the waves* 在波浪中嬉戲的海豚

sport car /ˈ· ·/ *n* [C] *AmE* a SPORTS CAR【美】跑車

sport coat /ˈ· ·/ *n* [C] *AmE* a SPORTS JACKET【美】〔男子作便服穿的〕外套

sport·ing /ˈsportɪŋ; ˈspɔːtɪŋ/ *adj* **1 a)** [only before noun 僅用於名詞前] related to or taking part in sports (有關或參加) 體育運動的: **sporting goods** *especially AmE* (=sports equipment)【尤美】體育用品 | **sporting event** (=occasion on which a sport is played) 體育比賽項目 **b)** related to or joining in country sports like hunting or horse racing 有關[從事]野外運動〈如打獵或賽馬〉的: *the sporting gentry* 喜歡野外運動的紳士們 **2** *BrE* fair and generous, especially in sports【英】有運動家風度的, 公正大度的: **it is sporting of sb** *It was sporting of him to admit that his last shot was out.* 他有運動家風度, 承認最後一槍打飛了。**3 a sporting chance** a fairly good chance of succeeding or winning 相當大的成功[取勝]機會: *Neil has a sporting chance of getting in the football team.* 尼爾有相當大的機會入選足球隊。—**sportingly** *adv*

spor·tive /ˈsportɪv; ˈspɔːtɪv/ *adj literary* enjoying fun and making jokes in a friendly way; PLAYFUL【文】嬉戲的, 歡鬧的 —**sportively** *adv* —**sportiveness** *n* [U]

sport jack·et /ˈ· ˌ··/ *n* [C] *AmE* a SPORTS JACKET【美】〔男子作便服穿的〕外套

sports /sports; spɔːts/ *adj* [only before noun 僅用於名詞前] **1** connected with sport or used for sport 有關體育活動的; 體育運動用的: *a sports field* 運動場 | *sports equipment* 運動裝備 | *sports clubs* (體育) 運動俱樂部 **2** on the subject of sport〔內容〕關於體育的: *When I buy a newspaper, I always read the sports page first.* 我買到報紙總是先看體育版。| *a sports commentator on television* 電視體育評論員

sports car /ˈ· ·/ *n* [C] a low fast car, often with a roof that can be folded back or removed 跑車〔車身低、車速快、通常車頂可以摺疊或移動的汽車〕

sports·cast /ˈspɔrtsˌkæst; ˈspɔːtskɑːst/ *n* [C] *AmE* a television broadcast of a sports match【美】電視的體育比賽播放 —**sportscaster** *n* [C]

sports cen·tre /ˈ· ˌ··/ *n* [C] *BrE* a building where many different types of indoor sports are played【英】體育運動中心, 體育館

sports coat /ˈ· ·/ *n* [C] a SPORTS JACKET〔男子作便服穿的〕外套

sports day /ˈ· ·/ *n* [C] *especially BrE* a day on which the children at a school have sports competitions【尤英】〔中小學生進行比賽的〕運動日; FIELD DAY (2) *AmE*【美】

sport shirt /ˈ· ·/ *n* [C] *AmE* a SPORTS SHIRT【美】〔男子作便服穿的〕運動衫

sports jack·et /ˈ· ˌ··/ *n* [C] a man's comfortable JACKET (1), usually made of TWEED, worn on informal occasions〔男子作便服穿的〕外套, 粗花呢夾克

sports·man /ˈspɔrtsmən; ˈspɔːtsmən/ *n plural* **sportsmen** /-mən; -mən/ [C] a man who plays several different sports, especially outdoor sports〔尤指戶外運動的〕運動員; 參加運動者 —see also 另見 SPORTSWOMAN

sports·man·like /ˈspɔrtsmənˌlaɪk; ˈspɔːtsmənlaɪk/ *adj* behaving in a fair, honest, and polite way when competing in sports〔在體育比賽中〕公平、誠實、有禮貌的; 有運動家風度[品格]的: *gentlemanly and sportsmanlike behaviour* 紳士般的、有運動家風度的行為

sports·man·ship /ˈspɔrtsmənˌʃɪp; ˈspɔːtsmənʃɪp/ *n* [U] behaviour that is fair, honest and polite in a game or sports competition 運動家風度[品格], 體育精神: **good/bad sportsmanship** *We try to teach the kids good sportsmanship.* 我們力求教育孩子們要有良好的體育精神。

sports schol·ar·ship /ˈ· ˌ···/ *n* [C] money given to some college students in America to pay for all or part of their education because they are good enough to play for one of the college's sports teams〔美國大學頒給運動成績優秀的學生的〕體育獎學金

sports shirt /ˈ· ·/ *n* [C] a shirt for men that is worn on informal occasions〔男子作便服穿的〕運動衫

sports·wear /ˈspɔrtsˌwɛr; ˈspɔːtsweə/ *n* [U] **1** clothes that are worn to play sports or when you are relaxing 運動服裝; 休閒服裝 **2** *AmE* clothes that are suitable for informal occasions【美】便服, 便裝

sports·wom·an /ˈspɔrtsˌwʊmən; ˈspɔːtsˌwʊmən/ *n plural* **sportswomen** /-ˌwɪmɪn; -ˌwɪmɪn/ [C] a woman who plays many different sports, especially outdoor sports〔尤指戶外運動的〕女運動員; 參加運動的女子

sport·y /ˈspɔrtɪ; ˈspɔːti/ *adj informal*【非正式】**1** designed to look attractive in a bright informal way 漂亮的, 花哨的, 瀟灑的: *a sporty jacket and skirt* 一套花哨的外套和裙子 **2** *especially BrE* good at and fond of sport【尤英】擅長[喜歡]運動的: *I'm not a very sporty person.* 我不是一個擅長運動的人。—**sportiness** *n* [U]

spot[1] /spɑt; spɒt/ *n* [C]

1 ►PLACE 地方◄ a particular place or area, especially a pleasant place where you spend time〔尤指休閒的〕地點, 場所: *an ideal spot for a picnic* 野餐的理想地點 | *We walked along the beach looking for a spot to sit.* 我們沿着海灘往前走, 想找個地方坐下。| **camping/swimming/holiday spot** (=a place that is suitable for a particular activity) 適合野營/游泳/度假的地方 *We found several good camping spots by the river.* 我們在河邊找到幾處很好的露營地點。| **the exact/very/same spot** (=the exact place where something happens)〔某事發生的〕準確地點 | **a sunny/shady spot** *These plants grow best in a sunny spot.* 這些植物在陽光充足的地方長得最好。—see 見 POSITION (USAGE) —see graph at 參見 LOCATION 圖表

2 ►AREA 面積◄ a usually round area on a surface, that is a different colour or is rougher, smoother etc than the rest〔圓〕點, 斑點: *Dalmatian dogs have white coats with black or brown spots.* 大麥町犬毛皮白色, 帶有黑色或棕色斑點。| **[+of]** *Her pink suit made a bright spot of colour against the white steps.* 她的粉紅色衣服在白色台階的襯托下形成一片亮麗的色彩。

3 ►MARK 痕跡◄ a small mark on something, especially one that is made by a liquid 污漬, 斑點: *There are a lot of grease spots on the shirt.* 襯衣上沾了許多油漬。| *spots of paint on the carpet* 地毯上的油漆斑點

4 on the spot if you do something on the spot, you do it immediately, often without thinking about it very carefully 立即, 馬上; 當場: *He bought the car on the spot.* 他立即買下了那輛汽車。| *The police could give you an on the spot fine.* 警察可以對你當場罰款。

5 be on the spot to be in the place where something is happening 在現場: *As the man on the spot, Coen was in a position to take vital decisions.* 作為在場唯一能作主的人, 科恩能夠作重大的決定。

6 ►MARK ON SKIN 皮膚上的斑點◄ a) a small round red area on someone's skin that shows that they are ill〔皮膚上的〕紅斑: *I was covered in spots when I had measles.* 我患麻疹時全身長滿了紅斑。**b)** *BrE* a small raised red mark on someone's skin, especially on their face; PIMPLE【英】〔尤指臉上紅色的〕丘疹; 粉刺: *This cream clears up teenage spots in days.* 這種乳膏用上幾天就能消除青少年臉上的粉刺。

7 ►POSITION 地位◄ a position in a competition, event, television programme etc〔在比賽、電視節目等中的〕地位, 位置: *The Bulldogs earned a spot in the semifinals.* 鬥牛犬隊贏得了半決賽資格。| *A bluegrass band has the second spot on the program.* 一支藍草鄉村樂隊表演第二個節目。| **guest spot** (=part of a television or radio programme showing someone who does not usually appear on the programme)〔電視或電台節目中的〕特邀嘉賓欄目: *a guest spot on the Johnny Carson show* 約翰尼·卡森節目中的客串表演

8 run/dance/hop etc on the spot to run etc in one place, without moving forwards or around the area 原地跑步/跳舞/跳躍等

9 weak spot a) a point at which someone or something is not very good 弱點, 不足(之處): *He'd look at my work and immediately find every weak spot.* 他會檢查我的工作, 並立即會發現每一點毛病。**b)** *AmE* if someone has a weak spot for something, they like it very much【美】〔對某物的〕特別喜愛, 偏愛

10 put sb on the spot to deliberately ask someone a question that is difficult or embarrassing to answer〔故意〕使某人處於難堪地位: *Reporters put the governor on the spot with questions about his involvement in the bribery scandal.* 記者們向州長提出一些關於他捲入賄賂醜聞的問題, 使他狼狽不堪。

11 in a spot *informal* in a difficult situation【非正式】處於困難境地: **put sb in a spot** *You've put us in one hell of a spot by telling them that, you know.* 你知道嗎, 你把那件事告訴他們, 使我們的處境非常糟糕。

12 bright spot something that is good in a bad situation 亮點, 困境中使人高興的事: **the one/only bright spot** *Being able to visit my folks was the one bright spot of the vacation.* 能夠看望親人, 是這個假期中唯一一件令人高興的事。

13 a spot of *BrE informal* a small amount of something【英, 非正式】一點點: *I could do with a spot of whisky.* 我可以喝一點點威士忌。| **a spot of bother** (=a small amount of trouble) 一點麻煩

14 ►ON CLOTH 在布上面◄ spots *BrE* small round areas that form a pattern on a piece of cloth; POLKA DOTS【英】〔指布上的〕圓點圖案, 斑點: *a dark blue dress with white spots* 帶白點的深藍色連衣裙

15 spots of rain *BrE* a few drops of rain【英】幾滴雨

16 ►LIGHT 燈◄ a SPOTLIGHT[1] (1) 聚光燈

17 five-spot/ten-spot etc *AmE spoken* a piece of paper money worth five dollars, ten dollars etc【美口】一張五美元/十美元等鈔票

18 ►ADVERTISEMENT 廣告◄ a short radio or television advertisement, especially one for a politician 廣告插播〔尤指為政客作的廣播或電視短廣告〕: *a 30-second spot on the local radio station* 在地方廣播電台插播的30秒短訊 —see also 另見 BEAUTY SPOT, BLACK SPOT, BLIND SPOT, **not change your spots** (CHANGE¹ (1)), G-SPOT, **high point/spot** (HIGH¹ (13)), **hit the spot** (HIT¹ (27)), **hot spot** (HOT¹ (30), **knock spots off** (KNOCK¹ (13)), **be rooted to the spot** (ROOT² (4)), **have a soft spot for** (SOFT (10)), TROUBLE SPOT

S3 **spot²** *v* [T]

1 ►NOTICE 注意到◄ to notice something, especially something that is difficult to see, or that you are looking for 看出, 認出; 找出: *Luckily, the enemy planes were spotted early.* 幸虧及早發現了敵機。| *I spotted a break in the fence and headed towards it.* 我看到籬笆上有個缺口, 便朝那裡走去。| **spot sb doing sth** *Meg spotted someone coming out of the building.* 梅格發現有人走出大樓。| **difficult/easy to spot** *Dick's very tall, so he's easy to spot in a crowd.* 迪克個子很高, 所以在人羣中容易被認出來。

2 ►RECOGNIZE 辨認出◄ to recognize the good or bad qualities in someone or something 發現, 辨認出〔某人或某事的特性〕: *You must learn to spot trouble ahead and prevent it.* 你一定要學會預先發現問題並加以防止。| **spot sb's potential** *Island Records were the first to spot his potential.* 海島唱片公司最早發現了他的潛質。

3 be spotted to have small round marks on the surface 〔表面〕有斑點, 有污漬: **[+with]** *The floor was spotted with paint.* 地板上有很多油漆的污漬。

4 ►GAME 比賽◄ *AmE* to give the other player in a game an advantage【美】〔在比賽中〕讓〔對手〕: **spot sb sth** *He spotted me six points and he still won.* 他讓了我六分, 但還是贏了。

spot³ *adj technical* for buying or paying immediately, not at some future time【術語】現貨的; 現付(款)的: **spot cash/price** *They won't take credit; they want spot cash.* 他們不賒賬, 他們要現錢。| *What's the spot price for oil?* 石油的現貨價是多少?

spot check /ˌ· ˈ·/ *n* [C] a quick examination of a few things or people from a group, to check whether everything is correct or satisfactory 抽樣檢查, 抽查: *spot checks by customs officers* 海關官員進行的抽查

spot·less /ˈspɑtlɪs; ˈspɒtləs/ *adj* **1** completely clean 一塵不染的, 乾乾淨淨的: *Joe's house is spotless.* 喬的房子收拾得很乾淨。**2 spotless reputation/record/character** a completely honest and good character 毫無瑕疵的名譽/記錄/品格: *Before his arrest, the suspect's record was spotless.* 嫌疑犯在被逮捕之前的記錄是完全清白的。—**spotlessly** *adv* —**spotlessness** *n* [U]

spot·light¹ /ˈspɑtˌlaɪt; ˈspɒtlaɪt/ *n* **1 a)** [C] a light with a very bright beam which can be directed at someone or something 聚光燈 —see picture at 參見 LIGHT¹ 圖 **b)** [singular] the round area of light made by this beam on the ground, stage etc 聚光燈照出的光圈: *Step into the spotlight so we can see you!* 走進光圈, 讓我們看得見你! **2 be in the spotlight** to receive a lot of attention in the newspapers, on television etc 受到報紙[電視等]經常注意: *Now that he's entered politics he is constantly in the spotlight.* 他既然進了政界, 就經常為公眾所矚目了。

spotlight² *v past tense and past participle* **spotlighted** *or* **spotlit** [T] **1** to direct attention to someone or something 使顯眼, 使突出, 使受注意: *The article spotlights the problems of the homeless.* 這篇文章突出報道了無家可歸者的種種問題。**2** to shine a strong beam of light on something 將聚光燈射向〔某物〕, 聚光照明 —**spotlit** /ˈspɑtˌlɪt; ˈspɒtlɪt/ *adj*

spot-on /ˌ· ˈ·◄/ *adj, adv BrE informal* exactly right【英, 非正式】完全正確的[地]: *Judith is always spot-on with her advice.* 朱迪斯的勸告總是完全正確的。

spot·ted /ˈspɑtɪd; ˈspɒtɪd/ *adj* [usually before noun 一般用於名詞前] having small round marks or DOTS on the surface〔表面上〕有圓點的, 有斑點的: *red and white spotted pyjamas* 有紅白色圓點的睡衣 —see picture on page A16 參見 A16 頁圖

spotted dick /ˌ·· ˈ·/ *n* [U] a boiled PUDDING (1) with CURRANTS which is eaten in Britain〔英國的〕葡萄乾布丁

spot·ter /ˈspɑtɚ; ˈspɒtə/ *n* [C] **bird/train etc spotter** *especially BrE* someone who spends time watching birds, trains etc【尤英】鳥類/火車等觀察者

spot·ty /ˈspɑtɪ; ˈspɒti/ *adj* **1** *BrE informal* having spots on your face【英, 非正式】〔臉上〕有粉刺的: *a spotty youth* 長粉刺的青年人 **2** *AmE* good only in some parts, but not in other parts; PATCHY【美】〔質量〕有好有壞的, 參差不齊的

spouse /spaus; spaʊs/ *n* [C] *formal* a husband or wife【正式】配偶〔指丈夫或妻子〕

spout¹ /spaut; spaʊt/ *n* [C] **1** a small tube or pipe on a container that you pour liquid out through 容器嘴, 壺嘴 **2 a spout of water/blood etc** a sudden strong stream of liquid which comes out of somewhere very fast 水柱/血柱等: *The whale blew a spout of water into the air.* 鯨向空中噴出一條水柱。—see also 另見 **water-spout** **3 up the spout** *BrE informal*【英, 非正式】**a)** if someone's plans have gone up the spout, they cannot succeed〔計劃等〕不成功的: *Her chances of studying medicine have gone up the spout.* 她學醫的機會已經告吹了。**b)** completely wrong 完全錯的: *His calculations are completely up the spout.* 他的計算完全錯誤。**c)** *old-fashioned* going to have a baby; PREGNANT【過時】懷孕的

spout² *v* **1 a)** [I always+adv/prep] if liquid or fire spouts from somewhere, it comes out very quickly in a powerful stream〔液體或火〕湧出; 噴出: **[+from]** *Blood was spouting from the wound in her arm.* 血從她手臂的傷口湧出來。**b)** [T] to send out liquid or flames very quickly in a powerful stream 噴出, 噴射〔液體或火焰〕: *a volcano spouting lava* 噴射着熔岩的火山 **2** also 又作 **spout off** [I,T] *informal* to talk a lot about something in a boring way, especially without thinking about what you are saying【非正式】喋喋不休[滔滔不絕]地說: **[+about]** *I'm tired of listening to Jim spouting about politics.* 吉姆滔滔不絕地談政治, 我都聽膩了。| **spout (off) sth** *It's no use spouting theories about education if you've never actually taught anyone.* 你如果從來沒有實際教過任何學生, 大談教育理論是不頂用的。**3** [I] if a WHALE spouts it sends out a stream of water from a hole in its head〔鯨〕噴水柱

sprain /spren; spreɪn/ *v* [T] to damage a joint in your body by suddenly twisting it 扭傷〔關節〕: *I fell down the steps and sprained my ankle.* 我摔下台階, 扭傷了腳踝。—**sprain** *n* [C]

sprang /spræŋ; spræŋ/ the past tense of SPRING

sprat /spræt; spræt/ *n* [C] a small European HERRING〔歐洲產的〕小西鯡

sprawl¹ /sprɔl; sprɔːl/ *v* **1** also 又作 **sprawl out** [I always+adv/prep] to lie or sit with your arms or legs stretched out in a lazy or careless way〔懶洋洋地〕伸開手腳躺[坐]着: **[+in/on etc]** *He just sprawls out in his chair and expects me to bring his dinner.* 他就這樣攤開四肢坐在椅子上, 等我來給他端上晚餐。| **be sprawled out** *The students were sprawled out on the grass.* 學生們伸開手腳躺在草地上。| **send sb sprawling** (=hit someone with such force that they fall over) 把某人打趴在地上 **2** [I always+adv/prep] if buildings or a town sprawl, they spread out over a wide area in an untidy and unattractive way〔建築羣或城鎮〕雜亂地延伸[擴展]: *An industrial estate sprawled across the valley.* 一個工業區雜亂無章地在山谷中延伸。

sprawl² *n* [singular] **1** a large area of buildings that are spread out in an untidy and unattractive way 雜亂無章

S

地擴展的大面積建築羣: *a vast sprawl of industrial development* 一大片肆意擴展的工業開發區 | **urban sprawl** *Los Angeles' huge urban sprawl* 洛杉磯市區無計劃的大規模擴張 **2** [singular] a position in which you have your arms or legs stretched out in a lazy or careless way 懶洋洋地伸開四肢躺臥的姿勢

spraw·ling /ˋsprɔlɪŋ; ˈsprɔːlɪŋ/ *adj* spreading over a wide area in an untidy or unattractive way 雜亂地延伸的, 無計劃地擴展的: *a sprawling metropolis* 一座雜亂無章地擴展的大城市

3 **spray¹** /spre; spreɪ/ *v* **1** [T] to make a stream of small drops of liquid come out of a small tube or several small holes 噴: **spray sb with sth** *She sprayed herself with perfume.* 她往自己身上噴香水。| **spray sth on/over sth** *Vandals had sprayed graffiti on the walls.* 破壞公物者在牆上亂噴亂塗一通。| **spray crops/plants** (=cover them with liquid to protect them from insects or disease) 給農作物/植物噴殺蟲藥 **2** [I always+adv/prep] if liquids or small bits spray somewhere they are quickly scattered through the air〔液體或碎屑〕飛濺出來: **[+over/around/from etc]** *Grass started spraying from the blades of the lawn mower.* 碎草開始從剪草機的刀片上飛濺出來。**3 spray (sb/sth with) bullets** to shoot many bullets from a gun quickly (向某人/某物) 開槍掃射: *Gunmen sprayed the crowd with bullets.* 持槍歹徒向人羣開槍掃射。

spray 噴

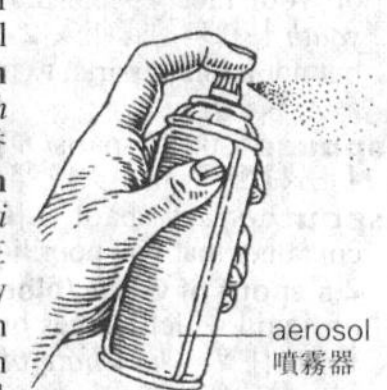

spray² *n*

1 ▶LIQUID 液體◀ [C,U] liquid which is forced out of a special container in a stream of very small drops 噴霧液體: **hair spray** (=spray which you put on your hair to keep it tidy) 噴髮定型劑 | **insect spray** (=spray used for killing insects) 殺蟲噴劑

2 ▶A CAN 一罐◀ [C] a can or other container with a special tube which forces liquid out in a stream of small drops 噴霧罐, 噴霧器: *Avoid sprays that contain harmful CFCs.* 避免使用裝着有害的含氯氟烴的噴霧器。

3 ▶FROM THE SEA 海上來的◀ [U] water in very small drops blown from the sea or a wet surface 浪花, 水花: *A thunderous plume of spray leapt half-way up the cliff.* 一大片浪花躥上懸崖的半腰, 發出雷鳴般的轟響。

4 ▶BRANCH 樹枝◀ [C] a small branch from a tree or plant used for decoration〔裝飾用的〕小樹枝: **[+of]** *sprays of holly* 冬青樹枝

5 ▶FLOWERS/JEWELS 花朵/珠寶◀ [C] an attractive arrangement of flowers or jewels 帶花[鑲有珠寶]的枝狀飾物

6 a spray of bullets/dust etc a lot of very small objects or bits moving quickly through the air 一陣槍彈/灰塵等

spray can /ˈ· ·/ *n* [C] a can from which paint is sprayed 噴漆罐

spray·er /ˋspreɚ; ˈspreɪə/ *n* [C] a piece of equipment used for spraying liquid, especially to protect crops from insects or disease〔尤指施殺蟲藥用的〕噴霧器

spray gun /ˈ· ·/ *n* [C] a piece of equipment held like a gun, which sprays liquid in very small drops 噴槍

spray paint /ˈ· ·/ *n* [U] paint that is sprayed from a can 噴漆 —**spray-paint** *v* [I,T]

2 2 **spread¹** /sprɛd; spred/ *v past tense and past participle* **spread**

1 ▶OPEN OR ARRANGE 打開或安排◀ also 又作 **spread sth ↔ out** [T] to open something so that it covers a bigger area, or arrange a group of things, so that they cover a flat surface 伸開, 展開, 張開, 鋪開: **spread sth on** *Let's spread the map out on the floor.* 我們把地圖攤開在地板上吧。| **spread sth over/across etc** *She spread the towel over the radiator to dry.* 她把毛巾鋪在暖氣管上烘乾。| *The market women had spread out their goods on the pavement.* 女商販在人行道上把貨物擺開。

2 ▶DISEASE/FEELING/PROBLEM/FIRE 疾病/感情/問題/火◀ [I,T] to increase, or be increased, and affect more and more people or affect a larger area (使) 傳播, (使) 蔓延: *The fire spread very quickly.* 大火迅速蔓延開來。| **[+through/to/across etc]** *Cholera is spreading through the refugee camps at an alarming rate.* 霍亂正以驚人的速度在難民營中傳播開來。| **spread sth** *She's the sort of woman who enjoys spreading bad feeling.* 她是那種喜歡散佈惡感的女人。

3 ▶INFORMATION/IDEAS 消息/思想◀ **a)** [I] to become known about or used by people more and more 變得廣為人知, 散佈: *News of the explosion spread swiftly.* 發生爆炸的消息迅速傳播開來。| **[+to/through/over etc]** *Buddhism spread to China from India.* 佛教從印度傳到中國。| **the word spread** (=the news became known by more and more people) 消息傳開 *The word spread that Louise had resigned.* 有傳聞說路易絲已經辭職了。| **spread like wildfire** (=become known very quickly) 不脛而走 **b)** [T] to tell a lot of people about something 散播, 散佈; 通知: **spread lies/rumours/gossip** *Andy loves spreading rumours about his colleagues.* 安迪很喜歡散播關於同事的謠言。| **spread the word** *Can you spread the word that the meeting is at 10.30?* 請你通知大家會議在十點半開始, 好嗎?

4 ▶PEOPLE/PLANTS/ANIMALS 人/植物/動物◀ [I always+adv/prep] to begin to live or grow in other areas or countries 分佈, 散佈: **throughout/over etc** *The Moors spread all over Southern Spain.* 摩爾人遍佈西班牙南部。

5 ▶SOFT SUBSTANCE 軟的物質◀ **a)** [T] to put a soft substance onto a surface in order to cover it 塗, 敷: **spread sth on/over** *He spread plaster on the walls.* 他往牆上塗灰泥。| **spread sth with sth** *Spread the toast thinly with butter.* 給烤麵包塗上薄薄的黃油。—see picture on page A11 參見 A11 頁圖 **b)** [I] to be soft enough to be put onto a surface in order to cover it〔夠軟〕容易塗敷: *If you warm up the butter it'll spread more easily.* 如果你把黃油加熱一下, 就更容易塗開。

6 ▶COVER A LARGE AREA 覆蓋大的面積◀ **a)** also 又作 **spread out** [I always+adv/prep] to cover or stretch over a large area 綿延; 擴展: **[+across/over etc]** *Leafy branches spread above her forming a canopy.* 葉子繁茂的樹枝在她頭頂散開形成一個罩篷。**b) be spread across/over etc** to exist or be present over a large area 遍佈, 散佈: *The population is fairly evenly spread across the country.* 這個國家的人口分佈相當均勻。

7 spread (out) your legs/arms/fingers etc to push your legs, fingers, arms etc as far apart as possible 張開雙腿/雙臂/手指等

8 ▶DO STH GRADUALLY 逐步進行某事◀ also 又作 **spread sth ↔ out** [T] to do something gradually over a period of time 將…分散於一段時間內: **spread sth over sth** *Could I spread the repayments over a longer period?* 我可以把分期還款的期限延長一些嗎?

9 ▶WORK/RESPONSIBILITY/MONEY 工作/責任/錢◀ [T] to share work, responsibility, or money among several people 分配, 分攤: *The work will be spread across the departments.* 這項工作將由各部門分擔。| **spread the load/burden** *If we type five pages each that should help spread the load.* 如果我們每人打五頁字, 那樣工作量就會分攤開了。

10 ▶EXPRESSION 表情◀ [I always+adv/prep] to gradually cover all of someone's face 滿臉流露: **[+across/over]** *A mischievous grin spread over her face.* 她滿臉調皮的微笑。

11 spread seeds/manure/fertilizer to scatter seeds, MANURE etc on the ground 撒種/施糞肥/施肥料

12 spread your wings to start to have an independent life 開始獨立生活: *A year spent studying abroad should allow him to spread his wings a bit.* 在外國留學一年,

他應當可以獨立一些了。

13 spread its wings if a bird or insect spreads its wings it stretches them wide〔鳥或昆蟲〕張開翅膀

14 spread a/the table (with) *old-fashioned* to put food and drink on a table【過時】〔在桌上〕擺上飯菜飲料

spread out *phr v* **1** [I] if a group of people spread out, they move apart from each other so that they cover a wider area〔人羣〕散開: *The detective ordered the officers to spread out and search the surrounding fields.* 探長命令警員散開, 搜查周圍的田野。**2** [T **spread** sth ↔ **out**] to open something out or arrange a group of things on a flat surface 打開, 攤開, 排開: *Sue spread out her notes on the kitchen table and began to write.* 蘇把筆記本打開放在廚房桌子上, 然後開始寫字。**3** [I] to cover or stretch over a large area 伸展, 延伸: *A lush green valley spread out below us.* 一片茂密翠綠的山谷在我們下面延伸。**4** [T **spread** sth ↔ **out**] to do something gradually over a period of time 將…分散在一段時間內: *You can spread out the cost over a year.* 你可以把費用分散在一年內支付。

spread² *n*

1 ►INCREASE 增長◄ [singular] the increase in the area, or number of people, affected by something, or in the number of people who do something 傳播; 擴展; 蔓延: **the spread of** *the spread of liberal ideas in the 19th century* 19世紀自由思想的傳播

2 ►SOFT FOOD 軟質食物◄ [C,U] a soft food which you spread on bread 塗麵包的醬: **cheese/chocolate etc spread** (=cheese, chocolate etc in a soft form) 乾酪醬/巧克力醬等

3 ►LARGE MEAL 豐盛的飯菜◄ [singular] *informal* a large meal for several guests on a special occasion【非正式】豐盛的飯菜, 宴會: *She organized a marvellous spread for the soiree afterwards.* 她後來為那次社交晚會舉行了盛大的筵席。

4 ►RANGE 範圍◄ [singular] a range of people or things 範圍; 廣度; 幅度: *We have a good spread of ages in the department.* 我們部門人員的年齡分佈很好。

5 double-page spread/centre spread a special article or advertisement in a newspaper or magazine, which covers two pages or covers the centre pages〔報刊中〕橫跨兩版的/中心頁跨頁的文章[廣告]

6 ►HAND/WINGS 手/兩翼◄ [U] the area covered when the fingers of a hand, or a bird's wings, are fully stretched 手指伸直時手的全長;〔鳥的〕兩翼全長, 翼展

7 a spread of land/water an area of land or water 一片土地/水域

8 ►FARM 農場◄ [C] *AmE* a large farm or RANCH【美】大農場; 大牧場

9 ►MONEY 錢◄ *technical* the difference between the buying price and the selling price of shares (SHARE² (5)) on the STOCK EXCHANGE【術語】〔股票的買入價和賣出價之間的〕差價, 差額 —see also 另見 MIDDLE-AGED SPREAD

spread·ea·gled /ˈsprɛdˌigld; spredˈiːgəld/ *adj* lying with arms and legs stretched out 伸開四肢躺着的: *He lay spreadeagled on the bed.* 他伸開四肢躺在牀上。

spread·sheet /ˈsprɛdˌʃit; ˈspredʃiːt/ *n* [C] *technical* a kind of computer PROGRAM that can show and calculate information about sales, taxes, profits etc【術語】電子數據表, 試算表〔能顯示和計算銷售、交稅、利潤等數據資料的電腦程序〕

spree /spri; spriː/ *n* [C] a short period of time doing something that you enjoy, especially spending money or drinking 作樂, 狂歡〔尤指花錢、喝酒等〕: **go (off) on a spree** *He's gone off on a drinking spree with his friends.* 他外出和朋友喝酒狂歡。| **a shopping/spending etc spree** *I'm going on a shopping spree to cheer myself up.* 我要去大買特買一番讓自己高興高興。

sprig /sprɪg; sprɪg/ *n* [C] a small stem or part of a branch with leaves or flowers on it 帶葉[花]的小枝: **[+of]** *a sprig of parsley* 一小枝帶葉的歐芹

spright·ly /ˈspraɪtlɪ; ˈspraɪtli/ *adj* an old person who is sprightly is still active and full of energy〔老人〕活躍的, 有活力的 —**sprightliness** *n* [U]

spring¹ /sprɪŋ; sprɪŋ/ *n* S2 W2

1 ►SEASON 季節◄ [C,U] the season between winter and summer when leaves and flowers appear 春天, 春季: *It was a cold, sunny day in early spring.* 那是早春裡寒冷而陽光燦爛的一天。| *the spring of 1933* 1933年春季 | *spring flowers* 春花

2 ►BED/CARS ETC 牀/汽車等◄ **a)** [C usually plural 一般用複數] something, usually a twisted piece of metal, that will return to its previous shape after it has been pressed down 彈簧; 發條 **b)** [U] the ability of a chair, bed etc to return to its normal shape after being pressed down 彈性, 彈力: *There's not much spring in this old sofa.* 這張舊沙發已經沒有多少彈性了。

3 ►WATER 水◄ [C] a place where water comes up naturally from the ground 泉, 泉源: *The islands are renowned for their thermal springs and sulphur baths.* 這些海島以其溫泉及硫磺浴而享有盛名。

4 with a spring in your step if you walk with a spring in your step, you move quickly and cheerfully 步伐輕快

5 ►SUDDEN JUMP 突然一跳◄ [singular] a sudden quick movement or jump in a particular direction 跳, 跳躍

spring² *v past tense* **sprang** /spræŋ; spræŋ/ also 又作 **sprung** /sprʌŋ; sprʌŋ/ *AmE*【美】, *past participle* **sprung**

1 ►MOVE SUDDENLY 突然移動◄ [I always+adv/prep] to move suddenly and quickly in a particular direction, especially by jumping 跳, 跳躍, 跳起: **[+out of/from/towards etc]** *Tom sprung out of bed and rushed to the window.* 湯姆從牀上跳起來衝到窗前。| *A kitten sprang from under the bush.* 一隻小貓從矮樹叢下躥了出來。| **spring to your feet** (=stand up suddenly) 突然站起

2 ►EXPRESSION/TEARS 表情/眼淚◄ [I always+adv/prep] to appear suddenly on someone's face or in their eyes〔在臉上或眼中〕突然出現, 冒出: **[+into/to]** *Tears sprang into her eyes as she started telling them what had happened.* 她開始向他們訴說發生了甚麼事時, 突然淚如泉湧。

3 ►MOVE BACK 復原◄ [I always+adv/prep] to move quickly back again after being pushed downwards or sideways 彈回原處, 反彈: **[+back/up]** *The branch sprang back and hit him in the face.* 樹枝彈回來打在他臉上。

4 spring to mind if someone or something springs to mind you immediately think of them 馬上想到: *Nobody's name actually springs to mind as an ideal candidate.* 的確一時想不出甚麼理想的人選。

5 spring into action also 又作 **spring to life** to suddenly become active 突然活躍起來: *The whole town would spring into action at carnival time.* 狂歡節時, 全鎮的人都會突然活躍起來。

6 spring into existence to suddenly begin to exist 突然出現: *A lot of small businesses sprang into existence during the 1980s.* 20世紀80年代突然冒出了許多小公司。

7 spring open/shut to open or close suddenly and quickly 突然打開/合上: *The lid of the box sprang open.* 盒蓋突然彈開。

8 spring a trap a) if an animal springs a trap, it makes the trap move and catch it〔動物〕觸發捕捉器〔而被捉〕 **b)** to make someone say or do something by tricking them 誘使某人說出[幹]某事

9 spring a leak if a boat or a container springs a leak, it begins to let liquid in or out through a crack or hole〔船或容器〕出現裂縫〔開始漏水〕

10 spring to sb's defence to quickly defend someone who is being criticized 迅速為某人辯護: *Charlene sprang immediately to her son's defence.* 夏琳馬上挺身而出為她兒子辯護。

11 spring to attention if soldiers spring to attention they stand suddenly upright〔士兵〕霍然立正

12 spring a surprise to make something unexpected or unusual happen 使突然發生, 使大吃一驚
13 ►PRISON 監獄◄ [T] *informal* to help someone escape from prison【非正式】幫助〔某人〕越獄: *A gangland boss was recently sprung from Dartmoor prison.* 一個黑社會頭目最近在別人幫助下從達特姆爾監獄逃跑。

spring from *phr v* [T] *spoken*【口】**1** to be caused by something 由…引起: *Her rudeness to other people springs from a basic insecurity.* 她對別人的不禮貌是由於她缺乏基本的安全感所致。**2 where did you/she etc spring from?** used to express surprise when you suddenly see someone who you thought was somewhere else 你/她等是從哪兒冒出來的?〔用於表示驚訝〕

spring sth **on** sb *phr v* [T] to tell someone some news that surprises or shocks them 向〔某人〕突然說〔某事, 令人驚訝或震驚〕

spring up *phr v* [I] to suddenly appear or start to exist 突然出現: *Fast-food restaurants are springing up all over town.* 突然市區到處都出現了快餐店。| *A strong wind seemed to have sprung up from nowhere.* 不知從哪兒突然颳來一陣強風。

spring·board /ˈsprɪŋˌbɔrd; ˈsprɪŋbɔːd/ *n* [C] **1** something that helps you to start doing something, especially by giving you ideas about how to do it〔工作的〕起點, 起步方法: **[+for]** *Teachers can use these ideas as a springboard for planning their own lessons.* 教師在備課時可以利用這些想法作為起點。**2** a strong board for jumping on or off, used when diving (DIVE[1] (1)) or doing GYMNASTICS〔跳水運動的〕跳板,〔體操運動的〕踏跳板

spring·bok /ˈsprɪŋˌbɑk; ˈsprɪŋbɒk/ *n* [C] a small DEER that can run fast and lives in South Africa 跳羚〔南非的一種小羚羊〕

spring break /ˌ· ˈ·/ *n* [C] *AmE* a holiday from college or university in the spring, that is usually two weeks long【美】春假〔大學裡在春天放的假, 通常為兩週〕

spring chick·en /ˌ· ˈ··/ *n* [C] **she's/you're no spring chicken** *humorous* used to say that someone is no longer young【幽默】她/你已經不再年輕了

spring-clean /ˌ· ˈ·◄/ *v* [I,T] to clean a house thoroughly, usually once a year〔通常一年一度對房屋的〕徹底打掃, 大掃除: **do the spring-cleaning** *Judith's busy doing the spring-cleaning.* 朱迪斯在忙於大掃除。—**spring-clean** *n* [singular] *BrE*【英】

spring fe·ver /ˌ· ˈ··/ *n* [U] a sudden feeling of energy and wanting to do something new and exciting that you have in the spring 春躁症〔指在春季突然覺得精力充沛、想嘗試新鮮刺激事物的心理狀態〕

spring on·ion /ˌ· ˈ··/ *n* [C] *BrE* a strong-tasting onion with a small white round part and a long green stem, usually eaten raw【英】大葱; SCALLION, GREEN ONION *AmE*【美】

spring roll /ˌ· ˈ·/ *n* [C] a type of Chinese food consisting of a piece of rolled PASTRY filled with vegetables and sometimes meat and cooked in oil 春卷; EGG ROLL *AmE*【美】

spring tide /ˌ· ˈ·/ *n* [C] a large rise and fall in the level of the sea at the time of the NEW MOON and the FULL MOON〔新月和滿月時的〕大潮, 滿潮, 朔望大潮

spring·time /ˈsprɪŋˌtaɪm; ˈsprɪŋtaɪm/ *n* [U] the time of the year when it is spring 春天, 春季: *Paris in the springtime* 春天的巴黎

spring train·ing /ˌ· ˈ··/ *n* [U] *AmE* the period during which a BASEBALL team gets ready for competition【美】〔棒球隊的〕賽前訓練

spring·y /ˈsprɪŋi; ˈsprɪŋi/ *adj* **1** something that is springy comes back to its former shape after being pressed or walked on 有彈性的, 有彈力的: *The turf felt springy underfoot.* 腳下的草皮踩起來有彈性。**2 springy step/walk** a way of walking which is quick and full of energy 輕快有力的步伐 —**springily** *adv* —**springiness** *n* [U]

sprin·kle[1] /ˈsprɪŋkl; ˈsprɪŋkəl/ *v* **1** [T] to scatter small drops of liquid or small pieces of something 灑〔小水滴〕; 撒〔小片固體〕: **sprinkle sth on/over sth** *She sprinkled perfume on the pillow.* 她往枕頭上灑香水。| **sprinkle sth with sth** *Sprinkle the pasta with cheese.* 給麵條撒些乾酪。—see picture on page A11 參見 A11 頁圖 **2 be sprinkled with jokes/quotations etc** to be full of jokes etc 插進了許多笑話/引語等: *Dr Krowik's conversation was liberally sprinkled with literary allusions.* 克勞威克博士在交談中用了大量的文學典故。**3 it is sprinkling** *AmE* if it is sprinkling, it is raining lightly【美】下着小雨

sprinkle[2] *n* [singular] **1** a sprinkling 少量, 一點: *Add a sprinkle of salt.* 放少量的鹽。**2** *AmE* a light rain【美】小雨

sprin·kler /ˈsprɪŋklə; ˈsprɪŋklə/ *n* [C] **1** a piece of equipment with holes, used for scattering water on grass or soil〔澆草地的〕灑水器 **2** a piece of equipment with holes that is on a ceiling and scatters water if there is a fire〔天花板上的〕自動噴水滅火裝置

sprin·kling /ˈsprɪŋklɪŋ; ˈsprɪŋklɪŋ/ *n* **a sprinkling of** a small quantity or amount of something 少量, 一點: *The hilltops were covered with a sprinkling of snow.* 山頂上覆蓋着薄薄的一層雪。

sprint[1] /sprɪnt; sprɪnt/ *v* [I] to run very fast for a short distance〔短距離〕快速奔跑, 衝刺: **[+along/across/up etc]** *Bill sprinted up the steps.* 比爾快速跑上台階。

sprint[2] *n* **1** [singular] a short period of running very fast 短距離的快速奔跑: **put on a sprint/make a sprint** (=run very quickly for a short distance) 全速短跑 **2** [C] a short race in which the runners run very fast over a very short distance 短距離賽跑, 短跑比賽: *the 100 metre sprint* 100 米短跑

sprint·er /ˈsprɪntə; ˈsprɪntə/ *n* [C] someone who runs in fast races over short distances 短跑運動員: *sprinter Linford Christie* 短跑運動員林弗德·克里斯蒂

sprite /spraɪt; spraɪt/ *n* [C] **1** a FAIRY (1), especially one who is graceful or who likes playing tricks on people 小精靈 **2** an image produced by a special type of computer, that is drawn in layers to look real〔電腦螢光幕上的多層次、有立體感的〕子圖形, 子畫面

spritz /sprɪts; sprɪts/ *v* [T] *AmE* to SPRAY a liquid in short bursts【美】噴〔液體〕: *Spritz a little water on the fern every day.* 每天給這棵蕨類植物噴一點水。—**spritz** *n* [C] *a spritz of hair spray* 噴灑噴髮定型劑

spritz·er /ˈsprɪtsə; ˈsprɪtsə/ *n* [C,U] a drink made with SODA WATER and white wine〔用汽水和白葡萄酒調製的〕汽酒

sprock·et /ˈsprɑkɪt; ˈsprɒkɪt/ *n* [C] **1** also 又作 **sprocket wheel** a wheel with a row of teeth (TOOTH (2)) for fitting into and turning a bicycle chain or a photographic film with holes〔自行車的〕鏈輪;〔電影放映機的〕輸片齒輪, 帶齒卷盤 **2** one of the teeth on a wheel of this kind 鏈輪〔輸片齒輪〕的齒

sprog /sprɑg; sprɒg/ *n* [C] *BrE humorous* a child or baby【英, 幽默】小孩; 嬰兒

sprout[1] /spraut; spraut/ *v* **1** [I] if leaves or BUDS sprout they appear and begin to grow〔樹葉或新芽〕開始長出來 **2** [I,T] if vegetables, seeds, or plants sprout they start to produce SHOOTS, or BUDS〔種子等〕發芽, 抽芽: *Keep the tray away from direct sunlight until the seeds begin to sprout.* 種子開始發芽之前, 花盆要放在沒有陽光直射的地方。| **sprout sth** *The plant had sprouted a few flower stalks.* 那棵植物長出了幾根花柄。**3** also 又作 **sprout up** [I always+adv/prep] to appear suddenly in large numbers 突然大量出現, 大量冒出: **[+in/throughout]** *Office blocks seem to be sprouting up everywhere.* 好像到處都有辦公大樓冒出來。**4** [T] to grow suddenly, or grow something suddenly, especially hair, horns, or wings〔尤指頭髮、角、翅膀等〕突然長出, 突然產生: *Jim seemed to have sprouted a beard overnight.* 吉姆好像一夜之間便長出了鬍子。

sprout[2] *n* [C] **1** a small green vegetable like a very small CABBAGE; BRUSSELS SPROUT 球芽甘藍 **2** a new growth on a plant; SHOOT[2] (1)〔植物的〕苗; 芽, 嫩枝 **3** [usually plural 一般用複數] *AmE* an ALFALFA seed which has grown a stem and is eaten【美】〔可食的〕苜蓿芽 **4** *AmE* a BEANSPROUT【美】豆芽

spruce[1] /sprus; spru:s/ *n* [C,U] a tree that grows in northern countries and has short leaves shaped like needles 雲杉

spruce[2] *v*

spruce up *phr v* [I,T] *informal* to make yourself or something look neater and tidier【非正式】把〔自己或某物〕打扮得整齊乾淨: *I'll just go upstairs and spruce up a bit before dinner.* 宴會之前我得上樓去打扮一下。| **spruce sb/sth ↔ up** *We need to spruce the house up a bit before we sell it.* 我們需要把房子稍微收拾一下才賣。

spruce[3] *adj* neat and clean 整齊乾淨的: *Mr Bailey was looking very spruce in a white linen suit.* 貝利先生穿着一身白色亞麻布衣服看起來真帥。—**sprucely** *adv*

sprung[1] /sprʌŋ; sprʌŋ/ a past tense and the past participle of SPRING

sprung[2] *adj* supported or kept in shape by SPRINGS 裝有彈簧的, 用彈簧支撐的: *a sprung mattress* 彈簧牀墊

spry /spraɪ; spraɪ/ *adj* a spry old person is active and cheerful〔老人〕充滿活力的, 開朗的: *a spry ninety-year old* 一位矯健的九十歲老人 —**spryly** *adv*

spud /spʌd; spʌd/ *n* [C] *informal* a POTATO【非正式】馬鈴薯, 土豆

spume /spjum; spju:m/ *n* [U] *literary* FOAM[1] (1) that forms on the top of waves when the sea is rough【文】〔海浪的〕泡沫, 浮沫

spun /spʌn; spʌn/ the past tense and past participle of SPIN

spunk /spʌŋk; spʌŋk/ *n* [U] **1** *informal* courage【非正式】膽量, 勇氣 **2** *BrE slang* SEMEN【英俚】精液 —**spunky** *adj*: *Clare's a spunky team captain.* 克萊爾是個有膽量的球隊隊長。

spur[1] /spɝ; spɜ:/ *n* [C] **1** a sharp pointed object on the heel of a rider's boot which is used to encourage a horse to go faster 馬刺 **2** a fact or event that makes you try harder to do something 激勵因素; 鼓舞; 鞭策: *Did your father's success act as a spur when you started in business?* 你開始從商時, 你父親的成功對你是一種鞭策嗎? **3 do sth on the spur of the moment** to do something suddenly, without thinking about it before you do it 一時衝動之下做某事: *On the spur of the moment she picked up the phone and called Mike.* 她一時衝動, 拿起話筒給邁克打電話。—see also 另見 SPUR-OF-THE-MOMENT **4** a piece of high ground which sticks out from the side of a hill or mountain 山嘴, 尖坡 **5** a railway track or road that goes away from a main line or road〔鐵路或公路的〕支線 **6** the stiff sharp part that sticks out from the back of a male chicken's leg〔公雞腿上的〕距

spur[2] *v* **spurred, spurring 1** also 又作 **spur on** [T] to encourage someone to try harder in order to succeed 激勵, 鼓勵: **spur sb (on) to** *It's unlikely that harsh criticism will spur a child on to greater efforts.* 嚴厲的批評不大可能激勵孩子作出更大的努力。| **spur sb into action** (=to make someone start doing something) 促使某人行動起來 **2** [T] to make an improvement or change happen faster 促進: *Lower taxes would spur investment and help economic growth.* 降低税率將刺激投資, 有助於經濟增長。**3** [I,T] to encourage a horse to go faster, especially by pushing it with special points on the heels of your boots〔尤指用馬刺〕策馬前進; 使〔馬〕快跑

spu·ri·ous /ˈspjurɪəs; ˈspjʊəriəs/ *adj* **1** a spurious statement, argument etc, is not based on facts or good reasoning and is likely to be incorrect〔聲明、論據等〕站不住腳的, 謬誤的: *a cosy and entirely spurious view of family life* 對家庭生活的美妙而虛幻的看法 **2** insincere 虛假的, 不誠實的: *spurious sympathy* 虛假的同情 —**spuriously** *adv* —**spuriousness** *n* [U]

spurn /spɝn; spɜ:n/ *v* [T] *especially literary* to refuse to accept something or to have a relationship with someone, especially because you are too proud【尤文】輕蔑地拒絕, 對...不屑一顧: *She spurned all offers of help.* 她輕蔑地拒絕一切幫助。| *a spurned lover* 被拋棄的戀人

spur-of-the-mo·ment /,· · · ˈ· ◂/ *adj* [only before noun 僅用於名詞前] a spur-of-the-moment decision or action is made or done suddenly without planning 出於一時衝動的

spurt[1] /spɝt; spɜ:t/ *v* **1** [I] if liquid or flames spurt from something they pour out of it quickly and suddenly〔液體或火焰〕噴出; 迸出: **[+from/out of]** *Water began spurting from a hole in the pipe.* 水開始從水管的裂口湧出來。**2** [T] to send out liquid or flames 噴出〔液體或火焰〕**3** [I always+adv/prep] to move somewhere very quickly 迅速行進; 衝刺: **[+towards/across]** *He spurted towards the finishing line.* 他向終點線衝刺。

spurt[2] *n* [C] **1** a sudden pouring out of liquid or flames〔液體或火焰的〕噴出; 湧出: **[+of]** *The fire sent up spurts of flame.* 火中躥出一股股火焰。| **in spurts** (=quickly for short periods) 突然一陣陣地 *The water came out of the tap in short spurts.* 水一陣陣地從水龍頭裡噴出。**2** a short sudden increase of activity, effort, or speed〔活動、努力或速度的〕突然增加; 迸發: **[+of]** *a sudden spurt of academic progress* 學業的突然進步 | **put on a spurt** (=to suddenly move more quickly for a short period) 衝刺 *Eric put on a spurt to try and catch up with the others.* 埃里克突然加速, 試圖趕上其他人。| **in spurts** (=in sudden short periods of effort) 短期的突然努力 *I tend to work in spurts.* 我經常會拚命地工作一陣子。

sput·ter /ˈspʌtɚ; ˈspʌtə/ *v* **1** [I] to make several sudden soft sounds like someone spitting (SPIT[1] (1)) 發出劈劈啪啪聲, 畢剝作響: *The engine began sputtering as the car climbed the hill.* 汽車上坡時, 引擎開始劈劈啪啪作響。**2** [I,T] to talk quickly in short confused phrases, especially because you are angry or shocked; SPLUTTER (1)〔因氣憤或震驚而〕語無倫次地說

spu·tum /ˈspjutəm; ˈspju:təm/ *n* [U] *technical* liquid in your mouth which you have coughed up from your lungs【術語】痰

spy[1] /spaɪ; spaɪ/ *n* [C] someone whose job it is to find out secret information about another country, organization, or group 間諜: *a British spy in World War II* 第二次世界大戰中的一名英國間諜 | *a spy film* 間諜片

spy[2] *v* **1** [I] to secretly collect information about an enemy country or an organization you are competing against 從事間諜活動; 祕密收集情報: **[+on]** *He was charged with spying on top-secret naval bases.* 他被指控刺探絕密的海軍基地情報。**2 spy on sb** to watch someone secretly 祕密監視某人: *Jean's always spying on the neighbours.* 簡總是窺探她的鄰居。**3** [T] *especially literary* to suddenly see someone or something, especially after searching for them【尤文】〔尤指通過搜索後〕突然看見, 突然發現: *Ellen suddenly spied her friend in the crowd.* 埃倫突然在人羣中看到了她的朋友。

spy sth ↔ **out** *phr v* [T] **1** to secretly find out information about something 暗中查明 **2 spy out the land** to secretly find out more information about a situation before deciding what to do〔作決定前〕暗中摸清情況

spy·glass /ˈspaɪˌglæs; ˈspaɪglɑ:s/ *n* [C] a small TELESCOPE used by sailors in the past〔舊時水手用的〕小型望遠鏡

sq the written abbreviation of 縮寫= SQUARE

squab·ble /ˈskwɑbl̩; ˈskwɒbəl/ *v* [I] to quarrel continuously about something unimportant〔為瑣事〕爭吵, 口角: **[+about/over]** *The kids are still squabbling about whose turn it is to wash the dishes.* 孩子們仍然在為該輪到誰洗碗而爭吵。—**squabble** *n* [C]

squad /skwɑd; skwɒd/ *n* [C] **1** a group of players from which a team will be chosen for a particular sports event〔為參加某體育比賽而組成的〕運動隊; 球隊: *the Italian World Cup squad* 代表意大利參加世界盃賽的球隊 **2** the police department responsible for dealing with a particular kind of crime〔警察的〕特別行動小組: **drugs/fraud/vice squad** *Officers of the narcotics squad raided* W3

S

the club. 緝毒小組的警員突擊搜查這個俱樂部。**3** a small group of soldiers working together as a unit〔士兵組成的〕班, 小隊: *a drill squad* 操練〔示範〕班 **4** *AmE* a group of CHEERLEADERS【美】啦啦隊 —see also 另見 DEATH SQUAD, FIRING SQUAD, FLYING SQUAD

squad car /'· ·/ *n* [C] a car used by police on duty; PATROL CAR 巡邏警車: *He was bundled into the back of a squad car.* 他被塞進巡邏警車的後座。

squad·dy, squaddie /ˈskwɑdɪ; ˈskwɒdi/ *n* [C] *BrE informal* a soldier who is not an officer【英, 非正式】士兵

squad·ron /ˈskwɑdrən; ˈskwɒdrən/ *n* [C] a military force consisting of a group of aircraft or ships 飛行中隊; 海軍分遣艦隊: *a squadron of bombers* 轟炸機中隊

squadron lead·er /'·· ,··/ *n* [C] an officer in the British AIRFORCE below a WING COMMANDER〔英國〕空軍少校〔中隊長〕

squal·id /ˈskwɑlɪd; ˈskwɒlɪ̇d/ *adj* **1** dirty and unpleasant because of a lack of care or money〔因無人料理或缺錢而〕污穢的, 骯髒的: *How can anyone live in such squalid conditions?* 人怎麼能住在如此污穢的環境中? | *a tiny squalid apartment* 骯髒的小套房 **2** involving low moral standards or dishonesty; SORDID (1) 道德敗壞的; 卑鄙的; 低賤的: *a squalid tale of sex and corruption* 涉及色情和腐敗的下流故事 —see also 另見 SQUALOR —**squalidly** *adv* —**squalidness** *n* [U]

squall¹ /skwɔl; skwɔːl/ *n* [C] a sudden strong wind, especially one that brings rain or snow 颮〔突起的狂風, 常夾有雨或雪〕: *A violent squall sank both ships.* 一陣強烈的颮把兩艘船都颳沉了。

S

squall² *v* [I] if a baby or child squalls, it cries noisily〔嬰兒或小孩〕大聲哭喊; 尖叫

squal·ly /ˈskwɔlɪ; ˈskwɔːli/ *adj* squally rain or snow comes with sudden strong winds 風狂雨暴的, 多颮的: *squally showers* 狂風暴雨

squal·or /ˈskwɑlə; ˈskwɒlə/ *n* [U] the condition of being SQUALID 污穢, 骯髒: *The refugees are forced to live in squalor.* 難民們被迫生活在骯髒的環境裡。

squan·der /ˈskwɑndə; ˈskwɒndə/ *v* [T] to spend money or use your time carelessly on things that are not useful 浪費, 揮霍: **squander sth on** *They squandered millions on that film.* 他們在那部電影上浪費了幾百萬。—**squanderer** *n* [C]

2 3 **square¹** /skwɛr; skweə/ *adj*

1 ►SHAPE 形狀◄ having four straight equal sides and 90° angles at the corners 正方形的, 四方形的: *a square flower bed* 正方形的花壇

2 ►ANGLE 角◄ forming a 90° angle 成直角的: *a square corner* 成直角的拐角 | *a square jaw* 方下巴 | *square shoulders* 寬肩膀

3 square metre/mile etc an area of measurement equal to a square with sides a metre long, a mile long etc 平方米/平方英里等: *about four square meters of ground* 大約四平方米的土地 | *There isn't a café within a square mile of here.* 這地方一平方英里內沒有咖啡館。

4 5 feet/2 metres etc square having the shape of a square with sides that are 5 feet, 2 metres etc long 五英尺/兩米見方等: *The room is six metres square.* 這個房間為六米見方。

5 ►LEVEL 水平的◄ parallel with a straight line 平行的, 水平的: **[+with]** *I don't think the shelf is square with the floor.* 我覺得這塊擱板與地面不平行。

6 a square deal honest and fair treatment from someone, especially in business 公平對待; 公平交易: *I try to give my workers a square deal, decent wages, and a clean room.* 我盡量對我的工人公平合理, 給他們像樣的工資和清潔的住房。—see also 另見 **hit sth fair and square** (FAIR² (2)), **tell sb fair and square** (FAIR² (3))

7 a square meal a good satisfying meal 豐盛的一頓飯

8 be all square to have the same number of points as your opponent in a competition 比分相同, 平局: *The teams were all square at the end of the first half.* 上半場結束時兩隊打成平局。

9 (all) square *informal* if two people are square they do not owe each other any money【非正式】〔彼此〕兩不欠賬的: *Here's your £10 back, that makes us square.* 還你10英鎊, 這樣我們誰也不欠誰的了。

10 ►UNFASHIONABLE 不合時尚的◄ *old-fashioned* boring and unfashionable【過時】古板的; 守舊的

11 a square peg in a round hole *informal* someone who is in a job or situation that is not suitable for them【非正式】不適宜做某工作的人; 與周圍環境格格不入的人 —**squareness** *n* [U]

square² *n* [C] 2

1 ►SHAPE 形狀◄ **a)** a shape with four straight equal sides with 90° angles at the corners 正方形, 四方形: *First of all, draw a square.* 首先, 畫一個正方形。—see picture at 參見 SHAPE¹ 圖 **b)** a piece of something in this shape (正)方形物: **[+of]** *a square of cloth* 一塊方布 —see picture on page A7 參見 A7 頁圖

2 ►IN A TOWN 在城鎮裡◄ **a)** a broad open area in the middle of a town usually in the shape of a square, or the buildings surrounding it 廣場; 廣場周圍的建築物: *There's a market in the square every Tuesday.* 每星期二廣場上有集市。**b) Square** used in addresses 廣場〔用於地址中〕: *She lives in Hanover Square.* 她住在漢諾威廣場。

3 be back to square one to be back in exactly the same situation that you started from, so that you have made no progress 退回起點〔毫無進展〕; 從頭開始: *Police have released the suspect and are now back to square one.* 警方釋放了那個嫌疑人, 現在又得從頭開始。

4 ►NUMBER 數字◄ the result of multiplying a number by itself 平方, 二次冪: *The square of 4 is 16.* 4的平方是16。—see also 另見 SQUARE ROOT

5 ►IN A GAME 在遊戲中◄ a space on a board used for playing a game such as CHESS〔棋盤等上的〕方格

6 ►PERSON 人◄ *old-fashioned* someone who is boring because they are not interested in the newest styles of music, clothes etc【過時】古板守舊的人; 老古板

7 ►TOOL 工具◄ a flat tool with a straight edge, often shaped like an L, used for drawing or measuring 90° angles 直角尺, 丁字尺, 曲尺 —see also 另見 SETSQUARE

8 be on the square *old-fashioned* to behave or speak honestly【過時】行為正直; 說話誠實: *Are you really on the square?* 你是真心的嗎?

square³ *v* [T]

1 ►MULTIPLY 乘◄ to multiply a number by itself 使〔某數〕自乘一次; 使〔某數〕成平方

2 ►IN A COMPETITION 在競賽中◄ to win the same number of points or games as your opponent 把〔比分〕拉平, 使〔比賽〕打成平局: *India won the second match to square the series at one each.* 印度隊贏了第二場, 使循環賽積分為一平。

3 ►PAY SB MONEY 付錢給某人◄ to pay money to someone in an official position, so that they do what you want 收買, 賄賂: *We'll have to square a few government officials, if we're going to get this scheme approved.* 我們要想使這個計劃得到批准, 就得買通幾位政府官員。

4 square your shoulders to push back your shoulders with your back straight, usually to show your determination 挺直肩膀〔以顯示決心〕

5 ►MAKE STH STRAIGHT 使某物變直◄ to make something straight or parallel 使...變直[變平行]

6 square the circle to attempt something impossible 嘗試做不可能的事

square sth ↔ **away** *phr v* [T usually passive 一般用被動態] *AmE* to finish something, especially by putting the last details in order【美】完成〔尤指做完最後細節〕: *Get your work squared away before you leave.* 把工作了結後才離開。

square off *phr v* [T] **1** [T **square** sth ↔ **off**] to make something square with straight edges 把...弄成方形 **2** [I] *AmE* to get ready to fight someone【美】擺好打鬥的

架勢

square up *phr v* **1** [I] to pay money that you owe 清賬; 結賬: *I'll pay for the drinks and you can square up later.* 我把飲料的錢付掉, 你可以過後再結算。**2** [I] *BrE* to get ready to fight someone【英】擺好打鬥的架勢 **3** [T **square up to** sb/sth] to deal with a difficult situation or person in a determined way 果敢地面對〔某人或困難的處境〕: *I admire the way she squared up to the problem.* 我欽佩她正視問題的勇氣。

square with *phr v* **1** [I,T not in progressive 不用進行式] if you square two ideas, statements etc with each other or if they square with each other they can be accepted together even though they seem different (使)〔兩種觀點、說法等〕一致: *Ben's story doesn't square with Jane's version.* 本的說法跟簡的不一致。| **square sth with sth** *How do you square fighting in a war, with being a Christian?* 你作為一名基督徒還去打仗, 這怎麼說得通呢? | **square sth with your conscience** (=make yourself believe that what you are doing is morally right) 使自己對某事感到心安理得 **2** [T **square** sth **with** sb] to arrange something with someone by persuading them to agree to it or allow it 取得〔某人的〕同意[認可]: *I'll take the day off if I can square it with my boss.* 我要是能徵得老闆的同意, 就休一天假。

square⁴ *adv* [only after verb 僅用於動詞後] **1** directly and firmly; SQUARELY 直接地; 果斷地: **square in the eye** *Look him square in the eye and say no.* 直視着他的眼睛說不。**2** [+to] at 90° to a line; SQUARELY (4) 成直角; 垂直地

square-bash·ing /ˈ· ˌ··/ *n* [U] *BrE informal* practice in marching as part of military training【英, 非正式】〔軍隊的〕操練步伐

square brack·ets /ˌ· ˈ··/ *n* [plural] *BrE* a pair of BRACKETS [ ], used for enclosing information【英】方括號

squared /skwɛrd; skweəd/ *adj* **1** divided into squares or marked with squares 方格的: *squared paper* 方格紙; 座標紙 **2 3/9/10 etc squared** the number 3, 9 etc multiplied by itself 數字 3/9/10 等的自乘: *3 squared equals 9.* 3 的平方是 9。

square dance /ˈ· ·/ *n* [C] a type of COUNTRY DANCE in which four pairs of dancers face each other in a square〔四對男女跳的〕方形舞

square knot /ˈ· ·/ *n* [C] *AmE* a double knot that will not come undone easily; REEF KNOT【美】方結, 平結〔一種不易鬆脫的雙結〕

square·ly /ˈskwɛrlɪ; ˈskweəli/ *adv* [only after verb 僅用於動詞後] **1** directly and firmly; SQUARE⁴ (1) 直接地, 堅定地: *He turned and faced her squarely.* 他轉過身來徑直地面對着她。**2** completely and with no doubt 完全地, 毫無疑問地: *The report puts the blame squarely on the government.* 這份報告毫不含糊地把責任歸在政府頭上。**3** straight on something and centrally 端端正正地: *Dr Soames jammed his hat squarely on his head.* 索姆斯博士把帽子端端正正地扣在頭上。**4** at 90° to a line; SQUARE⁴ (2) 成直角; 垂直地

square-rigged /ˌ· ˈ·◂/ *adj* a ship that is square-rigged has its sails set across it and not along its length〔船〕有橫帆裝置的

square root /ˌ· ˈ·/ *n* [C] the square root of a number is the number which, when multiplied by itself, equals that number 平方根: *The square root of nine is three.* 9 的平方根是 3。

squar·ish /ˈskwɛrɪʃ; ˈskweərɪʃ/ *adj* shaped almost like a square 近似方形的, 呈方形的

squash¹ /skwɑʃ; skwɒʃ/ *v* **1** [T] to press something into a flat shape, often breaking or damaging it 擠扁; 壓碎; 壓壞: *I don't want my hat getting squashed in your bag.* 我不想我的帽子在你的包裡給壓扁。| *Hey! You're squashing me!* 嗨, 你擠着我啦! **2** [I always+adv/prep, T always+adv/prep] to push yourself or something else into a space that is too small 擠進; 塞進: **[+into]** *Seven of us squashed into the car.* 我們中有七個人擠進了汽車。**3** [T] *informal* to use your power or authority to stop something that is causing trouble; QUASH【非正式】鎮壓, 壓制

squash 壁球

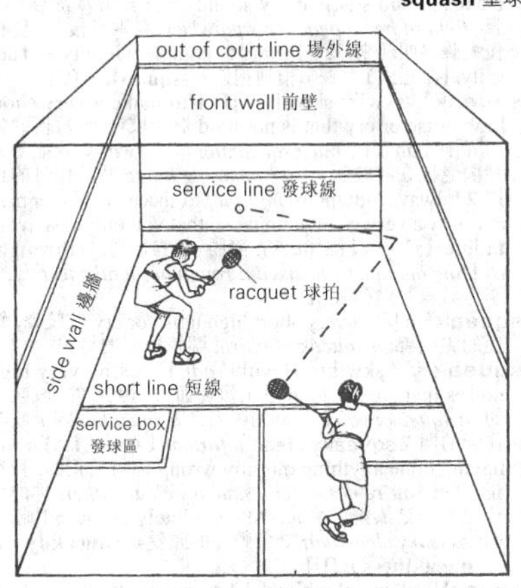

a squash court 壁球場

squash² *n* **1** [U] a game played by two people who use rackets (RACKET¹ (3)) to hit a small rubber ball against the four walls of a square court 壁球 **2 it's a squash** *spoken* used to say that there is not enough space for everyone to fit comfortably in【口】太擠了: *Sorry it's a squash with six in the car.* 對不起, 這輛車坐六個人太擠了。**3** [C,U] one of a group of large vegetables with solid flesh and hard skins, such as PUMPKINs and ZUCCHINI 南瓜屬植物〈如南瓜、西葫蘆〉—see picture on page A9 參見 A9 頁圖 **4** [U] *BrE* a drink made from fruit juice, sugar, and water【英】果汁飲料

squashed /skwɑʃt; skwɒʃt/ *adj* broken or made flat by being pressed hard 壓碎的; 壓扁的: *a bag of squashed tomatoes* 一袋壓爛了的番茄

squash rack·ets /ˈ· ˌ··/ *n* [U] SQUASH² (1) 壁球

squash·y /ˈskwɑʃɪ; ˈskwɒʃi/ *adj* soft and full of liquid 軟而多汁的: *squashy overripe tomatoes* 過熟發軟的番茄 —**squashiness** *n* [U]

squat¹ /skwɑt; skwɒt/ *v* **squatted, squatting** [I] **1** also 又作 **squat down** to sit with your knees bent under you, your bottom off the ground, and balancing on your feet 蹲, 蹲坐: **[+on/behind/in etc]** *Parsons squatted down beside the footprints to get a better look.* 帕森斯蹲在腳印旁, 以便看得更清楚。—see picture at 參見 CROUCH 圖 **2** to live in a building or on a piece of land without permission and without paying rent 擅自佔用建築物[空地]: *There are people squatting in the house next door.* 有人擅自居住在隔壁的房子裡。

squat² *adj* unattractively short and thick or low and wide 矮胖的; 粗矮的: *squat stone cottages roofed in slate* 矮寬的石板瓦屋頂的小石屋

squat³ *n* **1** [C] a squatting position 蹲坐; 蹲姿 **2** [singular] *BrE* a house that people are living in without permission and without paying rent【英】被擅自佔用的房子: *She lives in a draughty squat in Camden.* 她居住在卡姆登一間私佔的四周透風的房子裡。

squat·ter /ˈskwɑtɚ; ˈskwɒtə/ *n* [C] someone who lives in an empty building or on a piece of land without permission and without paying rent 擅自佔用建築物[空地]的人: *crudely built squatters' shacks* 私佔空地者搭建的簡陋的棚屋

S

squaw /skwɔ; skwɔː/ *n* [C] *old use* a word for a Native American woman, which many people think is offensive【舊】美洲土著女子〔許多人認為該詞具有冒犯性〕

squawk /skwɔk; skwɔːk/ *v* [I] **1** if a bird squawks, it makes a loud sharp angry sound〔鳥〕發出響亮的尖叫聲: *Behind her a peacock squawked.* 在她身後, 一隻孔雀大聲尖叫起來。**2** *informal* to complain loudly and angrily【非正式】大聲氣憤地抱怨 —**squawk** *n* [C]

squeak¹ /skwik; skwiːk/ *v* [I] **1** to make a very short high noise or cry that is not loud 發出吱吱聲[短促的尖叫聲]: *I can hear mice squeaking in the walls.* 我能聽到牆內老鼠在吱吱叫。| *a squeaking hinge* 吱吱作響的鉸鏈 **2** [always+adv/prep] *informal* to succeed, win, or pass a test by a very small amount so that you only just avoid failure【非正式】僥倖成功; 險勝; 勉強通過: [**+through/by**] *She only just squeaked through her maths test.* 她數學考試只是勉強及格。

squeak² *n* [C] a very short high noise or cry 吱吱聲, 短促的尖叫聲: *a squeak of alarm* 鬧鐘短促的響聲

squeak·y /ˈskwikɪ; ˈskwiːki/ *adj* **1** making very high noises that are not loud 發出短促而尖利聲音的; 吱吱叫的: *a squeaky voice* 尖利的嗓音 | *a squeaky door* 吱吱作響的門 **2 squeaky clean** *informal*【非正式】**a)** never having done anything morally wrong 品行端正的; 行為正直的: *You're not exactly squeaky clean either.* 你的品行也並不是無懈可擊的。**b)** completely clean 極其乾淨的: *squeaky clean hair* 非常乾淨的頭髮 —**squeakily** *adv* —**squeakiness** *n* [U]

squeal¹ /skwil; skwiːl/ *v* [I] **1** to make a long loud high sound or cry 發出長而尖銳的聲音[叫聲]: *squealing tires* 嘎吱作響的輪胎 | [**+with/in**] *The children squealed with delight.* 孩子們高興得尖叫了起來。**2 squeal (on sb)** *informal* to tell the police or someone in authority about someone you know who has done something wrong【非正式】舉報(某人); 告密

squeal² *n* [C] a long loud high sound or cry 長而尖銳的聲音[叫聲]: [**+of**] *Squeals of delight came from the children.* 孩子們發出高興的尖叫聲。| *a squeal of brakes* 剎車發出的刺耳的嘎吱聲

squeam·ish /ˈskwimɪʃ; ˈskwiːmɪʃ/ *adj* easily shocked, upset or easily made to feel sick by unpleasant sights 易受驚的; 易嘔吐的; 神經質的: *I could never be a nurse – I'm too squeamish.* 我永遠當不了護士——我太經不住刺激了。—**squeamishly** *adv* —**squeamishness** *n* [U]

squee·gee /ˈskwidʒi; ˈskwiːdʒiː/ *n* [C] a tool with a thin rubber blade and a short handle, used for removing or spreading a liquid on a surface 橡膠拖把, 橡膠刷帚

squeeze¹ /skwiz; skwiːz/ *v* **1** [T] to press something firmly inwards 壓; 擠; 捏; 榨: *Alice squeezed his arm affectionately.* 艾麗斯疼愛地捏了捏他的胳膊。| *Must you squeeze the toothpaste tube in the middle?* 你非得從中間擠牙膏不可嗎? —see picture on page A20 參見A20頁圖 **2** [T] to get liquid from something by pressing it 壓出; 擠出; 榨出〔液體〕: **squeeze sth out** *Try to squeeze a bit more out of the tube.* 盡量從筒裡再擠出一點兒。| **squeeze sth on/onto sth** *Squeeze a bit of lemon onto the fish.* 往魚上擠點檸檬。—see picture on page A11 參見A11頁圖 **3** [I always+adv/prep, T always+adv/prep] to try to make something fit into a space that is too small, or to try to get into such a space (使)擠進; 塞入: [**+into/through/past/between**] *Five of us squeezed into the back seat of the car.* 我們中有五個人擠進了汽車的後座。| *Move your chair and I'll try to squeeze past.* 挪一下你的椅子, 我盡量擠過去。| **squeeze sth into** *You'll never squeeze yourself into that dress.* 那件連衣裙你根本套不進去。**4 squeeze sth out of sb** to force someone to tell you something 強迫某人說出某事: *See if you can squeeze more information out of them.* 看看你能否逼他們說出更多的東西。**5 squeeze sb out (of sth)** to make it difficult for someone to continue in business, by attracting their customers〔通過吸引某人的顧客〕將某人擠出(某行業): *It's the big operators squeezing the independents out of the market.* 那些大企業正在把單獨經營者擠出市場。**6** [T] to manage to do something although you are very busy〔在很忙的時候〕設法安排〔做某事〕: **squeeze sth in/into** *How do you manage to squeeze so much into one day?* 你一天裡怎麼能有時間做那麼多事情? | **squeeze sb in** (=have time to see them) 擠出時間見某人 *I can squeeze you in at four o'clock.* 我能擠出時間在四點鐘見你。**7 squeeze in/into/through** to succeed, win, or pass a test by a very small amount so that you only just avoid failure 僥倖成功; 險勝; 勉強通過〔考試〕**8** [T] to strictly limit the amount of money that is available to a company or organization 緊縮〔公司或機構的〕資金; 使…經濟拮据: *The failure of the levy has squeezed the school district's budget.* 稅款徵收不利使學區預算撥款變得拮据。

squeeze² *n* **1 a (tight) squeeze** a situation in which there is only just enough room for things or people to fit somewhere 擁擠; 密集: *It'll be a squeeze with six people in the car.* 這輛汽車坐六個人會很擁擠。**2** [C] an act of pressing something firmly, usually with your hands 緊捏; 緊握; 擠壓: **give sb/sth a squeeze** *Marty gave her hand a little squeeze.* 馬蒂輕輕地捏了一下她的手。**3 a squeeze of lemon/lime etc** a small amount of juice obtained by squeezing a piece of fruit 擠出微量的檸檬汁/酸橙汁等 —see picture on page A7 參見A7頁圖 **4 a squeeze** a situation in which wages, prices, borrowing money etc are strictly controlled 拮据; 緊縮: *a credit squeeze* 信貸緊縮 **5 put the squeeze on sb** *informal* to try to persuade someone to do something【非正式】試圖說服某人 **6 your/her/his main squeeze** *AmE informal* someone's BOYFRIEND or GIRLFRIEND【美, 非正式】你/她/他的男[女]朋友

squeeze·box /ˈskwizˌbɑks; ˈskwiːzbɒks/ *n* [C] *informal* an ACCORDION【非正式】手風琴

squeez·er /ˈskwizɚ; ˈskwiːzə/ *n* [C] a small tool for squeezing juice from fruit such as LEMONs 榨汁器

squelch /skwɛltʃ; skweltʃ/ *v* [I] **1** to make a sucking sound by walking in soft wet mud〔在泥沼中走時〕發出咯吱咯吱聲: [**+through/along/up**] *We squelched up the sodden path.* 我們咯吱咯吱地走過浸透水的小路。—see picture on page A19 參見A19頁圖 **2** [T] *AmE* to stop something such as an idea from continuing to develop or spread【美】扼殺, 消除〔念頭等〕: *Such rigid teaching methods only serve to squelch kids' creativity.* 如此僵化的教學方法只會扼殺孩子的創造力。—**squelch** *n* [C]

squelch·y /ˈskwɛltʃɪ; ˈskweltʃi/ *adj* squelchy mud or ground is soft and wet and makes a sucking noise when you walk on it〔泥濘或地面〕軟濕的, 踩上去發出咯吱咯吱聲的

squib /skwɪb; skwɪb/ *n* [C] **1** a small exploding FIREWORK 小爆竹, 甩砲 **2** *literary* a short amusing piece of writing that attacks someone【文】諷刺短文 —see also 另見 **damp squib** (DAMP¹ (2))

squid /skwɪd; skwɪd/ *plural* **squid** *or* **squids** *n* [C] a sea creature with a long body and ten arms around its mouth 槍烏賊, 魷魚

squidg·y /ˈskwɪdʒɪ; ˈskwɪdʒi/ *adj BrE* soft and wet, like thick mud【英】〔像泥一樣〕軟而濕的

squif·fy /ˈskwɪfɪ; ˈskwɪfi/ *adj BrE old-fashioned* slightly drunk【英, 過時】微醉的

squig·gle /ˈskwɪgl̩; ˈskwɪgəl/ *n* [C] a short irregular line in writing or drawing that curls and twists 扭曲、不規則的短線: *I can't read the signature, it's just a squiggle.* 我看不懂這個簽名, 它只是一條歪歪扭扭的線。—**squiggly** *adj*: *squiggly lines* 彎曲的短線

squint¹ /skwɪnt; skwɪnt/ *v* [I] **1** to look at something with your eyes partly closed in order to see better 眯着眼睛看: *Anna squinted in the sudden bright sunlight.* 太陽光突然變強, 安娜眯起眼睛看。| [**+at**] *Squinting at the target, Mark took careful aim.* 馬克眯着眼睛, 認真瞄準靶子。**2** [not in progressive 不用進行式] to have a squint 患斜視(症)

S

squint² *n* [singular] **1** a condition of your eye muscles that makes each eye look in a different direction 斜視, 斜視症 **2 have/take a squint at sth** *informal* to look at something【非正式】看一眼某物; 瞟一眼某物

squire /skwaır; skwaıə/ *n* [C] **1** the man who in the past owned most of the land around a country village in England〔從前英國鄉村的〕大地主, 鄉紳 **2** a young man in the Middle Ages who learned how to be a KNIGHT[1] (1) by serving one〔中世紀〕騎士的隨從 **3** *BrE spoken* used by some men to address a man when they do not know his name【英口】先生〔某些男人對其不知道姓名的男性的稱呼〕

squirm /skwɝm; skwɜːm/ *v* [I] **1** to twist your body from side to side because you are uncomfortable or nervous〔因不舒服或緊張而〕扭動身體: *Stop squirming so I can finish doing your hair!* 別扭來扭去, 讓我把你的頭髮梳好! **2** to feel very embarrassed or ashamed 感到尷尬[慚愧]: **[+with]** *Greg turned red, squirming with guilt.* 格雷格的臉變紅了, 內疚得侷促不安。—**squirm** *n* [singular]

squir·rel¹ /ˋskwɝəl; ˈskwırəl/ *n* [C] a small animal with a long furry tail that climbs trees and eats nuts 松鼠

squirrel² *v* [T+away] *especially AmE* to keep something in a safe place to use later【尤美】儲存, 貯藏〔供以後使用〕

squir·rel·y /ˋskwɝəlı; ˈskwırəli/ *adj AmE informal* unable to stay still; RESTLESS【美, 非正式】靜不下來的; 焦躁不安的

squirt¹ /skwɝt; skwɜːt/ *v* **1** [I,T] if you squirt liquid or if it squirts, it is forced out of a narrow hole in a thin fast stream 使噴出; 射出; 噴射: *Water's squirting from about five different leaks.* 水正從五個不同的裂縫中噴出。| **squirt sth** *Squirt some oil in the lock.* 往鎖裡面噴些油。**2** [T] to hit or cover someone or something with a thin fast stream of liquid 向…噴射〔液體〕: **squirt sb/sth with sth** *Mom! Chad's squirting me with the hose!* 媽! 查德用水管噴我!

squirt² *n* [C] **1** a fast thin stream of liquid 噴射的液體, 細的噴流 —see picture on page A7 參見 A7 頁圖 **2 little squirt** *spoken* an insulting word for a short person, especially someone who is annoying you【口】小矮子, 小東西〔侮辱性用語〕: *You're just an ignorant little squirt.* 你只不過是個無知的小矮子!

squirt gun /ˋ· ·/ *n* [C] *AmE* a WATER PISTOL【美】玩具水槍

squish /skwıʃ; skwıʃ/ *v* **1** [I always+adv/prep] to make a soft sucking sound by moving in or through something soft and wet like mud 發出咯吱聲 —see picture on page A19 參見 A19 頁圖 **2** [I,T] *AmE informal* to SQUASH[1] something, or to become squashed【美, 非正式】(被) 擠扁; (被) 壓碎

squish·y /ˋskwıʃı; ˈskwıʃi/ *adj* soft and wet or full of liquid 濕軟的: *squishy mud* 濕軟的爛泥 —**squishiness** *n* [U]

Sr *BrE*【英】, **Sr.** *AmE*【美】**1** [only after noun 僅用於名詞後] the written abbreviation of 縮寫= SENIOR 老, 大: *Douglas Fairbanks, Sr.* 老道格拉斯·費爾班克斯 **2** [only before noun 僅用於名詞前] the written abbreviation of 縮寫= SEÑOR 先生: *Sr Lopez* 洛佩斯先生 **3** the written abbreviation of 縮寫= Sister, used in front of the name of a NUN 修女〔用於名字前〕: *Sr Bernadette* 貝爾娜德特修女 **4** *BrE* the written abbreviation of 縮寫= Sister, used in front of the name of a nurse【英】護士長〔用於名字前〕

SS /ˋɛs ɛs; ˈes es/ [only before noun 僅用於名詞前] the abbreviation of 縮寫= STEAMSHIP

3 **ssh** /ʃ; ʃ/ *interjection* used to ask for silence or less noise 噓〔用於要求別人保持安靜〕: *Ssh! You'll wake everybody up.* 噓! 你會把大家都吵醒的。

St *BrE*【英】also 又作 **St. 1** [only after noun or adjective 僅用於名詞或形容詞後] the written abbreviation of 縮寫= street 大街: *Wall St.* 華爾街 | *Church St* 教堂街 **2** the written abbreviation of 縮寫= SAINT 聖…: *St Luke's Gospel* (聖) 路加福音 **3 st** the written abbreviation of 縮寫= STONE[1] (6) 呫, 英石

-st /st; st/ *suffix* **1** forms written ORDINAL numbers with 1〔加在數字 1 後構成序數詞〕: *the 1st* (=first) *prize* 一等獎 | *my 21st birthday* 我的 21 歲生日 **2** *old use or biblical* another form of the suffix -EST (2)【舊或聖經】〔後綴 -est (2) 的另一種形式〕: *thou dost* (=you do) 你做

stab¹ /stæb; stæb/ *v* **stabbed, stabbing 1** [T] to push a knife into someone or something〔用刀〕刺, 戳, 捅: **stab sb to death** *Smith was found stabbed to death in a burning car.* 在一輛燃燒着的汽車中發現史密斯被人刺死了。| **stab sb in the heart/arm etc** *Luca stabbed her in the thigh with a breadknife.* 盧卡用一把麵包刀刺她的大腿。**2** [I,T] to make quick pushing movements with your finger or something pointed; JAB[1]〔用手指或尖的東西〕戳 **3 stab sb in the back** to do something that harms someone who likes and trusts you; BETRAY 背後中傷某人; 背叛某人 —see also 另見 STABBING

stab² *n* [C] **1** an act of stabbing or trying to stab someone 刺, 戳, 捅: *severe stab wounds* 嚴重的刺傷 | **[+at]** *He made a vicious stab at me with a broken bottle.* 他用破瓶子狠狠地朝我刺過來。**2 a stab of fear/disappointment/pain etc** a sudden sharp feeling of fear etc 一陣恐懼/失望/痛苦等: *A quick stab of excitement ran through him.* 他突然感到一陣興奮。**3 have/make a stab at (doing) sth** *informal* to try to do something【非正式】試圖[嘗試]做某事 **4 a stab in the back** an attack from someone you thought was a friend 背後中傷; 背叛: *One of them smiles in your face while the other one stabs you in the back.* 他們兩個中一人當面對你友好, 另一個人則在背後向你施放暗箭。

stab·bing¹ /ˋstæbıŋ; ˈstæbıŋ/ *adj* a stabbing pain is sharp and sudden, as if it had been made by a knife〔疼痛〕突然而劇烈的, 如刀刺的: *stabbing headaches* 刀刺般的頭痛

stabbing² *n* [C] a crime in which someone is stabbed 用利器傷人罪

sta·bil·i·ty /stəˋbılətı; stəˈbılǝti/ *n* [U] **1** the condition of being strong, steady and not changing 穩固, 穩定: **[+of]** *the stability of the dollar* 美元的穩固 | *a long period of political stability* 長期的政治穩定 **2** *technical* the ability of a substance to stay in the same state【術語】〔物質的〕穩定性 —opposite 反義詞 INSTABILITY

sta·bil·ize also 又作 **-ise** *BrE*【英】/ˋstebḷˌaız; ˈsteıbǝlaız/ *v* [I,T] to become firm, steady or unchanging, or to make something firm or steady (使) 穩固; (使) 穩定: *The patient's condition has now stabilized.* 病人的情況已經穩定下來了。—**stabilization** /ˌstebələˋzeʃən; ˌsteıbǝlaıˈzeıʃən/ *n* [U]

sta·bil·iz·er also 又作 **-iser** *BrE*【英】/ˋstebəˌlaızɚ; ˈsteıbǝlaızə/ *n* [C] **1** a chemical that helps something such as a food to stay in the same state〔食物等的〕穩定劑 **2** a piece of equipment that helps make something such as an aircraft, ship, or bicycle steady〔飛機、輪船或自行車的〕穩定器, 平衡器

sta·ble¹ /ˋstebḷ; ˈsteıbəl/ *adj* **1** steady and not likely to move or change 穩定的; 安定的; 不變的: *Be careful, that ladder isn't stable.* 小心, 那把梯子不穩。| *a stable marriage* 穩定的婚姻 | *a politically stable country* 政局穩定的國家 **2** calm, reasonable, and not easy to upset 平靜的; 穩重的: *Norman's a bit neurotic, but his wife's a very stable person.* 諾曼有點神經質, 但他的妻子是很穩重的人。**3** *technical* a stable substance tends to stay in the same chemical or ATOMIC state【術語】〔物質〕穩定的, 不易分解[變化]的 —opposite 反義詞 UNSTABLE —see also 另見 STABILITY —**stably** *adv* 3

stable² *n* [C] **1** *BrE* a building where horses are kept【英】馬廄, 馬房 **2** *AmE* a building where horses, cattle etc are kept【美】牲口棚 **3 a)** a group of racing horses that has one owner or trainer〔一位馬主或馴馬師所擁有的〕一羣賽馬 **b)** a group of people working for the same company or with the same trainer〔在同一家公

S

司工作或受同一教練訓練的〕一羣人: *actors from the same Hollywood stable* 同在一家荷里活公司旗下的演員 **4 shut/close the stable door after the horse has bolted** to try to prevent something when it is too late, and harm has already been done 亡羊補牢, 賊去關門

stable³ *v* [T] to put or keep a horse in a stable 置〔馬〕於馬房

sta·ble·boy /ˈstebḷˌbɔɪ; ˈsteɪbəlbɔɪ/ also 又作 **stable lad** /ˈ·· ·/ *BrE*【英】, **stableman** /ˈstebḷˌmæn; ˈsteɪbəlmæn/ *AmE*【美】*n* [C] a man or boy who works in a stable and looks after horses〔在馬房照顧馬匹的〕馬夫; 馬童

sta·ble·mate /ˈstebḷˌmet; ˈsteɪbəlmeɪt/ *n* [C] something or someone that is like other things or people 類似的事物: *ambient music and its stablemate techno* 氛圍音樂及與它相似的高技術音樂

sta·bles /ˈstebḷz; ˈsteɪbəlz/ *n* [plural] a stable or a group of stables 馬廐; 馬房

sta·bling /ˈsteblɪŋ; ˈsteɪblɪŋ/ *n* [U] space for horses to be stabled 拴馬處, 拴馬位; 馬廐

stac·cat·o /stəˋkɑto; stəˈkɑːtəʊ/ *adv* when music is played staccato the notes are cut short and do not flow smoothly〔音樂〕斷斷續續地; 不連貫地 —compare 比較 LEGATO —**staccato** *adj*

stack¹ /stæk; stæk/ *n* [C] **1** a neat pile of things one on top of the other〔疊放整齊的〕一疊, 一堆, 一摞: **[+of]** *a stack of papers* 一疊文件 | *stacks of dishes waiting to be washed* 一摞摞待洗的盤碟 **2** a large pile of grain, grass etc that is stored outside〔儲放於戶外的〕糧垛; 草堆 —see also 另見 HAYSTACK **3 a stack of/stacks of** *informal especially BrE* a large amount【非正式, 尤英】大量, 大批, 許多: *Mr. Truman has stacks of money.* 杜魯門先生有很多很多的錢。**4** a tall chimney 高大的煙囱 **5 the stacks** a part of a library where books are stored close together〔圖書館的〕書庫; 藏書書架 **6** a temporary store of information on a computer〔電腦臨時儲存資料的〕存貯棧; 棧式存貯 —see also 另見 **blow your top/stack** (BLOW¹ (20))

stack² *v* **1** also 又作 **stack up** [I,T] to form a neat pile or make things into a neat pile 整齊地堆起; (使) 成堆; 摞起: *These chairs are designed to stack easily.* 這些椅子設計得易於疊放在一起。| **stack sth** *Stack the books up against the wall.* 把圖書靠牆堆起來。| *a stacking hi-fi system* 組合式高保真音響系統 **2** [T usually passive 一般用被動態] to put piles of things on a place or in a place 把…堆放在〔某處〕; 堆滿: **[+with]** *The floor was stacked with boxes.* 地板上堆滿了箱子。**3 have the odds stacked against you** *informal* to be at a great disadvantage【非正式】處於非常不利的地位, 處於困境: *The home team can't win; the odds are stacked against them.* 主隊贏不了啦, 形勢對他們極為不利。**4 stack the cards** *BrE*【英】, **stack the deck** *AmE*【美】*informal* to arrange cards dishonestly in a game【非正式】洗牌作弊 **5** also 又作 **stack up** [I,T] if aircraft stack or are stacked around an airport, they are made to fly around it until they can land (使) 飛機在機場上空作定高分層盤旋〔等待着陸〕

stack up *phr v* [I] *informal* to have a particular appearance when compared with something else【非正式】比較, 比高低: **[+against]** *How does their product stack up against our own?* 他們的產品跟我們的產品相比怎麼樣?

stacked /stækt; stækt/ *adj informal* an offensive word meaning having large breasts【非正式】胸部豐滿的〔冒犯語〕

stack sys·tem /ˈ· ˌ··/ *n* [C] an arrangement of equipment for playing music, in which one piece stands on top of another 組合音響

stack-up /ˈ· ·/ *n* [C] a situation in which several aircraft are flying around an airport waiting to land〔數架飛機在機場上空等候着陸時的〕定高分層盤旋

sta·di·um /ˈstedɪəm; ˈsteɪdiəm/ *n plural* **stadiums** or **stadia** /-dɪə; -diə/ [C] a building for sports, consisting of a field surrounded by rows of seats〔有多層看台的〕體育場, 運動場: *a baseball stadium* 棒球場

staff¹ /stæf; stɑːf/ *n*

1 ►WORKERS 工作人員◄ **a)** [C, also+plural verb *BrE* 英] the people who work for an organization, especially a school or business〔尤指學校或公司的〕全體職員, 員工: *The school's staff is excellent.* 這所學校的教職員是優秀的。| *We now employ a staff of 25.* 我們現在雇了25名員工。| **member of staff** *complaints by members of staff about sick pay* 雇員關於病假工資的投訴 | **on the staff** (=being a member of staff) 成為一名職員 *It's good to have you on the staff.* 很高興你成為我們的職員。**b)** [plural] the members of such a group 職員, 人員: *Andrea's in charge of about 20 staff.* 安德烈婭負責管理約20名員工。| *a special car park for senior staff* 高級雇員專用的停車場

2 ►STICK 棍, 棒◄ [C] *plural* **staves** /stevz; steɪvz/ **a)** *old use* a long thick stick to help you walk【舊】手杖, 拐杖 **b)** a long thick stick that an official holds in some ceremonies 權杖

3 ►FLAG 旗◄ [C] a pole for flying a flag on; FLAGPOLE 旗杆

4 ►MUSIC 音樂◄ [C] the set of five lines that music is written on; STAVE¹ (1) 五線譜

5 the staff of life *literary* a basic food, especially bread【文】主食〔尤指麵包〕—see also 另見 GENERAL STAFF, GROUND STAFF

staff² *v* [T usually passive 一般用被動態] to provide the workers for an organization 為…配備職員: *The refuge is staffed mainly by volunteers.* 在避難所工作的主要是志願人員。—see also 另見 OVERSTAFFED, UNDERSTAFFED —**staffing** *n* [U]: *staffing levels* 人員配備水平

staff nurse /ˈ· ˌ·/ *n* [C] a British hospital nurse whose rank is just below a sister's (SISTER (2))〔英國〕醫院護士〔地位僅次於護士長〕

staff of·fi·cer /ˈ· ˌ···/ *n* [C] an officer who helps a military commander of a higher rank 參謀

staff ser·geant /ˈ· ˌ··/ *n* [C,U] a lower rank in the army or the US Air Force or Marines, or someone who has this rank〔美國空軍的〕中士;〔海軍陸戰隊的〕上士 —see table on page C6 參見 C6 頁附錄

stag /stæg; stæg/ *n* [C] **1** a fully grown male DEER 成年雄鹿, 牡鹿 **2** *BrE* someone who buys shares (SHARE² (5)) in a new company, hoping to sell them quickly and make a profit【英】認購新股並迅速拋出獲利者, 炒新股者 **3 go stag** *AmE informal* if a man goes stag he goes to a party without a woman【美, 非正式】〔指男子〕不帶女伴參加社交聚會 —see also 另見 STAG NIGHT, STAG PARTY

stage¹ /stedʒ; steɪdʒ/ *n*

1 ►TIME/STATE 時間/狀態◄ [C] a particular time or state that something reaches as it grows or develops 時期; 階段: *The plan is still in its early stages.* 這項計劃仍處於初期階段。| *the different stages of a child's development* 孩子成長的不同階段 | **at this stage** *It would be unwise to comment at this stage of the negotiations.* 在談判的這個階段發表評論是不明智的。| **stage by stage** (=gradually) 逐步地, 逐漸地 | **at a later stage** *The design may well be modified at a later stage.* 這個設計以後很可能要修改。—compare 比較 PHASE¹ (1), STEP¹ (4)

2 ►THEATRE 戲院◄ [C] the raised floor in a theatre on which plays are performed 舞台: **on stage** *She is on stage for most of the play.* 在這部戲裡, 大部分時間她都出場。| **stage left/right** (=from the left or right side of the stage) 從舞台的左側/右側 —see picture at 參見 THEATRE 圖

3 ►ACTING 表演◄ **the stage** acting as a profession 舞台生涯; 戲劇表演: **go on the stage** (=become an actor) 當演員

4 take centre stage/be at the centre of the stage to have everyone's attention, or to be very important 成為大家注意的中心; 非常重要: *Sally just loves to take center stage.* 莎莉就是喜歡吸引大家的注意。| *The hostage question has returned to the centre of the stage.* 人質問題再次成為人們關注的焦點。

5 ►PLACE 地方◄ [singular] a place where something important happens〔重大事件發生的〕地點, 場所: *Geneva has been the stage for many such conferences.* 日內瓦已成為眾多此類會議的舉辦地點。| *the European political stage* 歐洲政治舞台

6 set the stage for to prepare for something or make something possible 為…做準備; 使…成為可能: *Will this agreement merely set the stage for another war?* 這個協議是否只會釀成另一場戰爭?

7 he's/she's going through a stage *informal* used to say that someone young will soon stop behaving badly or strangely【非正式】他/她正在經歷成長階段〔指某些年輕人過了這個階段後, 很快就會改變不良或者奇怪的行為〕—see also 另見 LANDING STAGE

stage² *v* [T] to organize an event that people will come to see, or that you hope many people will notice 舉辦; 舉行: *We hope to stage four plays this season.* 我們希望在本季上演四部話劇。| *They'll be staging a Hockney exhibition.* 他們將舉辦一場霍克納畫展。| **stage a strike/demonstration/sit-in etc** *School teachers are staging a protest against the cuts.* 教師正在為反對減薪而舉行抗議活動。

stage·coach /ˋstedʒˏkotʃ; ˈsteɪdʒkəʊtʃ/ *n* [C] a closed vehicle pulled by horses that in former times carried passengers who paid to go to a particular place〔舊時的〕驛站馬車

stage di·rec·tion /ˈ· ·ˌ··/ *n* [C] a written instruction to an actor to do something in a play 舞台指示

stage door /ˌ· ˈ·◂/ *n* [C] the side or back door in a theatre, used by actors and theatre workers〔供演員及舞台工作人員使用的〕劇院側門[後門]

stage fright /ˈ· ·/ *n* [U] nervousness felt by someone who is going to perform in front of a lot of people 怯場

stage·hand /ˋstedʒˏhænd; ˈsteɪdʒhænd/ *n* [C] someone who works on a theatre stage, getting it ready for a play or for the next part of a play 舞台工作人員

stage-man·age /ˈ· ˌ··/ *v* [T] *informal* to organize a public event, such as a meeting, in a way that will give you the result that you want【非正式】對…進行幕後策劃[安排]: *The press conference was cleverly stage-managed.* 記者招待會安排得很巧妙。

stage man·ag·er /ˈ· ˌ···/ *n* [C] someone in charge of a theatre stage during a performance 舞台監督

stage name /ˈ· ·/ *n* [C] a name used by an actor instead of his or her real name〔演員的〕藝名

stage-struck /ˋstedʒˏstrʌk; ˈsteɪdʒstrʌk/ *adj* loving to see plays, or wanting very much to become an actor 愛看戲劇的; 渴望當演員的

stage whis·per /ˌ· ˈ··/ *n* [C] **1** an actor's loud WHISPER that other actors on the stage seem not to hear 舞台上的低聲旁白 **2** a loud WHISPER that is intended to be heard by everyone 有意使大家都能聽見的耳語: *"What's going on?" I demanded in a stage whisper.* "發生了甚麼事?"我用大家都能聽見的低聲問道。

stag·y /ˋstedʒɪ; ˈsteɪdʒi/ *adj* another spelling of STAGY stagy 的另一種拼法

stag·fla·tion /ˌstægˋfleʃən; stægˈfleɪʃən/ *n* [U] an economic condition in which there is INFLATION (=a continuing rise in prices) but many people do not have jobs and businesses are not doing well 停滯性通貨膨脹, 滯脹〔指出現通貨膨脹, 但許多人失業、商業蕭條的一種經濟狀況〕

stag·ger¹ /ˋstægɚ; ˈstægə/ *v* **1** [I always+adv/prep] to walk or move unsteadily, almost falling over 蹣跚; 搖搖晃晃地走: **[+away/into/down etc]** *The old man staggered drunkenly to his feet.* 老漢醉醺醺地搖晃着站了起來。| *Marcus came staggering through the door with his groceries.* 馬庫斯拿着食品雜貨搖搖晃晃地走進門。—see picture on page A24 參見 A24 頁圖 **2** [T usually passive 一般用被動態] to make someone feel very surprised or shocked 使〔某人〕驚愕[震驚]: *What staggered us was the sheer size of her salary.* 令我們感到驚愕的是她的巨額工資。**3** [T] to arrange people's working hours, holidays etc so that they do not all begin and end at the same time 錯開〔工作時間、假期等〕**4** [T] to start a race with each runner at a different place on a curved track 梯形起跑〔指環形跑道上運動員在不同的位置起跑〕

stagger² *n* [C usually singular 一般用單數] an unsteady movement of someone who is having difficulty in walking 蹣跚; 搖晃不穩的腳步

stag·gered /ˋstægɚd; ˈstægəd/ *adj* [not before noun 不用於名詞前] very surprised at something that has happened to you, or some news that you have heard that is hard to believe 非常吃驚的; 難以置信的: **[+by/at]** *I was staggered by the size of the phone bill.* 電話賬單上的金額使我感到非常吃驚。| **staggered to hear/see/find etc** *We were staggered to find that we were not entitled to any money.* 我們非常吃驚地發現我們無權得到一分錢。

stag·ger·ing /ˋstægərɪŋ; ˈstægərɪŋ/ *adj* very surprising, shocking, and almost unbelievable 令人吃驚[震驚]的; 令人難以置信的: *The cost was a staggering $10 million.* 費用竟高達 1000 萬美元。—**staggeringly** *adv*: *a staggeringly high phone bill* 費用高得驚人的電話賬單

stag·ing /ˋstedʒɪŋ; ˈsteɪdʒɪŋ/ *n* **1** [C,U] the activity or art of performing a play〔戲劇的〕上演, 演出; 演技: *a modern-dress staging of 'Hamlet'* 穿現代服裝演出的《哈姆雷特》**2** [U] movable boards and frames for standing on 腳手架; 台架, 棚架

staging a·re·a /ˈ·· ˌ···/ *n* [C] a place where soldiers meet and where military equipment is gathered before it is moved to another place〔軍隊的〕集結待命地區

staging post /ˈ·· ·/ *n* [C] a place where a stop is regularly made on a long journey〔長途旅行中的〕中途站: *Bahrain is a staging post on the flight from Britain to Australia.* 巴林是從英國飛往澳大利亞的中途站。—compare 比較 STOPOVER

stag·nant /ˋstægnənt; ˈstægnənt/ *adj* **1** stagnant water or air does not move or flow and often smells bad〔水或空氣〕不流動的, 靜止的; 有臭味的: *a stagnant pond* 一潭死水 **2** not changing, developing, or making progress; inactive 不發展的, 停滯(不前)的; 不活躍的: *Industrial output has remained stagnant.* 工業生產一直停滯不前。—**stagnancy** *n* [U] —**stagnantly** *adv*

stag·nate /ˋstægnet; stægˈneɪt/ *v* [I] to stop developing or making progress 停滯; 不發展: *a stagnating economy* 停滯不前的經濟 | *I don't want to spend the rest of my life stagnating in that office.* 我不想一輩子在那間辦公室裡毫無前途地幹下去。—**stagnation** /stægˋneʃən; stægˈneɪʃən/ *n* [U]: *economic stagnation* 經濟停滯

stag night /ˈ· ·/ *n* [C] *BrE* the night before a man's wedding, which he spends with his male friends, drinking or having a party【英】單身漢之夜〔指男子結婚前一個晚上, 和男性朋友共同度過這個夜晚, 一起喝酒或舉行派對〕

stag par·ty /ˈ· ˌ··/ *n* [C] a party for men only, especially on the night before a man's wedding〔尤指男子結婚前一晚舉辦的〕只限男人參加的社交聚會

stag·y, stagey /ˋstedʒɪ; ˈsteɪdʒi/ *adj* behaviour that is stagy is not natural and is like the way an actor behaves on a stage〔行為等〕不自然的; 演戲似的; 做作的: *a very stagy manner* 非常做作的舉止 —**stagily** *adv*

staid /sted; steɪd/ *adj* serious, old-fashioned, and boring in the way you live, dress, or work 嚴肅呆板的; 古板的; 枯燥的: *a staid old bachelor* 一個嚴肅呆板的老單身漢 | *staid attitudes* 古板的態度 —**staidly** *adv* —**staidness** *n* [U]

stain¹ /sten; steɪn/ *v* **1** [I,T] to accidentally make a mark on something, especially one that cannot be removed, or to be marked in this way 染污, 沾污; 留下難以清除的污跡: **[+with]** *teeth stained with nicotine from years of smoking* 因多年抽煙而被尼古丁熏黃的牙齒 | *Pale carpets stain too easily.* 淺色的地毯太容易沾污。—see picture on page A18 參見 A18 頁圖 **2** [T] to change the

S

colour of something, especially something made of wood, by using a special chemical or DYE 給〔某物, 尤指木製品〕染色[着色] **3 stain sb's name/honour/reputation etc** *literary* to damage the good opinion that people have about someone【文】玷污某人的名譽

stain² *n* **1** [C] a mark that is difficult to remove, especially one made by a liquid such as blood, coffee, or ink〔尤指液體做成的〕污跡, 污點: *There's a big stain on your tie.* 你的領帶上有一大塊污跡。| **blood/ink/wine etc stain** *How do you get wine stains out of a tablecloth?* 怎樣把桌布上的葡萄酒污跡洗掉? **2** [C,U] a chemical for darkening something, especially wood〔尤指木材的〕着色劑, 染色劑 **3 a stain on sb's character/reputation etc** something that makes people think that someone has done something wrong or illegal 某人性格/名聲等上的污點

stained glass /,· '·◂/ *n* [U] glass of different colours used for making pictures and patterns in windows, especially in a church〔尤指教堂窗戶上的〕彩色玻璃

stain·less /ˋstenlıs; 'steınləs/ *adj literary* without any sign of illegal or immoral behaviour【文】〔行為〕無污點的; 清白的; 無瑕疵的: *a lady of beauty, rank and stainless reputation* 一位有地位的清白無瑕的美麗女士

stainless steel /,·· '·/ *n* [U] a type of steel that does not RUST 不鏽鋼: *stainless steel cutlery* 不鏽鋼餐具

stair /stɛr; steə/ *n* **1 stairs** [plural] a set of steps built for going from one level of a building to another〔樓層之間的〕樓梯: **up/down the stairs** *Jerry ran up the stairs.* 傑里跑上樓梯。| **the top/head of the stairs** *Kate was standing at the top of the stairs.* 凱特站在樓梯的最上面。| **the foot of the stairs** (=the bottom) 樓梯下端 | **a flight of stairs** (=between two floors of a building)〔建築物兩層之間的〕一段樓梯 *The attic's up five flights of stairs.* 閣樓在第五層。—see also 另見 DOWNSTAIRS, UPSTAIRS² —see picture on page A4 參見 A4 頁圖 **2** [C] one of the steps in a set of stairs 樓梯的一級: *Lucy sat down on the bottom stair.* 露西坐在樓梯最下面的一級上。**3** [C] *especially literary* a set of stairs【尤文】階梯: *a steep winding stair to the tower* 通向塔樓陡峭而迴旋的階梯 **4 below stairs** *old-fashioned BrE* in the servants' part of a large house, in the past【過時, 英】〔舊時〕在傭人的住處

stair·case /ˋstɛr,kes; 'steəkeıs/ *n* [C] a set of stairs inside a building with its supports and the side parts that you hold on to〔包括扶手、欄杆的〕樓梯

stair·way /ˋstɛr,we; 'steəweı/ *n* [C] a staircase, especially a large or impressive one〔尤指大的或氣派的〕樓梯

stair·well /ˋstɛr,wɛl; 'steəwel/ *n* [C] the space going up through all the floors of a building, where the stairs go up 樓梯井

stake¹ /stek; steık/ *n*

1 ►SHARP POST 尖樁◄ [C] a pointed piece of wood, metal etc that is pushed into the ground to hold a rope, mark a particular place etc〔尖狀木頭或金屬等的〕樁; 柱

2 the stake a post to which a person was tied in former times to be killed by being burnt〔舊時捆綁並處死犯人的〕火刑柱: **burn sb at the stake** *Witches were often burnt at the stake.* 巫婆經常被綁在火刑柱上燒死。

3 have a stake in to have an important part or share in a business, plan etc so that you will gain if it succeeds 在〔公司、計劃等中〕有股份; 與…有利害關係: *a 33% stake in the business* 該公司33% 的股份 | *I just don't feel I have a stake in the country's future.* 我就是感覺不到我與國家的未來休戚相關。

4 be at stake if something that you value very much is at stake, you will lose it if a plan or action is not successful 瀕於險境; 處於成敗關頭: *If we lose the contract, hundreds of jobs are at stake.* 我們如果失去這項合同, 幾百人將瀕於失業的境地。

5 (be prepared to) go to the stake for/over sth to take great risks to protect or defend an idea, belief etc (準備) 為保護[捍衛]某事物冒巨大風險: *That's my opinion, but I wouldn't go to the stake for it.* 那是我的觀點, 但我不會冒大險去捍衛它。

6 ►RISK 風險◄ [C usually singular 一般用單數] money risked on the result of something, especially a horse race; BET² (1)〔尤指賽馬的〕賭注; 賭金

7 stakes [plural] money that people risk on the result of a game, race etc, all of which is taken by the winner〔遊戲、比賽等的〕賭金; 賭注: *We're playing for very high stakes here.* 我們這裡下的賭注都很大。

8 play for high stakes a) to risk a lot of money in a game〔在比賽中〕下大賭注 **b)** to be in a situation where you gain or lose a lot 處於利害攸關的境地

9 the popularity/fashion etc stakes a situation that can be considered as if it were a competition 聲望/時尚大賽: *Ben wouldn't score very highly in the popularity stakes.* 本的聲望不會很高。

10 pull up stakes *AmE*【美】, **up stakes** *BrE*【英】*informal* to leave your job or home【非正式】辭職; 離家; 搬家: *We're going to pull up stakes and move to Montana.* 我們打算把家搬到蒙大拿州去。

stake² *v* [T] **1** to risk money on a race or competition 把〔錢〕押下打賭: *Hargreave staked his whole fortune on one card game.* 哈格雷夫把他的全部財產都押在一場紙牌戲上。**2** to risk losing something that is valuable or important to you, if a plan or action is not successful 拿…去冒險: **stake sth on sb/sth** *The President is staking his reputation on these trade talks.* 總統把自己的聲譽都押在這些貿易談判上。| *I've staked all my hopes on you.* 我把我所有的希望都寄託在你身上了。**3** also 又作 **stake up** to fasten or strengthen something with stakes 用樁支撐; 把…繫在柱上: *Those young trees will have to be staked.* 那些小樹得用樁子支撐起來。**4** also 又作 **stake off** to mark or enclose an area of ground with stakes 用標樁標出[圍起]〔某一地區〕: *The muddiest corner of the field has been staked off.* 這塊地最泥濘的一角已用標樁圍了起來。**5 stake (out) a claim** to say publicly that you think you have a right to have or own something 公開聲明對…擁有所有權: *Joe staked his claim to the land where he found the gold.* 喬聲明擁有他發現黃金的那塊土地。

stake sth ↔ **out** *phr v* [T] *informal* to watch a place secretly and continuously【非正式】持續監視〔某處〕: *The vice squad have been staking out the club for weeks.* 警察緝捕隊已經對這個俱樂部監視了幾個星期。—**stake-out** *n* [C]

stake·hold·er /ˋstek,holdɚ; 'steık,həʊldə/ *n* [C] **1** someone chosen to hold the money that is risked by people on a race, competition etc and to give all of it to the winner 賭金保管人 **2** someone, usually a lawyer, who takes charge of a property during a quarrel or a sale〔爭執或銷售時的〕財產保管人〔常指律師〕

stal·ac·tite /stəˋlæktaıt; 'stæləktaıt/ *n* [C] a sharp pointed object hanging down from the roof of a CAVE, which is formed gradually by water that contains minerals as it drops slowly from the roof〔鐘乳洞中的〕鐘乳石, 石鐘乳

stal·ag·mite /stəˋlægmaıt; 'stæləgmaıt/ *n* [C] a sharp pointed object coming up from the floor of a CAVE, formed by drops from a stalactite〔鐘乳洞中的〕石筍

stale¹ /stel; steıl/ *adj* **1** bread or cake that is stale is no longer fresh or good to eat〔麵包、蛋糕〕不新鮮的; 變味的: **go stale** *This loaf has gone stale.* 這條麵包變味了。**2** air that is stale is not fresh or pleasant〔空氣〕不新鮮的; 污濁的 **3** news or jokes that are stale are no longer interesting or exciting〔新聞、笑話〕不再有趣的, 沒有新意的, 乏味的: *the same stale old jokes we've all heard before* 我們以前都曾聽過的那些老掉牙的笑話 **4** someone who is stale has no new ideas, interest, or energy, because they have been doing the same thing for too long〔因長期從事同一工作而〕疲沓的, 沒有生氣的: **feel/get/go stale** *I'm getting stale in this job – I need a change.*

這個工作我已經幹膩了, 需要換一換工作。—**staleness** *n* [U]

stale[2] *v* [I] *formal* to become less interesting or exciting【正式】變得疲沓[不再有趣]

stale·mate /ˋstelˏmet; ˈsteɪlmeɪt/ *n* [C,U] **1** a situation in which it seems impossible to settle an argument or disagreement, and neither side can get an advantage; DEADLOCK 僵局; 僵持: *The discussions with the miners' union ended in stalemate.* 同礦工工會的談判以陷入僵局告終。**2** a position in CHESS in which neither player can win〔國際象棋的〕和棋 —**stalemate** *v* [T]

stalk[1] /stɔk; stɔːk/ *n* [C] **1** a long narrow part of a plant that supports leaves, fruits, or flowers; stem〔植物的〕莖; 柄; 梗: *celery stalks* 芹菜梗 **2** a thin upright object 柄狀物: *a microphone on a short stalk* 短柄麥克風 **3 eyes out on stalks** *BrE informal* if your eyes are out on stalks you are surprised or shocked【英, 非正式】吃驚的, 震驚的

stalk[2] *v* **1** [T] to follow a person or animal quietly in order to catch or kill them〔為捉拿或殺死某人或某動物而〕悄悄地跟蹤; 潛近: *a tiger stalking its prey* 悄悄跟蹤獵物的老虎 | *We know the rapist stalks his victims at night.* 我們知道那個強姦犯在夜間偷偷地跟蹤受害人。**2** [I always+adv/prep] to walk in a proud or angry way, with long steps〔高傲或氣憤地〕大步地走: **[+out/off/away]** *Yvonne turned and stalked out of the room in disgust.* 伊馮娜轉身氣憤地大踏步走出了房間。

stalk·er /ˋstɔkɚ; ˈstɔːkə/ *n* [C] a criminal who follows a woman over a period of time in order to force her to have sex, or kill her〔伺機強姦或殺害婦女的〕暗中尾隨的罪犯

stalk·ing /ˋstɔkɪŋ; ˈstɔːkɪŋ/ *n* [U] the crime of following someone over a period of time in order to force them to have sex or kill them〔伺機強姦或殺害婦女的〕暗中尾隨犯罪

stalking horse /ˈ‥ ˌ·/ *n* [C] someone or something that hides someone's true purpose, especially a politician who says he wants his leader's job when the real plan is that another, more important politician should get it 掩護者; 障眼物;〔尤指競選中的〕掩護性候選人

S2 **stall[1]** /stɔl; stɔːl/ *n* **1** [C] a table or a small shop with an open front, especially outdoors, where goods are sold〔尤指戶外的〕貨攤, 攤位: *a market stall* 市場攤位 **2** [C] an enclosed area in a building for an animal 畜欄, 畜棚, 廐 **3** [C usually singular 一般用單數] an occasion when an engine stops working〔引擎〕停止運轉, 熄火: *The plane went into a stall.* 這架飛機進入了失速狀態。**4** [C usually plural 一般用複數] a seat in a row of fixed seats for priests and singers in some larger churches〔一些大教堂中的〕牧師[唱詩班]座位: *choir stalls* 唱詩班席位 **5 shower/toilet stall** a small enclosed private area for washing or using the toilet 淋浴間/廁所的小隔間 **6 the stalls** *BrE* the seats on the main level of a theatre or cinema【英】〔戲院、劇院的〕正廳座位: *a good seat in the front row of the stalls* 正廳前排的好座位 —see picture at 參見 THEATRE 圖

stall[2] *v* **1** [I,T] if an engine stalls or you stall it, it stops because there is not enough power or speed to keep it going〔引擎因動力或速度不足而〕停止運轉; 熄火; 使〔引擎〕停止運轉: *Stupid car! It always stalls on hills.* 破車! 總是在山坡上拋錨。| **stall sth** *An inexperienced pilot may easily stall a plane.* 沒有經驗的飛行員很容易會使飛機失速。**2** [I] *informal* to deliberately delay because you are not ready to do something, answer questions etc【非正式】故意拖延: *Quit stalling and answer my question!* 別拖延時間了! 快回答我的問題! **3** [T] *informal* to make someone wait or stop something from happening until you are ready【非正式】搪塞; 拖延: *Maybe we can stall the sale until the prices go up.* 也許我們可以拖到價格上漲時再出售。| *Dad's coming! Stall him for a minute while I hide this.* 爸爸來了! 把他拖住一會兒, 等我把這個藏起來。

stall·hold·er /ˋstɔlˏholdɚ; ˈstɔːlˌhəʊldə/ *n* [C] *BrE* someone who rents and keeps a market stall【英】攤主, 攤販

stal·lion /ˋstæljən; ˈstæljən/ *n* [C] a male horse kept for breeding 種馬 —compare 比較 MARE

stal·wart[1] /ˋstɔlwɚt; ˈstɔːlwət/ *n* [C] someone who works hard and is loyal to a particular organization or set of ideas〔某組織或思想的〕忠實擁護者: *Conservative party stalwarts* 保守黨的忠實擁護者

stalwart[2] *adj* **1 stalwart supporter/ally etc** a very loyal and strong supporter etc 忠實的擁護者/盟友等 **2** *formal* strong in appearance【正式】強壯的; 雄健的 —**stalwartly** *adv*

sta·men /ˋstemən; ˈsteɪmən/ *n* [C] *technical* the male part of a flower that produces POLLEN【術語】〔花的〕雄蕊

stam·i·na /ˋstæmənə; ˈstæmɪnə/ *n* [U] physical or mental strength that lets you continue doing something for a long time without getting tired 持久力, 耐力, 毅力: *You need stamina to be a long-distance runner.* 當長跑運動員需要有耐力。

stam·mer[1] /ˋstæmɚ; ˈstæmə/ *v* [I,T] to speak or say something with a lot of pauses and repeated sounds, either because you have a speech problem, or because you are nervous, excited etc 口吃地說, 結結巴巴地說: *Whenever he was angry he would begin to stammer slightly.* 他一生氣說話就開始有點結巴。—compare 比較 STUTTER[1] (1) —**stammerer** *n* [C] —**stammeringly** *adv*

stammer[2] *n* [C usually singular 一般用單數] a speech problem which makes someone speak with a lot of pauses and repeated sounds 結巴, 口吃: *He's got a bad stammer.* 他口吃非常嚴重。

stamp[1] /stæmp; stæmp/ *n* [C] S2

1 ►MAIL 郵件◄ also 又作 **postage stamp** *formal*【正式】a small piece of paper that you buy and stick onto an envelope or package before posting it 郵票: *a 29-cent stamp* 29 美分的郵票 | **a sheet/book of stamps** (=set of stamps that you buy) 一版/一本郵票

2 ►TOOL 工具◄ a tool for pressing or printing a mark or pattern onto a surface, or the mark made by this tool 印章, 圖章; 印記, 戳記: *a date stamp* 日期戳 | *a passport stamp* 護照印

3 the stamp of sth if something has the stamp of a particular quality, it clearly has that quality 具有…的特點[特徵]: **bear the stamp of sth** *The speech bore the stamp of authority.* 這個講話有權威性。

4 ►PAYMENT 支付, 付款◄ *BrE* a small piece of paper that is worth a particular amount of money and is bought and collected for something over a period of time【英】代幣券; 購物券: *television licence stamps* 電視機許可證代金券

5 ►TAX 稅◄ a piece of paper for sticking to some official papers to show that British tax has been paid 印花稅票〔在英國貼在官方文件上證明稅已交訖的票據〕

6 a man/woman of his/her stamp *formal* someone with a particular kind of character【正式】他/她這類人〔指具有某種特徵的人〕: *I wouldn't trust a man of his stamp.* 我不會相信他這種人。

7 an act of stamping, especially with your foot 跺; 跺腳, 頓足: *an angry stamp* 氣憤的跺腳

stamp[2] *v* 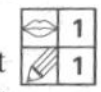

1 ►FOOT 腳◄ [I] to lift your foot off the ground and put it down hard on something 跺腳; 用力踩: **[+on]** *Marta shrieked and started stamping on the cockroach.* 瑪爾塔尖聲大叫, 並開始用力踩那隻蟑螂。| **stamp around** (=walk this way) 跺着腳到處走 *Just because you're mad you don't have to stamp around like that.* 你就算生氣也不必那樣來回跺腳。

2 stamp your foot to lift your foot off the ground and bring it down again very hard because you are angry〔氣憤地〕跺腳; 頓足: *"I will not!" yelled Bert, and* *stamped his foot.* "我不會的!" 伯特大喊道, 並氣憤地跺着腳。

3 stamp your feet to keep lifting each foot and bringing it down again very hard, to make a noise or because you are cold〔為發出聲響或因寒冷而〕跺腳: *She stood at the bus stop stamping her feet to keep warm.* 她站在公共汽車站那裡, 跺着腳以保持暖和。

4 ►MAKE A MARK 留下印記◄ [T] to put a pattern, sign or letters on something using a special tool 在…上面印蓋〔圖案、記號、字等〕: **stamp sth on sth** *Stamp the date on all the letters.* 在所有的信上加蓋日期〔戳〕。| **stamp sth with sth** *Your passport must be stamped with your entry date.* 你的護照上必須蓋上入境日期。

5 stamp on sb/sth *informal* to use force or your authority to stop someone from doing something, or stop something from happening【非正式】鎮壓[壓制]某人/某事: *Roberts stamped on every suggestion we made and then decided to end the project.* 羅伯茨壓制我們提出的每一項建議, 然後決定終止那個計劃。

6 ►AFFECT SB/STH 影響某人/某物◄ [T] to have an important or permanent effect on someone or something 對…有重要[永久性]的影響: **be stamped on sb's memory** *That awful experience is indelibly stamped on my memory.* 那個可怕的經歷給我留下了不可磨滅的記憶。| **stamp sb with sth** *His army years had stamped him with an air of brisk authority.* 多年的軍旅生涯使他養成了一種雷厲風行的作風。

7 stamp sb as sth to show that someone has a particular type of character 表明某人有某種特徵: *The latest scandal clearly stamped her as a liar.* 最近的醜聞清楚地說明她是個說謊者。

S

8 ►MAIL 郵政◄ [T] to stick a stamp onto a letter, parcel etc 在…上貼上郵票

stamp sth ↔ **out** *phr v* [T] **1** to prevent something bad from continuing 消除; 杜絕: *We aim to stamp out poverty in our lifetimes.* 我們的目標是在有生之年消除貧困。**2** to put out a fire by stepping hard on the flames 踏滅〔火〕**3** to make a shape or object by pressing hard on something using a machine or tool〔用機器或工具〕衝壓製成

stamp du·ty /ˈ· ˌ··/ *n* [U] a tax that must be paid in Britain on particular legal documents that have to be officially checked〔英國的〕印花稅

stamped ad·dressed en·ve·lope /ˌ· ·ˌ· ˈ···/ *n* [C] *BrE* an SAE; an envelope with your name, address and a stamp on it, which you send to a person or organization so that they can send you information【英】貼有郵票的回郵信封; SELF-ADDRESSED *AmE*【美】

stam·pede¹ /stæmˋpid; stæmˈpiːd/ *n* [C] **1** a sudden rush of frightened animals〔受驚動物的〕奔逃, 逃竄 **2** a sudden rush by a lot of people, all wanting to do the same thing or go to the same place〔人羣的〕蜂擁; 爭先恐後的行動: *stampede of producers offering her roles in their films* 爭先恐後請她拍影片的製片商 **3** *AmE* an entertainment event at which COWBOYs show their skills, and there are competitions, dancing etc【美】牛仔競技表演 —compare 比較 RODEO

stampede² *v* [I,T] **1** if animals stampede, they suddenly start running together, because they are frightened〔動物因受驚而〕奔逃, 逃竄: *a herd of stampeding buffalo* 一羣驚逃的水牛 **2 be/get stampeded** to be made frightened or worried so that you do something too quickly 因受驚嚇而蜂擁去做某事: **[+into]** *Don't get stampeded into any rash decisions.* 不要因驚慌失措而作出草率的決定。

stamp·ing ground /ˈ·· ˌ·/ *n* [C] **sb's stamping ground** a favourite place where someone often goes 某人常去的地方

stance /stæns; stɑːns/ *n* [C usually singular 一般用單數] **1** an opinion that is stated publicly〔公開表明的〕觀點; 立場; 看法: **[+on]** *an uncompromising stance on nuclear disarmament* 在核裁軍問題上的堅定立場 | **take/adopt a stance** *The President has adopted a tough stance on terrorism.* 總統對恐怖主義採取強硬的立場。**2** a position in which you stand, especially when doing a particular activity〔尤指在做某活動時的〕站姿: *A good relaxed stance is essential when skiing.* 滑雪時良好、放鬆的站姿是非常重要的。—compare 比較 POSTURE¹ (1)

stanch /stæntʃ; stɑːntʃ/ *v* [T] an American spelling of STAUNCH² staunch² 的美式拼法

stan·chion /ˋstæntʃən; ˈstɑːntʃən/ *n* [C] a strong upright bar used to support something 立柱, 支柱

---

1 1

stand¹ /stænd; stænd/ *v past tense and past participle* **stood** /stud; stʊd/

① **BE UPRIGHT** 直立, 站立
② **CAN'T STAND** 無法忍受
③ **ACCEPT/BEAR** 接受/忍受
④ **IN A PARTICULAR STATE/SITUATION** 處於某種狀態/境地
⑤ **CONTINUE/NOT CHANGE** 繼續/不改變
⑥ **NOT MOVED OR USED** 沒有移動或使用過
⑦ **FEELINGS/OPINIONS** 感覺/看法
⑧ **LEVEL/AMOUNT/VALUE/HEIGHT** 水平/數量/價值/高度
⑨ **BE RESPONSIBLE** 負責
⑩ **LAW** 法律
⑪ **BE PROUD/INDEPENDENT** 自豪/獨立
⑫ **COULD STAND** 需要; 應該
⑬ **OTHER MEANINGS** 其他意思

① **BE UPRIGHT** 直立, 站立

1 [I] to support yourself on your feet in an upright position 站立: *It looks like we'll have to stand – there are no seats left.* 看來我們只能站着 —— 沒有座位了。| *Can you see any better from where you're standing?* 在你站的地方是不是看得更清楚? | **stand and do sth** *Diane stood and waved until his car was gone.* 黛安娜站在那兒揮手, 直到他的汽車遠去。| **stand still** (=not move) 站着不動 *Stand still and let me wipe your face.* 站着別動, 讓我給你擦擦臉。| **stand there** (=stand and not do anything) 閒站着 *Don't just stand there – help me!* 不要光站在那裡, 幫幫我! | **stand on your toes/stand on tiptoe** (=support yourself on your toes) 踮着腳站着 *If you stand on tiptoe you can just about reach it.* 如果你踮起腳就差不多能夠着了。—see also 另見 STANDSTILL, **stand up**

2 ►STAND SOMEWHERE TO DO STH 站在某處做某事◄ [I always+adv/prep] to take a particular position or do something in particular while standing 站在某個位置; 站着做某事: *Everybody stand in a circle.* 大家站成一圈。| *You don't need to stand closer to the microphone.* 你不必站得離麥克風很近。| **[+at/beside/by etc]** *Ouida, you stand at the door and greet people.* 維達, 你站在門口迎接大家。| **stand on sth** *We used to get in trouble for standing on the seats.* 我們以前常因站在座位上而惹麻煩。| **stand somewhere doing sth** *They just* *stood there laughing.* 他們只是站在那兒笑。| **stand back/aside** (=step backwards or sideways) 向後站/靠邊站 *Stand back and give her some air!* 向後站，讓她透透氣！| **stand clear (of)** (=move away) 移開；不靠近 *Stand clear of the doors, please.* 請勿靠近門口。

3 ►RISE 起立◄ also 又作 **stand up** [I,T] to rise to an upright position, or to make someone do this（使）起立[站立]: *Suddenly, everyone stood up and cheered.* 突然，大家都站了起來大聲歡呼。| *Please stand and face the judge.* 請起立面對法官。| *Come on, stand up and say something.* 快，站起來，説點甚麼。| **stand sb (up) on sth** *Stand Molly up on a chair so she can see.* 讓莫莉站在椅子上，她就看得見了。

4 ►ON A BASE 在基礎上◄ [I,T always+adv/prep] to stay upright on a base or on an object, or to put something there（使）豎立[屹立]: *Few houses were left standing after the tornado.* 龍捲風過後，剩下沒倒的房子寥寥無幾。| *A green lamp stood on the leather-topped desk.* 皮面的桌子上擺着一盞綠色的枱燈。| *There's a parking lot where the theater once stood.* 以前劇院的位置現在是一個停車場。| **stand sth on/in/over etc** *Can you stand that pole in the corner for now?* 你能不能暫時把那根竿子立在角落裡？

5 stand to attention if soldiers stand to attention, they stand very straight and stiff to show respect〔士兵〕立正

6 stand on your head/hands to support yourself on your head or hands, with your feet in the air 用頭/手支撐倒立

7 stand in line *AmE* to wait to be able to do something until the people ahead of you have done it【美】排隊; queue up (QUEUE²) *BrE*【英】: *Gail has men standing in line wanting to go out with her.* 想跟蓋爾約會的男人排着隊（等候）。

8 stand fast/stand firm/stand your ground to refuse to be forced to move backwards 拒不後退；拒不讓步

② CAN'T STAND 無法忍受

9 [T] *usually spoken* to not like someone or something at all, or think that something is extremely unpleasant【一般口】不能忍受〔某人或某物〕: *I can't stand whiskey.* 威士忌我喝不了。| **can't stand the sight of** *I'm so mad, I can hardly stand the sight of him.* 我非常惱火，幾乎一看見他就討厭。| **can't stand to see/hear/do etc** *I can't stand to see good food going to waste.* 我不能忍受看到好好的食物被浪費。| **can't stand seeing/hearing/doing etc** *Lily can't stand working in an office.* 在辦公室工作，莉莉受不了。| **can't stand sb/sth doing** *I can't stand people dropping litter.* 我討厭人們亂扔垃圾。—see also 另見 **stand for** (STAND¹), **can't bear sb doing sth** (BEAR¹ (1))

③ ACCEPT/BEAR 接受/忍受

10 [I,T] to be able to accept or deal well with a difficult situation; TOLERATE 接受，對付；忍受: *I've had about as much as I can stand of your arguing!* 你們的爭吵我快要聽膩了！| *I don't know if I can stand the waiting any longer.* 再等下去，我不知道我是否受得了。| **stand sb doing sth** *How can you stand Marty coming home late all the time?* 你怎麼能容忍馬蒂總是晚回家？| **not stand any nonsense** *Get up to bed, and I won't stand any nonsense.* 上牀睡覺去吧，不許跟我胡鬧。—see graph at 參見 BEAR 圖表

11 ►BE GOOD ENOUGH 夠好的◄ [T] to be done or made well enough to be successful, strong, or useful for a long time 經得起，經受: **stand close examination** (=be proved to be correct, well made etc) 經得起仔細檢驗 *I suspect Murray's theory won't stand close examination.* 我懷疑默里的理論經受不住仔細檢驗。| **stand the test of time** (=stay strong) 經受時間的考驗 *It's nice to see their marriage has stood the test of time.* 很高興看到他們的婚姻經得起時間的考驗。

12 if you can't stand the heat, get out of the kitchen used to say that you should leave a job or situation if you cannot deal with its difficulties 受不了熱就別在廚房待着〔指如果對付不了困難，就應該離開〕

④ IN A PARTICULAR STATE/SITUATION 處於某種狀態/境地

13 [I always+adv/prep, linking verb 連繫動詞] to be in, stay in, or get into a particular state 處於[保持；進入]某種狀態: *Court stands adjourned until 2 p.m.* 法庭休庭至下午2點。| **as sth stands** *The law, as it stood, favoured the developers.* 從法律本身來看對開發商有利。| **the way things stand/as things stand** (=used when talking about the state that a situation has reached) 目前的狀況/就目前的情況看 *I'm not too thrilled with the way things stand at the moment.* 我對目前的情況並不感到很高興。| **where/how do things stand?** (=used to ask what is happening in a situation) 目前情況如何？*Where do things stand in terms of the budget?* 現在預算的情況怎麼樣？| **stand united/divided** (=agree or disagree completely) 意見統一/有分歧 *The committee stands divided on this issue.* 委員會在這個問題上有分歧。| **stand prepared/ready to do sth** (=be prepared to do something whenever it is necessary) 準備好做某事 | **stand together** (=stay united) 團結一致 *If we all stand together, they can't beat us.* 如果我們團結一致，他們就無法擊敗我們。| **stand in awe of sb** (=admire them, be afraid of them, or both) 敬畏某人

⑤ CONTINUE/NOT CHANGE 繼續/不改變

14 stand alone to continue to do something alone, without help from anyone else 繼續獨自做某事: *Harper stood alone in his refusal to sell to the railroad.* 哈珀獨自堅持着拒不賣給鐵路。

15 ►STILL EXIST 依然存在◄ [I not in progressive 不用進行式] to continue to exist, be correct, or be VALID 繼續存在；保持正確；保持有效: *My offer of a place to stay still stands.* 我願提供住處的意願仍沒有變。| *The court of appeal has ruled that the conviction should stand.* 上訴法庭的判決是維持原判。

16 stand still to not change or progress at all although time has passed 毫無變化；停滯不前: *Nothing stands still in the computer industry.* 在電腦業，一切都在不停地變化。| **time stands still** *Going back home, it's as if time has stood still and I'm ten years old.* 回到家裡，時光好像停頓了下來，而我才十歲。

17 stand your ground/stand firm/stand fast also 又作 **stand your guns** *AmE*【美】to refuse to change your opinions, intentions, or behaviour 堅持立場；拒不讓步: *Stand your ground, don't let them talk you into anything you don't want.* 要堅定，不要聽他們的勸説而做你自己不願做的事情。| **[+on/against]** *I call on you as citizens to stand firm against racism!* 我呼籲你們作為公民要堅決反對種族主義！

18 stand pat *AmE informal* to refuse to change a decision, plan etc【美，非正式】堅持不變: **[+on]** *Harry's standing pat on his decision to fire Janice.* 哈里堅持解雇賈妮絲的決定。

⑥ NOT MOVED OR USED 沒有移動或使用過

19 [I, linking verb 連繫動詞] to stay in a particular position, place, or state without being moved or used 停放在某位置，處於某狀態；沒有移動[使用]過: *The car's been standing in the garage for weeks.* 這輛汽車停放在車庫裡好幾個星期了。| **stand empty/idle** (=not being used) 空置/閒置 *scores of derelict houses standing empty* 幾十幢無人居住的廢棄房屋

20 ►LIQUID 液體◄ [I] a liquid that stands does not flow or is not made to move〔液體〕不流動；處於靜止狀態: *standing pools of marsh water* 一潭潭沼澤的積水

S

⑦ **FEELINGS/OPINIONS 感覺/看法**

21 know how/where you stand (with sb) to know how someone feels about you 知道某人對自己的看法: *Yvonne may be blunt, but you always know where you stand with her.* 伊馮娜也許有點遲鈍, 但你總能了解她對你有甚麼看法。

22 where sb stands someone's opinion about something, or the official rule about something 某人對某事的看法; 對某事的正式規定: **[+on]** *The voters want to know where you stand on abortion.* 選民們想知道你對墮胎的看法。

23 from where I stand according to what you know or feel 據我所知; 在我看來: *Well from where I'm standing, it seems like she's being unreasonable.* 我覺得她好像是不講道理的。

24 I stand corrected *spoken formal* used to admit that your opinion or something that you just said was wrong 【口, 正式】我承認錯誤〔用於承認自己的觀點或剛才說過的話是錯誤的〕

⑧ **LEVEL/AMOUNT/VALUE/HEIGHT 水平/數量/價值/高度**

25 [I always+adv/prep] to be at a particular level or amount 處於某水平[數量]: **[+at]** *Inflation currently stands at four percent.* 目前的通貨膨脹為百分之四。| *Your bank balance stands at $720.92.* 你的銀行存款為720.92美元。

26 [I always+adv/prep] to have a particular rank or position when compared to similar things or people〔與類似事物或人相比〕處於某等級[地位]: *I know your son stands high on the list of suitable candidates.* 我知道你兒子在合適的候選人名單中排在前面。| **stand in relation to** *How do their sales stand in relation to those of similar firms?* 他們的銷售額與類似的公司相比如何?

27 [I always+adv/prep, linking verb 連繫動詞] *usually written* to be a particular height【一般書面】高度為…: **stand four feet etc (high)/stand 20 metres etc (tall)** *The Eiffel Tower stands 300m high.* 埃菲爾鐵塔的高度為300米。

⑨ **BE RESPONSIBLE 負責**

28 [linking verb 連繫動詞] to take a particular responsibility 承擔某種職責: **stand guard (over)** *If you stand guard over our stuff, I'll run get the tickets.* 要是你來看管我們的東西, 我就跑過去買票。| **stand bail** (=pay money as a promise that someone will return to a court to be judged)〔為某人〕提供保釋金, 做保釋人 | **stand surety** (=be responsible for the results if someone else does not do what they promise to) 作擔保

⑩ **LAW 法律**

29 stand trial to be brought to a court of law to have your case examined and judged〔在法庭上〕受審: **[+for]** *Gresham will stand trial for murder.* 格雷沙姆將因謀殺罪而受審。

30 stand accused to be the person in a court of law who is being judged for a crime 被指控, 被控告: *Vincent Amis, you stand accused of murder.* 文森特·埃米斯, 你被指控犯有謀殺罪。

⑪ **BE PROUD/INDEPENDENT 自豪/獨立**

31 stand on your own (two) feet to be able to earn what you need without help from others 自立: *I'll think of him as equal when he's learnt to stand on his own two feet.* 當他學會了自立後, 我就對他平等看待。

32 stand tall *AmE* to be proud and feel ready to deal with anything【美】自豪; 自信

33 stand on your dignity to demand to be treated with respect 要求受到應有的禮遇; 保持自己的尊嚴[身分]: *Never one to stand on her dignity, Eva joined in with the fun.* 伊娃從來不愛擺架子, 她和大家一起玩了起來。

⑫ **COULD STAND 需要; 應該**

34 used to say very directly that it would be a good idea for someone to do something or for something to happen〔用於直言〕〔某人〕最好做〔某事〕;〔某事〕應該發生: **sb could stand to do sth** *You could stand to lose a few pounds.* 你最好能減肥幾磅。| **sth could stand another look/more attention etc** (=it ought to be looked at more closely) 某事物需要再仔細查看 *Your report could stand another read-through for typos.* 你的報告得再通讀一次, 看看是否有打印錯誤。

35 I could stand sth *AmE spoken humorous* used to say that you would like something【美口, 幽默】我想要某物: *I could stand another piece of pie!* 我想再吃一塊餡餅!

⑬ **OTHER MEANINGS 其他意思**

36 stand a chance/hope (of doing sth) to be likely to be able to do something or to succeed 有機會/有希望(做某事): *You'll stand a better chance of getting a job with a degree.* 你有了學位找到工作的機會就更大。| **not stand a chance** *I'm afraid she doesn't stand a chance.* 恐怕她沒有甚麼機會。| **stand little chance** (=not be likely to succeed) 成功的可能性不大 *The bill stands little chance of becoming law.* 這項議案幾乎沒有可能成為法律。

37 stand to gain/lose/win etc to be likely to do or have something 很可能獲得/失去/赢得等: *We stand to make a lot of money from the merger.* 通過這次合併, 我們很可能賺到一大筆錢。

38 do sth standing on your head to do something easily 輕而易舉地做某事: *Get Anne to help – she can fix things like that standing on her head.* 請安妮來幫忙, 她能輕而易舉地修理好那樣的東西。

39 stand on your head to do sth to make a great effort to do something 努力[竭力]去做某事: *You won't find me standing on my head to help him any more.* 你再也不會看到我盡力去幫助他了。

40 it stands to reason used to say that something should be completely clear to anyone who is sensible 顯然; 合乎情理: *If the thefts are all in the same area, it stands to reason it's the same kids doing it.* 如果盜竊都發生在同一地區, 那顯然是同一夥年輕人幹的。

41 ►ELECTION 選舉◄ [I] to try to become elected to a council, parliament etc 競選; 當候選人: *Who's standing for the Democrats in the 44th district?* 誰是第44區的民主黨候選人? —see also 另見 **stand against**

42 stand in sb's way/path to prevent someone from doing something 妨礙某人; 阻礙某人: *If you really want to marry Liam, I'm not going to stand in your way.* 你如果真的想跟利亞姆結婚, 我不會阻止你的。

43 stand sb in good stead to be very useful to someone when needed 需要時對某人很有用: *Now that I'm emigrating to the United States, my being able to speak English should stand me in good stead.* 我要移民去美國了, 我能講英語對我應該很有幫助。

44 stand sb a drink/meal etc to pay for something as a gift to someone; TREAT¹ (5) 請某人喝酒/吃飯等: *Come on, Jack, I'll stand you a drink if you like.* 來吧, 傑克, 我請你喝一杯。賞光嗎?

45 not stand on ceremony to not worry about the formal rules of polite behaviour 隨便; 不拘禮節: *Don't stand on ceremony – if you want a drink, have one.* 別客氣, 想喝酒就來一杯吧。

46 stand or fall by/on to depend on something for success 成敗取決於: *The whole project must stand or fall on the quality of its research.* 整個項目的成敗取決於研究的質量。

47 stand sth on its head to show that a belief, idea etc is completely untrue 證明〔信念、觀點等〕完全不真實, 把某事徹底推翻: *Galileo's discovery stood medieval thought on its head.* 伽利略的發現徹底推翻了中世紀的思想。

48 [I+**on/in**] *BrE* to accidentally step on or in something【英】意外地踩到: *Mind you don't stand on Fluffy's tail.* 小心別踩到弗拉菲的尾巴。—see also 另見 **make sb's hair stand on end** (HAIR (6)), **leave sb/sth standing** (LEAVE[1] (31)), **not have a leg to stand on** (LEG[1] (8))

stand against sb/sth *phr v* [T] to oppose a person, organization, plan, decision etc 反對: *If we don't stand against the cutbacks, they'll cut even more next year.* 我們如果不反對這次削減, 明年他們就會減得更多。

stand around *phr v* [I] to stand somewhere and not do anything〔無所事事地〕閒站着: *It's too cold to stand around out here – I'm going back inside.* 在外面閒站着太冷了, 我要進屋裡去了。

stand by *phr v* **1** [T] to not do anything to help someone or prevent something from happening 袖手旁觀: *We are not prepared to stand by and let them close our schools.* 我們不會袖手旁觀, 聽任他們關閉我們的學校。**2** [T **stand by** sth] to keep a promise, agreement etc, or to declare that something is still true 信守〔諾言〕; 遵守〔協定〕; 堅持: *I stand by what I said earlier.* 我堅持原先說的話。**3** [T **stand by** sb] to stay loyal to someone and support them, especially in a difficult situation〔尤指在困難情況下〕繼續忠於; 支持: *Wes needs to know we'll always stand by him.* 韋斯需要確定我們總是會支持他。**4** [I] to be ready to do something if necessary 準備行動: **be standing by** *A rescue boat is always standing by in case of trouble.* 一艘營救船隨時待命, 以防發生事故。| [**+for**] *Stand by for the countdown.* 請作好倒數準備。| **stand by to do sth** *Stand by to cue the commercial.* 請準備好插播廣告。—see also 另見 BYSTANDER, STANDBY

stand down *phr v* **1** [I] to agree to leave your position or to stop trying to be elected, so that someone else can have a chance 辭職; 退出競選: *I'm prepared to stand down in favor of a younger candidate.* 我準備退出競選, 讓位給一個年輕點的候選人。—see also 另見 **step down** (STEP[2]) **2** [I] to leave the WITNESS BOX in court 離開證人席 **3** [I,T **stand** sb ↔ **down**] *BrE* to send a soldier away from work after they have done their work for the day, or to stop working for the day; **go off duty** (DUTY (3))【英】撤走〔值過班的士兵〕;〔士兵〕下班[不值勤]

stand for sth *phr v* [T] **1** if a letter, number or sign stands for something, it represents it as a short form of a word, name, or idea 代表; 象徵; 意味着: *"My name is Dean E. Beller." "What does the E stand for?"* "我的名字是迪恩·E·貝勒。" "E代表的是甚麼?" **2** [usually in questions and negatives 一般用於疑問句和否定句] to allow something to continue to happen without complaining about it or trying to stop it 忍受; 容忍: *We will not stand for this sort of behavior, young man!* 小伙子, 我們不會容忍這種行為! | **stand for being** *I won't stand for being treated like a child.* 我不會容忍被別人當孩子對待。**3** to support a particular set of ideas, values, or principles 主張; 支持; 擁護: *I want to know what she stands for before I'll vote for her.* 在我投她的票之前, 我想知道她主張甚麼。

stand in *phr v* [I] to temporarily do someone else's job 暫時代替〔某人〕: [**+for**] *Can you stand in for Meg while she's on vacation?* 梅格休假期間, 你能暫時代替她嗎? —see also 另見 STAND-IN

stand out *phr v* [I] **1** to be very easy to see or notice by looking or sounding different from other things or people 顯眼; 突出: *I think black lettering will stand out best on a yellow sign.* 我認為黃色標誌上用黑色字體最醒目。| **stand out in a crowd** *Well, that dress will make you stand out in a crowd!* 好, 那件連衣裙會使你在人羣中很顯眼! **2 stand out a mile** to be very clear or noticeable 顯而易見; 極醒目: *They thought no one knew but it stood out a mile they were interested in each other.* 他們以為沒有人知道, 但他們互相有意思是明擺着的事。**3** to be clearly better or the best 顯然比…好; 最傑出: **stand out as** *Among mystery writers, P D James stands out as a superior storyteller.* 在偵探小說作家中, P·D·詹姆斯最突出, 是最好的小說家。| [**+from/among/above**] *Nathan stands out from the rest of the singers.* 內森從其他歌手中脫穎而出。—see also 另見 STANDOUT

stand out against sth *phr v* [T] to be strongly opposed to an idea, plan etc 堅決[強烈]反對: *We must stand out against bigotry.* 我們必須堅決反對偏見。

stand over sb *phr v* [T] to stand very close behind someone and watch as they work to make sure they do nothing wrong〔站在某人身後〕嚴密監督[監視]: *I can't concentrate with him standing over me like that.* 他那樣監視着我, 我無法專心工作。

stand to *phr v* [I,T **stand** sb ↔ **to**] *BrE* to order a soldier to move into a position so that they are ready for action, or to move into this position【英】命令〔士兵〕進入戰備狀態;〔士兵〕進入戰備狀態

stand up *phr v* **1** [I usually in progressive 一般用進行式] to stand 站立, 站: *Boy am I tired, I've been standing up all day.* 哎呀, 我真的累壞了, 我已經站了一整天。| **stand up straight** *Stand up straight, boy, don't slouch!* 站直, 孩子, 別沒精打采的! **2** [I always+ adv/prep] to stay healthy in a difficult environment or in good condition after a lot of hard use 耐久; 耐用; 經得起: [**+to**] *The trees stood up pretty well to the frosts this winter.* 這些樹經得起今年冬天的霜凍。**3** [I] to be proved to be true, correct, useful etc when tested 站得住腳; 證明真實[正確, 有用等]: **stand up under/to** *stand up under close scrutiny* 經得起仔細推敲 | **stand up in court** (=be successfully proved in a court of law) 在法庭上站得住腳 *Without a witness, the charges will never stand up in court.* 如果沒有證人, 這些指控在法庭上是絕對站不住腳的。**4** [T **stand** sb **up**] *informal* to not meet someone after you have promised to do something with them【非正式】未如約與…見面, 爽約: *I was supposed to go to a concert with Kyle on Friday, but he stood me up.* 我星期五本來要跟凱爾一起去聽音樂會的, 但他失約了。**5 stand up and be counted** to make it very clear what you think about something when this is dangerous or might cause trouble for you〔尤指對危險或可能引起麻煩的事物〕公開表明立場[態度] —see also 另見 STAND-UP

stand up for sb/sth *phr v* [T] to support or defend a person or idea when they are being attacked 支持; 保衛; 維護: *It's time we stood up for our rights.* 我們該維護自己的權利了。| *Didn't anyone stand up for James and say it wasn't his fault?* 難道沒有人支持詹姆斯, 說那不是他的過錯?

stand up to sb/sth *phr v* [T] to refuse to accept unfair treatment from a person or organization 拒絕接受〔某人或組織〕的不公平對待: *He'll respect you more if you stand up to him.* 如果你向他提出抗議, 他會更尊重你。

stand² *n*

1 ►FOR SUPPORT 作支撐用◄ [C] a piece of furniture or equipment for supporting something 架; 台; 座: *a music stand* 樂譜架 | *an umbrella stand* 傘架 | *Can we put another microphone stand here?* 我們可以在這裡再放一個話筒架嗎? | **coat-stand/hat-stand** (=for hanging coats or hats on) 衣架/帽架

2 ►FOR SELLING 作銷售用◄ [C] a small structure used for selling or showing things; STALL[1] (1) 售貨台[亭]; 貨攤, 攤位: *a hotdog stand* 熱狗攤 | *Come by our stand at the exhibition and see the new products.* 到我們在展覽會上設的攤位來看看新產品。—see also 另見 NEWSSTAND

3 ►OPINION/ATTITUDE 觀點/態度◄ [C usually singular 一般用單數] a position or opinion that you state firmly and publicly〔公開表明的〕堅定主張[立場]: **take a stand (on)** *The Labour Party has not taken a stand on the political position of the monarchy.* 工黨

S

還沒有就君主的政治地位表明立場。

4 ▶SPORTS GROUND 運動場◀ [C] also 又作 **stands** *plural* a building where people stand or sit to watch the game at a sports ground〔運動場裡的〕看台 —see also 另見 GRANDSTAND

5 ▶OPPOSE/DEFEND 反對/防禦◀ [C] a strong effort to defend yourself or to oppose something 防禦; 反抗, 抵抗: **make a stand** *In February 1916 the French army made a stand at Verdun.* 1916年2月, 法國軍隊在凡爾登進行了奮力的抵抗。| **make/mount a stand against** *Somebody's got to make a stand against the parish council.* 得有人站出來反對行政區議會。

6 ▶SPORTS GAME 體育比賽◀ [C] the period of time in which two batsmen (BATSMAN) are playing together in a game of CRICKET (2), or the points that they get〔在一局板球賽中兩個擊球員的〕持續堅守; 得分

7 the stand *AmE* a WITNESS BOX【美】證人席: **take the stand** *Will the next witness please take the stand?* 請下一位證人到證人席來。—see also 另見 ONE-NIGHT STAND

stand·a·lone /ˈstændəˌlon; ˈstændələʊn/ *adj technical* a standalone computer works on its own without being part of a NETWORK[1] (4)【術語】〔計算機〕獨立操作的

stan·dard¹ /ˈstændəd; ˈstændəd/ *n*

1 ▶LEVEL OF QUALITY 質量水平◀ [C often plural 常用複數, U] a level of quality, skill, ability or achievement by which someone or something is judged, that is considered to be necessary or acceptable in a particular situation 水平; 水準; 標準: *The airline has rigorous safety standards.* 這家航空公司有嚴格的安全標準。| **[+of]** *Inspections are meant to ensure the standard of teaching is acceptable.* 視察是為了確保教學水準合格。| **(of a) high/low standard** *Our students achieve very high standards of musical ability.* 我們的學生達到了很高的音樂水平。| *Articles of a low standard will not be accepted.* 質量差的論文不會被接受。| **set a standard** (=decide what people are expected to do) 制定標準 *The International Atomic Energy Agency sets standards for the industry.* 國際原子能機構為該行業制定標準。| **meet/reach/attain a standard** *They have to reach a certain standard or they won't pass.* 他們必須達到一定水準, 不然就無法通過。| **to standard** (=well enough) 合乎標準; 足夠好 *completing work to standard and on time* 合乎標準並準時完成工作 | **maintain standards** (=keep them the way they are) 保持水平; 保持水準 *After his early success, Cameron was unable to maintain such high standards.* 卡梅倫起初獲得了成功, 但他沒能把如此高的水平保持下去。| **above/below standard** (=better than usual, or not good enough) 超過/低於標準 *The accommodation here is really below standard.* 這裡的住宿條件實在低於標準。| **up to standard** (=good enough) 合乎[達到]標準 *Your recent work just hasn't been up to standard.* 你最近的工作就是沒有達到標準。| **raise/lower a standard** *We're not about to lower our standards just to make a cheaper product.* 我們不會為了製造更廉價的產品而降低我們的標準。| **let standards fall/drop/slip** (=allow them to get worse) 允許標準下降/下滑 *On no account must we let standards slip.* 我們無論如何也不能允許水準下滑。

2 ▶COMPARING 比較◀ [C usually plural 一般用複數] the ideas of what is good or normal that someone uses to compare one thing with another 標準; 規範; 規格: **by sb's standards** *They were all pretty excitable by our quiet English standards.* 按我們英國人性情平和的標準來看, 他們都相當容易激動。| **by any standard(s)** (=by anyone's opinion or values) 無論在誰看來; 不論以甚麼標準 *It's a deprived area by any standard.* 不論以甚麼標準來看, 那都是個貧困地區。

3 ▶MORAL RULE 道德準則◀ [C usually plural 一般用複數] rules for behaviour based on an idea of what is morally good and right 道德標準; 道德準則: *Nobody could live up to his standards.* 沒有人能夠達到他的道德標準。

4 ▶MEASUREMENT 計量, 測量◀ [C] a fixed official rule for measuring weight, purity, value etc〔重量、純度、價值等的〕標準, 基準: *an official government standard for the purity of silver* 白銀純度的政府法定標準

5 ▶SONG 歌曲◀ [C] a popular song that has been sung by many different singers〔很多歌星演唱過的〕流行歌曲

6 ▶FLAG 旗◀ [C] a flag used in ceremonies 儀式用旗幟: *the royal standard* 王室的旗幟

7 ▶MILITARY POLE 軍隊旗杆◀ [C] a pole with a picture or shape at the top carried in the past at the front of an army〔舊時軍隊的〕軍旗旗杆 —see also 另見 DOUBLE STANDARD, LIVING STANDARD

This graph shows some of the words most commonly used with the noun **standard**. 本圖表所示為含有名詞 standard 的一些最常用的詞組。

high standard
set a standard
meet a standard
to standard
low standard
maintain standards
reach/attain a standard
2 4 6 8 10 per million 每百萬

Based on the British National Corpus and the Longman Lancaster Corpus
據英國國家語料庫和朗文蘭卡斯特語料庫

standard² *adj* **1** accepted as normal or usual 正常的; 普通的; 普遍接受的: *We paid them the standard rate for the job.* 這工作我們付給他們標準的工錢。| **standard practice/procedure** (=the usual way of doing things) 例行的做法/程序 *Searching luggage at airports is now standard practice.* 在機場檢查行李現在已成為例行的做法。**2** regular and usual in shape, size, quality etc〔形狀、大小、質量等〕規則的; 標準的: *We make shoes in standard and wide sizes.* 我們做標準碼和加寬碼的鞋子。| *All these vans are made to a standard design.* 這些客貨兩用車都是按標準設計製造的。**3** a standard book, work, author etc is read by everyone studying a particular subject〔某一學科的書、作品、作者等〕公認為標準的; 有權威的 **4 standard English/spelling/pronunciation etc** *BrE* the form of English, spelling, pronunciation etc that most people in Britain use, and that is not limited to one area or group of people【英】標準英語/拼法/發音等 —see also 另見 NON-STANDARD, SUBSTANDARD

standard-bear·er /ˈ·· ˌ··/ *n* [C] **1** an important leader in a moral argument or political group 領導者; 倡導者; 領袖; 旗手 **2** a soldier who carried the STANDARD (=flag) at the front of an army〔軍隊的〕旗手

standard de·duc·tion /ˌ·· ·ˈ··/ *n* [C usually singular 一般用單數] *AmE* a fixed amount of the money you earn that you do not have to pay tax on【美】標準扣減額〔指收入中無需納稅的一筆固定金額〕

standard de·vi·a·tion /ˌ·· ··ˈ··/ *n* [C] *technical* a number in statistics (STATISTIC (1)) that shows how widely members of a mathematical set vary from the average set【術語】〔統計學上的〕標準差

standard-is·sue /ˌ·· ˈ··◂/ *adj* included in ordinary military equipment〔軍隊裝備〕標準配給的, 統一分發的

stan·dard·ize also 又作 **-ise** *BrE*【英】/ˈstændəˌdaɪz; ˈstændədaɪz/ *v* [T] to make all the things of one particular type the same as each other 使…標準化[統一規格]: *Attempts to standardize English spelling have never been successful.* 統一英語拼寫的嘗試從未成功過。—**standardization** /ˌstændədəˈzeʃən; ˌstændədaɪˈzeɪʃən/ *n* [U]

standard lamp /ˈ·· ·/ *n* [C] *BrE* a tall lamp that stands on the floor【英】落地燈; FLOOR LAMP *AmE*【美】—see picture at 參見 LIGHT¹ 圖

standard of liv·ing /ˌ‥ · ˈ‥/ *n* [C usually singular 一般用單數] the amount of wealth, comfort, and things that can be bought that a particular person, group, country etc has 生活水平, 生活水準: *a nation with a high standard of living* 生活水準高的國家

standard time /ˌ‥ ˈ·/ *n* [singular] the time to which all clocks in a particular area of the world are set 標準時間

stand·by, stand-by /ˈstændˌbaɪ; ˈstændbaɪ/ *n* **1** [C] something that is kept ready so that it can be used when needed 備用物: *Powdered milk is a good standby in an emergency.* 奶粉是緊急情況下很好的備用品。| *The hospital has a standby generator.* 這家醫院有備用發電機。**2 on standby** ready to help immediately if you are needed 隨時待命: *A special team of police were kept on standby.* 一支警察特遣隊隨時待命。**3** [U] the condition of being ready to travel on a plane if there are any seats left when it is ready to leave〔飛機乘客〕等候剩餘機票的, 候補的: *a cheap standby ticket* 便宜的剩餘機票 | **on standby** *All the seats are taken, but we can put you on standby.* 機位已滿, 但我們可以讓你做候補乘客。**4** [C] someone or something that you can always depend on or that will always be suitable 可依靠的人[事物]; 總是合適的人[事物]: *It's useful to have a little black dress as a standby.* 備一件黑色小禮服很有用。—see also 另見 **stand by** (STAND¹)

stand-in /ˈ· ·/ *n* [C] **1** someone who does the job or takes the place of someone else for a short time〔職位或工作的〕臨時替代者: *Gilbert failed to find a stand-in and so could not go to their dinner party.* 吉爾伯特找不到人臨時替代他, 因此無法參加他們的晚宴。**2** someone who takes the place of an actor for some scenes in a film〔電影中的〕替身 —see also 另見 **stand in** (STAND¹)

stand·ing¹ /ˈstændɪŋ; ˈstændɪŋ/ *adj* [only before noun 僅用於名詞前] **1** permanently agreed or arranged 永久的; 長期有效的; 常置的: *You have to pay standing charges whether or not you use the service.* 無論你是否使用這項服務, 你都必須交納固定費用。| **standing invitation** (=permission to visit someone whenever you like) 長期有效的邀請 **2 standing order(s) a)** an agreement to pay for something regularly from your bank account〔要求銀行定期付款的〕長期自動轉賬委託 **b)** a permanent rule that a committee, council etc follows when it meets〔委員會、議會等的〕議事規則 **3** done from a standing position 直立着做的; 站着做的: *The runners set off from a standing start.* 賽跑者站着起跑。| **standing ovation** (=when people stand up to CLAP¹ (1) after a performance) 起立鼓掌 **4 standing joke** something that happens often and that people make jokes about 經常引人發笑的笑話: *My spelling mistakes had become a standing joke in the office.* 我的拼寫錯誤已經成為辦公室裡講不厭的笑話。

standing² *n* [U] **1** someone's rank or position in a system, organization, society etc, based on what other people think of them 地位; 身分; 聲望: *The scandal will certainly damage the Governor's standing in the polls.* 醜聞肯定會損害州長在選舉中的聲望。| **high/low standing** *a lawyer of high standing* 名望高的律師 **2 of five/many etc years' standing** used to show the time during which something such as an agreement has existed〔協議等〕已經存在五年的/多年的等: *an arrangement of several years' standing* 執行了好幾年的安排

standing ar·my /ˌ‥ ˈ‥/ *n* [C] a professional, permanent army, rather than one that has been formed for a war 常備軍; 正規軍

standing com·mit·tee /ˈ‥ ˌ‥/ *n* [C] a group of people chosen by the British parliament or the US Congress to consider possible new laws〔英國議會或美國國會的〕常務委員會

standing or·der /ˌ‥ ˈ‥/ *n* [C,U] an arrangement by which a bank pays a fixed amount of money from your account every month, year etc〔要求銀行定期付款的〕長期自動轉賬委託 —compare 比較 DIRECT DEBIT

standing room /ˈ‥ ·/ *n* [U] space for standing in a theatre, sports ground etc〔戲院、運動場等的〕站位: **standing room only** (=no seats are left) 只有站位

stand·off /ˈstændˌɔf; ˈstændɒf/ *n* [C] a situation in which neither side in a fight or battle can gain an advantage〔戰鬥的〕僵持(狀態)

stand-of·fish /ˌstænd ˈɔfɪʃ; ˌstænd ˈɒfɪʃ/ *adj informal* rather unfriendly and formal【非正式】不友好的; 冷淡的; 疏遠的: *She was cold and stand-offish.* 她態度冷漠, 不甚友好。—**stand-offishly** *adv* —**stand-offishness** *n* [U]

stand·out /ˈstændˌaut; ˈstændaʊt/ *n* [C] *AmE* someone who is better at doing something or more attractive than other people in a group【美】突出的人; 引起注意的人: *In that class, Mary's a standout.* 瑪麗在那個班裡很是突出。—**standout** *adj*: *a standout performance* 一場出色的演出

stand·pipe /ˈstændˌpaɪp; ˈstændpaɪp/ *n* [C] a pipe that provides water in a public place in the street〔在街上給公共場所供水的〕豎管

stand·point /ˈstændˌpɔɪnt; ˈstændpɔɪnt/ *n* [C usually singular 一般用單數] a way of thinking about people, situations, ideas etc; POINT OF VIEW 立場; 觀點; 立足點: *the feminist standpoint* 女權主義立場 | **[+of]** *Let's look at this from the standpoint of the voters.* 讓我們從選民的角度來看待這個問題。

stand·still /ˈstændˌstɪl; ˈstændˌstɪl/ *n* [singular] a situation in which there is no movement or activity at all 靜止(狀態); 停頓, 停滯: **come to a standstill/bring sth to a standstill** *Strikers brought production to a standstill.* 罷工者使生產陷於停頓。| **at a standstill** *Traffic was at a standstill on the freeway.* 高速公路上的交通完全癱瘓了。

stand-up¹, standup /ˈstændˌʌp; ˈstændʌp/ *adj* [only before noun 僅用於名詞前] **1** stand-up COMEDY involves one person telling jokes as a performance〔喜劇〕單人説笑表演的: *a stand-up comedian* 從事單人説笑表演的喜劇演員 **2** done or intended to be used by people who are standing up 站着做的; 站着使用的: *We had a stand-up buffet.* 我們吃了一頓站着吃的自助餐。**3** a stand-up fight, argument etc is loud and violent〔打鬥、爭論等〕喧鬧而激烈的: *If it came to a stand-up fight, I wouldn't have a chance.* 要是硬碰起來, 我根本不是對手。**4** able to stay upright 能夠直立的: *a photo in a stand-up frame* 豎立相架中的照片 | *a stand-up collar* 直立的衣領 —see also 另見 **stand up**

stand-up² also 又作 **standup** *n* [U] stand-up COMEDY 單人説笑喜劇, 單口相聲: **do stand up** *Mark used to do stand up at Roxy's bar.* 馬克曾在羅克西的酒吧裡表演單口相聲。

stank /stæŋk; stæŋk/ the past tense of STINK

stan·za /ˈstænzə; ˈstænzə/ *n* [C] a group of lines in a repeated pattern forming part of a poem〔詩的〕節, 段

sta·ple¹ /ˈstepl̩; ˈsteɪpəl/ *n* [C] **1** a small piece of thin wire that is pushed into sheets of paper and bent over to hold them together 釘書釘 **2** a small U-shaped piece of metal with pointed ends, used to hold something in place U形釘 **3** a food that is needed and used all the time 常用食物; 主食: *staples like flour and rice* 麵粉和大米等主食 **4** *technical* the main product that is produced in a country【術語】〔一國的〕主要產品: *Bananas and sugar are the staples of Jamaica.* 香蕉和糖是牙買加的主要產品。

staple² *v* [T] to fasten two or more things together with a staple 用釘書釘把…釘住

staple³ *adj* [only before noun 僅用於名詞前] **1** forming the greatest or most important part of something 主要的; 最重要的: *Oil is Nigeria's staple export.* 石油是尼日利亞的主要出口產品。| *a staple ingredient of com-*

S

edy 喜劇最重要的成分 **2 staple diet a)** the food that you normally eat 主食: *They live on a staple diet of rice and vegetables.* 他們以大米和蔬菜為主食。**b)** something that is always being produced, seen, bought etc 經常製作[看到, 購買等]的東西: *television's staple diet of soap operas and quiz shows* 以肥皂劇和問答比賽為主的電視節目 **3** used all the time 常用的, 慣用的: *Marty's staple excuses* 馬蒂慣用的藉口

staple gun /ˈ·· ·/ *n* [C] a tool used for putting strong staples into walls U形釘槍

sta·pler /ˈsteplɚ; ˈsteɪplə/ *n* [C] a tool used for putting staples into paper 釘書機

star¹ /stɑr; stɑː/ *n* [C]

1 ▶IN THE SKY 在空中◀ a burning mass of gases in space that can be seen at night as a point of light in the sky 星; 恒星: *I lay on my back and looked up at the stars.* 我仰面躺着看天上的星星。—see also 另見 FALLING STAR, SHOOTING STAR

2 ▶PERFORMER 表演者◀ **a)** a famous and successful performer in entertainment or sport〔娛樂或體育的〕明星, 名角: **film/movie star** *There were pictures of film stars all over the walls.* 牆上掛滿了電影明星的照片。| **pop star** (=famous popular music singer) 流行歌星 | **big star** (=very famous performer) 大明星 *By the age of twenty she was already a big star.* 她二十歲時就已經是大明星了。| **star quality** (=something that makes you seem special, and likely to be a star) 明星氣質 | **rising star** (=someone who is becoming successful and famous) 嶄露頭角的明星, 新秀 *a rising star in the music world* 音樂界的後起之秀 **b)** someone who acts the part of the main character in a film or play〔電影或戲劇中的〕主角: *The star of his next movie was an unknown young actress.* 他下一部電影中的主角是一位名不見經傳的年輕女演員。| **the star part** (=the most important part in a film or play)〔電影或戲劇中〕最主要的角色 | **child star** (=a child who has an important part in a film) 童星 | **the star of the show** (=the person who gives the best performance in a play, film etc)〔電影、戲劇等中〕表演最精彩的演員 —see also 另見 STAR²

3 ▶SHAPE 形狀◀ **a)** a shape with four or more points which is supposed to look like a star in the sky 星狀, 星形: *A five-pointed star is called a pentagram.* 五個角的星稱為五角星。—see picture at 參見 SHAPE¹ 圖 **b)** a mark in this shape, used to draw attention to something written; ASTERISK 星號 **c)** a piece of cloth or metal in this shape, worn to show someone's rank or position〔表示級別或地位的〕星章

4 ▶HOTELS/RESTAURANTS 酒店/餐館◀ a mark used in a system for judging the quality of hotels and restaurants〔評判酒店和餐館質量等級的〕星(級): **three-star/four-star/five-star** *a two-star bed and breakfast* 提供住宿和次日早餐的兩星級旅館

5 the stars a) *informal* a HOROSCOPE (=description of what will happen to you in the future) that is printed in newspapers or magazines【非正式】〔報紙或雜誌上刊登的〕星象: **read your stars** *I never read my stars – I don't believe any of it anyway.* 我從來不看星象——反正我對它一點兒也不信。**b)** *literary* a force that controls what will happen in the future; FATE (2)【文】命運, 運氣: **written in the stars** (=decided by this) 命中注定的 —see also 另見 STAR-CROSSED

6 ▶SUCCESSFUL PERSON 成功的人◀ *informal* someone who is particularly successful at a job, course of study etc【非正式】〔在某工作、課程等中〕特別成功的人: *I was the star of my village because I won a place at the school in Nayoumi.* 我是我們村裡的明星, 因為我考上了在拿猶米的那所學校。| **a star player/performer/salesman etc** *the Academy's star pupil* 學院最優秀的學生 | **shining star** (=very successful person) 非常成功的人

7 you're/she's a star! *informal* used to say that someone is very good at something or thank someone for helping you【非正式】你/她(真是)太棒[太好]了!〔稱讚某人或感謝某人幫助時使用〕

8 star turn the main or best performer or event in a performance 主角; 最佳演員; 主要[最精彩]節目: *Our star turn was a fire-eating act.* 我們最精彩的節目是吞火表演。

9 star attraction the most interesting person or thing, that most people want to see 最有吸引力的人[事物]

10 see stars to see flashes of light, especially because you have been hit on the head 眼冒金星〔尤指因頭部被擊所致〕: *I felt a little dizzy and could see stars.* 我覺得有點頭暈, 眼冒金星。

11 have stars in your eyes to imagine that something you want to do is much more exciting or attractive than it really is 充滿不切實際的幻想 —see also 另見 STARRY-EYED

12 four star (petrol) *BrE* high quality petrol that has lead (LEAD³ (1)) in it【英】高質量含鉛汽油 —see also 另見 EVENING STAR, FIVE-STAR GENERAL, FOUR-STAR GENERAL, MORNING STAR, **guiding star** (GUIDING), **be born under a lucky/unlucky star** (BORN (10)), **reach for the stars** (REACH¹ (8)), **thank your lucky stars** (THANK (6))

star² **starred, starring** *v* **1** [I] to act the part of the main character in a film or play〔在電影或戲劇中〕擔任主角; 主演: **[+in]** *She will star in the Los Angeles production of 'Phantom' this year.* 今年她將擔任在洛杉磯上演的《歌劇魅影》的主角。**2** [T] if a film or play stars someone, that person acts the part of the main character 由…擔任主角; 由…主演: *a film starring Meryl Streep* 由梅麗史翠普主演的電影 **3 starring role** the most important acting part in a film, play etc〔電影、戲劇等中的〕主角 **4** to put an ASTERISK (=a star-shaped mark) next to something written 給…加上星號: *The starred items will be available from July.* 加星號的貨品將於七月份起有售。

star·board /ˈstɑrˌbɔrd; ˈstɑːbəd/ *n* [U] the side of a ship or aircraft that is on your right when you are facing forwards〔船舶或飛機的〕右舷, 右側 —**starboard** *adj* —opposite 反義詞 PORT (4)

starch¹ /stɑrtʃ; stɑːtʃ/ *n* **1** [U] a white substance that has no taste and forms an important part of foods such as grain, rice, and potatoes 澱粉 **2** [C,U] a food that contains this substance 含澱粉的食物: *Avoid fatty foods and starches.* 不要吃高脂肪和含澱粉的食物。**3** [U] a substance that is mixed with water and is used to make cloth stiff〔用於漿布的〕漿粉

starch² *v* [T] to make cloth stiff, using starch 給…上漿: *a starched white tablecloth* 漿洗過的白桌布

star cham·ber /ˌ· ˈ··/ *n* [C] a group of people that meets secretly and makes decisions that are important or judgements that are severe 星室法庭〔祕密地開會, 並作出重要決定或重判的團體〕; 專橫暴虐的團體

starch·y /ˈstɑrtʃɪ; ˈstɑːtʃi/ *adj* **1** containing a lot of STARCH¹ (1) 含大量澱粉的: *starchy foods* 含大量澱粉的食物 **2** very formal and correct in your behaviour 古板的; 拘謹的; 生硬的: *Not knowing what to say or do he became stiff and starchy.* 他不知道說甚麼和做甚麼, 顯得古板而又拘謹。—**starchily** *adv* —**starchiness** *n* [U]

star-crossed /ˈ· ·/ *adj literary* star-crossed lovers can never be happy because their situation prevents them from being together【文】〔戀人〕命運不佳的, 不幸的

star·dom /ˈstɑrdəm; ˈstɑːdəm/ *n* [U] the situation of being a famous performer 明星的地位: *Her triumphs were clouded by the loneliness of stardom.* 她的成功的喜悅被做明星的孤獨沖淡。| **shoot/rise to stardom** (=become famous very quickly) 迅速登上明星寶座

star·dust /ˈstɑrˌdʌst; ˈstɑːdʌst/ *n* [U] *literary* an imaginary magic substance like shiny powder【文】虛無縹緲之物〔想像中具有魔力的粉狀閃光物〕

stare¹ /stɛr; steə/ *v* [I] **1** to look at something or someone for a long time without moving your eyes 凝視; 盯着看: **[+out]** *Stop staring out of the window and do some work!* 別盯着窗外看了, 快做點事吧! | **[+at]** *What are you staring at?* 你在盯着看甚麼呢? | **stare into space**

(=look for a long time at nothing) 瞪着眼睛發愣, 出神 —see 見 GAZE¹ (USAGE) **2 be staring sb in the face** **a)** *informal* to be very clear and easy to see; be OBVIOUS【非正式】非常清楚而容易看見; 明顯的: *The solution is staring you in the face.* 解決辦法就明擺在你面前。**b)** to seem impossible to avoid 看來無法避免: *Defeat was staring us in the face.* 看來我們輸定了。—see also 另見 **stark staring mad** (STARK² (2))

stare sb out *BrE*【英】, **stare sb down** *AmE*【美】*phr v* [T] to look at someone for so long that they start to feel uncomfortable and look away 盯得〔某人〕不敢再對視

stare² *n* [C] a long steady look or a way of staring 盯視; 凝視: *a disapproving stare* 不贊成的目光 | *She ignored the stares of everyone around her.* 她不理會周圍所有人凝視的目光。| **hold sb's stare** (=not look away when someone is staring at you) 與某人對視

star·fish /ˈstɑrˌfɪʃ; ˈstɑːˌfɪʃ/ *n* [C] a flat sea animal that has five arms forming the shape of a star 海星

star·fruit /ˈstɑrˌfrut; ˈstɑːˌfruːt/ *n* [C] a pale green fruit that has a shape similar to a star 楊桃, 五斂子

star·gaz·er /ˈstɑrˌgezɚ; ˈstɑːˌgeɪzə/ *n* [C] **1** someone who studies ASTRONOMY or ASTROLOGY 天文學家; 占星家 **2** someone with ideas or plans that are impossible or not practical 空想家; 不切實際的人 —**stargazing** *n* [U]

star jump /ˈ· ·/ *n* [C usually plural 一般用複數] *BrE* one of a series of exercise jumps that you do from a standing position with your arms and legs pointing out at each side; JUMPING JACK【英】星狀跳躍, 跳躍運動〔健身動作, 從站立姿勢起跳, 四肢叉開〕

stark¹ /stɑrk; stɑːk/ *adj* **1** very simple and severe in appearance〔外表上〕簡陋的; 荒涼的: *In the cold dawn light the castle looked stark and forbidding.* 在黎明冰冷的光線下, 城堡看上去荒涼而令人生畏。| *the stark beauty of the New Mexico desert* 新墨西哥沙漠的荒涼之美 **2** unpleasantly clear and impossible to avoid; HARSH 明擺着的; 嚴峻的: **stark reality** *The film shows the stark realities of life in the slums.* 這部電影反映貧民窟裡嚴酷的生活現實。| **stark choice** *The Tories are facing a stark choice between cutting the deficit and maintaining benefits.* 保守黨面臨着減少赤字或保留救濟金的困難選擇。**3** [only before noun 僅用於名詞前] complete; total 完全的; 全然的; 十足的: *Jerry's eyes were wide open with a look of stark terror.* 傑里的眼睛睜得很大, 神色極度恐懼。| **in stark contrast to** (=completely opposite) 與…形成鮮明對照 *Their poverty was in stark contrast to the luxury all around them.* 他們的貧窮與周圍的奢華形成了鮮明的對照。—**starkly** *adv* —**starkness** *n* [U]

stark² *adv* **1 stark naked** *informal* not wearing any clothes at all; completely NAKED【非正式】一絲不掛的, 赤裸裸的 **2 stark raving mad** also 又作 **stark staring mad** *BrE* completely crazy【英】完全瘋了的

stark·ers /ˈstɑrkɚz; ˈstɑːkəz/ *adj* [not before noun 不用於名詞前] *BrE informal* not wearing any clothes; NAKED【英, 非正式】一絲不掛的, 赤裸裸的

star·less /ˈstɑrlɪs; ˈstɑːləs/ *adj* with no stars showing in the sky 無星的; 沒有星光的

star·let /ˈstɑrlɪt; ˈstɑːlɪ̈t/ *n* [C] a young actress who plays small parts in films and is hoping to become famous 常演配角而渴望成名的年輕女演員

star·light /ˈstɑrˌlaɪt; ˈstɑːlaɪt/ *n* [U] the light that comes from the stars, often considered to be romantic 星光〔常被認為有浪漫氣息〕

star·ling /ˈstɑrlɪŋ; ˈstɑːlɪŋ/ *n* [C] a greenish black bird that is very common in Europe (紫翅) 椋鳥〔常見於歐洲〕

star·lit /ˈstɑrˌlɪt; ˈstɑːˌlɪt/ *adj literary* made brighter by stars【文】星光照耀的: *a starlit night* 星光照耀的夜晚

Star of Da·vid /ˌstɑr əv ˈdevɪd; ˌstɑːr əv ˈdeɪvɪ̈d/ *n* [C usually singular 一般用單數] a star with six points that is strongly connected with Judaism or the state of Israel 大衞之星〔為猶太教和以色列國標誌的六角星〕

star·ry /ˈstɑrɪ; ˈstɑːri/ *adj* having many stars 佈滿星星的: *a starry winter sky* 滿天星斗的冬夜

starry-eyed /ˌ·· ˈ·◂/ *adj informal* happy and hopeful about things in a way that is silly or UNREALISTIC【非正式】過分樂觀的; 不切實際的: *a starry-eyed optimist* 不切實際的樂天派

Stars and Stripes /ˌ· · ˈ·/ *n* [singular] *AmE* the flag of the US【美】星條旗, 美國國旗

star sign /ˈ· ·/ *n* [C] one of the twelve signs of the ZODIAC (=the system that uses people's birth dates to say what will happen to them in the future)〔黃道十二宮之一的〕宮; 星座

Star-Span·gled Ban·ner /ˌ· ·· ˈ··/ *n* [singular] **1** the NATIONAL ANTHEM (=national song) of the US《星條旗永不落》,《星條旗之歌》〔美國國歌〕 **2** *AmE literary* the flag of the US【美, 文】星條旗, 美國國旗

star-stud·ded /ˈ· ˌ··/ *adj* including many famous performers 明星雲集的: *a star-studded cast* 明星雲集的演員陣容

start¹ /stɑrt; stɑːt/ *v* [S2] [W2]

1 ►BEGIN DOING STH 開始做某事◄ [I,T] to begin doing something 開始〔做某事〕: **start doing sth** *I've just started learning German.* 我剛開始學德語。| *We'd better start getting dressed soon.* 我們最好趕快穿好衣服。| **start to do sth** *When Tom heard this he started to laugh uncontrollably.* 湯姆在聽到這事時, 忍不住笑了起來。| *Things started to go wrong after we reached Cairo.* 我們到達開羅後, 情況開始不對勁了。| *Damn! It's just started to rain.* 該死! 開始下雨了。| **start sth** *Haven't you started that book yet?* 你開始讀那本書了沒有? | *There was so much to do we didn't know where to start.* 要做的事情太多了, 我們不知道從哪裡開始。| *Do start,* (=begin to eat a meal) *or it'll go cold.* 開始吃吧, 不然要涼了。| **[+from]** *Starting from point A draw a straight line down to point B.* 從A點開始, 畫一條直線至B點。| **start (off) with** (=deal with something as the first part of an activity) 從…開始做起 *Decorating the place was going to be a major job, and we decided to start with the kitchen.* 裝修這個地方是項大工程, 我們決定先從廚房開始做起。| **start (off) by doing** *Start by melting the butter in the frying pan.* 先在平底煎鍋裡把黃油融化。| **start again** (=begin doing something again) 又開始做某事 *Billy was afraid to say anything in case she started crying again.* 比利怕她又哭起來, 所以甚麼也不敢說。| **get started** (=start doing something, especially when you have not been able to do anything yet, or have been lazy) 開始幹; 着手做 *We'd better get started if we want to finish this job by midday.* 我們要想在中午前完成這項工作, 最好現在就開始幹。| **start from scratch** (=start a job or activity from the beginning) 從頭開始〔做某事〕 *They had to start from scratch redecorating the house.* 他們不得不從頭開始, 重新裝修房子。| **start afresh/anew** (=start doing something again better or differently) 重新開始 *Lisa saw the new job as a chance to start afresh.* 麗莎把這個新工作當作一次重新開始的機會。—see graph at 參見 COMMENCE 圖表

2 ►BEGIN HAPPENING 開始發生◄ also 又作 **start off** [I,T] to begin happening or make something begin happening (使) 開始發生: *Do you know what time the match starts?* 你知道比賽幾點鐘開始嗎? | **[+in]** *The marathon race starts in the city centre.* 馬拉松賽跑從市中心出發。| **start sth** *The avalanche was started by a rock fall on the higher slopes.* 雪崩是由高坡上一塊石頭滾落引起的。| **start sb doing sth** *The conversation he overheard had started him thinking.* 他無意中聽到的那段對話令他沉思起來。| **start with** *The festivities started with a huge fireworks display.* 慶祝活動一開始是大型煙花表演。| **starting from now/tomorrow/next week etc** *You have two minutes to answer the following questions starting from now.* 從現在開始, 你有兩分鐘時間回答下列問題。| **get started** (=start happening, especially after a delay)〔尤指在延誤後〕開始 *The match finally got started at 2.30 p.m.* 比賽最終於下午2時30分開始。

3 to start with a) used when talking about the beginning of a situation, especially when it changes later 起初, 開始時〔尤指情況後來發生變化〕: *I felt nervous to start with, but soon began to relax.* 我起初覺得有點緊張, 但很快就開始放鬆了。**b)** used to emphasize the first of a list of facts or opinions you are stating 首先, 第一〔用於強調所敘述的一系列事實、觀點等中的第一條〕: *We're not going on holiday this year; to start with we haven't got the money and then there's still a lot we need to do on the house.* 我們今年不去度假了, 首先, 我們沒有錢; 其次, 這房子還有很多事要我們去幹。—see 見 FIRSTLY (USAGE)

4 ►PERIOD OF TIME 一段時間◄ [I always+adv/prep, T always+adv/prep] if a fixed period of time starts in a certain way, or you start it in a certain way, it begins in that way 以某種方式開始: **[+badly/well]** *The season started badly for United when they lost their first three matches.* 賽季一開始聯隊就出師不利, 前三場比賽都輸掉了。| **start sth with/on etc** *Jerome always starts the day with a cup of coffee and a cigarette.* 傑羅姆每天起來總要來一杯咖啡和一根香煙。

5 be back where you started to have failed to do what you have been trying to do 試圖做某事失敗; 白費勁: *Liz hasn't got his address, so we're back where we started.* 利茲沒有他的地址, 所以我們是在白費工夫。

6 ►JOB/SCHOOL 工作/學校◄ [I,T] to begin a new job, or to begin going to school, college etc 開始(新的工作); 開始(上學): *The sales manager phoned this morning to ask if I could start next week.* 營業經理今天上午來電話, 問我能否下週上班。| **start school/college/work** *Simon's starting school in September.* 西蒙九月份就要開始上學了。

7 ►JOURNEY 旅程, 旅行◄ also 又作 **start off/out** [I] to begin a journey 啟程, 動身, 出發: *We'll have to start early to get to Edinburgh by midday.* 我們必須早早出發, 才能在中午之前到達愛丁堡。| **[+from]** *We start out from Harlow at seven.* 我們七點鐘從哈洛起程。

8 ►LIFE/PROFESSION 生活/職業◄ also 又作 **start off/out** [I always+adv/prep, T always+adv/prep] to begin your life or profession in a certain way 開始生活; 開始立業: **[+as/in]** *Rob started off as a salesman and now he's managing director.* 羅伯從一名推銷員開始做起, 現在成了總經理。| **start sth** *We started married life living in a caravan.* 我們剛結婚時住在一輛旅行拖車裡。

9 ►ROAD/RIVER 道路/河流◄ [I always+adv/prep] if a river, road etc starts somewhere it begins in that place 起源, 起始: **[+in/at]** *The Mississippi starts in Minnesota.* 密西西比河發源於明尼蘇達州。

10 ►CAR 汽車◄ also 又作 **start up** [I,T] if you start a car or engine or if it starts, it begins to work (使) 發動, (使) 開始運作, 啟動: *The car wouldn't start this morning.* 今天早上這輛車發動不起來。| **get the car/engine started** *He couldn't get his motorbike started.* 他的摩托車發動不起來。

11 ►PRICES 價格◄ [I always+adv/prep] if prices start at or from a particular figure, that is the lowest figure at which you can get or buy something〔價格等〕自...起: **[+at/from]** *Prices for bed and breakfast start at £15 a night.* 牀鋪宿夜加次日早餐的價錢由15英鎊起。

12 ►BUSINESS/CLUB 公司/俱樂部◄ also 又作 **start up** [T] to make something begin to exist 創辦; 建立: *Sally decided to start up a club for single mums in the neighbourhood.* 莎莉決定在鄰近的住宅區成立一個單親媽媽俱樂部。| **start a business/company/firm** *Bruno started his own plumbing business when he was only 24.* 布魯諾年僅24歲時就創辦了自己的管道設備公司。

13 start a family to have your first baby 生第一個孩子: *At 34 she thought it was about time they started a family.* 34歲那年, 她覺得他們應該生個孩子了。

14 start a fire to deliberately cause a fire 點火, 生火

15 start a fight/argument etc to deliberately cause a fight, argument etc 挑起打鬥/爭吵等: *Don't let him drink too much – he'll only start a fight with someone.* 別讓他喝太多的酒, 不然他只會找人尋釁打架。

16 start a rumour to tell other people something, usually something unpleasant or untrue 造謠, 散佈流言: *She wondered who could have started such a vicious rumour.* 她想知道是誰在散佈如此惡毒的謠言。

17 Don't (you) start! *BrE spoken* used to tell someone to stop complaining, arguing or annoying you【英口】別招人煩!〔用於叫某人停止抱怨、爭吵或騷擾〕: *"Mum, I don't like this ice-cream." "Oh, don't you start!"* "媽媽, 我不喜歡這冰淇淋。" "哦, 你別招我厭煩了!"

18 you started it! *spoken* used to tell someone that they caused an argument or problem【口】是你挑起來的!〔用於表示爭論或問題是某人引起的〕: *"Stop arguing with me Dave!" "It was you who started it."* "戴夫, 別再跟我爭論了!" "這是你先挑起的。"

19 start something/anything to begin causing trouble 惹麻煩, 闖禍: *I was worried in case my mate Ronnie started anything.* 我擔心萬一我的朋友羅尼惹出麻煩。

20 ►MOVE SUDDENLY 突然移動◄ [I] to move your body suddenly, especially because you are surprised or afraid〔尤指因吃驚或害怕〕突然移動; 驚起, 嚇一跳: *A loud knock at the door made her start.* 巨大的敲門聲把她嚇了一跳。| **[+from]** *Emma started from her chair and rushed to the window.* 埃瑪從椅子上驚跳起來, 向窗口衝去。

21 ►LIQUID 液體◄ [I always+adv/prep] if a liquid or substance starts from somewhere, it comes out quickly〔液體等〕湧出; 突然出現: *Blood started from the wound.* 血從傷口湧出。

22 start young to begin doing something when you are young 很年輕就開始(做某事): *"Marcia's only ten and she's already got a boyfriend." "Yes, they start young nowadays!"* "瑪西婭才十歲就已經有男朋友了。" "是啊, 現在的孩子早戀!"

start off *phr v* **1** [I,T] to begin happening or make something begin happening (使) 開始: **start sth ↔ off** *Richard started the discussion off by telling us about his experiences in Africa.* 理查德向我們講述了他在非洲的經歷, 作為討論的開場白。| *The match started off at a fast and furious pace.* 比賽一開始節奏急速, 戰況激烈。**2** [I] to begin a journey 啟程, 動身: *What time will we have to start off in the morning?* 我們必須早上幾點鐘動身? **3** [I] to move in a particular direction 朝〔某方向〕移動: *The bus started off slowly up the road.* 公共汽車慢慢地上路了。**4** [T **start** sb **↔ off**] to help someone begin an activity 幫助〔某人〕開始: *I tried to start the children off by giving them ideas for things to write about.* 我給孩子們提供一些題材, 幫助他們動筆。**5** [T **start** sb **↔ off**] *informal* to make someone get angry, or start laughing, by saying something【非正式】〔說某事〕使〔某人〕生氣[發笑]: *Don't mention Steve's name to Jenny; it'll only start her off!* 別跟珍妮提起史蒂夫的名字, 那只會惹她生氣! | **start sb off doing sth** *David's remarks started the girls off giggling.* 大衛的話令女孩們咯咯地笑了起來。

start sb **on** sth *phr v* [T] to make someone start doing something regularly, especially because it will be good for them 使開始有規則地做〔尤指做對某人有益的事〕: *We started Gemma on solid foods when she was four months old.* 吉瑪四個月大的時候, 我們開始餵她吃固體食物。

start on sth *phr v* [T] to begin doing something or using something 開始做; 開始使用: *Let's start on the wine shall we?* 我們開始喝酒好嗎? | *I guess it's time we started on the packing.* 我想我們該開始收拾行李了。

start on at sb *phr v* [T] to begin criticizing someone or complaining to them about something 開始批評, 開始抱怨: *Ray's wife started on at him about how he spent* *too much time in the pub.* 雷的太太開始抱怨他怎麼花那麼多的時間泡酒吧。

start over *phr v* [I] *AmE* to start doing something again from the beginning, especially because you want to do it better【美】重新開始, 從頭做起: *If you make a mistake when you're keying, just press delete and start over.* 如果鍵盤輸入出錯, 就按刪除鍵重新開始。

This graph shows how common the different grammar patterns of the verb **start** are. 本圖表顯示, 動詞 start 構成的不同語法模式的使用頻率。

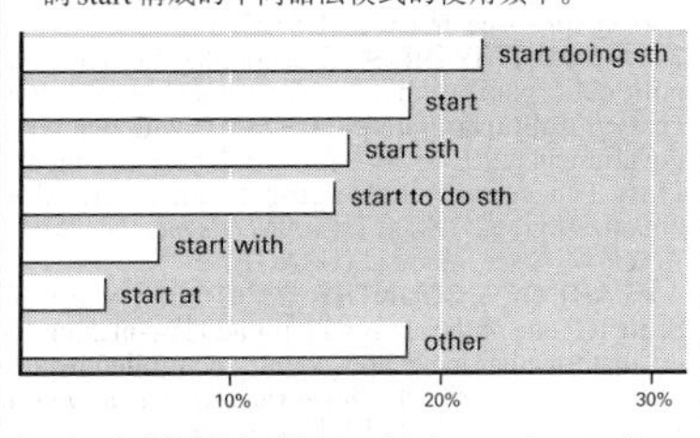

Based on the British National Corpus and the Longman Lancaster Corpus
據英國國家語料庫和朗文蘭卡斯特語料庫

S2 W3 **start²** *n*

1 ▶OF AN ACTIVITY/EVENT 用於活動/事件◀ [C usually singular 一般用單數] the beginning of an activity or event or the point at which it starts to develop〔活動或事件的〕開始, 開端; 起始點: **[+of]** *This fighting marked the start of more widespread civil unrest.* 這場戰鬥標誌着更廣泛的國內動蕩的開始。| *We arrived late and missed the start of the film.* 我們遲到了, 錯過了電影的開頭。| **(right) from the start** *We've had problems with this project right from the start.* 這個項目從剛一開始起我們就遇到許多難題。| **from start to finish** *The concert was a fiasco from start to finish.* 這場音樂會從頭到尾都很失敗。| **get off to a good/bad start** (=begin well or badly) 開始時很好 / 不好 *Chelsea got off to a good start, beating their opponents 5-0.* 切爾西隊開局順利, 以 5 比 0 擊敗對手。

2 ▶OF A PERIOD OF TIME 一段時間的◀ [C usually singular 一般用單數] the beginning of a fixed period of time 一段時間的開始: **the start of the year/day/season** *The start of the season was marred by the awful weather.* 這個季節一開始就給糟糕的天氣破壞了。| **get off to a good/bad start** *The day got off to a bad start when I missed the train.* 我那天誤了火車, 從一開始就不順利。

3 make a start (on sth) to begin doing something 着手〔做某事〕: *I guess it's time I made a start on the housework.* 我想我該着手做家務了。

4 ▶SPORT 體育運動◀ the start the place where a race begins〔比賽的〕起點; 起跑線: *The horses were all lined up at the start.* 馬匹在起跑線上各就各位。

5 ▶ADVANTAGE 優勢◀ [C usually singular 一般用單數] a situation in which you have an advantage over other people 優勢地位; 有利條件: *George was grateful to his parents for the start they'd given him.* 喬治感謝父母為他提供有利條件。| **a start in life** (=things that will help you to succeed in life) 人生中有利於成功的優勢 *Naturally we want to give our kids the best possible start in life.* 當然, 我們想給孩子們最好的人生起步條件。

6 ▶IN A RACE/COMPETITION 在賽跑/比賽中◀ [C usually singular 一般用單數] the amount of time or space by which one person is ahead of another, especially in a race or competition〔尤指在賽跑或比賽中的〕搶先之時間[距離]: *They decided to give the younger boys a sixty metre start.* 他們決定讓那些年齡小的男孩先跑六十米。| **[+on]** *The prisoners had a three hour start on their pursuers.* 囚犯們逃跑了三個小時後, 追捕的人才開始追。

7 ▶SUDDEN MOVEMENT 突然移動◀ [singular] a sudden movement of the body, usually caused by fear or surprise〔因恐懼或吃驚〕突然移動; 驚起: **with a start** *Ted woke up with a start and felt for the light switch.* 特德猛然驚醒過來, 摸索着找電燈開關。| **give you a start** (=frighten or surprise you) 令某人吃了一驚 *The sound of footsteps gave me quite a start.* 腳步聲嚇了我一大跳。

8 for a start used to emphasize the first of a list of facts or opinions you are stating 首先, 第一〔用於強調一系列事實或觀點的第一條〕: *Vincent should never have been picked for the team; for a start he has not had enough experience.* 文森特根本就不該入選球隊; 首先他經驗不足。—see also 另見 FALSE START, **in/by fits and starts** (FIT³ (6))

start·er /ˈstɑrtɚ; ˈstɑːtə/ *n* [C] **1** a person, horse, car etc that is in a race when it starts〔賽跑、賽馬、賽車等的〕參賽者[馬、汽車等]: *Of the eight starters, only three finished the race.* 參賽的八名選手中, 只有三名賽完全程。 **2 for starters** *informal* a phrase meaning to begin with, used to tell someone what should be done or said first【非正式】首先, 第一, 作為開頭: *Well, for starters, you'd better get an application form.* 哦, 首先, 你最好拿一張申請表。 **3** someone who gives the signal for a race to begin〔賽跑的〕發令員: *The starter fired his gun.* 發令員鳴響發令槍。| **under starter's orders** (=about to begin the race) 準備起跑 **4** a piece of equipment for starting a machine, especially an electric motor for starting an engine〔機器的〕起動裝置〔尤指使發動機起動的電動機〕 **5** *BrE* the first part of a meal; APPETIZER【英】〔一頓飯的〕第一道菜, 開胃小吃: *Would you like soup or melon as a starter?* 第一道菜你是要湯還是要甜瓜? —see also 另見 NONSTARTER, SELF-STARTER

starter home /ˈ·· ·/ *n* [C] *BrE* a small house or apartment bought by people who are buying their first home【英】起步房〔第一次置業者購買的小房子或小公寓〕

starter mo·tor /ˈ·· ˌ··/ *n* [C] a STARTER (4)〔機器的〕起動裝置 —see picture at 參見 ENGINE 圖

starter pack /ˈ·· ·/ *n* [C] the basic equipment and instructions that you need to start working, especially on a computer〔尤指電腦操作的〕啟動包, 基礎設備和指令

start·ing block /ˈ·· ·/ *n* [C] one of a pair of blocks fixed to the ground that a runner pushes their feet against at the start of a race 起跑器

starting gate /ˈ·· ·/ *n* [C] a gate or pair of gates that open to allow a horse or dog through at the start of a race〔賽馬或賽狗比賽的〕起跑閘

starting price /ˈ·· ·/ *n* [C] the last PRICE (=amount of money that is returned for money risked) that is offered just before a horse or dog race begins〔賽馬或賽狗的〕臨賽賠率, 賭率

start·le /ˈstɑrtḷ; ˈstɑːtl/ *v* [T] to make someone suddenly surprised or slightly shocked 使〔某人〕吃驚; 嚇〔某人〕一跳: *You startled me! I didn't hear you come in.* 你嚇了我一跳! 我沒有聽見你進來。| **startled to see/hear/learn etc** *I was startled to see Amanda there.* 我看到阿曼達在那裡, 吃了一驚。

start·ling /ˈstɑrtlɪŋ; ˈstɑːtlɪŋ/ *adj* very unusual or surprising 驚人的; 令人震驚的: *Paddy's words had a startling effect on the children.* 帕迪的話在孩子們身上產生了驚人的效果。—**startlingly** *adv*: *startlingly pale* 蒼白得驚人

start-up /ˈ· ·/ *adj* start-up costs are connected with beginning and developing a new business 創辦時的〔成本〕; 起始〔階段〕的: *a start-up budget of $90,000* 9 萬美元的創辦預算

starv·a·tion /stɑrˈveʃən; stɑːˈveɪʃən/ *n* **1** [U] suffering or death caused by lack of food 挨餓, 飢餓; 餓死: *people dying of starvation in the famine* 在饑荒中餓得瀕臨死亡的人 **2 starvation diet** *informal* very little food【非正式】極少量的食物 **3 starvation wages** extremely low wages 挨餓工資, 極低的工資

starve /stɑrv; stɑːv/ *v* [I,T] **1** to suffer or die because you do not have enough to eat, or to make someone else do this (使)挨餓; (使)餓死: *Thousands of people will starve if food doesn't reach the stricken city.* 如果食物不能運到那座受災的城市, 數以千計的人就要餓死。| **starve sth** *The dog looked like it had been starved.* 這隻狗看上去像是被餓壞了。| **starve to death** (=die from lack of food) 餓死 *They'll either die from the cold or starve to death.* 他們要麼將被凍死, 要麼將被餓死。**2** to not give or not be given something very important, for example love or money, with harmful results〔使某人〕得不到某物〈如愛或錢〉而受苦; 缺乏: **[+of]** *The schools are understaffed and starved of funds.* 學校師資不足, 資金匱乏。| **be starved for sth** *AmE* (=not get any at all)【美】得不到某物 *That poor kid's just starved for attention.* 那個可憐的孩子極需關注。**3 be starving** also 又作 **be starved** *especially AmE spoken*【尤美, 口】to be very hungry 感覺很餓, 餓極了: *You must be starving! Come and eat lunch.* 你肯定餓壞了！快來吃午飯吧。

starve sb **into** *phr v* [T] to force someone to do something, by preventing them from getting food or money 以飢餓迫使..., 使〔某人〕餓得只好做〔某事〕: *The miners were starved into submission.* 礦工們被餓得只好屈服。

starve sb **out** *phr v* [T] to force someone to leave a place by preventing them from getting food 使〔某人〕挨餓而被迫離開〔某處〕: *If we can't blast them out, we'll starve them out.* 如果不能把他們炸出來, 我們就把他們餓出來。

S

starve·ling /ˈstɑrvlɪŋ; ˈstɑːvlɪŋ/ *n* [C] *literary* a person or animal that is thin and unhealthy from lack of food【文】〔因飢餓而〕瘦弱不堪的人[動物]

starving /ˈstɑrvɪŋ; ˈstɑːvɪŋ/ *adj* **1** so hungry that you will die soon if you do not eat 飢餓的, 挨餓的: *pictures of starving children* 飢餓兒童的照片 | **the starving** (=people who are starving) 飢民 **2** [not before noun 不用於名詞前] *spoken* very hungry【口】很餓的: *Can we get something to eat – I'm absolutely starving.* 我們弄點吃的吧 —— 我餓極了。

stash¹ /stæʃ; stæʃ/ *v* [T always+adv/prep] *informal* to store something in a safe, often secret, place【非正式】儲藏, 存放, 藏匿: **stash sth away** *He has money stashed away in the Bahamas.* 他把錢藏在巴哈馬。| **[+in/under]** *You can stash your gear in here.* 你可以把你的工具存放在這裡。

stash² *n* [C] *informal* an amount of something that is kept in a secret place【非正式】隱藏的東西: **[+of]** *a stash of drugs* 藏匿的一批毒品

state¹ /stet; steɪt/ *n*

1 ►CONDITION 狀況◄ [C] the mental, emotional, or physical condition that someone or something is in at a particular time 狀況, 狀態, 情況, 情形: *Frankly I wouldn't trust his emotional state right now.* 坦白地說, 我不相信他目前的情緒狀態。| *Water exists in three states: liquid, gaseous, and solid.* 水有三種狀態: 液態、氣態和固態。| **in a bad/good etc state** *The roads are in a terrible state after the severe winter weather.* 嚴冬過後, 公路的路面情況極差。| **[+of]** *The driver was in a state of shock.* 司機處於休克狀態。| **not in a fit state to do sth** (=not healthy enough or in a good enough condition) 因健康狀況不佳而不適宜做某事 *David's in no fit state to go out yet.* 大衛健康狀況不佳, 仍不適宜外出。| **state of mind** (=the way you feel) 思想狀態; 心情 *Ames' dismissal had left him in a distressed state of mind.* 埃姆斯因被解雇而心煩意亂。| **be in a good/bad state of repair** (=not need repairing, or need repairing) 維修良好/亟待修葺 *The house we're buying is in a good state of repair.* 我們要買的房子維修得很好。| **a state of war** (=officially fighting another country) 戰爭[交戰]狀態 —see also 另見 STATE OF EMERGENCY

2 ►GOVERNMENT 政府◄ also 又作 **State** [singular, U] the government or political organization of a country 國家, 政府: *If elected, they want to cut back the powers of the state.* 如果當選, 他們要削減政府的權力。| *The State has allocated special funds for the emergency.* 國家已撥出專款應付緊急狀況。| **state employees/property/regulations etc** *limits on salary increases for state workers* 對政府職員加薪的限制 | **state-owned/state-funded/state-subsidized etc** (=owned, paid for etc by the government) 國有的/政府投資的/政府補貼的 *a state-funded community housing project* 政府資助的社區住房項目 | **matters of state** (=the business of the government) 國家大事 —see also 另見 POLICE STATE, WELFARE STATE —see 見 RACE¹ (USAGE)

3 ►A COUNTRY 國家◄ [C] a country considered as a political organization〔作為政治組織的〕國家: **democratic/totalitarian/one-party state** (=with that type of government) 民主/極權主義/一黨制的國家 | **member state** (=a country belonging to an international organization) 成員國, 會員國 *NATO's member states* 北約成員國 —see 見 RACE¹ (USAGE)

4 ►PART OF A COUNTRY 國家的一部分◄ also 又作 **State** [C] one of the areas with limited law-making powers that together make up a country controlled by a central government 州; 邦: *Queensland is one of the states of Australia.* 昆士蘭是澳大利亞的一個州。

5 ►CEREMONY 儀式◄ [U] the grand, official ceremonies and events connected with governments and rulers〔與政府和統治者有關的〕盛禮; 隆重儀式: **state visit** (=official visit to another country) 國事訪問 *the President's state visit to Moscow* 總統對莫斯科的國事訪問 | **state occasions** (=special public events) 隆重的盛典 *Their band often plays at the White House on state occasions.* 他們的樂隊經常在白宮的隆重盛典上演奏。| **in state** (=with a lot of comfort and public attention) 豪華地; 隆重地 *The empress travelled in state with all her ladies.* 女皇帶着她所有的貴族夫人、小姐隆重出行。—see also 另見 **lie in state** (LIE¹ (12))

6 the States *spoken* a word meaning the US, used especially by someone when they are outside the US【口】美國〔尤在美國境外時使用〕: *Which part of the States would you suggest I should visit?* 你會建議我去美國的哪個地方?

7 be in a state/get into a state *spoken* to be or become very nervous, anxious, or excited【口】處於/陷入緊張[焦慮、興奮]之中: *Mom and Dad were in a state when I didn't come home until very late.* 我很晚才回到家, 爸爸媽媽非常着急。

8 state of affairs a situation 情況, 局勢, 事態: *I must say this is a very unsatisfactory state of affairs.* 必須承認, 目前的局勢令人很不滿意。

9 the state of play a) the position reached in an activity or process that has not finished yet〔某一活動或過程的〕當前進展情況: *What is the state of play in the current negotiations?* 目前談判的最新情況怎麼樣? **b)** the score points that have been gained at one time in a sports game〔體育比賽在某一時刻的〕得分

state² *v* [T] **1** to formally give a piece of information or your opinion, especially by saying it clearly 陳述, 說明, 闡明: *Please state your name and address.* 請說出你的姓名和地址。| *The Government needs to clearly state its policy on UN intervention.* 政府需要就聯合國干預問題清楚地闡明其政策。| **[+(that)]** *The witness stated that he had not seen the woman before.* 證人說他以前從未見過那個女人。| **state the obvious** (=say something that is completely unnecessary because it is already clear) 陳述明顯的事實 **2** if a document, newspaper, ticket etc states information, it contains the information written clearly〔文件、報紙、票據等〕寫明: *The price of the tickets is stated on them.* 票價清楚地印在票上。

state at·tor·ney /ˌ· ·ˈ··/ *n* [C] *AmE* a lawyer who represents the state in court cases【美】州檢察官

state ben·e·fit /ˌ· ˈ···/ *n* [C,U] money given by the government in Britain to people who are poor, without a job, ill etc〔英國的〕政府救濟金

state court /ˈ· ·/ *n* [C] a court in the US which deals with legal cases that are concerned with state laws or a state's CONSTITUTION (1)〔美國的〕州法院

State De·part·ment /ˈ· ·,··/ *n* the American government department that deals with anything connected with foreign countries 美國國務院

state·hood /ˈstethud; ˈsteɪthʊd/ *n* [U] **1** the condition of being an independent nation 獨立國家的地位 **2** the condition of being one of the states making up a nation, such as the US〔美國等國的〕州 [邦] 的地位

State·house /ˈstet,haus; ˈsteɪthaʊs/ *n* [C usually singular 一般用單數] the building where the lawyers in a US state do their work〔美國的〕州議會大廈

state·less /ˈstetlɪs; ˈsteɪtləs/ *adj* not officially being a citizen of any country 無國籍的: *All stateless individuals were presumed to be lawless vagabonds.* 所有無國籍的人均被推定是沒有法律控制的流浪者。—**statelessness** *n* [U]

state line /,· ˈ·/ *n* [C] the line between two states in the US〔美國的〕州界線: *At the end of the trip we crossed the state line into California.* 行程最後, 我們跨過州界線進入加利福尼亞州。

state·ly /ˈstetlɪ; ˈsteɪtli/ *adj* **1** done slowly and with a lot of ceremony; formal 緩慢而莊嚴的; 正式的: *the stately progress of the procession* 隊伍緩慢而莊嚴的行進 **2** impressive in style and size; NOBLE¹ (2) 雄偉的; 高貴的; 堂皇的: *the stately trees of the pine forest* 松樹林裡的參天大樹

stately home /,·· ˈ·/ *n* [C] a large house in the countryside in Britain which has historical interest 豪華宅第〔英國有歷史價值的鄉村大宅〕

[2] [1] **state·ment¹** /ˈstetmənt; ˈsteɪtmənt/ *n* **1** [C] something you say or write publicly or officially to let people know your intentions or opinions, or to record facts〔正式的〕陳述; 聲明: *False statements on your tax form could land you in jail.* 在報稅表上作不實申報會把你送進監獄的。| **make a statement (about)** *Before we begin, I'd like to make a statement about my involvement.* 在我們開始之前, 我想就我和此事的關係作一聲明。| **issue a statement** (=write something that can be read in public or given to newspapers) 發表聲明 *The Congressman issued a statement to the press.* 這位國會議員向新聞界發表了一份聲明。| **get/take a statement** (=officially write down what someone says) 正式記錄〔某人的〕陳述 | **sworn statement** (=that you officially declare to be true) 經宣誓的證詞 **2** [C] a list showing amounts of money paid, received, owing etc and their total 結算表, 財務報表: *the company's annual financial statement to shareholders* 公司給股東的年度財務報表 | **bank statement** (=sent regularly from your bank about your account) 銀行賬戶結算單 **3** [U] *formal* the act of expressing something in words【正式】措詞; 表達: *The details of the agreement need more exact statement.* 這項協議中細節的措詞需要更加準確。

statement² *v* [T] *BrE* if an education authority statements a child who has special educational needs, they give a school additional money to help teach that child【英】〔教育部門〕為〔有特殊教育需要的學生〕向其所在學校提供額外教育經費 —**statemented** *adj*

state of e·mer·gen·cy /,· · ·ˈ···/ *n* [C] a situation that a government officially declares to be very dangerous, and in which it uses special laws so that it can react very quickly 緊急狀態: *There has been a call for the lifting of the state of emergency.* 有人呼籲解除緊急狀態。

state-of-the-art /,· · · ˈ·◂/ *adj* using the most modern and recently developed methods, materials, or knowledge 使用最先進技術的, 達到最新水平的: *state-of-the-art technology* 最先進的技術

state park /,· ˈ·/ *n* [C] a large park owned and managed by a US state, often in an area of natural beauty〔美國的〕州立公園

state·room /ˈstet,rum; ˈsteɪtrʊm/ *n* [C] one of the large rooms in a palace〔宮殿裡的〕豪華房間

State's at·tor·ney /,· ·ˈ··/ *n* [C] *AmE* STATE ATTORNEY【美】州檢察官

state school /ˈ· ,·/ *n* [C] a British school which receives money from the government and provides free education〔英國的〕公立學校

State's ev·i·dence /,· ˈ···/ *n AmE*【美】**turn State's evidence** if a criminal turns State's evidence, they give information in a court of law about other criminals〔罪犯向法庭〕提供對同案犯不利的證據;〔罪犯〕作為污點證人指控同黨; QUEEN'S EVIDENCE *BrE*【英】

State·side /ˈstet,saɪd; ˈsteɪtsaɪd/ *adj, adv AmE informal* a word meaning in the US or connected with the US, used by people when they are not in the US【美, 非正式】在美國; 美國的〔談話者不在美國時使用〕: *When were you last Stateside?* 你最近甚麼時候在美國?

states·man /ˈstetsmən; ˈsteɪtsmən/ *n* [C] a political or government leader, especially one who is respected as being wise, honourable, and fair〔尤指賢明公正的〕政治家 —**statesmanlike** *adj*: *a statesmanlike performance in dealing with the crisis* 在處理危機中表現出的政治家風範 —**statesmanship** *n* [U]

state tax /ˈ· ·/ *n* [C,U] *AmE* a tax in the US that is paid to the state rather than to the central government【美】州稅 —compare 比較 FEDERAL TAX

state troop·er /,· ˈ··/ *n* [C] *AmE* a member of a police force that is controlled by one of the US state governments who works anywhere in that state【美】州警察

state u·ni·ver·si·ty /,· ··ˈ···/ *n* [C] *AmE* a university in the US which receives money from a state to help pay its costs【美】州立大學

state·wide /ˈstetˋwaɪd; ˈsteɪtwaɪd/ *adj AmE* affecting an entire US state【美】影響全州的; 全州範圍的: *Regulations will be local rather than statewide.* 規章將適用於當地, 而不是整個州。

stat·ic¹ /ˈstætɪk; ˈstætɪk/ *adj* not moving, changing, or developing, especially when movement or change would be good 不動的; 不變化的; 不發展的; 靜 (止) 的: *Economists predict that house prices will stay static for a long period.* 經濟學家預測, 房價將長期保持穩定。—compare 比較 DYNAMIC¹ (2,3)

static² *n* [U] **1** noise caused by electricity in the air that blocks or spoils the sound from radio or TV 靜電干擾 **2** static electricity 靜電 **3** *AmE informal* complaints or opposition to a plan, situation, or action【美, 非正式】〔對計劃、狀況或行動的〕抱怨, 指責, 反對: *His promotion has caused a lot of static.* 他的晉升招致很多人的不滿。—**statically** /-klɪ; -kli/ *adv*

static e·lec·tri·ci·ty /,·· ··ˈ···/ *n* [U] electricity that is not flowing in a current, but collects on the surface of an object and gives you a small ELECTRIC SHOCK 靜電

stat·ics /ˈstætɪks; ˈstætɪks/ *n* [U] the science dealing with the forces that produce balance in objects that are not moving 靜力學 —compare 比較 **dynamics** (DYNAMIC² (1b))

sta·tion¹ /ˈsteʃən; ˈsteɪʃən/ *n* [1] [1]

1 ►TRAVEL 旅行◄ [C] **a)** a place where public vehicles regularly stop so that passengers can get on and off, goods can be loaded etc 車站: *the city bus station* 城市公共汽車站 | **train station** *especially AmE*【尤美】, **railway station** *especially BrE*【尤英】*It's time to meet Daddy at the train station.* 該去火車站接爸爸了。| **subway station** *AmE*【美】, **underground station** *BrE*【英】(=for trains that run under the ground) 地鐵站 **b)** the building or buildings at such a place 車站建築: *Is there a waiting room in the station?* 車站裡有候車室嗎? | *Grand Central Station* 中央火車站

2 ►ACTIVITY OR SERVICE 活動或服務◄ [C] a building or place that is a centre for a particular kind of service or activity 所; 站; 台; 局: **(police/fire) station** *You'll have to go with the officer to the station.* 你必須跟警察

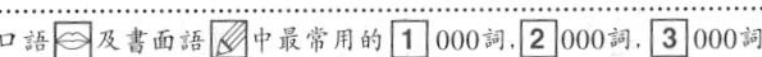
口語 及書面語 中最常用的 1 000詞, 2 000詞, 3 000詞

到警察局去。| **petrol station** *BrE*【英】, **gas station** *AmE*【美】(=where petrol is sold) 汽車加油站 | **polling station** (=where you vote in an election) 投票站 | **research station** *Frank spent six months at an arctic research station.* 弗蘭克在一個北極研究所度過了六個月。—compare 比較 ACTION STATIONS

3 ►BROADCASTING 廣播◄ [C] **a)** one of the many different signals you can receive on your radio or television, that a company broadcasts on〔電台或電視台的〕頻率, 台: *Tom tuned the radio to a country music station.* 湯姆把收音機調到一個鄉村音樂台。| **get/pick up a station** *I can't get many stations on this thing.* 這玩意能收到的頻道不是很多。**b)** an organization which makes television or radio broadcasts, or the building where this is done 電視台; 廣播電台: *That woman from the local TV station is here for your interview.* 當地電視台的那位女士來這裡採訪你。—compare 比較 CHANNEL[1] (1,2)

4 ►POSITION 位置◄ [C] a place where someone stands or sits in order to be ready to do something quickly if needed 崗位; 位置: *You're not to leave your station unless told.* 沒有命令, 你不得離開崗位。

5 ►FARMING 畜牧業◄ [C] a large sheep or cattle farm in Australia or New Zealand〔澳大利亞或新西蘭的〕大牧羊場; 大牧牛場

6 ►SOCIAL RANK 社會地位◄ [C] *old-fashioned* your position in society【過時】社會地位; 身分: **above your station** (=higher than your social rank) 高於自己的地位 *Don't get ideas above your station.* 不要有超越自己地位的想法。

7 ►MILITARY 軍事◄ [C] a small military establishment 軍隊小型的駐地; 基地

8 ►SHIPS 船◄ [U] *technical* a ship's position in relation to others in a group, especially a military ship【術語】〔船隻的, 尤指軍艦的〕編隊位置, 戰位

station² *v* [T usually passive 一般用被動態] to put someone in a particular place in order to do a particular job or military duty 部署〔某人〕於; 安置; 使駐紮: *He's still in the Army, stationed in Washington.* 他仍在部隊, 駐紮在華盛頓。| *Two guards were stationed at the back of the room.* 在房間的後面佈置了兩名衛兵。

sta·tion·a·ry /ˈsteʃənˌɛrɪ; ˈsteɪʃənəri/ *adj* standing still instead of moving 不(移)動的; 靜止的: *How did you manage to drive into a stationary vehicle?* 你是怎麼開的車, 竟會撞上一輛停着不動的車子?

station break /ˈ·· ·/ *n* [C] *AmE* a pause during a radio or television broadcast in the US, so that local stations can give their names【美】〔美國電台、電視台的〕廣播間歇〔在節目中途的間歇用以插播台名〕

sta·tion·er /ˈsteʃənɚ; ˈsteɪʃənə/ *n* [C] *BrE*【英】**1 stationer's** a shop that sells stationery 文具店 **2** someone in charge of a shop that sells stationery 文具商, 文具店店主

sta·tion·e·ry /ˈsteʃənˌɛrɪ; ˈsteɪʃənəri/ *n* [U] **1** materials that you use for writing, such as paper, pens, pencils etc 文具 **2** paper for writing letters on, usually with matching envelopes〔一般指有信封配套的〕信紙: *a letter on hotel stationery* 用酒店信紙寫的信

sta·tion-house /ˈ·· ˌ·/ *n* [C] *AmE old-fashioned* the local office of the police in a town, part of a city etc; POLICE STATION【美, 過時】〔城鎮等的〕警察(分)局

station mas·ter /ˈ·· ˌ··/ *n* [C] someone who is in charge of a train station 火車站站長

station wag·on /ˈ·· ˌ··/ *n* [C] *AmE* a large car with extra space at the back, with a door there for loading and unloading【美】客貨兩用車; ESTATE CAR *BrE*【英】

S2 W3 **sta·tis·tic** /stəˈtɪstɪk; stəˈtɪstɪk/ *n* **1 statistics a)** [plural] a collection of numbers which represent facts or measurements 統計數字[資料]: *Statistics on illness are used in planning health care.* 疾病統計數字被用於制定保健計劃。| *Statistics show that 35% of new businesses fail in their first year.* 統計資料顯示, 35% 的新企業在第一年即倒閉。**b)** [U] the science of dealing with and explaining such numbers 統計學: *Statistics is a branch of mathematics.* 統計學是數學的一個分支。**2** [singular] a single number which represents a fact or measurement 數據; 統計數字中的一項: *Is he aware of the statistic that women make up 40% of the work force?* 女性佔勞動力的 40%, 他知道這個數據嗎? —see also 另見 VITAL STATISTICS —**statistical** *adj*: *statistical evidence* 以統計數字表明的證據 —**statistically** /-klɪ; -kli/ *adv*: *The variation is not statistically significant.* 這一變化在統計學上是沒有顯著意義的。

stat·is·ti·cian /ˌstætəˈstɪʃən; ˌstætɪˈstɪʃən/ *n* [C] someone who works with statistics 統計學家; 統計員

sta·tive /ˈstetɪv; ˈsteɪtɪv/ *adj technical* a stative verb describes a state rather than an action or event, and is not usually used in PROGRESSIVE[1] (3) forms, for example 'belong' in the sentence 'this book belongs to me'【術語】〔動詞〕表示狀態的〔一般不用進行式, 如 this book belongs to me 中的 belong〕

stats /stæts; stæts/ *n* [plural] *informal* statistics【非正式】統計學

stat·u·a·ry /ˈstætʃuˌɛrɪ; ˈstætʃuəri/ *n* [U] *technical* statues【術語】雕像; 塑像; 雕塑作品: *a fine collection of Greek statuary* 一批精美的希臘雕塑收藏品

stat·ue /ˈstætʃu; ˈstætʃuː/ *n* [C] an image of a person or animal that is made in solid material such as stone or metal and is usually large 雕像; 塑像: *a bronze statue of a horse* 一座馬的銅像 | *People say Rome is a city with many statues.* 人們說羅馬是一座有很多雕像的城市。—compare 比較 SCULPTURE

stat·u·esque /ˌstætʃuˈɛsk; ˌstætʃuˈesk/ *adj* large and beautiful in a formal way, like a statue 雕像般端莊優美的: *a tall statuesque woman* 一個身材高大、端莊優美的女人

stat·u·ette /ˌstætʃuˈɛt; ˌstætʃuˈet/ *n* [C] a very small statue for putting on a table or shelf〔放在桌子或架子上的〕小雕像; 小塑像 —compare 比較 BUST[2] (1)

stat·ure /ˈstætʃɚ; ˈstætʃə/ *n* [C,U] *formal*【正式】**1** the degree to which someone is admired or regarded as important 名聲, 聲望: *Louis Armstrong was a musician of world stature.* 路易斯·阿姆斯特朗是一位享譽世界的音樂家。**2** someone's height or size 身高; 身材: *short in stature* 身材矮小

sta·tus /ˈstetəs; ˈsteɪtəs/ *n* **1** [C,U] the legal position or condition of a person, group, country etc〔人、組織、國家等的〕法律地位; 身分, 狀況: *What is her immigration status?* 她的移民狀況如何? | *Don't accept any money if it will affect your amateur status.* 如果會影響你的業餘選手身分的話, 就不要接受任何金錢。| **marital status** (=whether you are married or not) 婚姻狀況 *Please state your name, age and marital status.* 請說明你的姓名、年齡和婚姻狀況。W2 **2** [U] **a)** your social or professional rank or position, considered in relation to other people 社會地位; 專業資格; 職位: **high/low status** *high status businessmen* 地位高的商人 **b)** high social position that makes people recognize and respect you 重要地位; 重要身分: *Barnes has a great status in the community.* 巴恩斯在這個社區有很高的地位。| **status symbol** (=something that you have or own that you think shows high social status) 社會地位的象徵 *A secretary is a boss's status symbol.* 祕書是老闆的身分象徵。**3** [C] a situation at a particular time, especially in an argument, discussion etc〔尤指爭論、討論等的〕狀態; 狀況: *What's the status of the trade talks?* 貿易談判進行到何種程度了?

status quo /ˌstetəs ˋkwo; ˌsteɪtəs ˈkwəʊ/ *n* **the status quo** the state of a situation as it is 現狀: **maintain the status quo** (=not make any changes) 維持現狀 *Managers want to maintain the status quo because they're afraid to take risks.* 經理們想維持現狀, 因為他們害怕冒險。

stat·ute /ˈstætʃut; ˈstætʃuːt/ *n* [C] **1** a law passed by a parliament, council etc and formally written down 法

令, 法規; 成文法: **by statute** *Protection for the consumer is laid down by statute.* 保障消費者權益已在法令裡作了規定。**2** a formal rule of an institution or organization〔某機構、組織的〕條例; 章程: *College statutes forbid drinking on campus.* 大學校規禁止在校園內喝酒。

statute book /'·· ·/ *n not technical*【非術語】**the statute book** a real or imaginary written collection of the laws in existence 成文法典, 法令全書: **on the statute book** (=in operation) 在實施中 *The government would like to see this new law on the statute book as soon as possible.* 政府希望看到這項新法令儘快付諸實施。

statute law /'·· ·/ *n* [U] the whole group of written laws established by a parliament, council etc 成文法 —compare 比較 COMMON LAW²

statute of lim·i·ta·tions /,·· · ··'··/ *n* [C] *AmE technical* a law which gives the period of time within which action may be taken on a legal question or crime【美, 術語】訴訟時效法規;〔法律上的〕時效

stat·u·to·ry /ˈstætʃuˌtɔri; ˈstætʃʊtəri/ *adj* fixed or controlled by law 依照法令的; 法定的: *statutory employment rights* 法定就業權利 | *She's below the statutory age for school attendance.* 她還不到法定的入學年齡。—**statutorily** *adv*

statutory of·fence /,···· ·'·/ *n* [C] *AmE technical* a crime that is described by a law and can be punished by a court【美, 術語】法定罪行

statutory rape /,···· '·/ *n* [C] *law* the act of having sex with someone who is not allowed by law to have sex【法律】法定強姦罪〔指與未成年人發生性關係〕

staunch¹ /stɔntʃ; stɔːntʃ/ *adj* giving strong, loyal support to another person, organization, belief etc; STEADFAST 堅定的; 忠實可靠的: *They are staunch trade unionists.* 他們是堅定的工會主義者。| *a staunch friend and ally* 堅定可靠的朋友和盟友 —**staunchly** *adv* —**staunchness** *n* [U]

staunch² also 又作 **stanch** *AmE*【美】—*v* [T] to stop the flow of liquid, especially of blood from a wound 止住〔液體的〕流出; 使〔傷口〕止血: *The blood seemed to pour from the wound and I thought I would never staunch the flow.* 血好像從傷口裡不停地往外湧, 我以為再也止不住了。

stave¹ /stev; steɪv/ *n* [C] **1** the set of five lines on which music is written 五線譜 **2** one of the thin curved pieces of wood fitted close together to form the sides of a BARREL¹ (1)〔桶邊上弧形的〕桶板, 側板

stave² *v*

stave in *phr v past tense and past participle* **staved** *or* **stove** [I,T] to break something inwards or be broken inwards by something〔從外向裡〕打破, 砸破: **stave sth ↔ in** *The ship's side was stove in when it went onto the rocks.* 船撞到了岩石上, 船舷被撞穿了。

stave sth ↔ **off** *phr v past tense and past participle* **staved** [T] to keep someone or something from reaching you or affecting you for a period of time 擋開; 避開: *She'd brought some fruit on the journey to stave off hunger.* 她旅途上帶了些水果充飢。| *Amazingly, the protestors have staved off the army for three nights running.* 令人驚奇的是, 抗議者們已經連續三個晚上把軍隊擋住。

staves /stevz; steɪvz/ the plural of STAFF

S1 W1 **stay¹** /ste; steɪ/ *v*

1 ►IN A PLACE 在某處◄ [I] to stop and remain in a place rather than go or leave 停留, 逗留, 留下: **stay (for) an hour/a while etc** *Can't you stay a little longer?* 你能再多待一會兒嗎? | **stay late** *I had to stay later than planned at work.* 我不得不比原計劃晚了些才下班。| **stay here/there** *Stay right there! I'll be back in a minute.* 待在那兒別動! 我一會兒就回來。| **stay to dinner/stay for lunch** *Can you stay for supper?* 你能留下來吃晚飯嗎? | **stay behind** (=remain after others have gone)〔在別人走後〕留下來 *I stayed behind to help clean up after the party.* 聚會結束後, 我留下來幫助收拾東西。—see graph at 參見 REMAIN 圖表

2 ►IN A POSITION 處於某位置◄ [I, linking verb 連繫動詞] to continue to be in a particular position, place, or state, without changing 保持原狀, 維持: **stay calm/quiet/warm etc** *It's going to stay cold for the next few days.* 在接下來的幾天裡天氣仍然寒冷。| *You'd think he could stay sober for once.* 你可能會認為這一次他能保持清醒。| **[+away/back/on etc]** *Stay away from my daughter!* 不要纏着我女兒! | *Get out of this house and stay out!* 滾出這幢房子, 別再回來! | *You stay on this road for one mile before turning off.* 順着這條路走一英里, 然後拐彎。| **stay in/out** (=not leave your home, or remain away from home) 待在家裡/不在家中 *I won't have you staying out on a school night.* 第二天要上學, 我不許你晚上不回家。| **stay up** (=not go to bed) 熬夜, 不睡覺 *I stayed up late to watch the film.* 我為看那部電影很晚才睡覺。| **stay in a job** (=keep doing it) 繼續做某工作 *I don't know whether to stay in teaching or not.* 我不知道是否該繼續當教師。| **stay around** *informal* (=not leave someone)【非正式】不離開某人 *How do you know he'll stay around?* 你怎麼知道他會待在你身邊? | **stay up/down/the same etc** (=remain at the same level) 保持不跌/不漲/不變等 *House prices have stayed down for a whole year.* 房價一整年都沒有上漲。| **stay out of** *spoken* (=not get involved)【口】不要捲入 *Stay out of this, Ben, it's none of your business.* 本, 別捲入這件事, 這跟你無關。

3 ►LIVE SOMEWHERE 住在某處◄ [I] to live in a place for a while as a visitor or guest〔過訪或做客時〕留宿, 暫住: **[+at/with]** *We stayed at the hotel for four nights.* 我們在那家旅店住了四晚。| *My mother is staying with us this week.* 我母親這星期來我們家住。| **stay the night/stay overnight/stay over** (=stay from one evening to the next day) 過夜 *You can stay overnight if you don't want to drive home.* 你要是不想開車回家, 可以在這兒過夜。

4 stay put *spoken* to remain in one place and not move【口】待在原處, 不動: *You stay put in the car while I run into the store!* 我跑去商店, 你待在汽車裡別動!

5 be here to stay to become accepted and used by most people 被普遍接受[使用]; 成為風尚: *Do you think computers are here to stay?* 你認為電腦會得到廣泛使用嗎?

6 stay after school to remain at school after the day's classes are finished, often as a punishment 課後留在學校〔常作為懲罰〕

7 stay the course *informal* to finish something in spite of difficulties【非正式】堅持到底: *Working in sales is very demanding and not many of our people stay the course.* 做銷售非常費力, 我們的很多銷售員都不能堅持到最後。

8 ►STOP 停止◄ [I,T] *literary* to stop doing something, or stop someone from doing something【文】停止; 制止

9 stay! used to tell a dog not to move 別動!〔作為對狗的命令〕

stay on *phr v* [I] to continue to do a job or to study after the usual or expected time for leaving〔在通常或預定的時間後〕繼續留下工作[學習]: *"I thought your contract was done." "It is, but I'm staying on."* "我以為你的合同期滿了。" "是的, 但我繼續留下來。"

stay² *n* **1** [C usually singular 一般用單數] a limited time of living in a place 停留, 逗留, 暫住: *I met her towards the end of my stay in Los Angeles.* 我在洛杉磯暫住快要結束時結識了她。| *a short stay in the hospital* 短期住院 **2** [C,U] *law* the stopping or delay of an action because a judge has ordered it【法律】延緩, 延期, 推遲: **stay of execution** (=a delay of the punishment) 刑罰的緩期執行 **3** [C] a strong wire or rope used for supporting a ship's MAST (1) 支索〔支撐船桅的繩索、鋼索〕**4** [C] a short piece of plastic, bone, or wire used to keep a shirt COLLAR¹ (1) or a CORSET stiff〔襯衫衣領、緊身胸衣等的〕撐條 **5 stays** [plural] a CORSET〔婦女穿的〕緊身胸衣, 緊身褡

S

stay-at-home /ˈ· · ˌ·/ *n* [C] *informal* someone who always stays at home and never does exciting things【非正式】不愛出門的人; 深居簡出的人

stay·er /ˋsteɚ; ˈsteɪə/ *n* [C] *BrE* a horse or person who can keep going to the end of a long race, job etc【英】有耐力的馬[人]

stay·ing pow·er /ˈ·· ˌ··/ *n* [U] the ability or energy to keep doing something difficult until it is finished 耐力, 持久力: *They showed their staying power in the long-distance races.* 他們在長跑比賽中顯示了耐力。

St Ber·nard /ˌsent bɚˋnɑrd; sənt ˈbɜːnəd/ *n* [C] a large strong Swiss dog that was trained in the past to help find people who were lost in the snow 聖班納狗, 聖伯納狗〔一種瑞士大狗, 過去被訓練用來尋找在雪中迷路的人〕

STD /ˌɛs ti ˋdi; ˌes tiː ˈdiː/ *n* [U] **1** subscriber trunk dialling; the telephone system in Britain that allows people to connect their own LONG-DISTANCE calls〔英國的〕用戶直撥長途電話 **2** sexually transmitted disease; a disease that is passed on through having sex, such as AIDS, HERPES etc 性傳播疾病〈如愛滋病、疱疹等〉

std the written abbreviation of 縮寫= STANDARD

stead /stɛd; sted/ *n* **do sth in sb's stead** *formal* to do something that someone else usually does or was going to do【正式】代替某人做某事 —see also 另見 **stand sb in good stead** (STAND[1] (43))

stead·fast /ˋstɛdˌfæst; ˈstedfɑːst/ *adj literary* faithful and very loyal【文】忠實的, 忠誠的: **[+in]** *Harold remained steadfast in his Christian faith throughout his life.* 哈羅德一輩子虔誠地信奉基督教。—**steadfastly** *adv* —**steadfastness** *n* [U]

3 **stead·y[1]** /ˋstɛdɪ; ˈstedi/ *adj*

1 ►NOT MOVING 不移動的◄ firmly held in a particular position and not moving or shaking 穩定的, 牢固的, 不搖晃的: *Keep the camera steady while you take a picture.* 照相時把照相機拿穩。| **a steady hand** *You need a steady hand for such a delicate job.* 做這樣精細的工作手要穩。

2 ►CONTINUOUS 持續的◄ moving, happening, or developing in a continuous gradual way 平穩進行的; 持續的; 逐漸的: *a steady decline in manufacturing output* 製造業產量的持續下降 | *Paul has made steady progress this year.* 保羅今年有持續的進步。| **a steady stream of visitors/enquiries etc** *a steady stream of East Germans making their way through the new gap in the wall* 源源不絕地穿越柏林牆的新缺口過來的東德人

3 ►NOT CHANGING 不變的◄ a steady level, speed etc stays about the same〔水平、速度等〕平穩的, 固定不變的: *We were driving at a steady 60 mph.* 我們一直以60英里的時速行駛。

4 ►PERSON 人◄ someone who is steady is sensible and you can depend on them 穩健的, 靠得住的: *a steady worker* 可靠的工人

5 steady job/work/income a job or work that will definitely continue over a long period of time 穩定的職位/工作/收入

6 steady boyfriend/girlfriend someone that you have been having a romantic relationship with 關係固定的男朋友/女朋友

7 steady relationship a serious and strong relationship that continues for a long time 穩定的關係 —**steadily** *adv* —**steadiness** *n* [U]

steady[2] *v* **1** [T] to hold something steady or make it steady 拿穩, 扶穩; 使穩定[穩固]: **steady yourself** (=get back your balance in order to prevent yourself from falling) 使自己站穩 *He tried to steady himself by grabbing the tree.* 他抓住那棵樹, 試圖使自己站穩。**2** [I] to stop increasing or decreasing and remain about the same 停止升降, 穩定下來: *The dollar has steadied after early losses on the money markets.* 美元在貨幣市場經歷了早些時候的下跌之後, 現在已經穩定下來。**3 steady your nerves** to make yourself calm 使自己鎮定: *She had a brandy to steady her nerves.* 她喝了一杯白蘭地酒, 使自己鎮定下來。

steady[3] *adv* **go steady (with sb)** to have a long regular romantic relationship with a BOYFRIEND or GIRLFRIEND (與某人) 有固定的戀愛關係

steady[4] *n* [C] *AmE informal* a BOYFRIEND or GIRLFRIEND that someone has been having a romantic relationship with【美, 非正式】關係確定的男朋友[女朋友]: *Jill is Ray's steady.* 吉爾是雷的對象。

steady[5] *interjection BrE informal*【英, 非正式】**1** used when you want to tell someone to be careful or not to cause an accident 當心; 穩一點: *Steady! You nearly knocked me over.* 小心點! 你差點兒把我撞倒了。**2 Steady on!** used when you think that what someone is saying is too strong or extreme 說話當心點〔當某人說話太重或太極端時用作提醒〕: *Steady on! Derek's not that bad.* 說話小心點! 德里克沒有那麼壞!

steady state the·o·ry /ˌ·· ˈ· ˌ···/ *n technical* the idea that things in space have always existed and have always been moving away from each other as new atoms begin to exist【術語】(宇宙學中的) 穩恆狀態理論 —compare 比較 BIG BANG THEORY

steak /stek; steɪk/ *n* **1** [C,U] good quality BEEF (=meat from a cow), or a large thick piece of any good quality red meat 牛排;〔紅色肉類的〕肉排: *I like my steak rare.* 我喜歡牛排燒得生一點。**2** [U] *BrE* beef that is not of such good quality and is used in making CASSEROLEs etc【英】用來做燉鍋菜的質量一般的牛肉 **3 cod/salmon/tuna etc steak** [C] a large thick piece of fish 鱈魚/三文魚/金槍魚排

steak·house /ˋstekˌhaus; ˈsteɪkhaʊs/ *plural* **steakhouses** /-ˌhauzɪz; -haʊzɪz/ *n* [C] a restaurant that serves steak 牛排餐廳

steak tar·tare /ˌ· ·ˈ·/ *n* [U] steak that is cut into very small pieces and eaten raw, usually with a raw egg〔通常配生雞蛋供生吃的〕韃靼牛肉末

steal 偷

He stole her purse *BrE*【英】/wallet *AmE*【美】.
He robbed the woman (of her purse) *BrE*【英】/wallet *AmE*【美】. 他偷了那位女士的錢包。

steal[1] /stil; stiːl/ *v past tense* **stole** /stol; stəʊl/ *past participle* **stolen** /ˋstolən; ˈstəʊlən/ 3 3

1 ►TAKE STH 拿走某物◄ [I,T] to take something that belongs to someone else 偷, 竊取: **[+from]** *Some drug users steal from their own families to finance their habit.* 有些吸毒者偷自己家裡的錢來購買毒品。| **steal sth** *Sean has a long history of stealing cars.* 肖恩偷汽車有很長時間了。| **steal sth from sb** *He was accused of stealing ideas from a rival studio.* 他被指控盜用敵對設計室的概念。

2 ►MOVE SOMEWHERE 向某處移動◄ [I always+adv/prep] to move quietly without anyone noticing you 悄悄

地移動: [+into/across etc] *I tried to steal out of the room without waking Stefan.* 我盡量悄悄地溜出房間，免得吵醒斯特凡。

3 steal the show/limelight/scene to do something, especially when you are acting in a play, that makes people pay more attention to you than to other people〔尤指演戲時〕搶出風頭

4 steal a look/glance etc to look at someone or something quickly and secretly 偷偷地看一眼/瞥一眼等

5 ▶SPORT 體育運動◀ [I,T] to run to the next BASE[2] (8) in the game of BASEBALL before someone hits the ball〔在棒球比賽中〕偷(壘)

6 steal a kiss to kiss someone quickly when they are not expecting it 偷吻(一下)

7 steal sb's thunder to get the success and praise someone else should have got, by doing what they had intended to do 搶在別人前面做某事而獲得成功和讚賞; 搶別人的功勞

8 steal a march on sb to secretly or unexpectedly start something that someone else had planned to do, so that you gain an advantage over them 偷偷地[出其不意地]搶在某人前頭; 搶佔先機

9 steal sb's heart *literary* to make someone fall in love with you【文】使某人愛上自己; 獲得某人的歡心

USAGE NOTE 用法說明: STEAL

WORD CHOICE 詞語辨析: **steal, take, rob, burgle, burglarize, pick sb's pocket**

People **steal** things (from people, cars, houses, shops, banks etc). steal 用於從某人那裡，或從汽車、房屋、商店、銀行等中偷竊: *He's stolen my Walkman!* (NOT 不用 *stolen me* or 或 *robbed my Walkman*) 他偷了我的隨身聽。| *Someone stole his passport while he was asleep.* 他睡着時，有人把他的護照偷走了。

Take is also often used in this sense. take 也常常用來表達這個意思: *Someone's taken my wallet.* 有人把我的錢包偷走了。

People **rob** other people (of things) especially in a public place. rob 用於搶劫某人(身上的東西)，尤指在公共場所: *A man was robbed by three youths as he walked home from work yesterday.* 一名男子昨天下班回家時被三名青年搶劫。

People **rob** banks, or gas stations, but usually **burgle** (*BrE*) or **burglarize** (*AmE*) a house or office. 搶劫銀行或汽車加油站用 rob，但闖入別人房子或辦公室行竊，一般用 burgle【英】或 burglarize【美】: *At least 10 houses in the area had been burgled during the night.* 這個地區起碼有 10 戶住宅在夜間被盜。

If someone **picks your pocket**, they steal things from your pocket, usually when you are in a crowd of people. pick your pocket 指"扒竊，掏某人的腰包"，一般是在人多擁擠的地方。

steal² *n* [C] *informal*【非正式】**1 be a steal** to be very cheap 便宜極了: *At 20 bucks the camera was a steal.* 這台照相機只要 20 美元，實在太便宜了。—see 見 CHEAP[1] (USAGE) **2** the act of running to the next BASE[2] (8) in the game of BASEBALL before someone hits the ball〔棒球比賽中的〕偷壘

stealth /stɛlθ; stelθ/ *n* [U] the action of doing something very quietly, slowly, or secretly so that no one notices you 悄悄的行動，祕密行動: *Cats rely on stealth to catch their prey.* 貓悄無聲息地行動以捕捉獵物。| **by stealth** *They are trying to carry out their aims by stealth, after failing to impose them by law.* 他們的目標未能通過法律來達到，現正試圖祕密地實施。

stealth bomb·er /'· ˌ··/ *n* [C] an American military aircraft that cannot be discovered by RADAR instruments〔美國的〕隱形轟炸機

stealth·y /ˈstɛlθɪ; ˈstelθi/ *adj* moving or doing something quietly and secretly 悄悄的，鬼鬼祟祟的，偷偷的: *His eye caught a stealthy movement at the edge of the wood.* 他看到樹林邊有人悄悄地在移動。—**stealthily** *adv*

steam¹ /stim; stiːm/ *n* [U] 3

1 ▶GAS 氣體◀ the hot mist that water produces when it is boiled 蒸汽，水蒸氣: *Be careful of the steam from the kettle.* 小心水壺冒出來的蒸汽。

2 ▶MIST ON A SURFACE 表面的霧氣◀ the mist that forms on windows, mirrors etc when warm wet air suddenly becomes cold 水汽; 霧氣

3 ▶POWER 動力◀ power that is produced by boiling water to make steam, in order to make things work or move 蒸汽動力[壓力]: *The engines are driven by steam.* 發動機是由蒸汽驅動的。| **steam engine/train etc** (=an engine etc that works by the power produced by steam) 蒸汽機車/火車等

4 let off steam to get rid of your anger or excitement in a way that does not harm anyone by doing something active 發泄怒火; 宣泄激情: *PE is a good time for the kids to let off steam!* 體育課是孩子們宣泄過剩精力的好時機!

5 run out of steam to no longer have the energy or the desire to continue doing something, especially because you are tired〔尤指因疲勞而〕泄氣; 失去動力: *The home team began to run out of steam in the last quarter.* 主隊在最後一節開始泄氣了。

6 get/pick up steam a) if an engine gets up steam, it gradually starts to go faster〔指發動機〕逐漸加速 **b)** if plans, beliefs etc get up steam, they gradually become more important and more people become interested in them〔計劃、觀念等〕逐漸變得重要，逐漸得到關注

7 under your own steam if you go somewhere under your own steam, you get there without help from anyone else 靠自己的力量: *I'll get to the restaurant under my own steam.* 我會自己設法趕到那家餐館。

8 go full steam ahead with to do something with as much energy and eagerness as possible 全力以赴地做〔某事〕

9 ▶RAILWAY 鐵路◀ a railway system in which the trains use steam for power 使用蒸汽機車的鐵路系統: *the age of steam* 蒸汽機車時代

steam² *v* **1** [I] if something steams, steam rises from it, especially because it is hot 散發蒸汽; 冒熱氣: *a mug of steaming coffee* 一杯冒着熱氣的咖啡 **2** [T] to cook something in steam〔用蒸汽〕蒸: *Steam the vegetables lightly.* 把蔬菜稍蒸一下。**3** [I always+adv/prep] to travel somewhere in a boat or train that uses steam to produce power 乘汽船[蒸汽火車]旅行: [+into/from etc] *During the next two weeks, we steamed from port to port.* 在接下來的兩週裡，我們乘汽船到了一個又一個港口。**4 be steamed** *AmE spoken* to be very angry【美口】非常生氣

steam sth ↔ open/off *phr v* [T] to use steam to open an envelope or to remove a stamp from an envelope 用蒸汽把〔信封〕打開/把〔郵票〕揭下來

steam up *phr v* [I,T] to cover or become covered with steam (使)蒙上水汽: **steam sth ↔ up** *The warm room steamed up my glasses.* 溫暖的房間使我的眼鏡結了一層水汽。—see also 另見 STEAMED-UP

steam·boat /ˈstimˌbot; ˈstiːmbəʊt/ *n* [C] a boat that uses steam to produce power and is used for sailing along rivers and coasts 汽船，汽艇

steam clean /'· ·/ *v* [T] to clean something made of cloth by using a machine that produces steam 蒸汽洗滌

steam·ed-up /ˌ· '·/ *adj* [not before noun 不用於名詞前] *informal* excited and angry or worried【非正式】激動的; 生氣的; 焦慮的: *Don't get so steamed-up about it – it's not really important.* 別為這事生那麼大的氣，其實這無關緊要的。

steam·er /ˈstimə; ˈstiːmə/ *n* [C] **1** a STEAMSHIP 汽船，大輪船 **2** a container used to cook food in steam 汽鍋，蒸鍋

S

steam·ing /ˈstimɪŋ; ˈstiːmɪŋ/ *adv* **1 steaming hot** very hot 十分炎熱的; 滾燙的: *It was a steaming hot day.* 那天天氣很熱。**2** *ScotE* very drunk【蘇格蘭】大醉的, 爛醉的

steam i·ron /ˈ· ˌ··/ *n* [C] an electric iron that produces steam in order to make clothes easier to iron 蒸汽熨斗

steam·roll /ˈstimˌrol; ˈstiːmrəʊl/ *v* [T] *AmE* to steamroller【美】〔以權力、影響力〕強迫, 迫使; 強行

steam·roll·er¹ /ˈstimˌrolɚ; ˈstiːmˌrəʊlə/ *n* [C] a heavy vehicle with very wide wheels that you drive over road surfaces to make them flat 蒸汽壓路機

steamroller² *v* [T] *informal* to force someone to do what you want them to do, or to make sure something happens by using all your power and influence【非正式】〔以權力、影響力〕強迫, 迫使; 強行; STEAMROLL *AmE*【美】: *He steamrollered his bill through Parliament against fierce opposition.* 他不顧別人的強烈反對, 以高壓手段強行使這項法案在議會通過。

steam·ship /ˈstimˌʃɪp; ˈstiːmˌʃɪp/ *n* [C] a large ship that uses steam to produce power 汽船, 大輪船

steam shov·el /ˈ· ˌ··/ *n* [C] *AmE* a large machine that digs and moves earth in a large bucket【美】挖土機, 電鏟

steam·y /ˈstimɪ; ˈstiːmi/ *adj* **1** full of steam or covered in steam 充滿蒸汽的; 水汽覆蓋的: *steamy windows* 被水汽覆蓋的窗戶 **2** sexually exciting and slightly shocking 色情而狂放的: *a steamy love affair* 狂放的性關係

steed /stid; stiːd/ *n* [C] *poetic* a strong fast horse【詩】駿馬

2 3 **steel¹** /stil; stiːl/ *n* **1** [U] strong metal that can be shaped easily, consisting of iron and CARBON 鋼, 鋼鐵: *a bridge made of steel* 鋼鐵大橋 | **stainless steel** *stainless steel cutlery* 不鏽鋼餐具 **2** [U] the industry that makes steel 鋼鐵工業: *Sheffield is a major steel town.* 設菲爾德是主要的鋼鐵城市。**3 nerves of steel** the ability to be brave and calm in a dangerous or difficult situation 超人的膽量, 巨大的勇氣: *You need nerves of steel to be a racing driver.* 要做賽車手, 你必須具有超人的膽量和勇氣。**4** [C] a thin bar of steel used to sharpen knives〔磨刀用的〕鋼棒

steel² *v* [T] **steel yourself** to prepare yourself to do something that you know will be unpleasant or upsetting 使自己堅強起來〔去應付不愉快的事〕: **steel yourself to do sth** *Bob steeled himself to tell her about her father's death.* 鮑勃硬起心腸把她父親的死訊告訴了她。

steel band /ˌ· ˈ·/ *n* [C] a group of people who play a type of music from the West Indies, in which you hit different areas on drums made from metal oil BARRELs to produce different musical sounds 鋼鼓樂隊〔以金屬油桶製成的鼓為樂器, 演奏一種西印度羣島音樂的樂隊〕

steel gui·tar /ˌ· ·ˈ·/ *n* [C] a musical instrument with ten strings that is played using a steel bar and a PEDAL (=a bar you press with your foot) 鋼結他〔一種有十根弦、用鋼棒和踏板演奏的樂器〕

steel wool /ˌ· ˈ·/ *n* [U] a rough material made of fine steel threads, that is used to make surfaces smooth, remove paint etc 鋼絲絨, 鋼棉〔用於磨光表面、擦除油漆等〕—compare 比較 WIRE WOOL

steel·works /ˈstilˌwɝks; ˈstiːlwɜːks/ *n* [C] *plural* **steelworks** a factory where steel is made 煉鋼廠 —**steelworker** *n* [C]

steel·y /ˈstilɪ; ˈstiːli/ *adj* **1 steely determination/expression etc** an extremely strong and determined attitude, expression etc 堅定[鋼鐵般]的決心/表情等 **2** having a grey colour like steel 鋼一樣灰白的, 鋼灰色的: *a steely sky* 鋼灰色的天空

3 **steep¹** /stip; stiːp/ *adj* **1** a road, hill etc that is steep slopes at a high angle〔路、山等〕陡的, 陡峭的: *The road's too steep to ride up on a bike.* 這路太陡了, 騎自行車上不去。**2** steep prices, charges etc are unusually expensive〔價格、收費等〕過高的, 過分昂貴的: *landlords asking steep rents* 收租過高的房東 **3** a steep increase or rise in something is a very big increase〔增加、上升〕大幅度的; 急遽的: *a steep increase in the number of car thefts in the area* 該地區汽車盜竊案的急劇上升 **4 that's/it's a bit steep** *BrE spoken* used to say that a request or action is unreasonable【英口】那太不合理了〔指要求或行動〕: *They want us to work on New Year's Day? That's a bit steep!* 他們要我們在元旦上班? 這太過分了! —**steeply** *adv* —**steepness** *n* [U]

steep² *v* [I,T] **1 be steeped in history/tradition etc** to have a lot of a particular quality such as history etc 有豐富歷史/傳統等: *a town steeped in history* 歷史悠久的小城 **2** to put food in a liquid and leave it there so that it becomes soft or has the same taste as the liquid 浸泡〔食物〕: *Steep the raisins in sherry.* 把葡萄乾泡在雪利酒中。

steep·en /ˈstipən; ˈstiːpən/ *v* [I,T] if a slope, road etc steepens or something steepens it, it becomes steeper (使)變得陡峭

stee·ple /ˈstipl̩; ˈstiːpəl/ *n* [C] a tall pointed tower on the roof of a church〔教堂的〕尖塔

stee·ple·chase /ˈstipl̩ˌtʃes; ˈstiːpəltʃeɪs/ *n* [C] **1** a long race in which horses jump over gates, water etc 越野障礙賽馬 **2** a long race in which people run and jump over fences, water etc 障礙賽跑

stee·ple·jack /ˈstipl̩ˌdʒæk; ˈstiːpəldʒæk/ *n* [C] someone whose work is repairing towers, tall CHIMNEYs etc 尖塔、高煙囪等的修理工

steer¹ /stɪr; stɪə/ *v*

1 ►CAR/BOAT ETC 汽車/船等◄ [I,T] to control the direction a vehicle is going, for example by turning a wheel 操縱〔車、船的行駛方向〕; 駕駛〔車、船等〕: **[+for/towards etc]** *I tried to steer around the bollard.* 我試圖駕車繞過安全柱。| *We turned about and steered for Port of Spain.* 我們轉向朝西班牙港駛去。

2 ►CHANGE SB/STH 改變某人/某物◄ [T] to guide someone's behaviour or the way a situation develops without anyone noticing it 引導, 指導, 帶領〔某人的行為〕: **steer sb towards/away from** *We steered Noel towards less expensive hobbies.* 我們引導諾埃爾培養花錢較少的業餘愛好。| **steer the conversation** *Helen tried to steer the conversation away from school.* 海倫試圖把談話從學校這個話題上引開。

3 ►BE IN CHARGE OF 負責◄ [T always+adv/prep] to be in charge of an organization, team etc and make decisions that help it be successful, especially during a difficult time 掌管, 控制;〔尤指在困難時期〕帶領…度過: **steer sth through/to etc** *McKinney steered the company through the hard years of recession.* 麥金尼帶領公司度過經濟衰退的艱難歲月。

4 ►GUIDE SB TO A PLACE 引領某人到某處◄ to guide someone to a place, especially by putting your hand on their back, shoulder etc and gently pushing them 帶領, 引導〔尤指用手輕推某人的背或肩等〕: **steer sb towards/to etc** *Joel steered the visitors towards the backyard.* 喬爾領着客人們向後院走去。

5 steer clear (of) *informal* to try to avoid someone or something unpleasant or difficult【非正式】避開; 從…脱身: *Paul's in a bad mood, so I'd steer well clear if I were you.* 保羅現在情緒不好, 所以我要是你的話, 我就遠遠地躲着他。

6 steer a middle course to choose a course of action that is not extreme 選擇一條中間路線, 不走極端

steer² *n* [C] a young male cow that has had its sex organs removed〔閹過的〕小公牛 —compare 比較 BULLOCK, HEIFER

steer·age /ˈstɪrɪdʒ; ˈstɪərɪdʒ/ *n* [U] the part of a passenger ship where people who had the cheapest tickets used to travel in the past〔舊時的〕下等客艙, 統艙

steer·ing /ˈstɪrɪŋ; ˈstɪərɪŋ/ *n* [U] the parts of a car, boat etc that allow you to control its direction〔汽車、船等的〕轉向裝置, 操縱裝置: *power steering* 動力轉向裝置 | *The steering on this car is lighter.* 這輛汽車的轉向裝置比較輕。

steering com·mit·tee /'·· ·ˌ··/ *n* a committee that guides or directs a particular activity〔某項活動的〕指導委員會, 程序委員會

steering wheel /'·· ·/ *n* [C] a wheel that you turn to control the direction of a car 方向盤 —see picture on page A2 參見 A2 頁圖

steers·man /ˈstɪrzmən; ˈstɪəzmən/ *n* [C] someone who steers a ship 舵手

stein /staɪn; staɪn/ *n* [C] a tall cup for drinking beer, often decorated and with a lid〔常指有裝飾、帶蓋的〕啤酒杯 —see picture at 參見 CUP 圖

stel·lar /ˈstɛlɚ; ˈstelə/ *adj* [only before noun 僅用於名詞前] **1** *technical* connected with the stars【術語】星的, 星球的 —see also 另見 INTERSTELLAR **2** *AmE* done extremely well【美】非常出色的, 優秀的: **stellar performance** *Well, it wasn't exactly a stellar performance, was it Mike?* 哦, 那場演出並不算很出色, 對嗎, 邁克?

stem¹ /stɛm; stem/ *n* [C] **1** the long thin central part of a plant above the ground or the smaller parts that grow from it, from which leaves grow; STALK¹ (1)〔植物的〕莖; 梗; 柄 **2** the long thin part of a wine glass, VASE etc, between the base and the wide top〔葡萄酒杯、花瓶等的〕頸, 柄, 腳 **3** the narrow tube of a pipe used to smoke tobacco 煙斗柄 **4** the part of a word that stays the same when different endings are added to it, for example 'driv-' in 'driving' and 'driven' 詞幹〈如 driving 和 driven 中的 driv-〉 **5 from stem to stern** all the way from the front to the back, especially of a ship 從船頭到船尾; 從頭到尾; 到處

stem² *v* **stemmed, stemming** [T] **1 stem the tide/flow of** to stop something from spreading or developing 阻止…的擴散; 遏制…的發展: *The public apology was intended to stem the tide of complaints from viewers.* 公開道歉的目的是為了阻止觀眾大量的投訴。**2** *formal* to stop the flow of a liquid【正式】阻止〔液體的流動〕; 堵住; 止住: *stem the bleeding* 止住流血 **3 long-stemmed/short-stemmed etc** having a long stem, a short stem etc 長/短莖的; 高/矮腳的: *long-stemmed wine glasses* 高腳酒杯

stem from sth *phr v* [T not in progressive 不用進行式] to develop as a result of something else 源於…, 來自…; 由…發生: *Most of the difficulties stemmed from poor workmanship.* 麻煩大多是由於工藝差造成的。

stench /stɛntʃ; stentʃ/ *n* [C usually singular 一般用單數] **1** a very strong unpleasant smell 惡臭, 臭氣: *the stench of urine* 尿臭味 **2** something unpleasant that makes you believe that something very bad and dishonest is happening 歪風邪氣; 不誠實: **the stench of privilege/injustice etc** *The stench of corruption hangs over this whole affair.* 整件事籠罩着腐敗的邪氣。

sten·cil¹ /ˈstɛnsl; ˈstensəl/ *n* [C] a piece of plastic etc in which patterns or letters have been cut, or the decorative pattern or words made by putting paint or ink over this〔鏤有圖案或文字的〕模板, 型板; 刻字蠟紙; 用模板印製的文字[圖案]

stencil² *v* [T] to make a pattern, letters etc using a stencil 用模板製作; 用蠟紙印

Sten gun /ˈstɛn ˌgʌn; ˈsten ˌgʌn/ *n* [C] a small British SUBMACHINE GUN〔英國製造的〕斯特恩式輕機槍

sten·o /ˈstɛno; ˈstenəʊ/ *n* [C] *informal*【非正式】**1** [C] a stenographer 速記(打字)員 **2** [U] stenography 速記(法)

ste·nog·ra·pher /stəˋnɑgrəfɚ; stəˈnɒgrəfə/ *n* [C] *AmE or BrE old-fashioned* someone whose job is to write down what someone else is saying, using stenography, and then type a copy of it【美或英, 過時】速記(打字)員; SHORTHAND TYPIST *BrE*【英】

ste·nog·ra·phy /stəˋnɑgrəfɪ; stəˈnɒgrəfi/ *n* [U] *AmE or BrE old-fashioned* a system of writing quickly by using signs or shorter forms for letters, words, and phrases; SHORTHAND【美或英, 過時】速記(法)

sten·to·ri·an /stɛnˋtorɪən; stenˈtɔːriən/ *adj literary* a stentorian voice is very loud and powerful【文】〔聲音〕極其洪亮的

step¹ /stɛp; step/ *n* S2 W2

1 ▶MOVEMENT 移動◀ [C] the movement you make when you put one foot in front of the other when walking 腳步, 步: *With every step my bags seemed heavier.* 我每走一步都覺得行李越來越重。| **take a step** *Take two steps forward and one step back.* 向前走兩步, 再往後退一步。| **retrace your steps** (=go back the way you came) 順原路返回 | **direct/bend your steps** *literary* (=walk in a particular direction)【文】往某個方向走 *The sun was setting as he bent his steps towards home.* 他往家走時, 太陽開始落山了。

2 ▶ACTION 動作, 行動◀ [C] one of a series of things that you do in order to deal with a problem or to succeed〔一系列行動中的〕步驟; 措施: *Dole's first step will be to unite the party.* 多爾的第一步就是要把黨團結起來。| [+towards] *The talks are an important step towards reconciliation.* 談判是邁向和解的重要一步。| **take steps** (=take action) 採取措施 *We must take steps to make sure such an accident can never happen again.* 我們必須採取措施確保此類事故不會再次發生。| **a step forward** *The discovery of penicillin was a major step forward in the treatment of infections.* 青黴素的發現在治療感染方面前進了一大步。| **a step in the right direction** (=an action that is not complete, but is good as a beginning) 朝正確方向邁出的一步 | **step backward** (=something you do that makes a situation worse) 退步, 倒退 *Many teachers see an emphasis on written tests as a step backwards in education.* 很多教師認為, 強調筆試是教育的一個倒退。

3 ▶STAIR 樓梯◀ [C] a flat narrow piece of wood or stone, especially one in a series, that you put your foot on when you are going up or down in a building 梯級, 台階: *Jenny waited on the church steps.* 珍妮在教堂的台階上等着。| **flight of steps** (=set of steps) 一段台階 —see also 另見 DOORSTEP¹ (1)

4 ▶IN A PROCESS 在過程中◀ [C] a stage in a process or a position on a scale 階段; 進程; 等級, 級別: *Every year you go up one step on the salary scale.* 你的工資每年增長一級。| **every step of the way** (=continuously during every stage of something) 在每一個階段; 從頭到尾 *Pam's husband has supported her every step of the way.* 帕姆的丈夫自始至終一直支持她。| **a step up** *Nina's promotion is quite a step up for one so young.* 尼娜的晉升對於一個這麼年輕的人來說是相當大的一步。—compare 比較 STAGE¹ (1)

5 ▶DANCING 舞蹈◀ [C] a movement of your feet in dancing 舞步: *Wayne's learning the steps for the new routine.* 韋恩正在學習一套新的舞蹈動作。

6 mind *BrE*【英】**/watch your step a)** to be careful about what you say or how you behave 謹慎地說話[做事]: *You'll get into trouble if you don't watch your step.* 你要是不謹慎行事就會惹麻煩。**b)** to be careful when you are walking 小心行走: *Mind your step – the railing's loose.* 走路小心一點, 欄杆鬆了。

7 be/keep in step a) if people or their ideas are in step, they agree with each other or with what is usual, acceptable etc〔與他人〕一致/保持一致: *Suzie tries to keep in step with fashion.* 蘇西試圖緊跟時尚。**b)** to march with a group of people so that your right feet all go forward at the same time〔與他人〕步伐一致/保持步伐一致

8 be out of step a) if people or their ideas are out of step, they are different from the other people in a group〔與他人或他人的觀點〕不一致, 不合拍: *Joshua's out of step with modern life.* 喬舒亞與現代生活不合拍。**b)** if someone marching with a group is out of step, they are marching with their right foot going forward at a different time than everyone else〔與他人〕步伐不一致

9 ▶SOUND 聲音◀ [C] the sound you make when you set your foot down while walking 腳步聲: *I heard a step in the corridor.* 我聽到走廊裡有腳步聲。—compare 比較 FOOTSTEP

10 ▶DISTANCE 距離◀ [C] the short distance you move

when you take a step while walking 一步（的距離）: *There's a pub just a few steps down the road.* 順着這條路只有幾步遠就有一家酒吧。—compare 比較 PACE[1] (3)
11 fall into step to walk so that you are putting your right foot forward at the same time as the people you are walking with〔與他人〕步伐一致起來: *Mr. Jones soon fell into step beside her.* 瓊斯先生很快就跟她的步伐一致起來。
12 step by step slowly and gradually from one stage to the next 逐漸地，一步一步地: *Adam's learning the rules of chess step by step.* 亞當正在一步一步地學習國際象棋的規則。
13 be one step ahead to be better prepared for something or know more about something〔比某人〕準備充分; 了解更多: *A good teacher should always be one step ahead of his students.* 好教師應該總是比學生領先一步。
14 ►WAY SB WALKS 某人走路的方式◄ [C usually singular 一般用單數] the way someone walks, which often tells you how they are feeling 步態; 走路的姿勢: *Gianni's usual bouncy step* 加安妮總是生氣勃勃的步伐
15 steps [plural] *BrE* a STEPLADDER【英】活（動）梯（子），摺梯
16 ►EXERCISE 鍛鍊◄ [C,U] a type of exercise you do by walking onto and off a flat piece of equipment several inches high, or that piece of equipment itself 踏板運動; 踏板: *Beginners' step class 7 pm.* 踏板運動初級班晚上7點上課。
17 ►MUSIC 音樂◄ [C] *AmE* the difference in pitch (PITCH[1] (3)) between two musical notes that are separated by one key (KEY[2] (4)) on the piano【美】〔音樂中的〕音級; TONE[1] (8) *BrE*【英】

3 **step²** *v* **stepped, stepping** [I always+adv/prep]
1 ►TAKE ONE STEP 走一步◄ to raise one foot and put it down in front of the other one 跨步，邁步: **[+forward/back/down etc]** *Step aside, let the doctor through.* 站到一邊去，讓醫生過去。
2 ►WALK 步行◄ to walk a short distance〔短距離〕行走: **[+inside/outside etc]** *I stepped into the hall to wait.* 我走進大廳裡去等。| **step this way** (=come the way I am showing you) 往這邊走
3 ►STAND ON STH 站在某物上◄ to bring your foot down on something 踏，踩; TREAD[1] (1) *BrE*【英】: **[+in/on etc]** *I stepped in a puddle and got my shoes wet.* 我踩進一個水坑裡把鞋弄濕了。
4 step forward to come and offer help 前來提供幫助: *Police are appealing for witnesses to step forward.* 警方呼籲目擊者前來協助。
5 step out of line to behave badly by breaking rules or disobeying orders 行為出軌; 違反規矩[命令]
6 step on it/step on the gas *AmE spoken* to drive faster【美口】加速，加快; 踩油門: *If you don't step on it we'll miss the plane.* 你要是不加快速度，我們就趕不上飛機了。
7 step lively! *BrE spoken* used to tell someone to hurry【英口】快點〔用於催促某人〕—see also 另見 **step into the breach** (BREACH[1] (5))

step down also 又作 **step aside** *phr v* [I] to leave your job or official position 辭職; 下台; 讓位: **step down as sth** *Eve has stepped down as chairperson.* 伊芙已經辭去主席一職。| **step down in favour of sb/sth** *Lister is stepping down in favor of a younger man.* 利斯特準備退下來，讓位給一個更年輕的人。

step in *phr v* [I] to become involved in a discussion or disagreement, especially in order to stop the trouble; INTERVENE 介入，干涉，插手: *If the dispute continues, the government will have to step in.* 如果爭端繼續下去，政府將不得不進行干涉。

step out *phr v* [I] **1** *AmE* to go out for a short time【美】出去一會兒，暫時離開: *Molly just stepped out but she'll be back soon.* 莫莉剛出去一會兒，不過她很快就會回來。—see also 另見 POP[1] (1) **2** *old-fashioned* to start walking fast【過時】加快步伐，快走

step sth ↔ **up** *phr v* [T] to increase the amount of an activity or the speed of a process in order to improve a situation 使增加; 使上升; 使加快: *We will be stepping up production to meet the increased demand.* 為滿足需求的增長，我們將增加產量。

step- /stɛp; step/ *prefix* related not by birth but because a parent has remarried 繼的〔無血緣關係，但因父母一方再婚而構成親緣關係的〕: *my stepfather* (=not my real father, but a man who has married my mother) 我的繼父 | *her stepchildren* 她的繼子繼女

step·broth·er /ˈstɛpˌbrʌðɚ; ˈstepbrʌðə/ *n* [C] a boy or man whose father or mother has married your father or mother 繼父[繼母]的兒子

step-by-step /ˌ· · ˈ·◄/ *adj* [only before noun 僅用於名詞前] a step-by-step plan, method etc does things carefully and in a particular order 一步接着一步的; 循序漸進的

step·child /ˈstɛpˌtʃaɪld; ˈsteptʃaɪld/ *n* [C] a stepdaughter or stepson 繼女; 繼子〔妻子與前夫或丈夫與前妻所生的孩子〕

step·daugh·ter /ˈstɛpˌdɔtɚ; ˈstepdɔːtə/ *n* [C] a daughter that your husband or wife has from being married to someone else before 繼女〔妻子與前夫或丈夫與前妻所生的女兒〕

step·fa·ther /ˈstɛpˌfɑðɚ; ˈstepfɑːðə/ *n* [C] the man who is married to your mother but who is not your father 繼父

step·lad·der /ˈstɛpˌlædɚ; ˈstepˌlædə/ *n* [C] a LADDER with two sloping parts that are joined at the top and that can be folded flat 活（動）梯（子），梯凳

step·moth·er /ˈstɛpˌmʌðɚ; ˈstepmʌðə/ *n* [C] a woman who is married to your father but who is not your mother 繼母

step·par·ent /ˈstɛpˌpɛrənt; ˈstepˌpeərənt/ *n* [C] a stepfather or stepmother 繼父，後父; 繼母，後母

steppes /stɛps; steps/ *n* **the steppes** a large area of land without trees, especially an area in Russia, parts of Asia, and southeast Europe〔尤指俄羅斯、亞洲和東南歐部分地區的〕無樹木的大草原，乾草原

step·ping-stone /ˈ·· ·/ *n* [C] **1** something that helps you to progress towards achieving something especially in your work〔尤指工作上〕達到成功的手段，進身之階: *Think of this job as a stepping-stone to something better.* 把這個工作看作是通往更好工作的階梯。**2** one of a row of large flat stones that you walk on to get across a stream〔過河用的〕踏腳石

step·sis·ter /ˈstɛpˌsɪstɚ; ˈstepsɪstə/ *n* [C] a girl or woman whose father or mother has married your mother or father 繼父[繼母]的女兒

step·son /ˈstɛpˌsʌn; ˈstepsʌn/ *n* [C] a son that your husband or wife has from being married to someone else before 繼子〔妻子與前夫或丈夫與前妻所生的兒子〕

-ster /stɚ; stə/ *suffix* [in nouns 構成名詞] **1** someone who has a particular quality 有…特徵[品性]的人: *a youngster* (=a young person) 年輕人 **2** someone who is connected with, deals with, or uses a particular thing 與…有關的人; 參與…的人: *a trickster* (=someone who plays deceiving tricks) 騙子 | *a gangster* (=a member of a GANG)〔結成團夥的〕歹徒 | *a pollster* (=someone who carries out POLLS) 民意調查者

ster·e·o¹ /ˈstɛrɪo; ˈsteriəʊ/ *n* **1** [C] a machine for playing records, CDs etc that produces sound from two speakers (SPEAKER (3)) 立體聲音響器材 **2 in stereo** if music, a radio programme etc is in stereo, it is being played or broadcast using a system in which sound is directed through two speakers 用立體聲播放的: *This programme is being broadcast in stereo.* 本節目是用立體聲播放的。 3

stereo² also 又作 **ster·e·o·phon·ic** /ˌstɛrɪəˈfɑnɪk; ˌsteriəˈfɒnɪk◄/ *adj* using a system of sound recording or broadcasting in which the sound is directed through two speakers (SPEAKER (3)) to make it seem more real 立體聲的: *stereo recording* 立體聲錄音 —compare 比較 MONO², QUADRAPHONIC

ster·e·o·gram /ˋstɛrɪə͵græm; ˈsteriəgræm/ *n* [C] a picture that looks like a repeating pattern, but in which some people can see THREE-DIMENSIONAL objects 立體相片[圖片]

ster·e·o·scop·ic /͵stɛrɪəˋskɑpɪk; ͵steriəˈskɒpɪk◂/ *adj* a stereoscopic photograph, picture etc is made so that when you look at it through a special machine it looks solid 立體的, 有立體感的

stereo sys·tem /ˈ··· ͵··/ *n* [C] a set of equipment for playing music on, usually including a record player, CASSETTE PLAYER, and radio 立體聲音響設備

ster·e·o·type[1] /ˋstɛrɪə͵taɪp; ˈsteriətaɪp/ *n* [C] a fixed idea or image of what a particular type of person or thing is like 模式化的思想[形象]; 老一套; 舊框框: *racial stereotypes* 種族陳規 | [+of] *the stereotype of a woman who stays at home with the children* 待在家裡照看小孩的婦女的典型形象 —**stereotypical** /͵stɛrɪəˋtɪpɪkḷ; ͵steriəˈtɪpɪkəl◂/ *adj*

stereotype[2] *v* [T usually passive 一般用被動態] to decide, usually unfairly, that certain people have particular qualities or abilities because they belong to a particular race, sex, or social class 對…有老一套看法; 把…模式化: [+as] *Homeless people are often stereotyped as a bunch of alcoholics.* 無家可歸者經常被一律看成是一羣酗酒者。—**stereotyping** *n* [U]: *sexual stereotyping* 性的公式化 —**stereotyped** *adj*

ster·ile /ˋstɛrəl; ˈsteraɪl/ *adj* **1** not able to have babies 不能生育的: *She became sterile because of exposure to radiation.* 她因接觸輻射而失去了生育能力。—compare 比較 FERTILE (2) **2** completely clean and not containing any BACTERIA 無菌的, 消過毒的: *Operations must be carried out in a sterile environment.* 手術必須在無菌的環境下進行。**3** land that is sterile cannot be used for growing crops〔土地〕貧瘠的, 不毛的, 不長植物的 **4** lacking new ideas or imagination 缺乏新意念[想像力]的: *sterile thought* 缺乏新意的想法 —**sterility** /stɛˋrɪlətɪ; stəˈrɪlᵻti/ *n* [U]

ster·il·ize also 又作 **-ise** *BrE*【英】/ˋstɛrə͵laɪz; ˈsterᵻlaɪz/ *v* [T usually passive 一般用被動態] **1** to make something completely clean and kill any BACTERIA in it 給…消毒[殺菌]: *sterilized milk* 消毒牛奶 | *Sterilize the bottles with boiling water.* 用沸水把這些瓶子消毒。**2** to perform an operation that makes a person or animal unable to have babies 為…做絕育手術, 使…失去生殖能力 —**sterilizer** *n* [C] —**sterilization** /͵stɛrələˋzeʃən; ͵sterᵻlaɪˈzeɪʃən/ *n* [C,U]

ster·ling[1] /ˋstɝlɪŋ; ˈstɜːlɪŋ/ *n* [U] the standard unit of money in the United Kingdom, based on the pound 英國貨幣

sterling[2] *adj* **1 sterling silver/gold** silver or gold of a particular standard or pureness 標準純銀/純金 **2 sterling qualities/effort/character etc** *especially BrE* qualities etc that are excellent and dependable【尤英】優秀的品質/出色的努力/高尚的品德等

stern[1] /stɝn; stɜːn/ *adj* **1** strict in a very serious and often unpleasant way 嚴格的, 苛刻的: *a stern teacher* 嚴格的教師 | *groups calling for sterner penalties for drug offences* 呼籲對毒品犯罪施以更嚴厲懲處的團體 **2 stern look/expression/rebuke** something that someone says or does that expresses disapproval 嚴厲的神色/表情/指責 —**sternly** *adv* —**sternness** *n* [U]

stern[2] *n* [C usually singular 一般用單數] the back part of a ship 船尾, 艉部 —compare 比較 BOW[2] (2) —see picture at 參見 YACHT 圖

ster·num /ˋstɝnəm; ˈstɜːnəm/ *n* [C] *plural* **sternums** or **sterna** /-nə; -nə/ *technical* a BREASTBONE【術語】胸骨 —see picture at 參見 SKELETON 圖

ste·roid /ˋstɪrɔɪd; ˈstɪərɔɪd/ *n* [C] a chemical compound produced in the body, but also given as a drug by doctors for injuries and used illegally by people doing sports to improve their performance 類固醇, 甾族化合物

ster·to·rous /ˋstɝtərəs; ˈstɜːtərəs/ *adj* stertorous breathing makes a noisy sound〔呼吸〕打鼾的, 發出呼嚕聲的: *His breathing was stertorous but regular.* 他呼吸聲粗重但很均勻。

steth·o·scope /ˋstɛθə͵skop; ˈsteθəskəʊp/ *n* [C] an instrument used by doctors to listen to someone's heart or breathing 聽診器

stet·son /ˋstɛtsṇ; ˈstetsən/ *n* [C] *trademark* a tall hat with a wide BRIM (=edge), worn especially in the American West【商標】〔尤指在美國西部戴的〕史特森高頂寬邊帽 —see picture at 參見 HAT 圖

ste·ve·dore /ˋstivə͵dɔr; ˈstiːvᵻdɔː/ *n* [C] *AmE* someone whose job is loading and unloading ships【美】碼頭裝卸工, 搬運工; DOCKER *BrE*【英】

stew[1] /stu; stjuː/ *n* **1** [C] a cooked dish, made of meat and vegetables that are cooked slowly together in liquid 燉煮的菜餚: *beef stew* 燉牛肉 **2 in a stew** *informal* to be confused or anxious, especially because you are in a difficult situation【非正式】〔尤指因處於困境而〕困惑的; 焦慮的: *You're in a real stew about this interview, aren't you?* 你很擔心這次面試, 對嗎?

stew[2] *v* **1** [T] to cook something slowly in liquid 燉, 煨, 燜: *stewed apples* 燉蘋果 **2 stew (in your own juice)** *informal* to worry because of something bad that has happened or a mistake you have made【非正式】自作自受

stew·ard /ˋstuɚd; ˈstjuːəd/ *n* [C] **1** a man who serves food and drinks to the passengers on a plane or ship〔飛機、輪船上的〕男乘務員, 男服務員 **2** a man whose job is to look after a house and its lands, such as a farm〔房屋、田地的〕看管人 **3** a man who arranges the supply and serving of food in a club, college etc〔俱樂部、學校等的〕伙食管理員 **4** *BrE* someone who is in charge of a horse race, meeting, or other public event【英】〔賽馬、聚會或其他公共活動的〕負責人, 管事, 幹事 —see also 另見 SHOP STEWARD

S

stew·ard·ess /ˋstuɚdɪs; ˈstjuːədᵻs/ *n* [C] a woman who serves food and drinks to the passengers on a plane or ship〔飛機、輪船上的〕女乘務員, 女服務員

stew·ard·ship /ˋstuɚd͵ʃɪp; ˈstjuːədʃɪp/ *n* [U] the way in which someone controls and looks after an event or organization〔某活動或組織的〕管理方式

stewed /stud; stjuːd/ *adj* **1** [not before noun 不用於名詞前] *informal* drunk【非正式】喝醉酒的 **2** *BrE* tea that is stewed tastes too strong and bitter because it has been left too long before being drunk【英】〔茶因為時間久而〕泡得太濃的

stick[1] /stɪk; stɪk/ *v past tense and past participle* **stuck** /stʌk; stʌk/ [S2] [W3]

1 ►PUSH 推◄ [T always+adv/prep, I always+adv/ prep] if a pointed object sticks into something or you stick it into something, it is pushed into it 刺, 戳, 插: **stick sth in/into/through etc** *They stuck pins in the map to mark enemy positions.* 他們把針插在地圖上, 標出敵人的位置。| **stick in/through etc** *Joe had cactus spines sticking in his finger.* 仙人掌的刺扎進了喬的手指。

2 ►FIX 固定◄ [I,T] to fix something to something else with a sticky substance, or to become fixed to a surface 黏, 黏住, 貼上: *I can't get this stamp to stick.* 這張郵票我貼不上。| **stick sth to/in/on etc** *It took hours to stick all these photos in my album.* 把這些照片都貼進我的相冊花了好幾個小時。| **[+to]** *It was so hot his shirt was sticking to his back.* 天氣太熱, 他的襯衫都黏在背上了。

3 ►PUT 放置◄ [T always+adv/prep] *informal* to put something somewhere quickly and without thinking carefully; SHOVE[1] (2)【非正式】隨便擺放: **stick sth in/on/there etc** *Just stick your coat on that chair.* 把你的外衣放在那張椅子上就行了。

4 ►DIFFICULT TO MOVE 難以移動◄ [I] if something sticks it becomes fixed in one position so that it is difficult to move 卡住, 釘住: *This cupboard door keeps sticking.* 這扇櫃門老是卡住。

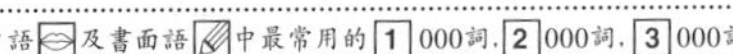

5 stick in sb's mind if something sticks in your mind, you remember it very well, especially because it is unusual or interesting〔尤因不同尋常或有意思而〕留在某人的腦海裡, 令某人記憶猶新: *What really sticks in my mind is how sad the woman looked.* 真正令我難忘的是那個女人悲傷的神情。
6 stick it [T usually in negatives 一般用於否定句] to continue to deal with a difficult or unpleasant situation 繼續應付困境; 堅持下去: *College is harder than I thought, I don't think I can stick it much longer.* 上大學比我想像的更難, 我想我是堅持不了多久了。
7 make sth stick *informal* to prove that someone is guilty【非正式】證明…有罪: *The police won't bring the case to court because they don't think they can make the charges stick.* 警方不會把這案件提交法院, 因為他們認為他們無法使指控成立。
8 you/they can stick sth *spoken* used to say angrily that you do not want what someone is offering you【口】留給你(們)/他們自己吧〔用於生氣地表示自己不要所給的東西〕: *You can stick your job if you won't pay me more than that!* 你如果不願意出更多的錢, 那就把這工作留給你自己幹吧!
9 be stuck fast to be fixed in one position and unable to move 牢牢黏住, 卡住不能移動: *His arm was stuck fast in the drainpipe.* 他的胳膊卡在排水管裡不能動了。
10 stick fast to a belief/idea etc to continue to believe something although it may be difficult 堅守某一信仰/觀點等: *Through it all Stella has stuck fast to her belief in the Communist system.* 經過了所有這一切, 斯特拉堅持對共產主義制度的信仰。
11 be stuck for *spoken* to be unable to think or to find something that you need to have【口】無法想出; 找不到〔需要的東西〕: *If you're stuck for a babysitter, Alison's always free.* 如果你找不到人照顧孩子, 阿莉森總是有空的。
12 stick in your throat *BrE*【英】**/stick in your craw** *AmE*【美】**a)** if a situation or someone's behaviour sticks in your throat, it is so annoying that you cannot accept it〔指某種處境或某人的行為〕使人難以接受 **b)** if words stick in your throat, you are unable to say what you want〔指言詞〕難以啟齒, 說不出口
13 ►NAME 名字◄ [I] if a name that someone has invented sticks, people continue to use it〔指綽號〕被繼續使用: *One newspaper dubbed him 'Eddie the Eagle' and the name stuck.* 一家報紙戲稱他為"老鷹埃迪", 這個綽號就被叫開了。
14 ►CARD GAME 紙牌戲◄ [I] to decide not to take any more cards in some card games 決定不再要牌: *I'm sticking.* 我不再要牌了。
15 can't stick *BrE spoken* to dislike someone or something very much【英口】極不喜歡; 無法忍受: *I can't stick her husband, he's always so rude.* 我無法忍受她的丈夫, 他總是那麼粗魯。| **can't stick sb doing sth** *Lena can't stick anybody reading over her shoulder.* 莉娜不喜歡別人在她背後一起閱讀。—see also 另見 **stick/poke your nose into** (NOSE¹ (4))

stick around *phr v* [I] *informal* to stay in the same place for a little longer, especially in order to wait for something that you expect to happen【非正式】〔在某處〕逗留, 待在…附近〔尤指等待某事發生〕: *Stick around, there'll be dancing later.* 不要走開, 一會兒有舞蹈。

stick at sth *phr v* [T] *BrE*【英】**1** to continue to study or work hard at something in a very determined way 堅持…, 繼續不懈地做…: **stick at it** *Just stick at it and you'll pass your exams easily.* 堅持下去, 你會輕易地通過考試的。**2 stick at nothing** *informal* to be willing to do anything, even if it is illegal, in order to achieve something【非正式】無所顧忌, 不擇手段: *Des'll stick at nothing to make money.* 德斯為了賺錢甚麼都做得出來。

stick by sb/sth *phr v* [T] **1** to continue to give your support to a friend who has problems 繼續支持〔有困難的朋友〕: *Samuel promised to stick by her, whatever happened.* 塞繆爾答應, 無論發生甚麼事他都會支持她。**2** to do what you said you would do or what you think you should do 堅持〔承諾等〕: **stick by a decision/promise etc** 堅持決定/堅守諾言等

stick sth **on** sb *phr v* [T] *informal* to prove or make it seem that someone is guilty of a crime【非正式】證明〔某人〕有罪; 誣告, 陷害: *They can't stick it on me – I wasn't even in the country at the time.* 他們無法誣告我, 我當時根本不在國內。

stick out 突出; 伸出

Peter's ears stick out.
彼得長着一副兜風耳。

Lucy stuck her tongue out.
露茜伸出舌頭。

stick out *phr v*
1 ►COME UP OR FORWARD 向上或向前突出◄ [I] if a part of something sticks out, it comes out further than the rest of a surface or comes out through a hole 突出; 突出來: *Francis wore glasses and his front teeth stuck out.* 弗朗西斯戴眼鏡, 門牙外突。| **stick out of/from/through** *Careful – there's a nail sticking out of that board.* 小心, 那塊板上有顆釘子突了出來。
2 ►PUT STH OUT 伸出某物◄ [T **stick** sth ↔ **out**] to deliberately make part of your body come forward or out from the rest of your body〔有意〕伸出〔身體的一部分〕, 探出: *Carl stuck his leg out and tripped the man up.* 卡爾伸出一條腿, 將那個男人絆倒。| **stick your tongue out** (=show your tongue in order to be rude to someone) 伸舌頭〔對某人無禮〕
3 stick it out to continue to the end of an activity that is difficult, painful, or boring〔把困難、棘手或枯燥的活動〕堅持到底: *The movie was really boring but we stuck it out.* 那部影片的確枯燥, 但我們還是堅持把它看完。
4 stick out like a sore thumb *informal* to look very unsuitable and different from everyone or everything around【非正式】礙眼, 惹人注目: *I'm not going to the party dressed like this, I'd stick out like a sore thumb.* 我不會穿成這個樣子去參加聚會, 那會顯得很礙眼。
5 it sticks out a mile *informal* used to say that a fact about someone's character or feelings is very clear and easily noticed【非正式】〔某人的性格或情緒〕很明顯, 顯而易見, 一目了然: *It always sticks out a mile when Jenny doesn't like someone, she just can't hide her feelings.* 珍妮不喜歡誰總是很明顯的, 她就是不會掩飾自己的感情。
6 stick your neck out *informal* to give your opinion about something when you know there is a risk that you may be wrong or that people may disagree with you【非正式】說冒風險[惹禍]的話

stick out for sth *phr v* [T] *informal* to refuse to accept less than what you asked for【非正式】堅持索取[要求]: *The unions are sticking out for a higher pay offer.* 工會堅持要求提高工資。

stick to sth *phr v* [T]
1 ►PROMISE/BELIEF 承諾/信仰◄ to do or keep doing what you said you would do or what you believe in 遵守, 信守; 堅持: *Just make a decision and stick to it.* 作個決定, 然後照着去做吧。| **stick to your decision/principles etc** *We have stuck to our election promises.* 我們遵守了我們競選時的承諾。

2 ►CONTINUE WITH SAME THING 繼續使用同一東西; 繼續做同一件事◄ to keep using or doing one particular thing and not change to anything else 繼續使用; 繼續做: *If you're driving, stick to soft drinks.* 你如果要開車, 那還是堅持喝軟性飲料。| *Reporters should stick to investigating the facts.* 記者應該繼續調查事實。
3 stick to it to continue to work or study in a very determined way in order to achieve something 堅持下去; 繼續做下去: *I hated practicing, but I stuck to it and now I can play pretty well.* 我討厭練習, 但還是堅持了下來, 現在我彈得很好了。
4 stick to the point/subject/facts to talk only about what you are supposed to be talking about or what is certain 緊扣主題/題目/事實: *We'll never finish this meeting if people don't stick to the point.* 如果大家不能緊扣主題, 我們這個會就永遠開不完。
5 stick to the path/road etc to stay on a marked path or road so that you do not get lost 沿着小徑/大路等走〔以免迷路〕
6 stick to the rules *informal* to do something exactly according to the rules【非正式】遵守規則
7 stick to your guns *informal* to refuse to change your mind about something even though other people are trying to persuade you that you are wrong【非正式】〔雖然受攻擊仍〕堅持自己的立場[觀點]
8 That's my story and I'm sticking to it. *spoken* used to say that you are not going to change any part of what you have already said【口】這就是我說的情況, 我堅持這一説法〔用於表示自己不會對已經説過的話作出任何改變〕

stick together *phr v* [I] *informal* if people stick together, they continue to support one another even when they have problems【非正式】互相支持; 團結一致: *If we stick together we've got a better chance.* 我們如果同心協力, 希望就更大。

stick up *phr v* **1** [I] if a part of something sticks up, it is raised up or points upward above a surface 向上突起; 豎起: *His hair stuck up as though he hadn't had time to comb it.* 他的頭髮都豎了起來, 好像他沒有時間梳理似的。| **[+from/out of/through etc]** *We could just see part of the boat sticking up out of the water.* 我們只能看見船的一部分露出水面。**2 stick 'em up** *slang* used to tell someone to raise their hands when threatening them with a gun【俚】〔被槍指着時〕舉起手來〔威脅語〕

stick up 豎起

Dad's hair sticks up.
爸爸的頭髮直豎着。

stick up for sb *phr v* [T] *informal* to defend someone who is being criticized, especially when no one else will defend them【非正式】為…辯護; 支持; 維護: *At least my friends stuck up for me.* 起碼我的朋友支持我。| **stick up for yourself** *She's always known how to stick up for herself.* 她總是知道如何保護自己。

stick with sb/sth *phr v* [T] *informal*【非正式】**1** to stay close to someone 緊跟; 跟…在一起, 不離開…: *If you don't want to get lost, you'd better stick with me.* 你如果不想迷路的話, 最好緊跟着我。**2** to continue doing or using something the way you did or planned to do before 繼續做[使用], 不放棄: *Let's stick with the original arrangements.* 我們按原先的安排去做吧。**3** to continue doing something, especially something difficult 堅持〔做某事, 尤指困難的事情〕: **stick with it** *Stick with it and you'll win through in the end.* 堅持下去, 你最終會成功的。**4** *informal* to remain in someone's memory【非正式】留在…的記憶裡: *One thing he said then has stuck with me ever since.* 他當時說的一件事我一直記憶猶新。

sticks 棍, 棒

chopsticks 筷子
drumsticks 鼓槌
stick 枝條
toothpicks 牙籤
shooting stick 摺疊座手杖
hockey stick 曲棍球棒
lacrosse stick 長曲棍球棒
walking stick 手杖
crook 曲柄杖

stick² *n* 3 3
1 ►FROM A TREE 來自樹上◄ [C] a long thin piece of wood that has fallen or been cut from a tree 柴枝, 枝條
2 ►FOR WALKING 供走路用◄ a long thin piece of wood or metal that you use to help you walk 手杖, 拐杖 —see also 另見 CANE¹ (1)
3 ►SPORT 體育運動◄ a long thin piece of wood that you use for hitting the ball in sports such as HOCKEY〔曲棍球等體育運動中使用的〕棍, 棒
4 ►FOR HITTING SB 用於打人◄ a long thin piece of wood that you use to hit someone or something〔打擊用的〕棍, 棒
5 stick of celery/dynamite etc a long thin piece of CELERY etc 一根芹菜/一條棍狀炸藥等
6 get (hold of) the wrong end of the stick *spoken* to misunderstand one small thing that makes you misunderstand everything about a particular situation【口】完全誤解
7 give sb stick *BrE spoken* to criticize someone for something they have done, sometimes in a humorous way【英口】批評某人; 嘲諷某人
8 (out) in the sticks very far from a town or city 遠離城鎮: *They live somewhere out in the sticks.* 他們住在遠離城市的某個地方。
9 ►CAR 汽車◄ *AmE informal* a STICK SHIFT【美, 非正式】〔汽車的〕變速桿, 換擋桿
10 up sticks *BrE spoken* if you up sticks, you move to a different area or house【英口】搬家, 遷居: *He'd upped sticks and moved to London.* 他搬家去了倫敦。
11 old stick *BrE old-fashioned* used to describe someone in a friendly way【英, 過時】某種類型的人〔用於友善地描述某人〕: *Ned's a good old stick.* 內德是個蠻不錯的傢伙。

stick·ball /ˈstɪkˌbɔl; ˈstɪkbɔːl/ *n* [U] a game like BASE-

S

BALL that is played in the street by children in the US, using a small ball and a stick 棍球〔美國兒童在街頭玩的類似棒球的遊戲〕

3 **stick·er** /ˈstɪkɚ; ˈstɪkə/ *n* [C] **1** a small piece of paper or plastic with a picture or writing on it that you can stick on to something〔有圖或文字的〕黏貼標籤, 貼紙 —compare 比較 LABEL[1] (1) —see picture at 參見 SIGN[1] 圖 **2** *BrE informal* someone who keeps trying to do something even when it becomes very difficult【英, 非正式】堅持不懈的人, 鍥而不捨的人

stick·ing point /ˈ·· ˌ·/ *n* [singular] the thing that prevents an agreement being made in a discussion〔談判中的〕癥結, 障礙: *The question of equal pay is likely to be the sticking point.* 同等報酬的問題可能成為癥結之所在。

stick in·sect /ˈ· ˌ··/ *n* [C] an insect with a long thin body that looks very like a small stick 竹節蟲

stick-in-the-mud /ˈ· · · ˌ·/ *n* [C] someone with old-fashioned attitudes who is not willing to try anything new 守舊的人, 墨守成規的人

stick·ler /ˈstɪklɚ; ˈstɪklə/ *n* **be a stickler for rules/punctuality etc** to think that rules etc are very important and that other people should behave according to them as well 堅持遵守規則/時間

stick-on /ˈ· ·/ *adj* [only before noun 僅用於名詞前] stick-on material has a sticky substance on its back so that you can stick it on to something 可黏貼的, 背後帶膠的: *stick-on sequins* 可黏貼的閃光裝飾片

stick·pin /ˈstɪkˌpɪn; ˈstɪkˌpɪn/ *n* [C] *AmE* a decorated pin worn as jewellery【美】裝飾別針

stick shift /ˈ· ·/ *n* [C] *AmE*【美】**1** a movable metal bar in a car that you use to control its gears〔汽車的〕變速桿, 換擋桿; GEAR LEVER *BrE*【英】**2** a car that uses a stick shift system to control its gears 使用變速桿系統的汽車 —compare 比較 AUTOMATIC[2] (2)

stick-to-it·ive·ness /ˌstɪk ˈtu ɪtɪvnɪs; stɪk ˈtuː ɪtɪvnɪs/ *n* [U] *AmE informal* the ability to continue doing something that is difficult or tiring to do【美, 非正式】堅忍不拔, 不屈不撓

stick-up /ˈ· ·/ *n* [C] *informal* a situation in which someone steals money from people in a bank, shop etc by threatening them with a gun【非正式】持槍搶劫

stick·y /ˈstɪki; ˈstɪki/ *adj*

1 ▶SWEETS/HONEY ETC 糖果/蜂蜜等◀ made of or covered with a substance that sticks to surfaces 黏性的, 黏的: *Jeremy's hands were sticky with jam.* 傑里米的手上都是黏糊糊的果醬。| *tea and sticky buns* 茶和黏牙的圓麵包

2 sticky label/tape etc *BrE* a LABEL[1] (1) etc that has glue on one side so that it sticks to surfaces【英】黏貼標籤/黏膠帶

3 ▶WEATHER 天氣◀ making you feel uncomfortable and very hot, wet, and dirty 濕熱得令人難受的: *a hot sticky day in August* 八月裡一個濕熱得令人難受的日子

4 ▶EMBARRASSING 令人尷尬的◀ *informal* a sticky situation, conversation, or event is embarrassing and makes you feel worried or nervous【非正式】〔情況、對話或事件〕令人尷尬的; 令人焦慮的: *We were in for a long, sticky evening.* 我們注定要經歷一個令人不安的漫漫長夜。

5 ▶DIFFICULT 困難的◀ a sticky situation, question, or problem is difficult or dangerous to deal with〔處境、問題等〕困難的, 棘手的: *The band now have a minder to get them out of sticky situations.* 樂隊現在有個保鏢幫助他們應付麻煩的情況。

6 ▶NOT HELPFUL 不肯幫忙的◀ *BrE* not willing to help you or do what you want【英】不肯幫忙的; 不大方的: *I asked him to lend me some money, but he was rather sticky about it.* 我要他借一點錢給我, 可是他不大樂意。

7 have sticky fingers *informal* to be likely to steal something【非正式】好偷竊的, 有偷竊習慣的

8 come to/meet a sticky end *BrE informal* to die violently especially because you have been doing something bad【英, 非正式】〔尤因做了壞事〕橫死; 不好的下場, 悲慘的結局: *The gangsters in his novels always come to a sticky end.* 他小說中的歹徒都沒有好下場。

9 be on a sticky wicket *BrE informal* to be in a situation that is difficult or that may become difficult【英, 非正式】處於困難的境遇, 處於不利的形勢 —**stickiness** *n* [U]

stiff[1] /stɪf; stɪf/ *adj* 3

1 ▶BODY 身體◀ if a part of your body is stiff or you are stiff, your muscles hurt and it is difficult to move 僵直的, 不靈活的; 疼痛的: *Arthritis makes your joints stiff and sore.* 關節炎令關節發僵疼痛。| **stiff neck/back/joint** *Alastair woke up with a stiff neck.* 阿拉斯泰爾一覺醒來感到頸部僵直。| **feel stiff** *I felt really stiff after playing basketball last week.* 我上星期打了籃球後感到身體發僵。

2 ▶DOOR/DRAWER ETC 門/抽屜等◀ difficult to move, bend or turn 難移動的; 難彎曲的; 難轉動的: *Pull hard – that drawer's very stiff.* 使勁拉, 那個抽屜很緊。

3 ▶PAPER/MATERIAL 紙/材料◀ hard and difficult to bend 硬的, 難摺疊的: *a sheet of stiff cardboard* 一張硬紙板

4 ▶MIXTURE 混合物◀ thick and almost solid, so that it is not easy to stir 稠的, 難攪拌的: *Beat the egg whites until stiff.* 把蛋白打到發稠。| *stiff dough* 硬麵團

5 ▶UNFRIENDLY 不友好的◀ unfriendly or very formal, so that other people feel uncomfortable 不友好的; 拘謹的: *He replied in a stiff, ironic voice.* 他用生硬、諷刺的口氣回答。

6 ▶VERY HARD 非常嚴厲的◀ more difficult, strict, or severe than usual 艱難的; 嚴格的; 嚴厲的: **stiff sentence/penalty/fine** *There's a stiff fine for speeding.* 超速駕駛要受重罰。| **stiff competition** *He'll be facing stiff competition for that job.* 要得到那份工作, 他將面臨激烈的競爭。

7 a stiff wind/breeze a fairly strong wind etc 強勁的風

8 a stiff drink/whisky etc a very strong alcoholic drink 烈性酒/威士忌等

9 keep a stiff upper lip to try to keep calm and not show your feelings in a situation when most people would become upset 保持沉着堅強; 咬緊牙關 —**stiffly** *adv* —**stiffness** *n* [U]

stiff[2] *adv* **1 bored/scared/worried stiff** *informal* extremely bored etc【非正式】極其膩煩/害怕/擔心: *As a child I was scared stiff of going down to the cellar.* 小時候, 我非常害怕到地下室去。**2 frozen stiff a)** extremely cold 非常寒冷的, 凍僵的: *Joey was frozen stiff after walking through the snow.* 喬伊在雪中步行後快凍僵了。**b)** cloth that has frozen stiff is hard because the water in it has become ice〔布〕凍得堅硬的

stiff[3] *n* [C] *slang*【俚】**1** the body of a dead person 死屍, 屍體 **2 working stiff** *AmE informal* an ordinary person who works to earn enough money to live【美, 非正式】〔掙錢謀生的〕普通人, 勞動者

stiff[4] *v* [T] *AmE informal* to not pay someone money that you owe them or that they expect to be given, especially by not leaving a tip (TIP[1] (2)) in a restaurant【美, 非正式】不給〔某人〕付錢; 不給〔侍者〕小費

stiff·en /ˈstɪfən; ˈstɪfən/ *v* **1** [I] to suddenly become unfriendly, angry, or anxious〔突然〕變得冷淡; 頓時強硬起來: *Francesca stiffened at his suggestion that it was her fault.* 他暗示那是她的過錯, 弗蘭切斯卡一下子就變得強硬起來。**2** [I,T] to become stronger and more determined (使) 變得更堅強[堅定]: *The advancing army met stiffening resistance.* 推進中的部隊遇到更加頑強的抵抗。| **stiffen sb's resolve** *His emotional speech was sure to stiffen their resolve.* 他那感人的演說一定會增強他們的決心。**3** [T] to make material stiff so that it will not bend easily 使〔材料〕變硬[堅挺]: *a spray to stiffen shirt collars* 能使衣領堅挺的噴劑 **4** [I] to become painful and difficult to move 變得酸痛[僵硬]: *His joints had stiffened.* 他的關節變得僵硬。

stiff-necked /ˌ· ˈ·◂/ *adj* proud and refusing to change or obey; OBSTINATE (1) 頑固而傲慢的, 倔強的

sti·fle /ˋstaɪfḷ; ˈstaɪfəl/ *v* **1** [I,T] to stop someone from breathing or be unable to breathe comfortably, especially because the air is too hot or not fresh (使)感到窒息, (使)透不過氣來: *He was almost stifled by the fumes.* 他差點被煙熏得喘不過氣來。**2** [T] to stop something from happening or developing 抑止, 阻止, 壓制: *rules and regulations that stifle initiative* 壓制積極性的規章制度 **3** [T] to stop a feeling from being expressed 強忍住, 壓抑〔感情〕: *He stifled an urge to hit her.* 他強忍住衝動, 沒有打她。| **stifle a yawn/smile/laughter etc** *Nancy stifled a yawn as the teacher's voice droned on.* 南希忍住呵欠, 聽老師不停地嘮叨。

stif·ling /ˋstaɪflɪŋ; ˈstaɪflɪŋ/ *adj* **1** a room or weather that is stifling is very hot and difficult to breathe in 〔房間、天氣〕悶熱的, 令人窒息的: *a stifling, crowded carriage* 悶熱擁擠的車廂 **2** a situation that is stifling stops you from developing your own ideas and character 〔境況〕令人窒息的; 壓制個性發揮的: *the stifling atmosphere of the court* 法庭上令人窒息的氣氛

stig·ma /ˋstɪgmə; ˈstɪgmə/ *n* **1** [singular,U] a strong feeling in society that a type of behaviour is shameful 恥辱, 羞辱, 見不得人的感覺: *There is a strong stigma attached to suicide.* 自殺被認為是非常見不得人的事情。| **the stigma of alcoholism/abortion etc** *The stigma of alcoholism makes it a more difficult problem to treat.* 酗酒的羞恥感使之變得更加難以治療。**2** [C] *technical* the top of the centre part of a flower that receives the POLLEN that allows it to form new seeds【術語】〔植物的〕柱頭

stig·ma·ta /ˋstɪgmətə; ˈstɪgmətə/ *n* [plural] the marks on Christ's body caused by nails, or similar marks on the bodies of some holy people 聖痕〔耶穌(受難時)身上的釘痕或其他一些聖人身上相似的傷痕〕

stig·ma·tize also 又作 **-ise** *BrE*【英】/ˋstɪgməˌtaɪz; ˈstɪgmətaɪz/ *v* [T] **be stigmatized** to be treated by society as if you should be ashamed of your situation or actions 被視為可恥: *People with handicaps shouldn't be stigmatized.* 身心上有缺陷的人不應該被人看不起。—**stigmatization** /ˌstɪgmətəˋzeɪʃən; ˌstɪgmətaɪˈzeɪʃən/ *n* [U]

stile /staɪl; staɪl/ *n* [C] a set of steps placed on either side of a fence so that people can climb over it 〔設於籬笆兩側供人跨越用的〕梯磴, 台階

sti·let·to /stɪˋlɛto; stəˈletəʊ/ *plural* **stilettos** or **stilettoes** *n* [C] **1** also 又作 **stiletto heel** /ˌ·ˌ·· ˈ·/ a high thin heel of a woman's shoe 〔女鞋上的〕細高跟 **2** a shoe that has this kind of heel 細高跟鞋 —see picture at 參見 SHOE[1] 圖

1 1 **still¹** /stɪl; stɪl/ *adv* **1** up to a particular point in time and continuing at that moment 還, 仍然: *Do you still play tennis?* 你還打網球嗎? | *With 30 minutes still to go, neither team had scored.* 還剩下30分鐘的時間, 兩個隊都沒有得分。**2** in spite of what has just been said or done 雖然如此, 儘管那樣, 然而: *Clare didn't do much work, but she still passed the exam.* 克萊爾學習上雖然沒花多大功夫, 但她仍然通過了考試。| [sentence adverb 句子副詞] *The hotel was terrible. Still, we were lucky with the weather.* 旅店很糟糕, 然而我們有幸遇上了好天氣。| **still and all** (=all the same) 不過; 依然; 畢竟 *Still and all, you have to admire her.* 不過, 你不得不佩服她。**3** even more extreme than the situation or thing that you have just described 更, 還要: *It's cold today, but it'll be still colder tonight.* 今天很冷, 但晚上會更冷。| *The first question is very difficult, and the second is more difficult still.* 第一個問題很難, 第二個問題則更難。**4** **still more/another/other etc** even more in amount 還有更多的/另外一個/別的等: *There were still more reasons why the programme shouldn't go ahead.* 這個節目之所以不應該繼續進行還有更多的原因。

USAGE NOTE 用法說明: STILL

WORD CHOICE 詞語辨析: **still, already, yet**

Still suggests surprise that something has continued for longer than you might expect. still 表示因為某事物持續時間比預期更久而感到驚訝: *After fifty lessons I still can't drive very well.* 我上了五十次課, 車還是開得不太好。

Already is usually used in positive sentences to express surprise that something has happened earlier than you thought it would. already 通常用於肯定句中, 表示對某事物發生得比預料中更早而感到驚訝: *Are they here already?* 他們已經到了?

Yet is used in negatives and questions to talk about things that you expect to happen, but have not happened or might not have happened. yet 用於否定句和疑問句中, 表示某事物預期應該發生但還未發生或可能還未發生: *I haven't had breakfast yet.* 我還沒有吃早餐。| *Has Bill arrived yet?* 比爾到了嗎?

Compare **yet** with **already** in a question. 比較疑問句中yet和already的區別: *Have you had lunch yet?* asks for information, while *Have you had your lunch already?* expresses surprise that lunch has already been eaten. Have you had lunch yet? (你吃過午飯了嗎?) 這句話是詢問信息, Have you had your lunch already? (你已經吃過午飯了?) 則表示感到驚訝。

Yet used instead of **still** in a positive sentence is rare and a little formal. 肯定句中用 yet 替代 still 的情況很少見, 而且較正式: *We have yet to hear the truth.* 我們還沒有聽到實情。| *The Council may yet surprise us.* 地方議會也許仍會令我們吃驚。In conversation, however, you are more likely to say something like 但在對話中, 更常用類似下面例句的說法: *We don't know the truth yet.* 我們仍然不知道實情。

GRAMMAR 語法

Still usually comes immediately before any negative word. still 通常直接出現在否定詞前: *She still isn't ready.* 她還沒有準備好。| *They still don't know.* 他們仍然不知道。| *A solution has still not been found* (or 或 *...still hasn't,* NOT 不用 *...has not still*). 目前還沒有找到解決的辦法。

Still usually comes immediately after a positive modal verb. still 通常緊跟在肯定的情態動詞後: *I can still remember* (NOT 不用 *still can remember*). 我仍然記得。| *He may still be there* (or 或 *...be still there...*). 他可能還在那裡。

Otherwise **still** comes after the verb **to be** and immediately before any main verb. still 還出現在動詞 to be 之後或直接用於其他主要動詞之前: *He's still eating* (NOT 不用 *still is eating*). 他還在吃。| *It's still wet outside.* 外面還是濕的。| *We still have time* (NOT 不用 *have still time*). 我們還有時間。| *I still love her.* 我依然愛她。

still² *adj* **1** not moving 靜止的, 不動的: *a still pool* 不流動的池塘 | **keep/stand/lie etc still** *Keep still while I tie your shoe.* 別動, 我給你繫鞋帶。**2** not windy 無風的: *a hot, still, airless day* 無風、悶熱的一天 **3** quiet, calm, and without any activity 寂靜的; 安寧的; 寧靜的: *It was so still you could have heard a pin drop.* 真靜啊, 靜得連掉下一根針都聽得見。**4** *BrE* a still drink does not contain gas【英】〔飲料〕不含氣體的 **5** **still waters run deep** used to say that someone who is quiet may have very strong feelings or a lot of knowledge 靜水流深〔指沉默寡言者可能有強烈的情感或豐富的知識〕—**stillness** *n* [U]

still³ *n* [C] **1** a photograph of a scene from a cinema film 〔電影的〕劇照; 定格畫面 **2** a piece of equipment for making alcoholic drinks out of grain or potatoes 〔做酒用的〕蒸餾器 **3** **the still of the night/evening etc** *lite-*

rary the calm and quiet of the night etc【文】夜間/傍晚等的寂靜

still⁴ *v* [T] *literary*【文】**1** to make someone or something become quiet or calm 使安靜, 使靜止: *The food stilled the baby's cries.* 嬰兒吃了食物便不哭了。**2** if a doubt or fear is stilled, it becomes weaker or goes away 使〔疑慮或恐懼〕減輕[消除]; 使平靜

still·birth /ˈstɪl͵bɝθ; ˈstɪlbɜːθ/ *n* [C,U] a birth in which the baby is born dead 死產, 死胎 —compare 比較 ABORTION, MISCARRIAGE

still·born /ˈstɪl͵bɔrn; ˈstɪlbɔːn/ *adj* **1** born dead 死產的: *a stillborn baby* 死產兒 **2** ending before having had a chance to start 未開始便結束的; 夭折的: *a stillborn romance* 夭折的羅曼史

still life /͵· ˈ·◂/ *plural* **still lifes** *n* [C,U] a picture of an arrangement of objects, especially flowers and fruit 靜物畫

stilt /stɪlt; stɪlt/ *n* [C usually plural 一般用複數] **1** one of two poles on which you can stand and walk high above the ground 高蹺: *A clown crossed the ring on stilts.* 一個小丑踩着高蹺走過圓形表演場。**2** one of a set of poles that support a building so it is raised above ground or water level〔將建築物撐離地面或水面的〕支撐物, 支材

stilt·ed /ˈstɪltɪd; ˈstɪltɨd/ *adj* a stilted style of writing or speaking is formal, and unnatural〔文體、言談〕呆板的, 生硬的, 不自然的: *a stilted conversation* 生硬的對話 —**stiltedly** *adv*

Stil·ton /ˈstɪltn̩; ˈstɪltən/ *n* [U] a kind of English cheese that is white with grey-blue marks and has a strong taste〔英國的〕斯提爾頓乾酪, 藍芝士

stim·u·lant /ˈstɪmjələnt; ˈstɪmjɨlənt/ *n* [C] **1** a drug or substance that makes you feel more active and full of energy 興奮劑[藥]; 引起興奮的物質: *Caffeine is a stimulant.* 咖啡因是一種興奮劑。| **[+to]** *a stimulant to appetite* 刺激食慾的興奮劑 | **stimulant effects/properties etc** *a drug with stimulant properties* 具有興奮劑性能的藥品 **2** something that encourages more of a particular activity; STIMULUS 刺激(物): *economic stimulants* 刺激經濟增長的措施 | **[+to]** *Travel can be a stimulant to learning.* 旅遊能夠成為刺激學習的因素。

stim·u·late /ˈstɪmjə͵let; ˈstɪmjɨleɪt/ *v* [T] **1** to encourage an activity to begin or develop further 刺激, 促使, 促進: *The discussions stimulated a free exchange of ideas.* 討論促進了思想的自由交流。| **stimulate growth/demand/the economy etc** (=make economic growth etc start or become stronger) 刺激增長/需求/經濟等 **2** to encourage someone by making them excited about and interested in something 激發, 鼓勵, 激勵: **stimulate sb to do sth** *An inspiring teacher can stimulate students to succeed.* 一個富有啟發性的教師可以激勵學生取得成功。**3** to make a plant or part of the body become active or stronger 使活躍; 使強壯: *Light stimulates plant growth.* 光會促進植物的生長。—**stimulative** /-͵letɪv; -lətɪv/ *adj* —**stimulation** /͵stɪmjəˈleʃən; ͵stɪmjɨˈleɪʃən/ *n* [U]

stim·u·lat·ing /ˈstɪmjə͵letɪŋ; ˈstɪmjɨleɪtɪŋ/ *adj* **1** exciting or full of new ideas 使人興奮的; 充滿新思想的: *We had a most stimulating conversation.* 我們進行了一次很有啟發性的談話。**2** making you feel more active and healthy 使人振奮的: *I find mountain air much more stimulating.* 我覺得山上的空氣非常使人振奮。

stim·u·lus /ˈstɪmjələs; ˈstɪmjɨləs/ *plural* **stimuli** /-laɪ; -laɪ/ *n* **1** [singular,U] something that helps a process to develop more quickly or more strongly 刺激(物), 促進因素: **[+to]** *The discovery of oil acted as a stimulus to the local economy.* 石油的發現促進了當地的經濟。**2** [C] something that causes a reaction in a plant or part of the body 使植物[人體]產生反應之物, 刺激物: *A reflex action is a response to a stimulus.* 反射行為是對刺激的一種反應。

sting¹ /stɪŋ; stɪŋ/ *v past tense and past participle* **stung** /stʌŋ; stʌŋ/ **1** [I,T] if an insect or a plant stings you, it causes a sharp pain and that part of your body swells 刺, 蜇, 叮: *Henry was stung by a bee at the picnic.* 亨利在野餐時被蜜蜂蜇了一下。**2** [I,T] to hurt or to make something hurt with a sudden sharp pain for a short time (使)刺痛, (使)產生〔短時間的〕劇痛: *The antiseptic might sting a little.* 這消毒劑可能會引起點刺痛。| *Chopping onions makes my eyes sting.* 切洋葱把我的眼睛辣得很痛。**3** [T usually passive 一般用被動態] if a remark or criticism stings, it makes you feel upset and embarrassed 使感到氣憤[尷尬]: *Days later she was still stung by the accusations.* 好多天後, 她仍因受到指控而感到氣憤。| **sting sb into (doing) sth** *Her harsh words stung him into action.* 她嚴厲的批評刺激他採取了行動。| **stinging rebuke/sarcasm etc** (=severe and strongly expressed criticism etc) 尖刻的指責/挖苦等

sting sb **for** sth *informal*【非正式】**1** *especially BrE* to charge someone too much for something【尤英】向〔某人〕索取過高的價錢, 在…上敲〔某人的〕竹槓: *The garage stung him for £300.* 汽車修理站敲了他 300 英鎊。**2** *BrE* to borrow money from someone【英】向〔某人〕借錢: *Can I sting you for a fiver?* 我能跟你借五英鎊嗎?

sting² *n*

1 ▶INSECT/ANIMAL 昆蟲/動物◀ [C] *BrE* a sharp needle-like part of an animal or insect's body that can be pushed through the skin of a person or animal, often leaving poison【英】刺, 螫刺, 螫針; STINGER *AmE*【美】

2 ▶WOUND 傷(口)◀ [C] a wound or mark made when an insect or plant stings you 刺傷處, 蜇傷處: *Rub ointment on to the wasp sting.* 把藥膏塗在黃蜂蜇傷的地方。

3 ▶PAIN 疼痛◀ [singular] a sharp pain in your eyes or skin, caused by being hit, smoke etc 刺痛, 劇痛: *the sting of salt in a wound* 鹽入傷口的劇痛

4 a sting in the tail an unexpected end to a story, suggestion etc, that makes the whole thing less pleasant for the person listening〔指故事或建議等的〕使人不快的結尾

5 take the sting out of to make something unpleasant easier to deal with 使不引起刺痛; 使不快的事較易應付: *She smiled to take the sting out of her words.* 她微笑着, 使自己的話不至於刺痛別人。

6 ▶CRIME 犯罪◀ [C] *AmE*【美】**a)** a situation in which criminals obtain a large amount of money by cheating someone; SWINDLE² 〔巨額〕詐騙 **b)** a situation in which the police catch criminals by pretending to be involved in criminal activity themselves〔警方假裝參與犯罪以抓獲罪犯的〕圈套

sting·er /ˈstɪŋɚ; ˈstɪŋə/ *n* [C] *AmE* the sharp needle-like part of an animal or insect's body that can be pushed through the skin of a person or animal, often leaving poison【美】刺, 螫刺, 螫針; STING² (1) *BrE*【英】

stinging net·tle /ˈ·· ͵··/ *n* [C] a wild plant with leaves that sting and leave red marks on the skin 帶刺蕁麻

sting·ray /ˈstɪŋ͵re; ˈstɪŋreɪ/ *n* [C] a large fish with a flat body and several sharp points on its back near its tail 刺魟

stin·gy /ˈstɪndʒɪ; ˈstɪndʒi/ *adj* **1** *informal* not generous, especially with money, when you can easily afford to be【非正式】吝嗇的, 小氣的: *Jim's too stingy to give money to charity.* 吉姆太小氣, 不願捐錢行善。**2** a stingy amount of something, especially food, is too small to be enough 極少量的, 不足的: *The helpings here are pretty stingy.* 這裡的一份食物量很少。—**stingily** *adv* —**stinginess** *n* [U]

stink¹ /stɪŋk; stɪŋk/ *past tense* **stank** /stæŋk; stæŋk/ *past participle* **stunk** /stʌŋk; stʌŋk/ *v* [I] **1** to have a strong and very unpleasant smell 散發惡臭, 發臭味: *That paint stinks!* 那種油漆味道難聞極了! | **[+of]** *The place stank of old fish.* 那地方有陳魚的臭味。| **it stinks** *It stinks of smoke in here.* 這裡有難聞的煙味。| **stink to high heaven** (=stink very much) 臭氣熏天 **2 it stinks!** *spoken* used to say that you do not like something【口】糟透了〔用於表示不喜歡某事物〕: *"What did you think of the* *show?" "It stank!"* "你覺得那演出怎麼樣?" "糟透了!" **3** to make you think that something dishonest has been done secretly 讓人感覺不對勁: *The whole business really stinks.* 這整件事讓人感覺很不對頭。

stink sth **out** *BrE*【英】, **stink** sth **up** *AmE*【美】*phr v* [T] to fill a place with a very unpleasant smell 使…充滿難聞的味道: *Those onions are stinking the whole house out.* 那些洋葱弄得滿屋子都是一股難聞的氣味。

stink² *n* [C] **1** a terrible smell 惡臭, 難聞的氣味: *What a stink!* 這味道真臭! | **[+of]** *a stink of rotten eggs* 變質雞蛋的臭味 **2 make/raise/cause etc a stink** to complain very strongly because you are annoyed about something 強烈抱怨; 大吵大鬧: *I'm going to kick up a stink if they don't get us onto a flight soon.* 如果他們不盡快安排我們上飛機, 我就要大鬧一場。**3 work/run/go like stink** *BrE* to work etc as fast and as well as you can【英】賣力地工作/奔跑/行走: *We had to work like stink to meet the deadline.* 為了能在最後期限之前完成, 我們不得不非常賣力地工作。

stink bomb /ˈ· ·/ *n* [C] a small container that produces an extremely bad smell when it is broken〔爆炸時發出惡臭的〕臭彈

stink·er /ˈstɪŋkɚ; ˈstɪŋkə/ *n* [C] *informal*【非正式】**1** something that is very difficult or unpleasant 非常困難[令人不快]的事: *This cold I've got is a real stinker.* 這次我得的感冒真是令人難受。**2** someone who behaves badly 行為惡劣的人, 非常無禮的人: *That son of theirs is a little stinker!* 他們的那個兒子是個討厭的小傢伙!

stink·ing /ˈstɪŋkɪŋ; ˈstɪŋkɪŋ/ *adj* **1** having a very strong unpleasant smell 臭的, 發(惡)臭味的: *an alley full of stinking garbage cans* 滿是發出惡臭的垃圾桶的巷子 **2** *spoken* used to emphasize what you are saying when you are angry【口】令人討厭的〔生氣時用以加強語氣〕: *Just keep your stinking money then.* 那你就留着你的臭錢吧。**3** [only before noun 僅用於名詞前] *informal, especially BrE* very unpleasant【非正式, 尤英】討厭的, 糟糕的: *Stinking weather we've had lately!* 最近的天氣真糟糕! | **a stinking cold** *I've got an absolutely stinking cold.* 我得了討厭的重感冒。**4 stinking rich** *informal* an expression meaning extremely rich, used especially when you think this is unfair【非正式】十分富有的, 非常有錢的〔尤用於表示這是不公平的〕**5 a stinking letter** *BrE* an angry letter in which you complain very strongly about something【英】言辭激烈的投訴信

stink·y /ˈstɪŋkɪ; ˈstɪŋki/ *adj informal* smelling unpleasant; SMELLY【非正式】難聞的, 有臭味的: *stinky socks* 臭襪子

stint¹ /stɪnt; stɪnt/ *n* [C usually singular 一般用單數] **1** a limited or fixed period of work or effort 固定的工作期限; 固定的工作量: **[+as]** *the beginning of her stint as waitress* 她做服務員的初期 | **do a stint** *Mark did a two-year stint in the army.* 馬克服過兩年的兵役。| **do your stint** (=do some work that other people also have to do and that you do not expect to enjoy much) 做自己的那份工作 *Has he done his stint at the bar yet?* 他在酒吧的那份工作做完了嗎? **2 without stint** *formal* very generously【正式】不吝惜地, 非常慷慨地: *Sarah gave of her time and money without stint.* 莎拉毫不吝惜地出了時間出了錢。

stint² *v* [I usually in negatives 一般用於否定句] to give or use too little of something 節制, 吝惜, 限量: **stint on sth** *You can't stint on the butter with that recipe.* 按那個食譜烹飪時, 可不能吝惜黃油。

sti·pend /ˈstaɪpɛnd; ˈstaɪpend/ *n* [C] an amount of money paid regularly to someone such as a priest or student as wages or money to live on〔尤指給牧師、學生等的〕薪俸, 薪金; 助學金

sti·pen·di·a·ry¹ /staɪˈpɛndɪˌɛrɪ; staɪˈpendiəri/ *adj* receiving a stipend 有薪俸的, 領薪金的

stipendiary² also 又作 **stipendiary ma·gis·trate** /·ˌ····ˈ···/ *n* [C] a MAGISTRATE in Britain who is paid by the state〔英國的〕領薪治安官, 領薪地方法官

stip·ple /ˈstɪpl; ˈstɪpəl/ *v* [T] to draw or paint a picture or pattern using short STROKE*s* or spots instead of lines 點畫; 點刻 —**stippled** *adj* —**stippling** *n* [U]

stip·u·late /ˈstɪpjəˌlet; ˈstɪpjᵊleɪt/ *v* [T] to say that something must be done, when you are making an agreement or offer〔在協議或提議中〕規定, 約定: *Vanessa clearly stipulated payment in advance.* 瓦內莎清楚地說明要預先付款。| **stipulate that sth be done** *Tony stipulated that all expenses be refunded.* 托尼講明所有的開支都必須報銷。

stip·u·la·tion /ˌstɪpjəˈleʃən; ˌstɪpjᵊˈleɪʃən/ *n* [C,U] a specific condition that is stated as part of an agreement 條款, 約定[規定]的條件: **[+that]** *Kay signed, with the stipulation that she would take 10% of the profits.* 凱簽字了, 附加的條件是她要得到利潤的10%。

stir¹ /stɝ; stɜː/ *v* S3 W3

stir 攪動

1 ▶MIX 混合◀ [T] to move a liquid or substance around with a spoon or stick in order to mix it together 攪, 攪拌, 攪動: *Stir the paint to make sure it is smooth.* 將油漆攪拌至均勻。| **stir sth in/into** *When the sauce has cooled, add the grated cheese and stir it in.* 調味汁冷卻後, 拌入磨碎的乳酪。

2 ▶FEELINGS 感情◀ a) [T] to make someone have a strong feeling or reaction 激發, 激起〔強烈的感情〕, 引起〔強烈的反應〕: *He was stirred by the man's enthusiasm.* 他被那個人的熱情所打動。| **stir sb's memory/imagination etc** *Her imagination was stirred by the scene.* 那場景激發了她的想像。| **stir memories/emotions etc** *The news stirred memories of their own persecution.* 該新聞喚起他們對自己受迫害的回憶。**b)** [I] a feeling stirs in you, you begin to feel it〔感情〕激起, 喚起, 挑起: *Excitement stirred inside her.* 她內心開始興奮起來。

3 ▶MOVE SLIGHTLY 微動◀ [I] **a)** to move slightly or change your position because you are uncomfortable or just before you wake up〔睡覺時〕輕輕地移動[挪動]: *I never stirred all night long.* 我睡覺整夜都一動也不動。**b)** to move slightly 微微地動: *Something stirred in the long grass.* 高高的草叢中有東西輕輕地動了一下。

4 ▶DO STH 做某事◀ [T] to make someone feel they must do something 激發, 激勵〔某人做某事〕: *The incident stirred them to action.* 該事件激勵他們行動起來。| **stir yourself** *especially BrE*【尤英】*He stirred himself to answer the door.* 他趕快去開門。

5 ▶CAUSE TROUBLE 導致麻煩◀ [I] *BrE informal* to cause trouble between people by spreading false or secret information【英, 非正式】〔通過散佈謠言〕搬弄是非, 挑撥: *Ben's always stirring!* 本總是搬弄是非!

6 ▶MAKE STH MOVE 使某物移動◀ [T] to make something move slightly 使輕輕地移動: *The wind stirred the fallen leaves.* 風吹動落葉。

stir sth ↔ **up** *phr v* [T] **1** to deliberately try to cause arguments or problems between people 惹起〔麻煩〕, 挑起〔爭吵〕: *The new leader was accused of stirring up trouble.* 新領導人被指責挑起事端。| **stir things up** *Dave's just trying to stir things up because he's jealous.* 戴夫只不過因為嫉妒而試圖搬弄是非。**2** to make something move around in the air or in water 攪起, 攪動, 使揚起: *The horse's hooves stirred up a lot of dust.* 馬蹄揚起很多塵土。

stir² *n* **1** [C usually singular 一般用單數] an act of stirring something 攪拌, 攪動: **give sth a stir** *Give that pan a stir, will you?* 把那個鍋攪一下, 行嗎? **2** [C usually singular 一般用單數] a feeling of excitement or annoyance 激動[煩惱]的感覺: **[+of]** *a stir of disapproval* 一陣不滿的騷動 | **create/cause a stir** *Plans for the motorway caused quite a stir among local residents.* 修建高速公路的計劃在當地居民中引起了相當大的轟動。

stir-cra·zy /ˌ·ˈ··◂/ *adj informal* extremely nervous and upset, especially because you feel trapped in a place【非正式】〔尤指因感覺被困在某處而〕極度緊張的, 神經失常的

stir-fry /ˈ··/ *v* [T] to cook something by mixing it in hot oil for a short time 炒〔菜〕, 爆炒: *stir-fried vegetables* 爆炒的蔬菜 —**stir-fry** *n* [C]

stir·rer /ˈstɝə; ˈstɜːrə/ *n* [C] *BrE informal* someone who likes to cause trouble between people by spreading false or secret information【英, 非正式】煽動者; 搬弄是非者; 搗亂分子

stir·ring /ˈstɝɪŋ; ˈstɜːrɪŋ/ *adj* producing strong feelings or excitement in someone; ROUSING 激動人心的, 令人振奮的: *stirring music* 激動人心的音樂 | *a stirring speech* 令人振奮的演講 —**stirringly** *adv*

stir·rings /ˈstɝɪŋz; ˈstɜːrɪŋz/ *n* **stirrings of love/doubt/rebellion etc** early signs that love etc is starting 愛情/疑慮/反叛等的先兆

stir·rup /ˈstɪrəp; ˈstɪrəp/ *n* [C] a ring of metal that hangs from each side of a horse's SADDLE[1] (1) for someone to put their foot in 馬鐙 —see picture at 參見 HORSE[1] 圖

stitch[1] /stɪtʃ; stɪtʃ/ *n*

1 ▶**SEWING** 縫紉◀ [C] one of the short pieces of thread that you can see in a piece of cloth where it has been sewn〔縫紉中的〕一針: *Some of the stitches have come out of this shirt sleeve.* 這件襯衫的袖子有幾針散開了。

2 ▶**WITH WOOL** 用毛線◀ [C] one of the small circles that join together to make a SWEATER etc, formed when you are knitting (KNIT (2)) with wool〔編結中的〕一針: **drop a stitch** (=lose a stitch because the wool has come off the needle) 漏掉一針

3 ▶**STYLE** 風格◀ [C,U] a particular way of sewing or knitting (KNIT[1] (2)) that makes a particular pattern 縫法, 針法; 編結法: *Purl and plain are the two main stitches in knitting.* 反織和平織是編織中的兩種主要織法。

4 ▶**FOR WOUND** 縫合傷口◀ [C] a piece of thread that fastens the edges of a wound together〔縫合傷口的〕縫線: *The cut needed 15 stitches.* 這傷口需要縫 15 針。| *He had three stitches in it.* 他在該處縫了三針。

5 ▶**PAIN** 疼痛◀ [singular] a sharp pain in the side of your body, that you can get by running or laughing very hard〔跑步或大笑引起的〕脅部的突然劇痛: *I can't go any faster – I have a stitch.* 我無法跑得更快了, 我覺得脅部劇痛。

6 **in stitches** laughing uncontrollably 忍不住大笑, 忍俊不禁: **have sb in stitches** (=make sb laugh) 使某人忍不住大笑 *Her jokes had us all in stitches.* 她的笑話使我們大家都忍俊不禁。

7 **not have a stitch on** *informal* to be wearing no clothes【非正式】一絲不掛, 赤身露體

8 **not have a stitch to wear** to not have any clothing that is suitable for a particular occasion〔在某一場合〕沒有甚麼衣服可穿

9 **a stitch in time (saves nine)** *spoken* used to say that it is better to deal with problems early than to wait until they get worse【口】一針及時, 可省九針; 及時處理, 事半功倍

stitch[2] *v* [T] to SEW two pieces of cloth together, or to sew a decoration onto a piece of cloth 縫, 縫合, 縫補; 縫綴: *She stitches the pieces together to make a quilt.* 她把小布塊縫在一起做成被子。| **stitch sth onto** *Nina stitched a flower onto the skirt.* 尼娜把一朵花縫在裙子上。

stitch up *phr v* [T] **1** [**stitch** sth ↔ **up**] to put stitches in cloth or a wound in order to fasten parts of it together 縫合, 縫攏: *She stitched up the cut and left it to heal.* 她把傷口縫好讓它癒合。**2** [**stitch** sth ↔ **up**] to get a deal or agreement completed satisfactorily so that it cannot be changed 圓滿地完成: *The deal was stitched up in minutes.* 那交易幾分鐘就完成了。**3** [**stitch** sb ↔ **up**] *BrE informal* to make someone seem guilty of a crime by providing false information; FRAME[2] (3)【英, 非正式】陷害, 誣陷: *George said he'd been stitched up.* 喬治說他是被人陷害的。

stitch·ing /ˈstɪtʃɪŋ; ˈstɪtʃɪŋ/ *n* [U] a line of stitches in a piece of material 針腳

stoat /stot; stəʊt/ *n* [C] a small thin animal with brown fur that is similar to a WEASEL, and kills other animals 掃雪, 短尾鼬, 白鼬

stocks 足枷

stock[1] /stɑk; stɒk/ *n*

1 ▶**SUPPLIES** 供應◀ [C] also 又作 **stocks** *plural* a supply of something that you keep and can use when you need to 儲備物, 備用物; 供應物: *stocks of flour and sugar* 儲備的麵粉和糖 | **build up a stock** *The country has been building up its stock of weapons.* 該國一直在加強其武器儲備。

2 ▶**IN A SHOP** 在商店◀ [C,U] a supply of a particular type of thing that a shop has to sell〔商店的〕存貨, 現貨: *Buy now while stocks last!* 欲購從速, 餘貨售完即止! | **out of/in stock** (=unavailable or available in a particular shop) 沒有貨/有現貨 *I'm sorry, that swimsuit is completely out of stock in your size.* 對不起, 你要的那種尺寸的游泳衣全賣光了。| **take stock** (=check and count the goods in a shop) 盤點存貨

3 ▶**FINANCE** 金融◀ **a)** [C] *technical* a SHARE[2] (5) in a company【術語】股份 **b)** [U] the total value of a company's shares (SHARE[2] (5))〔某公司的〕總股值

4 ▶**COOKING** 烹飪◀ [C,U] a liquid made by boiling meat or bones and vegetables, which is used to make soups etc 湯汁, 原湯〈如肉湯、骨頭湯等〉: *chicken stock* 原汁雞湯

5 ▶**AMOUNT AVAILABLE** 可利用的量◀ [singular] also 又作 **stocks** *plural* the total amount of something that is available to be used in a particular area 可供利用的數量, 總儲備量: *Cod stocks in the North Atlantic have dropped radically.* 北大西洋鱈魚的總量已大幅下降。

6 ▶**ANIMALS** 動物◀ [U] farm animals, especially cattle; LIVESTOCK 家畜, 牲畜〔尤指牛〕

7 **take stock (of sth)** to think carefully about the things that have happened in a situation in order to decide what to do next〔對形勢〕作出估計[判斷], 估量: *Turning 40 is a time to take stock of your life.* 到 40 歲了, 該檢討一下自己的人生了。

8 **be of peasant/Protestant/Scottish stock etc** to be related to a particular type of family in the past 出身於農民/新教徒/蘇格蘭家庭等

9 **sb's stock is high/low** if someone's stock is high or low, they are very popular or very unpopular 某人很受人/不受人喜愛; 某人的聲望高/低: *The government's stock was high just before the election.* 政府在選舉前夕聲望很高。

10 ▶**FLOWER** 花◀ [C] a plant with pink, white, or light purple flowers and a sweet smell 紫羅蘭

11 ▶**PLANT** 植物◀ **a)** a plant that you can cut stems off to make new plants grow 砧木; 苗木 **b)** a thick part of a stem onto which another plant can be added so that the two plants grow together 嫁接另一種植物於其上的枝幹, 根莖

12 ▶DOCUMENT 文件◀ [C] an official document promising that a government will pay back the money it has borrowed with a fixed amount of INTEREST[1] (4) 公債
13 a stock of jokes/knowledge/courage etc the jokes, knowledge etc that someone knows or has 一堆笑話/一套知識/一股勇氣等: *John seems to have an inexhaustible stock of funny stories.* 約翰似乎有講不完的滑稽故事。
14 the stocks a) a wooden structure in a public place to which criminals were fastened by their feet or hands in former times 足枷; 手枷〔舊時一種木製的刑具〕 **b)** a wooden structure in which a ship is held while it is being built〔造船用的〕船台
15 ▶ACTORS 演員◀ [C] *AmE* a STOCK COMPANY (2)【美】〔演出幾種不同保留劇目的〕專業劇團 | **summer stock** (=a group of actors who work together on several plays during the summer) 夏季劇團〔夏季在一起演出幾種不同劇目的一羣演員〕| **do stock** (=work as an actor in this group) 做專業劇團的演員 *Jim's doing stock in Northern California.* 吉姆正在北加州做專業劇團的演員。
16 ▶CLOTHING 衣服◀ [C] a wide band of cloth worn around the neck so that the ends hang in front of your chest, especially by some priests 領圈;〔尤指牧師衣領下的〕闊領帶 —see also 另見 **laughing stock** (LAUGH[1] (9)), **lock, stock, and barrel** (LOCK[2] (3)), ROLLING STOCK

stock[2] *v* [T] **1** if a shop stocks a particular product, it keeps a supply of it to be sold〔商店為銷售而〕儲備: *Do you stock English wines?* 你們備有英國葡萄酒出售嗎? **2** to provide a supply of something so that it is ready to use 供應, 提供: *The fridge was stocked with all the butter and eggs needed for the Christmas baking.* 冰箱裡存足了做聖誕糕餅所需的黃油和雞蛋。**3** to put fish in a lake or river〔在湖或河裡〕放養〔魚〕: **[+with]** *rivers stocked with trout* 放養鱒魚的河 —see also 另見 WELL-STOCKED

stock up *phr v* [I] to buy a lot of something to use when you need to 囤積, 貯存: **[+on]** *We stocked up on wine when we went to Paris.* 我們去巴黎時買了很多葡萄酒。

stock[3] *adj* **1 stock excuse/question/remark etc** an excuse etc that people often say or use, especially when they cannot think of anything more interesting or original 老一套的藉口/問題/評論等 **2** [only before noun 僅用於名詞前] kept in a shop as goods to be sold〔商店〕庫存的, 常備的: *shoes in all the stock sizes* 所有常備尺碼的鞋子

stock·ade[1] /stɑk`ed; stɒ'keɪd/ *n* [C usually singular 一般用單數] a wall or fence made of large upright pieces of wood, built to defend a place〔防禦用的〕柵欄, 圍樁

stockade[2] *v* [T] to put a stockade around a place in order to defend it 用柵欄防衛, 用圍樁圍住

stock·breed·er /`stɑk,bridɚ; 'stɒk,briːdə/ *n* [C] a farmer who breeds cattle 牲畜飼養人

stock·brok·er /`stɑk,brokɚ; 'stɒk,brəʊkə/ *n* [C] someone whose job is to buy and sell stocks (STOCK[1] (3)), bonds (BOND[1] (1)), and shares (SHARE[2] (5)) for other people 證券[股票]經紀人 —**stockbroking** *n* [U]

stock car /'· ·/ *n* [C] **1** a car that has been made stronger so that it can compete in a race where cars often crash into each other〔用普通車改裝的〕賽車 **2** *AmE* a railway carriage for cattle【美】〔火車的〕牲畜運載車廂

stock cer·tif·i·cate /'· ·,···/ *n* [C] *AmE* an official document that shows that you own shares (SHARE[2] (5)) in a company【美】股份證書, 股票, 股權證

stock com·pa·ny /'· ,···/ *n* [C] *AmE*【美】**1** a company whose money is divided into shares (SHARE[2] (5)) so that many people own a small part of it; JOINT-STOCK COMPANY 股份公司 **2** a group of actors who work together doing several different plays〔演出幾種不同保留劇目的〕一羣演員, 專業劇團

stock cube /'· ·/ *n* [C] a small piece of solid substance made of dried juices from meat and vegetables, that is mixed with water to make STOCK[1] (4)〔經脫水的〕粒狀湯料, 固體湯料

stock ex·change /'· ·,·/ *n* [C usually singular 一般用單數] **1** the business of buying stocks (STOCK[1] (3)) and shares (SHARE[2] (5)) 證券交易, 股票交易: *She made a fortune on the stock exchange.* 她買賣股票賺了一大筆錢。**2** a place where stocks and shares are bought and sold 證券[股票]交易所

stock·hold·er /`stɑk,holdɚ; 'stɒk,həʊldə/ *n* [C] *especially AmE* someone who owns stocks (STOCK[1] (3)) in a business【尤美】股票[證券]持有人, 股東; SHAREHOLDER *BrE*【英】

stock·i·nette /,stɑkɪn`ɛt; ,stɒkɪ'net/ *n* [U] *especially BrE* a soft cotton material that stretches, used especially for BANDAGES【尤英】鬆緊棉織物, 彈力棉織物〔尤用作繃帶〕

stock·ing /`stɑkɪŋ; 'stɒkɪŋ/ *n* [C usually plural 一般用複數] **1** a thin close-fitting piece of clothing that covers a woman's leg and foot (女式) 長筒襪 —compare 比較 PANTYHOSE, TIGHTS **2** *old-fashioned* a man's sock【過時】男襪 **3 in your stockinged feet** not wearing any shoes 只穿襪而不穿鞋的 —see also 另見 BODY STOCKING, CHRISTMAS STOCKING

stock-in-trade /,· · '·/ *n* [U] **1** words or behaviour that a particular type of person often uses 慣用言辭; 慣有行為; 慣用手段[伎倆]: *A pleasant manner is part of a politician's stock-in-trade.* 待人親切熱情是政治家慣用的策略之一。**2** *old-fashioned* the things you need to do your job【過時】經營某行業所需的一切

stock·ist /`stɑkɪst; 'stɒkɪst/ *n* [C] *BrE* a person, shop, or company that keeps a particular product or particular goods to sell【英】備有某種產品[貨物]供出售的商人[商店、公司], 零售商 (店)

stock·man /`stɑkmən; 'stɒkmən/ *n* [C] a man whose job it is to look after farm animals 畜牧工人, 飼養員

stock mar·ket /'· ,··/ *n* [C usually singular 一般用單數] the STOCK EXCHANGE 證券[股票]交易所, 證券市場

stock·pile[1] /`stɑk,paɪl; 'stɒkpaɪl/ *n* **[C+of]** a large supply of goods, weapons etc that are kept ready to be used in the future, especially when they may become difficult to obtain〔尤指為有可能短缺而準備的物資、武器等的〕貯存, 儲備

stockpile[2] *v* [T] to keep adding to a supply of goods, weapons etc that you are keeping ready to use if you need them in the future 貯存, 積聚〔物資、武器等〕: *The Superpowers are stockpiling nuclear arms.* 超級大國在加強他們的核武器貯備。

stock·pot /`stɑk,pɑt; 'stɒkpɒt/ *n* [C] a pot in which you make STOCK[1] (4) 湯鍋

stock·room /`stɑk,rum; 'stɒkrʊm/ *n* [C] a room for storing things in a shop or office〔商店或辦公室的〕倉庫, 儲藏室

stock-still /,· '·/ *adv* not moving at all 靜止地, 一動不動 (地): *Oscar stood stock-still and listened.* 奧斯卡站在那兒一動不動地聽着。

stock·tak·ing /`stɑk,tekɪŋ; 'stɒk,teɪkɪŋ/ *n* [U] *BrE* an occasion when you make a list of all the goods that you have a supply of at a particular time, especially in a shop【英】〔存貨的〕盤點, 清點存貨; INVENTORY (2) *AmE*【美】

stock·y /`stɑkɪ; 'stɒki/ *adj* a stocky person is short and heavy and looks strong〔人〕矮而結實的, 粗壯的 —**stockily** *adv* —**stockiness** *n* [U]

stock·yard /`stɑk,jɑrd; 'stɒkjɑːd/ *n* [C] a place where cattle, sheep etc are kept before being taken to a market and sold〔在運往市場出售之前臨時的〕牲畜圍欄

stodge /stɑdʒ; stɒdʒ/ *n* [U] **1** heavy food that makes you feel full very quickly 油膩易使人飽的食物 **2** *BrE informal* something written that is very dull and difficult to read【英, 非正式】乏味難懂的作品

stodg·y /`stɑdʒɪ; 'stɒdʒi/ *adj* **1** stodgy food is heavy and makes you feel full very quickly〔食物〕油膩易使人飽的 **2** *BrE informal* stodgy writing is dull and difficult to read【英, 非正式】〔作品〕乏味難懂的 **3** a stodgy person is dull and behaves rather formally〔人〕墨守成規的, 古板而乏味的 —**stodginess** *n* [U]

sto·gie /ˈstogɪ; ˈstəʊgi/ *n* [C] *AmE informal* a CIGAR, especially a thick cheap one【美, 非正式】雪茄〔尤指廉價的粗雪茄〕

sto·ic /ˈsto·ɪk; ˈstəʊɪk/ *n* [C] someone who does not show their emotions and does not complain when something unpleasant happens to them 堅忍克己的人; 不以苦樂為意的人; 恬淡寡慾的人; 禁慾(主義)者

sto·ic·al /ˈsto·ɪkḷ; ˈstəʊɪkəl/ *adj* also 又作 **stoic** not complaining or feeling unhappy when bad things happen to you 堅忍的; 不以苦樂為意的; 恬淡寡慾的; 禁慾的 —**stoically** /-kḷɪ; -kli/ *adv*

sto·i·cis·m /ˈsto·ɪˌsɪzəm; ˈstəʊɪ̣sɪzəm/ *n* [U] patience and calmness when bad things happen to you 堅忍(精神); 不以苦樂為意; 恬淡寡慾; 禁慾

stoke /stok; stəʊk/ also 又作 **stoke up** *v* [I,T] to add more coal or wood to a fire used for cooking or heating 添加〔煤、柴火等燃料〕; 給…添加〔燃料〕: **stoke sth with sth** *Stoke the furnace with wood.* 給爐子添加柴火。

stoke up *phr v* [T] **1** to add more coal or wood to a fire 添〔火〕: **stoke sth ↔ up** *Get the fire stoked up.* 把火添旺。**2 to stoke up fear/anger etc** to make a lot of people feel frightened etc about something 引發恐懼/憤怒等: *The leaflets stoked up a lot of fears of an invasion.* 傳單引起很多人對侵略的恐懼。**3 stoke up on/with a)** to eat a lot of food, for example because you will not eat again for a long time 飽餐一頓, 大吃一頓: *We stoked up on hot soup before going out in the snow.* 我們冒雪出門之前喝了很多熱湯。**b)** to buy a lot of something that you need 大量購置, 大量添置: *stoking up on warm clothing* 大量購置保暖的衣服

stoked /stokt; stəʊkt/ *adj AmE spoken* very excited about something good that is happening and that you did not expect【美口】〔因意外的驚喜而〕振奮的, 非常興奮的

stok·er /ˈstokɚ; ˈstəʊkə/ *n* [C] someone whose job is to put coal or other FUEL[1] (1) into a FURNACE 燒火工, 司爐, 火伕

stole[1] /stol; stəʊl/ the past tense of STEAL

stole[2] *n* [C] a long straight piece of cloth or fur that a woman wears across her shoulders 女用披肩, 長圍巾

sto·len /ˈstolən; ˈstəʊlən/ the past participle of STEAL: *stolen cars* 被盜的汽車 | *books stolen from libraries* 從圖書館偷出來的書

stol·id /ˈstɑlɪd; ˈstɒlɪ̣d/ *adj* someone who is stolid does not react to situations or seem excited by them when most people would react; IMPASSIVE 不易激動的; 麻木不仁的; 無動於衷的 —**stolidly** *adv* —**stolidness** also 又作 **stolidity** /stəˈlɪdətɪ; stəˈlɪdɪ̣ti/ *n* [U]

3 3 **stom·ach[1]** /ˈstʌmək; ˈstʌmək/ *n* [C] **1** the organ inside your body where food begins to be digested (DIGEST[1] (1)) 胃 —see picture at 參見 DIGESTIVE SYSTEM 圖 **2** the front part of your body, below your chest 腹部: *Andrew was lying on his stomach.* 安德魯俯臥着。**3 do sth on an empty stomach** to do something when you have not eaten 空着肚子做某事: *Don't go to work on an empty stomach.* 別空着肚子去工作。**4 have a strong stomach** to be able to see or do things that are unpleasant without feeling sick or upset 有很強的承受能力: *Don't watch that film unless you have a strong stomach.* 除非你忍受得了, 否則不要去看那部電影。**5 turn your stomach** to make you feel sick or upset 使某人感到噁心, 令某人翻胃: *The sight of the slaughtered cow turned my stomach.* 看到被宰殺的牛令我感到噁心。**6 have no stomach for a fight/task etc** to have no desire to do something because you do not like doing it etc 不想打架/沒興趣做某工作等

stomach[2] *v* [T usually in questions and negatives 一般用於疑問句和否定句] **1** to be able to accept something, especially something unpleasant; ENDURE 承受, 容忍, 忍耐 | **can't stomach** *Tracy couldn't stomach the idea of moving to Glasgow.* 特蕾西不能接受移居到格拉斯哥的主意。| **hard/difficult to stomach** *Rob found Cathy's attitude hard to stomach.* 羅布覺得卡西的態度令人難以忍受。**2** to eat something without becoming ill 吃…而不感到難受[不適]: *I can't stomach fried food.* 我不能吃油炸的食物。

stom·ach·ache /ˈstʌməkˌek; ˈstʌmək-eɪk/ *n* [C,U] pain in your stomach or near your stomach 胃痛; 肚子痛

stomach pump /ˈ·· ·/ *n* [C] a machine with a tube that doctors use to suck out the food etc inside someone's stomach, especially after they have swallowed poison 胃唧筒〔抽吸胃中食物等的醫療器具, 尤用於給服毒者洗胃〕

stomp /stɑmp; stɒmp/ *v* [I always+adv/prep] **1** to walk with heavy steps, especially because you are angry〔尤指因生氣〕跺腳, 重踩: *Alex stomped angrily up the stairs.* 亞歷克斯怒氣沖沖地重步走上樓梯。**2 sb's stomping ground** a favourite place where someone often goes 某人喜歡常去的地方

stone[1] /ston; stəʊn/ *n* 2 1

1 ►ON THE GROUND 在地上◄ [C] a small piece of rock of any shape, found on the ground 石子, 石塊, 石頭: *Round, flat stones are the best for skimming across water.* 圓圓扁扁的石子打水漂最好。

2 ►ROCK 石, 石料◄ [U] a hard mineral substance or rock 礦石; 石料: *honey colored stone* 蜜黃色的礦石 | *stone statues* 石像

3 ►JEWELLERY 珠寶◄ [C] a jewel 寶石: *gem stones* 寶石

4 ►FRUIT 水果◄ [C] *BrE* a large hard single seed at the centre of some fruits【英】〔某些果實中的〕核; PIT[1] (9) *AmE*【美】—compare 比較 PIP[1] (1)

5 ►MEDICAL 醫學的◄ [C] a ball of hard material that can form in organs such as your BLADDER or KIDNEYS〔器官如膀胱或腎臟中的〕結石

6 ►WEIGHT 重量◄ [C] *plural* **stone** or **stones** a measurement of weight used in Britain that is equal to 6.35kg 英石, 唡〔英國的重量單位, 等於6.35公斤〕—see table on page C4 參見 C4 頁附錄

7 a stone's throw (away) very close to something 投石可及的距離, 非常靠近, 附近: *The villa was only a stone's throw from the beach.* 該度假別墅離海灘很近。

8 be made of stone also 又作 **have a heart of stone** to not show any emotions or pity for someone 冷酷無情, 有一副鐵石心腸 —see also 另見 FOUNDATION STONE, PAVING STONE, STEPPING-STONE

stone[2] *v* [T] **1** to throw stones at someone or something 向…扔石頭, 用石頭擲擊: **stone sb to death** (=kill someone with stones, especially as a punishment in the past) 投擲石頭砸死某人〔舊時作為懲罰手段〕**2** *BrE* to take the stone out of fruit【英】去掉〔水果的〕核; PIT[2] (2) *AmE*【美】: *stoned dates* 去核的棗 **3 stone the crows!** also 又作 **stone me!** *BrE old-fashioned* used to express surprise or shock【英, 過時】哎呀, 啊〔表示驚訝或震驚〕

Stone Age /ˈ· ·/ *n* the earliest known time in human history, when only stone was used for making tools, weapons etc 石器時代 —compare 比較 BRONZE AGE, IRON AGE

stone-cold /ˌ· ˈ·◄/ *adj* **1** completely and unpleasantly cold 冰冷的, 完全涼的: *The body's stone-cold.* 屍體已經冰涼。**2 stone-cold sober** having drunk no alcohol at all 完全清醒的, 一點酒也沒有喝

stoned /stond; stəʊnd/ *adj* [not before noun 不用於名詞前] **1** *informal* feeling very excited or extremely relaxed because you have taken an illegal drug【非正式】〔吸食毒品後〕極度興奮[鬆弛]的 **2** very drunk 爛醉如泥的

stone dead /ˌ· ˈ·◄/ *adj* completely dead 完全死了的

stone deaf /ˌ· ˈ·◄/ *adj* completely unable to hear 完全聾的

stone-ground /ˈ· ·/ *adj* stone-ground flour is made by crushing grain between two MILLSTONES〔麵粉〕用石磨研磨的

stone·ma·son /ˈstonˌmesn̩; ˈstəʊnˌmeɪsən/ *n* [C] someone whose job is cutting stone into pieces to be used in buildings 石匠, 石工

stone·wall /ˌstonˈwɔl; ˌstəʊnˈwɔːl/ *v* [I] to delay a discussion, decision etc by talking a lot and refusing to answer questions〔用冗長的發言或拒絕回答問題的辦法〕拖延[阻礙]〔議事、作出決定等〕

stone·ware /ˈstonˌwɛr; ˈstəʊnweə/ *n* [U] pots etc that are made from a special hard clay 粗陶器

stone-washed /ˌ· ˈ·◂/ *adj* stonewashed JEANS etc have been made softer by a washing process in which they are beaten with stones〔牛仔褲等〕石洗的, 石磨的

stone·work /ˈstonˌwɝk; ˈstəʊnwɜːk/ *n* [U] the parts of a building that are made of stone, especially when they are decorative 建築物的石製部分〔尤指帶有裝飾的〕

stonk·ered /ˈstɑŋkɚd; ˈstɒŋkəd/ *adj AustrE informal* very tired【澳, 非正式】筋疲力竭的, 非常疲勞的

stonk·ing /ˈstɑŋkɪŋ; ˈstɒŋkɪŋ/ *adj BrE informal* surprisingly good【英, 非正式】好得出奇的, 非常好的: *He scored a stonking goal.* 他進了很漂亮的一球。

ston·y /ˈstonɪ; ˈstəʊni/ *adj* **1** covered by stones or containing stones 鋪着石頭的; 多石的; 石質的: *stony soil* 多石的土壤 **2** without emotion or pity 冷酷的, 無情的; 無同情心的: *stony faces* 冷酷的面孔 | *a stony silence* 事不關己的沉默 **3 fall on stony ground** if a request, suggestion, joke etc falls on stony ground, it is ignored or people do not like it 被忽視; 不受喜歡; 沒有引起反響 —**stonily** *adv*

stony-faced /ˌ·· ˈ·◂/ *adj* showing no emotion or friendliness 面無表情的, 冷漠的

stood /stʊd; stʊd/ the past tense and past participle of STAND[1]

stooge /studʒ; stuːdʒ/ *n* [C] **1** one of two performers who is the subject of the jokes made by the other performer〔作為另一演員引逗或打趣對象的〕配角 **2** *informal* someone who always does what someone else wants them to【非正式】唯命是從的人, 傀儡

stook·ie /ˈstʊkɪ; ˈstʊki/ *n* [C] *ScotE* a PLASTER CAST【蘇格蘭】石膏模型

stool /stul; stuːl/ *n* [C] **1** a seat without any supporting part for your back or arms 凳子: *a bar stool* 酒吧凳子 —see picture at 參見 CHAIR[1] 圖 **2** *technical* a piece of solid waste from your body【術語】大便, 糞便

stool·pi·geon /ˈstulˌpɪdʒən; ˈstuːlˌpɪdʒɪ̆n/ *n* [C] *AmE informal* someone, especially a criminal, who helps the police to catch another criminal; INFORMER【美, 非正式】〔警察的〕眼線; 用來誘捕罪犯的人; 告密者

stoop[1] /stup; stuːp/ *v* [I] **1** also 又作 **stoop down** to bend your body forwards and down 俯身, 彎腰: *The doorway was so low that Martin had to stoop to go in.* 門口很低, 馬丁不得不彎腰進去。 **2** to stand with your back and shoulders bent forwards 弓背, 彎腰曲背站立

stoop to sth *phr v* [T] to do something, even though you know it is morally wrong, because you think it will help you achieve something 降低道德標準去做…: *Ray would stoop to anything to get what he wants.* 雷為了得到自己想要的東西甚麼事都做得出來。| **stoop to doing sth** *I didn't expect you to stoop to lying.* 我沒料到你竟然會下賤到去撒謊。

stoop[2] *n* **1** [singular] if you have a stoop, your shoulders slope forward or seem too round 曲背; 彎腰: *Jeff's developed a stoop.* 傑夫有些駝背。 **2** [C] *AmE* a raised area at the door of a house, usually big enough to sit on【美】門廊, 門階

stooped /stupt; stuːpt/ *adj* having a stoop 彎腰的; 駝背的: *a stooped old man* 駝背的老人

stoop·ing /ˈstupɪŋ; ˈstuːpɪŋ/ *adj* stooping shoulders are bent forwards or have become too round〔肩膀〕彎曲的

S1 W1 **stop[1]** /stɑp; stɒp/ *v* **stopped, stopping**

1 ►NOT MOVE OR CONTINUE 不再移動或繼續◄ [I,T] to no longer move or continue to do something, or to make someone or something do this (使)停止, (使)停下來: *Stop, thief!* 站住, 小偷! | **stop sth** *Apply pressure to stop the bleeding.* 壓住傷口止血。| *You'll have to stop the generator, it's overheating.* 你得把發電機停下來, 機器過熱了。| **stop doing sth** *Lena's trying to stop smoking.* 莉娜正試圖戒煙。| **stop that/it** *spoken*【口】*Stop it! You're hurting me.* 住手! 你弄痛我了。| **stop short** (=stop walking suddenly) 突然止步, 突然停住腳步 | **stop and do sth** *People stopped and stared as she screamed at him.* 她對他尖叫時, 人們停下來盯着他們看。| **stop (dead)/stop in your tracks** (=stop walking or running very suddenly) 突然停止走[跑], 猛然止步 | **stop (sth) at/outside/in etc** *Jill stopped the car outside the post office.* 吉爾在郵局外面把汽車停下。| **stop on a dime** *AmE* (=stop very quickly)【美】迅速停止

2 ►PREVENT 防止, 阻止◄ [T] to prevent someone from doing something or something from happening 防止, 阻止, 阻擋: *I'm leaving home and you can't stop me.* 我要離開這個家, 你無法阻止我。| **stop sb (from) doing sth** *Lynn's parents tried to stop her seeing him.* 琳恩的父母企圖阻止她和他見面。| **there's nothing to stop sb** *There's nothing to stop you calling her to say you're sorry.* 你完全可以給她打個電話向她道歉。

3 ►END 結束◄ [I,T] to end or make something end (使)結束, (使)終止: *We'll go out when the rain stops.* 雨停了我們就出去。| **stop sth** *The referee stopped the fight.* 裁判終止了這場拳賽。| **[+at]** *The road stops at the farm.* 這條路通到農場就斷了。

4 ►PAUSE 暫停◄ [I] to pause in an activity, journey etc in order to do something before continuing 中止, 暫時停下來: **stop for sth** *We stopped for a drink on the way home.* 我們在回家的路上停下來喝點東西。| **stop to do sth** *Maya stopped to tie her shoelace.* 梅雅停下來繫鞋帶。| **stop to think/consider etc** *It's time we stopped to think about our next move.* 我們該停下來想一下我們下一步的行動了。

5 stop at nothing (to do sth) to be ready to do anything, even if it is cruel, dishonest, or illegal, to get what you want (做某事)不擇手段, (做某事)無所顧忌: *Franca will stop at nothing to get a part in the film.* 為了能在那部電影中扮演一個角色, 弗蘭卡會不擇手段。

6 stop short of (doing) sth to decide that you are not willing to do something wrong or dangerous, though you will do something similar that is less dangerous 決定不去做〔錯誤或危險的事情〕; 不願逾矩: *The US government supported sanctions but stopped short of military action.* 美國政府支持制裁, 但不願採取軍事行動。

7 ►STAY 停留◄ [I] *BrE informal* to stay somewhere for a short time, especially at someone's house【英, 非正式】〔尤指在某人家裡〕逗留, 短時間停留: *I won't sit down – I'm not stopping.* 我不坐了, 我不打算逗留。| **[+for]** *Can you stop for a chat?* 你能停下來聊聊天嗎?

8 ►WALKING/TRAVELLING 步行/旅行◄ [T] to go to someone and speak to them or make them stop when they are walking or travelling somewhere 使〔某人〕停下, 攔住, 截住: *Someone stopped me in the street and asked the way.* 有人在街上攔住我問路。| *If they try to get away, they'll be stopped at the border.* 他們要是企圖逃跑, 在邊境上將會被截住。

9 ►MONEY 錢◄ to prevent money from being paid after you agreed to pay it 停付; 扣留: **stop sth from sth** *Money for breakages will be stopped from your wages.* 損耗費將從你的工資中扣除。| **stop a cheque** (=tell your bank not to pay the money) 停止兌付支票

10 ►BLOCK 堵塞◄ [T] also 又作 **stop up** to block something such as a pipe so that water, smoke etc cannot go through it 堵塞, 塞住, 堵住

stop back *phr v* [I] *AmE* to go back to a place you have been to earlier【美】返回: *Can you stop back later? I'm real busy right now.* 你能過一會再來嗎? 我現在實在很忙。

stop by *phr v* [I,T] to make a short visit to a place or person, especially when you are on your way to somewhere else 順便拜訪, 順路探望: *Daniel stopped by the newsagent's on his way home.* 丹尼爾在回家的路上順便去了一趟報攤。

stop sth ↔ **down** *phr v* [T] to make the hole in a camera LENS (2) smaller so that less light gets in when you take a photograph〔攝影時〕縮小〔鏡頭的〕光圈

stop in *phr v* [I] *informal*【非正式】**1** to make a short visit to a place or person, especially when you are on your way to somewhere else 順便拜訪, 順路探望: **[+at]** *Let's stop in at Vera's on our way.* 我們順路去薇拉家坐坐吧。**2** *BrE* to stay at home【英】待在家裡: *I'm stopping in to wash my hair tonight.* 我今晚待在家裡洗頭。

stop off *phr v* [I] to make a short visit to a place during a journey, especially to rest or to see someone〔在旅途中〕中途停留: *Shall we stop off somewhere on the way to Cornwall?* 我們去康沃爾郡的路上要在哪裡逗留嗎? | **[+in/at etc]** *We stopped off in Santa Rosa for a day.* 我們在聖羅莎停留了一天。

stop out *phr v* [I] *BrE informal* to stay out later than usual【英, 非正式】待在外面, 晚歸: *Lizzie stopped out all night on Saturday.* 莉齊星期六整夜待在外面沒有回家。

stop over *phr v* [I] to make a short stay somewhere before continuing a long journey 中途作短暫停留: *The plane stops over in Dubai on the way to India.* 飛機飛往印度的途中在杜拜作短暫停留。

stop up *phr v* [I] *BrE informal* to stay up late【英, 非正式】熬夜, 遲睡: *Joe stopped up till 3 o'clock to watch the boxing.* 喬為看那場拳擊賽一直熬到三點鐘才睡覺。

S

This graph shows how common the different grammar patterns of the verb **stop** are. 本圖表所示為動詞 stop 構成的不同語法模式的使用頻率。

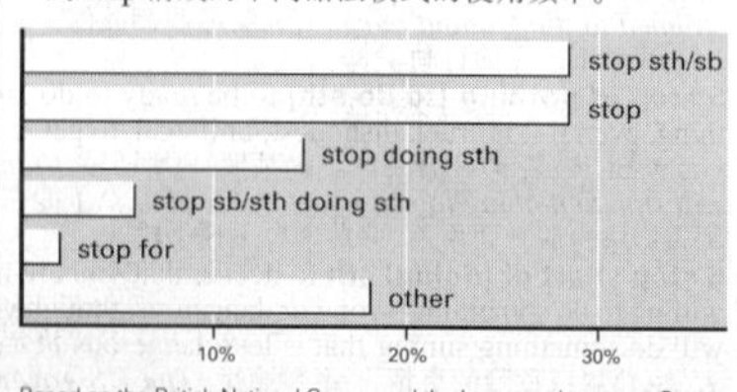

Based on the British National Corpus and the Longman Lancaster Corpus
據英國國家語料庫和朗文蘭卡斯特語料庫

3 3 **stop²** *n* [C]

1 bring sth to a stop to stop something moving or happening 使…停下來; 使…停止: *David brought the truck to a shuddering stop.* 戴維使卡車顫抖着停了下來。

2 come/roll to a stop if a vehicle, an activity etc comes to a stop, it stops moving or happening〔車輛、活動等〕停下來, 停止: *Work on the project has come to a stop because of lack of funding.* 因缺乏資金, 該項目已經停下來了。

3 ►DURING JOURNEY 旅途中◄ a time or place when you stop during a journey for a short time 中途停留(處): *Our first stop was Paris, and then we traveled on to Marseilles.* 我們旅行的第一站是巴黎, 接着我們又到了馬賽。| **make a stop** (=stop somewhere while travelling) 途中停留 *We only made two stops on the long drive down through France.* 我們開車穿越法國的漫長旅途中只作了兩次停留。

4 ►BUS/TRAIN 公共汽車/火車◄ a place where a bus or train regularly stops for people to get on and off 車站: *This is your stop, isn't it?* 你到站該下車了, 對嗎?

5 put a stop to sth to prevent something from continuing or happening 制止, 使…停下來: *The new law should put a stop to this tax evasion.* 新法例應該制止這種偷稅漏稅的行為。

6 pull out all the stops to do everything you possibly can to make something happen and succeed 竭盡全力; 全力以赴: *The Bianchis had pulled out all the stops for their daughter's wedding.* 比安奇夫婦為女兒的婚禮全力以赴。

7 ►MUSIC 音樂◄ **a)** a set of pipes on an ORGAN (2) that produce sound〔風琴的〕(一排) 音管 **b)** a set of handles that you push in or out in an organ to control the amount of sound it produces〔風琴的〕音栓

8 ►CONSONANT 子音◄ a consonant sound, like /p/ or /k/, made by stopping the flow of air completely and then suddenly letting it out of your mouth; PLOSIVE (閉) 塞音 —see also 另見 FULLSTOP

stop·cock /ˈstɑpˌkɑk; ˈstɒpkɒk/ *n* [C] a VALVE (1) that can be opened or closed with a TAP (=object you turn) to control the flow of a liquid in a pipe〔調節管道中液體流量的〕管門, 活栓, 閥門; TURNCOCK *BrE*【英】

stop·gap /ˈstɑpˌgæp; ˈstɒpgæp/ *n* [C] something or someone that you use for a short time until you can replace it with something better 臨時替代的物[人]; 補缺者: *a stopgap measure* 臨時措施

stop-go /ˌ· ˈ·◄/ *adj* **stop-go approach/policies etc** *BrE* a way of controlling the economy by restricting government spending for a period of time and then not restricting it so severely for a time【英】〔用作調控經濟的〕緊縮與膨脹交替的應變方法/政策等

stop·light /ˈstɑpˌlaɪt; ˈstɒplaɪt/ *n* [C] also 又作 **stoplights** *plural AmE* a set of coloured lights used to control and direct traffic; TRAFFIC LIGHTS【美】交通信號燈, 紅綠燈

stop·o·ver /ˈstɑpˌovɚ; ˈstɒpˌəʊvə/ *n* [C] a short stay somewhere between parts of a journey, especially on a long plane journey〔尤指長途飛行中的〕中途停留: *a two-day stopover in Hong Kong* 在香港逗留兩天

stop·page /ˈstɑpɪdʒ; ˈstɒpɪdʒ/ *n* **1** [C] a situation in which workers stop working for a short time as a protest 停工, 罷工: *time lost in disputes and stoppages* 因糾紛和停工損失的時間 **2** [C] something that blocks a tube or container 堵塞(物), 阻塞(物): *an intestinal stoppage* 腸堵塞 **3** [C,U] *BrE* the act of stopping something from moving or happening【英】停止, 中止, 阻止: *complete stoppages of production* 生產的完全停頓 | *stoppages due to injury* 因傷暫停 **4 stoppages** [plural] *BrE* money kept back from your wages by your employer in order to pay your tax, for your PENSION etc【英】〔從工資中的〕扣除部分, 扣除額

stop·per /ˈstɑpɚ; ˈstɒpə/ *n* [C] the thing that you put in the top part of a bottle to close it 瓶塞, 栓 —**stopper** *v* [T] —see picture at 參見 LABORATORY 圖

stopping dis·tance /ˈ·· ˌ··/ *n* [C,U] the distance that a driver is supposed to leave between their car and the one in front in order to be able to stop safely 安全車距

stop press /ˌ· ˈ·◄/ *n* [singular] late news added to a newspaper after the main part has been printed〔報紙開印後臨時插入的〕最新消息

stop·watch /ˈstɑpˌwɑtʃ; ˈstɒpwɒtʃ/ *n* [C] a watch used for measuring the exact time it takes to do something, especially to finish a race〔尤用於賽跑的〕秒錶, 跑錶

stor·age /ˈstɔrɪdʒ; ˈstɔːrɪdʒ/ *n* [U] **1** the act of keeping or putting something in a special place while it is not being used 儲存, 貯藏, 保管: *the storage of radioactive material* 放射性材料的存放 | **storage space/capacity** (=space etc for storing things) 貯存空間/容量 **2 in storage** if furniture or other goods are in storage, they are being kept in a special place until you need to use them〔家具等〕被存放着 **3** the price you pay for having goods or furniture stored 貯存費, 倉租 3

storage heat·er /ˈ·· ˌ··/ *n* [C] *BrE* a HEATER that stores heat at times when electricity is cheaper【英】電蓄熱器

store¹ /stɔr; stɔː/ *n* [C] 1

1 ►LARGE SHOP 大商店◄ a large place that sells many different kinds of goods 大商店: *At Christmas the stores stay open late.* 在聖誕節期間, 大商店營業到很晚。—see also 另見 CHAIN STORE, DEPARTMENT STORE, GENERAL STORE 1

2 ►SHOP 商店◄ *AmE* a place where goods are sold to the public; SHOP[1] (1)【美】商店, 店鋪: *There are about 60 different stores in the Fallbrook Mall.* 福爾布魯克購物中心有大約60家不同的商店。| **a shoe/clothing/grocery etc store** (=one that sells one type of goods) 鞋店/服裝店/(食品)雜貨店等 *She worked in a book store during college.* 她讀大學時在一家書店打工。| **go to the store** *I need to go to the store for some milk.* 我需要去商店買些牛奶。—see graph at 參見 SHOP[1] 圖表

3 ►SUPPLY 供應◄ a supply of something that you keep to use later 儲備, 貯存物: **[+of]** *Granny always had a special store of chocolate for us.* 奶奶總是特地為我們儲備一些巧克力。

4 ►PLACE TO KEEP THINGS 儲存物品的地方◄ a large building in which goods are stored so they can be used or sold later; WAREHOUSE 倉庫: *a grain store* 糧倉

5 be in store if something unexpected such as a surprise or problem is in store for someone, it is about to happen to them 將要發生, 就要出現: *He's got a few surprises in store if he thinks he can order us around.* 如果他認為他可以把我們差來遣去, 他將會感到有點吃驚。

6 stores [plural] **a)** supplies of food and equipment that are used by an army, navy etc 軍需品, 補給品 **b)** the building or room in an army camp, ship etc where these are kept〔軍營或船上等的〕補給品倉庫

7 set great store by sth to consider something to be very important 認為某事非常重要: *Anne sets great store by that training course.* 安妮非常重視那個培訓課程。

S3 W3 **store**[2] *v* [T] **1** also 又作 **store away** to put things away and keep them until you need them 貯藏, 儲存, 積蓄: *Squirrels are storing up nuts for the winter.* 松鼠正在為冬天儲存堅果。**2** to keep facts or information in your brain or a computer〔在頭腦或電腦中〕儲存〔事實或信息〕: *A mass of data is stored in the computer.* 大量數據存入了電腦。**3 store up trouble/problems etc** to behave in a way that will cause trouble for you later 製造麻煩/難題等: *Sarah is storing up problems for herself by lying to him.* 莎拉對他說謊是在為自己製造麻煩。

store brand /ˈ· ·/ *n* [C] *especially AmE* a type of goods that are produced for a particular shop and have the shop's name on them【尤美】商店品牌〔專為某商店生產並標有該商店店名的商品〕

store de·tec·tive /ˈ· ·,··/ *n* [C] someone who is employed in a large shop to watch the customers and to stop them stealing 店鋪偵探, 專抓在商店裡行竊者的人

store·front /ˈstɔrˌfrʌnt; ˈstɔːfrʌnt/ *n* [C] *AmE*【美】**1** the part of a store that faces the street〔臨街的〕店面, 鋪面 **2 storefront law office/church/school** a small law office etc in a shopping area〔購物區內〕臨街的小型律師事務所/教堂/學校

store·house /ˈstɔrˌhaus; ˈstɔːhaʊs/ *n* [C] **1 a storehouse of information/memories etc** something that contains a lot of information etc 信息/記憶等的寶庫 **2** *old-fashioned* a building where things are stored; WAREHOUSE【過時】倉庫, 棧房

store·keep·er /ˈstɔrˌkipɚ; ˈstɔːˌkiːpə/ *n* [C] *AmE* someone who owns or manages a shop【美】店主; SHOPKEEPER *BrE*【英】

store·room /ˈstɔrˌrum; ˈstɔːrʊm/ *n* [C] a room where goods are stored 貯藏室

sto·rey *BrE*【英】, **story** *AmE*【美】/ˈstɔrɪ; ˈstɔːri/ *n* [C] **1** a floor or level of a building〔建築物的〕層 **2 two-storey/five-storey etc** having two etc storeys 兩/五層樓等的

stor·ied /ˈstɔrɪd; ˈstɔːrid/ *adj* **1 two-storied/five storied etc** *AmE* having two etc storeys【美】有兩/五層樓等的 **2** [only before noun 僅用於名詞前] *literary* being the subject of many stories; FAMOUS【文】傳說[故事]中有名的

stork /stɔrk; stɔːk/ *n* [C] a tall white bird with long legs and a long beak (白)鸛

W3 **storm**[1] /stɔrm; stɔːm/ *n* **1** [C] a period of very bad weather when there is a lot of rain, strong winds, and often lightning 暴風雨: *crops damaged by recent heavy storms* 最近被暴風雨毀壞的莊稼 | **the storm broke** (=suddenly started) 暴風雨突然來臨 —see picture on page A13 參見 A13 頁圖 **2** [C usually singular 一般用單數] a situation in which people suddenly express very strong feelings about something that someone has said or done 感情的突然爆發, 迸發: *The governor found himself at the centre of a political storm.* 州長發現自己處於一場政治風暴的中心。| **a storm of protest/abuse/laughter etc** *Government plans for hospital closures provoked a storm of protest.* 政府關閉醫院的計劃激起了強烈的抗議。**3 take somewhere by storm a)** to be very successful in a particular place 在某地大獲成功: *The new show took London by storm.* 新劇轟動了倫敦。**b)** to attack a place using large numbers of soldiers and succeed in getting possession of it 大舉進攻並佔領某地, 直搗某地 **4 a storm in a teacup** an unnecessary expression of strong feelings about something that is very unimportant 茶杯裡的風波; 小題大做; 大驚小怪 **5 dance/sing/party up a storm** *AmE* to do something with all your energy【美】盡情地跳舞/唱歌/狂歡: *They're dancing up a storm in there.* 他們正在那裡盡情地跳舞。

storm[2] *v* **1** [T] to suddenly attack and enter a place using a lot of force 猛烈攻擊, 突然襲擊: *An angry crowd stormed the embassy.* 憤怒的人羣突然襲擊大使館。**2** [I always+adv/prep] to go somewhere in a noisy fast way that shows you are extremely angry 氣沖沖地走: **[+out of/into/off etc]** *Alan stormed out of the room.* 阿倫氣沖沖地走出房間。**3** [I,T] *literary* to shout something because you feel extremely angry【文】怒吼, 憤怒地喊叫: *"What difference does it make?" she stormed.* "那又怎麼樣?" 她嚷道。

storm cel·lar /ˈ· ,··/ *n* [C] *AmE* a place under a house where you can go to be safe during violent storms【美】暴風雨避難窖, 防風地窖

storm cloud /ˈ· ·/ *n* [C] **1** a dark cloud which you see before a storm 暴風雨前的烏雲, 暴風雲 **2** [usually plural 一般用複數] a sign that something very bad is going to happen 不祥的預兆, 凶兆: *Storm clouds are gathering over the East-West trade negotiations.* 烏雲正籠罩着東西方貿易談判。

storm door /ˈ· ·/ *n* [C] a second door that is fitted to the outside of a door in winter in the US to give protection against rain, snow etc〔美國的防雨、雪等用的〕外重門

storm lan·tern /ˈ· ,··/ *n* [C] a lamp which has a cover to protect the flame against the wind 防風燈

storm·troop·er /ˈstɔrmˌtrupɚ; ˈstɔːmˌtruːpə/ *n* [C] a member of a special group of German soldiers in the Second World War who were trained to be particularly violent〔第二次世界大戰中德國的〕衝鋒隊員, 突擊隊員

storm win·dow /ˈ· ,··/ *n* [C] a second window fitted to the outside of a window in winter in the US to give more protection against rain, snow etc〔美國的防雨、雪等用的〕外重窗

storm·y /ˈstɔrmɪ; ˈstɔːmi/ *adj* **1** stormy weather, sky etc is full of strong winds, heavy rain, and dark clouds 暴風雨的: *The sky was starting to look rather stormy.* 天空烏雲密佈, 暴風雨即將來臨。**2** a stormy relationship, meeting etc is full of strong and often angry feelings 激烈的, 衝動的; 多風波的: *a stormy meeting* 爭論激烈的會議 | *a stormy affair* 一波三折的事情

S2 W2 **sto·ry** /ˈstɔrɪ; ˈstɔːri/ *n* [C]

1 ►FOR ENTERTAINMENT 供娛樂◄ a description of how something happened, that is intended to entertain people, and may be true or imaginary〔真實或虛構的〕故事; 敘述; 描述: *the story of Cinderella* 灰姑娘的故事 | *Don't be frightened, Connie – it's only a story.* (=it is imaginary) 康妮, 別害怕, 這只是一個虛構的故事。| **[+about]** *a story about gangsters* 一個關於匪徒的故事 | **fairy/ghost/love story** *a true-life love story* 一個真實的

S

愛情故事 | **tell/read sb a story** *Mommy, will you read me a story?* 媽媽, 你能給我講一個故事嗎?
2 ▶EVENTS 事件◀ a description of the most important events in someone's life or in the development of something 事蹟; 記事; 史話: *the story of the railways* 鐵路史話 | *the Tina Turner Story*《天娜·端納傳記》| **sb's life story** *Nobody wants to hear your life story the first time you meet them.* 誰也不想在第一次見面時就聽你的生活經歷。
3 ▶NEWS 新聞◀ a report in a newspaper or news broadcast about a recent event〔報刊或廣播中的〕(新聞)報道: *a front-page story in 'The Times'*《泰晤士報》的頭版新聞報道 | **run a story** (=report an event) 刊登對某事件的報道 *'The Observer' ran a big story about the scandal.*《觀察家報》刊登了有關該醜聞的長篇報道。| **cover story** (=the main story in a magazine that is about the picture on the cover)〔雜誌的〕封面故事[專題報道] | **success story** *Calvin's life was a success story – from farm boy to business tycoon.* 卡爾文的一生是一個從農村孩子成為商業巨頭的成功故事。—see graph at 參見 NEWS 圖表
4 ▶OF A FILM/PLAY ETC 電影/戲劇等的◀ what happens in a film, play, or book; PLOT¹ (1)〔電影、戲劇、書的〕(故事)情節: *Tom Hanks was brilliant, but the story was boring.* 湯漢斯演技很出色, 但電影情節十分枯燥。
5 ▶EXCUSE 藉口◀ an excuse or explanation, especially one that you have invented〔尤指編造的〕藉口, 遁詞: *Where were you? And don't give me any story about working late!* 你去了哪裡? 不要給我找藉口, 說晚上加班甚麼的! | *Well that's my story* (=that is what I say happened), *and I'm sticking to it.* 哦, 這就是我要說的情況, 而且我堅持這一說法。
6 my/your side of the story the way that a particular person describes what happened 我/你對事情的描述: *Before we decide who is to blame, we want to hear your side of the story.* 在決定是誰的錯之前, 我們想聽一聽你對這件事情的描述。
7 ▶WHAT PEOPLE SAY 人們的說法◀ information which people tell each other, but which may be untrue; RUMOUR 傳聞, 傳說, 謠傳: *There are a lot of wild stories going around.* 有很多荒誕的謠言在流傳。| **so the story goes** (=people are saying this) 據說如此, 傳說是這樣 *He was having an affair with Julie, or so the story goes.* 他跟朱莉有曖昧關係, 至少大家是在這麼傳的。
8 it's a long story *spoken* used to tell someone that you do not want to give them all the details that a full answer to their question would need【口】說來話長〔表示不想講細節〕
9 it's the same story in/here/there etc used to say the same thing is happening in another place 這裡/那裡等也是同樣的情況: *Unemployment is falling in the US and it's the same story in Europe.* 美國的失業人數正在減少, 歐洲也是如此。
10 it's the same old story *spoken* used to say that the present bad situation has often happened before【口】又是那老一套〔表示目前糟糕的情況以前經常發生〕: *It's the same old story – too much work and not enough time.* 情況還是跟過去一樣——工作太多, 但時間不夠。
11 to cut a long story short *BrE spoken*【英口】, **to make a long story short** *AmE spoken*【美口】used when you want to finish a story quickly 長話短說; 簡而言之; 總之
12 but that's another story *spoken* used when you have mentioned something that you are not going to talk about on this occasion【口】那是另一回事了〔表示不打算談論所提及的某事〕
13 that's not the whole story *spoken* used to say that there are more details which people need to know in order to understand the situation【口】情況還不止這樣, 那還不是事情的全部
14 that's the story of my life *spoken* used after a disappointing experience to mean that similar disappointing things always seem to happen to you【口】我總是這樣倒霉〔在經歷失望的事情之後表示自己經常遭遇類似的不幸〕
15 end of story *BrE spoken* used to mean that there is nothing more to say about a particular subject【英口】就這樣〔表示對某話題再沒有甚麼好談論的了〕: *As far as I'm concerned Terry is still a friend, end of story.* 在我看來, 特里仍然是我的朋友, 就這麼簡單。
16 ▶A LIE 謊言◀ a word used by or to children meaning a lie 謊言, 假話〔兒語〕: **tell stories** *Have you been telling stories again?* 你又在說謊了嗎?
17 the American spelling of STOREY storey 的美式拼法 —see also 另見 SHORT STORY, **cock and bull story** (COCK¹ (3)), **hard-luck story** (HARD¹ (23)), SOB STORY

sto·ry·book¹ /ˈstɔrɪˌbʊk; ˈstɔːribʊk/ *n* [C] a book of stories for children〔為兒童編寫的〕故事書: *a creature standing in front of us like something out of a storybook* 一頭像是從故事書裡走出來的生物, 站在我們的面前

storybook² *adj* **a storybook ending/romance etc** an ending etc that is so happy or perfect that it is like one in a children's story 傳奇故事式的結局/愛情等: *I walked up the path in front of a lopsided storybook cottage.* 我走在一座村舍前的一條小路上, 那村舍歪歪斜斜的, 就像童話故事裡講的那種。

story line /ˈ·· ·/ *n* [C] the main set of connected events in a story; PLOT¹ (1) (故事)情節

sto·ry·tell·er /ˈstɔrɪˌtɛlɚ; ˈstɔːriˌtelə/ *n* [C] someone who tells stories, especially to children〔尤指給兒童〕講故事的人; 說書人

stoup /stup; stuːp/ *n* [C] **1** a container for holy water near the entrance to a church〔教堂入口附近的〕聖水鉢 **2** a glass or MUG¹ (1,2) used for drinking in former times〔舊時用的〕玻璃杯; 大酒杯, 圓筒形有柄大杯

stout¹ /staut; staʊt/ *adj* **1** fairly fat and heavy or having a thick body 胖的, 粗壯的: *a short, stout man* 體格粗壯的矮個子男人 | *She's gotten pretty stout since you last saw her.* 自從你上次見到她以來, 她變得富態了。—see 見 FAT¹ (USAGE) **2** *literary* strong and thick【文】粗壯的, 結實的: *a stout stick* 粗大的棍子 | *a stout pair of shoes* 一雙結實的鞋子 **3** *literary* brave and determined【文】勇敢的; 堅定的; 堅決的: **stout defence/support/resistance** *Michael offered his usual stout support.* 邁克爾一如既往地給予堅定的支持。—**stoutly** *adv*: *He stoutly maintained his innocence.* 他堅稱自己是無辜的。—**stoutness** *n* [U]

stout² *n* [U] a strong dark beer (烈性)黑啤酒

stout·heart·ed /ˌstautˈhɑrtɪd; ˌstaʊtˈhɑːtɪd◂/ *adj literary* brave and determined【文】勇敢的; 堅定的

stove¹ /stov; stəʊv/ *n* [C] **1** a thing used for heating a room or for cooking, which works by burning wood, coal, oil or gas〔炊事或取暖用的〕爐子, 火爐: *a wood-burning stove* 燒木柴的火爐 | *a camp stove* 野營火爐 —compare 比較 COOKER (1) **2** *AmE* the top of a COOKER【美】廚灶, 爐頭

stove² *v* the past tense and past participle of STAVE²

stove·pipe hat /ˌstovpaɪp ˈhæt; ˌstəʊvpaɪp ˈhæt/ *n* [C] *AmE* a tall black silk hat worn by men in the past【美】〔舊時的〕高筒窄邊男用絲絨大禮帽

stow /sto; stəʊ/ also 又作 **stow away** *v* [T always+adv/prep] to put or pack something tidily away in a space until you need it again 將…裝好收起: *You can stow your gear under the bed.* 你可以把你的工具裝好放在牀底下。
stow away *phr v* **1** [I] to hide on a ship or plane in order to travel secretly or without paying 偷乘〔船或飛機〕: *The boy was caught trying to stow away on a plane bound for India.* 那男孩在企圖偷乘一架開往印度的飛機時被捉住了。**2** [T **stow** sth ↔ **away**] to stow something 將…裝好收起 —see also 另見 STOWAWAY

stow·age /ˈstoɪdʒ; ˈstəʊɪdʒ/ *n* [C] space available on a boat for storing things〔船舶的〕裝載空間

stow·a·way /ˈstoəˌwe; ˈstəʊəweɪ/ *n* [C] someone who hides on a ship or plane in order to avoid paying or to travel secretly 無票偷乘船[飛機]者; 偷渡者

strad·dle /ˈstrædl; ˈstrædl/ *v* [T] **1** to sit or stand with your legs on either side of someone or something 跨坐; 跨立: *Joe sat straddling the beam.* 喬跨坐在橫梁上。**2** if something straddles a line, road, or river, part of it is on one side and part on the other side 橫跨…的兩邊, 跨越…的兩邊: *a little town straddling the frontier between France and Germany* 橫跨法德兩國邊境線的一座小城鎮 **3** to include different areas of activity 包括〔不同的活動領域〕: *Her job straddled marketing and public relations.* 她的工作包括市場營銷和公共關係兩個領域。

strafe /stref; streɪf/ *v* [T] to attack a place by flying low and firing many bullets 低空〔飛行〕掃射[襲擊]

strag·gle /ˈstrægl; ˈstrægəl/ *v* [I] **1** to move at a slower speed than the group you are with so that you remain at a distance behind them 掉隊, 落伍, 落後: [+in] *runners straggling in two hours after the leaders* 比領先者落後兩小時到達的賽跑者 **2** to move, grow, or spread out untidily in different directions 蔓延, 蔓生; 零亂地散佈: *thin, black, straggling hair* 稀疏、散亂的黑髮 | *Her handwriting straggled over the page.* 她的字跡毫無規則地散佈在那一頁紙上。

strag·gler /ˈstræglɚ; ˈstræglə/ *n* [C] someone who is too slow to stay with the others in a group so that they move along some distance behind 掉隊的人, 落伍者: *Wait for the stragglers to catch up.* 等那些掉隊的人趕上來。

strag·gly /ˈstræglɪ; ˈstrægəli/ *adj* growing untidily and spreading out in different directions 蔓延的; 散落的; 零亂的: *a straggly moustache* 蓬亂的小鬍子 —see picture on page A6 參見 A6 頁圖

S1 W2 **straight¹** /stret; streɪt/ *adv*

1 ►IN A STRAIGHT LINE 成直線地◄ moving in a straight line 筆直地, 成直線地: **straight ahead/at/down/in front of etc** *The book is on the table straight in front of you.* 那本書就在你面前的桌子上。| *She was looking straight at me.* 她直盯着我看。| *We're stuck in the middle of the road with this truck heading straight towards us.* 我們陷在路中間無法動彈, 這輛卡車朝我們直衝過來。| *She walked straight past me.* 她就從我身邊一直走了過去。| *Terry was so tired he couldn't walk straight.* 特里累得走路都走不穩了。| *The cat sat in front of him, its tail stretched out straight.* 那隻貓坐在他的前面, 尾巴伸得直直的。

2 ►IMMEDIATELY 立即◄ [+adj/adv] immediately or without delay 立即; 徑直, 不延誤地: **straight to/after/down/back etc** *Let's get straight down to business.* 我們直接談正題吧。| *Go straight home and tell your mother.* 馬上回家告訴你媽媽。| *We can meet straight after lunch.* 我們午飯後馬上就可以見面。

3 ►ONE AFTER THE OTHER 一個接一個◄ happening one after the other in a series, especially an unusually long series 連續地: *He's been without sleep now for three days straight.* 他已經連續三天沒有睡覺了。

4 ►SEE/THINK 看見/思考◄ if you cannot think or see straight, you cannot think or see clearly 清楚地: *Turn the radio down, I can't think straight.* 把收音機的音量調低點, 我思緒很亂。

5 tell sb straight/straight out *spoken* to tell someone something clearly without trying to hide your meaning【口】坦率地告訴某人: *She told him straight out that she wouldn't work on Saturday.* 她直率地對他說她不願意星期六上班。| **straight to his/her face** *I'll tell him straight to his face what I think of him.* 我會當着他的面坦白地告訴他我對他的看法。

6 go straight *informal* to stop being a criminal and live an honest life【非正式】改邪歸正, 重新做人: *Tony's been trying to go straight for about six months.* 托尼努力改邪歸正大約有六個月了。

7 straight off also 又作 **straight away** *BrE spoken* immediately or at once【英口】立即, 立刻, 馬上: *I guessed it was you straight off.* 我一下子就猜出是你。

8 straight up *BrE spoken*【英口】**a)** used to ask someone if they are telling the truth 真的嗎〔用於詢問某人是否在說實話〕: *"The shoes cost £250." "Straight up?"* "這雙鞋要 250 英鎊。" "是真的嗎?" **b)** used to emphasize that what you are saying is true 的確, 真的〔用於強調自己所說的是實話〕: *I don't know where she is, straight up.* 我不知道她在哪裡, 真的。

9 straight from the shoulder *AmE informal* expressed plainly and directly, without trying to avoid unpleasantness【美, 非正式】直截了當地, 坦誠地

10 damn straight *AmE spoken* used to explain that something is completely true or right【美口】絕對真實, 絕對正確: *Damn straight that's good.* 那絕對好。

straight² *adj* S2 W3

1 ►NOT BENDING OR CURVING 不彎曲的◄ something such as a line or road that is straight goes in one direction and does not bend or curve (筆) 直的: *Anne loved Rome with its open spaces and long straight avenues.* 安妮喜歡羅馬開闊的空地和筆直的大街。| **in a straight line** *After five beers I was incapable of walking in a straight line.* 五杯啤酒下肚, 我路都走不直了。| **straight hair** (=hair without curls) 直髮 —see picture on page A6 參見 A6 頁圖

2 ►LEVEL/UPRIGHT 平正的/豎直的◄ level, upright, or flat in position or shape 平正的, 端正的; 豎直的: *Stand up straight.* 站直。| *Is my tie straight?* 我的領帶繫得正嗎?

3 ►ONE AFTER ANOTHER 一個接一個的◄ immediately one after another in a series, especially in an unusually long series 一個接一個的, 連續的: *an amazing record of 43 straight wins* 連贏 43 場的驚人記錄

4 ►TIDY 整齊的◄ [not before noun 不用於名詞前] a room that is straight is clean and tidy and everything is in its proper place 整潔的, 整齊的, 有條理的: *I'm trying to get the room straight before your parents get here.* 我正設法在你父母到達前把房間收拾好。

5 ►TRUTHFUL 真誠的◄ honest and truthful 誠實的; 真實的: **be straight with sb** *Are you going to be straight with me or not?* 你是打算對我說老實話還是不? | **a straight answer** *It's difficult to get a straight answer out of him.* 很難得到他的坦率答覆。| **straight talk/honesty** *No more of this fancy playing with words – I want some straight talk here.* 不要再玩這種文字遊戲了 —— 我要聽實話。

6 get this/it straight *spoken* to understand the true facts about a situation【口】清楚無誤地了解情況; 弄清楚事實: *Let me get this straight – Tom sold the car and gave you the money?* 讓我先把這件事弄清楚 —— 湯姆賣掉了汽車, 把錢給了你, 對嗎?

7 set/put sb/sth straight (about) to make someone understand the true facts about a situation 使某人正確了解事實, 使某人弄清楚情況: *Tell him to ask Ruth – she'll put him straight.* 叫他去問露絲 —— 她會幫他把情況弄清楚的。| **set/put the record straight** *I'd like to put the record straight about Bill's resignation.* 我想弄清楚比爾辭職的事。

8 get/put/set things straight (between) *spoken* to deal with the small problems you have in your relationship with someone【口】說明情況; 理順〔與某人的〕關係: *I think it's best to get things straight from the start. This job is not easy.* 我認為最好從一開始就把事情說清楚。這份工作並不容易。

9 ►CHOICE/FIGHT 選擇/打鬥◄ a straight choice or contest involves only two possible choices or opponents〔選擇〕只有兩個可能的;〔競賽〕只涉及兩個對手的: *The election is seen as a straight fight between the Socialists and the ruling coalition.* 這次選舉被認為是社會黨人和執政聯盟之間的直接交鋒。| *How about a straight swap, my U2 album for this one?* 作個簡單直接的交換如何? 我的 U2 唱片換這一張。—see also 另見 STRAIGHTFORWARD (2)

10 ►NOT LIMITED 無限制的◄ simple and not limited by any conditions; STRAIGHTFORWARD (3) 簡單的; 無 (條

件) 限制的: *Did you do it? Just give me a straight yes or no.* 這是不是你幹的? 明確地回答我是或不是。
11 a straight face someone who has a straight face looks serious although they really want to smile or laugh 嚴肅的表情: **keep a straight face** *She looked so ridiculous it was hard to keep a straight face.* 她看上去很滑稽, 很難讓人忍得住笑。
12 ►ALCOHOLIC DRINKS 酒精飲料◄ alcoholic drinks that are straight have no water or ice or any other liquid added; NEAT (4) 純的, 不加水[冰、其他飲料]的: *I like my vodka straight.* 我喜歡喝純的伏特加酒。
13 ►NORMAL 正常的◄ *slang* someone who is straight behaves in a way that is accepted as normal by many people but which you think is dull and boring【俚】正經的; 枯燥的: *Dave's OK, but his wife is really straight.* 戴夫還不錯, 但他的妻子太一本正經了。
14 ►NOT OWING SB MONEY 不欠債的◄ [not before noun 不用於名詞前] no longer owing money to someone or being owed money by someone 不欠債的; 不被別人欠錢的: *If you give me £10 then we're straight.* 如果你給我十英鎊, 我們就誰也不欠誰了。
15 ►SEX 性行為◄ *slang* HETEROSEXUAL【俚】異性戀的
16 ►DRUGS 毒品◄ *slang* not using drugs【俚】不吸毒的

straight³ *n* **1** [C] *slang* someone who is attracted to people of the opposite sex【俚】異性戀者 **2** [C] *slang* someone who is not a drug user【俚】不吸毒的人 **3** [singular] *especially BrE* the straight part of a RACETRACK【尤英】跑道的直道 (部分) ; STRAIGHTAWAY *AmE*【美】**4 keep to/stray from the straight and narrow** *humorous* to live in an honest and moral way, or to fail to do this【幽默】循規蹈矩地/不循規蹈矩地生活; 安分守己/不安分守己

straight ar·row /ˌ· ˈ··/ *n* [C] *AmE informal* someone who never does anything illegal or unusual and exciting【美, 非正式】循規蹈矩的人, 安分守己的人

straight·a·way¹ /ˈstretəˌwe; ˌstreɪtəˈweɪ/ *adv* at once; immediately 立即, 立刻; 馬上: *Let's start work straightaway.* 我們立即開始工作吧。

straight·a·way² /ˈstretəˌwe; ˈstreɪtəweɪ/ *n* [singular] *AmE* the straight part of a RACETRACK【美】跑道的直道 (部分) ; STRAIGHT³ (3) *BrE*【英】

straight·en /ˈstretn̩; ˈstreɪtn/ *v* **1** also 又作 **straighten out** [I,T] to become straight or make something straight (使) 變直; 把…弄直: *Straighten your tie.* 把你的領帶弄直。| *The road twisted and turned and then straightened out.* 那條路先是彎彎曲曲的, 後來就變得筆直了。**2** also 又作 **straighten up** [I] to make your back straight, or to stand up straight after bending down 挺直身子, 直起身來 **3** also 又作 **straighten up** to make something tidy 把…弄整齊: *You can't go out till you straighten your room.* 你把房間整理好才能出去。

straighten sb/sth ↔ **out** *phr v* [T] **1** to settle a difficult situation by dealing with the things that are causing problems or confusion 解決〔問題〕; 清理, 整頓〔混亂情況〕: *There are a few things that need straightening out between us.* 我們之間有幾件事情需要弄清楚。**2** to deal with someone's bad behaviour or personal problems 使改好, 使變好: *We try to help these kids straighten themselves out and get back into school.* 我們試圖幫助這些孩子改邪歸正, 重新回去上學。

straighten up *phr v* [I] *AmE* to begin to behave well after behaving badly【美】改邪歸正, 重新做人: *You'd better straighten up, young lady!* 小姑娘, 你最好循規蹈矩一點!

straight·faced /ˌstretˈfest; ˌstreɪtˈfeɪst◄/ *adj* not showing by the expression on your face that you are really joking or doing something funny〔在開玩笑或做好玩的事時〕表情嚴肅的: *"I've never been so serious in all my life," Bart said straightfaced.* "我這輩子從來沒有如此認真過。" 巴特一本正經地說。—**straightfacedly** /-ˈfesədlɪ; -ˈfeɪsɨ̩dli◄/ *adv*

straight·for·ward /ˌstretˈfɔrwəd; ˌstreɪtˈfɔːwəd◄/ *adj* **1** honest about your feelings or opinions and not hiding anything 誠實的, 坦率的, 老實的: *Jack is tough, but always straightforward and fair.* 傑克很強硬, 但總是坦誠公正的。**2** simple and easy to understand 簡單的, 易懂的: *The system itself is perfectly straightforward.* 該系統本身非常簡單。**3** [only before noun 僅用於名詞前] not limited by any conditions 無條件限制的, 明確的: *a straightforward cash settlement* 直接的現金結算 —**straightforwardly** *adv* —**straightforwardness** *n* [U]

straight·jack·et /ˈstretˌdʒækɪt; ˈstreɪtˌdʒækɨ̩t/ *n* [C] another spelling of STRAITJACKET straitjacket 的另一種拼法

straight man /ˈ· ·/ *n* [C] a male entertainer who works with a COMEDIAN, providing him or her with opportunities to make jokes〔喜劇演員的〕男搭檔, 男配角

straight shoot·er /ˈ· ˌ··/ *n* [C] *AmE informal* an honest person who you can trust【美, 非正式】〔可以信賴的〕正派人, 老實人

straight tick·et /ˌ· ˈ··/ *n* [C] a vote in which someone chooses all the candidates of a particular political party in the US〔美國〕只投同一政黨所有候選人票的選票

straight·way /ˈstretˌwe; ˈstreɪt-weɪ/ *adv old use* STRAIGHTAWAY【舊】立即, 立刻, 馬上

strain¹ /stren; streɪn/ *n*
1 ►WORRY 焦慮◄ [C,U] worry caused by having to deal with a problem or work too hard over a long period of time 焦慮; 緊張: *The trial has been a terrible strain for both of us.* 法庭審判令我們兩人都非常焦慮。| **put a strain on sb/sth** *Nick's frequent trips were putting a strain on their marriage.* 尼克經常外出旅行使他們的婚姻關係趨於緊張。| **be under (a) strain** *I know you've been under a lot of strain lately.* 我知道你最近壓力很大。| **stresses and strains** (=problems and worries) 緊張和壓力 *the stresses and strains of everyday working life* 日常工作中的緊張和壓力
2 ►DIFFICULTY 困難◄ [C] a problem or difficulty that is caused when something is used more than is normal or acceptable 問題, 困難; 負擔; 緊張: *The drought has put a heavy strain on our water resources.* 乾旱給我們的水資源帶來了很重的負擔。
3 ►FORCE 力, 力量◄ [U] a force that pulls, stretches or pushes something 拉力, 張力, 推力: **[+on]** *The strain on the cables supporting the bridge is enormous.* 支撐橋梁的這些鋼纜拉力極強。| **under the strain** (=because of the force) 因受拉力 *The rope snapped under the strain.* 繩子因拉得太緊而斷了。
4 ►INJURY 損傷◄ [C,U] an injury to a muscle or part of your body caused by using it too much〔肌肉〕拉傷, 扭傷, 損傷: *a back strain* 背部扭傷 —compare 比較 SPRAIN
5 ►DISTRUST 不信任◄ [C,U] a situation in which two people, groups etc have stopped being friendly or trusting each other; TENSION (2)〔人或團體之間的〕不友好[不信任]狀態; 緊張: *the current strain in relations between the two countries* 目前兩國之間的緊張關係
6 ►PLANT/ANIMAL 植物/動物◄ [C] a breed or type of animal, plant etc 系, 品系, 品種, 類型: **[+of]** *trying to develop a new strain of wheat* 試圖開發小麥的新品種
7 the strains of sth *literary* the sound of music being played【文】曲調, 旋律: **[+of]** *the strains of the Blue Danube Waltz*《藍色多瑙河圓舞曲》的旋律
8 ►QUALITY 特點◄ [singular] a particular quality which people have, especially one that is passed from parents to children〔尤指遺傳的〕性格傾向, 氣質, 性情: **[+of]** *There's a strain of madness in his family.* 他一家都有瘋癲的傾向。
9 take the strain to pull on something such as a rope until it is tight, then keep it in that position 拉緊〔繩子等〕
10 ►WAY OF SAYING STH 說話的方式◄ [singular]

formal the meaning of what you are saying or writing, or the way it is expressed【正式】表達方式; 口吻, 語氣; 筆調: *a strain of bitterness in Young's later work* 楊後期作品中悲傷的筆調

strain² *v*

1 ►PART OF BODY 身體的一部分◄ [T] to injure a muscle or part of your body by making it work too hard〔因過分用力而〕拉傷, 扭傷, 損傷: *strain a muscle in your leg* 拉傷你的腿部肌肉 | *You'll strain your eyes trying to read in this light.* 在這樣的光線下看書會傷害眼睛。

2 ►EFFORT 努力◄ [I,T] to try very hard to do something using all your physical or mental strength 使勁, 竭力, 用盡全力: **strain to do sth** *The singer had to strain to reach the high notes.* 那位歌手費了很大的勁才唱到那高音。| **strain for sth** *Bill choked and gasped, straining for air.* 比爾噎住了, 使勁地喘息着吸氣。| **strain your ears/eyes** (=try very hard to hear or see) 費勁地聽/看 *I strained my ears, listening for any sound in the silence of the cave.* 我豎起耳朵, 試圖在寂靜的山洞裡聽到些聲音。| **strain yourself** (=try too hard) 努力過度 *Don't strain yourself! You need to rest more.* 別累壞了自己! 你需要更多的休息。

3 ►LIQUID 液體◄ [T] to separate solid things from a liquid by pouring the mixture through something with very small holes in it 濾, 過濾 —see picture on page A11 參見A11頁圖

4 ►BEYOND A LIMIT 超過限度◄ [T] to force something to be used to a degree that is beyond a normal or acceptable limit 使用…到超過正常限度, 使用…到極限: *The influx of refugees is straining our limited facilities.* 難民的湧入使我們有限的設施不堪重負。| **strain sth to the limit** *I tell you, my patience has been strained to the limit!* 我告訴你, 我的忍耐已經到了極限!

5 strain a friendship/relationship etc to behave in a way that causes problems in a friendship etc 損害友誼/關係等, 使友情/關係等出現問題: *Too many arguments about money can strain a relationship.* 因錢而發生過多的爭吵會使關係變得緊張。

6 ►PULL/PUSH 拉/推◄ [I] to pull hard at something or push hard against something 使勁拉[推], 繃緊: **[+against]** *Buddy's huge gut strained against the buttons on his shirt.* 巴迪的大肚子把他襯衫的鈕扣繃得緊緊的。| **[+at]** *a ship straining at its moorings* 把纜索拉得很緊的船

7 strain every nerve to try as hard as possible to do something 全力以赴: *a comedian straining every nerve to get a laugh* 竭力逗樂的喜劇演員

8 straining at the leash eager to be allowed to do what you want 急欲獲准做某事, 躍躍欲試: *30,000 troops straining at the leash and the generals locked in indecision* 三萬大軍躍躍欲試, 將軍卻在猶豫不決中

strained /strend; streɪnd/ *adj* **1** a situation or behaviour that is strained makes people feel nervous and uncomfortable, and unable to behave naturally; TENSE¹ (1) 緊張的; 不自在的: *I couldn't stand the strained atmosphere at dinner anymore.* 我再也忍受不了飯桌上的那種緊張氣氛了。**2** showing the effects of worry or too much work 心力交瘁的; 焦慮的; 疲憊的: *Dinah's face looked white and strained.* 黛娜臉色蒼白, 疲憊不堪。

strain·er /ˈstrenɚ; ˈstreɪnə/ *n* [C] a kitchen tool for separating solids from liquids 濾器, 濾網: *a tea strainer* 茶葉過濾網

strait¹ /stret; streɪt/ *n* [C] **1** also 又作 **straits** [plural] a narrow passage of water between two areas of land, usually connecting two seas 海峽, 狹窄的水道: *the Strait of Gibraltar* 直布羅陀海峽 **2 be in dire straits** to be in a difficult situation, especially a financial one, that could have very bad or dangerous results 陷於惡劣的困境中〔尤指財務困境〕: *If one of the family is in dire straits, we try to help each other out.* 家中如果有人陷入困境, 我們盡量互相幫助, 使其擺脱困難。

strait² *adj biblical* narrow and therefore usually difficult to pass through【聖經】狹窄的, 由於狹窄而難以通過的

strait·ened /ˈstretn̩d; ˈstreɪtnd/ *adj formal*【正式】**in straitened circumstances** in a difficult situation because of a lack of money 因經濟拮据而陷入困境: *an elderly spinster living in straitened circumstances* 窮困潦倒的老姑娘

strait·jack·et, straightjacket /ˈstretˌdʒækɪt; ˈstreɪtˌdʒækɪ̵t/ *n* [C] **1** a special piece of clothing that is used to control the movements of someone who is mentally ill and violent〔用於約束精神病人的〕約束衣, 緊身衣 **2** something such as a law or set of ideas that puts unfair limits on someone 約束, 不公平的限制〈如法律、思想等〉: *the straitjacket of censorship* 審查制度的約束

strait·laced /ˈstretˋlest; ˌstreɪtˈleɪst◄/ *adj* having strict, old-fashioned ideas about moral behaviour〔道德方面〕一本正經的; 守舊的, 古板的: *So then Sally and her straitlaced friend showed up and we all had to shut up.* 後來, 莎莉和她那個古板的朋友來了, 我們大家都不得不停止談話。

strand〔線、繩的〕股; 縷

strand /strænd; strænd/ *n* [C] **1** a single thin piece of thread, wire, hair etc〔線、繩、毛髮等的〕股; 縷: *a strand of yarn* 一股線 **2** one of the parts of a story, problem etc 故事的情節; 問題的一部分: *Plato draws all the strands of the argument together at the end.* 柏拉圖最後把各個論點歸結起來。

strand·ed /ˈstrændɪd; ˈstrændɪ̵d/ *adj* a person or vehicle that is stranded is unable to move from the place where they are〔人或交通工具〕被滯留的;〔船〕擱淺的: **leave sb/sth stranded** *The tide had gone out, leaving the boat stranded on the rocks.* 潮水退了, 小船擱淺在礁石上。| **[+in/on/at]** *There I was, stranded in Rome with no passport and no money.* 我當時就這樣被困在羅馬, 沒有護照, 也沒有錢。

strange¹ /strendʒ; streɪndʒ/ *adj* **1** unusual or surprising, especially in a way that is difficult to explain or understand 奇怪的, 不尋常的; 不可思議的: *a strange noise* 奇怪的噪聲 | *Does Geoff's behaviour seem strange to you?* 你覺得傑夫的行為奇怪嗎? | **that's strange** *spoken*【口】*That's strange. I was sure Jude was right here a second ago.* 真奇怪, 我敢肯定片刻鐘前裘德就在這裡。| **it's strange that/how** *It's strange that you've never met him.* 很奇怪, 你居然從來沒有見過他。| **there's something strange about** *There's something strange about that house.* 那所房子有點奇怪。| **strange to say** *BrE* (=strangely)【英】說來奇怪 *Strange to say, I was just thinking that myself.* 說來奇怪, 我自己剛才也是那麼想的。**2** someone or something that is strange is not familiar because you have not seen or met them before 陌生的, 不熟悉的: *all alone in a strange city* 獨自一人在一個陌生的城市裡 **3 feel strange** to feel unpleasant physically or emotionally 覺得不舒服: *Can you get me a glass of water? I feel a bit strange.* 你能幫我拿杯水嗎? 我覺得有點不舒服。—**strangeness** *n* [U]

S2 W2

strange² *adv* [only after verb 僅用於動詞後] *AmE* in a way that is different from what is normal【美】古怪地: *The cat's been acting really strange – I wonder if it's sick.* 這隻貓的行為怪怪的, 不知道是不是病了。

strange·ly /ˈstrendʒlɪ; ˈstreɪndʒli/ *adv* **1** in an unusual way 奇怪地, 不尋常地: *Mick's been acting very strangely lately.* 米克最近的行為很怪。| *a strangely shaped shell* 形狀奇特的貝殼 **2 strangely enough** [sentence adverb 句子副詞] used to say that although something seems unlikely, it is true 真奇怪〔表示某事雖然似乎不可能, 但卻是真的〕: *Strangely enough, I wasn't really that disappointed.* 真奇怪, 我並不是那麼失望。**3** in a way that is surprising or unexpected 令人吃驚地, 出乎意料地: *Her voice was strangely familiar.* 她的聲音出乎意料地熟悉。

strang·er /ˋstrendʒɚ; ˈstreɪndʒə/ *n* [C] **1** someone whom you do not know 陌生人: *Children must not talk to strangers.* 小孩子千萬不要同陌生人說話。| **perfect/complete/total stranger** (=used to emphasize that you do not know them) 根本不相識的人, 完全陌生的人 *A perfect stranger waved to me in the street this morning.* 今天上午, 一個我根本不認識的人在街上向我招手。**2 be no stranger to sth** to have had a lot of a particular kind of experience 有過很多某事的經歷, 對某事並不陌生: *My sister is no stranger to hard times.* 我的姐姐飽經磨難。**3** someone in a new and unfamiliar place 異鄉人; 外地人; 新來者: *"Where's the station?" "Sorry, I'm a stranger here myself."* "車站在哪裡?" "對不起, 我也不是本地人。" **4 Hello, stranger!** *spoken humorous* used to greet someone you have not seen for a long time【口, 幽默】你好, 陌生人! 嗨, 久違了! 〔用於跟好久不見的人打招呼〕

stran·gle /ˋstræŋgḷ; ˈstræŋgəl/ *v* [T] **1** to kill someone by pressing on their throat with your hands, a rope etc 扼死, 勒死, 絞死: *The victim had been strangled with a nylon stocking.* 受害者是被人用尼龍長襪勒死的。**2** to limit or prevent the growth or development of something 限制[阻止]...的成長[發展]; 扼殺: *UN sanctions are slowly strangling the economy.* 聯合國的制裁正在逐漸扼殺該國的經濟。—**strangler** *n* [C]

S

stran·gled /ˋstræŋgḷd; ˈstræŋgəld/ *adj* **strangled cry/gasp/sound etc** a cry etc that is suddenly stopped before it is finished 突然止住的哭泣/喘息/聲音等

stran·gle·hold /ˋstræŋglhold; ˈstræŋgəlhəʊld/ *n* **1** [C usually singular 一般用單數] complete control over a situation, organization etc 〔對局勢、組織等的〕完全控制: **have a stranglehold on** *firms have a stranglehold on the production of CDs* 完全控制了激光唱片生產的公司 | **break the stranglehold of sb** (=stop someone having complete control) 打破某人的完全控制 **2** [C] a strong hold around someone's neck that is meant to stop them from breathing 勒頸, 卡脖子

stran·gu·late /ˋstræŋgjəˌlet; ˈstræŋgjʊ̈leɪt/ *v* [I,T] if a part of your body strangulates or is strangulated, it becomes tightly pressed so that the flow of blood stops 絞扼, 絞窄, 扼住, 壓緊〔以阻止血流〕

stran·gu·la·tion /ˌstræŋgjəˋleʃən; ˌstræŋgjʊ̈ˈleɪʃən/ *n* [U] the act of killing someone by strangling them STRANGLE (1), or the fact of being killed in this way 扼死, 勒死, 絞死; 窒息而死

strap¹ /stræp; stræp/ *n* [C] a narrow band of strong material that is used to fasten, hang, or hold onto something 帶子: *a leather watch strap* 皮錶帶 | *a backpack with adjustable straps* 背帶長度可調整的背包 —see also 另見 CHINSTRAP, SHOULDER STRAP

strap² *v* **strapped, strapping** [T] **1** [always+adv/prep] to fasten something or somebody in place with one or more straps 用帶子束住, 捆綁: **strap sb/sth in/on/down etc** *Strap that saddle on good and tight.* 把那副馬鞍繫好綁緊。| **be strapped in** (=have a belt fastened around you in a car) 繫好安全帶 *Are the kids strapped in?* 孩子們繫好安全帶了嗎? **2** *BrE*【英】also 又作 **strap up** [often passive 常用被動態] to tie BANDAGES firmly round a part of your body that has been hurt 〔用繃帶〕包紮〔傷口〕; TAPE² (4) *AmE*【美】

strap·hang·ing /ˋstræpˌhæŋɪŋ; ˈstræpˌhæŋɪŋ/ *n* [U] *BrE informal* supporting yourself while standing in a moving bus, train etc by holding onto a strap that hangs from the roof【英, 非正式】〔乘車時〕拉着吊帶站着 —**straphanger** *n* [C]

strap·less /ˋstræplɪs; ˈstræpləs/ *adj* **strapless dress/gown** a dress that leaves your shoulders completely bare 露肩[無帶]連衣裙/晚裝

strapped /stræpt; stræpt/ *adj* **strapped (for cash)** *informal* having little or no money at the moment【非正式】錢不多的; 身無分文的: *Can you lend me ten dollars? I'm a little strapped for cash.* 你能借給我十美元嗎? 我身上現金不多了。

strap·ping /ˋstræpɪŋ; ˈstræpɪŋ/ *adj* [only before noun 僅用於名詞前] a strapping young man or woman is strong, tall, and looks healthy and active 身材高大的, 魁梧的; 強健的: *a strapping young man of 15 or so* 15 歲上下的壯小子

stra·ta /ˋstretə; ˈstrɑːtə/ *n* **1** the plural of STRATUM stratum 的複數形式 **2** a plural form often used instead of STRATUM 常用來代替 stratum 的複數形式

strat·a·gem /ˋstrætədʒəm; ˈstrætədʒəm/ *n* [C] *formal* a trick or plan to deceive an enemy or gain an advantage【正式】〔蒙蔽敵人或謀取利益的〕計謀, 策略; 花招

stra·te·gic /strəˋtidʒɪk; strəˈtiːdʒɪk/ also 又作 **stra·te·gic·al** /-dʒɪkḷ; -dʒɪkəl/ *adj* **1** done as part of a plan, especially in a military, business, or political situation 戰略(性)的; 策略(上)的: *UN forces have made a strategic withdrawal to regroup.* 聯合國部隊作了一次戰略性撤退, 以便重新部署。| *strategic bombing* 戰略轟炸 **2** useful or right for a particular purpose 〔對某特定目的〕有用的; 合適的: *Marksmen were placed at strategic points along the president's route.* 在總統經過路線的重要位置上安排了神槍手。**3** used in fighting wars 用於戰爭的: *secret purchases of strategic materials* 祕密購買戰略物資 | **strategic arms/weapons** (=weapons designed to reach an enemy country from your own) 戰略性武器 —**strategically** /-kḷɪ; -kli/ *adv* 3

strat·e·gist /ˋstrætədʒɪst; ˈstrætɪ̈dʒɪ̈st/ *n* [C] someone who is good at planning, especially military movements 善於策劃的人; 〔尤指〕戰略家

strat·e·gy /ˋstrætədʒɪ; ˈstrætɪ̈dʒi/ *n* **1** [U] the skill of planning in advance the movements of armies or equipment in a war 〔戰爭中的〕戰略; 戰略學 **2** [C] a well-planned series of actions for achieving an aim, especially success against an opponent 〔為實現某目標, 尤指為戰勝對手而制定的〕行動計劃; 計謀, 策略: *Our strategy was to defend and then counterattack.* 我們的策略是先防禦後反攻。| [+for] *a strategy for dealing with unemployment* 對付失業問題的行動計劃 **3** [U] skilful planning in general 戰略, 策略: *the need to focus on strategy for the entire company* 把注意力集中到公司整體策略的必要性 2

strat·i·fi·ca·tion /ˌstrætəfəˋkeʃən; ˌstrætɪ̈fɪ̈ˈkeɪʃən/ *n* **1** [C,U+of] the way that a society develops into different social classes 〔社會的〕分層, 階層形成 **2** [C,U] the way that different layers of earth, rock etc develop over time 層理; 地層 **3** [C,U] the position that different layers of something have in relation to each other 層疊(現象)

strat·i·fied /ˋstrætəˌfaɪd; ˈstrætɪ̈faɪd/ *adj* **1** having different social classes 有不同社會等級的, 分層的: *a stratified society* 等級社會 **2** having several layers of earth, rock etc 〔土壤、岩石等〕成層的: *stratified rock* 成層岩

strat·os·phere /ˋstrætəˌsfɪr; ˈstrætəsfɪə/ *n* **1 the stratosphere** the outer part of the air surrounding the Earth, starting at about ten kilometres above the Earth 平流層, 同溫層 **2 the fashion/pop music etc stratosphere** a very high position in fashion etc that makes you famous 最高檔次的時裝/流行音樂等

stra·tum /ˋstretəm; ˈstrɑːtəm/ *n plural* **strata** /-tə; -tə/ [C] **1** a layer of rock of a particular kind, especially one with different layers above and below it 岩層 **2** a layer of earth, such as one where tools, bones etc from an ancient civilization are found by digging 地層〈如考古層〉 **3** a social class in a society 社會階層

straw /strɔ; strɔː/ *n* **1 a)** [U] the dried stems of wheat or similar plants that are used for animals to sleep on, and for making things such as baskets, mats etc 〔乾的〕麥  3

稈, 稻草, 禾稈: *a straw hat* 草帽 **b)** [C] a single dried stem of wheat etc〔單根的〕麥稈, 稻草稈: *Some straws were sticking to his jacket.* 他的夾克衫上黏着幾根稻草稈。**2** [C] a thin tube of paper or plastic for sucking up liquid〔喝飲料用的〕吸管: *a boy happily drinking a chocolate milkshake through a straw* 高興地用吸管喝着巧克力奶昔的男孩 **3 the last straw/the straw that breaks the camel's back** the last problem in a series of problems that finally makes you give up, get angry etc 壓垮駱駝的最後一根稻草,〔一系列問題中〕最終使人無法承受的事, 終於使人不堪重負的因素 **4 a straw in the wind** *BrE* a sign of what might happen in the future【英】〔未來事態的〕跡象, 徵兆; 苗頭: *These stories of food riots may well be straws in the wind.* 這些因食物引起暴亂的傳聞很可能就是要出事的苗頭。**5 straw man** *AmE* a weak opponent or imaginary argument that can easily be defeated【美】稻草人; 不堪一擊的假想對手; 不值一駁的虛構論點 —see also 另見 **you can't make bricks without straw** (BRICK[1] (4)), **clutch at straws** (CLUTCH[1]), **draw the short straw** (DRAW[1] (26))

3 **straw·ber·ry** /ˈstrɔˌbɛrɪ; ˈstrɔːbəri/ *n* **1** [C] a soft red juicy fruit with small pale seeds on its surface, or the plant that grows this fruit 草莓〔指植物或其果實〕: *strawberries and cream* 奶油草莓 | *strawberry jam* 草莓果醬 —see picture on page A8 參見 A8 頁圖 **2** [U] a dark pink colour 紫紅色, 草莓色

strawberry blonde /ˌ··· ˈ·/ *n* [C] a woman with light reddish yellow hair 頭髮略帶紅色的金髮女子 **—strawberry blonde** *adj*

strawberry mark /ˈ··· ·/ *n* [C] a reddish mark on your skin at birth that never goes away; BIRTHMARK 莓狀痣; 紅色胎記

straw boat·er /ˌ· ˈ··/ *n* [C] *BrE* a stiff hat made of straw that is usually worn in summer【英】〔夏天戴的〕硬草帽

straw-col·oured /ˈ· ˌ··/ *adj* light yellow 淺黃色的, 麥稈色的

straw poll /ˌ· ˈ·/ also 又作 **straw vote** *n* [C] an unofficial test of people's opinions before an election, to see what the result is likely to be〔大選前為測驗民意進行的〕非正式投票

stray¹ /stre; streɪ/ *v* [I] **1** to leave the place where you should be without intending to 走離; 走失, 迷路: *a warship that had strayed into enemy waters* 誤入敵方水域的戰艦 **2** to begin to deal with a different subject than the main one, without intending to 偏離〔主題〕: **stray into/onto sth** *We're straying into ethnic issues here.* 我們現在偏離主題, 討論起種族問題來。| **stray from the subject/point/question** *Try not to stray from the point in your answers.* 你在回答中盡量不要離題。

stray² *adj* [only before noun 僅用於名詞前] **1** a stray animal walks around because it is lost or has no home〔動物〕走失的, 迷路的, 流浪的 **2** accidentally separated from other things of the same kind 離散的; 零落的: *A stray spark must have started the blaze.* 一定是一顆散落的火花引起了這場大火。| *a few stray wisps of hair* 幾縷散髮

stray³ *n* [C] **1** an animal that is lost and cannot find its home or has no home 走失[流浪]的動物 **2** *informal* someone or something that has become separated from others of the same kind【非正式】離開同類的人; 離開原位的東西 —see also 另見 **waifs and strays** (WAIF (2))

streak¹ /strik; striːk/ *n* [C] **1** a coloured line, especially one that is not straight or has been made accidentally 色條; 條痕; 斑紋: *Sue has blonde streaks in her hair.* 蘇的頭髮裡夾雜着幾縷金髮。**2** a part of someone's character that is different from the rest of their character 個性特徵, 特點: *Mel has a romantic streak in him.* 梅爾個性有點浪漫。| *a sadistic streak* 有點兒虐待狂 **3** a period of time during which you continue to be successful or to fail〔不斷成功或失敗的〕一段時期: *a streak of good luck* 一陣子好運氣 | **be on a winning/losing streak** (=have a period of time when you continue to win or lose) 一段時期連贏/連輸 *After a month-long losing streak we finally won a game.* 我們一連輸了一個月後, 終於贏了一場。**4 a streak of lightning** a long straight burst of LIGHTNING 一道閃電: **like a streak of lightning** (=very fast) 迅速地; 風馳電掣地 *The cat shot out the door like a streak of lightning.* 那隻貓閃電般地跑出門去。

streak² *v* **1** [I always+adv/prep] to run or fly somewhere so fast you can hardly be seen 飛速地跑[飛]: **[+across/along/down etc]** *Two jets streaked across the sky.* 兩架噴氣式飛機從空中迅速地飛過。**2** [T usually passive 一般用被動態] to cover something with streaks 使佈滿條紋: **[+with]** *Colin's face was streaked with tears.* 科林的臉上有一條條淚痕。**3** [I] to run across a public place with no clothes on to shock people 裸跑

streak·er /ˈstrikɚ; ˈstriːkə/ *n* [C] someone who runs across a public place with no clothes on to shock people 裸跑的人

streak·y /ˈstrikɪ; ˈstriːki/ *adj* marked with streaks 有條紋的; 有紋理的: *When I washed the shirt it went all streaky.* 我洗這件襯衫後, 它變得盡是條痕。

streaky ba·con /ˌ·· ˈ··/ *n* [U] *BrE* smoked or salted pig meat that has lines of fat between the meat【英】五花熏鹹肉; BACON *AmE*【美】

stream¹ /strim; striːm/ *n* [C] 3

1 ▶SMALL RIVER 小河◀ a natural flow of water that moves across the land and is narrower than a river 小河, 小溪: *a mountain stream* 山澗 —see also 另見 DOWNSTREAM, UPSTREAM

2 ▶CONTINUOUS SERIES 連續的系列◀ a long and almost continuous series of events, people, objects, etc〔事件、人、物等的〕一連串, 一系列, 流: **[+of]** *a stream of traffic* 川流不息的車輛 | *A steady stream of visitors came to the house.* 參觀這所房子的人絡繹不絕。| *a stream of abuse* 一連串的辱罵

3 ▶AIR/WATER 空氣/水◀ a current of water or air, or the direction in which it is flowing 水流(方向); 氣流(方向): *A stream of cold air rushed through the open door.* 一股冷風穿門而過。—see also 另見 GULF STREAM, JET STREAM

4 come on stream *technical* to start producing something such as oil, electricity, goods etc【術語】投入生產〔石油、電、貨品等〕: *The new plant will come on stream at the end of the year.* 新工廠將於年底投產。

5 go/swim against the stream to do or think something differently from what people in general do or think 反潮流; 不隨大流

6 ▶SCHOOL 學校◀ *especially BrE* a level of ability within a group of students of the same age【尤英】同齡學生按能力水平劃分的班[組]: *Caroline's in the top stream.* 卡羅琳在智力最高組。—see also 另見 BLOODSTREAM, STREAM OF CONSCIOUSNESS

stream² *v*

1 ▶POUR 傾注◀ [I always+adv/prep,T] to flow quickly and in great amounts, or to make something flow in this way; pour (使)奔流; (使)傾注; (使)湧流: **[+out/in/onto etc]** *Water came streaming out of the burst pipe.* 水從爆裂的水管中湧出來。| *Tears streamed down her cheeks.* 淚水順着她的臉頰流下來。

2 ▶FLOW 流動◀ [I always+adv/prep] to move in a continuous flow in the same direction 不斷地流動;〔朝同一方向〕湧: **[+out/across/past etc]** *The crowd streamed out of the football ground.* 人羣從足球場蜂擁而出。

3 ▶MOVE FREELY 自由移動◀ [I always+adv/prep, usually in progressive 一般用進行式] to move freely in a current of wind or water〔在風或水中〕自由飄動, 自由流動: **[+in/out/behind etc]** *Elise ran, her hair streaming out behind her.* 埃莉斯跑着, 頭髮向後飄動。

4 ►GIVE OUT LIQUID 流出液體◄ [I,T] to produce a continuous flow of liquid 流淌; 不斷地流出: [+**with**] *The onions made my eyes stream with tears.* 洋葱使我的眼睛直流淚水。
5 ►SCHOOL 學校◄ [T] *especially BrE* to put school children in groups according to their ability【尤英】將〔學生〕按能力水平分組[分班]; TRACK² (5) *AmE*【美】
6 a streaming cold *BrE* a very bad cold, with liquid flowing from your nose【英】會流鼻涕的重感冒

stream·er /ˋstrimɚ; ˈstriːmə/ *n* [C] **1** a long narrow piece of coloured paper, used for decoration at special occasions〔裝飾用的〕彩色紙帶, 飾帶 **2** a long narrow flag 長條旗

stream·line /ˋstrimˏlaɪn; ˈstriːmlaɪn/ *v* [T] **1** to form something into a smooth shape so that it moves easily through the air or water 使…成為流線型: *All these new cars have been aerodynamically streamlined.* 所有這些新汽車都被做成了流線型。**2** to make something such as a business, organization etc work more simply and effectively 精簡〔企業、組織等〕, 簡化使效率更高: *efforts to streamline the production process* 簡化生產過程以提高效率的努力 —**streamlined** *adj*

stream of con·scious·ness /ˏ· ˈ···/ *n* [U] the expression of thoughts and feelings in writing exactly as they pass through your mind, without the usual ordered structure they have in formal writing 意識流〔一種創作方式〕

1 1 **street** /strit; striːt/ *n* [C] **1** a public road in a city or town that has houses, shops etc on one or both sides 大街, 街道: *101 Oxford Street, London* 倫敦牛津街101號 | **street map** (=showing the names and positions of all the roads) 街道圖 | **street musicians** (=performing outdoors in towns) 街頭演奏音樂家 —see also 另見 HIGH STREET **2 the streets** a phrase meaning the roads of a city, used to mean a place where people live who have no home and where it is difficult to survive〔無家可歸的窮人居住的〕街頭: **on the streets** *young people living on the streets* 流落街頭的年輕人 **3 the man/woman in the street** the average person, who represents the general opinion about things 普通人, 一般人: *The man in the street wouldn't have a clue what a dongle is.* 一般人根本不知道一個硬件為何物。**4 (right) up your street** a job or course that is up your street is exactly right for you because you have the right skills and are interested in it〔指工作或課程因在某人的技能和興趣範圍內〕剛好適合某人 **5 one-way/two-way street** a process that fully involves the opinions and feelings of only one person or group, or of both people or groups 單方面/雙方參與的過程: *Trust is not a one-way street.* 信任不是單向的。**6 walk the streets** *old-fashioned* an expression meaning to be a PROSTITUTE【過時】當妓女, 賣淫 **7 streets ahead (of)** *BrE informal* much better than someone or something else【英, 非正式】比…好得多: *James is streets ahead of the rest of the class at reading.* 詹姆斯在閱讀方面遠遠超過班裡的其他同學。—see also 另見 BACKSTREET, **be on easy street** (EASY¹ (11)), STREET SMARTS

USAGE NOTE 用法說明: STREET

WORD CHOICE 詞語辨析: **street, road**

A **street** is in the middle of a town, and usually has shops and other buildings and pavements (*BrE* 英)/sidewalks (*AmE* 美). street是指城鎮的街道, 兩旁通常有商店等建築物和人行道: *a street corner* (NOT 不用 *road corner*) 街角

A **road** can be in the town or in the country, and usually leads to another town, or to another part of a town. road是指城鎮或鄉間的公路, 通常連接一個城鎮與另一城鎮或城鎮的一個地區與另一個地區: *the road to Birmingham* (NOT 不用 *street*) 往伯明翰的公路

BRE-AME DIFFERENCES 英國英語和美國英語的區別

British speakers often say **in a street or road** where American speakers say **on a street or road**. 英國人常在street或road前用介詞in, 美國人則常用on: *the shops in the High Street* 大街上的商店 (*BrE* 英) | *the stores on Main Street* 大街上的商店 (*AmE* 美) | *a house in Bristol Road* (*BrE* 英)在布里斯托爾路的一棟房子 | *a house on Boston Road* (*AmE* 美)在波士頓路的一棟房子

In spoken American English words like **street** are often left out especially when giving directions to numbered streets. 在美國口語中, 尤其在告訴別人如何去某條有編號的大街時, street等詞常被省去: *Where's the Empire State Building? At 34th and 5th.* 到帝國大廈怎麼走? 在三十四街和第五大街的交匯處。In British English this would be 英國英語則說: *At the junction of 34th Street and 5th Avenue.* 在三十四街和第五大街的交匯處。

street·car /ˋstritˏkɑr; ˈstriːtkɑː/ *n* [C] *AmE* a type of bus that runs on electricity along metal tracks in the road【美】有軌電車; TRAM *BrE*【英】

street-cred /ˋstrit ˏkrɛd; ˈstriːt kred/ also 又作 **street cred·i·bil·i·ty** /ˏ· ··ˈ···/ *n* [U] popular acceptance and approval among young people, especially because you know how to survive in a city〔在年輕人中認同的〕街頭信譽: *It'll wreck your street cred if you're seen helping the police.* 如果有人看到你幫助警察, 會損害你的街頭信譽。—**street-credible** /ˈ· ˏ···/ *adj*

street·lamp /ˋstritˏlæmp; ˈstriːtlæmp/ *n* [C] a streetlight 街燈, 路燈

street·light /ˋstritˏlaɪt; ˈstriːtlaɪt/ *n* [C] a light at the top of a tall post in the street 街燈, 路燈 —see picture on page A4 參見A4頁圖

street peo·ple /ˈ· ˏ··/ *n* [plural] people who have no home and live on the streets 無家可歸的人, 漂泊街頭的人

street smarts /ˈ· ·/ *n* [U] *AmE* the abilitiy to deal with difficult situations on the streets of a big city【美】在城市街頭應付困境的能力: *unsuspecting tourists with no street smarts whatsoever* 根本沒有城市街頭適應能力的、毫無提防的遊客

street style /ˈ· ·/ *n* [U] style connected with the clothes, music etc of ordinary young people〔衣服、音樂等的〕普通年輕人的風格, 大眾風格

street val·ue /ˈ· ˏ··/ *n* [C,U] the price for which a drug can be sold illegally to people〔毒品的〕街頭黑市行情[價格]: *The drugs haul had a street value of £100,000.* 這批毒品的黑市價格為十萬英鎊。

street·walk·er /ˋstritˏwɔkɚ; ˈstriːtˌwɔːkə/ *n* [C] *old-fashioned* a PROSTITUTE who stands on the street to attract customers【過時】〔街頭拉客的〕妓女

street·wise /ˋstritwaɪz; ˈstriːtwaɪz/ *adj informal* clever and experienced enough to deal with difficult situations on the streets of a big city【非正式】善於在街頭營生的; 圓滑世故能在城市街頭混得開的: *streetwise drug dealers overtaking the neighborhood* 稱霸街坊、常在街頭混的毒品販子

strength /strɛŋθ; streŋθ/ *n* 2 2
1 ►PHYSICAL STRENGTH 體力◄ [U] the physical power and energy that makes someone strong 體力, 力氣, 力量: *It took Susan weeks to regain her strength after the illness.* 蘇珊病癒後過了好幾個星期才恢復體力。| **the strength to do sth** *I don't have the strength to climb any further.* 我沒有力氣再往上爬了。| **with all your strength** *Diana pulled on the rope with all her strength.* 黛安娜用盡全身的力氣拉繩子。| **not know your own strength** (=not realize how strong you are) 沒有意識到自己的力量 —see also 另見 **outgrow your strength** (OUTGROW (4))

2 ▶OF AN OBJECT 某物體的◀ [U] how strong an object or structure is, especially its ability to last for a long time without breaking 強度: **[+of]** *I have doubts about the strength of that beam in the ceiling.* 我懷疑天花板上的那條橫梁的強度。

3 ▶OF CHARACTER 性格上的◀ [U] the ability to deal with difficult or unpleasant situations in a brave or determined way〔處理困境等的〕意志力: *moral strength* 道德力量 | **strength to do sth** *Where did you find the strength to keep trying?* 你不斷進行嘗試的意志力是從哪兒來的? | **strength of character** (=strong ability to deal with difficult situations) 性格的堅強 *the underlying strength of character behind Roosevelt's easy charm* 羅斯福平易近人的外表下潛在的堅強性格 | **inner strength** (=strength of spirit) 精神力量 *His troubles have bred in him an inner strength he'll never lose.* 他所經受的磨難使他產生出一種永遠不會喪失的精神力量。—see also 另見 **tower of strength** (TOWER¹ (3))

4 ▶OF FEELING/BELIEF/RELATIONSHIP 感情/信仰/關係的◀ [U] how strong a feeling, belief, or relationship is 堅強; 堅定; 強度: **[+of]** *We can't ignore the strength of public opinion.* 我們不能忽視公眾輿論的力量。| *the strength of family bonds* 家庭紐帶的力量 | **strength of feeling** *Don't underestimate the strength of feeling that the abortion issue will generate.* 不要低估墮胎問題將會引發的強烈情緒。| **strength of purpose** (=determination) 決心 *I began to feel my strength of purpose failing me.* 我開始覺得自己的決心在動搖。

5 ▶POLITICAL/MILITARY/ECONOMIC 政治/軍事/經濟(上)的◀ [U] political, military or economic power〔政治、軍事或經濟上的〕實力: **[+of]** *the strength of the US economy* 美國的經濟實力 | **a show of strength** (=an occasion when a country shows how powerful its army etc is)〔軍事等的〕實力顯示, 顯示力量

6 ▶OF A SUBSTANCE/MIXTURE 物質/混合物的◀ [C, U] how strong a substance or mixture is 強度; 濃度; 烈度: *The drug is available in two strengths.* 這種毒品有兩種不同的烈度。| **full-strength/half-strength/double-strength etc** *acid diluted to half-strength* 濃度被稀釋了一半的酸

7 ▶USEFUL QUALITY OR ABILITY 有用的特徵或能力◀ [C] a particular quality or ability that gives someone or something an advantage 強點, 長處, 優勢: *The great strength of our plan lies in its simplicity.* 我們這個計劃的最大長處在於它的簡單。

8 position of strength a position where you have an advantage over someone, especially in discussions〔尤指在討論中的〕優勢地位: *If we keep our nuclear weapons, we can negotiate from a position of strength.* 我們如果保存自己的核武器, 就能夠在談判中處於強勢地位。

9 ▶OF A TEAM/ARMY ETC 團隊/軍隊等的◀ [U] the number of people in a team, army etc 人力, 人數; 兵力: **below strength** *The police force is below strength at the moment.* 目前警力不足。| **in strength** (=in large numbers) 大批地, 大量地

10 ▶OF MONEY 金錢的◀ [U] the value of a country's money〔某國家貨幣的〕價值; 價格堅挺程度: **[+of]** *the strength of the dollar on the international money markets* 美元在國際貨幣市場上的強勢

11 ▶COLOUR/LIGHT 顏色/光線◀ [U] how strong a light or colour is〔光線或顏色的〕強度: *the strength of the beam of light* 光束的強度

12 ▶OF A WIND/CURRENT 風/水流的◀ [U] how strong a wind or current of water is〔風或水流的〕強度

13 go from strength to strength to have one success after another 不斷取得成功; 日益壯大: *Since the advent of the personal computer, the software industry has gone from strength to strength.* 自從有了個人電腦, 軟件業在不斷壯大。

14 on the strength of sth because of something that persuaded you 基於…; 受…的鼓勵: *I bought the book on the strength of your recommendation.* 我是因為聽了你的推薦才買這本書的。

15 give me strength *spoken* used when you are annoyed or angry about something【口】給我力量吧! 真叫人受不了!〔用於表示煩惱或生氣〕

strength·en /ˋstrɛŋθən; ˈstreŋθən/ *v* [W3]

1 ▶FEELING/BELIEF/RELATIONSHIP 感情/信仰/關係◀ [I,T] to become stronger or make something stronger (使) 變強, 加強; 使更堅固: *Our friendship has steadily strengthened over the years.* 我們的友誼逐年加深。| **strengthen sth** *Steve's opposition only strengthened her resolve to go ahead.* 史蒂夫的反對只有加強了她繼續下去的決心。

2 ▶TEAM/ARMY ETC 團隊/軍隊等◀ [T] to make an organization, army etc more powerful, especially by increasing the number or quality of the people in it 增強〔某組織或軍隊等的〕實力: *The team has been strengthened by the arrival of two Brazilian players.* 兩位巴西球員的到來增強了球隊的實力。

3 ▶MONEY 錢◀ [I,T] to increase in value or to increase the value of money〔貨幣〕增值; 增加〔貨幣的〕價值: *The pound has strengthened against other currencies.* 英鎊對其他貨幣的比值上升了。

4 ▶FINANCIAL SITUATION 財政狀況◀ [T] to improve the financial situation of a country or company 增強, 改善〔某國或公司的財政狀況〕: *measures to strengthen the economy* 增強經濟的措施

5 ▶STRUCTURE 結構◀ [T] to make something physically or structurally stronger 加固: *Metal supports were added to strengthen the outer walls.* 增加了金屬支架以加固外牆。

6 ▶PROOF/REASON 證據/理由◀ [T] to give support to a reason or an attempt to prove something 為…提供更有力的理由[證據]: *Evidence from independent witnesses would greatly strengthen your case.* 獨立證人的證詞會使你在案子中更加有利。

7 ▶WIND/CURRENT 風/水流◀ [I] to increase in force 加強, 增大: *The wind had strengthened during the night.* 風在夜裡颳得更大了。

stren·u·ous /ˋstrɛnjuəs; ˈstrenjuəs/ *adj* **1** needing great effort or strength 艱苦的, 須作出努力的, 要花功夫的: *a strenuous climb* 艱難的攀登 | *The doctor advised Ken to avoid strenuous exercise.* 醫生建議肯不要做劇烈運動。**2** active and determined 積極的; 堅決的: **make strenuous efforts** *the strenuous efforts the council is making to improve security* 地方議會為改進安全所作出的積極努力 **—strenuously** *adv*: *She strenuously denied the accusations.* 她極力否認那些指控。

strep throat /ˌstrɛp ˋθrot; ˌstrep ˈθrəʊt/ *n* [C,U] *informal* an illness in which your throat is very painful【非正式】鏈球菌性咽喉炎, 膿毒性咽喉炎

strep·to·coc·cus /ˌstrɛptəˋkɑkəs; ˌstreptəˈkɒkəs/ *n plural* **streptococci** /-kaɪ; -kaɪ/ [C] a BACTERIA that causes infections, especially in your throat 鏈球菌 **—streptococcal** *adj*

strep·to·my·cin /ˌstrɛptəˋmaɪsɪn; ˌstreptəʊˈmaɪsən/ *n* [U] a strong drug used in medicines to kill BACTERIA 鏈黴素

stress¹ /strɛs; stres/ *n* [S3] [W3] **1** [C,U] continuous feelings of worry about your work or personal life, that prevent you from relaxing 壓力; 憂慮; 緊張: *Your headaches are due to stress.* 你的頭痛是緊張造成的。| **under stress** *Janet's been under a lot of stress since her mother's illness.* 珍妮特自從母親生病以來承受了很大的壓力。| **stresses and strains** (=problems and worries) 緊張和壓力 | **stress-related** (=caused by stress) 與緊張有關的 *a stress-related illness* 與緊張有關的疾病 **2** [C,U] the physical force or pressure on an object 應力: *the stress exerted on an aircraft's wing* 施加於飛機機翼的應力 **3** [U] the

S

special attention or importance given to a particular idea, fact, or activity; EMPHASIS 強調; 重要性: **put/lay stress on** *Pugh laid particular stress on the need for discipline.* 皮尤特別強調紀律的必要性。**4** [C,U] the degree of force or loudness with which a part of a word is pronounced or a note in music is played, which makes it sound stronger than other parts or notes 重音, 重讀; 〔音樂中的〕加強

stress² *v* [T] **1** to emphasize a statement, fact, or idea 強調, 着重: *I can't stress enough the need for cooperation.* 無論我如何強調合作的必要性都不過分。**2** to pronounce a word or part of a word more forcefully or loudly 重讀: *The word 'machine' is stressed on the second syllable.* machine這個詞的第二個音節要重讀。

stressed /strɛst; strest/ *adj* **1** [not before noun 不用於名詞前] so worried and tired that you cannot relax 焦慮的, 緊張的, 無法放鬆的 **2** *technical* an object, especially a metal object, that is stressed has had a lot of pressure or force put on it【術語】〔尤指金屬物體〕受力的

stressed out /ˌ· ˈ·◂/ *adj informal* so worried and tired that you cannot relax【非正式】極度焦慮的; 非常緊張的, 壓力大的: *Rob looks so stressed out since he started this new job.* 羅布自從開始做這份新工作以來, 看上去一直非常緊張。

stress·ful /ˈstrɛsfəl; ˈstresfəl/ *adj* a job, experience, or situation that is stressful makes you worry a lot 充滿壓力的, 緊張的: *Moving to a new house is a very stressful experience.* 搬新家是件很勞心的事。

stress mark /ˈ· ·/ *n* [C] a mark that shows which part of a word is pronounced more forcefully 重音符號

stretch¹ /strɛtʃ; stretʃ/ *v*

1 ►MAKE STH BIGGER/LOOSER 使某物更大/更鬆◄ **a)** [I,T] to make something bigger or looser by pulling it, or to become bigger or looser as a result of being pulled (使) 變大; (使) 變鬆; 拉長: *My big, blue sweater has stretched completely out of shape.* 我那件藍色大毛線衫已經鬆得完全變了形。**b)** [I not in progressive 不用進行式] if material stretches, it can become bigger or longer when you pull it and then return to its original shape when you stop 可伸展, 可延伸, 有彈性: *Lycra shorts will stretch to fit you perfectly.* 萊卡短褲有彈性, 穿着很貼身。

2 ►ARM/BODY 手臂/身體◄ [I,T] to straighten your arms, legs, or body to full length 伸開, 張開, 伸展〔肢體〕: *Carl sat up in bed, yawned and stretched.* 卡爾在牀上坐了起來, 邊打呵欠邊伸懶腰。

3 ►MAKE STH TIGHT 使某物變緊◄ [T] to pull something so that it is tight 拉緊, 拽緊: *a rope stretched between two poles* 在兩根柱子間拉緊的繩子 | **stretch sth tight** *Stretch the canvas tight over the frame.* 把油畫布緊繃在畫框上。

4 ►IN SPACE 在空間上◄ [I always+adv/prep] to spread out or cover a large area of land 延伸, 綿延: **[+to/into/away]** *The desert stretched away as far as the eye could see.* 沙漠綿延, 一望無際。| *a line stretching around the block* 圍繞着街區的一條線

5 ►IN TIME 在時間上◄ [I always+adv/prep] to continue over a period of time 延續, 延伸: **[+into/on/over]** *a research program stretching over several years* 一個歷時數年的研究項目

6 ►RULE/LIMIT 規則/限制◄ [T] to allow something that would not normally be allowed by a rule or limit 放寬規則[限制]: *This once I'll stretch the rules and let you leave work early.* 這一次我就放寬規定讓你早下班。| **stretch a point** (=allow a rule to be broken) 破例; 放寬規定 *We'll stretch a point and let the baby travel free this time.* 我們這次破例讓嬰兒免費旅行。

7 stretch sb's patience/credulity etc to be almost beyond the limits of what someone can accept, believe etc 使某人難以忍受/相信等: **stretch sth to the limit** *Barry's behaviour has stretched my patience to the limit.* 巴里的行為已經使我忍無可忍。

8 ►ABILITIES 能力◄ [T] to make someone use all of their skill, abilities or intelligence 使〔某人〕施展才華: *The work's too easy. The students aren't being stretched enough.* 作業太容易, 沒有讓學生充分發揮出來。

9 be stretched (to the limit) to have hardly enough money or supplies for your needs 手頭拮据, 沒有足夠的錢[日用品]: *We're stretched at the moment, otherwise I'd offer to lend you some money.* 我們目前手頭拮据, 不然我會主動提出借一些錢給你。

10 stretch the truth to make something seem more important, bigger etc than it really is 誇大事實, 言過其實: **be stretching it** *He's a good player, but 'world class' is stretching it.* 他是一位優秀的選手, 但要説是"世界級的", 那就有點誇張了。

11 not stretch to sth if someone's money will not stretch to something, they cannot afford it 買不起某物, 支付不起某物的費用: *Our savings don't stretch to a vacation this year.* 今年我們的存款不夠去度假。

12 stretch your legs *informal* to go for a walk, especially after sitting for a long time【非正式】〔尤指久坐後〕伸伸腿; 散散步 —**stretchable** *adj*

stretch out *phr v* **1** [I always+adv/prep] *informal* to lie down, usually in order to sleep or rest【非正式】躺下〔睡覺或休息〕: *I'm just going to stretch out on the couch for ten minutes.* 我打算在沙發上躺十分鐘。**2** [T **stretch** sth ↔ **out**] to put out your hand, foot etc in order to reach something 伸出, 伸開〔手、腳等〕: *Jimmy stretched out his hand to take the candy.* 吉米伸出手去拿糖果。

stretch² *n*

1 ►LENGTH OF LAND/WATER 一片地域/水域◄ [C] an area of land or water, especially one that is long and narrow〔尤指長而窄的〕一片地域; 一片水域: **[+of]** *The boat rocked as it entered the stretch of rough water.* 船進入那段風浪大的水域後搖晃起來。| *a beautiful stretch of countryside* 一片鄉村美景 | **home/final/finishing stretch** (=the last part of a track before the end of a race) 臨近終點的一段跑道

2 ►TIME 時間◄ [C] a continuous period of time 連續的一段時間: **[+of]** *a stretch of three weeks without sunshine* 一連三個星期沒有陽光 | **at a stretch** (=without stopping) 不停地, 連續地 *I couldn't stand for hours at a stretch.* 我無法連續站立幾個小時。

3 ►BODY 身體◄ [C] the action of stretching a part of your body out to its full length, or a particular way of doing this 伸展動作; 〔肢體的〕伸展, 伸開, 張開: *The ski instructor showed us some special stretches.* 滑雪教練給我們示範了幾個特別的伸展動作。

4 ►MATERIAL 材料◄ [U] the ability a material has to increase in length or width without tearing 伸展性, 彈性: *This elastic has lost its stretch.* 這條鬆緊帶已經失去了彈性。—compare 比較 STRETCHY

5 not by any stretch of the imagination used to say that something cannot be true, even if you try very hard to imagine or believe it 無論怎樣想像都不〔表示某事怎麼想像或推想也不可能是真實的〕: *You wouldn't call him smart by any stretch of the imagination, but he did ok for himself.* 無論你如何想像, 也不能説他是聰明人, 但他自己生活得還可以。

6 ►JAIL 監獄◄ [C usually singular 一般用單數] *informal* a period of time spent in prison【非正式】服刑期, 徒刑

7 at full stretch *BrE*【英】**a)** using everything that is available 全力以赴, 竭盡所能: *The emergency services were at full stretch after the motorway pile-up.* 高速公路發生連環撞車事故之後, 緊急救護部門正全力以赴(進行處理)。**b)** with your body or part of your body stretched as far as possible 身體[肢體]伸直: *He dived and caught the ball at full stretch.* 他一個魚躍伸手把球接住。

stretch·er¹ /ˋstrɛtʃɚ; ˈstretʃə/ *n* [C] a covered frame for carrying someone who is too injured or ill to walk 擔架

stretcher² *v* [T always+adv/prep] to carry someone on a stretcher 用擔架抬送〔某人〕: **stretcher sb off/into etc** *Ward was stretchered off early in the game after a tackle by Townley.* 沃德在比賽初段遭湯利的一次阻截之後被擔架抬下了場。

stretcher-bear·er /ˈ·· ˌ·ˈ·/ *n* [C] someone, usually a soldier, who carries one end of a stretcher 抬擔架的人〔通常為士兵〕

stretch lim·o /ˋstrɛtʃ ˌlɪmo; ˈstretʃ ˌlɪməʊ/ also 又作 **stretch lim·ou·sine** /ˈ· ˌ···/ *n* [C] a very large comfortable car that has been made longer than usual 加長豪華轎車, 特大豪華轎車

stretch·mark /ˋstrɛtʃmɑrk; ˈstretʃmɑːk/ *n* [C usually plural 一般用複數] a mark left on your skin as a result of it stretching too much, especially during PREGNANCY〔尤指懷孕時留下的〕萎縮紋, 妊娠紋

stretch·y /ˋstrɛtʃɪ; ˈstretʃi/ *adj* material that is stretchy can stretch when you pull it and then return to its original shape 有彈性的, 可伸張的: *stretchy cotton leggings* 彈性棉護腿

strew /stru; struː/ *v past participle* **strewn** /strun; struːn/ or **strewed** [T usually passive 一般用被動態] **1** to scatter things around a large area 撒, 散播: **[+around/about/over]** *I found papers strewn all over the room.* 我發現整個房間散滿了文件。| **be strewn with** *The yard was strewn with garbage.* 院子裡到處散落着垃圾。**2** *literary* to lie scattered over something【文】散佈於, 點綴於: *Flowers strewed the path.* 花散落在小徑上。**3** **strewn with** containing a lot of something 充滿: *conversation liberally strewn with swear words* 充滿罵人話的談話

strewth /struθ; struːθ/ *interjection BrE and AustrE* used to express surprise, annoyance etc【英和澳】哎呀, 天哪〔表示驚訝、煩惱等〕

stri·at·ed /ˋstraɪetɪd; straɪˈeɪtɪ̈d/ *adj technical* having narrow lines or bands of colour; STRIPED【術語】有線條的, 有條紋的

stri·a·tion /straɪˋeʃən; straɪˈeɪʃən/ *n* [C usually plural 一般用複數] *technical* one of a number of narrow lines or bands of colour; STRIPE (1)【術語】線條, 條紋

strick·en /ˋstrɪkən; ˈstrɪkən/ *adj formal* very badly affected by trouble, illness, unhappiness etc【正式】受災的; 患病的; 受困擾的; 受苦的: *Supplies of medicine were rushed to the stricken city.* 藥品被迅速送往受災城市。| **[+by/with]** *stricken with a fatal disease* 患致命的疾病 | **poverty stricken** (=very poor) 非常貧窮的, 極度貧困的 *poverty stricken areas riddled with disease* 受疾病侵擾的極度貧困地區 | **panic stricken** (=filled with sudden terror) 驚慌失措的, 驚恐至極的 *Panic stricken crowds swarmed into the square.* 驚慌失措的人羣紛紛湧進廣場。| **grief stricken** *A grief stricken mother from Kansas wrote in to tell me of her tragedy.* 堪薩斯的一位悲痛欲絕的母親寫信來向我訴說她的悲劇。

[S] [3] **strict** /strɪkt; strɪkt/ *adj* **1** someone who is strict demands that rules should always be obeyed 嚴格的, 嚴厲的: *a strict teacher* 嚴格的老師 | **[+with]** *The Stuarts are very strict with their children.* 斯圖爾特夫婦待子女很嚴。| **[+about]** *This company is very strict about punctuality.* 這公司嚴格要求準時。**2** a strict order or rule is one that must be obeyed〔命令、規則〕必須嚴格遵守的: *You had strict instructions not to tell anybody.* 你得到嚴格指示不得告訴任何人。| **in the strictest confidence** (=it must be kept completely secret) 極其祕密地 *I'm telling you this in the strictest confidence.* 我告訴你這事, 你要嚴加保密。**3** [usually before noun 一般用於名詞前] exact and correct, but often unreasonably exact 嚴謹的; 精確的, 確鑿的: *He's using 'trust' in the strict legal sense.* 他是在嚴格的法律意義上使用 trust (信任) 這個詞。**4** **strict Muslim/vegetarian etc** someone who obeys all the rules of a particular religion, belief etc 不折不扣的穆斯林/素食者等 —**strictness** *n* [U]

strict·ly /ˋstrɪktlɪ; ˈstrɪktli/ *adv* **1** exactly and completely 完全地; 確切地: *That isn't strictly true.* 那並不全是真的。**2** **strictly speaking** used when you are using words or explaining rules in an exact and correct way 嚴格地說: *Strictly speaking, spiders are not insects, although most people think they are.* 嚴格地說, 蜘蛛不是昆蟲, 雖然大多數人都認為牠們是昆蟲。**3** only for a particular person or thing and no one else 嚴格限定地; 只限於某人[某物]: *This is strictly between us. Nobody else must know.* 此事僅限於我們知道, 不可告訴其他任何人。**4** in a way that must be obeyed 嚴格地, 嚴明地: *Discipline will be strictly enforced.* 我們將嚴格執行紀律。

stric·ture /ˋstrɪktʃɚ; ˈstrɪktʃə/ *n* [C often plural 常用複數] *formal*【正式】**1** a severe criticism 嚴厲批評 **2** **[+on/against]** a rule that strictly limits you morally or physically 約束; 限制; 束縛

stride¹ /straɪd; straɪd/ *v past tense* **strode** /strod; strəʊd/ *past participle* **stridden** /ˋstrɪdn̩; ˈstrɪdn/ [I always+adv/prep] to walk quickly with long steps 邁大步走, 大踏步走: **[+across/into/down]** *Clarice jumped off the porch and strode across the lawn.* 克拉麗斯從門廊上跳下, 大步走過草坪。

stride² *n*

1 ▶WALKING 走, 步行◀ [C] a long step 大步, 闊步: *Paco reached the door in only three strides.* 帕科三大步就走到門口。

2 ▶PATTERN OF STEPS 步態◀ [U] the pattern of your steps or the way you walk or run; GAIT 步法, 步態: *the runner's long, loping stride* 跑步者大步輕快的步法

3 ▶IMPROVEMENT 改進◀ [C] an improvement in a situation or in the development of something 進步, 進展, 發展: **make great/big/giant strides** *We've made great strides in medical technology this century.* 本世紀我們在醫療技術方面有了很大的進展。

4 get into your stride *BrE*【英】, **hit your stride** *AmE*【美】to become comfortable with a job so you can do it continuously and well〔做某工作〕開始上軌道, 駕輕就熟: *Once I get into my stride I can finish the essay in a few hours.* 我一旦寫順手, 幾個小時就能寫完那篇論文。

5 take sth in your stride to not allow something to annoy, embarrass, or upset you in any way 從容地對付: *Eva took all the setbacks in her stride.* 伊娃從容地應對所有的挫折。

6 put sb off their stride to make someone stop giving all their attention to what they are doing 使某人分心: *Knowing that Bob was watching the game really put me off my stride.* 知道鮑勃正在觀看比賽, 這使得我實在無法集中注意力。

7 (match sb) stride for stride to manage to be just as fast, strong, skilled etc as someone else even if they keep making it harder for you (設法與某人) 並駕齊驅

8 without breaking stride *especially AmE* without allowing something to interrupt or annoy you【尤美】不加停頓地; 心平氣和地: *Zeke dealt with the reporters' questions without breaking stride.* 齊克從容地應付了記者的提問。

9 strides [plural] *AustrE informal* trousers【澳, 非正式】褲子

stri·dent /ˋstraɪdn̩t; ˈstraɪdənt/ *adj* **1** a sound or voice that is strident is too loud and high and sounds unpleasant 刺耳的, 尖聲的: *the strident blaring of a military band* 軍樂隊刺耳的演奏聲 **2** forceful and determined 強烈的; 堅定的: *the strident demands of the American media* 美國媒體的強烈要求 —**stridently** *adv* —**stridency** *n* [U]

strife /straɪf; straɪf/ *n* [U] *formal* trouble between two people or groups; CONFLICT¹【正式】〔兩個人或團體之間的〕衝突, 糾紛, 爭鬥: *a time of political strife* 政治鬥爭的時代

S

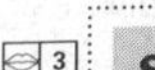

strike¹ /straɪk; straɪk/ *v past tense and past participle* **struck** /strʌk; strʌk/

① THINK/NOTICE 想/注意
② STOP WORK 停止工作
③ HIT 擊, 打
④ LIGHTNING 閃電
⑤ ATTACK/HARM 攻擊/傷害
⑥ EXPRESS AN OPINION/FEELING 表達觀點/感情
⑦ CLOCKS 時鐘
⑧ STRONG FEELINGS 強烈的感情
⑨ FIND 發現
⑩ DO STH 做某事
⑪ OTHER MEANINGS 其他意思

① THINK/NOTICE 想/注意

1 [T not in progressive 不用進行式] if a thought or idea strikes you, you suddenly realize that it is important, interesting, surprising, bad etc 突然意識到, 突然想到: *The funny side of the affair suddenly struck her.* 她突然意識到事情可笑的一面。| **it strikes sb that** *It struck Carol that what he'd said about Helen applied to her too.* 卡羅爾突然意識到他說海倫的那些話也適用於自己。| **be struck by** *We were struck by the generosity of even the poorest citizens.* 使我們深受感動的是, 甚至最貧窮的市民也慷慨大方。—see 見 OCCUR (USAGE)

2 strike sb as sth to seem to have a particular quality or feature 給某人…的印象: *His jokes didn't strike Jack as being very funny.* 傑克不覺得他的笑話很好笑。| *How did he strike you?* (=how did he seem to you?) 他給你的印象如何? | **it strikes sb as** *It strikes me as a great idea.* 我覺得這個主意好極了。| **strike sb as strange/odd/funny etc** *It struck me as odd at the time.* 我當時覺得這很古怪。

3 strike the eye to be particularly noticeable 顯眼, 醒目: *What strikes your eye at once is her gorgeous red hair.* 一下子吸引你注意力的是她那一頭美麗的紅髮。

② STOP WORK 停止工作

4 [I] to deliberately stop working for a time because of a disagreement about pay, working conditions etc 罷工: *The police are forbidden to strike.* 警察被禁止罷工。| **strike for** *We're striking for another two dollars an hour.* 我們為爭取每小時再加兩美元而罷工。

③ HIT 擊, 打

5 [I always+adv/prep,T] *formal* to hit or knock hard against something【正式】打, 擊, 撞: **strike (sth) against** *Then my shovel struck against something metallic.* 然後我的鏟子碰到一件像金屬的東西。| **strike sb/sth on** *A snowball struck him on the back of the head.* 一團雪球打中他的後腦勺。| **strike sth** *My foot struck a rock.* 我的腳碰到一塊石頭。| **be struck by sth** *The car had been struck by a falling tree.* 汽車被一棵倒下的樹砸中了。

6 ►WITH YOUR HAND 用手◄ [T] *formal* to deliberately hit someone or something hard, especially with your hand【正式】〔尤指用手〕打, 擊: *I wouldn't dream of striking a woman.* 我做夢也不會打女人。| *strike the bass drum* 打低音鼓 | **strike sth with** *He struck the table with his fist.* 他用拳頭砸桌子。| **strike a blow** *The blow was almost certainly struck with the left hand.* 那一拳幾乎可以肯定是用左手打的。| **strike home** (=hit something exactly where you were aiming to hit it) 擊中目標, 擊中要害 *His sword struck home deep into the bull's neck.* 他的劍正中目標, 深深地扎在公牛的脖子上。

7 strike a match/light to light a match by hitting it against a hard surface 劃火柴

④ LIGHTNING 閃電

8 [I,T] when LIGHTNING strikes something, it hits and damages it〔閃電〕擊中, 擊毀: *That old forked tree was once struck by lightning.* 那棵有杈的老樹曾經被閃電擊中過。

⑤ ATTACK/HARM 攻擊/傷害

9 [I] to attack quickly and suddenly 猛然攻擊, 突然襲擊: *When the snake strikes, its mouth opens wide.* 蛇發起攻擊時嘴張得很大。| *Police fear that the killer will strike again.* 警方擔心兇手會再次作案。| **strike at** *This law strikes at the most vulnerable groups in our society.* 這項法律打擊的是我們社會中最脆弱的羣體。| **strike at the heart of** *spending cuts that strike at the heart of socialized medicine* 給公費醫療以沉重打擊的削減開支

10 [I] if something unpleasant strikes, it suddenly happens〔不愉快的事〕突然發生: *Tragedy struck two days later when Tammy was in a serious car accident.* 兩天後悲劇突然發生, 塔米遭遇嚴重車禍。

11 [I] to do something that gives you an advantage or harms your opponent in a fight, competition etc 主動出擊, 搶佔優勢: *Brazil struck first with a goal in the third minute.* 巴西隊先發制人, 在第三分鐘時就進了一球。| **strike the first blow** (=gain the first advantage) 先發制人, 搶佔最初的優勢

12 strike a blow for to do something to help an idea, belief, or organization 以實際行動擁護〔某主意、信念或團體〕: *It's time we struck a blow for women's rights.* 我們以實際行動維護婦女權益的時候到了。

13 strike a blow at to have a harmful effect on people's behaviour or beliefs 危害, 傷害: *This latest research strikes a blow at the foundations of psychiatry.* 這項最新研究動搖了精神病學的基礎。

⑥ EXPRESS AN OPINION/FEELING 表達觀點/感情

14 strike a chord to express an opinion or idea that other people agree with or have sympathy with 引起共鳴, 打動: *Powell's angry speech struck a deep chord with his audience.* 鮑威爾憤怒的演說深深地打動了聽眾。

15 strike a happy/cheerful/cautious etc note to express a particular feeling or attitude 表達出高興/振奮/謹慎等的感情[態度]: *The article struck a conciliatory note.* 那篇文章表達了和解的姿態。| **strike the right note/a discordant note** (=express or fail to express what people are feeling) 說出大家的心聲/發出不和諧的聲音 *Her speech appeared to strike exactly the right note.* 她的演說似乎正好表達了大家的心聲。

16 strike home if something that you say strikes home, it has exactly the effect on someone that you intended 產生預期的效果: *Anna's criticism of his laziness really struck home.* 安娜批評他懶惰的確擊中了他的要害。

⑦ CLOCKS 時鐘

17 [I,T] when a clock strikes or strikes one, six etc, its bell sounds a certain number of times to show what the time is 敲鐘, 報時: *The church clock began to strike twelve.* 教堂的鐘開始敲十二下。| **strike the hour** (=strike when it is exactly one o'clock, two o'clock etc) 整點報時

⑧ **STRONG FEELINGS 強烈的感情**
18 strike terror/fear/a chill into sb's heart to make someone feel afraid 使某人感到恐懼/害怕/毛骨悚然: *The word 'cancer' still strikes terror into many hearts.* "癌症"這個詞仍然使很多人感到恐懼。
19 be struck dumb to be unable to speak, usually because you are very surprised〔常指吃驚得〕說不出話來: *When the Queen shook my hand, I was struck dumb.* 女王跟我握手, 我驚得一時說不出話來。

⑨ **FIND 發現**
20 strike gold/oil etc to suddenly find gold, oil etc, especially after you have been looking for it〔尤指經過挖掘〕找到黃金/石油等: *They finally struck gold in 1886.* 他們終於在1886年發現了金礦。
21 strike it rich/lucky to suddenly make a lot of money or have good luck 發橫財/交好運: *With her last book she's really struck it rich.* 她靠最近的那本書發了大財。

⑩ **DO STH 做某事**
22 strike a balance to give the correct amount of importance or attention to two opposing things 使達到平衡, 兩者兼顧: **strike the right balance** *The speech strikes the right balance between humour and seriousness.* 演説幽默而不失嚴肅, 恰到好處。
23 strike a bargain/deal to agree to do something if someone else does something for you 達成協議/交易: *The US and China have recently struck a deal over trade.* 美國和中國最近就貿易問題達成一項協議。
24 strike while the iron is hot [usually imperative 一般用祈使句] to do something immediately rather than waiting until a later time when you are less likely to succeed 趁熱打鐵, 趁機行事

⑪ **OTHER MEANINGS 其他意思**
25 ►LIGHT 光線◄ [T] to fall on a surface 射在〔某表面〕: *What happens when light strikes a glass lens?* 光射在玻璃鏡片上會怎麼樣?
26 be within striking distance to be very close to something or very near to achieving something 非常靠近〔某物〕; 即將實現〔某目標〕
27 strike a pose/an attitude to stand or sit with your body in a particular position 以某種姿勢站[坐]; 擺姿勢: *Eva walked to the middle of the room, turned, and struck a pose with her head to one side.* 伊娃走到房間中央, 轉過身來, 頭一歪擺了個姿勢。
28 strike sb/sth off/from to remove a name or a thing from a written list〔從名單〕上刪去某人/某物, 塗掉某人/某物: *We had to strike him off the short list.* 我們不得不從決選名單上刪去他的名字。
29 ►TENT/SAIL 帳篷/帆◄ [T] to take down a tent or sail 拆除〔帳篷或船帆〕: **strike camp** (=take down tents when leaving a camping place)〔離開野營地時〕拆除帳篷

strike back *phr v* [I] to attack someone who has attacked you first 回擊, 反擊: *The rebels struck back within hours.* 叛軍幾小時內進行了反擊。

strike sb ↔ **down** *phr v* [T] **1** to hit someone so hard that they fall down 將〔某人〕擊倒 **2** [usually passive 一般用被動態] to make someone die or become seriously ill 使喪命; 使病倒: *Hundreds died that winter, struck down by pneumonia.* 那年冬天數百人因患肺炎而死去。

strike off *phr v* **be struck off** *BrE* if a doctor, lawyer etc is struck off, their name is removed from the official list of people who are allowed to work as doctors etc【英】將〔醫生、律師等〕除名

strike on/upon sth *phr v* [T] **1** to discover something or have a good idea about something 發現; 想出: *At last I've struck on a plan that might work.* 最後, 我想出了一個可能行得通的計劃。**2 be struck on** *BrE informal* to think that something is good or well made【英, 非正式】喜歡, 認為…好: *I'm not very struck on these chocolates.* 我不是很喜歡這些巧克力。

strike out *phr v*
1 ►NAME 名字◄ [T **strike** sth ↔ **out**] to draw a line through something written on a piece of paper 劃掉, 刪去, 塗掉
2 ►WALK/SWIM 步行/游泳◄ [I always+adv/prep] to start walking or swimming in a particular direction, especially in a determined way〔朝某方向〕堅定地行進[游去]: *He decided to follow her, striking out in the same direction.* 他決定跟着她, 朝同一個方向堅定地走下去。
3 strike out on your/his/their own to start doing something new or living by yourself, without other people's help 開始獨立做新的事情; 開始獨立的生活: *Eric left the family business and struck out on his own.* 埃里克離開了家庭經營的業務, 自行創業。
4 ►NOT SUCCEED 不成功◄ [I] *informal especially AmE* to be unsuccessful at something【非正式, 尤美】不成功, 失敗: *"Did she say she'd go out with you?" "No, I struck out."* "她説願意跟你外出約會嗎?" "沒有, 我碰了釘子。"
5 ►BASEBALL 棒球◄ a) [I] to be unable to continue trying to hit the ball in BASEBALL, because you have already missed it three times 三擊不中出局 **b)** [T **strike** sb ↔ **out**] to put a player out in BASEBALL by making them fail to hit the ball three times 使〔某球員〕三擊不中出局

strike up *phr v* **1** [I,T] to begin playing a piece of music 開始演奏〔樂曲〕: **strike up the band** (=tell it to begin playing) 叫樂隊開始演奏 **2 strike up a friendship/relationship/conversation** to start to become friendly with someone 建立友誼/建立關係/交談起來

S

strike² *n* [C] (S3 W3)
1 ►STOP WORK 停止工作◄ a period of time when a group of workers deliberately stop working because of a disagreement about pay, working conditions etc 罷工; 罷課: **miners'/train/electricity etc strike** *During the teachers' strike, all the schools were closed.* 教師罷課期間, 所有的學校都關閉了。| **go on strike/on strike** *The Boston police went on strike in 1919.* 1919年波士頓警察罷工。| **be (out) on strike** *Within half an hour, all the drivers were out on strike.* 半個小時內, 所有的司機都罷工了。| **come out/go out on strike** (=start one) 開始罷工 | **call a strike** (=ask people to stop working) 號召舉行罷工 | **call off a strike** (=decide not to continue it) 停止罷工 | **strike action** *The mine-workers were solidly in favour of strike action.* 礦工們堅決支持罷工行動。| **general strike** (=involving most workers in the country) 總罷工, 全國大罷工
2 hunger/rent strike a time when someone refuses to eat or pay rent as a protest about something 絕食抗議/拒交房租: *a hunger strike by political prisoners* 政治犯的絕食抗議
3 ►ATTACK 打擊, 攻擊◄ a military attack, especially by aircraft dropping bombs 軍事打擊〔尤指空襲〕: **[+against/on]** *nuclear strikes on several targets* 對幾個目標進行的核打擊 | **launch a strike** *American aircraft carriers have launched several strikes.* 美國的航空母艦發動了數次襲擊。—see also 另見 FIRST STRIKE
4 oil strike the discovery of oil under the ground 石油的意外發現
5 ►SPORT 體育運動◄ a) a situation in BOWLING (1) in which you knock down all the PINS (=bottle shaped objects) with one of two balls〔保齡球〕一擊全倒 **b)** an attempt to hit the ball in BASEBALL in which you miss hitting the ball〔棒球〕好球

strike·bound /ˋstraɪkˏbaund; ˈstraɪkbaʊnd/ *adj* unable to move, travel, or happen because of a STRIKE[2] (1) 由於罷工而停頓的: *a strikebound port* 由於罷工而陷入停頓的港口

strike·break·er /ˋstraɪkˏbrekɚ; ˈstraɪkˌbreɪkə/ *n* [C] someone who takes the job of someone who is striking (STRIKE[1] (4)) 代替罷工者工作的人, 破壞罷工者 —compare 比較 BLACKLEG, SCAB (2) —**strikebreaking** *n* [U]

strike·out /ˋstraɪkˏaut; ˈstraɪkaʊt/ *n* [C] if the PITCHER (3) in BASEBALL throws a strikeout, he puts the player out by throwing three strikes (STRIKE[2] (5)) 〔棒球〕三擊不中 (擊球員) 出局 —see also 另見 **strike out** (STRIKE[1])

strike pay /ˈ· ·/ *n* [U] money paid to workers who are striking (STRIKE[1] (4)) by their union 〔工會在罷工期間給工人的〕罷工津貼

strik·er /ˋstraɪkɚ; ˈstraɪkə/ *n* [C] **1** someone who is striking (STRIKE[1] (4)) 罷工者; 罷課者 **2** a player in football whose main job is to kick a GOAL (2) 〔足球隊的〕前鋒 (隊員)

strik·ing /ˋstraɪkɪŋ; ˈstraɪkɪŋ/ *adj* **1** unusual or interesting enough to be noticed 驚人的, 顯著的: **a striking contrast** *a striking contrast between the luxury hotels and the ghettos just a block away* 豪華旅店和一個街區之隔的貧民窟之間的天壤之別 **2** someone who is striking is very attractive, often in an unusual way 吸引人的, 惹人注目的: *a dark man with striking features* 相貌動人的黝黑男子 —see also 另見 **be within striking distance** (STRIKE[1] (26)) —**strikingly** *adv*

3 2 **string[1]** /strɪŋ; strɪŋ/ *n*

1 ►THREAD 線◄ [C,U] a strong thread made of several threads twisted together, used for tying or fastening things 〔由幾股合成的〕線; 細繩; 帶子: *Can you find me some string to tie up this package?* 你能幫我找些繩子來捆這個包裹嗎? | *Puppets are worked by strings.* 木偶是用線來操縱的。| *a piece of string* 一根繩子

2 ►GROUP/SERIES 組/系列◄ [C] **a)** a number of similar things or events coming one after another 一連串, 一系列〔事件等〕: **[+of]** *a string of hit albums* 一系列非常成功的唱片 **b)** a group of similar things 一系列〔類似的事物〕: **[+of]** *She owns a string of health clubs.* 她擁有多家類似的健身俱樂部。**c)** *technical* a group of letters, words, or numbers, especially in a computer PROGRAM 【術語】〔尤指電腦程序中字符的〕串

3 a string of pearls/beads/onions several objects of the same kind connected with a thread 一串珍珠/珠子/洋葱

4 ►MUSIC 音樂◄ **a)** [C] one of the long thin pieces of wire, NYLON etc that is stretched across a musical instrument and produces sound 〔樂器上的〕弦 **b) strings** [plural] the people in an ORCHESTRA who play the instruments that have strings, such as VIOLIN*s* 樂隊的弦樂器演奏者〈如小提琴手〉

5 have sb on a string *informal* to be able to make someone do whatever you want 【非正式】操縱[支配]某人: *Susie has her mother on a string.* 蘇茜竟能任意支配她的母親。

6 no strings (attached) if an agreement or relationship has no strings, there are no special conditions or limits 〔協議或關係〕無附帶條件, 無任何限制: *The policy offers 15% interest with no strings attached.* 該保險單支付 15% 的利息, 不附帶任何條件。

7 pull strings to secretly use your influence with important people in order to get what you want or help someone else 暗中施加影響; 走後門: *Phil had to pull a few strings to get them to give me the job.* 菲爾只得動用一些私人關係, 讓他們把那份工作給我。| **pull sb's strings** (=control them) 控制某人, 操縱某人

8 have more than one string to your bow to have more than one skill, idea, plan etc that you can use if you need to 有後備技能[想法、計劃等]; 有兩手準備 —see also 另見 G-STRING, **hold/control the purse strings** (PURSE[1] (6))

string[2] *v past tense and past participle* **strung** /strʌŋ; strʌŋ/ [T] **1** to put things together onto a thread, chain etc 用〔線、鏈等〕穿起來: *beads strung on a silver chain* 穿在銀鏈上的珠子 **2** [always+adv/prep] to hang things in a line, high up, especially for decoration 懸掛〔尤指作為裝飾〕: **[+string sth up/along/across etc]** *Dad had strung brightly-colored lights up in the backyard.* 爸爸在後院裡掛起了鮮豔的彩燈。**3** to put a string or a set of strings onto a musical instrument 給〔樂器〕裝弦

string along *phr v informal* 【非正式】 **1** [T] to deceive someone for a long time by making them believe that you will help them, that you love them etc 哄騙; 吊〔某人〕胃口: *Timms will never pay you back; he's just stringing you along.* 蒂姆斯根本不會還錢給你, 他只是在哄騙你而已。**2** [I] *BrE* to go somewhere with someone for a short time, especially because you do not have anything else to do 【英】〔尤因找不到別的事情幹而〕跟隨, 暫與〔某人〕結伴: **[+with]** *If you're going into town, I'll string along with you.* 你如果進城, 我就和你結伴同行。

string sth ↔ **out** *phr v* [T] **1** [usually passive 一般用被動態] to spread something out in a long line 把…排成一條線, 使擺成一行: *The islands were strung out along the coastline.* 那些島嶼沿海岸線排成一行。—see also 另見 STRUNG-OUT **2** *informal* to make something last longer 【非正式】使拖長, 拉長: *The whole deal was strung out for a lot longer than necessary.* 整個交易被拖了很長時間。

string sth ↔ **together** *phr v* [T] **string two words/sentences together** to say something that makes sense to other people 說出令人聽懂的話: *He was so drunk he could hardly string two words together.* 他醉得幾乎連話都說不成句了。

string sth/sb ↔ **up** *phr v* [T] *informal* to kill someone by hanging them 【非正式】絞死, 吊死: *He should be strung up for what he did to that girl.* 就他對那個女孩的所作所為, 他應該被絞死。—see also 另見 STRUNG-UP

string bean /ˌ· ˈ·/ *n* [C] *especially AmE* a green bean with long thin pods (POD[1] (1)) that are eaten as food 【尤美】紅花菜豆; RUNNER BEAN *BrE* 【英】 —see picture on page A9 參見 A9 頁圖

stringed in·stru·ment /ˌ· ˈ···/ *n* [C] a musical instrument that produces sound from a set of strings (STRING[1] (4)), such as a VIOLIN 弦樂器〈如小提琴〉

strin·gent /ˋstrɪndʒənt; ˈstrɪndʒənt/ *adj* **1 stringent rule/test/condition** very strict and must be obeyed 嚴格的規則/測驗/條件: *stringent antinoise regulations* 嚴格的防噪音條例 **2** stringent economic conditions exist when there is a severe lack of money and strict controls on the supply of money 〔經濟狀況〕銀根緊的, 緊縮的 —**stringently** *adv* —**stringency** *n* [U]

string·er /ˋstrɪŋɚ; ˈstrɪŋə/ *n* [C] someone who regularly sends in news stories to a newspaper, but who is not employed by that newspaper 特約記者[通訊員]

string tie /ˌ· ˈ·/ *n* [C] a thick string worn around your neck and held in place by a decorative object, worn by men in the western US 〔美國西部男士戴的〕厚狹領結[帶], 繩領帶

string·y /ˋstrɪŋɪ; ˈstrɪŋi/ *adj* **1** meat, fruit, or vegetables that are stringy are full of thin pieces that are difficult to eat 纖維多的; 有筋的: *Scoop out the pumpkin's stringy fibres.* 用杓子把南瓜中的筋挖出來。**2** hair that is stringy is very thin and looks like string, especially because it is dirty 〔尤指毛髮因髒而〕呈線狀的: *old men with stringy beards leaning on walking sticks* 拄着拐杖、鬍鬚打綹的老人 **3** someone or a part of their body that is stringy is very thin so that their muscles show through their skin; WIRY 瘦的, 青筋畢露的: *I'd like to wring his stringy little neck!* 我要把他的細脖子擰斷!

strip[1] /strɪp; strɪp/ *v* **stripped, stripping**

1 ►TAKE OFF CLOTHES 脱衣服◄ also 又作 **strip off** [I,T] to take off your clothes or take off someone else's clothes 脱去 (…的) 衣服: *Jack stripped off and jumped into the shower.* 傑克脱掉衣服, 跳進淋浴間。| **strip sb**

The police stripped us all, looking for drugs. 警察剝光我們大家的衣服搜查毒品。| **stripped to the waist** (=not wearing any clothes on the top half of your body) 上身脱得精光的 | **strip down to your pants/socks etc** (=take off all your clothes except your pants etc) 脱得只剩內褲/襪子等 | **strip naked** (=remove all your clothes) 脱光所有的衣服

2 ►REMOVE A LAYER 除去一層◄ [T] to remove something that is covering the surface of something else 剝去, 除去: **strip sth off/from** *We need to strip the wallpaper off the walls first.* 我們得先把牆紙鏟掉。| **strip sth of** *a branch stripped of its bark* 剝去樹皮的樹枝

3 strip sb of sth to take away something important from someone as a punishment, for example their title, property, or power〔作為懲罰〕剝奪某人的頭銜、財產或權力: *Captain Evans was found guilty and stripped of his rank.* 埃文斯上尉被判有罪, 被免去了軍銜。

4 ►ENGINES/EQUIPMENT 發動機/設備◄ also 又作 **strip down** [T] to separate an engine or piece of equipment into pieces in order to clean or repair it; DISMANTLE 拆卸〔發動機或設備以進行清理或檢修〕

5 ►BUILDING/SHIP 建築物/輪船◄ [T] to remove everything that is inside a building, ship, car etc so that it is completely empty 搬走〔建築物、輪船、汽車等中的〕所有東西, 搬空: *The house was stripped by thieves.* 那所房子被盜賊洗劫一空。—see also 另見 ASSET STRIPPING

strip sth ↔ **away** *phr v* [T] to gradually get rid of habits, customs etc 逐漸擺脱〔習慣、風俗等〕: *Changes in society have stripped away men's role as protector and breadwinner.* 社會的變遷已使男人不再充當保護者和掙錢養家者的角色。

3 **strip**[2] *n* [C] **1** a long narrow piece of paper, cloth etc 條, 狹條狀物〔紙、布料等〕; *a strip of paper* 一張紙條 **2** a long narrow area of land 狹長的一塊土地: *a strip of sand between the cliffs and the sea* 懸崖和大海之間的一塊沙地 **3 do a strip** to take your clothes off, especially in a sexually exciting way as a form of entertainment 表演脱衣舞 **4** *AmE* a road with a lot of shops, restaurants etc along it【美】〔沿途有許多商店、餐館等的〕公路: *I could see the outline of the neon lights of the strip through the haze.* 從薄霧中我可以看到商業街上霓虹燈的輪廓。**5** *BrE* the clothes of a particular colour worn by a team【英】〔運動隊穿的某種顏色的〕運動服, 隊服: *Liverpool's famous red strip* 利物浦隊著名的紅色運動服 **6** a STRIP CARTOON 連環漫畫 —see also 另見 COMIC STRIP, LANDING STRIP, **tear sb off a strip** (TEAR[2] (9))

strip car·toon /ˌ· ˈ··/ *n* [C] *BrE* a series of drawings inside a row of small boxes tells a short story【英】連環漫畫; COMIC STRIP *AmE*【美】—compare 比較 CARTOON (1)

strip club /ˈ· ·/ *n* [C] a place where people go to see performers who take off their clothes to music 表演脱衣舞的夜總會

stripe /straɪp; straɪp/ *n* [C] **1** a line of colour, especially one of several lines of colour all close together 條紋, 線條: *a shirt with black and white stripes* 黑白條紋相間的襯衣 **2** a narrow piece of material worn on the arm of a uniform as a sign of rank〔軍服袖子上〕表示軍銜的條紋: *A sergeant has three stripes.* 軍士軍服上有三條槓。**3 earn your stripes** *informal* to do something to deserve a particular rank or position【非正式】〔為對得起某官職或地位而〕須作出努力

striped /straɪpt; straɪpt/ *adj* having lines or bands of colour 有不同顏色條紋的: *a blue and white striped T-shirt* 藍白條紋相間的 T 恤 —see picture on page A16 參見 A16 頁圖

strip joint /ˈ· ·/ *n* [C] *informal* a strip club【非正式】表演脱衣舞的夜總會

strip light·ing /ˈ· ˌ··/ *n* [U] lighting provided by long, white FLUORESCENT tubes, usually in public buildings rather than in houses〔通常在公共建築中的〕螢光燈管照明 —see picture at 參見 LIGHT[1] 圖

strip·ling /ˈstrɪplɪŋ; ˈstrɪplɪŋ/ *n* [C] *literary* a boy who is almost a young man【文】青年男子, 小伙子

strip mall /ˈ· ·/ *n* [C] *AmE* a small shopping centre that consists of a single row of shops with parking spaces in front of them【美】小型購物中心

strip min·ing /ˈ· ˌ··/ *n* [U] *especially AmE* a method of getting metal, coal etc by removing the earth from the surface of the ground, rather than by digging a passage under the ground【尤美】露天採礦 —compare 比較 OPENCAST

strip·per /ˈstrɪpɚ; ˈstrɪpə/ *n* [C] **1** someone, especially a woman, who takes off their clothes in a sexually exciting way in order to entertain people 表演脱衣舞者;〔尤指〕脱衣舞舞女 **2** a tool or liquid used to remove something from a surface 剝離表面物的器具; 清除表層物的液體: *paint stripper* 除漆劑

strip pok·er /ˌ· ˈ··/ *n* [C] a game of POKER (=card game) in which players that lose take off pieces of their clothing "剝豬玀"撲克牌戲〔輸者被罰剝去衣服〕

strip search /ˈ· ·/ *n* [C] a process in which you have to remove your clothes so that your body can be checked, usually for hidden drugs〔通常指為尋找隱藏的毒品而作的〕裸體搜查

strip show /ˈ· ·/ *n* [C] a form of entertainment where people, especially women, take off their clothes in a sexually exciting way 脱衣舞表演

strip·tease /ˈstrɪpˌtiz; ˈstrɪptiːz/ *n* [C,U] a performance in which someone, especially a woman, takes off their clothes in a sexually exciting way 脱衣舞（表演）—**striptease** *v* [I]

strip·y /ˈstraɪpɪ; ˈstraɪpi/ *adj BrE* STRIPED【英】有不同顏色條紋的

strive /straɪv; straɪv/ *v past tense* **strove** /strov; strəʊv/ *past participle* **striven** /ˈstrɪvən; ˈstrɪvən/ [I] *formal* to make a great effort to achieve something【正式】〔為獲得某物而〕努力, 奮鬥: **[+for/after]** *We must continue to strive for greater efficiency.* 我們必須繼續爭取提高效率。| **strive to do sth** *The film studio is striving to improve its public image.* 該電影製片廠正在努力改善其公眾形象。

strobe light /ˈstrob ˌlaɪt; ˈstrəʊb ˌlaɪt/ also 又作 **strobe** *n* [C] a light that flashes on and off very quickly, often used in places where you can dance〔常用於跳舞場所的〕頻閃閃光燈

strode /strod; strəʊd/ the past tense of STRIDE

stroke[1] /strok; strəʊk/ *n* [C] 3

1 ►ILLNESS 疾病◄ an occasion when a blood tube in your brain suddenly bursts or is blocked 卒中, 腦卒中; 中風: *He was paralyzed by a severe stroke.* 他因嚴重中風而癱瘓。| **have/suffer a stroke** *I'm afraid your aunt has had a slight stroke.* 你姑姑怕是患了輕度中風。

2 ►SWIMMING/ROWING 游泳/划船◄ **a)** one of a set of movements in swimming or rowing in which you move your arms or the OAR forward and then back repeatedly〔游泳或划船的〕一次划水: *She swam with strong steady strokes.* 她平穩地用力划水游泳。**b)** a style of swimming or rowing〔游泳的〕游法;〔划船的〕划法: *the back stroke* 仰泳 **c)** the person who sets the speed at which everyone in the boat rows〔指揮划槳速度的〕尾槳手, 領槳手

3 a) at a/one stroke with a single sudden action 一舉, 一下子: *Brian saw a chance of solving all his problems at one stroke.* 布萊恩找到一個可以一下子解決所有問題的機會。**b) a bold stroke** something that someone does to achieve something that seems very brave 勇敢的行動

4 ►A HIT 擊, 打◄ an action in which you hit someone with something such as a whip or thin stick 一擊, 一抽: *He cried out at each stroke of the whip.* 鞭子每抽一下, 他都叫出聲來。

5 on the stroke of seven/nine etc at exactly seven o'clock etc 在七點正/九點正等: *She arrived punctually on the stroke of five.* 她在五點正準時到達。

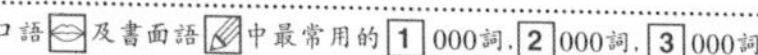

6 ▶CLOCK/BELL 時鐘/鈴◀ a single sound made by a clock giving the hours, or by a bell, GONG etc〔時鐘、鈴等報時的〕一次鳴響, 敲擊聲: *Maria appeared on the final stroke of the dinner gong.* 瑪麗亞在晚飯鈴敲最後一響時出現了。

7 a stroke of luck/fortune something lucky that happens to you unexpectedly 一樁意外的幸事/運氣: *By an amazing stroke of luck, I ran into her that very evening.* 非常幸運的是, 我就在那天晚上碰到了她。

8 a stroke of lightning a bright flash of lightning, especially one that hits something〔尤指擊中某物的〕閃電的一擊

9 a stroke of genius/inspiration etc a very good idea about what to do to solve a problem 聰明之舉/絕妙的主意等: *It was a stroke of genius to make her the party chairman.* 讓她做黨的主席實在是個聰明之舉。

10 ▶SPORT 體育運動◀ a hitting of the ball in games such as tennis, golf and cricket〔網球、高爾夫球、板球等的〕擊球; 一擊, 一抽: *learn to play the basic backhand strokes* 學打基本的反手擊球

11 ▶A MOVEMENT OF YOUR HAND 手的動作◀ a gentle movement of your hand over something 輕撫, 撫摸: **give sth a stroke** *She gave the dog a stroke.* 她撫摸了一下那隻狗。

12 ▶PEN/BRUSH 鋼筆/毛筆◀ **a)** a single movement of a pen or brush when you are writing or painting〔鋼筆或毛筆的〕一揮, 揮筆動作: *Max made a few quick decisive strokes with his brush.* 馬克斯用畫筆迅速、果斷地畫了幾筆。**b)** a line made by doing this 一筆, 一畫; 筆劃: *the thick downward strokes of the characters* 字體中那些向下的粗筆畫

13 with/at a stroke of the pen if you do something with a stroke of the pen, you do it by signing a piece of paper 大筆一揮〔簽字〕: *You cannot wipe out a thousand years of history at the stroke of a pen.* 你不能把一千年的歷史一筆勾掉。

14 not do a stroke (of work) *informal* to not do any work at all【非正式】甚麼〔工作〕也不做

15 put sb off their stroke *informal* to make someone stop giving all their attention to what they are doing【非正式】使某人分心: *Seeing Frank watching me put me off my stroke.* 發現弗蘭克在看我, 我無法專心。

16 ▶IN NUMBERS 在數字中◀ *BrE* used when you are saying a number written with the mark (/) in it【英】斜線〔號〕: *The serial number is seventeen stroke one.* (=17/1) 編號是 17/1。

stroke² *v* [T] **1** to move your hand gently over something 輕撫, 撫摸: *He reached out and stroked her cheek tenderly.* 他伸手輕柔地撫摸她的臉頰。—see picture on page A21 參見 A21 頁圖 **2** [always+adv/prep] to move something somewhere with gentle movements of your hand 用手輕輕地移動〔某物〕

stroll /strol; strəʊl/ *v* [I] to walk somewhere in a slow relaxed way 散步, 漫步, 閒逛, 溜達: **[+along/across/around]** *We strolled around the park for an hour or so.* 我們繞着公園閒逛了一個小時左右。—**stroll** *n* [C] —see picture on page A24 參見 A24 頁圖

stroll·er /ˈstrolɚ; ˈstrəʊlə/ *n* [C] *AmE* a small chair on wheels in which a small child sits and is pushed along【美】〔手推〕輕便嬰兒車; PUSHCHAIR *BrE*【英】—see picture at 參見 PRAM 圖

stroll·ing /ˈstrolɪŋ; ˈstrəʊlɪŋ/ *adj* [only before noun 僅用於名詞前] a strolling entertainer travels around the country giving informal performances on the way〔藝人〕巡迴的, 流浪的

strong /strɔŋ; strɒŋ/ *adj*

1 ▶PHYSICAL STRENGTH 體力◀ having a lot of physical power so that, for example, you can lift heavy things 強健的, 健壯的, 力氣大的: *He was a very strong man.* 他是個很強壯的人。| *her strong hands* 她那強有力的雙手

2 ▶THINGS 事物◀ not easily broken or destroyed 堅固的, 結實的, 不易損壞的: *a tall, strong tree* 一棵高而茁壯的樹 | *a pair of strong scissors* 一把結實的剪刀

3 ▶ABLE TO DEAL WITH DIFFICULTY 能夠對付困難◀ determined and able to deal with a difficult or upsetting situation〔處理困境時〕堅強的, 堅定的: *I wasn't sure whether I was strong enough to go to the funeral.* 我不知道我是否堅強得能去參加那個葬禮。| *My grandmother was a strong woman.* 我祖母是位堅強的女性。

4 ▶POWER 權力◀ having a lot of power or influence 強大的, 強有力的, 影響力大的: *Margaret Thatcher was certainly a strong leader.* 瑪格麗特·戴卓爾無疑是位強有力的領袖。| *a strong navy* 強大的海軍

5 ▶HEALTHY 健康的◀ healthy, especially after you have been ill〔尤指病後〕健康的, 強健的: *I don't think her heart is very strong.* 我認為她的心臟不太健康。| **have a strong constitution** (=be healthy and not easily become ill) 體質強壯; 健壯

6 ▶FEELINGS/OPINIONS 感情/觀點◀ strong emotions, opinions, beliefs etc are ones that you feel or believe a lot and are very serious about〔感情、觀點、信仰等〕強烈的, 堅定的, 不會動搖的: *The subject of abortion always arouses strong emotions.* 墮胎問題總會激起強烈的情緒。| *Harris has received strong support from her colleagues.* 哈里斯得到了同事們堅定的支持。| **strong sense of sth** *He has always had a strong sense of duty.* 他總是有強烈的責任感。

7 ▶AFFECT/INFLUENCE 影響◀ a strong desire, influence etc affects you very much〔慾望、影響等〕強烈的, 深刻的: *I was overcome by a strong desire to speak to her.* 我很想跟她講話, 不能自持。| *The temptation is very strong.* 那種誘惑力很強。

8 ▶RELATIONSHIP 關係◀ a strong relationship, friendship etc is very loyal and likely to last a long time〔關係、友情等〕忠誠的; 牢固的; 持久的: *There is a very strong bond between the two of us.* 我們兩人的關係非常牢固。| *He has strong links with the drugs trade.* 他與毒品貿易關係密切。

9 ▶ARGUMENT/REASON ETC 論據/理由等◀ a set of reasons that are likely to persuade other people that something is true or the correct thing to do 強有力的, 有說服力的: *There is strong evidence to support Evan's discrimination claim.* 埃文說有歧視, 他這樣說是有確鑿證據的。

10 ▶LIKELY 可能的◀ likely to succeed or happen〔成功或發生〕可能性大的: *She's a strong candidate for the party leadership.* 她是該黨領袖的有力候選人。| **strong possibility/probability/chance** *I think there's a strong possibility that the Cowboys will win.* 我認為牛仔隊獲勝的可能性極大。

11 ▶GROUP OF PEOPLE 小組, 團隊◀ a strong team or other group of people is very good at doing something 強有力的; 善於…的: *A strong cast was led by Leo McKern.* 強大的演員陣容由利奧·麥克恩率領。| *Germany has one of the strongest teams in the tournament.* 德國隊是錦標賽中最強的隊伍之一。

12 ▶GOOD AT 擅長…的◀ something that someone is strong on is the thing that they do well 擅長的: *Offence is where she's strong – her defensive play isn't good.* 她擅長進攻, 不善於防守。| **be sb's strong point/suit** *Tact never was my strong point.* 我一向不夠老練。| **be strong on** (=be good at doing something) 擅長做… *My family has always been strong on science.* 我們家的人一向在理科方面比較強。| **strong subject** (=something you are studying that you are good at) 擅長的學科 *French was always my strong subject.* 法語一直是我擅長的學科。

13 be in a strong position to be in a situation where you have power over other people or are likely to get what you want 處於優勢地位: *The party has never been more popular and is in a strong position to win the election.* 該黨從來沒有如此受歡迎, 很可能在大選中取勝。

14 ▶FOOD/DRINK 食物/飲料◀ having a lot of taste or

a lot of the substance that gives something its effect 強烈的; 味道濃的; 烈性的: *strong coffee* 濃咖啡 | *a strong curry* 很辣的咖喱 | **strong drink** (=alcoholic drinks) 烈性酒 *He hasn't touched strong drink for years.* 他很多年沒喝過烈性酒了。
15 ►TASTE/SMELL 味道/氣味◄ having a taste etc that you notice easily〔氣味〕強烈的; 味道重的: *This cheese has a very strong flavour.* 這乳酪味道很重。| *a strong smell of bonfires* 濃濃的篝火味
16 ►LIGHT/COLOUR 光/顏色◄ bright and easy to see 強烈的; 深的; 鮮明的: *The light was not very strong.* 光線不是很強。
17 strong wind/current/tide a wind etc that moves with great force 強風/急流/洶湧的潮水: *strong spring tides* 洶湧的春潮
18 strong language speech or writing that contains a lot of swearing 激烈的語言, 罵人的話: *This film is not suitable for children under 12 as it contains strong language.* 這部電影裡有髒話, 不適合 12 歲以下的兒童觀看。
19 strong accent the way that someone pronounces words that shows clearly that they come from a particular area or country 濃重的口音: *a strong German accent* 濃重的德國口音
20 strong nose/chin/features a nose etc that is large and noticeable, especially in an attractive way 好看的高鼻梁/好看的突下巴/輪廓分明的容貌: *She has the same strong features as her mother.* 她有跟她媽媽一樣輪廓分明的動人容貌。
21 a strong pound/dollar/mark etc a CURRENCY (=the type of money used in a country) that does not easily lose its value compared with other currencies 堅挺的英鎊/美元/馬克等
22 600/10,000 etc strong [only after number 僅用於數字後] used to give the number of people in a crowd or organization 人數達 600/10,000 等: *the 70,000 strong South African Domestic Workers Union* 有 70,000 名會員的南非國內工人協會
23 strong verb *technical* a verb that does not add a regular ending in the past tense, but may change a vowel 【術語】不規則變化的動詞
24 have a strong stomach to be able to watch something unpleasant without feeling sick or upset〔看到討厭的事情〕不感到噁心[煩惱]; 耐力強: *It's a very violent film. You'll need a strong stomach to sit through it.* 這部電影暴力鏡頭很多, 要把它看完你得耐得住才行。
25 be still going strong to continue to be active or successful, even after a long time〔長時間後〕仍然強壯; 繼續保持成功: *I'm glad to see that the printing classes are still going strong.* 我很高興地看到, 印刷課依舊很受落。
26 be a bit strong *especially BrE informal* to be too severe or extreme【尤英, 非正式】太嚴厲; 過分: *Describing him as 'evil' was a bit strong, I thought.* 我當時覺得, 說他"邪惡"有點過分了。—see also 另見 **come on strong** (COME¹) —**strongly** *adv*

strong-arm /ˈ· ·/ *adj* [only before noun 僅用於名詞前] *informal*【非正式】**strong-arm methods/tactics etc** methods etc that use force or violence, especially when this is not necessary〔尤指不必要的〕強制手段/策略等 —**strong-arm** *v* [T]

strong·box /ˈstrɔŋˌbɑks; ˈstrɒŋbɒks/ *n* [C] a box, usually made of metal, that can be locked and is used for keeping valuable things in 保險箱[櫃]

strong·hold /ˈstrɔŋˌhold; ˈstrɒŋhəʊld/ *n* [C] **1** an area where there is a lot of support for a particular way of life, political party etc〔某生活方式、政黨等〕備受支持的地方; 據點, 大本營: *The area is a Republican stronghold.* 該地區是共和黨的大本營。**2** *old-fashioned* a FORTRESS【過時】要塞, 堡壘

strong-mind·ed /ˌ· ˈ··◂/ *adj* not easily influenced by other people to change what you believe or want 意志堅強的, 果斷的, 堅定的: *You have to be pretty strong-minded to say "no" to him.* 你得很堅定才能對他說"不"。—**strong-mindedly** *adv* —**strong-mindedness** *n* [U]

strong room /ˈ· ·/ *n* [C] a special room in a bank, shop etc where valuable objects can be kept safely〔銀行、商店等貯藏貴重物品的〕保險庫

strong-willed /ˌ· ˈ·◂/ *adj* knowing exactly what you want to do and being determined to achieve it, even if other people advise you against it 意志堅強的, 堅決的

stron·ti·um /ˈstrɑnʃɪəm; ˈstrɒntiəm/ *n* [U] a soft metal that is one of the chemical elements (ELEMENT (1)) 鍶〔一種金屬元素〕

strop /strɑp; strɒp/ *n* [C] **1** a narrow piece of leather used for sharpening a RAZOR 磨剃刀用的皮帶, 革砥 **2 be in a strop** *BrE informal* to be annoyed about something【英, 非正式】因某事而煩惱

strop·py /ˈstrɑpɪ; ˈstrɒpi/ *adj BrE informal* bad-tempered and easily offended or annoyed【英, 非正式】脾氣壞的, 易生氣的: *Aaron, we won't go anywhere if you're going to be stroppy!* 艾倫, 如果你要發脾氣的話, 我們就哪兒也不去了! —**stroppily** *adv* —**stroppiness** *n* [U]

strove /strov; strəʊv/ the past tense of STRIVE

struck /strʌk; strʌk/ the past tense of STRIKE

struc·tur·al /ˈstrʌktʃərəl; ˈstrʌktʃərəl/ *adj* connected with the structure of something 結構(上)的, 構造(上)的: *structural damage* 建築結構方面的破壞 | *structural changes in the economy* 經濟的結構性變化 —**structurally** *adv*

structural en·gi·neer /ˌ··· ··ˈ·/ *n* [C] an engineer skilled in planning the building of large structures such as bridges〔設計橋梁等大型建築的〕結構工程師 —**structural engineering** *n* [U]

struc·tur·al·is·m /ˈstrʌktʃərəlɪzm̩; ˈstrʌktʃərəlɪzəm/ *n* [U] a method of studying language, literature, society etc in which you examine the different parts or ideas in a subject to find a common pattern 結構主義〔語言學、文學、社會學等學科採用的研究方法, 注重通過分析不同的部分或觀點以尋找共同的模式〕—**structuralist** *adj, n*

struc·ture¹ /ˈstrʌktʃɚ; ˈstrʌktʃə/ *n* S3 W2
1 ►PARTS FORMING A WHOLE 構成整體的部分◄ [U] the way in which the parts of something are connected with each other and form a whole 結構, 構造, 組織: *the structure of the brain* 大腦的結構 | *sentence structure* 句子結構
2 ►BUILDING/BRIDGE ETC 建築物/橋梁等◄ [C] a large building, bridge etc, especially one that has many parts〔尤指擁有多個部分的〕建築物, 結構物: *a six-storey concrete structure* 一座六層的混凝土建築物
3 ►PEOPLE/ORGANIZATIONS ETC 人/組織等◄ [C] the way in which relationships between people or groups are organized in a society or in an organization〔社會或組織中的〕關係結構, 體系: *the power structure of world politics* 世界政治的權力結構
4 ►ORGANIZED ACTIVITY 有組織的活動◄ [C,U] an activity that is carefully organized and planned 條理性的活動, 組織性的活動: *Children need some sort of structure to their day.* 兒童一天的生活需要有點條理性。—see also 另見 **career structure** (CAREER¹ (1))

structure² *v* [T] to arrange the different parts of something into a pattern or system in which each part is connected to the others 組織; 安排: *You need to structure your arguments more carefully.* 你需要更為仔細地組織好自己的論點。

stru·del /ˈstrudəl; ˈstru:dl/ *n* [C,U] a type of Austrian or German cake, made of PASTRY with fruit inside 果餡卷〔一種奧地利或德國糕點〕: *apple strudel* 蘋果餡卷

strug·gle¹ /ˈstrʌgl; ˈstrʌgəl/ *v* [I] **1** to try extremely hard to achieve something, even though it is very difficult and you have a lot of problems 奮鬥, 拼搏, 作出極大的努力: **struggle to do sth** *She's struggling to bring up a family on a very low income.* 她靠着微薄的收入艱難地供養一個家庭。| **[+for]** *a young artist struggling for rec-*

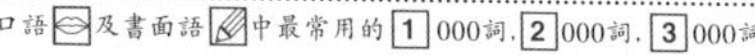

ognition 一位為獲得承認而奮鬥的青年藝術家 **2** to fight someone who is attacking you or holding you, especially so that you can escape〔尤指為逃脫而與他人〕搏鬥; 掙扎: **[+with]** *Liz struggled fiercely with her attacker.* 莉茲同攻擊她的人進行激烈的搏鬥。**3** if two people struggle, they fight each other for something, especially something one of them is holding 爭鬥, 爭搶: *They struggled briefly, then Ray grabbed the bag and ran.* 他們爭搶了一會, 後來雷抓住那個袋子跑了。**4** to move somewhere with great difficulty 艱難地〔向某處〕行進: **[+towards/into etc]** *Kim struggled out of the wreckage, her head bleeding badly.* 金艱難地從殘骸中爬了出來, 頭上血流不止。

struggle on *phr v* [I] to continue doing something that you find difficult, tiring etc 掙扎着堅持下去: *We've lost two of our best players, but we're struggling on.* 我們失去了兩名最好的運動員, 但我們仍努力堅持下去。

3 **struggle²** *n* [C] **1** a long hard fight to get freedom, political rights etc〔為爭取自由、政治權利等而進行的〕鬥爭, 奮鬥: *the nation's struggle for independence* 該國爭取獨立的鬥爭 | **power struggle** (=a fight to get power in a country or organization) 權力鬥爭 **2** a fight between two people for something, especially something one of them is holding 爭鬥, 爭搶: *After a short struggle I got the knife off him.* 經過短暫的搏鬥, 我從他手裡奪過了刀子。**3** an attempt to fight or escape from someone who is attacking you or holding on to you 搏鬥; 掙扎: *Police examined the body but found no signs of a struggle.* 警察檢查了屍體, 但沒有發現搏鬥的痕跡。**4 be a struggle** if an activity, job etc is a struggle for someone, they find it very difficult to do 是困難[費勁]的事: **[+for]** *Reading is a struggle for Tim.* 閱讀對蒂姆來説是件費勁的事。

strum /strʌm; strʌm/ *v* **strummed, strumming** [I,T] to play an instrument such as a GUITAR by moving your fingers up and down across its strings 彈奏, 撥弄〔結他等弦樂器〕

strum·pet /ˈstrʌmpɪt; ˈstrʌmpɪ̣t/ *n* [C] *old use* an insulting word meaning a woman who has sex for money【舊】妓女, 婊子

strung /strʌŋ; strʌŋ/ the past tense and past participle of STRING²

strung-out /,· ˈ·◂/ *adj* [not before noun 不用於名詞前] *informal*【非正式】**1** if you are strung-out on a drug, that drug is affecting you a lot, so that you cannot react normally 有吸毒癮的: **[+on]** *strung-out on heroin* 吸海洛因成癮的 **2** extremely tired and worried 精疲力竭的; 極其焦慮的

strung-up /,· ˈ·◂/ *adj BrE informal* very nervous, worried, or excited【英, 非正式】極其緊張[焦慮; 興奮]的

strut¹ /strʌt; strʌt/ *v* **strutted, strutting** [I] **1** to walk proudly with your head high and your chest pushed forwards, showing that you think you are important 趾高氣揚地走, 架子十足地走: **[+about/across etc]** *Ryan was strutting around the office, issuing orders.* 瑞安在辦公室裡趾高氣揚地走來走去, 發號施令。**2 strut your stuff** *informal* to show your skill at doing something【非正式】炫耀自己的本領: *Look at Dave strutting his stuff on the dance floor.* 看, 戴夫正在舞池裡大顯身手。

strut² *n* **1** [C] a long thin piece of metal or wood used to support a part of a building, the wing of an aircraft etc 支柱, 撐桿, 支桿 **2** [singular] a proud way of walking, with your head high and your chest pushed forwards 趾高氣揚的步態, 昂首闊步的樣子

strych·nine /ˈstrɪknin; ˈstrɪkniːn/ *n* [U] a very poisonous substance sometimes used in small amounts as a medicine 士的寧, 馬錢子鹼〔有毒, 微量可作藥用〕

stub¹ /stʌb; stʌb/ *n* [C] **1** the short part that is left when the rest of something long and thin, such as a cigarette or pencil, has been used 殘頭, 殘根; 煙蒂; 鉛筆頭 **2** the part of a ticket that is returned to you after it has been torn, as proof that you have paid 票根, 存根 **3** a piece of a cheque left in a cheque book as a record after the main part has been torn out 支票的存根

stub² *v* [T] **stub your toe** to hurt your toe by hitting it against something 使腳趾碰到〔某物〕

stub sth ↔ **out** *phr v* [T] to stop a cigarette burning by pressing the end of it against something 把〔香煙〕捻滅 —see picture at 參見 PUT 圖

stub·ble /ˈstʌbḷ; ˈstʌbəl/ *n* [U] **1** short stiff hairs that grow on a man's face if he does not SHAVE¹ (1) 鬍子茬, 鬚茬, 短鬚: **designer stubble** (=stubble that a man has to look fashionable) 時髦的短鬚 **2** short stiff pieces left in the fields after wheat, corn etc has been cut〔作物收割後遺留在地裡的〕殘莖, 茬(子) **—stubbly** *adj*

stub·born /ˈstʌbɚn; ˈstʌbən/ *adj* **1** determined not to change your mind, even when people think you are being unreasonable 固執的, 頑固的, 執拗的; 倔強的: **a stubborn streak** (=a stubborn part of your character) 個性中固執的傾向 *I knew you'd be too stubborn to listen!* 我早就知道你太固執, 不會聽的! | **stubborn as a mule** (=very stubborn) 非常執拗[固執] **2 stubborn opposition/persistence etc** very strong and determined opposition etc 頑強的抵抗/堅持不懈等: *The Broncos provided stubborn opposition throughout the whole game.* 在整場比賽中野馬隊進行了頑強的抵抗。**3** difficult to remove, deal with, or use 難以去除[對付; 使用]的: *stubborn stains* 很難洗掉的污漬 **—stubbornly** *adv* **—stubbornness** *n* [U]

stub·by /ˈstʌbɪ; ˈstʌbi/ *adj* short and thick or fat 短粗的, 矮胖的: *stubby little fingers* 短粗的小手指

stuc·co /ˈstʌko; ˈstʌkəʊ/ *n* [U] a type of PLASTER¹ (1) surface on the outside walls of buildings〔塗外牆用的〕灰泥

stuck¹ /stʌk; stʌk/ the past tense and past participle of STICK¹

stuck² *adj* [not before noun 不用於名詞前]

1 ▶FIXED 固定的◀ fixed in a particular position and impossible to move 卡住的, 無法移動的, 動不了的: *Sheila tried to open the window but it was stuck.* 希拉試圖打開窗戶, 可窗戶卡住了。| **get stuck** *The bus got stuck in the snow and we had to walk the rest of the way.* 公共汽車陷在雪中開不動了, 剩下的路我們只好步行了。| **get sth stuck** *Tommy got his head stuck between the railings.* 湯美的頭卡在欄杆之間動不了。

2 ▶DIFFICULTY 困難◀ unable to do any more of something that you are working on because it is too difficult 被難倒的, 困住的; 沒法進行下去的: *Can you help me with my homework Dad? I'm stuck.* 爸爸, 你能幫我做作業嗎? 我給難倒了。

3 ▶SITUATION 處境◀ unable to escape from an unpleasant or boring situation 無法擺脱困境的: **[+in/at]** *I wouldn't be able to stand being stuck in an office all day.* 我無法忍受整天被困在辦公室裡。| **[+with]** *I was stuck with my aunt all afternoon.* 我整個下午都被我姑姑纏住了。

4 be stuck with sth to have something you do not want because you cannot get rid of it 不得不接受某事物; 無法擺脱某事物: *We're renting the house, so we're stuck with this ugly wallpaper.* 我們將租用這房子, 所以不得不接受這難看的牆紙。

5 be stuck on sb *informal* to be attracted to someone【非正式】非常喜歡某人, 被某人吸引: *Jane's really stuck on the new boy in her class.* 簡真的很喜歡她班裡新來的那個男孩。

6 get stuck in *BrE spoken* to start doing something eagerly and with a lot of energy【英口】積極地開始做某事, 急切地做…: *Let's get stuck in and see if we can finish this by lunchtime.* 我們快開始幹吧, 看午飯前能否把這事做完。

stuck³ *n* [U] **be in stuck** *BrE informal* to be in trouble【英, 非正式】陷入麻煩

stuck-up /,· ˈ·◂/ *adj informal* proud and unfriendly because you think you are better and more important than other people【非正式】傲慢的, 自以為了不起的: *a stuck-up officious little man* 一個自命不凡、愛管閒事的小男人

stud 鞋底防滑凸起物

stud *BrE*【英】/ cleat *AmE*【美】防滑釘

spike 鞋釘

stud[1] /stʌd; stʌd/ *n*
1 ▶ON SHOES 在鞋上◀ [C] one of a set of small pointed pieces of metal or plastic that are fixed onto the bottom of a running shoe, football boot etc to stop you from slipping〔跑鞋、足球鞋等的〕鞋底防滑凸起物;〔鞋底的〕防滑釘
2 ▶IN YOUR EAR 在耳朵上◀ [C] a small, round EARRING 圓形小耳環, 螺栓式耳環, 耳釘 —see picture at 參見 JEWELLERY 圖
3 ▶DECORATION 裝飾◀ [C] a round piece of metal that is stuck into a surface for decoration 飾釘, 大頭釘: *a leather jacket with studs around the collar and cuffs* 領子和袖口有飾釘的皮夾克
4 ▶FOR A SHIRT 供襯衫用◀ [C] a small thing for fastening a shirt or collar that consists of two round, flat pieces of metal joined together by a bar 領扣, 飾鈕 —see also 另見 PRESS-STUD
5 ▶ANIMAL 動物◀ [C,U] animals such as horses that are kept for breeding 種畜; 種馬: *a stud farm* 種馬飼養場 | **put an animal out to stud** (=use the animal for breeding) 為配種而飼養某動物
6 ▶MAN 男人◀ [C] *informal* an insulting word for a man who has a lot of sexual partners and who is very proud of his sexual ability【非正式】為自己的性能力驕傲的男子, 亂搞性關係的男人〔侮辱性用語〕
7 ▶BOARD 木板◀ [C] *AmE* the kind of board that is used to make the frame of a house【美】板牆筋, 壁骨; 立柱

stud[2] *v* [T usually passive 一般用被動態] *literary* to cover a surface or area with many small things【文】覆蓋, 散佈於: *field studded with daisies* 雛菊遍地的田野

stud·book /ˈstʌdˌbʊk; ˈstʌdbʊk/ *n* [C] a list of names of race horses from which other race horses have been bred 賽馬血統記錄簿; 馬種系譜

stud·ded /ˈstʌdɪd; ˈstʌdɨd/ *adj* decorated with a lot of studs or small jewels etc 鑲滿飾鈕[寶石]的: *a studded leather belt* 鑲滿飾釘的皮帶

stu·dent /ˈstudn̩t; ˈstjuːdənt/ *n* [C] **1** someone who is studying at a school, university etc 學生, 學員: *a first year student at the University of Oslo* 奧斯陸大學一年級的學生 | **law/medical/engineering etc student** *A lot of art students live in this dorm.* 許多學藝術的學生住在這個宿舍。| **student teacher/nurse** (=someone who is learning to be a teacher or nurse) 實習教師/護士 | **A/B/C etc student** *AmE* (=someone who always earns A's etc for their work)【美】學業成績總是得 A/B/C 等的學生 —see also 另見 MATURE STUDENT **2 be a student of sth** to be very interested in a particular subject 對某學科非常感興趣: *Myles was a profound student of human nature.* 邁爾斯對研究人性非常感興趣。

student bod·y /ˌ.. ˈ../ *n* [C] *AmE* all of the students in a HIGH SCHOOL, college, or university, considered as a group【美】〔一所中學或大學的〕全體學生

student gov·ern·ment /ˌ.. ˈ.../ also 又作 **student council** /ˌ.. ˈ../ *n* [C] *AmE* an elected group of students in a HIGH SCHOOL, college, or university who represent the students in meetings and who organize school activities【美】學生自治會〔指中學或大學裡推選出來代表學生參加會議並組織學校活動的學生團體〕

student loan /ˌ.. ˈ./ *n* [C] a method of paying for your education in which students at a college or university borrow money from a bank or the government and repay it when they start working 學生貸款

students' u·nion /ˌ.. ˈ../ also 又作 **student union** *n* [C] **1** a building where students go to meet socially 學生活動大樓 **2** *BrE* an association of students in a particular college or university【英】〔大專院校的〕學生會

student teach·ing /ˌ.. ˈ../ *n* [U] *AmE* the period of time during which students who are learning to be teachers practise teaching in a school【美】教學實習; TEACHING PRACTICE *BrE*【英】

stud·ied /ˈstʌdɪd; ˈstʌdid/ *adj* a studied way of behaving is deliberate and often insincere because you have planned your behaviour carefully 經過深思熟慮的; 有意的; 裝模作樣的: *She spoke with studied politeness.* 她故作有禮地說話。

stu·di·o /ˈstudɪˌo; ˈstjuːdiəʊ/ *n* [C] 3
1 ▶FOR TELEVISION/RECORDS 供電視/錄音用◀ a room where television and radio programmes are made and broadcast or where music is recorded 錄音室, 播音室, 演播室: *a TV studio* 電視錄製室
2 ▶FILMS 電影◀ also 又作 **studios** a film company or the buildings it owns and uses to make its films 電影製片公司, 電影製片廠: *Depardieu is making a film with one of the big Hollywood studios.* 迪柏度正與荷里活的一家大製片公司合作拍攝一部電影。
3 ▶FOR PAINTING/PHOTOGRAPHY 供繪畫/攝影用◀ **a)** a room where a painter or photographer regularly works〔畫家、攝影師的〕工作室 **b)** a company that produces pictures or photographs 畫室; 照相館, 攝影室
4 ▶FOR DANCING 供舞蹈用◀ a room where dancing lessons are given or that dancers use to practise in 舞蹈練習廳
5 ▶APARTMENT 公寓◀ also 又作 **studio apartment** *AmE*【美】, **studio flat** *BrE*【英】a small apartment with one main room 單室公寓房

studio au·di·ence /ˌ... ˈ.../ *n* [C] a group of people who watch and are sometimes involved in a radio or television programme while it is being made〔廣播或電視節目的〕現場觀眾

stu·di·ous /ˈstudɪəs; ˈstjuːdiəs/ *adj* **1** spending a lot of time studying and reading 好學的, 勤奮的, 用功的: *a quiet studious young man* 文靜好學的年輕人 **2** careful in your work〔工作〕認真的, 仔細的, 小心的: *studious attention to detail* 認真注意細節 —**studiously** *adv* —**studiousness** *n* [U]

stud·y[1] /ˈstʌdɪ; ˈstʌdi/ *n* 3 2
1 ▶PIECE OF WORK 一項工作◀ [C] a piece of work that is done to find out more about a particular subject or problem, and usually includes a written report〔對某一課題或問題的〕研究: **[+of/into]** *We're doing a study into how much time people spend watching television.* 我們正在進行一項研究, 調查人們看電視所花的時間。| *a study of Australian wild birds* 一項對澳大利亞野生鳥類的研究 | **make/carry out/conduct a study** *a study of children's eating habits carried out in 1976* 1976 年對兒童飲食習慣進行的研究
2 ▶ROOM 房間◀ [C] a room in a house that is used for work or study 書房, 書齋
3 ▶SCHOOL WORK 功課◀ [U] the activity of studying 學習; 讀書: *Set aside a period of time specifically for study.* 專門留出一段時間來學習。
4 studies [plural] subjects that people study, especially several related subjects〔尤指幾個相關專業的〕學科; 學業: *the Department of Russian Studies* 俄語系

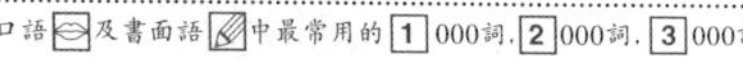

5 ▶**ART** 藝術◀ [C] a small detailed drawing, especially one that is done to prepare for a large painting〔繪畫的〕試畫, 習作: *Renoir's studies of small plants and flowers* 雷諾阿的小植物和花卉試畫
6 ▶**MUSIC** 音樂◀ [C] a piece of music, usually for piano, that is often intended for practice〔尤指鋼琴的〕練習曲
7 **be a study in sth** to be a perfect example of something 是…的最佳例子, 是…的典型: *His face was a study in incredulity.* 他的臉上完全是難以置信的神色。
8 **be in a brown study** *old-fashioned* to be thinking deeply about something【過時】在沉思中, 正在默想

study² *v* **studied, studying 1** [I,T] to spend time reading, going to classes etc in order to learn about a subject 學習, 攻讀: *I've been studying English for 6 years.* 我學英語已有6年了。| *I can't study with that music playing all the time.* 那音樂老在播放, 我無法學習。| **study to be a doctor/lawyer etc** *My brother's studying to be an accountant.* 我弟弟在讀會計。| **study for an exam/diploma etc** *I've only got three weeks left to study for my exams.* 我只剩下三個星期的學習時間為考試做準備。| **study under sb** (=be trained by a famous teacher) 師從某人, 跟某名師學習 *a psychologist who studied under Jung in Zurich* 曾在蘇黎世師從榮格的心理學家 —see 見 KNOW[1] (USAGE) **2** [T] to watch and examine something carefully over a period of time in order to find out more about it 仔細端詳, 仔細察看; 研究: *Goodall was studying the behavior of gorillas in the wild.* 古多爾在仔細觀察處於野生狀態的大猩猩的行為。| **study how/why/when etc** *studying how stress affects body chemistry* 研究壓力如何影響人體的化學反應 **3** [T] to spend a lot of time carefully examining a plan, document, problem etc 仔細研究〔計劃、文件、問題等〕: *I haven't had time to study the proposals yet.* 我還沒有時間去仔細研究那些提議。

study hall /'·· ·/ *n* [U] *AmE* a period of time during a school day in which a student does not have a class and usually goes somewhere to study【美】〔學校的〕自習時間, 自修(課)

stuff¹ /stʌf; stʌf/ *n* [U]
1 ▶**SUBSTANCE** 物質◀ *informal* a kind of substance or material【非正式】材料, 東西: *What's that stuff you're drinking?* 你喝的那是甚麼東西? | *The dress was made of silky stuff.* 那件衣服是用絲綢料子做的。
2 ▶**THINGS** 事物◀ *informal* a number of different things【非正式】幾種不同的物品, 東西: *How do you think you're going to fit all that stuff into a car?* 你認為怎樣才能把那些東西都裝進汽車裡呢?
3 ▶**SUBJECT** 話題◀ *informal* the subject of something such as a book, television programme, lesson etc【非正式】〔書、電視節目、課程等的〕題材, 話題: *What kind of stuff do you like to read?* 你喜歡讀哪一類的題材?
4 ▶**ACTIVITIES** 活動◀ all the activities that someone does〔某人從事的〕活動, 事情: *I've got so much stuff to do this weekend.* 我這個週末有很多事情要做。
5 **sb's stuff** *informal* things that belong to someone【非正式】某人的物品, 某人的所有物: *I'm leaving in an hour and I still haven't packed my stuff.* 我一小時後就要出發, 可我還沒有收拾東西呢。
6 ▶**EQUIPMENT** 設備◀ *informal* the equipment you need for a particular activity【非正式】做某事所需的東西: *Where's the camping stuff?* 野營用的東西在哪兒?
7 **the stuff of dreams/life/politics** exactly the kind of thing that dreams etc consist of 夢/生活/政治的內容: *an enchanting place – the very stuff of dreams* 一個迷人的地方 — 正如夢中所見的那樣
8 ▶**CHARACTER** 性格◀ the qualities of someone's character〔某人的〕本質, 品質: **the right stuff** (=qualities that make you able to deal with difficulties) 對付困難的能力 | **be made of sterner stuff** (=be more determined) 性格更加堅強 *I thought you were made of sterner stuff – don't just give up.* 我原以為你是個性格更堅強的人 — 別就這樣放棄了。
9 **do/show your stuff** to do what you are good at when everyone wants you to do it 拿出自己的本領, 顯身手: *Come on Gina, get on the dance floor and do your stuff!* 來吧, 吉娜, 到舞池裡一顯身手!
10 **that's the stuff!** *spoken* used to express approval of what someone is doing or saying【口】這就對啦! 好呀!〔用於對某人所做或所說的事情表示贊同〕
11 **stuff and nonsense** *spoken* used to say that you think something is stupid or untrue【口】胡說八道, 廢話 —see also 另見 **a bit of stuff** (BIT[1] (19)), **be hot stuff** (HOT[1] (18)), **kid's stuff** (KID[1] (4)), **know your stuff** (KNOW[1] (13)), **strut your stuff** (STRUT[1] (2))

stuff² *v* [T]
1 ▶**PUSH** 推◀ [always+adv/prep] to push something soft into a small space in a careless hurried way 填, 塞: **stuff sth into/in/up** *She stuffed two more sweaters into her bag.* 她又往袋子裡塞了兩件毛線衫。| **be stuffed with** *a huge picnic basket stuffed with delicacies* 塞滿美食的野餐大籃子 | **stuffed full of** *a briefcase stuffed full of papers* 裝滿文件的公文包
2 ▶**FILL** 裝滿◀ to fill something tightly with soft material, so that it becomes firm 填滿, 裝滿: *a pillow stuffed with feathers* 塞滿羽毛的枕頭
3 ▶**FOOD** 食物◀ to fill a chicken or another type of food, such as a TOMATO, with a mixture of bread, rice etc 給〔雞、番茄等〕填餡, 填料於〔食物〕
4 ▶**DEAD ANIMAL** 死的動物◀ to fill the skin of a dead animal in order to make the animal look real 填塞〔死動物〕的皮以做標本: *a stuffed parrot* 製成標本的鸚鵡
5 **stuff yourself** also 又作 **stuff your face** *informal* to eat so much food that you cannot eat anything else【非正式】吃飽, 吃足: **[+with]** *The kids have been stuffing themselves with candy.* 孩子們一直在吃糖果, 都吃飽了。
6 **get stuffed** *spoken* used to tell someone very rudely and angrily that you do not want to talk to them or accept their offer【口】走開, 不要煩了, 去你的吧〔以非常粗魯和生氣的語氣表示不想與某人交談或拒絕接受某人的提議〕: *He only offered me £10 for it, so I told him to get stuffed.* 他只出10英鎊想買下它, 所以我就叫他滾開。
7 **you/they can stuff sth** *spoken* used to say very angrily or rudely that you do not want what someone is offering【口】見你的鬼去吧〔非常氣憤或粗魯地表示不接受某人的提議〕: *Yeah? Well you can stuff your damn contract!* 是嗎? 那你就和你那該死的合同一起見鬼去吧!
8 ▶**GAME** 比賽◀ to defeat an opposing team easily 輕易擊敗〔對手〕: *We stuffed them, 15-2, 15-4, 15-3.* 我們以15比2, 15比4, 15比3輕取對手。

stuffed /stʌft; stʌft/ *adj* completely full, so that you cannot eat any more 吃飽了的: *No, no dessert, I'm stuffed.* 不, 不要甜點了, 我吃飽了。

stuffed an·i·mal /,· '···/ *n* [C] *AmE* a toy animal covered and filled with soft material【美】〔填充鬆軟材料的〕動物玩具; SOFT TOY *BrE*【英】

stuffed shirt /,· '·/ *n* [C] someone who behaves in a very formal way and thinks that they are important 神氣十足的人, 妄自尊大的人

stuffed-up /,· '·◂/ *adj* unable to breathe properly through your nose because you have a cold 鼻塞的, 〔因感冒鼻塞而〕無法正常呼吸的

stuff·ing /'stʌfɪŋ; 'stʌfɪŋ/ *n* [U] **1** a mixture of bread, onion, egg and HERBS that you put inside meat before cooking it 填在肉食中的餡; 〔肉食中的〕填料; DRESSING (2) *AmE*【美】: *sage and onion stuffing* 洋蘇葉和洋蔥填料 **2** soft material that is used to fill something such as a CUSHION〔墊子等中的〕填料, 充填物 —see also 另見 **knock the stuffing out of** (KNOCK[1] (10))

stuff·y /'stʌfɪ; 'stʌfi/ *adj* **1** a room or building that is stuffy does not have enough fresh air in it〔房間或建築物〕通風不好的, 空氣不新鮮的, 悶的: *It's getting stuffy in here – do you mind if I open the window?* 這裡有點兒

悶熱, 我打開窗戶行嗎? **2** someone who is stuffy is too formal and has old-fashioned ideas〔指人〕一本正經的, 古板的, 拘謹的 —**stuffily** *adv* —**stuffiness** *n* [U]

stul·ti·fy·ing /ˈstʌltəˌfaɪ-ɪŋ; ˈstʌltɪ̇faɪ-ɪŋ/ *adj* so boring that you feel as though you are losing your ability to think 使人呆滯的; 使人厭倦[遲鈍]的: *a stultifying exercise* 枯燥刻板的練習 —**stultify** *v* [T] —**stultification** /ˌstʌltəfəˈkeʃən; ˌstʌltɪ̇fɪ̇ˈkeɪʃən/ *n* [U]

stum·ble /ˈstʌmbḷ; ˈstʌmbəl/ *v* [I] **1** to hit your foot against something or put your foot down awkwardly while you are walking or running, so that you almost fall 絆腳, 絆跌, 絆了一下: *In her hurry she stumbled and spilled the milk all over the floor.* 匆忙中她絆了一下, 把牛奶全灑到地上。| **[+over/on]** *Vic stumbled over the step as he came in.* 維克進來時在台階上絆了一下。**2** to walk unsteadily and often almost fall 蹣跚而行, 踉蹌: **[+in/out/across etc]** *I finished the whisky and then stumbled upstairs and into bed.* 我喝完威士忌, 然後踉蹌地爬上樓倒在牀上了。**3** to stop or make a mistake when you are reading to people or speaking〔朗讀或說話時〕打結巴; 說錯: **[+over/at/through]** *I hope I don't stumble over any of the long words.* 但願我說那些長字眼時不結結巴巴。**4 stumbling block** a problem or difficulty that prevents you from achieving something 阻礙成功的困難[難題], 障礙物, 絆腳石: **[+to]** *a territorial dispute which is the main stumbling block to a peace settlement* 成為達成和平協議主要障礙的領土糾紛 —**stumble** *n* [C]

stumble on/across sth *phr v* [T] to discover something or meet someone by chance and unexpectedly 偶然發現[碰見]: *Boyce was killed because he stumbled across something he shouldn't have seen.* 博伊斯因偶然看到自己不應看到的事而被殺害了。

stump¹ /stʌmp; stʌmp/ *n* [C]

1 ►TREE 樹◄ the bottom part of a tree that is left in the ground after the rest of it has been cut down; TREE STUMP〔樹被砍下後留下的〕樹樁, 樹墩

2 ►SOMETHING BROKEN 打破的東西◄ the small useless part of something that remains after most of it has broken off or worn away 殘餘部分; 殘段; 殘根: *the stump of a broken tooth* 壞牙的殘根

3 ►ARM/LEG 胳膊/腿◄ the short part of someone's leg, arm etc that remains after the rest of it has been cut off 殘肢

4 ►IN SPORT 在體育運動中◄ one of the three upright sticks in CRICKET (2) that you throw the ball at〔板球〕三柱門的任何一柱

5 stump speech *AmE* a speech made while travelling around to get political support【美】巡迴政治演說

stump² *v* **1** [T] to ask someone such a difficult question that they are completely unable to think of an answer 把〔某人〕難住, 難倒: *trying to stump the teacher* 企圖把老師難倒 | **be stumped** *Nobody knows – even the experts are stumped.* 誰也不知道——連專家都被難住了。| **get/have sb stumped** *This question'll have them all stumped.* 這個問題會把他們都難住的。**2 [I+up/along/across]** to walk with heavy steps; STOMP 邁着沉重的步子走; 跺着腳走 **3** [T] to put a BATSMAN out of the game in CRICKET (2) by touching the stumps with the ball when he is out of the hitting area〔板球〕以球觸三門柱而使〔跑分的擊球員〕出局 **4** [I,T] *AmE* to travel around an area, meeting people and making speeches in order to gain political support【美】作巡迴政治演說: *I'm too old to keep stumping around the state.* 我太老了, 不能繼續在州內到處作巡迴演說了。

stump up *phr v* [I,T] *BrE informal* to pay money, even if it is difficult【英, 非正式】〔勉強地〕支付〔錢〕: *That's ten quid you owe me. Come on, stump up.* 你欠我十英鎊, 快掏錢吧。

stump·y /ˈstʌmpɪ; ˈstʌmpi/ *adj BrE* stumpy legs, fingers etc are short and thick in an unattractive way; STUBBY【英】〔腿、手指等〕短粗的, 敦實的

stun /stʌn; stʌn/ *v* **stunned, stunning** [T not in progressive 不用進行式] **1** to surprise or upset someone so much that they do not react immediately 使大吃一驚, 使震驚: *Sacha was too stunned by what had happened to say anything.* 薩莎對發生的事情感到十分震驚, 一時說不出話來。| **stunned silence** (=silence because everyone is too surprised to speak) 瞠目結舌 **2** to make someone unconscious for a short time 使〔某人〕短暫失去知覺, 使暈過去: *Thank God that punch only stunned you!* 感謝上帝, 那一拳只是把你打昏了而已!

stung /stʌŋ; stʌŋ/ the past tense and past participle of STING¹

stun gun /ˈ· ·/ *n* [C] a weapon that produces a very strong electric current and can be used to make animals or people unconscious〔使被擊中者暈眩的〕電擊槍

stunk /stʌŋk; stʌŋk/ a past tense and the past participle of STINK¹

stun·ner /ˈstʌnɚ; ˈstʌnə/ *n* [C] *old-fashioned* someone or something that is very attractive, especially a woman【過時】極具吸引力的人[物]; 〔尤指〕極漂亮的女人

stun·ning /ˈstʌnɪŋ; ˈstʌnɪŋ/ *adj* **1** extremely attractive or beautiful 極具吸引力的, 極漂亮的: *You look absolutely stunning in that dress.* 你穿上那件衣服, 看上去非常迷人。| *a stunning view* 非常美麗的景色 **2** very surprising or shocking 令人驚奇的, 令人震驚的: *stunning news* 令人震驚的新聞 —**stunningly** *adv*

stunt¹ /stʌnt; stʌnt/ *n* [C] **1** a dangerous action that is done to entertain people, especially in a film〔尤指電影中的〕特技表演, 絕技: *Not many actors do their own stunts.* 很多演員並不親自表演特技動作。**2** something that is done to attract people's attention, especially in advertising or politics〔尤指廣告或政治中的〕噱頭, 引人注目的花招: **publicity stunt** *Todd flew over the city in a hot air balloon as a publicity stunt.* 托德乘坐熱氣球從城市上空飛過, 作為一種宣傳花招。**3 pull a stunt** to do something that is silly or that is slightly dangerous 做愚蠢[驚險]的事: *Next time you pull a stunt like that don't expect me to get you out of trouble.* 下次你要再做那樣的蠢事, 別指望我幫你解圍。

stunt² *v* [T] to stop something or someone from growing to their full size or developing properly 抑制, 阻礙…的成長[發育]: *Lack of sunlight will stunt the plant's growth.* 缺乏陽光會阻礙植物的生長。

stunt man /ˈ· ·/ *n* [C] a man who is employed to take the place of an actor when something dangerous has to be done in a film〔電影中受雇替代男演員做驚險動作的〕男替身演員

stunt wom·an /ˈ· ˌ··/ *n* [C] a woman who is employed to take the place of an actress when something dangerous has to be done in a film〔電影中受雇替代女演員做驚險動作的〕女替身演員

stu·pe·fied /ˈstupəˌfaɪd; ˈstjuːpɪ̇faɪd/ *adj* so surprised, tired, or bored that you cannot think clearly〔因吃驚、疲勞或厭倦而〕目瞪口呆的: *a stupefied expression* 目瞪口呆的表情 —**stupefaction** /ˌstupəˈfækʃən; ˌstjuːpɪ̇ˈfækʃən/ *n* [U]

stu·pe·fy·ing /ˈstupəˌfaɪ-ɪŋ; ˈstjuːpɪ̇faɪ-ɪŋ/ *adj* making you feel extremely surprised, tired, or bored 令人非常吃驚[疲勞; 厭倦]的: *stupefying inefficiency* 令人驚訝的低效率 —**stupefy** *v* [T]

stu·pen·dous /stuˈpɛndəs; stjuːˈpendəs/ *adj* surprisingly large or impressive 巨大的; 驚人的; 了不起的: *a stupendous achievement* 了不起的成就 —**stupendously** *adv*

stu·pid /ˈstupɪd; ˈstjuːpɪ̇d/ *adj*  **1** showing a lack of good sense or good judgment; silly 愚蠢的, 傻的: *stupid mistakes* 愚蠢的錯誤 | *I was very drunk last night – I hope I didn't do anything stupid.* 我昨晚喝得爛醉, 希望我沒幹甚麼蠢事。| **it is stupid (of sb) to do sth** *It was stupid of me to lose my temper.* 我大發脾氣, 真是太愚蠢了。**2** having a low level of intelligence, so that you have difficulty learning or understanding things 笨的, 頭腦

遲鈍的: *Charlie understands perfectly well what you mean. He's not stupid.* 查利完全理解你的意思，他並不笨。**3** *informal* used when you are talking about something that makes you annoyed or impatient【非正式】惱人的，討厭的〔用以表示氣惱或不耐煩〕: *I can't get this stupid radio to work.* 我無法弄響這台討厭的收音機。**4** [singular] an insulting way of talking to someone who you think is being stupid 笨蛋，蠢貨〔侮辱性的說法〕: *No, stupid, don't do it like that!* 不，笨蛋，不要那樣做! **5 stupid with cold/sleep/shock etc** unable to think clearly because you are extremely tired, cold etc 凍得/睡得/驚得頭昏腦脹 —**stupidly** *adv*: *Stupidly I forgot my umbrella and ended up getting soaked.* 我糊塗得忘記帶雨傘了，結果淋得渾身都濕透了。

stu·pid·i·ty /stuˋpɪdətɪ; stjuːˈpɪdəti/ *n* **1** [C usually plural 一般用複數, U] behaviour or actions that show a lack of good sense or good judgment 愚蠢的行為: *all the horrors and stupidities of war* 戰爭中的所有恐怖事和愚蠢行為 **2** [U] the quality of being stupid or unintelligent 愚蠢，愚笨；糊塗

stu·por /ˋstupɚ; ˈstjuːpə/ *n* [C,U] a state in which you cannot think, speak, see or hear clearly, usually because you have drunk too much alcohol or taken drugs〔因過量喝酒或吸毒引起的〕昏迷，恍惚，不省人事: **drunken stupor** *We found him lying at the bottom of the stairs in a drunken stupor.* 我們發現他躺在樓梯口，醉得不省人事。

stur·dy /ˋstɝdɪ; ˈstɜːdi/ *adj* **1** someone who is sturdy is strong, short, and healthy looking〔指人〕健壯的，強健的，壯實的: *a sturdy young man* 健壯的小伙子 | *sturdy legs* 結實的雙腿 **2** an object that is sturdy is strong, well-made, and not easily broken〔指物〕結實的，堅實的，堅固的: *a sturdy wall* 堅固的牆 **3** determined and not easily persuaded to change your opinions 堅定的，堅決的，不易改變主意的: *They kept up a sturdy opposition to the plan.* 他們一直堅決反對那項計劃。—**sturdily** *adv* —**sturdiness** *n* [U]

stur·geon /ˋstɝdʒən; ˈstɜːdʒən/ *n* [C,U] a large fish, from which CAVIAR is obtained, or the flesh of this fish which can be eaten 鱘(魚)〔其卵可製魚子醬〕；鱘魚肉

stut·ter[1] /ˋstʌtɚ; ˈstʌtə/ *v* **1** [I,T] to speak with difficulty because you cannot stop yourself from repeating the first CONSONANT of some words; STAMMER[1] 結結巴巴地說: *"I'm D-d-david," he stuttered.* "我叫戴…戴…戴維。"他結結巴巴地說。**2** [I] if a machine stutters, it keeps making little exploding noises and does not work smoothly〔機器〕發出突突的噪聲，不順暢地運轉

stutter[2] *n* [singular] an inability to speak normally because you stutter 結巴，口吃: *a nervous stutter* 緊張性的口吃

sty /staɪ; staɪ/ *n* [C] **1** a place where pigs are kept; PIGSTY (2) 豬圈，豬欄 **2** also 又作 **stye** an infected place on the edge of your EYELID, which becomes red and swollen 瞼腺炎，麥粒腫

Sty·gi·an /ˋstɪdʒɪən; ˈstɪdʒiən/ *adj literary* unpleasantly dark【文】陰暗的；陰森森的: *the Stygian gloom* 陰森森的昏暗地區

S2 W1 **style**[1] /staɪl; staɪl/ *n*

1 ►WAY OF DOING/MAKING 做事/製作方式◄ [C] a particular way of doing something, designing something, or producing something, especially one that is typical of a particular period of time or of a particular group of people〔某個時期或某個團體的〕風格，作風: *styles of architecture* 建築風格 | *The Dutch created a completely new style of football.* 荷蘭人創造出一種全新的足球風格。| **Swedish/new/country etc style** (=done or made in a way that is typical of Sweden etc) 瑞典/新/鄉村等風格的 *a gangland-style killing* 黑社會式的謀殺 | *The cathedral is one of the earliest examples of the gothic style.* 這座大教堂是最早的哥特式建築之一。

2 ►WAY OF BEHAVING/WORKING 行為/工作方式◄ [C] the particular way that someone does something or deals with other people〔某人做事或待人的〕方式，特點: **[+of]** *an authoritarian style of leadership* 專斷的領導作風 | **management/teaching etc style** *an attempt to use Japanese management style in a European business* 在歐洲企業中使用日本管理方式的嘗試 | **it's not his/her style** (=it is not the way someone usually behaves) 那不是他/她的做事作風 *I can't ask a man out – it's just not my style.* 我不會請一個男士出去玩，那不是我做事的作風。| **like sb's style** (=approve of the way someone does things, used especially by someone in authority) 讚賞某人的做事作風〔尤作權威人士用語〕*I like your style, Simpson. I think you'll do well here.* 辛普森，我喜歡你做事的作風。我認為你在這兒會很有前途的。| **be more sb's style** *spoken* (=used as a joking way of saying that you prefer something that does not need as much skill or bravery as something that has been mentioned)【口】那才是我做的事〔玩笑用語，表示跟剛提及的事相比，自己更喜歡做不需要那麼多技巧或勇氣的事情〕*I don't think the parachuting weekend is for me – the art class is more my style.* 我認為週末去跳傘不適合我，上繪畫課才是我做的事。| **in true British/student etc style** (=in a way that is very typical of the behaviour of a particular type of person) 典型的英國人/學生等風格 *Then the sailors, in true navy style, drank a bottle of rum each.* 然後，那些水手們每人喝了一瓶朗姆酒，典型的水手風格。

3 ►DESIGN 設計◄ [C] the design of something, which decides what shape or appearance it will have〔某物的〕設計，款式: *Car styles have changed radically in the past 20 years.* 在過去20年裡，汽車的款式徹底地改變了。

4 ►FASHION 時裝◄ [C,U] a fashion in clothes or hair〔衣服或頭髮的〕流行式樣，款式: *70's styles look very odd today.* 70年代的時裝式樣今天看來很古怪。

5 ►WRITING/LITERATURE 寫作/文學◄ [C,U] the particular way someone uses words to express ideas, tell stories etc 文體，文風: *The stories are typical of Kelman's robust prose style.* 這些故事是凱爾曼一貫尖銳有力的散文文體。—see also 另見 STYLISTIC

6 ►ART/MUSIC/FILM 繪畫/音樂/電影◄ [C,U] the typical way that someone paints, writes music etc, or a typical way of painting etc from a particular period of time〔某人或某時期的〕風格: *a modern musician who composes in the style of Bach* 用巴赫風格作曲的現代音樂家

7 ►SPECIAL QUALITY 特徵◄ [U] a confident and attractive quality that makes people admire you, and that is shown in your appearance, or the way you do things 風度，氣派，格調: **have style** *You may not like her, but she certainly has style!* 你也許不喜歡她，但她確實有風度! —see also 另見 STYLISH

8 in style done in a way that people admire, especially because it is unusual, shows great determination, or involves spending a lot of money 有氣派；有風度；擺排場: **in great/grand/fine etc style** *Sampras won the title in fine style, not losing a single game.* 森柏斯沒輸過一場比賽，非常瀟灑地贏得了冠軍。—see also 另見 **cramp sb's style** (CRAMP[2] (2))

style[2] *v* [T] **1** to design clothing, furniture, or the shape of someone's hair in a particular way 設計，把…製作成某種式樣: *These shoes have been styled for maximum comfort.* 這雙鞋精心設計，力求達到最大限度的舒適。| **have sth styled** *She has her hair styled by Giorgio.* 她請喬治奧為她做頭髮。**2 style yourself Lord/Dr etc** *formal* to give yourself a particular title or name【正式】稱自己為勳爵/博士等: *They style themselves 'the terrible twins'.* 他們稱自己為"可怕的雙胞胎"。—see also 另見 SELF-STYLED

styling brush /ˈ‥ ˌ/ *n* [C] a heated brush used, especially by women, to make their hair a particular shape〔尤指女性用於做髮型的〕定型刷子

styl·ish /ˋstaɪlɪʃ; ˈstaɪlɪʃ/ *adj* attractive in a fashionable way 有風度[氣派]的；時髦的: *a stylish dresser* 穿着很

時髦的人 **—stylishly** *adv* **—stylishness** *n* [U]

styl·ist /ˋstaɪlɪst; ˈstaɪləst/ *n* [C] **1** someone who cuts or arranges people's hair as their job 髮型師 **2** someone who has carefully developed a good style of writing 文體家, 追求優美寫作風格的人

styl·is·tic /staɪˋlɪstɪk; staɪˈlɪstɪk/ *adj* related to the style of a piece of writing or art 寫作文體上的; 藝術風格上的 **—stylistically** /-klɪ; -kli/ *adv*

styl·is·tics /staɪˋlɪstɪks; staɪˈlɪstɪks/ *n* [U] the study of style in written or spoken language 文體學, 風格學

sty·lized also 又作 **-ised** *BrE*【英】/ˋstaɪ͵laɪzd; ˈstaɪlaɪzd/ *adj* drawn or written in an artificial style, that does not include natural detail〔繪畫或寫作〕程式化的: *a stylised picture of a car* 程式化的汽車圖形 **—stylize** *v* [T]

sty·lus /ˋstaɪləs; ˈstaɪləs/ *n* [C] **1** the small pointed part of a RECORD PLAYER, that touches the record〔唱機的〕唱針 **2** a pointed instrument used in the past for writing on WAX[1] (1)〔舊時在蠟板上寫字的〕尖筆, 鐵筆

sty·mie /ˋstaɪmɪ; ˈstaɪmi/ *v* [T] *informal* to prevent someone from doing what they have planned or want to do; THWART【非正式】阻礙, 妨礙, 使不能實施: *He desperately wanted to save his marriage, but felt stymied and doomed to fail* 他極想挽救自己的婚姻, 但感覺阻力很大, 注定要失敗。

Sty·ro·foam /ˋstaɪrə͵fom; ˈstaɪərə͵fəʊm/ *n* [U] *AmE trademark* a soft light plastic material that prevents heat or cold from passing through it, used especially to make containers【美, 商標】聚苯乙烯泡沫塑料; POLYSTYRENE *especially BrE*【尤英】: *a Styrofoam cup* 聚苯乙烯泡沫塑料杯

suave /swɑv; swɑːv/ *adj* someone who is suave is polite, confident, and relaxed, especially in an insincere way 溫文爾雅的; 自信而老於世故的: *a suave and sophisticated gentleman* 溫文爾雅的紳士 **—suavely** *adv* **—suavity, suaveness** *n* [U]

sub- /sʌb; sʌb/ *prefix* **1** under; below 在…下面的: *subzero temperatures* 零度以下的溫度 | *subsoil* (=beneath the surface)〔土壤的〕底土層 **2** less important or powerful than someone or something, or of lower rank than someone〔重要性或級別〕次於…, 低於…: *a subcommittee*〔委員會下設的〕專門小組 | *a sublieutenant* 陸軍少尉 **3** part of a bigger whole 分支: *a subsection* 分部 **4** used to say that something is like something else, but not as good or not real 仿, 近似的: *dreary rows of sub-Victorian villas* 幾排單調的仿維多利亞時代的花園別墅 **5** *technical* almost【術語】近於, 亞: *subtropical heat* 亞熱帶的高溫

S3 **sub**[1] /sʌb; sʌb/ *n* [C] *informal*【非正式】**1** a SUBMARINE 潛水艇 **2** a SUBSTITUTE in sports such as football〔足球等體育運動的〕替補隊員 **3** a SUBSCRIPTION 捐贈款; 會費 **4** *BrE* part of your wages that you receive earlier than usual because you need money【英】〔工資中的〕預支款; ADVANCE[1] (4) *AmE*【美】**5** *AmE* a long bread roll split open and filled with meat, cheese etc【美】潛艇[大型]三明治〔長麵包縱向切開, 中間夾肉、乾酪等〕**6** *AmE* a SUBSTITUTE TEACHER【美】代課教師 **7** *BrE* a SUBEDITOR【英】助理編輯, 文字編輯

sub[2] *v* **subbed, subbing** *informal*【非正式】**1** [I+**for**] to act as a SUBSTITUTE for someone 代替; 作替補隊員 **2** [T] *BrE* to give someone part of their wages earlier than usual or lend them money【英】預支工資給…, 預付; 借錢給…: *I subbed Fenella a tenner to get a decent bunch of flowers.* 我預付給費奈拉十英鎊, 去買一束像樣的鮮花。**3** [T] *BrE* to SUBEDIT something【英】審校〔文稿〕, 對〔稿件〕作文字加工

sub·al·tern /səbˋɔltɚn; ˈsʌbəltən/ *n* [C] a middle rank in the British army, or someone who has this rank〔英國〕陸軍中尉(軍銜)

sub-aq·ua /sʌb ˋækwə; sʌb ˈækwə/ *adj* [only before noun 僅用於名詞前] *BrE* related to sports that take place under water【英】水下運動的: *sub-aqua diving* 潛泳

sub·arc·tic /sʌbˋɑrktɪk; ͵sʌbˈɑːktɪk◂/ *adj* near or typical of the Arctic Circle 近北極圈的; 亞北極區的

sub·a·tom·ic /͵sʌbəˋtɑmɪk; ͵sʌbəˈtɒmɪk◂/ *adj* smaller than an atom or existing within an atom 亞原子的, 次原子的; 原子內的

sub·com·mit·tee /ˋsʌbkə͵mɪtɪ; ˈsʌbkə͵mɪti/ *n* [C] a small group formed from a committee to deal with a particular subject in more detail〔委員會下設的〕專門小組

sub·con·scious[1] /sʌbˋkɑnʃəs; sʌbˈkɒnʃəs/ *adj* subconscious feelings, desires etc are hidden in your mind and you do not know that you have them〔感覺、慾望等〕下意識的, 潛意識的: *a subconscious fear of failure* 對失敗的潛意識恐懼 **—subconsciously** *adv*

subconscious[2] *n* [singular] the part of your mind that has thoughts and feelings you do not know about; UNCONSCIOUS[2] 下意識, 潛意識

sub·con·ti·nent /sʌbˋkɑntənənt; ͵sʌbˈkɒntənənt/ *n* [C] **1** a very large area of land that is part of a CONTINENT 次大陸 **2 the subcontinent** *especially BrE* the area of land that includes India, Pakistan, and Bangladesh【尤英】印度次大陸〔包括印度、巴基斯坦和孟加拉國〕

sub·con·ti·nen·tal /͵sʌbkɑntəˋnɛntl; ͵sʌbkɒntəˈnentl◂/ *adj AmE* related to a subcontinent【美】次大陸的

sub·con·tract /sʌbˋkɑntrækt; ͵sʌbkənˈtrækt/ *v* [T] if a company subcontracts work, they pay other people to do part of their work for them 將〔已簽合約的工作〕分包[轉包]給〔他人〕: *We will be subcontracting most of the electrical work.* 我們將把大部分的電工活轉包出去。**—subcontract** /sʌbˋkɑntrækt; sʌbˈkɒntrækt/ *n* [C]

sub·con·trac·tor /͵sʌbˋkɑntræktɚ; ͵sʌbkənˈtræktə/ *n* [C] someone who does part of the work of another person or firm 分包者

sub·cul·ture /ˋsʌb͵kʌltʃɚ; ˈsʌb͵kʌltʃə/ *n* [C] a particular group of people within a society and their behaviour, beliefs, and activities, which many people disapprove of 亞文化羣; 亞文化: *the drug subculture of the inner city* 舊城區的吸毒亞文化羣

sub·cu·ta·ne·ous /͵sʌbkjuˋtenɪəs; ͵sʌbkjuːˈteɪniəs◂/ *adj technical* beneath your skin【術語】皮下的: *subcutaneous fat* 皮下脂肪 **—subcutaneously** *adv*

sub·di·vide /͵sʌbdəˋvaɪd; ͵sʌbdəˈvaɪd/ *v* [T] to divide into smaller parts something that is already divided 把〔分過的東西〕再分, 重分, 細分: *The house was subdivided into apartments about ten years ago.* 這房子大約十年前被細分成一間間的公寓房。

sub·di·vi·sion /͵sʌbdəˋvɪʒən; ͵sʌbdəˈvɪʒən/ *n* **1** [C,U] the act of dividing something that has already been divided, or the parts that result from doing this 再分, 進一步細分; 進一步分成的部分 **2** [C] *AmE* an area of land that has been subdivided for building houses on【美】〔為建房而劃分的〕一塊土地

sub·due /səbˋdu; səbˈdjuː/ *v* [T] **1** to stop a person or group from behaving violently, especially by using force 鎮壓, 制伏: *Police managed to subdue the angry crowd.* 警察設法控制憤怒的人羣。**2** *formal* to prevent your emotions from showing【正式】克制, 抑制〔情緒〕: *Frank subdued his grief in order to comfort Cathy.* 為安慰卡西, 弗蘭克抑壓住自己的悲痛。**3** *formal* to take control of a place by defeating the people who live there【正式】征服, 控制〔某地〕: *Napoleon subdued much of Europe.* 拿破侖征服了大半個歐洲。

sub·dued /səbˋdud; səbˈdjuːd/ *adj* **1** subdued lighting, colours etc are less bright than usual〔照明、顏色等〕柔和的, 不強烈的 **2** a person or sound that is subdued is unusually quiet〔人〕抑鬱的, 沉默寡言的, 悶悶不樂的;〔聲音〕壓低的: *Richard seems very subdued tonight.* 理查德今晚似乎很消沉。**3** an event or business activity that is subdued does not have as much excitement or interest as you would expect〔事件、生意〕冷清的, 沉悶的: *The housing market is fairly subdued.* 住房市場相當蕭條。

sub·ed·it /sʌbˋɛdɪt; ͵sʌbˈedət/ *v* [T] *BrE* to examine other people's writing for mistakes and make them correct【英】審校〔文稿〕, 對…作文字加工; COPYEDIT *AmE*【美】

sub·ed·i·tor /sʌb`ɛdɪtɚ; ˌsʌb'edɪ̵tə/ *n* [C] *BrE* someone whose job is to examine other people's writing, such as a newspaper article, and to change mistakes【英】助理編輯, 文字編輯

sub·group /`sʌbˌgrup; 'sʌbgruːp/ *n* [C] a separate, smaller, and sometimes less important part of a group 小團體, 小集團, 小分組

sub·head·ing /`sʌbˌhɛdɪŋ; 'sʌbˌhedɪŋ/ *n* [C] a short phrase used as a title for a small part within a longer piece of writing 副標題, 小標題

sub·hu·man /sʌb`hjumən; sʌb'hjuːmən/ *adj* behaving or thinking in a way that you do not expect from people, especially when this is very bad〔行為、思維〕低於人類的: *subhuman intelligence* 低於人的智能

sub·ject¹ /`sʌbdʒɪkt; 'sʌbdʒɪkt/ *n* [C]
1 ▶THING TALKED ABOUT 談論的東西◀ the thing you are talking about or considering in a conversation, discussion, book, film etc〔對話、討論、書、電影等的〕主題, 題目; 話題: *Subjects covered in this chapter are exercise and nutrition.* 本章討論的問題是運動和營養。| *Paul has strong opinions on most subjects.* 保羅在大多數的話題上觀點激烈。| **change the subject** (=start talking about something different) 改變話題 *Stop trying to change the subject!* 別想改變話題! | **get onto the subject (of)** (=start talking about it) 開始談論…話題 *How did we get onto the subject of drugs?* 我們是怎樣談起毒品這個話題的? | **get off the subject (of)** (=start talking about something else instead of what you were supposed to be talking about) 離開…話題〔而談論別的事情〕 *Somehow we got off the subject of homework altogether.* 不知怎的, 我們完全偏離了家庭作業的話題。| **be on the subject (of)** (=be talking about) 正在談論…話題 *While we're on the subject of money, have you got the £10 you owe me?* 既然我們談到了錢的問題, 你欠我的那10英鎊現在能還我嗎? | **be the subject of** (=be what is dealt with) 是…的主題 *Truffaut's childhood memories were the subject of his first film.* 楚浮的童年記憶是他第一部電影的主題。| **be a subject of/for debate/discussion etc** *Genetic engineering is very much a subject for debate.* 基因工程是個很有爭論的問題。
2 ▶ART 藝術◀ the thing you are dealing with when you paint a picture, take a photograph etc〔繪畫、攝影等的〕主題: *Monet loved to use gardens as his subjects.* 莫奈喜歡以花園作為繪畫的主題。
3 ▶SCHOOL 學校◀ an area of knowledge that you study at a school or university 學科, 科目; 課程: *My favourite subject at school was English.* 我上學時最喜歡的學科是英語。
4 ▶TEST 實驗◀ a person or animal that is used in a test 實驗對象, 接受實驗的人[動物]: *The subjects of this experiment were all men aged 18-35.* 本實驗的對象均為年齡在18至35歲的男性。
5 ▶GRAMMAR 語法◀ a noun, noun phrase, or PRONOUN that usually comes before a main verb and represents the person or thing that performs the action of the verb, or about which something is stated, such as 'She' in 'She hit John' or 'elephants' in 'Elephants are big'〔文法中的〕主詞, 主語〈如 She hit John 中的 she, 或 Elephants are big 中的 elephants〉—compare 比較 OBJECT¹ (6)
6 ▶COUNTRY 國家◀ someone who was born in a country that has a king or queen, or someone who has a right to live there〔君主國的〕臣民, 國民: *a British subject* 英國國民 —compare 比較 CITIZEN (2), NATIONAL²

subject² *adj* **1** [not before noun 不用於名詞前] likely to be affected by something, especially something unpleasant 易受…影響的; 易患…的: [+to] *areas subject to strong winds* 易受強風襲擊的地區 | *Kieran is subject to fits of depression.* 基蘭常患憂鬱症。**2 subject to** dependent on something else 取決於…, 有待於…: *Your planning application is subject to review by the local council.* 你的建房申請有待當地議會的審查。**3** [only before noun 僅用於名詞前] *formal* a subject country, state, people etc are strictly governed by another country【正式】〔國家、人民等〕被他人統治的, 受人管轄的

subject³ /səb`dʒɛkt; səb'dʒekt/ *v* [T] *formal* to force a country or group of people to be ruled by you and control them very strictly【正式】使隸屬, 使順從; 征服
subject sb/sth **to** sth *phr v* [T often passive 常用被動態] to force someone or something to experience something very unpleasant or difficult, especially over a long time 使遭受, 使經歷, 使蒙受: *Barker subjected his victim to a terrifying ordeal.* 巴克使其受害者遭受痛苦的折磨。| **be subjected to** *All our products are subjected to rigorous testing.* 我們所有的產品都經過嚴格的檢驗。

sub·jec·tion /səb`dʒɛkʃən; səb'dʒekʃən/ *n* [U] *formal*【正式】**1** the act of forcing a country or group of people to be ruled by you 征服, 鎮壓; 強行統治: *Rome was intent on the subjection of the world.* 羅馬曾試圖征服全世界。**2 in subjection (to)** strictly controlled by someone 被(某人)嚴格控制, 受(某人)支配: *Grandfather kept the whole household in subjection to his wishes.* 爺爺讓全家人都對他言聽計從。

sub·jec·tive /səb`dʒɛktɪv; səb'dʒektɪv/ *adj* **1** a statement, report, attitude etc that is subjective is influenced by personal opinion and can therefore be unfair 主觀的: *As a critic, his writing is far too subjective.* 作為評論家, 他的文章太主觀了。—opposite 反義詞 OBJECTIVE² (1) **2** [no comparative 無比較級] existing only in your mind or imagination 主觀想像的, 只存在於想像之中的: *our subjective perception of colours* 我們對顏色的主觀感知 **3** *technical* related to the subject in grammar【術語】〔文法中〕主詞的, 主語的 —**subjectively** *adv* —**subjectivity** /ˌsʌbdʒɛk`tɪvətɪ; ˌsʌbdʒek'tɪvɪ̵ti/ *n* [U]

subject mat·ter /'·· ˌ··/ *n* [U] what is being talked about in speech or writing, or represented in art〔講話、著作或藝術作品的〕題材; 內容: *The movie has been rated 'R' due to adult subject matter.* 這部電影因為它的成人題材而被列為限制級。

sub·join /ˌsʌb`dʒɔɪn; ˌsʌb'dʒɔɪn/ *v* [T+to] *technical* to add a sentence or phrase at the end of a statement【術語】〔在末尾〕增補, 補述, 添加〔一句話等〕

sub ju·di·ce /sʌb `dʒudɪsɪ; ˌsʌb 'dʒuːdɪsi/ *adv* [only after verb 僅用於動詞後] *law* a legal case being considered sub judice is now being dealt with by a court, and therefore is not allowed to be publicly discussed, for example in a newspaper【法律】〔司法案件〕在審理中的, 尚未裁決的; 〔因尚未裁決〕不准公諸於眾的

sub·ju·gate /`sʌbdʒəˌget; 'sʌbdʒʊgeɪt/ *v* [T] to defeat a person or group and make them obey you 使屈服, 征服, 降伏: *a subjugated people* 被征服的民族 —**subjugation** /ˌsʌbdʒə`geʃən; ˌsʌbdʒʊ'geɪʃən/ *n* [U]

sub·junc·tive /səb`dʒʌŋktɪv; səb'dʒʌŋktɪv/ *n* [C] a verb form or a set of verb forms in grammar, used in some languages to express doubt, wishes〔文法中〕假設語氣, 虛擬語氣: *In 'if I were you' the verb 'to be' is in the subjunctive.* 在 if I were you 中動詞 to be 是虛擬語氣。—compare 比較 IMPERATIVE¹ (3), INDICATIVE² —**subjunctive** *adj*

sub·lease /`sʌbˌlis; 'sʌb-liːs/ *n* [C] an agreement in which someone who rents property from its owner then rents that property to someone else 轉租, 分租 —**sublease** /sʌb`lis; sʌb'liːs/ *v* [I,T]

sub·let /sʌb`lɛt; sʌb'let/ *v* **subletted, subletting** [I,T] to rent to someone else a property that you rent from its owner 將〔租來的物業〕轉租, 分租 —**sublet** /`sʌblɛt; 'sʌblet/ *n* [C]

sub·lieu·ten·ant /ˌsʌblu`tɛnənt; ˌsʌb-lə'tenənt/ *n* [C] a middle rank in the Royal Navy, or someone who has this rank 海軍中尉 —see table on page C6 參見 C6 頁附錄

sub·li·mate /`sʌbləˌmet; 'sʌblɪ̵meɪt/ *v* [I,T] *technical* to use the energy that comes from sexual feelings to do something, such as work or art, that is more acceptable to your society【術語】使〔性慾〕轉化為社會接受的行為; 使昇華, 使高尚化

sub·li·ma·tion /ˌsʌbləˋmeʃən; ˌsʌblɨˈmeɪʃən/ *n* [U] **1** the process of sublimating (SUBLIMATE) 淨化, 高尚化 **2** *technical* the process of changing a solid substance to a gas by heating it and then changing it back to a solid in order to make it pure【術語】昇華, 純化

sub·lime¹ /səˋblaɪm; səˈblaɪm/ *adj* **1** excellent in a way that makes you feel extremely happy 卓越的, 超羣的; 令人讚嘆的: *We had a sublime view over the Mediterranean.* 我們在地中海上空看到令人嘆為觀止的景色。**2** not caring or thinking at all about the result of your actions 不顧後果的: *sublime insensitivity to other people's feelings* 完全不體察他人感情 —**sublimely** *adv* —**sublimeness** *n* [U] —**sublimity** /səˋblɪmətɪ; səˈblɪmɨti/ *n* [U]

sublime² *n* **1 the sublime** something that is excellent and makes you feel extremely happy 高尚, 崇高; 壯觀, 宏偉; 莊嚴: *The sublime, unlike beauty, can inspire awe.* 與美不同的是, 莊嚴使人敬畏。**2 from the sublime to the ridiculous** used to say that a serious and important thing or event is being followed by a silly thing or event〔指事物或事件〕從高超到荒謬, 從一個極端到另一個極端: *First Hamlet, now pantomime? That's going from the sublime to the ridiculous.* 演完《哈姆雷特》後現在演童話劇? 這太煞風景了。

sub·lim·i·nal /sʌbˋlɪmənl̩; sʌbˈlɪmɨnəl/ *adj* at a level of your mind that you are not conscious of 潛意識的, 下意識的; 潛在的: **subliminal messages** *Reverend Jones claims there are subliminal Satanic messages on that album.* 瓊斯牧師聲稱, 那張唱片中有潛在的邪惡信息。| **subliminal advertising** (=with hidden messages and pictures in it) 潛意識廣告

sub·ma·chine gun /ˌsʌbməˋʃin ˌgʌn; ˌsʌbməˈʃiːn gʌn/ *n* [C] a type of MACHINE GUN that is light and easily moved 衝鋒槍, 輕機槍

submarine 潛水艇

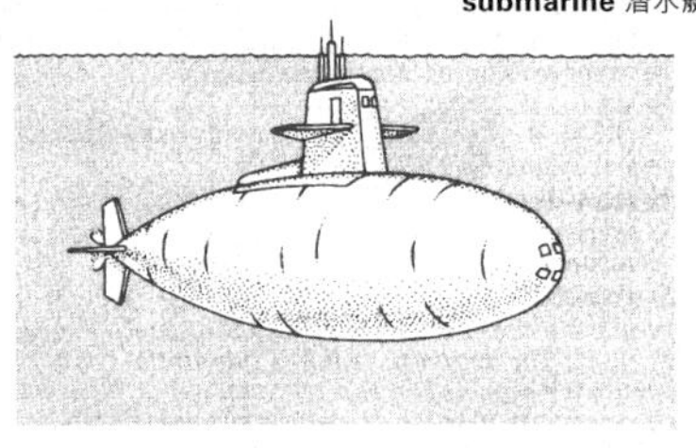

sub·ma·rine¹ /ˋsʌbməˌrin; ˈsʌbməriːn/ *n* [C] a ship, especially a military one, that can stay under water 潛(水)艇: *a nuclear submarine* 核潛艇

submarine² *adj technical* growing or used under the sea【術語】海底的, 海中的; 生於海底[海中]的; 海底使用的: *submarine plant life* 海生植物

sub·mar·i·ner /ˌsʌbməˋrinɚ; sʌbˈmærɪnə/ *n* [C] a sailor living and working in a submarine 潛水艇水手

submarine sand·wich /ˌ··· ˋ··/ *n* [C] *AmE* a SUB¹ (5)【美】潛艇[大型]三明治〔長麵包縱向切開, 中間夾肉、乾酪等〕

sub·merge /səbˋmɝdʒ; səbˈmɜːdʒ/ *v* **1** [I,T] to go under the surface of water, or to put something under water or another liquid (使) 潛入水中, (使) 沒入水中; (使) 浸沒; 淹沒: *The tunnel entrance was submerged by rising sea water.* 隧道入口被漲起的海水淹沒。**2** [T] to cover or completely hide something 完全掩蓋, 遮掩; 使完全消失: *Feelings she thought she'd submerged were surfacing again.* 她以為她已經掩飾的感情又顯露了出來。**3 submerge yourself in sth** to make yourself very busy doing something 埋頭於某事: *Alice submerged herself in work to try and forget about Tom.* 艾麗斯埋頭工作, 試圖忘記湯姆。—**submergence** *n* [U]

sub·merged /səbˋmɝdʒd; səbˈmɜːdʒd/ *adj* just under the surface of water or another liquid 在水下的, 沒入液體中的: *submerged rocks* 沒入水中的礁石

sub·mersed /səbˋmɝst; səbˈmɜːst/ *adj* submersed plants etc live under the water〔植物〕生長於水下的

sub·mer·si·ble /səbˋmɝsəbl̩; səbˈmɜːsɨbəl/ *n* [C] a vehicle that can travel under water 可潛入水中的交通工具

sub·mer·sion /səbˋmɝʃən; səbˈmɜːʃən/ *n* [U] the act of going under water, or the state of being completely covered in liquid 沒入水中, 浸沒, 淹沒

sub·mis·sion /səbˋmɪʃən; səbˈmɪʃən/ *n* **1** [U] the state of being completely controlled by a person or group, and accepting that you have to obey them 屈服, 屈從; 順從: **force/frighten etc sb into submission** *The prisoners were eventually starved into submission.* 囚犯們最終因飢餓被迫屈服了。| **in submission to** (=in obedience to) 順從…, 服從…, 聽從… *I offer my resignation in submission to your request.* 我按你的要求提交辭呈。**2** [C,U] the act of giving a plan, piece of writing etc to someone in authority for them to consider or approve, or the plan, piece of writing etc itself 提交(物), 呈遞(書): *The deadline for the submission of proposals is May 1st.* 提交建議的最後期限是 5 月 1 日。**3** [U] *formal* an opinion or thought that you state【正式】意見, 建議, 看法: **in my submission** *It is important, in my submission, that a wider view be taken.* 我認為持更開明的見解是很重要的。**4** [C] *law* a request or suggestion that is given to a judge for them to consider【法律】提交仲裁的要求; 提請考慮的建議 S2

sub·mis·sive /səbˋmɪsɪv; səbˈmɪsɪv/ *adj* always willing to obey someone even if they are unkind to you 服從的, 順從的; 恭順的: *Martin expects his wife to be meek and submissive.* 馬丁期望妻子溫順, 對他言聽計從。—**submissively** *adv* —**submissiveness** *n* [U]

sub·mit /səbˋmɪt; səbˈmɪt/ *v* **submitted, submitting** **1** [I,T] to obey someone when you have no choice about it because they have power over you 順從, 服從; 屈從: [+to] *I will not submit to your bullying.* 我不會屈服於你的欺侮。| **submit yourself to sb/sth** *Derek agreed to submit himself to questioning.* 德里克同意接受審問。**2** [T] to give a plan, piece of writing etc to someone in authority for them to consider or approve 呈送, 提交, 呈遞〔計劃等〕: *All applications must be submitted by Monday.* 所有申請必須在星期一前遞交。**3** [T] *formal* to agree to obey a person, group, or set of rules【正式】同意服從[遵守]: **submit sth to** *We are willing to submit to arbitration.* 我們願意接受仲裁。**4** [T] *formal* to suggest or say something【正式】建議, 主張: **submit that** *I submit that the jury has been influenced by the publicity in this case.* 我認為, 在本案的審理過程中, 陪審團受到了外界宣傳的影響。 S2 W3

sub·nor·mal /sʌbˋnɔrml̩; ˌsʌbˈnɔːməl◂/ *adj* less or lower than normal 比正常少的, 低於正常的: *subnormal temperatures* 低於正常的溫度

sub·or·bit·al /sʌbˋɔrbɪtl̩; sʌbˈɔːbɨtl/ *adj technical* making less than one complete ORBIT (=journey around the Earth)【術語】〔軌道〕不滿一整圈的, 亞軌道的: *a suborbital space flight* 亞軌道太空飛行

sub·or·di·nate¹ /səˋbɔrdnɪt; səˈbɔːdɨnət/ *adj* less important than something else, or in a lower position with less authority 次要的; 下級的; 從屬的: *a subordinate role on the committee* 委員會中次要的角色 | [+to] *a commission that is subordinate to the Security Council* 隸屬於安理會的委員會 —compare 比較 SUBSERVIENT

subordinate² *n* [C] someone who has a lower position and less authority than someone else in an organization 部下, 下級, 部屬

S

sub·or·di·nate³ /sə`bɔrdə͵net; sə'bɔːdɪ̵neɪt/ *v* [T] to put someone or something in a less important position 使處於次要地位, 使從屬於…: **subordinate sth to sb/sth** *Joe subordinated his wishes to those of the group.* 喬使自己的願望服從於全組的願望。—**subordination** /sə͵bɔrdə`neʃən; sə͵bɔːdɪ̵'neɪʃən/ *n* [U]

subordinate clause /·͵··· '·/ *n* [C] a DEPENDENT CLAUSE 從句, 從屬子句

sub·orn /sə`bɔrn; sə'bɔːn/ *v* [T] *law* to persuade someone to tell lies in a court of law or to do something else that is illegal, especially for money【法律】唆使; 收買〔某人〕作僞證[做其他非法的事] —**subornation** /͵sʌbɔr`neʃən; ͵sʌbɔː'neɪʃən/ *n* [U]

sub·plot /`sʌb͵plɑt; 'sʌbplɒt/ *n* [C] a PLOT (=set of events) that is less important than and separate from the main plot in a story, play etc〔小説、劇本等的〕次要情節, 從屬情節

sub·poe·na¹ /sə`pinə; sə'piːnə/ *n* [C] *law* a written order that you must come to a court of law and be a witness【法律】〔傳喚出庭的〕傳票

subpoena² *v past tense* **subpoenaed** [T] *law* to order someone to come to a court of law and be a witness【法律】用傳票傳喚〔某人〕出庭

sub-post of·fice /͵· '· ͵··/ *n* [C] a small British post office that has fewer services than a main post office〔英國的〕小郵局, 郵政所

sub·rou·tine /͵sʌbru`tin; ͵sʌbruː'tiːn/ *n* [C] a part of a computer PROGRAM containing a set of instructions for doing a small job that is part of a larger job〔電腦的〕子程序

sub·scribe /səb`skraɪb; səb'skraɪb/ *v* **1** [I] to pay money regularly to have copies of a newspaper or magazine sent to you 訂閱〔報紙或雜誌〕: **[+to]** *What newspaper do you subscribe to?* 你訂閱哪種報紙? **2** [I] *BrE* to pay money regularly to be a member of an organization or to help its work【英】定期繳納會員費; 定期捐款贊助: **[+to]** *Chris subscribes to an environmental action group.* 克里斯定期捐款給一個環保行動組織。**3** [T] *BrE* to give money regularly for a service【英】〔為某項服務〕定期交費: *People in the office subscribe £1 a week for coffee.* 辦公室的人每週出一英鎊支付咖啡的費用。**4** [T] *formal* to sign your name【正式】簽〔名〕: *Please subscribe your name to the document.* 請在文件上簽名。

subscribe for sth *phr v* [T] to agree to buy or pay for shares (SHARE² (5)) 認購〔股票〕: *Each employee may subscribe for up to £2,000 worth of shares.* 每個雇員可以認購價值不超過 2,000 英鎊的股票。

subscribe to sth *phr v* [T usually in questions and negatives 一般用於疑問句和否定句] if you subscribe to an idea, view etc, you agree with it or support it 同意, 贊同; 支持: *I have never subscribed to the view that schooldays are the happiest days of your life.* 我從來沒有同意過校園生活是人生最快樂的日子這個看法。

sub·scrib·er /səb`skraɪbɚ; səb'skraɪbə/ *n* [C] **1** someone who pays money regularly to receive copies of a newspaper or magazine〔報紙或雜誌的〕訂閱者, 訂戶 **2** *BrE* someone who pays money to be part of an organization or to help its work【英】〔某組織的〕會員; 〔某項活動的〕贊助者 **3** *BrE* someone who gives money regularly for a service【英】〔某項服務的〕用戶 **4** someone who signs their name on a document〔文件的〕簽名者

sub·scrip·tion /səb`skrɪpʃən; səb'skrɪpʃən/ *n* [C] **1** an amount of money you pay regularly, especially once a year, to receive copies of a newspaper or magazine 訂閱費 **2** *BrE* an amount of money you pay regularly to be a member of an organization or to help its work【英】會(員)費; 捐贈款

sub·sec·tion /sʌb`sɛkʃən; 'sʌbsekʃən/ *n* [C] a part of a SECTION 分部; 小節, 小段

2 **sub·se·quent** /`sʌbsɪ͵kwɛnt; 'sʌbsɪ̵kwənt/ *adj formal* coming after or following something else【正式】隨後的, 繼…之後的: *These skills were then passed on to subsequent generations.* 然後, 這些技術被傳給了後代。| **subsequent to** (=after) 在…之後 *events that happened subsequent to the accident* 在那場事故之後發生的事情 —compare 比較 CONSEQUENT

sub·se·quent·ly /`sʌbsəkwəntlɪ; 'sʌbsɪ̵kwəntli/ *adv formal* after an event in the past【正式】後來, 隨後, 接着: *The book was subsequently translated into 15 languages.* 那本書後來被翻譯成 15 種語言。 3

sub·ser·vi·ent /səb`sɝvɪənt; səb'sɜːviənt/ *adj* **1** someone who is subservient is too willing to do what other people want them to do 恭順的, 屈從的, 卑躬屈膝的 **2** *formal* less important than something else; SUBORDINATE【正式】次要的, 從屬的: **[+to]** *Your own needs must be subservient to those of the group.* 你個人的需要必須服從於小組的需要。—**subserviently** *adv* —**subservience** *n* [U]

sub·set /`sʌb͵sɛt; 'sʌbset/ *n* [C] a set that is part of a larger set 子集; 〔大套中的〕一小套

sub·side /səb`saɪd; səb'saɪd/ *v* [I] **1** if a feeling or noise subsides, it gradually decreases〔情緒、噪聲〕逐漸減弱; 平靜下來, 平息: *Simon waited until the laughter subsided.* 西蒙一直等到笑聲平息下來。**2** if a building subsides, it gradually sinks further into the ground〔建築物〕沉降, 下陷 **3** if land subsides, its surface sinks to a lower level〔土地〕塌陷, 下陷: *After the heavy rains, part of the road subsided.* 大雨過後, 部分路段塌陷了。**4** if bad weather conditions subside, they gradually return to a normal state〔惡劣天氣〕平息, 平靜下來: *Then the wind subsided, and all was quiet.* 後來風漸漸停了, 一切又恢復了平靜。

sub·si·dence /səb`saɪdn̩s; səb'saɪdəns/ *n* [C,U] the process by which land sinks to a lower level, or the state of land or buildings that have sunk〔建築物的〕沉降; 〔土地的〕塌陷, 下陷: *Is your house insured against subsidence?* 你給房子投保了沉降險嗎?

sub·sid·i·ar·i·ty /səb͵sɪdɪ`ærɪtɪ; səb͵sɪdi'ærɪ̵ti/ *n* [U] a word meaning a political POLICY (1) in which more power, for example to make decisions, is given to a smaller group of people, used especially about the European Community giving power to its member countries 權力下放政策, 權利自主(原則)〔尤指給予歐盟各成員國更多自主權的政策〕

sub·sid·i·a·ry¹ /səb`sɪdɪ͵ɛrɪ; səb'sɪdiəri/ *n* [C] a company that is owned or controlled by another company 子公司, 附屬公司: *a subsidiary of a US parent company* 美國總公司的一家子公司

subsidiary² *adj* connected with, but less important than, the main plan, subject, event etc 附帶的, 附屬的; 次要的: **[+to]** *The smaller workshops are subsidiary to the main conference.* 這些小規模的研討會是這次主要會議的附帶活動。

sub·si·dize also 又作 **-ise** *BrE*【英】/`sʌbsə͵daɪz; 'sʌbsɪ̵daɪz/ *v* [T] to pay part of the cost of something so that the buyer can pay less for it 給…津貼[補貼]: *Farming is partly subsidized by the government.* 農業得到政府的部分補貼。—**subsidizer** *n* [C] —**subsidization** /͵sʌbsədə`zeʃən; ͵sʌbsɪ̵daɪ'zeɪʃən/ *n* [U]

sub·si·dy /`sʌbsədɪ; 'sʌbsɪ̵di/ *n* [C] money that is paid by a government or organization to make prices lower, reduce the cost of producing goods etc〔政府或組織為平抑物價、降低生產成本等而發放的〕津貼, 補貼, 補助金: *international disagreement over trade subsidies* 有關貿易津貼的國際糾紛

sub·sist /səb`sɪst; səb'sɪst/ *v* [I] to stay alive on only small amounts of food or money〔以很少的食物或錢〕維持生活, 生存下去: **[+on]** *We had to subsist on bread and water.* 我們不得不靠麵包和水維持生存。

sub·sis·tence /səb`sɪstəns; səb'sɪstəns/ *n* [U] **1** the ability to live with very little money or food〔以很少的食物或錢〕維持生活; 生存, 生計: *Not even subsistence is possible in such conditions.* 在這種條件下連維持生存都不可能。**2** a small amount of money or food that is just enough to survive 僅夠維持生存的錢[食物]: **subsistence allowance** (=money given to you to live on) 僅夠維持最低限度生活的補貼[津貼] | **subsistence diet** (=only enough food to keep living) 僅夠維持生存的飲食 | **subsistence farmers** (=who produce just enough food to live on) 生產的糧食只夠自己食用的農民

subsistence crop /ˈ·ˈ·· ·/ *n* [C] a crop that is grown to be used by the farmer rather than to be sold〔農民生產只供自己食用的〕自給作物 —compare 比較 CASH CROP

subsistence lev·el /ˈ·ˈ·· ˌ··/ *n* [singular] a very poor standard of living, which only provides the things that are completely necessary and nothing more 勉強糊口的生活水平: *Many of the poorer farmers live at subsistence level.* 許多窮苦的農民只能過着勉強糊口的生活。

sub·soil /ˋsʌbˌsɔɪl; ˈsʌbsɔɪl/ *n* [U] the layer of soil between the surface and the lower layer of hard rock 下層土, 底土層, 心土

sub·son·ic /sʌbˋsɑnɪk; ˌsʌbˈsɒnɪk◂/ *adj* slower than the speed of sound 亞音速的: *subsonic flight* 亞音速飛行

sub·spe·cies /ˋsʌbˌspiʃiz; ˈsʌbˌspiːʃiːz/ *n* [C] a group of similar plants or animals that is smaller than a SPECIES〔動植物的〕亞種

3 **sub·stance** /ˋsʌbstəns; ˈsʌbstəns/ *n*

1 ▶MATERIAL 物質◀ [C] a type of solid or liquid that has particular characteristics 物質: *a sticky substance* 黏性物質, 膠黏物 | *radioactive substances* 放射性物質 | *Heroin is an illegal substance.* 海洛因是一種違禁品。

2 ▶IDEAS 思想◀ [singular,U] *formal* the most important ideas contained in an argument or piece of writing; ESSENCE (1)【正式】〔論點、著作的〕主旨, 主要內容; 真諦: **the substance of** *The substance of his argument was that too many people live below the poverty line.* 他的主要論點就是太多的人生活在貧困線之下。| **in substance** *What she said in substance was that the mayor must resign.* 她所說的中心意思就是市長必須辭職。

3 ▶IMPORTANCE 重要性◀ [U] *formal* importance, especially because of dealing with things that are necessary; SIGNIFICANCE【正式】重要性: *It was an entertaining speech, but without much substance.* (=without many important or serious ideas) 那是一篇吸引人的演講, 但是沒有多少實質內容。| **matters/issues of substance** *Instead of debating points of procedure, we should be discussing matters of substance.* 我們與其爭辯程序問題, 還不如討論一些實質性的東西。

4 ▶TRUTH 事實◀ [U usually in questions and negatives 一般用於疑問句和否定句] *formal* basic facts that are true【正式】事實: **[+to]** *There is no substance to the rumour that the princess is pregnant.* 公主懷孕的傳説是不真實的。| **without substance** (=untrue) 失實(的)

5 substance abuse *technical* the habit of taking too many drugs so that you are harmed by them【術語】藥物濫用

6 a man/woman of substance *literary* a rich man or woman【文】富人, 有財產的人

7 ▶REAL 真實的◀ [U] something that really exists that you can feel 真實存在的事物: *phantoms without substance* 不真實的幻影

sub·stan·dard /sʌbˋstændɚd; ˌsʌbˈstændəd◂/ *adj* not as good as the average, and not acceptable 低於標準的, 次等的: *substandard housing* 不夠標準的住房 —compare 比較 NON-STANDARD, STANDARD[2]

2 2 **sub·stan·tial** /səbˋstænʃəl; səbˈstænʃəl/ *adj* **1** large enough in amount or number to be noticeable or to have an important effect 大量的; 重要的; 有重要影響的: *The document requires substantial changes.* 該文件需要作重大修改。| *We have the support of a substantial number of parents.* 我們有許多家長的支持。**2** large enough to be satisfactory 多的; 可觀的: *a substantial salary* 可觀的薪水 | *a substantial breakfast* 豐盛的早餐 **3** large and strongly made 堅固的, 結實的: *a substantial mahogany desk* 堅固的紅木書桌 **4** *formal* having a lot of influence or power, usually because of wealth【正式】〔常指因富有而〕有影響力[權勢]的: *a very substantial family in the wool trade* 羊毛業中一個舉足輕重的家族

sub·stan·tial·ly /səbˋstænʃəlɪ; səbˈstænʃəli/ *adv* **1** when considering the most important parts 主要地; 大體上, 基本上: *There are one or two minor differences, but they're substantially the same text.* 這些文本有一兩處小的差異, 但他們大體上是一樣的。**2** very much 大量地; 可觀地: *substantially higher prices* 高出許多的價格

sub·stan·ti·ate /səbˋstænʃɪˌet; səbˈstænʃieɪt/ *v* [T] *formal* to prove the truth of something that someone has said, claimed etc【正式】證明, 證實: *Can you substantiate your claim in a court of law?* 你能在法庭上證明你聲稱的事是有根據的嗎? —**substantiation** /səbˌstænʃɪˋeʃən; səbˌstænʃiˈeɪʃən/ *n* [U]

sub·stan·tive[1] /səbˋstæntɪv; səbˈstæntɪv/ *adj* **1** *formal* dealing with things that are important or real【正式】實質的; 真實的, 實際的: **substantive discussions** (=in which important matters are discussed) 實質性的討論 **2** *technical* expressing existence, in grammar【術語】〔語法中〕表示存在的: *The substantive verb is 'to be'.* to be 是表示存在的動詞。**3** [only before noun 僅用於名詞前] *formal* real and continuing, rather than being only for a limited time【正式】永久的, 終身的: *the substantive rank of colonel* 終身的上校軍銜 —**substantively** *adv*

sub·stan·tive[2] /ˋsʌbstəntɪv; ˈsʌbstəntɪv/ *n* [C] *technical* a noun【術語】名詞 —**substantival** /ˌsʌbstənˋtaɪvl; ˌsʌbstənˈtaɪvəl◂/ *adj*

sub·sta·tion /ˋsʌbˌsteʃən; ˈsʌbˌsteɪʃən/ *n* [C] a place where electricity is passed on from the place that produces it into the main system 變電站, 變電所, 配電室

sub·sti·tute[1] /ˋsʌbstəˌtut; ˈsʌbstɪtjuːt/ *n* [C] **1** someone who does someone else's job for a limited period of time especially in a sports team or performance 代替者; 替補隊員[演員]: *The lead singer was ill and her substitute wasn't nearly as good.* 主唱歌手病了, 替代她的演員遠遠比不上她。**2** something new or different that you use instead of something else that you used previously 代替物, 替代品: *a sugar substitute* 糖的代用品 **3 be no substitute for sth** to not have the same good or desirable qualities as something or someone else 沒有…那樣好, 不如…稱心: *Vitamin pills are no substitute for healthy eating.* 維生素片不能替代健康飲食。

substitute[2] *v* **1** [T] to use something new or different instead of something else 用〔新的或不同的事物〕代替: **substitute sth for/with sth** *You can substitute yogurt for the sour cream.* 你可以用酸奶代替酸味奶油。**2** [I,T] to do someone's job until the person who usually does it is able to do it again 替代, 頂替; 替換: **[+for]** *Bill substituted for Larry who was off sick.* 拉里因病沒有上班, 比爾替了他。

substitute teach·er /ˌ··· ˈ··/ *n* [C] *AmE* a teacher who teaches a class when the usual teacher is ill【美】代課教師; SUPPLY TEACHER *BrE*【英】

sub·sti·tu·tion /ˌsʌbstəˋtuʃən; ˌsʌbstɪˈtjuːʃən/ *n* [C,U] someone or something that you use instead of the person or thing you would usually use, or the act of using them 代替的人[物]; 代替, 替換: *Coach Packard made two substitutions in the second half.* 帕卡德教練在下半場兩次換人。

sub·stra·tum /sʌbˋstretəm; ˌsʌbˈstrɑːtəm/ *n plural* **substrata** /-tə; -tə/ [C] **1** a layer that lies beneath another layer, especially in the earth〔尤指土壤的〕下層, 底(土)層: *a substratum of rock* 底層岩石 **2** *formal* a quality that is hidden【正式】隱藏的特點: *a substratum of truth in the argument* 該論據中隱含的真實性

sub·struc·ture /ˋsʌbˌstrʌktʃɚ; ˈsʌbˌstrʌktʃə/ *n* [C] **1** one of the structures (STRUCTURE[1] (3)) within a society or organization that combines with others to form a whole〔組成社會或機構的〕基礎, 下層結構 **2** a solid base under the ground that supports a building above the ground〔支持地面建築的〕基礎, 下層結構, 地下建築, 根基

S

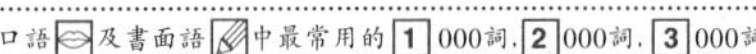
口語 及書面語 中最常用的 1 000詞, 2 000詞, 3 000詞

sub·sume /səb`sum; səb'sjuːm/ *v* [T] *formal* to include someone or something as a member of a group or type, rather than considering it separately【正式】把...歸入[納入]某一類: **subsume sb/sth under sth** *For the purpose of the survey, typists are subsumed under office workers.* 為了便於調查, 打字員被算作辦公室工作人員。

sub·ten·ant /sʌb`tɛnənt; ˌsʌb'tenənt/ *n* [C] someone who pays rent for an apartment, office etc to the person who is renting it from the owner〔公寓、辦公室等的〕轉租承租人, 次承租人 —**subtenancy** *n* [C,U]

sub·tend /səb`tɛnd; səb'tend/ *v* [T] *technical* to be opposite to a particular angle or ARC, and form the limits of it in GEOMETRY【術語】〔幾何中〕對向〔某角或某弧度〕

sub·ter·fuge /`sʌbtɚˌfjudʒ; 'sʌbtəfjuːdʒ/ *n* [C,U] *formal* a secret trick or slightly dishonest way of doing something, or the use of this【正式】花招, 詭計, 手段: *Sereni was lured to Moscow by subterfuge.* 塞麗妮被人施詭計引誘到了莫斯科。

sub·ter·ra·ne·an /ˌsʌbtə`reniən; ˌsʌbtə'reɪniən◂/ *adj* beneath the surface of the Earth 地下的, 地表下的: *subterranean passages* 地下通道

sub·text /`sʌbˌtɛkst; 'sʌbtekst/ *n* [C] a hidden or second meaning in something that someone says or writes 潛在含義, 字面下的意思, 潛台詞: *Whatever their text, the subtext is always this: political repression.* 不論他們的原文是甚麼, 潛台詞總是這四個字: 政治鎮壓。

sub·ti·tle /`sʌbˌtaɪtḷ; 'sʌbˌtaɪtl/ *n* [C] **1 subtitles** [plural] the words printed over a film in a foreign language to translate what is being said by the actors〔外國電影的〕字幕, 對白譯文: *a French film with English subtitles* 有英語字幕的法國電影 **2** a less important title below the main title in a book 副標題, 小標題 —**subtitle** *v* [I,T]

sub·ti·tled /`sʌbˌtaɪtḷd; 'sʌbˌtaɪtld/ *adj* having subtitles or a particular subtitle 有副標題的; 以...為副標題的

sub·tle /`sʌtḷ; 'sʌtl/ *adj* **1** not easy to notice or understand unless you pay careful attention 難以捉摸[理解]的; 微妙的, 細微的: *a subtle flavor of oranges* 少許的橙子味 | *The pictures are similar, but there are subtle differences between them.* 這些圖畫很相似, 但它們之間有細微的差別。**2** someone who is subtle uses indirect methods to hide what they really want or intend to do 含蓄的, 隱晦的: *Hugo didn't even try to be subtle about it – he stared right at her.* 休哥毫不含蓄——他直直地看着她。**3** clever, especially in order to deceive people 狡猾的, 狡詐的: *a subtle plan* 巧妙狡猾的計劃 **4** very clever in noticing and understanding things; SENSITIVE (1) 敏感的, 敏銳的; 有辨別力的: *a subtle mind* 敏銳的頭腦 —**subtly** *adv*

sub·tle·ty /`sʌtḷtɪ; 'sʌtlti/ *n* **1** [U] the quality of being subtle 敏銳, 機敏; 微妙, 巧妙; 狡猾: *She argued her case with considerable subtlety.* 她相當機敏地為自己的論點辯護。**2** [C usually plural 一般用複數] a thought, idea, or detail that is important but difficult to notice or understand 微妙的思想; 〔想法等中的〕細微之處: **[+of]** *Some of the subtleties of the language are lost in translation.* 語言中的一些微妙之處在譯文中丟失了。

sub·to·tal /`sʌbˌtotḷ; 'sʌbˌtəʊtl/ *n* [C] the total of a set of numbers, especially on a bill, that is added to other numbers to form a complete total〔尤指賬單上的〕小計, 部分累計數

sub·tract /səb`trækt; səb'trækt/ *v* [T] to take a number or an amount from something larger 減去, 減掉: **subtract sth from sth** *If you subtract 10 from 30 you get 20.* 30減去10等於20。—compare 比較 ADD (2), DEDUCT, MINUS[1] (1)

sub·trac·tion /səb`trækʃən; səb'trækʃən/ *n* [C] the act of subtracting 減; 減法 —compare 比較 ADDITION (4)

sub·trop·i·cal /sʌb`trɑpɪkḷ; ˌsʌb'trɒpɪkəl◂/ *adj* related to an area near to a tropical area, or typical of that area 副熱帶的, 亞熱帶的: *subtropical vegetation* 亞熱帶植物

sub·urb /`sʌbɝb; 'sʌbɜːb/ *n* [C] an area away from the centre of a town or city, where a lot of people live〔城鎮的〕郊區, 近郊, 城郊住宅區: **[+of]** *Blackheath is a suburb of London.* 布萊克希斯是倫敦的一個郊區。| **the suburbs** (=this type of area) 市郊, 市郊住宅區 *a naive kid from the suburbs* 一個來自市郊的天真孩子

sub·ur·ban /sə`bɝbən; sə'bɜːbən/ *adj* **1** related to a suburb, or in a suburb 郊區的, 市郊的: *suburban life* 郊區的生活 | *suburban streets with houses that all look the same* 房屋一模一樣的郊區街道 **2** boring and having very traditional beliefs and interests 乏味的; 古板的; 傳統的: *suburban attitudes* 狹隘的態度

sub·ur·ban·ite /sə`bɝbənˌaɪt; sə'bɜːbənaɪt/ *n* [C] someone who lives in a suburb 郊區居民, 住在郊區的人

sub·ur·bi·a /sə`bɝbɪə; sə'bɜːbiə/ *n* [U] **1** the behaviour, opinions, and ways of living that are typical of people who live in a suburb 郊區人的行為、觀念和生活方式; 郊區習俗: *middle-class suburbia* 郊區中產階級的生活方式 **2** suburban areas in general 郊區

sub·ven·tion /səb`vɛnʃən; səb'venʃən/ *n* [C] *formal* a gift of money for a special use【正式】〔特殊用途的〕資助金; 補貼費; 津貼

sub·ver·sion /səb`vɝʒən; səb'vɜːʃən/ *n* [U] secret activities that are intended to encourage people to oppose the government〔對政府的〕顛覆; 暗中破壞

sub·ver·sive[1] /səb`vɝsɪv; səb'vɜːsɪv/ *adj* ideas, activities etc that are subversive are often secret and intended to encourage people to oppose a government, religion etc〔對政府、宗教等〕顛覆性的: *subversive political activities* 顛覆性政治活動 —**subversively** *adv* —**subversiveness** *n* [U]

subversive[2] *n* [C] someone who is subversive 顛覆分子, 破壞分子

sub·vert /səb`vɝt; səb'vɜːt/ *v* [T] *formal*【正式】**1** to try to destroy the power and influence of a government or established system etc 顛覆; 暗中破壞〔現政府、現有制度等〕: *attempts to subvert the democratic process* 破壞民主進程的企圖 **2** to destroy someone's beliefs or loyalty 腐蝕; 敗壞; 使放棄〔信念、忠誠等〕

sub·way /`sʌbˌwe; 'sʌbweɪ/ *n* [C] **1** *BrE* a path for people to walk under a road or railway【英】〔公路或鐵路下的〕地下通道, 地下人行道; UNDERPASS *AmE*【美】**2** *AmE* a railway that runs under the ground【美】地下鐵道, 地鐵; UNDERGROUND[3] *BrE*【英】

sub-ze·ro /ˌ· `··◂/ *adj* below zero in temperature〔溫度〕零度以下的

suc·ceed /sək`sid; sək'siːd/ *v* S3 W2

1 ►NOT FAIL 沒有失敗◄ [I] to do what you have tried or wanted to do 成功, 達成: *I'm sure you'll succeed if you work hard.* 你只要努力, 我肯定你會成功的。| **succeed in doing sth** *Negotiators have not yet succeeded in establishing a ceasefire.* 談判者仍未達成停火協定。| **succeed only in doing sth** (=fail and do the opposite of what you had wanted) 取得相反的效果; 弄巧反拙 *You've only succeeded in upsetting your mother.* 你這樣反而弄得你媽媽不高興了。

2 ►HAVE A GOOD RESULT 取得好結果◄ [I] to have the result or effect something was intended to have 達到目的, 取得預期效果: *The anti-smoking campaign has only partly succeeded.* 反吸煙運動只是部分地獲得成功。

3 ►REACH A HIGH POSITION 升到高位◄ [I] to do well in your job, especially because you have worked hard at it for a long time〔在事業上〕取得成功, 功成名就: **[+as]** *I'm not sure he has the determination to succeed as an actor.* 我不敢肯定他有當一名出色演員的決心。| **[+in]** *Women need to be tough to succeed in the male-dominated world of business.* 在男性主宰的商界裡, 婦女必須堅強才能取得成功。

4 ►FOLLOW IN A POSITION 繼位◄ [I,T] to be the next person to take a position or rank after someone else 接替; 繼任; 繼承: **succeed sb as sth** *Gingrich will succeed Foley as speaker of the house.* 金里奇將接替福利擔任議院議長。

5 ►REPLACE 替代◄ [T] *formal* to come after and re-

place something else【正式】替代, 替換: *a new generation of computers designed to succeed their existing range* 為替代現有的電腦系列而設計的新一代電腦
6 nothing succeeds like success used to say that success often leads to even greater success 一事成, 事事成; 一順百順

suc·ceed·ing /sək`sidɪŋ; səkˈsiːdɪŋ/ *adj* coming after something else 隨後的, 接着的: *Over the succeeding weeks things went from bad to worse.* 在接下來的幾個星期裡, 情況越來越壞。

1 1 **suc·cess** /sək`sɛs; səkˈses/ *n* **1** [U] the achieving of something you have been trying to do, with a good result 成功, 勝利, 成就: *success in a highly competitive market* 在競爭激烈的市場中取勝 | *She puts her success down to hard work and good luck.* 她認為自己的成功是由於努力和幸運。| **have success in doing sth** *Did you have any success in persuading Adam to come?* 你勸説亞當來成功了嗎? **2** [C] something that has a good result or effect 成功的事, 達到目的的事: *The play was an overnight success.* 這部劇作一夜之間走紅。| **a great/huge/big success** *Kathy's wedding shower was a great success.* 凱西的結婚送禮會搞得極為成功。| **make a success of sth** *Dick's taken over a pub, I bet he makes a success of it.* 迪克接手開了一家酒吧, 我肯定他會取得成功。| **prove a success** (=become successful) 表明是成功的; 取得成功 **3** [C] someone who does very well in their job 成功者; 取得成就的人: **[+in]** *Janet is determined to be a success in whatever field she chooses.* 珍妮特下了决心, 不管自己選擇甚麼行業都要做個成功者。| **[+as]** *Tony's been a great success as our new coach.* 作為我們的新教練, 托尼一直幹得極為出色。**4 success story** someone or something that becomes successful in spite of difficulties 大獲成功的人[事物]; 成功的範例: *Ewing has turned the business into a success story.* 尤因把公司經營得很成功。

2 1 **suc·cess·ful** /sək`sɛsfəl; səkˈsesfəl/ *adj* **1** having the effect or result you intended 成功的; 如願以償的, 達到目的的: *Well, it wasn't a very successful meeting.* 哎, 那次會不大成功。| **successful in doing sth** *Were you successful in persuading him to change his mind?* 你勸他改變主意, 他聽了嗎? **2** a successful business, film etc makes a lot of money〔公司、影片等〕利潤豐厚的, 非常賺錢的: *The show's had a pretty successful run.* 這戲相當成功, 已連演多場。**3** a successful person earns a lot of money or is very well known and respected〔人〕有成就的; 賺錢多的; 出人頭地的: *luxury apartments for the successful young executive* 供飛黃騰達的年輕行政人員居住的豪華公寓 | **[+in]** *successful in politics* 在政壇上飛黃騰達 —opposite 反義詞 UNSUCCESSFUL —**successfully** *adv*

3 **suc·ces·sion** /sək`sɛʃən; səkˈseʃən/ *n* **1 in succession** happening one after the other without anything different happening in between 連續不斷; 一個接一個: *She won the championship four times in succession.* 她連續四次奪得冠軍。| **in close/quick succession** (=quickly one after the other) 一個緊接一個 **2 a succession of** a number of people or things of the same kind following, coming or happening one after the other 連續不斷的〔人或物〕: *A succession of visitors came to the door.* 登門造訪者接踵而來。**3** [U] the act of taking over an office or position, or the right to be the next to take it 接替, 繼承, 繼任; 繼承權: *If Prince Charles dies, the succession passes to his son.* 查爾斯王子如果去世, 繼承權就傳給他的兒子。| **succession to sth** *the queen's succession to the throne* 女王對王位的繼承 —compare 比較 ACCESSION (1)

suc·ces·sive /sək`sɛsɪv; səkˈsesɪv/ *adj* coming or following one after the other 連續的, 接連的, 相繼的: *The hockey team has had five successive victories.* 這支曲棍球隊已經連續五次獲勝了。—**successively** *adv*

suc·ces·sor /sək`sɛsɚ; səkˈsesə/ *n* [C] **1** someone who takes a position previously held by someone else 繼承人; 繼任者, 接班人: **[+as]** *His successor as chairman takes over next week.* 接替他擔任主席的人下週接任。**2** *formal* a machine, system etc that exists after another one in a process of development【正式】〔機器、操作系統等的〕換代產品, 接替的事物: *the transistor's successor, the microchip* 晶體管的換代產品, 微晶片 —opposite 反義詞 PREDECESSOR

suc·cinct /sək`sɪŋkt; səkˈsɪŋkt/ *adj approving* clearly expressed in a few words【褒】言簡意賅的, 簡明扼要的, 簡練的: *a very succinct explanation* 非常簡明的解釋 —**succinctly** *adv* —**succinctness** *n* [U]

suc·cor /`sʌkɚ; ˈsʌkə/ *n* [U] the American spelling of SUCCOUR succour 的美式拼法 —**succor** *v* [T]

suc·co·tash /`sʌkə,tæʃ; ˈsʌkətæʃ/ *n* [U] *AmE* a dish made from corn, beans, and TOMATO*es* cooked together【美】青玉米粒煮利馬豆〔用玉米、豆子和番茄一起煮成的食品〕

suc·cour¹ *BrE*【英】, **succor** *AmE*【美】/`sʌkɚ; ˈsʌkə/ *n* [U] *literary* help that is given to someone who is having problems【文】救濟, 援助, 救助

succour² *BrE*【英】, **succor** *AmE*【美】—*v* [T] *literary* to help someone who has problems【文】救濟, 援助, 救助: *succouring the needy* 救濟貧困的人們

suc·cu·bus /`sʌkjəbəs; ˈsʌkjʊbəs/ *n plural* **succubi** /-baɪ; -baɪ/ [C] *literary* a female devil that has sex with a sleeping man【文】〔傳説中與睡眠中的男子性交的〕女夢淫妖 —compare 比較 INCUBUS (2)

suc·cu·lent¹ /`sʌkjələnt; ˈsʌkjʊlənt/ *adj* **1** juicy and delicious 多汁美味的: *a succulent steak* 美味多汁的牛排 **2** *technical* a succulent plant has thick soft leaves or stems that can hold a lot of liquid【術語】〔植物〕莖葉肥厚多水分的, 肉質的 —**succulence** *n* [U]

succulent² *n* [C] *technical* a succulent plant such as a CACTUS【術語】肉質植物〈如仙人掌〉

suc·cumb /sə`kʌm; səˈkʌm/ *v* [I] *formal*【正式】**1** to stop opposing someone or something that is stronger than you, and allow them to take control 屈服, 屈從; 不再抵抗: *After an intense artillery bombardment the town finally succumbed.* 經過一番猛烈砲轟後, 該城鎮終於投降了。| **succumb to temptation** *Gina finally succumbed to temptation and had some ice cream.* 吉娜終於抵不住誘惑, 吃了一些冰淇淋。**2** if you succumb to an illness you become very ill or die of it 病情加重;〔因病而〕死

such¹ /sʌtʃ; sʌtʃ/ *predeterminer, determiner* **1** used to talk about a person, thing etc which is of the same kind as that which has already been mentioned 上述一類的, 諸如此類的, 這樣的, 這類的〔用於指已提到的人或事物〕: *Such behavior is just not acceptable in this school.* 此類行為在本校是絕對不能接受的。| *The rules make it quite clear what should be done in such a situation.* 條例中明確規定在這種情況下應當如何處理。| **[+as]** *It was against such a background as this that the President made his speech.* 總統正是在這種背景下發表演説的。**2 such as** used when giving an example of something 像, 諸如, 例如〔用於舉例〕: *The local community is still reliant on traditional industries such as farming and mining.* 當地社區仍然依賴務農和採礦之類的傳統產業。| *"There are lots of ways to increase productivity." "Such as?"* "提高生產力的途徑多得很。" "舉例來説呢?" | **people/things etc such as** *professional people such as bank managers and solicitors* 諸如銀行經理和事務律師一類的專業人士 **3 such a kind man/such tall women etc** used to emphasize how kind a man is, how tall particular women are etc 如此和善的男人/如此高大的女士等〔用於表示強調〕: *Did you have to buy such an expensive coat?* 你非得買這樣昂貴的外套嗎? | *You haven't invited Ron have you? He's such a bore.* 你沒有邀請羅恩吧? 他可是夠討厭的。| *I've seen an eagle before, but never at such close quarters.* 我以前見過老鷹, 但從來沒有離得這麼近地見過。| **[+(that)]** *It's such a tiny kitchen that I don't have to do much to keep it clean.* 這個廚房很小, 我不必太操勞就可以把它保持清潔 1 1

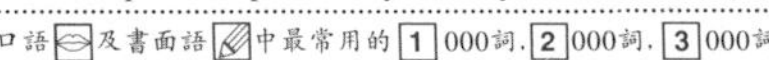

了。| *He's such an idiot, I don't even ask him to help any more.* 他這個人蠢得很，我根本不會再找他幫忙了。**4 or some such person/thing etc** a person, thing etc like the one just mentioned 或諸如此類的人/東西等: *He said she looked scruffy, or made some such helpful comment.* 他説她看上去邋裡邋遢，並作了一些諸如此類的有益的點評。**5 such as it is/such as they are etc** *especially spoken* used when you do not think that something is good enough or impressive enough【尤口】雖然它不過如此/雖然它們不怎麼樣等: *You're welcome to borrow my car such as it is.* 歡迎你借用我的汽車，雖然它不怎麼樣。**6 there's no such person/thing etc as** used to say that a particular person or thing does not exist 沒有…這樣的人/物等〔用於表示某一類人或物並不存在〕: *These days there's no such thing as a job for life.* 如今已經沒有終身職位這種事兒了。**7 such...as** *formal or literary* used to emphasize that there is a small amount of something or that it is of poor quality【正式或文】…的那些; …的那種〔用於強調某物數量不多或質量不好〕: *Such food as they gave us was warm and nutritious.* 他們給我們的那些食物是熱的，而且有營養。

such² *pron* **1** used to talk about a person, thing, etc that is of the same kind as that which has already been mentioned 這樣的人[事物], 上述的人[事物]〔用於指已提到的人或事物〕: *A Welsh victory had been predicted and such indeed was the result.* 有人預言威爾斯隊會獲勝，果然不出所料。**2 such...as/that** *formal or literary* used to give a reason or explanation for something【正式或文】到如此程度; 如此…以至〔用於給出理由或作解釋〕: *The nature of the job was such that he felt obliged to tell no one about it.* 那種工作的性質就如此，他覺得只好祕而不宣了。| *His manner was such as to offend everyone who he met.* 他態度如此惡劣，以至到處得罪人。**3 and such** *spoken* and people or things like that【口】以及諸如此類的人[物]: *It won't be anything special, just a few cakes and sandwiches and such.* 不會有甚麼特別的東西，只是幾塊蛋糕和三明治以及諸如此類的點心罷了。**4 not...as such** *spoken* used to say that something is not really what you are calling it【口】並不是真正的…, 並非名副其實的…〔用於表示某物名不副實〕: *There isn't a garden as such, just a little vegetable patch.* 那裡並不是一個真正的菜園，只是一小塊菜地罷了。**5 such...as** *formal* those people or things of a particular group or kind【正式】凡是…, 那些…: *Such of you as wish to leave may do so now.* 你們想走的現在都可以走了。

such and such /ˈ· · ˌ·/ *predeterminer spoken* a certain time, amount etc that is not named【口】某某; 這樣那樣的〔表示未具體指明的時間、數量等〕: *If they tell you to come on such and such a day, don't agree unless it's convenient.* 如果他們叫你在某一天來，你若不方便就不要答應。

such·like¹ /ˈsʌtʃˌlaɪk; ˈsʌtʃlaɪk/ *pron spoken* things of that kind【口】這一類的事物, 諸如此類的東西: *Do you enjoy plays, films and suchlike?* 你喜歡看戲劇、電影這類東西嗎?

suchlike² *adj* [only before noun 僅用於名詞前] *spoken* of that kind; SIMILAR【口】這一類的, 諸如此類的, 類似的: *tennis and baseball and suchlike summer sports* 網球、棒球以及類似的夏季運動

S3 **suck¹** /sʌk; sʌk/ *v* [I,T]
1 ►DRINK 喝◄ to take liquid into your mouth by tightening your lips into a small hole and using the muscles of your mouth to pull the liquid in 吸, 吮, 啜: **suck at sth** *a baby sucking at its mother's breast* 在媽媽懷裡吃奶的嬰兒 | **suck sth up** *Jennie sucked up the last bit of milkshake with her straw.* 詹妮用吸管喝完最後一點奶昔。
2 ►PUT IN MOUTH 放在嘴裡◄ to hold something in your mouth and pull on it with your tongue and lips 含在嘴裡吮食: *Don't suck your thumb, dear!* 不要吮大拇指，寶貝! | **suck on sth** *Lara's been sucking on that jawbreaker for half an hour.* 那塊圓硬糖羅拉已經吮了半個鐘頭了。
3 ►PULL 拉◄ to pull someone or something with great power and force to a particular place 抽, 吸; 以強大的吸力吞沒, 把…捲入: **[+down/into]** *Something got sucked down into the boiler and clogged it.* 有個東西給吸進了鍋爐裡，把它塞住了。| **suck sb under/along** *Be careful of rip tides! They'll suck you right under.* 當心急流! 它會把你直捲進海底的。
4 suck sb into sth to make someone become involved in a particular situation, event etc, especially a bad one 使某人捲入某事〔尤指壞事〕: *Gullible people can easily get sucked into religious cults.* 輕信的人很容易被引入邪教。
5 sth sucks *informal especially AmE* an impolite expression meaning that something is very bad in quality or that a situation is very bad【非正式，尤美】某事物真差勁, 某事物糟透了: *Her acting sucks.* 她的演技糟透了。
suck up *phr v* [I] *informal* to say or do a lot of nice things in order to make someone like you or to get what you want【非正式】奉承, 巴結, 拍馬屁: **suck up to sb** *He's always sucking up to the boss.* 他總是拍老闆的馬屁。

suck² *n* [C] an act of sucking 吸, 吮, 啜

suck·er¹ /ˈsʌkɚ; ˈsʌkə/ *n* [C]
1 ►PERSON 人◄ *informal* someone who is easily deceived, tricked, or persuaded to do something they do not want to do【非正式】容易上當受騙的人; 傻瓜: *You fell for that old line? Sucker!* 你居然相信了那一套騙人的老話? 真是大傻瓜!
2 be a sucker for sth to like something so much that you cannot refuse it 對某物入迷, 非常喜歡某物: *She's a real sucker for old movies.* 她非常愛看老電影。
3 ►PART OF AN ANIMAL 動物身體的部位◄ *not technical* a part of an insect or of an animal's body that it uses to hold on to a surface【非術語】〔動物的〕吸盤: *Tree frogs have suckers on their feet.* 樹蛙腳上有吸盤。
4 ►SWEET 甜的◄ *AmE* a LOLLIPOP (2)【美】棒棒糖
5 ►PLANT 植物◄ a part of a plant that grows from the root or lower stem of a plant to become a new plant 根出條〔從植物的根部或底部長出的新枝〕
6 ►RUBBER 橡膠◄ a flat piece of rubber that sticks to a surface by SUCTION 橡皮吸盤

sucker² *v*
sucker sb **into** sth *phr v* [T] *AmE* to persuade someone to do something they do not want to do, especially by tricking them or lying to them【美】騙〔某人〕去做〔某事〕: **sucker sb into doing sth** *Laurie got suckered into babysitting her little sister.* 勞里被哄去照看她的小妹妹。

suck·le /ˈsʌkl; ˈsʌkəl/ *v* **1** [T] to feed a baby or young animal with milk from the breast 給〔嬰兒或小動物〕餵奶, 哺乳: *a sheep suckling her lamb* 給羊羔哺乳的綿羊 **2** [I] if a baby or young animal suckles, it sucks milk from a breast〔嬰兒或小動物〕吮吸〔母乳〕, 吸奶 —compare 比較 BREASTFEED, NURSE² (6)

suck·ling /ˈsʌklɪŋ; ˈsʌklɪŋ/ *n* [C] *literary* a young human or animal still taking milk from its mother【文】乳兒; 乳獸

suckling pig /ˈ· · ·/ *n* [C] a young pig still taking milk from its mother, which is often cooked and eaten on special occasions 乳豬

su·crose /ˈsukros; ˈsuːkrəʊz/ *n* [U] *technical* the common form of sugar【術語】蔗糖 —compare 比較 FRUCTOSE, LACTOSE

suc·tion /ˈsʌkʃən; ˈsʌkʃən/ *n* [U] the process of removing air or liquid from an enclosed space so that another substance is sucked in, or so that two surfaces stick together〔對水或空氣的〕吸, 抽吸, 吸出

suction cap /ˈ· · ·/ *BrE*【英】, **suction cup** *AmE*【美】*n* [C] a small round piece of rubber or plastic that sticks to a surface by suction 吸盤, 吸杯

suction pump /ˈ· · ·/ *n* [C] a pump that works by removing air from an enclosed space, so that the substance to be pumped is sucked in 抽吸泵, 真空泵

2 3 **sud·den** /ˈsʌdn̩; ˈsʌdn/ *adj* **1** happening, coming, or done quickly and unexpectedly 突然的, 忽然的, 迅速而意外的: *I keep having sudden bouts of dizziness.* 我總是突然覺得一陣陣的眩暈。| *a sudden change in temperature* 溫度的突然變化 | *Marry you? Why, George, this is all so sudden!* 嫁給你? 啊喲, 喬治, 這太突然了! **2 (all) of a sudden** suddenly 突然地, 突如其來地, 猛然地: *We were driving along, when all of a sudden a car pulled straight out in front of us.* 我們正開着車子往前走, 冷不防一輛汽車在我們前面衝了出來。—**suddenness** *n* [U]

sudden death /ˌ·· ˈ·/ *n* [U] if a game goes into sudden death, it continues after its usual ending time until one player or team gains the lead and wins 突然死亡法〔指加賽時以先得分者為勝方的決勝方法〕

2 1 **sud·den·ly** /ˈsʌdn̩lɪ; ˈsʌdnli/ *adv* quickly and unexpectedly 迅速而意外地, 突然地, 突如其來地: *Suddenly there was a huge bang.* 突然傳來一聲巨響。| *George died very suddenly.* 喬治死得非常突然。

suds /sʌdz; sʌdz/ *n* [plural] **1** the mass of BUBBLEs (BUBBLE[1] (1)) formed on the top of water with soap in it 一團肥皂泡, 肥皂泡沫 **2** *AmE informal* beer【美, 非正式】啤酒 —**sudsy** *adj*

sue /su; sjuː/ *v* [I,T] to make a legal claim against someone, especially for an amount of money, because you have been harmed in some way〔尤指為要求賠償損失而〕控告, 起訴, 告…的狀: *If the builders don't fulfil their side of the contract, we'll sue.* 如果建築商一方不履行合同, 我們就要提出訴訟。| **sue sb for libel/negligence/malpractice etc** (=because of something they have done wrong) 控告某人誹謗/玩忽職守/瀆職等 *Elton John sued a newspaper for libel.* 艾頓莊控告一份報紙誹謗。| **sue sb for £100,000/damages** (=in order to get money) 對某人提起訴訟, 索賠10萬英鎊/索要賠償金 *I'll sue them for every penny they've got.* 被他們弄去的每一分錢我都要打官司拿回來。| **sue sb for divorce** (=in order to end a marriage) 對某人提出訴訟要求離婚

sue for sth *phr v* [T] *formal* to BEG or ask for something【正式】乞求, 要求: **sue for peace** *The rebels were forced to sue for peace.* 叛亂分子被迫要求和解。

suede /swed; sweɪd/ *n* [U] soft leather with a slightly rough surface〔外表略粗糙而料子柔軟的〕絨面革, 軟皮革: *suede shoes* 絨面革皮鞋 —see picture on page A16 參見A16頁圖

su·et /ˈsuɪt; ˈsuːɪ̯t/ *n* [U] hard fat from around an animal's KIDNEYs, used in cooking 動物腰部的板油, 硬脂肪油〔用於烹調〕—**suety** *adj*

1 1 **suf·fer** /ˈsʌfɚ; ˈsʌfə/ *v*

1 ▶PAIN 疼痛◀ [I,T] to experience physical or mental pain 感到疼痛, 遭受痛苦; 蒙受, 遭受: *At least he died suddenly and didn't suffer.* 起碼他死得很突然, 沒有遭受痛苦。| **[+from]** *Simon suffers from migraines.* 西蒙患有偏頭痛。| **I/you/she will suffer for it** (=will feel very ill or sore) 我/你/她會因此而吃苦頭 *I know I'll suffer for it in the morning, but give me another gin.* 我知道我明天早上會因此而難受, 不過, 還是再給我來一杯杜松子酒吧。

2 ▶BAD SITUATION 不好的形勢◀ [I,T] to be in a very bad situation that makes things very difficult for you 遭受困難, 吃苦頭, 受損害: *Small businesses have suffered financially during the recession.* 小公司在經濟不景氣期間遭受了經濟損失。| **suffer the consequences** (=be punished) 承擔後果, 受到懲罰 *If you break the law, you must be prepared to suffer the consequences.* 如果你犯法, 你就要準備為此承擔後果。

3 ▶EXPERIENCE 經歷◀ [T] if someone suffers an unpleasant or difficult experience, it happens to them 經受, 經歷〔不愉快或困難的事〕: **suffer a defeat** *The Democrats have just suffered a huge defeat in the polls.* 民主黨剛在選舉中遭到了慘敗。| **suffer damage/injury/loss** *The car suffered severe damage in the accident.* 汽車在事故中受到嚴重損壞。

4 ▶WORSE 更壞◀ [I] to become worse in quality because a bad situation is affecting something or because nobody is taking care of it 變差, 變壞, 變糟: *The ferry operators denied that safety would suffer if costs were cut.* 渡輪經營者否認降低成本就會影響安全的說法。

5 not suffer fools gladly to not be patient with people you think are stupid 對愚蠢的人沒有耐心, 不能耐着性子與蠢人相處

6 suffer sb to do sth *old use* to allow someone to do something【舊】允許某人做某事

suf·fer·ance /ˈsʌfrəns; ˈsʌfərəns/ *n* **on sufferance** *formal* if you live or work somewhere on sufferance, you are allowed to do it by someone who would rather you did not do it【正式】勉強〔被容許〕地: *Martha made it clear I was only staying with them on sufferance.* 瑪莎說得很清楚, 我只是勉強被容許和他們住在一起。

suf·fer·er /ˈsʌfərɚ; ˈsʌfərə/ *n* [C] someone who suffers, especially from a particular illness 受害者, 受苦者;〔尤指某種疾病的〕患者: *a huge increase in the number of asthma sufferers* 哮喘患者的劇增

suf·fer·ing /ˈsʌfrɪŋ; ˈsʌfərɪŋ/ *n* [C,U] physical or mental pain and difficulty, or an experience of this〔肉體或精神上的〕痛苦, 困難(的經歷): *the suffering of innocent people during a war* 無辜人民在戰爭期間遭受的痛苦

suf·fice /səˈfaɪs; səˈfaɪs/ *v* [not in progressive 不用進行式] **1** [I] *formal* to be enough【正式】足夠, 滿足…的需要: *A light lunch will suffice.* 少量的午餐就夠了。| **suffice to do sth** *Two examples should suffice to illustrate my point.* 舉兩個例子就足以說明我的觀點了。**2 suffice (it) to say (that)** used to say that the statement that follows is enough to explain what you mean, even though you could say more 只要說…就夠了: *Suffice to say it was a local person who called the police.* 就說是一個當地人給警方打的電話, 其他的就不必多說了。**3** [T] *formal* to be enough to satisfy someone【正式】足夠〔某人〕之用, 使滿足: *Just some bread and soup will suffice me.* 我只要點麵包和湯就夠了。

suf·fi·cien·cy /səˈfɪʃənsɪ; səˈfɪʃənsi/ *n formal*【正式】**1** [U] the state of being or having enough 足夠, 充足 **2 a sufficiency of** a supply that is enough 足夠的供應; 足夠的量: *Eating fruit should ensure a sufficiency of Vitamin C.* 吃水果應能保證維生素C的足量補充。

suf·fi·cient /səˈfɪʃənt; səˈfɪʃənt/ *adj formal* as much as is needed for a particular purpose; enough【正式】足夠的, 充足的: *We can only prosecute if there is sufficient evidence.* 我們只有在證據充足時才能提出起訴。| **sufficient to do sth** *His income is sufficient to keep him comfortable.* 他的收入足夠供他舒適地生活。| **[+for]** *There is sufficient food for everyone.* 有足夠的食物供所有人吃。—opposite 反義詞 INSUFFICIENT —see 見 ADEQUATE (USAGE) 2 2

suf·fix /ˈsʌfɪks; ˈsʌfɪks/ *n* [C] a letter or letters added to the end of a word to form a new word 後綴, 詞尾: *You can add the suffix 'ness' to the word 'kind' to form 'kindness'.* 在kind後加後綴ness可以構成kindness。—see also 另見 AFFIX —compare 比較 PREFIX[1] (1)

suf·fo·cate /ˈsʌfəˌket; ˈsʌfəkeɪt/ *v* **1** [I,T] to die or make someone die by preventing them from breathing (使)窒息而死, (使)悶死: *She rolled onto her baby and actually suffocated it!* 她翻身壓在嬰兒身上, 竟把它悶死了! **2 be suffocating** to feel uncomfortable because there is not enough fresh air 感到窒息, 感到呼吸困難: *Can you open a window? I'm suffocating.* 請你打開窗戶好嗎? 我覺得很悶。**3** [T] to prevent a relationship, plan, business etc from developing well or being successful 壓制, 扼殺, 阻礙: *Jealousy can suffocate any relationship.* 妒忌可以扼殺任何人際關係。—**suffocation** /ˌsʌfəˈkeʃən; ˌsʌfəˈkeɪʃən/ *n* [U]

suf·fra·gan /ˈsʌfrəgən; ˈsʌfrəgən/ *adj* [only before noun 僅用於名詞前] a suffragan BISHOP (1) helps another bishop of higher rank in their work〔指主教〕協助上級主教的, 副的 —**suffragan** *n* [C]

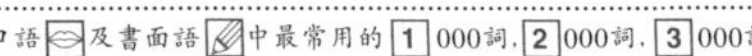

suf·frage /ˋsʌfrɪdʒ; ˈsʌfrɪdʒ/ *n* [U] the right to vote in national elections 選舉權, 投票權

suf·fra·gette /ˌsʌfrəˋdʒɛt; ˌsʌfrəˈdʒet/ *n* [C] a woman who tried to gain the right to vote for women especially as a member of a group in Britain or the US in the early 20th century 為婦女爭取選舉權的女子〔尤指 20 世紀初英國或美國某團體的成員〕

suf·fuse /səˋfjuz; səˈfjuːz/ *v* [T] *especially literary* if warmth, colour, liquid etc suffuses something or someone, it covers or spreads through them【尤文】〔溫暖、顏色、液體等〕充滿, 佈滿, 彌漫於: *The light of the setting sun suffused the clouds.* 夕陽映紅了浮雲。—**suffusion** /səˋfjuʒən; səˈfjuːʒən/ *n* [U]

S2 W3 **sug·ar¹** /ˋʃugɚ; ˈʃʊgə/ *n* **1** [U] a sweet white or brown substance that is obtained from plants and used to sweeten food and drinks 食糖〈如白糖、紅糖〉: *Do you take sugar in your coffee?* 你喝咖啡加糖嗎? **2** [C] the amount of sugar that a small spoon can hold 一茶匙的糖: *How many sugars do you want in your tea?* 你的茶裡要放幾茶匙糖? **3** *technical* one of several sweet substances formed in plants【術語】糖〔植物中形成的甜味物質〕—compare 比較 GLUCOSE **4** *BrE spoken* used to address someone you like very much【英口】親愛的, 心肝, 寶貝〔用於稱呼自己非常喜愛的人〕 **5 (oh) sugar!** *spoken especially BrE* used when you are very annoyed about something stupid that you have just done, or when something goes wrong【口, 尤英】(噢) 糟了! (哦) 真糟糕!〔用於因做了蠢事感到惱火或某事出了麻煩之時〕

sugar² *v* [T] **1** to add sugar or cover something with sugar; SWEETEN (1) 加糖於, 裹糖於…上: *Did you sugar my coffee?* 你給我的咖啡加糖了嗎? **2 sugar the pill** *especially BrE* to do something that makes an order, activity etc less unpleasant【尤英】把苦藥包上糖衣; 降低〔某項命令、活動等〕令人討厭的程度 —**sugared** *adj*: *sugared almonds* 糖杏仁

sugar beet /ˈ·· ·/ *n* [U] a vegetable that grows under the ground from which sugar is obtained; BEET (1)〔製糖用的〕甜菜, 糖蘿蔔

sug·ar·cane /ˋʃugɚˌken; ˈʃʊgəkeɪn/ *n* [U] a tall tropical plant from whose stems sugar is obtained 甘蔗

sugar-coat·ed /ˌ·· ˈ··◂/ *adj* **1** covered with sugar 裹糖的, 包有糖衣的 **2** made to seem better than something really is 粉飾過的: *I'm tired of hearing Fred's sugar-coated promises.* 我已經聽膩了弗雷德那些甜言蜜語的許諾。

sugar cube /ˈ·· ·/ *n* [C] a sugar lump 方糖

sugar dad·dy /ˈ·· ˌ··/ *n* [C] *informal* an older man who gives a young woman presents and money in return for her company and often for sex【非正式】〔以禮物和金錢換取年輕女人陪伴或性好處的〕老色迷, 闊乾爹, 甜爹

sugar lump /ˈ·· ·/ *n* [C] *especially BrE* a square piece of solid sugar【尤英】方糖

sugar ma·ple /ˈ·· ˌ··/ *n* [C] a kind of MAPLE tree that grows in North America whose SAP (=liquid from the tree) is used to make MAPLE SYRUP 糖槭〔產於北美, 其樹液可製成槭糖漿〕

sug·ar·y /ˋʃugərɪ; ˈʃʊgəri/ *adj* **1** containing sugar or tasting like sugar 含糖的, 甜的: *sugary snacks* 甜點心 **2** language, emotions etc that are sugary are too nice and seem insincere〔語言、情感等〕過於甜蜜的, 媚人的, 甜言蜜語的: *songs full of sugary sentiments about love* 充滿柔情蜜意的歌曲

S1 W1 **sug·gest** /səgˋdʒɛst; səˈdʒest/ *v* [T] **1** to tell someone your ideas about what they should do, where they should go etc 建議, 提議: *If this is not convenient, please suggest another date.* 要是這個日期不方便, 那就請另選一個日子吧。| **suggest doing sth** *John suggested going together in one car.* 約翰建議大家坐同一輛汽車去。| **suggest (that)** *She suggested that we write that into the contract.* 她建議我們把那一點寫進合同。| **can/may I suggest** (=used to politely suggest a different idea) 我可以提個建議…嗎?〔用於客氣地表示不同的想法〕*May I suggest that you see a financial advisor?* 我可否建議你去找個財政顧問諮詢一下? | **suggest how/where etc** *Can you suggest where to stay in Rio?* 你能建議在里約熱內盧住甚麼地方嗎? —see 見 PROPOSE (USAGE) **2** to tell someone about a suitable person for a job 推薦〔某職務的合適人選〕: **suggest sb for** *Mr Roberts Guarino has been suggested for the post of director.* 羅伯茨·瓜里諾先生已被推薦擔任主任一職。**3** to make someone think that a particular thing is true; INDICATE (1) 顯示, 間接表明; 暗示: *The actual number of rapes may be higher than the statistics suggest.* 實際的強姦數字可能要比統計資料所顯示的更高。| **[+(that)]** *There was nothing to suggest that she intended to kill herself.* 沒有任何跡象顯示她有意自殺。**4** to make someone have a new idea 使產生〔新想法〕; 啟發: **suggest sth to sb** *It was a magazine article that suggested the idea to me.* 是雜誌上的一篇文章使我產生這個想法的。**5 I'm not suggesting** *spoken* used to say that what you are going to say is not meant to criticize someone as much as it may seem【口】我並不是說〔用於表示自己並非要強烈批評某人〕: *I'm not suggesting that you are lying, but it is very misleading.* 我並不是說你在撒謊, 但你的話誤導性很強。**6** to remind someone of something or help them to imagine it 使人想起; 使人聯想到: *The stage was bare, with only the lighting to suggest a prison.* 舞台上空無一物, 只有燈光使人聯想到監獄。

sug·ges·ti·ble /səgˋdʒɛstəbl; səˈdʒestəbəl/ *adj* easily influenced by other people or by things you see and hear 易受影響的: **highly/very suggestible** *At that age, kids are highly suggestible.* 小孩在那種年齡非常容易受影響。

S1 W2 **sug·ges·tion** /səgˋdʒɛstʃən; səˈdʒestʃən/ *n* **1** [C] an idea, plan, or possibility that someone mentions 建議, 提議, 意見: **have a suggestion** *We've had several suggestions on a name for the baby.* 我們已經得到好幾個關於給寶寶取個甚麼名字的建議了。| **make a suggestion** *Can I just make one suggestion about how we might do this?* 關於如何做此事, 我能否提一個建議? | **[+that]** *He rejected my suggestion that we appoint Roger.* 他拒絕了我提出的我們應任命羅傑的建議。—see 見 PROPOSE (USAGE) **2 a suggestion of** a slight amount of something 微量的…; …的跡象: *There was just a suggestion of a smile on her face.* 她臉上微微露出一絲笑意。**3** [U] the act of telling someone your idea about what they should do 提議, 建議: **at sb's suggestion** (=because someone suggested something) 由於某人的提議, 根據某人的建議 *At her father's suggestion, she left Paris and returned home.* 根據父親的建議, 她離開巴黎回到了家中。| **open to suggestions** (=willing to listen to ideas) 願意聽取意見; 歡迎提建議 **4 suggestion that/of** [usually in questions and negatives 一般用於疑問句及否定句] a slight possibility 些微的可能, 細微的跡象: *There was never any suggestion of criminal involvement.* 沒有發現涉及犯罪的任何跡象。**5** [U] an indirect way of making you accept an idea, for example by HYPNOTISM 通過間接方式〈如催眠術〉作出的暗示, 示意

sug·ges·tive /səgˋdʒɛstɪv; səˈdʒestɪv/ *adj* **1** a remark, behaviour etc that is suggestive makes you think of sex〔話語、行為等〕挑動色情的, 性挑逗[暗示]的 **2** reminding you of something 暗示的; 示意的; 啟發的, 引起聯想的: **suggestive of sth** *an abstract painting suggestive of a desert landscape* 一幅使人聯想起荒漠景色的抽象畫 —**suggestively** *adv* **suggestiveness** *n* [U]

su·i·cid·al /ˌsuəˋsaɪdl; ˌsuːəˈsaɪdl◂/ *adj* **1** wanting to kill yourself 想自殺的, 有自殺傾向的: *After his wife left him he was suicidal.* 在妻子離他而去之後, 他很想自殺。| **suicidal tendencies** *For many years before treatment, Clare had suicidal tendencies.* 在治療前許多年, 克萊爾都有自殺傾向。**2** likely to lead to death 自殺性的; 可能導致死亡的: *the suicidal challenge of jumping over 50 cars on a motorcycle* 騎摩托車躍過 50 輛汽車的玩命逞強之舉 **3** likely to lead to a lot of damage or trouble 可能造成大破壞[麻煩]的: *It would be suicidal for the sena-*

tor to oppose this policy. 如果反對這項政策，這位參議員將會自毀前程。

su·i·cide /ˈsuəˌsaɪd; ˈsuːɨsaɪd/ *n* [C,U] **1** the act of killing yourself 自殺: **attempt suicide** (=try to kill yourself) 企圖自殺 | **commit suicide** (=kill yourself) 自殺 *Gill committed suicide last year after losing her job.* 吉爾去年失業之後自殺了。—see 見 KILL¹ (USAGE) **2 political/social suicide** something you do that ruins your good position in politics or society 斷送自己政治/社會前程之舉

suicide pact /ˈ··· ˌ·/ *n* [C] an arrangement between two or more people to kill themselves at the same time 自殺合約〔指兩人以上約定一起自殺〕

2 3 **suit¹** /sut; suːt/ *n* [C]

1 ▶CLOTHES 衣服◀ a set of clothes made of the same material, usually including a JACKET (=short coat) with trousers or a skirt 一套衣服〔通常包括用相同衣料做的短上衣和褲子或裙子〕: *a cream linen suit* 一套米色亞麻衣服 | *a grey winter suit* 一套灰色冬裝 —see also 另見 MORNING SUIT

2 jogging/swim suit a piece or pieces of clothing used for a special purpose 慢跑運動服/游泳衣 —see also 另見 BOILER SUIT, SHELL SUIT, WET SUIT

3 ▶CARDS 紙牌◀ one of the four types of cards in a set of playing cards 〔一副紙牌中的〕四種花色的牌中的任何一種

4 ▶LAW 法律◀ an argument brought to a court of law by a private person or company, not by the police or government; LAWSUIT 〔個人或公司而非警方或政府提出的〕訴訟; 訟案: **file suit** (=bring an argument to a court of law) 提出訴訟

5 sb's strong suit *especially AmE* something that you are good at【尤美】某人擅長的事, 某人的專長, 某人的特長: *Politeness is not his strong suit.* 他不擅長客套。

6 plead/press your suit *old use* to ask a woman to marry you【舊】〔向女子〕求婚 —see also 另見 **in your birthday suit** (BIRTHDAY (2)), **follow suit** (FOLLOW (15))

2 3 **suit²** *v* [T] **1** to be acceptable or CONVENIENT for a particular person or in a particular situation 適合; 中...的意; 對...方便: *Finding a date that suits us all is very difficult.* 很難找到一個對我們大家都合適的日期。| *Buy a database program to suit your needs.* 買個數據庫程序來滿足你的需要吧。| **suit sb (fine)** *spoken* (=be completely acceptable)【口】(很) 合某人的意; 對某人 (很) 合適 *"Eight o'clock?" "That suits me fine."* "八點鐘行嗎?" "行, 這對我很合適。" | **suit sb down to the ground** (=be exactly right for someone) 對某人非常合適 *Yup, this little car suits me down to the ground.* 好, 這輛小汽車對我再合適不過了。**2** [not in passive 不用被動態] to make someone look attractive 使顯得漂亮: *That coat really suits Paul.* 保羅穿那件外套真好看。| *Red suits you.* 你穿紅色很漂亮。—see 見 FIT¹ (USAGE)

3 well/best/ideally suited to have the right qualities to do something 非常適合〔做某事〕; 具備做某事的特質: *Dirk would be ideally suited to the job.* 德克做這工作再合適不過了。

4 suit yourself *spoken* used to tell someone they can do whatever they want to, even though it annoys you【口】隨你的便吧; 你想怎樣就怎樣吧: *"I don't really feel like going out after all." "Suit yourself."* "我還是不是特別想出去。" "隨你的便。"

5 suit sb's book *BrE informal* to fit well into someone's plans【英, 非正式】適合某人的計劃, 合某人的心意

suit sth **to** sth *phr v* [T] *formal* to make something exactly right for something else【正式】使〔某物〕適合於〔另一物〕: *Suit the punishment to the crime, I say.* 我說呀, 要按罪量刑。

suit·a·bil·i·ty /ˌsutəˈbɪlətɪ; ˌsuːtəˈbɪlɨti/ *n* [U] the degree to which something or someone has the right qualities for a particular purpose 合適, 適合, 適宜: **[+for]** *There's no doubt about Christine's suitability for the job.* 克里斯廷適合做這份工作, 這是毫無疑問的。

suit·a·ble /ˈsutəbḷ; ˈsuːtəbəl/ *adj* having the right qualities for a particular person, purpose, or situation 合適的, 適合的, 適宜的: *We are hoping to find a suitable school.* 我們希望能找到一所合適的學校。| **[+for]** *The house is not really suitable for a large family.* 這所房子不是很適合大家庭居住。| **suitable to do sth** *Would this be suitable to wear to Deb's wedding?* 穿這套衣服參加德布的婚禮合適嗎? —opposite 反義詞 UNSUITABLE —**suitableness** *n* [U] 2 2

suit·a·bly /ˈsutəblɪ; ˈsuːtəbli/ *adv* **1 suitably dressed/prepared/equipped etc** wearing the right clothes, having the right information, equipment etc for a particular situation 衣着得體/準備停當/裝備完善等: *We were relieved that Gordon had arrived at the wedding suitably dressed.* 看見戈登衣着得體地來參加婚禮, 我們都鬆了一口氣。**2 suitably impressed/amazed** showing the amount of feeling you would expect in a particular situation 合乎情理地佩服/吃驚: *The others were suitably impressed by the huge trout I caught.* 大家對我抓到的特大鱒魚表示欽佩, 也是合情合理的。

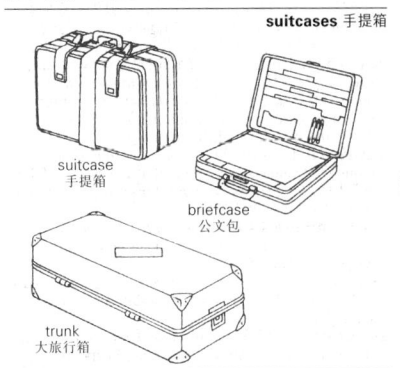

suitcases 手提箱

suitcase 手提箱

briefcase 公文包

trunk 大旅行箱

suit·case /ˈsutˌkes; ˈsuːtkeɪs/ *n* [C] a large case with a handle, used for carrying clothes and possessions when you travel 〔旅行用的〕手提箱

suite /swit; swiːt/ *n* [C]

1 ▶ROOMS 房間◀ a set of rooms, especially expensive ones in a hotel 〔旅館的〕套房〔尤指豪華套房〕: *a honeymoon suite* 蜜月套房 | **suite of rooms** *a suite of rooms for palace guests* 王室賓客套房

2 ▶FURNITURE 家具◀ *especially BrE* a set of matching furniture for a room【尤英】一套家具: *a pink bathroom suite* 一套粉紅色浴室家具 | **three-piece suite** (=a large seat and two chairs) 三件套家具〔一張長沙發加兩張單座沙發〕

3 ▶MUSIC 音樂◀ a piece of music made up of several short parts 〔音樂的〕組曲: *the Nutcracker Suite*《胡桃夾子組曲》

4 ▶POLITICS 政治◀ the people who work for, advise, or help an important person; RETINUE 〔要人的〕〔一批〕隨員, 隨從

5 ▶COMPUTERS 電腦◀ *technical* a group of related computer PROGRAMs that make a set【術語】〔電腦的〕程式組

suit·ing /ˈsutɪŋ; ˈsuːtɪŋ/ *n* [U] *technical* material used for making suits, especially woven wool【術語】西服衣料, 羊毛衣料

sui·tor /ˈsutɚ; ˈsuːtə/ *n* [C] *old use* a man who wants to marry a particular woman【舊】〔女子的〕追求者, 求婚者

sul·fate /ˈsʌlfet; ˈsʌlfeɪt/ *n* [C,U] the American spelling of SULPHATE sulphate 的美式拼法

sul·fide /ˈsʌlfaɪd; ˈsʌlfaɪd/ *n* [C,U] the American spell-

S

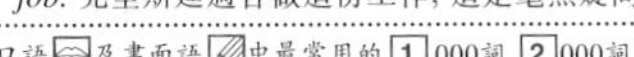

ing of SULPHIDE sulphide的美式拼法

sul·fur /ˋsʌlfɚ; ˈsʌlfə/ *n* [U] the American spelling of SULPHUR sulphur的美式拼法

sulfur di·ox·ide /,‥ ·ˋ‥/ *n* [U] the American spelling of SULPHUR DIOXIDE sulphur dioxide的美式拼法

sul·fu·ric a·cid /sʌl,fjʊrɪk ˋæsɪd; sʌl,fjʊərɪk ˈæsɪ̌d/ *n* [U] the American spelling of SULPHURIC ACID sulphuric acid的美式拼法

sul·fu·rous /ˋsʌlfərəs; ˈsʌlfərəs/ *adj* the American spelling of SULPHUROUS sulphurous的美式拼法

sulk¹ /sʌlk; sʌlk/ *v* [I] to show that you are annoyed about something by being silent and having an unhappy expression on your face 生悶氣, 慍怒: *Stuart's sulking because I told him he couldn't go out and play.* 斯圖爾特在生悶氣, 因為我不許他到外面去玩。

sulk² *n BrE*【英】**in a sulk** angry and silent 慍怒(的), 生着悶氣(的): *Neil's in a sulk because Paul won't play football with him.* 尼爾在生悶氣, 因為保羅不肯跟他踢足球。

sulk·y /ˋsʌlkɪ; ˈsʌlki/ *adj* **1** showing that you are sulking 生悶氣的, 繃着臉的: *a sulky frown* 鬱鬱不樂的皺眉 **2** tending to sulk 愛生悶氣的, 動輒不高興的: *a sulky child* 愛生悶氣的孩子 —**sulkily** *adv* —**sulkiness** *n* [U]

sul·len /ˋsʌlən; ˈsʌlən/ *adj* **1** silently showing anger or bad temper 悶悶不樂的, 慍怒的: *a look of sullen resentment* 滿臉的慍怒怨恨 **2** *literary* sky or weather that is sullen is dark and unpleasant【文】〔天空或天氣〕陰沉的 —**sullenly** *adv* —**sullenness** *n* [U]

sul·ly /ˋsʌlɪ; ˈsʌli/ *v* [T] *formal or literary* to spoil or reduce the value of something that was perfect【正式或文】弄髒, 玷污, 破壞: *a scandal that sullied his reputation* 玷污了他名譽的醜聞

sul·phate *BrE*【英】, **sulfate** *AmE*【美】/ˋsʌlfet; ˈsʌlfeɪt/ *n* [C,U] a SALT¹ (4) formed from SULPHURIC ACID 硫酸鹽: *copper sulphate* 硫酸銅

sul·phide *BrE*【英】, **sulfide** *AmE*【美】/ˋsʌlfaɪd; ˈsʌlfaɪd/ *n* [C,U] a mixture of sulphur with another substance 硫化物

sul·phur *BrE*【英】, **sulfur** *AmE*【美】/ˋsʌlfɚ; ˈsʌlfə/ *n* [U] an ELEMENT (=simple substance) especially in the form of a light yellow powder, used in drugs, explosives, and industry 硫, 硫磺

sulphur di·ox·ide *BrE*【英】, **sulfur dioxide** *AmE*【美】/,‥ ·ˋ‥/ *n* [U] a poisonous gas that is a cause of air POLLUTION in industrial areas 二氧化硫〔污染空氣的有毒氣體〕

sul·phu·ric ac·id *BrE*【英】, **sulfuric acid** *AmE*【美】/sʌl,fjʊrɪk ˋæsɪd; sʌl,fjʊərɪk ˈæsɪ̌d/ *n* [U] a powerful acid 硫酸

sul·phu·rous *BrE*【英】, **sulfurous** *AmE*【美】/ˋsʌlfərəs; ˈsʌlfərəs/ *adj* related to, full of, or used with sulphur 硫的, 含硫的

sul·tan /ˋsʌltn̩; ˈsʌltən/ *n* [C] a ruler in some Muslim countries 蘇丹〔某些穆斯林國家統治者的稱號〕

sul·ta·na /sʌlˋtænə; sʌlˈtɑːnə/ *n* [C] **1** a small pale RAISIN (=dried fruit) without seeds, used in baking〔做糕餅用的〕無籽小葡萄乾; GOLDEN RAISIN *AmE*【美】**2** also 又作 **Sultana** the wife, mother, or daughter of a sultan 蘇丹的女眷〔指其妻子、母親或女兒〕

sul·tan·ate /ˋsʌltn̩ɪt; ˈsʌltəneɪt/ *n* [C] **1** a country ruled by a sultan 蘇丹統治的國家, 蘇丹國: *the sultanate of Oman* 阿曼蘇丹國 **2** the position of a sultan, or the period of time during which he rules 蘇丹的職位; 蘇丹的統治期

sul·try /ˋsʌltrɪ; ˈsʌltri/ *adj* **1** weather that is sultry is unpleasantly hot with no wind〔天氣〕悶熱的 **2** a woman who is sultry makes other people feel strong sexual attraction to her〔女子〕風騷的, 性感迷人的: *a sultry look* 撩人的一瞥 —**sultriness** *n* [U]

3 **sum¹** /sʌm; sʌm/ *n*
2 **1 ▶MONEY 錢◀** [C] an amount of money 金額, 款項: **a large/small sum (of)** *Sid was left a large sum of money by his aunt.* 錫德的姑母給他遺留下一大筆錢。| **for the sum of** *It was mine for the sum of £20.* 我是花了20英鎊把它買來的。—see also 另見 LUMP SUM, **princely sum** (PRINCELY (1))

2 the sum of the total produced when you add two or more numbers together 和; 總和, 總數: *The sum of 6 and 4 is 10.* 6加4之和為10。

3 greater/more than the sum of its parts a group of things or people that is greater than the sum of its parts has a quality or effectiveness as a group that you would not expect from looking at each member〔總體的作用〕大於各部分的總和

4 ▶CALCULATION 計算◀ [C] *BrE* a simple calculation by adding, multiplying, dividing etc, especially one done by children at school【英】簡單的計算, 算術〔尤指小學生的加減乘除運算〕

5 do your sums *informal BrE* to calculate whether you have enough money to do something【非正式, 英】算一算是否有足夠的錢做某事: *Well I've done my sums, and I think I can afford a holiday.* 我已經算過了, 我想我有足夠的錢去度假。

6 in sum *old-fashioned* used before a statement that gives the main information about something in a few simple words【過時】總之, 簡而言之: *It was, in sum, a complete failure.* 總之, 這是一次徹底的失敗。—see also 另見 SUM TOTAL

sum² *v* **summed, summing**

sum up *phr v* **1** [I,T] to give the main information about a report, speech, TRIAL¹ (1) etc in a short statement at the end; SUMMARIZE 概括, 總結, 概述: **to sum up** *So, to sum up, we need to concentrate on staff training.* 因此, 概括地說, 我們需要集中精力提高員工的培訓。| **sum sth ↔ up** *The last chapter sums up the arguments.* 最後一章概括了全部論點。**2** [T **sum** sb/sth ↔ **up**] to form a judgment or opinion about someone or something 對…作出判斷; 對…形成意見: *Pat summed up the situation at a glance.* 帕特一眼就看清了當時的情勢。**3 that (about) sums it up** *spoken* used to say that you have said everything that is important about a subject【口】主要情況就是這樣 —see also 另見 SUMMING-UP

sum·ma cum lau·de /ˋsʌmə ,kʌm ˋlɔdɪ; ,sʌmə kʌm ˈlɔːdi/ *adj, adv AmE* the highest level of HONOURS given to American university or college students【美】〔給予美國大學生的〕最高榮譽 —compare 比較 CUM LAUDE

sum·mar·ize also 又作 **-ise** *BrE*【英】/ˋsʌmə,raɪz; ˈsʌməraɪz/ *v* [I,T] to make a short statement giving only the main information and not the details of a plan, event, report etc 總結, 概括, 概述: *Jack quickly summarized the main points of his plan.* 傑克很快地概述了他計劃中的要點。

sum·ma·ry¹ /ˋsʌmərɪ; ˈsʌməri/ *n* [C] a short statement that gives the main information about something, without giving all the details 總結, 摘要, 概要: *Please write a one-page summary of this report.* 請給這份報告寫一個一頁紙的摘要。| *a news summary* 新聞提要 | **in summary** *So, in summary, we've got to try to get further funding.* 因此, 概括地說, 我們必須努力爭取更多的資金。

summary² *adj* [only before noun 僅用於名詞前] *formal* done immediately, without paying attention to the usual processes, rules etc【正式】立即的; 速決的〔未顧及慣常的程序、規定等〕: *a summary execution* 立即處決 —**summarily** *adv*: *Franklin was summarily dismissed.* 富蘭克林被立即開除了。

sum·mat /ˋsʌmət; ˈsʌmət/ *pron dialect* a spoken form 2
of SOMETHING【方言】某事, 某物, 某種東西〔something的口語形式〕

sum·ma·tion /sʌmˋeʃən; səˈmeɪʃən/ *n* [C] *formal*【正式】**1** a summary; SUMMING-UP 總結, 概括, 概述 **2** the total amount or number you get when two or more things are added together 總和, 總數, 合計

sum·mer¹ /ˋsʌmɚ; ˈsʌmə/ *n* **1** [C,U] the time of the year 1
when the sun is hottest and the days are longest, be- 1

tween spring and autumn 夏天, 夏季: *Are you going on vacation this summer?* 今年夏天你去度假嗎? | *the summer of 1940* 1940 年夏季 | **be summer** *I'm so glad it's summer!* 夏天到了, 我很高興! | **summer clothes/sports etc** (=used or done in summer) 夏季衣服/運動等 *a summer dress* 一件夏裝 | **high summer** (=the hottest part of summer) 盛夏 **2 summer rental** [C] *AmE* a house or apartment that you rent only during the summer【美】夏季出租房〔只在夏天租用的房子或公寓〕**3 your 50/70 etc summers** *literary* a way of saying how old someone is【文】50 歲/70 歲等, 50 個/70 個等春秋: *looking younger than his 70 summers* 他看起來要比 70 高齡顯得年輕 —see also 另見 INDIAN SUMMER

summer² *v* [I] to spend the summer in a particular place〔在某地〕過夏天, 度夏

summer camp /ˈ·· ˌ·/ *n* [C,U] a place where children in the US can stay during the summer, and take part in various activities 夏令營

summer hol·i·days /ˌ·· ˈ···/ *n* [plural] *BrE* the period of time during the summer when schools and universities are closed【英】〔學校的〕暑假; SUMMER VACATION *AmE*【美】

sum·mer·house /ˈsʌmɚˌhaus; ˈsʌməhaʊs/ *n* [C] a building in your garden, where you can sit in warm weather〔花園中的〕涼亭, 涼棚

summer pud·ding /ˌ·· ˈ··/ *n* [C,U] a British sweet dish made from pieces of bread and fruit such as berries 夏令布丁〔用水果, 如漿果和麵包片做的英式甜品〕

summer school /ˈ·· ·/ *n* [C,U] courses you can take in the summer at a school, university, or college 暑期課程, 暑期學校, 暑期班

summer sol·stice /ˌ·· ˈ··/ *n* [singular] the longest day in the northern HEMISPHERE (=top half of the earth), around June 22nd 夏至〔北半球白天最長的一天, 在 6 月 22 日前後〕

sum·mer·time /ˈsʌmɚˌtaɪm; ˈsʌmətaɪm/ *n* [U] the season when it is summer 夏天, 夏季 —see also 另見 BRITISH SUMMER TIME

summer va·ca·tion /ˌ·· ·ˈ··/ *n* [U] *AmE* the period of time during the summer when schools and universities are closed【美】〔學校的〕暑假; SUMMER HOLIDAYS *BrE*【英】

sum·mer·y /ˈsʌmərɪ; ˈsʌməri/ *adj* suitable for, or reminding you of the summer 適合夏季的; 夏季的: *a light summery dress* 一件輕薄的夏裝

summing-up /ˌ·· ˈ·/ *n plural* **summings-up** [C] a statement giving the main facts but not the details of something, especially made by a judge at the end of a TRIAL¹ (1)〔尤指法官在審判結束時所作的〕總結, 總括性概述: *In his summing-up, the judge said it was dangerous to convict on this evidence alone.* 法官在總結中說, 單憑這點證據就宣判有罪是危險的。—see also 另見 **sum up** (SUM²)

3 **sum·mit** /ˈsʌmɪt; ˈsʌmɪ̬t/ *n* [C] **1** the top of a mountain 山頂: *The climbers reached the summit of Mount Everest yesterday.* 登山者昨天登上珠穆朗瑪峯的頂峯。—see picture on page A12 參見 A12 頁圖 **2** a set of meetings between the leaders of several governments 首腦會議, 最高級會議, 峯會: *the recent Geneva summit* 最近召開的日內瓦首腦會議 | **summit meeting** (=for a particular purpose) 首腦會議, 最高級會議; 高峯會 **3 the summit of** *formal* the greatest amount or highest level of something【正式】…的頂峯, …的極點: *the summit of scientific achievement* 科學成就的頂峯

sum·mon /ˈsʌmən; ˈsʌmən/ *v* [T] *formal*【正式】**1** to officially order someone to come to a meeting, a court of law etc 召集〔開會〕; 傳喚〔出庭〕: **summon sb to sth** *We were all summoned to a meeting with the principal.* 我們都被叫去和校長開會。| **summon sb to do sth** *They'll probably be summoning you to appear in court.* 他們也許要傳喚你出庭。**2** also 又作 **summon** sth ↔ **up** to make a great effort to use your strength, courage, energy etc 鼓起〔勇氣〕; 振作〔精神〕; 使出〔力氣〕: *Summoning all her strength, Julia gave one last pull.* 朱莉婭使盡全身力氣最後再拉了一次。| *I couldn't summon up the courage to ask you out until now.* 我直到現在才鼓起勇氣請你出來。**3 summon a meeting/conference etc** to arrange for a meeting to take place and order people to come to it; CONVENE 召開會議等

sum·mons¹ /ˈsʌmənz; ˈsʌmənz/ *n plural* **summonses** [C] an official order to appear in a court of law〔法庭的〕傳票: **serve a summons on sb** (=order someone to appear in court) 發出傳票傳喚某人出庭

summons² *v* [T usually passive 一般用被動態] to order someone to appear in a court of law 發傳票給〔某人〕, 傳喚, 傳訊: *I was summonsed to appear as a witness.* 我被傳喚出庭作證。

su·mo /ˈsumo; ˈsuːməʊ/ also 又作 **sumo wrest·ling** /ˌ·· ˈ··/ *n* [U] a Japanese form of wrestling (WRESTLE (1)), done by men who are very large 相撲〔日本的一種摔跤運動〕—**sumo wrestler** *n* [C]

sump /sʌmp; sʌmp/ *n* [C] **1** the lowest part of a DRAINAGE system where liquids or wastes remain〔排水系統的〕集液池, 污水坑 **2** *BrE* the part of an engine that contains the supply of oil【英】〔發動機的〕油盤, 潤滑油箱; OIL PAN *AmE*【美】

sump·tu·ous /ˈsʌmptʃuəs; ˈsʌmptʃuəs/ *adj* very impressive and expensive; LUXURIOUS 豪華的, 奢華的, 奢侈的: *a sumptuous banquet* 盛宴 —**sumptuously** *adv*: *sumptuously dressed in velvet* 身穿華貴天鵝絨衣服 —**sumptuousness** *n* [U]

sum to·tal /ˌ· ˈ··/ *n* **the sum total of** the whole amount of something, especially when this is less than expected or needed 全部〔東西〕; 總數, 總量, 總額〔尤用於表示比預料或所需的少〕: *Is that the sum total of what they've taught you?* 這就是他們教給你的全部東西了嗎?

S

Sun the written abbreviation of 縮寫= SUNDAY

sun¹ /sʌn; sʌn/ *n* **1** [singular] the large bright thing in the sky that gives us light and heat, and around which the Earth moves 太陽 —see picture at 參見 SOLAR SYSTEM 圖 **2** [U] the heat and light that come from the sun 太陽的熱和光, 陽光, 日光: *Too much sun is bad for you.* 過多的太陽光對你沒有好處。| **in the sun** *Tanya sat in the sun, reading a book.* 塔尼婭坐在陽光下看書。**3** [C] any star around which PLANETS move〔有行星的〕恒星 **4 catch the sun** *BrE*【英】, **get the sun** *AmE*【美】**a)** if someone catches or gets the sun, they become slightly red or brown because they have been outside in the sun〔人〕被曬黑 **b)** if a place or room catches or gets the sun, it is very bright and warm when the sun shines〔地方或房間〕陽光充足 **5 under the sun** used to emphasize that you are talking about something that includes very large numbers of ideas or things etc 世界上, 天(底)下〔用於表示強調〕: *Santos could talk about any subject under the sun.* 桑托斯可以談論世界上的任何話題。—see also 另見 **make hay while the sun shines** (HAY (3)) 2 1

sun² *v* **sunned, sunning** [T] **sun yourself** to sit or lie outside when the sun is shining 曬太陽: *a cat sunning itself on the patio* 在露台上曬太陽的貓

sun-baked /ˈ· ·/ *adj* made very hard and dry by the sun〔太陽〕曬乾的, 曬硬的: *the sun-baked earth of the western desert* 被太陽曬硬了的西部沙漠土地

sun·bathe /ˈsʌnˌbeð; ˈsʌnbeɪð/ *v* [I] to sit or lie outside in the sun, especially in order to become brown 沐日光浴, 曬太陽: *a good beach for sunbathing* 日光浴的理想海灘 —see 見 BATH² (USAGE)

sun·beam /ˈsʌnˌbim; ˈsʌnbiːm/ *n* [C] a beam of light from the sun that you can see because it is shining through a cloud〔一道〕日光, 陽光光束

sun·bed /ˈsʌnbɛd; ˈsʌnbed/ *n* [C] **1** a metal structure the size of a bed that you lie on to make your skin brown using light from special lamps 太陽燈浴浴牀 **2** a SUN LOUNGER〔室外用的〕輕便摺椅 —see also 另見 SUNLAMP

sun·belt /ˈsʌnbɛlt; ˈsʌnbelt/ *n* [singular] the southern or southwestern parts of the US, from Virginia to California 陽光地帶〔指美國南部或西南部從弗吉尼亞州至加利福尼亞州一帶〕

sun blind /ˈ· ·/ *n* [C] *BrE* the thing you pull down over a window to keep the sun out of a room【英】〔阻擋陽光照進室內的〕百葉窗, 遮陽簾

sun·block /ˈsʌnblɑk; ˈsʌnblɒk/ *n* [C,U] cream or oil that you rub into your skin, in order to completely stop the sun's light from burning you 防曬霜, 防曬油 —compare 比較 SUNSCREEN

sun·bon·net /ˈsʌn,bɑnɪt; ˈsʌnbɒnʒt/ *n* [C] a hat worn in the past by women as protection from the sun〔舊時的〕闊邊遮陽女帽

sun·burn /ˈsʌn,bɝn; ˈsʌnbɜːn/ *n* [U] the condition of having skin that is red and painful, as a result of spending too much time in the sun 曬傷,〔曬太陽過量而引起的〕皮膚灼痛 —**sunburned** also 又作 **sunburnt** *adj* —compare 比較 SUNTAN

sun cream /ˈ· ·/ *n* [C,U] *BrE* a cream or oil that you rub into your skin to stop the sun from burning you too much; SUNTAN LOTION【英】防曬霜, 防曬油

sun·dae /ˈsʌndɪ; ˈsʌndeɪ/ *n* [C] a dish made from ICE CREAM, fruit, sweet SAUCE, nuts etc 聖代冰淇淋, 新地〔一種加水果、糖漿、果仁等的冰淇淋〕: *a chocolate sundae* 巧克力聖代冰淇淋

Sun·day /ˈsʌndɪ; ˈsʌndi/ written abbreviation 縮寫為 **Sun** *n* [C,U] **1** the day between Saturday and Monday. In Britain, Sunday is considered the last day of the week, and in the US it is considered the first day of the week 星期日, 星期天〔在英國被看作是一週的最後一天, 在美國則被看作是一週的第一天〕: *I went to a concert last Sunday.* 上星期天我去聽了一場音樂會。| *We're going to a match on Sunday.* 我們星期天要去看比賽。| *Sunday nights are usually pretty quiet.* 星期天晚上一般都相當安靜。| **on Sundays** (=each Sunday) 每逢星期天, 在星期天 *Do you go to church on Sundays?* 你每個星期天都上教堂做禮拜嗎? | **a Sunday** (=one of the Sundays in the year)〔一年中的〕某個星期日 *My birthday is on a Sunday this year.* 我今年的生日是在一個星期天。| **the Sunday** *BrE* (=the Sunday of the week being mentioned)【英】所提及的一週的星期日 *Nan came on the Monday and left on the Sunday.* 南星期一來的, 星期天就走了。**2 Sunday best** your best clothes, worn only for special occasions or for church〔某人衣服中〕最好的衣服, 節日盛裝 **3 Sunday driver** an insulting word meaning someone who annoys other people by driving too slowly 星期日司機〔侮辱性用語, 指開車慢得令人厭煩的人〕—see also 另見 **never in a month of Sundays** (MONTH (7))

Sunday school /ˈ·· ·/ *n* [C,U] a place where children are taught about Christianity on Sundays 主日學校〔星期日對兒童進行基督教教育的場所〕

sun·deck /ˈsʌn,dɛk; ˈsʌndek/ *n* [C] a part of a ship where people can sit in the sun〔大船上供乘客坐在陽光下的〕日光甲板

sun·der /ˈsʌndɚ; ˈsʌndə/ *v* [T] *literary* to break something into parts, especially violently【文】〔尤指猛烈地〕將〔某物〕分開; 使碎開; 割開; 切開 —see also 另見 ASUNDER

sun·dial /ˈsʌn,daɪəl; ˈsʌndaɪəl/ *n* [C] an object used in the past for telling the time, by looking at the position of a shadow made on a stone circle by a pointed piece of metal〔舊時用以測量時間的〕日規, 日晷

sun·down /ˈsʌn,daun; ˈsʌndaʊn/ *n* [U] *old-fashioned* SUNSET (1)【過時】日落

sun·down·er /ˈsʌn,daunɚ; ˈsʌn,daʊnə/ *n* [C] *informal especially BrE* an alcoholic drink drunk in the evening【非正式, 尤英】〔黃昏時喝的〕日落酒

sun-drenched /ˈ· ·/ *adj* a sun-drenched place is one where the sun shines most of the time〔地方〕陽光充足的, 充滿陽光的: *sun-drenched tropical islands* 陽光充足的熱帶海島

sun·dress /ˈsʌn,drɛs; ˈsʌndres/ *n* [C] a dress that you wear in hot weather, that does not cover your arms, neck, or shoulders 太陽裙〔一種天熱時穿的無袖連衣裙〕

sun-dried /ˈ· ·/ *adj* [only before noun 僅用於名詞前] sun-dried food has been left in the sun to dry in order to give it a particular taste〔食物〕曬乾的: *sun-dried tomatoes*〔曬成的〕番茄乾

sun·dries /ˈsʌn,drɪz; ˈsʌndriz/ *n* [plural] *formal* small objects that are not important enough to be named separately【正式】雜物; 雜項 —see also 另見 SUNDRY

sun·dry /ˈsʌndrɪ; ˈsʌndri/ *adj* [only before noun 僅用於名詞前] *formal*【正式】**1 all and sundry** everyone, not just a few carefully chosen people 每個人〔而不是精心挑選的某些人〕: *In the 80s the economy was booming and banks dished out loans to all and sundry.* 在 80 年代, 經濟繁榮, 銀行貸款人人可得。**2** not similar enough to form a group; various 各種各樣的, 雜七雜八的: *pens, books, and other sundry articles* 鋼筆、書本及各種其他物品

sun·fish /ˈsʌn,fɪʃ; ˈsʌnfɪʃ/ *n* [C,U] a fish that lives in the sea and has a large round body 太陽魚, 棘臀魚〔一種海魚〕

sun·flow·er /ˈsʌn,flauɚ; ˈsʌn,flaʊə/ *n* [C] a very tall plant with a large yellow flower and seeds that can be eaten 向日葵

sung /sʌŋ; sʌŋ/ the past participle of SING

sun·glass·es /ˈsʌn,glæsɪz; ˈsʌn,glɑːsʒz/ *n* [plural] dark glasses that you wear to protect your eyes when the sun is very bright 太陽鏡, 墨鏡

sun god /ˈ· ·/ *n* [C] a god in some ancient religions who represents the sun or has power over it〔古代某些宗教信仰中的〕太陽神

sun hat /ˈ· ·/ *n* [C] a hat that you wear to protect your head from the sun〔闊邊〕遮陽帽 —see picture at 參見 HAT 圖

sunk /sʌŋk; sʌŋk/ the past tense and past participle of SINK[1]

sunk·en /ˈsʌŋkən; ˈsʌŋkən/ *adj* **1** [only before noun 僅用於名詞前] having fallen to the bottom of the sea 沉沒的, 沉在海底的: *a sunken ship* 一艘沉船 | *sunken treasure* 沉在海底的寶物 **2** [only before noun 僅用於名詞前] built or placed at a lower level than the surrounding floor, ground etc 低於周圍地面的, 沉降式的, 下沉式的: *a sunken bath* 低於地面的浴缸 | *a sunken garden* 沉降式花園 **3 sunken cheeks/eyes etc** cheeks or eyes that have fallen inwards, especially because you are old, or ill 凹陷的雙頰/兩眼等〔尤指因年老或患病所致〕

sun·lamp /ˈsʌn,læmp; ˈsʌnlæmp/ *n* [C] a lamp that produces a special light used for making your skin brown 太陽燈, 紫外線燈

sun·less /ˈsʌnlɪs; ˈsʌnləs/ *adj* having no light from the sun 無陽[日]光的: *the sunless depths of the ocean* 沒有陽光的海洋深處

sun·light /ˈsʌn,laɪt; ˈsʌnlaɪt/ *n* [U] natural light that comes from the sun 陽光, 日光: *bright sunlight* 燦爛的陽光 | *plants that need a lot of sunlight* 需要大量日光的植物

sun·lit /ˈsʌn,lɪt; ˈsʌnlɪt/ *adj* made brighter by light from the sun 陽光照耀的: *a sunlit garden* 陽光燦爛的花園

sun lounge /ˈ· ·/ *n* [C] *BrE* a room with large windows and often a glass roof, designed to let in lots of light【英】日光浴室〔窗戶很大, 房頂常用玻璃建造以吸收陽光〕; SUN PORCH *AmE*【美】

sun loun·ger /ˈ· ,··/ *n* [C] a light chair like a folding bed, that you can sit or lie on outside〔室外用的〕輕便摺椅

Sun·na, Sun·nah /ˈsunə; ˈsʊnə/ *n* **the Sunna** a set of Muslim customs and rules based on the words and acts of Muhammad〔伊斯蘭教根據穆罕默德言行建立的〕遜奈, 穆斯林言行規範

Sun·ni /ˈsunɪ; ˈsʊni/ *n* [C] a Muslim who follows one of the two main branches of the Muslim religion 遜尼派教

徒〔遜尼派是伊斯蘭教的兩支主要教派之一〕—compare 比較 SHIITE

sun·ny /ˋsʌnɪ; ˈsʌni/ *adj* **1** full of light from the sun 陽光充足的: *a sunny day* 陽光明媚的日子 | *a sunny room* 陽光充足的房間 **2** *informal* cheerful and happy【非正式】興高采烈的, 快樂的: *a sunny smile* 快活的微笑

sunny-side up /ˌ·· · ˈ·/ *adj* [not before noun 不用於名詞前] *AmE* an egg that is cooked sunny-side up is cooked in hot fat on one side only, and not turned over in the pan【美】〔煎蛋〕單面煎的, 只煎一面的

sun porch /ˈ· ·/ *n* [C] *AmE* a room with large windows and often a glass roof, designed to let in lots of light【美】日光浴室〔窗戶很大, 房頂常用玻璃建造以吸收陽光〕; SUN LOUNGE *BrE*【英】

sun·rise /ˋsʌnˌraɪz; ˈsʌnraɪz/ *n* [U] **1** the time when the sun first appears in the morning 日出(時分); 黎明; 拂曉: *We got up at sunrise.* 我們黎明時起牀。**2** the part of the sky where the sun first appears in the morning 晨曦, 朝霞: *sunrise over Mount Fuji* 富士山山頂的晨曦

sunrise in·dus·try /ˈ·· ˌ···/ *n* [C] an industry, such as ELECTRONICS or making computers, that uses modern processes and takes the place of older industries 朝陽工業, 新興工業〈如電子工業、電腦製造業等〉—compare 比較 HEAVY INDUSTRY

sun·roof /ˋsʌnˌruf; ˈsʌnruːf/ *n* [C] **1** a part of the roof of a car that you can open to let in air and light〔汽車的〕活動車頂, 滑動頂板 —see picture on page A2 參見 A2 頁圖 **2** a flat roof of a building where you can sit when the sun is shining〔可曬太陽的〕平屋頂, 樓頂平台

sun·screen /ˋsʌnˌskrin; ˈsʌnskriːn/ *n* [C,U] a cream or oil that you rub into your skin to stop the sun from burning you 防曬霜, 防曬油 —see also 另見 SUNBLOCK

sun·set /ˋsʌnˌsɛt; ˈsʌnset/ *n* **1** [U] the time of day when the sun disappears and night begins 日落(時分), 薄暮, 黃昏: **at sunset** *The builders stop work at sunset.* 建築工人傍晚時分收工。**2** [C,U] the part of the sky where the sun gradually disappears at the end of the day 晚霞, 落日餘暉: *We sat on the beach and watched the sunset.* 我們坐在海灘上觀看落日餘暉。

sun·shade /ˋsʌnˌʃed; ˈsʌnʃeɪd/ *n* [C] an object shaped like an UMBRELLA, used especially in the past as protection from the sun; PARASOL 太陽傘; 遮陽篷

3 **sun·shine** /ˋsʌnˌʃaɪn; ˈsʌnʃaɪn/ *n* [U] **1** a word meaning the light and heat that come from the sun, used when you want to say that this is pleasant 陽光, 日照: *Northern Ireland will start dry with some sunshine.* 北愛爾蘭一早天氣乾燥, 有些陽光。**2** *informal* happiness【非正式】快樂, 幸福: **ray of sunshine** *Zoe was the only ray of sunshine during those depressing months.* 在令人憂愁的那幾個月裡, 佐伊是唯一能帶來快樂的人。

sun·spot /ˋsʌnˌspɑt; ˈsʌnspɒt/ *n* [C] **1** *technical* a small dark area on the sun's surface【術語】〔太陽表面的〕黑子, 日斑 **2** *informal* a place where the sun shines a lot, that many people go to on holiday【非正式】陽光充沛的度假地

sun·stroke /ˋsʌnˌstrok; ˈsʌnstrəʊk/ *n* [U] fever, weakness etc caused by being outside in the sun for too long 日射病, 中暑

sun·tan /ˋsʌntæn; ˈsʌntæn/ *n* [C] attractively brown skin which you get when you spend a lot of time in bright sunlight; TAN² (2)〔皮膚的〕曬黑 —**suntanned** *adj* —compare 比較 SUNBURN

suntan lo·tion /ˈ·· ˌ··/ also 又作 **suntan oil** /ˈ·· ˌ·/ *n* [C, U] a cream or oil that you rub into your skin to stop the sun from burning you too much 防曬霜, 防曬油

sun·trap /ˋsʌnˌtræp; ˈsʌntræp/ *n* [C] a place that is sheltered and gets a lot of heat and light from the sun 避風向陽處: *Our terrace is a real suntrap.* 我們的露台真是個向陽避風的地方。

sun-up /ˈ· ·/ *n* [U] *old-fashioned* SUNRISE【過時】日出

sun-wor·ship·per /ˈ· ˌ···/ *n* [C] *informal* someone who likes to lie in the sun to get a SUNTAN【非正式】極愛日光浴的人

sup /sʌp; sʌp/ *v* **1** [T] to drink something, especially slowly in small amounts 一點點地喝, 呷: *Mrs Holliday was supping porridge in the back kitchen.* 霍利戴太太在後邊廚房裡慢慢地喝粥。**2** *old use* to eat supper【舊】吃晚飯 —**sup** *n* [C]

super- /supɚ; suːpə/ *prefix* more, larger, greater, or more powerful than usual 超, 特別, 過於: *a supertanker* (=a ship that can carry extremely large loads) 超級貨輪[油輪] | *superglue* 超強力膠水 | *super-rich film stars* 特別闊氣的電影明星 | *superheated steam* 過熱的蒸汽

su·per¹ /ˋsupɚ; ˈsuːpə/ *adj informal* extremely good; WONDERFUL【非正式】極好的, 了不起的: *It's a super place for a holiday.* 這是個度假的絕佳去處。| *That sounds super.* 那聽起來棒極了。| *What a super idea!* 這個主意好極了! 2

super² *n* [C] *informal* a SUPERINTENDENT (3)【非正式】看門人

super³ *adv AmE spoken* extremely【美口】十分, 非常, 極: *Sorry, I'm super tired, I have to turn in.* 對不起, 我累得很, 得上牀睡覺了。

su·per·a·bun·dance /ˌsupɚəˋbʌndəns; ˌsuːpərəˈbʌndəns/ *n formal*【正式】**a superabundance of** more than enough of something 過多, 過剩 —**superabundant** *adj*

su·per·an·nu·at·ed /ˌsupɚˋænjuˌetɪd; ˌsuːpərˈænjueɪtɪ̈d/ *adj formal* old and no longer useful or no longer able【正式】陳舊的; 過時無用的; 老弱無能的: *a load of superannuated computer equipment* 一大堆過時的電腦設備 | *superannuated Tory politicians* 老朽無能的保守黨政客

su·per·an·nu·a·tion /ˌsupɚˌænjuˋeʃən; ˌsuːpərænjuˈeɪʃən/ *n* [U] *technical especially BrE* money paid as a PENSION¹, especially from your former employer【術語, 尤英】〔尤指由前雇主支付的〕退休金

superannuation scheme /ˌ····ˈ·· ·/ *n* [C] *BrE* a type of PENSION PLAN that is paid for by your employer【英】〔由雇主支付的〕退休金方案

su·perb /suˋpɝb; sjuːˈpɜːb/ *adj* [no comparative 無比較級] extremely good; excellent 極好的, 超級的; 傑出的, 卓越的: *The food was superb.* 食物好極了。| *a superb performance* 極其精彩的演出 —**superbly** *adv*

su·per·bug /ˋsupɚˌbʌg; ˈsuːpəbʌg/ *n* [C] *not technical* a type of BACTERIA that cannot be killed by traditional drugs【非術語】〔不能用傳統藥物消滅的〕超級病菌

su·per·charg·er /ˋsupɚˌtʃɑrdʒɚ; ˈsuːpəˌtʃɑːdʒə/ *n* [C] *technical* a piece of equipment that increases the power of an engine by supplying air or FUEL¹ (1) at a pressure that is higher than normal【術語】〔發動機的〕增壓(助燃)器 —**supercharged** *adj*

su·per·cil·i·ous /ˌsupɚˋsɪlɪəs; ˌsuːpəˈsɪliəs◂/ *adj* behaving as if you think that other people are less important than you; HAUGHTY 高傲的, 傲慢的, 目中無人的: *She's got a supercilious way of speaking that makes me want to scream!* 她那種目中無人的講話態度讓我真想大叫! | *a supercilious smile* 傲慢的微笑 —**superciliously** *adv* —**superciliousness** *n* [U]

su·per·con·duc·tiv·i·ty /ˌsupɚˌkɑndʌkˋtɪvətɪ; ˌsuːpəkɒndʌkˈtɪvɪ̈ti/ *n* [U] the ability of some substances to allow electricity to flow through them very easily, especially at very low temperatures 超導(電)性

su·per·con·duc·tor /ˌsupɚkənˋdʌktɚ; ˌsuːpəkənˈdʌktə/ *n* [C] a substance that allows electricity to flow through it very easily, especially at very low temperatures 超導體

su·per·du·per /supɚˋdupɚ; ˌsuːpəˈduːpə◂/ *adj old-fashioned* extremely good; SUPER¹【過時】極好的, 極棒的, 了不起的

su·per·e·go /ˌsupɚˋigo; ˌsuːpərˈiːgəʊ/ *n* [C] *technical* a word meaning your conscience, used in Freudian PSYCHOLOGY【術語】〔弗洛伊德精神分析學中的〕超我 —compare 比較 EGO (3), ID

su·per·fi·cial /ˌsupɚˋfɪʃəl; ˌsuːpəˈfɪʃəl◂/ *adj* **1 ▶APPEARANCE 外表◀** seeming to have a particular appearance at first, although this is not true or real 表面(上)的: *Despite their superficial similarities, the two novels are in fact very different.* 這兩本小説儘管表面上有相似之處，但實際上很不相同。| *a superficial air of tranquility* 表面上平靜的氣氛 **2 ▶NOT LOOKING/STUDYING CAREFULLY 不仔細察看/研究的◀** not studying or looking at something carefully and only noticing the most obvious things 膚淺的，淺薄的，不深入的: *theories based on a superficial knowledge of Japanese business methods* 以對日本經營方法膚淺了解為基礎的理論 **3 ▶WOUND/DAMAGE 傷口/損傷◀** affecting only the surface of your skin or the outside part of something, and therefore not serious 表皮的，外部的，不嚴重的: *She escaped with only superficial cuts and bruises.* 她逃了出來，只是皮膚有幾處刮破和青腫。| **superficial examination/study etc** *Even a superficial inspection revealed grave flaws.* 即使從表面查看也看出了嚴重的缺點。**4 ▶PERSON 人◀** someone who is superficial does not think about things that are serious or important; SHALLOW[1] (2) 淺薄的，膚淺的: *a weak-minded and superficial husband who seemed only interested in football* 意志薄弱、頭腦簡單、只對足球感興趣的丈夫 **5 ▶NOT IMPORTANT 不重要的◀** superficial changes, difficulties etc are not important and do not have a big effect〔變化、困難等〕不重要的，影響不大的: *superficial changes in government policies on the environment* 政府在環境政策方面微不足道的改變 **6 ▶TOP LAYER 表層◀** existing in or connected with the top layer of something, especially soil, rock etc〔尤指土壤、岩石等〕表層的 —**superficially** *adv* —**superficiality** /ˌsupɚˌfɪʃɪˋælətɪ; ˌsuːpəfɪʃiˈæləti/ *n* [U]

su·per·flu·i·ty /ˌsupɚˋfluətɪ; ˌsuːpəˈfluːəti/ *n formal*【正式】**a superfluity of** a larger amount of something than is necessary 多餘；過多；過剩

su·per·flu·ous /suˋpɝfluəs; suːˈpɜːfluəs/ *adj formal* more than is needed or wanted; unnecessary【正式】多餘的；過剩的；不必要的: *We could all see what was going on, so the commentary was superfluous.* 我們都能看出正在發生的一切，所以那些解説是多餘的。—**superfluously** *adv* —**superfluousness** *n* [U]

su·per·glue /ˋsupɚglu; ˈsuːpəgluː/ *n* [U] *trademark* a very strong glue that sticks very quickly and is difficult to remove【商標】超強力膠水 —**superglue** *v* [T]

su·per·grass /ˋsupɚgræs; ˈsuːpəgrɑːs/ *n* [C] *BrE* a criminal who gives the police information about many other criminals, in order to get a less severe punishment【英】〔為獲得減刑而〕向警方提供有關其他犯罪分子情報的罪犯

su·per·he·ro /ˋsupɚˌhɪro; ˈsuːpəˌhɪərəʊ/ *n* [C] a character in stories who uses special powers, such as great strength or the ability to fly, to help people〔故事中以特異本領助人的〕超級英雄

su·per·high·way /ˋsupɚˌhaɪwe; ˈsuːpəˌhaɪweɪ/ *n* [C] *AmE* a very large road on which you can drive distances quickly【美】(超級)高速公路 —see also 另見 INFORMATION SUPERHIGHWAY

su·per·hu·man /ˌsupɚˋhjumən; ˌsuːpəˈhjuːmən◂/ *adj* much greater than ordinary human powers or abilities 超人的，超出常人能力的；非凡的: **superhuman effort/strength** *It will require a superhuman effort to get the job done on time.* 要按時完成這件工作需要付出非凡的努力。

su·per·im·pose /ˌsupərɪmˋpoz; ˌsuːpərɪmˈpəʊz/ *v* [T] **1** to put one picture, image, or photograph on top of another so that both can be partly seen 使〔圖畫、圖像、照片〕重疊，使疊加: **superimpose sth on/onto sth** *His face had been superimposed onto a different background.* 他的臉部被疊加到一個不同的背景上。**2** to combine two systems, ideas, opinions etc so that one influences the other 使〔兩種制度、思想、意見等〕相結合，使融合: *Eastern themes superimposed onto Western architecture* 與西方建築學融合的東方主題 —**superimposition** /ˌsupərɪmpəˋzɪʃən; ˌsuːpərɪmpəˈzɪʃən/ *n* [U]

su·per·in·tend /ˌsuprɪnˋtɛnd; ˌsuːpərɪnˈtend/ *v* [T] *formal* to be in charge of something, and control how it is done【正式】主管；監督；控制 —**superintendence** *n* [U]

su·per·in·tend·ent /ˌsuprɪnˋtɛndənt; ˌsuːpərɪnˈtendənt/ *n* [C] **1** someone who is officially in charge of a place, job, activity etc 主管人；負責人 **2** a middle rank in the British police, or someone who has this rank〔英國的〕警察長，警司 **3** *AmE* someone who is in charge of an apartment building【美】〔公寓樓的〕管房人；看門人；CARETAKER (1) *BrE*【英】**4** also 又作 **superintendent of schools** someone who is in charge of all the schools in a particular area in the US〔美國的〕地區教育主管

su·pe·ri·or[1] /səˋpɪrɪɚ; suːˈpɪəriə/ *adj* **1** having a higher position or rank than someone else 職位[級別]更高的；上級的: *I'll report you to your superior officer.* 我要把你的情況向你的上司投訴。| **a superior court** 上級法院 **2** better, more powerful, more effective etc than a similar person or thing, especially one that you are competing against 更好的；更強的；更有效的: *Fletcher's fitness and superior technique brought him victory.* 弗萊徹的體能和出色的技術使他取得了勝利。| **[+to]** *The new mark IV engine is superior to its rivals.* 新的 IV 型發動機強於其競爭產品。| **vastly superior** (=very much better than others) 比其他的好得多 **3** a word meaning of very good quality, used especially in advertising 質量上乘的，優質的〔尤用於廣告〕: *a superior wine* 優質[上等]葡萄酒 | *superior craftsmanship* 高超的手藝 **4** thinking that you are better than other people 有優越感的，高傲的，傲慢的: *He has such a superior attitude, I feel like spitting at him.* 他的態度如此傲慢，我真想往他的臉上吐唾沫。**5** *technical* higher in position; upper【術語】上面的，上部的: *the superior limbs* (=arms) 上肢 **6 Mother Superior** a title for the woman in charge of a group of NUNS 女修道院院長 —compare 比較 INFERIOR[1]

superior[2] *n* [C] someone who has a higher rank or position than you, especially in a job 上級，上司，長官: **sb's immediate superior** (=the person in a position directly above you) 某人的頂頭上司 —compare 比較 INFERIOR[2]

su·per·i·or·i·ty /səˌpɪrɪˋɔrətɪ; suːˌpɪəriˈɒrəti/ *n* [U] **1** the quality of being better, more skilful, more powerful etc than other things 優秀；優勢；優越: **[+over]** *the intellectual superiority of humans over other animals* 人類與其他動物相比所具有的智力優勢 | **[+in]** *US superiority in air power* 美國空軍的優勢 **2** an attitude that shows you think you are better than other people 優越感，驕傲自大: *Janet always spoke with an air of superiority.* 珍妮特說話時總帶着一種優越感。

su·per·la·tive[1] /səˋpɝlətɪv; suːˈpɜːlətɪv/ *adj* **1** excellent 最好的，最優秀的: *a superlative performance* 精彩絕倫的表演 **2** a superlative adjective or adverb expresses the highest degree of a particular quality〔形容詞或副詞〕最高級的: *The superlative form of 'good' is 'best'.* good 的最高級形式是 best。—compare 比較 COMPARATIVE[1] (4)

superlative[2] *n* **1 the superlative** the superlative form of an adjective or adverb〔形容詞或副詞的〕最高級(形式): *'Biggest' is the superlative of 'big'.* biggest 是 big 的最高級形式。**2** [C] a word in this form, used especially when expressing great praise or admiration〔尤指表示讚賞的〕最高級形式的形容詞[副詞]: **a string of superlatives** (=several superlative adjectives praising someone or something) 一連串的盛讚之詞

su·per·la·tive·ly /səˋpɝlətɪvlɪ; suːˈpɜːlətɪvli/ *adv* extremely 極其，非常: *superlatively happy* 極為高興

su·per·man /ˋsupɚˌmæn; ˈsuːpəmæn/ *plural* **supermen** /-mɛn; -men/ *n* [C] a man of unusually great ability or strength 超人〔具有超常能力或力量的人〕

3 **su·per·mar·ket** /ˋsupɚ͵mɑrkɪt; ˈsuːpə͵mɑːkɪ̈t/ *n* [C] a very large shop where customers can choose from a large number of different kinds of food and other regularly needed goods 超級市場

su·per·nal /suˋpɝnl; suːˈpɜːnl/ *adj formal* connected with the sky or heaven【正式】〔來自〕天上的; 天國的

su·per·nat·u·ral[1] /͵supɚˋnætʃrəl; ͵suːpəˈnætʃərəl◂/ *adj* impossible to explain by natural causes, and therefore seeming to involve the powers of gods or magic 超自然的; 奇異的; 神奇的: *supernatural forces* 超自然力量 —**supernaturally** *adv*

supernatural[2] *n* **the supernatural** supernatural events, powers, and creatures 超自然事件; 超自然力; 超自然體: *belief in the supernatural* 相信超自然力量

su·per·no·va /͵supɚˋnovə; ͵suːpəˈnəʊvə/ *n* [C] a very large exploding star〔天文中的〕超新星 —compare 比較 NOVA

su·per·nu·me·ra·ry /͵supɚˋnjumə͵rɛrɪ; ͵suːpəˈnjuːmərəri/ *n* [C] *formal* someone or something that is additional to the number of people or things that are needed【正式】多餘的人[物]; 額外的人[物] —**supernumerary** *adj*

su·per·pow·er /͵supɚˋpauɚ; ˈsuːpə͵paʊə/ *n* [C] a nation that has very great military and political power 超級大國

su·per·script /ˋsupɚ͵skrɪpt; ˈsuːpəskrɪpt/ *adj* written or printed above a number, letter etc 上角標的〔寫或印在數字、字母等上方或上角的〕—**superscript** *n* [C,U]

su·per·sede /͵supɚˋsid; ͵suːpəˈsiːd/ *v* [T often passive 常用被動態] if a new idea, product, or method supersedes another one, it becomes used instead because it is more modern or effective 替代, 取代: *Television superseded radio in the fifties.* 電視在五十年代取代了無線電廣播。

su·per·ser·ver /ˋsupɚ͵sɝvɚ; ˈsuːpə͵sɜːvə/ *n* [C] a very powerful computer that controls other computers〔電腦的〕超級服務器

su·per·son·ic /͵supɚˋsɑnɪk; ͵suːpəˈsɒnɪk◂/ *adj* faster than the speed of sound 超音速的: *supersonic aircraft* 超音速飛機 —compare 比較 SUBSONIC

su·per·star /ˋsupɚ͵stɑr; ˈsuːpəstɑː/ *n* [C] an extremely famous performer, especially a musician or film actor〔尤指音樂或電影中的〕超級巨星

su·per·sti·tion /͵supɚˋstɪʃən; ͵suːpəˈstɪʃən/ *n* [C,U] a belief that some objects or actions are lucky and some are unlucky, based on old ideas of magic 迷信: *the old superstition that walking under a ladder is unlucky* 認為在梯子下走不吉利的那種古老的迷信思想

su·per·sti·tious /͵supɚˋstɪʃəs; ͵suːpəˈstɪʃəs◂/ *adj* influenced by old-fashioned beliefs about luck and magic 迷信的 —**superstitiously** *adv*

su·per·store /ˋsupɚ͵stor; ˈsuːpəstɔː/ *n* [C] *BrE* a very large shop that sells many different types of goods, usually just outside a town【英】超級商場, 大型商場〔通常在市外, 出售各類商品的大型商店〕

su·per·struc·ture /ˋsupɚ͵strʌktʃɚ; ˈsuːpə͵strʌktʃə/ *n* [singular,U] **1** a structure that is built on top of the main part of something such as a ship or building〔船、建築物等的〕上部結構, 上部建築, 上層建築物 **2** *formal* political and social systems that are based on a simpler system【正式】〔包括政治和社會制度等的〕上層建築: *a superstructure of religion based on nature worship* 以自然崇拜為基礎的宗教上層建築

su·per·tank·er /ˋsupɚ͵tæŋkɚ; ˈsuːpə͵tæŋkə/ *n* [C] an extremely large ship that can carry large quantities of oil or other liquids 巨型油輪, 超級油輪

su·per·vene /͵supɚˋvin; ͵suːpəˈviːn/ *v* [I] *formal* to happen unexpectedly, especially in a way that stops or interrupts an event or situation【正式】意外發生〔尤指因而終止或干擾某事〕

su·per·vise /͵supɚˋvaɪz; ˈsuːpəvaɪz/ *v* [I,T] to be in charge of a group of workers or students and be responsible for making sure that they do their work properly 監督; 管理; 指導 —**supervisor** *n* [C] —**supervisory** /͵supɚˋvaɪzərɪ; ͵suːpəˈvaɪzəri◂/ *adj*: *She works there in a supervisory capacity.* 她在那裡擔任監督指導的工作。

su·per·vi·sion /͵supɚˋvɪʒən; ͵suːpəˈvɪʒən/ *n* [U] the act of supervising someone or something 監督; 管理; 指導; 主管: *The patient is improving, but still needs constant supervision.* 病人已在好轉, 但還需要不間斷地進行監護。| **under sb's supervision** *We work under the Chief Engineer's supervision.* 我們在總工程師的指導下進行工作。

su·pine /suˋpaɪn; ˈsuːpaɪn/ *adj formal*【正式】**1** lying on your back 仰臥的 —opposite 反義詞 PRONE (2) **2** allowing other people to make decisions instead of you in a way that seems very weak-minded 無所作為的; 消極的; 優柔寡斷的: *a supine and cowardly press, scared by government threats of censorship* 消極軟弱、被政府的審查威脅嚇破了膽的新聞界 —**supinely** *adv*

sup·per /ˋsʌpɚ; ˈsʌpə/ *n* [C,U] the last meal of the evening 晚飯, 晚餐

sup·plant /səˋplænt; səˈplɑːnt/ *v* [T] to take the place of a person or thing so that they are no longer used, no longer in a position of power etc 取代, 代替; 將…排擠掉: *Barker was soon supplanted as party leader.* 巴克在該黨中的領導地位很快就被人取代了。

sup·ple /ˋsʌpl̩; ˈsʌpəl/ *adj* **1** someone who is supple bends and moves easily and gracefully〔身體〕柔軟的, 靈活的: *She exercises every day to keep herself supple.* 她每天鍛鍊以保持身體靈活。**2** leather, skin, wood etc that is supple is soft and bends easily〔皮革、皮膚、木料等〕柔軟易彎的; 柔韌的 —**suppleness** *n* [U]

sup·ple·ment[1] /ˋsʌpləmənt; ˈsʌplɪ̈mənt/ *n* [C] **1** something that you add to something else to improve it or make it complete 增補物, 補充物, 補給品: *a dietary supplement* 飲食的補充物 **2** an additional part at the end of a book, or a separate part of a newspaper, magazine etc〔書的〕附錄; 補編; 補遺;〔報紙、雜誌的〕增刊: *the Sunday supplements* 星期天的增刊 **3** an amount of money that is added to the price of a service, hotel room etc〔服務、旅館房費等的〕附加費: *There is a £5 supplement for extra sheets and towels.* 額外的牀單和毛巾收附加費五英鎊。

sup·ple·ment[2] /ˋsʌplə͵mɛnt; ˈsʌplɪ̈ment/ *v* [T always+adv/prep] to add something, especially to what you earn or eat, in order to increase it to an acceptable level 補充, 增補, 增加: **supplement sth by/with** *Kia supplements her regular salary by tutoring in the evenings.* 基婭靠在晚上當家庭教師來補貼她固定的薪水。—**supplementation** /͵sʌpləmɛnˋteʃən; ͵sʌplɪ̈menˈteɪʃən/ *n* [U]

sup·ple·men·ta·ry /͵sʌpləˋmɛntərɪ; ͵sʌplɪ̈ˈmentəri◂/ *adj* provided in addition to what already exists 補充的, 增補的, 附加的: *There is a supplementary water supply in case the main supply fails.* 萬一主要供水系統出現故障, 還有補充供水。

sup·pli·ant /ˋsʌplɪənt; ˈsʌpliənt/ *n* [C] *literary* a supplicant【文】懇求者, 哀求者 —**suppliant** *adj*

sup·pli·cant /ˋsʌplɪkənt; ˈsʌplɪkənt/ *n* [C] *literary* someone who asks for something, especially from someone in a position of power or from God【文】懇求者, 哀求者, 祈求者〔尤指向有權者或上帝請求〕

sup·pli·cate /ˋsʌplɪ͵ket; ˈsʌplɪ̈keɪt/ *v* [I,T] *literary* to ask or pray for help from someone in power or from God【文】懇求, 祈求; 哀求〔有權勢者或上帝〕—**supplication** /͵sʌplɪˋkeʃən; ͵sʌplɪ̈ˈkeɪʃən/ *n* [U]: *Paolo knelt and bowed his head in supplication.* 保羅跪着在低頭祈禱。

sup·pli·er /səˋplaɪɚ; səˈplaɪə/ *n* [C] also 又作 **suppliers** a company that provides a particular product 供應商: *Continental is one of the world's biggest suppliers of grain.* 大陸公司是世界最大的穀物供應商之一。

sup·ply[1] /səˋplaɪ; səˈplaɪ/ *n* 3 2

1 ►AMOUNT AVAILABLE 可用量◄ [C] an amount of

S

something that is available to be used 供應量, 供給量: **[+of]** *a regular supply of fresh vegetables* 新鮮蔬菜的經常供應 | *More donors are needed as blood supplies are running low.* 由於血液供應不足, 需要更多的捐血者。

2 be in short supply if something is in short supply, there is very little of it available and it is difficult to get 供應不足, 不充裕: *Chocolate was in short supply during the war.* 戰爭期間巧克力供應不足。

3 gas/electricity/water supply a system that is used to supply gas etc 煤氣/電力/自來水供應(系統): **cut off a supply** (=stop the supply) 停止[中斷]供應 *During the drought some households had their water supply cut off.* 在乾旱期間有些住戶的自來水供應被中斷。

4 ►NECESSARY THINGS 必需品◄ supplies [plural] food, clothes and things necessary for daily life, especially for a group of people over a period of time 日用(必需)品〔尤指供一些人在一段時間內用的東西〕: *A convoy of trucks packed with vital medical supplies succeeded in reaching the town.* 一個滿載重要醫藥用品的卡車車隊成功抵達那個城鎮。

5 supply and demand [U] the relationship between the amount of goods for sale and the amount that people want to buy, especially the way it influences prices 供求關係

6 ►ACT OF SUPPLYING 供應◄ [U] the act or process of supplying something 供應, 供給, 補給: *The military government is trying to stop the supply of guns to the rebels.* 軍政府在試圖切斷叛軍的槍支補給。| *supply of oxygen to the brain* 對大腦的氧氣供應

7 supply ship/convoy/route etc a ship etc used for bringing or storing supplies 補給船/車[船]隊/路線等 —see also 另見 MONEY SUPPLY

3 3 **supply²** *v* [T] to provide people with something that they need or want, especially regularly over a long period of time 供應, 供給, 提供〔所需物品〕: **supply sb with sth** *US forces mounted a massive air operation to keep the city supplied with food.* 美軍進行大規模空運以保持那個城市的食品供應。| *An informer supplied the police with the names of those involved in the crime.* 一位告密者向警方告發了與罪案有牽連的人。| **supply sth to sb** *They were arrested for supplying drugs to street dealers.* 他們因給街頭毒品販子提供毒品而被逮捕。

supply-side e·co·nom·ics /ˌ·ˈ· ·,··ˈ··/ *n* [U] *technical* the idea that if the government reduces taxes, producers will be able to make more goods and this will improve a country's economic situation【術語】供應經濟學〔主張通過減稅以刺激生產和投資從而有利於國家經濟形勢的理論〕

supply teach·er /·ˈ· ˌ··/ *n* [C] *BrE* a teacher who does the work of another teacher who is ill, on a course etc【英】代課教師; SUBSTITUTE TEACHER *AmE*【美】

2 2 **sup·port¹** /səˋport; səˈpɔːt/ *v* [T]

1 ►AGREE WITH SB/STH 贊同某人/某事◄ to say that you agree with an idea, group, person etc and want them to succeed 支持; 贊成; 擁護: *The bill was supported by a large majority in the Senate.* 這項法案得到參議院裡大多數人的支持。| **support sb in sth** *We support the police wholeheartedly in their work against crime.* 我們全力支持警方打擊犯罪活動的工作。| **strongly support** (=support something very much) 大力支持

2 ►HOLD STH UP 撐起某物◄ to hold the weight of something, keep it in place, or prevent it from falling 支撐, 承受〔某物的重量〕: *The middle part of the bridge is supported by two huge towers.* 橋的中部由兩個巨型橋塔支撐着。| *I grabbed the rail to support myself.* 我抓住欄杆來支撐自己。

3 ►PROVIDE MONEY TO LIVE 提供生活費◄ to provide enough money for someone to pay for all the things they need 供養, 撫養, 資助: *She needs a high income to support such a large family.* 她需要一份高收入來養活這麼一大家子。| *It's difficult to support yourself on this salary.* 靠這份薪水來養活你自己是困難的。

4 ►GIVE MONEY TO STH 給某事物出錢◄ to encourage a group, organization or event etc by giving it money 出錢幫助, 為…提供資金, 資助: *Please support your local theatre, buy some tickets today!* 請資助本地的劇院, 今天就買幾張票吧!

5 ►HELP SB 幫助某人◄ to help someone by being sympathetic and kind to them during a difficult time in their life〔在困難時期〕幫助, 支持: *My wife supported me enormously when my mother died.* 我母親去世時, 我妻子給了我極大的安慰。

6 ►LAND 土地◄ if land can support people or animals, it is of good enough quality to grow enough food for them to live〔指土地提供足夠的食物〕養活, 維持〔人和動物的生命〕: *This land isn't fertile enough to support many cattle.* 這片土地不夠肥沃, 養不活許多牛。

7 ►A BAD HABIT 不良習慣◄ to get money in order to pay for a bad habit such as taking drugs 支付…的花費, 用錢維持〔不良習慣〕: *He stole from his mother's savings to support his drug habit.* 他偷母親的積蓄來維持自己的吸毒惡習。

8 ►PROVE STH 證明某事物◄ to show or prove that something is true or correct 證明, 證實: *The results support our original theory.* 這些結果證明了我們最初的理論。

9 ►SPORTS TEAM 運動隊◄ *especially BrE* to like a particular sports team and go to watch the games they play【尤英】為〔某運動隊〕捧場, 支持: *Trev supports Arsenal, but I like Spurs.* 特雷夫是阿仙奴隊的球迷, 而我喜歡熱刺隊。

10 ►BEAR STH 忍受某事◄ [usually in negatives 一般用於否定句] *formal* to be able to bear something; ENDURE【正式】忍受: *She could not support the heat any longer.* 她再也不能忍受這種酷熱了。—see also 另見 INSUPPORTABLE

support² *n* 2 2

1 ►APPROVAL 贊同◄ [U] approval and encouragement for an idea, plan etc 支持, 擁護, 贊同: *Local people have given us a lot of support in our campaign.* 當地人民對我們的運動給予了很多支持。| **in support of** *They signed a petition in support of the pay claim.* 他們在請願書上簽名支持這次的加薪要求。| **drum up support** (=get many people's approval) 爭取人們的支持 *The Americans used the story to drum up support for the stronger measures against Libya.* 美國人利用這個藉口爭取人們支持對利比亞採取更加強硬的措施。

2 ►SYMPATHY/HELP 同情/幫助◄ [U] sympathetic encouragement and help that you give to someone 同情; 鼓勵; 幫助: *Thanks for all your support at this difficult time.* 謝謝你們在這困難時刻所給予的一切幫助。—see also 另見 **moral support** (MORAL¹ (3))

3 ►HOLD STH UP 撐起某物◄ [C,U] something such as a piece of wood that presses up on something else to hold it up or in position 支撐物; 支柱; 支架; 支座: *The roof may need extra support.* 這個房頂需要額外的支撐物。| *the supports of a bridge* 橋梁的支座

4 ►INJURED PART OF BODY 身體的受傷部位◄ [C] something that you wear to hold a weak or damaged part of your body in the right place〔用以支撐身體虛弱或受傷部位等的〕支持(器), 托

5 ►PEOPLE WHO SUPPORT STH 支持某事的人◄ [U] the people who support a political party, an idea, a team etc〔某政黨、思想、球隊等的〕支持者, 擁護者: *There isn't much local support for the new candidate.* 新候選人得不到多少當地人的支持。

sup·por·ta·ble /səˋportəbl; səˈpɔːtəbəl/ *adj* [usually in negatives 一般用於否定句] *formal* possible to bear; TOLERABLE【正式】可忍受的

sup·port·er /səˋportɚ; səˈpɔːtə/ *n* [C] **1** someone who supports a particular person, group, or plan 支持者, 擁護者: **strong/firm/staunch supporter** *one of Clinton's staunchest supporters* 克林頓最堅定的支持者之一 | *supporters of animal rights legislation* 支持為動物權利立法的人們 **2** *especially BrE* someone who supports a 

sports team, especially by regularly going to watch them play; FAN[1] (1)【尤英】〔球隊的〕支持者, 球迷: *Manchester United supporters* 曼徹斯特聯隊的支持者

support group /ˈ·ˌ· ·/ *n* [C] a group of people who meet to help each other with a particular problem, for example ALCOHOLISM〔酗酒者等的〕互助組

sup·port·ing /səˋpɔrtɪŋ; səˈpɔːtɪŋ/ *adj* **1 supporting part/role/actor etc** a small part in a play or film, or the actor who plays such a part〔戲劇或電影中的〕配角/演配角的男演員等 **2 supporting wall/beam etc** a wall etc that supports the weight of something 支撐牆/梁等

sup·por·tive /səˋpɔrtɪv; səˈpɔːtɪv/ *adj approving* giving help or encouragement, especially to someone who is in a difficult situation【褒】支持的; 給予幫助和鼓勵的: *I can always count on Gail to be supportive when things go wrong.* 出問題時我總能依仗蓋爾的幫助。

1 1 **sup·pose**[1] /səˋpoz; səˈpəʊz/ *v* [T] **1 be supposed to do sth a)** used when saying what someone should or should not do, especially because of rules or what someone in authority has said 被期望做某事; 應該做某事: *You're supposed to ask the teacher if you want to leave the classroom.* 你如果要離開教室, 應該先問問老師。| *We're not supposed to smoke here.* 我們不應該在這裡抽煙。**b)** used when saying what people intended should happen, especially when it failed to happen 本應, 本該〔用於表示某事本應發生而沒有發生〕: *The new laws are supposed to prevent crime.* 這些新法令本應起到防止犯罪的作用。| *The meeting was supposed to take place on Tuesday, but we've had to postpone it.* 這會本應該星期二舉行, 但我們不得不把它推遲了。**2 be supposed to be sth** to be believed to be something by many people 被相信是…, 被認為…: *The castle is supposed to be haunted.* 這座城堡據說在鬧鬼。| *'Dirty Harry' is supposed to be one of Eastwood's best films.*《辣手神探》被認為是奇連依士活的最佳影片之一。**3** to think that something is probably true, based on what you know 認為, 料想, 猜想, 假定: *There were many more deaths than was first supposed.* 死亡人數要比早先預想的多得多。| **suppose (that)** *What makes you suppose we're going to sell the house?* 你憑甚麼認為我們準備把這房子賣掉? | **be generally supposed** (=most people think that something was probably fine) 被多數人認為, 一般認為 *Mr Tyke was generally supposed to have left the country.* 一般認為泰克先生已經離開這個國家了。| **There is no reason to suppose (that)** (=used to say that you think something is unlikely) 沒有理由推測〔表示某事不大可能〕*There's no reason to suppose her new book will be any better than her last one.* 沒有理由推測她的新書會比上一本好。**4** *formal* to expect that something will happen and base your plans on it【正式】假定, 預期; 以…為條件: *The company's plan supposes a steady increase in orders.* 公司的計劃是假定訂單將持續穩定地增加。

Frequencies of the verb **suppose** in spoken and written English 動詞 suppose 在英語口語和書面語中的使用頻率

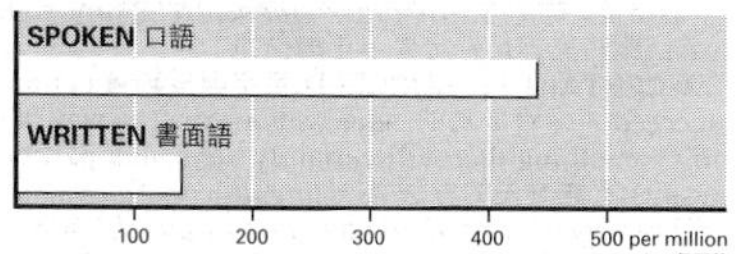

Based on the British National Corpus and the Longman Lancaster Corpus 據英國國家語料庫和朗文蘭卡斯特語料庫

This graph shows that the verb **suppose** is much more common in spoken English than in written English. This is because it is used in some common spoken phrases. 本圖表顯示, 動詞 suppose 在英語口語中的使用頻率遠遠高於書面語, 因為口語中一些常用的片語是由 suppose 構成的。

suppose (*adv*) **SPOKEN PHRASES**
含 suppose 的口語片語

5 I suppose *especially BrE*【尤英】**a)** used to say you think something is true, although you are uncertain about it 我想, 我認為〔用於認為某事真實, 但不敢肯定〕: **I suppose (that)** *I suppose he could have shot himself, but where would he have got the gun?* 我想他可能是開槍自殺的, 但他從哪裡弄到槍的? | *I suppose Philip will be late, as usual.* 我想菲利普照例又會遲到的。**b)** used when agreeing to let someone do something, especially unwillingly 我想〔尤用於表示勉強同意某人做某事〕: **I suppose so** *"Can we come with you?" "Oh, I suppose so."* "我們可以跟你一起去嗎?" "噢, 我看可以吧。" **c)** used when guessing that something is true 我猜想〔用於表示猜測〕: *She looked about 50, I suppose.* 我看她大約 50 歲。**d)** used when saying in an angry way that you expect something is true 我看〔用於生氣地表示預料某事真實〕: **I suppose (that)** *I suppose you thought you were being smart!* 我看你是自作聰明! **e)** used to say that you think that something is probably true, although you wish it was not and hope someone will tell you it is not 恐怕〔用於表示某事很可能真實, 雖然自己希望並非如此〕: **I suppose (that)** *I suppose it's too late to apply for that job now.* 恐怕現在申請那份工作已經太遲了。**6 suppose/supposing** used to ask someone to imagine what would happen if a particular situation existed 假設, 假定〔用於要某人設想如果某情況存在會發生甚麼事〕: *Look, suppose you lost your job tomorrow, what would you do?* 哎, 假設你明天丟掉了工作, 你會怎麼辦呢? **7 I don't suppose (that)** *especially BrE*【尤英】**a)** used to ask for something in a very polite way〔用於很禮貌地提出要求〕: *I don't suppose you'd give me a lift to the station?* 我能否順便搭你的車子去車站? **b)** used to say that you think it is unlikely something will happen 我以為不會〔用於表示某事不大可能發生〕: *I don't suppose I'll ever see her again.* 我想我再也不會見到她了。**8 who/what etc do you suppose** used to ask someone who, what etc they think did something, is something etc 你認為是誰/甚麼…: *Who on earth do you suppose could have done this?* 你認為到底是誰能幹出這種事來? **9 what's that supposed to mean?** used when you are annoyed by what someone has just said 這是甚麼意思?〔用於表示對某人剛說的話感到惱火〕: *"I'll bear your offer in mind." "Bear it in mind! What's that supposed to mean?"* "你的提議我會記在心上。" "記在心上! 那是甚麼意思?"

suppose[2] *conjunction especially spoken*【尤口】**1** used when imagining what the result would be if something happened; SUPPOSING 假設, 假定〔用於假設某事發生後帶來的後果〕: **suppose (that)** *It's not worth the risk, suppose your mother found out?* 不值得冒這個險, 萬一你媽媽發現了怎麼辦? **2** *informal* used to suggest something; SUPPOSING【非正式】〔用於提出建議〕: *Suppose we try to sort this out before we go.* 咱們盡量在走之前把這事解決了吧。

sup·posed /səˋpozd; səˈpəʊzd/ *adj* [only before noun 僅用於名詞前] claimed by other people to be true or real, although you do not think they are right 據說的, 假定的: *the supposed benefits and advantages of privatizing state industries* 所謂的國家工業私有化帶來的利益和優越性

sup·pos·ed·ly /səˋpozɪdlɪ; səˈpəʊzɪ̈dli/ *adv* used when saying what many people say or believe is true, especially when you disagree with them 據說, 據稱; 一般相信, 一般看來: *In April 1912 this supposedly unsinkable ship hit an iceberg.* 1912年4月, 這艘據稱不會沉沒的海輪撞上了冰山。[sentence adverb 句子副詞] *Supposedly, she's a rich woman.* 據推測, 她是個很有錢的女人。

sup·pos·ing /sə`pozɪŋ; sə'pəʊzɪŋ/ *conjunction* SUPPOSE[2] 假設, 假定

sup·po·si·tion /ˌsʌpə`zɪʃən; ˌsʌpə'zɪʃən/ *n* [C,U] something that you think is true even though you are not certain and cannot prove it 假定; 推測; 猜測: *His version of events is pure supposition.* 他對事件的說法純屬推測。| **supposition (that)** *The police are acting on the supposition that she took the money.* 警方正按照她偷了錢的推測採取行動。

sup·pos·i·to·ry /sə`pɑzəˌtorɪ; sə'pɒzǀtəri/ *n* [C] a small piece of solid medicine that is placed in someone's RECTUM or VAGINA〔放入直腸或陰道的〕栓劑, 坐藥 —compare 比較 PESSARY (1)

sup·press /sə`prɛs; sə'pres/ *v* [T] **1** to stop people from opposing the government, especially by using force〔尤指用武力〕鎮壓, 制止, 壓制: *The revolt was ruthlessly suppressed by the military.* 叛亂受到軍方的殘酷鎮壓。**2** to prevent important information or opinions from becoming known, especially from people who have a right to know 禁止發表〔消息、言論等〕, 查禁, 封鎖: *attempts by the Pentagon to suppress documents connected with the case* 五角大樓想封鎖與該案件有關文件的企圖 **3** to stop yourself from showing your feelings 抑制〔感情〕, 忍住: *Susan could hardly suppress a giggle.* 蘇珊差點忍不住要咯咯地笑出聲來。| *suppressed anger* 強忍的怒火 **4** to prevent something from growing or developing, or from working effectively 抑制〔生長、發展、起作用等〕: *The virus suppresses the body's immune system.* 這種病毒抑制身體的免疫系統。—**suppressible** *adj* —**suppression** /-`prɛʃən; -'preʃən/ *n* [U]: *the suppression of free speech* 壓制言論自由

sup·pu·rate /`sʌpjəˌret; 'sʌpjǀreɪt/ *v* [I] *technical* if a wound suppurates it produces or gives out PUS (=infected liquid)【術語】〔傷口〕化膿 —**suppuration** /ˌsʌpjə`reʃən; ˌsʌpjǀ'reɪʃən/ *n* [U]

su·pra·na·tion·al /ˌsuprə`næʃənḷ; ˌsuːprə'næʃənəl/ *adj* involving more than one country 超國家的, 多國的: *a supranational organization* 超國家組織

su·prem·a·cist /sə`prɛməsɪst; sə'preməsǀst/ *n* [C] someone who believes that their own particular group or race is better than any other〔某團體或種族〕至上主義者: *a white supremacist group* 白人至上主義者團體

su·prem·a·cy /sə`prɛməsɪ; sə'preməsi/ *n* [U] the position in which you are more powerful or advanced than anyone else 至高無上; 最高地位: *Japan's unchallenged supremacy in the field of electronics* 日本在電子領域未受到挑戰的最高地位

su·preme /su`prim; suː'priːm/ *adj* **1** having the highest position of power, importance, or influence〔權力、地位、重要性或影響力〕最高的, 至高無上的: *the Supreme Allied Commander in Europe* 歐洲盟軍最高司令 | **reign supreme** *where justice reigns supreme* 在正義主宰一切的地方 **2** [only before noun 僅用於名詞前] the greatest possible〔程度〕最大的, 極度的: *supreme courage in the face of terrible danger* 在極大危險面前表現出的高度勇氣 | **supreme effort** *It required a supreme effort to stop myself from giving up.* 我盡了最大努力才使自己沒有半途而廢。| **of supreme importance** *a matter of supreme importance* 極為重要的事情 **3 make the supreme sacrifice** to die for your country, for a principle etc 為國捐軀;〔為原則等〕犧牲

Supreme Be·ing /ˌ·ˌ ˈ··/ *n* [singular] *literary* God【文】上帝

Supreme Court /ˌ·ˌ ˈ·/ *n* [singular] the most important court of law in some countries or some states of the US〔一些國家或美國一些州的〕最高法院

su·preme·ly /su`primlɪ; suː'priːmli/ *adv* [+adj/adv] extremely or to the greatest possible degree 極度地; 極其: *a supremely talented player* 極有才能的選手

su·prem·o /sʊ`primo; suː'priːməʊ/ *n* [C] *BrE informal* someone who controls a particular activity, organization, or industry, and has unlimited powers【英, 非正式】〔具有無限權力的〕最高權威; 最高領導人

Supt. the written abbreviation of 縮寫= SUPERINTENDENT

sur·charge[1] /`sɝˌtʃɑrdʒ; 'sɜːtʃɑːdʒ/ *n* [C] money that you have to pay in addition to the basic price of something 附加費, 額外費用: **[+on]** *a 10% surcharge on airline tickets* 飛機票10%的附加費

surcharge[2] *v* [T] to make someone pay an additional amount of money 向〔某人〕收取附加費

sur·coat /`sɝˌkot; 'sɜːkəʊt/ *n* [C] a piece of clothing with no arms which was worn over ARMOUR (1) in the past〔古代穿在鎧甲外面的〕無袖罩袍

sure[1] /ʃʊr; ʃɔː/ *adj*

1 ►CERTAIN YOU KNOW STH 肯定知道某事◄ [not before noun 不用於名詞前] confident that you know something or that something is true or correct 確信的, 有把握的: *"What time does the show start?" "I'm not sure."* "表演甚麼時候開始?" "我拿不準。" | **sure (that)** *I'm sure there's a logical explanation for all this.* 我確信所有這些問題都是有合理解釋的。| *Are you sure you know how to get there?* 你肯定知道怎樣到那裡去嗎? | **[+of]** *You need to be sure of your facts before making any accusations.* 你在提出任何指控之前必須對自己所掌握的事實很有把握才行。| **[+about]** *"That's the man I saw in the building last night." "Are you quite sure about that?"* "那就是我昨晚在大樓裡看見的那個男人。" "你能完全肯定嗎?" | **not sure how/where/whether etc** *I'm not sure where Michael is, to be honest.* 老實說, 我拿不準邁克爾現在在哪兒。| **not sure if** *Mr Watkins isn't sure if he'll be able to come.* 沃特金斯先生不敢肯定他是不是能來。| **pretty sure** (=almost certain) 幾乎可以肯定 *I'm pretty sure Barbara still works there.* 我幾乎可以肯定芭芭拉還在那兒工作。

2 ►CERTAIN ABOUT YOUR FEELINGS 清楚自己的感覺◄ [not before noun 不用於名詞前] certain about what you feel, want, like etc〔對自己的感覺、要求、喜愛等〕肯定的, 確實的, 無疑的: *"Are you sure you really want a divorce?"* "你肯定你確實想要離婚嗎?"

3 make sure a) to find out if something is true or to check that something has been done〔把某事〕弄清楚, 查明: *"Did you lock the front door?" "I think so, but I'd better make sure."* "你鎖前門了嗎?" "我想是的, 但我最好還是去查看一下。" | **make sure (that)** *Emma peered into the room to make sure that Ruth was asleep.* 愛瑪往房間裡仔細查看, 要搞清楚露思確實是睡着了。**b)** to do something so that you can be certain of the result 設法確保: **make sure (that)** *I made sure that the rope was firmly fastened around his waist.* 我檢查了繩子, 確保其牢牢繫在他的腰部。| **make sure of sth** *Ben made sure of winning by betting on all the horses.* 本對所有的馬都下了注, 確保能贏。

4 ►CERTAIN TO BE TRUE 肯定(真實)的◄ certain to be true 肯定真實的, 肯定的, 確切的: **one thing is (for) sure** *One thing's for sure, we'll never be able to move this furniture on our own.* 有一點是肯定的, 我們自己絕對搬不動這些家具。| **sure sign/indication** (=a sign that something is certainly going to happen) 某事肯定會發生的徵兆/標誌 *Those black clouds are a sure sign of rain.* 那些黑雲是肯定要下雨的徵兆。

5 ►CERTAIN TO SUCCEED 肯定要成功◄ certain to succeed 肯定會成功的: **sure way/means** (=a way of doing something that will certainly achieve a particular result) 萬無一失的方法 *Arriving at work in pyjamas is a sure way of attracting attention to yourself!* 穿睡衣去上班肯定是惹人注目的一種做法! | **a sure bet** *AmE* (=something that is certain to succeed)【美】一定成功的事, 十拿九穩的事 | **a sure thing** *AmE* (=something that will definitely happen, win, succeed etc)【美】一定會發生的事; 肯定會贏[成功]的事

6 be sure of to be certain to get something or be certain that something will happen 一定會, 肯定會: *United must beat Liverpool to be sure of winning the championship.* 曼聯隊要穩拿冠軍就必須打敗利物浦隊。| *You can be*

sure of one thing – there'll be a lot of laughs. 有一點可以肯定——將會笑聲不斷。

7 sure of yourself confident in your own abilities and opinions, sometimes in a way that annoys other people 有自信心；〔過分〕自信：*Kids nowadays seem very sure of themselves.* 如今的小孩顯得非常自信。

8 be sure to do sth *spoken* used to tell someone to remember to do something【口】一定要做某事，務必要做某事〔用於告訴某人記住做某事〕：*Be sure to ring and let us know you've got back safely.* 一定要來個電話，讓我們知道你已經平安返回。

9 sure to do sth certain to happen or to do something〔某事〕一定會發生；肯定會做某事：*He's sure to get nervous and say something stupid.* 他肯定會精神緊張，説些蠢話。

10 (as) sure as hell *spoken especially AmE* used to emphasize a statement【口，尤美】絕對肯定〔用於強調〕：*I'm sure as hell not gonna do it.* 我絕對肯定不去做那件事。

11 to be sure *BrE spoken* used to admit that something is true, before saying something that is the opposite【英口】不能否認；誠然，固然〔用於要説相反意見之前〕：*Jamie's had his problems to be sure, but he's got potential.* 無可否認，傑米固然有他自己的問題，但他是有潛力的。

12 sure thing *AmE spoken* used to agree to something【美口】當然；沒問題：*"See you next week?" "Sure thing."* "下星期再見？" "當然。"

13 have/get a sure hold/footing if you have a sure hold or footing your hands or feet are placed firmly so they cannot slip 抓緊／站穩 —see also 另見 SURELY

14 sure as eggs are eggs *BrE old-fashioned* used to say that something is definitely true【英，過時】的的確確，千真萬確，毫無疑問 —**sureness** *n* [U]

Frequencies of the word **sure** in spoken and written English 單詞sure在英語口語和書面語中的使用頻率

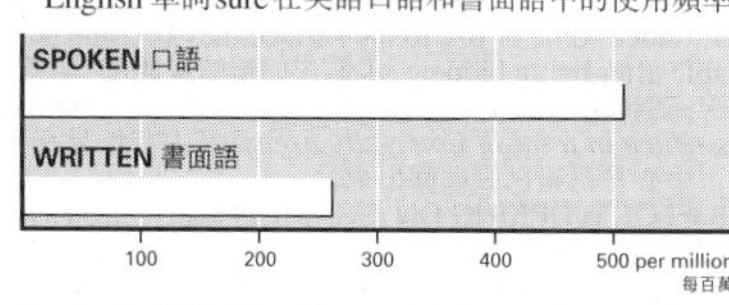

Based on the British National Corpus and the Longman Lancaster Corpus 據英國國家語料庫和朗文蘭卡斯特語料庫

This graph shows that the word **sure** is much more common in spoken English than in written English. This is because it has special uses in spoken English and is used in some common spoken phrases. 本圖表顯示，單詞sure在英語口語中的使用頻率遠遠高於書面語，因為它在口語中有特殊的用法，而且口語中一些常用片語是由sure構成的。

sure² *adv*

1 for sure *spoken*【口】**a)** certainly 肯定地，確切地：*No one knows for sure what really happened.* 沒有人確切地知道到底發生了甚麼事。**b)** used to emphasize that something is true 毫無疑問〔用於強調某事真實〕：*I know one person who won't be happy with the decision, that's for sure.* 我知道有一個人會對這個決定感到不高興，這一點毫無疑問。**c)** *AmE* used to agree with someone【美】當然；肯定〔用於表示同意〕

2 sure enough used to say that something did actually happen in the way that you said it would 果真，果然（如此）〔表示發生的事與預料的相符〕：*Sure enough Mike managed to get lost.* 邁克果然迷路了。

3 ▶USED TO SAY 'YES' 用於表示"是"◀ *spoken especially AmE* used to say 'yes' to someone【口，尤美】當然，好的：*"Can you give me a ride to work tomorrow?" "Sure."* "明天我可以順路搭你的車子上班去嗎？" "當然可以。"

4 ▶USED AS A REPLY 用作回答◀ *AmE spoken* used as a way of replying to someone when they thank you【美口】不（用）謝，不（用）客氣：*"Thanks for your help Karen." "Sure."* "謝謝你的幫助，卡倫。" "不用謝。"

5 ▶USED TO EMPHASIZE STH 用於強調某事◀ *AmE informal* used to emphasize a statement【美，非正式】必定，無疑：*Mom's sure gonna be mad when she gets home.* 媽媽回到家時一定會大為惱火。

6 ▶USED BEFORE STATEMENT 用於陳述的內容之前◀ *AmE spoken* used at the beginning of a statement admitting that something is true, especially before adding something very different【美口】的確，無可否認〔用於陳述的開始，承認某事真實，但往往接着補充不同看法〕：*Sure Joey's happy now, but will it last?* 喬伊現在的確是快樂的，但這能持久嗎？

sure·fire /ˈʃʊrˌfaɪr; ˈʃɔːfaɪə/ *adj* [only before noun 僅用於名詞前] *informal* certain to succeed【非正式】一定能成功的：*There's no surefire way to get rid of cockroaches.* 沒有甚麼方法一定能把蟑螂滅掉。| **surefire success** *I think the new show will be a surefire success with kids.* 我認為這個新節目一定會大受孩子們的歡迎。

sure·foot·ed /ʃʊrˋfʊtɪd; ˌʃɔːˈfʊtɪ̌d◂/ *adj* able to walk without sliding or falling in a place where it is not easy to do this 腳步穩的，不會摔倒的

sure·ly /ˈʃʊrlɪ; ˈʃɔːli/ *adv* **1** [sentence adverb 句子副詞] used to show that you think something must be true, especially when people seem to be disagreeing with you 想必，諒必〔尤用於當別人似乎不同意時〕：*You must have heard about the riots surely?* 想必你已經聽到發生騷亂的事了吧？| *There must surely be some explanation.* 肯定是有某種解釋吧。| *Surely we can't just stand back and let this happen?* 我們總不能袖手旁觀任由此事發生吧？**2 surely not** *spoken* used to show you cannot believe that something is true【口】決不可能，絕對不會〔用於表示不相信〕：*"The chairman's just handed in his resignation." "Surely not."* "主席剛遞交了辭呈。" "決不可能。" **3** *old-fashioned* certainly【過時】必定，無疑：*Such sinners will surely be punished.* 這樣的罪人必定會受到懲罰。**4** *AmE old-fashioned* used to say 'yes' to someone or to express agreement with them【美，過時】當然；可以〔用於表示同意〕 S1 W2

S

USAGE NOTE 用法説明：SURELY

WORD CHOICE 詞語辨析：**surely, certainly, sure, definitely, of course, naturally, obviously**

Surely is usually used to show that you believe something, and would be surprised if others did not agree. surely通常用於表示相信某事，並會對其他人不同意感到驚訝：*Surely they must realize that* (=I think they should realize that, and don't you agree?). 想必他們已認識到這一點了〔=我想他們應已認識到這一點，你説是吧？〕。| *They've gone home, surely* (=you seem to be still expecting to see them, but I'm sure they have gone). 他們諒必已經回家了〔=你似乎還在期待見到他們，但我敢肯定他們已經走了〕。| *He surely doesn't expect me to pay him immediately* (=I hope he doesn't expect this and I don't think he ought to). 他想必不會以為我會馬上付錢給他吧〔=我希望他不會這樣想，而且我認為他不應該這樣〕。

A sentence with **surely**, especially near the beginning, usually sounds like a question, even if nobody actually answers, and could easily be followed by a question tag. 句子裡〔尤其在接近句首的地方〕用surely時，通常聽起來像個問句，但並不要求真的給予回答。這種句子往往帶有一個附加疑問句：*Surely they know, don't they?* 他們想必知道，不是嗎？

Certainly is four times as frequent as **surely** in spoken English and shows that you strongly believe something, in spite of what others think. 在英語口語中，certainly的使用頻率是surely的四倍，表示你

堅決相信某事，而不管別人怎樣想：*He certainly doesn't expect me to pay him immediately* (=I know he doesn't expect the money now). 他肯定不認為我馬上付錢給他的〔=我知道他並不認為現在就會拿到那筆錢〕。| *She was amazed and I was certainly surprised too* (NOT *surely* because it would be strange to expect others to know how you feel). 她大為驚訝，我也着實吃了一驚〔不用 surely，因為不能期待別人知道你的感覺如何〕。

Certainly often suggests that there may also be a slight doubt or condition, even if it is not actually followed by **but**. certainly 常暗示可能同時包含輕微的疑問或條件，即使句子後面不一定跟用 but: *It's certainly very beautiful, but it's far too expensive.* 它無疑是很漂亮的，但實在太貴了。| *"He's a brilliant student, isn't he?" "Well, he certainly works very hard."* (=but I do not agree that he is brilliant) "他是個很聰明的學生，不是嗎？" "噢，他確實很勤奮。"〔=但我不認為他很聰明〕

In informal spoken American English **sure** is often used, especially just before the verb, with a similar meaning to **certainly**, but is often stronger and may show annoyance or impatience. 在非正式美國口語中，sure 常用在動詞前面，意義和 certainly 相似，但一般語氣較強，且可能表示惱火或不耐煩：*They sure are late* (=they're late and isn't that surprising/annoying?)! 他們確實遲到了〔=他們竟然遲到，這真讓人驚訝/惱火〕！

Definitely shows that you believe something so strongly that there is no doubt or question about it at all. definitely 表示對某事堅決相信，毫無疑問：*He's definitely the best player in the team.* 他無疑是隊裡最佳的選手。

Of course, **naturally**, and **obviously** show that you not only think something is true but also that it is not surprising. of course, naturally 和 obviously 表示認為某事不但真實，而且不足為奇：*They broke down on the way so of course they were late.* 他們的車子在路上壞了，所以他們自然遲到了。| *Naturally my mother loved me.* 我媽媽自然是愛我的。| *A vacation in Switzerland would obviously be expensive.* 在瑞士度假不用說會是很費錢的。

For information about using these words in answer to questions see **of course** (WORD CHOICE). 關於這些詞用於回答問題時的用法，請參閱 of course（詞語辨析）。

sur·e·ty /ˈʃʊrtɪ; ˈʃɔːrəti/ *n* [C,U] *law*【法律】**1** someone who will pay a debt, appear in court etc if someone else fails to do so 保證人，擔保人 **2 stand surety (for sb)** be responsible for paying a debt, appearing in court etc if someone else fails to do so 做（某人的）擔保人 **3** money someone gives to make sure that someone will appear in court〔交給法院保證出庭的〕保證金

surf[1] /sɝf; sɜːf/ *v* [I] **1** to ride on waves standing on a special board 衝浪：**go surfing** *When we were in Hawaii we went surfing every day.* 我們在夏威夷時每天都去衝浪。**2 surf the net** to look quickly through information on the computer INTERNET for anything that interests you 在互聯網上衝浪，上網瀏覽信息：*surfing the net with a high-speed modem* 用高速調制解調器在互聯網上瀏覽信息 —**surfer** *n* [C]

surf 衝浪

surf[2] *n* [U] the white substance that forms on top of waves as they move towards the shore 浪頭的白色泡沫

sur·face[1] /ˈsɝfɪs; ˈsɜːfɪs/ *adj* [only before noun 僅用於名詞前] appearing to be true or real, but not representing what someone really feels or what something is really like; SUPERFICIAL 表面（上）的；外表的：*The surface calm of the city was shattered by a massive explosion.* 這個城市表面的寧靜被巨大的爆炸聲打破了。| *surface resemblance* 外表相似

surface[2] *n* [C]

1 ▶WATER/LAND 水/陸◀ the top layer of an area of water or land〔水或陸地的〕表面，面：*the Earth's surface* 地球表面 | *Pieces of trash were floating on the surface of the river.* 一片片的垃圾漂浮在河面上。| *the surface of the road* 路面

2 ▶TOP LAYER 表層◀ the outside or top layer of an object〔物體的〕外層，表層，面：*a frying pan with a non-stick surface* 不黏（的煎）鍋

3 on the surface if someone or something is calm, nice etc on the surface, they seem that way until you know them better 表面上；外表上：*On the surface Mrs Lewis seemed nice enough but she had a nasty temper at times.* 劉易斯太太表面上顯得非常和藹可親，但有時脾氣很壞。

4 below/beneath/under the surface if an emotion or quality is below, beneath, under the surface, it is not easy to notice at first〔情感等〕隱藏的：*I sensed a lot of tension and jealousy beneath the surface.* 我感覺到表面之下隱藏着非常緊張和嫉妒的情緒。

5 come/rise to the surface if unpleasant feelings or attitudes come or rise to the surface they become noticeable after being hidden〔不愉快的情緒或態度〕顯露，顯現；表現出來：*Violence and prejudice have risen to the surface in a lot of inner-city areas.* 暴力和偏見在很多市中心貧民區已經顯露出來。

6 ▶FOR WORKING ON 供工作用的◀ an area on a desk, table etc used for working 桌面，枱面；〔某物的〕面：*Make sure all kitchen surfaces are clean and tidy.* 一定要把廚房所有表面都搞得清潔整齊。

7 ▶SIDE OF AN OBJECT 物體的面◀ *technical* one of the sides of an object【術語】〔物體的一個〕面：*How many surfaces does a cube have?* 立方體有幾個面？—see also 另見 **scratch the surface** (SCRATCH[1] (7))

surface[3] *v* **1** [I] to rise to the surface of water 浮出水面：*The bird dived and didn't surface for at least a minute.* 鳥潛入水裡，至少有一分鐘沒有浮出水面。**2** [I] if information or feelings surface, they become known after being hidden〔信息或情感〕顯露，暴露；公開：*A few personality clashes have surfaced within the department.* 這個部門裡的一些個人衝突已經公開化了。**3** [I] *humorous* to get up, especially after being in bed for a long time【幽默】〔尤指久睡後〕起牀：*Joe never surfaces before midday on Sunday.* 喬在星期天不睡到中午是不會起牀露面的。**4** [T] to put a surface on a road 給…鋪路面

surface a·re·a /ˈ·· ,···/ *n* [C] the area of the outside of an object that can be measured〔物體可量度的〕表面面積

surface mail /ˈ·· ˌ·/ *n* [U] the system of sending letters or packages by land or sea 陸路[水路]郵件，平（寄）郵（件）

surface ten·sion /ˌ·· ˈ··/ *n* [U] the way the MOLECULES in the surface of a liquid stick together so that the surface is held together 表面張力

surface-to-air /ˌ·· · ˈ·◂/ *adj* **surface-to-air-missile** a MISSILE (1) that is fired at planes from the land or from a ship 地[艦]對空導彈

surface-to-surface /ˌ... '...◂/ *adj* **surface-to-surface missile** a MISSILE (1) that is fired from land or a ship at another point on land or at another ship 地對地[艦]導彈; 艦對艦[地]導彈

surf·board /ˈsɝfˌbɔrd; ˈsɜːfbɔːd/ *n* [C] a long piece of plastic, wood etc that you stand on to ride the waves 衝浪板 —see picture at 參見 SURF 圖

sur·feit /ˈsɝfɪt; ˈsɜːfɪt/ *n formal*【正式】**a surfeit of sth** an amount of something that is too large or that is more than you need 過量的某物; 過度的某事物: *a surfeit of food and drink* 過量的食物和飲料

surf·ing /ˈsɝfɪŋ; ˈsɜːfɪŋ/ *n* [U] **1** the activity or sport of riding over the waves on a special board 衝浪(運動) **2 channel/cyber surfing** looking quickly from one television programme to another, or looking through the computer INTERNET for something that interests you〔為尋找有趣的東西〕頻繁更換電視頻道/網上衝浪

surge[1] /sɝdʒ; sɜːdʒ/ *v* **1** [I always+adv/prep] if a crowd of people surges, they suddenly move forward together very quickly〔人羣〕迅速湧動; 蜂擁向前: **[+forward/through etc]** *The crowd surged through the gates.* 人羣蜂擁通過各個進出口。**2** also 又作 **surge up** [I] if a feeling surges or surges up you begin to feel it very strongly〔情感〕湧起, 湧現: *Helpless rage surged up within me.* 無法抑制的怒火在我胸中湧起。**3** [I always+adv/prep] if a large amount of water surges, it moves very quickly and suddenly〔大水〕洶湧; 奔騰

surge[2] *n* [C usually singular 一般用單數] **1 a surge of** a sudden, large increase in a feeling〔情感〕激增; 湧現: *a surge of excitement* 一陣興奮 **2** a sudden increase in something such as demand, profit, interest etc〔需求、利潤、興趣等的〕急劇增加: **[+in]** *stores expecting the usual surge in demand as Christmas approaches* 期望着聖誕來臨時需求照例陡增的商店 **3** a sudden movement of a lot of people〔人羣的〕蜂擁: **[+of]** *a surge of refugees into the country* 湧入這個國家的難民潮

sur·geon /ˈsɝdʒən; ˈsɜːdʒən/ *n* [C] a doctor who does operations in hospital 外科醫生 —see also 另見 DENTAL SURGEON

S2 W3 **sur·ge·ry** /ˈsɝdʒərɪ; ˈsɜːdʒəri/ *n* **1** [U] medical treatment in which a surgeon cuts open your body to repair or remove something inside 外科手術: *major heart surgery* 心臟大手術 —see also 另見 COSMETIC SURGERY, PLASTIC SURGERY **2** [C,U] *especially AmE* the place where operations are done in a hospital【尤美】手術室; THEATRE (3) *BrE*【英】**3** [C] *BrE* a place where a doctor or DENTIST gives treatment【英】〔醫生或牙醫的〕診所; OFFICE *AmE*【美】**4** [U] *BrE* a regular period each day when people can see a doctor or DENTIST【英】門診時間; **office hours** (OFFICE (3)) *AmE*【美】: *Surgery is from 9am – 1pm on weekdays.* 週一至週五的門診時間為上午九時至下午一時。**5** [C] *BrE* a special period of time when people can see a MEMBER OF PARLIAMENT to discuss problems【英】〔議員的〕接待時間

sur·gi·cal /ˈsɝdʒɪkl̩; ˈsɜːdʒɪkəl/ *adj* [only before noun 僅用於名詞前] **1** connected with or used for medical operations 外科的; 外科手術的: *surgical techniques* 外科技術 **2 surgical stocking/collar etc** a STOCKING etc that someone wears to support a part of their body that is injured or weak 外科治療襪/領圈[護頸]等 —**surgically** /-klɪ; -kli/ *adv*: *The growth was surgically removed.* 用外科手術把腫瘤給切除了。

surgical spir·it /ˌ... ˈ../ *n* [U] *BrE* a type of alcohol used for cleaning wounds or skin【英】〔用以清洗傷口等的〕消毒用酒精; RUBBING ALCOHOL *AmE*【美】

surgical strike /ˌ... ˈ./ *n* [C] a carefully planned quick military attack intended to destroy something in a particular place without damaging the surrounding area 外科手術式打擊, 精確的軍事攻擊

sur·ly /ˈsɝlɪ; ˈsɜːli/ *adj* **surlier, surliest** bad-tempered, unfriendly, and often rude 脾氣暴躁的, 粗暴的: *Passengers complain of frequent delays and surly staff.* 乘客投訴航班經常延誤和工作人員粗暴無禮。—**surliness** *n* [U]

sur·mise /sɚˈmaɪz; səˈmaɪz/ *v* [T] *formal* to guess that something is true using the information you know already【正式】推測, 猜測, 臆測 —**surmise** *n* [C,U]

sur·mount /sɚˈmaunt; səˈmaʊnt/ *v* [T] *formal*【正式】**1** to succeed in dealing with a problem or difficulty; OVERCOME 克服〔困難〕: *a program designed to help couples surmount marital difficulties* 為幫助夫妻克服婚姻問題而設計的課程 **2** [usually passive 一般用被動態] to be above or on top of something 聳立於…之上; 在…頂上: *a stone tower surmounted by a tall spire* 有高聳塔尖的石塔 —**surmountable** *adj*

sur·name /ˈsɝˌnem; ˈsɜːneɪm/ *n* [C] the name that you share with your parents, or often with your husband if you are a married woman, and which in English comes at the end of your full name; LAST NAME 姓

sur·pass /sɚˈpæs; səˈpɑːs/ *v* [T] **1** to be even better or greater than someone or something else 超過; 勝過: *Gower became England's highest run scorer, surpassing Geoff Boycott's old record.* 高爾超過了傑夫·博伊科特的舊記錄, 成為英國得分最高的板球選手。| **surpass expectations/hopes/dreams** (=be better than you had expected, hoped etc) 比期望/希望/夢想的更好 **2 surpass yourself** an expression meaning to do something even better than you have ever done before, often used jokingly when someone has done something badly 超越自己〔表示比自己過去做得更好, 但常用於開玩笑, 表示做得很差〕: *You've really surpassed yourself this time!* 你這回真的超越自己了!

sur·pass·ing /sɚˈpæsɪŋ; səˈpɑːsɪŋ/ *adj* [only before noun 僅用於名詞前] *literary* much better than that of other people or things【文】出色的, 卓越的: *a picture of surpassing beauty* 一幅優美絕倫的畫作

sur·plice /ˈsɝplɪs; ˈsɜːplɪs/ *n* [C] a piece of clothing made of white material worn over other clothes by priests or singers in church〔教士或唱詩班成員穿的〕白色罩袍, 白色法衣

sur·plus[1] /ˈsɝpləs; ˈsɜːpləs/ *n* [C,U] **1** an amount of something that is more than what is needed or used 剩餘, 過剩; 剩餘額, 多餘的量: *Apply paste thinly to the back of the wallpaper taking care to remove any surplus.* 把糨糊薄薄地塗在牆紙背面, 注意抹去多餘的。| **[+of]** *an enormous surplus of crude oil* 大量過剩的原油 **2** the amount of money that a country or company has left after it has paid for all the things it needs 盈餘; 順差 —see also 另見 TRADE SURPLUS

S

surplus[2] *adj* **1** more than what is needed or used 過剩的, 剩餘的, 多餘的: *Companies are likely to continue laying off surplus staff well into the recovery.* 各公司很可能繼續解雇冗員, 直至經濟明顯復蘇。**2 be surplus to requirements** *formal* be no longer necessary【正式】不再需要: *Most of this furniture is now surplus to requirements.* 這些家具現在大多都用不着了。

sur·prise[1] /sɚˈpraɪz; səˈpraɪz/ *n* S3 W2

1 ▶EVENT 事件◀ [C] an unexpected or unusual event 意想不到的事; 不同尋常的事: *Joan! What a lovely surprise to see you again!* 瓊! 再次見到你真是驚喜萬分! | **surprise visit/announcement/attack etc** *Let's pay grandma a surprise visit.* 咱們去看望奶奶給她一個驚喜。| *US forces launched a surprise attack on the Panamanian capital.* 美軍對巴拿馬首都發動突襲。| **come as a surprise (to sb)** (=happen unexpectedly) 出乎(某人)意料, 使(某人)感到來得突然 *The news that George was leaving came as a surprise to everyone.* 喬治要離開的消息使大家都感到意外。| **it came as no surprise** (=you expected it would happen) 來得並不突然 *It came as no surprise when Sarah announced she was pregnant.* 莎拉宣布她懷孕時, 人們並不感到意外。| **there is a surprise in store for sb** (=something unexpected is going to happen to them) 將有意想不到的事發生在某人身上

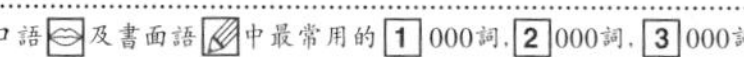
口語及書面語中最常用的 1 000詞, 2 000詞, 3 000詞

2 ►FEELING 感覺◄ [U] the feeling you have when something unexpected or unusual happens 驚奇, 驚訝, 詫異: *Imagine my surprise when she told me she'd been married twice already.* 當她告訴我她已結過兩次婚時, 想像一下我有多麼吃驚吧。| **get/have a surprise** *Harwich police got a nasty surprise yesterday when someone left a suspected unexploded bomb inside the police station.* 昨晚有人將一枚可疑的未爆的炸彈放在哈威治警察局內, 這使警方吃了一驚。| **in/with surprise** *She noticed with surprise the change in his appearance.* 她吃驚地注意到他外表的變化。| **much to my surprise** (=in a way that surprises you) 使我十分驚訝的是 *Much to my surprise they offered me the job.* 使我非常驚奇的是, 他們把那份工作給了我。

3 take sb by surprise to happen unexpectedly 出乎某人意料: *The heavy snowfall had taken us all by surprise.* 這場大雪使我們大家猝不及防。

4 take sb/sth by surprise to suddenly attack a place or an opponent when they are not ready 出其不意地襲擊某人/某地: *Rebel forces took the town by surprise.* 叛軍突襲了該鎮。

5 ►GIFT/PARTY ETC 禮物/聚會等◄ [C usually singular 一般用單數] an unexpected present, trip etc which you give to someone or organize for them, often on a special occasion 令某人意外驚喜的事物〈如禮物、旅行等〉: *I've got a little surprise waiting for you at home.* 我有一件讓你意想不到的禮物在家等着你。| *Jim's organized a trip to the opera as a surprise for his mum.* 吉姆安排去看歌劇, 要給媽媽一個驚喜。

6 surprise guest/visitor etc someone who arrives somewhere unexpectedly 不速之客

7 surprise! *spoken* used when you are just about to show someone something that you know will surprise them【口】有個你想不到的東西!〔用於即將給某人看令其驚奇的東西時〕

8 a) surprise, surprise used when saying in a joking way that you expected something to happen or be true 啊, 真出乎意料〔玩笑語, 用於表示自己預料某事屬實或將會發生〕: *The American TV networks are – surprise, surprise, full of stories about the royal divorce.* 真想不到! 美國各個電視網竟大事報道王室離婚的新聞。**b)** *spoken* used when you suddenly appear in front of someone who you know is not expecting to see you【口】沒想到吧?〔出其不意地突然出現在某人面前時說的話〕

9 ►METHOD 方法◄ [U] the use of methods which are intended to cause surprise 令人驚奇[感到意外]的方法: **an element of surprise** *An element of surprise is important to any attack.* 出其不意在任何進攻中是非常重要的。

surprise² *v* [T] **1** to make someone feel surprised 使驚奇, 使詫異, 使感到意外: *Paul's news surprised her.* 保羅的消息使她感到意外。| **it surprises sb to see/find/know etc** *It surprised them to see Jane up so early.* 他們看到簡那麼早起牀感到驚奇。| **it doesn't surprise me** *"Howard and Shari have split up." "I have to say it doesn't surprise me."* "霍華德和夏麗已經分手了。" "我得說這不足為奇。" | **what surprises sb is** *What surprised me most was that she didn't seem to care.* 最令我感到意外的是, 她好像毫不在乎。—see 見 SHOCK¹ (USAGE) **2** to find, catch, or attack someone when they are not expecting it, especially when they are doing something they should not be doing 出其不意地發現; 當場抓獲; 突然襲擊: **surprise sb doing sth** *A security guard surprised the burglars in the store room.* 一名保安員出其不意地在儲藏室當場抓住了小偷。

sur·prised /sə`praɪzd; sə'praɪzd/ *adj* having a feeling of surprise 吃驚的, 驚奇的, 驚訝的, 詫異的: *Mr Benson looked surprised when I told him I was leaving.* 當我告訴他我要離去時, 本森先生非常驚訝。| **[+at/by]** *We were all surprised at Sue's outburst.* 蘇突然情緒激動起來, 我們大家都很驚訝。| **surprised (that)** *Harry was surprised that Carl didn't say anything to defend himself.* 卡爾沒為自己作任何辯護, 這使哈里感到很驚奇。| **surprised to see/hear/learn etc** *I was pleasantly surprised to learn that I had passed.* 我知道自己已經通過, 感到非常驚喜。| **surprised look/expression** *She just sat there with a surprised expression on her face.* 她只是坐在那裡, 臉上帶着驚愕的表情。| **don't be surprised if...** *spoken* (=used when saying that something is likely to happen)【口】要是…不必感到驚奇〔用於表示很可能發生某事〕*Don't be surprised if they ask a lot of difficult questions.* 他們如果提出很多難以解答的問題, 你不要感到奇怪。| **I wouldn't be surprised** *spoken* (=used when saying that you expect something will happen)【口】我不會覺得意外, 我認為那是意料中的事 *"Do you think they'll get married?" "I wouldn't be at all surprised."* "你認為他們會結婚嗎?" "如果他們結婚, 我一點也不會感到吃驚。"

sur·pris·ing /sə`praɪzɪŋ; sə'praɪzɪŋ/ *adj* unusual or unexpected 令人驚奇的, 使人吃驚的, 出人意料的: *a surprising lack of communication between management and staff* 管理部門和職工之間令人吃驚地缺少溝通 | **it is surprising (that)** *It's not really surprising that only a few people came tonight.* 今晚只來了幾個人, 這並不十分出人意料。| **it is surprising how/what etc** *It's surprising how quickly those in the public eye fade.* 那些公眾人物轉眼就淡出了人們的視線, 快得令人吃驚。| **it is hardly/scarcely surprising** *It's hardly surprising that she won't talk to you after what you said to her.* 在你對她說了那些話以後, 她不願跟你說話就不足為奇了。

sur·pris·ing·ly /sə`praɪzɪŋlɪ; sə'praɪzɪŋli/ *adv* unusually or unexpectedly 驚人地, 使人吃驚地, 出人意料地: [+adj/adv] *The exam was surprisingly easy.* 這次考試簡單得出人意料。| **not surprisingly** [sentence adverb 句子副詞] *Not surprisingly, the UK has the highest divorce rate in the Community.* 毫不奇怪, 英國的離婚率在歐洲共同體中是最高的。

sur·real /sə`riəl; sə'rɪəl/ *adj* a situation or experience that is surreal is very strange, like something from a dream〔情況或經歷〕超現實的; 離奇的, 荒誕的: *American politics has always been more surreal than any satire.* 美國政治向來比任何諷刺作品都更加荒誕離奇。

sur·real·is·m /sə`riəlˌɪzəm; sə'rɪəlɪzəm/ *n* [U] 20th century art or literature in which the artist or writer connects unrelated images and objects in a strange way〔20世紀文學、藝術上的〕超現實主義 —**surrealist** *adj*: *a surrealist painting* 一幅超現實主義繪畫 —**surrealist** *n* [C]

sur·real·is·tic /səˌriəl`ɪstɪk; səˌrɪə'lɪstɪk◄/ *adj* **1** seeming very strange because of a combination of many unusual, unrelated events, images etc 夢幻般的; 離奇的; 超現實的 **2** connected with surrealism 超現實主義的 —**surrealistically** /-klɪ; -kli/ *adv*

sur·ren·der¹ /sə`rɛndɚ; sə'rendə/ *v* **1** [I] to say officially that you want to stop fighting because you realize that you cannot win 投降: *The terrorists were given ten minutes to surrender.* 恐怖分子被限定在十分鐘之內投降。| **surrender to sb** *The unit was forced to surrender to the enemy.* 這支部隊被迫向敵人投降。**2 surrender to sth** to allow yourself to be controlled or influenced by something 聽任…擺佈; 屈服於…: *Colette surrendered to temptation and took out a cigarette.* 科萊特經不起誘惑, 拿出了一根香煙。**3** [T] to give your soldiers or land to an enemy after they have beaten you in a battle〔向敵人〕交出〔部隊〕; 放棄〔土地〕: *The General had to surrender his troops.* 將軍不得不交出他的部隊。**4** [T] to give up something that is important or necessary, often because you feel forced to〔被迫〕放棄: *Critics feel that Boyer has surrendered his artistic identity in his later films.* 評論家們感到博耶在他後期的電影裡放棄了自己的藝術風格。**5** [T] *formal* to give something such as a ticket or a PASSPORT to an official【正式】〔向官員〕交出〔票證、護照等〕: **surrender sth to sb** *The court ordered Bond to surrender his passport to the authorities.* 法院命令邦德把護照交給當局。

surrender² *n* [singular,U] **1** the act of saying officially that you want to stop fighting because you realize that you cannot win 投降: **unconditional surrender** (=act of accepting total defeat) 無條件投降 **2** the act of allowing yourself to be controlled or influenced by something 屈服; 讓步: *a surrender to the forces of evil* 向惡勢力屈服

sur·rep·ti·tious /ˌsɝəpˈtɪʃəs; ˌsʌrəpˈtɪʃəs◂/ *adj* done secretly or quickly because you do not want other people to notice 祕密的, 偷偷摸摸的, 鬼鬼祟祟的: *Robert stole a surreptitious glance at Myrna to see her reaction.* 羅伯特偷偷掃了默娜一眼, 看看她的反應。—**surreptitiously** *adv* —**surreptitiousness** *n* [U]

sur·rey /ˈsɝɪ; ˈsʌri/ *n* [C] *AmE* a light carriage with two seats, which was pulled by a horse and was used in the past【美】〔舊時的〕雙座輕便馬車

sur·ro·gate /ˈsɝəget; ˈsʌrəgeɪt/ *adj* [only before noun 僅用於名詞前] a surrogate person or thing is one that takes the place of someone or something else 替代的, 代理的: *Uncle Giles became a sort of surrogate father to them after the accident.* 在那次事故以後賈爾斯叔叔便成了他們的代理父親。—**surrogate** *n* [C]

surrogate moth·er /ˌ··· ˈ··/ *n* [C] a woman who has a baby for another woman who cannot have one 代孕婦, 代母〔替不育婦女生育的婦女〕

2 **sur·round¹** /səˈraund; səˈraʊnd/ *v* [T] **1** [usually passive 一般用被動態] to be all around someone or something on every side 環繞, 圍繞: *The city is surrounded on all sides by hills.* 這個城市四面環山。| **be surrounded by sth** *Jill was sitting on the floor surrounded by boxes.* 吉爾坐在地板上, 周圍擺滿了箱子。**2 be surrounded by sb/sth** to have a lot of a particular kind of people or things near you 周圍有很多…; 被…圍住: *How can I work when I'm surrounded by idiots.* 周圍都是白痴, 叫我怎麼工作? **3** if police or soldiers surround a place they arrange themselves in positions all the way around it 包圍, 圍困〔某處〕: *We've got the place surrounded. Come out with your hands up.* 這個地方已被我們包圍了, 舉起手出來吧。**4** to be closely connected with a situation or event 與〔某情況或事件〕密切相關: *the controversy surrounding the group's 'Cop Killer' track* 圍繞着該演唱組《警察殺手》這首歌曲的爭論 **5 surround yourself with** to choose to have certain people or things near you all the time 和…在一起, 與…為伍: *David loved to surround himself with young people.* 大衛很喜歡和年輕人在一起。

surround² *n* [C] an area around the edge of something, especially one that is decorated or made of a different material 圍飾, 緣飾

sur·round·ing /səˈraundɪŋ; səˈraʊndɪŋ/ *adj* [only before noun 僅用於名詞前] near or around a particular place 附近的, 四周的: *the surrounding towns* 附近的城鎮 | *After the explosion the army sealed off the surrounding area.* 爆炸發生後, 軍隊封鎖了周圍地區。

sur·round·ings /səˈraundɪŋz; səˈraʊndɪŋz/ *n* [plural] the objects, buildings, natural things etc that are around a person or thing at a particular time 環境; 周圍的事物: *It took me a few weeks to get used to my new surroundings.* 我花了好幾個星期才適應這個新環境。

sur·tax /ˈsɝˌtæks; ˈsɜːtæks/ *n* [U] an additional tax on money you earn if it is higher than a particular amount〔對超過一定額的收入徵收的〕附加稅

sur·veil·lance /sɚˈveləns; səˈveɪləns/ *n* [U] the act of carefully watching a person or place because they may be connected with criminal activities〔對可疑的人或地方的〕監視; 盯梢: **keep sb/sth under surveillance** *Police are keeping the area under constant surveillance.* 警察在不間斷地監視這個地區。

3 3 **sur·vey¹** /ˈsɝve; ˈsɜːveɪ/ *n* [C] **1** a set of questions that you ask a large number of people in order to find out about their opinions or behaviour 調查: **to carry out/conduct a survey** (=do a survey) 進行調查 *a recent survey conducted by Manchester university into children's attitudes to violence on television* 曼徹斯特大學進行的關於兒童對電視暴力所持態度的新近調查 **2** an examination of a house or other building done especially for someone who wants to buy it〔尤指為購房者所做的〕房屋鑑定[查勘] **3** an examination of an area of land in order to make a map of it〔繪製地圖前對某地的〕勘測, 測量, 測繪 **4** a general description or report about a particular subject or situation〔對某一專題或形勢的〕概論, 概述: *a survey of modern English literature* 現代英國文學概論

sur·vey² /sɚˈve; səˈveɪ/ *v* [T] **1** [often passive 常用被動態] to ask a large number of people questions in order to find out their attitudes or opinions 調查: *Almost 60% of those surveyed said they supported the President's action.* 在被調查人中有將近60%的人支持總統的行動。**2** to look at or consider someone or something carefully, especially in order to form an opinion about them〔尤指為形成某種意見而〕審視, 仔細考慮: *He leaned back in his chair and surveyed her critically for a moment.* 他靠在椅子上, 挑剔地審視了她一番。**3** to examine the condition of a house or other building and make a report on it, especially for people who want to buy it〔尤指為購房者〕鑑定〔房屋〕**4** to examine and measure an area of land and record the details on a map 測量, 勘測, 勘定: *a surveying expedition* 一次勘測之行

survey course /ˈ·· ˌ·/ *n* [C] *AmE* a university course that gives an introduction to a subject for people who have not studied it before【美】〔大學裡介紹一門學科的〕概論課

sur·vey·or /sɚˈveɚ; səˈveɪə/ *n* [C] someone whose job is to examine the condition of a building, or to measure and record the details of an area of land〔建築物的〕鑑定人, 房產檢視員;〔土地〕測量員, 勘測員 —see also 另見 QUANTITY SURVEYOR

sur·viv·al /sɚˈvaɪvl̩; səˈvaɪvəl/ [U] *n* **1** the state of continuing to live or exist 繼續生存; 幸存: *His doctors said he had a 50-50 chance of survival.* 醫生說他有50%的生存機會。| *Our disregard for the environment threatens the long-term survival of the planet.* 我們對環境的漠視威脅着地球的長久存在。| **fight for survival** (=struggle or work hard in order to continue to exist) 為生存而奮鬥 *A lot of small companies are having to fight for survival.* 很多小公司正不得不為生存而奮鬥。**2 survival of the fittest** a situation in which only the strongest and most successful people or things continue to exist 適者生存 **3 a survival from** *especially BrE* something that has continued to exist from a much earlier period, especially when similar things have disappeared; RELIC【尤英】…時代的殘存物; 遺風; 遺跡 3

survival kit /ˈ··· ·/ *n* [C] a collection of things that you need to help you stay alive if you get hurt or lost 救生包, 救生箱〔裝有受傷或迷路時維持生命所必需的救生用品〕

sur·vive /sɚˈvaɪv; səˈvaɪv/ *v* **1** [I,T] to not die in an accident or war or from an illness〔經歷事故、戰爭或疾病後〕活下來, 倖存; 倖免於難: *Only 12 of the 140 passengers survived.* 在140名乘客中只有12人倖免於難。| **survive sth** *There are concerns that the refugees may not survive the winter.* 人們擔心那些難民可能熬不過冬天。**2** [I,T] to continue to exist in spite of many difficulties and dangers 經歷〔困難和危險後〕仍然存在; 保存下來: *A few pages of the original manuscript still survive.* 有幾頁原始手稿保存了下來。**3** [I,T] *often spoken* to continue to live normally and not be too upset by your problems【常口】從〔困難中〕挺過來; 掙扎着過下去: *I don't think I could survive another year as a teacher; it's just too stressful.* 再當一年教師我想我是挺不過去了, 壓力實在太大。| *"How are you?" "Oh, surviving!"* "你過得怎麼樣?" "噢, 湊合着過唄!" **4 survive on** to continue to live a normal life even though you have very little money〔靠很少錢〕繼續維持生活: *I don't know how you* 2 2

all manage to survive on Jeremy's salary. 我真不知道你們只靠傑里米的薪金是怎樣過活的。**5** [T] to live longer than someone else, usually someone closely related to you 比〔尤指親人〕活得更長, 比〔某人〕長壽: *Harry survived his wife by three months.* 哈里比他妻子多活了三個月。

sur·vi·vor /sə`vaɪvə; sə'vaɪvə/ *n* [C] **1** someone or something that still exists in spite of having been nearly destroyed or almost dead 生還者, 倖存者; 殘存物: **sole/lone survivor** (=only person who survives) 唯一生還者 *Major Hawkins was the lone survivor of the crash.* 霍金斯少校是這次墜機事件中的唯一生還者。**2** someone who manages to live their life without being too upset by problems 善於在困境中生存的人, 善於求存者: *Don't worry about Kurt; he's a survivor.* 不用為庫爾特擔心, 他善於在困境中生存。

sus·cep·ti·bil·i·ty /sə͵sɛptə`bɪlətɪ; sə͵septɪ̬'bɪlɪ̬ti/ *n* **1** [U] the condition of being easily affected or influenced by something 敏感; 易受影響(的狀況); 過敏性: *susceptibility to disease* 易於得病(的體質) **2 sb's susceptibilities** someone's feelings, especially when they are easily offended or upset 某人易受傷害的感情, 某人的敏感心理: *The policy has no regard for the susceptibilities of minority groups.* 這項政策忽視了少數民族的敏感心理。

sus·cep·ti·ble /sə`sɛptəbḷ; sə'septɪ̬bəl/ *adj* **1 susceptible to sth a)** likely to suffer from a particular illness or be affected by a particular problem 易得病的; 易受某事影響的: *Certain people are more susceptible to stress than others.* 有些人比其他人更受不了壓力。**b)** easily influenced or affected by something 易受…影響的: *Men are supposedly easily susceptible to feminine charms.* 男人據稱容易受女性魅力的誘惑。**2** *literary* tending to experience strong feelings easily and be easily influenced by other people; IMPRESSIONABLE【文】多情的; 易動情的: *a susceptible young boy* 容易動感情的少年 **3 susceptible of change/interpretation/analysis etc** *formal* able to be changed etc【正式】可以改變/解釋/分析等的

su·shi /`suʃɪ; 'suːʃi/ *n* [U] a Japanese dish consisting of pieces of raw fish on top of cooked rice 壽司〔一種在米飯上加生魚片的日本主食〕

2 3 **sus·pect¹** /sə`spɛkt; sə'spekt/ *v* [T not in progressive 不用進行式] **1** to think that something is probably true or likely, especially something bad 猜想, 懷疑, 覺得〔尤指壞事〕可能是事實: **suspect (that)** *She strongly suspected her husband had been lying.* 她覺得她丈夫很可能一直在說謊。| **suspect murder/foul play** (=suspect that someone has been murdered) 疑為謀殺 | **I suspect** *spoken*【口】: *It was a decision, I suspect, that he will later regret.* 這個決定我認為他以後會後悔的。**2** to think that someone is probably guilty 懷疑〔某人〕有罪, 認為〔某人〕有嫌疑: *Who do you suspect?* 你懷疑是誰? | **suspect sb of sth** *He's suspected of murder.* 他有殺人嫌疑。| **suspect sb of doing sth** *Pilcher was suspected of being a spy.* 皮爾徹被懷疑是間諜。**3** to distrust someone or doubt the truth of something 不信任, 不相信; 懷疑…的真實性: *I began to suspect his motives when he asked to borrow more.* 當他提出要借更多的錢時, 我開始懷疑起他的動機來了。

sus·pect² /`sʌspɛkt; 'sʌspekt/ *n* [C] someone who is thought to be guilty of a crime〔犯罪〕嫌疑人, 可疑分子: *Two suspects were arrested today in connection with the robbery.* 兩個與搶劫案有關的嫌疑人今天被捕了。

suspect³ *adj* **1** something that is suspect seems likely to have something wrong with it and should not be trusted, believed, or depended on 可疑的; 不可信任的; 不可靠的: *The evidence against the four Irishmen was highly suspect.* 指控那四個愛爾蘭人的證據很不可靠。| **highly suspect** 非常值得懷疑的 **2** [only before noun 僅用於名詞前] suspect packages, goods etc look as if they contain something illegal or dangerous〔包裹、貨物等〕可疑的: *Customs officers impounded the suspect crates.* 海關人員扣押了那些可疑的貨箱。

sus·pect·ed /sə`spɛktɪd; sə'spektɪ̬d/ *adj* **1 suspected terrorist/spy etc** someone the police believe is a TERRORIST etc〔被警方〕疑為恐怖分子/間諜等的人 **2 a suspected broken knee/heart attack etc** if you have a suspected broken knee etc, doctors think that you may have a broken knee etc 疑似膝部骨折/心臟病發等

sus·pend /sə`spɛnd; sə'spend/ *v* [T] **1** to officially stop something from continuing, especially for a short time 暫停, 中止: *Sales of the drug will be suspended until more tests are completed.* 這種藥品在完成進一步檢驗之前暫停銷售。**2** to make someone leave school, a job, or an organization temporarily, especially because they have broken the rules〔尤指因違反紀律〕使…暫時停學[停職]: **suspend sb from sth** *Dave was suspended from school for a week.* 戴夫被停學一個星期。**3** *formal* to hang something from something else【正式】懸, 掛, 吊: **suspend sth from sth** *The long fluorescent tubes were suspended from the ceiling.* 一支支長長的螢光管吊在天花板上。| **suspend sth by sth** *a ball suspended by a rope from a branch* 用繩子懸掛在樹枝上的球 **4 suspend judgment** to decide not to make a firm judgment about something until you know more about it 暫不作出判斷 **5 be suspended in** *technical* if something is suspended in a liquid or in air, it floats in it without moving【術語】懸浮在: *an insect suspended in a piece of amber* 懸浮在琥珀中的昆蟲

suspended an·i·ma·tion /·͵·· ··`··/ *n* [U] **1** a state in which someone's body processes are slowed down to a state almost like death 假死 **2** a feeling that you cannot do anything because you have to wait for what happens next 焦灼

suspended sen·tence /·͵·· `··/ *n* [C] a punishment given by a court in which the criminal will only go to prison if they do something else illegal within a particular period of time 緩刑: *a two-year suspended sentence* 緩刑兩年

sus·pend·er /sə`spɛndə; sə'spendə/ *n* [C] **1** *BrE* something that hangs down from a woman's underwear to hold STOCKINGS up【英】吊襪帶; GARTER (2) *AmE*【美】**2 suspenders** *AmE* two bands of cloth that go over your shoulders and fasten to your trousers to hold them up【美】〔男褲的〕吊帶, 背帶; braces (BRACE² (5)) *BrE*【英】

suspender belt /·`·· ·/ *n* [C] *BrE* a piece of women's underwear with suspenders joined to it【英】〔女用的〕吊襪束腰帶; GARTER BELT *AmE*【美】

sus·pense /sə`spɛns; sə'spens/ *n* [U] a feeling of excitement or anxiety when you do not know what will happen next 懸念; 焦慮; 緊張感: **in suspense** *The children waited in suspense to hear the end of the story.* 孩子們緊張地等着聽故事的結局。| **keep sb in suspense** *We were kept in suspense waiting for the results of the contest.* 我們焦急地等待比賽的結果。| **the suspense is killing me!** (=used when you are excited or anxious because you do not know what will happen) 我等得急死了!〔表示因不知接下來會發生甚麼事而感到緊張〕

sus·pen·sion /sə`spɛnʃən; sə'spenʃən/ *n* **1** [U] the act of officially stopping something from continuing for a period of time 暫停, 中止: **[+of]** *EC sanctions included suspension of the 1980 trade agreement and import limits on textiles.* 歐共體的制裁包括中止 1980 年的貿易協定和限制紡織品進口。**2** [C] the removal of someone from a team, job, school etc for a period of time, especially to punish them〔尤指作為處分〕暫時停職[停學]; 暫時〔從球隊等〕除名: *Sean McCarthy is set to return to football after a three match suspension.* 肖恩·麥卡錫在被罰停賽三場之後將再出場比賽。**3** [U] equipment fixed to the wheels of a vehicle to make it more comfortable on roads that are not smooth〔裝在車輪上以減少震動的〕懸架, 減震裝置 **4** [C] *technical* a liquid mixture consisting of very small pieces of solid material that are contained in the liquid but have not combined with it【術語】懸浮液; 懸浮體 —compare 比較 COLLOID **5** [U] the act of hanging something from something else 懸, 掛, 吊: *suspension cables* 懸纜

suspension bridge /'·'·· ·/ *n* [C] a bridge that is hung from strong steel ropes fixed to towers 懸索橋, 吊橋

sus·pi·cion /sə`spɪʃən; sə'spɪʃən/ *n* **1** [C,U] a feeling that someone is probably guilty of doing something wrong or dishonest 懷疑, 嫌疑: **have your suspicions** (=think you probably know who did something wrong) 心中有懷疑對象 *I'm not sure who took it, but I have my suspicions.* 我不能肯定是誰拿走了它, 但我心中有懷疑對象。| **have a sneaking suspicion** (=have a slight feeling that someone has done something wrong without having any definite information) 有點懷疑 | **arouse sb's suspicions** *Neighbours' suspicions were aroused by the bruises on the child's arms.* 孩子手臂上的傷痕引起了鄰居們的懷疑。**2 on suspicion of** because someone is thought to be guilty of a crime 因受到懷疑, 涉嫌: *She was arrested on suspicion of killing her boyfriend.* 她因涉嫌謀殺男友而被捕。**3 under suspicion** someone who is under suspicion of a crime is thought to be guilty of it 被懷疑犯了罪的, 有作案嫌疑的: **come/fall under suspicion** *Yet another politician came under suspicion of being in the pay of big business.* 又有一名政客涉嫌被大企業收買。**4 above/beyond suspicion** if someone is above or beyond suspicion, they definitely could not be guilty of a crime or have done something wrong 無可懷疑的, 沒有嫌疑的: *Just because she knew and liked Dysart did not mean that the man was necessarily above suspicion.* 僅僅因為她認識並喜歡戴薩特並不等於這個人就肯定沒有嫌疑。**5** [C,U] a feeling that you do not trust someone 不信任, 猜疑: *She always treated us with suspicion.* 她總是對我們疑神疑鬼的。| **look upon/regard sb with suspicion** *Anyone who expressed any kind of liberal opinion was regarded with deep suspicion.* 凡是表達過開明思想的人都受到極大的懷疑。**6** [C] a feeling that something has happened is true 疑心; 懷疑: *There is always a suspicion that the legal system is designed to suit lawyers rather than to protect the public.* 人們總是覺得, 法律制度的制定是為了迎合律師而不是為了保護公眾。| **suspicion (that)** *I had a suspicion she might be hurt.* 我隱約覺得她可能受到了傷害。**7 a suspicion of sth** a very small amount of something seen, heard, tasted etc 一點兒, 些微: *I could see the faintest suspicion of a tear in her eyes.* 我能看到她眼睛裡有一丁點淚水。

S3 **sus·pi·cious** /sə`spɪʃəs; sə'spɪʃəs/ *adj* **1** thinking that someone might be guilty of doing something wrong or dishonest, without being sure 懷疑的, 猜疑的: *His behaviour that day made the police suspicious.* 他那天的行為使警方產生了懷疑。| **[+of/about]** *I'm suspicious of Jen's intentions.* 我懷疑詹的動機。**2** making you think that something bad or illegal is happening 可疑的, 引起懷疑的: *Anyone who saw anything suspicious is asked to contact the police immediately.* 任何人看到可疑的事請立即與警方聯繫。| *They found a suspicious package under the seat.* 他們在座位底下發現了一個可疑的包裹。| *a suspicious-looking character* 一個形跡可疑的人物 | **in suspicious circumstances** *Her mother had died in suspicious circumstances.* 她母親的死亡情況可疑。—see also 另見 SUSPECT³ **3** feeling that you do not trust someone or that there is something wrong 感到懷疑的, 認為有問題的: **[+of]** *Both parents and pupils are deeply suspicious of the new exams.* 家長和學生都對這種新的考試深感懷疑。

sus·pi·cious·ly /sə`spɪʃəslɪ; sə'spɪʃəsli/ *adv* **1** in a way that shows you think someone has done something wrong or dishonest 懷疑地, 猜疑地: *Meg looked at me very suspiciously.* 梅格疑心重重地看着我。**2** in a way that makes people think that something bad or illegal is happening 可疑地, 值得懷疑地: *He saw two youths acting suspiciously outside the pub.* 他看到酒館外面兩個年輕人行動鬼祟, 形跡可疑。**3** in a way that shows you think there is probably something wrong with something 懷疑地: *They sat in silence, eyeing the food suspiciously.* 他們沉默地坐着, 懷疑地看着那些食物。**4 looks/sounds etc suspiciously like** *often humorous* used when saying that something is very like something else【常幽默】看起來/聽起來等十分像…: *That pen looks suspiciously like the one I lost last week!* 那枝筆看起來十分像我上星期丢失的那一枝!

suss /sʌs; sʌs/ *v* [T] *BrE informal* to realize something【英, 非正式】認識到, 明白; 發現: **suss (that)** *We soon sussed she wasn't telling the truth.* 我們很快就發現她沒有講真話。

suss sb/sth ↔ **out** *phr v* [T] *BrE informal* to understand the important things about someone or something, especially things they are trying to hide【英, 非正式】發現…的真相, 探明…的隱情: *She's bound to suss out the truth sooner or later.* 她遲早一定會了解真相的。

sussed /sʌst; sʌst/ *adj BrE informal* knowing all about someone or something【英, 非正式】對…完全了解的: *These boys are too sussed to believe their own hype.* 這些男孩甚麼都知道, 所以根本不相信他們自己天花亂墜的宣傳。| **get sth sussed** *It's so annoying, you get something sussed and then they change the rules.* 真煩人, 你剛把事情弄明白, 他們又改變規則了。

sus·tain /sə`sten; sə'steɪn/ *v* [T] W3

1 ▶MAKE STH CONTINUE 使某事繼續◀ to make something continue to exist over a period of time; MAINTAIN (1) 保持, 維持, 使持續: *The teacher tried hard to sustain the children's interest.* 老師努力保持孩子們的興趣。—see also 另見 SUSTAINED

2 ▶GIVE STRENGTH 給予力量◀ to make it possible for someone to stay strong or hopeful 使保持強壯; 使保持信心[希望]: *A good breakfast will sustain you all morning.* 豐富的早餐會使你整個上午保持精力充沛。| *They were sustained by the knowledge that help would come soon.* 他們知道援助很快就會到來, 因此得以支撐下去。

3 sustain damage/an injury/defeat/heavy losses etc *formal* to be damaged, hurt or defeated or lose a lot of soldiers, money etc【正式】遭受破壞/傷害/失敗/嚴重損失等: *Allied forces sustained heavy losses in the first few weeks of the campaign.* 盟軍在戰役的最初幾個星期中遭受慘重的損失。

4 ▶WEIGHT 重量◀ *formal* to hold up the weight of something【正式】支撐, 承受〔重量〕: *The floor wouldn't sustain the weight of a piano.* 這地板承受不了一架鋼琴的重量。

5 ▶IDEA 意見◀ *formal* to support an idea, argument etc【正式】支持〔某意見、論點等〕: *There was no proof to sustain his views.* 沒有證據支持他的觀點。

6 ▶LAW 法律◀ **objection sustained** *spoken* used by a judge when saying that someone was right to object to another person's statement【口】反對有效〔法官說的話, 表示某人提出的異議正當〕

sus·tain·a·ble /sə`stenəbl; sə'steɪnəbəl/ *adj* an action or process that is sustainable can continue or last for a long time 能長期保持的; 能長期維持的; 能持續的: *sustainable economic growth* 可持續的經濟增長

sus·tained /sə`stend; sə'steɪnd/ *adj* something that is sustained continues for a long time 持續的, 持久的: *Paula owes her success to sustained hard work.* 葆拉把她的成就歸功於堅持不懈的努力。| *sustained economic development* 持續的經濟發展

sus·te·nance /`sʌstənəns; 'sʌstənəns/ *n* [U] **1** *formal* food that keeps people strong and healthy; NOURISHMENT【正式】〔使人健康強壯的〕食物; 營養: *The children were thin and badly in need of sustenance.* 孩子們身體瘦弱, 極需營養。**2** *informal* food you feel you need because you are tired and hungry【非正式】〔因疲勞或飢餓而需要的〕食物: *I need sustenance! Let's go get some food!*

我需要補充一下！咱們去弄點吃的來！| *There's not much sustenance in a bag of crisps.* 一包油炸馬鈴薯片沒有甚麼營養。**3** the act of sustaining something 保持; 維持; 支持

su·tra /ˋsutrə; ˈsuːtrə/ *n* [C] a piece of Hindu or Buddhist holy writing〔印度教或佛教中的〕經

sut·tee /sʌˋti; ˈsʌtiː/ *n* [U] the ancient custom in the Hindu religion of burning a wife with her dead husband 殉夫自焚〔古時印度教中寡婦在亡夫火葬時與其俱焚的習俗〕

su·ture /ˋsutʃɚ; ˈsuːtʃə/ *n* [C,U] the act of sewing a wound together, or a stitch used in this〔傷口的〕縫合;〔傷口縫合的〕一針, 縫針 —**suture** *v* [T]

su·ze·rainty /ˋsuzərɪntɪ; ˈsuːzəreɪnti/ *n* [U] the right of a country or leader to rule over another country 宗主權, 宗主國的地位 —**suzerain** /-rɪn; -reɪn/ *n* [singular]

svelte /svɛlt; svelt/ *adj* someone, especially a woman, who is svelte is thin and graceful〔尤指女子〕身材苗條的, 修長的: *a svelte young lady* 身材苗條的年輕女子

Sven·ga·li /svɛnˋgɑlɪ; svenˈgɑːli/ *n* [C] a man who has the power to control people's minds and make them behave in a bad way 能控制別人思想並令其作惡的人

SW the written abbreviation of 縮寫= SOUTHWEST and SOUTHWESTERN

swab¹ /swɑb; swɒb/ *n* [C] **1** a small piece of material used by a doctor or nurse to clean a wound or take liquid from someone's body〔醫生或護士用以清潔傷口等的〕拭子, 藥棉棒: *a cotton swab* 棉籤 **2** a test using such a piece of material 用棉籤取樣所作的檢驗: *Take a swab of his throat, nurse.* 護士, 用棉籤從他的咽喉取樣做檢查。

S

swab² *v* **swabbed, swabbing** [T] **1** also 又作 **swab down** to clean something, especially the floors of a ship 擦洗〔尤指船上的地板〕 **2** also 又作 **swab out** to clean a wound with a piece of material〔用拭子等〕拭抹〔傷口〕

swad·dle /ˋswɑdḷ; ˈswɒdl/ *v* [T] *old-fashioned* to wrap a baby tightly to protect it【過時】用襁褓包裹〔嬰孩〕

swaddling clothes /ˈ·· ·/ *n* [plural] *old use* the pieces of cloth wrapped around babies to protect them【舊】襁褓

swag /swæg; swæg/ *n* **1** [U] *slang* the goods stolen when someone is robbed【俚】〔偷或搶來的〕贓物; 掠奪物 —compare 比較 LOOT¹ (1) **2** [C] a deep fold of material, especially in or above a curtain〔帳子、窗簾等的〕深褶子 **3** [U] *AustrE* a set of clothes and possessions wrapped in a cloth and carried by someone who is travelling on foot【澳】〔徒步旅行者的〕行囊, 包袱

swag·ger¹ /ˋswægɚ; ˈswægə/ *v* [I] **1** [always+adv/prep] to walk proudly, swinging your shoulders in a way that shows too much confidence 昂首闊步, 大搖大擺地走, 趾高氣揚地走: **[+down/in/out etc]** *He swaggered down the street with a foolish grin on his face.* 他大搖大擺地走在街道上, 臉上帶着傻笑。**2** *old-fashioned* to talk or behave in a very proud way; BOAST¹ (1)【過時】自我吹噓; 狂妄自大; 自鳴得意 —**swaggerer** *n* [C] —**swaggeringly** *adv*

swagger² *n* [singular,U] a way of behaving or walking that is too confident or unusually confident 趾高氣揚; 狂妄自大; 自鳴得意: *He combines the cocky swagger of Johnny Rotten with the animal sexuality of Prince.* 他身上兼有約翰尼·羅頓的狂妄與歌手王子的原始性感。

swain /swen; sweɪn/ *n* [C] *poetic* a young man from the country who loves a girl【詩】鄉下情郎

3 **swal·low¹** /ˋswɑlo; ˈswɒləʊ/ *v*

1 ►FOOD 食物◄ [T] to make food or drink go down your throat and towards your stomach 吞下, 嚥下〔食物或飲料〕: *He swallowed the last of his coffee and asked for the bill.* 他喝下最後一口咖啡, 要求結賬。

2 ►NERVOUSLY 緊張地◄ [I] to make this kind of movement with your throat, especially because you are nervous〔尤指因為心情緊張〕做吞嚥動作, 嚥口水: *Leo swallowed hard and walked into the interview.* 利奧使勁嚥了一口口水, 然後走進去面試。

3 ►BELIEVE/ACCEPT 相信/接受◄ [T] *informal* to immediately believe a story, explanation etc that is not actually true【非正式】輕信, 輕易接受〔不真實的解釋等〕: **swallow sth whole** (=believe something without asking questions) 對某事深信不疑; 全盤相信某事 *Her excuse was obviously a lie, but Eric swallowed it whole.* 她的辯解明顯是在撒謊, 但埃里克竟然全盤相信了。| **hard to swallow** (=difficult to believe) 難以置信 *I find those old superstitions hard to swallow.* 我覺得那些古老的迷信思想難以置信。

4 ►FEELINGS 感情◄ [T] to stop yourself from showing your feelings 使〔感情、想法等〕不流露: *Daisy tried hard to swallow her doubts.* 黛西盡力不露出自己的疑心。

5 swallow your pride to ignore your feelings and do something that is very embarrassing for you because you have no choice 忍辱含垢; 抑制羞恥感: *When Ken lost his job he had to swallow his pride and borrow money.* 肯失業的時候, 他不得不拋開面子去借錢。—see also 另見 **a bitter pill (to swallow)** (BITTER¹ (7))

swallow sb/sth **up** *phr v* [T usually passive 一般用被動態] **1** if something such as a company or a country is swallowed up by a large company, organization etc it becomes part of it and no longer exists on its own 吞併: *Their company was swallowed up by a multinational.* 他們的公司為一家跨國公司所吞併。**2** if something such as an amount of money is swallowed up by something else, it is made to disappear completely 耗盡〔金錢〕, 用盡: *I got a pay rise, but it was swallowed up by the increase in train fares.* 我加了工資, 但讓火車票漲價給完全抵消了。

swallow² *n* [C] **1** a small bird with a tail that comes to northern countries in the summer 燕子 **2** an act of making food go down your throat 吞, 嚥: *He downed his whisky in one swallow.* 他一口把威士忌喝完。

swallow dive /ˈ·· ·/ *n* [C] *BrE* a DIVE² (1) into water, that starts with your arms stretched out from the sides of your body【英】燕式跳水; SWAN DIVE *AmE*【美】

swam /swæm; swæm/ the past tense of SWIM¹

swa·mi /ˋswɑmɪ; ˈswɑːmi/ *n* [C] a Hindu religious teacher〔印度教的〕宗教教師

swamp¹ /swɑmp; swɒmp/ *n* [C,U] land that is always very wet or slightly covered with water 沼澤（地）—compare 比較 MARSH —**swampy** *adj*: *swampy ground* 濕地

swamp² *v* [T] **1** [usually passive 一般用被動態] to suddenly give someone a lot of work, problems etc to deal with 使陷入〔大量工作〕; 使面臨〔大量問題〕: **swamp sb with sth** *We've been swamped with calls since we put the ad in the paper.* 我們自從在報紙上登出廣告之後, 電話就多得應接不暇。**2** to suddenly cover something with a lot of water, especially in a way that causes damage〔驟然〕淹沒, 浸沒: *The shoreline was swamped by the high tides.* 海岸線被高漲的潮水淹沒了。

swan¹ /swɑn; swɒn/ *n* [C] a large white bird with a long graceful neck that lives on rivers and lakes 天鵝

swan² *v* **swanned, swanning** [I always+adv/prep] *BrE informal* to do things in a relaxed way that is not very responsible【英, 非正式】悠閒地工作; 馬馬虎虎地做事: **[+off/around]** *You can't just swan off to the cinema when you're supposed to be working!* 你可不能在上班時間溜出去看電影啊！

swan dive /ˈ· ·/ *n* [C] *AmE* a DIVE² (1) into water, that starts with your arms stretched out from the sides of your body【美】燕式跳水; SWALLOW DIVE *BrE*【英】

swank¹ /swæŋk; swæŋk/ *v* [I] *informal especially BrE* to behave or speak too confidently, especially to try and make other people admire you【非正式, 尤英】炫耀, 吹噓, 擺闊: *Stop swanking; you're not the only person who's got a flash car.* 別炫耀了, 又不是只有你一個人才有花哨的汽車。

swank² *n informal especially BrE*【非正式, 尤英】**1** [U] proud, confident behaviour that is intended to make people admire you, but is annoying 炫耀; 擺架子; 賣弄 **2** [C] someone who talks and behaves confidently in order to make people admire them 愛吹噓的人, 愛出風頭的人

swank³ *adj especially AmE* swanky【尤美】非常時髦的; 奢華的

swank·y /ˈswæŋkɪ; ˈswæŋki/ *adj informal*【非正式】**1** very fashionable or expensive; POSH 非常時髦的; 奢華的: *a really swanky reception* 很有排場的招待會 **2** *especially BrE* tending to act too confidently to get attention【尤英】愛出風頭的; 愛吹噓的; 愛擺闊的

swan·song /ˈswɑnˌsɔŋ; ˈswɒnsɒŋ/ *n* [C] the last piece of work or performance of a poet, painter etc〔詩人、畫家等的〕最後一個作品; 最後一次表演: *The 1992 tour was a swansong for the two Irish players.* 1992 年的巡迴比賽是這兩位愛爾蘭球員的告別演出。

3 **swap¹, swop** /swɑp; swɒp/ *v* **swapped, swapping** [I,T] **1** to exchange something with someone, especially so that each of you get what you want; TRADE² (1) 交換〔尤指雙方各得所需之物〕: *I liked her coat and she liked mine, so we swapped.* 我喜歡她的外套, 她也喜歡我的, 所以我們就交換了。| **swap sth for sth** *Adam swapped three of his stickers for three of Alex's.* 亞當用自己的三張貼紙跟亞歷克斯換了三張。| **swap sth with sb** *I swapped hats with Mandy.* 我和曼迪交換了帽子。| **swap sb sth for sth** *I'll swap you two of mine for one of yours.* 我可以用我的兩張換你的一張。**2 swap places** also 又作 **swap round** *BrE* to let someone sit or stand in your place, so that you can have their place【英】互換位置[座位]: *I want to sit by Val; can we swap places?* 我想坐在瓦爾旁邊, 我們可以互換座位嗎?

swap², swop *n* [C] *informal*【非正式】**1** [usually singular 一般用單數] an exchange of one thing for another 交換, 交易: *a swap of arms for hostages* 以武器交換人質 | **do a swap** *I like your doll better; let's do a swap.* 我更喜歡你的玩具娃娃, 咱們交換吧。**2** something that has been or may be exchanged 交換物; 可交換之物

swap meet /ˈ· ,·/ *n* [C] *AmE* an occasion when people meet to buy and sell used goods, or to exchange them【美】〔買賣或交換舊貨的〕二手貨集市

sward /swɔrd; swɔːd/ *n* [C] *literary* a piece of grassy land【文】一片草地[草皮]

swarf /swɔrf; swɔːf/ *n* [U] small bits of metal, plastic etc that are produced when you use a cutting tool〔金屬或塑料等的〕細屑, 切屑

swarm¹ /swɔrm; swɔːm/ *n* [C] **1** a large group of insects, especially BEES, or animals moving together 移動中的一羣昆蟲; 〔尤指〕蜂羣 **2** a crowd of people who are moving quickly〔迅速移動的〕人羣: **[+of]** *Swarms of tourists jostled through the square.* 一羣羣遊客熙熙攘攘地穿過廣場。

swarm 蜂羣

a swarm of bees
一羣蜜蜂

swarm² *v* [I] **1** [always+adv/prep] if people swarm somewhere, they go there as a large, uncontrolled crowd 成羣結隊地移動, 蜂擁, 湧往: **[+through/over/out etc]** *photographers swarming around the princess* 一窩蜂地擁到公主周圍的攝影記者們 **2** if BEES swarm they leave a HIVE (=place where they live) in a large group to look for another home〔蜜蜂〕成羣飛離蜂巢尋覓新巢

swarm with sb/sth *phr v* **be swarming with** to be full of a moving crowd of people or animals 擠滿〔移動的人羣或動物〕: *The museum was swarming with tourists.* 博物館裡擠滿了觀光客。

swar·thy /ˈswɔrðɪ; ˈswɔːði/ *adj* someone who is swarthy has dark skin that is considered unattractive〔人〕膚色黝黑的

swash·buck·ling /ˈswɑʃˌbʌklɪŋ; ˈswɒʃˌbʌkəlɪŋ/ *adj* enjoying adventures, sword fighting etc 喜歡冒險[鬥劍]的: *swashbuckling pirates* 冒險成性的海盜 —**swashbuckler** *n* [C]

swas·ti·ka /ˈswɑstɪkə; ˈswɒstɪkə/ *n* [C] an ancient sign consisting of a cross with each end bent at 90°, used in the twentieth century as a sign for the Nazi Party 卐字〔20 世紀時用作納粹黨的黨徽〕

swat /swɑt; swɒt/ *v* **swatted, swatting** [T] to hit an insect to try to kill it 重拍, 猛擊〔昆蟲〕—**swat** *n* [C]

swatch /swɑtʃ; swɒtʃ/ *n* [C] a piece of cloth that is used as an example of a type of material or its quality〔小塊〕布樣, 樣品

swathe¹ /sweð; sweɪð/ also 又作 **swath** /swɑθ; swɒθ/ *n* [C] **1** a long band of cloth 長布條: *swathes of cotton* 長條的棉布 **2** a line or area of grass or crops that has been cut by a machine or a cutting tool〔用機器、鐮刀等割出的〕一行草[作物] **3** any large area of land that is different from the land on either side of it〔與兩旁土地不同的〕大片土地: *Acid rain is now affecting great swathes of Western Europe.* 酸雨現正影響着西歐的廣大地區。**4 cut a swath through** if a fire, severe storm etc cuts a swath through a place, it destroys almost everything around it〔大火、暴風雨等〕把…夷為平地; 嚴重摧毀

swathe² *v* [T usually passive 一般用被動態] *literary*【文】**be swathed in sth** to be wrapped or covered in something, especially cloth 用某物包裹; 用某物覆蓋: *women swathed in expensive furs* 身穿名貴毛皮衣服的女士們

sway¹ /swe; sweɪ/ *v* **1** [I,T] to move slowly from one side to another (使) 搖擺, (使) 擺動, (使) 搖晃: *trees swaying gently in the breeze* 在微風中輕輕搖動的樹木 | **sway sth** *Melanie swayed her hips in time with the music.* 梅拉尼隨着音樂節拍扭動着臀部。**2** [T often passive 常用被動態] to influence someone who has not yet decided about something so that they change their opinion 影響〔某人〕; 使改變看法: *Don't allow yourself to be swayed by his promises.* 你可不要聽了他的許諾就改變主意呀。

sway² *n* [U] **1** swinging movement from side to side 搖擺, 擺動, 搖晃: *the sway of the ship* 船的搖晃 **2** *literary* power to rule or influence people; control【文】影響力; 支配; 統治: **hold sway** (=have great power or influence) 擁有大權; 有巨大影響力 *In medieval times the Church held great sway politically.* 在中世紀, 教會在政治上處於支配地位。

sway·back /ˈsweˌbæk; ˈsweɪbæk/ *n* [C usually singular 一般用單數] *AmE* a condition in which your back curves inward too much【美】脊椎前凸

swear /swɛr; sweə/ *v past tense* **swore** /swɔr; swɔː/ *past participle* **sworn** /swɔrn; swɔːn/ 2

1 ▶OFFENSIVE LANGUAGE 無禮的語言◀ [I] to use offensive language, especially because you are angry〔尤指因生氣〕詛咒, 咒罵, 用粗話罵人: *Don't swear in front of the children.* 不要在孩子們面前罵人。| **[+at]** *Rich tripped over the dog and swore at it.* 里奇被狗絆了一跤, 就咒罵起牠來。| **swear like a trooper** (=use very offensive language) 滿口髒話

2 ▶SERIOUS PROMISE 嚴肅的許諾◀ [T] to make a very serious promise 起誓保證: **swear to do sth** *Mona swore never to return home.* 莫娜發誓不再回家。| **swear (that)** *Victor swore he would get his revenge.* 維克托發誓要報仇。| **[+on/by]** *Do you swear on your honour never to tell anyone?* 你能以你的名譽發誓永遠不會告訴任何人嗎?

3 ▶PUBLIC PROMISE 公開承諾◀ [I,T] to make a public official promise, especially in a court of law〔尤指在法庭上〕宣誓, 起誓: **[+on]** *Witnesses have to swear on the Bible.* 證人必須用手按着《聖經》宣誓。| **swear an oath** *Before giving evidence you have to swear an*

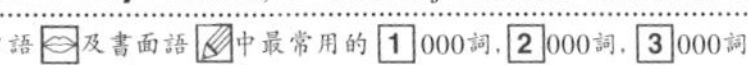

oath to tell the truth. 在提供證詞前，你必須宣誓保證說實話。| **swear allegiance** *Presidents must swear allegiance to the US constitution.* 總統必須宣誓效忠美國憲法。

4 ►STATE THE TRUTH 說真話或實話◄ [T not in progressive 不用進行式] *informal* to say that what you have said is the truth【非正式】保證〔自己說的是真話〕，鄭重說明：**swear (that)** *He says he was there all the time, but I swear I never saw him.* 他說他自始至終都在那裡，但我保證我根本沒有見到他。| **swear blind (that)** *informal* (=used to empasize you are telling the truth)【非正式】一口咬定〔自己說的是實話〕*She swore blind that she had never met the man.* 她一口咬定她從未見過那個男子。| **I could have sworn (that)** *informal* (=I was almost certain)【非正式】我幾乎可以肯定 *I could have sworn I left the keys on that table.* 我幾乎可以肯定是把鑰匙放在那張桌子上的。| **swear to God** *I never touched her I swear to God.* 我對上帝發誓我從未碰過她。

5 swear sb to secrecy/silence to make someone promise not to tell anyone what you have told them 使某人發誓保守祕密

swear by sth *phr v* [T not in progressive 不用進行式] *informal* to have great confidence in the effectiveness of something【非正式】極其信賴：*He swears by vitamin C pills, and says he never gets ill.* 他非常相信維生素C片，說他因此從不生病。

swear sb ↔ **in** *phr v* [T usually passive 一般用被動態] **1** to make someone promise publicly to be loyal to a country, official job etc 使〔某人〕宣誓就職：*The new governor was sworn in.* 新州長宣誓就職。| *the swearing-in ceremony* 宣誓就職儀式 **2** to make someone give an official promise in a court of law 使〔某人〕在法庭宣誓：*The jury had to be sworn in first.* 陪審團必須首先宣誓。

swear off sth *phr v* [T] to promise to stop doing something that is bad for you 承諾終止〔某種不良行為〕：*I'm swearing off alcohol after last night!* 昨晚之後，我保證戒酒了！

swear to *phr v* [T] **not swear to (doing) sth** to be unwilling to say that something is true because you are not sure about it 不能保證〔某事〕屬實：*I think it was Sue I saw, but I wouldn't swear to it.* 我覺得我看到的人是蘇，但我不敢保證是她。

swear word /ˈ· ·/ *n* [C] a word that is considered to be offensive or shocking by most people 詛咒語，粗話

sweat[1] /swɛt; swet/ *v*

1 ►LIQUID FROM SKIN 皮膚冒出的液體◄ [I] to have liquid coming out through your skin, especially because you are hot or frightened 出汗，流汗，冒汗：*I was sweating after the long climb.* 我長時間攀爬後出汗不止。| **sweat heavily/profusely** (=sweat a lot) 出大汗；流很多汗 | **sweat like a pig** *informal* (=sweat a lot)【非正式】汗流浹背，渾身臭汗 | **sweat buckets** *informal* (=sweat a lot)【非正式】汗如雨下，大汗淋漓

2 ►WORK 工作◄ [I] *informal* to work hard【非正式】辛苦工作，拚命幹活：*For years she had struggled and sweated to keep the family fed.* 多少年來，她為了養家糊口在拚命幹活。| **[+over]** *Tim really sweated over that thesis.* 蒂姆寫那篇論文可費勁了。| **sweat blood** (=work very hard) 拚命地幹

3 ►WORRY 擔心◄ [I] *informal* to be anxious, nervous, or worried about something【非正式】焦慮；精神緊張；擔心：*We were all really sweating as we waited for the results.* 我們在等待結果時心情真是緊張得很。| *Don't tell them yet – let them sweat a bit first!* 暫時不要告訴他們——先讓他們着急一下！

4 don't sweat it *AmE spoken* used to tell someone not to worry about something【美口】別擔心，別着急：*Don't sweat it, I'll lend you the money.* 不用擔心，我會借錢給你的。

5 don't sweat the small stuff *AmE spoken* used to tell someone not to worry about unimportant things【美口】不要為小事擔心

6 sweat bullets *AmE informal* to be very worried, anxious, or frightened【美，非正式】非常擔心；十分着急；非常害怕

7 ►PRODUCE LIQUID 產生液體◄ [I] if something such as cheese sweats, liquid from inside appears on its surface〔乳酪等〕表面滲出水分

8 ►COOK 烹調◄ [T] *BrE* to heat food gently in a little water or fat【英】用文火煮：*Sweat the vegetables until the juices run out.* 用文火煮這些蔬菜，直至熬出菜汁。

sweat sth ↔ **out** *phr v* [T] **1 sweat it out a)** to continue doing something until it is finished, even though it is difficult 堅持做完〔困難的工作〕：*You can't leave the course now. Just sweat it out until the summer.* 你現在不能放棄這門課程，堅持到夏季把它修完吧。**b)** to do hard physical exercise 吃力地鍛鍊身體：*They were sweating it out in the gym.* 他們正拚命地在健身房裡進行訓練。**2** to get rid of an illness by making yourself sweat a lot 通過發汗把〔疾病〕治好 **3 sweat your guts out** *informal* to work very hard, especially using physical effort【非正式】拚命工作〔尤指體力勞動〕：*I've sweated my guts out trying to get this shed built on time.* 為了爭取按時建好這間棚屋，我一直在拚命苦幹。**4 sweat sth out of sb** *AmE informal* to find out information from someone by asking lots of questions in a threatening way【美，非正式】反覆威逼某人說出某情況：*Finally they sweated the other names out of him.* 他們終於逼他說出了其他人的名字。

sweat sth ↔ **off** *phr v* [T] to lose weight by sweating a lot 通過大量流汗減輕〔體重〕：*He sweated off two pounds in the sauna.* 他通過洗桑那浴大量出汗，體重減輕了兩磅。

sweat[2] *n*

1 ►LIQUID ON SKIN 皮膚上的液體◄ [U] liquid that comes out through your skin when you are hot, frightened, or doing exercise 汗，汗水，汗液：*Ian came off the squash court dripping with sweat.* 伊恩大汗淋漓地走出壁球場。| **work up a sweat** (=to do physical exercise or hard work that makes you sweat) 因鍛鍊[辛苦工作]而流汗 | **break out in a sweat** (=start to sweat, especially because you are frightened)〔尤指因懼怕〕冒汗 *I was ready to kill the guy, and he didn't even break out in a sweat!* 我恨不得殺死那個人，而他竟然連汗也沒有冒！

2 get into a sweat about sth *informal* to become nervous or frightened about something【非正式】因某事而緊張[害怕]：*Don't get into such a sweat about it! It's only a test.* 不要為這事那麼緊張！這只不過是一次測驗。

3 a cold sweat a state of nervousness or fear, in which you start to sweat, even though you are not hot〔由於精神緊張或害怕出的〕一身冷汗：*I woke up from the nightmare in a cold sweat.* 我從噩夢中驚醒，出了一身冷汗。

4 no sweat *spoken* used to say that you can do something easily【口】一點也不難，毫不費力：*"Are you sure you can do it on time?" "Yeah, no sweat!"* "你有把握按時完成嗎？" "是的，沒問題！"

5 sweats [plural] *AmE informal*【美，非正式】**a)** clothes made of thick, soft cotton, worn especially for sport; SWEAT SUIT 運動服 **b)** trousers of this type; SWEAT PANTS 運動褲

6 the sweat of sb's brow *literary* the hard effort that someone has made in their work【文】〔某人所付出的〕艱苦努力

7 ►WORK 工作◄ [singular] *old-fashioned* hard work, especially when it is boring or unpleasant【過時】〔尤指枯燥或不愉快的〕艱苦的工作

8 (old) sweat *old-fashioned* someone who has a lot of experience, especially a soldier【過時】經驗豐富的人〔尤指老兵〕

sweat·band /ˈswɛtˌbænd; ˈswetbænd/ *n* [C] **1** a narrow band of cloth that you wear around your head or wrist to stop sweat running down when you are doing sport〔運動時纏在頭部或手腕的〕吸汗帶 **2** a narrow piece of cloth that you wear sewn or stuck in the inside of a hat 帽子內側的防汗帶

sweated la·bour *BrE*【英】, **sweated labor** *AmE*【美】/,.. '../ *n* [U] **1** hard work done for very low wages, especially in a factory〔尤指工廠的〕艱苦而工資低微的工作, 血汗勞動 **2** the people who do this work 在艱苦條件下工作的廉價勞工, 血汗勞工

sweat·er /ˈswɛtɚ; ˈswetə/ *n* [C] a piece of warm WOOLLEN or cotton clothing for the top half of your body that has long SLEEVEs and no buttons〔長袖〕毛線衣, 羊毛衫, 針織(套)衫, 運動衫; JUMPER (1) *BrE*【英】

sweat gland /'. ./ *n* [C] a small organ under your skin that produces sweat 汗腺

sweat pants /'. ./ *n* [plural] *AmE* thick cotton trousers, worn especially for sport【美】棉織厚長褲, 運動褲

sweat·shirt /ˈswɛtˌʃɝt; ˈswet-ʃɜːt/ *n* [C] a piece of thick cotton clothing with long SLEEVEs, worn on the top half of your body, especially for sport 棉織長袖衫, 長袖運動衫

sweat·shop /ˈswɛtˌʃɑp; ˈswet-ʃɒp/ *n* [C] a small business, factory etc where people work hard in bad conditions for very little money 血汗工廠〔工作條件惡劣而工資低微的小廠〕: *Sweatshops often employ female or immigrant workers.* 血汗工廠經常雇用婦女和移民勞工。

sweat suit /'. ./ *n* [C] *AmE* a set of clothes made of thick soft cotton, worn especially for sport【美】〔棉織〕運動套裝, 運動衣褲

sweat·y /ˈswɛtɪ; ˈsweti/ *adj* **1** covered with SWEAT[2] (1) 有汗的; 滿是汗的, 被汗水濕透的: *We came home hot and sweaty after the day's work.* 幹完一天工作之後, 我們熱得滿身是汗地回家。| *sweaty palms* 有汗的掌心 **2** smelling unpleasantly of SWEAT[2] 發汗臭味的: *sweaty socks* 有汗臭味的襪子 **3** unpleasantly hot or difficult so that you SWEAT[1] 悶熱的; 勞累的, 使人出汗的: *a sweaty August day* 八月裡悶熱的一天 | *a sweaty job* 吃力的工作 **4** cheese that is sweaty has drops of liquid on its surface〔乳酪〕表面滲出水分的

Swede /swid; swiːd/ *n* [C] someone who comes from Sweden 瑞典人

swede *n* [C,U] *BrE* a round yellow vegetable that grows under the ground【英】瑞典甘藍, 蕪菁甘藍; RUTABAGA *AmE*【美】

Swe·dish[1] /ˈswidɪʃ; ˈswiːdiʃ/ *n* [U] **1** the language spoken in Sweden 瑞典語 **2 the Swedish** the people of Sweden 瑞典人(總稱)

Swedish[2] *adj* from or connected with Sweden 瑞典的; 來自瑞典的; 與瑞典有關的

S3 W3 **sweep[1]** /swip; swiːp/ *v past tense and past participle* **swept** /swɛpt; swept/

1 ►CLEAN STH 把…弄乾淨◄ [T] to clean the dust, dirt etc from the floor or ground using a special brush 掃, 打掃, 清掃: *Bert swept the path in front of the house.* 伯特清掃門前的小路。| *Sweep the floor clean for me please.* 請幫我把地板打掃乾淨。—see picture at 參見 CLEAN[2] 圖

2 ►PUSH STH SOMEWHERE 把某物推到某處◄ [T always+adv/prep] **a)** to clean a surface by pushing something to a particular place or in a particular direction with a special brush 掃去, 拂去, 清除: *Could you sweep the snow off the patio for me?* 你能幫我把露台上的雪清除掉嗎? **b)** to move something to a particular place or in a particular direction with a brushing or swinging movement 捲走; 沖走; 移去; 颳走: *The wind swept the dead leaves away.* 風把枯葉颳走了。| *I swept the papers quickly into the drawer.* 我迅速地把那些文件塞進抽屜裡。

3 ►CROWD 人羣◄ [I always+adv/prep] if a group of people sweep somewhere, they quickly move there together 迅速地移動; 衝過: **[+through/along etc]** *The crowd swept through the gates of the stadium.* 人羣衝過體育場的大門。

4 ►PERSON 人◄ [I always+adv/prep] if someone sweeps somewhere, they move quickly and confidently, especially because they are impatient or like to seem important 昂首闊步地走: **[+into/through etc]** *Eva swept into the meeting and demanded to know what was going on.* 伊娃大步衝進會場, 要求知道正在發生甚麼事情。

5 ►WIND/WAVES ETC 風/浪等◄ [I always+adv/prep, T] if winds, waves, storms etc sweep a place or sweep through, across etc a place, they move quickly and with a lot of force〔風、浪、風暴等迅速猛烈地〕掃過, 掠過〔某地〕: **[+across/through etc]** *90 mile per hour winds swept across the plains.* 時速 90 英里的強風橫掃平原。| **sweep sth** *Thunderstorms swept the country.* 雷暴橫掃全國。

6 ►IDEA/FEELING 思想/感情◄ [I always+adv/prep,T] if an idea or feeling sweeps a group of people or sweeps across, over etc a group, it quickly becomes very popular with them 風行; (在…)迅速傳播: **[+across/through etc]** *The new dance craze swept through the teenage population.* 新的舞蹈時尚在青少年中風靡一時。| **sweep sth** *a wave of nationalism sweeping the country* 席捲全國的民族主義浪潮

7 sweep sb along/away a) if a crowd sweeps someone along or away it forces them to move in the same direction it is moving in〔人羣〕擁着某人向前: *I was swept away by the crowd and lost sight of Alyssa completely.* 我被人羣擁着往前走, 完全看不到阿麗莎了。**b)** if a feeling or idea sweeps you along or away, you are so involved or interested in it that you forget about other things〔感情、思想〕令某人着迷; 使某人深受影響: *19th century scientists swept along on the tide of Darwin's theories* 19 世紀深受達爾文理論思潮影響的科學家

8 sweep to victory/power to win something easily and in an impressive way 大獲全勝/一舉掌權: *Nixon and Agnew swept to victory with 47 million votes.* 尼克遜和阿格紐贏得 4700 萬張選票, 大獲全勝。

9 sweep the board to win everything that can be won, especially very easily〔尤指輕易地〕大獲全勝, 囊括全部獎項

10 ►FORM A CURVE 形成曲線◄ [I always+adv/prep] to form a long curved shape 蜿蜒; 延伸: **[+down/along etc]** *The hills swept down to the sea.* 山丘延綿, 伸到了海邊。

11 ►LOOK 看◄ [I always+adv/prep,T] to look quickly at all of something〔目光等〕掃視: *The General's eyes swept the horizon.* 將軍雙目掃視着地平線。| **[+over/across/around etc]** *Her eyes swept over Marcia appraisingly.* 她用評價的目光迅速打量着瑪西婭。

12 sweep sb off their feet to make someone feel suddenly and strongly attracted to you in a romantic way 把某人一下子迷住, 使某人神魂顛倒: *Jill's been swept off her feet by an older man.* 吉爾被一位年長男子迷住了。

13 sweep sth under the carpet also 又作 **sweep sth under the rug** *AmE*【美】to try to keep something a secret, especially something you have done wrong 掩蓋某事〔尤指錯事〕

sweep sth ↔ **aside** *phr v* [T] to refuse to pay attention to something someone says 拒不理會, 無視

sweep sth ↔ **away** *phr v* [T] **1** to completely destroy something or make something disappear 掃除; 消滅; 摧毀: *houses swept away by the floods* 被洪水摧毀的房屋 | *A sudden feeling of nostalgia swept all my anger away.* 突然的一陣懷舊情緒使我怒氣全消。**2 be swept away by** to be so interested or involved in something that you forget about other things 深受…感染, 被…打動: *We couldn't help being swept away by Bette's enthusiasm.* 我們都不禁被貝特的熱情打動了。

sweep sth ↔ **back** *phr v* [T] if you sweep your hair back, you pull it back from your face, especially so that it stays in that style 把〔頭髮〕梳向後面, 向後掠〔頭髮〕: **[+in/into]** *Kerry swept her hair back into a bun.* 凱麗把頭髮梳到後面盤成一個髻。

sweep up *phr v* **1** [I,T] to clean a place using a special brush, or to pick up dirt, dust etc in this way 打掃, 清掃: *The janitor was just sweeping up as I left the building.* 我離開大樓時, 看門人正在進行打掃。**sweep sth ↔ up** *Jan was left to sweep up the bits of paper and broken glass.* 簡被留下來清掃那些紙屑和碎玻璃。**2** [T **sweep** sb **↔ up**] to pick someone up in one quick movement 一下抱起〔某人〕: *Harriet swept the child up in her arms and stormed out.* 哈麗特一把抱起孩子, 怒氣沖沖地跑了出去。**3 sweep sb's hair up** to pull someone's hair back away from their face, especially so that it stays in that style 把某人的頭髮梳到後面

sweep² *n* **1** [C] a long swinging movement of your arm, a weapon etc 揮動: *With one sweep of his sword, he cut through the rope.* 他劍一揮, 把繩索砍斷了。**2** [C usually singular 一般用單數] *BrE* the act of sweeping something【英】打掃, 清掃: *The kitchen needs a good sweep.* 廚房需要好好打掃一下了。**3 the sweep of a)** a long curved line or area of land 長而彎曲的一段〔土地〕; 連綿彎曲的地帶: **[+of]** *the sweep of the hills in the distance* 遠處延綿的山丘 **b)** the quality that an idea, plan, piece of writing etc has of considering many different and important things〔思想、作品等的〕廣度, 範圍: *the grand sweep of Whitman's poetic vision* 惠特曼豐富的詩歌想像力 **4** [C usually singular 一般用單數] a search or attack that moves over a large area〔大面積的〕搜索, 搜查; 掃蕩 **5 sweeps** [singular] *AmE informal* a SWEEPSTAKE【美, 非正式】賭金全贏制 **6** [C] a CHIMNEYSWEEP 煙囱清潔工 —see also 另見 **clean sweep** (CLEAN¹ (12))

S

sweep·er /ˈswipɚ; ˈswiːpə/ *n* [C] **1** someone or something that sweeps 清掃者, 清潔工; 清掃機: *a road sweeper* 馬路清潔工; 馬路清掃機 **2** *BrE* a football player who plays in a position behind other defending players【英】〔足球運動的〕自由中衛

sweep·ing /ˈswipɪŋ; ˈswiːpɪŋ/ *adj* **1** affecting many things, or making a big difference to things 影響大的; 範圍廣的; 廣泛的: **sweeping changes/cuts etc** *sweeping changes that mean job cuts in every department* 意味着每個部門都要裁員的全面變更 | *sweeping proposals* 內容廣泛的建議 **2** lacking knowledge of or consideration for facts or details 籠統的; 總括性的: *sweeping statements* 總括性的說法 | **sweeping generalization** *You shouldn't make sweeping generalizations about women drivers.* 你不該對女性駕駛員一概而論。

sweep·ings /ˈswipɪŋz; ˈswiːpɪŋz/ *n* [plural] dirt, dust etc that is left to be swept up 掃攏的垃圾[塵土等]: *a pile of sweepings* 一堆掃攏的垃圾

sweep·stake /ˈswipˌstek; ˈswiːpsteɪk/ *n* [C] a type of betting (BET¹), in which the winner gets all the money risked by everyone else〔勝者可獲全部賭金的〕賭金全贏制: *a sweepstake on the horses* 賽馬中的賭金全贏制

S2 W3 **sweet¹** /swit; swiːt/ *adj*

1 ►TASTE 味道◄ having a taste like sugar 甜的, 味甜的: *This tea is too sweet.* 這茶太甜了。| *a sweet apple* 甜蘋果 | *sweet wine* 甜酒 —compare 比較 BITTER¹ (4), DRY¹ (9), SOUR¹ (1)

2 ►CHARACTER 性格◄ kind, gentle, and friendly 和藹的; 温柔的; 友好的: *a sweet smile* 和藹的微笑 | *How sweet of you to remember my birthday!* 你真好, 還記得我的生日! —see also 另見 SWEET-TEMPERED

3 ►CHILDREN/SMALL THINGS 小孩/小物品◄ *especially BrE* looking pretty and attractive; CUTE【尤英】漂亮的, 可愛的: *Your little boy looks very sweet in his new coat.* 你的小兒子穿着新外套真好看。

4 ►THOUGHTS/EMOTIONS 思想/感情◄ making you feel pleased, happy, and satisfied 令人愉悦的, 愜意的; 使人滿足的: *Revenge is sweet.* 報仇給人帶來快感。

5 ►SMELLS 氣味◄ having a pleasant smell; FRAGRANT 芳香的, 芬芳的: *sweet-smelling flowers* 氣味芳香的花朵

6 ►SOUNDS 聲音◄ pleasant to listen to 悦耳的, 動聽的: *She had a very sweet singing voice.* 她唱歌的聲音悦耳動聽。

7 have a sweet tooth to like things that taste of sugar 愛吃甜食

8 keep sb sweet *informal* to behave in a pleasant, friendly way towards someone, because you want them to help you later【非正式】討好某人, 巴結某人: *I'm trying to keep Angela sweet so that she'll lend me her notes.* 我在盡力向安傑拉獻殷勤, 好讓她把筆記借給我。

9 in your own sweet way if you do something in your own sweet way, you do it in exactly the way that you want to, without considering what other people say or think 只憑自己的意願; 不考慮別人; 自私地: *I'd rather carry on in my own sweet way, if you don't mind.* 如果你不介意, 我就按我的想法做下去了。

10 sweet deal *AmE* a really good deal【美】賺錢的交易; 十分合算的買賣

11 sweet FA also 又作 **sweet Fanny Adams** *BrE informal* used to say FUCK ALL (=nothing at all) when you want to avoid using the word 'fuck'【英, 非正式】一點兒也沒有〔fuck all 的委婉說法, 以避免使用 fuck 這個髒詞〕: *"How much did they pay you for that job?" "Sweet FA!"* "幹那件工作他們給了你多少報酬?""一分錢也沒有!"

12 sweet nothings things that lovers say to each other〔情侶之間的〕卿卿我我的話, 情話: *a couple whispering sweet nothings to each other* 悄悄地互相說着情話的情侶

13 be sweet on sb *old-fashioned* to be very attracted to or in love with someone【過時】鍾情於某人, 愛上某人 —see also 另見 **home sweet home** (HOME¹ (16)), **short and sweet** (SHORT¹ (9)), SWEETNESS —**sweetly** *adv*

This graph shows how common the nouns **sweet** and **candy** are in British and American English. 本圖表顯示名詞 sweet 和 candy 在英國英語和美國英語中的使用頻率。

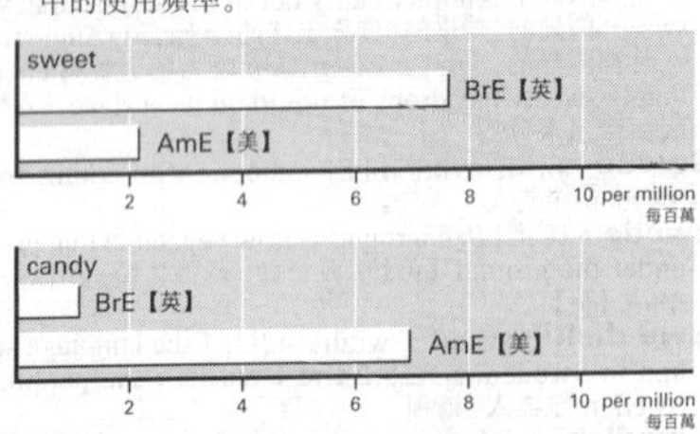

Based on the British National Corpus and the Longman Lancaster Corpus
據英國國家語料庫和朗文蘭卡斯特語料庫

In British English **sweet** is used to mean a small piece of sweet food made of sugar or chocolate. Americans use **candy** for this meaning. In British English **sweet** also means sweet food that is served at the end of a meal. Americans use **dessert** for this meaning. 在英國英語中, sweet 指用糖或巧克力做的糖果, 而美國英語則用 candy 表示此意。英國英語中 sweet 也可指餐後的甜食, 而美國英語則用 dessert。

sweet² *n* **1** [C] *BrE* a small piece of sweet food made of sugar or chocolate【英】糖果; CANDY *AmE*【美】: *Eating sweets is bad for your teeth.* 吃糖果對牙齒不好。**2** [C, U] *BrE* sweet food served at the end of a meal; DESSERT【英】〔餐後的〕甜食, 甜點: *Would you like a sweet, or some cheese and biscuits?* 你是喜歡來點甜食, 還是乾酪和餅乾? **3 (my) sweet** *old-fashioned* used when speaking to someone you love【過時】親愛的, 甜心〔用作愛稱〕: *Don't cry, my sweet.* 親愛的, 不要哭。 S2

sweet-and-sour /ˌ‥ˈ‥◂/ *adj* [only before noun 僅用於名詞前] a sweet-and-sour dish in Chinese cooking has both sweet and sour tastes together〔中國菜〕甜酸的, 糖醋的: *sweet-and-sour pork* 咕咾肉

sweet·bread /ˈswitˌbrɛd; ˈswiːtbred/ *n* [C] *old-fash-*

ioned a small organ from a sheep or young cow, used as food【過時】〔從羊或小牛身上取下供食用的〕胰臟, 雜碎

sweet·corn /ˈswitkɔrn; ˈswiːtkɔːn/ *n* [U] *BrE* the soft yellow seeds from MAIZE that are cooked and eaten【英】甜玉米〔可煮食〕; CORN (2b) *AmE*【美】

sweet·en /ˈswitn̩; ˈswiːtn/ *v* **1** [I,T] to make something sweeter, or become sweeter (使) 變甜; 加糖於: *Sweeten the mixture with a little honey.* 加點蜂蜜使混合料變甜。**2** also 又作 **sweeten** sb ↔ **up** [T] *informal* to try to persuade someone to do what you want, by giving them presents or money【非正式】〔通過送禮物或金錢〕籠絡, 討好: *We're going to have to sweeten them up if we want that contract.* 如果想簽上那份合同, 我們就得花錢籠絡他們一下。—see also 另見 SWEETENER (2) **3** [T] *literary* to make someone kinder, gentler etc【文】使和藹; 使溫和; 使溫柔: *Old age had not sweetened her.* 年老並沒有使她變得和藹可親。

sweetened con·densed milk /,·· ·'·· ·/ *n* [U] *especially AmE* milk that has been made thicker and sweeter, and is usually sold in cans【尤美】甜煉乳; CONDENSED MILK *BrE*【英】

sweet·ener /ˈswitn̩ɚ; ˈswiːtnə/ *n* **1** [C,U] a substance used to make something taste sweeter 甜味劑, 甜化劑: *No artificial sweeteners are used in this product.* 本產品沒有使用人造甜味劑。**2** [C] *informal* something that you give to someone to persuade them to do something【非正式】賄賂物, 籠絡物: *These tax cuts are just a pre-election sweetener.* 這些減稅措施只不過是選舉前用來籠絡人心的東西。

sweet gum /,· ˈ·/ *n* [C] a tree with hard wood and groups of seeds like PRICKLY balls, common in North America〔產於北美的〕楓香樹

sweet·heart /ˈswit,hɑrt; ˈswiːthɑːt/ *n* [C] **1** a way of addressing someone you love 親愛的, 甜心〔用作愛稱〕: *Come here, sweetheart.* 到這兒來, 親愛的。**2** an informal way of addressing a woman you do not know, which some women find offensive 甜心, 可愛的人〔對陌生女子的非正式稱呼, 有些女子認為這種稱呼帶有冒犯性〕**3** *old-fashioned* the person that you love【過時】情人, 戀人 —see also 另見 DARLING[1] (1), LOVE[2] (9)

sweet·ie /ˈswitɪ; ˈswiːti/ *n* [C] **1** *BrE informal* a word for a SWEET[2] (1), used by or to children【英, 非正式】糖果〔兒語〕**2** *BrE informal* something or someone that is small, pretty, and easy to love【英, 非正式】小巧[漂亮、可愛]的人[物]: *Look at that little dog – isn't he a sweetie!* 瞧那隻小狗 —— 牠多逗人喜愛! **3** *informal* a way of addressing someone you love【非正式】親愛的〔用作愛稱〕

sweetie pie /ˈ·· ·/ *n* [C] *AmE informal* a way of addressing someone you love【美, 非正式】親愛的, 寶貝〔用作愛稱〕

sweet·meat /ˈswit,mit; ˈswiːtmiːt/ *n* [C] *BrE old-fashioned* a SWEET[1] (1), or any food made of or preserved in sugar【英, 過時】糖果; 甜食; 蜜餞

sweet·ness /ˈswitnɪs; ˈswiːtn̩s/ *n* [U] **1** how sweet something is 甜度 **2 be all sweetness and light** to behave in a way that is very pleasant and friendly, especially when you do not normally behave like this〔尤指一反常態地〕和藹可親, 親切友善: *She's all sweetness and light when Paul's around.* 每當保羅在場時, 她就異常地和藹可親。

sweet pea /,· ˈ·/ *n* [C] a climbing plant with sweet-smelling flowers in pale colours 香豌豆

sweet pep·per /,· ˈ··/ *n* [C] a green, red, or yellow vegetable that is hollow with many seeds 甜椒; BELL PEPPER *AmE*【美】

sweet po·ta·to /,· ·ˈ··/ *n* [C] a vegetable that looks like a red potato, is yellow inside and tastes sweet 番薯, 紅薯, 白薯 —compare 比較 YAM (1) —see picture on page A9 參見 A9 頁圖

sweet roll /ˈ· ·/ *n* [C] *AmE* a small sweet PASTRY【美】小甜油酥點心

sweet-talk /ˈ· ·/ *v* [T] *informal* to try to persuade someone to do something by talking to them in a pleasant way【非正式】用甜言蜜語勸誘: **sweet-talk sb into doing sth** *I managed to sweet-talk her into driving me home.* 我終於用花言巧語哄得她開車送我回家。—**sweet talk** *n* [U]

sweet-temp·ered /,· ˈ··◂/ *adj* having a character that is kind and gentle 性情溫和的, 脾氣好的

sweet wil·liam /,swit ˈwɪljəm; ,swiːt ˈwɪljəm/ *n* [C,U] a plant with sweet-smelling flowers 美國石竹

swell[1] /swɛl; swel/ *v past tense* **swelled** *past participle* **swollen** /ˈswolən; ˈswəʊlən/

1 ►PART OF YOUR BODY 身體部位◄ [I] also 又作 **swell up** to gradually increase in size 腫, 腫脹: *Her ankle was already starting to swell.* 她的腳踝已經開始腫了。

2 ►PEOPLE 人◄ [T] to gradually increase in amount or number〔數量〕逐漸增加, 增多, 增大: *We asked them to come to the meeting to swell the numbers.* 我們叫他們來開會以增加出席的人數。| *The crowd swelled.* 人羣逐漸擴大。| **swell the ranks of sth** (=increase the number of people in a particular situation) 擴大…的隊伍; 增加…的人數 *School leavers are swelling the ranks of the unemployed.* 離校生正在不斷擴大失業者的隊伍。

3 ►SOUND 聲音◄ [I] *literary* to become louder【文】〔聲音〕增強, 變響亮: *Music swelled around us.* 音樂聲在我們四周逐漸增強。

4 ►SHAPE 形狀◄ [I,T] also 又作 **swell** (sth ↔) **out** to get or give something a full round shape (使) 鼓起, (使) 隆起: *The wind swelled the sails.* 風吹得船帆鼓了起來。

5 swell with pride/anger etc to feel very proud, angry etc 揚揚得意/怒氣沖沖等: *His heart swelled with pride as he watched his daughter collect her prize.* 他看着女兒領獎時心中充滿了自豪。

6 ►SEA 海◄ [I] to move suddenly and powerfully upwards 波濤洶湧 —see also 另見 GROUNDSWELL, SWOLLEN

swell[2] *n* **1** [singular] the way the sea moves up and down 海面的起伏, 浪湧: **heavy swell** (=very strong swell) 大浪濤, 猛烈的浪湧 *We didn't go sailing that day, as there was a heavy swell.* 那天我們沒有駕船出海, 因為海上浪濤很大。**2** [singular] an increase in sound level, especially in music; CRESCENDO (1)〔尤指音樂〕音量逐漸增強 **3** [singular] the roundness and fullness of something 膨脹; 鼓起; 隆起: *the firm swell of her breasts* 她豐滿堅挺的乳房 **4** [C] *old-fashioned* a fashionable or important person【過時】時髦人物; 頭面人物, 要人

swell[3] *adj AmE old-fashioned* very good【美, 過時】極好的, 第一流的: *You look swell!* 你看起來漂亮極了!

swell-head·ed /,· ˈ··◂/ *adj AmE informal* thinking that you are more important or clever than you really are【美, 非正式】自負的, 自命不凡的

swell·ing /ˈswɛlɪŋ; ˈswelɪŋ/ *n* **1** [C] an area of your body that has become larger than normal, because of illness or injury〔身體因患病或受傷產生的〕腫塊, 腫脹處: *a nasty swelling on my neck* 我頸部嚴重的腫塊 **2** [U] the condition of having swelled 膨脹; 腫脹: *The spider's bite can cause pain and swelling.* 蜘蛛的叮咬可能引起腫疼。

swel·ter /ˈswɛltɚ; ˈsweltə/ *v* [I] to feel unpleasantly hot 感到熱得難受, 熱得發昏: *sitting and sweltering in the classroom* 坐在教室裡熱得難受

swel·ter·ing /ˈswɛltərɪŋ; ˈsweltərɪŋ/ *adj* unpleasantly hot 熱得使人難受的: *Open a window; it's sweltering in here!* 打開一扇窗子吧; 這裡面熱得難受!

swept /swɛpt; swept/ the past tense and past participle of SWEEP

swept-back /,· ˈ·◂/ *adj* **1** hair that is swept-back is brushed backward from your face〔頭髮〕向後梳的 **2** swept-back wings on an aircraft look like the letter v〔飛機機翼〕後掠的, 後掠成 V 字形的

swerve /swɝv; swɜːv/ *v* [I] **1** to make a sudden sideways movement while moving forwards, especially in order to avoid hitting something〔尤指為了避免碰撞〕突然地轉向一邊: *Jo swerved to avoid a dog.* 喬為了避

S

免撞着狗而突然轉向一邊。| **[+across/off etc]** *The car swerved across the road and crashed into a wall.* 汽車突然轉向衝過馬路，撞在一堵牆上。—see picture on page A3 參見 A3 頁圖 **2** [usually in negatives 一般用於否定句] *formal* to change from an idea, course of action, purpose etc【正式】改變主意[做法，目的等]；背離：**[+from]** *He vowed he would not swerve from his declared aims.* 他發誓不會背離他公開宣布的目標。—**swerve** *n* [C]: *a swerve to the left* 向左急轉

swift¹ /swɪft; swɪft/ *adj* **1** happening quickly and immediately 迅速的；立刻的：*My letter received a swift reply.* 我的信得到迅速的答覆。**2** [only before noun 僅用於名詞前] moving, or able to move, very fast（能）迅速移動的；速度非常快的：*a swift runner* 跑得快的人 | **swift of foot** *literary* (=able to run fast)【文】跑得快的，健步如飛的 **3 be swift to do sth** to do something as soon as you can, without any delay 迅速做某事，立刻做某事：*They were swift to deny the accusations.* 他們立刻否認了那些指控。—**swiftly** *adv* —**swiftness** *n* [U]

swift² *n* [C] a small brown bird that has pointed wings, flies very fast, and is similar to a SWALLOW² (1) 雨燕

swig /swɪg; swɪg/ *v* **swigged, swigging** [T] *informal* to drink something in large mouthfuls, especially from a bottle【非正式】〔尤指直接從瓶子〕大口地喝，痛飲：*They sat there, swigging beer.* 他們坐在那裡大口大口地喝啤酒。—**swig** *n* [C]: *He took a large swig from the bottle.* 他從瓶子裡喝了一大口。

swill¹ /swɪl; swɪl/ *v* [T] **1** to wash an area by pouring a lot of water over it or into it〔用水〕沖洗，涮：**swill sth ↔ down/out** *Get a bucket to swill the yard down.* 去拿個桶來把院子沖洗沖洗。**2** *informal* to drink something in large amounts【非正式】大口地喝，痛飲：*He does nothing but swill beer all day.* 他一天到晚啥事也不做，只是拚命地喝啤酒。

swill² *n* **1** [U] food for pigs, mostly made of unwanted bits of human food 泔腳飼料，豬食 —see also 另見 PIGSWILL **2** [C] the act of washing something by pouring a lot of water over it 沖洗，涮

swim¹ /swɪm; swɪm/ *v past tense* **swam** /swæm; swæm/ *past participle* **swum** /swʌm; swʌm/ *present participle* **swimming**

1 ►MOVE THROUGH WATER 在水裡移動◄ [I] to move yourself through water using your arms, legs etc 游水，游泳：*My dad taught me to swim.* 我爸爸教我游泳。| *Exotic fish swam around in the tank.* 奇異的魚兒在缸裡游來游去。| **go swimming** (=swim for fun) 去游泳 —see 見 BATH² (USAGE)

2 ►IN A PARTICULAR AREA OF WATER 在某特定水域◄ [T] to get across a particular area of water by doing this 游過〔某水域〕，泅渡：*She was the first woman to swim the Channel.* 她是第一位游過英吉利海峽的女子。

3 ►A PARTICULAR STYLE 某種姿勢◄ [T] to use a particular style of swimming 游〔某一泳式〕：*She can swim breaststroke, backstroke, and crawl.* 她會游蛙泳、仰泳和自由泳。

4 ►NOT THINKING/SEEING PROPERLY 思維/視覺不清◄ [I] **a)** if your head swims, you start to feel confused or DIZZY (1) 發暈，眩暈：*My head was swimming after looking at that screen all day.* 我看了一整天螢屏之後覺得頭昏眼花。**b)** if something you are looking at swims, it seems to move because you feel DIZZY (1)〔因暈眩而覺得眼前物體〕旋轉：*The numbers swam before my eyes.* 那些數字在我眼前旋轉。

5 be swimming with sth also 又作 **be swimming in sth** to be very full of liquid or completely surrounded by liquid 浸[泡]在液體裡：*potatoes swimming in thick gravy* 泡在濃肉汁裡的馬鈴薯

6 swim with the tide to do or say the same things as most other people want because you do not want to seem different 順應潮流，隨大流，隨波逐流

7 swim against the tide to do or say different things from what most people do, because you do not mind being different 反潮流，不隨大流 —see also 另見 **sink or swim** (SINK¹ (17))

swim² *n* [C] **1** a period of time that you spend swimming 游泳：*Let's go for a swim.* 咱們游泳去吧。**2 in the swim** *informal* knowing about and involved in what is happening in modern life【非正式】了解並融入現代生活的；不脫離潮流的

swim·mer /ˈswɪmə; ˈswɪmə/ *n* [C] **a)** someone who swims well, often as a competitor 游泳者；游泳運動員：**good/strong swimmer** (=someone who swims well) 善於游泳者/游泳能手 **b)** someone who is swimming 正在游泳的人：*We watched the swimmers heading out across the lake.* 我們看着游泳的人向湖對岸游去。

swim·ming /ˈswɪmɪŋ; ˈswɪmɪŋ/ *n* [U] the sport of swimming 游泳（運動）：*Swimming is great exercise.* 游泳是項很好的鍛鍊。| *a swimming club* 游泳俱樂部 2

swimming bath /ˈ·· ·/ *n* [C] *BrE old-fashioned* a public swimming pool, usually indoors【英，過時】〔一般指室內的〕公共游泳池

swimming cos·tume /ˈ·· ˌ··/ *n* [C] *BrE* a piece of clothing worn for swimming, especially the kind worn by women【英】〔尤指女用〕游泳衣，泳裝

swim·ming·ly /ˈswɪmɪŋlɪ; ˈswɪmɪŋli/ *adv old-fashioned*【過時】**go swimmingly** if something you plan goes swimmingly, it happens without problems 順利地進行，一帆風順

swimming pool /ˈ·· ·/ *n* [C] a hole in the ground that has been built and filled with water for people to swim in; POOL¹ (1) 游泳池：*a house with a swimming pool* 有游泳池的房子

swimming suit /ˈ·· ·/ *n* [C] *AmE* a SWIMSUIT【美】游泳衣

swimming trunks /ˈ·· ·/ *n* [plural] *BrE* a piece of clothing like trousers with very short legs, worn by men for swimming【英】〔男用〕游泳褲

swim·suit /ˈswɪmˌsut; ˈswɪmsuːt/ *n* [C] a piece of clothing worn for swimming 游泳衣，泳裝

swimwear /ˈswɪmˌwɛr; ˈswɪmweə/ *n* [U] clothing used for swimming 游泳衣

swin·dle¹ /ˈswɪndḷ; ˈswɪndl/ *v* [T] to get money from someone by deceiving them 詐騙，欺詐，騙取〔錢財〕：**swindle sb out of sth** *He made a fortune swindling old ladies out of their life savings.* 他靠詐騙老年婦女的終生積蓄發了大財。

swindle² *n* [C] a situation where someone gets money by deceiving someone else 騙局；詐騙，騙取錢財：*a big tax swindle* 巨額稅款詐騙

swine /swaɪn; swaɪn/ *n* [C] **1** *plural* **swine** *or* **swines** *informal* someone who behaves very unpleasantly【非正式】下流坯，豬玀：*Leave her alone you filthy swine!* 不許你再纏着她，你這無恥的下流坯！**2** *old use* a pig【舊】豬

swine·herd /ˈswaɪnˌhɝd; ˈswaɪnhɜːd/ *n* [C] *old use* someone who looks after pigs【舊】養豬人，豬倌

swing¹ /swɪŋ; swɪŋ/ *v past tense and past participle* **swung** /swʌŋ; swʌŋ/ 3

1 ►MOVE BACKWARDS/FORWARDS 向後/向前移動◄ [I,T] to move backwards and forwards hanging from a fixed point, or to make something do this〔前後〕擺動，搖擺，搖蕩：*a sign swinging in the wind* 風中搖擺的招牌 | *The soldiers swung their arms as they marched.* 士兵們行進時擺動着雙臂。

2 ►MOVE IN A CURVE 成弧線移動◄ [I always+adv/prep, T always+adv/prep] to move quickly in a smooth curve, or to make something move like this（使）旋轉，（使）轉動；（使）轉彎：*The heavy gates swung shut.* 沉重的大門旋轉着關上了。| **swing sth through/into etc sth** *She swung the car into the drive.* 她把車子拐進了汽車道。| *Bradley swung himself up into the saddle.* 布拉德利跨上了馬鞍。

3 ►CHANGE 改變◄ [I,T] if emotions or opinions swing or something swings them, they change quickly to the

opposite of what they were（使）〔感情、意見等〕劇變，扭轉: *His mood could swing suddenly from great joy to complete despair.* 他的情緒可以從歡天喜地突然變成徹底絕望。
4 ▶ARRANGE STH 安排某事◀ [T] *informal* to make special arrangements for something to happen, especially something that is not usually allowed【非正式】設法做成，想法辦妥〔尤指通常不允許做的事〕: *I'll see if I can swing it so my wife can come on that business trip with me.* 我看這次出差能否設法把我太太也帶去。
5 ▶PLAY 遊戲◀ [I] to sit on a SWING² (1) and make it move backwards and forwards by bending and unbending your legs 蕩鞦韆: *The girl swung higher and higher.* 那個女孩鞦韆蕩得越來越高。
6 swing for sth *old-fashioned* to be killed by hanging (HANG¹ (3)) as a punishment for a crime【過時】〔因犯罪〕被絞死，被處以絞刑
7 swing both ways *informal* to be BISEXUAL【非正式】對男女兩性都有性慾，既搞異性戀也搞同性戀
8 the swinging sixties the years 1960 to 1969, thought of as a time when there was an increase in social and sexual freedom 放縱不羈的 60 年代〔20 世紀 60 年代被認為是社會自由和性自由高漲的年代〕
9 swing the lead *BrE old-fashioned* to avoid doing your work or duty, especially by pretending to be ill【英，過時】〔尤指以裝病〕逃避工作[責任] —see also 另見 **there's not enough room to swing a cat** (ROOM¹ (2))

swing around/round *phr v* **1** [I,T] to turn around quickly or make something turn around quickly, to face in the opposite direction（使）突然轉向;（使）突然轉身: *He swung around and yelled "that's a damn lie!"* 他猛地轉過身來大聲喊道:"那完全是謊言!" | **swing sth ↔ around/round** *In seconds they had swung the big gun around.* 他們在幾秒鐘內就調轉了大砲砲口的方向。**2** [I] if a wind swings around it changed direction suddenly and quickly〔風〕突然轉向，〔風向〕急變: *The wind swung round to the North-East.* 風突然轉向變為東北風。

swing by *phr v* [I,T] *AmE informal* to visit a place or person for a short time, usually for a particular purpose【美，非正式】〔常指為某目的〕短時探訪；順便過訪: **swing by sth** *I'll swing by the grocery store on my way home.* 我將在回家的路上順便到食品雜貨店去一趟。

[S3] **swing²** *n*
1 ▶SEAT WITH ROPES 有繩子的座位◀ [C] a seat hanging from ropes or chains, for children to play on 鞦韆: *kids playing on the swings in the park* 在公園裡蕩鞦韆的小孩子
2 ▶MOVEMENT 動作◀ [C] a swinging movement with your arm, leg etc especially made in order to hit something〔手臂、腿等的〕揮動，揮舞，揮擊: **take a swing at sth** *He took a swing at my head and missed.* 他揮拳向我頭部打來，但沒有打着。
3 ▶GOLF 高爾夫球◀ [singular] the swinging movement of your arms and body when you hit the ball in GOLF 揮桿擊球動作: *I spent months correcting my swing.* 我花了幾個月時間糾正我的揮桿擊球動作。
4 ▶CHANGE 變化◀ [C] a noticeable change, especially in opinions or ideas〔尤指意見或主意的〕明顯改變: *a big swing towards right-wing ideology* 向右翼思想的大轉變
5 ▶MUSIC 音樂◀ [U] JAZZ music of the 1930s and 1940s with a strong regular beat, usually played by a big band 搖擺樂〔流行於 20 世紀 30 和 40 年代的強節奏爵士樂，通常由大型樂隊演奏〕
6 get into the swing of sth *BrE* to become fully involved in an activity or situation【英】完全投入某事: *As soon as you get into the swing of it, you'll find it's quite easy.* 你一旦完全投入進去就會覺得它相當容易。
7 be in full swing if an event or process is in full swing it has reached its highest level of activity 正在熱烈進行中，正起勁: *The party was in full swing when the police burst in.* 晚會正進行得如火如荼的時候，警察闖了進來。
8 swings and roundabouts *BrE informal* used to say that every situation or decision has advantages and disadvantages【英，非正式】〔某種情況或決定〕有得也有失
9 go with a swing *BrE*【英】**a)** if a party or activity goes with a swing it is lively, enjoyable and successful〔聚會、活動等〕搞得活躍、歡快和成功 **b)** if music goes with a swing it has a strong beat and a clear tune that is easy to dance to〔音樂〕節奏強勁，曲調明快

swing-boat /ˈ· ·/ *n* [C] a large SWING² (1) shaped like a boat that two people can sit in〔可供兩人坐的〕船形鞦韆

swing bridge /ˌ· ˈ·/ *n* [C] *BrE* a bridge that can be swung to the side when tall ships need to pass through【英】平轉橋，平旋橋

swing door /ˌ· ˈ·/ *n* [C] a door that can be pushed open from either side, and swings shut afterwards 雙開式彈簧門 —see picture on page A15 參見 A15 頁圖

swinge·ing /ˈswɪndʒɪŋ; ˈswɪndʒɪŋ/ *adj BrE*【英】**swingeing cuts** very severe reductions in spending, especially by a government or organization; SWEEPING (1)〔尤指政府或組織的〕大量削減開支: *swingeing cuts in public spending* 公共開支的大幅度削減

swing·er /ˈswɪŋə; ˈswɪŋə/ *n* [C] *old-fashioned*【過時】**1** someone who is very active and fashionable, and goes to many parties, NIGHTCLUBs etc 活躍而時髦的人，常參加社交聚會去夜總會的人 **2** someone who has sexual relationships with many people 性濫交的人；放蕩的人

swing·ing /ˈswɪŋɪŋ; ˈswɪŋɪŋ/ *adj informal* exciting, fun, and enjoyable【非正式】令人興奮的，歡快的: *a swinging party* 熱鬧而有趣的聚會 —see also 另見 **the swinging sixties** (SWING¹ (8))

swing·om·e·ter /swɪŋˈɑmɪtə; swɪŋˈɒmɪtə/ *n* [C] *BrE informal* a special machine, used on television programmes during elections to show how much support each political party is getting as results become known【英，非正式】選票顯示器〔選舉時電視節目中用的一種特殊裝置，用以顯示各政黨所得的票數〕

swing set /ˈ· ·/ *n* [C] *AmE* a tall metal frame with swings (SWING² (1)) hanging from it, for children to play on【美】〔兒童玩耍的〕成套鞦韆

swing shift /ˈ· ·/ *n* [singular] *AmE informal* workers who work from 3 or 4 o'clock in the afternoon until 11 or 12 o'clock at night, or the system of working these times【美，非正式】〔三班制的〕中班〔通常從下午 3 或 4 點至晚上 11 點或 12 點〕；中班工人

swin·ish /ˈswaɪnɪʃ; ˈswaɪnɪʃ/ *adj BrE* extremely unpleasant or difficult to deal with【英】極討厭的；可鄙的；難對付的: *a swinish problem* 非常棘手的問題 | *swinish behaviour* 可鄙的行為

swipe¹ /swaɪp; swaɪp/ *v* **1** [I,T] to hit or to try to hit someone or something by swinging you arm very quickly〔揮臂〕重擊，猛擊: *Jim swiped Bob across the face.* 吉姆往鮑勃臉上猛摑了一巴掌。| **[+at]** *The woman swiped at the child.* 那個女人猛摑那個孩子。**2** [T] *informal* to steal something【非正式】偷竊: *Who's swiped my pen?* 誰偷了我的筆? **3** [T] to pull a special plastic card through a machine to record information on a computer 刷〔卡，把特製塑料磁卡劃過取讀器使電腦記下有關信息〕: *You need to swipe your card to get in the building.* 你必須刷過卡後才能進入這幢大樓。

swipe² *n* [C] **1** an act of hitting someone or something by swinging your arm very quickly〔揮臂〕重擊，猛擊: **take a swipe at** *He took a wild swipe at the policeman.* 他瘋狂地揮臂打那位警察。**2 take a swipe at** to publicly criticize someone in a speech or in writing〔口頭或書面〕公開批評，抨擊: *In her latest article she takes a swipe at her detractors.* 在最新的一篇文章裡，她公開抨擊詆毀她的人。

swirl¹ /swɜl; swɜːl/ *v* [I,T] to turn around quickly in a twisting circular movement, or make something do this（使）旋動，（使）打旋: *He swirled the brandy around in his glass.* 他旋動杯中的白蘭地酒。| *The river had be-*

come a swirling torrent. 河水已變成了翻滚的洪流。

swirl² *n* [C] **1** a swirling movement 旋動, 打旋: **[+of]** *a swirl of dust* 滚滚飛揚的塵土 **2** a twisting circular pattern 漩渦狀; 螺旋形

swish¹ /swɪʃ; swɪʃ/ *v* [I,T] to move or make something move quickly through the air with a smooth quiet sound (使) 發出刷刷[嗖嗖]聲; (使) 刷刷[嗖嗖]地移動: *Her skirt swished as she walked.* 她走動時裙子窸窣作響。| *The horse swished his tail.* 那匹馬刷刷地擺動着尾巴。 —**swish** *n* [singular]

swish² *adj BrE* fashionable and expensive-looking【英】時髦的; 豪華的: *a really swish apartment* 一套非常豪華的公寓

Swiss /swɪs; swɪs/ *adj* coming from or related to Switzerland 瑞士的; 與瑞士有關的

Swiss chard /ˌ· ˈ·/ *n* [U] CHARD 瑞士甜菜; 君蓬菜

swiss roll /ˌ· ˈ·/ *n* [C,U] *BrE* a long thin cake that is rolled up with JAM¹ (1) or cream inside【英】〔夾有果醬或奶油的〕卷筒夾心蛋糕, 瑞士卷

swiss steak /ˌ· ˈ·/ *n* [C,U] *AmE* a thick flat piece of BEEF covered in flour and cooked in a SAUCE【美】〔外蘸麵粉加調味汁烹調而成的〕瑞士牛排

switch off 關上開關

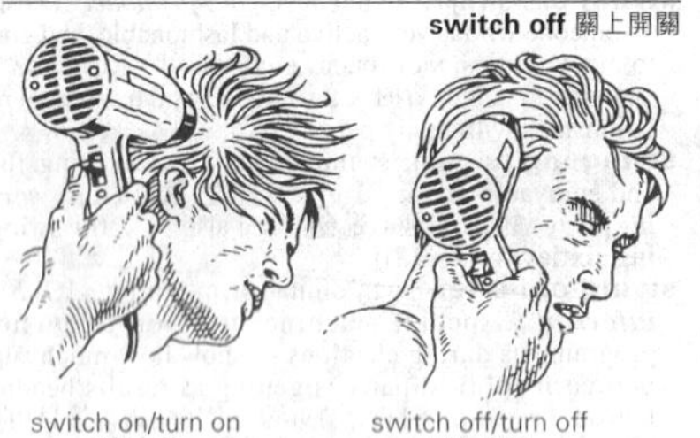

switch on/turn on 打開開關　　switch off/turn off 關上開關

switch¹ /swɪtʃ; swɪtʃ/ *v* **1** [I,T] to change from one thing to another, usually suddenly〔常指突然地〕轉換, 轉變, 改變: **[+to]** *He used to play tennis, but now he's switched to golf.* 他過去常打網球, 但現在改打高爾夫球了。| **switch sth to/from/away etc** *Duval switched easily and fluently from French to English.* 杜瓦爾流利自如地交替着講法語和英語。| **switch jobs/positions etc** (=change from one job or position to another) 改變工作/職位等 **switch sth to/from/away etc** *We can switch the meeting to Tuesday if you like.* 如果你願意的話, 我們可以把會議時間改到星期二。| **switch your attention** *Just switch your attention to the screen on your left.* 注意左邊的屏幕。**2** [T] to secretly remove one object and put another similar object in its place〔祕密地〕換掉, 替換: *Someone must have switched suitcases at the airport.* 一定有人在飛機場把手提箱掉了包。**3** [I] to help someone you work with who needs time away from the job by agreeing to work certain hours for them if they do the same for you〔與同事〕調換上班時間, 調班: **switch with sb** *Can you switch with me on Monday night?* 你星期一晚上可以和我調班嗎? **4** [T always+adv/prep] to change the way a machine operates by using a switch〔用開關〕改變〔機器的運轉〕, 轉換: *Switch the freezer to the 'extra cold' setting.* 把冰箱的冷凍室調到"特冷"擋。

switch off *phr v* **1** [I,T] to turn off a machine, electric light, radio etc by using a switch〔用開關〕關掉, 關上: *Don't forget to switch off when you've finished.* 用完後不要忘記關掉開關。| **switch sth ↔ off** *Can you switch the television off?* 請把電視機關掉好嗎? —see 見 OPEN² (USAGE) **2** [I] *informal* to stop listening or paying attention【非正式】不聽; 對...不加理睬[注意]: *He just switches off when you start talking to him.* 你要對他説話時, 他就不理不睬。

switch on *phr v* [I,T] to turn on a machine, electric light, radio etc by using a switch〔用開關〕開, 打開: **switch sth ↔ on** *Can you switch the light on?* 請你開燈好嗎? —see 見 OPEN² (USAGE)

switch over *phr v* [I] **1** to change completely from one method, product etc to another〔方法、產品等〕完全改變, 完全轉變: **[+from/to]** *A lot of banks are switching over to the new electronic system because it's more efficient.* 很多銀行正在改用新的電子系統, 因為它效率更高。**2** [I,T] *BrE* to change from one radio or television station to another【英】轉換〔電台或電視頻道〕: *Switch over if you don't like the programme.* 如果你不喜歡這個節目, 就換個台吧。

switch² *n* [C] **1** the part on a light, radio, machine etc that starts or stops the flow of electricity when you press it up or down〔電燈、收音機、機器等的〕開關; 電閘: **light switch** *a light switch* 電燈開關 | *the on/off switch* 開關鍵 | **throw a switch** (=pull a large switch) 扳動電閘 *He threw a switch and all the lights in the theatre came on.* 他一扳電閘, 戲院裡的燈全都亮了。**2** a complete, and usually sudden, change from one thing to another 驟變, 突變: *The switch to a free market economy will not be easy.* 向自由市場經濟轉變並不容易。| **that's a switch** *AmE* (=used to say that someone's behaviour is unusual for them)【美】那真不尋常〔用以指某人的行為一反往常〕*"Mark's doing the dishes tonight." "That's a switch!"* "馬克今晚要洗盤子。" "那可真不尋常!" **3** **make the switch** to secretly remove one object and put another similar object in its place〔偷偷地〕調換, 掉包: *The original painting has been replaced by a fake, and no one knows when the switch was made.* 這幅畫的原件被一件贋品替換了, 但沒有人知道是甚麼時候被掉包的。**4** a thin stick that bends easily 細軟的枝條: *a willow switch* 柳枝 3

switch·back /ˈswɪtʃˌbæk; ˈswɪtʃbæk/ *n* [C] **1** a road or track that goes up and down steep slopes and around sharp bends〔陡坡上公路或鐵路的〕之字形爬坡路段; 多急轉彎的道路 **2** a ROLLER COASTER〔遊樂場的〕環滑車, 過山車

switch·blade /ˈswɪtʃˌbled; ˈswɪtʃbleɪd/ *n* [C] *AmE* a knife with a blade inside the handle which springs out when you press a button【美】彈簧(小摺)刀; FLICK KNIFE *BrE*【英】

switch·board /ˈswɪtʃˌbɔrd; ˈswɪtʃbɔːd/ *n* [C] a central system used to connect telephone calls in an office building, hotel etc, or the people who operate the system 電話交換台, 電話總機; 總機接線員: *Hello switchboard? Can I have an outside line?* 喂, 總機嗎? 請接外線。| *switchboard operators* 交換台接線員 | **jam the switchboard** (=make too many calls for the switchboard to deal with) 電話太多使總機應接不暇

switch card /ˈ· ·/ also 又作 **switch** *n* [C] *BrE trademark* a plastic card from your bank that you use to pay for things and that allows the money to be taken straight from your account【英, 商標】〔銀行〕代支卡〔由銀行發放、供購物付款使用的一種塑料磁卡〕

switched-on /ˌ· ˈ·◂/ *adj old-fashioned* quick to notice new ideas and fashions【過時】緊跟時尚的, 對新觀念[時尚]敏感的

swiv·el¹ /ˈswɪvl; ˈswɪvəl/ **swivelled, swivelling** *BrE*【英】, **swiveled, swiveling** *AmE*【美】also 又作 **swivel around/round** *v* **1** [I,T] to turn something around that is fixed to a moving central point (使) 旋轉, (使) 轉動: *He swivelled the camera on the tripod to follow the riders.* 他轉動三腳架上的照相機追蹤拍攝那些騎手。**2** [I] to turn around quickly in this way〔迅速地〕旋轉, 轉動

swivel² *n* [C] a thing that joins two parts of something in such a way that one or both parts can turn around freely 旋轉接頭; 旋軸

swivel chair /ˈ·· ·/ *n* [C] a chair that turns around on a swivel 轉椅 —see picture at 參見 CHAIR¹ 圖

swiz, swizz /swɪz; swɪz/ *n BrE spoken*【英口】**what a**

swizz! used when something makes you feel cheated or disappointed 真是上當！真令人掃興！〔用於感到受騙或失望時〕

swiz·zle stick /ˈswɪzḷ ˌstɪk; ˈswɪzəl ˌstɪk/ *n* [C] a small stick for mixing drinks〔調飲料用的〕小棒；攪酒棒

swol·len¹ /ˈswolən; ˈswəʊlən/ the past participle of SWELL¹

swollen² *adj* **1** a part of your body that is swollen is bigger than usual because of illness or injury〔身體某部位〕腫起的，腫脹的；膨脹的：*He bandaged his swollen ankle.* 他用繃帶包紮腫起來的腳踝。**2** a river that is swollen has more water in it than usual〔河流〕漲滿的，漲水的 **3 have a swollen head/be swollen-headed** *BrE* to be too proud so that you think you are very clever or important【英】驕傲自滿，自負，自高自大

swoon /swun; swuːn/ *v* [I] **1** to feel so much excitement, happiness, or admiration that you almost faint 欣喜若狂；〔愛慕得〕神魂顛倒：*The audience was full of swooning girls.* 聽眾中有無數心醉神迷的女孩。**2** *old use* to become unconscious and fall down; FAINT² (1)【舊】失去知覺，昏倒 —**swoon** *n* [singular]

swoop¹ /swup; swuːp/ *v* [I] **1** if a bird or aircraft swoops it moves suddenly and steeply down through the air, especially to attack something〔鳥或飛機〕突然下落；向下猛衝，猛撲：**[+in/down etc]** *The hawk swooped and seized a rabbit.* 老鷹猛衝下來，抓住了一隻兔子。**2** to make a sudden, surprise attack 突然襲擊：**[+in/on etc]** *Police swooped in on gang hideouts in a series of raids.* 警方對歹徒藏身處進行了一系列的突擊搜捕。

swoop² *n* [C] **1** a swooping movement or action 向下猛衝；猛撲；飛撲 **2** a sudden surprise attack 突然襲擊：*Police hunting the killer arrested a man in a swoop on his flat last night.* 警方追捕殺人兇手，昨晚突擊搜查一公寓時逮捕了一名男子。—see also 另見 **at/in one fell swoop** (FELL⁴)

swoosh /swuʃ; swuːʃ/ *v* [I] to make a sound by moving quickly through the air〔在空氣中移動時〕發出嘩嘩聲，嗖嗖作響 —**swoosh** *n* [C]

swop /swɑp; swɒp/ another spelling of SWAP swap的另一種拼法

swords 劍，刀

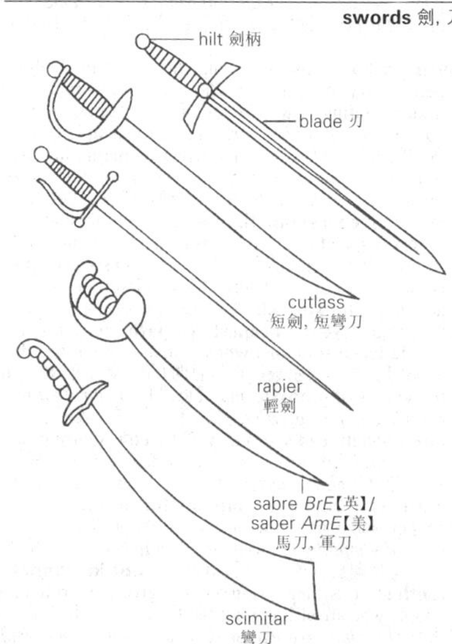

sword /sɔrd; sɔːd/ *n* [C] **1** a weapon with a long pointed blade and a handle 劍；刀 **2 put sb to the sword** *old use* to kill someone with a sword【舊】用刀劍殺死某人 **3 sword of Damocles** *literary* the possibility of something bad or dangerous happening at any time【文】德摩克利斯之劍〔喻指隨時可能有禍事或危險臨頭〕：*The treaty hung like a sword of Damocles over French politics.* 這個條約好像一把德摩克利斯之劍懸在法國政壇的頭上。—see also 另見 **cross swords (with)** (CROSS¹ (15))

sword dance /ˈ· ·/ *n* [C] a Scottish dance in which people dance between and around swords that are laid on the ground 劍舞〔一種蘇格蘭舞，圍着置於地上的刀劍或在其間起舞〕—**sword dancer** *n* [C] —**sword dancing** *n* [U]

sword·fish /ˈsɔrdˌfɪʃ; ˈsɔːdˌfɪʃ/ *n* [C] a large fish with a very long pointed upper jaw like a sword 劍魚

swords·man /ˈsɔrdzmən; ˈsɔːdzmən/ *n* [C] someone who fights with a sword or someone who is skilled in this 劍客，刀劍手

swords·man·ship /ˈsɔrdzmənˌʃɪp; ˈsɔːdzmənʃɪp/ *n* [U] skill in fighting with a sword 劍術，刀術

swore /swɔr; swɔː/ the past tense of SWEAR

sworn¹ /swɔrn; swɔːn/ the past participle of SWEAR

sworn² *adj* **1 sworn enemies** two people or groups of people who will always hate each other 不共戴天的死敵 **2 sworn statement/evidence/declaration** a statement etc that someone makes after officially promising to tell the truth 宣誓後發表的陳述/證詞/聲明

swot¹ /swɑt; swɒt/ *n* [C] *BrE informal* someone who spends too much time studying and seems to have no other interests【英，非正式】只知道讀書的人 —**swotty** *adj*

swot² *v* [I] *BrE informal* to study a lot in a short time, especially for an examination【英，非正式】〔尤指為準備考試臨時〕刻苦學習，下死功夫讀書；CRAM (3) *AmE*【美】：**[+for]** *I was busy swotting for my History exam.* 我正臨陣磨槍，準備歷史考試。

swot up *phr v* [I,T] *BrE* to study a subject a lot in a short time, especially to prepare for an examination【英】〔為準備考試〕刻苦學習〔某學科〕；臨時抱佛腳地學：**[+on]** *Jill's busy swotting up on German.* 吉爾正忙於溫習德語。| **swot sth ↔ up** *I've got to swot up French irregular verbs.* 我得用功學習法語的不規則動詞。

swum /swʌm; swʌm/ the past participle of SWIM¹

swung /swʌŋ; swʌŋ/ the past tense and past participle of SWING¹

syb·a·rit·ic /ˌsɪbəˈrɪtɪk; ˌsɪbəˈrɪtɪk◂/ *adj formal* wanting or enjoying expensive pleasures and comforts【正式】享受奢侈的，驕奢淫逸的 —**sybarite** /ˈsɪbəˌraɪt; ˈsɪbəraɪt/ *n* [C]

syc·a·more /ˈsɪkəˌmɔr; ˈsɪkəmɔː/ *n* [C] **1** a European tree that has leaves with five points and seeds with two parts like wings〔歐洲的〕西克摩槭樹 **2** an American PLANE TREE 美國梧桐(樹)，懸鈴木

syc·o·phant /ˈsɪkəfənt; ˈsɪkəfənt/ *n* [C] *formal* someone who praises important or powerful people insincerely in order to get something from them【正式】阿諛奉承者，諂媚者，拍馬屁者：*a dictator surrounded by sycophants* 被阿諛奉承者簇擁的獨裁者 —**sycophantic** /ˌsɪkəˈfæntɪk; ˌsɪkəˈfæntɪk◂/ *adj*: *a sycophantic smile* 諂笑

syl·la·ba·ry /ˈsɪləˌbɛrɪ; ˈsɪləbəri/ *n* [C] a list of syllables, sometimes represented as SYMBOLs 音節(符號)表

syl·lab·ic /sɪˈlæbɪk; səˈlæbɪk/ *adj* of or based on syllables 音節的；分音節的；由音節組成的：*syllabic stress* 音節重音 | *syllabic verse* 每行[每節]的音節數目固定的詩體

syl·la·ble /ˈsɪləbḷ; ˈsɪləbəl/ *n* [C] a word or part of a word which contains a single vowel sound 音節

syl·la·bub /ˈsɪləˌbʌb; ˈsɪləbʌb/ *n* [C,U] a sweet dish made with cream, wine or fruit juice, and usually eggs 乳酒凍〔一種用奶油、酒或果汁，經常還加雞蛋混合而成的甜食〕

syl·la·bus /ˈsɪləbəs; ˈsɪləbəs/ *n* [C] *plural* **syllabuses** or **syllabi** /-baɪ; -baɪ/ a plan that states exactly what students at a school or college should learn in a particular

S

subject〔某學科的〕教學大綱: *Dickens and Hardy are on this year's English syllabus.* 狄更斯和哈代的作品被列入今年的英語課程大綱。—compare 比較 CURRICULUM

syl·lo·gis·m /ˋsɪlə͵dʒɪzəm; ˈsɪlədʒɪzəm/ *n* [C] a statement with three parts, the first two of which prove that the third part is true, for example 'all men will die; Socrates is a man; therefore Socrates will die' 三段論法〔由大、小前提引出結論的推理, 如"凡人必死, 蘇格拉底是人, 因此蘇格拉底終將會死。"〕—**syllogistic** /͵sɪləˋdʒɪstɪk; ˌsɪləˈdʒɪstɪk◂/ *adj*

sylph /sɪlf; sɪlf/ *n* [C] **1** an attractively thin and graceful girl or woman 苗條高雅的女子 **2** an imaginary female spirit that, according to ancient stories lived in the air〔古代神話中空氣裡的〕女精靈

sylph·like /ˋsɪlf͵laɪk; ˈsɪlf-laɪk/ *adj literary* attractively thin and graceful【文】苗條而優雅的: *a sylphlike figure* 苗條的身材

syl·van /ˋsɪlvən; ˈsɪlvən/ *adj* in the forest or belonging to the forest; SILVAN 在森林中的; 森林的

sym- /sɪm; sɪm/ *prefix* the form used for SYN- before b, m, or p 前綴 syn- 用於字母 b, m 或 p 前的形式

sym·bi·o·sis /͵sɪmbaɪˋosɪs; ˌsɪmbaɪˈəʊsɪs/ *n* [U] **1** *formal* a relationship between people or organizations that depend on each other equally【正式】〔人與人之間或機構之間平等的〕互相依賴(關係) **2** *technical* the relationship between two different living things that depend on each other for particular advantages【術語】〔生物的〕共生(關係) —**symbiotic** /͵sɪmbaɪˋɑtɪk; sɪmbaɪˈɒtɪk◂/ *adj*: *a symbiotic relationship* 共生關係

3 **sym·bol** /ˋsɪmbl; ˈsɪmbəl/ *n* [C] **1** a picture or shape that has a particular meaning or represents an idea 象徵, 標誌: **[+of]** *The dove is a symbol of peace.* 鴿子是和平的象徵。**2** a letter, number, or sign that represents a sound, an amount, a chemical substance etc 符號, 記號, 標記: *'0' is the symbol for zero.* 0是零的符號。—see picture at 參見 SIGN[1] 圖 **3** someone or something that people think of as representing a particular quality or idea〔某一特性或思想的〕代表, 代表性的人[物]: *Space exploration provides a symbol of national pride.* 宇宙探索是民族自豪感的象徵。—see also 另見 SEX SYMBOL

sym·bol·ic /sɪmˋbɑlɪk; sɪmˈbɒlɪk/ also 又作 **sym·bol·i·cal** /-kl; -kəl/ *adj* used as a symbol, or containing symbols 象徵的, 象徵性的: *a symbolic painting* 一幅有象徵意義的畫 | **be symbolic of sth** *The snake is symbolic of evil.* 蛇是邪惡的象徵。—**symbolically** /-klɪ; -kli/ *adv*

sym·bol·is·m /ˋsɪmbl͵ɪzəm; ˈsɪmbəlɪzəm/ *n* [U] the use of symbols to represent something 象徵主義(手法): *religious symbolism* 宗教象徵主義

sym·bol·ize also 又作 **-ise** *BrE*【英】/ˋsɪmbl͵aɪz; ˈsɪmbəlaɪz/ *v* [T] **1** to be a symbol of something 象徵, 是...的象徵: *In Europe, the colour white symbolizes purity.* 在歐洲, 白色象徵純潔。**2** to represent something with a symbol 用符號代表, 用象徵物表示: *Peace is symbolised by a dove.* 和平用鴿子作為象徵。—**symbolization** /͵sɪmbləˋzeʃən; ˌsɪmbəlaɪˈzeɪʃən/ *n* [U]

symmetrical 對稱的

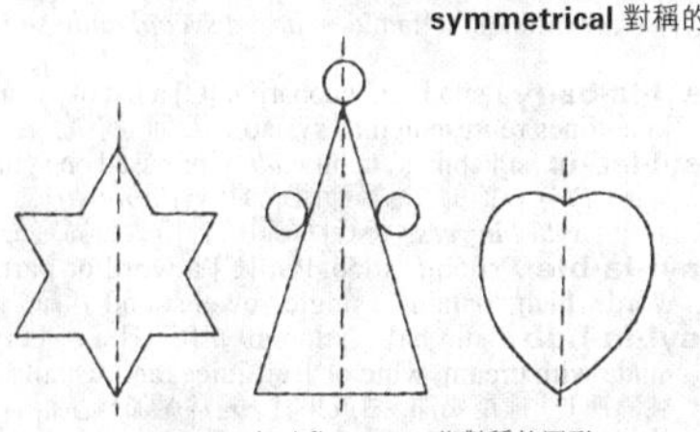

some symmetrical figures 一些對稱的圖形

sym·met·ri·cal /sɪˋmɛtrɪkl; sɪˈmetrɪkəl/ also 又作 **sym·met·ric** /sɪˋmɛtrɪk; sɪˈmetrɪk/ *adj* a thing or design that is symmetrical has two halves that are exactly the same shape and size 對稱的: *The leaves of most trees are symmetrical.* 大多數樹木的葉子是對稱的。—opposite 反義詞 ASYMMETRICAL —**symmetrically** /-klɪ; -kli/ *adv*

sym·me·try /ˋsɪmɪtrɪ; ˈsɪmɪtri/ *n* [U] exact likeness in size and shape between two sides of something 對稱(性): *the symmetry of the human body* 人體的對稱(性)

sym·pa·thet·ic /͵sɪmpəˋθɛtɪk; ˌsɪmpəˈθetɪk◂/ *adj* **1** willing to try to understand someone else's problems and give them any help they need 同情的; 有同情心的: *You're not being very sympathetic, Joan.* 瓊, 你沒有表現出很大的同情心。| **a sympathetic ear** (=willingness to listen to someone else's problems) 樂於傾聽別人的困難 *Paul's great if you need a sympathetic ear or advice.* 假如你想傾訴衷腸或徵求意見, 保羅最合適不過了。**2** [not before noun 不用於名詞前] willing to give approval and support to an aim or plan〔對某目的或計劃〕贊成的, 支持的: **[+to/towards]** *There is a group in the party sympathetic towards our aims.* 黨內有一批人贊成我們的目標。**3** providing the right conditions to make the results you want to happen 合意的; 合適的: *a sympathetic environment* 合適的環境 **4 sympathetic figure/character** *literary* someone in a book, play etc who the author intends you to like【文】〔書、戲劇等中〕令人喜愛的人物/角色 —**sympathetically** /-klɪ; -kli/ *adv*

sym·pa·thize also 又作 **-ise** *BrE*【英】/ˋsɪmpə͵θaɪz; ˈsɪmpəθaɪz/ *v* [I] **1** to feel sorry for someone because you understand their problems 同情, 憐憫; 體諒: *I sympathize; you need to know exactly what caused the accident.* 我非常同情, 你需要了解導致事故發生的確切原因。| **[+with]** *I sympathize with the plight of the homeless.* 我很同情無家可歸者的困境。**2** to support someone's ideas or actions 支持; 贊同: **[+with]** *Many workers sympathized with the striking miners.* 很多工人都支持那些正在罷工的礦工。

sym·pa·thiz·er also 又作 **-iser** *BrE*【英】/ˋsɪmpə͵θaɪzɚ; ˈsɪmpəθaɪzə/ *n* [C] someone who supports the aims of an organization or political party but does not belong to it 同情者; 支持者: *The anti-abortion rally attracted many sympathizers.* 反對人工流產的羣眾集會吸引了很多支持者。

sym·pa·thy /ˋsɪmpəθɪ; ˈsɪmpəθi/ *n* [U] **1** the feeling of being sorry for someone who is in a bad situation and understanding how they feel 同情; 同情心: *He wants your sympathy so he's pretending to be sick.* 他想得到你的同情, 所以在裝病。| **have/feel sympathy for sb** *I've a lot of sympathy for her; she brought up the children on her own.* 我非常同情她, 她是獨自把孩子們撫養成人的。| **have no sympathy for sb** (=feel that someone deserves something bad that is happening to them) 不同情某人〔認為某人是自作自受〕| **play on sb's sympathy** (=make someone feel sorry for you in order to gain an advantage for yourself)〔為得到好處而〕利用某人的同情 | **you have my deepest sympathy** *formal* (=used in a letter to someone whose close relative has died)【正式】謹向你表示最深切的慰問〔用於慰唁信中〕| **offer your sympathy** *formal*【正式】*She wrote a letter offering her sympathy.* 她寫了一封信去表示慰問。| **message/letter of sympathy** *The victim's parents have received thousands of messages of sympathy.* 罹難者的父母收到成千上萬封的慰問信。**2 be in sympathy with** also 又作 **have sympathy for** to agree with and support someone's aims and actions 贊同, 支持: *We have a lot of sympathy for your stand on lower taxes.* 我們非常支持你關於減稅的立場。**3 come out in sympathy (with sb)** to STRIKE[1] (4) in order to give support to other people who are striking 舉行罷工以示支持〔其他罷工的人〕: *The miners were on strike and the railwaymen came out in sympathy.* 礦工們罷工, 鐵路工人也舉行罷工表示支持。**4 sympathies** [plural] **a)** feelings of support and approval〔感情上的〕支持, 贊同: **sb's sympathies lie**

with *Anne's sympathies lie firmly with the Conservative Party.* 安妮在感情上是堅決支持保守黨的。**b)** a message of comfort to someone who is very upset because someone has died 唁函[電] —see also 另見 **tea and sympathy** (TEA (5)) **5** [U] a feeling that you understand someone because you are similar to them〔與某人的〕同感, 共鳴

sym·pho·ny /ˋsɪmfənɪ; ˈsɪmfəni/ *n* [C] a long piece of music usually in four parts written for an ORCHESTRA 交響樂, 交響曲: *Beethoven's Third Symphony* 貝多芬《第三交響曲》

symphony or·ches·tra /ˈ··· ˌ···/ *n* [C] a large ORCHESTRA (=group of musicians) 交響樂團

sym·po·si·um /sɪmˋpozɪəm; sɪmˈpəʊziəm/ *plural* **symposiums** *or* **symposia** /-zɪə; -ziə/ *n* [C] *formal*【正式】**1** a formal meeting in which people who know a lot about a particular subject have discussions about it 專題研討會; 討論會: *a symposium on neurological science* 神經病學研討會 **2** a group of articles on a particular subject collected together in a book 專題論文集

3 **symp·tom** /ˋsɪmptəm; ˈsɪmptəm/ *n* [C] **1** a physical condition which shows that you have a particular illness 症狀: *Symptoms include headaches and vomiting.* 症狀包括頭痛和嘔吐。| **[+of]** *the first symptoms of malaria* 瘧疾的早期症狀 **2** a sign that a serious problem exists〔嚴重問題存在的〕徵兆, 徵候: **[+of]** *The crime rate is a symptom of social unrest.* 這種犯罪率是社會不安定的一個徵兆。—see also 另見 **withdrawal symptoms** (WITHDRAWAL (5))

symp·to·mat·ic /ˌsɪmptəˋmætɪk; ˌsɪmptəˈmætɪk◂/ *adj* **1 be symptomatic of sth** *formal* if a situation or kind of behaviour is symptomatic of something, it shows that a serious problem exists【正式】是…徵兆; 表明…: *Her irritation seems symptomatic of something deeper.* 她的煩躁可能是更深刻問題的徵兆。**2** *technical* related to medical symptoms【術語】症狀的 —**symptomatically** /-klɪ; -kli/ *adv*

syn- /sɪn; sɪn/ *prefix* together; sharing 共, 同, 合: *a synthesis* (=combining of separate things) 合成

syn·a·gogue /ˋsɪnəˌgɔg; ˈsɪnəgɒg/ *n* [C] a building where Jewish people meet for religious worship〔猶太〕會堂, 猶太教堂

sync, synch /sɪŋk; sɪŋk/ *n informal*【非正式】**1 in sync** two or more parts of a machine, process etc that are in sync are working at the same rate 同步的; 協調的 **2 out of sync** two or more parts of a machine, process etc that are out of sync are not working at the same rate 不同步的; 不協調的

syn·chro·ni·city /ˌsɪŋkrəˋnɪsətɪ; ˌsɪŋkrəˈnɪsəti/ *n* [U] the fact of two or more events happening at the same time or place, when these events are believed to be connected in some way〔有關聯的事件的〕同時發生

syn·chro·nize also 又作 **-ise** *BrE*【英】/ˋsɪŋkrəˌnaɪz; ˈsɪŋkrənaɪz/ *v* **1** [T] to arrange for two or more actions to happen at exactly the same time 使同時發生, 使同步: *If we synchronize our attacks they'll cause more disruption.* 假如我們同時發動攻擊, 造成的破壞就會更大。**2 synchronize your watches** to make two or more watches or clocks show exactly the same time 校準〔兩個或多個〕鐘錶, 使鐘錶顯示同一時間 **3** [I,T] if the sound and action of a film synchronize or if you synchronize them, they go at exactly the same speed (使)〔電影〕聲畫同步, (使)〔影片的〕動作與聲音同步 —**synchronization** /ˌsɪŋkrənəˋzeʃən; ˌsɪŋkrənaɪˈzeɪʃən/ *n* [U]

synchronized swim·ming /ˌ··· ˈ··/ *n* [U] an activity in which swimmers move in patterns in the water to music 花式游泳

syn·chro·nous /ˋsɪŋkrənəs; ˈsɪŋkrənəs/ *adj* a synchronous signal on a computer is one in which the time between one BIT[1] (12) and the next is the same〔電腦信號〕同時的, 同步的

syn·co·pa·tion /ˌsɪŋkəˋpeʃən; ˌsɪŋkəˈpeɪʃən/ *n* [U] a RHYTHM in a line of music in which the beats (BEAT[2] (3)) that are usually weak are emphasized〔音樂的〕切分音, 切分節奏

syn·co·pe /ˋsɪŋkəpɪ; ˈsɪŋkəpi/ *n* [U] *technical*【術語】**1** the loss of consciousness when someone faints 暈厥 **2** a way of making a word shorter by leaving out of sounds or letters in the middle of it, for example changing 'cannot' to 'can't' 詞中省略, 中略〈如以 can't 代替 cannot〉

syn·di·cal·is·m /ˋsɪndɪklˌɪzəm; ˈsɪndɪkəlɪzəm/ *n* [U] a political system or belief whose aim is for workers to control industry 工團主義, 工聯主義〔以工人控制工業為目標的制度或主張〕—**syndicalist** *n* [C] —**syndicalist** *adj*

syn·di·cate[1] /ˋsɪndɪkɪt; ˈsɪndɪkɪt/ *n* [C] a group of people or companies who join together in order to achieve a particular aim 辛迪加, 商業財團, 企業聯合組織: *a syndicate of local industrialists* 一個由本地工業家組成的集團

syn·di·cate[2] /ˋsɪndɪˌket; ˈsɪndɪkeɪt/ *v* **1** [T] to arrange for written work, photographs etc to be sold to a number of different newspapers, magazines etc 安排出售〔文章、照片等〕給多家報刊發表: **be syndicated** *His column is syndicated throughout America.* 他的專欄文章同時在美國全國各地的報刊發表。**2** [I,T] to form into a syndicate (把…)組成辛迪加 —**syndication** /ˌsɪndɪˋkeʃən; ˌsɪndɪˈkeɪʃən/ *n* [U]

syn·drome /ˋsɪnˌdrom; ˈsɪndrəʊm/ *n* [C] **1** *technical* a set of physical or mental effects that show that someone has a particular disease【術語】綜合徵: *There is no satisfactory drug treatment for irritable bowel syndrome.* 腸道過敏綜合徵還沒有令人滿意的治療藥物。—see also 另見 DOWN'S SYNDROME **2** a set of qualities, events or behaviour that is typical of a particular kind of problem〔標明某類問題的〕一組典型特徵[事件, 行為]: *the syndrome of the bored middle-aged man* 感到厭煩的中年男性的種種典型表現

syn·er·gy /ˋsɪnɚdʒɪ; ˈsɪnədʒi/ *n* [U] *technical* additional energy that is produced by two people combining their energy and ideas【術語】〔兩個人的精力和思想結合後產生的〕協同作用, 增效作用

syn·od /ˋsɪnəd; ˈsɪnəd/ *n* [C] an important meeting of church members to make decisions concerning the church〔對教會重大問題作決定的〕教會會議

syn·o·nym /ˋsɪnəˌnɪm; ˈsɪnənɪm/ *n* [C] a word with the same meaning or nearly the same meaning as another word in the same language, such as 'sad' and 'unhappy' 同義詞, 近義詞〈如 sad 和 unhappy〉—compare 比較 ANTONYM

sy·non·y·mous /sɪˋnɑnəməs; sɪˈnɒnɪməs/ *adj* **1** a situation, quality, idea etc that is synonymous with something else is the same or nearly the same as another 相同的; 近似的: **[+with]** *She seems to think that being poor is synonymous with being lazy.* 她似乎認為, 貧窮和懶惰是相同的。**2** two words that are synonymous have the same or nearly the same meaning〔單詞〕同義的, 近義的 —**synonymously** *adv*

sy·nop·sis /sɪˋnɑpsɪs; sɪˈnɒpsɪs/ *n plural* **synopses** /-siz; -siːz/ [C+of] a short account of something longer, such as the story of a film, play, or book; SUMMARY[1]〔電影故事、戲劇、書等的〕提要, 概要, 梗概

syn·tac·tic /sɪnˋtæktɪk; sɪnˈtæktɪk/ *adj technical* related to syntax【術語】句法的: *The two sentences have the same syntactic structure.* 這兩個句子的句法結構相同。—**syntactically** /-klɪ; -kli/ *adv*

syn·tax /ˋsɪntæks; ˈsɪntæks/ *n* [U] *technical*【術語】**1** the rules of grammar that are used for ordering and connecting words to form phrases or sentences 句法; 句法結構 **2** the rules that describe how words and phrases are used in a computer language〔電腦語言中使用的〕句法規則, 語法 —compare 比較 MORPHOLOGY (1)

syn·the·sis /ˋsɪnθəsɪs; ˈsɪnθɪsɪs/ *n* **1** [C] something such as a substance or an idea, made by combining different

S

things 綜合物; 綜合體: [+of] *Their beliefs are a synthesis of Eastern and Western religions.* 他們的信仰是東西方宗教的綜合體。**2** [U] the act of combining separate things, ideas etc into a complete whole 合成; 綜合: *the synthesis of rubber from petroleum* 用石油來合成橡膠 **3** [C] the production of the sounds of speech or music by electronic means〔用電子手段對語音或音樂的〕合成

syn·the·size also 又作 **-ise** *BrE*【英】/ˋsɪnθəˏsaɪz; ˈsɪnθ¦saɪz/ *v* [T] to produce something by combining different things, especially to make something similar to a natural product by combining chemicals 綜合, 合成〔尤指用化學物質合成人造產品〕: *Many minerals have been synthesized chemically.* 很多種礦物是通過化學方法合成的。

syn·the·siz·er also 又作 **synthesiser** *BrE*【英】/ˋsɪnθəˏsaɪzə; ˈsɪnθ¦saɪzə/ *n* [C] an electrical instrument that produces the sounds of various musical instruments〔電子〕音響合成器, 電聲合成器 —see also 另見 SPEECH SYNTHESIZER

syn·thet·ic /sɪnˋθɛtɪk; sɪnˈθetɪk/ *adj* produced by combining different artificial substances, rather than being naturally produced 合成的, 人造的: *synthetic fabrics like nylon* 尼龍等人造纖維 —**synthetically** /-klɪ; -kli/ *adv*

syph·i·lis /ˋsɪflɪs; ˈsɪfəl¦s/ *n* [U] a very serious disease, passed on during sexual activity or from parent to child 梅毒

sy·phon /ˋsaɪfən; ˈsaɪfən/ *n* [C] another spelling of SIPHON siphon 的另一種拼法

sy·ringe¹ /ˋsɪrɪndʒ; s¦ˈrɪndʒ/ *n* [C] an instrument for taking blood from someone's body or putting liquid, drugs etc into it, consisting of a hollow plastic tube and a needle 注射器, 注射筒

syringe² *v* [T] to clean something with a syringe〔用注射器〕灌洗; 沖洗: *Get the doctor to syringe your ears.* 去找醫生把你的耳朵沖洗一下。

syr·up /ˋsɪrəp; ˈsɪrəp/ *n* [U] **1** sweet liquid, especially sugar and water 糖水: *canned fruit in syrup* 糖水水果罐頭 **2** thick sticky pale liquid made from sugar 糖漿: *golden syrup* 金黃色的糖漿 | *maple syrup* 槭糖漿 **3** medicine in the form of a thick sweet liquid 藥用糖漿, 含藥糖漿: *cough syrup* 咳嗽[止咳]糖漿

syr·up·y /ˋsɪrəpɪ; ˈsɪrəpi/ *adj* **1** thick and sticky like syrup or containing syrup 糖漿狀的; 含有糖漿的: *syrupy drinks* 糖漿似的飲料 **2** too sweet, nice or kind 太甜蜜的; 過於多情的: *Her voice was syrupy.* 她說話嗲聲嗲氣的。

S1 W1 **sys·tem** /ˋsɪstəm; ˈsɪst¦m/ *n*

1 ►RELATED PARTS 相關部分◄ [C] a group of related parts that work together as a whole for a particular purpose 系統: *They have an alarm system in the house.* 他們房子裡裝有報警系統。| *the body's immune system* 身體的免疫系統 | *the banking system in the US* 美國的銀行系統 | *the railway system* 鐵路系統

2 ►METHOD 方法◄ [C] an organized set of ideas, methods, or ways of working 體制, 制度; 一套辦法, 一套工作方法: [+of/for] *What is the system for marking pronunciation in the dictionary?* 這本詞典用甚麼系統注音?

3 ►THE BODY 身體◄ [C] your body considered as a set of working parts〔由各器官組成的〕整個身體: *All this overeating is bad for my system.* 這暴飲暴食對我身體有害。

4 ►COMPUTERS 電腦◄ [C] the way in which a computer or set of computers works〔電腦的〕工作系統[方式]: *a fault in the system* 系統中出的毛病 | *What software does the system use?* 這個系統用的是甚麼軟件? —see also 另見 OPERATING SYSTEM

5 the system *informal* the combination of official rules and powerful groups or organizations that seem to govern your life and limit your freedom【非正式】〔操縱個人生活、限制個人自由的〕既成秩序; 現行體制; 制度: *You can't beat the system in this company!* 本公司的制度違反不得!

6 get sth out of your system *informal* to do something that helps you get rid of unpleasant strong feelings【非正式】消除強烈的不快情緒: *I was furious, so I went for a run to get it out of my system.* 我氣壞了, 便去跑步發泄怒火。

7 ►ORDER 秩序◄ [U] the use of sensible and organized methods 條理; 秩序: *We need a bit more system in the way we organize our files.* 我們的檔案管理需要安排得更有條理些。

sys·te·mat·ic /ˏsɪstəˋmætɪk; ˌsɪst¦ˈmætɪk◄/ *adj* based on carefully organized methods; THOROUGH 有系統的, 有條理的, 仔細周到的: *The way they've collected their data is not very systematic.* 他們收集資料的方法條理性不夠。| *a systematic search of the building* 對大樓的徹底搜查 —**systematically** /-klɪ; -kli/ *adv*

sys·te·ma·tize also 又作 **-ise** *BrE*【英】/ˋsɪstəməˏtaɪz; ˈsɪst¦mətaɪz/ *v* [T] to put facts, numbers, ideas etc into a particular order 使條理化, 使系統化 —**systematization** /ˏsɪstəmətəˋzeʃən; ˌsɪst¦mətaɪˈzeɪʃən/ *n* [U]

sys·te·mic /sɪsˋtɛmɪk; sɪsˈtemɪk/ *adj technical* having an effect on the whole of something, especially a living thing【術語】影響全局的;〔尤指〕影響〔生物〕全身的: *systemic injection* 影響全身的注射 —**systemically** /-klɪ; -kli/ *adv*

systems an·a·lyst /ˈ·· ˌ···/ *n* [C] someone who studies business or industrial operations, and uses computers to plan them, improve them etc 系統分析員, 系統分析專家 —**systems analysis** /ˌ·· ·ˈ···/ *n* [U]

T,t

T, t /ti; tiː/ *plural* **T's** or **t's** **1** the 20th letter of the English alphabet 英語字母表的第二十個字母 **2 to a T** *informal* if something suits you to a T, it is exactly right for you【非正式】恰好, 精確地: *That dress suits you to a T.* 那件連衣裙你穿正合身。

TA /ˌti ˋe; ˌtiː ˈeɪ/ *n* [singular] the abbreviation of 縮寫= TERRITORIAL ARMY

S3 **ta** /tɑ; tɑː/ *interjection BrE informal* thank you【英, 非正式】謝謝

tab /tæb; tæb/ *n* [C]
1 ▶SMALL PIECE OF PAPER/CLOTH 小片紙/布◀ a small piece of paper, cloth etc that is fixed to the edge of something, especially giving information about it〔固定在某物邊緣, 尤指列出其有關信息的〕小紙條; 小布條; 小標籤
2 ▶ON A CAN 罐頭上◀ *AmE* a small piece of metal that you pull to open a can of drink【美】〔開罐的金屬〕小拉環
3 ▶IN A BAR/RESTAURANT 在酒吧/飯館◀ a system used in some bars, restaurants etc in which they keep a record of what you have bought and you pay for it later〔某些酒吧或飯館的〕賒賬制; 賬單: **put sth on a tab** *Don't worry about the meal. Put it on my tab.* 別擔心吃飯的事, 記在我的賬上。
4 keep tabs on sb *informal* to watch someone carefully to check what they are doing【非正式】密切注意某人, 監視某人的一舉一動: *The police have been keeping tabs on Rogers since he got out of prison.* 自從羅傑斯出獄以來, 警察一直在嚴密監視他。
5 pick up the tab to pay for something, especially when it is not your responsibility to pay〔尤指代他人〕付賬; 承擔費用: *Taxpayers pick up the tab for government mismanagement of the economy.* 納稅人為政府經濟管理不善而承擔損失。
6 ▶CIGARETTE 香煙◀ *slang* a cigarette【俚】香煙
7 ▶IN TYPING 打字機上◀ a TAB STOP 跳格鍵, 製表鍵
8 *slang* a solid form of the illegal drug LSD【俚】迷幻藥毒丸: *a tab of acid* 一粒迷幻藥毒丸

Ta·bas·co /təˋbæsko; təˈbæskəʊ/ also 又作 **tabasco sauce** /·ˌ·· ˈ·/*n* [U] *trademark* a very hot-tasting red liquid made from CHILLI (2) peppers, used in cooking【商標】〔烹調用的〕塔巴斯科辣醬汁

tab·by /ˋtæbɪ; ˈtæbi/ *n* [C] a cat with grey, brown, or orange marks on its fur〔毛皮上有灰色、褐色或橙色斑點的〕(虎) 斑貓 —**tabby** *adj*

tab·er·nac·le /ˋtæbɚˌnækl; ˈtæbənækəl/ *n* [C] **1 the tabernacle** the small tent in which the ancient Jews kept their most holy objects〔古代猶太人存放聖物的〕聖幕; 會幕 **2** a church or other building used by some Christian groups〔某些基督教派的〕教堂, 禮拜堂 **3** a box used for keeping holy bread and wine in Roman Catholic churches〔羅馬天主教堂裡存放聖餐用麵包和葡萄酒的〕聖體櫃

S1 W1 **ta·ble¹** /ˋtebḷ; ˈteɪbəl/ *n*
1 ▶FURNITURE 家具◀ a piece of furniture with a flat top supported by legs 桌子, 枱子: *a kitchen table* 廚房用桌 | **table lamp** (=made to be put on a small table) 枱燈 | **book a table** (=ask a restaurant to keep a table available for you)〔向飯館〕預訂餐桌 *I've booked a table for two for 8:00.* 我已經訂好八點鐘兩個人的餐桌。| **lay the table** *BrE*【英】**set the table** *especially AmE*【尤美】(=put knives, forks etc on a table before a meal) 佈置桌子〔指開飯前放餐具等〕| **clear the table** (=take all the empty plates, dishes etc off a table after eating)〔指飯後〕收拾桌子 | **at table** *BrE formal* (=sitting around a table having a meal)【英, 正式】就餐, 用餐 —see also 另見 COFFEE TABLE, HIGH TABLE
2 ▶LIST 表格◀ [C] a list of numbers, facts, or information arranged in rows across and down a page (一覽) 表, 表格; 單子: **table of contents** *The table of contents at the front will tell you which page it's on.* 前面的目錄會告訴你具體在哪頁。
3 ▶MATHS 數學◀ a list that young children learn, in which all the numbers between 1 and 12 are multiplied by each other 乘法表: **three/four etc times table** *He's 12 years old and still doesn't know his three times table.* 他 12 歲了, 卻還不會背三的乘法口訣。
4 on the table a) an offer, idea etc that is on the table has been officially suggested and you are considering it〔某事或某主意〕正式提交考慮, 被擺到桌面上: *The offer on the table at the moment is a 10% wage increase.* 此刻擺到桌面上的是增加 10% 工資的方案。**b)** *AmE* an offer, idea etc that is on the table is no longer being considered at the moment but will be dealt with in the future【美】〔某事或某主意〕目前被擱置〔留待以後考慮〕
5 turn the tables (on sb) to suddenly become stronger than the opponent who used to be stronger than you〔突然〕轉弱為強, 轉敗為勝: *Suddenly Harry felt that the tables had somehow been turned and that he was now the victim.* 突然間, 哈里覺得局勢莫名其妙地對他變得不利起來, 他現在成了被動挨打的。
6 under the table *informal* money that is paid under the table is paid secretly and illegally to get what you want【非正式】〔指金錢的〕非法支付: *payments made under the table to local officials* 對當地官員的賄賂
7 ▶GROUP 一羣人◀ the group of people sitting around a table〔飯桌上的〕一桌人, 同席的人: *His stories kept the whole table amused.* 他講的故事讓全桌人很開心。—see also 另見 **drink sb under the table** (DRINK² (2))

table² *v* [T] **1** *BrE* **table a proposal/question/demand etc** to suggest a proposal etc for other people to consider【英】提交議案/問題/要求等〔供討論〕**2** *AmE* **table a bill/measure/proposal etc** to leave an offer, idea etc to be dealt with in the future【美】擱置法案/措施/議案等, 把...留到以後處理

tab·leau /ˋtæblo; ˈtæbləʊ/ *n* [C] a group of people who do not speak or move arranged on stage to show a famous event 舞台造型〔由一羣人在舞台上塑造靜態畫面, 以表現著名事件〕

ta·ble·cloth /ˋtebḷˌklɔθ; ˈteɪbəlklɒθ/ *n* [C] a cloth used for covering a table 桌布 —see picture on page A15 參見 A15 頁圖

table d'hôte /ˋtɑbḷ dot; ˌtɑːbəl ˈdəʊt/ *n* [singular] a complete meal served at a fixed price in a hotel or restaurant〔價格固定的〕套餐

ta·ble·land /ˋtebḷˌlænd; ˈteɪbəl-lænd/ also 又作 **tablelands** *n* [C] *technical* a large area of high flat land; PLATEAU (1)【術語】台地, 高地

table lin·en /ˈ·· ˌ··/ *n* [U] all the cloths used during the meal〔席間所有的〕餐桌用布〈如枱布、餐巾、盆盤布墊等〉

table man·ners /ˈ·· ˌ··/ *n* [plural] the way in which someone eats their food, considered according to the usual rules of social behaviour about eating 進餐禮儀, 用餐時的禮節: *Piotr's got terrible table manners.* 皮埃特的餐桌禮儀糟透了。

table mat /ˈ·· ·/ *n* [C] a small mat that you put under a hot dish or plate〔放在熱食盤碟下的〕碗墊, 盤墊 —see picture on page A15 參見 A15 頁圖

ta·ble·spoon /ˋtebḷˌspun; ˈteɪbəlspuːn/ *n* [C] **1** *BrE* a large spoon used for serving food, or the amount held in it【英】大湯匙, 大調羹; 一大匙容量: *three tablespoons of sugar* 三大調羹白糖 **2** *AmE* a medium-sized spoon which you use for eating【美】〔進餐用的〕中號調羹 **3** *AmE* a spoon that holds exactly 1/128 of a US pint of liquid【美】〔剛好能盛放 1/128 美國品脫液體的〕茶匙 —see picture at 參見 SPOON[1] 圖

ta·ble·spoon·ful /ˈtebḷspunˌful; ˈteɪbəlspuːnfʊl/ *n plural* **tablespoonfuls, tablespoonsful** [C] the amount that a tablespoon holds 一大調羹容量: **[+of]** *two tablespoonsful of flour* 兩調羹麵粉

tab·let /ˈtæblɪt; ˈtæblɨ̣t/ *n* [C] **1** *especially BrE* a small round hard piece of medicine; PILL (1)【尤英】藥片: *three tablets a day before meals* 一日三片藥, 飯前服用 **2** a flat piece of soap 一塊肥皂 **3** a flat piece of stone or metal with words cut into it〔銘刻有文字的〕石匾, 金屬匾

table ten·nis /ˈ·· ˌ··/ *n* [U] an indoor game played on a table by two or four players who hit a small plastic ball to each other across a net; PING-PONG 乒乓球運動

ta·ble·ware /ˈtebḷˌwɛr; ˈteɪbəlweə/ *n* [U] the plates, glasses, knives etc used when eating a meal 餐具〔總稱〕

table wine /ˈ·· ˌ·/ *n* [C,U] a fairly cheap wine intended for drinking with meals 佐餐酒

tab·loid /ˈtæblɔɪd; ˈtæblɔɪd/ *n* [C] **1** *BrE* a newspaper that has a lot of stories about sex, famous people etc, and not much serious news【英】〔刊載大量有關性、名人軼事等報道的〕通俗小報: *The tabloids had the story splashed all over their front pages.* 各通俗小報都在頭版醒目位置刊載了這一報道。**2** a newspaper with a small page 小報〔開本小的報紙〕—compare 比較 BROADSHEET —**tabloid** *adj*: *the tabloid press* 小報新聞界

ta·boo[1] /tæˈbu; təˈbuː/ *adj* **1 taboo subject/area/word** a subject etc that people avoid because they think it is offensive or embarrassing 禁忌題材/禁區/禁忌語: *Death is still a taboo subject to some people.* 對某些人來說, 死亡仍然是一個忌諱的話題。**2** *technical* too holy or evil to be touched, or used【術語】〔因太神聖或太邪惡而〕禁止接觸的, 禁止使用的

taboo[2] *n plural* **taboos** [C,U] **1** a social custom which means a particular activity or subject must be avoided 禁忌, 忌諱: **[+about/on/against]** *a strong taboo against fighting in public* 嚴格禁止在公共場所打架 **2** a religious custom that FORBIDS a particular activity because it may offend God〔宗教方面的〕清規戒律

ta·bor /ˈtebɚ; ˈteɪbə/ *n* [C] a small DRUM[1] (1) 小鼓

tab stop /ˈ· ·/ *n* [C] a button on a computer or TYPEWRITER that you push, in order to move forward to a particular place on a line of text〔電腦或打字機上的〕跳格鍵, 製表鍵

tab·u·lar /ˈtæbjəlɚ; ˈtæbjɨ̣lə/ *adj* arranged in the form of a TABLE (=set of numbers arranged in rows across and down a page)〔列成〕表格的, 表格式的

tab·u·la ra·sa /ˌtæbjələ ˈrɑzə; ˌtæbjɨ̣lə ˈrɑːzə/ *n* [C usually singular 一般用單數] *Latin literary* your mind in its original state, before you have learned anything【拉丁, 文】心靈白板〔出生後未曾學習任何外界東西之前的心靈原始狀態〕

tab·u·late /ˈtæbjəˌlet; ˈtæbjɨ̣leɪt/ *v* [T] to arrange figures or information together in a set or a list so that they can be easily compared 把…製成表格; 以表格形式排列〔數字、資料等〕—**tabulation** /ˌtæbjuˈleʃən; ˌtæbjɨ̣ˈleɪʃən/ *n* [U]

tach·o·graph /ˈtækəˌgræf; ˈtækəgrɑːf/ *n* [C] a piece of equipment for recording the speed of a vehicle, the distance it has travelled etc 速度里程計

ta·chom·e·ter /təˈkɑmətɚ; tæˈkɒmɨ̣tə/ *n* [C] a piece of equipment used to measure the speed, at which the engine of a vehicle turns 轉速表, 速度表

ta·cit /ˈtæsɪt; ˈtæsɨ̣t/ *adj* tacit agreement, support etc is accepted or understood without actually being officially agreed 心照不宣的, 默認的: *a tacit agreement that no company would cut their prices* 各公司之間不削價的默契 —**tacitly** *adv* —**tacitness** *n* [U]

ta·ci·turn /ˈtæsəˌtɝn; ˈtæsɨ̣tɜːn/ *adj* speaking very little, so that you seem unfriendly 沉默寡言的, 不苟言笑的 —**taciturnly** *adv* —**taciturnity** /ˌtæsəˈtɝnətɪ; ˌtæsɨ̣ˈtɜːnɨ̣ti/ *n* [U]

tack[1] /tæk; tæk/ *n*

1 ►NAIL 針◄ [C] a small nail with a sharp point and flat top 平頭針, 大頭針

2 ►PIN 釘◄ [C] *AmE* a short pin with a large round flat top, for fixing notices to boards, walls etc【美】圖釘, 按釘; DRAWING PIN *BrE*【英】, THUMBTACK *AmE*【美】

3 change tack/try a different tack etc to do something completely different from what you were doing before, especially in order to achieve something 改變策略; 採取另一做法: *Rudy changed tack, his tone suddenly becoming friendly.* 魯迪改變了方式, 他的語氣突然變得友好起來。

4 ►SHIP 船◄ [C,U] the direction of a sailing ship, based on the direction of the wind and the position of its sails〔帆船的〕航行方向〔由風向和帆的位置決定〕: *Ships on the starboard tack have right of way.* 右舷搶風行駛的船有先行權。

5 ►SEWING 縫紉◄ [C] a long loose stitch used for fastening pieces of cloth together before SEWING them properly〔大針腳〕暫縫, 粗縫

6 ►UGLY OBJECTS 醜陋的雜物◄ [U] small objects that are very ugly and cheap, but are sold as decorations〔難看而廉價的〕小裝飾品; 劣質雜物: *souvenir shops full of tack* 廉價紀念品充斥的商店

7 ►HORSES 馬◄ [U] all the equipment you need for horse riding 馬具, 鞍轡

tack[2] *v* **1** [T always+adv/prep] to fasten something with a tack〔用圖釘〕把…釘上: **[+up]** *tacking notices up on the board* 把告示釘在板上 **2** [T] to fasten pieces of cloth together with long loose stitches, before SEWING them properly〔大針腳〕暫縫, 粗縫 **3** [I] to change the course of a sailing ship so that the wind blows against its sails from the opposite direction〔船〕搶風航行

tack sth **↔ on** *phr v* [T] *informal* to add something to something that already exists or is complete, especially in a way that looks badly planned【非正式】〔尤指笨拙、多餘地〕增補; 附加: *The environmental section of the bill was obviously tacked on afterwards.* 那個法案關於環境方面的內容顯然是後來粗糙地增補上去的。| *a little porch tacked on to the front of the house* 屋前加的小門廊

tack·le[1] /ˈtækḷ; ˈtækəl/ *v* 3 3

1 [T] to make a determined effort to deal with a difficult problem 處理, 對付〔難題〕: *It took twelve fire engines to tackle the blaze.* 用了十二輛消防車來對付那場烈火。

2 [T] to talk to someone in order to deal with a difficult problem〔為了解決難題〕與…交涉: **tackle sb about sth** *When I tackled Didi about it, she admitted he'd tried to do too much.* 當我與迪迪交涉此事時, 她承認他過於賣力了。

3 [I,T] **►SPORT** 體育運動◄ **a)** to try to take the ball away from an opponent in a game such as football or HOCKEY (1)〔足球或曲棍球〕把(…的)球搶走 —see picture on page A23 參見 A23 頁圖 **b)** to force someone to the ground so that they stop running, in a game such as American football or RUGBY〔美式足球或橄欖球比賽中〕摟抱並拽倒〔對方球員〕

4 [T] to fight against another person, organization etc 對付: *I certainly couldn't tackle both of them on my own.* 光我一個人當然對付不了他們兩個。

tackle[2] *n* **1** [C] **a)** the act of trying to take the ball from an opponent in a game of football or HOCKEY (1)〔足球或曲棍球〕阻截得球 **b)** [C] the act of stopping an opponent by forcing them to the ground, especially in American football or RUGBY〔尤指美式足球或橄欖球〕擒抱, 抱截〔通過拉倒對手來阻擋進攻〕**2** [C] a player in American football who stops other players by tackling them

阻截隊員〔美式足球的前線球員之一〕**3** [U] the equipment used in some sports, especially fishing〔體育〕器具〔尤指釣具〕**4** [U] *slang* a man's sexual organs【俚】男性性器官 **5** [C,U] ropes and PULLEYS (=wheels) used for moving a ship's sails, lifting heavy things etc 滑車, 滑輪組

tack·y /ˋtækɪ; ˈtæki/ *adj* **1** cheap looking and of very bad quality 模樣寒磣的; 劣質的: *tacky ornaments* 劣質廉價的飾品 **2** slightly sticky 發黏的: *The paint's still slightly tacky.* 油漆還有些黏。—**tackily** *adv* —**tackiness** *n* [U]

ta·co /ˋtɑko; ˈtɑːkəʊ/ *n* [C] a type of Mexican food consisting of a flat circle made of CORN (2) flour folded and filled with BEEF¹ (1), beans etc〔牛肉、豆子等作餡的〕墨西哥玉米薄餅卷

tact /tækt; tækt/ *n* [U] the ability to be polite and careful about what you say or do so that you do not upset or embarrass other people 得體; 乖巧; 機敏: *With great tact, Aunt Jo persuaded Theo to apologize.* 喬姨媽十分巧妙地説服了西奧去道歉。

tact·ful /ˋtæktfəl; ˈtæktfəl/ *adj* careful not to say or do anything that will upset or embarrass other people 乖巧的; 機敏的; 圓通的: *Sam maintained a tactful silence as she ranted on.* 她大叫大嚷個不停時, 山姆很老練, 一聲不吭。—**tactfully** *adv*: *Everyone tactfully refrained from mentioning his argument with the boss.* 大家都很乖巧, 避免提及他與老板的爭論。

tac·tic /ˋtæktɪk; ˈtæktɪk/ *n* **1** [C] a method that you use to achieve something 手法; 策略: *Salesmen employ all sorts of clever tactics to try and persuade you.* 推銷員用盡各種聰明的手法來努力説服你。| **delaying tactic(s)** (=something you do in order to give yourself more time) 拖延戰術[策略] | **strongarm tactics** (=the use of violence to achieve your aim) 武力手段[策略] **2** [C usually plural 一般用複數] the way in which military forces are arranged in order to win a battle 戰術

tac·tic·al /ˋtæktɪkḷ; ˈtæktɪkəl/ *adj* **1** done in order to achieve what you want at a later time, especially in a game or large plan 策略性的; 謀略性的: *a tactical move to avoid the threat of legal action* 為躲避可能的法律行動而採取的策略 **2 tactical error/mistake** a mistake that will harm your plans later 戰術失誤/錯誤: *Telling him your age was a tactical error.* 你把年齡告訴了他是一個策略性的錯誤。**3 tactical weapon/missile etc** a weapon etc that is only used over short distances〔只用於短距離的〕戰術性武器/導彈等: *tactical nuclear missiles* 戰術核導彈 **4** connected with the organizing of military forces in order to win battles 戰術上的 —**tactically** /-kḷɪ; -kli/ *adv*

tactical vot·ing /ˌ… ˈ../ *n* [U] the practice of voting for a political party that you do not support in order to prevent another party from winning an election 策略性投票〔為防止另一政黨贏得選舉而把票投給自己並不支持的一個政黨〕

tac·ti·cian /tækˋtɪʃən; tækˈtɪʃən/ *n* [C] someone who is very good at TACTICS 戰術家; 謀略家

tac·tile /ˋtæktḷ; ˈtæktaɪl/ *adj* connected with your sense of touch 觸覺的: *a tactile sensation* 觸覺

tact·less /ˋtæktlɪs; ˈtæktləs/ *adj* likely to upset or embarrass someone without intending to 不乖巧的, 不圓通的; 不明智的: *I wanted to know about the divorce, but thought it would be tactless to ask.* 我想知道離婚的事, 但又覺得這樣問欠妥當。| *a tactless remark* 不明智的話 —**tactlessly** *adv* —**tactlessness** *n* [U]

tad /tæd; tæd/ *n informal*【非正式】**a tad** *BrE dialect* a small amount, or to a small degree【英, 方言】少量; 輕微: *"Would you like some milk?" "Just a tad."* "你想要點牛奶嗎?" "就一點點。"

tad·pole /ˋtædˌpol; ˈtædpəʊl/ *n* [C] a small creature that has a long tail, lives in water, and grows into a FROG (1) or TOAD 蝌蚪

taf·fe·ta /ˋtæfɪtə; ˈtæfɪ̀tə/ *n* [U] a shiny stiff cloth made from silk or NYLON 塔夫綢

Taf·fy /ˋtæfɪ; ˈtæfi/ *n* [C usually singular 一般用單數] *BrE slang* a word for someone who is Welsh, often considered to be offensive【英俚】威爾斯人〔常被認為不禮貌的稱呼〕

taffy *n* [U] *especially AmE* a soft sweet usually made from sugar boiled brown【尤美】太妃糖, 乳脂糖

tag¹ /tæg; tæg/ *n* **1** [C] a small piece of paper, plastic etc, fixed to something to show what it is, who owns it, what it costs etc 標籤, 標牌: **name/identification/price tag** *Where's the price tag on this dress?* 這件衣服上的價格標籤在哪裡? **2** [U] a children's game in which one player chases and tries to touch the others〔兒童玩的〕捉人遊戲 **3** [C] a phrase such as 'isn't it?', 'won't it?', or "does she?', added to the end of a sentence to make it a question or to ask you to agree with it 附加疑問句 **4** [C] a metal or plastic point at the end of a piece of string or SHOELACE that prevents it from splitting〔繩子、鞋帶末端的〕金屬[塑料]包頭

tag² **tagged, tagging** *v* [T] **1** to fasten a tag onto something 給…加上標籤, 給…掛上標牌: *Tag the bottles now or we'll forget which one is which.* 現在給那些瓶子貼上標籤, 否則我們會忘了哪個是哪個。**2 be tagged as stupid/a failure etc** to be thought of in a particular way that is difficult for you to change〔難以改變地〕被看作是笨蛋/沒有出息的人等: *He quit after 4½ years because he didn't want to be tagged forever as a game show host.* 他幹了四年半後辭職了, 因為他不想讓人永遠把他看作是一個遊戲節目主持人。**3 Tag!** *spoken* used in a children's game when a player manages to touch someone they are chasing【口】捉到啦!〔兒童在玩捉人遊戲時的用語〕**4** *slang* to illegally paint your name or sign on a wall, vehicle etc【俚】〔在牆壁、汽車等上面違法〕塗寫〔名字或標記〕

tag along *phr v* [I] *informal* go somewhere with someone, especially when they do not want you to【非正式】〔尤指在對方並不情願的情況下〕跟着〔某人〕去: *Mom, I can't do anything with her tagging along all the time.* 媽媽, 她老是跟着我, 我甚麼也幹不了。

tag sth ↔ **on** *phr v* [T] to add something to something that already exists or is complete, especially in a way that looks badly planned 把…附加於…〔尤指安排不妥地多餘填加〕: *Why don't you just tag on a paragraph about the latest research?* 你何不在後面加上一段, 把最新的研究情況包括進去?

ta·glia·tel·le /tægljəˋtɛlɪ; ˌtægljəˈteli/ n [U] a kind of PASTA that is cut in very long, thin, flat pieces〔又長又薄的、扁平的〕意大利扁麵條 —see picture at 參見 PASTA 圖

tai chi /ˌtaɪ ˋtʃi; ˌtaɪ ˈtʃiː/ *n* [U] a Chinese form of physical exercise that trains your mind and body in balance and control 太極(拳)

tail¹ /tel; teɪl/ *n* (S2, W3)

1 ▶ANIMAL 動物◀ [C] the movable part at the back of an animal's body 尾巴: *The dog wagged its tail.* 狗搖擺尾巴。| *a fish's tail* 魚尾 —see picture at 參見 HORSE 圖

2 ▶AIRCRAFT 飛機◀ [C] the back part of an aircraft〔飛機的〕尾部 —see picture at 參見 AIRCRAFT 圖

3 ▶SHIRT 襯衫◀ [C] the bottom part of your shirt at the back, that you put inside your trousers〔襯衫的〕後下擺

4 ▶BACK PART 末尾部分◀ [C usually singular 一般用單數] the back part of something, especially something that is moving away from you 末尾部分; 後部〔尤指某種從你面前移開的東西〕: *We saw the tail of the procession disappearing round the corner.* 我們看到遊行隊伍的隊尾漸漸消失在拐角處。

5 tails a) [U] the side of a coin that does not have the head of the president, queen etc on it〔硬幣的〕反面: *Which side do you want, heads or tails?* 你要哪一面, 正面還是反面? —opposite 反義詞 **heads** (HEAD¹ (36)) **b)** [plural] a man's formal JACKET (1) with two long parts that hang down at the back〔男子的〕晚禮服, 燕尾服

6 ▶FOLLOW 跟蹤◀ [C] *informal* someone who is employed to watch and follow someone, especially a criminal【非正式】盯梢者: **put a tail on sb** (=order someone to follow another person) 派人跟蹤〔某人〕

7 sit/be on sb's tail *BrE informal* to follow another car too closely【英, 非正式】〔開車時〕與前面車輛距離太小; TAILGATE² *AmE*【美】

8 turn tail to run away because you are too frightened to fight or attack〔因不敢抵抗或攻擊而〕逃跑, 轉身逃走

9 the tail end of a queue/meeting etc the very last part of a QUEUE etc 隊列/會議等的末尾; 尾聲

10 with your tail between your legs embarrassed or unhappy because you have failed or been defeated〔因失敗或被打敗而〕夾着尾巴; 垂頭喪氣

11 the tail is wagging the dog *informal* used to say that an unimportant thing is wrongly controlling a situation【非正式】尾巴搖狗〔用來比喻本末倒置或主次顛倒〕—see also 另見 **nose to tail** (NOSE¹ (19)), **a sting in the tail** (STING² (4))

tail² *v* [T] *informal* to follow someone and watch what they do, where they go etc【非正式】跟蹤〔某人〕, 盯〔某人〕的梢

tail away *phr v* [I] to become quieter, thinner etc and then disappear 變得越來越靜/稀少; 逐漸消失: *The beach tailed away to nothing.* 沙灘逐漸消失得無影無蹤了。

tail back *phr v* [I] *especially BrE* to form a tailback【尤英】形成塞車

tail off *phr v* [I] to become gradually smaller or weaker, sometimes stopping completely 逐漸變小[弱]; 完全消失: *Our profits tailed off towards the end of the year.* 我們的利潤到年底幾乎減至零了。

tail·back /ˈtelˌbæk; ˈteɪlbæk/ *n* [C] *BrE* a line of traffic that is moving very slowly or not moving at all【英】〔因交通堵塞而形成的〕車輛長龍: *a five mile tailback on the M25* M25號公路上長達五英里的塞車長龍

tail·board /ˈtelˌbɔrd; ˈteɪlbɔːd/ *n* [C] a TAILGATE¹〔汽車後部向外向下開的〕後門, 尾門

T

tail·bone /ˈtelbon; ˈteɪlbəʊn/ *n* [C] the bone at the very bottom of your back; COCCYX 尾骨

tail·coat /ˈtelˌkot; teɪlˈkəʊt/ *n* [C] a coat worn by men to formal events such as weddings, that is short at the front and divides into two long pieces at the back〔男子在正式場合穿的〕燕尾服

tail·gate¹ /ˈtelˌget; ˈteɪlgeɪt/ n [C] *AmE* a door at the back of a vehicle that opens outwards and downwards【美】〔汽車後部向外向下開的〕後門, 尾門

tailgate² *v* [I,T] *especially AmE* to drive too closely behind another vehicle【尤美】〔開車時〕與前面車輛距離太小

tailgate par·ty /ˈ·· ˌ··/ also 又作 **tailgate** *n* [C] a party before an American football game where people eat and drink in the CARPARK of the place where the game is played 車尾大聚餐〔指美式足球開賽前人們在停車場就地吃喝的場面〕

tail-light /ˈ· ·/ *n* [C] one of the two red lights at the back of a vehicle〔車輛的紅色〕尾燈 —see picture on page A2 參見A2頁圖

tai·lor¹ /ˈtelɚ; ˈteɪlə/ *n* [C] someone who makes men's clothes specially measured to fit each customer〔為男顧客量體裁衣的〕裁縫

tailor² *v* [T] **tailor sth to your needs/requirements** to make something so that it is exactly right for your particular needs 根據特定需要製作…: *We can tailor the insurance policy according to your family's needs.* 我們可以根據你家庭的需要制定保險單。

tai·lored /ˈtelɚd; ˈteɪləd/ *adj* **1** a piece of clothing that is tailored is made to fit very well〔衣服〕定做的 **2** made to fit a particular need or situation 適合〔特定需要或情況〕的: *tailored financial advice* 配合個別需要的財務諮詢

tai·lor·ing /ˈtelərɪŋ; ˈteɪlərɪŋ/ *n* [U] the work of making men's clothes or the style in which they are made〔製做男裝的〕裁縫業; 裁縫手藝

tailor-made /ˌ·· ˈ·◂/ *adj* exactly right or suitable for someone or something 正好適合〔某人或某物〕的: **[+for]** *The job's tailor-made for John.* 這份工作正好適合約翰去做。

tail·piece /ˈtelˌpis; ˈteɪlpiːs/ *n* [C] a part added at the end of a book, story etc〔附加於書末或故事結尾處的〕附屬部分; 補白

tail pipe /ˈ· ·/ *n* [C] *AmE* the pipe that takes unwanted gases out of a vehicle's engine【美】〔車輛發動機的〕尾部排氣管, 尾噴管; EXHAUST² (1) *BrE*【英】

tail·spin /ˈtelˌspɪn; ˈteɪlˌspɪn/ *n* [C] an uncontrolled fall of a plane through the air, in which the back of the plane spins in a wider circle than the front〔飛機失控下墜時的〕尾旋

tail·wind /ˈtelˌwɪnd; ˈteɪlˌwɪnd/ *n* [C] a wind blowing in the same direction that a vehicle is travelling〔車輛等行駛時從後面吹來的〕順風

taint¹ /tent; teɪnt/ *v* [T usually passive 一般用被動態] to make someone or something seem less pure and desirable by relating it to something unpleasant 玷污, 敗壞〔某人的名譽〕; 弄髒〔某物〕: **be tainted by/with** *a political reputation tainted by association with the Mafia* 由於與黑手黨來往而被玷污的政治聲譽

taint² *n* [singular] the appearance of being related to something shameful or terrible 污點, 瑕疵; 腐壞: **[+of]** *court officials free from the taint of corruption* 一身清廉的法庭官員

taint·ed /ˈtentɪd; ˈteɪntɪ̣d/ *adj especially AmE* food or drink that is tainted is no longer safe because it has decayed or contains poison【尤美】〔食物或飲料〕腐壞的, 變質的, 有毒的: *tainted milk* 變質牛奶

take¹ /tek; teɪk/ *v past tense* took /tʊk; tʊk/ *past participle* taken /ˈtekən; ˈteɪkən/

① MOVE STH 移動某物
② DO SOMETHING 做某事
③ NEED STH 需要某物
④ SCHOOL/EXAMS 學校/考試
⑤ GET SOMETHING IN YOUR POSSESSION 取得某物
⑥ TAKE PART 參加
⑦ TAKE PLACE 發生
⑧ ACCEPT SOMETHING 接受某物
⑨ SPOKEN PHRASES 口語片語
⑩ OTHER MEANINGS 其他意思
⑪ PHRASAL VERBS 片語動詞

① MOVE STH 移動某物

1 [T] to move someone or something from one place to another 把〔某人或某物〕帶(走); 拿(走); 取(走); 搬(走): *Don't forget to take your bag when you go.* 你走的時候別忘了拿自己的包。| *Paul doesn't know the way – can you take him?* 保爾不認識路, 你能帶他去嗎? | **take sb/sth to** *We take the kids to school in the car.* 我們用車送孩子們上學。| *Our neighbor was taken away in a police car.* 我們的鄰居被一輛警車帶走了。| *Take the car to the garage to be repaired.* 把車送到修

理廠去修理一下。| **take sb sth** *Take your mother a cup of tea.* 給你媽拿杯茶去。| **take sb/sth with you** *I'll take the dogs with me when I go to the lake.* 我去湖邊時會把狗都帶上。—see 見 BRING (USAGE)

② DO SOMETHING 做某事

2 [T] a word meaning to do something, used with many different nouns to form a phrase that means 'do the actions connected with the nouns'〔與許多不同的名詞連用, 構成短語, 意義相當於"做與該名詞相關的動作"〕: *take a walk* 散步 | *take a bath* 洗澡 | *take a breath* 吸一口氣 | *take a vacation* 度假

③ NEED STH 需要某物

3 take (sb) 2 hours/6 months etc to need a particular amount of time to do something or for something to happen 花〔某人〕兩個小時/六個月等: *The journey takes three hours.* 這段路程要花三個小時。| **take 2 hours/6 months etc to do sth** *It took three hours to fix the washing machine.* 修理那台洗衣機花了三個小時。| *It took us half an hour to get there.* 我們花了半個小時到那兒。

4 ▶NEED MONEY/EFFORT/A QUALITY 需要錢/努力/某種品質◀ [T] to need a particular quality, amount of money, or effort, in order for you to do something or for something to happen〔為了做成某事或使某事發生〕需要〔某種特殊的品質、一定數量的錢或努力〕: *It takes strength and stamina to be a long-distance runner.* 要想成為一名長跑運動員, 需要體力和耐力。| **it takes sth to do sth** *It took a lot of courage to admit you were wrong.* 要承認自己錯了, 需要很大的勇氣。

5 ▶STH NEEDS STH〔某物〕需要〔某物〕◀ [T] if a machine, vehicle etc takes a particular kind of petrol, BATTERY (1) etc, you have to use that in it〔機器、車輛等〕需要使用〔某種特定的汽油、電池等〕: *The car only takes unleaded.* 這輛車只用無鉛汽油。

6 have what it takes *informal* to have the qualities needed to be successful【非正式】具有成功的天資[品質]: *Neil's got what it takes to be a great footballer.* 內爾具有成為一名偉大足球運動員的天賦。

④ SCHOOL/EXAMS 學校/考試

7 ▶STUDY STH IN SCHOOL 在學校學習◀ [T] to study a particular subject in a school or college, in order to do an examination〔在學校〕攻讀〔某一課程〕: *I only had to take 6 credits my senior year.* 我大四時只需修六個學分。

8 ▶TEACH 教書◀ [T] *BrE* to teach a particular group of students in a school or college【英】〔在學校〕教授〔某個班級〕: **take sb for sth** *Who takes you for French?* 誰教你們法語?

9 take an exam/test to do an examination or test 參加考試/測驗: *I had to take my driving test three times before I passed.* 我參加了三次駕駛考試才通過。

⑤ GET SOMETHING IN YOUR POSSESSION 取得某物

10 ▶STEAL 偷竊◀ [T] to steal something, or borrow something without someone's permission 偷竊〔某物〕;〔未經某人允許〕拿走〔某物〕: *The burglars took most of our jewellery.* 竊賊偷走了我們的大多數珠寶。| *She's taken my pen.* 她拿走了我的筆。—see 見 STEAL (USAGE)

11 ▶GET CONTROL 得到控制◀ [T] to get possession or control of something 擁有; 控制〔某物〕: *Enemy forces have taken the airport.* 敵軍已經控制了機場。| **take control/charge** *Ann took control of the division last month.* 安上個月接管了該部門。

12 ▶GET STH 得到某物◀ [T] to get something for yourself 把…據為己有: *Jim took all the credit, even though he hadn't done much of the work.* 吉姆把一切榮譽據為己有, 儘管他並未幹多少活。

13 take a seat to sit down 坐下

14 take the lead to take the leading position in a race, competition etc〔在比賽、競賽等中〕領先

15 ▶HOLD STH 拿着某物◀ [T] to get hold of something in your hands〔手裡〕拿着〔某物〕: *Let me take your jacket.* 把你的夾克給我。| *She took my arm as we walked down the street.* 我們沿街走着時, 她挽着我的手臂。

⑥ TAKE PART 參加

16 take part to do an activity, sport etc with other people 參加〔活動、體育運動等〕: *Greg was too sick to take part.* 格雷格病得太重, 沒法參加。| **take part in sth** *She was invited to take part in a TV debate.* 她被邀請參加一場電視辯論。

⑦ TAKE PLACE 發生

17 take place if an event takes place, it happens〔某一事件〕發生; 舉行: *The contest takes place every four years.* 該賽事每四年舉行一次。| *We don't know exactly what took place, but they both looked furious afterward.* 我們不知道到底出了甚麼事, 但他們倆事後都是一臉慍怒。—see 見 OCCUR (USAGE)

⑧ ACCEPT SOMETHING 接受某物

18 a) [T] to accept something that someone offers you 接受〔某人給的東西〕: *If I were you I'd take the job.* 我要是你的話, 我會接受聘請的。| **take it or leave it** *spoken* (=used to say that your offer will not change)【口】要不要隨你的便: *I'll give you £50 – take it or leave it.* 我給你 50 英磅 —— 要不要隨你的便。| **take sb's advice** *I took your advice and went to the doctor's.* 我聽從了你的建議, 去看過醫生。**b)** [T not in progressive 不用進行式] to be willing to accept that something is true and correct 樂意接受; 相信…是真的/正確的: *I refuse to take the blame.* 我不認為出錯的責任該由我承擔。| *Do they take credit cards in this shop?* 這家商店接受信用卡嗎? | **take sb's word for it** (=accept that what someone says is true) 相信某人説的是真的 *Don't take my word for it if you don't want – go back and see for yourself!* 如果你不樂意, 就別信我的話 —— 回去自己看看去吧!

19 take sth as read to accept that something is correct because you have no other choice〔因別無選擇而〕相信…是不會錯的: *We can take it as read that Judith will want to come.* 朱迪思會希望來, 我們可以肯定這是不會錯的。

20 ▶ACCEPT STH UNPLEASANT 接受令人不快的事◀ [T] *informal* to accept an unpleasant situation or someone's unpleasant behaviour without becoming upset【非正式】容忍, 忍受: *I can't take any more of his lies and deceit.* 我再也無法忍受他的謊言和欺騙了。| *Steve's tough – He can take it.* 史蒂夫很堅強 —— 他能承受此事。| **hard to take** *All this uncertainty is really very hard to take.* 這種種患得患失的心情實在難以忍受。

Frequencies of the verb **take** in spoken and written English 動詞take在英語口語和書面語中的使用頻率

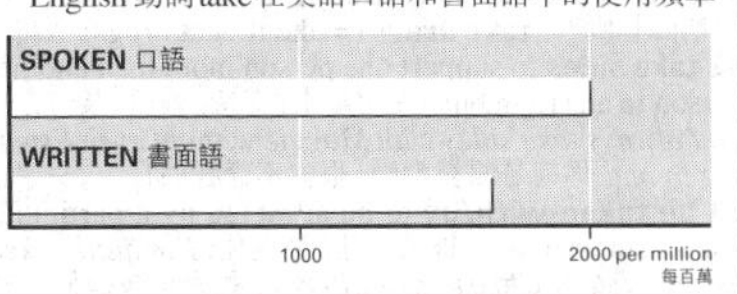

Based on the British National Corpus and the Longman Lancaster Corpus
據英國國家語料庫和朗文蘭卡斯特語料庫

This graph shows that the verb **take** is more common in spoken English than in written English. This is because it is used in some common spoken phrases. These are shown in the section marked SPOKEN PHRASES. 本圖表顯示, 動詞take在英語口語中的使用頻率高於書面語, 因為該詞用於一些常用口語片語中。這些片語出現在標有"SPOKEN PHRASES口語片語"的部分。

T

21 ▶**SUFFER STH** 忍受某事◀ [T] to experience something unpleasant because you cannot avoid it 不得已而接受; 忍受: *Staff have agreed to take a 2% pay cut.* 員工已經同意接受削減 2% 的薪水。

⑨ SPOKEN PHRASES 口語片語

22 take sb/sth (for example) used when you want to give an example of something you have just been talking about 以某人/某事為例; 舉例說明: *You don't need loads of qualifications – take me for example, I failed my exams, but still found a job.* 你不需要具備許多資格 —— 以我為例, 我考試沒有過關, 但還是找到了一份工作。

23 I take it (that) used to say that you expect someone will do something, know something etc 我想; 我認為: *I take it you've heard that Rick's resigned.* 我想你已聽說里克辭職了。

24 I take your point used when you are accepting that what someone has said is true 我同意你的觀點; 我相信〔你的話是正確的〕: *Mr Chairman, I take your point, but I also support Mr Baxter's view.* 主席先生, 我同意你的說法, 但我也支持巴克斯特先生的觀點。

25 take it from me used to persuade someone that what you are saying is true 請相信我的話, 我敢擔保: *Ken won't last long in this job, take it from me.* 這項工作, 肯不會幹長的, 相信我的話吧。

26 take a hike *especially AmE* used to tell someone to go away【尤美】叫〔某人〕離開: *Look, Buddy, I'm tired of your mouth. Why don't you take a hike.* 瞧! 老兄, 我對你的話已經厭煩了。你還是走人吧。

27 it takes all sorts (to make a world) used to show that you think what someone is doing, likes etc is very strange 世上甚麼人都有; 大千世界無奇不有

28 what do you take me for? used when someone has suggested you would do something and you want to say you would not do anything like that 你把我當甚麼人看了?: *I won't tell her the secret – what do you take me for?* 我不會把這祕密告訴她的 —— 你把我當甚麼人看了?

⑩ OTHER MEANINGS 其他意思

29 ▶**NUMBERS** 數字◀ [T] to subtract one number from another number 從…中減去: **take something from** *Take four from nine and what do you get?* 九減去四, 結果是多少?

30 ▶**HAVE SPACE FOR** 給…留有空地◀ [T not in progressive or passive 不用進行式或被動態] to have only enough space to contain a particular amount of something, or a particular number of things 能裝下, 能盛下, 能容納: *The car takes five people.* 這輛車能裝五個人。| *The shelf won't take any more books.* 書架上再也擺不下書了。

31 ▶**MEDICINE/DRUG** 藥, 藥品/毒品◀ [T] to take a drug into your body 服〔藥〕, 吃〔藥〕: *Do you want to take an aspirin for your headache?* 你頭痛, 要吃一片阿斯匹林嗎? | **take drugs** (=take illegal drugs) 吸毒

32 take sides to support one person more than another person in an argument 〔在辯論中〕支持, 偏袒〔某一方〕: *You always take sides with Maggie without even listening to me!* 你總是偏袒麥姬, 根本不聽我的!

33 be taken with/by to be attracted by a particular idea, plan or person 被吸引住, 被迷住: *I'm quite taken by the idea of Christmas in Berlin.* 我完全被這個在柏林過聖誕節的想法所吸引。

34 be taken ill/sick etc to suddenly become ill 突然病倒

35 ▶**SEX** 性◀ [T] *literary* if a man takes a woman, he has sex with her【文】和〔婦女〕發生性行為

36 ▶**EAT/DRINK** 吃/喝◀ [T] used in some phrases meaning to eat or drink something 吃; 喝〔用於某些短語中〕: **do you take sugar** (=do you take sugar in your tea or coffee) 你〔喝茶或喝咖啡時〕加糖嗎?

37 ▶**TAXI/BUS/TRAIN ETC** 計程車/公共汽車/火車等◀ [T] to go somewhere by taxi, bus, or train 乘坐〔計程車、公共汽車或火車〕: *We were too exhausted to walk so we took the bus.* 我們累得實在走不動了, 所以改乘公共汽車。

38 ▶**FEELINGS** 感覺◀ [T] to have or experience a particular feeling, used in some phrases 〔用於某些短語中, 表示一種特定的感覺〕: *Lin takes no interest in her work.* 琳對自己的工作毫無興趣。| **take pity on** (=help someone that you feel pity for) 同情, 可憐 *that nice young man who took pity on me and helped me with my bags* 那個同情我、幫我拿包的好小伙子 | **take offence** (=feel offended by something) 覺得被冒犯了 *Don't take offence. Roger says things like that to everybody.* 不要見怪, 羅傑跟誰說話都是那樣的。

39 take a picture/photograph to photograph someone or something 給…拍照: **[+of]** *I took several pictures of the cottage we stayed in.* 我給我們旅宿過的那間小農舍拍攝了好些照片。

40 ▶**WRITE** 寫◀ [T] to write down information that you have just been given 把〔剛剛得知的情況〕寫下, 記下: *Don't let me forget to take your address before you leave.* 你離開前別忘了給我留下地址。| *It might be a good idea to take notes during the lecture.* 聽講座時記筆記, 或許是個好辦法。

41 take sth seriously/lightly to consider someone or something in a particular way 認真地/不當回事地對待某人或某事: *It's not the kind of comment you take lightly, is it?* 不是能掉以輕心的那一類評論, 是嗎? | *I always take you seriously, don't I?* 我總是很認真地對待你, 不是嗎?

42 take sth well/badly to react well or badly when you find something out 對某事作出好/不好的反應: *"How did she take it when you told her?" "Er, not too well."* "你告訴她時, 她有甚麼反應?" "呃, 反應不是很好。"

43 ▶**TEST/MEASURE STH** 測試/測量某物◀ [T] to test or measure something 測試; 測量〔某物〕: *He took my temperature and blood pressure.* 他測量了我的體溫和血壓。

44 take sth to bits/pieces to divide something into its separate parts 拆開; 分解: *We had to take the radio to pieces to find out what was wrong with it.* 我們只好把收音機拆開, 以搞清楚裡面究竟出了甚麼故障。

45 take a bend/fence/corner etc [T] to try to get over or around something in a particular way 轉過彎道/柵欄/角落等: *We took the bend at over 60 and lost control.* 我們以 60 多英里的時速轉彎, 結果失去了控制。

46 ▶**SIZE** 尺寸, 型號◀ [T] to wear a particular size of clothes or shoes 穿…尺寸[號碼]的衣服[鞋子]: *I take size 6 shoes.* 我穿六碼的鞋。

47 ▶**STH WORKS** 某物起作用◀ [I] if a DYE (=colouring substance) or INJECTION (=medicine) takes, it is successful 〔染料或注射的藥物等〕起了作用, 有了效果

⑪ PHRASAL VERBS 片語動詞

take aback *phr v* [T] **be taken aback** to be very surprised about something 對…吃驚: *He seemed quite taken aback by the news.* 他好像對這一消息十分驚訝。

take after sb *phr v* [T not in progressive 不用進行式] to look or behave like an older relative 〔在外貌、行為等方面〕與〔某個長輩〕相像: *Jenni really takes after her mother.* 珍妮真的長得很像自己的母親。

take sb/sth **apart** *phr v* [T] **1** to separate something into pieces; DISMANTLE 拆開, 拆卸 **2 a)** to beat someone very easily in a game or sport 〔比賽中〕把…打得一敗塗地 **b)** to criticize someone very strongly 嚴厲批評; 把…駁得體無完膚

take away from sth *phr v* [T] to harm the good effect or success of something; DETRACT 減損; 貶低: *We won't allow a few troublemakers to take away from our enjoyment of the occasion.* 我們不會允許幾個製造麻煩的人影響我們在這次活動中獲得的樂趣。

take back *phr v* [T] **1 [take** sth ↔ **back]** to admit that you were wrong to say something 收回〔說錯的話〕:

I'm sorry I was rude, I take it all back. 對不起, 我太粗魯了, 我收回我說過的所有話。**2** [**take** sth ↔ **back**] to take something you have bought back to a shop because it is not suitable 退回〔從商店裡購買的貨物〕: *If the shirt doesn't fit, take it back.* 如果這件襯衣不合身, 拿去退貨吧。**3** [**take** sb **back**] to make you remember a time in the past 使回憶起: *Seeing those old pictures really took me back.* 看到那些老照片, 真的使我想起了過去。

take sth ↔ **down** *phr v* [T] **1** to separate a large structure or machine into pieces 把〔大件物品或機器〕拆開, 拆卸: *They're taking the scaffolding down next week.* 他們下週要把腳手架拆除。**2** to write something down 寫下, 記下: *Let me take down your name and number.* 讓我記下你的名字和號碼。**3** to lower your trousers, SHORTS (SHORT³ (2)) etc without actually removing them 褪下〔褲子等, 但不脱掉〕

take in *phr v* [T]

1 ▶PERSON 人◀ [**take** sb ↔ **in**] to let someone stay in your house, especially because they have nowhere else to stay 收留, 收容, 收養: *Brett's always taking in stray animals.* 布雷特總是收養那些走失的動物。

2 ▶INCLUDE 包括◀ [**take** sth ↔ **in**] if a price or cost takes in something it includes it〔價格或成本裡〕包括: *This price takes in the cost of all the accommodation and food.* 這個價格包括了食宿等一切費用。

3 take in a movie/show etc *AmE* to go to see a film, play etc【美】觀看電影/戲劇等

4 ▶CLOTHES 衣服◀ [**take** sth ↔ **in**] to make a piece of clothing narrower so that it fits you 改小〔衣服〕— opposite 反義詞 **let out** (4) (LET¹)

5 ▶UNDERSTAND/REMEMBER STH 理解/記住某事◀ [**take** sth ↔ **in**] to understand and remember new facts and information 領會, 理解; 記住: *I told Grandpa we were going away, but I don't think he took it in.* 我告訴爺爺我們要走了, 但我認為他並沒把話聽進去。

6 be taken in to be completely deceived by someone so that you believe a lie 被騙: *Don't be taken in by products claiming to help you lose weight in a week.* 不要被那些聲稱在一週內會幫你減肥的產品給騙了。

take off 脱去〔衣服〕;〔飛機〕起飛

He took his coat off. 他脱去了外衣。

The plane took off. 飛機起飛了。

take off *phr v*

1 ▶REMOVE STH 除掉某物◀ [T **take** sth ↔ **off**] to remove something, especially a piece of clothing 脱下, 脱去〔尤指衣服〕: *Take your coat off.* 脱掉你的外衣。| *I forgot to take off my make-up last night.* 我昨天晚上忘了卸妝。—opposite 反義詞 **put on**

2 ▶AIRCRAFT/SPACECRAFT 飛機/航天器◀ [I] to rise into the air at the beginning of a flight 起飛: *As the plane was taking off, I remembered I hadn't turned the iron off.* 飛機起飛時, 我才想起我沒有給熨斗斷電。

3 ▶COPY SB 模仿某人◀ [T **take** sb ↔ **off**] *informal* to copy the way someone speaks or behaves, in order to entertain people【非正式】為了逗笑模仿〔某人的談吐舉止〕

4 ▶HOLIDAY 假日◀ [T **take** sth **off**] to have a holiday from work on a particular day, or for a particular length of time〔在某日或某段時間〕休假: *I'm taking Thursday off to do some Christmas shopping.* 我星期四要休假, 去買一些聖誕禮物。

5 ▶SUCCESS 成功◀ [I] to suddenly start being successful 突然開始成功; 開始走紅: *I hear the business is really taking off.* 我聽説生意真的開始興隆了。

6 ▶LEAVE A PLACE 離開一個地方◀ [I] *informal* to leave somewhere suddenly, especially without telling anyone【非正式】〔尤指不打招呼就〕匆匆離開: *Clare just took off without saying goodbye.* 克萊爾沒有道別就離開了。

take on *phr v* [T] **1** [**take** sb **on**] to start to employ someone 開始雇用〔某人〕: *We're taking on 50 new staff this year.* 我們今年要雇用50名新員工。—see 見 HIRE¹ (USAGE) **2** [**take on** sth] to begin to have a particular quality or appearance 開始具有〔某種特徵、面貌等〕; 呈現; 露出: *His face took on a worried look.* 他的臉上開始露出焦慮的神情。| *These insects can take on the colour of their surroundings.* 這些昆蟲能夠呈現出與其周圍環境相同的顏色。**3** [**take** sb ↔ **on**] to start an argument or fight with someone 開始和…爭吵[鬥毆、較量等] **4** [**take** sth ↔ **on**] to agree to do some work or be responsible for something 接受〔工作等〕; 承擔〔責任等〕: *I'm worried about Doug, he's taking on too much work. He looks awful.* 我擔心道格, 他承擔的工作太多了。他的氣色很不好。

take out *phr v* [T]

1 ▶PERSON 人◀ [T **take** sb **out**] to take someone to a restaurant, cinema, club etc 帶〔某人〕出去〔到飯館、電影院、俱樂部等地〕: *We're taking my folks out for a meal next week.* 下週我們帶父母出去吃飯。

2 ▶GET STH 獲得某物◀ [**take** sth ↔ **out**] to arrange to get something officially, especially from an insurance company or a court of law 正式地獲得…;〔尤指從保險公司或法庭〕領到: *I'm thinking of taking out a life insurance policy.* 我正在考慮買一份人壽保險。| *They've taken out an ad in the local paper.* 他們在當地的報紙上登了一則廣告。

3 take it out of sb to make someone feel very tired 使某人筋疲力盡: *Having the flu really takes it out of you!* 患了流感會讓你真的覺得渾身沒有勁!

4 ▶ KILL/DESTROY 殺害/摧毀◀ [**take** sb/sth ↔ **out**] *informal* to kill someone, or destroy something【非正式】殺害〔某人〕; 摧毀〔某物〕: *The building was completely taken out by a bomb.* 那幢大樓被一顆炸彈完全摧毀了。

5 take sb out of themselves to make someone feel less worried about their problems 使某人減少煩惱

take sth **out on** sb *phr v* [T] **take it out on sb** to make someone suffer because you are feeling angry, tired etc 向〔某人〕發泄〔不滿等〕; 拿〔某人〕出氣: *Don't take it out on me, it's not my fault you've had a bad day.* 別把火發泄到我身上, 你今天不順心, 又不是我的錯。

take over *phr v* [I,T] to take control of something 接管; 接任; 接手: *Who will take over now that Ewing has resigned?* 尤因已經辭職, 誰將接替他呢? | **take** sth ↔ **over** *Will you take over the driving when we reach Madison.* 等我們到達麥迪遜後, 你來接着開車, 好嗎? —

see also 另見 TAKEOVER

take to sb/sth *phr v* [T not in passive 不用被動態] **1** to start to like someone or something 喜歡上…; 對…產生好感: *I took to Paul as soon as I met him.* 我一見到保羅, 就喜歡上了他。**2** to start doing something as a habit 染上…習慣/嗜好: *All this bad news is enough to make you take to drink.* 所有這種壞消息足以使你借酒消愁。| **take to doing sth** *Dee's taken to getting up at 6 and going jogging.* 迪伊開始習慣在六點起牀, 然後去慢跑。**3 take to your bed** to go to your bed and stay there 上牀〔休息〕

take up sth *phr v* [T]

1 ►ACTIVITY/SUBJECT 活動/主題◄ [T **take up** sth] to become interested in a particular activity or subject and spend time doing it 對〔某項活動或主題〕產生興趣; 開始花時間從事…: *Glenn has taken up pottery.* 格倫已開始喜歡上陶瓷製作。

2 ►JOB/RESPONSIBILITY 工作/責任◄ [**take up** sth] to start a new job or have a new responsibility 開始從事〔一項新的工作〕/開始擔當〔一項新的責任〕: *She took up her first teaching post in 1950.* 1950年, 她走上第一個教學崗位。

3 ►POSITION 位置◄ [**take up** sth] to put yourself in a particular position ready for something to happen, or so that you can see better 佔好位置以備…: *The runners took up their positions on the starting line.* 賽跑運動員已在起跑線上各就各位。

4 ►IDEA/SUGGESTION/SUBJECT 想法/建議/主題◄ [**take** sth ↔ **up**] to do something about an idea or suggestion that you have been considering 着手處理, 着手進行: *I'm going to take this matter up with my lawyer.* 我將找我的律師着手處理此事。

5 ►OFFER 建議◄ [**take** sth ↔ **up**] to accept an offer or CHALLENGE¹ (1) that someone has made 接受〔建議或挑戰〕: *Are you going to take up the challenge of lasting a whole week without arguing?* 堅持一週內不爭吵, 你打算接受這一挑戰嗎?

6 ►SPACE/TIME 空間/時間◄ [**take up** sth] if something takes up a particular amount of time or space it fills it 佔去〔時間或空間〕: *Writing the paper took up most of the weekend.* 寫那篇論文佔去了週末的大半時間。| *Your clutter takes up far too much space.* 你那些亂七八糟的東西佔去了太多地方。

7 take up arms to fight a battle using weapons 拿起武器〔去戰鬥〕

8 take up residence to start living somewhere 開始在〔某地〕安頓下來; 在…定居

9 ►CLOTHES 衣服◄ [**take** sth ↔ **up**] to reduce the length of a skirt or pair of trousers 收短〔裙子或褲子〕

10 ►CONTINUE AN ACTIVITY 繼續某項活動◄ [**take** sth ↔ **up**] to continue a story or activity that someone else started, or that you have started but had to stop 繼續講/做; 把…接着進行下去: *I'll take up the story where you left off.* 我將從你停下的地方把這個故事繼續講下去。

take sb **up on** sth *phr v* [T] to accept an invitation that someone has made 接受…邀請: *I'll take you up on that offer of a drink, if it still stands!* 我會接受你的邀請去喝一杯, 如果你說的話還算數!

take up with sb/sth *phr v* [T] **1** to become friendly with someone, especially someone who may influence you badly 開始與…親密交往〔尤指會有不良影響〕: *Sean's taken up with a bunch of lazy hoods.* 肖恩開始與一羣遊手好閒的惡棍交往。**2 be taken up with** to be very busy dealing with someone or something 忙於: *Jo's completely taken up with work at the moment.* 喬此刻正全神貫注地工作。

take upon *phr v* [T] **take it upon yourself to do sth** to decide to do something without permission or approval 擅自決定做〔某事〕: *Stefan took it upon himself to sell the car while I was away.* 我不在時斯蒂芬自作主張地把那輛車賣了。

take² *n* [C] **1** the act of a scene for a film or television programme〔電影或電視節目〕一次拍攝的鏡頭: *We had to do six takes for this particular scene.* 為了這個場景, 我們不得不拍了六個鏡頭。**2** [usually singular 一般用單數] the amount of fish or animals caught at one particular time 一次獲得的捕魚量; 捕獲量 **3** [usually singular 一般用單數] *informal especially AmE* the amount of money earned by a shop or business in a particular period of time【非正式, 尤美】營業額 **4 be on the take** *informal* to be willing to do something wrong in return for money【非正式】〔願意〕受賄, 貪贓枉法 **5 sb's take on sth** *AmE informal* someone's opinion about a situation or idea【美, 非正式】某人對某事的觀點[立場]:*What's your take on the Middle East issue?* 你對中東問題的立場是甚麼?

take·a·way /ˈtekəˌwe; ˈteɪkəweɪ/ *n* [C] *BrE*【英】**1** a meal that you buy at a shop or restaurant to eat at home〔商店或餐館的〕外賣食品; TAKE-OUT (1) *AmE*【美】: *Let's have a takeaway tonight.* 我們今晚買點東西帶回去吃吧。**2** a shop or restaurant that sells meals to be eaten somewhere else 外賣商店; 外賣餐館; TAKE-OUT (2) *AmE*【美】

take-home pay /ˈ· · ˌ·/ *n* [U] the amount of money that you receive after you have paid tax etc〔扣除稅款等後的〕實得工資

tak·en /ˈtekən; ˈteɪkən/ the past participle of TAKE¹

take-off /ˈ· ·/ *n* **1** [C,U] the time when a plane or ROCKET rises into the air〔飛機或火箭的〕起飛, 升空 **2** [C] the act of leaving the ground as you make a jump 起跳 **3** [C] an amusing performance that copies the way someone behaves〔對某人動作的〕滑稽模仿: *Suzie did a brilliant take-off of the principal.* 蘇茲模仿校長的動作, 學得惟妙惟肖。—see also 另見 **take off** (TAKE¹)

take-out /ˈ· ·/ *n* [C] *AmE*【美】**1** a meal that you buy at a shop or restaurant to eat at home〔商店或餐館的〕外賣食品; TAKEAWAY (1) *BrE*【英】**2** a shop or restaurant that sells cooked meals to be eaten somewhere else 外賣商店; 外賣餐館; TAKEAWAY (2) *BrE*【英】

take·o·ver /ˈtekˌovə; ˈteɪkˌəʊvə/ *n* [C] **1** the act of getting control of a company by buying most of its shares (SHARE² (5)) 購股兼併, 〔通過購買其大部分股票而實現對某企業的〕接管, 接收 | **takeover bid** (=an attempt to get control) 兼併要約, 盤進出價 **2** an act of getting control of a country or political organization, especially by using force〔尤指通過武力對某國或某政治組織的〕接管, 接收: *the communist takeover in Laos* 共產黨政權接管老撾

ta·ker /ˈtekə; ˈteɪkə/ *n* [C] **be no/few/not many takers** used to say that no-one accepted or wanted something that was offered 沒有/很少/不多〔某被提供的東西的〕接受者: *There have been a few takers so far, but the price is a big obstacle.* 目前已有幾個顧客, 但價格是個大的障礙。

take-up /ˈ· ·/ *n* [U] the rate at which people buy or accept something offered by a company, government etc〔對公司、政策等推出東西的〕認購率; 接受率: *Despite all the advertisements, the take-up has been slow.* 儘管做了那麼多廣告, 認購率還是很低。

tak·ings /ˈtekɪŋz; ˈteɪkɪŋz/ *n* [plural] the money that a shop gets from selling its goods〔商店〕收入, 營業額: *Someone broke in and stole the day's takings from the safe.* 有人入室行竊, 把當天的收入從保險櫃裡偷走了。

talc /tælk; tælk/ *n* [U] **1** talcum powder 滑石粉, 爽身粉 **2** a soft smooth mineral that feels like soap and is used for making paints, plastics, etc〔用來製造顏料、塑料等的〕滑石

tal·cum pow·der /ˈtælkəm ˌpaudə; ˈtælkəm ˌpaʊdə/ *n* [U] a fine powder which you put on your skin after washing to make it dry or smell pleasant 滑石粉, 爽身粉

tale /tel; teɪl/ *n* [C] **1** a story of imaginary events, especially of an exciting kind 故事: *tales of far-off lands* 異國他鄉的故事 **2** a spoken description of an event or situation that is often not completely true〔未必完全真實的〕陳述; 傳説, 傳聞: *tales of his life in post-war Berlin* 有關他在戰後柏林的生活傳聞 **3 tell tales** *especially BrE* to tell someone in authority something untrue, unfair, or unpleasant, often because you want to harm someone else【尤英】向上級誣告; 搬弄是非; TATTLE *AmE*【美】: *Samantha's been telling tales to the teacher again.* 薩曼莎又在對老師説別人的壞話了。**4 tale of misery/woe** a description of events that made you very unhappy 痛苦的/悲慘的故事 **5 live/survive etc to tell the tale** *humorous* to still be alive after a dangerous or unpleasant event【幽默】〔經歷危難後〕活下來/倖存等: *Yes, it's true. I've been to stay at my mother-in-law's and lived to tell the tale.* 是的, 是真的。我暫住在我岳母家, 總算度過來了。

3 3 **tal·ent** /ˈtælənt; ˈtælənt/ *n* **1** [C,U] a special natural ability or skill 天資, 天賦; 才能: *musical talent* 音樂天賦 | **[+for]** *She showed a talent for acting at an early age.* 她在很小的時候就顯示出演戲的天賦。| **a man/woman of many talents** (=someone who has the ability to do several things very well) 一個多才多藝的男人/女人 | **talent contest/show/competition** (=a competition in which people show how well they can sing, dance, tell jokes etc) 新秀選拔賽〔指通過唱歌、跳舞、講笑話等活動選拔出有演出才能的人〕**2** [U] people who have a special natural ability or skill 有才能的人, 天才, 才子: **footballing/golfing etc talent** (=people who are good at football, GOLF etc) 足球天才/高爾夫球天才等 *Britain has lost a lot of its footballing talent to clubs abroad.* 英國有許多足球天才流失到了國外的球隊。**3** [U] *BrE slang* sexually attractive people【英俚】性感的人, 尤物: *There's not much talent round here tonight.* 今晚這裡沒有多少尤物。

tal·ent·ed /ˈtæləntɪd; ˈtæləntɪ̵d/ *adj* very good at something such as singing, acting, or playing sports 有天資的, 有才能的: *a talented actor* 一名很有天賦的演員

talent scout /ˈ·· ·/ *n* [C] someone whose job is to find young people who are good at a sport or activity〔擅長於發掘體育或其他活動人才的〕人才發掘者, 新秀物色者〈如球探、星探〉

tal·is·man /ˈtelɪzmən; ˈtælɪ̵zmən/ *n plural* **talismans** [C] an object that is believed to have magic powers of protection 辟邪物, 護身符

1 1 **talk[1]** /tɔk; tɔːk/ *v*

1 ►CONVERSATION 交談◄ [I] to say things to someone, especially in a conversation 談話, 交談: **talk to** *Who was that you were talking to at the party?* 晚會上與你説話的那一位是誰? | **talk with** *Bob was talking with a pretty woman from the fire department.* 鮑勃正在與一名消防部門的漂亮女士談話。| **talk about/of** *We were talking about our childhoods and realized we both went to the same school.* 我們談起了各自的童年, 發現我倆上的是同一所學校。—see 見 SAY[1] (USAGE) | **get talking** (=start having a conversation) 開始交談 *Once they got talking nothing could stop them.* 他們一開始談起來, 便會沒完沒了。| **talk sport/politics etc** (=have a conversation about sport etc) 談論體育/政治等 *I can't stand it when you talk politics.* 你一談政治, 我就受不了。—see 見 SPEAK (USAGE)

2 ►SERIOUS SUBJECT 嚴肅話題◄ [I] to discuss something with someone, especially an important or serious subject 討論; 商談: *We need to talk before things get any worse.* 在事情變得更糟之前, 我們需要好好談一談。| **talk about/of** *Jenny and I have talked about getting married some day.* 我和珍妮已經談過了將來結婚的事。| **talk to** *I think I'm going to have to talk to a solicitor.* 我想我必須去跟律師討論一下。—see also 另見 **talk shop** (SHOP[1] (6))

3 ►SAY WORDS 説話◄ [I] to produce words in a language 説話: *Most babies start to talk by 18 months.* 大多數嬰兒最晚18個月大時開始説話。| *Who would ever believe that computers would be able to talk?* 誰會相信電腦居然會説話?

4 people will talk/people are talking *informal* used to emphasize that people will think you are doing something bad【非正式】人們會説閒話的/人們正在傳言: *Don't leave your car outside my house; people will talk.* 別把你的車停在我家外邊。人們會説閒話的。

5 ►SECRET INFORMATION 祕密情報◄ [I] to give someone important secret information because they force you to〔被迫〕説出內情, 吐露祕密; 招供: *Even after three days of interrogation, Maskell refused to talk.* 即使經過三天的審問, 馬斯凱爾仍然拒不開口。

6 not be talking *informal* if two people are not talking they refuse to talk to each other because they have argued【非正式】〔兩人因爭吵過而〕互不理睬: *It's been 3 weeks and they're still not talking.* 已經三週了, 他倆仍然互不理睬。

7 ►A SPEECH 演講◄ [I] to give a speech 演講; 談論: **talk on/about** *This morning Mrs Elliott will be talking about the best way to cultivate roses.* 今天上午, 愛略特夫人將介紹種植玫瑰花的最佳方法。

8 talk sense to give sensible opinions about things 説得有理: *He's a little old-fashioned but he talks a lot of sense.* 他的觀點有些陳舊, 但話都説得很有道理。

9 talk sense into to persuade someone to behave in a sensible way 以道理説服某人, 以理服人: *Will you see if you can talk some sense into him – he says he wants to join the army.* 你是否願意跟他談一談, 曉以利害 —— 他説他要參軍。

10 talk your way out of *informal* to escape from an unpleasant or embarrassing situation by giving explanations, excuses etc【非正式】依靠口才使〔自己〕擺脱困境: *I'd like to see you talk your way out of this one!* 我倒想看看你如何憑藉自己的口才擺脱這一困境!

11 talk the hind legs off a donkey *informal* to talk a lot, especially about unimportant things【非正式】嘮叨個沒完沒了

12 talk nineteen to the dozen *informal*【非正式】**talk a blue streak** *AmE*【美】to talk very quickly and without stopping 説話滔滔不絕, 口若懸河

13 talk turkey *informal AmE* to talk seriously about important things, especially in order to agree on something【非正式, 美】〔尤指為了達成某事〕嚴肅地商談: *"I'm ready to make a deal." "OK. Let's talk turkey."* "我是有意達成交易的。""好的, 我們認真談談。"

14 talking point a subject, problem, piece of news etc that many people are interested in〔很多人感興趣的〕話題, 論題

15 talk dirty *informal* to talk in a sexual way to someone in order to make them feel sexually excited【非正式】説下流話〔以使某人性興奮〕

16 talk tough *informal* to tell people very strongly what you want from them【非正式】説話口氣強硬

17 be talking through your hat *informal* to say silly or stupid things about something that you think you know a lot about【非正式】信口開河, 胡説八道

Frequencies of the verb **talk** in spoken and written English 動詞talk在英語口語和書面語中的使用頻率

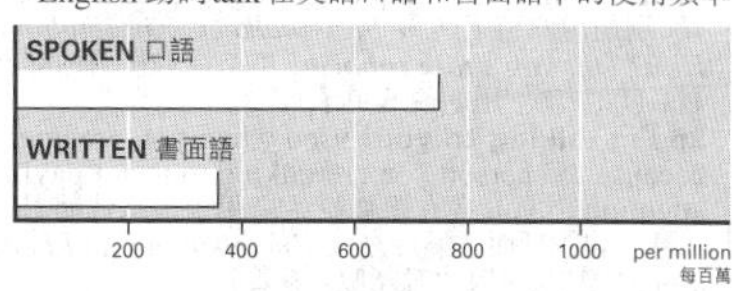

Based on the British National Corpus and the Longman Lancaster Corpus
據英國國家語料庫和朗文蘭卡斯特語料庫

This graph shows that the verb **talk** is much more common in spoken English than in written English. This is because it is used in a lot of common spoken phrases.
本圖表顯示, 動詞talk在英語口語中的使用頻率遠遠高於書面語, 因為口語中很多常用片語是由talk構成的。

T

talk (*v*) SPOKEN PHRASES
含 talk 的口語片語

18 what are you talking about? a) used when the person you are talking to has just said something stupid or annoying 你(們)在說些甚麼?〔用來指對方說的話顯得愚蠢或令人惱怒〕: *"I'm sorry – I didn't do the report because my cat hurt his paw." "What on earth are you talking about?"* "對不起, 我沒有準備好那份報告, 因為我的貓傷了爪子。" "你到底在說些甚麼?" **b)** used to ask someone what their conversation is about 你(們)在說些甚麼?〔用來問對方談論的話題〕

19 know what you are talking about to know a lot about a particular subject 對某一方面很了解, 是行家: *I worked in hotels for years, so I know what I'm talking about.* 我在酒店工作過多年, 所以我對這一行很了解。

20 talk about rich/funny/stupid etc used to emphasize that the person or thing you are talking about is very rich, funny, stupid etc 說到富有/可笑/愚蠢等〔用來強調所談論的人或物很富有、可笑、愚蠢等〕: *Talk about luck! That's the second competition he's won in a week!* 說到運氣! 這可是一週內他贏的第二次比賽!

21 talking of/about used to say more about a subject that someone has just mentioned 談到, 論及〔用來承接剛才的話題〕: *Talking of Venice, have you seen the masks I bought there last year?* 談到威尼斯, 你見過我去年在那兒買的那些面具嗎?

22 now you're talking used when you think someone's suggestion is a very good idea 你這話說得對了! 太對了! 正合我意!: *"We could go for a pizza instead." "Now you're talking."* "我們可以改吃比薩餅。" "正合我意!"

23 look who's talking/you're a fine one to talk/you can talk used to tell someone they should not criticize someone else because they are just as bad 虧你有臉說別人〔意即你沒資格批評別人, 你同別人一樣糟糕〕: *"Peggy shouldn't smoke so much." "Look who's talking!"* "佩吉不應該抽那麼多煙。" "你還有臉說別人!"

24 we're/you're talking (about) a) used to tell someone what will be necessary in order to do or get what they are asking you about 我們/你們需要〔用來告知對方為了滿足要求需要付出…〕: *If you want the job done properly you're talking £10,000 at least.* 如果你想妥善處理此事, 你至少需要付出 10,000 英鎊。**b)** used to explain something about a person or thing that is being discussed 我們/你們正在談論的是…〔用來解釋正在討論中的某人或某事〕: *Don't forget, we're talking about a country where millions are starving.* 別忘了, 我們正在談論的是一個有幾百萬人在挨餓的國家。

25 don't talk rubbish/nonsense/crap etc *especially BrE* used to tell someone that what they are saying is silly and completely wrong【尤英】別說傻話, 別胡說八道了: *The best goalkeeper in England! Him? Oh, don't talk rubbish!* 英格蘭最優秀的守門員! 就他? 噢, 別胡說八道了!

26 I'm talking to you! used when you are angry because the person you are talking to is not paying attention to you 我在跟你說話!〔用來表示你因對方未注意你說話而生氣〕: *Hey! I'm talking to you! Look at me!* 嘿! 我在跟你說話呢! 看着我!

talk around *phr v* [T] **1** [**talk** sb ↔ **around**] to persuade someone to change their opinion and agree with you 說服〔某人〕改變主意: *Leave Betty to me. I'll soon talk her around.* 把貝蒂交給我吧。我會很快讓她改變主意的。**2 talk around sth** to discuss a problem without really dealing with the important parts of it 不着邊際地談; 不得要領地談

talk back *phr v* [I] to answer someone rudely after they have criticized you or told you to do something 回嘴, 頂嘴: *I'd never let a child of mine talk back to me like that!* 我絕不允許我的孩子這樣跟我頂嘴!

talk sb/sth ↔ **down** *phr v* [T] **1** to give instructions on a radio to a PILOT[1] (1) so that they can bring an aircraft safely to the ground〔通過無線電跟飛行員通話以〕引導〔飛機〕安全着陸 **2** to make something that is successful or good seem worse than it really is 以言辭貶損; 貶低…: *It's just like the Labour Party to talk down the achievements of the health service reforms.* 這就像工黨喜歡貶低健康保健改革的成就一樣。**3** to persuade someone to come down from a high place when they are threatening to jump and kill themselves 說服〔想從高處跳下自殺的人〕下來

talk down to sb *phr v* [T] to talk to someone as if they were stupid when in fact they are not; PATRONIZE 以高人一等的口氣對〔某人〕說話: *You have to realize that kids aren't stupid; they know when they're being talked down to.* 你必須注意到孩子們並不傻; 他們知道甚麼時候你在用居高臨下的口氣跟他們講話。

talk sb **into** sth *phr v* [T] to persuade someone to do something 說服〔某人〕做〔某事〕: *She didn't want to come, but I talked her into it.* 她並不想來, 不過我把她說服了。| **talk sb into doing sth** *Try to talk Liz into buying a ticket.* 盡量說服莉茲買一張票吧。

talk sth ↔ **out** *phr v* [T] *informal* to talk about a problem in order to solve it【非正式】通過商談解決〔問題〕: *We need to spend a little time talking it out.* 我們需要花點時間談談, 以解決這件事。

talk sb **out of** sth *phr v* [T] *informal* to persuade someone not to do something【非正式】說服〔某人〕不去做〔某事〕: *Stuart was threatening legal action but I think his sister talked him out of it.* 斯圖爾特威脅說採取法律行動, 不過我想他姐姐已說服他不這樣做了。| **talk sb out of doing sth** *Can't you talk them out of selling the house?* 難道你不能說服他們不要賣掉那幢房子?

talk sth ↔ **over** *phr v* [T] to discuss a problem or situation with someone before you decide what to do〔在作出決定前與某人〕商量, 討論: *Don't worry, we have plenty of time to talk it over.* 別擔心, 我們有足夠的時間好好商量一下。| **[+with]** *Well obviously I wanted to talk it over with you first.* 當然啦, 我首先要與你就此事認真地談一談。

talk sth ↔ **through** *phr v* [T] to discuss all of something so that you are sure you understand it 把〔某事〕徹底說清楚: *I think we really need to talk this one through – there are so many things that could go wrong.* 我想我們真的有必要把這件事情說說清楚 —— 可能出錯的地方有許多。

talk² *n* S1 W1

1 ►CONVERSATION 交談◄ [C] a conversation 交談: **[+with/about]** *After a long talk, we decided to stop seeing each other.* 經過一次長談之後, 我們決定不再見面。| **have a talk** *Listen John, you're going to have a talk with Marty.* 聽着, 約翰, 你必須跟馬蒂談一談。

2 ►A SPEECH 講話◄ [C+about/on] a speech or LECTURE[1] (1) 講話, 演講; 講座, 報告: *a series of talks about literary theory* 關於文學理論的系列講座 | **give a talk** *Dr. Howard is giving a talk on homeopathy today.* 霍華德博士今天要作一次關於順勢療法的報告。

3 ►DISCUSSION 討論◄ talks [plural] formally organized discussions between governments, organizations etc〔政府、機構等之間的〕正式會談; 談判: *Peace talks* 和平談判 | *Talks with the rebels have failed yet again.* 與叛軍的談判再次破裂了。

4 ►TYPE OF CONVERSATION 說話的方式◄ [U] type of conversation 說話的方式: *Some people would say that kind of talk was treason!* 有些人會說, 那種講話的口吻簡直就是叛國! | **girls' talk/football talk/fighting talk etc** *All this football talk bores me stiff!* 全是足球行話, 煩死我啦!

5 be all talk *spoken* to always be talking about what you have done or what you are going to do without ever actually doing anything【口】說空話, 空談: *Don't be scared of Jake. He's all talk!* 別害怕傑克, 他全是放空砲!
6 be the talk of the town/company etc to be the person or thing that everyone is talking about because they are very interested, excited, shocked etc 街談巷議的話題; 眾人的談資: *Tim's been the talk of the department since his affair with Janice.* 蒂姆自從和賈尼絲有了曖昧關係之後, 成了整個部門的談資。
7 just talk/only talk *informal* a story, claim etc that is just talk or only talk is very likely to be untrue【非正式】閒話; 流言蜚語: *Everyone says he was a spy but if you ask me it's just talk.* 人人都說他曾當過間諜, 但如果要我說的話, 那不過是流言蜚語。
8 there's talk of used to say that a lot of people are talking about something that might happen in the future 有...的傳聞[傳言]: *There's talk of more factory closures in the area.* 有傳言說本地區有更多的工廠將關閉。—see also 另見 SMALL TALK, SWEET-TALK

talk·a·tive /ˈtɔlkətɪv; ˈtɔːkətɪv/ *adj* liking to talk a lot 愛說話的, 健談的, 多嘴的 —**talkativeness** *n* [U]

talk·er /ˈtɔkɚ; ˈtɔːkə/ *n* [C] *informal* someone who talks a lot or talks in a particular way【非正式】健談的人; 以某種方式說話的人: *What a talker that man is!* 那傢伙真是一個會講話的人! | *We need a persuasive talker and a good organizer.* 我們需要一個會做說服工作的人和一個優秀的組織者。

talk·ie /ˈtɔkɪ; ˈtɔːki/ *n* [C] *old-fashioned* a cinema film with sounds and words【過時】有聲電影 —see 另見 SILENT (4)

talking book /ˌ·· ˈ·/ *n* [C] a book that has been recorded for blind people to listen to〔供盲人使用的〕有聲讀物

talking head /ˌ·· ˈ·/ *n* [C] *informal* someone on television who talks directly to the camera, for example when reading the news【非正式】〔出現在電視屏幕上面對攝像機〕說話的人〈例如新聞播音員〉

talking-to /ˈ·· ·/ *n* **give sb a talking-to** *informal* to talk to someone angrily because you are annoyed about something they have done【非正式】申斥, 責罵; 給〔某人〕一頓教訓: *If you ask me, what that girl needs is a good talking-to.* 要是問我的話, 那姑娘需要狠狠地訓一頓。

talk show /ˈ· ·/ *n* [C] *AmE* a radio or television show on which famous people talk to each other and are asked questions【美】〔廣播或電視上的〕名人訪談節目, 脫口秀; CHAT SHOW *BrE*【英】

2 2 **tall** /tɔl; tɔːl/ *adj* **1** a person, building, tree etc that is tall has a greater than average height〔人、樓、樹等〕高於一般的; 高大的: **6 ft/2 metres etc tall** *I'm only five feet tall.* 我只有五英尺高。—see 見 HIGH[1] (USAGE) —see picture at 參見 HIGH[1] 圖 **2** *AmE* a tall drink has a small amount of alcohol mixed with a large amount of a non-alcoholic drink and is served in a tall glass【美】〔含少量酒精的飲料〕高腳杯的; 一大杯的 **3 be a tall order** *informal* if a request or piece of work is a tall order, it will be almost impossible for you to do【非正式】極難辦成的; 很難做到的: *Fixed by Monday? That's a tall order.* 星期一之前修好? 那可很難辦到。**4 tall story** *BrE*【英】, **tall tale** *AmE*【美】a story that is difficult to believe, because it makes events seem more exciting, dangerous etc than they really were 荒誕的故事; 難以置信的事: *Jim was full of tall stories about his travels.* 吉姆愛說旅行中碰見的荒誕不經的事。—see also 另見 **stand tall** (STAND[1] (32)), **walk tall** (WALK[1] (9)) —**tallness** *n* [U]

tall·boy /ˈtɔlˌbɔɪ; ˈtɔːlbɔɪ/ *n* [C] *BrE* a tall piece of wooden furniture containing several drawers【英】〔帶有好幾層抽屜的〕高腳櫥櫃; HIGHBOY *AmE*【美】

tal·low /ˈtælo; ˈtæləʊ/ *n* [U] hard animal fat used for making CANDLES〔用於製造蠟燭的〕硬動物脂肪

tal·ly[1] /ˈtælɪ; ˈtæli/ *n plural* **tallies** [C] **1** a record of how much you have spent, won, obtained etc so far〔花費的〕賬目;〔比賽等活動中贏得的〕積分, 得分: *England's tally at the moment is 15 points.* 英格蘭隊目前的積分是15分。| **keep a tally** (=write down or remember) 記錄〔賬單等〕**2** a special stick that was used in the past to show an amount of money owed, a quantity of goods delivered etc〔舊時用來記錄欠款、交貨數量等的〕記事木籤, 符木

tally[2] *v* **tallied, tallying 1** [I] if numbers or statements tally, they match each other exactly 符合; (完全) 吻合: *If the figures don't quite tally you might be missing an invoice.* 如果數目不完全吻合, 可能是你遺漏了一張發票。| **tally with** *Your account of the accident doesn't tally with the facts.* 你對這次事故的描述與事實不完全一致。**2** also 又作 **tally up** [T] to calculate the total number of points won, things done etc 計算〔得分、總數等〕

Tal·mud /ˈtælmud; ˈtælmʊd/ *n* **the Talmud** the collection of writings that make up Jewish law about religious and non-religious life 塔木德經〔規範猶太人宗教及世俗生活的法典〕

tal·on /ˈtælən; ˈtælən/ *n* [C] a sharp powerful curved nail on the feet of some birds that catch animals for food〔某些鳥強有力的〕利爪

tam·a·rind /ˈtæməˌrɪnd; ˈtæmərɪ̀nd/ *n* [C] a tropical tree, or the fruit of this tree 羅望子〔一種熱帶樹木〕; 羅望子的果實

tam·bour /ˈtæmbur; ˈtæmbʊə/ *n* [C] a circular wooden frame used to hold cloth firmly in place while patterns are being sewn (SEW) on to it; EMBROIDERY HOOP〔刺繡用的〕繃圈, 圓形繃架

tam·bou·rine /ˌtæmbəˈrin; ˌtæmbəˈriːn/ *n* [C] a circular musical instrument with small pieces of metal around the edge that makes a sound when you shake it〔鼓邊四周裝有小金屬片, 一搖發出聲響的〕鈴鼓

tame[1] /tem; teɪm/ *adj* **1** *informal* boring or unexciting and disappointing【非正式】平淡的; 枯燥乏味的; 令人失望的: *After all that hype, the film was a bit tame.* 經過鋪天蓋地的一陣宣傳, 那部電影還是怪沒勁的。**2** an animal that is tame has been trained to live with people〔動物〕馴服的; 由人馴養的 —**tamely** *adv* —**tameness** *n* [U]

tame[2] *v* [T] **1** to reduce the power or strength of something and prevent it from causing trouble 制服, 控制; 駕馭: *Over the years, a series of dams has tamed the might of the Colorado river.* 多年來通過一系列大壩的修建, 把科羅拉多河的兇猛給制服了。**2** to train a wild animal to obey you and not to attack people 馴服〔野生動物〕, 使馴化 —compare 比較 DOMESTICATE

tam-o'-shan·ter /ˌtæm əˈʃæntɚ; ˌtæm əˈʃæntə/ also 又作 **tam·my** /ˈtæmɪ; ˈtæmi/ *n* [C] a Scottish cap, usually made of wool, with a POMPOM (=small wool ball) in the centre 蘇格蘭式便帽〔一般用羊毛製成, 帽頂中央有一小絨球〕

tamp /tæmp; tæmp/ *v* [T always+adv/prep] also 又作 **tamp down** to press or push something down by lightly hitting it several times 壓實; 拍打...使堅實: *"Ah well," sighed Papa, absently tamping the tobacco down in his pipe.* "噢, 是的。" 爸爸一邊嘆氣, 一邊心不在焉地把煙斗裡的煙葉裝實。

Tam·pax /ˈtæmpæks; ˈtæmpæks/ *n plural* **Tampax** [C] *trademark* the name of a very common type of TAMPON【商標】丹碧絲〔一種常用的月經棉塞〕

tam·per /ˈtæmpɚ; ˈtæmpə/ *v*
tamper with sth *phr v* [T] to touch something or make changes to it without permission, especially in order to deliberately damage it 胡亂擺弄; 擅自篡改; 故意損壞: *How likely is it that the drugs could have been tampered with?* 藥品的成分被人擅自改變, 有多大可能呢? | *They just don't see the point in tampering with a system that's worked fine so far.* 他們不理解為甚麼要去破壞一套迄今一直運行不錯的系統。

tamper-ev·i·dent /ˈ·· ˌ···/ *adj BrE* a package or container that is tamper-evident is made so that you can see if someone has opened it before it is sold in the shops【英】商品包裝拆封後易於被識別的; TAMPER-RESISTANT *AmE*【美】

tamper-proof /ˈ·· ·/ *adj* a package or container that is tamper-proof is made in a way that prevents someone opening it before it is sold〔商品包裝〕防拆封的, 防撕扯封條的

tamper-re·sist·ant /ˈ·· ·ˌ··/ *adj AmE* TAMPER-EVIDENT【美】商品包裝拆封後易於被識別的

tam·pon /ˈtæmpɑn; ˈtæmpɒn/ *n* [C] a tube-shaped mass of cotton or similar material that a woman puts inside her VAGINA during her PERIOD〔婦女用的〕月經棉塞

tan¹ /tæn; tæn/ *v* **tanned, tanning 1** [I] if you tan, your skin becomes darker because you spend time in the sun〔皮膚〕曬黑: *People with fair skin usually don't tan very easily.* 皮膚白皙的人通常不容易曬得很黑。**2** [T] if the sun tans you, it makes your skin become darker 使曬黑〔皮膚〕**3** [T] to make animal skin into leather by treating it with TANNIN (=a kind of acid) 用鞣酸將〔獸皮〕製成皮革 **4 tan sb's hide** *old-fashioned* to hit someone a lot, as a punishment【過時】把某人狠揍一頓 **—tan** *adj AmE*【美】: *Did you see Lizzie? She's so tan!* 你看到利齊了嗎? 她曬得真黑!

tan² *n* **1** [U] a light yellowish brown colour 棕黃色, 黃褐色: *tan shoes* 棕黃色的鞋 —see picture on page A5 參見 A5 頁圖 **2** [C] the brown colour that someone with pale skin gets after they have been in the sun; SUNTAN〔被太陽曬成的〕棕褐色膚色: *I wish I could get a tan like that.* 但願我能曬成那樣的棕褐色膚色。**3** [C] an abbreviation of 縮寫= TANGENT (3)

tan·dem /ˈtændəm; ˈtændəm/ *n* [C] **1** a bicycle built for two riders sitting one behind the other〔兩人一前一後同騎的〕雙人自行車 **2 in tandem with** happening at the same time 同時發生: *Hastings' appointment in tandem with McDougan's should improve our sales expertise.* 哈斯汀和麥克道根的同時就任應該使我們的銷售水平得到提高。**3 work in tandem with** to work together with someone to get the best results 與〔某人〕協同工作, 聯合工作

tan·doo·ri /tɑnˋdurɪ; tænˈdʊəri/ *n* [U] a northern Indian method of cooking in a large closed clay pot 唐杜里烹飪法〔印度北部用密封大陶罐烹調的一種方法〕

tang /tæŋ; tæŋ/ *n* [singular] a strong sharp taste or smell 強烈刺鼻的味道: *the salty tang of the sea air* 帶強烈鹹味的海上空氣 **—tangy** *adj*: *tangy oranges* 味道濃烈的橙子

tan·gent /ˈtændʒənt; ˈtændʒənt/ *n* [C] **1 go/fly off at a tangent** *informal* to suddenly start thinking or talking about a completely new and different subject【非正式】突然離開原來的思路; 突然離題: *It's impossible to have a logical discussion with Rob because he keeps going off at a tangent.* 不可能跟羅布進行一次合乎邏輯的討論, 因為他老是不斷地突然離題。**2** *technical* a straight line that touches the outside of a curve but does not cut across it【術語】切線 **3** *technical* the FRACTION (2) calculated for an angle by dividing the length of the side that would be opposite it in a TRIANGLE with a RIGHT-ANGLE by the length of the side that would be next to it【術語】〔三角學中的〕正切 —compare 比較 COSINE, SINE

tan·gen·tial /tænˋdʒɛnʃəl; tænˈdʒenʃəl/ *adj* **1** *formal* tangential information, comments etc are only indirectly related to a particular subject【正式】〔情況、評論等〕不直接相干的; 略為觸及〔主題〕的 **2** *formal* tangential lines, roads etc move or go out in different directions; DIVERGENT【正式】〔線條, 道路等〕漫射開來的, 朝不同方向的, 分岔的 **3** *technical* like a tangent【術語】(像)切線的 **—tangentially** *adv*

tan·ge·rine /ˈtændʒəˌrin; ˌtændʒəˈriːn/ *n* [C] a small sweet fruit like an orange with a skin that comes off easily 橘子

tan·gi·ble /ˈtæŋdʒəbl̩; ˈtændʒɪbəl/ *adj* **1 tangible proof/results/benefits etc** proof, results, advantages etc that are easy to see so that there is no doubt 確鑿的證據/明顯的結果/實在的利益等: *Welfare reform has not yet brought any tangible benefits.* 福利改革還沒有帶來任何實在的好處。—opposite 反義詞 INTANGIBLE **2** *formal* able to be felt by touch【正式】可觸摸的, 可觸知的; 有形的 **—tangibly** *adv* **—tangibility** /ˌtændʒəˋbɪlətɪ; ˌtændʒɪˈbɪlɪti/ *n* [U]

tan·gle¹ /ˈtæŋgl; ˈtæŋgəl/ *v* [I,T] to become twisted together or make something become twisted together in an untidy mass (使)纏結在一起; (使)亂成一團: *My hair tangles easily.* 我的頭髮很容易纏在一起。| **tangle sth** *Somebody's tangled all these cables under my computer.* 有人把我電腦下面的線搞得亂成一團。

tangle with sb *phr v* [T] *informal* to argue or fight with someone【非正式】和…爭吵[打架]: *I wouldn't tangle with him if I were you.* 如果我是你的話, 是不會跟他爭吵的。

tangle² *n* [C] **1** a twisted mass of something such as hair or thread〔頭髮、線等的〕纏結, 糾結, 亂成一團: *Her hair was full of tangles after being out in the wind.* 在外面吹了風之後, 她的頭髮變得亂糟糟的。| **tangle of branches/weeds/threads etc** *We had to cut our way through a tangle of branches.* 我們不得不砍掉纏在一起的樹枝來開路前進。**2** a confused state 亂成一團, 紛亂, 混亂: *My emotions were in a complete tangle.* 我的情緒完全亂成一團了。**3** *informal* [+with] a quarrel or fight【非正式】爭吵; 打架

tan·gled /ˈtæŋgld; ˈtæŋgəld/ also 又作 **tangled up** *adj* **1** twisted together in an untidy mass 糾結的; 纏繞在一起的: *The telephone cord is all tangled up.* 電話線全纏在一起了。**2** complicated or made up of many confusing parts 複雜的; 混亂的; 亂糟糟的: *What she needed was time to sort out her tangled feelings.* 她需要時間來整理一下紛亂的心情。

tan·go¹ /ˈtæŋgo; ˈtæŋgəʊ/ *n plural* **tangos** [C] a lively dance from South America, or a piece of music for this dance 探戈舞; 探戈舞曲

tango² *v* [I] **1** to dance the tango 跳探戈舞 **2 it takes two to tango** *spoken* used to say that if a problem involves two people then both people are equally responsible【口】探戈舞得兩個人跳; 一個巴掌拍不響

tank¹ /tæŋk; tæŋk/ *n* [C] **1** a large container for storing liquid or gas〔盛放液體或氣體的〕大容器: *The hot water tank is leaking.* 熱水箱在漏水。| **fish tank** (=for keeping fish in) 魚缸 | **petrol tank** *BrE*【英】**/gas tank** *AmE*【美】(=part of a vehicle for holding petrol〔汽車的〕油箱 **2** also 又作 **tankful** the amount of liquid or gas held in a tank〔液體或氣體〕滿滿一箱的容量: *I'll do over 400 miles on a full tank.* 有滿滿一箱的油, 我可以跑四百多英里。**3** a heavy military vehicle that has a large gun and runs on two metal belts fitted over its wheels 坦克(車) **4** a large artificial pool for storing water 人工大蓄水池 —see also 另見 THINK-TANK, SEPTIC TANK

tank² *v*

tank up *phr v* [I] *especially AmE* to put petrol in your car so that the tank is full【尤美】〔給汽車〕加滿汽油

tan·kard /ˈtæŋkəd; ˈtæŋkəd/ *n* [C] a large metal cup, usually with a handle and lid, used for drinking beer〔通常有把手和杯蓋的〕大金屬啤酒杯 —see picture at 參見 CUP 圖

tanked up /ˌ· ˈ·/ also 又作 **tanked** /tæŋkt; tæŋkt/ *AmE*【美】*adj* [not before noun 不用於名詞前] *slang* drunk【俚】喝醉的: *Jim gets really funny when he's tanked.* 吉姆喝醉的時候真是滑稽可笑。

tank·er /ˈtæŋkə; ˈtæŋkə/ *n* [C] a vehicle or ship specially built to carry large quantities of gas or liquid, especially oil 油船, 油輪; 油罐車 —see also 另見 OIL TANKER

tank top /ˈ· ·/ *n* [C] **1** *BrE* a piece of clothing like a SWEATER but with no sleeves (SLEEVE (1))【英】〔像無袖套頭毛衣的〕緊身短背心 **2** *AmE* a piece of clothing like a shirt but with no sleeves (SLEEVE (1))【美】〔無袖〕運動背心

tanned /tænd; tænd/ *adj* having a darker skin colour because you have been in the sun〔皮膚〕被曬黑的 —see picture on page A6 參見A6頁圖

tan·ner /ˈtænɚ; ˈtænə/ *n* [C] **1** someone whose job is to make animal skin into leather by tanning (TAN¹ (3)) 鞣皮工, 製革工 **2** *BrE old use* SIXPENCE (=a coin)【英舊】六便士硬幣

tan·ne·ry /ˈtænərɪ; ˈtænəri/ *n* [C] a place where animal skin is made into leather by tanning (TAN¹ (3)) 鞣皮廠, 製革廠

tan·nin /ˈtænɪn; ˈtænɪ̣n/ also 又作 **tan·nic acid** /ˌtænɪk ˈæsɪd; ˌtænɪk ˈæsɪ̣d/ *n* [U] a reddish acid used in preparing leather, making ink etc 丹寧(酸), 鞣酸〔用於製革、製造墨水等〕

tan·noy /ˈtænɔɪ; ˈtænɔɪ/ *n* [C] *BrE trademark* a system for giving out information in public places by means of LOUDSPEAKERS【英, 商標】坦諾伊播音設備〔一種以擴音器向公眾發佈消息的播音設備〕: **over the tannoy** *What were they saying about flight delays over the tannoy?* 他們在廣播裡就航班延誤的事說了些甚麼?

tan·ta·lize also 又作 **-ise** *BrE*【英】/ˈtæntḷˌaɪz; ˈtæntəl-ˌaɪz/ *v* [T usually passive 一般用被動態] to show or promise something that someone really wants, but then not allow them to have it 使〔某人〕因想要卻得不到而乾着急; 逗引; 撩撥

tan·ta·liz·ing also 又作 **tantalising** *BrE*【英】/ˈtæntḷˌaɪzɪŋ; ˈtæntəl-aɪzɪŋ/ *adj* making you feel a strong desire to have something that you cannot have 逗引人的; 撩撥人的: *The tantalizing smell of warm bread wafted out of the shop.* 熱麵包誘人的味道從店裡飄出。—**tantalizingly** *adv*

tan·ta·lus /ˈtæntḷəs; ˈtæntəl-əs/ *n* [C] a case in which bottles of alcoholic drink can be locked up in such a way that they can be seen 上鎖透明酒櫃

tan·ta·mount /ˈtæntəˌmaunt; ˈtæntəmaʊnt/ *adj* **be tantamount to sth** if an action, suggestion, plan etc is tantamount to something, it is almost the same thing as it〔行動、建議、計劃幾乎〕等於某事, 相當於某事: *But that's tantamount to saying poor people are criminals!* 不過, 那等於是說窮人就是罪犯!

tan·trum /ˈtæntrəm; ˈtæntrəm/ *n* [C] a sudden moment of unreasonable bad temper and anger〔突然無理的〕脾氣發作: **have/throw a tantrum** *Some kid threw a tantrum in the middle of the store.* 有個孩子在商店裡大發脾氣。

Tao /tau; taʊ/ *n* [U] the natural force that unites all things in the universe, according to Taoism〔道家學說中的〕道

Taoi·seach /ˈtiʃək; ˈtiːʃək/ *n* **the Taoiseach** the title of the PRIME MINISTER of the Republic of Ireland〔愛爾蘭共和國的〕總理

Tao·is·m /ˈtauɪzəm; ˈtaʊɪzəm/ *n* [U] a way of thought developed in ancient China, based on the writings of Lao Tzu, emphasizing a natural and simple way of life 道家學說, 道教

3 **tap¹** /tæp; tæp/ *n*

1 ▶WATER/GAS 水/煤氣◀ [C] a piece of equipment for controlling the flow of water, gas etc from a pipe or container〔水、煤氣等管道或容器的〕龍頭, 閥門; FAUCET *AmE*【美】: **turn on the tap** (=so that water comes out of it) 打開(水)龍頭 *Carla, don't leave the taps running!* 卡拉, 別讓水龍頭開着空流! | **tap water** *In some countries, the tap water isn't safe enough to drink.* 在某些國家自來水不夠清潔, 不能直接飲用。| **cold/hot tap** (=the tap that cold or hot water comes from) 冷水龍頭/熱水龍頭 —see picture on page A10 參見A10頁圖

2 ▶BARREL 桶◀ [C] a specially shaped object used for letting liquid out of a BARREL¹ (1)〔桶的〕塞子

3 ▶A LIGHT HIT 輕輕的敲擊◀ [C] an act of hitting something lightly, especially to get someone's attention〔尤指為了引起某人注意而對某物的〕輕輕敲擊, 輕叩, 輕拍: **[+at/on]** *There was a tap at the door.* 有人輕輕地敲了一下門。| *Suddenly, I felt a tap on my shoulder and turned round to see Sheila there.* 突然, 我感覺到有人在我肩膀上輕輕拍了一下, 我轉過身一看是希拉。

4 on tap a) *informal* something that is on tap is ready to use when you need it【非正式】可隨時取用[使用]的: *We've got a lot of experts on tap to advise us.* 我們有很多專家可以隨時向我們提供諮詢。**b)** beer that is on tap comes from a BARREL¹ (1)〔桶裝啤酒〕可隨時旋開旋塞供飲用的

5 ▶DANCING 跳舞◀ also 又作 **tap dancing** [U] dancing in which you wear special shoes with pieces of metal on the bottom which make a loud sharp sound on the floor 踢踏舞

6 ▶TELEPHONE 電話◀ [C] an act of secretly listening to someone's telephone, using electronic equipment 電話竊聽

7 ▶TUNE 樂調◀ taps a song or tune played on the BUGLE at night in an army camp, and at military funerals〔軍營裡的〕熄燈號;〔軍隊的〕葬禮號

tap² *v* **tapped, tapping** 3

1 ▶HAND OR FOOT 手或腳◀ [I,T] to hit your hand or foot lightly against something, especially to get someone's attention or without thinking about it〔用手或腳〕輕敲, 輕叩, 輕拍: *She tapped her feet in time to the music.* 她和着音樂用腳輕敲着節拍。| **tap sth on/against etc** *He sat tapping his fingers on the arm of the chair.* 他坐着, 手指輕輕敲着椅子的扶手。| **[+on]** *I went up and tapped on the window.* 我走上前去, 輕輕叩了一下窗戶。| **tap sb on the arm/shoulder etc** *"Hey Paul," she said, tapping him on the shoulder.* "嘿, 保羅。"她一邊說着, 一邊拍了拍他的肩膀。—compare 比較 KNOCK¹ —see picture on page A20 參見A20頁圖

2 ▶ENERGY 能源◀ also 又作 **tap into** [T] to use or take what is needed from an energy supply or power supply 發掘, 開發〔能源或電力〕: *We have enormous reserves of oil still waiting to be tapped.* 我們有儲量巨大的石油有待開發。

3 ▶IDEAS 思想◀ [T] also 又作 **tap into** to make as much use as possible of the ideas, experience, knowledge etc that a group of people has 利用, 採用〔思想、經驗、知識等〕: *Honestly, we have a vast pool of practical experience, just waiting to be tapped.* 老實說, 我們有大量的實際經驗有待利用。

4 ▶TELEPHONE 電話◀ [T] to listen secretly to someone's telephone by using a special piece of electronic equipment 電話竊聽

5 ▶TREE 樹木◀ [T] to get liquid from the TRUNK of a tree by making a hole in it 在〔樹幹〕上鑿孔以取其液汁: *tapping rubber trees* 割開橡膠樹皮取膠乳

6 tap sb for sth *BrE informal* to get money from someone【英, 非正式】從某人處弄到錢: *Joey tapped me for a fiver.* 喬伊從我這兒弄走五英鎊。

tap sth ↔ **in** *phr v* [T] to put information, numbers etc into a computer, telephone etc by pressing buttons or keys 把〔信息、數據等〕敲入[鍵入, 輸入]〔電腦、電話等〕: *Tap in your password before you log on.* 登錄前請先輸入密碼。

tap·as /ˈtɑpəs; ˈtæpəs/ *n* [plural] small dishes of food eaten as part of the first course of a Spanish meal〔一種西班牙飯菜的〕餐前小吃

tap dan·cing /ˈ· ˌ··/ *n* [U] dancing in which you wear shoes with pieces of metal on the bottom, which make a sharp sound 踢踏舞 —**tap dance** *n* [C] —**tap dancer** *n* [C]

tape¹ /tep; teɪp/ *n* 3 3

1 ▶FOR RECORDING 用於錄製◀ a) [U] narrow plastic material covered with a special MAGNETIC substance, on which sounds, pictures, or computer information can be recorded and played〔可以錄音、錄像或錄製電腦信息的〕磁帶, 帶子: **on tape** (=recorded on tape) *We've got the film on tape.* 我們已把這部片子錄在帶子上了。| *I don't like the sound of my own voice on tape.* 我不喜歡

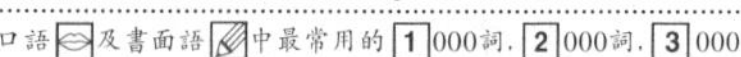

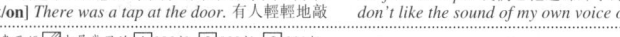

錄下來的我自己的聲音。**b)** [C] a special plastic box containing a length of tape that you can record sound on; CASSETTE（盒式）磁帶: *Turn the tape over when it's finished.* 磁帶放完時要翻一面。| *William lent me some of his Beatles tapes.* 威廉把他的一些"披頭四"音樂磁帶借給了我。| **blank tape** (=with nothing recorded on it) 空白磁帶 **c)** [C] a special plastic box containing a length of tape that you can record sound and pictures on; VIDEOTAPE（盒式）錄像帶: *Police have seized a number of magazines and tapes.* 警察繳獲了一些雜誌和錄像帶。
2 ►PIECE OF MUSIC/FILM 音樂帶子/影片帶子◄ [C] a recording of a performance, piece of music, speech etc on tape〔錄有演出、音樂、演講等的〕錄音帶: **[+of]** *I'd like a tape of the concert.* 我想要一盤音樂會的錄音帶。
3 ►STICKY MATERIAL 膠黏材料◄ [U] narrow length of sticky material used to stick things together 膠帶, 膠布; SELLOTAPE *BrE*【英】; SCOTCH TAPE *AmE*【美】: *a parcel fastened with tape* 用膠帶纏住的包裹
4 ►THIN PIECE OF MATERIAL 細長材料◄ [C,U] a long thin piece of material used for various purposes such as marking out an area of ground or to tie things together〔劃分地界或拴捆東西用的〕帶子, 線帶
5 the tape a string stretched out across the finishing line in a race and broken by the winner〔比賽終點衝刺的〕終點線
6 ►FOR MEASURING 用於測量◄ a TAPE MEASURE 捲尺 —see also 另見 RED TAPE

3 **tape[2]** *v*
1 ►RECORD STH 錄製某物◄ also 又作 **tape record** [I,T] to record sound or pictures onto a TAPE[1] (1)〔用磁帶〕錄音〔或錄像〕
2 ►FASTEN STH 拴緊某物◄ also 又作 **tape up** [T] to fasten a package, box etc with TAPE[1] (3)〔用膠帶〕拴住, 捆紮
3 ►STICK STH 黏連某物◄ [T] to stick something onto something else using TAPE[1] (3) 用〔膠布〕黏貼: *He had a picture of his girlfriend taped to the inside of his locker door.* 他把一張女朋友的相片貼在上鎖櫃門的內側。
4 ►INJURY 傷口◄ also 又作 **tape up** [T usually passive 一般用被動態] *especially AmE* to tie a BANDAGE[1] firmly around an injured part of someone's body【尤美】用〔繃帶〕包紮〔受傷部位〕; STRAP[2] (2) *BrE*【英】: *We've got a nurse to tape that up for you.* 我們找了一名護士來為你包紮傷口。
5 have sth/sb taped *BrE informal* to understand someone or something completely and have learned how to deal with them【英, 非正式】摸清某人/某事的底細: *You can't fool Liz – she's got you taped.* 你騙不了莉茲——她摸清了你的老底。

tape deck /ˈ· ·/ *n* [C] the part of a TAPE RECORDER that winds the tape, and records and plays back sound〔錄音機的〕錄音座

tape drive /ˈ· ·/ *n* [C] a small machine attached to a computer that passes information from a computer to a tape or from a tape to a computer〔電腦上的〕磁帶驅動器

tape mea·sure /ˈ· ˌ··/ *n* [C] a long narrow band of cloth or steel, marked with centimetres, metres etc, used for measuring something〔測量用的〕捲尺, 鋼捲尺

ta·per[1] /ˈtepɚ; ˈteɪpə/ *v* [I,T] also 又作 **taper off** to become gradually narrower towards one end（使）一端逐漸變得細小: *The jeans taper towards the ankle.* 牛仔褲的褲管從上到腳踝逐漸變窄。
taper off *phr v* [I] to decrease gradually 逐漸變少; 逐漸減弱: *Interest in the scandal seems to be tapering off.* 人們對那件醜聞的興趣似乎越來越小了。—**tapering** *adj*: *long tapering fingers* 細長的手指

taper[2] *n* [C] **1** [usually singular 一般用單數] a gradual decrease in the width of a long object〔長形物體的〕逐漸變細[變窄] **2** a very thin CANDLE 細蠟燭 **3** a piece of string covered in WAX[1] (1), used for lighting lamps and CANDLES〔點燈火和點蠟燭用的〕火煤

tape re·cord /ˈ· ·ˌ·/ *v* [T] to record sound using a tape recorder〔用錄音機〕錄〔音〕

tape re·cord·er /ˈ· ·ˌ··/ *n* [C] a piece of electrical equipment that can record sound on tape and play it back 盒式磁帶錄音機

tape re·cord·ing /ˈ· ·ˌ··/ *n* [C] something that has been recorded with a tape recorder 磁帶錄音: *The court heard secretly obtained tape recordings of the meeting.* 法庭聽取了祕密獲得的會議錄音。

ta·pered /ˈtepɚd; ˈteɪpəd/ *adj* having a shape that gets narrower towards one end 一端逐漸變得尖細的; 錐形的: *tapered sleeves* 錐形袖

tap·es·try /ˈtæpɪstrɪ; ˈtæpəstri/ *n* [C,U] heavy cloth or a large piece of cloth on which coloured threads are woven to produce a picture, pattern etc 掛毯, 壁毯: *the Bayeux Tapestry*〔法國〕巴約掛毯

tape·worm /ˈtepˌwɝm; ˈteɪpwɜːm/ *n* [C] a long flat PARASITE that lives in the bowels (BOWEL (1)) of humans and other animals 絛蟲〔腸內的一種寄生蟲〕

tap·i·o·ca /ˌtæpɪˈokə; ˌtæpiˈəʊkə/ *n* [U] small hard white grains made from the crushed dried roots of CASSAVA, used especially for making sweet dishes〔製作甜點心用的〕木薯澱粉(顆粒)

ta·pir /ˈtepɚ; ˈteɪpə/ *n* [C] an animal like a pig with thick legs, a short tail, and long nose, that lives in tropical America and Southeast Asia 貘〔一種像豬的動物, 腿粗, 尾短, 鼻長, 生活於熱帶美洲和東南亞〕

tap·pet /ˈtæpɪt; ˈtæpət/ *n* [C] *technical* an engine part that moves up and down and makes another part of the engine move, open, close etc【術語】〔發動機內的〕挺桿, 推桿

tap·root /ˈtæpˌrut; ˈtæpruːt/ *n* [C] the main root of a plant, that grows straight down and produces smaller side roots〔植物的〕主根

tar[1] /tɑr; tɑː/ *n* [U] **1** a black substance, thick and sticky when hot but hard when cold, used especially for making road surfaces〔尤指用於鋪路的〕柏油; 瀝青 —see also 另見 COAL TAR **2** a sticky substance that is formed by burning tobacco〔煙草的〕煙鹼, 焦油: **high/low/medium tar** *high tar cigarettes* 焦油含量高的香煙

tar[2] *v* **tarred, tarring** [T] **1** to cover a surface with tar 用瀝青覆蓋〔路面〕**2 be/get tarred with the same brush** to be blamed for someone else's faults or crimes 被認為有同樣缺點, 被看作一路貨色 **3 tar and feather** to cover someone in tar and feathers as a cruel unofficial punishment 把〔某人〕渾身塗上柏油再黏上羽毛以作為一種非官方的殘酷懲罰

ta·ra·ma·sa·la·ta /ˌtærəməsəˈlɑtə; ˌtærəməsəˈlɑːtə/ *n* [U] a Greek food consisting of a pink mixture made from fish eggs 希臘紅魚子醬

tar·an·tel·la /ˌtærənˈtɛlə; ˌtærənˈtelə/ *n* [C] a fast Italian dance, or the music for this dance 塔蘭台拉舞〔一種意大利快步舞〕; 塔蘭台拉舞曲

ta·ran·tu·la /təˈræntʃələ; təˈræntjʊlə/ *n* [C] a large poisonous SPIDER from Southern Europe and tropical America 塔蘭托大蜘蛛〔南歐及熱帶美洲的一種有毒的大蜘蛛〕

tar·dy /ˈtɑrdɪ; ˈtɑːdi/ *adj formal*【正式】**1** done later than it should have been done 遲的, 晚了的: *We apologize for our tardy response to your letter.* 來函遲遲未覆, 謹表歉意。**2** acting or moving slowly; SLUGGISH 行動緩慢的; 拖沓的 —**tardily** *adv* —**tardiness** *n* [U]

tare /tɛr; teə/ *n* **1** [usually singular 一般用單數] *technical* the weight of wrapping material in which goods are packed【術語】〔貨物的〕包裝材料的重量, 皮重 **2** [usually singular 一般用單數] *technical* the weight of an unloaded goods vehicle, used to calculate the actual weight of its goods【術語】空重; 車身重量 **3** [usually plural 一般用複數] *biblical* an unwanted plant growing in fields of grain; WEED[1] (1)【聖經】稗子, 莠草

tar·get[1] /ˈtɑrgɪt; ˈtɑːgət/ *n* [C] 3
1 ►OBJECT OF ATTACK 攻擊對象◄ an object, person, or place that is deliberately chosen to be attacked〔有意 2

攻擊的〕目標; 攻擊對象: **[+for/of]** *The docks are the main target for the bombing raids.* 碼頭區是轟炸襲擊的主要目標。| **soft/easy target** *Cars without security devices are an easy target for the thief.* 沒有安全裝置的汽車很容易成為盜賊的目標。| **prime target** (=a very likely target) 首要攻擊目標

2 ►AN AIM 目標◄ a result, such as a total, an amount, or a time, which you aim to achieve; GOAL (1) 想要達到的結果〈如總數、時限等〉; 想要實現的目標; 指標: *I've set myself a target of saving £20 a month.* 我給自己定了一個目標: 每月存上 20 英鎊。| **meet targets** (=achieve targets) 達到指標; 實現目標 *Dealers are under pressure to meet sales targets.* 經銷商們受到要完成銷售指標的壓力。| **on target** (=likely to achieve a target) 有可能實現目標 *We're on target for 3% inflation by 1996.* 我們有可能在 1996 年前把通貨膨脹控制到 3%。

3 ►SHOOTING 射擊◄ something that you practise shooting at, especially a round board with circles on it〔射擊的〕靶子: A *target 300 yards away* 300 碼以外的一個靶子 | **target practice** *The area is used by the army for target practice.* 這一地區被軍隊用來練習打靶。

4 target group/area/audience etc a limited group, area etc that a plan, idea etc is aimed at 特別針對的羣體/領域/聽眾等: *We need to clearly identify our target market.* 我們需要明確我們針對的市場。

5 be the target of criticism/complaints etc to be criticized, blamed, etc for something 成為批評/抱怨等的對象: *She's become the target of much criticism since the affair became public.* 自從那一曖昧關係公開之後, 她招來了很多批評。

target² *v* [T] **1** to aim something at a target 對…瞄準, 把…當作靶子: **target sth on/at** *missiles targeted on American and European cities* 瞄向美國和歐洲城市的導彈 **2** to make something have an effect on a particular limited group or area 以…為目標[對象]: **[+on/at]** *We want to target more welfare on the poorest groups in society.* 我們想給社會上最貧困的羣體提供較多的福利。**3** to choose someone or something as your target 把…選作目標: *It's clear that smaller, more vulnerable banks have been targeted.* 很明顯, 規模較小、力量較脆弱的銀行已被確定為目標。

tar·iff /ˋtærɪf; ˈtærɪ̣f/ *n* [C] **1** a tax on goods coming into a country or going out of a country〔對進口或出口商品徵收的〕關稅 **2** *especially BrE* a list of fixed prices, such as the cost of meals or rooms, charged by a hotel or restaurant【尤英】〔旅館或餐廳對房間或餐飲等固定收費項目的〕收費表, 價目表

tar·mac¹ /ˋtɑrˌmæk; ˈtɑːmæk/ *n* **1** also 又作 **tar·ma·cad·am** /ˌtɑrməˋkædəm; ˌtɑːməˈkædəm/ [U] a mixture of TAR and very small stones, used for making the surface of roads; ASPHALT〔鋪路用的〕柏油碎石, 瀝青和碎石的混合物 **2 the tarmac** an area covered with tarmac, especially where planes take off or land〔尤指飛機跑道用的〕鋪有柏油碎石的地面

tarmac² *v* [T] to cover a road's surface with tarmac 在〔路面上〕鋪柏油碎石

tar·nish¹ /ˋtɑrnɪʃ; ˈtɑːnɪʃ/ *v* **1** [T] if an event or fact tarnishes someone's REPUTATION, record, image etc, it makes it worse 玷污〔名譽〕; 損害〔形象〕: *a record tarnished by recent scandals* 被最近醜聞玷污的記錄 **2** [I,T] if metals such as silver, COPPER (1), or BRASS (1) tarnish, or if something tarnishes them, they become dull and lose their colour (使)〔銀器、銅器、黃銅器等金屬〕失去光澤, 變暗淡: *tarnished silver spoons* 失去光澤的銀匙

tarnish² *n* [singular, U] dullness of colour, or loss of brightness 顏色晦暗; 光澤變暗

ta·ro /ˋtɑro; ˈtɑːrəʊ/ *n* [C,U] a tropical plant grown for its thick root which is boiled and eaten 芋, 芋頭

tar·ot /ˋtæro; ˈtærəʊ/ *n* [singular,U] a set of 78 cards, used for telling what will happen to someone in the future 塔羅牌〔一套用於占卜的紙牌, 共 78 張〕

tar·pau·lin /tɑrˋpɔlɪn; tɑːˈpɔːlɪ̣n/ *n* [C,U] a heavy cloth prepared so that water will not pass through it, used to keep rain off things 防水帆布, 油布

tar·ra·gon /ˋtærəˌgɑn; ˈtærəgən/ *n* [U] the leaves of a small European plant used as a HERB 龍蒿〔一種歐洲植物, 其葉是用於烹調的香草〕: *chicken with tarragon* 龍蒿葉煮雞肉

tar·ry¹ /ˋtærɪ; ˈtæri/ *v* [I] *literary*【文】**1** to stay in a place, especially when you should leave; LINGER〔尤指應離開時〕逗留, 停留; 徘徊 **2** to delay or be slow in going somewhere 耽擱, 拖延

tar·ry² /ˋtɑrɪ; ˈtɑːri/ *adj* covered with TAR (=a thick black liquid) 塗了柏油的

tar·sus /ˋtɑrsəs; ˈtɑːsəs/ *n* [C] *technical* your ANKLE or one of the seven small bones in your ankle【術語】腳踝; 跗骨〔踝部的七塊小骨頭之一〕—**tarsal** *adj*

tart¹ /tɑrt; tɑːt/ *n* **1** [C,U] a PIE (1) without a top on it, containing something sweet〔頂部不用麵皮密封的〕甜餡餅 **2** [C] *informal* a woman whose appearance or behaviour makes you think that she is too willing to have sex【非正式】蕩婦 **3** [C] *slang* a PROSTITUTE【俚】妓女

tart² *adj* **1** food that is tart has a slightly sour taste that stings your tongue〔味道〕酸的: *a tart apple* 酸蘋果 **2 tart reply/remark etc** a reply, remark etc that is sharp and unkind 尖刻的回答/話等: *Her tart reply upset me.* 她那尖刻的回答令我很難受。—**tartly** *adv*: *Colin replied tartly that he hadn't invited me.* 柯林尖酸刻薄地說, 他並沒有邀請我。—**tartness** *n* [U]

tart³ *v*

tart sth ↔ **up** *phr v* [T] *BrE informal*【英, 非正式】**1** to try to make something more attractive by decorating it, often in a way that other people think is cheap or ugly 把…裝飾得刺眼而又俗氣: *All they've done for the party is to tart up the old church hall.* 他們為那次晚會所做的就是把那座舊教堂的大廳裝飾得俗不可耐。**2 tart yourself up** *often humorous* if a woman tarts herself up she tries to make herself look attractive, by putting on jewellery, MAKE-UP (1) etc【常幽默】把自己打扮得花枝招展

tar·tan /ˋtɑrtn̩; ˈtɑːtn/ *n* **1 a)** [U] woollen cloth, originally from Scotland woven with bands of different colours and widths that cross each other at right angles〔蘇格蘭〕格子花呢 —see picture on page A16 參見 A16 頁圖 **b)** [C] this pattern on other cloth 格子織物, 花格圖案: *Her skirt is a red and green tartan.* 她的裙子是紅綠相間花格圖案的。**2** [C] a special pattern of this type worn by a particular Scottish CLAN (=large family group)〔作為蘇格蘭某大家族標誌的〕格子花呢圖案: *the MacGregor tartan* 麥格雷戈家族的格子花呢圖案 —**tartan** *adj*: *a bright tartan shirt* 色彩鮮豔的格子襯衣

tar·tar /ˋtɑrtɚ; ˈtɑːtə/ *n* **1** [U] a hard substance that forms on your teeth 牙石, 牙垢 **2** [U] a reddish-brown substance that forms on the inside of wine barrels 酒石〔酒桶內壁上形成的一種赤褐色物質〕**3** [U] a white powder used in baking and in medicine 酒石英, 酒石酸氫鉀〔一種用於烘烤麵包糕點和醫藥的白色粉末〕**4** [C] *informal* someone who has a violent temper or is difficult to deal with【非正式】兇悍的人; 很難對付的人: *She's a real tartar.* 她真是一個悍婦。

tar·tare sauce /ˌtɑrtɚ ˋsɔrs; ˌtɑːtə ˈsɔːs/ *n* [U] a cold white SAUCE often eaten with fish, made from egg, oil, GHERKIN*s* and capers (CAPER² (1)) 塔塔醬, 蛋黃沙司〔吃魚時常用的一種調味醬〕

tar·tar·ic ac·id /tɑrˋtærɪk ˋæsɪd; tɑːˌtærɪk ˈæsɪ̣d/ *n* [U] a strong acid that comes from a plant and is used in preparing some foods and medicines 酒石酸〔用於製作某些食品和醫藥〕

tart·y /ˋtɑrtɪ; ˈtɑːti/ *adj especially BrE* wearing the kind of clothes that people think a PROSTITUTE would wear【尤英】穿着打扮很妖冶的

task /tæsk; tɑːsk/ *n* [C] **1** a piece of work that must be done, especially one that is difficult or unpleasant or that must be done regularly〔尤指困難或必須定期做的〕 

工作; 任務: **[+of]** *He was given the task of stacking the chairs in the auditorium.* 給他分派的任務是要把大禮堂的椅子堆放好。| *the grim task of identifying the dead* 辨認死者的令人生畏的工作 | *daily tasks* 日常工作任務 | **thankless task** (=a boring task that no one wants to do) 費力不討好的事, 苦差事 *Volunteers had the thankless task of distributing campaign leaflets.* 志願者們承擔了散發宣傳頁這件苦差事。**2** a piece of work that is difficult but very important〔困難但又很重要的〕工作: *Our main task is to improve the economy.* 我們的主要工作是改善經濟。**3 take someone to task** to tell someone that you strongly disapprove of something they have done〔為某人所做之事〕責備[嚴厲批評]某人

task force /'· ·/ *n* [C] **1** a group formed for a short time to deal with a particular problem〔為處理某一特定問題而暫時組成的〕工作組: *a citizens' task force formed to rejuvenate the area* 為使該地區重振活力而由居民組成的一支工作小組 **2** a military force sent to a place for a special purpose〔軍隊的〕特別行動小組, 特遣部隊

task·mas·ter /ˈtæskˌmæstɚ; ˈtɑːskˌmɑːstə/ *n* **be a hard/stern/tough taskmaster** to force people to work very hard or use a lot of effort 是一個嚴厲的監督人[監工, 工頭]

tas·sel /ˈtæsl; ˈtæsəl/ *n* [C] a mass of threads tied together into a round ball at one end and hung as a decoration on clothes, curtains etc 流蘇, 穗, 纓〔用作衣服、窗簾等的裝飾〕—**tasselled** *BrE*【英】also 又作 **tasseled** *AmE*【美】*adj*

S2 W2 **taste**[1] /test; teɪst/ *n*

1 ►FOOD 食物◄ [singular,U] the special feeling that is produced by a particular food or drink when you put it in your mouth 味道, 滋味: *Sugar has a sweet taste.* 糖有甜味。| *Has the milk gone sour? It's got a funny taste.* 牛奶變酸了嗎? 有一種怪味。| *the strong taste of the coffee* 濃郁的咖啡味道

2 ►JUDGEMENT 鑑賞力◄ [U] someone's judgement about what is good or suitable when they choose clothes, music etc〔對衣服、音樂等的〕鑑賞力; 品味; 趣味: **have (good) taste** (=make good judgements) 有(很好的)鑑賞力 *She has instinctive good taste.* 她天生就有不錯的鑑賞力。| **have bad/no taste** *Mick has really bad taste in clothes.* 米克穿衣服很不得體。

3 ►STH YOU LIKE 你喜歡的東西◄ [C,U] the type of thing that you tend to like 喜愛, 愛好; 口味: **[+for/in]** *His tastes in films and books were very different from her own.* 他在電影和書籍方面的志趣與她大不相同。| **have a taste for** *I've always had a taste for jazz and blues music.* 我一向喜愛爵士樂和勃魯斯音樂。| **to sb's taste** (=in a way that someone likes) 合某人的口味; 稱某人的心 *She had the whole house redecorated to her taste.* 她按照自己的品味把整座房子重新裝修。| **have no taste for** (=not like something at all) 一點都不喜歡...

4 ►SMALL AMOUNT 少量◄ [usually singular 一般用單數] a small amount of food or drink that you put in your mouth to try it〔食物、飲料的〕少量, 一小口: *Have a taste of this soup and see if it needs more salt.* 嚐一嚐這湯, 看看是否還需要加鹽。

5 ►WITH TONGUE 用舌頭◄ [U] the sense by which you know one food from another 味覺: *You need a good sense of taste to be a chef.* 要想成為一名廚師, 你需要具備良好的味覺。

6 be in bad/poor taste jokes, remarks etc that are in bad taste are unacceptable, especially because they upset someone〔笑話、講話等〕格調低的, 庸俗的: *I thought your terrorist joke was in pretty bad taste.* 我當時就認為你那個關於恐怖分子的笑話格調很庸俗。

7 a taste of fame/success etc a short experience of something that you want more of 對名望/成功等的〔短暫〕體驗

8 leave a bad/nasty taste in your mouth to feel angry or upset as a result of seeing or hearing something unpleasant 留下難受的滋味: *The way he spoke to those children left a nasty taste in my mouth.* 他對那些孩子說話的方式讓我覺得很不是滋味。

9 to taste a phrase meaning as much as is needed to make something taste the way you like, used in instructions for cooking 按照個人的口味, 適量地〔用於烹調的說明語〕: *Add salt and pepper to taste.* 隨個人口味適量加鹽和胡椒。

10 an acquired taste something that you like only after you have tried it several times 多嚐才會喜歡的東西: *Olives are something of an acquired taste.* 橄欖是一種需要多吃才會讓人喜歡的食物。

11 there is no accounting for taste used to say that you do not understand why someone has chosen something 人各有所好: *He's so nice – I don't see why you don't like him. But there's no accounting for taste.* 他這麼好, 我不明白你為甚麼不喜歡他。人可是各有所好呢。

taste[2] *v* **1** [I not in progressive 不用進行式] to have a particular kind of taste 有...的味道: **taste delicious/sweet/fresh etc** *The mangoes tasted delicious.* 那些芒果味美可口。| *This wine tastes too acidic.* 這葡萄酒味道太酸了。| **taste like** *This chicken tastes more like turkey.* 這雞肉的味道吃起來更像火雞肉。| *What does pumpkin taste like?* 南瓜吃起來是甚麼味道? | **taste of** *over-ripe cheese tasting of ammonia* 有氨水味的熟過了頭的乾酪 | **sweet-tasting/strong-tasting etc** (=having a sweet, strong etc taste) 味道甜的/味道濃烈的等 *strong-tasting coffee* 味道濃郁的咖啡 **2** [T] to put a small amount of food or drink into your mouth to see what it is like 嚐, 品嚐: *You'd better taste the soup to see if I put enough salt in it.* 你最好嚐一下那湯, 看看我是否放夠了鹽。| *Come on, just taste it!* 來, 嚐一嚐吧! **3** [T not in progressive 不用進行式] to experience the taste of food or drink 嚐出...的味道: *I can hardly taste what I'm eating because of my cold.* 因為感冒了, 我幾乎嚐不出食物的味道。**4 taste fame/freedom etc** to have a short experience of something that you want more of〔短暫地〕體驗到出名/自由等的滋味: *We had tasted success and wanted more.* 我們已經體驗到成功的滋味, 還想取得更大的成功。

USAGE NOTE 用法說明: TASTE

WORD CHOICE 詞語辨析: **taste, try, sample, savour** (*BrE* 英) **/savor** (*AmE* 美)

If you eat or drink a little of something just in order to find out its taste or flavour, you **taste** it. 嚐食物或飲料的滋味用 taste: *Have you tasted this wine yet?* 你品嚐過這種酒嗎? However, **taste** is much more often used in other meanings, where you receive the taste of something but do not actively search for it 然而, taste 有一種常見得多的用法, 指不主動尋找而察覺出味道: *Can you taste the spices in this dish?* 你能嚐出這道菜裡的香料嗎? | *This wine tastes great* (NOT 不用 *This wine is very good taste*). 這種酒十分香醇。

In fact most often people use the word **try** when they eat or drink something deliberately to see if they like it – not just what it tastes like, but also what it looks like, its smell etc. 其實, 品嚐食物或飲料, 不僅嚐它的味道, 還看它的樣子、聞它的氣味等, 最常用的詞是 try: *You must try this wine/our local dishes/the salmon.* 你得嚐一嚐這種酒/我們本地的菜/鮭魚。

You may also **sample** food or drink, that is try just a little, perhaps not a full dish or meal. 也可以淺嚐 (sample) 食物或飲料, 即不吃一整盤或一整餐: *You'll have a chance to sample all the cheeses of the region.* 你將有機會品嚐本地區的各種乾酪。

If you spend time enjoying the taste of something you **savour** it. savour 指專門花時間去享受美味: *Here you can relax, chat and savour a variety of local dishes.* 在這裡, 您可以休息、閒談、品嚐種種當地風味菜餚。

taste bud /ˋ· ·/ *n* [C usually plural 一般用複數] one of the small parts of the surface of your tongue which can tell the difference between foods according to their taste 味蕾

taste·ful /ˋtestfəl; ˈteɪstfəl/ *adj* made, decorated, or chosen with good TASTE¹ (2) 有鑑賞力的, 趣味高雅的: *a simple but tasteful arrangement of flowers* 簡單而顯得趣味高雅的插花 —compare 比較 TASTY —**tastefully** *adv*: *tastefully decorated* 裝飾得很大方 —**tastefulness** *n* [U]

taste·less /ˋtestlɪs; ˈteɪstləs/ *adj* **1** food or drink that is tasteless is unpleasant because it has no particular taste〔食品或飲料〕無味道的: *The vegetables were tasteless and soggy.* 這些蔬菜淡而無味, 濕乎乎的。**2 tasteless joke/remark/comment etc** a joke etc that is unacceptable in a particular situation 格調不高的笑話/話語/評論等 **3** made, decorated or chosen with bad TASTE¹ (2) 格調很低的, 庸俗的: *a tasteless outfit* 一套趣味庸俗的服裝 —**tastelessly** *adv* —**tastelessness** *n* [U]

tast·er /ˋtestɚ; ˈteɪstə/ *n* [C] **1** someone whose job is to test the quality of foods, teas, wines etc by tasting them 品嘗家, 試味專家: *a wine taster* 品酒師 **2** *informal* a small example of something that is provided so that you can see if you like it【非正式】〔檢驗某物的一份〕小樣: **[+of]** *Here's just a taster of what will be in print next month.* 這兒就有一份小樣, 從中可以看出下月將刊載些甚麼。

tast·ing /ˋtestɪŋ; ˈteɪstɪŋ/ *n* [C] an event that is organized so that you can try different foods or drinks to see if you like them〔食品或飲料的〕品嘗集會: *a wine and cheese tasting* 一次品嘗酒和乾酪的集會

tast·y /ˋtestɪ; ˈteɪsti/ *adj* **tastier, tastiest 1** food that is tasty has a good taste 味道好的, 味美可口的: *a wide selection of tasty cold meats* 多種可供選擇的味美可口的冷葷 —compare 比較 TASTEFUL **2** *informal* tasty news, GOSSIP etc is especially interesting and often connected with sex or surprising behaviour【非正式】〔新聞、傳聞等〕特別有趣的; 與桃色事件相關的 **3** *informal* a word meaning attractive, used especially by men about women【非正式】有吸引力的, 夠味兒的〔尤指男子形容女性〕: *She's well tasty.* 她真夠味兒。—**tastiness** *n* [U]

tat /tæt; tæt/ *n* [U] *BrE* things that are cheap and badly made【英】不值錢的東西; 質量低劣的東西 —see also 另見 TIT FOR TAT

[S3] **ta-ta** /ˋtɑˌtɑ; tæˈtɑː/ *interjection BrE informal* goodbye【英, 非正式】再見

ta·ter /ˋtetɚ; ˈteɪtə/ *n* [C] *informal* a potato【非正式】馬鈴薯

tat·tered /ˋtætɚd; ˈtætəd/ *adj* **1** clothes, books etc that are tattered are old and torn〔衣服、書等〕破舊的, 破爛的: *an old man in a tattered brown coat* 一個穿着一件棕色破舊外衣的老人 —see picture on page A18 參見 A18 頁圖 **2** dressed in old torn clothes 衣衫襤褸的

tat·ters /ˋtætɚz; ˈtætəz/ *n* [plural] **1** clothing or pieces of cloth that are old and torn 破舊衣服; 破布 **2 in tatters a)** a plan, policy etc that is in tatters is ruined or badly damaged〔計劃、政策等〕千瘡百孔的: *The government's income policy was in tatters.* 政府的收入政策徹底破產了。**b)** clothes that are in tatters are old and torn〔衣服〕破舊不堪的

tat·tie /ˋtætɪ; ˈtæti/ *n* [C] *ScotE* a potato【蘇格蘭】馬鈴薯: *neeps and tatties* 蕪菁甘藍和馬鈴薯

tat·ting /ˋtætɪŋ; ˈtætɪŋ/ *n* [U] a kind of LACE that you make by hand, or the process of making it〔手工〕梭織花邊; 梭織花邊工藝

tat·tle /ˋtætḷ; ˈtætl/ *v* [I] **1** *old-fashioned* to talk about small unimportant things, or about other people's private affairs; GOSSIP【過時】閒聊; 談論他人隱私 **2** if a child tattles, they tell a parent or teacher that another child has done something bad〔小孩〕打小報告 —**tattler** *n* [C]

tat·tle·tale /ˋtætḷˌtel; ˈtætlteɪl/ *n* [C] *AmE informal* a word meaning someone who tattles, used by or to children【美, 非正式】〔小孩中的〕打小報告者; 搬弄是非者〔兒語〕; TELLTALE² *BrE*【英】

tat·too¹ /tæˋtu; təˈtuː/ *n plural* **tattoos 1** [C] a picture or message that is permanently marked on your skin with a needle and ink〔皮膚上的〕文身: *a tattoo of a snake* 一條蛇的文身 **2** [C] an outdoor military show with music, usually at night〔常在夜間舉行的、有音樂伴奏的〕軍隊表演操 **3** [singular] a rapid continuous beating of drums, especially played as a military signal, or a sound like this〔尤指作為軍事信號的〕連續快速的擊鼓聲

tattoo² *v* [T] **1** to make a permanent picture or message on someone's skin with a needle and ink DYEs〔用針和墨水〕在〔皮膚上〕刺花紋, 文身 **2** to mark someone in this way 給〔某人〕刺花紋, 文身 —**tattooed** *adj*: *The Maori's face was heavily tattooed.* 那個毛利人的臉上刺有很多花紋。

tat·too·ist /tæˋtuɪst; təˈtuːɪst/ *n* [C] someone whose job is tattooing 專門替人文身的人, 文身師

tat·ty /ˋtætɪ; ˈtæti/ *adj* **tattier, tattiest** *informal especially BrE* untidy or in a bad condition; SHABBY【非正式, 尤英】不整潔的, 邋遢的; 破舊的: *tatty jeans* 破舊的牛仔褲 | *a few tatty old chairs* 幾把破舊的椅子 —**tattily** *adv* —**tattiness** *n* [C]

taught /tɔt; tɔːt/ the past tense and past participle of TEACH: *She taught English in Prague.* 她曾在布拉格教英語。

taunt¹ /tɔnt; tɔːnt/ *v* [T] to try to make someone angry or upset by saying unkind things or laughing at their faults or failures etc 激怒; 嘲弄; 奚落: **[+about/over]** *The other children taunted him about his weight.* 別的孩子嘲笑他體胖。—**tauntingly** *adv*

taunt² *n* [C often plural] a remark or joke intended to make someone angry or upset〔引人發怒或傷人感情的〕嘲弄, 譏笑: *The boy's taunts rang after her. 'Cry baby! Cry baby!'* 男孩的嘲笑還在她耳邊回響:"哭鼻子大王! 哭鼻子大王!"

taupe /top; təʊp/ *n* [U] a brownish grey colour 褐灰色 —**taupe** *adj*

Tau·rus /ˋtɔrəs; ˈtɔːrəs/ *n* **1** [singular] the second sign of the ZODIAC, represented by a BULL, and believed to affect the character and life of people born between April 21 and May 22 金牛宮〔黃道十二宮的第二宮〕**2** [C] someone who was born between April 21 and May 22 出生於金牛宮時段〔即 4 月 21 日至 5 月 22 日之間〕的人: *My husband's a Taurus.* 我的丈夫出生於金牛宮時段。

taut /tɔt; tɔːt/ *adj* **1** stretched tight 拉緊的, 繃緊的: *the taut strings of the guitar* 吉他繃緊的弦 | *The runners were crouching, muscles taut.* 賽跑運動員正蹲在地上, 肌肉繃得緊緊的。—opposite 反義詞 SLACK¹ (3) **2** showing signs of worry or anxiety; TENSE¹ (1) 憂慮的; 緊張不安的: *Catherine looked upset, her face taut.* 凱瑟琳顯得心緒不寧, 臉色緊張。

taut·en /ˋtɔtn̩; ˈtɔːtn/ *v* [I,T] to make something stretch tight, or to become stretched tight (使…) 拉緊, (使…) 繃緊

tau·tol·o·gy /tɔˋtɑlədʒɪ; tɔːˈtɒlədʒi/ *n* [C,U] a statement in which you unnecessarily say the same thing twice using different words, for example, 'He sat alone by himself.' 同義反覆, 贅述〈如: "他自己獨自坐着。"〉—**tautological** /ˌtɔtəˋlɑdʒɪkḷ; ˌtɔːtəˈlɒdʒɪkəl◂/ *adj* —**tautologically** /-kḷɪ; -kli/ *adv*

tav·ern /ˋtævɚn; ˈtævən/ *n* [C] **1** *BrE old use* a PUB where you can also stay the night【英舊】小旅店, 客棧 **2** word for a bar, often used in the name of a bar 酒館; 酒吧: *Murphy's Tavern* 墨菲酒館

taw·dry /ˋtɔdrɪ; ˈtɔːdri/ *adj* cheaply and badly made 廉價的, 不值錢的; 製作粗糙的: *tawdry jewellery and fake furs* 廉價珠寶和假冒毛皮 —**tawdriness** *n* [U]

taw·ny /ˋtɔnɪ; ˈtɔːni/ *adj* brownish yellow in colour 黃褐色的: *a lion's tawny fur* 獅子的黃褐色毛皮

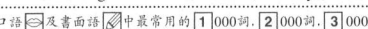

[S1] [W1] **tax¹** /tæks; tæks/ *n* **1** [C,U] an amount of money that you must pay to the government according to your income, property, goods etc that is used to pay for public services 稅, 稅款: *The government claimed it would lower taxes.* 政府宣稱將降低稅收。| [+on] *If you cash in the investment early, then you have to pay tax on that.* 如果你提早把投資兌現, 那麼你必須為此繳稅。| **before/after tax** (=before or after paying tax on something) 稅前/稅後 *What are you earning before tax?* 你納稅之前掙多少? | **tax burden** (=the total amount of tax paid by an average person) 〔平常人的〕納稅負擔 **2** [singular] *formal* something that uses a lot of your strength, PATIENCE etc【正式】沉重的壓力[負擔] —see also 另見 CAPITAL GAINS TAX, **corporation tax** (CORPORATION (3)), INCOME TAX, PROPERTY TAX, SALES TAX, VAT

tax² *v* [T] **1** to charge a tax on something 對…徵稅, 向…課稅: **heavily/lightly taxed** *Cigarettes are heavily taxed in Britain.* 在英國, 香煙要課以重稅。**2 tax a car/motorbike etc** *BrE* to pay the sum of money charged each year for using a vehicle on British roads【英】繳納〔汽車/摩托車的〕牌照稅 **3 tax sb's patience/strength etc** to use almost all of someone's patience, strength etc 使某人不耐煩/費盡力氣等: *The kids are really taxing my patience today.* 這些孩子今天真讓我夠受的。—see also 另見 TAXING —**taxable** *adj*: *taxable income* 應予課稅的收入

tax sb **with** sth *phr v* [T] *formal* to tell someone they have done something wrong, or blame them for it【正式】因…而責備〔某人〕; 為…而譴責〔某人〕

3 **tax·a·tion** /tæk`seʃən; tæk'seɪʃən/ *n* [U] **1** the system of charging taxes 徵稅, 課稅, 稅收(的制度): *the reform of taxation* 稅收改革 | **direct taxation** (=the taxing of income) 直接稅〔即所得稅〕| **indirect taxation** (=the taxing of the things people buy) 間接稅〔即商品或貨物稅〕**2** money collected from taxes 稅額, 稅款: *We'll have to consider even higher taxation in the next year or two.* 我們必須考慮在今後一兩年再提高稅額。

tax a·void·ance /'· ·,·· / *n* [U] legal ways of paying less tax 避稅〔以合法的方式少繳稅〕—compare 比較 TAX EVASION

tax brack·et /'· ,··/ *n* [C] a particular range of income levels on which the same rate of tax is paid 徵稅範圍〔按同一稅率繳納的收入範圍〕

tax break /'· ·/ *n* [C] *AmE* a special reduction in taxes that the government allows for a particular purpose【美】減稅優惠: *a tax break for insulating your home* 為將你住所隔熱保溫而給予的減稅優惠

tax-de·duc·ti·ble /,· '····◂/ *adj* tax-deductible costs can be taken off your total income before it is taxed〔在課稅前〕可從個人總收入中扣除的: *If you're self-employed, your travel expenses are tax-deductible.* 如果你是個體經營, 你的旅行開支可在計稅前從總收入中扣除。

tax-de·ferred /,· ·'·◂/ *adj AmE* not taxed until a later time【美】推遲扣稅的: *tax-deferred savings* 推遲扣稅的存款

tax disc /'· ·/ *n* [C] a small round piece of paper on a car WINDSCREEN in Britain that shows the driver has paid ROAD TAX 圓形納稅證〔貼在汽車的擋風玻璃上, 表示路稅已付〕

tax dodge /'· ·/ *n* [C] a legal way of paying less tax 避稅〔合法地少繳稅的方式〕

tax e·va·sion /'· ·,··/ *n* [U] illegal ways of paying less tax 逃稅〔以非法的方式少繳稅〕

tax ex·empt /,· ·'·◂/ *adj* tax exempt savings, income etc are not taxed 免稅的, 不收稅的

tax ex·ile /'· ,··/ *n* [C] someone who lives abroad in order to avoid paying high taxes in their own country〔為躲避在國內繳納高額稅款而移居國外的〕避稅者, 逃稅者

tax ha·ven /'· ,··/ *n* [C] a place where people go to live to avoid paying high taxes in their own country 逃稅者樂園, 避稅天堂〔指稅率低的地方, 許多人為躲避在國內繳納高額稅款而移居此地〕

tax·i¹ /`tæksɪ; 'tæksi/ *n* [C] a car and driver that you pay to take you somewhere; CAB (1) 出租車, 計程車 | **flag (down)/hail a taxi** (=wave or shout at a taxi to make it stop) 揮手攔下/叫住一輛出租車

taxi² *v* [I] if a plane taxis, it moves slowly along the ground before taking off or after landing〔飛機起飛前或着陸後〕在地面緩慢滑行

taxi·cab /`tæksɪ,kæb; 'tæksikæb/ *n* [C] a taxi 出租車

tax·i·der·mist /`tæksə,dɝmɪst; 'tæksɨdɜːmɨst/ *n* [C] someone whose job is taxidermy 動物標本剝製師

tax·i·der·my /`tæksə,dɝmɪ; 'tæksɨdɜːmi/ *n* [U] the art of specially preparing the skins of dead animals, birds or fish then filling them with a special material so that they look as though they are alive 動物標本剝製術

tax·ing /`tæksɪŋ; 'tæksɪŋ/ *adj* needing a lot of effort; DEMANDING 煩重的, 累人的; 費勁的: *The job is taxing but enjoyable.* 這項工作很累人, 但也很有樂趣。

tax in·spect·or /'· ·,··/ *n* [C] someone who works for the government, deciding how much tax a person or company should pay〔政府的〕稅務稽查員

taxi rank /'·· ·/ also 又作 **taxi stand** *n* [C] *BrE* a place where taxis wait to be HIRED【英】出租車候客點; CABSTAND *AmE*【美】

tax·man /`tæksmæn; 'tæksmæn/ *n* [C] **1** a tax collector or tax inspector 稅務員; 稅務稽查員 **2 the taxman** the government department that collects taxes〔政府的〕稅務部門

tax·on·o·my /tæks`ɑnəmɪ; tæk'sɒnəmi/ *n* [C,U] the process of organizing things such as plants or animals into different groups or sets that show their natural relationships〔動、植物等的〕分類學

tax·pay·er /`tæks,peɚ; 'tæks-peɪə/ *n* [C] a person or organization that pays tax 納稅人; 納稅單位

tax re·lief /'· ·,·/ *n* [U] *BrE* the right to not have to pay tax on part of what you earn【英】部分收入免稅權

tax re·turn /'· ·,·/ *n* [C] the form on which you have to give information so that your tax can be calculated 納稅申報單

tax shel·ter /'· ,··/ *n* [C] a plan or method that allows you to legally avoid paying tax 合法避稅手段

tax year /'· ·/ *n* [C] the period of 12 months in which your income is calculated for paying taxes. The tax year begins on April 6th in Britain, and January 1st in the US. 稅務年度〔計數所得稅的時段, 為期12個月, 在英國始於4月6日, 在美國始於1月1日〕

TB *BrE*【英】, **Tb** *AmE*【美】/,ti `bi; ,tiː 'biː/ *n* [U] tuberculosis; a serious infectious disease that affects your lungs and other parts of your body 結核(病)

T-ball /`ti ,bɔl; 'tiː bɔːl/ *n* [U] *trademark* an easy form of BASEBALL for young children; TEE-BALL【商標】〔一種供小孩玩的〕簡易棒球

T-bone steak /,ti bon `stek; ,tiː bəʊn 'steɪk/ *n* [C] a thinly cut piece of BEEF¹ (1) that has a T-shaped bone in it T字骨牛排

tbs, tbsp *n* [C] the written abbreviation of 縮寫= TABLESPOON: *1 tbs sugar* 一湯匙糖

tea /ti; tiː/ *n*

1 ►DRINK 飲料◄ [U] **a)** a hot brown drink made by pouring boiling water onto the dried leaves from a particular bush 茶: *Do you take milk and sugar in your tea?* 你的茶裡面放牛奶和糖嗎? **b)** [C] *especially BrE* a cup of tea【尤英】一杯茶: *Three teas and a coffee, please.* 請來三杯茶, 一杯咖啡。 1 2

2 mint/camomile etc tea a hot drink made by pouring boiling water onto the leaves or flowers of a particular plant, sometimes used as a medicine 薄荷茶/甘菊茶等〔用某些葉子或花泡的飲料〕

3 ►LEAVES 葉子◄ [U] the dried, finely cut leaves of a particular Asian bush, that is used for making tea 茶葉: *China tea* 中國茶葉 | *Ceylon tea* 錫蘭茶葉 | *tea plantations* 茶葉種植園

4 ►MEAL 飯餐◄ [U] *BrE*【英】**a)** a very small meal of cake or BISCUITs, eaten in the afternoon with a cup of tea

下午茶, 午後茶點 **b)** a large meal that is eaten early in the evening in some parts of Britain〔英國某些地方的分量大的〕傍晚茶 —compare 比較 DINNER, SUPPER —see also 另見 HIGH TEA

5 tea and sympathy *BrE* kindness and attention that you give someone when they are upset【英】對不幸者的安慰和同情

6 (not) for all the tea in China *informal* used to say that you would refuse to do something, whatever happened【非正式】絕對不, 無論如何都不: *I wouldn't do his job, not for all the tea in China.* 我無論如何都不會去幹他那份工作。—see also 另見 **not be your cup of tea** (CUP[1] (8))

tea·bag /ˈtibæg; ˈtiːbæg/ *n* [C] a small paper bag with tea leaves inside, used for making tea 袋泡茶, 茶包

tea break /ˈ· ·/ *n* [C] *especially BrE* a short pause from work in the middle of the morning or afternoon for a drink, a rest etc; COFFEE BREAK【尤英】喝茶休息時間〔上午或下午工作中間的短暫休息〕

tea cad·dy /ˈ· ˌ··/ *n* [C] a small metal box that you keep tea in 茶葉罐

tea·cake /ˈtiˌkek; ˈtiːkeɪk/ *n* [C] *BrE* a small flat round cake made of a bread-like mixture with RAISINS or CURRANTS in it【英】茶點心〔一種帶葡萄乾的小圓餅〕

1 2 **teach** /titʃ; tiːtʃ/ *past tense and past participle* **taught** /tɔt; tɔːt/ *v*

1 ►SCHOOL/COLLEGE ETC 學校/大學等◄ [I,T] to give lessons in a school, college, or university 教書; 講授: *Guy's been teaching in France for 3 years now.* 蓋伊已經在法國教了三年書。| **teach English/mathematics/history etc** *Janet teaches science at a local school.* 珍妮特在當地一所學校講授科學。| **teach sth to sb** *I'm teaching English to Italian students.* 我給一些意大利學生講授英語。| **teach school/college etc** *AmE* (=teach in a school etc)【美】教中、小學/大學 *My Dad taught school in New York.* 我爸在紐約一所學校教書。

2 ►SHOW SB HOW 教某人如何做◄ [T] to show someone how to do something 教〔某人〕做〔某事〕: **teach sb (how) to do sth** *My father taught me to swim.* 父親教我游泳。| *Hamad is teaching me how to play the guitar.* 哈馬德教我如何彈吉他。| **teach sb sth** *Can you teach me one of your card tricks?* 你能教我一點你的牌技嗎?

3 ►CHANGE SB'S IDEAS 改變某人的想法◄ [T] to show or tell someone how they should behave or what they should think 教導; 教育: **teach sb to do sth** *When I was young, children were taught to treat older people with respect.* 我小的時候, 人們教育孩子要尊重老人。| **teach sb sth** *The trouble is that parents don't teach their kids the difference between right and wrong.* 問題在於父母們不教自己的孩子分清是非。

4 ►EXPERIENCE SHOWS STH 經驗説明了某事◄ [T] if an experience or situation teaches you something, it helps you to understand something about life〔經驗〕使〔某人〕明白: **teach sb to do sth** *Poverty taught us to appreciate the little things in life.* 貧窮教會了我們要珍惜生活中的小東西。

5 that'll teach you! *spoken* used when something unpleasant has just happened to someone because they ignored your warning【口】這下你知道了吧!: **that'll teach you to do sth** *That'll teach you to park your car in a restricted area!* 這下你知道不應該把車停放在禁止停車區域了吧!

6 teach sb a lesson *informal* to punish someone to make sure that they will not behave badly again【非正式】教訓某人: *Next time he comes home drunk lock him out, that'll teach him a lesson.* 下次他再醉醺醺地回家, 就把他關在門外, 那會給他一個教訓的。

7 you can't teach an old dog new tricks used to say that older people often do not want to change the way they do things 老傢伙不會接受新東西的, 積習難改

8 teach your grandmother (to suck eggs) *BrE* to give someone advice about something that they already know【英】班門弄斧

USAGE NOTE 用法説明: TEACH

WORD CHOICE 詞語辨析: **teach, instruct, coach, tutor, train, educate**

Teach is the general word for helping a person or group of people to learn something. teach 泛指"教": *He teaches German at a local school.* 他在當地一所學校教德語。| *Mom taught me to drive.* 媽媽教我開車。

If you **instruct** someone you usually teach them, especially in a practical way and about a practical skill. instruct 指教導、指導, 尤指教授實用的技巧: *First of all you'll be instructed in the use of the safety equipment.* 首先, 將教你們如何使用安全設備。

In British English you can **coach** a person, often outside the ordinary educational system, and often in a particular subject that they need additional help with. 在英國英語中, coach 指針對某一特定學科的額外指導、輔導, 這種指導通常在普通教育系統之外進行: *She coaches kids in advanced mathematics, usually in their homes.* 她通常是到孩子們的家裡給他們輔導高等數學。In American English, you **tutor** someone when they need help learning a particular subject. 在美國英語中, 針對某一特定學科的個別輔導的用詞是 tutor: *tutoring in reading and arithmetic* 輔導閱讀和算術。People also may **coach** a person or team to become better in a sport. coach 也指在體育運動方面的執教、擔任教練: *Greg's coaching the football team this year.* 格雷格今年執教這支足球隊。

You can **train** a person or group of people, especially in particular skills and knowledge, up to a necessary level for a job. train 是訓練、培訓人的意思, 尤其是訓練特定的技能和知識, 以滿足一定層次的工作需要: *It takes several years to train a doctor.* 培養一名醫生需要花費好幾年時間。| *Soldiers are trained to kill.* 士兵受訓殺敵。You can also **train** an animal. train 也指訓練動物: *The dogs are trained to attack any stranger that comes near.* 狗受訓攻擊任何靠近的陌生人。

Educate means to teach people over a long period of time, in all kinds of knowledge (not just school subjects). **Educating** someone is sometimes compared with **training** them in skills for jobs. educate 指長期地、全面地教育, 不僅指學科的教育, 有時與工作技能的培訓 (training) 對比: *He was educated at Eton.* 他在伊頓公學受過教育。| *Parents should educate their children in how to behave.* 父母們應該教育自己的孩子注意行為舉止。| *The government's campaign aims to educate everyone about AIDS.* 政府的宣傳活動旨在教育大家對愛滋病有所了解。

GRAMMAR 語法

Teach is not usually used with **about** except when it is transitive. 除了在作及物動詞時, teach 通常不與 about 連用: *Children need to be taught about drugs.* 有必要給孩子們講解毒品方面的知識。| *She taught us about the new computer system* (but NOT 但不用 *She taught about the new computer system*). 她給我們講解有關這套新的電腦系統的情況。

Remember the past tense and past participle forms are **taught**, never *teached*. 記住其過去式和過去分詞是 taught, 從不用 teached。

teach·er /ˈtitʃɚ; ˈtiːtʃə/ *n* [C] someone whose job is to teach 教師, 老師, 教員: *Miss Tindale's my favourite teacher.* 廷德爾小姐是我最喜歡的老師。 1 1

teacher's pet /ˌ·· ˈ·/ *n* [singular] *informal* a child who everyone thinks is the teacher's favourite student and is therefore disliked by the other students【非正式】〔為其他學生所反感的〕老師的寵兒, 老師寵愛的學生

tea chest /ˈ· ·/ *n* [C] a large wooden box that used to

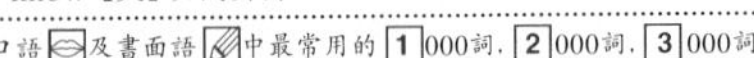

have tea in it, often used afterwards for moving and storing things 茶葉箱〔裝運茶葉的大木箱, 常用來搬運或儲存其他東西〕

teach·ing /ˈtitʃɪŋ; ˈtiːtʃɪŋ/ *n* [U] **1** the work or profession of a teacher 教學工作; 教學事業: *She's thinking of going into teaching.* (=becoming a teacher) 她在考慮從事教學工作。| *a teaching career* 教學生涯 | **teaching practice** *BrE*【英】, **student teaching** *AmE*【美】(=a period of teaching done by someone who is training to be a teacher) 教學實習 **2** also 又作 **teachings** [plural] the moral, religious, or political ideas spread by a particular person or group〔道德、宗教、政治等方面的〕教義; 學說: *the teachings of Gandhi* 甘地的學說

teaching hos·pi·tal /ˈ·· ˌ···/ *n* [C] a hospital where medical students receive practical training from experienced doctors 教學醫院

tea cloth /ˈ· ·/ *n* [C] *BrE*【英】**1** a TEA TOWEL 茶巾 **2** a small piece of material used to cover a tea-table〔鋪在茶几上的〕小桌布

tea co·sy /ˈ· ˌ··/ *n* [C] a thick cover that you put over a TEAPOT to keep the tea hot〔用以保溫的〕茶壺套

tea·cup /ˈtiˌkʌp; ˈtiːkʌp/ *n* [C] a cup that you serve tea in 茶杯 —see also 另見 **storm in a teacup** (STORM[1] (4))

tea gar·den /ˈ· ˌ··/ *n* [C] a large area of land used for growing tea; tea PLANTATION (1) 茶葉種植園

tea·house /ˈtiˌhaus; ˈtiːhaʊs/ *n* [C] a special house in China or Japan where tea is served, often as part of a ceremony〔中國及日本的〕茶館, 茶樓, 茶室

teak /tik; tiːk/ *n* **1** [U] a very hard, yellowish brown wood that is used for making ships and good quality furniture 柚木木材 **2** [C] the South Asian tree that this wood comes from 柚木(樹)

teal /til; tiːl/ *n* **1** [C] a small wild duck 小野鴨 **2** [U] a greenish blue colour 綠光暗藍色

tea·leaf /ˈtiˌlif; ˈtiːliːf/ *n* [C] **1 tealeaves** [plural] the small, finely cut pieces of leaf used for making tea 茶葉 **2** *BrE slang* a thief【英俚】賊, 小偷

team[1] /tim; tiːm/ *n* [C] **1** a group of people who play a game or sport together against another group〔遊戲或體育運動的〕隊; 小組: *There are nine players on a baseball team.* 一支棒球隊有九名隊員。| [also+plural verb *BrE* 英]: *Our team are winning.* 我們的球隊目前領先。| **play for a team** *Tim plays for the national volleyball team.* 蒂姆為國家排球隊效力。| **in a team** *BrE*【英】, **on a team** *AmE*【美】: *Is Mario going to be on the team this year?* 馬里奧今年會在該隊打球嗎? | **make the team** *AmE* (=be chosen for a team)【美】入選球隊 **2** a group of people who have been chosen to work together to do a particular job 工作隊, 工作組: **[+of]** *a team of twelve scientists* 由十二名科學家組成的工作組 **3** two or more animals that are used to pull a vehicle〔同拉一輛車的〕一組動物

team[2] *v*

team up *phr v* [I] to join with someone in order to work on something 結成一隊; 合作: **[+with]** *You can team up with one other class member if you want.* 如果你願意的話, 你可以與班裡一個同學組成一隊。

team-mate also 又作 **teammate** *especially AmE*【尤美】/ˈ· ·/ *n* [C] someone who plays in the same team as you 隊友

team spir·it /ˌ· ˈ··/ *n* [U] willingness to work with other people as part of a team 團隊精神

team·ster /ˈtimstɚ; ˈtiːmstə/ *n* [C] *AmE* someone whose job is to drive a TRUCK[1] (1)【美】卡車司機

team·work /ˈtimˌwɝk; ˈtiːmwɜːk/ *n* [U] the ability of a group of people to work well together 合作, 協作, 配合

tea par·ty /ˈ· ˌ··/ *n* [C] **1** a small party in the afternoon at which tea, cake etc is served (午後)茶會 **2 be no tea party** *AmE informal* to be very difficult or unpleasant to do【美, 非正式】很難做; 令人不愉快的

tea·pot /ˈtiˌpɑt; ˈtiːpɒt/ *n* [C] a container for making and serving tea, which has a handle and a SPOUT[1] (1) 茶壺

tear[1] /tɪr; tɪə/ *n* **1** [C] a drop of salty liquid that flows from your eye when you are crying 眼淚, 淚水: *Tears just rolled down his face.* 他簡直是淚流滿面。| *tear-stained cheeks* 淚水沾濕的雙頰 | **(be) in tears** (=crying) 哭泣, 流淚 *My wife actually broke down in tears telling me.* 我妻子實際上是流着眼淚告訴我的。| **burst into tears** (=suddenly start crying) 突然大哭起來 *Bridget burst into tears and ran out.* 布里奇特突然大聲哭着跑了出去。| **be close to tears/be on the verge of tears** (=be almost crying) 眼淚快要奪眶而出 | **fight back tears** (=try very hard not to cry) 努力克制着不哭出來 | **bring tears to sb's eyes** (=make someone almost cry) 使〔某人〕禁不住流淚 *It's music that'll bring tears to the eyes of grown men.* 這種音樂使男子漢也禁不住流起淚來。| **reduce sb to tears** (=make someone cry, especially by being unkind to them) 逼得〔某人〕流淚 | **shed tears** (=cry because you are sad) 灑淚, 揮淚 *Few of us shed any tears when Miss Crabbe left.* 克拉布小姐走的時候, 我們當中沒有幾個人流淚的。| **tears of joy/laughter etc** *Tears of gratitude shone in his eyes.* 他的眼裡閃動着感激的淚水。**2 it'll (all) end in tears** *BrE spoken* used to warn someone that what they are doing will have an unpleasant result and cause unhappiness【英口】〔警告某人〕不會有好結果的, 不會有好下場的 —see also 另見 **bore sb to tears** (BORE[2] (1)), **shed crocodile tears** (CROCODILE (4))

tear[2] /tɛr; teə/ *v past tense* **tore** /tɔr; tɔː/ *past participle* **torn** /tɔrn; tɔːn/

tear out 撕下

1 a) ►PAPER/CLOTH 紙/布◄ [T] to damage something such as paper or cloth by pulling it too hard or letting it touch something sharp 撕破; 扯破; 劃破; 戳破: *Oh no! I've torn my T-shirt.* 哦, 不! 我把T恤衫扯破了。| **tear sth on sth** *Be careful you don't tear your sleeve on that nail.* 小心, 別讓你的袖子被那釘子劃了。| **tear sth out/off/away etc** (=remove something by tearing it away from something else) 把〔某物〕撕開/撕掉/扯掉 *Someone's torn the last page out.* 有人把最後一頁給撕掉了。| **tear a hole in sth** *"Oh Rick, you've torn a hole in your best pants."* "哎, 里克, 你這條最好的褲子給劃了一道口子。" | **tear sth to shreds/pieces** (=tear something so much that it is in small pieces) 把…撕成碎片 *The contract lay on the ground, torn to shreds.* 合同被撕成碎片, 扔在地上。| **tear sth open** (=to open something very quickly by tearing it) 撕開; 拆開 *Lister grabbed the envelope and tore it open to see if he'd got the job.* 里斯特搶過信封後撕開, 看他是不是獲得了那份工作。**b)** [I] if paper or cloth tears, a hole appears in it, or it splits, because it has been pulled too hard or has touched something sharp〔紙或布〕破裂, 被撕裂; 被扯破: *Careful, the paper is very old and tears easily.* 小心點, 那紙很舊了, 很容易撕破。

2 ►MOVE QUICKLY 快速移動◄ [I always+adv/prep] to move somewhere very quickly, especially in a dangerous or careless way〔尤指以危險的、粗心大意的方式〕疾馳; 飛跑; 狂奔: **[+away/up/past etc]** *The way the big kids tear around the garden on their bikes, it's dangerous for the little ones.* 那些大孩子在花園裡騎着自行車到處亂闖, 這對小一點的孩子是很危險的。

3 ►REMOVE STH 除掉某物◄ [T always+adv/prep] to pull something violently from the place where it is fixed or held〔猛烈地〕撕扯; 拔掉; 掀掉: **tear sth from/away etc** *The wind tore the door from its hinges.* 風把門從鉸鏈上給颳掉了。

4 tear loose to escape from something that is holding you by moving violently 掙脫束縛: *The dog tore loose and ran off.* 那條狗掙脫束縛跑掉了。
5 be torn between to be unable to decide between two people or things, because you want both 左右為難, 難以取捨: *I'm torn between getting a new car and going on vacation.* 我既想買一輛新車, 又想去度假, 這真讓我左右為難。
6 be torn by sth a) to feel very worried, guilty, anxious etc because you are affected by a strong emotion or feeling〔心理或情感上〕被折磨; 對...感到憂慮: *I was torn by conflicting impulses.* 相互衝突的慾望折磨着我。**b)** if a country or family is torn by an argument, war etc, it is very badly affected by it〔國家或家庭〕飽受〔戰爭、爭吵等的〕折磨: a *nation torn by war and riots* 一個飽受戰爭和動亂之苦的民族
7 tear sb/sth to shreds/pieces to criticize someone or something very severely 對〔某人〕嚴厲批評或駁斥; 對〔某事〕大事挑剔: *In the end the prosecutor's case was torn to shreds by Russell's lawyer.* 最後, 原告的論據被拉舍爾的律師駁得體無完膚。
8 ▶MUSCLE 肌肉◀ [T] to damage a muscle or LIGAMENT (=a strong band connected to your muscles) 使〔肌肉或韌帶〕撕裂, 受傷
9 tear sb off a strip/tear a strip off sb *BrE informal* to criticize someone angrily because they have done something wrong【英, 非正式】怒斥某人, 嚴厲譴責某人
10 tear sb limb from limb *humorous* to attack someone in a very violent way【幽默】痛打〔某人〕; 猛烈攻擊〔某人〕: *When I get hold of the person responsible, I'll tear them limb from limb.* 等我抓到肇事者, 我會痛打他一頓的。
11 tear your hair out *informal* to be very anxious or angry about something【非正式】對〔某事〕極其擔憂或憤怒: *I've been tearing my hair out sorting out these wedding arrangements.* 我一直在急着要把婚禮的安排整理出一個頭緒來。
12 be in a tearing hurry *BrE* to be doing something very quickly, especially because you are late【英】〔尤指遲於規定時刻〕非常匆忙〔地做某事〕
13 tear sb's heart out to make someone feel extremely upset 使心碎; 使極其難受: *She's so lonely – it's tearing my heart out.* 她是如此孤獨, 這讓我心裡難受極了。
14 that's torn it! *BrE spoken* used when something bad has happened that stops you from doing what you intended to do【英口】這下完了; 這下倒霉了: *That's torn it! I've left my keys in the car!* 這下完了! 我把鑰匙忘在車上了!

tear sb/sth **apart** *phr v* [T] **1** to make someone feel extremely unhappy or upset 使心裡不快; 使極其難受: *It tears me apart to see them argue.* 看到他們爭吵, 我難受極了。**2** to cause serious arguments in an organization, group etc 使〔機構、團體等〕嚴重內訌, 分裂: *Scandal is tearing the government apart.* 醜聞使政府面臨分裂。**3** to break something into many small pieces, especially in a violent way〔尤指粗暴地〕把...撕成碎片: *a carcass torn apart by wolves* 被狼羣撕碎的屍體

tear at sb/sth *phr v* [T] to pull violently at someone or something 撕扯: *The children were screaming and tearing at each other's hair.* 孩子們尖叫着, 互相抓扯着對方的頭髮。

tear away *phr v* **1** [I] to suddenly start moving very quickly〔突然迅速地〕離開: *The car tore away into the distance.* 汽車突然加速, 迅速消失在遠方。**2 tear yourself away (from)** to leave a place or person very unwillingly because you have to 依依不捨地離開: *Could you please tear yourself away from the TV and help me for a minute.* 勞駕你先別看電視了, 來幫我一下。

tear sth ↔ **down** *phr v* [T] to knock down a large building or part of a building 推倒, 拆毀〔建築物〕: *It's time some of these old apartment blocks were torn down.* 這裡有些舊的住宅樓該拆了。

tear into sb/sth *phr v* [T not in passive 不用被動態] **1** to attack someone by hitting them very hard 猛攻; 向...猛撲: *boxers tearing into each other* 拳擊手相互猛攻對方 **2** to criticize someone very strongly, especially unfairly〔尤指不公正地〕猛烈抨擊〔某人〕: *All I said was that she could maybe try harder and she really tore into me.* 我只不過說她也許得更努力一些, 她倒真的向我開起火來了。

tear off *phr v* **1** [T **tear** sth ↔ **off**] to remove your clothes as quickly as you can 迅速脫掉〔衣服〕: *Ben tore off his coat and dived in to rescue the child.* 本迅速脫掉外衣, 跳下水去救那個孩子。**2** [I] to suddenly start moving very quickly 突然迅速走開[離開]: *I must tear off to the store before it closes.* 我必須在關門前趕到商店。**3** [T **tear** sth ↔ **off**] *BrE informal* to write something in a short time【英, 非正式】匆匆寫成: *I tore off a letter.* 我匆匆寫就了一封信。

tear up 撕碎

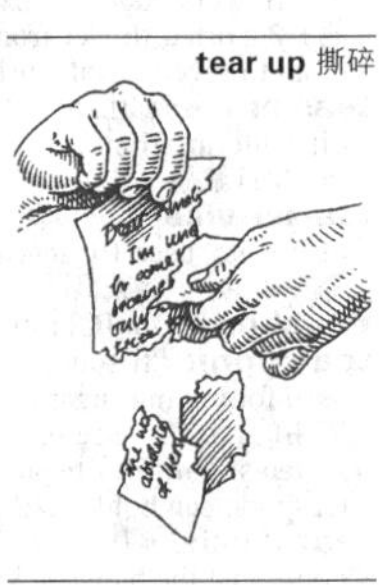

tear sth ↔ **up** *phr v* [T] **1** to destroy a piece of paper or cloth by breaking it into small pieces 把〔紙或布〕撕碎: *Crying, she tore up his letter.* 她邊哭邊把他的信給撕碎了。**2** to damage or ruin a place, especially by behaving violently〔尤指舉止粗暴地〕搗毀, 破壞〔某個地方〕: *football fans tearing up the grounds* 足球迷們搗毀場地 **3 tear up an agreement/contract etc** to suddenly decide to stop being restricted by a contract etc 撕毀協議/合同等

tear³ /tɛr; teə/ *n* [C] a hole in a piece of cloth, paper etc where it has been torn〔布、紙等〕撕破的地方; 裂口 — see also 另見 **wear and tear** (WEAR² (4))

tear·a·way /ˈtɛrəˌwe; ˈteərəweɪ/ *n* [C] *informal* a young person who behaves badly and often gets into trouble【非正式】小流氓, 暴徒; 愛惹禍的小伙子: *One night some young tearaways set fire to the De Corizo house.* 一天夜裡, 幾個小流氓放火燒了德·科里佐家的房子。

tear·drop /ˈtɪrˌdrɑp; ˈtɪədrɒp/ *n* [C] *especially literary* a single drop of salty liquid from your eye【尤文】淚滴, 淚珠

tear·ful /ˈtɪrfʊl; ˈtɪəfəl/ *adj* crying a little or almost crying 哭泣的; 將要哭泣的: *a tearful reunion at the airport* 機場上一次滿含淚水的團聚 —**tearfully** *adv*

tear gas /ˈtɪr gæs; ˈtɪə gæs/ *n* [U] a gas that stings your eyes, used by the police to control crowds 催淚瓦斯, 催淚彈 —**teargas** *v* [T]

tear·jerk·er /ˈtɪrˌdʒɝkɚ; ˈtɪəˌdʒɜːkə/ *n* [C] *informal* a film, book, story etc that makes you feel very sad【非正式】使人悲傷流淚的電影[圖書, 故事等]

tea·room /ˈtiˌrum; ˈtiːruːm/ *n* [C] a restaurant where tea and light meals are served〔供應茶和點心的〕茶館, 茶室

tease¹ /tiz; tiːz/ *v* **1** [I,T] to make jokes and laugh at someone in order to have fun by embarrassing them, either in a friendly way or in an unkind way 戲弄, 逗弄; 拿...取笑[開玩笑]: *Don't get upset, I was only teasing.* 別介意, 我只是在開玩笑。| **tease sb** *Kids often tease each other.* 孩子們經常互相開玩笑。| **tease sb about** *I was teased about my weight as a child.* 我小的時候別人老取笑我長得胖。**2** [T] to deliberately annoy an animal〔故意地〕逗弄; 激怒〔動物〕: *Stop teasing the cat!* 別再招惹那隻貓了! **3** [I,T] to deliberately make someone sexually excited without intending to have sex with them 挑逗, 撩撥〔使某人性興奮〕**4** [T] *AmE* to comb your hair in the opposite direction to which it grows, so that it looks thicker【美】回梳, 逆梳〔以使頭髮顯得濃密〕; BACKCOMB *BrE*【英】

T

tease out *phr v* [T] **1 tease sth out of sb** to persuade someone to tell you something that they do not want to tell you 哄騙〔某人〕說出〔某事〕 **2 [tease** sth ↔ **out]** to gently loosen or straighten hairs or threads that are stuck together 把〔纏繞在一起的毛髮或線繩〕輕輕弄鬆[弄直]: *She teased out the knots in her hair.* 她把頭髮裡的結弄開了。

tease² *n* [C] *informal*【非正式】**1** someone who enjoys making jokes at people, and embarrassing them, especially in a friendly way 愛開玩笑的人, 愛戲弄別人的人〔尤指以無惡意的方式〕: *Don't take any notice of Joe – he's a big tease.* 千萬不要搭理喬 —— 他可特別愛戲弄人。**2** someone who deliberately makes you sexually excited, but has no intention of having sex with you 性挑逗者

tea·sel /ˋtizl; ˈtiːzəl/ *n* [C] **1** a plant with PRICKLY leaves and flowers 起絨草, 川續斷〔一種葉子和花都帶刺的植物〕**2** a dried flower from this plant, used for brushing cloth to give it a soft surface 曬乾的起絨草花

teas·er /ˋtizɚ; ˈtiːzə/ *n* [C] *informal*【非正式】**1** a very difficult question, especially in a competition〔尤指競賽中的〕難題 **2** a TEASE² 愛戲弄別人的人; 性挑逗者

tea ser·vice /ˈ· ˌ··/ *n* [C] a matching set of cups, plates, teapot etc, used for serving tea〔包括茶杯、茶碟和茶壺等在內的〕一套茶具

tea shop /ˈ· ·/ *n* [C] a TEAROOM 茶館

tea·spoon /ˋtiˌspun; ˈtiːspuːn/ *n* [C] **1** a small spoon used for mixing sugar into tea, coffee etc〔攪拌茶、咖啡等用的〕茶匙 —see picture at 參見 SPOON¹ 圖 **2** also 又作 **tea·spoon·ful** /ˋtispunful; ˈtiːspuːnfʊl/ the amount a teaspoon can hold 一茶匙容量

teat /tit; tiːt/ *n* [C] **1** *BrE* the rubber part on a baby's bottle that the baby sucks milk from【英】〔嬰兒奶瓶上的〕橡皮奶頭; NIPPLE (3) *AmE*【美】**2** one of the small parts on a female animal's body that her babies suck milk from〔雌性動物的〕奶頭, 乳頭

tea tow·el /ˈ· ˌ··/ *n* [C] *BrE* a cloth for drying cups, plates etc, after you have washed them【英】〔用來擦乾洗過的杯盤等的〕拭布; 茶巾; DISH TOWEL *AmE*【美】—see picture on page A10 參見 A10 頁圖

tea trol·ley /ˈ· ˌ··/ *n* [C] *BrE* a small table on wheels, that you serve food and drinks from【英】〔用來端食品和飲料的〕小餐車

tea urn /ˈ· ·/ *n* [C] a large metal container with a TAP¹ (1) used for heating the water to make tea〔燒水泡茶用的〕大茶壺, 茶炊

tea·zel, teazle /ˋtizl; ˈtiːzəl/ *n* [C] another spelling of TEASEL teasel 的另一種拼法

tech /tɛk; tek/ *n* [C] *BrE informal* a TECHNICAL COLLEGE【英, 非正式】技術學院

tech·ie /ˋtɛkɪ; ˈteki/ *n* [C] *AmE informal* a TECHNICIAN (1)【美, 非正式】技術人員

tech·ni·cal /ˋtɛknɪkḷ; ˈteknɪkəl/ *adj*

1 ►INDUSTRY/SCIENCE 工業/科學◄ connected with practical knowledge, skills, or methods, especially in industrial or scientific work 技術的, 技能的; 工藝的: *technical experts* 技術專家 | *technical training* 技術訓練 —see 見 TECHNIQUE (USAGE)

2 ►LANGUAGE 語言◄ using words in a special way that is difficult for most people to understand because it is connected with one particular subject 技術性的; 與技術或專業相關的: *technical terms* 術語

3 technical problem/hitch a problem involving the way an engine or system works 技術故障, 機件故障

4 ►ACCORDING TO RULES 根據規則◄ according to the exact details in a set of rules 嚴格根據規則的; 嚴格遵循某些規章的: *a technical infringement of the rules* 一次法律意義上的違規

5 ►IN MUSIC/ART 在音樂/藝術方面◄ concerning the special skill of doing something difficult, especially in music, art, sport etc〔尤指在音樂、藝術、體育運動等方面〕技巧卓越的: *Navratilova's technical mastery of the game* 娜拉蒂露娃對網球運動技巧的出色掌握

technical col·lege /ˈ··· ˌ··/ *n* [C] a college in Britain where students who have finished school study for further qualifications especially in practical subjects〔英國實用科目方面的〕專科學院, 技術學院

tech·ni·cal·i·ty /ˌtɛknɪˋkælətɪ; ˌteknḷˈkæləti/ *n* [C] **1 technicalities** [plural] details of a system or process that you need a special knowledge to understand 技術細節: *Can you explain the technicalities of laser printing?* 你能不能解釋一下激光打印的技術細節? **2** a small detail in a law or a set of rules, especially one that forces you to make a decision that seems unfair〔法律或規則上的〕細則〔尤指迫使人作出看似不公平決定的細則〕: *A legal technicality meant Tollitt had to be released, although the evidence was against him.* 根據法律上的一項細則, 必須釋放托利特, 儘管證據對他不利。| **on a technicality** (=only because of a technicality) 因法律[規則]的細節 *Wild lost the competition on a technicality.* 懷爾德因規則的一項細節而輸掉了那場比賽。

tech·ni·cally /ˋtɛknɪkḷɪ; ˈteknɪkli/ *adv* **1** [sentence adverb 句子副詞] according to the exact details of rules, laws etc; STRICTLY (1) 嚴格根據法律地; 嚴格遵循規則地: *Technically, I'm not supposed to do this, but we're short-staffed.* 按說, 我不應該這樣做, 但我們實在是缺少人手。**2** [+adj/adv] showing the special skills connected with a particular activity 技巧上; 與技巧有關地: *a technically brilliant pianist* 一位技巧卓越的鋼琴家 **3 technically possible/impossible/difficult etc** possible etc using the scientific knowledge that is available now 技術上是可能的/不可能的/困難的

tech·ni·cian /tɛkˋnɪʃən; tekˈnɪʃən/ *n* [C] **1** a skilled scientific or industrial worker 技師, 技術人員: *a laboratory technician* 一名實驗室技術人員 —see 見 TECHNIQUE (USAGE) **2** someone who is very good at the skills of a particular sport, art etc〔運動、藝術等〕精於技巧者; 巧匠: *Whether he was a great artist or not, Dali was a superb technician.* 無論達里是不是一名偉大的藝術家, 他確是一名卓越的技巧大師。

Tech·ni·col·or /ˋtɛknɪˌkʌlɚ; ˈteknɪkʌlə/ *n* [U] *trademark* a type of colour film process used for the cinema【商標】〔電影的〕彩色印片法

tech·ni·col·our *BrE*【英】**, technicolor** *AmE*【美】/ˋtɛknɪˌkʌlɚ; ˈteknɪkʌlə/ *adj* [only before noun 僅用於名詞前] *humorous* having many very bright colours, usually too bright【幽默】色彩(過分)鮮豔的, 豔麗多彩的

tech·nique /tɛkˋnik; tekˈniːk/ *n* [C] **1** a special skill or way of doing something, especially one that has to be learned 技巧; 手法: *new techniques for producing special effects in movies* 製作電影特別效果的一些新技法 **2** [U] the level of skill or the set of skills that someone has 技術水平; 技能: *a footballer with brilliant technique* 一名技術高超的足球運動員

USAGE NOTE 用法說明: TECHNIQUE

WORD CHOICE 詞語辨析: **technique, technology, technical, technician, expert, high tech**

A **technique** [C] is a specific way of doing something, usually involving some skill. It may or may not be scientific or involve machines. 可數名詞 technique 指技巧、技術, 它不一定與科學或機器有關: *a teaching/management/propaganda technique* 教學/管理/宣傳技巧 | *a new technique that allows us to see inside the human body* 一種使我們得以看到人體內部的新技術

Technique [U] is the way you do something practical or skilful. 不可數名詞 technique 指做某實用或要求專門技巧的事情的水平、技能: *She's a wonderful skater, her technique is superb.* 她是一名了不起的滑冰高手, 她的水平是一流的。

Technology (usually [U]) is the general use of scientific knowledge for practical purposes, usually seen in actual machines or in industry. technology 一般用作不可數名詞，泛指針對實用目的的科學知識，通常體現於具體的機器或工業方面: *high technology* (NOT 不用 *high techniques*) 高科技 | *Computer/medical technology is changing the world* (NOT 不用 *the technology is changing the world*). 電腦／醫學技術正在改變着世界。| *An examination of the wrecked ship will tell us something about the technology of the past* (NOT 不用 *technique*). 通過對遇難船隻的檢查，我們將會明白有關前人科技的一些東西。

Something that is **technical** often relates to detailed practical knowledge of something involving science, technology, or machines. technical 往往與科學技術或機械的具體知識相關: *a technical report on the plane crash* (=describing exactly what went wrong with the plane) 關於飛機墜毀的技術性報告〔詳細描述失事飛機的問題所在〕| *The train is delayed due to a technical fault.* 火車因為技術故障而誤點。| *technical progress/subjects/information/help/expertise* 技術進步／題材／情報／幫助／知識

More generally **technical** matters may involve knowledge about any job or subject that only someone specially trained would usually have. 較廣義的 technical 指與必須經過專門訓練才能掌握的任何工作或學科有關的知識: *a technical point of law* 一個專業性的法律觀點 | *a technical grammatical term* 一個語法專業術語 | *a highly technical question* 一個高度專業性的問題

Someone who works with and mends scientific equipment or machines is a **technician**. Someone who knows all about a particular subject of any sort is an **expert** (NOT 不用 *a technical*). technician 是指在工作中使用科學設備或機器並會對其進行修理的技術人員。expert (專家) 是指通曉某一學科的人。

A machine, process or industry may be **high tech** (=using the latest scientific ideas, especially electronic) (but NOT 但不用 *high technical*). high tech 形容機器、工序、工業等，指使用最新科學思想尤其是電子學的高科技: *Surgeons now use the latest in high tech medical equipment.* 外科醫生們現在使用最新的高科技醫療設備。| *high tech computer companies* 高科技電腦公司

SPELLING 拼寫

Technique is never spelt *technic* or *tecnique*. technique 不能拼寫成 technic 或 tecnique。

tech·no /ˋtɛkno; ˈteknəʊ/ *n* [U] a type of popular electronic dance music with a fast, strong beat 高技術音樂〔一種節奏快而強勁的電子舞蹈音樂〕

techno- /tɛknə; teknə/ *prefix* **1** concerning TECHNOLOGY 表示與技術相關的: *technocracy* (=rule by skilled specialists) 技術專家統治 | *technophobia* (=dislike of computers, machines etc) 技術恐懼〔指不喜歡電腦、機器等〕 **2 techno-literacy/techno-babble/techno-theorist etc** connected with electronic equipment such as computers 對電腦的通曉／技術套語[行話]／電腦理論家等: *techno-literacy* (=skill in using computers) 會用或通曉電腦

tech·noc·racy /tɛkˋnɑkrəsɪ; tekˈnɒkrəsi/ *n* [C,U] a social system in which people with a lot of scientific or technical knowledge have a lot of power 技術專家統治〔一種科學技術人材掌握大量權力的社會制度〕

tech·no·crat /ˋtɛknə͵kræt; ˈteknəkræt/ *n* [C] a highly skilled scientist who has a lot of power in industry or government 技術專家官員，在工業或政府內有很大權力的技術專家

tech·no·lo·gi·cal /͵tɛknəˋlɑdʒɪkḷ; ͵teknəˈlɒdʒɪkəl◂/ *adj* related to technology 技術的; 科技的; 工藝的: *The steam engine was the greatest technological advance of the 19th century.* 蒸汽機是 19 世紀最偉大的科技進步。—**technologically** /-kḷɪ; -kli/ *adv*: *technologically developed countries* 科技發達國家

tech·nol·o·gist /tɛkˋnɑlədʒɪst; tekˈnɒlədʒɪst/ *n* [C] someone who has special knowledge of technology 技術專家; 工藝學專家

tech·nol·o·gy /tɛkˋnɑlədʒɪ; tekˈnɒlədʒi/ *n* **1** [C,U] knowledge about scientific or industrial methods or the use of these methods 科技; 工藝; 工業技術: *nuclear technology* 核工業技術 | *the application of modern technologies to agriculture* 現代科技在農業上的應用 —see 見 TECHNIQUE (USAGE) **2** [U] machinery and equipment used or developed as a result of this knowledge 技術設備; 技術應用: *The factory uses the very latest technology.* 工廠使用了最新的技術設備。 S2 W1

tech·no·phobe /ˋtɛknə͵fob; ˈteknəfəʊb/ *n* [C] someone who does not like modern machines, such as computers 〔指不喜歡電腦等現代機器的〕技術恐懼者 —**technophobia** /͵tɛknəˋfobɪə; ͵teknəˈfəʊbiə/ *n* [U]

ted·dy bear /ˋtɛdɪ bɛr; ˈtedi beə/ also 又作 **teddy** *BrE* 【英】 *n* [C] a soft toy in the shape of a bear 玩具熊

teddy boy /ˈ·· ·/ *n* [C] a member of a group of young men in Britain in the 1950's who had their own special style of clothes and music〔指英國 20 世紀 50 年代在衣着打扮和音樂愛好方面都很獨特的〕男阿飛

te·di·ous /ˋtidɪəs; ˈtiːdiəs/ *adj* boring, tiring, and continuing for a long time 枯燥乏味的; 冗長的: *a tedious lecture* 一次很枯燥的講座 —**tediously** *adv* —**tediousness** *n* [U]

te·di·um /ˋtidɪəm; ˈtiːdiəm/ *n* [U] the quality of being tedious 枯燥乏味; 冗長: *She hated the tedium of life in a small country village.* 她很厭煩小鄉村裡枯燥乏味的生活。

tee[1] /ti; tiː/ *n* [C] **1** a small object, used in GOLF to hold the ball above the ground before you hit it〔高爾夫球運動中用來放置球的〕球座 —see picture on page A23 參見 A23 頁圖 **2** a flat, raised area from which you hit the ball in a game of GOLF〔高爾夫球運動中的〕開球區, 發球區

tee[2]

tee off *phr v* **1** [I] to hit the ball off the tee in a game of GOLF〔從高爾夫球球座上〕開球, 發球 **2** [T **tee** sb **off**] *AmE informal* to make someone angry【美, 非正式】使〔某人〕生氣, 激怒: *His attitude really tees me off.* 他的態度真的惹惱了我。**3** [T **tee off on** sb] *AmE informal* to be angry with someone or criticize them【美, 非正式】責罵; 嚴厲地批評〔某人〕

Tee-ball /ˈ· ·/ *n* [U] another spelling of T-BALL t-ball 的另一種拼法

teed off /͵· ˈ·/ *adj AmE slang* annoyed or angry; FED UP 【美俚】惱怒的, 發怒的

teem /tim; tiːm/ also 又作 **teem down** *v* [I] *BrE* to rain very heavily【英】下大雨: *It's been teeming down all day.* 一整天都在下着大雨。

teem with sth *phr v* [T not in passive 不用被動態] to be full of people, animals etc 充滿〔人或動物等〕: **be teeming with** *Times Square was teeming with theatergoers.* 時代廣場上擠滿了看戲的人。

teem·ing /ˋtimɪŋ; ˈtiːmɪŋ/ *adj* full of people, animals, etc that are all moving around 充滿〔人或動物等〕的; 擁擠的; 萬頭攢動的: **teeming city/streets/market etc** *the teeming streets of Cairo* 萬頭攢動的開羅街道

teen[1] /tin; tiːn/ *adj informal*【非正式】[only before noun 僅用於名詞前] teenage 少年的, 十幾歲的: *a teen magazine* 一本少年雜誌

teen[2] *n* [C] *AmE informal* a teenager【美, 非正式】少年, 十幾歲的孩子

teen·age /ˋtin͵edʒ; ˈtiːneɪdʒ/ also 又作 **teen·aged** /ˋtin͵edʒd; ˈtiːneɪdʒd/ *adj* [only before noun 僅用於名詞前] aged between 13 and 19, or concerning someone of that age 少年的, 十幾歲的〔13 到 19 歲之間的〕: *my teenage daughter* 我那十多歲的女兒

teen·ag·er /ˋtin͵edʒɚ; ˈtiːneɪdʒə/ *n* [C] also 又作 **teen** *AmE informal*【美, 非正式】someone who is between 13 and 19 years old 少年, 十幾歲的孩子〔13 到 19 歲之

T

間的孩子〕: *a TV sex education series aimed at teenagers* 一部針對少年的性教育電視系列片 —see 見 CHILD (USAGE)

teens /tinz; tiːnz/ *n* [plural] the period of your life when you are between 13 and 19 years old 少年時期; 13 到 19 歲之間的階段: **be in your teens** *They were in their teens when they first met.* 他們初次見面時都才十多歲。

tee·ny /ˋtinɪ; ˈtiːni/ *adj informal* very small; TINY【非正式】很小的, 小小的

tee·ny·bop·per /ˋtinɪˌbɑpɚ; ˈtiːniˌbɒpə/ *n* [C] *old-fashioned* a girl between the ages of about 9 and 14, who is very interested in popular music, teenage fashions etc【過時】〔年齡在大約 9 至 14 歲之間、熱衷於流行音樂、少年時尚等的〕時髦少女

tee·ny wee·ny /ˋtinɪ ˋwinɪ; ˌtiːni ˈwiːni◂/ also 又作 **teen·sy ween·sy** /ˌtinzɪ ˋwinzɪ; ˌtiːnzi ˈwiːnzi◂/ *adj informal* a word meaning very small, used especially by or to children【非正式】小小的; 一點點的〔尤指兒語〕

tee·pee /ˋtipi; ˈtiːpiː/ *n* [C] another spelling of TEPEE tepee 的另一種拼法

tee shirt /ˈ· ˌ·/ *n* [C] another spelling of T-SHIRT t-shirt 的另一種拼法

tee·ter /ˋtitɚ; ˈtiːtə/ *v* [I] **1** to stand or move unsteadily as if you are going to fall 站立不穩; 搖搖欲墜; 蹣跚行走: **[+on/along/across etc]** *She teetered along in her high-heeled shoes.* 她穿着高跟鞋踉踉蹌蹌地走着。**2 be teetering on the brink/edge of** to be very close to an extreme and dangerous situation 瀕臨〔危險形勢〕: *teetering on the brink of revolution* 革命前夕

teeter-tot·ter /ˈ·· ˌ··/ *n* [C] *AmE* a large toy like a board on which two children sit, one at each end; SEESAW[1]【美】蹺蹺板

teeth 牙齒

wisdom tooth 智慧齒
molar 臼齒
front tooth/incisor 門齒
canine tooth 犬齒

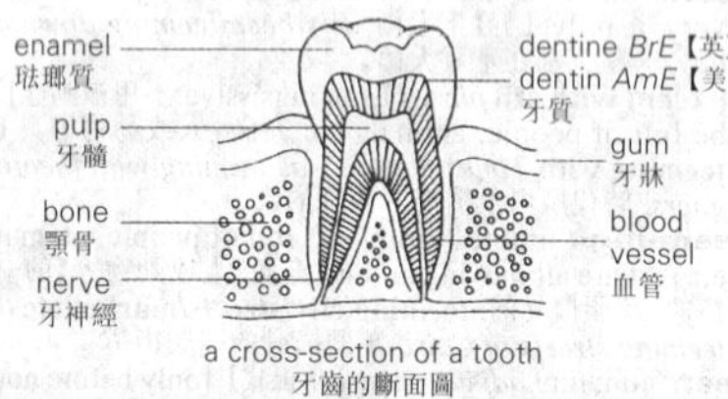

a cross-section of a tooth
牙齒的斷面圖

teeth /tiθ; tiːθ/ *n* the plural of TOOTH

teethe /tið; tiːð/ *v* [I] **be teething** if a baby is teething, its first teeth are growing〔嬰兒〕長乳牙 —**teething** *n* [U]

teething troub·les /ˈ·· ˌ··/ *n* [plural] small problems that a company, product, system etc has at the beginning〔公司、產品、系統等〕開始階段的困難: *a few teething troubles with the new computer system* 這套新的電腦系統在啟用階段遇到的幾個問題

tee·to·tal /tiˋtotl̩; ˌtiːˈtəʊtl◂/ *adj* never drinking alcohol 滴酒不沾的 —**teetotalism** *n* [U]

tee·to·tal·ler *BrE*【英】, **teetotaler** *AmE*【美】/tiˋtotl̩ɚ; tiːˈtəʊtələ/ *n* [C] someone who never drinks alcohol 滴酒不沾的人: *There was a time when no self-respecting pop star would admit to being a non-smoking teetotaller.* 曾經有一段時間, 所有自尊自重的明星都不願承認自己是煙酒不沾的人。

TEFL /ˋtɛfəl; ˈtefəl/ *n* [U] the teaching of English as a foreign language 作為外語的英語教學 —compare 比較 TESOL

Tef·lon /ˋtɛflɑn; ˈteflɒn/ *n* [U] *trademark* a plastic that stops things from sticking to it, often used in making pans【商標】特氟隆, 聚四氟乙烯〔一種不易黏的塑料, 常用於平底鍋製造中〕

tel the written abbreviation of 縮寫= TELEPHONE NUMBER

tele- /tɛlɪ; teli/ *prefix* **1** at or over a long distance 遠(距離): *a telescope* (=for seeing a long way) 望遠鏡 | *telecommunications* 電信, 長途通信 | *telepathy* (=sending of thought messages) 通靈術 | *teleshopping*(=using a computer in your home to order goods) 電腦購物(法) **2** by or for television 由電視; 為電視: *a teleplay* 電視劇 | *a telerecording* 電視屏幕錄像

tel·e·cast /ˋtɛləˌkæst; ˈtelikɑːst/ *n* [C] a broadcast on television 電視廣播

tel·e·com·mu·ni·ca·tions /ˌtɛləkəˌmjunəˋkeʃənz; ˌtelikəmjuːnɪ̈ˈkeɪʃənz/ *n* [plural] the process or business of sending and receiving messages by telephone, radio, television etc 電信〔指用電話、無線電、電視等發送和接收信息〕: *a telecommunications satellite* 通信衛星

tele·com·mut·er /ˋtɛləkəˌmjutɚ; ˈtelikəˌmjuːtə/ *n* [C] someone who works for a company at home using a computer connected to the main office 遠距離工作者〔指在家裡通過使用與公司辦公室相連接的電腦而工作的人〕 —**telecommuting** *n* [U]

tel·e·gram /ˋtɛləˌgræm; ˈtelɪ̈græm/ *n* [C] a message sent by telegraph 電報, 電文; WIRE[1] (6) *AmE*【美】: *telegrams of congratulations* 賀電

tel·e·graph[1] /ˋtɛləˌgræf; ˈtelɪ̈grɑːf/ *n* **1** [U] an old-fashioned method of sending messages using radio or electrical signals〔舊時用無線電或電信號發送信息的〕電報 **2** [C] a piece of equipment that receives or sends messages in this way 電報機 —see also 另見 BUSH TELEGRAPH —**telegraphic** /ˌtɛləˋgræfɪk; ˌtelɪ̈ˈgræfɪk◂/ *adj* —**telegraphically** /-klɪ; -kli/ *adv*

telegraph[2] *v* **1** [I,T] to send a message by telegraph (給…)發電報, 發電文: *Once he knew where we were, Lewis telegraphed every few hours.* 一知道了我們所在的地方, 劉易斯每隔幾小時便發來一份電報。**2** [T] *informal* to let people clearly see what you intend to do without saying anything【非正式】流露; 暴露〔意圖〕: *Sampras rather telegraphed that shot.* 森柏斯這球要怎麼打, 毫不含糊。

te·leg·ra·pher /təˋlɛgrəfɚ; tɪ̈ˈlegrəfə/ *n* [C] someone whose job is to send and receive messages by telegraph 電報員, 報務員

tel·e·graph·ese /ˌtɛləgræˋfiz; ˌtelɪ̈grəˈfiːz/ *n* [U] the style of language used in TELEGRAM*s* in which you only include the really necessary words 電報文體

te·leg·ra·phist /təˋlɛgrəfɪst; tɪ̈ˈlegrəfɪ̈st/ *n* [C] a telegrapher 電報員, 報務員

telegraph line /ˈ··· ˌ·/ *n* [C] a telegraph wire 電報線

telegraph pole /ˈ··· ˌ·/ *n* [C] *BrE* a tall wooden pole for supporting telephone wires【英】電話線杆; TELEPHONE POLE *AmE*【美】

telegraph post /ˈ··· ˌ·/ *n* [C] *BrE* a telegraph pole【英】電話線杆

telegraph wire /ˈ··· ˌ·/ *n* [C] a wire for sending messages by TELEGRAPH[1] 電報線

te·leg·ra·phy /təˋlɛgrəfɪ; tɪ̈ˈlegrəfi/ *n* [U] *technical* the process of sending messages by TELEGRAPH[1]【術語】電報通訊(術)

tel·e·ki·nes·is /ˌtɛləkɪˋnisɪs; ˌtelikɪˈniːsɪs/ *n* [U] the ability to move physical objects using only the power of your mind 心靈致動〔僅憑心靈的力量可移動物體的能力〕

tel·e·mar·ket·ing /ˌtɛləˋmɑrkɪtɪŋ; ˌteliˈmɑːkɪ̈tɪŋ/ *n* [U] a method of selling things in which you telephone people to see if they want to buy something 電話推銷(術) —compare 比較 TELESALES —**telemarketer** *n* [C]

te·lem·e·try /təˋlɛmətrɪ; tɪ̆ˈlemɪ̆tri/ *n* [U] *technical* the use of special scientific equipment to measure something and send the results somewhere by radio【術語】遙測

tel·e·ol·o·gy /tɛlɪˋalədʒɪ; ˌteliˈɒlədʒi/ *n* [U] the belief that all natural things and events were specially planned for a particular purpose 目的論〔認為自然界一切事物均被有意安排以達到某種目的〕—**teleological** /ˌtɛlɪəˋladʒɪkəl; ˌteliəˈlɒdʒɪkəl◂/ *adj*

tel·e·path·ic /ˌtɛlɪˋpæθɪk; ˌtelɪ̆ˈpæθɪk◂/ *adj* **1** having a mysterious ability to know what other people are thinking 有心靈感應能力的: *How did he know that? He must be telepathic.* 他怎麼知道那件事的? 他一定有心靈感應。**2** connected with or sent by telepathy 與心靈感應相關的; 以心靈感應術傳送的: *telepathic messages* 以心靈感應術傳遞的信息

te·lep·a·thy /təˋlɛpəθɪ; tɪ̆ˈlepəθi/ *n* [U] the communication of thoughts directly from one person's mind to someone else's without speaking, writing, or signs 傳心術, 心靈感應術

S1 W2 **tel·e·phone¹** /ˋtɛləˌfon; ˈtelɪ̆fəʊn/ *n* **1 the telephone** the system of communication that you use to have a conversation with someone in another place; PHONE¹ (1) 電話: *The telephone was invented by Alexander Graham Bell.* 電話是由亞歷山大·格雷厄姆·貝爾發明的。| *a telephone conversation* 一次電話交談 | **by telephone** *Reservations can be made by telephone.* 可以通過電話預訂。**2** [C] the piece of equipment that you use when you are speaking to someone by telephone; PHONE¹ (2) 電話機: *The telephone is ringing.* 電話鈴響了。| *the cost of installing telephones* 安裝電話的費用 **3 be on the telephone a)** to be talking to someone using the telephone 正在打電話: *I was on the telephone when he came in.* 他進來時, 我正在打電話。**b)** to have a telephone in your home, office etc〔在家裡、辦公室裡等〕有電話 **4** [C] the part of a telephone that you hold close to your ear and mouth; RECEIVER (1) 電話筒; 聽筒 —**telephonic** /ˌtɛləˋfanɪk; ˌtelɪ̆ˈfɒnɪk◂/ *adj*

USAGE NOTE 用法說明: TELEPHONE

WORD CHOICE 詞語辨析: words related to the telephone 與 telephone 有關的詞

Telephone can be used as a noun or a verb, as can the short form **phone**, which is four times more common in spoken English. telephone可用作名詞或動詞, 其縮寫形式 phone 亦如此。phone 在口頭英語中使用的頻率是 telephone 的四倍。

If someone phones you, you **have or receive a call** (NOT 不用 *a telephone*) from them. have a call 或 receive a call 指接到一個電話。

If you want to **phone** a friend or **call** them (or **ring** them **(up)** (*BrE*), **give** them **a ring** (*BrE*)/**call**), you **dial** their **(phone) number**. 給朋友打電話 (phone, call, ring ... up【英】, 或 give ... a ring【英】/call), 需撥 (dial) 他的電話號碼 (phone number)。

If you are phoning **long distance**, you will need to dial the **code** (*BrE*)/**area code** (*AmE*) (=number) for the region or country where they live, as well as their **local** number. 打長途電話 (long distance), 需撥區號 (code【英】/area code【美】) 和本地的號碼 (local number)。

All these numbers are found in the **phone book** or **directory** (*BrE*), or by phoning **directory enquiries** (*BrE*)/**information** (*AmE*). 電話號碼可以在電話號碼簿 (phone book/directory【英】) 中找到, 也可以在尋號台 (directory enquiries【英】/information【美】) 找到。

If you have a problem **getting through** to the person you are phoning, you may ring the **operator** for help. 電話接通是 get through。接不通電話時可以找接線員 (operator) 幫忙。

When you phone someone, their phone will **ring**, and if they are at home they will answer by **picking up the phone** (or technically the **receiver**, or on cordless phones the **handset**). 你給人打電話時, 他的電話鈴聲會響 (ring) 起來。如果他在家, 他會拿起電話 (pick up the phone) 來聽; 嚴格地說是拿起聽筒 (receiver 或無繩電話的 handset)。

If they are busy they may ask you to **phone/call/ring back** later or to **hold on**, or more officially and in American English **hold** (=wait). 如果他正忙着, 他會讓你待會再打 (phone/call/ring back) 或等一下 (hold on, 正式用語或美式英語是 hold)。

If they do not want to speak to you, or have finished speaking to you, they may **hang up** (=replace the receiver or switch off the handset). 如果聽電話的人不想跟你談, 或者已經談完了, 他會掛斷電話 (hang up)。

If someone is already **on the phone** when you call them, their number is **engaged** (*BrE*)/**busy** (*AmE*). 如果打電話時對方正在通話 (on the phone), 電話會佔線 (engaged【英】/busy【美】)。

If someone does not want to receive any calls, they may **leave their phone off the hook** (=the receiver is not in its proper place) so that no calls will get through. 不想接電話的人會把電話摘下來 (leave the phone off the hook), 那麼甚麼電話都接不通。

A telephone in a public place is a **public phone** or **payphone**, often placed in a **phone/call box** (*BrE*) or **phone booth** (*AmE*). 在公共場所的電話是公用電話 (public phone) 或投幣電話 (payphone), 它常設置在電話亭 (phone/call box【英】, 也叫 phone booth【美】) 裡。

GRAMMAR 語法

You **(tele)phone** a place or a person, NOT *to* them. telephone 的賓語是一個地方或人, 不加 to: *Please phone Mary/the hospital.* 請給瑪麗/醫院打電話。But you often speak of being **on the phone to** someone. 但可以說 on the phone to ...。

telephone² *v* [I,T] *BrE formal* to speak to someone by telephone; PHONE²【英, 正式】(給...) 打電話: *Mr Dodd telephoned to say he was ill.* 多德先生打電話說他病了。

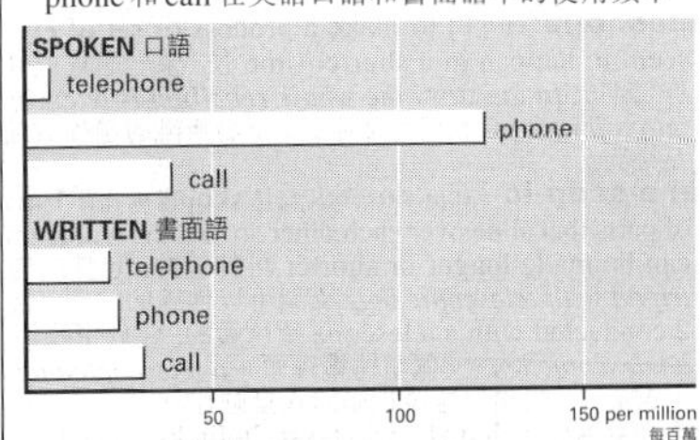
Frequencies of the verbs **telephone**, **phone** and **call** in spoken and written English 動詞 telephone, phone 和 call 在英語口語和書面語中的使用頻率

Based on the British National Corpus and the Longman Lancaster Corpus
據英國國家語料庫和朗文蘭卡斯特語料庫

This graph shows that it is much more usual in spoken English to use the verbs **phone** or **call** rather than **telephone**, which is formal and is therefore much more common in written English than in spoken English. 本圖表顯示, 在英語口語中, 動詞 phone 和 call 的使用頻率遠遠高於 telephone, 後者屬正式用語, 故而在英語書面語中更加常用。

T

telephone book /'··· ˌ·/ *n* [C] a TELEPHONE DIRECTORY 電話號碼簿

telephone box /'··· ˌ·/ *BrE*【英】, **telephone booth** *AmE*【美】*n* [C] an enclosed structure containing a telephone that can be used by the public 公用電話亭[間]

telephone call /'··· ˌ·/ *n* [C] an attempt to speak to someone by telephone 電話: *There's a telephone call for you, Mr Baron.* 巴倫先生, 有電話找你。

telephone di·rec·to·ry /'··· ·ˌ···/ *n* [C] a book containing an alphabetical list of the names, addresses, and telephone numbers of all the people in a particular area 電話號碼簿

telephone ex·change /'··· ·ˌ·/ *n* [C] a central building or office where telephone calls are connected to other telephones 電話交換台; 電話局

telephone num·ber /'··· ˌ··/ *n* [C] the number that you DIAL² to telephone a particular person or place 電話號碼

telephone pole /'··· ˌ·/ *n* [C] *AmE* a tall wooden pole for supporting telephone wires【美】電話線杆; TELEGRAPH POLE *BrE*【英】

te·leph·o·nist /tə'lɛfənɪst; tə̇'lefənə̇st/ *n* [C] *BrE* someone whose job is to connect telephone calls at a SWITCHBOARD or telephone exchange【英】接線員, 話務員 —compare 比較 OPERATOR (1)

te·le·pho·to lens /ˌtɛləfoto 'lɛnz; ˌteləfəʊtəʊ 'lenz/ *n* [C] a special camera LENS (2) used for taking clear photographs of things that are far away〔拍攝遠處物體用的〕長焦距鏡頭, 攝遠鏡頭: *a time before the advent of chequebook journalism and telephoto lenses* 在媒體出高價徵集名人隱私和攝遠鏡頭問世之前的時代

tel·e·print·er /'tɛlɪˌprɪntə; 'telə̇ˌprɪntə/ *n* [C] a machine for writing TELEX messages that you are sending, and for printing messages received 電傳打字機; TELETYPEWRITER *AmE*【美】

Tel·e·prompt·er /'tɛlɪˌprɑmptə; 'telə̇ˌprɒmptə/ *n* [C] *trademark* a machine that helps someone speaking on television by showing them the words of their speech on a screen【商標】〔在屏幕上為電視講話人映出講稿的〕電子提詞機

tel·e·sales /'tɛlɪselz; 'teliseɪlz/ *n* [U] the practice of telephoning people in order to try to sell them things 電話銷售, 電話售貨 —compare 比較 TELEMARKETING

tel·e·scope¹ /'tɛləˌskop; 'telə̇skəʊp/ *n* [C] a piece of scientific equipment shaped like a tube, used for making distant objects look larger and closer 望遠鏡: *the 250-ft Lovell telescope at Jodrell Bank* 焦德雷爾·班克的250英尺直徑的洛弗爾望遠鏡 —see also 另見 RADIO TELESCOPE

telescope² *v* [T] to make a process or set of events seem to happen in a shorter time 使〔某一過程或某事件〕縮短: *In the story the whole rebellion is telescoped into a few days.* 在這個故事裡, 整場叛亂的過程被縮短為幾天。

tel·e·scop·ic /ˌtɛlə'skɑpɪk; ˌtelə̇'skɒpɪk◂/ *adj* **1** made of parts that slide over each other so that the whole thing can be made longer or shorter 可伸縮的; 套疊式的: *a tripod with telescopic legs* 支架可以伸縮的一個三腳架 **2** connected with a telescope 望遠鏡的; 關於望遠鏡的: *a telescopic lens* 一個望遠鏡鏡頭 | *a telescopic picture of Mars* 一張用望遠鏡拍攝的火星圖片

tel·e·text, Teletext /'tɛləˌtɛkst; 'telitekst/ *n* [U] a system of broadcasting written information on television 電視文字播送

Tel·e·type /'tɛlɪˌtaɪp; 'telitaɪp/ *n* [C] *trademark* a TELEPRINTER【商標】電傳打字機

tel·e·type·writ·er /ˌtɛlɪ'taɪpraɪtə; ˌteli'taɪpraɪtə/ *n* [C] *AmE* a TELEPRINTER【美】電傳打字機

tel·e·vise /'tɛləˌvaɪz; 'telə̇vaɪz/ *v* [T] to broadcast something on television 用電視播放: *The game will be televised live on ABC tonight.* 這場比賽今晚將由美國廣播公司現場直播。

tel·e·vi·sion /'tɛləˌvɪʒən; 'telə̇ˌvɪʒən/ *n* **1** [C] also 又作 **television set** *formal* a thing shaped like a box with a screen, on which you can watch programmes; TV【正式】電視(機): *a 16 inch colour television* 一台16英寸的彩色電視機 **2** [U] a way of broadcasting pictures and sounds in the form of programmes that people can watch 電視播放(技術): *Who invented television?* 電視播放技術是誰發明的? | *television and radio journalism* 電視廣播新聞事業 **3** [U] the programmes broadcast in this way; TV 電視節目: **watch television** *In the evenings I like to relax and watch television.* 晚上, 我喜歡放鬆下來, 看看電視節目。| **television programme/show/commercial etc** *the television news* 電視新聞 **4 on (the) television** broadcast or being broadcast on television 在電視上播放: *What's on television tonight?* 今晚有甚麼電視節目? **5** [U] the business of making and broadcasting programmes on television 電視廣播業: *Jean works in television.* 瓊從事電視廣播。| **television producer/reporter/newsreader etc** *a television film-crew* 一支電視影片工作組

television li·cence /'···· ˌ··/ *n* [C] an official piece of paper that you need to buy in Britain in order to legally use a television in your home〔英國的〕電視機使用許可證

tel·e·work·er /'tɛlɪˌwɝkə; 'teliwɜːkə/ *n* [C] someone who works from home using a computer, FAX etc 家庭辦公者〔指在家裡使用電腦、傳真機等辦公的人〕

tel·ex¹ /'tɛlɛks; 'teleks/ *n* **1** [U] the system of sending messages from one business to another on the telephone network, by SATELLITE (1) etc 電傳, 電傳打字: **by telex** *We'll send you the reply by telex.* 我們將通過電傳給您回覆。**2** [C] a message sent in this way 通過電傳收發的信息

telex² *v* [I,T] to send a message, piece of information etc to someone using a telex 用電傳將〔信息〕傳給〔某人〕

tell off 斥責

tell /tɛl; tel/ *v past tense and past participle* **told** /told; təʊld/

1 ►SAY/INFORMATION 説/信息◄ [T] to give someone facts or information about something 把〔某事〕告訴〔某人〕; 説, 講: **tell sb (that)** *She wrote to tell me she couldn't come.* 她寫信告訴我她不能來了。| *Don't tell me you've forgotten my birthday again.* 不要對我説你又忘了我的生日。| *Police will not name the body until the relatives have been told.* 在告知親屬之前, 警察是不會公佈死者的身分的。| **tell sb who/why/what etc** *There is a sign telling you where the emergency exits are.* 有標誌告訴你緊急出口在哪裡。| **tell sb about sth** *Harry's been telling me all about his last vacation.* 哈里一直在給我講有關他上次度假的事。| **tell sb sth** *Tell me your name and address.* 告訴我你的名字和住址。| *Can you tell me the quickest way to Manchester?* 你能告訴我去曼徹斯特最快的方式嗎? | **tell a story/joke/secret/lie** *When I was young my father told me stories about the war.* 我小的時候, 我父親給我講過那次戰爭中的故事。| **tell the truth** *If Dan is telling the truth, the others are in* *danger.* 如果丹講的是真話, 那其他那些人就有危險。| **tell sb straight** (=tell someone the true facts or your true feelings) 直截了當地告訴某人 *I told her straight I wasn't coming.* 我直截了當地告訴她, 我不來了。—see 見 SAY[1] (USAGE)

2 ▶ORDER 命令◀ [T] to say that someone must do something; order 命令; 給…下命令: **tell sb to do sth** *The teacher told all the children to sit down quietly.* 老師要所有孩子都安安靜靜地坐下。| **tell sb what/how etc** *Don't tell me how to behave in public!* 不用你告訴我在公共場合該怎樣怎樣! | *Stop trying to tell me what to do all the time.* 別老是想命令我該做甚麼。| **tell sb (that)** *All the hostages were told that they had to lie on the floor.* 所有的人質被告知必須躺在地板上。| **do as you are told** (=obey) 按照告訴你的去做 *These kids will never do as they're told.* 這些孩子從來不按照要求去做。

3 tell yourself to remind yourself of the facts of a situation because it is difficult to accept or because it worries you 提醒自己; 叮囑自己: *I keep telling myself there is nothing I could have done to save him.* 我不斷告訴自己, 我實在是無力去救他。

4 ▶RECOGNIZE THE SIGNS 辨別跡象◀ [I,T not in progressive 不用進行式] to know something or be able to recognize something because of certain signs that show this 知道; 看出; 認出: *Yes, I do dye my hair. How can you tell?* 是的, 我的確經常染頭髮。你怎麼看出來的? | **tell (that)** *Even though it was so dark I could still tell it was you.* 儘管光線這麼暗, 我還是能認出這就是你。| **tell when/how etc** *It's hard to tell how long the job will take.* 很難說這工作要花多長時間。| **tell by/from** *You can tell by the way it walks that the dog has been injured.* 從這隻狗走路的樣子可以判斷出牠受傷了。| **tell a mile off** (=know very easily) 很容易看出 *You could tell a mile off that he was lying.* 很容易看出, 他是在撒謊。

5 ▶RECOGNIZE DIFFERENCE 識別◀ [T not in progressive 不用進行式] to be able to see how one person or thing is different from another 識別, 辨別, 分辨: **tell sth from sth** *Amateurs may be unable to tell the fake from the original painting.* 業餘愛好者也許識別不了真跡與贗品。| **tell sb and sb apart** *It's almost impossible to tell Jackie and Moira apart since they had their hair cut.* 由於傑基和莫伊拉都把頭髮剪了, 所以幾乎不可能把她倆區別開來。| **tell the difference** *Margarine and butter? I can't tell the difference.* 人造黃油和普通黃油? 我說不出它們有甚麼區別。

6 ▶WARN 警告◀ [T usually in past tense 一般用過去式] to warn someone that something bad might happen 警告; 告誡: **tell sb (that)** *I told you it was a waste of time talking to him.* 我早就告訴過你, 跟他談話是在浪費時間。| **tell sb to do sth** *My mother told me not to trust Robert.* 我媽媽告誡我不要相信羅伯特。

7 ▶BE A SIGN OF STH 顯示某種情況◀ [T not in progressive or passive 不用進行式或被動態] to give information in ways other than talking which helps you know or understand more about a situation 顯示; 提示; 說明: **tell sb (that)** *The bleeper tells you you've left your lights on.* 嘟嘟聲提示你忘了關燈。| **tell sb what/why etc** *The red light tells you when the machine is ready to use.* 紅燈提示你, 機器已可以使用。| **tell sb about sth** *What do these fossils tell us about our ancestors?* 這些化石說明了我們祖先的甚麼情況?

8 tell the time *BrE*【英】, **tell time** *AmE*【美】 to be able to know what time it is by looking at a clock 從鐘錶上讀出時間

9 ▶AFFECT 影響◀ [I not in progressive 不用進行式] to have an effect on someone, especially a harmful one 產生影響〔尤指有害的影響〕: *His years in the army certainly tell in his attitude to his work.* 他的多年軍旅生涯當然會影響他對自己工作的態度。| **tell on sb** *These late nights are really beginning to tell on her.* 這些天的熬夜真的開始在影響她了。| *The stress of work told on their marriage.* 工作的緊張影響了他倆的婚姻生活。—see also 另見 TELLING

10 ▶BAD BEHAVIOUR 不良行為◀ [I] *informal* to tell someone in authority about something wrong that someone has done【非正式】告發, 舉報: *I'm going to tell, if you don't stop messing around.* 如果你還是到處瞎混, 我就要告發你。| **tell on sb** *If you promise not to tell on me I'll put the money back where I found it.* 如果你答應不去告發我, 我就把這些錢放回到原處。

11 tell tales *BrE* to say something that is not true about someone else, especially to cause them trouble【英】誣衊; 搬弄是非: *Have you been telling tales again?* 你是不是又搬弄是非了? | **tell tales on sb** *an unpopular child, always telling tales on the other children* 一個不招人喜歡的、總愛給其他孩子打小報告的小孩子 —see also 另見 TELLTALE[2]

12 tell sb where to get off *informal* to tell someone angrily that you are not interested in them, what they want etc【非正式】嚴厲斥責〔某人〕; 使〔某人〕碰一鼻子灰: *"Did you give him the money?" "No, I told him where to get off."* "你把那錢給他了嗎?" "沒有。我讓他碰了一鼻子灰。"

13 all told altogether, when everyone or everything has been counted 總共, 合計, 總括起來: *There must have been eight cars in the accident, all told.* 這次大概總共有八輛車出了事故。

14 ▶VOTES 票數◀ [T] *technical* to count the votes in an election【術語】數, 計算〔選票〕—see also 另見 SAY[2] (1)

Frequencies of the verb **tell** in spoken and written English 動詞 tell 在英語口語和書面語中的使用頻率

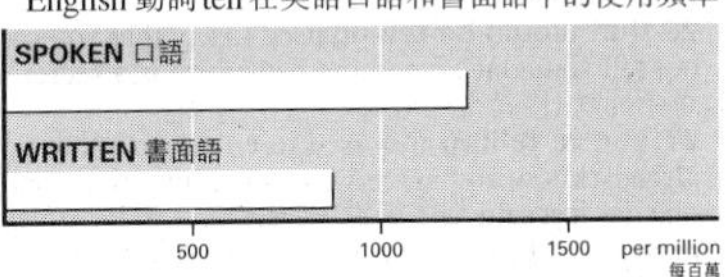

Based on the British National Corpus and the Longman Lancaster Corpus
據英國國家語料庫和朗文蘭卡斯特語料庫

This graph shows that the verb **tell** is more common in spoken English than in written English. This is because it is used in a lot of common spoken phrases.
本圖表顯示, 動詞 tell 在英語口語中的使用頻率遠遠高於書面語, 因為口語中很多常用片語是由 tell 構成的。

tell (*v*) **SPOKEN PHRASES**
含 tell 的口語片語

15 I'll tell you what used when you are suggesting or offering something 我的建議是, 我的主張是: *I tell you what, we'll get you something to eat on the way.* 我的建議是, 我們給你準備一點在路上吃的東西。

16 I told you so used when you have warned someone about a possible danger that has now happened and they have ignored your warning 我告誡過你吧; 我原來說對了吧

17 to tell (you) the truth used to emphasize that you are being very honest 老實說, 實話對你講: *I don't really want to go out, to tell the truth.* 老實說, 我並不是真的想出去。

18 I can tell you/I'm telling you used to emphasize that what you are saying is true even though it may be difficult to believe 我可以肯定地說/我說的沒錯; 聽我說: *I'm telling you Sheila, I've never seen anything like it in my life.* 聽我說, 希拉, 我這輩子從來沒見過這樣的事。

19 tell me used before asking a question 告訴我〔用於提問之前〕: *Tell me, what do you think of the new boss?* 告訴我, 你對這位新老闆有甚麼看法?

20 I'll tell you something/one thing/another

thing used when giving your opinion about something, especially to someone you disagree with 我來講一點, 我來發表一下我的觀點〔尤用於表示反對〕: *I'll tell you one thing – you'll never get me to vote for him.* 我告訴你 — 你休想讓我投他的票。
21 I couldn't tell you used to tell someone that you do not know the answer to their question 我不清楚, 我沒法說: *"How much would a rail ticket cost?" "I couldn't tell you, I always drive."* "一張火車票要花多少錢?" "沒法說。我總是自己開車。"
22 I can't tell you a) used to say that you cannot tell someone something because it is a secret 不能告訴你〔因為保密〕: *"Where are you taking me?" "I can't tell you, it would spoil the surprise."* "你要把我帶到哪兒去?" "不能告訴你, 不然那一份驚奇就沒了。" **b)** used to say that you cannot express your feelings or describe something properly 無法表達; 無法形容: **I can't tell you how/what etc** *I just can't tell you how worried I've been.* 我簡直無法形容我一直是多麼擔心。
23 don't tell me used to interrupt someone because you know what they are going to say or because you want to guess 別告訴我〔用於打斷對方的話, 表示已經知道他要說甚麼或要猜他要說甚麼〕: *"I'm sorry I'm late but..." "Don't tell me – the car broke down again?"* "對不起, 我遲到了, 不過..." "不會又是車子壞了吧?"
24 John/she etc tells me (that) used to say what someone has told you 約翰/她等告訴我: *Mike tells me you found a job.* 麥克告訴我, 你找到了一份工作。
25 I'm not telling(you) used to say that you refuse to tell someone something 我不會告訴你的
26 that would be telling used to say that you cannot tell someone something because it is a secret 那可不能講〔因為是祕密〕
27 you're telling me used to emphasize that you already know and agree with something that someone has just said 那還用說! 你說得完全對!: *"It's hot in here." "You're telling me!"* "這裡面很熱。" "那還用說!"
28 tell me about it used to say that you already know how bad something is, especially because you have experienced it yourself 我早就知道了! 我也有同感!: *"I've been so tired lately." "Yeah, tell me about it!"* "我近來一直感到很累。" "是呀, 我也是這樣!"
29 you never can tell/you can never tell used to say that you cannot be certain about what will happen in the future 說不準; 對〔某事〕沒有把握
30 there's no telling what/how etc used to say that it is impossible to know what has happened or what will happen next 不可能知道是甚麼/將發生甚麼事: *She's desperate. There's no telling what she'll try next.* 她不顧一切了, 不知道她下一步會做甚麼。
31 tell me another used when you do not believe what someone has told you 我不信, 哪有這種事

tell against sb *phr v* [T no passive 無被動態] *BrE formal* if a bad quality or feature tells against you, it makes you unsuccessful in what you are trying to achieve【英, 正式】對...有不利影響, 不利於...: *She has the figure of a model but her height really tells against her.* 她具有模特兒的身材, 但她的身高真的對她不利。

tell sb/sth **apart** *phr v* [T not in progressive 不用進行式] to be able to see which person or thing is which, even though they are very similar 區分, 辨別: *I've never been able to tell the twins apart.* 我從來都不能區別出那對雙胞胎。| **[+from]** *It's difficult to tell the forged stamp apart from the real one.* 很難把假的郵票與真的郵票區別開來。

tell of sb/sth *phr v* [T] *especially literary* to describe the details of an event or person【尤文】描述, 敘述: *The poem tells of the deeds of a famous warrior.* 這首詩描述了一位著名武士的壯舉。

tell sb ↔ **off** *phr v* [T] **1** to talk angrily to someone because they have done something wrong 斥責; 訓誡: **be/get told off** *Do your homework or you'll get told off again.* 做你的家庭作業吧, 不然你又要挨罵了。| **tell sb off for doing sth** *My dad told me off for swearing.* 我爸因為我罵人而訓斥我。**2** *formal* to separate a group of people from a larger group, in order to do special work or tasks【正式】〔為擔當特殊工作或任務而〕抽調出〔一部分人〕; 派出: *Ten soldiers were told off to dig ditches.* 十名士兵被抽調去挖壕溝。

tell·er /ˈtɛlɚ; ˈtelə/ *n* [C] **1** someone whose job is to receive and pay out money in a bank 銀行出納員 **2** someone who counts votes 清點選票的人, 點[計]票員

tell·ing /ˈtɛlɪŋ; ˈtelɪŋ/ *adj* **1** having a great or important effect; SIGNIFICANT (1) 有力的; 有效的; 有重大影響的: a *telling argument* 有說服力的論點 —see also 另見 TELL (9) **2** a remark that is telling shows what you really think although you may not intend it to 顯露內心活動的, 流露真實思想的 —**tellingly** *adv*

telling-off /ˌ.. ˈ./ *n* **give sb a telling-off** to talk angrily to someone because they have done something wrong 責備, 斥責: *They gave the children a good telling-off.* 他們給了那羣孩子一頓痛罵。—see also 另見 **tell off** (TELL)

tell·tale[1] /ˈtɛltel; ˈteltеɪl/ *adj* **telltale signs/marks etc** signs that clearly show something that is unpleasant or is supposed to be secret 泄露祕密的, 暴露內情的: *the telltale scars of injecting heroin* 注射過海洛因的明顯痕跡

telltale[2] *n* [C] *BrE* a word used by children, meaning a child who tells adults about other children's secrets or bad behaviour【英】愛搬弄是非的小孩; 打小報告者〔兒語〕; TATTLETALE *AmE*【美】

tel·ly /ˈtɛlɪ; ˈteli/ *n* [C,U] *BrE informal* television【英, 非正式】電視; 電視機: **on telly** *Is there anything good on telly tonight?* 今晚電視上有甚麼好節目嗎? 3

te·me·ri·ty /təˈmɛrətɪ; təˈmerəti/ *n* [U] *formal* unreasonable confidence that is likely to offend someone【正式】魯莽; 冒失; 不自量力: **have the temerity to do sth** *I was amazed that you had the temerity to ask the question.* 我感到很驚訝, 你竟冒失地提出那個問題。

temp[1] /tɛmp; temp/ *n* [C] an office worker who is only employed temporarily〔辦公室的〕臨時雇員

temp[2] *v* [I] to work as a temp 做臨時雇員: *Carol's temping until she can find another job.* 卡羅爾在能找到另一份工作之前一直在做臨時雇員。

tem·per[1] /ˈtɛmpɚ; ˈtempə/ *n*

1 ▶TENDENCY TO BE ANGRY 容易發怒◀ [C,U] a tendency to become angry suddenly 壞脾氣: *That temper of hers will get her into trouble one of these days.* 她的那種脾氣早晚會讓她碰到麻煩的。| *If he can't control his temper, he should give up teaching.* 如果他控制不住自己的脾氣, 他就應該放棄教書工作。| **quick/fiery/violent temper** *Be careful, he's got a pretty violent temper.* 小心點, 他的脾氣非常暴躁。| **tempers become frayed** (=people become angry) 人們變得暴躁 *Tempers were becoming frayed as the day went on.* 隨着這天時間過去, 大家的火氣變得越來越大。

2 ▶SHORT ANGRY FEELING 短時間的怒氣◀ [singular,U] an uncontrolled feeling of anger that lasts for a short time〔煩躁的〕情緒;〔難以控制的〕怒氣: **be in a temper** *It's no use talking to him when he's in a temper.* 他心情煩躁時跟他談是沒有用的。| **be in a foul/awful temper** (=be angry) 發怒 | **a fit of temper** (=a quick expression of anger) 突發的一頓脾氣 *Pete hit his brother in a fit of temper.* 皮特一氣之下打了他的弟弟。| **fly into a temper** (=suddenly become very angry) 突然大發脾氣 | **temper tantrum** (=sudden angry behaviour like that of a small child) 耍小孩子脾氣

3 lose your temper to suddenly become so angry that

you cannot control yourself 發脾氣, 生氣: *"Stop it," Helen shouted at the children, trying not to lose her temper.* "住手。"海倫朝孩子們大聲嚷道, 盡量不讓自己發脾氣。

4 keep your temper to stay calm when it would be easy to get angry 捺住性子, 不讓脾氣發作: *I was finding it increasingly difficult to keep my temper.* 我發現越來越難控制住自己的脾氣了。

5 good-tempered/foul tempered etc having a good, bad temper etc 脾氣好的/脾氣糟的

6 temper! temper! *spoken* used humorously to tell someone not to get angry【口】別生氣啦! 別生氣啦!〔幽默用法〕

7 ▶ATTITUDE 態度◀ [singular] *formal* the general attitude that people have in a particular place at one time【正式】〔某時某地人們普遍的〕態度, 看法: **[+of]** *the temper of life in Renaissance Italy* 文藝復興時期意大利人的生活態度 —see also 另見 BAD-TEMPERED, EVEN-TEMPERED, ILL-TEMPERED

temper² *v* [T] **1** to make metal as hard as is needed by heating it and then putting it in cold water 使〔金屬〕變堅韌, 鍛煉, 使回火: *tempered steel* 回火鋼 **2** *formal* to make something difficult or unpleasant more acceptable or pleasant【正式】使緩和; 使容易接受

tem·pe·ra /ˋtɛmpərə; ˈtempərə/ *n* [U] a method of painting in which the colour is mixed with a thick liquid such as egg 蛋彩畫法

tem·pe·ra·ment /ˋtɛmprəmənt; ˈtempərəmənt/ *n* [C, U] the emotional part of someone's character, especially how likely they are to be happy, angry etc; DISPOSITION (1) 氣質, 性情, 性格, 稟性: *a sunny temperament* 快活的性格

tem·pe·ra·men·tal /ˌtɛmprəˋmɛntḷ; ˌtempərəˈmentl◂/ *adj* **1** likely to suddenly become upset, excited, or angry 喜怒無常的; 易興奮的; 易怒的: *It's difficult to work for someone who's so temperamental.* 為一個如此喜怒無常的人工作, 真是困難啊。**2** a machine, system etc that is temperamental does not always work properly〔機器、系統等〕性能不穩定的 **3** related to the emotional part of someone's character 氣質的, 性情的, 性格的: *serious temperamental differences between the couple* 那對夫婦之間嚴重的性格不合 —**temperamentally** *adv*

tem·pe·rance /ˋtɛmprəns; ˈtempərəns/ *n* [U] **1** the practice of never drinking alcohol for moral or religious reasons 戒酒; 禁酒〔因道德或宗教原因〕: *the Victorian virtues of thrift, temperance, and hard work* 節儉、戒酒、勤奮等這些維多利亞時代的美德 **2** *formal* sensible control of the things you say and do, especially the amount of alcohol you drink【正式】〔對言行, 尤指飲酒的〕自我克制, 節制

tem·pe·rate /ˋtɛmprɪt; ˈtempərɨt/ *adj* **1 temperate climate/region** a type of weather or a part of the world that is never very hot or very cold 溫和的氣候; 溫帶地區: *the temperate zone, north and south of the tropics* 熱帶以北和以南的溫帶地區 **2** *formal* behaviour that is temperate is calm and sensible【正式】〔行為〕溫和的, 心平氣和的; 自我節制的 —see also 另見 INTEMPERATE (1)

tem·pe·ra·ture /ˋtɛmprətʃɚ; ˈtempərətʃə/ *n* **1** [singular] a measure of how hot or cold a place or thing is 溫度, 氣溫: *The temperature of the water was just right for swimming.* 這水溫剛好適合游泳。| **a temperature of 20°/100° etc** *Water boils at a temperature of 100°C.* 水在攝氏100度達到沸點。| **the temperature rises/goes up** (=it gets hotter) 溫度上升 | **high/low temperatures** *a material that can withstand high temperatures* 一種耐高溫的材料 | **rise/fall etc in temperature** *a gradual rise in ocean temperatures* 海洋溫度的逐步上升 | **room temperature** (=normal, comfortable temperature of a room) 室溫, 常溫 *Let the mixture cool to room temperature.* 讓混合物的溫度降到室溫。| **air/water/body temperature** *You mustn't let the body temperature drop too low.* 你千萬不要讓體溫降得太低。| **the temperature falls/drops etc** (=it gets colder) 溫度下降 *The temperature in New York dropped to minus 10° last night.* 紐約的溫度昨晚降到了零下十度。| **temperature change** *a great temperature change from last week* 上週以來氣溫的大幅度變化 | **constant temperature** (=a temperature that does not change) 恒溫 *The refrigerator keeps your food at a constant temperature.* 電冰箱以恒溫狀態保存食物。
2 sb's temperature the temperature of your blood 某人血液的溫度: **take sb's temperature** (=measure their temperature) 量某人的體溫 *The nurse took my temperature.* 護士給我量過體溫。| **have/run a temperature** (=have a temperature that is higher than normal) 發燒 *Susie has a temperature and has gone to bed.* 蘇思發燒, 已經上牀歇着去了。**3** [C] the temperature of a situation is the way people are reacting, for example whether they are behaving angrily or calmly〔人們反應的〕情緒; 氣氛: *Be careful what you say, the temperature's a bit hot in there.* 小心你的說話, 那兒的氣氛有些緊張。

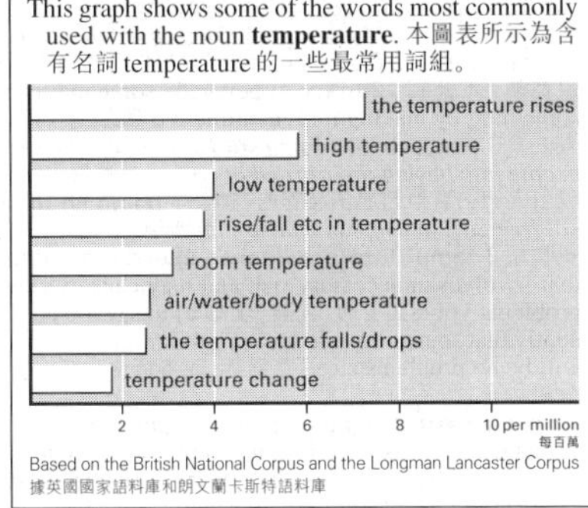
This graph shows some of the words most commonly used with the noun **temperature**. 本圖表所示為含有名詞temperature的一些最常用詞組。

Based on the British National Corpus and the Longman Lancaster Corpus
據英國國家語料庫和朗文蘭卡斯特語料庫

tem·pest /ˋtɛmpɪst; ˈtempɨst/ *n* [C] *literary* a violent storm【文】暴風雨; 暴風雪

tem·pes·tu·ous /tɛmˋpɛstʃuəs; temˈpestʃuəs/ *adj* **1** a tempestuous relationship or period of time includes many strong emotions〔關係〕強烈情感錯雜的;〔時代〕風雲變幻的: *a tempestuous marriage* 愛恨交加的婚姻關係 **2** *literary* a tempestuous sea or wind is very rough and violent; STORMY【文】〔大海〕波濤洶湧的;〔天氣〕狂風暴雨的: *lost in the dark tempestuous night* 迷失在狂風暴雨的黑夜裡 —**tempestuously** *adv* —**tempestuousness** *n* [U]

tem·plate /ˋtɛmplɪt; ˈtempleɪt/ *n* [C] **1** a thin sheet of plastic or metal in a special shape or pattern used to help cut other materials in a similar shape〔切割材料時用的塑料或金屬〕模板, 型板, 樣板 **2** *technical* a system for arranging information on a computer screen【術語】〔在電腦上整理信息用的〕模板

tem·ple /ˋtɛmpḷ; ˈtempəl/ *n* [C] **1** a building where people go to WORSHIP¹ (1), in the Hindu, Buddhist, Sikh, Mormon, or modern Jewish religions 廟宇, 寺院; 聖殿 **2** [usually plural 一般用複數] one of the two fairly flat areas on each side of your forehead 太陽穴 —see picture at 參見 HEAD¹ 圖

tem·po /ˋtɛmpo; ˈtempəʊ/ *n* [C] **1** the speed at which music is played or should be played〔音樂演奏的〕速度 **2** the speed at which something happens; PACE〔事情進展的〕節奏; 步調: *the easy tempo of island life* 島上生活的輕鬆節奏

tem·po·ral /ˋtɛmpərəl; ˈtempərəl/ *adj formal*【正式】**1** related to or limited by time 關於時間的; 受時間限制的; 短暫的: *the temporal character of human existence* 人生的短促 **2** related to practical instead of religious

T

affairs〔與宗教相對應的〕塵世的, 世俗的: *The Church has no temporal power in the modern state.* 在現代國家裡, 教會沒有世俗權力。

tem·po·ra·ry /ˋtɛmpəˏrɛrɪ; ˈtempərəri/ *adj* **1** lasting for only a limited period of time 暫時的, 臨時的: *A lot of work now is temporary or part-time.* 現在有很多工作都是臨時的或兼職的。| *The accident caused a temporary disability.* 事故造成了暫時的殘疾。**2** intended to be used for only a limited period of time 短期的, 短暫的: *The council have placed us in temporary accommodation.* 委員會給我們安排了臨時住處。—compare 比較 PERMANENT[1], PROVISIONAL (1) —**temporariness** *n* [U] —**temporarily** / ˋtɛmpəˏrɛrəlɪ; ˈtempərərɨli/ *adv*: *The library is temporarily closed for repairs.* 圖書館暫時關閉, 以便維修。

tem·po·rize also 又作 **-ise** *BrE*【英】/ˋtɛmpəˏraɪz; ˈtempəraɪz/ *v* [I] *formal* to delay or avoid making a decision in order to gain time【正式】〔為爭取時間而〕拖延

tempt /tɛmpt; tempt/ *v* [T] **1** to make someone want to have or do something, even though they know they really should not 引誘, 誘使: *If you leave valuables in your car it will tempt thieves.* 如果你把貴重物品留在車上, 那是在引誘小偷。| **be tempted** *I'm tempted to buy that dress even though it's expensive.* 儘管那件套裙很貴, 我還是動了心想買。**2** to try to persuade someone to do something by making it seem attractive 慫恿; 引誘〔某人去做〕: **tempt sb into doing sth** *The ads hope to tempt people into buying their brand of coffee.* 那些廣告希望吸引人們去買他們那個品牌的咖啡。| **tempt sb to do sth** *free gifts to tempt people to join* 吸引人們參加的免費贈品 **3 tempt fate/providence a)** to do something that involves unnecessary risk and may cause serious problems 冒〔不必要的〕危險; 玩命 **b)** to say too confidently that something will have a good result, that there will be no problems etc 言之過甚, 說事情會有好結果、會順利等

T

temp·ta·tion /tɛmpˋteʃən; tempˈteɪʃən/ *n* **1** [C,U] a strong desire to have or do something even though you know you should not 引誘, 誘惑: **temptation to do sth** *There might be a temptation to cheat if students sit too close together.* 如果同學們坐得太近, 那有可能誘使他們去作弊。| **resist/overcome (the) temptation** (=not do something, even though you want to) 抵擋/戰勝誘惑 | **give in to (the) temptation** (=do something although you know you should not) 經不住誘惑 *I finally gave in to the temptation and had a cigarette.* 我終於經不住誘惑, 抽了一支煙。**2** [C,U] something that makes you want to have or do something, even though you know you should not 很有誘惑力的東西: *Having candy in the house is a great temptation!* 在屋裡放糖果, 那多有誘惑力!

temp·ting /ˋtɛmptɪŋ; ˈtemptɪŋ/ *adj* something that is tempting seems very good and you would like to have it or do it 誘人的, 吸引人的: *a tempting job offer* 一次很誘人的工作機會 | *That pie looks tempting!* 那餡餅看上去太誘人了! | **it is tempting to do sth** *It's tempting to just ignore her when she's this upset.* 看她這麼心煩意亂, 真想不去理她。—**temptingly** *adv*

temp·tress /ˋtɛmptrɪs; ˈtemptrɨs/ *n* [C] *old-fashioned* a woman who makes a man want to have sex with her【過時】引誘男人的女子, 妖婦

tem·pus fu·git /ˏtɛmpəs ˋfjudʒɪt; ˈtempəs ˈfjuːdʒɨt/ *Latin* a phrase meaning 'time flies'; used to say that time passes very quickly【拉丁】光陰似箭, 時光易逝

ten /tɛn; ten/ *number* **1** 10 十 —see table on page C1 參見 C1 頁附錄 **2 ten to one** *informal* used to say that something is very likely【非正式】十之八九, 極有可能, 多半會: *Ten to one he'll have forgotten all about it tomorrow.* 他明天多半會把這事忘得一乾二淨。**3 be ten a penny** *BrE informal* to be very common and therefore not special or unusual【英, 非正式】很普通, 很平常, 不稀罕 —see also 另見 **a dime a dozen** (DIME (2)) **4 ten out of ten** *BrE* used in schools to give a perfect mark, or humorously to praise someone【英】〔學校〕給打了滿分; 得了滿分〔稱讚人的幽默說法〕: *You get ten out of ten for effort, Simon.* 西蒙, 你因為努力得了滿分。—**tenth** *number*

ten·a·ble /ˋtɛnəbl̩; ˈtenəbəl/ *adj* **1** a belief, argument etc that is tenable is reasonable and can be defended successfully〔信仰、論點等〕有道理的, 站得住腳的 —opposite 反義詞 UNTENABLE **2 be tenable for** a job or position that is tenable for a particular length of time will continue for that length of time〔工作或職位〕可保持一段時間的; 可擔任一段時間的

te·na·cious /tɪˋneʃəs; tɨˈneɪʃəs/ *adj* determined to do something and unwilling to stop trying even when the situation becomes difficult 堅持的; 堅韌不拔的; 頑強的 —**tenaciously** *adv* —**tenaciousness** or **tenacity** /tɪˋnæsətɪ; tɨˈnæsɨti/ *n* [U]

ten·an·cy /ˋtɛnənsɪ; ˈtenənsi/ *n* **1** [C] the period of time that someone rents a house, land etc〔住房、土地等的〕租賃期, 租用期: *a six-month tenancy* 六個月的租賃期限 **2** [C,U] the right to use a house, land etc that is rented〔住房、土地等的〕租賃權, 租用權

ten·ant /ˋtɛnənt; ˈtenənt/ *n* [C] someone who lives in a house, room etc and pays rent to the person who owns it 房客; 租戶

tenant farm·er /ˏ·· ˈ··/ *n* [C] someone who farms land that is rented from someone else 佃農, 佃戶

ten·ant·ry /ˋtɛnəntrɪ; ˈtenəntri/ *n* **the tenantry** *old use* all the farmers who rent land from the same person in one place【舊】〔在同一地區向同一地主租地耕種的〕佃戶, 承租人

tend /tɛnd; tend/ *v* 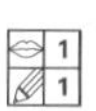

1 tend to do sth to often do a particular thing, especially something that is bad or annoying, and to be likely to do it again 易於; 往往會做某事〔尤指不好的事〕: *Sally tends to interfere in other people's business.* 莎利經常會干涉別人的事情。| *The car does tend to overheat.* 這車確實很容易過熱。

2 tend towards sth to have a particular quality or feature more than others 有…的趨勢; 傾向於…: *Charles tends towards obesity.* 查爾斯有肥胖的趨勢。

3 tend bar *especially AmE* to serve customers in a store, bar etc【尤美】〔在商店、酒吧等處〕接待顧客: *Theresa tends bar at the Irish Lion.* 特麗莎在"愛爾蘭獅"酒吧做招待。

4 ►LOOK AFTER 照料◄ also 又作 **tend to** [T] *old-fashioned* to look after someone or something【過時】照顧, 照料: *a shepherd tending sheep on the hillside* 在山坡上照料羊羣的牧羊人

5 ►MOVE/DEVELOP 移動/發展◄ [I always+adv/prep] *formal* to move or develop in a particular direction【正式】朝〔某一特定方向〕移動; 發展: **[+upwards/downwards]** *Interest rates are tending upwards.* 利率有提高的趨勢。

ten·den·cy /ˋtɛndənsɪ; ˈtendənsi/ *n* [C] **1** a PROBABILITY that you will develop, think or behave in a certain way〔發育、思想、行為等的〕傾向: **[+to/towards]** *Some people may inherit a tendency to alcoholism.* 有些人可能天生有酗酒的傾向。| **have a tendency to do sth** (=often do something and be more likely to do it than other people) 傾向於做某事, 往往會做某事 *Jean's nice but she has a tendency to talk too much.* 瓊人倒不錯, 就是往往太嘮叨了。**2 artistic/alcoholic etc tendencies** particular skills, weaknesses or desires that make someone behave in a particular way 藝術的氣質/酗酒的危險: *kids with criminal tendencies* 有犯罪傾向的孩子 **3** a general change or development in a particular direction 趨勢, 趨向: **[+for]** *We've noticed a growing tendency for people to work at home instead of in offices.* 我們注意到一種趨勢, 越來越多的人在家裡工作而不是在辦公室裡上班。| **[+to/towards]** *There has been a general tendency towards conservation and recycling.* 總的趨勢一直是着眼於保護和回收。**4** [also+plural verb *BrE* 英] a group within a political party that supports ideas that 

are usually more extreme than those of the main party〔政黨內部觀點往往較為極端的〕激進派: *the growing fascist tendency* 日益增長的法西斯極端勢力

ten·den·tious /tɛn`dɛnʃəs; tenˈdenʃəs/ *adj* a tendentious speech, remark, book etc expresses a strong opinion that is intended to influence people〔演講、評論、書籍等的觀點〕有強烈傾向性的, 鼓動色彩濃厚的

ten·der¹ /ˈtɛndɚ; ˈtendə/ *adj*
1 ▶MEAT/VEGETABLES 肉食/蔬菜◀ easy to cut and eat, especially because they have been well cooked 嫩的; 軟的; 易燉爛的〔尤指烹飪恰到好處〕: *tender beef* 嫩牛肉 —opposite 反義詞 TOUGH
2 ▶PART OF YOUR BODY 身體的某一部分◀ a tender part of your body is painful if someone touches it 疼痛的, 一觸即痛的: *My arm is still tender where I bruised it.* 我手臂碰傷的地方仍然很痛。
3 ▶GENTLE 溫柔的◀ gentle and careful in a way that shows love 溫柔的; 體貼入微的; 慈愛的: *Sam's voice was full of tender concern.* 山姆的話語裡充滿了體貼入微的關懷。| *a tender look* 含情脈脈的一瞥
4 tender loving care *usually spoken* sympathetic treatment and a lot of attention【一般口】體貼入微的關懷
5 tender blossoms/plants etc plants etc that are easily damaged 嬌弱的花朵/幼嫩的植株
6 tender age *humorous or literary* the time when you are young or inexperienced【幽默或文】年幼時期; 未成熟時期: *I don't know that your jokes are suitable for someone of my tender age!* 我不知道你那些笑話對於我這樣年幼的人來說是不是合適! | **at the tender age of** *Nicholas was sent to boarding school at the tender age of seven.* 尼古拉斯在年僅七歲時就被送往寄宿學校。—**tenderly** *adv* —**tenderness** *n* [U]

tender² *n* [C] **1** a formal statement of the price you would charge for doing a job or providing goods or services 投標(書): **put sth out to tender** (=ask for statements of the price for doing a particular job) 招標承辦某事 **2** a small boat that takes people or supplies between the shore and a larger boat〔來往於岸邊和大船之間運送人員或補給品的〕駁運船; 補給船; 交通艇 **3** part of a steam train used for carrying coal and water for the train〔蒸汽火車的〕煤水車 —see also 另見 BARTENDER, LEGAL TENDER

tender³ *v* **1** [I] to make a formal offer to do a job or provide goods and services at a particular price 投標〔承辦某事〕: **[+for]** *tendering for a road building contract* 投標承接一項公路修建合同 **2** [T] *formal* to give or show something to someone【正式】遞呈, 呈交; 提出: *tender a proposal* 提出一項方案 | **tender your resignation** (=officially say that you are going to leave your job) 正式遞交辭呈 **3** [T] *old-fashioned* to give money as a payment【過時】付款, 償還

ten·der·foot /ˈtɛndɚˌfʊt; ˈtendəfʊt/ *n* [C] *AmE informal*【美, 非正式】**1** someone who has just arrived at a place where life is much harder than they are used to 新到艱苦地區的人; 還沒吃過苦的新來者 **2** an inexperienced beginner 沒有經驗的新手, 初學者: *a political tenderfoot* 政界的新手

tender-heart·ed /ˌ·· ˈ··◂/ *adj* very kind and gentle 心腸軟的, 溫柔慈善的: *She was too tender-hearted to refuse.* 她心腸太軟, 拒絕不了。—**tender-heartedly** *adv* —**tenderheartedness** *n* [U]

ten·der·ize also 又作 **-ise** *BrE*【英】/ˈtɛndəˌraɪz; ˈtendəraɪz/ *v* [T] to make meat softer and easier to eat by preparing it in a special way〔通過特殊處理〕把〔肉〕烹製得嫩嫩的

ten·der·loin /ˈtɛndɚˌlɔɪn; ˈtendəlɔɪn/ *n* [U] meat that is soft and easy to eat, cut from each side of the backbone of cows or pigs〔牛或豬背腰處的〕嫩肉, 裡脊肉: *pork tenderloin* 豬裡脊肉

ten·don /ˈtɛndən; ˈtendən/ *n* [C] a thick strong string-like part of your body that connects a muscle to a bone〔連接肌肉和骨頭的〕腱

ten·dril /ˈtɛndrɪl; ˈtendrəl/ *n* [C] **1** a thin leafless curling stem by which a climbing plant fastens itself to a support〔攀緣植物的〕卷鬚 **2** a thin curling piece of hair 鬈髮: *Ralph pushed the damp tendrils of hair out of his eyes.* 拉爾夫把幾綹濕鬈髮從眼前撥開。

ten·e·ment /ˈtɛnəmənt; ˈtenəmənt/ *n* [C] a large building divided into apartments, especially in the poorer areas of a city〔尤指城市貧民區的〕公寓大樓

ten·et /ˈtɛnɪt; ˈtenət/ *n* [C] a principle or belief, especially one that is part of a larger system of beliefs 教義; 信念, 信條: *the tenets of Buddhism* 佛教的教義

ten·fold /ˈtɛnfold; ˈtenfəʊld/ *adj, adv* ten times as much or as many of something 十倍的: *Company turnover has risen tenfold to $550 million.* 公司營業額上升了九倍, 達到5.5億美元。

ten-gal·lon hat /ˌ· ·· ˈ·/ *n* [C] a tall hat made of soft material with a wide BRIM, worn especially by COWBOYS〔尤指美國牛仔戴的〕寬邊高頂軟帽

ten·ner /ˈtɛnɚ; ˈtenə/ *n* [C] *BrE informal* £10 or a ten-pound note【英, 非正式】十英鎊; 十英鎊鈔票: *Can you lend me a tenner?* 你能借給我十英鎊嗎?

tennis 網球

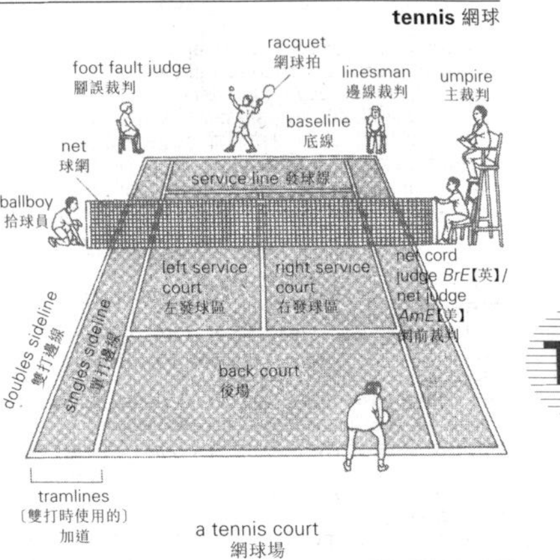

a tennis court
網球場

ten·nis /ˈtɛnɪs; ˈtenəs/ *n* [U] a game for two people or two pairs of people who use rackets (RACKET¹ (3)) to hit a small soft ball backwards and forwards over a net 網球(運動)

tennis court /ˈ·· ·/ *n* [C] the four-sided area that you play tennis on 網球場

tennis el·bow /ˌ·· ˈ··/ *n* [U] a medical problem in which your elbow is very painful 網球肘〔一種肘部十分疼痛的疾病〕

tennis shoe /ˈ·· ·/ *n* [C] a strong shoe used for sports 網球(運動)鞋

ten·on /ˈtɛnən; ˈtenən/ *n* [C] an end of a piece of wood, that has been cut to fit exactly into a MORTISE in order to form a strong joint 榫頭, 榫舌

ten·or /ˈtɛnɚ; ˈtenə/ *n* **1** [C] a man with a singing voice that can reach the range of notes just below the lowest woman's voice 男高音(歌手): *the famous tenor, Luciano Pavarotti* 著名男高音盧契亞諾·巴伐洛提 **2** [singular] the part of a piece of music this person sings 高音聲部: *Can you sing the tenor?* 你能唱出高音聲部嗎? **3** [C] a musical instrument with the same range of notes as the singer 次中音樂器 **4 the tenor of a)** *formal* the general way in which an event or process takes place【正式】一般趨向; 一般(發展)進程: *The general tenor of the debate was stressful.* 那場辯論的總的過程充滿了緊張氣氛。**b)** the general meaning of something written or spoken〔文章或講話的〕大意, 要旨: *the theological*

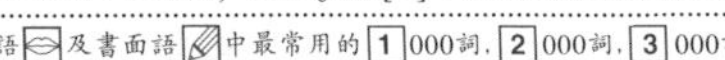

tenor of his speech 他講話中神學方面的要旨

ten·pin /ˋtɛnˌpɪn; ˈtenˌpɪn/ *n* [C] one of the ten bottle-shaped wooden objects that you try to knock down in BOWLING (1)〔保齡球運動中作為滾擊目標的〕瓶形木柱，木瓶

tenpin bowl·ing /ˌ·· ˈ··/ *n* [U] *BrE* an indoor sport in which you roll a heavy ball along a floor to knock down bottle-shaped wooden objects【英】保齡球，十柱滾木球運動; BOWLING *AmE*【美】

tense¹ /tɛns; tens/ *adj* **1** feeling very nervous and worried because of something bad that might happen 緊張的; 焦慮的: *The robbers were tense as they waited the long minutes for the van to arrive.* 劫匪們在運鈔車到來之前的漫長等待中一直十分緊張。| **tense moment/atmosphere etc** *Marion spoke, eager to break the tense silence.* 瑪麗安説着話，一心想要緩和緊張沉默的氣氛。**2** unable to relax your body or part of your body because your muscles feel tight〔肌肉〕緊張的; 繃緊的: *Massage is great if your neck and back are tense.* 如果你的頸部和背部肌肉緊張的話，按摩一下是很管用的。—see also 另見 TENSION —**tensely** *adv* —**tenseness** *n* [U]

tense² *v* [I,T] also 又作 **tense up** to make your muscles tight and stiff, or to become tight and stiff 使〔肌肉〕繃緊; 僵直: *Relax, and try not to tense up so much.* 放鬆，試着不要繃得這麼緊。| *She felt how his body tensed with anger.* 她感覺到他的身體因憤怒而繃得緊緊的。

tense³ *n* [C,U] any of the forms of a verb that show the time, continuance or completion of an action or state that is expressed by the verb. 'I am' is in the present tense, 'I was' is past tense, and 'I will be' is future tense.〔動詞的〕時態〔"I am" 是現在時態，"I was" 是過去時態，而 "I will be" 是將來時態〕

tensed up /ˌ· ˈ·/ *adj* [not before noun 不用於名詞前] *informal* feeling so nervous or worried that you cannot relax【非正式】緊張不安的: *Why are you so tensed up?* 你為甚麼這樣緊張不安?

ten·sile /ˋtɛnsḷ; ˈtensaɪl/ *adj* able to be stretched 可伸展[拉長]的: *tensile rubber* 有伸縮性的橡膠

tensile strength /ˌ·· ˈ·/ *n* [U] *technical* the ability of a particular kind of steel, CONCRETE² etc to bear pressure or weight【術語】抗拉強度

ten·sion /ˋtɛnʃən; ˈtenʃən/ *n*

1 ►NERVOUS FEELING 緊張感覺◄ [U] a nervous worried feeling that makes it impossible for you to relax 緊張; 焦慮; 焦急: *The tension was becoming unbearable, and I wanted to scream.* 這種緊張再也忍受不了，我真想尖聲大叫。

2 ►NO TRUST 不信任◄ [C usually plural 一般用複數, U] the feeling that exists when people or countries do not trust each other and may suddenly attack each other〔人與人、國家與國家之間的〕緊張關係，緊張局勢: *attempts to ease racial tensions in inner cities* 緩和市中心貧民區種族之間緊張關係的努力

3 ►DIFFERENT INFLUENCES 不同的影響力◄ [singular] a situation in which different needs, forces or influences pull in different directions and make the situation difficult〔需求、勢力或影響力間的〕衝突; 緊張狀況: [+**between**] *In business there's always a tension between the needs of customers and shareholders.* 在商業活動中，顧客和股東的需求之間始終存在着矛盾。

4 ►TIGHTNESS 繃緊◄ [U] tightness or stiffness in a wire, rope, muscle etc〔電線、繩子、肌肉等的〕拉緊，繃緊: *Tension in the neck muscles can cause headaches.* 頸部肌肉的緊張會導致頭痛。

5 ►FORCE 力量◄ [U] the amount of force that stretches something 張力，拉力: *This wire will take 50 pounds tension.* 這根金屬線能承受50磅的張力。

tent /tɛnt; tent/ *n* [C] a shelter consisting of a sheet of cloth supported by poles and ropes, used especially for camping 帳篷: **pitch a tent** (=put up a tent) 搭帳篷 —see also 另見 OXYGEN TENT

ten·ta·cle /ˋtɛntəkḷ; ˈtentɪ̵kəl/ *n* [C] one of the long thin parts of a sea creature such as an OCTOPUS, which it uses for holding things〔海洋動物如章魚等的〕觸手，觸角，觸鬚 —see picture at 參見 OCTOPUS 圖

ten·ta·tive /ˋtɛntətɪv; ˈtentətɪv/ *adj* **1** not definite or certain, because you may want to change your mind 不確定的; 暫定的; 試探性的: *We've fixed a tentative date for the meeting.* 我們暫定了一個開會的日期。**2** done without confidence 躊躇不決的，猶豫的: *a tentative smile* 勉強的笑容 —**tentatively** *adv*: *Albi knocked tentatively and entered.* 阿爾比猶猶豫豫地敲了一下門，然後走了進去。—**tentativeness** *n* [U]

ten·ter·hooks /ˋtɛntɚˌhʊks; ˈtentəhʊks/ *n* **be on tenterhooks** to feel nervous and excited because you are waiting for something〔因等待而〕緊張不安: *She had been on tenterhooks all night, expecting Joe to return at any moment.* 她一晚上都焦慮不安，期待着喬隨時回來。

tenth¹ /tɛnθ; tenθ/ *n* 10th 第十

tenth² *n* [C] one of ten equal parts of something 十分之一

ten·u·ous /ˋtɛnjuəs; ˈtenjuəs/ *adj* **1 tenuous link/relationship/evidence** a link etc that seems weak or doubtful 薄弱的環節/曖昧的關係/無力的證據: *a tenuous link with my past* 與我過去的微弱的聯繫 **2** *literary* very thin and easily broken【文】纖細的; 易碎的 —**tenuously** *adv* —**tenuousness** *n* [C]

ten·ure /ˋtɛnjɚ; ˈtenjə/ *n* [U] **1** the right to stay permanently in a teaching job at university〔大學教師的〕終身職位 **2** *formal* the period of time when someone has an important job【正式】〔重要職位的〕任期: *throughout his tenure in office* 在他的整個任期內 **3** *law* the legal right to live in a house or use a piece of land for a period of time【法律】〔房屋的〕居住權;〔土地的〕使用期

te·pee /ˋtipi; ˈtiːpiː/ *n* [C] a round tent used by Native Americans〔美洲土著人使用的〕圓錐形帳篷

tep·id /ˋtɛpɪd; ˈtepɪ̵d/ *adj* **1** tepid liquid is slightly warm, especially in a way that seems unpleasant〔液體〕微溫的，微熱的〔尤指溫度不合適的〕: *I politely sipped my tepid coffee.* 我斯文地啜飲着微熱的咖啡。—see picture at 參見 HOT¹ 圖 **2** a feeling, reaction etc that is tepid shows a lack of excitement or interest〔感覺〕不夠熱情的;〔反應〕冷淡的: *The critics' reaction to the play was tepid.* 評論家對該劇的反應冷淡。—see also 另見 LUKEWARM —**tepidly** *adv* —**tepidness** or **tepidity** /tɪˋpɪdətɪ; teˈpɪdɪ̵ti/ *n* [U]

te·qui·la /təˋkilə; tɪ̵ˈkiːlə/ *n* [C,U] a strong alcoholic drink made in Mexico from the CACTUS plant 特奎拉酒〔一種用墨西哥產植物龍舌蘭製成的烈酒〕

ter·cen·te·na·ry /ˌtɝˋsɛntəˌnɛrɪ; ˌtɜːsenˈtiːnəri/ *n* [C] the day or year exactly 300 years after a particular event 300週年(紀念日)

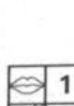

term¹ /tɝm; tɜːm/ *n* [C]

① ONE WAY OF REGARDING SOMETHING 看待某事的一種方式
② WORDS/LANGUAGE 字詞/語言
③ PERIOD OF TIME 時段
④ CONDITIONS/AGREEMENT 條件/協議
⑤ RELATIONSHIP 關係
⑥ OTHER SENSES 其他意思

① ONE WAY OF REGARDING SOMETHING 看待某事的一種方式
1 in financial/artistic/psychological etc terms if you describe or consider something in financial etc terms, you are mainly interested in the financial etc side of it 就金融/藝術/心理學等而言: *In artistic terms, the film was revolutionary.* 從藝術角度來看，這部電影具有革命性。| *the enormous cost of war, in human terms* 就人的生命而言戰爭的高昂代價
2 in terms of if you explain or judge something in terms of a particular fact or event, you are only interested in its connection with that fact or event 在…方面，從…方面來說；根據…來解釋: *US foreign policy tended to see everything in terms of the Vietnam war.* 美國的外交政策往往根據越南戰爭的角度來看待一切。| *In terms of customer satisfaction, the policy cannot be criticized.* 說到顧客的滿意情況，這個政策無可挑剔。
3 in sb's terms according to one person's set of opinions 在某人看來，根據某人的觀點: *In their terms, cutting government spending is the most important thing.* 根據他們的觀點，削減政府開支是最重要的事情。
4 in real terms a change of a price or cost in real terms has been calculated to include the effects of other changes such as price rises〔價格或費用的〕實際變化情況: *Our wages have gone down in real terms over the past year.* 我們的工資實際上比去年降低了。

② WORDS/LANGUAGE 字詞/語言
5 ►WORD/EXPRESSION 字詞/詞組◄ [C] a word or expression that has a particular meaning, especially in a technical or scientific subject 專門名詞；術語: **medical/legal/scientific term** *Contusion is the medical term for a bruise.* "挫傷"一詞是磕碰受傷的醫學名稱。
6 a term of abuse/endearment etc a word or expression used to insult someone, say you love them etc 罵人的詞/表示愛意的詞: *To an islander, tourist was just about the worst term of abuse.* 對一個島上居民來說，遊客差不多是最尖酸刻薄的詞。
7 in glowing terms/in strong terms if you describe something in glowing terms or say something in strong terms, you show that you admire something very much or that you are very angry 以十分讚許的口吻/以強烈的措辭: *I complained to the manager in the strongest possible terms.* 我以最強烈的措辭向經理投訴。
8 in no uncertain terms in a clear and usually angry way〔通常帶着怒氣〕直截了當地: *He told me in no uncertain terms not to park near his house.* 他直截了當地告訴我，別把車停在他家附近。—see also 另見 **a contradiction in terms** (CONTRADICTION (3))

③ PERIOD OF TIME 時段
9 ►SCHOOL/UNIVERSITY 中小學/大學◄ [C] *BrE* one of the three periods that the school or university year is divided into【英】學期〔一學年分為三學期〕: **summer/autumn/spring term** *The main exams are at the end of the summer term.* 主要的考試都安排在夏季學期的期末。| **term time** (=during the term) 在學期內 *Teachers often feel overworked in term time.* 教師們在學期內經常覺得工作擔子過重。—see also 另見 HALF-TERM —compare 比較 SEMESTER
10 in the long/short/medium term considered over a period from now until a long etc time in the future 就長期/短期/中期而言: *The company's prospects look good in the long term.* 公司的遠景看好。
11 ►TIME IN A JOB 工作的時間◄ [C] a period of time for which someone is elected to an important government job, or that a government has power〔當選重要政府職務的〕任期，期限: **term of office/term in office** *The president hopes to be elected to a second term of office.* 總統希望第二屆連任當選。
12 prison/jail term etc a period of time that someone must spend in prison 服刑期限: *The terrorists each received a 30 year prison term.* 每一名恐怖分子被判30年監禁。
13 ►BUSINESS 商務◄ [singular] the period of time that a contract, LOAN¹ (1) etc continues for〔合同等的〕有效期限: *We're trying to extend the term on our mortgage.* 我們正在設法延長抵押的期限。
14 ►END OF BUSINESS AGREEMENT 商務協議的終止◄ [singular] *technical* the end of the period of a business agreement【術語】〔商務協議的〕終止期: *The policy reaches its term next year.* 這份保險單在明年終止。
15 ►HAVING A BABY 生孩子◄ [U] *technical* the end of the period of time when a woman is PREGNANT【術語】分娩期，足月（分娩）—see also 另見 LONG-TERM, SHORT-TERM

④ CONDITIONS/AGREEMENT 條件/協議
16 ►CONDITIONS 條件◄ terms [plural] **a)** the conditions of an agreement, contract, or legal document〔協議、合同或法律文件的〕條款: *Under the terms of the agreement, Hong Kong goes back to China in 1997.* 根據協議條款，香港於1997年回歸中國。**b)** the conditions under which you agree to buy or sell something 付款條件；購買[出售]條件: *I bought this car on very reasonable terms.* 我以非常合理的價格買了這輛車。| **on easy terms** (=a way of paying for something gradually in small amounts) 以分期付款的方式
17 on your (own) terms according to the conditions that you ask for 按照自己的條件: *If I agree to do this it will be on my own terms.* 如果我同意做這事，就要按我的條件來辦。
18 terms of reference the agreed limits of what an official committee or report has been asked to study〔對某一官方委員會或報告的〕授權範圍；研究事項

⑤ RELATIONSHIP 關係
19 be on good/bad terms to have a friendly relationship or bad relationship with someone 關係好/關係不好: [+with] *We're on good terms with all our neighbours.* 我們與所有的鄰居關係都好。| *He had been on bad terms with his father for years.* 他多年來一直與父親關係不好。
20 be on speaking terms to be able to talk to someone and have a friendly relationship with them, especially after a quarrel〔尤指吵架後〕關係好，友好地相互說話: *They were barely on speaking terms.* 他們關係不好，相互之間幾乎不說話。

⑥ OTHER SENSES 其他意思
21 come to terms with sth to accept an unpleasant situation or event and no longer feel upset or angry about it 與…妥協，對…讓步；接受〔不愉快的事〕: *It's hard to come to terms with being unemployed.* 很難接受失業這個現實啊。
22 on equal terms/on the same terms having the same advantages, rights, or abilities as anyone else 在平等的條件下/在相同的條件下: *US companies want to be able to compete on equal terms with their overseas rivals.* 美國的公司想要在平等的條件下與他們的海外對手展開競爭。
23 be thinking/talking in terms of to be considering doing something, buying something, arranging something etc 正考慮做某事；正打算做某事: *She's talking in terms of resigning.* 她正打算辭職。| *I was just thinking in terms of a small party.* 我只打算搞一次小型聚會。
24 ►NUMBER/SIGN 數字/符號◄ [C] *technical* one of the numbers or signs used in a mathematical calculation【術語】〔數學運算中的〕項

term² *v* [T usually passive 一般用被動態] to use a particular word or expression to name or describe something 把…稱為，把…叫做: **be termed sth** *This condition is sometimes termed RSI, or repetitive strain injury.*

這種疾病有時稱為RSI, 即重複性勞損。| *The meeting could hardly be termed a success.* 這次會議很難説是一次成功的會議。

ter·ma·gant /ˋtɝməgənt; ˈtɜːməgənt/ *n* [C] *literary* a noisy woman who often quarrels with people【文】悍婦, 潑婦 —**termagant** *adj*

ter·mi·nal[1] /ˋtɝmənl̩; ˈtɜːmɪ̵nəl/ *adj* **1** a terminal illness cannot be cured, and causes death 不治之症的: *terminal cancer* 晚期癌症 **2 terminal decline/decay** the state of becoming worse and worse and never getting better 越來越糟; 一蹶不振: *Britain's industrial base seems in a terminal decline.* 英國的工業基礎彷彿日薄西山。**3 terminal boredom** *humorous* the feeling of being extremely bored【幽默】極度的沉悶 **4** [only before noun 僅用於名詞前] *technical* existing at the end of something【術語】終端的, 末端的, 末尾的: *terminal buds* 頂芽 —**terminally** *adv*: *terminally ill* 患不治之症的; 病入膏肓的

terminal[2] *n* [C] **1** a big building where people wait to get onto planes, buses, or ships, or where goods are loaded on〔飛機、公共汽車、輪船或貨物運輸的〕集散站; 終點站: *Terminal 4 at Heathrow airport* 希思羅機場的4號集散站 **2** a piece of computer equipment consisting of at least a keyboard and a screen, that you use for putting in or taking out information from a large computer〔電腦的〕終端; 終端設備 **3** one of the points at which you can connect wires in an electrical CIRCUIT〔電路的〕端子

ter·mi·nate /ˋtɝmə͵net; ˈtɜːmɪ̵neɪt/ *v* [I,T] *formal* if something terminates, or if you terminate it, it ends【正式】(使) 結束, (使) 終止: *His contract was terminated immediately they found out who he was.* 他們發現他的身分後便立即終止了與他訂的合同。

ter·mi·na·tion /͵tɝməˋneʃən; ͵tɜːmɪ̵ˈneɪʃən/ *n* [C,U] **1** [C] *technical* a medical operation to end the life of a developing child before it is born; ABORTION【術語】終止妊娠 **2** *formal* the act of ending something, or the end of something【正式】結束, 終止, 停止: *You may face a reduction or termination of benefits.* 你可能會面臨津貼的減少或停發。

ter·mi·nol·o·gy /͵tɝməˋnɑlədʒɪ; ͵tɜːmɪ̵ˈnɒlədʒi/ *n* [C, U] the technical words or expressions that are used in a particular subject 術語, 專門用語: *scientific terminology* 科學術語 —**terminological** /͵tɝmɪnəˋlɑdʒɪkl̩; ͵tɜːmɪ̵nəˈlɒdʒɪkəl◂/ *adj*

ter·mi·nus /ˋtɝmənəs; ˈtɜːmɪ̵nəs/ *n* [C] the station or stop at the end of a railway line or bus service〔鐵路、公共汽車線路的〕終點站

ter·mite /ˋtɝmaɪt; ˈtɜːmaɪt/ *n* [C] an insect that eats and destroys wood from trees and buildings 白蟻

term·ly /ˋtɝmlɪ; ˈtɜːmli/ *adj BrE* happening each TERM (=one of the three periods in the school or university year)【英】每學期發生[舉行]的

term pa·per /ˈ· ͵··/ *n* [C] *AmE* a long piece of written work by a US school or college student, that is the most important piece of work in their course【美】學期論文

tern /tɝn; tɜːn/ *n* [C] a black and white sea-bird that has long wings and a tail with two points 燕鷗〔一種海鳥〕

ter·race /ˋtɛrɪs; ˈterɪ̵s/ *n* [C]

1 ►HOUSES 房屋◄ *especially BrE* a row of houses that are joined to each other, or a street with one of these rows in it【尤英】〔互相連接的〕一排房屋, 排屋;〔排屋面對的〕街道: *21 Chestnut Terrace* 栗樹街21號

2 ►PLACE YOU CAN SIT 可以坐的地方◄ an area, especially next to a hotel or restaurant, where people can sit outside to eat or drink〔尤指旅館或餐館人們可以坐在室外吃喝的〕露天平台

3 ►FOOTBALL 足球◄ the terraces [plural] *BrE* the wide steps that the people watching a football match can stand on【英】〔足球賽觀眾站立的〕看台

4 ►FLAT ROOF 平的屋頂◄ a flat roof used as an outdoor living area〔用作室外起居的〕屋頂平台

5 ►FLAT LAND 平地◄ a flat area cut out of a slope, usually one in a series that rise up the slope, that is often used to grow crops〔修在坡地上的〕梯田; 階地

terraced house /͵·· ˈ·/ *n* [C] *BrE* a house which is part of a row of houses that are joined together【英】排屋中的一棟房屋; ROW HOUSE *AmE*【美】—see picture on page A4 參見 A4 頁圖

ter·ra·cot·ta /ˋtɛrəˋkɑtə; ͵terəˈkɒtə◂/ *n* [U] hard reddish-brown baked CLAY 赤陶土: *a terracotta pot* 赤陶罐子

ter·ra fir·ma /͵tɛrə ˋfɝmə; ͵terə ˈfɜːmə/ *n* [U] *Latin, usually humorous* land rather than sea or air【拉丁, 一般幽默】大地, 陸地: *We were glad to be back on terra firma again.* 我們很高興又踏上了陸地。

ter·rain /tɛˋren; teˈreɪn/ *n* [C,U] a word meaning a particular type of land, for example, hilly, rough etc 地形, 地勢; 地面: *rocky terrain* 多石的地形

ter·ra·pin /ˋtɛrəpɪn; ˈterəpɪ̵n/ *n* [C] a small TURTLE (=animal with four legs and a hard shell) that lives in water in warm areas 水龜〔生活在温暖水域中的一種小龜〕

ter·rar·ium /təˋrɛrɪəm; təˈreəriəm/ *n* [C] a large glass container that you grow plants in as a decoration〔栽培裝飾性植物所用的〕大玻璃盆, 陸棲植物育養箱

ter·res·tri·al /təˋrɛstrɪəl; tɪ̵ˈrestriəl/ *adj technical*【術語】**1** connected with the Earth rather than with the moon or other planets 地球的 —see also 另見 EXTRATERRESTRIAL[2] **2** living on or connected with land rather than water 陸地的; 陸生的, 陸棲的 **3 terrestrial TV/broadcasting/channels etc** TV etc that is broadcast from the earth rather than from SATELLITES (=special equipment in outer space) 地面的〔而不是衛星的〕電視/廣播/頻道等 —**terrestrially** *adv*

ter·ri·ble /ˋtɛrəbl̩; ˈterɪ̵bəl/ *adj* **1** extremely severe in a way that causes harm or damage 劇烈的; 厲害的; 非常嚴重的: *a terrible accident* 一次嚴重事故 | *The poor lad took a terrible beating.* 那可憐的少年遭到一頓毒打。**2** making you feel afraid or shocked 可怕的, 駭人的; 令人震驚的: *There was a terrible noise and the roof caved in.* 隨着一陣可怕的聲音, 房頂坍塌了。**3** *informal* extremely bad; AWFUL[1] (1)【非正式】很糟的, 極差的: *The hotel was absolutely terrible.* 這家旅館糟糕透了。| *I'm a terrible cook.* 我做的飯菜差極了。 1 3

ter·ri·bly /ˋtɛrəblɪ; ˈterɪ̵bli/ *adv* **1** [+adj/adv] *especially BrE* very; extremely【尤英】很, 非常, 極度: *We were terribly worried.* 我們非常擔心。| *I'm terribly sorry to have kept you waiting.* 非常抱歉, 讓您久等了。**2** very badly; severely 非常糟地; 嚴重地: *The little boy missed his mother terribly.* 那小男孩太想念媽媽了。 

ter·ri·er /ˋtɛrɪɚ; ˈteriə/ *n* [C] a small active type of dog that was originally used for hunting 㹴〔一種原來用於狩獵的小犬〕

ter·rif·ic /təˋrɪfɪk; təˈrɪfɪk/ *adj* **1** *informal* very good, especially in a way that makes you feel happy and excited【非正式】極好的, 極棒的; 非常愉快的: *We had a terrific time on holiday.* 我們度假時玩得特別愉快。| *I feel terrific!* 我感到特別開心！**2** very large in size or degree〔尺寸或程度〕極其巨大的, 大得驚人的: *Suddenly, there was a terrific bang!* 突然"砰"的一聲巨響！

ter·rif·i·cally /təˋrɪfɪklɪ; təˈrɪfɪkli/ *adv* [+adj/adv] *informal* very; extremely【非正式】非常; 極度: *It's terrifically difficult for working parents to find adequate child care.* 雙職工父母要找到妥善的託兒服務, 真是非常的困難。

ter·ri·fied /ˋtɛrə͵faɪd; ˈterɪ̵faɪd/ *adj* very frightened 非常害怕的, 極度驚恐的: *a terrified animal* 一頭受驚的動物 | **[+of]** *I'm terrified of heights.* 我有恐高的毛病。| **[+at]** *Mark was terrified at the thought of parachuting.* 馬克一想到跳傘就害怕得要命。| **terrified (that)** *We were both terrified that the bridge would collapse.* 我們兩人都很害怕橋會塌掉。

ter·ri·fy /ˋtɛrə͵faɪ; ˈterɪ̵faɪ/ *v* [T] to make someone extremely afraid 使害怕, 使恐懼: *Her husband's violence* *terrified her.* 她丈夫的暴力行為讓她感到害怕。

ter·ri·fy·ing /ˋtɛrə͵faɪɪŋ; ˈterɪ̇faɪ-ɪŋ/ *adj* extremely frightening 極其可怕的, 駭人聽聞的: *The hostages suffered a terrifying ordeal.* 人質們遭受了極其可怕的折磨。—**terrifyingly** *adv*

ter·rine /tɛˋrin; teˈriːn/ *n* [C,U] a dish made of cooked meat, fish etc, formed into a LOAF shape and served cold; PÂTÉ〔用肉類、魚類等做成塊狀, 用作冷盤的〕肉醬

ter·ri·to·ri·al¹ /͵tɛrəˋtɔrɪəl; ͵terɪ̇ˈtɔːriəl◂/ *adj* **1** [no comparative 無比較級] related to land that is owned or controlled by a particular country〔某國家的〕領土的; 屬地的 **2** *technical* territorial animals, birds etc guard the area of land that they consider to be their own【術語】〔獸類、鳥類等〕守衛自身活動地域的; 領域性的 —**territoriality** /͵tɛrə͵tɔrɪˋælətɪ; ͵terɪ̇tɔːriˈælɪ̇ti/ *n* [U]

territorial² often 常作 **Territorial** *n* [C] a member of the British Territorial Army 英國國防義勇軍的成員

Territorial Ar·my /͵····ˋ··/ *n* **the Territorial Army** a military force of people in Britain who train as soldiers in their free time; TA〔業餘時間接受軍訓的〕英國國防義勇軍 —compare 比較 NATIONAL GUARD

territorial wa·ters /͵····ˋ··/ *n* [plural] the sea near a country's coast, which that country has legal control over〔某一國的〕領海

2 **ter·ri·to·ry** /ˋtɛrə͵torɪ; ˈterɪ̇təri/ *n*

1 ▶GOVERNMENT LAND 政府土地◀ [C,U] land that is owned or controlled by a particular government, ruler, or military force 領土, 版圖, 領地: *We crossed the river into enemy territory.* 我們渡河進入敵軍的領地。

2 ▶TYPE OF LAND 某一類土地◀ [U] land of a particular type〔某種特定的〕地區, 地方: *an expedition through previously unexplored territory* 一次穿越未經勘探的地區的探險

3 US Territory land that belongs to the United States, but is not a state〔美國的〕屬地

4 ▶EXPERIENCE 經驗◀ [U] a particular area of experience or knowledge〔經驗或知識的〕領域: *The company is moving into unfamiliar territory with this new software.* 該公司正通過這種新開發的軟件進入一個陌生的領域。

5 ▶ANIMAL 動物◀ [C,U] the area that an animal, bird etc regards as its own and will defend against other animals〔獸類、鳥類等的〕地盤, 領域

6 ▶BUSINESS 商務◀ [C,U] an area of business, especially in selling, for which someone is responsible〔商務活動、尤指商業銷售的〕地區: *I'm in charge of the metropolitan Chicago territory.* 我負責芝加哥大都市地區的銷售活動。

7 come/go with the territory to be a natural and accepted part of a particular job, situation, place etc 在某種工作、情況中難免碰到的事: *I'm a cop – so I could get shot – it goes with the territory.* 我是警察, 所以我有可能吃槍彈——那恐怕是工作中難免碰到的事情。

ter·ror /ˋtɛrɚ; ˈterə/ *n*

1 ▶FEAR 恐懼◀ [U] a feeling of extreme fear 恐懼, 驚恐: *Paul screamed, the terror bursting out of him.* 保爾尖聲大叫, 恐懼表露無遺。| **in terror** (=very frightened) 驚恐地 *The people fled in terror.* 人們驚恐而逃。| **live in terror of** (=be very frightened of someone or something) 非常害怕〔某人或某事〕*After being bullied, Steven lived in terror of going to school.* 被人欺負後, 史蒂文非常害怕去上學。| **sheer terror** *There was a look of sheer terror on his face.* 他的臉上有一種非常恐怖的表情。| **in terror of your life** (=very frightened that you will be killed) 害怕丟命

2 ▶VIOLENT ACTION 暴力行動◀ [U] violent action for political purposes; TERRORISM 恐怖活動; 恐怖主義: *The resistance movement started a campaign of terror.* 抵抗運動開始搞恐怖活動。

3 ▶FRIGHTENING SITUATION 可怕的情況◀ [C] an event or situation that makes people feel extremely frightened, especially because they think they may die〔尤指令人擔憂生命安危的〕可怕的事[情況]: *The hostages suffered untold terror.* 人質們遭受無法言喻的驚恐。

4 ▶PERSON 人◀ [C] *informal* a very annoying person, especially a child【非正式】討厭的人〔尤指孩子〕: *That Johnson kid's a real terror!* 約翰遜家的那個孩子真是混世魔王!

5 hold no terrors for sb *formal* to not frighten or worry someone【正式】不讓人害怕; 不讓人焦慮: *Death held no terrors for me.* 死亡並不讓我感到恐懼。—see also 另見 **reign of terror** (REIGN¹ (2)), **a holy terror** (HOLY (4)), **strike terror into sb's heart** (STRIKE¹ (18))

ter·ror·is·m /ˋtɛrə͵rɪzəm; ˈterərɪzəm/ *n* [U] the use of violence such as bombing, shooting or KIDNAPPING to obtain political demands 恐怖主義: *The government is determined to combat international terrorism.* 政府決心同國際恐怖主義作鬥爭。

ter·ror·ist /ˋtɛrə͵rɪst; ˈterərɪ̇st/ *n* [C] someone who uses violence such as bombing, shooting etc to obtain political demands 恐怖分子: *Two of the terrorists were shot dead.* 恐怖分子中有兩名被擊斃。| **terrorist attack/activity** *Twenty people were killed in the latest terrorist attack.* 有二十人死於最近的那次恐怖主義襲擊。—compare 比較 GUERRILLA, PARTISAN² (2)

ter·ror·ize also 又作 **-ise** *BrE*【英】/ˋtɛrə͵raɪz; ˈterəraɪz/ *v* [T] to deliberately frighten people by threatening to harm them, especially so they will do what you want 恐嚇…: *Many people have been terrorized into leaving their homes.* 許多人遭到恐嚇, 離開了家園。

ter·ry·cloth /ˋtɛrɪ͵klɔθ; ˈteriklɒθ/ also 又作 **ter·ry** /ˋtɛrɪ; ˈteri/ *n* [U] a type of thick cotton cloth with uncut threads on both sides, used to make TOWEL*s*, bath mats etc 毛圈織物; 毛巾布 —see picture on page A16 參見 A16 頁圖

terse /tɝs; tɜːs/ *adj* a terse reply, message etc uses very few words and often shows that you are annoyed〔回答、信息等〕簡短的〔常表示厭煩等〕: *Derek's terse reply ended the conversation.* 德里克的簡短回答使談話終止了。—**tersely** *adv*: *"Continue!" he said tersely.* "繼續!" 他簡短地說道。—**terseness** *n* [U]

ter·tia·ry /ˋtɝʃɪ͵ɛrɪ; ˈtɜːʃəri/ *adj technical* third in place, degree, or order【術語】第三位的; 第三級的; 第三代的

tertiary ed·u·ca·tion /͵··· ··ˋ··/ *n* [U] *formal* education at a college, university etc; HIGHER EDUCATION【正式】高等教育, 大學教育

Te·ry·lene /ˋtɛrəlin; ˈterɪ̇liːn/ *n* [U] *BrE trademark* a light strong artificial cloth【英, 商標】滌綸〔一種人造纖維織物〕

TESL /ˋtɛsl̩; ˈtesəl/ *n* [U] the Teaching of English as a Second Language 作為第二語言的英語教學

TESOL /ˋtɛsɑl; ˈtesɒl/ *n* [U] *especially AmE* the teaching of English to speakers of other languages【尤美】向說其他語言的人講授英語, 作為外語的英語教學

tes·sel·la·ted /ˋtɛsl̩͵etɪd; ˈtesɪ̇leɪtɪ̇d/ *adj technical* made of small flat pieces in various shapes and colours that fit together to form a pattern【術語】用小塊東西鑲嵌成花紋的

test¹ /tɛst; test/ *n* [C] S1 W1

1 ▶EXAM 考試◀ a set of questions, exercises or practical activities to measure someone's skill, ability, or knowledge 測驗, 測試; 考查, 考試: **spelling/driving/biology etc test** *How did you do on your maths test?* 你數學測驗考得怎麼樣? | **pass/fail a test** *She passed her driving test when she was 17.* 她 17 歲時通過了駕車考試。| **do/take/sit a test** (=take part in it) 參加考試 *The thought of taking the test terrifies me.* 一想到參加考試, 我就害怕。| **[+on]** *We have a test on irregular verbs tomorrow.* 我們明天測驗不規則動詞。| **test result** *When do you get your test results back?* 你甚麼時候拿回你的考試成績?

2 ▶MEDICAL 醫學的◀ **a)** a short medical examination on a part of your body, or to find out what is wrong with you〔醫學〕檢查; 化驗: *an eye test* 視力檢查 | **run a test** (=do one quickly) 對…作出快速的檢查 *We'll just run some tests on your blood sample.* 我們將對你的血液樣本很快做出檢查。| **test results** *I'm still waiting for my test results from the hospital.* 我還在等待醫院的化驗結果。**b)** equipment for carrying out a medical test 醫療檢查設備: *a pregnancy test* 懷孕檢查設備

3 ►FOR CHECKING STH 檢驗某物◄ a process used to find out whether equipment works correctly, or whether something contains a particular substance 檢驗; 試驗: *nuclear weapons tests* 核武器試驗 | **a test for sth** (=a test to find sth) 對某物的檢驗 *a test for chemicals in the water* 對水中化學物質的檢驗 | **test site/equipment/procedure** *We went to the test site in Nevada.* 我們前往內華達的試驗場地。

4 ►DIFFICULT SITUATION 艱難處境◄ a situation in which the qualities of someone or something are clearly shown 考驗: **a test of character/strength etc** *The problems she faced were a real test of character.* 她面臨的那些問題是對她的品格的一次真正考驗。| **put sb/sth to the test** (=find out how good someone or something is) 使某人/某事得到考驗 *Living together will soon put their relationship to the test.* 一起生活會很快使他們的關係得到考驗。

5 stand the test of time to be good enough, strong enough etc to last for a long time 經受時間的考驗: *Our friendship has stood the test of time.* 我們的友誼經受住了時間的考驗。

6 ►STANDARD 標準◄ something that is used as a standard to judge or examine something else〔判斷或檢驗某事的〕標準, 試金石: *It's difficult to know what's a good test of love.* 很難說甚麼是檢驗愛情的試金石。—see also 另見 TEST CASE

7 ►SPORT 體育運動◄ *BrE*【英】the short form of 縮略式= TEST MATCH —see also 另見 BREATH TEST, MEANS TEST, SMEAR TEST

This graph shows some of the words most commonly used with the noun **test**. 本圖表所示為含有名詞 test 的一些最常用詞組。

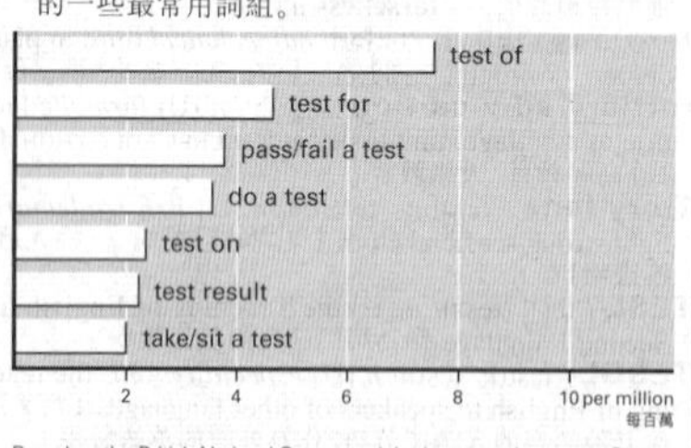

Based on the British National Corpus and the Longman Lancaster Corpus
據英國國家語料庫和朗文蘭卡斯特語料庫

T

3 2 **test**[2] *v*

1 ►EXAM 考試◄ [T] to ask someone spoken or written questions, or make them do a practical activity, to find out what they know about a subject 測驗, 測試; 考查: **test sb on** *We're being tested on grammar tomorrow.* 我們明天要測驗語法。| **test sth** *We'll have to test his knowledge of computers.* 我們得測試一下他的電腦知識。

2 ►MEDICAL 醫學的◄ a) [T] to give someone a short medical examination on a part of their body, or to find out what is wrong with them 檢查〔身體的某個部分〕, 給…體檢: *I must have my eyes tested.* 我必須檢查一下我的視力。| **test sb for sth** *I'm going to test you for diabetes.* 我給你檢查一下, 看有沒有糖尿病。**b)** to get a particular result when a medical test is done on you 化驗結果為…: *He tested positive for HIV.* 他的愛滋病病毒化驗結果呈陽性。

3 ►MACHINE/PRODUCT 機器/產品◄ [T] to use something for a short time to see if it works properly 試驗; 檢驗: *testing nuclear weapons* 試驗核武器 | **test sth on sb/sth** (=use something on someone or something to test it) 在某人/某物身上做試驗 *None of this range of cosmetics has been tested on animals.* 這一化妝品系列從未在動物身上試驗過。

4 ►FIND OUT 查出◄ [T] to examine something in order to find out something about it 檢查, 查看: *Test the cake to see if it's done.* 檢查一下糕點, 看看是否做好了。| **test sth for sth** *testing ore samples for quality* 檢查礦石樣品的質量

5 ►BE DIFFICULT 困難的◄ [T] to be so difficult that all of someone or something's good qualities will be needed to do it 考驗, 考查: *The next six months will test your powers of leadership.* 接下來的六個月將考驗你的領導能力。—see also 另見 TESTING

6 ►OIL/GAS 石油/天然氣◄ [I,T] to search for oil, gas etc by carrying out tests 勘探, 探測: **[+for]** *testing for oil* 探測石油

7 test the water to check people's reaction to a plan before you decide to do anything 試探〔人們對某項計劃的〕反應: *We'll have to test the water before we ban smoking in the staffroom.* 我們禁止在職工休息室吸煙之前, 得先看看大夥的反應。—see also 另見 **tried and tested** (TRIED[2])

tes·ta·ment /ˈtɛstəmənt; ˈtestəmənt/ *n* [C] *formal*【正式】**1 a testament to sth** something that shows or proves something else very clearly 對某物的證明[證據]: *The aircraft's safety record is an impressive testament to its designers' skill.* 飛機的安全記錄是對其設計師技能的一個有力證明。**2** a WILL[2] (2) 遺囑 —see also 另見 NEW TESTAMENT, OLD TESTAMENT —**testamentary** /ˌtɛstəˈmɛntərɪ; ˌtestəˈmentəri◂/ *adj*

test ban /ˈ· ·/ *n* [C] an agreement between countries to stop testing NUCLEAR WEAPONS 禁止核武器試驗協定

test card /ˈ· ·/ *n* [C] a pattern or picture that is shown on television when there are no programmes〔檢測電視上圖案或畫面效果的〕測試卡

test case /ˈ· ·/ *n* [C] a legal case that establishes a particular principle and is then used as a standard which other similar cases can be judged against 判例案件〔確定某種判決準則、供其他類似案件作判決依據的案件〕

test cer·tif·i·cate /ˈ· ·,···/ *n* [C] *BrE* the official paper that proves that a car is legally safe enough to drive【英】〔汽車的〕安全證明書

test drive /ˈ· ·/ *n* [C] an occasion when you drive a car to see if it works correctly or if you like it so that you can decide if you want to buy it〔汽車的〕試驗駕駛, 試車 —**test-drive** *v* [T]

test·er /ˈtɛstɚ; ˈtestə/ *n* [C] a small bottle of PERFUME[1] (1) etc, in a shop, for customers to try〔商店裡供顧客試用的〕試用品〈如香水等〉

tes·ti·cle /ˈtɛstɪkl̩; ˈtestɪkəl/ *n* [C] one of the two round organs that produce SPERM in a male, that are enclosed in a bag of skin behind and below the PENIS 睾丸

tes·ti·fy /ˈtɛstəˌfaɪ; ˈtestɨfaɪ/ *v* **1** [I,T] to make a formal statement of what is true, especially in a court of law〔尤指在法庭上〕作證: **[+that]** *Can you testify that you saw the defendant at the scene of the crime?* 你能作證你看見被告在犯罪現場嗎? | **[+against]** *It would not be easy to testify against people you know.* 要作證指控你相識的人, 真是不容易啊。| **[+for]** *Vicky agreed to testify for the accused.* 維基同意為被告作證。**2** [I,T] *formal* to be a clear sign that something is true【正式】證明, 證實: **[+to]** *Mrs Parson's nervous behaviour testified to the strain she was under.* 帕森夫人的緊張行為證明了她承受的壓力有多大。**3** [I] *AmE* to stand up and tell people about how God has helped you in your life【美】作見證〔指基督徒向人訴說上帝的恩典〕

tes·ti·mo·ni·al /ˌtɛstəˈmonɪəl; ˌtestɨˈməʊniəl/ *n* [C] **1** a formal written statement describing someone's character and abilities〔對某人品格和能力的〕證明書, 推薦

信 —see also 另見 REFERENCE (4) **2** something that is given or done to someone to show thanks, praise, or admiration 感謝信; 表揚信; 獎狀; 獎勵: *a testimonial dinner* 一次表示謝意的宴會

tes·ti·mo·ny /ˋtɛstəˏmonɪ; ˈtestɪ̵mənɪ/ *n* [C,U] **1** a formal statement that something is true, such as the one a WITNESS makes in a court of law〔法庭上的〕證詞: *Barker's testimony is crucial to the prosecution's case.* 巴克的證詞對控告方的證據起到關鍵的作用。**2** a fact or situation that shows or proves something very clearly 證據; 證明: **[+to/of]** *These results are a testimony to your hard work.* 這些成果證明了你的辛勤勞動。

test·ing /ˋtɛstɪŋ; ˈtestɪŋ/ *adj* a testing situation, experience etc is difficult to deal with 很難對付的, 棘手的: *a testing time in their relationship* 他們的關係經受考驗的時刻

testing ground /ˈ·· ·/ *n* [C] **1** a place where machines, cars etc are tried to see if they work properly〔機器、汽車等的〕測試場; 試驗地 **2** a situation or problem in which you can try new ideas and methods to see if they work〔新思想、新方法的〕試驗機會: *Eastern Europe has become a testing ground for high speed privatization.* 東歐已經成為高速私有化的試驗場。

tes·tis /ˋtɛstɪs; ˈtestɪ̵s/ *n plural* **testes** /-tiz; -tiːz/ [C] *technical* a TESTICLE【術語】睾丸

test match /ˈ· ·/ *n* [C] a CRICKET (2) or RUGBY match that is played between the teams of different countries 板球[橄欖球]的國際比賽

tes·tos·ter·one /tɛsˋtɑstəˏron; teˈstɒstərəʊn/ *n* [U] the chemical in males that gives them their male qualities 睾丸素, 睾丸甾酮

test pi·lot /ˈ· ˏ··/ *n* [C] a pilot who flies new aircraft in order to test them〔新飛機的〕試飛員

test tube /ˈ· ·/ *n* [C] a small glass container that is shaped like a tube and is used in chemistry 試管 —see picture at 參見 LABORATORY 圖

test-tube ba·by /ˈ· · ˏ··/ *n* [C] *not technical*【非術語】**1** a baby born as a result of ARTIFICIAL INSEMINATION〔人工授精產下的〕試管嬰兒 **2** a baby that started to develop from an egg removed from a woman's body and was then put back inside the woman to continue developing〔體外受精後再移植入母體而產下的〕試管嬰兒

tes·ty /ˋtɛstɪ; ˈtesti/ *adj* impatient and easily annoyed; IRRITABLE 不耐煩的; 急躁的: *a testy old man* 一位脾氣暴躁的老頭 | *testy remarks* 不耐煩的話 —**testily** *adv*: *"You can't!" Ralph interrupted him testily.* "你不可以!" 拉爾夫不耐煩地打斷了他的話。—**testiness** *n* [U]

tet·a·nus /ˋtɛtənəs; ˈtetənəs/ *n* [U] a serious illness caused by BACTERIA that enter your body through cuts and wounds and make your muscles, especially your jaw, go stiff; LOCKJAW 破傷風

tetched /tɛtʃt; tetʃt/ *adj AmE spoken* slightly crazy【美口】神經有點不正常的, 瘋瘋癲癲的

tetch·y /ˋtɛtʃɪ; ˈtetʃi/ *adj* likely to get angry or upset easily 急躁的; 容易生氣的: *Jane's a bit tetchy this morning, watch what you say to her.* 簡今天上午有點犯急, 你跟她說話得小心點。—**tetchily** *adv* —**tetchiness** *n* [U]

tête-à-tête¹ /ˈtet ə ˋtet; ˌteɪt ɑː ˈteɪt/ *n* [C] *French* a private conversation between two people【法】〔兩人之間的〕私下交談: *have a cosy tête-à-tête* 作一次溫馨的促膝交談

tête-à-tête² *adv* [only after verb 僅用於動詞後] *French* if two people meet, speak, or eat tête-à-tête they are together in private【法】〔兩人之間〕私下地

teth·er¹ /ˋtɛðɚ; ˈteðə/ *n* [C] **1** a rope or chain that an animal is tied to so that it can only move around within a limited area〔拴牲畜用的〕繫繩, 拴鏈 **2 be at the end of your tether** to be so worried, tired etc, that you feel you can no longer deal with a difficult or upsetting situation 忍無可忍; 走投無路; 一籌莫展: *Morel was at the end of his tether, too exasperated to answer.* 莫雷爾忍無可忍, 氣得無言以對。

tether² *v* [T] to tie an animal to a post so that it can only move around within a limited area 拴住, 繫住〔牲畜〕

tetra- /tɛtrə; tetrə/ *prefix* having four of something 表示"四": *a tetrahedron* (=solid shape with four sides) 一個四面體

Teu·ton·ic /tjuˋtɑnɪk; tjuːˈtɒnɪk/ *adj* **1** *humorous* having qualities that are thought to be typical of German people【幽默】〔品質等〕日耳曼人所獨具的; 典型德國人風格的: *Teutonic efficiency* 日耳曼人的效率 **2** connected with the ancient German peoples of northwestern Europe〔古代西北歐的〕條頓民族的

Tex-mex /ˋtɛks mɛks; ˈteks meks/ *adj AmE informal* connected with the music, cooking etc of Mexican-American people【美, 非正式】〔音樂、烹飪等〕墨西哥裔美國人的: *a Tex-Mex restaurant* 一家墨西哥裔美國人餐館

text /tɛkst; tekst/ *n* **1** [U] the writing that forms the main part of a book, magazine etc rather than the pictures or notes〔書、雜誌等的〕正文〔區別於圖片、注釋等〕; 文字: *There ought not to be too much text in children's books.* 兒童書籍裡不應該有太多的文字。**2** [U] any written material 文字材料: *One disk can store the equivalent of 500 pages of text.* 一張磁碟能夠儲存相當於 500 頁的文字材料。**3 the text of sth** the exact words of a speech, article etc〔演說、文章等的〕原文: *Only 'The Times' printed the full text of the President's speech.* 只有《泰晤士報》刊載了總統演說的全文。**4** [C] a book or other piece of writing that is connected with learning or intended for study 課本, 教科書; 教材: **a set text** (=a book that must be studied for an examination)〔考試指定的〕必讀課本 *'Hamlet' is a set text for this year's English exam.* 《哈姆雷特》是今年英語考試的必讀課本。**5** [C] a short piece from the Bible that someone reads and talks about〔某人誦讀並講述的一小段〕聖經經文 S2 W1

text·book¹ /ˋtɛkstˏbʊk; ˈtekstbʊk/ *n* [C] a book that contains information about a subject that people study 教科書, 教材, 課本: *a biology textbook* 一本生物學教材 —see also 另見 COURSEBOOK

textbook² *adj* [only before noun 僅用於名詞前] done or happening exactly as something should be done or as it should happen 合乎規範的; 完善的: *That shot of Becker's was superb – textbook stuff.* 貝克爾那一球打得真棒, 無懈可擊! | **textbook case/example** *The advertising campaign was a textbook example of how to sell a product.* 這項廣告宣傳活動是如何銷售產品的一個範例。

tex·tile /ˋtɛkstḷ; ˈtekstaɪl/ *n* [C] **1** a word used mainly in business for woven material that is made in large quantities 紡織品: *Their main exports are textiles, especially silk and cotton.* 他們的主要出口商品是紡織品, 尤其是絲綢和棉布。| **textile industry/market etc** *a textile factory* 一家紡織廠 **2 textiles** *plural* the industry involved in making cloth 紡織業

tex·tu·al /ˋtɛkstʃuəl; ˈtekstʃuəl/ *adj* concerning the way that a book, magazine etc is written〔書、雜誌等〕正文的, 原文的: *a detailed textual analysis* 詳細的文本分析

tex·ture /ˋtɛkstʃɚ; ˈtekstʃə/ *n* [C,U] **1** the way a surface, substance, or material feels when you touch it, especially how smooth or rough it is〔尤指光滑或粗糙的〕手感, 質感, 質地: *the smooth texture of silk* 絲綢的光滑質感 | *a soil with a loose sandy texture* 鬆散的沙質土壤 **2** *literary* the way the different parts are combined in a piece of writing, music, art etc in order to make a particular impression on you; CHARACTER (2)【文】〔寫作、音樂、藝術等作品的〕神韻, 風神格調: *the rich texture of Shakespeare's English* 莎士比亞筆下的英語之豐富神韻 —**textural** *adj* —**texturally** *adv*

tex·tured /ˋtɛkstʃɚd; ˈtekstʃəd/ *adj* **1** having a surface that is not smooth 質地粗糙的: *textured wallpaper* 質地粗糙的牆紙 **2 coarse-textured/smooth-textured/fine-textured etc** having a texture that is smooth etc 質地粗糙的/質地光滑的/質感緻密的等: *heart-shaped,* *rough-textured leaves* 質地粗糙的心形樹葉

textured vege·ta·ble pro·tein /ˌ·· ˌ··· ˈ··/ *n* [U] a substance made from beans, used instead of meat; TVP 結構性植物蛋白, 植物組織蛋白

-th /θ; θ/ *suffix* **1** forms ORDINAL numbers, except with 1, 2, or 3〔構成除一、二、三之外的序數詞〕第〔幾〕: *the 17th of June* 6月17日 | *a fifth of the total* 總數的五分之一 —see also 另見 -ND, -RD, -ST **2** *old use or biblical*【舊或聖經】another form of the suffix -ETH 後綴 -eth 的另一種拼法: *he doth* (=does) 他做

Tha·lid·o·mide /θəˋlɪdəˏmaɪd; θəˈlɪdəmaɪd/ *n* [U] *trademark* a drug given to people to make them calm, until it was discovered that it harmed the development of the arms and legs of unborn babies【商標】反應停, 酞胺哌啶酮〔原用作鎮靜劑, 發現它有害於胎兒四肢的發育後停用〕

1 1 **than¹** /ðən; ðən; *strong* 強讀 ðæn; ðæn/ *conjunction* **1 higher than/cheaper than etc** used when comparing two things that are different to introduce the second thing 比…更高/更廉價等〔用於兩個事物的比較, 引入第二個事物〕: *The cost of the repairs was a lot cheaper than I thought.* 維修費用比我所想的要便宜許多。**2 would rather/would sooner...than...** used to say that you prefer one thing to another 寧願…而不願…: *If it's alright by you I'd rather walk than go by car.* 如果你沒有問題的話, 我寧願走路, 而不願乘車。**3 hardly/scarcely/no sooner etc...than...** used to say that something had only just happened when something else happened 一…就…: *No sooner had I mailed the letter than I realized she'd changed address.* 我剛寄出那封信, 就記起她已更改了地址。**4** *informal* except【非正式】除…之外: *They left me with no option than to resign.* 除了辭職, 他們沒有給我任何選擇。

1 1 **than²** *prep* **1 higher/more expensive than** used when comparing two things that are different to introduce the second thing 比…更高/更昂貴等〔用於兩個事物的比較, 引入第二個事物〕: *Miranda has always been more intelligent than her two brothers.* 米蘭達一直比她的兩個兄弟更聰明。| *Richard's marrying a woman who's older than his own mother.* 理查德要跟一個比自己母親還年長的女人結婚。| *The new tax system will definitely affect some people more than others.* 新的稅收體制將對一些人產生比較明顯的影響。**2 more/less/fewer etc than** used when comparing two different amounts, numbers etc to introduce the second amount or number 比…多/少等: *The programme doesn't last any longer than an hour.* 該節目長度不超過一個小時。| *He's been unemployed for more than 18 months now.* 他到現在已經失業十八個多月了。| *It's a beautiful dress but it's much more than I can afford.* 這件連衣裙很漂亮, 不過太貴了。

thane /θen; θeɪn/ *n* [C] a man who fought for the King but was below the rank of a KNIGHT¹ (1) in early English history〔英國早期歷史上為國王服兵役, 地位低於騎士的〕大鄉紳

1 2 **thank** /θæŋk; θæŋk/ *v* [T] **1** to tell someone that you are pleased and grateful for something they have done, or to be polite about it 感謝, 向…表示謝意: *Remember to thank Uncle Robin when you see him.* 你見到羅賓大叔別忘了向他致謝。| **thank sb for** *Meg and Jo ran to thank their aunt for the presents.* 梅格和喬跑過去感謝姨媽給他們送禮物。| **thank sb for doing sth** *I must write and thank him for sending the cheque.* 我必須寫信感謝他送來了支票。**2 thank God/goodness/heavens** used to show that you are very glad about something 感謝上帝, 謝天謝地: *Thank God that's over! I've never been so nervous in my life!* 感謝上帝, 那終於結束了! 我一生中從來沒有這麼緊張過! | **[+for]** *"Your son is safe!" "Thank heavens for that!"* "你的兒子安全了!" "那真要謝天謝地了!" —see 見 GOD (USAGE) **3 have sb to thank (for sth)** used when saying who is responsible for something helpful or, humorously, who is responsible for something unhelpful 因某事感謝某人; 因某事責怪某人〔幽默用法〕: *I have Phil to thank for getting me my first job.* 我得感謝菲爾幫我找到了我的第一份工作。| *And who do I have to thank for that mess on my desk?* 我的桌上那麼亂, 是誰幹的好事? **4 only have yourself to thank (for sth)** *spoken* used to say that you are responsible for something bad that has happened to you【口】只能怪自己, 咎由自取: *She has only herself to thank if she doesn't have any friends.* 如果說她沒有任何朋友, 那只能怪她自己。**5 sb won't thank you (for doing something)** used to tell someone that another person will be annoyed because of what they have done 某人不會(因你做了某事而)感謝你的: *I know you're just trying to help, but he won't thank you for telling him how to do it.* 我知道你只不過是想幫幫他的忙, 但他不會因為你告訴他如何辦而感謝你的。**6 thank your lucky stars** *spoken* used to tell someone that they are very lucky, especially because they have avoided an unpleasant or dangerous situation【口】多虧自己的運氣好: *You should thank your lucky stars I got here when I did!* 多虧你運氣好, 當時我剛巧來到這兒。**7 you'll thank me** *spoken* used to tell someone not to be annoyed with you for doing or saying something, because it will be helpful to them later【口】你將來會感謝我的: *You'll thank me for this one day, Laura.* 勞拉, 你將來會曉得我是一片好心的。**8 I'll thank you to do sth** *spoken formal* used to tell someone in an angry way not to do something because it is annoying you【口, 正式】請〔不要做某事〕好不好〔語氣含有怒意〕: *I'll thank you to mind your own business.* 我請你別管閒事好不好? —see also 另見 THANK YOU

thank·ful /ˋθæŋkfəl; ˈθæŋkfəl/ *adj* [not before noun 不用於名詞前] grateful and glad about something that has happened, especially because without it the situation would be much worse 感謝的, 感激的; 為…感到高興的: **[+for]** *I'll be thankful for a good night's sleep after the week I've had.* 在經歷了這樣的一週之後, 我能好好地睡上一個晚上就感激不盡了。| **thankful (that)** *You should be thankful that you have me to look after you.* 有我來照料你, 你應該高興才是。| **thankful to do sth** *I was thankful to make any sort of progress at all.* 能取得一點進步, 我感到欣慰。—see also 另見 **be thankful for small mercies** (MERCY (5)) —**thankfulness** *n* [U]

thank·ful·ly /ˋθæŋkfəlɪ; ˈθæŋkfəli/ *adv* **1** [sentence adverb 句子副詞] used to say that you are glad that something has happened, especially because a difficult situation has ended or been avoided 高興地, 欣慰地: *Thankfully, I managed to pay off all my debts before we got married.* 感到欣慰的是, 在我們結婚前, 我已設法還清了所有債務。**2** feeling grateful and glad about something, especially because a difficult situation has ended or been avoided 滿懷感激地〔尤指困境已過去或避免〕: *We came in and collapsed thankfully onto our beds.* 我們進到屋裡, 謝天謝地, 終於可以癱倒在牀上了。

thank·less /ˋθæŋklɪs; ˈθæŋkləs/ *adj* **1** a thankless job is difficult and you do not get any praise for doing it 吃力不討好的, 為人作嫁的: **a thankless task** *Cooking for the family every day is a thankless task.* 每天給家裡人做飯是一件費力不討好的事。**2** *literary* a thankless person is not grateful【文】〔指人〕不知感激的, 忘恩負義的: *a thankless child* 一個忘恩負義的孩子 —**thanklessly** *adv*

thanks¹ /θæŋks; θæŋks/ *interjection* **1** used to tell someone that you are grateful for something they have given you or done for you; THANK YOU 感謝, 謝謝: *"Pass the salt, please ... thanks."* "請把鹽遞過來…謝謝"。| **thanks for (doing) sth** *I'd love to go to the party. Thanks for asking me.* 我非常願意去參加晚會。謝謝邀請了我。| *Thanks for the ride home – see you tomorrow!* 謝謝開車送我回家。明兒見! | **thanks a lot** *informal*【非正式】: *Thanks a lot for the drink.* 多謝你請我喝酒。| **many thanks** (=often used in a formal business letter) 非常感謝〔常用於正式商務信函〕*Dear Mr Williams, Many* thanks for the articles you sent me last week. 親愛的威廉姆斯先生，非常感謝您上週給我寄來的文章。**2** used as a polite way of accepting something that someone has offered you 謝謝〔表示禮貌地接受〕: *"Do you want another cup of coffee?" "Oh, thanks."* "你還想要一杯咖啡嗎?" "呃，謝謝!" **3 fine thanks** *spoken* used when politely answering someone's question【口】很好，謝謝〔禮貌地回答某人的問候〕: *"Hi, Bill, how are you?" "Fine, thanks."* "嗨，比爾，你可好嗎?" "很好，謝謝。" **4 no thanks** used to say politely that you do not want something 不用，謝謝〔禮貌地謝絕〕: *"How about some cake?" "Oh, no thanks, I'm on a diet."* "來點蛋糕怎麼樣?" "哦，不用，謝謝，我在節食。"

thanks² *n* [plural] **1** the things you say or do to show that you are grateful to someone 道謝的話; 道謝的舉動: *Joe got up and left without a word of thanks.* 喬起身離開了，一句感謝的話也沒有說。**2 thanks to a)** used to say that someone has done something very helpful or useful 歸功於: *Thanks to Germaine's tireless efforts, the concert was a huge success.* 多虧傑曼努力不懈，音樂會獲得了巨大成功。—see 見 OWING (USAGE) **b)** used to say, angrily or humorously that someone has caused a problem 歸咎於〔憤怒的或幽默的語氣〕: *It was supposed to be a surprise, but thanks to your big mouth she knows all about it now.* 本來打算來一次驚喜的，但是，就怪你多嘴，她現在甚麼都知道了。**c)** used to say that something good is caused by something else 由於，因為: *Thanks to the warm Autumn, our fuel bills have been very low.* 由於今年秋季溫暖，我們的燃料費一直很低。**3 no thanks to** *spoken* an expression meaning 'in spite of', used when someone should have helped you but did not【口】不是因為〔某人〕才...〔表示儘管某人本該幫忙卻沒有〕: *It was no thanks to you that we managed to win the game.* 我們不是因為你才最終贏得了那場比賽。—see also 另見 VOTE OF THANKS

Thanks·giv·ing /ˌθæŋks`ɡɪvɪŋ; ˌθæŋks'ɡɪvɪŋ◂/ *n* [U] a public holiday in the US in November, when families have a large meal together and celebrate the origins of their country 感恩節〔美國11月份的一個公共假日〕

thanksgiving *n* [C,U] an expression of thanks to God〔對上帝的〕感恩

thank you /'· ·/ *interjection* **1** used to tell someone that you are grateful for something they have given you or done for you; THANKS 謝謝你，多謝: *Margaret handed him the butter. "Thank you," said Samuel.* 瑪格麗特把黃油遞給了他。"謝謝你，" 塞繆爾說。| *Thank you very much, Brian.* 非常感謝你，布萊恩。| **thank you for (doing) sth** *It's good to see you, Mr. Mathias. Thank you for coming.* 很高興見到您，馬賽厄斯先生。謝謝您的光臨。| *Dear Grandma, thank you for the lovely shirt you sent me for Christmas.* 親愛的外婆，謝謝您在聖誕節給我寄來的那件漂亮的襯衫。**2** used as a polite way of saying that you would like something that someone has offered 謝謝你〔禮貌地表示接受某事〕: *"Can I give you a lift into town?" "Oh, thank you."* "搭我的車進城好嗎?" "噢，謝謝你。" **3** used when politely answering someone's question 謝謝你〔禮貌地回答某人的問候〕: *"How was your trip to Paris?" "Very pleasant, thank you."* "你的巴黎之行怎麼樣?" "非常愉快。謝謝。" **4 no thank you** used to say politely that you do not want something 不用，謝謝〔禮貌地表示謝絕〕: *"Would you like some more coffee?" "No, thank you, I'm fine."* "再來點咖啡嗎?" "不用了，謝謝，我夠了。" **5** used at the end of a sentence when telling someone firmly that you do not want their help or advice and are slightly annoyed by it 多謝啦!〔略帶氣憤地謝絕提供的幫助或建議〕: *I can manage quite well on my own, thank you!* 我自己完全能做好，多謝你啦!

thank-you¹ *adj* **thank-you letter/note/card etc** a short letter etc in which you thank someone 感謝信/便條/卡片等

thank-you² *n* [C] something you say or do in order to thank someone 道謝的話; 道謝的舉動: *This present's a thank-you for helping me last week.* 這份禮物是為了感謝你上週幫了我的忙。

that¹ /ðæt; ðæt/ *determiner plural* **those** /ðoz; ðəʊz/ **1** used to talk about a person, thing, idea etc that has already been mentioned or that the person you are talking to knows about already 那，那個; 那些〔指已經提到或已經知道的人、事物、想法等〕: *Who was that man I saw you with last night?* 我看到昨天晚上跟你在一起的那個人是誰? | *Those flowers that you gave me lasted over a week.* 你給我的那些花擱了一個多星期都沒有枯萎。| *Later that day the news was being broadcast all over the world.* 那天晚些時候，世界各地的廣播都報道了這一消息。| *How much is that hat in the window?* 櫥窗裡的那頂帽子多少錢? | *The lawyer was expensive, but at that stage we wanted to make sure everything went smoothly.* 請律師是很貴的，但已經到了那一步，我們想要保證一切事情都進展順利。**2** used to talk about the person or thing that is farthest from you, or the situation that is not happening at the moment 那，那個; 那些〔指離你最遠的人或物或尚未發生的情況〕: *That party of hers was great but this one will be even better.* 她那次聚會辦得不錯，但這一次會更好。| *So many cakes to choose from – I'll take that one over there.* 有這麼多糕點可供選擇 —— 我要那邊的那一塊。| *Look at those men in that car. What on earth are they doing?* 瞧那輛車上的那些人。他們究竟在幹甚麼?

that² *pron plural* **those 1** used to talk about a person, thing, idea etc that has already been mentioned or that the person you are talking to already knows about 那，那個; 那些〔指已經提到或已經知道的人、事物或想法等〕: *Pregnant! Who told you that?* 懷孕啦! 誰告訴你的? | *Where did you get those? I've been looking for some shoes just like that.* 你是在哪兒買那雙鞋子的? 我一直就在找那樣的鞋子。| *So that's why you don't like him.* 所以，那就是你為甚麼不喜歡他的原因。| *I wish you wouldn't say things like that.* 我希望你不要說那樣的話。| **with that** (=after doing that) 隨後，隨即 *She slammed the book on the table and with that ran out of the room.* 她把書摔在桌子上，隨後跑出了房間。**2** used to talk about the person or thing that is farthest from you, the situation that is not happening at the moment etc 那個人; 那事物〔指離你最遠的人或物或尚未發生的情況〕: *No, that's your desk, this one's mine.* 不，那才是你的課桌，這個是我的。| *Those were great years at college, but I think that I'm even happier now.* 那些是大學時代的美好時光，不過我覺得我現在還要快樂一些。**3** *formal* used when talking about a particular person or thing, especially one which is a particular type or kind【正式】〔特定的〕那一個; 那一類: *In my opinion the finest wines are those from France.* 我認為，最好的葡萄酒要數法國產的那些。| **that of** *Rupert's manner was that of someone accustomed to mixing with aristocracy.* 魯珀特的舉止態度屬於那種習慣與貴族打交道的人。**4 that's life/men/politics etc** *spoken* used to say that someone's actions are typical of a particular group of people, situation etc【口】那便是生活/男人/政治等: *"I washed all my clothes only to find I'd left a £20 note in the pocket." "That's life I suppose."* "我把所有的衣服都洗了，結果發現口袋裡留了一張20英鎊的鈔票。" "我想，人生就是這樣!" | *We go out for a romantic meal and all he wants to do is talk about football. That's men for you.* 我倆出去是為了享受浪漫的一頓飯，但他只想談論足球。男人就是這樣! **5 at that** *especially spoken* used to give more information, about something mentioned before【尤口】此外，而且: *He'll have to buy a new car and a big one at that. There are 8 children in his family.* 他不得不買一輛新車，而且要買一輛大的。他家裡有八個孩子。**6 and (all) that** *BrE spoken* and similar people or things【英口】等等，諸如此類: *There were lots of sandwiches and pies and that but I wasn't really hungry.* 有很多的三明治、餡餅等東西，不過我不很餓。**7 that is (to**

say) *spoken* used to correct something that you have just said or written【口】也就是說，即〔用於更正〕: *I know how to operate a computer. That is, I thought I did until I saw this one.* 我知道如何操作電腦。也就是說，在看到這一台之前，我想我是知道的。**8 that's a clever dog/that's a good girl** *spoken* used to praise children or animals【口】這才是好乖乖/這才是好姑娘: *You've eaten all your supper–that's a good boy!* 你把晚飯全吃完了——這才是乖孩子！**9 that's it** *spoken* used when you are angry about a situation and you do not want it to continue【口】完了，就這樣〔表示憤怒〕: *That's it. I'm not taking any more. You can keep your rotten job.* 就這樣。我是受不了。你可以繼續幹那沒有勁的活。**10 that's that** *spoken* used to say you will not change a decision【口】就這麼定了，就這樣吧〔表示決心堅定〕: *I refuse to go and that's that!* 我不會去的。就是這樣！

Frequencies of the pronoun **that** in spoken and written English 代名詞 that 在英語口語和書面語中的使用頻率

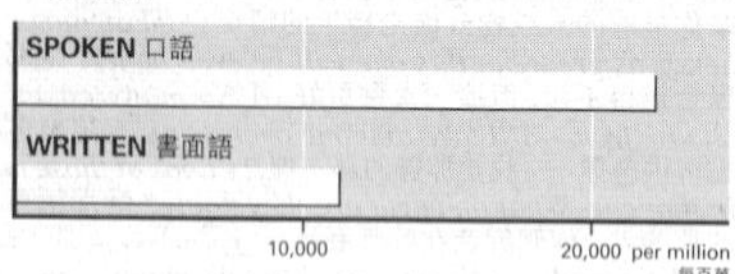

Based on the British National Corpus and the Longman Lancaster Corpus
據英國國家語料庫和朗文蘭卡斯特語料庫

This graph shows that the pronoun **that** is more common in spoken than in written English. This is because it is used a lot in conversation to refer to something that has already been mentioned, or when talking about the person or thing that is farthest from you, or a situation in the past. It is also used in some common spoken phrases. 本圖表顯示，代名詞 that 在英語口語中的使用頻率遠遠高於書面語，因為該詞經常用於會話中，指代前面已經提及過的事物，離自己很遠的人或物，或者是過去的事情。它還用於一些常用的口語片語中。

1 1 **that³** /ðət; ðət; *strong* 強讀 ðæt; ðæt/ *conjunction* **1** used after verbs, nouns and adjectives to introduce a CLAUSE (2) which gives more information, a reason, an explanation etc〔用在動詞、名詞或形容詞後引入包含信息、理由、解釋等的子句〕: *If she said that she'd come, she'll come.* 如果她說過她要來，她就會來的。| *The rules state that only the goal keeper can handle the ball.* 規則規定，只有守門員才能用手觸球。| *Is it true that the Robinsons are emigrating?* 羅賓遜一家要移居國外，這是真的嗎？| *The fact that he is your brother-in-law should not affect your decision.* 他是你的姐夫，但這一事實不應該影響你的決定。**2 a) so big/tall etc that...** very big, very tall etc with the result that something happens or someone does something 如此大/高等…〔用在 so 之後，表示結果〕: *She's so tall that she has to have her clothes made for her.* 她長得這麼高，所以不得不定做衣服。**b) such a big man/such a tall house etc that** a very big man, a very tall house etc with the result that something happens or someone does something 如此一個大個子男人/如此一幢高房等〔用在such之後，表示結果〕: *He's such a miserable so-and-so that none of the nurses like helping him.* 他是一個讓人非常討厭的傢伙，沒有哪個護士願意幫助他。**3** used as a RELATIVE PRONOUN like 'who', and 'which'〔用作關係代名詞，相當於 who 或 which〕: *Did you know the man that bought the sportscar?* 你認識那個買了跑車的男子嗎？| *There are lots of things that I need to buy before the trip.* 我在旅行前有許多東西需要去買。**4** used with objects of a PREPOSITION in a CLAUSE (2)〔在子句中用作介詞的受詞〕: *The police have found the gun that she was shot with.* 警察已經找到打死她的那支槍。| *There's Betty, my sister that I've been telling you about.* 那就是貝蒂，我多次對你說過的我的妹妹。**5 the year/time etc that** the year, the time etc when something happened〔某事發生的〕那一年/那一時刻等: *The day that my father died, I was on holiday in Greece.* 我父親去世的那一天，我正在希臘度假。**6** used to introduce a clause after a SUPERLATIVE¹ (2)〔用來引入最高級形容詞或副詞後的子句〕: *Veronica is the most boring person that I've ever met.* 韋洛尼卡是我遇見過的最討厭的人。| *He was the greatest boxer that ever lived.* 他是歷史上最偉大的拳擊手。**7** *formal* in order that, or so that something may happen or someone may do something【正式】為了，以便〔表示目的或可能的結果〕: *We pray that he may recover soon.* 我們祈願他早日康復。**8** *literary* used when you wish that something would happen, that you could do something etc【文】〔用來引導對某種事情的願望〕: *Oh, that I could fly.* 我要是能飛就好了！—see also 另見 **so (that)** (so² (2))

USAGE NOTE 用法說明: THAT

SPOKEN-WRITTEN 口語－書面語

In conversation it is not usual for **that** to actually be used in a *that* clause after a verb or adjective. This is especially true after the commonest verbs taking such clauses in spoken English – **think, say, know, see,** and after common adjectives like **sure, confident, afraid, sorry, aware, glad**. 在對話中，that 實際上往往並不用於動詞或形容詞後的 that 子句中。在口頭英語中，在諸如 think, say, know, see 等最常用的帶這一類子句的動詞和 sure, confident, afraid, sorry, aware, glad 等形容詞後，尤其如此: *I think Stuart's gone crazy.* 我想斯圖亞特已經發瘋了。| *I'm afraid it could be there for six months.* 我想這會持續六個月。

In written English there are differences between different styles of writing. **That** is hardly ever left out in academic writing, where in any case the commonest verbs are not the same as in spoken English, but are words like **show, ensure**. 在書面英語中，不同的文體之間是有差異的。在學術性寫作中，that 很少被省略掉，無論如何，學術性文字中最常用的動詞不是口頭英語中的那些，而是 show, ensure 等詞: *Empirical data show that similar processes can be guided quite differently.* 實際觀察得來的數據表明，類似的過程可以用完全不同的方法來引導。| *It is important that both groups are used in the experiment.* 重要的是，兩組都必須接受實驗。

In newspapers **that** is used at least twice as much as it is left out. 在報刊中，使用that的時候比被省略的時候至少要多出一倍: *The police say that they don't have the time to worry about marijuana.* 警察說，他們沒有時間去操心大麻的事。But in fiction it is left out more than it is kept in. 但是在小說中，被省掉的時候多於被保留的時候: *I'm sorry I hit you just now!* 對不起，我剛才打了你。

GRAMMAR 語法

That is more often left out when the subject of the *that* clause is the same as the subject of the main clause, or where it is a pronoun. 當 that 子句的主詞與主句的主詞一樣時，或者子句開頭是代名詞時，that 更多是被省略掉: *I think I'll make a shopping list.* 我想我要開一張購物清單。| *They were glad she'd gone out.* 他們很高興她已經出去了。But 但是，*I suspect that John was a bit drunk.* 我懷疑約翰有點兒醉了。

That is usually put in if the main verb is passive, or where the *that* clause does not immediately follow the verb. 如果主句動詞是被動語態，或者 that 子句不是緊跟在主句動詞後，通常要使用 that: *I was told that he had arrived.* 我被告知，他已經到了。| *They warned him that it was dangerous.* 他們警告他，這很危險。

PUNCTUATION 標點符號

That does not usually immediately follow a comma. *Who* and *which* may follow a comma in relative clauses that add information but do not restrict the meaning, but *that* is not used in these clauses. 一般來說, that 不直接跟在逗號之後。who 和 which 在關係子句中可以跟在逗號之後, 補充説明情況, 但並無限制性意義, 而 that 不用在這類子句中。Look at this restrictive clause 試看下面的限制性子句: *She visited her brother who/that lives in Detroit* (=she has more than one brother, and the relative clause with *who/that* tells us which one). 她探訪了她那位住在底特律的兄弟〔她有不止一個兄弟, 而關係子句告訴了我們是哪一個〕。Compare this non-restrictive clause 試比較下面的非限制性子句: *She visited her brother, who lives in Detroit* (=she has only one brother, and the relative clause, which cannot begin with *that*, just adds further information about him). 她探訪了她的兄弟, 他住在底特律〔她只有一個兄弟, 這裡的關係子句不能以 that 開始, 它只是補充了有關他的情況〕。

1 2 **that**[4] /ðæt; ðæt/ *adv* [+adj/adv] **1 that long/many etc** *spoken* used to say how long or how many, especially because you are showing the size, number etc with your hands【口】那麼長/那麼多等〔尤指通過手勢比劃來表示大小、數目等〕: *The fish was that long, give or take an inch or two.* 那條魚有那麼長, 相差不超過一兩英寸。| *He missed hitting the car in front by that much.* 他險些撞到前面那輛車, 就差那麼一點點。**2 not that long/many** *spoken* used when you mean fairly short, only a few etc【口】沒有那麼長/那麼多〔用來表示較短、較少等〕: *Will's not that tall, considering he's 16 already.* 威爾不很高, 他已經16歲了。| **not all that** *The film wasn't all that good really.* 那部電影實際上不怎麼好看。**3 that long/many etc (that)** *BrE spoken* so long, so many etc that something happens, someone does something etc【英口】那麼長/那麼多等...〔表示程度、結果等〕: *She was that tired that she had to go upstairs and rest.* 她疲倦極了, 只好上樓去休息。| *I've eaten that much, I think I'm going to be sick.* 我已吃了那麼多, 我想我會反胃的。

thatch[1] /θætʃ; θætʃ/ *v* [I,T] to make the roof of a building with dried STRAW (=strong stems), REEDs etc 用茅草、蘆葦等覆蓋〔屋頂〕—**thatched** *adj*: *a thatched cottage* 茅屋, 茅舍 —**thatcher** *n* [C]

thatch[2] *n* **1** [C] a roof made of dried STRAW, REEDs etc 茅草屋頂 **2** [U] STRAW or REEDs used to make a roof〔用以蓋屋頂的〕茅草; 蘆葦 **3** [singular] *humorous* a thick untidy pile of hair on someone's head【幽默】濃密的亂髮

thaw[1] /θɔ; θɔː/ *v* **1** [I,T] also 又作 **thaw out** if ice or snow thaws or is thawed, it becomes warmer and turns into water〔冰雪〕融化: *The lake thawed in March.* 3月裡, 湖水解凍了。| **it thaws** (=ice and snow melt)〔冰、雪〕融化 *It thawed overnight.* 一夜之間冰雪就融化了。**2** also 又作 **thaw out** [T] to let frozen food unfreeze until it is ready to cook 解凍〔冷凍食品〕: *Thaw frozen meat in its packet and then cook as soon as possible.* 先讓凍肉在包裝盒裡解凍, 然後盡快烹煮。**3** [I] to become friendlier and less formal〔態度〕變得溫和、親熱: *After a few glasses of wine Robert began to thaw a little.* 幾杯酒過後, 羅伯特開始變得比較溫和了。

thaw[2] *n* **1** [singular] a period of warm weather during which snow and ice melt 融雪期; 化冰期; 解凍期: *The thaw begins in March.* 解凍期在3月份開始。**2** [C] an improvement in relations between two countries after a period of unfriendliness〔兩國之間經歷一段不和時期之後的關係〕緩和, 改善

the- /θɪ; θi/ *prefix* another form of the prefix THEO- 前綴 theo- 的另一種拼寫

the[1] /ðə; ðə; *before vowels* 元音前作 ðɪ; ði; *strong* 強讀 ði; ðiː/ *definite article, determiner* **1** used to refer to a particular thing or person when everyone knows which thing or person you are talking about, or because only one such person or thing exists〔用來指大家知道正在談論的或唯一存在的某一特定的事物或人〕: *I've got two cats now; the black and white one's called Rosie and the ginger one's called Joseph.* 我現在有兩隻貓了, 黑白相間的那一隻名叫羅絲, 姜黃色的那隻名叫約瑟夫。| *The audience clapped and cheered.* 觀眾鼓掌歡呼。| *Take these letters to the post office, will you.* 把這些信件拿到郵局去, 好嗎? | *The sky was gray and overcast.* 天空灰蒙蒙、陰沉沉的。| *They're holding an election later in the year.* 他們要在下半年舉行選舉。| *the tallest building in the world* 世界上最高的建築 | **the United States/the Aegean Sea etc** (=used before the names of certain countries, seas etc) 美國/愛琴海等〔用於某些國家、海洋名稱之前〕| **His Holiness the Pope/the Defense Minister etc** (=used as part of someone's title) 教皇(陛下)/國防部長(閣下)等〔用於某些人的頭銜中〕| **the Smiths/the Kings/the Mitchells etc** *especially spoken* (=used before the name of a family to refer to all the members of that family)【尤口】史密斯一家/金一家/米切爾一家等〔用於某個家庭的姓氏之前, 指全家的所有成員〕**2** used to refer to something that everyone knows because it happens in nature or is a part of daily life〔用來指自然界或日常生活中大家都知道的某事〕: *We drove through the night to get to New Orleans in time.* 我們徹夜驅車, 及時地趕到了新奧爾良。| *Ella's been complaining about the traffic keeping her awake at night.* 埃拉一直在抱怨來往車輛讓她晚上睡不着覺。| *We would ask tenants to switch off the water supply before vacating the property.* 我們要求房客在搬出前先把自來水關掉。**3** used to refer to a part of the body or to someone or something that belongs to someone〔用來指某人身體的某一部位或屬於某人的某一東西〕: *She hit him on the* (=his) *ear.* 她打了他一記耳光。| *How's the* (=your) *arm?* 手臂怎麼樣了? | *The* (=my) *car broke down again today.* 今天車又拋錨了。| **the wife** *spoken* (=used especially by men to refer to their own wife or to another man's wife and considered to be offensive by some women)【口】那婆娘〔尤為男人用來指自己的或別人的妻子, 一些婦女認為這是冒犯用語〕**4** used before an adjective to make it into a noun when you are referring to all the people who that adjective describes〔用在形容詞前, 指某一類人〕: *We need more sheltered accommodation for the elderly.* 我們需要為老年人提供更多的安身之所。| **the rich/the poor** *She devoted her life to helping the poor.* 她畢生都在幫助窮人。| **the wounded/the disabled/the physically handicapped etc** *parking facilities for the disabled* 殘疾人專用停車設施 | **the Germans/the Japanese/the British** (=used to refer to all the people from a particular country) 德國人/日本人/英國人〔用來指某一國的全體人民〕**5** *especially spoken* used before an adjective to make it into a noun when you are referring to a situation that that adjective describes【尤口】〔用在形容詞前, 指某一類情況〕: *Her behaviour is verging on the manic.* 她的行為近於瘋狂。| **the impossible/the ridiculous/the insane** *Come on now, that's asking for the impossible.* 得了吧, 那是強人所難。**6** used before a singular noun to make it general〔用於單數名詞前, 表示泛指〕: *The condor is in danger of extinction.* 兀鷲有瀕於滅絕的危險。| *The computer has revolutionized office work.* 電腦使辦公室工作發生了革命性變化。**7** used before a plural noun to refer generally to a particular kind of thing〔用於複數名詞前, 表示泛指〕: *I find it easier to get up when the mornings are lighter.* 晨光更明亮的時候, 我覺得更容易起牀。| *The shops are always packed just before Christmas.* 聖誕節前幾天, 商店裡總是擠滿了人。**8** used before activities that people do, especially musical activities, but usually not including sports〔用於人的活動前, 尤用於音樂活動前, 但一般不包括體育運動〕: *Fiona's learning the flute.* 菲奧納正在學吹長笛。| *He plays the violin.* 他會拉小

提琴。**9 the flu/the measles/the mumps** *spoken* used before the names of certain not very serious illnesses【口】流感/麻疹/腮腺炎〔用於某些不太嚴重的疾病名稱前〕: *Amy's off school with the measles.* 艾米因患麻疹而告假了。**10** *spoken* used before referring to a particular day, date, or month【口】〔用於某一特定的日期或月份前〕: *Tuesday the thirteenth of April* 4月13日星期二 | *We moved house in the first week of July.* 我們是在7月份的第一個星期裡搬家的。| *The meeting was scheduled for the Thursday.* 會議定在星期四。**11** used to refer to a period of time that lasts ten or a hundred years〔用來指十年或一百年的一個時期〕: **the twenties/the thirties/the forties etc** *There was a severe recession in the mid-twenties.* 20年代中期曾有過一次嚴重的經濟衰退。| **the sixteen-hundreds/the seventeen-hundreds/the eighteen-hundreds** *the great novelists of the nineteen-hundreds* 20世紀的偉大小說家 **12 by the metre/by the dozen/by the handful etc** used before the names of measurements when describing how something is calculated, sold, or used〔用於量度名稱之前〕論米/論打/論手捧等〔來計算、銷售或使用〕: *This cloth is sold by the metre.* (=it is measured in metres in order to calculate its price) 這布匹論米賣〔按米尺度量來計算價格〕。| *We get paid by the hour.* 我們按小時計報酬。**13** used before a noun, especially in negative sentences to show an amount or degree needed for a particular purpose〔用於名詞前、尤用於否定句中, 表示所需要的量或程度〕: *I haven't the time to talk just now.* 我現在沒有時間談話。| *Eric didn't even have the common sense to send for a doctor.* 埃里克甚至連去請醫生的常識都沒有。**14** used before the name of a thing that represents a particular activity〔用於某一物體名詞前, 表示某一特定的活動〕: *Rupert took to the bottle* (=began to drink a lot of alcohol) *after his wife died.* 魯珀特在妻子死後開始貪杯愛酒。| *He's already been under the knife* (=had a medical operation) *twice this year.* 他今年已經是兩次開刀做手術了。**15** *spoken* used with strong pronunciation before a noun to show that it is the best, most famous etc person or thing of its kind【口】〔用於名詞之前, 表示某一類人或事物中最好的、最有名的, 發音要重讀〕: *"Apparently Paul McCartney's singing at the club tonight." "Not the Paul McCartney surely!"* "據我所知保羅·麥卡尼今晚上要在俱樂部演唱了。" "當然不是那個保羅·麥卡尼!" **16** *spoken* used when describing someone or something when you are angry, jealous, surprised etc【口】〔用於形容某人或某事, 表示憤怒、嫉妒、吃驚等〕: *He's stolen my parking space, the bastard!* 他偷佔了我的停車位, 這個臭傢伙! | *I can't get this drawing pin out, the stupid thing.* 我沒法取出這顆圖釘, 這破爛玩意兒! | *"Jamie's won a holiday in Hawaii." "The lucky devil!"* "傑米贏得了去夏威夷度假的機會。" "這傢伙真走運!" **17** *spoken* used in certain phrases that express anger, surprise etc【口】〔用於某些短語中, 表示憤怒、吃驚等〕: *What the hell are you doing here?* 你究竟在這裡搞甚麼? | *For the love of God what will the boy do next!* 上帝知道那孩子下一步還會幹些甚麼!

USAGE NOTE 用法說明: THE

GRAMMAR 語法

The is not used with uncountable or plural nouns when you mean 'all' of something in general, or when what you are talking about is not already specifically known about by the reader or listener. 當泛指某事物的"總體"時, 或者當談論的事還沒有為讀者或聽者具體知曉時, the不與不可數名詞或複數名詞一起使用: *I love life/rock music/wine/ice cold beer/silk shirts/bananas.* 我喜愛生活/搖滾樂/葡萄酒/冰鎮啤酒/綢襯衫/香蕉。| *We sat around eating cheese and crackers and listening to rock music.* 我們隨意地坐着, 一邊吃着乾酪和餅乾, 一邊聽着搖滾樂。

The is used if you are mentioning specific things that are already known to the reader or listener 如果你提到的具體事物是讀者或聽者已經知曉的, 要用the: *We drank the beer and the wine and watched the video* (=the beer etc that I just told you about or that you know about). 我們一邊喝着啤酒和葡萄酒, 一邊看着錄像〔那些啤酒或葡萄酒是我剛告訴過你的或者你本來就知道的〕。

The is also used whenever you use an *of* phrase, relative clause, superlative etc, to say more specifically what kind of thing you mean. 在使用of短語、關係從句、最高級等以更具體地說出你所意指的某種事物時, 也要用 the: *I love the life of a writer/the food that you cook/the best things in life.* 我喜愛作家的生活/你做的那些食品/生活中最美好的東西。

The is not usually used at all in the following situations (though in a few specific cases it may be if the noun is restricted as just described). 在下列情況下, 通常不用 the〔然而在少數具體情況下, 如果名詞像上述那樣受到限制的話, 也可以用 the〕:

1. With many times of day and night and days, months etc, especially after **at, by,** and **on**. 表示白天、晚上、星期、月份等時, 尤其在at, by和on之後: *at sunset/noon/by night/on Monday* 在夕陽西下時/在中午時分/在晚上前/在星期一 (Compare 比較 *during the night/on the Monday after Christmas* 在那天晚上/在聖誕節後的那個星期一) Compare also 再比較以下兩句: *Last week was awful* (=the one just before now) and *The last week was awful* (=the last week of my vacation etc some time ago). 上週糟糕透了〔指現在之前的那一週〕/最後一週糟糕透了〔指先前度假中等的最後一週〕。

2. When you give dates in speech you say 講話中提到日期時要說: *June the third* (*BrE* 英)/*June third* (*AmE* 美) or *the third of June* 6月3日, but you would write 但寫作時則用: *June 3rd*

3. When you are talking about meals, especially after **at, before, during, after, for,** and the verb **have**. 在談論飯餐時, 尤其在at, before, during, after, for之後和動詞 have之後: *after/at/before/during breakfast* 早餐之後/吃早餐時/早餐之前/早餐期間 | *coffee for breakfast* 咖啡當早餐 | *When do you have breakfast?* 你甚麼時候吃早飯? | *Lunch is at one.* 午飯在一點吃。(Compare 比較 *The breakfast she gave us was good.* 她給我們準備的早餐很不錯。)

4. In many fixed expressions such as 在許多固定片語裡, 諸如: *by car/bus etc* 坐汽車/公共汽車 | *at/to school/university etc* 在學校/在大學/去上學/去上大學 | *in/to bed/prison/church* 在牀上/在監獄裡/在教堂裡/上牀/進監獄/上教堂 | *arm in arm* 手臂挽着手臂 | *face to face* 面對着面 | *husband and wife* 夫妻 | *from beginning to end* 自始至終

5. With names of languages and most diseases 指語言和大多數疾病的名稱時: *She speaks Greek.* 她說希臘語。| *He's got cancer/flu/mumps/a cold.* 他患了癌症/流感/腮腺炎/感冒。In informal spoken English, however, people often use **the** before the names of several common diseases. 然而, 在非正式的口頭英語中, 人們經常在一些常見疾病名稱前使用the: *He has got the flu/the mumps.* 他患了流感/腮腺炎。

6. With names of airports and railway stations 指機場、火車站的名稱時: *I'm arriving at Heathrow airport/Grand Central Station.* 我將到達希思羅機場/中央大火車車站。

7. With many names of streets, places, countries, mountains etc 指街道、地點、國家、山脈等時: *Madison Avenue/Oxford Street/New York/Texas/Hol-*

land/Mount Fuji. 麥迪遜大街／牛津街／紐約／德克薩斯／荷蘭／富士山 (compare 比較 *This isn't the New York I remember* 這不是我記憶中的紐約。)

8. However, some such names always contain **the**. 然而，有些這類名稱總是含有 the: *The Strand, The Bronx, The Hague, The Sudan* 斯特蘭德大街，布朗克斯區，海牙，蘇丹 This includes especially the names of countries that are plural or contain the word *state, republic* etc 這尤其包括名稱是複數或含有state, republic等詞的國家: *The Netherlands, the USA, the UK, the Irish Republic.* 荷蘭，美國，英國，愛爾蘭共和國

9. **The** is usually needed with names of hotels and restaurants if they do not end in *'s.* 如果旅館或餐館的名稱不是以 's 結尾，通常需要用 the: *The Hilton/The Grand Hotel/The Mandarin.* 希爾頓酒店／貴賓酒店／曼德琳酒店 Also with names of rivers, seas, and groups of mountains. 另外，用於河流、海洋和山脈的名稱: *The Ganges/The Atlantic/The Rockies* 恆河／大西洋／落基山脈

the² *adv* **1** used in comparisons to show that two things happen together〔用於比較，表示兩件事同時發生〕: *The more he eats the fatter he gets.* 他吃得越多就越胖。| *"When do you want this done?" "The sooner the better."* "你想要這事甚麼時候辦成?" "越早越好。" **2** used in comparisons to show that someone or something has more or less of a particular quality than before〔用於比較，表示某人或某物與過去相比的某一品質〕: **the better/the worse** *You'll feel all the better for having some time away from work.* 你如能離開工作一段時間，就會感覺好一些。| **none the wiser** (=not knowing more about something than before) 仍然弄不明白 *Her lengthy explanation left me none the wiser.* 她冗長的解釋還是讓我弄不明白。**3** used in front of adjectives and adverbs to emphasize that something is as big, good etc as it is possible to be〔用於形容詞或副詞前，強調某事盡可能的程度〕: *He likes you the best.* 他最喜歡你。| *I had the greatest difficulty understanding her.* 我費了好大的勁才明白她的意思。

theatre 劇場

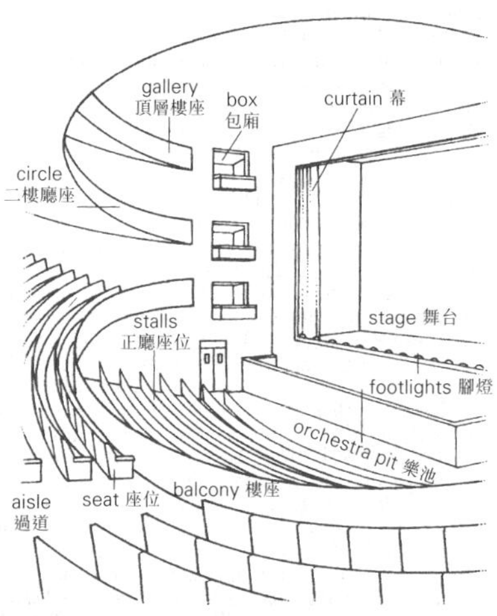

gallery 頂層樓座
box 包廂
curtain 幕
circle 二樓廳座
stalls 正廳座位
stage 舞台
footlights 腳燈
orchestra pit 樂池
aisle 過道
seat 座位
balcony 樓座

2 2 **thea·tre** *BrE*【英】, **theater** *AmE*【美】/ˈθɪətə; ˈθɪətə/ *n* **1 ▶BUILDING 建築物◀** [C] a building or place with a stage where plays are performed 劇場，戲院: *an open-air theatre* 露天劇場 | *the Mercury Theater* 墨丘利劇院
2 ▶PLAYS 戲劇◀ [U] **a)** plays as a form of entertainment 戲劇: *I enjoy theater and swimming.* 我喜歡看戲和游泳。| **the theatre** *He's really interested in literature and the theatre.* 他對文學和戲劇真的很感興趣。| **good theatre** (=effective entertainment) 具有娛樂性 *Yeats' plays are great poetry but they are not good theatre.* 葉慈的劇作都是偉大的詩篇，但不能用來消閒解悶。**b)** the work of acting in, writing, or organizing plays 戲劇事業; 劇作，劇本: *classes in theater and music* 戲劇音樂班 | *She's been working in the theatre for over thirty years.* 她從事戲劇工作已有三十餘載。
3 ▶IN A HOSPITAL 在醫院◀ [C,U] a special room in a hospital where medical operations are done〔醫院裡的〕手術室; OPERATING THEATRE *BrE*【英】
4 ▶AREA 區域◀ [C] a large area where a war is being fought 戰區; 戰場: *the Pacific theater during World War II* 第二次世界大戰期間的太平洋戰區
5 ▶PLACE TO SEE A FILM 看電影的地方◀ [C] *AmE AustrE* a building where films are shown【美，澳】電影院; CINEMA (1) *BrE*【英】, MOVIE THEATER *AmE*【美】

thea·tre·go·er *BrE*【英】, **theatergoer** *AmE*【美】/ˈθɪətəˌgoə; ˈθɪətəˌgəʊə/ *n* [C] someone who regularly watches plays at the theatre 戲院常客，戲迷: *Ken's a keen theatregoer.* 肯是一個狂熱的戲迷。

theatre-in-the-round /ˌ‥ · · ˈ·/ *n* [U] the performance of a play on a central stage with the people watching sitting in a circle around it〔舞台在正中央、觀眾坐在四周的〕圓形劇場; 圓形劇場戲劇技法

theatre weap·ons /ˈ‥ ˌ‥/ *n* [plural] *technical* weapons, especially MISSILEs that can only be fired a few hundred kilometres【術語】戰術武器〔尤指射程只有幾百公里的導彈〕

the·at·ri·cal /θɪˈætrɪkḷ; θiˈætrɪkəl/ *adj* **1** connected with the performing of plays 劇場的，劇院的; 戲劇的; 演劇的: *comic and theatrical skills* 喜劇演藝技能 **2** behaving in a loud or very noticeable way that is intended to get people's attention 戲劇性的; 誇張的: *He took her hand and kissed it in a theatrical gesture.* 他捧起她的手，用一種誇張的姿勢吻了一下。—**theatrically** /-kḷɪ; -kli/ *adv*

the·at·ri·cals /θɪˈætrɪkḷz; θiˈætrɪkəlz/ *n* [plural] **1** *BrE informal* deliberately emotional behaviour so that people will notice you【英，非正式】戲劇性行為; 誇張行為: *We can do without all these theatricals, Andrew!* 安德魯，我們不需要這些裝模作樣! **2** performances of plays 戲劇表演: *amateur theatricals* 業餘戲劇表演

thee /ði; ðiː/ *pron old use* the object¹ (6) form of THOU; you【舊】汝，爾〔thou 的受格〕

theft /θɛft; θeft/ *n* **1** [U] the crime of stealing 盜竊罪: *Car theft is on the increase.* 汽車盜竊犯罪越來越多。**2** [C] an act of stealing something 偷竊，偷盜: *There have been a number of thefts in the area.* 幾宗偷竊案在該地區發生。| **[+of]** *the theft of £150 from the office* 從辦公室偷走 150 英鎊

their /ðɚ; ðə; *strong* 強讀 ðɛr; ðeə/ *determiner* [possessive form of *they* 的所有格形式] **1** of or belonging to them 他們的; 她們的; 它們的: *They washed their faces and went to bed.* 他們洗過臉，就上牀睡覺了。| *The twins spend all their time together.* 那對雙胞胎總是呆在一起。**2** used to avoid saying 'his' or 'her' after words like 'anyone', 'no one', 'everyone' etc〔用在 anyone, no one, everyone 等詞後，泛指〕人人，大家: *Everyone is entitled to their own opinion.* 人人都可以有自己的意見。—compare 比較 HIS¹ —see 見 EACH¹ (USAGE) 1 1

theirs /ðɛrz; ðeəz/ *pron* [possessive form of *they* they 的所有格形式] **1** of or belonging to the people or things that have already been mentioned〔對已經提到過的人或事物〕他們的; 她們的; 它們的〔東西〕: *When our washing machine broke, our neighbours let us use theirs.* 我 3

T

們的洗衣機壞了的時候, 鄰居讓我們用他們的。| *They shared the prize money with a friend of theirs.* 他們與他們的一位朋友分享那筆獎金。**2** used to avoid saying 'his' or 'hers' after words like 'anyone', 'no one', 'everyone' etc〔用在 anyone, no one, everyone 等詞後, 泛指〕人人, 大家: *Everyone wants what is theirs by right.* 人人都想得到權利賦予他們的東西。—compare 比較 HIS[2]

the·is·m /ˈθiːɪzəm; ˈθiːɪzəm/ *n* [U] *technical* the belief that a personal God exists and that He has made His existence known to people through the Bible, church, dreams etc【術語】〔基督教的〕一神論 —**theistic** /θiˈɪstɪk; θiːˈɪstɪk/ *adj* —**theistically** /-klɪ; -kli/ *adv*

them¹ /ðəm; ðəm; *strong* 強讀 ðɛm; ðem/ *pron* **1** the object form of 'they' 他們; 她們; 它們〔they 的賓格〕: *Has anyone seen my keys? I can't find them anywhere.* 有人見到我的鑰匙嗎? 我到處都找不到。| *The police were very helpful when I spoke to them.* 當我向警察說明情況後, 他們很幫忙。—see 見 ME (USAGE) **2** used to avoid saying 'him' or 'her' after words like 'anyone', 'no one', 'everyone' etc〔用在 anyone, no one, everyone 等詞後, 泛指〕那人, 那些人: *If anyone phones, tell them I'll be back later.* 如果有人打電話來, 就說我要過一會兒才回來。

them² / ðɛm; ðem/ *determiner spoken* sometimes used to mean those, although most people think this is incorrect【口】那些〔多數人認為這是不正確的用法〕: *Can I have some of them biscuits, Mum?* 媽媽, 我可以吃一點那些餅乾嗎?

the·mat·ic /θɪˈmætɪk; θɪˈmætɪk/ *adj* concerned with a particular THEME 主題的; 專題的; 題目的: *thematic consistency* 主題的連貫性

theme /θim; θiːm/ *n* [C] **1** the main subject or idea in a piece of writing, speech, film etc 主題: *The book's theme is the conflict between love and duty.* 本書的主題是愛情與職責之間的衝突。**2** a short simple tune that is repeated and developed in a piece of music 主調; 主旋律: *Freia's theme in Wagner's opera* 瓦格納歌劇中的弗雷雅主旋律 **3** *AmE* a short piece of writing on a particular subject that you do for school【美】〔為某一特定學科寫作的〕作文, 短論文: *Your homework is to write a two-page theme on pollution.* 你們的家庭作業是就污染問題寫一篇兩頁的作文。**4 theme music/song/tune** music or a song that is often played during a film or musical play or at the beginning and end of a television or radio programme 主題音樂/主題歌/主調: *The kids were singing the theme song from 'The Brady Bunch'.* 孩子們唱着《布雷迪一家》中的主題歌。

theme park /ˈ· ·/ *n* [C] a type of park where you can have fun riding on big machines such as a ROLLER COASTER and the BIG WHEEL, but where the whole park is based on one subject such as water or space travel 主題公園

theme par·ty /ˈ· ˌ··/ *n* [C] *BrE* a party where everyone has to dress in a particular way connected with a particular subject【英】主題晚會: *a wild West theme party* "西部荒野"主題晚會

them·selves /ðəmˋsɛlvz; ðəmˈselvz/ *pron* **1** the reflexive form of 'they' 他們自己; 她們自己; 它們自己〔they 的反身代名詞〕: *The kids seem very pleased with themselves – what have they been doing?* 孩子們自得其樂, 似乎非常高興——他們一直在幹些甚麼? | *Our neighbours have just bought themselves a jacuzzi.* 我們那些鄰居剛剛都給自家買了一個漩水式浴缸。**2** used to emphasize the pronoun 'they', a plural noun etc 自己, 自身〔用於強調〕: *Doctors themselves are the first to admit the treatment has side effects.* 醫生們自己首先承認說, 這種治療方法有副作用。**3** used after words like 'everyone', 'anyone', 'no one' etc when you talk about someone already mentioned and you do not know what sex they are or it is not important〔用於 everyone, anyone, no one 等詞後, 泛指〕他們自己; 他們親自: *Someone told me they'd actually seen the accident happen themselves.* 有人告訴我說他們的確目擊了那場事故的發生。**4 in themselves** used to say that ideas or situations only become important, serious etc when you consider other related ideas or situations 本身, 自身; 就本身而言: *None of the witnesses' statements prove anything in themselves, but together they are quite conclusive.* 沒有哪一個證人的證詞本身能證明甚麼, 但把它總括起來, 結論卻相當明顯。**5 (all) by themselves a)** alone 單獨地, 獨自地: *It is a sad fact that many pensioners now live by themselves.* 許多領取養老金的人現在都是獨自生活, 這是一個令人悲哀的事實。**b)** without help 全靠自己地: *Did the children make the model all by themselves?* 孩子們是全靠自己做那個模型的嗎? **6 (all) to themselves** if people have something to themselves, they do not have to share it with anyone 完全屬於自己的: *In the new house the children will have a room to themselves.* 在新房子裡, 孩子們將有一間屬於自己的房間。**7 not be/feel themselves** if people are not themselves, they do not feel or behave in the way they usually do because they are nervous, upset or ill〔因神經緊張、煩惱、生病等而〕表現反常/心神不定

then¹ /ðɛn; ðen/ *adv* **1** at a particular time in the past or future 當時, 那時; 到時候, 屆時: *It was then that I realised she'd tricked me.* 直到那個時候我才意識到她騙了我。| *I used to go to school with Mavis Butterwick, or Mavis O'Brien as she then was.* 我曾經同梅維絲·巴特韋克一道上學, 她當時名叫梅維絲·奧布賴恩。| *The furniture is being delivered next week so until then we'll have to sit on the floor.* 家具下週才送來, 所以在此之前, 我們只好坐在地板上。| **from then on** (=starting at that time) 從那時開始 *They met in 1942 and from then on they were firm friends.* 他們1942年相識, 從那時開始, 他們一直是好朋友。| **just then** *Silently she closed the door. Just then she heard a noise.* 她默不作聲地關上了門, 就在那時, 她聽到一陣嘈雜聲。| **back then** (=a long time ago in the past, when things were different) 回首往事, 當年 *Back then we spent holidays in Blackpool.* 當年我們曾在布萊克普爾度假。| **then and only then** *Tidy your room, then and only then can you go out with Mike.* 先整理好了你的屋子, 這樣, 也只有這樣, 你才可以跟麥克一塊兒出去。**2** next; after something has happened 接下來, 然後: *You're doing it all wrong. Mix the flour and butter and then add the eggs.* 你弄錯了。是先把麵粉和黃油攪拌好, 然後加入雞蛋。| *First the passengers and then the stewards jumped from the wreckage.* 先是乘客, 然後是乘務人員從失事的船上跳了下來。**3** used to say that because of what you know about the situation, something else is probably true 那麼: *Still in your pyjamas? Have you just got out of bed then?* 你還穿着睡衣? 那麼你是剛起牀嘍? | **if...then...** *If $x = 3$ and $y = 5$ then $xy = 15$.* 假定x=3, y=5, 那麼 xy=15。**4 but then (again)** *especially spoken* used to say that although something is true something else is also true which makes the first thing seem less important【尤口】不過話又說回來: *I don't spend much but then I don't really go out much.* 我花費不大, 不過話又說回來, 我實際上並不怎麼出去。**5** *spoken* used at the end of questions, statements etc, especially to agree with someone or to make people aware that you are speaking【口】那麼好吧〔用在句末, 尤表示贊同或引人注意〕: *So, what do you do then?* 這麼說來, 你是幹甚麼的? | *Right then, shall we start?* 那好吧, 我們開始吧? | *"Mom, will you play tennis with me?" "Get the balls out then."* "媽媽, 你跟我一塊兒打網球好嗎?" "那好吧, 把球拿出來吧。" **6** *especially spoken* used when giving your opinion or advice about something【尤口】那, 那就: *If you're going to go then go.* 如果你打算去, 那就去吧。| *"He's boring, rude and arrogant." "Then divorce him."* "他令人厭煩, 而且粗魯傲慢。" "那就跟他離婚吧。" **7** so that something happens or so that someone does something 這樣, 這樣一來: *Wear a big hat and dark glasses then no one will recognize you.* 戴上一頂大帽子和一副墨鏡, 這樣, 就沒有人會認出你來了。**8** used in a list of things when you have remembered something else you want to add 另外, 還有: *I do all the washing and cleaning and then there's the ironing too.* 所有的洗滌清理工作都是我在做, 另外還有熨燙的活。**9 then and there** also 又作 **there and then** immediately 立即, 當場: *I expected to have to wait a few days, but they issued the passport then and there.* 我原以為得等上幾天時間, 但他們當場就辦好了護照。—see also 另見 **now and then** (NOW¹ (6))

then² *adj* **the then President, Director etc** the President, Director etc at a particular time in the past 當時的總統/主任等: *secretary to the then Head of Light Entertainment* 那時的娛樂節目負責人的祕書

thence /ðɛns; ðens/ *adv formal*【正式】**1** from there 從那兒, 從那裡: *We went by boat to Trieste, and thence by train to Prague.* 我們先坐船去的里雅斯特, 然後從那兒坐火車去布拉格。**2** for that reason 因為那個緣故; 因而

thence·forth /ˌðɛnsˋfɔrθ; ðensˈfɔːθ/ also 又作 **thence·forward** /ˌðɛnsˋfɔrwəd; ðensˈfɔːwəd/ *adv formal* starting from that time【正式】從那時起: *Thenceforth he made his life in England.* 從那時起, 他開始在英格蘭謀生。

theo- /θɪə; θɪə/ also 又作 **the-** *prefix* concerning God or gods 神的: *theology* (=study of religion) 神學

the·oc·ra·cy /θɪˋɑkrəsɪ; θiˈɒkrəsi/ *n* [C] a social system or state controlled by religious leaders 神權政治; 神權政體 —**theocratic** /ˌθiəˋkrætɪk; ˌθiːəˈkrætɪk◂/ *adj*: *the imposition of a theocratic State* 強迫實行神權政體

the·od·o·lite /θɪˋɑdḷˌaɪt; θiˈɒdəlaɪt/ *n* [C] a piece of equipment used by a land SURVEYOR for measuring angles 經緯儀〔土地丈量人員用來測量角度的一種儀器〕

the·o·lo·gian /ˌθiəˋlodʒən; ˌθiːəˈləʊdʒən/ *n* [C] someone who has studied theology 神學家, 神學研究者

theological col·lege /..ˋ...,..ˋ../ *BrE*【英】, **theological seminary** /ˌ.... ˋ..../ *AmE*【美】*n* [C] a college for training people to become priests or church ministers 神學院〔訓練人們成為牧師或教會神職人員的學院〕

the·ol·o·gy /θɪˋɑlədʒɪ; θiˈɒlədʒi/ *n* **1** [U] the study of religion and religious ideas and beliefs 神學: *He studied theology at college.* 他在大學讀神學。**2** [C,U] a particular system of religious beliefs and ideas 宗教信仰體系: *According to Muslim theology there is only one God.* 根據穆斯林的宗教信仰體系, 神只有一個。—**theological** /ˌθiəˋlɑdʒɪkḷ; ˌθiːəˈlɒdʒɪkəl◂/ *adj*: *theological debate* 神學辯論 —**theologically** /-klɪ; -kli/ *adv*

theo·rem /ˋθiərəm; ˈθɪərəm/ *n* [C] *technical* a statement, especially in mathematics, that you can prove by reasoning【術語】〔尤指數學中依據推理可以證明的〕定理

theo·ret·i·cal /ˌθiəˋrɛtɪkḷ; θɪəˈretɪkəl/ also 又作 **theo·ret·ic** /ˌθiəˋrɛtɪk; θɪəˈretɪk/ *adj* **1** concerned with the study of scientific ideas rather than with practical uses of science or practical experience〔科學〕理論的: *theoretical physics* 理論物理 —compare 比較 PRACTICAL¹ (1) **2** a theoretical situation or condition is supposed to exist but does not really exist 理論上的; 推想的, 臆測的: *Equality between men and women in our society is still only theoretical.* 在我們這個社會裡, 男女之間的平等仍然停留在理論上。| *a theoretical risk of an explosion* 臆測的爆炸的風險

theo·ret·i·cally /ˌθiəˋrɛtəkəlɪ; θɪəˈretɪkli/ *adv* [sentence adverb 句子副詞] **1** used to say what is supposed to happen in a particular situation when the opposite is true 根據推測來看, 按道理講: *Theoretically, Damian's the boss, but I coordinate the team on a day-to-day basis.* 按理說, 達米安是老闆, 但全隊日常的協調工作是由我來做的。**2** according to a scientific idea that has not been proved to be true in a practical way 在理論上; 從理論上說: *It is theoretically possible for computers to be programmed to think like humans.* 對電腦進行編程, 使它像人一樣思考, 這在理論上是可能的。

theo·rist /ˋθiərɪst; ˈθɪərɨst/ also 又作 **theo·re·ti·cian** /ˌθiərəˋtɪʃən; ˌθɪərəˈtɪʃən/ *n* [C] someone who develops ideas within a particular subject that explain why particular things happen or are true 理論家: *a leading economic theorist* 傑出的經濟學理論家

theo·rize also 又作 **-ise** *BrE*【英】/ˋθiəˌraɪz; ˈθɪəraɪz/ *v* [I+about/on, T+that] to think of a possible explanation for an event or fact 建立理論; 闡釋

theo·ry /ˋθiərɪ; ˈθɪəri/ *n* **1** [C] an idea or set of ideas that is intended to explain something about life or the world, especially one that has not yet been proved to be true 學說: *Darwin's theory of evolution* 達爾文的進化論 | **theory that** *the theory that light is made up of waves* 光是由波組成的這一學說 **2** [U] the general principles or ideas of a subject, especially a scientific subject 理論: *Freudian theory has had a great influence on psychology.* 弗洛伊德理論對心理學有着巨大的影響。**3 in theory** something that is true in theory is not actually true although it is supposed to be 理論上, 從理論上來說: *In theory, a child could live on breast milk for ever, but this is hardly practical.* 理論上, 一個孩子可以永遠靠母乳養活, 但這實際上行不通。**4** [C] an idea that someone thinks is true but for which they have no proof 猜想; 假設: **theory that** *Detectives are working on a theory that his murderer was someone he knew.* 偵探的調查基於一個猜想, 即謀殺他的人是他認識的。**5** [U] the set of rules on which a practical subject or skill is based 原理; 學理: *musical theory* 樂理

ther·a·peu·tic /ˌθɛrəˋpjutɪk; ˌθerəˈpjuːtɪk◂/ *adj* **1** intended to help treat or cure an illness 有助於治療的: *Nettles contain vitamins that have a therapeutic value.* 蕁麻含有幾種具治療價值的維生素。**2** making you feel calm and relaxed 使人鎮靜的; 使人放鬆的: *I find swimming very therapeutic.* 我覺得游泳能鬆弛神經。—**therapeutically** /-klɪ; -kli/ *adv*

ther·a·peu·tics /ˌθɛrəˋpjutɪks; ˌθerəˈpjuːtɪks/ *n* [U] *technical* the part of medical science concerned with the treatment and cure of illness【術語】治療學

ther·a·pist /ˋθɛrəpɪst; ˈθerəpɨst/ *n* [C] someone who has been trained to give a particular form of treatment for physical or mental illness 治療專家, 理療師: *a speech therapist* 語言治療師

ther·a·py /ˋθɛrəpɪ; ˈθerəpi/ *n* [C,U] **1** the treatment of an illness or injury over a fairly long period of time, especially without using drugs or operations〔尤指不使用藥物或不施行手術的〕療法, 治病術 **2** the treatment or examination of someone's mental problems by talking to them for a long time about their feelings; PSYCHOANALYSIS〔通過長時間言談來治療或了解病人的心理問題的〕心理療法; 精神分析: **be in therapy** (=be having therapy) 接受心理療法 *Rob was in therapy for several years.* 羅布接受心理治療已有好幾年了。—see also 另見 OCCUPATIONAL THERAPY, SPEECH THERAPY

there¹ /ðɛr; ðeə/ *pron* **1 there is/there are/there must be** used to say that something exists 有〔表示存在〕: *Is there life after death?* 死後有生命存在嗎? | *There's no special way of doing it – you just have to mix the dough slowly.* 做這沒有甚麼特別的方法 —— 你只需要把麵團慢慢地和好。| *There must be some explanation for such outlandish behaviour.* 如此怪異的行為, 一定事出有因。| **there seems/appears to be** *There seems to be some mistake. I've never met you before in my life.* 大概弄錯了吧, 我以前從來沒有見過你。| **there exists/there remains etc** *formal*【正式】*There remains the possibility that mistakes have been made.* 仍然有這個可能: 有人出了差錯。**2 there was/there were etc** used to say that something happened〔表示過去某事發生的〕有過: *Suddenly there was a loud crash as the clock fell to the floor.* 突然傳來一聲巨響, 鐘掉到了地板上。| *There were several fights outside the stadium but no one was hurt.* 在體育場外面發生了好幾宗打鬥事件, 但無人受傷。

there² /ðɛr; ðeə/ *adv* **1** in or to a particular place 在那裡; 往那裡: *Sit there and wait until the teacher's finished.* 坐在那兒, 等到老師完了事。| *Scotland? I've always* *wanted to go there.* 蘇格蘭？我一直想去那兒。| *Don't just stand there – do something!* 別光站在那兒 —— 做點甚麼事吧！| **out/in/under etc there** *I know there's a mouse under there somewhere.* 我知道在那下面的甚麼地方有一隻老鼠。| **over there** *How are you getting on over there in Paris?* 你在巴黎那邊過得怎麼樣？—compare 比較 HERE¹ (1) **2** if something is there, it exists 那裡，那兒：*The chance was there, but I didn't take it.* 機會來臨了，不過我沒有抓住。| *All the food is there to be eaten so please enjoy it.* 所有的食品放在那兒就是讓人吃的，所以請享用吧。| *When asked why he climbed Everest, Mallory just said "Because it was there."* 當問到他為甚麼要攀登珠穆朗瑪峯時，馬洛里只是說"因為它就在那兒。" **3** *spoken* used to say which statement, idea or reason you agree with, you want to say something about etc【口】在那一點上，有關那一點：*"I believe we are all products of our environment." "I'm sorry but I disagree with you there."* "我認為我們全是環境的產物。""對不起，在這一點上我並不同意你的看法。" **4** *spoken* used to get someone's attention when you are speaking to them or to make them notice someone or something【口】〔用來引起某人注意〕：*Hey, you there! Watch out!* 喂！說你呢！小心！| *Hi there, I haven't seen you in ages.* 嗨！好久都沒看到你了。| *There goes the phone again. It's not stopped ringing all morning.* 電話鈴又響了。整個上午都在響個不停。**5 get there a)** to arrive in a particular place 到達那兒：*Most of the food had been eaten by the time I got there.* 等我到那兒時，已經沒剩下多少吃的了。**b)** *spoken* to succeed in doing something【口】成功地做某事，得以：*It took me a lot of time and effort to qualify as a doctor but I got there in the end.* 為了成為一名合格的醫生，我花費了大量的時間和精力，不過最終我還是成功了。**6 be there (for sb)** *spoken* to be ready to help someone or be kind to them when they have problems【口】隨時樂於幫助（某人）：*That's what I loved about my father – he was always there for me.* 這便是我那麼愛我的父親的原因 —— 因為他總是願意幫我一把。**7 he's/she's not all there** *spoken* a phrase used to describe someone who is not very intelligent and seems slightly crazy, used when you want to avoid saying this directly【口】他/她有點不對勁〔以比較含蓄的方式說某人不是很聰明，有一點瘋癲〕 **8 there and back** the distance, cost etc there and back is the total distance or cost of the journey to a place, added to the distance or cost of the return〔旅程、旅費等的〕往返，來回：*The journey's not too bad – only four hours there and back.* 旅途上不算太糟 —— 來回只花了四個小時。**9 there and then** also 又作 **then and there** immediately 在彼時彼地，當場，立即：*I thought I'd have to wait but they offered me the job there and then.* 我原以為我得等着，但他們當場就把那份工作給了我。**10 there's a good boy/there's a clever dog etc** *spoken* used to praise a child or animal【口】這才是乖孩子/這才是小乖乖 **11 there you are/go** *spoken*【口】**a)** used to be polite when giving something to someone 行啊；給你〔給某人某物時的禮貌用語〕：*"Can I have two bottles of beer please?" "There you are, that'll be £3.20 please."* "請來兩瓶啤酒。""給，請付 3.20 英鎊。" **b)** used when someone is upset, complains etc, to tell them that what has happened is typical or they should have expected it 根本不足為奇；原本就是這麼回事〔對某人難受、抱怨時用的回答〕 **12 that book there/those shoes there etc** *spoken* used when showing or pointing to where something is【口】那邊那本書/那邊那雙鞋等〔用來表示某物所在的地方〕：*Can you pass me that wine glass there?* 你能把那邊那個酒杯遞給我嗎？| **that there book/those there shoes etc** (=a form of this expression that is sometimes used although most people think it is incorrect) 那本書/那雙鞋等〔這種表達形式有時候有人使用，但大多數人認為是不正確的用法〕 *It was those there holes in the road which made me fall down.* 是路上的那些坑使我摔倒了。

there³ /ðɛr; ðeə/ *interjection* used to express success, satisfaction, sympathy etc 瞧好啦〔用來表示成功、滿意、同情等〕：*There! I've done it! I've resigned.* 瞧！我已經做了！我已經辭職了。| *It only lasted a week but there! What can you expect for £2 an hour.* 只幹了一週時間就打住了！一小時兩英鎊，你能有甚麼指望？| **there, there!** (=used to comfort someone who is crying) 好啦！好啦！〔用來安慰哭泣的人〕 *There, there, don't get so upset!* 好啦，好啦，別這麼難過啦！

there·a·bouts /ˌðɛrəˋbauts; ˌðeərəˈbaʊts/ also 又作 **there·a·bout** /-ˋbaut; -ˈbaʊt/ *adv AmE* near a particular time, place, number etc, but not exactly【美】接近〔某一時間、地點、數目等〕；近乎；大約；左右：**or thereabouts** *These houses were built in 1930 or thereabouts.* 這些房子是在 1930 年左右修建的。

there·af·ter /ðɛrˋæftɚ; ðeərˈɑːftə/ *adv formal* after a particular event or time; afterwards【正式】其後，此後：*10,000 men had volunteered by the end of September; thereafter, approximately 1,000 men enlisted each month.* 到 9 月底時已有 10,000 人志願加入，此後，每個月差不多有 1,000 人應徵入伍。

there·by /ðɛrˋbaɪ; ðeəˈbaɪ/ *adv formal* with the result that something else happens【正式】藉此，由此：*He became a citizen in 1978, thereby gaining the right to vote.* 他在 1978 年成為公民，由此獲得了投票權。

there·fore /ˋðɛrˌfɔr; ˈðeəfɔː/ *adv formal* as a result of something that has just been mentioned【正式】因此，為此，所以：*The dollar has gone down against the yen, therefore Japanese goods are more expensive for Americans.* 美元兑日元的匯率下跌了，因此日本商品對美國人來說漲價了。—see 見 THUS (USAGE)

there·in /ðɛrˋɪn; ðeərˈɪn/ *adv formal*【正式】**1** in that place, or in that piece of writing 在那裡；在那篇文章[那本書]裡：*See Thompson, 1983, and the references cited therein.* 見湯普森 (1983) 以及該書裡引用的參考資料。**2 therein lies** used to say that something is caused by or comes from a particular situation 此即，緣此〔用以說明某事是由某種情況引起〕：*The treaty was imposed by force, and therein lay the cause of its ineffectiveness.* 該條約是通過武力強加於人的，它所以執行不力的原因就在於此。

there·in·af·ter /ˌðɛrɪnˋæftɚ; ˌðeərɪnˈɑːftə/ *adv law* later in the same official paper, statement etc【法律】在〔同一正式文件、聲明等的〕下文；以下

there·of /ðɛrˋɑv; ðeərˈɒv/ *adv formal* concerning something that has just been mentioned【正式】其；其中：*States differ in standards for products and the labelling thereof.* 各州產品的標準不同，其標籤也不同。

there·on /ðɛrˋɑn; ðeərˈɒn/ *adv formal*【正式】**1** on the thing that has just been mentioned 在那件事情上 **2** THEREUPON 隨即；就此，在其上

there·to /ðɛrˋtu; ðeəˈtuː/ *adv formal* concerning an agreement or piece of writing that has just been mentioned【正式】關於〔已提及的協議、文字資料等〕的：*the treaty and any conditions attaching thereto* 該條約及其所附的任何條件

there·un·der /ðɛrˋʌndɚ; ðeərˈʌndə/ *adv formal*【正式】**1** under something that has just been mentioned 在其下，在那一點下面 **2** according to a document, law, or part of an agreement that has just been mentioned 根據〔文件、法律或協議中的〕那一點

there·up·on /ˌðɛrəˋpɑn; ˌðeərəˈpɒn/ *adv formal*【正式】**1** immediately after something else has happened, and usually as a result of it; then 隨即，隨後；於是：*Thereupon the whole audience stood up and began cheering.* 於是，全體觀眾起立，開始歡呼。**2** concerning a subject that has just been mentioned 就此，在其上：*I have read your article, and wish to comment thereupon.* 我讀過你的文章，並且想就此作一番評論。

therm /θɝm; θɜːm/ *n* [C] a measurement of heat equal to 100,000 British Thermal Units, used in Britain for measuring how much gas someone has used 撒姆〔一種

測量熱量的單位, 相當於100,000英制熱單位, 在英國用於測算某人所使用的煤氣量〕

therm- /θɝm; θɜːm/ *prefix* another form of the prefix THERMO- 前綴 thermo- 的另一種拼法

ther·mal[1] /ˋθɝml̩; ˈθɜːməl/ *adj* [only before noun 僅用於名詞前] **1** concerned with or caused by heat 熱的; 熱量的; 由熱引起的: *thermal energy* 熱能 | *thermal conductivity* 熱導率 **2** thermal water is heated naturally under the earth〔水〕天然溫熱的: *thermal springs* 溫泉 **3** thermal clothing is made from special material to keep you warm in very cold weather〔衣服〕保溫的, 保暖的: *thermal underwear* 保暖內衣

thermal[2] *n* [C] **1** a rising current of warm air used by birds〔鳥在飛翔過程中常借用的〕上升的熱氣流 **2 thermals** [plural] *informal* special warm clothing, especially underwear【非正式】保暖型衣服〔尤指保暖內衣〕

ther·mi·on·ics /ˌθɝmɪˋɑnɪks; ˌθɜːmiˈɒnɪks/ *n* [U] *technical* the part of science that deals with the flow of ELECTRONs from heated metal【術語】熱離子學

thermo- /θɝmo; θɜːməʊ/ also 又作 **therm-** *technical prefix* concerning heat【術語】熱的; 與溫度有關的: a *thermostat* (=for controlling temperature) 恒溫器 | *thermostable* (=not changing when heated) 熱穩定的

ther·mo·dy·nam·ics /ˌθɝmodaɪˋnæmɪks; ˌθɜːməʊdaɪˈnæmɪks/ *n* [U] the science that deals with the relationship between heat and other forms of energy 熱力學

ther·mom·e·ter /θəˋmɑmətɚ; θəˈmɒmɪ̣tə/ *n* [C] a piece of equipment that measures the temperature of the air, of your body etc 溫度計, 寒暑表; 體溫計: *The thermometer was reading over 100°C.* 溫度計上的讀數超過了攝氏100度。

ther·mo·nu·cle·ar /ˌθɝmoˋnuklɪɚ; ˌθɜːməʊˈnjuːkliə◂/ *adj* thermonuclear weapons use a NUCLEAR reaction, involving the splitting of atoms, to produce very high temperatures and a very powerful explosion 熱核的: *a thermonuclear device* 熱核武器

ther·mo·plas·tic /ˌθɝmoˋplæstɪk; ˌθɜːməʊˈplæstɪk◂/ *n* [C,U] *technical* a plastic that is soft and bendable when heated but hard when cold【術語】熱塑性塑料〔加熱時柔軟可彎曲但在低溫時堅硬的塑料〕

ther·mos /ˋθɝməs; ˈθɜːməs/ also 又作 **thermos flask** /ˈ‥ ·/ *n* [C] *trademark* a special container like a bottle, that keeps drinks hot or cold【商標】保溫瓶 —see picture at 參見 FLASK 圖

ther·mo·set·ting /ˋθɝmoˌsɛtɪŋ; ˈθɜːməʊˌsetɪŋ/ *adj technical* thermosetting plastic becomes hard and unbendable after it has been heated【術語】〔指塑料〕加熱後即硬化的, 熱固的

ther·mo·stat /ˋθɝməˌstæt; ˈθɜːməstæt/ *n* [C] an instrument used for keeping a room or a machine at a particular temperature〔使房間或機器保持一定溫度的〕恒溫器 —see picture at 參見 ENGINE 圖

the·sau·rus /θɪˋsɔrəs; θɪˈsɔːrəs/ *n plural* **thesauruses** or **thesauri** /-raɪ; -raɪ/ [C] a book in which words are put into groups with other words that have similar meanings 分類詞典, 分類詞匯編

these /ðiz; ðiːz/ the plural of THIS

the·sis /ˋθisɪs; ˈθiːsɪ̣s/ *n plural* **theses** /-siz; -siːz/ [C] **1** a long piece of writing about a particular subject that you do as part of an advanced university degree such as an MA or a PhD 論文〔指大學的高級學位論文, 如文學碩士論文或哲學博士論文〕: *Writing a thesis on dance clubs is not as strange as it seems.* 寫一篇研究舞蹈俱樂部的論文似乎奇怪, 其實不然。**2** *formal* an idea or theory that tries to explain why something happens【正式】〔設法解釋某事的〕論點: *Their main thesis is that inflation is caused by increases in the money supply.* 他們的主要論點是, 通貨膨脹是因為貨幣供應增加而引起的。

thes·pi·an /ˋθɛspɪən; ˈθespiən/ *n* [C] *formal or humorous* an actor【正式或幽默】演員 —**thespian** *adj*: *Aidan turns all his thespian charm on the beautiful Tara.* 艾丹竭盡他的演技才能來追求漂亮的塔拉。

they /ðe; ðeɪ/ *pron* [used as the subject of a verb 用作句子主詞] **1** used to talk about two or more people or things that have been mentioned already or that the person you are talking to already knows about 他們; 她們; 它們: *Bob and Sue sold everything they owned and they now run a bar in Spain.* 鮑勃和蘇把他們擁有的一切東西都變賣了, 他倆現在在西班牙開了一家酒吧。**2 they say/think etc** *especially spoken* used to say what people in general think or believe【尤口】據說/據信: *They say his wife ran off with a younger man.* 他的妻子據說跟一個小伙子跑了。**3** *especially spoken*【尤口】**a)** the government, the police, the people who control an organization etc 他們〔泛指政府、警察或控制某一機構的人等〕: *I see they're threatening to put up taxes again.* 我明白他們又在威脅要提高稅收。**b)** all the people in a group, such as all doctors, all scientists, all teachers etc 他們〔泛指醫生、教師等某一團體中的所有人〕: *Apparently she has something they call 'glue ear'.* 看來她患了醫生們稱為"分泌性中耳炎"的耳疾。**4** used to avoid saying 'he' or 'she' after words like 'anyone', 'no one', 'everyone' etc〔用在 anyone, no one, everyone 等詞後, 泛指那些人〕: *If anyone has any information related to the crime will they please contact the police.* 任何人如果掌握有關這一案件的情況, 請與警方聯繫。—see 見 HE (USAGE)

they'd /ðed; ðeɪd/ **1** the short form of 縮略式= 'they had': *If only they'd been there.* 他們當時要在那兒就好了。**2** the short form of 縮略式= 'they would': *It's a pity my parents didn't come, they'd have enjoyed it.* 很遺憾, 我的父母沒有來, 要不然他們會很開心的。

they'll /ðel; ðeɪl/ the short form of 縮略式= 'they will': *They'll be tired after the long journey.* 他們在這次長途旅行後會很疲勞的。

they're /ðer; ðɚ; *strong* 強讀 ðɛɚ; ðeə/ the short form of 縮略式= 'they are': *They're going to Crete next week.* 他們下週要去克里特。

they've /ðev; ðeɪv/ *especially BrE*【尤英】the short form of 縮略式= 'they have', used especially in verb compounds〔尤用在動詞複合結構中〕: *They've had a lot of trouble with their car.* 他們的車子經常出毛病。| *They really need the money, because they've a new baby to think of now.* 他們確實需要那筆錢, 因為他們現在得顧及剛出生的孩子。

thi·am·in /ˋθaɪəˌmɪn; ˈθaɪəmiːn/ also 又作 **thi·a·mine** /-mɪn; -miːn/ *n* [U] a natural chemical in some foods, that you need in order to prevent particular illnesses 硫胺素, 維生素B₁

thick 厚的

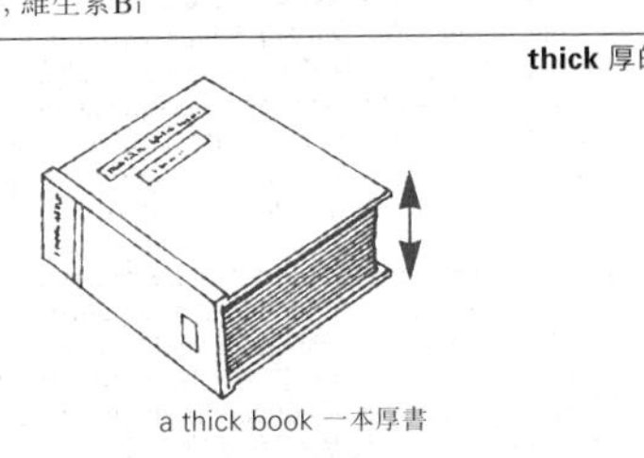

a thick book 一本厚書

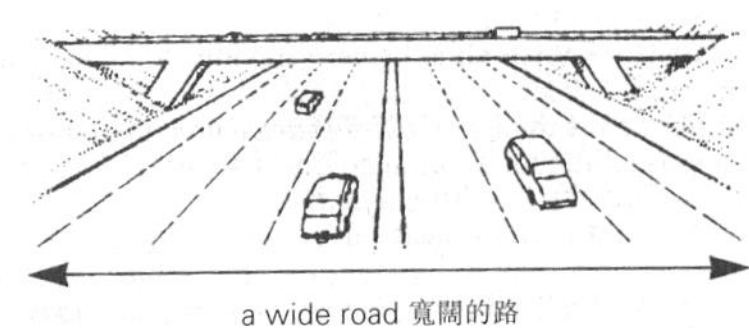

a wide road 寬闊的路

thick[1] /θɪk; θɪk/ *adj*
1 ▶THINGS 物體◀ a) measuring a particular amount,

especially more than usual, between two surfaces or sides 厚的: *a thick oak door* 一扇厚重的橡木門 | *Wrap your baby in a thick towel or blanket.* 把你的嬰兒裹在厚的毛巾或毛毯裡面。| **3 feet/1 cm/two inches etc thick** *In some places, the walls are over two meters thick.* 在某些地方, 牆壁有兩米多厚。| **[+with]** (=forming a thick layer) *The staircase was crumbling, and thick with dust.* 樓梯搖搖欲墜, 積着厚厚的灰塵。**b)** measuring more around the middle than usual 粗的; 粗大的: *Connect the battery using a thick cable.* 用一根粗電纜線把電池組連接起來。—opposite 反義詞 THIN

2 ►PERSON 人◄ *BrE informal* stupid【英, 非正式】愚笨的: *Don't think I can't see what's going on – I'm not that thick.* 別以為我不明白正在發生的事, 我沒那麼蠢。| *He's a nice guy, but he's a bit thick.* 他是個不錯的傢伙, 只是有點兒笨。| **(as) thick as two short planks** (=very stupid) 愚笨之極

3 ►LIQUID 液體◄ not solid, but moving or flowing slowly 稠的; 濃的: *For a thicker gravy, add more flour.* 要想肉汁濃一點, 就再加些麵粉。| *thick porridge* 稠粥

4 ►SMOKE/CLOUD ETC 煙/雲等◄ filling the air, and difficult to see through or breathe in 濃密的; 不清明的: *At the scene of the riot, thick black smoke is still pouring from burning tires.* 在暴亂的現場, 熊熊燃燒的輪胎仍然冒着濃密的黑煙。| *thick fog* 濃霧 | **[+with]** *The air was thick with exhaust fumes.* 空氣中廢氣瀰漫。

5 be thick on the ground to be present or available in large amounts or numbers 大量隨處可見: *Cheap houses aren't as thick on the ground as they used to be.* 廉價房不再像從前那樣隨處可見了。—opposite 反義詞 **be thin on the ground** (THIN¹ (12))

6 ►VOICE 口音◄ a) clearly belonging to a particular place or part of the country〔某地的口音〕濃重的; 重濁的: **a thick German/Yorkshire/Brazilian etc accent** *TV viewers will get just one more chance to hear his thick Scottish accent.* 電視觀眾將還有一次機會聽到他那濃重的蘇格蘭口音。**b)** not as clear or high as usual, for example because someone has been crying〔聲音〕沙啞的; 低沉的: *Bill's voice was thick and gruff.* 比爾說話粗聲粗氣。

7 ►TREES/BUSHES ETC 樹木/灌木等◄ growing very close together, or having a lot of leaves, so there is not much space in between 茂密的; 繁茂的: *The little animal tried to hide in the thick undergrowth.* 那頭小獸試圖躲藏在茂密的矮灌木叢中。| *a thick forest* 密林

8 ►HAIR/FUR ETC 頭髮/毛皮等◄ forming a deep, soft covering 濃密的: *She ran her fingers through her thick brown hair.* 她用手指揉搓她那濃密的褐色頭髮。

9 be (as) thick as thieves if two people are as thick as thieves, they are very friendly with each other and seem to share a lot of secrets 非常親密: *I don't trust those two. Lately they've been as thick as thieves.* 我不信任那兩個傢伙, 他倆近來一直很親密。

10 give sb a thick ear/get a thick ear *BrE spoken* to hit someone or be hit on the head, as a punishment【英口】打某人的頭部/頭部被打: *Any more cheek from you and you'll get a thick ear.* 你再這樣放肆, 會挨耳光的。

11 have a thick skin to not care if people criticize you or do not like you 臉皮厚; 抱着無所謂的態度 —see also 另見 THICK-SKINNED

12 be thick with sb to be very friendly with someone 與某人非常友好

13 (it's) a bit thick *BrE old-fashioned* used to say something is a little unfair or annoying【英, 過時】不怎麼公平; 有點讓人氣憤 —**thickly** *adv*

thick² *adv* **1** if you spread, cut etc something thick, you spread or cut it in a way that produces a thick layer or piece〔某物被抹或被切得〕厚: *peanut butter spread thick* 抹得很厚的花生醬 **2 thick and fast** arriving or happening very frequently, in large amounts or numbers 大量而急速地; 頻繁且迅猛地: *Competition entries have been coming in thick and fast.* 參加比賽的作品紛至沓來。—see also 另見 **lay it on thick** (LAY²)

thick³ *n* **1 be in the thick of sth** to be involved in the busiest, most active, most dangerous etc part of a situation 在〔最繁忙、最活躍、最危險的情況〕之中: *Following his recent operation, Governor Brown hopes to be back in the thick of the action as soon as possible.* 在經過最近的手術之後, 布朗州長希望盡可能快地重新投入工作。**2 through thick and thin** in spite of any difficulties or problems 患難與共; 同甘共苦: **stick together through thick and thin** *As kids we promised to stick together through thick and thin.* 小時候我們曾許下諾言, 患難與共, 團結一致。

thick·en /ˈθɪkən; ˈθɪkən/ *v* [I,T] to become thick, or make something thick 加厚; 變厚; 使濃; 使密集: *The fog was beginning to thicken.* 霧開始變濃了。| **thicken sth** *You can thicken a sauce by adding cornstarch.* 你可以添加玉米粉使調味汁變濃。—see also 另見 **the plot thickens** (PLOT¹ (3))

thick·en·er /ˈθɪkənɚ; ˈθɪkənə/ also 又作 **thick·en·ing** /ˈθɪkənɪŋ; ˈθɪkənɪŋ/ *n* [C,U] a substance used to thicken a liquid〔使液體變稠的〕增稠劑

thick·et /ˈθɪkɪt; ˈθɪkɪ̵t/ *n* [C] a group of bushes and small trees 灌木叢

thick-head·ed /ˌ· ˈ··◂/ *adj informal* extremely stupid【非正式】愚笨之極的: *He's so thick-headed he can't understand the simplest instructions.* 他愚笨極了, 連最簡單的指令都理解不了。

thick·ness /ˈθɪknɪs; ˈθɪknɪ̵s/ *n* **1** [C,U] how thick something is 厚度: *The length of nails you need depends on the thickness of the plank.* 你所需要的釘子長度取決於木板的厚度。**2** [C] a layer of something〔某東西的〕層: **[+of]** *Wrap the cake in two thicknesses of greaseproof paper.* 用兩層防油紙包蛋糕。

thick·o /ˈθɪko; ˈθɪkəʊ/ *n* [C] *informal* someone who is very stupid【非正式】笨蛋, 傻瓜

thick·set, thick-set /ˌθɪkˈsɛt; ˌθɪkˈset◂/ *adj* having a wide strong body; STOCKY〔身體〕粗壯的; 粗實的: *a short thickset man* 一名矮而粗壯的男子

thick-skinned /ˌ· ˈ·◂/ *adj* not easily offended by other people's criticism or insults 厚臉皮的; 不易傷害的: *a thick-skinned insurance salesman* 一位厚臉皮的保險推銷員

thief /θif; θiːf/ *n plural* **thieves** /θivz; θiːvz/ [C] someone who steals things, especially without using violence 小偷, 賊: *a car thief* 盜車賊 | *Leaving ground floor windows open will encourage thieves.* 讓底樓的窗戶敞開着, 那是在招引小偷。—compare 比較 BURGLAR, ROBBER —see also 另見 **be (as) thick as thieves** (THICK¹ (9))

thiev·e·ry /ˈθivərɪ; ˈθiːvəri/ *n* [U] *formal* thieving【正式】偷竊行為

thiev·ing /ˈθivɪŋ; ˈθiːvɪŋ/ *n* [U] *informal especially BrE* the practice of stealing things【非正式, 尤英】偷竊行為 —**thieving** *adj*: *He's a nasty thieving good-for-nothing.* 他是一個卑鄙齷齪、慣愛偷摸、毫無用處的傢伙。

thiev·ish /ˈθivɪʃ; ˈθiːvɪʃ/ *adj literary* like a thief【文】賊頭賊腦的, 賊眉鼠眼的

thigh /θaɪ; θaɪ/ *n* [C] the top part of your leg, between your knee and your HIP¹ (1) 大腿, 股 —see picture at 參見 BODY 圖

thim·ble /ˈθɪmbl̩; ˈθɪmbəl/ *n* [C] a small metal or plastic cap used to protect your finger when you are sewing〔縫紉時用來保護手指的〕頂針, 針箍

thim·ble·ful /ˈθɪmbl̩ˌfʊl; ˈθɪmbəlfʊl/ *n* [C+of] *informal* a very small quantity of liquid【非正式】〔液體的〕少量, 些微

thin¹ /θɪn; θɪn/ *comparative* 比較級 **thinner** *superlative* 最高級 **thinnest** *adj*

1 ►NOT THICK 不厚的◄ having a very small distance or a smaller distance than usual between two sides or two flat surfaces 薄的; 細的: *a thin nylon rope* 一條細的尼龍繩 | *She's only wearing a thin summer jacket.* 她只

穿了一件很薄的夏季短上衣。| *two thin slices of bread* 兩薄片麵包 | *The road was covered with a thin layer of ice.* 路面上覆蓋着一層薄薄的冰。| **paper thin** (=very thin) 薄如紙的; 非常薄的 *Keep your voice down, the walls are paper thin.* 小點兒聲, 這些牆很薄。—opposite 反義詞 THICK¹ (1)

thin 薄的; 細的

a thin book 一本薄書

a narrow street 窄窄的街道

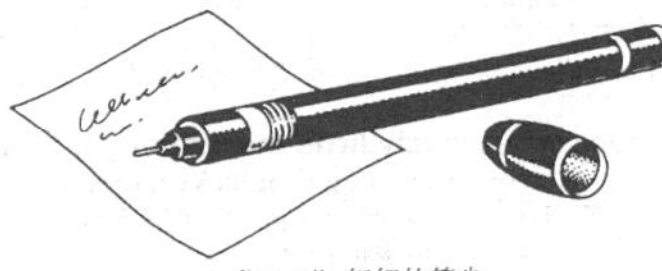
a fine nib 細細的筆尖

2 ▶NOT FAT 不肥胖的◀ having little fat on your body〔身體〕瘦的: *Larry was tall and thin with dark brown hair.* 拉里又高又瘦, 長着一頭深褐色的頭髮。| *I wish my legs were thinner.* 但願我的腿再瘦一點。—opposite 反義詞 FAT¹ (1)
3 ▶LIQUID 液體◀ a liquid that is thin flows very easily because it has a lot of water in it〔液體〕稀的; 淡的: *thin paint* 稀的油漆
4 ▶SMOKE/MIST 煙/霧靄◀ smoke or mist that is thin is easy to see through〔煙或霧靄〕稀薄的, 淡薄的: *The fog is quite thin in places.* 在某些地方, 霧很稀薄。—opposite 反義詞 THICK¹ (4)
5 ▶AIR 空氣◀ air that is thin is more difficult to breathe than usual because it has less OXYGEN in it〔空氣〕稀薄的: *the thinner air high in the mountains* 高山上較為稀薄的空氣
6 ▶VOICE 話音◀ a thin voice is high and unpleasant to listen to 尖聲細氣的; 刺耳難聽的: *a thin cracked singing voice* 尖細刺耳的歌聲
7 ▶SOUND 聲音◀ a thin sound is unpleasantly weak〔聲音〕微弱而聽着難受的: *the thin mewing of a bedraggled kitten* 一隻渾身濕漉漉的小貓刺耳的喵喵聲 —opposite 反義詞 FULL¹ (15)
8 ▶HAIR/PLANTS 毛髮/植物◀ hairs or plants that are thin have spaces between them〔毛髮或植物〕稀疏的: *a thin straggly beard* 稀稀拉拉的鬍子 | *thin vegetation* 稀疏的植被
9 ▶EXCUSE/ARGUMENT/EXPLANATION 藉口/論據/解釋◀ a thin excuse, argument, or explanation is not good or detailed enough to persuade you that it is true〔藉口、論據或解釋〕貧乏的; 空泛的; 不能令人信服的
10 ▶INFORMATION/DESCRIPTION 信息/描述◀ a piece of information or a description that is thin is not detailed enough to be useful or effective〔信息或描述〕不夠充分的; 不夠有效的: *The evidence for Viking settlements in America is pretty thin.* 有關北歐海盜在美洲定居的證據很不充分。
11 the thin end of the wedge *especially BrE spoken* an expression meaning something that you think is the beginning of a harmful development【尤英, 口】糟糕事情的開始: *These job cuts are just the thin end of the wedge.* 這次裁員只是開始, 好戲還在後頭。
12 be thin on the ground if a particular type of person or thing is thin on the ground, there are very few available 不是隨處可見的, 少有的: *Taxis seem to be thin on the ground.* 計程車好像為數不多。
13 be having a thin time (of it) *spoken* to be in a difficult situation, especially one in which you do not have enough money【口】過窘迫日子〔尤指錢不夠用〕
14 be (skating) on thin ice to be in a situation in which you are likely to upset someone or cause trouble 容易使人反感; 容易招惹麻煩: *I think the people who argue that discoveries in genetics should be commercially protected are on thin ice.* 有些人主張遺傳學上的種種發現應該得到商業上的保護, 我認為這些人是在招惹麻煩。
15 disappear/vanish into thin air to disappear or vanish completely in a mysterious way 神祕地消失不見
16 thin on top *informal* an expression meaning having little hair on your head used when you want to avoid saying this【非正式】頭上稀疏〔一種表示某人頭髮稀少的含蓄說法〕—see also 另見 THINLY —**thinness** *n* [U]

USAGE NOTE 用法說明: THIN
WORD CHOICE 詞語辨析: **thin, slim, slender, lean, skinny, underweight, emaciated, narrow**

Thin is a general word to describe people who have little or no fat on their bodies (opposite *fat*), but it often sounds a little negative. thin 泛指身體瘦, 瘦削(其反義詞是 fat), 但往往含一點貶義。

If you want to make clear that someone is **thin** in a pleasant way, you say they are **slim** or (less common) **slender**. 如果要說某人瘦得很喜人, 用 slim 或〔不太常用的〕slender: *I wish I were as slim as you.* 但願我有你那麼苗條。| *with a slim build and long slender legs* 有着苗條的身段和修長的腿

You can also say **lean** (=thin in a strong and healthy way). 形容瘦而健康的, 可以說 lean: *a lean, muscular body* 沒多餘脂肪、肌肉發達的身體

If someone is a bit too thin they are **skinny** (informal), **underweight** (the technical word), or (worst of all) **emaciated**. 形容太瘦的人可以用 skinny〔非正式用法〕、underweight〔術語〕, 最嚴重是 emaciated〔骨瘦如柴〕: *He looks skinny as a rake.* 他瘦得像一把耙子。| *skinny fashion models* 纖瘦的時裝模特兒。| *The doctor says I'm a little underweight since my illness.* 醫生說我自從生病以來體重有點過輕了。| *the emaciated bodies of the famine victims* 饑民皮包骨的身體

Thin (opposite **thick**) can also be used for things if the distance through them is not very big. thin 也指物體細、薄(其反義詞是 thick): *a thin post/wire/dress/slice of cheese* 一根細柱子/一條細電線/一件薄連衣裙/薄薄的一片乾酪

Narrow is usually used to describe something that is not very wide from side to side. narrow 一般用來形容物體狹窄: *a narrow road/bed/gap* 窄路/窄牀/窄縫 However, in a few contexts, especially where something is both long and narrow, **thin** can be used in this sense too. 然而在少數情況下, thin 也可表示狹長: *a thin stripe/strip of tape/a dress with very thin straps* 細長的條紋/細長的錄音磁帶/吊帶非常細長的連衣裙

thin² *adv* so as to be thin 薄地; 細地: *Don't cut the bread so thin.* 別把麵包切得這麼薄。
thin³ *v* **thinned, thinning** [T] **1** also 又作 **thin out** to

make more room for plants to grow by removing the weaker ones 使〔植物〕稀疏，給…間苗: *thinning out the carrots* 給胡蘿蔔間苗 **2 thin the ranks** if something thins the ranks of a group of people, there are less of them as a result of it 減少人員: *Illness had thinned our ranks.* 疾病使我們人員減少了。**3** to make a liquid weaker by adding water or another liquid 使〔液體〕稀釋;（使）變淡: *This paint needs thinning.* 這種油漆需要稀釋。

thin out *phr v* [I] if a crowd thins out the people gradually separate and leave so there are fewer of them〔擁擠的人羣〕變稀少；散去: *By midnight the crowd outside the theatre was starting to thin out.* 到半夜時分，劇院外面的人羣開始散去了。

thine[1] /ðaɪn; ðaɪn/ *pron old use* yours【舊】你的；你們的

thine[2] *determiner old use* a word meaning your, used before a word beginning with a vowel or 'h'; THY【舊】你的；你們的〔用在元音或 h 開頭的單詞前〕

thing /θɪŋ; θɪŋ/ *n*

1 ▶IDEA/ACTION/FEELING/FACT 思想/行動/感覺/事實◀ [C] anything that you can think of as a single item, for example an idea, an action, a feeling, or a fact〔任何單一的〕事情: *The important thing is for us to tell the truth.* 重要的事情是我們要講出真相。| *What a stupid thing to do.* 做的是一件多麼蠢的事。| *A horrible thing happened yesterday.* 昨天發生了一件可怕的事。| **do the right/decent/honourable etc thing** *I kept wondering if I was doing the right thing.* 我一直在想我是不是在做正確的事情。

2 ▶OBJECT 物體◀ [C] an object 物體；東西: *On top of the box there was a thing like a long handle.* 在盒子頂端有一個像長柄的東西。| *I need to pop into the supermarket to get a few things.* 我需要馬上趕到超市去買幾樣東西。—see 見 MACHINE[1] (USAGE)

3 ▶SITUATION 情況◀ things [plural] life in general and the way it is affecting people 情況；形勢: *How are things with you?* 你們的情況怎麼樣？| *Things could be worse.* 情況有可能更糟。| *Things are going really well at the moment.* 此刻的形勢真的很好。

4 there is no such thing used to emphasize that something does not really exist or happen 根本不存在這樣的事情: *"There's no such thing as love," that's what she said.* "根本不存在愛這種東西。"她是這麼說的。

5 not know a thing/not feel a thing/not see a thing etc to know, feel etc nothing 甚麼都不知道/甚麼都感覺不到/甚麼都看不見等: *I can't feel a thing – my mouth is completely numb.* 我甚麼都感覺不到——我的嘴完全麻木了。| *She doesn't do a thing to help around the house.* 她在家裡甚麼事都不動手幫忙。

6 make a (big) thing out of sth to make something seem more important than it really is, by getting angry, excited etc〔由於氣憤、激動等〕把事情鬧大了: *OK, so we disagree, but let's not make a big thing out of it.* 好吧，就算咱們意見不一致，也別把事情鬧大了。

7 the last thing sb wants/expects etc something that someone does not want, expect etc at all 根本不想要/不敢指望的事等: *The last thing I felt like doing was dancing.* 我最不想做的事便是跳舞。

8 ▶EQUIPMENT 設備◀ [C] *especially BrE* the tools, equipment, clothes etc that you need for a particular job, sport etc【尤英】〔某一工作或體育活動所需的〕用品；設備；物件: *I left my swimming things at home.* 我把游泳的那些用品忘在家裡了。

9 ▶AT THE END 在最終◀ last thing at the end of a day, afternoon, evening etc〔某一天、某一下午或晚上等的〕最後事情: *He always polished his shoes last thing at night.* 他在晚上的最後一件事總是擦鞋子。

10 ▶AT THE BEGINNING 在開始◀ first thing at the beginning of a day, morning, afternoon etc〔某一天、某一上午或下午等的〕開頭第一件事情: *I'll phone you first thing Monday morning.* 星期一上午第一件事，我就給你打電話。

11 ▶CLOTHES/POSSESSIONS 衣服/所屬物品◀ things [plural] *especially BrE* clothes and possessions【尤英】衣服等所屬物品: *Pack your things. We're leaving.* 把你的衣物等裝好。我們馬上出發。

12 all things considered having considered all the facts about something 所有情況考慮進來；綜合考慮起來: *All things considered, the team didn't do too badly.* 總的來說，該隊的表現不算太差。

13 among other things used when you are giving one fact, reason, effect etc but want to suggest that there are many others 除了其他很多事情外，還…: *This led, among other things, to the resignation of the Director.* 這導致了局長的辭職，以及其他許多事情。

14 make things easy/difficult to deliberately make it easy, difficult etc for someone to do something 故意使事情變得容易，方便/為難: [+for] *He could make things difficult for you if he chooses.* 他可以給你製造麻煩，如果他想那樣做的話。

15 be onto a good thing *informal* to be in a situation that is very helpful, comfortable, or profitable for you【非正式】處於非常有利的形勢: *When they offered to pay for her travel as well she realized she was onto a good thing.* 當他們提出還要為她支付旅費時，她意識到自己有好事了。

16 the done thing *informal* the way of behaving or doing something that is socially acceptable【非正式】符合社會習俗的事情: *You can't serve beer with the meal. It's not the done thing.* 吃飯時是不能供應啤酒的，這不符合習俗。

17 poor thing/lovely little thing/funny little thing etc a person or animal that is unlucky, attractive, funny etc 可憐的傢伙/可愛的小傢伙/可笑的小傢伙等: *You poor thing.* 你這個可憐的傢伙。

18 the (latest) thing *informal* the thing that is popular or fashionable at the moment【非正式】時下流行的東西: *Platform heels are the thing at the moment.* 厚底高跟鞋是時下流行的東西。

19 be a thing of the past to no longer exist or happen 昨日黃花: *Good manners seem to be a thing of the past.* 良好的禮貌似乎已是昨日黃花了。

20 do your own thing *informal* to do something in the way that you like instead of copying other people or following strict rules【非正式】按照自己的方式做事，走自己的路: *Do you prefer a structured exercise class, or do you like to do your own thing?* 你是較喜歡一種有組織的練習課，還是喜歡按自己的方式去做？

21 have a thing about *informal* to have very strong and often unreasonable feelings about someone or something【非正式】對〔某人或某事〕非常反感〔常指抱有成見〕: *He's got a real thing about people smoking.* 他對人們吸煙真的很反感。

22 breakfast things/dinner things etc *BrE* the plates, dishes etc used for a particular meal【英】早餐後的那一攤子〔碗筷碟盤等〕/晚餐後的那一攤子等: *I'll just wash up the breakfast things.* 我得把早餐後的那一攤子全部洗乾淨。

23 taking one thing with another *BrE* considering all the facts【英】綜合考慮起來: *Taking one thing with another, I think it's a good scheme.* 綜合考慮起來，我認為這是一個不錯的計劃。

24 be all things to all men to behave in a way that makes everyone like you 八面玲瓏，面面俱到: *You must stop trying to be all things to all men.* 你千萬不要再試圖八面玲瓏了。

25 the shape of things to come the way in which things will probably happen or develop in the future 未來事情的形態；未來的發展趨勢: *Perhaps shopping by computer is the shape of things to come.* 也許，通過電腦購物是未來的發展趨勢。

26 in all things in every situation 在一切事情上；在各種情況下: *She believes in being honest in all things.* 她認為在一切事情上都應該誠實。

Frequencies of the noun **thing** in spoken and written English 名詞 thing 在英語口語和書面語中的使用頻率

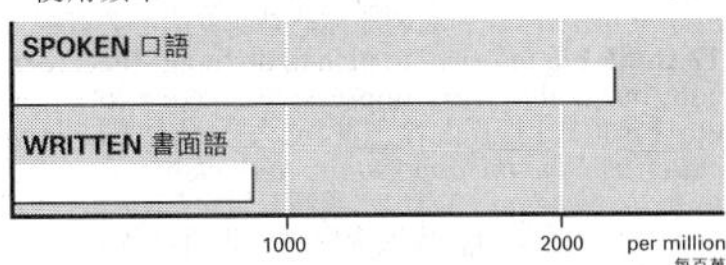

Based on the British National Corpus and the Longman Lancaster Corpus 據英國國家語料庫和朗文蘭卡斯特語料庫

This graph shows that the noun **thing** is much more common in spoken English than in written English. This is because it is used in a lot of common spoken phrases. 本圖表顯示, 名詞 thing 在英語口語中的使用頻率遠遠高於書面語, 因為口語中有很多常用片語是由 thing 構成的。

thing (*n*) **SPOKEN PHRASES**
含 thing 的口語片語

27 the thing is used when explaining a problem or the reason for something 目前的問題是, 事情的原委是: *The thing is, I can't afford to buy a car.* 問題是, 我買不起一輛車。
28 thing to do something that someone does 所做的事: *That was a really stupid thing to do.* 那真是做了一件蠢事。
29 thing to say a remark 所說的話: *What a strange thing to say!* 多麼奇怪的話!
30 light bulb thing/handle thing/switch thing etc used when you do not know the correct name for something 叫燈泡甚麼的東西/叫把手甚麼的東西/叫開關甚麼的東西等〔用於不知道某物正確名稱之時〕: *Is that it – that handle thing under the shelf?* 是那個嗎 —— 架子下面那個叫把手甚麼的東西?
31 for one thing used to give one reason for something 其中一個原因是: *I wouldn't work abroad. I don't like travelling for one thing.* 我不願在國外工作。一個原因是, 我不喜歡旅行。
32 it is a good thing (that) used to say that it is lucky or good that something has happened 這是一件幸運的事[好事]: *It's a good thing we brought some food with us.* 我們隨身帶了一些食品, 真不錯。
33 that sort/kind of thing used to mean 'other things of the same type', without giving more examples 那一類的事情: *Oh, we spent the time reading, listening to the radio, that kind of thing.* 噢, 那段時間我們所做的就是讀書、聽收音機之類的事情。
34 and things used to mean 'and other things', without giving more examples 等 (其他) 東西: *They sell jewellery and things, but it's all cheap stuff.* 他們賣珠寶首飾等東西, 不過全是些便宜貨。
35 the thing with used to say what the problem with someone or something is〔某人或某事的〕問題所在: *That's the thing with him, isn't it? You can't trust him.* 那便是他的問題所在, 不是嗎? 你不能信任他。
36 just one of those things used to say that something unpleasant or unlucky cannot be prevented 沒辦法的一件倒霉事: *It wasn't really the driver's fault, it was just one of those things.* 那實際上不是駕駛員的錯, 那只是沒辦法的一件倒霉事。
37 it's (just) one thing after another used to say that a lot of unpleasant or unlucky things keep happening to you (簡直) 是接二連三的倒霉事, 禍不單行: *Train strikes, computer problems, illness – it's just one thing after another!* 鐵路工人罷工, 電腦出故障, 生病 —— 真是禍不單行!
38 just the thing/the very thing exactly the thing that you want or that is necessary 正是想要的東西; 正是需要的東西: *"Would this help?" "That's just the thing I was looking for."* "這個有用嗎?" "這正是我在找的東西。"
39 what with one thing and another used to explain that you have not done something because you have been too busy 忙了這個又要忙那個; 忙這忙那地: *Well, what with one thing and another, we never got round to getting it fixed.* 唉, 忙了這個又要忙那個, 我們根本沒有時間來修理這個東西。
40 the way things are/stand used to say that because of the present situation you must do or cannot do something 目前的情況是: *The way things are we can't possibly afford a vacation this year.* 從目前的情況看來, 我們今年不可能有錢去度假。
41 it's no bad thing used to say that even though an event seems to be unlucky it does actually help 這算不上甚麼壞事: *We had to sell the car, although it was no bad thing really because it was too expensive to run.* 我們不得不把那輛車賣掉, 因為開車太花錢了, 所以這實際算不上是甚麼壞事。
42 of all things used to show that you are surprised or shocked by something that someone has done or said 偏偏, 真沒想到: *And for breakfast he had curry, of all things!* 真沒想到, 他早餐竟然吃咖喱!
43 it's one thing to..., it's another thing to..., used to say that doing one thing is very different from doing another thing 做…是一回事, 做…則是另一回事: *It's one thing to play a computer game; it's quite another thing to write your own programs.* 玩電腦遊戲是一回事, 自己編寫程序則完全是另一回事。
44 sb did/said etc no such thing used to say angrily that someone did not do or say something 某人根本沒做這樣的事/沒說這樣的話等: *"Jane says that you took the money out of the cash box." "I did no such thing!"* "簡說你從錢櫃裡拿了錢。" "我絕沒有做過這種事!"
45 (do) the...thing *AmE* used to talk about an activity and everything that is involved with it【美】(做) …方面的事: *Jody tried the college thing but finally dropped out.* 喬迪嘗試了一下大學生活, 但最終還是輟學了。

thing·a·ma·jig /ˈθɪŋəməˌdʒɪɡ; ˈθɪŋəmɪ̵dʒɪɡ/ also 又作 **thing·a·ma·bob** /ˈθɪŋəməˌbɑb; ˈθɪŋəmɪ̵bɒb/ **thing·y** /ˈθɪŋɪ; ˈθɪŋi/ *n* [C] *spoken* used when you cannot remember or do not know the name of the person or thing you want to mention【口】某人; 某物〔用來指記不清或不知道你要提及的某人的名字或某東西的名稱〕: *Have you got the thingamajig for opening the wine?* 你有開酒瓶的那個玩意嗎?

think¹ /θɪŋk; θɪŋk/ *past tense and past participle* **thought** /θɔt; θɔːt/ *v* 

1 ▶OPINION/BELIEF 觀點/信念◀ [T] to have an opinion or belief about something 認為; 以為: **think (that)** *I think that she should have paid the money back.* 我認為她應該償還那筆錢。| *Harry thought it was a lousy idea.* 哈里認為那是一個很糟的主意。| *I didn't think anyone would believe me.* 我以為沒有人會相信我。| *I remember thinking their behaviour was strange.* 我記得曾經認為他們的行為很奇怪。| *Well, Tom, what do you think?* 呃, 湯姆, 你怎麼認為? | **think of sb/sth as sth** (=think that someone or something is something) 認為某人/某物是… *We now think of the car as being essential rather than a luxury.* 我們現在認為汽車是很重要的, 而不是甚麼奢侈品。| **think sb/sth (to be) sth** *We all thought her very intelligent.* 我們當時都認為她很聰明。| **think it right/important etc** *formal*【正式】*Do you think it right for the government to cut funding in this way?* 你認為政府以這種方式削減經費是正確的嗎? | **be thought to be (doing sth)** *formal*【正式】*They are thought to be receiving arms from the Republic.* 有人認為他們正從該共和國那兒得到武器。
2 ▶USE YOUR MIND 用你的思想◀ [I] to use your mind

to solve something, decide something etc 思考; 思慮; 考慮: *We must think very carefully before we decide what to do.* 在決定做甚麼之前, 我們必須十分慎重地考慮。| *Wait a minute, I'm thinking.* 等一下, 我正在思考。| **[+about/of]** *She lay awake thinking about the money.* 她躺在那兒, 心裡想着那筆錢。| *I tried not to think of Richard or what he was doing.* 我盡量不去想理查德或者他在幹甚麼。| **think deeply** (=think carefully, for a long time) 沉思, 深思 *They clearly haven't thought very deeply about the possible consequences.* 很明顯, 他們對可能的後果並未作過深入的思考。

3 ►HAVE AN IDEA 有一個想法◄ [T] to have an idea or thought in your mind, especially one that appears suddenly 想, 想到: *And then I thought: "Why the hell shouldn't I?"* 然後我想:"我究竟為甚麼不應該呢?"| *"I certainly am in luck!" Katy thought.* "我當然是幸運的嘍!"凱蒂想道。

4 think of/about doing sth to consider the possibility of doing something 考慮做某事的可能性: *I had never thought of becoming an actor.* 我從未考慮過要當一名演員。| *We did think about buying a flat in London.* 我們確實考慮過要在倫敦買一套房子。

5 think better of it to not do something that you had planned to do, because you realize that it is not a good idea 認為還是不做的好: *He started to say something, then thought better of it.* 他開口想說點甚麼, 繼而覺得還是不說為好。

6 think nothing of (doing sth) to do something easily or without complaining, even though other people would find it difficult 認為(做某事)沒有甚麼困難: *The people here think nothing of walking ten miles to collect firewood.* 這裡的人認為走十英里路去打柴算不上甚麼困難事。

7 think for yourself to have ideas and thoughts of your own rather than believing what other people say 獨立思考: *Parents have to teach their children to think for themselves.* 父母們必須教育孩子自己動腦筋。

8 think sth to yourself to have a thought in your mind, but not tell it to anyone 自己心裡想着某事: *I thought to myself, when I'm 60, Patrick will still only be in high school.* 我暗自思忖, 當我60歲時, 帕特里克還只在中學讀書。

9 think twice (before doing sth) to think very carefully before deciding to do something, because you know about the dangers or problems (在做某事之前)再三考慮, 慎重思考: *I'll think twice before taking out such a large loan again.* 在再一次借出這麼一大筆貸款之前, 我會慎重考慮的。

10 think again to think of a new idea or plan because you realize that you cannot use the first one that you thought of 重新考慮: *If we can't have the car we'll have to think again about how to get there.* 如果沒有車, 我們得重新考慮如何去那兒。

11 think aloud/think out loud to say what you are thinking, without talking to anyone in particular 自言自語: *Oh, sorry; I guess I was thinking out loud.* 噢, 對不起, 我想我是在自言自語。

12 think a lot of sb/think highly of sb to admire or respect someone 佩服某人/看重某人: *I can assure you, the management thinks very highly of you.* 我可以肯定地告訴你, 管理層非常看重你。

13 think the world of sb to like or love someone very much 非常喜愛某人: *He thinks the world of those children.* 他非常喜愛那些孩子。

14 think badly of sb to disapprove of someone or what they have done 不贊同某人; 看不慣某人的所為: *Please don't think badly of me. I had no choice.* 請不要看不起我。我當時沒有選擇。

15 not think much of to think that someone or something is bad, useless etc 認為〔某人或某事〕不好[無用]: *I don't think much of that new restaurant.* 我對那家新飯館評價不高。

16 think the best/worst of sb to consider someone's actions in a way that makes them seem as good as possible or as bad as possible 對某人的行為往最好處想/最壞處想: *Ellie's the type of person that always thinks the best of people.* 埃利屬於那種總是認為人心盡善的人。

17 think big *informal* to plan to do things that are difficult, but will be very impressive, make a lot of profit etc【非正式】打算大幹一番, 立大志: *We had money, materials, and the opportunity to think big. It was up to us to do something with it.* 我們有資金, 有原料, 也有大幹一番的機會。得失成敗全取決於我們自己。

18 think on your feet to answer questions or think of ideas quickly, without preparing in advance 思路敏捷: *A good teacher can think on her feet.* 一名優秀的教師頭腦靈活, 能隨機應變。

19 think to do sth *literary* to try to do something【文】設法做某事: *They had thought to deceive me.* 他們想騙我。

Frequencies of the verb **think** in spoken and written English 動詞 think 在英語口語和書面語中的使用頻率

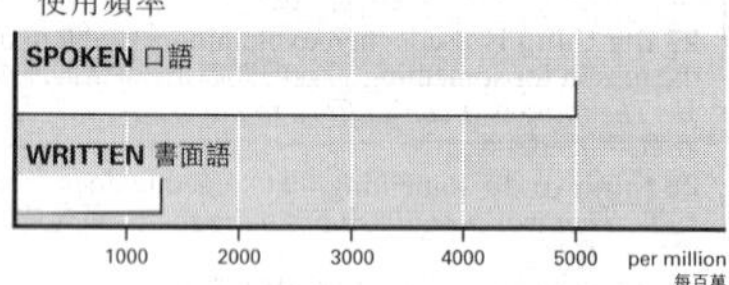

Based on the British National Corpus and the Longman Lancaster Corpus 據英國國家語料庫和朗文蘭卡斯特語料庫

This graph shows that the verb **think** is much more common in spoken English than in written English. This is because it is used in a lot of common spoken phrases. 本圖表顯示, 動詞think在英語口語中的使用頻率遠遠高於書面語, 因為口語中很多常用片語是由think構成的。

think (*v*) **SPOKEN PHRASES**
含 think 的口語片語

20 I think used when you are saying that you believe something is true, although you are not sure 我認為; 我想: *Mary is in the garden, I think.* 我想瑪麗在花園裡。| *I don't think Ray will mind.* 我認為雷不會介意的。

21 I think I'll used when saying what you will probably do 我想我將會: *I think I'll go into town today.* 我想我今天要進城去。

22 I think so/I don't think so/I think not used when answering a question, to say that you believe something is true or not true 我認為如此/我不認為如此/我認為不是: *"Is Jenny still living in Manchester?" "I think so."* "珍妮還住在曼徹斯特嗎?""我想是吧。"

23 I thought (that) a) used when you are politely suggesting something to do 我想〔用於禮貌地建議做某事〕: *I thought we could meet for lunch.* 我想我們可以一起吃頓午飯。| *I thought we'd go swimming tomorrow.* 我想我們明天可以去游泳。**b)** used to say what you thought or believed was true, although you were not sure 我原以為: *I thought he was honest, but I was wrong.* 我原以為他誠實, 但我錯了。

24 I should/would think used when you are saying that you believe something is probably true 依我說; 依我認為: *We'll need about six yards of material, I should think.* 依我認為, 我們需要大約六碼的材料。

25 I can't think who/where/what used to say that you cannot remember or understand something 我想不起/想不明白是誰/是在哪裡/是甚麼: *I can't think where I left my keys.* 我想不起我把鑰匙忘在哪裡了。| *I can't think why she ever married him.* 我想不明白她為甚麼居然嫁給了他。

26 do you think (that)...? a) used when you are asking someone politely to do something for you〔用於禮貌地請某人為你做某事〕: *Do you think you could help me move these boxes?* 您能不能幫我搬一下這些箱子? **b)** used to ask someone's opinion〔用來徵求某人的意見〕: *Do you think I need to bring a jacket?* 你認為我有必要帶一件夾克嗎?
27 who/what etc do you think? a) used to ask someone's opinion 你認為誰/甚麼〔用來徵求某人的意見〕: *Who do you think will win?* 你認為誰會贏? **b)** used when asking someone angrily about something〔用於氣憤地責問某人〕: *What do you think you're doing with that computer?* 你以為你在用那台電腦幹些甚麼? | *Where do you think you're going?* 你以為你要去哪裡呢?
28 (now I) come to think of it used when you are adding something more to what you have said, because you have just remembered it, or realized it (現在我) 回想起來: *My father looked worried and, now I come to think of it, so did my brother.* 我父親當時很焦慮, 現在我回想起來, 我哥哥當時也是那樣。
29 who would have thought? used to say that something is very surprising 誰會想到呢?〔表示非常吃驚〕: *Who would have thought she'd end up dancing for a living?* 誰會想得到呢, 她最終竟靠跳舞謀生?
30 I thought as much used to say that you are not surprised by what you have just found out 我已經意料到, 我已看出個大概〔表示並不吃驚〕: *"Andy failed his driving test." "I thought as much when I saw his face."* "安迪沒有通過駕駛考試。" "我看到他的表情時便已猜出個大概。"
31 just think! used to ask someone to imagine or consider something 試着想一想: *Just think – we could be millionaires!* 試着想一想 —— 我們竟有可能成為百萬富翁! | **[+of]** *It would be lovely, but just think of the expense!* 是很不錯, 但想一想那費用!
32 you would have thought (that)/you would think (that) used to say that you expect something to be true, although it is not 你本來會以為.../你會以為...〔表示預期的事沒發生〕: *You would have thought the school would do more to help a child like Craig.* 你本來會以為學校會做更多的事去幫助像克雷格這樣的孩子。
33 anyone would think (that) used to say that someone behaves as if a particular thing were true, although it is not 誰都會以為...: *Anyone would think he owns the place, the way he talks!* 誰都會以為他擁有那個地方, 瞧他說話的那副樣子!
34 I wasn't thinking/I didn't think used as a way of saying you are sorry because you have upset someone 我沒想清楚〔用於道歉〕: *Sorry, I shouldn't have said that. I wasn't thinking.* 對不起, 我不該說那樣的話。那些話是衝口而出的。
35 to think (that)...! used to show that you are very surprised about something 真沒想到...!: *To think that we lived next door to him and never realised what he was up to!* 真沒想到我們住在他的隔壁, 竟從不知道他在幹甚麼勾當!
36 think nothing of it used when someone has thanked you for doing something, to say politely that you did not mind doing it 算不上甚麼事; 不用謝
37 if you think..., you've got another think coming! used to tell someone that if they think someone is going to do something, they are wrong 如果你認為..., 那你就大錯特錯了!: *If you think I'm going to wait around for you, you've got another think coming!* 如果你認為我會百般無聊地等你, 那你就大錯特錯了!
38 when you think about it used to say that you realize something when you consider a fact or subject 你〔思考某一事實或主題時〕會意識到...; 其實: *When you think about it, most of the things you worry about in life aren't that important.* 其實你生活中擔心的大多數事情都不那麼重要。
39 that's what you/they etc think! used to say that you strongly disagree with someone 那是你的/他們等的看法!〔表示你強烈反對某人的看法〕

think back *phr v* [I] to think about things that happened in the past 回想起; 追憶: **[+on/to]** *When I think back to those nights, it is the crunch of snow and the warm lights from the windows that I remember.* 當我回想起那些夜晚時, 我記得的是踩在雪地上的咯吱聲和從窗戶裡映照出來的溫暖燈光。

think of sb/sth *phr v* [T] **1** to produce a new idea, name, suggestion etc by thinking 想出〔新主意、名字、建議等〕: *They're still trying to think of a name for the baby.* 他們還在想方設法給那個嬰兒取個名字。| *Can you think of anyone else who could do it?* 你能不能想出還有誰可以做這事? **2** to remember a name or fact 想起, 回憶起: *No, I can't think of the name of the hotel either.* 不, 我也想不起那家酒店叫甚麼。**3** to behave in a way that shows that you want to treat other people well 對〔某人〕關懷: *It was very good of you to think of me.* 感謝你的關懷。| *He never thinks of others, only of himself.* 他從來不關心別人, 只關心他自己。**4 what do you think of...?** used to ask what someone's opinion is about something 你怎麼認為...?〔用來問詢某人對某事的看法〕: *So what do you think of this new manager then?* 那麼, 你對這位新來的經理持甚麼看法?

think sth ↔ **out** *phr v* [T] to think about something carefully, considering all the possible problems, results etc 把〔某事〕考慮好: *He had spoken on the spur of the moment, without thinking things out first.* 他當場說了那番話, 根本沒有把事情首先考慮好。

think sth ↔ **over** *phr v* [T] to think about something carefully 認真考慮〔某事〕: *Why don't you think it over for a while, and give me a call in a couple of days.* 你何不認真地考慮一下, 過一兩天再給我打電話來。

think sth ↔ **through** *phr v* [T] to think carefully about the possible results of doing something 認真地考慮〔做某事可能產生的結果〕: *Having thought it through, I listed the pros and cons and made my decision.* 我把此事通盤想了一番, 把贊同的和反對的意見都列了出來, 然後作出了自己的決定。

think sth ↔ **up** *phr v* [T] to produce a new idea, name etc by thinking hard about something 想出, 構思出〔主意、名字等〕: *We laugh at the absurdity of these laws and wonder how anyone ever thought them up.* 我們對這些法律的荒謬感到可笑, 搞不懂怎麼會有人想出這些東西來。

think² *n* **have a think** to think about a difficulty or question 想一想, 想一下: *I don't know whether I'll go to the party, I'll have a think and let you know.* 我不知道我是否去參加那個聚會, 我得想一想, 然後再告訴你。

think·er /ˈθɪŋkɚ; ˈθɪŋkə/ *n* [C] someone who is famous for their important work in a subject such as science or PHILOSOPHY 思想家: *Einstein was one of the world's great thinkers.* 愛因斯坦是世界上偉大的思想家之一。

think·ing¹ /ˈθɪŋkɪŋ; ˈθɪŋkɪŋ/ *n* [U] your opinion about something or your attitude towards it 想法, 看法; 態度: *The Administration's thinking changed as the war progressed.* 隨着戰爭的進展, 本屆政府的態度改變了。| **to my way of thinking** (=in my opinion) 依我所想, 依我看來 *Well, to my way of thinking, they should have done that years ago.* 唉, 依我看來, 他們在幾年前就應該做那件事了。| **put on your thinking cap** *informal* (=think seriously about a problem, in order to try and solve it)【非正式】開動你的腦筋; 認真地想一想

thinking² *adj* [only before noun 僅用於名詞前] a thinking person is intelligent and tries to think carefully about important subjects 有思想的; 認真思考的: *No thinking person would seriously disagree with this point of view.*

沒有哪一個有思想的人會強烈反對這一觀點。

think-tank /ˈ· ·/ *n* [C also+plural verb] a committee of people with experience in a particular subject that an organization or government establishes to produce ideas and give advice 智囊團〔為某個機構或政府就某方面問題出謀劃策的委員會〕: *a right-wing political think-tank* 一個右翼的政治智囊團

thinly /ˈθɪnlɪ; ˈθɪnli/ *adv* **1** in a way that has a very small distance between two sides or two flat surfaces 很薄地: *thinly sliced bread* 切得很薄的麵包片 **2** scattered or spread over a large area, with a lot of space in between 稀疏地: *Sow the radish seeds thinly.* 把蘿蔔籽撒播得稀一些。| **thinly populated/settled etc** *The mountain regions are more thinly populated than the lowlands.* 高山地區比低地地區人煙稀少。**3 thinly disguised/concealed etc** if something or someone is thinly disguised etc, you can easily see what it really is 偽裝/隱瞞不夠巧妙的; 很容易識破的: *moralism thinly disguised as fiction* 明顯地以小説形式出現的説教

thin·ner /ˈθɪnə; ˈθɪnə/ *n* [U] a liquid such as TURPENTINE that you add to paint to make it less thick〔松節油等添加到油漆中的〕稀釋液

thin-skinned /ˌ· ˈ·◂/ *adj* too easily offended or upset by criticism 臉皮薄的; 一批評就臉紅的

third[1] /θɜd; θɜːd/ *number* 3rd 第三: **third time lucky** *spoken* used when you have failed to do something twice and hope to be successful the third time【口】第三次會交好運〔指前兩次均已失敗而希望第三次取得成功〕

third[2] *n* [C] **1** one of three equal parts of something 三分之一 **2** the lowest type of degree that is given by a British university〔英國大學裡頒發的〕第三等學位, 三級榮譽學位

third class /ˌ· ˈ·◂/ *n* [U] **1** a cheap class of mail in the US, usually used for sending advertisements 三等郵件〔美國的一種廉價郵件, 通常用來寄送廣告〕**2** a THIRD[2] (2) 第三等學位, 三級榮譽學位 **3** *old use* the cheapest and least comfortable part of a train or ship【舊】〔火車最廉價的〕三等車廂; 〔輪船的〕三等艙 —**third-class** *adj, adv*: *We travelled third-class to Marseilles.* 我們坐三等艙去馬賽。

third de·gree /ˌ· ·ˈ·◂/ *n* **give sb the third degree** *informal* to ask someone a lot of questions in order to get information from them【非正式】〔為獲得信息而〕嚴厲盤問某人: *I got home after midnight and Dad gave me the third degree.* 我半夜以後才回家, 爸爸嚴厲盤問我一番。

third-degree burn /ˌ· ·· ˈ·/ *n* [C] the most serious kind of burn, that goes right through your skin 三度燒傷〔最為嚴重的一種燒傷, 傷及皮下深層〕

third par·ty /ˌ· ˈ··◂/ *n* [C] *law* someone who is not one of the two main people involved in an agreement or legal case, but who is affected by it in some way【法律】〔協議或法律案件中的〕第三方: *third party insurance* 第三方保險

third per·son /ˌ· ˈ··◂/ *n* **1 the third person** a form of a verb or PRONOUN that is used for showing the person, thing or group that is being mentioned〔動詞或代詞的〕第三人稱: *'He', 'she', 'it' and 'they' are third person pronouns.* he, she, it 和 they 都是第三人稱代詞。**2 in the third person** a story in the third person is told as the experience of someone else, using the pronouns 'he', 'she' or 'they' 以第三人稱形式〔指使用代詞"他"、"她"或"他們"來講述故事〕—see also 另見 FIRST PERSON, SECOND PERSON

third-rate /ˌ· ˈ·◂/ *adj* of very bad quality 三流的; 劣質的: *a third-rate hotel* 一家三流酒店

Third World /ˌ· ˈ·◂/ *n* **the Third World** the poorer countries of the world that are not industrially developed 第三世界〔指世界上工業不發達的貧窮國家〕—**Third World** *adj*: *Third World problems* 第三世界問題

thirst[1] /θɜst; θɜːst/ *n* **1** [singular] the feeling of wanting or needing a drink 渴, 口渴: **quench your thirst** (=get rid of your thirst by drinking something) 止渴; 解渴 *a thirst-quenching drink* 一種止渴的飲料 | **work up a thirst** (=do work or exercise that makes you thirsty) 幹得/鍛鍊得口渴 *I really worked up a thirst during that game.* 我在那場比賽中真的累得十分口渴。| **raging thirst** (=an extremely strong thirst) 火燒火燎的口渴, 口乾舌燥 **2** [U] the state of not having enough to drink 飲水不足, 缺水: *Half of the animals had died of thirst.* 有一半的動物死於飲水不足。**3 a thirst for knowledge/excitement/power etc** *literary* a strong desire for knowledge etc【文】對知識/刺激/權力等的渴望: *These new immigrants had a thirst for education.* 這些新來的移民渴望獲得教育。

thirst[2] *v* [I] *old use* to be thirsty【舊】感到口渴; 渴望, 渴求

thirst for/after sth *phr v* [T] *literary* to want something very much【文】渴望, 渴求〔某物〕: *young men thirsting for adventure* 渴望冒險的年輕人

thirst·y /ˈθɜstɪ; ˈθɜːsti/ *adj* **1** needing to drink or feeling that you want a drink 渴的, 口渴的: *Can I have a glass of water, I'm really thirsty.* 我能喝一杯水嗎? 我真的很口渴。| **thirsty work** (=work that makes you want a drink) 使人口渴的工作 *All this digging is thirsty work.* 這種不斷的挖掘是使人口渴的工作。**2 thirsty for knowledge/power** *literary* having a strong desire for knowledge etc【文】渴望知識/權力 **3** *literary* fields or plants that arc thirsty need water【文】〔田地或植物〕乾旱的; 缺水的 —**thirstily** *adv*

thir·teen /θɜˈtin; ˌθɜːˈtiːn◂/ *number* 13 十三

thir·teenth[1] /θɜˈtinθ; ˌθɜːˈtiːnθ/ *n* 13th 第十三

thirteenth[2] *n* [C] one of thirteen equal parts of something 十三分之一

thir·ty /ˈθɜtɪ; ˈθɜːti/ *number* **1** 30 三十 **2 the thirties** the years from 1930 to 1939 30 年代〔1930 年至 1939 年〕**3 in your thirties** aged between 30 and 39 在三十多歲年紀: **in your early/late thirties** (=below or above 35) 在 30 到 35 歲之間/在 35 到 39 歲之間 **4 in the thirties** if the temperature is in the thirties, it is between 30° and 39° 在三十多度〔指温度在 30° 至 39° 之間〕: **in the high/low thirties** *a hot day, with temperatures in the low thirties* 氣温三十度出頭的熱天 —**thirtieth** *adj*

thir·ty·some·thing /ˈθɜtɪˌsʌmθɪŋ; ˈθɜːtiˌsʌmθɪŋ/ *n* [C] *informal* someone in their thirties who is well educated with a good job, plenty of money etc【非正式】三十多歲的成功人士: *a glossy new magazine aimed at thirtysomethings* 一份針對三十多歲成功人士、用有光紙印刷的新雜誌 —**thirtysomething** *adj*: *a thirtysomething lawyer* 一名三十多歲事業有成的律師

this[1] /ðɪs; ðɪs/ *determiner plural* **these** /ðiz; ðiːz/ **1** used to talk about a person, thing, idea etc that has already been mentioned or that the person you are talking to already knows about 這, 這個〔指已經提到的或已知的人、物、主意等〕: *Wait till you hear this joke.* 等着, 你來聽聽這個笑話。| *What is the purpose of your visit to this country?* 你訪問這個國家的目的是甚麼? | *There will be another meeting later this week.* 本週晚些時候還將有一個會議。| *How can we help these poor children?* 我們怎樣才能幫助這些窮孩子? | *If we carry on at this rate we'll be bankrupt by the end of the week.* 如果我們以這種進度繼續下去的話, 我們到不了週末就會破產。**2** used to talk about the person or thing nearest to you or the time that is soonest etc 這, 這個〔指人或事物最靠近的一個或時間最近的一個〕: *I'm going to visit my Mum this Wednesday.* 這個週三我要去看我媽。| *I'll look in these rooms if you look in all the rest.* 我來看看這些房間, 你去看其餘的所有房間。| *I'm surprised you like that photo – I prefer this one.* 真想不到你喜歡那張照片 —— 我更喜歡這張。**3** *spoken* used in stories, jokes etc when you mean a person or thing, especially when you do not know their name【口】〔用於故事或笑話等中〕某一個〔人或事物〕: *When am I going to meet this boyfriend of yours?*

我甚麼時候能看到你的這一位男朋友? | *I met this really weird guy tonight.* 我今晚遇到一個真的很怪異的傢伙。 **4 this minute/second** immediately 立刻, 馬上: *I want to see you in my office this minute!* 我要你立即到辦公室裡來見我!

1 1 **this²** *pron plural* **these 1** used to talk about a person, thing, idea etc that has already been mentioned or that the person you are talking to knows about already 這, 這個〔指已經提到的或已知的人、物、主意等〕: *Where did you find these?* 你在哪裡找到這些的? | *This is terrible. What on earth are we going to do?* 真糟糕。我們究竟該怎麼辦呢? | *If you think that's funny wait till you hear this.* 如果你認為那很可笑, 那就等着聽聽這件事吧。**2** used to talk about the person or thing nearest to you, the time that is soonest etc 這, 這個〔指人或事物最靠近的一個或時間最近的一個〕: *These are your coats, aren't they?* 這些是你的外衣, 是嗎? | *That might be a much prettier dress but I feel more comfortable in this.* 那一件可能要漂亮得多, 但我覺得穿着這一件要舒服些。**3 a)** *informal* used to introduce someone to someone else【非正式】這一位〔用於介紹某人〕: *Sam, this is my sister, Liz.* 山姆, 這位是我的妹妹麗茲。**b)** used when you have answered the telephone and you want to give your name〔用於接電話説出自己的名字時〕: *"Can I speak to Joan please?" "This is Joan speaking."* "請問瓊在嗎?" "我就是瓊。" **4** a particular time 某一時刻: *I thought he would have been back before this.* 我以為他會在這之前回來的。| *Well young lady, what time do you call this?* 唉, 年輕的女士, 你説這是甚麼時候了? **5 this, that and the other** also 又作 **this and that** *especially spoken* various different things, subjects etc【尤口】形形色色的東西; 各種不同的話題: *"What have you two been gossiping about all evening?" "Oh this, that and the other."* "你們倆整個晚上一直在嘮叨些甚麼?" "哦, 這樣那樣的雜事。" **6 what's (all) this?** *spoken* used to ask what is happening, what someone's problem is etc【口】出甚麼事了? 怎麼了?: *What's this? Crying again?* 怎麼了? 又哭了?

this³ *adv* [+adj/adv] **this big/many etc** *spoken* used to say how big or how many, especially because you are showing the size, number etc with your hand【口】這麼大/多〔表示有多大或有多少的程度, 尤其在用手勢表示大小、數目等時〕: **this big/tall etc** *The table's about this high and this wide.* 那桌子大約有這麼高, 這麼寬。| **this much/many** *Do you know he cut this much off my fringe without even asking me!* 你可知道, 他連問都不問我一下就把我的劉海剪去這麼多!

this·tle /ˋθɪsḷ; ˈθɪsəl/ *n* [C,U] a wild plant with prickly leaves and purple or white furry flowers 薊〔一種葉片帶刺、開紫色或白色毛茸狀花朵的野生植物〕

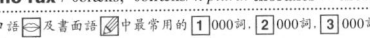

thistle 薊

this·tle·down /ˋθɪsḷˌdaun; ˈθɪsəldaʊn/ *n* [U] the soft light feathery substance fastened to thistle seeds that helps them to float in the air 薊種子冠毛〔薊種子上的軟翅, 可幫助種子飄浮空中〕

thith·er /ˋðɪðɚ; ˈðɪðə/ *adv old use* in that direction【舊】向那邊, 到那邊

tho' /ðo; ðəʊ/ *adv* a short form of 縮略式= 'though'

thong /θɔŋ; θɒŋ/ *n* [C] **1** a long thin piece of leather used to fasten something or as part of a whip 皮帶子;〔皮鞭的〕梢 **2 thongs** [plural] *AmE* a type of shoe that you hold on with your toes【美】平底人字拖鞋; FLIPFLOPS *BrE*【英】—see picture at 參見 SHOE¹ 圖 **3** a pair of KNICKERS or the bottom half of a BIKINI that has a single string instead of the back part 短襯褲;〔後面狹窄如帶子的〕比基尼泳裝褲

tho·rax /ˋθoræks; ˈθɔːræks/ *n plural* **thoraxes** *or* **thoraces** /-rəsiz; -rəsiːz/ [C] **1** *technical* the part of your body between your neck and your waist【術語】〔人的〕胸(部), 胸廓 **2** the part of an insect's body between its head and its ABDOMEN (2)〔昆蟲的〕胸(節) —**thoracic** /θɔˋræsɪk; θɔːˈræsɪk/ *adj*

thorn /θɔrn; θɔːn/ *n* **1** [C] a sharp point that grows on the stem of a plant such as a rose〔植物莖上的〕刺 **2** [C, U] a bush or tree that has thorns 帶刺的灌木, 荊棘 **3 a thorn in your side** someone or something that annoys you or causes problems for a long period of time 長時間使人苦惱或招來麻煩的人[事], 肉中刺: *He's been a thorn in the side of the party leadership for years.* 他多年來一直是該黨領導層的肉中刺。

thorn·y /ˋθɔrnɪ; ˈθɔːni/ *adj* **1 thorny question/problem/point/issue** a question etc that is complicated and difficult 棘手的問題/難題等: *The thorny question of redundancies will have to be tackled sooner or later.* 裁減冗員這一棘手問題遲早必須給以解決。 **2** a thorny bush, plant etc has thorns〔灌木、植物等〕有刺的, 多刺的 —**thorniness** *n* [U]

thor·ough /ˋθɝo; ˈθʌrə/ *adj* **1** including every possible detail 徹底的; 全面的; 詳盡的: *My doctor gave me a thorough check-up.* 我的醫生給我做了一次全面的檢查。| *I made very thorough notes of the meeting.* 我對那次會議作了非常詳盡的筆記。**2** careful to do things properly so that you avoid mistakes 仔細的; 縝密的: *Our mechanics will check everything, they're very thorough.* 我們的機械師要對一切東西進行檢查, 他們的工作是非常仔細的。 **3 a thorough pest/nuisance/mess** used to emphasize the bad qualities of someone or something 徹頭徹尾的討厭鬼/十足的麻煩/混亂不堪 —see also 另見 THOROUGHLY —**thoroughness** *n* [U]

thor·ough·bred /ˋθɝoˌbrɛd; ˈθʌrəbred/ *n* [C] **1** a horse that has parents of the same very good breed 純種馬 **2** someone who seems to do something naturally to a very high standard 天才: *If we are talking about batsmen, Gower is a thoroughbred.* 要談論擊球手, 高爾是匹千里馬。

thor·ough·fare /ˋθɝoˌfɛr; ˈθʌrəfeə/ *n* **1** [C] the main road through a place such as a city or village 大街, 大道: *The motel was off the main thoroughfare.* 那家汽車旅館不靠大馬路。**2 no thoroughfare** a written sign used to tell people that they cannot go on a particular road or path 此路不通; 禁止通行〔標牌用語〕

thor·ough·go·ing /ˋθɝoˋgo·ɪŋ; ˌθʌrəˈgəʊɪŋ◂/ *adj* **1** very thorough and careful 徹底的; 仔細的: *a thoroughgoing inspection of the site* 對現場的徹底檢查 **2** [only before noun 僅用於名詞前] a thoroughgoing action or quality is complete 完全的, 十足的: *the thoroughgoing materialism of this generation* 這一代人十足的物質主義

thor·ough·ly /ˋθɝolɪ; ˈθʌrəli/ *adv* **1** completely 完全地; 極度地: *She sat in her room feeling thoroughly miserable.* 她坐在房間裡, 感到痛苦極了。| *I thoroughly enjoyed the play this evening.* 我非常喜歡今天晚上演出的這部劇。**2** carefully, so that nothing is forgotten 徹底地; 仔細地; 詳盡地: *to clean a room thoroughly* 徹底地打掃房間

those /ðoz; ðəʊz/ the plural of THAT

thou¹ /θau; θaʊ/ *n* [C] *spoken* a thousand or a thousandth【口】一千; 一千分之一: *They paid about sixty nine thou for it.* 他們花了大約六萬九千塊買它。

thou² /ðau; ðaʊ/ *pron old use* a word meaning you, used as the subject of a sentence【舊】汝, 爾〔用作主語〕—see also 另見 HOLIER-THAN-THOU

though¹ /ðo; ðəʊ/ *conjunction* **1** used to introduce a statement that makes the other main statement seem surprising or unlikely 雖然, 儘管: *Though he was only twelve he could run faster than any kid in the school.* 儘管他只有十二歲, 他卻比學校裡的任何孩子都跑得快。| **though old/tired etc** *His childhood, though poverty stricken, had been a happy one.* 他的童年生活雖然貧 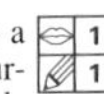

困, 卻也很幸福。| **old though it is/tired though he was etc** *Odd though it may seem, I actually like housework.* 儘管可能說來奇怪, 我實際上喜歡做家務活。**2** used to add a fact or opinion which makes what you have just said seem less serious, less important etc 可是, 不過, 然而: *These samosas are great, though there's not much meat in them.* 這些油炸三角肉餃味道真不錯, 雖然裡面肉沒有多少。| *The offenders were dealt with firmly though fairly.* 違規者受到了嚴厲的, 不過也是很公平的處理。**3 as though** as if 好像, 彷彿: *The lights were on as though everyone had left in a hurry.* 燈還亮着, 好像大家是匆匆離去的。—see also 另見 ALTHOUGH, **even though** (EVEN[1] (6))

though² *adv* [sentence adverb 句子副詞] *especially spoken* used at the end of a CLAUSE (2) to add a fact or opinion which makes what you have just said seem less important, or to add a very different fact or opinion etc【尤口】可是, 不過, 然而〔用在從句末〕: *Yeah, a Rolex for £150 is a great bargain. Is it real though?* 是呀, 150 英鎊買一隻勞力士錶是很划算。不過那是真的嗎? | *Two heart attacks in a year. It hasn't stopped him smoking though.* 一年兩次心臟病發作, 可是那也沒讓他把煙戒掉。

thought¹ /θɔt; θɔːt/ past tense and past participle of THINK[1]

thought² *n*

1 ►STH YOU THINK ABOUT 你想到的某事◄ [C] something that you think of, remember, or realize; idea 思想, 想法; 觀念: *I was just going to pick up the phone when a sudden thought made me hesitate.* 我正要去拿電話, 這時, 一個突然出現的想法使我猶豫起來。| **[+of]** *a traveller's thoughts of home* 遊子對家的思念 | **the thought (that)** *I'm bothered by the thought that I might not have a job next year.* 一想到我明年可能沒有工作, 我就煩着呢。| **have a thought** (=suddenly think of something) 突然想起某事 *I've just had a thought – why don't we invite Judith?* 我剛剛有了一個想法 —— 我們何不把朱迪思請來呢? | **the thought crossed my mind** (=I considered it) 我心裡有這個想法 *"Do you think we should cancel the holiday?" "The thought had crossed my mind."* "你認為我們應該取消這次度假嗎?" "我也這樣想過。" | **a/the thought occurs to sb** (=someone thinks of something) 某人想起了某事 *The thought has just occurred to me, that we should get some insurance.* 我是剛剛才有這個想法的, 我們應該買些保險。| **the very thought (of)** (=used when a thought produces strong feelings) 一想到… *The very thought of moving to New York filled him with dread.* 一想到遷居紐約, 他心裡便充滿了恐懼。| **sobering thought** (=a serious and worrying thought) 發人深省的想法, 令人憂慮的想法 *It's a sobering thought that this country spends more on weapons than on education.* 這個國家花在武器上的錢比花在教育上的錢多, 這真讓人憂慮。| **dark thoughts** (=evil or sad thoughts) 邪惡的想法; 悲哀的想法 *You must put such dark thoughts out of your mind.* 你必須把這種邪惡的想法從心裡弄掉。| **cannot bear the thought of** (=be unable to accept an idea) 無法接受…的想法 *Louis could not bear the thought of being parted from her.* 路易斯無法接受要與她分手的想法。

2 ►ACT OF THINKING 思考行為◄ [U] the act of thinking 想, 思考; 思維: **lost/deep in thought** (=thinking so much that you do not notice what is happening around you) 陷入思索中/在沉思中 *Derek was staring out of the window, lost in thought.* 德里克凝視着窗外, 陷入了沉思。| **thought process** (=the way people's minds work) 思維方式 *Piaget helped teachers to understand children's thought processes.* 皮亞傑幫助教師們了解孩子的思維方式。

3 ►CAREFUL CONSIDERATION 認真考慮◄ [U] careful and serious consideration 考慮, 思索: *With more thought and care this would have been a first class essay.* 如果再認真琢磨一下, 這本來應該是一篇一流的散文。| **give sth thought** (=think carefully about sth) 認真考慮某事 *I've been giving your proposal a lot of thought.* 我一直在認真地考慮你的提議。

4 that's a thought! *spoken* used to say that someone has made a good suggestion【口】那是一個好主意!: *"Why don't you ask Walter's advice?" "That's a thought! – I'll phone him right away."* "你為甚麼不徵求一下沃爾特的意見?" "那是個好主意! —— 我這就給他打電話。"

5 it's just a thought *spoken* used to say that what you have just said is only a suggestion and you have not thought about it very much【口】僅僅是一個想法而已: *I was wondering if your brother could help us – it was just a thought.* 你哥哥是否能幫咱們的忙呢? —— 那只是一個想法而已。

6 ►SUGGESTION 建議◄ [C] a suggestion or opinion about something 建議; 意見: **[+on]** *Do you have any thoughts on how we should spend the money?* 你有沒有甚麼建議, 我們應該怎樣花這筆錢?

7 ►INTENTION 意圖◄ [C,U] intention or hope of doing something 意圖, 打算; 希望: **[+of]** *I had no thought of gaining any personal advantage.* 我當時未曾想到要獲得任何個人的好處。

8 ►CARING ABOUT STH 關心某事◄ [C,U] a feeling of worrying or caring about something 對…的擔心; 關心: **[+for]** *Louis went back into the blazing building with no thought for his own safety.* 路易斯又回到熊熊燃燒的大樓裡, 根本沒有考慮到自身的安全。| **you are always in my thoughts** (=used to tell someone that you think about them and care about them a lot) 我一直在想着你; 我一直在關心着你

9 sb's thoughts turn to sth if your thoughts turn to something, you start to think about it 轉而開始想到某事: *Debbie's thoughts had turned to more serious matters.* 德比轉而思考一些更重大的問題。

10 spare a thought for used to tell someone that they should think about someone who is in a worse situation than they are〔用於要求別人〕給〔某人〕一點關心: *Spare a thought for the homeless.* 給無家可歸的人一點關心。

11 don't give it another thought *spoken* used to tell someone politely not to worry after they have told you they are sorry【口】別把它放在心上, 不要再往心裡去〔禮貌地告訴某人不要因為歉意而心裡過不去〕

12 it's the thought that counts *spoken* used to say that someone's actions are very kind even if they have only done something small or unimportant【口】〔也許實效微小但〕情意勝過一切

13 ►WAY OF THINKING 思想方法◄ [U] a way of thinking that is typical of a particular group, period of history etc〔某一團體的〕思想(方法);〔某一歷史時期的〕思潮: *ancient Greek thought* 古希臘思想 —see also 另見 **perish the thought** (PERISH (3)), SECOND THOUGHT, **school of thought** (SCHOOL[1] (8))

thought·ful /ˈθɔtfəl; ˈθɔːtfəl/ *adj* **1** serious and quiet because you are thinking a lot 認真思考的, 沉思的; 若有所思的: *a thoughtful expression* 若有所思的表情 **2** always thinking of the things you can do to make people happy or comfortable 想得周到的; 體貼的, 關心的: *You'll like Paul, he's very thoughtful.* 你會喜歡保羅的, 他非常體貼人。| **[+of]** *It was really thoughtful of you to remember my birthday.* 你真是體貼人, 還記得我的生日。—**thoughtfully** *adv* —**thoughtfulness** *n* [U]

thought·less /ˈθɔtlɪs; ˈθɔːtləs/ *adj* forgetting about the needs and feelings of other people because you are thinking about what you want 欠考慮的; 不為他人着想的, 自私的: *rash and thoughtless actions* 輕率的自私行動 | **it is thoughtless of sb to do sth** *It's so thoughtless of John to smoke when there's a baby around.* 約翰真是不為別人着想, 旁邊有一個嬰兒, 他竟然還抽煙。—**thoughtlessly** *adv* —**thoughtlessness** *n*

thought-out /ˌ· ˈ·◂/ *adj* **carefully/well/badly thought-out** planned and organized carefully, well etc 考慮仔細的/周密的/不周的: *a carefully thought-out* *speech* 字斟句酌的演講

thou·sand /ˈθauzn̩d; ˈθaʊzənd/ *number* **1** 1000 一千 —see 見 HUNDRED (USAGE) **2 thousands** a lot 許許多多; 數以千計: **[+of]** *There were thousands of people at the concert.* 有數以千計的人出席這次音樂會。—**thousandth** *adj*

thral·dom *BrE*【英】, **thralldom** *AmE*【美】/ ˋθrɔldəm; ˈθrɔːldəm/ *n* [U] *literary* the state of being a slave; SLAVERY【文】奴役; 奴隸制度

thrall /θrɔl; θrɔːl/ *n* **in sb's thrall** *literary* controlled or strongly influenced by someone or something【文】在某人的奴役[束縛, 控制]之下: *The magic of the evening held them in thrall.* 那個晚會的魅力征服了他們。

thrash¹ /θræʃ; θræʃ/ *n* **1** [singular] a violent movement from side to side 劇烈的擺動; 不斷的揮動 **2** [C] *old-fashioned* a loud noisy party【過時】鬧哄哄的聚會 **3** [U] *informal* a type of ROCK¹ (2) music with very loud fast electric guitar playing【非正式】刺耳搖滾樂

thrash² *v* **1** [T] to beat someone violently in order to punish them 毒打; 痛打: *My poor brother used to get thrashed for all kinds of minor offences.* 我那可憐的哥哥曾經因為各種雞毛蒜皮的違規行為而常常挨打。**2** [I always+adv/prep] to move or make something move from side to side in a violent or uncontrolled way 猛烈擺動; 翻騰: **[+about/around]** *The fish were thrashing about in the bottom of the boat.* 魚在船的底艙裡亂蹦亂跳。**3** [T] *informal* to defeat someone very easily in a game【非正式】〔比賽中〕輕易地把…擊敗: *Brazil thrashed Italy 5-0.* 巴西隊以五比零輕取意大利隊。

thrash sth ↔ **out** *phr v* [T] to discuss a problem thoroughly with someone until you find an answer 徹底討論〔直到找出解決辦法〕; 商討: *We spent the whole day trying to thrash out a solution.* 我們花了一整天時間反覆研究, 盡力找出一個解決辦法。

thrash·ing /ˈθræʃɪŋ; ˈθræʃɪŋ/ *n* [C] **give/get a thrashing a)** to beat someone or be beaten violently as a punishment 痛打/被痛打: *If you speak to your mother like that again, you'll get a thrashing.* 如果你再那樣跟你的母親說話, 你會挨一頓痛打的。**b)** to defeat someone or be defeated easily in a game〔比賽中〕輕易地擊敗…; 被…輕易地擊敗

thread¹ /θrɛd; θred/ *n*

1 ►COTTON/SILK ETC 棉/絲綢等◄ [C,U] a long thin string of cotton, silk etc used to SEW or weave cloth〔縫衣服的〕線, 細線: *Have you got a needle and thread?* 你有針線嗎?

2 ►IDEAS 思想◄ [singular] the connection between the different parts of an explanation, story etc 思路, 頭緒; 貫穿的主線: *a common thread running through all the poems* 把所有詩歌貫穿起來的一條共同主線 | **lose the thread** (=stop understanding how ideas or events are connected) 失去頭緒; 中斷思路 *I'm sorry, I've lost the thread of your argument.* 對不起, 我失去了頭緒, 不能理解你的論證。

3 pick up the threads to begin something again after a long period, especially a relationship or way of life〔尤指某種關係或生活方式中斷很長時間後〕再繼續下去: *It's difficult to pick up the threads when you've been travelling for so long.* 你已經旅行了這麼長的時間, 要恢復原來的生活方式是很困難的。

4 ►LIGHT/SMOKE ETC 光/煙等◄ [C] *literary* a long thin line of something【文】線一樣細長的東西: **[+of]** *The Colorado River is just a thread of silver, 4000 feet below.* 在下面4000英尺處的科羅拉多河就像一條銀色的細線。

5 ►ON A SCREW 在螺釘上◄ [C] a continuous raised line of metal that winds around the curved surface of a screw 螺紋 —see picture at 參見 SCREW¹ 圖

6 threads [plural] *old fashioned, especially AmE* clothes【過時, 尤美】衣服 —see also 另見 **hang by a thread** (HANG¹ (5))

thread² *v* [T] **1** to put a thread or string through a hole 穿線於: *Williams threaded the rope through the karabiner and attached it to the safety point.* 威廉姆斯把繩索穿在登山鐵環裡, 然後固定在樁子上。| **thread a needle** (=push a thread through the hole in a needle) 穿針(引線) **2** to put a film, tape etc correctly through parts of a camera, PROJECTOR or TAPE RECORDER 把〔膠卷、磁帶等〕裝放〔在照相機、錄音機等裡面〕**3** to connect objects by pushing a string through a hole in them 用線把…串連起來: *Thread the beads on a string and make a necklace.* 用線把珠子串連起來, 做成一根項鏈。**4 thread your way through/into etc** to move through a place by carefully going around things that are blocking your way 小心〔避開障礙物〕穿過/進入〔某地〕等: *She came towards me, threading her way through the traffic.* 她小心地避過車輛行人, 朝我走過來。

thread·bare /ˈθrɛdˌbɛr; ˈθredbeə/ *adj* **1** clothes, carpets etc that are threadbare are very thin and in bad condition because they have been used a lot〔衣服、地毯等〕破舊的; 磨得很薄的: *a threadbare old sofa* 一張用得很舊的沙發 —see picture on page A18 參見A18頁圖 **2 threadbare excuse/argument/joke etc** an excuse etc that is no longer effective because it has been used too much 陳舊的託辭/論點/笑話等

threat /θrɛt; θret/ *n* **1** [C,U] a statement that you will cause someone pain, unhappiness, or trouble 威脅, 恐嚇: *Your threats don't scare me!* 你的那些威脅嚇不倒我! | **[+of]** *the threat of strike action* 採取罷工行動的威脅 | **make/issue a threat against** *Threats have been made against the book's author.* 有人對那本書的作者發出恐嚇。| **give in to threats** (=do what someone wants because they threaten you) 屈服於威脅 *The government will not give in to terrorist threats.* 政府不會屈服於恐怖分子的威脅。| **carry out a threat** (=do what you threatened to do) 把威脅付諸行動 | **empty threat** (=a threat to do something that you cannot really do) 虛張聲勢的威脅 *Take no notice – they're empty threats.* 不要在意 — 那些是虛張聲勢的威脅。| **death/bomb etc threat** *Police are investigating death threats made against the singer.* 警察正在調查針對那名歌手的死亡威脅。| **under threat of** *Mancini claims he was forced to carry out their orders under threat of death.* 曼西尼聲稱自己是在死亡的威脅下才被迫執行他們的命令的。**2** [C usually singular 一般用單數] the possibility that something very bad will happen〔災難等〕壞事發生的可能: **[+of]** *There's a serious threat of famine.* 饑荒爆發的可能性極大。| **be under threat of closure/attack etc** (=be likely to be closed, attacked etc) 有可能遭到關閉/攻擊等 *The factory is still under threat of closure.* 這家工廠仍然有關閉的可能。**3** [C usually singular 一般用單數] someone or something that is regarded as a possible danger 可能會帶來危險的人[事]: **[+to]** *Automation presents the biggest threat to the workforce.* 自動化給勞動大軍帶來最大的威脅。| **pose a threat** *Nuclear weapons continue to pose a threat.* 核武器繼續構成威脅。 2 2

threat·en /ˈθrɛtn̩; ˈθretn/ *v* **1** [T] to say that you will cause someone pain, unhappiness, or trouble if they do not do what you want 威脅, 恐嚇〔某人〕: **threaten to do sth** *Every time they quarrel, Jan threatens to leave.* 他倆每次吵架時, 簡都威脅說要離開。| **threaten sb with sth** *We were threatened with the sack if we didn't cooperate.* 我們被威脅, 不合作就會被解雇。| **threaten sb** *It's no use threatening me – I won't do it.* 威脅我是沒有用的 — 我不會幹這個的。| **threaten sth** *The unions are threatening a one-day strike.* 工會威脅說要舉行一天的罷工。| **threaten that** *He's threatening that if he doesn't get his way, he'll resign.* 他威脅說, 如果他不能如願以償的話, 他就辭職。**2** [T] to be likely to harm or destroy something 威脅到; 危害到: *Poaching threatens the survival of the rhino.* 偷獵危及犀牛的生存。**3** [I, T] if something threatens to cause an unpleasant situation, it seems likely that it will cause it〔不利的事〕將要發生;〔某事〕可能引起〔不利的後果〕: **threaten sb/** 2 2 sth with *Large areas of the jungle are now threatened with destruction.* 大片的熱帶叢林現在面臨毀滅的危險。| **threaten to do sth** *The incident threatens to ruin his chances in the election.* 這一事件可能會粉碎他在這次選舉中當選的機會。

threat·en·ing /ˋθrɛtṇɪŋ; ˈθretn-ɪŋ/ *adj* **1** talking or behaving in a way that is intended to threaten someone〔言行〕帶有威脅口氣的: *His voice sounded threatening.* 他的話音裡帶有威脅的口氣。**2** making threats 威脅（性）的, 恐嚇（性）的: *a threatening letter* 一封恐嚇信 —**threateningly** *adv*

1 **three** /θri; θriː/ *number* **1** 3 三 **2 the three R's** *old-fashioned* used when talking about children's education to mean reading, writing and ARITHMETIC【過時】〔兒童教育的〕三 R 技能〔指讀、寫、算三項基本技能〕

three-cor·nered /ˌ· ˈ··◂/ *adj* **1** having three corners 三角的, 有三個角的 **2 three-cornered contest/fight** a competition which involves three people or groups 涉及三方的競爭／角逐

three-D, 3-D /ˌθri ˋdi; ˌθriː ˈdiː◂/ *adj* a three-D film or picture is made so that it appears to be three-dimensional 三維的, 立體的 —**three-D** *n* [U]: *a film in 3-D* 一部立體電影

three-day e·vent /ˌ· · ˈ·/ *n* [C] *BrE* a horse-riding competition that takes place for three days【英】三日馬術賽

three-di·men·sion·al /ˌ· ·ˈ···◂/ *adj* **1** having or seeming to have length, depth, and height（似）有三維的, 立體的: *a three-dimensional structure* 三維結構 **2** a three-dimensional character in a book, film etc, seems like a real person〔書、電影等中的人物〕有立體感的; 逼真的

three·fold /ˋθriˋfold; ˈθriːfəʊld/ *adj* three times as much or as many 三倍的 —**threefold** *adv*

three-half·pence /· ˈ··/ *n* [U] *BrE old use* one and a half old pence【英舊】一個半便士

three-leg·ged race /ˌ· ˈ·· ·/ *n* [C] a race in which two people run together, and one person has their right leg tied to the other person's left leg 綁腿賽跑, 二人三足賽跑〔一種兩人為一組的賽跑, 其中一人的右腿與另一人的左腿綁在一起〕

three-line whip /ˌ· · ˈ·/ *n* [C] an order from a leader of a British political party telling MPs in that party that they must vote in a particular way 緊急通知〔指英國政黨領袖要求本黨議員必須按照指示投票〕

three·pence /ˋθrɪpəns; ˈθrepəns/ *n* [U] *BrE old use* three old pence【英舊】三便士

three·pen·ny bit /ˌθripɛnɪ ˋbɪt; ˌθrepəni ˈbɪt/ *n* [C] a small coin used in Britain before 1971 that was worth three old pence〔1971 年之前在英國使用的〕三便士小硬幣

three-piece suit /ˌ· · ˈ·/ *n* [C] a suit that consists of a JACKET (1), WAISTCOAT, and trousers made from the same material 三件套的西裝〔包括上衣、背心和褲子〕

three-piece suite /ˌ· · ˈ·/ *n* [C] *especially BrE* two chairs and a SOFA covered in the same material【尤英】三件套的沙發

three-ply /ˈ· ·/ *adj* three-ply wood, wool, TISSUE (1) etc consists of three layers or threads〔木板等〕三層的;〔線等〕三股的

three-point turn /ˌ· · ˈ·/ *n* [C] a way of turning your car so that it faces the opposite way, by driving forwards, backwards, and then forwards again 三點轉向〔指把汽車前駛、後退再前駛以轉為相反方向的方法〕

three-quar·ter /· ˈ··/ *adj* [only before noun 僅用於名詞前] three quarters of the full size, length etc of something〔大小、長度等〕四分之三的: *a three-quarter violin* 一把四分之三大小的小提琴 | **a three-quarter length coat** (=one that ends a little above your knees) 長及膝蓋以上的外套

three-quar·ters /· ˈ··/ *n* [plural] an amount equal to three of the four equal parts that make up a whole 四分之三: **[+of]** *three-quarters of an hour* 四十五分鐘

three-ring cir·cus /ˌ· · ˈ··/ *n* [singular] *AmE informal* a place or situation that is confusing because there is too much activity【美, 非正式】亂哄哄的地方[場面]: *I don't know how you can work in that office – it's like a three-ring circus.* 我不知道你怎麼能夠在那樣的辦公室裡工作 —— 那裡就像一個鬧哄哄的大馬戲團。

three R's /ˌθri ˋɑrz; ˌθriː ˈɑːz/ *n* **the three R's** *old-fashioned* reading, writing, and ARITHMETIC (=working with numbers), considered as the basic things that children must learn【過時】〔兒童必須學會的〕三 R 技能〔指讀、寫、算〕

three·score /ˋθriskɔr; ˈθriːskɔː/ *number old use* 60【舊】六十 —see also 另見 SCORE[3] (1)

three·some /ˋθrisəm; ˈθriːsəm/ *n* [C usually singular 一般用單數] *informal* a group of three people or things【非正式】三人一組; 三件一套

three-star /ˈ· ·/ *adj* a three-star hotel, restaurant etc is officially judged to be of a good standard〔賓館、飯店等〕三星級的

three-wheel·er /ˌ· ˈ··◂/ *n* [C] a car that has three wheels 三輪汽車

thren·o·dy /ˋθrɛnədɪ; ˈθrenədi/ *n* [C] *literary* a funeral song for someone who has died【文】輓歌, 哀歌

thresh /θrɛʃ; θreʃ/ *v* [I,T] to separate the grain from the rest of corn, wheat etc, by beating it with a special tool or machine（給）〔玉米、小麥等〕脫粒; 打穀 —**thresher** *n* [C] —compare 比較 THRASH[2]

threshing ma·chine /ˈ·· ·ˌ·/ *n* [C] a machine used for separating the grain from the rest of corn, wheat etc〔給玉米、小麥等脫粒的〕打穀機, 脫粒機

thresh·old /ˋθrɛʃold; ˈθreʃhəʊld/ *n* [C] **1** the entrance to a room or building, or the area of floor at the entrance 門檻 **2** the level at which something starts to happen or have an effect〔某事開始發生或產生效果的〕閾, 限度: *my boredom threshold* 我忍受煩悶的限度 | **pain threshold** (=the amount of pain you can suffer before you react to it) 痛覺閾〔指能忍受疼痛的限度〕| **have a high pain threshold** (=be able to suffer a lot of pain before you react) 痛覺閾高〔指忍受疼痛的能力高〕| **have a low pain threshold** (=not be able to suffer much pain before you react) 痛覺閾低〔指忍受疼痛的能力低〕**3 on the threshold of** at the beginning of a new and important event or development 在〔重要事件等〕的開端: *All Europe stands on the threshold of an era of prosperity.* 整個歐洲都處在一個繁榮時期的開端。

threw /θru; θruː/ the past tense of THROW[1]

thrice /θraɪs; θraɪs/ *adv old use* three times【舊】三倍; 三次

thrift /θrɪft; θrɪft/ *n* [U] *old-fashioned* wise and careful use of money, so that none is wasted【過時】節省, 節儉 —see also 另見 SPENDTHRIFT

thrift shop /ˈ· ·/ *n* [C] *AmE* a shop that sells used goods, especially clothes, often in order to get money for a CHARITY (2)【美】〔常為慈善機構籌募經費, 尤其出售舊衣服的〕廉價舊貨店

thrift·y /ˋθrɪftɪ; ˈθrɪfti/ *adj* using money carefully and wisely 節省的, 節儉的: *hard-working, thrifty folk* 勤勞節儉的人們 —**thriftily** *adv* —**thriftiness** *n* [U]

thrill[1] /θrɪl; θrɪl/ *n* **1** [C] a sudden strong feeling of excitement and pleasure, or the thing that makes you feel this〔突然強烈的〕激動; 狂喜: **get a thrill out of** *Even though I've been acting for years, I still get a thrill out of going on stage.* 儘管我多年來一直在演出, 但一上舞台我仍然感到十分激動。| **give sb a thrill** *Pete reckons that using guns gives him a thrill.* 皮特認為使用槍會給他一種刺激感。| **the thrill of (doing sth)** (=the excitement you get from something)〔做某事獲得的〕興奮感 *the thrill of travelling at speed* 駕車飛馳的興奮感 | **do sth for the thrill of it** (=do something for excitement and not for any serious reason) 為了尋求刺激而做某事 **2 thrills and spills** the excitement and danger involved in an activity, especially a sport〔尤指體育運動中的〕驚險刺激 —see also 另見 **cheap thrill** (CHEAP¹ (5))

thrill² *v* **1** [T] to make someone feel excited and happy 使興奮, 使衝動: *The magic of his music continues to thrill audiences.* 他那魔法般的音樂繼續使聽眾感動。**2** [I] to feel excited 感到激動: [**+to**] *Thrill to the magic of the world's greatest guitarist.* 感受世界上最偉大的吉他手的魅力。

thrilled /θrɪld; θrɪld/ *adj* [not before noun 不用於名詞前] very excited, happy, and pleased 非常激動的, 興奮的, 高興的: *We were so thrilled to hear about the baby.* 聽到那個嬰兒的消息, 我們非常高興。| **thrilled to bits** (=very thrilled) 興奮得不得了

thrill·er /ˋθrɪlɚ; ˈθrɪlə/ *n* [C] a book or film that tells an exciting story about murder or crime〔關於謀殺或犯罪的〕驚險小說; 驚險電影

thril·ling /ˋθrɪlɪŋ; ˈθrɪlɪŋ/ *adj* interesting and exciting 引人入勝的; 令人激動的: *a thrilling climax to the championship* 爭奪冠軍的緊張高潮 —**thrillingly** *adv*

thrive /θraɪv; θraɪv/ *v past tense* **thrived** or **throve** /θrov; θrəʊv/ [I] *formal* if something such as a company or plant thrives, it becomes very successful or very strong and healthy【正式】興旺, 欣欣向榮; 茁壯成長: *tree ferns that still thrive in tropical rainforests* 在熱帶雨林裡仍然長勢旺盛的桫欏 | *a free-market economy in which businesses can thrive* 使企業得以蓬勃發展的自由市場經濟

thrive on sth *phr v* [T] to enjoy or be successful in conditions that other people, businesses etc find difficult or unpleasant 樂意做〔別人覺得難做或不樂意做的事〕;〔在其他人、企業等認為困難或不利的環境中〕成功: *I wouldn't want that much pressure, but she seems to thrive on it.* 我不願承擔那麼多的壓力, 但她好像樂在其中。

thri·ving /ˋθraɪvɪŋ; ˈθraɪvɪŋ/ *adj* a thriving company, business etc is very successful 欣欣向榮的, 興旺發達的: *a thriving tourist industry* 欣欣向榮的旅遊業

3 3 **throat** /θrot; θrəʊt/ *n* [C] **1** the passage from the back of your mouth to the top of the tubes that go down to your lungs and stomach 喉嚨, 咽喉 —see picture at 參見 HEAD¹ 圖 **2** the front of your neck 喉部, 頸前部: *She fingered the pearls at her throat.* 她用手指撥弄着脖子上的珍珠。**3 clear your throat** to make a noise in your throat, especially before you speak, or in order to get someone's attention〔說話前或引人注意時〕清一下嗓子 **4 force/ram sth down sb's throat** *informal* to force someone to accept or listen to your ideas and opinions【非正式】強迫某人接受/聽從自己的意見 **5 be at each other's throats** if two people are at each other's throats, they are fighting or arguing 互相打鬥; 激烈爭吵 **6 cut your own throat** to behave in a way that is certain to harm you, especially because you are proud or angry〔尤指因驕傲或發怒而〕自己害自己; 自尋死路 —see also 另見 **bring a lump to sb's throat** (LUMP¹ (4)), **have a frog in your throat** (FROG (2)), **jump down sb's throat** (JUMP¹ (9)), **stick in your throat** (STICK¹ (12))

throat·y /ˋθrotɪ; ˈθrəʊti/ *adj* making a low rough sound when you speak or sing〔說話或唱歌時〕聲音低沉的, 聲音沙啞的 —**throatily** *adv* —**throatiness** *n* [C,U]

throb¹ /θrɑb; θrɒb/ *v* [I] **throbbed, throbbing 1** if a part of your body throbs, you get a regular feeling of pain in it〔身體的某一部分〕抽痛: *Her foot was throbbing with pain.* 她的腳在陣陣抽痛。**2** if music or a machine throbs it makes a sound with a strong regular beat〔音樂或機器〕有規律地顫動發聲 **3** if your heart throbs, it beats faster or more strongly than usual〔心臟急速強烈地〕跳動, 搏動

throb² *n* [C] a low, strong, regular beat or sensation 顫動; 震動; 跳動: *the throb of distant drums* 遠處鼓聲的震動 —see also 另見 HEARTTHROB

throes /θroz; θrəʊz/ *n* [plural] **in the throes of** in the middle of a very difficult situation 處於…的困境之中: *a country in the throes of a profound economic crisis* 一個深陷於經濟危機之中的國家 —see also 另見 DEATH THROES

throm·bo·sis /θrɑmˋbosɪs; θrɒmˈbəʊsɪs/ *n* [C,U] *technical* a serious medical problem caused by a CLOT² (1) forming in your blood, especially in your heart【術語】血栓形成

throne /θron; θrəʊn/ *n* **1** [C] a special chair used by a king or queen at important ceremonies〔君王的〕寶座, 御座 **2 the throne** the position and power of being a king or queen 王位, 帝位; 王權, 君權: **be on the throne** (=be ruling)〔君主〕在位 *in 1913 when George V was on the throne* 1913 年喬治五世在位的時候 | **come to the throne** (=become king or queen)〔君主〕繼位, 登基 | **be next in line to the throne** (=be the person who will become king or queen when the present one dies) 身為儲君

throng¹ /θrɔŋ; θrɒŋ/ *n* [C] *literary* a large group of people in one place; crowd【文】一大羣人; 人羣: *a milling throng of excited spectators* 一羣到處亂轉、激動不已的觀眾 | **the throng** *She got lost in the throng.* 她在人羣中迷路了。

throng² *v* **1** [I always+adv/prep,T] if people throng a place, they go there in large numbers〔人羣〕蜂擁; 羣集; 擠滿〔某地〕: *tourists still thronging the bars and restaurants* 仍然擠滿在酒吧和餐館裡的遊客 **2 be thronged with** if a place is thronged with people, it is very crowded with them〔某地〕被…擠滿: *streets thronged with Christmas shoppers* 擠滿了聖誕購物者的街道

throt·tle¹ /ˋθrɑtl̩; ˈθrɒtl/ *v* [T] **1** to hold someone's throat very tightly so that they cannot breathe; STRANGLE (1) 掐〔某人的〕脖子, 把〔某人〕勒得透不過氣來; 使窒息(而死) **2** to make it difficult or impossible for something to succeed 阻擋; 壓制; 扼殺: *These policies are throttling individual initiative and effort.* 這些政策是在扼殺個人的進取和努力。

throttle back *phr v* [I,T] to reduce the amount of petrol or oil flowing into an engine, in order to reduce speed 減少〔流進發動機的〕汽油以減速

throttle² *n* [C] *technical*【術語】**1** a piece of equipment that controls the amount of petrol, oil etc going into a vehicle's engine〔控制汽車發動機油量的〕節流閥, 油門(桿) **2 at full throttle** as fast as possible in your car, boat etc〔汽車、船隻等〕油門大開地; 全速地

through¹ /θru; θruː/ *prep* **1** entering something such as a door, passage, tube, or hole at one end or side and leaving it at the other 穿過, 貫穿; 從一端到另一端: *They were suddenly plunged into darkness as the train went through the tunnel.* 當火車穿過隧道時, 他們一下子陷入了黑暗之中。| *The ball went flying through the window.* 球從窗戶飛穿了過去。| *As the water passes through the filter a lot of dirt is taken out.* 水在流過過濾器時, 過濾掉大量的污物。**2** going into an area, group etc and moving across it or within it 穿過, 通過〔某一地區、人羣等〕: *He had to push his way through the crowd to get to her.* 他得擠過人羣, 才能到達她那兒。| *The new ring road stops all the traffic driving through the centre of town.* 新的環城路使穿越城市中心的所有交通都受到了限制。| *gliding noiselessly through the air* 無聲地滑過空中 —see picture on page A1 參見 A1 頁圖 **3** if you see something through glass, a window etc, you are on one side of the glass etc and it is on the other 透過〔玻璃、窗戶等〕: *I could see her through the window.* 我能透過窗戶看到她。| *Through the mist she could just make out his silhouette.* 透過霧靄, 她只能看到他身體的輪廓。**4** passing a place where you are supposed to stop〔在應該停下的地方〕闖過: *The driver had gone straight through the traffic lights and hit an oncoming car.* 那名司機徑直闖過交通燈, 撞上了一輛迎面駛來的汽車。| *Once through passport control your luggage will be searched.* 過了護照檢查站, 你的行李就要接受檢查。**5** cutting, breaking or making a hole from one side of something to the other 切斷, 斷開; 鑿穿: *Not only did the drill pierce the wood but it went straight through the table underneath too!* 那鑽頭不僅鑽穿了木頭, 還徑直鑽進了木頭下面的桌子! | *The goat had eaten right through the rope.* 那頭山羊徑直啃斷了繩子。**6** during and to the end of a period of time 在整個期間; 自始至終: *Sometimes I go to bed at 5 a.m. and sleep right through the day.* 有時候我早上 5 點上牀, 然後睡一個白天。| *I wouldn't worry about Joe, he's just going through a difficult period.* 我不擔心喬, 他正在經歷一個困難時期。**7** if you get through a difficult situation or experience you deal with it successfully 戰勝〔困境〕; 成功地渡過: *I've no idea how I managed to get through my exams last year.* 我不知道我去年是如何通過考試的。| *He has lots of friends which really helped him through the divorce.* 他有很多的朋友, 這真的幫他渡過了離婚這一關。**8 look through/search through/go through etc** to do something from beginning to end and include all parts of it 徹底地查看/搜尋/檢查: *In the dress rehearsal he'll go through the play one final time.* 在最後彩排時, 他要對全劇最後再審查一遍。| *I've searched through all my documents and I still can't find my passport.* 我找遍了我的所有文件, 但仍然找不到我的護照。**9** because of someone or something 由於, 因為: *How many working days were lost through sickness last year?* 去年因為員工生病損失了多少個工作日? | *Through your incompetence many of the hotel's regular guests have taken their business elsewhere.* 由於你的無能, 酒店的許多常客已把生意帶到其他地方去了。**10 get through/go through** to use a lot of something 大量用[消費]〔某物〕: *You wouldn't believe how many packets of cigarettes she gets through.* 你不會相信她抽多少盒煙。**11** using a particular person, organization etc to help you achieve something 通過, 經由: *I got my first job through an employment agency.* 我通過一家職業介紹所獲得了我的第一份工作。**12 May through June/Wednesday through Friday etc** *AmE* from May until June, from Wednesday until Friday etc【美】從 5 月到 6 月/從星期三到星期五等: *The store is open Monday through Saturday.* 商店從星期一到星期六都開門。—see 見 INCLUSIVE (USAGE) **13** if you go through a country, you travel across it 在…旅行; 遊遍: *It was while we were travelling through Africa that we decided to settle over there.* 正是在遊歷非洲期間, 我們決定在那邊定居。**14** if a law passes through a parliament, it is agreed and accepted as a law〔法律在議會的〕通過: *The bill's passage through Congress was not a smooth one.* 該議案在國會的通過不是很順利的。—see also 另見 THRU

through² *adv* **1** from one end or side of something to the other 穿過; 通過: *Let me through – I'm a doctor!* 讓我過去吧 —— 我是醫生! **2 read/think/talk etc sth through** to read, think etc about something very carefully from beginning to end 認真徹底地閱讀/想想/談談: *If you think it through – we have no choice but to agree to his demands.* 如果你認真徹底地想一想 —— 我們沒有選擇, 只有同意他的要求。**3 get through/come through/pull through etc** to deal with a difficult situation or experience successfully 渡過(難關)/戰勝(困難)/堅持下來等: *I don't know why you worry about exams – you'll sail through as usual.* 我不知道你為甚麼擔心考試 —— 你會像平常一樣順利通過的。| *Doctors are unsure about whether she'll pull through.* 她是否會挺得過來, 醫生們沒有把握。**4 get through/make it through etc** to reach a person, place etc after a difficult journey〔艱難地〕到達, 抵達: *It's snowing too heavily, you'll never get through.* 雪下得太大了, 你根本去不了的。| [+to] *After days of effort, rescue teams have finally made it through to the survivors.* 經過幾天的努力, 營救隊終於到了倖存者那兒。**5 wet through/cooked through etc** *informal* very wet, cooked completely etc【非正式】濕透了/熟透了: *You're wet through. What on earth have you been doing?* 你濕透了。你到底幹甚麼去了? **6 get through/be through** *BrE* to be connected to someone by telephone【英】〔打電話〕接通了: [+to] *I managed to get through to her after several attempts.* 我試了好幾次, 終於接通了她的電話。| **put sb through** (=connect someone by telephone to someone else) 給〔某人〕接通〔電話〕 *"Can I speak to Mr Henry please?" "I'm putting you through sir."* "請問亨利先生在嗎?" "我這就給你接過去, 先生。" **7 go through to London/Paris etc** if something such as a train goes through to London it continues as far as London 通往倫敦/巴黎等 **8 through and through** if someone is a particular type of person through and through, they are completely that type of person 完完全全地, 徹底地: *I'll say one thing for Sandra – she's a professional through and through.* 我要為桑德拉說一句 —— 她完完全全是專家。

through³ *adj* **1 be through (with sb/sth)** *informal*【非正式】**a)** to have finished doing something, using something etc 完成〔某事〕; 用完〔某東西〕: *I'm not through just yet – I should be finished in an hour.* 我還沒有做完 —— 一個小時後該做完了吧。**b)** to no longer be having a relationship with someone 與〔某人〕關係完結: *That's it! Simon and I are through.* 就這樣! 我和西蒙的關係完結了。**c)** to have stopped doing something or using something that is bad or that you do not like 戒除, 戒掉〔惡習〕: *He says he's through with drugs but it's just not that easy.* 他說他已戒掉了毒品, 但事情沒有那麼容易。**2 through train/road** a train or road by which you can reach a place, without having to use other trains or roads 直達火車/直通路

through·out¹ /θruˋaut; θruːˈaʊt/ *prep* **1** in every part of a particular area, place etc 遍及; 在…各處: *a large international organization with offices throughout the world* 在世界各地設有辦事處的一家大型國際機構 **2** during all of a particular period, from the beginning to the end 在整個期間; 自始至終: *He had misled the court throughout the trial.* 在整個審判過程中, 他一直在誤導法庭裡所有的人。

throughout² *adv* [usually at the end of a sentence 一般用於句尾] **1** in every part of a particular area, place etc 到處, 各個地方: *The house is in excellent condition with fitted carpets throughout.* 這幢房子條件極好, 到處都鋪了地毯。**2** during all of a particular period, from the beginning to the end 在整個期間; 自始至終: *He managed to remain calm throughout.* 他自始至終勉力保持鎮靜。

through·put /ˋθruˏput; ˈθruːpʊt/ *n* [U] the amount of work, materials etc that can be dealt with in a particular period of time〔在一定時間內的〕工作量; 吞吐量; 處理能力: *an airport with a weekly throughput of 100,000 passengers* 一週旅客吞吐量達 100,000 的機場

through·way /ˋθruˏwe; ˈθruːweɪ/ *n* [C] *AmE* a THRUWAY【美】高速公路

throve /θrov; θrəʊv/ *old-fashioned*【過時】the past tense of THRIVE

throw¹ /θro; θrəʊ/ *v past* **threw** /θru; θruː/ *past participle* **thrown** /θron; θrəʊn/

1 ►THROW A BALL/STONE ETC 扔球/石等◄ [I,T] to make an object such as a ball move quickly through the air by moving your hand quickly 投, 扔, 拋, 擲: **throw sth at/to/towards etc** *Someone threw a stone at the car.* 有人朝那輛汽車扔了一塊石頭。| *Cromartie throws the ball back to the pitcher.* 克羅馬蒂把球又扔回給投手。| **throw sb sth** *Throw me that towel, would you.* 請把那塊毛巾扔給我。

2 ►PUT STH CARELESSLY 隨意放置某物◄ [T always+adv/prep] to put something somewhere quickly and carelessly 隨手扔下〔某物〕: **throw sth on/onto/down etc** *Don't just throw your clothes on the floor – pick them up!* 不要隨手把衣服扔在地板上 —— 把它們撿起來!

3 ►PUSH ROUGHLY/VIOLENTLY 粗魯地/猛烈地推◄ [T always+adv/prep] to push someone or something roughly and violently in a particular direction or into a particular position〔粗魯和猛烈地〕把…推向, 拋向: **throw sth ↔ open** *Smelling smoke, she threw open all the windows.* 她聞到煙的味道, 便用力推開所有的窗戶。| **throw sb into the air** *Patrick was thrown into the air by the force of the explosion.* 爆炸的威力把帕特里克拋到了空中。| **throw sb to the ground** *The guards threw Biko to the ground and started kicking him.* 衛兵們猛力地把比科推倒在地, 開始用腳踢他。

4 ►MAKE SB FALL 使某人倒下◄ [T] **a)** to make your opponent fall to the ground in WRESTLING or JUDO〔摔跤或柔道比賽中〕把〔對手〕摔倒在地 **b)** if a horse throws its rider it makes them fall onto the ground〔馬〕把〔騎手〕拋落在地

5 throw yourself at/on/into/down etc to move or jump somewhere suddenly and with a lot of force 突然猛力地撲向/跳到/衝進/撲倒等: *I managed to open the door by throwing myself at it.* 我用身體撞開了門。

6 ►MOVE HANDS/HEAD ETC 移動手/頭等◄ [T always+ adv/prep] to suddenly and quickly move your hands, arms, head etc into a new position 急伸, 將〔手、臂、頭等〕猛動: **throw sth back/up/around etc** *I threw my arms around her and kissed her.* 我猛地把她摟住並親吻她。

7 throw sb into prison/jail to suddenly put someone in prison 把〔某人〕投進監獄: *Anyone who opposes the regime is liable to be thrown in jail.* 任何反對該政權的人都有可能被投進監獄。

8 throw sb out of work/office etc to suddenly take away someone's job or position in authority 突然把〔某人〕解雇/解職等: *Nixon was thrown out of office, following the Watergate scandal.* 在水門醜聞後, 尼克遜被迫辭去職務。

9 throw sb into confusion/chaos/disarray etc to suddenly make a group of people very confused and uncertain about what they should do 突然使〔人們〕陷入困惑/混亂等中: *Everyone was thrown into confusion by this news.* 這一消息突然使大家茫然不解。

10 ►CONFUSE SB 使某人困惑◄ [T] to confuse or shock someone, especially by suddenly saying something〔尤指突然說出的話〕使人困惑; 使人震驚: **throw sb completely** *This handsome young stranger said "Hello, Maria," – it threw me completely.* 這位年輕英俊的陌生人說, "你好, 瑪麗婭。" —— 這話讓我完全怔住了。

11 be thrown back on to be forced to have to depend on your own skills, knowledge etc 被迫依靠〔自己的技能、知識等〕: *Once again we were thrown back on our own resources.* 我們再一次被迫依靠自己的力量解決困難。

12 throw suspicion/doubt on to make people think that someone is probably guilty or that something may not be true 使人們對…產生懷疑: *new discoveries that throw doubt on some basic scientific assumptions* 使人們對一些基本科學假設產生懷疑的新發現

13 throw sb a look/glance/smile etc to quickly look at someone with a particular expression that shows how you are feeling 朝某人看了一下/掃了一眼/笑了一下等

14 throw a fit/scene/tantrum etc to react in a very angry way 大發一通脾氣: *I can't tell my parents – they'd throw a fit!* 我不能告訴我爸媽 —— 他們會大發脾氣的!

15 throw questions/a remark to ask a lot of questions or suddenly say something 不斷地提問題/突然說出一句話: *They kept throwing awkward questions at me.* 他們不斷地向我提出一些令人尷尬的問題。

16 throw a switch/handle/lever to make a large machine or piece of electrical equipment start or stop working by moving a SWITCH[2] (1) 推一下開關/把手/控制桿〔使大型機器或電器設備啟動或停止〕

17 throw a party to organize a party and invite people 舉辦一次聚會

18 throw yourself into sth to start doing an activity eagerly and using a lot of time and effort 積極投入到某項事中去: *Since her husband died, she's thrown herself into her work.* 自從丈夫去世後, 她積極投身到工作之中。

19 throw dice/a six/a four etc to roll DICE or to get a particular number by rolling dice 擲骰子/擲了個六點/擲出四點: *You have to throw a six to start.* 你必須擲一個六點才能開始。

20 throw money at *informal* to try to solve a problem by spending a lot of money but without really thinking about the problem【非正式】靠大量花錢〔以解決某個問題, 但沒經過深思熟慮〕

21 throw good money after bad/throw money down the drain to waste money by spending it on something that has already failed 花冤枉錢/花的錢打水漂了

22 throw your weight around to use your position of authority to tell people what to do in an unreasonable way 耀武揚威, 作威作福: *He's the sort of insensitive bully who enjoys throwing his weight around.* 他是那種毫無同情心的惡霸, 喜歡到處耀武揚威。

23 throw your weight behind to publicly support a plan, person etc and use your power to make sure they succeed 公開支持…; 作為…的後盾: *The party leadership is throwing its weight behind the campaign.* 黨的領導層公開支持這項活動。

24 throw cold water on to say that a plan, suggestion etc is unlikely to succeed 給〔計劃、建議等〕潑冷水

25 throw light on to make something easier to understand by providing new information〔提供新資料〕使…更易理解: *startling revelations that throw new light on Elvis, the man* 有助於重新認識埃爾維斯其人的驚人發現

26 throw a light/shadows/rays [T] to make light, shadows etc fall on a particular place 發出光亮/投射影子/發射光束: *The trees threw long, dark shadows across the cornfield.* 樹木在玉米地裡投下長長的黑影。

27 throw the book at *informal* to punish someone as severely as possible or charge them with as many offences as possible【非正式】盡量從嚴懲罰〔某人〕; 盡量從嚴指控〔某人〕所犯的罪行

28 throw caution to the wind(s) to ignore the risks and deliberately behave in a way that may cause trouble or problems 不顧一切風險; 故意冒險行事

29 ►DELIBERATELY LOSE 故意輸掉◄ [T] to deliberately lose a fight or sports game that you could have won 故意輸掉〔搏鬥或體育比賽〕

30 throw sth (back) in sb's face to be unkind to someone after they have been kind to you or helped you 以怨報德; 忘恩負義

31 throw a punch/a left/a right etc to try to hit someone with your hand in a fight 打〔某人〕一拳/一記左拳/一記右拳

32 throw yourself at sb *informal* to try very hard to attract someone's attention because you want to have a sexual relationship with them【非正式】努力引起某人的注意〔因為想與其發生性關係〕

33 throw your hat into the ring to officially announce that you will compete or take part in something〔正式宣布〕參加角逐[參與某事]

34 throw the baby out with the bath water to get rid of good useful parts of a system, organization etc when you are changing it in order to try and make it better〔在改革某系統、機構等時〕把優良東西連同糟粕部分一起扔棄

35 ►POT 陶罐◄ [T] to make a clay object such as a bowl, using a POTTER'S WHEEL〔在陶輪上〕製作〔陶器〕, 把…拉成坯

36 throw your voice to use a special trick to make your voice seem to be coming from a different place from the place you are standing〔利用口技〕使嗓音讓人聽來似乎來自他處 —see also 另見 **be thrown in at the deep end** (DEEP[1] (16))

T

throw sth ↔ **away** *phr v* [T] **1** to get rid of something that you do not want or need 扔掉，拋棄〔某物〕: *I shouldn't have thrown away the receipt.* 我不應該扔掉那張收據的。**2** to lose or waste something good that you have, for example a skill or an opportunity 浪費掉〔本領〕；錯過〔機會〕: *This could be the best chance you'll ever have. Don't throw it away!* 這或許是你能得到的最好機會。別白白地錯過了！

throw in sth *phr v* [T] **1** [**throw** sth ↔ **in**] to add something to what you are selling, without increasing the price 免費添加，額外奉送: *We paid $2000 for the boat, with the trailer and spares thrown in.* 我們花了 2000 美元買那隻船，拖車和備用件是額外贈送的。**2** [**throw** sth ↔ **in**] if you throw in a remark, you say it suddenly without thinking carefully 隨口說〔話〕 **3 throw in the sponge/towel** *informal* to admit that you have been defeated【非正式】認輸，承認失敗

throw sb/sth ↔ **off** *phr v* [T] **1** [**throw** sth ↔ **off**] to take off a piece of clothing in a quick, careless way 匆匆脫下〔衣服〕: *He threw off his sweater.* 他匆匆脫掉毛衣。**2** [**throw** sth ↔ **off**] to get free from something that has been limiting your freedom 擺脫〔束縛〕: *In 1845 they finally threw off the yoke of foreign rule.* 1845年，他們最終擺脫了外國統治的枷鎖。**3** [**throw** sth ↔ **off**] if you throw off a slight illness such as a COLD² (2), you succeed in getting better 擺脫〔感冒等小病〕 **4** [**throw** sb/sth ↔ **off**] to escape from someone or something that is chasing you 甩掉，擺脫掉〔追趕者〕: **throw sb off the scent** (=make someone who is following you unable to find where you have gone) 甩掉跟蹤的尾巴；擺脫跟蹤者 *If we cross the stream it might throw them off the scent.* 我們如果跨過小溪，有可能甩掉他們的追蹤。**5** [**throw** sth ↔ **off**] to produce large amounts of heat, light, RADIATION etc 散發出，放射出〔熱、光、輻射等〕: *The engine was throwing off so much heat that the air above it shimmered with haze.* 發動機散發出太多的熱量，使它上面霧濛濛地一片。

throw sth ↔ **on** *phr v* [T] to put on a piece of clothing quickly and carelessly 匆匆穿上〔衣服〕

throw sth ↔ **open** *phr v* [T] **1** to allow people to go into a place that is usually kept private 對公眾開放〔某地〕: *plans to throw the Palace open to the public* 把這座宮殿對公眾開放的計劃 **2** to allow anyone to take part in a competition or a discussion 使〔競賽或討論〕對公眾開放

throw sb/sth ↔ **out** *phr v* [T] **1** [**throw** sth ↔ **out**] to get rid of something that you do not want or need, especially when you are tidying〔尤指打掃時〕扔掉，拋掉〔不想要的東西〕: *We usually throw out all our old magazines.* 我們通常把所有的舊雜誌全部扔掉。**2** [**throw** sb ↔ **out**] to make someone leave a place, school, or organization etc quickly, especially because they have been behaving badly or made you angry 攆走；解雇〔某人〕: *Nick got thrown out of college in the second year for taking drugs.* 因為吸毒尼克在二年級時被大學開除了。| **throw sb out on the street** (=make someone leave their house immediately, even if they have nowhere else to live) 把〔某人〕趕出家門 **3** [**throw** sth ↔ **out**] if parliament or another official or political organization throws out a plan or suggestion, they refuse to accept it and make it legal, especially after voting〔議會或某個政治機構〕拒絕接受〔計劃或提議〕: *The bill was thrown out by the Senate.* 該議案遭到參議院的拒絕。**4** [**throw** sth ↔ **out**] if something throws out smoke, heat, dust etc, it produces a lot of it and fills the air with it 散發出〔大量煙霧、熱量、灰塵等〕: *huge trucks throwing out noxious fumes from their exhausts* 排氣管中散發出大量有毒煙霧的大型卡車

throw sb **over** *phr v* [T] *old-fashioned* to end a romantic relationship with someone【過時】斷絕與〔某人〕的戀愛關係

throw sb/sth **together** *phr v* [T] **1** [**throw** sth ↔ **together**] to make something such as a meal quickly and not very carefully 匆匆張羅出〔飯菜等〕: *There's lots of food in the fridge – I'm sure I can throw something together.* 冰箱裡有許多食物——我有把握能很快地做出一點吃的東西來。**2** [**throw** sb ↔ **together**] if a situation throws people together, it makes them meet and know each other 使〔人們〕相遇相識；使偶然相聚在一起

throw up *phr v* **1** [I,T] to bring food or drink up from your stomach out through your mouth because you are ill or drunk etc; VOMIT¹〔因生病或醉酒等〕嘔吐，嘔出: *Georgia was bent over the basin, throwing up.* 喬治亞趴在洗臉盆邊嘔吐。—see 見 SICK¹ (USAGE) **2** [T **throw** sth ↔ **up**] to produce new ideas, problems, or new people 產生〔新思想、新問題〕；帶來〔新人〕: *It wasn't a long meeting, but it did throw up some interesting suggestions.* 會議時間並不長，卻提出了一些有意思的建議。**3** [T **throw** sth ↔ **up**] if a vehicle, runner etc throws up dust, water etc, they make it rise into the air as they move along〔汽車、跑步者等經過時〕揚起〔灰塵等〕；濺起〔水等〕 **4** [T **throw** sth ↔ **up**] *informal* to suddenly leave your job, your home etc【非正式】突然辭去〔工作〕；拋棄〔家庭〕: *I can't just throw up everything and come and live with you.* 我不可能拋棄一切，過來與你一同生活。

throw² *n* [C] **1** an act of throwing something such as a ball 投，扔，拋，擲: *The throw went straight to Marinelli on first base.* 那一投徑直朝第一壘的馬里內利飛去。**2** the distance which something is thrown 投擲的距離: *a throw of over eighty metres* 投出八十多米的距離 **3** the result of throwing something in a game such as darts (DART² (1)) or DICE¹ (1) 投擲飛標／骰子等的結果 **4 £5/£10/50p etc a throw** *BrE informal* £5, £10 etc each【英，非正式】每個的價格是五英鎊／十英鎊／五十便士等

throw·a·way /ˈθroə͵we; ˈθrəʊəweɪ/ *adj* **1 throwaway remark/line/comment etc** a short remark etc that is said quickly and without careful thought 脫口而出的話／即興的台詞／信口開河的評論: *a comedy act full of short throwaway lines* 充滿簡短即興台詞的喜劇節目 **2 throwaway cup/plate/razor etc** a cup, plate etc that has been produced cheaply so that it can be thrown away after it has been used; DISPOSABLE (1)〔杯子／盤子／剃鬚刀等〕用後即扔的；一次性使用的 **3 the throwaway society** used to show disapproval when talking about modern societies in which products are not made to last a long time 一次性物品充斥的社會〔表達對現代社會的不滿〕

throw·back /ˈθro͵bæk; ˈθrəʊbæk/ *n* [C usually singular 一般用單數] something that is similar to or is a result of something that happened in the past 復舊；返祖現象: **be a throwback to** *This year's fashions are a throwback to the 1950s.* 今年的時裝是 20 世紀 50 年代流行的款式東山再起。

throw-in /ˈ· ·/ *n* [C] the act of throwing the ball back onto the field in football, after it has gone over the line at the side of the field〔足球踢出邊線後的〕擲邊線球 — see picture on page A23 參見 A23 頁圖

thru /θru; θruː/ *adj, adv AmE informal*【美，非正式】a short form of 縮略式= THROUGH —**thru** *prep*

thrum /θrʌm; θrʌm/ *v* **thrummed, thrumming** [I,T] to make a low sound like something beating or shaking 低沉地嗡嗡作響: *the deep thrumming of the engine* 發動機低沉的隆隆聲

thrush /θrʌʃ; θrʌʃ/ *n* **1** [C] a brown bird with spots on its front 鶇 **2** [U] an infectious disease that affects the VAGINA or mouth 鵝口瘡，口腔念珠菌病；念珠菌性陰道炎

thrust¹ /θrʌst; θrʌst/ *v past tense and past participle* **thrust** [T] **1** to push something somewhere with a sudden or violent movement 猛推，猛塞: **thrust sth into/back** *The man thrust a package into Jake's hand and ran away.* 那名男子把一包東西塞進傑克的手裡，然後跑開了。**2 have sth thrust upon you** to be forced to accept something that you did not expect or want〔被迫〕接受不指望得到或不想要的東西; 身不由己 **3** [I+at] to make a sudden movement forward with a sword or knife〔用劍或刀〕刺, 戳

thrust sth ↔ **aside** *phr v* [T] to refuse to think about something 把〔某事〕拋在一邊; 拒絕考慮〔某事〕: *Our complaints were thrust aside and ignored.* 我們的投訴被拋在一邊, 無人理睬。

thrust² *n* **1** [C] a sudden strong movement that pushes forward 猛衝, 猛刺; 推進: *the quick thrust of his sword* 他運劍猛刺 **2 the thrust** the main meaning or most important part of what someone says or does〔說話或做事的〕要旨, 中心點: *the main thrust of Clinton's healthcare reforms* 克林頓的健康醫療改革的要旨 **3** [U] *technical* the force of an engine that pushes something such as a plane forward【術語】〔發動機推進飛機等的〕推力, 推進力

thru·way, throughway /ˈθruˌwe; ˈθruːweɪ/ *n* [C] *AmE* a wide road for fast traffic that you pay to use【美】〔路面寬闊的〕付費高速公路

thud¹ /θʌd; θʌd/ *n* [C] the low sound made by a heavy object hitting something else〔重物碰擊其他東西時發出的〕砰然聲, 低沉聲: *His head hit the wall with a dull thud.* 他的頭碰在牆上, 發出低沉的一聲。

thud² *v* **thudded, thudding** [I] to hit or fall onto something with a low sound〔砰地一聲〕碰擊; 掉落〔在某物上〕

thug /θʌg; θʌg/ *n* [C] a violent man 惡棍, 暴徒: a *bunch of thugs* 一羣暴徒 —**thuggery** *n* [U]

thumb¹ /θʌm; θʌm/ *n* [C] **1** the part of your hand that is shaped like a thick short finger and helps you to hold things〔手的〕拇指: *a baby sucking its thumb* 吮吸拇指的嬰兒 **2** the part of a GLOVE that fits over your thumb〔手套的〕拇指部分 **3 be all (fingers and) thumbs** *informal* to be unable to do things neatly and carefully with your hands【非正式】笨手笨腳: *Would you do up these buttons for me? I seem to be all thumbs today.* 幫我扣上這些鈕扣好嗎? 今天我感覺笨手笨腳的。**4 give sth the thumbs up/down** *informal* to officially accept or reject a plan, suggestion etc【非正式】正式接受/拒絕〔計劃、建議等〕: *The project had been given the thumbs up and we could now get started.* 這項工程已經獲得批准, 我們現在可以開始了。**5 be under sb's thumb** to be so strongly influenced by someone that they control you completely 完全在某人的控制下; 在某人的巨大影響之下 —see also 另見 **stick out like a sore thumb** (STICK¹), **rule of thumb** (RULE¹ (9))

thumb² *v* **1 thumb a lift** *BrE informal*【英, 非正式】**thumb a ride** *AmE informal*【美, 非正式】to persuade a driver of a passing car to stop and take you somewhere, by putting your hand out with your thumb raised〔伸出手並豎起拇指向過路的車〕請求搭車 **2 thumb your nose at** to show that you do not respect rules, laws etc or you do not care what someone thinks of you 蔑視〔規則、法律等〕; 不在乎〔別人對自己的看法〕: *a chance to thumb his nose at authority* 一次讓他可以表現蔑視權力的機會

thumb through sth *phr v* [I,T] to look through a book, magazine etc quickly 匆匆翻閱, 瀏覽〔圖書、雜誌等〕: *thumbing through the pages of a gardening catalogue* 瀏覽園藝用品目錄

thumb in·dex /ˈ· ˌ··/ *n* [C] a series of U-shaped cuts in the edge of a large book, usually showing the letters of the alphabet, that help you find the part you want〔在一本厚書的邊緣上通常標有字母的〕拇指索引, 書邊挖月索引

thumb·nail¹ /ˈθʌmˋnel; ˈθʌmneɪl/ *adj* **thumbnail sketch/description** a short description giving only the main facts about something 簡略的描述

thumbnail² *n* [C] the nail on your thumb 拇指甲

thumb·screw /ˈθʌmˌskru; ˈθʌmskruː/ *n* [C] an instrument used in the past to punish or TORTURE² (1) people by crushing their thumbs 拇指拶子〔舊時的一種刑具〕

thumb·tack /ˈθʌmˌtæk; ˈθʌmtæk/ *n* [C] *AmE* a short pin with a broad flat top used especially for fixing notices on walls【美】圖釘, 按釘; DRAWING PIN *BrE*【英】—see picture at 參見 PIN¹ 圖

thump¹ /θʌmp; θʌmp/ *v* **1** [T] *informal* to hit someone very hard with your hand closed【非正式】捶打, 重擊: *If you don't shut up, I'm going to thump you!* 如果你不住嘴的話, 我就要狠狠揍你! —see picture on page A20 參見 A20 頁圖 **2** [I always+adv/prep,T] to make a dull loud sound by beating or falling against a surface 發出重擊聲; 嘭地作響: [**+against/on/into**] *the dog's tail thumping against the floor* 狗尾巴擊打着地板的聲音 **3** [I] if your heart thumps, it beats very quickly because you are frightened or excited〔心臟因恐懼或激動〕砰砰地跳

thump² *n* **1** [C] the dull sound that is made when something hits a surface 重擊聲; 嘭的一聲: *We heard a loud thump and then a scream from upstairs.* 我們聽到樓上傳來砰的一聲, 然後是一聲尖叫。**2 give sb a thump on the back/head etc** *especially BrE* to hit someone on the back, head etc【尤英】給某人的背上/頭上等一記重擊

thump·ing /ˈθʌmpɪŋ; ˈθʌmpɪŋ/ also 又作 **thumping great/big** *adj* [only before noun 僅用於名詞前] *BrE informal* very big【英, 非正式】非常大的, 極大的: *Mulroney swept to power with a thumping majority.* 穆羅尼以壓倒性的多數票當選執政。

thun·der¹ /ˈθʌndɚ; ˈθʌndə/ *n* **1** [U] the loud noise that you hear during a storm, usually after a flash of lightning 雷聲: **clap of thunder** (=one sudden noise of thunder) 一聲霹靂 **2** [singular] a loud, deep noise like thunder 雷鳴般的響聲, 轟隆聲: *the thunder of gunfire* 砲火的轟鳴聲 **3 a face like thunder** looking very angry 滿面怒容 —see also 另見 BLOOD-AND-THUNDER, **steal sb's thunder** (STEAL¹ (7))

thunder² *v* **1 it thunders** if it thunders, there is a loud noise in the sky, usually after a flash of lightning 打雷 **2** [I always+adv/prep] to move in a way that makes a very loud noise 轟隆隆地移動: *The children came thundering downstairs.* 孩子們轟隆隆地走下樓梯。| [**+against/onto**] *The sea thundered against the rocks.* 海水轟然地撞擊着礁石。**3** [T] to shout loudly and angrily 憤怒地大聲叫嚷, 怒吼

thun·der·bolt /ˈθʌndɚˌbolt; ˈθʌndəbəʊlt/ *n* [C] **1** a flash of LIGHTNING and a noise of thunder together, which hits something〔擊中某東西的〕雷電 **2** a sudden event or piece of news that shocks you 晴天霹靂般的事件; 令人震驚的消息 **3** an imaginary weapon of thunder and lightning, used by gods to punish people 霹雷〔神懲罰人所用的一種雷電武器〕

thun·der·clap /ˈθʌndɚˌklæp; ˈθʌndəklæp/ *n* [C] a single loud noise of thunder 雷聲, 雷鳴

thun·der·cloud /ˈθʌndɚˌklaud; ˈθʌndəklaʊd/ *n* [C] a large dark cloud that you see before or during a storm〔暴風雨來臨之前或暴風雨期間所看到的〕雷雨雲

thun·der·ing /ˈθʌndərɪŋ; ˈθʌndərɪŋ/ *adj, adv BrE old-fashioned* very bad, severe etc【英, 過時】非常壞的, 嚴重的: *That's a thundering great lie!* 那是一個極大的謊言!

thun·der·ous /ˈθʌndərəs; ˈθʌndərəs/ *adj* extremely loud 響聲極大的, 雷鳴般的: *thunderous applause* 雷鳴般的掌聲 —**thunderously** *adv*

thun·der·storm /ˈθʌndɚˌstɔrm; ˈθʌndəstɔːm/ *n* [C] a storm with thunder and lightning 雷暴

thun·der·struck /ˈθʌndɚˌstrʌk; ˈθʌndəstrʌk/ *adj* [not before noun 不用於名詞前] extremely surprised or shocked 極其震驚的, 嚇得目瞪口呆的: *Jeff was staring at me thunderstruck. "You mean it's been stolen?" he gasped.* 傑夫目瞪口呆地看着我。"你的意思是說它被偷走了?" 他喘息着說。

thun·der·y /ˈθʌndərɪ; ˈθʌndəri/ *adj* thundery weather is the type of weather that comes before a thunderstorm

〔天氣〕雷暴前的

Thurs·day /ˈθɝzdɪ; ˈθɜːzdi/ written abbreviation 縮寫為 **Thur.** or **Thurs.** *n* [C,U] the day between Wednesday and Friday. In Britain, Thursday is considered the fourth day of the week, and in the US it is considered the fifth day of the week 星期四, 週四: *We went to the theatre last Thursday.* 我們上週四去看戲了。| *I'll phone you on Thursday.* 我星期四給你打電話。| *Christmas Day is on a Thursday this year.* 今年的聖誕節是個星期四。| **Thursday morning/evening etc** *Shall we go to a film Thursday night?* 星期四晚上我們去看電影好嗎?| **on Thursdays** (=each Thursday) 每個星期四, 每週四 *I go to night school on Thursdays.* 我每個週四去上夜校。| **the Thursday** *BrE* (=the Thursday of the week being mentioned)【英】提及的星期的週四 *Angela's arriving on the Thursday and leaving on the Sunday.* 安傑拉週四到達, 週日離開。

1 **thus** /ðʌs; ðʌs/ *adv formal*【正式】**1** [sentence adverb 句子副詞] as a result of something that you have just mentioned; HENCE 因此, 因而, 從而: *Most of the evidence was destroyed in the fire. Thus it would be almost impossible to prove him guilty.* 多數證據已毀於火災, 因而要證明他有罪, 幾乎是不可能的。**2** in this manner or way 以此種方式; 如此, 這樣: *He sold his car and used the money thus obtained to fly to Rio.* 他賣掉自己的汽車, 用所得的錢坐飛機去了里約熱內盧。**3 thus far** until now 到此為止, 迄今: *Her political career thus far had remained unblemished.* 她的政治生涯至今還沒有一絲污點。

USAGE NOTE 用法說明: THUS

WORD CHOICE 詞語辨析: **thus, so, therefore, consequently, for this reason, as a result**

Thus is a little old-fashioned and only used in very formal English. thus 有點舊式, 僅用於非常正式的文體。In court you might hear 在法庭裡可能聽見: *They had no offer of finance, and thus were unable to achieve completion* (=they did not get the money so they could not buy the house). 他們無法提供資金, 因而未能完成交易。

In spoken English you usually use **so**. 口語中一般用 so: *I don't use the language much, so I tend to forget it* (NOT 不用 *thus*). 那門語言我用得不多, 所以往往會遺忘。

In formal speech and writing **therefore** will usually be used or, especially at the beginning of a sentence, **consequently**, **for this reason**, or **as a result** 在正式的口頭語和書面語中, 一般用 therefore, consequently, for that reason 或 as a result, 後三者在句子的開頭尤其常用: *The country was beautiful. Consequently I decided to return the next year./I therefore decided to return the next year.* 那個國家很美麗, 因此我決定第二年再回到那兒。

thwack¹ /θwæk; θwæk/ *n* [C] a short loud sound like something hitting a hard surface 拍打(聲); 重擊(聲)

thwack² *v* [T] to hit someone or something making a short loud sound 拍打; 重擊

thwart¹ /θwɔrt; θwɔːt/ *v* [T] *formal* to prevent someone from doing what they are trying to do【正式】阻撓, 阻礙: *My plans were thwarted by the intervention of the police.* 我的計劃因警察的干預而受到阻撓。| *thwarted ambition* 受挫的雄心

thwart² *n* [C] *technical* a seat fixed across a ROWING BOAT【術語】〔划船上的〕座板

thy /ðaɪ; ðaɪ/ *determiner old use* your【舊】你的: *We praise thy name, O Lord.* 主啊, 我們讚美你的聖名。

thyme /taɪm; taɪm/ *n* [U] a plant used for giving food a special taste 百里香〔用作食物的調味品〕

thy·roid /ˈθaɪrɔɪd; ˈθaɪrɔɪd/ also 又作 **thyroid gland** /ˈ·· ,·/ *n* [C] an organ in your neck that produces substances that affect the way you develop and behave 甲狀腺

thy·self /ðaɪˈsɛlf; ðaɪˈself/ *pron old use* yourself【舊】你自己

ti /ti; tiː/ *n* [singular] the seventh note in a musical SCALE¹ (8) according to the SOL-FA system 全音階的第七音

ti·a·ra /taɪˈɛrə; tiˈɑːrə/ *n* [C] a piece of jewellery like a small CROWN¹ (1a), that a woman wears on her head on formal occasions〔婦女在正式場合佩戴的〕冕狀寶石頭飾: *a diamond tiara* 冕狀鑽石頭飾

tib·i·a /ˈtɪbɪə; ˈtɪbiə/ *n plural* **tibiae** /-bɪˌi; -bi-iː/ *or* **tibias** [C] *technical* a bone in the front of your leg【術語】脛骨 —see picture at 參見 SKELETON 圖

tic /tɪk; tɪk/ *n* [C] a sudden, uncontrolled movement of a muscle in your face, usually because of a nervous illness〔一般因神經疾病造成面部肌肉的〕抽搐

tick¹ /tɪk; tɪk/ *n* **1** [C] a mark (✓) written next to an answer, something on a list etc, to show that it is correct or has been dealt with〔在答案旁邊或名單上標明正確或已經處理的〕勾號(✓); CHECK² (9) *AmE*【美】: *Put a tick in the box if you agree with this statement.* 如果你同意這種說法, 就在方格內打一個勾號。**2** [C] a very small animal like an insect that lives under the skin of other animals and sucks their blood〔動物身上的〕蜱, 壁虱 **3** [singular] the short repeated sound that a clock or watch makes every second〔鐘錶發出的〕滴答聲 —see picture on page A19 參見A19頁圖 **4** [singular] *spoken especially BrE* a very short time【口, 尤英】一瞬間, 一剎那: **in a tick** (=soon) 立刻, 馬上 *I'll be with you in a tick.* 我馬上就過來。**5 on tick** *informal old-fashioned* if you get something on tick, you arrange to take it now and pay later【非正式, 過時】賒購, 賒賬

tick² *v* **1** [I] if a clock or watch ticks, it makes a short sound every second〔鐘錶〕發出滴答聲 **2** [T] *BrE* to mark a test, list of questions etc with a tick, usually to show that something is correct【英】給〔試卷、問題等〕打勾號; CHECK¹ (5) *AmE*【美】: *Tick the box next to the statement that best describes you.* 在最符合你的那種說法旁邊的框內打上勾號。**3 what makes sb tick** *informal* the thoughts, desires, opinions etc that give someone their character or make them behave in a particular way【非正式】形成某人的性格或影響他的行為的思想[慾望、見解等]

tick away/by *phr v* **1** [I] if time ticks away or by, it passes, especially when you are waiting for something to happen〔尤指等待某事發生時〕時光在流逝, 時間一點一點地過去: *We're going to have to make a decision – time's ticking away.* 我們必須馬上做出決定 —— 時間正在一分一秒地過去。**2** [T **tick** sth ↔ **away**] if a clock or watch ticks away the hours, minutes etc, it shows them as they pass〔鐘錶〕以滴答聲表示〔小時、分鐘等的〕流逝

tick sb/sth ↔ **off** *phr v* [T] **1** *BrE informal* to tell someone angrily that you are annoyed with them or disapprove of them【英, 非正式】責備, 怒斥〔某人〕: *The teacher ticked us off for talking in class.* 因為在課堂上說話, 老師責備了我們。**2** *BrE* to mark the things on a list with a tick to show that they are finished or have been dealt with【英】給…打勾號〔表明…已經完成或已作處理〕: *She should have ticked off Miss Vine's name on her list.* 她本應把瓦因小姐的名字從名單上勾掉。**3** *AmE informal* to annoy someone【美, 非正式】使生氣, 激怒

tick over *phr v* [I] *BrE*【英】**1** if a vehicle's engine ticks over, it works slowly without moving the vehicle〔汽車發動機〕空轉, 慢轉 **2** if a system, business etc ticks over, it continues working but without producing very much or without much happening〔某一系統、公司等〕在慢吞吞地延續; 進展緩慢; 停滯: *The business is just about ticking over.* 公司的業務無大進展。

tick·er /ˈtɪkɚ; ˈtɪkə/ *n* [C] *informal* your heart【非正式】心臟

ticker tape /ˈ·· ·/ *n* **1** [U] long narrow paper on which information is printed by a special machine〔一種特別的機器打印信息時用的窄長條〕紙帶 **2 ticker tape pa-**

rade *AmE* an occasion when someone important or famous arrives in an American city and pieces of paper are thrown from high buildings to welcome them【美】拋扔紙帶的迎賓式〔當某要人或名人抵達某城市時人們從高樓上扔出紙片的歡迎儀式〕

tick·et¹ /ˈtɪkɪt; ˈtɪkɨt/ *n* [C]

1 ▶CINEMA/BUS/TRAIN ETC 電影院/公共汽車/火車等◀ a printed piece of paper which shows that you have paid to enter a cinema, travel on a bus, plane etc〔進電影院或乘坐公共汽車、飛機等的〕票; 入場券: **theatre/train/airline ticket** *The plane ticket only cost $170.* 飛機票只花了170美元。—see also 另見 SEASON TICKET

2 ▶DRIVING OFFENCE 駕駛違章◀ a printed note ordering you to pay money because you have done something illegal while driving or parking your car〔駕車或停車時因違章而收到的〕罰款通知: *a parking ticket* 停車罰款通知

3 ▶IN SHOPS 在商店◀ a piece of paper fastened to something in a shop that shows its price, size etc〔商店裡貨物的〕標籤; 價格標籤

4 ▶ELECTION 選舉◀ [singular] *especially AmE*【尤美】**a)** a list of the people supported by a particular political party in an election〔政黨的〕候選人名單: *He withdrew his name from the Democratic ticket.* 他從民主黨候選人名單中撤了出來。**b)** the ideas that a political party supports in an election〔政黨在選舉中支持的〕政見; 綱領: *He fought the election on an openly racist ticket.* 他以公開的種族主義觀點參加選舉。

5 ticket to success/fame etc *especially AmE* a way of getting success etc【尤美】成功/出名等的手段: *The part in the movie was his ticket to stardom.* 他在這部電影裡扮演一個角色, 因而成為明星。

6 be just the ticket *old-fashioned* to be exactly what is needed【過時】正是所需要的東西 —see also 另見 MEAL TICKET, DREAM TICKET

ticket² *v* [T] **1** to fasten a small piece of paper onto something to show its price, size etc 加標籤於; 標明〔價格、尺碼等〕**2** *AmE* to give someone a ticket for parking their car in the wrong place【美】對〔某人〕發出停車違章通知單 **3 be ticketed for** to be intended for a particular use, purpose, job etc 被指定, 被指派〔為某種用途、目的、工作等〕: *These cars have been ticketed for sale abroad.* 這些汽車被指定銷往國外。

ticket tout /ˈ·· ˌ·/ *n* [C] *BrE* someone who sells tickets outside a theatre or sports ground at a high price because there are not many available【英】倒票的人, 黃牛; SCALPER *AmE*【美】

tick·ing /ˈtɪkɪŋ; ˈtɪkɪŋ/ *n* [U] a thick strong cotton cloth used for making MATTRESS and PILLOW¹ (1) covers〔用於製作牀墊套或枕套的〕結實型厚棉布

ticking off /ˌ·· ˈ·/ *n* **give sb a ticking off** *BrE informal* to tell someone that you disapprove of something they have done【英, 非正式】斥責, 責備 —see also 另見 **tick off** (TICK²)

tick·le¹ /ˈtɪkḷ; ˈtɪkəl/ *v* **1** [T] to rub someone's body gently with your fingers in order to make them laugh〔用手指輕觸某人的身體〕使覺得癢; 搔〔某人的〕癢癢 —see picture on page A20 參見A20頁圖 **2** [I,T] if something touching your body tickles you, it makes you want to rub your body because it is uncomfortable (使) 發癢; (使) 感到癢: *Mommy, this blanket tickles.* 媽媽, 這毛毯讓人感到癢癢。**3** [T] if a situation, remark etc tickles you, it amuses or pleases you〔情況、講話等〕使開心; 使高興: *I was tickled by her description of the wedding.* 我聽了她對婚禮的描述感到很開心。| **be tickled pink** (=be very pleased or amused) 非常開心, 覺得非常有趣 *She was tickled pink to see you in the paper!* 她非常高興在報紙上看到你的大名! **4 tickle sb's fancy** *old-fashioned* if something tickles your fancy, it seems interesting and makes you want to do it【過時】勾起了某人的興趣: *The idea of appearing in a film rather tickled his fancy.* 想到要在電影裡出頭露面, 這讓他躍躍欲試。**5 tickle the ivories** *old-fashioned* to play the piano【過時】彈鋼琴

tickle² *n* [singular] **1** a slight sore feeling which makes you want to cough or rub yourself; ITCH² (1) 癢, 發癢: *I've got a tickle in my throat that won't go away.* 我的嗓子發癢, 總好不了。**2 give sb a tickle** to rub someone lightly with your fingers in order to make them laugh 搔某人癢癢

tick·lish /ˈtɪklɪʃ; ˈtɪklɪʃ/ *adj* **1** someone who is ticklish is sensitive to tickling 對癢敏感的, 怕癢的 **2** *informal* a ticklish situation or problem must be dealt with very carefully, especially because you may offend or upset people【非正式】〔情況或問題〕需小心對付的, 棘手的: *You'll have the ticklish task of explaining to Rita why she hasn't been promoted.* 你得來處理這個棘手的問題, 向麗塔解釋她為甚麼沒有得到晉升。—**ticklishly** *adv* —**ticklishness** *n* [U]

tick-tack-toe /ˌ· · ˈ·/ *n* [U] *AmE* a children's game in which two players draw X's or O's in a pattern of nine squares【美】三連畫圈打叉遊戲, 劃井遊戲〔一種由兩人在九個方格內填寫"×"或"○"的兒童遊戲〕; NOUGHTS AND CROSSES *BrE*【英】

tick-tock /ˌtɪk ˈtɑk; ˌtɪk ˈtɒk/ *n* [singular] the noise that a large clock makes when it ticks〔大鐘發出的〕滴答聲

ticky-tacky /ˌtɪkɪ ˈtækɪ; ˌtɪki ˈtæki◂/ also 又作 **ticky-tack** /-ˈtæk; -ˈtæk/ *n* [U] *AmE informal* a material, especially for building, that is cheap and of low quality【美, 非正式】廉價劣質的材料〔尤指建築材料〕—**ticky-tacky** *adj*

tid·al /ˈtaɪdḷ; ˈtaɪdl/ *adj* connected with the regular rising and falling of the sea 潮汐的, 潮水的: *a tidal pool* 潮潭

tidal wave /ˈ·· ·/ *n* [C] **1** a very large ocean wave that flows over the land and destroys things 海嘯 **2** a very large amount of a particular kind of feeling or activity happening at one time〔感情或活動的〕浪潮: *a tidal wave of public condemnation* 公眾譴責的浪潮

tid·bit /ˈtɪdˌbɪt; ˈtɪdˌbɪt/ *n* [C] *AmE*【美】**1** a small piece of food that tastes good 少量的精美食品, 珍饈; TITBIT *BrE*【英】**2** a small piece of interesting information, news etc 花絮, 趣聞; TITBIT *BrE*【英】: *tidbits of gossip* 閒話趣聞

tid·dler /ˈtɪdlɚ; ˈtɪdlə/ *n* [C] *BrE informal* a very small fish【英, 非正式】很小的魚

tid·dly, tiddley /ˈtɪdḷɪ; ˈtɪdli/ *adj BrE informal*【英, 非正式】**1** slightly drunk 微醉的 **2** very small 很小的: *a tiddly little insect* 一隻很小的昆蟲

tid·dly·winks /ˈtɪdḷɪˌwɪŋks; ˈtɪdliwɪŋks/ *n* [U] a children's game in which you try to make small round pieces of plastic jump into a cup by pressing one edge with a larger piece 彈塑料片遊戲〔一種以大塑料圓片壓小塑料圓片, 使其彈跳落入杯中的兒童遊戲〕

tide¹ /taɪd; taɪd/ *n* **1** [C usually singular 一般用單數] the regular rising and lowering of the level of the sea 海潮, 潮汐: *driftwood on the beach, brought in by the tide* 被潮水帶到沙灘上的漂木 | **the tide is in/out** (=the sea is at a high or low level) 潮漲/潮落 —see also 另見 HIGH TIDE, LOW TIDE **2** [C] a current of water caused by the tide 潮水: *Strong tides make swimming dangerous.* 大的潮水使游泳很危險。**3** [C usually singular 一般用單數] the way in which events, opinions etc are developing 潮流, 趨勢: **the tide turns against** (=people's opinions change so that they no longer approve of someone or something)〔輿論〕趨勢朝不利於…的方向轉變 *The tide of public opinion seems to be turning against the President.* 公眾輿論的趨勢看來在朝不利於總統的方向轉變。| **swim with/against the tide** (=support or oppose what most people think) 隨大流/反潮流 | **stem the tide** (=prevent something from developing and getting worse) 阻止…的進一步惡化 *efforts to stem the tide of hysteria caused by the shootings* 努力阻止槍殺引起的歇斯底里惡化 **4** [singular] a large number of people or things moving along together 潮水般的人流; 洪流: *the tide of refugees crossing the border* 跨越邊界的難民流 | **stem the tide** (=stop this movement) 阻止人流; 阻止潮流 **5 Christmastide/eveningtide/morningtide etc** *old use* a particular time of the year or day【舊】聖誕節期間/晚上時間/早晨時光

tide²

tide sb **over** *phr v* [T] to help someone through a difficult period 幫助〔某人〕渡過難關: *I can give you enough money to tide you over until next month.* 我可以給你足夠的錢讓你堅持到下個月。

tide-mark /ˈ· ·/ *n* [C] **1** a mark left on the shore by the sea, that shows how high the water was〔潮水在海岸上留下的最高〕潮痕 **2** *BrE informal* a dirty mark left around the inside of a bath that shows how high the water was【英, 非正式】〔浴缸裡水位留下的〕垢痕

tide pool /ˈ· ·/ *n* [C] *AmE* a small area of water left among rocks by the sea when the tide goes out【美】〔潮水退走後在礁石間留下的〕潮水潭; ROCK POOL *BrE*【英】

tide·wa·ter /ˈtaɪdˌwɔtə; ˈtaɪdˌwɔːtə/ *n* **1** [U] water that flows onto the land when the tide rises to a very high level〔大潮時湧上陸地的〕潮水 **2** [U] water in the parts of rivers that are affected by tides〔江河裡的〕潮水 **3** [C] *AmE* an area of land at or near the sea coast【美】沿海陸地, 濱海地區

tide·way /ˈtaɪdˌwe; ˈtaɪdweɪ/ *n* [C] *AmE*【美】**1** a narrow area of water through which the tide flows〔潮水流經的〕潮路 **2** a strong current flowing through a tideway〔經潮路流過的〕強潮流

tid·ings /ˈtaɪdɪŋz; ˈtaɪdɪŋz/ *n* [plural] *old use* news【舊】消息: **good/glad tidings** (=good news) 佳音, 喜訊

ti·dy¹ /ˈtaɪdɪ; ˈtaɪdi/ *adj especially BrE*【尤英】**1** a room, house, desk etc that is tidy is neatly arranged with everything in the right place〔房間、房子、書桌等〕整潔的, 整齊的: **neat and tidy** *Ellen's room always looks neat and tidy.* 艾倫的房間看上去總是乾淨整潔。**2** someone who is tidy keeps their house, clothes etc neat and clean〔人〕整潔的, 愛整齊的: *I've always been a naturally tidy person.* 我天生愛乾淨, 始終如此。**3 a tidy sum/profit** *informal* a large amount of money【非正式】一大筆錢/利潤: *We sold the house for a tidy sum and moved south.* 我們把那座房子賣了一大筆錢, 然後移居到了南方。—**tidily** *adv* —**tidiness** *n* [U]

tidy² also 又作 **tidy up** *v* [I,T] *especially BrE* to make a place look tidy【尤英】使整潔, 整理, 收拾: *You're not allowed to go out until you tidy up your room.* 你在整理好房間之前, 不准出去。| **tidy up after** (=tidy a place after someone has made it untidy) 收拾被人弄得很髒亂的地方 *I'm tired of tidying up after you boys.* 你們這些男孩子常常把這裡弄得又髒又亂, 我真懶得去收拾。

tidy sth **away** *phr v* [T] *BrE* to put something back in the place where it should be【英】收拾好放回原處: *Let's tidy these papers away.* 我們把這些文件收拾起來吧。

tidy³ *n* [C] **desk/car/sink tidy** *BrE* a container for putting small objects in, used to keep your desk, car etc tidy【英】桌子上/汽車裡/洗滌槽旁邊用來放零星雜物的容器

2 3 **tie¹** /taɪ; taɪ/ *v*

1 ▶STRING/ROPE 線/繩索◀ a) [T] to fasten one thing to another with a piece of string, rope etc〔用線、繩索等〕繫, 紮, 拴, 捆: **tie sth to/behind/onto etc** *Tie this label onto your suitcase.* 把這個標籤拴在衣箱上。| **tie sb to sth** *They tied him to a lamp-post and beat him up.* 他們把他捆在一根燈柱上, 然後狠狠地揍他。| **tie sb's hands/feet** (=tie them together) 捆住某人的手/腳 **b)** also 又作 **tie up** [T] to fasten a piece of string, rope etc around something to keep it closed or keep all its parts together 把…捆起來[縛在一起]: **tie sth with sth** *The package had been tied with strong green string.* 那包東西是用結實的綠色繩子捆起來的。| **[+around/over/under etc]** *I'll just tie my hair back out of my eyes.* 我只需把頭髮繫在後邊, 不擋住眼睛就行。| **tie sth in bunches/bundles etc** *tie the sticks up in bundles* 把那些棍子一束一束捆起來 | **tie your hair back** (=fasten your hair to the back of your head so that it does not reach your face) 把頭髮繫在腦後 **c)** [T] to make a knot in a piece of string, rope etc, for example to fasten shoes or other clothes 把〔線、繩索等〕打結; 繫上: **tie sb's shoelaces** *Can you tie your shoelaces by yourself?* 你自己會繫鞋帶嗎? | **tie a knot/bow** *She pulled the ribbon tightly and tied a bow.* 她把絲帶拉緊, 打了一個蝴蝶結。**d)** [I] to be fastened using pieces of string, RIBBON (1) etc 用帶子、絲帶等繫牢: *The dress ties at the back.* 這件連衣裙是在背後繫帶的。

2 ▶GAME/COMPETITION 比賽/競賽◀ also 又作 **be tied** [I] if two players, teams etc tie or are tied in a game or competition, they finish it with an equal number of points〔在比賽或競賽中雙方〕得分相同, 打成平局: **[+with]** *At the end of the season, we were tied with the Tigers.* 在本賽季結束時, 我們與泰格爾隊得分相同。| **tie for first/second place** *Woosnam and Lyle tied for fourth place on 264.* 伍斯納姆和萊爾並列第四, 總桿數都是264。

3 be tied to a) to be connected with something or dependent on it 聯繫在一起; 依附於: *The flat is tied to the job.* 住房是與工作聯繫在一起的。**b)** to be unable to leave the situation, place, job etc that you are in 束縛, 約束, 限制: *a housewife tied to the kitchen all day* 整天被束縛在廚房裡的家庭主婦

4 tie the knot *informal* to get married【非正式】結婚

5 tie yourself (up) in knots *BrE informal* to become very confused when you are trying to explain something【英, 非正式】〔解釋某事時〕自己給自己搞糊塗了, 自己把自己難住了

6 sb's hands are tied if someone's hands are tied, they cannot do what they want because of particular conditions, rules etc〔因某種條件、規則等〕某人無法做想做的事: *Team manager, Ron Jones, would like to buy some new players, but his hands are tied at the moment.* 球隊經理羅恩·瓊斯想買幾名新球員, 但現在不能隨心所欲。

7 tie one on *AmE slang* to get drunk【美俚】喝醉

tie sb **down** *phr v* [T] **1** to stop someone from being free to do the things they want to do 束縛, 牽制〔某人〕: *He wouldn't marry her because he didn't want to feel tied down.* 他不願意娶她, 因為他不想有被拴住的感覺。**2 tie yourself down (to sth)** to make a promise or agreement that restricts what you do 使自己受到〔許諾或協議的〕約束: *I'm happy to do the job, but I don't want to tie myself down to a particular date.* 我很樂意做這份工作, 不過我不想給自己定下一個具體的日期。

tie in *phr v* [I+with] **1** if one idea or statement ties in with another one, it helps to prove the same thing 同…一致, 與…相符: *Marsden's conclusions tie in with our theory perfectly.* 馬斯登的結論與我們的理論完全相符。**2** to happen at the same time as something else 與…同時發生: *We've planned the broadcast to tie in with the bicentenary celebrations.* 我們已計劃使這次廣播與二百週年紀念活動同時進行。

tie up *phr v*

1 ▶PERSON 人◀ [T **tie** sb ↔ **up**] to tie someone's arms, legs etc so that they cannot move 把〔某人〕捆綁起來: *The intruders tied Kurt up and put him in the closet.* 闖進庫爾特家裡的強盜把他捆綁起來, 然後關進壁櫥裡面。

2 ▶OBJECT 物體◀ [T **tie** sth ↔ **up**] to fasten something together by using string or rope 把〔某物〕捆綁起來

3 ▶BUSY 忙◀ be tied up to be so busy that you cannot do anything else 忙得脫不開身: *I can't see you tomorrow – I'm going to be tied up all day.* 我明天沒法見你——我會一整天忙得脫不開身的。

4 ▶TRAFFIC 交通◀ be tied up *especially AmE* if traffic is tied up, it is blocked and cannot move freely【尤美】〔交通〕阻塞, 動彈不得

5 ▶MONEY 錢◀ be tied up if your money is tied up in something, it is all being used for that thing and you cannot use it for anything else〔錢用於某項事情上而〕不能動用: **[+in]** *My money's all tied up in the house.* 我

的錢全投在房子上而不能動用。

6 ▶ARRANGEMENTS 安排◀ [T **tie** sth ↔ **up**] to finish arranging all the details of something such as an agreement or a plan 訂妥〔協議或計劃〕; 安排好〔細節〕: *We'd better tie up the details with a solicitor.* 我們最好讓律師把這些細節安排好。

7 be tied up with to be very closely connected with something 與…有密切聯係: *Christianity in Africa is tied up with its colonial past.* 非洲的基督教與非洲的殖民歷史有密切的關係。

8 tie up loose ends to do the things that are necessary in order to finish a piece of work 做收尾的工作: *I just have to tie up a few loose ends before I go on vacation.* 我只要處理完幾件收尾的工作就去度假。

9 ▶BOAT 船◀ [I] to tie a boat to something 〔船〕繫泊: *We tied up alongside a barge.* 我們把船繫泊在一艘駁船旁邊。

tie² *n* [C]

1 ▶MEN'S CLOTHES 男式服裝◀ a long narrow piece of cloth that you wear around your neck, tied in a special knot in front 領結, 領帶; —see also 另見 BLACK-TIE, BOW TIE

2 ▶CONNECTION/RELATIONSHIP 聯繫/關係◀ a relationship between two people, groups, or countries that connects them 〔人與人、團體與團體、國家與國家之間的〕關係, 聯繫: *close economic ties between the two countries* 那兩個國家之間密切的經濟聯繫

3 ▶FOR CLOSING STH 用來捆紮某物◀ a piece of string, wire etc used to fasten or close something such as a bag 〔用來捆紮某物的〕繩子, 帶子

4 ▶RESULT 結果◀ [usually singular 一般用單數] the result of a game, competition, or election in which two or more people get the same number of points, votes etc 〔比賽、競賽或選舉中〕分數相同; 票數相同; 平局, 平手: **end in a tie** *The match ended in a tie.* 這場比賽以平局告終。

5 ▶GAME 體育比賽◀ *BrE* one game, especially of football, that is part of a larger competition 【英】較大型比賽中的一場〔尤指足球賽中的〕: *the fourth round tie of the FA cup* 足總杯第四輪比賽

6 ▶PREVENT YOU FROM DOING STH 阻止做某事◀ something that forces you to stay in one place, job etc or prevents you from being free to do what you want 束縛, 羈絆; 牽累, 累贅: *If you're the sort of person who enjoys travelling, young children can be a tie.* 如果你是那種喜好旅遊的人, 小孩子可能是個累贅。

7 ▶RAILWAY 鐵路◀ *AmE* a heavy piece of wood or metal supporting a railway track 【美】軌枕, 枕木; SLEEPER (4) *BrE* 【英】

tie·break·er /ˋtaɪˌbrekɚ; ˈtaɪˌbreɪkə/ also 又作 **tie·break** /ˋtaɪbrek; ˈtaɪbreɪk/ *n* [C] **1** an additional question in a game or QUIZ, used to decide who will win when two people have the same number of points 〔遊戲或搶答賽的〕決勝題 **2** the final game of a set (SET² (5)) in tennis when each player has won six games 〔網球比賽中各勝六局後的〕決勝局

tied cot·tage /ˌ· ˈ··/ *n* [C] *BrE* a house that a farm worker rents from a farmer while he is working in that farm 【英】〔農場工人受雇於農場期間從農場主那兒租住的〕契約屋, 雇工農舍

tied house /ˌ· ˈ·/ *n* [C] *BrE* a PUB that can only sell the beer made by a particular company 【英】〔只出售某公司所產啤酒的〕特約經銷酒館

tie-dye /ˈ· ·/ *v* [T] to tie string around parts of a piece of material and colour it with DYE (=coloured liquid) in order to make a special pattern 紮染〔把布料捆紮後再用染料染色以形成特別的圖案〕—see picture on page A16 參見 A16 頁圖

tie-in /ˈ· ·/ *n* [C] a product such as a record, book, or toy that is connected with a new film, TV show etc 關聯性產品〔指與一部新電影、電視劇等有關的唱片、圖書或玩具〕

tie-pin /ˈ· ·/ *n* [C] a thing used for keeping a man's TIE² (1) fastened to his shirt or as a decoration 領帶別針

tier /tɪr; tɪə/ *n* [C] **1** one of several rows of seats that rise one behind another 〔階梯式座位的〕一排, 一列 **2** one of several levels in an organization or system 〔機構或系統的〕層次; 等級: *The company has three tiers of management.* 該公司有三個管理層次。**3 two-tiered/three-tiered etc** having two, three etc layers 有兩層的/有三層的等: *a three-tiered wedding cake* 三層的婚禮蛋糕

tie-up /ˈ· ·/ *n* [C] *informal* 【非正式】 **1** an agreement to become business partners 〔公司的〕聯營; 聯合: **[+with]** *IBM's tie-up with Auspex System Inc* IBM與Auspex 系統合夥公司的聯營 **2** *BrE* a close connection between two or more things, especially when one causes the other 【英】〔因果〕關係, 聯繫: **[+between]** *the tie-up between class interests and politics* 階級利益與政治之間的關係 **3** *AmE* a situation in which traffic is prevented from moving or there is a problem which prevents a system or plan from working 【美】〔交通的〕阻塞; 〔系統或計劃的〕停頓, 停滯不前 —see also 另見 **tie up** (TIE¹)

tiff /tɪf; tɪf/ *n* [C] a slight argument between two people who are in love 〔情侶之間的〕口角, 吵嘴: *Dave's had a tiff with his girlfriend.* 戴夫同女友吵了嘴。

tif·fin /ˋtɪfɪn; ˈtɪfən/ *n* [U] *BrE old use or IndE* a light meal eaten in the morning or the middle of the day 【英舊或印】上午的茶點小吃; 午餐

ti·ger /ˋtaɪgɚ; ˈtaɪgə/ *n* [C] a large strong animal that has yellow and black lines on its body and is a member of the cat family 虎, 老虎 —see also 另見 **paper tiger** (PAPER² (4))

tiger lil·y /ˈ·· ˌ··/ *n* [C] a LILY (=flower) that has large orange flowers with black spots 卷丹(花)

tiger moth /ˈ·· ·/ *n* [C] a type of MOTH (=flying insect) with black stripes on its wings 燈蛾

tight¹ /taɪt; taɪt/ *adj* [S2] [W3]

1 ▶CLOTHES 衣服◀ fitting a part of your body very closely, especially in a way that is uncomfortable 緊身的, 貼身的: *tight trousers* 緊身褲 | *My shoes were far too tight and I was in agony by the time I got home.* 我的鞋太夾腳, 等我走回家時, 已痛苦不堪了。| **be a tight fit** (=only just fits someone) 剛好合身 *The top is rather a tight fit.* 上面剛剛合身。—see also 另見 SKIN-TIGHT, TIGHT-FITTING

2 ▶PULLED/STRETCHED 拉/繃◀ string, wire, cloth etc that is tight has been pulled or stretched firmly so that it is straight or cannot move 拉緊的, 繃緊的: **pull sth tight** *Pull the thread tight.* 把線拉緊。| *The bandage must be tight enough to stop the bleeding.* 繃帶必須拉緊, 才能止住流血。

3 ▶FIRMLY FIXED/FASTENED 固定/拴或繫得很牢◀ something such as a screw or lid that is tight is firmly fixed and is difficult to move 緊的, 牢的: *Check that the screws are tight.* 查看一下螺絲釘是否擰緊了。

4 a tight hold/grip a firm hold on something 緊緊抓住: *His mother kept a tight hold on his hand.* 他的母親一直緊緊地抓住他的手。

5 ▶STRICT CONTROL 嚴格控制◀ controlled very strictly and firmly 〔控制〕嚴格的, 嚴密的: *Spending is kept within very tight limits.* 開銷受到非常嚴格的限制。| *Security was very tight for the president's visit.* 為了總統的來訪, 保安工作做得非常嚴密。| **keep a tight rein on** (=control someone or something very strictly) 嚴格控制住〔某人或某物〕| **run a tight ship** (=manage a company, organization etc very effectively by having strict rules) 對〔公司、組織機構等〕嚴格管理

6 ▶MONEY 錢◀ *informal* 【非正式】 **a)** if money is tight, you do not have enough of it 手頭緊的, 手頭拮据的: **money is tight/things are tight** *Money was tight and he needed a job badly.* 他手頭很拮据, 急需找到工作。**b)** someone who is tight is not generous and tries very hard to avoid spending money; MEAN² (2) 花錢小氣的, 吝嗇的 —see also 另見 TIGHT-FISTED

7 ►LITTLE TIME 少量時間◄ if time is tight, it is difficult for you to do everything you need to do in the time available〔時間〕緊的: **tight schedule/deadline** (=one that gives you very little time to do or finish something) 排得滿滿的日程表/緊張的期限 *a tight deadline* 緊張的期限 | *It'll be a bit tight, but we should just get there and back in time.* 時間是有點緊，但我們應該可以趕到那兒並及時地趕回來。
8 ►LITTLE SPACE 少量空間◄ if space is tight, there is only just enough space to fit something into a place 填滿的, 塞滿的, 擠滿的: **a tight squeeze/fit** (=a situation where there is only just enough space for things or people to fit) 擠得滿滿的/貼得緊緊的狀況 *It was a tight squeeze, but somehow we all got into the car.* 已經擠得滿滿的，但無論怎樣我們還是全都擠進了車裡。
9 ►CLOSE TOGETHER 緊密地在一起◄ placed or standing very close together 緊密的, 緊緊的: *She wore her hair in a tight bun.* 她把頭髮緊緊地盤成一個髻。
10 ►CLOSE RELATIONSHIP 親密關係◄ a tight group of people, countries etc have a close relationship with each other and are closely connected with each other〔人與人、國家與國家等之間〕關係密切的
11 ►CHEST/STOMACH ETC 胸/胃等◄ feeling painful or uncomfortable, because you are ill or worried 憋悶的; 不適的: *He had been complaining of a tight chest and sore throat.* 他當時一直在抱怨胸口悶、嗓子疼。
12 ►SMILE/EXPRESSION/VOICE ETC 笑容/表情/聲音等◄ showing that you are annoyed, or upset 顯得生氣的; 不高興的: *Her mother gave a tight, forced smile.* 她的母親很不自然地勉強笑了一下。—see also 另見 TIGHT-LIPPED
13 ►BEND/TURN 轉彎/轉向◄ very curved so that it turns very quickly to another direction 轉得很急的: *Careful now, there's a tight bend coming up.* 現在小心點，馬上有個急轉彎。
14 **in a tight corner/spot** *informal* in a difficult situation【非正式】處境困難的: *I'm always willing to help a friend in a tight spot.* 我總是願意幫助處境困難的朋友。
15 ►PLAY/PERFORMANCE 表演/演出◄ performed very exactly, with no unnecessary pauses 準確的, 緊湊的, 一氣呵成的: *a tight, well-rehearsed production* 經過充分排練, 一氣呵成的演出
16 ►GAME/COMPETITION 比賽/競賽◄ a tight game, competition etc is one in which the teams, competitors etc all play well and it is not easy to win 緊張激烈的; 不相上下的, 勢均力敵的: *It was a tight match, with the winning goal scored in the final minute.* 那是一場難分難解的比賽, 在最後一分鐘才打進決定勝負的一球。
17 ►DRUNK 醉的◄ [never before noun 不用於名詞前] *old-fashioned informal* drunk【過時, 非正式】喝醉的 —see also 另見 AIRTIGHT, WATERTIGHT —**tightly** *adv*: *Marie held the baby tightly in her arms.* 瑪麗把嬰兒緊緊地抱在懷中。—**tightness** *n* [U]

tight² *adv* very firmly or closely; tightly 緊緊地, 牢牢地: **hold tight** *Hold tight to the safety rail.* 把安全桿抓緊。| **keep sth tight shut** *I kept my eyes tight shut and hoped they would go away.* 我緊閉雙眼，希望他們會走開。—see also 另見 **sit tight** (SIT (5)), **sleep tight** (SLEEP[1] (4))

tight·en /ˈtaɪtn̩; ˈtaɪtn/ also 又作 **tighten up** *v* **1** [T] to close or fasten something firmly by turning it 使變緊; 使更牢固: *Tighten up the screws.* 把螺絲擰緊。| *You'll need to tighten the lid on the jar.* 你得把罐子上的蓋擰緊。**2** [I,T] if you tighten a rope, wire etc, or if it tightens, it is stretched or pulled so that it becomes tight 繃緊, 拉緊〔繩子、線等〕: *When you tighten guitar strings the note gets higher.* 你把吉他的弦繃緊一點，音就會變高。**3** [I, T] to become stiff or make a part of your body become stiff (使)〔身體的某一部分〕變得僵硬, 變得僵直: *I can feel my neck tightening up.* 我能感覺到自己的脖子正變得僵硬起來。**4** [T] to make a rule, law, or system more strict 使〔規則、法律或制度〕更嚴格; 加緊, 加強: **tighten up on** *measures aimed at tightening up on security* 旨在加強保安的措施 **5 tighten your hold/grip on** to hold someone or something more firmly 更緊地抓住〔某人或某物〕: *Sarah tightened her grip on my arm.* 莎拉更緊地抓住我的手臂。**6 tighten your belt** *informal* to try to spend less money than you used to【非正式】勒緊褲帶; 設法更節儉地過日子: *When Maureen lost her job, we had to tighten our belts.* 莫琳失業之後, 我們不得不勒緊褲帶過日子。

tight-fist·ed /ˌtaɪt ˈfɪstɪd; ˌtaɪt ˈfɪstɪ̈d◄/ *adj informal* not generous with money; STINGY【非正式】〔花錢〕非常小氣的, 吝嗇的 —**tight-fistedness** *n* [U]

tight-fit·ting /ˌ· ˈ··◄/ *adj* fitting very closely or tightly〔衣服〕緊身的; 貼身的;〔蓋子〕嚴密的, 嚴實的: *a tight-fitting skirt* 一條緊身的女裙 | *saucepan with a tight-fitting lid* 蓋子嚴實的深平底鍋

tight-knit /ˌ· ˈ·◄/ *adj* [only before noun 僅用於名詞前] **1** a tight-knit group of people are closely connected with each other 緊密團結的: *a tight-knit island community* 一個緊密團結的島上社區 **2** *AmE* a tight-knit plan is very carefully arranged so that nothing can go wrong【美】〔計劃〕周密的

tight-lipped /ˌtaɪt ˈlɪpt; ˌtaɪt ˈlɪpt◄/ *adj* **1** unwilling to talk about something 不願說話的, 緘默的: *Diplomats are remaining tight-lipped about the negotiations.* 外交官們對談判的情況仍然閉口不談。**2** with your lips tightly pressed together because you are angry〔因為生氣〕緊閉雙唇的

tightly-knit /ˌ·· ˈ·◄/ *adj* TIGHT-KNIT 緊密團結的; 計劃周密的

tight·rope /ˈtaɪtˌrop; ˈtaɪt-rəʊp/ *n* [C] **1** a rope or wire high above the ground that someone walks along in a CIRCUS (1)〔馬戲團表演用的〕鋼絲, 繃索 **2 walk a tightrope** to be in a difficult situation in which you must be careful about what you say or do 走鋼絲〔比喻處境困難, 言行必須謹慎〕

tights /taɪts; taɪts/ *n* [plural] **1** *BrE* a piece of women's clothing that fits closely around your feet and legs and up to your waist, made of very thin material【英】女用連褲襪; PANTYHOSE *AmE*【美】—see picture on page A17 參見 A17 頁圖 **2** a similar piece of clothing that is coloured and cannot be seen through, worn especially by dancers〔尤指舞蹈演員穿的〕緊身衣

tight·wad /ˈtaɪtˌwɑd; ˈtaɪtwɒd/ *n* [C] *informal especially AmE* someone who hates to spend or give money【非正式, 尤美】吝嗇鬼, 守財奴: *My allowance is very small – Dad's a real tightwad.* 我的零用錢很少 —— 爸爸真是個吝嗇鬼。

ti·gress /ˈtaɪgrɪs; ˈtaɪgrɪ̈s/ *n* [C] a female tiger 母虎, 雌老虎

tike /taɪk; taɪk/ *n* [C] another spelling of TYKE tyke的另一種拼法

til, 'til /tɪl; tɪl/ a short form of 縮略式= TILL[1]

til·de /ˈtɪldə; ˈtɪldə/ *n* [C] a mark (˜) placed over the letter 'n' in Spanish to show that it is pronounced /nj/〔西班牙語中置於字母 n 之上的〕顎化音符號

tile¹ /taɪl; taɪl/ *n* **1** [C] a flat square piece of baked clay or other material, used for covering roofs, floors etc〔屋頂、地板等上面用的〕瓷磚, 地磚: *bathroom tiles* 浴室瓷磚 **2** [C] a thin curved piece of baked clay used for covering roofs〔蓋屋頂用的〕瓦, 瓦片 **3 go out on the tiles** *BrE informal* to go out drinking, dancing etc for enjoyment【英, 非正式】縱情玩樂, 花天酒地

tile² *v* [T] to cover a roof, floor etc with tiles 鋪瓦於〔屋頂〕; 貼地磚於〔地面等〕—**tiled** *adj*: *a tiled floor* 鋪了地磚的地面 —**tiler** *n* [C]

til·ing /ˈtaɪlɪŋ; ˈtaɪlɪŋ/ *n* [U] a set of tiles used to cover a roof, floor etc〔一套〕瓦; 瓷磚; 地磚

till¹ /tɪl; tɪl/ *prep, conjunction especially spoken* until【尤口】直到: *I didn't learn to drive till I was thirty three.* 我直到三十三歲才學開車。| *The shop's open till nine o'clock* *most evenings.* 這家商店大多數晚上要營業到九點。

till² /tɪl; tɪl/ *n* [C] *BrE* a machine used in shops, restaurants etc for calculating the amount of you have to pay, and storing the money【英】〔商店、飯館等的〕現金出納機; REGISTER[1] (5) *AmE*【美】—see also 另見 **be caught with your fingers in the till** (FINGER[1] (8))

till³ *v* [T] *old use* to prepare land for growing crops【舊】耕〔地〕, 犁〔地〕

till·age /ˈtɪlɪdʒ; ˈtɪlɪdʒ/ *n* [U] *old use* the activity of preparing land for growing crops【舊】耕作, 耕地

til·ler /ˈtɪlə; ˈtɪlə/ *n* [C] a long handle fastened to the RUDDER (=part that controls the direction) of a boat〔控制船舶方向的〕舵柄 —see picture at 參見 YACHT 圖

tilt¹ /tɪlt; tɪlt/ *v* **1** [I,T] to move or make something move into a position where one side is higher than the other (使) 傾斜, (使) 翹起: *The table tilted suddenly, spilling all the drinks.* 桌子突然傾斜, 飲料全都灑了出來。**2** [T] to move your head or chin upwards or to the side 仰起〔頭, 下巴〕; 使〔頭, 下巴〕側偏, 偏向: *Jodi tilted her head and looked thoughtful.* 喬迪仰起頭, 一副若有所思的樣子。**3** [T] to influence an opinion or situation so that people prefer one person, belief etc 使傾向於, 使偏向於: *This new evidence may tilt the balance of opinion in his favour.* 這一新的證據可能使輿論有利於他。

tilt at sb *phr v* [T] **1** to attack someone by what you say or write 抨擊〔某人〕 **2** *old use* to move quickly on a horse towards someone, in order to attack them with a LANCE【舊】騎馬持矛衝向〔某人〕

tilt² *n* **1 at full tilt** as fast as possible 全速地: *We rode down the hill at full tilt.* 我們騎着馬全速衝下山去。**2** [C,U] a movement or position in which one side of something is higher than the other 傾斜, 傾側 **3** [C] a spoken or written attack on someone or something〔口頭或文字的〕抨擊, 攻擊

tim·ber /ˈtɪmbə; ˈtɪmbə/ *n* **1** [U] *especially BrE* wood used for building or making things, or the trees that produce this wood【尤英】木材, 原木; 〔可作木材的〕樹木; LUMBER[2] (2) *AmE*【美】**2** [C] a wooden beam, especially one that forms part of the main structure of a house〔尤指構成房屋主要結構的〕棟木, 大梁 **3 timber!** *spoken* used to warn people that a tree being cut down is about to fall【口】倒啦! 避開!〔用來警告人們所伐樹木快要倒下〕—see also 另見 HALF-TIMBERED W3

tim·ber·line /ˈtɪmbəˌlaɪn; ˈtɪmbəlaɪn/ *n* [singular] *technical*【術語】**1** the height above the level of the sea beyond which trees will not grow 林木線〔指樹木生長的海拔高度上限〕 **2** the northern or southern limit in the world beyond which trees will not grow 樹木生長線〔指南半球或北半球樹木生長的緯度上限〕

tim·bre /ˈtɪmbə; ˈtæmbə/ *n* [C,U] the quality of the sound made by a particular instrument or voice〔樂器或嗓音的〕音質, 音品, 音色

tim·brel /ˈtɪmbrəl; ˈtɪmbrəl/ *n* [C] *old use* a TAMBOURINE【舊】鈴鼓

time¹ /taɪm; taɪm/ *n*

① TIME 時間
② TIME SHOWN ON A CLOCK 時刻
③ OCCASION 場合
④ HOW OFTEN 頻度
⑤ TIME WHEN STH HAPPENS 某事發生的時間
⑥ TIME WHEN STH SHOULD HAPPEN 某事應發生的時間
⑦ SUITABLE TIME 合適的時機
⑧ PERIOD OF TIME 一段時間
⑨ GOOD TIME/BAD TIME ETC 好時光/壞時光等
⑩ PERIOD IN HISTORY 歷史階段
⑪ TIME NEEDED TO DO STH 做某事所需的時間
⑫ AVAILABLE TIME 可利用的時間
⑬ SLOWLY/QUICKLY 慢/快
⑭ MODERN 現代
⑮ IN TIME 及時
⑯ HOW MANY 多少
⑰ COMPARISONS 比較
⑱ GRADUALLY/EVENTUALLY 逐漸/最終
⑲ MUSIC 音樂
⑳ LIKE/DISLIKE 喜歡/不喜歡
㉑ OTHER MEANINGS 其他意思

① TIME 時間

1 [U] something that is measured in minutes, hours, years etc using clocks 時間: *a machine that can travel through time* 可以穿越時間的機器 | *The basic unit of time, the second, was redefined in 1967.* 1967年, 時間的基本單位——秒——被重新作出定義。| **time passes/goes by** *Time goes by so quickly these days.* 這些天時間過得真快。

② TIME SHOWN ON A CLOCK 時刻

2 [singular] a particular point in time shown on a clock in hours and minutes 時間, 時刻〔指鐘錶上顯示的具體時間〕: *What time is it?* 幾點了? | **what time do you make it?** *BrE*【英】**/what time do you have?** *AmE*【美】(=used to ask someone with a watch what time it is) 你的錶幾點了? | **have you got the time?** *BrE*【英】**/do you have the time?** *AmE*【美】(=used to ask someone if they know what time it is) 你知道幾點鐘了嗎? | **tell the time** *BrE*【英】**/tell time** *AmE*【美】(=be able to know what time it is by looking at a clock) 講出鐘錶上的時間, 識鐘錶: *He's ten years old and he still can't tell the time.* 他已經十歲了, 但還認不出鐘錶上的時間。| **look at the time** *spoken* (=used when it is later than you thought it was)【口】看看已經幾點了〔表示已經很晚了〕 *Oh look at the time – we'd better get moving.* 哦, 瞧已經幾點了——我們最好動身吧。

3 keep good/perfect etc time if a clock or watch keeps good or perfect time, it works very well〔鐘錶〕走得很準

4 ►IN PART OF THE WORLD 世界某地◄ [U] the time in one particular part of the world, or the time used in one particular area〔某一特定地區的〕時間: *Eastern Standard Time* 東部標準時間 | *British Summer Time* 英國夏令時間 | **local time** *We will be arriving in New York at 3 am local time.* 我們將在當地時間凌晨三點抵達紐約。

③ OCCASION 場合

5 [C] an occasion when something happens or someone does something 次, 回: **every/each time** *It was the only time I ever saw her lose her temper.* 那是唯一一次我看見她發脾氣。| *Every time I meet her I always forget her name.* 每次見到她時, 我總忘了她的名字。| **next time** *Give us a call next time you're in town.* 下次你進城時, 請給我們來個電話。| **this time** *I won't report you this time but don't do it again.* 我這次不告發你, 但別再做這事了。| **the last time** *When was the last time you were ill?* 你最近一次生病是在甚麼時候? | **one time** (=once) 有一次 *I came home one time and found that someone had smashed all the windows.* 我有一次回家, 發現有人把所有窗戶都給砸碎了。

④ HOW OFTEN 頻度

6 three/four/ten etc times used to say how often something happens 三次/四次/十次等: *I must have called you about five times.* 我差不多給你打過五次電話。| *How many times have you visited the US?* 你去過美國多少次? | *We visit him two or three times a month.* 我們每個月去看他兩三次。

7 nine times out of ten/99 times out of 100 used to say that something is almost always true or almost always happens 十之八九: *Nine times out of ten she's right.* 她十之八九是對的。

8 all the time continuously or very often 一直, 始終; 十分經常: *It's a really useful book – I use it all the time.* 真是一本很有用的書 ── 我總在用它。

9 most of the time very often or almost always 大多數時候: *Most of the time they seem to just sit around watching TV.* 大多數時候他們似乎只是閒坐着看電視。

10 the whole time if something happens the whole time, especially something annoying, it happens continuously 老是, 總是〔尤指惱人的事〕: *The baby was crying the whole time.* 那嬰兒老是哭個不停。

11 time after time/time and time again happening often over a long period, especially in a way that is annoying 反覆多次; 一而再, 再而三: *I've told her time after time not to bring that dog in here.* 我已反覆多次告訴她不要把那條狗帶到這裡來。

12 at times sometimes but not usually 有時, 偶爾: *At times I wonder if it's worth all the effort.* 有時候我會想, 這一切努力是否值得。

13 from time to time sometimes, but not regularly or very often 偶爾, 有時: *I still see her from time to time.* 我偶爾還是會去見她。

14 half the time *especially spoken* if something happens half the time, especially something annoying, it happens quite often【尤口】經常〔尤指惱人的事〕: *Half the time they don't even bother to answer my letters.* 他們經常甚至不願給我回信。

15 at no time used to say strongly that something never happened or should never happen 在任何時候都不(應該), 從來沒有: **at no time do/did etc** *At no time did I tell you that you could use my car.* 我從沒告訴過你, 說你可以用我的車子。

16 at all times used especially in official notices or announcements to say what always happens or should always happen (應該) 隨時, 總是〔尤用於正式告示或通知〕: *Identification badges must be worn at all times.* 表示身份的徽章必須隨時佩戴。

⑤ TIME WHEN STH HAPPENS 某事發生的時間

17 [C,U] the particular minute, hour, day etc when something happens or someone does something〔某事發生或某人做某事的〕具體時刻: *What time did you get to bed?* 你是幾點上牀的? | *Her note didn't give the time of the meeting.* 她的通知沒有給出會議的具體時間。| *We both left college at around the same time.* 我們兩人是差不多同時離開大學的。| **by the time** *By the time you get this letter I'll be in Canada.* 等你拿到這封信的時候, 我已經在加拿大了。| **opening/closing time** (=the time when a shop, bar etc opens)〔商店、酒吧等的〕開門/關門時間 | **arrival/departure time** (=the time when a train, plane etc leaves)〔火車、飛機等的〕到達/出發時間: *Departure times for all flights to Spain are subject to delay.* 所有飛往西班牙的航班離港時間都可能推遲。| **lunch/dinner/break etc time** (=the time when you usually have lunch etc) 午飯/晚餐/中間休息時間 | **at any one time** (=at any particular time) 在任何時候, 隨時 *There are always at least two nurses on duty at any one time.* 任何時候至少有兩名護士在值班。| **this time tomorrow/last week etc** *This time tomorrow I'll be getting on a plane to Dallas.* 明天這個時候我將登上飛往達拉斯的飛機。

⑥ TIME WHEN STH SHOULD HAPPEN 某事應發生的時間

18 [singular] the time when you should do something, when something should happen, or when something is expected to happen〔應該做某事或某事應該發生的〕時間, 時候: **it's time to do sth** *Come on kids, it's time to go home.* 來吧, 孩子們, 該回家了。| **it's time sb did sth/was doing sth** (=used when saying that someone should do something soon) 某人不久該做某事: *It's time we had a party.* 我們該舉行一次聚會了。| **it's time for** *The voters felt it was time for a change.* 選民們認為到了該有改變的時候了。

19 it's about time *especially spoken* used to say strongly that you think something should happen soon or should already have happened【尤口】到了該做某事的時候: *It's about time he got himself a proper job.* 他該給自己找一份合適的工作。

20 and about time too/not before time *spoken* used when you are annoyed because someone arrives late or something happens later than you expected or than was arranged【口】早就到時間了/已經晚了: *"Here's Helen!" "And about time too – where has she been?"* "海倫來了!" "她早該到了 ── 她上哪兒去了?"

21 on time arriving or happening at the correct time or the time that was arranged 準時, 按時: *These buses are never on time.* 這些公共汽車從來就不準時。| **right/bang/dead on time** (=at exactly the right time) 準時, 一分不差地: *Our train arrived bang on time.* 我們的火車一分不差地準時到達。

22 ahead of/behind time earlier or later than the time when a piece of work should be finished, someone should arrive somewhere etc〔某項工作完成或某人到達的〕時間提前/晚了: *The dam was completed two years ahead of time.* 水壩提前兩年竣工。

23 call time *BrE* to tell the customers in a PUB that it is time to stop drinking【英】到點了〔酒館告訴顧客到打烊的時間了〕

⑦ SUITABLE TIME 合適的時機

24 [C,U] a suitable or convenient time for something to happen or someone to do something〔合適的或方便的〕時間: **good/bad time** (=a convenient or inconvenient time) 合適的/不合適的時間: *I'm afraid you've caught me at a bad time – Can you call back later?* 你在這個時候找我恐怕不合適 ── 能不能稍後再打來? | **not be the time/be hardly the time** *This is hardly the time to ask him for a loan.* 這不是向他借貸的時機。| **come at the right/wrong time** *The pay rise came at just the right time.* 加薪來得正是時候。

25 there's no time like the present *especially spoken* used to say that now is a good time to do something【尤口】再沒有比現在更好的時機: *If you're thinking of buying a house, there's no time like the present.* 你如果想買房子, 再沒有比現在更好的時機了。

26 the time is ripe (for) used to say that the conditions are suitable now for something to happen〔某事發生的〕時機[條件]已經成熟: *The time is ripe for a peace*

settlement. 達成和平協議的時機已經成熟。
27 when the time comes when something that you expect to happen actually happens, or when something becomes necessary 當預期發生的事確實發生了; 必要時: *I'm sure she'll make the right choice when the time comes.* 我敢肯定, 必要時她會做出正確的選擇。

⑧ PERIOD OF TIME 一段時間

28 [singular] a period of time during which something happens or someone does something 一段時間; 某段日子: *I enjoyed my time as a student.* (=the period when I was a student) 我在學生時代日子過得挺快活的。| **for a long time/for some time etc** *The cheering went on for quite some time.* 歡呼聲持續了好一陣子。| **a long time ago/some time ago** *All this happened a very long time ago, before you were born.* 這一切都發生在很久以前, 你那時還沒有出生。| **time of year/day etc** *It should be pretty out there at this time of the year.* 在一年中的這個時候, 那裡的景色應該是不錯的。
29 at the time at a particular moment or period in the past, especially when the situation is very different now 當時: *It seemed like a good idea at the time.* 在當時, 這似乎是一個好主意。| *I was living in Phoenix at the time.* 我當時住在菲尼克斯。
30 at one time at some time in the past but not now 曾經有一個時期, 一度: *This used to be a very pretty valley at one time.* 這裡曾經是一處非常美麗的山谷。
31 at this time *AmE* at this particular moment【美】此時此刻: *I don't really want to start up any new relationships at this time.* 我真的不想在這個時候開始有甚麼新的戀愛關係。
32 for the time being for a short period of time from now, but not permanently 眼下, 暫時: *You can stay in the spare room for the time being.* 你可以暫時住在那間空房間裡。
33 for a time for a fairly short time, until something happens to change the situation 有一段較短的時間: *For a time we all lived together peacefully. Then the trouble started.* 曾經有一段時間, 我們大家和睦地住在一起。然後, 麻煩開始來了。| *Peter lived in Italy for a time.* 彼得曾在意大利住過一段時間。
34 for some time for a fairly long time 好長一段時間, 較長時間: *I hadn't seen my family for some time.* 我已有好長一段時間沒見到家人了。
35 for hours/months etc at a time for a period that continues for several hours, months etc 連續幾個小時/幾個月: *Alex is happy to read for hours at a time.* 亞列克斯連續讀幾個小時的書, 樂在其中。
36 for any length of time for more than just a short time 稍長一段時間: *He seemed unable to keep the same job for any length of time.* 他好像不能將同一份工作幹得稍微長久一點。
37 from time out of mind *literary* for a very long time【文】很長時間, 很久

⑨ GOOD TIME/BAD TIME ETC 好時光/壞時光等

38 [C] a good time, bad time, difficult time, etc is a period or part of your life when you have good, bad, difficult etc experiences〔好的、倒霉的、艱難的〕時光, 時日, 歲月: *This was the happiest time of her life.* 這是她一生中最幸福的時光。| **have a good/great/fantastic time** (=enjoy yourself a lot) 玩得很高興/高興極了/特別高興: *Thanks for the meal – we both had a really good time.* 謝謝這頓美餐 —— 我倆真的過得很開心。| **good/bad/hard etc times** *It's best to forget the bad times and just remember the good ones.* 最好忘掉不愉快的歲月, 只記住美好的歲月。

⑩ PERIOD IN HISTORY 歷史階段

39 [C] also 又作 **times** [plural] — a particular period in history〔歷史上的〕時代, 時期: **Roman/Greek/ancient etc times** *a tradition that goes back to Medieval times* 可以追溯到中世紀的一種傳統 | *The film takes us back to the time of the American War of Independence.* 這部電影把我們帶回到了美國獨立戰爭時期。| **our time(s)** (=the present period in history) 我們的時代 *peace in our time* 我們這個時代的和平

⑪ TIME NEEDED TO DO STH 做某事所需的時間

40 [C,U] the amount of time that it takes you to do something〔做某事需要花費的〕時間: *How much time will it take you to finish your essay?* 你完成這篇文章需要花多少時間? | **journey time/travel time** *The Channel tunnel has cut the journey time from London to Paris by as much as 3 hours.* 海峽隧道使倫敦到巴黎的旅行時間減少了三個小時。
41 take time if doing something takes time, it needs a long period of time 需要時間, 花費時間: *Learning a language isn't easy – it takes time.* 學一門語言不容易 —— 這需要時間。
42 ►IN A RACE 比賽中◄ [C] the amount of time taken by a runner, swimmer etc in a race〔比賽中花費的〕時間: *the fastest time in the world this year over 400 metres* 今年世界上400米跑的最快時間
43 have (the) time to have enough time to do something 有足夠時間〔做某事〕: **[+for]** *Do you have time for a coffee?* 你有時間喝杯咖啡嗎? | **have time to do sth** *I don't have time to talk to you right now.* 我現在沒有時間同你談話。| *She hung up before I had time to say sorry.* 我還沒來得及道歉, 她就掛斷了電話。
44 make/find time to arrange your plans so that you have enough time to do something 抽出/找出時間: *You should try and make time to see a doctor.* 你應該盡量抽出時間去看醫生。
45 there is time there is enough time for someone to do something 有足夠時間〔做某事〕: *We thought we'd do some shopping after lunch, if there's time.* 我們想, 如果有時間的話, 午飯後去買點東西。| **there is time (for sb) to do sth** *We had to leave at once – there wasn't even time to pack.* 我們當時必須馬上動身 —— 甚至連打點行李的時間都沒有。

⑫ AVAILABLE TIME 可利用的時間

46 [U] the amount of time that is available for you to do something〔可以利用的〕時間: *You'd better hurry up – we don't have much time.* 你最好快點 —— 我們沒有多少時間了。| *Time is running out in the hostage crisis.* 解決這次人質危機的時間不多了。| **sb's time** (=the time they have available) 某人可以利用的時間 *I seem to spend most of my time on the phone.* 我好像把大多數時間都花在打電話上了。| **precious time** (=time that is valuable because there is not much available) 寶貴的時間 *Hurry up – we're wasting precious time.* 快一點 —— 我們在浪費寶貴的時間。
47 have all the time in the world used to say that you have as much time as you want in which to do something 要多少時間就有多少時間, 有的是時間
48 time's up *spoken* used in competitions and examinations to tell people that there is no more time left【口】時間到, 沒有時間了〔用於競賽和考試中〕
49 be out of time an expression used on television and radio programmes when saying that there is no more time left〔電視和電台節目中說的〕時間到了,〔節目〕要結束了: *Sorry, we're out of time – I'll have to stop you there.* 對不起, 時間到了 —— 我們不得不就此打住。

⑬ SLOWLY/QUICKLY 慢/快

50 take your time a) to do something slowly or carefully without hurrying 不用急; 慢慢來: *There's no need to rush back – just take your time.* 不用急着趕回來 —— 慢慢來吧。**b)** to do something more slowly than seems reasonable 慢吞吞, 拖拉: *The builders are certainly tak-*

ing their time with our roof! 這些建築工人在建屋頂時肯定在磨洋工！

51 in no time at all/in next to no time very quickly or soon, especially in a way that is surprising 立刻，馬上〔尤指快得令人吃驚〕: *Jed got the car fixed in no time at all.* 傑德馬上就把那輛車修理好了。

52 make good time if you make good time on a journey, you travel quickly, especially more quickly than you expected〔旅途中〕快速行進〔尤指比預期的要快〕: *There wasn't much traffic, so we made good time.* 交通流量不大，所以我們一路快速行進。

53 there's no time to lose used to say that you must do something quickly because there is very little time 沒有可以損失的時間；必須抓緊時間

54 with time to spare sooner than expected or necessary 還有剩餘的時間〔指比預期的要快〕: *There was very little traffic, and we got to the airport with time to spare.* 路上沒有多少車輛，因此我們去到機場後還有富餘時間。

55 time is of the essence *formal* used to say that it is important that something is done quickly【正式】時間是關鍵；時間上得快點

56 time is money used to say that wasting time or delaying something costs money 時間就是金錢，一寸光陰一寸金

⑭ MODERN 現代

57 ahead of your time someone who is ahead of their time uses the newest ideas and methods, which are later used by many other people 走在時代的前面；〔思想或方法〕超前，創新: *Matisse was well ahead of his time in his use of colour.* 馬蒂斯在運用色彩方面大大超前於他那個時代。

58 ahead of its time a machine, system etc that is ahead of its time has a very modern and advanced design〔機器、制度等〕很現代化，很先進；超前: **way ahead of its time** (=a long way ahead of its time) 大大領先於同時代 *The car, which featured a turbo-charged engine and disc-brakes, was way ahead of its time.* 這種車配備了渦輪增壓發動機和盤式制動器，在當時遙遙領先於時代。

⑮ IN TIME 及時

59 in 10 days/five years/a few minutes' etc time ten days, five years etc from now 十天/五年/幾分鐘等後: *Don't worry, we'll be at the hospital in a couple of minutes' time.* 不要擔心，我們幾分鐘後就趕到醫院。

60 in time a) early or soon enough to do something 及時〔做某事〕: **in time to do sth** *Brian usually gets home in time to bath the children.* 布賴恩通常會及時趕回家裡給孩子們洗澡。| **just in time** *"Did you catch your plane?" "Yes – we got there just in time."* "你趕上飛機了嗎?" "是的 —— 我們剛剛趕上。" | **in good time/in plenty of time** (=early, so that you do not have to rush or you have enough time to get ready) 及早，盡早；及時 *Let me know in good time if you need any help.* 你如果需要幫助，請盡早告訴我。**b)** after a certain period of time, especially after a gradual process of change and development 過一段時間，遲早: *Don't worry – I'm sure things will get better in time.* 不要擔心 —— 情況肯定遲早會有好轉的。

⑯ HOW MANY 多少

61 one/three/a few etc at a time separately, or in groups of three, a few etc together at the same time 一次一個/三個/幾個等: *We had to see the nurse one at a time.* 我們必須一個一個地去見護士。| *He dragged himself along a few steps at a time.* 他幾步一停地拖着腳往前走。

⑰ COMPARISONS 比較

62 five/ten/many etc times used to say how much bigger, better etc one thing is than another 五倍/十倍/很多倍等: *Their garden is three times bigger than ours.* 他們的花園比我們的要大三倍。| *Sue earns five times as much as I do.* 蘇掙的錢是我的五倍。

63 the best/biggest etc...of all time the best, biggest etc of a particular kind of person or thing that has ever existed 有史以來最好的/最大的...: *the most successful movie of all time* 有史以來最賣座的一部電影

⑱ GRADUALLY/EVENTUALLY 逐漸/最終

64 all in good time used to tell someone to be patient because something they are waiting for will certainly happen eventually, and probably quite soon 完全來得及；快了；別急〔告訴某人他期待的事肯定最終會發生，而且也許即將發生〕

65 it's (only) a matter/question of time used to say that something will definitely happen at some time in the future, but you do not know when 這（只不過）是時間問題〔指某事肯定會發生〕: *That road's dangerous – it's only a matter of time before someone gets killed.* 那條路很危險 —— 早晚會有人在那裡喪命。

66 (only) time will tell used to say that it will eventually become clear whether or not something is true, right etc, at some time in the future（只有）時間會說明一切: *I don't know if she's the best choice for the job – only time will tell.* 我不知道她是不是擔任這項職務的最佳人選 —— 時間會說明一切。

67 over time if something happens over time, it happens gradually during a long period 漸漸地，慢慢地: *Over time her husband's mood seemed to change.* 漸漸地，她丈夫的情緒似乎有所改變。

68 with time/given time after a certain period of time, especially after a gradual process of change and development 隨着時間的推移；逐漸地: *I guess things will improve with time.* 我想情況會逐漸改善的。

69 time heals all wounds used to say that things you are worried or upset about will gradually disappear as time passes 時間會醫治一切創傷

⑲ MUSIC 音樂

70 ►MUSIC 音樂◄ [U] the number of beats (BEAT[2] (4)) in each bar (BAR[1] (6)) in a piece of music〔音樂的〕拍子，節拍: *Waltzes are usually in three-four time.* 華爾茲舞通常是四分之三拍。

71 in time to if you do something in time to a piece of music, you do it using the same RHYTHM and speed as the music 合着〔音樂的〕節拍: *She began moving her body in time to the music.* 她開始合着音樂的節拍晃動身體。

72 keep time to play a piece of music using the right RHYTHM and speed 按節拍〔演奏音樂〕

73 keep/beat time to show the RHYTHM and speed that a piece of music should be played at to a group of musicians, using your hands〔用手〕打着節拍

74 in/out of time (with) if you are in or out of time with someone who is playing a piece of music, you are or are not following the same RHYTHM and speed as them 合着/不合〔別人演奏的節拍〕

⑳ LIKE/DISLIKE 喜歡/不喜歡

75 have a lot of time for *informal* to like or admire someone or something【非正式】喜歡；欽佩；對...非常感興趣

76 not have much time for/have no time for *informal* to dislike and not want to waste your time on someone or something【非正式】不喜歡，討厭〔某人或某事〕；不想在...上浪費時間: *She's always complaining – I've got no time for people like that.* 她總愛發牢騷 —— 我可不喜歡那樣的人。

㉑ OTHER MEANINGS 其他意思

77 before your time a) something that is before your time happened before you were born, before you started working or living somewhere etc 在...出生[開始工作，

到某地生活]之前; 早於…的時代: *The Beatles were a bit before my time.* 披頭四樂隊略早於我的時代。**b)** if you do something before your time, you do it before the time when most people usually do it in their lives 過早: *She's growing old before her time.* 她過早地開始衰老了。
78 in my/your etc time during the period of time when you were living in a particular place or working in a particular company etc 我/你〔在某地〕生活[工作]的那個年代: *Of course in my time we didn't have all these computers.* 當然啦, 在我那個年代, 我們可沒有這些電腦。
79 in your own time if you do work or studying in your own time, you do it outside normal school or work hours 在自己的時間裡, 在業餘時間裡
80 in your own good time *informal* when you are ready【非正式】在自己作好準備之時, 在自己認為方便之時: *I'll speak to him about it in my own good time.* 我在方便的時候會跟他說這事的。
81 (sb's) time is up *spoken* used to say that someone has to stop doing something, because they have done it for long enough【口】〔某人做某事〕該結束了: *OK kids! Time's up – get out of the pool.* 好啦, 孩子們! 游夠了——從池子裡出來吧。
82 sb's time is up/sb's time is drawing near someone is going to die soon 某人快要死了/某人活不長了
83 be near her time *old-fashioned* if a woman is near her time, she is going to have a baby soon【過時】〔女人〕即將分娩
84 time is on your side used to say that someone is young enough to be able to wait before doing something or until something happens 你還年輕, 有的是時間
85 against time if you work against time to do something, you try to do it even though you have very little time 爭分奪秒, 盡快
86 time was (when) used to say that there was a time when you used to be able to do something, when something used to happen etc 曾經有一個時候…: *Time was when you could buy a new car for less than $500.* 曾經有一段時間, 用不了 500 美元就可以買一輛新車。
87 pass the time of day (with sb) to say hello to someone and have a short talk with them (與某人) 打招呼, (與某人) 寒暄
88 ►PRISON 牢房◄ do time to spend a period of time in prison 坐牢服刑
89 time and a half one and a half times the normal rate of pay 相當於平時一倍半的工資 —see also 另見 BIG TIME, FULL TIME, HALF TIME, PART-TIME, **at the best of times** (BEST[3] (12)), **it is high time** (HIGH[1] (20)), **bide your time** (BIDE (1)), **in the fullness of time** (FULLNESS (1)), **kill time** (KILL[1] (9)), **lose time** (LOSE[1] (14)), **mark time** (MARK[1] (11)), **move with the times** (MOVE[1] (19)), **in the nick of time** (NICK[1] (1)), **for old times' sake** (OLD (18)), **once upon a time** (ONCE[1] (14)), **play for time** (PLAY[1] (16)), **at the same time** (SAME[1] (3)), **sign of the times** (SIGN[1] (9)), **a stitch in time (saves nine)** (STITCH[1] (9)), **have a whale of a time** (WHALE[1] (2))

time[2] *v* [T] **1** [usually passive 一般用被動態] to arrange or choose that something should happen at a particular time 安排…的時間, 選好…的時間: *You timed your arrival well; we're just going to eat.* 你來得正好; 我們剛要吃飯。| **be timed to do sth** *The bomb was timed to go off in the rush-hour.* 炸彈設定在人流高峯時刻爆炸。| **be timed for sth** *The next show is timed for 8 o'clock.* 下一個節目定在 8 點。**2** to measure how fast someone or something is going, how long it takes to do something etc 測定…的速度; 記錄…所需的時間: *We timed our journey: it took two and a half hours.* 我們算了一下旅程的時間: 一共花了兩個半小時。| **time sb/sth at** *Christie was timed at 10.02 seconds.* 克里斯蒂用了 10.02 秒的時間。| **time how long** *Time how long it takes me to swim 4 lengths.* 測試一下我游兩個來回要花多長時間。**3** to hit a ball or make a shot at a particular moment 看準〔擊球、射門或投籃〕的時間: *a perfectly timed smash* 時間卡得很準的扣球 | **time sth well/badly etc** *Baggio timed that pass beautifully.* 巴治奧那個球傳得正是時候。—see also 另見 ILL-TIMED, MISTIME, WELL-TIMED

time and mo·tion stud·y /ˌ· · ˈ·· ˌ··/ *n* [C] a study of working methods to find out how effective they are 時間和動作研究〔指對工作方法的有效程度進行的一種研究〕

time bomb /ˈ· ·/ *n* [C] **1** a bomb that is set to explode at a particular time 定時炸彈 **2** a situation that is likely to become a very serious problem 潛在的嚴重問題: *the time bomb of youth unemployment* 年輕人失業的潛在問題

time cap·sule /ˈ· ˌ··/ *n* [C] a container that is filled with objects from a particular time, so that people in the future will know what life was like then 時代文物錦囊, 當代史料儲存器〔用來存放某個時代的物件, 以供後人了解當時的生活情況〕

time card /ˈ· ·/ *n* [C] a piece of card on which the hours you have worked are recorded by a special machine 工作時間記錄卡, 考勤卡

time clock /ˈ· ·/ *n* [C] a special clock that records the exact time when someone arrives at and leaves work 上下班記時鐘, 考勤鐘

time-con·sum·ing /ˈ· ·ˌ··/ *adj* taking a long time to do 耗費時間的; 曠日持久的: *an expensive, complex, and time-consuming process* 一個昂貴、複雜、費時的過程

time-hon·oured /ˈ· ˌ··/ *adj* a time-honoured method, custom etc is one that has existed for a long time〔方法、習俗等〕古老的, 歷史悠久的: *the time-honoured patterns of sheep-grazing and cultivation* 歷史悠久的牧羊和耕種方式

time·keep·er /ˈtaɪmˌkipɚ; ˈtaɪmˌkiːpə/ *n* [C] **1** someone who officially records the times taken to do something, especially at a sports event〔尤指體育賽事中的〕計時員 **2 good/bad timekeeper a)** someone who is good or bad at arriving at work at the right time 上班準時/不準時的人 **b)** a watch or clock that is good or bad at showing the right time 時間準/不準的鐘[錶] —**timekeeping** *n* [U]

time lag /ˈ· ·/ also 又作 **time lapse** *n* [C] the period of time between two connected events〔兩個相關聯事件之間的〕時間間隔, 時間差: *There is a considerable time lag between the planning stage and the final product.* 在規劃階段和最終成品之間有相當大的時間間隔。

time-lapse /ˈ· ·/ *adj* time-lapse photography makes a very slow process seem to happen much faster〔攝影〕延時的, 定時的〔以高速顯示非常緩慢的過程的攝影技術〕

time·less /ˈtaɪmlɪs; ˈtaɪmləs/ *adj* **1** remaining beautiful, attractive etc and not becoming old-fashioned 萬古長新的; 永不過時的: *the timeless beauty of Venice* 威尼斯萬古不變的美 **2** *literary* continuing for ever【文】永恆的, 恒久的: *the timeless universe* 永恆的宇宙 —**timelessly** *adv* —**timelessness** *n* [U]

time lim·it /ˈ· ˌ··/ *n* [C] the longest time that you are allowed in which to do something 時限, 期限: *the legal time limit for abortions* 墮胎的法定期限

time·ly /ˈtaɪmlɪ; ˈtaɪmli/ *adj* done or happening at exactly the right time 適時的, 及時的: *a timely intervention* 及時的干預 | **timely reminder** (=one that makes you remember something at the right time) 讓人及時想起某事的東西

time ma·chine /ˈ· ·ˌ·/ *n* [C] an imaginary machine in which people can travel backwards or forwards in time 時間機器〔一種想像中的機器, 人們可以乘坐它到過去或未來〕

time off /ˌ· ˈ·/ *n* [U] time when you are officially allowed not to be at work or studying〔正式規定的〕休假, 放假: **take/have etc time off** *If you're feeling tired* *you should take some time off.* 你如果覺得累，就應休一段時間的假。

time out /ˌ· ˈ·/ *n* [C] **1 take time out** *informal* to rest or do something different from your usual job or activities【非正式】〔日常工作或活動中〕暫停休息 **2** *technical* a short break during a sports match when the teams can rest, get instructions from their manager etc【術語】〔體育比賽過程中的〕暫停

time·piece /ˈtaɪmˌpis; ˈtaɪmpiːs/ *n* [C] *old use* a clock or watch【舊】鐘; 錶

tim·er /ˈtaɪmɚ; ˈtaɪmə/ *n* [C] **1** an instrument that you use to measure time, when you are doing something such as cooking 定時器: *Set the timer on the cooker for three minutes.* 把飯鍋上的定時器定為三分鐘。—see also 另見 EGG-TIMER **2 part-timer/full-timer** someone who works part or all of a normal working week 兼職人員/全職人員

times /taɪmz; taɪmz/ *prep* multiplied by 乘，乘以: *Two times two equals four. (2×2=4)* 二乘二等於四。

time-sav·ing /ˈ· ˌ··/ *adj* designed to reduce the time usually needed to do something 節省時間的，省時的: *a time-saving device* 一種可以節省時間的裝置 —**time-saver** *n* [C]

time·scale /ˈtaɪmˌskel; ˈtaɪmskeɪl/ *n* [C] the period of time it takes for something to happen or be completed 時標，時段〔某事發生或完成所需要的時間段〕

time-serv·er /ˈtaɪmˌsɝvɚ; ˈtaɪmˌsɜːvə/ *n* [C] *informal* someone who does the least amount of work possible【非正式】工作上混時間的人，得過且過的人 —**time-serving** *adj n* [U]

time·share /ˈtaɪmʃɛr; ˈtaɪmʃeə/ *n* [C] a holiday home that you buy with other people so that you can each spend a period of time there every year〔每年分時段與別人共享的〕分時享用的度假住房 —**timeshare** *adj*

time-shar·ing /ˈ· ˌ··/ *n* [U] **1** *technical* the art of dealing with more than one computer PROGRAM at the same time【術語】〔電腦同時有不止一個程序在運轉的〕分時操作，時間共享 **2** the practice of owning a timeshare 分時享用度假住房

time sheet /ˈ· ·/ *n* [C] a piece of paper on which the hours you have worked are written or printed 工作時間記錄單，考勤單

time sig·nal /ˈ· ˌ··/ *n* [C] a sound on the radio that shows the exact time〔收音機發出的〕報時信號

time sig·na·ture /ˈ· ˌ···/ *n* [C] two numbers at the beginning of a line of music that tell you how many beats (BEAT[2] (4)) there are in a BAR[1] (6)〔樂譜開頭用以表示節拍數的〕拍號

time switch /ˈ· ·/ *n* [C] an electronic control that can be set to start or stop a machine at a particular time 計時開關，定時開關

time·ta·ble[1] /ˈtaɪmˌtebl; ˈtaɪmˌteɪbəl/ *n* [C] *BrE*【英】**1** a list of the times at which buses, trains, planes, etc arrive and leave〔公共汽車、火車、飛機等的〕運行時間表，時刻表; SCHEDULE *AmE*【美】**2** a list of the times of classes in a school, college etc〔學校裡的〕課程表; SCHEDULE *AmE*【美】**3** a plan of events and activities, with their dates and times; SCHEDULE〔活動計劃的〕時間表，日程表

timetable[2] *v BrE*【英】**1** [T usually passive 一般用被動態] to plan that something will happen at a particular time in the future; SCHEDULE 為…安排[確定]時間: **timetable sth for** *The meeting has been timetabled for 2 o'clock.* 會議已經定在2點開。**2** [I,T] to arrange the times at which classes will take place in a school or college〔學校裡〕安排課程時間表: *Timetabling is the responsibility of the deputy head.* 安排課程時間表是副校長的職責。

time warp /ˈ· ·/ *n* [C] **1 be (caught/stuck) in a time warp** to have not changed even though everyone or everything else has 固步自封，僵化不變: *The whole college seems stuck in some 1960s time warp!* 整個大學固步自封，似乎還停留在20世紀60年代的某個時候! **2** an imaginary situation in which the past or future becomes the present〔幻想中的〕時間異常，時空錯亂

time-worn /ˈtaɪmˌwɔrn; ˈtaɪmwɔːn/ *adj* something time-worn is old and has been used a lot 陳舊的; 年久而殘破的: *timeworn phrases* 用濫了的語句

time zone /ˈ· ·/ *n* [C] one of the 24 areas that the world is divided into, each of which has its own time 時區

tim·id /ˈtɪmɪd; ˈtɪmɪ̥d/ *adj* not having courage or confidence 膽小的，膽怯的; 羞怯的: *a timid smile* 羞澀的一笑 | *a policy that is both timid and inadequate* 一項既無膽識又不完善的政策 —**timidly** *adv* —**timidity** /tɪˈmɪdətɪ; tɪ̥ˈmɪdɪ̥ti/ *n* [U]

tim·ing /ˈtaɪmɪŋ; ˈtaɪmɪŋ/ *n* [U] **1** a word meaning the time, day etc when someone does something or when something happens, especially when you are considering how suitable this is 時間的選擇，時機的掌握: **good/bad/perfect etc timing** *Ah good timing! I was just thinking I needed a coffee.* 啊，真是好時候! 我剛巧在想要一杯咖啡呢。| *What perfect timing! I was just finishing my work as you arrived to pick me up.* 時間真是恰到好處! 你來接我的時候，我剛把工作做完。**2** the way in which electricity is sent to the SPARK PLUGs in a car engine〔汽車發動機內電傳送到火花塞的〕時間配合，時間同步

tim·o·rous /ˈtɪmərəs; ˈtɪmərəs/ *adj formal* lacking confidence and easily frightened【正式】膽怯的; 缺乏自信的; 易受驚嚇的: *She was no helpless, timorous female.* 她決不是柔弱膽怯的女性。—**timorously** *adv* —**timorousness** *n* [U]

tim·pa·ni /ˈtɪmpənɪ; ˈtɪmpəni/ *n* [U] a set of KETTLEDRUMS〔一組〕定音鼓

tim·pa·nist /ˈtɪmpənɪst; ˈtɪmpənɪ̥st/ *n* [C] someone who plays the timpani 定音鼓手

tin[1] /tɪn; tɪn/ *n* **1** [U] a soft white metal that is often used to cover and protect iron and steel 錫: *a tin box* 錫盒 **2** [C] *BrE* a small metal container in which food or drink is sold【英】罐頭; CAN *especially AmE*【尤美】: *a sardine tin* 沙丁魚罐頭 | *a tin of beans* 一罐豆子 —see picture at 參見 CONTAINER 圖 **3** [C] a metal container with a lid in which food can be stored〔存放食物的〕金屬盒: *a biscuit tin* 餅乾盒 **4** [C] *BrE* a metal container in which food is cooked【英】〔烹飪食物的〕器皿; PAN[1] (2) *AmE*【美】: *a bread tin* 麵包烤模

tin[2] *adj* **1** made of TIN 錫製的，鍍錫的: *a tin mug* 錫杯 | *a tin soldier* 錫兵 **2 have a tin ear** *AmE informal* to be unable to hear the difference between musical notes【美，非正式】不能辨別樂音，五音不辨 **3 tin god** *informal* someone gets much more admiration and respect than they really deserve【非正式】被盲目崇拜的人，浪得虛名的人

tinc·ture /ˈtɪŋktʃɚ; ˈtɪŋktʃə/ *n* [C,U] [+of] *technical* a medical substance mixed with alcohol【術語】酊劑〔藥物與酒精的混合物〕

tin·der /ˈtɪndɚ; ˈtɪndə/ *n* [U] dry material that burns easily and can be used for lighting fires 引火物，火絨，火種

tin·der·box /ˈtɪndɚˌbɑks; ˈtɪndəbɒks/ *n* **1** [C usually singular 一般用單數] a place or situation that is dangerous and where there could suddenly be a lot of fighting or problems 危機四伏的地區[形勢]: *Racial tension was high, and the southern states were a real tinderbox.* 種族關係緊張，南方各州真是一個火藥桶。**2** [C] a box containing things needed to make a flame, used in former times〔舊時取火用的〕火絨盒

tinder-dry /ˌ·· ˈ·◂/ *adj* extremely dry and likely to burn very easily 極乾燥易燃的: *The whole forest is tinder-dry.* 整座森林都乾燥，容易失火。

tin·foil /ˈtɪnˌfɔɪl; ˈtɪnfɔɪl/ *n* [U] thin shiny metal that bends like paper and is used for covering food etc〔用於包裹食物等的〕錫箔，錫紙

ting /tɪŋ; tɪŋ/ *n* [C] a high clear ringing sound 叮噹聲: *the ting of a bell* 鐘發出的叮噹聲 —**ting** *v* [I,T]

ting-a-ling /ˌ· · ˈ·◂/ *n* [C] *informal* the high clear ringing sound that is made by a small bell【非正式】〔小鈴發出的〕玎璫聲, 叮噹聲

tinge¹ /tɪndʒ; tɪndʒ/ *n* [C] a very small amount of a colour, emotion, or quality 淡淡的色調; 些許, 一點, 一絲〔情緒、特質等〕: **[+of]** *a tinge of sadness in her voice* 她聲音裡的一絲悲傷

tinge² *v* [T+with] to give something a small amount of a particular colour, emotion, or quality 着淡色於…; 使帶有一點…〔情緒、特質等〕

tinged /tɪndʒd; tɪndʒd/ *adj* **tinged with** showing a small amount of a colour, emotion or quality 略帶一點〔顏色、情緒、特質等〕的: *black hair tinged with grey* 略帶灰色的黑髮

tin·gle /ˈtɪŋgḷ; ˈtɪŋgəl/ *v* [I] **1** if a part of your body tingles, you feel a slight uncomfortable feeling, especially on your skin〔尤指皮膚〕感到刺痛, 刺癢: **[+with]** *My cheeks were tingling with the cold.* 我的臉頰凍得刺痛。**2 tingle with excitement** to feel very excited 感到很激動 —**tingle** *n* [C]: *A nervous tingle ran down her spine.* 一陣令人不安的刺癢沿着她脊背往下擴散。

tin hat /ˌ· ˈ·/ *n* [C] a metal hat worn by soldiers〔士兵的〕鋼盔

tin·ker¹ /ˈtɪŋkɚ; ˈtɪŋkə/ *n* [C] **1** someone who travels from place to place selling things or repairing metal pots, pans etc〔遊走四方的〕小販; 補鍋匠 **2** *BrE old-fashioned* a disobedient or annoying young child【英, 過時】頑童, 小淘氣 **3 not give a tinker's curse/cuss** *BrE spoken*【英口】**not give a tinker's damn** *AmE spoken*【美口】to not care about something at all〔對…〕毫不在乎

tinker² *v* [I+with] to make small changes to something in order to repair it or make it work better〔隨便馬虎地〕修理, 修補; 擺弄: *It's no use just tinkering with the legislation.* 對立法只是小修小補, 那是沒用的。

tin·kle¹ /ˈtɪŋkḷ; ˈtɪŋkəl/ *n* [C usually singular 一般用單數] **1** a light ringing sound 叮噹聲, 玎璫聲: *She could hear the tinkle of coffee cups.* 她可以聽到咖啡杯發出的叮噹聲。—see picture on page A19 參見 A19 頁圖 **2 give sb a tinkle** *BrE informal* to call someone on the telephone【英, 非正式】給某人打電話: *I'll give you a tinkle tomorrow.* 我明天給你打電話。**3 have a tinkle** an expression meaning to URINATE (=pass water from your body), used especially by or to children 撒尿, 尿尿〔尤為兒語〕

tinkle² *v* [I,T] to make light ringing sounds or to make something do this (使) 發出叮噹聲[玎璫聲]: *a tinkling bell* 叮叮噹噹的鈴聲

tinned /tɪnd; tɪnd/ *adj BrE* tinned food is sold in a TIN¹ (2) and can be kept for a long time before it is opened【英】〔食品〕罐裝的: *tinned tomatoes* 罐頭番茄

tin·ni·tus /tɪˈnaɪtəs; ˈtɪnɪtəs/ *n* [U] *technical* an illness in which you hear noises, especially ringing, in your ears【術語】耳鳴 (症)

tin·ny /ˈtɪnɪ; ˈtɪni/ *adj* **1** a tinny sound is unpleasant to listen to, like small pieces of metal hitting each other〔聲音〕尖細的, 像薄金屬碰撞聲的 **2** a tinny metal object is badly or cheaply made〔金屬製品〕廉價的, 粗製的, 質量差的

tin o·pen·er /ˈ· ˌ···/ *n* [C] *BrE* a tool for opening tins【英】開罐器, 罐頭刀; CAN OPENER *especially AmE*【尤美】—see picture on page A10 參見 A10 頁圖

Tin Pan Al·ley /ˌ· · ˈ··/ *n* [U] *informal* the people who produce popular music and their way of life【非正式】流行音樂製作者; 流行音樂界

tin·plate /ˈtɪnˌplet; ˈtɪnpleɪt/ *n* [U] very thin sheets of iron or steel covered with tin 鍍錫鐵皮, 馬口鐵

tin-pot /ˈ· ·/ *adj* [only before noun 僅用於名詞前] a tin-pot person, organization, etc is not very important, although they think that they are〔人、組織機構等〕卑微而又自負的: *a tin-pot dictator* 無足輕重卻自我陶醉的獨裁者

tin·sel /ˈtɪnsḷ; ˈtɪnsəl/ *n* [U] **1** thin strings of shiny paper used as decorations, especially at Christmas〔尤指聖誕節期間裝飾用的〕錫箔紙, 閃光紙 **2** something that seems attractive but is not valuable or important 花哨而無用的東西, 華而不實的東西: *the tinsel and glamour of Hollywood* 好萊塢的浮華和魅力

tin shears /ˈ· ·/ *n* [plural] *AmE* heavy scissors for cutting metal【美】〔切割金屬的〕大剪刀; snips (SNIP¹ (1)) *BrE*【英】

tint¹ /tɪnt; tɪnt/ *n* [C] **1** a small amount of a particular colour 淡淡的色澤; 色調: *autumn tints* 淡淡的秋色 **2** artificial colour, used to slightly change the colour of your hair 染髮劑: *She had put red tints in her hair.* 她把自己的頭髮染成了淡紅褐色。

tint² *v* [T] **1** to slightly change the colour of someone's hair using artificial colour〔用染髮劑〕稍微改變〔頭髮〕的顏色 **2** to give hair an artificial colour 給〔頭髮〕染成人工的顏色

tin·tack /ˈtɪnˌtæk; ˈtɪntæk/ *n* [C] a short nail made of iron and covered with tin 鍍錫小鐵釘

tint·ed /ˈtɪntɪd; ˈtɪntɪ̣d/ *adj* [only before noun 僅用於名詞前] tinted glass is coloured, rather than completely transparent〔玻璃〕有色的

tin·tin·nab·u·la·tion /ˌtɪntɪˌnæbjəˈleʃən; ˌtɪntɪ̣næbjʊ̣ˈleɪʃən/ *n* [C,U] *literary* the sound of bells【文】鈴聲; 叮噹聲, 玎璫聲

ti·ny /ˈtaɪnɪ; ˈtaɪni/ *adj* extremely small 極小的, 微小的: *a tiny baby* 很小的嬰兒 | *The opium farmers receive only a tiny fraction of this sum.* 種植鴉片的農民們從這筆錢中只拿到極小的一部分。

-tion /ʃən; ʃən/ *suffix* (in nouns 構成名詞) another form of the suffix -ION 後綴 -ion 的另一種形式

tip¹ /tɪp; tɪp/ *n*

1 ▶END 末端◀ [C] the end of something, especially something pointed 末端, 末梢; 尖端; 頂點: *Use the tip of the brush to paint fine lines.* 用畫筆的尖端來繪細線。| *The tip of her nose was red.* 她的鼻尖是紅的。—see also 另見 FINGERTIP

2 ▶MONEY 錢◀ [C] a small amount of additional money that you give to someone, such as a WAITER or a taxi driver 小費, 賞錢: *Did you leave a tip?* 你留下小費了嗎? | *a 10% tip* 10% 的小費

3 ▶ADVICE 忠告◀ [C] a helpful piece of advice 有用的勸告, 忠告, 建議: **[+on]** *Steve gave me some useful tips on how to take good pictures.* 就如何拍好照片, 史蒂夫給了我一些很有用的建議。

4 ▶WASTE 垃圾◀ [C] *BrE* an area where unwanted waste is taken and left; DUMP² (1)【英】垃圾場: *a rubbish tip* 垃圾棄置場

5 ▶UNTIDY 不整潔◀ [singular] *BrE informal* an extremely dirty or untidy place【英, 非正式】極不乾淨[極不整潔]的地方: *Your room's a real tip! When are you going to clean it?* 你的房間簡直成垃圾堆了! 你打算甚麼時候打掃打掃?

6 on the tip of your tongue if a word, name etc is on the tip of your tongue, you know it but cannot remember it 就在嘴邊〔但記不起來了〕

7 the tip of the iceberg a small sign of a problem that is much larger 冰山的一角; 重大問題顯露出表面的一小部分: *The official statistics are probably only the tip of the iceberg.* 官方的統計數字可能只反映問題的一小部分。

8 ▶HORSE RACE 賽馬◀ [C] *informal* special information about which horse will win a race【非正式】〔關於賽馬中哪匹馬會贏的〕特別情報, 內部情報

tip² *v* **tipped, tipping**

1 ▶FALL 倒下◀ [I,T] also 又作 **tip over/up** to fall or turn over, or make something do this (使) 倒下; (使) 傾翻: *Careful you don't tip the milk jug over!* 你小心點, 別把牛奶罐弄翻了! | *If you lean on the table, it'll tip up.* 如果你斜靠在桌子上, 它會翻的。

2 ▶POUR 傾倒◀ [T] to pour something from one place or container into another 把…從一個容器倒入另一容器;

傾倒; 傾卸: **tip sth out/into/onto etc** *She weighed out the flour and tipped it out into a bowl.* 她稱了麵粉, 然後把它倒進一個碗裡。

3 ►LEAN 傾斜◄ [I,T] to lean at an angle instead of being level or straight, or to make something do this (使)傾斜, (使)傾側: *Sit still and don't tip the chair back.* 坐定了, 別把椅子往後傾斜。

4 ►MONEY 錢◄ [I,T] to give an additional amount of money to someone such as a WAITER or taxi driver 給〔服務員或出租車司機等〕小費, 給賞錢: *Did you remember to tip the waiter?* 你記得給服務員小費了嗎? —see picture on page A15 參見A15頁圖

5 ►LIKELY TO SUCCEED 可能成功的◄ [T usually passive 一般用被動態] *especially BrE* to say who you think is most likely to be successful at something【尤英】認為…最有可能成功: **tip sb as/for** *She's been tipped for promotion.* 有人認為她可能得到提升。| **tip sb/sth to do sth** *a horse that was tipped to win* 被認為有可能贏的賽馬

6 ►COVER 覆蓋◄ be tipped with to have one end covered in something 頂端覆蓋着…: *arrows tipped with poison* 頂端塗有毒藥的箭

7 it's tipping down *BrE spoken* it is raining【英口】天正下着雨

8 tip the balance/scales to give a slight advantage to someone or something 使平衡局面發生傾側; 使稍微有利於…: *Your support tipped the balance in our favour.* 你們的支持使整個局面對我們有利。

9 tip the scales at to weigh a particular amount before a BOXING or WRESTLING match〔參加拳擊或摔跤比賽前〕稱得重量為…: *He tips the scales at 180 pounds.* 他稱得重量為180磅。

10 tip sb the wink *BrE informal* to give someone secret information【英, 非正式】給某人祕密消息

11 tip your hat to *AmE* to show that you think someone is very good, helpful, successful etc【美】向…致敬

tip sb ↔ off *phr v* [T] to give someone a secret warning or piece of information, especially to the police about illegal activities 向…提出祕密警告; 〔尤指給警察〕通風報信: *The police must have been tipped off.* 警察一定事先得知了風聲。

tip-off /ˈ· ·/ *n* [C] *informal* a warning that something is going to happen, especially to the police about illegal activities【非正式】祕密的警告; 〔尤指給警察的〕通風報信, 密報: *Acting on an anonymous tip-off, police raided the house.* 警察根據匿名提供的情報採取行動, 搜查了那所房子。

Tipp-Ex /ˈtɪp ɛks; ˈtɪp eks/ *n* [U] *BrE trademark* white liquid that is used to cover over mistakes in writing, typing etc【英, 商標】"迪美斯"牌修正液[塗改液]; WHITEOUT *AmE*【美】

tipp·ex /ˈtɪpɛks; ˈtɪpeks/ *v* [T+**out**] *BrE* to cover over a mistake in writing, typing etc, using white liquid【英】用修正液[塗改液]塗改

tip·ple /ˈtɪpl; ˈtɪpəl/ *n informal especially BrE*【非正式, 尤英】**favourite tipple** someone's favourite alcoholic drink〔某人〕最喜愛喝的酒

tip·pler /ˈtɪplɚ; ˈtɪplə/ *n* [C] *informal especially BrE* someone who drinks alcohol【非正式, 尤英】飲烈酒者, 酒徒

tip·ster /ˈtɪpstɚ; ˈtɪpstə/ *n* [C] someone who gives information about which horse is likely to win a race〔提供賽馬信息的〕情報販子

tip·sy /ˈtɪpsɪ; ˈtɪpsi/ *adj informal* slightly drunk【非正式】微醉的 —**tipsily** *adv* —**tipsiness** *n* [U]

tip·toe¹ /ˈtɪpˌto; ˈtɪptəʊ/ *n* **on tiptoe(s)** if you stand on tiptoe you stand on your toes, in order to make yourself taller 踮着腳: *Anita stood on tiptoe and tried to see over the wall.* 阿妮塔踮着腳尖, 想看到牆那邊。

tiptoe² *v* [I] to walk quietly and carefully on your toes 踮着腳走, 躡手躡腳地走: **[+across/down etc]** *He tiptoed across the hall and followed her into the kitchen.* 他躡手躡腳地穿過走廊, 跟着她進了廚房。—see picture on page A24 參見A24頁圖

tip-top /ˌ· ˈ·◂/ *adj informal* excellent【非正式】非常好的, 頂呱呱的: **in tip-top condition/shape etc** *The car's in tip-top condition.* 這輛車的狀況非常好。

ti·rade /ˈtaɪred; taɪˈreɪd/ *n* [C] a long angry speech criticizing someone or something 抨擊性的長篇演說: *He launched into a tirade against the church.* 他發表了一篇抨擊教會的演說。

tire¹ /taɪr; taɪə/ *v* **1** [I,T] to start to feel tired or make someone feel tired (使)感到累, (使)感到疲勞: *As we neared the summit, we were tiring fast.* 當接近山頂時, 我們越來越累, 快不行了。**2 tire of sth** to become bored with something 對某事感到厭煩: *Sooner or later he'll tire of politics.* 遲早他會厭煩政治的。**3 never tire of doing sth** to do something so much that it annoys other people 不厭其煩地做某事〔因此令人厭煩〕: *She never tires of telling everyone how wonderful her new house is.* 她不厭其煩地告訴每個人, 說她的新房子是如何如何的好。

tire sb ↔ **out** *phr v* [T] to make someone very tired 使精疲力盡, 使疲勞不堪

tire² *n* [C] the American spelling of TYRE tyre的美式拼法

tired /taɪrd; taɪəd/ *adj* **1** feeling that you want to sleep or rest 睏倦的; 疲倦的, 累的: *I'm so tired I could sleep for a week.* 我累極了, 簡直能睡上一個星期。| *She can't come tonight – she says she's too tired.* 她今晚不能來了 — 她說她太累。**2** bored with something because it is no longer interesting, or has become annoying 厭煩的, 厭倦的: **tired of doing sth** *I'm tired of watching television, let's go for a walk.* 我看電視都看膩了, 我們出去走走吧。| **[+of]** *I was getting tired of all her negative remarks.* 我對她那一整套消極言論感到越來越厭煩了。**3 tired out** very tired, especially after a lot of hard work, travelling etc〔尤指在幹了大量繁重工作、旅行等之後〕精疲力竭的 **4 tired (old) subject/joke etc** a subject, joke etc that is boring because it is too familiar 枯燥乏味[老一套]的話題/笑話等 —see also 另見 DOG-TIRED, **be sick (and tired) of sth** (SICK¹ (4)) —**tiredness** *n* [U] —**tiredly** *adv*

tire·less /ˈtaɪrlɪs; ˈtaɪələs/ *adj* working very hard in a determined way without stopping 不知疲倦的, 孜孜不倦的: *the tireless efforts of the rescue workers* 營救工作人員堅持不懈的努力 —**tirelessly** *adv*

tire·some /ˈtaɪrsəm; ˈtaɪəsəm/ *adj* making you feel annoyed or impatient 煩人的, 令人厭煩的: *the whole tiresome business of filling out the forms* 填寫表格這一整套煩人的事

tir·ing /ˈtaɪrɪŋ; ˈtaɪərɪŋ/ *adj* making you feel that you want to sleep or rest 令人睏倦的; 令人疲勞的, 令人感到累的: *We've all had a very tiring day – let's go to bed.* 大家今天都很累 — 我們上牀睡覺吧。

ti·ro /ˈtaɪro; ˈtaɪərəʊ/ *n* [C] someone who is only beginning to learn something 新手, 生手, 初學者

'tis /tɪz; tɪz/ *poetical*【詩】the short form of 縮略式= 'it is'

tis·sue /ˈtɪʃu; ˈtɪʃuː/ *n* **1** [C] a piece of soft thin paper, used especially for blowing your nose on 紙巾, 面巾紙: *a box of tissues* 一盒面巾紙 **2** also 又作 **tissue paper** [U] light thin paper used for wrapping, packing etc〔包裝等用的〕薄紙, 綿紙 **3** [U] the material forming animal or plant cells〔動植物細胞的〕組織: **plant/lung/brain etc tissue** 植物/肺/腦組織 **4 a tissue of lies** a story or account that is completely untrue 一派謊言

tit /tɪt; tɪt/ *n* [C] **1** *informal* an offensive word for a woman's breast【非正式】〔女人的〕乳房, 奶子〔冒犯用語〕**2** *BrE slang* a stupid person【英俚】傻瓜, 笨蛋 **3 get on sb's tits** *BrE slang* to annoy someone a lot【英俚】讓某人非常厭煩 **4** a small European bird 山雀〔歐洲的一種小鳥〕

ti·tan, Titan /ˈtaɪtn̩; ˈtaɪtn/ *n* [C] a very strong or important person; GIANT² (4) 巨人, 大力士; 泰斗, 大師; 鉅子

ti·tan·ic /taɪˋtænɪk; taɪˈtænɪk/ *adj* very big, strong, impressive etc 巨大的; 力大無比的; 重大的: *a titanic struggle* 大搏鬥

ti·ta·ni·um /taɪˋtenɪəm; taɪˈteɪniəm/ *n* [U] a strong, light, and very expensive metal 鈦〔一種金屬元素〕

tit·bit /ˋtɪtˌbɪt; ˈtɪtˌbɪt/ *n* [C] *especially BrE*【尤英】**1** a small piece of food 少量的精美食品, 珍饈; TIDBIT *AmE*【美】**2 titbit of information/gossip/news etc** *plural* a small but interesting piece of information etc 趣聞/花絮/花邊消息等

titch /tɪtʃ; tɪtʃ/ *n* [singular] *BrE* a humorous or insulting way of addressing a small person【英】矮個子, 小不點〔對身材矮小的人的幽默或侮辱性的稱呼語〕

titch·y /ˋtɪtʃɪ; ˈtɪtʃi/ *adj BrE informal* extremely small【英, 非正式】極小的

tit·fer /ˋtɪtfɚ; ˈtɪtfə/ *n* [C] *BrE old-fashioned slang* a hat【英, 過時, 俚】帽子

tit for tat /ˌ· · ˋ·/ *n* [U] *informal* something bad that you do to someone because they have done something bad to you【非正式】一報還一報, 以眼還眼

tithe /taɪð; taɪð/ *n* [C usually plural 一般用複數] a tax paid to the church, in former times 什一稅〔舊時支付給基督教會的一種稅〕

tit·il·late /ˋtɪtḷˌet; ˈtɪtɪleɪt/ *v* [T] if a picture or a story titillates someone, it makes them feel sexually excited or interested 使感到性興奮; 使感到有趣: *the usual pin-ups to titillate the readers* 照例提供的讓讀者感到性刺激的女人圖片 —**titillating** *adj* —**titillation** /ˌtɪtḷˋeʃən; ˌtɪtɪˈleɪʃən/ *n* [U]

tit·i·vate, tittivate /ˋtɪtəˌvet; ˈtɪtɪveɪt/ *v* [I,T] *informal* to make yourself pretty or tidy【非正式】打扮, 裝飾, 梳整 —**titivation** /ˌtɪtəˋveʃən; ˌtɪtɪˈveɪʃən/ *n* [U]

3 1 **ti·tle** /ˋtaɪtḷ; ˈtaɪtl/ *n* **1** [C] the name given to a particular book, painting, play etc〔書籍、圖畫、戲劇等的〕題目, 標題: *The title of this play is 'Othello'.* 這部劇作的標題是《奧賽羅》。**2** [C] a book〔某一本〕書: *His novel was one of last year's best-selling titles.* 他的小說是去年的暢銷書之一。**3** [C] **a)** a name such as 'Sir' or 'Professor', or letters such as 'Mrs' or 'Dr', that are used before someone's name to show their rank or profession, whether they are married etc〔表明某人地位或職業的〕頭銜, 稱謂 **b)** a name that describes someone's job or position〔表示某人工作的〕職位, 職稱: *Her official title is editorial manager.* 她的正式職位是編輯部經理。**4** [singular,U] *technical* the legal right to own something【術語】所有權: [+to] *He has title to the land.* 他擁有那塊土地的所有權。**5** [C] the position of being the winner of an important sports competition〔重大體育比賽中的〕冠軍: *Navratilova won a record number of Wimbledon titles.* 娜拉蒂露娃創記錄地贏得了很多次溫布頓網球賽冠軍。

ti·tled /ˋtaɪtḷd; ˈtaɪtld/ *adj* having a title such as 'lord', DUKE, EARL etc 有貴族頭銜的, 有爵位的

title deed /ˋ·· ·/ *n* [C] a piece of paper giving legal proof that someone owns a particular property 房地產契據, 產權證

title hold·er /ˋ·· ˌ··/ *n* [C] **1** a person or team that is the winner of an important sports competition〔體育比賽的〕冠軍; 冠軍隊 **2** someone who owns a title deed 房地產契據持有人, 產權人

title page /ˋ·· ·/ *n* [C] the page at the front of a book which shows the book's name, writer etc〔圖書的〕書名頁, 扉頁

title role /ˋ·· ·/ *n* [C] the main acting part in a play, which is the same as the name of the play〔主角與劇作名稱一樣的〕劇名角色

tit·mouse /ˋtɪtˌmaus; ˈtɪtmaʊs/ *n* [C] a small European bird 山雀〔歐洲的一種小鳥〕

tit·ter /ˋtɪtɚ; ˈtɪtə/ *v* [I] to laugh quietly in a high voice, especially because you are nervous〔尤指緊張時〕竊笑; 傻笑: *At the word 'breast' some of the class tittered.* 聽到"乳房"這個詞, 班上的一些同學吃吃地笑了起來。—**titter** *n* [C]

tittle-tat·tle /ˋtɪtḷ ˌtætḷ; ˈtɪtl ˌtætl/ *n* [U] unimportant conversation about other people and what they are doing; GOSSIP[1] (1)〔關於別人的〕閒聊; 閒言碎語

tit·ty /ˋtɪtɪ; ˈtɪti/ *n* [C] *slang* a woman's breast; TIT【俚】〔女人的〕乳房, 奶子

tit·u·lar /ˋtɪtʃələ; ˈtɪtʃʊlə/ *adj* [only before noun 僅用於名詞前] **titular head/leader/monarch etc** someone who is the official leader or ruler of a country but who does not have real power or authority 掛名的頭目/沒有實權的領導/有名無實的君主等

tiz·zy /ˋtɪzɪ; ˈtɪzi/ also 又作 **tizz** /tɪz; tɪz/ *n* [singular] *informal*【非正式】**in a tizzy** feeling worried, nervous, and confused 焦慮不安, 心慌意亂

T-junc·tion /ˋti ˌdʒʌŋkʃən; ˈtiː ˌdʒʌŋkʃən/ *n* [C] *BrE* a place where two roads meet and form the shape of the letter T【英】〔道路的〕T形交叉, 丁字路口

TLC /ˌti ɛl ˋsi; ˌtiː el ˈsiː/ *n* [U] *informal* tender loving care; kindness and love that you show someone to make them feel better and happier【非正式】親切的關愛

TM[1] a written abbreviation of 縮寫= TRADEMARK

TM[2] /ˌti ˋɛm; ˌtiː ˈem/ an abbreviation of 縮寫= TRANSCENDENTAL MEDITATION

TNT /ˌti ɛn ˋti; ˌtiː en ˈtiː/ *n* [U] a powerful explosive 梯恩梯〔一種烈性炸藥〕

to[1] /tə; tə, *before vowels* 元音前作 tʊ; tʊ; *strong* 強讀 tu; tuː/ **1** [used before a verb to show that it is the infinitive 用於動詞前表示是不定式, but not before 但不用於 **can, could, may, might, will, would, shall, should, must,** or 或 **ought** 之前。The following senses show the patterns in which **to** is used. 下列義項表明了 to 的各種用法。] **2** used after verbs〔用於動詞後〕: *He lived to be 90.* 他活到了 90 歲。| *I used to live in New York.* 我曾經住在紐約。| *He wants to leave.* 他想離開。| *Let her leave if she wants to.* 她如果想走, 就讓她走吧。| *They allowed the hostages to go.* 他們允許人質離開。| *He told his men to shoot.* 他叫他的手下人射擊。| *He told them not to.* 他告訴他們不要這樣。**3** [used after 用於 **how, where, who, whom, whose, which, when, what,** or 或 **whether** 之後]: *I know where to go but I don't know how to get there.* 我知道去甚麼地方, 但我不知道怎樣去那兒。| *She wondered whether or not to go.* 她不知道是不是該去。| *She wondered whether to go or not.* 她不知道是該去呢, 還是不該去。| *Would you tell me when to leave?* 你能告訴我甚麼時候動身嗎? **4** used after nouns〔用於名詞後〕: *an attempt to make a joke* 試圖開一個玩笑 | *I haven't got the qualifications to apply.* 我沒有資格申請。| *There seemed to be no reason to stay.* 似乎沒有留下的理由。**5** after adjectives〔用於形容詞後〕: *That's very easy to say.* 那是很容易說的。| *I'm glad to say she's making a good recovery.* 我很高興地說, 她正恢復得很不錯。| *We are sorry to announce the cancellation of the flight to Geneva.* 我們很抱歉地通知大家, 飛往日內瓦的航班被取消。**6** used to refer to, or to emphasize a particular verb〔用於指稱或強調某一動詞〕: *'To find' takes a direct object.* to find 要加直接賓語。| *It would be best to wear waterproof clothing.* 最好是穿上防水服。| *What I really should have done was to say "no" straightaway.* 我當時真正應該做的是直截了當地說"不"。**7** used to show that someone intends to do something〔用於表示某人想做某事〕: *They left early to catch the train.* 為了趕火車他們很早就動身了。| *She wore a large hat to keep the sun off her head.* 她戴了一頂很大的帽子, 不讓自己的頭曬到太陽。| *I've taken some money out of the bank to buy Christmas presents.* 我從銀行裡取了一些錢好買聖誕禮物。**8** used after **too**+adjective〔用於 too+形容詞後〕: *It's too cold to go out.* 天太冷了, 沒法出去。| *Jim's too honest to play a trick like that.* 吉姆太老實了, 他不會那樣搞惡作劇的。**9** used after an adjective and **enough**〔用於形容詞和 enough 之後〕: *I reckon it's warm enough to wear a T shirt.* 我想天氣夠暖和了, 穿一件 T 恤衫就行。| *It's cold enough to snow.* 1 1

T

天狗冷的，會下雪的。**10** used to introduce a statement〔用於引導陳述句〕: *To be quite honest, I've never even heard of him.* 老實說，我壓根兒就沒有聽說過他。| *To put it another way, how are you going to get the cash to pay for it?* 換一種問法，你打算如何搞到現金來買這東西？| *To begin with, let's look at Chapter 3.* 首先，讓我們來看第三章。**11** used after the pattern **There is**+noun〔用於 There is+名詞這一句型之後〕: *There were plenty of things to eat.* 可以吃的東西很多。| *There's also the cost to consider.* 還有成本也要考慮到。

to[2] /tu; tuː/ *adv* **1** if you push a door to, or something moves a door to, it closes〔門〕在關上的位置: *The wind blew the door to.* 風把門吹得關上了。**2 come to** if someone comes to, they become awake or conscious after being asleep or unconscious 蘇醒過來: *John didn't come to for half-an-hour after falling and hitting his head.* 約翰摔了一跤把頭給撞了，過了半個小時才蘇醒過來。

1 1 **to[3]** /tə; tə, *before vowels* 元音前作 tu; tʊ; *strong* 強讀 tu; tuː/ *prep* **1** in a direction towards 向，朝，到，往: *the road to London* 通往倫敦的路 | *a journey to China* 中國之行 | *She stood up and walked to the window.* 她站起來走到窗口。| *Sam threw the ball to his little sister.* 山姆把球扔向他的小妹妹。**2** in a direction from a particular person or thing 在…方，位於…方向: *Chongqing is about 150 miles to the south of Chengdu.* 重慶位於成都以南大約 150 英里處。| *I was sitting to the left of the President.* 我當時坐在總統的左邊。**3** in order to be in a particular place or area 到…去: *We're hoping to go to Istanbul for our holidays this year.* 我們希望今年去伊斯坦布爾度假。| *Don't forget; we're going to Eve's for supper tomorrow night.* 別忘了，我們明晚要去伊夫家裡吃晚飯。| *I usually go to bed at 11p.m.* 我通常晚上 11 點上牀睡覺。| *"Where's Emily?" "She's gone to the loo."* "艾米莉在哪兒？" "她去洗手間了。" **4** in order to be in a particular situation, or in a particular physical or mental state 為了到…情況；為了到達…身體[精神]狀態: *After two difficult years the company is now on the road to recovery.* 在渡過兩年困難期之後，該公司目前正在復蘇中。| *She sang the baby to sleep.* 她唱歌哄嬰兒入睡。| *The mob stoned her to death.* 這羣暴徒用石頭砸死了她。| *Wait until the lights change to green.* 等到變成綠燈為止。**5** reaching as far as a particular thing 達到〔某事物〕: *The water came right up to our knees.* 水一直漲到了我們的膝部。**6** in a position in which two things are touching〔相互之間〕貼着，緊挨着: *The paper stuck firmly to the wall.* 那紙緊緊地貼在牆上。| **cheek to cheek** *They danced cheek to cheek.* 他倆臉貼着臉跳舞。**7** facing something or in front of it 對着，面對着: *I sat with my back to the engine.* 我背對發動機坐着。| **face to face** *We stood face to face.* 我們面對面站着。| **back to back** *The two houses were back to back.* 那兩座房子背向而立。**8** until and including 直到〔並包括在內〕: *She can already count from one to twenty.* 她已經能從一數到二十了。| *They stayed from Friday night to Sunday morning.* 他們從星期五晚上一直待到星期天早上。| *It's ten kilometres from here to Angers.* 從這裡到昂熱有十公里。| **from beginning to end** *She read the novel from beginning to end.* 她從頭到尾地讀了這部小說。| **a nine-to-five job** (=a typical job in which you begin work at nine o'clock and finish at five o'clock) 朝九晚五的工作 **9** used to show the person or thing to which actions or words are directed or to whom things belong〔用於指出行動或語言的對象；用於指出東西的擁有者〕: *This is a letter to Mildred from George.* 這是喬治寫給米爾德里德的一封信。| *Have you told all your news to John?* 你把全部消息都告訴約翰了嗎？| *You have no right to this land.* 你對這塊土地沒有所有權。| *Will they give you an office to yourself?* 他們會給你一間屬於自己的辦公室嗎？**10** used to show the person or thing that is affected by an action 對，對於〔用來指出受行動影響的人或事物〕: *a danger to your health* 對你健康的威脅 | *She's very kind to animals.* 她對動物很仁慈。| *What have you done to the radio? It's not working.* 你是怎麼擺弄這台收音機的？它現在不響了。| *There's always an element of risk to starting up a new business.* 創業總會有風險的。**11** working for someone, or being a part of something that is necessary to make it work 為…〔工作〕；是…的〔一部分〕: *Have you seen the key to the back door?* 你見過開後門的那把鑰匙嗎？| *Rona's secretary to the managing director.* 羅娜是總經理的祕書。**12** used when comparing two things, numbers etc 與…相比，相對於…而言: *I know he's successful but he's nothing to what he could have been.* 我知道他有成就，但與他本來可取得的成就相比，這一點算不了甚麼。| *England beat Scotland by two goals to one.* 英格蘭隊以二比一擊敗了蘇格蘭隊。**13** used especially after verbs such as 'seem', 'feel', 'sound' to show how things affect, concern, or influence someone 至於，對於〔尤用於 seem, feel, sound 等動詞後，表示影響到或涉及某人〕: *The whole thing sounds very suspicious to me.* 整個事情在我聽來都非常可疑。| *Tickets cost £10 each and to some people that's a lot of money.* 每張票十英鎊，對於某些人來說，這是個大數目。**14** according to a particular feeling or attitude 合乎〔某一看法或態度〕: **to your liking/taste etc** *The decor wasn't really to our liking.* 這種裝飾實在不合我們的口味。| **to your advantage** (=in a way that will help you or be good for you) 對你有利的 *You could use this information to your advantage.* 你可以利用這條信息。| **to your knowledge** (=according to what you know) 就你所知道的 *Brookner has not to my knowledge written any books since this one.* 據我所知，布魯克納自從寫了這本書以後就再也沒有寫過別的書。**15 to your surprise/annoyance/delight** in a way that makes you feel a particular emotion 讓你吃驚/氣惱/高興的是: *Much to her surprise she passed the exam with distinction.* 讓她十分驚奇的是，她以出眾的成績通過了考試。| *To our amazement she climbed on the desk and started removing her clothes.* 讓我們大為吃驚的是，她竟爬到桌子上，開始脫衣服了。**16** *especially spoken* forming something or being one of the separate parts that makes something up【尤口】形成，組成: *We're only getting eight francs to the pound at the moment.* 現在我們用一英鎊只能兑換八法郎。| *There are sixteen ounces to every pound.* 一磅有十六盎司。| **there's more to sb/sth than meets the eye** (=used to say that a person or situation is more complicated than they seem to be) 某人/某事比看上去複雜得多 **17** used when adding one number to another or when thinking about two facts at the same time 加〔數目〕；還有，以及: *Add fifty to seventy-five.* 七十五再加上五十。| *In addition to all Ron's other problems his father died yesterday.* 除了其他所有那些問題，羅恩還有一件事，他父親昨天去世了。**18** used to show that there is a certain amount of time before an event or before a particular time 在…之前還有〔時間〕: *Only two weeks to Christmas.* 離聖誕節只有兩個星期。| *How long is it to dinner?* 到開晚飯還有多長時間？| **ten to five/twenty to one etc** (=ten minutes, twenty minutes etc before a particular hour) 差 10 分到 5 點/差 20 分到 1 點等 **19** used between two numbers when you try to guess an exact number …至…之間〔用來估計數字〕: *There must have been between eighteen to twenty thousand people at the concert.* 那場音樂會上一定有一萬八千到兩萬人。| *He drowned in 10 to 12 feet of water.* 他淹死在 10 到 12 英尺的水深處。**20** used when saying what the chances of something happening are or giving the ODDS in betting (BET[1] (1)) 比〔用於表示某事發生的可能或打賭中的輸贏比率〕: *It's 100-1 he'll lose.* 他輸定了。| *Seagram is running at 11-8.* 西格拉姆的賠率是 11 比 8。

toad /tod; təʊd/ *n* [C] a small animal that looks like a large FROG and lives mostly on land 蟾蜍，癩蛤蟆

toad-in-the-hole /ˌ· · · ˈ·/ *n* [U] a British dish made of SAUSAGEs cooked in a mixture of eggs, milk, and flour 麵裹烤香腸〔一種英國菜〕

toad·stool /ˈtodˌstul; ˈtəʊdstuːl/ *n* [C] a wild plant like a MUSHROOM, that can be poisonous（毒）蕈

toad·y¹ /ˋtodɪ; ˈtəʊdi/ *n* [C] *informal* someone who pretends to like an important person so that they will help you【非正式】諂媚者, 馬屁精

toady² *v* [I] to pretend to like an important person so that they will help you 諂媚, 奉承, 拍馬屁: **[+to]** *toadying to the boss* 拍老闆的馬屁

to and fro¹ /ˌtu ənd ˋfro; ˌtuː ənd ˈfrəʊ/ *adv* if someone or something moves to and fro, they move in one direction and then back again 來來往往地, 往復地: *People walking to and fro on the promenade.* 步行大道上人來人往。—**to-and-fro** *adj*

to and fro² *n* [U] *informal* continuous movement of people or things from place to place【非正式】〔人或東西的〕來來往往, 川流不息 —see also 另見 TOING AND FROING

3 **toast¹** /tost; təʊst/ *n* **1** [U] bread that has been heated so that it is brown on both sides and no longer soft 烤麵包〔片〕, 吐司: *We had toast for breakfast.* 我們早餐吃的是烤麵包片。**2** [C] an occasion when you ask people to all drink something in order to thank someone, wish someone luck etc〔為答謝或祝福某人而進行的〕祝酒, 乾杯: **propose a toast** (=ask people to drink a toast) 提議乾一杯 **3 warm as toast** comfortably warm 温暖舒適: *They sat near the fire, warm as toast.* 他們坐在火邊, 温暖又舒適。**4 be the toast of Broadway/Hollywood etc** to be very popular and praised by many people for something you have done in a particular field of work 百老匯/好萊塢等的大名人 —see also 另見 FRENCH TOAST

toast² *v* [T] **1** to drink a glass of wine, etc to thank someone, wish someone luck etc 為…舉杯祝酒: *We toasted our success with champagne.* 我們用香檳酒慶祝自己的成功。**2** to make bread or other food brown by placing it close to heat 烘, 烤〔麵包或其他食品〕: *toasted cheese sandwiches* 烘烤乾酪三明治 **3** to sit yourself near a fire to make yourself warm〔坐在火邊〕使暖和

toast·er /ˋtostɚ; ˈtəʊstə/ *n* [C] a machine you use for toasting bread 烤麵包機 —see picture on page A10 參見 A10 頁圖

toasting fork /ˈ‥ ˌ/ *n* [C] a long fork used to hold bread over a fire to toast it〔烤麵包等用的〕烤叉

toast·mas·ter /ˋtostˌmæstɚ; ˈtəʊstˌmɑːstə/ *n* [C] someone who introduces the speakers at a formal occasion such as a BANQUET (=large formal meal)〔在宴會等正式場合中介紹演講者的〕(宴會) 主持人

toast·y /ˋtostɪ; ˈtəʊsti/ *adj AmE informal* warm and comfortable【美, 非正式】暖烘烘的, 温暖舒適的

to·bac·co /təˋbæko; təˈbækəʊ/ *n* [U] the dried brown leaves that are smoked in cigarettes, pipes etc 煙葉, 煙草

to·bac·co·nist /təˋbækənɪst; təˈbækənɪst/ *n* [C] *BrE*【英】**1** someone who has a shop that sells tobacco, cigarettes etc 煙草店老闆, 煙草經銷商 **2 tobacconist's** a shop that sells tobacco, cigarettes etc 煙草銷售店, 煙店

to·bog·gan¹ /təˋbɑgən; təˈbɒgən/ *n* [C] a light wooden board with a curved front, used for sliding down hills covered in snow 平底木板雪橇

toboggan² *v* [I] to slide down a hill on a toboggan 坐平底木板雪橇滑行

to·by jug /ˋtobɪ ˌdʒʌg; ˈtəʊbi dʒʌg/ *n* [C] a container for drinking from, shaped like a fat man wearing a hat (人形) 小酒杯〔形如頭戴帽子的胖人〕

toc·ca·ta /təˋkɑtə; təˈkɑːtə/ *n* [C] a piece of music, usually for piano or organ, that is played very quickly 托卡塔〔一種用鋼琴或管風琴快速演奏的樂曲〕

toc·sin /ˋtɑksɪn; ˈtɒksɪn/ *n* [C] *literary* a signal of danger that is made by ringing a bell【文】警鈴, 警鐘

tod /tɑd; tɒd/ *n* **on your tod** *BrE slang* by yourself【英俚】獨自, 自個兒

1 1 **to·day¹** /təˋde; təˈdeɪ/ *adv* **1** on the day that is happening now 今天, 今日: *I couldn't go shopping yesterday so I'll have to go today.* 我昨天沒能去買東西, 所以今天我必須去。| *Ed has his music lesson today.* 埃德今天有音樂課。| **today week/a week today** *BrE* (=one week from today)【英】距今天一週之後, 下週的今天 *We're going on holiday today week.* 我們一週之後要去度假。—see picture at 參見 DAY 圖 **2** at the present time 現今, 現在, 時下: *Students today seem to know very little about geography.* 如今的學生似乎對地理知識掌握得很少。

today² *n* [U] **1** the day that is happening now 今天, 今日 —see picture at 參見 DAY 圖: *Today is my birthday!* 今天是我的生日！| *Have you read today's paper yet?* 你看過今天的報紙了嗎? **2** the present period of time 現今, 現在, 眼下: *Today's computers are becoming much smaller and lighter.* 現在的電腦正變得越來越小、越來越輕了。| *The children of today have more choices than their parents.* 現在的孩子比他們的父母有更多的選擇。

tod·dle /ˋtɑdl̩; ˈtɒdl/ *v* [I] if a small child toddles, it walks with short, unsteady steps〔學步小孩〕蹣跚行走

tod·dler /ˋtɑdlɚ; ˈtɒdlə/ *n* [C] a very young child who is just learning to walk 剛學走路的小孩 —see 見 CHILD (USAGE)

tod·dy /ˋtɑdɪ; ˈtɒdi/ *n* [C] a hot drink made with WHISKY, sugar, and hot water 甜熱酒〔由威士忌加糖和熱水調製而成〕

to-do /təˋdu; təˈduː/ *n* [singular] *informal* unnecessary excitement or angry feelings about something; FUSS¹ (2)【非正式】騷動, 喧鬧; 大驚小怪: *What a to-do there was when I said I didn't want to be married in a church!* 我說我不想在教堂裡舉行婚禮, 就引起了那麼大的騷動！

toe¹ /to; təʊ/ *n* [C] **1** one of the five movable parts at the 3
end of your foot 腳趾: *He stubbed his toe on a rock.* 他的腳趾碰在了一塊石頭上。| **big toe** (=the largest of your toes) 大腳趾 **2** the part of a shoe or sock that covers the front part of your foot〔鞋或襪的〕足尖部 —see picture at 參見 SHOE¹ 圖 **3 step on sb's toes** *AmE*【美】**tread on sb's toes** *BrE*【英】to offend someone, especially by becoming involved in something that they are responsible for〔尤指因涉足別人負責的範圍而〕得罪某人, 觸犯某人: *He's new in the department and will have to be careful not to step on anyone's toes.* 他是這個部門新來的, 必須小心謹慎, 不要得罪任何人。**4 keep sb on their toes** to make sure that someone is ready for anything that might happen 使某人隨時準備行動; 使某人保持警覺: *She certainly keeps the children on their toes!* 她的確讓孩子們保持警覺！**5 make sb's toes curl** to make someone feel very embarrassed or uncomfortable about something 使某人感到尷尬; 使某人感到不舒服 **6 touch your toes** to bend downwards so that your hands touch your toes 躬身用手摸腳趾 —see also 另見 **from head to toe** (HEAD¹ (2)), **from top to toe** (TOP¹ (20))

toe² *v* [T] **toe the line** to do what other people in a job or organization say you should do, whether you agree with them or not〔不管同意與否〕聽從命令; 服從紀律; 按規定行事: *You toe the line or you don't stay on the team!* 你要聽從命令, 否則你就別待在隊裡！

toe·cap /ˋtokæp; ˈtəʊkæp/ *n* [C] a piece of metal or leather that covers the front part of a shoe〔鞋前部的〕外包頭, 鞋頭

toe·hold /ˋtoˌhold; ˈtəʊhəʊld/ *n* **1** [singular] your first involvement in a particular activity, from which you can develop and become stronger〔事業發展、增強的〕初步的立腳點: *The company has gained a toehold in the competitive computer market.* 該公司在競爭激烈的電腦市場站穩了腳根。**2** [C] a small hole in a rock where you can put your foot when you are climbing〔攀登時可容納一隻腳的〕小的立足點

toe·nail /ˋtoˌnel; ˈtəʊneɪl/ *n* [C] the hard part that covers the top of each of your toes 腳趾甲 —see picture at 參見 FOOT¹ 圖

toe·rag /ˋtoræg; ˈtəʊræg/ *n* [C] *BrE spoken* an offensive word for someone you dislike【英口】臭小子; 臭娘們〔冒犯用語〕: *That toerag cheated me!* 那個臭小子騙了我！

toff /tɑf; tɒf/ *n* [C] *BrE old-fashioned* someone who is rich or has a high social position【英, 過時】有錢人; 上流社會的人

tof·fee /ˈtɑfɪ; ˈtɒfi/ *n* [C,U] **1** a sticky sweet brown substance that you can eat, made by boiling sugar, water, and butter together, or a piece of this substance 太妃糖 **2 can't do sth for toffee** *BrE informal* to be very bad at doing something【英, 非正式】根本幹不了某事, 完全無法勝任某事: *He can't sing for toffee!* 他根本就不會唱歌!

toffee ap·ple /ˈ·· ˌ··/ *n* [C] an apple covered with toffee and put on a stick 太妃糖蘋果〔蘋果外裹有太妃糖, 插於棍上〕

toffee-nosed /ˈ·· ·/ *adj BrE informal* a toffee-nosed person thinks that they are better than other people because of their social position【英, 非正式】勢利的, 好擺架子的, 自命不凡的: *He's a toffee-nosed little creep!* 他是個自命不凡的小人!

to·fu /ˈtofu; ˈtəʊfuː/ *n* [U] a soft white food like cheese, that is made from SOY BEANs 豆腐

tog[1] /tɑg; tɒg/ *n* [C] **1 togs** [plural] *informal* clothes【非正式】衣服 **2** *technical* a unit for measuring the warmth of QUILTs etc【術語】托格〔測量被子保暖性的單位〕

tog[2] *v*

tog yourself **up/out** *phr v* [T] *informal* to put on clothes for a particular occasion or activity【非正式】〔為出席特殊場合或活動而〕給〔自己〕打扮, 使〔自己〕穿得漂亮

to·ga /ˈtogə; ˈtəʊgə/ *n* [C] a long loose piece of clothing worn by people in ancient Rome 托加袍〔古羅馬人穿的寬鬆長袍〕

to·geth·er[1] /təˈgɛðɚ; təˈgeðə/ *adv*

1 ►MAKE ONE THING 製作一種東西◄ if you want to put two or more things together, you join them so that they form a single subject or group 結合起來: *Mix the butter and sugar together.* 把黃油和糖攪拌在一起。| *He added all the numbers together.* 他把所有的數目加在一起。| *We stuck the pieces together again.* 我們把那些碎片又重新黏合在一起。| *The model was held together with string.* 那個模型用繩子拴在一起。

2 ►IN ONE PLACE 在一個地方◄ if you keep, collect etc things together, you keep or collect them all in one place 到一起, 集攏着: *I gathered all my favourite paintings together.* 我把我喜愛的所有畫都收集到了一起。

3 close/packed/crowded etc together if people or objects are close together, packed together etc, they are placed very near to each other 緊挨在一起/塞在一起/擠在一起: *The climbers were sitting huddled together for warmth.* 登山者們擠成一團取暖。| *Her ornaments were all bunched together at one end of the shelf.* 她的那些裝飾品全都束在一起, 放在書架的一端。

4 ►AGAINST EACH OTHER 相互◄ if you rub, bang etc things together, you rub or bang them against each other 相互, 彼此: *Max was rubbing his hands together with glee.* 馬克斯高興地搓着雙手。| *Knock the brushes together to clean them.* 把刷子互相拍拍弄乾淨。

5 ►WITH EACH OTHER 共同◄ if two or more people are together or do something together, they are with each other or do something with each other 共同; 一齊, 一塊兒: *We were at school together.* 我們曾經在同一所學校上學。| *Let's all stay together or someone might get lost.* 我們全都待在一塊兒, 以防有人走失。| *They've decided to spend more time together.* 他們決定花更多的時間在一起。| *I hear George and his wife have got back together.* 我聽說喬治和他妻子復婚了。| **all together (now)** *spoken* (=used when you are asking a group of people to say or do something together)【口】(現在) 大家一起上 *Right, men. All together now...Push!* 好的, 夥計們。現在大家一起上…推!

6 ►IN AGREEMENT 一致地◄ if people are together, come together etc they are or become united and work with each other 團結一致地, 齊心協力地, 合作地: *Together we can win.* 團結一致, 我們就能取勝。| *We must work closely together on this one.* 這回我們必須密切合作。| *bring the two sides in the dispute together* 使糾紛雙方達成和解

7 ►AT THE SAME TIME 同時◄ at the same time 同時, 一齊: *Why do all the bills always come together?* 為甚麼賬單總是一下子同時來呢? | *You should have used both the tools together.* 你應該同時使用這兩種工具。

8 together with in addition to; at the same time as 和…一起, 連同: *Just bring it back to the store, together with your receipt.* 把它連同收據一起拿回到店裡來就行了。

9 ►WITHOUT STOPPING 不停地◄ *old use* without interruption【舊】不間斷地, 接連地: *It rained for four days together.* 雨接連下了四天。—see also 另見 **get your act together** (ACT[1] (5)), **hold together** (HOLD[1]), **piece sth together** (PIECE[2]), **pull together** (PULL[1])

together[2] *adj spoken* someone who is together always thinks clearly and does things in a very sensible, organized way【口】思路清晰的, 處事明智的, 條理井然的: *I admire Rosie – she's such a together person.* 我佩服羅茜, 她是一位如此鎮靜自若的人。

to·geth·er·ness /təˈgɛðɚnɪs; təˈgeðənɪ̤s/ *n* [U] the feeling you have when you are part of a group of people who have a close relationship with each other 和睦團結; 親密無間: *I really miss the togetherness we felt at college.* 我真懷念我們在大學時那種親密無間的感覺。

tog·gle /ˈtɑgl; ˈtɒgəl/ *n* [C] **1** a small piece of wood or plastic that is used as a button on coats, bags etc〔用作外衣、背包等鈕扣的〕栓扣, 棒形鈕扣 —see picture at 參見 FASTENER 圖 **2** something on a computer that lets you change from one operation to another〔電腦上的〕雙態元件〔使一種操作轉換為另一種操作的鍵等元件〕

toggle switch /ˈ·· ·/ *n* [C] *technical* a small part on a machine that is used to turn electricity on and off by moving it up or down【術語】〔上下開閉電源的〕撥動開關

toil[1] /tɔɪl; tɔɪl/ *v* [I always+adv/prep] **1** also 又作 **toil away** to work very hard for a long period of time 長時間地苦幹, 辛苦勞作: **[+at/over]** *I've been toiling away at this essay all weekend.* 我整個週末一直在辛苦地寫這篇文章。**2** to move slowly and with great effort 吃力地慢行, 跋涉: **[+up/through/against etc]** *They toiled slowly up the hill.* 他們吃力地慢慢爬上了山。

toil[2] *n* [U] *formal*【正式】**1** hard unpleasant work done over a long period 長時間的辛苦勞作: *a life of toil* 一生辛勞 **2 the toils of** *literary* if you are caught in the toils of an unpleasant feeling or situation, you are trapped by it【文】困境; 困惑; 迷惑

toi·let /ˈtɔɪlɪt; ˈtɔɪlɪ̤t/ *n* **1** [C] a large bowl that you sit on to get rid of waste liquid or waste matter from your body 抽水馬桶, 便池: *He flushed the toilet.* 他放水沖了馬桶。**2** [C] *especially BrE* a room or building containing a toilet【尤英】廁所, 洗手間, 衛生間; BATHROOM (2) *AmE*【美】: *public toilets* 公共廁所 **3 go to the toilet** *BrE* to pass waste liquid or waste matter from your body【英】上廁所: *Mummy, I need to go to the toilet!* 媽媽! 我得去上廁所! **4** [U] *old-fashioned* the act of washing and dressing yourself【過時】梳洗, 打扮

toilet bag /ˈ·· ·/ *n* [C] a bag in which you keep things such as soap, TOOTHPASTE etc when travelling〔旅行時帶着的〕梳洗用具袋; SPONGE BAG *BrE*【英】—see picture at 參見 BAG[1] 圖

toilet pa·per /ˈ·· ˌ··/ *n* [U] soft thin paper used for cleaning yourself after you have used the toilet 衛生紙, 手紙

toi·let·ries /ˈtɔɪlɪtrɪz; ˈtɔɪlɪ̤triz/ *n* [plural] things such as soap and TOOTHPASTE that are used for washing yourself 梳洗用具; 梳妝用品

toilet roll /ˈ·· ·/ *n* [C] *BrE* toilet paper that is wound around a small tube【英】衛生卷紙

toilet-train·ing /ˈ·· ˌ··/ *n* [U] the act of teaching a child to use a toilet〔教孩子〕使用便盆的訓練 —**toilet-train** *v* [T] —**toilet-trained** *adj*

toilet wa·ter /ˈ·· ˌ··/ *n* [U] a kind of PERFUME (=pleasant smelling liquid) that does not have a very strong smell 花露水

to·ing and fro·ing /ˌtuɪŋ ənd ˋfroɪŋ; ˌtuːɪŋ ənd ˈfrəʊɪŋ/ *n* [U] **1** movement backwards and forwards many times between two or more places 來來回回, 往復多次 **2** a lot of activity that does not help you to do something 瞎忙; 忙亂: *After much toing and froing they finally reached a decision.* 忙亂了一陣之後他們終於作出了決定。

to·ken[1] /ˈtokən; ˈtəʊkən/ *n* [C] **1** a round piece of metal that you use instead of money in some machines〔在某些機器上用來代替錢的〕金屬代幣 **2** *formal* something that represents a feeling, fact, event etc【正式】象徵, 標誌: **a token of your gratitude/respect/appreciation etc** *Please accept this gift as a small token of our appreciation.* 區區薄禮, 略表謝意。—see also 另見 **by the same token** (SAME[1] (8)) **3 book/record/gift token** *BrE* a special piece of paper that you can exchange for a book, record etc in a shop【英】〔商店的〕購書禮券/唱片禮券/禮券; GIFT CERTIFICATE *AmE*【美】: *a £10 book token* 一張價值十英鎊的購書券

token[2] *adj* [only before noun 僅用於名詞前] **1** a token action, change etc is only done so that someone can pretend that they are dealing with a problem 裝門面的; 裝模作樣的: *The government thinks it can get away with token gestures on environmental issues.* 關於解決環境保護的問題, 政府以為做點表面文章就能掩人耳目。| **token black/woman etc** (=someone who is included in a group to make everyone think that it has all types of people in it, when this is not really true)〔放進某些團體以示公正的〕裝點門面的黑人/婦女等 **2** done as a first sign that an agreement, promise etc will be kept and that more will be done later 象徵性的〔指為了表示守信而做, 並將會做得更多〕: *A small token payment will keep the bank happy.* 一小筆象徵性的付款會讓銀行感到滿意。

to·ken·ism /ˋtokənˌɪzəm; ˈtəʊkənɪzəm/ *n* [U] actions that are intended to make people think that an organization deals fairly with people or problems when in fact it does not 裝點門面, 做表面文章

told /told; təʊld/ the past tense and past participle of TELL

tol·e·ra·ble /ˋtɑlərəbl̩; ˈtɒlərəbəl/ *adj* **1** a situation that is tolerable is not very good, but you are able to accept it〔狀況〕可接受的, 過得去的, 尚好的: *The apartment is really too small, but it's tolerable for the time being.* 這套公寓真的太小了, 不過暫時還過得去。**2** unpleasant or painful and only just able to be accepted 令人不快[痛苦], 僅僅可以忍受的: *The heat in this room is barely tolerable.* 這房間裡熱得簡直無法忍受。

tol·e·ra·bly /ˋtɑlərəblɪ; ˈtɒlərəbli/ *adv* [+adj/adv] fairly, but not very much 相當; 尚可: *We were tolerably happy for the first year.* 第一年, 我們還算比較幸福。

tol·e·rance /ˋtɑlərəns; ˈtɒlərəns/ *n* **1** [U] willingness to allow people to do, say, or believe what they want without criticizing them 忍受, 容忍; 寬容: **[+of/towards]** *tolerance towards religious minorities* 對宗教上的少數派所持的寬容態度 **2** [C,U] the degree to which someone can suffer pain, difficulty etc without being harmed or damaged〔痛苦、困難等的〕忍受程度, 忍耐力: **[+of/to]** *Many old people have a very limited tolerance to cold.* 許多老年人特別怕冷。**3** [C,U] *technical* the amount by which the size, weight etc of something can change without causing problems【術語】〔某物在大小、重量等方面的〕公差〔偏離公差則不能正常工作〕

tol·e·rant /ˋtɑlərənt; ˈtɒlərənt/ *adj* allowing people to do, say, or believe what they want without punishing or criticizing them 寬容的; 容忍的: *Luckily, my parents were tolerant of my choice of music.* 幸運的是, 我的父母對我選擇音樂持寬容態度。

tol·e·rate /ˋtɑləˌret; ˈtɒləreɪt/ *v* [T] **1** to allow people to do, say, or believe something without criticizing or punishing them 容忍, 容許; 寬容: *We simply will not tolerate vigilante groups on our streets.* 我們根本不容許在我們的街道上出現治安聯防小組。**2** to be able to accept something unpleasant or difficult, even though you do not like it 忍受; 忍耐: *Many workers said they couldn't tolerate the long hours.* 許多工人都說他們無法忍受長時間的工作。

tol·e·ra·tion /ˌtɑləˋreʃən; ˌtɒləˈreɪʃən/ *n* [U] willingness to allow people to believe what they want without being punished 容忍 (精神); 寬容 (態度): *a long history of religious toleration* 宗教寬容的漫長歷史

toll[1] /tol; təʊl/ *n* [C] **1** the money you have to pay to use a particular road, bridge etc〔道路、橋樑等的〕通行費 **2** [usually singular 一般用單數] the number of people killed or injured in a particular accident, by a particular illness etc〔事故、疾病等造成的〕傷亡人數: **death toll** *The death toll has risen to 83.* 死亡人數已上升到83人。**3 take its toll (on)** to have a very bad effect on something or someone over a long period of time 對…產生嚴重的不良影響: *Years of smoking have taken their toll on his health.* 多年的吸煙已嚴重損害了他的健康。**4** the sound of a large bell ringing slowly 大鐘緩慢的敲擊聲

toll[2] *v* [I,T] if a large bell tolls, or you toll it, it keeps ringing slowly, especially to show that someone has died〔尤表明某人已死而緩慢持續地〕敲 (鐘), 鳴 (鐘)

toll·booth /ˋtolˌbuθ; ˈtəʊlbuːθ/ *n* [C] a place where you pay to drive on a road, bridge etc〔道路、橋樑等徵收通行費的〕收費亭[處]

toll-bridge /ˈ· ·/ *n* [C] a bridge that you pay to drive across 收費橋

toll-free /ˌ· ˈ·◂/ *adv AmE* if you telephone a particular number toll-free, you do not have to pay for the call【美】〔打某個電話號碼時〕無需付費的, 免費的 —**toll-free** *adj*: *Call this toll-free number for details!* 詳情請撥打這個免費電話號碼!

toll·gate /ˋtolˌget; ˈtəʊlgeɪt/ *n* [C] a gate across a road, at which you have to pay money before you can drive any further〔公路上收通行費的〕收費站, 收費處

toll road /ˈ· ·/ *n* [C] a road that you pay to use 收費道路

toll·way /ˋtolwe; ˈtəʊlweɪ/ *n AmE* a large long road that you pay to use【美】收費長途公路

tom /tɑm; tɒm/ *n* [C] *informal* a TOMCAT【非正式】雄貓, 公貓

tom·a·hawk /ˋtɑməˌhɔk; ˈtɒməhɔːk/ *n* [C] a light AXE[1] (1) used by Native Americans〔北美印第安人用的〕輕斧, 戰斧

to·ma·to /təˋmeto; təˈmɑːtəʊ/ *n plural* **tomatoes** [C] a round soft red fruit eaten raw or cooked as a vegetable 番茄, 西紅柿 —see picture on page A9 參見A9頁圖 S3

tomb /tum; tuːm/ *n* [C] a grave, especially a large one above ground〔尤指較大的〕墳, 墓, 塚: *the tomb of the Unknown Soldier* 無名戰士墓

tom·bo·la /ˋtɑmbələ; tɒmˈbəʊlə/ *n* [U] *BrE* a game in which you buy a ticket with a number on it in order to try and win a prize【英】"擔保樂"〔一種摸彩遊戲〕

tom·boy /ˋtɑmˌbɔɪ; ˈtɒmbɔɪ/ *n* [C] a girl who likes playing the same games as boys 野丫頭, 假小子〔指喜歡像男孩子那樣打鬧的女孩子〕: *I was just coming out of my tomboy stage.* 我剛度過我的野丫頭階段。

tomb·stone /ˋtumˌston; ˈtuːmstəʊn/ *n* [C] a stone that is put on a grave and shows the dead person's name, dates of birth and death etc; GRAVESTONE 墓石, 墓碑

tom·cat /ˋtɑmkæt; ˈtɒmkæt/ *n* [C] a male cat 雄貓, 公貓

tome /tom; təʊm/ *n* [C] *literary* a large heavy book【文】大部頭書, 厚本書: *hefty leather-bound tomes of uncertain age* 沉重的、年代不詳的皮裝大部頭書

tom·fool /ˌtɑmˋful; ˌtɒmˈfuːl◂/ *adj* very silly 極傻的, 笨透的: *That was a tomfool thing to do!* 那件事做得愚蠢透頂!

tom·fool·e·ry /ˌtɑmˋfulərɪ; tɒmˈfuːləri/ *n* [U] silly

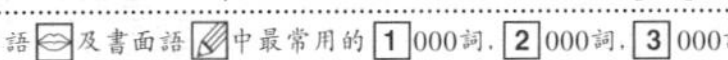

behaviour 愚蠢行為

tom·my gun /ˈtɑmɪ ˌgʌn; ˈtɒmi gʌn/ *n* [C] *informal* a small gun that can fire many bullets very quickly【非正式】湯姆式衝鋒槍, 輕機槍

1 2 **to·mor·row¹** /təˈmɔro; təˈmɒrəʊ/ *adv* on or during the day after today (在) 明天: *Our class is going to London tomorrow.* 我們全班明天要去倫敦。| **a week tomorrow** also 又作 **tomorrow week** *BrE*【英】(=a week from tomorrow) 明天之後一週 *James's new job starts a week tomorrow.* 詹姆斯的新工作從明天算起一週之後開始。

tomorrow² *n* **1** [U] the day after today 明天: *I'll see you at tomorrow's meeting.* 在明天的會上再見吧。—see picture at 參見 DAY 圖 **2** the future, especially the near future 來日, 未來〔尤指不久的將來〕: *The computers of tomorrow will be smaller and more powerful.* 未來的電腦將更小巧, 功能將更強大。**3 do sth like there's no tomorrow** do something very quickly and carelessly, without worrying about the future 不考慮將來地做某事: *Rita's spending money like there's no tomorrow.* 麗塔花起錢來根本不考慮將來。

tom-tom /ˈ· ·/ *n* [C] a long narrow drum you play with your hands〔一種狹長的〕手鼓, 長筒鼓

3 **ton** /tʌn; tʌn/ *n* [C] **1** *plural* **tons** or **ton** a unit for measuring weight, equal to 2240 pounds or 1016 kilos in Britain, and 2000 pounds or 907.2 kilos in the US 英噸〔2240 磅或 1016 公斤〕; 美噸〔2000 磅或 907.2 公斤〕—compare 比較 TONNE —see table on page C3 參見 C3 頁附錄 **2 tons of** *informal* a lot of【非正式】大量的: *We've bought tons of beer for the party tonight.* 我們已經為今晚的聚會買了大量啤酒。**3 weigh a ton** *informal* to be very heavy【非正式】非常重: *Your bag weighs a ton!* 你的包重得不得了! **4 do a ton** *BrE informal* to drive at 100 miles an hour【英, 非正式】以每小時 100 英里的速度駕駛 **5 come down on sb like a ton of bricks** *informal* to get very angry with someone about something they have done【非正式】對某人大發脾氣

ton·al /ˈtonḷ; ˈtəʊnl/ *adj* **1** connected with tones of colour or sound 色調的; 音調的: *The tonal range she uses is wide and varied.* 她使用的音域寬廣, 富於變化。**2** *technical* a piece of music that is tonal is based on a particular KEY² (4)【術語】〔音樂〕調性的 —opposite 反義詞 ATONAL

ton·al·i·ty /toˈnæləti; təʊˈnæləti/ *n* [C,U] *technical* the character of a piece of music that depends on the KEY² (4) of the music and the way in which the tunes and harmonies (HARMONY (1)) are combined【術語】〔音樂的〕調性

2 **tone¹** /ton; təʊn/ *n*

1 ►VOICE SHOWING FEELING 表明情感的說話聲◄ [C] [plural] the way your voice sounds that shows how you are feeling, or what you mean〔說話的〕語氣, 口氣; 腔調: *"Why would I lie?" Nora asked in an injured tone.* "我為甚麼要撒謊?" 諾拉用委屈的口氣問道。| *She spoke in warm tones about her family.* 她以溫暖的語氣談論她的家庭。| **tone of voice** *spoken* (=used about someone's rude or angry way of speaking)【口】說話的腔調〔帶有粗魯或慍怒〕*I don't like your tone of voice.* 我不喜歡你說話的腔調。| **don't take that tone with me** *spoken* (=do not speak to me in that rude or unpleasant way)【口】別用那種口吻跟我說話

2 ►SOUND 聲音◄ [C,U] the quality of a sound especially the sound of a musical instrument or someone's voice〔尤指樂器或某人說話的〕音調; 音色, 音質: *Your piano has a beautiful tone.* 你這架鋼琴音色很美。| **in tone** (=having a particular tone) 在音質上 *Margaret's voice was shrill in tone.* 瑪格麗特尖聲尖氣地說話。| **deep-toned/even-toned/shrill-toned etc** (=having a low, calm etc tone) 聲音低沉/平和/很尖等的 *My father spoke in an even-toned voice.* 我父親以平和的聲音說話。

3 ►GENERAL FEELING/ATTITUDE 一般的感覺/態度◄ [singular,U] the general feeling or attitude expressed in a piece of writing, activity etc〔作品、活動等的〕基調, 格調; 氣氛: *Sara had kept the tone of the meeting businesslike.* 莎拉一直使會議保持着務實的氣氛。| **set the tone** (=establish the general attitude or feeling of an event, activity etc) 確定基調 *Unfortunately, their disagreement set the tone for the whole evening.* 不幸的是, 他們的不和籠罩着整個晚會。

4 ►SOCIALLY ACCEPTABLE 社會可以接受的◄ [U] the degree to which something is considered polite, interesting, socially acceptable etc 風氣; 格調, 情調: *The formal setting gave a certain tone to the evening.* 正規拘謹的環境使晚會帶上了某種氣氛。| **lower/raise the tone** *That horrible building lowers the whole tone of the neighborhood.* 那棟難看的建築物降低了周圍的格調。

5 ►COLOUR 顏色◄ [C] one of the many types of a particular colour, each slightly darker, lighter, brighter etc than the next 色調, 色彩的層次: *The entire painting was in tones of blue.* 整幅畫都是藍色調。—see also 另見 TWO-TONE

6 ►ELECTRONIC SOUND 電子聲音◄ [C] a sound made by electronic equipment, such as a telephone〔電話等發出的〕電子聲音: *Please leave a message after the tone.* 請在提示音後留言。| **dial/busy** *AmE*【美】/**engaged** *BrE*【英】**tone** (=the sound you hear on a telephone that means you can dial, it is busy etc)〔電話的〕撥號音/忙音 —see also 另見 DIALLING TONE

7 ►BODY 身體◄ [U] *technical* how firm and strong your muscles, skin etc are【術語】〔肌肉、皮膚等的〕強健, 健康狀況: *Swimming improves your muscle tone.* 游泳會使你的肌肉更強健。

8 ►MUSIC 音樂◄ [C] *technical* the difference in PITCH² (3) between two musical notes that are separated by one KEY² (4) on the piano【術語】音程, 音級; STEP¹ (17) *especially AmE*【尤美】

9 ►VOICE LEVEL 語音調子◄ [C] *technical* the PITCH¹ (3) of someone's voice as they speak【術語】〔說話的〕聲調; 語調: *The Chinese language has several tones.* 漢語有幾種聲調。

tone² *v* [T] to improve the strength and firmness of your skin, muscles etc 使〔皮膚、肌肉等〕更強健, 使更健康: *It cleanses and tones your skin.* 它清潔你的皮膚, 使之更加健康。

tone sth ↔ **down** *phr v* [T] **1** to reduce the effect of a speech or piece or writing, so that people will not be offended 緩和…語氣: *His advisers told him to tone down his speech.* 他的顧問們告訴他要緩和講話的語氣。**2** to make a colour less bright 使〔顏色〕暗淡, 柔和

tone sth/sb ↔ **up** *phr v* [T] to make your body or part of your body feel healthier and stronger 使更健康, 使更強健: *Aerobics really tones up your muscles.* 增氧健身法的確會使你的肌肉更加強健。

tone-deaf /ˌ· ˈ·◂/ *adj* unable to tell the difference between different musical notes 不會辨別音調的: *the tone-deaf morons in today's pop groups* 在今天的流行音樂樂隊裡五音不辨的蠢才

tone lan·guage /ˈ· ˌ··/ *n* [C] *technical* a language such as Chinese in which the way a sound goes up or down affects the meaning of the word【術語】聲調語言〔聲調的高低會影響單詞意思的語言, 如漢語〕

tone·less /ˈtonlɪs; ˈtəʊnləs/ *adj* a toneless voice does not express any feelings〔聲音〕單調的, 平板的: *"I'm sorry," he said, in a flat toneless voice.* "對不起。" 他以一種平淡的聲調說道。—**tonelessly** *adv*

tone po·em /ˈ· ˌ··/ *n* [C] a piece of music written to represent an idea, scene, or story 交響詩, 音詩〔表達思想、場面、故事的音樂作品〕

ton·er /ˈtonɚ; ˈtəʊnə/ *n* [U] **1** a type of ink used in computer PRINTERs, PHOTOCOPIERs etc〔電腦打印機、複印機等用的〕增色劑, 色粉 **2** a liquid that you put on your face to make your skin feel good〔抹在臉上的〕潤膚水

tongs /tɔŋz; tɒŋz/ *n* [plural] a tool that consists of two moveable bars joined at one end, used to pick up an object 夾子, 鉗子, 鑷子 —see picture at 參見 LABORATORY 圖

3 3 **tongue** /tʌŋ; tʌŋ/ *n*
1 ▶MOUTH 嘴◀ [C] the soft, moveable part inside your mouth that you use for tasting, eating, and speaking 舌, 舌頭: *Joe ran his tongue over his dry lips.* 喬用舌頭舔舔乾燥的嘴唇。| *The dog panted, his tongue hanging out in the heat.* 那隻狗在酷暑中把舌頭伸在外面, 喘着粗氣。| **stick your tongue out** (=put your tongue outside your mouth as a rude gesture) 伸出舌頭〔不禮貌的表示〕 *Kim stuck her tongue out at the teacher.* 金不禮貌地朝老師伸出舌頭。
2 sharp/eloquent/silver/acid etc tongue if you have a sharp, silver etc tongue, you speak in a way that shows your anger, use beautiful language etc 尖刻/流利/動聽/尖酸等的話: *Gina's sharp tongue will get her into trouble one day.* 吉娜說話尖酸刻薄, 總有一天會給自己惹上麻煩的。| **rough-tongued/sharp-tongued/silver-tongued etc** (=speaking in an angry, beautiful etc way) 說話憤怒/尖刻/動聽等的 *He was clever and acid-tongued.* 他伶牙俐齒的, 老愛挖苦人。
3 tongue in cheek if you say something with your tongue in your cheek, you say it as a joke〔說話〕不當真地; 開玩笑地 —see also 另見 TONGUE-IN-CHEEK
4 slip of the tongue a mistake in something you say 說漏了嘴, 說錯了話, 口誤: *Did I say $100? It must have been a slip of the tongue.* 我說過 100 美元嗎? 那一定是口誤。
5 bite your tongue to stop yourself saying something because it is better not to 停止說話, 保持緘默: *I wanted to argue but I had to bite my tongue.* 我想辯駁, 但又不得不保持緘默。| **bite your tongue!** (=used to tell someone angrily that they should not say the type of thing they have just said) 閉上你的嘴!, 別再說了!
6 Cat got your tongue? also 又作 **Lost your tongue?** *spoken* used to ask someone why they are not talking【口】怎麼不說話了?
7 get your tongue around *informal* to be able to say a difficult word or phrase【非正式】說出〔某個拗口的詞或短語〕: *I can't get my tongue around the names of these Welsh towns.* 這些威爾斯城鎮的名字很拗口, 我唸不出來。
8 ▶LANGUAGE 語言◀ *literary* a language【文】語言; 方言: *Anton lapsed into his own tongue when he was excited.* 安東激動的時候就說自己的家鄉話了。—see also 另見 MOTHER TONGUE, **native tongue** (NATIVE[1] (3))
9 watch your tongue! *spoken* used to tell someone that they should not have said something rude【口】注意你的話!
10 ▶FOOD 食物◀ [U] the tongue of a cow or sheep, cooked and eaten cold〔牛、羊等動物可供冷食的〕舌頭
11 trip/roll off the tongue *humorous* if a name, phrase etc trips or rolls off your tongue, it is easy or pleasant to say【幽默】〔名字、片語等〕流暢地講出: *Agatha Boglewood: it doesn't exactly trip off the tongue does it?* 阿加莎·博格爾伍德: 說起來並不那麼容易, 是吧?
12 ▶SHAPE 形狀◀ [C] something that has a long thin shape 舌狀物: [+of] *tongues of fire* 火舌
13 ▶SHOE 鞋◀ the part of a shoe that lies on top of your foot, under the part where you tie it 鞋舌 —see picture at 參見 SHOE[1] 圖
14 loosen sb's tongue if something, such as alcohol loosens your tongue, it makes you talk a lot〔喝酒等〕使某人話多, 使某人管不住嘴: *Tongues loosened by drink, they told me what I needed to know.* 他們喝了酒話多, 結果把我需要知道的都告訴了我。
15 find your tongue to speak after being silent because you were afraid or shy〔因害怕或害羞而沉默之後〕終於開口說話: *Dana finally found his tongue and told them how he'd hated his first day at school.* 達納終於開口說話了, 他告訴他們, 他是多麼討厭上學的第一天。
16 hold your tongue! *old-fashioned spoken* used to angrily tell someone to stop speaking【過時, 口】閉嘴!, 不要講話!
17 wagging tongues if you talk about tongues wagging, you mean that people are talking about someone in an unkind way 風言風語, 說長道短: *Angela's divorce will certainly set tongues wagging.* 安傑拉的離婚肯定會讓人們說三道四的。
18 keep a civil tongue in your head *spoken* used when you think someone should speak politely【口】說話要講禮貌〔認為別人說話粗魯時使用〕
19 speak with forked tongue *humorous* to tell lies【幽默】說謊
20 speak in tongues to speak using strange words as part of a religious experience 說別國的話, 說其他民族的話〔一種宗教體驗〕
21 tongue and groove joint *technical* a way of joining two pieces of wood【術語】〔兩塊木頭的〕舌槽式接合 —see also 另見 **on the tip of your tongue** (TIP[1] (6)), **give sb the rough side of your tongue** (ROUGH[1] (18))

tongue de·press·or /ˈ· ·,··/ *n* [C] *AmE* a little flat piece of wood a doctor uses to hold down your tongue while examining your throat【美】〔醫生檢查病人喉嚨時用的〕壓舌板; SPATULA *BrE*【英】

tongue-in-cheek /,· · ˈ·◂/ *adj* a tongue-in-cheek remark, comment etc is said as a joke〔講話、評論等〕不可當真的, 開玩笑的: *a splendidly tongue-in-cheek account of their first meeting* 對他們第一次見面的情景所作的天花亂墜的、不可當真的描述 —**tongue-in-cheek** *adv*: *I believe he said this tongue-in-cheek.* 我認為他說的這一點是開玩笑。

tongue-tied /ˈ· ·/ *adj* unable to speak easily to other people, especially because you feel embarrassed〔尤指因感到難堪而〕張口結舌的, 說不出話的: *He sat tongue-tied, like a shy schoolboy.* 他笨嘴拙舌地坐在那裡, 活像個害羞的小學生。

tongue twist·er /ˈ· ,··/ *n* [C] a word or phrase that is difficult to say quickly and correctly 繞口的詞語[句子], 繞口令

ton·ic[1] /ˈtɑnɪk; ˈtɒnɪk/ *n* **1** [C,U] also 又作 **tonic water** a clear bitter tasting drink that is mixed with alcoholic drinks such as GIN or VODKA 奎寧水: *a gin and tonic* 加奎寧水的杜松子酒 **2** [C usually singular 一般用單數] *BrE* something that improves your health, strength, or confidence【英】增進健康[增強信心]的東西: *The holiday was a real tonic.* 那次度假確實讓人精神煥發。**3** [C] a medicine that is designed to give you more energy or strength when you feel tired 強身劑, 補藥: *a herbal tonic* 滋補性草藥 **4** [C usually singular 一般用單數] *technical* the first note in a musical SCALE[1] (8)【術語】〔音階中的〕主音

tonic[2] *adj formal* giving you energy and strength【正式】強身健體的, 有利於健康的: *Sea air has a tonic quality.* 海洋空氣有增進健康的作用。

to·night[1] /təˈnaɪt; təˈnaɪt/ *adv* on or during the night of today (在)今晚: *I've been really tired all day so I think I'll go to bed early tonight.* 我整天都覺得累極了, 所以今晚想早點上牀睡覺。| *at 9 o'clock tonight* 在今晚 9 點鐘 1 2

tonight[2] *n* [U] the night of today 今晚: *Tonight is a very special occasion.* 今晚是個非同尋常的場合。| *tonight's news bulletin* 今晚的新聞發佈

ton·nage /ˈtʌnɪdʒ; ˈtʌnɪdʒ/ *n* [C,U] **1** the size of a ship or the amount of goods it can carry, shown in TONs〔表示船舶大小的〕噸位; 載重噸位 **2** the total number of TONs that something weighs〔以噸計的〕總重量, 總噸數

tonne /tʌn; tʌn/ *n plural* **tonnes** *or* **tonne** [C] a metric unit for measuring weight, equal to 1000 kilograms 公噸〔等於 1000 公斤〕—see table on page C3 見 C3 頁附錄

tons /tʌnz; tʌnz/ *adv informal* very much【非正式】非常, 極其: *I feel tons better after a rest.* 休息之後, 我感覺好多了。

ton·sil /ˈtɑnsḷ; ˈtɒnsəl/ *n* [C] one of two small round

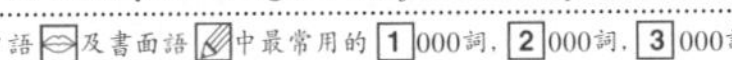

tools 工具

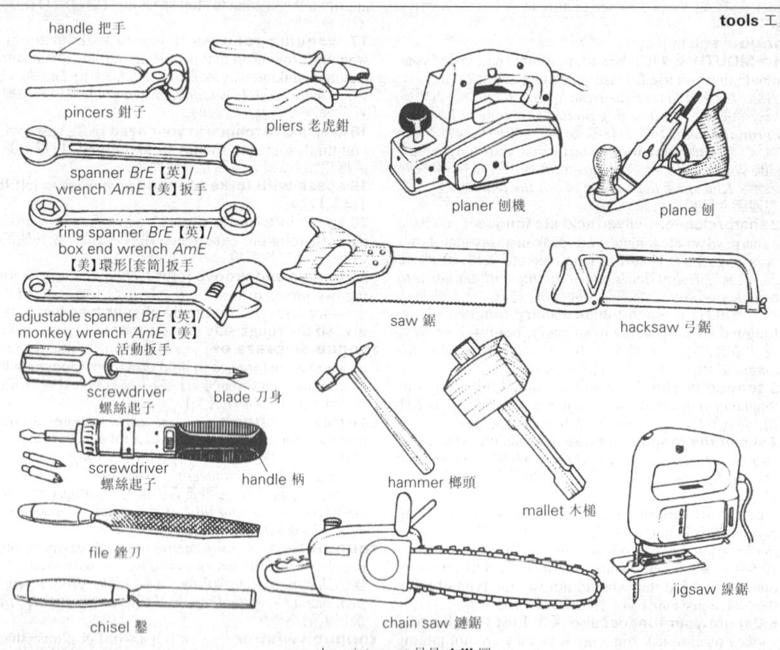

see also picture at 另見 **drill** 圖

pieces of flesh at the sides of the throat near the back of the tongue 扁桃體, 扁桃腺: *She had to have her tonsils out.* 她得把扁桃體切除。—see picture at 參見 RESPIRATORY 圖

ton·sil·li·tis /ˌtɑnsḷˈaɪtɪs; ˌtɒnsḷˈlaɪtḷs/ *n* [U] a serious infection of the tonsils 扁桃體炎, 扁桃腺炎

ton·so·ri·al /tɑnˋsɔrɪəl; tɒnˈsɔːriəl/ *adj humorous* connected with cutting hair【幽默】理髮的; 理髮師的: *a display of tonsorial perfection* 理髮師精湛手藝的展示

ton·sure /ˋtɑnʃə; ˈtɒnʃə/ *n* **1** [U] the act of removing all the hair from the top of your head to show that you are a MONK〔出家為僧的〕削髮〔儀式〕**2** [C] the top part of your head that has had the hair removed for this reason〔出家僧人的〕頭頂剃光部分,〔出家僧人的〕光頂 —**tonsured** *adj*

ton-up /ˈ· ·/ *adj BrE old-fashioned*【英, 過時】**ton-up driver/biker etc** someone who likes to drive very fast 喜歡開快車的駕駛員/喜歡騎快車的自行車手等

1 1 **too** /tu; tuː/ *adv* **1** [+adj/adv] more than is reasonable, possible, or necessary 太, 過分: *That music is too loud, turn the radio down.* 那音樂太鬧了, 把收音機關小一點。| **too much/little/many etc sth** *There's too much talking! Open your books and get down to work.* 話太多了! 打開書本, 開始學習吧。| **much/far/a little etc too** *Amanda is much too young to get married.* 阿曼達太年輕了, 還不能結婚。| **too tall/old etc for** *That crossword is too difficult for me.* 那個拼字遊戲對我來說太難了。| **too good/hot/big (a sth) to do sth** *My coffee is too hot to drink.* 我的咖啡太燙, 沒法喝。| *A free cruise to Acapulco – that's too good an opportunity to miss.* 免費乘船遊覽阿卡普爾科——那真是一個太好的機會, 不能錯過。**2** [at the end of a sentence or clause 用於句子或子句的末尾] also 也, 亦, 還: *It's a nutritious meal and cheap too!* 這是富於營養的一餐飯, 而且還很便宜。| *Sheila wants to come too.* 希拉也想來。—compare 比較 EITHER **3** [+adj/adv] very 很, 非常: *Dinner shouldn't be too long. Would you like a drink first?* 晚餐應該不會等得很久的。你要不要先喝上一杯? | *You shouldn't have bought flowers. You're too kind.* 你不必買花的。你太好了。**4 all too/only too** used to say that something is very easy to do, happens very often etc when it should not 很, 極, 非常: *Sadly this kind of attack is becoming all too common these days.* 現在這種襲擊太常見了, 令人悲哀。**5** used to emphasize that you are angry, surprised, or agree with something〔用於強調憤怒、吃驚或贊同某事〕: *"They've just built another car park next to the supermarket." "About time too."* "他們剛在超市旁邊修建了另外一個停車場。" "是該修了。" **6 I am/he is/you are etc too** *informal especially AmE* used to emphasize that you disagree with what someone has said about you【非正式, 尤美】我/他/你等其實[一定]...〔用於斷然表示不同意〕: *"You're not smart enough to use a computer." "I am too!"* "你腦子不夠機靈, 不會用電腦。" "我其實可以!"

took /tuk; tʊk/ the past tense of TAKE

tool¹ /tul; tuːl/ *n* [C] **1** something such as a hammer that you hold in your hand and use to do a particular job 工具: *Rob didn't have the right tool to repair the engine.* 羅布沒有合適的工具來修理發動機。**2** something such as a piece of equipment or skill that is useful for doing your job 器具; 技能: *Television is an important tool for the modern teacher.* 對於現代的教師來說, 電視是一種重要的工具。| **tools of the trade** *The poet is a craftsman and words are the tools of his trade.* 詩人是工匠, 文字是他這一行必不可少的工具。**3** someone who is used unfairly by someone else 被人利用的工具; 爪牙; 傀儡: **[+of]** *The king was merely a tool of the military government.* 這位國王只不過是軍人政府的傀儡。**4** *ta-*

boo slang a PENIS (=the male sex organ)【諱, 俚】陰莖, 雞巴 —see also 另見 **down tools** (DOWN⁴ (3))

tool² *v* [I+along/down] *AmE informal* to drive along a street, especially for fun【美, 非正式】〔尤指悠閒地〕駕駛車輛

tool up *phr v* [I,T **tool** sth ↔ **up**] to prepare a factory for production by providing the necessary tools and machinery〔以必要的工具和機器等〕裝備〔工廠〕: *tooled up to produce light weapons* 裝備工廠以生產輕型武器

tooled /tuld; tuːld/ *adj* tooled leather has been decorated using a special tool〔皮革〕手工壓花的

tool kit /'· ·/ *n* [C] a set of various tools 工具包, 工具箱

tool shed /'· ·/ *n* [C] a small wooden building in a garden, where tools are kept〔園圃裡的〕工具房

toot¹ /tut; tuːt/ *v* [I,T] **1** *especially BrE* if you toot your car horn, or if it toots, it makes a short, high sound【尤英】(使)〔汽車喇叭〕發嘟嘟聲: *The taxi driver was angrily tooting his horn.* 那位計程車司機在憤怒地按着喇叭。**2** *AmE slang* to take COCAINE up through your nose【美俚】〔通過鼻孔〕吸入(可卡因)

toot² *n* [C] a short high sound, made especially by a car horn〔汽車喇叭發出的〕嘟嘟聲

2 2 **tooth** /tuθ; tuːθ/ *n plural* **teeth** /tiθ; tiːθ/ [C]

1 ►IN MOUTH 在嘴裡◄ one of the hard white objects in your mouth that you use to bite and CHEW your food 牙, 牙齒: *Brush your teeth twice a day.* 每天刷牙兩次。| *I'm going to the dentist to have a tooth out.* 我要去找牙醫拔牙。| **cut a tooth** (=grow a new tooth) 長新牙 *The baby's cutting a tooth.* 那個嬰兒在長新牙了。| *The Doberman sank its teeth into his leg.* 那隻多伯曼狗咬住了他的大腿, 牙齒深深陷在肉裡。

2 ►ON A TOOL ETC 在工具等上面◄ one of the pointed parts that sticks out from the edge of a comb, SAW² (1), COG (1), etc〔梳子、鋸子等的〕齒

3 fight tooth and nail to try with a lot of effort or determination to do something 竭盡全力; 堅決: *We fought tooth and nail to get our plans accepted.* 我們竭盡全力爭取使我們的計劃被採納。

4 get your teeth into *informal* to start to do something with eagerness and energy【非正式】開始認真處理; 急迫地想開始做〔某事〕: *I can't wait to get my teeth into the new course.* 我真想馬上開始新的課程。

5 in the teeth of a) in spite of opposition or danger from something 不顧〔反對或危險〕: *The new law was passed in the teeth of public protest.* 這項新的法律儘管遭到公眾的抗議可還是通過了。**b)** against a stormy wind 頂着〔暴風〕: *sailing in the teeth of a storm* 頂着暴風雨航行

6 set sb's teeth on edge if a sound, taste etc sets your teeth on edge, it makes you feel physically uncomfortable〔聲音、味道等〕使某人感到不舒服: *That scraping really sets my teeth on edge.* 那種刮擦聲真讓我受不了。

7 ►LAW 法律◄ **have teeth** if a law, regulation etc has teeth, or if you give it teeth, it has the power to force people to obey it〔法律、法規等〕具有效力: *The agreement works because it has teeth.* 這個協議並非一紙空文, 因為它是有法律效力的。

8 sharp-toothed/saw-toothed/fine-toothed etc having sharp parts that stick out of the edge, etc 尖牙利齒/鋸齒般/細齒等的: *a fine-toothed comb* 一把細齒梳子 —see also 另見 **armed to the teeth** (ARMED (1)), **cut your teeth on sth** (CUT¹ (16)), **by the skin of your teeth** (SKIN¹ (5)), **be a kick in the teeth** (KICK² (4)), **lie through your teeth** (LIE² (1)), **have a sweet tooth** (SWEET¹ (7)), **take the bit between your teeth** (BIT¹ (17))

tooth·ache /ˈtuθˌek; ˈtuːθ-eɪk/ *n* [C,U] a pain in a tooth 牙痛

tooth·brush /ˈtuθˌbrʌʃ; ˈtuːθbrʌʃ/ *n* [C] a small brush for cleaning your teeth 牙刷 —see picture at 參見 BRUSH¹ 圖

tooth·less /ˈtuθləs; ˈtuːθləs/ *adj* **1** having no teeth 沒有牙齒的: *a toothless smile* 開口一笑, 露出沒有牙齒的嘴巴 **2** a law that is toothless has no power to make someone obey it〔法律〕無效的, 無約束力的, 不起作用的: *Without legal sanctions it is toothless.* 沒有法律上的認可, 這是無約束力的。

tooth·paste /ˈtuθˌpest; ˈtuːθpeɪst/ *n* [U] a substance used to clean your teeth 牙膏

tooth·pick /ˈtuθˌpɪk; ˈtuːθˌpɪk/ *n* [C] a very small pointed stick for removing bits of food that are stuck between your teeth 牙籤

tooth pow·der /'· ,··/ *n* [U] a special powder used to clean your teeth 牙粉

tooth·some /ˈtuθsəm; ˈtuːθsəm/ *adj humorous* tasting good; DELICIOUS【幽默】味道好的, 美味可口的: *the less toothsome corners of English cuisine* 英國烹調中不那麼可口的方面

tooth·y /ˈtuθɪ; ˈtuːθi/ *adj* **toothy smile/grin** a smile in which you show a lot of teeth 露齒的笑

toot·le /ˈtutl̩; ˈtuːtl/ *v* [I] *BrE*【英】**1** *old-fashioned* to move slowly in a car【過時】〔汽車〕緩慢地行駛 **2** to play an instrument such as a FLUTE without producing any particular tune〔長笛等樂器〕連續發出不成音調的聲音

toots /tʊts; tʊts/ *n* [C] *AmE old-fashioned* a way of addressing a woman, sometimes considered offensive【美, 過時】娘們〔該稱呼有時被認為具有冒犯性〕: *Hey toots! How're you doing?* 嘿, 娘們! 過得怎麼樣?

toot·sie /ˈtʊtsɪ; ˈtʊtsi/ *n* [C] **1** *AmE spoken* a way of addressing a woman, sometimes considered offensive【美口】娘們〔該稱呼有時被認為具有冒犯性〕**2 tootsies** [plural] *informal* a word meaning toes, used especially by or to children【非正式】腳趾〔尤為兒語〕

top¹ /tɑp; tɒp/ *n* [C] 

1 ►THE HIGHEST PART 最高部分◄ the highest part of something 頂部, 頂端, 上端: **the top of** *Place the mixture in the top of the oven.* 把混合物放在烤箱的上半部分。| *The top of the mountain is covered with snow.* 山頂覆蓋着白雪。| *I filled the glass right to the top.* 我把杯子一直斟滿為止。| *She could only just see over the tops of their heads.* 她僅僅能越過他們的頭頂看後邊。| **at the top (of sth)** *Write your name at the top of the page.* 在頁面的上端寫下你的名字。| *I stood at the top of the stairs.* 我站在樓梯頂端。| **the very top** (=the highest part) 最上端 *The book I wanted was at the very top of the stack.* 我想要的那本書在那堆書的最上面。| **up the top** *spoken* (=at or near the top of a tree, mountain etc)【口】在[靠近]...的頂端 *You'll see it when you get up the top of the hill.* 你到山頂時就會看到的。| **tree top/roof-top/hill-top etc** *the white cliff-tops in the distance* 遠處白色的峭壁頂端 —opposite 反義詞 BOTTOM¹ (1)

2 ►UPPER SURFACE 上方表面◄ the flat upper surface of an object〔物體的〕上面: *papers spread all over the top of piano* 攤放在鋼琴上面的報紙 | *The table has a glass top.* 這桌子是玻璃桌面。

3 ►BEST POSITION 最佳位置◄ **the top** the best, most successful, or most important position in an organization, company, group etc〔機構、公司、團體等中的〕最好位置; 最重要的職位; 最高位: *He started life at the bottom and worked his way up to the top.* 他從最低層幹起, 然後一步步升到了最高層。| *the cult of secrecy at the top* 上層對保密的熱中 | **the top of** *people who are near the top of the wages league* 差不多最高工資的人 | **(at the) top of the class/division etc** (=the best in a list or in an order of things) 在班上/在部門裡等名列前茅 *We came top of our group three years running.* 我們連續三年在小組裡名列榜首。| **top of the range** *informal* (=an expression meaning one of the best or most expensive, used especially in advertising)【非正式】最佳[最貴]的產品〔尤廣告上使用〕*a perfectly smooth ride, as you would expect from the top of the range product* 行駛絕對平穩, 正如你對頂尖產品所期望的那樣 | **the top of the tree** *informal* (=the highest position in a profession)【非正式】〔在某一行業中〕高居首位; 達到頂峯 *By now Vivien Westwood had reached the top of the fashion tree.* 此

時, 費雯·威斯特伍德已達時裝界的頂峯。—opposite 反義詞 BOTTOM¹ (5)
4 be (at the) top of the list/agenda something that is at the top of the list etc will be dealt with or discussed first 是名單上/議事日程上首要考慮的〔事情〕: *Defence isn't always at the top of the political agenda!* 國防不總是政治議程上首要考慮的事!
5 on top a) on the highest point or surface of something 在最上面, 在頂部: *Sprinkle some Parmesan on top and grill.* 在面上撒一些帕爾馬乾酪, 然後加以燒烤。| *a hat with a red pompom on top* 頂部有一個紅色小絨球的帽子 | **on top of** *There's $10 on top of the refrigerator.* 冰箱上面有十美元。| **one on top of the other** also 又作 **on top of one another** (=in a pile) 一個一個地碼成一堆 *The workmen were stacking the crates on top of one another.* 工人們把那些板條箱一個挨一個地碼起來。—opposite 反義詞 UNDERNEATH **b)** in the most successful or important position in business, a game etc〔在商務、體育比賽等中〕處於領先地位, 佔上風: *The All Blacks stayed on top throughout the match.* "全黑"隊整場比賽一直領先。**c)** on the highest part of your head 在頭頂部: *Cut it short on top, please.* 請把頭頂上的頭髮剪短。
6 on top of if something dangerous or threatening is on top of you, it is very near you〔危險或威脅〕非常接近, 逼近: *The truck was almost on top of us.* 那輛卡車幾乎把我們撞倒。**a)** if something bad happens to you on top of something else, it happens when you have other problems 除...之外〔還有其他煩惱〕: *On top of everything else, I now owe my parents $10,000 for the fines!* 除了其他一切之外, 我現在還因為那些罰金欠了父母 10,000 美元。**b)** in complete control of a job, situation etc 完全控制着...; 對...摸得一清二楚: *Don't worry; I'm back on top of things now.* 不要擔心, 我現在又完全控制了局面。
7 come out on top to win a difficult struggle or argument, especially one that has lasted for a long time〔尤指經過長期努力後〕獲得成功: *It's very difficult to predict who will come out on top.* 很難預測誰將最後勝出。
8 get on top of if work, a problem etc gets on top of you, it begins to make you feel unhappy and upset〔工作、問題等〕壓得人受不了: *Things are starting to get on top of him.* 事情開始壓得他受不住了。
9 on top of the world *informal* extremely happy【非正式】極其高興的: *When I heard she'd been released I felt on top of the world!* 聽説她已被釋放, 我感到高興極了!
10 ►COVER 蓋子◄ something that you put on a pen, bottle etc to close it, especially something that you push or turn〔筆〕帽;〔瓶〕蓋: *You've left the top off the toothpaste again!* 你又沒有蓋上牙膏蓋! | *Where's the top of this pen?* 這筆帽到哪去了? | **bottle/pen etc** *milk bottle tops* 牛奶瓶蓋子 —see also 另見 SCREW TOP
11 ►CLOTHES 衣服◄ a piece of clothing that you wear on the upper part of your body 上衣, 上裝: *her stripy top* 她那件條紋上衣 | *a skirt with a matching top* 一條配有上裝的裙子 | *slip your pyjama top off* 脱掉你的睡衣上裝
12 ►PLANT 植物◄ the part of a fruit or vegetable where it was attached to the plant, or the leaves of a plant whose root you can eat〔植物的〕頂梢部分;〔根部可食用的植物的〕葉子: *Cut the tops off the tomatoes.* 把番茄的莖葉削掉。| *carrot tops* 胡蘿蔔莖葉
13 the top of the milk *BrE* the creamy part that rises to the top of a bottle of milk【英】〔瓶裝牛奶最上面的〕頂層乳
14 ►STREET/FIELD ETC 街道/田地等◄ the part of the street or of a piece of land that is the furthest away either from you or from the most important entrance to it〔街道或田地的〕最遠處; 末端, 盡頭: *I waited at the top of East Street.* 我在東街的盡頭等着。
15 the top of the table the part of a long dinner table where the most important people sit〔長條形餐桌上地位最高的人坐的〕餐桌首席, 上席, 上座 —see also 另見 TOP TABLE
16 off the top of your head *informal* if you answer a question or provide information off the top of your head, you do it immediately without checking the facts【非正式】立即, 馬上; 不加思索地〔回答問題、提供信息〕: *Just off the top of my head I'd say there were about 50.* 要馬上說的話, 我說大約有 50 個。
17 sing/shout at the top of your voice to sing etc as loudly as you possibly can 放開嗓子唱歌/叫喊: *We yelled at the tops of our voices.* 我們敞開嗓門叫喊着。
18 from the top *spoken* an expression meaning from the beginning, used especially in the theatre【口】從頭, 從最開始〔尤用於戲劇〕: *Alright. Once more from the top. Action!* 好的。從頭再來一遍。開始!
19 from top to bottom if you clean or search somewhere from top to bottom, you do it very thoroughly 徹底地〔清理、尋找等〕
20 from top to toe if a person is dressed or covered in something from top to toe, they are completely dressed or covered in it 從頭到腳, 完完全全〔指穿衣服或被覆蓋〕: *expensive Parisian couture from top to toe* 從頭到腳一身昂貴的巴黎時裝
21 the top and bottom of *BrE spoken* the general result or meaning of a situation, expressed in a few words【英口】〔用三言兩語概括的某情況的〕結果; 實質: *He's trying to embarrass you, that's the top and bottom of it.* 他想讓你難堪, 那便是他所作所為的本意。
22 not have much up top *BrE spoken* to be not very intelligent【英口】不怎麼精明, 沒甚麼頭腦
23 tops *BrE spoken* used after a number to say that it is the highest possible amount of money you will get【英口】〔用於一筆錢的數目後表示可能得到的〕最高數目: *You'll make £200 from it, £250 tops.* 你會從中賺到 200 英鎊, 最高還可賺到 250 英鎊。
24 be (the) tops *old-fashioned informal* to be the best【過時, 非正式】是最好, 為最佳
25 ►TOY 玩具◄ a child's toy that spins around on its point when the child twists it 陀螺
26 spin like a top to spin or turn round very quickly 很快地轉動: *The impact sent me spinning like a top.* 這一撞使我暈頭轉向。
27 sleep like a top *BrE* to sleep very deeply and well【英】睡得很香, 熟睡

top² *adj* [only before noun 僅用於名詞前]
1 ►HIGHEST 最高◄ at the top; highest 頂端的; 最高的: *the top button of his shirt* 他襯衫最上面的那顆紐扣 | *I can dive off the top board.* 我能從最高那層跳板上跳水。| *Sprinkle cheese over the top layer of tomatoes.* 在最上面一層的番茄上撒些乾酪。| **top floor** *Andrew lives on the top floor.* 安德魯住在頂層。| **top priority** *We are giving the matter top priority.* 我們優先處理這件事情。| **the top 50/third/20% etc** *She is among the top 5% of earners in this country.* 她在這個國家屬於收入最高的 5% 這一行列。| *We weren't even in the top 100 companies.* 我們甚至還沒有進入前 100 家大公司的行列。—opposite 反義詞 BOTTOM² (1)
2 top left/right/centre expressions meaning the picture at or nearest the top of the pages on the left or right or in the centre, used in magazines and newspapers 左上/右上/中間頂端〔指報刊雜誌等圖片在頁面上的位置〕: *Top right: Silk Blouse £95 from Harrods.* 右上圖: 哈羅茲的女式絲綢襯衫, 價格 95 英鎊。
3 ►BEST 最佳◄ best or most successful 最佳的, 最好的; 最成功的: *one of our top tennis players* 我們最優秀的網球運動員之一 | *a top New York salon* 紐約的一家頂級美容院 | *people in top jobs* 工作職位最高的人 | *top quality ingredients* 優質配料 | *She got top marks.* 她獲得了最高分。| **be on top form** (=to be doing something that you are good at especially well) 處於最佳狀態 *Our team's on top form at the moment.* 我們隊此時處於最佳狀態。
4 top speed the fastest speed a vehicle can move at

〔交通工具的〕最高速, 全速: *We chased after them at top speed.* 我們以最快速度追趕他們。

5 top copy a piece of written material that is produced first and from which copies have been or can be made 〔書面材料的〕正本

6 the top brass *informal* people in positions of high rank, especially in the army, navy etc【非正式】達官貴人;〔尤指〕高級軍官

7 top dog *informal* the person in the highest or most important position especially after a struggle or effort【非正式】〔尤指經過競爭和努力而〕奪魁者; 居高位的人

8 ►HIGH SOCIAL CLASS 上層社會◄ *old-fashioned informal* from the highest social class【過時, 非正式】上層社會的: *a top people's magazine* 上層社會人士的一份雜誌

top³ *v* **topped, topping** [T]

1 ►BE HIGHER 更高◄ to be higher or more than something 高於; 超過: *Their profits have reportedly topped £1,000,000 this year.* 據報道, 他們的利潤今年已超過1,000,000英鎊。

2 top an offer/bid etc to offer more money than someone else 超過某一開價/標價等: *A rival company has topped our offer by $5 million.* 同我們競爭的一家公司以500萬美元超過了我們的開價。

3 ►BE BETTER 更好◄ if you top someone else's remarks or actions you say or do something better, funnier or more exciting 優於, 勝過: **top that** *And we also met Michael Jackson. Bet you can't top that!* 況且我們還見過米高積遜。我敢說沒有比這更帶勁的事情了!

4 top the bill/charts etc to come first in a list or in an order of things 在名單/列表等上面成為第一名: *Their party topped the poll in only 12 seats.* 他們的政黨在選舉中只獲得12個席位。—see also 另見 CHART-TOPPING

5 be topped by sth if something, especially an article of clothing, a mountain, or a building, is topped by something else, it has that thing on its top 某物在…的頂部: *roofs topped by fat chimneys* 矗立着粗大煙囪的房頂 | *trellis-topped brick walls* 牆頭搭了棚的磚牆

6 topped with cream/onions etc with cream etc on the top …上面蓋了一層奶油/洋蔥等: *spicy new pizzas topped with curry sauce* 澆了一層咖喱醬的新式香辣比薩餅 —see also 另見 TOPPING

7 to top it all *spoken* in addition to other bad things that have happened to you【口】更有甚者, 更糟糕的是: *To top it all I lost my job.* 更糟糕的是, 我還丟了工作。

8 top and tail *BrE* to cut the top and bottom off a piece of fruit or a vegetable【英】削掉〔水果或蔬菜〕的根和葉; 去掉…的兩端

9 ►REACH THE TOP 達到頂點◄ *literary* if you top a rising piece of ground, you reach the top of it【文】到達…的頂部; 上升到…的頂點: *Our wagon topped the crest of the hill and we gasped at the view before us.* 馬車到達了山頂, 我們對眼前的景色驚嘆不已。

10 top yourself *BrE slang* to kill yourself deliberately【英俚】自殺

top sth ↔ **off** *phr v* [T] to complete something successfully by doing a last action or adding a last detail 〔完成一個行動或增加最後一點細節從而〕圓滿地完成〔某事〕: *Let's top off the evening with a drink.* 咱們喝上一杯來圓滿地結束今晚的活動。| *A cherry on each cake would top them off nicely.* 每塊蛋糕上加一顆櫻桃就大功告成了。

top out *phr v* [I] if something such as a price that is increasing tops out, it reaches its highest point and stops rising 〔價格等達到最高點後〕不再上升: *Do you think interest rates have topped out now?* 你認為利率現在已經上升到最高點了嗎?

top sth/sb ↔ **up** *phr v* [T] *especially BrE*【尤英】**1** to fill a partly empty container with liquid 注滿〔半空的容器〕: *I'll just top up the coffee pot.* 我把咖啡壺裝滿就行。**2** to put more drink in someone's glass or cup 給〔某人的杯子〕加滿: *Can I top you up?* 我給你的杯子加滿好嗎? **3** to increase the level of something slightly so as to bring it back to the level you want 稍微增加〔某物〕以回復到想要達到的水平: *Top up your tan this winter!* 今冬把你的皮膚曬得更漂亮! —see also 另見 TOP-UP

to·paz /ˋtopæz; ˈtəʊpæz/ *n* [C,U] a transparent yellow jewel or the mineral that it is cut from 黃玉; 黃玉礦

top-class /ˌ· ˈ·◂/ *adj* being the best, most skilful etc 最優秀的, 第一流的: *top-class athletes such as Linford Christie* 像林福德·克里斯蒂那樣的頂尖運動員 | *a top-class restaurant* 一流的餐館

top·coat /ˋtɑpˌkot; ˈtɒpkəʊt/ *n* **1** [C,U] the last layer of paint that is put on a surface 〔油漆的〕外塗層 **2** [C] *old-fashioned* a warm long coat【過時】長大衣, 寬大衣

top-down /ˌ· ˈ·◂/ *adj BrE* a top-down plan etc is one in which you start with a general idea of what you want and then add the details later【英】〔規劃等〕從總體構思到具體細節的; 自上而下的: *adopting a top-down managerial philosophy* 採納一套自上而下的管理理念

top-drawer /ˌ· ˈ·◂/ *adj informal* of the highest quality or social class【非正式】最優質的; 社會最上層的, 上流社會的: *top-drawer entertainment* 上流社會的娛樂

top-dress·ing /ˋtɑpˌdrɛsɪŋ; ˌtɒpˈdresɪŋ/ *n* [C,U] *technical* a layer of FERTILIZER that is spread over land【術語】〔撒在土地上的〕表層肥料, 頂肥

to·pee, topi /toˋpi; ˈtəʊpiː/ *n* [C] a hard hat for protecting your head in tropical sunshine 〔熱帶地區的〕太陽帽

top-flight /ˌ· ˈ·◂/ *adj* most successful, skilful, or important 最成功的; 第一流的; 最重要的: *They've hired a really top-flight sales team.* 他們雇用了一支真正稱得上第一流的銷售隊伍。

top gear /ˌ· ˈ·/ *n* [U] **1** the highest GEAR of a car, bus etc 〔汽車等的〕高速擋: **in top gear** *The car will cruise at 80 mph in top gear.* 這輛車在高速擋能以每小時80英里的速度平穩地行駛。**2 be in top gear** to be at the highest level of activity 處於最活躍的狀態: *The party's election campaign is now in top gear.* 該黨的選舉活動現在進行得如火如荼。

top-gross·ing /ˈ· ˌ··/ *adj* a top-grossing film earns more money than any other film at a particular time 〔電影〕票房收入高的

top hat /ˌ· ˈ·/ *n* [C] a man's tall black or grey hat, now worn only on formal occasions 〔僅在正式場合戴的〕男子高頂大禮帽 —see picture at 參見 HAT 圖

top-heav·y /ˌ· ˈ··◂/ *adj* **1** too heavy at the top and therefore likely to fall over 上重下輕的, 頭重腳輕的 **2** an organization that is top heavy has too many managers compared to the number of ordinary workers 〔機構等〕高層管理人員過多的: *burdened by a top-heavy bureaucracy* 在高層管理人員過多的官僚機構的重負下

to·pi /toˋpi; ˈtəʊpiː/ *n* [C] another spelling of TOPEE topee 的另一種拼法

to·pi·a·ry /ˋtopɪˌɛrɪ; ˈtəʊpiəri/ *n* [U] trees and bushes cut into the shapes of birds, animals etc, or the art of cutting them in this way 〔把喬木或灌木修剪成鳥、獸的形狀的〕樹木整形(術)

top·ic /ˋtɑpɪk; ˈtɒpɪk/ *n* [C] a subject that people talk or write about 〔講話或寫作的〕話題, 論題, 題目: *The environment is a popular topic these days.* 近來環境是一個很流行的話題。| **topic of conversation** *The wedding has been the only topic of conversation for weeks!* 那次婚禮是幾週以來唯一的話題! W2

top·ic·al /ˋtɑpɪkḷ; ˈtɒpɪkəl/ *adj* a story, subject, problem etc that is topical is interesting because it deals with something that is important at the present time 熱門話題的; 當前受到關注的: *a new TV comedy dealing with topical issues* 一部反映熱門問題的新電視喜劇 —**topically** /-kḷɪ; -kli/ *adv* —**topicality** /ˌtɑpɪˋkælətɪ; ˌtɒpɪˈkæləti/ *n* [U]

top·knot /ˋtɑpˌnɑt; ˈtɒpnɒt/ *n* [C] a way of arranging your hair, often tied with RIBBONS, on top of your head 頂髻

top·less /ˋtɑplɪs; ˈtɒpləs/ *adj* a woman who is topless is not wearing any clothes on the upper part of her body, so that her breasts are bare〔婦女〕無上裝的, 上身裸露的: *topless sunbathing* 上身裸露的日光浴 | **topless bar/show** (=one in which the women serving or performing are topless) 雇用袒胸女招待的酒吧/女子袒胸表演

top-lev·el /,· '··◂/ *adj* [only before noun 僅用於名詞前] involving the most powerful people in a country, organization etc 最高階層的, 最高級的: *Top-level talks are to be held between the heads of state.* 最高級會談將在兩國元首之間舉行。

top·most /ˋtɑp,most; ˈtɒpməʊst/ *adj* [only before noun 僅用於名詞前] the topmost part of something is its highest part 最高的; 最上面的; 絕頂的: *The topmost branches were still bathed in sunlight.* 頂端的枝椏仍然沐浴在陽光下。

top-notch /,· '·◂/ *adj informal* having the highest quality or standard【非正式】最高級的; 頂呱呱的; 第一流的: *I was lucky and got myself a job with a top-notch company.* 我當時很幸運, 在一家頂尖的公司找到了一份工作。

to·pog·ra·phy /toˋpɑgrəfɪ; təˈpɒgrəfi/ *n* [U] **1** the science of describing an area of land, or making maps of it 地貌學; 地形測繪學 **2** [+of] the shape of an area of land, including its hills, valleys etc 地形, 地貌 —**topographer** *n* [C] —**topographical** /,tɑpəˋgræfɪkl; ˌtɒpəˈgræfɪkəl◂/ *adj*

top·per /ˋtɑpɚ; ˈtɒpə/ *n* [C] *informal* a TOP HAT【非正式】男子高頂大禮帽

top·ping¹ /ˋtɑpɪŋ; ˈtɒpɪŋ/ *n* [C,U] something you put on top of food to make it look nicer or taste better〔加在食品上面使之更好看或更好吃的〕配料, 澆頭: *a pizza with extra cheese topping* 額外加了乾酪配料的比薩餅

topping² *adj BrE old-fashioned* excellent【英, 過時】極好的, 頂呱呱的

top·ple /ˋtɑpl; ˈtɒpəl/ *v* **1** [I,T] to become unsteady and then fall over, or to make something do this (使) 不穩而倒下, (使) 倒塌: **[+over]** *A stack of plates swayed, and began to topple over.* 一大堆盤子搖晃着, 然後開始倒塌了。**2** [T] to take power away from a leader or government, especially by force; OVERTHROW¹ (1)〔尤指通過暴力〕從…奪取政權; 推翻: *This scandal could topple the government.* 這一醜聞有可能使政府倒台。

top-rank·ing /,· '··◂/ *adj* most powerful and important within an organization 最高級別的: *top-ranking diplomats* 最高級別的外交官

top-rat·ed /,· '··◂/ *adj informal* very popular with the public【非正式】受歡迎的: *a top-rated TV show* 大受歡迎的電視節目

top round /ˋ· ·/ *n* [U] *AmE*【美】〔牛肉的〕大腿肉; TOPSIDE¹ *BrE*【英】

top-se·cret /,· '··◂/ *adj* top-secret documents or information must be kept completely secret〔文件或情報〕絕密的: *a top-secret military code* 絕密軍事代碼

top·side¹ /ˋtɑpˋsaɪd; ˈtɒpsaɪd/ *n* [U] *BrE* high quality BEEF cut from the upper leg of the animal【英】〔牛肉的〕大腿肉; TOP ROUND *AmE*【美】

topside² also 又作 **top·sides** /-ˋsaɪdz; -saɪdz/ *adv AmE* towards or onto the DECK (=upper surface) of a boat or ship【美】朝向甲板; 在甲板上

top·soil /ˋtɑp,sɔɪl; ˈtɒpsɔɪl/ *n* [U] the upper level of soil in which most plants have their roots 表土層; 耕作層

top·spin /ˋtɑp,spɪn; ˈtɒp,spɪn/ *n* [U] the turning movement of a ball that has been hit or thrown in such a way that it spins forward〔球的〕上旋

top·sy-tur·vy /ˋtɑpsɪ ˋtɝvɪ; ˌtɒpsi ˈtɜːvi◂/ *adj informal* in a state of complete disorder or confusion【非正式】亂七八糟的, 一團糟的: *He left his room all topsy-turvy.* 他的房間完全是一團糟。

top tab·le /,· '··/ *n* [C] *BrE* a table at a formal meal, for example at a wedding, where the most important people sit【英】〔正式宴會上重要人物坐的〕首席餐桌; HEAD TABLE *AmE*【美】

top-up /ˋ· ·/ *n* [C] *BrE* an amount of liquid that you add to a glass, cup etc in order to make it full again【英】加至滿杯的量: *Would you like a top-up?* 您來一個滿杯好嗎?

tor /tɔr; tɔː/ *n* [C] *BrE* a rocky hill【英】多岩石的小山

Tor·ah /ˋtɔrə; ˈtɔːrə/ *n* [singular] all the writings and teachings concerned with Judaism, especially the first five books of the Jewish Bible 托拉〔指猶太教的全部律法教條, 尤指《猶太聖經》的首五卷書〕

torch 手電筒

torch¹ /tɔrtʃ; tɔːtʃ/ *n* [C] **1** *BrE* a small electric lamp that you carry in your hand【英】手電筒; FLASHLIGHT *AmE*【美】: *We shone our torches around the walls of the cavern.* 我們用手電筒照山洞的四周洞壁。**2** a long stick with burning material at one end that produces light 火把; 火炬: *the Olympic torch* 奧林匹克火炬 | *a torchlight procession* 火炬遊行隊伍 **3 carry a torch for** *old-fashioned* to secretly love and admire someone【過時】暗戀〔某人〕

torch² *v* [T] *informal* to deliberately make a building start to burn【非正式】故意點燃: *Rioters torched several abandoned cars.* 暴徒放火燒毀了幾輛被遺棄的汽車。

torch·light /ˋtɔrtʃ,laɪt; ˈtɔːtʃlaɪt/ *n* [U] **1** *BrE* the light produced by a torch【英】手電筒光 **2** the light produced by burning torches 火炬光

tore /tɔr; tɔː/ the past tense of TEAR²

to·re·a·dor /ˋtɔrɪə,dɔr; ˈtɒriədɔː/ *n* [U] the person who fights bulls (BULL¹ (1)) in a Spanish BULLFIGHT〔西班牙鬥牛的〕鬥牛士

tor·ment¹ /ˋtɔrmɛnt; ˈtɔːment/ *n* **1** [U] severe mental or physical suffering, often lasting a long time〔精神或肉體上的〕折磨, 痛苦: **in torment** *She lay awake all night in torment.* 她一晚都沒有睡着, 在痛苦中煎熬。**2** [C] someone or something that makes you suffer 使人痛苦的人[物]

tor·ment² /tɔrˋmɛnt; tɔːˈment/ *v* [T] **1** to make someone suffer a lot, especially so that they feel guilty or very unhappy 折磨, 使痛苦; 使苦惱: *Seth was tormented by feelings of guilt.* 塞思備受負罪感的折磨。| *tormented by hunger* 飽受飢餓的折磨 **2** to deliberately treat someone cruelly by annoying them or hurting them 騷擾; 煩擾: *The older boys would torment him whenever they had the chance.* 那些年歲較大的男孩子一有機會就騷擾他。—**tormentor** *n* [C]

torn /tɔrn; tɔːn/ the past participle of TEAR² —see picture on page A18 參見 A18 頁圖

tor·na·do /tɔrˋnedo; tɔːˈneɪdəʊ/ *n plural* **tornadoes** *or* **tornados** [C] an extremely violent storm consisting of air that spins very quickly and causes a lot of damage 龍捲風 —compare 比較 HURRICANE, CYCLONE

tor·pe·do¹ /tɔrˋpido; tɔːˈpiːdəʊ/ *n plural* **torpedoes** [C] a long narrow weapon that is fired under the surface of the sea and explodes when it hits something 魚雷

torpedo² *v* [T] **1** to attack or destroy a ship with a torpedo 用魚雷攻擊[摧毀] **2** to stop something such as a plan from succeeding 破壞〔計劃等〕; 使失敗: *New threats of violence have effectively torpedoed the peace talks.* 新的暴力威脅實質上破壞了和平談判。

tor·pid /ˋtɔrpɪd; ˈtɔːpɪ̈d/ *adj formal* not active because you are lazy or sleepy, or making you feel like this【正式】(使人) 遲鈍的, (使人) 懶散的; (使人) 昏昏欲睡的, 有氣無力的: *a torpid mind* 遲鈍的思維 | *the heavy torpid warmth of the evening air* 夜晚滯重的、暖洋洋的空氣 —**torpidly** *adv*

tor·por /ˋtɔrpɚ; ˈtɔːpə/ *n* [singular,U] *formal* a state of being not active because you are lazy or sleepy【正式】

〔因懶散或睏倦而〕不活躍: *stirring the wasps from their winter torpor* 把黃蜂從冬天的慵懶中攪醒 —**torpidity** /tɔrˋpɪdətɪ; tɔːˈpɪdʒti/ *n* [U]

torque /tɔrk; tɔːk/ *n* [U] *technical* the force or power that makes something turn around a central point, especially in an engine【術語】〔尤指發動機的〕轉矩, 力矩

tor·rent /ˋtɔrənt; ˈtɒrənt/ *n* [C] **1** a large amount of water moving very rapidly and strongly in a particular direction〔水的〕湍流, 急流: **a raging torrent** (=a very violent torrent) 洶湧的急流 *After five days of heavy rain the Telle river was a raging torrent.* 經過五天的大雨之後, 泰勒河成了洶湧的急流。**2 torrent of abuse/criticism/protest etc** a lot of insults, criticism etc that someone suddenly receives 連珠砲似的痛罵/批評/抗議等: *a torrent of protest over the proposed tax* 針對擬議稅收的抗議浪潮

tor·ren·tial /tɔˋrɛnʃəl; tɒˈrenʃəl/ *adj* **torrential rain** very heavy rain 傾盆大雨

tor·rid /ˋtɔrɪd; ˈtɒrɪ̣d/ *adj* **1** involving strong emotions, especially of sexual love〔尤指性愛〕熱烈的;〔情慾〕熾烈的: *a torrid love affair* 狂熱的風流韻事 **2** *literary* torrid weather is very hot【文】〔天氣〕灼熱的, 炎熱的: *the torrid desert sun* 沙漠中灼熱的太陽

tor·sion /ˋtɔrʃən; ˈtɔːʃən/ *n* [U] *technical* the twisting of a piece of metal【術語】〔金屬的〕扭轉, 扭曲

tor·so /ˋtɔrso; ˈtɔːsəʊ/ *n* [C] **1** your body, not including your head, arms, or legs〔頭和四肢除外的〕人體軀幹: *Police have found the headless torso of a woman.* 警察發現了一名婦女的無頭軀體。**2** a STATUE of a torso 人體軀幹雕像

tort /tɔrt; tɔːt/ *n* [C] *law* an action that is wrong but not criminal and can be dealt with in a CIVIL (3) court of law【法律】〔不構成刑事罪的〕民事侵權行為

tor·til·la /tɔrˋtijə; tɔːˈtiːjə/ *n* [C] a piece of thin flat bread made from corn or wheat flour from Mexico〔墨西哥的一種〕薄玉米餅, 玉米粉圓餅

tor·toise /ˋtɔrtəs; ˈtɔːtəs/ *n* [C] a slow-moving land animal that can pull its head and legs into the hard round shell that covers its body 陸龜 —compare 比較 TURTLE

tor·toise·shell /ˋtɔrtəsˌʃɛl; ˈtɔːtəsʃel/ *n* **1** [U] a hard, shiny brown and white material made from the shell of a tortoise 龜甲; 玳瑁殼 **2** [C] a cat that has yellow, brown, and black marks on its fur 花斑家貓 **3** [C] a BUTTERFLY that has brown and orange wings〔翅膀呈褐色和橙色的〕蛺蝶

tor·tu·ous /ˋtɔrtʃuəs; ˈtɔːtʃuəs/ *adj* **1** a tortuous path, stream, road etc has a lot of bends in it and is therefore difficult to travel along 彎彎曲曲的; 曲折的: *a tortuous path over the mountains to Kandahar* 翻山越嶺通往坎大哈的一條蜿蜒小徑 **2** complicated and long and therefore confusing 轉彎抹角的, 繞圈子的; 複雜的; 令人費解的: *The book begins with a long, tortuous introduction.* 這本書的開頭是一篇冗長的、令人費解的前言。—**tortuously** *adv* —**tortuousness** *n* [U]

tor·ture[1] /ˋtɔrtʃɚ; ˈtɔːtʃə/ *n* [C,U] **1** an act of deliberately hurting someone in order to force them to tell you something, to punish them, or to be cruel 拷打, 拷問; 酷刑: *He died after five days of excruciating torture.* 在經歷五天的嚴刑拷打後, 他死了。**2** severe physical or mental suffering〔身心所受的〕折磨, 煎熬: *Hearing her practice the violin is torture!* 聽她練小提琴, 簡直是受罪!

torture[2] *v* [T] **1** to deliberately hurt someone to force them to give you information, to punish them, or to be cruel 拷打, 拷問; 對…施以酷刑: *Political opponents of the regime may be tortured.* 反對該政權的政治犯可能要受酷刑。**2** if a feeling or knowledge tortures you, it makes you suffer mentally 使〔精神上〕受到折磨; 使痛苦; 使苦惱: *tortured by guilt* 因內疚而感到痛苦 —**torturer** *n* [C]

To·ry /ˋtɔrɪ; ˈtɔːri/ *n* [C] a member of the British Conservative Party〔英國的〕保守黨成員, 托利黨人: *a lifelong Tory* 一名終身的保守黨黨員 | *Tory principles* 保守黨的各項原則

Tory Par·ty /ˈ·· ˌ··/ *n* [singular] another name for the British Conservative Party 托利黨〔英國保守黨的別稱〕

toss[1] /tɔs; tɒs/ *v*

1 ▶THROW 扔◀ [T] to throw something, especially something light, with a quick gentle movement of your hand 扔, 擲, 拋〔尤指輕快地拋較輕的東西〕: **toss sth into/down/out of etc** *Toss that book over here, will you?* 把那本書扔過來, 好嗎? | **toss sth to sb** *"Catch!" said Sandra, tossing her bag to him.* "接着!"桑德拉一邊說着, 一邊把包扔給他。| **toss sb sth** *Frank tossed her the newspaper.* 弗蘭克把報紙扔給了她。

2 ▶MOVE 移動◀ [I,T] to move and turn around continuously in a violent or uncontrolled way, or make something do this (使)動來動去; (使)翻轉不停: **toss sth about/around** *Our small boat was tossed about like a cork.* 我們的小船像軟木塞一樣顛簸不停。| **toss and turn** (=keep changing your position in bed because you cannot sleep) 輾轉反側 *I've been tossing and turning all night.* 我整個晚上翻來覆去睡不着。

3 ▶THROW A FLAT OBJECT 拋扔扁平的物體◀ [T] *BrE* to throw a flat object upwards so that it turns over in the air before it falls again【英】把〔扁平的物體〕拋向空中使其翻轉落下; FLIP[1] (2) *AmE*【美】: *tossing pancakes on Pancake Day* 薄煎餅日那天拋薄餅

4 ▶A COIN 硬幣◀ also 又作 **toss up** [I,T] *especially BrE* to make a coin go upwards and spin in the air, as a way of deciding something【尤英】把(硬幣)拋向空中〔以決定某事〕; FLIP[1] (2) *especially AmE*【尤美】: *They tossed a coin to decide who would go first.* 他們拋硬幣以決定誰先走。| **toss (up) for it** *Well we can't make up our minds; we'll just have to toss for it.* 既然我們無法下定決心, 那就只好拋硬幣來決定了。

5 ▶IN COOKING 烹調過程中◀ [T] to cover food in a liquid by shaking it around in the liquid〔在液體中〕搖晃, 攪拌〔食物〕: *Toss the carrots in some butter before serving.* 用一些黃油把胡蘿蔔攪拌一下, 然後端上桌子。

6 toss your head to move your head back suddenly, often with a shaking movement showing anger 把頭往後一仰〔表示氣憤〕: *He tossed his head angrily and left the room.* 他氣憤地把頭往後一仰, 離開了房間。

7 toss your cookies *AmE spoken* to VOMIT[1]【美口】嘔吐

toss off *phr v* **1** [T **toss** sth ↔ **off**] to produce something quickly and without much effort 輕而易舉地完成〔某事〕: *one of those painters who can toss off a couple of pictures before breakfast* 那種能夠在早餐之前輕鬆地完成一兩幅繪畫的畫家 **2** [T **toss** sth ↔ **off**] *old-fashioned* to drink something quickly【過時】將…一飲而盡: *He tossed off a few whiskies.* 他一口氣喝下幾杯威士忌酒。**3** [I,T **toss** sb ↔ **off**] *BrE taboo* to MASTURBATE【英諱】手淫

toss[2] *n* [C] **1** the act of throwing a coin in the air to decide something 拋硬幣〔決定某事〕: *The toss of a coin decided who would serve first.* 通過拋硬幣決定誰首先發球。**2** a sudden backwards movement of your head, so that your hair moves 猛一仰頭: *"I'll see," the nurse said, with an officious toss of her head.* 這名護士猛一仰頭, 以發號施令的口吻說: "我來看看。" **3 win/lose the toss** *especially BrE* to win or lose the right to make a choice at the beginning of a game or race, according to the result of tossing a coin【尤英】〔在比賽等開始時〕拋硬幣贏了/輸了 **4** the act of gently throwing something〔輕輕的〕拋, 扔, 投: *Will distracted me and I missed the toss.* 威爾分散了我的注意力, 我因而沒有投中。**5 not give a toss** *BrE spoken* to not care about something at all【英口】根本不在乎: *I really couldn't give a toss what Dermot thinks.* 我真的根本就不在乎德莫特是怎麼想的。—see also 另見 **argue the toss** (ARGUE (5))

toss-up /ˈ· ·/ *n* **1 it's a toss-up** *spoken* used when you do not know which of two things will happen, or which of two things to choose【口】這件事尚未分曉[難以定奪]: *"I don't know who'll get the job – it's a toss-up between*

Carl and Steve."“我不知道誰會得到這份工作——卡爾和史蒂夫兩人的機會不相上下。” **2** [C usually singular 一般用單數] *BrE* an act of tossing a coin in order to decide something【英】拋硬幣〔決定某事〕

tot¹ /tɑt; tɒt/ *n* [C] **1** *informal* a very small child【非正式】小娃娃 **2** *especially BrE* a small amount of an alcoholic drink【尤英】少量酒

tot² *v* **totted, totting**

tot sth ↔ **up** *phr v* [T] *informal* to add together numbers or amounts of money in order to find the total【非正式】把〔數字或錢〕加起來: *The waiter quickly totted up the bill.* 服務生很快便把賬單算好了。

to·tal¹ /ˈtotḷ; ˈtəʊtl/ *adj* **1** [only before noun 僅用於名詞前] complete, and affecting or including everything 完全的, 徹底的: *The sales campaign was a total disaster.* 那次促銷活動完全是一場災難。| *a total ban on cigarette advertising* 徹底禁止香煙廣告 **2 total number/amount/cost etc** the number, amount etc that is the total 總數/總量/總成本等: *total sales of 200,000 per year* 每年200,000的銷售總額

total² *n* [C] **1** the final number or amount of things, people etc when everything has been counted 總數, 總量, 總額: *If you add 30 and 45 the total is 75.* 30加45, 總數是75。| **a total of** *They were jailed for a total of thirty years.* 他們在監牢裡總共被關了三十年。| **in total** *There were probably about 40 people there in total.* 那裡總共可能有40人左右。| **the sum total** (=the whole of an amount when everything is considered together) 全部, 總數 **2 grand total a)** the final total, including all the totals added together 總計 **b)** *humorous* used when you think the final total is small【幽默】〔自認為很小的〕總數: *I earned a grand total of $4.15.* 我總共才掙了四塊一毛五。

total³ *v* **totalled, totalling** *BrE*【英】, **totaled, totaling** *AmE*【美】**1** [T, linking verb 連繫動詞] to reach a particular total 總數為, 總共達: *losses totalling $3 million* 總計達300萬美元的損失 **2** [T] *AmE informal* to damage a car so badly that it cannot be repaired【美, 非正式】徹底毀壞〔汽車〕: *Chuck ran into a telephone pole and totaled his dad's new Toyota.* 查克撞到一根電線杆上, 把他爸爸那輛新豐田車撞得粉碎。

total sth ↔ **up** *phr v* [T] to find the total number or total amount of something by adding 求得…的總數, 把…相加起來: *At the end of the game total up everyone's score to see who has won.* 在遊戲結束時, 把每個人的總分加起來, 看看是誰贏了。

to·tal·i·tar·i·an /toˌtæləˈtɛrɪən; təʊˌtælḷˈteəriən/ *adj* based on a political system in which ordinary people have no power and are completely controlled by the government 極權主義的: *a totalitarian régime* 極權主義政權 —**totalitarianism** *n* [U]

to·tal·i·ty /toˈtælətɪ; təʊˈtælḷti/ *n* [U] *formal*【正式】**1** the whole of something 整體, 全部: **in its totality** (=as a complete thing) 作為一個整體, 從整體上 *It's essential that we look at the problem in its totality.* 重要的是, 我們應從整體上看待這個問題。**2** a total amount 總數, 總額

to·tal·i·za·tor also 又作 **-isator** /ˈtotḷəˌzetə; ˈtəʊtəlaɪˌzeɪtə/ *n* [C] *BrE formal* a TOTE² 【英, 正式】〔賽馬的〕賭金計算器

to·tal·ly /ˈtotlɪ; ˈtəʊtli/ *adv* completely 完全地, 徹底地: *That's a totally different matter.* 那是一件完全不同的事情。| *It's like learning a totally new language.* 這就好像在學一門全新的語言。| *a totally unexpected situation* 完全沒有預料到的情況

tote¹ /tot; təʊt/ also 又作 **tote around** *v* [T] *informal especially AmE* to carry something, especially regularly【非正式, 尤美】〔尤指經常性地〕隨身攜帶: *having to tote around heavy textbooks* 不得不隨身攜帶着厚重的課本

tote² *n* [C] a machine that adds together the amounts of money BET on a race and divides it among the winners〔賽馬的〕賭金計算器

tote bag /ˈ· ,·/ *n* [C] *AmE* a large bag for carrying things【美】〔裝東西的〕大袋子 —see picture at 參見 BAG¹ 圖

to·tem /ˈtotəm; ˈtəʊtəm/ *n* [C] an animal, plant etc that is thought to have a special spiritual connection with a particular tribe, especially in North America, or a figure made to look like the animal etc 圖騰; 圖騰形象 —**totemic** /toˈtɛmɪk; təʊˈtemɪk/ *adj*

totem pole /ˈ·· ·/ *n* [C] **1** a tall wooden pole with one or more totems cut or painted on it, made by the Native Americans of northwest North America〔北美土著的〕圖騰柱 **2 low man on the totem pole** *AmE* someone of low rank in an organization or business【美】〔在機構或公司中〕級別較低的人

to·to /ˈtoto; ˈtəʊtəʊ/ —see 見 IN TOTO

tot·ter /ˈtɑtə; ˈtɒtə/ *v* [I] **1** to walk or move unsteadily from side to side as if you are going to fall over 搖搖晃晃, 跌跌撞撞: *Lorrimer swayed a little, tottered, and fell.* 洛里墨歪了一下, 然後搖搖晃晃地倒了下去。—see picture on page A24 參見A24頁圖 **2** if a political system or organization totters, it becomes less strong and is likely to stop working〔政治制度或機構〕搖搖欲墜

tou·can /ˈtukæn; ˈtuːkən/ *n* [C] a tropical American bird with bright feathers and a very large beak 巨嘴鳥〔熱帶美洲的一種鳥〕

tou·ch¹ /tʌtʃ; tʌtʃ/ *v*

① FEEL SB/STH PHYSICALLY 觸到某人/某物
② AFFECT SB'S FEELINGS 影響某人的感情
③ USE/HANDLE 使用/觸摸
④ DEAL/ATTEND TO 處理
⑤ HAVE AN EFFECT ON 產生影響
⑥ OTHER MEANINGS 其他意思

① FEEL SB/STH PHYSICALLY 觸到某人/某物

1 [T] to put your hand or another part of your body on something or someone so that you can feel them〔手或身體其他部位〕觸到, 摸到, 碰到: *Small children are constantly moving and wanting to touch everything.* 小孩子總是不斷地活動, 甚麼都想摸一摸。| *She couldn't bear the thought of touching a dead body.* 要去觸摸一具死屍, 她連想都不敢想。

2 to put your hand or any part of your body on someone in a sexual way〔因性慾而〕接觸〔別人的身體〕: *Ben hadn't touched her yet. Hadn't even kissed her.* 本沒有碰過她, 甚至還沒有吻過她。| *She bent over me, touching me with her lips.* 她朝我俯過身來, 吻了我一下。

3 [T] to put your hand on someone in order to show them kindness or affection 撫摸〔表示親切、憐愛等〕: *He put his hand out to touch the young man's shoulder.* 他伸出手, 碰了一下那位小伙子的肩膀。| *He was a remote man who hardly ever played with or even touched his children.* 他是個孤僻的人, 難得跟自己的孩子一起玩, 也不去愛撫他們。

4 [I,T] if two things are touching, they reach each other so that there is no space between them 觸碰; 觸及; 接觸: *I sat facing him, our knees touching.* 我面向他坐, 我倆的膝蓋相互靠着。| **touch sth** *The little boy's legs were too short to touch the ground.* 那個小男孩的兩條腿太短了, 夠不着地面。

5 not touch sb to not hit someone or hurt them physically 不傷害某人〔身體〕: *The older boys swore they hadn't touched the child.* 那些年長的男孩子發誓說沒有打過那個小孩。

② **AFFECT SB'S FEELINGS** 影響某人的感情
6 [T] to make someone feel upset, sympathetic, interested etc 使感到難受[同情, 有趣等]: *His harsh words had obviously touched her although she tried not to show it.* 她儘管竭力不表現出來, 但對他那些苛刻的言辭明顯地感到難受。| *Politics didn't touch me an awful lot those days.* 在那些日子裡, 政治對我的影響並不很大。
7 touch a nerve to mention a subject that makes someone feel upset, or angry 觸到某人的痛處: *I think you touched a nerve when you brought up the subject of divorce.* 我認為, 你提及離婚這個話題是觸到了痛處。
8 be touched by sth to feel grateful for or pleased about something nice that someone does 被某事感動, 打動: *I was very touched by his kind letter.* 我被他那封親切的信深深打動了。—see also 另見 TOUCHING

③ **USE/HANDLE** 使用/觸摸
9 not touch sth a) ▶OBJECT/POSSESSION 物體/財產◀ to not use or handle something 不使用[不接觸]某物: *I've never touched a penny of that money.* 那筆錢我從來沒有用過一分。| *He has a car but I'm sure he wouldn't let you touch it.* 他有一輛車, 但我敢說他是不會讓你用的。| **Don't touch (sth)** *spoken* (=used when you are warning someone not to handle or touch something because it is dangerous or not allowed)【口】不准碰〔警告語〕*"Don't touch that switch!" his father shouted.* "不要碰那個開關!" 他父親嚷道。**b) ▶FOOD/DRINK** 食品/飲料◀ to not eat or drink the thing mentioned 不吃; 不喝: *She went to school without touching her breakfast.* 她沒吃早飯就上學去了。| *He rarely ever touches alcohol, except at Christmas.* 除了在聖誕節, 他平常幾乎不喝酒。| **not/never touch the stuff** (=not drink alcohol) 不喝/從不喝酒 *My grandfather was an alcoholic and as a result my father never touched the stuff.* 我祖父酗酒成性, 因此我父親滴酒不沾。

④ **DEAL/ATTEND TO** 處理
10 ▶PRACTICAL MATTER/SITUATION 實際的問題/情況◀ [T] to deal with or become involved with a particular matter, situation or problem 處理; 參與: *He was the only lawyer who would touch the case.* 他是唯一願意處理此案的律師。| *He's a walking disaster! Everything he touches goes wrong.* 他真是一個災星! 他涉及的每一件事都會出錯。
11 not touch sth to not do any work on or give any time to something which needs work or attention 沒有做某事; 沒有關注某事: *The garden looks awful – I'm afraid I haven't touched it for weeks.* 花園看上去亂糟糟的 —— 我恐怕有好幾個禮拜沒有清理它了。
12 wouldn't touch sth/sb (with a bargepole) *BrE*【英】**ten-foot pole** *AmE*【美】used as a way of saying that you think something or someone is bad in some way and you do not want to get or advise getting involved with them〔因趨利避害而〕不想與某事/某人有瓜葛; 不建議別人與其有瓜葛: *I wouldn't touch that house with a bargepole – it's almost falling down.* 我才不想管那座房子呢 —— 它都快要倒塌了。

⑤ **HAVE AN EFFECT ON** 產生影響
13 [T] to have an effect on someone or something so that it changes or influences them 對…有影響: *They had lived in such isolation that the outside world had barely touched them.* 他們生活在這麼孤零零的環境裡, 外面的世界對他們幾乎沒有影響。
14 be touched by sth to be affected by a particular quality 受…的影響; 帶有…的特性: *All the family were touched by a common genius.* 全家人都帶有一種共同的天賦。| *There was no denying that his motivation was touched by self interest.* 不可否認的是, 他的動機裡帶有自私的成分。
15 [T] if an expression such as a smile touches your face, your face has that expression for a short time〔臉上〕露出, 閃現〔笑容等〕: *A rare frown touched his normally placid face.* 他那通常平靜的臉上出現了難得一見的皺眉。

⑥ **OTHER MEANINGS** 其他意思
16 [T] to concern a particular subject, situation, or problem 涉及, 關係到: *Though the question touched a new vein, Nelson answered promptly.* 儘管這個問題涉及一個新的方向, 納爾遜還是迅速地作了回答。
17 nothing/no one to touch sth/sb, nothing/no one that can touch sth/sb nothing or no one that is as good as something or someone 沒有甚麼/沒有人能比得上: *She's a brilliant tennis player – there's no one else here to touch her.* 她是一名傑出的網球選手 —— 這裡沒有誰能比得上她。| *You can listen to a recording of a concert but nothing can touch actually being there.* 你可以聽音樂會的錄音, 不過這根本無法與在現場聽相比。
18 touch bottom a) to reach the ground at the bottom of a sea, river etc 下降到[碰到]〔海、河等的〕底部: *He swam down and down but could not touch bottom.* 他往下面游啊游, 但還是碰不到底。**b)** to reach the lowest level or worst condition 達到最低點; 落到最壞的地步: *After weeks of uncertainty, morale in the company has touched bottom.* 經過幾週的不穩定之後, 公司的士氣已經跌落到最低點。
19 touch wood *especially BrE* used when you have just said that you have been lucky in some way in the past, because this expression is traditionally supposed to help your good luck to continue【尤英】摸摸木頭就運氣好〔英國民俗認為說這話能使好運氣延續下去〕: *I haven't been ill yet this winter – touch wood.* 我今年冬天還沒有生過病 —— 摸摸木頭就運氣好。

touch down *phr v* [I] if an aircraft touches down, it lands on the ground〔飛機等〕降落, 着陸: *We all sighed with relief when the plane finally touched down safely.* 當飛機最終安全着陸時, 我們全都鬆了一口氣。

touch sb **for** sth *phr v* [T] *informal* to persuade someone to give or lend you something, especially money【非正式】求某人給[借]某物〔尤指錢〕: *Can I touch you for a fiver until next week?* 我能向你借五塊錢, 等下週再還嗎?

touch sth ↔ **off** *phr v* [T] to cause a difficult situation or violent events to begin 使產生〔困境〕; 引發〔暴力事件〕: *The government's actions touched off a storm of protest.* 政府的行動激發了抗議風暴。

touch on/upon sth *phr v* [T] to mention or deal with a particular subject briefly when talking or writing〔說話或寫作時〕簡略地提到, 提及: *There is one factor we have not touched on, so far, in talking about personality.* 在討論個性方面, 有一個因素我們迄今還未談到。

touch sth **up** *phr v* [T] to improve something by changing it or adding to it slightly 修改, 改進, 潤色: *The speech he finally gave had been touched up by his staff.* 他最後所作的發言是經他的工作班子潤色過的。| *She quickly touched up her lipstick.* 她很快地添補了一點唇膏。

touch sb **up** *phr v* [T] to touch someone in a sexual way when you should not 對〔異性〕動手動腳: *He had a reputation for touching up his secretaries.* 他因為對自己的祕書動手動腳而名聲不好。

T

touch² *n*

1 ►SENSE 感覺◄ [U] the sense that you use to discover what something feels like, by putting your hand or another part of your body on it 觸覺: *Visually impaired people orient themselves by touch.* 視力有障礙的人通過觸覺確定自己的方位。| **to the touch** *Natural fabrics feel much nicer to the touch.* 天然纖維摸起來感覺要好得多。

2 ►ACT OF TOUCHING 觸摸行為◄ [C usually singular 一般用單數] what you do when you put your hand or another part of your body on or against something or someone either deliberately or not 觸, 碰, 摸: *A smile, a friendly gesture, a touch – any of these can be of an enormous help.* 一個微笑, 一個友好的姿態, 一下觸摸——任何這些行為都可能有巨大的幫助。| *I couldn't move. The slightest touch hurt.* 我不能動。輕輕的碰一下都疼。| **at the touch of a button** (=used to emphasize how easily something practical can be done) 只需按一下鍵鈕〔用以強調某事很容易做成〕*We can contact people on the other side of the world at the touch of a button nowadays.* 今天, 我們只需按一下按鈕就能與遠在天涯海角的人聯繫上。

3 ►FEEL SB/STH 感覺某人/某物◄ [C usually singular 一般用單數] the way that someone or something feels and the effect they have on your body〔觸摸的〕感覺: *She longed to see him again and feel his touch.* 她渴望着能再次見到他, 感受他的撫摸。| *The child recoiled from the thought of the cold slimy touch of the snake's body.* 一想到蛇身那種冷冰冰、黏糊糊的感覺, 這孩子退縮了。

4 be in touch to speak especially on the telephone, or write to someone about something〔尤指通過電話或寫信〕聯繫: *I'll be in touch when I get back from Paris.* 我從巴黎回來後就可以聯繫上了。| **[+with]** *My officials have been in touch with the department concerning their comments.* 我手下的官員已經與提出意見的那個部門聯繫上了。

5 get in touch to write or speak to someone on the telephone in order to tell them something〔寫信或打電話〕取得聯繫: *We'll get in touch as soon as we know the results of the test.* 我們一知道測試的結果就盡快進行聯繫。| **[+with]** *You can get in touch with me at the office if necessary.* 如果必要的話, 你可以在辦公室與我取得聯繫。

6 keep/stay in touch to speak or write to someone when you can no longer see them as often as you used to 保持聯繫: **[+with]** *Our neighbours are moving away but I hope that we'll still keep in touch with each other.* 我們的鄰居要搬走了, 不過我希望我們仍然會保持聯繫。

7 lose touch to no longer speak or write to someone because they do not live near you, work with you etc 失去聯繫: **[+with]** *I've lost touch with most of my friends from college.* 我與大學時代的大多數朋友已經失去了聯繫。

8 put sb in touch with sb to give someone the name, address, or telephone number of a person or organization they need 安排某人與某人聯繫: *Your doctor should be able to put you in touch with a specialist.* 你的醫生應該能夠安排你與一位專科醫生取得聯繫。

9 be/keep/stay in touch with sth to have the latest information, knowledge, and understanding about a subject 獲得某方面的最新情況[知識, 了解等]: *Through the media we are able to keep in touch with events on the other side of the world almost as they happen.* 通過媒體, 我們幾乎立即就能夠了解到在世界另一端發生的事件。

10 be out of touch with sth/lose touch with sth to no longer have the correct information or a good understanding about a subject 不再了解某事, 與某事已很生疏: *Government ministers are often being accused of being out of touch with real life.* 政府部長們經常被指責與實際生活脫節。

11 ►DETAIL/ADDITION 細節/補充◄ [C] a small detail that improves or completes something〔細節上的〕潤色, 修飾, 點綴: *The flowers on every table were a very nice touch.* 每張桌子上擺放的花是非常美麗的點綴。| *She was just adding the final touches to her speech.* 她正在給她的演講作最後的潤色。| **finishing touch/touches** *The necklace was the finishing touch to her wedding outfit.* 那串項鏈是她結婚禮服的點睛之筆。

12 ►WAY OF DOING STH 做某事的方式◄ [C] a particular way of doing something 手法, 風格, 技巧: *A more sensitive touch is needed in our approach to this problem.* 我們解決這一問題需要一種更加細膩的技巧。| *The room was decorated with a very artistic touch.* 這個房間的裝飾很有藝術風格。

13 a touch of sth a very small amount of something 少量某物, 一點兒某物: *"I'm afraid I don't agree," said Hazel, with a touch of irritation.* 黑兹爾略帶氣憤地說: "我恐怕不同意。" | *She had a touch of fever in the night.* 她晚上稍微有點發燒。

14 a touch cold/strange/unfair etc slightly cold, strange etc 有點冷/奇怪/不公平等的: *He sounded a touch upset when I spoke to him on the phone.* 我在電話裡跟他說話時, 他似乎有點不高興。

15 lose your touch to lose your ability to do something 失去〔做某事的〕能力: *He's been playing so badly recently that it seems he's losing his touch.* 他最近的表演一直很差勁, 他似乎失去了功力。—see also 另見 **the common touch** (COMMON¹ (8)), **a soft touch** (SOFT (11))

touch-and-go /ˌ· · ˈ·/ *adj informal* in a touch-and-go situation, there is a serious risk that something bad could happen【非正式】一觸即發的, 危險的; 沒有把握的: *It was touch-and-go whether the doctor would get there on time.* 醫生能否會按時趕到那兒是沒有把握的。

touch·down /ˈtʌtʃˌdaʊn; ˈtʌtʃdaʊn/ *n* [C] **1** the moment at which a plane or SPACECRAFT lands〔飛機、航天器等的〕降落, 着陸 **2** an act of touching the ball down on the ground behind your opponent's GOAL (3) in RUGBY〔橄欖球賽中越過對方底線的〕觸地得分 **3** an act of moving the ball across the opposing team's GOAL LINE in American football〔美式足球賽中的〕持球過底線得分 —see picture on page A22 參見 A22 頁圖

tou·ché /tuˈʃe ˈtuːʃeɪ/ *interjection* used when you want to emphasize in a humorous way that someone has made a very good point during an argument 說得好, 說到點子上了〔用於強調某人在辯論中論點有力的一種幽默說法〕: *"You should be ashamed." "So should you." "Touché," he replied, not at all put out.* "你應該感到羞恥。" "你也應該如此。" "說得好!" 他回答說, 一點也不覺得惱怒。

touched /tʌtʃt; tʌtʃt/ *adj* [not before noun 不用於名詞前] **1** feeling happy and grateful because of someone's actions 高興的; 感激的; 受感動的: *We were deeply touched by their present.* 他們送來禮物, 我們非常感激。| **touched that** *Cathryn was touched that Sarah had come to see her off.* 令凱瑟琳感動的是, 莎拉來為她送行了。—see also 另見 TOUCH¹ (8) **2** *informal* slightly strange in your behaviour【非正式】行為有點古怪的: *He seems a bit touched to me!* 我覺得他的行為顯得有點古怪!

touch foot·ball /ˈ· ˌ··/ *n* [U] *AmE* a type of American football in which you touch the person with the ball instead of tackling (TACKLE¹ (3)) them【美】觸身式橄欖球〔美式足球的變種, 持球球員被對方接觸到就不得再跑, 但不允許擒抱持球球員〕

touch·ing¹ /ˈtʌtʃɪŋ; ˈtʌtʃɪŋ/ *adj* making you feel pity, sympathy, sadness etc 令人同情的; 感人的; 傷感的: *a touching reunion of father and son* 感人的父子團聚情景 —see also 另見 TOUCH¹ (6) —**touchingly** *adv*

touching² *prep formal* concerning【正式】關於, 有關: *matters touching the conduct of diplomacy* 有關外交事務的問題

touch·line /ˈtʌtʃˌlaɪn; ˈtʌtʃlaɪn/ *n* [C] a line along each of the two longer sides of a sports field, especially in football〔尤指足球場的〕邊線

touch·pa·per /ˈtʌtʃ,pepɚ; ˈtʌtʃ,peɪpə/ *n* [C] a piece of slow-burning paper, that you light in order to start a FIREWORK burning〔引發煙花爆竹用的〕導火線, 火絨線: *Light the blue touchpaper, then retire to a safe distance.* 點燃藍色的火絨線, 然後退到安全距離之外。

touch·stone /ˈtʌtʃ,ston; ˈtʌtʃstəʊn/ *n* [C] something used as a test or standard 試金石; 檢驗標準: **[+of]** *Pupil behaviour was seen as 'the touchstone of quality' of the school system.* 學生的行為表現被認為是學校系統的"質量檢驗標準"。

touch-tone phone /ˈ· · ,·/ *n* [C] a telephone that produces different sounds when different numbers are pushed 按鈕式電話機

touch-type /ˈ· ·/ *v* [I] to be able to use a TYPEWRITER without having to look at the letters while you are using it〔不用看鍵盤上的字母而〕邊閱讀邊打字

touch·y /ˈtʌtʃɪ; ˈtʌtʃi/ *adj* **1** easily becoming offended or annoyed 過分敏感的; 易動怒的: *Since his girlfriend left him, he's been very touchy.* 自從女朋友離開他後, 他一直動不動就來脾氣。**2 touchy subject/question etc** a subject etc that needs to be dealt with very carefully 需小心對待的話題/問題等: *Asking about a reporter's sources can be a touchy business.* 要使一名記者透露他的消息來源, 需要非常謹慎。—**touchily** *adv* —**touchiness** *n* [U]

2 **tough¹** /tʌf; tʌf/ *adj*
3 **1 ▶DIFFICULT** 困難的◀ difficult to do or deal with, and needing a lot of effort and determination 難辦的, 棘手的; 費力的: *Life as a single mother can be tough and depressing.* 單身母親的生活可能會艱難而令人沮喪。| *a tough decision* 艱難的決定 | *The reporters were asking a lot of tough questions.* 記者們問了許多難以回答的問題。

2 ▶STRONG PEOPLE 堅強的人◀ able to live through difficult or severe conditions 堅強的, 頑強的; 能吃苦耐勞的: *The men who work on the oil rigs are a tough bunch.* 在石油鑽塔上工作的那些人是一羣能吃苦耐勞的人。| **as tough as nails/as tough as old boots** (=very tough) 非常堅強的; 能吃大苦的 *He's as tough as nails – a good man to have on the mountain rescue team.* 他非常堅強 —— 是山區營救隊的得力成員。

3 ▶STRONG THING 堅固的東西◀ not easily broken or made weaker 結實的, 不易破損的; 堅固的: *a very tough, hard-wearing cloth* 非常結實、耐磨損的布料

4 ▶DETERMINED 堅定的◀ very determined or strict 堅定的; 強硬的; 嚴格的: *Congress is taking a tough anti-inflation line.* 國會正在採取一條強硬的反通貨膨脹的路線。| **get tough with** (=punish or deal with someone in a determined and strict way) 以強硬的方式懲罰[對付] *It's time to get tough with drunk drivers.* 該對醉酒司機採取強硬手段了。| **be tough on** (=treat someone very strictly) 嚴格對待; 嚴格對付 *My mother was tougher on my older sister than she was on me.* 我母親對我姐姐比對我要嚴厲一些。| *It's time to get tough on crime.* 到了該嚴厲打擊犯罪的時候了。| **tough nut/cookie/customer** *informal* (=someone who is very determined to do what they want and not what other people want)【非正式】〔態度堅決〕很難對付的人/傢伙/顧客

5 ▶FOOD 食物◀ difficult to cut or eat 切不下的; 咬不動的; 不嫩的, 老的: *The meat was tough and hard to chew.* 這肉太硬, 很難嚼動。| *the tough outer leaves of the cabbage* 洋白菜外面那幾層老菜葉 —opposite 反義詞 TENDER¹

6 ▶ANGRY/NOT SORRY 生氣的/不同情的◀ *spoken* used when you do not have any sympathy with someone【口】氣憤的/不憐憫的: **tough!** *"I'm getting wet." "Tough! You should've brought your umbrella."* "我淋濕了。" "活該! 你本該帶着雨傘的。" | *She didn't tell us she was coming, so if this screws up her plans that's just tough.* 她沒有告訴我們她要來, 所以, 如果這打亂了她的計劃, 也是活該。

7 tough luck *spoken*【口】**a)** also 又作 **tough shit** *taboo*【諱】used when you do not have any sympathy for someone's problems 活該倒霉: *Well, that's just their tough luck. It was their mistake.* 唉, 活該他們倒霉。那是他們自己的錯。**b)** *BrE* used when you feel sympathy about something bad that has happened to someone【英】倒霉的, 可憐的〔表示同情〕: *You didn't get the job? Oh, tough luck.* 你沒有得到那份工作? 噢, 真不走運。

8 ▶VIOLENT PERSON 粗暴的人◀ likely to behave violently and having no gentle qualities 粗暴的, 兇惡的; 滅絕人性的: *tough young thugs looking for trouble* 像凶神惡煞、到處滋事的年輕暴徒

9 ▶VIOLENT AREA 暴力地區◀ a tough part of a town has a lot of crime or violence〔城區〕暴力犯罪多發的, 治安很差的: *tough areas of Chicago* 芝加哥治安很差的地區

10 ▶UNFORTUNATE 不幸的◀ unfortunate in a way that seems unfair 不幸的; 不公平的: **[+on]** *It's really tough on him – his wife divorces him, then he has all these problems at work.* 他真是不幸 —— 妻子與他離了婚, 接着工作上又出現了這麼多問題。

11 tough love *AmE* love and strictness at the same time【美】嚴厲和愛的結合 —**toughly** *adv* —**toughness** *n* [U]

tough² *n* [C] *old-fashioned* someone who often behaves in a violent way【過時】暴徒, 惡棍

tough³ *v* **tough it out** to manage to stay in a difficult situation by being determined 渡過難關, (從困境中) 挺過來: *We toughed it out, knowing the boss would soon be leaving.* 我們堅定地挺了過來, 知道老闆快要離任的。

tough·en /ˈtʌfn̩; ˈtʌfən/ also 又作 **toughen up** *v* [I,T] to become tougher or make someone or something tougher (使) 變堅韌; (使) 變堅強: *toughened glass* 強化玻璃 | *Three years in the army toughened him up.* 三年的軍隊生活使他變得堅強起來。

tou·pée /tuˈpe; ˈtuːpeɪ/ [C] a small artificial piece of hair that some men wear over a place on their heads where the hair no longer grows〔男子用來遮蓋禿髮處的〕假髮

tour¹ /tʊr; tʊə/ *n* [C] **1** a journey for pleasure, during which you visit several different towns, areas etc〔觀 2
光〕旅遊, 旅行: *a bicycle tour* 騎自行車旅遊 | **[+round/around/of]** *a 10-day tour of China* 中國十日遊 —see also 另見 PACKAGE TOUR **2** a short trip through a place to see it〔對某地的〕參觀, 遊覽: **[+of/round/around]** *a guided tour around the Kennedy Space Center* 有嚮導陪同的甘迺迪太空中心遊覽 **3** a planned journey made by musicians, a sports team etc in order to perform or play in several places 巡迴演出; 巡迴比賽: **[+of]** *the England cricket team's tour of India* 英格蘭板球隊在印度的巡迴比賽 | **on tour** *The Moscow Symphony Orchestra is here on tour.* 莫斯科交響樂團巡迴演出, 來到此地。| **a leg of a tour** (=one part of it) 巡迴演出的一站 *the first leg of U2's European tour* U2 演唱組歐洲巡迴演出的第一站 **4** a period during which you go to live somewhere, usually abroad, to do your job, especially military work 外地工作期〔尤指在海外的軍方工作〕: *a two-year tour in Vietnam* 在越南的兩年派駐期 **5 tour of inspection** an official visit to a place, institution, group etc in order to check its quality or performance〔官員的〕視察訪問, 巡察

tour² *v* [I,T] to visit somewhere on a tour 遊覽, 觀光: *We're touring the Greek islands this summer.* 我們今年夏天要去遊覽希臘諸島。

tour de force /ˌtʊr də ˈfɔrs; ˌtʊə də ˈfɔːs/ *n* [singular] something that is done very skilfully and successfully, in a way that impresses people 絕技, 絕活, 拿手好戲: *His speech to the Democratic Convention was a tour de force.* 他在民主黨大會上的演說精彩極了。

tour·is·m /ˈtʊrɪzm̩; ˈtʊərɪzəm/ *n* [U] the business of providing things for people to do, places for them to stay etc while they are on holiday 旅遊業, 觀光業: *The country depends on tourism for most of its income.* 該國的大部分收入依靠旅遊業。

tour·ist /ˈtʊrɪst; ˈtʊərɪst/ *n* [C] someone who is travel- 3 ling or visiting a place for pleasure 遊客, 遊人, 觀光客: *Cambridge is always full of tourists in the summer.* 劍橋在夏季總是擠滿了遊客。

tourist at·trac·tion /'·· ·,··/ *n* [C] a place or event that a lot of tourists go to 旅遊勝地; 旅遊盛事: *The Statue of Liberty is a major tourist attraction.* 自由女神像是一處重要的旅遊景點。

tourist class /'·· ·/ *n* [U] the cheapest standard of travelling conditions on a plane, ship etc〔飛機、輪船等上面最廉價的〕旅遊艙, 經濟艙

tourist of·fice /'·· ,··/ also 又作 **tourist in·for·ma·tion of·fice** /,·· ··'·· ,··/ *n* [C] an office that gives information to tourists in an area 旅遊信息諮詢處

tourist trap /'·· ,·/ *n* [C] a place that many tourists visit, but where drinks, hotels etc are more expensive 敲遊客竹槓的地方〈如餐飲店、旅店等〉

tour·ist·y /'tʊrɪstɪ; 'tʊərɪ̩sti/ *adj informal*【非正式】**1** a place that is touristy is unpleasantly full of tourists and the things that attract tourists 擠滿遊客的, 充滿吸引遊客的東西的: *Benidorm is too touristy for me.* 貝尼多姆對我來説遊客太多了一點。**2** a touristy activity is unpleasantly typical of the things that tourists do〔活動〕像旅遊似的; 走馬觀花似的: *The boat trip was kind of touristy, but we did get to see a lot.* 那次乘船旅行有點走馬觀花似的, 不過我們還是看到了不少風景。

tour·na·ment /'tɝnəmənt; 'tʊənəmənt/ *n* [C] **1 tennis/chess/badminton etc tournament** a competition in which players compete against each other in a series of games until there is one winner 網球/國際象棋/羽毛球等錦標賽 **2** a competition to show courage and fighting skill between soldiers in the Middle Ages〔中世紀的〕騎士比武大會

tour·ni·quet /'tɝnɪ,kɛt; 'tʊənɪkeɪ/ *n* [C] a band of cloth that is twisted tightly around an injured arm or leg to stop it bleeding 止血帶

tour of du·ty /,· · '··/ *n* [C] a period of time when you are working in a particular place or job, especially abroad while you are in the army etc 工作期;〔尤指軍隊中派駐海外的〕服役期

tour op·e·rat·or /'· ,····/ *n* [C] *BrE* a company that arranges travel tours【英】旅遊公司, 旅行社

tou·sle /'taʊzḷ; 'taʊzəl/ *v* [T] to make someone's hair look untidy 弄亂〔頭髮〕

tou·sled /'taʊzḷd; 'taʊzəld/ *adj* tousled hair or a tousled appearance looks untidy〔頭髮〕蓬亂的; 蓬頭垢面的: *She had just awakened, her eyes sleepy and her hair tousled.* 她剛睡醒, 一副睡眼惺忪、頭髮蓬亂的樣子。

tout[1] /taʊt; taʊt/ *v* **1** [T] to praise something or someone in order to persuade people that they are important or worth a lot 讚揚; 吹捧: *the much touted delights of England in the spring* 眾口交譽的英格蘭春天的樂趣 | **be touted as sth** *Bates was widely touted as the next Olympic star.* 貝茨被大家預測為下一屆奧林匹克之星。**2** [I, T] *especially BrE* to try to persuade people to buy goods or services you are offering【尤英】兜售, 推銷〔商品或服務〕: **tout for business/custom** (=look for customers) 拉生意/招徠顧客 **3** [I,T] *AmE* to give someone information about a horse in a race【美】(向…) 提供賽馬情報

tout[2] *n* [C] *BrE*【英】**1** someone who buys tickets for a concert, sports match etc and sells them at a very high price 票販子, 黃牛黨; SCALPER *AmE*【美】**2** someone who tries to sell goods or services to people passing on the street 沿街兜售者, 拉生意者

tow[1] /to; təʊ/ *v* [T] to pull a vehicle or ship along behind another vehicle using a rope or chain 牽引, 拖, 拉〔車或船〕: *The ship had to be towed into the harbor.* 那艘輪船不得已被拖進了港口。

tow[2] *n* **1** [C] an act of pulling a vehicle behind another vehicle using a rope or chain 牽引, 拖, 拉〔車船等〕: *Can you give us a tow?* 你能幫我們拖一下嗎? **2 in tow** *informal* following closely behind someone or something【非正式】緊跟在後: *Hannah arrived with her four kids in tow.* 漢納來了, 她的四個孩子緊跟在後面。**3 take sth in tow** to connect a rope or a chain to a vehicle or ship so that it can be towed〔用繩索或鏈條〕拖着〔車或船〕**4 on tow** *BrE* a vehicle that is on tow is being pulled along by another vehicle【英】〔車〕被拖着走

to·wards /tɔrdz; tə'wɔːdz/ *especially BrE*【尤英】, **to·ward** /tɔrd; tə'wɔːd/ *especially AmE*【尤美】*prep* **1** moving, looking, or pointing in a particular direction 向(着), 朝(着): *He noticed two policemen coming towards him.* 他覺察到兩名警察正朝他走來。| *All the windows face toward the river.* 所有的窗戶都朝向河。| *He was standing with his back towards me.* 他背對我站着。—see picture on page A1 參見 A1 頁圖 **2** if you do something towards something, you do it in order to achieve it 為了 (…目的): *These negotiations are the first step toward reaching an agreement.* 這些談判是為了達成一項協議而邁出的第一步。| *The council is constantly working towards racial and sexual equality.* 該委員會正不斷努力爭取種族和性別上的平等。**3** a feeling, attitude etc towards something is how you feel or what you think about it 對於; 關於〔指感覺、態度等〕: *Brian's attitude towards his work has always been very positive.* 布萊恩對工作的態度總是非常積極主動的。**4** money put, saved, or given towards something is used to pay for it〔錢〕用於支付…: *A lot of the donations will be put towards repairing the church roof.* 捐款中的很大部分將用於維修教堂的屋頂。**5 a)** just before a particular time 快要到〔某個時刻〕: *Toward the end of the afternoon it began to rain.* 快到傍晚時, 天下起雨來了。**b)** near a particular place 接近〔某一地方〕: *As you get towards the coast you notice more and more hotels and restaurants.* 快接近海邊時, 你會注意到有許許多多的旅館和飯店了。

tow·a·way zone /'toəwe ,zon; 'təʊəweɪ ,zəʊn/ *n* [C] *AmE* an area where cars are not allowed to park, and from which they can be taken away by the police【美】禁止停車區〔違章車有可能被警察拖走〕

tow·bar /'tobɑr; 'təʊbɑː/ *n* [C] a metal bar on the back of a car for towing (TOW[1]) a CARAVAN (1) or boat〔用以牽引車、船等的〕牽引槓

tow·el[1] /'taʊəl; 'taʊəl/ *n* [C] a piece of cloth that you use for drying your skin or for drying things such as dishes 毛巾, 紙巾; 抹布: *a bath towel* 浴巾 —see also 另見 PAPER TOWEL, TEA TOWEL, **throw in the towel** (THROW[1])

towel[2] *v* [T] *AmE* also 又作 **towel down** to dry yourself using a towel【美】用毛巾擦乾 —see also 另見 TOWELLING

tow·el·ette /,taʊə'lɛt; ,taʊə'let/ *n* [C] a small piece of soft wet paper that you use to clean your hands or face 小毛巾; 濕餐巾紙

tow·el·ling *BrE*【英】, **toweling** *AmE*【美】/'taʊəlɪŋ; 'taʊəlɪŋ/ *n* [U] thick soft cloth, used especially for making towels or BATHROBES 毛巾布 —see picture on page A16 參見 A16 頁圖

towel rail /'·· ·/ also 又作 **towel rack** *n* [C] a bar or frame on which towels can be hung, especially in a bathroom〔尤指浴室裡的〕毛巾架

tow·er[1] /'taʊɚ; 'taʊə/ *n* [C] **1** a tall narrow building either built on its own or forming part of a castle, church etc 塔; 塔樓: *They rebuilt the church tower in the 1870s.* 他們在19 世紀 70 年代重修了那座教堂的鐘樓。**2** a tall structure, often made of metal, used for signalling, broadcasting etc〔發送信號或廣播等用的〕鐵塔, 塔狀建築物: *an air traffic control tower* 空中交通管制塔 **3 tower of strength** someone who gives you a lot of help, sympathy, and support when you are in trouble〔在遇到麻煩時〕可依靠的人; 力量的支柱: *Her father was a tower of strength to her when her marriage broke up.* 她的婚姻破裂時, 父親成了她可以依靠的支柱。—see also 另見 COOLING TOWER, **ivory tower** (IVORY (6)), WATER TOWER

tower² *v* [I] **1** to be much taller than the people or things around you〔比周圍的人或物體〕高出許多; 高聳, 屹立: [**+about/over**] *Graham was 6 ft 5, and towered over the rest of us.* 格雷厄姆身高六英尺五英寸, 比我們其餘的人都要高出許多。**2** to be much better than any other person or organization that does the same thing as you〔比…〕優秀許多; 高踞〔於…之上〕: [**+about/over**] *Mozart towers over all other composers.* 莫扎特高踞於其他所有作曲家之上。

tower block /'‥ ˌ/ *n* [C] *BrE* a tall building containing apartments or offices【英】〔作公寓或辦公用的〕高層建築

tower computer /ˌ‥ ·'‥/ *n* [C] a computer in the shape of a tall box 塔式電腦 —see picture on page A14 參見A14頁圖

tow·er·ing /'tauərɪŋ; 'taʊərɪŋ/ *adj* [only before noun 僅用於名詞前] **1** very tall 高大的, 高聳的: *great towering cliffs* 宏偉高聳的峭壁 **2** much better than other people of the same kind; OUTSTANDING (1) 出眾的, 傑出的: *a towering genius of his time* 他那個時代一名傑出的天才 **3 in a towering rage** very angry 怒氣沖天

tow·head /'toˌhɛd; 'təʊhed/ *n* [C] someone with very light-coloured hair 亞麻色頭髮的人 —**towheaded** *adj*

tow·line /'tolaɪn; 'təʊlaɪn/ *n* [C] a TOWROPE 拖索, 縴繩

1 1 **town** /taun; taʊn/ *n*

1 ▶PLACE 地方◀ [C] a large area with houses, shops, offices etc where people live and work, that is smaller than a city and larger than a village〔大於村莊、小於城市的〕鎮, 城鎮, 市鎮: *an industrial town in the Midlands* 英格蘭中部地區的一座工業城鎮 | *the town of Norwalk, Connecticut* 康涅狄格州諾沃克鎮

2 ▶MAIN CENTRE 主要中心◀ [U] the business or shopping centre of a town〔市鎮的〕商業中心區, 鬧市區: *We're going into town tonight to see a film.* 我們今晚要去市中心看電影。| *They have a small apartment in town.* 他們在市中心有一套不大的公寓房。

3 ▶PEOPLE 人們◀ [singular] all the people who live in a particular town 鎮民, 市鎮居民: *The whole town turned out to watch the procession.* 全鎮的人都出來觀看遊行隊伍。

4 ▶WHERE YOU LIVE 居住地◀ [U] *AmE* the town or city where you live【美】〔居住的〕城鎮; 城市: *Cam left town about an hour ago, he should be out at the farm by now.* 卡姆大約一個小時前離開城裡, 他現在應該在城外的農場上了。| **out of town** *I'll be out of town for about a week.* 我將離開城裡大約一個星期。| **in town** *Guess who's in town? Jodie's sister!* 猜猜誰到城裡來了? 喬迪的妹妹! | **be from out of town** (=live in a different town than the one you are in) 來自另一個城鎮 *Do you know of a good place to eat? I'm from out of town.* 你能介紹個吃飯的好地方嗎? 我是外地人。

5 ▶VILLAGE 村莊◀ [C] *AmE* several houses forming a small group around a church, shops etc【美】鄉鎮, 集鎮; VILLAGE *BrE*【英】: *Rowayton is a small town of around 4000 people.* 羅威頓是一個大約有4000人的小鄉鎮。

6 ▶NOT COUNTRY 不是鄉下◀ the town life in towns and cities in general 城鎮生活, 城市生活〔統稱〕: *Which do you prefer, the town or the country?* 城市生活與鄉村生活, 你較喜歡哪一種?

7 go to town (on) *informal* to do something in a very eager or thorough way, often spending a lot of money【非正式】拚命地幹〔某事〕; 花大錢〔做某事〕: *Angela really went to town on buying things for her new house.* 安傑拉在為自己的新房子買東西時真是捨得花錢。

8 go/be out on the town *informal* to go to restaurants, bars, theatres etc for entertainment in the evening【非正式】〔晚間去娛樂場所〕尋歡作樂

9 town and gown *BrE* used to describe the situation in which the people living in a town and the students in a town seem to be separate and opposing groups【英】〔分成兩派、相互對立的〕城鎮居民和學生 —see also 另見 GHOST TOWN, **blow town** (BLOW¹ (11)), MARKET TOWN, NEW TOWN, **paint the town red** (PAINT² (6))

town cent·re /ˌ· '‥/ *n* [C] *BrE* the main business area in the centre of a town【英】市中心, 城裡商業區; DOWNTOWN *AmE*【美】

town clerk /ˌ· '·/ *n* [C] an official who keeps records, advises on legal matters etc〔主管檔案、提供法律事務諮詢等工作的〕鎮書記

town coun·cil /ˌ· '‥/ *n* [C] *BrE* a group of people who are responsible for public areas and services, such as roads, parks etc, in a particular town【英】〔負責管理某一城鎮公共事務的〕鎮議會, 市議會 —**town councillor** *n* [C]

town cri·er /ˌ· '‥/ *n* [C] someone employed in former times to walk around the streets of a town, shouting news, warnings etc〔昔日受雇沿街〕大聲宣讀公告的人

town hall /ˌ· '·/ *n* [C] a public building used for a town's local government 市政廳, 鎮公所, 鎮政府辦公樓

town house /'· ·/ *n* [C] **1** a house in a town or city, especially a fashionable one in a central area 市鎮住宅〔尤指市鎮中心區的新式住宅〕**2** a house in a town that belongs to someone who also owns a house in the countryside〔在鄉間擁有住所者的〕市內住宅: *the Duke's town house in Mayfair* 公爵在梅菲爾的市內住宅 **3** *AmE* a house in a group of houses that share one or more walls【美】〔邊牆共用的〕排屋, 連棟房屋

town·ie /'taunɪ; 'taʊni/ *n* [C] *informal* someone who lives in a town or city and does not know anything about life in the countryside【非正式】〔對鄉村生活一無所知的〕城裡人

town meet·ing /ˌ· '‥/ *n* [C] *AmE* a meeting at which the people who live in a town discuss subjects or problems that affect their town【美】鎮民大會

town plan·ning /ˌ· '‥/ *n* [U] the study of the way towns work, so that roads, houses, services etc can be provided as effectively as possible 城鎮規劃

town·ship /'taunʃɪp; 'taʊnʃɪp/ *n* [C] **1** a town in Canada or the US that has some local government〔加拿大或美國享有一定地方行政權的〕鄉, 鎮區 **2** a town in South Africa where black citizens live〔過去南非的〕黑人居住的城市, 鎮: *the black township of Soweto* 黑人城鎮索韋托

towns·peo·ple /'taunzˌpipl̩; 'taʊnzˌpiːpəl/ also 又作 **towns·folk** /-fok; -fəʊk/ *n* [plural] **1** all the people who live in a particular town 城鎮居民: *the proud townspeople of Semer Water* 塞默－沃特城自豪的居民們 **2** people who live in towns and not in the country 鎮民, 城裡人

tow·path /'toˌpæθ; 'təʊpɑːθ/ *n* [C] a path along the side of a CANAL or river used especially in former times by horses pulling boats〔運河或河流兩岸昔日供馬拉船的〕曳船道, 縴路

tow·rope /'toˌrop; 'təʊrəʊp/ also 又作 **towline** *n* [C] a rope or chain used for pulling vehicles along 拖索, 拖纜, 縴繩

tow·truck /'toˌtrʌk; 'təʊtrʌk/ *n* [C] *AmE* a strong vehicle that can pull cars behind it【美】拖運車, 牽引車; BREAKDOWN TRUCK *BrE*【英】

tox·ae·mi·a *BrE*【英】, **toxemia** *AmE*【美】/tɑks'imɪə; tɒk'siːmiə/ *n* [U] a medical condition in which your blood contains poisons 毒血症

tox·ic /'tɑksɪk; 'tɒksɪk/ *adj* containing poison, or caused by poisonous substances 有毒的; 由有毒物質引起的: *toxic fumes* 有毒煙氣 | *a toxic waste dump* 有毒廢物棄置場 —**toxicity** /tɑks'ɪsətɪ; tɒk'sɪsəti/ *n* [U]

tox·i·col·o·gy /ˌtɑksɪ'kɑlədʒɪ; ˌtɒksɪ'kɒlədʒi/ *n* [U] the science and medical study of poisons and their effects 毒物學, 毒理學

toxic shock syn·drome /ˌ‥ '· ˌ‥/ *n* [U] a serious illness that causes a high temperature and is thought to be connected with the use of TAMPONS 中毒性休克綜合徵〔嚴重疾病, 患者發高燒, 被認為與使用月經棉塞有關〕

toxic waste /ˌ‥ '·/ *n* [C,U] waste products from industry that are harmful to people, animals, or the environment 有毒（工業）垃圾

tox·in /ˋtɑksɪn; ˈtɒksən/ *n* [C] a poisonous substance, especially one that is produced by BACTERIA and causes a particular disease 毒素〔尤指細菌產生的致病物質〕

toy¹ /tɔɪ; tɔɪ/ *n* [C] **1** an object for children to play with 玩具: *some toys for the baby* 給嬰兒的一些玩具 | **toy boat/car/truck etc** *Davey wanted some toy soldiers for Christmas.* 戴維想要一些玩具兵作為聖誕禮物。| **soft/cuddly toy** *BrE* (=a toy that looks like an animal and is covered in fur)【英】軟毛動物玩具／讓人想摟抱的動物玩具 **2** an object that you buy because it gives you pleasure and enjoyment 小玩藝兒, 小擺設: *The food mixer is her latest toy.* 食品攪拌器是她最近買來的小玩藝兒。

toy² *v*

toy with sth *phr v* [T] **1** to think about an idea or possibility, usually for a short time and not very seriously〔通常指短暫而不認真地〕考慮: **toy with the idea of doing sth** *I've been toying with the idea of going to Japan to visit them.* 我一直打算去日本探訪他們, 只是從來沒有認真地想過。**2** to play with an object, often while you are thinking about something else 擺弄, 戲耍〔常指一邊想其他事情一邊擺弄〕: *Elsa toyed with her coffee cup.* 艾爾莎擺弄着自己的咖啡杯。

toy³ *adj* [only before noun 僅用於名詞前] a toy animal or dog is a type of dog that is specially bred to be very small〔動物〕體形非常小的: *a toy poodle* 小小的長鬈毛狗

toy boy /ˈ· ·/ *n* [C] *informal* a young man who is having a sexual relationship with an older woman【非正式】〔與年齡較大的婦女有性關係的〕小男人, 小情人

trace¹ /tres; treɪs/ *v* [T]

1 ►FIND SB/STH 發現某人/某物◄ to find someone or something that has disappeared by searching for them carefully 仔細找尋: *She had given up all hope of tracing her missing daughter.* 她已經放棄了一切尋找到失蹤女兒的希望。

2 ►ORIGINS 來源◄ to find the origins of something, or where something came from 追溯; 追查: **trace sth (back) to** *The style of these paintings can be traced back to early medieval influences.* 這些繪畫的風格可以追溯到中世紀早期的影響。

3 ►HISTORY/DEVELOPMENT 歷史/發展◄ to study or describe the history, development, or progress of something 研究…的歷史; 探索…的發展; 追尋…的軌跡: *Sondheim's book traces the changing nature of the relationship between men and women.* 桑德海姆的這本書探索了男人與女人之間關係變化着的本質。

4 ►COPY 謄寫◄ to copy a drawing, map etc by putting a piece of transparent paper over it and then drawing the lines you can see through the paper〔用透明紙在圖上〕描摹, 描繪

5 ►DRAW 勾畫◄ to draw real or imaginary lines on the surface of something, usually with your finger or toe〔用手指或腳趾在物體表面〕畫〔線〕; 留下〔印跡〕: **trace sth on/in/across** *Rosie's fingers traced a delicate pattern in the sand.* 羅絲用手指在沙地上留下了精美的圖案。

6 trace a call to use special electronic equipment to find out who made a telephone call〔利用特殊的電子設備〕追查打電話的人 —**traceable** *adj*

trace² *n*

1 ►SIGN OF STH 某物的跡象◄ [C,U] a small sign that shows that someone or something was present or existed 蹤跡, 痕跡, 跡象: **no trace** *There was no trace of anyone having entered the room since then.* 沒有任何跡象表明有人在那以後進過這間屋子。| **all trace** *Petra's lost all trace of her German accent.* 佩特拉已完全沒有德國口音。| **any trace** *Officers were unable to find any trace of drugs.* 警察未能找到毒品存在的任何跡象。| **disappear/vanish/sink without trace** (=disappear completely, without leaving any sign of what happened) 消失/隱沒/沉沒得無影無蹤 *The Roanoke colony vanished without trace.* 羅阿諾克殖民地消失得無影無蹤了。

2 ►SMALL AMOUNT 小量◄ [C] a very small amount of a quality, emotion, substance etc that is difficult to see or notice 微量; 痕量: **[+of]** *I saw the faintest trace of a smile cross Sandra's face.* 我看到在桑德拉的臉上閃過一絲微笑。| *traces of poison* 微量毒素

3 ►TELEPHONE 電話◄ [C] *technical* a search to find out where a telephone call came from, using special electronic equipment【術語】〔利用特殊電子設備對電話的〕追查, 追蹤: *The police were able to put a trace on the call.* 警察能夠追查到電話是從甚麼地方打過來的。

4 ►INFORMATION RECORDED 記錄的信息◄ [C] the mark or pattern made on a SCREEN or on paper by a machine that is recording an electrical signal〔記錄電信號的機器在屏幕或紙上作的〕描記線: *This trace shows the heartbeat.* 這條描記線顯示了心臟跳動的情況。

5 kick over the traces to stop following the rules of a social group and do what you want 掙脫羈絆, 擺脫約束

6 ►CART/CARRIAGE 大車/馬車◄ [C] one of the two pieces of leather, rope etc by which a cart or carriage is fastened to the animal that is pulling it〔大車或馬車上的〕挽繩

trac·er /ˋtresɚ; ˈtreɪsə/ *n* [C] a bullet that leaves a line of smoke or flame behind it 曳光彈

trac·e·ry /ˋtresərɪ; ˈtreɪsəri/ *n* [C,U] **1** *technical* the curving and crossing lines of stone in the upper parts of some church windows【術語】〔教堂窗戶上部的〕窗花格 **2** *literary* an attractive pattern of lines that cross each other【文】線條交錯的美麗圖案: *the delicate tracery of the bare branches against the sky* 在天空襯托下光禿禿的枝椏交錯成的細緻圖案

tra·che·a /ˋtrekɪə; trəˈkiːə/ *n* [C] *technical* the tube that takes air from your throat to your lungs【術語】氣管 —see picture at 參見 RESPIRATORY 圖

trach·e·ot·o·my /ˌtrekɪˋɑtəmɪ; ˌtrækiˈɒtəmi/ *n* [C] *technical* an operation to cut a hole in someone's throat so that they can breathe【術語】氣管切開術

tra·cho·ma /trəˋkomə; trəˈkəʊmə/ *n* [U] *technical* a painful illness that affects the transparent covering over your eyes【術語】沙眼〔一種眼病〕

trac·ing /ˋtresɪŋ; ˈtreɪsɪŋ/ *n* [C] a copy of a map, drawing etc made by tracing (TRACE¹ (4)) it 描摹

tracing pa·per /ˈ·· ˌ··/ *n* [U] strong transparent paper used for tracing (TRACE¹ (4)) 描圖紙

track¹ /træk; træk/ *n*

1 ►ROAD 道路◄ [C] a narrow road with a rough uneven surface that cars can travel on〔路面粗糙不平的、可行車的〕小道, 窄路: *The road leading to the farm was little more than a rough track.* 通往農場的道路基本上只是一條凹凸不平的小路。| *a deeply-rutted cart track* 車轍很深的小道

2 ►PATH 小徑◄ [C] a narrow path, especially one made by people or animals frequently walking in the same place〔尤指經常行走踩出來的〕小路, 小徑: *a mountain track* 山間小路 | *The track led through dense forest.* 小徑穿過茂密的森林。

3 ►FOR RACING 用於比賽◄ [C] a circular course around which runners, cars etc race, often with a specially prepared surface 跑道: *To run a mile, you have to run four circuits of the track.* 要跑完一英里, 你必須沿着跑道跑四圈。—see also 另見 DIRT TRACK

4 ►RAILWAY 鐵路◄ [C] the two metal lines along which trains travel or the narrow strip of land to which they are fixed; RAILWAY LINE〔鐵路的〕軌道, 鐵路線: *The track was damaged in several places.* 這條鐵路線有好幾處地方都毀壞了。—see picture at 參見 TUNNEL¹ 圖

5 tracks [plural] a line of marks left on the ground by a moving person, animal, or vehicle〔人、獸等的〕足跡, 痕跡;〔車輛的〕軌跡, 車轍: *We followed the tyre tracks across a muddy field.* 我們順着車胎的轍印穿過一片泥濘的田野。| *The tracks, which looked like a fox's, led into*

the woods. 這些看上去像狐狸足跡的痕跡延伸到樹林裡。
6 be on the right/wrong track to think in a way that is likely to lead to a correct or incorrect result 思路正確/錯誤: *He's not interested in her at all – you're on the wrong track there.* 他對她根本不感興趣 —— 你在這一點上想錯了。
7 ►MUSIC/SONG 音樂/歌曲◄ [C] one of the songs or pieces of music on a record, CASSETTE, or CD〔唱片、錄音帶或CD上的〕一首歌; 一支曲子: *There's a great Miles Davis track on side two.* 在第二面有邁爾斯·戴維斯的一首名曲。
8 keep/lose track of to pay attention to someone or something so that you know where they are or what is happening to them, or to fail to do this 掌握/失去…的線索; 了解/不了解…的動態: *It's difficult to keep track of all the new discoveries in genetics.* 要全面掌握遺傳學的新發現是困難的。
9 stop (dead) in your tracks to suddenly stop, especially because something has frightened or surprised you〔尤指因驚嚇而〕突然停下: *Fay stopped in her tracks and pointed at the house.* 費伊突然停了下來, 指着那座房子。
10 cover/hide your tracks to be careful not to leave any signs that could let people know where you have been or what you have done because you want to keep it a secret 掩蓋/隱匿自己的行蹤[活動]: *We don't know where Ford is, he's been very clever in covering his tracks.* 我們不知道福特在哪兒, 他非常狡猾, 來無影去無蹤的。
11 be on the track of to hunt or search for someone or something 追蹤, 追尋: *Police are on the track of a gang that has robbed five post offices in the last month.* 警察正在追蹤過去一個月裡搶劫了五家郵局的一幫匪徒。
12 ►SPORT 體育運動◄ [U] *AmE*【美】**a)** sport that involves running on a track 徑賽運動: *The next year he didn't run track or play football.* 第二年他沒有參加徑賽運動, 也沒有踢足球。**b)** all the sports in an ATHLETICS competition such as running, jumping, or throwing the JAVELIN 田徑運動: *a famous track star* 田徑運動名星 | *She went out for track in the spring.* (=she joined the school's track team) 她在春季加入了學校的田徑隊。
13 I'd better make tracks *spoken* used to say you must leave a place, especially when you do not want to leave【口】我得馬上離開〔尤指自己並不想離開〕: *I'd love to stay, but it's time we started making tracks.* 我倒很想留下, 不過我們該離開了。
14 ►DIRECTION 方向◄ [C] the direction or line taken by something as it moves〔物體移動的〕方向; 行動路線: [+of] *islands that lie in the track of North Atlantic storms* 位於北大西洋風暴運行路線上的島嶼
15 ►ON A VEHICLE 交通工具上◄ [C] an endless metal band driven by the wheels of a vehicle such as a BULLDOZER that allows it to move over uneven ground〔車輛的〕履帶
16 ►FOR RECORDING 錄音用的◄ [C] a band on a TAPE[1] (1) on which music or information can be recorded〔錄音帶的〕音軌, 磁跡: *Sergeant Pepper was recorded on eight tracks.*《佩珀中士》是用八軌磁帶錄音的。
17 be on track *spoken* to be likely to achieve the result you want【口】有可能獲得〔想要的結果〕: *We're still on track for 10% growth.* 我們仍然有可能達到 10% 的增長率。
18 get off the track *spoken* to begin to deal with a new subject rather than the main one which was being discussed【口】偏離正題, 離題: *Don't get off the track, we're looking at this year's figures not last year's.* 別偏離正題了, 我們關注的是今年的數字, 而不是去年的。— see also 另見 **off the beaten track** (BEATEN (3)), ONE-TRACK MIND, **be from the wrong side of the tracks** (WRONG[1] (14))

track² *v*
1 ►SEARCH 搜尋◄ [T] to search for a person or animal by following the marks they leave behind them on the ground, their smell etc 追蹤, 跟蹤: **track sb to sth** *The dogs tracked the wolf to its lair.* 狗追蹤那隻狼一直到牠的巢穴。
2 ►AIRCRAFT/SHIP 飛行器/輪船◄ [T] to follow the movements of an aircraft or ship by using RADAR〔用雷達〕跟蹤〔飛機或輪船〕: *a tracking station* 跟蹤站
3 ►CAMERA 攝像機◄ [I+in/out] to move a film or television camera away from or towards a scene in order to follow the action that you are recording〔電影或電視攝像機〕跟蹤攝影, 移動攝影
4 ►RECORD 唱片◄ [I] if a PICK-UP (4) tracks, it moves in the grooves (GROOVE[1] (1)) on a record〔唱針在唱片紋道中〕移動
5 ►SCHOOL 學校◄ [T] *AmE* to put school children in groups according to their ability【美】把〔學生〕按能力分組; STREAM[2] (5) *BrE*【英】
6 ►MARK 印跡◄ [T] *AmE* to leave behind a track of something such as mud or dirt when you walk【美】留下…的足印: *Which of you boys tracked mud all over the kitchen floor?* 是你們中哪個男孩子在廚房地板上到處留下帶泥的腳印? —**tracker** *n* [C] *a police tracker dog* 搜索用警犬

track sb/sth ↔ **down** *phr v* [T] to find someone or something that is difficult to find by searching or making inquiries in several different places 追蹤到; 追查到: *I finally managed to track down the book you wanted in a shop near the station.* 我在車站附近的一家書店裡終於找到了你想要的那本書。

track and field /ˌ· ·ˈ·/ *n* [U] *AmE* sports such as running and jumping【美】田徑運動; ATHLETICS *BrE*【英】
track·ball /ˈtrækˌbɔl; ˈtrækbɔːl/ *n* [C] a small ball connected to a computer, that you turn in order to move the CURSOR 跟蹤球〔一種與電腦連接的用來控制光標移動的小球〕
tracker dog /ˈ·· ·/ *n* [C] a dog that has been specially trained to follow and find people 搜索用警犬
track e·vent /ˈ· ·ˌ·/ *n* [C] *AmE* a running race【美】徑賽項目
tracking sta·tion /ˈ·· ˌ··/ *n* [C] a place from which objects moving in space, such as SATELLITES and ROCKETS, can be recognized and followed〔對在太空中運行的人造衛星、火箭等進行識別、追蹤的〕跟蹤站
track·lay·er /ˈtrækˌleə; ˈtrækˌleɪə/ *n* [C] *AmE* a workman who builds or repairs railway tracks【美】〔鐵路〕鋪軌工人; 養路工; PLATE-LAYER *BrE*【英】
track meet /ˈ· ·/ *n* [C] *AmE* a sports event consisting of competitions in running, jumping etc【美】田徑運動會
track rec·ord /ˈ· ˌ··/ *n* [singular] all the things that a person or organization has done in the past, which show how good they are at doing their job, dealing with problems etc〔個人或機構在工作、解決問題等方面的〕成績記錄, 業績記錄: *We're looking for someone with a proven track record in selling advertising.* 我們正在尋找一位在廣告銷售業績方面有良好記錄的人。
track·suit /ˈtrækˌsut; ˈtræksuːt/ *n* [C] *BrE* loose clothes consisting of trousers and a JACKET (1), worn especially for sport【英】寬鬆式運動衣褲, 田徑服
tract /trækt; trækt/ *n* [C] **1 digestive/reproductive/urinary etc tract** a system of connected organs that have one main purpose in a part of your body〔身體器官系統中的〕消化道/生殖道/泌尿道等 **2** a large area of land〔土地的〕一大片: *vast tracts of woodland* 大片林地 **3** *formal* a short piece of writing, especially about a moral or religious subject【正式】〔尤指道德或宗教題材的〕短文, 小冊子: *a tract on the dangers of drink* 一本關於飲酒之種種危險的小冊子
trac·ta·ble /ˈtræktəbl; ˈtræktəbəl/ *adj formal* easy to control or deal with【正式】易控制的; 易對付的: *Separating a problem into separate chunks often makes it more tractable.* 把一個問題分成不同的幾大部分往往會使它更容易處理。—opposite 反義詞 INTRACTABLE —**tractability** /ˌtræktəˈbɪlətɪ; ˌtræktəˈbɪləti/ *n* [U]
trac·tion /ˈtrækʃən; ˈtrækʃən/ *n* [U] **1** the process of treat-

T

ing a broken bone with special medical equipment that pulls it〔治療骨折用的〕牽引術: **be in traction** (=be receiving this kind of treatment) 接受牽引治療 *He was in traction for weeks after the accident.* 事故後他接受了幾個星期的牽引治療。**2** the force that prevents something such as a wheel sliding on a surface〔防止車輪在路面滑動的〕附着摩擦力: *The tires were bald and lost traction on the wet road.* 那些輪胎都用禿了, 在濕的路面上失去了附着摩擦力。**3** the type of power needed to make a vehicle move, or to pull a heavy load〔使汽車或重物等移動的〕牽引力

trac·tor /ˈtræktɚ; ˈtræktə/ *n* [C] a strong vehicle with large wheels, used for pulling farm machinery 拖拉機, 牽引車

trade¹ /tred; treɪd/ *n*

1 ►BUYING/SELLING 買/賣◄ [U] the activity of buying, selling, or exchanging goods within a country or between countries 買賣, 交易, 貿易: *There has been a marked increase in trade between East and West.* 東西方之間的貿易已經有了明顯的增長。| **the arms trade** (=the buying and selling of weapons) 武器買賣, 軍火生意 —see also 另見 BALANCE OF TRADE, FREE TRADE, SLAVE TRADE

2 the hotel/banking/tourist etc trade the business done by banks, hotels etc 酒店業/銀行業/旅遊業等: *My husband worked in the jewellery trade all his life.* 我丈夫一輩子都在珠寶行業工作。

3 ►AMOUNT OF BUSINESS 營業額◄ [U] business activity, especially the amount of goods or products that are sold 營業額, 交易量: *A lot of pubs nowadays do most of their trade at lunch-times.* 現在的許多小酒館, 大多數生意都是在午飯時。—see also 另見 **do a roaring trade** (ROARING (3))

4 ►JOB/WORK 職業/工作◄ [C] a particular job, especially one needing special skill with your hands〔尤指需要特殊手工技巧的〕職業; 手藝: *In those days people would leave school at fourteen to learn a trade.* 在那些年代, 人們十四歲時便輟學去學一門手藝。| **be sth by trade** (=be trained to do a particular job) 職業是〔幹某種工作〕 *My grandfather was a plumber by trade.* 我祖父的職業是管子工。| **tools of your trade** (=the things that you need to do your job) 幹某項工作所需的工具 —see 見 JOB (USAGE)

5 the trade a particular kind of business, and the people who are involved in it 某一行業和從事該行業的人: *I could get Ron to look at your car for you; he works in the trade.* 我可以讓羅恩為你看看車子, 他是幹這行的。

6 passing trade people who go into a shop, restaurant etc because they see it, but are not regular customers 過路客生意: *Souvenir shops rely mainly on passing trade.* 紀念品商店主要做的是過路客生意。—see also 另見 STOCK-IN-TRADE, JACK-OF-ALL-TRADES, **tricks of the trade** (TRICK¹ (5))

trade² *v* **1** [I,T] to buy and sell goods, services etc 做買賣, 進行貿易, 從事交易: **[+with]** *Britain built up her wealth by trading with other countries.* 英國通過與其他國家進行貿易而積累起財富。| **[+in]** *These companies trade mainly in furs and animal skins.* 這些公司主要從事動物毛皮的交易。| **trade sth** *Salesmen traded the new products all over the country.* 推銷員們在全國各地推銷這些新產品。| **trading partner** (=a country that buys your goods and sells their goods to you) 貿易夥伴（國）**2** [I] to exist and operate as a business 做生意, 開展業務: *The firm now trades under the name Lanski and Weber.* 這家公司現在使用蘭斯基和韋伯的名稱開展業務。| **cease trading** (=stop being a business) 結束業務 **3** [T usually passive 一般用被動態] *technical* to buy or sell something on the STOCK EXCHANGE【術語】從事〔股票〕交易: *Over a million shares were traded during the day.* 那天成交了一百多萬股。**4 trade insults/blows etc** *informal* to insult or hit each other during an argument or fight【非正式】對罵/對打等 **5** [I,T] *especially AmE* to exchange something you have for something someone else has【尤美】用…交換…, 互相交換: **trade sth for** *I'll trade my Roberto Clemente card for your Hank Aaron one.* 我用我的羅伯托·克萊蒙特棒球卡換取你的漢克·阿倫棒球卡。| *We traded necklaces.* 我們互相交換了項鏈。| **I'll trade you** *spoken* (=used to say you want to exchange something)【口】我要與你交換東西 *"I have peanut butter and jelly today." "Trade you. I have cream cheese."* "我今天有花生醬和果醬。""與你交換吧。我有奶油乾酪。"

trade sth ↔ **down** *phr v* [T] *especially AmE* to sell something such as a car in order to buy one that costs less【尤美】賣出〔某物〕以買進較廉價的同類物

trade sth ↔ **in** *phr v* [T] to give something such as a car to the person you are buying a new one from, so that you pay less 以〔某物〕折價換購同類的新貨物: *He traded his old car in for a new model.* 他把舊車折價換購了一輛新的款式。—see also 另見 TRADE-IN

trade sth ↔ **off** *phr v* [T] to balance one situation or quality against another, in order to produce an acceptable result 在…和…之間取得平衡: *We have to trade off the cost of research against the danger that our competitors will overtake us.* 我們必須在控制研究成本和保持競爭力之間取得平衡。—see also 另見 TRADE-OFF

trade on/upon sth *phr v* [T] to use a situation or someone's kindness in order to get an advantage for yourself 利用〔某一形勢或某人的善良〕: *If you ask me they're just trading on Sam's good nature.* 如果你問我的話, 他們只不過是在利用薩姆的善良本性。

trade up *phr v* [I,T] to give a used item, such as a car, for a similar item which is more expensive or valuable 以〔舊物〕折價換購〔同類中更貴或更有價值的貨物〕: **trade up sth** *Diego's traded up his old car for a more expensive model.* 迪戈把他那輛舊車折價換購了一款更貴的車。

trade def·i·cit /ˈ· ˌ···/ also 又作 **trade gap** *n* [C] the amount by which the value of what a country buys from abroad is more than the value of what it sells 貿易赤字, 貿易逆差

trade dis·count /ˈ· ˌ··/ *n* [C] a special reduction in the price of goods sold to people who are going to sell the goods in their own shop or business 同行折扣, 批發折扣

trade fair /ˈ· ·/ *n* [C] a large event when several companies show their goods or services in one place, to try to sell them 交易會

trade gap /ˈ· ·/ *n* [C] TRADE DEFICIT 貿易赤字

trade-in /ˈ· ·/ *n* [C] *AmE* a used item, often a car, given to reduce the price of the new one that you are buying【美】〔以舊物折價抵銷新物部分價格的〕折價貼換交易; PART-EXCHANGE *BrE*【英】: *Are you going to give your Ford as a trade-in?* 你打算以折價貼換的形式賣掉你的福特車嗎? | **trade-in price/value/figure** *The trade-in value of the car is roughly $3000.* 這輛汽車的折價貼換價值大約是3000美元。

trade·mark /ˈtredˌmɑrk; ˈtreɪdmɑːk/ *n* [C] **1** a special name, sign, or word that is marked on a product to show that it is made by a particular company〔公司生產某一產品的〕商標, 註冊商標 **2** a particular way of behaving, dressing etc by which someone or something can be easily recognized〔某人或某物在行為、穿着等方面很容易被識別出來的〕標記, 特徵: *The striped T-shirt became the comedian's trademark.* 那件帶條紋的T恤衫成了這位喜劇演員的穿着特徵。

trade name /ˈ· ·/ *n* [C] a name given to a particular product, that helps you recognize it from other similar products; BRAND NAME〔某種產品的〕商標名, 商品名

trade-off /ˈ· ·/ *n* [C] an acceptable balance between two opposing things that you want〔兩種對立因素之間的〕平衡; 妥協; 協調: *There has to be a trade-off between quality and quantity if we want to keep prices low.* 如果我們想要保持低價格的話, 必須在質量和數量之間進行協調。

trade price /ˈ· ·/ *n* [C] the price at which goods are sold to shops by the companies that produce them 批發價格, 同行價格

trad·er /ˋtredɚ; 'treɪdə/ *n* [C] someone who buys and sells goods 商人, 買賣人, 經商者

trade route /ˈ· ·/ *n* [C] a way across land or sea often used by traders' vehicles, ships etc 商隊路線; 商船航線; 貿易路線; 貿易航線

trade school /ˈ· ˌ·/ *n* [C] *especially AmE* a school where people go in order to learn a particular trade (TRADE[1] (4)) 【尤美】職業學校

trade se·cret /ˌ· ˈ··/ *n* [C] **1** a piece of secret information about a particular business, that is only known by the people who work there〔只有商家內部人知道的〕行業祕密: *The Coca-Cola formula is a well kept trade secret.* 可口可樂的配方是一個保守很嚴的行業祕密。**2** *informal* a piece of information about how to do or make something, that you do not want other people to know【非正式】祕密: *Could you give me the recipe for that 'coq au vin' or is it a trade secret?* 你能把那道"紅酒燴雞"的食譜給我嗎? 難道那是一個祕密不成?

trades·man /ˋtredzmən; 'treɪdzmən/ *n* [C] **1** *especially BrE* someone who buys and sells goods, especially in a shop【尤英】商人, 買賣人,〔尤指商店裡的〕零售商, 店主 **2** *especially BrE* someone who goes to people's houses to sell or deliver goods【尤英】上門推銷員; 送貨員 **3** *especially AmE* someone who works at a job or trade (TRADE[1] (4)) that involves skill with your hands【尤美】手藝人; 技工

Trades U·nion Con·gress /ˌ· ·· ˈ··/ *n* the TUC〔英國的〕工會代表大會; 工會聯合會

trade sur·plus /ˌ· ˈ··/ *n* [C] *technical* the amount by which the value of the goods that a country sells to other countries is more than the value of what it buys from them【術語】貿易盈餘〔指一個國家的出口商品總值超過進口總值〕

trade u·nion /ˌ· ˈ··/ also 又作 **trades union** *BrE*【英】*n* [C] an organization, usually in a particular trade or profession, that represents workers, especially in meetings with employers〔某一行業的〕工會; LABOR UNION *AmE*【美】—**trade unionist** *n* [C]

trade wind /ˈ· ·/ *n* [C] a tropical wind that blows continually towards the EQUATOR from either the northeast or the southeast 信風, 貿易風〔指從東北或東南方向不停地吹向赤道的熱帶風〕

trading es·tate /ˈ·· ·ˌ·/ *n* [C] *BrE* an area of land, often at the edge of a city, where there are small factories and businesses【英】工商業區, 工業園區〔通常位於市郊〕

trading post /ˈ·· ·/ *n* [C] a place where people can buy and exchange goods in a country area, especially in the US or Canada in the past〔尤指昔日美國或加拿大的〕貿易站: *a remote trading post in the Yukon* 育空地區一處偏遠的貿易站

2 2 **tra·di·tion** /trəˋdɪʃən; trə'dɪʃən/ *n* **1 a)** [C] a belief, custom, or way of doing something that has existed for a long time 傳統: *Christmas traditions* 聖誕傳統 | **[+of]** *a long tradition of wine-making* 悠久的釀酒傳統 | **tradition that** *the tradition that the eldest son inherits the property* 長子繼承財產的傳統 —see 見 HABIT (USAGE) **b)** [U] beliefs or customs like this in general 傳統信仰; 傳統習俗: *The British are lovers of tradition.* 英國人很看重傳統。| **by tradition** *By tradition, it is the bride's parents who pay for the wedding.* 根據傳統習俗, 由新娘的父母支付婚禮的費用。**2** [C,U] the way in which things are done in a particular country, group of people etc 傳統方式, 慣例, 老規矩: *the Western tradition in art* 西方的藝術傳統方式 | *It had become a tradition in our house to stay up all night at New Year.* 在新年時守夜已成了我們家的慣例。| **break with tradition** (=stop doing something in the way it has always been done) 打破傳統, 打破老規矩 *Breaking with family tradition, they decided not to send Laura to boarding school.* 他們打破家庭的老規矩, 決定不送勞拉上寄宿學校。**3 be in the tradition of** to have the same features as something that has been made or done in the past 沿襲…的傳統: *His paintings are very much in the tradition of Picasso and Matisse.* 他的繪畫在很大程度上沿襲了畢加索和馬蒂斯的傳統。

tra·di·tion·al /trəˋdɪʃənḷ; trə'dɪʃənəl/ *adj* **1** being part of the traditions of a country or group of people 傳統的; 習俗的; 慣例的: *Kumar gave the traditional Hindu greeting.* 庫瑪按照印度習俗打招呼。| *traditional music* 傳統音樂 | **it is traditional (for sb) to do sth** *It is traditional for the bridegroom to make a speech.* 按照慣例, 新郎要致辭。**2** following ideas and methods that have existed for a long time, without being interested in anything new or different; CONVENTIONAL 傳統的; 因襲的; 守舊的: *I went to a very traditional school.* 我上的是一所非常守舊的學校。—**traditionally** *adv* 3 1

tra·di·tion·al·is·m /trəˋdɪʃənḷˌɪzəm; trə'dɪʃənəlɪzəm/ *n* [U] belief in the importance of TRADITIONs and customs 傳統主義, 崇尚傳統

tra·di·tion·al·ist /trəˋdɪʃənḷɪst; trə'dɪʃənəl-ɪst/ *n* [C] someone who respects TRADITION and does not like change 傳統主義者, 崇尚傳統者; 墨守成規者 —**traditionalist** *adj*

tra·duce /trəˋdjus; trə'djuːs/ *v* [T] *formal* to deliberately say things that are untrue or unpleasant【正式】誹謗, 中傷, 詆毀

traf·fic[1] /ˋtræfɪk; 'træfɪk/ *n* [U] **1** the vehicles moving along a road or street〔道路或街道上的〕車輛交通: *The noise of the traffic kept me awake.* 道路上車輛的噪音使我無法入睡。| **heavy traffic** (=a large amount of traffic) 擁擠的交通 *We were stuck in heavy traffic for more than an hour.* 我們在擁擠的交通中被堵了一個多小時。**2** the movement of aircraft, ships, trains etc from one place to another〔飛機、輪船、火車等的〕往來, 交通: *air traffic control* 空中交通管制 **3** *formal* the movement of people or goods by aircraft, ships, or trains【正式】〔飛機、輪船或火車等運送人或貨物的〕交通運輸: **[+of]** *Most long-distance traffic of heavy goods is done by ships.* 大多數重型貨物的長途運輸都是使用輪船的。**4** the secret buying and selling of illegal goods〔祕密進行的〕非法買賣, 非法交易: *drugs traffic* 毒品買賣 | **[+in]** *traffic in firearms* 非法軍火交易 1 2

traffic[2] *v past tense and past participle* **trafficked**

traffic in sth *phr v* [T] to buy and sell illegal goods〔非法地〕販賣, 交易: *Lewis was found guilty of trafficking in drugs.* 劉易斯販賣毒品, 被判有罪。

traffic calm·ing /ˈ·· ˌ··/ *n* [U] *BrE* changes made to a road to stop people driving too fast along it【英】〔路面上設置的阻止駕車速度過快的〕交通減速路障

traffic cir·cle /ˈ·· ˌ··/ *n* [C] *AmE* a raised circular area that cars must drive around, where three or more roads join【美】環形交叉路口, 環島; ROUNDABOUT[1] (1) *BrE*【英】

traffic cone /ˈ·· ˌ·/ *n* [C] a plastic marker in the shape of a CONE that is put on the road to show where repairs are being done 錐形交通路標〔放在路面上表示該段道路正在維修〕

traffic cop /ˈ·· ˌ·/ *n* [C] *AmE informal*【美, 非正式】**1** a police officer who stands in the road and directs traffic〔站在馬路上指揮交通的〕交通警察 **2** a police officer who stops drivers who drive in an illegal way〔阻截違章駕車司機的〕交通巡警

traffic court /ˈ·· ˌ·/ *n* [C] *AmE* a court in a town or city in the US that deals with people who have done something illegal while driving【美】交通法庭

traffic is·land /ˈ·· ˌ··/ *n* [C] a raised area in the middle of the road where people can wait for traffic to pass〔馬路中間的〕安全島

traffic jam /ˈ·· ˌ·/ *n* [C] a long line of vehicles on a road that cannot move, or that can only move very slowly 交通阻塞, 塞車: *We were stuck in a traffic jam on the freeway for two hours.* 我們在高速公路上碰上了交通阻塞, 被堵了兩個小時。

T

traf·fick·er /ˈtræfɪkɚ; ˈtræfɪkə/ *n* [C] someone who buys and sells illegal goods, especially drugs 做非法買賣的人〔尤指毒品販子〕

traf·fick·ing /ˈtræfɪkɪŋ; ˈtræfɪkɪŋ/ *n* [U] the buying and selling of illegal goods, especially drugs〔尤指毒品的〕非法買賣, 非法交易: *drug trafficking* 毒品販賣

traffic lights /ˈ·· ˌ·/ *n* [C] special lights at a place where roads meet, that control the traffic by means of red, yellow, and green lights 交通信號燈, 紅綠燈

traffic school /ˈ·· ˌ·/ *n* [C] *AmE* a class that teaches you about driving laws, that you can go to instead of paying money for something you have done wrong while driving【美】交通法規學校〔違章司機可以上這種學校而免交罰金〕

traffic war·den /ˈ·· ˌ··/ *n* [C] *BrE* someone whose job is to check that vehicles have not parked illegally on the streets【英】〔市區負責監控車輛停放的〕交通督導員

tra·ge·di·an /trəˋdʒidɪən; trəˈdʒiːdiən/ *n* [C] *formal* an actor or writer of tragedy【正式】悲劇演員; 悲劇作家

tra·ge·dy /ˈtrædʒədɪ; ˈtrædʒədi/ *n* **1** [C,U] a very sad event, that shocks people because it involves death 悲劇性事件, 慘劇, 慘案: *Tragedy struck the family when their two-year old son died of leukemia.* 悲劇降臨到這個家庭, 他們兩歲的兒子因白血病死了。**2** [C] *informal* something that seems very sad and unnecessary because something will be wasted, lost, or harmed【非正式】〔因浪費、失去或傷害而造成的〕不幸; 遺憾: *It's a tragedy to see so much talent going to waste.* 看到這麼多的天賦浪費掉, 真是可惜啊。**3 a)** [C] a serious play or book that ends sadly, especially with the death of the main character 悲劇作品: *'Hamlet' is one of Shakespeare's best known tragedies.*《哈姆雷特》是莎士比亞最有名的悲劇作品之一。**b)** [U] this type of plays or books 悲劇〔文學類別之一〕: *an actor specializing in tragedy* 一名擅長演悲劇的演員

tra·gic /ˈtrædʒɪk; ˈtrædʒɪk/ *adj* **1** a tragic event or situation makes you feel very sad 悲慘的, 不幸的: *Lillian Board's death at 22 was a tragic loss for the world of British athletics.* 利蓮·波德22歲時就死了, 這對英國田徑界來說是一個不幸的損失。**2** [only before noun 僅用於名詞前] connected with tragedy in books or plays 悲劇的: *a great tragic actor* 一名偉大的悲劇演員 | **tragic hero** (=the main character in a tragedy) 悲劇主角 **3 tragic flaw** a weakness in the character of the main person in a tragedy that causes their own problems and usually death 悲劇性缺陷〔指悲劇主人公性格上的弱點, 這些弱點引發諸多問題, 通常會導致自身毀滅〕: *Jealousy is Othello's tragic flaw.* 妒忌是奧賽羅的悲劇性缺陷。

tra·gic·ally /ˈtrædʒɪklɪ; ˈtrædʒɪkli/ *adv* in a very sad or unfortunate way 悲慘地, 不幸地: [sentence adverb 句子副詞] *Tragically, her dancing career ended only six months later.* 很不幸的是, 她的舞蹈生涯僅在六個月後就結束了。| [+adj/adv] *Alan died tragically young.* 很不幸, 艾倫年紀輕輕就去世了。

tra·gi·com·e·dy /ˌtrædʒɪˋkɑmədɪ; ˌtrædʒɪˈkɒmədi/ *n* [C, U] a play or a story that is both sad and funny 悲喜劇 — **tragicomic** /ˌtrædʒɪˋkɑmɪk; ˌtrædʒɪˈkɒmɪk◂/ *adj*

trail¹ /trel; treɪl/ *v* **1** [I,T always+adv/prep] if something trails behind you, or if you trail it behind you, it gets pulled behind you as you move along 拖, 拉; 拖在後面: **[+across/in/through]** *She walked slowly along the path, her skirt trailing in the mud.* 她慢慢地沿着小徑走着, 裙子拖在泥地上。| **trail sth in/on/through** *Rees was leaning out of the boat trailing his hand through the water.* 里斯把身體傾斜在船外邊, 讓手在水裡蕩着。**2** also 又作 **trail along** [I always+adv/prep] to walk slowly, especially because you are tired or bored, and often following other people〔尤指因疲倦或厭煩〕慢吞吞地走(在後面): **[+behind/around]** *Susie trailed along behind her parents.* 蘇絲慢吞吞地走在她父母的身後。**3** [I,T usually in progressive 一般用進行式] to be losing in a game, competition, or election〔體育比賽、競賽或選舉中〕落後於: *The Democrats are still trailing in the latest poll.* 在最近的民意調查中, 民主黨仍然落在後面。| **trail (sb) by** *At the end of the first half Bolton were trailing by two goals to nil.* 在上半場結束時, 保頓隊以零比二落後。**4** [T] to follow a person or animal by looking for signs that they have gone in a particular direction 跟蹤, 追蹤: *Police trailed the gang for several days.* 警察花了好幾天的時間跟蹤那幫傢伙。—see also 另見 TRAILER

trail away/off *phr v* [I] if someone's voice trails away or off, it becomes gradually quieter and then stops〔說話的聲音〕逐漸變小, 減弱: *She trailed off, silenced by the look Kris gave her.* 她看到克里斯給她的眼色, 說話的聲音越來越小, 終於默不作聲了。

trail² *n* [C] **1 be on sb's trail** to be finding out where someone has gone in order to find or catch them 跟蹤, 追蹤〔某人〕: *Police believe they are on the trail of a dangerous killer.* 警方相信他們追蹤的是一名危險的殺手。| **be hard/hot on sb's trail** (=be close to finding someone you are trying to catch) 緊追不捨〔並即將發現某人〕**2 while the trail is still hot** if you chase someone while the trail is still hot, you follow them soon after they have left〔某人〕剛離開〔就隨後追趕〕**3** the track or smell of a person or animal by which it can be hunted or followed〔人或動物的〕足跡, 蹤跡; 嗅跡: *The hunters lost the tiger's trail in the middle of the jungle.* 獵人們在叢林中找不到那隻老虎的蹤跡了。**4** a rough path across open country or through a forest 小路, 小徑: *The trail led over Boulder Pass before descending to a lake.* 那條小路穿過博爾德山口, 然後向下通向一個湖。**5 trail of blood/dust etc** a line or series of marks left by someone or something that is moving 血跡/塵土等的痕跡: *They left a trail of muddy footprints on the living room carpet.* 他們在客廳的地毯上留下了一長串泥濘的腳印。| **trail of destruction** (=damage left by a moving storm or army)〔暴風雨或軍隊過後留下的〕毀壞痕跡, 斷壁殘垣 **6 a trail of broken hearts/unpaid bills etc** *humorous* a series of unhappy people or bad situations all caused by the same person【幽默】〔某人留下的〕一串破碎的心/一大摞未支付的賬單等: *He left a trail of broken hearts, of deserted women behind him.* 他留下一長串破碎的心, 一個個被遺棄的婦人。—see also 另見 **blaze a trail** (BLAZE¹ (4))

trail·blaz·er /ˈtrelˌblezɚ; ˈtreɪlˌbleɪzə/ *n* [C] someone who is the first to discover or develop new methods of doing something 開路人; 先驅, 創始人: *a trailblazer in the field of medical research* 醫學研究領域的先驅

trail·er /ˈtrelɚ; ˈtreɪlə/ *n* [C] **1** *AmE* a vehicle that can be pulled behind a car, used for living and sleeping in during a holiday【美】〔度假期間拖在汽車後面的、用作起居和睡覺的〕活動房屋; CARAVAN (1) *BrE*【英】**2** a vehicle that can be pulled behind a vehicle, used for carrying something such as a boat or large piece of equipment 拖車, 掛車 **3** *especially BrE* an advertisement for a new film or television show, usually consisting of small scenes taken from it【尤英】〔電影、電視節目的〕新片預告, 預告片

trailer park /ˈ·· ·/ also 又作 **trailer court** *n* [C] *AmE* an area where TRAILER*s* are parked and used as people's homes【美】拖車式活動房屋停車場

trail·ing /ˈtrelɪŋ; ˈtreɪlɪŋ/ *adj* a trailing plant grows along the ground or hangs down〔植物〕蔓生的: *ivy and other trailing plants* 常春藤及其他蔓生植物

train¹ /tren; treɪn/ *n* [C]

1 ►RAILWAY 鐵路◄ a number of connected carriages pulled by an engine along a railway line 火車, 列車: *Jeff just missed the six o'clock train.* 傑夫剛好錯過了六點鐘的那班火車。| **[+to]** *I caught the early train to Bruges.* 我趕早班火車去了布魯日。| **by train** *It's more relaxing to travel by train.* 坐火車旅行讓人更為放鬆。| **train driver/journey/service** *There's no train service between here and Wales.* 這裡與威爾斯之間沒有通火車。—see also 另見 BOAT TRAIN

2 ▶SERIES 系列◀ train of a series of connected events, actions etc 一系列, 一連串〔相關事件、行動等〕: *That one incident sparked off a whole train of events.* 那一次事件引發了一連串事件。
3 train of thought a connected series of thoughts developing in your mind 一連串想法; 思路: *The phone rang and interrupted my train of thought.* 電話鈴響了, 打斷了我的思路。
4 set sth in train *formal* to make something start happening【正式】使…開始啟動: *Plans to modernize have been set in train.* 現代化的計劃已經開始啟動。
5 bring sth in its train *formal* if an action or event brings something in its train, that thing happens as a result of it【正式】引發〔某事〕: *a decision that brought disaster in its train* 帶來災難的一項決定
6 ▶PEOPLE/ANIMALS 人/動物◀ a long line of moving people, animals, or vehicles〔行進中的〕行列, 隊列: *a camel train* 一支駝隊
7 ▶DRESS 裙子◀ a part of a long dress that spreads out over the ground behind the person who is wearing it 長裙拖在地上的下擺, 拖裾: *a wedding dress with a long train* 下擺很長的結婚禮服
8 ▶SERVANTS 僕從◀ a group of servants or officers following an important person, especially in former times〔尤指舊時重要人物的〕隨行人員, 隨從

train² *v* **1** [I,T] to teach someone or be taught the skills of a particular job or activity (接受) 訓練; (被) 培訓: **[+as]** *Nadia trained as a singer under a famous professor of music.* 納迪亞曾在一位音樂名教授的指導下接受歌手的訓練。| **train sb in** *Soldiers trained in hand-to-hand combat.* 接受過徒手格鬥訓練的士兵。| **train to do sth** *Hugh's training to be a doctor.* 休正在接受培訓, 準備當醫生。—see 見 TEACH (USAGE) **2** [T] to teach an animal to do something or to behave correctly 訓練〔動物〕: **train sth to do sth** *These dogs are trained to detect explosives.* 這些狗受過訓練, 能搜尋爆炸物。| *a well-trained puppy* 訓練有素的小狗 **3** [I,T] to prepare for a sporting event or tell someone how to prepare for it, especially by exercising〔為準備體育賽事而〕訓練, 操練: **[+for]** *Brenda spends two hours a day training for the marathon.* 布蓮達為了馬拉松比賽每天訓練兩個小時。**4** [T] to aim a gun, camera etc at someone or something 把〔槍、照相機等〕對準, 瞄準: **train sth on/at** *The firemen trained their hoses on the burning building.* 消防人員把水管對準那幢燃燒着的建築物。**5** [T] to make a plant grow in a particular direction by bending, cutting, or tying it 使〔植物〕按照特定方向生長 —**trained** *adj*: *a highly trained technician* 技巧嫻熟的技術人員 —**trainable** *adj* —see also 另見 TRAINING

train·bear·er /ˈtrenˌbɛrɚ; ˈtreɪnˌbeərə/ *n* [C] someone who holds the train (TRAIN¹ (7)) of a dress, especially at a wedding〔尤指婚禮中牽新娘婚紗的〕牽紗者, 挽裙裾者

train·ee /trenˈi; ˌtreɪˈniː◂/ *n* [C] someone who is being trained for a job 接受工作培訓的人; 實習生: *The new trainees will start next week.* 新一批實習生下週開始上班。| **trainee reporter/engineer/salesman etc** *a trainee hairdresser* 實習美髮師

train·er /ˈtrenɚ; ˈtreɪnə/ *n* [C] **1** someone who trains people or animals for sport, work etc 教練 (員); 馴獸師: *a teacher trainer* 培訓教師的人 **2** *BrE* a type of strong shoe that you wear for sport【英】運動鞋, 跑鞋; SNEAKER *AmE*【美】—see picture at 參見 SHOE¹ 圖

train·ing /ˈtrenɪŋ; ˈtreɪnɪŋ/ *n* **1** [singular,U] the process of training or being trained 訓練, 培訓; 受訓: **[+in]** *On the course we received training in every aspect of the job.* 在培訓課上, 我們接受了有關工作的全面訓練。| *a training manual* 培訓手冊 **2** [U] special physical exercises that are part of a plan for keeping someone fit and healthy〔保持體形的〕訓練, 鍛鍊: *Lesley does weight training twice a week.* 萊斯利一週進行兩次器械訓練。| **be in/out of training** (=be fit or not fit for a sport) 正處於良好/不佳的競技狀態 *The champion is in training for his next fight.* 這位冠軍正在為下一場比賽進行訓練。—see also 另見 SPRING TRAINING

training col·lege /ˈ‥ ˌ‥/ *n* [C,U] *BrE* a college for adults that gives training for a particular profession【英】〔為成人開設的〕職業培訓學院: *a teacher training college* 師範學院 | *a training college for pilots* 飛行學院

train set /ˈ· ·/ *n* [C] a toy train with railway tracks〔包括鐵軌在內的〕玩具火車

train spot·ter /ˈ· ˌ‥/ *n* [C] *BrE*【英】**1** someone who collects the numbers of railway engines and other information about them for fun〔作為娛樂愛好〕收集火車機車號碼等的人 **2** someone who you think is boring and only interested in unimportant details 無聊的人; 只關心芝麻小事的人 —**trainspotting** *n* [U]

traipse /treps; treɪps/ *v* [I always+adv/prep] *informal* to walk somewhere slowly and unwillingly when you are tired【非正式】閒蕩: **[+up/down/around etc]** *I've been traipsing round the shops all morning.* 我整個上午一直在逛商店。

trait /tret; treɪt/ *n* [C] *formal* a particular quality in someone's character【正式】〔人性格中的〕特性, 品質: *Anne's generosity is one of her most pleasing traits.* 安妮的慷慨是她最受人喜愛的品性之一。

trai·tor /ˈtretɚ; ˈtreɪtə/ *n* [C] someone who is not loyal to their country or friends 賣國者; 叛徒, 背叛者: *He was hanged as a traitor.* 他因叛國罪被絞死。| *a traitor to the cause of women's rights* 女權運動的背叛者

trai·tor·ous /ˈtretərəs; ˈtreɪtərəs/ *adj especially literary* not loyal to your country or friends【尤文】賣國的; 叛變的, 背叛的 —**traitorously** *adv*

tra·jec·to·ry /trəˈdʒɛktərɪ; trəˈdʒektəri/ *n* [C] *technical* the curved path of an object that is fired or thrown through the air【術語】〔物體射向或拋向空中形成的〕軌道, 軌跡; 彈道

tram /træm; træm/ also 又作 **tram·car** /ˈtræmˌkɑr; ˈtræmkɑː/ *n* [C] *especially BrE* an electric vehicle for carrying passengers, which moves along the streets on metal tracks【尤英】有軌電車; STREETCAR *AmE*【美】

tram·lines /ˈtræmˌlaɪnz; ˈtræmlaɪnz/ *n* [plural] *BrE*【英】**1** the metal tracks in the road that trams run along 有軌電車的軌道 **2** *BrE informal* a pair of parallel lines at the edge of a tennis court【英, 非正式】〔網球場兩側供雙打時用的〕加道 —see picture at 參見 TENNIS 圖

tram·mels /ˈtræml̩z; ˈtræməlz/ *n* [plural] *formal* something that limits or prevents free movement, activity, or development【正式】限制, 拘束, 束縛, 妨礙: *an urge to shake off the trammels of respectability* 一種想擺脫禮俗束縛的願望 —see also 另見 UNTRAMMELLED

tramp¹ /træmp; træmp/ *n* [C] **1** someone who has no home or job and moves from place to place, often asking for food or money 流浪者, 遊民: *a group of tramps huddled around a fire* 圍坐在火邊的一羣流浪漢 **2** a long or difficult walk (長途) 跋涉: *It was a long tramp home through the snow.* 那天冒雪走回家, 是一次長途跋涉。**3** *old-fashioned especially AmE* a woman who has too many sexual partners【過時, 尤美】蕩婦 **4 the tramp of** the sound of heavy walking …沉重的腳步聲: *the steady tramp of soldiers' feet on the road* 士兵們走在路上發出的沉重腳步聲

tramp² *v* [I always+adv/prep,T] to walk around or through somewhere with firm or heavy steps 用重重的腳步走 (過): **tramp sth** *I've tramped the streets all day looking for work.* 我一整天走遍大街小巷, 尋找工作。| **[+across/over/up etc]** *Who's been tramping all over the floor in muddy shoes?* 誰穿着沾滿泥的鞋子在地板上到處亂踩?

tram·ple /ˈtræmpl̩; ˈtræmpəl/ *v* [I always+adv/prep, T] **1** to step heavily on something so that you crush it with your feet 踩, 踐踏: **[+on/over/through etc]** *You trampled on my beautiful flowerbeds!* 你踩壞了我那些美麗的花壇! | **trample sb/sth underfoot** *She dropped her jacket* *and it was trampled underfoot.* 她的外衣掉在地上，被踩在脚下。| **trample sb to death** (=kill someone by stepping heavily on them) 踩死某人 *Several people were nearly trampled to death in the rush to get out.* 大家往外衝的時候，好幾個人差點被踩死。**2 trample on sth/trample sth underfoot** to behave in a way that shows that you do not care about someone's rights, hopes, ideas etc 侵犯；無視〔某人的權利、願望、想法等〕: *The colonial government had trampled on the rights of the native people.* 殖民政府侵犯了本土人民的權利。

tram·po·line /ˌtræmpəˋlin; ˈtræmpəliːn/ *n* [C] a piece of equipment that you jump up and down on as a sport, made of a sheet of material tightly stretched across a metal frame 蹦牀，彈牀〔一種體育用具〕—**trampoline** *v* [I] —**trampolining** *n* [U]

trance /træns; trɑːns/ *n* [C] **1** a state in which you behave as if you were asleep but are still able to hear and understand what is said to you 恍惚狀態: *a hypnotic trance* 催眠後的恍惚狀態 **2** a situation in which you are thinking about something so much that you do not notice what is happening around you 恍惚；出神，發呆: **be in a trance** *What's the matter with you? You've been in a trance all day!* 你怎麼啦？一整天都恍恍惚惚的！

tran·quil /ˋtræŋkwɪl; ˈtræŋkwɪl/ *adj* pleasantly calm, quiet, and peaceful 平靜的，寧靜的，安謐的: *a tranquil village scene* 寧靜的鄉村景色 —**tranquilly** *adv* —**tranquillity** *BrE*【英】, **tranquility** *AmE*【美】/træŋˋkwɪlətɪ; træŋˈkwɪləti/ *n* [U]: *the tranquillity of the Tuscan countryside* 托斯卡尼鄉下的寧靜

tran·quil·lize also 又作 **-ise** *BrE*【英】, **tranquilize** *AmE*【美】/ˋtræŋkwɪˌlaɪz; ˈtræŋkwəlaɪz/ *v* [T] to make a person or animal calm or unconscious by using a drug〔用藥物〕使〔人或動物〕鎮靜[昏迷]

tran·quil·lizer also 又作 **-iser** *BrE*【英】, **tranquilizer** *AmE*【美】/ˋtræŋkwɪˌlaɪzə; ˈtræŋkwəlaɪzə/ *n* [C] a drug used to reduce nervous anxiety and make you calm 鎮靜劑，安定藥

trans- /træns; træns/ *prefix* **1** on or to the far side of something; across 在[到]…的另一邊；橫穿，橫貫: *transatlantic flights* 橫跨大西洋的航班 | *the trans-Siberian railway* 西伯利亞橫貫鐵路 **2** between two things or groups; INTER- 在…之間的: *trans-racial fostering* 異族收養 **3** shows a change 表示變化: *He's been transformed by the experience.* 那次經歷改變了他。| *the transmutation of base metal into gold* 賤金屬變為黃金

trans·act /trænzˋækt; trænˈzækt/ *v* [I,T] *formal* to do business【正式】辦理（業務），做（交易）: *Most deals are transacted over the phone.* 大多數交易是在電話上做成的。

S3 W3 **trans·ac·tion** /trænzˋækʃən; trænˈzækʃən/ *n formal*【正式】**1** [C] a business deal（一筆）交易；（一件）事務: *The bank charges a fixed rate for each transaction.* 銀行對辦理的每一筆交易收取一定的費用。| *financial transactions* 金融業務 **2** [U] the process of doing business〔業務等的〕辦理；執行: *the transaction of his public duties* 執行他的公共職責 **3 transactions** [plural] discussions that take place at the meetings of a society, or a written record of these〔學會等的〕討論，議事；議事錄，公報

trans·at·lan·tic /ˌtrænzətˋlæntɪk; ˌtrænzətˈlæntɪk◂/ *adj* [only before noun 僅用於名詞前] **1** crossing the Atlantic Ocean 橫跨大西洋的: *transatlantic flights* 橫跨大西洋的航班 **2** involving countries on both sides of the Atlantic Ocean 大西洋兩岸國家的: *a transatlantic agreement* 大西洋兩岸國家的一項協定 **3** on the other side of the Atlantic Ocean 大西洋彼岸的: *one of America's transatlantic military bases* 美國在大西洋彼岸的軍事基地之一

trans·cei·ver /trænsˋsivə; trænˈsiːvə/ *n* [C] a radio that can both send and receive messages 無線電收發兩用機

tran·scend /trænˋsɛnd; trænˈsend/ *v* [T] *formal* to go above or beyond the limits of something【正式】超越；超過，超出: *The desire for peace transcended political differences.* 對和平的渴望超越了政治上的分歧。

tran·scen·dent /trænˋsɛndənt; trænˈsendənt/ *adj formal* going far beyond ordinary limits【正式】超常的，卓越的，出類拔萃的: *the transcendent genius of Mozart* 莫扎特的卓越天才 —**transcendently** *adv*

tran·scen·den·tal /ˌtrænsɛnˋdɛntl; ˌtrænsenˈdentl◂/ *adj* experiences or ideas going beyond human knowledge, understanding, and experience 超出人類知識範圍的；超出一般經驗的 —**transcendentally** *adv*

tran·scen·den·tal·is·m /ˌtrænsɛnˋdɛntl̩ˌɪzəm; ˌtrænsenˈdentəl-ɪzəm/ *n* [U] the belief that knowledge can be obtained by studying thought and not necessarily by practical experience 先驗論〔認為無需通過實踐經驗，只憑研究思想即可獲得知識的哲學觀點〕—**transcendentalist** *n* [C]

transcendental med·i·ta·tion /ˌ···· ··ˈ··/ *n* [U] a method of becoming calm by repeating special religious words in your mind 超脫禪定（法）

trans·con·ti·nen·tal /ˌtrænzkɑntəˋnɛntl̩; ˌtrænzkɒntɪˈnentl/ *adj* crossing a CONTINENT 橫貫大陸的: *a transcontinental railway* 一條橫貫大陸的鐵路

tran·scribe /trænˋskraɪb; trænˈskraɪb/ *v* [T] *formal*【正式】**1** to write an exact copy of something 謄寫，抄寫: *transcribing an ancient manuscript* 抄寫一本古代手稿 **2** to write down something exactly as it was said 逐字逐句記錄，記下〔所說的話〕: *A secretary transcribed the witnesses' statements.* 祕書記下了證人的口供。**3** *technical* to represent speech sounds with special PHONETIC letters【術語】用音標記下〔語音〕，標註〔音標〕**4** [+into] *formal* to change a piece of writing into the alphabet of another language【正式】把〔一篇文字〕用另一種語言的字母寫出[記下] **5** to arrange a piece of music for a different instrument or voice 改編〔一段音樂使適於其他樂器演奏或用其他聲調演唱〕: **transcribe sth for sth** *a piece transcribed for piano* 改編成鋼琴曲的一首樂曲 **6** to copy recorded music, speech etc from one system to another, for example from TAPE[1] (1) to CD 複製，轉錄〔音樂、話語等，如從錄音帶轉換成光碟〕

tran·script /ˋtrænˌskrɪpt; ˈtrænskrɪpt/ *n* [C] **1** an exact written or printed copy of something 抄本，副本；轉錄本: [+of] *A transcript of the tapes was presented in court as evidence.* 那些錄音帶的文字本被呈交法庭作為證據。**2** *AmE* an official document of a college or university that has a list of a student's classes and the results they received【美】〔大學的〕學生成績單

tran·scrip·tion /trænˋskrɪpʃən; trænˈskrɪpʃən/ *n* **1** [U] the act or process of transcribing something 抄寫；記錄；轉錄；標音: *Pronunciation is shown by a system of phonetic transcription.* 發音用音標系統表示。**2** [C] an exact written or printed copy of something; transcript 抄本，副本，文字記錄

tran·sept /ˋtrænsɛpt; ˈtrænsept/ *n* [C] one of the two parts of a church that are built out from the main area of the church to form a cross shape〔建在教堂主體兩邊以呈十字形的〕耳堂

trans·fer[1] /trænˋsfɝ; trænsˈfɜː/ *v* **transferred, transferring**

1 ►PERSON 人◄ [I,T] to move or arrange for someone to move from one place or job to another, especially within the same organization 轉移（地方）；調動（工作）〔尤指在同一機構中〕: **transfer sb to** *They're transferring me to the Edinburgh office.* 他們要把我調往愛丁堡辦事處。

2 ►THING/ACTIVITY 東西/活動◄ [T] *formal* to move something from one place or position to another【正式】搬運；遷移: **transfer sth (from sth) to** *Transfer the cookies to a wire rack to cool.* 把小甜餅放到金屬絲製的架子上冷卻。| *We're transferring production to Detroit.* 我們正在把生產移到底特律。

3 ►MONEY 錢◄ [T] to move money from the control of one account or institution to another 把〔錢〕轉到另一賬戶上: *I'd like to transfer £500 into my current* *account.* 我想把 500 英鎊轉到我的支票活期賬戶上。| *Will I be able to transfer my pension rights?* 我能把我的退休金轉賬嗎?

4 transfer your affection/loyalty etc to change from loving or supporting one person to loving or supporting a different one 移情於別人/轉而支持別人: [+**to**] *I immediately transferred my support to the other candidate.* 我立即轉而支持另一位候選人。

5 ▶PROPERTY 財產◀ [T] *law* to officially give property or money to someone else【法律】把〔財產〕轉讓給另一人: *The assets were transferred into his wife's name.* 那些資產轉讓到了他妻子的名下。

6 transfer power/responsibility/control (to) to officially give power etc to another person or organization 轉讓權力/責任/控制權(給…): *transferring control of public land to the states* 把公共土地控制權轉讓給各州

7 ▶PLANE 飛機◀ [I,T] to change from one plane to another during a journey, or arrange for someone to do this 轉機; 轉乘, 改乘: *You'll have to transfer at Los Angeles.* 你必須在洛杉磯轉機。

8 ▶RECORDING 錄音◀ [T] to copy recorded information, music etc from one system to another, for example from TAPE[1] (1) to CD 錄製, 轉錄〔信息、音樂等, 如從錄音帶轉換成光碟〕: *I decided to transfer the files onto floppy disk.* 我決定把這些文件轉錄到軟盤上去。— **transferable** *adj*: *Airline tickets are not transferable.* 飛機票不得轉讓。

2 **trans·fer²** /ˈtrænsfɝ; ˈtrænsfɜː/ *n* **1 a)** [C,U] the process by which someone or something moves or is moved from one place, job etc to another〔地點的〕轉移;〔工作的〕調動: *Penny's applied for a transfer to another part of the company.* 彭尼已申請調到公司的其他部門工作。| *data transfer* 資料傳送 **b)** [C] someone or something that has been moved in this way 已調動的人; 已轉移的東西 **2 transfer of power** a process by which the control of a country is taken from one person or group and given to another 權力的轉讓[過渡]: *the peaceful transfer of power in South Africa* 南非權力的和平過渡 **3** [C] *especially BrE* a drawing, pattern etc that can be stuck or printed onto a surface【尤英】〔可黏貼或印製的〕圖畫, 圖案; DECAL *especially AmE*【尤美】**4** [C] *especially AmE* a ticket that allows a passenger to change from one bus, train etc to another without paying more money【尤美】〔公共汽車、火車等的〕轉乘票證

trans·fer·ence /trænsˈfɝəns; ˈtrænsfərəns/ *n* [U] *formal* a process by which someone or something is moved from one place, position, job etc to another【正式】調任, 調職; 轉移; 轉讓

transfer fee /ˈ·· ·/ *n* [C] *BrE* the money that is paid to one football club by another for the transfer of a player【英】〔足球員的〕轉會費

transfer list /ˈ·· ·/ *n* [C] a list of the football players at one club who can transfer to other clubs〔足球員的〕轉會名單

trans·fig·ure /trænsˈfɪgjɚ; trænsˈfɪgə/ *v* [T] *literary* to change the way someone or something looks, especially so that they become more beautiful【文】使變形, 使改觀; 美化: *a face transfigured with joy* 因喜悅而容光煥發的臉 —**transfiguration** /ˌtrænsfɪgjəˈreʃən; trænsˌfɪgəˈreɪʃən/ *n* [C,U]

trans·fix /trænsˈfɪks; trænsˈfɪks/ *v* [T] *literary* to make a hole through something or someone with a sharp pointed weapon【文】刺穿, 戳破, 釘住

trans·fixed /trænsˈfɪkst; trænsˈfɪkst/ *adj* [not before noun 不用於名詞前] unable to move because you are very shocked, frightened etc〔因震驚、害怕等〕不能動彈的; 驚呆的: *Joe stood transfixed when I told him the terrible news.* 當我把這可怕的消息告訴喬時, 他驚呆了。

3 **trans·form** /trænsˈfɔrm; trænsˈfɔːm/ *v* [T] to completely change the appearance, form, or character of something or someone, especially in a way that improves it 使改觀, 使變形; 使轉化: **transform sth into** *In the last 20 years Korea has been transformed into an advanced industrial power.* 在最近的 20 年裡, 韓國已變成一個先進的工業強國。| **transform sb/sth** *Put yourself in the hands of our experts, who will transform your hair and makeup.* 你把自己交給我們的專家吧, 他們會使你的髮型和化妝徹底改觀。—**transformable** *adj*

trans·for·ma·tion /ˌtrænsfɚˈmeʃən; ˌtrænsfəˈmeɪʃən/ *n* [U] a complete change in someone or something〔徹底的〕改變, 改觀: *In recent years the film industry has undergone a complete transformation.* 近年來, 電影業發生了徹底的改變。

trans·form·er /trænsˈfɔrmɚ; trænsˈfɔːmə/ *n* [C] a piece of equipment for changing electricity from one VOLTAGE to another 變壓器

trans·fu·sion /trænsˈfjuʒən; trænsˈfjuːʒən/ *n* [C,U] *formal* the process of putting blood from one person into another person's body【正式】輸血: *A blood transfusion saved his life.* 輸血挽救了他的性命。

trans·gress /trænsˈgrɛs; trænzˈgres/ *v* [I,T] *formal* to do something that is against the rules of social behaviour or against a moral principle【正式】違背, 違反〔社會規範或道德準則〕: *Those who have transgressed against custom must be punished.* 那些違背了習俗的人必須受到懲罰。—**transgressor** *n* [C] —**transgression** /-ˈgrɛʃən; -ˈgreʃən/ *n* [C,U]

tran·si·ent¹ /ˈtrænʃənt; ˈtrænziənt/ *adj formal*【正式】**1** continuing only for a short time; TRANSITORY 短暫的, 轉瞬即逝的, 一時的: *transient fashions* 短暫的時尚 **2** passing quickly through a place or staying there for only a short time 逗留時間很短的; 流動性的: *a transient population of gold prospectors* 探尋黃金的流動人口 — **transience, transiency** *n* [U]

transient² *n* [C] *AmE* someone who has no home and moves around from place to place; TRAMP[1] (1)【美】流浪者; 遊民

tran·sis·tor /trænˈzɪstɚ; trænˈzɪstə/ *n* [C] **1** a small piece of electronic equipment in radios, televisions etc that controls the flow of electricity 晶體管, 電晶體 **2** a transistor radio 晶體管收音機, 電晶體收音機

tran·sis·tor·ize also 又作 **-ise** *BrE*【英】/trænˈzɪstəˌraɪz; trænˈzɪstəraɪz/ *v* [T] *technical* to put transistors into something so that it can be made smaller【術語】裝晶體管於; 使電晶體化

transistor ra·di·o /·,·· ˈ···/ *n* [C] a small radio that has transistors in it instead of valves (VALVE (3)) 晶體管收音機, 電晶體收音機

tran·sit /ˈtrænsɪt; ˈtrænsɪt/ *n* **1** [U] the process of moving goods or people from one place to another〔人或貨物的〕運輸: **in transit** (=in the process of being moved) 在運輸過程中 *goods damaged in transit* 在運輸中受損的貨物 **2** [C,U] *technical* the movement of a PLANET or moon in front of a larger object in space, such as the sun【術語】凌(日)〔行星或月球在太陽等較大天體前面經過〕

transit camp /ˈ·· ,·/ *n* [C] a place where REFUGEES stay before moving to somewhere more permanent〔難民暫居的〕過境營地, 臨時難民營

tran·si·tion /trænˈzɪʃən; trænˈzɪʃən/ *n* [C,U] *formal* the act or process of changing from one form or state to another【正式】過渡; 轉變, 變遷: *the band's gradual transition from hard rock hipsters to kings of pop* 樂隊從趕時髦的硬搖滾樂手向流行音樂之王的逐漸轉變 | **in transition** (=in the process of changing) 在演變之中 *The book takes an interesting look at a marriage in transition.* 這本書描寫一段變化中的婚姻關係, 引人入勝。 3

tran·si·tion·al /trænˈzɪʃənl; trænˈzɪʃənəl/ *adj* **1 transitional stage/period etc** a period during which something is changing from one state or form into another 過渡階段/時期等: *maintaining law and order in the transitional period between governments* 在兩屆政府過渡時期維持法治和秩序 **2 transitional government** a government that is temporary during a period of change 過渡政府 —**transitionally** *adv*

tran·si·tive /ˋtrænsətɪv; ˈtrænsɪ̣tɪv/ *adj technical* a transitive verb must have an object, for example the verb 'break' in the sentence 'I broke the cup'. Transitive verbs are marked [T] in this dictionary.【術語】〔動詞〕及物的〔如在句子 I broke the cup 中的 break。本辭典的及物動詞均標以 [T]〕—compare 比較 DITRANSITIVE, INTRANSITIVE —**transitive** *n* [C] —**transitively** *adv*

transit lounge /ˈ·· ˌ·/ *n* [C] an area in an airport where passengers can wait〔機場的〕中轉候機廳

tran·si·to·ry /ˋtrænsəˌtorɪ; ˈtrænzɪ̣tərɪ/ *adj* continuing or existing for only a short time; TRANSIENT 短暫的, 一時的

transit vi·sa /ˈ·· ˌ··/ *n* [C] a VISA (=special document) that allows someone to pass through one country on their way to another 過境簽證

trans·late /trænsˋlet; trænsˈleɪt/ *v* **1** [I,T] to change speech or writing into another language 翻譯, 把〔話語或文字〕譯成〔另一種語言〕: *Robin doesn't speak German so I'll have to translate.* 羅賓不會講德語, 所以我得翻譯。| **translate sth (from sth) into** *We translated the text from Italian into English.* 我們把文字從意大利語譯成了英語。—compare 比較 INTERPRET (2) **2** [I] to be changed from one language into another (被) 翻譯: *Most poetry doesn't translate easily.* 大多數詩歌都是不容易翻譯的。**3** [T] to change something from one form into another 把…變成另一種形狀, 轉化為…: **translate sth into** *We're hoping to translate our ideas into action.* 我們希望把自己的思想轉化為行動。—**translatable** *adj*

trans·la·tion /trænsˋleʃən; trænsˈleɪʃən/ *n* **1** [C,U] the act of translating something or something that has been translated 翻譯; 翻譯作品: *a translation of Aristotle's 'Ethics'* 亞里士多德的《倫理學》譯本 | **translation (from sth) into** *translation from Latin into English* 由拉丁語到英語的翻譯 | **in translation** *I've only read "Madame Bovary" in translation.* 我只讀過《包法利夫人》的翻譯本。| **be lost in translation** (=be no longer effective when translated) 在翻譯中丟失了 *Much of the book's humour has been lost in translation.* 這本書的很多幽默之處在翻譯中丟失了。**2** [U] *formal* the process of changing something into a different form【正式】轉化: *the translation of ideas into deeds* 思想轉化為行動

trans·la·tor /trænsˋletɚ; trænsˈleɪtə/ *n* [C] someone who changes speech or writing into a different language 翻譯 (者), 譯員 —compare 比較 INTERPRETER

trans·lit·e·rate /trænsˋlɪtəˌret; trænzˈlɪtəreɪt/ *v* [T] to write a word, sentence etc in the alphabet of a different language or writing system 把〔詞、句子等〕用另一種語言的字母[另一種書寫系統]寫出 —**transliteration** /ˌtrænslɪtəˋreʃən; trænzˌlɪtəˈreɪʃən/ *n* [C,U]

trans·lu·cent /trænsˋlusn̩t; trænzˈluːsənt/ *adj* not transparent, but clear enough to allow light to pass through 半透明的: *translucent paper* 半透明紙 —**translucence** *n* [U]

trans·mi·gra·tion /ˌtrænsmaɪˋgreʃən; ˌtrænzmaɪˈgreɪʃən/ *n* [U] *technical* the time when the soul passes into another body after death, according to some religions【術語】〔死後靈魂的〕輪迴, 轉世

trans·mis·sion /trænsˋmɪʃən; trænzˈmɪʃən/ *n* **1** [U] the process of sending out of electrical signals, messages etc, by radio or similar equipment〔電子信號、信息等的〕發送, 播送: *We apologize for the break in transmission earlier in the programme.* 我們為節目初期出現的播放中斷表示歉意。**2** [C] *formal* something that is broadcast on television, radio etc【正式】〔電視、廣播等的〕播送節目 **3** [C] the parts of a vehicle that take power from the engine to the wheels〔汽車的〕傳動裝置, 變速器: *My car has automatic transmission.* 我的汽車具有自動傳動裝置。**4** [U] *formal* the process of sending or passing of something from one person, place, or thing to another【正式】傳遞, 傳播: *the transmission of disease* 疾病的傳播

trans·mit /trænsˋmɪt; trænzˈmɪt/ *v* **transmitted, transmitting 1** [I,T] to send out electric signals, messages etc by radio or other similar equipment; broadcast 發送, 播送, 播放〔電子信號、信息等〕: *The US Open will be transmitted live via satellite.* 美國公開賽將通過衛星現場直播。**2** [T] to send or pass something from one person, place or thing to another 傳送, 傳遞, 傳播: *an infection transmitted by mosquitoes* 由蚊子傳播的一種傳染病 —see also 另見 SEXUALLY TRANSMITTED DISEASE **3** [T] *technical* if an object or substance transmits sound or light, it allows sound or light to travel through or along it【術語】傳播〔聲音或光〕

trans·mit·ter /trænsˋmɪtɚ; trænzˈmɪtə/ *n* [C] equipment that sends out radio or television signals〔發送無線電或電視信號的〕發射機, 發報機

trans·mog·ri·fy /trænsˋmɑgrəˌfaɪ; trænzˈmɒgrɪ̣faɪ/ *v* [T] *humorous* to change the shape of something completely, as if by magic【幽默】〔變魔術般〕完全改變

trans·mute /trænsˋmjut; trænzˈmjuːt/ *v* [T] *formal* to change one substance or type of thing into another【正式】使變化; 把…變成…: *Alchemists tried to transmute lead into gold.* 煉金術士試圖把鉛變成金。—**transmutable** *adj* —**transmutation** /ˌtrænsmjuˋteʃən; ˌtrænzmjuːˈteɪʃən/ n [C,U]

tran·som /ˋtrænsəm; ˈtrænsəm/ *n* [C] **1** a bar of wood above a door, separating the door from a window above it〔門的〕橫檔, 橫楣 **2** a bar of wood or stone across a window, dividing the window into two parts〔把窗戶分隔為二的〕過梁 **3** *AmE* a small window over a door or over a larger window【美】門頂窗; 楣窗; 氣窗; FANLIGHT *BrE*【英】

trans·par·en·cy /trænˋspɛrənsɪ; trænˈspærənsi/ *n* **1** [C] a piece of photographic film through which light can be shone to show a picture on a large screen; SLIDE[2] (4) 幻燈片 **2** [U] the quality of glass, plastic etc that makes it possible for you to see through it〔玻璃、塑料等的〕透明 (性)

trans·par·ent /trænˋspɛrənt; trænˈspærənt/ *adj* **1** something that is transparent allows light to pass through it, so that you can see the things through it 透明的: *Plain glass is transparent.* 普通玻璃是透明的。| *a transparent silk blouse* 透明的絲綢女襯衫 —compare 比較 OPAQUE, TRANSLUCENT **2** a lie, excuse etc that is transparent does not deceive people〔謊言、藉口等〕騙不了人的; 顯而易見的 **3** *formal* speech or writing that is transparent is clear and easy to understand【正式】〔講話或文字〕含意清楚的 —**transparently** *adv*

tran·spi·ra·tion /ˌtrænspəˋreʃən; ˌtrænspɪ̣ˈreɪʃən/ *n* [U] *technical* the process of transpiring (TRANSPIRE (3))【術語】蒸騰 (作用)

tran·spire /trænˋspaɪr; trænˈspaɪə/ *v* **1 it transpires that** *formal* if it transpires that something is true, people find out that it is true【正式】泄露, 被人所知: *It now transpires that he kept all the money for himself.* 他把所有的錢都據為己有, 這點現在已大白於天下了。**2** [T] to happen 發生: *Let's wait and see what transpires.* 讓我們等着瞧會發生甚麼事吧。**3** [I,T] *technical* when a plant transpires, it gives off water from its surface【術語】〔植物〕蒸騰

trans·plant¹ /trænsˋplænt; trænsˈplɑːnt/ *v* [T] **1** to move a plant from one place and plant it in another 移植, 移栽〔植物〕**2** to move an organ, piece of skin etc from one person's body to another 移植〔器官、皮膚等〕**3** *formal* to move something or someone from one place to another【正式】搬運, 搬遷, 遷移 —**transplantation** /ˌtrænsplænˋteʃən; ˌtrænsplɑːnˈteɪʃən/ *n* [U]

trans·plant² /ˋtrænsplænt; ˈtrænsplɑːnt/ *n* [C,U] **1** the operation of transplanting an organ, piece of skin etc〔器官、皮膚等〕移植 (手術): *heart transplant surgery* 心臟移植外科 **2** the organ etc that is transplanted in this type of operation 移植的器官, 移植物 —compare 比較 IMPLANT

trans·po·lar /træns`polɚ; ˌtrænz'pəʊlə◂/ *adj* across the area around the North or South Pole 穿越北極[南極]的; 穿越極地的

trans·pond·er /træn`spɑndɚ; træn'spɒndə/ *n* [C] *technical* a piece of radio or RADAR equipment that sends out a particular signal when it receives a signal telling it to do this【術語】發射機應答器

trans·port¹ /`trænsport; 'trænspɔːt/ *n* **1** [U] a system for carrying passengers or goods from one place to another〔旅客或貨物的〕運輸, 運送; TRANSPORTATION (2) *AmE*【美】: **public transport** (=buses, trains etc) 公共交通 *Public transport in Prague was excellent.* 布拉格的公共交通很好。**2** [U] a method of travelling from one place to another 交通工具, 運輸途徑: *It's easier to get to the college if you have your own transport* (=car, bicycle etc). 如果你有自己的交通工具, 要去學院就容易了。| **means of transport** *Horses provided the only means of transport.* 馬匹曾是唯一的交通工具。**3** [U] the process or business of taking goods from one place to another 運輸(過程); 運輸(業務); TRANSPORTATION (1) *AmE*【美】: [+of] *The transport of freight by air is very expensive.* 航空貨運是非常昂貴的。**4** [C] a ship or aircraft for carrying soldiers or supplies〔運送士兵或供給品的〕運輸船; 運輸機 **5 be in a transport of delight/joy etc** *literary* to be feeling very strong emotions of pleasure, happiness etc【文】感到非常高興/快樂等

trans·port² /træns`port; træn'spɔːt/ *v* [T] **1** to take goods, people etc from one place to another in a vehicle 運輸, 運送〔貨物、人等〕: *Transporting goods by rail reduces pollution.* 通過鐵路運輸貨物可以減少污染。| **transport sb/sth to** *You will be transported to the resort by coach.* 將用遊覽車把你們運送到度假勝地。**2 be transported back/into etc** to imagine that you are in another place or time because of something that you see or hear〔想像中〕被帶回到/被帶入〔另一地點或時間等〕: *Walking around the town, I was transported back to my youth.* 我在城裡到處走着, 好像回到了青少年時代。**3** to send a criminal to a distant country as a punishment in former times〔舊時〕流放, 放逐〔犯人〕**4 be transported with delight/joy etc** *literary* to feel very strong emotions of pleasure, happiness etc【文】欣喜若狂, 喜不自勝 —**transportable** *adj*

trans·por·ta·tion /ˌtrænspɚ`teʃən; ˌtrænspɔː'teɪʃən/ *n* [U] **1** the process or business of taking goods from one place to another 運輸(過程); 運輸(業務): *the transportation of dangerous chemicals by road* 通過公路運輸危險的化學品 **2** *AmE* a system for carrying passengers or goods from one place to another【美】〔旅客或貨物的〕運輸, 運送; TRANSPORT¹ (1) *BrE*【英】**3** *old use* the punishment of sending a criminal to a distant country【舊】〔犯人的〕流放, 放逐

transport caf·e /'·· ˌ·'·/ *n* [C] *BrE* a cheap restaurant beside a main road, used mainly by drivers of heavy vehicles【英】〔主要為重型貨車司機服務的〕路邊廉價餐館; TRUCK STOP *AmE*【美】

trans·port·er /træns`portɚ; træn'spɔːtə/ *n* [C] a long vehicle that can carry one or more other vehicles〔運載其他車輛的〕長型貨車

transport plane /'·· ˌ·/ *n* [C] a plane that is used especially for carrying military equipment or soldiers〔尤指運送軍事設備或士兵的〕運輸機

transport ship /'·· ˌ·/ *n* [C] a ship used especially for carrying soldiers〔尤指運送士兵的〕運輸船

trans·pose /træns`poz; træn'spəʊz/ *v* [T] *technical*【術語】**1** *formal* to change the order or position of two or more things【正式】變換, 調換〔順序或位置〕**2** to write or perform a piece of music in a musical KEY² (4) that is different from the one that it was first written in 使〔樂曲〕變調, 移調 —**transposition** /ˌtrænspə`zɪʃən; ˌtrænspə'zɪʃən/ *n* [C,U]

trans·put·er /træns`pjutɚ; trænz'pjuːtə/ *n* [C] *technical* a powerful computer MICROCHIP that can deal with very large amounts of information very fast【術語】〔能迅速處理大量信息的, 功率強大的〕電腦微晶片

trans·sex·u·al /ˌtræns`sɛkʃuəl; træn'sekʃuəl/ *n* [C] someone who wants to be or look like a member of the opposite sex, especially by having a medical operation〔尤指通過醫學手術〕欲改變性別者, 易性癖者 —**transsexual** *adj* —**transsexualism** *n* [U]

tran·sub·stan·ti·a·tion /ˌtrænsəbˌstænʃɪ`eʃən; ˌtrænsəbstænʃi'eɪʃən/ *n* [U] *technical* the belief of some Christians that the bread and wine in the MASS (=a religious ceremony) become the actual body and blood of Christ【術語】變體〔有些基督徒認為在彌撒上的麵包和葡萄酒實際上變成耶穌基督的肉和血的一種論點〕

trans·verse /træns`vɝs; trænz'vɜːs/ *adj* [no comparative 無比較級] *technical* lying or placed across something【術語】橫向的, 橫斷的: a *transverse beam* 橫梁

trans·ves·tite /træns`vɛstaɪt; trænz'vestaɪt/ *n* [C] someone who enjoys dressing like a person of the opposite sex 有異性裝扮癖的人, 愛穿異性服裝的人 —**transvestite** *adj* —**transvestism** *n* [U]

trap¹ /træp; træp/ *n* [C]

1 ▶FOR ANIMALS 用於動物的◀ a piece of equipment for catching animals〔捕捉動物的〕夾子, 羅網, 陷阱: *a mouse caught in a trap* 被夾子夾住的老鼠 | **set a trap** (=prepare it) 設置陷阱, 佈下圈套 —see also 另見 MOUSETRAP

2 ▶BAD SITUATION 惡劣的處境◀ an unpleasant or difficult situation that is difficult to escape from 圈套; 困境: *Amanda felt that marriage was a trap.* 阿曼達覺得婚姻是一個陷阱。

3 ▶CLEVER TRICK 聰明的計策◀ a clever trick that is used to catch someone or to make them do or say something that they did not intend to 計謀, 策略; 陷阱: **fall/walk into a trap** *Hopefully, the thief will fall right into our trap.* 如果順利的話, 那個賊會恰好落入我們設置的圈套。| **lay a trap (for)** (=arrange a trap for someone) 為…設下圈套

4 fall into the trap of doing sth to do something that seems good at the time but is not sensible or wise 做〔某事〕不明智: *Don't fall into the trap of investing all your money in one place.* 不要把你所有的錢都投資到一個地方, 那樣做並不明智。

5 keep your trap shut *spoken* to not say anything about things that are secret【口】不把…說出去, 不泄密: *Just keep your trap shut, and we won't get into trouble.* 你只要不說出去, 我們就不會有麻煩。

6 shut your trap! *spoken* a rude way of telling someone to stop talking【口】閉上你的嘴!

7 ▶VEHICLE 車輛◀ a light vehicle with two wheels, pulled by a horse 雙輪輕便馬車: *a pony and trap* 小馬拉的雙輪輕便馬車

8 ▶SPORT 體育運動◀ *AmE* a place on a GOLF COURSE where there is sand, and from which it is difficult to hit the ball【美】〔高爾夫球場的〕沙坑; BUNKER (3) *BrE*【英】

9 ▶DOG RACE 賽狗◀ a special gate from which a dog is set free at the beginning of a GREYHOUND race〔賽狗開始時放狗出籠的〕閘欄 —see also 另見 BOOBY TRAP, DEATH TRAP, POVERTY TRAP, SPEED TRAP

trap² *v* [T]

1 ▶IN A DANGEROUS PLACE 在危險的地點◀ [usually passive 一般用被動態] to prevent someone from escaping from a dangerous place 困住, 關住; 使陷於危險中: *Twenty miners were trapped underground.* 二十名礦工被困在地下。

2 ▶IN A BAD SITUATION 在惡劣的處境中◀ **be trapped** to be in a bad situation from which you cannot escape 使陷於困境: *Julia felt trapped in a dead end job.* 朱莉婭覺得工作沒有出路, 陷於困境。

3 ▶ANIMAL 動物◀ to catch an animal or bird using a trap 用陷阱捕獵〔獸或鳥〕

4 ▶CATCH SB 抓住某人◀ to catch someone by forcing them into a place from which they cannot escape 把〔某人〕困住〔以便捕捉〕; 使陷入羅網: *The police trapped the terrorists at a roadblock.* 警察在設有路障的地方圍困恐怖分子。

5 ►TRICK SB 欺騙某人◄ to trick someone so that you make them do or say something that they did not intend to 誘騙, 誘使: **trap sb into (doing) sth** *I was trapped into signing a confession.* 我被誘騙在供詞上簽了字。

6 ►CRUSH 壓扁◄ to get a part of your body crushed between two objects 被夾住; 被壓扁: *a four-year-old who had trapped his fingers in the door* 手指被夾在門裡的一個四歲小孩 | *pain from a trapped nerve in the back* 因背上一根神經被壓迫而引起的疼痛

7 ►GAS/WATER ETC 氣/水等◄ to hold and keep gas, water etc so that it can be used later 把〔氣、水等〕儲存; 留存: *solar panels that trap the sun's heat* 把太陽熱量儲存起來的太陽能電池板

trap·door /ˋtræpdɔr; ˈtræpdɔː/ *n* [C] a small door that covers an opening in a roof or floor 〔房頂的〕活動天窗; 〔地板的〕活板門

tra·peze /træˋpiz; trəˈpiːz/ *n* [C] a short bar hanging from two ropes high above the ground, used by ACROBATS 〔雜技運動員用的〕空中吊槓, 空中鞦韆

tra·pe·zi·um /trəˋpiziəm; trəˈpiːziəm/ *n* [C] *technical* 【術語】**1** *BrE* a shape with four sides, of which only two are parallel 【英】梯形 **2** *AmE* a shape with four sides of which none are parallel 【美】不規則四邊形 —see picture at 參見 SHAPE 圖

trap·e·zoid /ˋtræpəˌzɔɪd; ˈtræpɪzɔɪd/ *n* [C] *technical* 【術語】**1** a shape with four sides, of which none are parallel 不規則四邊形 **2** *AmE* a shape with four sides of which only two are parallel 【美】梯形 —see picture at 參見 SHAPE 圖

trap·per /ˋtræpɚ; ˈtræpə/ *n* [C] someone who traps wild animals, especially for their fur 〔尤指為獲取毛皮的〕設陷阱捕獸者

trap·pings /ˋtræpɪŋz; ˈtræpɪŋz/ *n* [plural] things such as clothes, possessions etc that show someone's rank, success, or position 〔表明某人官職或地位的〕服飾; 標誌: **[+of]** *all the trappings of fame* 表示名望的各種標誌

Trap·pist /ˋtræpɪst; ˈtræpɪst/ *n* [C] a member of a Roman Catholic religious society whose members never speak 〔羅馬天主教中緘默無言的〕特拉普派修士

trap·shoot·ing /ˋtræpˌʃutɪŋ; ˈtræpˌʃuːtɪŋ/ *n* [U] the sport of shooting at special clay objects fired into the air 飛靶射擊

3 **trash¹** /træʃ; træʃ/ *n* [U] **1** *AmE* waste material that will be thrown away 【美】廢物, 垃圾; RUBBISH *BrE* 【英】—see graph at 參見 RUBBISH¹ 圖表 **2** *informal* something that is of very poor quality 【非正式】質量粗劣的東西: *There's a lot of trash on TV these days.* 近來電視上有大量粗製濫造的東西。**3** *informal especially AmE* a very insulting word for people who you think do not deserve your respect 【非正式, 尤美】廢物〔極具侮辱性的用語, 指不值得尊敬的人〕

trash² *v* [T] *informal* to destroy something completely, either deliberately or by using it too much 【非正式】〔因故意或過分使用而〕搗毀, 破壞: *The place got trashed last time we had a party!* 我們上一次舉行聚會的時候把這個地方搞得亂七八糟的!

trash·can /ˋtræʃˌkæn; ˈtræʃkæn/ *n* [C] *AmE* 【美】**1** a large container with a lid for holding waste material from people's homes 垃圾桶; DUSTBIN *BrE* 【英】**2** a container for waste paper etc in a public place 廢紙簍; 公用垃圾箱; LITTER BIN *BrE* 【英】

trash com·pac·tor /ˈ· ·ˌ··/ *n* [C] *AmE* a machine that presses waste material together into a very small mass 【美】垃圾壓實機

trashed /træʃt; træʃt/ *adj AmE spoken* 【美口】**1** very drunk 爛醉的: *We went out and got trashed last night.* 我們昨晚外出喝酒, 喝得爛醉。**2** completely destroyed 完全毀壞的: *We need a new map – this one's trashed.* 我們需要一張新地圖 —— 這張已完全毀壞了。

trash·y /ˋtræʃɪ; ˈtræʃi/ *adj* of extremely bad quality 質量極其粗劣的; 毫無價值的: *trashy novels* 垃圾小說, 毫無價值的小說 —**trashiness** *n* [U]

trau·ma /ˋtrɔmə; ˈtrɔːmə/ *n* **1** [C] a very unpleasant and upsetting experience 痛苦的經歷: *the trauma of an attack or rape* 遭到襲擊[強姦]的痛苦經歷 **2** [U] a mental state of extreme shock caused by a very frightening or unpleasant experience 心理創傷: *compensation for the emotional trauma he had suffered since childhood* 對他童年以來所受感情創傷的補償 **3** [C,U] *technical* injury 【術語】損傷, 外傷: *the hospital's trauma unit* 醫院的外傷科

trau·mat·ic /trɔˋmætɪk; trɔːˈmætɪk/ *adj* a traumatic experience is so shocking and upsetting that it affects you for a long time 〔經歷〕痛苦難忘的, 造成精神創傷的: *The death of his son was the most traumatic event in Stan's life.* 兒子的死是斯坦一生中最痛苦難忘的事。—**traumatically** /-klɪ; -kli/ *adv*

trau·ma·tized also 又作 **-ised** *BrE* 【英】/ˋtrɔməˌtaɪzd; ˈtrɔːmətaɪzd/ *adj* so shocked by something that you are unable to forget it or to continue your life as normal 精神上受到創傷的, 痛苦難忘的: *totally traumatized by his war experiences* 因其戰爭經歷而在精神上完全受到創傷

trav·ail /ˋtrævel; ˈtræveɪl/ *n* [U] *old use* 【舊】**1** also 又作 **travails** [plural] very tiring work 很累人的工作, 苦活 **2 in travail** a woman who is in travail is feeling the pain of giving birth 〔婦女〕分娩的陣痛

trav·el¹ /ˋtrævl; ˈtrævəl/ *v* **travelled, travelling** *BrE* 【英】**traveled, traveling** *AmE* 【美】

1 ►JOURNEY 旅途◄ a) [I] to go from one place to another, or to several places, especially to distant places 〔尤指長途〕旅行: *If I had a lot of money I'd travel.* 我如果有很多的錢, 就外出去旅行。| *They're travelling down from Edinburgh on Monday.* 他們星期一要從愛丁堡來。| **travel by train/car etc** *We travelled by train across Eastern Europe.* 我們乘火車遊歷了東歐。| **travel widely** (=go to many different places) 到過很多地方 | **travel around** (=go to different places over a period of time) 〔在某段時間裡〕四處漫遊 *I met Tim while I was travelling around.* 在我四處漫遊期間, 遇見了蒂姆。| **travel light** (=without taking many bags) 輕裝旅行 **b) travel the world/country** to go to most parts of the world or most parts of a particular country 周遊世界/周遊全國

2 well-travelled/widely travelled having travelled to many different countries 到過很多地方的, 遊歷很廣的

3 ►DISTANCE 距離◄ [I,T] to go a particular distance or at a particular speed 走過〔某距離〕; 〔以某速度〕行進: *The train was travelling at 100 mph.* 火車前進的速度是每小時 100 英里。| *They travelled 200 miles on the first day.* 他們第一天走了 200 英里。

4 ►FOOD/WINE 食品/酒◄ travel well to remain in good condition when taken long distances 經得起長途運輸而保持優良品質

5 ►LIGHT/SOUND 光/聲音◄ [I] to move at a particular speed or in a particular direction 〔以某一速度或朝某一方向〕前進: *Light travels faster than sound.* 光速比音速快。

6 ►FOR BUSINESS 用於商務◄ [I] to go from place to place to sell and take orders for your company's products 作旅行推銷, 四處兜售商品: **[+for]** *My wife travels for a London firm.* 我妻子為倫敦一家公司做旅行推銷。

7 ►MOVE QUICKLY 快速移動◄ [I] *informal* to go very fast 【非正式】快速行進, 飛馳: *That motorbike was really travelling.* 那輛摩托車開得真快。

8 ►NEWS 消息◄ [I] to be passed quickly from one place to another 很快地傳播開來: *News travels fast.* 消息傳得很快。

9 ►SPORT 體育運動◄ [I] *technical* to run while you are holding the ball in BASKETBALL【術語】〔籃球比賽中〕持球走，帶球跑

USAGE NOTE 用法說明: TRAVEL

WORD CHOICE 詞語辨析: **travel** (*n,v*), **sb's travels, journey, trip, voyage, flight**

Travel [U] is only used for the general activity of moving from place to place. travel〔不可數〕只用於泛指從某地去另一地: *He came home after years of foreign travel.* 他在國外旅行多年後回到了家。The *-ing* form of the verb **travel** is also used widely with a similar meaning. travel 的 -ing 形式也用得廣泛，表達類似的意義: *I do a bit of travelling abroad* (NOT 不用 *travel(s)*). 我經常去國外走走。| *travel/travelling expenses* 旅行花費 | *air travel/travelling by air* 航空旅行

If someone moves from place to place over a period of time, you talk about **their travels**. 如果某人在某段時間裡到處走，可用 travels: *Did you go to Rome during your travels?* 你在旅行期間去羅馬了嗎? | *He's on his travels again.* 他又旅行去了。

A particular time spent and distance covered when you go somewhere is a **journey**, especially if it is long or travelled regularly. journey 表示去某地所花的時間和旅行的距離，尤指較長距離的或定期的旅行: *I get tired of the journey to work every day.* 我厭煩了每天去上班的那段路程。| *The journey to Darjeeling was awful – I was sick all the way* (NOT 不用 *travel*). 前往大吉嶺的那段路太糟糕了——我一直想吐。

A journey to a place and back that is not made regularly, and is perhaps short, is a **trip**. 表示非定期的，也許較短的往返旅行，則用 trip: *This is my first trip abroad.* 這是我第一次出國旅行。| *The kids are going on a trip to the castle.* 孩子們要去那座城堡走一趟。| *How long does the trip take?* 來回要花多長時間? (*travel* would not be used in any of these).〔travel 不用於這些句子中〕。

A journey by sea or in space is a **voyage**, and by plane a **flight**. You **take** a **flight** or **trip** and **make** or **go** on a **voyage** or **journey** (but NOT 但不用 *a travel*). 海上旅行或太空旅行的用詞是 voyage，乘飛機旅行是 flight。與 flight 或 trip 搭配的動詞是 take; 與 voyage 或 journey 搭配的動詞是 make 或 go。

GRAMMAR 語法

Travel (*v*) is not often used transitively travel 通常不用作及物動詞 except when you are talking about 下列說法除外: *travelling the country/the world* 走遍全國/世界。Otherwise it is usually intransitive and a preposition is used with the place involved. 其他情況通常用作不及物動詞，要用介詞連接所指地點: *He travels a lot/all over the world.* 他遊歷甚廣/他遊遍世界。| *We travelled to Paris/in India/through many foreign countries* (NOT 不用 *travelled many countries*). 我們去了巴黎/在印度旅行/遊歷了許多國家。

travel² *n* [U] **1** the act or activity of travelling 旅行; 移動; 運動: *Snow has disrupted travel in many parts of the country.* 該國很多地方都下雪，影響了交通。**2 travels** [plural] journeys, especially to places that are a long way away〔尤指長途的〕旅行，遊歷: *Tell us more about your travels.* 給我們多講講你的旅行經歷。| **be off on your travels** *informal* (=be travelling for pleasure)【非正式】外出旅遊 *Are you off on your travels again this summer?* 你今年夏天又要外出旅遊嗎?

travel a·gen·cy /ˈ·· ˌ···/ *n* [C] an office or company that arranges travel and holidays for people 旅行社

travel a·gent /ˈ·· ˌ··/ *n* [C] someone who owns or works in a travel agency 旅行代理人，開辦旅行社的人

trav·el·a·tor /ˈtrævəletɚ; ˈtrævəleɪtə/ *n* [C] another spelling of TRAVOLATOR travolator 的另一種拼法

travel bu·reau /ˈ·· ˌ··/ *n* [C] a TRAVEL AGENCY 旅行社

trav·el·ler *BrE*【英】, **traveler** *AmE*【美】/ˈtrævlɚ; ˈtrævələ/ *n* [C] **1** someone who is on a journey or someone who travels often 旅客，旅行者; 經常旅行的人: *Rail travellers will suffer as a result of fare increases.* 鐵路旅客將會因票價上漲而吃苦頭。**2** *BrE* someone who travels around from place to place in a CARAVAN as a way of life【英】坐旅行拖車過漂泊生活的人 —compare 比較 GYPSY

traveller's cheque *BrE*【英】, **traveler's check** *AmE*【美】/ˈ··· ˌ·/ *n* [C] a special cheque that can be exchanged for the money of a foreign country 旅行支票

trav·el·ling *BrE*【英】, **traveling** *AmE*【美】/ˈtrævlɪŋ; ˈtrævəlɪŋ/ *adj* **1 travelling musician/circus etc** a musician etc that goes from place to place in order to work or perform 巡迴演出的音樂家/馬戲團等 **2 travelling rug/clock etc** a clock etc designed to be used when you are travelling 旅行用毛毯/時鐘等 **3 travelling people/folk** travellers (TRAVELLER (2)) 過漂泊生活的人

travelling sales·man *BrE*【英】, **traveling salesman** *AmE*【美】/ˌ··· ˈ··/ *n* [C] someone who goes from place to place, selling their company's products 旅行[巡迴]推銷員

trav·el·ogue also 又作 **travelog** *AmE*【美】/ˈtrævəˌlɔg; ˈtrævəlɒg/ *n* [C] a film or talk that describes travel in a particular country, or a particular person's travels 旅行記錄片; 旅行見聞講座

travel-sick /ˈ·· ·/ *adj* feeling ill because you are travelling in a vehicle 暈車的; 暈船的; 暈飛機的: *Many children get travel-sick on long journeys.* 許多孩子在作長途旅行時都會頭暈。—**travel sickness** *n* [U]

tra·verse¹ /trəˈvɝs; ˈtrævɜːs/ *v* [T] *formal* to move across, over, or through something【正式】跨過，穿過，橫越，橫穿: *They traversed the desert slowly.* 他們緩慢地穿過沙漠。

trav·erse² /ˈtrævɝs; ˈtrævɜːs/ *n* [C] *technical* a sideways movement across a very steep slope in mountain-climbing【術語】〔爬山時的〕斜向攀上[下]〔陡坡〕: *the traverse of the mountain's north face* 斜向攀登山的北坡

trav·es·ty /ˈtrævɪstɪ; ˈtrævɪ̈sti/ *n* [C] an extremely bad example of something; especially one that is very unfair or morally wrong and has the opposite result to the one it should have 歪曲模仿，曲解; 嘲弄: *O'Brien described his trial as a travesty of justice.* 奧布賴恩把對他的審訊描述成是對司法的嘲弄。

trav·o·la·tor, travelator /ˈtrævəletɚ; ˈtrævəleɪtə/ *n* [C] *BrE formal* a flat moving band of material on the floor, that people can step onto so that they do not have to walk, especially in airports【英，正式】〔尤指機場的〕自動人行道

trawl¹ /trɔl; trɔːl/ *v* [I,T] **1** to search through a lot of documents, lists, etc in order to find out information〔在大量文件、名單等中〕搜尋〔資料〕: **[+through]** *I'll have to trawl through all my lecture notes again.* 我不得不把所有講座筆記再翻一遍。**2** to fish by dragging a special wide net behind a boat 以拖網捕魚: *trawling the bay for herring* 在海灣裡用拖網捕鯡魚

trawl² *n* [C] **1** an act of searching through a lot of documents, lists etc in order to find something〔在大量文件、名單等中的〕搜尋 **2** a wide net that is pulled along the bottom of the sea to catch fish 拖網 **3** a TRAWL LINE 排鈎繩

trawl·er /ˈtrɔlɚ; ˈtrɔːlə/ *n* [C] a fishing boat that trawls 拖網漁船

traw·ler·man /ˈtrɔlɚˌmæn; ˈtrɔːləmən/ *n* [C] someone who works on a trawler 拖網漁民; 拖網漁船工人

trawl line /ˈ· ·/ *n* [C] *AmE* a long fishing line to which many smaller lines are fastened【美】排鈎繩〔掛有許多小釣線的長的釣線〕

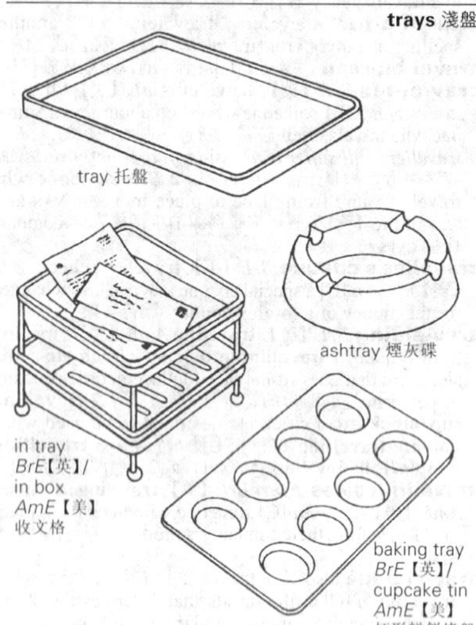

tray /tre; treɪ/ *n* [C] **1** a flat piece of plastic, metal, or wood, with raised edges, used for carrying things such as plates, food etc〔淺〕盤, 托盤: *The waiter brought drinks on a tray.* 服務員用托盤端來飲料。**2** *especially BrE* a flat open container with three sides used for holding papers, documents etc on a desk【尤英】〔辦公桌上存放文件等的〕格子: **in tray** (=for holding documents you still have to deal with)〔放置待處理文件的〕收文格 | **out tray** (=for holding documents you have dealt with)〔放置已處理文件的〕發文格 —see also 另見 BAKING TRAY

treach·e·rous /ˈtrɛtʃərəs; ˈtretʃərəs/ *adj* **1** someone who is treacherous cannot be trusted because they are disloyal and secretly intend to harm you 背信棄義的, 不忠的, 陰險的: *a treacherous plot to overthrow the leader* 一項推翻領導人的陰謀 **2** ground or conditions that are treacherous are particularly dangerous because you cannot see the dangers 暗藏危險的: *There are treacherous currents in the bay.* 海灣中有暗流。—**treacherously** *adv*

treach·e·ry /ˈtrɛtʃərɪ; ˈtretʃəri/ *n* **1** [U] behaviour that is not loyal to someone who trusts you, especially when this helps their enemies 背信棄義, 不忠, 背叛: *the treachery of those who plotted against the king* 那些陰謀叛亂的人對國王的不忠 **2** [C usually plural 一般用複數] a disloyal action against someone who trusts you 背叛行為; 欺騙行為

trea·cle /ˈtrikḷ; ˈtriːkəl/ *n* [U] *BrE*【英】**1** a thick sweet black sticky liquid that is obtained from the sugar plant and used in cooking 糖蜜; MOLASSES *AmE*【美】**2** GOLDEN SYRUP 糖漿: *a treacle tart* 糖漿餡餅

trea·cly /ˈtriklɪ; ˈtriːkli/ *adj BrE*【英】**1** thick and sticky, like treacle 稠的, 黏的; 糖蜜似的: *treacly black mud* 又稠又黑的泥濘 **2** expressing feelings of love or fondness in a way that seems insincere 過分多情的; 討好的

tread[1] /trɛd; tred/ *v past tense* **trod** /trɑd; trɒd/ *past participle* **trodden** /ˈtrɑdn; ˈtrɒdn/

1 ►STEP IN/ON 踩到裡面/上面◄ [I always+adv/prep] *BrE* to put your foot on or in something while you are walking; STEP【英】踩, 踏: **[+in/on]** *Sorry – did I tread on your foot?* 對不起——我踩到你的腳了嗎? | *Be careful not to tread on that broken glass.* 小心別踩到那塊碎玻璃上。

2 ►CRUSH 壓扁◄ **a)** [T] *BrE* to press or crush something into the floor or ground with your feet【英】用力踩; 踩爛; TRACK[2] (6) *AmE*【美】: **tread sth into/onto/over** *Stop treading mud all over my clean kitchen floor!* 不要在我乾淨的廚房地板上到處踩上泥! | *Bits of the broken vase got trodden into the carpet.* 破花瓶的一些碎片被踩進了地毯裡面。**b) tread grapes** to crush GRAPEs with your feet in order to produce the juice from which wine is made 用腳踩爛葡萄〔以釀酒〕

3 tread carefully/warily/cautiously etc to be very careful about what you say or do in a difficult situation 步步為營, 言行謹慎: *We can't risk the talks breaking down – we'll have to tread carefully.* 我們不能冒談判破裂的風險——我們必須步步為營。

4 tread a path *formal* to take a particular action or series of actions【正式】採取某種[系列]行動: *Anyone who makes such serious allegations is treading a very dangerous path.* 任何人提出如此嚴重的指控, 都要冒極大的風險。

5 tread water a) to stay floating upright in deep water by moving your legs as if you were riding a bicycle〔游泳時〕踩水 **b)** to make no progress in a particular situation, especially because you are waiting for something to happen〔尤指因等待某事發生而〕裹足不前

6 tread the boards *humorous* to work as an actor【幽默】當演員, 演戲

7 ►WALK 走路◄ [I always+adv/prep,T] *literary especially BrE* to walk【文, 尤英】行走, 步行: *David trod wearily along behind the others.* 大衛疲憊地走在別人的後面。—see also 另見 **step/tread on sb's toes** (TOE[1] (3))

tread[2] *n* **1** [C,U] the pattern of lines on the part of a tyre that touches the road 輪胎胎面花紋 **2** [C] the part of a stair that you put your foot on〔樓梯的〕梯面, 踏步板 **3** [singular] the particular sound that someone makes when they walk 腳步聲, 走路聲: *I could hear our father's heavy tread outside the door.* 我能聽到門外父親沉重的腳步聲。

trea·dle /ˈtrɛdḷ; ˈtredl/ *n* [C] a flat piece of metal or wood that you move with your foot to turn a wheel in a machine〔機器上踩踏使輪子轉動的〕踏板

tread·mill /ˈtrɛd,mɪl; ˈtred,mɪl/ *n* **1** [singular] work or a way of life that seems very boring because you always have to do the same things 單調而枯燥的工作[生活] **2** [C] a MILL[1] (1) worked in the past by prisoners treading on steps fixed to a very large wheel〔過去用以懲罰犯人的〕踏車

trea·son /ˈtrizṇ; ˈtriːzən/ *n* [U] the crime of being disloyal to your country or its government, especially by helping its enemies or trying to remove the government using violence 叛國(罪), 通敵(罪): **[+against]** *an act of treason against the state* 叛國行為 | **commit treason** (=do something that is treason) 犯叛國罪 | **high treason** (=treason of the worst kind) 嚴重叛國罪

trea·son·a·ble /ˈtrizṇəbḷ; ˈtriːzənəbəl/ also 又作 **trea·son·ous** /-zṇəs; -zənəs/ *adj* a treasonable offence can be punished as treason 叛逆的, 叛國的: *a treasonable act against the head of state* 針對國家元首的一次叛逆行動

trea·sure[1] /ˈtrɛʒɚ; ˈtreʒə/ *n* **1** [U] a store of gold, silver, jewels etc 金銀財寶, 寶藏: *buried treasure* 埋在地下的財寶 | **treasure chest** (=box containing treasure) 珠寶箱 **2** [C] a very valuable and important object such as a painting or ancient document 珍寶, 珍品: *the art treasures of the Louvre* 羅浮宮的藝術珍品 **3** *informal old-fashioned* [singular] someone who is very useful or important to you【非正式, 過時】很有用的人, 得力幫手: *Our housekeeper is a real treasure.* 我們的管家真是個難得的好幫手。

treasure[2] *v* [T] to treat something as being very special, important, or valuable 珍藏, 珍惜, 珍視: *Thank you; I shall treasure this gift always.* 謝謝您; 我會永遠珍惜這件禮物的。| *treasured memories of happier days* 對幸

福日子的珍貴回憶

treasure hunt /ˈ·· ˌ·/ *n* [C] a game in which you have to find something that has been hidden by answering questions that are left in different places 尋寶遊戲〔通過解答留在不同地點的問題來找到隱藏的東西〕

trea·sur·er /ˈtrɛʒərə; ˈtreʒərə/ *n* [C] someone who is in charge of the money for an organization, club, political party etc〔團體、機構等的〕司庫, 財務主管

treasure trove /ˈtrɛʒə ˌtrov; ˈtreʒə trəʊv/ *n* [U] *BrE law* valuable objects, coins etc that are found where they have been hidden or buried, which are not claimed by anyone【英, 法律】被發現埋藏的無主財寶

trea·su·ry /ˈtrɛʒərɪ; ˈtreʒəri/ *n* **1 the Treasury** a government department that controls the money that the country collects and spends〔政府的〕財政部: *a senior civil servant at the Treasury* 財政部的一位高級公務員 **2** [C] a place where money or valuable objects are kept in a castle, church, PALACE etc〔城堡、教堂、宮殿等的〕金庫, 寶庫

treat¹ /trit; triːt/ *v* [T]

1 ▶BEHAVE TOWARDS SB 對待某人◀ [always+adv/prep] to behave towards someone in a particular way 對待, 看待: **treat sb like/as** *She treats me like one of the family.* 她把我當作家人來看待。| *Even though they were much younger, we treated them as equals.* 他們即便年輕得多, 我們還是平等地對待他們。| **badly treated/well treated** *The prisoners were well treated by their guards.* 囚犯受到衛兵很好的對待。| **treat sb with respect/contempt/kindness etc** *Despite her seniority, Margot was never treated with much respect.* 馬戈特儘管是長輩, 但從未受到多少尊重。| **treat sb like dirt/a dog** (=treat someone unkindly and without respect) 把某人不當人看待/當狗看待

2 ▶DEAL WITH STH 處理某事◀ [always+adv/prep] to deal with or discuss something in a particular way 處理; 討論: **treat sth as** *Please treat this information as completely confidential.* 這項資料請絕對保密。| **treat sth favourably/seriously/carefully etc** *Any complaint about safety standards must be treated very seriously.* 任何有關安全標準的投訴意見必須十分認真地對待。

3 ▶MEDICAL 醫學的◀ to try to cure an illness or injury by using drugs, hospital care, operations etc 治療, 醫治: *Nowadays malaria can be treated with drugs.* 如今, 瘧疾可以用藥物醫治。

4 ▶REGARD 看待◀ [always+adv/prep] to regard an idea, subject, statement etc in a particular way 把…看作; 看待: **treat sth as** *She treats everything I say as some kind of joke.* 她把我說的每一件事都當成是玩笑。

5 ▶BUY STH FOR SB 為某人買某物◀ to buy something special for someone that you know they will enjoy 請客, 款待, 招待: **treat sb to sth** *We treated Mom to lunch at the Savoy.* 我們在薩伏伊酒店請媽媽吃午飯。| **treat yourself to sth** (=buy yourself something special) 自己花錢享受某物 *I treated myself to a new dress.* 我給自己買了一條新連衣裙。

6 ▶PROTECT/CLEAN 保護/清理◀ to put a special substance on something or use a chemical process in order to protect, clean, or preserve it 為…塗上保護層;〔用化學方式〕處理; 清理: *It is possible to treat sewage so that it can be used as fertilizer.* 可以對污水進行處理, 使之可以用作肥料。—see also 另見 TRICK OR TREAT

treat with sth *phr v* [T] *formal* to try to reach an official agreement with someone【正式】與…協商[談判、交涉]

treat of sth *phr v* [T] *formal* if a book, article etc treats of something, it is about that subject【正式】〔著作、文章等就某主題〕探討, 論述

treat² *n* **1** [C] something special that you give someone or do for them because you know they will enjoy it〔給某人的〕特別待遇, 款待, 招待: *Steven took his son to the zoo as a birthday treat.* 史蒂文帶兒子去動物園慶祝生日。**2** [singular] an unexpected event that gives you a lot of pleasure 意外的樂事, 幸事: *I really miss everyone, and getting a letter from home is a big treat.* 我真的很想念大家, 收到家裡的來信成了我的一大樂事。**3 my treat** *spoken* used to tell someone that you will pay for something such as a meal for them【口】我來付錢, 我請客: *Let's go out for dinner – my treat this time.* 咱們出去吃飯吧——這次由我來請客。**4 go down a treat** *BrE informal* if something goes down a treat, people like it very much【英, 非正式】深受喜愛: *Brightly coloured building blocks always go down a treat with toddlers.* 色彩鮮豔的積木總是深得幼童的喜愛。**5 look/work a treat** *BrE informal* to look very good or work very well【英, 非正式】看上去很好/工作得很出色: *The sports ground looked a treat, with all the flags flying.* 運動場看上去很漂亮, 到處都是彩旗飄揚。

treat·a·ble /ˈtritəbl̩; ˈtriːtəbəl/ *adj* a treatable illness or injury can be helped with drugs or an operation〔病或傷〕可醫治的

trea·tise /ˈtritɪs; ˈtriːtl̩s/ *n* [C+**on**] a serious book or article about a particular subject 專著, 專題論文: *a treatise on medical ethics* 論述醫學倫理的專著

treat·ment /ˈtritmənt; ˈtriːtmənt/ *n* S3 W1

1 ▶MEDICAL 醫學的◀ [C,U] a method that is intended to cure an injury or illness 治療; 療法: [+**for**] *The best treatment for a cold is to rest and drink lots of fluids.* 治療感冒的最佳方法是休息和多喝流質。| **give sb treatment** *She was given emergency treatment by paramedics.* 她接受了護理人員的緊急治療。| **receive treatment** *receiving treatment for skin cancer* 接受皮膚癌治療 | **respond to treatment** (=get better when you are treated) 有療效

2 ▶BEHAVIOUR TOWARDS SB 對待某人的行為◀ [U] a particular way of behaving towards someone or of dealing with them 對待(方式), 待遇: [+**of**] *Henchard's cruel treatment of his wife* 亨恰德對妻子的虐待 | **special/preferential treatment** (=when one person is treated better than another) 特殊的待遇/優待 *The two young princes were not singled out for special treatment at school.* 兩位年輕的王子在學校裡並沒有享受特殊待遇。| **give sb the full treatment** *informal especially BrE* (=treat someone in a very special way and give them a lot of attention)【非正式, 尤英】給某人特殊的禮遇

3 ▶OF A SUBJECT 有關某一主題◀ [C,U] a particular way of dealing with or talking about a subject〔針對某一主題的〕討論, 論述: *I didn't think the film gave the issue serious enough treatment.* 我認為這部電影對那個問題並沒有給予足夠嚴肅的闡述。

4 ▶CLEAN/PROTECT 清理/保護◀ [U] a process by which something is cleaned, protected etc 處理〔指清理、保護等的過程〕: *the treatment of waste oils and solvents* 對廢棄油料及溶劑的處理

treat·y /ˈtritɪ; ˈtriːti/ *n* **1** [C] a formal agreement between two or more countries or governments〔國家或政府間的〕條約: *the Treaty of Versailles* 凡爾賽條約 | **peace treaty** *A peace treaty was signed between the US and Vietnam.* 美國和越南簽訂了一項和平條約。**2** [U] *technical* formal agreement between two people, especially to buy a house【術語】〔尤指為了購房, 兩人之間簽訂的〕協議, 協定 W2

treb·le¹ /ˈtrɛbl̩; ˈtrebəl/ *predeterminer* three times as big, as much, or as many as something else 三倍的, 三重的: *They sold the house for treble the amount they paid for it.* 他們以購進價的三倍出售了這所房子。

treble² *v* [I,T] to become three times as big in amount, size, or number, or to make something increase in this way (使)成三倍: *Their profits have trebled in the last two years.* 他們的利潤在最近兩年裡增加了兩倍。

treble³ *n* **1** [U] the upper half of the whole range of musical notes〔音樂的〕最高音部 —compare 比較 BASS¹ (3) **2** [C] a boy with a high singing voice 能唱最高音部的男孩子 —**treble** *adj, adv*: *a clear treble voice* 嘹亮的高音

treble clef /ˌ·· ˈ·/ *n* [C] *technical* a sign (𝄞) at the beginning of a line of written music which shows that the note written on the bottom line of the STAVE[1] (1) is an E above MIDDLE C【術語】高音譜號 —see picture at 參見 MUSIC 圖

tree /tri; triː/ *n* [C] **1** a very tall plant that has a wooden trunk, branches, and leaves, and lives for many years 樹(木), 喬木: *We planted an orange tree in the backyard.* 我們在後院種了一棵柑橘樹。| *Children love to climb trees.* 小孩喜愛爬樹。**2** a drawing with many branching lines that shows how several things are related to each other 樹形圖; 家譜圖 —see also 另見 FAMILY TREE **3 be out of your tree** *informal* to not be thinking in a sensible or practical way【非正式】不理智的, 傻裡傻氣的 —see also 另見 CHRISTMAS TREE, **the top of the tree** (TOP[1] (3)), **it doesn't grow on trees** (GROW (9)), **be up a gum tree** (GUM TREE (2))

tree fern /ˈ· ·/ *n* [C] a large tropical FERN 桫欏〔一種高大的熱帶木本蕨類植物〕

tree·house /ˈtrihaus; ˈtriːhaʊs/ *n* [C] a wooden structure built in the branches of a tree for children to play in〔供孩童玩的〕樹上小屋

tree·less /ˈtriləs; ˈtriːləs/ *adj* a treeless area has no trees in it 無樹木的

tree line /ˈ· ·/ *n* [singular] the TIMBERLINE 林木線

tree-lined /ˈ· ·/ *adj* a tree-lined road has trees on both sides〔道路兩旁〕植有樹木的

tree sur·ge·ry /ˈ· ˌ···/ *n* [U] the treatment of damaged trees, especially by cutting off branches 樹木整形(術), 樹木修補(術)

tree·top /ˈtritɑp; ˈtriːtɒp/ *n* [C usually plural 一般用複數] the branches at the top of a tree 樹梢: *looking out over the treetops* 從樹梢上方望出去

tree-trunk /ˈ· ·/ *n* [C] the thick central part of a tree 樹幹

tre·foil /ˈtrifɔɪl; ˈtriːfɔɪl/ *n* [C] **1** a type of small plant that has leaves which divide into three parts 三葉植物 **2** a pattern in the shape of these leaves 三葉形

trek[1] /trɛk; trek/ *v* **trekked, trekking** [I always+adv/prep] to make a long and difficult journey, especially on foot 艱苦跋涉〔尤指徒步長途旅行〕: **[+in/across etc]** *trekking in the Himalayas* 在喜馬拉雅山地區的艱苦跋涉

trek[2] *n* [C] **1** a long and difficult journey especially on foot〔尤指徒步的〕長途艱苦旅行: *the long trek to the Pole* 前往極地的長途跋涉 **2** *informal* a distance that seems long when you walk it【非正式】〔顯得很漫長的〕一段路程: *I'm afraid it's a bit of a trek to the station.* 到車站怕有一大段路程吧。

trel·lis /ˈtrɛlɪs; ˈtrelɪ̇s/ *n* [C] a frame made of long narrow pieces of wood that cross each other, used to support climbing plants〔用以支撐攀緣植物的〕棚, 架

trem·ble /ˈtrɛmbḷ; ˈtrembəl/ *v* [I] **1** to shake slightly in a way that you cannot control, especially because you are upset or frightened〔尤指因難受或受到驚嚇而〕顫抖, 發抖, 戰慄: *His lip started to tremble and then he started to cry.* 他的嘴唇開始顫抖, 然後就哭了起來。| **tremble with anger/fear etc** *I stood there trembling with humiliation and rage.* 我站在那兒, 因屈辱和憤怒而發抖。**2** to shake slightly〔輕微地〕搖晃, 震顫: *The whole house trembled as the train went by.* 火車經過時, 整座屋子都在震顫。**3** if your voice trembles, it sounds nervous and unsteady〔說話聲〕緊張, 發抖 **4** to be worried or frightened about something 焦慮, 擔憂; 擔驚受怕: **I tremble to think what/how** *I tremble to think what will happen when she finds out.* 一想到她發現真相後會發生的事, 我就不寒而慄。—**tremble** *n* [C] —**trembly** *adj*

tre·men·dous /trɪˈmɛndəs; trɪˈmendəs/ *adj* **1** very big, fast, powerful etc 巨大的; 極快的; 強有力的: *a tremendous explosion* 猛烈的爆炸 | *I learned a tremendous amount in a short time.* 我在短時間內學到了大量東西。**2** excellent 極好的, 特棒的: *She's got a tremendous voice, hasn't she?* 她有一副絕好的嗓子, 不是嗎?

trem·o·lo /ˈtrɛməˌlo; ˈtreməlәʊ/ *n* [C] rapidly repeated musical notes〔音樂中的〕顫音, 震音

trem·or /ˈtrɛmɚ; ˈtremə/ *n* [C] **1** a small EARTHQUAKE in which the ground shakes slightly〔大地的〕輕微震動: *an earth tremor* 小地震 **2** a slight shaking movement that you cannot control, especially because you are ill, weak, or upset〔尤指因生病、虛弱或激動而不能控制的〕顫抖, 發抖: *He was left with a slight tremor in his hand after his stroke.* 中風之後, 他的手有點輕微的顫抖。

trem·u·lous /ˈtrɛmjələs; ˈtremjɪ̇ləs/ *adj literary* shaking slightly, especially because you are nervous【文】〔尤指因緊張而〕顫抖的, 微微發抖的: *a tremulous voice* 顫抖的嗓音 —**tremulously** *adv*

trench /trɛntʃ; trentʃ/ *n* [C] **1** a long narrow hole dug into the surface of the ground 壕溝; 溝渠: *Plant your roses in a trench filled with manure.* 把玫瑰種植在填滿肥料的溝裡。**2** a deep trench dug in the ground as a protection for soldiers 戰壕, 塹壕: *the trenches of World War I* 第一次世界大戰時的塹壕 **3** *technical* a long narrow valley in the ground beneath the sea【術語】海溝: *the Marianas Trench in the Pacific Ocean* 太平洋中的馬里亞納海溝

tren·chant /ˈtrɛntʃənt; ˈtrentʃənt/ *adj* expressed very strongly, effectively, and directly without worrying about offending people 尖銳的, 尖刻的, 直言不諱的: *a trenchant attack on the principle of 'political correctness'* 對"政治正確性"原則的尖銳抨擊 —**trenchantly** *adv* —**trenchancy** *n* [U]

trench coat /ˈ· ·/ *n* [C] a military style raincoat with a belt〔有腰帶的〕軍用雨衣

trench·er /ˈtrɛntʃɚ; ˈtrentʃə/ *n* [C] a wooden plate used in former times for serving food〔舊時用來盛食物的〕木盤

trench war·fare /ˌ· ˈ··/ *n* [U] a method of fighting in which soldiers from opposing armies are in TRENCHes facing each other 塹壕戰

trend /trɛnd; trend/ *n* [C] **1** a general tendency in the way a situation is changing or developing 趨勢, 趨向, 傾向, 動向: **[+in]** *recent trends in education* 教育的最新動向 | **[+towards]** *The current trend is towards more part-time employment.* 現行的趨勢是更多的人在兼職。| **reverse a trend** (=make a trend go in the opposite direction) 使趨勢逆轉, 扭轉趨勢 *These figures reverse the trend of spending increases.* 這些數字表示開支增加的趨勢得到了扭轉。| **underlying trend** (=the trend over a long period of time) 基本趨勢, 長期趨勢 **2 set the trend** to start doing something that other people copy 開創潮流: *'Rambo' set the trend for a whole wave of violent action movies.*《第一滴血》開創了暴力動作影片的新潮流。

trend·set·ter /ˈtrɛndˌsɛtɚ; ˈtrendˌsetə/ *n* [C] someone who starts a new fashion or makes it popular 開創新潮流的人; 開創新風的人 —**trendsetting** *adj*

trend·y[1] /ˈtrɛndɪ; ˈtrendi/ *adj* influenced by the most fashionable styles and ideas 時髦的; 受新潮思想影響的: *He's a trendy photographer in Santa Monica.* 他在聖莫尼卡工作, 是思想新潮的攝影師。—**trendily** *adv* —**trendiness** *n* [U]

trendy[2] *n* [C] *BrE informal* someone who is trendy because they want other people to think they are very modern【英, 非正式】時髦人物; 思想新潮的人: *young trendies with left-wing ideas* 有左翼思想的新潮年輕人

tre·pan /trɪˋpæn; trɪˈpæn/ *v* [T] to cut a round piece of bone out of your SKULL (=head) as part of a medical operation 在〔顱骨〕施行環鑽術〔即在顱骨上開圓形的洞, 是一種外科手術〕

trep·i·da·tion /ˌtrɛpəˈdeʃən; ˌtrepɪ̇ˈdeɪʃən/ *n* [U] a feeling of anxiety or fear about something that is going to happen 恐懼不安, 惴惴不安: *With some trepidation, I opened the door.* 我有些惴惴不安地打開了門。

tres·pass[1] /ˈtrɛspəs; ˈtrespəs/ *v* [I+on] **1** to go onto someone's private land without their permission 未經許

可進入私人宅地，擅自進入 **2** *old use* to do something wrong; SIN[2]【舊】做壞事 —**trespasser** *n* [C]

trespass on sth *phr v* [T] to unfairly use more than you should of someone else's time, help etc, for your own advantage 過多佔用〔別人的時間〕; 過多利用〔別人的幫助〕: *It would be trespassing on their hospitality to accept any more from them.* 要是再接受他們的款待，就太過意不去了。

trespass[2] *n* **1** [C,U] the offence of going onto someone's land without their permission 擅自進入私人宅地，非法進入: *prosecute him for trespass* 起訴他擅入禁地 **2** [C] *biblical* something you have done that is morally wrong; SIN【聖經】過錯，罪過

tress·es /ˋtrɛsɪz; ˈtresɨz/ *n* [plural] *literary* a woman's beautiful long hair【文】〔女人的〕漂亮長髮

tres·tle /ˋtrɛsl̩; ˈtresəl/ *n* [C] *especially BrE* an A-shaped frame used as one of the two supports for a temporary table【尤英】〔用來支撐臨時性桌面的〕支架，擱凳

trestle ta·ble /ˈ·· ˌ··/ *n* [C] *especially BrE* a temporary table made of a long board supported on trestles【尤英】〔臨時性的〕擱板桌

trews /truz; truːz/ *n* [plural] a pair of trousers, especially with a TARTAN pattern 褲子〔尤指有蘇格蘭格子花呢圖案的褲子〕

trey /tre; treɪ/ n [C] *AmE* a playing card or the side of a DICE with three marks on it【美】三點的紙牌;〔骰子〕刻有三點的一面: *I have two pairs, treys and sevens.* 我有兩對牌，一對三點和一對七點。

tri- /traɪ; traɪ/ *prefix* three; three times 表示"三"，"三次"，"三倍": *trilingual* (=speaking three languages) 説三門語言的 | *triangle* (=a shape with three sides) 三角形

tri·ad /ˋtraɪæd; ˈtraɪæd/ *n* [C] **1** [singular] a Chinese secret criminal group 三合會〔華人黑社會組織〕**2** a group of three people or things that are related or similar to each other 三人組合; 三種事物的組合

tri·al[1] /ˋtraɪəl; ˈtraɪəl/ *n*

1 ▶COURT 法庭◀ [C,U] a legal process in which a court of law examines a case to decide whether someone is guilty of a crime 審判，審理: *a murder trial* 一宗謀殺案的審判 | *The defendant has a right to a fair trial.* 被告有權利得到公正的審判。| **stand trial/be on trial (for)** (=be judged in a court of law) 接受審判/因…受到審判 *Brady was on trial for assault.* 布雷迪因襲擊他人而受到審判。| *a bank employee who is due to stand trial on embezzlement charges* 因被控侵吞公款而將受到審判的一名銀行職員 | **come to trial** *formal* (=when a case is brought to a court of law)【正式】提交法庭審判 *By the time the case comes to trial he will have spent a year behind bars.* 到這個案子提交法庭審判時，他已經在監獄裡過了一年。—see also 另見 SHOW TRIAL

2 ▶TEST 試驗◀ [C,U] **a)** a process of testing to find out whether something works effectively and is safe 試驗，試用: *a new drug that is undergoing clinical trials* 正在接受臨牀試驗的一種新藥 **b)** a short period during which you use something or employ someone to find out whether they are satisfactory for a particular purpose or job 試驗期，試用期: **take/have sth on trial** (=test something without having to buy it first) 把〔某物〕拿來試用 *Take the vacuum cleaner on trial for a week; if you don't like it you pay nothing.* 把那個真空吸塵器拿去試用一週; 你如果不滿意的話，不必付錢。| **trial period** *The security system will be reviewed after a three-month trial period.* 這套安全系統在經過三個月試用期後將進行復查。

3 by trial and error if you do something by trial and error, you test many different methods of doing something in order to find the best 反覆試驗〔以得出最佳效果〕: *You'll find out by trial and error which flowers grow best.* 你通過反覆試驗就會發現哪些花長得最好。

4 ▶WORRY/ANNOY 焦慮/厭煩◀ be a trial (to) to be very worrying or annoying to someone〔令某人〕焦慮[厭煩]: *My brothers and I were always a real trial to my parents.* 父母親總為我們幾個兄弟憂心。

5 trials and tribulations difficulties and troubles 艱難困苦: *After many trials and tribulations we reached our destination.* 歷經艱難困苦後我們終於到達了目的地。

6 ▶SPORTS 體育運動◀ trials [plural] *BrE* a sports competition that tests a player's ability【英】預賽，選拔賽

trial[2] *v* [T] to thoroughly test something to see if it works correctly or is effective〔全面徹底地〕測試，試驗，試用: *These techniques were trialled by teachers in 300 schools.* 教師們在 300 所學校裡試用過這些技巧。

trial run /ˌ·· ˈ·/ *n* [C] an occasion when you test a new method or system to see if it works well 試行; 試驗; 試車; 試航: *This year is something of a trial run for the new service.* 今年可以説是新的服務項目的試行年。

trials bike /ˈ·· ·/ *n* [C] *BrE* a type of MOTORCYCLE that you can ride on very rough ground【英】〔可以在非常崎嶇不平的路面上行駛的〕越野摩托車

tri·an·gle /ˋtraɪˌæŋgl̩; ˈtraɪæŋgəl/ *n* [C] **1** a flat shape with three straight sides and three angles 三角形 —see picture at 參見 SHAPE[1] 圖 **2** something that is shaped like a triangle 三角形物體: *a triangle of land* 一塊三角地 **3** a musical instrument made of metal bent in the shape of a triangle, that you hit to make a ringing sound 三角鐵〔一種打擊樂器〕**4** *AmE* a flat plastic object with three sides that has one angle of 90° and is used for drawing angles【美】〔直角〕三角板，三角尺; SET-SQUARE *BrE*【英】

tri·an·gu·lar /traɪˋæŋgjələ; traɪˈæŋgjɨlə/ *adj* **1** shaped like a triangle 三角形的 **2** involving three people or teams 三者之間的: *a triangular sporting competition* 一次由三方參加的體育比賽

tri·an·gu·la·tion /ˌtraɪæŋgjəˋleʃən; traɪˌæŋgjɨˈleɪʃən/ *n* [U] a method of finding your position by measuring the lines and angles of a triangle on a map 三角測量法

triangulation sta·tion /···ˈ·· ˌ··/ *n* [C] *formal* a TRIG POINT【正式】三角點〔在山頂上通常用石塊標誌的一個點，用以測定你在地圖上所處的位置〕

tri·ath·lon /traɪˋæθlən; traɪˈæθlən/ *n* [C] a sports competition in which competitors run, swim, and cycle long distances 三項全能運動〔賽跑、游泳、自行車〕

trib·al /ˋtraɪbl̩; ˈtraɪbəl/ *adj* connected with a tribe or tribes 部落的: *a tribal dance* 部落舞蹈 | *tribal warfare* 部落戰爭

trib·al·is·m /ˋtraɪbl̩ɪzm̩; ˈtraɪbəl-ɪzəm/ *n* [U] **1** the state of being organized into tribes 部落制度 **2** behaviour and attitudes that are based on strong loyalty to your tribe 部落意識[習性]

tribe /traɪb; traɪb/ *n* [C] **1** a social group consisting of people of the same race who have the same beliefs, customs, language etc, and usually live in one particular area ruled by a chief 部落，部落社會: *the tribes living in the Amazonian jungle* 生活在亞馬遜熱帶叢林裡的部落 —see 見 RACE[1] (USAGE) **2** a group of related animals or plants 族，羣〔動植物的一類〕: *the cat tribe* 貓族 **3** *humorous* a large family【幽默】大家庭: *We were only expecting Jack and his wife, but the whole tribe turned up.* 我們只想着傑克和他的妻子會來，但結果是全家大小都來了。

tribes·man /ˋtraɪbzmən; ˈtraɪbzmən/ *n* [C] a man who is a member of a tribe 部落男性成員

tribes·wom·an /ˋtraɪbzˌwumən; ˈtraɪbzˌwʊmən/ *n* [C] a woman who is a member of a tribe 部落女性成員

trib·u·la·tion /ˌtrɪbjəˋleʃən; ˌtrɪbjɨˈleɪʃən/ *n* [C,U] *formal* serious trouble or a serious problem【正式】苦難，艱難: *the tribulations of his personal life* 他個人生活中的種種艱辛 —see also 另見 **trials and tribulations** (TRIAL[1] (5))

tri·bu·nal /trɪˋbjunl̩; traɪˈbjuːnl/ *n* [C] a type of court that is given official authority to deal with a particular situation or problem 特別法庭; 審理委員會: *The case of your redundancy will be heard by an independent* *tribunal.* 一個獨立的審理委員會將處理有關你們裁員的案子。

trib·une /ˈtrɪbjun; ˈtrɪbjuːn/ *n* [C] an official in ancient Rome who was elected by the ordinary people to protect their rights〔古羅馬由普通人民選出的〕護民官, 保民官

trib·u·ta·ry¹ /ˈtrɪbjəˌtɛrɪ; ˈtrɪbjʊtəri/ *n* [C] a stream or river that flows into a larger river〔河流的〕支流

tributary² *adj formal* having a duty to pay TRIBUTE (3)【正式】需交納貢賦的

trib·ute /ˈtrɪbjut; ˈtrɪbjuːt/ *n* **1** something that you say, do, or give in order to express your respect or admiration for someone〔向某人表示敬慕而獻出的〕禮品, 贈品; 頌詞: **pay tribute to** (=praise and thank someone publicly) 公開讚揚和感謝 *I'd like to pay tribute to the party workers for all their hard work.* 我謹對黨內工作人員的辛苦工作表示讚揚和感謝。**2 be a tribute to** to be a clear sign of the good qualities that someone or something has〔某種優良品質的〕標示, 證明: *It was a tribute to her teaching methods that so many children passed the test.* 這麼多孩子通過了考試, 這就是對她的教學方法的一種證明。**3** [C,U] a payment of goods or money by one ruler or country to another more powerful one〔一國向強國交付的〕貢品, 貢賦, 貢金 **4 floral tribute** flowers sent to a funeral 敬獻給葬禮的鮮花

trice /traɪs; traɪs/ *n* **in a trice** *BrE literary* very quickly【英, 文】一剎那, 瞬間

tri·ceps /ˈtraɪsɛps; ˈtraɪseps/ *n* [C] the large muscle at the back of your upper arm〔手臂上的〕三頭肌

3 **trick¹** /trɪk; trɪk/ *n* [C]

1 ►DECEIVING SB 欺騙某人◄ something you do in order to deceive someone 騙局, 花招, 詭計: *He pretended to be ill, but it was just a trick.* 他假裝生病了, 不過那只是一個花招。| *a clever trick to cheat the authorities* 欺騙當局的詭計

2 dirty/rotten/mean trick an unkind or unfair thing to do 下流的/無恥的/卑鄙的詭計: *He didn't turn up? What a rotten trick!* 他沒有露面? 多麼無恥的詭計!

3 ►JOKE 玩笑◄ something you do to surprise someone and to make other people laugh 惡作劇: *I'm getting tired of your silly tricks.* 我對你那些愚蠢的惡作劇感到厭煩了。| **play a trick on sb** *The girls were always playing tricks on their teacher.* 這些女孩子總是捉弄她們的老師。

4 do the trick *spoken* if something does the trick it solves a problem or provides what is needed to get a good result【口】奏效, 達到預期效果: *A bit more flour should do the trick.* 再來一點麵粉應該就可以了。

5 ►CLEVER METHOD 巧妙辦法◄ a clever way of doing something that works very well 訣竅; 技巧, 技法: *The trick is to bend your knees as you catch the ball.* 訣竅是接球時要屈膝。| **tricks of the trade** (=clever methods used in a particular job) 某一行工作的訣竅 *a salesman who knew all the tricks of the trade* 一個對本行業訣竅全都通曉的推銷員

6 use every trick in the book to use every clever or dishonest method that you know to achieve what you want 使出各種絕招, 使出渾身解數: *Ed used every trick in the book to get that contract.* 埃德使出渾身解數得到了那份合同。

7 sb can teach/show you a trick or two *informal* used to say that someone knows a lot more than you【非正式】〔某人〕可以教你一兩招, 〔某人〕比你懂得多

8 be up to your (old) tricks *informal* to be doing the same dishonest things that you have often done before【非正式】耍 (老) 花招: *Watch out for Joe, he's up to his old tricks again.* 小心喬, 他又要耍老花招了。

9 ►MAGIC 魔術◄ a skilful set of actions that seem like magic, done to entertain people 戲法, 把戲: *We spent the next hour performing card tricks.* 我們在接下來的一個小時裡表演紙牌戲法。

10 a trick of the light a strange effect of the light that changes the way things look or makes you see something that is not really there 燈光引起的錯覺: *For a moment I thought you were Duncan, but it was just a trick of the light.* 有那麼一會兒, 我以為你就是鄧肯, 不過那只是燈光在捉弄人罷了。

11 ►CARDS 紙牌◄ the cards played or won in one part of a game of cards〔紙牌遊戲中出的或贏的〕一圈牌, 一墩牌: *He won the first three tricks easily.* 他輕鬆地贏了頭三圈牌。

12 ►HABIT 習慣◄ **have a trick of doing sth** to have a habit of using a particular expression or of moving your face or body in a particular way 有〔使用某句口頭禪或以特別的方式活動臉部或身體〕的習慣: *She had this trick of raising her eyebrows at the end of a question.* 她有一個習慣, 在提問結束時總要揚起眉頭。

13 never miss a trick *informal* to always know exactly what is happening even if it does not concern you【非正式】對所發生的事無所不曉; 了如指掌: *Dave's found out. He never misses a trick, does he?* 戴夫已經知道了。他從不漏過一點東西, 是嗎?

14 how's tricks? *spoken* used to greet someone in a friendly way【口】近來如何?〔寒暄語〕: *Hello Bill! How's tricks?* 你好, 比爾! 近來怎麼樣?

15 turn a trick *AmE slang* to have sex with someone for money【美俚】賣淫 —see also 另見 CONFIDENCE TRICK, HAT-TRICK

trick² *v* **1** [T] to deceive someone in order to get something from them or to make them do something 欺騙, 誘騙, 哄騙: *He knew he'd been tricked, but it was too late.* 他知道自己被騙了, 但為時已晚。| **trick sb into doing sth** *Clients were tricked into believing their money was being invested.* 客戶們被騙了, 以為他們的錢正用於投資。| **trick sb out of** *The corporation was tricked out of $20 million.* 那家公司被騙走了 2000 萬美元。**2 be tricked out with/in** *literary* to be decorated with something【文】裝飾, 打扮: *a hat tricked out with ribbons* 一頂用緞帶作裝飾的帽子

trick³ *adj* **1 trick photography** photography that cleverly changes the way things look 特技攝影 **2 trick question** a question which seems easy to answer but has a hidden difficulty 看似容易其實困難的問題 **3 trick knee/ankle etc** *AmE* a joint that is weak and can suddenly cause you problems【美】軟弱無力會突然撐不住的膝關節/腳踝骨等

trick·e·ry /ˈtrɪkərɪ; ˈtrɪkəri/ *n* [U] the use of tricks to deceive or cheat people 耍花招, 欺騙, 哄騙

trick·le¹ /ˈtrɪkl̩; ˈtrɪkəl/ *v* [I always+adv/prep] **1** if liquid trickles somewhere, it flows slowly in drops or in a thin stream 滴, 淌; 涓涓地慢流: **[+down/into/out]** *The tears trickled down her cheeks.* 淚水一滴一滴地從她面頰上流下。**2** if people, vehicles, goods etc trickle somewhere, they move there slowly in small groups or amounts〔人、車輛、貨物等〕緩慢而零星地移動: **[+in/into/away]** *The first few fans started to trickle into the stadium.* 最早到達的幾位球迷開始三三兩兩地走進體育場。

trickle² *n* [singular] **1** a thin slow flow of liquid 涓涓細流: *The water in the stream had been reduced to a trickle.* 溪流中的水已減少成涓涓細流了。**2** a movement of people, vehicles, goods etc into a place in very small numbers or amounts 小批的移動, 少量的移動: *Recent legislation has reduced immigration to a trickle.* 最近的立法已使移民減少到很小數量。

trickle charg·er /ˈ·· ˌ··/ *n* [C] a piece of equipment used to put electricity into a car BATTERY (1)〔汽車電池的〕點滴式充電器, 連續補充充電器

trickle-down ef·fect /ˌ·· ˈ· ˌ·/ *n* [singular] a belief that additional wealth gained by the richest people in society will have a good economic effect on the lives of everyone 滴入效應〔一種認為社會中最富有的一批人獲得的額外財富會對每一個人的生活產生良好經濟效應的理論〕

trick or treat /ˌ· · ˈ·/ *v* **go trick or treating** if children go trick or treating, they go from house to house on HALLOWE'EN saying 'trick or treat' in order to get small presents "不請吃就搗蛋"〔萬聖節前夕孩子們挨家逐戶索要小禮物時說的話〕

trick·ster /ˈtrɪkstɚ; ˈtrɪkstə/ *n* [C] someone who deceives or cheats people 騙子: **confidence trickster** *a slick, fast-talking confidence trickster* 一名花言巧語、口若懸河、欺詐錢財的騙子

trick·y /ˈtrɪkɪ; ˈtrɪki/ *adj* **1** a tricky job is difficult to do because it is complicated and needs great care 困難的; 複雜的; 需慎重對待的: *Finding the electrical fault was really tricky.* 查找電路故障真是複雜, 需要謹慎。**2** a tricky situation is difficult to deal with and is full of problems 難對付的, 棘手的; 問題很多的: *I find myself in a very tricky situation.* 我發覺自己處境十分難堪。**3** a tricky person is likely to deceive you; CRAFTY 狡猾的; 會耍花招的, 詭計多端的 —**trickiness** *n* [U] —**trickily** *adv*

tri·col·our *BrE*【英】, **tricolor** *AmE*【美】/ˈtraɪˌkʌlɚ; ˈtrɪkələ/ *n* [C] a flag with three equal bands of different colours, especially the national flags of France or Ireland 三色旗〔有三條寬度相等的色帶的旗, 尤指法國或愛爾蘭的國旗〕

tri·cy·cle /ˈtraɪsɪkl̩; ˈtraɪsɪkəl/ *n* [C] a bicycle with three wheels, especially for young children〔尤指幼兒騎的〕三輪自行車[腳踏車]

tri·dent /ˈtraɪdn̩t; ˈtraɪdənt/ *n* [C] **1** a weapon with three points that looks like a large fork 三叉戟〔一種武器〕**2 Trident** a type of NUCLEAR weapon sent from a SUBMARINE[1]〔由潛艇發射的一種核武器〕三叉戟導彈

tried¹ /traɪd; traɪd/ the past tense and past participle of TRY[1]

tried² *adj* **tried and tested/trusted** a tried and tested method has been used successfully many times 經實踐反覆證明的, 屢試不爽的: *tried and tested safety procedures* 經實踐反覆證明的安全守則 | *a tried and trusted formula* 一個屢試不爽的公式

tri·en·ni·al /traɪˈɛnɪəl; traɪˈeniəl/ *adj* happening every three years 三年一次的

tri·er /ˈtraɪɚ; ˈtraɪə/ *n* [C] *informal* someone who always makes a great effort, even if they do not often succeed【非正式】〔不計成敗〕盡心竭力[埋頭苦幹]的人

trif·fid /ˈtrɪfɪd; ˈtrɪfɪ̵d/ *n* [C] an imaginary plant that grows very large, moves about, and attacks people 巨型三裂植物〔想像中的一種植物, 能到處行走, 攻擊人類〕

tri·fle¹ /ˈtraɪfl̩; ˈtraɪfəl/ *n* **1 a trifle** *formal* slightly; rather【正式】有點兒, 稍稍: *You seem a trifle nervous.* 你似乎有點兒緊張。**2** [C] *old-fashioned* something unimportant or not valuable【過時】瑣碎事; 無價值的東西: *I don't know why you waste your money on such trifles.* 我不明白你為甚麼把錢浪費在這一類雞毛蒜皮的小事上。**3** [C, U] a cold sweet dish that consists of layers of cake, fruit, JELLY (1), CUSTARD (1), and cream 蛋糕甜食〔一種由蛋糕、水果、果凍、牛奶蛋糊、奶油等層層構成的冷甜食〕

trifle² *v*

trifle with sb/sth *phr v* [T] to treat someone or something without proper respect or seriousness 輕視, 小看, 隨便對待: *The boss is not a man to be trifled with.* 這位老闆不是一個可以小看的人。

tri·fling /ˈtraɪflɪŋ; ˈtraɪflɪŋ/ *adj* unimportant or of little value 不重要的, 微不足道的: *a trifling matter* 小事 | *a trifling sum* 一小筆錢

trig·ger¹ /ˈtrɪgɚ; ˈtrɪgə/ *n* [C] **1** the part of a gun that you press with your finger to fire it〔槍的〕扳機 | **pull/squeeze the trigger** *He aimed carefully and squeezed the trigger.* 他仔細地瞄準, 然後扣動了扳機。—see picture at 參見 GUN[1] 圖 **2 be the trigger (for)** to be the thing that quickly causes a serious problem 成為引發〔嚴重問題〕的因素: *Even a minor incident could be the trigger for renewed fighting.* 即便是一件小事, 也有可能成為重新開戰的導火線。

trigger² also 又作 **trigger off** *v* [T] to make something happen very quickly, especially a series of violent events 引發, 激發〔尤指一系列暴力事件〕: *The assassination triggered off a wave of rioting.* 這次暗殺事件引發了一輪暴亂。| **trigger a feeling/memory** (=make you suddenly feel or remember something) 使人突然覺得/突然記起 *The song triggered many happy memories.* 那首歌勾起許多幸福的回憶。

trigger-hap·py /ˈ‥ ˌ‥/ *adj informal* much too willing to shoot at people【非正式】隨便就開槍的: *He nearly got shot by some trigger-happy cop.* 他差點被某個亂開槍的警察射中。

trig·o·nom·e·try /ˌtrɪgəˈnɑmətrɪ; ˌtrɪgəˈnɒmɪ̵tri/ *n* [U] the part of mathematics that is concerned with the relationship between the angles and sides of TRIANGLES〔數學中的〕三角學 —**trigonometrical** /ˌtrɪgənəˈmɛtrɪkl̩; ˌtrɪgənəˈmetrɪkəl/ *adj*

trig point /ˈtrɪg ˌpɔɪnt; ˈtrɪg pɔɪnt/ *n* [C] *BrE* a point often marked by a stone block on top of a hill, used for measuring your position on a map【英】三角點〔在山頂上通常用石塊標誌的一個點, 用以測定你在地圖上所處的位置〕

trike /traɪk; traɪk/ *n* [C] *informal* a TRICYCLE【非正式】三輪自行車

tril·by /ˈtrɪlbɪ; ˈtrɪlbi/ *n* [C] *especially BrE* a man's soft FELT[2] hat【尤英】〔一種男人戴的〕軟氈帽

tri·lin·gual /traɪˈlɪŋgwəl; ˌtraɪˈlɪŋgwəl◂/ *adj* able to speak or use three languages 會三種語言的

trill¹ /trɪl; trɪl/ *v* [I,T] **1** to sing with repeated short high notes 用顫音唱; 發出顫音: *birds trilling in the trees* 在樹上囀鳴的鳥 **2** to say something in a pleasant high cheerful voice 以悅耳歡樂的高嗓音說話: *"Have a nice time, darling," she trilled.* "玩得開心點, 親愛的。"她歡快地高聲叫道。

trill² *n* [C] **1** *technical* a musical sound made by quickly going up and down several times between two notes a SEMITONE apart【術語】〔音樂的〕顫音 **2** a sound like this, especially one made by a bird〔尤指鳥的〕囀鳴聲, 啼囀聲 **3** *technical* a speech sound produced by quickly moving the end of your tongue against the top part of your mouth when you say 'r'【術語】〔發 r 音時發出的〕顫音

tril·lion /ˈtrɪljən; ˈtrɪljən/ *number, quantifier* **1** one million million; 1,000,000,000,000 一萬億 **2** also 又作 **trillions** *informal* a very large number of something【非正式】大量, 巨額

tri·lo·bite /ˈtraɪləˌbaɪt; ˈtraɪləbaɪt/ *n* [C] a small simple sea creature that lived millions of years ago and is now a FOSSIL (1) 三葉蟲〔一種生活於海洋的古生物〕

tril·o·gy /ˈtrɪlədʒɪ; ˈtrɪlədʒi/ *n* [C] a group of three connected plays, books, films etc about the same characters〔戲劇、圖書、電影等的〕三部曲: *the second part of a trilogy* 三部曲中的第二部

trim¹ /trɪm; trɪm/ **trimmed, trimming** *v* [T]

1 ▶**CUT** 剪◀ to make something look neater by cutting small pieces off it 修剪: *Your hair needs trimming.* 你的頭髮需要修剪了。| *Can you trim the hedge?* 你能修剪一下樹籬嗎?

2 ▶**REDUCE** 減少◀ to remove parts of a plan to reduce its cost 削減: *We need to trim the Defence budget by a further £500m.* 我們有必要把國防預算再削減五億英鎊。

3 ▶**DECORATE** 裝飾◀ [usually passive 一般用被動態] to decorate the edges of clothes by adding a piece of different material 裝飾, 點綴〔衣服的邊緣部分〕: **trim sth with** *a dress trimmed with lace* 飾有花邊的連衣裙

4 ▶**SAIL** 航行◀ to move the sails of a boat into a position that makes the boat go faster 調整船帆使航行加快

5 trim your sails *informal* to spend less money【非正式】減少開支

trim sth ↔ **off** *phr v* [T] to cut small pieces off something so that it looks neater 去掉〔細碎部分, 使之更整齊〕: *Trim off the ragged edges.* 剪去不整齊的邊緣。

trim² *adj* **1** thin, attractive, and healthy looking 修長的, 健康好看的: *I play tennis regularly to keep trim.* 我定期

打網球, 以保持體形。| *a trim figure* 勻稱的身材 **2** neat and well looked after 整齊的, 整潔的: *a trim suburban garden* 整潔的郊區花園

trim³ *n* **1** [singular] an act of cutting something to make it look neater 修剪: *My beard needs a trim.* 我的鬍子需要修剪了。**2 be in (good) trim** *informal* to be in good physical condition【非正式】處於良好狀態: *The team is in good trim for the match.* 球隊為這場比賽已做好了準備。**3** [singular, U] additional decoration on a car, piece of clothing etc〔汽車等的〕額外裝飾: *1983 Ford Escort, metallic black with white trim* 一輛配以白色飾邊的 1983 年產黑色福特"護駕者"車 **4** [U] the degree to which an aircraft is level in relation to the horizon 飛機相對於地平線的傾斜度

tri·ma·ran /ˌtraɪmə`ræn; ˈtraɪmərӕn/ *n* [C] a sailing boat that has three separate but connected parts that float on the water 三體帆船

tri·mes·ter /traɪ`mɛstɚ; trɪˈmestə/ *n* [C] **1** *AmE* one of three periods of equal length that the year is divided into in some schools【美】〔有些學校實行的一年三學期制的〕一學期; TERM[1] (9) *BrE*【英】**2** one of the three-month periods of a PREGNANCY 三月期〔懷孕的三個為期三個月的階段之一〕

trim·mer /`trɪmɚ; ˈtrɪmə/ *n* [C] a machine for cutting the edges of HEDGEs, LAWNs etc 修剪器; 剪草機

trim·mings /`trɪmɪŋz; ˈtrɪmɪŋz/ *n* [plural] **1** pieces of material used to decorate clothes〔衣服的〕裝飾品, 花飾: *the fur trimmings on a hat* 帽子上的毛皮裝飾品 **2** the small pieces that are left after you have cut something larger 剪下來的細小碎片: *hedge trimmings* 從樹籬上修剪下來的細枝碎葉 **3 all the trimmings** *BrE informal* all the other types of food that are traditionally served with the main dish of a meal【英, 非正式】〔主菜的〕全部配菜: *Christmas dinner with all the trimmings* 有各種配菜的聖誕晚餐

trin·i·ty /`trɪnətɪ; ˈtrɪnɪ̈ti/ *n* **1 the Trinity** the union of Father, Son, and Holy Spirit in one God according to the Christian religion〔基督教關於聖父、聖子、聖靈合一的〕三位一體 **2** [C] *literary* a group of three people or things【文】三人一組; 三件東西一組; 三合一

trin·ket /`trɪŋkɪt; ˈtrɪŋkɪ̈t/ *n* [C] a piece of jewellery or a small pretty object that is not worth much money 廉價珠寶; 小件飾物: *a shop selling little trinkets and souvenirs* 一家銷售小件飾物和紀念品的商店

tri·o /`trio; ˈtriːəʊ/ *n plural* **trios** [C] **1** a group of three people or three connected things 三人一組; 三件一套: [**+of**] *He was met by a trio of smiling executives.* 迎接他的是三位面帶笑容的主管。**2** a group of three singers or musicians who perform together 三重唱[奏]團 **3** a piece of music for three performers 三重唱(曲); 三重奏(曲) —compare 比較 DUET, QUARTET

S2 W2 **trip¹** /trɪp; trɪp/ *n* **1** [C] a journey to a place and back again〔往返〕旅行, 外出: *Did you have a good trip?* 你外出一趟還好嗎? | **make a trip** *I couldn't carry everything at once, so I had to make several trips.* 我不能一次就扛走所有的東西, 所以不得不來回跑幾趟。| **go on/take a trip** *We're thinking of taking a trip to the mountains.* 我們正在考慮去山裡旅行一趟。| **coach/boat trip** *a boat trip up the Thames* 沿泰晤士河而上的一次乘船旅行 | **business/school/skiing etc trip** *a business trip to Japan* 去日本出差 | **day trip** (=a pleasure trip done in one day) 一日遊 —see 見 TRAVEL (USAGE) **2** [C] *slang* the experiences someone has while their mind is affected by a drug such as LSD【俚】〔吸毒時經歷的〕幻覺: *a bad trip* 不舒服的一陣迷幻感覺 **3** [C] an act of falling as a result of hitting something with your foot 絆倒 **4** [singular] *AmE slang* a person or experience that is amusing and very different from normal【美俚】讓人開心的奇人; 奇妙有趣的體驗: *She's a real trip.* 她真是個妙人。—see also 另見 **ego trip** (EGO (2)), ROUND TRIP

trip² *v*

1 ►FALL 倒下◄ also 又作 **trip up** [I] to hit something with your foot while you are walking or running so that you fall or almost fall 絆倒: *I didn't push him, he tripped.* 我沒有推他, 他自己絆倒的。| [**+over**] *Pick up that box or someone will trip over it.* 把那個箱子撿起來, 不然會把人絆倒的。

2 ►MAKE SB FALL 使某人倒下◄ also 又作 **trip sb up** [T] to make someone fall by putting your foot in front of them when they are moving 把〔某人〕絆倒: *Baggio was clearly tripped inside the penalty area.* 巴治奧在禁區裡很明顯是被人絆倒的。

3 ►WALK/DANCE 走路/跳舞◄ [I always+adv/prep] *literary* to walk or run with quick light steps as if you are dancing【文】輕快地走; 小跑: **trip along/over/down etc** *a little girl tripping along the lane* 輕快地沿着小巷走的小姑娘

4 trip off the tongue to be easy to say or pronounce 很容易說出[發音]: *Monofluorophosphate! It doesn't exactly trip off the tongue, does it?* 單氟磷酸鹽! 不容易上口, 是嗎?

5 trip a switch/wire to accidentally make an electrical system operate by moving part of it〔偶然地〕觸動開關/線路: *Alarm bells were ringing so I must have tripped a switch on my way in.* 警鈴都響起來了, 所以一定是我在進來的時候不小心觸動了開關。

6 ►DRUG 毒品◄ also 又作 **trip out** [I] *slang* to experience the effects of an illegal drug such as LSD【俚】〔服用迷幻藥等後〕產生幻覺

7 trip the light fantastic *humorous* to dance【幽默】跳舞

trip up *phr v* **1** [T **trip** sb **up**] to trick someone into making a mistake 使〔某人〕犯錯誤: *The questions look simple, but they're designed to trip you up.* 這些問題看上去很簡單, 但它們的本意就是為了迷惑人。**2** [T **trip** sb **up**] to make someone fall by putting your foot in front of them when they are walking 使〔某人〕絆倒 **3** [I] to hit something with your foot while you are walking so that you fall 絆倒 **4** [I] to make a mistake 犯錯誤, 出差錯: [**+over**] *It's easy to trip up over some of the regulations.* 很容易在一些規定上出差錯。

tri·par·tite /traɪ`partaɪt; traɪˈpɑːtaɪt/ *adj formal*【正式】**1 tripartite agreement/alliance etc** involving three groups or nations 三方之間的協定/聯盟等 **2** having three parts 由三部分組成的: *a tripartite structure* 由三部分組成的結構

tripe /traɪp; traɪp/ *n* [U] **1** the stomach of a cow or pig used for food〔供食用的〕牛肚; 豬肚 **2** *informal* something that has been said or written which is stupid or untrue【非正式】瞎說[瞎寫]的東西; 廢話, 蠢話: *Why do you read such tripe?* 你為甚麼看這種蹩腳的東西?

trip·le¹ /`trɪpl; ˈtrɪpəl/ *adj* [only before noun 僅用於名詞前] **1** having three parts or involving three members 有三部分的, 有三個成員的: *a triple alliance* 三方同盟 **2 triple circle/line/coil etc** a set of three circles etc 三重圓/線/圈等 **3 triple murder/killing etc** the murder etc of three people 三重謀殺/殺害

triple² *v* [I,T] to become three times as much or as many, or to make something do this (使)成為三倍, 增加兩倍: *The company has tripled in size in the last twenty years.* 在最近二十年裡, 該公司在規模上已擴大了兩倍。| **triple sth** *We should triple our profits next year.* 我們明年應該使利潤增長兩倍。

triple³ *n* [C] a hit of the ball in BASEBALL that allows the BATTER[2] (3) to get to the third BASE[2] (8)〔棒球中的〕三壘打

triple jump /ˈ·· ·/ *n* [singular] an ATHLETICS event in which you try to jump as far as you can by jumping with one foot, then onto the other foot, and finally with both feet 三級跳遠

trip·let /`trɪplɪt; ˈtrɪplɪ̈t/ *n* [C] one of three children born at the same time to the same mother 三胞胎中的一個 —compare 比較 COUPLET

trip·lex /`trɪplɛks; ˈtrɪpleks/ *n* [C] *AmE* an apartment which has rooms on three floors of a building【美】三層一套的公寓房

Triplex *n* [U] *BrE trademark* a special type of safety glass used in car windows【英, 商標】〔汽車窗戶上的〕三層安全玻璃, 夾層玻璃

trip·li·cate /ˋtrɪplə͵ket; ˈtrɪplɨkɨt/ *n* **in triplicate** if a document is written in triplicate, there are three copies of it〔文件的〕一式三份

tri·pod /ˋtraɪpɑd; ˈtraɪpɒd/ *n* [C] a support with three legs, used for a camera, TELESCOPE[1] etc〔照相機、望遠鏡等的〕三腳架 —see picture at 參見 LABORATORY 圖

trip·per /ˋtrɪpɚ; ˈtrɪpə/ *n* [C] *BrE old-fashioned* someone visiting a place on a short pleasure trip for one day【英, 過時】〔一日遊的〕遊客: **day tripper** *The beach was crowded with day trippers.* 沙灘上擠滿了一日遊的遊客。

trip·tych /ˋtrɪptɪk; ˈtrɪptɪk/ *n* [C] *technical* a picture, especially a religious one, painted on three pieces of wood that are joined together【術語】三聯畫〔在三塊相連的木板上的繪畫, 尤指宗教題材繪畫〕

trip·wire /ˋtrɪp͵waɪr; ˈtrɪp͵waɪə/ *n* [C] a wire stretched across the ground as part of a trap〔陷阱在地面上繃緊的〕絆腳線, 觸發線

tri·reme /ˋtraɪrim; ˈtraɪriːm/ *n* [C] an ancient warship with three rows of OARs on each side〔古代的〕三列划槳戰船

tri·sect /traɪˋsɛkt; traɪˈsekt/ *v* [T] *technical* to divide a line, angle etc into three equal parts【術語】把〔線、角等〕分成三等份

tri·state /ˋtraɪstet; ˈtraɪsteɪt/ *adj AmE* related to a group of three states in the US【美】三個州的, 三州之間的

trite /traɪt; traɪt/ *adj* a trite remark, idea etc has been used so often that it seems boring and not sincere〔話〕老一套的;〔思想〕陳腐的: *a dull speech full of trite clichés* 充滿陳詞濫調的枯燥演講 —**triteness** *n* [U]

tri·umph¹ /ˋtraɪəmf; ˈtraɪəmf/ *n* **1** [C] an important victory or success, especially after a difficult struggle〔尤指艱苦戰鬥後獲得的〕勝利, 成功: *Winning the championship represents a personal triumph for the team's manager.* 贏得冠軍標誌着該隊領隊的成功。| **[+over]** *a brave man's triumph over adversity* 一位勇者戰勝逆境 **2** a feeling of pleasure and satisfaction that you get from victory or success 勝利[成功]的喜悅: *yells of triumph* 勝利的歡呼 **3** [C] a very successful example of something 傑出的模範, 榜樣: *The gallery is a triumph of design.* 這個畫廊是卓越設計的典範。

triumph² *v* [I] to gain a victory or success, especially after a difficult struggle 戰勝, 獲勝: **[+over]** *We know that in the end we shall triumph over evil.* 我們知道, 我們最終將戰勝邪惡。

tri·um·phal /traɪˋʌmfl; traɪˈʌmfəl/ *adj* [only before noun 僅用於名詞前] done or made in order to celebrate a triumph 為慶祝勝利而進行的[製作的]: *a triumphal procession* 慶祝勝利的遊行 | *a triumphal arch* 一座凱旋門

tri·um·phal·is·m /traɪˋʌmflɪzəm; traɪˈʌmfəlɪzəm/ *n* [U] the expression of being too proud about a victory and too pleased about your opponent's defeat〔因勝利而〕耀武揚威; 趾高氣揚

tri·um·phant /traɪˋʌmfənt; traɪˈʌmfənt/ *adj* **1** having gained a victory or success 勝利的, 成功的: *the triumphant army* 得勝的軍隊 **2** expressing pleasure and pride because of your victory or success〔因勝利或成功而〕洋洋得意的; 耀武揚威的 —**triumphantly** *adv*: *"I've done it!" he shouted triumphantly.* "我成功了!" 他得意洋洋地喊道。

tri·um·vir·ate /traɪˋʌmvərɪt; traɪˈʌmvɨrɨt/ *n* [C] *formal* a group of three very powerful people who share control over something【正式】三頭政治, 三雄執政

triv·et /ˋtrɪvɪt; ˈtrɪvɨt/ *n* [C] **1** a metal support, placed under a hot pot or dish to protect the surface of a table〔桌面上放置滾燙菜鍋或菜盤的〕金屬柗架 **2** a support for holding a pot over a fire〔放在火上支撐炊具的〕三腳架

triv·i·a /ˋtrɪvɪə; ˈtrɪviə/ *n* [plural] **1** unimportant or useless details 瑣事; 微不足道的細節: *I'm not going to waste my time on such trivia.* 我不打算把時間浪費在這一類瑣事上。**2** detailed facts about past events, famous people, sport etc used in QUIZ games〔問答遊戲中有關歷史事件、名人或體育運動等的〕詳細知識, 細節

triv·i·al /ˋtrɪvɪəl; ˈtrɪviəl/ *adj* **1** unimportant or of little value 微不足道的, 沒有甚麼價值的: *I'm sorry to bother you with what must seem a trivial problem.* 用一個似乎微不足道的問題打擾您, 我感到抱歉。| *a trivial sum* 很小的一筆錢 **2** ordinary 普通的, 平常的: *trivial everyday duties* 普通的日常事務 —**trivially** *adv*

triv·i·al·i·ty /͵trɪvɪˋælətɪ; ͵trɪviˈælɨti/ *n* **1** [U] the fact of being not at all important or serious 瑣碎; 平凡 **2** [C] something that is very unimportant 瑣事: *Don't waste your time on trivialities.* 別把時間浪費在雞毛蒜皮的小事上。

triv·i·al·ize also 又作 **-ise** *BrE*【英】/ˋtrɪvɪəl͵aɪz; ˈtrɪviəlaɪz/ *v* [T] to make an important subject seem less important than it really is 使顯得瑣碎[平凡]: *The article trivializes the whole issue of equal rights.* 這篇文章使整個有關平等權利的問題顯得瑣碎無聊。—**trivialization** /͵trɪvɪəlaɪˋzeʃən; ͵trɪviəlaɪˈzeɪʃən/ *n* [U]

Trivial Pur·suit /͵··· ·ˋ·/ *n* [U] *trademark* a game in which people have to answer questions about many different subjects【商標】難題答問棋賽〔一種參與者必須回答許多不同題材問題的遊戲〕

tro·chee /ˋtroki; ˈtrəʊkiː/ *n* [C] *technical* a unit in poetry consisting of one strong or long beat followed by one weak or short beat, as in 'father'【術語】〔英語詩歌的〕揚抑格, 長短格

trod /trɑd; trɒd/ the past tense of TREAD[1]

trod·den /ˋtrɑdn̩; ˈtrɒdn/ the past participle of TREAD[1]

trog·lo·dyte /ˋtrɑglə͵daɪt; ˈtrɒglədaɪt/ *n* [C] someone living in a CAVE[1], especially in very ancient times〔尤指遠古時代的〕穴居人

troi·ka /ˋtrɔɪkə; ˈtrɔɪkə/ *n* [C] **1** a Russian carriage pulled by three horses side by side〔俄羅斯的〕三駕馬車 **2** a group of three people working together, especially in government〔尤指政府中的〕三人組, 三頭政治

Tro·jan /ˋtrodʒən; ˈtrəʊdʒən/ *n* **work like a Trojan** to work very hard 非常勤奮地工作

troll /trol; trəʊl/ *n* [C] an imaginary creature in ancient Scandinavian stories, like a very large or very small ugly person〔古代斯堪的納維亞傳說中的〕山精; 巨人; 侏儒

trol·ley /ˋtrɑlɪ; ˈtrɒli/ *n* [C] **1** *especially BrE* a large metal basket or frame on wheels that you push along, used for carrying bags, shopping etc【尤英】購物手推車; CART[1] (2) *AmE*【美】: *a supermarket trolley* 超級市場的購物手推車 **2** *BrE* a small table on very small wheels from which food and drinks are served【英】〔送食品飲料的〕手推車; CART[1] (3) *AmE*【美】: *a tea trolley* 茶具車 **3** *AmE* an electric vehicle for carrying passengers which moves along the street on metal tracks【美】有軌電車; TRAM *BrE*【英】**4** a TROLLEYBUS 無軌電車 **5** the part of an electric vehicle that connects it to the electric wires above〔電車與其上方電線相連接的〕觸輪 **6 be off your trolley** *BrE humorous* to be crazy【英, 幽默】瘋瘋癲癲, 失去理智

trol·ley·bus /ˋtrɑlɪ͵bʌs; ˈtrɒlibʌs/ *n* [C] a bus that gets its power from electric wires above the street 電車, 無軌電車

trol·lop /ˋtrɑləp; ˈtrɒləp/ *n* [C] **1** *old-fashioned* an offensive word for a very untidy woman【過時】邋遢女人〔冒犯用語〕**2** an offensive word for a sexually immoral woman 行為不檢的女人, 蕩婦

trom·bone /trɑmˋbon; trɒmˈbəʊn/ *n* [C] a large musical instrument made of metal which you blow into and which has a long tube that you slide in and out to change the notes 長號, 伸縮喇叭〔一種樂器〕

trom·bon·ist /trɑmˋbonɪst; trɒmˈbəʊnɨst/ *n* [C] a musician who plays a trombone 長號手, 長號演奏者

3 2

troop¹ /trup; tru:p/ *n* **1 troops** [plural] soldiers, especially in organized groups 部隊; 軍人: *Troops were sent in to stop the riots.* 派部隊進來制止暴亂。**2 troop movements/concentrations** movements or gatherings of troops 部隊調動/集結 **3** [C] a group of soldiers, especially on horses or in tanks (TANK¹ (3))〔一支部隊, 尤指〕騎兵連; 裝甲連 **4** [C] a group of people or wild animals, especially when they are moving〔尤指行進中的〕一羣人; 一羣動物 **5** [C] a group of about 32 SCOUTs led by an adult〔由成人帶領 32 人一隊的〕童子軍中隊 —compare 比較 TROUPE

troop² *v* [I always+adv/prep] to move together in a group 成羣結隊地移動: **[+into/along/out etc]** *We all trooped into the meeting.* 我們全都一起走進會場。

troop car·ri·er /ˈ· ˌ···/ *n* [C] a ship, aircraft, or vehicle used for carrying soldiers 運兵船;〔運送軍人的〕運輸機; 運兵車

troop·er /ˈtrupə; ˈtru:pə/ *n* **1** [C] the lowest ranking soldier in the part of the army that uses tanks (TANK¹ (3)) or horses〔軍階最低的〕裝甲兵; 騎兵 **2 swear like a trooper** to swear a lot 滿口粗話 **3** [C] a member of a state police force in the US〔美國的〕州警察

troop·ship /ˈtrupˌʃɪp; ˈtru:pˌʃɪp/ *n* [C] a ship used for carrying a large number of soldiers 部隊運輸船, 運兵船

trope /trop; trəʊp/ *n* [C] *technical* a FIGURE OF SPEECH【術語】比喻

tro·phy /ˈtrofɪ; ˈtrəʊfi/ *n* [C] **1** a prize for winning a race or other competition, especially a silver cup or a PLAQUE (2)〔比賽等贏得的〕獎杯, 獎牌: *the Football League Trophy* 足球聯賽獎杯 **2** something that you keep to show something successful that you have done, especially in war or hunting〔尤指戰爭或狩獵中的〕戰利品; 獵獲物; 勝利紀念品: *A lion's head was among the trophies of his African trip.* 在他的非洲之行的戰利品中有一個獅子頭。

T

trop·ic /ˈtrɑpɪk; ˈtrɒpɪk/ *n* **1** [C] one of the two imaginary lines around the world, either the Tropic of Cancer which is 23 ½° north of the EQUATOR, or the Tropic of Capricorn which is 23 ½° south of the EQUATOR〔赤道以北或以南的〕回歸線 —see picture at 參見 EARTH¹ 圖 **2 the tropics** the hottest part of the world, which is between the two tropics 熱帶

trop·i·cal /ˈtrɑpɪkl̩; ˈtrɒpɪkəl/ *adj* **1** coming from or existing in the hottest parts of the world 熱帶的: *the tropical rain forests* 熱帶雨林 | **tropical medicine** (=study of diseases that are common in hot countries) 熱帶醫學 **2** weather that is tropical is very hot and wet〔天氣〕濕熱的: *a steamy tropical night* 一個悶熱潮濕的夜晚

trot¹ /trɑt; trɒt/ *v* **trotted, trotting 1** [I] if a horse trots, it moves fairly quickly with each front leg moving at the same time as the opposite back leg〔馬〕小跑 **2** [I always+adv/prep] **a)** to run fairly slowly, taking short steps 小跑, 慢跑: *William trotted along happily beside his parents.* 威廉在父母旁邊高興地一路小跑。**b)** *spoken* to walk or go somewhere【口】走, 去〔某地〕: *I'm just trotting down to the shops.* 我正要去商店。

trot sth ↔ **out** *phr v* [T] *informal* to give opinions, excuses, reasons etc that you have used too often to seem sincere【非正式】重複說〔老一套的東西〕: *Steve trotted out the same old excuses.* 斯蒂夫重複的又是老一套藉口。

trot² *n* **1** [singular] the movement of a horse at trotting (TROT¹) speed〔馬的〕小跑: *We set off at a brisk trot.* 我們以輕快的步伐出發了。**2** [C] a ride on a horse at trotting (TROT¹) speed 騎馬小跑: *I'm going for a trot down the lane.* 我要沿着小路騎馬慢跑。**3** [singular] a fairly slow way of running in which you take short steps 慢跑, 快步: **break into a trot** (=increase your speed to a trot) 開始小跑 **4 on the trot** *BrE informal*【英, 非正式】**a)** one after the other 一個接一個地: *Sally's won three races on the trot.* 莎莉連續贏了三項比賽。**b)** busy doing something 馬不停蹄地忙於某事: *I've been on the trot all day.* 我整天都在馬不停蹄地忙着。**5** [C] *AmE* a book of translations or answers used by students; a CRIB¹ (4b)【美】〔學生用來作弊的〕譯本; 答案 **6 the trots** *humorous* DIARRHOEA【幽默】腹瀉, 跑肚

troth /trɔθ; trəʊθ/ *n old use*【舊】**1 by my troth** used when expressing an opinion strongly 請相信我; 我保證; 我發誓〔用以表示強烈的意見〕**2 in troth** truly; INDEED 真的, 的確 —see also 另見 **plight your troth** (PLIGHT²)

Trot·sky·ite /ˈtrɑtskɪˌaɪt; ˈtrɒtskiaɪt/ also 又作 **Trot·sky·ist** /-skɪɪst; -skiɨst/ *n* [C] someone who believes in the political ideas of Leon Trotsky, especially that the working class should take control of the state 托洛茨基主義者, 托派分子 —**Trotskyite** *adj*

trot·ter /ˈtrɑtə; ˈtrɒtə/ *n* [C] a pig's foot, cooked and used as food〔用作食物的〕豬蹄

trou·ba·dour /ˈtrubəˌdur; ˈtru:bədɔ:/ *n* [C] a type of singer and poet who travelled around the PALACEs and castles of Southern Europe in the 12th and 13th centuries〔12, 13 世紀周遊於南歐一帶宮殿和城堡的〕行吟詩人

troub·le¹ /ˈtrʌbl̩; ˈtrʌbəl/ *n*

1 ►PROBLEMS 問題◄ [C,U] problems that make something difficult, spoil your plans, make you worry etc 麻煩; 煩擾; 憂慮: *Every time there's trouble, I have to go along and sort it out.* 每次有麻煩時, 我都得堅持下去, 把問題化解掉。| **[+with]** *They're having a lot of trouble with the new baby.* 新生的嬰兒給他們添了許多麻煩。| **trouble doing sth** *I never have any trouble getting to sleep.* 我從來不會失眠。| **what's the trouble?** *spoken* (=used to ask someone what is causing a particular problem)【口】出甚麼麻煩了? 怎麼了? | **the trouble is** *spoken* (=used when explaining why something is impossible or difficult)【口】麻煩是, 問題是 *I'd like to give you the money now – the trouble is, I don't get paid till Friday.* 我倒想現在就把錢給你, 但麻煩的是, 我要到星期五才發薪。| **sb's troubles** (=all the problems that you have in your life) 生活中的種種問題 *Because I'm a good listener people often come to me with their troubles.* 人們有麻煩就往往來找我, 因為我善於傾聽。| **teething troubles** (=small problems at the beginning) 初始階段遇到的小問題 *After a few teething troubles, the new system worked perfectly.* 這套新系統在開始階段出了幾個小問題, 後來就運轉得非常好。

2 ►FAULT 過錯◄ the trouble with *spoken* used when explaining what is unsatisfactory about something or someone【口】過錯, 不足, 缺點: *The trouble with you is that you don't listen.* 你的缺點是不好好聽講。| *That's the trouble with lasagne – it takes so long to make.* 那便是鹵汁寬麵條的麻煩之處 — 需要花太長的時間來做。

3 ►HEALTH 健康◄ [U] a problem that you have with your health 毛病: **[+with]** *He sometimes has trouble with his breathing.* 他有時候呼吸系統有毛病。| **heart/stomach/skin etc trouble** *Irene's at home today with stomach trouble.* 艾琳今天因犯胃病待在家裡了。

4 ►MACHINE/SYSTEM 機器/系統◄ [U] something that is wrong with a machine, vehicle, or system〔機器、車輛等的〕故障, 毛病: *engine trouble* 發動機故障 | **[+with]** *trouble with the central heating system* 中央供暖系統的毛病

5 ►BAD SITUATION 惡劣處境◄ [U] a difficult or dangerous situation 困境, 險境: **be in trouble** *an SOS from a ship in trouble* 一艘遇險輪船發出的求救信號 | **get/run into trouble** *The company ran into trouble when it tried to expand too quickly.* 這家公司擴展業務的步伐太快, 陷入了困境。| **in serious/deep/big trouble** *If you connect the wrong wires to the power supply, you'll be in deep trouble.* 如果你把線接錯了電源, 你會惹出大麻煩的。

6 be asking for trouble *informal* to take risks or do something stupid that is likely to cause problems【非正式】自尋麻煩, 自討苦吃: *You're just asking for trouble if you don't get those brakes fixed.* 你如果不把那些煞車修好, 你簡直就是在自討苦吃。

7 ►EFFORT 努力◄ [U] an amount of effort and time that is needed to do something, especially when it is inconvenient for you to do it 麻煩, 費事; 不方便: **put sb**

to a lot of trouble (=make someone use a lot of time and effort) 給某人添了很多麻煩 *I'm sorry, I didn't mean to put you to so much trouble.* 對不起, 我並不是有意要給你添這麼多的麻煩。| **take the trouble to do sth** (=make a special effort to do something) 費[盡]力地做某事 *The teacher took the trouble to learn all our names on the first day.* 第一天老師就努力地記住我們所有人的名字。| **go to/take a lot of trouble** (=use a lot of time and effort doing something carefully) 不厭其煩地〔做某事〕| **save sb the trouble (of doing sth)** (=make it unnecessary for sb to do sth) 為某人省去了(做某事)的麻煩 *I thought if I phoned you, it would save you the trouble of writing a letter.* 我當時想, 如果我給你打電話, 就不用麻煩你寫信了。| **be more trouble than it's worth** *spoken* (=when something takes too much time and effort to do)【口】太花時間, 太費事 *I find that making my own clothes is more trouble than it's worth.* 我覺得自己做衣服廢時失事。

8 no trouble/it's no trouble *spoken* used to say that you are very willing to do something because it is not inconvenient for you【口】一點也不麻煩

9 be no trouble *informal* if someone is no trouble, they do not annoy or worry you【非正式】〔某人〕不會添麻煩: *You can leave the children with me. They're no trouble.* 你可以把孩子們留給我照管。他們不會給我添麻煩的。

10 ▶ARGUMENT/VIOLENCE 爭論/暴力◀ also 又作 **troubles** [plural] a situation in which people quarrel or fight with each other 糾紛; 騷亂, 動亂: *The trouble started when the police tried to break up the demonstration.* 警察試圖驅散這次遊行示威, 結果騷亂爆發了。| *the recent troubles in Northern Ireland* 最近發生在北愛爾蘭的騷亂 | **cause/make trouble** (=deliberately cause trouble) 惹麻煩/闖禍 *Don't give him another drink or he'll start causing trouble.* 別讓他再喝了, 不然他會開始惹出麻煩來的。

11 ▶BLAME 責怪◀ [U] a situation in which someone in authority is angry with you or is likely to punish you 惹出麻煩的處境: *There'll be trouble when your father finds out what you've done.* 要讓你父親發現你幹了甚麼, 麻煩就來了。| **be in trouble (with)** *My brother's in trouble with the police again.* 我弟弟又惹上警察的麻煩了。| **get into trouble** *Don't copy my work or we'll both get into trouble.* 不要抄我的作業, 不然我們兩人都會有麻煩的。

12 get sb into trouble a) to put someone into a situation in which they are likely to be punished 給某人惹來麻煩: *Diane told a lie rather than get her friend into trouble.* 為了保護朋友, 黛安娜說了謊話。**b)** *old-fashioned* to make a woman PREGNANT【過時】使女人懷孕

Frequencies of the noun **trouble** in spoken and written English 名詞 trouble 在英語口語和書面語中的使用頻率

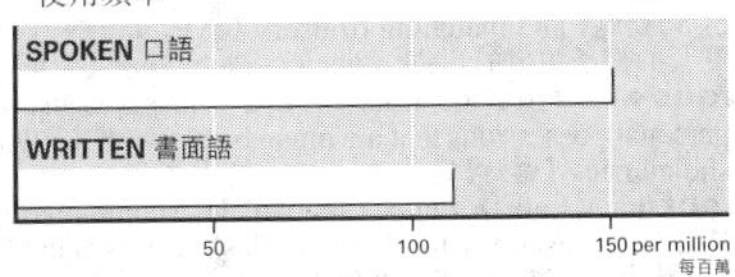

Based on the British National Corpus and the Longman Lancaster Corpus
據英國國家語料庫和朗文蘭卡斯特語料庫

This graph shows that the noun **trouble** is more common in spoken English than in written English. This is because it is used in some common spoken phrases. These are marked '*spoken*' in the entry. 本圖表顯示, 名詞 trouble 在英語口語中的使用頻率遠遠高於書面語, 這是因為該詞用於一些常用的口語片語中。在詞條裡, 這些片語用"【口】"標示。

USAGE NOTE 用法說明: TROUBLE

WORD CHOICE 詞語辨析: **trouble** (*n,v*), **problem**, **troubles**, **troubled**, **worried**, **bother**

Trouble [usually U] is usually used to talk about the worry etc that people have in some situations (especially when there is some specific difficulty). trouble〔一般作不可數名詞〕通常用來指人們在某些情況下〔尤指在有某種具體困難時〕產生的憂慮、擔心等: *Her back is giving her a lot of trouble* (=pain). 她的背給她帶來不少痛苦。| *Do you have much trouble with the kids?* (=*do they behave badly?*) 孩子們給你惹了很多麻煩嗎? | *Thanks for your trouble* (=effort). 你辛苦了。

When you speak of a **problem** [C], you are thinking more of a person, thing, or situation that is difficult (either for things or people). problem〔可數名詞〕指造成困難的人、事或情況: *Acid rain is an increasing environmental problem.* 酸雨是一個日趨嚴重的環境問題。| *my biggest problem* (NOT 不是 *my best trouble*) 我最大的問題

In many situations a **problem** is a source of **trouble**, so there are some contexts where both words may be used. 在許多情況下 problem (問題) 就是 trouble (麻煩) 的根源。所以這兩個詞有時可以互換: *What's the trouble/problem?* 怎麼了? | *I had a bit of trouble/a bit of a problem.* 我有了一點麻煩。| *the trouble/problem with my car* 我車子的麻煩 However sometimes there is a clear difference in meaning. 然而, 有時候兩者在意思上有着明顯的差別: *There's trouble in the bar* (perhaps means people are fighting). 酒吧裡有麻煩了〔也許意味着有人在毆鬥〕。But *There's a problem in the bar* (perhaps means there is no beer left). 酒吧裡出了點問題〔也許意味着沒有啤酒了〕。

In some contexts only **problem** can be used. You can *solve* problems but not trouble(s). Something may *pose* a problem but not trouble. In spoken English **trouble** is frequent only in certain phrases. 有時只能用 problem。可以用 solve problems (解決問題), 但不能用 solve trouble(s); 某事可能 pose a problem (引起問題), 但不能 pose trouble(s)。在英語口語中 trouble 僅僅常用於某些短語中: *The (only) trouble is/was...* (唯一的) 麻煩是... | *This/that is/was the trouble.* 這/那正是麻煩所在。| *...Just don't cause any trouble...* 只要不惹任何麻煩... | *...have (no) trouble with...* 有[沒有]...的麻煩 | *be in (real/a lot of) trouble* 陷入(真正的/大量的) 麻煩中 | *...get into trouble...* ...陷入麻煩...

Problem is more common in technical or formal contexts, **trouble** in informal or conversational ones. problem 在術語或正式語境中用得較為普遍, 而 trouble 則較多地用於非正式或對話語境中: *the nuclear problem* 核問題 | *the problem with BCCI is more common* 國際商業信貸銀行的問題更為普遍。But you are more likely to say 不過更有可能說: *tummy trouble* 肚子痛 | *The trouble with Paul is that he has no sense of humour.* 保羅的問題在於他沒有幽默感。

Troubles (plural) is used with a much more specific meaning either for all the things that worry a person, or all the difficulties of an organization or country. troubles〔複數〕可用來更具體地指某人所焦慮的一切事情或某一組織或國家的所有困難: *money troubles* 經濟困難 | *the troubles besetting the government* 困擾政府的麻煩 | *the troubles in Northern Ireland* 北愛爾蘭的麻煩 But you would say 但人們會說: *world/traffic problems* (NOT 不用 *troubles*) 世界/交通問題

Trouble (*v*) and **troubled** (*adj*) are not very common in ordinary spoken English. trouble〔動詞〕

T

和 troubled〔形容詞〕在普通的口頭英語中用得並不很普遍: *I was worried about my work* (in writing you might perhaps use *troubled*). 我很擔心我的工作〔寫作時也許會用 troubled 代替 worried〕。| *Don't bother me while I'm watching TV.* 我看電視時不要煩我。| *My car had a problem* (NOT 不用 *was troubled*). 我的車子出了點問題。

GRAMMAR 語法

Usually someone *has trouble* (NOT *troubles*) doing something (NOT *has trouble to do it*). 一般用 has trouble〔不用 troubles〕doing something〔不用 has trouble to do it〕。

You may be *in trouble* (NOT *in a trouble/troubles*). 可以用 in trouble〔不用 in a trouble/troubles〕。

trouble² *v* **1** [T] if a problem troubles you, it makes you feel worried 使憂慮, 使苦惱: *You must talk to your daughter and find out what's troubling her.* 你必須跟女兒談談, 弄清楚甚麼事在讓她苦惱。**2** [T] *formal* to ask someone to do something for you when it is inconvenient for them【正式】麻煩〔某人〕, 給〔某人〕添麻煩: *I promise not to trouble you again.* 我保證不再給你添麻煩了。**3 may I trouble you?/sorry to trouble you** *spoken formal* used when politely asking someone to do something for you or give you something【口, 正式】我可以麻煩您一下嗎?/對不起, 麻煩您一下: *Sorry to trouble you, but could you tell me the way to the station, please.* 對不起, 麻煩您一下, 請問到車站怎麼走? | *May I trouble you for the salt?* 麻煩你遞一下鹽好嗎? | *Can I trouble you to close the door.* 麻煩你把門關上。**4 not trouble to do sth** to not do something because it needs too much effort 不用費神[操心]做某事: *They never troubled to ask me what I would like.* 他們從來不費神問我喜歡甚麼。**5** [T] if a medical problem troubles you, it causes you pain or makes you suffer 使疼痛, 使不舒服: *Roy has been troubled by a stomach ulcer for months.* 羅伊已被胃潰瘍折磨好幾個月了。

troub·led /ˋtrʌbl̩d; ˈtrʌbəld/ *adj* **1** feeling worried or anxious 憂慮的; 煩惱的, 苦惱的: *Benson looked troubled when he heard the news.* 本森聽到這消息時面露憂色。—see 見 TROUBLE (USAGE) **2** having many problems 問題叢生的, 混亂的: *These are troubled times for the coal industry.* 對於煤炭工業來說, 現在是多事之秋。

trouble-free /ˌ·· ˈ·◂/ *adj* causing no difficulty or worry 沒有困難的; 沒有問題的; 沒有憂慮的: *Since we changed our car we've had two years of trouble-free motoring.* 自從換了這輛車後, 我們開了兩年都沒出過故障。

troub·le·mak·er /ˋtrʌbl̩ˌmekɚ; ˈtrʌbəlˌmeɪkə/ *n* [C] someone who deliberately causes problems, especially by complaining or making people argue with each other 惹事生非者, 搗蛋鬼: *a handful of troublemakers who are damaging the club's reputation* 毀壞俱樂部名聲的一羣惹事生非者

troub·le·shoot·er /ˋtrʌbl̩ˌʃutɚ; ˈtrʌbəlˌʃuːtə/ *n* [C] someone who is employed by a company to deal with serious problems〔公司雇用的〕處理難題的人

troub·le·some /ˋtrʌbl̩səm; ˈtrʌbəlsəm/ *adj* causing you trouble or anxiety, over a long period of time 引起麻煩的; 令人煩惱[討厭]的: *a troublesome child* 煩人的孩子

trouble spot /ˈ·· ˌ·/ *n* [C] a place where trouble often happens, especially war or violence〔尤指經常發生戰爭或暴力的〕麻煩地區, 不安定地區: *Extra police were drafted in to patrol late-night trouble spots.* 又徵召了一些警察在後半夜經常出事的地區巡邏。

trough /trɔf; trɒf/ *n* [C] **1** a long narrow open container that holds water or food for animals〔餵動物的〕食槽, 飲水槽 **2** the hollow area between two waves in the sea or between two hills〔海中的〕浪谷, 波谷;〔山間的〕槽谷 **3** a short period of low activity, low prices etc in something that is continuously measured over a longer period〔商業活動、價格等的〕低谷期, 蕭條期: *the peaks and troughs of economic cycles* 經濟週期中的高峯和低潮 **4** *technical* a long area of fairly low pressure on a weather map between two areas of high pressure【術語】〔氣象圖上標示的〕低壓槽

trounce /trauns; traʊns/ *v* [T] to defeat someone completely 徹底打敗, 擊潰: *We were trounced 13-0.* 我們以 0 比 13 的比分被打得一敗塗地。

troupe /trup; truːp/ *n* [C] a group of singers, actors, dancers etc who work together 演出團, 劇團, 歌舞團

troup·er /ˋtrupɚ; ˈtruːpə/ *n* [C] *informal* someone who has a lot of experience of work in the entertainment business【非正式】從事娛樂業多年的人, 老演員, 老藝人

trouser press /ˈ·· ·/ *n* [C] a piece of equipment that you can keep your trousers in to keep them flat and smooth〔使褲子保持平整不皺的〕壓褲器

trou·sers /ˋtrauzɚz; ˈtraʊzəz/ *n* [plural] a piece of clothing that covers the lower half of your body, with a separate part fitting over each leg 褲子: *I need a new pair of trousers for work.* 我需要一條新的工作褲。| *short trousers* 短褲 —**trouser** *adj* [only before noun 僅用於名詞前]: *The tickets are in my trouser-pocket.* 票在我的褲子口袋裡。—see also 另見 **wear the trousers** (WEAR¹ (8)), **catch sb with their trousers down** (CATCH¹ (3)) —see picture on page A17 參見 A17 頁圖

This graph shows how common the nouns **trousers** and **pants** are in British and American English. 本圖表所示為名詞 trousers 和 pants 在英國英語和美國英語中的使用頻率。

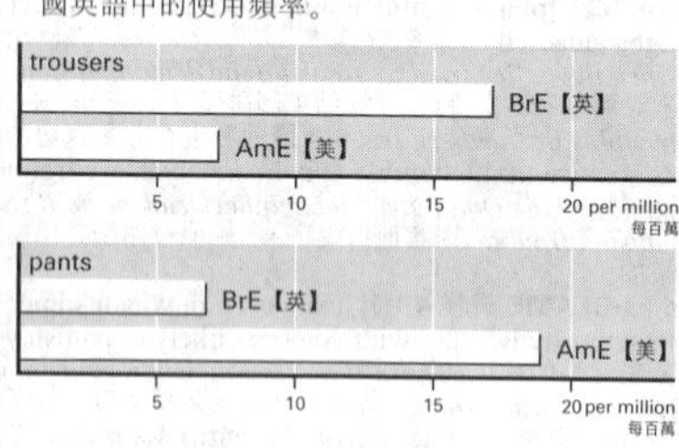

Based on the British National Corpus and the Longman Lancaster Corpus
據英國國家語料庫和朗文蘭卡斯特語料庫

In British English **trousers** is used to mean a piece of clothing that covers the lower half of your body, with a separate part fitting over each leg. In American English **pants** is used for this meaning. **Pants** is commonly used in British English to mean underwear, but Americans use the word **underwear**. 在英國英語中, trousers 用來指褲子。在美國英語中, 褲子是 pants。pants 在英國英語中普遍用來指內褲, 而美國人則用 underwear 指內褲。

trouser suit /ˈ·· ·/ *n* [C] *BrE* a woman's suit consisting of a JACKET and matching trousers【英】〔女子的上衣與配套的褲子組成的〕長褲套裝; PANTSUIT *AmE*【美】

trous·seau /truˋso; ˈtruːsəʊ/ *n* [C] *old-fashioned* the personal possessions that a woman brings with her when she marries【過時】嫁妝

trout /traut; traʊt/ *n* **1** *plural* **trout** [C,U] a common river-fish, often used for food, or the flesh of this fish 鱒魚〔一種河魚〕; 鱒魚肉 **2 old trout** *BrE spoken* an unpleasant or annoying old person, especially a woman【英口】老傢伙; 老厭物〔尤指老婦人〕

trove /trov; trəʊv/ *n* —see 見 TREASURE TROVE

trow·el /ˋtrauəl; ˈtraʊəl/ *n* [C] **1** a garden tool like a very small SPADE 小泥鏟, 小鏟子〔一種園藝工具〕 **2** a small tool with a flat blade, used for spreading CEMENT on bricks etc〔泥瓦匠使用的〕瓦刀, 鏝刀, 抹子

troy weight /ˋtrɔɪ ˌwet; ˈtrɔɪ weɪt/ *n* [U] a British weights system, used in former times for weighing gold, silver etc〔英國舊時稱量金銀等用的〕金衡制

tru·an·cy /ˈtruənsɪ; ˈtruːənsi/ *n* [U] the practice of deliberately staying away from school without permission 逃學, 曠課

tru·ant /ˈtruənt; ˈtruːənt/ *n* [C] **1** a student who stays away from school without permission 逃學者, 曠課生 **2 play truant** *BrE* to stay away from school without permission【英】逃學, 曠課 —**truant** *v* [I]

truce /trus; truːs/ *n* [C] an agreement between enemies to stop fighting or arguing for a short time, or the period for which this is arranged 休戰, 停戰(協定); 停止爭辯(協議): **call a truce** (=announce a truce) 宣布休戰 *The People's Liberation Movement called a truce for the elections.* 人民解放運動組織宣布在選舉期間休戰。

3 3 **truck[1]** /trʌk; trʌk/ *n* **1** [C] a large road vehicle used to carry goods 貨車, 卡車; LORRY *BrE*【英】: *The trucks were loaded at the docks.* 這些卡車在碼頭上裝貨。**2** [C] *BrE* a railway vehicle that is part of a train and carries goods【英】〔鐵路的〕貨車; CAR[1] (3) *AmE*【美】: *coal trucks* 運煤車 **3** [C] a simple piece of equipment on wheels used to move heavy objects 手推車, 手拉車 **4 have no truck with sb** to avoid speaking or doing business with someone 不與…打交道, 不同…來往

truck[2] *v especially AmE*【尤美】**1** [T] to take something somewhere by truck 用貨車裝運 **2** [I always+adv/prep] *informal* to go, move, or travel【非正式】去, 移動, 行進: **truck along/down etc** *We were trucking on down to Jack's place.* 我們在去傑克家的路上。**3 get trucking** *informal* to leave【非正式】離開, 上路

truck·er /ˈtrʌkɚ; ˈtrʌkə/ *n* [C] *AmE* a truck driver【美】貨車司機

truck farm /ˈ· ·/ *n* [C] *AmE* an area for growing vegetables and fruit for sale【美】商品果蔬農場; MARKET GARDEN *BrE*【英】

truck·ing /ˈtrʌkɪŋ; ˈtrʌkɪŋ/ *n AmE*【美】**1** [U] the business of taking goods from place to place by road 貨車運輸業 **2 keep on trucking** *spoken* used to encourage someone to continue what they are doing【口】繼續幹下去〔鼓勵人的話〕

truck·le /ˈtrʌkḷ; ˈtrʌkəl/ *v*

truckle to sb/sth *phr v* [T] *old-fashioned* to do what someone tells you in a way that seems weak【過時】屈從, 對…唯命是從

truckle bed /ˈ·· ˌ·/ *n* [C] *BrE* a low bed on small wheels, that you can slide under a larger bed【英】〔不用時可推入大牀下的〕裝有腳輪的矮牀; TRUNDLE BED *AmE*【美】

truck·load /ˈtrʌkˌlod; ˈtrʌkləʊd/ *n* [C] the amount that fills a truck 貨車裝載量

truck stop /ˈ· ·/ *n* [C] *AmE* a cheap place to eat on a main road, used mainly by TRUCK[1] (1) drivers【美】〔主要為貨車司機服務的〕路邊廉價餐館; TRANSPORT CAFE *BrE*【英】

truc·u·lent /ˈtrʌkjələnt; ˈtrʌkjʊlənt/ *adj* bad-tempered and always willing to argue with people 脾氣暴躁的; 好鬥的, 尋釁的: *Most people resented his truculent manner.* 大多數人都不滿他那尋釁好鬥的作派。—**truculently** *adv* —**truculence** *n* [U]

trudge[1] /trʌdʒ; trʌdʒ/ *v* [I always + adv/prep] to walk with slow, heavy steps, especially because you are tired〔尤指因疲倦而〕艱難地走, 步履沉重地走: **trudge home/along/through etc** *The old man trudged home through the snow.* 老人步履艱難地穿過雪地走回了家。—see picture on page A24 參見 A24 頁圖

trudge[2] *n* [singular] a long tiring walk 長途疲憊的步行, 長途跋涉

1 1 **true[1]** /tru; truː/ *adj*

1 ▶NOT FALSE 不假的◀ based on facts and not imagined or invented 符合事實的, 真的, 真實的: *No, honestly, it's a true story.* 不, 老實說, 這是一個真實的故事。| **it is true (that)** *Is it true that you're leaving?* 你是真的要走了嗎? | **be true of sb** *Babies need a lot of sleep and this is particularly true of newborns.* 嬰兒需要大量的睡眠, 新生兒尤其如此。—opposite 反義詞 FALSE

2 the true value/seriousness/nature etc the real value etc of something rather than what seems at first to be correct 真正的價值/嚴重性/本性等: *I didn't realize the true seriousness of the problem until I checked the fuel gauge.* 我直到檢查了燃料表後才意識到這個問題的真正嚴重性。| *The house was sold for only a fraction of its true value.* 這房子賣出去了, 價格比它真正的價值低得多。

3 ▶REAL FEELINGS 真實的感情◀ your true emotions, beliefs, opinions etc are the ones that you really have and not the ones that you pretend to have〔情感、信仰、意見等〕真實的, 實際的: *Her true motives only emerged later.* 她真實的動機是後來才顯露出來的。

4 ▶ADMITTING STH 承認某事◀ *spoken* used when you are admitting that something is true, but saying that in spite of this something else is also true【口】誠然, 固然, 的確〔用來承認某事的真實性, 但同時指出另一事情也真實〕: *"He's very hard-working." "True, but I still don't think he's the right man for the job."* "他工作非常勤奮。" "的確如此, 不過我還是認為他不是這項工作的合適人選。"

5 true love/courage/freedom etc the type of love etc that is strong and has all the qualities that it should have 真正的愛情/勇氣/自由等: *True courage includes the recognition of your own fear.* 真正的勇氣包括承認自己的恐懼。

6 come true if wishes, dreams etc come true, they happen in the way that someone has said or hoped that they would〔願望、夢想等〕實現, 成真: *By 1975 the worst economic predictions had come true.* 到 1975 年, 對經濟最糟糕的預測已經成為現實。—see also 另見 **a dream come true** (DREAM[1] (5))

7 ▶LOYAL 忠心的◀ faithful and loyal to someone, whatever happens 忠實的, 忠貞的: **[+to]** *Throughout the whole ordeal, she remained true to her husband.* 在整個磨難時期, 她對丈夫忠貞不渝。

8 true friend/believer/sportsman etc someone who behaves in the way that a good friend etc should behave 真正的朋友/信仰者/體育愛好者等: *You find out who your true friends are at times like this.* 在這種時候, 你會發現哪些人才是你真正的朋友。

9 true to form/type used to say that someone is behaving in the bad way that you expect them to〔不良行為〕一如既往: *True to form, Henry turned up late.* 像往常一樣, 亨利很晚才露面。

10 true to life a book, play, description etc that is true to life seems very real and natural; REALISTIC〔圖書、戲劇、描述等〕逼真的, 活靈活現的

11 true to your word doing exactly what you have promised to do 說話算數, 履行諾言: *True to his word, John arrived promptly at 2 o'clock.* 約翰說話算數, 在兩點鐘時就準時來了。

12 be true to your principles/beliefs etc to behave according to the principles that you claim to believe in 忠實於原則/信仰等: *He remains true to the traditions of his profession.* 他一直忠實於他這一行業的傳統。

13 only (too true) used to say that you know something is true, especially when you do not like it 千真萬確的〔用來表示知道某事是真的, 尤指不喜歡的事〕: *It is only too true that people are judged by their accents.* 人們以口音來判斷人, 這簡直再真實不過了。

14 true mammal/fish/plant etc having all the qualities of a particular class of object, animal, plant etc according to an exact description of it 真正的哺乳動物/魚類/植物等〔表示合乎嚴格的定義, 有某類的全部特徵〕: *Despite its appearance, the whale is a true mammal.* 儘管有那樣的外表, 鯨是真正的哺乳動物。

15 ▶STRAIGHT/LEVEL 直的/平的◀ [not before noun 不用於名詞前] *technical* fitted, placed, or formed in a way that is perfectly flat, straight, correct etc【術語】〔安裝、放置等〕端正的; 正確的: *If the door's not true, it won't close properly.* 這門如果安得不正, 就關不嚴。

16 sb's aim is true if your aim is true, you hit the thing

T

that you were throwing or shooting at〔投擲、射擊等〕命中目標
17 (there's) many a true word spoken in jest used to say that when people are joking they sometimes say things that are true and important 玩笑中也有不少實話 —see also 另見 **be too good to be true** (GOOD[1] (23)), **show yourself in your true colours** (COLOUR[1] (11)), **not ring true** (RING[2] (5)), TRULY, TRUTH

true² *adv* **1** in an exact straight line 端正地; 筆直地: *The arrow flew straight and true to its target.* 箭筆直地射中了目標。**2** *old use* truthfully【舊】真實地, 確實地 **3** *technical* if a type of animal breeds true, the young animals are exactly like their parents【術語】〔動物〕子代與親代完全相同地, 與原種相同地, 純種地

true³ *n* **out of true** not completely straight, level, or balanced 不直; 不平; 不正: *The walls are slightly out of true.* 牆壁稍微有點不平。

true-blue /ˌ· ˈ·◂/ *adj* **1** *BrE informal* believing completely in the ideas of the British CONSERVATIVE PARTY【英, 非正式】忠於保守黨思想的: *a true-blue Tory* 忠誠的保守黨黨員 **2** *AmE* completely loyal to a person or idea【美】非常忠誠的, 忠心耿耿的: *a true-blue friend* 忠心耿耿的朋友

true-heart·ed /ˌ· ˈ··◂/ *adj literary* faithful; loyal【文】忠實的; 忠心的

true-life /ˌ· ˈ·◂/ *adj* [only before noun 僅用於名詞前] based on real facts and not invented 以事實為依據的〔而不是虛構的〕: *a true-life adventure* 一次真實的冒險活動

true·love /ˈtruˌlʌv; ˈtruːlʌv/ *n* [C] *poetic* the person that you love【詩】愛人, 戀人, 心上人

true north /ˌ· ˈ·/ *n* [U] north as it appears on maps, calculated as a line through the centre of the earth rather than by using the MAGNETIC POLE 真北〔地圖上的北方, 即根據地球中軸線而不是用磁極計算的正北方〕

T

truf·fle /ˈtrʌfl; ˈtrʌfəl/ *n* [C] **1** a black or light brown FUNGUS that grows underground, and is a very expensive food 塊菌〔生長於地下的一種很昂貴的食用真菌〕**2** a soft creamy sweet made with chocolate 巧克力軟糖: *a rum truffle* 朗姆酒心巧克力軟糖

tru·is·m /ˈtruɪzəm; ˈtruːɪzəm/ *n* [C] a statement that is clearly true, so that there is no need to say it 自明之理, 不言而喻的話: *His speech was just a collection of clichés and truisms.* 他說的只不過是一堆陳詞濫調和不言而喻的話。

W3 **tru·ly** /ˈtrulɪ; ˈtruːli/ *adv* [+adj/adv] **1** used to emphasize that the way you are describing something is really true 真實地, 確實地: *There was a truly beautiful view from the bedroom.* 從臥室望出去的風景確實很美。| *a truly amazing story* 確實令人驚異的故事 | *Truly, this is an honour.* 的確, 這是一項榮譽。**2** *formal* sincerely【正式】誠摯地, 真誠地: *I am truly sorry.* 我真的感到抱歉。**3** in an exact or correct way 準確地; 正確地: *A spider cannot truly be described as an insect.* 準確地說, 蜘蛛不能算是昆蟲。**4 well and truly** *especially spoken* completely; totally【尤口】徹底地, 完全地: *We were well and truly trapped.* 我們完全被困住了。**5 really and truly** *spoken* used to emphasize that something is definitely true【口】的的確確地, 千真萬確地〔用於強調〕: *I couldn't believe we were really and truly going at last.* 我無法相信我們終於真的可以走了。**6 yours truly a)** used at the end of a business letter, before the signature 你忠實的〔用於公文書信結尾, 簽名前〕—see also 另見 **yours faithfully, yours sincerely** (YOURS (3)) **b)** *informal humorous* used to mean yourself【非正式, 幽默】本人, 我自己: *So, yours truly was left to clean up.* 於是, 留下我自己來收拾殘局。

trump¹ /trʌmp; trʌmp/ *n* [C] **1** a card from the SUIT (=one of the four types of cards in a set) that has been chosen to have a higher value than the other suits in a particular game〔牌戲中的〕王牌, 將牌 **2 trumps** [plural] also 又作 **trump** *AmE*【美】the SUIT[1] (3) chosen to have a higher value than the other suits in a particular game 王牌的花色: *Hearts are trumps.* 紅桃是王牌。**3 come up trumps/turn up trumps** to provide what is needed, especially unexpectedly and at the last moment〔在最後時刻意外地〕提供需要之物: *Paul came up trumps and managed to borrow a car for us.* 保羅送來及時雨, 為我們借到了一輛汽車。

trump² *v* [T] to play a trump that beats someone else's card in a game〔牌戲中〕打出王牌贏〔別人的牌〕
trump sth ↔ **up** *phr v* [T] to use false information to make someone seem guilty of a crime 捏造〔罪名〕, 假造〔罪證〕: *They had trumped the whole thing up to get rid of him.* 為了除掉他, 他們捏造了所有罪證。—see also 另見 TRUMPED-UP

trumped-up /ˌ·ˈ·◂/ *adj* **trumped-up charges/evidence etc** false information that has been used to make someone seem guilty of a crime 捏造的罪名/證據等: *Dissidents were routinely arrested on trumped-up charges.* 異己經常因捏造的罪名被逮捕。

trump·e·ry /ˈtrʌmpərɪ; ˈtrʌmpəri/ *adj old use* not valuable【舊】毫無價值的

trum·pet¹ /ˈtrʌmpɪt; ˈtrʌmpɪ̣t/ *n* **1** [C] a musical instrument that you blow into, which consists of a curved metal tube that is wide at the end with three buttons to change the note 喇叭, 小號〔一種銅管樂器〕**2** [singular] the loud noise that an ELEPHANT makes 大象的吼聲 —see also 另見 **blow your own trumpet** (BLOW[1] (21))

trumpet² *v* **1** [T] to tell everyone about something that you are proud of, in an annoying way 吹噓, 大肆宣揚: *She's always trumpeting her son's achievements.* 她總是到處吹噓兒子的成就。**2** [I] if an ELEPHANT trumpets, it makes a loud noise〔大象〕吼叫

trun·cate /ˈtrʌŋket; trʌŋˈkeɪt/ *v* [T] *formal* to make something shorter【正式】把…截短 —**truncation** /trʌŋˈkeʃən; trʌŋˈkeɪʃən/ *n* [U]

trun·cat·ed /trʌŋˈketɪd; trʌŋˈkeɪtɪ̣d/ *adj* made shorter than before, or shorter than usual 縮短了的

trun·cheon /ˈtrʌntʃən; ˈtrʌnʃən/ *n* [C] *especially BrE* a short thick stick that police officers carry as a weapon【尤英】警棍 —compare 比較 NIGHTSTICK *AmE*【美】

trun·dle /ˈtrʌndl; ˈtrʌndl/ *v* [I always+adv/prep,T] to move slowly along on wheels, or to make something do this by pushing or pulling it (使) 慢慢地移動[滾動]: *Two large wagons trundled by.* 兩輛大馬車緩慢地駛過。

trundle bed /ˈ·· ˌ·/ *n* [C] *AmE* a low bed on wheels that you can slide under a larger bed【美】〔不用時可推入大牀下的〕裝有腳輪的矮牀; TRUCKLE BED *BrE*【英】

trunk /trʌŋk; trʌŋk/ *n* [C] **1** the thick central wooden stem of a tree 樹幹 **2** *AmE* the part at the back of a car where you can put bags, tools etc【美】〔汽車後部的〕行李箱; BOOT[1] (3) *BrE*【英】**3** the very long nose of an ELEPHANT 象鼻 **4 trunks** [plural] a piece of clothing like very short trousers, worn by men for swimming 男式游泳褲 **5** *technical* the main part of your body, not including your head, arms, or legs【術語】〔人體的〕軀幹 **6** a very large box made of wood or metal, in which clothes, books etc are stored or packed for travel 大箱子, 大旅行箱 —see picture at 參見 SUITCASE 圖

trunk call /ˈ· ·/ *n* [C] *BrE old-fashioned* a telephone call between places that are a long distance apart【英, 過時】長途電話

trunk road /ˈ· ·/ *n* [C] *BrE* a main road used for travelling long distances【英】幹道

truss¹ /trʌs; trʌs/ *v* [T] **1** also 又作 **truss up** to tie someone's arms, legs etc very firmly with rope so that they cannot move 捆, 紮, 綁〔人的手腳, 使人動彈不得〕: *They trussed up their victim and left him for dead.* 他們把受害人捆綁起來, 把他當作死屍一樣。**2** to prepare a chicken, duck etc for cooking by tying its legs and wings into position 捆紮〔雞、鴨等的腿、翅以便烹煮〕

truss² *n* [C] **1** a special belt worn to support a HERNIA (=medical problem that affects the muscles below your stomach)〔患疝病者用的〕疝帶 **2** a frame supporting a roof or bridge〔支撐屋頂或橋梁的〕桁架, 構架

1 **trust**[1] /trʌst; trʌst/ *n*
2 **1 ►BELIEF 相信◄** [U] a strong belief in the honesty, goodness etc of someone or something 信任, 信賴, 相信: *an agreement made on the basis of mutual trust* 在相互信任基礎上達成的一項協議 | **put your trust in** *You shouldn't put your trust in a man like that.* 你不應該相信那樣的一個男人。| **betray sb's trust** (=do something that shows someone should not have trusted you) 辜負某人的信任

2 take sth on trust to believe that something is true without having any proof 憑空相信: *I just had to take it on trust that he would deliver the money.* 我只好希望他守信用, 會把那筆錢送來。

3 ►FINANCIAL ARRANGEMENT 金融安排◄ [U] an arrangement by which someone has legal control of your money or property, especially until you are old enough to use it〔金錢或財產的〕信託, 託管〔尤指為少年兒童代管〕: **hold sth in trust** *The money your father left you will be held in trust until you are 21.* 你父親給你留下的這筆錢將委託他人代管, 直至你滿 21 歲。

4 ►ORGANIZATION 機構◄ [C usually singular 一般用單數] an organization or group that has control over money that will be used to help someone else 信託機構: *a charitable trust* 慈善信託機構 —see also 另見 TRUST FUND

5 a position of trust a job or position in which you have been given the responsibility of making important decisions 重任, 要職

6 ►COMPANIES 公司◄ [C] *especially AmE* a group of companies that illegally work together to reduce competition and control prices【尤美】托拉斯〔企業為減少競爭和操縱價格而非法形成的組合〕: *anti-trust laws* 反托拉斯法 —see also 另見 **breach of trust** (BREACH[1] (2)), UNIT TRUST

2 **trust**[2] *v*
3 **1 ►HONEST PEOPLE 誠實的人◄** [T] to believe that someone is honest and will not harm you, cheat you etc 信任, 相信: *I trusted Max, so I lent him the money.* 我相信馬克斯, 所以我把錢借給了他。| **trust sb to do sth** *Can they be trusted to look after the house?* 能信任他們會把房子照管好嗎? | **trust sb completely/implicitly** *You must trust her implicitly and do everything she says.* 你必須絕對地信任她, 一切按照她所說的去做。| **not trust sb an inch** *BrE informal* (=not trust someone at all)【英, 非正式】一點都不信任某人 —opposite 反義詞 DISTRUST

2 ►DEPEND ON FACTS 取決於事實◄ [T] to be sure that something is true or will happen 對…有把握, 信得過: *I wouldn't trust any information I get from them.* 從他們那兒獲得的任何信息我都信不過。| **trust sth to do sth** *You can't trust the trains to run on time.* 你不能指望火車會準時。

3 trust sb's judgement to think that someone is likely to make the right decisions 相信某人的判斷

4 trust you/him/them etc (to do sth)! *spoken* used to say that someone has behaved in a bad way that is typical of them【口】你/他/他們等肯定(要做某事)!〔指做不好的事〕: *Trust you to be late!* 知道你肯定要遲到!

5 I trust (that) *spoken formal* used to say politely that you hope something is true【口, 正式】我希望…: *I trust that your family is well.* 我希望你的家人都好。

6 trust sb with sth to believe that someone would be careful with something valuable or dangerous if you gave it to them 放心地把〔某物〕交給〔某人〕: *Would you trust that kid with a hammer?* 把鐵錘交給那個孩子, 你放心得下嗎? —see also 另見 TRUSTING, **tried and tested/trusted** (TRIED)

trust in sth/sb *phr v* [T] *formal* to believe in someone or something【正式】相信; 信仰: *We trust in God.* 我們信仰上帝。

trust to sth *phr v* [T] **trust to luck/chance/fate etc** to hope that luck etc will help you, usually because there is nothing else you can do 依靠運氣/機會/命運等, 聽其自然, 聽天由命

trust·ee /trʌsˈtiː; ˌtrʌsˈtiː◂/ *n* [C] **1** someone who has control of money or property that is in a TRUST[1] (3) for someone else〔金錢或財產的〕受託人 **2** a member of a group that controls the money of a company, college, or other organization〔公司、學院等的〕理事, 董事會成員 2

trust·ee·ship /trʌsˈtiʃɪp; trʌsˈtiːʃɪp/ *n* **1** [C,U] the job of being a trustee 受託人的職位; 理事[董事]職位 **2** [U] government of an area by a country or countries that are given authority by the United Nations 託管〔聯合國委託某國或某幾國管理某地區〕

trust·ful /ˈtrʌstfəl; ˈtrʌstfəl/ *adj* ready to trust other people 容易相信他人的 —**trustfully** *adv* —**trustfulness** *n* [U]

trust fund /ˈ· ·/ *n* [C] money belonging to someone that is controlled for them by a trustee 信託基金

trust·ing /ˈtrʌstɪŋ; ˈtrʌstɪŋ/ *adj* willing to believe that other people are good and honest 容易相信他人的, 輕信的: *Sara's trusting nature led her to believe Tony's lies.* 莎拉輕信的性格使她相信了托尼的謊言。

trust·wor·thy /ˈtrʌstˌwɝðɪ; ˈtrʌstˌwɜːði/ *adj* someone who is trustworthy can be trusted and depended upon; DEPENDABLE 值得信賴的, 可靠的 —**trustworthiness** *n* [U]

trust·y /ˈtrʌstɪ; ˈtrʌsti/ *adj* [only before noun 僅用於名詞前] *old use or humorous* a trusty weapon, vehicle, animal etc is one that you have had for a long time and can depend on【舊或幽默】〔武器、車輛、動物等〕久經考驗的, 可靠的: *his trusty sword* 他那把歷久彌堅的劍 | *My trusty old car will get us home.* 我那輛經久耐用的舊車將載我們回家。

truth /truθ; truːθ/ *n* 1

1 ►TRUE FACTS 事實◄ the truth the true facts about something, as opposed to what is untrue, imagined, or guessed 真實, 真相, 實情: **[+about]** *We never found out the truth about Mike's past.* 我們從未搞清楚邁克的來歷。| **tell the truth** *How can we be sure that she's telling the truth?* 我們怎麼能確信她說的是實情? | **be the truth** *It's the truth. She really did it.* 這是真的。的確是她幹的。| **get to the truth** (=find out what really happened) 弄清真相 *Only after several days of questioning did the police finally get to the truth.* 經過好幾天的審問以後, 警方才最終查明了真相。| **the truth of the matter** *Reforms were promised, but the truth of the matter is that nothing has changed.* 改革的許諾已經作出, 但事情的真實情況是, 甚麼都沒有改變。 2

2 ►BEING TRUE 真實性◄ [U] the state or quality of being true 真實性: *Do you think there's any truth in these rumours?* 你認為這些謠傳有甚麼真實性嗎? | **a grain of truth** (=a small amount of truth) 些許真實性 *There wasn't a grain of truth in what he said.* 他的話一點真實性都沒有。

3 ►IMPORTANT IDEAS 重要思想◄ [C usually plural 一般用複數] *formal* an important fact or idea that is accepted as being true【正式】真理: *the fundamental truths about mankind* 關於人類的基本真理

4 to tell (you) the truth *spoken* used when giving your personal opinion or admitting something【口】老實說, 實話對你說: *Well, to tell you the truth, I've never really liked her.* 唉, 實話對你說吧, 我從來就沒有真正喜歡過她。

5 if (the) truth be known used when telling someone the real facts about a situation, or your real opinion 如果要把事實說出來的話: *If the truth be known, that was the main reason why we left.* 如果要實話實說, 那便是我們離開的主要原因。

6 nothing could be further from the truth used to say that something is definitely not true 那絕對不是事實

7 the gospel truth if you think something is the gospel

truth, you believe completely that it is true 絕對的真理: *I thought everything my teachers told me was the gospel truth.* 我曾認為老師們告訴我的一切都是絕對真理。

8 in (all) truth *old-fashioned* in fact; really【過時】事實上; 的確: *In truth, I did not mind whether we went or not.* 事實上, 當時我們去不去我都無所謂。

9 the truth will out *old-fashioned* used to say that even if you try to stop people from knowing something, they will find out in the end【過時】真相終會大白的 —see also 另見 HALF-TRUTH, **home truths** (HOME[3] (6)), **the moment of truth** (MOMENT (11))

truth drug /ˈ· ·/ *BrE*【英】, **truth serum** /ˈ· ,··/ *AmE*【美】*n* [C,U] a drug that is supposed to make people tell the truth 吐真藥〔一種據說能使人吐露真言的藥〕

truth·ful /ˈtruθfəl; ˈtru:θfəl/ *adj* **1** someone who is truthful does not usually tell lies 誠實的, 一向說實話的: *a truthful child* 一個從不說謊的孩子 **2** a truthful statement gives the true facts about something 真實的, 如實的 —**truthfully** *adv* —**truthfulness** *n* [U]

1 1 **try¹** /traɪ; traɪ/ *v*

1 ►ATTEMPT 試圖◄ [I,T] to attempt to do or get something 試, 嘗試; 試圖; 努力: **try to do sth** *Don't shout at him; he's only trying to help.* 別對他大叫大嚷的; 他只是想幫忙。| **try sth** *Roberts tried a shot at goal.* 羅伯茲試着射門。| **try and do sth** *You must try and control your temper.* 你必須盡量控制自己的脾氣。| **try** *Tim may not be good at math but at least he tries.* 蒂姆的數學也許不是很好, 但至少他很努力。| **try doing sth** (=try to do something) 試着做〔某事〕*I'm going to try cooking a paella this evening.* 我打算今晚上試着做一道西班牙肉菜飯。| **try hard/desperately** (=make a lot of effort to do something) 極力/拚命地努力 *Sharon tried hard to keep a straight face.* 雪倫拚命忍住笑。| **try your best/hardest** (=make as much effort as possible to do something) 盡最大努力 *I'll try my best to finish the work for this evening.* 我會盡最大努力完成今晚的工作。| **try and try** (=keep making an effort to do something) 試了又試; 一再努力 *He tried and tried to make her stay but she refused.* 他一再努力挽留她, 但遭到了她的拒絕。| **try as you might** (=used to say that someone is making a lot of effort to do something) 儘管努力了 *Try as I might, I could not overcome my fear of heights.* 我儘管努力了, 但還是無法克服恐高症。| **it wasn't for lack/want of trying** (=used to say that if someone does not achieve something it is not because they have not tried) 並不是因為沒有努力 *If Simon doesn't get through his accountancy exams it won't be for lack of trying.* 如果西蒙通不過會計考試, 那並不是因為他沒有努力。| **you couldn't do sth if you tried** *spoken* (=used to say that someone does not have the skill or ability to do something)【口】再努力也做不了〔某事〕*My Dad couldn't fix a car if he tried.* 我爸爸再努力也修不了車。

2 ►TEST/USE 試驗/使用◄ [T] to do or use something for a short while to discover if it is suitable, enjoyable etc 試一下; 試驗; 試用: *It works really well – you should try it.* 這東西真的很好使 — 你應該試試。| **try doing sth** *Try taking deep, slow breaths.* 試着慢慢地做深呼吸。| **try sth on sb/sth** *Scientists are trying the new drugs on rats.* 科學家們在老鼠身上試驗這些新藥。| **try sb on sth** *Petra's trying the baby on solid foods.* 彼德拉試着讓嬰兒吃些固體食品。| **try something new/different** (=do or use something that is different from what you usually do or use) 嘗試新的/不同的東西 *a different kind of holiday for those who are willing to try something new* 為那些願意嘗試新玩法的人設計的一種另類假日 | **try sth for size** (=put on a piece of clothing to find out whether it fits you) 試穿〔衣服〕看是否合身

3 ►FOOD/DRINK 食品/飲料◄ [T] to taste food or drink to find out if you like it 嚐一嚐, 品嘗: *You must try that home-made apple pie.* 你一定要嚐一嚐那自製的蘋果餡餅。—see 見 TASTE (USAGE)

4 ►TRY TO FIND SB/STH 試圖找到某人/某物◄ [I,T] to go to a place or person, or call them, in order to find something or someone 問〔某人〕; 去〔某地〕找; 試一試; 找一找: *"Where's the glue?" "Try Charles; maybe he knows."* "膠水在哪兒?" "去問問查爾斯, 他也許知道。" | *We tried several hotels before finding one with two single rooms.* 我們試着找了好幾家旅館之後才找到一家有兩個單人房間的。| *I'm sorry, but Ms Bouvier is out of the office. Could you try again later.* 對不起, 布維爾女士不在辦公室。請稍後再打來。

5 ►DOOR/WINDOW 門/窗戶◄ [T] to try to open a door, window etc in order to see if it is locked 試着打開〔門、窗等〕: *I tried the top drawer but it was locked.* 我試着打開最上面那格抽屜, 但它上了鎖。| **try the lock/latch/handle** (=try to open a door, window etc by moving or pushing a lock etc) 轉動鎖/閂/把手〔來開門窗等〕

6 ►LAW 法律◄ [T usually passive 一般用被動態] to examine and judge a legal case, or someone who is thought to be guilty of a crime in a court 審判, 審理: *Lansman was tried for murder.* 蘭斯曼因謀殺罪受到審判。

7 try sb's patience/temper/nerves etc to make someone feel impatient, angry, nervous etc 考驗某人的耐心/脾氣/神經等: *The constant noise from next door was trying my nerves to the utmost.* 隔壁那沒完沒了的噪聲使我的神經都要崩潰了。| **it's enough to try the patience of a saint** *spoken* (=used to say that something or someone is very annoying)【口】〔令人煩擾的事或人〕連聖人也受不了 *These computer crashes are enough to try the patience of a saint.* 這些電腦故障讓聖人也受不了。

8 try your hand at sth to try a new activity in order to see whether it interests you or whether you are good at it 對某事作新的嘗試: *You ought to try your hand at portrait painting.* 你應該嘗試一下肖像畫。

9 try your luck to try to achieve something or get something you want, usually by taking a risk 試一試運氣: *After his singing career failed so miserably in England, he decided to try his luck abroad.* 他在英國的演唱事業慘敗之後, 決定去國外碰碰運氣。

This graph shows how common the different grammar patterns of the verb **try** are. 本圖表所示為動詞 try 構成的不同語法模式的使用頻率。

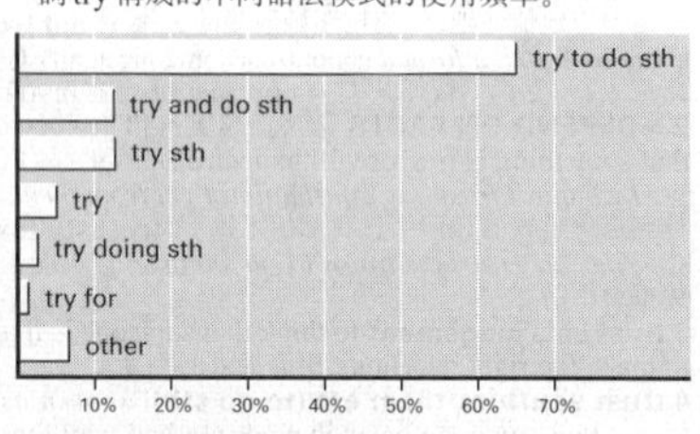

Based on the British National Corpus and the Longman Lancaster Corpus
據英國國家語料庫和朗文蘭卡斯特語料庫

try for sth *phr v* [T] *BrE* to try to get something you really want such as a job, prize, or a chance to study somewhere【英】試圖獲得; 爭取, 謀求: *Alison's trying for a job as a research assistant.* 艾莉森正在爭取一份研究助理的工作。

try sth ↔ **on** *phr v* [T] **1** to put on a piece of clothing to see if it fits you or if it suits you 試穿; 試戴: *She tried the shoes on but they were too small.* 她試穿了那些鞋, 但都太小了。**2 try it on** *BrE spoken* to behave badly in order to find out how bad you can be before people become angry【英口】〔故意表現惡劣以〕試探, 刺探: *During your first few days' teaching the kids will probably try it on just to see how you react.* 在你剛開始教學的幾

天裡，孩子們可能會故意搗蛋，試探你的反應。

try sth ↔ **out** *phr v* [T] **1** to test something such as a method or a piece of equipment to see if it is effective or works properly 試用；試驗；檢驗：*Jamie could hardly wait to try out his new bike.* 傑米迫不及待地想試一下他那輛新自行車。**2** to practise a skill in order to improve it 練習〔技巧〕：**try sth out on sb/sth** *She enjoyed trying her French out on Jean-Pierre.* 她喜歡找讓·皮埃爾練習法語。

try out for sth *phr v* [T] *AmE* to try to be chosen as a member of a team, for a part in a play etc【美】參加選拔；爭取成為〔團隊的一員等〕：*Joan tried out for the school basketball team.* 瓊參加了校籃球隊的選拔。

3 **try²** *n* [C] **1** [usually singular 一般用單數] an attempt to do something 嘗試，試：*She didn't manage to break the record, but it was a good try.* 她沒有能夠打破紀錄，但這不失為一次很好的嘗試。| **have a try** *Let me have a try; I might be able to open it.* 讓我試一試；我或許能打開。| **give it a try** *I'm not sure I can make him change his mind, but I'll give it a try.* 我不敢保證我能使他改變主意，不過我會試一下。| **worth a try** *My idea may not work, but it's worth a try.* 我的主意也許行不通，但值得一試。**2 give sth/sb a try** to try using or doing something to see if it is suitable or successful, or to ask if someone can help you 試一下某事/試一下向某人求助：*Shall we give that Tibetan restaurant a try?* 我們要不要嚐一下那家藏民飯館？**3** four points won by putting the ball on the ground behind the opponents' GOAL LINE in RUGBY〔橄欖球賽中〕在對方球門線後帶球觸地得四分

try·ing /ˈtraɪ-ɪŋ; ˈtraɪ-ɪŋ/ *adj* annoying or difficult in a way that makes you feel worried, tired etc 令人難受的；惱人的；困難的：*That child is very trying.* 那個孩子非常磨人。—see also 另見 TRY[7]

try·out /ˈtraɪaʊt; ˈtraɪaʊt/ *n* [singular] *AmE* a time when people who want to be in a sports team, activity etc are tested, so that the best can be chosen【美】〔體育隊的成員等的〕挑選，選拔；TRIAL[1] (6) *BrE*【英】：*Cheerleading tryouts will be held on Friday afternoon.* 星期五下午將進行啦啦隊選拔。

try-out /ˈ· ·/ *n* [C] *BrE* a period of time spent trying a new method, tool, machine etc to see if it is useful【英】〔新方法、工具、機器等的〕試用期；試驗期

tryst /trɪst; trɪst/ *n* [C] *old use or humorous*【舊或幽默】**1** an arrangement between lovers to meet in a secret place or at a secret time〔情人的〕幽會 **2** a place where lovers meet secretly 幽會處

tsar, tzar, czar /tsɑr; zɑː/ *n* [C] a male ruler of Russia before 1917〔1917年以前統治俄國的〕沙皇

tsa·ri·na, tzarina, czarina /tsɑˈrinə; zɑːˈriːnə/ *n* [C] a female ruler of Russia before 1917, or the wife of a tsar〔1917年以前統治俄國的〕女沙皇；沙皇皇后

tsar·ism, tzarism, czarism /ˈtsɑrɪzm̩; ˈzɑːrɪzəm/ *n* [U] a system of government controlled by a tsar, especially the system in Russia before 1917〔尤指1917年以前俄國的〕沙皇制度；沙皇統治 —**tsarist** *n* [C] —**tsarist** *adj*

tset·se fly, tzetze fly /ˈtsɛtsɪ flaɪ; ˈtetsi flaɪ/ *n* [C] an African fly that sucks the blood of people and animals and spreads serious diseases 舌蠅，采采蠅〔非洲一種吸吮人和動物血液並傳播嚴重疾病的蒼蠅〕

T-shirt, tee-shirt /ˈti ˌʃɝt; ˈtiː ʃɜːt/ *n* [C] a soft, usually cotton shirt that stretches easily, has short SLEEVES and no collar T恤（衫），短袖運動衫：*She was wearing jeans and a T-shirt.* 她穿着牛仔褲和T恤衫。

tsp the written abbreviation of 縮寫= TEASPOON: *1 tsp of salt* 一茶匙鹽

T-square /ˈti ˌskwɛr; ˈtiː skweə/ *n* [C] a large T-shaped piece of wood or plastic used to draw exact plans or pictures〔畫圖用的〕丁字尺

tsu·na·mi /tsuˋnɑmɪ; tsʊˈnɑːmi/ *n* [C] *technical* a TIDAL WAVE【術語】海嘯

tub /tʌb; tʌb/ *n* [C]

1 ▶CONTAINER 容器◀ **a)** a small container made of paper or plastic with a lid, in which food is bought or stored〔盛食物的〕小鉢：*a tub of margarine* 一小鉢人造黃油 **b)** a large round container without a lid, used for washing, storing things in etc 盆，缸：*There were roses in tubs on the balcony.* 在陽台上的大盆裡種有玫瑰花。

2 ▶BATH 洗澡◀ *AmE* a large container in which you sit to wash yourself; BATHTUB【美】浴缸

3 ▶AMOUNT 數量◀ also 又作 **tubful** the amount of liquid, food etc that a tub can contain 一鉢/一盆的容量：*We ate a whole tub of ice-cream.* 我們吃了整整一盒冰淇淋。

4 ▶BOAT 船◀ *humorous* an old boat that travels slowly【幽默】行駛緩慢的舊船，老爺船

5 ▶PERSON 人◀ *AmE informal* someone who is short and fat【美，非正式】矮胖子：*Their children are all tubs.* 他們的孩子全都是矮胖子。

tu·ba /ˈtjubə; ˈtjuːbə/ *n* [C] a very large musical instrument, consisting of a curved metal tube, larger than a TRUMPET[1] (1) which you blow into and which produces a very deep sound 大號〔一種銅管樂器〕

tub·by /ˈtʌbɪ; ˈtʌbi/ *adj informal* short and slightly fat, with a round stomach; PLUMP[1] (1)【非正式】矮胖的，大腹便便的 —see 見 FAT[1] (USAGE)

tube /tub; tjuːb/ *n* 3 3

tubes 管子，筒

rubber tubing
橡皮管

a cardboard tube
硬紙板筒

1 ▶PIPE FOR LIQUID 液體輸送管◀ [C] a round pipe made of metal, glass, rubber etc, especially for liquids or gases to go through〔輸送液體或氣體的〕圓管，管子 —see also 另見 INNER TUBE, TEST TUBE

2 ▶CONTAINER 容器◀ [C] a narrow container made of plastic or soft metal and closed at one end, that you press between your fingers in order to push out the soft substance that is inside〔裝有柔軟物質的〕軟管：*a tube of toothpaste* 一管牙膏

3 ▶IN YOUR BODY 在人體內◀ [C] a tube-shaped part inside your body〔身體內的〕管，道：*the bronchial tubes* 支氣管

4 ▶TRAINS 列車◀ **the tube** *BrE* the system of trains that run under the ground in London【英】地下鐵道，地鐵：*Smoking is forbidden on the Tube.* 地鐵裡禁止吸煙。| *a tube station* 地鐵站 | **by tube** *It's quicker by tube.* 坐地鐵要快一些。—compare 比較 SUBWAY (2) —see also 另見 UNDERGROUND[3]

5 go down the tubes *informal* if a situation goes down the tubes, it quickly becomes ruined or spoiled【非正式】被毀滅；被破壞：*I wasn't going to sit and watch my career go down the tubes.* 我不會坐視我的事業被毀掉。

6 ▶TELEVISION 電視◀ **the tube** *AmE informal* the television【美，非正式】電視

7 ▶ELECTRICAL EQUIPMENT 電子設備◀ [C] *technical* the part of a television that creates the picture; CATHODE RAY TUBE【術語】電視機顯像管；陰極射線管

tu·ber /ˈtubɚ; ˈtjuːbə/ *n* [C] a round swollen part that grows below the ground on the stem of certain plants such as the potato, from which new plants grow〔馬鈴薯等植物的〕塊莖 —**tuberous** *adj*

tu·ber·cu·lar /tuˋbɝkjələ; tjuːˈbɜːkjələ/ also 又作 **tuberculous** /-kjələs; -kjələs/ *adj* connected with tuberculosis 結核病的

tu·ber·cu·lo·sis /tuˌbɝkjəˋlosɪs; tjuːˌbɜːkjəˈləʊsɪs/ *n* [U] a serious infectious disease that affects many parts of your body, especially your lungs; TB 結核病〔尤指肺結核〕

tube top /ˈ· ·/ *n* [C] *AmE informal* a piece of women's clothing that goes around your chest and back to cover your breasts but does not cover your shoulders or stomach

T

【美, 非正式】〔婦女的〕管狀胸褡; 抹胸; BOOB TUBE *BrE* 【英】

tub·ing /ˈtubɪŋ; ˈtjuːbɪŋ/ *n* [U] tubes in general, especially when connected together into a system〔尤指連成一個系統的〕管道, 管子: *rubber tubing* 橡皮管

tub-thump·ing /ˈ·,··/ *adj* [only before noun 僅用於名詞前] *BrE informal* trying to persuade people about your opinions in a loud and forceful way【英, 非正式】〔設法說服人時〕大喊大叫的, 氣焰逼人的: *a tub-thumping speech* 慷慨激昂的演講 —**tub-thumping** *n* [U] —**tub-thumper** *n* [C]

tu·bu·lar /ˈtubjələ˞; ˈtjuːbjʊ̈lə/ *adj* **1** made of tubes or in the form of a tube 用管子做成的; 管狀的: *tubular metal furniture* 用金屬管製作的家具 **2** *AmE* a word meaning very good or excellent, used especially by young people【美】非常出色的, 挺好的〔尤為年輕人使用〕

TUC /ˌti ju ˈsi; ˌtiː juː ˈsiː/ *n* the abbreviation of 縮寫= Trades Union Congress; the association of British trade unions〔英國的〕工會代表大會; 工會聯合會

tuck¹ /tʌk; tʌk/ *v* **1** [T always+adv/prep] to push the edge of a piece of cloth or paper into something so that it looks tidier or stays in place 把〔衣服或紙張〕塞進〔某處〕: **tuck sth into/under** *Nick was tucking his shirt into his trousers when she walked in.* 她走進去的時候, 尼克正把襯衫下擺塞進褲子裡。**2** [T always+adv/prep] to put something into a small space, especially in order to protect or hide it 把…收藏起來: **tuck sth behind/under/into sth** *I tucked the letter into my bag.* 我把那封信塞進包裡。**3** [T] to put a TUCK (=a special fold) in a piece of clothing 在〔衣服裡〕縫褶子

tuck sth ↔ **away** *phr v* [T] **1 be tucked (away) somewhere a)** if a place is tucked away it is in a quiet area〔某處所〕隱藏在〔寂靜的地方〕: *The inn was tucked away in a remote mountain village.* 那家客棧隱藏在一個偏遠的山村裡。**b)** if someone or something is tucked away they are hidden or difficult to find 躲藏, 隱藏; 被收藏: *The key to the cellar was tucked away at the back of the shelf.* 地窖的鑰匙被藏在架子的背後。**2** *informal* to store something, especially money, in a safe place【非正式】把某物〔尤指錢〕收藏在安全處: *Over the years, she had tucked away over £2,000.* 這些年來, 她一共攢了兩千多英鎊。**3** *informal* to eat a lot of food, usually quickly and with enjoyment【非正式】大吃〔尤指狼吞虎咽地美美地吃〕: *I watched as he tucked away a huge plate of pie.* 我看着他狼吞虎咽地吃完了一大盤餡餅。

tuck in *phr v* **1** [I] *informal especially BrE* to eat eagerly【非正式, 尤英】大吃: *Come on everyone, tuck in!* 來吧, 各位, 大吃一頓吧! **2** [T **tuck** sb ↔ **in**] to make a child comfortable in bed by arranging the sheets around them 幫助〔孩子〕蓋好被子安睡: *I'll come up and tuck you in in a minute.* 我一會兒上來幫你蓋好被子。**3** [T **tuck** sth ↔ **in**] to put the edge of a piece of clothing, paper etc inside something so that it looks tidier or stays in place 把〔衣服、紙張等〕塞進〔某處〕: *The blanket was too short to tuck in at the bottom.* 毯子太短了, 底端塞不進去。**4** [T **tuck** sth ↔ **in**] to move a part of your body inwards so that it does not stick out so much 使〔身體的某一部分〕緊貼身體: *When you dive, keep your elbows tucked in.* 你在跳水的時候要夾緊肘部。

tuck into sth *phr v* [T] *informal* to eat something eagerly【非正式】大吃, 狼吞虎咽地吃: *They were tucking into the Christmas turkey.* 他們狼吞虎咽地吃着聖誕火雞。

tuck sb ↔ **up** *phr v* [T] **1** to make a child comfortable in bed by arranging the sheets around them 幫助〔孩子〕蓋好被子安睡 **2 be tucked up** *informal* to be lying or sitting in bed【非正式】臥[坐]在牀上: *He was tucked up in bed doing a crossword.* 他坐在牀上玩縱橫填字謎遊戲。

tuck² *n* **1** [C] a narrow flat fold of cloth sewn into a piece of clothing for decoration or to give it a special shape〔衣服的〕褶, 縫褶 **2** [U] *BrE old-fashioned* a word for cakes, sweets etc used especially by schoolchildren【英, 過時】糖果糕點〔此詞多為小學生使用〕**3** [C] a small medical operation done to make your face or stomach look flatter and younger〔臉部或腹部的〕整容小手術: *tiny tucks behind her ears* 她耳朵背後的細微整容

tuck·er¹ /ˈtʌkə˞; ˈtʌkə/ *v*

tucker sb **out** *phr v* [T] *AmE informal* to make someone very tired【美, 非正式】使非常疲乏: *The kids were tuckered out after the walk.* 孩子們在步行之後疲倦極了。

tucker² *n* [U] *AustrE, NZE informal* food【澳, 新西蘭, 非正式】食物 —see also 另見 **your best bib and tucker** (BIB (3))

-tude /tud; tjuːd/ *suffix* (in nouns 構成名詞) another form of the suffix -ITUDE 後綴 -itude 的另一種形式: *disquietude* (=anxiety) 憂慮不安 | *desuetude* 廢棄不用

Tu·dor /ˈtudə˞; ˈtjuːdə/ *adj* connected with the period in British history between 1485 and 1603〔英國歷史從1485-1603年〕都鐸王朝的; 都鐸王室的: **Tudor house/buildings/architecture etc** (=built in the style used in the Tudor period) 都鐸式房子/大樓/建築等 *a rambling Tudor house overlooking the river* 一幢俯瞰河面的大而無當的都鐸式房屋

Tues·day /ˈtuzdɪ; ˈtjuːzdi/ written abbreviation 縮寫為 **Tue.** or **Tues.** *n* [C,U] the day between Monday and Wednesday. In Britain, Tuesday is considered the second day of the week, and in the US it is considered the third day of the week 星期二: *We moved in last Tuesday.* 我們上星期二搬進來的。| *The results come out on Tuesday.* 結果在星期二出來。| *His birthday is on a Tuesday this year.* 今年他的生日是在一個星期二。| **Tuesday morning/evening etc** *Let's go out for a meal Tuesday night.* 星期二晚上我們出去吃飯吧。| **on Tuesdays** (=each Tuesday) 每週二 *I usually stay in on Tuesdays.* 週二我通常在家。| **the Tuesday** *BrE* (=the Tuesday of the particular week being mentioned)【英】〔指提及的某週的〕星期二 *We went out on the Tuesday.* 那個星期二我們出去了。

tuft /tʌft; tʌft/ *n* [C] a bunch of hair, feathers, grass etc growing or held closely together at their base〔頭髮、羽毛、草等的〕一束, 一簇: *a few scrawny goats chewing at tufts of grass* 幾隻正在咀嚼簇簇青草的骨瘦如柴的山羊

tuft·ed /ˈtʌftɪd; ˈtʌftɪ̈d/ *adj* with a tuft or tufts 有簇飾的; 有羽冠的: *a tufted duck* 一隻長着羽冠的鴨子

tug¹ /tʌg; tʌg/ *v* **tugged, tugging** [I,T] also 又作 **tug at** to pull with one or more short, quick pulls〔迅猛地〕拉, 拖, 拽: *She kept tugging insistently at Alan's sleeve.* 她執意不住地拽艾倫的袖子。

tug² *n* [C] **1** also 又作 **tug boat** /ˈ· ·/ a small strong boat used for pulling or guiding ships into a port, up a river etc 拖船 **2** [usually singular 一般用單數] a sudden strong pull 猛拉, 拖, 拽: *He gave the rope a sharp tug and I fell sprawled on the deck.* 他猛地拉了一下繩子, 我四腳朝天地倒在甲板上。

tug-of-war /ˌ· · ˈ·/ *n* [singular] **1** a test of strength in which two teams pull against each other on a rope 拔河賽 **2** a situation in which two people or groups try very hard to get or keep the same thing 激烈的爭奪: *The children are trapped in an emotional tug-of-war when their parents quarrel.* 當父母吵架時, 孩子們陷入了情感上的激烈鬥爭。

tu·i·tion /tuˈɪʃən; tjuˈɪʃən/ *n* [U] **1** teaching, especially in small groups〔尤指學生人數不多的〕教學, 講課: *I had to have extra tuition in maths.* 我不得不上數學的補習課。| **tuition fees** (=the money you pay for being taught) 學費 **2** *AmE* the money you pay for being taught【美】學費: *When I started college, tuition was $350 a quarter.* 我開始唸大學的時候, 學費是一個學期350美元。

tu·lip /ˈtuləp; ˈtjuːlɪ̈p/ *n* [C] a brightly coloured flower that is shaped like a cup and grows from a BULB (2) in spring 鬱金香(花)

tulle /tul; tjuːl/ *n* [U] a thin soft silk or NYLON material like a net〔絲綢或尼龍的〕薄紗, 絹網

tum·ble¹ /ˋtʌmbl; ˈtʌmbəl/ *v* [I] **1** [always+adv/prep] to fall quickly and suddenly downwards, especially with a rolling movement 倒下, 跌倒, 摔倒; 滾下; 翻滾: [**+over/backwards/down**] *She lost her balance and tumbled backwards.* 她失去了平衡, 朝後倒去。**2** [always+adv/prep] to move in an uncontrolled way 莽莽撞撞地行動; 胡亂地走: [**+into/through**] *The kids tumbled out of the car.* 孩子們一窩蜂地下了車。**3** if prices or figures tumble, they go down suddenly and by a large amount〔價格或數字〕猛跌, 暴跌: *Stock market prices have tumbled over the past week.* 股市價格在過去的一週裡猛跌。**4** [always+adv/prep] if someone's hair tumbles down, it is long and thick and has curls〔長而鬈曲的濃髮〕垂下, 垂落: *Long blonde hair tumbled about her face.* 金色的長髮垂落在她的臉上。**5** *AmE* to do TUMBLING【美】翻跟斗, 空翻

tumble to sth *phr v* [T] *informal* to suddenly understand or realize something【非正式】忽然明白: *It was a long time before she tumbled to what I meant.* 過了很久她才忽然明白我的意思。

tumble² *n* [C] a fall, especially from a high place〔尤指從高處〕倒下, 跌倒, 摔倒 —see also 另見 ROUGH-AND-TUMBLE

tum·ble·down /ˋtʌmbḷˏdaun; ˈtʌmbəldaʊn/ *adj* [only before noun 僅用於名詞前] **tumbledown building/house/cottage etc** old and beginning to fall down, often in a way that seems attractive 搖搖欲墜的大樓/房子/小屋等: *a row of tumbledown labourer's cottages* 一排搖搖欲墜的勞工小屋

tumble dry·er /ˌ·· ˈ··/ *n* [C] *BrE* a machine that uses hot air to dry clothes after they have been washed; DRYER【英】衣服烘乾機

tum·bler /ˋtʌmblɚ; ˈtʌmblə/ *n* [C] **1** a glass with a flat bottom and no handle 無柄的平底玻璃杯 —see picture at 參見 GLASS¹ 圖 **2** also 又作 **tumblerful** /-ful; -fʊl/ the amount of liquid that this type of glass can contain 一平底玻璃杯的容量: *Jack must have had about six tumblers of whisky last night.* 傑克昨晚上一定喝了差不多六杯威士忌。**3** *old-fashioned* someone who performs special movements such as doing SOMERSAULTs (=a jump in which you turn over completely in the air); ACROBAT【過時】雜技演員

tum·ble·weed /ˋtʌmbḷˏwid; ˈtʌmbəlwiːd/ *n* [U] a plant that grows in the desert areas of North America and is blown from place to place by the wind〔北美沙漠地區的〕風滾草

tum·bling /ˋtʌmblɪŋ; ˈtʌmblɪŋ/ *n* [U] a sport similar to GYMNASTICS but with all the exercises done on the floor 翻騰運動〔與體操相似的運動, 但所有動作是在地上做的〕

tu·mes·cent /tuˋmɛsṇt; tjuːˈmesənt/ *adj technical* swollen or swelling【術語】腫脹的, 腫大的 —**tumescence** *n* [U]

tu·mid /ˋtumɪd; ˈtjuːmɪ̣d/ *adj technical* a tumid part of the body is swollen【術語】〔身體某一部分〕腫脹的, 腫大的 —**tumidity** /tuˋmɪdətɪ; tjuːˈmɪdɪ̣ti/ *n* [U]

tum·my /ˋtʌmɪ; ˈtʌmi/ *n* [C] a word for STOMACH, used especially by or to children 肚子〔尤為兒語〕: *Touch your head and pat your tummy.* 摸摸自己的腦袋, 拍拍自己的肚子。| **tummy bug/upset** (=an illness of the stomach that makes you feel sick) 胃病/肚子難受

tu·mour *BrE*【英】, **tumor** *AmE*【美】/ˋtumɚ; ˈtjuːmə/ a mass of diseased cells in your body that have divided and increased too quickly 腫瘤: *a brain tumour* 腦瘤 | **malignant/benign tumour** (=dangerous/harmless tumour) 惡性/良性腫瘤 —**tumourous** *adj*

tu·mult /ˋtumʌlt; ˈtjuːmʌlt/ *n* [C,U] *formal*【正式】**1** a state of confusion, noise, and excitement, often caused by a large crowd〔通常由一大羣人引起的〕混亂, 騷亂; 吵鬧, 喧嘩: *His announcement was drowned in the tumult.* 他的宣讀被淹沒在一片喧嘩聲中。| **in tumult** (=in a state of confusion or change) 混亂/動蕩之中 *The whole country is in tumult.* 全國一片混亂。**2** a state of mental confusion caused by strong emotions such as anger, sadness etc〔思想上的〕波動, 激動: **in tumult** (=anxious, confused, or unhappy) 焦急不安, 心煩意亂 *His mind was in tumult.* 他心裡煩躁不安。

tu·mul·tu·ous /tuˋmʌltʃuəs; tjuːˈmʌltʃuəs/ *adj* **1** full of activity, confusion, or violence 混亂的, 騷亂的, 亂哄哄的: *the tumultuous weeks leading up to the revolution* 革命爆發前混亂的幾個星期 **2** very loud 嘈雜的, 吵鬧的, 喧嘩的: *Tumultuous applause rang through the hall.* 整個大廳裡掌聲雷動。—**tumultuously** *adv*

tu·mu·lus /ˋtumjələs; ˈtjuːmjɪ̣ləs/ *n* [C] a very large pile of earth put over a grave by people in former times〔古時的〕墳頭

tu·na /ˋtunə; ˈtjuːnə/ *n* **1** [C] a large sea fish caught for food 金槍魚〔一種食用海魚〕**2** [U] the flesh of this fish, usually sold cooked in tins 金槍魚肉〔通常以熟食罐裝形式銷售〕

tun·dra /ˋtʌndrə; ˈtʌndrə/ *n* [U] the large flat areas of land in the north of Russia, Canada etc, where it is very cold and there are no trees 凍原, 苔原

tune¹ /tun; tjuːn/ *n* [C] **1** a series of musical notes that are played or sung one after the other to make a pattern of sound that is usually pleasant to listen to 調子, 曲調, 旋律: *I recognize that tune but I can't remember the name of the song.* 我記得那個調子, 但忘記了那首歌的名稱。**2 in tune** playing or singing the correct musical note 合調: *Sadie can't sing in tune.* 薩迪唱歌不入調。**3 out of tune** playing or singing higher or lower than the correct musical note 走調: *That old piano's completely out of tune.* 那架舊鋼琴完全走調了。**4 be in tune with/out of tune with** to be able or unable to realize, understand, or agree with what someone else thinks or wants 與…協調(一致)/不協調: *Many politicians are totally out of tune with the needs of ordinary people.* 許多政客完全不考慮普通人的需要。**5 to the tune of $1000/£2 million etc** *informal* used to emphasize how large an amount or number is【非正式】達到 1000 美元/200 萬英鎊等〔用來強調數量或數目大〕: *We're already in debt to the tune of £5,000.* 我們已經欠下高達 5,000 英鎊的債了。—see also 另見 **call the tune** (CALL¹ (25)), **change your tune** (CHANGE¹ (13)), **dance to sb's tune** (DANCE² (6)) S3

tune² *v* [T] **1** to make a musical instrument play at the right PITCH¹ (3) 為〔樂器〕調音: *Someone's coming tomorrow to tune the piano.* 明天會有人來給鋼琴調音。**2** to make an engine work as well as possible 把〔發動機〕調到最佳運轉狀態 **3** to make a radio or television receive broadcasts from a particular place 把〔收音機或電視機〕調到某一頻道; 收聽; 收看: *The radio was tuned to a classical station.* 收音機被調到了一個古典音樂台。| **stay tuned to (sth)** (=continue watching or listening to the same radio station or television programme) 繼續收聽或收看〔同一個電台或電視節目〕*Stay tuned for the latest news from Washington.* 請繼續收聽來自華盛頓的最新消息。**4 finely tuned sense/perception/ balance etc** a very careful and skilful way of judging something, understanding situations etc 細緻的理解/深入的認識/微妙的平衡等: *She had a finely tuned sense of right and wrong.* 她對是非有細緻入微的理解。

tune in *phr v* [I,T] **1** to watch or listen to a broadcast on radio or television 收聽(廣播); 收看(電視): *60 million people tuned in to watch the Royal Wedding.* 有 6,000 萬人收看了這次王室婚禮。| **tune sth ↔ in (to sth)** *Tune the radio in to KCRW.* 把收音機調到 KCRW 電台。**2 tuned in** able to realize or understand what is happening or what other people are thinking 了解, 熟悉〔情況或別人的想法等〕: *She doesn't seem very tuned in to these new developments.* 她對這些新的動態似乎不很了解。

tune out *phr v* [I,T] *informal especially AmE* to ignore or stop listening to someone【非正式, 尤美】不理

T

睬, 置之不理: *She tuned out after I said no extra money was involved.* 我説起沒有額外追加的錢款之後, 她便不加理睬了。| **tune sb/sth ↔ out** *I learned to tune out the background noise.* 我學會了對背景雜音聽而不聞。

tune up *phr v* **1** [I] when musicians tune up, they prepare their instruments to play at the same PITCH[1] (3) as each other〔音樂家演奏前〕把樂器調好音 **2** [T **tune** sth **↔ up**] to make a musical instrument play at the right PITCH[1] (3) 給〔樂器〕調好音

tune·ful /ˋtunfʊl; ˈtjuːnfəl/ *adj* pleasant to listen to 悦耳動聽的, 曲調優美的: *tuneful melodies from light opera* 輕歌劇悦耳動聽的旋律 —**tunefully** *adv* —**tunefulness** *n* [U]

tune·less /ˋtunlɪs; ˈtjuːnləs/ *adj* not having a pleasant tune 不合調的, 不悦耳的: *tuneless humming* 不成曲調的亂哼哼 —**tunelessly** *adv*

tun·er /ˋtunɚ; ˈtjuːnə/ *n* [C] the part of a radio or television that you can change to receive different TV stations and radio stations〔電視機或收音機上的〕調諧器

tune-up /ˈ· ·/ *n* [C] the process of making small changes to an engine so that it works as well as possible〔發動機的〕微調保養

tung·sten /ˋtʌŋstən; ˈtʌŋstən/ *n* [U] a hard metal that is one of the ELEMENT*s* (=simple substances) used in making steel 鎢〔一種硬金屬元素〕

tu·nic /ˋtunɪk; ˈtjuːnɪk/ *n* [C] **1** a long loose piece of clothing worn in former times, usually without sleeves (SLEEVE (1)) or a belt〔古人穿的一種〕〔無袖〕長袍 **2** *BrE* a specially shaped short coat worn by soldiers, police officers etc as part of a uniform【英】〔士兵、警察等穿的〕緊身短上衣

tuning fork /ˈ·· ·/ *n* [C] a small U-shaped steel instrument that makes a particular musical note when you hit it〔為樂器調音用的〕音叉 —see picture at 參見 FORK[1] 圖

tuning peg /ˈ·· ·/ *n* [C] a wooden screw used for tightening the strings on a VIOLIN, GUITAR etc〔小提琴、吉他等上面的〕調音弦軸, 琴栓 —see picture at 參見 PEG[1] 圖

tunnel 隧道

3 **tun·nel**[1] /ˋtʌnl̩; ˈtʌnl/ *n* [C] **1** a passage that has been dug under the ground for cars, trains etc to go through〔汽車、火車等通行的〕隧道 **2** a passage under the ground that animals have dug to live in〔動物挖掘的〕地道, 坑道

tunnel[2] *v* **tunnelled, tunnelling** *BrE*【英】, **tunneled, tunneling** *AmE*【美】[I always+adv/prep,T] to dig a long passage under the ground 挖掘〔隧道, 地道〕: [**+under/through etc**] *tunneling through hard rock* 掘隧道穿過堅硬的岩石 | **tunnel your way into/through/under etc** (=move somewhere by digging a passage) 掘隧道進入/穿過; 在…下面掘隧道 *The prisoners tunneled their way under the fence.* 囚犯們在柵欄下面挖了一條地道。

tunnel vi·sion /ˌ·· ˈ··/ *n* [U] **1** the tendency to only think about one part of something such as a problem or plan, instead of considering all the parts of it 狹隘的眼光, 一孔之見, 井蛙之見: *He had the paranoia and tunnel vision of the knee-jerk patriot.* 他具有盲目的愛國者那種多疑和狹隘。**2** a condition in which someone's eyes are damaged so that they can only see things that are straight ahead 管狀視〔視力受損而只能直視前方的物體〕

tun·ny /ˋtʌnɪ; ˈtʌni/ *n* [C,U] a British form of the word TUNA tuna 的英式拼寫

tup·pence /ˋtʌpəns; ˈtʌpəns/ *n* [C,U] a British spelling of TWOPENCE twopence 的英式拼法

tup·penny /ˋtʌpənɪ; ˈtʌpni/ *adj* [only before noun 僅用於名詞前] a British spelling of TWOPENNY twopenny 的英式拼法

Tup·per·ware /ˋtʌpɚˌwɛr; ˈtʌpəweə/ *n* [U] *trademark* a type of plastic container that closes very tightly and is used to store food【商標】"特百惠"塑料容器〔帶緊蓋, 用來存放食物等〕

tur·ban /ˋtɝbən; ˈtɜːbən/ *n* [C] a long piece of cloth that you wind tightly round your head, worn by men in parts of North Africa and Southern Asia and sometimes by women as a fashion〔北非、南亞地區男性纏在頭上的〕頭巾; 女用頭巾

tur·bid /ˋtɝbɪd; ˈtɜːbɪd/ *adj formal* turbid water or liquid is dirty and muddy【正式】〔水或液體〕混濁的, 不清的: *the silty, turbid waters of the Congo river* 淤泥阻塞、混濁不清的剛果河河水 —**turbidity** /tɝˋbɪdətɪ; tɜːˈbɪdəti/ *n* [U]

tur·bine /ˋtɝbɪn; ˈtɜːbaɪn/ *n* [C] an engine or motor in which the pressure of a liquid or gas moves a special wheel around 渦輪機, 透平機 —see also 另見 GAS TURBINE, WIND TURBINE

tur·bo·charg·er /ˋtɝboˌtʃɑrdʒɚ; ˈtɜːbəʊˌtʃɑːdʒə/ also 又作 **turbo** *n* [C] a system that makes a vehicle more powerful by using a turbine to force air and petrol into the engine under increased pressure 渦輪增壓器: *The 2.4 litre turbo diesel is the top-seller.* 2.4升的渦輪增壓器柴油車是最暢銷的。—**turbocharged** *adj*

tur·bo·jet /ˋtɝboˌdʒɛt; ˈtɜːbəʊdʒet/ *n* [C] **1** a powerful engine that makes something, especially an aircraft, move forwards, by forcing out hot air and gases at the back 渦輪噴氣發動機 **2** an aircraft that gets power from this type of engine 渦輪式噴氣飛機

tur·bo·prop /ˋtɝboˌprɑp; ˈtɜːbəʊprɒp/ *n* [C] **1** a turbine engine that drives a PROPELLER 渦輪螺旋槳發動機 **2** an aircraft that gets power from this type of engine 渦輪式螺旋槳飛機

tur·bot /ˋtɝbət; ˈtɜːbɒt/ *n* [C,U] a large flat European fish 大菱鮃〔歐洲產的一種扁平的大魚〕

tur·bu·lence /ˋtɝbjələns; ˈtɜːbjələns/ *n* [U] **1** irregular and violent movements of air or water that are caused by the wind〔由風造成的空氣或水的〕湍流; 不穩定的強氣流: *The flight was very uncomfortable because of turbulence.* 由於遇上不穩定的強氣流, 這次飛行很不舒服。**2** a political or emotional situation that is very confused〔政治或情感上的〕騷亂, 騷動: *A period of political turbulence followed the civil war.* 內戰之後是一段政治動蕩的時期。

tur·bu·lent /ˋtɝbjələnt; ˈtɜːbjələnt/ *adj* **1** a turbulent situation or period of time is one in which there are a lot of sudden changes and often wars or violence 騷亂的, 動亂的: *The Reformation was one of the most turbulent periods in English history.* 新教改革是英國歷史上最為動盪的時期之一。**2** turbulent air or water moves around a lot because of the wind 風大浪高的; 狂風大作的: *turbulent weather conditions* 狂風大作的天氣狀況 **3** turbulent crowds or people are noisy and violent〔人羣〕騷動的; 暴戾的: *the turbulent populace of the city's teeming ghettos* 該市擁擠的貧民窟裡騷動不安的人們

turd /tɝd; tɜːd/ *n* [C] **1** *informal* a slightly rude word for a piece of the solid waste material you pass from your body【非正式】大便〔稍微粗俗的用語〕**2** *taboo* an insulting word for an unpleasant person【諱】混蛋, 臭小子: *You stupid little turd!* 你這個愚蠢的臭小子!

tu·reen /tuˋrin; tjʊˈriːn/ *n* [C] a large dish with a lid used for serving soup or vegetables〔盛湯用的〕大蓋碗, 湯碗

turf[1] /tɝf; tɜːf/ *n* **1** [U] a surface that is made up of soil and a thick covering of grass 草皮: *the springy turf of the lawn* 草坪上有彈性的草皮 **2** *plural* **turfs** *or* **turves** /tɜvz; tɜːvz/ [C] *BrE* a square piece of turf cut out of the ground【英】一塊草皮; SOD[1] (4) *AmE*【美】**3 the turf** the sport of horse racing, or the track on which horses race 賽馬(運動); 賽馬跑道: *devotees of the turf* 賽馬愛好者 **4** [U] *AmE informal* an area that you think of as being your own【美, 非正式】〔自己劃定的〕地盤: *They resented these strangers invading their turf.* 他們對這些陌生人侵入他們的地盤感到憤怒。| **turf war** (=a fight or argument over the things you think belong to you) 地盤之爭, 地盤爭奪戰 **5** [C,U] *AmE, IrishE* a soft brown substance like earth that is used for burning instead of coal, especially in Ireland; PEAT【美, 愛爾蘭】〔尤指愛爾蘭的〕泥炭, 泥煤

turf² *v* [T] to cover an area of land with TURF[1] (1) 用草皮覆蓋〔某塊地〕

turf sb/sth ↔ **out** *phr v* [T] *BrE informal* to get rid of someone or something【英, 非正式】趕走〔某人〕; 扔掉〔某物〕: *He's been turfed out of the golf club for bad behaviour.* 他因為行為不端而被逐出了這家高爾夫俱樂部。

turf ac·coun·tant /ˈ· ·,··/ *n* [C] *BrE* someone who has a business where people can BET[1] (1) on the results of horse races, football games etc; BOOKMAKER【英】〔經營賽馬、足球比賽等賭博的〕莊家

tur·gid /ˈtɜdʒɪd; ˈtɜːdʒɪd/ *adj* **1** turgid writing or speech is boring and difficult to understand〔寫作或講話〕枯燥乏味的; 很難理解的: *The whole play is turgid, amateurish drivel.* 整場戲枯燥乏味, 全是業餘水準的廢話。**2** *formal* full and swollen with liquid or air【正式】〔因有液體或空氣〕鼓得滿滿的; 腫脹的 **—turgidly** *adv* **—turgidity** /tɜˋdʒɪdətɪ; tɜːˈdʒɪdɪti/ *n* [U]

Turk /tɜk; tɜːk/ *n* [C] someone from Turkey 土耳其人

tur·key /ˈtɜkɪ; ˈtɜːki/ *n* **1** [C] a bird that looks like a large chicken and is often eaten at Christmas and at Thanksgiving 火雞 **2** [U] the meat from a turkey eaten as food 火雞肉: *roast turkey* 烤火雞肉 **3** [C] *AmE informal* someone who is silly or stupid【美, 非正式】傻瓜, 笨蛋: *That guy's a real turkey.* 那傢伙真是個笨蛋。**4** *AmE informal* an unsuccessful film or play【美, 非正式】〔電影、戲劇等的〕失敗之作 **5 talk turkey** *informal especially AmE* to talk seriously about details, especially in business【非正式, 尤美】認真地談論〔細節, 尤指商務談判〕—see also 另見 COLD TURKEY

Turk·ish¹ /ˈtɜkɪʃ; ˈtɜːkɪʃ/ *n* [U] the language of Turkey 土耳其語

Turkish² *adj* from or connected with Turkey 土耳其的; 土耳其人的

Turkish bath /,·· ˈ·/ *n* [C] a health treatment that involves sitting in a very hot steamy room 土耳其浴, 蒸汽浴: *I walked into the club and it was like a Turkish bath!* 我走進俱樂部, 裡面簡直就像蒸汽浴一樣!

Turkish cof·fee /,·· ˈ··/ *n* [C,U] very strong black coffee that you drink in small cups with sugar 土耳其咖啡〔一種不加奶的濃烈咖啡〕

Turkish de·light /,·· ·ˈ·/ *n* [U] a type of sweet made from firm JELLY (1) that is cut into pieces and covered in sugar or chocolate〔外包糖粉或巧克力的〕土耳其軟糖

tur·me·ric /ˈtɜmərɪk; ˈtɜːmərɪk/ *n* [U] yellow powder used to give a special colour or taste to food, especially CURRY[1] 薑黃根粉〔用作食品調色或調味之用, 尤用於咖喱〕

tur·moil /ˈtɜmɔɪl; ˈtɜːmɔɪl/ *n* [U, singular] a state of confusion, excitement, and trouble 混亂, 騷亂, 動亂: *The country is in complete turmoil.* 這個國家陷入一片混亂之中。

T

turn¹ /tɜn; tɜːn/ *v*

① CHANGE DIRECTION/POSITION 改變方向/位置
② COLOUR 顏色
③ AGE/TIME 年齡/時間
④ CHANGE 改變
⑤ PAGE 書頁
⑥ VEHICLE 車輛
⑦ OTHER MEANINGS 其他意思

① CHANGE DIRECTION/POSITION 改變方向/位置

1 a) ►**YOUR BODY** 人的身體◄ [I] to move your body so that you are looking in a different direction 轉過身, 翻身: *Ricky turned and walked away.* 里克轉身走了。| [**+around/round/away etc**] *I turned around quickly to see if someone was following.* 我迅速轉過身來, 看看是否有人在後面跟着。| *Dan turned away so Brody couldn't see the fear in his eyes.* 丹轉過身去, 這樣布洛迪就看不到他眼中的恐懼了。| **turn to do sth** *She turned to look back at him as she got on the plane.* 她登上飛機時轉過身來回看了他一眼。| *He turned to face Kim with tears in his eyes.* 他轉過身來面對着基姆, 眼裡噙滿了淚水。| **turn on your heel** (=turn away suddenly) 突然轉身 *Brigitte glared at him, turned on her heel, and stomped out of the room.* 布麗吉特瞪了他一眼, 然後轉過身跺着腳走出了房間。**b)** ►**OBJECT** 物體◄ [T] to move something so that it is pointing or aiming in a different direction 轉動〔某物〕; 使〔某物〕對準或瞄準〔某一方向〕: *Turn the vase so the crack doesn't show.* 轉一下花瓶, 這樣裂縫就不會露出來了。| *The firemen turned the hose on the burning building.* 消防隊員把水管對準正在燃燒的大樓。| **turn sth to face sth** *I turned the chair to face him and began to talk.* 我轉過椅子, 面朝着他開始說話。

2 ►**ROAD/RIVER/PATH ETC** 路/河流/小徑等◄ [I] to curve in a particular direction〔向某方向〕轉彎: *The river turns east and flows down out of the mountains.* 河流折向東邊, 然後從山裡流了出來。| *a small path twisting and turning through the woods* 曲折蜿蜒穿過樹林的一條小徑

3 ►**MOVE AROUND CENTRAL POINT** 沿中心點轉動◄ [I,T] to move around a central or fixed point, or make something move in this way (使) 旋轉, 轉圈: *The wheel creaked as it turned.* 輪子在旋轉的時候嘎吱作響。| **turn sth** *Turn the handle as far as it will go to the right.* 向右轉動手柄直到轉不動為止。

② COLOUR 顏色

4 ►**OBJECT** 物體◄ [linking verb 連繫動詞] to become a different colour 變色: *The clothes all turned pink in the wash.* 衣服在洗滌過程中全變成粉紅色了。| *The leaves turned red, orange, and yellow in the autumn air.* 樹葉在秋季變成了紅、橙、黃幾種顏色。—see 見 BECOME (USAGE)

5 ►**PERSON** 人◄ [linking verb 連繫動詞] if a person turns a particular colour, their skin looks that colour because they feel ill, embarrassed etc〔因生病、尷尬等人的皮膚〕變色: *Vy turned white when she saw all the blood on the floor.* 看到地板上全是血, 維伊臉都變白了。| *Every time Inge speaks to Hans, he turns bright red.* 每次英格跟漢斯說話時, 他的臉都會變得通紅。

6 ►**HAIR** 頭髮◄ [linking verb 連繫動詞] if your hair turns grey or white, it becomes that colour because you are getting older〔因年老頭髮〕變色: *Her face was lined and her hair was already turning grey.* 她的臉上有了

皺紋，頭髮也變成灰白色了。

③ **AGE/TIME 年齡/時間**

7 ▶AGE 年齡◀ [linking verb 連繫動詞] if someone turns a particular age, they become that age 到達〔某年齡〕: *"How old is Dennis?" "He's just turned 40."* "丹尼斯有多大了?" "他剛滿40歲。"

8 ▶TIME 時間◀ [linking verb 連繫動詞] if it has turned a particular time, that time has just passed 到達〔某時間〕: *"What time is it?" "It's just turned 3:00."* "甚麼時間了?" "剛三點鐘。"

④ **CHANGE 改變**

9 turn nasty/mean/violent etc to suddenly become angry, violent etc 突然變得憤怒/卑鄙/兇暴等: *One day the dog just turned nasty and bit me.* 一天，那隻狗一怒之下咬了我。| *The police are worried that the situation could turn violent.* 警察擔憂的是有可能會出現暴力行動。—see 見 BECOME (USAGE)

10 turn cold/nasty if the weather turns cold or nasty, it suddenly becomes cold, unpleasant etc 〔天氣〕變冷/變壞: *The forecast says it's going to turn nasty.* 預報說天氣會變得很糟糕。

11 ▶ACTIVITY 活動◀ [I] to stop one activity and start something completely different 改變; 轉向: **[+to]** *Our laughter turned to horror when we realized Jody really was hurt.* 當我們意識到喬迪真的受傷了，我們的笑聲一下變成了恐懼。| *Many people here have turned to solar power as an alternative to electricity.* 這裡的許多人轉用太陽能替代電能。

12 actor turned politician/football player turned author etc someone who has done one job and then does something completely different 演員變成了政治家/足球運動員變成了作家等

13 turn traitor to be disloyal to a person, group, or idea that you have strongly supported before 成了叛徒: *Ramirez's lieutenant turned traitor and told the military where he was hiding.* 拉米雷斯的助手叛變了，把他藏身的地方告訴了軍方。

⑤ **PAGE 書頁**

14 [T] if you turn a page in a book, you move it so that you can read the next page 翻動〔書頁〕—see also 另見 **turn to** (TURN¹)

⑥ **VEHICLE 車輛**

15 [I,T] if you turn a vehicle or it turns, it changes direction (使)〔汽車〕轉向, 拐彎: **[+into/off/left/right]** *Turn left at the next light.* 在下一個紅綠燈向左轉。| *The car in front of me turned into a driveway.* 我前面的那輛車拐彎上了一條私用車道。| **turn sth around/into** *Jason turned the car around while I brought the suitcases.* 賈森在我去拿衣箱時把車子調了頭。

⑦ **OTHER MEANINGS 其他意思**

16 ▶INJURY 受傷◀ [T] if you turn your ankle, you twist it in a way that injures it; SPRAIN 扭傷〔踝關節〕: *Is it bad? No, I just turned my ankle on the step.* 很嚴重嗎? 不，我只是在台階上扭了腳踝。

17 ▶MILK 牛奶◀ [I] if milk turns, it becomes sour 〔牛奶〕變酸

18 turn your back (on) a) to refuse to help or give sympathy to someone when they need it 對…置之不理; 對…撒手不管: *How can you turn your back on your own mother?* 你怎麼能對自己的母親撒手不管呢? **b)** to deliberately stop being involved in something that used to be very important for you 不再參與〔某事〕: *Isn't it hard to turn your back on tennis after so many years at the top?* 這麼多年你一直處在最高峯，現在決定不再打網球了，難道不感到難受嗎? **c)** to turn so that your back is pointing towards someone or something 轉身背對着〔某人或某物〕: *He turned his back on her and spoke quietly into the phone.* 他轉過身背對着她，對着話筒輕聲說話。| *As soon as you turn your back on these kids, they're acting like maniacs again!* 你剛轉過身不理這些孩子，他們又發狂似地鬧開了!

19 turn sth inside out a) to pull a piece of clothing, bag etc so that the inside is facing outwards 把〔衣服、口袋等〕裡朝外翻: *Just turn the bag inside out to make sure there's nothing left in it.* 只需把口袋裡朝外翻，確保裡面沒有留下任何東西。**b)** also 又作 **turn sth upside down** to search everywhere for something, in a way that makes a place very untidy 到處搜尋〔某物〕，翻了個底朝天: *The thieves had turned the house upside down looking for the papers.* 小偷把屋子翻了個底朝天，想尋找那些文件。

20 turn (people's) heads if something turns people's heads, they are surprised by it 讓(人)吃驚: *Yes, it did turn a few heads when he moved back to the village.* 是的，他搬回村裡居住，着實讓一些人吃了一驚。

21 turn sb's head to be attractive in a romantic or sexual way to a particular person 使〔某人〕愛慕: *You mean that horrible old man actually managed to turn Jo's head?* 你指的是那個可怕的老頭，竟然使喬愛上了他?

22 have turned the corner to have done the most difficult part of something, so that the rest looks fairly easy 已經渡過了最困難的階段 —see also 另見 **turn a blind eye** (BLIND¹ (2)), **turn the other cheek** (CHEEK¹ (6)), **sb would turn in their grave** (GRAVE¹ (3)), **not turn a hair** (HAIR (8)), **turn your hand to** (HAND¹ (10)), **turn over a new leaf** (LEAF¹ (3)), **turn your nose up (at)** (NOSE¹ (6)), **turn the tables (on sb)** (TABLE¹ (5)), **turn tail** (TAIL¹ (8))

turn against sb/sth *phr v* [T] to decide that you do not like someone or agree with something any more 轉而討厭; 轉而反對: *Public opinion in Panama turned against him.* 巴拿馬的輿論轉而反對他。

turn sb **against** sb/sth *phr v* [T] to make someone not to like someone any more or not to agree with something any more 使與…為敵; 離間…: *After the divorce, Dave accused Christina of turning the kids against him.* 離婚後，戴夫指責克里斯蒂娜挑唆孩子們與他作對。

turn around also 又作 **turn round** *BrE*【英】*phr v* **1** [T **turn** sth ↔ **round**] to complete the process of making a product or providing a service 完成; 提供; 生產出: *We can turn around a batch of 50 pressings in two hours.* 我們能夠在兩小時內壓製出50張唱片。**2** [T **turn** sth ↔ **round**] to manage an unsuccessful business so well that it becomes successful again 使〔業務〕好轉: *In under three years she had completely turned the company around.* 在不到三年的時間裡，她已完全使公司的業務好轉起來。**3 turn around and say/tell** *spoken* to tell someone something that they think is unfair or unreasonable【口】反而說/講〔不合理的話〕: *I complained about it but they just turned round and said it was my own fault.* 我投訴時，他們卻說是我自己的過錯。

turn away *phr v* **1** [T **turn** sb ↔ **away**] to refuse to let someone into a place such as a theatre, cinema etc, because there is no more space 〔戲院等因滿座〕不讓…進入: *They turned about 1,000 people away at the Arena because all the tickets were gone.* 因為所有的票都已賣光了，他們把大約1,000人拒在阿里納劇院之外。**2** [I,T] to refuse to give someone sympathy, help, or support 拒絕給…同情[援助, 支持]: *Europe cannot in good conscience turn away from these refugees.* 歐洲拒絕援助這些難民，不能無愧於心。| **turn sb ↔ away** *I can't turn her away. She's my brother's child.* 我不能拒絕她。她是我的姪女。

turn back *phr v* **1** [I] to go in the opposite direction 折回，掉轉頭: *It was late afternoon when we finally decided it was time to turn back.* 下午晚些時候，我們最終決定該往回走了。| *One of the boats had to turn back* *because it was taking in water.* 其中的一隻船因為進水而不得不折回來了。**2** [T **turn** sb ↔ **back**] to tell someone to go in the opposite direction, often because there is danger ahead〔常指因前方有危險〕使…折返: *We were turned back at the border because of the fighting.* 因為戰火, 我們在邊境處被迫折返。**3 turn back the clock a)** if you want to turn back the clock, you wish you had the chance to do something again so you could do it better 回復到從前; 重新有機會做〔某事〕: *"I'd like to be able to turn back the clock and make things right with Brett," said Gloria.* "我希望能夠有機會回到從前, 與布雷特重歸於好。" 格洛麗亞説道。**b)** to do something the way it was done at an earlier time, especially when that is worse than the way it is done now 回到過去的老一套, 倒退: *legislation that turns back the clock on human rights* 人權立法的倒退

turn down *phr v* [T] **1** [**turn** sth ↔ **down**] to make a machine such as an oven, radio etc produce less heat, sound etc 調低〔機器的熱度、音量等〕: *Can you please turn the TV down? I can't hear myself think!* 請你把電視的聲音關小一點行嗎? 我沒法靜下心來思考! **2** [**turn** sb/sth ↔ **down**] to refuse an offer, request, or invitation 拒絕〔建議、要求、邀請等〕: *Pauline's turned down offers from several different law firms.* 保利拒絕了好幾家律師事務所提出的建議。| *Jimmy offered to marry her again, but she'd already turned him down three times.* 傑米再向她求婚, 但她已經三次拒絕了他。—see 見 REFUSE[1] (USAGE)

turn in *phr v* **1** [T **turn** sth ↔ **in**] to give something back to the person that owns it, especially when it has been lost or borrowed 交回, 交還〔尤指失物或借來的東西〕: *Make sure to turn your security badge in before you leave the company.* 在離開公司之前一定要交回保安徽章。| [+**to**] *My wallet was turned in to the police two days after it was stolen.* 我的錢包在被盜後兩天被交還給了警察。**2** [T **turn** sth ↔ **in**] *especially AmE* to give a piece of work to a teacher, your boss etc【尤美】交〔作業給老師〕; 交〔已完成的工作給老闆〕: *Have you all turned in your homework from last night?* 你們全都交了昨晚的家庭作業沒有? **3** [T **turn** sb ↔ **in**] to tell the police who or where a criminal is〔向警方〕告發〔罪犯〕: *Margrove's wife finally turned him in after months of silence.* 在沉默了幾個月後, 馬格洛夫的妻子最終向警方告發了他。**4** [I] to go to bed 上牀睡覺: *Well, I think I'll turn in. I've got to get up early.* 呃, 我想我要去睡覺了。我得早起。

turn into sth *phr v* **1** [T] to become something different, or make someone or something do this 使…變成; 把…變成: **turn into sth** *In a few weeks, the caterpillar will turn into a butterfly.* 幾週之後, 毛蟲就會變成蝴蝶了。| *The sofa turns into a bed.* 沙發變成了牀。| **turn sth into sth** *Lieutenant, do you have to turn everything into a question?* 中尉, 你甚麼樣的事都得提問嗎? | **turn sb into sth** *You'll never turn me into a salesman, Dad. I'm not made for it.* 爸爸, 你千萬別指望我會成為推銷員。我天生不是那塊料。**2** [T] to change by magic from one thing into another, or make something do this〔通過魔法〕變成; 使…變成: **turn into sth** *In a flash of light, the prince turned into a frog.* 一陣閃光之後, 王子變成了一隻青蛙。| **turn sb/sth into sth** *The fairy godmother turned the pumpkin into a coach.* 仙姑把那隻南瓜變成了一輛馬車。**3** [T] if one season turns into another season, it changes gradually from one to the next〔季節〕變化, 轉換: *The snows melted, and winter turned into spring.* 積雪融化, 冬去春來。**4 days turned into weeks/months turned into years etc** used to say that time passed slowly while you waited for something to happen 幾天之後又是幾週/幾個月之後又是幾年〔用於表示等待某事發生時日子過去〕: *Weeks turned into months, and still there was no letter from Renata.* 幾週之後又是幾月, 但仍然沒有雷納塔的來信。

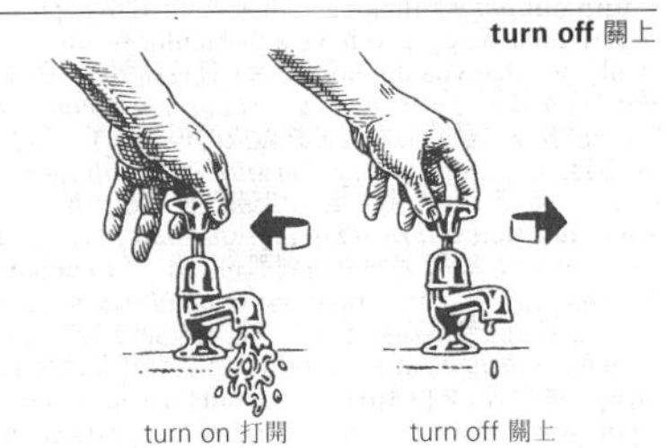

turn off *phr v* **1** [T **turn** sth ↔ **off**] to stop the supply of water, gas etc from flowing by turning a handle or TAP as far as it will go 關掉〔自來水、煤氣等的〕開關: *Turn off the hot water.* 把熱水關掉。| *They've turned the gas off for a couple of hours.* 他們已把煤氣關閉幾個小時了。**2** [T **turn** sth ↔ **off**] to make a machine or piece of electrical equipment such as a television, car, light etc stop operating by pushing a button, turning a key etc 關閉〔電視機、汽車引擎、電燈等〕: *Don't forget to turn off the lights when you leave.* 離開時別忘了關燈。| *Turn the TV off now.* 現在把電視機關了。**3** [I,T] to leave one road, especially a large one, and drive along another one 離開〔某條路, 尤指大路〕而轉上另一條路: **turn off at/near etc** *I'm sure we should have turned off at the last exit.* 我敢肯定地説, 我們該在上一個出口駛出。| **turn off sth** *Gill turned off the A10 and started heading west.* 吉爾離開 A10 號公路, 開始奔西而去。—see also 另見 TURN-OFF **4** [T **turn** sb ↔ **off**] to do something that makes someone decide they do not like something 使〔人〕不喜歡: *Don't oversell the product. If your salespeople are pushy, they'll turn the customer off.* 推銷產品不要沒有分寸。你們的推銷員如果咄咄逼人, 會讓顧客不喜歡的。**5** [T **turn** sb ↔ **off**] to do something that makes someone feel that they are not attracted to you in a sexual way 使喪失性的吸引力: *It really turns me off when Richard wears his smelly socks to bed.* 理查德穿着他的臭襪子上牀, 真讓我倒胃口。

turn on *phr v* **1** [T **turn** sth ↔ **on**] to make the supply of water, gas etc start flowing from something by turning a handle or TAP[1] (1) 打開〔自來水、煤氣等的〕開關: *I turned the water on in the shower.* 我打開了淋浴間的水龍頭。| *We'll be turning on the gas in about an hour.* 我們在大約一小時後開啟煤氣。**2** [T **turn** sth ↔ **on**] to make a machine or piece of electrical equipment such as a car, television, light etc start operating by pushing a button, turning a key etc 啟動〔汽車〕, 打開〔電視機、電燈等〕: *Could you turn on the light, please?* 請把燈打開好嗎? | *When I turned the engine on it made a funny noise.* 當我啟動發動機時, 它發出了異常的聲音。—see 見 OPEN[2] (USAGE) **3** [T **turn on** sb] to suddenly attack someone or treat them badly, using physical violence or unpleasant words 突然襲擊〔某人〕; 惡劣地對待〔某人〕: *Peter turned on Rae with eyes blazing and screamed, "Get out of my sight!"* 彼得用充滿怒火的雙眼看着雷高聲叫道: "從我面前滾開!" **4** [T **turn on** sth] if a situation, event, argument turns on a particular thing or idea, it depends on that thing in order to work 取決於, 依…而定: *The negotiations turned on getting the Italian delegation to agree.* 談判取決於能否獲得意大利代表團的同意。**5** [T **turn** sb **on**] to make someone feel sexually excited 使感到性刺激: *A lot of guys are turned on by the idea of women in uniform.* 許多傢伙一想到穿着制服的女性就感到十分刺激。—see also 另見 TURN-ON **6** [T **turn** sb **on to** sth] to make someone become interested in a product, idea etc 使產生興趣: *Mark's that friend of mine who turned me on to classical music.* 馬克就是那位使我對古典音樂產生興趣的朋友。

T

turn out *phr v* **1** [linking verb 連繫動詞] to happen in a particular way, or to have a particular result, especially one that you did not expect 最後結果是, 最終成為: *I hate the way my hair turned out. The colour's all wrong.* 我不喜歡我的頭髮最終做成的那個樣子。顏色完全不對勁。| *Don't worry, I'm sure it will all turn out fine.* 不要擔心, 我敢肯定一切最終會好起來的。| **it turns out that** *It turned out that she didn't get the job in the end.* 結果是, 她沒有得到那份工作。| **turn out to be** *That guy we met turned out to be Maria's second cousin.* 我們遇到的那個傢伙原來是瑪麗亞的堂弟。| *His statement turned out to be false.* 他說的那番話後來證明是一派謊言。**2** [T **turn** sth ↔ **out**] if you turn out a light, you stop the flow of electricity to it by pushing a button, pulling a string etc 關上, 關掉〔電燈〕: *Don't forget to turn out the lights when you go!* 你走的時候不要忘了關燈! **3** [T **turn** sb ↔ **out**] to force someone to leave a place 驅逐, 趕走: *Benjamin turned his son out of the house without any money.* 本傑明把兒子趕出了家門, 沒給他一分錢。**4** [I] if people turn out for an event, they gather together to see it happen〔為看熱鬧〕蜂擁而出: *Crowds of people turned out to watch the filming of the final scene of Rocky.* 人羣蜂擁而至, 前來觀看《洛奇》這部電影最後一場戲的拍攝。—see also 另見 TURNOUT **5** [T **turn** sth ↔ **out**] to produce or make something 生產, 製造: *The factory turns out 300 units a day.* 這家工廠一天生產 300 台。**6 well/beautifully/badly turned out** to be dressed in good, beautiful etc clothes 衣着很好/很漂亮/很差勁: *elegantly turned-out young ladies* 衣着雅致的年輕女士

turn over *phr v* **1** [T **turn** sb ↔ **over to** sb] to bring a criminal to the police or other official organization 把〔犯人〕交給〔警方等〕: *The FBI caught Rostov and turned him over to the CIA.* 聯邦調查局拘捕了羅斯托夫並把他移交給中央情報局。**2** [T **turn** sth ↔ **over to** sb] to give someone the right to own or the responsibility for something such as a plan, business, piece of property etc 把〔所有權〕交給〔某人〕; 交託〔某人〕負責〔某事〕: *I'm turning the shop over to my son when I retire.* 我退休時就把商店託付給兒子去經營。| *When you leave, the project will be turned over to Mathias.* 你離開時, 這項工程就交給馬賽厄斯來負責。**3** [T **turn over** sth] if a business turns over a particular amount of money, it makes that amount in a particular period of time 營業額達到: *We were turning over $1,500 a week when business was good.* 生意好的時候, 我們一週的營業額可達 1,500 美元。**4** [I] *BrE* to turn a page in a book or a sheet of paper to the opposite side【英】〔書頁或紙張〕翻過 **5** [I] *BrE to* change the CHANNEL[1] (1) on a television【英】變換電視頻道: *I hate this programme. Can we please turn over?* 我討厭這個節目。請問能換個頻道嗎? **6 turn sth over in your mind** to think about something carefully, considering all the possibilities 認真考慮某事, 從多方面考慮某事: *I turned Zeke's comments over in my mind for a long time that night.* 我那天晚上很長時間都在反覆思考澤克的評語。

turn to *phr v* **1** [T **turn to** sb/sth] to try to get help, advice, or sympathy from someone or by doing something 求助於, 求教於: *Nobody seems to understand. I don't know who to turn to.* 似乎沒有人明白這個。我不知道該向誰求教。| *Paul turned to drink* (=drinking alcohol) *to try to forget his problems at work.* 保羅借酒澆愁, 想忘掉工作中的問題。**2** [T **turn to** sth] to look at a particular page in a book 翻到〔書中的某頁〕: *Turn to page 655 for more information on this subject.* 翻到 655 頁就可以知道有關這一論題的更多情況。**3 turn your attention/thoughts/efforts etc to sth** to begin to think about or do something different from what you have been doing 開始注意到/想到/致力於某事 **4** [I] *old-fashioned* to begin to work hard【過時】開始努力工作: *We'll really have to turn to in order to finish this on time.* 為了按時完成工作, 我們真的必須開始努力幹了。

turn up *phr v* **1** [T **turn** sth ↔ **up**] to make a machine such as an oven, radio etc produce more heat, sound etc 調大, 開大〔熱度、音量等〕: *Turn the oven up to 220°C.* 把爐子調高到 220°C。| *Turn up the radio!* 把收音機開大聲一點! **2** [I] to suddenly appear after having been lost or searched for 突然露面, 重新出現: *I couldn't find my watch for ages, but then one day it turned up in a coat pocket.* 我有好長時間找不着手錶了, 但有一天, 它在一件外衣的口袋裡出現了。**3** [I always+adv/prep] to arrive at a place 到達, 來到: *Steven turned up late as usual.* 史蒂文像往常一樣來遲了。**4** [I] if an opportunity or situation turns up, it happens, especially when you are not expecting it〔機會或情況〕突然發生, 不期而至: *Don't worry, I'm sure a job will turn up soon.* 不要着急, 我敢肯定工作不久就會有的。**5** [T **turn** sth ↔ **up**] to find something by thoroughly searching for it〔經過徹底搜尋〕發現, 發掘出: *The police investigation hasn't turned up any new evidence.* 警方的調查還沒有發現任何新的證據。**6** [T **turn** sth ↔ **up**] *BrE* to shorten a skirt, trousers etc by folding up the bottom and SEWING it【英】〔把裙腳、褲腳捲起縫上〕改短... —see also 另見 **come up trumps/turn up trumps** (TRUMP[1] (3))

turn upon sb *phr v* [T] to suddenly attack someone or treat them badly, using physical violence or unpleasant words 突然襲擊; 惡劣對待

1 1

turn² *n*

1 it is sb's turn if it is your turn to do something, it is the time when you can or should do it, because you are one of a number of people doing the same activity in a particular order 輪到某人〔做某事〕: *It's your turn. Roll the dice.* 輪到你了。擲骰子吧。| **sb's turn to do sth** *I think it's our turn to drive the kids to school this week.* 我想這週該輪到我們開車送孩子們上學了。**2 take turns** also 又作 **take it in turns** *BrE* if many people take turns doing work or playing a game, they each do it one after the other in order to share work or play fairly【英】輪流, 依次: *You'll have to take turns being captain of the team.* 你們得輪流當球隊的隊長。| **take turns doing sth** *We took turns doing the driving on the way up to Canada.* 在往北去加拿大的途中, 我們輪流開車。| **take turns to do sth** *brainstorming sessions where we all took turns to throw in ideas* 我們都輪流獻計獻策的攻關會議

3 in turn a) as a result of something 因此, 因而: *Interest rates were cut, and in turn, share prices rose.* 利率降了, 因而股票價格漲了。**b)** one after the other, especially in a particular order 輪流地, 依次地: *He asked each of us in turn to describe how alcohol had affected our lives.* 他要我們每個人依次描述一下酒是如何影響自己的生活的。

4 ►VEHICLE 車輛◄ [C] the act of changing direction in a vehicle, or making it do this〔車輛的〕轉向, 使轉彎: **make a left/right turn** *Make a left turn after the bank.* 過了銀行後向左拐。

5 ►ACT OF TURNING STH 轉動某物的動作◄ [C] the act of turning something completely around a fixed point 轉動, 旋轉: *Tighten it another two or three turns.* 再給它轉緊兩三圈。

6 ►ROAD 道路◄ [C] the place where one road goes in a different direction from another〔道路的〕轉彎處, 交叉處: *According to the map, we missed our turn back there at the light.* 從地圖來看, 我們錯過了在交通燈那兒轉彎。

7 the turn of the century the beginning of a century 世紀之交: *At the turn of the century, new technologies will already be in place.* 到世紀之交時, 新的技術將已經投入使用了。

8 take a turn for the worse/better to suddenly become worse or better 突然變得更糟/更好: *Paul's health took a turn for the worse on Tuesday.* 保羅的健康狀況

在星期二突然惡化起來。

9 turn of events a change in what is happening, especially an unusual one 事態的變化〔尤指不同尋常的變化〕: *The General's agreement to the peace talks is a welcome but unexpected turn of events.* 將軍同意和談, 這是值得歡迎的, 但也是未曾預料到的事態變化。

10 turn of phrase a) a particular way of saying something; expression 言談方式; 說法; 措辭: *I've never liked that turn of phrase – when people say 'I won't detain you any longer'.* 我從來就不喜歡"我不再耽誤你的時間了"這種說法。**b)** the ability to say things in a clever or funny way 巧妙風趣的口才: *Kate has a witty turn of phrase.* 凱特的言談妙趣橫生。

11 on the turn a) if the TIDE is on the turn, it is starting to come in or go out〔潮水〕在漲[落] **b)** starting to change, or in the process of changing 開始轉變, 正在轉變: *I began to think that maybe my luck was on the turn.* 我開始想我的運氣也許正在變。**c)** *especially BrE* if milk, fish, or other food is on the turn, it is starting to become sour【尤英】〔牛奶、魚等食品〕開始變酸

12 speak out of turn to say something you should not say in a particular situation, especially because you do not have enough authority to say it 說不該說的話〔尤指超越本分說話〕: *I hope I'm not speaking out of turn, sir, but I don't think this is the best way to proceed.* 我希望我沒有冒昧無禮, 先生, 但我認為這並不是最好的做法。

13 do sb a good/bad turn to do something that is helpful or unhelpful for someone 做有利/有損於某人的行為: *You'll be doing me a good turn by driving Max home tonight.* 你今晚開車送馬克斯回家, 就是幫了我一個大忙。

14 at every turn if something happens at every turn, it happens again and again 每一回; 總是; 處處: *We were frustrated at every turn in our efforts to get money for the project.* 我們努力想為這個項目籌錢, 但總是處處碰壁。

15 by turns if someone shows different feelings or qualities by turns, they change from one to another 輪流地, 依次〔表現某些情感或特質〕: *That evening he was silly, witty, and mournful by turns.* 那天晚上, 他先是傻乎乎的, 然後變得妙趣橫生, 最後又悲從心來。

16 turn of mind *literary* the way that someone usually thinks or feels【文】性情; 習性, 天性: *He was of a melancholy turn of mind.* 他性情憂鬱。

17 done/cooked to a turn to be perfectly cooked 烹調得恰到好處

18 one good turn deserves another used to say that if someone does something nice for you, you should do something nice for them to thank them 好心應該得到好報; 以德報德

19 take a turn in/on etc *old-fashioned* to walk somewhere just for pleasure【過時】悠閒地散步, 閒逛: *I think they're out taking a turn in the gardens.* 我想他們正在花園裡悠閒地散步。

20 give sb a turn *old-fashioned* to frighten someone【過時】驚嚇〔某人〕

21 have a turn *BrE old-fashioned* to feel slightly ill or faint【英, 過時】感覺有點不舒服; 有點頭昏

turn·a·bout /ˈtɝnəˌbaut; ˈtɜːnəbaʊt/ *n BrE*【英】[C usually singular 一般用單數] **1** a complete change in someone's opinions or ideas〔觀點或思想的〕徹底改變, 變卦: *an extraordinary turnabout in public opinion* 輿論的異常轉變 **2 turnabout is fair play** *AmE* used to say that because someone else has done something you can do it too【美】一人一遭, 天公地道; 以其人之道還治其人之身乃是公道

turn·a·round /ˈtɝnəˌraund; ˈtɜːnəraʊnd/ *n* [C usually singular 一般用單數] *especially AmE* a TURNROUND【尤美】收到某物、處理並送回所需的時間; 好轉, 轉機;〔觀點或思想的〕徹底改變

turn·coat /ˈtɝnˌkot; ˈtɜːnkəʊt/ n [C] someone who stops supporting a political party or group and joins the opposing side 叛黨者, 變節者: *Casson was pilloried as a turncoat and a traitor.* 卡森因叛黨變節而臭名昭彰。

turn·er /ˈtɝnɚ; ˈtɜːnə/ *n* [C] someone who uses a LATHE (=special tool) to make shapes out of wood or metal 車工, 旋工

turn·ing /ˈtɝnɪŋ; ˈtɜːnɪŋ/ *n* [C] *BrE* a road that connects with the one you are on【英】從所在的路分出的路;〔道路的〕拐彎處; TURN[2] (6) *AmE*【美】: *Take the first turning on the left.* 到第一個拐彎處就向左拐。

turning cir·cle /ˈ·· ˌ··/ *n* [C] the smallest space in which a vehicle can drive around in a circle 回轉圓〔汽車能轉彎的最小行車圈〕

turning point /ˈ·· ·/ *n* [C] the time when an important change starts, especially one that improves the situation 轉折點; 關鍵時刻: *The Battle of El Alamein was a turning point in the war.* 阿拉曼戰役是這次戰爭中的一個轉折點。

tur·nip /ˈtɝnɪp; ˈtɜːnɪ̥p/ *n* [C,U] a large round pale yellow vegetable that grows under the ground, or the plant that produces it 蕪菁 —see picture on page A9 參見 A9 頁圖

turn·key[1] /ˈtɝnki; ˈtɜːnkiː/ *n* [C] *old use* a JAILER【舊】監獄看守

turnkey[2] *adj* [only before noun 僅用於名詞前] ready to be used immediately 立即可以使用的: *low-cost turnkey systems for retail applications* 低成本的、馬上可以交付使用的零售應用系統

turn-off /ˈ· ·/ *n* **1** [C] a smaller road that leads off a main road 岔路, 支路 **2** [singular] *informal* something that makes you lose interest in something, especially sex【非正式】〔尤指在性方面〕使人失去興趣的東西: *The music was a real turn-off so we left.* 那音樂真是讓人倒胃口, 所以我們就離開了。—see also 另見 **turn off** (TURN[1])

turn-on /ˈ· ·/ *n* [singular] *informal* something that makes you feel excited, especially sexually【非正式】〔尤指在性方面〕使人感到興奮的東西: *I found the whole thing a real turn-on.* 我覺得這整件事真的讓人感到興奮。—see also 另見 **turn on** (TURN[1])

turn·out /ˈtɝnˌaut; ˈtɜːnaʊt/ *n* **1** [singular] the number of people who go to a party, meeting, or other organized event〔聚會、會議等〕出席人數, 到場人數: *Despite the rain, there was a good turnout.* 儘管下雨, 到場的人數還是不少。**2** [singular] the number of people who vote in an election〔選舉中的〕投票人數: **high turnout** (=a lot of people voting) 高投票率 *Feelings about the election were strong, which ensured a high turnout.* 這次選舉羣情鼎沸, 從而確保了高投票率。—see also 另見 **turn out** (TURN[1]) **3** [C] *AmE* a place at the side of a narrow road where cars can wait to let others pass【美】〔窄路上的〕避車道

turn·o·ver /ˈtɝnˌovɚ; ˈtɜːnˌəʊvə/ *n* **1** [singular] the amount of business done in a particular period, measured by the amount of money earned 營業額: *an annual turnover of £5.6 million* 560 萬英鎊的年營業額 **2** [singular] the rate at which people leave an organization and are replaced by others 人事變動率, 人員流動率: *Low pay accounts for the high turnover of staff.* 低薪金是職員流動率高的原因。**3** [singular] the rate at which a particular type of goods is sold〔貨物的〕銷售量, 成交量: *Supermarkets depend on a high turnover at low prices.* 超市依賴於低價格和高銷售量。**4** [C] a small fruit PIE (1) 水果小餡餅: *an apple turnover* 蘋果餡餅 **5** [C] *AmE* a situation in a game of American football or basketball in which something happens so that one team loses the ball and the other team gets it【美】〔美式足球或籃球中的〕失球,〔球的〕易手

turn·pike /ˈtɝnˌpaɪk; ˈtɜːnpaɪk/ *n* [C] **1** *AmE* a large road for fast traffic, especially one that drivers have to pay to use【美】〔尤指需要付費的〕高速公路: *the New Jersey Turnpike* 新澤西付費高速公路 **2** *BrE* a road in Britain in the 18th century that travellers had to pay to use【英】〔18 世紀英國的一種〕付費公路, 收稅路

T

turn·round /ˋtɝn͵raund; ˈtɜːnraʊnd/ *BrE*【英】, **turnaround** *especially AmE*【尤美】*n* [C] **1** the time it takes to receive something, deal with it and send it back, especially on a plane, ship etc 收到某物、處理並送回所需的時間〔尤指使用飛機、輪船等〕: *Some drivers are on a bonus for fast turnround and deliveries.* 一些司機因周轉快、送貨快而獲得獎金。—see also 另見 **turn around** (TURN[1]) **2** [usually singular 一般用單數] a complete change from a bad situation to a good one 好轉, 轉機: *This year's profits will confirm the company's remarkable turnaround.* 今年的利潤將證實該公司的情況已有明顯好轉。**3** [usually singular 一般用單數] a complete change in someone's opinion or ideas〔觀點或思想的〕徹底改變, 轉變; TURNABOUT (1) *BrE*【英】: *a turnround in government policy* 政府政策的徹底轉變

turn sig·nal /ˋ· ͵··/ *n* [C] *AmE* one of the lights on a car that flash to show which way the car is turning【美】〔汽車上的〕轉向指示燈; INDICATOR (2) *BrE*【英】

turn·stile /ˋtɝn͵staɪl; ˈtɜːnstaɪl/ *n* [C] a small gate that spins around and only lets one person at a time go through an entrance〔入口處的〕旋轉式柵門: *We're getting far more spectators through the turnstiles than last year.* 我們吸引進場的觀眾大大超過去年。

turn·ta·ble /ˋtɝn͵tebl; ˈtɜːn͵teɪbəl/ *n* [C] **1** the round flat surface on a RECORD PLAYER that you put records on〔唱機的〕轉盤, 唱盤 **2** a large flat round surface on which railway engines are turned around〔鐵路機車掉轉方向的〕轉車台

turn-up /ˋ· ·/ *n* **1** [C] *BrE* the bottom of a trouser leg that is folded up for decoration or to make it shorter【英】〔褲腿的〕捲起部分, 捲邊; CUFF *AmE*【美】—see picture on page A17 參見 A17 頁圖 **2 a turn up for the book(s)** *BrE informal* an unexpected and surprising event【英, 非正式】意想不到的事, 突發事件: *Keith's buying the drinks – that's a turn up for the books!* 基思請喝飲料呢 —— 那可是沒料到啊!

tur·pen·tine /ˋtɝpən͵taɪn; ˈtɜpəntaɪn/ *n* [U] a type of oil used for making paint more liquid or removing it from clothes, brushes etc 松節油

tur·pi·tude /ˋtɝpə͵tud; ˈtɜːpɪ̈tjuːd/ *n* [U] *formal* evil【正式】邪惡, 墮落: *gross moral turpitude* 道德淪喪

turps /tɝps; tɜːps/ *n* [U] *BrE informal* turpentine【英, 非正式】松節油

tur·quoise /ˋtɝkwɔɪz; ˈtɜːkwɔɪz/ *n* **1** [C,U] a valuable greenish-blue stone or a jewel that is made from this 綠松石; 綠松石首飾 **2** [U] a greenish-blue colour 綠松石色, 青綠色 —**turquoise** *adj* —see picture on page A5 參見 A5 頁圖

tur·ret /ˋtɝɪt; ˈtʌrɪ̈t/ *n* [C] **1** a small tower on a large building, especially a CASTLE (1)〔尤指城堡的〕小塔樓 **2** the place on a TANK (=army vehicle) from which guns are fired〔坦克上的〕砲塔 —**turreted** *adj*

tur·tle /ˋtɝtl̩; ˈtɜːtl/ *n* [C] **1** an animal that lives mainly in water and has a soft body covered by a hard shell 海龜, 龜 **2 turn turtle** a ship or boat that turns turtle turns upside down〔船〕傾覆

tur·tle·dove /ˋtɝtl̩͵dʌv; ˈtɜːtldʌv/ *n* [C] a type of bird that makes a pleasant soft sound and is sometimes used to represent love 斑鳩

tur·tle·neck /ˋtɝtl̩͵nɛk; ˈtɜːtlnek/ *n* [C] *AmE* a type of sweater with a high, close-fitting band that folds down as a collar【美】高領套頭毛線衫; POLO NECK *BrE*【英】: *wearing a tweed skirt and a turtleneck sweater* 穿着一條粗花呢裙和一件高領毛衣 —**turtlenecked** *adj*

turves /tɝvz; tɜːvz/ *n* [plural] the plural of TURF[1] (2)

tush[1] /tʌʃ; tʌʃ/ *interjection old use* used to say that something is not worth considering【舊】呸, 啐〔表示輕蔑等〕

tush[2] /tʊʃ; tʊʃ/ *n* [C] *AmE slang* the part of your body that you sit on; BOTTOM[1] (7)【美俚】屁股

tusk /tʌsk; tʌsk/ *n* [C] one of a pair of very long pointed teeth, that stick out of the mouth of animals such as ELEPHANTS〔大象等動物的〕長牙, 獠牙

tus·sle[1] /ˋtʌsl̩; ˈtʌsəl/ *n* [C] *informal* a struggle or fight using a lot of energy, especially one in which you pull or push someone rather than hit them【非正式】搏鬥〔尤指互相揪扯而不動手打人〕: *After quite a tussle I finally wrenched the letter from him.* 經過好一陣撕扯, 我終於從他手上奪走了那封信。

tussle[2] *v* [I+with] *informal* to fight or struggle without using any weapons, by pulling or pushing someone rather than hitting them【非正式】〔不持武器地〕揪扯, 搏鬥: *tussling with the other boys in the queue* 與隊列中其他男孩揪扯

tus·sock /ˋtʌsək; ˈtʌsək/ *n* [C] a small thick mass of grass 一簇草, 叢生草

tut[1] /tʌt; tʌt/ *interjection* a sound that you make by touching the top of your mouth with your tongue in order to show disapproval 咂嘴聲, 嘖嘖聲〔表示不贊同〕—**tut** *n* [C]

tut[2] *v* [I] to express disapproval by making a tut sound 嘖嘖〔表示不贊同〕: *The nurses rushed in, tutting with irritation.* 護士們衝了進去, 氣得直咂嘴。

tu·te·lage /ˋtutl̩ɪdʒ; ˈtjuːtɪ̈lɪdʒ/ *n* [U] *formal*【正式】**1** the state or period of being taught or looked after by someone 受指導 (期); 受監護 (期): **under sb's tutelage** (=being taught by someone) 在某人的指導下 *Under Sir Edward's meticulous tutelage, I soon developed a discriminating taste.* 在愛德華爵士的細心指導下, 我很快培養了鑑別能力。**2** regular teaching over many years or months 經年累月的定期教導[指導] **3** responsibility for someone's education, actions or property 監護, 保護

tu·tor[1] /ˋtutɚ; ˈtjuːtə/ *n* [C] **1** someone who teaches one pupil or a small group, and is paid directly by them 家庭教師, 私人教師: *a reading tutor* 指導閱讀的家庭教師 **2** a teacher in a British university or college〔英國大學裡的〕助教, 導師: *She was my tutor at Durham.* 她是我在達勒姆大學時的導師。

tutor[2] *v* [T+in] to teach someone as a tutor 給…當家庭教師; 指導 —see 見 TEACH (USAGE)

tu·to·ri·al[1] /tuˋtɔrɪəl; tjuːˈtɔːriəl/ *n* [C] a period of teaching and discussion with a tutor, especially in a British university〔尤指英國大學裡的〕導師輔導 (時間): *the tutorial system* 導師制

tutorial[2] *adj* connected with a tutor or their work 家庭教師的; 助教的; 大學導師的; 輔導的, 指導的

tut·ti frut·ti /͵tutɪ ˋfrutɪ; ͵tuːti ˈfruːti/ *n* [U] a type of ICE CREAM that has very small pieces of fruit and nuts in it 什錦水果堅果冰淇淋

tut-tut[1] /ˋtʌt ˋtʌt; ͵tʌt ˈtʌt/ *interj* a sound made by touching the top of the mouth with the tongue twice, in order to show disapproval 咂嘴聲, 嘖嘖聲〔表示不贊同〕

tut-tut[2] *v* [I] to express disapproval by saying tut-tut 嘖嘖〔表示不贊同〕

tu·tu /ˋtutu; ˈtuːtuː/ *n* [C] a short skirt made of many folds of stiff material worn by BALLET dancers 芭蕾舞裙〔芭蕾舞演員穿的短裙〕

tu-whit tu-whoo /tu ˋhwɪt tu ˋhwu; tə ͵wɪt tə ˈwuː/ *n* [C] the sound made by an OWL 嘟噎嘟嗚〔貓頭鷹叫聲〕

tux /tʌks; tʌks/ *n* [C] *informal* a tuxedo【非正式】男式無尾禮服

tux·e·do /tʌkˋsido; tʌkˈsiːdəʊ/ *n* [C] **1** a man's JACKET (1) that is usually black, worn on formal occasions〔在正式場合穿的〕男式無尾禮服上衣 **2** a man's suit that includes this type of jacket 一套男式無尾禮服

TV /͵ti ˋvi; ͵tiː ˈviː◂/ *n* [C,U] television 電視: **TV programme/series/drama/star etc** *a new TV series about exploration* 一部關於探險的新電視系列片 | *Jonathan Ross, the TV personality* 電視名人喬納森·羅斯 | **on TV** *Did you see it on TV? What a game!* 你在電視上看到了嗎? 多精彩的比賽! | *a TV in every room* 每個房間一台電視機

TV din·ner /͵·· ˋ··/ *n* [C] a meal that is sold already prepared, so that you just need to heat it before eating〔只需加熱即可食用的〕電視便餐

TVP /ˌti vi ˋpi; ˌtiː viː ˈpiː/ *n* [U] the abbreviation of 縮寫 = TEXTURED VEGETABLE PROTEIN

twad·dle /ˋtwɑdḷ; ˈtwɒdl/ *n* [U] *informal* something that someone has said or written that you think is stupid; nonsense【非正式】〔說的或寫的〕無聊話，廢話: *a load of self-indulgent twaddle* 大量自我陶醉的廢話

twain /twen; tweɪn/ *prep old use*【舊】**1** two 二，兩，雙 **2 never the twain shall meet** used to say that two things are so different that they can never exist together 兩者永遠合不到一起

twang¹ /twæŋ; twæŋ/ *n* [C usually singular 一般用單數] **1** a quality in the way someone speaks, produced when the air used to speak passes through your nose as well as your mouth 鼻音: *a rural twang* 鄉下鼻音 **2** a quick ringing sound like the one made by pulling a very tight wire and then suddenly letting it go 撥弦聲

twang² *v* [I,T] if you twang something or if it twangs, it makes a quick ringing sound by being pulled and then suddenly let go (使)發出撥弦聲; (使)發出"嘣"的一聲: *She twanged the guitar strings.* 她撥弄吉他弦，發出嘣嘣聲。

twas /twɑz; twɒz/ *poetic*【詩】= it was

twat /twɑt; twɒt/ *n* [C] *BrE taboo*【英諱】**1** a stupid or unpleasant person 蠢人，討厭鬼 **2** the female sex organ 屄〔女性性器官〕

tweak /twik; twiːk/ *v* [T] **1** to suddenly pull or twist something 捏，擰: *Matthew tweaked her nose.* 馬修捏了她的鼻子。**2** to make small changes to a machine, vehicle, or system in order to improve the way it works 對〔機器、汽車或系統〕作小小的改進: *Of course the programme still needs tweaking to maximize efficiency.* 當然這套程序仍然需要作小小的改進才能發揮最高效率。—**tweak** *n* [C usually singular 一般用單數]

twee /twi; twiː/ *adj BrE* something that is twee looks too pretty or perfect【英】太花哨的; 過分豔麗的; 完美得過分的: *That picture of little cottages with lace curtains is rather twee.* 那張有網眼紗簾的小屋圖畫有點造作。

tweed /twid; twiːd/ *n* [U] **1** rough WOOLLEN cloth woven from threads of different colours, used mostly to make jackets (JACKET (1)), suits, and coats 粗花呢 —see picture on page A16 參見 A16 頁圖 **2 tweeds** [plural] a suit of clothes made from this type of cloth 粗花呢套裝

tweed·y /ˋtwidɪ; ˈtwiːdi/ *adj* **1** *BrE* wearing tweed clothes in a way that is thought to be typical of the British upper class【英】愛穿粗花呢服裝的; 典型英國上層階級的: *the epitome of the tweedy country squire* 愛穿粗花呢服裝的鄉紳典型 **2** made of tweed or like tweed 粗花呢(似)的

tween /twin; twiːn/ *prep poetic* between【詩】在…之間

tweet /twit; twiːt/ *v* [I] to make the short high sound of a small bird〔小鳥〕啾啾地叫 —**tweet** *n* [C]

tweet·er /ˋtwitɚ; ˈtwiːtə/ *n* [C] a SPEAKER (=piece of equipment) through which the high sounds from a STEREO etc are made louder 高頻揚聲器 —compare 比較 WOOFER

twee·zers /ˋtwizɚz; ˈtwiːzəz/ *n* [plural] a small tool that has two narrow pieces of metal joined at one end, used to pull or move very small objects 鑷子，小鉗子: *plucking her eyebrows with a pair of tweezers* 用一副鑷子拔她的眉毛

tweezers 鑷子

twelfth /twɛlfθ; twelfθ/ *n* [C] one of 12 equal parts of something 十二分之一

twelve /twɛlv; twelv/ *number* 12 十二

twelve-month /ˋ· ·/ *n* [C] *old-fashioned* a year【過時】一年

twen·ty /ˋtwɛntɪ; ˈtwenti/ *number* **1** 20 二十 **2 the twenties** also 又作 **the 20's** the years from 1920 to 1929 20年代〔指1920年–1929年〕: *a photo showing how the street looked in the early twenties* 一張展現20年代初期這條街道風貌的照片 **3 be in your twenties** to be aged between twenty and twenty nine〔年齡〕在20多歲時: *She met him when she was in her twenties.* 她20多歲時認識了他。

twenty-first /ˌ·· ˈ·◂/ *n* [C usually singular 一般用單數] your twenty-first BIRTHDAY or the celebration you have for it 二十一歲生日; 二十一歲生日慶祝會

twenty-one /ˌ·· ˈ·◂/ *n* [U] *AmE* a card game, usually played for money【美】二十一點牌戲〔一種賭博遊戲〕; PONTOON (1) *BrE*【英】

twenty-twenty vi·sion, 20/20 vision /ˌ·· ·· ˈ··/ *n* [U] the ability to see perfectly 極好的視力; 正常視力: *To be a pilot you must have twenty-twenty vision.* 要想當飛行員，你必須具有極好的視力。

twenty-two, .22 /ˌtwɛntɪˋtu; ˌtwentiˈtuː/ *n* [C] a gun that fires small bullets, used for hunting small animals .22口徑的獵槍

twerp /twɝp; twɜːp/ *n* [C] *informal* a stupid or annoying person【非正式】蠢人; 討厭鬼

twice /twaɪs; twaɪs/ *predeterminer* two times 兩次; 兩倍 —see also 另見 **once bitten, twice shy** (ONCE¹ (17)), **once or twice** (ONCE¹ (7)), **think twice** (THINK¹ (9))

twid·dle¹ /ˋtwɪdḷ; ˈtwɪdl/ *v* [T] **1** also 又作 **twiddle with** to move or turn something around with your fingers many times, especially because you are bored〔尤指因為厭煩而反覆地用手指〕捻弄，擺弄 **2 twiddle your thumbs** *informal*【非正式】**a)** to do nothing while you are waiting for something to happen 閒着無事，閒得無聊 **b)** to join your fingers together and move your thumbs in a circle around each other, because you are bored〔因無聊厭煩而把〕兩手的手指互扣，旋轉大拇指 —**twiddle** *n* [C]

twiddle² *n* [C] a small twist or turn, especially in a decorative pattern〔尤指裝飾圖案中的〕小旋轉，小迴轉

twiddly /ˋtwɪdlɪ; ˈtwɪdli/ *adj* **twiddly bit** *spoken* used to talk about a small part of an object without naming it【口】小東西〔用來代替正確名稱，指物體的一小部分〕: *Where's the twiddly bit for the top?* 放在上面的那個小東西到哪去了?

twig¹ /twɪg; twɪg/ *n* [C] a small very thin stem of wood that grows from a branch on a tree〔樹枝上的〕細枝，嫩枝 —**twiggy** *adj*

twig² *v* [I,T] *BrE informal* to suddenly realize something about a situation【英，非正式】突然懂得: *Do you mean he still hasn't twigged?* 你的意思是指他仍舊沒有明白?

twi·light /ˋtwaɪˌlaɪt; ˈtwaɪlaɪt/ *n* **1** [U] the small amount of light in the sky as the day ends 暮色，黃昏的天色: *It appeared shadowy and insubstantial in the twilight.* 暮色中顯得陰影模糊，虛幻不清。**2** [U] the time when day is just starting to become night 黃昏時分，薄暮時分 **3** [singular] the period just before the end of the most active part of someone's life〔人生的〕暮年時期: *the twilight of her acting career* 她演藝生涯的晚期 | **twilight years** (=the last ones of your life)〔人生的〕暮年，晚年 **4 twilight world** *literary* a strange situation involving mystery, dishonesty etc【文】朦朧世界; 陰暗世界: *the twilight world of espionage* 間諜活動的陰暗世界

twi·lit /ˋtwaɪˌlɪt; ˈtwaɪlɪt/ *adj literary* lit by twilight【文】暮色下的: *the twilit gray of the sea* 暮色下灰暗的海面

twill /twɪl; twɪl/ *n* [U] strong cloth woven to produce parallel sloping lines across its surface 斜紋織物: *grey twill trousers* 灰色的斜紋褲子

twin¹ /twɪn; twɪn/ *n* [C] one of two children born at the same time to the same mother 雙胞胎中的一個: *My brother and I look so alike that people often think we are twins.* 我和我的兄弟長得太像了，人們經常認為我們是雙胞胎。| **twin sister/brother/daughters etc** *Meet my twin sister.* 認識一下我的孿生妹妹。—see also 另見 IDENTICAL TWIN, SIAMESE TWIN

twin² *adj* [only before noun 僅用於名詞前] **1 twin prob-**

lems/goals etc happening at the same time and related to each other 兩個同時出現、密切相關的問題/目標等: *a policy to combat the twin problems of poverty and unemployment* 解決貧困和失業這兩個密切相關問題的一項政策 **2 twin beds/engines etc** two similar things that are intended to be used as a pair 成對的(單人)牀/雙引擎等 —see also 另見 TWINSET, TWIN TOWN, TWIN TUB —see picture at 參見 BED 圖

twin³ *v* [T usually passive 一般用被動態] *BrE* to form a relationship between two similar towns in different countries in order to encourage visits between them【英】〔不同國家的兩個類似城市〕結為姐妹城市: [+with] *Harlow in England is twinned with Stavanger in Norway.* 英國的哈洛與挪威的斯塔萬格結成了姐妹城市。—see also 另見 TWIN TOWN

twin bed /,· '·/ *n* [C] **1** [usually plural 一般用複數] one of a pair of beds in a room for two people 雙人房間中的對牀之一 **2** *AmE* a bed for one person【美】單人牀 —**twin-bedded** *adj*: *twin-bedded rooms* 有兩張牀的雙人房間

twine¹ /twaɪn; twaɪn/ *n* [U] strong string made by twisting together two or more threads or strings 兩[多]股的線: a *bundle of papers tied up with twine* 用雙股線捆紮起來的一摞文件

twine² *v* [I,T] to wind or twist around something else 纏繞, 盤繞; 捻: **twine sth around sth** *She twined her fingers round the empty cup.* 她手指交叉地捧着那個空杯子。| [+around] *Ivy twined around the balcony.* 常春藤纏繞着陽台。

twin-en·gined /,twɪn `ɛndʒɪnd; ,twɪn 'endʒɪnd◂/ *adj* a twin-engined aircraft has two engines〔飛機〕雙引擎的

twinge /twɪndʒ; twɪndʒ/ *n* [C] **1** a sudden feeling of slight pain 一陣刺痛: *I felt a twinge in my back.* 我感到背部一陣刺痛。**2 a twinge of guilt/jealousy/fear etc** a sudden slight feeling of guilt etc 感到一陣內疚/嫉妒/恐懼等: *John felt a twinge of regret as he walked away.* 約翰走開的時候感到一陣後悔。

twin·kle¹ /`twɪŋkḷ; 'twɪŋkəl/ *v* [I] **1** if a star or light twinkles, it shines in the dark, quickly changing from bright to faint 閃爍, 閃耀: *The lights of the town twinkled below us.* 小鎮的燈光在我們下方閃爍。**2** if someone's eyes twinkle, they have a cheerful expression〔眼睛〕閃閃發光: [+with] *Don's eyes twinkled with laughter.* 唐的雙眼因歡笑而閃閃發光。**3 in the twinkling of an eye** *old-fashioned* very quickly【過時】轉眼間, 瞬間, 霎時

twinkle² *n* [C usually singular 一般用單數] **1 a twinkle in your eye** an expression in your eyes that shows you are happy or amused 眼睛裡閃爍着愉悦的光芒: *"I can get that at home!" she said with a twinkle in her eye.* "我家裡有!"她說道, 眼裡閃爍着喜悦的光芒。**2 when you were just a twinkle in your father's eye** before you were born 在你還未出世的時候 **3** a small bright shining light that becomes brighter and then fainter 閃爍的光

twin·set /`twɪn,sɛt; 'twɪnset/ *n* [C] *BrE* a woman's SWEATER and CARDIGAN that are meant to be worn together【英】女裝兩件套毛衣〔由套頭毛衣和開襟衫組成〕: *twinset and pearls* 珍珠和女裝兩件套毛衣

twin town /,· '·/ *n* [C] *BrE* a town that has formed a relationship with a similar town in another country in order to encourage visits between them【英】〔與外國某個類似城市結成的〕姐妹城: *Oxford's twin town is Bonn.* 牛津的姐妹城是波恩。

twin tub /,· '·/ *n* [C] *BrE* a type of WASHING MACHINE with one part for washing and one for spin-drying (SPIN-DRYER)【英】雙缸洗衣機

twirl¹ /twɝl; twɜːl/ *v* [I,T] to turn around and around or make something do this (使)旋轉; (使)轉動; (使)纏繞: [+around/round] *twirling around the dance floor* 圍繞着舞池旋轉 | **twirl sth around/round** *He twirled the gun round in his hand.* 他轉動手上的槍。

twirl² *n* [C] a sudden quick spinning movement 快速的旋轉, 轉動 —**twirly** *adj*

twist¹ /twɪst; twɪst/ *v*

1 ►BEND 彎曲◄ [T] to bend and turn something several times, especially in order to make something or to tie it to something 扭, 擰; 扭轉成; 使彎曲: **twist sth into/around etc** *She twisted the wire into the shape of a star.* 她把金屬絲扭成了星星的形狀。

2 ►MOVE 移動◄ [I] to turn a part of your body around or change your position by turning 扭動(身體): *He twisted to try and get free of the ropes.* 他扭動着身體, 設法掙脱掉繩子。

3 ►TURN 轉動◄ [T] to turn something using your hand〔用手〕轉動, 旋動: **twist sth off** *Jack twisted the cap off the bottle.* 傑克旋開了瓶上的蓋子。

4 ►WIND 盤繞◄ [T always+adv/prep] to wind something in a particular way 盤繞, 纏繞; 捻, 搓: **twist sth round/around** *She twisted the streamers round the banisters.* 她把那些飾帶纏繞在樓梯扶手上。| **twist sth together** *Twist the two ends of the wire together.* 把這根電線的兩頭繞在一起。

5 ►ROAD/RIVER 道路/河流◄ [I] if a road, river etc twists, it changes direction in a series of curves 盤旋; 蜿蜒: *The track twisted into the hills.* 小道蜿蜒進入了山區。

6 ►WORDS 詞語◄ [T] to change the true or intended meaning of a statement, especially in order to get some advantage for yourself; DISTORT 歪曲, 曲解: *Every time I try to discuss the situation, he twists what I say.* 每次我想要討論形勢時, 他總要歪曲我說的話。

7 twist your wrist/ankle/knee to hurt your wrist etc by pulling or turning it too suddenly while you are moving 扭傷手腕/踝關節/膝蓋

8 twist and turn a) if a path, road, stream etc twists and turns, it has a lot of bends in it〔道路、溪流等〕彎彎曲曲, 蜿蜒 **b)** if a person or animal twists and turns, they make twisting movements〔人或動物〕曲折地行走; 扭動身體: *The snake twisted and turned through the mud.* 那條蛇蠕動身體穿過泥地。

9 twist sb's arm a) *informal* to persuade someone to do something they do not want to do【非正式】強迫某人做某事, 向某人施加壓力: *I'm sure he'll come to the party if you twist his arm.* 如果你給他施加一點壓力, 我敢說他會來參加聚會的。**b)** to bend someone's arm upwards behind their back in order to hurt them 把某人的手臂反扭到背後 **c) twist my arm!** *spoken* used humorously to accept an invitation, a drink etc【口】敢強迫我!〔接受邀請、喝酒等; 一種幽默用法〕: *Oh, go on, twist my arm! I'll have a red wine.* 好啊, 繼續來吧, 敢強迫我喝酒! 那我就喝杯紅酒。—see also 另見 **twist/wrap sb around your little finger** (FINGER¹ (13)), **twist/turn the knife** (KNIFE¹ (4))

twist² *n* [C] **1** a twisting action or movement 扭, 擰, 捻, 搓: *Give that lid a twist – it's coming loose.* 擰一下那個蓋子——它快要鬆脱了。**2** a bend in a river or road〔河流或道路的〕彎子 **3** an unexpected change in the meaning of a situation or in the progress of a series of events〔形勢或事態的〕意外轉折: *The story ends with a strange twist – the detective turns out to be the murderer.* 這個故事的結尾有一個奇特的轉折——那偵探原來就是殺人兇犯。| **a twist of fate/fortune** *By an amazing twist of fate, we met again in Madrid five years later.* 命運巧合得令人驚奇, 我們五年以後又在馬德里相遇了。**4** a small piece of something that is twisted into a particular shape 搓捻成某一形狀的東西: [+of] *a twist of tobacco* 煙葉卷 | *a twist of lemon* 檸檬卷片 **5 round the twist** *BrE* crazy【英】發瘋的: **drive/send sb round the twist** (=make someone angry by continuously doing something) 不斷做某事逼得某人發怒 **6 the twist** a popular fast dance in the 1960s in which you twist your body from side to side〔流行於20世紀60年代的〕扭擺舞 —**twisty** *adj*: *a twisty road* 一條彎彎曲曲的路 —see also 另見 **get your knickers in a twist** (KNICKERS (3))

twist·ed /ˈtwɪstɪd; ˈtwɪstɪd/ *adj* **1** bent in many directions, so that it has lost its original shape 扭曲的, 變形的: *a mass of twisted wreckage* 一堆變形的殘骸 **2** seeming to enjoy things that are cruel or shocking, in a way that is not normal〔興趣〕反常的, 變態的: *Whoever sent those letters has a twisted mind.* 寄那些信的人有變態心理。

twist·er /ˈtwɪstɚ; ˈtwɪstə/ *n* [C] **1** *BrE informal* someone who cheats other people【英, 非正式】騙子, 奸詐的人 **2** *AmE informal* a TORNADO【美, 非正式】龍捲風

twit /twɪt; twɪt/ *n* [C] *informal* a stupid or silly person【非正式】笨蛋, 傻瓜

twitch[1] /twɪtʃ; twɪtʃ/ *v* **1** [I,T] if a part of someone's body twitches, it makes a small, sudden, uncontrolled movement〔身體的某個部分〕顫動, 抽動, 抽搐: *My eye won't stop twitching.* 我的眼皮跳個不停。**2** [T] to move something quickly and suddenly 猛拉, 急扯: *Sarah twitched the reins, and we moved off.* 莎拉猛地一拉韁繩, 我們出發了。

twitch[2] *n* [C] **1** a quick movement of a muscle that you cannot control〔肌肉的〕抽搐, 顫動: *a nervous twitch* 神經性抽搐 **2** a sudden, quick movement 猛的一拉, 一動: *A twitch of the line means you've caught a fish.* 線猛的一動, 意味着你釣着魚了。

twitch·y /ˈtwɪtʃɪ; ˈtwɪtʃi/ *adj* **1** behaving in a nervous way because you are anxious about something 焦急的; 緊張的: *Why are you so twitchy today?* 你今天為何如此焦躁不安? **2** repeatedly making sudden small movements 反覆抽動的, 抽搐的; 痙攣性的: *a cat with a twitchy tail* 尾巴老是抽動的貓

twit·ter[1] /ˈtwɪtɚ; ˈtwɪtə/ *v* [I] **1** if a bird twitters, it makes a lot of short high sounds〔鳥〕鳴囀, 啾啾叫, 吱吱叫: *the twittering of larks overhead* 頭上啾啾叫着的雲雀 **2** if a woman twitters, she talks very quickly and nervously in a high voice〔婦女〕嘁嘁喳喳地說話

twitter[2] *n* **1** [singular] the short, high sounds that birds make〔鳥的〕鳴囀聲, 啾啾聲, 吱吱聲 **2 be all of a twitter** also 又作 **be in a twitter** to be excited and nervous 很興奮; 很緊張: *She's been all of a twitter since her daughter's engagement.* 自從她女兒訂婚以來, 她一直興奮得不得了。—**twittery** *adj*

twixt /twɪkst; twɪkst/ *prep old use* between【舊】在…之間

two /tu; tuː/ *number* **1** 2 二 **2 put two and two together** to guess the meaning of something you have heard or seen 根據現有情況推論, 綜合起來判斷: *I didn't call to say I'd be late, but she put two and two together when she heard the weather reports.* 我沒打電話說要遲到, 但她聽天氣預報便知道了。**3 that makes two of us** *spoken* used to tell someone that you are in the same situation and feel the same way【口】我們兩人的情況一樣; 我跟你有同感: *"Well, I don't want to be the one to tell him." "That makes two of us."* "唉, 我不想充當去告訴他的那個人。" "彼此彼此。" **4 two can play at that game** *spoken* used to tell someone that they will not have an advantage over you by doing something because you can do it too【口】這一套你會我也會 **5 two cents (worth)** [plural] *AmE informal* your opinion or what you want to say about a subject【美, 非正式】〔對所討論問題的〕意見, 觀點: *Everyone had to get in their two cents worth.* 每個人都得發表自己的意見。**6 for two cents** *AmE spoken* used when you are describing angrily what you would like to do to change a situation【美口】恨不得〔用於憤怒地表示要做某事〕: *For two cents I'd kick him out.* 我恨不得把他踢出去。**7 two bits** *AmE informal* twenty five CENTS, or a coin that is worth this amount of money【美, 非正式】25 美分 (硬幣), 二毛五 **8 two's company, three's a crowd** used to say that it is better to leave two people alone to spend time with each other 兩人成伴, 三人不歡 —see also 另見 **don't care two hoots** (HOOT[1] (5)), **be in two minds about** (MIND[1] (6)), **two of a kind** (KIND[1] (8)), **be two a penny** (PENNY (11)), **it takes two to tango** (TANGO[2] (2))

two-bit /ˈ· ·/ *adj informal* not at all good or important【非正式】差勁的; 微不足道的, 不重要的: *She's just a two-bit movie star.* 她只是一名末流的電影明星。

two-di·men·sion·al /ˌ· ·ˈ···◂/ *adj* **1** a two-dimensional character in a book, play etc does not seem like a real person〔書本或劇中的人物〕描寫沒有深度的; 沒有真實感的 **2** flat 二維的, 平面的: *a two-dimensional shape* 平面形狀

two-edged /ˌ· ˈ·◂/ *adj* **1** having disadvantages or bad effects that are less easy to see than the good effects 優劣混雜的〔缺點不及優點明顯的〕: *the two-edged triumphs of technology* 有利有弊的技術成就 | **a two-edged sword** (=with as many bad results as good ones) 雙刃刀, 雙鋒刀 *Strong leadership is a two-edged sword.* 強有力的領導是一把雙刃刀。**2** having two edges that can cut 雙刃的

two-faced /ˌ· ˈ·◂/ *adj informal* changing what you say according to who you are talking to, in a way that is insincere and unpleasant【非正式】兩面派的, 虛偽圓滑的: *He came out of the affair as a two-faced hypocrite.* 他在那件事上終於顯出偽君子兩面派的嘴臉。

two·fold /ˈtufold; ˈtuːfəʊld/ *adj* **1** two times as much or as many of something 兩倍的: *a twofold increase in the incidence of TB* 結核病發病率呈兩倍的增加 **2** having two important parts 有兩部分的; 雙重的: *The reasons for the collapse are twofold.* 倒塌的原因是雙重的。—**twofold** *adv*

two-hand·ed /ˌ· ˈ··◂/ *adj* **1** using both hands to do something 用雙手操作的: *the tennis star's famous two-handed backhand* 那位網球名星著名的雙手反手擊球 **2** a two-handed tool is used by two people together〔工具〕兩人操作的

two-line whip /ˌ· · ˈ·/ *n* [C] a written order given to members of the British Parliament about how they should vote on a particular subject〔發給英國議員就某一議題如何投票的〕書面通知

two-man /ˈ· ·/ *adj* designed to be used by two people 為二人設計的; 限於二人使用的: *a two-man tent* 雙人帳篷

two-one, 2-1 /ˌtu ˈwʌn; ˌtuː ˈwʌn/ *n* [C] the higher of two levels of a second-class university degree in Britain 英國大學學位中第二類中較高的一級, 二級一等

two·pence, tuppence /ˈtʌpəns; ˈtʌpəns/ *n BrE*【英】**1** [U] an amount of money worth two pence 兩便士 **2** [C] a British coin in former times that was worth two pence〔英國舊時的〕兩便士硬幣 **3 not care twopence** *old-fashioned* to not care at all about something or someone【過時】一點也不在乎

two·pen·ny /ˈtuˌpɛnɪ; ˈtʌpəni/ *adj BrE old-fashioned*【英, 過時】**1** [only before noun 僅用於名詞前] costing two pence; TUPPENNY 值兩便士的 **2 twopenny-halfpenny** worth almost nothing 幾乎沒有價值的, 一文不值的

two-per·cent milk /ˌ· ·· ˈ·/ *n* [U] *AmE* milk that has had about half the fat removed【美】半脫脂牛奶; SEMI-SKIMMED *BrE*【英】

two-piece /ˌ· ˈ·◂/ *adj* [only before noun 僅用於名詞前] a two-piece suit consists of a matching JACKET (1) and trousers〔衣服〕兩件套的〔指相配的短上衣和褲子〕

two-ply /ˈ· ˌ·/ *adj* consisting of two threads or layers 雙股的; 兩層的: *two-ply wool* 雙股毛線 | *two-ply tissues* 雙層紙巾

two seat·er /ˌ· ˈ··◂/ *n* [C] a car, aircraft etc with seats for two people 雙座汽車; 雙座飛機

two-sid·ed /ˌ· ˈ··◂/ *adj* having two different parts 兩方面的, 雙重的: *a two-sided problem* 一個雙重問題 —see also 另見 ONE-SIDED, MANY-SIDED

two·some /ˈtusəm; ˈtuːsəm/ *n* [C usually singular 一般用單數] two people who work together or spend a lot of time together〔兩人組成的〕一對, 一雙; 搭檔: *the talented comedy twosome, French and Saunders* 才華橫溢的喜劇搭檔弗倫奇和桑德斯

two-star /ˈ· ·/ *adj* [only before noun 僅用於名詞前] a

level of quality used to judge hotels, restaurants etc, that shows they are of a medium standard〔旅館、飯館等〕二星級的, 中檔的

two-step /ˈ· ·/ *n* [singular] a dance with long sliding steps or the music for this type of dance 兩步舞; 兩步舞曲

two-stroke /ˈ· ·/ *adj* a two-stroke engine is one in which there is a single up-and-down movement of a PISTON〔發動機〕二衝程的

two-time /ˈ· ·/ *v* [T] *informal* to have a secret relationship with someone who is not your regular partner【非正式】背着…偷情; 對〔戀人〕不忠: *If you're two-timing me, I'll kill you I swear!* 如果你背着我偷情, 我發誓會殺了你！—**two-timer** *n* [C]

two-tone /ˈ· ·/ *adj* **1** two-tone furniture, clothes etc are made of material in two colours〔家具、衣服等〕兩色的, 雙色的: *two-tone shoes* 雙色鞋 **2** making two different sounds 發雙音的

two-two, 2-2 /ˌ· ˈ·/ *n* [C] the lower of two levels of a second-class university degree in Britain 英國大學學位中第二類中較低的一級; 二級二等: *She got a 2-2 in French.* 她有個二級二等的法語學位。

two-way /ˌ· ˈ·◂/ *adj* **1** moving or allowing movement in both directions 雙向的; 可雙向通行的: *two-way traffic* 雙向行駛的車輛交通 | *two-way trade* 雙向貿易 **2** two-way radio both sends and receives messages〔無線電〕收發兩用的

two-way mir·ror /ˌ· · ˈ··/ *n* [C] glass that looks like a mirror from one side, but that you can see through from the other〔從一面看是鏡子, 從反面看是透明的〕雙向鏡

two-way street /ˌ· · ˈ·/ *n* [C usually singular 一般用單數] *AmE informal* a situation that depends on two people working well together【美, 非正式】依靠兩人和睦相處的關係: *Marriage has to be a two-way street.* 婚姻之道在於相互溝通。

-ty /tɪ; ti/ *suffix* [in nouns 構成名詞] another form of the suffix -ITY 後綴 -ity 的另一種拼寫: *certainty* (=being certain) 確定

ty·coon /taɪˋkun; taɪˈkuːn/ *n* [C] someone who is successful in business or industry and has a lot of money and power〔工商界的〕巨頭, 大亨: *Millionaire computer tycoon, Alan Sugar.* 電腦業巨頭百萬富翁艾倫·休格。

ty·ing /ˋtaɪ-ɪŋ; ˈtaɪ-ɪŋ/ the present participle of TIE

tyke /taɪk; taɪk/ *n* [C] **1** *spoken BrE* a child who is behaving badly【口, 英】淘氣的孩子, 小淘氣 **2** *AmE* a small child【美】小孩子 **3** *BrE informal* someone from Yorkshire【英, 非正式】約克郡人

tym·pa·num /ˋtɪmpənəm; ˈtɪmpənəm/ *n* [C] *technical* an EARDRUM【術語】鼓膜

type[1] /taɪp; taɪp/ *n* **1** [C] one member of a group of people or things that have similar features or qualities 類型, 種類: *There have been several incidents of this type in recent weeks.* 最近幾週已經發生好幾宗類似事件了。| *Buy the right shampoo for your hair type.* 買適合你髮質的洗髮劑。| **[+of]** *She's the type of person I admire.* 她是我欣賞的那一類人。**2** [U] printed letters 印刷字體: *italic type* 斜體字 **3** [C,U] a small block with a raised letter on it that is used to print with, or a set of these〔印刷用的〕活字 **4** [C] someone with particular qualities or interests 某種類型的人: *the sporty type* 愛好運動的人 **5 be sb's type** *especially spoken* to be the kind of person someone is sexually attracted to【尤口】在性方面對某人有吸引力的那類人: *He wasn't my type really.* 他實際上不是對我有吸引力的那種人。

type[2] *v* **1** [T] to print a document on a piece of paper using a TYPEWRITER〔用打字機〕打字: *Does the report need to be typed?* 那份報告需要打出來嗎？**2** [I] to write using a TYPEWRITER or a computer〔用打字機或電腦〕寫, 打字: *He types with two fingers.* 他用兩個手指打字。**3** [T] *technical* to find out what type a plant, disease etc is【術語】找出〔植物、疾病等〕的類型, 把…分類

type·cast /ˋtaɪpˌkæst; ˈtaɪpkɑːst/ *v* [T] **1** to always give an actor the same type of character to play 總是給〔演員〕分配同一類型的角色: *He always gets typecast as the villain.* 他總是被分派去演壞蛋。**2** to give someone a particular type of job, activity etc to do, because you think it suits their character 給〔某人〕分派〔合乎其性格的工作、活動等〕

type·face /ˋtaɪpˌfes; ˈtaɪpfeɪs/ *n* [C] a group of letters, numbers etc of the same style and size, used in printing〔印刷用的〕字體

type·script /ˋtaɪpˌskrɪpt; ˈtaɪpˌskrɪpt/ *n* [C] a copy of a document, made using a TYPEWRITER〔用打字機打出的〕原稿, 打字稿

type·set·ter /ˋtaɪpˌsɛtɚ; ˈtaɪpˌsetə/ *n* [C] a person or machine that arranges the letters, words etc on a page or SCREEN[1] (1) for printing 排字工; 排字機

type·set·ting /ˋtaɪpˌsɛtɪŋ; ˈtaɪpˌsetɪŋ/ *n* [U] the job or activity of arranging TYPE[1] (3) for printing 排字〔工作〕—**typeset** *v* [T]

type·writ·er /ˋtaɪpˌraɪtɚ; ˈtaɪpˌraɪtə/ *n* [C] a machine that prints letters of the alphabet onto paper 打字機

type·writ·ten /ˋtaɪpˌrɪtn; ˈtaɪpˌrɪtn/ *adj* written using a TYPEWRITER 用打字機打出的: *three sides of typewritten notes* 三頁打字稿

ty·phoid /ˋtaɪfɔɪd; ˈtaɪfɔɪd/ also 又作 **typhoid fe·ver** /ˌ·· ˈ··/ *n* [U] a serious infectious disease that is caused by dirty food or drink 傷寒: *a sudden outbreak of typhoid* 傷寒的突然爆發

ty·phoon /taɪˋfun; ˌtaɪˈfuːn◂/ *n* [C] a very violent storm in tropical areas in which the wind moves in circles 颱風

ty·phus /ˋtaɪfəs; ˈtaɪfəs/ *n* [U] a serious infectious disease carried by insects that live on the bodies of people and animals 斑疹傷寒

typ·i·cal /ˋtɪpɪkl; ˈtɪpɪkəl/ *adj* **1** having the usual features or qualities of a particular group or thing 典型的, 有代表性的: *a typical British summer* 典型的英國夏季 | **[+of]** *This painting is fairly typical of his early work.* 這幅畫在他早期作品中是相當典型的。**2** behaving or happening in the usual way 表現出個性的, 一向如此的: **[+of]** *It was typical of him to get angry about it.* 他因此發怒了, 這表現了他的個性。**3 typical!** *spoken* used to show that you are annoyed when something bad happens again【口】老是這樣！〔表示氣憤〕

typ·i·cally /ˋtɪpɪklɪ; ˈtɪpɪkli/ *adv* **1** in a way that a person or group is generally believed to behave 典型地, 有代表性地: *It's a typically British bureaucratic response.* 這是典型的英國官僚式的回答。**2** in the way that a particular type of thing usually happens 一向, 向來, 通常: *The disease typically takes several weeks to appear.* 這種病通常要等幾個星期才發作。

typ·i·fy /ˋtɪpəˌfaɪ; ˈtɪpɪfaɪ/ *v* [T not in progressive 不用進行式] **1** to be a typical example of something 是…的典型: *the arrogance that typifies this government's approach* 這個政府在處事上典型的傲慢態度 **2** to be a typical part or feature of something 是…的一部分; 是…的一向特徵: *the long complicated sentences that typify legal documents* 法律文件一向具有的長而複雜的句子

typ·ing /ˋtaɪpɪŋ; ˈtaɪpɪŋ/ *n* [U] the activity of using a TYPEWRITER to write something 打字〔工作〕: *I've got a lot of typing to do today.* 我今天有大量的打字工作要做。

typing pool /ˈ·· ·/ *n* [C] a group of typists in a large office who type letters for other people〔大辦公室裡的〕打字組

typ·ist /ˋtaɪpɪst; ˈtaɪpɪst/ *n* [C] **1** a secretary whose main job is to TYPE letters 打字員 **2** someone who uses a TYPEWRITER 打字者: *I'm a slow typist.* 我打字很慢。

ty·po /ˋtaɪpo; ˈtaɪpəʊ/ *n* [C] *informal* a small mistake in the way something has been typed (TYPE[2] (2)) or printed【非正式】打字錯誤; 排印錯誤

ty·pog·ra·pher /taɪˋpɑgrəfɚ; taɪˈpɒgrəfə/ *n* [C] **1** someone who designs TYPEFACEs 設計印刷字體的人 **2** a COMPOSITOR 排字工

ty·po·graph·ic /ˌtaɪpəˋɡræfɪk; ˌtaɪpəˈɡræfɪk◂/ also 又作 **ty·pograph·i·cal** /-fɪkḷ; -fɪkəl/ *adj* connected with typography 排印的; 印刷文字設計的 —**typographically** /-kḷɪ; -kli/ *adv*

ty·pog·ra·phy /taɪˋpɑɡrəfɪ; taɪˈpɒɡrəfi/ *n* [U] **1** the work of preparing written material for printing 排印 **2** the arrangement, style and appearance of printed words 印刷文字設計

ty·ran·ni·cal /tɪˋrænɪkḷ; tʒˈrænɪkəl/ *adj* **1** behaving in a cruel and unfair way towards someone you have power over 暴虐的, 專橫的: *a tyrannical father* 專橫的父親 **2** tyrannical rules or laws etc are based on a system in which a single ruler uses their power unfairly 專制的: *the tyrannical laws relating to debtors* 針對債務人的苛刻法律

tyr·an·nize also 又作 **-ise** *BrE*【英】/ˋtɪrəˌnaɪz; ˈtɪrənaɪz/ *v* [T] to use power over someone cruelly or unfairly 對…施以暴政; 專橫地對待: *a family tyrannized by their grandfather* 一個受到祖父專橫管制的家庭

ty·ran·no·sau·rus /tɪˌrænəˋsɔrəs; tʒˌrænəˈsɔːrəs◂/ also 又作 **tyrannosaurus rex** /·ˌ···ˈ·/ *n* [C] a very large, flesh-eating DINOSAUR 霸王龍〔一種大型食肉恐龍〕

tyr·an·nous /ˋtɪrənəs; ˈtɪrənəs/ *adj old-fashioned* TYRANNICAL【過時】暴虐的, 專制的

tyr·an·ny /ˋtɪrənɪ; ˈtɪrəni/ *n* **1** [U] unfair and strict control over someone 暴虐, 專橫: *He longed to escape from the tyranny of his aunt.* 他渴望擺脱姨媽的專橫管制。**2** [C,U] government by one person or a small group that has gained power unfairly and uses it cruelly 暴政, 苛政, 專制統治 **3 the tyranny of fashion/the clock etc** the way that fashion etc limits people's freedom to do things the way they want to do 潮流/時間等的殘酷無情〔比喻潮流等限制人們的自由〕**4** [C often plural 常用複數] a cruel or unfair action that limits someone's freedom 暴行: *the tyrannies of Louis XVI's court* 路易十六朝廷的暴行

ty·rant /ˋtaɪrənt; ˈtaɪərənt/ *n* [C] **1** a ruler who has complete power and uses it in a cruel and unfair way 暴君, 專制君主: *Caligula and Nero, the two great tyrants* 加利古拉和尼祿這兩個大暴君 **2** someone who has power over other people, and uses it cruelly or unfairly 暴君似的人; 專橫的人

tyre *BrE*【英】, **tire** *AmE*【美】/taɪr; taɪə/ *n* [C] **1** a thick, round band of rubber that fits around the wheel of a car, bicycle etc 輪胎: **a flat tyre** (=one that has lost all its air) 癟輪胎 —see also 另見 SPARE TYRE —see picture on page A2 參見 A2 頁圖 **2** a round band of metal that fits around the outside of a wooden wheel〔木輪上的〕輪箍 3

tzar /tsɑr; zɑː/ *n* [C] another spelling of TSAR tsar 的另一種拼法 —**tzarist** *adj*

tza·ri·na /tsɑˋrinə; zɑːˈriːnə/ *n* [C] another spelling of TSARINA tsarina 的另一種拼法

tzar·is·m /ˋtsɑrɪzəm; ˈzɑːrɪzəm/ *n* [U] another spelling of TSARISM tsarism 的另一種拼法

tze·tze fly /ˋtsɛtsɪ ˌflaɪ; ˈtetsi flaɪ/ *n* [C] another spelling of TSETSE FLY tsetse fly 的另一種拼法

T

U,u

U, u /ju; juː/ *plural* **U's, u's** *n* [C] the 21st letter of the English alphabet 英語字母表的第二十一個字母

U /ju; juː/ *n* **1** [C] a letter used in Britain to officially show that a film is suitable for people of any age U級電影〔英國的一種電影標籤, 指適合各種年齡的觀眾觀看〕 **2** [C] a mark used in schools and examinations to show that your work or behaviour is extremely bad〔表示在學校的表現或考試成績〕"很差勁"的符號 **3** [C] *BrE* a GRADE[1] (5) given in an examination to show that the work is too bad to be marked at all【英】極差〔考試的評分〕**4** [singular] *AmE old-fashioned*【美, 過時】an abbreviation for 縮寫= university: *Indiana U* 印第安納大學

u·biq·ui·tous /juˋbɪkwətəs; juːˈbɪkwɪ̈təs/ *adj formal or humorous* seeming to be everywhere【正式或幽默】普遍存在的, 無處不在的: *We were tormented in the outback by the ubiquitous Australian fly.* 在內地, 我們被無處不在的澳大利亞蒼蠅所折磨。—**ubiquitously** *adv* —**ubiquity** *n* [U]

U-boat /ˋju ˌbot; ˈjuː bəʊt/ *n* [C] a German SUBMARINE, especially one that was used in the Second World War〔尤指第二次世界大戰期間所用的〕德國潛艇

ud·der /ˋʌdɚ; ˈʌdə/ *n* [C] the part of a female cow, goat etc that hangs down between its back legs and that produces milk〔母牛、母山羊等的〕乳房

UFO /ˋjuˌfo; ˈjuːfəʊ/ *n* [C] Unidentified Flying Object; a strange object in the sky, sometimes thought to be a SPACESHIP from another world 不明飛行物, 幽浮物〔空中的神祕飛行物體, 有時被認為是來自另一個星球的宇宙飛船〕

ugh /ʊx; ʊx/ *interjection* used to show strong dislike 哎, 呀〔表示強烈厭惡〕: *Ugh! This medicine tastes awful!* 哎! 這藥味道真噁心!

ug·ly /ˋʌglɪ; ˈʌgli/ *adj* **1** extremely unattractive and unpleasant to look at 醜陋的; 難看的: *He's just so ugly!* 他就是這麼醜! | *heavy, ugly furniture* 笨重醜陋的家具 | **ugly as sin** (=very ugly) 非常醜陋 **2** making you feel frightened, nervous, or threatened 可怕的, 恐怖的: *There were ugly scenes as rival gangs started attacking each other.* 敵對團夥互相打起來, 場面很可怕。**3 rear its ugly head** to appear and start to cause problems〔不好的東西〕抬頭, 冒頭: *Scandal has reared its ugly head yet again.* 流言蜚語又抬頭了。**4 ugly duckling** [C] someone who is less attractive, skilful etc than other people when they are young, but who becomes beautiful and successful later 醜小鴨〔小時難看笨拙、日後變得好看和有出息的人〕—**ugliness** *n* [U]

UHF /ˌju etʃ ˋɛf; ˌjuː eɪtʃ ˈef/ *n* [U] ultra-high frequency; a range of radio waves (WAVE[1] (3)) that produces a very good quality of sound 超高頻

uh huh /ʌ ˋhʌ; ʌ ˈhʌ/ *interjection informal* used to show that you understand or agree with what someone is saying to you【非正式】嗯〔表示理解或贊同〕: *"He's what, six years old?" "Uh huh."* "他甚麼, 六歲了?" "嗯。"

UHT milk /ˌju etʃ ti ˋmɪlk; ˌjuː eɪtʃ tiː ˈmɪlk/ *n* [U] *BrE* milk that has been heated to a very high temperature to preserve it【英】超高温消毒牛奶

uh-uh /ˋʌ ʌ; ˈʌ ʌ/ *interjection informal* used to say no【非正式】啊, 哦〔表示否定〕

UK /ˌju ˋke; ˌjuː ˈkeɪ◂/ *n* the abbreviation of 縮寫= United Kingdom 聯合王國

u·ke·le·le /ˌjukəˋlelɪ; ˌjuːkəˈleɪli/ *n* [C] a musical instrument with four strings, like a small GUITAR 尤克萊利琴〔一種類似結他的四弦琴〕

-ular /julɚ; jʊ̈lə/ *suffix* [in adjectives 構成形容詞] of or concerning something ...的; 關於...的: *glandular fever* 腺熱, 傳染性單核細胞增多症 | *tubular steel* 管形鋼

ul·cer /ˋʌlsɚ; ˈʌlsə/ *n* [C] a sore area on your skin or inside your body that may BLEED or produce poisonous substances 潰瘍: *stomach ulcers* 胃潰瘍 —**ulcerous** *adj*

ul·cer·ate /ˋʌlsəˌret; ˈʌlsəreɪt/ *v* [I,T] to form an ulcer, or become covered with ulcers (使)形成潰瘍; (使)潰爛 —**ulcerated** *adj* —**ulceration** /ˌʌlsəˋreʃən; ˌʌlsəˈreɪʃən/ *n* [U]

-ule /jul; juːl/ *suffix* [in nouns 構成名詞] *technical* a small type of something【術語】小型物: *a granule* (=small grain) 小粒, 細粒

ul·na /ˋʌlnə; ˈʌlnə/ *n* [C] *technical* the inner bone of your lower arm, on the side opposite to your thumb【術語】尺骨 —see picture at 參見 SKELETON 圖

ul·te·ri·or /ʌlˋtɪrɪɚ; ʌlˈtɪəriə/ *adj* **ulterior motives/purpose etc** reasons for doing something that you deliberately hide in order to get an advantage for yourself 別有用心的動機/目的等: *In some countries, Peace Corps volunteers were suspected of having ulterior motives, such as spying for the CIA.* 在一些國家, 和平隊志願者被懷疑別有用心, 例如為中情局當間諜。

ul·ti·mate[1] /ˋʌltəmɪt; ˈʌltɪ̈mɪ̈t/ *adj* [only before noun 僅用於名詞前] **1** better, bigger, worse etc than all other objects of the same kind〔同類中〕最出色的; 最糟糕的: *the ultimate sports car* 最棒的跑車 **2** an ultimate aim, purpose etc is the final and most important one〔目標等〕最終的; 首要的: *Complete disarmament was the ultimate goal of the conference.* 全面裁軍是這次會議的最終目標。**3** an ultimate decision, responsibility etc is one that you cannot pass on to someone else〔決定、責任等〕最大的, 最高的: *Ultimate responsibility lies with the President.* 總統肩負着最大的責任。

ultimate[2] *n* **the ultimate in stupidity/luxury/technology etc** something that shows the highest possible level of stupidity etc 極端的愚蠢/極度的奢侈/尖端技術等: *This video-sound system is the ultimate in home entertainment technology.* 這種音像系統是家庭娛樂技術的尖端。

ul·ti·mate·ly /ˋʌltəmɪtlɪ; ˈʌltɪ̈mɪ̈tli/ *adv* [sentence adverb 句子副詞] after everything or everyone else has been done or considered 最後; 最終: *Ultimately the decision rests with the child's parents.* 最終要由孩子的父母作出決定。

ul·ti·ma·tum /ˌʌltəˋmetəm; ˌʌltɪ̈ˈmeɪtəm/ *n* [C] a threat saying that if someone does not do what you want by a particular time, you will do something to punish them 最後通牒, 哀的美敦書: **give sb an ultimatum** *Well, give him an ultimatum: either he pays by Friday or he finds somewhere else to live.* 好吧, 給他下個最後通牒: 要麼在星期五之前付款, 要麼另找住處。

ultra- /ʌltrə; ʌltrə/ *prefix* **1** *technical* above in a range; beyond【術語】外; 超: *ultrasound* (=too high to hear) 超聲 —compare 比較 INFRA- **2** extremely 極(度): *an ultramodern building* 極現代的建築 | *an ultracautious approach* 極其謹慎的辦法

ul·tra-high fre·quen·cy /ˌ‥ ˋ‥ ˌ‥/ *n* [U] = UHF 超高頻

ul·tra·ma·rine /ˌʌltrəməˋrin; ˌʌltrəməˈriːn◂/ *n* [C,U] a very bright blue colour 佛青色, 深藍色 —**ultramarine** *adj*

ul·tra·son·ic /ˌʌltrəˋsɑnɪk; ˌʌltrəˈsɒnɪk◂/ *adj* ultrasonic sound waves are too high for humans to hear〔聲波〕超聲的

ul·tra·sound /ˋʌltrəˌsaund; ˈʌltrəsaʊnd/ *n* **1** [U] sound that is too high for humans to hear, and is often used in medical processes 超聲（波） **2** [C] a medical process using this type of sound that produces an image of something inside your body, especially a baby〔醫學中的〕超聲波檢查

ul·tra·vi·o·let /ˌʌltrəˋvaɪəlɪt; ˌʌltrəˈvaɪələ̥t◂/ *adj* **1** ultraviolet light is beyond the purple end of the range of colours that people can see 紫外（線）的 **2** [only before noun 僅用於名詞前] an ultraviolet lamp, treatment etc uses this light to treat skin diseases or make your skin darker 利用紫外線的

u·lu·la·tion /juljəˋleʃən; juːljʊ̈ˈleɪʃən/ *n* [C] *literary* a long low sound made with your voice【文】呼喊（聲）；嚎叫（聲）—**ululate** /ˋjuljəˌlet; ˈjuːljʊ̈leɪt/ *v* [I]

um /ʌm; ʌm/ *interjection* used when you cannot immediately decide what to say next 嗯〔說話時表示猶豫〕: *Um, yeah, I guess so.* 嗯，是的，我猜是這樣。

um·ber /ˋʌmbɚ; ˈʌmbə/ *n* [C,U] a brown colour like earth 棕土色；赭色 —**umber** *adj*

um·bil·i·cal cord /ʌmˋbɪlɪkḷ ˌkɔrd; ʌmˈbɪlɪkəl ˌkɔːd/ *n* [C] a long narrow tube of flesh that joins an unborn baby to its mother 臍帶

um·bil·i·cus /ʌmˋbɪlɪkəs; ʌmˈbɪlɪkəs/ *n* [C] *technical* the small hollow place on your stomach; NAVEL【術語】臍，肚臍

um·brage /ˋʌmbrɪdʒ; ˈʌmbrɪdʒ/ *n* **take umbrage (at)** to be offended by something that someone has done or said（為…）生氣，（因…）見怪: *James took umbrage at Mrs Dubose's remarks.* 詹姆斯為杜博斯太太說的話而生氣。

um·brel·la /ʌmˋbrɛlə; ʌmˈbrelə/ *n* [C] **1** a circular folding frame covered in cloth that you hold above you when it is raining 雨傘 —compare 比較 SUNSHADE, PARASOL **2 umbrella organization** an organization that includes many smaller groups〔有眾多附屬團體的〕傘狀組織[機構] **3 umbrella term/word** a word whose meaning includes many different types of a particular object〔包括多種含義的〕綜合術語/詞 **4** the protection given by a powerful country, army, a weapons system etc 保護（傘）: *the political umbrella of the United Nations* 聯合國的政治庇護

umbrella 雨傘

um·laut /ˋʊmlaʊt; ˈʊmlaʊt/ *n* [C] a sign (¨) written over a German vowel to show how it is pronounced〔標在德語元音上方的〕變音符號（¨），曲音符號

ump /ʌmp; ʌmp/ *n* [C] *AmE spoken* an umpire【美口】裁判員

um·pire¹ /ˋʌmpaɪr; ˈʌmpaɪə/ *n* [C] the person in some sports who makes sure that the players obey the rules 裁判員 —see picture at 參見 TENNIS 圖

umpire² *v* [I,T] to be the umpire for a game or competition（給…）當裁判

ump·teen /ˋʌmpˈtin; ˌʌmpˈtiːn◂/ *determiner informal* a large number of【非正式】無數的；許許多多的: *There seemed to be umpteen rules and regulations to learn.* 似乎有許許多多的規章制度要學習。—**umpteenth** *number*

'un /ən; ən/ *pron BrE spoken*【英口】**good 'un/bad 'un etc** a short form of 簡略式= one, used to say that someone or something is bad, good etc 一個好/壞人[東西]: *He's a bad 'un.* 他是個壞傢伙。| *Those apples are little 'uns.* 那都是些小蘋果。

UN /ˌju ˋɛn; juː ˈen/ *n* [singular] the United Nations; an international organization that tries to find peaceful solutions to world problems 聯合國

un- /ʌn; ʌn/ *prefix* [especially in adjectives and adverbs 尤構成形容詞和副詞] **1** shows a negative, a lack, or an opposite; not 不〔表示"否定"、"缺乏"、"相反"之意〕: *unfair* 不公平的 | *unhappy* 不高興的 | *unfortunately* 不幸地 **2** [especially in verbs 尤構成動詞] shows an opposite〔表示做相反的動作〕: *to undress* (=take your clothes off) 脫去衣服

un·a·bashed /ˌʌnəˋbæʃt; ˌʌnəˈbæʃt◂/ *adj* not ashamed or embarrassed, especially when doing something unusual or rude 不害臊的，不怕羞的；滿不在乎的: *She stared at him with unabashed curiosity.* 她好奇地盯着他看，一點也不害臊。

un·a·bat·ed /ˌʌnəˋbetɪd; ˌʌnəˈbeɪtɪ̥d◂/ *adj, adv* continuing without becoming any weaker or less violent 不減弱的[地]；不衰退的[地]: *The storm continued unabated throughout the night.* 暴風雨持續了一夜，絲毫沒有減弱。| *his unabated ambition* 他那銳氣不減的抱負

un·a·ble /ʌnˋebḷ; ʌnˈeɪbəl/ *adj* not able to do something 不能…的；不會…的: **be unable to do sth** *Many passengers were unable to reach the lifeboats.* 許多乘客無法到達救生艇。 [3] [2]

un·a·bridged /ˌʌnəˋbrɪdʒd; ˌʌnəˈbrɪdʒd◂/ *adj* a piece of writing, speech etc that is unabridged is in its full form without being made shorter〔文章、演講等〕未刪節的，全文的: *the complete and unabridged works of Dickens* 不加節略的狄更斯全集

un·ac·cept·a·ble /ˌʌnəkˋsɛptəbḷ; ˌʌnəkˈseptəbəl◂/ *adj* **1** something that is unacceptable is so wrong or bad that you think it should not be allowed 不能接受的: *unacceptable levels of unemployment* 不能接受的失業水平 **2 the unacceptable face of** the bad or unfair part of a system, activity etc …難以接受的一面: *property speculation, the unacceptable face of capitalism* 房地產投機，資本主義不可接受的一面 —**unacceptably** *adv*

un·ac·com·pa·nied /ˌʌnəˋkʌmpənɪd; ˌʌnəˈkʌmpənid◂/ *adj* **1** someone who is unaccompanied has no one with them 無人陪伴的；無隨從的: *Unaccompanied children are not allowed on the premises.* 無人陪伴的兒童不得入內。**2** an unaccompanied singer or musician sings or plays alone 無伴奏的: *a piece for unaccompanied voices* 一段適於清唱的曲子 **3 unaccompanied bags/luggage etc** bags, cases etc that are sent on a plane, train etc without their owner 託運的包裹/行李等

un·ac·count·a·ble /ˌʌnəˋkaʊntəbḷ; ˌʌnəˈkaʊntəbəl◂/ *adj formal*【正式】**1** very surprising and difficult to explain 莫名其妙的；無法解釋的；不可理解的: *Patrick's disappearance was quite unaccountable.* 帕特里克的失蹤相當令人費解。**2** not having to explain your actions or decisions to anyone else〔對本身的行為或決定〕不用解釋的: *It is not acceptable that the governors of this institution should be largely unaccountable.* 令人不能接受的是這一機構的主管人員竟然可以在多數情況下獨斷專行。—**unaccountably** *adv*

un·ac·count·ed /ˌʌnəˋkaʊntɪd; ˌʌnəˈkaʊntɪd◂/ *adj* something or someone that is unaccounted for cannot be found or their absence cannot be explained 失蹤的；不明去向的: *Two people are still unaccounted for after the floods.* 有兩人在洪水過後仍下落不明。

un·ac·cus·tomed /ˌʌnəˋkʌstəmd; ˌʌnəˈkʌstəmd◂/ *adj formal*【正式】**1 unaccustomed to** not used to something 對…不習慣的: *a country boy, unaccustomed to city ways* 不習慣城市生活方式的鄉下男孩 **2** [only before noun 僅用於名詞前] not usual, typical, or familiar 不尋常的；非慣例的；不熟悉的: *unaccustomed physical exertion* 超常的體力付出 **3 unaccustomed as I am (to)** *spoken formal* used before saying something in front of a lot of people【口，正式】儘管我不習慣於〔用於當眾講話時〕

un·ac·knowl·edged /ˌʌnəkˋnɑlɪdʒd; ˌʌnəkˈnɒlɪdʒd◂/ *adj* **1** not generally or publicly known for something that should be rewarded, thanked, or praised 未被公認的；未被承認的；未答謝的；未受讚揚的: *Women's work in the home tends to be both unpaid and unacknowledged.* 婦女料理家務往往既得不到報酬，也不被讚揚。**2 the unacknowledged leader/authority etc** a leader etc who is not officially or publicly recognised 自封的[未經正式認可的]領導/權威等: *Grandma was the unacknowledged boss of the family.* 祖母當時是非正式的一家之主。**3** ignored or not noticed 未受到注意[重視]的: *The tap on the door went unacknowledged for some time.* 輕輕的敲門聲過了好一陣子才有人回應。

un·a·dopt·ed /ˌʌnəˋdɑptɪd; ˌʌnəˈdɒptɨ̣d◂/ *adj BrE* an unadopted road must be repaired by the people who live along it and not by a town council【英】〔道路〕不由地方當局承擔保養的

un·a·dul·te·rat·ed /ˌʌnəˋdʌltəˌretɪd; ˌʌnəˈdʌltəreɪtɨ̣d◂/ *adj* **1** not mixed with other less pure substances 不攙雜的, 純的 **2** [only before noun 僅用於名詞前] complete or total 完全的; 十足的: *What unadulterated nonsense!* 真是一派胡言!

un·af·fect·ed /ˌʌnəˋfɛktɪd; ˌʌnəˈfektɨ̣d◂/ *adj* **1** not changed or influenced by something 未改變的; 未受影響的: **[+by]** *The northwest was unaffected by the drought.* 西北部沒有受到乾旱影響。**2** *approving* natural in the way you behave【褒】〔舉止〕不裝腔作勢的, 自然的: *her easy, unaffected manner* 她那從容、自然的舉止 —**unaffectedly** *adv*

un·aid·ed /ʌnˋedɪd; ʌnˈeɪdɨ̣d/ *adj, adv* without help 無助的[地]; 獨立的[地]: *It was the first time she had walked unaided since her illness.* 這是她生病以來第一次獨立行走。

un·al·loyed /ˌʌnəˋlɔɪd; ˌʌnəˈlɔɪd◂/ *adj literary* not mixed with anything else【文】不攙雜的; 純的: *unalloyed happiness* 純真的幸福

un·al·ter·a·ble /ʌnˋɔltərəbḷ; ʌnˈɔːltərəbəl/ *adj formal* not possible to change【正式】不可變更[改變]的: *an unalterable fact* 不可改變的事實 —**unalterably** *adv*

un·am·big·u·ous /ˌʌnæmˋbɪgjuəs; ˌʌnæmˈbɪgjuəs◂/ *adj* a statement, instruction etc that is unambiguous is clear and easy to understand because it can only mean one thing 清楚的, 明確的, 不含糊的: *a brief, unambiguous description of the problem* 對該問題簡潔明確的表述 —**unambiguously** *adv*

un-A·mer·i·can /ˌ·‧ˈ···◂/ *adj* not loyal to generally accepted American customs and ways of thinking〔習俗、思維方式等〕不合美國的; 非美國的: **un-American activities** (=political activity believed to be harmful to the US) 非美活動〔被認為不利於美國的政治活動〕

u·na·nim·i·ty /ˌjunəˋnɪmɪtɪ; ˌjuːnəˈnɪmɨ̣ti/ *n* [U] *formal* a state or situation of complete agreement among a group of people【正式】一致同意

u·nan·i·mous /juˋnænəməs; juːˈnænɨ̣məs/ *adj* **1** a unanimous decision, statement etc is one that everyone agrees with〔決定、聲明等〕一致通過的, 無異議的 **2** agreeing completely about something 一致同意的: **unanimous that** *The jury was unanimous that the defendant was guilty.* 陪審團一致同意被告有罪。—**unanimously** *adv*

un·an·nounced /ˌʌnəˋnaunst; ˌʌnəˈnaʊnst◂/ *adj, adv* happening without anyone expecting or knowing about it 出人意料的[地]; 未經通報的[地]: *We arrived unannounced.* 我們未經通報就到了。

un·an·swer·a·ble /ʌnˋænsərəbḷ; ʌnˈɑːnsərəbəl/ *adj* **1** definitely true and therefore impossible to argue against 無可辯駁的: *an unanswerable case in law* 無法申辯的法律案件 **2** an unanswerable question is one that seems to have no possible answer or solution〔問題〕無法回答的, 沒有答案的

un·ap·peal·ing /ˌʌnəˋpilɪŋ; ˌʌnəˈpiːlɪŋ◂/ *adj* not pleasant or attractive 無吸引力的: *an unappealing bowl of watery soup* 一碗淡而無味的稀湯

un·ap·proach·a·ble /ˌʌnəˋprotʃəbḷ; ˌʌnəˈprəʊtʃəbəl◂/ *adj* seeming unfriendly and therefore difficult to talk to 不可親的, 冷淡的, 難以接近的: *Jo appeared, looking grim and unapproachable.* 喬出現了, 表情陰冷, 無法接近。

un·ar·gu·a·ble /ʌnˋɑrgjuəbḷ; ʌnˈɑːgjuəbəl/ *adj* something that is unarguable is definitely true or correct 不容置疑的; 無可爭辯的 —**unarguably** *adv*

un·armed /ʌnˋɑrmd; ʌnˈɑːmd◂/ *adj* not carrying any weapons 未帶武器的, 徒手的: **unarmed combat** (=fighting without weapons) 徒手格鬥

un·a·shamed /ʌnəˋʃemd; ˌʌnəˈʃeɪmd◂/ *adj* not feeling embarrassed or ashamed about something that people might disapprove of 不害羞的; 恬不知恥的: *the unashamed luxury of our marble bath* 我們家裡大理石浴缸的恣意奢華 —**unashamedly** *adv*

un·asked /ʌnˋæskt; ʌnˈɑːskt/ *adj, adv* **1** if a question is unasked, no one asks it, often because they are embarrassed〔常因不便過問而〕未被問及的[地] **2** if you do something unasked, you do it without anyone asking or inviting you to 未被要求的[地]; 未受邀請的[地]: *Jerry entered unasked, and stood by the fire.* 傑里主動走進來, 站在爐火旁邊。| **unasked for** *hundreds of pounds in unasked for donations* 自發捐贈的數百英鎊

un·as·sail·able /ˌʌnəˋseləbḷ; ˌʌnəˈseɪləbəl◂/ *adj formal* not able to be criticized, attacked, or made weaker【正式】不容置疑的; 攻不破的: *an unassailable argument* 無懈可擊的論據

un·as·sum·ing /ˌʌnəˋsumɪŋ; ˌʌnəˈsjuːmɪŋ◂/ *adj* showing no desire to be noticed or given special treatment; MODEST 謙遜的, 不擺架子的: *an unassuming middle-class family* 謙遜的中產階級家庭

un·at·tached /ˌʌnəˋtætʃt; ˌʌnəˈtætʃt◂/ *adj* **1** not involved in a romantic relationship; SINGLE[1] (3) 未戀愛的; 單身的: *Sure, he's handsome, but is he unattached?* 沒錯, 他挺帥, 可他是否單身呢? **2** not connected or fastened to anything 無關係的; 非附屬的; 獨立的

un·at·tain·a·ble /ˌʌnəˋtenəbḷ; ˌʌnəˈteɪnəbəl◂/ *adj* impossible to achieve 達不到的: *an unattainable goal* 達不到的目標

un·at·tend·ed /ˌʌnəˋtɛndɪd; ˌʌnəˈtendɨ̣d◂/ *adj* left alone without anyone in charge 無人照看[負責]的: *unattended luggage* 無人照看的行李 | **leave sb/sth unattended** *Children should not be left unattended in the playground.* 孩子們在遊樂場不應該沒人照管。

un·at·trac·tive /ˌʌnəˋtræktɪv; ˌʌnəˈtræktɪv◂/ *adj* **1** not attractive, pretty, or pleasant to look at 無吸引[誘惑]力的; 不漂亮的: *an unattractive man* 沒有魅力的男子 **2** not good or desirable 不好的; 討厭的: *the unattractive aspects of nationalism* 民族主義令人生厭的方面 —**unattractively** *adv*

un·au·tho·rized /ʌnˋɔθəˌraɪzd; ʌnˈɔːθəraɪzd/ also 又作 **-ised** *BrE*【英】*adj* without official approval or permission 未經授權[批准]的: *laws to prevent unauthorized photocopying* 防止擅自影印的法律

un·a·vail·a·ble /ˌʌnəˋveləbḷ; ˌʌnəˈveɪləbəl/ *adj* [not before noun 不用於名詞前] **1** not able to be obtained 得不到的: *Funding for the new school is unavailable.* 無法得到新學校的資金。**2** not able or willing to meet someone 沒空的: *I'm sorry, the principal is unavailable just now.* 對不起, 校長這會兒沒空。

un·a·vail·ing /ˌʌnəˋvelɪŋ; ˌʌnəˈveɪlɪŋ/ *adj literary* not successful or effective【文】徒勞的; 無益的, 無用的: *unavailing efforts* 徒勞

un·a·void·a·ble /ˌʌnəˋvɔɪdəbḷ; ˌʌnəˈvɔɪdəbəl/ *adj* impossible to prevent 不可避免的: *There are now fears that war is unavoidable.* 人們現在擔心戰爭不可避免。—**unavoidably** *adv*: *Molly was unavoidably delayed.* 莫莉不得已被耽擱了。

un·a·ware /ˌʌnəˋwɛr; ˌʌnəˈweə/ *adj* not noticing or realizing what is happening 未覺察到的; 未意識到的: **[+of]** *Mike seems unaware of the trouble he's causing.* 邁克看來還未意識到他所惹的麻煩。| **unaware that** *She remained unaware that she was being watched.* 她一直未察覺到自己在被監視。—**unawareness** *n* [U]

un·a·wares /ˌʌnəˋwɛrz; ˌʌnəˈweəz/ *adv* **1 take/catch sb unawares** to happen or to do something in a way that someone was not expecting and so was not prepared for 讓某人措手不及: *Caught unawares like that, I was* *unable to think of an excuse.* 冷不防被人這樣抓住，我甚麼藉口也想不出來了。**2** *formal* without noticing【正式】不知不覺地；無意中：*We had walked unawares over the border.* 我們無意中越了界。

un·bal·anced /ʌnˋbælənst; ˌʌnˈbælənst/ *adj* **1** someone who is unbalanced seems slightly crazy〔人〕精神失常[錯亂]的 **2** a report, argument etc that is unbalanced is unfair because it emphasizes one opinion too much〔報告、論點等〕有失公允的，片面的 **3** a relationship that is unbalanced is not equal because one person has more influence, power etc〔關係〕不平衡的，不平等的

un·bear·a·ble /ʌnˋbɛrəbl̩; ʌnˈbeərəbəl/ *adj* too unpleasant, painful, or annoying to bear; INTOLERABLE 忍受不了的；承受不住的；無法容忍的：*Their constant arguments were unbearable.* 他們持續不斷的爭論讓人無法忍受。—**unbearably** *adj*: *an unbearably hot day* 熱得讓人無法忍受的一天

un·beat·a·ble /ʌnˋbitəbl̩; ʌnˈbiːtəbəl/ *adj* **1** something that is unbeatable is the best of its kind〔同類中〕無與倫比的：*unbeatable prices* 無與倫比的價格 **2** a team, player etc that is unbeatable cannot be defeated 打不垮的，無法擊敗的

un·be·com·ing /ˌʌnbɪˋkʌmɪŋ; ˌʌnbɪˈkʌmɪŋ◂/ *adj old-fashioned*【過時】**1** clothes that are unbecoming do not make you look attractive〔衣服等〕不相配的；不合身的；難看的：*a blouse in an unbecoming green colour* 顏色難看的綠色襯衫 **2** behaviour that is unbecoming is shocking or unsuitable〔行為〕不合禮節的，不得體的：**[+to]** *conduct unbecoming to a teacher* 與教師身分不相稱的行為

un·be·known /ˌʌnbɪˋnon; ˌʌnbɪˈnəʊn/ also 又作 **unbeknownst** [sentence adverb 句子副詞] **unbeknown to sb** without that person knowing about it 不為某人所知的：*Unbeknown to him, his wife had been trying to phone him all morning.* 他不知道的是，他妻子一上午都在想方設法打電話給他。

un·be·lief /ˌʌnbɪˋlif; ˌʌnbə̇ˈliːf/ *n* [U] *formal* a lack of belief or a refusal to believe in a religious faith【正式】無信仰；不信(宗教) —compare 比較 DISBELIEF

3 **un·be·lie·va·ble** /ˌʌnbɪˋlivəbl̩; ˌʌnbə̇ˈliːvəbəl◂/ *adj* **1** extremely surprising 極其驚人的：*Dealers were paying unbelievable prices for her paintings.* 商人開出驚人的高價來收購她的畫。**2** very difficult to believe and therefore probably untrue 不可信的，難以相信的：*Yvonne's excuse for being late was totally unbelievable.* 伊馮娜遲到的理由根本不可信。—**unbelievably** *adv*: *an unbelievably bad movie* 糟糕透頂的電影

un·be·liev·er /ˌʌnbəˋlivɚ; ˌʌnbə̇ˈliːvə◂/ *n* [C] someone who does not believe in a particular religion 不信教者

un·bend /ʌnˋbɛnd; ʌnˈbend/ *v* **1** [I,T] to become straight or make something straight (把…)弄直 **2** [I] to relax and start behaving in a less formal way 放鬆；變得隨意：*She'd be a lot more likeable if she'd unbend a little.* 她如果放鬆一點，會變得更可愛。

un·bend·ing /ʌnˋbɛndɪŋ; ʌnˈbendɪŋ/ *adj* unwilling to change your opinions, decisions etc 不妥協的；固執的：*a stern, unbending man* 嚴厲而又固執的男子

un·bi·ased /ʌnˋbaɪəst; ʌnˈbaɪəst/ *adj* able to make a fair judgment, especially because you are not influenced by your own or other people's opinions 不偏不倚的；無偏見的；公正的：*With all the publicity surrounding the case, it's going to be hard to find an unbiased jury.* 這個案件已經鬧得沸沸揚揚，要找一個不偏不倚的陪審團將很困難。

un·bid·den /ʌnˋbɪdn̩; ˌʌnˈbɪdn/ *adv literary* without being asked for, expected, or invited【文】未被要求的；意想不到的；未受邀請的

un·blem·ished /ʌnˋblɛmɪʃt; ˌʌnˈblemɪʃt/ *adj* not spoiled by any mistake or bad behaviour 無瑕疵的；清白的：*an unblemished reputation* 清白的名聲

un·born /ʌnˋbɔrn; ˌʌnˈbɔːn◂/ *adj* not yet born 未出生的：*an unborn child* 未出生的孩子

un·bos·om /ʌnˋbuzəm; ˌʌnˈbʊzəm/ *v* [T] *literary* **unbosom yourself to** to tell someone about the things that are worrying you【文】向〔某人〕吐露心事，向〔某人〕傾訴心曲

un·bound·ed /ʌnˋbaʊndɪd; ʌnˈbaʊndə̇d/ *adj formal* extreme or without any limit【正式】無邊際的，無限的：*unbounded energy* 無限的能量

un·bri·dled /ʌnˋbraɪdl̩d; ʌnˈbraɪdld/ *adj literary* not controlled and too extreme or violent【文】放縱的，不受控制的；激烈的：*unbridled passion* 奔放的熱情

un·bro·ken /ʌnˋbrokən; ʌnˈbrəʊkən/ *adj* continuing without being broken or interrupted 未破損的，完整的；未中斷的：*an unbroken silence* 未打破的沉寂 | *the unbroken prosperity of the last 25 years* 過去25年的持續繁榮

un·buck·le /ʌnˋbʌkl̩; ˌʌnˈbʌkəl/ *v* [T] to unfasten the BUCKLE on something 解開…的搭扣：*He unbuckled his belt.* 他解開了皮帶的搭扣。

un·bur·den /ʌnˋbɝdn̩; ˌʌnˈbɜːdn/ *v* [T] **1 unburden yourself/your heart** to tell someone your problems, secrets etc so that you feel better 吐露心事；傾訴衷腸：*Jane unburdened herself of a terrible secret.* 簡講出了一個可怕的祕密。| **[+to]** *He felt an urge to unburden his heart to this stranger.* 他迫切地想向這個陌生人傾訴衷腸。**2** *literary* to take a heavy load away from someone【文】卸去…的負擔

un·called-for /ʌnˋkɔld ˌfɔr; ʌnˈkɔːld fɔː/ *adj informal* behaviour or remarks that are uncalled-for are unfair or unsuitable【非正式】〔行為、評論等〕不公正的，不合適的：*That comment was totally uncalled-for.* 那番評論毫無道理。

un·can·ny /ʌnˋkænɪ; ʌnˈkæni/ *adj* very strange and difficult to explain 離奇的；不可思議的：*an uncanny coincidence* 不可思議的巧合 —**uncannily** *adv*

uncared for /ʌnˋkɛrd ˌfɔr; ʌnˈkeəd ˌfɔː/ *adj* not looked after or not looked after properly 沒人照顧的；未得到適當照顧的：*The dogs looked hungry and uncared for.* 這幾隻狗看起來又餓又缺乏照顧。

un·ceas·ing /ʌnˋsisɪŋ; ʌnˈsiːsɪŋ/ *adj* never stopping 不停的；不斷的：*an unceasing barrage of questions* 沒完沒了的連珠砲似的問題 —**unceasingly** *adv*

un·ce·re·mo·ni·ous /ˌʌnsɛrəˋmonɪəs; ˌʌnserə̇ˈməʊniəs◂/ *adj* without paying any attention to politeness or good manners 無禮的；隨便的：*Philippa finished her meal with unceremonious haste.* 菲莉帕狼吞虎嚥地吃完了飯。—**unceremoniously** *adv* —**unceremoniousness** *n* [U]

un·cer·tain /ʌnˋsɝtn̩; ʌnˈsɜːtn/ *adj* **1** [not before noun 不用於名詞前] not sure or feeling doubt 不確定的；不能斷定的：*Lee moved awkwardly and looked uncertain.* 李動作笨拙，看起來很遲疑。| **[+how/what/where etc]** *She hesitated, uncertain what to do next.* 她猶豫不決，拿不定主意下一步做甚麼。**2** likely to change, often in a way that is bad 無常的，易變的：*My whole future now seemed uncertain.* 我的整個未來現在看起來變化無常。**3** [not before noun 不用於名詞前] not definite or decided 未確定的：*Our holiday plans are still uncertain.* 我們的度假計劃仍未確定。**4 in no uncertain terms** if you tell someone something in no uncertain terms, you tell them very clearly without trying to be polite 直截了當地：*I told Colin in no uncertain terms what I thought of him.* 我直截了當地告訴科林我對他的看法。—**uncertainly** *adv* —**uncertainty** *n* [C,U]

un·chal·lenged /ʌnˋtʃælɪndʒd; ʌnˈtʃælə̇ndʒd/ *adj* **1** accepted and believed by everyone and not doubted 未引起爭論的；無異議的，未引起質疑的：*Roy's authority was unchallenged.* 羅伊的權威未受到挑戰。**2** someone who goes somewhere unchallenged is not stopped and asked who they are or what they are doing〔人〕未受到盤查的；順利的：*How did the prisoners manage to get to the outer fence unchallenged?* 那些犯人是如何順利到達外層圍欄的？

un·chang·ing /ʌnˋtʃendʒɪŋ; ʌnˈtʃeɪndʒɪŋ/ *adj* always staying the same 不變的, 恆定的

un·char·ac·ter·is·tic /ʌnˌkærəktəˋrɪstɪk; ʌnˌkærɨ̧ktəˈrɪstɪk◂/ *adj* not typical of someone or something and therefore surprising 不典型的, 不表示〔某人或某物的〕特性的: **[+of]** *It's uncharacteristic of her to be late.* 她不是常遲到的人。—**uncharacteristically** /-klɪ; -kli/ *adv*

un·char·i·ta·ble /ʌnˋtʃærətəbl; ʌnˈtʃærɨ̧təbəl/ *adj* unkind or unfair in the way you judge people 苛刻的, 不寬厚的; 不公正的; 挑剔的: *It's very uncharitable to say Phillip's problems are all his own fault.* 說菲利普的問題都是他自己的錯, 這未免太苛刻了。

un·chart·ed /ʌnˋtʃartɪd; ʌnˈtʃɑːtɨ̧d/ *adj literary*【文】**1** not marked on any maps 地圖上沒有標明的: *The ship arrived at a previously uncharted island.* 船到達了一個以前地圖上沒有標明的海島。**2 uncharted waters/territory** a situation or activity that you have never experienced or tried before 未知的水域/領域: *This new operation was uncharted territory for the surgeons.* 這種新手術對外科醫生來說是個未知的領域。

un·checked /ʌnˋtʃɛkt; ˌʌnˈtʃekt◂/ *adj* **1** an unchecked activity, illness etc develops and gets worse because it is not controlled or stopped〔活動、疾病等〕未受抑制的, 未受制止的: *We cannot allow such behaviour to continue unchecked.* 我們不能允許這樣的行為繼續下去而不加制止。**2** not tested for quality, safety etc 未經檢查[檢驗]的: *The goods should not have left the factory unchecked.* 產品不該在未經檢驗的情況下出了廠。—see also 另見 CHECK

un·civ·i·lized also 又作 **-ised** *BrE*【英】/ʌnˋsɪvḷˌaɪzd; ʌnˈsɪvɨ̧laɪzd/ *adj* **1** uncivilized behaviour is rude or socially unacceptable 野蠻的; 不文明的: *uncivilized incidents of racial violence* 野蠻的種族暴力事件 **2 an uncivilized hour** *informal* extremely early in the morning【非正式】一大清早

un·cle /ˋʌŋkl; ˈʌŋkəl/ *n* [C] **1** the brother of your mother or father, or the husband of your aunt 伯[叔, 舅]父; 姑[姨]丈 —see picture at 參見 FAMILY 圖 **2** a man whose brother or sister has a child 伯[叔, 舅]父: *Enrique was very excited about becoming an uncle.* 恩里克就要當伯伯[叔叔, 舅舅]了, 非常興奮。**3** used as a name for a man who is a close friend of your parents 叔叔; 伯伯〔用於稱呼父母的男性好朋友〕**4 say uncle** *AmE spoken* used by children to tell someone to admit they have been defeated【美口】討饒, 認輸〔兒童用語, 用於要求某人認輸、承認失敗〕—see also 另見 **talk like a dutch uncle** (DUTCH[2] (3))

un·clean /ʌnˋklin; ˌʌnˈkliːn◂/ *adj* **1** *biblical* morally or spiritually bad【聖經】不純潔的; 骯髒的; 邪惡的: *an unclean spirit* 邪惡的精靈 **2** unclean food, animals etc are those that must not be eaten, touched etc in a particular religion〔宗教上認為〕〔食物〕不宜食用的;〔動物〕不可接觸的 —**uncleanness** *n* [U]

un·clear /ʌnˋklɪr; ˌʌnˈklɪə◂/ *adj* **1** difficult to understand or be sure about, so that there is doubt or confusion 難懂的; 不清楚的; 不肯定的: *The terms of the contract are very unclear.* 合同的條款非常含糊不清。**2 be unclear about** to not understand something clearly 對…含糊不清: *I'm rather unclear about what I'm supposed to be doing here.* 我不太明白自己該在這兒做些甚麼。

Uncle Sam /ˌʌŋkḷ ˋsæm; ˌʌŋkəl ˈsæm/ *n* [singular] *informal* the US, or the US government, sometimes represented by the figure of a man with a white BEARD and tall hat【非正式】山姆大叔〔美國或美國政府的綽號, 有時用一個戴着高帽的白鬍子老頭的畫像指代〕

Uncle Tom /ˌʌŋkḷ ˋtam; ˌʌŋkəl ˈtɒm/ *n* [C] *AmE* a black person who is too friendly or respectful to white people, used in a disapproving way by other black people【美】湯姆叔叔〔指對白人必恭必敬的黑人, 黑人用此語常含不贊同的意味〕

un·clothed /ʌnˋkloðd; ʌnˈkləʊðd/ *adj formal* not wearing clothes or not covered by clothes; NAKED【正式】未穿衣服的, 赤裸的

un·coil /ʌnˋkɔɪl; ˌʌnˈkɔɪl/ *v* [I,T] if you uncoil something, or if it uncoils, it stretches out straight, after being wound around in a circle 解開〔捲着的東西〕;(使) 展開: *Slowly the snake uncoiled.* 蛇慢慢地伸展開盤着的身體。

un·com·fort·a·ble /ʌnˋkʌmfə·təbḷ; ʌnˈkʌmftəbəl/ *adj* **1** not feeling physically comfortable, or not making you feel comfortable 不舒服的; 不舒適的: *This sofa is so uncomfortable.* 這張沙發太不舒服了。**2** unable to relax because you are embarrassed 不自在的; 不安的: *an uncomfortable silence* 令人不安的沉寂 —**uncomfortably** *adv*

un·com·mit·ted /ˌʌnkəˋmɪtɪd; ˌʌnkəˈmɪtɨ̧d◂/ *adj* not having decided or promised to support a particular group, political belief etc 未作承諾的; 不受約束的; 未表態的; 中立的: *A large proportion of voters remain uncommitted.* 一大部分選民尚未表態。

un·com·mon /ʌnˋkamən; ʌnˈkɒmən/ *adj* rare or unusual 罕見的; 不平常的: *Violent crimes against the elderly are fortunately very uncommon.* 針對老年人的暴力犯罪幸好非常罕見。| **it is not uncommon for sb to do sth** *It is not uncommon nowadays for students to have bank loans.* 學生獲銀行貸款如今已不足為奇。—see 見 RARE (USAGE)

un·com·mon·ly /ʌnˋkamənlɪ; ʌnˈkɒmənli/ *adv* [+adj/adv] *old-fashioned* very【過時】非常: *That's uncommonly kind of you.* 你真是太好了。

un·com·plain·ing /ˌʌnkəmˋplenɪŋ; ˌʌnkəmˈpleɪnɪŋ◂/ *adj* willing to accept a difficult or unpleasant situation without complaining 順從的; 沒有怨言的, 不訴苦的: *A dog can make a wonderful, uncomplaining walking companion.* 狗可以成為稱心如意的散步夥伴。—**uncomplainingly** *adv*

un·com·pre·hen·ding /ˌʌnkamprɪˋhɛndɪŋ; ˌʌnkɒmprɪˈhendɪŋ/ *adj* not understanding what is happening 不理解的 —**uncomprehendingly** *adv*

un·com·pro·mis·ing /ʌnˋkamprəˌmaɪzɪŋ; ʌnˈkɒmprəmaɪzɪŋ/ *adj* unwilling to change your opinions or intentions 不妥協的, 不讓步的; 堅定的: *an uncompromising opponent of democratic reform* 民主改革的堅決反對者 —**uncompromisingly** *adv*

un·con·cern /ˌʌnkənˋsɝn; ˌʌnkənˈsɜːn/ *n* [U] an attitude of not caring about something that other people worry about 漠不關心, 冷漠: *In view of the deepening crisis, we are surprised at the government's apparent unconcern.* 鑑於日益嚴重的危機, 我們對政府表現出來的漠不關心感到驚訝。

un·con·cerned /ˌʌnkənˋsɝnd; ˌʌnkənˈsɜːnd/ *adj* **1** not worried about something because you think it does not affect you 不關心的; 不憂慮的: **[+about]** *Many large companies seem totally unconcerned about the environment.* 許多大公司似乎絲毫不把環境問題放在心上。**2** not interested in a particular aim or activity 不感興趣的: **[+with]** *unconcerned with making a profit* 不注重贏利 —**unconcernedly** /-ndlɪ; -nɨ̧dli/ *adv*

un·con·di·tion·al /ˌʌnkənˋdɪʃənəl; ˌʌnkənˈdɪʃənəl◂/ *adj* not limited by or depending on any conditions 不加限制的; 無條件的: *the unconditional release of all political prisoners* 所有政治犯的無條件釋放 | **unconditional surrender** *The Allies declared they would accept nothing less than unconditional surrender.* 同盟國聲明他們只接受無條件投降。—**unconditionally** *adv*

un·con·firmed /ˌʌnkənˋfɝmd; ˌʌnkənˈfɜːmd◂/ *adj* **unconfirmed report/story/rumour etc** a report etc that has not been proved or supported by official information 未經證實的報道/故事/傳聞等: *We've received unconfirmed reports of an explosion in central London.* 我們收到一些未經證實的報道, 說倫敦中心發生了爆炸。

un·con·scion·a·ble /ʌnˋkanʃənəbḷ; ʌnˈkɒnʃənəbəl/ *adj formal* much more than is reasonable or acceptable

【正式】不合理的; 過度的; 難以接受的: *an unconscionable amount of suffering* 極大的痛苦 —**unconscionably** *adv*

un·con·scious¹ /ʌnˋkɑnʃəs; ʌnˈkɒnʃəs/ *adj* **1** unable to see, move, feel etc in the normal way because you are not conscious 不省人事的, 失去知覺的: *She was found alive but unconscious.* 她被發現還活着, 但失去了知覺。| **knock/beat sb unconscious** *Murphy was attacked and beaten unconscious.* 默菲遭到攻擊, 被打得不省人事。**2** a feeling or thought that is unconscious is one that you have without realizing it〔感覺、想法〕無意識的; 不自覺的: *an unconscious need to be loved* 一種無意識的被愛的需要 —compare 比較 SUBCONSCIOUS¹ **3 be unconscious of** to not realize the effect of something you have said or done 未意識到..., 未覺察到...: *Doreen appeared to be unconscious of the amusement she had caused.* 多琳似乎並未意識到是她把大家逗樂了。**4** an action that is unconscious is not deliberate〔動作〕無意的 —**unconsciously** *adv* —**unconsciousness** *n* [U]

unconscious² *n* **the/sb's unconscious** the part of your mind in which there are thoughts and feelings that you do not realize you have; SUBCONSCIOUS² 無意識/某人的潛意識

un·con·sid·ered /ˌʌnkənˋsɪdəd; ˌʌnkənˈsɪdəd◂/ *adj* **1** unconsidered remarks or actions are made without thinking about the possible results〔評論或行動〕未經思考的, 輕率的 **2** *formal* not important or not noticed【正式】不重要的; 未被注意的: *unconsidered trifles* 瑣碎的小事

un·con·sti·tu·tion·al /ˌʌnkɑnstəˋtuʃənḷ; ˌʌnkɒnstɪ̵ˈtjuːʃənəl/ *adj* not allowed by the CONSTITUTION (=set of rules or principles by which a country or organization is governed) 違反憲法的: *the debate over whether flag-burning is an unconstitutional form of protest* 關於焚燒國旗是否屬於違反憲法的抗議形式的爭論 —**unconstitutionality** /ˌʌnkɑnstəˌtuʃənˋæləti; ˌʌnkɒnstɪ̵tjuːʃəˈnælɪ̵ti/ *n* [U]

un·con·trol·lable /ˌʌnkənˋtroləbḷ; ˌʌnkənˈtrəʊləbəl◂/ *adj* **1** uncontrollable emotions, desires or actions are ones that you cannot control or stop〔情感、慾望或動作〕控制不住的, 管束不了的: *I felt an uncontrollable urge to scream.* 我感到一種控制不住的要尖叫的衝動。**2** someone who is uncontrollable behaves badly and will not obey anyone〔人〕無法無天的 **3** situations or conditions that are uncontrollable cannot be changed〔情況〕失控的; 難以挽回的

un·con·trolled /ˌʌnkənˋtrold; ˌʌnkənˈtrəʊld◂/ *adj* uncontrolled emotions or behaviour continue because you are not trying to stop or control them 不加約束的; 無抑制的: *uncontrolled weeping* 放聲大哭

un·con·ven·tion·al /ˌʌnkənˋvɛnʃənḷ; ˌʌnkənˈvenʃənəl◂/ *adj* very different from the way people usually behave, think, dress etc 非常規的, 不落俗套的: *unconventional political views* 異乎尋常的政治觀點

un·co·op·er·a·tive /ˌʌnkoˋɑpəˌretɪv; ˌʌnkəʊˈɒpərətɪv◂/ *adj* not willing to work with or help someone 不願合作的, 不配合的: *The immigration authorities were brusque and uncooperative.* 移民當局粗暴而又不合作。

un·co·ordi·nat·ed /ˌʌnkoˋɔrdṇˌetɪd; ˌʌnkəʊˈɔːdɪ̵neɪtɪ̵d◂/ *adj* **1** someone who is uncoordinated is not good at physical activities because they cannot control their movements effectively; CLUMSY〔動作〕不協調的; 笨拙的: *I was always too uncoordinated to be good at tennis.* 我總是太笨手笨腳了, 所以打不好網球。**2** a plan or operation that is uncoordinated is not well organized with the result that the different parts of it do not work together effectively〔計劃、行動〕不協調的

un·cork /ʌnˋkɔrk; ʌnˈkɔːk/ *v* [T] to open a bottle by removing its CORK¹ (2) 拔去〔瓶子〕的塞子 —see picture on page A15 參見A15頁圖

un·count·a·ble /ʌnˋkaʊntəbḷ; ʌnˈkaʊntəbəl/ *adj* a noun that is uncountable has no plural form and means something which cannot be counted or regarded as either singular or plural, for example 'water', or 'beauty'. In this dictionary uncountable nouns are marked [U]; MASS NOUN〔名詞〕不可數的〔如water, beauty等, 在本辭典中不可數名詞以[U]標示〕

un·couth /ʌnˋkuθ; ʌnˈkuːθ/ *adj* behaving and speaking in a way that is rude or socially unacceptable〔言語、行為〕粗魯的, 不文明的: *rough, uncouth men* 粗暴無禮的男人 —**uncouthly** *adv* —**uncouthness** *n* [U]

un·cov·er /ʌnˋkʌvɚ; ʌnˈkʌvə/ *v* [T] **1** to find out about something that has been kept secret 發現, 破獲, 揭露: *Customs officials uncovered a plot to smuggle weapons into the country.* 海關官員發現了一個走私武器入境的陰謀。**2** to remove the cover from something 揭開...的蓋子, 移去...的覆蓋物

un·crit·i·cal /ʌnˋkrɪtɪkḷ; ʌnˈkrɪtɪkəl/ *adj* unable or unwilling to see faults in something or someone 無鑑別力的; 不加批評的: **[+of]** *John's mother is totally uncritical of his behaviour.* 約翰的母親對他的行為完全不加批評。—**uncritically** /-klɪ; -kli/ *adv*

un·crowned /ʌnˋkraʊnd; ˌʌnˈkraʊnd◂/ *adj* **the uncrowned king/queen of** the person who is thought to be the best or most famous in a particular activity〔某活動〕的無冕之王/后, ...最出色者: *Martina Navratilova, the uncrowned queen of women's tennis* 瑪蒂娜·娜拉蒂露娃, 女子網球王后

un·crush·a·ble /ʌnˋkrʌʃəbḷ; ʌnˈkrʌʃəbəl/ *adj* **1** material or cloth that is uncrushable is easy to keep smooth〔布料等〕揉不皺的 **2** very determined and not easily discouraged 堅強的, 壓不垮的: *her uncrushable will to survive* 她那求生的堅強意志

unc·tu·ous /ˋʌŋktʃuəs; ˈʌŋktʃuəs/ *adj formal* too friendly and praising people too much in a way that seems very insincere【正式】甜言蜜語的, 假殷勤的, 諂媚的: *There is something smug and unctuous about him.* 他這人有點沾沾自喜, 虛情假意。—**unctuously** *adv* —**unctuousness** *n* [U]

un·curl /ʌnˋkɝl; ˌʌnˈkɜːl/ *v* [I,T] to stretch out straight from a curled position, or to make something do this (使)伸直; (使)變直

un·cut /ʌnˋkʌt; ˌʌnˈkʌt◂/ *adj* **1** a film, book etc that is uncut has not been made shorter, for example by having violent or sexual scenes removed〔影片、書籍等〕未刪節[剪輯]的: *the uncut version of 'Lady Chatterley's Lover'*《查泰萊夫人的情人》的未刪節版本 **2** an uncut jewel that is still in its natural form has not been cut into a particular shape〔寶石〕未經雕琢的: *uncut gem stones* 未經琢磨的寶石

un·daunt·ed /ʌnˋdɔntɪd; ʌnˈdɔːntɪ̵d/ *adj* not afraid of continuing to try to do something in spite of difficulties or danger 無畏的, 大膽的, 不泄氣的: **[+by]** *Undaunted by the enormity of the task, they began rebuilding the village.* 他們不畏任務艱巨, 開始重建村莊。

un·de·ceive /ˌʌndɪˋsiv; ˌʌndɪˈsiːv/ *v* [T] *formal* to tell someone what the real facts are when they have previously believed something that was untrue【正式】使不再受騙; 使明真相, 使醒悟

un·de·cid·ed /ˌʌndɪˋsaɪdɪd; ˌʌndɪˈsaɪdɪ̵d/ *adj* **1** [not before noun 不用於名詞前] not having made a decision about something important 未決定的: **[+about]** *A third of the electorate remain undecided about how they will vote.* 三分之一的選民仍未決定投票意向。| **[+what/which/whether etc]** *Nadine was undecided whether or not to go to college.* 納丁尚未決定是否去上大學。**2** a game or competition that is undecided has no definite winner〔比賽〕未定局的 —**undecidedly** *adv*

un·de·mon·stra·tive /ˌʌndɪˋmɑnstrətɪv; ˌʌndɪˈmɒnstrətɪv/ *adj* not showing your feelings of love or friendliness, especially by not touching or kissing people 含蓄的, 感情不外露的〔尤指不觸摸或吻別人〕

un·de·ni·a·ble /ˌʌndɪˋnaɪəbḷ; ˌʌndɪˈnaɪəbəl◂/ *adj* definitely true or certain 不可否認的, 無可爭辯的: *undeniable proof* 確證 —**undeniably** *adv*

under- /ʌndɚ; ʌndə/ *prefix* **1** too little 不足: *under-*

development 欠發達 | *undercooked cabbage* 未煮熟的洋白菜 **2** going underneath something 在...下面: *an underpass* 地下通道 **3** inner; beneath others 內部的; 在...之下: *undergarments* 內衣 **4** less important or lower in rank〔重要性或等級〕次的, 低的: *a head gardener and three under-gardeners* 一個主管園丁和三個輔助園丁

un·der¹ /ˈʌndə; ˈʌndə/ *prep*
1 ►BELOW 在...下面◄ directly below something, or covered by it 在...下面, 在...底下; 在...裡面: *Write your name under your picture.* 在你的照片下面寫上名字。| *She was carrying her handbag under her arm.* 她胳膊下夾着個手提包。| *I could see something glittering under the water.* 我能看見水裡有東西在閃閃發光。
2 ►LESS THAN 少於◄ less than a particular number, amount, age, or price〔數字、數量、年齡或價格〕低於, 少於, 在...以下: *gifts for under ten dollars* 不到十美元的禮物 | *nursery education for children under five* 五歲以下兒童的幼兒教育 | *I spend just under four hours a day seeing customers.* 我一天接待顧客所花的時間將近四小時。| **be under age** (=not be old enough to drink, have sex etc legally) 未成年; 未及法定年齡 *You're not allowed in the bar if you're under age.* 未成年者不准進酒吧。
3 be under construction/discussion/attack etc to be in the process of being constructed, discussed etc 在建設/討論/攻擊中等: *The possibility of replacing the computers remains under consideration.* 更換電腦的可能性仍在考慮之中。| *The National Health Service is very much under attack from the Tory government.* (英國) 國民保健制度遭到保守黨政府的猛烈抨擊。
4 ►CONTROLLED 被控制的◄ being controlled by a particular leader, government, system etc 在...指揮[支配, 管理]下: *foreign policy under Kohl*〔前德國總理〕科爾指導下的外交政策 | *The Los Angeles Philharmonic is under the baton of Esa-Pekka Salonen.* 洛杉磯愛樂樂團由埃薩-佩卡·薩洛寧擔任指揮。
5 ►LAW/AGREEMENT 法律/協議◄ according to a particular agreement, law etc 根據..., 依照...: *an exemption under Article 85* 根據第85條作出的豁免
6 ►AFFECTED BY 受...的影響◄ being affected by particular conditions or situations 在...影響下: *She's been under a lot of pressure at work.* 她工作中有很大壓力。| *driving under the influence of alcohol* 酒後開車 | *The solicitor has said that under no circumstances must I pay it.* 律師說我無論如何都不需要付款。
7 be under (sb's) control/influence/spell etc if someone or something is under someone's control etc, they control or influence it 在(某人)控制/影響/吸引等之下: *I'm glad to see that you have everything under control.* 很高興看到一切都在你控制之中。| *She seems to be coming under Gina's influence.* 她似乎在受吉娜的影響。
8 ►CLASS/GROUP 類別/組◄ if an object, book, name etc is under a particular letter, list, system etc, that is where you can find it or that is the group it belongs to 在...類別下, 屬於...之類: *The baby's records are filed under the mother's last name.* 嬰兒的檔案記錄歸在母親的姓下。
9 ►POSITION AT WORK 工作職位◄ if people are under someone in authority, they work for that person and have a lower position 在...手下工作, 在...的管轄下: *Guerrero works under him directly.* 格雷羅直接在他手下工作。
10 be under an impression/delusion to believe something is true, especially when you are wrong in believing it 留下印象/錯覺: *I was under the impression that he was going on vacation that week.* 我的印象是他那週在休假。
11 be under anaesthesia/sedation/treatment etc to be treated by a doctor using a particular drug or method 在麻醉/鎮靜/治療等中
12 ►DIFFERENT NAME 別名◄ if you write something under another name, you write it using a name that is not your real name 用〔某個名字〕; 假託...: *Eric Blair wrote under the name of George Orwell.* 埃里克·布萊爾用喬治·奧韋爾的名字寫作。

USAGE NOTE 用法說明: UNDER
WORD CHOICE 詞義辨析: **under, underneath, below, beneath**

Under is the most common word used to talk about one thing being placed or moving directly under another, or being covered by it. 表示一物在另一物的正下方或在其中, under 是最常用的一個詞: *I found it under the table/cushion.* 我發現它在桌子[墊子]下面。| *The railway runs directly under the main street.* 鐵路在主街的正下方穿過。| *Just push the note under the door.* 把便條直接塞在門下。| *The police all wear bullet-proof vests under their shirts.* 警察襯衣裡面都穿上防彈背心。

Underneath is often used intead of **under** to slightly emphasize the idea of covering, touching, or hiding. 強調"遮蓋"、"接觸"、"藏匿"之意時, 常用 underneath 而不用 under: *He keeps his money in a secret safe underneath the floor boards.* 他把錢保存在地板下面一個祕密的保險櫃中。| *I wonder what's underneath that cover?* 我想知道那個蓋子下面藏了甚麼? | *a creature that makes its nest underneath desert rocks* 把窩築在沙漠岩石底下的動物。

You use **under** to talk about something that is covered by something that is also all around it, but you would not use **underneath** so often in this way. under 用以表示處於某物之下並為之包圍, underneath 則不常這麼用: *Sea lions can travel much faster under water.* 海獅在水中行進的速度要快得多。

Beneath can also be used in all these ways, but is a little old-fashioned or literary. beneath 含以上三種用法, 但有點過時或較常用於文學作品中。In a romantic story, for example, you might read 浪漫故事中偶可遇見這種用法: *They strolled hand in hand beneath the summer moon.* 他們手拉着手, 在夏日的月光下徜徉。

Below suggests that one thing is in a lower position than another, perhaps a little to one side or in front. below 表示一物處於另一物的下方, 位置稍微靠邊或靠前: *Jed and Jackie live in the apartment below us.* 傑德和傑姬住在我們樓下的公寓。| *There was a lake below the village, further down the valley.* 在村莊下面, 山谷更低處有一個湖。

under² *adv* **1** in or to a place below something or covered by it 在下面; 往下面; 在底下: *He crawled under the blankets.* 他在毯子下面爬。**2** less in age, number, amount etc than the age etc mentioned〔年齡、數量等〕低於, 少於: *Children twelve and under must be accompanied by an adult.* 十二歲及以下兒童必須有大人陪伴。

un·der·a·chiev·er /ˌʌndərəˈtʃivə; ˌʌndərəˈtʃiːvə/ *n* [C] someone who does not do as well as they could do, especially at school 未能充分發揮(學習)潛力者, 學習成績不理想者 **—underachieve** *v* [I] **—underachievement** *n* [U]

un·der·age /ˌʌndəˈedʒ; ˌʌndərˈeɪdʒ◄/ *adj* too young to legally buy alcohol, drive a car, vote etc 未成年的, 未及法定年齡的: *underage drinking* 未成年飲酒

un·der·arm¹ /ˈʌndəˌɑrm; ˈʌndərɑːm◄/ *adv* if you throw a ball underarm, you throw it without moving your arm above your shoulder〔擊球時〕低手地, 用手不過肩地; UNDERHAND² *AmE*【美】—see picture on page A23 參見 A23 頁圖

underarm² *adj* **underarm deodorant/antiperspirant** a substance which smells pleasant that you put under your arms 腋下除臭劑/止汗劑

un·der·bel·ly /ˈʌndəˌbɛlɪ; ˈʌndəˌbeli/ *n literary*【文】**1** the weakest or most easily damaged part of a country, plan etc 易受攻擊的區域; 最薄弱部分: *regional warfare* *tearing at the country's underbelly* 攻擊該國薄弱地區的局部戰爭 **2** the stomach of an animal such as a fish〔動物的〕下腹部〈如魚肚〉

un·der·brush /ˋʌndɚˏbrʌʃ; ˈʌndəbrʌʃ/ *n* [U] *especially AmE* bushes, small trees etc growing under and around larger trees in a forest; UNDERGROWTH【尤美】〔長在樹林中大樹下的〕下層灌木叢, 矮樹叢

un·der·cap·i·tal·ize also 又作 **-ise** *BrE*【英】/ˏʌndɚˋkæpɪtḷˏaɪz; ˌʌndəˈkæpɪtl-aɪz/ *v* [T usually passive 一般用被動態] to not give a business enough money with the result that it cannot operate effectively 對〔企業〕投資不足

un·der·car·riage /ˋʌndɚˏkærɪdʒ; ˈʌndəˌkærɪdʒ/ *n* [C] the wheels of an aircraft and the structure that holds them〔飛機的〕起落架 —see picture at 參見 AIRCRAFT 圖

un·der·charge /ˏʌndɚˋtʃɑrdʒ; ˌʌndəˈtʃɑːdʒ/ *v* [I,T] to charge too little or less than the correct amount of money for something (對…)少要價, 少收…的價錢: **undercharge sb by £1/$2 etc** *They undercharged me by about two dollars.* 他們少要了我大約兩美元。—opposite 反義詞 OVERCHARGE (1)

un·der·class /ˋʌndɚˏklæs; ˈʌndəklɑːs/ *n* [singular] the lowest social class, consisting of people who are very poor 下層社會, 最低階層

un·der·class·man /ˏʌndɚˋklæsmən; ˌʌndəˈklɑːsmən/ *n* [C] *AmE* a student in the first two years of school or college【美】低年級學生〔指大學或中學的一、二年級學生〕

un·der·clothes /ˋʌndɚˏkloðz; ˈʌndəkləʊðz/ also 又作 **un·der·clo·thing** /-ˏkloðɪŋ; -ˌkləʊðɪŋ/ *n* [plural] clothes that you wear next to your body under your other clothes; UNDERWEAR 內衣

un·der·coat /ˋʌndɚˏkot; ˈʌndəkəʊt/ *n* [C] a layer of paint that you put onto a surface before you put the final layer on 內[底]塗層

un·der·cov·er /ˋʌndɚˋkʌvɚ; ˌʌndəˈkʌvə◂/ *adj* [only before noun 僅用於名詞前] used or employed secretly, in order to catch criminals or find out information 暗中進行的; 祕密幹的: *an undercover operation* 祕密行動

un·der·cur·rent /ˋʌndɚˏkɝənt; ˈʌndəˌkʌrənt/ *n* [C] **1** a feeling, especially of anger or dissatisfaction, that people do not express openly 潛伏的情緒〔尤指憤怒、不滿〕: **[+of]** *He sensed an undercurrent of resentment among the crowd.* 他覺察到人羣中有潛在的怨恨。**2** a hidden and often dangerous current of water that flows under the surface of the sea or a river〔河、海中的〕暗流

un·der·cut /ˏʌndɚˋkʌt; ˌʌndəˈkʌt/ *v* [T] to sell goods or services more cheaply than another company 削價與…搶生意

un·der·de·vel·oped /ˏʌndɚdɪˋvɛləpt; ˌʌndədɪˈveləpt◂/ *adj* **1 underdeveloped country/region etc** a country, region etc that is poor and where there is not much modern industry 不發達的國家/地區等 —compare 比較 **developing country** (DEVELOPING) **2** not having grown or developed as much as is usual or necessary 發育不全的: *a skinny, underdeveloped child* 骨瘦如柴、發育不全的孩子

un·der·dog /ˋʌndɚˏdɔg; ˈʌndədɒg/ *n* [C] **1 the underdog** the person or team in a competition that is expected to lose 處於劣勢的人[隊];〔競賽中〕可能會輸的人[隊] **2** a person, country etc that is weak and is always treated badly 弱者; 弱國

un·der·done /ˋʌndɚˋdʌn; ˌʌndəˈdʌn◂/ *adj* meat that is underdone is not completely cooked〔肉〕未煮透的; 半生不熟的 —compare 比較 OVERDONE

un·der·dressed /ˏʌndɚˋdrɛst; ˌʌndəˈdrest◂/ *adj* wearing clothes that are too informal for a particular occasion 穿着過於隨便的

un·der·em·ployed /ˏʌndərɪmˋplɔɪd; ˌʌndərɪmˈplɔɪd◂/ *adj* working in a job where you cannot use all your skills or where there is not enough work for you to do 大材小用的, 未能人盡其才的; 就業不足的

un·der·es·ti·mate[1] /ˋʌndɚˋɛstəˏmet; ˌʌndərˈestɪmeɪt/ *v* **1** [I,T] to think that something is smaller, cheaper, less important etc than it really is (對…)估計不足, 低估; 看輕: *People often underestimate the importance of training.* 人們常常低估培訓的重要性。**2** [T] to think that someone is not as good, clever, or skilful, as they really are 輕視, 小看〔某人〕: *Don't underestimate Manville – he's a skilful campaigner.* 不要小看曼維爾——他可是個出色的活動家。

un·der·es·ti·mate[2] /ˋʌndɚˋɛstəmɪt; ˌʌndərˈestɪmɪt/ *n* [C] a guessed amount or number that is too low 估量過低; 低估: *14% may be an underestimate.* 14%也許是估計不足。

un·der·ex·pose /ˋʌndərɪkˋspoz; ˌʌndərɪkˈspəʊz/ *v* [T] to not let enough light reach the film when you are taking a photograph 使〔底片〕曝光不足

un·der·fed /ˏʌndɚˋfɛd; ˌʌndəˈfed/ *adj* not given enough food to eat 未吃飽的; 餵食不足的

un·der·felt /ˋʌndɚˋfɛlt; ˈʌndəfelt/ *n* [U] *BrE* soft material that you put between a CARPET[1] (1) and the floor【英】地毯墊氈〔置於地板與地毯之間的軟材料〕

un·der·foot /ˏʌndɚˋfʊt; ˌʌndəˈfʊt/ *adv* **1** under your feet where you are walking 在腳下: **wet/dry/firm etc underfoot** *The wet wood is very slippery underfoot.* 腳下的濕木頭很滑。**2 trample sb/sth underfoot a)** to crush someone or something on the ground by stepping heavily on them 把某人/某物踩在腳下 **b)** to completely destroy someone or something 徹底毀滅某人/某物

un·der·fund /ˏʌndɚˋfʌnd; ˌʌndəˈfʌnd/ *v* [T] **be underfunded** to not be provided with enough money 資金不足: *The childcare program is seriously underfunded.* 兒童保育計劃的資金嚴重不足。—**underfunding** *n* [U]

un·der·gar·ment /ˋʌndɚˏgɑrmənt; ˈʌndəˌgɑːmənt/ *n* [C] *old-fashioned* a piece of underwear【過時】內衣

un·der·go /ˏʌndɚˋgo; ˌʌndəˈgəʊ/ *v past tense* **underwent** /-ˋwɛnt; -ˈwent/ *past participle* **undergone** /-ˋgɔn; -ˈgɒn/ [T not in passive 不用被動態] if you undergo a change, an unpleasant experience etc, it happens to you, or is done to you 經歷, 經受; 遭受: *She's undergoing surgery.* 她正在接受手術。| *The company underwent several major changes.* 公司經歷了幾次重大變化。

un·der·grad·u·ate /ˏʌndɚˋgrædʒuɪt; ˌʌndəˈgrædʒuɪt◂/ *n* [C] *especially BrE* a student who is doing a university course for a first degree【尤英】〔尚未取得學位的〕大學(本科)生 —compare 比較 GRADUATE[1] (1)

un·der·ground[1] /ˋʌndɚˋgraʊnd; ˈʌndəgraʊnd/ *adj* **1** below the surface of the earth 地下的: *an underground passage* 地下通道 **2** [only before noun 僅用於名詞前] an underground group, organization etc is secret and illegal〔組織、機構等〕祕密的, 不合法的: *an underground terrorist organization* 地下恐怖主義組織

un·der·ground[2] /ˋʌndɚˋgraʊnd; ˌʌndəˈgraʊnd/ *adv* **1** under the earth's surface 在地(面)下: *nuclear waste buried deep underground* 深埋在地下的核廢料 | *The prairie dog burrows underground.* 草原犬鼠會打地洞。**2 go underground** to start doing something secretly, or hide in a secret place 轉入地下; 隱匿: *The ANC was forced to go underground when the government arrested its leaders.* 在政府逮捕其領導人之後, 非洲國民大會被迫轉入地下。

un·der·ground[3] /ˋʌndɚˋgraʊnd; ˈʌndəgraʊnd/ *n* **the Underground a)** *BrE* a railway system under the ground【英】地下鐵路, 地鐵; SUBWAY (2) *AmE*【美】: *a map of the London Underground* 倫敦地鐵圖 **b)** an illegal group working in secret against the rulers of a country 反政府的非法地下組織; 祕密團體

un·der·growth /ˋʌndɚˏgroθ; ˈʌndəgrəʊθ/ *n* [U] bushes, small trees, and other plants growing around and under bigger trees〔長在大樹下的〕下層灌木叢, 矮樹叢: *Some-*

thing rustled in the undergrowth. 有東西在下層灌木叢中沙沙作響。

un·der·hand¹ /ˌʌndɚˋhænd; ˌʌndəˈhænd◂/ also 又作 **un·der·hand·ed** /ˌʌndɚˋhændɪd; ˌʌndəˈhændɪ̵d/ *adj* dishonest and done secretly 欺詐的; 祕密進行的: *underhand dealings* 祕密[私下]交易 —**underhandedly** *adv* —**underhandedness** *n* [U]

underhand² *adv AmE* if you throw a ball underhand, you throw it without moving your arm above your shoulder; UNDERARM¹【美】〔擊球〕用手不過肩地, 低手地

un·der·lay /ˋʌndɚˏle; ˈʌndəleɪ/ *n* [C,U] a large piece of material put under a CARPET¹ (1)〔地毯下的〕墊料, 墊層

un·der·lie /ˌʌndɚˋlaɪ; ˌʌndəˈlaɪ/ *v past tense* **underlay** /-ˋle; -ˈleɪ/ *past participle* **underlaid** /-ˋled; -ˈleɪd/ [T] *formal* to be the real cause of or reason for something【正式】構成…的真正起因: *Social problems and poverty underlie much of the crime in today's big cities.* 社會問題和貧困是當今大城市許多犯罪的根本原因。

un·der·line /ˌʌndɚˋlaɪn; ˌʌndəˈlaɪn/ *v* [T] **1** to draw a line under a word to show that it is important 在…之下劃線〔以示重要〕**2** to show that something is important 強調; 使突出: *This tragic incident underlines the need for immediate action.* 這一悲劇事件表明有必要立即採取行動。

un·der·ling /ˋʌndɚlɪŋ; ˈʌndəlɪŋ/ *n* [C] an insulting word for someone who has a low rank 下屬, 部下; 走卒〔侮辱性用詞〕

3 **un·der·ly·ing** /ˌʌndɚˋlaɪɪŋ; ˌʌndəˈlaɪ-ɪŋ/ *adj* **underlying reason/cause/aim etc** the reason, cause etc that is the most important, although it is not easily noticed 根本的理由/原因/目標等: *the underlying causes of her depression* 她意志消沉的根本原因

un·der·manned /ˌʌndɚˋmænd; ˌʌndəˈmænd◂/ *adj* not having enough workers 人員不足的

un·der·men·tioned /ˌʌndɚˋmɛnʃənd; ˌʌndəˈmenʃənd◂/ *adj formal*【正式】**1** mentioned later in the same piece of writing 下述的: *Please supply me with the undermentioned goods.* 請給我供應下述貨物。**2 the undermentioned** the people or things that are mentioned in the list that is written immediately below 下列的人員[物品]: *The undermentioned will report for duty.* 下列人員將前來報到。

un·der·mine /ˌʌndɚˋmaɪn; ˌʌndəˈmaɪn/ *v* [T] **1** to gradually make someone or something less strong or effective 逐漸削弱[損害]: *She tried to undermine his authority at every opportunity.* 她試圖利用一切機會來削弱他的權威。| *economic policies that threaten to undermine the health care system* 可能會損害衛生保健制度的經濟政策 **2** to gradually take away the earth from under something 挖去…(底下)的土

2 **un·der·neath¹** /ˌʌndɚˋniθ; ˌʌndəˈniːθ/ *prep, adv* **1** directly under or below another object, used especially when one thing is covering or hiding another 在…下面; 在…底下〔尤指某物覆蓋或藏着另一物〕: *It's near where the railway goes underneath the road.* 它在臨近鐵路從路下通過的地方。| *A translation was written underneath.* 譯文寫在下面。—see 見 UNDER¹ (USAGE) —see picture on page A1 參見 A1 頁圖 **2** if someone is nice, shy etc underneath, they really are nice etc even though their behaviour shows a different character〔人〕本質上: *She seems aggressive, but underneath she's pretty shy.* 她看起來咄咄逼人, 實際上卻相當靦腆。

underneath² *n BrE*【英】**the underneath** the bottom surface of something, or the part of something that is below or under something else 下面; 下部; 底部, 底層: *We need to paint the underneath with a rust preventer.* 我們需要用防鏽漆把底部刷一下。

un·der·nour·ished /ˌʌndɚˋnɝɪʃt; ˌʌndəˈnʌrɪʃt◂/ *adj* unhealthy and weak because you have not had enough food 營養不足的 —**undernourishment** *n* [U]

un·der·paid /ˌʌndɚˋped; ˌʌndəˈpeɪd◂/ *adj* earning less money than you deserve for your work 所得工資不足[過低]的: *Teachers are generally overworked and underpaid.* 教師一般都工作過度, 報酬過低。—**underpay** *v* [T]

un·der·pants /ˋʌndɚˏpænts; ˈʌndəpænts/ *n* [plural] **1** *BrE* a short piece of underwear worn by men under their trousers【英】〔男用〕襯褲, 內褲 —see picture at 參見 UNDERWEAR 圖 **2** *AmE* a short piece of underwear of this type, worn by men or women【美】〔男或女用的〕內褲, 襯褲

un·der·pass /ˋʌndɚˏpæs; ˈʌndəpɑːs/ *n* [C] a road or path that goes under another road or a railway 地下通道; 下穿交叉道; 高架橋下的通道

un·der·pay /ˋʌndɚˋpe; ˌʌndəˈpeɪ/ *v past tense and past participle* **underpaid** /-ˋped; -ˈpeɪd/ [T] to pay someone too little for their work 付給…過低的工資

un·der·pin /ˌʌndɚˋpɪn; ˌʌndəˈpɪn/ *v* [T] **1** to give strength or support to an idea, belief etc 鞏固, 支持〔想法、信念等〕: *A solid basis of evidence underpins their theory.* 基礎堅實的證據鞏固了他們的理論。**2** to put a solid piece of metal under something such as a wall in order to make it stronger 加固〔牆等〕的基礎 —**underpinning** *n* [C,U]

un·der·play /ˌʌndɚˋple; ˌʌndəˈpleɪ/ *v* [T] **1** to make something seem less important than it really is 淡化[貶低]…的重要性, 使顯得不如實際重要 **2 underplay your hand** to discuss something with someone without telling them everything about your plans, abilities etc 不動聲色地小心行事, 不露鋒芒

un·der·priv·i·leged /ˋʌndɚˋprɪvəlɪdʒd; ˌʌndəˈprɪvɪ̵lɪdʒd◂/ *adj* very poor, with worse living conditions, educational opportunities etc than most people in society 貧困的; 社會地位低下的; 下層社會的

un·der·rate /ˋʌndɚˋret; ˌʌndəˈreɪt/ *v* [T] to think that someone or something is less good, effective, skilful etc than they really are 看輕; 低估: *a much underrated novel* 評價過低的小説

un·der·re·sourced /ˌʌndərɪˋsɔrst; ˌʌndərɪˈzɔːst/ *adj* not provided with enough money, equipment etc〔資金、設備等〕供應不足的

un·der·score /ˌʌndɚˋskɔr; ˌʌndəˈskɔː/ *v* [T] *especially AmE*【尤美】**1** to emphasize something so that people pay attention to it 強調 **2** to draw a line under a word or phrase to show that it is important; UNDERLINE 在〔單詞、片語〕底下劃線〔以示強調〕

un·der·sea /ˋʌndɚˋsi; ˈʌndəsiː/ *adj* [only before noun 僅用於名詞前] happening or existing below the surface of the sea 海底的; 海面下的; 在海面下進行的: *undersea exploration* 海底探險

un·der·sec·re·ta·ry /ˌʌndɚˋsɛkrəˏtɛrɪ; ˌʌndəˈsekrətəri/ *n* [C] **1** someone who is in charge of the daily work of a British government department〔英國的〕政務次官 **2** *AmE* a very important official in a government department who is one position in rank below the SECRETARY【美】副部長; 副國務卿

un·der·sell /ˌʌndɚˋsɛl; ˌʌndəˈsel/ *v past tense and past participle* **undersold** /-ˋsold; -ˈsəʊld/ [T] **1** to sell goods at a lower price than someone else 以低於〔他人〕的價格出售; 廉價出售 **2** to make other people think that someone or something is less good, effective, skilful etc than they really are 讓人輕視; 過於自謙; 過低評價: *I think he undersold himself at the interview.* 我認為他在面試時過於自謙。

under-served /ˌ·· ˈ·◂/ *adj AmE* not getting enough care and help from the government【美】〔政府〕關照不足的, 服務不周到的: *the under-served communities of the inner city* 未獲充分關照的舊城區貧民

un·der·sexed /ˌʌndɚˋsɛkst; ˌʌndəˈsekst◂/ *adj* having less desire to have sex than is normal 性慾不強的, 性冷淡的

un·der·shirt /ˋʌndɚˏʃɝt; ˈʌndəʃɜːt/ *n* [C] *AmE* a piece of underwear with or without arms, worn under a shirt

U

【美】內衣; 汗衫, 汗背心; VEST[1] (1) *BrE*【英】

un·der·side /ˈʌndɚˌsaɪd; ˈʌndəsaɪd/ *n* [singular] **the underside** the bottom side or surface of something 下側; 下面; 底部

un·der·signed /ˌʌndɚˋsaɪnd; ˈʌndəsaɪnd/ *adj formal*【正式】**the undersigned** the person or people who have signed a piece of writing, used especially in formal letters〔尤指正式信件的〕簽名者, 署名人

un·der·sized /ˈʌndɚˋsaɪzd; ˌʌndəˈsaɪzd◂/ also 又作 **un·der·size** /-ˋsaɪz; -ˈsaɪz◂/ *adj* smaller than usual, or too small 小於一般尺寸的; 太小的

un·der·staffed /ˌʌndɚˋstæft; ˌʌndəˈstɑːft◂/ *adj* not having enough workers, or fewer workers than usual 人員不足的, 人手不夠的

1 1 **un·der·stand** /ˌʌndɚˋstænd; ˌʌndəˈstænd/ *v past tense and past participle* **understood** /-ˋstʊd; -ˈstʊd/ [not in progressive 不用進行式]

1 ►MEANING 意思◄ [I,T] to know the meaning of what someone is telling you, or the language that they speak 懂; 理解; 明白: *She doesn't understand English – try Spanish.* 她不懂英語——試試西班牙語吧。| *I'm sorry, I don't understand. Can you explain that again?* 對不起, 我不明白。你能再解釋一遍嗎? | **understand perfectly** *I understand perfectly, the children must be in bed by 8 o'clock.* 我很清楚, 孩子們8點前必須上牀睡覺。

2 ►FACT/IDEA 事實/想法◄ [I,T] to know or realize how a fact, process, situation etc works, especially through learning or experience〔尤指通過學習或經歷〕了解; 熟悉: *I don't really understand the political situation in Northern Ireland.* 我真的不了解北愛爾蘭的政治形勢。| **understand how/why/where etc** *You don't need to understand how computers work to be able to use them.* 你不必熟悉電腦的工作原理, 會用就行。| **fully understand** *How the drug actually works isn't fully understood.* 這種藥的實際作用尚未完全了解。

3 ►PERSON 人◄ [I,T] to know and sympathize with how someone feels, and why they behave the way they do 理解, 諒解; 同情: *My parents just don't understand me.* 我父母就是不理解我。| *Don tried to understand.* 唐試圖去諒解。| **understand how/what etc** *I understand how you feel, but I think you're over-reacting.* 我理解你的感受, 但我認為你的反應過頭了。| **understand sb doing sth** *I can understand her wanting to live alone and be independent.* 我能理解她想獨自生活, 不再依賴別人。

4 I understand (that) *spoken formal* used to say that someone has told you that something is true【口, 正式】獲悉; 聽說: *I understand that you'll be coming to work here soon.* 我聽說你很快要來這兒工作了。

5 make yourself understood to be able to express simple things in another language〔用外語〕表達自己的意思: *I'm not very good at German, but I can make myself understood.* 我的德語不太好, 但我能表達自己的意思。

6 do you understand? *spoken* used when you are telling someone what they should or should not do, especially when you are angry with them【口】明白了嗎?〔用於告誡〕: *Never speak to me like that again! Do you understand?* 別再那樣子對我說話! 明白了嗎?

7 be understood *formal* used to say that something has been agreed and there is no need to discuss it【正式】〔某事〕已商定: **be understood that** *I thought it was understood that if we worked late we'd get paid double.* 我原以為已經商定, 我們加班就會得到雙份報酬。

8 understand sth/sb to mean sth accept something as having a particular meaning 領會某事/某人的含義: *In this document, 'children' is understood to mean people under 14.* 在本文件中, "兒童"是指14歲以下的人。

9 give sb to understand sth *formal* to make someone believe that something is true, something is going to happen etc, without telling them this directly【正式】〔不直接說明而〕使某人相信某事: *I was given to understand that the property was in good condition.* 我得到的感覺是房子保養得好。

This graph shows how common the different grammar patterns of the verb **understand** are. 本圖表所示為動詞 understand 構成的不同語法模式的使用頻率。

understand sth
understand how/why/where etc
understand (that)
understand
understand sth/sb to mean sth
understand sb doing sth
other
10% 20% 30% 40% 50%

Based on the British National Corpus and the Longman Lancaster Corpus
據英國國家語料庫和朗文蘭卡斯特語料庫

un·der·stand·a·ble /ˌʌndɚˋstændəbl̩; ˌʌndəˈstændəbəl/ *adj* **1** able to be understood; COMPREHENSIBLE 可懂的; 易於理解的: *The announcement was barely understandable.* 通告幾乎看不懂。**2** understandable behaviour, reactions etc seem normal and reasonable because of the situation you are in〔行為、反應等〕可以理解的, 合情理的: *Her anger was entirely understandable in the circumstances.* 她的憤怒在當時情況下是完全可以理解的。—**understandably** *adv*

un·der·stand·ing[1] /ˌʌndɚˋstændɪŋ; ˌʌndəˈstændɪŋ/ *n* 
1 [C usually singular 一般用單數] a private, unofficial agreement〔私底下、非正式的〕協議, 協定: **come to/reach an understanding** *I thought we had come to an understanding on this matter.* 我認為我們在這件事上已達成了協議。| **on the understanding that** (=on the condition that) 以…為條件 *I lent him the money on the strict understanding that he paid it back next month.* 我借錢給他, 條件是他必須在下個月歸還。**2** [singular,U] knowledge about something, based on learning or experience 了解; 熟悉: **have an understanding of** *The present Industry Secretary has only a limited understanding of economics.* 現任工業部長對經濟學所知有限。**3** [singular,U] sympathy towards someone's character and behaviour 諒解; 同情: *Mutual understanding is important in all relationships.* 互相諒解在所有關係中都是重要的。**4** [U] the way in which you judge the meaning of something 領會; 理解: [+of] *According to my understanding of the letter, it means something quite different.* 根據我對該信的理解, 它表示的意思完全不同。**5** [U] the ability to know and learn; INTELLIGENCE (1) 理解力; 智力: *beyond a child's understanding* 超出了孩子的理解力

understanding[2] *adj* sympathetic and kind about other people's problems 能諒解的, 寬容的: *Luckily, I have a very understanding boss.* 幸運的是, 我有一個非常通情達理的上司。

un·der·state /ˈʌndɚˋstet; ˌʌndəˈsteɪt/ *v* [T] to describe something in a way that makes it seem less important than it really is 沒有如實地陳述; 淡化: *This report understates the seriousness of the situation.* 這個報告沒有如實陳述形勢的嚴峻。

un·der·state·ment /ˈʌndɚˌstetmənt; ˌʌndəˈsteɪtmənt/ *n* **1** [C] a statement that is not strong enough to express how good, bad, impressive etc something really is 不充分的陳述, 輕描淡寫的陳述: *To say the movie was bad is an understatement.* 說這電影不好是低調的說法。**2** [U] a way of describing things as being less good, bad, important etc than they really are 輕描淡寫; 少說, 少報

un·der·stood /ˌʌndəˋstʊd; ˌʌndəˈstʊd/ the past tense and past participle of UNDERSTAND

un·der·stud·y¹ /ˋʌndəˌstʌdɪ; ˈʌndəˌstʌdi/ *n* [C] an actor who learns a part in a play so that they can act if the usual actor is ill 預備演員, 替角

understudy² *v* [T] to be an understudy for a particular actor in a play 充當〔某演員〕的替角

un·der·sub·scribe /ˌʌndəsəbˋskraɪb; ˌʌndəsəbˈskraɪb/ *v* [T] **be undersubscribed** if an activity, sale, service etc is undersubscribed, not many people want it 參加者[訂戶, 用戶]不足

3 **un·der·take** /ˌʌndəˋtek; ˌʌndəˈteɪk/ *v past tense* **undertook** /-ˋtʊk; -ˈtʊk/ *past participle* **undertaken** /-ˋtekən; -ˈteɪkən/ [T] *formal*【正式】**1** to accept that you are responsible for a piece of work, and start to do it 着手做; 承擔, 接受: *She undertook full responsibility for the new changes.* 她為新變化承擔全部責任。**2 undertake to do sth** to promise or agree to do something 答應做某事; 同意做某事: *He undertook to pay the money back in six months.* 他保證六個月內還款。

un·der·tak·er /ˌʌndəˋtekə; ˈʌndəteɪkə/ *n* [C] *BrE* someone whose job is to arrange funerals; FUNERAL DIRECTOR【英】承辦喪葬者, 殯儀員

un·der·tak·ing /ˌʌndəˋtekɪŋ; ˌʌndəˈteɪkɪŋ/ *n* **1** [C usually singular 一般用單數] an important job, piece of work, or activity that you are responsible for 任務; 事業: *Starting a new business can be a risky undertaking.* 創辦新企業是一項有風險的事情。**2** [C] *formal* a promise to do something【正式】許諾, 保證: *an undertaking to respect people's privacy* 尊重人們隱私的承諾 **3** [U] the business of an undertaker 喪葬事宜; 殯儀業

under-the-coun·ter /ˌ.. . ˈ..◂/ *adj informal* under-the-counter goods are bought or sold secretly, especially because they are illegal【非正式】〔商品〕暗中[私下]成交的; 違法交易的

un·der·tone /ˋʌndəˌton; ˈʌndətəʊn/ *n* **1** a feeling or quality that is not directly expressed but can still be recognized 潛在的情感;〔隱約的〕含意: **[+of]** *There was an undertone of sadness in her letter.* 她的信中流露出傷感的情緒。**2** [C] a quiet voice or sound 低聲, 低音 —see also 另見 OVERTONE

un·der·tow /ˋʌndəˌto; ˈʌndətəʊ/ *n* [singular] the water current under the surface that pulls back towards the sea when a wave comes onto the shore〔海浪衝上岸後退回去時形成的〕回流, 退浪

un·der·used /ˌʌndəˋjuzd; ˌʌndəˈjuːzd◂/ *adj* something that is underused is not used as much as it could be 未充分利用的

un·der·val·ue /ˋʌndəˋvælju; ˌʌndəˈvæljuː/ *v* [T] to think that someone or something is less important or valuable than they really are 小看, 輕視; 低估: *She felt that the company undervalued her work.* 她覺得公司低估了她的工作。

un·der·wa·ter /ˋʌndəˌwɔtə; ˌʌndəˈwɔːtə◂/ *adj* [only before noun 僅用於名詞前] below the surface of an area of water, or able to be used there 水下的; 水下(使)用的: *underwater cameras* 水下攝影機 —**underwater** *adv*

underwater 水下的

swimming underwater 潛泳

un·der·way /ˌʌndəˋwe; ˌʌndəˈweɪ/ *adj* [not before noun 不用於名詞前] **1** happening now 在進行中的: *Plans to merge the two companies are already underway.* 合併兩家公司的計劃已經在實施中。| **get underway** (=start happening) 開始進行, 啟動 **2** something such as a boat or train that is underway is moving〔船、火車等〕在行進中的 —see also 另見 **under way** (WAY¹ (67))

underwear 內衣

camisole 貼身胸衣

body *BrE*【英】/ body suit *AmE*【美】女式緊身衣

vest *BrE*【英】/ undershirt *AmE*【美】背心

boxer shorts 平腳短褲

underpants/pants *BrE*【英】內褲

knickers *BrE*【英】/ panties *AmE*【美】女用短襯褲

bra 乳罩

un·der·wear /ˋʌndəˌwɛr; ˈʌndəweə/ *n* [U] clothes that you wear next to your body under your other clothes 內衣; 襯衣

un·der·weight /ˋʌndəˋwet; ˌʌndəˈweɪt/ *adj* weighing less than is expected or usual 重量不足的; 標準重量以下的 —opposite 反義詞 OVERWEIGHT —see 見 THIN (USAGE)

un·der·went /ˌʌndəˋwɛnt; ˌʌndəˈwent/ the past tense of UNDERGO

un·der·whelm /ˌʌndəˋwɛlm; ˌʌndəˈwelm/ *v* [T] *humorous* to not be very impressive【幽默】未給…留下深刻印象

un·der·world /ˋʌndəˌwɝld; ˈʌndəwɜːld/ *n* [singular] **1** the criminals in a particular place and the criminal activities they are involved in〔某地的〕罪犯; 黑社會; 犯罪活動 **2** the place where the spirits of the dead are believed to live, especially in Ancient Greek stories〔尤指古希臘神話中的〕地獄, 陰間

un·der·write /ˌʌndəˋraɪt; ˌʌndəˈraɪt/ *v past tense* **underwrote** /-ˋrot; -ˈrəʊt/ *past participle* **underwritten** /-ˋrɪtn̩; -ˈrɪtn/ [T] **1** *formal* to support an activity, business plan etc with money, so that you are financially responsible for it【正式】(同意)負擔〔活動、商業計劃等〕的費用, 以金錢支持: *The government has agreed to underwrite the project with a grant of £5 million.* 政府同意撥款五百萬英鎊資助該項目。**2** *technical* to be responsible for an insurance agreement【術語】為…保險

un·der·writ·er /ˋʌndəˌraɪtə; ˈʌndəˌraɪtə/ *n* [C] someone who makes insurance contracts 保險商; 保險業務受理人

un·de·served /ˌʌndɪˋzɝvd; ˌʌndɪˈzɜːvd◂/ *adj* undeserved criticism, praise etc is unfair because you do not deserve it 不該受的; 冤枉的; 不應得的: *She had an undeserved reputation for making trouble.* 她有個愛惹麻煩的名聲真是冤枉。

un·de·sir·a·ble /ˌʌndɪˋzaɪrəbl; ˌʌndɪˈzaɪərəbəl◂/ *adj formal* something or someone that is undesirable is not welcome or wanted because they may affect a situation or person in a bad way【正式】不受歡迎的; 不合意的; 討厭的: *The incident could have undesirable consequences for the government.* 這事件會給政府帶來不良的後果。

un·de·sir·a·bles /ˌʌndɪˋzaɪərəbl̩z; ˌʌndɪˈzaɪərəbəlz/ *n* [plural] people who are considered to be immoral, criminal, or socially unacceptable 不良分子; 不受歡迎的人

un·de·vel·oped /ˌʌndɪˋvɛləpt; ˌʌndɪˈveləpt◂/ *adj* not yet developed 不發達的; 未成熟的; 未開發的 —compare 比較 UNDERDEVELOPED

un·did /ʌnˋdɪd; ʌnˈdɪd/ the past tense of UNDO

un·dies /ˋʌndɪz; ˈʌndiːz/ *n* [plural] *informal* underwear 【非正式】內衣, 襯衣

un·dig·ni·fied /ʌnˋdɪgnəˌfaɪd; ʌnˈdɪgnɪ̈faɪd/ *adj* behaving in a way that is embarrassing or makes you look silly 不莊重的; 有損尊嚴的; 不像樣子的: *Sally made an undignified exit with her bathrobe clutched about her.* 莎莉裹着浴衣不雅觀地退了出去。

un·di·lut·ed /ˌʌndaɪˋlutɪd; ˌʌndaɪˈluːtɪ̈d◂/ *adj literary* an undiluted feeling is very strong and not mixed with any other feelings 【文】〔感情〕未淡化的; 沒有攙雜的; 純真的: *undiluted joy* 濃濃的樂趣

un·dis·charged /ˌʌndɪsˋtʃɑrdʒd; ˌʌndɪsˈtʃɑːdʒd◂/ *adj technical* 【術語】**1** an undischarged debt is one that has not been paid 〔債務〕未償清的 **2 an undischarged bankrupt** someone who still owes money and is not legally allowed to stop repaying their debt 債務未償清的破產者

un·dis·crim·i·nat·ing /ˌʌndɪˋskrɪməˌnetɪŋ; ˌʌndɪˈskrɪmɪ̈neɪtɪŋ/ *adj* not having the ability to see a difference in value between two people or things, and therefore unable to make judgments about them 無鑑別力的; 區別不了的; 不加區別的

un·dis·guised /ˌʌndɪsˋgaɪzd; ˌʌndɪsˈgaɪzd◂/ *adj* clearly shown and not hidden 公開的; 坦率的; 不加掩飾的: *undisguised contempt* 不加掩飾的蔑視

un·di·sput·ed /ˌʌndɪˋspjutɪd; ˌʌndɪˈspjuːtɪ̈d◂/ *adj* **1** known to be definitely true 無可爭辯的, 毫無疑問的: *They talk about an after-life as if it were an undisputed truth.* 他們談論來世就好像這是無可置疑的事實。**2** accepted by everyone 公認的: *The brand has now become the undisputed market leader.* 這個牌子現已成為公認的市場主導。

un·dis·turbed /ˌʌndɪˋstɝbd; ˌʌndɪˈstɜːbd◂/ *adj* not interrupted or moved 沒受到干擾的; 未被動過的: *At last I was able to work undisturbed.* 我終於可以不受干擾地工作了。| *The documents lay undisturbed for years.* 文件有數年未曾動過。

un·di·vid·ed /ˌʌndɪˋvaɪdɪd; ˌʌndɪˈvaɪdɪ̈d◂/ *adj* complete 完整的; 全部的: **undivided attention** *Please give the matter your undivided attention.* 請專心處理這件事。

un·do /ʌnˋdu; ʌnˈduː/ *v past tense* **undid** /-ˋdɪd; -ˈdɪd/ *past participle* **undone** /-ˋdʌn; -ˈdʌn/ [T] **1** to unfasten something that is tied or wrapped 解開, 打開, 鬆開〔某物〕: *She carefully undid the parcel.* 她小心翼翼地打開了包裹。—see 見 OPEN² (USAGE) **2** to try to remove the bad effects of something you have done 消除…的壞影響: *Well, the mistake has been made now and can't be undone.* 唉, 錯已鑄成, 無可挽回。

un·do·ing /ʌnˋduɪŋ; ʌnˈduːɪŋ/ *n* **be sb's undoing** to cause someone's shame, failure etc 是某人蒙羞[失敗]的原因[禍根]: *In the end gambling was his undoing.* 最後, 賭博是他墮落的原因。

un·done /ʌnˋdʌn; ˌʌnˈdʌn◂/ *adj* [not before noun 不用於名詞前] **1** not fastened 解開的, 鬆開的: **come undone** (=become unfastened) 鬆開了 *One of your buttons is coming undone.* 你的一個鈕扣要鬆開了。**2 leave sth undone** not finish something 未完成某事 **3** *old use* destroyed and without hope 【舊】毀掉的; 完蛋了的: *I am undone! My secret has been discovered!* 我完了! 祕密已經被揭穿!

3 **un·doubt·ed** /ʌnˋdaʊtɪd; ʌnˈdaʊtɪ̈d/ *adj* definitely true or known to exist 毋庸置疑的; 肯定的: *her undoubted talent* 她那毋庸置疑的天才 —**undoubtedly** *adv*: *That is undoubtedly true.* 那是千真萬確的。

un·dreamed-of /ʌnˋdrimd ɑv; ʌnˈdriːmd -ɒv/ also 又作 **undreamt-of** /ʌnˋdrɛmt-; ʌnˈdremt-/ *adj* much more or much better than you could imagine 夢想不到的, 想像不到的: *undreamed-of wealth* 意外的財富 | *These technological advances were undreamt-of even 20 years ago.* 這些技術進步甚至在20年前還是不可想像的。

un·dress¹ /ʌnˋdrɛs; ʌnˈdres/ *v* [I,T] to take your clothes off, or take someone else's clothes off 脱去〔…的〕衣服

undress² *n* [U] *formal* a state in which you are wearing few or no clothes 【正式】穿衣很少; 裸體: *The dancers walked around in various stages of undress.* 舞蹈員身穿各式暴露的裝束走來走去。

un·dressed /ʌnˋdrɛst; ˌʌnˈdrest◂/ *adj* **1** [not before noun 不用於名詞前] not wearing any clothes 不穿衣服的, 裸體的: **get undressed** (=take your clothes off) 脱去衣服 **2** an undressed wound has not been covered to protect it 〔傷口〕未包紮的

un·due /ʌnˋdu; ˌʌnˈdjuː◂/ *adj* [only before noun 僅用於名詞前] *formal* more than is reasonable, suitable, or necessary 【正式】不適當的; 過度的, 過分的: *We managed to get through Customs without undue difficulty.* 我們沒費多大周折便通過了海關。

un·du·late /ˋʌndjəˌlet; ˈʌndjʊ̈leɪt/ *v* [I] *formal* to move or be shaped like waves that are rising and falling 【正式】起伏, 波動: *undulating hills* 起伏的山巒 —**undulation** /ˌʌndʒəˋleʃən; ˌʌndjʊ̈ˈleɪʃən/ *n* [C,U]

un·du·ly /ʌnˋdulɪ; ʌnˈdjuːli/ *adv formal* too extreme or too much 【正式】過度地, 過分地: *Perhaps I have been unduly severe in my judgment of him.* 也許我對他的評價過於嚴厲了。

un·dy·ing /ʌnˋdaɪɪŋ; ʌnˈdaɪ-ɪŋ/ *adj* [only before noun 僅用於名詞前] continuing for ever 不朽的; 永恆的: *They declared their undying love for each other.* 他們宣稱永遠愛對方。

un·earth /ʌnˋɝθ; ʌnˈɜːθ/ *v* [T] **1** to find out the truth about something 揭露; 發現: *The reporter had unearthed some important secrets about her.* 記者發現了有關她的一些重要祕密。**2** to find something after searching for it, especially something that has been buried in the ground 發掘, 掘出〔尤指埋藏於地下的東西〕

un·earth·ly /ʌnˋɝθlɪ; ʌnˈɜːθli/ *adj* **1** very strange and unnatural 奇異的, 不自然的: *I felt an unearthly presence in the room.* 我感覺房間裡怪怪的。**2 unearthly hour/time etc** *informal* very early or very late and therefore extremely inconvenient 【非正式】早[晚]得不合理的時間等: *We had to set off at some unearthly hour of the morning.* 我們得天沒亮就動身。—**unearthliness** *n* [U]

un·ease /ʌnˋiz; ʌnˈiːz/ *n* [U] a feeling of nervousness and anxiety that makes you unable to relax 不自在; 心神不寧

un·eas·y /ʌnˋizɪ; ʌnˈiːzi/ *adj* **1** nervous, anxious, and unable to relax because you think something bad might happen 心神不安的, 憂慮的, 不自在的: *Katie felt uneasy about what she had done.* 凱蒂對自己所做的事感到憂心忡忡。—see 見 NERVOUS (USAGE) **2** an uneasy period of time is one when people have agreed to stop fighting or arguing, but which is not really calm 不穩定的; 不安定的: *An uneasy peace descended on the area.* 一種不穩定的和平降臨到這個地區。**3** not comfortable, peaceful, or relaxed 不舒服的; 不踏實的; 不安的: *She eventually fell into an uneasy sleep.* 她最後睡着了, 但睡得並不踏實。| *an uneasy conscience* 不安的良心 —**uneasily** *adv* —**uneasiness** *n* [U]

un·eat·able /ʌnˋitəbl̩; ʌnˈiːtəbəl/ *adj* a word meaning unpleasant or unsuitable to eat, that some people think is incorrect; INEDIBLE 不可食的; 不適合食用的〔有些人認為這詞不正確〕

un·e·co·nom·ic /ˌʌnikəˋnɑmɪk; ˌʌniːkəˈnɒmɪk◂/ *adj* **1** not making enough money or profit 賺錢不多的; 利潤不大的, 沒有效益的: *Uneconomic mines will have to be closed.* 沒有效益的礦井將不得不關閉。**2** uneconomical 不經濟的, 浪費的

un·e·co·nom·ic·al /ˌʌnikəˋnɑmɪkl̩; ˌʌniːkəˈnɒmɪkəl/

adj using too much effort, money or materials 不經濟的; 浪費的: *The project was considered uneconomical and shelved.* 這個項目被認為太浪費而擱置起來。—**uneconomically** /-klɪ; -kli/ *adv*

un·ed·u·cat·ed /ʌn`ɛdʒəˌketɪd; ʌn'edjʊkeɪtɪ̈d/ *adj* not educated to the usual level, or showing that someone is not well educated 沒受過教育的; 未受過良好教育的; 沒有教養的: *ignorant and uneducated opinions* 無知無識的觀點

un·e·mo·tion·al /ˌʌnɪ`moʃənl̩; ˌʌnɪ'məʊʃənəl◂/ *adj* not showing your feelings 不流露感情的; 冷漠的: *He remained completely unemotional as the judge read out the sentence.* 法官宣讀判決時, 他仍然無動於衷。

un·em·ploy·able /ˌʌnɪm`plɔɪəbl̩; ˌʌnɪm'plɔɪəbəl◂/ *adj* not having the skills or qualities needed to get a job〔由於缺乏必要技能或素質而〕不能被雇用的

2 3 **un·em·ployed**[1] /ˌʌnɪm`plɔɪd; ˌʌnɪm'plɔɪd◂/ *adj* without a job 未被雇用的, 失業的

unemployed[2] *n* **the unemployed** [plural] people who have no job 失業者: **the long-term unemployed** (=people who have not had a job for a long time) 長期失業者

2 2 **un·em·ploy·ment** /ˌʌnɪm`plɔɪmənt; ˌʌnɪm'plɔɪmənt/ *n* [U] **1** the number of people in a country who do not have a job 失業人數: *levels of unemployment* 失業率 | **high unemployment** (=lots of people without a job) 高失業率 **2** the fact of having no job 失業: *Closure of the plant will mean unemployment for 500 workers.* 這家工廠的倒閉意味着 500 個工人要失業。**3** *AmE informal* money paid regularly by the government to people who have no job【美, 非正式】失業救濟金

unemployment ben·e·fit /··'·· ˌ···/ *BrE*【英】, **unemployment com·pen·sa·tion** /··'·· ··ˌ··/ *AmE*【美】— *n* [U] money paid regularly by the government to people who do not have a job 失業津貼; 失業救濟金

un·end·ing /ʌn`ɛndɪŋ; ʌn'endɪŋ/ *adj* something unpleasant or tiring that is unending seems as if it will continue for ever 無休止的, 不停的, 不斷的: *an unending struggle to survive* 無休止的掙扎求存

un·en·du·ra·ble /ˌʌnɪn`djʊrəbl̩; ˌʌnɪn'djʊərəbəl◂/ *adj formal* too unpleasant, painful etc to bear【正式】不可容忍的, 難以忍受的: *The pain was unendurable.* 疼痛無法忍受。

un·en·vi·a·ble /ʌn`ɛnvɪəbl̩; ʌn'enviəbəl/ *adj* difficult and unpleasant 艱難的; 令人不快的; 尷尬的: **unenviable task** *the unenviable task of informing the victim's relations* 通知受害人親屬的為難差事

un·e·qual /ʌn`ikwəl; ʌn'iːkwəl/ *adj* **1** not equal in number, amount, or level〔數目、數量或水平〕不相等的, 不相同的: **of unequal size/length etc** *two posts of unequal length* 不同長度的兩根柱子 | **be unequal in size/weight etc** *The baskets were unequal in weight and looked likely to topple.* 籃子的重量不一, 看來要倒下。**2** unfairly treating different people or groups in different ways 不平等的, 不公正的; 不均勻的: *an unequal contest* 不公平的競賽 | *the unequal distribution of wealth* 財富的分配不均 **3 be unequal to the task/job etc** to not have enough strength, ability etc to do something 不勝任任務/工作等 —**unequally** *adv*

un·e·qualled *BrE*【英】, **unequaled** *AmE*【美】/ʌn`ikwəld; ʌn'iːkwəld/ *adj* better than any other 無可比擬的, 無與倫比的: *The school's success rate is unequalled in the area.* 該校的成功率在本地區首屈一指。

un·e·quiv·o·cal /ˌʌnɪ`kwɪvəkl̩; ˌʌnɪ'kwɪvəkəl◂/ *adj formal* completely clear and without any possibility of doubt【正式】明確的; 毫不含糊的: *His answer was an unequivocal "No".* 他的回答是毫不含糊的"不"。—**unequivocally** /-klɪ; -kli/ *adv*

un·er·ring /ʌn`ɝɪŋ; ʌn'ɜːrɪŋ/ *adj* always exactly right 一貫準確的, 毫無偏差的: **unerring accuracy/judgement etc** *Max hit the target with unerring accuracy.* 馬克斯準確無誤地擊中了目標。—**unerringly** *adv*

un·eth·i·cal /ʌn`ɛθɪkl̩; ʌn'eθɪkəl/ *adj* not obeying rules of moral behaviour, especially those concerning a profession 不道德的〔尤指違反職業道德〕: *It is considered highly unethical for a psychiatrist to have a relationship with a patient.* 精神科醫生與患者發生關係被認為是極不道德的。—**unethically** /-klɪ; -kli/ *adv*

un·e·ven /ʌn`ivən; ʌn'iːvən/ *adj* **1** not smooth, flat, or level 不平坦的, 崎嶇的: *The ground was very uneven in places.* 這地上有些地方非常不平坦。**2** not regular 不規則的; 不勻的: *His breathing had become uneven.* 他的呼吸變得不均勻。**3** not equal or equally balanced 不平等的; 不平衡的: *an uneven contest* 實力不對等的競賽 **4** good in some parts and bad in others 不穩定的, 不一致的: *a rather uneven performance* 頗不穩定的演出 —**unevenly** *adv* —**unevenness** *n* [U]

un·e·vent·ful /ˌʌnɪ`vɛntfəl; ˌʌnɪ'ventfəl◂/ *adj* with nothing exciting or unusual happening 平淡的; 平靜的; 平凡的: *a quiet, uneventful life in a small town* 小鎮中寧靜平淡的生活 —**uneventfully** *adv* —**uneventfulness** *n* [U]

un·ex·am·pled /ˌʌnɪg`zæmpl̩d; ˌʌnɪg'zɑːmpəld◂/ *adj formal* better than anything else of the same type; EXCEPTIONAL (1)【正式】絕無僅有的; 無先例的, 空前的

un·ex·ci·ting /ˌʌnɪk`saɪtɪŋ; ˌʌnɪk'saɪtɪŋ◂/ *adj* ordinary and slightly boring 平淡的; 單調的: *a good quality but unexciting wine* 一種優質但味道淡的葡萄酒

un·ex·pect·ed /ˌʌnɪk`spɛktɪd; ˌʌnɪk'spektɪ̈d◂/ *adj* an unexpected event, remark etc is one that is surprising because you were not expecting it 想不到的, 意外的; 突然的: *Her angry outburst was totally unexpected.* 她的勃然大怒完全出人意料。—**unexpectedly** *adv* —**unexpectedness** *n* [U]

un·ex·plained /ˌʌnɪk`splend; ˌʌnɪk'spleɪnd◂/ *adj* something that is unexplained is something you cannot understand because you do not know the reason for it 無法解釋的; 莫名其妙的; 原因不明的: *her unexplained death* 她莫名其妙的死亡

un·ex·pur·gat·ed /ʌn`ɛkspɚˌgetɪd; ʌn'ekspəgeɪtɪ̈d/ *adj* an unexpurgated book, play etc is complete and has not had parts that might offend people removed〔書、劇本等〕完整的, 未刪節的

un·fail·ing /ʌn`felɪŋ; ʌn'feɪlɪŋ/ *adj* always there, even in times of difficulty or trouble 經久不衰的, 永恒的, 始終可靠的: *His unfailing good humour made him popular with everyone.* 他那始終不變的好脾氣使他受到大家的歡迎。—**unfailingly** *adv*

un·fair /ʌn`fɛr; ˌʌn'feə◂/ *adj* **1** not right or fair 不公平的, 不公正的: *It's so unfair – Mary gets more money for less work!* 太不公平了——瑪麗做的事少, 拿的錢卻多! **2** not giving a fair or equal opportunity to everyone〔機會〕不平等的, 不均等的: *an unfair advantage* 不平等的優勢 | *American workers feel threatened by unfair competition from abroad.* 美國工人感受到來自國外的不平等競爭的威脅。**3 unfair dismissal** a situation in which someone is illegally dismissed from their job 非法解雇 —**unfairly** *adv* —**unfairness** *n* [U]

un·faith·ful /ʌn`feθfəl; ʌn'feɪθfəl/ *adj* **1** someone who is unfaithful has sex with someone who is not their wife, husband, or usual partner〔對妻子、丈夫或伴侶〕不忠的, 有外遇的: [+to] *Edward discovered that Leonie had been unfaithful to him.* 愛德華發現莉奧妮對自己不忠。**2** not loyal to a principle, person etc〔對原則、人等〕不忠誠的, 不守信的 —**unfaithfully** *adv* —**unfaithfulness** *n* [U]

un·fal·ter·ing /ʌn`fɔltərɪŋ; ʌn'fɔːltərɪŋ/ *adj formal* strong, determined, and not becoming weaker【正式】堅決的; 堅定的: *His gaze was direct and unfaltering.* 他的凝視直接而又堅定。—**unfalteringly** *adv*

un·fa·mil·i·ar /ˌʌnfə`mɪljɚ; ˌʌnfə'mɪliə◂/ *adj* not known to you 不熟悉的, 不了解的: [+to] *The name was unfamiliar to me.* 我對這個名字不熟悉。| [+with] *Voters are unfamiliar with the real issues.* 投票者對真正的議題並不了解。—**unfamiliarity** /ˌʌnfəmɪlɪ`ærətɪ; ˌʌnfəmɪli'ærɪ̈ti/ *n*

un·fash·ion·a·ble /ʌnˋfæʃənəbḷ; ʌnˈfæʃənəbəl/ *adj* not popular or fashionable at the present time 不流行的; 不時髦的, 過時的: *an unfashionable old dress* 過時的舊連衣裙 | *His ideas have been unfashionable for some time.* 他的想法已經相當過時。

un·fas·ten /ʌnˋfæsṇ; ʌnˈfɑːsn/ *v* [T] to undo something such as a button, belt, rope etc 解開〔鈕扣、帶子、繩子等〕: *She unfastened her blouse.* 她解開了襯衫。

un·fath·om·a·ble /ʌnˋfæðəməbḷ; ʌnˈfæðəməbəl/ *adj literary* too strange or mysterious to be understood【文】莫測高深的, 難解的: *the unfathomable mysteries of human nature* 人性的不解之謎 —**unfathomably** *adv*

un·fa·vou·ra·ble *BrE*【英】, **unfavorable** *AmE*【美】/ʌnˋfevrəbḷ; ʌnˈfeɪvərəbəl/ *adj* **1** unfavourable conditions, situations etc are not as good as they should be or usually are 不適宜的; 不利的: *unfavourable weather* 不適宜的天氣 **2** expressing disapproval 反對的; 不同意的: *That new television series has had unfavourable reviews.* 那部新電視連續劇得不到好評。—**unfavourably** *adv*

un·feel·ing /ʌnˋfilɪŋ; ʌnˈfiːlɪŋ/ *adj* not sympathetic towards other people's feelings 無情的, 冷酷的, 冷漠的: *an unfeeling college bureaucracy* 冷漠的大學官僚主義 —**unfeelingly** *adv*

un·fet·tered /ʌnˋfɛtəd; ʌnˈfetəd/ *adj formal* not restricted by laws or rules【正式】不受〔法規〕約束的; 自由的: *free and unfettered trade* 自由、不受約束的貿易

un·fin·ished /ʌnˋfɪnɪʃt; ʌnˈfɪnɪʃt/ *adj* not completed 未竟的, 未完成的: *She looked away, leaving her sentence unfinished.* 她眼望別處, 話在中途打住。| **unfinished business** (=something that has to be done or dealt with that you have not yet done) 未竟之事

un·fit /ʌnˋfɪt; ʌnˈfɪt/ *adj* **1** not in a good physical condition〔身體上〕不健康的, 體格不佳的: *She never gets any excercise – she must be really unfit.* 她從不鍛鍊——身體一定不好。| **[+for]** *He was found to be medically unfit for overseas duty.* 他體格檢驗不合格, 不能到海外執行任務。**2** not good enough for a particular purpose 不合適的, 不適宜的; 不勝任的: **[+for]** *unfit for public office* 不適宜擔任公職 | **unfit for human habitation/consumption** *dwellings unfit for human habitation* 不適宜人類居住的住處

un·flag·ging /ʌnˋflægɪŋ; ʌnˈflægɪŋ/ *adj* continuing strongly and never becoming tired or weak 持久的; 不倦的; (經久) 不衰的: **unflagging energy/interest etc** *We couldn't have done it without your unflagging enthusiasm.* 沒有你毫不減退的熱情, 我們不可能完成它。—**unflaggingly** *adv*

un·flap·pa·ble /ʌnˋflæpəbḷ; ʌnˈflæpəbəl/ *adj informal* having the ability to stay calm and not get upset, even in difficult situations【非正式】臨危不亂的, 鎮定自若的: *My unflappable assistant worked steadily on as the argument raged around her.* 儘管周圍有激烈的爭論, 我那處亂不驚的助手仍從容地繼續工作。—**unflappably** *adv*

un·flinch·ing /ʌnˋflɪntʃɪŋ; ʌnˈflɪntʃɪŋ/ *adj* not changing or becoming weaker, even in a very difficult or dangerous situation 堅定的, 不畏縮的: *unflinching courage* 無畏的勇氣 —**unflinchingly** *adv*

un·fo·cused, unfocussed /ʌnˋfokəst; ʌnˈfəʊkəst/ *adj* **1** not dealing with or paying attention to the important ideas, causes etc 無焦點的; 不專心的: *The discussion was becoming unfocused.* 討論變得漫無目的。**2** eyes that are unfocused are open, but are not looking at anything〔張大着的眼睛〕甚麼都不看的;〔目光〕茫然的

un·fold /ʌnˋfold; ʌnˈfəʊld/ *v* [I,T] **1** to open something that was folded 展開, 打開, 攤開〔捲着的東西〕: *Chiara unfolded the map and spread it on the table.* 基婭拉攤開地圖, 把它鋪在桌子上。**2** if a story, plan etc unfolds, it becomes clearer as you hear or learn more about it〔故事、計劃等〕逐漸明確; 逐漸呈現; 展示: *As the tale unfolds we learn more about Max's childhood.* 隨着故事的展開, 我們對馬克斯的童年了解得更多。

un·fore·see·a·ble /ˌʌnfɔrˋsiəbḷ; ˌʌnfɔːˈsiːəbəl/ *adj* an unforeseeable event, situation etc could not have been expected 不可預見的; 預料不到的

un·fore·seen /ˌʌnfɔrˋsin; ˌʌnfɔːˈsiːn◂/ *adj* an unforeseen situation is one that you did not expect to happen 預料不到的, 意料之外的: *unforeseen delays* 出乎意料的延遲 | **unforeseen circumstances** *Due to unforeseen circumstances, the play has been cancelled.* 由於意料不到的一些情況, 這部戲取消了。

un·for·get·ta·ble /ˌʌnfəˋgɛtəbḷ; ˌʌnfəˈgetəbəl◂/ *adj* an unforgettable experience, sight etc affects you so strongly that you will never forget it, especially because it is particularly good or beautiful〔尤指因經歷、景色等極其美好而〕難以忘懷的: *The colours of New England in the fall are unforgettable.* 新英格蘭秋天的繽紛色彩令人難忘。—**unforgettably** *adv*

un·for·giv·a·ble /ˌʌnfəˋgɪvəbḷ; ˌʌnfəˈgɪvəbəl◂/ *adj* an unforgivable action is so bad or cruel that you cannot forgive the person who did it 不可原諒的; 不可饒恕的: *Her husband had deceived her, and this was unforgivable.* 她丈夫欺騙了她, 這是不可原諒的。—**unforgivably** *adv*

un·for·giv·ing /ˌʌnfəˋgɪvɪŋ; ˌʌnfəˈgɪvɪŋ◂/ *adj* someone who is unforgiving does not forgive people easily〔人〕不原諒人的; 無情的

un·formed /ˌʌnˋfɔrmd; ˌʌnˈfɔːmd◂/ *adj* not yet completely developed 未成形的; 未充分發展的: *The foetus's fingers and toes are as yet unformed.* 胎兒的手指和腳趾尚未成形。

un·for·tu·nate[1] /ˌʌnˋfɔrtʃənɪt; ʌnˈfɔːtʃənɪt/ *adj* **1** happening because of bad luck and often having serious or dangerous results 不幸的; 倒霉的: *an unfortunate accident* 不幸的事故 | *his unfortunate death at the height of his career* 他在事業巔峯時的不幸去世 **2** an unfortunate situation is one that you wish was different or had never happened 可嘆的; 令人遺憾的: *an unfortunate turn of events* 事態發生的讓人遺憾的變化 | **most unfortunate** *formal* (=very unfortunate)【正式】非常不幸; 真遺憾 *It's most unfortunate that your father can't come to the wedding.* 真遺憾, 你父親不能來參加婚禮。**3** *formal* unfortunate behaviour, remarks etc make people feel embarrassed or offended【正式】不適宜的, 不得體的; 粗野的: *I thought his choice of music was a little unfortunate.* 我認為他挑選的音樂有點不恰當。 

unfortunate[2] *n* [C] *literary* someone who has no money, home, job etc【文】不幸的人

un·for·tu·nate·ly /ʌnˋfɔrtʃənɪtlɪ; ʌnˈfɔːtʃənɪ̥tli/ *adv* [sentence adverb 句子副詞] used when you are mentioning a fact that you wish were not true 不幸地; 令人遺憾地: *Unfortunately, you were out when we called.* 很遺憾, 我們打電話時你出去了。 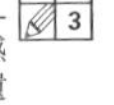

un·found·ed /ʌnˋfaʊndɪd; ʌnˈfaʊndɪ̥d/ *adj* statements, feelings, opinions etc that are unfounded are wrong because they are not based on true facts 沒有事實根據的; 無稽的; 虛幻的: *Fears about the side-effects are largely unfounded.* 對副作用的擔心大多沒有事實根據。

un·fre·quent·ed /ˌʌnfrɪˋkwɛntɪd; ˌʌnfrɪˈkwentɪ̥d◂/ *adj formal* not often visited by many people【正式】人跡罕至的; 冷落的: *an unfrequented spot* 人跡罕至的地方

un·frock /ʌnˋfrɑk; ʌnˈfrɒk/ *v* [T usually passive 一般用被動態] to remove someone from their position as a priest as a punishment for behaviour or beliefs that the church does not approve of 免去〔牧師或神父〕的聖職 —**unfrocked** *adj*

un·ful·filled /ˌʌnfʊlˋfɪld; ˌʌnfʊlˈfɪld◂/ *adj* **1** a wish, desire, hope etc that is unfulfilled has not been achieved 未實現的; 未達到的: *All her own dreams and ambitions remained unfulfilled.* 她所有的夢想和抱負仍未實現。**2** someone who is unfulfilled feels they could be achieving more in their job, relationship etc〔人在工作、關係等上〕未得到滿足的: *Her job left her feeling unfulfilled and unappreciated.* 她的工作使她感到壯志未酬, 懷才不遇。

un·furl /ʌn`fɝl; ʌn'fɜːl/ *v* [T] to unroll and open a flag, sail etc 打開, 展開〔旗、帆等〕

un·fur·nished /ʌn`fɝnɪʃt; ʌn'fɜːnɪʃt/ *adj* an unfurnished room, house etc has no furniture in it 無家具設備的

un·gain·ly /ʌn`genlɪ; ʌn'geɪnli/ *adj* moving in a way that does not look graceful〔動作〕笨拙的; 難看的; 不優雅的: *I had been a tall, ungainly teenager with a bad haircut and National Health glasses.* 我十幾歲時個子高, 動作笨拙, 髮型難看, 還戴着國民保健制度免費提供的眼鏡。—**ungainliness** *n* [U]

un·glued /ʌn`glud; ʌn'gluːd/ *adj* **come unglued** *AmE informal*【美, 非正式】**a)** to become extremely upset or angry about something 煩惱不堪; 異常憤怒: *Pat came unglued when I told him about the accident.* 當我把事故告訴帕特時, 他不安極了。**b)** if your plans come unglued, they do not work well〔計劃〕落空

un·god·ly /ʌn`gadlɪ; ʌn'gɒdli/ *adj* **1** [only before noun 僅用於名詞前] *informal* an ungodly time or noise is unreasonable and annoying【非正式】〔時間或噪音〕不合情理的, 惱人的, 不適當的: *Why did you wake me up at such an ungodly hour?* 你怎麼在這個時候把我叫醒? **2** *literary* showing a lack of respect for God【文】不敬神的, 不虔誠的

un·gov·er·na·ble /ʌn`gʌvənəbḷ; ʌn'gʌvənəbəl/ *adj* **1** *formal* feelings that are ungovernable are impossible to control【正式】〔感情〕難控制的: **ungovernable temper** (=extreme anger that cannot be controlled) 難以控制的暴怒 **2** a country or area that is ungovernable is one in which the people cannot be controlled by the government, the police etc〔國家或地區〕難統治[控制]的

un·gra·cious /ʌn`greʃəs; ʌn'greɪʃəs/ *adj* not polite or friendly, especially towards someone who has said they are sorry to you or are being friendly to you〔尤指對已經道歉或表示友好的人〕無禮的; 粗野的 —**ungraciously** *adv*

un·grate·ful /ʌn`gretfəl; ʌn'greɪtfəl/ *adj* not expressing thanks for something that someone has given to you or done for you 忘恩負義的; 不領情的: *Don't be so ungrateful!* 不要如此忘恩負義! —**ungratefully** *adv* —**ungratefulness** *n* [U]

un·guard·ed /ʌn`gardɪd; ʌn'gɑːdɪ̣d/ *adj* **1** an unguarded remark, statement etc is one that you make carelessly without thinking of the possible effects〔說話、聲明等〕粗心大意的; 不慎重的, 輕率的 **2 in an unguarded moment** at a time when you are not paying attention to what you are doing or saying 一不留神; 一不小心: *In an unguarded moment, I told her I was leaving.* 我一不留神, 告訴她我要走了。

un·guent /`ʌŋgwənt; 'ʌŋgwənt/ *n* [C] *literary* an oily substance used on your skin; OINTMENT【文】油膏, 軟膏

un·hand /ʌn`hænd; ʌn'hænd/ *v* [T] *old use* to stop holding someone you have caught【舊】放開〔某人〕: *Unhand me, sir!* 放了我吧, 先生!

un·hap·pi·ly /ʌn`hæpɪlɪ; ʌn'hæpɪ̣li/ *adv* **1** in a way that shows you are not happy 不高興地: *Zack looked at her unhappily.* 扎克不高興地看着她。**2** [sentence adverb 句子副詞] *old-fashioned* used when you are mentioning a fact that you wish were not true; UNFORTUNATELY【過時】不幸地, 令人遺憾地: *Unhappily, she was not able to complete the course.* 很遺憾, 她不能完成這門課程。

3 3 **un·hap·py** /ʌn`hæpɪ; ʌn'hæpi/ *adj* **unhappier, unhappiest 1** not happy 不幸福的; 不快樂的: *If you're so unhappy, why don't you change jobs?* 你要是這麼不快樂, 為甚麼不換換工作? **2** feeling worried or annoyed because you do not like what is happening in a situation 憂愁的; 不滿的: **[+about]** *We were unhappy about the press reports of the demonstration.* 我們對有關遊行示威的新聞報道感到不滿。| **[+with]** *If you're unhappy with your results, you can always take the exam again.* 你如果對成績不滿意, 不論甚麼時候都可以重考。**3** *formal* an unhappy remark, situation etc is unsuitable or unlucky【正式】不適當的; 不幸運的: *an unhappy turn of phrase* 不恰當的措辭 | *an unhappy coincidence* 不幸的巧合 —**unhappily** *adv* —**unhappiness** *n* [U]

un·harmed /ʌn`harmd; ʌn'hɑːmd/ *adj* [not before noun 不用於名詞前] not hurt or harmed 未受傷〔害〕的; 無恙的, 平安的: *They managed to escape unharmed.* 他們得以平安脫險。

un·health·y /ʌn`hɛlθɪ; ʌn'helθi/ *adj* **1** likely to make you ill 對健康有害的; 不衛生的: *unhealthy living conditions* 不利於健康的生活條件 **2** not healthy 不健康的: *unhealthy children who don't get enough exercise* 鍛鍊不足的不健康的孩子 **3** unhealthy skin, hair etc shows that you are ill or not healthy〔皮膚、頭髮等〕顯出病態的, 顯得不健康的: *an unhealthy pale complexion* 蒼白的病容 **4** behaviour that is unhealthy is not normal and may be harmful〔行為〕反常的; 病態的: **an unhealthy interest in** *Gareth had an unhealthy interest in death.* 加雷思對死亡有種病態的興趣。—**unhealthily** *adv* —**unhealthiness** *n* [U]

un·heard /ʌn`hɝd; ˌʌn'hɜːd/ *adj* [not before noun 不用於名詞前] not listened to 沒聽到的; 不予傾聽的: **go unheard** *Her cries for help went unheard.* 沒有人聽到她的呼救聲。

unheard-of /·`· ·/ *adj* something that is unheard-of is so unusual that it has not happened or been known before 前所未聞的; 空前的: *It's unheard-of for anyone to pass the exam so young.* 從未聽說過有人這麼年輕就通過了考試。

un·heed·ed /ʌn`hidɪd; ʌn'hiːdɪ̣d/ *adj literary* noticed but not listened to, accepted, or believed【文】沒有受到注意的, 被忽視的: **go unheeded** *Her prayers went unheeded.* 她的祈禱並無效驗。

un·help·ful /ʌn`hɛlpfəl; ʌn'helpfəl/ *adj* not willing or able to help in a situation and sometimes making it worse 不予幫助的; 不起幫助作用的, 無用的: *The authorities are being particularly unhelpful.* 當局尤其不予幫助。—**unhelpfully** *adv* —**unhelpfulness** *n* [U]

un·her·ald·ed /ʌn`hɛrəldɪd; ʌn'herəldɪ̣d/ *adj formal* not previously announced or mentioned【正式】未事先宣布的; 未預告的

un·hinge /ʌn`hɪndʒ; ʌn'hɪndʒ/ *v* [T] to make someone become mentally ill 使〔某人〕精神失常, 使錯亂: *The terrible experience seemed to have unhinged him slightly.* 這一可怕的經歷似乎使他有點精神失常了。—**unhinged** *adj*

un·hip /ʌn`hɪp; ʌn'hɪp/ *adj slang* unfashionable【俚】不時髦的

un·hitch /ʌn`hɪtʃ; ʌn'hɪtʃ/ *v* [T] **1** to unfasten something that is joined to something else 解開; 放鬆 **2 get unhitched** *AmE informal* to get divorced (DIVORCE[1] (1))【美, 非正式】離婚, 離異

un·ho·ly /ʌn`holɪ; ʌn'həʊli/ *adj* **1** [only before noun 僅用於名詞前] *informal* unreasonable and annoying【非正式】不合理的; 惹人討厭的: *The kids were making an unholy noise in the playroom.* 孩子們在遊戲室發出討厭的吵嚷聲。**2** not holy or not respecting what is holy 不神聖的; 不虔敬的; 褻瀆的 **3 unholy alliance** an unusual agreement between two people or organizations who would not normally work together, usually for a bad purpose 邪惡的同盟

un·hoped-for /ʌn`hopt ˌfɔr; ʌn'həʊpt fɔː/ *adj* much better than had been expected 沒有料到的, 出乎意料的: *unhoped-for success* 意外的成功

un·hur·ried /ʌn`hɝɪd; ʌn'hʌrid/ *adj* done slowly and calmly 不慌不忙的, 從容不迫的; 悠閒的: *He began to sketch with precise, unhurried strokes.* 他開始不慌不忙、一絲不苟地畫起素描來。—**unhurriedly** *adv*

un·hurt /ʌn`hɝt; ʌn'hɜːt/ *adj* [not before noun 不用於名詞前] not hurt 未受傷害的: *He was shaken and frightened, but unhurt.* 他受到驚嚇, 但沒有受傷。

u·ni /`junɪ; 'juːni/ *n* [C] *BrE, AustrE spoken* university【英, 澳, 口】大學

uni- /junɪ; juːnɪ̣/ *prefix* one; single 單, 一: *unidirectional* 單向(性)的

UNICEF /ˋjunɪsɛf; ˈjuːn$_{\text{ɪ}}^{\text{ə}}$sef/ *n* United Nations International Children's Fund; an organization that helps children in the world suffering from disease, HUNGER etc 聯合國兒童基金會

u·ni·corn /ˋjunɪˏkɔrn; ˈjuːn$_{\text{ɪ}}^{\text{ə}}$kɔːn/ *n* [C] an imaginary animal like a white horse with a long straight horn growing on its head〔傳說中似白馬的〕獨角獸

u·ni·cy·cle /ˋjunɪˏsaɪkḷ; ˈjuːniˏsaɪkəl/ *n* [C] a vehicle that is like a bicycle but has only one wheel 獨輪(自行)車

un·i·den·ti·fied /ˏʌnaɪˋdɛntɪˏfaɪd; ˏʌnaɪˈdent$_{\text{ɪ}}^{\text{ə}}$faɪd◂/ *adj* an unidentified person or thing is one that you do not recognize, do not know the name of etc 未辨別出來的; 身分不明的: *An unidentified man was spotted near the scene of the crime.* 有人在犯罪現場附近發現了一個身分不明的男子。

u·ni·fi·ca·tion /ˏjunəfəˋkeʃən; ˏjuːn$_{\text{ɪ}}^{\text{ə}}$f$_{\text{ɪ}}^{\text{ə}}$ˈkeɪʃən/ *n* [U] the act of combining separate countries to make a single country with one government〔國家的〕統一: *the unification of Germany* 德國的統一

3 **u·ni·form¹** /ˋjunəˏfɔrm; ˈjuːn$_{\text{ɪ}}^{\text{ə}}$fɔːm/ *n* [C,U] **1** a particular type of clothing worn by all the members of a group or organization such as the police, the army etc〔警察、軍人等穿的〕制服: *school uniform* 校服 **2 be in uniform a)** to be wearing a uniform 穿着制服 **b)** to be a member of the army, navy etc 做一名軍人, 當兵

uniform² *adj* being the same in all its parts or among all its members 全部相同的, 一致的: *a plank of uniform width* 一塊寬度均勻的木板 —**uniformly** *adv*

u·ni·formed /ˋjunəˏfɔrmd; ˈjuːn$_{\text{ɪ}}^{\text{ə}}$fɔːmd/ *adj* wearing a uniform 穿制服的: *uniformed police officers* 穿制服的警察

u·ni·form·i·ty /ˏjunəˋfɔrmətɪ; ˏjuːn$_{\text{ɪ}}^{\text{ə}}$ˈfɔːm$_{\text{ɪ}}^{\text{ə}}$ti/ *n* [U] the quality of being or looking the same as all other members of a group 相同(性); 統一(性); 一致(性): *the dull uniformity of the houses in the area* 該地區的房屋千篇一律

u·ni·fy /ˋjunəˏfaɪ; ˈjuːn$_{\text{ɪ}}^{\text{ə}}$faɪ/ *v* [T] **1** to combine the parts of a country, organization etc to make a single unit 統一〔國家、組織等〕, 使成一體: *Spain was unified in the 16th century.* 西班牙是在16世紀統一的。**2** to change a group of things so that they are all the same 使相同, 使一致

u·ni·lat·e·ral /ˏjunɪˋlætərəl; ˏjuːn$_{\text{ɪ}}^{\text{ə}}$ˈlætərəl◂/ *adj formal* a unilateral action or decision is done by only one of the groups involved in a situation【正式】〔行動或決定〕一方的, 單邊的; 單方面的: *a unilateral declaration of independence* 單方面宣布獨立 | **unilateral disarmament** (=the process of a country getting rid of its own NUCLEAR weapons without waiting for other countries to do the same) 單方面(核)裁軍 —compare 比較 BILATERAL, MULTILATERAL —**unilateralism** *n* —**unilaterally** *adv*

un·i·ma·gin·a·ble /ˏʌnɪˋmædʒɪnəbḷ; ˏʌnɪˈmædʒ$_{\text{ɪ}}^{\text{ə}}$nəbəl◂/ *adj* not possible to imagine 不能想像的, 想像不到的: *an unimaginable amount of money* 想像不到的款額

un·i·ma·gin·a·tive /ˏʌnɪˋmædʒɪnətɪv; ˏʌnɪˈmædʒ$_{\text{ɪ}}^{\text{ə}}$nətɪv◂/ *adj* **1** lacking the ability to think of new or unusual ideas 缺乏想像力的 **2** too ordinary and boring 平淡的, 無趣的: *an unimaginative shop window display* 單調的櫥窗陳設 **3** an unimaginative solution to a problem does not work very well because it does not involve any new or intelligent ideas 無新意的; 無創見的: *unimaginative housing policies* 無創意的住房政策

un·im·paired /ˏʌnɪmˋpɛrd; ˏʌnɪmˈpeəd◂/ *adj* not damaged by an unpleasant or unlucky experience 未受損的: *She survived the accident with her sight unimpaired.* 她從事故中倖存下來, 視力也未受損傷。

un·im·pea·cha·ble /ˏʌnɪmˋpitʃəbḷ; ˏʌnɪmˈpiːtʃəbəl◂/ *adj formal* so good or definite that criticism or doubt is impossible【正式】無可指摘的, 無懈可擊的; 不容置疑的; 可靠的: *unimpeachable moral principles* 無可指摘的道德原則 —**unimpeachably** *adv*

un·im·por·tant /ˏʌnɪmˋpɔrtṇt; ˏʌnɪmˈpɔːtənt◂/ *adj* not important 不重要的: *Women's issues were assumed to be unimportant, especially in the political arena.* 婦女的問題總被認為無關緊要, 特別是在政治舞台上。

un·im·pressed /ˏʌnɪmˋprɛst; ˏʌnɪmˈprest/ *adj* not thinking that someone or something is good, interesting, unusual etc 沒有印象的; 未受感動的: *Jay seemed unimpressed by the array of finery.* 傑伊似乎不為一系列的華麗服飾所動。

un·im·pres·sive /ˏʌnɪmˋprɛsɪv; ˏʌnɪmˈpresɪv◂/ *adj* someone or something that is unimpressive is not as good, large, important, skilful etc as you expected or as they are supposed to be 給人印象不深的; 不惹人注意的; 平淡的: *The new building is singularly unimpressive.* 新大樓非常不起眼。

un·in·formed /ˏʌnɪnˋfɔrmd; ˏʌnɪnˈfɔːmd◂/ *adj* not having enough knowledge or information 無知的; 不了解情況的: *uninformed criticism* 無根據的批評 —see also 另見 INFORMED

un·in·hab·it·a·ble /ˏʌnɪnˋhæbɪtəbḷ; ˏʌnɪnˈhæb$_{\text{ɪ}}^{\text{ə}}$təbəl◂/ *adj* **1** an uninhabitable place is impossible to live in 不能居住的 **2** an uninhabitable house or apartment is too dirty, cold etc to live in〔房子或公寓〕不適於居住的〈如太骯髒、太冷等〉—opposite 反義詞 HABITABLE

un·in·hab·it·ed /ˏʌnɪnˋhæbɪtɪd; ˏʌnɪnˈhæb$_{\text{ɪ}}^{\text{ə}}$t$_{\text{ɪ}}^{\text{ə}}$d◂/ *adj* an uninhabited place does not have anyone living there 無人居住的; 杳無人跡的: *an uninhabited island* 杳無人跡的荒島

un·in·hib·it·ed /ˏʌnɪnˋhɪbɪtɪd; ˏʌnɪnˈhɪb$_{\text{ɪ}}^{\text{ə}}$t$_{\text{ɪ}}^{\text{ə}}$d◂/ *adj* expressing your feelings easily without feeling embarrassed 不受約束的; 無拘無束的; 隨意的: *uninhibited laughter* 開懷大笑 —**uninhibitedly** *adv*

un·i·ni·ti·at·ed /ˏʌnɪˋnɪʃɪˏetɪd; ˏʌnɪˈnɪʃieɪt$_{\text{ɪ}}^{\text{ə}}$d◂/ *n* **the uninitiated** [plural] people who do not have special knowledge or experience of something 無某種專業知識[經驗]者: *To the uninitiated, this will make little sense.* 對非專業人士來說, 這並無甚麼意義。—**uninitiated** *adj*

un·in·spired /ˏʌnɪnˋspaɪrd; ˏʌnɪnˈspaɪəd◂/ *adj* not showing any imagination 缺乏創見的, 沒有想像力的; 平凡的: *an uninspired performance* 毫無創意的演出

un·in·spir·ing /ˏʌnɪnˋspaɪrɪŋ; ˏʌnɪnˈspaɪərɪŋ/ *adj* not at all interesting or exciting 引不起興趣的; 不令人振奮的: *an uninspiring piece of architecture* 一幢呆板的建築

un·in·tel·li·gi·ble /ˏʌnɪnˋtɛlədʒəbḷ; ˏʌnɪnˈtel$_{\text{ɪ}}^{\text{ə}}$dʒ$_{\text{ɪ}}^{\text{ə}}$bəl◂/ *adj* impossible to understand 難以理解的, 晦澀難懂的: *Eva muttered something unintelligible.* 伊娃咕噥了些無人能懂的話。—**unintelligibly** *adv*

un·in·ten·tion·al /ˏʌnɪnˋtɛnʃənḷ; ˏʌnɪnˈtenʃənəl◂/ *adj* not said or done deliberately 不是故意的, 無心的: *I know she upset you, but I'm sure it was unintentional.* 我知道她惹你心煩, 但我肯定這不是故意的。—**unintentionally** *adv*

un·in·terest·ed /ʌnˋɪntərɪstɪd; ʌnˈɪntr$_{\text{ɪ}}^{\text{ə}}$st$_{\text{ɪ}}^{\text{ə}}$d/ *adj* not interested 不感興趣的; 不關心的: [+**in**] *Kevin seems uninterested in learning anything.* 凱文似乎對學任何東西都不感興趣。—compare 比較 DISINTERESTED

un·in·ter·rupt·ed /ˏʌnɪntəˋrʌptɪd; ˏʌnɪntəˈrʌpt$_{\text{ɪ}}^{\text{ə}}$d◂/ *adj* continuous 不間斷的, 連續的: *a long, uninterrupted sleep* 長時間的不間斷的睡眠 —**uninterruptedly** *adv*

un·in·vit·ed /ˏʌnɪnˋvaɪtɪd; ˏʌnɪnˈvaɪt$_{\text{ɪ}}^{\text{ə}}$d◂/ *adj* not having been asked for 未被邀請的: *uninvited guests* 不速之客

un·in·vit·ing /ˏʌnɪnˋvaɪtɪŋ; ˏʌnɪnˈvaɪtɪŋ◂/ *adj* an uninviting place seems unattractive or unpleasant〔地方〕無吸引力的; 令人討厭的: *an uninviting, desolate landscape* 一派索然無味的荒涼景象

u·nion /ˋjunjən; ˈjuːnjən/ *n* **1** [C] an organization formed by workers to protect their rights; TRADE UNION 工會: *the air traffic controllers' union* 空中交通調度員工會 **2** a group of countries or states with the same central government 聯邦; 聯盟: *the Soviet Union* 蘇維埃聯盟, 蘇聯 **3** [singular,U] *formal* the act of joining two or more things together or the state of being joined together【正式】聯

合, 合併; 結合: *The artist's work shows the perfect union of craftsmanship and imagination.* 這位藝術家的作品表現出技藝和想像力的完美結合。| **[+with]** *Scotland's union with England in 1603* 1603年蘇格蘭與英格蘭的合併 **4** [singular,U] *formal* marriage【正式】結婚, 婚姻

u·nion·is·m /ˈjunjənɪzm̩; ˈjuːnjənɪzəm/ *n* [U] belief in the principles of TRADE UNIONs 工會主義; 工聯主義

U·nion·ist /ˈjunjənɪst; ˈjuːnjənɪst/ *n* [C] a member of a political party that wants Northern Ireland to remain part of the United Kingdom〔主張北愛爾蘭仍與英國保持統一的〕統一黨黨員 **—Unionism** *n* [U]

u·nion·ize also 又作 **-ise** *BrE*【英】/ˈjunjənˌaɪz; ˈjuːnjənaɪz/ *v* [I,T] if workers unionize or are unionized, they become members of a TRADE UNION (使)成立工會; (使)加入工會 **—unionization** /ˌjunjənəˈzeʃən; ˌjuːnjənaɪˈzeɪʃən/ *n* [U]

Union Jack /ˌ·· ˈ·/ *n* [C] the national flag of Great Britain and Northern Ireland 聯合王國國旗, 英國國旗

u·nion suit /ˈ·· ˌ·/ *n* [C] *AmE* woollen underwear that covers the whole body【美】連衣褲; COMBINATIONs *BrE*【英】

3 2 **u·nique** /juˈnik; juːˈniːk/ *adj* **1** [no comparative 無比較級] being the only one of its kind 獨一無二的; 獨特的: *Each person's fingerprints are unique.* 每個人的指紋都是不同的。**2** *informal* unusually good and special【非正式】極好的; 難得的, 不同尋常的; 特別的: *a unique opportunity to travel* 難得的旅行機會 **—uniquely** *adv*: *an actor uniquely suited to the part* 唯一適合該角色的演員 **—uniqueness** *n* [U]

USAGE NOTE 用法說明: UNIQUE

WORD CHOICE 詞語辨析: **unique, only**

If you want to say that something has features or qualities that make it different from anything else, especially when this makes it better, you say it is **unique**. unique表示某物具有獨特之處, 尤其是使之變得更為優秀: *His interpretation of the original screenplay is quite unique.* 他對這部原創電影劇本的解讀確有獨到之處。| *a style of folk art unique to these tribespeople* (=they are the only people who do it). 這些部落人獨具的民間藝術風格。

If you want to say that there is just one of something available in a particular place at a particular time out of all the others that may exist, you say it is the **only** one. only 表示在某時某地獨有的: *She was the only woman doctor in the district.* 她是該區唯一的女醫生。| *After the attack, only one building was left standing.* 攻擊過後, 只有一棟樓還矗立着。

GRAMMAR 語法

Before a singular noun **unique** usually follows *a*, **only** often follows *the*. 用在單數名詞前, unique前面通常加a; only 經常前面加 the: *This is a unique opportunity/the only opportunity I'll get.* 這是一次難得的機會/我能得到的唯一機會。

Many people think it is not correct to say something is *fairly* or *rather unique*, or *very unique*, as if **unique** can only be used in sense one. However, native speakers will often say this, because they are using **unique** in sense two to mean **unusual** or **special**. 許多人認為說某事fairly或rather unique, 或very unique不正確, 似乎unique只能用於釋義1。然而母語為英語的人常這樣說, 他們用的是unique釋義2的意思, 即"難得的"或"特別的"。

u·ni·sex /ˈjunəsɛks; ˈjuːnɪseks/ *adj* intended for both men and women 不分男女的, 男女皆適用的: *a unisex hairdressing salon* 男女通用的美髮廊

u·ni·son /ˈjunəsn̩; ˈjuːnɪsən/ *n* **1 in unison a)** if people speak in unison, they say the same words at the same time 一起〔說〕; 齊聲: *"No way!" the twins replied in unison.* "不行!"雙胞胎異口同聲地回答。**b)** if two groups, governments etc do something in unison they do it together because they agree with each other 共同〔做某事〕, 一致: *Management and workers must act in unison to compete with foreign business.* 管理層和員工必須行動一致, 與外國企業競爭。**2** [C] a way of singing or playing music in which everyone plays or sings the same tune〔音樂中的〕齊奏; 齊唱

u·nit /ˈjunɪt; ˈjuːnɪt/ *n* [C]

1 ▶PART 部分◀ a thing, person or group that is regarded as one single whole part of something larger 單位, 單元〔指構成更大整體的人、物、羣體〕: *The family is the smallest social unit.* 家庭是社會最小的基本單位。

2 ▶GROUP 團體◀ a group of people working together as part of the structure of a larger group, organization, company etc 科; 室; 部門: *She works in the emergency unit at the hospital.* 她在醫院的急診室工作。

3 ▶FOR MEASURING 用於計量◀ an amount or quantity of something used as a standard of measurement〔計量用的〕單位: **[+of]** *The dollar is the basic unit of currency in the US.* 美元是美國的基本貨幣單位。| *The patient was given 2 units of blood.* 給病人輸了兩單位的血。

4 ▶FURNITURE 家具◀ a piece of furniture such as a cupboard, especially one that can be fitted to others of the same type〔家具的〕組合件, 一套中的一件: **kitchen/office/storage unit** (=a unit designed for the kitchen etc) 廚房/辦公室/貯藏設備組合件

5 ▶PART OF A MACHINE 機器的部分◀ a piece of machinery which is part of a larger machine〔機械的〕部件, 元件: **control/filter/cooling unit** *The cooling unit must be replaced.* 冷卻元件必須更換。

6 ▶PART OF A BOOK 書的部分◀ one of the numbered parts into which a TEXTBOOK (=a book used in schools) is divided〔教科書中的〕單元

7 ▶PRODUCT 產品◀ *technical* a single complete product made by a company【術語】一台[一套]成品: *The factory's output is now up to 150,000 units each month.* 這家工廠的產量現已上升到每月15萬台。

8 ▶SCHOOL/UNIVERSITY 學校/大學◀ *AmE* an amount of work that a student needs to do in a particular course【美】〔課程的〕學習量

9 ▶APARTMENT 公寓◀ *AmE* a single apartment in a larger building【美】〔大樓中的〕一套住房

10 ▶NUMBER 數字◀ a) *technical* the smallest whole number; the number 1【術語】最小整數,〔數字〕1 **b)** any whole number less than ten 十以下的整數, 個位數: *hundreds, tens, and units* 百位數、十位數和個位數

U·ni·ta·ri·an /ˌjunəˈtɛrɪən; ˌjuːnɪˈteəriən◂/ *adj* connected with a Christian group that believes its members should be free to believe what they want〔基督教中主張信仰自由的〕一位論教派的 **—unitarian** *n* [C]

u·nite /juˈnaɪt; juːˈnaɪt/ *v* [I,T] to join together with other people, organizations to achieve something 聯合, 團結: *two nations that are united by a bond of friendship* 以友誼的紐帶聯合起來的兩個民族 | **[+in/against/behind]** *In a crisis, party members will always unite behind their leader.* 在危機中, 黨員總會團結起來支持他們的領導人。| **unite to do sth** *We must unite to fight against racism.* 我們必須聯合起來反對種族主義。

u·nit·ed /juˈnaɪtɪd; juːˈnaɪtɪd/ *adj* **1** joined or closely connected by feelings, aims etc 團結的, 聯合的, 統一的: *working for a united Europe* 致力於建設一個統一的歐洲 **2** involving or done by everyone 共同的, 一致的: *a united effort to clean up the environment* 共同努力使環境清潔 **—unitedly** *adv*

United Na·tions /·ˌ·· ˈ··/ *n* [singular] an international organization that tries to find peaceful solutions to world problems 聯合國

unit price /ˈ·· ˌ·/ *n* [C] the price that is charged for each single thing or quantity that is sold 單價

unit trust /ˌ·· ˈ·/ *n* [C] *BrE* a company through which you can buy shares (SHARE[2] (5)) in many different businesses【英】單位投資信託公司, 共同基金; MUTUAL FUND *AmE*【美】

u·ni·ty /ˈjunətɪ; ˈjuːnɪti/ *n* **1** [singular,U] a situation in which a group of people or countries work together for a particular purpose 團結; 聯合; 一致: *European unity* 歐洲的團結 **2** [U] the quality of being complete 整體(性); 協調(性): *The design has a pleasing unity and appearance.* 該設計具有一種悅人的整體感和外觀。**3** [U] *technical* the number 1【術語】〔數字〕1

Univ *n* a written abbreviation of 縮寫 = university

u·ni·ver·sal /ˌjunəˋvɝsl; ˌjuːnəˈvɜːsəl◂/ *adj* **1** done by all the members of a group 全體(做)的, 一致的: *There was universal agreement on the issue of sex education.* 關於性教育問題, 大家的意見是一致的。**2** involving or understood by everyone in the world 普遍的, 一般的: *a topic of universal interest* 人人都感興趣的話題 **3** true or suitable in every situation 通用的; 萬能的: *a universal truth* 舉世公認的真理 —**universally** *adv* —**universality** /ˌjunəvɝˋsæləti; ˌjuːnəvɜːˈsæləti/ *n* [U]

universal joint /ˌ···· ˈ·/ *n* [C] a part in a machine, at the point where two other parts join together, that can turn in all directions〔機器的〕萬向接頭

u·ni·verse /ˋjunəˌvɝs; ˈjuːnəvɜːs/ *n* [singular] **1 the universe** all space, including all the stars and PLANETS 宇宙; 天地萬物; 萬象 **2** the place where a particular person lives or works, including the people they know〔某人生活或工作的〕活動領域: **be the centre of sb's universe** (=be the most important thing to someone) 是某人生活的中心

u·ni·ver·si·ty /ˌjunəˋvɝsəti; ˌjuːnəˈvɜːsəti◂/ *n* [C,U] an educational institution at the highest level, where you study for a DEGREE 大學: **go to university** (=study at a university) 上大學

un·just /ʌnˋdʒʌst; ˌʌnˈdʒʌst◂/ *adj* not fair or reasonable 非正義的; 不公平的; 不公正的; 不合理的: *unjust laws* 不公正的法律 —**unjustly** *adv*

un·just·i·fi·a·ble /ʌnˋdʒʌstəˌfaɪəbl; ʌnˈdʒʌstəfaɪəbəl/ *adj* completely wrong and unacceptable 錯誤的; 不能接受的: *Poisoning the earth's atmosphere is ecologically and morally unjustifiable.* 污染地球大氣在生態上和道德上都是錯誤的。—**unjustifiably** *adv*

un·just·i·fied /ʌnˋdʒʌstəˌfaɪd; ʌnˈdʒʌstəfaɪd/ *adj* criticism, bad treatment etc that is unjustified is unfair〔批評、處理等〕不合理的, 不公正的: *I think your criticisms of Mr Ward are completely unjustified.* 我認為你對沃德先生的批評完全缺乏公正。

un·kempt /ʌnˋkɛmpt; ˌʌnˈkempt◂/ *adj* not neat or tidy 不整潔的, 凌亂的: *an unkempt garden* 亂糟糟的花園

un·kind /ʌnˋkaɪnd; ˌʌnˈkaɪnd◂/ *adj* nasty, unpleasant, or cruel 不仁慈的; 不和善的; 刻薄的: *an unkind remark* 刻薄的說話 | [+to] *Her husband is very unkind to her.* 她丈夫對她非常刻薄。—**unkindly** *adv* —**unkindness** *n* [U]

un·know·ing /ʌnˋnoɪŋ; ʌnˈnəʊɪŋ/ *adj* [only before noun 僅用於名詞前] *formal* not realizing what you are doing or what is happening; UNAWARE【正式】不知道的; 沒察覺的: *Buying the stolen property made her an unknowing accomplice to the crime.* 購買贓物使她無意中成了犯罪活動的共犯。—**unknowingly** *adv*

un·known¹ /ʌnˋnon; ˌʌnˈnəʊn◂/ *adj* **1** not known about 不知道的, 未知的: *a voyage through unknown territory* 穿越未知海域的航行 | *The murderer's identity remains unknown.* 謀殺者的身分仍然不明。**2** not famous 不知名的: *an unknown artist* 無名藝術家 **3 unknown to sb** without someone knowing 不為某人所知的: *Unknown to the general public, peace negotiations were already taking place.* 公眾還不知道, 和平談判已在進行中。—see also 另見 UNBEKNOWN **4 be an unknown quantity** if someone or something is an unknown quantity, you do not know what their abilities are or how they are likely to behave 是未被人所了解的人[物]

unknown² *n* **1** [C] someone who is not famous 不出名的人: *At that point in her career she was still an unknown.* 她那時仍是個無名小卒。**2 the unknown a)** a place that is not known about or that has not been visited by humans 不為人知[人類尚未到達]的地方: *The astronauts began their journey into the unknown.* 宇航員開始了探索未知世界的旅行。**b)** things that you do not know or understand 未知事物: *a fear of the unknown* 對未知的恐懼

un·law·ful /ʌnˋlɔfəl; ʌnˈlɔːfəl/ *adj law* not legal【法律】不合法的, 非法的, 違法的 —**unlawfully** *adv*

un·lead·ed /ʌnˋlɛdɪd; ʌnˈledəd/ *adj* unleaded petrol does not contain any LEAD³ (1) so is less harmful to the environment〔汽油〕不含鉛的, 無鉛的

un·learn /ʌnˋlɝn; ˌʌnˈlɜːn/ *v* [T] *informal* to deliberately forget something you have learned【非正式】設法忘記〔已學會的東西〕, 拋棄: *It's difficult to unlearn bad driving habits.* 很難改掉不好的駕駛習慣。

un·leash /ʌnˋliʃ; ʌnˈliːʃ/ *v* [T] **1** to suddenly let a strong force, feeling etc have its full effect 釋放出, 發泄〔力量、感情等〕: *forces of change unleashed by the war* 戰爭釋放出來的變革力量 **2** to let a dog run free after it has been held on a LEASH¹ (1) 解開皮帶以放開狗

un·leav·ened /ʌnˋlɛvənd; ʌnˈlevənd/ *adj* unleavened bread is flat because it is not made with YEAST〔麵包〕未經發酵的

un·less /ʌnˋlɛs; ʌnˈles/ *conjunction* used when one thing will only happen or be true as long as another thing happens or is true 如果不…; 除非…: *Milk quickly turns sour unless it's refrigerated.* 牛奶如果不冷藏, 很快就會變酸。| *Unless some extra money is found, the theatre will close.* 要是不能額外弄一些錢, 劇院將要關閉。

USAGE NOTE 用法說明: UNLESS

WORD CHOICE 詞語辨析: **unless, if…not, if, provided/providing that**

You do not use **unless** about something that did not happen or you know is not true, but you can use **if…not** in this way. 某事沒發生或明知某事不真實時, 不用 unless, 但可用 if…not。For example, you could not use **unless** in these sentences 例如下列句子中均不能用 unless: *She would have died if the doctor hadn't operated immediately* (=but they did). 醫生如果不是立即給她做了手術〔實際做了〕, 她就死定了。| *If he wasn't such an idiot* (=but he is), *he would understand.* 他如果不是個大傻瓜〔他就是〕, 他會明白的。

You use **unless** about something that *could* happen if something else does not happen or is not done, or if something *could* be true. unless 表示如果另一事不發生, 或沒有做, 或可能是真的, 那麼某事很可能會發生: *Unless the doctors operate immediately, she'll die./She'll die unless the doctors operate immediately* (=the doctors have not operated yet, and may or may not do). 醫生如果不立即給她做手術〔醫生還沒有做, 可能做, 也可能不做〕, 她會死去的。| *Unless he's a complete idiot, he'll understand* (=he may or may not be a complete idiot). 他如果不是個大傻瓜, 他會明白的〔他可能是也可能不是個大傻瓜〕。

Unless and **if…not** can both be used to say that what you will do depends on something else happening. unless 和 if … not 均可表示要做的事情取決於另一事的發生: *Unless he comes soon, I'm going without him.* | *If he doesn't come soon, I'm going without him.* 他如果不馬上來, 我就自己走了。

You use **provided (that)** or **providing (that)** when the condition is that something definitely happens or is definitely true. provided (that) 或 providing (that) 用於某事肯定會發生或一定是真實的時候: *Providing the weather's OK, we'll make the trip next Saturday.* 天氣如果可以, 我們下週六就去旅行。

You often use **unless** to add a condition that you think of after you have finished speaking. unless 還常用於表示說話後又想起來的某個附加條件: *We'll go there next Saturday – unless it's raining of course.* 我們下週六會去那裡 — 當然是如果不下雨的話。

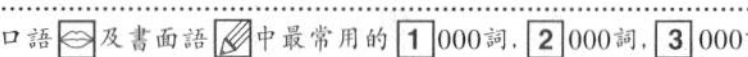
口語 及書面語 中最常用的 1 000詞, 2 000詞, 3 000詞

un·let·tered /ʌnˋlɛtəd; ʌnˈletəd/ *adj formal* unable to read or uneducated【正式】文盲的; 未受教育的

un·li·censed /ʌnˋlaɪsənst; ʌnˈlaɪsənst/ *adj* without a LICENSE (=official document that gives you permission to do or have something) 沒有執照的; 未得到許可證的: *unlicensed firearms* 未取得許可證的火器 | *unlicensed traders* 沒有營業執照的商人

3 **un·like**[1] /ʌnˋlaɪk; ˌʌnˈlaɪk◂/ *prep* **1** completely different from a particular person or thing 不像…; 和…不同: *In his jeans and T-shirt, Charles looked most unlike a lawyer.* 查爾斯身穿牛仔褲和T恤衫, 看上去一點兒也不像個律師。**2** not at all typical of something or someone 不是…的特點: *It's unlike Beth to drink so much, I wonder if she's all right.* 貝思喝這麼多可不像她平時的樣子, 我不知道她有沒有事。

unlike[2] *adj literary* not alike; different【文】不同的; 不相似的

2
2 **un·like·ly** /ʌnˋlaɪklɪ; ʌnˈlaɪkli/ *adj* **1** not likely to happen 未必會發生的, 不大可能的: *Donna might come, but it's very unlikely.* 唐娜也許會來, 不過這不大可能。| **it is unlikely that** *It's unlikely that the thieves will be caught.* 這夥竊賊被抓住的可能性不大。| **in the unlikely event of** (=if something which is unlikely happens) 萬一 *In the unlikely event of a fire, passengers should move to the top deck.* 萬一發生火警, 乘客應到頂層甲板上去。**2** not likely to be true 不大可能是真的, 靠不住的: *an unlikely story* 不大真實的報道 **3 unlikely couple** two people who are having a relationship but do not seem suitable for each other 不般配的一對

un·lim·i·ted /ʌnˋlɪmɪtɪd; ʌnˈlɪmɪ̈tɪ̈d/ *adj* **1** without a fixed limit 無界限的; 無限制的: *unlimited credit* 無限的貸款 **2** very large amount 數量極大的, 無數的: *an unlimited variety of cookies* 種類繁多的甜餅乾

un·list·ed /ʌnˋlɪstɪd; ʌnˈlɪstɪ̈d/ *adj* **1** not shown on an official STOCK EXCHANGE list〔證券〕未上市的 **2** *AmE* not in the list of numbers in the telephone DIRECTORY【美】電話號碼不列入電話簿的; EX-DIRECTORY *BrE*【英】

un·lit /ʌnˋlɪt; ˌʌnˈlɪt◂/ *adj* dark because there are no lights 未被照明的, 未點亮的: *an unlit stairway* 未亮燈的樓梯

un·load /ʌnˋlod; ʌnˈləʊd/ *v*

1 ▶VEHICLE/SHIP 車/船◀ a) to remove a load from a vehicle, ship etc 從〔車、船等〕卸下〔貨物〕: **unload sth from sth** *The driver unloaded some boxes from the back of the truck.* 司機從卡車後部卸下了幾隻箱子。**b)** [I,T] if a vehicle, ship etc unloads, the goods that it carries are removed from it〔車、船等〕卸〔貨〕: *The ship is unloading at the dock right now.* 船目前在碼頭卸貨。

2 ▶GUN 槍、砲◀ [I,T] to remove the bullets or shells (SHELL[1] (2,3)) from a gun〔從槍、砲中〕退出子彈[彈殼]

3 ▶CAMERA 照相機◀ to remove the film from a camera〔從照相機中〕退出膠卷

4 ▶GET RID OF 除去◀ [T] *informal*【非正式】**a)** to get rid of something illegal or not very good by selling it quickly 把〔非法或不是很好的東西〕脫手, 拋售; 傾銷: **unload sth on/onto** *Hundreds of cheap videos were unloaded on the British market.* 數百種廉價錄像帶在英國市場上拋售。**b)** to get rid of work or responsibility by giving it to someone else 擺脫, 推卸〔工作或責任〕: **unload sth on/onto sb** *Don't let him unload his problems onto you.* 別讓他把他的問題都推到你身上。

un·lock /ʌnˋlɑk; ʌnˈlɒk/ *v* [T] **1** to unfasten the lock on a door, box etc 開…的鎖 **2 unlock the secret of** to discover the most important facts about something 揭開…的祕密

un·looked-for /ʌnˋlʊkt ˏfɔr; ʌnˈlʊkt fɔː/ *adj informal* not expected【非正式】出乎意料的, 意外的

un·loose /ʌnˋlus; ʌnˈluːs/ *v* [T] *formal* to untie or unfasten something【正式】解開, 鬆開: *She unloosed her hair.* 她把頭髮鬆開。

un·loved /ʌnˋlʌvd; ʌnˈlʌvd/ *adj* not loved by anyone 無人喜愛的

un·love·ly /ʌnˋlʌvlɪ; ʌnˈlʌvli/ *adj literary* ugly【文】不可愛的, 醜陋的

un·luck·y /ʌnˋlʌkɪ; ʌnˈlʌki/ *adj* **1** having bad luck 不幸的; 不走運的, 不順利的: *He gambled frequently, but was usually unlucky.* 他經常賭博, 但往往運氣不佳。| **[+with]** *We were unlucky with the weather this weekend. It rained constantly.* 我們真不走運, 這個週末天公不作美, 不停地下雨。**2** happening as a result of bad luck 倒霉的: **it is unlucky (for sb) that** *It was unlucky for Stephen that the boss happened to walk in just at that moment.* 史蒂文真倒霉, 碰巧老闆在那一刻走了進來。**3** causing bad luck 不吉的, 不祥的 —**unluckily** *adv*

un·made /ʌnˋmed; ˌʌnˈmeɪd◂/ *adj* an unmade bed is not tidy because the sheets, BLANKETS etc have not been arranged since someone slept in it〔牀〕未鋪好的

un·man·age·a·ble /ʌnˋmænɪdʒəbḷ; ʌnˈmænɪdʒəbəl/ *adj* difficult to control or deal with 難控制的; 難處理的; 難辦的

un·man·ly /ʌnˋmænlɪ; ˌʌnˈmænli/ *adj* not thought to be suitable for or typical of a man 不適於男子的; 非男子漢的, 柔弱的

un·manned /ʌnˋmænd; ˌʌnˈmænd◂/ *adj* a machine, vehicle etc that is unmanned does not have a person operating or controlling it〔機器、車輛等〕無人駕駛[操縱]的: *an unmanned spacecraft* 無人駕駛的太空船

un·man·ner·ly /ʌnˋmænəlɪ; ʌnˈmænəli/ *adj formal* not polite; rude【正式】沒有禮貌的; 粗野的: *a rough, unmannerly security guard* 粗魯無禮的保安員

un·marked /ʌnˋmarkt; ˌʌnˈmɑːkt◂/ *adj* something that is unmarked has no words or sign on it to show where or what it is 未做標記的; 沒有標誌的: *an unmarked grave* 未做標記的墳墓 | *an unmarked police car* 無標誌的警車

un·mar·ried /ʌnˋmærɪd; ˌʌnˈmærid◂/ *adj* not married; SINGLE[1] (3) 未婚的; 獨身的: *unmarried mothers* 未婚母親

un·mask /ʌnˋmæsk; ʌnˈmɑːsk/ *v* [T] to make known the hidden truth about someone 揭露; 暴露〔真相〕: *Sherlock Holmes once again unmasked the murderer.* 夏洛克·福爾摩斯又一次揭露了殺人犯。

un·matched /ʌnˋmætʃt; ˌʌnˈmætʃt◂/ *adj literary* better than any other【文】無可比擬的, 無與倫比的: *a woman of unmatched beauty* 美貌絕倫的女子

un·men·tion·a·ble /ʌnˋmɛnʃənəbḷ; ʌnˈmenʃənəbəl/ *adj* too shocking or embarrassing to talk about〔因太震驚或尷尬而〕說不出口的

un·men·tion·a·bles /ʌnˋmɛnʃənəbḷz; ʌnˈmenʃənəbəlz/ *n* [plural] *old-fashioned* underwear【過時】內衣, 襯衣

un·mis·tak·a·ble, unmistakeable /ˌʌnməˋstekəbḷ; ˌʌnmɪ̈ˈsteɪkəbəl◂/ *adj* familiar and easy to recognize 不會弄錯的; 清楚明白的, 顯然的: *the unmistakable smell of rotting eggs* 明顯的臭雞蛋味 —**unmistakably** *adv*

un·mit·i·gat·ed /ʌnˋmɪtəˏgetɪd; ʌnˈmɪtɪ̈geɪtɪ̈d/ *adj* [only before noun 僅用於名詞前] **unmitigated disaster/failure etc** something that is completely bad 十足的災難/失敗等: *The tour was an unmitigated disaster.* 那次旅行完全是一場災難。

un·moved /ʌnˋmuvd; ʌnˈmuːvd/ *adj* [not before noun 不用於名詞前] feeling no pity, sympathy, or sadness, especially in a situation where most people would feel this 無動於衷的, 冷漠的: *Richard remained unmoved throughout the funeral.* 理查德在整個葬禮期間, 一直無動於衷。

un·named /ʌnˋnemd; ˌʌnˈneɪmd◂/ *adj* an unnamed person, place, or thing is one whose name is not known publicly 不知其名的: *The journalist cited an unnamed source in parliament.* 記者援引議會中一位不透露姓名的消息提供者。

un·nat·u·ral /ʌnˋnætʃərəl; ʌnˈnætʃərəl/ *adj* **1** different from what you would normally expect 不正常的, 反常的: *It seems unnatural for a child to prefer the company of adults.* 小孩子寧願與大人為伍, 這似乎不大正常。**2**

different from anything produced by nature 不自然的: *Her hair was an unnatural orange colour.* 她的頭髮是不自然的橘黃色。**3** different from normal human behaviour in a way that seems morally wrong〔行為〕違反常理的; 違背人道的: *unnatural sexual practices* 變態的性行為—**unnaturally** *adv*

un·ne·ces·sa·ry /ʌnˋnɛsəˌsɛrɪ; ʌnˈnesəsəri/ *adj* **1** not needed or more than is needed 不必要的; 多餘的: *I'm trying to cut down on all my unnecessary spending.* 我正在嘗試削減所有不必要的開支。**2** a remark or action that is unnecessary, is unkind or unreasonable〔說話或行動〕刻薄的; 無理的 —**unnecessarily** /ʌnˋnɛsəˌsɛrəlɪ; ʌnˈnesəsərəli/ *adv: I don't want to worry you unnecessarily.* 我不想給你徒添煩惱。

un·nerve /ʌnˋnɝv; ˌʌnˈnɜːv/ *v* [T] to upset or frighten someone so that they lose their confidence or their ability to think clearly 使氣餒; 使不知所措: *Her first encounter with the boss unnerved her.* 她第一次與老闆相遇時嚇得不知所措。—**unnerving** *adj*

un·no·ticed /ʌnˋnotɪst; ʌnˈnəʊtɪ̣st/ *adj, adv* without being noticed 不被注意的[地]: *Elsa stood unnoticed at the edge of the crowd.* 埃爾莎悄悄地站在人羣的邊緣。| **go/pass unnoticed** *His remark went unnoticed by everyone except me.* 他的話除了我別人都沒注意到。

un·num·bered /ʌnˋnʌmbɚd; ˌʌnˈnʌmbəd◂/ *adj* **1** not having a number 未編號的: *an unnumbered Swiss bank account* 未編號的瑞士銀行賬戶 **2** *literary* too many to be counted【文】(多得) 不可勝數的

un·ob·served /ˌʌnəbˋzɝvd; ˌʌnəbˈzɜːvd/ *adj, adv* not noticed 未受注意的[地]: *Ruth slipped out of the meeting unobserved.* 露思溜出會議而不被察覺。

un·ob·tain·a·ble /ˌʌnəbˋtenəbḷ; ˌʌnəbˈteɪnəbəl◂/ *adj* impossible to get 不能得到的, 弄不到的: *Fresh fruit was unobtainable in the winter.* 新鮮水果在冬季弄不到的。

un·ob·tru·sive /ˌʌnəbˋtrusɪv; ˌʌnəbˈtruːsɪv◂/ *adj* not attracting attention and therefore not likely to be noticed 不引人注目的, 不顯眼的: *a quiet unobtrusive student* 文靜而不引人注目的學生 —**unobtrusively** *adv*

un·oc·cu·pied /ʌnˋɑkjəˌpaɪd; ʌnˈɒkjʊ̣paɪd/ *adj* **1** a seat, house, room etc that is unoccupied has no one in it〔座位、房屋等〕未被佔用的, 空着的: *We moved in right away, as the flat was unoccupied.* 因為房子沒人住, 我們立刻搬了進去。**2** an unoccupied country or area is not controlled by the enemy during a war〔國家、地區在戰爭中〕未被 (敵人) 佔領的, 未淪陷的: *The family fled to unoccupied France.* 一家人逃到了未淪陷的法國。

un·of·fi·cial /ˌʌnəˋfɪʃəl; ˌʌnəˈfɪʃəl◂/ *adj* **1** without formal approval and permission from the organization or person in authority 非官方[非正式]批准的: *unofficial experiments carried out in secret laboratories* 在祕密實驗室進行的未經正式批准的實驗 **2** not made publicly known as part of an official plan 非正式公佈的: *The President made an unofficial visit to the Senator's house on Cape Cod.* 總統去那位參議員在科德角的房子進行了一次不公開的訪問。—**unofficially** *adv*

un·or·ga·nized also 又作 **-ised** *BrE*【英】/ʌnˋɔrgənˌaɪzd; ʌnˈɔːgənaɪzd/ *adj* people who are unorganized do not have an organization, TRADE UNION, group etc to help or support them 未組織起來的; 沒有組織的—compare 比較 DISORGANIZED

un·or·tho·dox /ʌnˋɔrθəˌdɑks; ʌnˈɔːθədɒks/ *adj* unorthodox beliefs or methods are different from what is usual or accepted by most people〔信念或方法〕非常規的; 非正統的: *a tennis player with an unorthodox style* 風格獨特的網球手

un·pack /ʌnˋpæk; ʌnˈpæk/ *v* **1** [I,T] to take everything out of a box or SUITCASE 打開〔盒子或手提箱〕取出〔物品〕: *Let's go upstairs and unpack.* 我們上樓去打開箱子吧。**2** [T] *technical* to change information in a computer so that it is easier to understand but takes up more space【術語】解壓〔壓縮的電腦信息〕

un·paid /ʌnˋped; ˌʌnˈpeɪd◂/ *adj* **1** an unpaid bill or debt has not been paid 未支付的; 未償還的 **2** done without receiving payment 不收報酬的; 無償的: *unpaid voluntary work* 無報酬的志願工作

un·pal·at·a·ble /ʌnˋpælətəbḷ; ʌnˈpælətəbəl/ *adj formal*【正式】**1** an unpalatable fact or idea is very unpleasant and difficult to accept〔事實或想法〕使人不快的; 令人討厭的; 難以接受的: *We were trying to avoid the unpalatable truth – that the whole plan had failed.* 我們正設法迴避這一使人不快的事實 —— 整個計劃失敗了。**2** unpalatable food tastes unpleasant 難吃的, 不可口的 —**unpalatably** *adv*

un·par·al·leled /ʌnˋpærəˌlɛld; ʌnˈpærəleld/ *adj formal* greater or better than all others【正式】無比的, 無雙的; 空前的: *a period of unparalleled economic prosperity* 一段經濟空前繁榮的時期

un·par·don·a·ble /ʌnˋpɑrdṇəbḷ; ʌnˈpɑːdnəbəl/ *adj formal* unpardonable behaviour is completely unacceptable【正式】不可寬恕的, 不可原諒的: *Your behaviour was unpardonable!* 你的行為不可饒恕! —**unpardonably** *adv*

un·pick /ʌnˋpɪk; ʌnˈpɪk/ *v* [T] to take out stitches from a piece of cloth or KNITTING 拆去〔衣料或編結物上〕的針腳[縫線]

un·placed /ʌnˋplest; ˌʌnˈpleɪst◂/ *adj BrE* not one of the first three to finish in a race or competition【英】〔在比賽中〕未獲前三名的, 無名次的, 落選的

un·pleas·ant /ʌnˋplɛzṇt; ʌnˈplezənt/ *adj* **1** not pleasant or enjoyable 使人不愉快的, 不合意的, 討厭的: *the unpleasant side-effects of the drug* 這種藥討厭的副作用 | *an unpleasant surprise* 令人不快的驚奇事 **2** not kind and friendly 不友善的, 不客氣的: *Our neighbours are extremely unpleasant.* 我們的鄰居極不友善。—**unpleasantly** *adv*

un·pleas·ant·ness /ʌnˋplɛzṇtnɪs; ʌnˈplezəntnɪ̣s/ *n* [U] trouble or arguments 不愉快的事; 爭執: *I hate all this unpleasantness.* 我討厭所有這些爭執。

un·plug /ʌnˋplʌg; ʌnˈplʌg/ *v* [T] to disconnect a piece of electrical equipment by taking its PLUG[1] (1a,c) out of a SOCKET (1) 拔去…的 (電源) 插頭: *Unplug the TV before you go to bed.* 睡前拔下電視的插頭。—see picture at 參見 PLUG[2] 圖

un·plumbed /ʌnˋplʌmd; ˌʌnˈplʌmd◂/ *adj* **the unplumbed depths of** something that is not known about because it has never been examined or explored 未經探究的…深處: *the unplumbed depths of the ocean* 未經探究的海洋深處

un·pop·u·lar /ʌnˋpɑpjəlɚ; ʌnˈpɒpjʊ̣lə/ *adj* not liked by most people 不受歡迎的, 不得人心的: *an unpopular decision* 不得人心的決定 | *He was very unpopular at school.* 他在學校裡非常不受歡迎。—**unpopularity** /ʌnˌpɑpjəˋlærətɪ; ʌnˌpɒpjʊ̣ˈlærɪ̣ti/ *n* [U]

un·pre·ce·dent·ed /ʌnˋprɛsəˌdɛntɪd; ʌnˈpresɪ̣dentɪ̣d/ *adj* never having happened before, or never having happened so much 空前的, 前所未有的: *unprecedented price increases* 前所未有的價格上漲 —**unprecedentedly** *adv*

un·pre·dict·a·ble /ˌʌnprɪˋdɪktəbḷ; ˌʌnprɪˈdɪktəbəl◂/ *adj* **1** something that is unpredictable changes a lot so it is impossible to know what will happen〔因改變太多而〕無法預測的: *The weather in Britain is very unpredictable.* 英國的天氣變幻莫測。**2** someone who is unpredictable tends to change their behaviour or ideas suddenly so that you never know what they are going to do or think〔人〕反覆無常的, 捉摸不透的

un·pre·ju·diced /ʌnˋprɛdʒədɪst; ʌnˈpredʒʊ̣dɪ̣st/ *adj* willing to consider different ideas and opinions 無偏見的, 公正的

un·pre·pared /ˌʌnprɪˋpɛrd; ˌʌnprɪˈpeəd◂/ *adj* not ready to deal with something 無準備的: **[+for]** *Doug was unprepared for the boredom that followed his retirement.* 道格對退休以後的乏味無聊沒有準備。

un·pre·pos·sess·ing /ˌʌnpripəˋzɛsɪŋ; ˌʌnpriːpəˈzesɪŋ/ *adj formal* not very attractive or noticeable【正式】不吸引人的; 不引人注意的

un·pre·ten·tious /ˌʌnprɪˋtɛnʃəs; ˌʌnprɪˈtenʃəs◂/ *adj approving* not trying to seem better, more important etc than you really are【褒】不炫耀的, 不招搖的; 不裝模作樣的: *an unpretentious restaurant* 簡樸的餐館 —**unpretentiously** *adv* —**unpretentiousness** *n* [U]

un·prin·ci·pled /ʌnˋprɪnsəpḷd; ʌnˈprɪnsǝpəld/ *adj formal* not caring about whether what you do is morally right; UNSCRUPULOUS【正式】不講道德的, 不擇手段的

un·print·a·ble /ʌnˋprɪntəbḷ; ʌnˈprɪntəbəl/ *adj* words that are unprintable are very rude or shocking〔詞語因粗魯或駭人聽聞而〕不宜刊印的, 不能印刷的

un·pro·duct·ive /ˌʌnprəˋdʌktɪv; ˌʌnprəˈdʌktɪv◂/ *adj* not producing any good results 無結果的, 徒勞的: *I've had a very unproductive week.* 我度過了毫無收益的一週。

un·pro·fes·sion·al /ˌʌnprəˋfɛʃənḷ; ˌʌnprəˈfeʃənəl◂/ *adj* someone who is unprofessional does not behave according to the standard that is expected in a particular profession or activity 違反行業準則的: *Johnson was fired for unprofessional conduct.* 約翰遜因為有違反職業道德的行為而被開除了。—**unprofessionally** *adv*

un·prof·it·a·ble /ʌnˋprɑfɪtəbḷ; ʌnˈprɒfǝtəbəl/ *adj* **1** making no profit 無利潤的: *unprofitable businesses* 無利可圖的買賣 **2** *formal* bringing no advantage or gain【正式】無益的, 徒勞的: *It would be unprofitable to commit yourself to any firm plans at the moment.* 現在承諾做任何確實的計劃都是無益的。

un·prompt·ed /ʌnˋprɑmptɪd; ʌnˈprɒmptǝd/ *adj formal* unprompted actions are things that you do without anyone asking you to【正式】未經鼓動的; 未經提示的; 自發的

un·pro·nounce·a·ble /ˌʌnprəˋnaʊnsəbl; ˌʌnprəˈnaʊnsəbəl◂/ *adj* an unpronounceable word or name is very difficult to say〔單詞或名字〕難發音的

un·pro·tect·ed /ˌʌnprəˋtɛktɪd; ˌʌnprəˈtektǝd◂/ *adj* **1** something that is unprotected could hurt someone or be damaged 無保護的; 無掩護的, 沒有防衛的: *Unprotected machinery can be dangerous.* 無保護的機器可能很危險。**2 unprotected sex** sex without a CONDOM 不用安全套的性交

un·pro·ven /ʌnˋpruvən; ˌʌnˈpruːvən, *ScotE*【蘇格蘭】-ˈprəvən; -ˈprəvən/ *adj* not tested, and not shown to be definitely true 未經檢驗的; 未經證實的: *unproven allegations* 未經證實的指控

un·pro·voked /ˌʌnprəˋvokt; ˌʌnprəˈvəʊkt◂/ *adj* unprovoked anger, attacks etc are directed at someone who has not done anything to deserve them〔憤怒、攻擊等〕無端的, 無緣無故的: *The assault was completely unprovoked.* 這次攻擊完全是無緣無故的。

un·qual·i·fied /ʌnˋkwɑləˌfaɪd; ʌnˈkwɒlǝfaɪd/ *adj* **1** not having the right knowledge, experience, or education to do something 無資格的; 不合格的: **unqualified to do sth** *I feel unqualified to advise you.* 我覺得自己沒有資格向你提出忠告。**2 unqualified success/approval etc** success etc that is complete and without any criticism 極大的成功/無條件的同意等: *The play was an unqualified success.* 這部劇取得了全面的成功。

un·ques·tion·a·ble /ʌnˋkwɛstʃənəbḷ; ʌnˈkwestʃənəbəl/ *adj* impossible to doubt; certain 不成問題的, 無可置疑的; 確實的 —**unquestionably** *adv*

un·ques·tioned /ʌnˋkwɛstʃənd; ʌnˈkwestʃənd/ *adj* something that is unquestioned is accepted or believed by everyone 無爭議的; 公認的: *the monarch's unquestioned right to rule* 公認的君主統治權

un·ques·tion·ing /ʌnˋkwɛstʃənɪŋ; ʌnˈkwestʃənɪŋ/ *adj* an unquestioning faith, attitude etc is very certain and without doubts〔信念、態度等〕無疑問[異議]的: *an unquestioning belief in God* 對上帝的深信不疑 | *unquestioning loyalty* 絕對的忠誠 —**unquestioningly** *adv*

un·qui·et /ʌnˋkwaɪət; ʌnˈkwaɪǝt/ *adj literary* tending to make you feel nervous【文】焦慮的, 不安的: *His unquiet gaze moved away from her.* 他不安的注視從她身上移開了。

un·quote /ʌnˋkwot; ʌnˈkwəʊt/ *adv* see 見 **quote...unquote** (QUOTE[1] (4))

un·rav·el /ʌnˋrævḷ; ʌnˈrævəl/ *v* **unravelled, unravelling** *BrE*【英】, **unraveled, unraveling** *AmE*【美】**1** [I,T] if you unravel threads or if they unravel, they become separated 解開, 拆散〔線等〕; 散開 **2** [T] to understand or explain something that is very complicated 理解; 解釋, 闡明: *It is difficult to unravel complex human emotions.* 很難闡明複雜的人類感情。

un·rea·da·ble /ʌnˋridəbḷ; ʌnˈriːdəbəl/ *adj* **1** an unreadable book or piece of writing is difficult to read because it is boring or complicated〔因平淡無味或複雜而〕難讀懂的 **2** unreadable writing is so untidy that you cannot read it; ILLEGIBLE 字跡模糊的, 難以辨認的

un·real /ʌnˋriəl; ˌʌnˈrɪəl◂/ *adj* **1** [not before noun 不用於名詞前] an experience, situation etc that is unreal seems so strange that you think you must be imagining or dreaming it 不真實的, 虛幻的: *The evening was so bizarre that it was beginning to seem unreal.* 那個晚上如此離奇, 似乎如夢幻一般。**2** not related to real things that happen 假的; 虛擬的: *Exam questions often deal with unreal situations.* 考試題常常討論一些虛擬的情景。**3** *spoken* very exciting; excellent【口】很刺激的, 極棒的: *Our trip to Disneyland was unreal.* 我們的迪士尼樂園之旅棒極了。—**unreality** /ˌʌnrɪˋælətɪ; ˌʌnrɪˈælǝti/ *n* [U]

un·rea·lis·tic /ˌʌnriəˋlɪstɪk; ˌʌnrɪəˈlɪstɪk◂/ *adj* unrealistic ideas, hopes are not based on facts 不現實的, 不切實際的: *Predictions that Labour would win the election began to look unrealistic.* 關於工黨會在大選中獲勝的預言開始顯得不切實際。| **it is unrealistic to do sth** *It is unrealistic to expect children to sit still for hours.* 指望孩子們安安靜靜地坐上幾個小時, 那是不切實際的。| **be being unrealistic** *John, I think you're being totally unrealistic – we'll never be ready by then.* 約翰, 我認為你完全是在做白日夢——我們到那時根本不可能準備好。—**unrealistically** /-kḷɪ; -kli/ *adv*

un·rea·son·a·ble /ʌnˋriznəbḷ; ʌnˈriːzənəbəl/ *adj* **1** behaving in an unfair, unpleasant, or stupid way 不講理的; 超越情理的, 過分的: *Will thinks I'm being unreasonable in not lending him the car.* 威爾認為我不借車給他有點過分。**2** an unreasonable belief, request, action etc is wrong or unfair〔信念、要求、行動等〕不合理的; 荒謬的: **it is unreasonable to do sth** *I think it's unreasonable to expect you to work Sundays.* 我認為期望你星期天工作是沒有道理的。| **make unreasonable demands** *Get assertive if your boss makes unreasonable demands.* 如果老闆提出無理的要求, 你不要讓步。**3** unreasonable prices, costs etc are too high〔價格、成本等〕過高的 —opposite 反義詞 REASONABLE —**unreasonably** *adv* —**unreasonableness** *n* [U]

un·rea·son·ing /ʌnˋriznɪŋ; ʌnˈriːzənɪŋ/ *adj formal* an unreasoning feeling is one that is not based on fact or reason【正式】缺乏理智的; 不講理的

un·rec·og·niz·a·ble also 又作 **-isable** *BrE*【英】/ʌnˋrɛkəgˌnaɪzəbḷ; ʌnˈrekəgnaɪzəbəl/ *adj* someone or something that is unrecognizable has changed or been damaged so much that you do not recognize them 不能識別的, 認不出來的: *They've built so many new buildings that the town centre was unrecognisable.* 他們蓋了那麼多新大樓, 鎮中心都認不出來了。

un·rec·og·nized also 又作 **-ised** *BrE*【英】/ʌnˋrɛkəgˌnaɪzd; ʌnˈrekəgnaɪzd/ *adj* **1** someone who is unrecognized for something they have done has not received the admiration or respect they deserve 未被承認的: *one of the great unrecognized jazzmen of the 1930s* 未得到承認的 20 世紀 30 年代傑出爵士樂演奏者之一 **2** not noticed or not thought to be important 不被注意的; 遭到輕視的: **go unrecognized** *Domestic violence went unrecognized for years.* 家庭暴力問題已多年未引起人們

的注意。

un·re·cord·ed /ˌʌnrɪˋkɔrdɪd; ˌʌnrɪˈkɔːdɪ̈d◂/ *adj* not written down or recorded 未寫下來的; 未記錄的; 未登記的: **go unrecorded** *Many of the complaints have gone unrecorded.* 許多投訴都未作記錄。

un·re·fined /ˌʌnrɪˋfaɪnd; ˌʌnrɪˈfaɪnd◂/ *adj* **1** [no comparative 無比較級] an unrefined substance has not been separated from the other substances that it is combined with in its natural form 未精製的; 未提煉的: *unrefined oil* 原油 | *unrefined sugar* 粗糖 **2** *formal* not polite or educated【正式】不優雅的; 無教養的 —opposite 反義詞 REFINED

un·re·gen·e·rate /ˌʌnrɪˋdʒɛnərɪt; ˌʌnrɪˈdʒenərɪ̈t◂/ *adj formal* making no attempt to change your bad habits or bad behaviour【正式】不改悔的, 不思改過的; 頑固不化的: *an unregenerate liar* 不改悔的說謊者

un·re·lat·ed /ˌʌnrɪˋletɪd; ˌʌnrɪˈleɪtɪ̈d◂/ *adj* **1** not connected to each other in any way 無關的, 不相關的: *The police think that the two incidents are unrelated.* 警方認為這兩件事件互不相關。**2** people who are unrelated are not members of the same family 無親戚關係的; 非親屬的

un·re·lent·ing /ˌʌnrɪˋlɛntɪŋ; ˌʌnrɪˈlentɪŋ◂/ *adj formal* an unpleasant situation that is unrelenting continues for a long time without stopping【正式】〔討厭的情況〕持續的; 不斷的: *the unrelenting pressures of the job* 持續的工作壓力 | *two days of unrelenting rain* 連續下了兩天的雨 —see also 另見 RELENT, RELENTLESS —**unrelentingly** *adv*

un·re·li·a·ble /ˌʌnrɪˋlaɪəbl̩; ˌʌnrɪˈlaɪəbəl◂/ *adj* unable to be trusted or depended on 不可信賴的; 不可靠的: *The car's becoming very unreliable.* 這部汽車變得非常不牢靠了。| **unreliable witness** (=someone who may not tell the truth in a court) 不可靠的證人 —opposite 反義詞 RELIABLE

un·re·lieved /ˌʌnrɪˋlivd; ˌʌnrɪˈliːvd◂/ *adj* an unpleasant situation that is unrelieved continues for a long time because nothing happens to change it〔討厭的情況〕未減輕的; 未解除的; 無變化的: *unrelieved pain* 未減輕的疼痛 —see also 另見 RELIEVE —**unrelievedly** /-ˋlivdlɪ; -ˈliːvɪ̈dli/ *adv*

un·re·mark·a·ble /ˌʌnrɪˋmɑrkəbl̩; ˌʌnrɪˈmɑːkəbəl◂/ *adj formal* not especially beautiful or interesting【正式】不引人注意的, 不顯著的; 平凡的: *unremarkable buildings* 不起眼的建築物

un·re·mit·ting /ˌʌnrɪˋmɪtɪŋ; ˌʌnrɪˈmɪtɪŋ◂/ *adj formal* an action or effort that is unremitting continues for a long time and probably will not stop【正式】〔行動或努力〕不間斷的; 無休止的: *lives of unremitting drudgery* 無休止的苦工生活 —**unremittingly** *adv*

un·re·peat·a·ble /ˌʌnrɪˋpitəbl̩; ˌʌnrɪˈpiːtəbəl◂/ *adj* **1** something that someone says that is unrepeatable is too rude or offensive for you to want to say it again〔說話因粗俗或冒犯而〕不宜重複的: *Tim's comment was unrepeatable.* 蒂姆的評論不便重複。**2** unable to be done again 不能重做的

un·re·pent·ant /ˌʌnrɪˋpɛntənt; ˌʌnrɪˈpentənt◂/ *adj* not feeling ashamed of behaviour, or beliefs that other people may disapprove of 不改悔的, 不悔悟的; 頑固的: *an unrepentant right-winger* 頑固不化的右翼分子

un·rep·re·sen·ta·tive /ˌʌnrɛprɪˋzɛntətɪv; ˌʌnreprɪˈzentətɪv/ *adj* **1** not typical of a group or type, and therefore not giving you any information about the other members of the same group or type 不能代表的; 不典型的: **[+of]** *This painting is unrepresentative of the rest of her work.* 這幅畫不代表她其餘的作品。**2** an unrepresentative government only has a few members from a variety of social groups, so that the opinions of many people are ignored〔政府〕不代表全體民意的

un·re·quit·ed /ˌʌnrɪˋkwaɪtɪd; ˌʌnrɪˈkwaɪtɪ̈d◂/ *adj* **unrequited love** romantic love that you feel for someone, but that they do not feel for you 單戀, 單相思

un·re·served /ˌʌnrɪˋzɝvd; ˌʌnrɪˈzɜːvd◂/ *adj* complete and without any doubts 無保留的; 完全的, 充分的 —**unreservedly** /-ˋzɝvɪdlɪ; -ˈzɜːvɪ̈dli/ *adv*: *The company apologized unreservedly for its mistake.* 公司坦誠地為其錯誤道了歉。

un·re·solved /ˌʌnrɪˋzɑlvd; ˌʌnrɪˈzɒlvd◂/ *adj* an unresolved problem or question has not been answered or solved 未解答的; 未解決的

un·res·pon·sive /ˌʌnrɪˋspɑnsɪv; ˌʌnrɪˈspɒnsɪv/ *adj* **1** not reacting to something or affected by it 無反應的; 不受影響的: **[+to]** *The disease is unresponsive to conventional treatment.*這種病常規療法不起作用。**2** not reacting to what people say to you 不作出答覆的; 無反應的; 冷淡的: *She remained still and unresponsive.* 她一動不動, 沒有任何反應。

un·rest /ʌnˋrɛst; ʌnˈrest/ *n* [U] a social or political situation in which people protest and tend to behave violently 不安寧; 動亂; 騷動: *The country was in a state of unrest.* 該國處於動亂之中。| **social/civil/political etc unrest** *These drastic measures were necessary to prevent further social unrest.* 這些嚴厲措施對防止進一步的社會動亂是必需的。

un·re·strained /ˌʌnrɪˋstrend; ˌʌnrɪˈstreɪnd◂/ *adj* not controlled or limited 無限制的; 無拘束的; 自由自在的: *unrestrained laughter* 放聲大笑 —**unrestrainedly** *adv*

un·ripe /ʌnˋraɪp; ˌʌnˈraɪp/ *adj* unripe fruit, grain etc is not fully developed or ready to be eaten 未成熟的, 生的: *green, unripe peaches* 青色的生桃子

un·ri·valled *BrE*【英】, **unrivaled** *AmE*【美】/ʌnˋraɪvl̩d; ʌnˈraɪvəld/ *adj formal* better than any other【正式】無敵的, 無雙的: *an unrivalled collection of Chinese art* 無與倫比的中國藝術珍品

un·ruf·fled /ʌnˋrʌfl̩d; ʌnˈrʌfəld/ *adj approving* calm and not upset by a difficult situation【褒】平靜的; 沉着的: *The Under-Secretary remained completely unruffled.* 那位副部長一直保持鎮定自若。

un·ru·ly /ʌnˋrulɪ; ʌnˈruːli/ *adj* **1** behaving in an uncontrolled or violent way〔行為〕難駕馭的, 難控制的; 粗暴的: *unruly children* 難管教的孩子 **2** unruly hair is untidy〔頭髮〕亂蓬蓬的 —**unruliness** *n* [U]

un·sad·dle /ʌnˋsædl̩; ʌnˈsædl/ *v* [T] **1** to remove the SADDLE (=leather seat) from a horse 給〔馬〕卸鞍 **2** if a horse unsaddles someone, it throws them off its back; UNSEAT〔馬〕把〔某人〕摔下來, 使墜馬

un·said /ʌnˋsɛd; ʌnˈsed/ *adv* **be left unsaid** if something is left unsaid, you do not say it although you might be thinking it〔話〕未說出口: *Some things are better left unsaid.* 有些事不說出來更好。—**unsay** /ʌnˋse; ʌnˈseɪ/ *v* [T]

un·san·i·ta·ry /ˌʌnˋsænəˌtɛrɪ; ˌʌnˈsænɪ̈təri/ *adj especially AmE* conditions or places that are unsanitary are very dirty and likely to cause disease; INSANITARY【尤美】不衛生的; 有礙健康的

un·sa·vour·y *BrE*【英】, **unsavory** *AmE*【美】/ʌnˋsevərɪ; ʌnˈseɪvəri/ *adj* unpleasant or morally unacceptable 令人不快的;〔道德上〕令人厭惡的: *I hope that ends the whole unsavoury business.* 我希望這會結束整樁令人討厭的事情。| **unsavoury light** *The latest revelations show the actor in a very unsavoury light.* 最近的新發現使那個演員的可惡之處暴露無遺。| **unsavoury character** (=an unpleasant and dishonest person) 缺德的小人

un·scathed /ʌnˋskeðd; ʌnˈskeɪðd/ *adj* [not before noun 不用於名詞前] not hurt by a bad or dangerous situation 沒有受傷的, 未遭受傷害的: *Faye walked away from the accident completely unscathed.* 費伊在事故中脫險, 安然無恙。

un·scram·ble /ʌnˋskræmbl̩; ʌnˈskræmbəl/ *v* [T] to change a television SIGNAL or a message that has been sent in CODE (=a deliberately confusing way) so that it can be seen or read 解讀〔電視信號〕; 譯出〔密電碼〕

unscrew 旋開

He tried to unscrew the lid.他試圖旋開蓋子。

un·screw /ʌnˋskru; ʌnˈskruː/ *v* [T] **1** to undo something by twisting it 擰開, 旋開〔某物〕 **2** to take the screws out of something 從〔某物〕旋出螺絲

un·script·ed /ˌʌnˋskrɪptɪd; ˌʌnˈskrɪptɪ̈d◂/ *adj* an unscripted broadcast, speech etc is not written or planned before it is actually made〔廣播、演講等〕不用稿子的; 不事前準備的

un·scru·pu·lous /ʌnˋskrupjələs; ʌnˈskruːpjɪ̈ləs/ *adj* behaving in an unfair or dishonest way 不擇手段的; 不講道德的; 無恥的: *a cunning and unscrupulous politician* 狡猾而不擇手段的政客 —**unscrupulously** *adv* —**unscrupulousness** *n* [U]

un·sea·son·a·ble /ʌnˋsizn̩əbl̩; ʌnˈsiːzənəbəl/ *adj* unseasonable weather is unusual for the time of year〔天氣〕不合時令[季節]的

un·seat /ʌnˋsit; ʌnˈsiːt/ *v* [T] **1** to remove someone from a position of power or strength 使退位; 使退職: *You'll see – we'll unseat the President at the next election.* 你瞧着吧——下次選舉我們就會把總統趕下台。**2** if a horse unseats someone, it throws them off its back〔馬〕把〔某人〕摔下來

un·seed·ed /ʌnˋsidɪd; ˌʌnˈsiːdɪ̈d◂/ *adj* not chosen as a SEED (=someone with a numbered rank in a competition), especially in a tennis competition〔尤指網球比賽中〕未被挑選為種子選手的

un·see·ing /ʌnˋsiɪŋ; ˌʌnˈsiːɪŋ◂/ *adj especially literary* not noticing anything even though your eyes are open【尤文】視而不見的: *Jack gazed unseeing out of the window.* 傑克視而不見地盯着窗外。—**unseeingly** *adv*

un·seem·ly /ʌnˋsimlɪ; ʌnˈsiːmli/ *adj formal* unseemly behaviour is not polite or not suitable for a particular occasion【正式】〔行為〕不體面的; 不合禮節的; 不得體的: *Ann thought it unseemly to kiss her husband in public.* 安認為當眾與丈夫接吻不太合適。—**unseemliness** *n* [U]

un·seen[1] /ʌnˋsin; ˌʌnˈsiːn◂/ *adj formal* not noticed or seen【正式】未被看見[察覺]的; 未受注意的 —**unseen** *adv*: *She crept out of the building unseen.* 她躡手躡腳地從建築物裡走出來, 沒讓人看見。

unseen[2] *n* [C] *BrE* a piece of writing in a foreign language that you have not seen before and that you must translate into your own language in an examination【英】〔考試中〕需即席翻譯成本國語的文章

un·set·tle /ʌnˋsɛtl̩; ʌnˈsetl/ *v* [T] to make someone feel upset or nervous 使心緒不寧; 使擔憂: *The sudden changes unsettled Judy.* 突如其來的變化使朱迪心神不寧。—**unsettling** *adj*

un·set·tled /ʌnˋsɛtl̩d; ʌnˈsetld/ *adj*
1 ►SITUATION 形勢◄ making people feel uncertain about what will happen 動蕩不定的; 不穩定的: *the unsettled times during the war* 戰爭期間的不穩定時期
2 ►FEELING 感情◄ worried or excited about something so that you feel upset or nervous 心煩意亂的; 不安的: *Children feel unsettled if their parents divorce.* 父母如果離婚, 孩子們會感到心神不安。
3 ►ARGUMENT OR DISAGREEMENT 爭論或分歧◄ still continuing without reaching any agreement 未定的; 未解決的: *The dispute between teachers and governors remains unsettled.* 教師與學校董事之間的爭議仍然沒有解決。
4 ►WEATHER 天氣◄ changing a lot in a short period of time 變幻莫測的; 易變的
5 ►STOMACH 胃◄ making you feel uncomfortable and a little sick 不舒服的, 稍感不適的: *My stomach's a bit unsettled after all that rich food.* 吃了那麼多油膩食物之後, 我的胃覺得有點不舒服。

un·sha·kea·ble, unshakable /ʌnˋʃekəbl̩; ʌnˈʃeɪkəbəl/ *adj* unshakable faith, beliefs etc are very strong and cannot be destroyed or changed〔信仰、信念等〕不可動搖的, 堅定不移的

un·shav·en /ʌnˋʃevən; ʌnˈʃeɪvən/ *adj* a man who is unshaven has very short hairs growing on his face because he has not shaved (SHAVE[1] (1))〔男子〕未剃鬚的, 未修面的

un·sight·ly /ʌnˋsaɪtlɪ; ʌnˈsaɪtli/ *adj* unpleasant to look at 不悅目的, 難看的, 不雅觀的: *unsightly power stations ruining the landscape* 大煞風景的醜陋的發電站 —**unsightliness** *n* [U]

un·skilled /ʌnˋskɪld; ˌʌnˈskɪld◂/ *adj* **1** an unskilled worker has not been trained for a particular type of job〔工人〕無特殊技能的, 未受專門訓練的: **unskilled labour** (=people who have no special training) 非熟練工人 **2** unskilled work, jobs etc do not need people with special skills〔工作等〕無需特殊技能的 —compare 比較 SKILLED

un·so·cia·ble /ʌnˋsoʃəbl̩; ʌnˈsəʊʃəbəl/ *adj* not liking to be with people or to go to social events 不愛交際的, 不合羣的 —see also 另見 UNSOCIAL

un·so·cial /ʌnˋsoʃəl; ˌʌnˈsəʊʃəl◂/ *adj* **work unsocial hours** also 又作 **work unsociable hours** to work very early in the morning, during the night etc when most people do not work 非正常工作時間〔即早班、夜班等〕

un·solved /ʌnˋsɑlvd; ˌʌnˈsɒlvd◂/ *adj* a problem, mystery, or crime that is unsolved has never been solved 未解決的

un·so·phis·ti·cat·ed /ˌʌnsəˋfɪstɪˌketɪd; ˌʌnsəˈfɪstɪ̈keɪtɪ̈d◂/ *adj* **1** having little knowledge or experience of modern fashionable things, and showing this by the way you talk or behave 不諳世故的, 天真無邪的: *an unsophisticated boy from the provinces* 來自外省的天真男孩 **2** unsophisticated tools, methods, or processes are simple, without many of the features of more modern ones〔工具、方法、過程〕不複雜的, 簡單的

un·sound /ʌnˋsaʊnd; ˌʌnˈsaʊnd◂/ *adj* **1** unsound arguments, methods etc are not based on fact or reason〔論點、方法等〕謬誤的; 無根據的: *ideologically unsound* 觀念上謬誤的 **2** an unsound building or structure is in bad condition〔建築物或結構〕不安全的, 不穩固的 **3 of unsound mind** *formal* mentally ill and not responsible for your actions【正式】心智不健全的

un·speak·a·ble /ʌnˋspikəbl̩; ʌnˈspiːkəbəl/ *adj* **1** unspeakable actions or people are extremely bad 壞得無法形容的, 壞透了的: *the unspeakable atrocities in Bosnia* 在波斯尼亞發生的難以形容的暴行 **2** *literary* unspeakable feelings are so extreme that it is impossible to describe them【文】〔感覺〕難以形容的: *unspeakable terror* 無法形容的恐怖 —**unspeakably** *adv*

un·spoiled /ʌnˋspɔɪld; ˌʌnˈspɔɪld◂/ also 又作 **un·spoilt** /-ˋspɔɪlt; -ˈspɔɪlt◂/ *especially BrE*【尤英】*adj* **1** *approving* an unspoiled place has not been changed for a long time, especially by new roads, buildings etc【褒】〔地方〕長時間未發生變化的; 未喪失原有自然美的 **2** someone who is unspoiled has not changed in spite of the good or bad things that have happened to them〔人〕未受影響的; 未被寵壞的: *She remained unspoilt by her success.* 她雖然事業有成, 卻依然保持本色。

un·sta·ble /ʌnˋstebl̩; ʌnˈsteɪbəl/ *adj* **1** dangerous and likely to fall over because not balanced or properly supported 不穩固的; 不牢靠的 **2** likely to change suddenly and perhaps become worse 易變的; 動蕩不定的: *an unstable economy* 不穩定的經濟 **3** someone who is unstable changes very suddenly so that you do not know how they will react or behave〔人〕反覆無常的, 動搖不定的 **4** an unstable chemical is likely to separate into simpler compounds〔化合物〕不穩定的

un·stint·ing /ʌnˋstɪntɪŋ; ʌnˈstɪntɪŋ/ *adj* unstinting support, help, agreement etc is complete and given willingly〔支持、幫助、協議等〕慷慨的, 大方的 —**unstintingly** *adv*

un·stop /ˌʌnˋstɑp; ˌʌnˈstɒp/ *v* [T] if you unstop a pipe, DRAIN[2] (1) etc, you remove something that is blocking it 除去〔管道、下水道等〕的堵塞物

un·stop·pa·ble /ʌnˋstɑpəbl̩; ʌnˈstɒpəbəl/ *adj* unable to be stopped 制止不住的, 阻止不了的: *Once Janet gets an idea, she's unstoppable.* 珍妮特一旦拿定主意, 誰也擋不住她。

un·stuck /ˌʌnˋstʌk; ˌʌnˈstʌk◂/ *adj* **come unstuck a)** if something comes unstuck, it becomes separated from something that it was stuck to 脱落; 鬆開 **b)** *BrE informal* if someone comes unstuck, something that they are doing starts to go wrong【英, 非正式】出毛病; 失靈; 失敗

un·stud·ied /ʌnˋstʌdɪd; ˌʌnˈstʌdid/ *adj formal* an unstudied quality seems natural and is not a result of effort or practice【正式】非造作的, 自然的: *unstudied grace* 自然的優雅

un·suit·able /ʌnˋsjutəbl̩; ˌʌnˈsuːtəbəl/ *adj* not having the right qualities for a particular person, purpose, or situation 不合適的; 不適宜的: **[+for]** *Those books are quite unsuitable for children.* 那些書對兒童頗不適宜。| *beaches judged unsuitable for swimming* 被斷定為不適合游泳的海灘

un·sul·lied /ʌnˋsʌlɪd; ʌnˈsʌlid/ *adj literary* not spoiled【文】未受污染的, 潔淨的: *unsullied lush vegetation and wide open spaces* 潔淨而又繁茂的草木和廣闊的空地

un·sung /ʌnˋsʌŋ; ˌʌnˈsʌŋ◂/ *adj* not praised or famous for something you have done although you deserve to be 應該而未被讚頌的: **unsung hero** *Liam was an unsung hero during the crisis.* 利亞姆是這次危機期間默默無聞的英雄。

un·sure /ʌnˋʃur; ˌʌnˈʃʊə◂/ *adj* **1** not certain about something or about what you have to do 無把握的; 不確知的: *If you are unsure about the operation, ask your doctor to explain it.* 你如果對手術無把握, 請醫生講解一下。**2 unsure of yourself** to lack confidence 缺乏自信: *Chris seemed nervous and unsure of herself.* 克里斯顯得緊張, 缺乏自信。

un·sur·passed /ˌʌnsɚˋpæst; ˌʌnsəˈpɑːst◂/ *adj* a skill, quality, or achievement that is unsurpassed is better than all the others〔技能、品質或成就〕無與倫比的, 超羣的: *Her knowledge of the subject is unsurpassed.* 她對這一學科的知識無人能比。

un·sus·pect·ing /ˌʌnsəˋspɛktɪŋ; ˌʌnsəˈspektɪŋ◂/ *adj* not knowing that something bad is about to happen 不懷疑的, 無疑心的: *unsuspecting victims* 無提防之心的受害人

un·swerv·ing /ʌnˋswɝvɪŋ; ʌnˈswɜːvɪŋ/ *adj* an unswerving belief or attitude is one that is very strong and never changes〔信念、態度〕堅定不移的: **unswerving in sth** *Liz was unswerving in her determination to be a journalist.* 利兹堅決要成為一名記者。| **unswerving loyalty/admiration** *Nina has always shown unswerving loyalty to the family.* 尼娜總是對家庭表現出絕對的忠誠。

un·tan·gle /ʌnˋtæŋgl̩; ˌʌnˈtæŋgəl/ *v* [T] **1** to undo pieces of string etc that are twisted together 解開〔糾結〕: *fisherman untangling their nets* 正在解開纏結的魚網的漁民 **2** to make something less complicated 理順, 整理〔某物〕

un·tapped /ʌnˋtæpt; ˌʌnˈtæpt◂/ *adj* an untapped RESOURCE[1], market etc has not yet been used〔資源、市場等〕未開發的; 未利用的

un·ten·a·ble /ʌnˋtɛnəbl̩; ʌnˈtenəbəl/ *adj* an untenable THEORY, argument etc is impossible to defend against criticism〔理論、論點等〕站不住腳的; 不堪一擊的: **untenable position** *The scandal left the President in an untenable position.* 醜聞使總統無可辯白。

un·thin·ka·ble /ʌnˋθɪŋkəbl̩; ʌnˈθɪŋkəbəl/ *adj* impossible to accept or imagine 不能接受的; 難以置信的; 難以想像的: *It would have been unthinkable ten years earlier to choose a woman as party leader.* 10年前選婦女作黨領袖是難以想像的。

un·think·ing /ʌnˋθɪŋkɪŋ; ʌnˈθɪŋkɪŋ/ *adj* not thinking about the effects of something you say or do 不考慮後果的 —**unthinkingly** *adv*

un·ti·dy /ʌnˋtaɪdɪ; ʌnˈtaɪdi/ *adj especially BrE*【尤英】**1** not neat; MESSY (1) 不整潔的, 凌亂的: *an untidy room* 凌亂的房間 **2** someone who is untidy does not keep their house, possessions etc neat〔人〕不整齊的, 無條理的 —**untidily** *adv* —**untidiness** *n* [U]

un·tie /ʌnˋtaɪ; ʌnˈtaɪ/ *v* [T] to undo the knots in something or undo something that has been tied 解開〔結或捆着之物〕—**untied** *adj*: *walking about with shoelaces untied* 鞋帶不繫四處走

un·til /ənˋtɪl; ʌnˈtɪl/ *prep, conjunction* **1** used to say that something stops happening or someone stops doing something at a particular time or when something else happens; TILL[1] 直到…為止: *Gary was working for IBM until 1969, when he got a job at Sperry.* 加里為國際商業機器公司一直工作到1969年, 接着他在斯佩里公司找到了一份工作。| *Black people were denied the vote in the US until well into the 1950s.* 美國黑人直到20世紀50年代才獲得選舉權。| **up until** *This ticket is valid up until the 12th of March.* 這張票的有效期一直到3月12日。**2** used to say that you should stop travelling at a particular place 直到〔某地〕: *Stay on the train until Birmingham, and then change for Peterborough.* 坐火車一直到伯明翰, 然後換乘到彼得巴勒的車。

un·time·ly /ʌnˋtaɪmlɪ; ʌnˈtaɪmli/ *adj* **1 untimely death/end etc** a death etc that is much earlier than usual or expected 過早死亡/結束等 **2** not suitable for a particular occasion or time 不適時的; 不合時宜的 —**untimeliness** *n* [U]

un·tir·ing /ʌnˋtaɪrɪŋ; ʌnˈtaɪərɪŋ/ *adj approving* never stopping while working hard or trying to do something【褒】不倦的; 堅持不懈的: *untiring efforts to help the homeless* 堅持不懈地致力於幫助無家可歸的人 —**untiringly** *adv*

U

un·to /ˋʌntu; ˈʌntuː/ *prep old use* to【舊】對, 向: *Thanks be unto God.* 感謝上帝。

un·told /ʌnˋtold; ˌʌnˈtəʊld◂/ *adj* too much or too many to be measured（多得）數不清的; 不可計量的: **untold misery** *The floods have caused untold misery to hundreds of homeowners.* 洪水給數以百計的家庭造成了不可估量的痛苦。| **untold damage** *The scandal has done untold damage to his reputation.* 醜聞給他的名聲造成了極大的損害。

un·touch·a·ble /ʌnˋtʌtʃəbl̩; ʌnˈtʌtʃəbəl/ *adj* **1** someone who is untouchable is in such a strong position that they cannot be affected by, or punished for, anything〔人因地位牢固而〕碰不得的; 不受影響的: *He was the boss's husband and therefore untouchable.* 他是老闆的丈夫, 因而碰不得。**2** belonging to the lowest social group, especially in the Hindu CASTE system 賤民的〔尤指印度種姓制度最低層者〕—**untouchable** *n* [C]

un·touched /ʌnˋtʌtʃt; ˌʌnˈtʌtʃt◂/ *adj* untouched food has not been eaten〔食物〕未動過的, 未吃[喝]過的: *The food looked so awful that it was left untouched.* 食物看起來太糟糕了, 結果原封未動。

un·to·ward /ʌnˋtɔrd; ˌʌntəˈwɔːd/ *adj* **anything/nothing untoward** *formal* something or nothing that is unexpected, unusual, or not wanted【正式】有/沒有意外[異常, 不幸]: *We walked past the house but didn't notice anything untoward.* 我們走過那棟房子, 但沒有注意到任何反常的情況。

un·tram·melled *BrE*【英】, **untrameled** *AmE*【美】/ʌnˋtræmḷd; ʌnˈtræməld/ *adj formal* without any limits

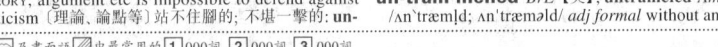

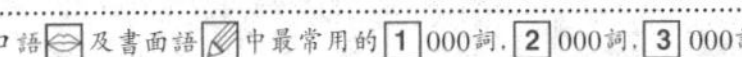

【正式】不受限制的, 不受妨礙的

un·treat·ed /ʌnˋtritɪd; ʌnˈtriːtɪ̣d/ *adj* **1** an untreated illness or injury has not had medical attention〔疾病、傷處〕未予治療的 **2** harmful substances that are untreated have not been made safe〔有害物質〕未經處理的: *untreated sewage* 未處理過的污水

un·tried /ʌnˋtraɪd; ˌʌnˈtraɪd◂/ *adj* **1** not having any experience of doing a particular job 無經驗的, 不熟練的: *a young and untried minister* 年輕而無經驗的部長 **2** not yet tested to see whether it is successful 未經試驗的: *a relatively new and untried method* 相當新穎但未經試驗的方法

un·true /ʌnˋtru; ʌnˈtruː/ *adj* **1** a statement that is untrue does not give the right facts; false 不真實的, 假的 **2** *literary* someone who is untrue to their husband, wife etc is not faithful to them【文】不忠的

un·truth /ʌnˋtruθ; ʌnˈtruːθ/ *n* [C] *formal* a word meaning a lie, used because you want to avoid saying this directly【正式】謊言, 假話〔委婉語〕

un·truth·ful /ʌnˋtruθfəl; ʌnˈtruːθfəl/ *adj* dishonest or not true 不誠實的; 不真實的 —**untruthfully** *adv*

un·used¹ /ʌnˋjuzd; ˌʌnˈjuːzd◂/ *adj* not being used, or never used 不在使用的; 未用過的: *unused office blocks* 空着的辦公大樓

un·used² /ˌʌnˋjust; ʌnˈjuːst/ *adj* **unused to** not experienced in dealing with something 不習慣於…: *a sensitive man unused to publicity* 不習慣於拋頭露面的敏感的人 | **unused to doing sth** *Maggie was unused to being told what to do.* 瑪吉不習慣被人呼來喚去。

un·u·su·al /ʌnˋjuʒuəl; ʌnˈjuːʒuəl/ *adj* **1** different from what is usual or ordinary 異常的, 不平常的: *The cake has a very unusual flavor.* 那塊蛋糕有一種異乎尋常的味道。| **it is unusual to do sth** *It is unusual to find diamonds of this size.* 很難得發現這樣大小的鑽石。| **it is unusual for sb to do sth** *Earlier last century, it was unusual for women to have a career.* 上世紀初, 婦女就業是很少有的。—see 見 RARE (USAGE) **2** interesting or attractive because of being different 獨特的, 與眾不同的: *Alan's artwork is very unusual.* 艾倫的工藝品非常獨特。

un·u·su·al·ly /ʌnˋjuʒuəlɪ; ʌnˈjuːʒuəli/ *adv* **1** **unusually hot/difficult etc** more hot etc than is usual 異常地熱/困難等 **2** in an unusual way 異乎尋常地: *The house was unusually quiet.* 那所房子異常地安靜。

un·ut·ter·a·ble /ʌnˋʌtərəbḷ; ʌnˈʌtərəbəl/ *adj formal* an unutterable feeling is too extreme to be expressed in words【正式】〔感受〕無法用言語表達的: *unutterable sadness* 難以形容的憂傷 —**unutterably** *adv*

un·var·nished /ʌnˋvɑrnɪʃt; ʌnˈvɑːnɪʃt/ *adj* [only before noun 僅用於名詞前] **1** plain and without additional decoration or description 未加修飾的, 直率的: *the unvarnished truth* 不經修飾的真相 **2** without any VARNISH (=a transparent substance like paint, used to protect the surface of wood etc) 未上清漆的

un·veil /ʌnˋvel; ˌʌnˈveɪl/ *v* [T] **1** to show or tell people something that was previously kept secret 透露; 揭露: *Reagan unveiled a series of budget cuts totaling $44 billion.* 列根透露了總計440億美元的一系列預算削減。**2** to remove the cover from something, especially as part of a formal ceremony〔尤指舉行儀式時〕揭去…上的覆蓋物: *The Queen unveiled a statue of Prince Albert.* 女王為艾伯特親王塑像揭幕。—**unveiling** *n* [C]

un·versed /ʌnˋvɝst; ˌʌnˈvɜːst/ *adj formal*【正式】**unversed in sth** without any knowledge or experience of something 對某事不了解[無經驗]: *unversed in city ways* 不熟悉城市(生活)方式

un·voiced /ʌnˋvɔɪst; ˌʌnˈvɔɪst◂/ *adj* **1** not expressed in words 未用語言表達的, 沒説出來的: *unvoiced fears* 未説出來的恐懼 **2** *technical* unvoiced CONSONANTS are produced without moving the VOCAL CORDS【術語】清音的, 無聲的: */d/ and /g/ are voiced consonants, and /t/ and /k/ are unvoiced.* /d/ 和 /g/ 是濁輔音, 而 /t/ 和 /k/ 是清輔音。

un·waged /ʌnˋwedʒd; ˌʌnˈweɪdʒd◂/ *adj BrE* not having a paid job; UNEMPLOYED【英】沒有工資收入的, 失業的

un·want·ed /ʌnˋwɑntɪd; ʌnˈwɒntɪ̣d/ *adj* not wanted or needed 不需要的, 多餘的: *an unwanted pregnancy* 不希望有的懷孕

un·war·rant·ed /ʌnˋwɔrəntɪd; ʌnˈwɒrəntɪ̣d/ **unwarrantable** *adj* done without good reason, and therefore annoying 沒有根據的; 無正當理由的: *unwarranted interference in our affairs* 對我們事務的無理干涉

un·wa·ry /ʌnˋwɛrɪ; ʌnˈweəri/ *adj* not knowing about possible problems or dangers, and therefore easily harmed or deceived 不警惕的, 粗心的〔因而容易受傷或受騙〕: **the unwary** (=people who are unwary) 粗心大意的人 —**unwarily** *adv* —**unwariness** *n* [U]

un·wel·come /ʌnˋwɛlkəm; ʌnˈwelkəm/ *adj* **1** something that is unwelcome is not wanted, especially because it might cause embarrassment or problems 不想要的: *unwelcome publicity* 不受歡迎的宣傳 **2** unwelcome guests, visitors etc are people that you do not want in your home〔客人等〕不受歡迎的, 討厭的

un·well /ʌnˋwɛl; ʌnˈwel/ *adj* [not before noun 不用於名詞前] *formal* ill, especially for a short time【正式】〔尤指短時間的〕不舒服的, 有病的 —see 見 SICK¹ (USAGE)

un·wield·y /ʌnˋwildɪ; ʌnˈwiːldi/ *adj* **1** an unwieldy object is big and heavy and difficult to carry〔物體〕龐大的, 笨重的, 難以搬運的 **2** an unwieldy system, argument, or plan is difficult to control or manage because it is too complicated〔因太複雜而〕難操縱的; 難控制的: *unwieldy bureaucracy* 難以控制的官僚機構 —**unwieldiness** *n* [U]

un·will·ing /ʌnˋwɪlɪŋ; ʌnˈwɪlɪŋ/ *adj* **1** [not before noun 不用於名詞前] not wanting to do something and refusing to do it 不願意的, 不樂意的: **unwilling to do sth** *They were unwilling to fund a project that had little chance of success.* 他們不願意為一個不大可能成功的項目提供資金。**2** [only before noun 僅用於名詞前] not wanting to do something but doing it 勉強(做)的, 不情願的: *an unwilling helper* 不情願的助手 —**unwillingly** *adv*

un·wind /ʌnˋwaɪnd; ʌnˈwaɪnd/ *v past tense and past participle* **unwound** /-ˋwaund; -ˈwaʊnd/ **1** [I] to relax and stop feeling anxious 放鬆, 鬆弛: *I love cooking. It helps me unwind.* 我喜歡烹飪, 這可以讓我放鬆下來。**2** [I,T] to undo something that has been wrapped around something else 解開; 展開〔捲起的東西〕

un·wit·ting·ly /ʌnˋwɪtɪŋlɪ; ʌnˈwɪtɪŋli/ *adv* in a way that shows you do not know or realize something 不知情地; 未意識到地: *Friedmann had unwittingly stumbled upon a vital piece of evidence.* 弗里德曼無意中發現一個極重要的證據。—**unwitting** *adj* [only before noun 僅用於名詞前]: *an unwitting accomplice* 不知情的同謀

un·wont·ed /ʌnˋwontɪd; ʌnˈwəʊntɪ̣d/ *adj* [only before noun 僅用於名詞前] *formal* unusual and not what you expect to happen【正式】不尋常的, 異常的: *"Good day" he cried with unwonted good humour.* "日安", 他帶着難得的好興致大聲説。

un·world·ly /ʌnˋwɝldlɪ; ʌnˈwɜːldli/ *adj* not interested in money or possessions 對錢財不感興趣的; 脱俗的, 超凡的

un·wound /ʌnˋwaund; ʌnˈwaʊnd/ the past tense and past participle of UNWIND

un·writ·ten /ʌnˋrɪtn̩; ʌnˈrɪtn/ *adj* known about and understood by everyone but not formally written down 非書面的; 不成文的: **unwritten rule/law** *It was an unwritten law among my friends that we never told our mothers what we did.* 我們從不把所做的事告訴母親, 這在我的朋友中是一種不成文的規定。

un·zip /ʌnˋzɪp; ˌʌnˈzɪp/ *v* [T] to unfasten the ZIP on a piece of clothing, bag etc 拉開…的拉鏈

up- /ʌp; ʌp/ *prefix* **1** making something higher 使升級, 使較高: *to upgrade a job* (=make it higher in importance) 提高工作的重要性 **2** [especially in adverbs and adjectives 尤構成副詞和形容詞] at or towards the top or beginning of something 在[向]…高處[源頭]的: *uphill* 上坡的; 往上坡 | *upriver* (=nearer to where the river starts) 在上游的; 向上游 **3** [especially in verbs 尤構成動詞] taking something from its place or turning it upside down 使起來〔離開原位〕; 使顛倒過來: *an uprooted tree* 被連根拔起的樹 | *She upended the bucket.* 她把水桶倒了過來。**4** [especially in adjectives and adverbs 尤構成形容詞和副詞] at or towards the higher or better part of something 在[向]更高處; 在[向]更好處: *up-market* (=suitable for the higher social groups) 高檔的; 適合高消費階層的 —compare 比較 DOWN-

1 1 **up¹** /ʌp; ʌp/ *adv* **1** towards a higher position from the floor, ground, or bottom of something 從下往上地, 向上地: *She picked her pen up off the floor.* 她從地板上撿起鋼筆。| *Can you lift that box up onto the shelf for me?* 你能幫我把那個箱子提起來放到架子上去嗎? | *After swimming for several seconds underwater he came up for air.* 他在水下游了幾秒鐘後, 浮上來換氣。| **up you come** *spoken* (=used especially to children when lifting them)【口】你上來了〔尤抱起兒童時用語〕**2** at or in a high position 在高處: *John's up in his bedroom.* 約翰在樓上他的臥室裡。| *The plane was flying 30,000 feet up.* 飛機在30,000英尺高空飛行。**3** into an upright or raised position 處於或趨於直立的位置, 起來: *Everyone stood up for the National Anthem.* 奏國歌時每個人都起立。| *Mick turned his collar up against the biting winds.* 米克翻起衣領抵擋刺骨的寒風。**4** in or towards the North 在[向]北方: *We're going to fly up to Scotland from London.* 我們將從倫敦向北飛往蘇格蘭。| *They live up North.* 他們住在北方。**5** towards someone so that you are near, or in the place where they are 向; 靠近: *He came right up and asked my name.* 他徑直走過來問我的名字。| *A man sidled up to her and asked for money.* 一個男子悄悄地走過來向她討錢。**6** increasing in loudness, strength, level of activity etc〔聲音、力量、水平等〕由小變大, 由低變高: *Can you turn the telly up a bit?* 你能把電視機調大聲點嗎? | *Competition between these two companies is really hotting up.* 這兩家公司的競爭真的愈來愈激烈了。**7** so as to be completely finished or used so that there is nothing left …完; …光: *Our savings are all used up.* 我們的積蓄都用光了。| *She won't eat up her vegetables.* 她吃不完自己的蔬菜。**8** so as to be in small pieces or divided into equal parts 成碎片; 平分: *They divided up the money.* 他們把錢分了。| *The plane hit the mountainside and broke up on impact.* 飛機撞在山坡上撞了個粉碎。**9** so as to be firmly fastened, covered, or joined〔拴、蓋、連接〕緊地; 牢牢地: *Mr Cain was boarding up the windows.* 凱恩先生正用木板封緊窗戶。**10** so as to be brought or gathered together 在一起, 合起來: *Let's just add up these figures quickly.* 讓我們快把這些數字加起來吧。| *Could you collect up the pens?* 你能把那些鋼筆收攏在一起嗎? **11** if a surface or part of something is a particular way up, it is on top 朝上: **right side up/right way up** (=with the part that is going to be used, or that has words or pictures on it on top) 正面朝上 *Put the playing cards right side up on the table.* 把紙牌正面朝上放在桌上。**12** so as to receive attention 提出 (以引起注意): *The question of a pay rise came up again during the meeting.* 增加工資的問題又在會議上提了出來。**13** above and including a certain amount or level 在…及以上: *Power was lost from the tenth floor up.* 10樓及以上沒有電。| *Children of twelve up must pay full fare.* 12歲及以上兒童必須購全票。**14 up and down a)** higher and lower 一上一下; 起伏地: *The crowd were jumping up and down and screaming excitedly.* 人羣跳上跳下, 激動得尖聲喊叫。| **look sb up and down** (=look at someone in order to judge their appearance or character) 上下打量某人; 審視 *Maisie looked her rival critically up and down.* 梅奇挑剔地上下打量着對手。**b)** backwards and forwards 來來回回; 往返地: *Ralph paced up and down the room looking agitated.* 拉爾夫在屋裡踱來踱去, 顯得焦慮不安。**15 up to a)** up to and including a certain amount or level 多達, 至多…: *Up to six people* (=any number between one and six) *can sleep in the caravan.* 篷車最多可以睡六個人。**b)** also 又作 **up till** if something happens up to a certain time, date etc it happens until that time〔時間上〕一直到: *She continued to care for her father up to the time of his death.* 她一直照顧父親直到他去世。**c)** clever, good, or well enough for a particular purpose or in order to do something 勝任〔工作等〕; 有資格做; 適於: *I'm afraid Tim just isn't up to the job* (=not good enough to do it properly). 我恐怕蒂姆幹不了這份工作。| *Gemma isn't really up to long walks at the moment* (=too ill to do them). 傑瑪眼下真的走不了這麼長的路。| **up to doing** *My German isn't up to translating that letter.* 我的德語還不足以翻譯那封信。**d)** if something is up to a particular standard it is good enough to reach that standard 達到〔標準〕: *The new CD is not up to the group's usual standard.* 新推出的雷射唱片沒有達到該演唱組通常的水準。**e)** doing something secret or something that you shouldn't be doing 幹祕密或不應該幹的事: *The children are very quiet; I wonder what they're up to.* 孩子們很安靜, 我不知道他們在搞甚麼鬼。| **up to no good** (=doing something wrong or illegal) 做壞事 *I'll bet that Joe and his mates are up to no good as usual.* 我敢肯定喬和他的同夥跟往常一樣在幹壞事。**16 it's up to you** *spoken* used to tell someone that they must make a decision themselves【口】由你作主, 取決於你: *"Shall we have red wine or white?" "It's up to you."* "我們要紅酒還是白酒?" "由你決定吧。" **17 up to your ears/eyes/neck in** *informal* deeply involved in a difficult or illegal situation【非正式】深陷於…; 埋頭於…: *Rona and Colin are up to their ears in debt* (=they owe a lot of money). 羅娜和科林債台高築。**18 up the workers!/up the reds! etc** *spoken* used to express support and encouragement for a particular group of people or for a sports team【口】工人加油! / 紅隊加油!

up² *prep* **1** towards or in a higher place 向[在]…上: *We climbed slowly up the hill.* 我們緩緩地爬上山。| *The water was getting up my nose.* 水嗆入我的鼻子裡。**2** towards or at the top or far end of 向[在]…頂上; 向[在]…的遠端: *Her office is up those stairs.* 她的辦公室在樓上。| *They live just up the road* (=further along the road from here). 他們就住在路的那一邊。**3** if you sail or go up a river you go towards its SOURCE¹ (4) 向…的上游: *a boat trip up the Bosphorus* 乘船逆博斯普魯斯而上 **4** *BrE spoken* used to mean to or at a particular place, although most people think this is incorrect【英口】到[在]…地方〔多數人認為此用法不正確〕: *Do you fancy going up the town?* 你想過到城裡去嗎? **5 up yours!** *spoken taboo* used to insult someone when they have done or said something that annoys you【口諱】去你的!〔用於被某人做的事或說的話激怒時〕: *"You'll never get promoted, you're not good enough." "Up yours!"* "你永遠別想得到提升, 你不夠資格。" "去你的!" 1 1

up³ *adj* **1** [not before noun 不用於名詞前] not in bed 起牀的, 沒睡覺的: *Are the kids still up?* 孩子們還沒睡嗎? **2** [not before noun 不用於名詞前] if a road is up, its surface is being repaired〔路面〕正在翻修的 **3** [not before noun 不用於名詞前] if a computer system is up, it is working〔電腦系統〕正在工作的, 運行的 —opposite 反義詞 DOWN³ (5) **4** [not before noun 不用於名詞前] if a number, level, or amount is up, it is higher than before〔數目、水平、數量〕上漲的: *Inflation is up by 2 %.* 通貨膨脹上漲2%。| [+on] *Profits are up on last year.* 利潤與去年比較增加了。| **two goals up/three points up** (=having two goals, three points etc more than your opponents) 領先兩球 / 三分 *United were a goal up at half time.* 聯隊在上半場結束時領先一球。**5** [not before noun 不用於名詞前] if a ball is up in tennis or similar sports, it has only hit the ground once and therefore can be hit back by the opponent〔網球等在被擊回前〕只落

地一次的 **6 be up and about** *informal* to be well enough to walk about and have a normal life after you have been in bed because of an illness or accident【非正式】病後能起牀走動 **7 be up to here (with)** *spoken* to be very upset and angry because of a particular situation or person【口】(對…) 感到氣憤: *I'm up to here with this job; I'm resigning!* 這份工作我幹夠了; 我要辭職! **8 be up and down** if someone is up and down, they sometimes feel well or happy and sometimes do not〔情緒〕波動不定: *Jason's been very up and down since his girlfriend left him.* 自從女朋友離開他以後, 賈森的情緒就很不穩定。**9 be up against** to have to deal with a difficult situation or fight an opponent 面臨, 必須對付〔困境或對手〕: *He came up against a lot of problems with his previous boss.* 上一個老闆給他不少麻煩。| **be up against it** *Murphy will be really up against it when he faces the reigning champion this afternoon.* 今天下午要面對本屆冠軍, 真夠墨菲受的。**10 be up before** *informal* to appear in a court of law because you have been accused of a crime【非正式】出庭受審: *He was up before the Magistrates court charged with grievous bodily harm.* 他被控犯有嚴重人身傷害罪而在地方法庭受審。**11 be up for a)** to be intended for a particular purpose 用於…的: *The house is up for sale.* 這房現供出售。| *Even the most taboo subjects were up for discussion.* 連最禁忌的話題也供討論了。**b)** to appear in a court of law because you have been accused of a crime〔因被控有罪而〕出庭受審: *Ron's up for drinking and driving next week.* 羅恩因酒後開車將於下週出庭受審。**12 be (well) up on/in/with** *informal* to know a lot about something【非正式】非常熟悉〔某事〕; 精通 **13** *spoken* if something is up, someone is feeling unhappy because they have problems, or there is something wrong in a situation【口】出事的; 發生不快的: *I could tell by the look on Joan's face that something was up.* 看瓊的臉色, 我就知道出事了。| **[+with]** *Is something up with Julie? She looks really miserable.* 朱莉出了甚麼事? 她看起來真的很痛苦。| **what's up?** *What's up? Why are you crying?* 怎麼啦? 你為甚麼哭? **14 not be up to much** *spoken* to not be of a very good quality or standard【口】不太好: *The food in that restaurant isn't up to much.* 那家餐館的飯菜不怎麼樣。**15** [not before noun 不用於名詞前] *informal* if a period of time is up, it is finished【非正式】到期的: *The President may be asked to resign before his four-year term is up.* 四年任期不到, 總統就可能被要求辭職。**16** [not before noun 不用於名詞前] *informal* when food or drink is up it is ready to be eaten or drunk【非正式】〔飯菜〕準備好的: *Dinner's up!* 晚飯準備好了! **17 be up and running** if a new system or process is up and running, it is working properly〔新系統、新程序〕運行正常: *The New York office was up and running in about half the time it took us in Paris.* 只用了我們在巴黎所花時間的一半, 紐約辦事處的工作就安排就緒了。**18 up to speed** knowing the necessary latest information or situation 跟上形勢, 不落伍: *getting top-level managers up to speed on developments in on-line services* 使高層管理人員掌握在線服務的最新發展

up⁴ *n* **1 be on an up** *spoken* to feel happy, especially after being upset and unhappy【口】開心〔尤指憂傷過後〕: *Kevin seems to be on an up at the moment; I hope it lasts.* 凱文眼下似乎很開心, 我希望這種好心情能保持下去。**2 ups and downs** *informal* the mixture of good and bad experiences that happen in any situation or relationship【非正式】盛衰; 浮沉; 苦樂: *We have our ups and downs like all couples.* 我們有苦有樂, 跟所有的夫妻一樣。**3 on the up and up** *informal*【非正式】**a)** *BrE* improving and becoming more successful, especially financially【英】〔尤指經濟上〕走上坡路, 蒸蒸日上 **b)** *AmE* not hiding anything; HONEST【美】坦誠的; 誠實的

up⁵ *v* **1** [T] to increase the amount or level of something 提高; 增加: *They've upped their offer by a further 5%.* 他們把出價又提高了5%。**2 up and ...** if you up and do something, you suddenly start to do something different or surprising 突然開始〔做某事〕: **up and leave** *Without saying another word, he upped and left.* 他沒再説一句話, 突然站起來走了。

up-and-com·ing /ˌ· · ˈ··◂/ *adj* [only before noun 僅用於名詞前] likely to be successful or popular 有希望的, 有前途的: *an up-and-coming band from Manchester* 來自曼徹斯特的大有前途的樂隊

up-and-un·der /ˌ· · ˈ··/ *n* [C] a situation in RUGBY when the ball is kicked forwards high into the air, and the players all rush towards the place where the ball lands〔橄欖球的〕過頂高球

up·beat /ˋʌpˏbit; ˈʌpbiːt/ *adj* cheerful and making you feel that good things will happen 樂觀的; 歡笑的: *a comedy film with an upbeat ending* 以皆大歡喜為結局的喜劇電影

up·braid /ʌpˋbred; ˌʌpˈbreɪd/ *v* [T] *formal* to tell someone angrily that they have done something wrong【正式】責備, 申斥〔某人〕

up·bring·ing /ˋʌpˏbrɪŋɪŋ; ˈʌpˌbrɪŋɪŋ/ *n* [singular] the care and training that parents give their children when they are growing up 撫育, 養育; 培養: *Mike had had a strict upbringing.* 邁克從小家教很嚴。

up·chuck /ˋʌpˏtʃʌk; ˈʌptʃʌk/ *v* [I] *AmE informal* to bring food or drink up from your stomach and out through your mouth because you are ill or drunk; VOMIT¹【美, 非正式】嘔吐

up·com·ing /ˋʌpˏkʌmɪŋ; ˈʌpˌkʌmɪŋ/ *adj* [only before noun 僅用於名詞前] happening soon 即將來臨的; 即將發生的: *the upcoming elections* 即將來臨的選舉

up·coun·try /ˌʌpˋkʌntrɪ; ˌʌpˈkʌntri◂/ *adj* from an area of land without many people or towns, especially in the middle of a country 來自內地的〔尤指一國的中部, 人或城鎮不多的地區〕: *upcountry people* 內地人 —**upcountry** *adv*

up·date¹ /ʌpˋdet; ʌpˈdeɪt/ *v* [T] **1** to add the most recent information to something 為…提供最新信息; 更新: *The files need updating.* 檔案需要更新。**2** to make something more modern in the way it looks or operates 使現代化

up·date² /ˋʌpdet; ˈʌpdeɪt/ *n* [C] the most recent news about something 最新消息: **[+on]** *the latest update on the Whitewater affair* 有關白水事件的最新消息

up·end /ˌʌpˋɛnd; ʌpˈend/ *v* [T] to turn something over so that it is standing upside down 顛倒, 倒放〔某物〕

up·front /ˌʌpˋfrʌnt; ˌʌpˈfrʌnt/ *adj* [not before noun 不用於名詞前] behaving or talking in a direct and honest way〔行為、談話〕坦率的, 誠實的: *Mo's very upfront with him about their relationship.* 莫在他們的關係上跟他很坦誠。—see also 另見 **up front** (FRONT¹ (15))

up·grade /ˌʌpˋgred; ˌʌpˈgreɪd/ *v* **1** [I,T] to make a computer or other machine better and able to do more things (使)〔電腦等〕升級 **2** [T] to give someone a more important job 提升〔某人〕, 給〔某人〕升職 **3** [T] to be given a better seat on a plane than the one you paid for 飛機座位提級, 升艙 —opposite 反義詞 DOWNGRADE —**upgrade** /ˋʌpgred; ˈʌpgreɪd/ *n* [C]

up·heav·al /ʌpˋhivḷ; ʌpˈhiːvəl/ *n* [C,U] **1** a very big change that often causes problems 激變, 劇變; 動亂: *political upheaval* 政治動亂 **2** a very strong movement upwards, especially of the earth〔尤指地的〕隆起

up·hill¹ /ˋʌpˈhɪl; ˌʌpˈhɪl◂/ *adj* **1** towards the top of a hill 上坡的, 上山的: *an uphill climb* 向山上爬 **2** an uphill battle, struggle, job etc is very difficult and needs a lot of effort〔戰鬥、鬥爭、工作等〕艱難的, 費力的

uphill² *adv* towards the top of a hill 往上坡; 往山上

up·hold /ʌpˋhold; ˌʌpˈhəʊld/ *v past tense and past participle* **upheld** /-ˋhɛld; -ˈheld/ [T] **1** to defend or support a law, system, or principle so that it is not made weaker 支持, 維護〔法規、制度或原則〕: *They want to uphold traditional family values.* 他們想堅持傳統的家庭價值觀念。**2** if a court upholds a decision made by another court, it states that the decision was correct〔法庭〕維持〔原判〕—**upholder** *n* [C]

up·hol·ster /ʌpˋholstɚ; ʌpˈhəʊlstə/ *v* [T] to cover a chair with material 為〔椅子〕裝墊子[套子] —**upholstered** *adj*

—**upholsterer** *n* [C]

up·hol·ster·y /ʌpˋholstərɪ; ʌpˈhəʊlstəri/ *n* [U] **1** material used to cover chairs 椅子套; 墊襯料 **2** the process of covering chairs with material 座椅的加套裝飾

up·keep /ˋʌpˌkip; ˈʌpkiːp/ *n* [U+**of**] the care needed to keep something in good condition 保養, 維修

up·lands /ˋʌpləndz; ˈʌpləndz/ *n plural* the parts of a country that are away from the sea and are higher than other areas 高地; 高原; 山地 —**upland** *adj*: *upland forests* 山地森林

up·lift[1] /ˋʌpˌlɪft; ˈʌplɪft/ *n* [U] a sudden happy feeling 振奮

up·lift[2] /ʌpˋlɪft; ʌpˈlɪft/ *v* [T] *formal*【正式】**1** to make someone feel more cheerful 使〔某人〕振奮, 鼓舞 **2** to make something higher 舉起, 抬起, 抬高〔某物〕

up·lift·ed /ʌpˋlɪftɪd; ʌpˈlɪftɪ̈d/ *adj* **1** feeling happier 振奮的 **2** *literary* raised upwards【文】被提[抬]起的

up·lift·ing /ʌpˋlɪftɪŋ; ʌpˈlɪftɪŋ/ *adj* making you feel more cheerful 令人振奮的

up·mar·ket /ˌʌpˋmɑrkɪt; ˌʌpˈmɑːkɪ̈t◂/ *adj* connected with people who belong to a high social class or who have a lot of money 適合高消費階層的; 高檔的; UPSCALE *AmE*【美】: *an upmarket fashion retailer* 高檔時裝零售商 —compare 比較 DOWNMARKET

up·on /əˋpɑn; əˈpɒn/ *prep formal*【正式】= on: *an honour bestowed upon the association* 授予該協會的榮譽 | *We are completely dependent upon your help.* 我們完全依賴你的幫助。—see also 另見 **once upon a time** (ONCE[1] (14)) —see picture on page A1 參見A1頁圖

up·per[1] /ˋʌpɚ; ˈʌpə/ *adj* [only before noun 僅用於名詞前] **1** in a higher position than something else〔位置〕較上的, 較高的, 上面的: *the upper lip* 上唇 **2** near or at the top of something 靠近頂部的; 在頂部的: *The monkeys live in the upper branches.* 猴子生活在靠近樹梢的樹枝上。**3 have/gain the upper hand** to have more power than someone else, so that you are able to control a situation 佔上風; 處於有利地位; 控制: *Police have gained the upper hand over the drug dealers in the area.* 警察打擊該地區的毒品販子, 處於上風。**4** more important than other parts or ranks in an organization, system etc 較高級的, 上級的: **the upper echelons** (=the most important and most senior members of an organization) 最高層 **5 the upper limit** the highest limit 上限, 最大限度: *sounds that are at the upper limit of our hearing capability* 處在我們聽力極限的聲音 **6** further from the sea or further north than other parts of an area 上游的; 北部的: **the upper reaches** (=the parts of a river that are the furthest from the sea) 上游 *the upper reaches of the Nile* 尼羅河的上游 —see also 另見 **keep a stiff upper lip** (STIFF[1] (9))

upper[2] *n* [C] **1** the top part of a shoe that covers your foot 鞋面, 鞋幫: *leather uppers* 皮鞋幫 —see picture at 參見 SHOE[1] 圖 **2 uppers** [plural] *slang* illegal drugs that make you feel happy and give you a lot of energy; AMPHETAMINE【俚】興奮劑; 安非他明 **3 be on your uppers** *BrE old-fashioned* to have very little money【英, 過時】一貧如洗

upper case /ˌ·· ˈ·◂/ *n* [U] *technical* letters written in capitals (A, B, C) rather than in small form (a, b, c)【術語】大寫字母

upper class /ˌ·· ˈ·◂/ *n* [C] **the upper class** the group of people who belong to the highest social class 上流社會, 上層社會: *upper class families* 上流階層家庭 —**upper class** *adj*

up·per·class·man /ˌʌpɚˋklæsmən; ˌʌpəˈklɑːsmən/ *n* [C] *AmE* a student in the last two years at a school or university【美】〔中學或大學的〕高年級學生 —compare 比較 UNDERCLASSMAN

up·per·class·wom·an /ˌʌpɚˋklæswʊmən; ˌʌpəˈklɑːswʊmən/ *n* [C] *AmE* a female student in the last two years of school or university【美】高年級女生

upper crust /ˌ·· ˈ·◂/ *n* [singular] *informal* the group of people who belong to the highest social class【非正式】上流社會, 上層社會 —**upper-crust** *adj*

up·per·cut /ˋʌpɚˌkʌt; ˈʌpəkʌt/ *n* [C] a way of hitting someone in which you swing your hand upwards into their chin 上鉤拳

Up·per House /ˌ·· ˈ·/ *n* [singular] a group of elected representatives in a country, that is smaller and less powerful than the country's LOWER HOUSE 上議院

up·per·most /ˋʌpɚˌmost; ˈʌpəməʊst/ *adj* **1 uppermost in your mind** if something is uppermost in your mind, you think about it a lot because it is very important to you 心目中最主要的: *It is Tom's safety that is uppermost in our minds.* 湯姆的安全是我們心中最牽掛的事。**2** more important than other things 最重要的, 壓倒一切的: *As he looked at her, curiosity was his uppermost feeling.* 他望着她時, 最主要的感覺是好奇。**3** higher than anything else 最高的: *the uppermost leaves on the tree* 樹上最高處的葉

upper school /ˈ·· ·/ *n* [C] the classes of a school in Britain that are for older pupils, usually aged 14 to 18〔英國學校中為14至18歲學生開設的〕大齡班

up·pi·ty /ˋʌpətɪ; ˈʌpɪ̈ti/ also 又作 **up·pish** /ˋʌpɪʃ; ˈʌpɪʃ/ *BrE*【英】*adj informal* behaving as if you are more important than you really are【非正式】傲慢的, 盛氣凌人的: *Now, don't start getting uppity with me, young man.* 好了, 別對我這麼傲慢, 年輕人。

up·right[1] /ˋʌpˌraɪt; ˈʌp-raɪt/ *adj* **1** standing straight up 垂直的, 筆直的 **2** always behaving in an honest way 正直的, 誠實的: *decent, upright citizens* 正派誠實的公民 —**uprightness** *n* [U]

upright[2] *adv* **1** sitting or standing with your back straight 筆直地: **sit/stand bolt upright** *He sat bolt upright, startled by the scream.* 他挺直地坐着, 被尖叫聲嚇呆了。**2** if something is pulled, held etc upright, it is put into a position in which it is standing straight up 豎直地

upright[3] *n* [C] a long piece of wood or metal that stands straight up and supports something〔木頭或金屬的〕直立支撐物

upright pi·an·o /ˌ·· ·ˈ··/ *n* [C] a piano with strings that are set in an up and down direction 豎[立]式鋼琴

up·ris·ing /ˋʌpˌraɪzɪŋ; ˈʌpˌraɪzɪŋ/ *n* [C] an occasion when a group of people use violence to try to change the rules, laws etc in an institution or country 起義, 暴動: *the 1956 Hungarian uprising* 1956年的匈牙利起義

up·riv·er /ˌʌpˋrɪvɚ; ˌʌpˈrɪvə/ *adv* away from the sea towards the place where a river begins 向上游; 從上游

up·roar /ˋʌpˌrɔr; ˈʌp-rɔː/ *n* [singular, U] a lot of noise or angry protest about something 喧囂; 吵鬧; 騷動: **be in an uproar** *The house was in an uproar, with babies crying and people shouting.* 房子裡嬰兒在哭, 人們在喊叫, 一片喧鬧。

up·roar·i·ous /ʌpˋrɔrɪəs; ʌpˈrɔːriəs/ *adj* very noisy, because a lot of people are laughing or shouting 喧鬧的, 人聲鼎沸的 —**uproariously** *adv*

up·root /ʌpˋrut; ˌʌpˈruːt/ *v* [T] **1** to pull a plant and its roots out of the ground 把〔植物〕連根拔起 **2** to make someone leave their home for a new place, especially when this is difficult or upsetting 使〔某人〕遷移他處居住: *My father was in the army, so every two years we were uprooted and moved again.* 我父親在軍隊中, 所以每隔兩年我們就要搬遷一次。

ups-a-dai·sy /ˋʌps ə ˋdezɪ; ˈʌps ə ˌdeɪzi/ *interjection* another spelling of OOPS-A-DAISY oops-a-daisy 的另一種拼法

up·scale /ˋʌpˌskel; ˈʌpskeɪl/ *adj AmE* connected with people from a high social class who have a lot of money; UPMARKET【美】適合高消費階層的, 高檔的

up·set[1] /ʌpˋsɛt; ʌpˈset/ *v past tense and past participle* **upset** [T] **1** to make someone feel unhappy or worried 使〔某人〕心煩意亂, 使生氣: *I'm sorry, I didn't mean to upset you.* 對不起, 我不是故意惹你不高興的。**2** to change a plan or situation in a way that causes problems 打亂, 攪亂〔計劃、形勢等〕: *The delicate ecological balance of the area was upset.* 該地區脆弱的生態平衡被打亂了。**3**

to push something over without intending to〔無意地〕打翻, 弄翻〔某物〕: *He upset a bottle of ink over the map.* 他把一瓶墨水打翻在地圖上。**4 upset sb's stomach** to make someone feel sick 使某人腸胃不適 **5 upset the apple cart** completely spoil someone's plans 破壞某人的計劃 —**upsetting** *adj*

up·set² /ˈʌpˌsɛt; ˈʌpset/ *n* **1** [C] an unexpected problem or difficulty 意外的挫折: *Despite this upset, the General decided to go ahead with the attack.* 儘管有此變故, 將軍還是決定發起攻擊。**2** an occasion when a person or team surprisingly beats a stronger opponent in a competition, election etc〔比賽、競選等中〕意外的擊敗: *It was a major upset when the young skater took the gold medal.* 那個年輕的滑冰選手奪得金牌, 這可真是個出乎意料的結果。**3 stomach/tummy upset** an illness that affects the stomach and makes you feel sick 腸胃/肚子不適 **4** [C,U] worry and unhappiness caused by an unexpected problem〔因意外問題引起的〕煩惱

up·set³ /ʌpˋsɛt; ˌʌpˈset◂/ *adj* **1** [not before noun 不用於名詞前] unhappy and worried because something unpleasant or disappointing has happened 不快的, 心煩意亂的, 煩惱的: **[+about/by/over etc]** *She was still upset about the argument she'd had with Harry.* 她依然為跟哈里發生的爭論而感到煩惱。| **upset that** *Dad was very upset that you didn't phone.* 你沒打電話來, 爸爸很不高興。**2 an upset stomach/tummy** an illness that affects the stomach and makes you feel sick 腸胃/肚子不適

up·shot /ˈʌpˌʃɑt; ˈʌpʃɒt/ *n* **the upshot (of)** the final result of a situation 結果, 結局: *The upshot was that Jane decided to leave home.* 結局是簡決定離家出走。

up·side¹ /ˈʌpˌsaɪd; ˈʌpsaɪd/ *n* [singular] *especially AmE* the positive part of a situation that is generally bad【尤美】〔不利局面中〕好的一面, 積極面: *The upside of the whole thing is that we got a free trip to Jamaica.* 整個事情的好處是我們免費去了一趟牙買加。

upside² *prep* **upside the head/face etc** *AmE informal* on the side of someone's head etc【美, 非正式】在頭/臉等的側面

up·side down /ˌ·· ˈ·/ *adv* **1** with the top at the bottom and the bottom at the top 倒置地, 顛倒地: *You've hung that picture upside down!* 你把那幅畫倒掛了! **2** disorganized or untidy 混亂地, 亂七八糟地 —see also 另見 **turn sth upside down** (TURN¹ (19b))

up·stage¹ /ˈʌpˋstedʒ; ˌʌpˈsteɪdʒ◂/ *v* [T] to do something that takes people's attention away from someone else who is more important 將他人注意力從〔某人〕引向自己; 搶〔更重要人物〕的鏡頭: *All the big name stars were upstaged by twelve-year-old Katy Rochford.* 所有的大明星都被十二歲的凱蒂·羅奇福特搶去了風頭。

upstage² *adv* towards the back of the stage in a theatre 朝着舞台後方 —**upstage** *adj*

2 **up·stairs¹** /ʌpˋstɛrz; ˌʌpˈsteəz◂/ *adv* **1** towards a higher floor in a building, using the stairs 往樓上: *Lucy came rushing upstairs after her sister.* 露西追着妹妹跑上樓。—opposite 反義詞 DOWNSTAIRS (1) **2** on an upper floor in a building, especially a house 在樓上: *My office is upstairs on the right.* 我的辦公室在樓上的右邊。—compare 比較 DOWNSTAIRS (1) —see also 另見 **kick sb upstairs** (KICK¹ (10)) —**upstairs** *adj*: *an upstairs window* 樓上的窗戶

upstairs² *n* [singular] **1 the upstairs** one or all of the upper floors in a building 樓層 **2 not have much upstairs** to not be very intelligent 不太有頭腦 **3 the man upstairs** *informal* God【非正式】上帝

up·stand·ing /ʌpˋstændɪŋ; ˌʌpˈstændɪŋ/ *adj formal*【正式】**1** honest and responsible 誠實的, 正直的: *an upstanding citizen* 正直的公民 **2** tall and strong 高大強壯的

up·start /ˈʌpˌstɑrt; ˈʌpstɑːt/ *n* [C] someone who is new in their job and behaves as if they are more important than they really are 暴發戶; 新貴; 自命不凡的傢伙: *an impudent young upstart* 粗魯無禮的年輕新貴 —**upstart** *adj*

up·state /ˈʌpˌstet; ˈʌpsteɪt/ *adj AmE* [only before noun 僅用於名詞前] in the northern part of a particular state【美】州的北部地區的: *upstate New York* 紐約州的北部地區 —**upstate** *adv*

up·stream /ˈʌpˋstrim; ˌʌpˈstriːm◂/ *adv* along a river, in the opposite direction from the way the water is flowing 向上游; 逆流(地) —**upstream** *adj* —opposite 反義詞 DOWNSTREAM

up·surge /ˈʌpsɝdʒ; ˈʌpsɜːdʒ/ *n* [C] **1** a sudden increase 猛增, 急劇上升: **[+in]** *There's been an upsurge in complaints about the police.* 對警察的投訴猛然增多。**2** sudden strong feelings〔情緒的〕高漲, 激發: **[+of]** *Adolescence is marked by an upsurge of sexual feeling.* 青春期的特點是性感覺驟增。

up·swing /ˈʌpˌswɪŋ; ˈʌpˌswɪŋ/ *n* [C] an improvement or increase in the level of something 進步; 改進; 改善; 上升: *an upswing in the economy* 經濟的回升

up·take /ˈʌpˌtek; ˈʌpteɪk/ *n* **1 be slow/quick on the uptake** *informal* to be slow or fast at learning or understanding things【非正式】領會[理解]慢/快 **2** [C,U] *technical* the rate at which a substance is taken into a system, machine etc【術語】吸收, 攝取(率): *the uptake of food and oxygen into an organism* 有機體對食物和氧氣的吸收

up·tem·po /ˌ· ˈ··◂/ *adj* moving or happening at a fast rate 快速度的: *music with an up-tempo beat* 快節奏的音樂

up·tight /ˈʌpˌtaɪt; ˈʌptaɪt/ *adj informal* behaving in an angry way because you are feeling nervous and worried【非正式】〔行為因緊張不安而〕憤怒的

up-to-date /ˌ· · ˈ·◂/ *adj* **1** modern or fashionable 現代的; 時髦的: *up-to-date ideas on education* 有關教育的現代理念 | **bring sth up-to-date** (=make something more modern) 使某事物更新潮 **2** including all the newest information 包含最新信息的: *up-to-date news* 最新消息 | *an up-to-date map* 包含最新資料的地圖 | **keep/bring sb up-to-date** (=give someone all the newest information about something) 給某人提供〔有關某事物的〕全部最新信息

up-to-the-min·ute /ˌ· · · ˈ··◂/ *adj* **1** including all the newest information 包含最新信息的: *up-to-the-minute financial information* 最新金融信息 **2** very modern or fashionable 最新式的; 最時髦的

up·town /ˈʌpˌtaun; ˌʌpˈtaʊn◂/ *adv AmE* towards the northern areas of a city, especially the areas where people have more money【美】向城市的北部〔尤指有錢人的住宅區〕—**uptown** *adj*: *an uptown bar* 非商業區酒吧 —**uptown** *n* [U]

up·trend /ˈʌpˌtrɛnd; ˈʌptrend/ *n* [C] a period of time when business or economic activity increases〔經濟方面〕向上[好轉]的趨勢

up·turn /ˈʌpˌtɝn; ˈʌptɜːn/ *n* [C] an increase in the level of something 好轉; 上升, 提高: **[+in]** *an upturn in the housing market* 房產市場的好轉

up·turned /ˌʌpˋtɝnd; ˈʌptɜːnd◂/ *adj* **1** turning upwards at the end 朝上翹的, 向上翻的: *an upturned nose* 翹鼻子 **2** turned upside down 翻轉的, 倒置的: *upturned tables* 翻轉的桌子

up·ward /ˈʌpwɚd; ˈʌpwəd/ *adj* [only before noun 僅用於名詞前] **1** moving or pointing towards a higher position 向上的: *an upward movement of the hand* 手的向上運動 **2** increasing to a higher level 升高的, 上升的: *the upward trend in house prices* 房價的上升趨勢 —opposite 反義詞 DOWNWARD

upwardly mo·bile /ˌ··· ˈ··/ *adj* moving up through the social classes and becoming richer 向較高社會階層流動的, 向上爬的 —**upward mobility** *n* [U]

up·wards /ˈʌpwɚdz; ˈʌpwədz/ also 又作 **upward** *adv AmE*【美】**1** moving or pointing towards a higher position 向上, 朝上: *Hold the gun so that it points upwards.* 握住槍, 使槍口朝上。—opposite 反義詞 DOWNWARDS **2** increasing to a higher level 上升: *Salary scales have been moving steadily upwards.* 薪金級別一直在穩步上升。—opposite 反義詞 DOWNWARDS **3** more than a particular amount, time etc〔數量、時間等〕...以上: *children of 14* *and upwards* 14歲及14歲以上的兒童 | **upwards of** *informal*【非正式】*The waiting time for an operation can be upwards of two years.* 等待手術的時間可達兩年以上。

u·ra·ni·um /ju`reniəm; jʊˈreɪniəm/ *n* [U] a heavy white metal that is an ELEMENT (=simple substance), is RADIOACTIVE, and is used to produce NUCLEAR power and weapons 鈾(元素)

U·ra·nus /`jurənəs; ˈjʊərənəs/ *n* [singular] **1** the PLANET seventh in order from the sun 天王星〔太陽系第七個行星〕—see picture at 參見 SOLAR SYSTEM 圖 **2** the ruler of the universe, in ancient Greek stories 烏拉諾斯〔古希臘神話中的宇宙的統治者〕

ur·ban /`ɝbən; ˈɜːbən/ *adj* [only before noun 僅用於名詞前] connected with a town or city 城市的, 都市的: *urban crime* 城市犯罪 | *the urban population* 城市人口

ur·bane /ɝ`ben; ɜːˈbeɪn/ *adj* behaving in a relaxed and confident way in social situations 溫文爾雅的, 彬彬有禮的: *Garroway's easy, urbane charm* 蓋洛韋從容而溫文爾雅的魅力 —**urbanely** *adv* —**urbanity** *n* [U]

ur·ban·ize also 又作 **-ise** *BrE*【英】/`ɝbən,aɪz; ˈɜːbənaɪz/ *v* [T] to build houses, towns etc in the countryside 使城市化, 使都市化 —**urbanization** /,ɝbənə`zeʃən; ,ɜːbənaɪˈzeɪʃən/ *n* [U]

urban myth /,.. ˈ./ *n* [C] a well-known story that many people believe, about an unusual or terrible event that has happened to an ordinary person 都市神話〔指發生在普通人身上的不尋常或恐怖的事〕

urban re·new·al /,.. .ˈ../ *n* [U] the process of improving poor city areas by building new houses, shops etc 舊城區改建, 城市更新[美化]

urban sprawl /,.. ˈ./ *n* [U] the spread of city buildings and houses into an area that was countryside 城區〔向鄉村的〕擴展

ur·chin /`ɝtʃɪn; ˈɜːtʃɪ̩n/ *n* [C] *old-fashioned* a small dirty untidy child【過時】衣衫髒亂的小孩 —see also 另見 SEA URCHIN

Ur·du /`ɝdu; ˈʊəduː/ *n* [U] the official language of Pakistan, also used in India 烏爾都語〔巴基斯坦的官方語言, 也通行於印度〕

-ure /jɚ; jə/ *suffix* [in nouns 構成名詞] the action of doing something, or condition of being treated in a particular way 表示"動作"或"動作之結果": *the closure* (=closing) *of the factory* 工廠的關閉 | *exposure* 暴露; 曝光

u·re·thra /ju`riθrə; jʊˈriːθrə/ *n* [C] *technical* the tube through which waste liquid flows from your BLADDER and through which the SEMEN of males flows【術語】尿道

urge¹ /ɝdʒ; ɜːdʒ/ *v* [T] **1** to strongly advise someone to do something 催促, 力勸〔某人〕: **urge sb to do sth** *Brown urged her to reconsider her decision.* 布朗極力勸說她重新考慮她的決定。| **urge that** *I urge that you read this report carefully.* 我勸你仔細看看這份報告。**2** *formal* to strongly suggest that something should be done【正式】極力主張; 強調; 強烈要求: *The UN has urged restraint in the current crisis.* 聯合國極力主張在當前危機中要保持克制。| **urge sth on/upon sb** *This course of action was urged upon us by all parties.* 這個行動是各方力促我們作出的。**3** [always+adv/prep] to make someone or something move by shouting, pushing them etc 推進; 驅策: **urge sb/sth into/forward** *Daniel urged the horses forward with a whip.* 丹尼爾用馬鞭策馬前進。

urge sb ↔ **on** *phr v* [T] to encourage a person or animal to work harder, go faster etc 激勵〔人〕; 驅策〔動物〕: *Urged on by the crowd, the Italian team scored two more goals.* 受到觀眾的激勵, 意大利隊又進了兩球。

urge² *n* [C] a strong wish or need 強烈的慾望; 迫切的要求; 衝動: *sexual urges* 性衝動 | **urge to do sth** *I felt a sudden urge to scream.* 我突然很想大聲喊叫。

ur·gent /`ɝdʒənt; ˈɜːdʒənt/ *adj* **1** very important and needing to be dealt with immediately 緊急的, 急迫的, 需迅速處理的: *an urgent message* 緊急的消息 | **be in urgent need of** *in urgent need of medical attention* 急需醫療 **2** *formal* done or said in a way that shows that you want something to be dealt with immediately【正式】強求的; 急切的: *an urgent whisper* 急切的私語 —**urgency** *n* [U]: *a matter of great urgency* 極為迫切的問題 —**urgently** *adv*

u·ric /`jurɪk; ˈjʊərɪk/ *adj* related to URINE 尿的

u·ri·nal /`jurənḷ; ˈjʊərɪ̩nəl/ *n* [C] **1** a type of toilet that men use that is fixed onto the wall〔附牆的〕男用小便盤 **2** a building or room containing urinals 小便處[所]

u·ri·na·ry /`jurə,nɛrɪ; ˈjʊərɪ̩nəri/ *adj technical* connected with urine or the parts of your body through which urine passes【術語】尿的; 泌尿器官的

u·ri·nate /`jurə,net; ˈjʊərɪ̩neɪt/ *v* [I] *technical* to make urine flow out of your body【術語】排尿 —**urination** /,jurə`neʃən; juərɪ̩ˈneɪʃən/ *n* [U]

u·rine /`jurɪn; ˈjʊərɪ̩n/ *n* [U] the liquid waste that comes out of your body when you go to the toilet 尿

urn /ɝn; ɜːn/ *n* [C] **1** a decorated container, especially one that is used for holding the ashes (ASH (3)) of a dead body 甕;〔尤指〕骨灰甕 **2** a metal container that holds a large amount of tea or coffee〔金屬的〕大茶壺; 大咖啡壺

US /,ju `ɛs; ,juː ˈes◂/ *n* also 又作 **USA** /,ju ɛs `e; ,juː es ˈeɪ◂/ the United States of America 美國 —**US** *adj*: *the US Navy* 美國海軍

us /əs; əs, *strong* 強讀 ʌs; ʌs/ *pron* **1** the object form of 'we' we (我們) 的受格: *Do you think Dave saw us?* 你認為戴夫看見我們了嗎? | *The house is too small for us now.* 這房子現在對我們來說太小了。| *Emilio bought us a drink.* 埃米里奧請我們喝一杯。**2** *BrE spoken* used instead of 'me', although most people think this incorrect【英口】我〔用於代替 me, 然而多數人認為這種用法不正確〕: *Give us a kiss.* 吻我一下。| *Lend us a pound, will you?* 借我一英鎊好嗎? —see 見 ME (USAGE) [S1] [W1]

us·a·ble /`juzəbḷ; ˈjuːzəbl/ *adj* something that is usable is in a suitable state to be used 可用的

us·age /`jusɪdʒ; ˈjuːsɪdʒ/ *n* **1** [C,U] the way that words are used in a language〔語言的〕慣用法: *a book on modern English usage* 關於當代英語用法的書 **2** [U] the way in which something is used, or the amount of it that is used 使用方法; 使用量

use¹ /juz; juːz/ *v* [T] [S1] [W1]

1 ▶USE STH 使用某物◀ if you use a particular tool, method, service, ability etc, you do something with that tool, by means of that method etc, for a particular purpose 用; 使用; 應用: *Can I use your phone?* 我可以用一下你的電話嗎? | *More people are using the library than ever before.* 使用圖書館的人比以往多。| *I can't tell you what to do – you must use your own discretion.* 我不能告訴你要做甚麼——你必須運用你自己的判斷力。| **use sth for doing sth** *We use this room for keeping all our junk in.* 我們用這房間存放所有的廢舊雜物。| **use sth as** *My mother uses old socks as dusters.* 我母親用舊襪子當抹布。| **use force** (=use violent methods) 使用武力

2 ▶AMOUNT OF STH 某物的數額◀ to take something from a supply of food, gas, money etc with the result that there is less left 耗費, 消費〔某物〕: *We use about £40 worth of electricity a month.* 我們每月耗去大約價值40英鎊的電。

3 ▶USE A PERSON 利用人◀ to make someone do something for you in order to get something you want 利用〔某人〕: **use sb to do sth** *Smugglers use innocent people to carry drugs through customs.* 走私販子利用無辜的人把毒品帶過海關。| **use sb for your own ends** *Gerald had been using her for his own ends.* 傑拉爾德一直在利用她來達到自己的目的。

4 ▶AN ADVANTAGE 優勢◀ to take advantage of a situation 利用〔優勢〕: **use sth for** *Gordon used his family's wealth for his own publicity.* 戈登利用家財使自己出名。| **use sth to do sth** *She used her position as manager to get jobs for her friends.* 她利用自己的經理職位為朋友謀職。

5 could use *spoken* if you say you could use something, you mean you would really like to have it【口】想要; 真想: *I could use a drink.* 我真想喝一杯。

6 ▶PRODUCT 產品◀ to buy a particular product regularly 定期購買〔某商品〕: *I always use the same deodorant.* 我總是用同一種除臭劑。
7 ▶WORD 言詞◀ to say or write a particular word or phrase 使用〔詞語〕: *an expression that would never be used in polite conversation* 從來不在禮貌談話中使用的用語
8 ▶DRUGS 毒品◀ to regularly take illegal drugs 吸食〔毒品〕
9 ▶NAME 名字◀ to call yourself by a name that is not yours in order to keep your name secret 用〔假名〕: *Grant had checked into a Miami hotel using a false name.* 格蘭特用假名入住邁阿密的一家旅館。

use sth ↔ **up** *phr v* [T] to use all of something 用完, 用光: *Don't use up all the hot water.* 別把熱水都用完。

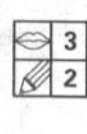
use² /jus; juːs/ *n* **1** [C] a way in which something can be used, or a purpose for which it can be used 用法; 用途: *Robots have many different uses in modern industry.* 機器人在現代工業中有許多不同的用途。**2** [singular, U] the act of using something or the amount that is used 使用; 用量: **[+of]** *the increasing use of computers in education* 教育上電腦的使用日益增多 | *the poet's use of metaphor* 詩人對隱喻的使用 **3 make use of** to use something that is available in order to achieve something or get an advantage for yourself 利用, 使用: *Not enough people are making use of the children's play scheme.* 沒有足夠的人使用兒童娛樂計劃。| *The artist makes use of scrap iron in her sculpture.* 那位藝術家把廢鐵使用在其雕塑中。| **make good use of** (=get as much advantage as possible from something) 充分利用 *We must make the best possible use of the resources we have.* 我們必須充分利用我們現有的資源。**4 put sth to (good) use** to use knowledge, skills etc for a particular purpose (好好) 利用: *an opportunity to put her medical training to good use* 讓她所受的醫學培訓能派上用場的機會 **5** [U] the ability or right to use something 運用能力; 使用權: *Joe's given me the use of his office till he gets back.* 喬讓我使用他的辦公室直到他回來。| *He lost the use of both legs as a result of the accident.* 他因事故而雙腿殘廢了。**6 be no use** also 又作 **be of no use** *formal* to be completely useless【正式】沒用處: *This map's no use – it doesn't show the minor roads.* 這張地圖沒用 ── 它沒有標明小路。| **be (of) no use to sb** *Have this sweater – it's of no use to me any more.* 帶上這件毛線衫吧 ── 我用不着了。**7 it's no use doing sth** *spoken* used to tell someone not to do something because it will have no effect【口】做某事沒用: *It's no use arguing with her – she won't listen.* 跟她爭論沒有用 ── 她不會聽的。**8 it's no use!** *spoken* used to say that you are going to stop doing something because you do not think it will be successful【口】白搭!〔用於表示停止做某事因認為不會成功〕: *Oh, it's no use! I can't fix it.* 唉, 算了吧! 我修不好它。**9 what's the use (of)?** *spoken* used to say that something seems to be a waste of time【口】(...) 有甚麼用?〔用於表示做某事是浪費時間〕: *What's the use of getting so angry?* 生這麼大氣有甚麼用? **10 be in use** a machine, place etc that is in use is being used〔機器、場所等〕在使用中: *All the machines are in use at the moment.* 眼下所有的機器都在使用中。**11 for the use of** provided for a particular person or group of people to use 供...用: *This parking lot is for the use of employees only.* 本停車場僅供員工使用。**12 come into use/go out of use** to start or stop being used 開始使用/停止使用: *New printing techniques have recently come into use.* 新的印刷技術最近開始投入使用。**13 out of use** a machine, place etc that is out of use is not being used〔機器、場所等〕廢棄不用, 不再使用 **14 be of use** *formal* to be useful【正式】有用: *I wondered if this book might be of use to you.* 我不知道這本書對你是否有用。**15 have no use for** to have no respect for someone or something 厭惡, 不喜歡: *She has no use for people who are always complaining.* 她討厭老是抱怨的人。**16 he/she/it has its uses** *spoken often humorous* used to say that something or someone can sometimes be useful【口, 常幽默】他/她/它自有其用處 **17** [C] one of the meanings of a word, or the way that a particular word is used〔某個詞的〕(一項) 詞義; 用法

use³ *v negative form of* **usedn't, usen't** *old-fashioned BrE*【過時, 英】**used to do sth** if something used to happen, it happened regularly or all the time in the past, but does not happen now 過去常做某事: *I used to go to the cinema a lot, but I never get the time now.* 我過去常看電影, 但現在根本沒有時間看了。| *Beth used to like rock 'n' roll when she was young.* 貝思年輕時喜歡搖滾樂。| **used to** *"Do you play golf?" "No, but I used to."* "你打高爾夫球嗎?" "不打, 但過去常打。" | **did not use to** also 又作 **used not to** *BrE old-fashioned*【英, 過時】過去不: *I'm surprised to see you smoking. You didn't use to.* 看見你抽煙我很驚訝。你過去是不抽的。| *The shops usedn't to open on Sundays.* 這些商店過去在星期天是不營業的。| **used to be** (=something was true in the past but is not true now) 過去是 *She used to be such a happy lively girl.* 她過去可是個活潑快樂的姑娘。| **did there use to be?** also 又作 **used there to be?** *formal*【正式】過去有嗎?: *Did there use to be a hotel on that corner?* 過去那個拐角處有家旅館嗎?

used /just; juːst/ *adj* **be used to** to have experienced something so that it no longer seems surprising, difficult, strange etc 習慣於〔某事物〕: *Lady Whitton wasn't used to people disagreeing with her.* 惠頓夫人不習慣別人跟她意見相左。| **get used to** *I'm sure I'll get used to the hard work.* 我肯定會習慣這項艱苦的工作。

used /juzd; juːzd/ *adj* **1 used cars/clothes etc** cars, clothes etc that have already had an owner; SECOND-HAND 舊汽車/衣服等: *a used car salesman* 二手車推銷員 **2** dirty as a result of use 用髒了的: *a used tissue* 髒紙巾

use·ful /ˈjusfəl; ˈjuːsfəl/ *adj* **1** helping you to do or get what you want 有用的; 有益的: *useful information* 有用的信息 | *Dean's a really useful person to have around when things go wrong.* 遇上甚麼事時, 迪安確實是個好幫手。| **useful to sb** *information that may be useful to the enemy* 可能對敵人有用的情報 | **useful for sth** *These yellow stickers are useful for leaving messages.* 這些黃色黏貼標籤可用於留言。| **prove useful** (=be useful in a particular situation) 派上用場 *Clive's experience in the building trade proved useful for re-roofing the garage.* 克萊夫在建築業的經歷在給車庫換屋頂時派上了用場。| **make yourself useful** (=help someone) (給人) 幫忙 *Can I do anything to make myself useful?* 我能幫上甚麼忙嗎? | **come in useful** (=be useful in a particular situation) 用得着 *Keep that, it might come in useful later.* 留着那東西, 也許以後用得上。**2** *BrE informal* satisfactory【英, 非正式】令人滿意的: *The England cricket team scored quite a useful total.* 英格蘭板球隊的總得分很令人滿意。—**usefully** *adv*

use·ful·ness /ˈjusfəlnɪs; ˈjuːsfəlnɪ̈s/ *n* [U] the state of being useful 有用; 實用性: **outlive its usefulness** (=not be useful any more) 不再有用

use·less /ˈjuslɪs; ˈjuːsləs/ *adj* **1** not useful or effective in any way 無用的; 無效的: *This bag is useless – it has a hole in it.* 這個袋子沒用了 ── 上面有個洞。| *a useless piece of information* 一則無用的情報 | **completely/totally/utterly useless** *At that time, art was considered a completely useless activity.* 那時, 藝術被認為是一項全然無用的活動。| **useless for** *It's a nice watch, but it's useless for scuba diving.* 手錶挺好看, 但戴水肺潛水時不能用。| **it is useless to do sth** *It was useless to complain.* 抱怨是沒有用的。**2** *informal* unable or unwilling to do anything properly【非正式】差勁的, 無能的: *Don't ask Tim to fix it. He's completely useless.* 別叫蒂姆來修理, 他根本不行。—**uselessly** *adv* —**uselessness** *n* [U]

us·er /ˈjuzɚ; ˈjuːzə/ *n* [C] someone or something that uses a product, service etc 使用者, 用戶: *road users* 道路使用者 —see also 另見 END USER

user fee /ˈ· · ˌ·/ *n* [C] *AmE* a tax on a service provided for the public【美】使用費〔一種服務稅〕

user friend·ly /ˌ·· ˈ··◂/ *adj* easy to use or operate 易使用[操作]的: *a user friendly guide to computing* 電腦操作便利指南 —**user-friendliness** *n* [U]

user in·ter·face /ˌ·· ˈ···/ *n* [C] the part of a computer PROGRAM or SOFTWARE package that contains the commands and operations for the person using the computer〔電腦〕用戶接口, 使用者界面

ush·er¹ /ˋʌʃɚ; ˈʌʃə/ *n* [C] **1** someone who shows people to their seats at a theatre, cinema, wedding etc〔劇院、戲院、婚禮等的〕引座員, 迎賓員, 招待員 **2** *BrE* someone who works in a law court whose job is to make sure there is no trouble【英】〔法院的〕庭警

usher² *v* [T] to help someone to get from one place to another, especially by showing them the way 引, 領; 招待: **usher sb into/to** *The guard ushered him into the room.* 警衛領他進入房間。

usher in sth *phr v* [T] to be the start of something new 宣告, 開創: *The Stockholm Conference ushered in a new era of international co-operation.* 斯德哥爾摩會議開創了國際合作的新紀元。

ush·er·ette /ˌʌʃɚˋɛt; ˌʌʃəˈret/ *n* [C] *especially BrE* a woman who works in a cinema, showing people to their seats【尤英】〔電影院的〕女引座員, 女服務員

usu the written abbreviation of 縮寫= USUALLY

u·su·al /ˋjuʒʊəl; ˈjuːʒuəl/ *adj* **1** the same as what happens most of the time or in most situations 通常的; 慣常的; 平常的: *I'll meet you at the usual time.* 我將在往常一樣的時間見你。| *Gina was her usual cheerful self.* 吉娜跟以前一樣快樂。| **it is usual for sb to do sth** *Is it usual for lectures to start so early?* 講座通常這麼早就開始嗎? | **better/more etc than usual** *It seemed colder than usual in the house.* 房子裡似乎比平時冷。**2 as usual** in the way that happens or exists most of the time 像往常一樣, 照例: *As usual, they'd left the children at home with Susan.* 像往常一樣, 他們把孩子留在家裡跟蘇珊在一起。**3 as per usual** *spoken* used to say that something bad that often happens has just happened again【口】〔壞事〕照常發生: *Matthew was drunk as per usual.* 馬修像往常一樣又喝醉了。**4 the usual** *spoken* the drink that you usually have【口】常喝的飲料

u·su·al·ly /ˋjuʒʊəlɪ; ˈjuːʒuəli/ *adv* used when describing what happens on most occasions or in most situations 通常地; 慣常地, 平常地: *I'm usually in bed by 11.30.* 我通常11:30以前上牀睡覺。| *Women usually live longer than men.* 女人通常比男人長壽。—see picture at 參見 FREQUENCY 圖

u·sur·er /ˋjuʒərɚ; ˈjuːʒərə/ *n* [C] *formal* someone who lends money to people and makes them pay too high a rate of INTEREST¹ (4)【正式】放高利貸者

u·su·ri·ous /juˋʒʊrɪəs; juːˈzjʊəriəs/ *adj formal* a usurious price or rate of INTEREST¹ (4) is unfairly high【正式】〔價格或利息〕過高的

u·surp /juˋzɝp; juːˈzɜːp/ *v* [T] *formal* to take someone else's power, position, job etc when you do not have the right to【正式】篡奪, 奪取〔權力、地位、工作等〕: *his deep jealousy at the thought of another man usurping his role as father* 想到另一個人奪走他身為父親的角色時他那深深的嫉妒 —**usurper** *n* [C] —**usurpation** /ˌjuzɚˋpeʃən; ˌjuːzɜːˈpeɪʃən/ *n* [U]

u·su·ry /ˋjuʒərɪ; ˈjuːʒəri/ *n* [U] *formal* the practice of lending money to people and making them pay unfairly high rates of INTEREST¹ (4)【正式】放高利貸

u·ten·sil /juˋtɛnsḷ; juːˈtensəl/ *n* [C] a tool or object with a particular use, especially in cooking 器皿, 用具〔尤指烹調用具〕: *kitchen utensils* 廚房用具

u·te·rus /ˋjutərəs; ˈjuːtərəs/ *n plural* **uteri** /-raɪ; -raɪ/ or **uteruses** [C] *technical* the organ in a woman or female MAMMAL where babies develop; WOMB【術語】子宮 —**uterine** /-raɪn; -raɪn/ *adj*

u·til·i·tar·i·an /ˌjutɪləˋtɛrɪən; juːˌtɪlə̇ˈteəriən/ *adj* **1** *formal* useful and practical rather than being used for decoration【正式】有用的; 實用的: *ugly utilitarian buildings* 醜陋但實用的建築物 **2** *technical* based on a belief in utilitarianism【術語】功利主義的; 實利主義的 —compare 比較 MATERIALISTIC

u·til·i·tar·i·an·is·m /ˌjutɪləˋtɛrɪənɪzṃ; juːˌtɪlə̇ˈteəriənɪzəm/ *n* [U] *technical* the belief that an action is good if it helps the greatest possible number of people【術語】功利主義; 實利主義

u·til·i·ty /juˋtɪlətɪ; juːˈtɪlə̇ti/ *n* **1** [usually plural 一般用複數] *especially AmE* a service such as gas or electricity provided for people to use【尤美】公用事業〈如煤氣、電力等〉: *Does your rent include utilities?* 你的房租包括公用事業費嗎? **2** [U] *formal* the amount of usefulness that something has【正式】效用, 實用

utility pole /·ˈ··· ˌ·/ *n* [C] *AmE* a tall wooden pole for supporting telephone and electric wires【美】〔木製〕電線杆

utility room /·ˈ··· ˌ·/ *n* [C] a room in a house where washing machines, FREEZERs etc are kept〔放置洗衣機、冰箱等的〕雜用室, 家用器具存放室

u·til·ize also 又作 **-ise** *BrE*【英】/ˋjutḷˌaɪz; ˈjuːtə̇laɪz/ *v* [T] *formal* to use something effectively【正式】利用, 使用: *a heating system that utilizes solar energy* 利用太陽能的供暖系統 —**utilizable** *adj* —**utilization** /ˌjutḷaɪˋzeʃən; ˌjuːtə̇laɪˈzeɪʃən/ *n* [U]

ut·most¹ /ˋʌtˌmost; ˈʌtməʊst/ *adj* **the utmost importance/respect/care etc** the greatest possible importance etc 極度的重要/尊敬/關心等: *a matter of the utmost importance* 極重要的事情

utmost² *n* [singular] **1** the most that can be done 極度, 極限, 最大可能: *Both runners had pushed themselves to the utmost.* 兩個賽跑運動員都盡了最大努力。**2 do your utmost** to try as hard as you can to achieve something 竭盡全力: *We've done our utmost to make the process as simple as possible.* 為使工序盡可能簡單, 我們已盡了全力。

u·to·pi·a /juˋtopɪə; juːˈtəʊpiə/ *n* [C,U] an imaginary perfect world where everyone is happy 烏托邦〔想像中的完美世界〕—**utopian** *adj*

ut·ter¹ /ˋʌtɚ; ˈʌtə/ *adj* [only before noun 僅用於名詞前] **utter failure/rubbish/fool etc** a complete failure etc 徹頭徹尾的失敗/廢物/傻瓜等: *What an utter waste of time!* 完全是浪費時間! | *We all watched in utter amazement.* 我們都萬分驚奇地看着。

utter² *v* [T] *formal or literary*【正式或文】**1** to make a sound with your voice, especially with difficulty〔吃力地〕發出〔聲音〕: *The wounded prisoner uttered a groan.* 受傷的囚犯發出一聲呻吟。**2** to say things 講; 説出: *Uttering a stream of filthy curses, Medlock stomped away.* 梅德洛克不乾不淨地咒罵了一通後, 跺着腳走了。

ut·ter·ance /ˋʌtərəns; ˈʌtərəns/ *n formal*【正式】**1** [C] something you say 言論, 言辭: *Politicians are judged by their public utterances.* 人們根據政治家公開的言論來評判他們。**2 give utterance to** to express something in words〔用言辭〕表達 **3** [U] the action of saying something 發聲; 説話; 表達

ut·ter·ly /ˋʌtɚlɪ; ˈʌtəli/ *adv* completely or totally 完全地, 十足地: *You look utterly miserable.* 你看起來難受極了。

ut·ter·most /ˋʌtɚˌmost; ˈʌtəməʊst/ *adj literary or formal* UTMOST¹【文或正式】極度的

U-turn /ˋjuˌtɝn; ˈjuː tɜːn/ *n* [C] **1** a turn that you make in a car, on a bicycle etc, so that you go back in the direction you came from〔汽車、自行車等的〕U形轉彎, 180度掉頭 **2** *informal* a complete change of ideas, plans etc【非正式】〔觀念、計劃等的〕徹底改變, 180度大轉變: *a government U-turn on economic policy* 政府在經濟政策上180度的大改變

u·vu·la /ˋjuvjələ; ˈjuːvjə̇lə/ *n* [C] *technical* a small soft piece of flesh which hangs down from the top of your mouth at the back【術語】懸雍垂, 小舌

u·vu·lar /ˋjuvjəlɚ; ˈjuːvjə̇lə/ *n* [C] a CONSONANT sound that you make with the back of your tongue touching, or nearly touching, your uvula〔輔音的〕小舌音 —**uvular** *adj*

V,v

V, v /vi; viː/ **1** *plural* **V's, v's** the 22nd letter of the English alphabet 英語字母表的第二十二個字母 **2** the number 5 in the system of ROMAN NUMERALS〔羅馬數字的〕5

V *n* [C usually singular 一般用單數] something that has a shape like the letter V V字形物: *She cut the material into a V.* 她把材料裁成V字形。

v 1 the written abbreviation of 縮寫= VERB **2** *informal*【非正式】the written abbreviation of 縮寫= VERY

v. the British abbreviation of 英國英語縮寫= VERSUS, used when talking about games in which two teams or players play against each other, or in the names of legal trials (TRIAL[1] (1))〔體育比賽或法庭審訊中〕〔一方〕對〔另一方〕; vs *AmE*【美】: *the England v. Australia cricket match* 英格蘭對澳大利亞的板球比賽

vac /væk; væk/ *n* [C usually singular 一般用單數] *BrE informal* a university VACATION[1] (2)【英, 非正式】〔大學的〕假期

3 **va·can·cy** /ˋvekənsɪ; ˈveɪkənsi/ *n* **1** [C] a room that is not being used in a hotel and is available for someone to stay in〔旅館中的〕空房間: *'No vacancies', the sign read.* 告示牌上寫着"客滿"。**2** [C] a job that is available for someone to start doing〔職位〕空位, 空缺: *Judge Ginsburg is to fill the vacancy on the US supreme court.* 金斯伯法官將填補美國最高法院的空缺。| **[+for]** *vacancies for drivers* 司機的空缺 **3** [U] lack of interest or thought 無聊; 心靈空虛; 失神: *His mouth fell open and the look of vacancy returned.* 他的嘴張着, 又顯出了茫然若失的神情。

va·cant /ˋvekənt; ˈveɪkənt/ *adj* **1** a vacant seat, room etc is empty and available for someone to use〔座位、房屋等〕空的, 未被佔用的: *Only a few apartments were still vacant.* 只有幾套公寓仍然空着。**2** *formal* a vacant job or position in an organization is available for someone to start doing【正式】〔工作或職位〕空缺的: **fall vacant** (=become vacant) 出缺 **3 vacant expression/smile/stare etc** an expression that shows that someone is not thinking about anything 茫然的表情/微笑/凝視等 **4 situations vacant** the part of a newspaper where jobs are advertised〔報紙上的〕招聘欄 —**vacantly** *adv*: *Cindy was staring vacantly into space.* 辛迪茫然地凝視着天空。

vacant lot /ˌ‥ ˈ‥/ *n* [C] *especially AmE* an area of land that is not being used and on which nothing has been built, especially in a city【尤美】〔尤指城市中的〕空地

vacant pos·ses·sion /ˌ‥ ‥ˈ‥/ *n* [U] *BrE technical*【英, 術語】**house/flat with vacant possession** a home or other building whose previous owner has left, so that the new owner can move into it immediately〔原房主搬離後, 新房主可立即遷入的〕閒置房屋/公寓

va·cate /ˋveket; vəˈkeɪt/ *v* [T] *formal*【正式】**1** to leave a job or position so that it is available for someone else to do 辭〔職〕, 騰出〔職位〕**2** to leave a seat, room etc so that someone else can use it 空出, 搬出: *Guests must vacate their rooms by 11 o'clock.* 客人必須於11點前騰出房間。

2 3 **va·ca·tion¹** /veˋkeʃən; vəˈkeɪʃən/ *n* **1** [C] *especially AmE* a holiday, or time spent not working【尤美】假期, 休假: **on vacation** *They're on vacation for the next two weeks.* 未來兩週他們要去度假。—see graph at 參見 HOLIDAY[1] 圖表 **2** [C] one of the periods of time when universities are closed〔大學的〕假期 —see also 另見 LONG VACATION **3** [U] *formal* the act of leaving a place【正式】〔工作的〕辭去; 〔房屋等的〕騰出

vacation² *v* [I] *AmE* to go somewhere for a holiday【美】度假, 休假: **[+in/at]** *The Bernsteins are vacationing in Europe.* 伯恩斯坦一家正在歐洲度假。

va·ca·tion·er /veˋkeʃənɚ; vəˈkeɪʃənə/ *n* [C] *AmE* someone who has gone somewhere for a holiday【美】度假者; HOLIDAYMAKER *BrE*【英】

vac·cin·ate /ˋvæksn̩ˌet; ˈvæksɪ̬neɪt/ *v* [T] to protect someone from a disease by putting a small amount of a substance containing that disease into their body 給…接種疫苗, 給…打預防針: **vaccinate sb against sth** *All children should be vaccinated against measles.* 所有兒童都應接種疫苗以預防麻疹。—see also 另見 IMMUNIZE, INOCULATE —**vaccination** /ˌvæksn̩ˋeʃən; ˌvæksɪ̬ˈneɪʃən/ *n* [C,U]

vac·cine /vækˋsin; ˈvæksiːn/ *n* [C,U] a substance which contains the VIRUS that causes a disease and is used to protect people from that disease 疫苗: *a polio vaccine* 天花[小兒麻痺]疫苗 —compare 比較 SERUM (1)

vac·il·late /ˋvæsl̩ˌet; ˈvæsɪ̬leɪt/ *v* [I] to continue to change your opinions, ideas etc; WAVER (2) 猶豫, 躊躇, 拿不定主意: *The administration is still vacillating over the Health Care issue.* 行政部門在保健問題上仍然舉棋不定。—**vacillation** /ˌvæsəˋleʃən; ˌvæsɪ̬ˈleɪʃən/ *n* [C,U]

va·cu·i·ty /væˋkjuətɪ; vəˈkjuːɪ̬ti/ *n* [U] *formal* a lack of intelligent, interesting, or serious thought【正式】空虛; 茫然; 愚蠢

vac·u·ous /ˋvækjuəs; ˈvækjuəs/ *adj formal*【正式】**1** a vacuous look or expression shows no sign of any feelings or intelligence〔神情或表情〕茫然的; 空洞的; 沒有思想感情的 **2** a vacuous life or existence seems to have no useful purpose〔生活等〕空虛的, 無聊的, 漫無目的的 —**vacuously** *adv* —**vacuousness** *n* [U]

vac·u·um¹ /ˋvækjuəm; ˈvækjuəm/ *n* **1** [C] a space that is completely empty of all gas, especially one from which all the air has been taken away 真空 **2** [singular] a situation in which someone or something is missing or lacking, especially one that causes problems or makes you feel unhappy 失落感; 空虛(感): *Her husband's death left a vacuum in her life.* 丈夫的去世使她的生活變得空虛。| **power/political etc vacuum** *Nixon's departure from office created a political vacuum.* 尼克遜的離任造成了一個政治真空狀態。**3 in a vacuum** existing completely separately from other people or things and having no connection with them 在真空狀態中; 與外界隔絕 **4** [C] *old-fashioned* a vacuum cleaner【過時】真空吸塵器

vacuum² *v* [I,T] to clean a place using a vacuum cleaner 用真空吸塵器打掃 —see picture at 參見 CLEAN[2] 圖

vacuum clean·er /ˈ‥ ˌ‥/ *n* [C] a machine that cleans floors by sucking up the dirt from them 真空吸塵器; HOOVER *BrE trademark*【英, 商標】

vacuum flask /ˈ‥ ˌ‥/ *BrE old-fashioned n* [C] a special container that keeps liquids hot or cold; THERMOS【英, 過時】保溫瓶, 熱水瓶

vacuum-packed /ˈ‥ ˌ‥/ *adj* vacuum-packed food is surrounded by plastic from which most of the air has been removed, so that the food will stay fresh for longer〔食物〕真空包裝的

vacuum pump /ˈ‥ ˌ‥/ *n* [C] a pump for removing gas or air from an enclosed space 真空泵

vacuum tube /ˈ‥ ˌ‥/ *n* [C] *AmE* a VALVE (3)【美】真空管

vag·a·bond /ˋvægəˌbɑnd; ˈvægəbɒnd/ *n* [C] *especially literary* someone who has no home but travels from place to place【尤文】流浪者, 漂泊者 —compare 比較 VAGRANT

va·ga·ries /ˋvegərɪz; ˈveɪgəriz/ *n* [plural] *formal* unusual or unexpected events, changes, ideas etc, that have an effect on your life【正式】〔事件、想法等〕不可捉摸[異

常]的變化: *the vagaries of the English weather* 英國天氣的變幻無常

va·gi·na /və`dʒaɪnə; və'dʒaɪnə/ *n* [C] the passage from a woman's outer sexual organs to her WOMB 陰道 —**vaginal** *adj*

va·gran·cy /`vegrənsɪ; 'veɪgrənsi/ *n* [U] the criminal offence of living on the street and BEGGING from people 遊蕩罪

va·grant /`vegrənt; 'veɪgrənt/ *n* [C] *formal* someone who has no home or work, especially someone who begs【正式】流浪者, 乞丐

vague /veg; veɪg/ *adj* **1** unclear because someone does not give enough details or does not say exactly what they mean 含糊的, 不明確的, 不清楚的: *vague promises of support* 含糊其辭表示支持的承諾 | **[+about]** *Maria was very vague about her plans for the future.* 瑪麗亞對自己未來的打算很不明確。**2 have a vague idea/feeling/recollection etc that** to think that something might be true or that you remember something, although you cannot be sure 隱約地想到/感到/憶起等 **3** not having a clear shape or form; INDISTINCT 模糊不清的: *The vague shape of a figure loomed through the mist.* 薄霧中隱隱出現一個模糊的人影。—**vagueness** *n* [U]

vague·ly /`veglɪ; 'veɪgli/ *adv* **1** slightly 稍微: *There was something vaguely familiar about him.* 對他稍微有點熟悉。**2** in a way that shows you are not thinking about what you are doing 心不在焉地: *He smiled vaguely at the ceiling.* 他心不在焉地笑看着天花板。**3** not exactly 不精確地; 不確切地; 不完全地: *vaguely round* 略有點兒圓

vain /ven; veɪn/ *adj* **1** someone who is vain is very proud of their good looks, abilities, or position; CONCEITED 自負的, 自視過高的 **2 in vain** without success in spite of your efforts 徒勞, 無結果: *I tried in vain to get Sue to come with us.* 我想帶蘇一起來, 結果白費心機。**3 vain attempt/hope/effort etc** an attempt, hope etc that fails to achieve the result you wanted 徒勞的嘗試/希望/努力等 **4 vain threat/promise etc** *literary* a threat, promise etc that is not worrying because the person cannot do what they say they will【文】空洞的威脅/承諾等 **5 take sb's name in vain** *humorous* to talk about someone, while they are not there, especially in a way that shows a lack of respect for them【幽默】〔趁其不在場而〕輕慢地談論某人 **6 take the Lord's name in vain** *old use* to swear using the words 'God', 'Jesus' etc【舊】褻瀆上帝之名 —**vainly** *adv*: *The instructor struggled vainly to open his parachute.* 教官拚命想打開降落傘, 但沒有成功。—see also 另見 VANITY

vain·glo·ri·ous /ven`glorɪəs; veɪn'glɔːriəs/ *adj literary* too proud of your own abilities, importance etc【文】非常自負的; 極度虛榮的 —**vaingloriously** *adv* —**vainglory** *n* [U]

val·ance /`væləns; 'væləns/, **valence** *n* [C] **1** a narrow piece of cloth that hangs from the edge of a shelf or from the frame of a bed to the floor〔裝飾櫥櫃、牀沿等的〕掛簾, 短帷幔, 掛布 **2** *especially AmE* a narrow piece of cloth above a window, covering the RAIL the curtains hang on【尤美】〔窗簾上端的〕布帷幔; PELMET *BrE*【英】

vale /vel; veɪl/ *n* [C] **1** *especially literary* a broad low valley【尤文】谷; 山谷 **2 the vale of tears/misery etc** *literary* used to mean the difficulties of life【文】塵世, 現世

val·e·dic·tion /ˌvælə`dɪkʃən; ˌvælǝ'dɪkʃən/ *n* [C,U] *formal* the act of saying goodbye, especially in a formal speech【正式】〔尤指正式演講中的〕告別

val·e·dic·to·ri·an /ˌvælədɪk`torɪən; ˌvælǝdɪk'tɔːriən/ *n* [C] *AmE* the student who has received the best marks all the way through school, and usually makes a speech【美】致告別辭的畢業生代表〔通常為成績最優者〕

val·e·dic·to·ry /ˌvælə`dɪktərɪ; ˌvælǝ'dɪktəri◂/ *adj formal* connected with saying goodbye, especially on a formal occasion【正式】〔尤指在正式場合中〕告別的: *a valedictory speech* 告別辭

va·lence¹ /`veləns; 'veɪləns/ *n* [C] *especially AmE* valency【尤美】原子價, 化合價

va·lence² /`væləns; 'væləns/ *n* [C] another spelling of VALANCE valance 的另一種拼法

va·len·cy /`velənsɪ; 'veɪlənsi/ *n* [C] *technical especially BrE* a measure of the power of atoms to combine together to form compounds【術語, 尤英】原子價, 化合價

val·en·tine /`væləntaɪn; 'væləntaɪn/ *n* [C] **1** someone you love or think is attractive, that you send a card to on St Valentine's Day (February 14th) (在聖瓦倫丁節〔2月14日〕向之贈送賀卡的) 情人: *Be my valentine.* 做我的情人吧。**2** a card you send to someone on St Valentine's Day 在聖瓦倫丁節贈送給某人的賀卡, 情人卡

valet¹ /`vælɪt; 'vælǝt/ *n* [C] **1** a male servant who looks after a man's clothes, serves his meals etc〔男子的〕貼身男僕, 男僕從 **2** *BrE* someone who cleans the clothes of people staying in a hotel【英】〔為旅館客人洗衣服的〕服務員 **3** *AmE* someone who parks your car for you at a hotel or restaurant【美】〔旅館或餐廳中〕為客人泊車的人: *valet service* 停車服務

valet² *v* [T] *BrE* to clean someone's car【英】洗車: *a valeting service* 洗車服務

valiant /`væljənt; 'væliənt/ *adj* very brave, especially in a difficult situation〔尤指在困境中〕勇敢的, 英勇的: *a valiant attempt to break the world record* 破世界紀錄的勇敢嘗試

val·id /`vælɪd; 'vælǝd/ *adj* **1** a valid ticket, document, or agreement can be used legally or is officially acceptable, especially for a fixed period of time or according to certain conditions 有效的: *a valid passport* 有效的護照 | *Your return ticket is valid for three months.* 你的回程票有效期為三個月。**2 valid reason/argument/criticism etc** a reason, argument etc that is based on what is true or sensible, and so should be accepted or treated in a serious way 正當的[有根據的]理由/論點/批評等: *His point about staff shortages was a valid one.* 他的關於員工短缺的觀點是有根據的。—**validity** /və`lɪdətɪ; və'lɪdǝti/ *n* [U]: *I would question the validity of that statement.* 我要質疑那個聲明的有效性。

val·i·date /`væləˌdet; 'vælǝdeɪt/ *v* [T] *formal* to prove that something is true or correct, or to make a document or agreement officially and legally acceptable【正式】證實; 使生效; 使合法化 —**validation** /ˌvælə`deʃən; ˌvælǝ'deɪʃən/ *n* [C,U]

va·lise /və`lis; və'liːz/ *n* [C] *old-fashioned* a small SUITCASE【過時】小旅行袋

Val·i·um /`vælɪəm; 'væliəm/ *n* [U] a drug to make people feel calmer and less anxious 安定〔一種鎮靜劑〕

val·ley /`vælɪ; 'væli/ *n* [C] an area of land between two lines of hills or mountains, usually with a river flowing through it 谷; 山谷〔常有河流流過〕: *the San Fernando valley* 聖費爾南多谷地

val·our *BrE*【英】, **valor** *AmE*【美】/`vælɚ; 'vælə/ *n* [U] *literary* great courage, especially in war【文】〔尤指在戰爭中的〕勇猛, 勇武 —see also 另見 **discretion is the better part of valour** (DISCRETION (3))

val·u·a·ble /`væljuəbl; 'væljuəbəl/ *adj* **1** worth a lot of money 值錢的, 貴重的: *a valuable painting* 一幅名貴的畫 **2** valuable help, advice etc is very useful because it helps you to do something〔幫助、勸告等〕有價值的, 有用的 **3** important because there is only a limited amount available 寶貴的, 珍貴的: *I won't waste any more of your valuable time.* 我不再浪費你的寶貴時間了。

val·u·a·bles /`væljuəblz; 'væljuəbəlz/ *n* [plural] things that you own that are worth a lot of money, such as jewellery, cameras etc〔珠寶、照相機等〕貴重物品: *Guests should leave their valuables in the hotel safe.* 客人應把貴重物品存放在旅館的保險櫃中。

val·u·a·tion /ˌvælju`eʃən; ˌvælju'eɪʃən/ *n* [C,U] a judgement about how much something is worth, how effective or useful a particular idea or plan will be etc 估價; 評價: **put a valuation on** *The valuation they put on the house was far too high.* 他們對房子的估價太高。

val·ue¹ /ˈvælju; ˈvælju:/ *n* [U]

1 ►MONEY 錢◄ [C,U] the amount of money that something is worth 價值: *The alterations doubled the value of the house.* 改建使房子的價值翻了一番。| **increase/go down etc in value** *Shares can go down as well as go up in value.* 股票的價值會上升, 也會下跌。| **market value** (=the amount of money that something can usually be sold for) 市場價值, 市價, 市值 *We paid a price that was well above the market value.* 我們付出的價錢遠遠高於市價。| **of value** (=worth a lot of money) 值錢的 *The thieves took nothing of value.* 小偷沒偷走任何值錢的東西。| **street value** (=the value of drugs when they are sold illegally) 〔毒品的〕黑市價 | **hold its value** (=continue to be worth the same amount of money) 保值 *It's a beautiful carpet – it should hold its value.* 這地毯很漂亮 — 應該能保值。—see 見 WORTH (USAGE)

2 be good/excellent etc value *BrE*【英】also 又作 **be (good) value for money** used to say that you get a lot of something or that its quality is good, considering the price you pay for it 很划算 —see 見 CHEAP¹ (USAGE)

3 be bad/poor etc value *BrE* used to say that you do not get much of something or its quality is not very good, considering the price you pay for it【英】不划算: *I thought £10 for a record that only lasts 14 minutes was incredibly poor value.* 我認為花 10 英鎊買一張只有14分鐘的唱片太不值了。

4 ►IMPORTANCE/USEFULNESS 重要性/有用性◄ [U] the importance or usefulness of something 重要性, 用處, 益處: **of great/little value** *His research has been of little practical value.* 他的研究沒多大實用價值。| **sentimental value** (=importance that something has for you because someone you like gave it to you, because it reminds you of the past etc) 情感價值

5 ►PRINCIPLES 準則◄ values [plural] your principles about what is right and wrong, or your ideas about what is important in life 準則; 價值觀(念): *Western liberal values* 西方的自由價值觀

6 ►AMOUNT 數額◄ [C] *technical* a mathematical quantity shown by a letter of the alphabet or sign【術語】〔由字母或符號表示的〕(數)值: *Let x have the value 25.* 設 x 的值為 25。

7 ►MUSIC 音樂◄ [C] the length of a musical note 音符長度, 時值

8 curiosity/novelty/snob etc value a quality something has that makes it seem interesting or desirable because it is different, new, or typical of high class people 〔某物所呈現出的〕在趣味性/新奇性/虛榮性等方面的價值

9 family values an expression meaning the belief that the family is very important, used especially by politicians 家庭觀念 —see also 另見 FACE VALUE

value² *v* [T] **1** to think that something is important to you 尊重, 重視: *I value your advice.* 我很重視你的意見。| *a valued friend* 看重的朋友 **2** [usually passive 一般用被動態] to decide how much money something is worth, by comparing it with similar things 估價, 計算…的價格: **value sth at** *We decided to get the house valued.* 我們決定給房子估估價。| *Paintings valued at over $200,000 were stolen from her home.* 幾幅估價為二十多萬美元的畫從她家裡被盜走了。

value-ad·ded tax /ˌ.. .. ˈ./ *n* [U] VAT 增值稅

value judg·ment /ˈ.. ˌ../ *n* [C] a decision or judgment about how good something is, based on opinions not facts 價值判斷〔根據見解而不是根據事實所作的判斷〕

val·u·er /ˈvæljuɚ; ˈvæljuə/ *n* [C] someone whose job is to decide how much money things are worth 估價者; 鑑定人

valve /vælv; vælv/ *n* [C] **1** a part of a tube or pipe that opens and shuts like a door to control the flow of liquid, gas, air etc passing through it 閥, 活門; 瓣(膜): *the valves of the heart* 心臟瓣膜 —see picture at 參見 BICYCLE¹ 圖 **2** the part on a TRUMPET¹ (1) or similar musical instrument that you press to change the sound of the note 〔樂器上的〕活塞, 栓塞 **3** *BrE* a closed glass tube used to control the flow of electricity in old radios, televisions etc【英】電子管, 真空管; VACUUM TUBE *AmE*【美】—see also 另見 BIVALVE, SAFETY VALVE

vamoose /væˋmus; vəˈmu:s/ *interjection AmE old-fashioned* used to tell someone to go away【美, 過時】〔用於叫某人〕走開

vamp¹ /væmp; væmp/ *n* [C] *old-fashioned* a woman who uses her sexual attractiveness to make men do things for her【過時】利用色相勾引男子為其效勞的女子; 女騙子

vamp² *v*

vamp sth ↔ **up** *phr v* [T] *informal* to make a story, music etc seem more exciting by adding things to it【非正式】〔通過補充〕編造〔故事、音樂等〕; 使…翻新

vam·pire /ˋvæmpaɪr; ˈvæmpaɪə/ *n* [C] an evil spirit that is believed to suck people's blood by biting their necks 吸血鬼〔傳說中咬破人脖子吸血的鬼魂〕

vampire bat /ˈ.. ./ *n* [C] a south American BAT that sucks the blood of other animals 〔南美的〕吸血蝙蝠

van /væn; væn/ *n* [C] **1** a vehicle used especially for carrying goods, which is smaller than a TRUCK and has a roof and usually no windows at the sides (廂式) 小型貨車: *a delivery van* 運貨車 | *a van driver* 小型貨車司機 **2** *especially BrE* a railway carriage with a roof and sides, used especially for carrying goods【尤英】帶篷蓋的鐵路貨車; 行李車: *a luggage van* 行李車 —see also 另見 GUARD'S VAN

van·dal /ˋvændl; ˈvændl/ *n* [C] someone who deliberately damages things, especially public property 故意破壞〔公共〕財物者

van·dal·is·m /ˋvændḷˌɪzəm; ˈvændəl-ɪzəm/ *n* [U] the crime of deliberately damaging things, especially public property 故意破壞〔公共〕財物的行為

van·dal·ize also 又作 **-ise** *BrE*【英】/ˋvændḷˌaɪz; ˈvændəl-aɪz/ *v* [T] to damage or destroy things deliberately, especially public property 故意破壞〔財物, 尤指公物〕

vane /ven; veɪn/ *n* [C] a flat blade that is moved by wind or water to produce power to drive a machine 〔風車、螺旋槳等的〕翼, 葉片: *the vanes of a propellor* 螺旋槳的葉片 —see also 另見 WEATHER VANE

van·guard /ˋvænˌgɑrd; ˈvængɑ:d/ *n* **1 in the vanguard** in the most advanced position of development 在前沿: *In the 19th century, Britain was in the vanguard of industrial progress.* 在 19 世紀, 英國是工業發展的前驅。**2 the vanguard** [singular] the leading position at the front of an army or group of ships moving into battle, or the soldiers who are in this position 〔軍隊或艦隊的〕前衛, 前鋒

va·nil·la¹ /vəˋnɪlə; vəˈnɪlə/ *n* [U] a substance used to give a special taste to ICE CREAM, cakes etc, made from the beans of a tropical plant 香草精, 香子蘭精

vanilla² *adj* having the taste of vanilla 香草味的: *vanilla ice cream* 香草冰淇淋 | *vanilla essence* 香精

van·ish /ˋvænɪʃ; ˈvænɪʃ/ *v* [I] **1** to disappear suddenly, especially in a way that cannot easily be explained 突然不見, 消失〔尤指以一種不易解釋的方式〕: *When I turned round again, the boy had vanished.* 當我再回頭時, 那個男孩已經不見了。| **vanish into thin air** (=disappear completely in a very mysterious way) 化為烏有 | **vanish without trace/vanish off the face of the earth** (=disappear so that no sign remains) 消失得無影無蹤 **2** to suddenly stop existing 滅絕: *Many species in South America have vanished completely.* 南美的許多物種已經滅絕。**3 do a vanishing act** *informal* to suddenly disappear, especially when someone is looking for you【非正式】突然消失〔尤指當有人在尋找你時〕

vanishing point /ˈ... ˌ./ *n* [singular] *technical* the point in the distance, especially on a picture, where parallel lines seem to meet【術語】消失點〔尤指透視畫中平行線的會聚點〕

van·i·ty /ˈvænətɪ; ˈvænɨ̍ti/ *n* [U] **1** too much PRIDE in yourself, so that you are always thinking about yourself and your appearance 虛榮(心); 自負 **2 the vanity of sth** *literary* the lack of importance of something compared to other things that are much more important【文】某事物的無用[無價值]: *The poem warns of the vanity of mental ambition.* 這首詩提醒世人, 不付諸實踐的抱負毫無用處。

vanity case /ˈ··· ˌ·/ *n* [C] a small bag used by a woman for carrying MAKE-UP etc〔女性放置化妝品的〕小手袋, 小手提包[盒]

vanity plate /ˈ··· ˌ·/ *n* [C] *AmE* a car NUMBERPLATE that has a special combination of numbers or letters, for example the first letters of the driver's names【美】特別車牌〈如由司機姓名首字母組合而成〉

vanity press /ˈ··· ˌ·/ also 又作 **vanity pub·lish·er** /ˈ··· ˌ···/ *n* [C usually singular 一般用單數] a company that writers pay to print their books 由作者自費出版書籍的出版社

vanity ta·ble /ˈ··· ˌ··/ *n* [C] *AmE*【美】梳妝台; a DRESSING TABLE *BrE*【英】

van·quish /ˈvæŋkwɪʃ; ˈvæŋkwɪʃ/ *v* [T] *literary* to defeat someone or something completely【文】徹底征服, 擊敗

van·tage point /ˈvæntɪdʒ ˌpɔɪnt; ˈvɑːntɪdʒ pɔɪnt/ *n* [C] **1** a good position from which you can see something〔能觀察某物的〕有利位置: *From my vantage point on the hill, I could see the whole procession.* 從山上的有利位置, 我可以看到整個遊行隊伍。**2** a way of thinking about things that comes from your own particular situation; POINT OF VIEW 見解, 觀點: *speaking from his vantage point as a major developer* 從他作為主要開發者的觀點來說

vap·id /ˈvæpɪd; ˈvæpɨ̍d/ *adj formal* lacking intelligence, interest, or imagination【正式】缺少靈性的; 乏味的, 平庸的: *vapid piped music* 乏味的管樂 —**vapidly** *adv* —**vapidness** *n* [U] —**vapidity** /vəˈpɪdətɪ; væˈpɪdɨ̍ti/ *n* [U]

va·por /ˈvepɚ; ˈveɪpə/ *n* [C,U] the American spelling of vapour vapour 的美式拼法

va·por·ize also 又作 **-ise** *BrE*【英】/ˈvepəˌraɪz; ˈveɪpəraɪz/ *v* [I,T] to change into a vapour, or to make something do this (使)蒸發, (使)變成蒸汽: *Water vaporizes when it boils.* 水沸騰時就變成蒸汽。—**vaporization** /ˌvepərəˈzeʃən; ˌveɪpəraɪˈzeɪʃən/ *n* [U]

va·pour *BrE*【英】, **vapor** *AmE*【美】/ˈvepɚ; ˈveɪpə/ *n* **1** [C,U] a mass of small drops of a liquid which float in the air, for example because the liquid has been heated 蒸汽, 水汽, 〔某種液體的〕蒸氣: *water vapour* 水蒸氣 **2 the vapours** [plural] *old use* a condition when you suddenly feel faint【舊】突然眩暈感 —**vaporous** *adj*

vapour trail *BrE*【英】, **vapor trail** *AmE*【美】/ˈ·· ·/ *n* [C] the white line that is left in the sky by a plane〔飛機在高空飛行時產生的〕霧化尾流

var·i·a·ble[1] /ˈvɛrɪəbl̩; ˈveəriəbəl/ *n* [C] **1** something that may be different in different situations, so that you cannot be sure what will happen 易變的事, 可變因素: *There are too many variables in the experiment to predict the result accurately.* 實驗中可變因素太多, 難以準確預測結果。**2** *technical* a mathematical quantity which can represent several different amounts【術語】〔數學中的〕變量, 變數 —compare 比較 CONSTANT[2]

variable[2] *adj* **1** likely to change often 易變的, 多變的: *the variable nature of the English climate* 英國氣候的多變性 | *Consumer preferences are so variable that planning is almost impossible.* 消費者的愛好如此易變, 要計劃幾乎是不可能的。**2** sometimes good and sometimes bad; UNEVEN 時好時壞的: *The team's performance has been very variable lately.* 這個隊近來的成績時好時壞。**3** able to be changed 可變的: *The machine has variable temperature settings.* 這台機器設有調溫裝置。—**variably** *adv* —**variability** /ˌvɛrɪəˈbɪlətɪ; ˌveəriəˈbɪlɨ̍ti/ *n* [U]

var·i·ance /ˈvɛrɪəns; ˈveəriəns/ *n* [U] *formal*【正式】**1 be at variance with** if two people or things are at variance with each other, they do not agree or are very different 與…有分歧; 與…大相徑庭: *Tradition and culture are often at variance with the needs of modern living.* 傳統和文化常常與現代生活的需要不相符合。**2** the amount by which two or more things are different or by which they change 差異, 不一致

var·i·ant /ˈvɛrɪənt; ˈveəriənt/ *n* [C] **1** something that is slightly different from the usual form of something 變體: **[+on]** *a variant on the archetypal Hollywood hero* 荷里活典型英雄的變體 **2** *technical* a slightly different form of a word or phrase【術語】〔同一詞或短語的〕異體: *regional spelling variants in British and American English* 英國英語和美國英語中地域性的不同拼法 —**variant** *adj*: *a variant form of the word* 詞的異體, 異體字

var·i·a·tion /ˌvɛrɪˈeʃən; ˌveəriˈeɪʃən/ *n* **1** [C,U] a difference or change from the usual amount or form of something〔數量或形式的〕變化, 變動: **[+in]** *There are wide regional variations in house prices.* 房價的地域性差異很大。**2** [C] something that is done in a way that is different from the way it is usually done〔做事方式的〕變更: **[+on]** *an interesting variation on the theme of betrayal and revenge* 對背叛與復仇這一主題的趣味性變更 **3** [C] one of a set of short pieces of music, each based on the same simple tune〔音樂中的〕變奏(曲): *Bach's Goldberg Variations* 巴赫的《哥德堡變奏曲》 W2

var·i·cose veins /ˌværɪkos ˈvenz; ˌværɨ̍kəʊs ˈveɪnz/ *n* [plural] a medical condition in which the VEINS in your leg become swollen and painful〔腿部的〕靜脈曲張

var·ied /ˈvɛrɪd; ˈveərid/ *adj* consisting of or including many different kinds of things or people, especially in a way that seems interesting 各種各樣的, 形形色色的: *The work's very varied.* 這項工作內容繁多。| *human nature, in all its many and varied forms* 形形色色的人性 | *products as varied as car bumpers and cigarette filters* 各式各樣的產品, 如汽車的保險槓和香煙的過濾嘴

var·ie·gat·ed /ˈvɛrɪˌgetɪd; ˈveərɪgeɪtɨ̍d/ *adj* **1** a variegated plant, leaf etc has different coloured marks on it〔植物〕雜色的; 斑駁的: *variegated ivies* 雜色的常春藤 **2** *formal* consisting of a lot of different types of thing【正式】多樣化的

var·ie·ga·tion /ˌvɛrɪˈgeʃən; ˌveərɨ̍ˈgeɪʃən/ *n* [U] marks of varied colours, especially in plants〔尤指植物的〕雜色; 斑駁

va·ri·e·ty /vəˈraɪətɪ; vəˈraɪəti/ *n* S2 W1

1 a variety of a lot of a particular type of things that are different from each other 種種: *The girls come from a variety of different backgrounds.* 女孩們的出身背景各異。| **a wide variety of** *The T-shirts are available in a wide variety of colors.* T恤有各種各樣顏色可供選擇。

2 ►DIFFERENCES 差異◄ [U] the differences within a group, set of actions etc that make it interesting 多樣化, 變化: **add variety to** (=make something more interesting) 給…增加趣味性 *There was little she could do to add variety to her daily routine.* 她無法給單調的日常生活增添些趣味。

3 ►PLANT/ANIMAL 植物/動物◄ [C] a type of plant or animal that is different from others in the same group〔動、植物的〕種類, 品種: **[+of]** *a new variety of apple* 新品種的蘋果

4 ►TYPE OF PERSON/THING 人/物的類型◄ [C usually singular 一般用單數] *often humorous* a particular type of person or thing【常幽默】〔人或物的〕類型: **of the... variety** *The men are mostly of the noble, long-suffering husband variety!* 男人大多屬於高尚、刻苦耐勞的丈夫類型!

5 variety is the spice of life used to say that doing a lot of different things, meeting different people etc is what makes life interesting 變化是生活的調味品

6 ►ENTERTAINMENT 娛樂◄ [U] a type of entertainment for theatre or television that includes a lot of different short performances〔劇院或電視的〕綜藝節目

variety store /-'··· ,-/ *n* [C] *AmE* a shop that sells many different kinds of goods, often at low prices【美】雜貨店

var·i·ous /ˋvɛrɪəs; 'veəriəs/ *adj* [usually before noun 一般用於名詞前] several different 各種各樣的: *available in various colours* 各種顏色的應有盡有

var·i·ous·ly /ˋvɛrɪəslɪ; 'veəriəsli/ *adv* **variously described/estimated etc** used to introduce a number of different descriptions, amounts etc, that people have made or used about something 各種不同描述/估價等的: *His fortune has been variously estimated at between $1 and $2 billion.* 對他的財產有各種不同的估價, 從10億到20億美元不等。

var·let /ˋvɑrlɪt; 'vɑːlɪ̵t/ *n* [C] *old use* a bad man【舊】無賴, 惡棍

var·mint /ˋvɑrmɪnt; 'vɑːmɪ̵nt/ *n* [C] *old-fashioned* someone, especially a child, who causes a lot of trouble【過時】老闖禍的人〔尤指頑童〕

var·nish¹ /ˋvɑrnɪʃ; 'vɑːnɪʃ/ *n* [C,U] **1** a clear liquid that is painted onto things, especially things made of wood, to protect them and give them a hard shiny surface〔尤指刷在木製品上的〕清漆, 罩光漆 **2 the varnish** the clear shiny surface of something that has been covered in this liquid〔塗清漆後產生的〕光澤的表面 —compare 比較 LACQUER¹ (1)

varnish² *v* [T] to cover something with varnish 給…塗上清漆

var·si·ty /ˋvɑrsətɪ; 'vɑːsɪ̵ti/ *n* [C,U] **1** *AmE* the main team that represents a university, college, or school in a sport【美】〔大專院校體育比賽中的〕代表隊, 校隊: *the varsity football team* 大學足球代表隊 —compare 比較 JUNIOR VARSITY **2** *BrE old-fashioned* a university, especially Oxford or Cambridge【英, 過時】大學〔尤指牛津大學或劍橋大學〕

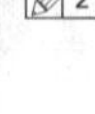

var·y /ˋvɛrɪ; 'veəri/ *v* **1** [I] if several things of the same type vary, they are all different from each other（彼此）相異, 存在不同之處: **vary greatly/considerably/enormously** *Teaching methods vary greatly from school to school.* 各家學校的教學方法大不相同。| **vary in price/quality/size** *flowers that vary in color and size* 色彩和大小各異的花朵 | **varying degrees of** *varying degrees of success* 不同程度的成功 **2** [I] to change often 多變, 變化無常: *Quentin's mood seems to vary according to the weather.* 昆廷的情緒似乎隨天氣而變化。| **it varies** *"What do you normally have for lunch?" "Well, it varies from day to day."* "你午飯通常吃甚麼?" "噢, 每天都不一樣。" **3** [T] to regularly change what you do or the way that you do it 經常改變, 使多樣化: *My doctor said I should vary my diet more.* 醫生說我應該使日常飲食更為多樣化。—see also 另見 VARIED

vas·cu·lar /ˋvæskjələ; 'væskjɡ̵lə/ *adj technical* connected with the tubes through which liquids flow in the bodies of animals or in plants【術語】〔動物〕脈管的;〔植物〕維管的: *the vascular system* 維管系統

vase /ves; vɑːz/ *n* [C] a glass or baked clay container used to put flowers in or for decoration 花瓶,〔裝飾用的〕瓶

va·sec·to·my /vəsˋɛktəmɪ; və'sektəmi/ *n* [C,U] a medical operation to cut the small tube that carries a man's SPERM so that he is unable to produce children 輸精管切除術

Vas·e·line /ˋvæsḷ,in; 'væsɪ̵liːn/ *n* [U] *trademark* a soft clear substance used for various medical and other purposes【商標】凡士林

vas·sal /ˋvæsḷ; 'væsəl/ *n* [C] **1** a man in the MIDDLE AGES who was given land to live on by a lord in return for promising to work or fight for him〔中世紀的〕封臣, 家臣〔對國君或領主效忠, 作為回報獲封土地者〕**2** *formal* a country that is controlled by another country【正式】(附) 屬國: *a vassal state* 附庸國

vast /væst; vɑːst/ *adj* **1** extremely large 巨大的, 廣大的, 廣闊的: *vast areas of rainforest* 廣闊的雨林地區 | **vast expense** *A huge palace was constructed at vast public expense.* 用巨額公費建起了一座龐大的宮殿。| **in vast numbers** *The refugees came across the border in vast numbers.* 大量難民越過邊界。**2 the vast majority/bulk of** used when you want to emphasize that something is true about almost all of a group of people or things …的絕大多數: *The vast majority of young people don't take drugs.* 絕大多數年輕人不吸毒。—**vastness** *n* [U]

vast·ly /ˋvæstlɪ; 'vɑːstli/ *adv* very much 非常: *This film is vastly superior to his last one.* 這部影片遠比他上一部優秀。

VAT /,vi e ˋti; ,viː eɪ 'tiː/ *n* [U] value added tax; a tax added to the price of goods and services in Britain and the EU 增值稅

vat /væt; væt/ *n* [C] a very large container for storing liquids such as WHISKY or DYE, when they are being made〔釀酒、盛染料用的〕大缸, 大桶

Vat·i·can /ˋvætɪkən; 'vætɪkən/ *n* **the Vatican a)** the large PALACE in Rome where the Pope (=head of the Roman Catholic Church) lives and works 梵蒂岡〔羅馬教廷所在地〕**b)** the government of the Pope 羅馬教廷: *The Vatican is taking a hard line on birth control.* 羅馬教廷在節育的問題上採取強硬路線。

vau·de·ville /ˋvɔdə,vɪl; 'vɔːdəvɪl/ *n* [U] *AmE* a type of theatre entertainment, popular from 1880 to 1950, in which there were many short performances of different kinds, including singing, dancing, jokes etc【美】歌舞雜耍表演, 綜藝節目〔盛行於1880年至1950年的一種劇院娛樂形式, 有演唱、舞蹈、笑話等〕

vault¹ /vɔlt; vɔːlt/ *n* [C] **1** also 又作 **vaults** [plural] a room with thick walls and a strong door where money, jewels etc are kept to prevent them from being stolen or damaged〔貴重財物的〕保管庫, 保險庫 **2** also 又作 **vaults** [plural] a room where people from the same family are buried, often under the floor of a church〔常指教堂地下的〕墓穴, 地下墓室 **3** a jump over something 撐竿跳 —see also 另見 POLE VAULT **4** a roof or CEILING (1) that consists of several ARCH*es* that are joined together, especially in a church〔尤指教堂的〕拱頂

vault² also 又作 **vault over** *v* [T] to jump over something in one movement, using your hands or a pole to help you〔尤指以手撐物或撐竿〕跳躍: *He vaulted over the fence and ran off into the night.* 他躍過籬笆, 消失在夜色之中。—**vaulter** *n* [C]

vault·ed /ˋvɔltɪd; 'vɔːltɪ̵d/ *adj* **vaulted roof/ceiling etc** a roof, ceiling etc that consists of several ARCH*es* which are joined together 拱狀屋頂/頂篷等

vault·ing¹ /ˋvɔltɪŋ; 'vɔːltɪŋ/ *n* [U] arches in a roof〔屋頂的〕拱; 拱形圓頂

vaulting² *adj* **vaulting ambition** *literary* the desire to achieve as much as possible【文】極度的野心

vaulting horse /'·· ·/ *n* [C] *BrE* a large wooden box used for jumping over in GYMNASTICS【英】跳馬〔體育運動器械〕

vaunt /vɔnt; vɔːnt/ *v* **much-vaunted** a much-vaunted achievement is one that people often say is very good, important etc, especially with too much pride 大肆吹噓的, 過分誇耀的〔尤指因過於驕傲〕: *Reagan's much vaunted economic miracle* 列根那被過譽的經濟奇蹟

VCR /,vi si ˋɑr; ,viː siː 'ɑː/ *n* [C] *especially AmE* video cassette recorder; a machine which is used to record television programmes or to play VIDEOTAPE*s*【尤美】錄像機; VIDEO¹ (3) *BrE*【英】

VD /,vi ˋdi; ,viː 'diː/ *n* [U] venereal disease; a disease that is passed from one person to another during sex 性病, 花柳病

VDU /,vi di ˋju; ,viː diː 'juː/ *n* [C] visual display unit; a machine like a television that shows the information from a computer or WORD PROCESSOR〔電腦或文字處理器的〕視頻顯示器

've /v; v, əv/ the short form of 縮略式= 'have': *We've finished.* 我們已經完成了。

veal /vil; viːl/ *n* [U] meat from a CALF (=a young cow) 小牛肉

vec·tor /ˋvɛktɚ; ˈvektə/ *n* [C] *technical*【術語】**1** a quantity that has a direction as well as a size, usually represented by an ARROW (2) 矢量, 向量 **2** the course taken by a plane 飛機航線, 航道

Ve·da /ˋvedə; ˈveɪdə/ *n* [plural] the oldest writings of the Hindu religion《吠陀》〔印度教最古老的文獻〕

vee·jay /ˌviˋdʒe; ˌviːˈdʒeɪ/ *n* [C] a VIDEO JOCKEY 電視音樂節目主持人

veep /vip; viːp/ *n* [C] *AmE informal* VICE PRESIDENT【美, 非正式】副總統

veer /vɪr; vɪə/ *v* [I] **1** [always+adv/prep] to change direction suddenly 突然改變方向, 轉向: **[+off/away/across etc]** *The car veered sharply to the right and crashed.* 小轎車向右猛地一拐撞了車。**2** [always+adv/prep] to change suddenly to a very different belief, opinion, or subject〔信仰、觀點或主題等〕突然改變: **[+towards/away from etc]** *The country's leaders seemed to veer towards nationalism.* 該國的領導人似乎突然轉向了民族主義。**3** *technical* if the wind veers in a particular direction, it changes round to that direction【術語】〔風向〕順轉

veg[1] /vɛdʒ; vedʒ/ *n* [plural] *BrE informal* vegetables【英, 非正式】蔬菜: *fruit and veg* 水果和蔬菜

veg[2] *v*

veg out *phr v* [I] *informal* to relax by doing something that needs very little effort, such as watching television【非正式】放鬆

ve·gan /ˋvɛgən; ˈviːgən/ *n* [C] someone who does not eat meat, fish, eggs, cheese, or milk 純素食者, 嚴格的素食主義者〔肉、魚、蛋、乳酪、牛奶均不吃的人〕—**vegan** *adj*: *a vegan diet* 純素食者的飲食

ve·ge·bur·ger /ˋvɛdʒɪˌbɝgɚ; ˈvedʒiˌbɜːgə/ *n* [C] *BrE* a BURGER made with vegetables, beans etc, but no meat【英】素漢堡(包)

vege·ta·ble /ˋvɛdʒətəbl̩; ˈvedʒtəbəl/ *n* **1** [C,U] a plant such as a CABBAGE, CARROT, or potato which is eaten raw or cooked and is usually not sweet 蔬菜: *vegetable oil* 植物油 | **green vegetables** *citrus fruits and fresh green vegetables* 柑橘類水果與新鮮的綠色蔬菜 —see picture on page A9 參見 A9 頁圖 **2** [C] *informal* someone who cannot think or move because their brain has been damaged in an accident【非正式】植物人

vegetable mar·row /ˌ··· ˈ··/ *n* [C] a MARROW (2) 西葫蘆〔葫蘆科蔬菜〕

veg·e·tar·i·an /ˌvɛdʒəˋtɛrɪən; ˌvedʒəˈteəriən◂/ *n* [C] someone who eats only vegetables, bread, fruit, eggs etc and does not eat meat or fish 素食主義者 —compare 比較 VEGAN —**vegetarian** *adj*: *a vegetarian restaurant* 素餐館

veg·e·tar·i·an·is·m /ˌvɛdʒəˋtɛrɪənɪzəm; ˌvedʒəˈteəriənɪzəm/ *n* [U] the practice of not eating meat or fish 素食主義

veg·e·tate /ˋvɛdʒəˌtet; ˈvedʒəteɪt/ *v* [I] not to do anything and feel bored because there is nothing interesting for you to do 無所事事地生活, 過枯燥呆板的生活: *I got fed up with vegetating at home.* 在家裡過懶散單調的生活, 我真膩煩極了。

veg·e·ta·tion /ˌvɛdʒəˋteʃən; ˌvedʒəˈteɪʃən/ *n* [U] plants in general, especially in one particular area〔尤指某一地區的〕植物, 草木〔總稱〕: *There was little vegetation on the island.* 島上幾乎沒有甚麼植物。

veg·gie /ˋvɛdʒɪ; ˈvedʒi/ *n* [C] *informal*【非正式】**1** *BrE* a VEGETARIAN【英】素食主義者 **2** *AmE* a VEGETABLE (1)【美】蔬菜

vehe·ment /ˋviəmənt; ˈviːəmənt/ *adj* showing very strong feelings or opinions 感情強烈的; 意見激烈的: *a vehement attack on the President's budget proposals* 對總統預算提案的激烈反對 —**vehemently** *adv*: *Dan vehemently denies the charges.* 丹斷然否認指控。—**vehemence** *n* [U]

ve·hi·cle /ˋviɪkl̩; ˈviːɪkəl/ *n* [C] **1** *especially formal* a thing such as a car, bus etc that is used for carrying people or things from one place to another【尤正式】運載工具; 車輛: *"Is this your vehicle, sir?" asked the policeman.* "這是你的車嗎, 先生?" 警察問道。| *a heavy goods vehicle* 重型貨車 **2 vehicle for (doing) sth** something that you use in order to achieve something or as a way of spreading your ideas, expressing your opinions etc 媒介(物); 用作…的工具: *The government used the press as a vehicle for its propaganda.* 政府把新聞媒體用作宣傳的工具。

ve·hic·u·lar /viˋhɪkjəlɚ; viːˈhɪkjʊlə/ *adj formal* connected with road vehicles【正式】車輛的: *vehicular traffic* 車輛交通

veil[1] /vel; veɪl/ *n* [C] **1** a thin piece of material worn by women to cover their faces at formal occasions such as weddings, or for religious reasons 面紗 **2 the veil** the system in Islamic countries in which women must keep their faces covered in public places〔伊斯蘭教國家的婦女在公共場所〕戴面紗的習俗 **3 draw a veil over** deliberately not to talk about something that happened in the past because it is unpleasant or embarrassing 把…掩蓋起來; 避而不談〔不愉快或難堪的事〕: *I think it's better if we draw a veil over the whole sorry affair.* 我認為最好避而不談這件不愉快的事。**4 veil of secrecy/deceit/silence etc** something that stops you knowing the full truth about a situation 蒙着神祕/虛假/靜默等的色彩: *A veil of mystery surrounds Kelly's death.* 凱利的死籠罩着一層神祕的色彩。**5 veil of mist/cloud etc** a thin layer of mist, cloud etc that covers something so that you cannot see it clearly 一層薄霧/雲等 **6 take the veil** *old-fashioned* to become a NUN【過時】當修女

veil 面紗

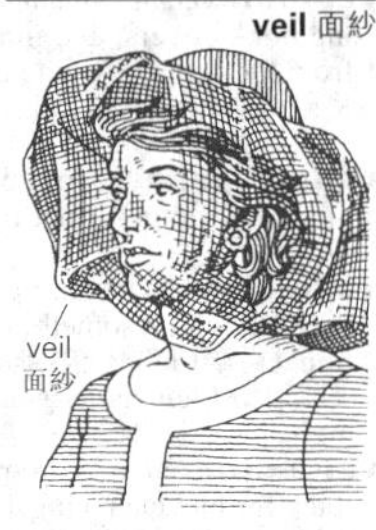

veil[2] *v* [T] **1 be veiled in mystery/secrecy** if something is veiled in mystery etc, very little is known about it and it seems mysterious 隱在神祕/祕密之中 **2** to cover something with a veil 以面紗掩蓋

veiled /veld; veɪld/ *adj* **veiled criticism/threats/hints etc** criticisms, threats etc that are hidden because you do not say directly what you think or mean 含蓄的批評/威脅/暗示等: **thinly veiled** (=only slightly hidden) 幾乎不加遮掩的 *thinly veiled threats of retaliation* 幾乎不加掩飾的報復恫嚇

vein /ven; veɪn/ *n* **1** [C] one of the tubes through which blood flows to your heart from other parts of your body 靜脈 —compare 比較 ARTERY (1) **2** [C] **a)** one of the thin lines on a leaf or on the wing of an insect〔植物的〕葉脈;〔昆蟲的〕翅脈 **b)** one of the thin lines on a piece of wood, cheese, MARBLE (1) etc〔木頭、乾酪、大理石等的〕紋理, 紋路 **3** [C] a thin layer of a valuable metal or mineral which is contained in rock 礦脈; 岩脈; 礦層: *a rich vein of silver*〔蘊藏量〕豐富的銀礦脈 **4** [singular] a particular style or way, especially when speaking or writing about something〔尤指說話、寫作的〕風格; 方式: **in the same vein/in a similar vein** *His second novel is in very much the same vein as the first.* 他的第二部小說跟第一部風格幾乎一模一樣。| **in a serious/light-hearted vein** *The rest of the speech was in a more light-hearted vein.* 演講的餘下部分語調輕鬆多了。**5 a vein of humour/malice etc** a small amount of a particular quality 一絲幽默/惡意等: **a rich vein** *There's a rich vein of humour running through her stories.* 她的故事透出濃濃的幽默感。

veined /vend; veɪnd/ *adj* having a pattern of thin lines on its surface that looks like veins 有紋理的: *black-veined marble* 有黑色紋理的大理石

ve·lar /ˈvilə; ˈviːlə/ *adj* a velar CONSONANT such as /k/ or /g/ is pronounced with the back of your tongue close to the soft part at the top of your mouth 軟顎音的〈例如 /k/ 或 /g/〉 —**velar** *n* [C]

Vel·cro /ˈvɛlkro; ˈvelkrəʊ/ *n* [U] *trademark* a material used for fastening clothes, which sticks together when you press a piece with a rough surface against a piece with a soft surface【商標】維可牢搭鏈, 尼龍黏帶 —see picture at 參見 FASTENER 圖

veldt, veld /vɛlt; velt/ *n* **the veldt** the high flat area of land in South Africa that is covered in grass and has few trees〔南非高原上的〕草原

vel·lum /ˈvɛləm; ˈveləm/ *n* [U] a material used for making book covers, and in the past for writing on, made from the skins of young cows, sheep, or goats〔用小牛皮或小羊皮製的〕精製皮紙, 犢[羊]皮紙〔用作書皮或在過去用於書寫〕

ve·lo·ci·pede /vəˈlɑsə,pid; vɪ̍ˈlɒsɪ̍piːd/ *n* [C] a kind of bicycle, used in former times〔舊時用的〕自行車, 腳踏車

ve·lo·ci·ty /vəˈlɑsətɪ; vɪ̍ˈlɒsɪ̍ti/ *n* **1** [C,U] *technical* the speed at which something moves in a particular direction【術語】〔沿一定方向的〕速度: *the velocity of light* 光速 | *a high velocity bullet* 高速子彈 **2** [U] *formal* a high speed【正式】高速

vel·o·drome /ˈvɛlə,drom; ˈvelədrəʊm/ *n* [C] a circular track for bicycle racing〔圓形賽道的〕腳踏車賽車場

ve·lour, velours /vəˈlur; vəˈlʊə/ *n* [U] heavy cloth which has a soft surface like velvet 棉絨; 絲絨

vel·vet /ˈvɛlvɪt; ˈvelvɪ̍t/ *n* [U] cloth with a soft surface on one side which is used for making clothes, curtains etc 天鵝絨, 絲絨 —see picture on page A16 參見 A16 頁圖

vel·ve·teen /,vɛlvəˈtin; ,velvɪ̍ˈtiːn◂/ *n* [U] cheap material which looks like velvet 平絨, 棉天鵝絨

vel·vet·y /ˈvɛlvɪtɪ; ˈvelvɪ̍ti/ *adj* looking, feeling, tasting or sounding smooth and soft 柔軟光滑的; 圓潤輕柔的: *His voice had a wonderful velvety sound.* 他的嗓音輕柔圓潤, 美妙極了。

ve·nal /ˈvinl̩; ˈviːnl/ *adj formal* using power in a dishonest or unfair way and accepting money as a reward for doing this【正式】〔利用職權〕貪污[受賄]的; 腐敗的 —compare 比較 VENIAL —**venally** *adv* —**venality** /viˈnælətɪ; viːˈnælɪ̍ti/ *n* [U]

vend /vɛnd; vend/ *v* [T] *formal or law* to sell something【正式或法律】出售

ven·det·ta /vɛnˈdɛtə; venˈdetə/ *n* [C] **1** a quarrel which continues for a long time in which one group or person tries to harm another because they feel angry about something that happened in the past 世仇; 宿怨: *The two sides have been engaged in a bitter private vendetta against each other.* 雙方積怨甚深, 彼此懷有深仇大恨。**2** a quarrel that has continued for a long time between two families who try to kill each other because of murders in the past; a FEUD 家族間的血仇, 族際仇殺

vending ma·chine /ˈ‥ ‥,‥/ *n* [C] a machine that you can get cigarettes, chocolate, drinks etc from by putting in a coin〔投幣式〕自動售貨機

vend·or /ˈvɛndə; ˈvendə/ *n* [C] **1** someone who sells things 小販: **news-vendor/ice-cream vendor etc** (=someone who sells ice-creams, newspapers etc in the street) 報販/售冰淇淋的小販等 | **street vendor** *I could hear the shouts of the street vendors.* 我能聽見街頭小販的叫賣聲。**2** *law* someone who is selling something such as a house or an area of land【法律】〔房地產的〕賣主, 賣方

ve·neer[1] /vəˈnɪr; vɪ̍ˈnɪə/ *n* **1** [C,U] a thin layer of good quality wood that covers the outside of a piece of furniture which is made of a cheaper material 飾面薄板, 鑲板〔鑲嵌於用廉價材料製成的家具表面的優質薄木板〕: *walnut veneer* 胡桃木鑲板 **2 a veneer of** *formal* behaviour that hides someone's real character or feelings【正式】〔掩飾真實性格或感情的〕舉止; 虛飾: *a veneer of self-confidence* 貌似自信

veneer[2] *v* [T+**with/in**] to cover something with a veneer 貼鑲板於〔某物的表面〕, 鑲飾

ven·e·ra·ble /ˈvɛnərəbl̩; ˈvenərəbəl/ *adj* **1** *formal or humorous* a venerable person or thing is very old and respected because of their age, experience, historical importance etc【正式或幽默】〔由於年齡、經驗〕令人尊敬的; 年高德劭的; 〔因歷史意義等〕神聖莊嚴的, 珍貴的: *venerable financial institutions such as the Bank of England* 像英格蘭銀行那樣歷史悠久的金融機構 **2 the Venerable... a)** the title given to a priest with the rank of ARCHDEACON in the Church of England 最尊敬的...〔英國國教中對副主教的尊稱〕 **b)** the title given by the Roman Catholic Church to a dead person who is very holy but not yet a SAINT (1) 最聖潔的...〔天主教對非常聖潔但還不是聖徒的已故者的稱號〕

ven·e·rate /ˈvɛnə,ret; ˈvenəreɪt/ *v* [T] *formal* to treat someone or something with great respect, especially because they are old or connected with the past【正式】尊敬, 崇拜, 敬重: *The Chinese venerate their ancestors.* 中國人尊敬自己的祖先。—**veneration** /,vɛnəˈreʃən; ,venəˈreɪʃən/ *n* [U]

ve·ne·re·al dis·ease /vəˈnɪrɪəl dɪ,ziz; vɪ̍ˈnɪəriəl dɪ,ziːz/ *n* [C,U] VD 性病, 花柳病

Ve·ne·tian blind /və,niʃən ˈblaɪnd; və,niːʃən ˈblaɪnd/ *n* [C] a set of long flat bars of plastic or metal which can be raised or lowered to cover a window 百葉窗簾 —see picture at 參見 BLIND[3] 圖

ven·geance /ˈvɛndʒəns; ˈvendʒəns/ *n* **1** [U] something violent or harmful that you do to someone in order to punish them for harming you, your family etc 報仇, 報復, 復仇: *Hamlet is driven by a desire for vengeance after his father is killed.* 父親被殺之後, 哈姆雷特被復仇的願望所驅使。**2 with a vengeance** if something is done with a vengeance, it is done much more than is expected or normal 過度地; 猛烈地: *The music started up again with a vengeance.* 音樂再度響起, 更加激昂。

venge·ful /ˈvɛndʒfəl; ˈvendʒfəl/ *adj literary* very eager to punish someone who has harmed you【文】有復仇心理的; 圖謀報復的, 復仇的: *a vengeful God* 復仇之神 —**vengefully** *adv*

ve·ni·al /ˈvinɪəl; ˈviːniəl/ *adj formal* a venial fault, mistake etc is not very serious and can therefore be forgiven【正式】〔錯誤等〕輕微的; 可原諒的: *a venial sin* 可饒恕的罪孽 —compare 比較 VENAL

ven·i·son /ˈvɛnəzn̩; ˈvenɪ̍zən/ *n* [U] the meat of a DEER 鹿肉

Venn di·a·gram /ˈvɛn ˌdaɪəgræm; ˈven ˌdaɪəgræm/ *n* [C] a picture that shows the relationship between a number of things by using circles that OVERLAP each other〔用彼此重疊的圓表示若干事物之間關係的〕維恩圖

ven·om /ˈvɛnəm; ˈvenəm/ *n* [U] **1** a liquid poison that some snakes, insects etc produce and that they use when biting or stinging another animal or insect〔蛇、昆蟲等的〕毒液 **2** extreme anger or hatred 痛恨, 怨恨, 憎恨: *There was real venom in her voice.* 她的聲音中有着切齒怨恨。

ven·om·ous /ˈvɛnəməs; ˈvenəməs/ *adj* **1** full of extreme hatred or anger 充滿怨恨的: *a venomous look* 充滿怨恨的表情 **2** a venomous snake, insect etc produces poison to attack its enemies〔蛇、昆蟲等〕有毒的, 分泌毒液的 —**venomously** *adv*

ve·nous /ˈvinəs; ˈviːnəs/ *adj* related to the VEINS (=tubes that carry the blood) in your body 靜脈的

vent[1] /vɛnt; vent/ *n* [C] **1** a hole or pipe through which gases, smoke, liquid etc can enter or escape from an enclosed space or a container〔供氣體或液體流通的〕孔口; 通風孔; 排氣道: *an air vent* 通風孔 **2 give vent to** *formal* to do something to express a strong feeling, especially of anger【正式】抒發〔強烈感情〕, 發泄〔尤指怒火〕: *Joshua gave vent to his anger by kicking the chair.* 喬舒亞踢椅子以發泄怒氣。**3** *technical* the small hole through which small animals, birds, fish, and snakes get rid of waste matter from their bodies【術語】〔小動物、鳥、魚、蛇的〕肛門 **4** *technical* a narrow straight opening at the bottom of a jacket or coat, at the sides or back【術語】衣服底部的開衩

vent² *v* [T] to do something to express your feelings, especially anger, often in a way that is unfair〔指常用不公正的方式〕發泄〔感情, 尤指怒火〕: **vent sth on sb** *Paul had a bad day at work and vented his anger on his family.* 保羅整天工作不順心, 就把怒氣發泄到家人身上。

ven·ti·late /ˋvɛntḷˌet; ˈventɪ̣leɪt/ *v* [T] **1** to let fresh air into a room, building etc 使通風: **well-ventilated/poorly ventilated etc** *a well-ventilated kitchen* 通風良好的廚房 **2** *formal* to express your opinions or feelings about something【正式】發表〔意見或看法〕; 表達〔感情〕: *Doctrinal issues were never ventilated.* 教義的問題從未討論過。—**ventilation** /ˌvɛntḷˋeʃən; ˌventɪ̣ˈleɪʃən/ *n* [U]: *Workers complained about the factory's lack of ventilation.* 工人抱怨工廠缺乏通風設施。| *a ventilation system* 通風系統

ven·ti·la·tor /ˋvɛntḷˌetɚ; ˈventɪ̣leɪtə/ *n* [C] **1** a thing designed to let fresh air into a room, building etc 通風裝置; 排氣風扇, 送風機 **2** a piece of equipment that pumps air into and out of someone's lungs when they cannot breathe without help 人工呼吸機

ven·tri·cle /ˋvɛntrɪkḷ; ˈventrɪkəl/ *n* [C] *technical*【術語】**1** one of the two spaces in the bottom of your heart that pump blood out into your body 心室 —compare 比較 ATRIUM (1) **2** a small hollow place in your body or in your brain〔人體內的〕腔室; 腦室

ven·tril·o·quis·m /vɛnˋtrɪləˌkwɪzəm; venˈtrɪləkwɪzəm/ *n* [U] the art of speaking without moving your lips, so that the sound seems to come from someone else 口技, 腹語術 —**ventriloquist** *n* [C]

ven·ture¹ /ˋvɛntʃɚ; ˈventʃə/ *n* [C] a new business activity that involves taking risks 風險項目, 風險投資; 冒險事業: *a commercial venture* 商業冒險 | **joint venture** (=an agreement between two companies to do something together) 合資企業

venture² *v formal*【正式】**1** [I always+adv/prep] to risk going somewhere when it could be dangerous 冒風險〔去某處〕, 冒險: **[+out/through/into etc]** *Today's the first time I've ventured out of doors since my illness.* 自生病以來, 今天是我第一次冒險走到室外。**2** [T] to say something although you are afraid of how someone may react to it 敢於說, 大膽表示: **venture to do sth** *Nobody ventured to say a word.* 沒人敢說一句話。| **venture an opinion** (=say what you think) 大膽提出意見 *If I may venture an opinion, I'd say the plan needs more thought.* 我斗膽提一點意見, 我認為對這個計劃需多加思量。**3** [T] to take the risk of losing something; GAMBLE¹ (1) 冒失去…的風險; 以…作為賭注: **venture sth on sth** *Jeff ventured his whole fortune on one throw of the dice.* 傑夫把全部財產全押在這次的擲骰子上。**4 nothing ventured, nothing gained** used to say that you cannot achieve anything unless you take a risk 不入虎穴, 焉得虎子

venture on/upon sth *phr v* [T] to try to do something that involves risks 冒險做〔有風險或危險的事〕: *Now is not the time to venture on such an ambitious project.* 現在不是承擔這種野心勃勃的項目的時候。

venture cap·i·tal /ˈ‥ ˌ‥ˈ/ *n* [U] money that is lent to someone so that they can start a new business 風險資本

ven·ture·some /ˋvɛntʃɚsəm; ˈventʃəsəm/ *adj especially literary*【尤文】**1** a venturesome person is always ready to take risks〔人〕好冒險的; 大膽的 **2** a venturesome action involves taking risks〔行動〕有風險的 —**venturesomeness** *n* [U]

ven·ue /ˋvɛnju; ˈvenjuː/ *n* [C] a place where something such as a concert or a meeting is arranged to take place 舉辦地點, 舉行場所, 會場: *the venue for the latest round of talks* 舉行最新一輪談判的地點

Ve·nus /ˋvinəs; ˈviːnəs/ *n* [singular] the PLANET second in order from the sun and nearest to the Earth 金星 —see picture at 參見 SOLAR SYSTEM 圖

Venus fly·trap /ˌvinəs ˋflaɪtræp; ˌviːnəs ˈflaɪtræp/ *n* [C] a plant that catches and eats insects 捕蠅草

ve·ra·ci·ty /vəˋræsətɪ; vəˈræsɪ̣ti/ *n* [U] *formal* the quality of being true or of telling the truth【正式】誠實; 真實; 講實話 —**veracious** *adj*

ve·ran·da, verandah /vəˋrændə; vəˈrændə/ *n* [C] an open area with a floor and a roof that is built on the side of a house on the ground floor〔房屋側面有屋頂和地板的〕走廊, 遊廊: *Hannah sat sewing in the shade on the veranda.* 漢娜坐在遊廊的陰涼處做針線活。

verb /vɝb; vɜːb/ *n* [C] a word or group of words that is used to describe an action, experience, or state, for example 'come', 'see', 'be', 'put on' 動詞: *to conjugate a verb* 列舉動詞的詞形變化 —see also 另見 AUXILIARY VERB, PHRASAL VERB

verb·al /ˋvɝbḷ; ˈvɜːbəl/ *adj* **1** spoken, not written 口頭的, 非書面的: *a verbal agreement* 口頭協議 —opposite 反義詞 NONVERBAL **2** connected with words or using words 與言辭有關的, 用言辭的; 文字上的: *verbal skill* 使用言辭的技能 | *verbal abuse* 惡言, 謾罵 **3** related to a verb 動詞的

verb·al·ize also 又作 **-ise** *BrE*【英】/ˋvɝbḷˌaɪz; ˈvɜːbəlaɪz/ *v* [I,T] *formal* to express something in words【正式】用言語表達: *He couldn't verbalize his fears.* 他無法用言語表達他的恐懼。

verb·al·ly /ˋvɝbḷɪ; ˈvɜːbəli/ *adv* in spoken words and not in writing 口頭地, 口頭上

verbal noun /ˌ‥ ˈ‥/ *n* [C] a noun that describes an action or experience and has the form of a PRESENT PARTICIPLE. For example 'building' is a verbal noun in 'The building of the bridge was slow work', but simply a noun in 'The bank was a tall building'; GERUND 動名詞〔動詞的現在分詞形式作名詞用〕—see also 另見 NOUN

ver·ba·tim /vɚˋbetɪm; vɜːˈbeɪtɪ̣m/ *adj, adv* repeating the actual words that were spoken or written 逐字的[地], 一字不差的[地]: *a verbatim account of our conversation* 對我們談話內容的逐字報道

ver·bi·age /ˋvɝbɪɪdʒ; ˈvɜːbi-ɪdʒ/ *n* [U] *formal* too many unnecessary words in speech or writing【正式】〔說話或寫作的〕冗詞, 囉唆; 贅語: *eliminate irrelevant verbiage* 刪去無關的冗詞

ver·bose /vɚˋbos; vɜːˈbəʊs/ *adj formal* using or containing too many words【正式】囉唆的; 累贅的; 冗長的: *a verbose sermon* 喋喋不休的說教 —compare 比較 VERBAL —**verbosely** *adv* —**verboseness** or **verbosity** /vɚˋbɑsətɪ; vɜːˈbɒsɪ̣ti/ *n* [U]

ver·bo·ten /vəˋbotn̩; vəˈbəʊtən/ *adj German* not allowed; forbidden【德】不允許的; 被禁止的: *Being impolite to grown-ups was absolutely verboten in our household.* 我們家絕對不允許對成年人無禮。

ver·dant /ˋvɝdn̩t; ˈvɜːdənt/ *adj literary* verdant land is covered with freshly growing green grass and plants【文】〔土地〕長滿青翠草木的: *verdant fields* 青翠的田野

ver·dict /ˋvɝdɪkt; ˈvɜːdɪkt/ *n* [C] **1** an official decision made by a JURY in a court of law about whether someone is guilty or not guilty of a crime〔法庭上陪審團作出的〕裁決, 裁定: *a majority verdict of 10 to 2* 一項10比2的多數裁決 | **return a verdict** *formal* (=give a verdict)【正式】作出裁決 | **reach a verdict** (=make a decision) 作出裁定 *After a week the jury had still not reached a verdict.* 一週過去了, 陪審團仍未作出裁決。**2** an official decision or opinion made by a person or group that has authority〔由當權者作出的〕正式決定; 正式意見: *The panel will be giving their verdict tomorrow.* 專責小組明天將提出正式意見。—see also 另見 OPEN VERDICT **3** *informal* an opinion or decision about something【非正式】意見; 決定: **[+on]** *What's your verdict on the movie?* 你覺得那部電影怎麼樣?

ver·di·gris /ˋvɝdɪˌgris; ˈvɜːdɪ̣griː/ *n* [U] a greenish-blue substance that forms a thin layer on COPPER (1) or BRASS

(1) that is kept in wet conditions〔銅器等的〕銅綠

ver·dure /ˋvɝdʒɚ; ˈvɜːdʒə/ *n* [U] *literary* the bright green colour of grass, plants, trees etc, or the plants themselves【文】草木的青翠; 青翠的草木

verge¹ /vɝdʒ; vɜːdʒ/ *n* [C] **1** *especially BrE* the edge or border of a road or path etc【尤英】〔路等的〕邊緣, 邊界: *the grass verge* 草地的邊緣 **2 be on the verge of** to be about to do something 瀕於, 即將: *Jessica was on the verge of tears.* 傑西卡幾乎就要哭了。| *scientists on the verge of a major breakthrough* 即將取得重大突破的科學家

verge² *v*

verge on/upon sth *phr v* [T] to be very close to a harmful or extreme state 接近, 瀕於: **verge on madness/panic/chaos etc** *Daniela's strange behaviour sometimes verges on madness.* 丹尼拉的怪異行為有時近乎瘋狂。| **verging on the impossible/ridiculous** (=almost impossible etc) 近乎不可能/荒謬

ver·ger /ˋvɝdʒɚ; ˈvɜːdʒə/ *n* [C] *especially BrE* someone whose job is to look after the contents of a church and perform small duties like showing people where to sit【尤英】教堂司事[堂守]

ver·i·fy /ˋvɛrəˌfaɪ; ˈverɪfaɪ/ *v* **verified, verifying** [T] **1** to find out if a fact, statement etc is correct or true; check 查證; 核實: **verify sth with sb** *These details must be verified with the Home Office.* 這些細節必須向內政部核實。| **verify that** *The bank will have to verify that you are the owner of the property.* 銀行必須核實你是該財產的所有者。**2** to state that something is true; CONFIRM 證實; 確認: *The prisoner's statement was verified by several witnesses.* 犯人的供述得到幾個證人的證實。—**verifiable** *adj* —**verification** /ˌvɛrɪfɪˋkeʃən; ˌverɪfɪˈkeɪʃən/ *n* [C,U]: *the verification of scientific laws* 科學定律的驗證

ver·i·ly /ˋvɛrəlɪ; ˈverɪli/ *adv biblical* really【聖經】真實地, 確實

ver·i·si·mil·i·tude /ˌvɛrəsəˋmɪləˌtud; ˌverɪsɪˈmɪlɪtjuːd/ *n* [U] *formal* the quality of a piece of art, a performance etc that makes it seem like something real【正式】貌似真實; 逼真

ver·i·ta·ble /ˋvɛrətəbḷ; ˈverɪtəbəl/ *adj formal* a word used to emphasize a comparison that you think is correct【正式】名副其實的: *The male bird is a veritable rainbow of colors.* 雄鳥色彩斑斕, 如彩虹一般。—**veritably** *adv*

ver·i·ty /ˋvɛrətɪ; ˈverɪti/ *n* [C usually plural 一般用複數] *formal* an important principle or fact about life, the world etc, that is true in all situations【正式】重要的真理[準則、事實]: *one of the eternal verities* 基本的道德準則之一; 永恆的真理之一

ver·mi·cel·li /ˌvɝməˋsɛlɪ; ˌvɜːmɪˈseli/ *n* [U] Italian PASTA (=food that is made from a mixture of flour, eggs, and water) that is shaped into very thin strings and cooked in boiling water〔意大利〕細麵條 —see picture at 參見 PASTA 圖

ver·mil·lion /vɚˋmɪljən; vəˈmɪljən/ *n* [U] a bright reddish-orange colour 朱紅色, 鮮紅色 —**vermillion** *adj*

ver·min /ˋvɝmɪn; ˈvɜːmɪn/ *n* [plural] **1** small animals or birds that destroy crops, spoil food etc, and are difficult to control 害獸; 害鳥: *a barn infested with vermin* 遭害獸侵擾的穀倉 —compare 比較 PEST **2** insects that live on people's or animals' bodies, bite them, and drink their blood〔寄生在人或動物身上並吸血的〕寄生蟲: *a bed alive with vermin* 滿是寄生蟲的牀鋪 **3** unpleasant people who cause problems for society 危害社會的人, 害人蟲, 敗類: *He thinks all beggars are vermin.* 他認為所有的乞丐都是寄生蟲。

ver·min·ous /ˋvɝmɪnəs; ˈvɜːmɪnəs/ *adj* **1** full of insects that bite you 長滿寄生蟲的: *the tramp's verminous old coat* 流浪乞丐滿是虱子的舊外套 **2** very unpleasant or nasty 污穢的, 討厭的: *verminous blackmail letters* 言語污穢的敲詐信

ver·mouth /ˋvɝməθ; ˈvɜːməθ/ *n* [U] a drink made from wine that has strong-tasting substances added to it, usually drunk before a meal 味美思酒, 苦艾酒

ver·nac·u·lar /vɚˋnækjəlɚ; vəˈnækjʊlə/ *n* [C usually singular 一般用單數] the language spoken in a country or area, especially when it is not the official language〔尤指非官方語言的〕本國語; 本地語, 土話, 方言 —**vernacular** *adj*

ver·nal /ˋvɝnḷ; ˈvɜːnl/ *adj* [only before noun 僅用於名詞前] *literary or technical* connected with the spring season【文或術語】春季的, 與春天有關的

ver·ru·ca /vəˋrukə; vəˈruːkə/ *n* [C] a small hard infectious thing that can be painful and grows on the skin on the bottom of your foot〔腳底生的〕疣, 肉贅; WART *AmE*【美】

versa —see 見 VICE VERSA

ver·sa·tile /ˋvɝsətɪl; ˈvɜːsətaɪl/ *adj approving*【褒】**1** good at doing a lot of different things and able to learn new skills quickly and easily 多才多藝的: *a very versatile performer* 多才多藝的表演者 **2** having many different uses 有多種用途的, 多功能的, 萬用的: *Nylon is a versatile material.* 尼龍是一種有多種用途的材料。—**versatility** /ˌvɝsəˋtɪlətɪ; ˌvɜːsəˈtɪlɪti/ *n* [U]

verse /vɝs; vɜːs/ *n* **1** [C] a set of lines that forms one part of a song 一節歌詞: *Let's sing the last verse again.* 我們把最後一節再唱一遍吧。—compare 比較 CHORUS¹ (1) **2** [C] a set of lines of poetry that forms one part of a poem, and that usually has a pattern that is repeated in the other parts 詩節: *Learn the first two verses of the poem.* 把這首詩的頭兩節記住。**3** [U] words arranged in the form of poetry 詩; 詩體; 韻文: *a book of comic verse* 一本滑稽詩集 —compare 比較 PROSE —see also 另見 BLANK VERSE, FREE VERSE **4** [C] one of the numbered groups of sentences that make up each CHAPTER (=numbered part) of a book of the Bible〔《聖經》中標有數碼的〕節 —see also 另見 **give/quote chapter and verse** (CHAPTER (5))

versed /vɝst; vɜːst/ *adj* **be (well) versed in** to know a lot about a subject or to be skilled in doing something 精通…, 通曉…, 對…造詣很深: *a woman well versed in the art of diplomacy* 熟諳外交藝術的婦女

ver·si·fi·ca·tion /ˌvɝsəfəˋkeʃən; ˌvɜːsɪfɪˈkeɪʃən/ *n* [U] *technical* the particular pattern that a poem is written in【術語】詩體; 詩律

ver·sion /ˋvɝʒən; ˈvɜːʃən/ *n* [C] **1** a copy of something that has been changed slightly so that it is different from the thing being copied〔同一種物件稍有不同的〕樣式, 型號; 複製件, 變體: **[+of]** *The dress is a cheaper version of one seen at the Paris fashion shows.* 這套服裝是巴黎時裝展上看到的那一款的廉價複製品。| **old/first/later etc version of** *This is a sophisticated version of the old tripod camera.* 這是老式三角架相機中的精緻款式。**2** a description of an event given by one person, especially when it is compared with someone else's description of the same thing〔某人對某一事件作出的〕描述; 說法, 講法: **[+of]** *The two newspapers gave different versions of what happened.* 兩家報紙對發生的事說法不一。**3** a play, film, piece of music etc that is slightly different from the book, piece of music etc on which it is based〔依據書、音樂等稍作改編的戲劇、電影、音樂等的〕版本; 改編本: **[+of]** *an abridged version of the play* 該劇的節略本 **4 an English/Japanese/Spanish version** an English etc translation of a book, poem, or other piece of writing 英文/日文/西班牙文譯本: **[+of]** *an English version of a German play* 德語劇本的英譯本

ver·so /ˋvɝso; ˈvɜːsəʊ/ *n* [C] *technical* a page on the left-hand side of a book【術語】〔書的〕左頁 —compare 比較 RECTO —**verso** *adj*

ver·sus /ˋvɝsəs; ˈvɜːsəs/ written abbreviation 縮寫為 **v** *or* **vs** *prep* **1** used to show that two people or teams are against each other in a game or court case〔比賽或訴訟中〕…對…: *the New York Knicks versus the Los Angeles Lakers* 紐約尼克斯隊對洛杉磯湖人隊 | *the Supreme*

Court decision in Roe versus Wade 最高法院關於羅對韋德訴訟案的裁決 **2** used when comparing the advantages of two different things, ideas etc 與...相對; 與...相比: *The Finance Minister must weigh up the benefits of a tax cut versus those of increased public spending.* 財政部長必須權衡是減稅還是增加公共開支更有利。

ver·te·bra /ˈvɝtəbrə; ˈvɜːtʃbrə/ *n plural* **vertebrae** /-brɪ; -bri/ [C] one of the small hollow bones down the centre of your back 脊椎, 椎骨 —**vertebral** *adj*

ver·te·brate /ˈvɝtəˌbret; ˈvɜːtʃbrʃt/ *n* [C] a living creature that has a BACKBONE (1) 脊椎動物 —compare 比較 INVERTEBRATE —**vertebrate** *adj*

ver·tex /ˈvɝtɛks; ˈvɜːteks/ *n plural* **vertices** /-təˌsiz; -tʃsiːz/ *or* **vertexes** [C+of] *technical*【術語】**1** the angle opposite the base of a shape such as a PYRAMID, CONE, TRIANGLE etc〔圓錐體、三角形等的〕頂角 **2** the point where the two lines of an angle meet〔一個角兩線相交的〕頂點 **3** the highest point 最高點: *the vertex of an arch* 拱門的頂

ver·ti·cal[1] /ˈvɝtɪkl; ˈvɜːtɪkəl/ *adj* **1** pointing straight up and down in a line and forming an angle of 90 degrees with the ground or with another straight line 垂直的; 直立的: *a vertical line* 垂直線 | *blue and green vertical stripes* 藍綠相間的豎條 | *a sheer, vertical cliff* 陡直的峭壁 **2** having a structure in which there are top, middle, and bottom levels 立體式的, 各種層次的, 從上到下的: *a vertical power relationship between top decision makers and the rest of the organization* 從高層決策者到機構其餘人員的立體式權力關係 —compare 比較 HORIZONTAL —**vertically** /-klɪ; -kli/ *adv*

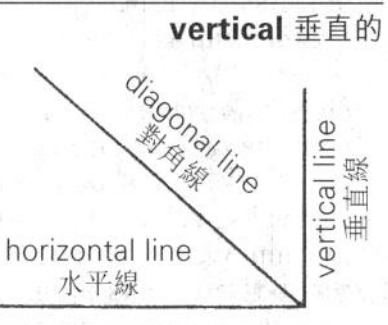

vertical[2] *n* **the vertical** the direction of something that is vertical 垂直方向; 垂直物, 垂直線: *an angle of about 30 degrees off the vertical* 距垂直線大約 30° 的角度

ver·tig·i·nous /vɝˈtɪdʒənəs; vɜːˈtɪdʒʃnəs/ *adj formal* a vertiginous place or position makes you feel ill because it is so high【正式】高得令人眩暈的; 感到眩暈的: *a vertiginous drop to the valley below* 直達谷底的令人眩暈的下落

ver·ti·go /ˈvɝtɪˌgo; ˈvɜːtɪgəʊ/ *n* [U] a sick DIZZY (1) feeling caused by looking down from a very high place〔因從高處俯視而產生的〕眩暈, 頭暈

verve /vɝv; vɜːv/ *n* [U] the quality of being cheerful and exciting which is shown in the way someone does something 活力; 熱情: *Cziffra played the Hungarian dances with great verve.* 席夫拉熱情洋溢地演奏匈牙利舞曲。

ve·ry[1] /ˈvɛrɪ; ˈveri/ *adv* **1** [+adj/adv] used to emphasize an adjective or adverb or to add force to an expression〔用於強調所修飾的形容詞或副詞, 或加強語氣〕很, 非常: *"Can I help you with those bags?" "Thanks, that's very nice of you."* "我能幫你提那些包嗎?" "謝謝, 你真是太好了。" | *It feels very cold up in the bedrooms.* 臥室裡冷極了。| *I feel a lot better today thanks very much.* 我今天好多了, 非常感謝。| *We must be aware of the very real problems that these people face.* 我們必須清楚這些人面臨的非常現實的問題。| *The traffic's moving very slowly this morning.* 今天早上路上來往的車輛開得很慢。| *James was very much hoping you'd be able to come to the wedding.* 詹姆斯非常希望你能來參加婚禮。| **the very same** (=used to emphasize the fact that one thing is exactly the same as something else) 完全相同的, 一模一樣的 *She was wearing the very same shoes as me.* 她穿的鞋跟我的一模一樣。**2** [+adj] used to emphasize superlative adjectives〔用於形容詞最高級前以加強語氣〕: *We only use the very best ingredients.* 我們只用最最好的配料。| *He might have told you he wasn't coming at the very least.* 他本來至少應該告訴你他不來了。| *This is the very last time I lend you money.* 這是我最後一次借錢給你。**3 your very own** used to emphasize the fact that something belongs to one particular person and to no one else〔強調某物歸某人所有〕完全屬於某人自己的: *She was thrilled at the idea of having her very own toys to play with.* 想到能玩完全屬於自己的玩具, 她感到極為興奮。**4 not very a)** used before a quality to mean exactly the opposite of that quality〔表示相反〕絕不, 根本不: *The teacher wasn't very pleased* (=was angry) *when she saw a dead mouse on the desk.* 看到桌子上有一隻死老鼠時, 老師很是惱火。**b)** only slightly 不很, 不大, 稍微: *"Was the play interesting?" "Not very."* "這齣戲好看嗎?" "不怎麼好看。"

very[2] *adj* [only before noun 僅用於名詞前] used to emphasize a noun〔用以加強名詞的語氣〕正是那一個的, 正是的: *He died in this very room.* 他就是在這個房間裡去世的。| **this very minute** (=now) 就現在 *You'd better start doing some work this very minute.* 你最好現在就開始幹點活。| **the very thought** (=just thinking about something) 一想到... *The very thought of food makes me feel ill.* 一想到食物, 我就覺得不舒服。| **the very idea!** (=used to express shock at what someone says or suggests) 虧你想得出來!〔對某人所說的表示震驚〕*Of course you shouldn't travel on your own at that time of night. The very idea!* 你當然不該在夜裡那個時候獨自外出。虧你想得出來! | **the very thing** (=used to describe an object or idea that is exactly right for a particular purpose) 正是它〔表示某物或意見正是所需要的〕*This gadget is the very thing for turning stiff taps.* 這個小玩意正好用來擰過緊的龍頭。

very high fre·quen·cy /ˌ... ˈ.../ *n* [U] VHF 甚高頻

Very light /ˈvɛrɪ ˌlaɪt; ˈvɪəri laɪt/ *n* [C] *trademark* a bright light produced by a kind of burning bullet that is fired into the air as a signal that a ship needs help【商標】維利式(彩色)信號彈, 閃光信號彈〔船隻求助時所發的信號彈〕

Very pis·tol /ˈ.. ˌ../ *n* [C] the gun from which a Very light is shot 維利式(彩色)信號槍

ves·pers /ˈvɛspɚz; ˈvespəz/ *n* [U] the evening service in some types of Christian church 晚禱

ves·sel /ˈvɛsl; ˈvesəl/ *n* [C] **1** *formal* a ship or large boat【正式】船; 艦: *a fishing vessel* 漁船 **2** *old use or formal* a container for holding liquids【舊或正式】〔盛液體用的〕容器, 器皿 **3** *technical* a tube that carries blood through your body, such as a VEIN, or that carries liquid through a plant【術語】〔人體的〕血管; 脈管; 〔植物的〕導管

vest[1] /vɛst; vest/ *n* [C] **1** *BrE* a piece of underwear without SLEEVE*s* that you wear under a shirt【英】內衣背心, 汗衫; UNDERSHIRT *AmE*【美】—see picture at 參見 UNDERWEAR 圖 **2** *AmE* a piece of clothing without arms that has buttons down the front and is usually worn under a JACKET, especially by men as part of a suit【美】馬甲, 西裝背心; WAISTCOAT *BrE*【英】**3** a piece of special clothing without SLEEVE*s* that is worn to protect your body 防護用背心: *a bullet-proof vest* 防彈背心

vest[2] *v*

vest in *phr v* [T] **1** [**vest** sth **in** sb] to give someone the official legal right to use power, property etc 授予, 賦予, 給予〔某人法律權力〕: **be vested in** *In most countries the right to make new laws is vested in the people's representatives.* 在大多數國家, 民眾代表都被授予制訂新法律的權力。**2** [**vest in** sb/sth not in passive 不用被動態] if property, power etc vests in someone, it belongs to them legally or officially〔財產、權力等〕歸屬於: *In former times this power vested in the Church.* 在過去, 這一權力屬於教會。

vest sb **with** sth *phr v* [T] *formal* to give someone the official or legal right to use power, property etc【正式】授予〔某人〕使用〔某種權力或財產等〕的權利

ves·tal vir·gin /ˌvɛstl ˈvɝdʒɪn; ˌvestl ˈvɜːdʒʃn/ *n* [C] a young unmarried woman who had duties in one of the ancient Roman temples 維斯太貞女〔在古羅馬廟宇中侍奉的年輕未婚女子〕

vested in·terest /,·· '··/ *n* [C] **1** if you have a vested interest in something happening, you have a strong reason for wanting it to happen because you will get an advantage from it 既得利益: *The tobacco companies have a vested interest in claiming that smoking isn't harmful.* 煙草公司聲稱抽煙無害，因當中有其既得利益。**2 vested interests** [plural] the groups of people who have a vested interest in something 既得利益集團: *The new reforms were opposed by both vested interests and welfare groups.* 新的改革既受到既得利益集團的反對，也受到福利團體的反對。

ves·ti·bule /ˋvɛstə,bjul; ˈvestəbju:l/ *n* [C] *formal*【正式】**1** a wide passage or small room inside the front door of a public building〔公共建築物前門內的〕門廳，前廳 **2** *AmE* the enclosed passage at each end of a railway carriage that connects it with the next carriage【美】〔火車車廂與另一車廂之間的〕通廊，連廊

ves·tige /ˋvɛstɪdʒ; ˈvestɪdʒ/ *n* [C] *formal*【正式】**1** a small part or amount of something that still remains when most of it no longer exists 痕跡，遺跡；殘餘: **[+of]** *The new law removed the last vestiges of royal power.* 新法律掃除了王權的最後殘餘。**2** the smallest possible amount of a quality or feeling 一點兒，絲毫: **[+of]** *There's not a vestige of truth in the story.* 這個故事毫無真實性可言。

ves·ti·gi·al /vɛsˋtɪdʒɪəl; veˈstɪdʒiəl/ *adj* **1** *technical* a vestigial part of the body has never developed completely or has almost disappeared because it is no longer used【術語】〔器官等〕退化的: *Some snakes have vestigial legs.* 某些蛇有退化了的腳。**2** *formal* remaining as a sign that something existed after most of it has disappeared【正式】殘餘的，殘留的，遺跡的: *vestigial traces of a past civilization* 昔日文明的遺跡 **—vestigially** *adv*

vest·ment /ˋvɛstmənt; ˈvestmənt/ *n* [C often plural 常用複數] a piece of clothing worn by priests during church services〔神職人員主持宗教儀式時穿的〕法衣，祭服；禮儀服

ves·try /ˋvɛstrɪ; ˈvestri/ *n* [C] a small room in a church where the priest and CHOIR change into their vestments and where holy plates, cups etc are stored〔教堂的〕法衣室，聖具室〔供放置各種聖器以及穿法衣用〕

3 **vet¹** /vɛt; vet/ *n* [C] **1** someone who is trained to give medical care and treatment to sick animals 獸醫; VETERINARIAN *AmE*【美】**2** *AmE informal* a VETERAN (1)【美，非正式】退伍軍人: *a Vietnam vet* 越戰退伍軍人

vet² *v* [T] **1** *BrE* to check someone's past activities, relationships etc in order to make sure they are suitable for a particular job, especially one that involves dealing with secret information【英】審查〔某人過去的活動、親屬關係等〕: *The candidates are vetted by Central Office.* 候選人受到中央辦公室的審查。**2** to check a report or speech carefully to make sure it is acceptable 檢審〔報告或演講等〕

vetch /vɛtʃ; vetʃ/ *n* [C] a plant with small flowers, often used to feed farm animals 巢菜，野豌豆

vet·e·ran /ˋvɛtərən; ˈvetərən/ *n* [C] **1** someone who has been a soldier, sailor etc in a war 經歷過戰爭的老軍人，老水兵，退伍軍人: *D Day veterans* 參加過二次大戰中盟軍諾曼底登陸的老兵 | *a veteran of the Second World War* 第二次世界大戰時的老兵 **2** someone who has had a lot of experience of a particular activity 老手，〔在某方面〕經驗豐富的人: *a veteran traveller* 富有經驗的旅行家 | **[+of]** *a veteran of the anti-apartheid movement* 反對種族隔離的老戰士 | **veteran politician/campaigner/statesman etc** (=someone who has been a politician etc for a long time) 老資格的政客/活動家/政治家等 *veteran Soviet politician Andrei Gromyko* 資深的（前）蘇聯政治家安德雷·葛羅米柯

veteran car /,··· '·/ *n* [C] *BrE* a car built before 1905【英】〔1905年前製造的〕老爺車

vet·e·ri·na·ri·an /,vɛtərəˋnɛrɪən; ˌvetərəˈneəriən/ *n* [C] *AmE* someone who is trained to give medical care and treatment to sick animals; VET¹ (1)【美】獸醫

vet·e·ri·na·ry /ˋvɛtərə,nɛrɪ; ˈvetərənəri/ *adj* [only before noun 僅用於名詞前] *technical* connected with the medical care and treatment of sick animals【術語】獸醫的: *veterinary science* 獸醫學

veterinary sur·geon /ˈ····· ,··/ *n* [C] *BrE formal* a VET¹ (1)【英，正式】獸醫

ve·to¹ /ˋvito; ˈvi:təʊ/ *v* **vetoed, vetoing** [T] **1** to officially refuse to allow something to happen, especially something that other people or organizations have agreed 否決〔他人或其他組織已贊同之事〕: *The president vetoed a tax increase on gasoline last week.* 總統上週否決了增收汽油稅的議案。**2** to refuse to accept a particular plan or suggestion 不同意；反對〔某個計劃或建議〕: *Jenny wanted to invite all her friends, but I quickly vetoed that idea.* 珍妮想把她的朋友都請來，但我馬上對此表示反對。

veto² *n plural* **vetos** [C,U] a refusal to give official permission for something, or the right to refuse to give such permission 否決（權）: **[+on]** *There is the threat of a presidential veto on this legislation.* 存在着總統可能否決這項立法的威脅。| **power/right of veto** *They exercised their right of veto in the Security Council to prevent the resolution being passed.* 他們在安理會行使了否決權，阻止那項決議通過。

vex /vɛks; veks/ *v* [T] *old-fashioned* to make someone feel annoyed or worried【過時】使惱怒；使煩惱

vex·a·tion /vɛksˋeʃən; vekˈseɪʃən/ *n* **1** [U] *formal* the feeling of being worried or annoyed by something【正式】煩惱，苦惱；惱火 **2** [C] *old-fashioned* something that worries or annoys you【過時】令人煩惱[惱火]的事

vex·a·tious /vɛksˋeʃəs; vekˈseɪʃəs/ *adj old-fashioned* making you feel annoyed or worried【過時】令人惱火[煩惱]的 **—vexatiously** *adv*

vexed /vɛkst; vekst/ *adj* **1** **[+at/with]** *old-fashioned* annoyed or worried【過時】惱火的；煩惱的 **2 vexed question/issue** a complicated problem that has caused a lot of arguments and is difficult to solve 引起爭論的問題，棘手的問題: *the vexed question of how to deal with hunger-strikers* 如何對付絕食抗議者這一難題

V-for·ma·tion /ˋvi fɔr,meʃən; ˈvi: fɔ:,meɪʃən/ *n* [C] if birds or planes fly in a V-formation, they form the shape of the letter V as they fly〔鳥或飛機成羣飛行時的〕V形隊形；人字形隊列

VGA /,vi dʒi ˋe; ˌvi: dʒi: ˈeɪ/ *n* [singular] Video Graphics Array; a standard of GRAPHICS (=pictures and letters) on a computer screen that has many different colours and is of a high quality 視頻圖形陣列

VHF /,vi ɛtʃ ˋɛf; ˌvi: eɪtʃ ˈef/ *n* [U] *technical* very high frequency; radio waves that move very quickly and produce good sound quality【術語】〔無線電的〕甚高頻

vi·a /ˋvaɪə; ˈvaɪə/ *prep* **1** travelling through a place on the way to another place 經過；取道: *We flew to Athens via Paris.* 我們經由巴黎飛往雅典。**2** using a particular person, machine etc to send something 通過〔某人或某機器等〕傳送〔某物〕；借助於: *I sent a message to Kitty via her sister.* 我通過基蒂的妹妹給她帶去一封信。

vi·a·ble /ˋvaɪəbl; ˈvaɪəbəl/ *adj* **1** a viable plan or system can work successfully〔計劃或系統〕切實可行的: **a viable proposition/alternative/method etc** *Nuclear energy is only one viable alternative to coal or gas.* 核能只是煤或天然氣其中一種可行的替代物。| **economically/commercially viable** *The project is not economically viable.* 這個項目從經濟效益來看是不可行的。**2** *technical* able to continue to live or to develop into a living thing【術語】能存活的；能生長發育的 **—viably** *adv* **—viability** /,vaɪəˋbɪlətɪ; ˌvaɪəˈbɪləti/ *n* [U]: *the long term viability of the company* 公司長期存在的可能性

vi·a·duct /ˋvaɪə,dʌkt; ˈvaɪədʌkt/ *n* [C] a long high bridge across a valley that has a road or railway on it〔架於山谷上的公路或鐵路〕高架橋

vi·al /ˋvaɪəl; ˈvaɪəl/ *n* [C] a PHIAL 小瓶；小藥瓶

vi·ands /ˈvaɪəndz; ˈvaɪəndz/ *n* [plural] *old use* food【舊】食物

vibes /vaɪbz; vaɪbz/ *n* [plural] *informal*【非正式】**1** the good or bad feelings that a particular person, group of people, or situation seems to produce and that you react to 感應, 共鳴: **good/bad/strange vibes** *I'm getting strange vibes from this guy, I think he's maybe lying to us.* 這傢伙給我的感覺怪怪的, 我想他可能在對我們說謊。**2** a VIBRAPHONE 電顫琴

vi·brant /ˈvaɪbrənt; ˈvaɪbrənt/ *adj* **1** exciting and full of activity and energy 令人興奮的; 充滿活力的, 精力充沛的, 活躍的: *Hong Kong is a vibrant, fascinating city.* 香港是個富有活力的迷人城市。**2** a vibrant light or colour is bright and strong〔光或顏色〕明亮的; 鮮豔的: *vibrant paintings of bullfights* 色彩鮮豔的鬥牛畫 —**vibrancy** *n* [U] —**vibrantly** *adv*

vi·bra·phone /ˈvaɪbrəˌfon; ˈvaɪbrəfəʊn/ *n* [C] an electronic musical instrument that consists of metal bars that you hit to produce a sound 電顫琴〔一種打擊樂器〕

vi·brate /ˈvaɪbret; vaɪˈbreɪt/ *v* [I,T] to shake or make something shake continuously with small fast movements (使) 顫動; (使) 震動; (使) 振動: *We could feel the floor vibrating to the beat of the music.* 我們能感覺到地板隨音樂的節拍而顫動。| *The vocal cords vibrate as air passes over them.* 聲帶在氣流通過時產生振動。

vi·bra·tion /vaɪˈbreʃən; vaɪˈbreɪʃən/ *n* [C,U] **1** a continuous slight shaking movement 顫動, 振顫; 震動: *You can feel the vibrations of the ship's engine.* 你能感覺到船上發動機的震動。**2 vibrations** [plural] VIBES (1) 感應, 共鳴

vi·bra·to /vɪˈbrɑto; vɪˈbrɑːtəʊ/ *n* [U] a way of singing or playing a musical note so that it goes up and down very slightly in PITCH[1] (3)〔演唱或演奏的〕顫動效果, 顫音

vi·brat·or /ˈvaɪbretɚ; vaɪˈbreɪtə/ *n* [C] a piece of electrical equipment that produces a small shaking movement, used especially in MASSAGE or to get sexual pleasure 振動器;〔尤指按摩或獲取性快感時用的〕振動按摩器; 顫震器

vic·ar /ˈvɪkɚ; ˈvɪkə/ *n* [C] a priest in the Church of England who is in charge of a church in a particular area〔英國國教的〕教區牧師

vic·ar·age /ˈvɪkərɪdʒ; ˈvɪkərɪdʒ/ *n* [C] a house where a vicar lives 教區牧師的住宅

vi·car·i·ous /vaɪˈkɛrɪəs; vɪˈkeəriəs/ *adj* [only before noun 僅用於名詞前] experienced by watching or reading about someone else doing something, rather than by doing it yourself 間接體驗他人感受的; 產生同感[共鳴]的: **vicarious pleasure/satisfaction/excitement etc** *the vicarious pleasure that parents get from their children's success* 父母因子女的成功而獲得同樣的快樂 —**vicariously** *adv*

3 **vice** /vaɪs; vaɪs/ *n* **1** [U] evil or criminal activities that involve sex or drugs〔涉及性或毒品的〕罪惡, 邪惡行徑; 不道德行為: **vice ring** (=a group of criminals involved in vice) 犯罪團夥 *The police have smashed a vice ring in Chicago.* 警察搗毀了芝加哥的一個犯罪團夥。**2** [C] a bad habit 惡習: *Smoking is my only vice.* 吸煙是我唯一的惡習。**3** [C] a bad or immoral quality in someone's character〔性格上的〕缺陷, 弱點; 劣根性: *the vice of greed* 貪婪的劣根性 —opposite 反義詞 VIRTUE **4** usually 一般作 **vise** *AmE*【美】[C] a tool that holds an object firmly so that you can work on it using both your hands 老虎鉗, 台鉗

vice- /vaɪs; vaɪs/ *prefix* the person next in official rank below someone, who can represent them or act instead of them〔指人〕副; 代 (理): *the Vice-President of the USA* 美國副總統 | *the vice-captain of the cricket team* 板球隊的副隊長

vice-ad·mi·ral /ˌ· ˈ···◂/ *n* [C] a high rank in the British or US navy, or someone who has this rank〔英、美海軍中的〕中將的軍銜; 海軍中將 —see table on page C6 參見C6頁附錄

vice-chan·cel·lor /ˌ· ˈ···/ *n* [C] **1** someone who is in charge of a British university〔英國負主管之責的〕大學(副) 校長 —compare 比較 CHANCELLOR (2) **2** someone who is next in rank to the CHANCELLOR (=person in charge) of a university in the US〔美國的〕大學副校長

vice·like /ˈvaɪsˌlaɪk; ˈvaɪslaɪk/ *adj* **a vicelike grip** a very firm hold 像老虎鉗一般的緊握, 抓牢

vice pres·i·dent /ˌ· ˈ···/ *n* [C] **1** the person who is next in rank to the president of a country and who is responsible for the president's duties if he or she is ill 副總統 **2** *AmE* someone who is responsible for a particular part of a company【美】〔公司等負責某個部門的〕副總裁: *our executive vice president for marketing* 主管營銷的執行副總裁

vice·roy /ˈvaɪsrɔɪ; ˈvaɪsrɔɪ/ *n* [C] a man who was sent by the king or queen to rule another country, especially in the British Empire〔尤指在英帝國時期由國王或女王派去管理另一國家的〕總督: *the viceroy of India* 印度總督

vice squad /ˈ· ·/ *n* [C usually singular 一般用單數] the part of the police force that deals with crimes involving sex or drugs〔處理與性、吸毒等有關的案件的〕警察緝捕隊

vice ver·sa /ˈvaɪsɪ ˈvɝsə; ˌvaɪs ˈvɜːsə/ *adv* used when the opposite of a situation you have just described is also true 反過來也是如此, 反之亦然: *Anything the men wanted the women didn't, and vice versa.* 男人想要的東西女人不想要, 反之亦然。

vi·cin·i·ty /vəˈsɪnətɪ; vɪ̈ˈsɪnɪ̈ti/ *n* **1 in the vicinity (of)** in the area around a particular place 在…附近: *The car was found abandoned in the vicinity of Waterloo Station.* 汽車被發現棄置在滑鐵盧車站附近。**2 in the vicinity of** *formal* close to a particular amount or measurement【正式】在…左右, 大約…: *a price somewhere in the vicinity of £25,000* 大約 25,000 英鎊的價格

vi·cious /ˈvɪʃəs; ˈvɪʃəs/ *adj* **1** violent and dangerous, and likely to hurt someone 兇險的; 會造成傷害的: *a vicious attack* 兇狠的攻擊 | *a vicious criminal* 兇暴的罪犯 | *Keep away from that dog, he can be vicious.* 離那隻狗遠點, 它很兇猛。**2** cruel and deliberately trying to hurt someone's feelings or make their character seem bad 狠毒的, 惡意的: *Sarah can be quite vicious at times.* 莎拉有時相當狠毒。| **vicious attack/campaign/rumour etc** *Senator Logan launched a vicious attack on the president and his advisors.* 參議員洛根對總統及其顧問發動了一場惡毒的攻擊。**3** unpleasantly strong or severe 劇烈的; 惡劣的: *a vicious gust of wind* 一股很猛烈的風 | *a vicious headache* 劇烈的頭痛 —**viciously** *adv*: *He twisted her arm viciously.* 他兇狠地擰她的胳膊。—**viciousness** *n* [U]

vicious cir·cle /ˌ·· ˈ··/ *n* [singular] a situation in which one problem causes another problem that then causes the first problem again, so that the whole process continues to be repeated 惡性循環

vi·cis·si·tudes /vəˈsɪsəˌtudz; vɪ̈ˈsɪsɪ̈tjuːdz/ *n* [plural] *formal* the continuous changes and problems that affect a situation or someone's life【正式】〔影響某種局面或個人生活的〕改變, 變遷; 興衰: *the vicissitudes of married life* 婚後生活的變化

vic·tim /ˈvɪktɪm; ˈvɪktɪ̈m/ *n* [C] **1** someone who has been attacked, robbed, or murdered 受害者; 犧牲者: *In most sexual offences the attacker is known to the victim.* 在大多數性侵犯事件中, 施暴者是受害者認識的人。| **rape/murder etc victim** *Most homicide victims are under 30.* 大多殺人案的受害者不足 30 歲。**2** someone who suffers because they are affected by a bad situation or by an illness〔惡劣情況的〕受災者;〔疾病的〕患者: *a victim of circumstances* 環境的受害者 | **famine/earthquake/flood victims** *a massive aid program for the famine victims* 對遭受饑荒者的大規模援助計劃 | **polio/cholera/AIDS victim** *Many cholera victims were being left to die.* 許多霍亂患者被置於等死的境地。**3** something that 2 2

is badly affected or destroyed by a situation or action 犧牲品: **fall victim to** (=become a victim of something) 成為...的犧牲品 *Vital public services have fallen victim to budget cuts.* 一些重要的公眾服務項目成了削減預算的犧牲品。**4 be a victim of its own success** to be badly affected by some unexpected results of being very successful 因成功而反受其害: *The once-peaceful village has attracted so many tourists that it has become a victim of its own success.* 那個曾經寧靜的村子吸引了如此眾多的遊客, 結果反受其害。**5 sacrificial victim** a person or animal that is killed and offered as a SACRIFICE[1] (3) (=gift) to a god 獻祭用的人[牲畜], 犧牲品 **6 fashion/style victim** *informal* someone who always wears the newest fashions whether it suits them or not【非正式】盲目追求時尚者

vic·tim·ize also 又作 **-ise** *BrE*【英】/ˋvɪktɪm͵aɪz; ˈvɪktɨmaɪz/ *v* [T] to treat someone unfairly, especially because you dislike their beliefs or the race they belong to〔尤指因厭惡某人的信仰或所屬的人種而〕不公正地對待, 使受害; 迫害: *The sacked men claim they have been victimized because of their political activity.* 被解雇者聲稱他們是由於自己的政治活動而受到迫害。—**victimization** /͵vɪktɪməˋzeʃən; ͵vɪktɨmaɪˈzeɪʃən/ *n* [U]

vic·tor /ˋvɪktɚ; ˈvɪktə/ *n* [C] *formal* the winner of a battle, game, competition etc【正式】〔戰鬥、比賽等中的〕得勝者, 勝利者: *After the game the victors returned in triumph.* 得勝者賽後凱旋而歸。

Vic·to·ri·an[1] /vɪkˋtorɪən; vɪkˈtɔːriən/ *adj* **1** connected with the period from 1837-1901 when Victoria was Queen of England 英國維多利亞(女王)時代的 **2** having the strict moral attitudes typical of the society of this period〔道德標準〕維多利亞(女王)時代特有的: *Victorian prudery* 維多利亞女王時代的那種故作正經

Victorian[2] *n* [C] an English person living in the period when Queen Victoria ruled 維多利亞(女王)時代的人

vic·to·ri·ous /vɪkˋtorɪəs; vɪkˈtɔːriəs/ *adj* having won a victory 得勝的, 勝利的, 戰勝的: *The victorious team held the trophy aloft.* 得勝的球隊把獎盃高高舉起。| *We were confident that the Allies would emerge victorious.* (=finally win) 我們確信盟軍最終一定能獲勝。—**victoriously** *adv*

 2 **vic·to·ry** /ˋvɪktərɪ; ˈvɪktəri/ *n* [C,U] **1** the success you achieve by winning a battle, game, race etc 勝利, 成功, 贏: *The streets were full of crowds, all celebrating an Italian victory.* 街上的人羣熙熙攘攘, 都在慶祝在意大利的勝利。| **[+over]** *A great shot by Johnson gave the Lakers victory over the Celtics.* 約翰遜一記漂亮的投球使湖人隊戰勝了凱爾特人隊。| **win a victory** *The Republicans won three election victories in a row.* 共和黨一連三次在大選中獲勝。| **sweep to victory** (=win easily and impressively) 輕而易舉大獲全勝 *Olson scored four times as the Rams swept to victory.* 奧爾森四次進球, 使公羊隊在比賽中大獲全勝。| **resounding victory** (=a very great victory) 大勝, 大捷 —opposite 反義詞 DEFEAT[1] (1) **2 be a victory for common sense** to be the most sensible way of settling a quarrel, which is not regarded as favourable to either side 常理獲勝, 不偏不倚的裁決 —see also 另見 PYRRHIC VICTORY

vict·ual /ˋvɪtl̩; ˈvɪtl/ *v* [T] to supply a large number of people with food 為〔數量眾多的人〕供應食物

vict·uals /ˋvɪtl̩z; ˈvɪtlz/ *n* [plural] *old use* food and drink【舊】食物和飲料

vi·cu·ña /vɪˋkjunə; vɪˈkjuːnə/ *n* **1** [C] a large South American animal related to the LLAMA, from which soft wool is obtained 駱馬〔產於南美, 與美洲駝近緣, 以其柔軟的毛而著稱〕**2** [U] the cloth made from this wool 駱馬毛織品

vi·de·li·cet /vɪˋdɛləsɪt; vɨˈdiːlɨset/ *adv Latin formal* VIZ【拉丁, 正式】即, 也就是

1 2 **vid·e·o**[1] /ˋvɪdɪ͵o; ˈvɪdiəʊ/ *n* **1** [C] a copy of a film or television programme recorded on VIDEOTAPE〔電影或電視節目在錄像帶上的〕錄影, 錄像: *I've borrowed the video of 'Gone with the Wind'.* 我把《亂世佳人》的錄像片借來了。| *a video shop* 出租錄像帶的商店 **2** [C, U] a VIDEOTAPE 錄像帶: *Have we got a blank video anywhere?* 我們哪裡有空白的錄像帶嗎? | **on video** *'Jurassic Park' is now available on video.*《侏羅紀公園》的錄像帶現已有售。**3** [C] *BrE* a VIDEO CASSETTE RECORDER【英】(盒式磁帶)錄像機 —see picture on page A14 參見 A14 頁圖 **4** [U] the process of recording and showing television programmes, films, real events etc using video equipment 錄影, 錄像〔錄製和播放電視節目、電影、真實事件等的過程〕: *Interactive learning has been greatly advanced by the introduction of video.* 錄像的引進極大地促進了互動式教學。

video[2] *v* [T] to record a television programme, film, or a real event on a VIDEOTAPE; TAPE[2] (1) 把〔電視節目、電影或真實事件等〕錄在錄像帶[錄影帶]上: *Could you video 'The Elvis Presley Story' for me at 8.00?* 你能幫我錄下8點鐘的《埃爾維斯·皮禮士利的故事》嗎? | *They got a friend to video the wedding.* 他們找了一位朋友把婚禮場面錄下來。

video[3] *adj* **1** [only before noun 僅用於名詞前] related to or used in the process of recording and showing pictures on television 電視的, 視頻的, 映像的: **video equipment/recording/system etc** *The VHS and Beta video systems are not compatible.* VHS 和 Beta 錄像系統互不兼容。—compare 比較 AUDIO **2** using VIDEOTAPE 用錄像磁帶[錄影帶]的: *a video recording* 錄影, 錄像

video ar·cade /ˈ··· ·͵·/ *n* [C] *AmE* a public place where there are a lot of VIDEO GAMES that you play by putting money in the machines【美】電子遊戲室

video cam·e·ra /ˈ··· ͵···/ *n* [C] a special camera that can be used to film events using VIDEOTAPE 攝像機

video cas·sette /͵··· ·ˈ·/ *n* [C] a VIDEOTAPE 盒式錄像帶, 錄像(磁)帶

video cas·sette re·cord·er /͵··· ·ˈ· ·͵··/ *n* [C] a machine used to record television programmes or show videos (VIDEO[1] (1))(盒式磁帶)錄像機; VCR *especially AmE*【尤美】, VIDEO[1] (3) *BrE*【英】

video con·fe·ren·cing /ˈ··· ͵····/ *n* [U] a system that allows people to communicate with each other by sending pictures and sounds electronically 電視會議, 視像會議(系統)

vid·e·o·disc /ˋvɪdɪo͵dɪsk; ˈvɪdiəʊ͵dɪsk/ *n* [C] a round flat piece of plastic from which films can be played in the same way as from a VIDEOTAPE〔激光〕視盤, 錄像盤, 影碟

video game /ˈ··· ͵·/ *n* [C] a game in which you move images on a screen by pressing electronic controls 電視遊戲

vid·e·og·ra·phy /͵vɪdɪˋɑgrəfɪ; ͵vɪdiˈɒgrəfi/ *n* [U] *formal* the art of recording events with a VIDEO CAMERA【正式】攝像 —**videographer** *n* [C]

video jock·ey /ˈ··· ͵··/ *n* [C] someone who introduces short VIDEO films on television, especially those showing performances of popular music; VJ〔尤指播放流行音樂的〕電視短片節目主持人

vid·e·o nas·ty /͵··· ˈ··/ *n* [C] *BrE informal* a VIDEO that includes very violent scenes【英, 非正式】兇殺錄像片, 暴力錄影片

vid·e·o·phone /ˋvɪdɪo͵fon; ˈvɪdiəʊfəʊn/ *n* [C] a type of telephone that allows you to see the person you are talking to on a machine like a television 視像電話

video re·cord·er /ˈ··· ·͵··/ *n* [C] a VIDEO CASSETTE RECORDER (盒式磁帶)錄像機

vid·e·o·tape[1] /ˋvɪdɪo͵tep; ˈvɪdiəʊteɪp/ *n* [C,U] a long narrow band of MAGNETIC material in a flat plastic container, on which films, television programmes etc can be recorded 盒式錄像帶, 錄像(磁)帶

videotape[2] *v* [T] to record a television programme, film etc on a videotape; VIDEO[2] 把〔電視節目、電影等〕錄在錄像帶[錄影帶]上

Vid·e·o·tex /ˋvɪdɪo͵tɛks; ˈvɪdiəʊ͵teks/ *n* [U] *trademark* a form of communication that allows information to be exchanged using a television system【商標】〔通過電視傳送的〕可視圖文(系統), 電傳視訊

vie /vaɪ; vaɪ/ *v* **vied, vying** [I] to compete very hard with someone in order to get something〔為獲得某物與某人〕競爭〔某事〕: **[+for]** *Simon and Julian were vying for her attention all through dinner.* 西蒙和朱利安整頓飯都在爭着吸引她的注意力。| **vie with sb to do sth** *The major record companies are vying with each other to sign the group.* 兩家主要唱片公司互相競爭, 都想與這個樂隊簽約。

view 視野, 景色

She had a wonderful view from her hotel window.
她的酒店房間窗外景色優美。

view¹ /vju; vjuː/ *n*

1 ►OPINION 觀點◄ [C] what you think or believe about something 觀點, 意見, 看法, 想法: **[+on/about]** *We'd like to find out young people's views on religion.* 我們想了解年輕人對宗教的看法。| **in my/your etc view** (=I, you etc think) 依我/你等之見 *In my view, what this country needs is a change of government.* 依我看, 這個國家需要的是換個政府。| **point of view** (=opinion) 觀點, 意見 *No one seemed to want to listen to my point of view.* 看來沒有人想聽我的意見。| **express the view that** (=say you think that) 表達…的看法 *The chairman expressed the view that it would be better not to increase investments.* 董事長表達自己的看法, 認為最好不要增加投資。| **take the view that** (=have the opinion that) 持…的觀點 *The judge took the view that a prison sentence would not be appropriate in this case.* 法官認為判決入獄對這一案件並不恰當。

2 ►WAY OF CONSIDERING 思考方式◄ [C usually singular 一般用單數] a way of considering or understanding something 思考[理解]的方式[方法], 考慮: **[+of]** *Has your view of the role of women changed since you got married?* 自結婚以來, 你對婦女所起作用的看法改變了嗎? | *James always did have a rather romantic view of life.* 詹姆斯對生活一向有一種相當浪漫的想法。| **an inside view** (=based on actual experience in an organization, group etc) 局內人的看法 *Healey's autobiography gives the reader an inside view of the Labour party.* 希利的自傳給讀者一種工黨內部人士的看法。| **clear view** (=a definite and specific idea about something) 明確的想法 *Before doing anything you need to have a clear view of the kind of book you want to write.* 在開始之前, 你需要對要寫甚麼類型的書有明確的計劃。| **take a dim/poor view of** (=disapprove) 不贊成 *She takes a pretty dim view of her son's recent behaviour.* 她對兒子近來的所行所為很不贊成。

3 ►SIGHT 視覺◄ [C,U] what you are able to see or the possibility of seeing it 能[可能]看見的東西; 視力; 視野; 視線: **have a good/bad/wonderful etc view (of)** (=be able to see a lot, very little etc) 看得見/看不見/看得非常清楚 *We had a really good view of the whole stage from where we were sitting.* 從我們坐的位置看, 整個舞台盡收眼底。| **be in view** (=can be seen from where you are) 在視野中 *She waited until the whole island was in view and then took a photograph.* 她一直等到看得見整個島後才拍了一張照片。| **come into view** (=begin to be seen) 出現在視野中 *As we rounded the bend in the river the castle came into view.* 我們繞河灣而行, 城堡就在眼前。| **in full view of** (=happening where people can see it clearly) …都清楚看見 *Francine screamed and slapped her husband in full view of all the guests.* 弗朗辛尖聲大叫, 當着所有客人的面給了丈夫一記耳光。| **block sb's view** (=stop someone from seeing something) 擋住某人的視線 *There was a tall guy sitting in front of me, blocking my view completely.* 有個高個子坐在我的前面, 把我的視線全擋住了。| **bird's eye view** (=a view seen from above) 鳥瞰 *We've got a bird's eye view of the football stadium from our office window.* 從我們辦公室的窗口可以鳥瞰足球場。

4 ►SCENERY 景色◄ [C] the whole area, especially a beautiful place, that you can see from somewhere 風景, 景色: *a spectacular view across the valley* 峽谷另一邊的壯麗景色 | **spoil the view** (=make a view look less beautiful) 煞風景 *A huge nuclear reactor now spoils the view of the coastline.* 一個龐大的核反應堆使海岸的風景大打折扣。

5 ►PICTURE 圖片◄ [C] a photograph or picture showing a beautiful or interesting place 風景照; 風景畫: *The book contains over fifty scenic views of Cambridge.* 該書有五十多幅劍橋的風景照。

6 be on view if paintings, photographs etc are on view, they are in a public place where people can go to look at them〔畫作、照片等〕在展覽[陳列]: *The Toulouse Lautrec posters are currently on view at the Hayward gallery.*〔法國畫家〕圖盧茲·勞特累克的招貼畫正在海華德美術館展出。

7 in view of used to introduce the reason for your decision or action 鑑於, 考慮到, 由於: *In view of Sutton's recent conduct the club has decided to suspend him until further notice.* 考慮到薩頓近來的表現, 俱樂部決定暫停其會員資格, 直至另行通知。

8 with a view to doing sth because you are planning to do something in the future 打算做某事: *We bought the cottage with a view to moving there when we retired.* 我們買了一間小屋, 打算退休後搬去住。

9 have sth in view to have something in your mind as an aim 作某事的打算: *He wants to find work, but he has nothing particular in view.* 他想找工作, 但沒有甚麼具體的打算。

10 take the long view (of) to think about the effect that something will have in the future rather than what happens now 對…作長遠打算

view² *v* **1** [T] *formal* to look at something, especially because you are interested【正式】〔尤指出於興趣〕看, 查看, 觀察: **view sth from** *The buildings are much more impressive when viewed from the other side of the river.* 從河的另一邊看, 這些大樓要雄偉得多。| **view a house/apartment/property** (=go to see the inside of a house etc which you are interested in buying)〔因有興趣購買而〕看房子/公寓/房產 | **view an exhibition/a garden etc** (=walk around it and look at it) 參觀展覽/花園等 *Thousands of tourists came to view the gardens every year.* 每年有成千上萬的遊客參觀這些花園。**2** [T always+adv/ prep] to regard something in a particular way〔從某種方面〕考慮: *Viewed from a financial standpoint, the show was a failure.* 從經濟的觀點看, 演出是不成功的。| **view sth as** *Conflict is viewed as an inevitable part of the child-parent relationship.* 衝突被視為子女與父母之間關係不可避免的一部分。| **view sth with caution/enthusiasm/horror etc** *Offers of rides from strangers should always be viewed with suspicion.* 如果有陌生人主動提出讓你搭車, 你一定要有戒備心理。**3** [I,T] *formal* to watch a television programme, film etc【正式】看〔電視、電影等〕: *an opportunity to view the film before it goes on general release* 觀看尚未公映的影片的一次機會

view·er /ˈvjuɚ; ˈvjuːə/ *n* [C] **1** someone who watches television 電視觀看者, 電視觀眾: *The new series has gone down well with viewers.* 這個新系列片很受電視觀眾的歡迎。**2** a small box with a light in it used to look at SLIDES (=colour photographs on special film) 看片器〔用於看幻燈片的內置燈的小箱子〕

view·find·er /ˈvju,faɪndɚ; ˈvjuː,faɪndə/ *n* [C] the small square of glass on a camera that you look through to see exactly what you are photographing〔照相機的〕取景器 —see picture at 參見 CAMERA 圖

view·point /ˈvju,pɔɪnt; ˈvjuːpɔɪnt/ *n* [C] **1** a particular way of thinking about a problem or subject 觀點, 看法, 見解: **from a different/practical/religious etc viewpoint** *From an ecological viewpoint, the new motorway has been a disaster.* 從生態學的角度看, 這條新公路是個災難。**2** a place from which you can see something 觀察點

vig·il /ˈvɪdʒəl; ˈvɪdʒ$_{\text{ɪ}}^{\text{ə}}$l/ *n* [C,U] **1** a period of time, especially during the night, when you stay awake in order to pray or remain with someone who is ill〔尤指為禱告或守護病人的〕守夜, 值夜: **keep (a) vigil** *For three weeks Jeff kept a vigil while his son lay in a coma.* 兒子昏迷期間, 傑夫一連三週日夜守護。**2** a silent political protest in which people wait outside a building, especially during the night〔尤指夜間〕靜坐抗議: **hold a vigil** *Over 2,000 demonstrators held a candlelit peace vigil in front of the US embassy.* 二千多名示威者在美國大使館前舉行了一次燭光和平靜坐抗議。

vig·i·lance /ˈvɪdʒələns; ˈvɪdʒ$_{\text{ɪ}}^{\text{ə}}$ləns/ *n* [U] careful attention that you give to what is happening, so that you will notice any danger or illegal activity 警惕, 警戒: *Constant vigilance is essential to combat drug-smuggling.* 始終保持警惕是打擊毒品走私所必需的。

vig·i·lant /ˈvɪdʒələnt; ˈvɪdʒ$_{\text{ɪ}}^{\text{ə}}$lənt/ *adj* giving careful attention to what is happening, so that you will notice any danger or illegal activity 警惕的, 警覺的, 警戒的: *Please remain vigilant at all times and report anything suspicious.* 請隨時保持警惕, 遇到可疑情況隨時報告。—**vigilantly** *adv*

vig·i·lan·te /,vɪdʒəˈlæntɪ; ,vɪdʒ$_{\text{ɪ}}^{\text{ə}}$ˈlænti/ *n* [C] a member of an unofficial group of people who join together to catch or punish criminals, usually because they think the police are ineffective〔非官方的〕治安維持會成員

vi·gnette /vɪnˈjɛt; vɪˈnjet/ *n* [C] **1** a short description in a book or play showing the typical features of a person or situation〔書本或劇本中對人物或場景的〕簡介 **2** a small drawing or pattern placed at the beginning of a book or CHAPTER (1)〔書的扉頁上或某章節前的〕小裝飾圖案

vig·or /ˈvɪgɚ; ˈvɪgə/ *n* [U] the American spelling of VIGOUR vigour 的美式拼法

vig·o·rous /ˈvɪgərəs; ˈvɪgərəs/ *adj* **1** using a lot of energy and strength or determination 強有力的; 積極的: *Vigorous efforts will be made to find alternative employment for those made redundant.* 將積極為失業人士另找一份職業。| *Your dog needs at least 20 minutes of vigorous exercise every day.* 你的狗每天需要進行至少20分鐘的激烈運動。**2 a vigorous opponent/defender etc** someone who opposes or defends something strongly 頑強的反對者/捍衛者等: *a vigorous campaigner for human rights* 爭取人權的頑強鬥士 **3** strong and very healthy 強健的, 精力旺盛的: *a vigorous man in the prime of life* 一個精力充沛的壯年男子 —**vigorously** *adv*: *Boil vigorously for five minutes.* 用猛火煮5分鐘。

vig·our *BrE*【英】, **vigor** *AmE*【美】/ˈvɪgɚ; ˈvɪgə/ *n* [U] physical and mental energy and determination 活力, 精力; 氣勢, 魄力: *He set about his task with renewed vigour.* 他恢復了體力, 開始了工作。

Vi·king /ˈvaɪkɪŋ; ˈvaɪkɪŋ/ *n* [C] one of a race of Scandinavian people in the 8th to 10th centuries who sailed in ships to attack areas along the coasts of northern and western Europe 北歐海盜, 維京人〔公元8到10世紀時乘船劫掠北歐和西歐海岸的斯堪的納維亞人的一支〕

vile /vaɪl; vaɪl/ *adj* **1** *informal* very unpleasant or nasty【非正式】壞透的; 討厭的: *This soup is vile.* 這湯太難喝了。| *She has a vile temper.* 她的脾氣太糟了。**2** evil 可恥的; 邪惡的: *a vile slander* 卑鄙的誹謗 —**vilely** *adv* —**vileness** *n* [U]

vil·i·fy /ˈvɪlə,faɪ; ˈvɪl$_{\text{ɪ}}^{\text{ə}}$faɪ/ *v* [T] *formal* to say bad things about someone, especially things that are not true, in order to influence other people against them【正式】誣蔑, 中傷, 誹謗 —**vilification** /,vɪləfəˈkeʃən; ,vɪl$_{\text{ɪ}}^{\text{ə}}$f$_{\text{ɪ}}^{\text{ə}}$ˈkeɪʃən/ *n* [C]: *his vilification by the popular press* 通俗報刊對他的中傷

vil·la /ˈvɪlə; ˈvɪlə/ *n* [C] **1** a big country house with large gardens〔帶有大花園的鄉間〕別墅 **2** *BrE* a house in another country that you can rent for your holidays【英】〔國外的可出租的〕度假別墅: *a holiday villa* 一幢度假別墅 **3** an ancient Roman house with its own farm〔古羅馬帶有農場的〕莊園, 邸宅

vil·lage /ˈvɪlɪdʒ; ˈvɪlɪdʒ/ *n* [C] **1** *BrE* a very small town in the countryside【英】鄉村, 村莊: **village school/sports/life** *The village fête happens every year in May.* 鄉村遊樂會在每年的五月舉行。**2 the village** the people who live in a village 全體村民: *The whole village came to the wedding.* 全村的人都來參加婚禮。

village green /,·· ˈ·/ *n* [C] an area of grass in the middle of an English village〔英國〕村鎮(公用)綠地

village id·i·ot /,·· ˈ···/ *n* [C] someone living in a village who is very stupid and does not understand the modern world 鄉巴佬, 鄉下傻子

vil·lag·er /ˈvɪlɪdʒɚ; ˈvɪlɪdʒə/ *n* [C] someone who lives in a village 村民

vil·lain /ˈvɪlən; ˈvɪlən/ *n* [C] **1** the main bad character in a film, play, or story〔電影、戲劇或小說中的〕主要反面人物, 反派角色 **2** *BrE informal* a bad person or criminal【英, 非正式】壞人; 罪犯:*Watch him – he's a bit of a villain!* 提防他——他不是好人! **3 the villain of the piece** *often humorous* the person or thing that has caused all the trouble in a particular situation【常幽默】首犯, 主要肇事者; 為害的事物: *The CIA is commonly regarded as the villain of the piece.* 中央情報局被普遍視為惹禍者。

vil·lain·ous /ˈvɪlənəs; ˈvɪlənəs/ *adj* **1** *literary* evil【文】邪惡的: *He gave a villainous leer.* 他不懷好意地瞥了一眼。**2** *informal* unpleasant or nasty【非正式】壞透的; 討厭的: *a villainous smell* 討厭的氣味

vil·lain·y /ˈvɪlənɪ; ˈvɪləni/ *n* [U] evil or criminal behaviour 惡行; 罪惡的行為

-ville /vɪl; vɪl/ *suffix old-fashioned slang, especially AmE*【過時, 俚, 尤美】**dullsville/squaresville etc** a place or thing that is dull etc 令人厭倦的地方[事物等]: *This party is really dullsville.* 這個聚會真是無聊極了。

vil·lein /ˈvɪlɪn; ˈvɪl$_{\text{ɪ}}^{\text{ə}}$n/ *n* [C] a poor farm worker in the Middle Ages who was given a small piece of land in return for working on the land of a rich lord〔中世紀的〕農奴; 佃農 —compare 比較 PEASANT (1)

vim /vɪm; vɪm/ *n* [U] *old-fashioned* energy【過時】精力, 活力: *bursting with vim and vigour* 精神煥發

vin·ai·grette /,vɪnəˈgrɛt; ,vɪn$_{\text{ɪ}}^{\text{ə}}$ˈgret/ *n* [U] a mixture of oil, VINEGAR, salt, and pepper that you put on a SALAD〔油、醋、鹽、胡椒混合成的〕沙拉[沙律]調味汁

vin·di·cate /ˈvɪndə,ket; ˈvɪnd$_{\text{ɪ}}^{\text{ə}}$keɪt/ *v* [T] *formal*【正式】**1** to prove that someone or something is right or true; JUSTIFY 證明…正確[屬實]: **vindicate an idea/method/decision** *Your decision not to resign has been fully vindicated.* 事實充分證明你不辭職的決定是正確的。**2** to prove that someone who was blamed for something is in fact not guilty 證明…清白; 為…辯護, 為…辯白: *The outcome of the trial vindicates Howells completely.* 庭審結果徹底證明了豪厄爾斯的清白。—**vindication** /,vɪndəˈkeʃən; ,vɪnd$_{\text{ɪ}}^{\text{ə}}$ˈkeɪʃən/ *n* [singular,U]: *Improved economic growth is seen as a vindication of government policies.* 人們認為經濟增長加快證明了政府決策的正確。

vin·dic·tive /vɪnˈdɪktɪv; vɪnˈdɪktɪv/ *adj* deliberately cruel and unfair, especially to someone who has harmed you 報復(性)的; 懷恨在心的; 惡意的: *After the divorce Joan's ex-husband became increasingly vindictive.* 離婚後, 瓊的前夫變得越來越惡毒了。—**vindictively** *adv*: *"That'll teach her," he thought vindictively.* "這對她倒是個教訓。" 他惡狠狠地想道。—**vindictiveness** *n* [U]

vine /vaɪn; vaɪn/ *n* [C] **1** a plant that produces GRAPES 葡萄屬植物; 葡萄藤 **2** *technical* any plant that has thin twisting stems and grows up walls or posts or along the ground【術語】藤本植物, 攀緣植物

vin·e·gar /ˋvɪnɪgɚ; ˈvɪnɪgə/ *n* [U] an acid tasting liquid made from MALT or wine that is used to improve the taste of food or to preserve it 醋

vin·e·gar·y /ˋvɪnɪgərɪ; ˈvɪnɪgəri/ *adj* **1** tasting of vinegar 酸的 **2** bad-tempered and always ready to say unkind things 尖酸的; 刻薄的; 乖戾的

vine·yard /ˋvɪnjɚd; ˈvɪnjəd/ *n* [C] a piece of land where VINES are grown in order to produce wine 葡萄園

vi·no /ˋvino; ˈviːnəʊ/ *n* [U] *informal* wine【非正式】(葡萄)酒

vi·nous /ˋvaɪnəs; ˈvaɪnəs/ *adj formal*【正式】**1** connected with wine (似)酒的; 有酒味的; 由酒引起的 **2** having the colour of red wine 有紅葡萄酒顏色的

vin·tage¹ /ˋvɪntɪdʒ; ˈvɪntɪdʒ/ *adj* **1** vintage wine is good quality wine made in a particular year〔某特定年份中釀製的酒〕佳釀的 **2** showing all the best or most typical qualities of something 最好的; 最典型的: *His latest film is vintage Spielberg.* 史匹堡最近的一部電影是他的代表作。**3** *often humorous* old【常幽默】舊式的, 老式的: *Our plane was a vintage Cessna.* 我們的飛機是一架老式的塞斯納小型飛機。**4 vintage year a)** a year when a good quality wine was produced 美酒釀成的年份 **b)** a year when something of very good quality was produced 某高品質事物的出產年份: *1963 was not a vintage year for movies.* 1963年是電影業不景氣的一年。

vintage² *n* [C] a particular year in which a wine is made 酒的釀造年份: *1961 was a very good vintage.* 1961年是釀酒的好年份。

vintage car /,·· ˈ·/ *n* [C] *BrE* a car made between 1919 and 1930【英】〔1919–1930年間製造的〕老爺車

vint·ner /ˋvɪntnɚ; ˈvɪntnə/ *n* [C] someone who buys and sells wines 酒商

vi·nyl /ˋvaɪnɪl; ˈvaɪnḷl/ *n* [U] **1** a type of strong plastic 乙烯基(塑膠): *a vinyl chair* 乙烯基製的椅子 | *vinyl flooring* 乙烯基地板材料 **2** a word for records that are played on a RECORD PLAYER, used when comparing them to CDs or TAPES (塑膠)唱片: *This album is no longer available on vinyl.* 這張專輯的塑膠唱片版已買不到了。

vi·o·la /vɪˋolə; viˈəʊlə/ *n* [C] a musical instrument like a VIOLIN but larger and with a lower sound 中提琴

vi·o·late /ˋvaɪəˌlet; ˈvaɪəleɪt/ *v* [T] **1** to disobey or do something against an official agreement, law, principle etc 違背, 違反; 侵犯: *practices that violate health and safety regulations* 違反健康與安全條例的做法 | *The arrest and detention of the protestors violated their civil liberties.* 逮捕和拘留抗議者是侵犯了他們的公民自由。**2** *formal* to break open a grave, or force your way into a holy place without showing any respect【正式】〔用暴力〕打開〔墳墓〕; 強行進入〔聖地〕; 褻瀆: *The thieves violated the graves searching for gold.* 盜賊們為尋找黃金而掘開了墳墓。**3 violate the peace/privacy of** *literary* to suddenly spoil a place or situation so that it is no longer peaceful or private【文】破壞…的和平/驚擾…的獨處 **4** *literary* to force a woman to have sex; RAPE【文】強姦 —**violator** *n* [C]

vi·o·la·tion /ˌvaɪəˋleʃən; ˌvaɪəˈleɪʃən/ *n* [C,U] **1** an action that breaks a law, agreement, principle etc 違背, 違反〔官方協議、法律、原則等〕: *human rights violations* 違反人權 | **[+of]** *violations of the ceasefire* 違反停火協議 | **in violation of** *The court's ruling is in violation of the UN Charter.* 法院的裁決違反了聯合國憲章。| *a violation of the 3-second rule in basketball* 違反了籃球的三秒規則 **2** [C,U] *formal* an action that causes harm or damage by treating someone or their possessions without respect【正式】侵害; 妨害; 妨礙: **[+of]** *I felt her visits were a violation of my privacy.* 我認為她幾次三番地來妨礙了我的私生活。| *He regarded the burglary as a violation of his home.* 他把這次偷盜視為對他住宅的侵害。

vi·o·lence /ˋvaɪələns; ˈvaɪələns/ *n* [U] **1** behaviour that is intended to hurt other people physically〔指傷害他人身體的〕暴力(行為): *There is too much sex and violence shown on television.* 電視上性和暴力場面太多了。| *sporadic outbreaks of violence* 零星發生的暴力事件 | *robbery with violence* 暴力搶劫 | **domestic violence** (=violence between family members) 家庭暴力 | **act of violence** *acts of violence against the new immigrants* 針對新移民的暴力行為 | **resort to violence** (=use violence when nothing else is effective) 訴諸暴力 **2** an angry way of speaking or reacting〔言語或反應的〕憤怒; 激烈: *She spoke with a violence that surprised them both.* 她言辭激烈, 令他們倆都很驚訝。**3** extreme force 極大[強烈]的力量: *the violence of the wind* 猛烈的風 **4 do violence to** *formal* to spoil something【正式】破壞, 對…損害 S2 W2

vi·o·lent /ˋvaɪələnt; ˈvaɪələnt/ *adj* S3 W3

1 ►ACTION 動作, 行為◄ involving actions that are intended to injure or kill people, by hitting them, shooting them etc 暴力的; 暴力引起的: *violent crimes such as murder or rape* 如謀殺或強姦的暴力犯罪 | *violent clashes between the police and demonstrators* 警察和示威者之間發生的暴力衝突 | **violent death** (=murder) 慘死 *He met a violent death at the hands of the mob.* 他慘死在暴徒手中。

2 ►PERSON 人◄ likely to attack, hurt, or kill other people 狂暴的, 兇暴的: *My father was a violent and dangerous man.* 我父親脾氣暴躁, 是個危險人物。| **turn/get violent** (=suddenly become violent)〔突然〕變得暴躁不安 *Keep the handcuffs on the prisoner in case he turns violent.* 別打開犯人的手銬, 以防他突然變得狂暴。

3 ►ARGUMENT/WORDS 論據/言辭◄ showing very strong angry emotions or opinions〔情緒、意見等〕憤怒的; 激烈的: *They had a violent quarrel over Dave's drinking.* 他們為戴夫喝酒而暴吵了一頓。| *His speech was full of violent denunciations of the government's promises.* 他的發言滿篇都是對政府承諾的猛烈譴責。

4 ►EMOTIONS 情緒◄ strong and very difficult to control 極端的; 暴躁的: *She has a violent temper.* 她脾氣暴躁。| *They took a violent dislike to each other.* 他們彼此極端厭惡。

5 violent film/play/drama a film etc that shows a lot of violent actions 暴力影片/戲/劇

6 violent storm/earthquake/explosion etc a storm etc that happens with a lot of force 強烈的風暴/地震/爆炸等

7 a violent headache/fit/coughing etc a physical feeling or reaction that is very painful or difficult to control 劇烈的頭痛/痙攣/咳嗽等

8 ►COLOUR 顏色◄ extremely bright〔色彩〕強烈的, 非常明豔的: *Her cheeks turned a violent red colour.* 她的雙頰騰地通紅。—**violently** *adv*: *She became violently aggressive.* 她變得咄咄逼人, 氣勢洶洶。| *Matthew trembled violently.* 馬修顫抖得很厲害。

vi·o·let /ˋvaɪəlɪt; ˈvaɪəlḷt/ *n* [C] **1** a small plant with sweet-smelling dark purple flowers 紫羅蘭 —see also 另見 SHRINKING VIOLET **2** [C,U] a colour between purple and blue 藍紫色 —**violet** *adj* —see picture on page A5 參見A5頁圖

vi·o·lin /ˌvaɪəˋlɪn; ˌvaɪəˈlɪn/ *n* [C] the smallest instrument in the group of wooden musical instruments that are played by pulling a special stick across wire strings 小提琴 —**violinist** *n* [C]

vi·o·lin·cel·lo /viəlɑnˋtʃɛlo; ˌvaɪələnˈtʃeləʊ/ *n* [C] a CELLO 大提琴

VIP /ˌvi aɪ ˋpi; ˌviː aɪ ˈpiː/ *n* [C] a very important person; someone who is very famous or powerful and is treated with special care and respect 要人; 大人物: *the VIP lounge at the airport* 機場貴賓休息室

vi·per /ˋvaɪpɚ; ˈvaɪpə/ *n* [C] **1** a small poisonous snake 蝰蛇〔小毒蛇〕 **2** *literary* someone who behaves in a nasty way and harms other people【文】陰險惡毒的人

vi·ra·go /vəˋrego; vəˈrɑːgəʊ/ *n* [C] *formal* a BAD-TEMPERED woman with a loud voice【正式】潑婦, 悍婦

vi·ral /ˋvaɪrəl; ˈvaɪərəl/ *adj* connected with or caused by a VIRUS 病毒(性)的, 病毒引起的: *viral pneumonia* 病毒性肺炎

vir·gin[1] /ˋvɝdʒɪn; ˈvɜːdʒən/ *n* [C] **1** someone who has never had sex 處女 **2 the Virgin Mary** the mother of Jesus 聖母馬利亞

virgin[2] *adj* **1 virgin land/forest/soil etc** land etc that is still in its natural state and has not been used or changed by people 處女地/原始森林/未開墾地等: **virgin snow** (=fresh and not spoiled) 初雪 **2** [only before noun 僅用於名詞前] without sexual experience 貞潔的: *a virgin bride* 貞潔的新娘

vir·gin·al /ˋvɝdʒɪnl; ˈvɜːdʒənəl/ *adj* like a virgin 處女(般)的

vir·gin·als /ˋvɝdʒɪnlz; ˈvɜːdʒənəlz/ *n* [plural] a small square musical instrument like a piano with no legs, popular in the 16th and 17th centuries 維金納琴〔16和17世紀流行的一種小方形鋼琴狀樂器, 無支架〕

virgin birth /ˌ‥ ˈ·/ *n* [singular] the birth of Jesus, which Christians believe was caused by God, not by sex between a man and a woman 聖靈感孕〔基督徒相信的耶穌基督的誕生方式〕

vir·gin·i·a creep·er /vɚˌdʒɪnjə ˋkripɚ; vəːˌdʒɪniə ˈkriːpə/ *n* [C,U] a garden plant that grows up walls and has large leaves that turn deep red in autumn 五葉地錦〔一種攀爬於牆, 秋天葉子會變紅的大葉植物〕; WOODBINE *AmE*【美】

vir·gin·i·ty /vɚˋdʒɪnətɪ; vəˈdʒɪnəti/ *n* [U] the condition of never having had sex 童貞, 處女狀態: **lose your virginity** (=have sex for the first time) 失去童貞 *She was 17 when she lost her virginity.* 她17歲時失去童貞。—compare 比較 CHASTITY

Vir·go /ˋvɝgo; ˈvɜːgəʊ/ *n* **1** [singular] the sixth sign of the ZODIAC, represented by a young woman, and believed to affect the character and life of people born between August 23 and September 22 室女宮〔黃道十二宮的第六宮〕 **2** [C] someone who was born between August 23 and September 22 生於室女宮時段〔8月23日至9月22日〕的人

vir·ile /ˋvɪrəl; ˈvɪraɪl/ *adj* **1** looking or behaving in a way that is typical of a man by being strong, brave, full of energy etc and therefore sexually attractive 有男子氣概的; 充滿陽剛活力的: *He had a muscular and virile body.* 他長得身強體壯, 威武雄健。**2** virile qualities and actions show typically male strength and energy〔特質和行動〕強勁的; 強健的; 雄渾的: *virile sports such as rugby* 像橄欖球這樣的典型男子運動項目

vi·ril·i·ty /vəˋrɪlətɪ; vəˈrɪləti/ *n* [U] **1** the typically male quality of being strong, brave, and full of energy, in a way that is sexually attractive 雄壯; 男子氣概 **2** the ability of a man to have sex; POTENCY〔男性〕生殖能力

vi·rol·o·gy /vaɪˋrɑlədʒɪ; vaɪəˈrɒlədʒi/ *n* [U] the scientific study of VIRUS*es* or of the diseases caused by them 病毒學

vir·tu·al /ˋvɝtʃuəl; ˈvɜːtʃuəl/ *adj* **1 virtual peace/darkness/destruction etc** something that is so nearly complete peace etc that any difference is unimportant 實際上的和平/黑暗/毀滅等: *We have achieved virtual perfection in sound reproduction.* 我們在聲音複製方面已經取得實際上的完美效果。| **be a virtual certainty/impossibility etc** (=be almost certain, impossible etc) 幾乎是肯定/不可能的等 *Car ownership is a virtual necessity when you live in the country.* 住在鄉下, 擁有汽車幾乎是必要的。**2 virtual leader/prisoner etc** someone who is in fact a leader, prisoner etc but not officially one 事實上的領袖/囚犯等: *The president was so much under his wife's influence that she was the virtual ruler of the country.* 總統受妻子的影響之大, 以至她成了國家實際上的統治者。

vir·tu·al·ly /ˋvɝtʃuəlɪ; ˈvɜːtʃuəli/ *adv* so nearly that any difference is not important; ALMOST 實際上, 事實上; 差不多: *Many species of wild animals have virtually disappeared from the face of the earth.* 許多野生動物物種實際上已經從地球上消失了。| *Virtually all the children come to school by bus.* 幾乎所有兒童都是乘公共汽車來上學的。

virtual re·al·i·ty /ˌ‥ ·ˈ‥/ *n* [U] an image produced by a computer that surrounds the person looking at it and seems almost real 虛擬現實

vir·tue /ˋvɝtʃu; ˈvɜːtʃuː/ *n* **1** [U] *formal* moral goodness of character and behaviour【正式】善; 德: *a man of the highest virtue* 品德極為高尚的人 —opposite 反義詞 VICE **2** [C] a particular good quality in someone's character 美德; 德行: *Among her many virtues are loyalty, courage and truthfulness.* 忠誠、勇敢和坦率是她諸多美德中的一部分。**3** [C,U] an advantage that makes something better or more useful than something else 優點, 長處: *Free trade has a number of virtues.* 自由貿易有許多優點。| **the virtue of** *The Johnson plan has the virtue of flexibility.* 約翰遜的計劃的優點是具靈活性。**4 by/in virtue of** *formal* by means of or as a result of something【正式】憑藉; 由於, 因為: *She became a British citizen by virtue of her marriage.* 她藉着結婚而成了英國公民。**5 make a virtue of necessity** to get an advantage out of doing something that you have to do 爽爽快快[心甘情願]地做非做不可的事

vir·tu·os·i·ty /ˌvɝtʃuˋɑsətɪ; ˌvɜːtʃuˈɒsəti/ *n* [U] *formal* a very high degree of skill in performing【正式】〔表演方面的〕精湛技巧, 高超技藝: *the violinist's incredible virtuosity* 小提琴演奏家那不可思議的精湛技巧

vir·tu·o·so /ˌvɝtʃuˋoso; ˌvɜːtʃuˈəʊsəʊ/ *n* [C] someone who is a very skilful performer, especially in music〔尤指音樂上的〕大演奏家, 藝術大師: *a virtuoso performance* 名家表演

vir·tu·ous /ˋvɝtʃuəs; ˈvɜːtʃuəs/ *adj* **1** *formal* behaving in a very honest and moral way【正式】有德行的; 正直的: *Thomas Dunlop was a virtuous man and a leader in the community.* 托馬斯·鄧洛普為人正直, 是社區的領導。**2** too satisfied with your own good behaviour and showing this in a way that annoys other people 自命清高的; 自以為高尚的: *She threw up her hands in virtuous indignation.* 她雙手揮過頭頂, 顯出自以為是的憤慨。—**virtuously** *adv* —**virtuousness** *n* [U]

vir·u·lent /ˋvɪrulənt; ˈvɪrələnt/ *adj* **1** *formal* virulent emotions or speeches are full of hatred and very strongly expressed【正式】〔情感或言辭〕充滿仇恨的, 刻毒的, 惡毒的: *virulent anti-Semitism* 惡毒的反猶太主義 **2** a poison, disease etc that is virulent is very dangerous and affects people very quickly〔毒藥、疾病等〕劇毒的, 迅速致命的: *a virulent form of malaria* 惡性瘧疾 —**virulence** *n* [U]: *the virulence of an epidemic* 流行病的致命性 —**virulently** *adv*

vi·rus /ˋvaɪrəs; ˈvaɪərəs/ *n* **1** [C] a very small living thing, smaller than BACTERIA, that causes infectious illnesses 病毒: *the common cold virus* 普通感冒病毒 | *virus infections* 病毒感染 **2** [C] the illness caused by a virus 病毒性疾病: *She's got some virus.* 她患上病毒性疾病。**3** [C,U] a set of instructions secretly put into a computer, that can destroy information stored in the computer〔電腦〕病毒

vi·sa /ˋvizə; ˈviːzə/ *n* [C] an official mark put on your passport by the representative of a foreign country, that gives you permission to enter, pass through, or leave that country〔護照上的〕簽證: **tourist/exit/entry visa** *She came here on a tourist visa, but it has expired.* 她是

持旅遊簽證來這裡的, 但簽證已經到期。—**visa** *v* [I]

vis·age /ˈvɪzɪdʒ; ˈvɪzɪdʒ/ *n* [C] *literary* a face【文】臉; 面容

vis-à-vis /ˌviz ə ˈvi; ˌviːz ɑː ˈviː/ *prep formal* in relation to or in comparison with something or someone【正式】關於, 對於; 同…相比: *the bargaining position of the worker vis-à-vis the employer* 雇員和雇主相比的討價還價的能力

vis·ce·ra /ˈvɪsərə; ˈvɪsərə/ *n* [plural] *technical* the large organs inside your body, such as your heart, lungs, stomach etc【術語】內臟, 臟腑〈如心、肺、胃等〉

vis·ce·ral /ˈvɪsərəl; ˈvɪsərəl/ *adj* **1** *literary* visceral beliefs and attitudes are the result of strong feelings rather than careful thought【文】〔信仰、態度〕出自內心的, 發自肺腑的: *Thatcher's visceral dislike of the European Monetary System* 戴卓爾對歐洲貨幣體系發自肺腑的厭惡 **2** *technical* connected with the viscera【術語】內臟的

vis·cid /ˈvɪsɪd; ˈvɪsɪd/ *adj* VISCOUS 黏性的

vis·count /ˈvaɪkaunt; ˈvaɪkaʊnt/ *n* [C] a British NOBLEMAN with a rank between that of an EARL and a BARON〔英國的〕子爵

vis·count·cy /ˈvaɪkauntsɪ; ˈvaɪkaʊntsi/ *n* [C] the rank or title of a viscount 子爵的地位[頭銜]

vis·count·ess /ˈvaɪkauntɪs; ˈvaɪkaʊntɪs/ *n* [C] the wife of a viscount, or a woman who has the rank of a viscount 子爵夫人; 女子爵

vis·cous /ˈvɪskəs; ˈvɪskəs/ *adj technical* a viscous liquid is thick and sticky and does not flow easily【術語】〔液體〕黏滯的, 黏性的 —**viscosity** /vɪsˈkɑsətɪ; vɪˈskɒsɪti/ *n* [U]

vise /vaɪs; vaɪs/ *n* [C] the usual American spelling of VICE (4) vice (4) 的一般美式拼法

vis·i·bil·i·ty /ˌvɪzəˈbɪlətɪ; ˌvɪzɪˈbɪlɪti/ *n* [U] **1** how far it is possible to see, especially when this is affected by weather conditions〔尤指受天氣狀況影響時的〕能見度; 視程: *Visibility is down to 20 metres due to heavy fog.* 由於有濃霧, 能見度降至 20 米。| **good/poor visibility** *The search for survivors was abandoned because of poor visibility.* 由於能見度低, 對倖存者的搜尋工作已經放棄。**2** the fact of something being easy to see 清晰度, 明顯度

vis·i·ble /ˈvɪzəbl; ˈvɪzɪbəl/ *adj* **1** something that is visible can be seen 看得見的; 可見的: *The outline of the mountains was clearly visible.* 羣山的輪廓清晰可見。**2** an effect that is visible is strong enough to be noticed〔影響〕明顯的; 顯然的; 可察覺的: *There is a visible change in attitudes to working women.* 人們在對待勞動婦女的態度上有了明顯的變化。| *She showed visible signs of annoyance.* 她顯然有些不高興。**3** someone who is visible is always on television, in the newspapers etc〔經常在電視上、報紙上等〕露面的: *highly visible politicians* 高度曝光的政治家

vis·i·bly /ˈvɪzəblɪ; ˈvɪzɪbli/ *adv* in a way that is easy to see or notice 顯然, 明顯地, 顯而易見地: *He was visibly shaken by her accusation.* 她的指控顯然使他大為震驚。

vi·sion /ˈvɪʒən; ˈvɪʒən/ *n*

1 ▶SIGHT 視力◀ [U] your ability to see 視力: *With my new glasses my vision is perfect!* 戴上新配的眼鏡, 我的視力好極了! | *Tears blurred her vision.* 淚水模糊了她的視線。| **field of vision** (=the area in which you are able to see things) 視野 *As the cars overtake you, they are temporarily outside your field of vision.* 汽車超車時, 他們就暫時離開了你的視野。| **20-20 vision** (=perfect vision) 極好的視力

2 ▶IDEA 概念◀ [C] a picture in your mind of a possible situation or scene〔對一可能情況或場景的〕構想, 設想; 念頭: **[+of]** *He conjured up a vision of a world without national divisions.* 他想像出一個沒有國界的世界的景象。| **have visions of** (=think a situation is likely to happen) 有…的念頭, 認為…會發生 *The airport bus broke down and Tim had visions of missing his plane.* 機場班車壞了, 蒂姆覺得這下可趕不上飛機了。

3 ▶IN A DREAM 在夢中◀ [C] something that you seem to see, especially in a dream, as part of a powerful religious experience〔尤指夢中有關宗教的經歷〕幻想; 幻覺; 夢幻: *She had a vision in which Jesus appeared before her.* 她在夢幻中看見耶穌出現在她面前。

4 ▶FUTURE PLANS 未來的計劃◀ [U] the knowledge and imagination that are needed in planning for the future with a clear purpose 遠見卓識: *At last we have a leader with vision and strong principles.* 我們終於有了一個有遠見、原則性強的領導。

5 a vision of innocence/beauty etc *literary* something you see which shows a particular quality or attitude【文】天真/美麗等的形象

6 ▶TELEVISION 電視◀ [U] the quality of a picture that you can see on a television〔電視〕圖像(質量): *interference affecting sound and vision* 對聲音和圖像的干擾

vi·sion·a·ry¹ /ˈvɪʒənˌɛrɪ; ˈvɪʒənəri/ *adj* **1** having clear ideas of what the world should be like in the future 有遠見的, 有眼光的: *Le Corbusier was a great visionary architect.* 勒·柯布西耶是一個有真知灼見的建築師。**2** existing only in someone's mind and unlikely to ever exist in the real world 夢幻中的; 空想的

visionary² *n* [C] **1** someone who has clear ideas and strong feelings about the way something should be in the future 有預見的人; 有遠見的人: *a visionary with a passionate belief in liberty* 一個崇尚自由、有遠見卓識的人 **2** a holy person who has visions (VISION (3)) 看見神靈顯現的人; 有幻覺的人

vis·it¹ /ˈvɪzɪt; ˈvɪzɪt/ *v* **1** [I,T] to go and spend time in a place or with someone, especially for pleasure or interest 參觀, 遊覽; 拜訪, 訪問: *"Do you live here?" "No, we're just visiting".* "你們住在這裡嗎?" "不, 我們只是來旅遊的。" | **visit sth** *We hope to visit the Grand Canyon on our trip.* 我們希望旅途中能去遊覽大峽谷。| **visit sb** *Aunt Jane usually visits us for two or three weeks in the spring.* 簡姑媽通常在春天到我們家住上兩三週。| **[+in/on/at/with]** *AmE*【美】: *When you are visiting in Washington, be sure to see the Air and Space Museum.* 到華盛頓時, 一定要去航空與航天博物館看看。**2** [T] to go to see a doctor, lawyer etc in order to get treatment or advice 去〔醫生、律師等〕處就診[諮詢] **3** [T] to go to a place in order to examine it officially 視察, 巡視: *The building inspector is visiting the new housing project.* 建築監察員正在視察這個新的住房項目。**4** [I] *AmE* to talk socially with someone【美】敍談, 閒談: **[+with]** *While Mom visited with Phyllis we played in the yard.* 媽媽跟菲莉絲聊天時, 我們在院子裡玩耍。

S2 W1

visit sth **on** sb/sth *phr v* [T] *especially biblical* to do something to punish someone or show them that you are angry【尤聖經】懲罰某人〔表示憤怒〕: *God's wrath will be visited on sinners.* 上帝一定會懲罰罪人。

USAGE NOTE 用法說明: VISIT

WORD CHOICE 詞語辨析: visit, go to, go and see, have been to, come and see

Visit is slightly formal. More often you would say you **go to** a place or **go and see/go to see** a place or a person. visit 為略顯正式的用語。表示去某地或到某處觀光或探望某人時, 更為常用的是 go to 或 go and see/go to see。You might write 可寫作: *We visited the Grand Canyon* (我們遊覽了大峽谷) or 或 *I visited my mother* (我去探望了母親) but in spoken English you are more likely to say 但在口語中更可能這樣說: *We went to the Grand Canyon* or 或 *I went to see my mother.* Note that you would also say 注意, 還可以說: *I've been to Hong Kong several times* (我已去過香港好幾次了) and 和 *When you are in Tokyo you must come and see me* (你來東京時一定要來看我)。

3 **visit²** *n* [C] **1** an occasion when someone visits a place or person 遊覽; 參觀; 拜訪: **[+to]** *a visit to New York* 遊覽紐約 | **on a visit** *We're just here on a short visit.* 我們來這兒只是短期逗留。| **pay sb a visit** *I must pay our new neighbors a visit.* 我必須拜訪一下新鄰居。| **have a visit from** *I've just had a visit from the police.* 警察剛到我這裡來過。| **flying visit** (=a very short visit) 短暫訪問 *We made a flying visit to my mother's to pick up the wedding presents.* 我們匆匆去了母親家一趟, 拿結婚禮物。**2** an occasion when you see a doctor, lawyer etc for treatment or advice 就診; 法律諮詢: **pay a visit** *I must pay a visit to the dentist.* 我得去看牙醫。| **home visit** (=when a doctor comes to your home)〔醫生〕出診, 探視 **3** *AmE* an occasion when you talk socially with someone, or the time you spend doing this【美】敍談; 閒談的時間: *Barbara and I had a nice long visit.* 巴巴拉和我作了一次愉快的長談。

vis·i·ta·tion /ˌvɪzəˋteʃən; ˌvɪzɪ̵ˈteɪʃən/ *n* [C] **1** *formal* an official visit, usually made in order to examine something or someone【正式】視察, 巡視: *a parental visitation of the school* 家長對學校的造訪 **2** *literary* an event that is believed to be God's punishment for something【文】天譴, 天禍: **[+of]** *visitations of plague, famine, and war* 瘟疫、饑荒及戰爭等天譴 **3** *humorous* a long visit from someone that you do not want to see【幽默】令人討厭的過長的拜訪

visiting card /ˈ··· ·/ *n* [C] a small card with your name printed on it that people used to give to the people they visited 名片

visiting fire·man /ˌ··· ˈ··/ *n* [C] *especially AmE* an important visitor that you need to entertain in a special way【尤美】〔需給予特別招待的〕貴賓

visiting hours /ˈ··· ·/ *n* [plural] the times during which you can visit people who are ill in hospital〔醫院的〕探望時間

visiting pro·fes·sor /ˌ··· ·ˈ··/ *n* [C] a university teacher who has come from another university to teach for a period of time 客座教授

2
2 **vis·it·or** /ˋvɪzɪtɚ; ˈvɪzɪ̵tə/ *n* [C] someone who comes to visit a place or a person 觀光者, 參觀者; 訪問者, 探望者: *They were expecting visitors and had cleaned the house.* 他們把房子打掃得乾乾淨淨, 等待着來客。| *travel tips for visitors to the USA* 給旅美遊客的旅行提示 —see also 另見 HEALTH VISITOR

visitors' book /ˈ··· ·/ *n* [C] a book, especially in a church or other important building, in which visitors write their names and addresses〔尤指教堂或其他重要建築的〕來客登記簿

vi·sor /ˋvaɪzɚ; ˈvaɪzə/ *n* [C] **1** the part of a HELMET (=protective hard hat) that can be lowered to protect your face〔頭盔上可移下來保護臉部的〕面甲, 臉盔 **2** *AmE* the curved part of a cap that sticks out in front above your eyes【美】帽舌; PEAK¹ (4) *BrE*【英】—see picture at 參見 CAP¹ 圖 **3** a flat piece of material above the front window inside a car that can be pulled down to keep the sun out of your eyes; SUN VISOR〔汽車擋風玻璃內上方的〕遮陽板 **4** a curved piece of plastic that you wear on your head so that it sticks out above your eyes and protects them from the sun 護目鏡;〔遮陽〕眼罩

vis·ta /ˋvɪstə; ˈvɪstə/ *n* [C] **1** *literary* a far view of beautiful scenery, especially looking between rows of trees, buildings etc【文】〔尤指從成排樹木或建築等中間看出去的〕長條形景色, 遠景: *The balcony commanded a vista of the harbour.* 從陽台上海港的景色一覽無遺。**2** the possibility of new experiences, ideas, events etc〔對新經歷、想法、事件等的〕展望: *Exchange programs open up new vistas for students.* 交流項目為學生拓展了新的前景。

3 **vi·su·al** /ˋvɪʒuəl; ˈvɪʒuəl/ *adj* connected with seeing 視覺的, 視力的: *visual identification of the subject by a witness* 證人對物件的視覺辯認 | *a powerful visual impact* 強大的視覺效果

visual aid /ˌ··· ˈ·/ *n* [C] something such as a map, picture, film etc that helps people understand, learn, or remember information 直觀教具〈如地圖、圖片、電影等〉

visual arts /ˌ··· ˈ·/ *n* [plural] art such as painting, SCULPTURE etc that you look at, as opposed to literature or music that you read or hear 視覺藝術〈如繪畫、雕塑等〉

visual dis·play u·nit /ˌ··· ·ˈ· ˌ··/ *n* [C] VDU〔電腦或文字處理器的〕視頻顯示器

vi·su·al·ize also 又作 **-ise** *BrE*【英】/ˋvɪʒuəlˌaɪz; ˈvɪʒuəlaɪz/ *v* [T] to form a picture of someone or something in your mind; IMAGINE 設想, 想像: *Try to visualize a successful future.* 試着設想一個成功的未來。| **visualize sb doing sth** *Somehow I can't visualize myself teaching adults.* 不知怎的, 我想像不出自己教成年人的情景。| **visualize how/what etc** *It's hard to visualize how these tiles will look in our bathroom.* 很難想像這些瓷磚鋪在我們浴室裡會是甚麼樣子。—**visualization** /ˌvɪʒuələˋzeʃən; ˌvɪʒuəlaɪˈzeɪʃən/ *n* [U]

vi·su·al·ly /ˋvɪʒuəlɪ; ˈvɪʒuəli/ *adv* **1** in appearance 表面上, 外觀上: *a visually stunning production* 看起來極好的生產情況 **2 visually impaired/handicapped** unable to see normally 視力受損的/有缺陷的: *She teaches visually impaired children.* 她給有視力障礙的孩子講課。**3** if you explain something visually, you let people see it by using pictures or films, or by showing real things〔用圖畫、電影或實物〕直觀地〔解釋某物〕: *The process is easy to understand when it is demonstrated visually.* 用直觀演示, 這個過程就容易理解了。

vi·tal /ˋvaɪtl̩; ˈvaɪtl/ *adj* **1** extremely important and necessary for something to succeed or exist 極其重要的, 必不可少的: *Choosing the right equipment is vital.* 挑選合適的設備極其重要。| **[+to]** *Such measures are vital to national security.* 這些措施對國家安全是必不可少的。| **[+for]** *Regular exercise is vital for your health.* 經常鍛鍊對健康非常重要。| **it is vital that** *It is vital that you keep accurate records.* 保持準確的記錄非常重要。| **vital importance** *The industry is of vital importance to the national economy.* 工業對國家經濟極其重要。| **play a vital role** *Richardson played a vital role in the team's success.* 理查森對本隊的成功起了極重要的作用。**2** full of energy in a way that is exciting and attractive 有生命力的; 充滿活力的, 生機勃勃的: *The drawings were crude but wonderfully vital.* 這些圖畫雖然粗糙, 但充滿驚人的活力。| *a strong, vital man* 一個身體強壯、朝氣勃勃的男子 **3** [only before noun 僅用於名詞前] necessary in order to keep you alive 維持生命所必需的: *the body's vital processes* 基本的生命活動 | *the vital organs* (=heart, brain etc) 要害器官〈如心、腦等〉

vi·tal·i·ty /vaɪˋtælətɪ; vaɪˈtælɪ̵ti/ *n* [U] **1** great energy and cheerfulness 精力; 活力: *Despite her eighty years Elsie was full of vitality.* 儘管已八十歲了, 埃爾西依然充滿活力。**2** the ability of an organization, country etc to continue working effectively〔組織、國家等的〕生命力: *The process of restructuring has injected some much-needed vitality into the company.* 重組為公司注入了一些急需的生命力。

vi·tal·ly /ˋvaɪtl̩ɪ; ˈvaɪtl-i/ *adv* in a very important or necessary way 極大地: *The way we treat our planet now will vitally affect the future of the human race.* 我們現在對待地球的方式將極大地影響人類的未來。| **vitally important** (=extremely important) 極其重要的 *It's vitally important that you all attend the meeting.* 你們都要參加會議, 這極為重要。

vi·tals /ˋvaɪtl̩z; ˈvaɪtlz/ *n* [plural] *old use* the parts of your body that are necessary to keep you alive, such as your heart and lungs【舊】〔維持生命的〕重要器官〈如心、肺等〉

vital sta·tis·tics /ˌ·· ·ˈ··/ *n* [plural] **1** *BrE humorous* a woman's chest, waist, and HIP measurements【英, 幽默】婦女的三圍（尺寸）〔指腰圍、胸圍和臀圍〕**2** figures that show the number of births, deaths, marriages etc within a population 人口動態統計〔指對出生、死亡、婚姻等人口資料的統計〕

vit·a·min /ˈvaɪtəmɪn; ˈvɪtəmᵻn/ *n* [C] a natural substance found in food that is necessary for good health 維生素, 維他命: *Milk is rich in vitamins.* 牛奶富含維生素。| *vitamin pills* 維生素片 | **vitamin A/B/C etc** (=a particular type of vitamin) 維生素A/B/C *Lack of vitamin A can cause blindness.* 缺乏維生素A可導致失明。

vi·ti·ate /ˈvɪʃɪˌet; ˈvɪʃieɪt/ *v* [T usually passive 一般用被動態] *formal* to make something less effective or spoil it 【正式】削弱〔某物〕的效能; 破壞, 損害: *The conclusions were vitiated by doubts concerning the scientific evidence.* 由於科學根據上存疑, 結論無效。—**vitiation** /ˌvɪʃɪˈeʃən; ˌvɪʃiˈeɪʃən/ *n* [U]

vit·i·cul·ture /ˈvɪtɪˌkʌltʃɚ; ˈvɪtᵻkʌltʃə/ *n* [U] the study or practice of growing GRAPEs for making wine〔為釀酒的〕葡萄栽培(學); 葡萄栽培術

vit·re·ous /ˈvɪtrɪəs; ˈvɪtriəs/ *adj* made of or looking like glass 玻璃做的; 玻璃(狀)的

vit·ri·fy /ˈvɪtrəˌfaɪ; ˈvɪtrᵻfaɪ/ *v* [I,T] *technical* if a substance vitrifies or is vitrified, it changes into glass【術語】(使)成玻璃, (使)玻璃化 —**vitrification** /ˌvɪtrɪfəˈkeʃən; ˌvɪtrᵻfᵻˈkeɪʃən/ *n* [U]

vit·ri·ol /ˈvɪtrɪəl; ˈvɪtriəl/ *n* [U] **1** *literary* very cruel remarks that are intended to hurt someone's feelings【文】尖刻[刻薄]的話; 諷刺 **2** *old-fashioned* SULPHURIC ACID【過時】硫酸

vit·ri·ol·ic /ˌvɪtrɪˈɑlɪk; ˌvɪtriˈɒlɪk◂/ *adj* vitriolic language is very cruel and intended to hurt someone's feelings〔言語〕尖刻的, 辛辣的: *a vitriolic attack on homosexuals* 對同性戀者的刻薄攻擊 —**vitriolically** /-klɪ; -kli/ *adv*

vitro *n* —see 見 IN VITRO

vi·tu·pe·ra·tion /vaɪˌtupəˈreʃən; vɪˌtjuːpəˈreɪʃən/ *n* [U] *formal* angry and cruel criticism【正式】謾罵, 咒罵, 辱罵: *the subject of daily vituperation and abuse* 每日辱罵的對象

vi·tu·pe·ra·tive /vaɪˈtupəˌretɪv; vɪˈtjuːpərətɪv/ *adj formal* full of angry and cruel criticism【正式】謾罵的, 充滿辱罵的

vi·va¹ /ˈvaɪvə; ˈvaɪvə/ *n* [C] *BrE informal* a spoken examination taken at the end of a university course; VIVA VOCE【英, 非正式】〔大學中一門課程結束時的〕口試, 口頭測驗

viva² *interjection* used to show that you approve of someone and want them to continue to exist or be successful 萬歲!〔表示讚許或祝願的歡呼聲〕: *Viva Eliot!* 艾略特萬歲!

vi·va·ce /vɪˈvatʃɪ; vɪˈvɑːtʃi/ *adj, adv* music that is vivace is played quickly and with a lot of energy〔音樂〕活潑的[地], 輕快的[地]

vi·va·cious /vaɪˈveʃəs; vᵻˈveɪʃəs/ *adj* a woman who is vivacious has a lot of energy and a happy attractive manner〔女性〕活潑的, 快活的, 生氣勃勃的: *a vivacious and outgoing personality* 活潑外向的個性 —**vivaciously** *adv* —**vivaciousness** *n* [U] —**vivacity** /vaɪˈvæsətɪ; vᵻˈvæsᵻti/ *n* [U]

vi·var·i·um /vaɪˈvɛrɪəm; vaɪˈveəriəm/ *n* [C] a place indoors where animals are kept in conditions that are as similar as possible to their natural environment〔模擬自然生態環境的〕動物飼養室

viv·a voc·e /ˌvaɪvə ˈvosɪ; ˌvaɪvə ˈvəʊsi/ *n* [C] *BrE formal* a VIVA¹【英, 正式】口試, 口頭測驗

viv·id /ˈvɪvɪd; ˈvɪvᵻd/ *adj* **1** vivid memories, dreams, descriptions etc are so clear that they seem real〔記憶、夢境、描述等〕生動的; 逼真的; 清晰的: *a vivid account of their journey across the desert* 對他們穿越沙漠旅行的生動記述 **2 vivid imagination** an ability to imagine unlikely situations very clearly 活躍的想像力 **3** vivid colours or patterns are very bright〔色彩、圖案〕鮮豔的; 鮮明的: *The lake was a vivid blue.* 湖水湛藍。—**vividly** *adv*: *I can vividly remember the day we met.* 我能清楚地記得我們相遇的那一天。—**vividness** *n* [U]

viv·i·sec·tion /ˌvɪvəˈsɛkʃən; ˌvɪvᵻˈsekʃən/ *n* [U] the practice of cutting open the bodies of living animals in order to do medical or scientific tests on them〔為做醫學或科學實驗而進行的〕動物活體解剖 —**vivisectionist** *n* [C]

vix·en /ˈvɪksn̩; ˈvɪksən/ *n* [C] **1** a female FOX¹ (1) 雌狐 **2** *old-fashioned* a BAD-TEMPERED woman【過時】悍婦, 潑婦 —**vixenish** *adj*

viz /vɪz; vɪz/ *adv formal* used to introduce specific details that make your meaning clearer; NAMELY【正式】即, 也就是, 就是說

vi·zier /vɪˈzɪr; vᵻˈzɪə/ *n* [C] an important politician in certain Muslim countries in the past 維齊爾〔舊時某些伊斯蘭國家的高官、大臣〕

VJ /ˌvi ˈdʒe; ˌviː ˈdʒeɪ/ *n* [C] a VIDEO JOCKEY〔尤指播放流行音樂的〕電視音樂節目主持人

V-neck /ˈvi nɛk; ˈviː nek/ *n* [C] an opening for the neck shaped like the letter V, in a piece of clothing V形(衣)領, 雞心領 —**V-necked** *adj*: *a V-necked sweater* 雞心領毛線衫 —see picture on page A17 參見A17頁圖

vo·cab /ˈvokæb; ˈvəʊkæb/ *n* [U] *informal* VOCABULARY (5)【非正式】詞彙表

vo·cab·u·la·ry /vəˈkæbjəˌlɛrɪ; vəˈkæbjᵍləri/ *n* **1** [C,U] all the words that someone knows, learns, or uses〔一個人學會或使用的〕詞彙量, 語彙: *Considering he's only six, he has an excellent vocabulary.* 考慮到他只有六歲, 他的詞彙量已經相當大了。| **wide/limited vocabulary** (=a large or small vocabulary) 豐富/有限的詞彙量 | **increase/extend/build up/enrich your vocabulary** *You should read more literature to enrich your vocabulary.* 你應該多看些文學作品, 以豐富你的詞彙量。**2** [C,U] the words that are typically used when talking about a particular subject 專業詞彙, 術語: *Most technical jobs use a specialized vocabulary.* 許多技術性工作要用專業詞彙。| **[+of]** *the vocabulary of politics* 政治學詞彙 **3** [C] all the words in a particular language〔某種語言的〕詞彙 **4 the word failure/compromise etc is not in sb's vocabulary** used to say that someone never thinks of accepting failure etc 某人的詞彙中沒有失敗/妥協等詞語〔指從不接受失敗、妥協等〕**5** [C] a list of words with explanations of their meanings, in a book for learning foreign languages〔外語教科書中有釋義的〕詞彙表 **6** [C,U] a list of the codes (CODE¹ (7)) or terms (TERM¹ (5)) used in a computer system〔電腦系統的〕詞彙表, 符號集

vo·cal¹ /ˈvokl̩; ˈvəʊkəl/ *adj* **1** protesting or complaining strongly and loudly about something 強烈反對的, 大聲抱怨的; 直言不諱的, 說話不客氣的: *a vocal critic of the government* 對政府直言不諱的批評者 **2** [only before noun 僅用於名詞前] connected with the voice 聲音的; 使用嗓音的: *The song suited the singer's vocal range.* 這首歌適合這位歌手的音域。—**vocally** *adv*

vocal² *n* [C usually plural 一般用複數] the part of a piece of music that is sung rather than played on an instrument〔音樂的〕歌唱部分〔相對於樂器演奏部分〕: *vocals by John Lennon and Paul McCartney* 約翰·連儂和保羅·麥卡尼的演唱

vocal cords, vocal chords /ˈ·· ·/ *n* [plural] thin pieces of muscle in your throat that produce sounds when you are speaking 聲帶 —see picture at 參見 BODY 圖

vo·cal·ist /ˈvoklɪst; ˈvəʊkəlᵻst/ *n* [C] someone who sings popular songs, especially with a band〔尤指與樂隊配合演唱流行歌曲的〕歌手 —compare 比較 INSTRUMENTALIST

vo·ca·tion /voˈkeʃən; vəʊˈkeɪʃən/ *n* **1** [C] a job that you do because you have a very strong feeling that doing this job is the purpose of your life, and especially because you want to help other people〔指自己非常熱愛的〕工作, 職業, 使命: *Teaching isn't just a job – it's a vocation.* 教書並不單單是一份工作——它是一種使命。| **find your vocation** *She felt that she had found her vocation when she began writing children's books.* 她開始創作兒童文學時, 才感到自己找到了所熱愛的工作。—see 見 JOB (USAGE) **2** [C,U] a special ability to do a particular job or activity, especially one that gives service to other people〔尤指從事某種服務性行業的〕素質, 才能: [+for] *He has a vocation for teaching.* 他有教書的稟賦。**3** [C,U] a strong belief that you have been chosen by God to be a priest or a NUN; CALLING 神召; 天職, 〔宗教上的〕使命感: *a vocation for the priesthood* 當牧師的使命感

vo·ca·tion·al /voˈkeʃənl; vəʊˈkeɪʃənəl/ *adj* **vocational training/guidance/course etc** training etc that teaches you the skills you need to do a particular job 職業培訓/指導/課程等

voc·a·tive /ˈvɑkətɪv; ˈvɒkətɪv/ *n* [C] *technical* a particular form of a noun in certain languages, used when speaking or writing to someone【術語】〔某些語言中的〕呼格; 呼格詞 —**vocative** *adj*

vo·cif·er·ate /voˈsɪfəˌret; vəˈsɪfəreɪt/ *v* [I] *formal* to shout loudly, especially when complaining【正式】〔尤指抱怨地〕大叫大嚷 —**vociferation** /voˌsɪfəˈreʃən; vəˌsɪfəˈreɪʃən/ *n* [C, U]

vo·cif·er·ous /voˈsɪfərəs; vəˈsɪfərəs/ *adj formal*【正式】**1** expressing your opinions loudly and strongly〔表述自己觀點時〕大聲的, 激昂的: *vociferous protesters* 吵吵嚷嚷的抗議者 **2** vociferous opinions are loudly and strongly expressed〔意見〕大聲疾呼地提出的: *a vociferous debate* 大叫大嚷的辯論 —**vociferously** *adv* —**vociferousness** *n* [U]

vod·ka /ˈvɑdkə; ˈvɒdkə/ *n* [U] a strong clear alcoholic drink from Russia 伏特加〔俄羅斯出產的烈酒〕

vogue /vog; vəʊg/ *n* [singular, U] if something is the vogue, it is popular or fashionable for a period of time 時尚; 流行: [+for] *the vogue for childbirth at home* 在家中分娩的時尚 | **be in vogue/be the vogue** *Short skirts are very much in vogue just now.* 短裙目前非常流行。

vogue word /ˌ· ˈ·/ *n* [C] a word that is fashionable for a short period of time 時髦詞, 時興詞

voice¹ /vɔɪs; vɔɪs/ *n*

1 ►SPEAKING 說話◄ [C,U] the sounds that you make when you speak 說話聲, 嗓音: *He recognized her voice instantly.* 他立刻聽出了她的聲音。| *I could hear voices in the next room.* 我能聽見隔壁房間裡的說話聲。| **a loud/deep/soft/husky etc voice** *a child with a squeaky voice* 說話尖聲尖氣的小孩 | **angry/excited/worried etc voice** *the angry voices of disgruntled passengers* 不滿意的乘客發出的憤怒聲 | **in a deep/angry etc voice** *He spoke in a pleasantly deep voice.* 他說話聲音深沉, 非常悅耳。| **a small voice** (=a quiet and shy voice) 小聲, 輕柔而羞怯的聲音 | **sb's tone of voice** (=the quality of someone's voice which expresses their attitude) 某人的語氣[聲調] *I could tell from his tone of voice that he was not impressed.* 我能從他的語氣中聽出他不感興趣。| **raise your voice** (=speak more loudly, especially in an angry way)〔尤指生氣地〕提高嗓門 *I know what you're saying – there's no need to raise your voice.* 我明白你的意思 —— 你沒必要提高嗓門。| **lower/drop your voice** (=speak more quietly) 放低聲音 *She moved closer and lowered her voice so Alex wouldn't hear.* 她往前湊了湊, 放低了聲音, 這樣亞歷克斯就聽不見了。| **keep your voice down** *spoken* (=used to tell someone to speak more quietly)【口】小聲點 | **at the top of your voice** (=shouting as loudly as you can) 扯着喉嚨, 放開嗓子〔喊叫〕*I could hear him screaming and yelling at the top of his voice.* 我能聽到他扯着嗓子又喊又叫。| **sb's voice breaks** (=when a boy's voice becomes deeper like a man's) 某人的嗓子變聲 *He was 13 and his voice was already starting to break.* 他 13 歲, 嗓子已經開始變聲了。—see 見 NOISE¹ (USAGE)

2 deep-voiced/husky-voiced etc having a voice that is deep etc 嗓音低沉的/沙啞的等

3 ►ABILITY TO SPEAK 說話能力◄ [U] the ability to use your voice 嗓子; 發聲能力: *You won't have any voice left if you keep shouting like that.* 這麼大喊大叫下去, 你會喊壞嗓子的。| **close your voice** (=be unable to speak because you have a sore throat) 無法發聲〔因嗓子疼而無法講話〕

4 ►SINGING 歌唱◄ a) [C,U] the quality of sound you produce when you sing〔唱歌的〕聲音, 音質: *a young man with a fine singing voice* 音色優美的青年 | **be in good voice** (=be singing well) 唱得好 **b)** [C] a person singing 演唱者: *a piece written for six voices and piano* 為六聲部和鋼琴譜的曲子

5 ►OPINION 意見◄ a) [singular,U] the right or ability to express an opinion, to vote, or to influence decisions 表達意見權; 發言權; 投票權; 影響力: **have a voice (in)** *It is important that parents should have a voice in deciding how their children are educated.* 重要的是父母應有權決定其子女受甚麼樣的教育。| **give voice to** (=express opinions or feelings openly) 公開表達〔意見、感情〕*Only Hartman dared to give voice to their discontent.* 只有哈特曼敢於公開表達他們的不滿情緒。**b)** [C] an opinion or wish that is expressed〔表達出的〕意見; 願望: *The government should listen to the voice of the black community.* 政府應該聽取黑人社區的呼聲。| **dissenting voices** (=people expressing disagreement) 不滿的聲音 | **add/lend your voice etc** (=express your support for something) 對…表示聲援, 支持 *Carter lent his powerful voice to the call for disarmament.* 卡特積極響應裁軍的呼籲。| **raise your voice against** (=oppose something publicly) 公開反對 *Not a voice was raised against the plan.* 沒有一個人反對這項計劃。| **make your voice heard** (=express your opinion so that people notice it) 發表意見〔讓別人注意〕

6 speak with one voice if a group of people speak with one voice, they all express the same opinion 異口同聲, 一致地

7 ►REPRESENTATIVE 代表◄ [singular] a person, organization, newspaper etc that expresses the opinions or wishes of a group of people 喉舌, 代言人: *Martin Luther King had become the voice of the Civil Rights Movement.* 馬丁·路德·金已成為民權運動的代言人。

8 the voice of reason/sanity/experience etc opinions or ideas that are reasonable, sensible, based on experience etc 合理的想法/明智的意見/經驗之談等: *"Marriage is a very risky business." "Ah, there speaks the voice of experience!"* "結婚是件冒險的事。" "啊, 這真是經驗之談呀!"

9 inner voice thoughts or feelings which you do not express but which seem to warn you or advise you 內心的想法[感覺]: *My inner voice told me to be cautious.* 我內心的感覺告訴我要小心謹慎。

10 active/passive voice *technical* the form of a verb that shows whether the subject of a sentence does an action or has an action done to it【術語】主動/被動語態

voice² *v* [T] **1** to tell people your opinions or feelings about a particular subject 表達, 吐露: **voice opinions/doubts etc** *He voiced several objections to the plan.* 他對這項計劃提出幾點反對理由。**2** *technical* to produce a sound with a movement of the VOCAL CORDS as well as the breath【術語】把…發成濁音

voice box /ˈ· ·/ *n* [C] *not technical* the part of your throat that you use to produce sounds when you speak; LARYNX【非術語】喉(頭)

voiced /vɔɪst; vɔɪst/ *adj technical* voiced sounds are made using the VOCAL CORDS. For example /d/ and /g/ are voiced consonants【術語】(發) 濁音的〈如/d/和/g/皆為濁輔音〉

voice·less /ˈvɔɪslɪs; ˈvɔɪsləs/ *adj technical* voiceless sounds are made without using the VOCAL CORDS. For example /p/ and /k/ are voiceless consonants【術語】(發) 清音的〈如/p/和/k/為清輔音〉

voice mail /ˈ· ·/ *n* [U] a system in which spoken messages are recorded onto a computer so that someone can listen to them later 語音信箱, 留言信箱

voice-o·ver /ˈ· ··/ *n* [C] an explanation or remarks that are spoken on a television advertisement or film by someone who cannot be seen〔電視廣告、電影的〕畫外音, 解說

voice print /ˈ· ·/ *n* [C] the sound of a particular person's voice recorded on a machine, which can be used to check who that person is〔某人嗓音的〕聲紋; 聲印

void¹ /vɔɪd; vɔɪd/ *adj* **1** *law* a contract or official agreement that is void is not legal and has no effect; NULL AND VOID【法律】〔合同或正式協議〕無效的, 沒有法律效力的 **2 be void of** *formal* to completely lack something【正式】毫無...的, 缺乏...的: *Her eyes were void of all expression.* 她的眼睛空洞無神。

void² *n* [C usually singular 一般用單數] **1** a feeling of great sadness that you have when someone you love dies or when something is taken from you 空虛感; 孤寂感: *Their son's death left a painful void in their lives.* 兒子的死給他們的生活留下了痛苦的孤寂感。**2** an empty area of space where nothing exists 空處, 空間: *the void between atoms* 原子之間的空隙 | *She looked over the cliff into the void.* 她從懸崖邊上望下去, 下面一片虛空。**3** a situation in which something important or interesting that previously existed is no longer present 空白, 空虛: *Many women re-enter the workforce after raising a family to fill a void in their lives.* 許多婦女把孩子養大後重新加入勞動大軍, 以填補生活中的空虛。

void³ *v* [T] **1** *law* to make a contract or agreement void so that it has no legal effect【法律】使〔契約或協議〕無效; 使作廢 **2 void the bladder/bowels** *formal* to pass waste liquid or solid matter from your body【正式】排空膀胱/大腸

voi·là /vwa`la; vwɑːˈlɑː/ *interjection French* used when suddenly showing something to someone【法】瞧!〔用於突然把某物展示給某人時〕: *Voilà! Your birthday cake!* 瞧! 你的生日蛋糕!

voile /vɔɪl; vɔɪl/ *n* [U] a very light almost transparent cloth made of cotton, wool, or silk 巴里紗〔一種用棉、毛或真絲織成的輕質近乎透明的薄紗〕

vol. the written abbreviation for 縮寫=VOLUME

vol·a·tile /ˈvɑlətl; ˈvɒlətaɪl/ *adj* **1** a volatile situation is likely to change suddenly and without much warning 易變的, 動盪不定的: *a volatile economic environment* 不穩定的經濟環境 **2** someone who is volatile can suddenly become angry or violent 易激動的; 易發作的; 易怒的 **3** a volatile liquid or substance changes easily into a gas 易揮發的 —**volatility**/ˌvɑləˈtɪlətɪ; ˌvɒləˈtɪlɪ̈ti/ *n* [U]

vol-au-vent /ˌvol o `vã; ˌvɒl əʊ ˈvɒn/ *n* [C] *French* a small round piece of PASTRY that is filled with chicken, vegetables etc【法】〔一種以雞肉、蔬菜等為餡的〕肉餡油酥餅

vol·can·ic /vɑl`kænɪk; vɒlˈkænɪk/ *adj* **1** connected with or caused by a volcano 火山的; 由火山作用引起的: *black volcanic sand* 黑火山砂 **2** happening or reacting suddenly and violently 暴烈的, 猛烈的: *a man of volcanic passions* 性情暴烈的人

vol·ca·no /vɑl`keno; vɒlˈkeɪnəʊ/ *n plural* **volcanoes** *or* **volcanos** [C] a mountain with a large hole at the top, through which hot rocks, LAVA, and ash sometimes rise into the air from inside the earth 火山: *Pompeii was destroyed when the volcano erupted in 79AD.* 龐貝為公元79年的火山爆發所毀。| **active volcano** (=a volcano that may explode at any time) 活火山 | **dormant volcano** (=a volcano that is not active at present) 休眠火山 | **extinct volcano** (=a volcano that is no longer active) 死火山

vole /vol; vəʊl/ *n* [C] a small animal like a mouse with a short tail that lives in fields and woods and near rivers 田鼠

vo·li·tion /vo`lɪʃən; vəˈlɪʃən/ *n* [U] *formal* the power to choose or decide something without being forced to do it【正式】意志力; 決斷: **of your own volition** (=because you want to do something, not because you are forced to do it) 出於某人自己的意志 *Helena left the company of her own volition.* 海倫娜自願離開了公司。

vol·ley¹ /ˈvɑlɪ; ˈvɒli/ *n* [C] **1** a large number of shots fired from guns at the same time〔槍砲等的〕羣射, 齊射: **[+of]** *a volley of bullets* 子彈齊射 **2** a lot of questions, insults, attacks etc that are all said or made at the same time〔質問、辱罵、攻擊等的〕連發; 迸發: **[+of]** *a volley of abuse* 一陣辱罵 | *a volley of blows* 一頓狠揍 **3** a hit in TENNIS, a kick in football etc when the player hits or kicks the ball before it touches the ground〔網球着地前的〕截擊, 攔擊;〔足球落地前的〕截踢, 凌空球 —see picture on page A23 參見A23頁圖 **4** a lot of objects that are thrown through the air at the same time 齊發, 羣擲: **[+of]** *a volley of stones* 一陣石頭亂砸

volley² *v* **1** [I,T] to hit or kick a ball before it touches the ground, especially in TENNIS or football 截擊〔球〕; 截踢〔球〕: *Ince volleyed the ball over the net.* 恩斯凌空抽射, 皮球高出球門。**2** [I] if a large number of guns volley, they are all fired at the same time〔槍砲〕羣射, 齊鳴

vol·ley·ball /ˈvɑlɪˌbɔl; ˈvɒlibɔːl/ *n* **1** [U] a game in which two teams hit a ball backwards and forwards over a high net with their hands and do not allow it to touch the ground 排球 (運動) **2** [C] the ball used in this game 排球

volt /volt; vəʊlt/ *n* [C] *technical* a unit for measuring the force of an electric current【術語】伏特, 伏〔電壓單位〕

volt·age /ˈvoltɪdʒ; ˈvəʊltɪdʒ/ *n* [C,U] *technical* electrical force measured in volts【術語】電壓, 伏特數: *a high voltage fence* 通了高壓電的圍欄

volte-face /ˈvɑltˌfɑs; ˌvɒlt ˈfæs/ *n* [C usually singular 一般用單數] *formal* a change to a completely opposite opinion or plan of action【正式】〔意見、行動計劃等的〕完全改變, 大轉變, 180度大轉彎

volt·me·ter /ˈvoltˌmitɚ; ˈvəʊltˌmiːtə/ *n* [C] an instrument for measuring voltage 伏特計, 電壓表

vol·u·ble /ˈvɑljəbl; ˈvɒljʊ̈bəl/ *adj formal*【正式】**1** talking a lot 健談的: *a voluble spokesman* 口若懸河的發言人 **2** a voluble speech, explanation etc uses a lot of words and is spoken quickly〔講話等〕滔滔不絕的; 流利的: *She broke into voluble and perfect Italian.* 她突然說起一口流利而純正的意大利語來。—**volubly** *adv* —**volubility** /ˌvɑljəˈbɪlɪtɪ; ˌvɒljʊ̈ˈbɪlɪ̈ti/ *n* [U]

vol·ume /ˈvɑljəm; ˈvɒljuːm/ *n* 

1 ►SPACE FILLED 充滿的空間◄ [C,U] the amount of space that a substance or object contains or fills 容量; 體積; 容積: *The volume of the container measures 100,000 cubic metres.* 這個集裝箱的容量是10萬立方米。| *an instrument for measuring the volume of a gas* 測量氣體體積的儀器

2 ►AMOUNT 數量◄ [C,U] the total amount of something, especially when it is large or increasing〔尤指巨大的或正在增加的〕量, 總量: *The volume of traffic on the roads has increased dramatically in recent years.* 近年來公路交通量急劇增加。| *the volume of trade* 貿易量

3 ►SOUND 聲音◄ [U] the amount of sound produced by a television, radio etc 音量; (音) 響度: *Can you turn the volume down on the stereo.* 把立體聲音響的音量調小一點。

4 ►BOOK 書籍◄ a) [C] one of the books into which a very long book is divided〔書的〕卷, 冊: *the M-Mon volume of the encyclopedia* 百科全書的M-Mon卷 **b)** [C] *formal* a book【正式】書籍: *a volume of poetry* 詩集 —see also 另見 **speak volumes** (SPEAK (11))

vo·lu·mi·nous /vəˈlumənəs; vəˈluːmɪ̈nəs/ *adj formal*【正式】**1** a voluminous piece of clothing is very large and loose〔衣服〕寬大的, 寬鬆的: *a voluminous cloak* 寬大的斗篷 **2** voluminous books, documents etc are very long and contain a lot of detail〔書籍、文件等〕多卷的; 篇幅長的, 大部頭的: *He took voluminous notes during the lecture.* 他在聽課時作了大量筆記。**3** a voluminous container is very large and can hold a lot of things〔容器〕大的; 容量大的: *a voluminous suitcase* 一個能裝很多東西的手提箱

vol·un·ta·ry¹ /ˈvɑlənˌtɛrɪ; ˈvɒləntəri/ *adj* **1 voluntary work/service etc** work etc that is done by people who do it because they want to, and without expecting any money for it 義務工作/服務等: *When she retired she* 3 did a lot of voluntary work for the Red Cross. 她退休後為紅十字會做了大量的義務工作。| **on a voluntary basis** *Participants in the experiment took part on a voluntary basis.* 參加實驗的人員都是自願的。**2 voluntary organization/society/institution etc** an organization etc that is organized or supported by people who give their money, services etc because they want to and without expecting reward 志願組織/團體/機構等: *a voluntary organization providing help for the elderly* 一個為老年人提供幫助的志願組織 **3 voluntary worker/helper/assistant etc** someone who works without expecting or receiving payment 志願人員/幫手/助手等 **4** done willingly and without being forced 自願的, 志願的; 自發的: *The suspect has given the police his voluntary cooperation.* 嫌疑犯自願與警方合作。| *Workers are being encouraged to take voluntary redundancy.* 工人被鼓勵自願離職。—compare 比較 COMPULSORY **5** *technical* voluntary movements of your body are controlled by you【術語】〔身體活動〕自如的, 隨意的 —opposite 反義詞 INVOLUNTARY —**voluntarily** /ˌvɑlənˋtɛrılı; ˈvɒləntərᶾli/ *adv*: *She wasn't fired – she left voluntarily.* 她不是被解雇的 —— 她是自願離職的。

voluntary² *n* [C] a piece of music, usually for the ORGAN (2), written to be played in church〔教堂中的〕(風琴) 演奏曲

vol·un·teer¹ /ˌvɑlənˋtır; ˌvɒlənˈtıə/ *n* [C] **1** someone who does something without being paid, or who is willing to offer to help someone 志願者, 自願參加者, 願做志願人員者: *Most of the relief work was done by volunteers.* 許多救援工作是由志願人員做的。| *I need some volunteers to clean up the kitchen.* 我需要幾名志願者來收拾一下廚房。**2** someone who offers to join the army, navy, or air force 志願兵

volunteer² *v* **1** [I,T] to offer to do something without expecting any reward, usually something that other people do not want to do 自願〔做某事〕; 自告奮勇, 自願效勞: **volunteer to do sth** *The company volunteered to donate fifty trucks to help the war effort.* 公司主動捐獻五十輛卡車支援戰事。| **[+for]** *Sidcup volunteered for guard duty.* 西德卡普自告奮勇去站崗。| **volunteer your services/help/advice** *I volunteered my services as a teacher.* 我自願去當老師。**2** [T] to tell someone something without being asked 自動說出〔某事〕: *Michael volunteered the information before I had a chance to ask.* 我還未來得及發問, 邁克爾就自動把情況說了。**3** [I] to offer to join the army, navy, or airforce 志願服役, 志願參軍: *When war broke out, my father volunteered immediately.* 戰爭一爆發, 我父親立即志願從軍。**4** [T] to say that someone else will do a job even though they may not want to 讓…做…: **volunteer sb for sth** *Mum volunteered Dave for washing-up duties.* 媽媽讓戴夫負責洗刷餐具。

vo·lup·tu·a·ry /vəˋlʌptʃuˌɛrı; vəˈlʌptʃuəri/ *n* [C] *literary* someone who enjoys physical, especially sexual, pleasure and having expensive possessions【文】驕奢淫逸的人; 酒色之徒

vo·lup·tu·ous /vəˋlʌptʃuəs; vəˈlʌptʃuəs/ *adj* **1** a woman who is voluptuous has large breasts and a soft curved body〔女性〕妖嬈的, 豐滿的, 性感的 **2** expressing strong sexual feeling or sexual pleasure 色情的; 勾起情慾的: *a voluptuous gesture* 挑逗的姿勢 **3** *literary* something that is voluptuous gives you pleasure because it looks, smells, or tastes good【文】令人愉悅的, 給感官以快感的: *the voluptuous fragrance of a summer garden* 夏季花園中散發出的令人心曠神怡的芬芳 —**voluptuously** *adv* —**voluptuousness** *n* [U]

vom·it¹ /ˋvɑmıt; ˈvɒmᶾt/ *v* [I,T] to bring food or drink up from your stomach out through your mouth, because you are ill 嘔吐; 嘔出, 吐出 —see 見 SICK¹ (USAGE)

vomit² *n* [U] food or other substances that come up from your stomach and through your mouth when you vomit 嘔吐物, 吐出物

voo·doo /ˋvudu; ˈvuːduː/ *n* [U] magical beliefs and practices used as a form of religion, especially by people in Haiti〔尤指海地人信仰的〕伏都教 (巫術)

voodoo e·co·nom·ics /ˌ‥ ‥ˈ‥/ *n* [U] *AmE* economic ideas that seem attractive but that do not work effectively over a period of time【美】華而不實的經濟學 (觀點)

vo·ra·cious /vəˋreʃəs; vəˈreıʃəs/ *adj* **1** eating or wanting large quantities of food 貪吃的; 食量大的: *Pigs are voracious feeders.* 豬的食量很大, 需要餵很多飼料。| **a voracious appetite** *Kids can have voracious appetites.* 小孩子會有大胃口。**2** extremely eager to read books, gain knowledge etc 求知慾極強的: *a voracious reader* 求知慾極強的讀者 —**voraciously** *adv* —**voraciousness** *n* [U] —**voracity** /-ˋræsətı; -ˈræsᶾti/ *n* [U]

vor·tex /ˋvɔrtɛks; ˈvɔːteks/ *n* [C] *literary*【文】**1** a mass of wind or water that spins rapidly and pulls things into its centre〔風或水形成的〕旋風; 旋渦 **2** [usually singular 一般用單數] a situation that has a powerful effect on people's lives and that influences their behaviour, even if they did not intend it to〔無法控制的對生活有巨大影響的〕形勢; 處境: **[+of]** *a black vortex of paranoia* 妄想症的黑色旋渦

vo·ta·ry /ˋvotərı; ˈvəʊtəri/ *n* [C] *formal* someone who regularly practises a particular religion【正式】信徒, 崇拜者

vote¹ /vot; vəʊt/ *n*

1 ►CHOICE 選擇◄ [C] a choice or decision that you make by voting in an election or meeting 投票所作的選擇[決定]: *The Democratic Party is counting on your vote.* 民主黨期望您投他們的票。| **[+for/against]** *There were 402 votes for Mr Williams, and 372 against.* 402 票支持威廉姆斯先生, 372 票反對。| **cast your vote** (=vote in a political election)〔在政治性選舉中〕投票 —see also 另見 CASTING VOTE

2 ►ELECTION 選舉◄ [C] an act of voting, when a group of people vote in order to decide or choose something 投票, 表決: *The results of the vote were surprising – 80% of workers favoured strike action.* 表決結果令人驚訝 —— 80%的工人贊成罷工行動。| **take/have a vote (on)** *We couldn't decide who to give the prize to so we took a vote on it.* 我們無法決定誰應該得獎, 於是投票表決。| **put sth to the vote** (=decide something by voting) 把某事訴諸表決 *Let's put it to the vote. All those in favor raise your hands.* 讓我們投票表決, 贊成的舉手。

3 ►RESULT 結果◄ [singular] the result of a vote 投票[表決]結果: *a very close vote* 票數很接近的表決結果 | *The motion was passed by a vote of 215 to 84.* 動議以 215 票對 84 票通過。

4 ►PAPER 紙◄ [C] the piece of paper which you use to make your vote 選票: *Party members were up all night counting the votes.* 黨員們通宵清點選票。

5 ►NUMBER OF VOTES 得票數◄ [singular] the total number of votes made in an election or the total number of people who vote〔選舉中的〕得票總數; 投票人數: *The Republicans increased their share of the vote.* 共和黨增加了在得票總數中所佔的份額。| *policies designed to win the African-American vote* (=all the votes of African-Americans) 旨在贏得非裔美國人選票的各項政策

6 the vote the right to vote in political elections〔政治上的〕選舉權, 投票權: *In France women didn't get the vote until 1945.* 在法國, 婦女到 1945 年才獲得選舉權。

7 sth gets my vote *spoken* used to say that you are ready to support something【口】我支持某事: *Anything that will mean a better deal for our children gets my vote.* 凡對我們的子孫有好處的事我都贊成。

vote² *v*

1 ►MAKE A CHOICE 作出選擇◄ [I,T] to show by marking a paper or raising your hand which person you want to elect or whether you support a particular plan 投票, 表決: *In 1918 British women got the right to vote.* 1918 年, 英國婦女獲得了選舉權。| **vote for sb** *I voted for the Labour candidate in the last election.* 我在上次選舉中

投票支持工黨候選人。| **[+on]** *If we can't agree, we'll have to vote on it.* 意見如果不能統一的話, 我們就得投票表決。| **vote to do sth** *Congress voted to increase foreign aid by 10%.* 國會表決通過增加10%的對外援助。| **vote for/in favour of/against sth** *53% of Danes voted in favour of the Maastricht treaty.* 53%的丹麥人投票贊成《馬斯特里赫特條約》。| **vote sth ↔ down** (=defeat a plan, law etc by voting) 否決 | **vote sth ↔ through** (=approve a plan, law etc by voting) 表決通過; 投票贊成〔計劃、法案等〕| **vote Democrat/Socialist/Republican etc** *I've voted Democrat all my life.* 我一生都在投民主黨的票。

2 ►ELECT 選舉◄ [T] to elect or dismiss someone by voting 選出, 選上; 使落選: **vote sb in/out** (=elect or dismiss someone from a position of power) 使某人當選/落選 *With policies like that he'll be voted out in the next election.* 執行這樣的政策, 他在下次選舉中非落選不可。| **vote sb into power/office/parliament etc** *Callaghan had been voted into office.* 卡拉漢獲選擔任公職。

3 ►PRIZE 獎勵◄ [T] to choose someone or something for a particular prize by voting for them 投票評選: *'Schindler's List' was voted 'Film of the Year'.*《舒特拉的名單》被選為"年度最佳電影"。

4 ►MONEY 錢款◄ [T] if a parliament, committee etc votes a sum of money for something, they decide by voting to provide money for that particular purpose〔議會、委員會等通過投票〕同意提供〔款項〕: *Parliament has voted £20 million extra funding for road improvements.* 國會投票通過另撥2,000萬英鎊用於改善道路。

5 vote sth a success/the best etc if people vote something a success etc, they all agree that it is a success 一致認為某事物是成功/最好的等: *Tom's party was voted a great success by everyone there.* 在場的人都認為湯姆的聚會辦得非常成功。

6 ►SUGGEST 建議◄ [T] *informal* to suggest something【非正式】提議: **[+that]** *I vote that we go to the movies.* 我提議一起去看電影。

7 vote with your feet to show that you do not support a decision or action by leaving a place or organization 以退席[退出組織]表示不支持〔某決定、行動等〕

vote of cen·sure /,· · '··/ *n* [C] a process in which members of parliament vote in order to blame the government for something〔國會議員對政府的〕不信任投票

vote of con·fi·dence /,· · '···/ *n* [C] **1** a formal process in which people vote in order to show that they support someone or something, especially the government〔尤指對政府的〕信任票: *a unanimous vote of confidence* 全體一致的信任票 **2** something that you do or say that shows you support someone and approve of their actions 贊同[支持]的表示

vote of no con·fi·dence /,· · · '···/ *n* [C] **1** a formal process in which people vote in order to show that they do not support someone or something, especially the government 不信任票, 不信任表決 **2** something that you do or say that shows that you do not support someone 不贊同[不支持]的表示

vote of thanks /,· · '·/ *n* **propose a vote of thanks** *especially BrE* to make a short formal speech in which you thank someone, especially at a public meeting or a formal dinner【尤英】〔尤指在公眾集會或正式晚宴上〕致答謝辭, 鳴謝

vot·er /ˋvotɚ; ˈvəʊtə/ *n* [C] someone who votes or has the right to vote, especially in a political election〔尤指政治性選舉中的〕選舉人, 投票人, 選民; 有投票權的人: *The party's policies do not appeal to the voters.* 該黨的政策不受選民歡迎。| *Tory voters* 投保守黨票的選民 —see also 另見 FLOATING VOTER

voting booth /'·· ·/ *n* [C] *AmE* an enclosed place where you can make your vote secretly【美】〔投票站裡供祕密寫選票用的〕投票亭, 寫票處; POLLING BOOTH *BrE*【英】

voting ma·chine /'·· ·,·/ *n* [C] a machine that records votes as they are made 投票機, 選票計算機

vo·tive /ˋvotɪv; ˈvəʊtɪv/ *adj technical* given or done to a promise made to God or to a SAINT【術語】〔對上帝或聖徒〕謝恩的; 還願的: *votive offerings* 謝恩奉獻物, 還願的奉獻物

vouch /vautʃ; vaʊtʃ/ *v*

vouch for sb/sth *phr v* [T] **1** to say that you believe that someone will behave well and that you will be responsible for their behaviour, actions etc 為〔某人的行為等〕作擔保: *I can vouch for my son, officer.* 我可以為兒子作保, 長官。**2** to say that you firmly believe that something is true or good because of your experience or knowledge of it 為〔某事〕作擔保, 保證: *I'll vouch for the quality of the report. I read it last night.* 我為報告的質量作保, 我昨晚看過。

vouch·er /ˋvautʃɚ; ˈvaʊtʃə/ *n* [C] **1** a kind of ticket that can be used instead of money for a particular purpose 代金券, 憑證: *a travel voucher* 旅行代金券 —see also 另見 LUNCHEON VOUCHER **2** an official statement or RECEIPT that is given to someone to prove that their accounts are correct or that money has been paid 收據, 收條; 憑單 ⊖ 3

vouch·safe /vautʃˋsef; vaʊtʃˈseɪf/ *v* [T] *formal*【正式】**1** to offer, give, or tell something to someone in a way that shows you trust them 惠予, 賜予: *insights into the future vouchsafed by God* 上帝賜予的對未來的洞察力 **2** to make it certain that something will be safe 確保…的安全: *political arrangements that vouchsafe peace* 確保和平的政治性安排

vow¹ /vau; vaʊ/ *n* [C] a serious promise 誓言; 誓約: *marriage vows* 結婚誓言 | **vow to do sth** *a vow to avenge his brother's death* 為他兄弟的死報仇的誓言 | **take/make a vow** *She made a vow never to tell anybody what she had heard.* 她起誓決不把聽到的告訴任何人。| **keep/break a vow** (=do or not do what you promised) 信守/違反誓言 | **vow of silence** (=a promise made to God that you will never speak again)〔向上帝〕立誓保持沉默[緘口保密] *monks who take the vow of silence* 立沉默之誓的僧侶 | **under a vow of** (=having promised to do something) 發過誓要… *nuns under the vow of chastity* 立誓保持貞潔的修女

vow² *v* [T] **1** *especially literary* to make a serious promise to yourself or someone else【尤文】立誓, 起誓: **vow to do sth** *He vowed to kill his wife's lover.* 他發誓要殺死妻子的情人。| **vow (that)** *I vowed that I would never drink again.* 我發誓絕不再喝酒了。**2** *formal* to make a religious promise that you will give something to God, the church etc【正式】〔向上帝、教會等〕立誓奉獻

vow·el /ˋvauəl; ˈvaʊəl/ *n* [C] **1** one of the human speech sounds that you make by letting your breath flow out without closing any part of your mouth or throat 元音 **2** a letter of the alphabet used to represent a vowel. In English the vowels are a, e, i, o, u, and sometimes y. 元音字母〔英語的元音字母為 a, e, i, o, u, 有時也包括 y〕

vox pop /,vɑks ˋpɑp; ,vɒks ˈpɒp/ *n* [U] *BrE informal* opinions expressed by ordinary people when they are asked questions about a particular subject during a television, radio, or newspaper report【英, 非正式】〔電視、電台或報紙就某主題採訪的〕普通民眾的觀點, 公眾輿論; 街頭民意調查

voy·age¹ /ˋvɔɪ·ɪdʒ; ˈvɔɪ-ɪdʒ/ *n* [C] a long journey in a ship〔乘船的長途〕航行: *The voyage from England to India used to take six months.* 過去從英國航行到印度要用六個月。

voyage² *v* [I] *literary* to make a long journey in a ship【文】航行, 航海 —see 見 TRAVEL (USAGE)

voy·ag·er /ˋvɔɪ·ɪdʒɚ; ˈvɔɪ-ɪdʒə/ *n* [C] *literary* someone who makes long and often dangerous journeys on the sea【文】航海者; 海上探險者

voy·eur /,vwɑˋjɚ; vwɑːˈjɜː/ *n* [C] **1** someone who gets sexual pleasure from secretly watching other people's sexual activities 窺淫狂者, 窺淫癖者 **2** someone who enjoys watching other people's private behaviour or suffering

喜歡窺探別人隱私的人 —**voyeurism** *n* [U] —**voyeuristic** /ˌvwɑjəˋrɪstɪk; ˌvwɑːjəˈrɪstɪk◂/ *adj* —**voyeuristically** /-klɪ; -kli/ *adv*

VP /ˌvi ˋpi; ˌviː ˈpiː/ the abbreviation of 縮寫= Vice President

vs /ˋvɝsəs; ˈvɜːsəs/ a written abbreviation of 縮寫= VERSUS

V sign /ˋvi ˌsaɪn; ˈviː saɪn/ *n* [C] **1** a sign meaning peace or victory made by holding up the first two fingers of your hand with the front of the hand facing forwards V字手勢, 勝利[和平]手勢〔手掌向外, 伸出食指及中指做成V字形〕 **2** *BrE* a rude sign made by holding up the first two fingers of your hand with the back of your hand facing towards another person【英】V字輕蔑侮辱手勢, 粗魯[下流]的手勢〔手背向外豎起食指及中指〕

vul·can·ize also 又作 **-ise** *BrE*【英】/ˋvʌlkənˌaɪz; ˈvʌlkənaɪz/ *v* [T] to make rubber stronger using a special chemical treatment〔通過化學處理〕使〔橡膠〕硫化; 把〔橡膠〕強化 —**vulcanization** /ˌvʌlkənaɪˋzeʃən; ˌvʌlkənaɪˈzeɪʃən/ *n* [U]

vul·gar /ˋvʌlgɚ; ˈvʌlgə/ *adj* **1** remarks, jokes etc that are vulgar deal with sex in a very rude and offensive way〔言語、玩笑等〕低俗的, 卑下的 **2** impolite and showing bad manners 無禮的, 粗俗的, 粗野的: *vulgar habits* 粗鄙的習慣 **3** *especially BrE* not showing good judgment about what is beautiful or suitable【尤英】庸俗的, 低級的: *a vulgar display of wealth* 庸俗地炫耀財富 —**vulgarly** *adv*

vulgar fraction /ˌ·· ˈ··/ *n* [C] *BrE old-fashioned* a FRACTION that is written as one number above a line and one number below it, and not as a DECIMAL【英, 過時】普通分數〔以分數式而不是以小數點表示〕; COMMON FRACTION *AmE*【美】

vul·gar·i·ty /vʌlˋgærətɪ; vʌlˈgærəti/ *n* **1** [U] the state or quality of being vulgar 庸俗, 粗俗, 粗鄙 **2 vulgarities** [plural] vulgar remarks, jokes etc 粗俗的話[玩笑等]

vul·gar·ize also 又作 **-ise** *BrE*【英】/ˋvʌlgəˌraɪz; ˈvʌlgəraɪz/ *v* [T] *formal* to spoil the quality or lower the standard of something that is good【正式】使庸俗化; 降低〔美好事物〕的水準 —**vulgarization** /ˌvʌlgəraɪˋzeʃən; ˌvʌlgəraɪˈzeɪʃən/ *n* [U]

Vul·gate /ˋvʌlget; ˈvʌlgeɪt/ *n* **the Vulgate** the Latin Bible commonly used in the Roman Catholic Church 拉丁文本《聖經》〔天主教普遍使用的文本〕

vul·ne·ra·ble /ˋvʌlnərəbl; ˈvʌlnərəbəl/ *adj* **1** someone who is vulnerable is easily harmed or hurt emotionally, physically, or morally 感情脆弱的; 易受傷的: *a vulnerable young child* 易受傷害的小孩 **2** a place, thing, or idea that is vulnerable is easy to attack 易受攻擊[責難]的: **[+to]** *The fort was vulnerable to attack from the north.* 該堡壘易從北面受到攻擊。| *a theory vulnerable to criticism* 易受批評的理論 —**vulnerably** *adv* —**vulnerability** /ˌvʌlnərəˋbɪlɪtɪ; ˌvʌlnərəˈbɪləti/ *n* [U]: *the vulnerability of airports to terrorist activity* 易受恐怖分子襲擊的機場

vul·ture /ˋvʌltʃɚ; ˈvʌltʃə/ *n* [C] **1** a large bird that eats dead animals 禿鷲 **2** someone who uses other people's troubles for their own advantage 壓榨別人的人, 盤剝弱者的人, 殘酷劫掠者

vul·va /ˋvʌlvə; ˈvʌlvə/ *n* [C] the outer part of a woman's sexual organs 女陰, 外陰

vy·ing /ˋvaɪ-ɪŋ; ˈvaɪ-ɪŋ/ the present participle of VIE

W,w

W, w /ˈdʌbl̩ju; ˈdʌbəlju:/ *plural* **W's, w's** *n* [C] **1** the 23rd letter of the English alphabet 英語字母表的第二十三個字母 **2** the written abbreviation of 縮寫= WEST or WESTERN **3** the written abbreviation of 縮寫= WATT

wack·y /ˈwækɪ; ˈwæki/ *adj informal* silly in an exciting or amusing way【非正式】瘋瘋癲癲的; 古怪的, 荒唐的 —**wackiness** *n* [U]

wad¹ /wɑd; wɒd/ *n* [C] **1** a thick pile of pieces of paper or thin material〔紙或輕薄材料的〕一疊; 一沓: *a wad of dollar bills* 一疊美元鈔票 —see picture on page A7 參見A7頁圖 **2** a thick soft mass of material that has been pressed together〔壓在一起的〕一團〔軟材料〕: *a wad of gauze* 一團紗布 **3** a piece of tobacco that you hold in your mouth 一小塊〔嚼用煙草〕

wad² *v*

wad sth ↔ **up** *phr v* [T] *AmE* to press something such as a piece of paper or cloth into a small tight ball【美】把〔紙或布等〕壓成一團

wad·ding /ˈwɑdɪŋ; ˈwɒdɪŋ/ *n* [U] soft material used for packing or to protect a wound 軟填料;〔醫用〕敷料

wad·dle /ˈwɑdl̩; ˈwɒdl/ *v* [I] to walk with short steps, swinging from one side to another like a duck〔似鴨子般〕搖搖擺擺地走: **[+along/around etc]** *Julie came waddling up the path, eight months pregnant.* 朱莉挺着八個月的大肚子, 一搖一擺地從路上走來。—**waddle** *n* [singular]

wade /wed; weɪd/ *v* [I+**across/through**,T] to walk through water that is not deep 蹚水, 涉水

wade in *phr v* [I] *BrE informal* to interrupt someone or become involved in something in an annoying way【英, 非正式】干涉, 介入, 插手: *I wish you wouldn't always wade in with your opinion.* 我希望你不要總是插進來提意見。

wade through sth *phr v* [T] to read or deal with a lot of boring papers or written work 吃力地閱讀; 費力地完成〔乏味的文件或文章〕: *Look at this pile of paperwork I have to wade through!* 瞧這一大堆煩人的文書, 我必須把它完成! —see picture on page A24 參見A24頁圖

wad·er /ˈwedɚ; ˈweɪdə/ *n* [C] **1** a bird that walks around in water to find its food and has long legs and a long neck〔腿頸俱長, 在水中覓食的〕涉禽 **2 waders** [plural] high rubber boots that you wear for walking in water〔涉水用的〕高統防水膠靴

wading bird /ˈ·· ˌ·/ *n* [C] a WADER (1) 涉禽

wad·ing pool /ˈ·· ·/ *n* [C] *AmE* a PADDLING POOL【美】嬉水池

wa·fer /ˈwefɚ; ˈweɪfə/ *n* [C] **1** a very thin BISCUIT (1) 威化餅乾, 薄脆餅 **2** a thin round piece of bread eaten with wine in the Christian religious ceremony of COMMUNION (2)〔基督教聖餐時與酒一起吃的〕聖餅

wafer-thin /ˌ·· ˈ·◂/ *adj* extremely thin 極薄的: *wafer-thin chocolates* 薄片巧克力

waf·fle¹ /ˈwɑfl̩; ˈwɒfəl/ *n* [C] **1** a thin flat cake, marked with a pattern of deep squares〔帶四方深紋的〕華夫餅, 奶蛋烘餅 **2** [U] *informal especially BrE* talk or writing that uses a lot of words but says nothing important【非正式, 尤英】胡扯, 冗長而空洞的話: *His exam answer was a load of old waffle.* 他的考試答卷簡直是廢話連篇。

waffle² *v* [I] *informal*【非正式】**1** also 又作 **waffle on** *especially BrE* to talk or write using a lot of words but without saying anything important【尤英】嘮叨, 廢話, 空話連篇: *Stop waffling and get to the point.* 別嘮叨了, 說正題吧。**2** *AmE informal* to be unable to decide what action to take【美, 非正式】猶豫不決: **[+over]** *Karl waffles over every darn decision!* 卡爾在每一個該死的決定上都舉棋不定!

waffle i·ron /ˈ·· ˌ··/ *n* [C] a piece of kitchen equipment used to cook waffles 華夫餅烤模

waf·fle·stomp·er /ˈwɑflˌstɑmpɚ; ˈwɒfəlˌstɒmpə/ *n* [C usually plural 一般用複數] *AmE* a type of very heavy walking boot【美】厚底旅行靴

waft /wɑft; wɑ:ft/ *v* [I always+adv/prep] to move gently through the air〔在空氣中〕飄蕩: **[+up/along/off etc]** *Cooking smells wafted up from downstairs.* 燒菜的氣味從樓下飄了上來。

wag¹ /wæg; wæg/ *v* [I,T] **1** to shake your finger or head repeatedly, especially to show disapproval〔反覆〕搖動〔手指或頭, 尤指表示不贊同時〕: **wag your finger** *"You naughty girl!" Mom said, wagging her finger at me.* "你這個淘氣的丫頭!"媽媽對我擺了擺手指說道。**2** If a dog wags its tail, it moves it repeatedly from one side to the other〔狗〕搖〔尾巴〕 **3 tongues wag** *informal* used to say that people are talking in a disapproving way about someone else's behaviour【非正式】〔對某人行為〕議論紛紛: *You'll have to stop visiting that woman – tongues are starting to wag.* 你不要再到那個女人那裡去了——有人開始說閒話了。

wag² *n* **1** [C usually singular 一般用單數] a wagging movement 搖動, 擺動 **2** [C] *old-fashioned* someone who talks or does something in a clever and amusing way【過時】愛說笑[逗樂]的人: *Some wag had drawn a face on the wall.* 愛逗樂的人在牆上畫了個臉形。—see also 另見 CHINWAG, WAGGISH

wage¹ /wedʒ; weɪdʒ/ *n* **1** [singular] also 又作 **wages** [plural] money you earn that is paid according to the number of hours, days, or weeks that you work〔按小時、日、週所計的〕工資, 薪金: *The job's not very exciting, but he earns a good wage.* 工作無甚趣味, 但他工資賺得不少。| **wage increase** also 又作 **wage rise** *BrE*【英】*The wage increases will come into effect in June.* 六月將開始加薪。| **daily/weekly etc wage** *a weekly wage of $250* 週薪250美元 | **wage levels/rates** (=fixed amounts of money paid for particular jobs)〔特定工作的固定〕工資級別/率 —compare 比較 SALARY —see 見 PAY² (USAGE) **2 a living wage** money you earn for work that is enough to pay for the basic things that you need to live 夠基本生活的工資 **3 wage freeze** an action taken by a company, government etc to stop wages increasing〔公司、政府等的〕工資凍結 **4 wage claim** the amount of money demanded by workers as an increase in wages 增加工資的要求 W3

wage² *v* [T] to be involved in a war against someone, or a fight against something 發動〔戰爭、鬥爭〕; 進行: **wage war (on)** *The police are waging war on drug pushers in the city.* 警方正在市內開展一場打擊毒販的鬥爭。| **wage a campaign/struggle/fight etc** *The struggle for political liberty waged throughout the 18th century.* 爭取政治自由的鬥爭貫穿了整個18世紀。

wage-earn·er /ˈ· ˌ··/ *n* [C] **1** someone who works for wages, often someone who works with their hands〔常指從事體力勞動的〕工人, 勞動者: *Both wage-earners and salaried officials were protected by the new regulations.* 勞動者和受薪的高級職員都得到了新規定的保護。**2** someone in a family who earns money for the rest of the family 家庭中賺錢的人

wage-pack·et /ˈ·ˌ··/ *n* [C] *BrE* an envelope that contains your wages【英】工資袋

wa·ger¹ /ˈwedʒɚ; ˈweɪdʒə/ *n* [C] *old-fashioned* an agree-

W

ment in which you win or lose money according to the result of something such as a race; BET² (1)【過時】打賭

wager² *v* [T] *old-fashioned*【過時】**1** to agree to win or lose an amount of money on the result of something such as a race 押賭注, 打賭: **wager sth on** *Stipes wagered all his money on an unknown horse.* 斯蒂普斯把他所有的錢都押在一匹不知名的馬上。**2 I'll wager** used to say that you are so sure that something is true that you are willing to risk money on it 我敢打賭〔表示你肯定某事是真實的〕: *I'll wager that boy's never worked in his life!* 我敢打賭這男孩從沒有工作過!

wag·gish /ˈwægɪʃ; ˈwægɪʃ/ *adj* a waggish person makes clever and amusing jokes, remarks etc 愛開玩笑的, 詼諧的 —**waggishly** *adv* —**waggishness** *n* [U]

wag·gle /ˈwægl; ˈwægəl/ *v* [I,T] to move something up and down or from side to side with short quick movements 使上下[左右]搖動[擺動]: *Can you waggle your ears?* 你能使自己的耳朵來回擺動嗎? —**waggle** *n* [C]

wag·on also 又作 **waggon** *BrE*【英】/ˈwægən; ˈwægən/ *n* [C] **1** a strong vehicle with four wheels, used for carrying heavy loads and usually pulled by horses〔一般由馬拉的〕四輪運貨車 **2** *BrE* a large open container pulled by a train, used for carrying goods【英】〔無頂的〕鐵路貨車 **3 be on the wagon** *informal* to not drink alcohol any more【非正式】戒酒 **4 fall off the wagon** *informal* to start drinking alcohol again after you have decided to stop【非正式】開酒戒, 又喝起酒來 —see also 另見 PADDY WAGON

wagon train /ˈ··· ·/ *n* [C] a long line of wagons and horses used by the people who moved to the West of America in the 19th century〔19 世紀向美國西部移民時用的〕馬車隊

wag·tail /ˈwæg,tel; ˈwægteɪl/ *n* [C] a small European bird that moves its tail quickly up and down when it walks 鶺鴒〔歐洲一種小鳥, 行走時尾巴上下擺動〕

waif /wef; weɪf/ *n* [C] **1** someone who is pale and thin, especially a child, and looks as if they do not have a home〔蒼白瘦弱的〕無家可歸者〔尤指小孩〕: *a grubby little waif huddled by the door* 蜷縮在門旁的邋遢的流浪兒 | **waif-like** (=very thin) 很瘦的 *teenage girls trying to emulate waif-like fashion models* 仿效瘦骨嶙峋的時裝模特兒的少女們 **2 waifs and strays** children or animals, who do not have a home 無家可歸的人[動物]: *She loved cats, and would take any waifs and strays into her home.* 她喜歡貓, 會把所有無家可歸的貓都帶回家去養着。

wail /wel; weɪl/ *v* **1** [T] to say something in a loud, sad, and complaining way 大聲哭叫: *"But what shall I do?" Bernard wailed.* 伯納德哭叫着說: "那我怎麼辦呢?" **2** [I] to cry out with a long, high sound, especially because you are very sad or in pain〔尤指因悲傷或痛楚而〕慟哭, 痛哭: **weeping and wailing** *weeping and wailing with grief* 悲痛地慟哭起來 **3** [I] to make a long, high sound 呼嘯, 哀鳴: *The wind wailed in the chimney.* 風在煙囪裡呼嘯。—**wail** *n* [C]: *the wail of police sirens* 警笛的尖嘯

wain·scot /ˈwenskət; ˈweɪnskət/ *n* [C] **1** a SKIRTING BOARD 踢腳板, 壁腳板; BASEBOARD *AmE*【美】**2** also 又作 **wainscotting** a wooden covering, especially on the lower half of the walls of an old house〔舊式房子中牆壁下半部的〕牆裙, 護牆板 —**wainscotted** *adj*

waist /west; weɪst/ *n* [C] **1** the narrow part in the middle of the human body 腰, 腰部: *wearing a belt around his waist* 他腰間繫着一根腰帶 | **from the waist up/down** (=in the top or bottom half of your body) 上身/下身 *Lota was paralysed from the waist down.* 洛塔下身癱瘓。| **stripped to the waist** (=not wearing any clothes on the top half of your body) 上身赤裸的 | **slim-waisted/narrow-waisted/thick-waisted etc** (=having a thin, thick etc waist) 苗條/窄小/粗大等的腰身 —see picture at 參見 BODY 圖 **2** the part of a piece of clothing that goes around this part of your body〔衣服的〕腰身部分 **3** *technical* the middle part of a ship【術語】〔船的〕中部; 甲板中部

waist·band /ˈwest,bænd; ˈweɪstbænd/ *n* [C] the part of a skirt, trousers etc that fastens around your waist 腰帶, 褲帶, 裙帶 —see picture on page A17 參見 A17 頁圖

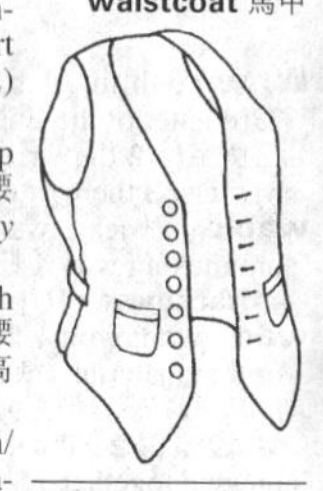
waistcoat 馬甲

waist·coat /ˈwest,kot; ˈweɪskəʊt/ *n* [C] *BrE* a piece of clothing without arms that you wear over a shirt【英】馬甲,〔西服〕背心; VEST¹ (2) *AmE*【美】

waist-deep /,· ˈ·◂/ *adj, adv* deep enough to reach your waist 齊腰深的[地]: *waist-deep in muddy water* 在齊腰深的泥水中

waist-high /,· ˈ·◂/ *adj, adv* high enough to reach your waist 齊腰高的[地]: *waist-high grass* 齊腰高的草

waist·line /ˈwest,laɪn; ˈweɪstlaɪn/ *n* **1** [singular] the amount you measure around the waist, especially used to judge how fat or thin you are 腰圍: *a trim waistline* 苗條的腰身 | **watch your waistline** (=to be careful about what you eat so you do not get fat) 注意你的腰圍, 控制體重 **2** the position of the waist of a piece of clothing〔衣服的〕腰身部分

wait¹ /wet; weɪt/ *v*

1 ►DELAY/NOT START STH 延遲/未開始某事◄ [I] to not do something or go somewhere until something else happens, someone arrives etc 等, 等候, 等待: *Hurry up! Everyone's waiting.* 快點!大家在等着呢。| *Wait right here until I come back.* 就在這兒等, 直到我回來。| **wait for sth/sb** *We had to wait over an hour for the bus.* 我們不得不花一個多小時等候公共汽車。| **wait until** *They'll just have to wait until I'm ready.* 他們得等到我準備好。| **wait for 3 hours/2 weeks etc** *Where have you been? I've been waiting for ages.* 你去哪裡了? 我等了好久。| **wait to do sth** *Are you waiting to use the phone?* 你在等着用電話嗎? | **keep sb waiting** (=make someone wait, especially by arriving late)〔尤指遲到而〕使某人一直等候 *I'm sorry to have kept you waiting.* 我真抱歉讓你一直等着。

2 ►EXPECT STH TO HAPPEN 期待某事發生◄ [I] to expect something to happen that has not happened yet 期待, 盼望: *"Have you heard about the job?" "No, I'm still waiting."* "你聽到那份工作的消息嗎?" "沒有, 我一直在期待着呢。" | **wait for sth** *I'm still waiting for my test results.* 我還在等測驗結果。| **wait for sb to do sth/wait for sth to happen** *I'm just waiting for him to realize how stupid he's been.* 我在等着他意識到自己有多麼笨。

3 wait a minute/second/moment etc *spoken*【口】**a)** used to stop someone for a short time when they are leaving or starting to do something 等一下, 慢着〔用於拖延某人離開或開始做某事〕: *Wait a second, I'll get my coat and come with you.* 等一等, 我拿上大衣和你一起去。**b)** used to interrupt someone, especially because you do not agree with what they are saying 且慢〔用於打斷別人的話, 尤其是你反對的話〕: *Wait a minute! That's not what we agreed!* 且慢!我們同意的可不是那樣! **c)** used when you suddenly remember or notice something 別忙〔用於突然想起或注意到某事〕: *Wait a moment, I'm sure I know her name.* 別忙, 我肯定知道她的姓名。

4 I can't wait/I can hardly wait *informal*【非正式】**a)** used when you feel excited and impatient about something that is going to happen soon 我急着/等不及〔用於對即將發生的事感到興奮和迫不及待〕: *We're going to Australia on Saturday – I can't wait!* 我們星期六去澳大利亞——我都等不及了! | **sb can't wait to do sth** *Tina can't wait to get home.* 蒂娜急着回家。| [**+for**] *I can't wait for my vacation.* 我迫不及待要放假。**b)** *spoken humorous* used to say that something seems likely to be very boring【口, 幽默】我等不及了〔用於表示某事看來

十分乏味〕: *A lecture on transformational grammar? I can hardly wait.* 有關轉換語法的講座? 我可等不及了。
5 sth can/can't wait used to say that something is not, or is very urgent 某事不急[可以等着]/特急[刻不容緩]: *"What's so important? Can't it wait till tomorrow?" "No, it can't."* "甚麼事這麼重要? 不能等到明天嗎?" "不行, 此事迫在眉睫。"
6 wait and see *especially spoken* used to say that someone should be patient because they will find out about something later【尤口】等着瞧〔用於叫某人耐心等待事情的結果〕: **sb will have to wait and see** *You'll have to wait and see what Father Christmas brings you.* 你們必須耐心等待, 看看聖誕老人會給你們帶來甚麼東西。
7 wait until/till *spoken* used when you are excited about telling or showing someone something【口】等到...〔用於興奮地告訴某人某事或向某人展示某物〕: *Wait till you see Gaby's new house!* 等到你看到蓋比的新家再說!
8 be waiting if something is waiting for you, it is ready for you to use, collect etc 等着〔表示某東西已準備好, 可供使用、提取等〕: *The report was typed up and waiting when they came back from coffee.* 他們喝完咖啡回來, 報告已經打印好。
9 wait your turn to stay calm until it is your turn to do something, instead of trying to move ahead of other people〔冷靜地〕等候輪到你〔做某事〕
10 sth is (well) worth waiting for *spoken* used to say that something is very good, even though it takes a long time to come【口】某事值得等〔表示某事很好, 值得久等〕: *Their new album was well worth waiting for.* 他們的新唱片等待已久, 是值得的。
11 (just) you wait *spoken* used to warn or threaten someone【口】你等着〔用於警告或威脅某人〕: *I'll get you back for what you've done, just you wait.* 你等着, 我會跟你算賬。
12 what are you waiting for? *spoken* used to tell someone to do something immediately【口】你還在等甚麼?〔用於叫某人馬上做某事〕: *Well, what are you waiting for? Go and apologize.* 唷, 你還在等甚麼呀? 道歉去。
13 what are we waiting for? *spoken* used to say in a cheerful way that you think everyone should start doing something immediately【口】我們還在等甚麼呀?〔高興地表示你認為大家應立即做某事〕
14 wait for it *spoken*【口】**a)** used just before you tell someone something that is funny or surprising 且聽這個〔用於表示要說的話有趣或使人吃驚〕: Guess *how much he won? Wait for it – $400,000!* 猜猜他贏了多少? 聽着 —— 40 萬美元! **b)** used to tell someone not to do something until the correct time because they seem very impatient to do it now〔用於告訴焦急的人〕等適當的時機到來再說
15 wait your chance/opportunity (to do sth) to wait until you have the best conditions to succeed in doing something 等待機遇/時機(做某事): *Wilson was merely waiting his chance to get revenge.* 威爾遜只是在伺機報復。
16 be waiting in the wings to be ready to do something if it is necessary or if a suitable time comes 正時刻準備着〔做某事, 如果有需要或時機適當〕
17 wait on tables/wait at table *BrE formal*【英, 正式】, **wait tables** *AmE*【美】to serve food to people at their table in a restaurant〔在餐廳裡〕侍候進餐
18 wait dinner/lunch etc (for sb) *AmE* to delay a meal until someone arrives【美】等(某人)吃晚飯/午飯: *Don't wait dinner for me, I'll be home late.* 別等我吃飯, 我要晚回家。
19 (play) a waiting game to do nothing deliberately and wait to see what other people do, in order to get an advantage for yourself 待機而動

wait around also 又作 **wait about** *BrE*【英】*phr v* [I] to stay in the same place and do nothing while you are waiting for something to happen, someone to arrive etc〔無所事事地〕等待: *We waited around at the stage door to try and see the stars.* 我們在劇場後門等, 想看看這些明星。

wait behind *phr v* [I] to stay somewhere after other people have left〔待他人走後〕留下來: *Paolo waited behind to speak to her alone.* 保羅留下來和她單獨說話。

wait in *phr v* [I] *BrE* to stay at home and wait there for someone to arrive【英】在家等候〔某人到來〕: *I have to wait in for the repair man.* 我得在家等修理工來。

wait on sb/sth *phr v* [T] **1** to serve food to someone at their table, especially in a restaurant〔尤指在餐館〕侍候〔客人〕進餐 **2** to wait for a particular event, piece of information etc, especially before doing something or making a decision〔尤指在做某事或決定前〕等待〔某事件或消息〕: *We're waiting on the blood test results.* 我們在等血液化驗結果。**3 wait on sb hand and foot** *often humorous* to do everything for someone while they do nothing【常幽默】無微不至地侍候某人: *His wife waits on him hand and foot.* 他妻子侍候得他無微不至。

wait sth ↔ **out** *phr v* [T] if you wait out an event or period or time, especially an unpleasant one, you wait for it to finish 耐心等待〔尤指討厭的事件、時期或時間〕結束: *Let's find a place where we can wait out the storm.* 讓我們找一個地方躲避暴風雨。

wait up *phr v* [I] **1** to wait for someone to return before you go to bed 等候着〔某人〕不睡: **[+for]** *Don't wait up for me – I'll be very late.* 不要熬夜等我, 我要很晚才回來。**2 Wait up!** *AmE* used to tell someone to stop, so that you can talk to them or go with them【美】〔叫別人〕停下片刻〔讓自己趕上或跟他說話〕; 等一等!

This graph shows how common the different grammar patterns of the verb **wait** are. 本圖表所示為動詞 wait 構成的不同語法模式的使用頻率。

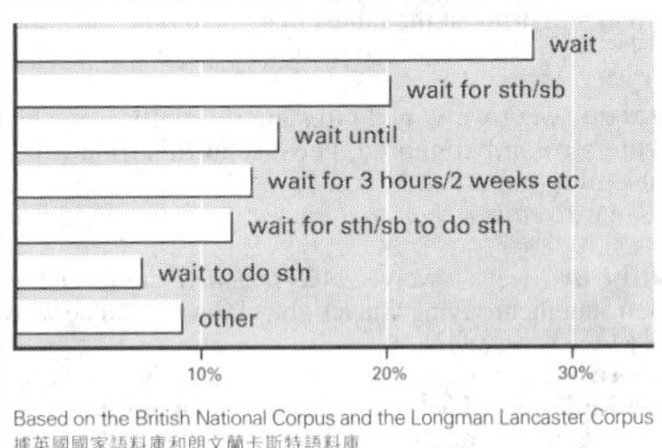

Based on the British National Corpus and the Longman Lancaster Corpus
據英國國家語料庫和朗文蘭卡斯特語料庫

USAGE NOTE 用法說明: WAIT
WORD CHOICE 詞語辨析: **wait for, await, wait, expect, look forward to**

If you **wait for** someone to come or for something to happen, you delay doing something or change what you are doing until they come or it happens. Often you do not do other things because you are **waiting**. wait for 指等候某人到來或某事發生, 表示你推遲做某事, 或改變正在做的工作直到某人到來或某事發生, 結果常常因等候而甚麼也沒有做: *Why are you standing there? I'm waiting for John (to come).* 你為甚麼站在那兒? 我在等約翰(來)。| *I'm waiting to use that machine.* 我在等着用那台機器。**Await** is a much more formal word for **wait for**. await 比 wait for 正式得多。

If you **expect** someone or something, you are sure that the person will come or that the event will happen, but you do not necessarily change what you are doing now because of this. expect 指期待某人會來或某事會發生, 你肯定那人會來或那事會發生, 而你不必為此而改變正在做的事: *We're expecting a cold winter.* 我們預料會有一個寒冷的冬

天。| *What kind of result are you expecting?* 你期待的是一種甚麼結局?

Waiting is something you do; **expecting** is a state of mind. waiting (等待) 是你在做的事; expecting (期待) 則是一種思想狀態。

If you are expecting something good to happen and feel happy about it, you **look forward to** it 如果你期待某種好事發生, 並且為此而感到高興, 適當的用語是look forward to (盼望): *I'm looking forward to seeing him again.* 我盼望再次見到他。

GRAMMAR 語法

You **wait for** something (NOT *wait it*). But you **await** something (NOT *await for it*). 表示等待某事用 wait for it〔不用 wait it〕, 或用 await it〔不用 await for it〕。

wait² *n* [singular] a period of time in which you wait for something to happen, someone to arrive etc 等候[等待]的時間: **[+for]** *We then faced a six-month wait for the results to arrive.* 結果出來前, 我們要等候六個月。—see also 另見 **lie in wait** (LIE¹ (6))

wait·er /ˋwetɚ; ˈweɪtə/ *n* [C] a man who serves food and drink at the tables in a restaurant〔餐館的〕男服務員, 男侍應生 —see picture on page A15 參見A15頁圖

wait·ing list /ˈ··ˌ·/ *n* [C] a list of people who have asked for something but who must wait before they can have it 等候者名單〔等候所要得到事物者的名單〕: *a two-year waiting list* 一份要等兩年的等候者名單

waiting room /ˈ··ˌ·/ *n* [C] a room for people to wait in, for example to see a doctor, take a train etc 等候室; 候診室; 候車室

wait·ress /ˋwetrɪs; ˈweɪtrɨs/ *n* [C] a woman who serves food and drink at the tables in a restaurant〔餐館的〕女服務員, 女侍應生 —see picture on page A15 參見A15頁圖

waive /wev; weɪv/ *v* [T] to state officially that a right, rule etc can be ignored, because at this time it is not useful or important 宣布放棄〔權利〕; 宣布取消〔規則〕: *She waived her right to a lawyer.* 她放棄了聘請律師的權利。

waiv·er /ˋwevɚ; ˈweɪvə/ *n* [C] *technical* an official written statement saying that a right, claim etc can be waived【術語】棄權聲明書

wake¹ /wek; weɪk/ *v past tense* **woke** /wok; wəʊk/ *or* **waked** *AmE*【美】*past participle* **woken** /ˋwokən; ˈwəʊkən/ *or* **waked** *AmE*【美】[I,T] also 又作 **wake up** to stop sleeping, or to make someone stop sleeping 睡醒, 醒來; 喚醒, 弄醒: *James usually wakes up early.* 詹姆斯通常醒得早。| *I'll wake you up when it's time to leave.* 到要走的時候我會叫醒你。| *Try not to wake the baby.* 別把寶寶吵醒。

wake up *phr v* [I,T] **1** to start to listen or pay attention to something 開始聽着, 開始注意: **Wake up!** (=give me your attention) 注意 *Wake up at the back there!* 後面的人注意! **2 wake up and smell the coffee** *AmE spoken* used to tell someone to recognize the truth or reality of something【美口】〔用於叫某人〕面對現實, 正視事實

wake (up) to *phr v* [T] **1** to experience something as you are waking up 醒來後發現: *Nancy woke to the sound of birds outside her window.* 南茜醒來後聽見窗外的鳥叫聲。**2** to start to realize and understand a danger, an idea etc 開始覺察[認識]到〔危險、想法等〕: *It's time you woke up to the fact that it's a tough world out there.* 外面是冷酷的世界, 你該認識到這個事實了。

wake² *n* [C] **1 in the wake of** if something, especially something bad, happens in the wake of an event, it happens afterwards and usually as a result of it〔尤指不好的事〕緊隨…而來; 作為…的結果: *Famine followed in the wake of the drought.* 旱災帶來的是饑荒。**2 in sb's/sth's wake** behind or after someone or something 緊跟某人/某物後面: *The car left clouds of dust in its wake.* 汽車開過, 後面揚起陣陣灰塵。**3** the time before a funeral when friends and relatives meet to remember the dead person〔葬禮前的〕守靈 **4** the track made behind a boat as it moves through the water〔船開過後留下的〕航跡, 尾流

wake·ful /ˋwekfəl; ˈweɪkfəl/ *adj* **1 a)** unable to sleep 不能入睡的, 失眠的: *lying wakeful in the hot night* 天氣酷熱, 晚上躺下, 不能入睡 **b)** a wakeful period of time is one when you cannot sleep 失眠的〔時間〕**2** *formal* ready to do whatever is necessary【正式】戒備的, 警覺的 —**wakefulness** *n* [U]

wak·en /ˋwekən; ˈweɪkən/ also 又作 **waken up** *v* [I,T] *formal* to wake, or to wake someone【正式】醒來; 喚醒: *She gently wakened the sleeping child.* 她輕輕地叫醒熟睡中的小孩。

wak·ey-wak·ey /ˌwekɪ ˋwekɪ; ˌweɪki ˈweɪki/ *interjection BrE spoken* used to tell someone in a joking way to wake up【英口】醒醒〔用於以開玩笑形式喚醒某人〕

wak·ing /ˋwekɪŋ; ˈweɪkɪŋ/ *adj* **waking hours/life/day etc** all the time when you are awake 醒着的時刻/生活/日子等: *How his face haunted her every waking moment!* 在她醒着的每一刻, 他的面容總在她心中纏繞不去!

walk¹ /wɔk; wɔːk/ *v*

1 ▶MOVE ALONG 往前走◀ [I] to move along putting one foot in front of the other 走, 行走: *We must have walked ten miles today.* 今天我們想必已經走了十英里。| **[+along/around/up etc]** *How long does it take to walk into town?* 進城要走多久? | *walk down the street* 走在街上 | **walk back/ home** *Marcus and I walked back through the park.* 我和馬庫斯穿過公園走回去。| **walk up to/walk over to** (=to go towards someone or something)〔向某人或物〕走過去 *She just walked up to him and slapped his face.* 她走到他面前, 給了他一個耳光。—see picture on page A24 參見A24頁圖

2 ▶WALK ACROSS A PLACE 走過某處◀ [T] to walk in order to get somewhere, across a particular area or distance〔為到某處而〕走過〔一個地方或一段距離〕: *I parked the car and walked the rest of the way.* 我停好汽車, 步行了剩下的路。

3 walk the dog to take a dog for a walk 遛狗: *Grandma's out walking the dog.* 祖母外出遛狗去了。

4 walk sb home/to school etc to walk somewhere with someone to make sure that they are safe 送某人回家/到學校等: *It's late – I'll walk you home.* 天色已晚——我送你回家。

5 go walking to walk for pleasure and exercise, especially in the countryside〔尤指在鄉間〕散步, 徒步旅行: *Rhys and I went walking in Snowdonia last summer.* 去年夏天我和里斯在斯諾多尼亞公園徒步旅行。

6 walk it *spoken*【口】**a)** to make a journey by walking 徒步旅行: *If the last bus has gone, we'll have to walk it.* 如果末班車已過, 我們只得走回去了。**b)** *BrE* to succeed or win something easily【英】輕易取勝: *We thought it would be a tough match but in fact we walked it, winning 5–0.* 我們本以為這是一場硬仗, 但實際上我們以 5:0 輕易取勝。

7 walk free to leave a court of law without being punished or sent to prison 無罪釋放: *the case of a teenage vandal who walked free from court* 一個故意破壞公物的少年被無罪釋放的案件

8 walking pace the speed that you normally walk at 步速

9 walk tall to be proud and confident because you know that you have not done anything wrong〔沒有做壞事所以〕光明磊落, 理直氣壯

10 walk on eggs/eggshells to treat someone vey carefully because they easily become very angry〔對待易怒的人〕小心翼翼, 如履薄冰

11 ▶HEAVY OBJECT 重物◀ [T] to move a heavy object slowly by moving first one side and then the other 將〔重物〕一步一步地挪動

12 walk the plank a) to be forced to walk along a board

laid over the side of the ship until you fall off into the sea〔被迫〕走跳板〔直到掉進海裡〕**b)** *AmE informal* to be dismissed from your job【美, 非正式】被解雇

13 walk on air to feel extremely happy 得意洋洋, 感到飄飄然

14 walk sb off their feet *BrE* to make someone tired by making them walk too far【英】使某人走得精疲力竭

walk away *phr v* **[I+from] 1** to leave a bad situation, instead of trying to make it better 逃避〔困境〕: *You can't just walk away from 15 years of marriage!* 你不能就這樣一走了之, 放棄15年的婚姻! **2** to come out of an accident or very bad situation without being harmed 從〔事故或險情中〕平安脱身: *Miraculously both drivers walked away unscathed.* 兩名司機奇蹟般死裡逃生, 安然無恙。

walk away with sth *phr v* to win something easily 輕易贏得: *She knew all the answers and walked away with the prize.* 她知道所有的答案, 輕而易舉地贏得了獎品。

walk in *phr v* [I,T] **1** to enter a building or room especially unexpectedly or without being invited 突然[擅自]闖入: *You can't just walk in here whenever you feel like it!* 你不能就這樣擅自闖入這裡! | **walk in the door** *I walked in the door and caught him at it.* 我走進屋, 撞見他在搗蛋。| **walk in off the street** (=visit someone such as a doctor without having previously arranged to see them) 未經預約拜訪〔醫生等〕 *People can walk in off the street and get confidential pregnancy counselling.* 人們可以不經預約隨時前來得到保密的妊娠咨詢。**2 walk in dirt/leaves etc** to make mud, leaves etc stick to the floor by walking over it when you have mud, leaves etc on your shoes〔屋裡〕踩進泥巴/樹葉等

walk in on sb *phr v* [T] to go into a place and interrupt someone who you did not expect to be there 進入〔某地〕出乎意料地撞上〔某人〕: *Arriving home early one day, she walked in on her husband and his mistress.* 一天她提早回家, 撞上了丈夫和他的情婦。

walk into sth *phr v* [T] **1** to hit an object accidentally as you are walking along〔意外地〕撞着〔某物〕: **walk straight/right/bang etc into** *Zeke wasn't looking where he was going and walked straight into a tree.* 澤科走路不看路, 徑直撞到了樹上。**2** if you walk into an unpleasant situation, you become involved in it without intending to〔無意地〕陷入〔尷尬局面〕**3** if you walk into a job, you get it very easily 輕易得到〔工作〕: *Nowadays you can't expect to leave university and walk into a job.* 如今你不能指望一出大學校門就輕易地得到一份工作。**4** to make yourself look stupid when you could easily have avoided it if you had been more careful〔由於不慎〕招致〔麻煩〕: **walk straight/right into** *You walked right into that one!* 那是你疏忽大意造成的!

walk off *phr v* [I] **1** to leave someone by walking away from them, especially in a rude or angry way〔尤指粗魯或憤怒地〕離開〔某人〕: *Don't just walk off when I'm trying to talk to you!* 你別急着走, 我想跟你說話! **2 [walk** sth ↔ **off]** if you walk off an illness or unpleasant feeling, you go for a walk to make it go away 用散步來消除〔病痛或不快〕: *Let's go out – maybe I can walk off this headache.* 我們出去走走 ── 或許我頭就不痛了。| **walk off dinner/a meal etc** (=go for a walk so that your stomach feels less full) 走路幫助消化, 消食

walk off with sth *phr v* [T] to take or steal something, especially in a relaxed or confident way〔輕鬆或自信地〕偷走〔某物〕: *Thieves walked off with two million dollars' worth of jewellery.* 小偷拿走了價值二百萬美元的珠寶。| *Lottery winners can walk off with a cool £18 million.* 彩票中獎者能輕而易舉地拿走足足1800萬英鎊。

walk over sb *phr v* [T] to treat someone badly by always making them do what you want them to do 刻薄[輕蔑]地對待〔某人〕: **walk all over sb** *It's terrible – she lets her kids just walk all over her.* 太可怕了 ── 她就這樣聽任孩子們的擺佈。

walk out *phr v* [I] **1** to go outside 走出去: **[+into]** *Payton walked out into the cold morning air.* 佩頓走了出去, 走到清晨的寒冷空氣中。**2** to leave a place suddenly, especially because you disapprove of something〔尤指由於反對某事而〕突然離開, 退席: *Mike walked out after a row with one of his colleagues.* 與一名同事大吵之後邁克退席了。**3** to stop working as a protest 罷工〔以示抗議〕: *The electricians have walked out, and will stay out until their demands are met.* 電工舉行罷工, 並將堅持到他們的要求得到滿足為止。**4 walk out (with)** *old use* to have a romantic relationship with someone【舊】與…談情說愛

walk out on sb/sth *phr v* [T] **1** to leave your husband, wife etc suddenly 突然遺棄〔丈夫、妻子等〕: *When she was three months pregnant, Pete walked out on her.* 她懷孕三個月時, 彼得把她扔下不顧。**2** to stop doing something you have agreed to do or that you are responsible for 不履行〔答應了或有責任做的事〕: *"I never walk out on a deal," Dee said.* 迪說: "我從不違背協議。"

walk sth ↔ **through** *phr v* [T] to practise something 排練: *Let's walk through scene two to see how long it takes.* 讓我們排練第二場, 看看需要多長時間。| **walk sb through sth** *I'll walk you through the procedure before you do it on your own.* 在你單獨做之前, 我將把步驟給你演示一下。

walk² *n* **1** [C] a journey that you make by walking, especially for exercise or enjoyment〔鍛鍊作用的〕步行; 散步: *It's a long walk. Maybe we should get the bus.* 走着去很遠, 或許我們要搭乘公共汽車。| **go for a walk** *"What did you do yesterday?" "Nothing much – I went for a walk in the park".* "昨天你做了甚麼?" "沒做甚麼 ── 只是到公園散步。" | **take/have a walk** *She takes a short walk every day before breakfast.* 她每天早餐前都去散散步。| **take sb for a walk** *Why don't we take the kids for a walk?* 我們為甚麼不帶孩子們去散步呢? | **walk to/through/across etc** *a short walk through the castle grounds* 穿過城堡的短途步行 | **long/short/five-mile/ten-minute etc walk** *I would put on heavy boots and go for long walks.* 我將穿上厚底靴作長途步行。**2** [C] a fixed ROUTE¹ (1) that you walk, especially through an attractive or interesting area 步行的路徑〔尤指要經過勝地〕: *There are some particularly interesting walks to the north of the city.* 城市北部有一些有趣的散步場所。**3** [U] the way someone walks 步態: *You can often recognize people by their walk.* 你往往可以從走路的姿態辨認出一個人。**4 take a walk** *especially AmE spoken* used to rudely tell someone to go away or to stop talking nonsense【尤美, 口】走開〔用於粗魯地叫某人離開或停止說廢話〕, 快走: *"Harry's here to see you". "Well, tell him to take a walk."* "哈里來看你了。" "嗯, 叫他滾吧。" —see also 另見 WALK OF LIFE, **sponsored walk** (SPONSORED)

walk·a·bout /ˈwɔkəˌbaut; ˈwɔːkəbaʊt/ *n* [C] **1** *BrE informal* an occasion when an important person walks through a crowd, talking informally to people【英, 非正式】〔重要人物〕走入人羣與他們閒聊: **go on a walkabout** *The Prince went on a walkabout near the war memorial.* 王子走進戰爭紀念碑附近的人羣中和他們閒談。**2 go walkabout** *BrE spoken humorous* to disappear【英口, 幽默】消失: *My watch seems to have gone walkabout again.* 我的手錶看來又沒了。

walk·a·way /ˈwɔkəˌwe; ˈwɔːkəweɪ/ *n* [C] *AmE informal* an easy victory【美, 非正式】輕易取得的勝利; WALKOVER *BrE*【英】

walk·er /ˈwɔkɚ; ˈwɔːkə/ *n* [C] **1** *especially BrE* someone who walks for pleasure or exercise; HIKER【尤英】〔散步或鍛鍊的〕步行者: *a keen hill-walker* 熱衷於走山路的人 **2 a fast/slow etc walker** someone who walks fast, slowly etc 走路走得快/慢的人 **3** a piece of equipment for helping someone to walk; ZIMMER FRAME 助行架

walk·ies /ˈwɔkɪz; ˈwɔːkiz/ *n* [plural] *BrE spoken* used to tell a dog that you are going to take it for a walk【英

口]〔對狗用語〕散步: *Come on, Shep! Walkies!* 快點, 謝普! 散步去!

walk·ie-talk·ie /ˈwɔkɪˌtɔkɪ; ˌwɔːkiˈtɔːki/ *n* [C] one of a pair of radios that you can carry with you, and use to speak to the person who has the other radio 步話機, 無線電對講機

walk-in /ˈ· ·/ *adj* [only before noun 僅用於名詞前] big enough for a person to walk inside 大得能容人走進的: *a walk-in closet* 大得能容人走進去的壁櫥

walk·ing¹ /ˈwɔkɪŋ; ˈwɔːkɪŋ/ *n* [U] **1** *especially BrE* the activity or sport of going for walks, especially in the countryside; go hiking (HIKE¹ (1))【尤英】〔尤指在鄉村〕徒步旅行: **go walking** *We went walking near Cambridge last weekend.* 上週末我們在劍橋附近散步。**2** the sport of walking long distances as fast as you can without actually running〔體育運動〕快步行走, 競走

walking² *adj* [only before noun 僅用於名詞前] **1 walking shoes/boots** shoes or boots that are strong and comfortable, because they are intended for walking long distances〔用於長途步行的〕輕便鞋/靴 —see picture at 參見 BOOT¹ 圖 **2 walking holiday/tour etc** *especially BrE* a holiday etc in which you walk a lot, especially in the countryside; hiking trip (HIKING)【尤英】〔尤指在鄉村〕徒步旅行的假日/遊覽等 **3 walking dictionary/encyclopaedia** *humorous* someone who knows a lot, and always has the information that you want【幽默】活字典/百科全書〔形容博學的人〕 **4 walking disaster (area)** *humorous* someone who always drops things, has accidents, makes mistakes etc【幽默】活災區〔形容經常丟三落四, 發生事故、犯錯等的人〕

walking pa·pers /ˈ·· ˌ··/ *n* [plural] **give sb their walking papers** *AmE* to tell someone that they must leave a place or a job【美】〔給某人的〕解雇通知書, 辭退書 —see also 另見 **be given/get your marching orders** (MARCH¹ (5))

walking stick /ˈ·· ·/ *n* [C] **1** a stick that is used to support someone, especially an old person, while they walk〔尤指老人步行用的〕手杖, 拐杖 —see picture at 參見 STICK² 圖 **2** *AmE* a STICK INSECT【美】竹節蟲

Walk·man /ˈwɔkmən; ˈwɔːkmən/ *n* [C] *trademark* a small CASSETTE PLAYER with HEADPHONES, that you carry with you so that you can listen to music; PERSONAL STEREO【商標】〔帶耳機的〕隨身聽

walk of life /ˌ· · ˈ·/ *n* [C] the position in society someone has, especially the type of job they have〔尤指因工作性質決定的〕社會階層: **from every walk of life/from all walks of life** *The club has members from every walk of life, from plumbers to doctors.* 俱樂部有從管子工到醫生的社會各階層人士。

walk-on /ˈ· ·/ also 又作 **walk-on part** /ˈ· · ˌ·/ *n* [C] a small acting part with no words to say in a play or film, or an actor who has a part like this〔戲劇或影片的〕跑龍套角色; 無台詞的小角色

walk·out /ˈwɔkˌaut; ˈwɔːk-aʊt/ *n* [C] an occasion when people stop working or leave somewhere as a protest〔表示抗議的〕罷工; 退席, 退會: **stage a walk-out** *The Irish delegation staged a walk-out in protest.* 愛爾蘭代表退席以示抗議。—see also 另見 **walk out** (WALK¹)

walk·o·ver /ˈwɔkˌovɚ; ˈwɔːkˌəʊvə/ *n* [C] *informal* a very easy victory【非正式】輕易取得的勝利; WALKAWAY *AmE*【美】—see also 另見 **walk over** (WALK¹)

walk-up /ˈ· ·/ *n* [C] *AmE informal*【美, 非正式】**1** a tall building with apartments in it that does not have an ELEVATOR (1) 無電梯的公寓大樓 **2** an apartment, office etc in a building like this 無電梯大樓裡的公寓房間[辦公室]

walk·way /ˈwɔkˌwe; ˈwɔːkweɪ/ *n* [C] an outside path, often above the ground, built to connect two parts of a building or two buildings〔連接建築物兩部分或兩座建築間的〕走道, 人行通道: *a covered walkway* 有篷的人行通道

S1 W1 **wall¹** /wɔl; wɔːl/ *n* [C]

1 ►AROUND AN AREA 圍着一個區域◄ an upright flat structure made of stone or brick, that divides one area from another〔用石頭或磚砌成、把區域分開的〕牆; 圍牆: *The garden was surrounded by a high brick wall.* 一堵高高的磚牆把花園圍起來。

2 ►IN A BUILDING 在建築物中◄ one of the sides of a room or building〔房間或建築物的〕牆壁: *We decided to paint the walls blue.* 我們決定把牆壁漆成藍色。

3 ►TUBE/CONTAINER 管子/容器◄ the side of something hollow, such as a pipe or tube〔中空物如管子或管道的〕內壁, 隔層: *The walls of the blood vessels had been damaged.* 血管壁已經受損。

4 wall of fire/water etc a tall mass of something such as fire or water, that prevents anything getting through〔阻止他物通過的高大〕火牆/水牆等: *A wall of fire was advancing through the forest.* 一道火牆在森林中蔓延開來。

5 wall of silence a situation in which nobody will tell you what you want to know〔你想知道某事卻〕無人回應, 沉默: *The police investigation was met with a wall of silence.* 警方的調查處處碰壁, 沒人回答。

6 go up the wall *BrE spoken* to become very angry【英口】非常惱火; 狂怒: *My mum went up the wall when I told her I wanted to leave school.* 我告訴媽媽我想輟學, 她聽了勃然大怒。

7 drive sb up the wall *spoken* to annoy someone very much【口】使某人非常惱火: *I wish she'd stop muttering – it drives me up the wall!* 我希望她不要嘮叨下去——快把我逼瘋了!

8 go to the wall *informal* if a company goes to the wall, it fails, especially because of financial difficulties【非正式】〔尤指公司因財政困難而〕破產, 倒閉

9 these four walls *spoken* the room that you are in, especially considered as a private place【口】在屋裡〔尤指私人地方〕; 私下裡: *I don't want anything that I have said repeated outside these four walls.* 我不想我在這間屋裡說的任何話傳出去。

10 be climbing/crawling up the wall *informal to be* feeling extremely anxious, dissatisfied, and impatient, especially because you are waiting for something or cannot do something you want to do【非正式】〔尤指因等待某事或不能做某事而〕極度焦急, 不滿, 不耐煩; 心煩意亂: *Last time I gave up smoking I was crawling up the wall within a few hours.* 上次我戒煙才幾小時, 便開始心煩意亂。

11 walls have ears used to warn people to be careful what they say, because other people, especially enemies, could be listening 隔牆有耳〔用於警告人們說話時要注意, 以防備他人, 尤指敵人聽見〕

12 hit the wall *informal* to reach the point of greatest physical tiredness when doing a sport【非正式】運動時身體疲勞度達到極限 —see also 另見 **have your back to the wall** (BACK² (20)), **bang your head against a brick wall** (BANG² (5)), **the writing is on the wall** (WRITING (7)), OFF-THE-WALL

wall² *v*

wall sth ↔ **in** *phr v* [T] to surround an open area with walls 用牆圍住: *They decided to wall the garden in.* 他們決定用牆把花園圍起來。

wall sth ↔ **off** *phr v* [T] to keep one area or room separate from another, by building a wall 用牆〔把一個區域或房間〕隔開: *The control room is walled off by soundproof glass.* 控制室用隔音玻璃隔開。

wall sb/sth ↔ **up** *phr v* [T] **1** to fill in a doorway, window etc with bricks or stone〔通道、窗等〕用磚石堵上: *The entrance had long since been walled up.* 入口處早就堵死了。**2** used to say that someone is a prisoner 監禁〔用於說某人是囚犯〕: *I can't bear the thought of her walled up in a cell.* 一想到她被關押在牢房裡, 我就無法忍受。

wal·la·by /ˈwɑləbɪ; ˈwɒləbi/ *n* [C] an Australian animal like a small KANGAROO〔澳大利亞的〕沙袋鼠

wal·lah, walla /ˈwɑlɑ; ˈwɒlə/ *n* [C] *IndE, PakE* someone who does a particular kind of job or duty【印, 巴】從事某種工作的人: *the medical wallahs* 醫務工作者

wall·chart /ˈwɔltʃɑrt; ˈwɔːltʃɑːt/ *n* [C] a large piece of paper with information on it that is fastened to a wall 掛圖

walled /wɔld; wɔːld/ *adj* [only before noun 僅用於名詞前] **walled garden/city/town etc** a garden etc that has a wall around it 有圍牆的園子/城市/市鎮等

wal·let /ˈwɑlɪt; ˈwɒlɪ̣t/ *n* [C] **1** a small flat leather case that you carry in your pocket, for holding paper money etc〔裝鈔票等的〕錢包, 皮夾子; BILLFOLD *AmE*【美】—compare 比較 PURSE¹ (2) —see picture at 參見 PURSE¹ 圖 **2** a long leather case for official documents 公事包

wall-eyed /ˌ· ˈ·◂/ *adj AmE* having eyes that seem to point to the side, rather than straight forwards【美】斜視的

wall·flow·er /ˈwɔlˌflauɚ; ˈwɔːlˌflaʊə/ *n* [C] **1** *informal* someone at a party, dance etc who is not asked to dance or take part in the activities【非正式】壁花〔譬喻在聚會、舞會中沒被邀請跳舞或參加活動的人〕**2** a sweet-smelling garden plant with yellow and red flowers 牆頭花, 桂竹香〔庭園植物, 氣味清香, 開黃色和紅色的花〕

wal·lop¹ /ˈwɑləp; ˈwɒləp/ *v* [T] *informal* to hit someone or something very hard【非正式】猛擊〔某人或某物〕

wallop² *n* [C] *informal* a hard hit, especially with your hand【非正式】〔尤指用手〕狠揍

wal·lop·ing¹ /ˈwɑləpɪŋ; ˈwɒləpɪŋ/ *n spoken*【口】**give sb/get a walloping** to hit someone repeatedly as a punishment 給某人/遭到一頓痛打〔以示懲罰〕

walloping² *adj* [only before noun 僅用於名詞前] **walloping great/big** *spoken* very big【口】非常大的: *a walloping great house in the country* 鄉間一棟非常大的房子

wal·low¹ /ˈwɑlo; ˈwɒləʊ/ *v* [I] **1 wallow in self-pity/despair/defeat etc** to seem to enjoy being sad etc, especially because you get sympathy from other people 沉湎於自憐/絕望/失敗等〔尤因為得到他人的同情〕: *Stop wallowing in self-pity, and do something positive.* 不要再自嘆自憐, 做點正經事吧。**2** if an animal wallows, it rolls around in mud, water etc for pleasure〔動物快樂地在泥、水等中〕打滾: *hippos wallowing in the mud* 在泥漿中打滾的河馬 **3** if a ship or boat wallows, it moves with difficulty through a rough sea〔船舶在大浪中〕顛簸着前進

wallow² *n* **1 a wallow in sth** an act of wallowing in something 沉溺於某事: *She indulged in a wallow in self-pity.* 她老是愛顧影自憐。**2** [C] a place where animals go to wallow, especially in mud〔動物經常去打滾的〕泥沼

wall paint·ing /ˈ· ˌ··/ *n* [C] a picture that has been painted directly onto a wall, especially a FRESCO 壁畫

wall·pa·per¹ /ˈwɔlˌpepɚ; ˈwɔːlˌpeɪpə/ *n* [C,U] paper that you stick onto the walls of a room in order to decorate it 壁紙, 牆紙

wallpaper² *v* [T] to put wallpaper onto the walls of a room 給〔房間〕糊牆紙

Wall Street /ˈ· ·/ *n* **1** a street in New York which is the most important financial centre in America 華爾街〔紐約市的一條街, 是美國最重要的金融中心〕: *Wall Street jitters caused by the Gulf War* 海灣戰爭引起美國金融界的緊張不安 **2** the American STOCK MARKET 美國股票市場

wall-to-wall /ˌ· · ˈ·◂/ *adj* **1** [only before noun 僅用於名詞前] covering the whole floor 鋪滿整個地板的: *wall-to-wall carpeting* 鋪滿整個地板的地毯 **2** *informal* filling all the space or time available, especially in a way you do not like【非正式】〔尤指不情願地〕佔滿所有空間[時間]的, 無所不在的, 無孔不入的: *wall-to-wall advertising on TV* 電視上沒完沒了的廣告

wal·ly /ˈwɑlɪ; ˈwɒli/ *n* [C] *BrE informal* someone who behaves in a silly way【英, 非正式】無能的人, 笨蛋: *Stop being such a wally!* 別犯傻了!

wal·nut /ˈwɔlˌnʌt; ˈwɔːlnʌt/ *n* **1** [C] a nut that you can eat, shaped like a human brain 胡桃, 核桃: *coffee and walnut cake* 咖啡和核桃蛋糕 **2** [C] also 又作 **walnut tree** a tree that produces this type of nut 胡桃樹 **3** [U] the wood from a walnut tree, often used to make furniture〔常用於製做家具的〕胡桃木

wal·rus /ˈwɔlrəs; ˈwɔːlrəs/ *n* [C] a large sea animal with two long TUSKS (=like teeth) coming down from its head 海象

waltz¹ /wɔlts; wɔːls/ *n* [C] **1** a fairly slow dance with a strong regular beat 華爾茲舞 **2** a piece of music intended for this type of dance 華爾茲舞曲, 圓舞曲: *a Strauss waltz* 史特勞斯圓舞曲

waltz² *v* **1** [I] to dance a waltz 跳華爾茲舞 **2** [I+adv/prep always] *informal* to walk somewhere calmly and confidently【非正式】神態自若地走: **[+in/into/up to]** *Jeff just waltzed up to the bar and helped himself to a drink.* 傑夫悠閒地走進酒吧, 自斟自飲起來。

waltz off with sth *phr v* [T] *informal* to take something without permission or without realizing that you have done this【非正式】偷走; 悄悄拿走: *Joe must have waltzed off with my jacket!* 肯定是喬偷走了我的外套!

waltz through sth *phr v* [T] *informal*【非正式】**waltz through an exam/test etc** to do an exam, test etc very well without any difficulty 輕而易舉地通過考試/測驗

wam·pum /ˈwɑmpəm; ˈwɒmpəm/ *n* [U] **1** shells put into strings, belts etc, used in the past as money by Native Americans〔舊時北美印第安人作貨幣用的〕貝殼串[貝殼帶] **2** *AmE informal* money【美, 非正式】錢

wan /wɑn; wɒn/ *adj especially literary* looking pale, weak, or tired【尤文】蒼白的; 虛弱的; 倦怠的: *She gave a wan smile.* 她慘淡地笑了一下。—**wanly** *adv*

wand /wɑnd; wɒnd/ *n* [C] **1** a thin stick you hold in your hand to do magic tricks〔表演魔術用的〕魔杖 **2** a tool that looks like a thin stick 細棒狀工具: *a mascara wand* 染睫毛筆

wan·der¹ /ˈwɑndɚ; ˈwɒndə/ *v* S 3

1 ►MOVE WITHOUT A DIRECTION 無目的的行進◄ [I,T] to move slowly across or around an area, without a clear direction or purpose〔在某地方〕徘徊; 閒逛; 漫步: **wander in/through/around etc** *I'll just wander around the mall for half an hour.* 我要在商場閒逛半個小時。| **wander sth** *Nomadic tribes wander these deserts.* 遊牧民族在這些沙漠裡四處流浪。

2 ►MOVE AWAY 離開◄ also 又作 **wander off** [I] to move away from where you are supposed to stay〔從應該逗留的地方〕離開: *Don't let any of the kids wander off.* 不要讓任何一個小孩走散。

3 ►CHANGE THE SUBJECT 改變話題◄ [I] to start to talk about something not connected with the main subject that you were talking about before 離題: **[+from/off]** *Pastor Riker started to wander from the point.* 賴克牧師開始偏離話題了。

4 ►MIND/THOUGHTS 精神/注意力◄ [I] If your mind, thoughts etc wander, you no longer pay attention to something, especially because you are bored or worried〔精神、注意力等因厭倦或焦慮而〕不集中, 走神: *I'm sorry, my mind was wandering. What did you say?* 對不起, 我有點走神。剛才你說甚麼?

5 sb's mind is wandering used to say that someone has become unable to think clearly, especially because they are old〔尤因年老而〕頭腦糊塗

6 ►ROAD/RIVER 道路/河流◄ [I] if a road or a river wanders somewhere, it does not go straight but in curves〔河流、道路等〕蜿蜒曲折: **[+through/across/along]** *The Missouri river wanders across several states.* 密蘇里河蜿蜒曲折地流經幾個州。—**wanderer** *n* [C]

wander² *n* [singular] a short relaxed walk 漫步: **go for/take a wander** *Let's take a wander down to the shops.* 我們蹓躂到商店去吧。

wan·der·ings /ˈwɑndərɪŋz; ˈwɒndərɪŋz/ *n* [plural] *literary* journeys to places where you do not stay for very long【文】〔在短暫停留的地方〕漫遊: *his wanderings through the Australian outback* 他在澳大利亞內地的漫遊

wan·der·lust /ˈwɑndɚˌlʌst; ˈwɒndəlʌst/ *n* [singular, U] a strong desire to travel to different places〔想到不同地方去的〕旅遊慾

wane¹ /wen; weɪn/ *v* [I] **1** if something such as power, influence, or a feeling wanes, it becomes gradually less strong or less important〔權力、影響或感覺〕逐漸減弱; 逐漸變小: *My enthusiasm for the project was waning.* 我對這計劃的熱情逐漸淡下去了。**2** when the moon wanes, you gradually see less of it〔月亮〕虧, 缺 —compare 比較 WAX² (4)

wane² *n* **on the wane** becoming smaller, weaker, or less important 正在減小[減弱], 日漸衰敗: *By the 5th century, the power of the Roman Empire was on the wane.* 到5世紀時, 羅馬帝國逐漸衰落。

wan·gle /ˈwæŋgḷ; ˈwæŋgəl/ *v* [T] *informal* to get something, or arrange for something to happen, by cleverly persuading or tricking someone【非正式】用巧計獲得〔某物〕[辦成〔某事〕]; 哄騙: **wangle sth out of sb** *In the end she wangled an invitation out of them.* 最終她施小計從他們手中弄到了一張請帖。| **wangle it for sth to happen** *I managed to wangle it for us all to go.* 我設法使我們大家都去。| **wangle your way out of sth** (=get out of a difficult or unpleasant situation in this way) 用計謀擺脱某事〔困境或尷尬局面〕—**wangle** *n* [singular]

wank¹ /wæŋk; wæŋk/ *v* [I] *BrE taboo* to MASTURBATE【英諱】行手淫

wank² *n* [singular] *BrE taboo* an act of MASTURBATION【英諱】手淫

wank·er /ˈwæŋkɚ; ˈwæŋkə/ *n* [C] *BrE taboo* someone who you think is stupid or unpleasant【英諱】笨蛋; 討厭的人

wan·na /ˈwɑnə; ˈwɒnə/ *spoken*【口】**1** a short form of 縮略式= want to **2** a short form of 縮略式= want a

wan·na·be /ˈwɑnəbi; ˈwɒnəbi/ *n* [C] *informal* someone who wants to be like someone famous or have money and power【非正式】仿效名人或富人的人 —compare 比較 **would-be**

want¹ /wɑnt; wɒnt/ *v* [not usually in progressive 一般不用進行式]

1 ▶DESIRE 渴望◀ [T] to have a desire for something 想要〔某物〕: *I want a drink.* 我想喝杯酒。| *What do you want for your birthday?* 你生日想要甚麼禮物? | **want to do sth** *Do you want to go to Kay's party?* 你想出席凱的聚會嗎? | **want sb to do sth** *I don't want Linda to hear about this.* 我不想讓琳達聽到這事。| **want sth of sb** *formal* (=want someone to do something)【正式】想讓某人做某事 *I wish I knew what he wanted of me.* 我希望我能知道他想要我做甚麼。

2 ▶NEED 需要◀ [T] to need something 需要〔某物〕: *Do you still want these magazines, or can I throw them out?* 你還需要這些雜誌嗎, 要不我就把它們扔掉了? | **want to do sth** *You only want to use a little glue.* 你只需要用一點膠水。| **want sth done** *I want that letter typed today.* 我要那封信在今天打好。| **what sb wants with sth** (=what someone needs something for) 某人想要某物〔做…〕*What do you want with a tool kit?* 你要工具箱幹甚麼? | **want doing** *especially BrE informal* (=need to be done)【尤英, 非正式】需要做… *The carpet really wants cleaning.* 這塊地毯真的需要清洗了。

3 ▶ASK FOR SB 要求見某人◀ [T] to ask for someone to come and talk to you, or to come to a particular place 要求〔某人〕到來; 要求與〔某人〕談話; 要〔某人〕到某地來: *You're wanted on the phone.* 有你的電話。

4 ▶SHOULD 應該◀ [T] *spoken especially BrE* ought or should【口, 尤英】理應, 應該: **want to do sth** *You want to see a doctor about that cough.* 你應該找醫生看一下咳嗽。

5 ▶LACK 缺少◀ [I,T] *formal* to suffer because you do not have something【正式】缺少〔某物, 因而受苦〕: *In many poorer countries, people still want basic food and shelter.* 在許多較貧困的國家, 人們仍然缺少基本的食物和住房。

6 want in/out *informal*【非正式】**a)** *especially AmE* to want to go in to or out of a place【尤美】想要進/出〔某處〕: *The cat wants out.* 這隻貓要出去。**b)** to want to take part in a plan or stop being involved 想參加/退出〔計劃〕: *If you want out, say so now.* 如果你想退出, 現在就説。—see also 另見 WANTED, WANTING, **waste not, want not** (WASTE² (7))

Frequencies of the verb **want** in spoken and written English 動詞 want 在英語口語和書面語中的使用頻率

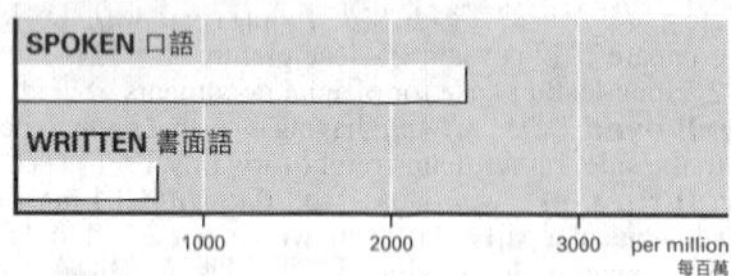

Based on the British National Corpus and the Longman Lancaster Corpus 據英國國家語料庫和朗文蘭卡斯特語料庫

This graph shows that the verb **want** is much more common in spoken English than in written English. This is because it used in a lot of common spoken phrases. 本圖表顯示, 動詞 want 在英語口語中的使用頻率遠遠高於書面語, 因為口語中很多常用片語是由 want 構成的。

want (*v*) **SPOKEN PHRASES**
含 want 的口語片語

7 I want/I don't want 我想要/我不想要: *I want a new coat.* 我想要一件新上衣。| *I don't want to go out tonight.* 今晚我不想出去。**8 what do you want?** used to ask, often in a slightly rude way, what someone wants you to give them, do for them etc 你想要甚麼?〔用於詢問(有一點不客氣)某人想要你給他甚麼或讓你替他做甚麼等〕: *What do you want now? I'm busy.* 這會兒你想要甚麼?我忙着呢。| *What do you want – chocolate or vanilla?* 你想要甚麼, 是巧克力還是香草冰淇淋? **9 do you want...?** used when offering something to someone 你想不想要…?〔用於給某人某物時〕: *Do you want a drink?* 你想喝杯酒嗎? | *Do you want me to come with you?* 你想我和你一起去嗎? **10 who wants...? a)** used to say that you do not like something, do not think that it is worth doing etc 誰想要…?〔表示你不喜歡某物, 認為某事不值得去做等〕: *Who wants to go to a noisy disco anyway?* 算了吧, 誰想去嘈雜的的士高舞廳! **b)** used when offering something to a group of people 誰想要…?〔用於給一羣人某物時〕: *Who wants a cup of coffee?* 誰想來杯咖啡? **11 if you want** used when someone suggests doing something, to say that you will do it, although you do not especially want to 如果你想要的話〔用於表示自己會做對方建議的事, 雖然不太樂意〕: *"Hey, shall we go to the beach?" "If you want."* "嘿, 我們去海濱怎麼樣?" "如果你想去的話。" **12 I want you to do something** used to tell someone to do something 我想讓你去做某事〔用於告訴某人做某事〕: *I want you to go and get me a newspaper.* 我想讓你去拿一份報紙給我。**13 want...?** used when offering something to someone 要…好嗎?〔用於給某人某物時〕: *Want a game of chess?* 想下盤棋嗎? **14 what I want** used to explain or say exactly what it is that you want 我想要…〔用於確切解釋或説明你想要的東西〕: *What I want is a car that's cheap and reliable.* 我想要的就是一輛既便宜又結實的汽車。**15 all I want** used to say that you only want something simple or small, and you think it is fair to ask for it 我只想要〔用於索求簡單或小的物品, 而且你認為提出的要求是合理的〕: *Look, all I want is a decent job. It's not much to ask for, is it?* 我只想要一份過得去的工作。這個要求不高, 不是嗎? **16 you don't want** used to advise someone not to do something (你)不要…〔用於勸別人不要做某事〕: *You don't want to go there, it's much too crowded.* 你不要到那兒去, 太擁擠了。**17 I just wanted to say/know etc** used to politely say something, ask about something etc 我只想説/知道等〔用於彬彬有禮地説某事、探詢某事等〕: *I just wanted to check that the meeting is still on next week.* 我只是想核實一下會議是否仍在下星期開。**18 it's/that's just what I (always) wanted** used to say that you like a present you have just been given very much 正是我所需要的〔用於表示你非常喜歡他人送的禮物〕

want for sth *phr v* [T] **1** to not have something that you need 缺少〔所需之物〕: *Say what you like, my kids never wanted for anything.* 不管你怎麼説, 我的孩子從來就甚麼都不缺。

want² *n*

1 ►LACK 缺乏◄ [C,U] *formal* something that you need but do not have【正式】需要〔但缺乏〕的東西: **for want of sth** (=because of a lack of something) 因缺乏某物 *People often take casual jobs in catering for want of any alternative.* 人們常幹承辦宴席的臨時工, 因為別無選擇。| **satisfy a want** (=give someone what they need) 滿足某人所需

2 ►SITUATION WITHOUT FOOD/MONEY 缺乏食物/金錢的處境◄ [U] a situation in which you do not have enough food, money, clothes etc〔食品、金錢、衣服等的〕匱乏; 貧困: *They had lived all their lives in want.* 他們一輩子都生活在窮困之中。

3 for want of a better word/term/phrase used to say that there is no exact word to describe what you are talking about 沒有更貼切的詞語/術語/成語等〔常表示詞不達意〕: *a feeling that, for want of a better word, we call love* 那種感情無以名之, 我們稱它為"愛情"

4 for want of anything better (to do) if you do something for want of anything better, you do it only because there is nothing else you want to do 既然沒有更好的〔辦法做某事〕

5 not for want of trying/asking etc used to say that you should have got what you wanted because you tried very hard or asked for it many times 並非沒有盡力/請求等〔用於表示應該得到想要的東西, 因為曾努力嘗試或多番請求〕: *Well, if he doesn't get the job it won't be for want of trying!* 好吧, 如果他得不到那份工作, 那並非是他沒有盡力!

6 be in want of sth *formal* to need something【正式】需要某事物: *a creaking house, in want of repair* 房子嘎吱作響, 需要修葺

want ad /'· ·/ *n* [C] *AmE* CLASSIFIED AD【美】分類廣告

want·ed /ˈwɑntɪd; ˈwɒntɪ̆d/ *adj* someone who is wanted is being looked for by the police 被警方追捕的, 被通緝的: *He is wanted in connection with the murder of a teenage girl.* 他因涉嫌謀殺一名少女而被警方通緝。

want·ing /ˈwɑntɪŋ; ˈwɒntɪŋ/ *adj* [not before noun 不用於名詞前] **1 be found wanting** proven not to be good enough for a particular purpose 證明不夠標準; 證明不夠資格: *Traditional solutions had been tried and found wanting.* 嘗試過傳統的辦法但發現行不通。**2 wanting in sth** *formal* not having enough of something【正式】某物不足; 缺少某物: *wanting in grace and tact* 缺乏風度和機敏 **3** *formal* lacking or missing【正式】缺少的; 找不到的: *A certain humanity is wanting in big cities.* 在大城市少了一些人情味。

wan·ton /ˈwɑntən; ˈwɒntən/ *adj* **1** wanton cruelty, destruction etc deliberately harms someone or damages something for no reason〔殘暴、破壞等〕恣意的, 惡意的: *an act of wanton aggression* 肆無忌憚的侵略行為 **2** *old-fashioned* a wanton woman is considered immoral because she has sex with a lot of men【過時】〔婦女〕淫蕩的 **3** *formal* uncontrolled【正式】不受拘束的: *wanton jungle growth* 熱帶叢林繁茂的生長 —**wantonly** *adv* —**wantonness** *n* [U]

3 1 **war** /wɔr; wɔː/ *n*

1 ►WAR IN GENERAL 一般意義上的戰爭◄ [U] fighting between two or more countries or opposing groups within a country, involving large numbers of soldiers and weapons〔兩國或多國之間的〕戰爭; 內戰: *Cambodia has been ravaged by war for the past 20 years.* 在過去20年裡, 柬埔寨飽受戰爭的蹂躪。| **war breaks out** (=war begins) 戰爭爆發 *War broke out in September of 1939.* 1939年9月爆發了戰爭。| **be at war (with)** *In 1920 Poland and Russia were still at war.* 到1920年, 波蘭和俄國仍在交戰。| **declare war (on sb)** (=announce publicly and officially that you are going to fight a war) 向〔某人〕宣戰 | **go to war (with)** (=start to fight a war with another country) 與〔他國〕開戰 | **wage war (on/against)** (=start and continue a war, especially for a long period)〔尤指長時期地〕與…進行戰爭 | **the outbreak of war** (=the start of fighting in a war) 戰爭的爆發

2 ►A PARTICULAR WAR 某次戰爭◄ [C] a particular period of time when countries fight with soldiers and weapons 某段戰爭時期: *Do you remember the last war?* 你還記得上次戰爭嗎? | **the Vietnam/Seven Years/First World etc War** *America's defeat in the Vietnam War* 美國在越戰中的失敗 | [**+with/against**] *Iran's seven year war with Iraq* 伊朗與伊拉克之間的七年戰爭 | **win/lose a war** *tactical errors that made France lose the war* 導致法國戰敗的戰術性錯誤 | **fight a war** *Britain has fought two wars in Europe this century.* 本世紀英國在歐洲打過兩場大仗。| **war between** *The war between England and France was to last another 50 years.* 英格蘭和法國之間的戰爭那時還將持續50年。| **a nuclear war** *Both countries wanted to avoid a nuclear war.* 兩國都想避免一場核戰爭。| **a war hero** (=a brave soldier) 戰鬥英雄 | **a war veteran** (=a former soldier) 老兵, 老戰士, 退伍軍人

3 ►AGAINST CRIME/DISEASE ETC 同犯罪/疾病等鬥爭◄ [C,U] a struggle over a long period of time to control something harmful〔為防止有害事物的蔓延而進行長時期的〕鬥爭: [**+against/on**] *the State's war on drugs* 國家針對毒品的鬥爭

4 ►FOR POWER/CONTROL 為了權力/控制◄ [C,U] a situation in which a person or group is fighting for power, influence, or control〔人或團體為權力、影響、控制進行的〕鬥爭; 競爭: *No one wants to start a trade war here.* 沒有人想在這裡開展一場貿易戰。

5 This means war! *spoken humorous* used to say that you are ready to fight about something【口, 幽默】這意味着戰爭!〔表示你已準備為某東西而鬥爭, 爭論〕

6 the war *especially BrE* the Second World War【尤英】第二次世界大戰

7 between the wars the period between the First and Second World Wars 兩次大戰〔指第一次和第二次世界大戰〕之間

8 look like you have been in the wars *BrE spoken* to look injured or damaged【英口】像是受了創傷或損傷 — see also 另見 CIVIL WAR, COLD WAR, PRICE WAR, PRISONER OF WAR, WAR OF ATTRITION, WAR OF NERVES, WAR OF WORDS, WARRING

This graph shows some of the words most commonly used with the noun **war**. 本圖表所示為含有名詞 war 的一些最常用詞組。

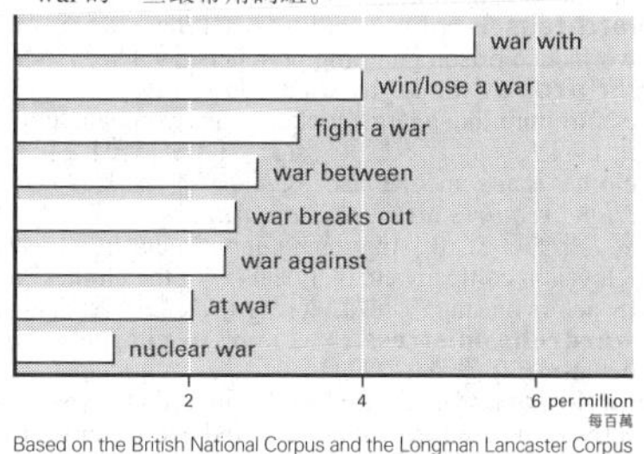

Based on the British National Corpus and the Longman Lancaster Corpus 據英國國家語料庫和朗文蘭卡斯特語料庫

war·ble /ˈwɔrbḷ; ˈwɔːbəl/ *v* **1** [I] to sing with a high continuous but rapidly changing sound, the way a bird does 高聲婉轉地唱;〔鳥〕囀鳴 **2** [I, T] *humorous* to sing【幽默】唱: *Ned warbled a serenade.* 內德唱了一首小夜曲。

war·bler /ˈwɔrblɚ; ˈwɔːblə/ *n* [C] **1** a bird that can make musical sounds 鳴禽 **2** *humorous* a singer, especially one who does not sing very well【幽默】歌手〔尤指唱得不好的〕

war bride /ˈ· ·/ *n* [C] a woman who marries a foreign soldier who is in her country because there is a war 戰時新娘〔指戰時嫁給在自己國家作戰的外國軍人的婦女〕

war cab·i·net /ˌ· ˈ···/ *n* [C] a group of important British politicians who meet to make decisions during a war〔英國〕戰時內閣

war chest /ˈ· ·/ *n* [C] *informal* the money that a government has available to spend on war【非正式】戰爭基金

war crime /ˈ· ·/ *n* [C] an illegal and cruel act done during a war 戰爭罪行 —**war criminal** *n* [C]

war cry /ˈ· ·/ *n* [C] a shout used by people fighting in a battle to show their courage and frighten the enemy〔作戰時顯示勇氣和嚇唬敵人的〕喊殺聲 —see also 另見 BATTLE CRY

-ward /wɚd; wəd/ *suffix* [in adjectives 構成形容詞] towards a particular direction or place 朝特定方向[地方]: *our homeward journey* 我們歸家的旅程 | *a downward movement* 向下的運動

3 **ward¹** /wɔrd; wɔːd/ *n* [C] **1** a large room in a hospital where people who need medical treatment stay〔醫院內的〕病房, 病室: *She's in charge of three different wards.* 她負責三間不同的病房。| **maternity/general/geriatric etc ward** (=a ward for people with a particular medical condition) 產科/普通/老年等病房 **2** *BrE* one of the small areas that a city has been divided into for the purpose of local elections【英】〔城市的〕選區 —compare 比較 CONSTITUENCY (2) **3** *law* someone, especially a child, who is under the legal protection of another person or of a law court【法律】受監護的人〔尤指兒童〕: *a ward of court* 受法院監護的人

ward² *v*

ward sth **off** *phr v* [T] to do something to prevent something such as an illness, danger, or attack from harming you 防止〔疾病、危險、攻擊等〕, 抵擋: *a spell to ward off evil spirits* 避邪的咒語

war dance /ˈ· ·/ *n* [C] a dance performed by tribes in preparation for battle or to celebrate a victory〔原始部落作戰前或戰後慶祝勝利跳的〕戰舞

war·den /ˈwɔrdṇ; ˈwɔːdn/ *n* [C] **1** an official whose job is to make sure that rules are obeyed〔監督法規執行的〕監察員 **2** *AmE* the person in charge of a prison【美】監獄長; GOVERNOR (3) *BrE*【英】**3** *BrE* someone who takes care of a building and the people in it, for example a place such as a home for old people【英】〔建築物的〕看守人; 監管員 —see also 另見 CHURCHWARDEN, GAME WARDEN, TRAFFIC WARDEN

ward·er /ˈwɔrdɚ; ˈwɔːdə/ *n* [C] *BrE* someone who works in a prison guarding the prisoners【英】監獄看守人

ward·ress /ˈwɔrdrɪs; ˈwɔːdrɪ̈s/ *n* [C] *BrE* a woman who works in a prison guarding prisoners【英】監獄女看守

war·drobe /ˈwɔrdˌrob; ˈwɔːdrəʊb/ *n* **1** [C] *BrE* a piece of furniture like a large cupboard that you hang clothes in【英】大衣櫃, 大衣櫥; CLOSET¹ (2) *AmE*【美】**2** [C] the clothes that someone has〔某人擁有的〕服裝: *Princess Diana requires an extensive wardrobe.* 戴安娜王妃需要大批的服裝。**3** [singular] a department in a theatre, television company etc that deals with the clothes worn by actors on stage〔劇院、電視台等的〕戲裝管理部門: **a wardrobe mistress** (=woman in charge of this department) 戲裝女管理員

ward·room /ˈwɔrdˌrum; ˈwɔːdrʊm/ *n* [C] the space in a WARSHIP where the officers live and eat, except for the captain〔軍艦上除艦長外的軍官使用的〕軍官起居室

-wards /wɚdz; wədz/ also 又作 **-ward** *especially AmE*【尤美】*suffix* [in adverbs 構成副詞] towards a particular direction or place 向〔某方向或地方〕, 朝: *We're travelling northwards.* 我們向北方前進。| *The plane plunged earthwards.* 飛機朝地面俯衝。

-ware /wɛr; weə/ *suffix* [in U nouns 構成不可數名詞] **1** articles made of a particular material, especially for use in the home〔尤指在家中使用的〕物品, 器皿: *glassware* (=glass bowls, glasses, etc) 玻璃器皿〔玻璃碗、玻璃杯等〕| *silverware* (=silver dishes, knives, etc) 銀器; 銀餐具〔銀盤、銀刀叉等〕**2** articles used in a particular place for the preparation or serving of food 製作或盛食物的用具: *ovenware* (=dishes for use in the OVEN) 烤箱用器皿 | *tableware* (=plates, glasses, knives, etc) 餐具〔盤、玻璃杯、刀等〕**3** things used in operating a computer〔用於操作電腦的〕...物件: *software* (=PROGRAMS) 軟件 | *liveware* (=people who operate computers) 人件〔操作電腦的人員〕

war ef·fort /ˈ· ˌ··/ *n* [singular] things done by all the people in a country to help when that country is at war〔全國人民的〕戰備

ware·house /ˈwɛrˌhaus; ˈweəhaʊs/ *n* [C] a large building for storing large quantities of goods 倉庫, 貨棧

wares /wɛrz; weəz/ *n* [plural] things that are for sale, usually not in a shop〔一般不在商店內出售的〕商品, 貨物: *the market trader's wares* 集市商販出售的貨物

war·fare /ˈwɔrˌfɛr; ˈwɔːfeə/ *n* [U] **1** a word meaning the activity of fighting in a war, used especially when talking about particular methods of fighting 戰爭狀態〔尤指作戰的方式〕: **nuclear/chemical/trench warfare** *the terrible prospect of large-scale nuclear warfare* 大規模核戰爭的可怕前景 | **guerrilla warfare** (=warfare by small groups of fighters in mountains, forests etc)〔山區、森林等裡的〕游擊戰 **2** a continous struggle between groups, countries etc〔集團、國家等之間的〕鬥爭, 衝突: *political warfare* 政治(宣傳)戰 —see also 另見 **psychological warfare** (PSYCHOLOGICAL (3))

war game /ˈ· ˌ·/ *n* [C] **1** an activity in which soldiers fight an imaginary battle in order to test military plans 軍事演習 **2** a game played by adults in which models of soldiers, guns, horses etc are moved around a table〔成人玩的〕戰棋, 戰爭遊戲〔有戰士、槍砲、戰馬等模型〕

war·head /ˈwɔrˌhɛd; ˈwɔːhed/ *n* [C] the explosive part at the front of a MISSILE (1) 導彈的彈頭

war·horse /ˈwɔrˌhɔrs; ˈwɔːhɔːs/ *n* [C] **1** *informal* a soldier or politician who has been in their job a long time, and enjoys dealing with all the difficulties involved in it【非正式】〔愛處理難題的〕老兵; 資深政治家 **2** a horse used in battle 軍馬, 戰馬

war·like /ˈwɔrˌlaɪk; ˈwɔːlaɪk/ *adj* **1** liking war and being skilful in it 好戰的; 善戰的: *a warlike nation* 好戰的國家 **2** threatening war or attack 以戰爭相威脅的: a *warlike stance* 以戰爭相威脅的態度

war·lock /ˈwɔrˌlɑk; ˈwɔːlɒk/ *n* [C] a man who has magical powers, especially evil powers〔尤指有邪惡力量的〕男巫, 術士

war·lord /ˈwɔrlɔrd; ˈwɔːlɔːd/ *n* [C] a military leader, especially an unofficial one fighting against a government or king 軍閥

warm¹ /wɔrm; wɔːm/ *adj*

1 ►BE WARM 溫暖的◄ slightly hot, especially pleasantly 暖的, 溫熱的: *a warm bath* 溫水浴 | *I hope we get some warmer weather soon.* 我希望天氣很快就會回暖。| **keep sth warm** (=stop something from becoming cold) 防止某物變冷 *I've put your dinner in the oven to keep it warm.* 我把飯菜放進烤箱裡保溫。—see picture at 參見 HOT¹ 圖

2 ►FEEL WARM 感到暖和◄ feeling slightly hot, or making you feel this way〔感到〕暖和的, 溫暖的: *Are you warm enough?* 你身上暖和嗎? | **keep warm** (=wear enough clothes not to feel cold)〔穿足夠的衣服以〕保暖, 不感到冷 *Make sure you keep warm!* 記得穿暖和點!

3 ►CLOTHES/BUILDINGS 衣服/建築物◄ clothes or

buildings that are warm can keep in heat or keep out cold〔衣服或建築物〕保暖的, 防寒的: *Here, put on your nice warm coat.* 來, 穿上這件非常保暖的上衣。
4 ►FRIENDLY 友善的◄ friendly in a way that makes you feel comfortable 熱情的, 熱忱的: *a warm, reassuring smile* 熱情而親切的微笑 | **a warm welcome** *Please give a warm welcome to our special guest!* 請熱烈歡迎我們的嘉賓!
5 ►COLOUR 色調◄ colours that are warm are red, yellow, orange, and similar colours〔紅、黃、橙及類似顏色〕暖色調的
6 as warm as toast pleasantly warm 暖烘烘的
7 ►CORRECT 正確的◄ used especially in games to say that someone is near to guessing the correct answer or finding a hidden object〔尤指遊戲中〕即將猜中〔答案〕的; 快要找到〔隱藏物〕的: *You're getting warmer.* 你快要猜中了。—opposite 反義詞 COLD[1] (13)
8 make it/make things warm for sb *informal* to cause problems for someone in order to punish them【非正式】〔為懲罰而〕給某人出難題, 使某人為難
9 warm scent/trail a smell or path that has been made recently, which a hunter can easily follow〔獵人容易追尋的〕新近留下的氣味/足跡
10 ►ANGRY/EXCITED 發怒的/激動的◄ *AmE* fairly angry or excited【美】怒氣沖沖的; 相當激動的: *The atmosphere in the meeting grew warm.* 會議的氣氛變得激烈起來。—**warmness** *n* [U]

warm² *v* also 又作 **warm up**
1 [T] to make someone or something warm or warmer 使某人[某物]暖和[更暖]: *Here, warm yourself by the fire.* 喂, 到爐火旁來取暖吧。**2** [I] to be heated 變熱: **[+in/by/on]** *There's some soup warming in the pot.* 鍋裡盛着湯, 正在熱起來。

warm to sb/sth *phr v* [T] **1** to begin to like something, or someone you have just met 對〔剛接觸的某物或某人〕有好感: *Bruce didn't warm to him as he had to Casey.* 布魯斯對他不像對凱西那樣有好感。**2** to become more eager or excited about something 對〔某物〕更加熱心: **warm to a theme/subject/ topic etc** *The more she spoke, the more she warmed to her subject.* 這話題她越說越起勁。

warm up *phr v*
1 ►MAKE WARM 使溫暖◄ [I,T] to become warm or to make someone or something warm 變暖; 使〔某人或某物〕暖和: **warm sb/sth ↔ up** *A brandy should warm you up.* 喝點白蘭地你就會暖和起來。| *If you're ready for your dinner I'll warm it up.* 如果你準備吃飯, 我就把飯菜熱一熱。
2 ►DO EXERCISES 鍛鍊◄ [I] to do gentle physical exercises to prepare your body for dancing, sport etc〔舞蹈、運動前〕做準備動作: *The athletes are warming up before the race.* 運動員正在做賽前的熱身運動。
3 ►MACHINE/ENGINE 機器/引擎◄ [I,T] if you warm up a machine or engine or it warms up, it becomes ready to work properly 預熱〔使有效工作〕
4 ►PARTY 聚會◄ [I,T] if a party warms up, it starts to become enjoyable〔聚會〕熱烈[興奮]起來: *Don't go, things are just starting to warm up.* 別走, 一切剛開始熱鬧起來。
5 ►BECOME CHEERFUL 變得活躍◄ [I,T] to become cheerful, eager, and excited, or to make someone feel this way (使) 變得活躍[激動, 興奮]: **warm sb ↔ up** *He warmed up the audience by telling them a few jokes.* 他先說了幾個笑話, 使觀眾的情緒興奮起來。—see also 另見 **like death warmed up/over** (DEATH (9))

warm up to sth *phr v* [T] *AmE* to warm to someone or something【美】〔對剛接觸的人或物〕產生好感

warm³ *n* **the warm** *especially BrE* a place that is warm【尤英】暖和的地方: *Come into the warm!* 到這暖和的地方來!

warm⁴ *adv* **wrap up warm** to put on enough clothes so that you do not feel cold 穿戴暖和〔以防寒〕

warm-blood·ed /ˌ· ˈ··◂/ *adj* animals that are warm-blooded have a body temperature that remains fairly high whether the temperature around them is hot or cold〔動物〕溫血的, 恒溫的 —compare 比較 COLD-BLOODED

warmed o·ver /ˌ· ˈ··◂/ *adj AmE*【美】**1** food that is warmed over has been cooked before and then heated again for eating〔食物冷卻後〕重新加熱的 **2** an idea or argument that is warmed over has been used before and is not interesting or useful any more〔意見、論點〕重複的〔不再有趣或有用〕—see also 另見 **like death warmed up/over** (DEATH (9))

war me·mo·ri·al /ˈ· ·ˌ···/ *n* [C] a MONUMENT (1) put up to remind people of those killed in a war 戰爭[陣亡將士]紀念碑

warm front /ˌ· ˈ·/ *n* [C] *technical* an expression used especially in weather reports meaning the front edge of a mass of warm air coming towards a place【術語】暖鋒〔尤用於天氣預報中〕

warm-heart·ed /ˌ· ˈ··◂/ *adj* friendly, kind, and always willing to help 友好的, 熱心腸的: *a warm-hearted landlady* 熱情的女房東 —compare 比較 COLD-HEARTED —**warm-heartedly** *adv* —**warm-heartedness** n [U]

warm·ing¹ /ˈwɔrmɪŋ; ˈwɔːmɪŋ/ *adj* making you feel pleasantly warm 使人感到暖熱的: *a warming cup of cocoa* 一杯使人身上暖烘烘的熱可可

warming² *n* [U] an act of making something warm or warmer 加溫: **global warming** (=the increase in the temperature of the Earth's air) 地球氣溫變暖 *global warming caused by pollution* 污染引起的全球變暖

warming pan /ˈ·· ·/ *n* [C] a metal container with a long handle, used in the past to hold hot coals for warming beds〔舊時用來暖牀的〕長柄炭爐, 暖牀器

warm·ly /ˈwɔrmlɪ; ˈwɔːmli/ *adv* **1** in a friendly way 友好地, 親切地: *Teri greeted the visitor warmly.* 特里友好地迎接來客。**2** in a way that makes something or someone warm 使某物[某人]溫暖: *Pat wrapped the baby up warmly.* 帕特把嬰兒裹得暖暖的。| **dress warmly** (=so you do not become cold) 穿得暖 **3** eagerly 熱切地: *"Do you like dancing?" "Love it," said Mary warmly.* "你喜歡跳舞嗎?"瑪麗熱切地說: "喜歡。" **4** *AmE* slightly angrily【美】微怒地: *I may have spoken too warmly.* 我可能說話時帶着點怒氣。

war·mon·ger /ˈwɔrˌmʌŋgɚ; ˈwɔːˌmʌŋgə/ *n* [C] someone, especially a politician, who is eager to start a war to achieve an aim 戰爭販子〔尤指熱衷於發動戰爭的政客〕—**warmongering** *adj* —**warmongering** *n* [U]

warmth /wɔrmθ; wɔːmθ/ *n* [U] **1** a feeling of being warm 溫暖: *the warmth of the sun* 太陽的溫暖 **2** friendliness and happiness 友好; 熱情: *the warmth of her smile* 她微笑中的熱情

warm-up /ˈ· ·/ *n* [C] a set of gentle exercises you do to prepare your body for dancing, sport etc 熱身〔跳舞、運動等前做的一套準備活動〕

warn /wɔrn; wɔːn/ *v* [I,T] **1** to tell someone that something bad or dangerous may happen, so that they can avoid it or prevent it 警告, 告誡; 提醒: *"Be careful, the rocks are slippery," Alex warned.* 亞歷士提醒說: "小心, 岩石滑溜。" | **warn sb about** *I warned him about those stairs.* 我提醒他要注意那幾級樓梯。| **warn (sb) of** *You were warned of the risks involved.* 請你注意所涉及的危險。| **warn sb not to do sth** *I warned you not to walk home alone.* 我告誡你不要一個人走回家。| **warn sb (that)** *We warned them that there was a bull in the field.* 我們提醒他們, 田裡有一頭公牛。**2** to tell someone about something before it happens so that they are not worried or surprised by it 預先通知〔某人以免焦慮或驚訝〕: *Can you warn your mother you're going to be back late?* 你能否事先告訴你媽媽說你準備晚點回去? 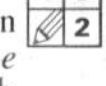 S3 W2

warn sb **↔ against** sth *phr v* [T] to advise someone not to do something because it may have dangerous or unpleasant results〔因可能有危險或產生不良結果而〕告誡〔某人〕不要做〔某事〕: *Her financial adviser warned* *her against such a risky investment.* 她的財務顧問告誡她不要進行風險那麼大的投資。| **warn sb against doing sth** *The police have warned tourists against going to remoter regions.* 警察告誡旅遊者不要到邊遠地區去。

warn sb **off** *phr v* [T] **1** to tell someone to go away or not come near something, using threats〔用威脅手段〕警告〔某人〕離開[不要接近]〔某物〕: *The farmer waved his stick in the air to warn us off his land.* 農夫在空中揮動木杖警告我們離開他的田地。**2** to advise someone to go away or to avoid something 勸告〔某人〕走開[避開某事]: **warn sb off doing sth** *I tried to warn her off going out with him.* 我試着告誡過她不要與他交往。

3 2 **warn·ing** /ˈwɔrnɪŋ; ˈwɔːnɪŋ/ *n* **1** [C,U] something, especially a statement, that tells you that something bad, annoying, or dangerous might happen〔因可能發生某種不幸、討厭或危險的事而發出的〕警告; 告誡: *the government health warning on packs of cigarettes* 香煙包上的政府健康警告 | **warning against** *The police issued a warning against speeding.* 警察發出警告, 不得超速行駛。| **warning of** *a warning of floods* 洪水警報 | **warning to sb** *a warning to pregnant women not to drink alcohol* 孕婦不要飲酒的警告 | **give a warning** *We were given no warning of possible delays at the airport.* 我們沒有得到飛機可能誤點的通告。| **a warning cry/sign/look etc** *Do not ignore warning signs such as tiredness and headaches.* 不要忽視諸如疲勞、頭痛等警告性的徵兆。| **without warning** *Without warning, the soldiers started firing into the crowd.* 沒有發出警告, 士兵就向人羣開槍了。| **advance warning** (=warning before something happens) 預先警告 **2** [C] a statement telling someone that if they continue to behave in an unsatisfactory way, they will be punished 通知〔告訴某人如繼續他的不好行為, 將受到懲罰〕: **give a warning** *I'm giving you a final warning – don't be late again.* 我最後警告你一次 —— 不要再遲到了。**3 give fair warning** to tell someone about something long enough before it happens so that they can be ready 給予合理通知〔某事發生前先告訴某人, 讓他有足夠時間準備〕

war of at·tri·tion /ˌ· · ˈ··/ *n* [C] a struggle in which you harm your opponent in a lot of small ways, so that they become gradually weaker 消耗戰

war of nerves /ˌ· · ˈ·/ *n* [C] an attempt to make an enemy worried, and to destroy their courage by threatening them, spreading false information etc〔利用恐嚇、散佈假情報等手段, 使敵人憂慮並削弱對方戰鬥意志的〕神經戰, 心理戰

war of words /ˌ· · ˈ·/ *n* [C] a public argument between politicians etc〔政治家等之間的〕論戰, 口仗

warp¹ /wɔrp; wɔːp/ *v* **1** [I,T] to bend or twist and to be no longer in the correct shape, or to make something do this (使) 扭曲; (使) 變形: *The door's been warped or something, it won't close properly.* 門變了形或甚麼的, 關不嚴了。**2** to have a bad effect on someone so that they think strangely about things 使〔思想〕反常; 使有偏見: *Henry's view of women had been warped by a painful divorce.* 亨利有過痛苦的離異經歷, 使他對婦女產生了偏見。

warp² *n* **1 the warp** *technical* the threads used in weaving cloth that go from the top to the bottom【術語】經紗〔織布中用的從上到下的線〕—compare 比較 WEFT **2** [singular] a part of something that is not straight or in the right shape〔某物的一部分〕彎曲; 變形 —see also 另見 TIME WARP

war paint /ˈ· ·/ *n* [U] **1** paint that some tribes put on their bodies and faces before going to war〔某些部落在打仗前〕塗在身上[臉上]的顏料 **2** *humorous* MAKE-UP (1)【幽默】化妝品: *Josie's just putting on her war paint.* 喬希正在化妝。

war·path /ˈwɔrˌpæθ; ˈwɔːpɑːθ/ *n informal*【非正式】**be on the warpath** to be angry and looking for someone to fight or punish 怒氣沖沖地尋人打架, 尋釁

warped /wɔrpt; wɔːpt/ **1** someone who is warped has ideas or thoughts that most people think are unpleasant or not normal〔想法或思想〕怪誕的: *a warped mind* 怪誕的心態 | **have a warped sense of humour** (=think strange and unpleasant things are funny) 有怪異的幽默感 **2** something that is warped is bent or twisted so that it is not in the correct shape〔某物〕彎曲的; 變形的

war·rant¹ /ˈwɔrənt; ˈwɒrənt/ *n* **1** [C] written permission from a court of law allowing the police to take a particular action〔法院授權警方採取行動的〕令狀: **[+for]** *The magistrate issued a warrant for his arrest.* 地方法官發出了對他的逮捕令。| **search warrant** (=permission to go into someone's house to look for something) 搜查令, 搜查證 —see also 另見 DEATH WARRANT **2** [U] *formal* good enough reason for doing something; JUSTIFICATION【正式】〔做某事的〕充分理由, 正當理由 —see also 另見 UNWARRANTED

warrant² *v* **1** [T] to be a good enough reason for something 使有充分理由: *This tiny crowd does not warrant such a large police presence.* 這一小羣人, 沒有理由出動這麼多警察。**2** to promise that something is true; GUARANTEE¹ (1) 保證〔某物是真的〕**3** [I,T] *old-fashioned* used to say that you are sure about something【過時】〔用於對某物表示〕肯定: *I'll warrant we won't see him again.* 我敢斷言, 我們不會再見到他了。

warrant of·fic·er /ˈ·· ˌ···/ *n* [C] a middle rank in the army, air force, or US Navy〔陸軍、空軍〕准尉;〔美國海軍〕二級准尉 —see table on page C6 參見 C6 頁附錄

war·ran·ty /ˈwɔrəntɪ; ˈwɒrənti/ *n* [C] a written promise that a company makes to replace or fix a product if it breaks or does not work properly〔產品的〕保證書: *a five-year anticorrosion warranty* 五年的防腐保證書 —compare 比較 GUARANTEE² (3), SECURITY (4)

war·ren /ˈwɔrɪn; ˈwɒrən/ *n* [C] **1** the underground home of rabbits 野兔的地下洞穴 **2** a place with so many streets, rooms etc that it is difficult to know the correct way around it〔因街道、房間過多〕容易迷失的地方: *a warren of alleyways* 迷宮般的小胡同

war·ring /ˈwɔrɪŋ; ˈwɔːrɪŋ/ *adj* [only before noun 僅用於名詞前] at war or fighting each other 交戰的, 敵對的: **warring factions** (=groups of people fighting each other) 交戰的派別

war·ri·or /ˈwɔrɪɚ; ˈwɒriə/ *n* [C] a soldier or man experienced in fighting, especially in the past〔尤指昔日的〕武士, 戰士, 勇士: *a noble warrior* 忠勇的戰士

war·ship /ˈwɔrˌʃɪp; ˈwɔːˌʃɪp/ *n* [C] a ship with guns that is used in a war 戰艦, 軍艦

wart /wɔrt; wɔːt/ *n* [C] **1** a small hard raised part on someone's skin〔皮膚上的〕肉贅, 疣 —see also 另見 VERRUCA **2 warts and all** *informal* including all the faults or unpleasant things【非正式】包括一切缺點: *Well, you married him – warts and all.* 好了, 你好歹已經嫁給他了。—**warty** *adj*

wart·hog /ˈwɔrtˌhɑg; ˈwɔːthɒg/ *n* [C] an African wild pig with long front teeth that stick out of its mouth 疣豬〔非洲的一種野豬, 嘴上長着一對長長的獠牙〕

war·time /ˈwɔrˌtaɪm; ˈwɔːtaɪm/ *adj* happening or existing during the time when a country is at war 戰時的: *a film set in wartime France* 一部以戰時法國為背景的電影 —**wartime** *n* [U] —opposite 反義詞 PEACETIME

war-torn /ˈ· ·/ *adj* [only before noun 僅用於名詞前] a war-torn country, city etc is being destroyed by war, especially war between opposing groups from the same country 受戰爭蹂躪的〔國家、城市等, 尤指內戰〕

war wid·ow /ˈ· ˌ··/ *n* [C] a woman whose husband has been killed in a war 戰爭中失去丈夫的寡婦

war·y /ˈwɛrɪ; ˈweəri/ *adj* someone who is wary is careful because they think something might be dangerous or harmful〔人〕小心翼翼的, 謹慎的: **be wary of (doing) sth** *I'm a bit wary of driving in this fog.* 在這樣的濃霧中開車我要小心一點。—**wariness** *n* [U] —**warily** *adv*: *"I want to ask you a favor." "What is it?" Mike said* *warily.* “我想請你幫個忙。” “甚麼事呀?” 邁克小心翼翼地回答。

war zone /ˈ· ·/ *n* [C] an area where a war is being fought 戰區; 交戰地帶

was /wəz; wəz; *strong* 強讀 wɑz; wɒz/ the first and third person singular of the past tense of BE be的第一和第三人稱單數過去式

1 3 **wash¹** /wɑʃ; wɒʃ/ *v*

1 ▶WASH SOMETHING 洗某物◀ [T] to clean something using soap and water〔用肥皂和水〕洗, 洗滌: *I'm just going to wash my hands.* 我正準備去洗手。| *This shirt needs washing.* 這件襯衫該洗洗了。| **wash the dishes** *It's your turn to wash the dishes.* 該輪到你洗碗碟了。

2 ▶WASH YOURSELF 洗澡◀ [I] to clean yourself with soap and water 洗澡: *Amy washed and went to bed.* 艾美洗過澡就睡覺去了。

3 ▶FLOW 流動◀ [I always+adv/prep, T always+adv/prep] if a liquid or something carried by a liquid washes or is washed in a particular direction, it flows there〔液體向某方向〕流動;〔某物被液體〕沖走, 沖刷: **[+against/away etc]** *The waves washed against the shore.* 浪濤拍打着海岸。| **wash sth away/against/down etc** *Floods had washed away the topsoil.* 洪水把表土沖掉了。| **wash ashore** (=be brought to the shore by waves)〔被浪〕沖上岸 *debris washed ashore by the tide* 被潮水沖上岸的碎片

4 sth doesn't/won't wash *spoken* used to say that you do not believe or accept someone's explanation, reason, attitude etc【口】不相信, 不接受〔某人的闡述、理由、態度等〕: *I'm sorry but all his charm just doesn't wash with me.* 對不起, 他的魅力我就是接受不了。

5 wash your hands of sth to refuse to be responsible for something anymore 對某事不願再管: *I've washed my hands of the whole affair.* 整個事情我已經不再過問了。

6 wash your dirty linen in public to discuss something unpleasant or embarrassing in public 把醜事公開; 使家醜外揚

7 wash your mouth out! *spoken* used when someone has just sworn or said something rude, to tell them they should not have spoken that way【口】嘴巴乾淨點!〔用於告誡說了髒話的人〕

8 wash well/badly to be easy or difficult to clean using soap and water〔用肥皂和水〕耐洗/不耐洗: *Silk doesn't wash well.* 絲綢不耐洗。—see also 另見 **wash up**

wash sth ↔ **down** *phr v* [T] **1** to clean something large using a lot of water 用大量水沖洗〔大的物體〕: *Can you wash down the driveway?* 你能沖洗車道嗎? **2** to drink something to help you swallow food or medicine〔借助飲料〕將〔食物或藥物〕吞下: **wash sth down with sth** *steak and chips washed down with red wine* 一邊吃牛排和炸薯條, 一邊喝紅葡萄酒

wash sth ↔ **off** *phr v* **1** [T] to clean dirt, dust etc from the surface of something with water〔用水將某物表面的污垢、塵埃等〕洗淨 **2** [I] if a substance washes off, you can remove it from the surface of something by washing〔物質〕能從某物表面洗掉: *Will this paint wash off?* 這漆能洗掉嗎?

wash sth ↔ **out** *phr v* **1** [T] to wash something quickly to get rid of the dirt in it 迅速洗淨: *I'll just wash out my paint rags first.* 我要先把抹油漆的碎布洗乾淨。**2** [I] if a substance washes out, you can remove it from a material by washing it〔物質能從某材料上〕洗掉 **3 be washed out** if an event is washed out, it cannot continue because of rain〔因下雨〕使〔活動〕無法繼續; 取消: *The summer fair was washed out by the English weather.* 英國夏季的雨使集市取消了。—see also 另見 WASHED-OUT, WASHOUT

wash over sb *phr v* [T] if a feeling washes over you, you suddenly feel it very strongly〔感覺〕突然襲來: *A feeling of relief washed over her as the plane landed.* 飛機着陸時, 她如釋重負。

wash up *phr v* **1** [I,T] *especially BrE* to wash plates, dishes, knives etc【尤英】洗餐具 —see also 另見 WASHING-UP —see picture at 參見 CLEAN² 圖 **2** [I] *AmE* to wash your hands【美】洗手: *Go wash up before dinner.* 飯前去洗手。**3** [T **wash** sth ↔ **up**] if waves wash something up, they bring it to the shore〔波浪〕把〔某物〕沖到岸邊: *His body was washed up the next morning.* 第二天早晨他的屍體被波浪沖到了岸邊。—see also 另見 **wash ashore** (WASH¹ (3)), WASHED UP

USAGE NOTE 用法說明: WASH

GRAMMAR 語法

You do not usually use the expression **wash yourself** unless a special effort is needed 除非需要特別費勁, 通常不使用 wash yourself 這種表達方式: *He washed/had a wash, dressed, and fixed breakfast.* 他洗了澡, 穿好衣服, 然後準備早餐。| *Several children in the class still can't wash themselves.* 班上有幾名學生仍然不會自己洗澡。

wash² *n*

1 ▶ACT OF CLEANING 洗◀ [C] an act of cleaning something using soap and water〔用肥皂和水的〕洗, 清洗: *Those drapes need a wash.* 這些布簾該洗了。| **have a wash** *I'll just have a quick wash before we go.* 走之前我趕緊洗一下澡。

2 in the wash waiting to be washed, being washed, or drying 待洗; 正在洗; 正在乾: *Your blue shirt's in the wash – you'll have to wear another one.* 你的藍襯衫正在洗 —— 你得穿另一件襯衫。| **shrink/fade/get damaged etc in the wash** *I'm afraid your black sweater shrank in the wash.* 我恐怕你的黑色毛線衫洗後縮水。

3 it'll all come out in the wash *spoken* used to tell someone not to worry about a problem because it will be solved in the future【口】最後會得到圓滿解決〔用於告訴某人不要為問題而擔憂〕

4 ▶BOAT 船◀ [singular, U] the movement of water caused by a passing boat〔船駛過後的〕尾流

5 ▶SEA/RIVER 海/河◀ the wash of the movement or sound made by flowing water 水的流動[聲音]: *the wash of the waves against the rocks* 浪濤衝擊岩石的聲音

6 ▶SKIN 皮膚◀ [C] a liquid used to clean your skin 洗面乳; 沐浴液: an *anti-bacterial face wash* 抗菌洗面乳

7 ▶COLOUR 顏料◀ [C] a very thin transparent layer of paint or colour 極薄的一層油漆[顏料]

8 ▶CLOTHES 服裝◀ [singular, U] *AmE* clothes that need to be washed, are being washed, or have just been washed【美】待洗[正在洗, 洗好了]的衣服; WASHING *BrE*【英】: **do the wash** (=wash dirty clothes) 洗衣服 | **hang the wash out** (=put it on the washing line)〔在晾衣繩上〕晾曬衣服

9 ▶RIVER 河流◀ also 又作 **dry wash** [C] *AmE* a river in a desert that usually has no water in it【美】沙漠中一般乾涸的河

10 *n* [singular] the area of land that is sometimes covered by the sea 淺水灘 —see picture on page A12 參見 A12 頁圖

wash·a·ble /ˈwɑʃəbḷ; ˈwɒʃəbəl/ *adj* **1** something that is washable can be washed without being damaged 可洗的; 耐洗的: *washable cushion covers* 可洗的坐墊套 | **machine washable** *machine washable wool* 可機洗的羊毛織物 **2** paint, ink etc that is washable will come out of cloth when you wash it〔漆、墨水等〕洗後會掉色的

wash·ba·sin /ˈwɑʃˌbesṇ; ˈwɒʃˌbeɪsən/ *n* [C] *BrE* a container like a small SINK² used for washing your hands and face【英】(洗)臉盆

wash·board /ˈwɑʃˌbɔrd; ˈwɒʃbɔːd/ *n* [C] a piece of metal with a slightly rough surface, used in the past for rubbing clothes on when you are washing them〔舊時洗衣服用的〕搓板, 洗衣板

wash·cloth /ˈwɑʃˌklɔθ; ˈwɒʃklɒθ/ *n* [C] *AmE* a small square cloth used for washing your hands and face【美】

〔洗臉、洗手用的〕毛巾; FACECLOTH *BrE*【英】

wash·day /ˈwɑʃˌde; ˈwɒʃdeɪ/ *n* [C,U] *old-fashioned* the day each week when you wash your clothes【過時】〔每星期固定的〕洗衣日

washed-out /ˌ· ˈ·◂/ *adj* **1** not brightly coloured any more usually as a result of being washed many times〔多次洗滌後〕褪了色的: *a washed-out shade of blue* 褪淡的藍色 **2** feeling weak and looking unhealthy because you are very tired〔因疲勞而〕筋疲力盡的, 面色蒼白的: *Debbie's looking a bit washed-out.* 黛比看上去臉色有點蒼白。—see also 另見 **wash out** (WASH[1])

washed-up /ˌ· ˈ·◂/ *adj* if a person or an organization is washed-up, they will never be successful again〔人或組織〕徹底失敗的; 不再有希望的: *washed-up ex-members of the Board* 不會再有建樹的董事會前任成員 —see also 另見 **wash up** (WASH[1])

wash·er /ˈwɑʃɚ; ˈwɒʃə/ *n* [C] **1** a thin flat ring of plastic, metal, rubber etc that is put over a BOLT[1] (2) before the NUT[1] (2) is put on, or between two pipes, to make a tighter joint 墊圈〔塑料、金屬、橡膠等做的扁環, 置於螺母和螺栓或兩條管子之間, 使之接得更緊〕 **2** *informal* a WASHING MACHINE【非正式】洗衣機

washer-dr·yer also 又作 **washer-drier** *BrE*【英】/ˌ·· ˈ··/ *n* [C] a machine that washes and dries clothes 洗衣乾衣兩用機

wash·er·wom·an /ˈwɑʃɚˌwʊmən; ˈwɒʃəˌwʊmən/ *n* [C] a woman in the past whose job was to wash other people's clothes〔舊時的〕洗衣女工

2 **wash·ing** /ˈwɑʃɪŋ; ˈwɒʃɪŋ/ *n* [singular, U] *BrE* clothes that need to be washed, are being washed, or have just been washed【英】待洗[正在洗; 洗好了]的衣服; WASH[2] (8) *AmE*【美】: **do the washing** (=wash dirty clothes) 洗衣服 | **put the washing out** (=hang it on a washing line) 晾衣服

washing day /ˈ·· ·/ *n* [C] WASHDAY〔每週固定的〕洗衣日

washing line /ˈ·· ·/ *n* [C,U] *BrE* a piece of string stretched between two poles that you hang wet clothes on so that they become dry; CLOTHESLINE【英】晾衣繩

washing liq·uid /ˈ·· ˌ··/ *n* [C,U] soap in the form of a liquid used for washing clothes 洗衣液

washing ma·chine /ˈ·· ·ˌ·/ *n* [C] a machine for washing clothes 洗衣機 —see picture on page A10 參見A10頁圖

washing pow·der /ˈ·· ˌ··/ *n* [C,U] *BrE* soap in the form of a powder used for washing clothes【英】洗衣粉

washing so·da /ˈ·· ˌ··/ *n* [U] a chemical that is added to water to clean very dirty things 洗滌鹼〔放入水中, 用來清洗很髒的東西〕

washing-up /ˌ·· ˈ·/ *n* [U] *BrE*【英】**1** the washing of plates, dishes, knives etc 洗餐具; dishes *AmE*【美】: **do the washing-up** *It's your turn to do the washing-up, Conrad.* 康拉德, 輪到你來洗餐具了。**2** the dirty pans, plates, dishes, knives etc that have to be washed 待洗的餐具; dishes *AmE*【美】: *a pile of washing-up* 一堆要洗的餐具

washing-up liq·uid /ˌ··ˈ· ˌ··/ *n* [U] *BrE* a liquid soap for washing plates, knives etc【英】〔洗餐具用的〕洗滌劑; DISHWASHING LIQUID *AmE*【美】—see picture on page A10 參見A10頁圖

wash·out /ˈwɑʃˌaʊt; ˈwɒʃ-aʊt/ *n* [C] *informal*【非正式】**1** a failure 失敗: *The picnic was a total washout – nobody turned up!* 野餐徹底失敗——沒人來! **2** an occasion when heavy rain washes the soil away from a place〔大雨把泥土〕沖刷, 沖蝕 —see also 另見 **wash out** (WASH[1])

wash·room /ˈwɑʃˌrum; ˈwɒʃrʊm/ *n* [C] *AmE* a word meaning a room where you use the toilet, used to avoid saying this directly【美】廁所〔委婉用語〕

wash·stand /ˈwɑʃˌstænd; ˈwɒʃstænd/ *n* [C] a table in a bedroom used in the past for holding the things needed for washing your face〔舊時放在臥室中的〕臉盆架, 盥洗台

wash·tub /ˈwɑʃˌtʌb; ˈwɒʃtʌb/ *n* [C] a large bowl used in the past for washing clothes in〔舊時的〕洗衣盆

was·n't /ˈwɑznt; ˈwɒzənt/ the short form of 縮略式= 'was not': *Jason wasn't at the party.* 賈森沒有出席聚會。

WASP /wɑsp; wɒsp/ *n* [C] *especially AmE* White Anglo-Saxon Protestant; an American whose family was originally from northern Europe and who is therefore considered to be part of the most powerful group in society【尤美】盎格魯-撒克遜裔的白人新教徒; 北歐裔美國人〔被看作屬於社會上的高等階層〕

wasp /wɑsp; wɒsp/ *n* [C] a thin black and yellow flying insect that can sting you 黃蜂

wasp·ish /ˈwɑspɪʃ; ˈwɒspɪʃ/ *adj* bad-tempered and cruel in the things that you say 脾氣暴躁、語言尖刻的: *waspish remarks* 惡毒的評論 —**waspishly** *adv* —**waspishness** *n* [U]

was·sail /ˈwɑsel; ˈwɒseɪl/ *v* [I] *old use* to enjoy yourself eating and drinking at Christmas【舊】〔聖誕節時〕吃喝取樂 —**wassail** *n* [U]

wast /wəst; wəst; *strong* 強讀 wɑst; wɒst/ *v* **thou wast** *old use* you were【舊】你是〔第二人稱單數過去式〕

wast·age /ˈwestɪdʒ; ˈweɪstɪdʒ/ *n* [U] **1 a)** the loss or destruction of something, especially in a way that is not useful or sensible 耗費〔尤指浪費〕; 損耗 **b)** the amount that is lost or destroyed 耗費量; 損耗量: *high levels of wastage in the fast-food industry* 快餐業的高消耗量 **2 natural wastage** *BrE* a reduction in the number of workers because of people leaving, retiring (RETIRE (1)) etc and not because they have lost their jobs【英】〔因離職、退休等而〕自然減員

waste[1] /west; weɪst/ *n*

1 ►BAD USE 使用不當◄ [singular, U] things such as money or skills that should be used and are not, or that are not used effectively〔金錢或技能的〕浪費: *waste in government departments* 政府部門的浪費 | **[+of]** *Being unemployed is such a waste of your talents.* 失業簡直是埋沒了你的才能。

2 be a waste of time/money/effort etc to be not worth the time, money etc that you use because there is little or no result 完全是浪費時間/金錢/力氣等: *We should never have gone – it was a total waste of time.* 我們真不該去——那是白費時間。

3 go to waste to be wasted 被浪費掉: *Don't let all this food go to waste.* 別讓這些食物白白浪費掉。

4 ►UNWANTED MATERIALS 廢料◄ [U] unwanted materials or substances that are left after you have used something〔使用某東西產生的〕廢棄物: *It's a good idea to recycle household waste.* 回收利用家庭廢棄物是個好主意。| **industrial/chemical etc waste** *Industrial waste has found its way into the water supply.* 工業廢物已滲入到水源中了。

5 a waste of space *spoken* someone who has no good qualities【口】一無是處的人: *That woman is a complete waste of space!* 那個女人簡直糟透了!

6 ►LAND 土地◄ [C usually plural 一般用複數] *especially literary* a large empty or useless area of land【尤文】大片荒地: *the icy wastes of Antarctica* 南極洲大片冰封的荒地 —see also 另見 WASTELAND

waste[2] *v* [T]

1 ►NOT USE SENSIBLY 不理智地使用◄ to use more money, time, energy etc than you should, or use it in a way that is not useful or sensible 濫用; 浪費〔金錢、時間、精力等〕: *Leaving the heating on all the time wastes electricity.* 讓暖氣整天開着是浪費電力。| **waste sth on** *Don't waste your money on that junk!* 不要為這個破爛浪費金錢!

2 waste your breath *spoken* to say something that has no effect【口】白費唇舌: *Don't try to reason with Paul – you're wasting your breath.* 不要跟保羅講理了——你是白費唇舌。

3 waste no time (in) doing sth to do something as quickly as you can because it will help you〔因對自己有幫助而〕不失時機地做某事: *Sandy wasted no time in getting to know the boss's daughter.* 桑迪急切地想認識

老闆的女兒。

4 be wasted on sb if something is wasted on someone they are too stupid or unsuitable to be able to use or enjoy it〔某物〕浪費在某人身上〔因那人太笨或不會使用或欣賞〕: *Her words of advice were wasted on me.* 她的勸告對我不起任何作用。

5 be wasted in sth if someone is wasted in a job etc, they are not using all of their abilities〔工作等上〕才能沒充分利用: *Hannah's wasted in that clerical job.* 漢娜幹文書工作是大材小用。

6 ►BECAUSE OF ILLNESS 因病◄ if an illness wastes someone, they become thinner and weaker〔疾病〕使〔身體〕消瘦, 使虛弱 —see also 另見 WASTED (3), WASTING

7 waste not, want not *spoken* used to say that if you use what you have carefully, you will not be left with nothing later【口】勤儉節約, 吃穿不愁

8 ►HARM SB 傷害某人◄ *slang especially AmE* to kill someone, severely injure them, or defeat them【俚, 尤美】殺死[嚴重打傷; 打敗]某人

waste away *phr v* [I] to gradually become thinner and weaker, usually because you are ill〔通常因有病而〕逐漸消瘦[衰弱]

3 **waste³** *adj* **1** waste materials, substances etc are unwanted because the good part of them has been removed〔材料、物資等〕廢棄的, 無用的 **2** used for holding or carrying away materials and substances that are no longer wanted 盛廢物的; 運走廢物的: *a waste pipe* 排污管; 廢氣排放管 | *a waste tank* 垃圾箱 **3** waste land is empty or not fit to be used〔土地〕荒蕪的; 無用的 —see also 另見 WASTE¹ (6), WASTELAND, **lay waste** (LAY¹(8))

waste·bas·ket /ˈwest,bæskɪt; ˈweɪst,bɑːskɨt/ *n* [C] *especially AmE* a small container, usually indoors, into which you put unwanted paper etc【尤美】〔一般用於室內的〕廢紙簍 —see picture at 參見 BASKET 圖

wast·ed /ˈwestɪd; ˈweɪstɨd/ *adj* **1 a wasted journey/trip/phone-call etc** an action that is unsuccessful because it has no helpful result 無用的行程/旅遊/電話等: *I'm sorry, you've had a wasted journey; Mr Newton isn't here.* 對不起, 讓你白跑了一趟; 牛頓先生不在這裡。**2** *slang* very drunk or affected by drugs【俚】爛醉的; 被毒品麻醉的 **3** very tired and weak-looking 疲勞的; 衰弱的

waste dis·pos·al /ˈ· ·,··/ *n especially BrE*【尤英】**1** also 又作 **waste disposal un·it** /ˈ· ··· ,··/ [C] a machine connected to the waste pipe of a kitchen SINK that cuts solid waste into small pieces 廢物處理裝置〔與廚房水槽廢水管連接的機器, 可把廚房垃圾碾碎〕; GARBAGE DISPOSAL *AmE*【美】**2** [U] the process or system of getting rid of unwanted materials or substances 廢物處理過程[系統]; DISPOSAL (1) *AmE*【美】: *the waste disposal plant* 廢物處理廠

waste·ful /ˈwestfəl; ˈweɪstfəl/ *adj* using things such as money, energy, or work in a way that wastes them 揮霍的; 浪費的: *It's wasteful to throw so much away.* 扔掉這麼多東西真是浪費。—**wastefully** *adv*: *Half the wood's energy is wastefully burned.* 燃燒的木材有一半能量白白地浪費了。—**wastefulness** *n* [U]

waste·land /ˈwest,lænd; ˈweɪstlænd/ *n* [C,U] land that is empty, ugly, and not used for anything 不毛之地, 荒地: **an industrial wasteland** (=with empty, ruined old factories) 工業廢址

waste pa·per /,· ˈ··◄/ *n* [U] paper that has been thrown away, especially because it has already been used〔尤指用過的〕廢紙

waste·pa·per bas·ket /ˈwest,pepə ˈbæskɪt; ,weɪstˈpeɪpə ,bɑːskɨt/ *n* [C] a small container, usually indoors, into which you put unwanted paper etc 廢紙簍 —see picture at 參見 BASKET 圖

waste prod·uct /ˈ· ,··/ *n* [C] something useless, such as ASH or gas, that is produced in a process that produces something useful〔生產過程中產生的〕廢物〈如灰燼、氣體〉: *The waste products of combustion are fed into the car's exhaust.* 燃燒產生的廢氣輸送入汽車排氣管。

wast·er /ˈwestə; ˈweɪstə/ *n* [C] **1** someone who wastes their time, money etc in a stupid way 造成〔時間、金錢等〕浪費的人 **2 time-waster** someone or something that uses up too much time 浪費過多時間的人[物]: *Waiting in lines is such a time-waster.* 排隊等候真是浪費時間。

wast·ing /ˈwestɪŋ; ˈweɪstɪŋ/ *adj* **wasting disease** a wasting disease is one that gradually makes you become thinner and weaker〔使人日益消瘦、虛弱的〕消耗性疾病

was·trel /ˈwestrəl; ˈweɪstrəl/ *n* [C] *literary* someone who wastes their time, money etc【文】浪費時間、金錢的人

watch¹ /wɑtʃ; wɒtʃ/ *v* S1 W1

1 ►LOOK AT 看◄ [I,T] to look at and pay attention to something that is happening 觀看, 注視: *Do you want to join in or just sit and watch?* 你是想加進來, 還是只坐在一旁觀看呢? | **watch sb/sth** *Harriet watched the man with interest as he walked in.* 這個人走進來時, 哈麗特饒有興味地看着他。| **watch sb do/doing sth** *Jack watched them slowly climb the wall.* 傑克看着他們慢慢地攀牆而上。| **watch television/a video/a film etc** *The Presidential debate was watched by over 10 million people.* 一千多萬人觀看了這場總統競選辯論。| **watch what/how/when etc** *Watch how I do it.* 注意看我怎麼做。—see picture at 參見 SEE¹ 圖

2 ►BE CAREFUL 小心◄ [T] to be careful with something 留心〔某事〕: **watch (that)** *Watch the milk doesn't boil over.* 當心不要讓牛奶煮溢。| **watch what/how/where etc** *Watch what you're doing with that knife!* 用那把刀時要當心! | **watch your weight** (=be careful not to get fat) 注意保持體重[不讓發胖]

3 ►LOOK AFTER 照顧◄ [T] to look after someone or something so that nothing bad happens to them 照顧〔某人或某物〕: *Can you watch the kids for a couple of hours tonight?* 今晚你能照看孩子幾小時嗎?

4 ►SECRETLY 暗中◄ [T] to secretly watch a person or place 監視〔某人或某地〕; 看守: *I feel like I'm being watched.* 我感覺像是有人監視着我。

5 watch yourself to control how you behave or what you do 自我克制, 謹慎: *I have to watch myself when it comes to eating chocolate.* 說到吃巧克力, 我必須克制自己。

6 watch your step *informal* used to warn someone to be careful, especially about making someone angry【非正式】做事謹慎小心〔用於警告某人, 尤指不要惹怒他人〕: *You'd better watch your step or you'll be in trouble again.* 你最好小心謹慎一些, 否則又要自討沒趣。

7 watch the clock *informal* to keep checking to see if it is time to stop what you are doing, instead of doing it【非正式】老在看鐘〔等待下班〕

8 watch this space *informal* an expression used especially in newspapers to tell people to wait because things are going to develop further【非正式】等待事態的發展〔尤用於報紙〕

9 watch the world go by to spend time looking at what is happening around you〔花時間〕觀察周圍發生的一切: *Bill likes to sit in the park and watch the world go by.* 比爾喜歡坐在公園裡觀察周圍發生的事。

10 watch the time to make sure you know what time it is to avoid being late for something 留意時間〔以免耽誤某事〕

Frequencies of the verb **watch** in spoken and written English 動詞 watch 在英語口語和書面語中的使用頻率

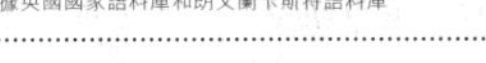

Based on the British National Corpus and the Longman Lancaster Corpus
據英國國家語料庫和朗文蘭卡斯特語料庫

W

This graph shows that the verb **watch** is more common in spoken English than in written English. This is because it is used in some common spoken phrases. 本圖表顯示, 動詞 watch 在英語口語中的使用頻率遠遠高於書面語, 因為口語中一些常用片語是由 watch 構成的。

watch (*v*) SPOKEN PHRASES
含 watch 的口語片語

11 watch it! a) used to tell someone to be more careful, especially in a dangerous situation〔尤指在危險情況下告訴某人〕小心！留神！: *Watch it! You nearly knocked my head off with that ladder!* 小心點！你差點讓那把梯子砸開我的頭了！ **b)** used to threaten someone (給我) 當心點！〔用於威脅某人〕: *Just watch it, right, or I'll get you!* 你可要當心點, 否則我就要給你顏色看！ **12 watch yourself** used to warn someone to be careful not to hurt themselves, get into danger etc 當心〔告誡某人要小心, 不要受傷或陷入危險境地〕: *Hey, watch yourself, that's very hot!* 嘿, 你要當心, 那東西很燙！ **13 watch this/just watch** used to make someone watch you while you do something 留神〔用於使別人注意你正在做的事〕: *Watch this! I'm going to balance this bottle on my nose.* 看呀！我要把這個瓶子在我鼻子上放穩。 **14 you watch** used to tell someone to watch something because you know what is going to happen 你看〔用於告訴某人注意某事, 因為你知道將要發生甚麼事〕: *You watch. Every time she goes out he follows her.* 你看, 每次她一出去, 他就跟在她後面。 **15 watch what you're doing** used to tell someone to do something more carefully 做某事要更小心: *Watch what you're doing! You're spilling it everywhere.* 做事小心點, 你灑得到處都是。 **16 watch your mouth** used to tell someone rudely or angrily to be careful what they say 說話當心點〔用於粗魯或憤怒地告訴某人要小心說話〕: *You'd better watch your mouth, young man!* 年輕人, 你說話該注意點！

watch for *phr v* [T] to wait and be ready for something 等待〔某事〕; 期待: *The prisoners watched for a chance to escape.* 犯人等待逃跑的機會。

watch out *phr v* [I usually in imperative 一般用於祈使句] *spoken* used to tell someone to be careful【口】小心〔用於提醒某人〕: *Watch out! There's a car coming.* 注意！有輛車開過來了。

watch out for sth/sb *phr v* [T] **1** to keep looking and waiting for someone or something 留意〔某人或某物〕: *Watch out for a tall man in a black hat.* 注意一個戴黑帽子的高個子男人。 **2** to be careful of something 小心〔某事〕, 提防: *You have to watch out for fast traffic along here.* 當心這裡來往的快車。

watch over sb/sth *phr v* [T] to guard or take care of someone or something 看守, 照顧〔某人或某事〕: *a shepherd watching over his sheep* 照看羊羣的牧羊人

S3 W3 **watch²** *n*

1 ►CLOCK 計時器◄ [C] a small clock that you wear on your wrist or carry in your pocket 錶, 手錶; 懷錶: *My watch has stopped.* 我的錶停了。

2 ►ACT OF WATCHING 注視◄ [singular, U] the act of watching something carefully in order to warn people of any danger 仔細注視〔一旦出現危險便警告他人〕, 監視: **keep watch** *I kept watch while the others slept.* 別人睡覺時我值班。

3 keep a (close) watch on a) to check a situation carefully so that you always know what is happening and are ready to deal with it 密切注視〔某情況, 以了解發生的事, 並準備處理〕: *UN forces are keeping a close watch on the area.* 聯合國部隊正密切注視着該地區的形勢。 **b)** to watch someone carefully, either because you think they may be doing something illegal, or in order to make sure they are safe 嚴密監視〔某人, 因認為他從事非法活動或為了保護他〕: *Police kept a 24-hour watch on the house.* 警方24小時嚴密監視着這座房子。

4 keep a watch out for to look carefully in order to try and find someone or something, while you are doing other things 做其他事時仔細留意, 以便找到某人[某物]

5 be on the watch (for) to be looking and waiting for something that might happen or someone you might see 注意〔可能發生的事或可能看到的人〕: *You should always be on the watch for pickpockets.* 你應該隨時注意提防扒手。

6 ►PEOPLE 人們◄ [C] a group of people employed to guard or protect someone or something 警衛; 看守人

7 ►GUARDING STH 看守某物◄ [C,U] a fixed period of the day or night when a group of people must look carefully for any signs of danger or attack〔白天或夜間的〕值班時間: *the first watch* 第一班 | **be on watch** *Who's on watch tonight?* 今晚誰值班?

8 the watches of the night *poetical* a period of the night when you are awake【詩】夜晚醒着的時候

9 the (night) watch the group of policemen in former times who were responsible for keeping a town or city safe at night〔昔日負責城鎮夜間安全的〕巡夜警察—see also 另見 NEIGHBOURHOOD WATCH

watch·band /ˈwɑtʃˌbænd; ˈwɒtʃbænd/ *n* [C] *AmE*【美】a WATCHSTRAP *BrE*【英】錶帶

watch·dog /ˈwɑtʃˌdɔg; ˈwɒtʃdɒg/ *n* [C] **1** a committee or person whose job is to make sure that companies do not do anything illegal or harmful〔確保公司沒有從事非法或有害活動的〕監察委員會; 監察人員: *a consumer watchdog* 保護消費者權益的監督員 **2** a dog used for guarding property 看門狗

watch·ful /ˈwɑtʃfəl; ˈwɒtʃfəl/ *adj* careful to notice what is happening, in case anything bad happens 留心的; 警惕的, 提防的: *watchful for any signs of activity* 隨時注意活動的跡象 | **keep a watchful eye on** *Pam kept a watchful eye on the time.* 帕姆是個守時的人。—**watchfully** *adv* —**watchfulness** *n* [U]

watch·ing brief /ˈ.. ˌ./ *n* [C] *law* instructions to a lawyer to watch a case that their client is not directly involved in【法律】讓律師出庭旁聽與委託人無直接關係的案件的委託書

watch·mak·er /ˈwɑtʃˌmekɚ; ˈwɒtʃˌmeɪkə/ *n* [C] someone who makes or repairs watches (WATCH² (1)) and clocks 鐘錶匠; 鐘錶製造[修理]工

watch·man /ˈwɑtʃmən; ˈwɒtʃmən/ *n* [C] *old-fashioned* someone whose job is to guard a building or place; SECURITY GUARD【過時】〔看守建築物或一個地方的〕守門人; 警衛

watch·strap /ˈwɑtʃˌstræp; ˈwɒtʃstræp/ *n* [C] *BrE* a piece of leather or metal for fastening your watch to your wrist【英】〔皮革或金屬的〕錶帶; WATCHBAND *AmE*【美】

watch·tow·er /ˈwɑtʃˌtauɚ; ˈwɒtʃˌtauə/ *n* [C] a high tower used for guarding a place, from which you can see things that are happening 崗樓, 瞭望塔

watch·word /ˈwɑtʃˌwɝd; ˈwɒtʃwɜːd/ *n* [singular] a word or phrase that explains what people should do in a particular situation 口號; 標語; 格言: *The watchword is caution.* 口號是"小心謹慎"。

wa·ter¹ /ˈwɔtɚ; ˈwɔːtə/ *n* [U]

1 ►LIQUID 液體◄ **a)** the clear colourless liquid that falls as rain, fills lakes and rivers, and is necessary for life to exist 水: *This reservoir supplies the whole city with water.* 這個水庫供應全城的用水。| *The prisoners were given only bread and water.* 囚犯只獲提供麵包和水。| **seawater/bathwater/rainwater** (=a particular type of water) 海水/洗澡水/雨水 —see also 另見 FRESHWATER, SALTWATER **b)** the supply of water to homes, factories etc through pipes and TAPS〔給家庭、工廠等的〕供水: **running water** (=water that flows, not kept in a container or pool) 自來水 *All rooms have hot and cold running water.* 每個房間都有冷熱自來水供應。| **water shortage** (=a situation when there is not much water available) 缺水

2 ►AREA OF WATER 水域◄ **a)** an area of water such as a lake, river etc〔湖、河等〕水域: *the water's edge* 水邊 | *Denzel dived into the water and swam towards her.* 登齊爾跳入水中朝她游去。| **by water** (=by boat) 乘船; 由水路 *We can transport the goods by water.* 我們可以經水路運輸貨物。**b)** the surface of a lake, river etc〔湖泊、河流等〕水面: *What's that floating on the water?* 漂浮在水面上的是甚麼東西? | **underwater/under water** *a camera designed for use under water* 用於水下拍攝的照相機

3 waters [plural] **a)** the water in a particular lake, river etc〔特定湖泊、河流等的〕水體: *the waters of the Amazon* 亞馬遜河的河水 **b)** an area of sea near or belonging to a particular country〔某國的〕領海, 海域: *the coastal waters of Alaska* 阿拉斯加近海水域 **c)** water containing minerals from a natural spring 礦泉水: **take the waters** (=drink the waters because you think it is good for your health)〔為保健而〕喝礦泉水

4 keep your head above water *informal* to avoid trouble, especially because of lack of money【非正式】避免陷入困境〔尤指經濟困境〕: *The firm is barely keeping its head above water.* 公司只不過在勉強維持。

5 be (like) water off a duck's back *informal* if advice, warnings, or rude remarks are like water off a duck's back to someone, they have no effect on them【非正式】〔忠告、警告、粗話等對某人〕毫無影響, 不起作用

6 be (all) water under the bridge *especially spoken* in the past, forgotten, and not worth worrying about【尤口】是過去[已忘記; 不值得擔心]的事: *Look, it's all water under the bridge now. Let's leave it behind us.* 現在一切已成過去, 讓我們把它忘記吧。

7 be all water under the bridge used to say that a situation has changed, especially over a long period of time or since a particular event 形勢發生了變化〔尤指經過一段長時間或某特殊事件後〕

8 deep/murky/unknown etc waters a situation that is unfamiliar or dangerous 不熟悉[危險]的情況

9 waters break when a PREGNANT woman's waters break, liquid flows out of her body just before the baby is ready to be born 羊水破了〔孕婦即將生產〕

10 high/low water the highest or lowest level of the sea and some rivers; TIDE〔海和一些河的〕漲潮/退潮

11 water on the brain/knee etc liquid that collects around the brain, knee etc as the result of a disease〔因疾病〕腦部/膝關節等的積水

12 make/pass water *formal* to URINATE【正式】小便

13 make water if a ship makes water, water gets inside it because of a LEAK[2] (1)〔因船漏而〕進水 —see also 另見 SODA WATER, TOILET WATER, **in deep water** (DEEP[1] (13)), **take to sth like a duck to water** (DUCK[1] (4)), **of the first water** (FIRST (30)), **like a fish out of water** (FISH[1] (3)), **not hold water** (HOLD[1] (41)), **get into hot water** (HOT[1] (8)), **muddy the waters** (MUDDY[2] (2)), **pour cold water on** (POUR (7)), **still waters run deep** (STILL[2] (5)), **test the water** (TEST[2] (7)), **tread water** (TREAD[1] (5))

3 **water[2]** *v*

1 ►PLANT/LAND 植物/土地◄ [T] to pour water on an area of land, a plant etc, especially in order to make things grow 給…澆水; 灌溉: *You must water the garden, it's very dry.* 你得給園子澆水, 太乾了。

2 eyes water if your eyes water, tears (TEAR[1] (1)) come out of them because of cold weather, pain etc〔因天寒、疼痛等〕眼睛流淚: *Chopping onions always makes my eyes water.* 切洋葱總使我眼睛流淚。—see also 另見 MOUTH-WATERING, **make your mouth water** (MOUTH[1] (10))

3 ►ANIMAL 動物◄ [T] to give an animal water to drink 給〔牲畜〕飲水

4 ►BY RIVER 江河流經◄ [T usually passive 一般用被動態] *technical* if an area is watered by a river, the river flows through it and provides it with water【術語】〔江河〕流經並給〔某地區〕供水: *Colombia is watered by several rivers.* 有幾條江河流經哥倫比亞。

5 ►WEAKEN LIQUID 把液體稀釋◄ [T] to add water to a drink in order to make it weaker than it should be 加水沖淡; 稀釋: *Someone had been watering the beer.* 有人在啤酒裡攙了水。

water sth ↔ **down** *phr v* [T usually passive 一般用被動態] **1** to make a statement, report etc less forceful by removing parts that may offend people〔刪去聲明或報告等中可能冒犯人的部分〕減弱〔其作用〕, 削弱 —see also 另見 WATERED-DOWN **2** to add water to a liquid, especially for dishonest reasons; DILUTE[1] (1) 往〔液體〕中攙水〔尤指出於不誠實的原因〕

wa·ter·bed /ˈwɔtɚˌbɛd; ˈwɔːtəbed/ *n* [C] a bed made of rubber and filled with water 水牀

water bird /ˈ·· ·/ *n* [C] a bird that swims or walks in water 水鳥, 水禽

water bis·cuit /ˈ·· ˌ··/ *n* [C] a hard BISCUIT (1) made from flour and water 淡味硬餅乾〔用水和麵粉製成〕

wa·ter·borne /ˈwɔtɚˌbɔrn; ˈwɔːtəbɔːn/ *adj* spread or carried by water 由水傳播的; 由水運送的: *waterborne diseases such as cholera* 由水傳播的疾病, 如霍亂

water bot·tle /ˈ·· ˌ··/ *n* [C] **1** a bottle used for carrying drinking water 水瓶, 水壺 **2** a HOT-WATER BOTTLE 熱水袋

water buf·fa·lo /ˈ·· ˌ···/ *n* [C] a large black animal like a cow with long horns, used for pulling vehicles and farm equipment in Asia 水牛〔在亞洲地區用於拉車和耕具〕

water bug /ˈ·· ·/ *n* [C] *AmE informal* a small insect that lives in or on water【美, 非正式】水蝽, 划蝽

water butt /ˈ·· ·/ *n* [C] *especially BrE* a BARREL[1] (1) used for collecting rainwater【尤英】〔接雨水用的〕水桶

water can·non /ˈ·· ˌ··/ *n* [C] a machine that sends out water at high pressure, used by police against crowds of people〔警察用於驅散人羣的〕高壓水砲

water chest·nut /ˈ·· ˌ··/ *n* [C] a white fruit like a nut from a plant grown in water, used in Chinese cooking 荸薺

water clos·et /ˈ·· ˌ··/ *n* [C] *old-fashioned* a wc (=a toilet)【過時】廁所

wa·ter·col·our /ˈwɔtɚˌkʌlɚ; ˈwɔːtəˌkʌlə/ *n* **1** [C usually plural 一般用複數, U] paint that you mix with water and use for painting pictures 水彩顏料 **2** [C] a picture painted with watercolours 水彩畫

wa·ter·course /ˈwɔtɚˌkɔrs; ˈwɔːtəkɔːs/ *n* [C] **1** a passage with water flowing through it, that can be natural or built〔天然或人工的〕水道; 河道; 渠道 **2** a flow of water such as a river or underground stream 河; 地下河

wa·ter·cress /ˈwɔtɚˌkrɛs; ˈwɔːtəkres/ *n* [U] a small plant with strong tasting green leaves that grows in water 水田芥〔水生植物, 葉辛辣〕

wa·tered-down /ˌ·· ˈ·◂/ *adj* **1** a watered-down statement, plan etc is much weaker and less effective than a previous plan etc〔聲明、計劃等比原先〕減弱了的, 打了折扣的: *a watered-down version of the original* 削弱了的形式 **2** a watered-down drink, especially an alcoholic drink, has had water added to it, especially in order to cheat people〔尤指欺騙顧客而把酒〕用水稀釋的; 沖淡了的

watered silk /ˌ·· ˈ·/ *n* [U] a silk that looks as if it is covered with shiny waves 波紋綢

wa·ter·fall /ˈwɔtɚˌfɔl; ˈwɔːtəfɔːl/ *n* [C] water that falls straight down over a cliff or big rock 瀑布 —see picture on page A12 參見A12頁圖

water foun·tain /ˈ·· ˌ··/ *n* [C] a DRINKING FOUNTAIN 噴泉式飲水器

wa·ter·fowl /ˈwɔtɚˌfaul; ˈwɔːtəfaʊl/ *n plural* **waterfowl** [C,U] a bird that swims in water, such as a duck, GOOSE[1] (1) etc 水鳥, 水禽

wa·ter·front /ˈwɔtɚˌfrʌnt; ˈwɔːtəfrʌnt/ *n* [C usually singular 一般用單數] a part of a town or an area of land that is next to the sea, a river etc〔城市的〕濱水地區; 水邊土地

wa·ter·hole /ˈwɔtə͵hol; ˈwɔːtəhəʊl/ *n* [C] a small area of water in a dry country, where wild animals go to drink〔乾旱地區野生動物飲水的〕水池，水坑

water ice /ˈ·· ·/ *n* [C,U] *BrE* a SORBET【英】冰糕

water·ing can /ˈ··· ·/ *n* [C] a container used for pouring water on garden plants, with a long tube at the front 灑水壺

watering hole /ˈ··· ·/ *n* [C] *humorous* a bar or other place where people go to drink alcohol【幽默】酒吧；人們常去飲酒的地方：*a favorite watering-hole of Ernest Hemingway* 恩斯特·海明威最喜歡去喝酒的地方

watering place /ˈ··· ·/ *n* [C] **1** a small area of water in a dry country, where wild animals go to drink〔乾旱地區野生動物去飲水的〕小水池，水坑 **2** a place with a spring of MINERAL WATER where people went in the past to be cured of various diseases; a SPA (1)〔昔日的〕礦泉療養地

watering pot /ˈ··· ·/ *n* [C] *AmE* a watering can【美】灑水壺

water jump /ˈ·· ·/ *n* [C] an area of water that horses or runners have to jump over during a race or competition〔賽馬中的〕水溝障礙；〔障礙賽跑中的〕水池

wa·ter·less /ˈwɔtəlɪs; ˈwɔːtələs/ *adj* with no water for people or animals to drink 無水的；乾的

water lev·el /ˈ·· ͵··/ *n* [U] the height to which water has risen or fallen 水位，水平面

water lil·y /ˈ·· ͵··/ *n* [C] a plant that floats on the surface of water and has large white, yellow, or pink flowers 睡蓮

wa·ter·line /ˈwɔtə͵laɪn; ˈwɔːtəlaɪn/ *n* **the waterline** the level that water reaches on the side of a ship〔船的〕吃水線

wa·ter·logged /ˈwɔtə͵lɑgd; ˈwɔːtəlɒgd/ *adj* **1** an area that is waterlogged is flooded with water and cannot be used〔地方〕水浸的，水澇的 **2** a boat that is waterlogged is full of water and could soon sink〔船〕灌滿水〔將沉〕的

water main /ˈ·· ·/ *n* [C] a large underground pipe that carries the public supply of water to houses and other buildings〔地下的〕主輸水管，供水總管道

wa·ter·mark /ˈwɔtə͵mɑrk; ˈwɔːtəmɑːk/ *n* [C] **1** a design that is put into paper and can only be seen when you hold it up to the light〔紙張上的〕水印（圖案）：*Banknotes have a watermark to prevent forgery.* 鈔票上有水印圖案以防偽造。**2 high/low watermark a)** a line showing the highest or lowest levels of the sea or a river〔海或河的〕高／低水位標誌 **b)** a period of great success or failure 輝煌／低谷時期：*the high watermark of the Roman Empire* 羅馬帝國的鼎盛時期

water mead·ow /ˈ·· ͵··/ *n* [C] a field near a river, which is often flooded〔河邊常被水淹的〕浸水草地

wa·ter·mel·on /ˈwɔtə͵mɛlən; ˈwɔːtə͵melən/ *n* [C,U] **1** a large round fruit with hard green skin, juicy red flesh, and a lot of black seeds 西瓜 —see picture on page A8 參見A8頁圖 **2 swallow a watermelon seed** *AmE informal* to become PREGNANT【美，非正式】懷孕

water me·ter /ˈ·· ͵··/ *n* [C] a piece of equipment that measures how much water is used 水表，水量計

wa·ter·mill /ˈwɔtə͵mɪl; ˈwɔːtə͵mɪl/ *n* [C] a MILL[1] (1) that has a big wheel that is turned by the flow of water 水磨〔河水流動推動輪子轉動〕

water moc·ca·sin /ˈ·· ͵···/ *n* [C] a poisonous North American snake that lives in water 棉口蛇，水蝮蛇〔生活在北美洲水中的一種毒蛇〕

water pipe /ˈ·· ͵·/ *n* [C] a pipe used for smoking tobacco, that consists of a long tube and a container of water; HOOKAH 水煙筒

water pis·tol /ˈ·· ͵··/ *n* [C] a toy gun that shoots water 玩具水槍

water po·lo /ˈ·· ͵··/ *n* [U] a game played by two teams of swimmers with a ball 水球運動

water pow·er /ˈ·· ͵··/ *n* [U] power obtained from moving water, used to produce electricity or to make a machine work〔可發電或使機器運轉的〕水力，水能

wa·ter·proof¹ /ˈwɔtə͵pruf; ˈwɔːtəpruːf/ *adj* waterproof clothing or material does not allow water to go through it〔衣服或材料〕防水的，不透水的

waterproof² *n* [C usually plural 一般用複數] *BrE* a piece of clothing such as a coat, that prevents you from getting wet【英】防水層

water rat /ˈ·· ·/ *n* [C] a small animal like a large mouse that lives in holes near water and can swim〔生活在水邊的〕水鼠

water-re·pel·lent /ˈ·· ·͵··/ *adj* cloth or clothes that are water-repellent are specially treated with chemicals so that water runs off them〔織物或衣服經化學品處理而〕抗水的

water re·sis·tant /ˈ·· ·͵··/ *adj* something that is water-resistant does not allow water to go through easily, but does not keep all water out 抗水的〔但不完全防水〕：*a watch that is water resistant to a depth of 50 metres* 一隻防水50米的手錶

wa·ter·shed /ˈwɔtə͵ʃɛd; ˈwɔːtəʃed/ *n* [C] **1** an event or period when important changes or improvements happen in history or in someone's life〔在歷史或人生中的〕轉折點；重要關頭：**[+in]** *The 1932 election represented a watershed in American politics.* 1932年的選舉是美國政治的轉折點。—compare 比較 TURNING POINT **2 the (9 o'clock) watershed** *BrE* the time in the evening after which television programmes that are not suitable for children may be shown【英】〔晚上九點起成人電視節目可以播放的〕分水嶺〔時間〕 **3** the high land separating two river systems 分水嶺，分水線

wa·ter·side /ˈwɔtə͵saɪd; ˈwɔːtəsaɪd/ *n* [singular] the edge of a lake, river etc 湖邊；河邊；水邊 —**waterside** *adj*: *a waterside restaurant* 一家湖濱餐館

water ski·ing /ˈ·· ͵··/ *n* [U] a sport in which you SKI over water while being pulled by a boat 滑水運動，水橇運動 —**water ski** *v* [I] —**water skier** *n* [C]

water sof·ten·er /ˈ·· ͵···/ *n* **1** [U] a chemical used for removing unwanted minerals from water 軟水劑 **2** [C] a piece of equipment used to do this 硬水軟化器

water-sol·u·ble /ˈ·· ͵···/ *adj* a water-soluble substance becomes part of a liquid when mixed with water 能溶解於水的

water sports /ˈ·· ͵·/ *n* [plural] sports played on or in water 水上運動

wa·ter·spout /ˈwɔtə͵spaʊt; ˈwɔːtəspaʊt/ *n* [C] **1** a pipe that water flows through 噴水嘴 **2** a type of storm over the sea in which a violent circular wind pulls water into a tall twisting mass 水龍卷，海龍卷 —compare 比較 TORNADO

water sup·ply /ˈ·· ·͵·/ *n* [U] the water provided for a building or area, or the system of lakes, pipes etc through which it flows〔建築物或地區的〕供水；供水系統

water ta·ble /ˈ·· ͵··/ *n* [C] the level below the surface of the ground where there is water 地下水位

wa·ter·tight /ˈwɔtə͵taɪt; ˈwɔːtətaɪt/ *adj* **1** something that is watertight does not allow water to pass through it 不透水的，水密的：*watertight boxes* 不透水的箱子 **2 watertight plan/case/argument etc** a plan etc that is made so carefully that there is no chance of any mistakes or problems 周密的計劃／證據確鑿的起訴／無懈可擊的論據等：*The police can't do anything, he's got a watertight alibi.* 警方毫無辦法，他不在犯罪現場的申辯無懈可擊。

water tow·er /ˈ·· ͵··/ *n* [C] a very tall structure supporting a large container into which water is pumped in order to supply water to surrounding buildings〔自來水〕水塔

water va·pour *BrE*【英】, **water vapor** *AmE*【美】/ˈ·· ͵··/ *n* [U] water in the form of gas in the air 水汽，水蒸氣

water vole /ˈ·· ·/ *n* [C] *BrE* a small animal like a large mouse that lives in holes near water and can swim; WA-

TER RAT【英】水鼠

wa·ter·way /ˈwɔtəˌwe; ˈwɔːtəweɪ/ *n* [C] a river or CANAL (1) that boats travel on 水路, 航道: *inland waterways* 內河航道

wa·ter·wings /ˈwɔtəˌwɪŋz; ˈwɔːtəˌwɪŋz/ *n* [plural] two bags filled with air that are attached to your arms when you learn to swim〔學習游泳時套在兩臂上的〕雙翼形充氣浮袋

wa·ter·works /ˈwɔtəˌwɜks; ˈwɔːtəwɜːks/ *n* [plural] **1** the system of pipes and artificial lakes used to clean and store water before it is supplied to a town〔城鎮的〕供水系統 **2 turn on the waterworks** *spoken* to start crying in order to get someone's sympathy【口】〔為贏得某人同情〕哭起來 **3** *informal or humorous* the system of organs and tubes inside your body that remove URINE (=liquid waste) from it【非正式或幽默】人體泌尿系統

wa·ter·y /ˈwɔtərɪ; ˈwɔːtəri/ *adj* **1** weak and pale in colour〔顏色〕淡的; 蒼白的: *a watery sun* 淡淡的陽光 **2** full of water 充滿水的: *a watery fluid* 含大量水分的液體 **3** related to water 與水有關的: *Watery gurgles came from the tank.* 從儲水池傳來水的汩汩聲。**4** watery food or drink contains too much water and does not taste good〔食物或飲料〕稀薄的; 含水太多的: *watery soup* 稀湯 **5 a watery grave** *literary* if someone comes to a watery grave, they drown【文】葬身水底

watt /wɑt; wɒt/ *n* [C] a measure of electrical power 瓦(特)〔電的功率單位〕

watt·age /ˈwɑtɪdʒ; ˈwɒtɪdʒ/ *n* [singular, U] the power of a piece of electrical equipment measured in watts〔電器的〕瓦(特)數

wat·tle /ˈwɑtl; ˈwɒtl/ *n* [U] **1** a material used for making fences consisting of small sticks on a frame of rods〔用作籬笆的〕編條構架 **2 wattle and daub** a mixture of this material and mud or clay used in the past to make the walls of houses〔舊時的〕抹灰籬笆牆, 枝條泥巴牆 **3** a piece of red flesh that grows from the head or neck of a bird like the TURKEY (1)〔禽鳥, 如火雞頭上或頸部的〕肉垂 **4** an Australian tree with small yellow flowers; ACACIA〔澳洲產的〕金合歡樹

Wave /wev; weɪv/ *n* [C] *AmE informal* a woman who is a member of a US navy VOLUNTEER[1] (2) group【美, 非正式】〔美國海軍〕志願緊急服役婦女隊隊員

wave[1] /wev; weɪv/ *n*

1 ▶ON THE SEA 海上的◀ [C] a line of raised water that moves across the surface of the sea 海浪, 波濤: *Dee watched the waves breaking on the rocks.* 迪伊看着海浪拍打着岩石。

2 ▶OF YOUR HAND 關於手的◀ [C usually singular 一般用單數] a movement of your hand or arm from side to side 揮手; 招手

3 ▶OF LIGHT/SOUND 關於光/聲的◀ [C] the form in which some types of energy such as light and sound move 光波; 聲波: *radio waves* 無線電波 —see also 另見 LONG WAVE, MEDIUM WAVE, SHORT WAVE

4 ▶SUDDEN INCREASE 激增◀ [C] **a)** a sudden increase in a particular type of behaviour or activity, especially an unpleasant one〔尤指令人討厭的行為或活動的〕突然增加, 高潮: **[+of]** *a new wave of terrorist bombings* 一輪新的恐怖分子炸彈襲擊浪潮 | **crime wave** (=a sudden increase in crime) 犯罪率激增 **b)** a sudden increase in the number of people or things arriving at the same time 同時到達的人數[事物]激增: **[+of]** *a new wave of immigrants* 一股新的移民潮 **c)** a group of soldiers, aircraft etc that attack together 一批士兵[飛機]的同時攻擊: **[+of]** *The next wave of troops went over the ridge.* 部隊的下一波攻擊越過山嶺。**d)** a sudden strong feeling that spreads from one person to another 突發並互相影響的強烈情緒: **[+of]** *A wave of panic swept through the crowd.* 一陣恐慌情緒在人羣中蔓延。

5 in waves if something happens in waves, a short period of activity is followed by a pause〔中間略有停頓的〕一陣一陣: *The pain swept over him in waves.* 一陣一陣的疼痛掃過他的全身。

6 ▶OF HAIR 頭髮的◀ [C] a part of your hair that has an even curved shape〔頭髮的〕鬈曲

7 make waves *informal* to cause problems【非正式】製造麻煩: *With so many jobs being cut, Parker didn't want to make waves.* 由於那麼多工作被砍掉, 帕克不想再製造麻煩。

8 the waves *literary* the ocean【文】大海

wave[2] *v* 3 3

1 ▶HAND 手◀ [I,T] to move your hand or arm from side to side in order to greet someone or attract their attention 揮手〔問候〕, 招手: *Toyah waved her hand regally.* 托亞威儀堂堂地揮手。| **wave to/at sb** *Tommy waved to us as he came across the field.* 湯姆穿過田地時朝我們揮手。| **wave sth at sb** *Lee waved his fist at me angrily.* 李朝我憤怒地揮動着拳頭。| **wave sth around/about** *BrE*【英】: *Stop waving your arms about.* 別揮動手臂了。| **wave sb goodbye/wave goodbye to sb** (=to say goodbye to someone by waving to them)〔向某人〕揮手告別 *Wave bye-bye to Granny.* 向奶奶揮手告別。

2 ▶SIGNAL 信號◀ [T always+adv/prep] to show someone where to go by waving your hand in that direction 對〔某人〕揮手以示方向: **wave sb through/on/away** *A guard waved me away from the fence.* 警衛揮手示意我離開圍欄。

3 ▶MAKE STH MOVE 使某物移動◀ [T] to hold something and move it from side to side 揮動〔某物〕: *The magician waved his wand and the door opened.* 魔術師一揮魔杖, 門就開了。| **wave sth under/about/at etc** *Trudie waved a $50 bill under his nose.* 特魯迪拿着一張 50 美元的鈔票在他鼻子底下晃了晃。

4 ▶MOVE SMOOTHLY 平穩移動◀ [I] to move smoothly up and down, or from side to side 上下起伏; 左右搖晃: *flags waving in the wind* 旗幟迎風飄揚

5 wave sth goodbye *informal* to be forced to accept that something you want will not happen【非正式】與某事揮別〔被迫接受不如意的結局〕: *A 3-0 defeat means United have waved their promotion chances goodbye.* 3:0 的失敗意味着聯隊失去了晉級的機會。

6 ▶HAIR 頭髮◀ [I,T] if hair waves or is waved, it grows in loose curls (使) 呈波浪形, (使) 變曲

wave sth ↔ **aside** *phr v* [T] to refuse to accept someone's opinion or idea because you do not think it is important 對〔某人的意見、主意〕不屑一顧: *Nancy waved aside our objections.* 南希對我們的反對置之不理。

wave sb/sth ↔ **down** *phr v* [T] to signal to the driver of a car to stop by waving your arm at them 揮手示意停車

wave sb **off** *phr v* [T] to wave goodbye to someone as they leave〔某人離開時〕揮手告別

wave·band /ˈwevˌbænd; ˈweɪvbænd/ *n* [C] a set of radio waves of similar length which are used to broadcast radio programmes〔無線電的〕波段

wave·length /ˈwevˌlɛŋθ; ˈweɪvleŋθ/ *n* [C] **1** the size of a radio wave used to broadcast a radio signal〔無線電的〕波長 **2** the distance between two waves of energy such as sound or light〔聲波、光波等的〕波長 **3 be on the same wavelength/on a different wavelength** *informal* to have the same or different opinions and feelings as someone else【非正式】〔與其他人的觀點、感情〕相投/不合: *We just aren't on the same wavelength when it comes to politics.* 說到政治, 我們就意見不相近了。

wa·ver /ˈwevə; ˈweɪvə/ *v* [I] **1** to be or become weak and uncertain 減弱; 動搖: *His voice wavered.* 他的聲音變弱了。| **waver in sth** *Harris never wavered in his loyalty to the cause.* 哈里斯對事業的忠誠是堅定不移的。**2** to not make a decision because you have doubts 猶豫不決; 躊躇: *wavering voters* 猶豫不決的選民 | **waver between (doing)** *Maya wavered between accepting and refusing his offer.* 是接受還是拒絕他的建議, 瑪雅猶豫不決。**3** to move unsteadily first in one direction then in another 搖曳, 搖擺: *reflections wavering in the water of* *the lake* 在湖水中搖曳的倒影 —**waverer** *n* [C] *We must persuade the waverers to vote with us.* 必須說服猶豫不決的人投票支持我們。—**waveringly** *adv*

wav·y /ˈwevɪ; ˈweɪvi/ *adj* **1** wavy hair grows in waves〔頭髮〕鬈曲的 —see picture on page A6 參見 A6 頁圖 **2** a wavy line or edge has smooth curves in it 波形的, 波紋的 —**waviness** *n* [U]

wax[1] /wæks; wæks/ *n* [U] **1** a solid material made out of fats or oils used to make CANDLES, polish etc〔製造蠟燭、上光等用的〕蠟: *wax crayon* 蠟筆 **2** a natural sticky substance in your ears 耳垢 —see also 另見 BEESWAX

wax[2] *v*

1 ▶FLOOR/FURNITURE 地板/家具◀ [T] to put a thin layer of wax on a floor or surface etc in order to polish it 給〔地板或表面等〕上蠟

2 ▶MOON 月亮◀ [I] when the moon waxes, it grows larger〔月亮〕漸圓, 漸滿

3 wax romantic/eloquent/lyrical etc *literary* to speak in a romantic way【文】浪漫/滔滔不絕/熱情奔放地說: *Mitch would wax eloquent on the subject of cars.* 說到汽車, 米奇滔滔不絕。

4 wax and wane *literary* to increase and then decrease【文】興衰, 榮枯

5 ▶LEGS 腿◀ [T] to put a thin layer of wax on your arms or legs in order to remove hairs〔在手臂或腿上〕塗一層薄蠟以去除體毛

waxed pa·per /ˌ· ˈ··/ also 又作 **wax·pa·per** /ˈwæksˌpepɚ; ˈwæksˌpeɪpə/ *n AmE* [U] paper with a thin layer of wax on used to wrap food【美】〔包食品的〕蠟紙; GREASEPROOF PAPER *BrE*【英】

wax·en /ˈwæksn̩; ˈwæksən/ *adj literary*【文】**1** pale and shiny like wax〔像蠟般〕蒼白的; 光滑的 **2** made of or covered in wax 蠟製的; 塗蠟的

wax·work /ˈwæksˌwɝk; ˈwækswɜːk/ *n* [C] **1 waxworks** *BrE*【英】**wax museum** *AmE*【美】a place where you pay to see models of famous people made of wax〔名人〕蠟像館 **2** a model of a person made of wax 蠟像

wax·y /ˈwæksɪ; ˈwæksi/ *adj* **1** made of or covered in wax 蠟製的; 塗蠟的 **2** looking or feeling like wax 似蠟的; 感覺像蠟的: *waxy petals* 像蠟做的花瓣 —**waxiness** *n* [U]

way[1] /we; weɪ/ *n*

① METHOD 方法
② MANNER 方式
③ ROAD/PATH 道路/路線
④ DIRECTION 方向
⑤ DISTANCE 距離
⑥ TIME 時間
⑦ BEHAVIOUR 舉止
⑧ ATTITUDE TO A SITUATION 對形勢的態度
⑨ WHAT YOU WANT 想要的東西
⑩ PREVENT/BLOCK STH 妨礙/阻止某事
⑪ DEVELOPMENT/PROGRESS 發展/前進
⑫ SITUATION/CONDITION 情況/條件
⑬ MAKE WAY 讓路
⑭ GIVE WAY 屈服
⑮ ON THE WAY 在途中
⑯ EITHER WAY 無論怎樣
⑰ SPOKEN PHRASES 口語片語
⑱ OTHER MEANINGS 其他意思

① METHOD 方法

1 [C] a method of doing something〔做事的〕方法: *These vegetables can be cooked in several different ways.* 這些蔬菜可用幾種不同的方法烹煮。| *At that time, the Pill was the easiest way of ensuring effective contraception.* 那時候口服避孕藥是最簡便有效的避孕方法。| *I've altered the way I teach science.* 我改變了我教科學科的方法。| *I'll tell her in my own time and in my own way.* 我將在我方便的時候以我的方式告訴她。| **way of doing sth** *I've got no way of contacting him at all.* 我沒有辦法和他聯繫上。| **way to do sth** *What's the right way to say this in English?* 這句話英語該怎麼說? | **way to go about sth** *I think you're going about this the wrong way.* 我覺得你這麼做, 方法不對。

2 one way or another *spoken* using one of several possible methods, although you do not yet know which one【口】用某種方法〔雖然不知道用哪一種〕: *We'll find the money, one way or another.* 我們無論如何會找到錢。

3 ways and means special methods for doing something, especially something secret or illegal 特殊的辦法〔尤指祕密或非法的〕: *There are ways and means of getting drugs in prison.* 在監獄內有各種辦法獲得毒品。—see also 另見 WAYS AND MEANS COMMITTEE

4 way out/around a possible method of solving a problem or difficult situation 解決問題[困難]的辦法: *I just can't see any way out of this mess.* 我真看不出有甚麼辦法來擺脫這種困境。| *There's no way around it – we'll have to tell Mom.* 我們不得不告訴媽媽——一點辦法也沒有。—see also 另見 WAY OUT, **take the easy way out** (EASY[1] (6))

5 way into television/publishing etc a possible method of getting a job in television etc, especially when this is difficult 進入電視界/出版界等的辦法〔尤指不容易進入〕: *She thought that working in the box office might be a way into the theatre.* 她覺得在票房工作或許是進入戲劇界的一種途徑。

② MANNER 方式

6 [C] a manner in which something can happen or be done, especially when there are several〔某事發生或做成的〕方式〔尤指有幾個方式〕: *I don't see it that way at all.* 我根本不那麼看。| *Look at the way he's dressed!* 看看他的打扮! | *Not all birds of prey suffered in this way (by eating insecticide), but many did.* 並非所有猛禽都遭受這種不幸 (指食用了殺蟲劑), 但有許多確實如此。| **in more ways than one** *spoken* (=in several ways)【口】不止一種方式 *This will benefit the company in more ways than one.* 這將在多方面對本公司有利。

7 that's no way to do sth *spoken* used to tell someone that they should not be doing something in a particular manner【口】不能用這種方式做某事: *That's no way to speak to your father!* 不能這樣跟你父親說話!

③ ROAD/PATH 道路/路線

8 [C] the road, path etc that you must follow in order to get to a particular place〔去某處的〕路, 道路: **[+to]** *Is this the way to Crouch End?* 到克勞奇角是走這條路嗎? | **lose your way** *We lost our way in the forest.* 我們在森林裡迷了路。| **know the way** *I hope Eric knows the way.* 我希望艾力克知道怎樣走。

④ DIRECTION 方向

9 [C] a particular direction from where you are now

〔特定的〕方向: *Which way is north?* 哪邊是北? | *Walk this way.* 這邊走。| *"Where's the lift?" "It's this way."* "電梯在哪兒?" "在這邊。" | **show sb/lead the way** *Could you just show me the way?* 你能告訴我怎麼走嗎?

10 on sb's way in the direction that someone is going 在某人要去的路上, 順路: *I'll give you a lift – it's on my way.* 你可以搭我的車 —— 我順路。

11 out of sb's way not in the direction that someone is going 不在某人要去的路上, 不順路: *You can't take me home – it's miles out of your way.* 你不能帶我回家 —— 我家離你走的路線還很遠呢。—see also 另見 OUT-OF-THE-WAY (1)

⑤ DISTANCE 距離

12 [singular] also 又作 **ways** *AmE informal* a distance, especially a long one【美, 非正式】路程〔尤指遠距離〕: *We have a ways to go yet.* 我們還要走很遠的路。| **a long way** *I was still a long way from home.* 我離家還很遠。| **all this way** *It would be too bad to come all this way and not see them.* 從老遠來卻沒有看見他們, 太不走運了。| **all the way down/across/through etc** (continuing for the full distance or length of something) 一直, 不停地 *Did you really swim all the way across?* 你真的是一直游過去的嗎? | **way beyond** (=much further) 高得多; 遠得多 *This achieves temperatures way beyond what is necessary.* 這樣達到的溫度比需要的高得多。

⑥ TIME 時間

13 [singular] a length of time, especially a long one〔尤指長的〕時段:*The two events were a long way apart.* 兩次事件之間隔了很長時間。

⑦ BEHAVIOUR 舉止

14 [C] a particular manner or style of behaving〔特殊的〕樣子; 神態: *He had an annoying way of picking his nails.* 他剔指甲的樣子讓人討厭。| *We all have our funny little ways.* 我們每個人都有些有趣的小動作。| **be (just) sb's way** *informal* (=be the way in which someone usually behaves, especially when this is unusual)【非正式】〔尤指某人不尋常的〕作風 *Oh, don't worry, that's just her way.* 噢, 別着急, 那正是她的作風。| **change/mend your ways** (=stop behaving badly) 改變作風〔停止錯誤的行為〕*Jamieson resolved to change his ways.* 傑米森決心改正。—see also 另見 **see the error of your ways** (ERROR (3))

⑧ ATTITUDE TO A SITUATION 對形勢的態度

15 [C] one of the possible ways of thinking about a situation, or one of many parts of it 思考某情況的方法; 某情況的一方面: **in a way** *In a way, it's kind of nice to be working alone.* 在某種程度上講, 獨自一個人工作相當不錯。| **in one way** *Well, in one way you're right, but it's not as simple as that.* 噢, 在某方面你是對的, 但是事情並非那麼簡單。| **in some ways** *In some ways, I'd rather he wasn't involved at all.* 從某些方面說, 我寧願他根本沒有牽涉進去。| **in no way** (=used to say that you should definitely not think about a situation in this way) 無論如何不, 決不〔用於表示你絕對不認同某觀點〕*This should in no way be seen as a defeat.* 這絕對不能看作是一種挫折。

⑨ WHAT YOU WANT 想要的東西

16 get your (own) way to do what you want to, even though someone else wants something different 隨心所欲〔雖然別人要求的不同〕: *You shouldn't let the children always get their own way.* 你不能總是讓孩子想怎樣就怎樣。

17 if I had my way *spoken* used before telling someone how you think something should be done【口】如果由我來處理〔用於告訴某人你認為某事應怎樣做〕: *Of course, if I had my way, they'd all be shot!* 當然, 要是由我來處理, 他們都該槍斃!

18 have it your own way! *spoken* used to tell someone in an annoyed way that you agree to what they want【口】按你的意思辦吧!〔用於生氣地表示同意某人的要求〕

19 go your own way to do what you want to do, make your own decisions etc 按自己的意願行事

20 have your (wicked) way with sb *old-fashioned* to persuade someone to have sex with you【過時】勸某人與自己發生性關係

⑩ PREVENT/BLOCK STH 妨礙/阻止某事

21 be in the way/in sb's way to be in a place or position that prevents someone or something else from moving freely 擋住去路; 礙事: *There was a large truck blocking the way.* 有一輛大卡車擋在路上。| *Get out of my way!* 讓開, 別擋我的路! | **[+of]** *Can you move that box? It's in the way of the door.* 你能搬開那隻箱子嗎? 它擋着進門的路。

22 get in the way of to prevent someone from doing something, or prevent something from happening 妨礙〔某人做某事〕; 阻止〔某事發生〕: *You mustn't let your social life get in the way of your studies.* 你不可以讓社交生活影響你的學業。

23 not stand in sb's way to not try to stop someone from doing something they want to do 不阻止某人做想做的事: *If you want to leave home, I'm not going to stand in your way.* 如果你想離家過獨立生活, 我不會阻止你的。

⑪ DEVELOPMENT/PROGRESS 發展/前進

24 have come a long way to have developed or changed a lot 進步[變化]很大: *Psychiatry has come a long way since the 1920s.* 自 20 世紀 20 年代以來, 精神病學進展很大。

25 have a long way to go to need to develop or change a lot in order to reach a particular standard〔為達到某標準〕仍有許多事要做: *Mac's still got a long way to go before he'll make a manager.* 想當上經理, 邁克仍有很長的路要走。

⑫ SITUATION/CONDITION 情況/條件

26 the way things are *spoken* used to describe the situation that you are in now【口】目前所處的情況: *The way things are at the moment, I don't think we're going to be able to go on vacation at all.* 根據目前的情況, 我認為我們不能休假了。

27 be in a bad way *BrE informal* to be very ill, injured, or upset【英, 非正式】病重, 嚴重受傷; 心煩意亂

⑬ MAKE WAY 讓路

28 make way a) to move to one side so that someone or something can pass 給〔某人或某物〕讓路〔以便其通過〕: **[+for]** *The crowd stepped aside to make way for the riders.* 人羣避到一旁, 讓路給騎馬的人。**b)** to be removed so that something newer or better can take your place 讓位〔給更新[更好]的事物〕: **[+for]** *Several houses were demolished to make way for the rail link.* 拆除了幾棟房子, 好騰出地方來建鐵路連線。

29 make your way a) to move towards something, especially when this takes a long time 走向〔某物, 尤指要用一段長時間〕: *We made our way down the hill towards the town.* 我們下山朝城裡走去。**b)** to slowly become successful in a particular job, activity, profession etc〔在工作、活動或職業中〕慢慢成功起來: *Gradually, Henderson began to make his way in politics.* 亨德森逐漸在政界有所建樹。

30 make/find your own way *informal* to go somewhere without the other people in your group【非正式】獨自一人去某處: *You'll have to make your own way to the pub.* 你得獨自一個人去酒吧。

⑭ **GIVE WAY 屈服**
31 to break because of too much weight or pressure〔因重量或壓力過多而〕坍塌; 垮掉: *The floor eventually gave way.* 地板最終塌了。
32 to have your place taken by something newer, better, or different 被〔更新、更好或不同的事物〕取代: **[+to]** *Steam trains finally gave way to electricity.* 蒸汽火車最終讓位給電氣火車。| *After a while my anger gave way to depression.* 過了一會兒, 我的怒氣變成了沮喪。
33 to agree to do what someone else wants to do, instead of what you wanted to do 讓步; 屈服: *Alison's too stubborn to give way.* 艾麗森太固執己見, 決不讓步。
34 *BrE* to allow vehicles to pass in front of you when you are driving【英】讓其他車輛先行; YIELD¹ (5) *AmE*【美】: *You must give way to traffic coming from the right.* 你必須讓右方駛來的車輛先行。

⑮ **ON THE WAY 在途中**
35 on your/the way (to) while travelling from one place to another 在途中: *Why don't you stop by our place on your way to Boston?* 在你去波士頓的途中, 為甚麼不順道來我們這兒? | **on your way in/out/home etc** *Could you mail these letters on your way downtown?* 你在去城裡的路上能把這幾封信寄走嗎?
36 be on the/its way to be arriving soon 即將到達: *There's a letter on its way to you.* 你很快會收到一封信。| *More changes are on the way.* 將會發生更多的變化。
37 be on your way *spoken* to be leaving one place in order to go somewhere else【口】離開〔某處〕去另外一些地方
38 be well on the way to to have almost finished changing from one state or situation to another, especially a better one〔尤指更好的改變〕行將完成: *The new building is well on the way to being finished.* 新大樓即將竣工。| *Jen is now well on the way to recovery.* 詹即將康復。
39 on/along the way while developing from one situation or part of your life to another 在〔生命中一個階段到另一個階段〕期間: *She had progressed smoothly through school and university, picking up several academic awards on the way.* 她順利完成中學和大學學業, 幾次因為成績優異而獲獎。
40 have a baby on the way *informal* to be PREGNANT【非正式】懷孕

⑯ **EITHER WAY 無論怎樣**
41 either way *spoken* used to say that something will be the same, whichever of two possible choices you make【口】無論怎樣〔用於表示有兩個選擇, 但不論選哪一個, 結果都一樣〕: *Either way, it's going to be expensive.* 不管怎樣, 都很費錢。

42 within two feet/ten years/one hour etc either way if a measurement is within two feet, ten years etc either way, it may be two feet etc more or less than the correct amount〔測量的誤差〕在兩英尺/十年/一小時等之內: *Your answer must be within a centimetre either way.* 答案的誤差必須小於一厘米。
43 could go either way if a situation could go either way, both results are equally possible 兩個結果都有可能: *The election could go either way.* 選舉雙方任何一方都可能獲勝。

⑰ **SPOKEN PHRASES 口語片語**
44 by the way used before saying something that is not connected with the main subject you were talking about before 附帶[順便]説〔用於轉入與剛才説的主題無關的事物〕: *By the way, have you seen my umbrella anywhere?* 順便問問, 你在甚麼地方見過我的傘嗎?
45 no way! a) used to say that you will definitely not do something 不!〔表示斷然拒絕做某事〕: *"Can I borrow your car?" "No way!"* "我能借用你的汽車嗎?" "不行!" | *No way am I going to help him.* 我決不去幫他。| **no way José!** (=used to emphasize that you will not do something) 絕對不做!〔用於強調〕 **b)** *especially AmE* used to say that you do not believe something or are very surprised by it【尤美】不會吧; 不可能!〔表示不相信或驚訝〕: *She's 45? No way!* 她45歲了?不會吧! **c)** used to say that something is not possible or cannot be done〔用於表示〕不可能〔完成某事〕: *There's no way we're going to get this finished on time.* 我們絕對不可能按時完成這項工作。
46 way out/over/across etc *AmE* a long distance out, over etc【美】離開〔某處〕一大段路程: *"Where's the meter?" "It's way the hell over there."* "停車計時收費器在哪兒?" "在那邊很遠的地方。"
47 in a big way very much 十分; 大量地: *My little brother's into cars in a big way.* 我弟弟對汽車非常入迷。
48 by a long way by a large amount or difference 遠遠地; ...得多: *He was the best in the group, by a long way.* 他是團隊中最好最好的。
49 no two ways about it used to say that something is definitely true, especially something unpleasant〔尤指令人討厭的事情〕就是這樣, 千真萬確
50 you can't have it both ways used to say that you cannot have the advantages from both of two different possible decisions or actions 你不能兩全其美, 兩者兼得: *You're either going to have to work harder or settle for lower grades – you can't have it both ways!* 你要麼今後更加努力, 要麼甘願拿更低的分數 —— 你不可能兩者兼得。
51 be with sb all the way to agree with someone completely 完全同意某人〔的意見〕: *I'm with you all the way on this salary issue, Joe.* 喬, 在工資這個問題上, 我完全同意你。
52 to my way of thinking used before telling someone your opinion 依我看; 我認為: *To my way of thinking, it ought to be banned altogether.* 我認為這應該全部取締。
53 have sth in the way of to have particular amounts or types of something〔某物〕有一定的量[種類]: *They don't have much in the way of leisure facilities.* 他們沒有多少休閒設施。
54 have a way of doing sth used to say that something usually happens in a particular way, especially when this is unpleasant or inconvenient〔尤指不愉快或不方便的事〕總是以某種形式發生: *These things have a way of turning up when you least expect them.* 這些事情總發生在我們最意料不到的時候。
55 get sth out of the way to finish, or deal with something, especially something difficult or unpleasant 完成[處理]某事〔尤指困難的或不愉快的事〕: *I'd rather have the interview in the morning and get it out of the way!* 我寧願上午面試, 趕緊結束這件事!
56 every which way a) *BrE* every possible method【英】每一種可能的辦法, 想盡辦法: *We tried every which way we could think of, but it couldn't be done.* 我們絞盡腦汁, 但還是做不了。 **b)** *AmE* in all directions【美】四面八方, 到處: *When I came back there was popcorn flying every which way!* 當我回來的時候, 爆玉米花蹦得到處都是!
57 that's the way used to tell someone that they are doing something correctly or well, especially when you are showing them how 就這麼做〔尤用於指導某人時, 告訴他做法正確〕: *Now bring your foot gently off the clutch – that's the way.* 現在把你的腳慢慢地移開離合器踏板 —— 對了, 就這麼做。
58 come sb's way if something comes your way, you get or experience it, especially unexpectedly or by chance〔某人〕得到[經歷]某事〔尤指不期而遇或偶然的事情〕: *You must make the most of the opportunities that come your way.* 你必須充分利用碰到的機會。
59 way to go! *AmE* used to tell someone that they have

done something very well, or achieved something special【美】幹得好!〔用於讚賞某人做得不錯或取得特別的成果〕

60 (that's/it's) always the way! used to say that things always happen in the way that is least convenient 總是這樣!〔用於表示事情總是以讓人感到最不方便的方式發生〕: *The train was delayed – always the way when you're in a hurry!* 火車誤點了——總是越急越誤點!

61 across/over the way on the opposite side of the street 在〔路的〕對面: *They live across the way from us at number 23.* 他們住在我們對面的23號。

62 down your/London etc way in your area, the area of London etc 在你住的地區/在倫敦〔附近〕等

63 way out! *AmE* an expression meaning that something is very good or exciting, used especially in the 1970s【美】非常新奇[時髦]!〔尤用於20世紀70年代〕

64 get into the way of doing sth *BrE* to start to do something regularly【英】開始習慣於做某事: *I never got into the way of carrying my passport around with me.* 我不習慣隨身帶着護照。

65 go all the way (with sb) to have sex with someone〔與某人〕性交

⑱ OTHER MEANINGS 其他意思

66 lead the way a) to walk at the front of a group of people 引路, 帶路: *We set off in single file with Lawrence leading the way.* 我們排成單列縱隊出發, 由勞倫斯在前面帶路。**b)** to develop or discover something before other people 領先〔發明或發現〕, 帶頭: *a group that is leading the way in cancer research* 在癌症研究方面取得領先地位的一個小組

67 be under way a) to be happening or being done 正在發生; 在進行中: *Plans are under way for a new link road.* 建造一條新中繼公路的計劃正在進行之中。| **get under way** (=start happening) 開始發生[進行] *I'll wait till the campaign gets under way properly.* 我將等到戰役真正打響。| **be well under way** (=be definitely happening, and too late to stop or change) 進行已久〔停止或改變已太晚〕 *By the mid-sixties, the process of change was well under way.* 到60年代中期, 變革已成定局。**b)** to be moving forwards 前進中: *The boat gave a lurch, and we were under way.* 船搖晃了一下, 我們開船了。

68 split sth two/three etc ways also 又作 **divide sth two/three etc ways** to divide something into two, three etc equal parts 將〔某物〕平分/分三等份: *We'll split the cost between us five ways.* 我們五個人平分費用。

69 by way of a) as a form of something, or instead of something 當作, 用作, 作為: *We had sandwiches by way of a meal.* 我們吃三明治, 算是一頓飯了。| *I'd just like to make a few comments by way of introduction.* 我想說幾句作為開場白。**b)** if you travel by way of a place, you go through it 經由〔某地〕, 經過: *We went by way of London.* 我們途經倫敦。

70 way around/round a particular order or position that something should be in〔某物屬於某個〕次序[位置]: *Which way round does this skirt go?* 這條裙子該放在哪兒? | **right/wrong way around** *Make sure you get the slides the right way around.* 查看一下, 確保幻燈片方向正確。

71 know your way around to be familiar with a place, system, or organization 熟悉某個地點[系統; 機構]

72 have a way with to have a special ability to do something 有〔特殊〕能力〔做某事〕: *David seemed to have a way with children.* 大衛看來跟孩子打交道很有一手。

73 go out of your way to do sth to do something that you do not have to do and that involves making an effort 特地[不怕麻煩地]做某事: *She went out of her way to be kind to the newcomer.* 她特意對新來的人示好。

74 go some way towards doing sth to help something to happen 有助於某事發生: *These donations will go some way towards repairing the damage.* 這些捐款將有助於彌補損失。

75 go your separate ways a) to start doing different things, having different interests etc, from someone you used to be friends with〔與朋友〕各走各路: *After leaving college, we went our separate ways.* 大學畢業以後, 我們就分道揚鑣了。**b)** to end a marriage or relationship 結束婚姻[感情關係]: *John and I have gone our separate ways now.* 我和約翰現在已經離婚。

76 keep out of sb's way to avoid someone 避開某人

77 in sb's own way used when you want to say that someone thinks, feels, or does something, although other people might think that they do not 其實, 實際上: *He seems harsh, I know, but in his own way he's quite caring.* 我知道, 他看來嚴厲, 但他其實是非常關心人的。

78 Way used in the names of roads 道〔用於道路名稱〕: *Abercrombie Way* 阿伯克尤比大道

79 put sb in the way of (doing) sth *old-fashioned BrE* to give someone the opportunity to do or get something【過時, 英】給某人以〔做某事或得到某物〕的機會 —see also 另見 **in the family way** (FAMILY (6)), **go the way of all flesh** (FLESH[1] (10)), HALFWAY, **out of harm's way** (HARM[1] (6)), ONE-WAY, **the parting of the ways** (PARTING[1] (3)), **pave the way for** (PAVE (2)), **pay your way** (PAY[1] (12)), RIGHT OF WAY, **rub sb up the wrong way** (RUB[1] (9)), **see your way (clear) to** (SEE[1] (48)), TWO-WAY, **where there's a will there's a way** (WILL[2] (5))

way[2] *adv* **1** by a large amount 大大地: **way above/below/out etc** *Her IQ is way above average.* 她的智商遠遠高於平均水平。| *Your guess was way out, he's actually thirty-eight.* 你猜得太離譜了, 他實際上是三十八歲。| **way back** (=a long time ago) 很久以前 *We first met way back in the 70s.* 我們早在70年代就初次見面了。**2** very far 很遠: **way ahead/behind/back** *American companies are way ahead when it comes to biotechnology.* 在生物技術方面, 美國公司遙遙領先。| **way off/a ways off** *AmE* (=far from where you are)【美】離得很遠 *Way off in the distance I could see snowcapped mountains.* 我能看到遠處的高山, 山峯白雪皚皚。| **way out in/past/beyond** (=far from the nearest town or from the point you mention)〔與最近的城鎮或所提及的地點〕距離甚遠 *O'Connell lives way out in the desert.* 奧康奈爾居住在遙遠的沙漠裡。**3** *AmE informal* very【美, 非正式】非常, 很: *"Hey, check out my new bike." "Way cool!"* "嘿, 看看我的新自行車。" "棒極了!"

way·far·er /ˈweˌfɛrɚ; ˈweɪˌfeərə/ *n* [C] *literary* a traveller who walks from one place to another【文】徒步旅行者 —**wayfaring** *adj* [only before noun 僅用於名詞前]

way·lay /ˌweˈle; weɪˈleɪ/ *v past tense and past participle* **waylaid** /-ˈled; -ˈleɪd/ [T] to stop someone so that you can talk to them, rob them, or attack them〔為了說話而〕攔截〔某人〕; 攔路搶劫[伏擊]

way of life /ˌ· · ˈ·/ *n plural* **ways of life** [C] **1** the way someone lives, or the way people in a society usually live 生活方式: *The tribesmen's traditional way of life is under threat.* 部落人的傳統生活方式受到了威脅。| **the American/British etc way of life** (=the life typical of Americans, British people etc) 美國人/英國人等〔典型〕的生活方式 **2** a job or interest that is so important that it affects everything you do 生活中重要的事情〔工作或興趣〕: *Nursing isn't just a job; it's a whole way of life.* 護理不只是工作, 而是生活。

way out /ˌ· ˈ·/ *n* [C] *BrE*【英】**1** a door or a passage through which you can leave a building; EXIT〔建築物的〕出口, 太平門 **2** a way of getting away from a difficult or unpleasant situation 出路, 擺脫困難的辦法 —see also 另見 **take the easy way out** (EASY[1] (6)), **way out** (WAY[1] (4))

way-out /ˌ· ˈ·◂/ *adj informal* very modern, and unusual or strange【非正式】時髦的; 不尋常的; 新奇的: *I like jazz, but not the way-out stuff.* 我喜歡爵士音樂, 但不喜歡出格的東西。

-ways /wez; weɪz/ *suffix* [in adverbs 構成副詞] in a particular direction 朝…方向: *leaning sideways* (=leaning to the side) 向一側傾斜

Ways and Means Com·mit·tee /,· · ·'· ·,··/ *n* [C] *AmE* a group of representatives in the government of a US state or in Congress who must find money for the government to spend【美】〔美國州政府、國會中負責稅收、貿易政策等的〕歲入委員會

way·side /ˈweˌsaɪd; ˈweɪsaɪd/ *n* [singular] *literary* the side of a road or path【文】路邊 —see also 另見 **fall by the wayside** (FALL[1] (23))

way sta·tion /'· ,··/ *n* [C] *AmE* a place between the main stations of a railway where a train stops【美】〔火車停靠的〕小站

way·ward /ˈwewəd; ˈweɪwəd/ *adj* behaving in a way that is different from other people and that causes problems 怪僻的〔因而招致麻煩〕; 倔強的: *a wayward teenager* 任性的少年 —**waywardly** *adv* —**waywardness** *n* [U]

wa·zoo /wəˈzu; wəˈzuː/ *n* [C] *AmE informal* your bottom【美, 非正式】屁股

WC /ˌdʌblju ˈsi; ˌdʌbəljuː ˈsiː/ *n* [C] water closet; a word for toilet used especially on signs in public places 廁所〔尤用於公共場所廁所的標記〕

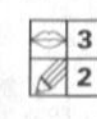

we /wi; wi; *strong* 強讀 wi; wiː/ *pron* [used as the subject of a sentence 用作句子的主詞] **1** I and one or more others 我們: *We were all amazed when we heard the news.* 我們聽到這個消息都目瞪口呆。| *Shall we* (=you and I) *have a coffee, Ted?* 泰德, 我們喝杯咖啡好嗎? | *Can we* (=I and the others) *go now, sir?* 先生, 我們現在可以走嗎? **2** *formal* used by a king or queen in official language to mean I【正式】寡人, 朕〔國王或女王在正式場合的自稱〕: *We are not amused.* 朕不覺得好笑。**3** used by a writer or a speaker to mean you (the reader or listener) and them 我們〔作者或說話人使用, 指讀者或聽眾和自己〕: *We saw in the previous chapter how this situation had arisen.* 在上一章裡我們看到這種情況是怎樣發生的。**4** used especially to children and people who are ill to mean you 我們〔尤用於與兒童或病人談話, 實際指對方〕: *And how are we feeling today, Mr Robson?* 羅布森先生, 我們今天感覺如何? **5** *formal* people in general【正式】人, 人類, 人們: *Do we have the right to destroy the planet?* 人們有權去破壞地球嗎?

weak /wik; wiːk/ *adj*

1 ▶PHYSICALLY 身體上◀ not physically strong 虛弱的, 不夠強壯的: *The illness had left her feeling tired and weak.* 疾病使她感到疲憊而虛弱。| **[+with]** *Nina was weak with hunger.* 妮娜餓得沒有氣力。| **weak heart/bladder/eyes etc** (=that do not work properly) 衰弱的心臟/膀胱/眼睛等

2 ▶CHARACTER 性格◀ easily influenced by other people because you cannot make decisions by yourself 意志薄弱的; 無決斷力的: *a weak and indecisive man* 軟弱而優柔寡斷的男人

3 ▶NOT GOOD AT 不精通◀ not having much ability or skill in a particular activity or subject 〔在某活動或學科的能力、技能〕差的; 弱的: *a weak backhand* 差勁的反手擊球 | **[+at/in]** *Julie's always been weak in science.* 朱莉的理科總是弱項。

4 ▶LEADERS/COUNTRIES/ORGANIZATIONS ETC 領導人/國家/組織等◀ not having much power or influence 無權力的; 無影響力的: *weak trade unions* 無影響力的工會 | *a weak leader* 軟弱的領導人

5 ▶ARGUMENT/EXPLANATION/STORY ETC 論據/闡述/描述等◀ not having the power to persuade or interest people 無說服力的; 不吸引人的: *The play was well-acted but the plot was weak.* 戲演得很好, 但情節乏味。

6 ▶INDUSTRY/COMPANY ETC 工業/公司等◀ not successful financially 〔金融上〕疲軟的; 蕭條的: *a weak economy* 不景氣的經濟 | *The pound was weak against the dollar.* 英鎊對美元的匯率疲軟。

7 ▶BUILDINGS/OBJECTS 建築物/實物◀ unable to support a lot of weight 不牢固的: *a weak bridge* 不牢固的橋梁

8 ▶DRINK/LIQUID 飲料/液體◀ containing a lot of water or having little taste 稀薄的; 味淡的: *weak tea* 淡茶

9 ▶LIGHT/SOUND 光線/聲音◀ difficult to see or hear 暗淡的; 微弱的: *a weak radio signal* 微弱的無線電信號

10 weak point/spot a part of something or of someone's character that can easily be attacked or criticized 〔物〕薄弱環節; 〔人〕弱點: **[+in]** *Agassi soon found the weak spots in Stich's game.* 阿加斯很快發現了斯蒂克的弱點。

11 weak at the knees not feeling well or strong, especially because you have had a sudden surprise or because you have seen someone you love 〔尤指因意外或遇見愛慕的人而〕兩腿發軟的: *His quick smile sent her weak at the knees.* 他歡快的笑容使她兩腿酥軟。

12 weak smile a slight smile, especially because you are not very happy 〔尤指不很高興而〕微微的一笑

13 a weak moment a time when you can be persuaded more easily than usual 意志薄弱的時刻: *David caught me at a weak moment and I lent him £10.* 大衛趁我心軟的時候, 讓我借給了他10英鎊。

14 weak in the head *informal* stupid or silly【非正式】愚蠢的; 頭腦遲鈍的

15 weak chin/jaw a weak chin or jaw is not very well developed and people often think it suggests a weak character 單薄的下巴〔常被認為是性格懦弱的象徵〕

16 weak verb *technical* a verb that forms the past tense and past participle in a regular way【術語】弱動詞〔過去式和過去分詞是規則形式的動詞〕

17 weak consonant/syllable a weak CONSONANT or syllable is not emphasized 弱輔音; 弱音節 —see also 另見 WEAKER SEX —**weakly** *adv*: *"I'm sorry," she said, smiling weakly.* "對不起," 她淡淡地一笑說。| *He sank down weakly on the sofa.* 他虛弱地癱倒在沙發裡。

weak·en /ˈwikən; ˈwiːkən/ *v*

1 ▶MAKE LESS POWERFUL 減弱◀ [I,T] to make someone or something less powerful or less important, or to become less powerful 使〔某人或某物〕變弱; 削弱; 減弱: *Russia's influence on African affairs has weakened.* 俄羅斯對非洲事務的影響已經減弱。

2 ▶PHYSICALLY 體能上◀ [I,T often passive 常用被動態] to make someone lose their physical strength, or to become physically weak 使〔某人〕虛弱, 使衰弱: *Julia was weakened by her long illness.* 朱莉亞長期生病, 身體衰弱。

3 ▶BUILDING/OBJECT 建築物/實物◀ [T] to become less strong and less able to support a lot of weight 〔使〕不結實: *The explosion severely weakened the foundations of the house.* 爆炸使那座房屋的地基受到嚴重的毀壞。

4 weaken sb's determination/resolve to make someone less determined 動搖某人的決心[決定]: *The opposition she encountered did nothing to weaken her resolve.* 反對意見絲毫沒有動搖她的決心。

5 ▶BECOME LESS CERTAIN 變得不肯定◀ [I] to become less determined, especially so that you change your opinion and accept someone else's (變得) 不堅決〔尤指改變自己的主張而聽從別人〕; (變得) 猶豫: *I think Mum's weakening about us going to that party.* 我覺得媽媽心軟下來了, 也許會讓我們去參加聚會。

6 ▶MONEY 金錢◀ [I,T] if a particular country's money or a company's SHARE[2] (5) prices weaken or are weakened, their value is reduced 使〔某國貨幣或公司股票的價格〕疲軟

weak·er sex /'·· ,·/ *n* **the weaker sex** an expression meaning women, that is now usually considered offensive 女性〔現在通常認為是冒犯用語〕

weak-kneed /,· '·◂/ *adj informal* lacking courage and unable to make your own decisions【非正式】懦弱的; 缺乏決斷力的

weak·ling /ˋwiklɪŋ; ˈwiːk-lɪŋ/ *n* [C] someone who is not physically strong 體格不強壯的人

weak·ness /ˋwiknɪs; ˈwiːknʒs/ *n*

1 ▶PHYSICAL 身體的◀ [U] the state of being physically weak 虛弱, 衰弱, 不強壯: *weakness in the muscles* 肌肉軟弱無力

2 ▶LACK OF DETERMINATION 缺乏決心◀ [U] lack of determination shown in someone's behaviour〔某人行為〕軟弱; 懦弱: **sign of weakness** *Most people saw her sensitivity as a sign of weakness.* 許多人把她的敏感看作是懦弱的表現。

3 ▶LACK OF POWER 缺乏權力◀ [U] lack of power and influence 缺乏權力[影響力]: *the weakness of the Trade Union movement in post-Thatcher Britain* 戴卓爾時代後的英國工會運動的衰落

4 ▶CHARACTER/DESIGN ETC 性格/設計等◀ [U] a fault in someone's character or in a system, organization, design etc〔性格或系統、組織、設計等的〕缺點, 弱點: *We spent two hours analyzing the team's strengths and weaknesses.* 我們花了兩個小時分析隊伍的強項和不足。| *a structural weakness in the aircraft* 飛機結構上的缺陷

5 ▶IDEA, PLAN ETC 想法、計劃等◀ [C] a part of something that can easily be attacked or criticized 薄弱環節: **[+in]** *We finally found a weakness in their case.* 我們終於在他們的論據中找到了漏洞。

6 a weakness for sth if you have a weakness for something, you like it very much even though it may not be good for you〔對不太好事物的〕癖好, 嗜好: *Ryan's always had a weakness for fast cars.* 瑞安總是偏愛跑車。

weak-willed /,· '·◂/ *adj* someone who is weak-willed cannot make decisions easily〔人〕優柔寡斷的

weal /wil; wiːl/ *n* [C] a red swollen mark on the skin where someone has been hit〔皮膚上被打後的〕紅腫, 傷痕

wealth /wɛlθ; welθ/ *n* **1** [U] a large amount of money and possessions 錢財, 財富: *The country's wealth comes from its oil.* 這個國家的財富來自石油。**2 a wealth of experience/knowledge/resources etc** a large number or amount of experience etc 豐富的經驗/知識/資源等

wealth·y /ˋwɛlθɪ; ˈwelθi/ *adj* **1** having a lot of money, possessions etc, especially because your family has owned them for a long time 富裕的, 富有的: *wealthy landowners* 有錢的地主 **2 the wealthy** people who have a lot of money, possessions etc 有錢人, 富人

wean /win; wiːn/ *v* [I,T] to gradually stop feeding a baby or young animal on its mother's milk and start giving it ordinary food 使〔嬰兒或幼小動物〕斷奶: *Some infants are weaned at six months.* 有些嬰兒六個月時就斷奶了。

wean sb **off** sth *phr v* [T] to make someone gradually stop doing something you disapprove of 使〔某人〕逐漸戒除〔做你不贊成的事〕: *I'm still trying to wean my daughter off sugary snacks.* 我仍在試圖使女兒改掉吃甜點的習慣。

wean sb **on** sth *phr v* [T] **be weaned on** to be influenced by something from a very early age 從幼年起便受〔某物〕影響: *Like many of his generation, he was weaned on the Bible.* 跟許多同齡人一樣, 他是在《聖經》的影響下長大的。

weap·on /ˋwɛpən; ˈwepən/ *n* [C] **1** something that you use to fight with, such as a knife, bomb, or gun 武器: *The crowd picked up sticks and bottles to use as weapons.* 羣眾撿起棍子和瓶子作為武器。| **lethal weapon** (=one that can kill) 致命的武器 **2** a type of behaviour, knowledge of a particular subject etc that you can use against someone when you are in a difficult situation〔身處困境時用來對付某人的〕手段: *The only weapon she could use against him was guilt.* 她用以對付他的唯一手段是喚起他的內疚。

weap·on·ry /ˋwɛpənrɪ; ˈwepənri/ *n* [U] a word meaning weapons, used especially when talking about particular types of weapons〔尤用於指某類〕武器: *nuclear weaponry* 核武器

wear¹ /wɛr; weə/ *v past tense* **wore** /wɔr; wɔː/ *past participle* **worn** /wɔrn; wɔːn/ S1 W1

1 ▶ON YOUR BODY 在身上◀ [T] to have something such as clothes, shoes, or jewellery on your body 穿〔衣服、鞋子〕, 戴〔首飾〕: *I'm going to wear a black dress and my diamond earrings.* 我準備穿黑衣裙, 戴鑽石耳環。| *Why aren't you wearing your glasses?* 你為甚麼不戴眼鏡? | **wear a seatbelt** (=put it around yourself) 繫上安全帶 | **wear blue/black/red etc** *I rarely wear bright colors.* 我很少穿色彩豔麗的衣服。| **wear sth to a party/dance/ interview etc** *You can't wear jeans to the opera.* 你不能穿牛仔褲去歌劇院。

2 ▶HAIR 毛髮◀ [T] to have your hair or BEARD in a particular style or shape 蓄〔鬚〕, 留〔髮〕: *Fay wore her hair in a ponytail.* 費伊束着馬尾辮。

3 ▶BECOME DAMAGED 損壞◀ [I] to become thinner or weaker after continuous use〔經不斷使用而〕磨損; 磨壞: *The stair carpet has worn in places.* 樓梯上的地毯很多處已磨損。

4 ▶HOLE 洞◀ [T] to change the shape or condition of something by using it a lot or gradually damaging it〔因長期使用而〕造成〔變形等〕: **wear a hole/groove/gap etc in sth** *You've worn a hole in these socks.* 你的襪子上已經磨出了一個洞。

5 wear well to remain in good condition without becoming broken or damaged after a period of time 經久耐用: *The concrete buildings of the 60s haven't worn well.* 60 年代的水泥樓房已顯得破舊。

6 ▶EXPRESSION 表情◀ [T] to have a particular expression on your face 面露〔某種表情〕: **wear a frown/smile/grin** *Harry's face wore a broad grin.* 哈里的臉上掛着興高采烈的笑容。

7 sth is wearing thin if an excuse, explanation, opinion etc is wearing thin, it has been used so often that you no longer believe or accept it〔藉口、解釋、意見等因使用過多而〕難以令人相信[接受]: *Neil says he has to work late again – I think that excuse is wearing thin.* 尼爾說他又得工作到很晚──我覺得那個藉口用得太多, 不可置信。

8 wear the trousers *BrE*【英】, **wear the pants** *AmE*【美】*informal* to be the person in a family who makes the decisions【非正式】是一家之主

9 not wear sth *BrE spoken* used to say that you will not allow or accept something【英口】〔用於表示對某事情〕不能容忍: *Jane came home after 2 a.m. – I'm not wearing that.* 簡凌晨兩點多才回家──我不能容忍這樣。

10 wear your heart on your sleeve *informal* to show your true feelings openly【非正式】公開流露自己的感情 —**wearable** *adj*

wear away *phr v* [I,T] to gradually damage something or make it get thinner or weaker by using it, rubbing it etc 使磨損; 使磨薄; 使磨掉: **wear sth ↔ away** *The cliff face is being worn away by the sea.* 海水逐漸把懸崖表面磨薄了。

wear down *phr v* **1** [I,T] to gradually become smaller or make something smaller, for example by rubbing it or using it a lot (使) 逐漸變小, 磨耗, 磨薄: *My shoes have worn down at the heel.* 我的鞋後跟已經磨損了。**2** [T] to make someone physically weaker or less determined 削弱〔某人的〕體力[決心]: **wear sb ↔ down** *Haig's bullying was wearing me down.* 黑格的欺侮使我逐漸垮下來。

wear off *phr v* [I] **1** if pain or the effect of something wears off, it gradually stops〔疼痛或某種效果〕逐漸減少[消失]: *The effects of the anaesthetic were starting to wear off.* 麻醉劑的效果開始逐漸消退。**2 the novelty wears off** used to say that you stop feeling interested or excited about something because it is no longer

W

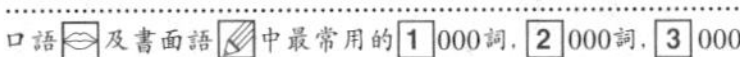
口語 及書面語 中最常用的 1 000詞, 2 000詞, 3 000詞

new 新鮮感慢慢消失

wear on *phr v* [I] if time wears on, it passes very slowly, especially when you are waiting for something to happen〔時間〕慢慢地過去〔尤用於等待某事發生時〕: *As the night wore on there was still no news of the missing plane.* 長夜漫漫, 仍然沒有失蹤飛機的消息。

wear out *phr v* [I,T] **1** to cause a lot of damage to something by using it a lot or for a long time so that it can no longer be used〔因過度或長期使用而〕磨損, 用壞: *Damn! My camera batteries have worn out.* 該死的! 我照相機裡的電池已經沒電了。| **wear sth ↔ out** *I've worn out the soles of my shoes.* 我的鞋底已經磨穿了。**2** to make someone feel extremely tired; EXHAUST[1] (1) 使〔某人〕精疲力竭: **wear sb ↔ out** *Two nights without sleep have worn me out.* 兩夜沒睡, 我已疲憊不堪。| **wear yourself out** *The baby has stopped crying. I think he's worn himself out.* 寶寶不哭了, 我想他是哭累了。—see also 另見 WORN-OUT

wear² *n* **1** [U] damage caused by continuous use over a long period〔因長期使用而〕磨損; 損壞: *The carpet is showing signs of wear.* 地毯已有磨損的痕跡了。**2** [U] the amount of use an object, piece of clothing etc has had, or the use you can expect to get from it〔物品、衣服等的〕耐用性, 經久性: *Considering the wear it's had, your coat's in good condition.* 你的外套穿了那麼久, 看上去還過得去。| **have/get a lot of wear out of sth** *You'll get a lot of wear out of a canvas tent.* 帆布帳篷能使用很長時間。| **a lot of wear is left in sth** (=it is still useful or can still be worn) 仍然有用; 還能穿 **3 sportswear/evening wear/childrens' wear etc** the clothes worn for a particular occasion or activity, or by a particular group of people 運動服/晚裝/童裝等: *a new range of casual wear* 新系列的休閒服 | *the menswear department* 男裝部 | *footwear* (=shoes) 鞋 **4 wear and tear** the amount of damage you expect to be caused to furniture, cars, equipment etc when they are used for a long period of time〔家具、汽車、設備等使用了一段長時間後的〕損耗, 磨損: **normal/everyday wear and tear** *The washer should last for ten years allowing for normal wear and tear.* 洗衣機在正常磨損的情況下可使用十年。—see also 另見 **the worse for wear** (WORSE[1] (8))

wear·er /ˈwɛrɚ; ˈweərə/ *n* [C] someone who wears a particular type of clothing, jewellery, etc〔服裝、珠寶等的〕穿戴者, 佩帶者: *Contact lens wearers often get red eyes.* 戴隱形眼鏡的人常患紅眼。

wear·ing /ˈwɛrɪŋ; ˈweərɪŋ/ *adj* making you feel tired or annoyed 使人疲倦的; 令人厭煩的: *The constant arguments at home are very wearing.* 家裡不斷的爭論真煩人。

wear·i·some /ˈwɪrɪsəm; ˈwɪərisəm/ *adj formal* making you feel bored, tired, or annoyed【正式】令人厭煩的; 使人疲倦的; 讓人討厭的: *a wearisome task* 乏味的任務

wear·y¹ /ˈwɪrɪ; ˈwɪəri/ *adj* **1** very tired, especially because you have been doing something for a long time〔尤指因長期做某事而〕筋疲力盡的, 非常疲勞的: *I just feel weary – I wish I didn't have to work nights.* 我感到疲憊不堪 — 我希望不必挑燈夜戰了。| *a weary smile* 疲倦的笑容 | **weary of doing sth** *I'm weary of arguing all the time.* 我對老是爭辯感到厭倦。**2** *especially literary* making you very tired【尤文】令人厭倦的: *a long and weary march* 令人疲倦的長途步行 —**wearily** *adv*: *Alice sighed wearily.* 愛麗絲疲倦地嘆息。—**weariness** *n* [U]

weary² *v* [I,T] *formal* to become very tired or make someone very tired【正式】非常疲倦; 令〔某人〕厭倦: *Amanda wouldn't admit how much the children wearied her.* 阿曼達不願承認孩子們讓她煩心。| **weary of doing** *Smoking is bad for you, as experts never weary of reminding us.* 專家不厭其煩地提醒我們, 抽煙不利於健康。

wea·sel¹ /ˈwizl; ˈwiːzəl/ *n* [C] a small thin furry animal that kills and eats rats and birds 鼬, 黃鼠狼

weasel² *v*

weasel out *phr v* [I] *informal* to avoid doing something you should do by using clever or dishonest excuses【非正式】逃避〔責任〕,〔狡猾地〕逃脫: **[+of]** *We made a deal and you can't weasel out of it.* 我們達成了協議, 你不能藉故反悔。

weasel word /ˈ·· ˌ·/ *n* [C] *informal* a word used instead of another word because it is less direct, honest, or clear【非正式】滑頭話, 狡辯之辭

weath·er¹ /ˈwɛðɚ; ˈweðə/ *n* **1** [singular, U] the temperature and other conditions such as sun, rain, and wind 天氣, 氣象: **the weather** *What was the weather like on your vacation?* 在你假期裡的天氣情況怎樣? | **hot/wet/cold etc weather** *a spell of very dry weather* 一段非常乾燥的天氣 | **weather forecast** (=a report saying what the weather is expected to be like in the near future) 天氣預報 | **weather permitting** (=if the weather is good enough) 如果天氣好 *I'm playing golf this afternoon – weather permitting.* 天氣好的話 — 我今天下午就去打高爾夫球。| **weather pattern** (=the way the weather usually is or changes over a long period of time)〔一段長時間的〕天氣模式 | **weather map/chart** *The weather map shows a ridge of high pressure coming in from the Atlantic.* 氣象圖顯示一股高氣壓正從大西洋到來。| **weather report** (=description of weather conditions on radio or television)〔電台或電視廣播的〕氣象報告 —see picture on page A13 參見 A13 頁圖 **2 the weather** *informal* the description of what the weather will be like in the near future, on radio, television, in newspapers etc【非正式】〔電台、電視廣播或報紙刊登的〕天氣預報: *I always watch the weather after the news.* 新聞之後我一定要看天氣預報。**3 in all weathers** in all types of weather, even when it is very hot or cold 無論天氣好壞: *There are homeless people sleeping on the streets in all weathers.* 不論甚麼天氣都有無家可歸的人露宿街頭。**4 under the weather** *informal* slightly ill【非正式】身體不大舒服: *You look a bit under the weather.* 你看來身體不太好。**5 keep a weather eye on** to watch a situation carefully so that you notice anything unusual or unpleasant 密切注視, 時刻警惕〔不尋常或令人不安的事情〕—see also 另見 **make heavy weather of sth** (HEAVY[1] (12))

weather² *v* **1** [I,T] if rock, wood etc weathers, or if wind, sun, rain etc weathers them, they change colour or shape over a period of time (使)〔岩石、木等〕受風雨侵蝕: *a badly weathered statue* 一尊被風雨剝蝕得很厲害的雕像 **2** [T] to come through a very difficult situation safely 平安地渡過〔難關〕: **weather the storm** *Many small firms did not weather the storm of the recession.* 許多小公司經受不住經濟衰退的衝擊。

weath·er·board /ˈwɛðɚˌbɔrd; ˈweðəbɔːd/ *n* **1** [U] *BrE* boards covering the outer walls of a house【英】〔房屋外牆上的〕護牆板, 封簷板; CLAPBOARD *AmE*【美】**2** [C] a board or set of boards fixed across the bottom of a door, to prevent water from getting inside〔門底的〕防水板, 擋雨板

weath·er·bound /ˈwɛðɚˌbaund; ˈweðəbaʊnd/ *adj* unable to move or travel because of bad weather 因天氣不好而受阻的

weather cen·tre *BrE*【英】, **weather bureau** *AmE*【美】/ˈ·· ˌ··/ *n* [C] a place where information about the weather is collected and where reports are produced 氣象中心, 氣象局

weath·er·cock /ˈwɛðɚˌkɑk; ˈweðəkɒk/ *n* [C] a WEATHER VANE in the shape of a COCK[1] (1) 風標, 風信雞

weath·er·man /ˈwɛðɚˌmæn; ˈweðəmæn/ *n* [C] a man on television or radio who tells you what the weather will be like〔電視台或電台的〕氣象報告員

weath·er·per·son /ˈwɛðɚˌpɝsn; ˈweðəpɜːsən/ *n* [C] someone on television or radio who tells you what the weather will be like〔電視台或電台的〕氣象報告員

weath·er·proof /ˈwɛðɚˈpruf; ˈweðəpruːf/ *adj* weatherproof clothing or material can keep out wind and rain 〔衣物或材料〕防風雨的; 不受氣候影響的 —**weather-proof** *v* [T]

weather ship /ˈ·· ·/ *n* [C] a ship at sea which reports on weather conditions 〔海上的〕氣象觀測船

weather sta·tion /ˈ·· ˌ··/ *n* [C] a place or building used for studying and recording weather conditions 氣象站

weather strip /ˈ·· ·/ *n* [C] a thin piece of plastic or other material put along the edge of a door or window to keep out cold air 〔門、窗的〕擋風雨的密封條 —**weather stripping** *n* [U]

weather vane /ˈ·· ·/ *n* [C] a metal thing fixed to the top of a building that blows around to show the direction the wind is coming from 風標

weave[1] /wiv; wiːv/ *v past tense* **wove** /wov; wəʊv/ *past participle* **woven** /ˈwovən; ˈwəʊvən/

1 ►CLOTH 布◄ [I,T] to make threads into cloth by crossing them under and over each other on a LOOM[1], or to make cloth in this way 織; 織〔布〕: *hand-woven scarves* 幾條手織圍巾

2 ►MAKE STH 製造某物◄ [T] to make something by twisting pieces of something together 編, 織: *traditional basket weaving* 傳統的籃子編織 | **weave sth together** *Fir branches were woven together to make garlands.* 用冷杉樹枝編成幾個花環。

3 ►STORY 故事◄ [T] to invent a complicated story or plan 編造〔故事或計劃〕: *What I like is how he weaves elaborate plots.* 我喜歡他筆下精巧多變的布局。

4 get weaving *BrE spoken* used to tell someone to hurry up and start doing something 【英口】趕快〔用於告訴某人趕快開始做某事〕

5 ►MOVE 移動◄ *past tense and past participle* **weaved** [I always+adv/prep, T always+adv/prep] to move somewhere by turning and changing direction a lot 迂迴[穿插]行進: [**+through/across etc**] *cyclists weaving in and out of the traffic* 在車水馬龍之中穿梭的騎車人 | **weave your way** *Cindy weaved her way through the crowd.* 辛迪在人羣中穿插着往前走。

weave[2] *n* [C] the way in which a material is woven, and the pattern formed by this 織法; 編織式樣: *a fine weave* 精織法

weav·er /ˈwivɚ; ˈwiːvə/ *n* [C] someone whose job is to weave cloth 織布工

web /wɛb; web/ *n* [C] **1** a net of thin threads made by a SPIDER to catch insects 蜘蛛網: **spin a web** (=make a web) 織網 —see also 另見 COBWEB —see picture at 參見 SPIDER 圖 **2 a web of sth** a closely related set of things that can be very complicated 錯綜複雜的一套…: *a web of lies* 一套謊言 **3** pieces of skin that connect the toes of ducks and some other birds, and help them to swim well 〔鴨子等的〕蹼 **4 the web** the network of computers that forms the Internet 〔構成互聯網的〕電腦網絡

webbed /wɛbd; webd/ *adj* webbed feet or toes have skin between the toes 〔趾間〕有蹼的

web·bing /ˈwɛbɪŋ; ˈwebɪŋ/ *n* [U] strong woven material in narrow bands, used for supporting seats etc 〔支撐椅子等的〕結實的帶狀織物

web-foot·ed /ˌ· ˈ··◄/ *adj* also 又作 **web-toed** having toes that are joined by pieces of skin 有蹼足的

web off·set /ˌ· ˈ··/ *n* [U] a method of printing using one continuous roll of paper 卷筒紙膠印

Wed a written abbreviation of 縮寫= WEDNESDAY

we'd /wɪd; wid; *strong* 強讀 wid; wiːd/ **1** the short form of 縮略式= we had: *We'd better go now.* 我們最好現在就走。**2** the short form of 縮略式= we would: *We'd rather stay.* 我們寧願留下來。

wed /wɛd; wed/ *v past tense and past participle* **wedded** or **wed** [I,T not in progressive 不用進行式] a word meaning to marry, used especially in literature or newspapers 娶; 嫁; 結婚〔尤用於文學或報刊中〕

wed·ded /ˈwɛdɪd; ˈwedɪ̈d/ *adj* **1 sb's (lawful) wedded husband/wife** *formal* someone's legal husband or wife 【正式】某人的（合法）丈夫/妻子 **2 be wedded to** to believe strongly in a particular idea or way of doing things 執着於〔某種思想或做法〕的, 堅持…的: *They're still very wedded to the idea of public ownership.* 他們仍然極力堅持公有制的思想。

wed·ding /ˈwɛdɪŋ; ˈwedɪŋ/ *n* [C] **1** a marriage ceremony, especially one with a religious service 〔尤指有宗教儀式的〕婚禮: **wedding present/reception/cake etc** *Careful with that vase! It was a wedding present.* 當心那隻花瓶！那是結婚禮物。**2 (hear the sound of) wedding bells** *spoken* used to say that you think it is likely that two people will get married 【口】好事近了〔用於表示認為兩個人將要結婚〕: *I reckon it's wedding bells for Tony and Jane.* 我想東尼和簡要結婚了。 S2 W3

wedding break·fast /ˈ·· ˌ··/ *n* [C usually singular 一般用單數] *BrE* a special meal after a wedding ceremony 【英】婚禮後的喜宴, 婚宴

wedding chap·el /ˈ·· ˌ··/ *n* [C] a building used in the US for wedding ceremonies 〔美國〕結婚教堂

wedding dress /ˈ·· ·/ also 又作 **wedding gown** *n* [C] a long white dress worn at a traditional wedding 婚紗

wedding ring /ˈ·· ·/ *n* [C] a ring worn on the third finger of your left hand to show that you are married 結婚戒指

wedge[1] /wɛdʒ; wedʒ/ *n* [C] **1** a piece of wood, metal etc that has one thick edge and one pointed edge and is used especially for keeping a door open or for splitting wood 〔木頭、金屬等的〕楔子〔尤用於抵住門或劈開木頭〕 **2** a piece of food shaped like this 楔形〔食物〕: *a wedge of chocolate cake* 一塊楔形的巧克力蛋糕 | *Garnish with lemon wedges.* 用楔形檸檬片裝飾。**3 drive a wedge between** to make the relationship between two people or groups worse 造成〔兩個人或團體〕之間的不和: *Their divorce has driven a wedge between the two families.* 他們的離婚導致了雙方家庭的不和。—see also 另見 **the thin end of the wedge** (THIN[1] (11))

wedge[2] *v* **1** [T always+adv/prep] to force something firmly into a narrow space 把…擠入: **wedge sth behind/under/in etc** *Cloth wedged in the cracks failed to block out the drafts.* 塞到縫隙裡的布擋不住風。| **wedged in** (=stuck in a small space) 擠入〔窄小的空間〕 *I was wedged in between Tom and Amy on the back seat.* 在後座上我被夾在湯姆和艾米中間。**2 wedge sth open/shut** to put something under a door, window etc to make it stay open or shut 用楔子把某物〔門窗等〕抵住讓它開着/關着

wed·lock /ˈwɛdlɑk; ˈwedlɒk/ *n* [U] *old use* 【舊】 **1 born out of wedlock** if a child is born out of wedlock, its parents are not married when it is born 非婚生的 **2** the state of being married 已婚狀態

Wednes·day /ˈwɛnzdɪ; ˈwenzdi/ written abbreviation 縮寫為 **Wed** or 或 **Weds** *n* [C,U] the day between Tuesday and Thursday. In Britain, Wednesday is considered the third day of the week, and in the US it is considered the fourth day of the week 星期三〔在英國被看作是一星期的第三天, 在美國則被看作是一星期的第四天〕: *She'll arrive on Wednesday.* 她將於星期三到達。| *It happened Wednesday afternoon.* 這事發生在星期三下午。| *They left last Wednesday.* 他們是上星期三離開的。| **on Wednesdays** (=each Wednesday) 每星期三 *We play tennis on Wednesdays.* 我們每星期三打網球。| **a Wednesday** (=one of the Wednesdays of the year) 一年中的某個星期三 *My birthday's on a Wednesday this year.* 我今年的生日在一個星期三。| **the Wednesday** *BrE* (=the Wednesday of the week being mentioned) 【英】〔話中所指的這個星期的〕星期三 *They're arriving on the Wednesday, and leaving just after Christmas.* 他們會在那週的星期三到, 過了聖誕節後就走。

Weds a written abbreviation of 縮寫= Wednesday

wee[1] /wi; wiː/ *adj* [usually before noun 一般用於名詞前] **1** *ScotE or informal* very small 【蘇格蘭或非正式】很小的: *a wee kitten* 小貓 **2 a wee bit** *informal* to a small degree【非正式】有些, 有點: *I'm a wee bit tired.* 我有點累了。**3 the wee (small) hours** *ScotE and AmE* the early hours of the morning, just after midnight【蘇格蘭和美】凌晨〔午夜後不久〕; SMALL HOURS *BrE*【英】

wee² *v* [I] *BrE spoken* a word meaning to pass water from your body, used by or to children; URINATE; WEE-WEE【英口】尿尿, 撒尿〔兒語〕—**wee** *n* [singular, U]: *Do you want a wee?* 你要尿尿嗎?

weed¹ /wid; wiːd/ *n* **1** [C] a wild plant growing where it is not wanted and that prevents crops or garden flowers from growing properly 野草, 雜草, 莠草 **2** [U] a plant without flowers that grows on water in a large green floating mass 海藻, 水草 **3** [C] *BrE informal* someone who is weak【英, 非正式】孱弱的人: *Nigel's such a weed, isn't he?* 奈傑爾弱不禁風, 是不是啊? **4 the weed** *informal* cigarettes or tobacco【非正式】香煙; 煙草 **5** [U] *old-fashioned* CANNABIS【過時】大麻 **6 (widow's) weeds** *old use* black clothes worn by a woman whose husband has died【舊】〔寡婦穿的黑色〕喪服

weed² *v* [I,T] to remove unwanted plants from a garden or other place 除去雜草

weed sb/sth ↔ **out** *phr v* [T] to get rid of people or things that are not very good 淘汰〔不合格的人或物〕: *Unsuitable recruits were soon weeded out.* 不合格的新兵很快就遭淘汰了。

weed·kil·ler /ˈwidˌkɪlɚ; ˈwiːdˌkɪlə/ *n* [C,U] poison used to kill unwanted plants 除草劑

weed·y /ˈwidɪ; ˈwiːdi/ *adj informal*【非正式】**1** full of unwanted wild plants 雜草叢生的 **2** *BrE* physically weak or having a weak character【英】瘦弱的; 懦弱的: *a weedy little man with glasses* 戴眼鏡的矮個子瘦弱男人

S1 W1 **week** /wik; wiːk/ *n* [C] **1** a period of seven days and nights, usually measured in Britain from Monday to Sunday and in the US from Sunday to Saturday 星期, 週〔共七天, 在英國從星期一至星期日; 在美國從星期日至星期六〕: *The flight to Accra goes twice a week.* 飛往阿克拉的航班每星期兩次。| *See you next week.* 下星期見。**2** any period of seven days and nights 連續七天, 一週: *The training program lasts three weeks.* 培訓課程歷時三週。**3** the part of the week when you go to work, usually from Monday to Friday; WORKING WEEK 工作週〔通常由星期一至星期五〕: *a 35-hour week* 每週工作35小時 | *I don't see her much during the week.* 在上班時間我不常見到她。**4 Monday week/Tuesday week etc** *BrE* a week after the day that is mentioned【英】星期一/星期二後一週等: *We're off to Spain Sunday week.* 我們星期日後一週去西班牙。**5 a week on Monday etc** *BrE*【英】, **a week from Monday etc** *AmE*【美】a week after the day that is mentioned 星期一後一週等: *The Reids are coming for dinner a week from Sunday.* 里兹一家星期日後一週來吃飯。| *Keith's coming home two weeks on Saturday.* 基思星期六後兩週回家。**6 week after week** also 又作 **week in week out** *usually spoken* continuously for many weeks【一般口】連續幾個星期, 一週又一週: *I just seem to do the same things week in week out.* 一週又一週, 我好像在反覆做相同的工作。

week·day /ˈwikˌde; ˈwiːkdeɪ/ *n* [C] any day of the week except Saturday and Sunday 工作日〔星期一到星期五中某天〕

S1 W2 **week·end¹** /ˈwikˋɛnd; ˌwiːkˈend/ *n* [C] **1** Saturday and Sunday (and sometimes also Friday evening), especially when considered as time when you do not work 週末〔指星期六和星期日, 有時亦包括星期五晚上, 尤指不用工作的時間〕: *Are you doing anything nice this weekend?* 這個週末你有甚麼好的安排? | **a long weekend** (=Saturday and Sunday, and also Friday or Monday, or both) 長週末〔指星期六和星期日, 加上星期五及[或]下星期一〕 *We're going for a long weekend to EuroDisney.* 我們準備到歐洲迪士尼去度一個長週末。| **at the weekend/at weekends** *BrE*【英】: *I never work at weekends.* 週末我從不工作。| **on the weekend/on weekends** *AmE*【美】: *What are you doing on the weekend?* 週末你準備幹甚麼? | **weekend cottage/cabin etc** (=a place in the country where you spend your weekends) 週末度假村舍/小屋等 **2** a holiday from Friday evening until Sunday evening〔自星期五晚至星期日晚的〕週末假期: *You've won a weekend for two in Paris!* 你贏得兩人週末到巴黎度假的機會! —see also 另見 **dirty weekend** (DIRTY¹ (2))

weekend² *v* [I always+adv/prep] to spend the weekend somewhere〔到某處〕度週末: *We're weekending on the coast.* 我們正在海濱度週末。

week·end·er /ˈwikˋɛndɚ; ˌwiːkˈendə/ *n* [C] someone who spends time in a place only at weekends 外出度週末的人, 週末來客

week·long /ˈwikˌlɑŋ; ˈwiːklɒŋ/ *adj* [only before noun 僅用於名詞前] continuing for a week 持續一週: *a weeklong seminar* 持續一週的研討會

week·ly¹ /ˈwiklɪ; ˈwiːkli/ *adj* happening once a week or every week 一週一次的, 每週的: *a weekly current affairs programme* 每週的時事節目 | *twice-weekly flights to Hong Kong* 每週兩次飛往香港的航班 —**weekly** *adv*: *The magazine is published weekly.* 這本雜誌是週刊。

weekly² *n* [C] a magazine that appears once a week 週刊: *a popular news weekly* 受歡迎的新聞週刊

week·night /ˈwiknaɪt; ˈwiːknaɪt/ *n* [C] any night apart from Saturday or Sunday 工作日夜晚〔星期一到星期五中某夜〕

wee·nie /ˈwinɪ; ˈwiːni/ *n* [C] *AmE informal*【美, 非正式】**1** a type of SAUSAGE; a WIENER (1) 法蘭克福香腸, 熏肉香腸: *a weenie roast* 法蘭克福烤腸 **2** a word meaning someone who is weak, afraid, or stupid, used especially by children 膽小鬼, 笨蛋〔尤兒語〕

wee·ny /ˈwinɪ; ˈwiːni/ *BrE*【英】, **weensie** /ˈwinzɪ; ˈwiːnzi/ *AmE*【美】*adj spoken* extremely small【口】極小的 —see also 另見 TEENY WEENY

weep /wip; wiːp/ *v past tense and past participle* **wept** /wɛpt; wept/ **1** [I,T] *formal or literary to* cry, especially because you feel very sad【正式或文】〔尤因悲傷〕哭泣, 流淚: *James broke down and wept.* 詹姆斯控制不住感情, 哭了起來。| **weep bitterly** (=cry a lot) 大哭 **2 I could have wept** *spoken* used to say that you felt very disappointed about something【口】〔對某事〕大失所望: *I could have wept when we lost by one point.* 我們輸了一分時, 我大失所望。**3** [I] if a wound weeps, liquid comes out of it〔傷口〕滲出液體 —**weep** *n* [singular]

weep·ie /ˈwipɪ; ˈwiːpi/ *n* [C] another spelling of WEEPY² weepy² 的另一種拼法

weep·ing /ˈwipɪŋ; ˈwiːpɪŋ/ *adj* **weeping willow/birch etc** a tree with branches that hang down towards the ground 垂柳/樹枝低垂的白樺等

weep·y¹ /ˈwipɪ; ˈwiːpi/ *adj informal* tending to cry a lot【非正式】動不動就哭的, 眼淚汪汪的: *feeling emotionally exhausted and weepy* 覺得感情崩潰, 只想哭

weepy², weepie *n* [C] *informal* a film or story that seems to be deliberately intended to make you cry【非正式】〔電影或故事〕催人淚下的

wee·vil /ˈwivl̩; ˈwiːvəl/ *n* [C] a small insect that spoils grain, flour etc by eating it〔吃穀物、麵粉等的〕象甲, 象鼻蟲

wee-wee /ˈ· ·/ *v* [I] *spoken* a word meaning to pass water from your body, used by or to children; URINATE【口】尿尿, 撒尿〔兒語〕—**wee-wee** *n* [singular, U]

weft /wɛft; weft/ *n* **the weft** *technical* the threads in a piece of cloth that are woven across the threads that go from top to bottom; WOOF²【術語】緯, 緯紗 —compare 比較 WARP² (1)

weigh /we; weɪ/ *v*

1 ►BE A PARTICULAR WEIGHT 有一定重量◄ [linking verb 連繫動詞] to have a particular weight 重〔若干〕, 重量是...: *Our Christmas turkey weighed 16 pounds.* 我們的聖誕火雞重16磅。| *How much do you weigh?* 你體重是多少?

2 ►MEASURE THE WEIGHT 測出重量◄ [T] to use a

W

machine to find out what something or someone weighs 稱…的重量: *Have you weighed yourself lately?* 你最近稱過體重嗎?

3 weigh a ton to be very heavy 非常重: *These books weigh a ton!* 這些書真重!

4 ▶CONSIDER/COMPARE 斟酌/比較◀ [T] to consider something carefully so that you can make a decision about it 認真考慮〔某事〕; 權衡: *Tim weighed the alternatives in his mind.* 蒂莫在腦中權衡着可能的選擇。| **weigh sth against sth** *We have to weigh the costs of the new system against the benefits it will bring.* 我們在衡量新系統帶來的好處時, 必須考慮到它的費用。—see also 另見 **weigh up** (WEIGH)

5 weigh your words to think very carefully about what you say because you do not want to say the wrong thing 〔因不想說錯話而〕字斟句酌, 推敲

6 ▶INFLUENCE 影響◀ [I always+adv/prep] *formal* to influence a result or decision【正式】(對結局或決定)有影響: **[+with]** *Her evidence weighed quite strongly with the judge.* 法官非常重視她的證詞。| **weigh against/in favour of** *a new argument that weighed heavily in Mark's favour* 對馬克非常有利的新論據

7 weigh anchor to raise an ANCHOR and sail away 起錨; 啟航

weigh sb/sth ↔ **down** *phr v* [T usually passive 一般用被動態] **1** to make someone or something bend or feel heavy under a load 使〔某人〕感到沉重; 壓彎〔某物〕, 壓下, 壓倒: *Sally was weighed down with shopping bags.* 莎莉提着購物袋頗感費力。**2** to feel worried about a problem or difficulty 〔因問題[困難]而〕感到焦慮: *a family weighed down with grief* 因悲傷而感到沮喪的家庭

weigh in *phr v* [I] **1** to have your weight tested before taking part in a fight or a horse race 〔拳擊手或騎師在賽前〕稱體重 —see also 另見 WEIGH-IN **2 weigh in (with)** *informal* to add a remark to a discussion or an argument【非正式】〔討論或爭辯時〕提出〔論點〕: *Each member weighed in with their own opinion.* 每個成員都提出了各自的觀點。

weigh on sb/sth *phr v* [T] to make someone worried or give them problems 使〔某人〕煩惱; 使陷入困境: *Yvonne's responsibilities were beginning to weigh on her.* 伊芳承擔的責任開始使她憂愁。| **weigh on sb's mind** *I'm sure there's something weighing on his mind.* 我肯定他有心事。| **weigh heavily** *responsibilities that weighed heavily on young shoulders* 在年輕肩膀上壓着的重擔

weigh sth ↔ **out** *phr v* [T] to measure an amount of something by weight 稱出〔某物的〕重量: *I watched as he weighed out half a pound of coffee beans and ground them up.* 我看着他稱出半磅咖啡豆, 並將它磨碎。

weigh sb/sth **up** *phr v* [T] **1** to consider a choice carefully so that you can make a decision 仔細考慮, 權衡: *We're just weighing up the pros and cons of the two deals.* 我們正在仔細考慮兩筆交易的利弊。**2** to form an opinion about someone by watching them, talking to them etc 〔通過觀察、談話等〕評估〔某人〕: *I can't quite weigh Marilyn up.* 我弄不清瑪里琳的為人。

weigh·bridge /ˈweˌbrɪdʒ; ˈweɪˌbrɪdʒ/ *n* [C] a machine for weighing vehicles and their loads, with a flat area that you drive the vehicle onto 〔稱車輛的〕橋秤, 地磅

weigh-in /ˈ· ·/ *n* [C usually singular 一般用單數] a check on the weight of a BOXER (1) or a JOCKEY¹ before a fight or a horserace 〔拳擊手或騎師在賽前的〕稱體重 —see also 另見 **weigh in** (WEIGH)

1 **weight¹** /wet; weɪt/ *n*

2 **1 ▶WHAT SB/STH WEIGHS** 某人/某物的重量◀ [C, U] how heavy something is when measured by a particular system 〔某物的〕重量: *The average weight of a baby at birth is just over seven pounds.* 嬰兒出生時的平均重量僅僅高於七磅。

2 ▶HOW FAT 有多胖◀ [U] how heavy and especially how fat someone is 〔某人的〕體重〔尤指肥胖〕: *A lot of teenage girls are obsessed about their weight.* 許多少女為體重所困擾。| **put on weight** (=get fatter) 體重增加 | **lose weight** (=get thinner) 體重減輕 | **watch your weight** (=be careful about what you eat so that you do not get fat) 節食減肥 | **have a weight problem** (=be too fat) 體重過重, 太胖 —see also 另見 OVER-WEIGHT; UNDERWEIGHT

3 ▶HEAVINESS 重◀ [U] the fact of being heavy 重: *The weight of her boots made it hard for Sue to run.* 蘇穿着沉重的靴子, 很難奔跑。| **under the weight of** (=supporting something heavy) 在…的重壓下 *Karen staggered along under the weight of her backpack.* 卡倫背着沉重的背包, 蹣跚而行。

4 ▶HEAVY THING 重物◀ [C] something that is heavy 重東西: *Omar can't lift heavy weights because of his bad back.* 奥馬爾因背部有毛病, 提不起重東西。

5 ▶FOR MEASURING QUANTITIES 測量分量◀ [C] a piece of metal weighing a particular amount that is balanced against something else to measure what it weighs 砝碼, 秤砣

6 ▶FOR EXERCISE 用於鍛鍊◀ [C] a piece of metal that weighs a certain amount and is lifted by people who want bigger muscles or who are competing in lifting competitions 槓鈴 —see also 另見 WEIGHTLIFTING

7 ▶SYSTEM 制度◀ [C,U] a system of standard measures of weight 重量單位制; 衡制: *metric weight* 公衡制 | *weights and measures* 度量衡

8 ▶RESPONSIBILITY/WORRY 責任/憂慮◀ [C] something that causes you a lot of worry 重壓, 負擔: **[+on]** *Since Jane's been sick, I've had to carry the full weight of running the school.* 自從簡生病以來, 我不得不承擔起管理學校的全部重任。

9 a weight off your mind something that solves a problem and makes you feel happier 除去心理負擔: *Selling the house was a great weight off my mind.* 賣掉房子去掉了我心頭的一塊大石。

10 ▶IMPORTANCE 重要性◀ [U] the influence or importance that something has when you are forming a judgment or opinions 〔作出判斷或形成意見時某物的〕影響; 重要性: *The weight of evidence against her led to her conviction.* 對她不利的重要證據致使她被定罪。| **carry weight** (=have influence) 有影響 *Una's opinion doesn't carry much weight around here.* 尤納的意見在這裡沒有多少影響。| **add weight to** *His declining health added weight to the argument that the king should abdicate.* 國王身體日趨衰弱, 這更加證明他應該退位這種說法是對的。| **attach weight to** (=think that something is important) 重視

11 throw your weight about/around *informal* to use your position of authority to tell people what to do in an unpleasant and unreasonable way【非正式】指手畫腳; 濫用權勢

12 throw your weight behind to use all your power and influence to support someone 〔用權力和影響力〕支持〔某人〕: *The US has thrown its weight behind the new leader.* 美國利用其影響支持這位新領導人。

13 pull your weight to do your full share of work 做好分內事: *Some people in the office hadn't been pulling their weight.* 辦公室裡有些人沒有盡本分做好工作。

14 take the weight off your feet *spoken* used to tell someone to sit down【口】坐下: *Come in, take the weight off your feet.* 進來, 坐坐吧。

15 weight of numbers the combined strength, influence etc of a large group 〔一個大羣體〕聯合起來的勢力[影響]: *They are likely to win this battle through sheer weight of numbers.* 他們純靠人多勢眾可能贏得這場戰鬥。

16 summer-weight/winter-weight a piece of clothing that is summer-weight or winter-weight, is made of material that is suitable for summer or winter 夏服/冬裝〔用適合夏天或冬天穿的布料縫製〕

17 ▶SCIENCE 科學◀ [C,U] *technical* the amount of

force with which an object is pulled down by GRAVITY (1)【術語】〔作用在物體上的〕重力 —see also 另見 **dead weight** (DEAD¹ (29))

weight² *v* [T] to add something heavy to something or put a weight on it, especially in order to keep it in place 加重量於〔某物, 以使穩固不動〕, 使變重: *fishing nets weighted with lead* 墜有鉛錘的魚網

weight·ed /ˈwetɪd; ˈweɪtɪ̈d/ *adj* **weighted in favour/against** producing conditions that are favourable or unfavourable to one particular group〔對某集團〕有利/不利的: **[+against]** *The voting system is weighted against the smaller parties.* 這種選舉制度對小黨派不利。| **weighted in favour of** *a pay increase heavily weighted in favour of the lower paid staff* 對低收入人員很有利的加薪

weight·ing /ˈwetɪŋ; ˈweɪtɪŋ/ *n* [singular, U] *BrE* additional money that you get paid because of the high cost of living in a particular area【英】〔因生活在某個生活費用高的地區而得到的〕額外津貼: *a London weighting* 倫敦地區的額外補貼

weight·less /ˈwetlɪs; ˈweɪtləs/ *adj* having no weight, especially when you are floating in space or water〔尤指在太空或水中〕失重的; 沒有重量的 —**weightlessly** *adv* —**weightlessness** *n* [U]

weight·lift·ing /ˈwet,lɪftɪŋ; ˈweɪt,lɪftɪŋ/ *n* [U] **1** the sport of lifting specially shaped weights (WEIGHT¹ (6)) 舉重運動 **2** also 又作 **weight training** *BrE* the activity of lifting specially shaped weights as a form of exercise【英】舉重〔鍛鍊〕—**weightlifter** *n* [C]

weight·y /ˈwetɪ; ˈweɪti/ *adj* **1** important and serious 重要的; 嚴肅的: *weighty reasons for change* 改變的重要理由 **2** *especially literary* heavy【尤文】沉重的 —**weightily** *adv* —**weightiness** *n* [U]

weir /wɪr; wɪə/ *n* [C] **1** a low structure built across a river or stream to control the flow of water 攔河壩, 堰 **2** a wooden fence built across a stream to make a pool where you can catch fish 魚梁〔溪流上用以捕魚的木柵欄〕

2 **weird** /wɪrd; wɪəd/ *adj* **1** *informal* unusual and different from anything you have seen or heard before; BIZARRE【非正式】古怪的, 奇異的: *Mike's got a really weird sense of humour.* 邁克有一種怪異的幽默感。| **weird and wonderful** *Tom's full of weird and wonderful ideas.* 湯姆滿腦子稀奇古怪的念頭。**2** very strange, mysterious, or frightening 非常奇怪的; 神祕的; 可怕的: *A weird green glow lit the sky.* 神祕的綠光照亮了天空。—**weirdly** *adv* —**weirdness** *n* [U]

weird·o /ˈwɪrdo; ˈwɪədəʊ/ also 又作 **weird·ie** /ˈwɪrdɪ; ˈwɪədi/ *n* [C] *informal* someone who behaves strangely, wears unusual clothes etc【非正式】〔行為、衣着等〕怪異的人: *Jenny's going out with a real weirdo.* 珍妮正和一個十分古怪的人交往。

welch /wɛltʃ; welʃ/ *v* [I] another spelling of WELSH² welsh² 的另一種拼法

3 2 **wel·come¹** /ˈwɛlkəm; ˈwelkəm/ *v* [T] **1** to say hello in a friendly way to someone who has just arrived 歡迎〔剛到達的人〕: *The Queen welcomed the President as he got off the plane.* 總統走下飛機, 女王上前迎接。**2** to accept an idea, suggestion etc happily 樂於接受〔某種思想、建議等〕: *Henri doesn't welcome intrusions into his privacy.* 亨利不希望有人干擾他的私生活。| *The college welcomes applications from people of all races.* 學院歡迎任何種族的人申請入學。**3 welcome sb/sth with open arms a)** to be very glad that someone has come 熱情歡迎某人的到來 **b)** to be very happy to accept something 樂於接受某事

2 3 **welcome²** *adj* **1** someone who is welcome is gladly accepted in a place〔某人〕受歡迎的: *I had the feeling I wasn't really welcome.* 我感覺到我其實不受歡迎。| **make sb welcome** (=make someone feel that you are pleased they have come) 使人感到受歡迎; 款待某人 **2** something that is welcome is pleasant and enjoyable, especially because it is just what you need or want〔某物尤因正需要而〕令人愉悦的: *a welcome break from the pressures of work* 及時的從工作壓力中解脱出來的休息 | *A cup of tea would be very welcome.* 來杯茶非常不錯。**3 be welcome to** *spoken* used to say that someone can have something if they want it, because you certainly do not want it【口】可以隨意擁有〔某物, 因為説話者不需要〕: *If Rob wants that job he's welcome to it!* 羅布如果想要那份工作, 就請他隨時來吧！**4 be welcome to do sth** *spoken* used to invite someone to do something if they would like to【口】可隨意做某事〔用於邀請某人做某事〕: *You're welcome to stay for lunch.* 你用不着客氣, 請留下來吃午飯。**5 you're welcome!** *spoken, especially AmE* a polite way of replying to someone who has just thanked you for something【口, 尤美】不用謝; 別客氣〔用於回答別人的感謝〕: *"Thanks for the coffee." "You're welcome."* "謝謝你的咖啡。" "別客氣。"

welcome³ *n* [C] **1** a greeting you give to someone when they arrive 歡迎, 迎接: *Mandela got a tremendous welcome at the airport.* 曼德拉在機場受到熱烈歡迎。| **extend a welcome to** *formal* (=welcome someone)【正式】歡迎某人 **2 give sb/sth a warm welcome a)** to welcome someone in a very friendly way 熱烈歡迎某人 **b)** to gladly accept an idea, suggestion etc 欣然接受〔意見、建議等〕**3 outstay/overstay your welcome** to stay at someone's house longer than they want you to 因作客時間太久而不再受歡迎

welcome⁴ *interjection* **1** an expression of greeting to a guest or someone who has just arrived 歡迎〔用於對客人或剛剛到達的人表示歡迎〕: **[+to]** *Welcome to London!* 歡迎到倫敦來！| *Welcome back – it's good to see you again.* 歡迎歸來 —— 再次見到你很高興。| **welcome home** (=used when someone has been away and returns home) 歡迎你回家 **2 welcome to the club** *spoken* used to make someone feel better when they are in a bad situation, by telling them you are already in that situation【口】彼此彼此〔用來安慰某人, 指大家都倒霉〕

welcome wag·on /ˈ.. ,../ *n* [C] *AmE* someone or something that welcomes someone who has just arrived in a new place【美】歡迎新來的人[物]: *The company is bringing out the welcome wagon for the new sales recruits.* 公司為新推銷員舉行迎新活動。

wel·com·ing /ˈwɛlkəmɪŋ; ˈwelkəmɪŋ/ *adj* a person or place that is welcoming makes you feel happy and relaxed when you meet them or arrive there〔人或地方〕殷勤的, 親切的; 賞心悦目的: *a welcoming smile* 迎人笑臉 | *The room was bright and welcoming.* 房間明亮如晝, 令人心曠神怡。| **welcoming committee/party** (=group of people who welcome someone) 歡迎委員會/迎賓會

weld¹ /wɛld; weld/ *v* **1** [I,T] to join metals by melting them and pressing them together when they are hot, or to be joined in this way 焊接〔金屬〕, 熔接 **2** [T always+adv/prep] to join or unite people into a single, strong group 使〔人〕團結〔成一個強大集體〕: *A person of vision was needed to weld the various political factions together.* 需要一個有遠見卓識的人把各個政治派別團結起來。—compare 比較 FORGE¹ (3), SOLDER²

weld² *n* [C] a joint that is made by welding two pieces of metal 焊接點[處]

weld·er /ˈwɛldɚ; ˈweldə/ *n* [C] someone whose job is to weld things 焊工

wel·fare /ˈwɛl,fɛr; ˈwelfeə/ *n* [U] **1** health, comfort, and happiness; WELL-BEING 幸福, 健康; 福祉: *Our only concern is the children's welfare.* 我們唯一關心的是孩子的幸福。**2** help that is provided, especially by government organizations for people with social or financial problems〔尤指政府機構提供的〕福利: *The company's welfare officer deals with employees' personal problems.* 公司負責福利的工作人員處理雇員的個人問題。| *welfare services* 福利機構 **3** *especially AmE* money paid by the government to people who are very poor, unemployed etc【尤美】〔政府對窮人、失業者等發放的〕救濟金: **on welfare** *Most of the people in this neighborhood are on welfare.* 這住宅區的大多數人都領取福利救濟。—compare 比較 SOCIAL SECURITY

welfare state /,.. '.·/ *n* **1 the welfare state** a system by which the government provides money, free medical care etc for people who are unemployed or too old to work 福利制度 **2** [C] a country with such a system 福利國家

wel·far·is·m /ˈwɛl,fɛrɪzm̩; ˈwelfeərɪzəm/ *n* [U] a way of life in which someone does not work, but accepts money from the government and makes no attempt to improve their situation 福利生活〔指一個人不工作, 而接受政府救濟, 卻不想改變這種狀況〕, 福利主義

wel·kin /ˈwɛlkɪn; ˈwelkɪn/ *n poetical* the sky【詩】蒼穹

we'll /wɪl; wil; *strong* 強讀 wil; wiːl/ the short form of 縮略式= we will or 或 we shall

well¹ /wɛl; wel/ *adv comparative* 比較級 **better** *superlative* 最高級 **best**

1 ▶SATISFACTORILY 滿意地◀ in a successful or satisfactory way 順利地; 令人滿意地: *Did you sleep well?* 你睡得好嗎? | *James reads well for his age.* 對詹姆斯這個年齡來說, 他的閱讀能力算不錯了。| **fairly/moderately/pretty well** (=quite well) 不錯/還可以/相當好 | **go well** (=happen in the way you planned or hoped) 成功〔與計劃或期望的一樣〕*I was really pleased that the concert had gone so well.* 音樂會辦得如此成功, 我真高興。

2 well-organized/well-educated etc organized, educated etc to a high standard 組織完善的/受過良好教育的等

3 do well a) to be successful, especially in work or business〔尤指工作或生意〕成功: *Elizabeth's done well for herself – a well-paid job, a nice house and a sports car.* 伊莉莎白事業有成 —— 高薪的工作、美好的住房, 還有跑車。**b)** if someone who has been ill is doing well, they are becoming healthy again〔病人〕康復: *The operation was successful and the patient is doing well.* 手術成功, 病人正在康復中。

4 ▶THOROUGHLY 徹底地◀ in a thorough way 徹底地, 充分地: *Mix the flour and butter well.* 把麵粉和黃油攪拌好。

5 as well as in addition to something else 又, 也, 還: *They own a house in Provence as well as a villa in Spain.* 他們在普羅旺斯有一棟房子, 在西班牙也有一座別墅。| **as well as doing sth** *The organization encourages members to meet on a regular basis, as well as providing them with financial support.* 該機構鼓勵成員經常聚會, 還給他們提供財政支持。

6 as well in addition to something or someone else〔除某事或某人外〕還: *We're going to the cinema tonight, why don't you come along as well?* 我們今晚去看電影, 你為甚麼不一起去?

7 may/might/could well do/be sth used to say that something is likely to happen or is likely to be true〔表示某事〕可能發生; 可能真實: *What you say may well be true.* 你說的或許是真實的。| *You could try the drugstore, but it may well be closed by now.* 你可以到藥店去試試, 但是現在它可能關門了。

8 may/might/could (just) as well do sth a) *informal* used when you do not particularly want to do something but you decide to do it【非正式】〔做某事〕倒也無妨〔用於表示做不大想做的事〕: *I suppose we may as well get started.* 我想我們不妨開始吧。**b)** used to mean that another course of action would have an equally good result 倒不如..., 還是...較好〔用於表示另一個行動也可能產生相同的好結果〕: *The taxi was so slow, we might just as well have gone on the bus.* 計程車開得那麼慢, 我們還不如乘公共汽車呢。

9 ▶EMPHASIZING STH 強調某事◀ **a) well before/behind/down etc** a long way or a long time before, behind etc〔很長一段時間或路程〕以前/以後等: *It was well after 12 o'clock when they arrived.* 12點過了好一陣子他們才到。| *Stand well back from the bonfire.* 站得離篝火遠遠的。**b) well pleased/well aware etc** very pleased etc 非常滿意/充分了解等: *I'm well aware of the problems involved.* 我充分了解所涉及的問題。| *Pardoe was well pleased with his day's work.* 帕多對自己一天的工作感到很滿意。| **well worth (doing) sth** *The amphitheatre is well worth a visit.* 圓形露天競技場很值得一看。**c)** [+adj] *BrE spoken* used to emphasize an adjective that describes how someone feels or what sort of situation they are in【英口】相當, 很〔強調某人感情或所處形勢的形容詞〕: *Our boss came out of the meeting looking well fed-up.* 我們老闆帶着很厭倦的表情走出會場。**d) well and truly** completely 完全地: *I went out and got well and truly drunk.* 我到外面喝得酩酊大醉。

10 know full well to know or realize something very well〔對某事〕十分了解: *You know full well what I mean.* 你完全清楚我的意思。

11 speak/think well of to talk about someone in an approving way or to have a favourable opinion of them 稱讚〔某人〕/重視〔某人〕: *Sue has always spoken well of you.* 蘇經常稱讚你。

12 well done!/well played! used to praise someone when you think they have done something very well 幹得好! 真棒!〔用於讚揚某人做事做得好〕

13 be well in with *informal* to have a friendly relationship with someone, especially someone important【非正式】〔尤指同要人〕關係密切: *Paul's well in with the boss these days.* 保羅這段日子跟老闆很要好。

14 be well out of *BrE spoken* to be lucky to no longer be involved in a particular situation【英口】幸而不受牽連; 幸而擺脫了: *She's well out of that marriage, her husband was a brute!* 她的婚姻幸好結束了, 她丈夫是個惡棍!

15 be well up in/on *informal especially BrE* to know a lot about a particular subject【非正式, 尤英】對〔某個科目〕非常熟悉: *Geoff's well up on the latest technological developments.* 傑弗對最新的科技發展瞭如指掌。

16 as well sb might/may used to say that there is a good reason for someone's feelings or reactions〔某人〕原該如此〔用於表示某人的感受或行為有充分的理由〕: *Marilyn looked guilty when she saw me, as well she might.* 瑪麗蓮見到我時顯得感到內疚 —— 本該如此。

17 do well by *informal* to treat someone generously【非正式】慷慨對待〔某人〕

well² *interjection* 

1 ▶EMPHASIZING STH 強調某事◀ used before a statement or question to emphasize it 好, 嗯〔用在陳述或問題之前以示強調〕: *Well, I think it's a good idea, I don't care what anyone else says.* 好, 我覺得這是一個好主意, 我不在乎別人說甚麼。| *Well, all I can say is it's a bloody waste of taxpayer's money!* 是啊, 我只能說, 這是對納稅人的錢的極大浪費! | **well then** *"James doesn't want to come to the cinema with us." "Well then, let's go on our own."* "詹姆斯不想和我們一起去看電影。" "那麼我們就自己去吧。"

2 ▶PAUSING 停頓◀ used to pause or give yourself time to think before saying something 唔, 噢〔用於停頓片刻或使自己在說某事前有時間考慮〕: *Mary's been a bit depressed and, well, I was worried she might do something stupid.* 瑪莉有點沮喪, 哦, 我擔心她也許會幹甚麼傻事。| *Well, let's see now, I could book you in for an appointment next Thursday.* 嗯, 我們看一下, 我能給你預約在下星期四。| **well I mean** *Well, I mean the whole idea just sounds crazy to me.* 唉, 我是說整個想法聽起來真是不可思議。

3 ▶ACCEPTING A SITUATION 接受某種局面◀ also 又作 **oh well** used to show that you accept a situation even though you feel disappointed or annoyed about it 好吧; 算了〔對不愉快的事表示接受〕: *Well, I did my best, I can't do any more than that.* 算了, 我已經盡力, 不能做得比這更好了。| *Oh well, we'll just have to cancel*

W

the holiday I suppose. 唉，算了，我想我們不得不取消這次休假。

4 ►SHOWING SURPRISE 表示驚訝◄ also 又作 **well, well (,well)** used to express surprise or amusement 哎呀，喲〔表示驚訝或興趣〕：*Well, so Steve's a senior manager now is he?* 喲，這麼説史蒂夫現在是高級經理了？| *Well, well, well, I didn't think I'd see you here Sue.* 哎呀，哎呀，我沒有想到在這裡見到你，蘇。

5 ►SHOWING ANGER 表示生氣◄ used to express anger or disapproval 嗯，噯〔表示生氣或不同意〕：*Well, you'd think at least she might have phoned to say she wasn't coming!* 嗯，本以為她至少會打電話來説她不來了！| **well honestly/well really** *"They were playing music next door until 4 a.m." "Well honestly, you'd think they'd show a bit more consideration."* "隔壁鄰居播放音樂到淩晨四點。" "説實在的，本以為他們會顧及一下別人。"

6 ►FINAL REMARK 結束語◄ used to show that you are about to finish speaking or stop doing an activity 好了，好啦〔表示結束發言或停止做某事〕：*Well, that's all for today, I'll see you all tomorrow.* 好啦，今天就到此為止，我們明天見。

7 ►EXPRESSING DOUBT 表示懷疑◄ used to express doubt or the fact that you are not sure about something 哦〔表示懷疑或對某事並無把握〕：*"I reckon Mike Whelan is worth a place in the England side." "Well, he's not a very consistent player is he?"* "我認為邁克·韋爾蘭應該入選英格蘭隊。" "哦，他的狀態不大穩定，對不?"

8 ►AGREEING 同意◄ **very well** used to show that you agree with or accept a suggestion, invitation etc 好吧〔表示同意或接受提議、邀請等〕：*"I think plain wallpaper would look better in this room." "Very well then, if you insist."* "我覺得這房間用素淨的壁紙較好。" "好吧，如果你堅持的話。"

9 ►CONTINUING A STORY 接續故事◄ used to connect two parts of a story that you are telling people especially in order to make it seem more interesting 對了，於是〔用以接續所説的兩部分，尤為使故事更有趣〕：*You know that couple I was telling you about the other day? Well, the police came round and arrested them both!* 你知道那天我告訴你的那對夫妻嗎?對了，警察來過並把他倆都抓走了！

10 ►DEMANDING AN EXPLANATION 要求解釋◄ **Well?** used to demand an explanation or answer when you are angry with someone 是嗎?〔生某人氣時，要求對方解釋或回答〕：*Mrs Hawkins says she saw you hanging around the town centre with some of your mates last night. Well?* 霍金斯太太説她昨晚看見你和幾個朋友在鎮中心蹓躂，是不是呢?

Frequencies of the word **well** in spoken and written English 單詞 well 在英語口語和書面語中的使用頻率

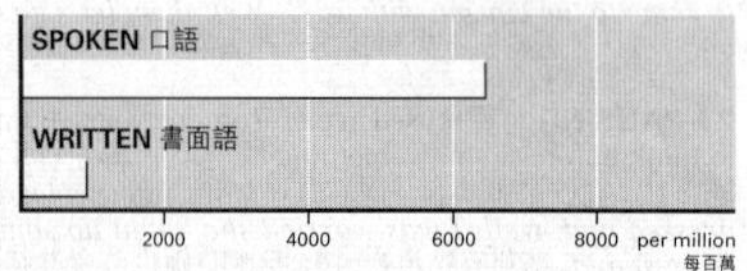

Based on the British National Corpus and the Longman Lancaster Corpus
據英國國家語料庫和朗文蘭卡斯特語料庫

This graph shows that **well** is much more common in spoken English than in written English. This is because it has several uses as an interjection in spoken English and is used in a lot of common spoken phrases.
本圖表顯示，單詞 well 在英語口語中的使用頻率遠遠高於書面語，因為作為感嘆詞，well 在口語中有幾種用法，並且口語中很多常用片語是由 well 構成的。

1 **well**[3] *adj comparative* 比較級 **better** /ˈbɛtə; ˈbetə/ *superlative* 最高級 **best** /bɛst; best/ **1** healthy 健康的：*"How are you?" "Very well thanks."* "你身體怎樣?" "很好，多謝關心。" | **look/feel well** *You're looking well, the vacation obviously did you good.* 你看來氣色不錯，很明顯，休假對你大有益處。| **get well soon** (=used to say that you hope someone soon feels better) 祝你早日恢復健康 **2 it is just as well (that)** *spoken* used to say that things have happened in a way that is fortunate or desirable【口】正好，幸好：*It's just as well I couldn't go to the funeral, I think I'd have found it too upsetting.* 幸好我不能去參加葬禮，我覺得葬禮太令人沮喪了。**3 it's/that's all very well but...** *spoken* used to say that you think something is not really satisfactory or acceptable, even if someone else thinks it is【口】...是好的，可是...〔表示對某事不真正滿意或接受〕：*"They said Maria should go to bed and rest." "That's all very well but who's going to look after the children?"* "他們説瑪麗亞應上牀休息。" "好倒是好，可是誰去照料孩子呢?" **4 it might be as well** *spoken* used to give someone advice or make a helpful suggestion【口】最好...〔給某人勸告或提出有用的意見〕：*It might be as well to leave him on his own for a few hours.* 最好讓他獨自待上幾個鐘頭。**5 that's/it's all well and good** *spoken especially BrE* used to say that you accept or approve of one part of a situation or thing but not of another part【口，尤英】固然好〔表示對某情況或事情部分接受或同意〕：*Going off on foreign holidays is all well and good but you've got to get back to reality sometime.* 到國外度假固然好，但日後你必須回到現實中來。**6 all is well/all is not well** *formal used* to say that a situation is satisfactory or not satisfactory【正式】〔情況〕令人滿意／不滿意：*All is not well with their marriage.* 他們的婚姻不美滿。**7 all's well that ends well** used after a situation has ended in a satisfactory way 結果好就一切都好〔用於表示情況有令人滿意的結果〕 **8** [not before noun 不用於名詞前] *literary* happy and comfortable【文】滿意的；舒服的：*We're very well where we are thank you.* 我們待的地方很不錯，謝謝。

well[4] *n* [C] **1** a deep hole in the ground from which people take water 井：*She lowered her bucket into the well.* 她把水桶放到井裡。| **sink a well** (=dig a well) 掘井 **2** an OIL WELL 油井 **3** an enclosed space in a building which goes straight up and down and surrounds a lift, stairs etc〔建築物中的〕電梯井道；樓梯井 —see also 另見 STAIRWELL **4** *BrE* the space in front of a judge in a court of law【英】〔法庭中位於法官前面的〕律師席

well[5] *v* also 又作 **well up** [I] *especially literary*【尤文】 **1** if liquids well or well up, they start to flow〔液體〕湧溢，開始流淌：*I felt tears well up in my eyes.* 我意識到淚水奪眶而出。**2** if feelings well or well up, they start to get stronger〔情緒〕變得強烈：*Anger welled up within him.* 他怒火中燒。

well-ad·just·ed /ˌ· ·ˈ··◄/ *adj* emotionally healthy and able to deal well with the problems of life 能適應環境的，性格健全的

well-ad·vised /ˌ· ·ˈ·◄/ *adj* **you would be well-advised to do sth** used when you are strongly advising someone to do something that will help them avoid trouble 你應該做某事〔用於強烈忠告某人做某事，以避免麻煩〕：*You would be well-advised to accept this settlement rather than go to court.* 你應該接受這種解決辦法而不是對簿公堂。

well-ap·point·ed /ˌ· ·ˈ··◄/ *adj formal* a well-appointed house, hotel etc has very good furniture and equipment【正式】〔房屋、旅館等〕設備完善的；陳設齊全的

well-bal·anced /ˌ· ˈ··◄/ *adj* **1** a well-balanced meal or DIET[1] (1) contains all the things you need to keep you healthy〔飲食〕營養均衡的 **2** a well-balanced person is sensible and is not controlled by strong emotions; STABLE[1] (2)〔人〕理智的；頭腦清醒的

well-be·haved /ˌ· ·ˈ·◄/ *adj* behaving in a polite or socially acceptable way 行為端正的；彬彬有禮的：*a well-*

behaved child 行為端正的孩子 | *The crowd was noisy but well-behaved.* 這羣人吵吵鬧鬧, 但循規蹈矩。

well-be·ing /,· '··/ *n* [U] a feeling of being comfortable, healthy, and happy 舒適; 健康; 幸福: **[+of]** *We are responsible for the care and well-being of patients.* 我們負責照顧病人, 為病人的健康負責。| **physical/social/economic etc well-being** *the economic well-being of the country* 該國的經濟繁榮 | **a sense of well-being** (=a feeling of being satisfied with your life) 幸福的感覺

well-born /,· '·◂/ *adj formal* born into a rich or UPPER CLASS family【正式】出身優裕的; 出身高貴的

well-bred /,· '·◂/ *adj old-fashioned* very polite, behaving or speaking as if you come from a family of high social class【過時】有修養的, 有教養的: *the epitome of a well-bred Englishwoman who never shows her feelings* 感情含蓄、教養良好的英國淑女的典範

well-brought-up /,· · '·◂/ *adj* a child who is well-brought-up has been taught to be polite and to behave well〔兒童〕從小受良好教育的

well-built /,· '·◂/ *adj* someone who is well-built is big and strong 體格健壯的, 結實的

well-cho·sen /,· '··◂/ *adj* carefully chosen 精心挑選的: **well-chosen words** (=suitable for a particular situation) 恰如其分的話語

well-con·nect·ed /,· ·'··◂/ *adj* knowing or being related to powerful and socially important people 與顯貴人物有關係的, 和有社會地位的人有來往的

well-dis·posed /,· ·'·◂/ *adj* feeling friendly towards a person or positive about an idea or plan〔對人〕親切的;〔對想法或計劃〕表示贊同的: **[+to/towards]** *The management is not well-disposed towards technical innovation.* 資方對技術革新不予支持。

well-doc·u·ment·ed /ˌwɛl ˋdɑkjəmɛntɪd; ˌwel-ˈdɒkjʊmentɪd/ *adj* well-documented events, behaviour etc definitely exist and people have written a lot about them〔確實存在的事件、行為等〕被大量記述的: *the well-documented problems faced by prisoners' families* 歷歷可考的犯人家庭面對的問題

well-done /,· '·◂/ *adj* food that is well-done, especially meat, has been cooked thoroughly〔尤指肉〕熟透的, 煮透的 —compare 比較 RARE (2) —see also 另見 **well done!** (WELL[1] (12))

well-dressed /,· '·◂/ *adj* wearing attractive, fashionable, and usually expensive clothes 衣着考究的, 穿着入時的

well-earned /,· '·◂/ *adj* something that is well-earned is something you deserve because you have worked hard 應得的: *It's time for a well-earned rest.* 這是應該有的休息。

well-en·dowed /,· ·'·◂/ *adj informal or humorous*【非正式或幽默】**1** a woman who is well-endowed has large breasts〔婦女〕乳房大的 **2** a man who is well-endowed has a large PENIS (=sex organ)〔男人〕生殖器大的

well-es·tab·lished /,· ·'··◂/ *adj* established for a long time and respected 歷史悠久、享有盛譽的: *a well-established law firm* 久負盛名的律師事務所

well-fa·voured /,· '··◂/ *adj old-fashioned* good-looking【過時】好看的, 漂亮的 —compare 比較 ILL-FAVOURED

well-fed /,· '·◂/ *adj* regularly eating plenty of good healthy food, especially if this has made you a little fat 吃得好的; 胖胖的

well-found·ed /,· '··◂/ *adj* a belief, feeling etc that is well-founded is based on facts or good judgment〔信仰、感覺等〕有事實根據的; 基於準確判斷的

well-groomed /,· '·◂/ *adj* having a very neat, clean appearance 穿戴整潔的: *a well-groomed businesswoman* 穿着整齊的女商人

well-ground·ed /,· '··◂/ *adj* **1 well-grounded in** fully trained in an activity or skill〔行動或技巧〕訓練有素的: *The soldiers were well-grounded in survival skills.* 士兵們的求生技能熟練。**2** WELL-FOUNDED 有充分根據的: *well-grounded suspicions* 有憑有據的懷疑

well-heeled /,· '·◂/ *adj informal* rich and usually of a high social class【非正式】富裕的; 有社會地位的

well-hung /,· '·◂/ *adj informal or humorous* a man who is well-hung has a large PENIS (=sex organ)【非正式或幽默】〔男人〕陰莖很大的

wel·lie /ˋwɛlɪ; ˈweli/ *n* [C] *BrE informal* a wellington【英, 非正式】防水橡膠靴 —see also 另見 WELLY

well-in·formed /,· ·'·◂/ *adj* knowing a lot about a particular subject or about many subjects〔對某一問題〕非常熟悉的;〔在數門學科上〕知識淵博的: **[+about]** *They seemed to be remarkably well-informed about the royal family.* 他們似乎對皇室家庭的事情知之甚多。

wel·ling·ton /ˋwɛlɪŋtən; ˈwelɪŋtən/ also 又作 **wellington boot** /,··· '·/ *n* [C] *BrE* a long rubber boot that stops your feet getting wet; RUBBER BOOT【英】長統橡膠雨靴, 防水橡膠靴 —see picture at 參見 BOOT[1] 圖

well-in·ten·tioned /,· ·'··◂/ *adj* trying to be helpful, but failing or actually making things worse 出於好心的〔但結果失敗〕: *well-intentioned grandparents who interfere between parents and children* 一片好心, 在父母和孩子之間瞎攙和的祖父母

well-kept /,· '·◂/ *adj* **1** a well-kept building or garden is very well cared for and looks neat and clean〔建築物或花園〕悉心照管的 **2** a well-kept secret is known only to a few people〔祕密〕嚴守的

well-known /,· '·◂/ *adj* known by a lot of people 眾所周知的: *It's a well-known fact that smoking can cause lung cancer.* 眾所周知, 抽煙會引起肺癌。| *This is probably their best-known song.* 這可能是他們最著名的歌曲。| **[+for]** *Mother Teresa is well-known for her work with the poor.* 德蘭修女因為幫助窮人而聞名。—see 見 FAMOUS (USAGE)

well-man·nered /,· '··◂/ *adj* polite and having very good manners (MANNER (3)) 有禮貌的; 行為端正的: *the perfect well-mannered host* 完美無瑕、彬彬有禮的主人 —opposite 反義詞 ILL-MANNERED

well-mean·ing /,· '··◂/ *adj* intending or intended to be helpful, but not succeeding 本意良好的, 好心好意的〔但不成功〕: *a well-meaning but misguided attempt to reconcile the couple* 出於好意想使夫妻言歸於好但不明智的做法 —see also 另見 **he/she means well** (MEAN[1] (16))

well-meant /,· '·◂/ *adj* something you say or do that is well-meant is intended to be helpful, but does not have the result you intended〔說話或行動〕出於好意的〔但結果失敗〕: *His comments were well-meant but a little tactless.* 他說的話出於好意但太直率了。—see also 另見 **he/she means well** (MEAN[1] (16))

well·ness /ˋwɛlnɪs; ˈwelnɪs/ *n* [U] *AmE* the state of being healthy【美】健康: *a wellness program to promote a healthy lifestyle* 提倡健康生活方式的"健康"計劃

well-nigh /'· ·/ *adv BrE formal or AmE* almost, but not quite【英, 正式或美】幾乎, 近乎: *The company has existed for well-nigh 200 years.* 公司成立近 200 年了。| **well-nigh impossible** *Getting them to agree would be well-nigh impossible.* 使他們同意幾乎不可能。

well-off /,· '·◂/ *adj comparative* 比較級 **better-off**, *superlative* 最高級 **best-off** **1** having more money than many other people, or enough money to have a good standard of living 有錢的; 境遇好的: *The government claims that people are better off than they were five years ago.* 政府聲稱人民的生活比五年前改善了。**2 well-off for** having plenty of something, or as much of it as you need〔某物〕充裕的, 有許多的: *We're well-off for supermarkets in this area.* 我們這個地區有許多超級市場。**3 you don't know when you're well-off** *spoken* used to tell someone that they are more fortunate than they realize【口】你身在福中不知福 —opposite 反義詞 BADLY-OFF

well-oiled /,· '·◂/ *adj* **1 a well-oiled machine** an organization or system that works very well〔機構或系統〕運作正常的 **2** *informal* drunk【非正式】喝醉的

well-paid /,· '·◂/ *adj* providing or receiving good wages 薪金優厚的, 高薪的: *a well-paid job* 高薪工作 | *well-*

paid managers 薪金豐厚的經理

well-pre·served /ˌ· ·ˈ·◂/ *adj humorous* someone who is well-preserved still looks fairly young although they are getting old【幽默】〔人〕身體保養得好的; 不見老的

well-read /ˈwɛlˋrɛd; ˌwel ˈred◂/ *adj* having read many books and knowing a lot about different subjects 博覽羣書的; 知識淵博的

well-round·ed /ˌ· ˈ··◂/ *adj* **1** someone who is well-rounded has had a wide variety of experiences in life 生活閱歷豐富的 **2** well-rounded education or experience of life is complete and varied〔教育或生活經驗〕全面的, 多方面的: *She has a well-rounded background in management.* 她在管理方面有豐富的經驗。**3** a woman who is well-rounded has a pleasantly curved figure; SHAPELY〔婦女的體型〕勻稱的; 豐滿的

well-spok·en /ˌ· ˈ··◂/ *adj* speaking in a clear and polite way, and with an ACCENT (=way of pronouncing words) that is socially approved of 談吐文雅的; 字正腔圓的

well·spring /ˈwɛlˌsprɪŋ; ˈwelˌsprɪŋ/ *n* [C+**of**] *literary* a never-ending supply of a personal quality【文】〔人的品性〕源源不斷的供應, 源泉: *There was a well-spring of courage within her which she could continually draw upon.* 在她身上有不竭的勇氣。

well-stacked /ˌ· ˈ·◂/ *adj informal or humorous* a woman who is well-stacked has very large breasts【非正式或幽默】乳房豐滿的

well-stocked /ˌ· ˈ·◂/ *adj* having a large supply and variety of things 備貨充足的; 貯貨豐富的: *a well-stocked pantry* 備貨充足的食品儲藏室

well-thought-of /ˌ· ˈ· ·◂/ *adj* liked and admired by other people 受人喜歡的; 受人尊敬的: *Her work is well-thought-of in academic circles.* 她的工作在學術界受到普遍好評。

well-thought-out /ˌ· · ˈ·◂/ *adj* carefully and thoroughly planned 縝密計劃的; 精心設計的: *a well-thought-out strategy* 深思熟慮的策略

well-thumbed /ˌ· ˈ·◂/ *adj* a well-thumbed book, magazine etc has been used a lot〔書籍、雜誌等〕翻舊了的, 常用的

well-timed /ˌ· ˈ·◂/*adj* said or done at the most suitable moment 時機合適的; 及時的: *My arrival wasn't very well-timed.* 我來得不太是時候。

well-to-do /ˌ· · ˈ·◂/ *adj* **1** rich and with a high social position 富有的; 有地位的: *well-to-do families* 有錢人家 **2 the well-to-do** people who are rich 富人

well-tried /ˌ· ˈ·◂/ *adj* **well-tried method/principle etc** a method or principle that has been used many times before and has always been successful 經反覆驗證、行之有效的方法/原理等

well-turned /ˌ· ˈ·◂/ *adj* a well-turned phrase or sentence is carefully expressed〔片語或句子〕措詞巧妙的

well-turned-out /ˌ· · ˈ·◂/ *adj* someone who is well-turned-out wears fashionable clothes and looks attractive 穿着入時的

well-versed /ˌ· ˈ·◂/ *adj* knowing a lot about something 精通的; 熟知的: [**+in/on**] *well-versed in matters of national security* 精通國家安全事務

well-wish·er /ˈ· ˌ··/ *n* [C] someone who does something to show that they admire someone and want them to succeed, be healthy etc 表示良好祝願的人, 祝福者: *many messages of support from well-wishers* 眾多來自祝福者表示支持的祝辭

well-wom·an /ˌ· ˈ··/ *adj* [only before noun 僅用於名詞前] providing medical care and advice for women, to make sure that they stay healthy 婦女保健的: *a well-woman clinic* 婦女保健診所

well-worn /ˌ· ˈ·◂/ *adj* **1** worn or used for a long time 穿舊了的; 使用了長時間的: *a well-worn jacket* 穿舊了的外衣 **2** a well-wom argument, phrase etc has been repeated so often that it is no longer interesting or effective〔理由、習語等〕陳腐的: *well-worn excuses* 陳腐的藉口

wel·ly /ˈwɛlɪ; ˈweli/ *n* [C] *BrE infomal*【英, 非正式】**1** a WELLINGTON (=kind of boot) 防水橡膠靴 **2 give it some welly!** *spoken* used to tell someone to put more effort into something they are doing【口】加油!努力幹!

Welsh /wɛlʃ; welʃ/ *n* **1** [U] the original language of Wales 威爾斯語 **2 the Welsh** people from Wales 威爾斯人 —**Welsh** *adj*

welsh, welch /wɛlʃ; welʃ/ *v* [I+**on**] *informal*【非正式】**1** to avoid paying money or your debts 賴賬; 躲債 **2** to not do something you have promised to do for someone〔對某人〕食言: *He gave us his solemn word and then he welshed on us.* 他對我們信誓旦旦, 然後卻翻悔。

USAGE NOTE 用法說明: WELSH
POLITENESS 禮節
Some Welsh people consider this verb to be offensive . 某些威爾斯人認為這個動詞具有冒犯性。

Welsh dres·ser /ˌ· ˈ··/ *n* [C] *BrE* a piece of wooden furniture consisting of drawers and cupboards in the lower part and shelves on top【英】〔下部為抽屜和碗櫥、上部為擱板的〕威爾斯式餐具櫃; HUTCH (2) *AmE*【美】

Welsh rare·bit /ˌwɛlʃ ˋrɛrbɪt; ˌwelʃ ˈreəbɪt/ also 又作 **Welsh rabbit** /ˌ· ˈ··/ *n* [C,U] a dish of cheese melted on bread 威爾斯乾酪烤麵包

welt /wɛlt; welt/ *n* [C] **1** a raised mark on someone's skin where they have been hit〔被打後的〕腫塊; 傷痕 **2** a piece of leather around the edge of a shoe, to which the top and bottom of the shoe are stitched〔鞋面和鞋底間的〕沿條, 貼邊

wel·ter /ˈwɛltɚ; ˈweltə/ *n* **a welter of** a large and confusing number of different details, emotions etc〔細節〕雜亂無章;〔思緒〕起伏: *The researchers were inundated with a welter of information.* 研究人員陷入一大堆雜亂無章的資料之中。

wel·ter·weight /ˈwɛltɚˌwet; ˈweltəweɪt/ *n* [C] a BOXER (1) who is heavier than a LIGHTWEIGHT[1] (2) but lighter than a MIDDLEWEIGHT 次中量級拳擊手

wench /wɛntʃ; wentʃ/ *n* [C] *old use or humorous* a girl or young woman, especially a servant【舊或幽默】姑娘, 少婦〔尤指女僕〕

wend /wɛnd; wend/ *v* **wend your way** *especially literary* to move or travel slowly from one place to another【尤文】緩慢地走[移動]: *The procession wended its way through the streets.* 隊伍緩緩地走過了街道。

wen·dy house /ˈwɛndɪ ˌhaus; ˈwendi ˌhaʊs/ *n* [C] *BrE* a small house for children to play in【英】兒童遊戲屋; PLAY HOUSE *AmE*【美】

Wens·ley·dale /ˈwɛnzlɪdel; ˈwenzlideɪl/ *n* [U] a white cheese that does not have a very strong taste, originally from Yorkshire〔原產約克郡, 味道不很濃的〕文斯利代爾乾酪

went /wɛnt; went/ the past tense of GO

wept /wɛpt; wept/ the past tense and past participle of WEEP

we're /wɪr; wɪə/ the short form of 縮略式= we are

were /wɚ; wə; *strong* 強讀 wɝ; wɜː/ *negative short form* 否定縮略式為 **weren't** /wɝnt; wɜːnt/ the past tense of BE

were·wolf /ˈwɪrˌwulf; ˈweəwʊlf/ *n* [C] a person who, in some stories, sometimes changes into a WOLF〔故事中的〕狼人, 會變成狼的人

wert /wɝt; wɜːt/ *v* **thou wert** *old use* you were【舊】你是

West /wɛst; west/ *n* **the West 1** the western part of the world and the people that live there, especially Western Europe and North America 西方世界〔尤指西歐和北美〕**2** the western part of the US〔美國〕西部地區 —compare 比較 MIDWEST, WEST COAST

west[1] *n* [singular, U] **1** the direction towards which the sun goes down, and which is on the left of someone who is facing north 西, 西面: **from/towards the west** *A strong* *wind was blowing from the west.* 正在颳強烈的西風。| **to the west of** *Birmingham is to the west of Leicester.* 伯明翰位於萊斯特的西面。**2 the west** the western part of a country or area〔某國或地區的〕西部

west² *adj* [only before noun 僅用於名詞前] **1** in the west or facing the west 在西方的; 朝西的: *the west door of the church* 教堂的西門 | *West Africa* 西非 **2** a west wind comes from the west〔風〕來自西面的

west³ *adv* **1** towards the west 朝西, 向西: *The room faces west.* 房間朝西。**2 go west** *BrE old-fashioned humorous*【英, 過時, 幽默】**a)** to die 死, 歸西 **b)** to be damaged or ruined 壞了, 完蛋了

west·bound /ˈwɛstˌbaund; ˈwestbaʊnd/ *adj* travelling or leading towards the west 向西行的

West Coast /ˈ· ·/ *n* **the West Coast** the western coastal states of the US〔美國〕西海岸

West Coun·try /ˈ· ˌ··/ *n* **the West Country** the southwest part of England 英格蘭的西南部

West End /ˌ· ˈ·◂/ *n* **the West End** the western part of central London where there are large shops, theatres, expensive hotels etc〔大商店、劇院、高級旅館等集中的〕倫敦西區

west·er·ly /ˈwɛstɚlɪ; ˈwestəli/ *adj* **1** towards or in the west 向西方的; 在西方的: *We set off in a westerly direction.* 我們出發往西去。**2** a westerly wind comes from the west〔風〕從西邊吹來的

west·ern¹, Western /ˈwɛstɚn; ˈwestən/ *adj* from or connected with the west part of the world or of a country〔世界〕西方的;〔國家〕西部的: *The Russian ballet is making a tour of Western Europe.* 俄羅斯芭蕾舞團正在西歐巡迴演出。

western² *n* [C] a film about life in the 19th century in the American West〔描寫19世紀美國西部生活的〕西部電影

West·ern·er /ˈwɛstɚnɚ; ˈwestənə/ *n* [C] **1** someone who lives in or comes from the western part of the world 西方人 **2** *AmE* someone who lives in or comes from the western part of the US【美】〔美國的〕西部人

west·ern·ize also 又作 **-ise** *BrE*【英】/ˈwɛstɚˌnaɪz; ˈwestənaɪz/ *v* [T] to bring customs, business methods etc that are typical of Europe and the US to other countries 使〔風俗、經營方式等〕西化 —**westernization** /ˌwɛstɚnaɪˈzeʃən; ˌwestənaɪˈzeɪʃən/ *n* [U]

west·ern·ized also 又作 **-ised** *BrE*【英】/ˈwɛstɚˌnaɪzd; ˈwestənaɪzd/ *adj* copying the customs, behaviour etc typical of the US or Europe〔風俗、行為等〕西化的

western medi·cine /ˌ·· ˈ··/ *n* [U] the type of medical treatment that is standard in the WEST (1) 西方醫學 —compare 比較 ALTERNATIVE MEDICINE

west·ern·most /ˈwɛstɚnˌmost; ˈwestənməʊst/ *adj* [no comparative 無比較級] furthest west 最西的

West In·di·an /ˌ· ˈ···/ *adj* from or connected with the West Indies 來自西印度羣島的; 與西印度羣島有關的

west·ward /ˈwɛstwɚd; ˈwestwəd/ *adj* going towards the west 向[朝]西的 —**westward, westwards** *adv*

wet¹ /wɛt; wet/ *adj*

1 ▶WATER/LIQUID 水/液體◀ covered in or full of liquid 濕的, 潮的: *wet grass* 濕草 | *My shirt's all wet!* 我的襯衫濕透了! | **[+with]** *His face was wet with sweat.* 他滿臉汗水。| **get (sth) wet** *Try not to get your feet wet.* 盡量別把你的腳弄濕。| **wet through** (=completely wet) 濕透 | **soaking/sopping/dripping wet** (=extremely wet) 極濕的, 濕淋淋的 *soaking wet socks* 濕淋淋的襪子

2 ▶WEATHER 天氣◀ rainy 多雨的, 下雨的: *wet weather* 下雨的天氣 | *It's very wet outside.* 外面雨很大。

3 the wet a) rainy weather 雨天: *Come in out of the wet.* 快進來免得淋雨。**b)** wet ground〔下雨後的〕濕地: *Don't trail your coat in the wet!* 別在濕地上拖着大衣!

4 ▶PAINT/INK ETC 油漆/墨水等◀ not yet dry 未乾的: *Careful, the paint's still wet.* 注意, 油漆未乾。

5 ▶PERSON 人◀ **a)** *BrE informal* unable to make decisions or take firm actions【英, 非正式】〔人〕猶豫不決的; 軟弱的: *Don't be so wet! Just tell them you don't want to go.* 別那麼優柔寡斷, 就告訴他們你不想去。**b) be all wet** *AmE informal* to be completely wrong【美, 非正式】大錯特錯

6 wet behind the ears *informal* very young and without much experience of life【非正式】年幼而沒有經驗的; 乳臭未乾的 —**wetly** *adv* —**wetness** *n* [U]

wet² *v past tense* **wet** *or* **wetted** [T] **1** to make something wet 把〔某物〕弄濕: *Wet your hair and apply the shampoo.* 弄濕頭髮, 倒上洗髮劑。**2** to make yourself, your clothes, or your bed wet because you pass water from your body by accident 尿濕; 遺尿: **wet yourself** *I nearly wet myself I was so scared.* 我嚇得幾乎屁滾尿流。**3 wet your whistle** *old-fashioned* to have an alcoholic drink【過時】喝點酒

wet·back /ˈwɛtˌbæk; ˈwetbæk/ *n* [C] *AmE* an offensive word for someone from Mexico who has come to the US illegally【美】濕背人〔冒犯語, 指由墨西哥進入美國的偷渡客〕

wet bar /ˈ· ·/ *n* [C] *AmE* a small bar with equipment for making alcoholic drinks, in a house, hotel room etc【美】〔家庭、旅館房間等的〕小酒吧

wet blan·ket /ˌ· ˈ··/ *n* [C] *informal* someone who tries to spoil other people's fun【非正式】掃興的人, 潑冷水的人

wet dream /ˌ· ˈ·/ *n* [C] a sexually exciting dream that a man has, resulting in an ORGASM 夢遺, 夢中遺精

wet fish /ˌ· ˈ·/ *n* [U] *BrE* fresh uncooked fish that is on sale in a shop【英】〔商店出售的〕鮮魚

wet-look /ˈ· ·/ *adj* [only before noun 僅用於名詞前] wet-look clothes have a shiny surface so that they look as if they are wet〔衣服〕表面閃光發亮的〔看起來像濕的一樣〕

wet nurse /ˈ· ·/ *n* [C] *old use* a woman who is employed to give her breast milk to another woman's baby【舊】奶媽, 乳母

wet-nurse *v* [T] to give someone too much care and attention as if they were a child 溺愛〔某人〕

wet suit 潛水服

wet suit /ˈ· ·/ *n* [C] a piece of clothing, usually made of rubber, that underwater swimmers wear to keep warm〔潛水者穿的〕保暖橡皮服; 潛水服

wet·ting a·gent /ˈ·· ˌ··/ *n* [C] a chemical substance which, when spread on a solid surface, makes it hold liquid〔塗於固體表面、使其容易被液體潤濕的〕潤濕劑

wetting so·lu·tion /ˈ·· ·ˌ··/ *n* [C,U] a liquid used for storing contact lenses (CONTACT LENS) in, or for making them more comfortable to wear〔隱形眼鏡用的〕護理液

we've /wɪv; wiv; *strong* 強讀 wiv; wiːv/ the short form of 縮略式 = we have

whack¹ /hwæk; wæk/ *v* [T] *informal*【非正式】**1** to hit someone or something hard 猛擊, 重擊〔某人或某物〕: *Ow! You whacked me with your elbow!* 哎唷! 你的手肘撞到我! **2** *spoken* to put something somewhere【口】把

某物置於某處: *Just whack it under the grill for a couple of minutes.* 就把它放在烤架下幾分鐘。

whack² *n* [C] *especially spoken*【尤口】**1** the act of hitting something hard or the noise this makes 重擊(聲) **2 have a whack at** to try to do something 試着做〔某事〕 **3 do your whack** *BrE* to do a fair or equal share of a job or activity【英】做你應做的一份〔工作或活動〕: *I've done more than my whack of the driving – it's your turn.* 我已經開了好半天車——該輪到你了。**4 (the) full whack** *BrE* the full amount【英】總量, 全額: *You don't have to pay full whack if you're unemployed.* 如果你沒有工作, 就不必付全部款額。**5 at/in one whack** *AmE* all on one occasion【美】一下子: *Steve lost $500 at one whack.* 史蒂夫一下子損失了 500 美元。**6 out of whack** *AmE* if a system, machine etc is out of whack, the parts are not working together correctly【美】〔系統、機器等〕有毛病, 不正常

whacked /hwækt; wækt/ *adj* [not before noun 不用於名詞前] *informal*【非正式】**1** also 又作 **whacked out** very tired 精疲力竭的 **2 whacked out** *AmE* behaving strangely, especially because of having too much alcohol or drugs【美】〔因醉酒、吸毒而〕行為怪異的

whack·ing /ˋhwækɪŋ; ˈwækɪŋ/ *adj* **whacking great** *BrE spoken* very big; WHOPPING【英口】巨大的, 極大的: *We got a whacking great gas bill this morning.* 今天上午我們收到一張數額巨大的煤氣賬單。

whack·y /ˋhwækɪ; ˈwæki/ *adj* another spelling of WACKY wacky 的另一種拼法

whale 鯨

whale¹ /hwel; weɪl/ *n* [C] **1** a very large animal that lives in the sea and looks like a fish, but is actually a MAMMAL 鯨 **2 have a whale of a time** *informal* to enjoy yourself very much【非正式】玩得非常愉快

whale² *v* **whale into** *AmE* to start attacking someone【美】開始攻擊〔某人〕

whale·bone /ˋhwel͵bon; ˈweɪlbəʊn/ *n* [U] a hard substance taken from the upper jaw of whales, used in the past for making women's clothes stiff〔舊時用以保持婦女衣服挺括的〕鯨鬚

whal·er /ˋhwelɚ; ˈweɪlə/ *n* [C] **1** someone who hunts whales 捕鯨者 **2** a boat which goes to hunt whales 捕鯨船

whal·ing /ˋhwelɪŋ; ˈweɪlɪŋ/ *n* [U] the activity of hunting whales 捕鯨(業)

wham /hwæm; wæm/ *interjection* **1** used to describe the sound of something suddenly hitting something else very hard〔形容某物突然撞擊他物的聲音〕砰, 嘭: *The car went wham into the wall.* 砰的一聲, 汽車撞到牆上。**2** used to express the idea that something very unexpected suddenly happens〔用於表示某事〕突如其來: *Life is going along nicely and then, wham, you lose your job.* 生活過得美滿舒適, 突然間, 你失業了。

wham·my /ˋhwæmɪ; ˈwæmi/ *n* [C] **put the whammy on sb** to use magic powers to make someone have bad luck 以魔力使某人倒運 —see also 另見 DOUBLE WHAMMY

wharf /hwɔrf; wɔːf/ *n* [C] *plural* **wharfs** or **wharves** a place built on the edge of a sea or river, where ships can be tied up to load and unload goods〔起卸貨物用的〕碼頭; 停船處

1 1 **what¹** /hwɑt; wɒt/ *predeterminer, determiner, pron* **1** used when asking questions about a thing or person, or a kind of thing or person that you do not know anything about 甚麼〔用於疑問句, 指某一或某種未知的事物或人〕: *What are you doing?* 你在做甚麼? | *What colour is the new carpet?* 新地毯是甚麼顏色的? | *"What do you do?" "I'm a teacher."* "你是幹甚麼的?" "我是教師。" | *What's your new boss like?* 你的新老闆是個怎樣的人? | *What do you mean, you want to spend Christmas alone?* 你是甚麼意思, 你想一個人過聖誕節? **2** used especially in indirect questions to talk about things or information …的事情〔尤用於間接問句, 指所說的事或信息〕: *I believe what he told me.* 我相信他對我說的話。| *Show me what you bought then.* 那麼給我看看你買的東西。| *They're discussing what to do next.* 他們正在討論下一步要做甚麼。| *I don't know what you think but if you ask me it's a waste of time.* 我不知道你怎麼想, 但是你如果問我, 我認為那是浪費時間。| *She gave him what money she had.* (=all the money she had, although she did not have much) 她把她僅有的錢給了他。**3** *spoken* used at the beginning of a statement to emphasize what you are going to say【口】…的是…〔用在陳述句的開始, 強調準備說的內容〕: *What that kid needs is some love and affection.* 那小孩需要的是關愛。| *What we'll do is leave a note for Mum to tell her we won't be back till late.* 我們要做的是給媽媽留一張便條, 告訴她我們要很晚才回來。**4 what?** *spoken*【口】**a)** used to ask someone to repeat something they have just said because you didn't hear it properly 甚麼?〔因沒有聽清楚, 要求對方重複所說的話〕: *"Have you got a pen I could borrow?" "What?"* "你有鋼筆我可以借用一下嗎?" "你說甚麼?" **b)** used during conversations when you have heard someone talking to you and want to tell them to continue 甚麼?〔用於談話中, 希望對方繼續說下去〕: *"Elaine!" "What?" "Are you coming?"* "伊萊恩!" "甚麼?" "你來嗎?" **c)** used to show that you are surprised by what someone has said 真的?〔對他人所說的表示驚訝〕: *"My wallet's missing." "What?"* "我的錢包丟了。" "真的嗎?" **5** *spoken* used at the beginning of a sentence to show that you think something is very good, very bad etc【口】多麼, 何等〔用在句子的開頭, 表示某事很好或很壞等〕: *What a lovely day !* (=the weather is good) 多好的天氣! | *What a horrible thing to do!* 做這種事真可怕! **6 what about...?** *spoken*【口】**a)** used to make a suggestion …怎麼樣?〔用於提出建議〕: *What about Czechoslovakia for a holiday?* 到捷克斯洛伐克度假去怎麼樣? | **what about doing** *What about going to a movie this evening?* 今晚去看電影怎麼樣? **b)** used to introduce a new person or thing into a conversation …怎麼樣〔在交談中說到新人或事〕: *What about Patrick? What's he doing nowadays?* 帕特里克怎麼樣? 他現在在幹甚麼? | *We've chosen the food, now, what about the wine?* 我們已經選了食品, 那麼, 葡萄酒怎麼辦? **7 I tell you what** *spoken* used to make an offer or suggestion【口】我有個主意, 你聽我說〔用於提出建議或意見〕: *I tell you what, I'll give you £20 for it.* 你聽我說, 那件東西我給你 20 英鎊。**8 guess what!** *spoken* used before telling someone some exciting or surprising news【口】猜猜發生了甚麼事!〔用於說出令人感到驚訝的事情前〕: *Guess what! Jane's getting married.* 猜猜發生甚麼事了! 簡要結婚了。**9 what (...) for?** *spoken*【口】**a)** why? 為甚麼?: *"She's decided to work part-time." "What for ?"* "她決定去兼職。" "為甚麼?" **b)** used to ask what purpose something has〔某物〕有何用?: *What's this gadget for?* 這個小玩意兒是幹甚麼用的? **10** *spoken* used to give yourself time to think before guessing a number or amount【口】嗯, 哦〔猜測數目或數量前給自己時間考慮〕: *You're looking at, what, about £4000 for a decent second-hand car.* 一輛性能尚可的二手車得花你, 嗯, 大約 4,000 英鎊。**11 what's his/her/its name** also 又作 **what d'you call him/her/it** *spoken* used when talking about a person or thing whose name you cannot immediately remember【口】那個甚麼來着〔說到某人或某物時一時記不起名稱〕: *The hospital have just got a, what d'you call it, er... a new scanner.* 醫院剛買了一台新的叫甚麼來着, 嗯…掃描器。**12 (and) what's more** *spoken* used when adding something to what you have already said, especially when it is exciting or interesting【口】而且, 更有甚者〔尤用於加上令人興奮或有趣的一點〕: *These deter-*

gents are environmentally friendly, what's more, they're relatively cheap. 這些洗滌劑有利環保，而且，價格還相當便宜。**13 what's what** *spoken* what a situation is really like as opposed to what people say it is like, or what they try and make you believe【口】事情的真相: *Shirley's been there before, she'll tell you what's what.* 雪莉以前到過那裡，她會告訴你是怎麼一回事。**14 what the hell/devil/blazes...?/what in God's name/heaven's name...?** *spoken* used to ask in an extremely angry or surprised way what is happening, what someone is doing etc【口】究竟甚麼…？到底甚麼…？〔用極生氣或驚訝的口吻問〕: *What the hell do you think you're doing?* 你究竟認為自己在幹甚麼？| *What in God's name will she think of next?* 接下來她到底會想到甚麼？**15 what the hell!** *spoken* used to say that you have decided to do something even though it is very expensive, difficult etc【口】管他呢！〔表示決定做某事，雖然昂貴、困難等〕: *Oh, what the hell! It's your birthday, let's have champagne!* 噢，管他呢！今天是你的生日，我們喝香檳酒吧！**16 ...or what?** *spoken* used to show that you are impatient when asking a question or because you think there is only one possible answer to the question【口】還是別的甚麼？〔發問時表示不耐煩或認為只有一個答案〕: *Are you coming then, or what?* 那麼你是來還是不來？| *Is that work going to be finished by Friday or what?* 那工作會在星期五完成還是在別的甚麼時間完成？**17 so what?** *spoken* used to say that you do not care about something or to tell someone angrily that something does not concern them【口】那有甚麼了不起？〔對事情表示不關心或生氣地告訴某人事情與他無關〕，那又怎樣？: *"Your room looks a real mess Tracey." "So what?"* "特雷西，你房間看起來凌亂不堪。" "那又怎麼樣？" **18 you what?** *spoken*【口】**a)** used to ask someone to repeat something they have just said, in a way people think is not polite 你說甚麼？〔用於讓對方重複一遍，人們認為這樣說不禮貌〕: *"Could you get the butter out of the fridge?" "You what?"* "請把黃油從冰箱裡拿出來好嗎？" "你說甚麼？" **b)** used to show that you are surprised 你說甚麼？〔表示驚訝〕: *"I got the job!" "You what?"* "我獲得那份工作啦！" "你說甚麼？" **19 what if...** *spoken*【口】**a)** used to make a suggestion 如果…怎麼樣〔用於提出建議〕: *What if we go and see a film tomorrow night?* 我們明天晚上去看電影，你覺得怎麼樣？**b)** used to ask what will happen, usually if an unpleasant or frightening situation happens 如果…將會怎樣〔用於問將會發生甚麼，通常是令人不快或驚恐的事〕: *What if we get burgled while we're on holiday?* 我們度假時，家裡被盜怎麼辦？**20 ...and what have you** *spoken* used at the end of a list of things to mean other things of a similar kind【口】等等；這一類東西〔用於物品清單末尾，表示還有類似的東西〕: *The shelves were crammed with books, documents, and what have you.* 書架上塞滿了書本、文件等一類東西。**21 have what it takes** *spoken* to have the right qualities or skills in order to succeed【口】具備成功的必要條件: *I reckon Jordi's got what it takes to be an international footballer.* 我認為喬迪已具備作為世界級足球員的條件。**22 what's with a)** *AmE spoken* used to ask a person or group of people who are behaving strangely or violently, why they are behaving in this way【美口】怎麼啦〔用於詢問某人或一羣人為甚麼他行為怪異或粗暴〕: *What's with you people?* 你們這些人怎麼啦？**b)** used to ask the reason for something 怎麼回事: *What's with the free sandwiches and beer?* 白吃三明治，白喝啤酒，是怎麼回事？**23 what of it?** *spoken* used to say that you do not care about something or to tell someone angrily that something does not concern them【口】那又有甚麼關係？〔用於表示對事情不關心或生氣地告訴某人事情與他無關〕: *"I hear you've just got a new car." "Yes, what of it?"* "我聽說你剛買了輛新汽車。" "是的，那又怎麼樣呢？" **24 now what?** *spoken* used to ask what is going to happen next, what you should do etc【口】下一步會怎樣；下一步怎麼辦？

Frequencies of **what** in spoken and written English
英語口語和書面語中 what 的使用頻率

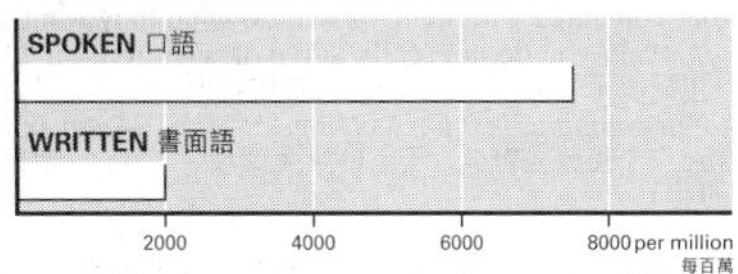

Based on the British National Corpus and the Longman Lancaster Corpus
據英國國家語料庫和朗文蘭卡斯特語料庫

This graph shows that **what** is much more common in spoken English than in written English. This is because it is used to ask questions, and it is used in a lot of common spoken phrases. 本圖表顯示，what 在英語口語中的使用頻率遠遠高於書面語，因為該詞經常用於問句中，而且口語中很多常用片語是由 what 構成的。

what² *adv* **1** used especially in questions to ask to what degree or in what way something matters〔尤用於問句〕到甚麼程度；在哪方面: *What do you care about it?* (=I don't think you care at all) 你對這事恐怕沒有甚麼要關心的吧？| *We may be a little late, but what does it matter?* 我們可能會晚到一會兒，但那有甚麼關係呢？**2 what with** *spoken* used to introduce a list of reasons that have made something happen or have made someone feel a particular way【口】〔用於列舉引起某事或某種感受的原因〕因為，由於: *What with neighbours, relatives, and friends there, the house was overflowing with people.* 由於有鄰居、親屬及朋友在那裡，房子裡人滿為患。

what·cha·ma·call·it /ˈwɑtʃəməˌkɔlɪt; ˈwɒtʃəməˌkɔːlɪt/ *n* [C] *spoken* a word you use when you cannot remember the name of something【口】叫甚麼東西來着〔忘記該東西的名稱時用〕: *I've broken the whatchamacallit on my bag.* 我把袋子上的甚麼東西弄壞了。

what·ev·er¹ /hwɑtˈɛvə; wɒtˈevə/ *determiner, pron* **1** any or all of the things that are wanted, needed, or possible 任何…的事物；甚麼…都: *Help yourself to whatever you want.* 儘請隨意。| *Jake's dad told him he could have whatever he wanted for Christmas.* 傑克的爸爸告訴他聖誕節他想要甚麼禮物都行。**2** used to say that it is not important what happens, what you do etc because it does not change the situation 無論甚麼，不管甚麼: *Whatever I suggest, he always disagrees.* 無論我提甚麼建議，他總是不同意。| *The building must be saved whatever the cost.* 不論花多少錢，這座建築物必須保留。| **whatever you do** *spoken*【口】: *Don't, whatever you do, let anyone see that letter.* 無論如何，你不要讓任何人看那封信。**3** *spoken* used to say that you do not know the exact meaning or name of someone or something【口】…甚麼來着〔用於表示你不知道某人的姓名或某事的真正意思〕: *Why don't you invite Steve, or whatever he's called, to supper?* 你為甚麼不邀請那個叫史蒂夫還是甚麼的人來吃晚飯？**4 ... or whatever** *spoken* used after naming things on a list to mean other things of the same kind【口】任何類似的東西〔用於物品清單之後〕: *Anyone seen carrying boxes, bags, or whatever was stopped by the police.* 誰要是帶盒子、袋子甚麼的，被警察看見了都給截查。| **...and whatever else** *Bring waterproof clothing, boots, and whatever else.* 帶上防水衣、靴子，以及諸如此類的東西。**5** *spoken* used to show that you are angry or surprised when making a statement or asking a question【口】究竟是甚麼〔用於述說事情或提出問題時表示生氣或驚訝〕: *Whatever can he mean?* 他能是甚麼意思？| **whatever next!** (=used to show surprise) 還要甚麼！〔表示驚訝〕*"Joan's learning Sanskrit." "Whatever next!"* "瓊在學梵文。" "她還要學甚麼！" **6** *spoken* used to tell someone that you do not care or are not interested when they ask you something【口】隨便怎樣，無所謂〔用於回答別人的問題，表示不感興趣〕: *"Shall I*

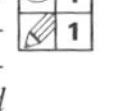

call you tonight or tomorrow?" "Whatever." "我是今晚還是明天打電話給你?" "由你。" **7 whatever you say/whatever you think** *spoken* used to tell someone that you agree with them or will do what they want, often when you do not really agree or want to do it【口】〔用於表示贊成, 往往是勉強的贊成〕隨你説/想: *"I want to go camping, just for a change." "OK, whatever you say."* "我想去野營, 只是想換換環境。" "好, 一切聽你的。"

Frequencies of **whatever** in spoken and written English 英語口語和書面語中whatever的使用頻率

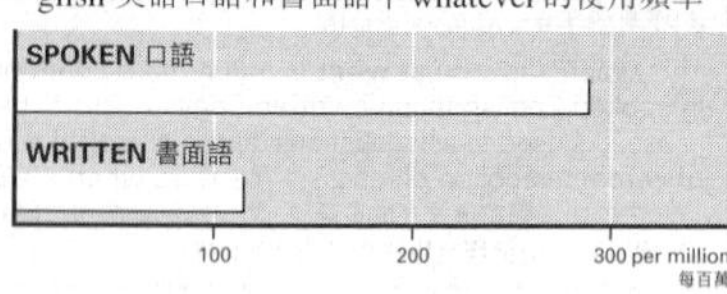

Based on the British National Corpus and the Longman Lancaster Corpus
據英國國家語料庫和朗文蘭卡斯特語料庫

This graph shows that **whatever** is more common in spoken English than in written English. This is because it is used in a lot of common spoken phrases. 本圖表顯示, whatever在英語口語中的使用頻率遠遠高於書面語, 因為口語中很多常用片語是由whatever構成的。

whatever² *adv* used to emphasize a negative statement; WHATSOEVER 絲毫; 任何〔用於強調否定句〕: *She gave no sign whatever of what she was thinking.* 她在想甚麼, 毫無跡象可循。

whatever³ *adj* **1** of any possible kind 任何的: *I'll take whatever help I can get.* 我得到甚麼幫助我都接受。 **2** of some kind, but you are not sure what ...甚麼樣的〔但你不肯定是甚麼〕: *Ellen's refusing to come, for whatever reason.* 不知甚麼原因, 艾倫不願來了。

what·not /ˈhwɑtˌnɑt; ˈwɒtnɒt/ *n* **1 and whatnot** *spoken* an expression used at the end of a list of things when you do not want to give the names of everything【口】〔用於物品清單末尾, 不把物品一一列舉時〕諸如此類的東西; 等等: *Put your bags, cases and whatnot in the back of the car.* 把你的袋子、盒子等等放到汽車後座。 **2** [C] a piece of furniture with shelves used especially in the 19th century to show small pretty objects〔19世紀放小玩意的〕陳設架, 古董架

whats·it /ˈhwɑtsɪt; ˈwɒtsɪ̥t/ *n* [C] *spoken* a word you use when you cannot think of the word you want【口】那個甚麼玩意兒〔指説不出名稱的小東西〕: *Try and undo the screw to get the whatsit off.* 試着鬆開螺絲, 把那個小玩意兒拆下來。

2 **what·so·ev·er** /ˌhwɑtsoˈɛvɚ; ˌwɒtsəʊˈevə/ *adv* used to emphasize a negative statement; WHATEVER 絲毫〔用於強調否定句〕: *Political factors played no part whatsoever in this decision.* 在這項決定中, 政治因素絲毫沒起作用。

wheat /hwit; wiːt/ *n* [U] **1** the grain that bread is made from 小麥麥粒 **2** the plant that this grain grows on 小麥(植物): *a field of wheat* 小麥地 **3 separate the wheat from the chaff** to choose the good and useful things or people and get rid of the others 分清好壞; 去蕪存菁

wheat·germ /ˈhwitˌdʒɝm; ˈwiːtdʒɜːm/ *n* [U] the centre of a grain of wheat 小麥胚芽

wheat·meal /ˈhwitmil; ˈwiːtmiːl/ *n* [U] *especially BrE* a brown flour made from whole grains of wheat【尤英】全麥麵粉

whee /hwi; wiː/ *interjection* used by children to express happiness or excitement 喲; 好啊〔兒童用以表示高興或激動〕

whee·dle /ˈhwidl̩; ˈwiːdl/ *v* [I,T] to try to persuade someone by saying pleasant things which you do not mean 哄騙; 〔用甜言蜜語〕騙取: *a wheedling voice* 哄騙的口吻 | **wheedle sb into doing sth** *He wheedled me into paying.* 他哄騙我讓我付錢。| **wheedle sth from/out of sb** *She managed to wheedle an extra day's pay out of him.* 她用花言巧語從他那裡多騙了一天的報酬。

wheel¹ /hwil; wiːl/ *n* [C]

1 ►ON A VEHICLE 車輛上的◄ [C] one of the round things under a car, bus, bicycle etc that turn when it moves〔汽車、公共汽車、自行車等的〕車輪 —see picture on page A2 參見A2頁圖

2 ►IN A MACHINE 機器上的◄ [C] a flat round part in a machine that turns round when the machine operates 機輪: *a gear wheel* 齒輪

3 ►FOR CONTROLLING A VEHICLE 用於控制車船等◄ [C] the piece of equipment in the shape of a wheel that you turn to make a car, ship etc move in a particular direction〔汽車、輪船等的〕方向盤: **at/behind the wheel** (=driving a car etc) 在駕駛〔汽車等〕| **take the wheel** (=drive instead of someone else) 替他人駕駛 —see also 另見 STEERING WHEEL

4 on wheels with wheels on the bottom 帶輪的: *a table on wheels* 帶輪的桌子

5 wheels/set of wheels *spoken* a car【口】汽車: *Like my new wheels?* 喜歡我的新車嗎?

6 wheels within wheels *spoken* used to say that a situation is complicated and difficult to understand because it involves processes and decisions that you know nothing about【口】錯綜複雜的情況; 複雜的形勢 —see also 另見 **oil the wheels** (OIL² (2)), **put your shoulder to the wheel** (SHOULDER¹ (8)), **put a spoke in sb's wheel** (SPOKE² (2))

wheel² *v* **1** [T always+adv/prep] **a)** to push something that has wheels 推動〔帶輪子的東西〕: **wheel sth out/down/into** *She wheeled her bike into the garage.* 她把自行車推到車庫裡。**b)** to move someone or something that is in an object with wheels, such as a WHEELCHAIR or a CART¹ (1) 用〔輪椅或手推車等〕運送〔某人或某物〕: *The nurse wheeled him into the ward.* 護士把他推進病房。 **2** [I] if birds or planes wheel they fly around in circles〔鳥或飛機〕盤旋 **3 [I+around/round]** to turn around suddenly 突然轉身: *She wheeled around and started yelling at us.* 她突然轉身, 開始衝着我們大喊起來。 **4 wheel and deal** to do a lot of complicated and sometimes slightly dishonest deals, especially in politics or business〔尤指在政治或商業上〕投機取巧; 玩弄手段

wheel sb/sth ↔ **out** *phr v* [T] *informal* to publicly show someone or something, and use them to help you achieve something【非正式】〔為幫助自己達成某事而〕提出〔某人〕; 推出〔某物〕: *The party always wheels out the same old celebrities whenever they need to raise money.* 每當需要募集資金的時候, 該黨總是推出這幾位老名人。

wheel·bar·row /ˈhwilˌbæro; ˈwiːlˌbærəʊ/ *n* [C] a small CART¹ (1) that you use outdoors to carry things, with a single wheel and two handles 獨輪手推車

wheel·base /ˈhwilˌbes; ˈwiːlbeɪs/ *n* [C] *technical* the distance between the front and back AXLES of a vehicle【術語】〔車輛前後軸的〕軸距

wheel·chair /ˈhwilˈtʃɛr; ˈwiːltʃeə/ *n* [C] a chair with wheels used by people who cannot walk 輪椅 —see picture at 參見 CHAIR¹ 圖

wheel clamp /ˈ· ·/ *n* [C] a metal object that is fastened to the wheel of an illegally parked car 車輪鎖夾〔鎖住非法停放汽車的車輪的裝置〕; DENVER BOOT *AmE*【美】— **wheel-clamp** *v* [T]

wheeled /hwild; wiːld/ *adj* having wheels 有輪子的

wheeler-deal·er /ˌ·· ˈ··/ *n* [C] someone who does a lot of complicated, often dishonest deals, especially in business or politics 善於投機取巧的人〔尤指在政治或商業上〕: *She was a real wheeler-dealer, sometimes loving the thrill of doing deals.* 她真是一個工於心計的人, 有時覺得談生意很帶勁。

wheel·house /ˈhwilˌhaus; ˈwiːlhaʊs/ *n* [C] the place

on a ship where the CAPTAIN stands at the WHEEL[1] (3)〔船上的〕駕駛室, 操舵室

wheel·ie /ˋhwilɪ; ˈwiːli/ *n* [C] **do a wheelie** *informal* to balance on the back wheel of a bicycle that you are riding【非正式】〔自行車前輪離地的〕後輪平衡特技

wheelie bin /ˈ·· ·/ *n* [C] *BrE* a large container with wheels that you put household waste into【英】大型輪式垃圾箱〔棄置家庭垃圾用〕

wheel·ing and deal·ing /ˌ·· · ˈ··/ *n* [U] activities that involve a lot of complicated and sometimes dishonest deals, especially in business or politics〔尤指在商業或政治上的〕投機取巧; 使用手段

wheel·wright /ˋhwilˌraɪt; ˈwiːlraɪt/ *n* [C] someone who made and repaired the wooden wheels of vehicles pulled by horses in the past〔舊時〕製作或修理馬車木輪的匠人

wheeze[1] /hwiz; wiːz/ *v* [I] to breathe with difficulty, making a whistling sound in your throat and chest 氣喘吁吁, 發出呼哧聲

wheeze[2] *n* [C] **1** the act or sound of wheezing 氣喘; 氣喘聲 **2** *old-fashioned or humorous* a clever and amusing idea or plan【過時或幽默】巧妙的主意; 把戲

wheez·y /ˋhwizɪ; ˈwiːzi/ *adj* wheezing or making a wheezing sound 氣喘的; 發出喘息聲的: *You sound wheezy.* 你氣喘吁吁。| *a wheezy cough* 呼哧呼哧的咳嗽 —**wheezily** *adv* —**wheeziness** *n* [U]

whelk /hwɛlk; welk/ *n* [C] a small sea animal that has a shell and can be eaten 蛾螺

whelp[1] /hwɛlp; welp/ *n* [C] a young animal, especially a dog or lion 幼獸〔尤指狗崽或幼獅〕

whelp[2] *v* [I] *old-fashioned* if a dog or lion whelps, it gives birth【過時】〔狗、獅〕產仔

when[1] /hwɛn; wen/ *adv, conj* **1** at what time 甚麼時候: *When is Tara coming?* 塔拉甚麼時候來? | *Do you know when she will arrive?* 你知道她甚麼時候到嗎? | *When did you hear about it?* 你甚麼時候聽到這消息的? **2** at the time that 當…時候: *Things were different when I was young.* 我年輕的時候情況並不一樣。| *The dog jumped up when he whistled.* 聽到他的口哨聲, 狗跳了起來。| *When I give the signal, turn off the light.* 當我發出信號時, 就關燈。| *When completed the tunnel will be the longest in the world.* 完工後, 這隧道將是世界上最長的。**3 day/time/afternoon when** the day, time etc on or at which 那天/時/下午: *There are times when I wonder what you're talking about.* 有幾次我不知道你在說甚麼。**4** considering that 考慮到: *Why do you want a new job when you've got such a good one already?* 既然你已經有了這麼好的工作, 為甚麼還要找新的工作? **5** even though or in spite of the fact that 雖然; 儘管: *They kept digging when they must have known there was no hope.* 他們雖然明知沒有希望, 但還是在不停地挖。

when[2] *pron* **1 since when** used in questions to mean since what time 從甚麼時候〔用於問句〕: *Since when has it been any of your business what I do?* 從甚麼時候起我做的事和你有關係呢? **2** which time 那時: *next May, by when the new house should be finished* 明年五月, 到那時新房子應該建成了

whence /hwɛns; wens/ *adv, pron old use* from where【舊】從哪裡: *Whence came this man?* 這個人從哪兒來的? —compare 比較 WHITHER

when·ev·er /hwɛnˋɛvɚ; wenˈevə/ *adv, conj* **1** every time that a particular thing happens 每當: *Whenever we come here we see someone we know.* 我們每次來這兒都會見到熟人。| *If you feed a baby whenever he is hungry, you will have less difficulty with him later.* 每當嬰兒餓的時候你就餵他, 以後你就容易帶他了。**2** at any time 任何時候: *I'd like to see you whenever it's convenient.* 在你方便的時候我想和你見面。**3** *spoken* used when it does not matter what time something happens, or when you do not know the exact time something happens【口】無論甚麼時候〔用於事情發生的時間並不重要或不確定時〕: *"Should I come over around six?" "Whenever."* "我六點左右來行嗎?" "甚麼時候都行。"

where /hwɛr; weə/ *adv, conjunction* S1 W1 **1** at, to, or from a particular place or position 在哪裡[某處]; 往哪裡[某處]; 從哪裡[某處]: *Where do you live?* 你住在哪裡? | *I asked Lucy where she was going.* 我問露西她去哪兒。| *Where are you going to put it?* 你會把它放到甚麼地方? | *Sit where you like.* 你愛坐哪兒就坐哪兒。—see 見 POSITION (USAGE) **2** in, towards, or from a particular situation or at a particular point in a speech, argument etc〔發言、爭論等〕在哪情況; 在哪一點: *Now where was I? Oh yes, I was telling you about taking mother to the airport.* 我說到哪兒了? 哦, 是的, 我正告訴你我帶着母親到機場。| *Where will all this fighting and bloodshed end?* 這一切衝突、流血, 結果會是甚麼樣? **3** used at the beginning of a sentence in which the second part expresses the opposite, or something different from the first part〔用於句子開頭, 表示與第二部分的情況相反或不同〕: *Where most people saw nothing but a hardened criminal, Audrey saw a lonely and desperate man.* 許多人只看見一個冷酷無情的罪犯, 但奧德麗卻看到一個孤獨而絕望的男人。

where·a·bouts[1] /ˌhwɛrəˋbaʊts; ˌweərəˈbaʊts◂/ *adv spoken* used to ask in what general area something or someone is【口】在哪一帶〔用於疑問句, 不要求準確地點〕: *Whereabouts do you live?* 你住在哪一帶?

where·a·bouts[2] /ˋhwɛrəˌbaʊts; ˈweərəbaʊts/ *n* [U] the place or area where someone or something is〔某人或某物的〕去向; 行蹤: **sb's whereabouts** *His family refused to reveal his whereabouts.* 他的家人拒絕說出他的去向。| **the whereabouts of** *the whereabouts of the missing documents* 丟失文件的下落

where·as /hwɛrˋæz; weərˈæz/ *conj* S2 W2 **1** used to say that although something is true of one thing, it is not true of another 但是; 卻〔用於說某事不適用於所有情況〕: *Why are some cancers cured by chemotherapy alone, whereas others are unaffected by drugs?* 為甚麼有些癌症僅用化療就能治癒, 而有些用藥物卻不起作用呢? **2** *law* used at the beginning of an official document to mean because of a particular fact【法律】鑑於〔用於文件的開首〕

where·at /hwɛrˋæt; weərˈæt/ *conj formal*【正式】**1** used when something happens immediately after something else, or as a result of something happening; WHEREUPON 隨即; 於是 **2** at a particular place; WHERE (1) 在那裡

where·by /hwɛrˋbaɪ; weəˈbaɪ/ *adv formal* S3 by means of which or according to which【正式】由此; 藉以: *a law whereby the wearing of seat belts becomes compulsory* 強制繫安全帶的法律

where·fore /ˋhwɛrˌfɔr; ˈweəfɔː/ *adv, conj old use*【舊】**1** used to ask why something has happened 為甚麼〔某事發生〕: *Wherefore comest thou?* 汝因何至此? **2** for that reason 為此, 因此: *Skills are the art of doing, wherefore they must be taught by practical example.* 技能是實踐的藝術, 因此必須用實例來教。—see also 另見 **whys and wherefores** (WHY[3])

where·in /hwɛrˋɪn; weərˈɪn/ *adv, conj literary* in which place or part【文】在哪裡; 在哪方面: *the clay ovens wherein some farm wives still bake bread* 有些農婦仍然用來烘烤麵包的泥窯 | *Wherein lies the difficulty?* 困難在哪兒?

where·of /hwɛrˋɑv; weərˈɒv/ *adv, conj old use* of which【舊】關於那個: *Theirs are the houses whereof I speak.* 我所說的是他們的房子。

where·on /hwɛrˋɑn; weərˈɒn/ *adv, conj old use* on which【舊】在那上面: *The sparrow flitted to the statue, whereon it perched.* 麻雀輕快地飛到塑像那裡, 在上面歇息。

where·so·ever /ˌhwɛrsoˋɛvɚ; ˌweəsəʊˈevə/ *adv, conj literary* another word for WHEREVER【文】wherever 的同義詞

where·to /hwɛrˋtu; weəˈtuː/ *adv, conj old use* to which place【舊】向哪裡

where·u·pon /ˌhwɛrəˋpɑn; ˌweərəˈpɒn/ *conj* used when

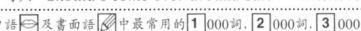

something happens immediately after something else, or as a result of something happening 馬上; 於是: *Molly banned her from the dining room, whereupon Bridget burst into tears.* 莫莉不准布麗奇特進飯廳, 她於是大哭起來。

wher·ev·er /hwɛrˋɛvɚ; weərˈevə/ *adv* **1** to or at whatever place, position, or situation 無論去哪裡; 無論在任何地方; 無論甚麼情況下: *If you could go wherever you wanted to in the world, where would you go?* 如果世界上任何地方你想去就能去的話, 你會去哪兒? | *Sleep wherever you like.* 你愛睡哪兒都可以。| **... or wherever** (=used to emphasize that you are talking about any place and not a specific place) 還是別的甚麼地方〔用於強調所述的不是一個特定的地方〕 *There has been an increase in crime whether it be in Britain, France, Germany, or wherever.* 不論是在英國、法國、德國, 還是別的甚麼地方, 犯罪活動均有所增加。**2 wherever possible** when it is possible to do something 只要有可能〔做某事〕: *Wherever possible jobs are given to local people.* 只要有可能, 工作都提供給當地人。**3** used at the beginning of a question to show surprise 究竟在哪兒〔用在問話前面, 表示驚訝〕: *Wherever did you get that idea?* 那個念頭你究竟是從哪兒來的? **4 wherever that may be** used to say that you do not know where a place or town is or have never heard of it〔表示不知道某地方或城鎮的所在或從沒有聽説過〕: *Rita lives in Horwich now, wherever that may be.* 麗塔現在住在霍里奇, 我不知道那個地方在哪兒。

where·with·al /ˋhwɛrwɪð͵ɔl; ˈweəwɪðɔːl/ *n* **the wherewithal to do sth** the money you need in order to do something 做某事所需的金錢: *We don't have the wherewithal to pay for a big wedding.* 我們沒有舉行盛大婚禮所需的金錢。

whet /hwɛt; wet/ *v* [T] **1 whet sb's appetite (for sth)** if an experience whets your appetite for something, it increases your desire for it 引起某人(做某事)的慾望: *The trip to Paris has whetted my appetite for travel.* 巴黎之旅激起了我的旅遊興趣。**2** *literary* to make the edge of a blade sharp【文】〔將刃〕磨快

wheth·er /ˋhwɛðɚ; ˈweðə/ *conj* **1** used when talking about a choice you have to make or about two different possibilities 是否〔用於表示兩種可能性中的選擇〕: *He asked me whether she was coming.* 他問我她是否來。| *The decision whether to see her was mine alone.* 看不看她由我自己拿主意。| **whether or not** *I couldn't decide whether or not to go to the party.* 我拿不定主意參不參加這個聚會。**2** used to say that something definitely will or will not happen whatever the situation is 不管, 不論〔用於表示無論發生哪種情況, 某事肯定發生或不發生〕: *I'm sure we'll see each other again soon whether here or in New York.* 我深信我們不久會再見面的, 不是在這裡就是在紐約。| **whether... or not** *Whether you like it or not, you're going to have to face him one day.* 不管你樂意還是不樂意, 總有一天你必須面對他。

W

USAGE NOTE 用法説明: WHETHER

GRAMMAR 語法

Whether and **if** are often used in similar contexts. However, **whether** is usually used for **if** when you also use the word **or** especially at the beginning of a sentence. whether 和 if 常用在相似的語境裡。然而, 在句子中與 or 連用, 尤其在句子開頭時, 就常用 whether 代替 if。People say 人們常説: *Whether you see her or not, phone me later.* 不論你有沒有見到她, 過一會打電話給我。| *If you see her, phone me.* 如果你見到她, 打電話給我。

If can usually be used instead of **whether** with clauses following some verbs and adjectives 與一些動詞或形容詞後面的從句連用時, if 通常替代 whether: *I wonder whether/if she can come.* 我不知道她是否能來。| *He wasn't sure whether/if he could come* (NOT 不用 *...whether could he come*). 他不敢肯定他是否能來。But you use **whether** (NOT **if**) before infinitives 但是, 在不定式前用 whether (不用 if) : *The question is whether to go or stay.* 問題是去還是留下。**Whether** is also used after prepositions. whether 也用在介詞之後: *It depends on whether he's ready or not.* 這取決於他是否準備好了。It is also used after nouns 它也用在名詞之後: *It's your decision whether you go or stay.* 去還是留要你自己拿主意。

You often use **whether** with **... or not** sentences, for example 常用whether...or not的句型, 如: *You're coming whether you like it or not.* 不管你樂意還是不樂意, 你都要來。| *We have to decide whether or not to support this proposal.* 我們得決定是否支持這項提案。

SPELLING 拼法

Note the spelling is **whether** (NOT *weather*). *Weather* (=sunshine, snow etc) is a completely different word. 注意拼法是 whether 而不是 weather, weather (天氣) 是完全不同的詞。

whet·stone /ˋhwɛt͵ston; ˈwetstəʊn/ *n* [C] a stone used to make the blade of cutting tools sharp 磨刀石

whew /hwju; hjuː/ *interjection* used when you are surprised, very hot, or feeling glad that something bad did not happen; PHEW 喲, 唷, 哎呀〔表示驚訝、感到炎熱或高興某種壞事竟然沒有發生〕: *Whew, that man has some temper!* 唷, 那個人的脾氣真大!

whey /hwe; weɪ/ *n* [U] the watery liquid that is left after the solid part has been removed from sour milk〔酸牛奶中去掉凝乳部分後剩下的〕乳清

which /hwɪtʃ; wɪtʃ/ *determiner, pron* **1** used to ask or state what people or things you mean when a choice has to be made 哪一個; 哪些〔用於選擇疑問句中〕: *Which of these books is yours?* 這些書中哪本是你的? | *Ask him which one he wants.* 問問他想要哪一個。| *Karen comes from either Los Angeles or San Francisco, I can't remember which.* 卡倫不是來自洛杉磯就是來自三藩市, 我記不清是哪個地方了。**2** used to show what specific thing or things you mean ...的那個〔用於指明事物〕; ...的那些: *Did you see the letter which came today?* 你看到今天來的那封信了嗎? | *This is the book which I told you about.* 這就是我跟你説過的那本書。**3** used especially in written language after a COMMA, to add more information about a specific thing or things, or about the first part of the sentence〔尤用於書面語, 放在逗號後, 説明某物或句子開頭部分〕: *The train, which takes only two hours, is quicker than the bus, which takes three.* 火車比公共汽車快, 火車只用兩小時, 公共汽車卻要三小時。| *The police arrived, after which the situation became calmer.* 警察到了, 隨後形勢就平靜下來。| **in which case** (=used to talk about a situation that you have just mentioned) 在那種情況下〔用於指剛提及的情況〕 *She may have missed the train, in which case she won't arrive for another hour.* 她可能沒有趕上火車, 那樣再過一個小時她也到不了。**4 which is which** used to say that you cannot tell the difference between two very similar people or things 誰是誰; 哪個是哪個〔用於指無法區別兩個相似的人或物〕: *They look so alike it's difficult to tell which is which.* 他們長得非常像, 很難分清誰是誰。

USAGE NOTE 用法説明: WHICH

FORMALITY 正式程度

As subject of a relative clause which restricts the meaning of a noun, **that** is used more often than **which** in informal English. 在非正式英語中, 限制名詞含義的關係子句, 用 that 作主語比用 which 作

主語普遍: *the street market which/that is held near my house* 我家附近的集市
In informal or spoken English, you can often leave out **that** or **which**. For example, you are likely to say 在非正式或口頭英語中, 常可省略 that 或 which, 例如, 可能會說: *Did you get the things you wanted?* 你拿到了想要的東西嗎? rather than 而不說: *Did you get the things that/which you wanted?*
The form **to which** is very formal. to which 的形式極其正式: *He would lunch in one of the clubs to which he belonged.* 他參加了幾家俱樂部, 經常在其中一家吃中飯。You would more usually say 英語平常的說法是: *...one of the clubs (that) he belonged to*
In relative clauses that add information but do not restrict the meaning of what comes before, you usually use **which**, especially after a comma 在補充信息但不限制先前的意思的關係從句中, 尤其在逗號之後, 通常用 which: *He's always really rude, which is why people tend to avoid him.* 他老是粗魯不堪, 所以人們總是躲着他。

which·ev·er /hwɪtʃˈɛvɚ; wɪtʃˈevə/ *determiner, pron* **1** used to say that it does not matter what thing you choose, what you do etc because it does not change the situation or someone's intention 無論哪個; 無論哪些: *You can have whichever you like best.* 你可以拿你最喜歡的。| *Whichever way you look at it this is disastrous news for the shipping industry.* 無論你怎麼看, 對航運業而言, 這是駭人聽聞的消息。**2** used to talk about a specific thing, method etc ...的那一個〔說及特定的事情、方法等〕: *I'll use whichever remedy the vet recommends.* 我將用獸醫推薦的那一種治療法。

whiff /hwɪf; wɪf/ *n* [C] **1** a very slight smell or something 一陣氣味: **[+of]** *a whiff of garlic* 一股大蒜味 | **get/catch a whiff of** *As she walked past, I caught a whiff of her perfume.* 當她走過時, 我聞到她身上的一股香水味。**2 a whiff of danger/adventure/freedom etc** a slight sign that something dangerous, exciting etc might happen 些微危險/冒險/自由等的跡象: *At the first whiff of trouble he was off like a shot.* 一有麻煩的跡象, 他馬上躲開了。

whif·fy /ˈhwɪfɪ; ˈwɪfi/ *adj BrE informal* having an unpleasant smell【英, 非正式】發出臭氣的

Whig /hwɪg; wɪg/ *n* [C] a member of a British political party of the 18th and early 19th centuries which wanted to limit royal power, and later became the Liberal Party 輝格黨黨員〔輝格黨是 18 世紀及 19 世紀初期英國的一個政黨, 主張限制王室權力, 後成為自由黨〕

while¹ /hwaɪl; waɪl/ *conjunction* **1** during the time that something is happening 當...時, 在...時: *They arrived while we were having dinner.* 他們來的時候, 我們正在吃飯。| *He got malaria while travelling in Africa.* 他在非洲旅行時患上了瘧疾。**2** if something happens while something else is happening, it happens at the same time as it 與...同時(發生): *He was so tired he fell asleep while reading the newspaper.* 他疲憊不堪, 看着報紙就睡着了。**3** used to emphasize the difference between two situations, activities etc 卻; 但是; 而〔用於強調兩種情況、活動等之間的差別〕: *That region has plenty of natural resources while this one has none.* 那個地區自然資源豐富, 這個地區卻一點也沒有。**4** used to show that you partly agree with, or accept something but not completely 雖然, 儘管〔表示部分同意或接受某事〕: *While she is a likeable girl she can be extremely difficult to work with.* 她雖然是一個可愛的姑娘, 但有時很難與她共事。

while² *n* **a while** a period of time, especially a short one 一段時間, 〔尤指〕一會兒: *Can you wait a while or do you have to leave right now?* 你能等一會兒還是現在必須就走? | **a short/little while** *Bob's only been working here a short while.* 鮑勃在這裡只工作了很短的一段時間。| **for a while** *He sat for a while, thinking about what Janice had said to him.* 他坐了一會兒, 思忖着賈妮絲跟他說過的話。| **quite a while** (=a fairly long time) 相當長的一段時間 | **all the while** (=all the time) 一直, 始終 —see also 另見 **once in a while** (ONCE¹ (8)), **it's worth your while** (WORTH¹ (5))

while³ *v* **while away the hours/evening/days etc** to spend time in a pleasant and lazy way 消磨時間/夜晚/日子等: *We whiled away the summer evenings talking and drinking wine.* 我們聊天、喝酒來打發夏日的夜晚。

whilst /hwaɪlst; waɪlst/ *conj especially BrE formal* WHILE¹【尤英, 正式】當...時; 與...同時; 卻; 儘管 S2 W2

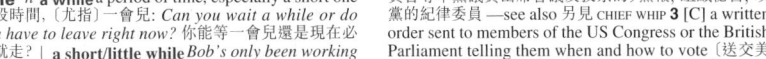

whim /hwɪm; wɪm/ *n* [C] a sudden feeling that you would like to do something or have something, especially when there is no particularly important or good reason 突發的念頭, 一時的興致: **on a whim** (=because of a whim) 興之所至 *I went to visit her on a whim.* 我心血來潮就去看她了。| **at the whim of** *The palace decor kept changing at the whim of the princess.* 宮殿的裝飾隨着公主的心意不斷更換。| **a passing whim** (=one that will soon be forgotten) 短暫的念頭 | **sb's every whim** *I was spoiled. My every whim was catered to.* 我被寵壞了, 我的每一個怪念頭都得到迎合。

whim·per /ˈhwɪmpɚ; ˈwɪmpə/ *v* [I] to make low crying sounds, or to speak in this way 嗚咽, 啜泣; 抽噎地說: *The dog whimpered in the corner.* 狗在角落處嗚咽地叫。| *"Okay," he managed to whimper.* 他啜泣着說: "好的。" —**whimper** *n* [C]

whim·si·cal /ˈhwɪmzɪkḷ; ˈwɪmzɪkəl/ *adj* unusual or strange and often amusing 古怪的; 異想天開的: *a whimsical smile* 古怪的笑 —**whimsically** /-klɪ; -kli/ *adv* —**whimsicality** /ˌhwɪmzəˈkælətɪ; ˌwɪmzɪˈkæləti/ *n* [U]

whim·sy /ˈhwɪmzɪ; ˈwɪmzi/ *n* **1** [U] a way of thinking or behaving that is unusual, strange, and often amusing 古怪〔而往往好笑的〕想法; 古怪[荒誕]行徑 **2** [C] a strange idea or desire that does not seem to have any sensible purpose 離奇的想法, 怪念頭: *This room, by some architectural whimsy, completely unbalanced the house.* 由於建築上的一些奇思怪想, 這房間使整棟房屋完全失去了均衡感。

whine /hwaɪn; waɪn/ *v* [I] **1** to complain in a sad, annoying voice about something 哀訴; 嘀咕: *For goodness sake stop whining, it's not much further to go.* 千萬不要抱怨了, 沒有多少路要走了。| **[+about]** *Mark always seems to be whining about his job.* 馬克好像總是對自己的工作埋怨個沒完。**2** to make a long high sound because you are in pain or unhappy 〔因痛楚或不愉快而〕悲鳴, 哀叫: *a dog whining outside the door* 門外一條哀叫的狗 **3** if a machine whines, it makes a continuous high sound 〔機器〕發出嘎嘎響 —**whine** *n* [C] *the whine of the plane's engine* 飛機引擎的嗡嗡聲 —**whiner** *n* [C]

whinge /wɪndʒ; wɪndʒ/ *v* [I] *BrE or AustrE* to keep complaining in an annoying way【英或澳】嘮叨; 嘀咕: *Stop whingeing and get on with it!* 不要嘀嘀咕咕個沒完, 繼續幹下去! —**whinge** *n* [C] —**whinger** *n* [C] *People with genuine grievances are being dismissed as whingers.* 真正受委屈的人被當作發牢騷者解雇了。

whin·ny /ˈhwɪnɪ; ˈwɪni/ *v* [I] if a horse whinnies, it NEIGHS (=makes the sound that horses makes) quietly 〔馬〕輕聲嘶叫 —**whinny** *n* [C]

whip¹ /hwɪp; wɪp/ *n* **1** [C] a long thin piece of rope or leather with a handle used for making animals move or punishing people 〔趕牲口或懲罰人用的〕鞭子: **crack a whip** (=make a loud noise with a whip) 甩響鞭 **2** [C] a member of the US Congress or the British Parliament who is responsible for making sure that the members of their party attend and vote 〔美國國會或英國議會中負責督導本黨議員出席會議及投票的〕黨鞭; 組織祕書; 政黨的紀律委員 —see also 另見 CHIEF WHIP **3** [C] a written order sent to members of the US Congress or the British Parliament telling them when and how to vote 〔送交美國國會或英國議會議員有關投票事宜的〕書面通知 —see

whip 鞭子

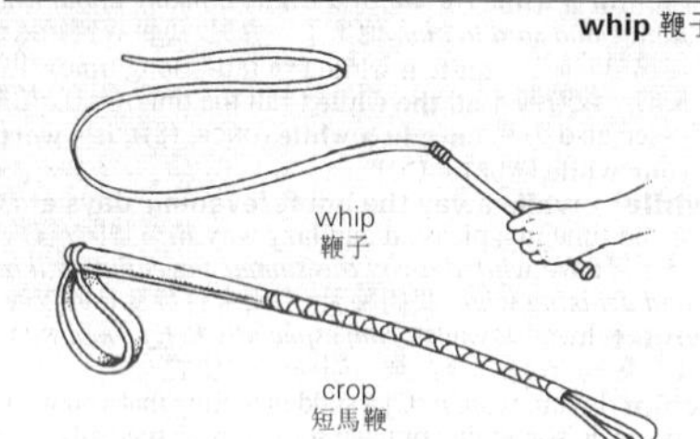

also 另見 TWO-LINE WHIP, THREE-LINE WHIP **4 chocolate whip/strawberry whip etc** [C,U] *BrE* a sweet dish made from the white part of eggs and chocolate or fruit, beaten together to make a smooth, light mixture【英】〔蛋清、巧克力或水果攪拌而成的〕巧克力／草莓甜點等 —see also 另見 **crack the whip** (CRACK[1] (20)), **give sb a fair crack of the whip** (FAIR[1] (11))

whip², **whipped, whipping** *v* **1** [T] to hit someone with a whip 鞭打〔某人〕 **2** [I always+adv/prep] [T always+adv/prep] to move quickly and violently, or to make something do this 迅速[猛地]移動: **[+across/around/past etc]** *The wind whipped across the plain.* 大風掃過平原。| **whip sth about/around** *The branches were being whipped about in the storm.* 樹枝在狂風中四處搖曳。| **whip around/round** (=turn around quickly) 快速轉身 *Suddenly, he whipped around and glared at them.* 突然之間, 他轉過身來, 對着他們怒目而視。**3** [T always+adv/prep] to move or remove something with a quick sudden movement 突然移動[挪開]〔某物〕: **[+away/off/out etc]** *He whipped out a gun.* 他突然抽出槍來。**4** [T] also 又作 **whip up** to mix cream or the clear part of an egg very hard until it becomes stiff 攪打〔奶油或蛋清〕使成糊狀 —see also 另見 WHISK[1], BEAT[1] (7) **5 have the whip hand** to have power and control over someone 支配[控制]某人 **6** [T] to make a TOP[1] (25) spin by using a piece of string fixed to a stick 抽〔陀螺並使之轉動〕 **7** [T] *BrE informal* to steal something【英, 非正式】偷走〔某物〕

whip through sth *phr v* [T] *informal especially BrE* to finish a job very quickly【非正式, 尤英】快速做完: *I can whip through all the cleaning in about half an hour.* 在大約半小時之內, 我能很快地把所有清潔工作做完。

whip up *phr v* [T] **1 whip up support/anger/enthusiasm etc** to deliberately try to make people feel or react strongly 引發支持／煽起憤怒／激起熱情等: *The rally was organised to whip up support for the independence campaign.* 組織羣眾集會以激起對獨立運動的支持。| **whip up a crowd** *a speech designed to whip up the crowd* 意在鼓動民眾的演講 **2** [**whip** sth ↔ **up**] to quickly make something to eat 匆匆做好〔飯菜〕: *I just had time to whip up a light salad before I went out again.* 我在再次外出前正好有時間匆匆做一份清淡的沙律。

whip·cord /ˈhwɪpˌkɔrd; ˈwɪpkɔːd/ *n* [U] **1** a strong type of CORD[1] (1) 鞭繩〔一種結實的細繩〕 **2** a strong woollen material 馬褲呢

whip·lash /ˈhwɪpˌlæʃ; ˈwɪp-læʃ/ *n* [C,U] a neck injury caused when your head moves forward and back again suddenly and violently, especially in a car accident 鞭抽式損傷〔尤指汽車事故中頸椎過度屈伸損傷〕

whipped cream /ˌ· ˈ·/ *n* [U] cream that has been beaten until it is thick, eaten on sweet foods〔作為甜點食用的〕攢奶油

whip·per·snap·per /ˈhwɪpɚˌsnæpɚ; ˈwɪpəˌsnæpə/ *n* [C] *old-fashioned* a young person who is too confident and does not show enough respect to older people【過時】妄自尊大的年輕人, 傲慢無禮的小子

whip·pet /ˈhwɪpɪt; ˈwɪpɪt/ *n* [C] a small thin racing dog like a GREYHOUND〔賽跑用的〕小靈狗

whip·ping /ˈhwɪpɪŋ; ˈwɪpɪŋ/ *n* [C usually singular 一般用單數] a punishment given to someone by whipping them; WHIP[2] (1)〔作為懲罰的〕鞭笞; 鞭刑

whipping boy /ˈ·· ·/ *n* [singular] someone or something that is blamed for someone else's mistakes; SCAPEGOAT 代人受過者, 替罪羊

whipping cream /ˈ·· ˌ·/ *n* [U] a type of cream that becomes very stiff when you beat it 可打稠製作攢奶油的奶油

whip·poor·will /ˌhwɪpɚˈwɪl; ˈwɪpʊəˌwɪl/ *n* [C] a small North American bird which makes a noise that sounds like its name 三聲夜鷹〔一種產於北美洲的小鳥〕

whip·py /ˈhwɪpɪ; ˈwɪpi/ *adj* long, thin, and easy to bend 鞭子似的; 易彎曲的

whip-round /ˈ· ·/ *n* **have a whip-round** *BrE informal* if a group of people have a whip-round, they all give some money so that they can buy something together【英, 非正式】〔一羣人〕湊錢〔買某物〕: *We're having a whip-round to get Sandy something for her birthday.* 我們正在湊錢買生日禮物送給桑迪。

whir /hwɝ; wɜː/ *v* [I] another spelling of WHIRR whirr 的另一種拼法

whirl¹ /hwɝl; wɜːl/ *v* **1** [I,T] to spin around very quickly, or to make something do this 急轉; 迅速旋轉: **[+about/around/toward etc]** *The snowflakes whirled around as they fell to the ground.* 雪花打着轉飄落到地面。| **whirl sth about/around/away etc** *Jim whirled the bike around.* 吉姆飛快地騎着自行車。**2** [I] if your head is whirling, your mind is full of thoughts and ideas, and you feel very confused or excited 暈眩; 〔思緒〕混亂

whirl² *n* [C usually singular 一般用單數] **1** a whirling movement 旋轉, 回旋: *a whirl of dust* 捲起的塵土 **2 give sth a whirl** *informal* to try something that you are not sure you are going to like or be able to do【非正式】嘗試〔不知道是否會喜歡或做得到的〕某事 **3** [singular] a lot of activity of a particular kind 接連不斷的某類活動: *the mad social whirl around Christmas* 聖誕節期間紛亂繁忙的社交活動 **4 be in a whirl** to feel very excited or confused about something〔對某事感到〕十分興奮; 一片混亂

whir·li·gig /ˈhwɝlɪˌgɪg; ˈwɜːlɪˌgɪg/ *n* [C] **1** a toy that spins; TOP[1] (25) 旋轉式玩具; 陀螺 **2** a MERRY-GO-ROUND (1) 旋轉木馬

whirl·pool /ˈhwɝlˌpul; ˈwɜːlpuːl/ *n* [C] a powerful current of water that spins around and can pull things down into it 漩渦

whirl·wind /ˈhwɝlˌwɪnd; ˈwɜːlˌwɪnd/ *n* [C] **1** an extremely strong wind that moves quickly with a circular movement, causing a lot of damage 旋風, 龍捲風; TORNADO, TWISTER (2) *AmE*【美】 **2 a whirlwind romance/tour etc** something that happens much more quickly than usual 旋風式戀愛／旅行等〔指發生的速度很快〕 **3 a whirlwind of activity/emotions etc** a situation in which you experience a lot of different activities or emotions one after another 一連串的活動／激情等

whirr /hwɝ; wɜː/ **whirred, whirring** *v* [I] to make a fairly quiet, regular sound, like the sound of a bird or insect moving its wings very fast〔像鳥或昆蟲快速拍動翅膀一樣〕呼呼作響; 啪啪作響: *Cameras whirred and reporters scribbled.* 照相機刷刷地響, 記者匆匆地記錄。—**whirr** *n* [C usually singular 一般用單數] —see picture on page A19 參見 A19 頁圖

whisk¹ /hwɪsk; wɪsk/ *v* [T] to mix liquid or soft things very quickly so that air is mixed in, especially with a fork or a whisk〔尤指用叉或攪拌器〕攪打

whisk sb/sth ↔ **away** *phr v* [T] **1** to take or remove something very quickly 迅速拿開〔某物〕: *He whisked the letter away before I could read it.* 他沒等我看就匆匆把信拿走了。**2** to take someone quickly away from a place 將〔某人〕急忙送離〔某地〕: *At the end of the concert the band was whisked away to a secret location.* 音樂會結束時, 樂隊被匆匆送往一個祕密場所。

whisk sb **off** *phr v* [T] to take someone quickly away from a place; whisk away 將〔某人〕急忙送離〔某地〕

whisk² *n* [C] **1** a small kitchen tool made of curved pieces of wire used for beating eggs, cream etc〔攪拌雞蛋、奶油等的〕攪拌器 —see picture on page A11 參見 A11 頁圖 **2** [usually singular 一般用單數] a quick light sweeping movement 掃; 拂, 撣: **[+of]** *The cow brushed away the flies with a whisk of its tail.* 這頭母牛甩動尾巴拂去蒼蠅。

whisk broom /ˈ· ·/ *n* [C] *AmE* a small stiff BROOM (1) that you use to brush clothes【美】〔刷衣服用的〕撣帚; 小笤帚

whis·ker /ˈhwɪskɚ; ˈwɪskə/ *n* [C] **1** one of the long, stiff hairs that grow near the mouth of a cat, mouse etc〔貓、老鼠等嘴邊的〕鬚 **2 whiskers** [plural] the hair that grows on a man's face〔男人的〕連鬢鬍子, 頰鬚, 髯鬚 **3 do sth by a whisker/come within a whisker** *informal* to only just fail or just manage to do something【非正式】〔做某事〕險些…: *We came within a whisker of defeat.* (=were almost defeated) 我們差點戰敗了。—**whiskery** *adj*

whis·key /ˈhwɪskɪ; ˈwɪski/ *n* [C,U] a strong alcoholic drink made in Ireland or the US from grain, or a glass of this〔愛爾蘭或美國生產的〕威士忌酒; 一杯威士忌酒

3 **whis·ky** /ˈhwɪskɪ; ˈwɪski/ *n* [C,U] a strong alcoholic drink made in Scotland from grain such as BARLEY, or a glass of this〔蘇格蘭產〕威士忌酒; 一杯威士忌酒

3 **whis·per¹** /ˈhwɪspɚ; ˈwɪspə/ *v* **1** [I,T] to speak or say something very quietly, using your breath rather than your voice 悄聲說; 低語; 耳語: *What are you two whispering about over there?* 你們兩人在那邊嘀咕甚麼? | **whisper sth to sb** *James leaned over to whisper something to Michael.* 詹姆斯俯身跟邁克爾低聲說了點甚麼。 **2** [T+that] to say or suggest something privately or secretly〔私下或祕密地〕傳說〔某事〕: *Some White House staff were whispering that the President was no longer in control.* 一些白宮職員在竊竊私語, 說總統不再掌權了。

whisper² *n* [C] **1** a very quiet voice, when you are whispering 低語; 耳語: **in a whisper** *"They're coming," he said in an excited whisper.* 他壓低聲音激動地說: "他們來了。" **2** a piece of news or information that has not been officially announced; RUMOUR 傳聞; 謠言: *The first whisper of the redundancies came from the newspapers.* 最初的裁員消息來自報紙。| **[+that]** *I've heard a whisper that he's going to resign.* 我聽到一個傳聞, 說他準備辭職。**3 a whisper of wind/silk etc** *literary* a low soft sound made by wind etc【文】〔風、絲綢等〕輕柔的颯颯聲

whis·per·ing cam·paign /ˈ··· ·,·/ *n* [C] an attack on someone that is made by privately spreading criticism about them 造謠活動〔指私下散佈謠言攻擊某人〕

whist /hwɪst; wɪst/ *n* [U] a card game for four players in two pairs, in which each pair tries to win the most tricks (TRICK¹ (11))〔由四人組成兩方對打的〕惠斯特紙牌戲

whist drive /ˈ· ·/ *n* [C] a meeting to play whist between several pairs of partners who change opponents 惠斯特紙牌戲比賽

whis·tle¹ /ˈhwɪsḷ; ˈwɪsəl/ *v*

1 ▶HIGH SOUND 高聲◀ [I,T] to make a high or musical sound by blowing air out through your lips 吹口哨; 用口哨吹奏〔曲調〕: *Adam whistled happily as he walked along.* 亞當一邊走一邊愉快地吹着口哨。| **whistle a song/tune** *I heard this song on the radio and I've been whistling it all day.* 我在收音機裡聽過這首歌, 然後整天用口哨吹它的曲調。| **whistle to sb** (=to get their attention) 向某人吹口哨〔以引起對方注意〕 *Adrian whistled to them but they didn't seem to hear him.* 阿德里安向他們吹口哨, 可是他們看來沒有聽見。

2 ▶USE A WHISTLE 用哨子◀ [I] to make a high sound by blowing into a whistle 吹哨子: *The referee whistled and the game began.* 裁判哨聲一響, 比賽開始了。

3 ▶GO/MOVE FAST 快速運動◀ [I always+adv/prep] to move quickly with a whistling sound 呼嘯着行進: *Bullets and shells were whistling overhead.* 子彈和砲彈在頭頂呼嘯而過。

4 ▶STEAM TRAIN/KETTLE 蒸汽火車/水壺◀ [I] to make a high sound when air or steam is forced through a small hole 鳴汽笛; 響壺哨

5 ▶BIRD 鳥◀ [I] to make a high, often musical sound〔鳥〕囀鳴

6 whistle in the dark *informal* to try to show that you are brave when really you are afraid【非正式】借吹口哨壯膽, 故作鎮定: *Her fine words had been so much whistling in the dark.* 她的豪言壯語都是虛張聲勢。

7 you can whistle for it *BrE spoken* used to tell someone that there is no chance of them getting what they have asked for【英口】空指望; 一定得不到〔想要的東西〕

8 not be whistling Dixie *AmE spoken* to be saying something because it is true, not just because you wish it was true【美口】認真的〔表示某物是真的, 並非出於個人願望〕: *Hey, this is good – and I'm not just whistling Dixie.* 嘿, 這個好 —— 我不是鬧着玩的。

whistle² *n* [C] **1** a small object that produces a high whistling sound when you blow into it 哨子: **blow a whistle** *Wait till the referee blows his whistle.* 等到裁判吹響哨子。—see also 另見 PENNY WHISTLE **2** a high sound made by blowing a whistle, by blowing air out through your lips, or when air or steam is forced through a small opening 口哨聲; 哨子聲; 汽笛聲 —see also 另見 WOLF WHISTLE **3** the sound of something moving quickly through the air 呼嘯聲: *the whistle of the wind in the trees* 風吹過樹林的呼嘯聲 —see also 另見 **blow the whistle on** (BLOW¹ (22)), **as clean as a whistle** (CLEAN¹ (19)), **wet your whistle** (WET² (3))

whistle-blow·er /ˈ·· ,··/ *n* [C] someone who tells people in authority or the public about dishonest or illegal practices in business, government etc〔將企業、政府等中的欺詐或非法行為揭發出來的〕告發者, 告密者 —see also 另見 **blow the whistle on** (BLOW¹ (22)) —**whistle-blowing** *n* [U]

whistle-stop /ˈ·· ·/ *n* [C] *AmE* a town where trains stop only if there are passengers who want to get on or off【美】〔遇有乘客想上、下火車才停的〕小鎮

whistle-stop tour /,·· · ˈ·/ *n* [C] a very quick trip around a place 短暫的旅行訪問: *a whistle-stop tour of the United States* 對美國作短暫的旅行訪問

Whit /hwɪt; wɪt/ *n* [C,U] *especially BrE* WHITSUN【尤英】聖靈降臨節

whit *n* **not a whit** *old use* not at all【舊】一點不, 毫不

white¹ /hwaɪt; waɪt/ *adj* **1** having the colour of milk, salt or snow 白的; 白色的; 雪白的: *white paint* 白油漆 —see picture on page A5 參見 A5 頁圖 **2** looking pale, because of illness, strong emotion etc〔因疾病、感情激動等而面色〕蒼白的; 無血色的: **white with anger/fear etc** *Her face was white with fear.* 她嚇得臉色發白。| **white as a sheet** (=extremely pale because you are frightened, ill etc)〔因驚慌、生病等〕面色蒼白 **3 a)** belonging to a race with pale skin〔人〕白種的 **b)** of or for white people 白人的; 白人用的: *a white neighborhood* 白人居住區 **4** white coffee has milk or cream in it〔咖啡〕加牛奶[奶油]的 —opposite 反義詞 BLACK¹ (3) **5** white wine is a very pale yellow or pale green colour〔白葡萄酒〕淡黃色的; 淺綠色的 —**whiteness** *n* [U] 1 1

white² *n* **1** [U] the colour of milk, salt, and snow 白色 **2** [C] someone who belongs to a pale-skinned race 白種人, 白人: *The party got a lot of support from South Africa's whites.* 該政黨得到眾多南非白人的支持。**3** [C+of] the white part of your eye 眼白 **4** [C,U] the transparent part of an egg that surrounds the YOLK (=yellow part) 蛋清, 蛋白 **5 whites** [plural] **a)** white clothes, sheets etc, which are separated from dark colours when they are washed〔洗滌時要跟深色衣物分開的〕白色衣服[牀單]等 **b)** *especially BrE* white clothes that are worn for some sports, such as TENNIS【尤英】〔做某些運動, 如 

口語及書面語中最常用的 1 000詞, 2 000詞, 3 000詞

打網球時穿的〕白色運動服

white ant /ˌ· ˈ·/ *n* [C] a TERMITE 白蟻

white·bait /ˈhwaɪtˌbet; ˈwaɪtbeɪt/ *n* [U] very young fish of several types, used as food 銀魚〔數種供食用的魚類之幼魚〕: *deep-fried whitebait* 油炸銀魚

white blood cell /ˌ· ˈ· ·/ *n* [C] one of the cells in your blood which fights against infection; LEUCOCYTE 白細胞, 白血球 —compare 比較 RED BLOOD CELL

white·board /ˈhwaɪtˌbɔrd; ˈwaɪtbɔːd/ *n* [C] a large board with a white, smooth surface used in classrooms for writing on〔教室裡表面白色而光滑, 書寫用的〕白板 —compare 比較 BLACKBOARD —see picture at 參見 BOARD[1] 圖

white-bread /ˈ· ·/ *adj AmE informal* ordinary and traditional in your opinions and way of life【美, 非正式】〔意見和生活方式〕平淡無奇的, 恪守傳統的; 典型白人中產階級口味的: *a white-bread family* 典型白人中產階級家庭

white·caps /ˈhwaɪtˌkæps; ˈwaɪtkæps/ *n* [plural] *AmE* WHITE HORSES【美】白浪

white-col·lar /ˌ· ˈ··◂/ *adj* **1** white-collar workers work in offices, banks etc as opposed to people who work in factories, mines etc〔在辦公室、銀行等工作的〕白領階層的〔與在工廠、礦山等工作的人相比〕**2 white-collar crime** crimes involving white-collar workers, for example when someone secretly steals money from the organization they work for〔偷盜公款等〕白領罪行 —compare 比較 BLUE-COLLAR, PINK-COLLAR

white cor·pus·cle /ˌ· ˈ···/ *n* [C] a WHITE BLOOD CELL 白細胞, 白血球

white dwarf /ˌ· ˈ·/ *n* [C] *technical* a hot star, near the end of its life, that is more solid but less bright than the sun【術語】白矮星 —compare 比較 RED GIANT

white el·e·phant /ˌ· ˈ···/ *n* [C] something that is completely useless, although it may have cost a lot of money 昂貴而無用的東西

white flag /ˌ· ˈ·/ *n* [C] a sign that you accept that you have been defeated〔投降用的〕白旗: **wave/show the white flag** (=accept defeat) 揮動/舉起白旗〔投降〕*There was no question of the Republicans throwing in the towel or showing the white flag.* 共和黨黨員不會認輸, 這是毫無疑問的。

white flour /ˌ· ˈ·/ *n* [U] wheat flour from which the BRAN (=outer layer) and WHEAT GERM (=inside seed) have been removed〔去掉麥麩及麥胚的〕精白麵粉 —compare 比較 WHOLEMEAL

white goods /ˈ· ·/ *n* [plural] a word used especially in business meaning large pieces of equipment used in the home, for example washing machines and REFRIGERATORS 大型家用電器〔此詞尤用於商業, 指洗衣機、冰箱等〕—compare 比較 BLACK GOODS

White·hall /ˈhwaɪtˌhɔl; ˈwaɪthɔːl/ *n* [U] **1** the British government, especially the government departments rather than parliament or the Prime Minister 英國政府〔尤指政府部門而不是議會或首相〕**2** the street in London where many of the government departments are 白廳〔英國很多政府部門所在的倫敦的一條街道〕

white heat /ˌ· ˈ·/ *n* [U] the very high temperature at which a metal turns white 白熱〔金屬變成白色的高温〕—see also 另見 WHITE-HOT

white hors·es /ˌ· ˈ··/ *n* [plural] *BrE* waves in the sea or on a lake that are white at the top【英】白浪; WHITECAPS *AmE*【美】

white-hot /ˌ· ˈ·◂/ *adj* white-hot metal is so hot that it shines white〔金屬〕白熱的

White House /ˈ· ·/ *n* **the White House 1** the President of the US and the people who advise him 美國總統〔及其顧問人員〕**2** the official home in Washington DC of the President of the US 白宮〔美國總統官邸, 在華盛頓特區〕

white knight /ˌ· ˈ·/ *n* [C] a person or company that puts money into a business in order to save it from being controlled by another company〔為某公司提供資金使其免受其他公司控制的〕救星, 救急的人或公司

white-knuck·led /ˌ· ˈ··◂/ *adj* anxious or afraid 神經緊張的; 害怕的

white lead /ˌhwaɪt ˈlɛd; ˌwaɪt ˈled/ *n* [U] a poisonous compound of lead with CARBON (1) and oxygen, used in the past in house paint〔以前用於油漆的〕鉛白

white lie /ˌ· ˈ·/ *n* [C] *informal* a lie that you tell in order to avoid hurting someone's feelings【非正式】善意的謊話; 無傷大雅的謊言

white light·ning /ˌ· ˈ··/ *n* [U] *AmE slang* MOONSHINE (=illegal strong alcohol)【美俚】非法釀造的烈酒

white ma·gic /ˌ· ˈ··/ *n* [U] magic used for good purposes 善意的法術, 白法術, 白魔術 —compare 比較 BLACK MAGIC

white meat /ˈ· ·/ *n* [U] meat that is pale in colour, especially from some types of cooked bird, for example chicken 白肉〔尤指某些家禽煮熟的肉〕—compare 比較 RED MEAT

whit·en /ˈhwaɪtn̩; ˈwaɪtn/ *v* [I,T] to become more white, or to make something do this 使更白; 變白; 漂白; 刷白

whit·en·er /ˈhwaɪtnɚ; ˈwaɪtnə/ also 又作 **whit·en·ing** /ˈhwaɪtnɪŋ; ˈwaɪtnɪŋ/ *n* [C,U] a substance used to make something more white 增白劑

white noise /ˌ· ˈ·/ *n* [U] noise coming from a radio or television which is turned on but not tuned (TUNE[2] (3)) to any programme 白噪聲〔收音機或電視機沒有調到有廣播節目的頻道而發出〕

white-out /ˈhwaɪtˌaut; ˈwaɪtaʊt/ *n* **1** [C] weather conditions in which there is so much cloud or snow that you cannot see anything 乳白天空〔一種天氣現象, 因雲或冰雪太多而使人眼花繚亂〕**2** [U] *AmE* TIPP-EX【美】修正液, 塗改液

White Pag·es /ˌ· ˈ··/ *n* **the White Pages** the white part of a telephone DIRECTORY in the US with the names, addresses, and phone numbers of people with telephones 白頁電話簿〔美國的電話簿, 刊登電話用戶的姓名、地址和電話號碼〕—compare 比較 YELLOW PAGES

White Pa·per /ˌ· ˈ··/ *n* [C] an official report from the British government, explaining their ideas and plans concerning a particular subject before a new law is introduced 白皮書〔英國政府就某一問題在立法前所作的正式報告〕—compare 比較 GREEN PAPER

white pep·per /ˌ· ˈ··/ *n* [U] a white powder made from the crushed inside of a PEPPERCORN which gives a slightly hot taste to food 白胡椒粉

white sale /ˈ· ·/ *n* [C] *AmE* a period when sheets, TOWELS etc, are sold for a lower price【美】〔牀單、毛巾等〕家用織物的削價銷售期

white sauce /ˌ· ˈ·/ *n* [C,U] a thick white liquid made of flour, milk, and butter which is sometimes eaten with meat and vegetables 白汁, 白汁沙司〔用麵粉、牛奶和黃油做成, 有時拌着肉和蔬菜吃〕

white slav·e·ry /ˌ· ˈ···/ *n* [U] *old-fashioned* the practice or business of taking girls to a foreign country and forcing them to be PROSTITUTES【過時】販賣婦女到外國為娼

white space /ˌ· ˈ·/ *n* [U] *AmE informal* free time【美, 非正式】自由時間; 閒暇時間

white spir·it /ˌ· ˈ··/ *n* [U] *BrE* a chemical liquid made from petrol, used for making paint thinner, removing marks on clothes etc; TURPENTINE【英】〔稀釋油漆等用的〕石油溶劑油

white su·prem·a·cy /ˌ· ·ˈ···/ *n* [U] the belief that white people are better than other races and that other races should be kept at a lower social level 白人至上〔認為白人比其他人種優越, 應把其他人種限制在社會低層的看法〕—**white supremacist** *n* [C]

white-tailed deer /ˌ· · ˈ·/ *n* [C] a common North American DEER with a long tail that is partly white〔產於北美, 長尾巴部分呈白色的〕白尾鹿

white-tie /ˌ· ˈ·◂/ *adj* a white-tie social occasion is a very formal one at which the men wear white BOW TIES and tails (TAIL[1] (5b))〔非常正式的社交場合〕繫白領結、穿燕尾服的 —compare 比較 BLACK-TIE

white trash /ˌ· ˈ·/ *n* [U] *AmE informal* an insulting expression meaning white people who are poor and uneducated【美, 非正式】〔冒犯語〕窮苦白人

white·wall /ˈhwaɪtˌwɔl; ˈwaɪtwɔːl/ *n* [C] *AmE* a car tyre that has a wide white band on its side【美】胎壁上有寬闊白色環子的輪胎, 白胎壁輪胎

white·wash¹ /ˈhwaɪtˌwɑʃ; ˈwaɪtwɒʃ/ *n* **1** [C,U] a report or examination of events that hides the true facts about something so that the person who is responsible will not be punished 掩飾真相; 粉飾 **2** [U] a white liquid mixture used especially for painting walls〔尤指刷牆用的〕石灰水 **3** [C] an easy win in sport〔在體育運動中〕輕而易舉的勝利

whitewash² *v* [T] **1** to hide the true facts about a serious accident or illegal action 掩飾〔嚴重意外或非法行為的真相〕; 粉飾 **2** to cover something with whitewash 用石灰水粉刷〔某物〕 **3** to defeat an opponent in sport easily〔在體育運動中〕輕鬆擊敗〔對手〕

white·wa·ter /ˌhwaɪtˈwɔtɚ; ˌwaɪtˈwɔːtə◂/ *n* [U] a part of a river that looks white because the water is running very quickly over rocks; RAPIDS〔河水撞擊岩石後的〕白浪; 湍流: *whitewater canoeing* 激流中划獨木舟

white wed·ding /ˌ· ˈ··/ *n* [C] a traditional wedding at which the woman being married wears a long white dress 新娘披白色婚紗的婚禮

whit·ey /ˈhwaɪtɪ; ˈwaɪti/ *n* [C,U] *AmE slang an* insulting word for a white person or white people in general, used especially by black people【美俚】白鬼〔尤用於黑人稱白人〕

whith·er /ˈhwɪðɚ; ˈwɪðə/ *adv old use*【舊】**1** a word meaning 'to which', used when talking about places 去何處; 往哪兒: *the place whither he went* 他去的那個地方 **2** a word meaning 'where' …的地方 **3** *formal* a word used to ask what the future of something will be or how it will develop【正式】向何處去〔用於問某事的未來或發展〕: *Whither European Union?* 歐洲聯盟何去何從? —compare 比較 WHENCE

whit·ing /ˈhwaɪtɪŋ; ˈwaɪtɪŋ/ *n* [C] a black and silver fish that lives in the sea and can be eaten 牙鱈〔一種可食用的海魚〕

whit·ish /ˈhwaɪtɪʃ; ˈwaɪtɪʃ/ *adj* almost white in colour 帶白色的

Whit·sun /ˈhwɪtsn̩; ˈwɪtsən/ *n* [C,U] **1** also 又作 **Whit Sun·day** /ˌ· ˈ··/ the seventh Sunday after Easter, when Christians celebrate the HOLY SPIRIT coming down from heaven; PENTECOST² 聖靈降臨節〔復活節後第七個星期日〕 **2** also 又作 **Whit·sun·tide** /ˈhwɪtsənˌtaɪd; ˈwɪtsəntaɪd/ the period around Whitsun 聖靈降臨週

whit·tle /ˈhwɪtl; ˈwɪtl/ *v* [I,T] to cut a piece of wood into a particular shape by cutting off small pieces with a small knife 削〔木頭〕

whittle sth ↔ **away** *phr v* [T] to gradually reduce the amount or value of something 削減, 削弱: *centralizing measures that had whittled away the powers of local government* 削弱了地方政府權力的中央集權措施

whittle sth ↔ **down** *phr v* [T] to gradually make something smaller by taking parts away 逐漸減少, 縮小: *I've whittled down the list of people from 30 to 16.* 我已經把名單上的人由 30 人減少到 16 人。

whizz¹ also 又作 **whiz** *especially AmE*【尤美】/hwɪz; wɪz/ *v* [I] **1** [always+adv/prep] *informal*【非正式】**a)** to move very quickly, often making a sound like something rushing through the air 颼颼地飛馳: **[+by/around/past]** *Martin whizzed by us on his bicycle.* 馬丁騎着自行車颼的一聲從我們身邊經過。**b)** to do something very quickly 迅速地做完〔某事〕: *Let's just whizz through it one more time.* 讓我們快速再幹一遍。**2** *AmE spoken* to URINATE【美口】撒尿 —see also 另見 GEE WHIZ

whizz² also 又作 **whiz** *especially AmE*【尤美】*n* **1** [C] *informal* someone who is very fast, intelligent, or skilled in a particular activity【非正式】快手, 高手, 能人: *a whiz on the computer* 電腦高手 **2** *AmE spoken* [singular] an act of urinating (URINATE)【美口】撒尿

whizz-bang, whizbang /ˌhwɪzˈbæŋ; ˌwɪzˈbæŋ/ *n* [C] *AmE informal* something that is noticed a lot because it is very good, loud, or fast【美, 非正式】非同尋常[引人注目]的東西: *a whizzbang of a stereo* 引人注目的立體聲音響

whizz-kid also 又作 **whizkid** *especially AmE*【尤美】/ˈhwɪzkɪd; ˈwɪzkɪd/ *n* [C] *informal* a young person who is very skilled or successful at something【非正式】神童; 年輕有為的人: *financial whizzkids in the City* 該市的年輕理財能手

who /hu; huː/ *pron* **1** used in questions to ask what person or people 誰, 甚麼人〔用於問句〕: *Who's that woman over there?* 在那邊的那個女人是誰? | *Did they find out who stole the money?* 他們查明是誰偷錢的了嗎? | *Who did you stay with?* 你和誰住在一起? **2** used in a question or statement to show what person or people you are talking about …的人〔用於問句或陳述句, 指代提及的人〕: *Do you know the people who live over the road?* 你認識住在馬路對面的人嗎? | *A postman is a man who delivers letters.* 郵遞員是送信的人。**3** used especially in written language after a COMMA, to add more information about a person or people 他, 她; 他們, 她們〔尤用於書面語, 置於逗號之後, 以提供更多關於某人的資料〕: *I discussed it with my brother, who is a lawyer.* 我和我弟弟商討了此事, 他是律師。**4 who are you to...?** used to say that someone should not judge someone or something because they have faults themselves or do not have the necessary experience 你憑甚麼…?〔指某人不應提出批評, 因他本身也有缺點或沒有所需的經驗〕: *Who am I to say how you should bring up your kids; I don't have any.* 我憑甚麼告訴你應該如何養育孩子; 我一個孩子都沒有。**5 who's who** the people within a particular organization or group and how important each person is, what their job is etc 誰是誰〔某組織或團體的人, 各人的地位、職位等〕: *I'm just getting to know who's who in the department.* 我正在了解部門每個人的情況。

USAGE NOTE 用法說明: WHO

FORMALITY 正式程度

Except in very formal English, **who** is used instead of **whom** as an object in all kinds of questions. 除了在非常正式的英語中, who 可替代 whom 在所有問句中用作賓語: *Who did you see?* 你看見了誰? | *I wonder who she married in the end.* 我想知道最終她和誰結婚。| *Who was she dancing with?* 她在和誰跳舞? Compare the much more formal 試和正式得多的英語相比: *With whom was she dancing?* 她在和誰跳舞?

The same is true when **who** is used in relative clauses that add information but do not restrict the meaning of the noun they follow, often after a comma. 在增加信息而不限制前面名詞的關係從句裡, 一般也用who 替代 whom, 這時 who常用在逗號之後: *This is Jed, who you haven't met before/who I work for* (=this is Jed, and I work for him). 這是傑德, 你以前沒有見過他/他是我的老闆。

In relative clauses that restrict the meaning of the noun, even **who** is rare as an object in informal or spoken English. Instead, **that** or nothing is used. 在非正式或口頭英語中, 限制名詞含義的關係從句的賓詞, 連 who 也不常用, 一般用 that 或甚麼都不用: *I'm the person (that) you need to see/speak to* (NOT 不用 *which*). 我就是你需要見的人/你要跟某人談話, 那人就是我。It would be very formal to say 極正式的說法: *... to whom you need to speak.* 你要與其談話的…。However, **whom** must be used immediately after a preposition, and you can avoid this by rephrasing your sentence. 然而, whom 必

須緊跟在介詞之後，改用其他措辭可避免這個現象。For example, instead of saying 例如，與其說：*To whom are you sending that letter?* It is much more natural to say 不如改用較自然的說法：*Who are you sending that letter to?* 那封信你寄給誰？

You can also use **that** instead of **who** when it is the subject of a relative clause. who 作為關係從句的主語時，也可用 that 替代：*I hate people who/that can't stop talking.* 我討厭嘮嘮叨叨的人。

GRAMMAR 語法

You can use **who** or **that** when a word for a group of people like **family** or **team** is followed by a plural verb (N.B. this is only usual in British English). 當 family 或 team 等表示一羣人的詞後跟複數動詞形式時，可用 who 或 that（注意，這種用法只常見於英國英語中）：*a family who quarrel among themselves* 一個吵吵鬧鬧的家庭。When such words are followed by a singular verb, you usually use **which** or **that** 當這類詞後跟單數動詞形式時，通常用 which 或 that: *a team which/that has won most of its games* 一支常勝的隊伍

whoa /hwo; wəʊ/ *interjection* a command given to a horse to make it stop 吁！〔用於吆喝馬停下〕

who·dun·it, whodunnit /hu`dʌnɪt; ˌhuːˈdʌnɪ̆t/ *n* [C] *informal* a book, film etc about a murder case, in which you do not find out who did the murder until the end【非正式】〔追查誰是兇手的〕偵探小說[影片]

2 **who·ev·er** /hu`ɛvɚ; huːˈevə/ *pron* **1** used to say that it does not matter who does something, is in a particular place etc 不管是甚麼人；無論是誰：*I'll take whoever wants to go.* 誰想去我就帶誰去。| **...or whoever** (=used to emphasize that you are talking about anyone and not about a specific person) 隨便誰〔用於強調所指是任何人〕*You could ask Gary or Jane or whoever really.* 你可以問加里或簡，或隨便誰都可以。**2** used to talk about a specific person or people〔用於指特定的人〕：*Whoever is responsible for this will be punished.* 對此事有責任的人將受到懲罰。**3** used at the beginning of a question to show surprise or anger 到底是誰，究竟是誰〔置於問句開頭，表示驚訝或生氣〕：*Whoever would do a thing like that to an old woman?* 究竟是誰會對一位老太太做出那樣的事？**4 whoever she/he may be** used to say that you do not know who someone is〔表示你不知道某人是誰〕：*You've got a message from someone called Tony Gower, whoever he may be.* 一個名叫東尼·高爾的人給你一個口信，但不清楚他究竟是甚麼人。

1 1 **whole¹** /hol; həʊl/ *adj* **1** all of something; ENTIRE 全部的，整個的：You *have your whole life ahead of you!* 你還年輕，來日方長！| *His whole attitude bugs me.* 他的整個態度讓我討厭。| **the whole school/country/village etc** (=all the people in a school, country etc) 全校/全國/全村等（的人）*The whole school meets together once a week.* 全校師生每星期集會一次。| **the whole thing** (=everything about a situation) 事情的全部 *The whole thing just makes me sick.* 整個事件令我作嘔。—see also 另見 **the whole of 2 a whole variety/series/range etc** used to emphasize that there are a lot of things of the same type 各種類/系列/範疇等〔用於強調同一類中包含很多東西〕：*a whole series of embarrassing defeats* 一連串令人尷尬的失敗 **3** complete and not divided or broken into parts 完整的；沒有破碎的：*Place a whole onion inside the chicken.* 把整個洋葱放在雞裡。**4 the whole point (of)** an expression meaning the main idea or reason for something, used especially to emphasize this and make it completely clear〔某事的〕中心思想〔尤用於強調和闡明〕；宗旨：*I thought the whole point of the meeting was to decide which offer to accept.* 我以為會議的目的是決定接受哪一種提議。**5 in the whole (wide) world** an expression meaning 'anywhere' or 'at all', used to emphasize a statement 普天之下〔用於強調陳述句〕：*You're my best friend in the whole wide world!* 世上只有你是我最好的朋友！**6 go the whole hog** *informal* to do something as completely or as well as you can, without any limits【非正式】徹底地幹；盡力而為：*I'm gonna go the whole hog and have a live band at the barbecue.* 我準備全力以赴，在燒烤野餐上安排現場樂隊表演。**7 go the whole nine yards** *AmE spoken* to continue doing something until it is completely done and everything has been settled, even if this is difficult【美口】〔事情雖然困難，但仍〕全部完成 —see also 另見 WHOLLY, **a whole new ball game** (BALL GAME (3)), **the whole shebang** (SHEBANG), **the whole shooting match** (SHOOTING MATCH), —**wholeness** *n* [U]

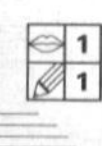

whole² *n* **1 the whole of** all of something, especially something that is not a physical object 整個，全部〔尤用於非實物〕：*The whole of the morning was wasted trying to find the documents.* 為了設法找到這些文件，整個上午給浪費了。**2 on the whole** used to say that something is generally true 總的看來，總體而言：*On the whole, life was much quieter after John left.* 總的說來，自從約翰離開之後，生活變得平靜多了。**3 as a whole** used to say that all the parts of something are being considered 整個來看〔用於表示所有部分都已考慮〕：*This rule does not only apply to seniors, but to the school as a whole.* 這項規定不僅僅適用於畢業班的學生，而是適用於全校。**4** [C usually singular 一般用單數] something that consists of a number of parts, but is considered as a single unit 整體〔某物包含數部分，但被當作一個單位〕：*Two halves make a whole.* 兩個一半構成全部。

whole·food /`hol͵fud; ˈhəʊlfuːd/ *n* [C,U] food that is considered healthy because it is in a simple natural form〔沒有加工的〕營養食品；天然食品

whole-heart·ed /͵· ˈ··◂/ *adj* **whole-hearted support/approval/effort etc** involving all your feelings, interest etc 全力支持/衷心讚許/全力以赴等：*enjoying the whole-hearted support of both governments* 得到兩國政府的全力支持 —**whole-heartedly** *adv*

whole·meal /`hol͵mil; ˈhəʊlmiːl/ *adj BrE* wholemeal flour or bread uses all of the grain, including the outer layer【英】〔麵粉或麵包〕全麥的；WHOLE WHEAT *AmE*【美】

whole note /`· ·/ *n* [C] *AmE* a musical note which continues for as long as two HALF NOTES【美】全音符；SEMIBREVE *BrE*【英】—see picture at 參見 MUSIC 圖

whole num·ber /͵· ˈ··/ *n* [C] a number such as 0, 1, 2 etc or –1, –2 etc; INTEGER 整數

whole·sale¹ /`hol͵sel; ˈhəʊlseɪl/ *n* [U] the business of selling goods in large quantities, especially at low prices 批發，躉售 —compare 比較 RETAIL¹

wholesale² *adj* **1** connected with the business of selling goods in large quantities, usually at low prices 批發的；整批賣的：*a wholesale price* 批發價 **2** affecting almost everything or everyone, and often done without any concern for the results 大規模的〔常包含不考慮結果而做某事的意思〕：*There will be no wholesale changes but a gradual modernization.* 不會有大規模變化，但會逐步現代化。—**wholesale** *adv*: *I can get it for you wholesale.* 我可以為你以批發價買它。

whole·sal·er /`hol͵selɚ; ˈhəʊl͵seɪlə/ *n* [C] someone who sells goods wholesale 批發商：*This profit covers the wholesaler's overheads.* 這項利潤包括批發商的經常開支。

whole·some /`holsəm; ˈhəʊlsəm/ *adj* **1** likely to make you healthy 對健康有益的：*well-balanced wholesome meals* 營養均衡的保健餐 **2** considered to have a good moral effect 在道德上有益的：*games that are just good clean wholesome fun* 增進身心健康的娛樂活動 —**wholesomeness** *n* [U]

whole wheat /`· ·/ *adj AmE* whole wheat flour etc uses all of the grain, including the outer layer【美】〔麵粉等〕全麥的；WHOLEMEAL *BrE*【英】

who'll /hul; huːl/ the short form of 縮略式= who will

whol·ly /`holɪ; ˈhəʊl-li/ *adv* [often with negatives 常與否定詞連用] *formal* completely【正式】完全地：*a wholly* *satisfactory solution* 完全滿意的解決 | *This seems to me a not wholly convincing argument.* 我看來這不是一個令人十分信服的論據。

whom /hum; huːm/ *pron* the object form of WHO, used especially in formal speech or writing 誰, 甚麼人〔who 的受格形式, 尤用於正式説話或書面語裡〕: *a neighbour with whom I shared a garden* 與我共享花園的鄰居 | *She brought with her three friends, none of whom I had ever met before.* 她帶來三位朋友, 沒有一位是我以前見過的。

whomp /hwɑmp; wɒmp/ *v* [T] *spoken*【口】**1** to hit someone very hard with your hand closed; PUNCH¹ (1) 用拳痛打〔某人〕**2** to defeat another team easily 輕易地擊敗〔另一隊〕

whoop /hup; wuːp/ *v* [I] **1** to shout loudly and happily〔高興地〕大叫, 歡呼 **2 whoop it up** *informal* to enjoy yourself very much, especially in a large group【非正式】〔尤指在一羣人中〕玩得很痛快; 狂歡 —**whoop** *n* [C] *whoops of victory* 勝利的歡呼

whoop-de-do /ˌhup dɪ ˋdu; ˌwuːp diː ˈdu/ *n* [C] *AmE spoken* a noisy party or celebration【美口】喧鬧的聚會[慶祝會]

whoo·pee¹ /ˈhwuˋpi; wʊˈpiː/ *interjection* a shout of happiness 哈哈! 好呀!〔高興的喊叫〕

whoop·ee² /ˈhwʊpɪ; ˈwʊpi/ *n* **make whoopee a)** *BrE old-fashioned* to go out and enjoy yourself【英, 過時】〔外出〕狂歡作樂 **b)** *AmE old-fashioned* to have sex【美, 過時】性交

whoopee cush·ion /ˈ·· ˌ··/ *n* [C] a rubber CUSHION¹ (1) filled with air that makes a funny noise when you sit on it〔橡膠製, 坐在上面會發出聲響的〕放屁坐墊

whoop·ing cough /ˈhupɪŋ ˌkɒf; ˈhuːpɪŋ kɒf/ *n* [U] an infectious disease that especially affects children, and makes them cough and have difficulty breathing 百日咳〔尤影響兒童的一種傳染病〕

whoops /hups; wʊps/ *interjection* **1** used when someone has fallen, dropped something, or made a small mistake 哎喲〔某人跌倒、掉了東西或出小差錯時用語〕: *Whoops! I nearly dropped it.* 哎喲! 我差點把它掉了。**2 whoops-a-daisy** used when someone, usually a child, falls down 起來吧, 沒事啦!〔通常用於兒童摔倒時〕

whoosh¹ /hwʊʃ; wʊʃ/ *n* [C usually singular 一般用單數] a soft sound like air or water moving quickly 呼的一聲, 嗖的一聲: *a sudden whoosh of flame and then a big bang* 火苗突然呼的一聲躥了起來, 然後一聲巨響

whoosh² *v* [I always+adv/prep] *informal* to move very fast with a soft rushing sound【非正式】〔呼呼地〕飛快移動

whop /hwɑp; wɒp/ *v* [T] *informal especially AmE* WHUP【非正式, 尤美】大獲全勝

whop·per /ˈhwɑpɚ; ˈwɒpə/ *n* [C] *informal*【非正式】**1** something unusually big 龐然大物, 特大的東西: *The fish Mike caught was a real whopper!* 邁克捉到的這條魚大得嚇人! **2** a lie 謊話

whop·ping /ˈhwɑpɪŋ; ˈwɒpɪŋ/ also 又作 **whopping great** /ˈ·· ·/ *adj* [only before noun 僅用於名詞前] *spoken* very large【口】極大的, 異常大的: *a whopping fee* 一筆巨額費用

who're /ˈhuɚ; ˈhuːə/ the short form of 縮略式= who are

whore /hɔr; hɔː/ *n* [C] **1** an offensive word for a woman who has sex for money; PROSTITUTE 妓女〔冒犯用詞〕**2** *taboo* an offensive word for a woman who has many sexual partners【諱】淫婦

whore·house /ˈhɔrˌhaus; ˈhɔːhaʊs/ *n* [C] *informal* a place where men can pay to have sex; BROTHEL【非正式】妓院, 窰子

whor·ing /ˈhɔrɪŋ; ˈhɔːrɪŋ/ *n* [U] *old-fashioned* the activity of having sex with a PROSTITUTE【過時】嫖妓: *drinking, gambling and whoring* 吃喝嫖賭

whorl /hwɝl; wɜːl/ *n* [C] **1** a pattern made of a line that curls outwards in circles that get bigger and bigger 渦; 螺旋狀 **2** a circular pattern of leaves or flowers on a stem〔莖部的葉或花的〕輪生體

who's /huz; huːz/ the short form of 縮略式= who is or 或 who has

whose /huz; huːz/ *determiner, pron* **1** used to ask which person or people a particular thing belongs to〔用於問物品屬於〕誰的: *Whose house is this?* 這是誰的房子? | *Whose is this car?* 這輛汽車是誰的? **2** used to show the relationship between a person or thing and something that belongs to that person or thing 他(們)的; 她(們)的; 它(們)的〔表示人與物間的關係〕: *That's the man whose house has burned down.* 就是那個男人的房子被燒毀了。| *a new laptop computer whose low cost will make it attractive to students* 新型可攜式電腦價格低廉, 對學生有吸引力 S2 W1

who·so·ev·er /ˌhusoˋɛvɚ; ˌhuːsəʊˈevə/ *pron old use* WHOEVER (1)【舊】無論誰

who've /huv; huːv/ the short form of 縮略式= who have

whup /hwʌp; wʌp/ *v* [T] *informal especially AmE* to defeat someone easily in a sport or fight【非正式, 尤美】〔在體育運動或打鬥中〕大獲全勝: *We whupped them!* 我們打敗了他們!

why¹ /hwaɪ; waɪ/ *adv, conj* **1** for what reason 為甚麼: *Why do you say that?* 你為甚麼那麼説? | *Why should we bother waiting any longer?* 我們為甚麼還要費工夫等下去? | *I can't think why he would do such a thing.* 我不明白他為甚麼做這種事。| **why ever...?** (=used to add force to a question) 究竟為甚麼...?〔用於加強問句語氣〕*Why ever would he come specially to visit us?* 他究竟為甚麼專程來探望我們? **2 why not...? a)** used to make a suggestion 為甚麼不...?〔用於提出建議〕: *Why not make your own Christmas cards instead of buying them?* 你為甚麼不自己做聖誕賀卡而要去買呢? | *Why don't you contact Eric – he may be able to help?* 你為甚麼不與艾力克聯絡 —— 他也許可以給你提供幫助呢? **b)** used to show that you agree with a suggestion or idea 幹嘛不?〔表示同意某建議或想法〕: *"It might be nice to see a film this afternoon." "Yes, why not?"* "今天下午去看電影也許不錯。" "對, 是不錯。" **3 why on earth...?** *spoken* used to ask in a surprised way why something has happened【口】到底為甚麼...?〔用於驚異地問某事為何發生〕: *But why on earth didn't you ask me to help?* 你到底為甚麼不叫我幫忙? **4 why the hell...?** *spoken* used to ask in a very angry way why something has happened【口】〔生氣地問〕究竟為甚麼...?: *Why the hell did you buy it in the first place?* 你當初究竟為甚麼去買它? **5 why oh why...?** *spoken* used to show that you very much regret something you did【口】為甚麼要...?〔表示很後悔做了某事〕: *Why oh why did I say those horrible things?* 我為甚麼會那樣胡言亂語? **6 why me/her?** *spoken* used to ask why something has been done, given etc to you or someone else【口】為甚麼是我/她?: *Why me? Why can't someone else drive you?* 怎麼是我呢? 為甚麼別人不能開車送你? S1 W1

Frequencies of **why** in spoken and written English
英語口語和書面語中 why 的使用頻率

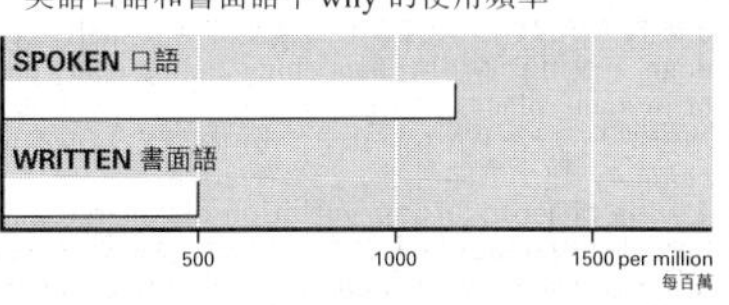

Based on the British National Corpus and the Longman Lancaster Corpus
據英國國家語料庫和朗文蘭卡斯特語料庫

This graph shows that **why** is much more common in spoken English than in written English. This is because it is used in questions and in some common spoken phrases. 本圖表顯示, why 在英語口語中的使用頻率遠遠高於書面語, 因為該詞經常用於疑問句中, 而且口語中一些常用片語是由 why 構成的。

W

why² *interjection especially AmE* used to show that you are surprised or annoyed【尤美】哎呀!嗨!〔表示驚訝或生氣〕: *Why, where on earth can Don have got to!* 嗨,唐究竟去了哪兒呢?

why³ *n* **the why(s) and the wherefore(s)** the reasons or explanations for something 緣故, 理由: *I'm not interested in the whys and the wherefores, just tell me what it will cost.* 我對前因後果不感興趣, 就告訴我這東西要多少錢。

wick /wɪk; wɪk/ *n* [C] **1** the piece of thread in a candle that burns when you light it 蠟燭芯 —see picture at 參見 CANDLE 圖 **2** a long piece of material in an oil lamp that sucks up oil so that the lamp can burn〔油燈的〕燈芯 **3 get on sb's wick** *BrE spoken* to annoy someone【英口】激怒某人

wick·ed /ˈwɪkɪd; ˈwɪkɨd/ *adj* **1** behaving in a way that is morally wrong; evil 邪惡的; 缺德的: *the wicked stepmother in 'Hansel and Gretel'*《漢塞爾和格蕾特爾》中傷天害理的繼母 **2** *informal* behaving badly in a way that is amusing; MISCHIEVOUS【非正式】淘氣的; 惡作劇的: *Carl had a wicked grin on his face as he crept up behind Ellen.* 卡爾躡手躡腳地走到艾倫後面, 臉上現出調皮的笑容。**3** *spoken* very good; excellent【口】棒的; 極好的: *That's a wicked bike!* 這輛自行車真棒! —**wickedly** *adv* —**wickedness** *n* [U]

wick·er /ˈwɪkɚ; ˈwɪkə/ *adj* [only before noun 僅用於名詞前] made from thin dry branches or REEDs woven together 柳條[蘆葦桿]编的: *a wicker basket* 柳條籃

wick·er·work /ˈwɪkɚˌwɝk; ˈwɪkəwɜːk/ *n* [U] objects made from wicker 柳條編製品

wick·et /ˈwɪkɪt; ˈwɪkɨt/ *n* [C] one of two sets of three wooden sticks that are stuck in the ground in a game of CRICKET (2), which the BOWLER tries to hit with the ball〔板球的〕三柱門 —see also 另見 **be on a sticky wicket** (STICKY (9))

wicket gate /ˈ·· ˌ·/ *n* [C] *old use* a small door or gate that is part of a larger one【舊】〔大門上的〕小門, 邊門

wicket keep·er /ˈ·· ˌ··/ *n* [C] a player who stands behind the wicket in CRICKET (2)〔板球運動中的〕三柱門守門員

wide¹ /waɪd; waɪd/ *adj*

1 ►DISTANCE 距離◄ a) measuring a large distance from one side to the other 寬的, 寬闊的: *a hat with a wide brim* 寬邊帽子 —opposite 反義詞 NARROW¹ (1) **b) five metres/two miles etc wide** measuring five metres etc from one side to the other 五米寬/兩英里寬等: *The door's three feet wide.* 門三英尺寬。—see picture at 參見 THICK¹ 圖

2 ►VARIETY 種類◄ including or involving a large variety of different people, things, or situations〔包括或涉及的人、物或形勢等〕廣泛的; 範圍大的; 廣闊的: *a man with a wide experience of foreign affairs* 外交事務經驗豐富的人 | **wide range/variety/selection etc** *We stock a wide range of furnishing materials.* 我們備有各種各樣的裝飾材料。

3 ►IN MANY PLACES 在許多地方◄ [usually before noun 一般用於名詞前] happening among many people or in many places 眾多的; 廣泛的〔發生於許多人中或地方的〕: *The Whitewater scandal received wide publicity.* 白水醜聞引起了公眾廣泛的關注。

4 wide difference/gap/variation etc a large and noticeable difference 巨大的差別/差距/變化等: *the ever-wider gap between the richest and poorest countries* 最富國與最窮國之間日益加大的差距

5 the wider issues/view/context etc the more general features of a situation, rather than the specific details 概貌/概觀/概況等: *We also have a wider aim: the restoration of democracy.* 我們也有一個總目標: 恢復民主。

6 ►EYES 眼睛◄ *especially literary* wide eyes are fully open, especially when someone is very surprised, excited, or frightened【尤文】〔眼睛〕睜大的〔尤指某人非常吃驚、興奮或恐懼〕: *Her eyes grew wide in anticipation.* 她睜大着眼睛期待着。

7 give sb/sth a wide berth *especially BrE* to avoid someone or something【尤英】對某人/某物敬而遠之

8 the big wide world *especially spoken* places outside the small familiar place where you live【尤口】〔在熟識的小天地以外的〕廣闊世界: *Soon you'll leave school and go out into the big wide world.* 很快你就要離開學校, 進入社會。

9 nationwide/city-wide etc happening or existing all over the nation, city etc 全國的/全市的等: *a countrywide problem* 全國的問題 —see also 另見 WIDELY, WIDTH

USAGE NOTE 用法說明: WIDE

WORD CHOICE 詞語辨析: **wide, broad, big, large, wide-ranging**

Wide is the most usual word to describe something that measures a long distance from one side to another. 形容寬的物體, wide 是最常用的詞: *a wide road/lake/doorway/entrance/staircase* 寬闊的馬路/湖/門道/入口/樓梯。You also use **wide** to express how much something measures from side to side. wide 也可用來表示某物的寬度: *The gap was only a few inches wide.* 裂縫才幾英寸寬。

Broad is often used about parts of the body. broad 常用於描述身體各個部位的寬度: *broad shoulders/hips* 寬肩膀/肥臀 | *a broad nose/forehead.* 大鼻子/寬額頭。**Broad** often suggests that something is wide in a good or attractive way. broad 常表示某物令人心曠神怡地“寬廣”或“寬闊”: *a broad sunny avenue running through the middle of the town* 穿過市中心的一條寬闊明亮的大道

Sometimes you may need to think whether you really mean **wide** or **broad**, or just **big** or **large** (=wide in all directions) 有時需要考慮想表達的確切含意是wide還是broad, 是big還是large (各個方向都寬): *a wide carpet/field* 寬地毯/寬廣的田野 or 或 *a large carpet/field?* 大地毯/大片田野

Wide-ranging means covering a lot of different subjects or including a lot of different ideas. wide-ranging 意為“覆蓋面大的; 廣泛的”: *a wide-ranging review/report/speech* 全面的回顧; 內容廣泛的報告/講話

wide² *adv* **1 a)** a door or window that is wide open is open as fully as it can be〔門或窗〕大開; 敞開 **b)** if someone's eyes or mouth are wide open, they are open as far as possible, especially when they are surprised〔尤指吃驚時嘴或眼〕張得很大地 **c)** if a competition, election etc is wide open, it is possible for anyone to succeed〔競賽、選舉等〕沒有一個參賽者有必勝把握: *After Milan's win the championship is wide open.* 米蘭獲勝後, 不知鹿死誰手。**2** opening or spreading as much as possible 充分地張開: *The door opened a little wider.* 門開得再大一點。| **open/spread sth wide** *Spiro spread his arms wide in a welcoming gesture.* 斯皮諾伸開雙臂, 做出歡迎的姿勢。| **wide apart** *Sandy stood with his back to the fire, legs wide apart.* 桑迪背對着火, 雙腳叉開站着。**3** not hitting the point you were aiming at 未擊中目標: *One of the guards fired at us but the shot went wide.* 一名衛兵向我們開槍, 但打歪了。**4 wide awake** completely awake 毫無睡意, 完全醒着 —see also 另見 **far and wide** (FAR¹ (1)), **off the mark/wide of the mark** (MARK² (11))

wide-an·gle lens /ˌ· ·· ˈ·/ *n* [C] a camera LENS (2) that lets you take photographs with a wider view than normal〔照相機的〕廣角鏡

wide boy /ˈ· ·/ *n* [C] *BrE informal* a man who makes money in dishonest ways and uses it to buy expensive clothes, cars etc【英, 非正式】〔用騙來的金錢購買昂貴衣物、汽車等的〕騙子: *Cockney wide boys trying to sell you something* 想賣東西給你的倫敦東區的騙子

W

wide-eyed /ˌ· ˈ·◂/ *adj, adv* **1** with your eyes wide open, especially because you are surprised or frightened〔尤因驚訝或恐懼而〕睜大着眼睛（地）**2** too willing to believe, accept, or admire things because you do not have much experience of life; NAIVE 天真的[地], 單純的[地]

wide·ly /ˈwaɪdlɪ; ˈwaɪdli/ *adv* **1** in a lot of different places or by a lot of people 廣泛地: *widely publicized events* 廣為宣傳的事件 | *an author who had travelled widely in the Far East* 一位遊歷過遠東很多地方的作者 **2** varying to a large degree 差異很大: *The quality of the applicants varies widely.* 申請人的素質差異很大。**3 widely read a)** read by a lot of people 讀者眾多的: *a widely read magazine* 一本讀者眾多的雜誌 **b)** having read many different books 博覽羣書的: *She's very widely read.* 她博覽羣書。

wid·en /ˈwaɪdn̩; ˈwaɪdn/ *v* [I,T] **1** to become wider or make something wider（使）變寬: *They're widening the road.* 他們正在拓寬馬路。**2** to become larger in degree or range, or make something do this（使）〔程度〕增加;（使）〔範圍〕擴大: *The gap between income and expenditure has widened to 11%.* 收入和支出之間的差距擴大到了 11%。| *They are trying to widen the discussion to include environmental issues.* 他們正設法把這次討論擴大到環境問題。—opposite 反義詞 NARROW² (1)

wide-rang·ing /ˌ· ˈ··◂/ *adj* including a wide variety of subjects, things, or people 範圍大的, 廣泛的: *a wide-ranging discussion* 內容廣泛的討論 | *wide-ranging proposals to improve the rail network* 改善鐵路網的各種提議

wide·spread /ˈwaɪdˈsprɛd; ˈwaɪdspred/ *adj* existing or happening in many places or situations, or among many people 分佈廣的; 廣泛流傳的: *the widespread use of chemicals in agriculture* 農業上化學品的廣泛使用

wid·get /ˈwɪdʒɪt; ˈwɪdʒɨt/ *n* [C] **1** *spoken* a small piece of equipment that you do not know the name for【口】〔不知其名的〕小裝置 **2** *informal* a word meaning an imaginary product that a company might produce【非正式】〔某公司的〕虛構產品: *Company A produces 6000 widgets a month at a unit price of $0.33.* A 公司每月生產 6,000 件產品, 每件單價 0.33 美元。

wid·ow /ˈwɪdo; ˈwɪdəʊ/ *n* [C] **1** a woman whose husband has died and who has not married again 寡婦, 遺孀: *Mr Castle's widow, Anne, described the sentence as 'obscene'.* 卡索爾先生的遺孀安妮認為那句話"下流"。**2 football widow/golf etc widow** *humorous* a woman whose husband spends all his free time watching football, playing golf etc【幽默】〔丈夫沉溺於足球、高爾夫球等而被冷落的〕足球/高爾夫球寡婦

wid·owed /ˈwɪdod; ˈwɪdəʊd/ *adj* having become a widow or widower 守寡的; 成為鰥夫的: *She was widowed at the age of 25.* 她 25 歲時成了寡婦。

wid·ow·er /ˈwɪdəwɚ; ˈwɪdəʊə/ *n* [C] a man whose wife has died and who has not married again 鰥夫

wid·ow·hood /ˈwɪdoˌhʊd; ˈwɪdəʊhʊd/ *n* [U] the time when you are a widow 守寡, 孀居

width /wɪdθ; wɪdθ/ *n* **1** [C,U] the distance from one side of something to the other〔從一邊到另一邊的〕寬度: *What's the width of the desk?* 這張書桌的寬度是多少? | **in width** *It's about 6 metres in width.* 它大約 6 米寬。—compare 比較 BREADTH, LENGTH —see picture at 參見 LENGTH 圖 **2** [C] a piece of a material that has been measured and cut〔裁剪了的〕料子: *four widths of curtain material* 四幅窗簾布料子

wield /wild; wiːld/ *v* [T] **1 wield power/influence/authority etc** to have a lot of power or influence, and be ready to use it 有權力/影響/權威等〔並隨時使用〕: *The Church wields immense power in Ireland.* 在愛爾蘭, 教會具有很大的權力。**2** to hold a weapon or tool that you are going to use 拿起〔武器或工具〕: *She had her car windows smashed by a gang wielding baseball bats.* 一夥揮舞棒球球棒的人把她的汽車玻璃窗砸碎了。

wie·ner /ˈwinɚ; ˈwiːnə/ also 又作 **wie·nie, weenie** /ˈwinɪ; ˈwiːni/ *n* [C] *AmE*【美】**1** a type of SAUSAGE 法蘭克福香腸 **2** *informal* someone who does something stupid【非正式】蠢人, 傻瓜 **3** a word used by children meaning a PENIS 小雞雞, 雞巴〔兒童用語, 指陰莖〕

wife /waɪf; waɪf/ *plural* **wives** /waɪvz; waɪvz/ *n* [C] the woman that a man is married to 妻子: *Have you met his wife?* 你見到他妻子了嗎?

wife·ly /ˈwaɪflɪ; ˈwaɪfli/ *adj old-fashioned* connected with qualities that are supposed to be typical of a good wife【過時】賢慧的; 具備好妻子美德的

wig /wɪg; wɪg/ *n* [C] artificial hair that you wear on your head 假髮

wig·gle¹ /ˈwɪgl̩; ˈwɪgəl/ *v* [I,T] to move with small movements from side to side or up and down, or make something move like this〔動作較小地〕擺動; 扭動: *Henry wiggled his toes.* 亨利扭動他的腳趾。

wiggle² *n* [C] **1** a small movement from side to side or up and down 擺動; 扭動: *a wiggle of the hips* 屁股的扭動 **2 get a wiggle on!** *AmE spoken* used to tell someone to do something more quickly【美口】趕快!趕緊!〔用於告訴某人更快地做某事〕

wig·gly /ˈwɪglɪ; ˈwɪgəli/ *adj informal* a wiggly line is one that has small curves in it; WAVY (2)【非正式】〔線〕波浪形的

wight /waɪt; waɪt/ *n* [C] *old use* a person【舊】人

wig·wam /ˈwɪgwɑm; ˈwɪgwæm/ *n* [C] a tall tent in which some Native Americans used to live〔北美印第安人居住的帳篷式〕棚屋

wild¹/waɪld; waɪld/ *adj*

1 ►PLANTS/ANIMALS 植物/動物◄ living in a natural state, not changed or controlled by humans 野生的; 未經栽培的; 未經馴化的: *wild flowers* 野花 | *a wild rabbit* 野兔 | **grow wild** *daffodils growing wild in the meadow* 草地上野生的黃水仙

2 ►EMOTIONS 感情◄ feeling or expressing strong uncontrolled emotions, especially anger, happiness, or excitement 感情強烈的〔尤指生氣、高興或激動〕: *wild laughter* 狂笑 | **[+with]** *wild with excitement* 興奮不已

3 go wild a) to behave in a very excited way〔行為〕瘋狂: *The crowd went wild as soon as Jackson stepped onto the stage.* 傑克遜一走上舞台, 人羣就騷動起來。**b)** to get very angry 狂怒

4 ►CRAZY 瘋狂的◄ behaving in an uncontrolled, sometimes violent way〔行為〕兇悍的; 瘋狂的: *She's great fun, but a bit wild.* 她是一個有趣的人, 但有點狂。| *Jack had a wild look in his eyes.* 傑克眼中流露出狂野的神色。

5 ►ENJOYABLE 有趣的◄ *informal* very enjoyable and exciting【非正式】十分有趣的; 棒極了的: *That was a really wild party last night!* 昨晚的那個聚會真是棒極了!

6 be wild about to be very interested in or excited about something 對〔某物〕極喜愛; 着了魔似的: *My son's wild about racing cars.* 我兒子對賽車如醉如痴。

7 ►WITHOUT CAREFUL THOUGHT 未經仔細考慮◄ done or said without much thought or care, or without knowing all the facts〔做事或說話〕輕率的; 缺乏根據的: *wild accusations* 誣告 | **a wild guess** *I just made a wild guess and it turned out to be right.* 我只是胡亂猜測, 結果卻猜對了。

8 run wild a) if a garden or plant runs wild, it grows uncontrollably because no one is looking after it〔因沒人照料, 園子〕荒蕪,〔植物〕蔓長 **b)** if children run wild, they do what they like because they are not controlled by an adult〔兒童〕肆無忌憚, 無法無天

9 beyond your wildest dreams beyond anything you imagined or hoped for 超出想像的: *an invention that was to change our lives beyond our wildest dreams* 一項超乎我們想像改變我們生活的發明

10 ►WEATHER 天氣◄ violent and strong 猛烈的; 狂暴的: *wild winds* 狂風

11 ►CARD GAMES 牌戲◄ a card that is wild can be

used to represent any other card in a game〔紙牌〕百搭的 —see also 另見 WILD CARD (1) —**wildly** *adv*: *The crowd ran wildly through the streets.* 人羣瘋狂地在街道上跑。| *wildly inaccurate statements* 極不準確的話 —**wildness** *n* [U]

wild² *n* **1 in the wild** in natural and free conditions, not kept or controlled by humans 處於野生狀態: *There are very few pandas living in the wild now.* 現在只有極少數的大熊貓處於野生狀態。**2 the wilds of Africa/Alaska etc** areas where there are no towns and not many people live 非洲/阿拉斯加州等的偏僻地區〔人煙稀少的地區〕

wild boar /ˌ· ˈ·/ *n* [C] a large wild pig with long hair〔長毛〕野豬

wild card /ˈ· ˌ·/ *n* [C] **1** a playing card that can represent any other card〔紙牌遊戲中的〕百搭牌 **2** *technical* a sign that can represent any letter in some computer commands【術語】〔電腦中的〕通配符 **3** someone that you do not know well, so that you cannot guess how they will behave in certain situations〔因不了解而〕無法猜度的人

wild·cat¹ /ˈwaɪldˌkæt; ˈwaɪldkæt/ *n* [C] a type of cat that looks similar to a large pet cat and lives in mountains, forests etc〔生活在山區、森林等的〕野貓

wildcat² *v* [I] *AmE* to look for oil in a place where nobody has found any yet【美】勘探〔石油〕—**wildcatter** *n* [C]

wildcat strike /ˌ·· ˈ·/ *n* [C] an occasion when people suddenly and unofficially stop working in order to protest about something 野貓式罷工〔指未經工會批准的突然罷工〕

wil·de·beest /ˈwɪldəˌbist; ˈwɪldəbiːst/ *n* [C] a large Southern African animal with a tail and curved horns; GNU 牛羚, 角馬〔產於南非〕

wil·der·ness /ˈwɪldɚnɪs; ˈwɪldənɪ̵s/ *n* [C usually singular 一般用單數] **1** a large area of land that has never been developed or farmed 荒野, 不毛之地: *a bleak wilderness of undrained marshes* 一片荒涼的未經排乾的沼澤 **2** any place where there is no sign of people or their effect 杳無人煙的地方: *That garden is a wilderness.* 那個花園裡一片荒蕪。| *The south side of the city had become a lawless wilderness.* 這個城市的南部已成為法紀蕩然的蠻荒地區。**3 in the wilderness** away from the centre of power and activity, especially political activity 離開權力和活動的中心;〔尤指政治上的〕在野狀態: *his return to office after several years in the wilderness* 他在野數年後的再度掌權

wilderness a·re·a /ˈ··· ˌ···/ *n* [C] an area of public land in the US where no buildings or roads are allowed to be built〔美國不允許在內建房、築路的〕公共莽原區

wild·fire /ˈwaɪldˌfaɪr; ˈwaɪldfaɪə/ *n* [U] —see 見 **spread like wildfire** (SPREAD¹ (3a))

wild·fowl /ˈwaɪldˌfaul; ˈwaɪldfaʊl/ *n* [plural] birds, especially ones that live near water〔尤指水邊的〕野禽

wild-goose chase /ˌ· ˈ· ˌ·/ *n* [C] a situation where you are looking for something that does not exist or that you are very unlikely to find, so that you waste a lot of time 徒勞之舉, 白費氣力的追逐

wild·life /ˈwaɪldˌlaɪf; ˈwaɪldlaɪf/ *n* [U] animals and plants growing in natural conditions 野生生物: *a wildlife park* 野生動物園 | *studying the wildlife* 研究野生生物

wild rice /ˌ· ˈ·/ *n* [U] the seed of a type of grass that grows in parts of North America and China〔生長在南美部分地方和中國的〕菰米

wiles /waɪlz; waɪlz/ *n* [plural] clever talk or tricks used to persuade someone to do what you want 花言巧語; 巧計: *She used all her wiles to coax a young man to help her escape.* 她用了各種花言巧語哄騙一個年輕人幫助她逃脫。

wil·ful *BrE*【英】, **willful** *AmE*【美】/ˈwɪlfəl; ˈwɪlfəl/ *adj* **1** continuing to do what you want, even after you have been told to stop 任性的; 固執的: *a wilful child* 任性的孩子 **2 wilful damage/disobedience/exaggeration etc** deliberate damage etc, when you know that what you are doing is wrong 故意損害/違抗/誇大其詞等 —**wilfully** *adv* —**wilfulness** *n* [U]

wi·li·ness /ˈwaɪlɪnɪs; ˈwaɪlinɪ̵s/ *n* [U] the quality of being WILY 詭計多端; 狡詐

will¹ /wɪl; wɪl/ [modal verb 情態動詞] *v* **1** used to express the simple future tense 將, 會, 要〔用於表示簡單將來式〕: *A meeting will be held next Tuesday at 3 p.m.* 下星期二下午三點將召開一個會議。| *What time will she arrive?* 她會甚麼時候到達? | *When will you be leaving for America?* 你準備甚麼時候起程去美國? **2** used to show that you are willing or ready to do something 願; 要〔用於表示願意、準備做某事〕: *I will come up and help you clear the attic in a moment.* 我馬上來幫你清理頂樓。| *Alma won't come to the party I'm sure.* 我敢肯定阿爾瑪不會參加這次聚會。| *Dr Weir will see you now.* 韋爾醫生現在要給你看病了。**3** used to ask someone to do something 請…好嗎〔用於請求某人做某事〕: *Will you phone me later?* 你過一會再給我打電話好嗎? | *Shut the door will you?* 把門關上, 好嗎? **4** used to say what always happens in a particular situation or what is generally true 總是, 慣於〔表示某事經常發生或總是如此〕: *Oil will float on water.* 油總是浮在水上。| *Accidents will happen.* 事故總是會發生的。**5** used like 'can' to show what is possible 能〔表示可能性〕: *This car will hold five people comfortably.* 這輛汽車能舒舒服服地坐五個人。**6** used like 'must' to show what you think is likely to be true 可能; 大概〔表示某事可能是真的〕: *That will be Tim coming home now.* 現在到家的大概是蒂姆。**7** used to order or tell someone angrily to do something 必須, 一定〔氣憤地命令某人做某事〕: *Will you two shut up for God's sake!* 天啊, 你們倆住嘴! **8** used to offer something to someone or to invite them to do something 要不要〔提供某物給某人或邀請某人做某事〕: *Will you be staying the night?* 你在這裡過夜好嗎? **9** used to describe someone's habits, especially when you find them strange or annoying 老是〔用於描述某人的習性, 尤指奇異或惱人的〕: *Trish will keep asking damn silly questions.* 特里斯老是不停地問一些十分愚蠢的問題。**10 I will** *spoken* used during a wedding ceremony to show that you agree formally to marry【口】〔婚禮時表示〕我願意〔娶[嫁]〕

will² *n*

1 ►DETERMINATION 決心◄ [C,U] determination to do something that you have decided to do, even if this is difficult 意志, 毅力: *Children sometimes have very strong wills.* 孩子有時有很強的意志力。| **the will to live/fight/succeed etc** *The survivors never lost the will to live.* 倖存者從未喪失求生的意志。| **iron will** (=very strong determination) 鋼鐵般的意志 | **a battle/clash of wills** (=when two people who both have strong wills oppose each other) 意志的較量 —see also 另見 FREE WILL, STRONG-WILLED, WEAK-WILLED

2 ►LEGAL DOCUMENT 法律文件◄ [C] a legal document that says who you want your money and property to be given to after you die 遺囑: **make a will** *Have you made a will yet?* 你的遺囑立好了嗎?| **in sb's will** *My grandmother left me these jewels in her will.* 祖母在她的遺囑中把這些首飾留給了我。

3 ►WHAT SB WANTS 某人的意願◄ [singular] what someone wants to happen in a particular situation〔某人的〕意願, 意旨: *I wish he'd stop trying to impose his will on others.* 我希望他不要企圖把自己的意願強加於其他人。| *obedience to God's will* 服從上帝的意旨 | **against your will** *The prisoner was made to sign a confession against his will.* 犯人被強迫在供狀上簽了字。

4 with the best will in the world *spoken* used to say that something is not possible, however much you want to do it【口】不管用意是多麼的好〔用於表示某事不可能〕: *With the best will in the world, I don't see what more I can do.* 儘管我煞費苦心, 也不知道還能再做點甚麼。

5 where there's a will there's a way *spoken* used to

say that if you really want to do something, you will find a way to succeed【口】有志者事竟成

6 at will whenever you want and in whatever way you want 隨心所欲: *a terrifying creature that could change its shape at will* 一隻可任意改變形狀的可怕怪物

7 with a will in an eager and determined way 起勁地; 熱情地; 誠心誠意

will³ *v* **1** [T] to try to make something happen by thinking about it very hard 設法用意志力驅使〔某事發生〕: **will sb to do sth** *She was willing herself not to cry.* 她極力使自己不要哭出來。**2** [T] to officially give something that you own to someone else after you die 立遺囑把〔財產〕遺贈〔某人〕 **3** [I,T] *old use* to want something to happen【舊】希望, 想要〔某事發生〕: *The King wills it.* 國王希望如此。

will·ful /ˈwɪlfəl; ˈwɪlfəl/ *adj* the American spelling of WILFUL wilful 的美式拼法

wil·lie /ˈwɪli; ˈwɪli/ *n informal*【非正式】**1 get the willies** to feel nervous or frightened 緊張不安; 心驚膽戰 **2 give sb the willies** to make someone feel nervous or frightened 使某人緊張[害怕]: *It gives me the willies to even think about plastic surgery.* 一想到整形外科, 我就不寒而慄。**3** [C] another spelling of WILLY willy 的另一種拼法

will·ing /ˈwɪlɪŋ; ˈwɪlɪŋ/ *adj* **1 be willing (to do sth)** to be prepared to do something, or have no reason to not want to do it 樂意〔做某事〕的; 沒有理由不想做的: *How much are they willing to pay?* 他們願意付多少錢? | **quite/perfectly willing** *I told them I was perfectly willing to help.* 我告訴他們, 我非常願意幫忙。**2 willing helper/worker etc** someone who is eager to help etc and does not have to be persuaded 熱心的幫手/積極肯幹的工人等: *60% of voters said they would willingly pay higher taxes for better health care.* 60%的選民表示, 為了得到更好的醫療保健, 他們樂意交納更高的稅款。—**willingly** *adv* —**willingness** *n* [U]

will o' the wisp /ˌ· · · ˈ·/ *n* [C usually singular 一般用單數] **1** a blue moving light that can be seen over wet ground at night 磷火; 鬼火 **2** someone that you can never completely depend on, or something that you can never achieve 捉摸不定的人; 實現不了的事

wil·low /ˈwɪlo; ˈwɪləʊ/ *n* [C,U] a type of tree that has long thin branches and grows near water, or the wood from this tree 柳樹; 柳木

wil·low·y /ˈwɪləwɪ; ˈwɪləʊi/ *adj* tall, thin, and graceful 苗條的; 婀娜多姿的: *She was pale and willowy with the most amazing violet eyes.* 她臉色蒼白、身材修長、有一雙驚人的藍紫色眼睛。

will·pow·er /ˈwɪlˌpaʊɚ; ˈwɪlˌpaʊə/ *n* [U] the ability to control your mind and body in order to achieve something that you want to do 毅力; 意志力: *It took all his willpower to remain calm.* 他竭盡全力才能保持鎮定。

wil·ly, willie /ˈwɪlɪ; ˈwɪli/ *n* [C] *BrE informal* a PENIS【英, 非正式】陰莖

willy-nil·ly /ˈwɪlɪ ˈnɪlɪ; ˌwɪli ˈnɪli/ *adv* if something happens willy-nilly, it happens whether you want it to or not 不管願不願意; 無論想不想要: *The Church is being forced, willy-nilly, to make clear its position on homosexuality.* 不管願不願意, 教會被迫表明對同性戀的立場。

wilt¹ /wɪlt; wɪlt/ *v* [I] **1** if a plant wilts, it bends over because it is too dry or old〔植物〕枯萎; 凋謝 —see picture on page A18 參見A18頁圖 **2** *informal* to feel weak, tired, or upset, especially because you are too hot【非正式】〔因太熱而〕萎靡不振[疲倦; 無精打采]

wilt² *v old use* **thou wilt** you will【舊】你將

wil·y /ˈwaɪlɪ; ˈwaɪli/ *adj* clever at getting what you want, especially by tricking people 詭計多端的; 狡詐的: *a wily politician* 老奸巨猾的政客 —**wiliness** *n* [U]

wimp¹ /wɪmp; wɪmp/ *n* [C] *informal*【非正式】**1** someone who has a weak character and is afraid to do something difficult or unpleasant 懦弱無用的人: *Don't be such a wimp!* 別那麼窩囊! **2** a man who is thin and physically weak 瘦弱的男人 —**wimpish, wimpy** *adj*

wimp² *v*

wimp out *phr v* [I] *spoken* to not do something that you intended to do, because you do not feel brave enough, strong enough etc【口】〔因缺乏勇氣、力量等〕不敢做〔想做的事〕

wim·ple /ˈwɪmpl̩; ˈwɪmpəl/ *n* [C] a piece of cloth that a NUN wears over her head〔修女戴的〕頭巾

win¹ /wɪn; wɪn/ *v past tense and past participle* **won** /wʌn; wʌn/ *present participle* **winning** S1 W1

1 ►COMPETITION/RACE 競賽/比賽◄ [I,T] to be the best or first in a competition, game, election etc〔在競賽、遊戲、選舉等中〕獲勝, 贏: *Who do you think will win the next election?* 你認為誰會在下一次競選中獲勝? | **win at sth** *I never win at cards.* 我玩紙牌從來贏不了。| **win by a mile/10 points etc** *We won by just one point.* 我們只贏了一分。| **win hands down** (=win very easily) 輕易獲勝

2 ►PRIZE 獎; 獎品◄ [T] to get something as a prize for winning in a competition or game 贏得, 獲得〔獎品〕: *How does it feel to have won the gold medal?* 獲得金牌的感覺如何? | *She won £160 on the lottery.* 她中彩券得了160英鎊。

3 ►GET/ACHIEVE 取得/獲得◄ [T] to get or achieve something that you want because of your efforts or abilities〔經努力或憑能力〕獲得, 博得〔某物〕: *Do you think he will win the Republican nomination?* 你認為他會獲得共和黨的提名嗎?| **win sb sth** *Those tactics won't win them any votes.* 那些策略不會給他們贏得任何選票。| **win sb's approval/trust/love etc** *Proposals for an out-of-town shopping mall have won the approval of the city council.* 在城外建一座購物中心的提案得到市議會的批准。| **win sb's heart** (=make them love you) 贏得某人的愛情

4 you win *spoken* used to agree to what someone wants after you have tried to persuade them to do something else【口】聽你的; 照你的做〔在試圖說服某人後, 表示同意他的要求〕: *OK, you win – we'll go to the movie.* 好, 聽你的 —— 我們看電影去。

5 you can't win *spoken* used to say that there is no satisfactory way of dealing with a particular situation【口】沒法子〔用於表示沒有令人滿意的方法處理某情況〕: *You can't win, can you? You either work late and upset Jenny, or go home and risk your job.* 你沒有法子, 是吧? 你要麼工作到深夜, 惹得珍妮不高興; 要麼冒着失業的危險回家去。

6 you can't win them all *spoken* used to show sympathy when someone has had a disappointing experience【口】你不可能事事都成功〔對某人失意表示同情〕

7 win the day to finally be successful in a discussion or argument; TRIUMPH² 〔在討論或爭論中〕最終獲得勝利: *Common sense won the day, and the development plans were dropped.* 常識最終獲勝, 發展規劃取消了。—see also 另見 **win the toss** (TOSS² (3)), WINNER, WINNING

win sb ↔ **round/around** *phr v* [T] to win someone over 說服〔某人〕; 把〔某人〕爭取過來

win sb/sth ↔ **back** *phr v* [T] to succeed in getting back something or someone that you had before 重新獲得〔某物或某人〕, 把…贏回來: *How can I win back her trust?* 我怎麼能重新贏得她的信任?

win out *phr v* [I] to win through〔經歷困難後〕終於成功

win sb ↔ **over** *phr v* [T] to get someone's support or friendship by persuading them or being nice to them〔通過勸說或示好以〕獲得〔某人的支持或友誼〕, 把〔某人〕爭取過來: *We'll be working hard over the next ten days to win over the undecided voters.* 我們將在接下來的十天努力, 把猶豫未決的選民爭取過來。

win through *phr v* [I] to eventually succeed in spite of problems〔經歷困難後〕終於成功: *As in most of his films, it's the good guys who win through in the end.* 正如在他的大多數電影裡一樣, 好人最終獲得勝利。

USAGE NOTE 用法説明: WIN

WORD CHOICE 詞語辨析: **win, beat, defeat**

You can **win** a game, race, competition, election etc (NOT **gain**). 在遊戲、比賽、競賽、選舉中獲勝的用詞是 win（不用 gain）。After the event you can say 事後可以説 *I've won!* 我贏了！A country can **win** a battle or war (NOT **gain**). 一個國家贏得戰役或戰爭用 win（不用 gain）。As a result you can also **win** a victory, championship, prize, scholarship, or a seat in the Senate. 於是贏得勝利[錦標賽, 獎品, 獎學金, 參議院議席]也用 win。—see also 另見 **gain** WORD CHOICE

When you win a game etc, you **beat** the other person or the other team or, more formally, you could say **defeat** 在運動比賽等中獲勝, 打敗了其他人或其他隊用 beat, 較為正式地可以用defeat: *We beat their team by ten points.* (NOT 不用 *won*) 我們以十分的優勢擊敗了他們的隊。| *He beat all his opponents/rivals for the seat.* 他擊敗所有對手／敵手, 獲得這個席位。

When a country wins a war it **defeats** its enemies (**beat** can be used informally) 一個國家在戰爭中獲勝, 就是打敗了 (defeat) 它的敵人〔beat 是非正式用語〕: *The Americans defeated the British in 1781.* 美國人在1781 年打敗了英國人。

3 **win**[2] *n* [C] a success or victory, especially in sport〔尤指在體育比賽中的〕勝利, 贏: *We've had two wins so far this season.* 這個賽季開始以來, 我們贏了兩場。| **[+over]** *In the under-16 event England had their first win over Germany, by 2-1.* 在 16歲以下的比賽項目中, 英格蘭隊以 2:1 的成績第一次戰勝了德國隊。—see also 另見 NO-WIN SITUATION

wince /wɪns; wɪns/ *v* [I] **1** to suddenly change the expression on your face as a reaction to something painful or upsetting 皺眉蹙眼〔因疼痛或不安導致面部表情突然改變〕: *Sandra winced as the dentist started to drill.* 牙醫開始鑽牙時, 仙杜拉皺眉蹙額。**2** to suddenly feel very uncomfortable or embarrassed because of something that happens, something you remember etc〔因發生或記起某事而突然〕感到不安; 畏縮: **wince at the thought/idea/memory** *I still wince at the thought of that terrible evening.* 一想起那可怕的夜晚, 我仍然不寒而慄。—**wince** *n* [singular]

win·cey·ette /ˌwɪnsɪˋɛt; ˌwɪnsiˈet◂/ *n* [U] *BrE* light material with a soft surface, used especially for clothes you wear in bed; FLANNELETTE【英】〔尤指做睡衣的〕棉織薄法蘭絨

winch[1] /wɪntʃ; wɪntʃ/ *n* [C] a machine with a rope or chain for lifting heavy objects 絞車; 起貨機

winch[2] *v* [T always+adv/prep] to lift something or someone up using a winch 用絞車提（起）; 用起貨機吊（起）: **winch sth out/from etc** *He was winched out of the sinking boat just in time.* 他被及時地從下沉的船中吊出來。

wind[1] /wɪnd; wɪnd/ *n*

1 ►AIR 空氣◄ [C,U] moving air, especially when it moves strongly or quickly in a current 風: *a 70-mile-an-hour wind* 時速 70 英里的風 | *branches swaying in the wind* 枝條在風中擺舞 | **the wind blows** *A gentle wind was blowing through the trees.* 一陣微風吹過樹林。| **strong/high winds** *The forecast is for strong winds and heavy rain.* 天氣預報報道會出現狂風暴雨。| **a gust of wind** (=a short strong wind) 一陣強風 *A sudden gust of wind blew the door shut.* 突然一陣強風把門關上了。| **east/west/north/south wind** (=coming from the east etc) 東／西／北／南風 | **a gentle/soft/light wind** *A soft wind teased a tendril of her hair.* 和風拂動着她的一綹頭髮。| **a bitter/chill/biting wind** (=a very cold wind) 刺骨的寒風 | **the wind is up/gets up** (=blows more strongly) 風勢漸大 | **the wind drops** (=blows less strongly) 風勢漸弱 *We'll wait till the wind drops before we put the tent up.* 我們等風勢減弱後再把帳篷支起來。—see also 另見 HEADWIND —see picture on page A13 參見A13 頁圖

2 get/have wind of *informal* to hear or find out about something secret or private, especially if you learn it accidentally or unofficially【非正式】〔尤指偶然地或非正式地〕聽到…的風聲; 獲得…的線索: *Jeremy, I don't want that reporter getting wind of this.* 傑里米, 我不想那名記者獲得這方面的線索。

3 ►BREATH 呼吸; 氣息◄ [U] your ability to breathe without difficulty〔正常〕呼吸能力: **get your wind (back)** (=be able to breathe normally again, for example after running)〔跑步等後〕恢復正常呼吸, 喘過氣來 | **knock the wind out of** (=hit someone in the stomach so that they cannot breathe for a moment)〔打[撞]某人的腹部〕使透不過氣來 —see also 另見 SECOND WIND, WINDPIPE

4 take the wind out of sb's sails *informal* to make someone lose their confidence, especially by saying or doing something unexpected【非正式】〔尤指以意想不到的言語或行動〕使某人喪失信心

5 see which way the wind is blowing to find out what the situation is before you do something or make a decision〔做事或做決定前〕觀望形勢; 看風向

6 be in the wind used to say that something is happening or going to happen, but not many people know what it is〔某事〕正在進行中; 即將發生〔但知道的人很少〕

7 the winds of change/freedom/public opinion etc events and changes that have started to happen and will have important effects, and that cannot be stopped〔有重要影響而不可遏止的〕〕改革／自由／輿論的趨勢

8 get the wind up/put the wind up sb *BrE informal* to become anxious or frightened, or to make someone feel this way【英, 非正式】(使) 某人擔驚受怕; (使) 某人受到驚嚇: *The threat of legal action will be enough to put the wind up them.* 用法律行動作威脅足以使他們心驚膽戰。

9 ►IN YOUR STOMACH 在胃中◄ [U] *BrE* the condition of having air or gas in your stomach, or the air or gas itself【英】腸胃氣脹; 胃氣, 腸氣; GAS *AmE*【美】: *I can't drink beer, it gives me wind.* 我不能喝啤酒, 它會令我腸胃氣脹。

10 the winds/the wind section all the musicians who play WIND INSTRUMENTS in a band〔樂隊中的〕管樂部, 管樂組

11 ►TALK 交談◄ [U] *informal* useless talk that does not mean anything【非正式】空談, 空話 —see also 另見 WINDY, **break wind** (BREAK[1] (43)), **an ill wind (that blows nobody any good)** (ILL[1] (5)), **sail close to the wind** (SAIL[1] (6)), **a straw in the wind** (STRAW (4))

wind[2] /waɪnd; waɪnd/ *v past tense and past participle* **wound** /waʊnd; waʊnd/ **1** [I always+adv/prep, T always+adv/prep] to turn or twist something repeatedly, especially around something else〔尤指繞着他物〕纏繞, 捲繞: **wind sth around/round** *Wind the wires around those pins there.* 把金屬絲繞在那邊的那些銷釘上。| **wind sth forward/back** *Can you wind the video back a little way – I want to see that bit again.* 請你把錄像往後倒一點 —— 我想再看看那一小段。| **[+around/round]** *Make sure the thread winds evenly around the bobbin.* 確保線均勻地繞在線軸上。—see also 另見 REWIND **2** also 又作 **wind up** [T] to turn something such as a handle or part of a machine around and around, especially in order to make something move or start working〔為使某物移動或起動而〕搖動〔把手等〕, 轉動; 給〔機器〕上發條: *What time is it? I forgot to wind my watch.* 幾點了? 我忘記給錶上發條。| *It was one of those old gramophones that you have to wind up.* 那是一台手搖的老式唱機。| **wind sth down/up** *BrE*【英】: *Would you mind winding down the window?* 請把窗戶搖下來好嗎? **3** [I always+adv/prep] if a road, track, river etc winds, it has many smooth bends and is usually very long〔道路、軌道、河流等〕蜿蜒; 曲折前進: **wind (its way) through/along** *Highway*

99 winds its way along the coast. 99號公路沿着海岸彎彎曲曲地延伸。—see also 另見 WINDING

wind down *phr v* **1** [T **wind** sth ↔ **down**] to gradually reduce the work of a business or organization so that it can be closed down completely 使〔業務〕逐步結束; 使〔組織〕停止運作 —compare 比較 **wind up** (2) **2** [I] to rest and relax after a lot of hard work or excitement〔緊張工作或興奮之後〕平靜下來; 放鬆: *I find it difficult to wind down after a day at work.* 一天工作之後, 我覺得很難讓自己平靜下來。

wind up *phr v* **1** [I, T **wind** sth ↔ **up**] bring an activity, meeting etc to an end 使〔活動、會議等〕結束: *OK, just to wind up, could I summarize what we've decided?* 好了, 該結束了, 我來把我們的決定做個總結好嗎? | *It's time to wind things up – I have a plane to catch.* 該結束了 — 我還得趕飛機。**2** [T **wind** sth ↔ **up**] to close down a company or organization 結束〔公司、機構〕: *Our operations in Jamaica are being wound up.* 我們在牙買加的業務正準備結束。—compare 比較 WIND DOWN[1] **3** [I, linking verb 連繫動詞] *informal* to unintentionally get into an unpleasant situation or place as a result of something you have done【非正式】〔無意間〕捲入; 牽涉到: [+with/in/at etc] *You know you're going to wind up in court over this.* 你知道你終歸會因此對簿公堂。| **wind up doing** *I wound up wishing I'd never come.* 我最後真希望我從未來過。| **wind up drunk/dead/ill etc** *You keep driving like that and you'll wind up dead.* 你老是那樣開車, 到頭來就得一命嗚呼。**4** [T **wind** sb ↔ **up**] *BrE* to deliberately say or do something in order to annoy someone, especially because you enjoy annoying them【英】故意惹惱〔某人, 尤因你喜歡這樣做〕, 愚弄: *Stupid! They're only winding you up.* 傻瓜! 他們只是在拿你開心。—see also 另見 WOUND-UP

wind[3] /waɪnd; waɪnd/ *n* [C] a bend or turn 彎曲; 轉動: **give sth a wind** *Give that crank another wind, will you?* 你再搖一下那個曲柄, 好嗎?

wind[4] /wɪnd; wɪnd/ *v* [T] to make someone have difficulty in breathing 使〔某人〕喘不過氣: **be winded** *"Is he OK?" "Yeah, I think he's just winded."* "他沒事吧?" "沒事, 我想他只不過是喘不過氣來。"

wind·bag /ˈwɪnd,bæg; ˈwɪndbæg/ *n* [C] *informal* someone who talks too much; GASBAG【非正式】誇誇其談的人; 喋喋不休的人; 話匣子

wind·break /ˈwɪnd,brek; ˈwɪndbreɪk/ *n* [C] a fence, line of trees, or wall that is intended to protect a place from the wind 擋風籬[牆]; 防風林

wind break·er /ˈwɪnd ˌbrekɚ; ˈwɪnd ˌbreɪkə/ *AmE*【美】, **windcheat·er** /ˈwɪnd,tʃitɚ; ˈwɪnd,tʃiːtə/ *BrE old-fashioned*【英, 過時】*n* [C] a type of coat that is made specially to keep the wind out 風衣, 防風上衣 —see picture at 參見 COAT[1] 圖

wind chime /ˈwɪnd ˌtʃaɪm; ˈwɪnd tʃaɪm/ *n* [C] long thin pieces of metal or glass hanging together in a group that make musical sounds when the wind blows 風鈴

wind·ed /ˈwɪndɪd; ˈwɪndɪ̈d/ *adj* unable to breathe easily, because you have been running or you have been hit in the stomach〔因跑步或腹部被打而〕呼吸困難的; 喘不過氣的

wind·fall /ˈwɪnd,fɔl; ˈwɪndfɔːl/ *n* [C] **1** an amount of money that you get unexpectedly 意外之財: *Jackpot pools winner Salters toasted his £2 million windfall at his Edinburgh home.* 累積獎金得主索特爾斯在愛丁堡的家中慶祝他獲得兩百萬英鎊的橫財。| **windfall gain/profit etc** (=high profits that you did not expect to make) 意外的巨大收穫/巨額利潤等 **2** a piece of fruit that has fallen off a tree 被風吹落的果實

wind·ing /ˈwaɪndɪŋ; ˈwaɪndɪŋ/ *adj* having a twisting turning shape 彎曲的; 蜿蜒的: *a winding path* 彎彎曲曲的小路 —see also 另見 WIND[2] (3)

winding sheet /ˈwaɪndɪŋ ˌʃit; ˈwaɪndɪŋ ʃiːt/ *n* [C] *old use* a SHROUD[1] (1)【舊】裹屍布

wind in·stru·ment /ˈwɪnd ˌɪnstrəmənt; ˈwɪnd ˌɪnstrʊ̈mənt/ *n* [C] a musical instrument that you play by blowing through it 管樂器

wind·jam·mer /ˈwɪnd,dʒæmɚ; ˈwɪnd,dʒæmə/ *n* [C] a large sailing ship of the type that was used for trade in the 19th century〔19世紀貿易用的〕大帆船

wind·lass /ˈwɪndləs; ˈwɪndləs/ *n* [C] a machine for pulling or lifting heavy objects 絞車

wind·mill /ˈwɪnd,mɪl; ˈwɪnd,mɪl/ *n* [C] **1** a building or structure with parts that turn around in the wind, used for producing electrical power or crushing grain 風車; 風力磨坊 **2** *BrE* a toy consisting of a stick with curved pieces of plastic at the end that turn around when they are blown【英】玩具風車; PINWHEEL *AmE*【美】

win·dow /ˈwɪndo; ˈwɪndəʊ/ *n* [C] **1** an opening in the wall of a building, car etc that lets in light and air, and is usually covered with glass〔建築物、汽車等上的〕窗; 窗戶; 櫥窗: *Do you mind if I open the window?* 我開窗可以嗎? | *looking at the Christmas displays in the shop windows* 觀看櫥窗裡的聖誕陳列品 —see picture on page A2 參見A2頁圖 **2** one of the separate areas on a computer screen where different processes or PROGRAMS are operating〔電腦屏幕上顯示不同程式正在操作的〕視窗 **3** a short period of time that is available for a particular activity〔某種活動能進行的〕短暫時限 **4 go out (of) the window** *informal* to disappear completely or no longer have any effect【非正式】完全消失; 不起作用: *One glass of wine, and all my good intentions went out the window.* 一杯酒讓我所有善意都白費了。**5 window of opportunity** a lucky opportunity to do something that you will not always be able to do 難逢的良機

window box /ˈ·· ·/ *n* [C] a long narrow box in which you can grow plants outside your window〔狹長形的〕窗台花箱, 窗口花壇

window clean·er /ˈ·· ˌ··/ *n* [C] someone whose job is to clean windows 窗戶清潔工

window dress·er /ˈ·· ˌ··/ *n* [C] someone whose job is to arrange goods attractively in shop windows〔商店的〕櫥窗設計[佈置]人

window dress·ing /ˈ·· ˌ··/ *n* [U] **1** something that is intended to give people a favourable idea about your plans or activities, and to stop them seeing the true situation 粉飾門面; 弄虛作假: *All these glossy pamphlets are just window dressing – the fact is that the new mall will ruin the environment.* 所有這些五光十色的小冊子只不過是用來裝飾門面而已 — 事實是新商場將破壞環境。**2** the art of arranging goods in a shop window so that they look attractive to customers〔商店的〕櫥窗佈置[裝飾]術

win·dow·pane /ˈwɪndo,pen; ˈwɪndəʊpeɪn/ *n* [U] a single whole piece of glass in a window〔整塊〕窗玻璃

Win·dows /ˈwɪndoz; ˈwɪndəʊz/ *n* [U] *trademark* a system produced by the Microsoft Corporation for organizing information on a personal computer, which can run several PROGRAMS in separate areas of the computer screen【商標】〔美國微軟公司生產的〕視窗〔一種電腦操作系統〕

window seat /ˈ·· ˌ·/ *n* [C] **1** a seat next to the window on a bus, plane etc〔公共汽車、飛機等的〕靠窗座位 **2** a seat directly below a window 窗檻下的座位

window shade /ˈ·· ˌ·/ *n* [C] *AmE* BLIND[3] (1)【美】窗簾; 遮簾

window-shopping /ˈ·· ˌ··/ *n* [U] the activity of looking at goods in shop windows without intending to buy them 瀏覽商店櫥窗; 逛街看商店櫥窗〔不打算購物〕— **window-shopper** *n* [C]

win·dow·sill /ˈwɪndo,sɪl; ˈwɪndəʊ,sɪl/ *n* [C] a shelf fixed along the bottom of a window 窗台, 窗沿 —see picture on page A4 參見A4頁圖

wind·pipe /ˈwɪnd,paɪp; ˈwɪndpaɪp/ *n* [C] the tube through which air passes from your mouth to your lungs 氣管

wind·screen /ˈwɪnd,skrin; ˈwɪndskriːn/ *n* [C] *BrE* the large window at the front of a car, bus etc【英】〔汽車等前部的〕擋風玻璃; WINDSHIELD *AmE*【美】—see picture on page A2 參見A2頁圖

windscreen wip·er /ˈ·· ˌ··/ *n* [C] *BrE* a long thin piece of metal with a rubber edge that moves across a windscreen to remove rain【英】〔汽車擋風玻璃上的〕刮水器, 雨刷; WINDSHIELD WIPER *AmE*【美】—see picture on page A2 參見A2頁圖

wind·shield /ˈwɪndˌʃild; ˈwɪndʃiːld/ *n* [C] **1** *AmE* a windscreen【美】擋風玻璃 —see picture on page A2 參見A2頁圖 **2** a piece of glass or clear plastic fixed at the front of a MOTORCYCLE〔摩托車前面的〕擋風玻璃, 透明擋風板

windshield wip·er /ˈ·· ˌ··/ *n* [C] *AmE* a windscreen wiper【美】〔汽車擋風玻璃上的〕刮水器, 雨刷 —see picture on page A2 參見A2頁圖

wind·sock /ˈwɪndˌsɑk; ˈwɪndsɒk/ *n* [C] a tube of material fastened to a pole at airports to show the direction of the wind 風向袋, 〔筒狀〕風標

wind·storm /ˈwɪndˌstɔrm; ˈwɪndstɔːm/ *n* [C] a period of bad weather when there are strong winds but not much rain〔少雨的〕風暴

wind-surf 帆板運動

wind-surf·ing /ˈwɪnd ˌsɝfɪŋ; ˈwɪnd ˌsɜːfɪŋ/ *n* [U] the sport of sailing across water by standing on a board and holding on to a large sail 帆板運動, 風帆滑浪〔運動〕—**wind-surfer** *n* [C] —**wind-surf** *v* [I]

wind·swept /ˈwɪndˌswɛpt; ˈwɪndswept/ *adj* **1** a place that is windswept is often windy because there are not many trees or buildings to protect it〔地方〕迎風的; 無遮擋的: *windswept moors* 當風的沼澤地 **2** hair, clothes etc that are windswept have been blown around by the wind〔頭髮、衣服等〕被風吹亂[散]的

wind tun·nel /ˈwɪnd ˌtʌnl; ˈwɪnd ˌtʌnl/ *n* [C] a large enclosed passage where aircraft are tested by forcing air past them〔測驗飛機的〕風洞

W

wind tur·bine /ˈwɪnd ˌtɝbɪn; ˈwɪnd ˌtɜːbaɪn/ *n* [C] a modern WINDMILL (1) for providing electrical power 風力渦輪機

wind-up /ˈwaɪnd ʌp; ˈwaɪnd ʌp/ *n* [C] *BrE informal* something you say or do to deliberately make someone angry or worried【英, 非正式】為了激怒人故意說的話[做的事]

wind·ward[1] /ˈwɪndwɚd; ˈwɪndwəd/ *adj, adv* **1** towards the direction from which the wind is blowing 迎風的[地], 向風的[地] **2** pointing towards the wind 頂風(的): *the windward side of the boat* 船的迎風一邊 —opposite 反義詞 LEEWARD

windward[2] *n* [U] the place from which the wind is blowing 迎風面, 向風面: *We sailed to windward across Oyster Bay.* 我們逆風航行, 橫渡奧伊斯特灣。

3 **wind·y** /ˈwɪndɪ; ˈwɪndi/ *adj* **1** with a lot of wind blowing 多風的, 風大的: *It's too windy for a picnic.* 今天風太大, 不適合野餐。**2** getting a lot of wind 當風的; 受大風吹刮的: *a windy hillside* 風很大的山坡 **3** windy talk is full of words that sound impressive but do not mean much 誇誇其談的; 空話連篇的: *the politician's windy generalizations* 政客誇誇其談的概括 —**windily** *adv* —**windiness** *n* [U]

wine[1] /waɪn; waɪn/ *n* [C,U] **1** an alcoholic drink made from GRAPES, or a type of this drink 葡萄酒: *a glass of white wine* 一杯白葡萄酒 | *a delicious Californian wine* 醇香味美的加利福尼亞葡萄酒 **2** an alcoholic drink made from another fruit or plant 果酒: *elderflower wine* 接骨木果酒 **3 wine, women and song** *old-fashioned* a pleasant, enjoyable life of dancing, drinking etc【過時】醇酒、美人、情歌〔指縱情歡樂的生活〕, 聲色犬馬

wine[2] *v* [T] **wine and dine** to entertain someone well with a meal, wine etc 以酒宴款待: *Hawksworth wined and dined potential clients.* 霍克斯沃思設宴招攬客戶。

wine bar /ˈ· ·/ *n* [C] *BrE* a place that serves mainly wine and light meals【英】〔主要供應葡萄酒和小食的〕酒吧

wine cool·er /ˈ· ˌ··/ *n* [C] **1** *AmE* a drink made with wine, fruit juice, and water【美】果汁清涼酒〔由葡萄酒、果汁和水調配而成的飲料〕**2** a special container that you put a bottle of wine into to make it cool 鎮酒冰壺

wine vin·e·gar /ˌ· ˈ···/ *n* [U] a type of VINEGAR made from sour wine, used in cooking〔烹調用〕葡萄酒醋

wing[1] /wɪŋ; wɪŋ/ *n* [C]

1 ►BIRDS 鳥類◄ a) one of the parts of a bird's or insect's body that it uses for flying〔鳥、昆蟲的〕翅膀, 翼: *a butterfly with beautiful markings on its wings* 翅膀上有美麗花紋的蝴蝶 | **flap its wings** (=move them up and down) 拍動翅膀 *vultures circling overhead, lazily flapping their wings* 兀鷲緩緩地拍動雙翅, 在頭頂上盤旋 **b)** the meat on the wing bone of a chicken, duck etc, used as food〔用作食物的〕翅膀〔如雞翅、鴨翅等〕: *spicy chicken wings* 香辣雞翅

2 ►PLANE 飛機◄ one of the large flat parts that stick out from the side of a plane and help to keep it in the air〔飛機的〕機翼 —see picture at 參見 AIRCRAFT 圖

3 ►BUILDING 建築物◄ one of the parts of a large building, especially one that sticks out from the main part〔尤指建築物的〕側翼; 側廳; 耳房, 廂房: *the east wing of the palace* 宮殿的東廂房 | *She works in the hospital's maternity wing.* 她在醫院的婦產科工作。

4 ►POLITICS 政治◄ a group within a political party or similar organization, whose members share particular opinions and aims, especially when these are different from those of most people in the organization〔觀點與政黨、組織中大多數人不一致的〕派別, 派(系): *She's on the liberal wing of the Republican Party.* 她是共和黨內的自由派。—see also 另見 LEFT WING, RIGHT WING

5 ►SPORT 體育運動◄ a) someone who plays on the far left or far right of the field in games like football〔足球等運動中的〕邊鋒, 側翼隊員 **b)** the far left or right part of the field 運動場的邊沿

6 ►CAR 汽車◄ *BrE* the part of a car's body that covers the wheels【英】〔汽車的〕擋泥板, 翼子板; FENDER (2) *AmE*【美】—see picture on page A2 參見A2頁圖

7 take sb under your wing to give help and protection, especially to someone younger or less experienced 將某人置於自己的庇護下〔尤指對年輕或經驗不足的人〕

8 (waiting) in the wings ready to take action or ready to be used when the time is right 準備行動〔只等待時機成熟〕; 隨時可以使用: *There's a whole series of tax-cutting measures waiting in the wings.* 有一整套減稅方案準備出台。

9 ►THEATRE 劇場◄ the wings [plural] the parts at either side of a stage where the actors are hidden from view〔舞台的〕側面

10 be on the wing *literary* if a bird is on the wing, it is flying【文】〔鳥〕在飛行中, 飛翔

11 take wing *literary* to fly away【文】飛走

12 get your wings to pass the necessary flying exams and become a pilot〔當飛行員前〕通過必要的飛行考試

wing[2] *v* **1** [I always+adv/prep] *especially literary* to fly【尤文】飛行, 飛: *a flock of geese winging down the coast from Iceland* 沿着冰島海岸南飛的一羣雁 **2 wing its**

way a) to fly 飛行, 飛: *planes winging their way to exotic destinations* 飛機飛往充滿異國情調的目的地 **b)** to be sent quickly from one place to another〔從一地〕快速送〔到另一地〕: *Our special first prize will soon be winging its way towards you.* 我們的特等頭獎將很快地送給你。**3** [T] to wound a person or bird in the arm or wing 弄傷〔人的〕手臂; 打傷〔鳥的〕翅膀 **4 wing it** *AmE spoken* to do something without planning or preparation【美口】臨時湊成; 即席而為: *I didn't have time to prepare for the meeting – I'll just have to wing it.* 這次會議我沒有時間準備 —— 我只好見機行事。

wing chair /ˈ· ·/ *n* [C] a comfortable chair that has a high back and pieces pointing forward on each side 翼狀靠背扶手椅

wing col·lar /ˌ· ˈ··/ *n* [C] a type of shirt collar for men that is worn with very formal clothes〔男裝禮服的襯衫的〕燕子領

wing com·mand·er /ˈ· ·ˌ··/ *n* a rank in the Royal Air Force〔英國皇家空軍的〕空軍中校 —see table on page C7 參見 C7 頁附錄

wing·ding /ˈwɪŋˌdɪŋ; ˈwɪŋˌdɪŋ/ *n* [C] *AmE old-fashioned* a party【美, 過時】狂歡會; 熱鬧的聚會

winge /wɪndʒ; wɪndʒ/ *v* another spelling of WHINGE whinge 的另一種拼法

winged /wɪŋd; wɪŋd/ *adj* having wings 有翼的; 有翅膀的: *winged insects* 有翅的昆蟲

wing·er /ˈwɪŋɚ; ˈwɪŋə/ *n* [C] **1** a player in games such as football, whose position is on the far left or far right of the field〔足球運動等的〕邊鋒 —see also 另見 WING¹ (5) **2 right-winger/left-winger** someone who belongs to the RIGHT WING or LEFT WING² of a political group〔政治羣體中的〕右翼分子/左翼分子

wing mir·ror /ˈ· ˌ··/ *n* [C] a mirror fixed to the side of a car〔汽車的〕側鏡 —see picture on page A2 參見 A2 頁圖

wing nut /ˈ· ·/ *n* [C] a NUT¹ (2) for fastening things, which has sides that stick out to make it easier to turn 蝶形螺母

wing·span /ˈwɪŋˌspæn; ˈwɪŋspæn/ *n* [C] the distance from the end of one wing to the end of the other 翼展, 翼幅〔兩翼展開時的寬度〕

wing·tip /ˈwɪŋtɪp; ˈwɪŋtɪp/ *n* [C] **1** the point at the end of a bird's or a plane's wing〔鳥、飛機的〕翼尖, 翼梢 **2** *AmE* a type of man's shoe with a pattern of small holes on the toe【美】〔腳尖處有孔的〕拷花男皮鞋

wink¹ /wɪŋk; wɪŋk/ *v* **1** [I,T] to close and open one eye quickly, usually to communicate amusement or a secret message 眨〔一隻眼〕, 使眼色〔常用於示意〕: **[+at]** *Joel winked at me, and I realized he was joking.* 喬爾向我眨眼示意, 我明白他是在開玩笑。**2** [I] to shine with a light that flashes on and off〔光〕閃爍, 明滅: *the winking lights of buoys out to sea* 海上的浮標發出的閃爍燈光

wink 眨〔一隻眼〕

wink at sth *phr v* [T] to pretend not to notice something bad or illegal, in a way that suggests you approve of it 對〔壞事、非法的事〕睜一隻眼閉一隻眼, 假裝沒有看見

wink² *n* **1** [C] a quick opening and closing of your eye, usually as a signal between people 眨眼〔示意〕: *a conspiratorial wink* 詭祕地眨一下眼 **2 not get a wink of sleep/not sleep a wink** not be able to sleep at all 無法入睡 **3 tip sb the wink** to secretly warn someone about something or give them information 暗中警告某人[向某人透露消息] **4 quick as a wink** *AmE* very quickly【美】很快地 —see also 另見 FORTY WINKS, **a nod's as good as a wink** (NOD² (3))

wink·ers /ˈwɪŋkɚz; ˈwɪŋkəz/ *n* [plural] *BrE informal* the small usually orange lights on a car that flash on the right or left to show that the car is turning【英, 非正式】〔汽車左右兩邊表示拐彎的橙色〕頻閃信號燈, 方向指示燈; BLINKERS (3) *AmE*【美】

win·kle¹ /ˈwɪŋkḷ; ˈwɪŋkəl/ *n* [C] a small sea animal that lives in a shell and is used for food〔可食用的〕蛾螺; 玉黍螺

winkle² *v*

winkle sth/sb ↔ **out** *phr v* [T] **1** to make someone leave somewhere 把〔某人〕趕出〔某地〕: *Government critics were winkled out of their positions of influence.* 批評政府的人士被解除了重要職位。**2** to discover something such as information 發現〔消息等〕: *Candy was very good at winkling out secrets.* 坎迪極善於刺探祕密。

winkle pick·er /ˈ·· ˌ··/ *n* [C usually plural 一般用複數] *BrE* a type of man's shoe with very pointed toes, popular in the 1950's【英】〔流行於 20 世紀 50 年代的〕男式尖頭皮鞋

win·ner /ˈwɪnɚ; ˈwɪnə/ *n* [C] **1** a person or an animal that has won something 獲勝者〔人或動物〕: *a Nobel prize winner* 諾貝爾獎得主 | *Sid backed a winner at this year's Derby.* 西德下注買中了今年打比賽馬中獲勝的馬。**2** *informal* someone or something that is likely to be very successful【非正式】可望成功的人[事]: *That idea's a real winner.* 那個主意的確好。| **be onto a winner** (=be selling, producing etc something that is very likely to be successful) 銷售[生產]極有市場的物品 S3 W2

win·ning /ˈwɪnɪŋ; ˈwɪnɪŋ/ *adj* [only before noun 僅用於名詞前] very pleasant and attractive in a way that makes everyone like you 可愛的; 迷人的: *a winning smile* 迷人的微笑

winning post /ˈ·· ˌ·/ *n* [singular] *especially BrE* the place where a horse race ends【尤英】〔賽馬的〕終點柱

win·nings /ˈwɪnɪŋz; ˈwɪnɪŋz/ *n* [plural] money that you win in a game or by betting (BET¹ (1))〔在比賽或打賭中〕贏得的錢

win·now /ˈwɪno; ˈwɪnəʊ/ *v* [T] to blow the CHAFF (=outer part) away from grain 簸去〔穀殼〕

wi·no /ˈwaɪno; ˈwaɪnəʊ/ *n* [C] *informal* someone who drinks a lot of cheap alcohol and lives on the streets【非正式】〔露宿街頭的〕醉鬼, 酒鬼: *accosted by winos asking for money* 被酒鬼搭訕要錢

win·some /ˈwɪnsəm; ˈwɪnsəm/ *adj literary* pleasant and attractive, especially in a simple, direct way【文】迷人的; 令人喜歡的: *a winsome smile* 迷人的微笑

win·ter¹ /ˈwɪntɚ; ˈwɪntə/ *n* [C,U] the season after autumn and before spring 冬季, 冬天: *the cold Canadian winters* 加拿大寒冷的冬天 | *the winter of 1942* 1942 年冬季 | **in (the) winter** *It usually snows here in winter.* 這兒冬天一般會下雪。| **winter coat/shoes etc** (=designed for cold weather) 冬衣/冬鞋等 S2 W2

winter² *v* [I always+adv/prep] to spend the winter somewhere〔在某處〕過冬: *Swallows winter in Africa or India.* 燕子在非洲或印度過冬。

win·ter·ize /ˈwɪntəraɪz; ˈwɪntəraɪz/ *v* [T] *AmE* to prepare your car, house etc for winter conditions【美】在〔汽車、房屋等〕內裝禦寒設備

winter sol·stice /ˌ·· ˈ··/ *n* [singular] the shortest day of the year in the Northern Hemisphere, usually around December 22nd 冬至〔在北半球, 一年中白晝最短的一天, 通常在12月22日左右〕

winter sports /ˌ·· ˈ·/ *n* [plural] sports that take place on snow or ice, such as skiing (SKI²) 冬季運動〔例如滑雪〕

win·ter·time /ˈwɪntɚˌtaɪm; ˈwɪntətaɪm/ *n* [U] the winter season when the weather is cold 冬季; 冬天

win·try /ˈwɪntrɪ; ˈwɪntri/ also 又作 **win·ter·y** /ˈwɪntrɪ; ˈwɪntəri/ *adj* like winter, or typical of winter, especially because it is cold 冬天似的; 寒冷的: *a wintry night* 寒冬的晚上

wipe¹ /waɪp; waɪp/ *v* 

1 ►CLEAN/RUB 清理/擦◄ [T] **a)** to rub a surface with

a cloth in order to remove dirt, liquid etc 擦, 拭, 揩: *I wiped the table with a damp cloth.* 我用一塊濕布擦桌子。| **wipe your eyes** (=stop crying or remove tears from your face) 擦乾眼淚, 停止哭泣 **b)** to clean something by rubbing it against a surface 擦乾淨〔某物〕: *She wiped her hands on the back of her jeans.* 她雙手在牛仔褲後面抹了抹。

2 ►REMOVE DIRT 去除污垢◄ [T always+adv/prep] to remove liquid, dirt, or marks by wiping 擦掉〔水、污垢、印跡等〕: *Wipe any dirt from round the cap before unscrewing it.* 把四周的塵土擦掉再把蓋子擰開。| **wipe sth off/away from** *I'll just wipe all these crumbs off the table.* 我會把桌子上的麵包屑擦掉。

3 ►COMPUTER/TAPE 電腦/磁帶◄ [T] to remove all the information that has been stored on a TAPE[1] (1a), VIDEO[1] (1,2), or computer DISK 抹掉〔磁帶上的錄音或錄像、磁盤上的信息〕

4 ►FORGET 忘卻◄ [T] to try to forget an unhappy or upsetting experience 忘記; 抹掉〔不愉快或令人不安的經歷〕: *I tried to wipe the whole experience from my mind.* 我設法忘記整個經歷。

5 wipe the floor with *informal* to defeat someone completely in a competition or argument【非正式】〔在比賽、辯論中〕把〔某人〕打得大敗

6 wipe the slate clean to agree to forget about mistakes or arguments that happened in the past 把以往的錯誤[爭論]一筆勾銷

7 wipe the smile/grin off sb's face *informal* to make someone less pleased or satisfied, especially because they are annoying you【非正式】使某人高興不起來〔尤指因對方觸怒了你〕: *Tell him how much it'll cost – that should wipe the smile off his face!* 告訴他要花多少錢——那樣他就笑不出來了!

8 wipe sth off the face of the earth/off the map to destroy something completely so that it no longer exists 徹底毀滅某物: *Another few years and this species could be wiped off the face of the earth.* 過不了幾年, 這物種可能從地球上徹底消失。

9 ►PLATES/CUPS ETC 盤子/杯子等◄ [I,T] *BrE* to dry plates, cups etc that have been washed【英】〔把洗過的碟子、杯子等〕擦乾: *You wash, I'll wipe.* 你洗, 我來擦。

wipe sth ↔ **down** *phr v* [T] to completely clean a surface using a wet cloth〔用濕布把表面〕擦乾淨

wipe out *phr v* **1** [T **wipe** sb/sth ↔ **out**] to destroy, remove, or get rid of something completely 徹底毀滅〔某物〕, 勾銷, 去除: *Half the population was wiped out by plague.* 鼠疫奪走了一半人的生命。**2** [T **wipe** sb ↔ **out**] *informal* to make you feel extremely tired【非正式】使疲憊不堪: *The heat had wiped us out.* 炎熱使我們精疲力竭。—see also 另見 WIPED OUT **3** [I] *AmE* to fall or hit another object when driving a car, bicycle etc【美】〔開車、騎自行車時〕翻跌下來; 撞上某物

wipe sth ↔ **up** *phr v* [T] to remove liquid from a surface using a cloth〔用布〕揩乾: *I hastily wiped up the milk I had spilled.* 我連忙把灑出來的牛奶擦乾淨。—see picture at 參見 CLEAN² 圖

wipe² *n* [C] **1** a wiping movement with a cloth 擦, 拭, 揩: *An occasional wipe with a soft cloth will keep the surface shiny.* 時不時用軟布擦一擦, 將使表面保持光亮。| **give sth a wipe** *Give the baby's nose a wipe, would you?* 擦擦這孩子的鼻子, 行嗎? **2** a special piece of wet material that you use to clean something and then throw away〔用完即棄〕濕抹布: *antiseptic wipes* 抗菌抹布

wiped out /ˌ· ˈ·/ *adj* [not before noun 不用於名詞前] *informal* extremely tired; EXHAUSTED (1)【非正式】疲憊不堪的

wip·er /ˈwaɪpɚ; ˈwaɪpə/ *n* [C] a WINDSCREEN WIPER or WINDSHIELD WIPER 擋風玻璃刮水器

S3 W3 **wire¹** /waɪr; waɪə/ *n* **1** [U] thin metal in the form of a thread 金屬絲[線]: *String wasn't strong enough, so we used wire.* 線不夠結實, 所以我們用了金屬絲。| *a wire fence* 金屬絲網 **2** [C] a piece of metal like this, usually covered in plastic, used for taking electricity from one place to another 電線 **3 get your wires crossed** to become confused about what someone is saying because you think they are talking about something else 弄不清某人說的話; 誤會 **4 right down to the wire** *informal* with very little time left before something must be finished or completed【非正式】〔完成某事的〕期限將近; 接近截止期 **5** [C] *AmE* a piece of electronic recording equipment, usually worn secretly on someone's clothes【美】竊聽器〔一般祕密地戴在衣服上〕 **6** [C] *AmE* a TELEGRAM【美】電報—see also 另見 LIVE WIRE, WIRY

wire² *v* [T] **1** also 又作 **wire up** to connect wires to something, especially in an electrical system 給〔電氣系統的某物〕連上電線: *Check that the plug has been wired up properly.* 檢查一下插頭的電線是否已經接好。**2** to fasten two or more things together using wire 用金屬絲把〔兩件或兩件以上的東西〕捆紮在一起: *The poles had all been wired together.* 已經用金屬絲把杆子捆在一起了。**3** to send money electronically from one bank to another〔通過銀行〕電匯〔錢〕 **4** *AmE* to send a TELEGRAM to someone【美】〔給某人〕打電報 —see also 另見 WIRING

wire cut·ters /ˈ· ˌ··/ *n* [plural] a special tool like very strong scissors, used for cutting wire 鋼絲鉗; 鐵絲剪

wired /waɪrd; waɪəd/ *adj* **1** also 又作 **wired up** fitted with hidden electronic recording equipment for listening to people's conversations 裝有竊聽器的: *Careful what you say – the room could be wired.* 說話注意——房間裡可能裝有竊聽器。**2** *AmE informal* very excited or nervous; TENSE[1] (1)【美, 非正式】極其興奮的; 極其緊張的 **3** *AmE informal* very active and excited, because you have taken a drug【美, 非正式】〔因吸食毒品而致〕神經興奮的

wire-haired /ˌ· ˈ·◄/ *adj* a wire-haired dog has fur that is stiff not soft〔狗〕粗毛的; 硬毛的: *a wire-haired terrier* 硬毛㹴

wire·less /ˈwaɪrlɪs; ˈwaɪələs/ *n* [C,U] *old-fashioned especially BrE* a radio【過時, 尤英】無線電收音機

wire net·ting /ˌ· ˈ··/ *n* [U] wires that have been woven together to form a net, used especially for fences 金屬絲網; 鐵絲網〔尤用於籬笆〕

wire·tap /ˈwaɪrˌtæp; ˈwaɪətæp/ *v* [T] to secretly listen to other people's telephone conversations, by fixing something to the wires of their phone〔在某人的電話線路上〕搭線竊聽 —**wiretap** *n* [C] —**wiretapping** *n* [U]

wire wool /ˌ· ˈ·/ *n* [U] a mass of very thin pieces of wire, used for cleaning pans〔洗鍋盤用的〕鋼絲絨

wir·ing /ˈwaɪrɪŋ; ˈwaɪərɪŋ/ *n* [singular] **1** the network of wires that form the electrical system in a building〔建築物中〕供電系統的線路: *faulty wiring* 出毛病的線路 | *The wiring needs to be replaced.* 供電線路需要更換。**2** a length of wire that is used for making a network for electricity〔電氣線路的〕配線; 佈線: *copper wiring* 銅線

wir·y /ˈwaɪrɪ; ˈwaɪəri/ *adj* **1** someone who is wiry is thin but has strong muscles〔人〕瘦而結實的 **2** hair that is wiry is stiff and curly〔毛髮〕硬而鬈曲的 —**wiriness** *n* [U]

wis·dom /ˈwɪzdəm; ˈwɪzdəm/ *n* [U] **1** good sense and judgment, based especially on your experience of life〔尤指基於生活閱歷的〕智慧; 明斷: *a man of great wisdom* 才智卓越的人 | **question the wisdom of** *formal* (=say that you think something is not sensible)【正式】懷疑…是否明智 *I would question the wisdom of lending him such a large sum of money.* 借給他這麼一大筆錢, 我懷疑這是否明智。**2** knowledge gained over a long period of time through learning or experience 知識, 學問: *the collected wisdom of many centuries* 許多世紀積累的知識 **3 received/conventional wisdom** a belief that is generally thought to be true 普遍的看法, 傳統的信念: *The received wisdom is that boys mature more slowly than girls.* 人們普遍認為男孩子比女孩子晚熟。**4 in his/her (infinite) wisdom** used to say jokingly that

you do not understand why someone has decided to do something 以他/她(無限的)智慧〔含戲謔意味，表示不明白某人為何決定做某事〕: *The boss, in her infinite wisdom, has decided to reorganize the whole office yet again.* 老闆無比英明，又決定重新安排整個辦公室。

wisdom tooth /'·· ·/ *n* [C] one of the four large teeth at the back of your mouth that do not grow until you are an adult 智齒，智牙 —see picture at 參見 TEETH 圖

wise¹ /waɪz; waɪz/ *adj*

1 ►DECISION/IDEA ETC 決定/意見等◄ wise decisions and judgements are based on good sense and experience; sensible〔決定和判斷〕明智的；有才智的；有判斷力的: *I think that would be a wise precaution.* 我覺得那會是一種明智的預防措施。| **be wise to do sth** *I think you were wise to leave when you did.* 我認為你當時就走很明智。

2 ►PERSON 人◄ someone who is wise makes good decisions, gives good advice etc, especially because they have a lot of experience of life〔人因閱歷豐富而〕英明的；有智慧的: *a wise old man* 睿智的老人 | **older and wiser** (=having learned from the experiences of life) 智慧隨年齡增長而增加 | **wise in the ways of** *formal* (=knowing a lot about something)【正式】〔對某方面〕知識豐富的

3 get wise to/be wise to *informal* to realize that someone is being dishonest【非正式】知道，了解〔某人不誠實〕: *I've got wise to his little tricks now.* 現在我已經看透他的小把戲了。—see also 另見 **wise up** (WISE²)

4 be none the wiser *informal* to not understand something, even after it has been explained【非正式】〔解釋後〕還是不明白，仍然不懂: *Charlie explained how the system works, but I'm still none the wiser.* 查理解釋了系統是如何運作的，可是我還是不明白。

5 no-one will be any the wiser *spoken* used to say that no-one will find out about something bad someone has done【口】沒有人會知道〔某人做了壞事〕: *Just put it back on the shelf, and no-one will be any the wiser.* 就把它放回架子上，沒人會知道。

6 wise guy *informal especially AmE* an annoying person who thinks they know more than they really do【非正式，尤美】自作聰明的人: *OK, wise guy, shut up and listen for a minute!* 好了，萬事通，你先別說，留神聽一會兒！

7 act wise *AmE spoken* to speak or behave in a rude way【美口】說話[行為]粗魯

8 be wise after the event to know how a mistake could have been avoided, after it has been made 事後聰明 —see also 另見 WISDOM, **sadder but wiser** (SAD (6)) —**wisely** *adv*: *Invest the money wisely.* 明智地投資這筆錢。| *He nodded wisely.* 他點點頭，一副睿智的樣子。

wise² *v*

wise up *phr v informal*【非正式】**1** [I] to realize the unpleasant truth about a situation 知道〔不愉快的真相〕，了解: *Wise up, Vic – he's cheating you!* 明白嗎，威克——他是在騙你！**2** [T **wise** sb **up (to)**] *especially AmE* to make someone realize the unpleasant truth about a situation【尤美】使〔某人〕知道〔不愉快的真相〕

wise³ *n* **1 price-wise/time-wise etc** *especially spoken* concerning or connected with prices etc【尤口】(有關)價格/時間等的: *Time-wise we're not doing too badly.* 時間方面我們做得還可以。**2 crosswise/lengthwise etc** in a direction across something, along the length of something etc 橫向地/縱向地等: *Cut the carrots lengthwise.* 將胡蘿蔔縱向切開。**3** [singular] *old use* a way or manner【舊】方式；方法: *They are in no wise to blame.* 他們根本不該受到責備。—see also 另見 STREETWISE

wise·a·cre /'waɪz,ekɚ; 'waɪzeɪkə/ *n* [C] *informal especially AmE* an annoying person who thinks they know more than they really do【非正式，尤美】自以為是的人，自作聰明的人

wise·crack /'waɪz,kræk; 'waɪzkræk/ *n* [C] a clever funny remark or reply 俏皮話；妙語 —**wisecrack** *v* [I]

wish¹ /wɪʃ; wɪʃ/ *v*

1 ►WANT STH IMPOSSIBLE 希望不可能的事◄ [T] to want something to be true although you know it is either impossible or unlikely 希望〔不可能或可能性很小的事〕: **wish (that)** *I wish I didn't have to go to work today.* 但願我今天不用上班。| **wish to goodness** *spoken* (=wish very much)【口】極其希望 *I wish to goodness they'd hurry up!* 我真希望他們能快點！

2 ►WANT TO DO STH 想做某事◄ [I,T] *formal* to want to do something【正式】想做〔某事〕: **wish to do sth** *I wish to make a complaint.* 我想投訴。| **if you wish** *You may leave now, if you wish.* 你想離開現在就可以離開。| **(just) as you wish** (=used to tell someone you will do what they want) 正如你願意的〔告訴某人會按其意思做事〕*"I'd like it ready by six." "Just as you wish, sir."* "我希望六點鐘準備就緒。""先生，聽您的。"

3 ►HAPPINESS/LUCK ETC 幸福/幸運等◄ [T] to say that you hope someone will have good luck, a happy life etc 祝，祝願〔某人好運、幸福等〕: **wish sb sth** *We wish you a Merry Christmas and a Happy New Year!* 我們祝你聖誕快樂、新年幸福！| *Wish me luck!* 祝我走運吧！| **wish sb well** (=hope that good things happen to someone) 祝福〔某人〕*They wished me well in my new job.* 他們祝我新的工作一切順利。

4 I don't wish to interfere/be nosy etc *spoken* used to show you are sorry if what you are going to say upsets or annoys someone【口】我無意干涉/多管閒事等〔如果將要說的話令某人不安或煩惱，用於道歉〕: *I don't wish to seem ungrateful, but it's not quite what I expected.* 我不想表現得不領情，可是那的確不是我期望的樣子。

5 I (only) wish I knew *spoken* used to emphasize that you do not know something, and you wish you did know【口】我知道就好了〔用於強調不知道某事〕: *"Where on earth have they gone?" "I wish I knew!"* "他們到底去哪兒啦？""我知道就好了！"

6 I/you wish! *spoken* used to say that something is not true, but you wish it was【口】但願如此！〔表示某事不是事實，但你希望是真的〕: *"Oh no, you're quite thin really." "I wish!"* "噢，不，你真的很瘦了。""真是瘦就好了！"

7 wouldn't wish sth on/upon sb *spoken* used to say that something is very unpleasant【口】不想某事發生在某人身上〔表示此事討厭、可怕〕: *It's so painful, you wouldn't wish it on your worst enemy, honestly!* 太痛苦了，坦白說，就是你的死敵你也不願他這樣。

wish for sth *phr v* [T] **1 the best/nicest etc that you would wish for** used to emphasize that something is as good, nice etc as it could possibly be 最理想的: *It was as fine an afternoon as you could wish for.* 這個下午難得的晴朗。| *He had everything a child could possibly wish for.* 他擁有一個孩子可能想得到的一切。**2** [I] to ask silently for something you want and hope that it will happen 默默期盼: *Her only hope now was to wish for a miracle.* 現在她的唯一希望是默默盼禱有奇蹟出現。

wish sth ↔ **away** *phr v* [T] to want something unpleasant to disappear, without doing anything about it 希望〔不愉快的事〕自行消失: *You can't just wish your problems away, you know!* 你知道，你不能一廂情願，希望問題自動解決！

USAGE NOTE 用法說明: WISH

WORD CHOICE 詞語辨析: **wish, want**

In sentences where both can be used, **wish** sounds much more formal than **want**. 在兩者都可以用的句子中，wish 比 want 正式得多。In a conversation you might say 在會話中可說: *I want to write to him but I don't know his address.* 我想給他寫信，可是不知道他的地址。| *They want us to come to dinner.* 他們想要我們去吃晚飯。But speaking officially you might say 但正式場合則說: *You may leave if*

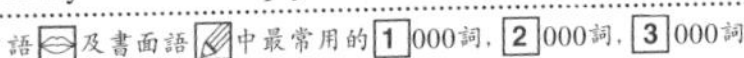

you wish. 你想走就請便吧。You are more likely to see **wish** on official forms and notices. 在正式表格及通告中, 會更多地用 wish。

GRAMMAR 語法

An infinitive after **wish, want,** or **hope** must always have *to* with it. wish, want 及 hope 後的不定式必須帶 to: *I want/hope to see you soon.* (NOT 不用 *...want see you...*)我想/希望不久就見到你。| *I wish to speak* (NOT 不用 *wish speak*). 我想要發言。

Wish and **hope**, unlike **want**, are not used with a direct object. wish 和 hope 與 want 不同, 不能與直接賓語連用: *Everybody wants a happy life* (NOT 不用 *wishes* or 或 *hopes*, but you could say 但可以說: *Everybody wishes to have a happy life/hopes for a happy life.* 每個人都想要/渴望過幸福的生活。)

Wish and **hope** (but NOT **want**) are both used with *that* clauses, but the verbs in them usually have to be in different tenses. wish 和 hope〔而不是 want〕均與 that 引導的從句連用, 然而從句中的動詞時態通常卻不同: *I hope (that) you will be happy* (NOT 不用 *wish* or 或 *want*). 我希望你會幸福。| *I wish (that) you could be happy.* 我祝願你幸福。(For the difference in meaning see 意思的差異見 **hope** WORD CHOICE). These are the main tenses used after **wish** 以下是用於 wish 後面的主要時態:

If you wish a particular situation existed at this moment, you use the past tense 如果希望此時某特定情況存在, 使用過去式: *I wish I knew/had my own house.* 但願我了解/擁有自己的房子。| *He wished it were Tuesday already.* 他但願今天已經是星期二。In informal British English it is common to use *was* instead of *were* in sentences like the last, but in American English *was* would be considered incorrect here. 在非正式英國英語中, 上句中的 were 通常可用 was 代替, 但是在美國英語中, 此處如果用 was, 則被認為是不正確的。

If you wish a situation would exist in the future, you use *could* 如果希望某情景在未來出現, 那就用 could: *I wish I could have my own house* (NOT 不用 *I wish I'll have my own house* or 或 *I wish I would...* or 或 *I wish if I could...*). 我希望我能擁有自己的房子。

If you wish a situation had existed or something had happened in the past, you use the past perfect 如果希望某情況已經存在, 或某事在過去已經發生, 那就用過去完成式: *I wish I had been alive in the twenties.* 我希望生活在20年代。| *I wish I'd had a chance to talk to you before you left.* 我想在你離開前能有機會和你談談 (可惜沒有)。

If you wish something would happen at this moment or at some time in the future, you use **would** or **could** 如果希望某事在此時或將來某時發生, 則用 would 或 could: *I wish you could/would come* (*could*=but something is stopping you 但目前有事阻止你來; *would*=but you don't want to 會來, 但你不想來). 我希望你能/會來。| *He wished the problem could be solved* (NOT 不用 *...problem be solved*). 他希望問題會得到解決。| *I wish you wouldn't go out every night.* 我希望你不要每天晚上都出去。

W

3 **wish²** *n* [C]

1 ▶DESIRE 願望◀ a feeling of wanting to do something, or wanting something to happen 希望; 願望: *It's important to respect the wishes of the patient.* 尊重病人的意願極為重要。| **a wish to do sth** *She had expressed a wish to see the children.* 她表達了要見孩子的願望。

2 ▶THING YOU WANT 希望發生的事/想要的東西◀ something that you want to have or to happen 想要的東西; 希望發生的事: *She wanted a new bike for Christmas, and she got her wish.* 她想在聖誕節得到一輛新自行車, 她如願以償了。| *the wishes of the majority* 大多數人的意願 | **dearest/greatest wish** (=what you want most of all) 最想要的/最大的願望 *His dearest wish was to become a father.* 他最大的願望是當爸爸。| **sb's wish is granted/fulfilled** (=they get what they want) 某人如願以償 | **sb's wish comes true** (=they get what they want, especially in a surprising and unexpected way) 某人的願望成真〔尤指通過令人吃驚或意想不到的途徑〕| **last wish/dying wish** (=something that you say you want just before you die) 臨終遺願

3 against sb's wishes if you do something against someone's wishes, you do it even though you know they do not want you to〔做事〕違反某人的意願: *She had left school against her mother's wishes.* 她違反母親的願望, 輟學了。| **go against sb's wishes** (=do something against their wishes) 與某人的意願相違

4 have no wish to do sth *formal* used to emphasize that you do not want or intend to do something【正式】無意做某事〔用於強調〕: *I have no wish to speak to her ever again.* 我再也不願意跟她說話了。

5 best wishes a) used in cards to say that you hope someone will be happy 最好的祝願〔賀卡中的祝辭〕: *best wishes for your married life* 致以新婚最好的祝願 **b)** used as a greeting at the end of a letter 祝好〔用於信件末尾的祝辭〕

6 ▶SILENT REQUEST 默禱◀ a silent request for something to happen as if by magic 默禱, 祈求; 許願: **make a wish** *I closed my eyes and made a wish.* 我閉上眼睛許了個願。

7 your wish is my command *especially humorous* used to say that you will do whatever someone asks you to do【尤幽默】悉聽尊命

wish·bone /ˈwɪʃ͵bon; ˈwɪʃbəʊn/ *n* [C] the breast bone from a cooked chicken etc, which two people pull apart to decide who will make a wish 叉骨, 如願骨〔煮熟的雞等的胸骨, 由兩人同時拉扯, 以決定由誰許願〕

wish·ful think·ing /͵.. ˈ../ *n* [U] the false belief that something will happen just because you want it to 如意算盤; 痴心妄想

wish·ing well /ˈ.. ͵./ *n* [C] a WELL⁴ (1) or pool of water that people throw coins into while making a wish〔投幣許願的〕許願井

wish list /ˈ. ./ *n* [C] *informal, especially AmE* all the things that you want in a particular situation【非正式, 尤美】〔在某情況中的〕願望清單

wish·y-wash·y /ˈwɪʃɪ ͵wɑʃɪ; ˈwɪʃi ͵wɒʃi/ *adj informal*【非正式】**1** a wishy-washy person does not have firm or clear ideas and seems unable to decide what they want〔人〕優柔寡斷的; 沒有明確目標的: *a bunch of wishy-washy liberals* 一羣沒有清晰目標的自由主義者 **2** colours that are wishy-washy are pale, not strong or dark〔色彩〕淡的; 弱的; 淺的

wisp /wɪsp; wɪsp/ *n* [C] **1 wisp of hair/hay/grass etc** a thin piece of hair etc that is separate from the rest 一縷頭髮/一把乾草/一束青草等: *A wisp of hair had escaped from under her hat.* 在她的帽子下面露出一縷頭髮。—see picture on page A7 參見 A7 頁圖 **2 wisp of smoke/cloud etc** a small thin line of smoke etc that rises upwards 一縷輕煙/一絲浮雲等 —see also 另見 WILL O' THE WISP —**wispy** *adj*

wis·te·ri·a /wɪsˈtɪrɪə; wɪˈstɪəriə/ *n* [C,U] a climbing plant with purple or white flowers 紫藤〔一種攀緣植物, 開紫色或白色花〕

wist·ful /ˈwɪstfəl; ˈwɪstfəl/ *adj* feeling rather sad and thoughtful, especially because of something that you would like but can no longer have〔尤指因心愛之物不復存在而〕惆悵的; 思念的; 依依不捨的: *wistful memories of her lost youth* 對她逝去青春的惆悵回憶 —**wistfully** *adv* —**wistfulness** *n* [U]

wit /wɪt; wɪt/ *n*

1 ▶AMUSING 娛人的◀ [U] the ability to say things that are clever and amusing〔說話〕機智風趣: *a woman* *of great wit and charm* 說話風趣、風韻動人的女人 | **quick/dry/sharp wit** *His sharp wit had them all smiling.* 他的機智詼諧使所有人笑不攏嘴。

2 ▶AMUSING PERSON 說話風趣的人◀ [C] someone who is able to say clever and funny things 說話風趣詼諧的人: *Oscar Wilde was a famous wit.* 奧斯卡·王爾德是著名的說話風趣的人。

3 wits [plural] your ability to think quickly and make the right decisions 機智: *It was a tricky situation – I had to use all my wits to extricate myself.* 形勢微妙 —— 我得費盡心機才能脱身。| **keep/have your wits about you** (=be ready to think quickly and do what is necessary in a difficult situation)〔在困難的情況下〕保持頭腦清醒, 隨機應變

4 have the wit to do sth to be clever enough to know the right thing to do 足夠明智, 作出正確決定〔做某事〕

5 frighten/scare sb out of their wits *informal* to frighten someone very much【非正式】嚇壞某人

6 at your wits' end very worried, because you have tried everything possible to solve a problem 智窮計盡, 束手無策

7 not beyond the wit of *often humorous* not too difficult for someone to do【常幽默】有做某事的才智: *It's surely not beyond the wit of man to come up with a solution.* 人類要想出解決方法肯定沒有困難。

8 to wit *old use* that is to say ; NAMELY【舊】即, 就是 — see also 另見 **a battle of wits** (BATTLE[1] (5)), HALF-WIT, **live by your wits** (LIVE[1] (9)), OUTWIT, QUICK-WITTED, WITTY —**witless** *adj*

witch /wɪtʃ; wɪtʃ/ *n* [C] **1** a woman who is supposed to have magic powers, especially to do bad things〔尤指做壞事的〕女巫, 巫婆 **2** *informal* an insulting word for an old or unpleasant woman【非正式】醜老太婆〔惡語〕—see also 另見 BEWITCH

witch 女巫, 巫婆

witch·craft /ˈwɪtʃˌkræft; ˈwɪtʃkrɑːft/ *n* [U] the use of magic to make things happen 巫術; 魔法

witch-doc·tor /ˈ· ˌ··/ *n* [C] a man who is believed to have magic powers and the ability to cure people of diseases, especially in some parts of Africa〔尤指非洲某些地區的〕巫醫

witch-ha·zel /ˈ· ˌ··/ *n* [C,U] a substance used for treating small wounds on the skin, or the tree that produces it〔用於治療傷口的〕金縷梅酊劑; 金縷梅 (樹)

witch-hunt /ˈ· ·/ *n* [C] a deliberate attempt, often based on false information, to find and punish people in a society or organization whose opinions are regarded as wrong or dangerous 迫害: *McCarthy's Communist witch-hunts* 麥卡錫對共產黨人的政治迫害

witch·ing hour /ˈ·· ˌ·/ *n* [singular] *literary* the time, especially in the middle of the night, when strange or magic things are believed to happen【文】〔尤指夜半〕怪事發生的時刻

1 1 **with** /wɪð; wɪð/ *prep* **1** near someone or something, or in someone's presence 在〔某人或某物〕附近; 與〔某人〕在一起: *I saw Bob in town with his girlfriend.* 我在城裡看見鮑勃與他的女朋友在一起。| *Mix the powder with boiling water.* 用開水把粉末調和。**2** having, possessing, or showing a particular thing, quality or feeling 具有; 帶有; 顯出〔某物、某種特性或感情〕: *a book with a green cover* 一本有綠色封面的書 | *Jack beamed with pleasure when he heard the news.* 傑克在聽到這消息後笑逐顏開。| **complete with** *The mixer comes complete with instructions and a guarantee.* 攪拌機帶有使用說明書和保證書。**3** including 包括…在內: *With a tip, the meal cost $30.* 包括小費在內, 這頓飯花了30美元。**4** by means of something or using it 用; 以; 藉: *Eat your melon with a knife and fork.* 用刀、叉吃甜瓜。| *What will you buy with the money?* 你會用這筆錢買甚麼? **5** used to show the idea of filling, covering, or containing something〔表示填充、覆蓋、含有的概念〕: *Her boots were covered with mud.* 她的靴子上滿是污泥。| *Fill the bowl with sugar.* 把這個碗裝滿糖。**6** concerning, or in the case of 關於; 對於; 至於: *Be careful with that glass.* 小心那隻玻璃杯。| *Britain's trade with Japan* 英國與日本之間的貿易 | *He's in love with you.* 他愛上了你。**7** supporting or liking someone or something 支持, 贊同〔某人或某物〕: *Some opposition MPs voted with the Government.* 一些反對黨的議員投票支持政府。| *You're either with me or against me.* 你要麼支持我, 要麼反對我。**8** against or opposing someone 反對; 與〔某人〕對立: *Stop fighting with your brother!* 不要和弟弟打架! | *We're competing with foreign businesses.* 我們在和外國公司競爭。**9** in the same direction as someone or something 與〔某人、某物〕方向一致: *We sailed with the wind.* 我們順風航行。**10** at the same time or rate as something else 與〔某物〕同時; 隨着: *This wine improves with age.* 這種酒越陳越醇。**11** used when comparing two things or considering the relationship between them 與…相比; 考慮到〔兩物的關係〕: *Compared with other children of the same age, Robert's very tall.* 和同年齡的其他孩子相比, 羅伯特長得很高。**12** used in some expressions to show that one person or thing separates from another〔用於表示〕分離: *Joan doesn't want to part with the money.* 瓊不想花掉這筆錢。| *a complete break with tradition* 與傳統徹底決裂 **13** in spite of 儘管; 雖然: *With all his faults, I still like him.* 他儘管有許多缺點, 仍然討我喜歡。**14** because of or considering the fact of 因為; 考慮到: *They were trembling with fear.* 他們嚇得直發抖。| *With John away there's more room in the house.* 因為約翰不在, 家裡寬敞了一些。**15** used to express a strong wish or command〔用於表達強烈的願望和命令〕: *Down with school!* 打倒學校! | *Off to bed with you!* 上牀睡覺去! **16 with it** *informal*【非正式】**a)** dressing in fashionable clothes and knowing about new ideas 衣着時髦; 認識新思想: *I can't get over how with it your mother is.* 你媽媽多麼時髦, 我感到驚訝極了! **b)** lively and able to understand things 生氣勃勃的, 機靈的: *I'm sorry I'm not feeling very with it today.* 對不起, 我今天有點遲鈍。—see also 另見 WITH-IT **17 with you** *informal*【非正式】**a)** understanding someone's explanation about something 聽懂某人的話: *I'm sorry, I'm not really with you; could you repeat what you just said.* 對不起, 我沒有聽懂; 請你重複一遍剛才所說的話。**b)** supporting someone by agreeing with what they say or do 支持, 同意〔對人所說、所為〕: *I'm with Harry all the way on this one.* 在這一方面我一直完全支持哈里。**18 with that** also 又作 **at that** used to say that something happens immediately after something else 隨即; 接着: *He gave a little wave and with that he was gone.* 他輕輕地揮了一下手, 隨即就走了。

with·al /wɪˈðɔl; wɪˈðɔːl/ *adv old use* besides; together with this【舊】此外; 而且; 又

with·draw /wɪðˈdrɔ; wɪðˈdrɔː/ *v past tense* **withdrew** /-ˈdru; -ˈdruː/ *past participle* **withdrawn** /-ˈdrɔn; -ˈdrɔːn/ ✎2

1 ▶MONEY 金錢◀ [T] to take money out of a bank account 提取〔銀行存款〕: **withdraw sth from** *Liz withdrew $100 from her account.* 莉茲從她的賬戶上提取了100美元。

2 ▶TAKE AWAY 取走, 拿走◀ [T] to remove something or take it away or take it back, often because of an official decision〔常因正方決定而〕撤回, 撤銷, 收回: *a government decision to withdraw funding* 政府撤銷提供資金的決定 | *One of the minority parties had withdrawn its support for Chancellor Kohl.* 一個少數黨已經不再支持科爾總理了。| **withdraw sth from** *She with-*

W

drew a document from her briefcase. 她從公文包中取出一份文件。| **withdraw sth from sale/from the market** (=stop selling it)〔從銷售/市場中〕收回某物; 停止銷售 *The drug has been withdrawn from the market for further tests.* 該藥已從市場上收回, 以便作進一步的化驗。

3 withdraw a remark/accusation to say that a remark that you made earlier was completely untrue; RETRACT 撤回評論/撤銷指控: *The newspaper has agreed to withdraw its allegations.* 報社已同意撤回其指控。

4 ►NOT TAKE PART 不參加◄ **a)** [I] to no longer take part in or belong to an organization 退出〔組織〕: **[+from]** *calls for Britain to withdraw from the European Union* 要求英國退出歐洲聯盟的呼聲 **b)** [I,T] to no longer take part in an activity, race etc, or to prevent someone from doing this (使) 不參加〔活動、比賽等〕: **[+from]** *Injury forced Clare to withdraw from the event.* 克萊爾因傷被迫退出比賽。| **withdraw sth/sb from** *Ted withdrew his horse from the race.* 泰德讓他的馬退出了這次比賽。

5 ►LEAVE 離開◄ **a)** [I] to leave a place, especially in order to be alone or go somewhere quiet 離開〔尤指想獨處或悄悄地去某處〕: *We withdrew to the garden for a private talk.* 我們退到花園裡進行祕談。**b)** [I,T] if an army withdraws or is withdrawn, it leaves a place, especially in order to avoid defeat〔尤指軍隊避免戰敗而〕撤退

6 ►STOP COMMUNICATING 停止交流◄ [I] to become quieter, less friendly, and more concerned about your own thoughts 變得冷漠; 離羣索居: **[+into/from]** *The little girl seemed to withdraw into a private world.* 小女孩看來要把自己封閉起來。

3 **with·draw·al** /wɪð`drɔəl; wɪð'drɔːəl/ *n*

1 ►MONEY 金錢◄ [C,U] the act of taking money from a bank account, or the amount you take out〔從銀行賬戶中〕提款; 提款額

2 ►ARMY 軍隊◄ [C,U] the act of moving an army, weapons etc away from the area where they were fighting 撤軍; 撤退; 撤回: **[+of/from]** *the withdrawal of all UN forces from the region* 所有聯合國部隊從該地區撤退

3 ►REMOVAL/ENDING 移走/終結◄ [U] the removal or stopping of something such as support, an offer, or a service〔對支持、建議、服務等的〕取消, 收回: **[+of]** *withdrawal of government aid* 取消政府的資助

4 ►STOP TAKING PART 停止參與◄ [U] the act of no longer taking part in an activity or being a member of an organization 退出〔活動或組織〕: **[+from]** *Germany's withdrawal from the talks* 德國退出談判

5 ►DRUGS 毒品◄ [U] the period after you have given up a drug that you were dependent on, and the mental and physical effects that this process involves 脫癮 (過程), 戒毒: **withdrawal symptoms** (=the painful or unpleasant effects caused by withdrawal) 脫癮症狀〔因脫癮而引起的痛苦或不適〕

6 ►STATEMENT 陳述◄ [U] the act of saying that something you previously said was in fact untrue 取消, 撤銷: **[+of]** *the withdrawal of all allegations* 撤銷所有指控

with·drawn /wɪð`drɔn; wɪð'drɔːn/ *adj* very shy and quiet, and concerned only about your own thoughts 孤僻的; 內向的; 沉默寡言的

with·er /`wɪðɚ; 'wɪðə/ *v* also 又作 **wither away** [I,T] if plants wither they become drier and smaller and start to die〔植物〕枯萎, 乾枯

with·ered /`wɪðɚd; 'wɪðəd/ *adj* **1** a withered plant has become drier and smaller and is dead or dying〔植物〕枯萎的, 乾枯的 **2** a withered person looks thin and weak and old〔人〕枯槁的; 憔悴的 **3** a withered arm or leg has not developed properly and is thin and weak〔胳膊或腿〕發育不全的; 萎縮的

with·er·ing /`wɪðərɪŋ; 'wɪðərɪŋ/ *adj* **a withering look/remark etc** a look, remark etc that makes someone feel stupid, embarrassed, or lose confidence 咄咄逼人的眼色/尖刻的言語等: *She gave him a withering glance.* 她咄咄逼人地瞥了他一眼。—**witheringly** *adv*

with·ers /`wɪðɚz; 'wɪðəz/ *n* [plural] the highest part of a horse's back, above its shoulders 鬐甲〔馬肩甲骨間隆起的部分〕—see picture at 參見 HORSE[1] 圖

with·hold /wɪð`hold; wɪð'həʊld/ *v past tense and past participle* **withheld** /-`hɛld; -'held/ [T] **1** to refuse to let someone have something, especially until something else is done 拒絕給予〔尤指直至某事完成〕, 扣留: *I withheld payment until they had completed the work.* 他們工作完成以後我才付錢。**2 withhold facts/evidence/information** to refuse to give information 隱瞞事實/證據/信息: *Ian was accused of withholding vital information from the police.* 伊恩被控向警方隱瞞關鍵情報。

with·hold·ing tax /·'·· ,·/ *n* [C,U] *AmE* money that is taken out of your wages as tax【美】〔工資中〕扣除的所得稅

with·in /wɪð`ɪn; wɪð'ɪn/ *adv, prep* **1 a)** before a certain period of time has passed 在〔某時間過去〕前: *Ray left suddenly promising to be back within the hour.* 雷伊突然離開, 他答應一小時內回來。**b)** during a certain period of time 在〔某段時間〕之內: *Her car has been broken into three times within a month.* 在一個月內, 她的汽車被盜竊三次。| **within the space of...** *Within the space of a year three of the town's biggest factories have closed down.* 在一年內, 城裡最大的廠家已有三家倒閉了。**2** inside a certain area and not beyond it 在…範圍以內: *Children must remain within the school grounds during the lunch break.* 午飯時間孩子必須留在校園裡。| **within 20 metres/50 kilometres/10 miles of etc** (=less than twenty metres, fifty kilometres etc from a particular place)〔離某地〕不出 20 米/50 公里/10 英里等 *We are now within two kilometres of the centre of Istanbul.* 我們現在離伊斯坦布爾市中心不到兩公里。| **apply/enquire within** (=used on notices and advertisements especially when someone is trying to sell something) 入內面洽/查詢〔通告和廣告用語, 尤指在出售物品時〕*Baby rabbits for sale. Enquire within.* 有小兔子出售, 請入內洽詢。**3** inside a society, organization, or group of people 在〔社會、組織或一羣人〕裡面: *There have been a lot of changes within the department since I joined.* 自我加入後, 部門內發生了很多變化。| **from within** *an attempt to reform the system from within* 從內部改革體制的嘗試 **4** according to particular limits or rules 在〔限制、規則〕之內: *We have to operate within a very tight budget.* 我們必須在極其嚴格的預算之內經營。| *This clause is no longer valid within the terms of the new settlement.* 在新協議的條款下, 這條款不再有效。**5 within sight/earshot etc** if something is within sight, earshot etc you can see or hear it 在視線/聽力等範圍內 **6 within reach a)** near, so that people can get there without difficulty 在…附近, 距離…不遠: *We live within easy reach of the shops.* 我們住在離商店不遠的地方。**b)** near enough to be picked up or touched when you stretch out your hand 伸手可及: *The key was hanging from a hook on the wall, just within my reach.* 鑰匙掛在牆上的鈎子上, 我伸手就夠到。**7 a play within a play/a university within a university etc** a small place, thing etc which exists inside a bigger place or thing of the same kind 戲中戲/大學中大學等

with-it /'· ·/ *adj old-fashioned* fashionable and modern in the way that you dress, think etc【過時】〔衣着、思想等〕時髦的, 時興的 —see also 另見 **with it** (WITH)

with·out /wɪð`aʊt; wɪð'aʊt/ *adv, prep* **1** lacking something, especially something that is basic or necessary 缺乏; 沒有〔尤指基本或必要之物〕: *We had to survive without light or heating for a whole month.* 整個月沒有照明、沒有暖氣, 我們也得活下去。| **can't do without** (=unable to live or work without something) 沒有〔某物〕無法生活[工作] *We can't do without hot water for too long.* 我們不能太長時間沒有熱水。**2** not doing or having something, or not showing a particular feeling, especially when it is considered normal or polite 不，不曾: *He had gone out without his parents' permission.* 他沒經父母的同意便出去了。| **without doing** *How dare you do such a thing without consulting me?* 你沒有和我商量，竟敢做這樣的事？| **without so much as...** (=used to say that someone does not do something that they should do) 連…也不；甚至於不〔用於表示某人沒有做應做的事〕*Without so much as a word of thanks Bowen turned and went back into the office.* 連一個謝字也不說，鮑恩轉身回到了辦公室。**3** not being with someone, or not having them to help you, especially someone you like or need 無〔某人，尤指喜歡或需要的人〕相伴[相助]: *She found it hard to face up to the prospect of life without Ken.* 沒有肯恩，她覺得很難面對未來的生活。**4** if something happens without something unpleasant happening, it happens in a way that is pleasant or easy〔某事〕在沒有〔不愉快事情〕的情況下〔發生〕: *I managed to get through the exam without too much trouble.* 在沒太多困難的情況下我考試及格了。**5 without wanting to/without wishing to** used before a criticism, complaint, or other statement to make it less definite 不想/不願意…〔用於批評、投訴或其他句子之前，以示婉轉〕: *Without wanting to sound too boastful, I think we have the best television programmes in the world.* 不想太吹牛，我覺得我們有世界上最精彩的電視節目。**6** *old use* outside【舊】在外面

with·stand /wɪθˋstænd; wɪðˈstænd/ *v past tense and past participle* **withstood** /-ˋstʊd; -ˈstʊd/ [T] **1** to be strong enough to remain unharmed by something such as great heat or cold, great pressure etc 耐受，承受〔酷熱、嚴寒、高壓等〕: *a type of desert bush that can withstand extremes of temperature* 一種能耐受温差懸殊的沙漠灌木 | **withstand the test of time** (=still be important, effective etc after a long time) 經得起時間的考驗 *theories that have withstood the test of time* 經得起時間考驗的理論 **2** to defend yourself against attack, and successfully oppose someone or something 抵擋；頂住: *withstanding a heroic doomed attack by six allied divisions* 頂住了盟軍六個師注定失敗的英勇進攻

wit·less /ˋwɪtlɪs; ˈwɪtləs/ *adj* **1** not very intelligent or sensible; silly 無才智的；愚蠢的: *if I catch the witless yobs who did this* 要是我抓住幹這件事的愚蠢無賴 **2 scare sb witless** to make someone very frightened 把某人嚇壞 —**witlessly** *adv* —**witlessness** *n* [U]

2 3 **wit·ness¹** /ˋwɪtnɪs; ˈwɪtnɨs/ *n* **1** [C] someone who sees a crime or an accident and can describe what happened〔罪行或事故的〕目擊者: *Police have appealed for witnesses to come forward.* 警方呼籲目擊者作證。**2** [C] someone in a court of law who tells what they saw or what they know about a crime〔法庭上的〕證人: *One witness claimed to have seen the gun.* 一位證人聲稱曾見過這枝槍。**3 bear witness** *formal* to show or prove that something is true or that something happened in the past【正式】證明〔某事是事實〕，證實〔過去的事〕: *The temples and theatres all bear witness to the city's former greatness.* 廟宇和劇場都證明了這個城市以前的輝煌。**4** [C] someone who is present when an official paper is signed and who signs it to prove this〔正式文件的簽署的〕見證人，連署人: **witness to** *a witness to a will* 遺囑的見證人 **5 be witness to** *formal* to be present when something happens, and watch it happening【正式】是…的目擊者: *We were witness to the worst excesses of the military.* 我們目擊了最惡劣的軍事暴行。**6** [C,U] *AmE* a public statement of strong Christian belief, or someone who makes such a statement【美】見證〔表示篤信基督教的公開聲明〕；見證人〔作這種見證的人〕

witness² *v* **1** [T] to see something happen, especially a crime or accident, because you are present when it happens 目擊，親眼看見〔尤指罪行或事故發生〕: *Police are appealing to any driver who may have witnessed the accident.* 警方正呼籲曾目睹這事故的司機協助。**2** [T] **a)** to experience important events or changes because you are there when they are happening 親自經歷〔重要事件或變遷〕: *We witnessed the break-up of the former Soviet Union.* 我們親身經歷了前蘇聯的解體。**b)** if a time or place witnesses an event, the event happens during that time or in that place 是發生〔某事件〕的時間[地點]: *The 1980s witnessed increasing unemployment throughout Europe.* 20世紀80年代是全歐洲失業日益加劇的年代。**3** [T] to be present when someone signs an official document, and sign it yourself to show this〔在正式文件上〕連署；在〔正式文件〕上簽署作證: *Will you witness my signature?* 你願意在我的簽字旁連署嗎？**4** [T] **a)** to be a sign or proof of something 表明；是〔某事〕的證明: *the rise in crime, as witnessed by our overcrowded prisons* 擁擠不堪的監獄證明犯罪的增多 **b)** used to give an example that proves something you have just mentioned〔用於給剛提及的事舉例〕作證: *Poor school grades don't prove much – witness Dana's amazing success in business.* 學校成績不好説明不了甚麼 —— 戴納驚人的經商成就即是明證。**5** [I] *AmE* to speak publicly about your strong Christian beliefs【美】見證〔公開表示篤信基督教〕

witness to sth *phr v* [T] to formally state that something is true or happened 證實；證明〔某事〕: *Her principal was called to witness to her good character.* 她的校長被傳喚來證明她優良的品德。| **witness to doing sth** *The driver witnessed to having seen the man enter the building.* 司機作證説，他看到此人進入那棟建築物。

witness box *BrE*【英】, **witness stand** *AmE*【美】/ˈ‥ ˌ/ *n* [C] the place in a court of law where a witness stands to answer questions〔法庭的〕證人席，證人台

wit·ter /ˋwɪtɚ; ˈwɪtə/ also 又作 **witter on** *v* [I] *informal* to talk a lot in a boring way or about something unimportant【非正式】絮叨；囉嗦: **[+about]** *I'm sick of her wittering on about New Men.* 她絮叨新派男子的事我聽得厭煩透了。

wit·ti·cis·m /ˋwɪtəˌsɪzəm; ˈwɪtɨsɪzəm/ *n* [C] a clever amusing remark 妙語；俏皮話；詼諧語

wit·ty /ˋwɪtɪ; ˈwɪti/ *adj* using words in a clever and amusing way 説話風趣的；妙趣橫生的: *a witty speaker* 講話風趣的人 | *witty remarks* 妙語 —**wittily** *adv* —**wittiness** *n* [U]

wives /waɪvz; waɪvz/ the plural of WIFE

wiz·ard /ˋwɪzɚd; ˈwɪzəd/ *n* [C] **1** a man who is supposed to have magic powers 巫師，術士 **2** someone who is very good at something 能手，奇才: *a financial wizard* 理財能手 | **[+at]** *Ben's a real wizard at chess.* 班恩是十足的國際象棋能手。

wizard 巫師，術士

wiz·ard·ry /ˋwɪzɚdrɪ; ˈwɪzədri/ *n* [U] impressive ability at something or an impressive achievement 傑出的才能[成就]: *The best thing about the movie is the sheer wizardry of the special effects.* 電影中最精彩的部分是非凡的特技。

wiz·ened /ˋwɪznd; ˈwɪzənd/ *adj* a wizened person, fruit etc is small and thin and has skin with a lot of lines and WRINKLES〔人、水果等〕乾瘦的；乾癟的: *wizened old Frenchmen playing boules in the square* 在廣場上玩滾木球遊戲的乾瘦的法國老人

wk the written abbreviation of 縮寫= WEEK

woad /wod; wəʊd/ *n* [U] a blue DYE (=colouring substance) used in ancient times to colour people's bodies〔古代用以染身的〕靛藍〔染料〕

wob·ble /ˋwɑbḷ; ˈwɒbəl/ *v* **1** [I,T] to move unsteadily from side to side, or make something do this 搖晃; 使〔某物〕搖擺: *The pile of bricks wobbled and fell.* 一堆磚搖搖晃晃, 然後倒了。| *His fat thighs wobbled as he ran along.* 他跑起步來, 肥胖的大腿不住顫動。| **wobble sth** *Stop wobbling the table with your foot.* 別用腳把桌子弄得搖搖晃晃。**2** [I always+adv/prep] to go in a particular direction while moving unsteadily from side to side 搖晃不穩〔朝某方向走〕: **[+off/along/across etc]** *Cindy wobbled along the street on her bike.* 辛迪騎着自行車在街上搖搖晃晃地走。**3** *AmE* to be unsure whether to do something【美】猶豫不決: *The President appeared to wobble over sending the troops in.* 對於是否出兵總統顯得猶豫不決。—**wobble** *n* [C]

wob·bly¹ /ˈwɑblɪ; ˈwɒbli/ *adj* **1** moving unsteadily from side to side 搖擺的; 顫動的: *a wobbly table* 搖搖晃晃的桌子 **2** *informal* feeling weak and unable to keep your balance【非正式】〔身體因虛弱而〕震顫: *I've gone all wobbly – I think I'll sit down.* 我渾身乏力——我想我要坐下來。**3** a wobbly voice is weak and shakes, especially when you feel frightened or upset〔聲音〕顫抖的〔尤因感到害怕或不安時〕

wobbly² *n* [C] *BrE informal*【英, 非正式】**throw a wobbly** to suddenly become very angry or frightened 勃然大怒; 大驚失色

wodge /wɑdʒ; wɒdʒ/ *n* [C] *BrE informal* a thick, solid piece or large amount of something【英, 非正式】〔某物的〕一大塊; 大量: *a wodge of ten pound notes* 一大沓十英鎊鈔票

woe /wo; wəʊ/ *n* **1** *literary* [U] great sadness【文】悲傷; 悲哀: *a tale of woe* 悲傷的故事 **2 woes** [plural] *formal* the problems and troubles affecting someone【正式】困難; 難題: *They tend to blame all of Africa's woes on colonialism.* 他們傾向把非洲的所有災難歸咎於殖民主義。**3 woe betide** *especially humorous* used to warn someone that there will be trouble if they do something【尤幽默】將要遭殃〔用於警告某人, 要是做某事會有麻煩〕: *Woe betide anyone who smokes in our house!* 誰在我們房子裡抽煙誰倒霉!

woe·be·gone /ˈwobɪˌgɔn; ˈwəʊbɪgɒn/ *adj especially literary* looking very sad【尤文】愁眉苦臉的: *Her woebegone expression made him feel protective.* 她滿臉愁容, 令他動了呵護之心。

woe·ful /ˈwofəl; ˈwəʊfəl/ *adj* **1** very bad or serious; DEPLORABLE 極壞的, 糟透的: *a woeful lack of information* 信息極其匱乏 **2** *literary* very sad; PATHETIC【文】悲哀的; 可憐的: *The little girl looked up at him with woeful eyes.* 小女孩用憂鬱的眼神仰望着他。—**woefully** *adv*: *woefully inadequate facilities* 設施嚴重不足

wog /wɑg; wɒg/ *n* [C] *BrE taboo* a very offensive word for a black person【英諱】外國佬〔對黑人的冒犯語〕

wok /wɑk; wɒk/ *n* [C] a wide pan shaped like a bowl, used in Chinese cooking〔烹調中國菜時用的〕鐵鍋; 鑊 —see picture at 參見 PAN¹ 圖

woke /wok; wəʊk/ the past tense of WAKE¹

wok·en /ˈwokən; ˈwəʊkən/ the past participle of WAKE¹

wolds /woldz; wəʊldz/ *n* [plural] *BrE* a word for an area of hilly countryside, especially used in the names of places【英】丘陵地區; 荒野〔尤用於地名〕: *the Yorkshire Wolds* 約克郡丘陵地區

wolf¹ /wʊlf; wʊlf/ *n plural* **wolves** /wʊlvz; wʊlvz/ [C] **1** a wild animal that looks like a large dog and lives and hunts in groups 狼: *a pack of wolves* 一羣狼 **2 a wolf in sheep's clothing** someone who seems to be friendly but is in fact, unpleasant etc 披着羊皮的狼〔指偽裝友善的人〕**3 cry wolf** to keep asking for help that you do not really need, with the result that when you do need help people do not believe you 喊"狼來了"〔指人不斷發假警報, 到真正需要幫忙時, 沒有人相信〕: *Jurgen's cried wolf one too many times. I'm sick of it!* 尤爾根多次謊報情況, 我感到煩透了! **4 keep the wolf from the door** to earn just enough money to buy the basic things you need 勉強維持生計: *Between us, we earn just enough to keep the wolf from the door.* 我們賺的錢勉強夠維持生計。—see also 另見 LONE WOLF —**wolfish** *adj*: *a wolfish grin* 獰笑

wolf² also 又作 **wolf down** *v* [T] *informal* to eat something very quickly, swallowing it in big pieces【非正式】狼吞虎嚥地吃

wolf·hound /ˈwʊlfˌhaʊnd; ˈwʊlfhaʊnd/ *n* [C] an extremely large dog〔大〕狼狗

wol·fram /ˈwʊlfrəm; ˈwʊlfrəm/ *n* [U] TUNGSTEN 鎢

wolf whis·tle /ˈ· ,··/ *n* [C] a way of whistling that men sometimes use to show that they think a woman is attractive〔男人對美貌女子吹的〕挑逗口哨 —**wolf-whistle** *v* [I]

wolves /wʊlvz; wʊlvz/ the plural of WOLF

wom·an /ˈwʊmən; ˈwʊmən/ *n plural* **women** /ˈwɪmɪn; ˈwɪmɪn/

1 ►FEMALE 女性◄ [C] an adult female person 成年女子, 婦人: *I was talking to a woman I met on the flight.* 我正在和在飛機上相遇的一個女子交談。| *married women* 已婚婦女 | **a woman priest/driver etc** *How long will it be until we have a woman President?* 需要多長時間我們才會有一位女總統? | **women's clothes/organization etc** *Kate works for a popular women's magazine.* 凱特在一家受歡迎的婦女雜誌社工作。—see 見 MAN¹ (USAGE)

2 ►FORM OF ADDRESS 稱呼形式◄ *spoken* a rude way of addressing a woman when you are angry, annoyed etc【口】婆娘〔生氣、煩惱時對婦女的粗魯稱呼〕: *Pull yourself together, woman!* 振作起來, 你這個婆娘!

3 another woman/the other woman *informal* a woman that a man is having a sexual relationship with, even though he is married to someone else【非正式】已婚男人的情人/情婦: *I'm sure he's got another woman.* 我敢肯定他有情婦。

4 ►GENERAL TERM 一般用語◄ [singular] *formal* women in general【正式】〔泛稱〕女人: *A woman's work is never done.* 女人的工作永遠幹不完。

5 ►PARTNER 伴侶◄ also 又作 **the old woman** [singular] *spoken* expressions meaning your girlfriend or wife, which many women find offensive【口】女朋友; 老婆〔許多婦女認為這是冒犯語〕: *Did he bring his woman with him?* 他帶老婆來了嗎?

6 businesswoman/spokeswoman etc a woman who has a particular kind of job 女商人/女發言人等: *a spokeswoman for the charity* 慈善團體的女發言人

7 be your own woman to make your own decisions and be in charge of your own life, without depending on anyone else 獨立自主; 不依賴他人

8 woman of easy virtue/woman of the night *old-fashioned* a PROSTITUTE¹ (1)【過時】娼妓

9 ►SERVANT 傭人◄ [C] a female servant or person who does works for you in your house 女傭; 女僕 —see also 另見 **make an honest woman of** (HONEST (8)), OLD WOMAN, **wine, women and song** (WINE¹ (3)), **be a man/woman of the world** (WORLD¹ (26))

wom·an·hood /ˈwʊmənˌhʊd; ˈwʊmənhʊd/ *n* [U] **1** the state of being a woman, not a man or a girl 女子成年〔的狀態〕**2** *formal* women in general【正式】〔泛稱〕女人 —compare 比較 MANHOOD

wom·an·ish /ˈwʊmənɪʃ; ˈwʊmənɪʃ/ *adj* a womanish man looks or behaves in a way that is supposed to be typical of women〔男人的外表或行為〕女人氣的; 女人腔的

wom·an·izer also 又作 **iser** *BrE*【英】/ˈwʊmənˌaɪzə; ˈwʊmənaɪzə/ *n* [C] a man who has sexual relationships with many different women 玩弄女性的男人 —**womanize** *v* [I] —**womanizing** *n* [U]

wom·an·kind /ˈwʊmənˋkaɪnd; ˈwʊmənkaɪnd/ *n* [U] women considered together as a group 女性, 婦女〔總稱〕—compare 比較 MANKIND

wom·an·ly /ˈwʊmənlɪ; ˈwʊmənli/ *adj approving* behaving, dressing etc in a way that is thought to be typical of or suitable for a woman【褒】〔行為、衣着等〕有女子氣質的; 女人特有的: *her soft womanly curves* 她的女性特有的柔滑曲線 —**womanliness** *n* [U]

womb /wum; wuːm/ *n* [C] the part of a female's body where her baby grows before it is born 子宮

wom·bat /ˈwɑmbæt; ˈwɒmbæt/ *n* [C] an Australian animal like a small bear whose babies live in a pocket of skin on its body 毛鼻袋熊〔產於澳大利亞〕

wom·en /ˈwɪmɪn; ˈwɪmɪn/ the plural of WOMAN

wom·en·folk /ˈwɪmɪnˌfok; ˈwɪmɪnfəʊk/ *n* [plural] all the women in a particular family or society〔某個家庭或社會中的〕(全體) 婦女

wom·en's lib /ˌ·· ˈ·/ also 又作 **women's lib·e·ra·tion** /ˌ·· ··ˈ··/ *n* [U] *old-fashioned* all the ideas, actions, and politics connected with giving women the same rights and opportunities as men【過時】婦女解放運動 —**women's libber** *n* [C]

women's move·ment /ˈ·· ˌ··/ *n* **the women's movement** all the women who are involved in the aim of improving the social, economic, and political position of women and of ending sexual DISCRIMINATION (1) 婦女(解放) 運動, 女權運動

women's re·fuge /ˌ·· ˈ··/ *n* [C] a special place where women and their children can go to escape being physically hurt by their husband, partner etc〔收容遭到丈夫、伴侶等虐待的婦女及其子女的〕婦女避難所

women's room /ˈ·· ·/ *n* [C] *especially AmE* a public TOILET (2) for women【尤美】女洗手間; 公共女廁所

won /wʌn; wʌn/ the past tense and past participle of WIN[1]

won·der[1] /ˈwʌndə; ˈwʌndə/ *v* [I,T] **1** to think about something that you are not sure about and try to guess what is true, what will happen etc〔對某事〕感到疑惑; 想要知道: **wonder who/what/how etc** *I wonder how James is getting on.* 我想知道詹姆斯的近況。| *What are they going to do now, I wonder?* 我想知道他們現在準備做甚麼。| **wonder if/whether/why** *I wonder if I'll recognize Philip after all these years.* 過了這些年, 我不知道是否還認得菲利普。| **it makes you wonder** *especially spoken*【尤口】: *Patrick's reaction made me wonder if he knew more than he'd told me.* 帕特里克的反應使我懷疑他是否只告訴我一部分。**2 I wonder if/whether** *spoken* used to ask politely for something【口】我不知道是否〔用於禮貌地詢問某事〕: *I wonder if I might have a glass of water?* 我可不可以要一杯水? **3 I was wondering if/whether a)** *spoken* used to politely ask someone to help you【口】我想知道〔用於禮貌地請求幫助〕: *I was wondering if I could borrow your car?* 請問我能否借一下你的汽車? **b)** used to ask someone politely if they would like to do something 不知可不可以〔禮貌地請求他人做某事〕: *I was wondering if you'd like to come to dinner.* 不知道你是否願意來吃晚飯。**4** [I,T] to feel surprised and unable to believe something〔對某事〕感到驚訝〔不能相信〕: **[+about/at]** *Sometimes I wonder about his behaviour.* 有時我對他的行為感到驚訝。| **[+how]** *I wonder how he dares to show his face after last night!* 昨晚之後他竟然還敢露面, 我覺得奇怪! | **I don't wonder** *BrE spoken* (=I am not surprised)【英口】我不覺得奇怪 *I don't wonder you're tired after the day you've had.* 你經過那樣的一天之後感到疲乏, 我覺得很正常。| **I shouldn't wonder** *BrE spoken* (=I would not be surprised about something)【英口】我覺得不足為奇 *He'll come back soon enough, I shouldn't wonder.* 他會很快回來, 我對此一點也不覺得奇怪。 **5** [I,T] to doubt or question whether something is true 懷疑〔某事的真實性〕: *"Is she serious?" "I wonder."* "她是認真的嗎?" "我看不一定。" | **wonder if/whether** *Ken says such stupid things that I wonder if he's got any sense at all!* 肯恩說出這種蠢話來, 我不知道他究竟還有沒有理智!

wonder[2] *n*

1 ►ADMIRATION 讚賞◄ a) [U] a feeling of surprise and admiration for something very beautiful or new to you〔對漂亮或新事物的〕驚嘆; 驚奇; 詫異: *The sight of the Taj Mahal filled us with wonder.* 看見泰姬陵, 我們充滿了驚嘆之情。**b)** [C] something that makes you feel surprise and admiration 奇事; 奇跡, 奇觀: *technological wonders* 技術奇跡 | *the Seven Wonders of the World* 世界七大奇觀

2 (it's) no wonder/small wonder/little wonder *especially spoken* used to say that you are not surprised by something【尤口】並不奇怪/不足為奇/十分自然: *No wonder you've got a headache, the amount you drank last night.* 昨晚你喝得太多, 頭痛不足為怪。

3 ►SURPRISING 驚訝◄ it's a wonder (that) *especially spoken* used to say that something is very surprising【尤口】令人驚奇的是: *It's a wonder Louise remembered to come, she's so scatty.* 真想不到路易斯那麼健忘, 居然記得來。

4 do/work wonders to be very effective in solving a problem 創造奇跡/取得驚人成效

5 ►CLEVER PERSON 聰明人◄ [singular] *BrE* someone who is clever at doing difficult things【英】奇才, 奇人: *Philip's a wonder, the way he manages on his own.* 菲利普真是奇才, 甚麼問題他都能獨自解決。

6 wonders will never cease! *spoken humorous* used to show you are surprised and pleased about something【口, 幽默】真是無奇不有 —see also 另見 **chinless wonder** (CHINLESS (3)), **nine days' wonder** (NINE (3))

wonder[3] *adj* [only before noun 僅用於名詞前] very good and effective 極好的; 靈驗的: *a new wonder drug* 新的靈丹妙藥

won·der·ful /ˈwʌndəfəl; ˈwʌndəfəl/ *adj* **1** making you feel very happy 令人高興的; 使人愉快的: *We had a wonderful time in Spain.* 我們在西班牙過得極為愉快。**2** making you admire someone or something very much〔某人、某物〕令人驚嘆的; 奇妙的: *It's wonderful what doctors can do nowadays.* 當今醫生能做的着實令人稱奇。—**wonderfully** *adv*

won·der·ingly /ˈwʌndərɪŋlɪ; ˈwʌndərɪŋli/ *adv* in a way that shows admiration, surprise, and pleasure 驚嘆地; 不可思議地; 令人高興地

won·der·land /ˈwʌndəˌlænd; ˈwʌndəlænd/ *n* [U] an imaginary place in stories〔故事中的〕仙境, 奇境

won·der·ment /ˈwʌndəmənt; ˈwʌndəmənt/ *n* [U] *literary* a feeling of pleasant surprise or admiration【文】驚嘆; 驚奇

won·drous /ˈwʌndrəs; ˈwʌndrəs/ *adj poetical* good or impressive in a surprising way【詩】奇妙的; 令人驚嘆的

won·ga /ˈwɑŋgə; ˈwɒŋgə/ *n* [U] *BrE slang* money【英俚】金錢

wonk /wɑŋk; wɒŋk/ *n* [C] *AmE informal* someone who works hard and is very serious【美, 非正式】用功而嚴肅的人: *policy wonks surrounding the President* 總統四周一本正經的政策專家

won·ky /ˈwɑŋkɪ; ˈwɒŋki/ *adj BrE informal* unsteady or not straight or level【英, 非正式】不穩的; 歪斜的; 不平的: *a wonky table* 搖搖晃晃的桌子

won't /wont; wəʊnt/ the short form of 縮略式= will not

wont[1] /wont; wəʊnt/ *n old-fashioned*【過時】**as is sb's wont** used to say that it is someone's habit to do something 就像某人慣常那樣〔表示某人慣於做某事〕: *He spoke for too long, as is his wont.* 他說話總是這樣發表長篇大論。

wont[2] *adj formal*【正式】**be wont to do sth** to be likely to do something 慣於做某事

wont·ed /ˈwʌntɪd; ˈwəʊntɪd/ *adj* [only before noun 僅用於名詞前] *old-fashioned* usual【過時】通常的

woo /wu; wuː/ *v* [T] **1** to try to persuade someone to buy something from you, vote for you etc 努力說服〔顧客、選民等〕: *The politicians will be wooing the voters before the election.* 選舉前政治家都盡力爭取選民的支持。**2** *old-fashioned* to try to persuade a woman to love you and marry you【過時】〔向女子〕求愛; 求婚 —**wooer** *n* [C]

2 2 **wood** /wʊd; wʊd/ *n* **1** [C,U] the material that trees are made of 木; 木材; 木料: *Put some more wood on the fire.* 往火上再添些木柴。| *a polished wood floor* 擦得光亮的木地板 | **soft/hard wood** *Pine is a soft wood.* 松木是軟質木材。**2** [C] also 又作 **the woods** a small forest 樹林; 林地: *a walk in the woods* 在樹林裡散步 **3** [C] one of a set of four GOLF CLUBS with wooden heads 木頭球棒〔棒頭為木製的高爾夫球棒〕 **4 not be out of the wood(s) yet** *informal* used to say that there are likely to be more difficulties before things improve【非正式】仍未脱離困[險]境: *It's been going well lately, but we're not totally out of the woods yet.* 情況最近有所好轉, 但我們仍未完全擺脱困境。**5 not see the wood for the trees** to not notice what is important about something because you give too much of your attention to small details 見樹不見林〔指着重細節而忽略重要部分〕—see also 另見 **dead wood** (DEAD[1] (30))

wood·bine /ˈwʊd,baɪn; ˈwʊdbaɪn/ *n* [U] **1** *poetical* HONEYSUCKLE【詩】忍冬〔一種攀緣植物〕 **2** *AmE* VIRGINIA CREEPER【美】五葉地錦

wood·block /ˈwʊd,blɑk; ˈwʊdblɒk/ *n* [C] **1** a piece of wood with a shape cut on it, used for printing〔印刷用的〕木刻印版 **2** a block of wood used in making a floor〔鋪地板用〕木板, 木塊

wood·carv·ing /ˈwʊdkɑrvɪŋ; ˈwʊdkɑːvɪŋ/ *n* [C,U] the process of shaping wood with special tools, or a piece of art produced in this way 木雕; 木雕藝術品

wood·chuck /ˈwʊd,tʃʌk; ˈwʊdtʃʌk/ *n* [C] a GROUNDHOG 土撥鼠

wood·cock /ˈwʊd,kɑk; ˈwʊdkɒk/ *n* [C] a brown bird that lives in woods〔樹林中的〕丘鷸

wood·craft /ˈwʊd,kræft; ˈwʊdkrɑːft/ *n* [U] the practical knowledge of woods and forests 森林生活技巧; 森林知識

wood·cut /ˈwʊd,kʌt; ˈwʊdkʌt/ *n* [C] **1** a picture that you make by pressing a shaped piece of wood and a colouring substance onto paper 木版畫 **2** a WOODBLOCK (1) 木刻印版

wood·cut·ter /ˈwʊd,kʌtɚ; ˈwʊd,kʌtə/ *n* [C] someone whose job is to cut down trees in a forest 伐木者

wood·ed /ˈwʊdɪd; ˈwʊdɪd/ *adj* having woods or covered with trees 多樹木的; 長滿樹木的: *densely wooded hills* 樹木茂盛的山崗

3 3 **wood·en** /ˈwʊdn̩; ˈwʊdn/ *adj* **1** made of wood 木製的: *a wooden bench* 木頭長櫈 **2** not showing enough expression, emotion, or movement, especially when performing in public〔尤指公開表演時〕呆板的; 木訥的; 笨拙的: *a rather wooden performance* 相當呆板的表演 —**woodenly** *adv* —**woodenness** *n* [U]

W

wooden-head·ed /,·· ˈ··◂/ *adj informal* stupid and slow to understand things【非正式】愚蠢的; 遲鈍的

wooden spoon /,·· ˈ·/ *n* [C] a large wooden spoon used in cooking〔烹調用的〕木匙 —see picture at 參見 SPOON[1] 圖

wood·land /ˈwʊd,lænd; ˈwʊdlənd/ also 又作 **woodlands** *plural n* [U] an area of land covered with trees 林地; 林區

wood·louse /ˈwʊd,laus; ˈwʊdlaʊs/ *n plural* **woodlice** /-laɪs; -laɪs/ [C] a small grey insect that lives under wood, stones etc〔生活在木頭、石塊等處的〕潮蟲, 土鼈

wood·peck·er /ˈwʊd,pɛkɚ; ˈwʊd,pekə/ *n* [C] a bird with a long beak that it uses to make holes in trees 啄木鳥

wood·pile /ˈwʊd,paɪl; ˈwʊdpaɪl/ *n* [C] a pile of firewood 木柴堆

wood pulp /ˈ· ·/ *n* [U] wood crushed into a soft mass, used for making paper〔造紙用〕木漿

wood·shed /ˈwʊd,ʃɛd; ˈwʊdʃed/ *n* [C] a place for storing wood for burning 柴棚, 柴房

woods·man /ˈwʊdzmən; ˈwʊdzmən/ *n plural* **woodsmen** /-mən; -mən/ [C] someone who works in a forest cutting down trees etc 伐木人

wood·sy /ˈwʊdzɪ; ˈwʊdzi/ *n AmE informal* connected with the woods【美, 非正式】與樹林有關的: *a woodsy smell* 樹林的氣味

wood·wind /ˈwʊd,wɪnd; ˈwʊd,wɪnd/ also 又作 **the woodwind** *n* [C,U] the group of musical instruments that you play by blowing and pressing keys (KEY[2] (3)) 木管樂器 —**woodwind** *adj*

wood·work /ˈwʊd,wɝk; ˈwʊdwɜːk/ *n* [U] **1** *BrE*【英】, **wood·work·ing** /ˈwʊd,wɝkɪŋ; ˈwʊdwɜːkɪŋ/ *AmE*【美】 the skill or activity of making wooden objects 木工手藝; 木工活 **2** the parts of a house or room that are made of wood〔房屋或房間〕木建部分: *The woodwork needs painting.* 木建部分需要油漆。**3 crawl/come out of the woodwork** if people you don't like crawl out of the woodwork, there suddenly seems to be a lot of them〔令你討厭的人〕突然紛紛出現; 大羣露面: *When they heard about the funeral, suddenly all our weird relatives came crawling out of the woodwork.* 當聽到喪葬的事後, 我們所有奇怪的親戚都突然跑了出來。

wood·worm /ˈwʊd,wɝm; ˈwʊdwɜːm/ *n* [C] **1** a small insect that makes holes in wood 蛀木蟲, 木蠹 **2** [U] the damage that is caused to wood by this creature 蛀木蟲害

wood·y /ˈwʊdɪ; ˈwʊdi/ *adj* **1** a plant that is woody has a stem like wood〔植物〕木莖的; 木質的 **2** a woody area of land has a lot of trees growing on it〔地方〕樹木茂盛的

woof[1] /wuf; wʊf/ *interjection* a word used for describing the sound a dog makes 汪汪〔形容狗的吠聲〕—**woof** *v* [I] *informal*【非正式】

woof[2] /wuf; wuːf/ *n* [C] WEFT 緯紗, 緯線

woof·er /ˈwʊfɚ; ˈwuːfə/ *n* [C] a LOUDSPEAKER (1) that produces deep sounds 低音喇叭, 低音揚聲器 —compare 比較 TWEETER

woof·ter /ˈwʊftɚ; ˈwʊftə/ *n* [C] *BrE slang* an offensive word for a man who speaks or behaves in a way that is considered typical of HOMOSEXUALS【英俚】〔因言談舉止被認為是〕同性戀的男子〔冒犯語〕

wool /wʊl; wʊl/ *n* [U] **1** the soft thick hair that sheep and some goats have on their body 羊毛 **2** material made from wool 毛織物: *Is this coat wool?* 這件大衣是毛料的嗎? | **wool jacket/carpet/blanket etc** *a pure wool skirt* 純毛裙子 **3** thread made from wool that you use for knitting (KNIT[1] (1)) clothes 毛線, 絨線 **4 pull the wool over sb's eyes** to deceive someone by not telling the truth 蒙騙某人 —see also 另見 COTTON WOOL, DYED-IN-THE-WOOL, WIRE WOOL

wool·len *BrE*【英】, **woolen** *AmE*【美】/ˈwʊlən; ˈwʊlən/ *adj* [only before noun 僅用於名詞前] made of wool 羊毛製的, 毛料的 —see picture on page A16 參見A16頁圖

wool·lens *BrE*【英】, **woolens** *AmE*【美】/ˈwʊlənz; ˈwʊlənz/ *n* [plural] clothes made from wool, especially wool that has been knitted (KNIT[1] (1)) 毛料衣服; 〔尤指〕針織毛線衣 —see also 另見 WOOLLY[2]

wool·ly[1] *BrE*【英】, **wooly** *AmE*【美】/ˈwʊlɪ; ˈwʊli/ *adj* **1** made of or feeling like wool 羊毛製的; 像羊毛的: *a woolly hat* 羊毛帽子 **2** not showing clear thinking〔思想〕不清楚的; 混亂的: *a woolly argument* 思路混亂的論點 —**wooliness** *n* [U]

woolly[2] *n* [C usually plural 一般用複數] *BrE* a piece of clothing made of wool, especially wool that has been knitted (KNIT[1] (1))【英】毛料服裝; 〔尤指〕針織毛線衣: *winter woollies* 冬季毛衣

woolly-head·ed /,·· ˈ··◂/ *adj* not able to think clearly 頭腦糊塗的; 思想混亂的

woo·zy /ˈwuzɪ; ; ˈwuːzi/ *adj informal* feeling weak and unsteady; DIZZY (1)【非正式】虛弱的; 眩暈的

wop /wɑp; wɒp/ *n* [C] a very offensive word for someone who is Italian 意大利佬〔嚴重的冒犯語〕

word¹ /wɝd; wɜːd/ *n*

① LANGUAGE/STH YOU SAY OR WRITE 語言/所說或所寫的東西
② TALK/DISCUSSION 談話/討論
③ INFORMATION/NEWS 信息/新聞
④ ORDER/DECISION 命令/決定
⑤ PROMISE 諾言
⑥ OTHER MEANINGS 其他意思

① LANGUAGE/STH YOU SAY OR WRITE 語言/所說或所寫的東西

1 [C] the smallest unit of language that people can understand if it is said or written on its own〔最小的語言單位〕字; 詞; 單詞: *Write an essay of about five hundred words.* 寫一篇大約五百字的文章。| *There were a lot of words in the film I couldn't understand.* 影片中有許多詞我聽不懂。| *It's not a word I often use.* 這不是我常用的詞。| *I know the tune, but not the words.* 我熟悉曲調, 但不知道歌詞。| **a word for** (=a word that means) …意思的一個字 *"Casa" is the Italian word for house.* casa是意大利語"房屋"的意思。| **sb's words** (=what someone says) 某人所言 *Those are the editor's words, not mine.* 那都是編輯的話, 不是我的。| **in your own words** *Tell us exactly what happened in your own words.* 你自己對我們說, 到底發生了甚麼事情。

2 not believe/hear/understand a word to not believe etc what someone says or writes〔對某人所說、所寫〕一點都不相信/聽不到/不了解: *He says he played in a jazz group, but I don't believe a word of it.* 他說他在一隊爵士樂隊中表演過, 但我一點都不信。| *Stuart didn't understand a word of that stuff on genetics either.* 那些有關遺傳學的東西, 斯圖爾特也一點兒都不懂。| *Can you speak up, we can't hear a word.* 你能大聲點說嗎, 我們甚麼都聽不見。

3 put your feelings into words to express what you want to say clearly 用語言表達感覺: *I'm not very good at putting my feelings into words, but I'll try to explain.* 我不善表達, 但我會設法解釋。

4 find the words to choose the words that express your feelings or ideas clearly 用恰當的語言表達: *She only wished she could find the words to express her affection for the old man.* 她只希望能用恰當的語言表達對這位老人的感情。

② TALK/DISCUSSION 談話/討論

5 have a word (with) *especially spoken* to talk to someone quickly, especially because you need their advice about something or you want to tell them to do something【尤口】與〔某人〕說幾句話〔尤因要徵求對方的意見或叫對方做事〕: *Could I have a word with you after the meeting?* 會後我們可否談談? | **have/exchange a few words** (=have a short conversation) 進行簡短的談話 | **have a quick/brief word (with)** (=have a short conversation) 簡短交談 *We managed to have a quick word before the others arrived.* 在其他人到來之前, 我們談了幾句。

6 want a (little) word *spoken* to want to speak to someone, especially in order to criticize or warn them【口】想和某人談話〔尤指批評或警告對方〕: *The boss wants a little word with you.* 老闆要跟你談一下。

7 a word/a few words a short talk for a particular purpose〔為某目的〕作簡短交談: **a word of advice/warning/encouragement etc** *Could you give the boys a few words of encouragement?* 你能鼓勵男孩子們幾句嗎?

8 not say/breathe a word to not say anything about something to anyone because it is a secret〔因守祕密〕絕口不談; 堅守祕密: *Don't say a word about the party to Dad.* 不要跟父親說聚會的事。

9 have/drop a word in sb's ear to say something to someone privately especially in order to arrange something that would otherwise have been difficult〔尤指為事情順利進行〕祕密地告訴某人〔某事〕: *Don't worry – I've dropped a word in his ear – everything's settled.* 別擔心 —— 我已經和他通了氣 —— 一切都已安排妥當。

10 have/exchange words (with) an expression meaning to quarrel, used to avoid saying this directly〔委婉語〕與…吵架; 和…吵嘴: *I saw Gwen after the meeting. We had words.* 會後我見到格溫, 我們吵了起來。

③ INFORMATION/NEWS 信息/新聞

11 [singular, U] a piece of news or a message 一則新聞[消息]: **word gets out/around** (=people hear about something) 消息傳開; 人們聽說 *If word of the Royal visit gets out, we'll have the press here in force.* 如果王室到訪的消息傳開, 這裡就會有大批的記者。| **The word is (that)/word has it (that)** (=people are saying that) 人們都在說 *The word is that Ben is leaving after Christmas.* 大家都在說班恩聖誕節後離開。| **no word from** *There's been no word from Susan since July.* 自七月以來, 蘇珊一點消息也沒有。| **send/bring word** (=send or bring a message) 送來/帶來消息 *The mayor sent word he'd be late.* 市長派人傳話說, 他要晚來。| **spread/pass the word** (=tell other people the news) 傳播消息

④ ORDER/DECISION 命令/決定

12 the last/final word a) the power to decide whether or how to do something〔做不做或如何做某事的〕最後決定權: *The final word rests with the board.* 最後決定取決於董事會。| **have the last/final word** *My boss has the final word on hiring staff.* 雇用員工問題, 我的老闆說了算。**b)** the last statement or speech in a discussion or argument〔討論、爭論中〕最後的話: **have the last/final word** *Why must you always have the last word in any argument?* 為何你爭論甚麼總要一爭到底, 說最後那句話?

13 [C usually singular 一般用單數] an order to do something〔做某事的〕命令: *On the word 'go' I want you to start running.* 一聽到"起步", 我希望你馬上起跑。| **give the word** *Captain Rix gave the word and we moved forward.* 里克斯船長發出命令, 我們向前航行。

⑤ PROMISE 諾言

14 my/sb's word a sincere promise 我的/某人的諾言: **give sb your word** (=promise someone very sincerely that you will do something)〔真誠地〕對某人保證〔會做某事〕| **keep your word** *Gail kept her word and returned all the money.* 佳兒履行了她的諾言, 把錢如數歸還。| **be as good as your word** (=do exactly what you have promised to do) 按承諾行事, 踐諾 | **a man of his word/woman of her word** (=a man or woman who does what they have promised to do) 一諾千金的人

15 take sb at their word to choose to believe what someone has said even though it is possible they do not mean it 相信某人的話〔儘管它不一定是真話〕: *Geoff said we could call him any time, so let's take him at his word.* 傑弗說我們隨時可以找他, 所以我們姑且相信他吧。

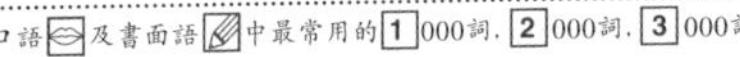

16 take my word for it *spoken* used to say that someone should accept what you say as true【口】相信我的話〔用於告訴某人應該信任你〕: *The business is doing very well. You can take my word for it.* 買賣進展順利。你可以相信我的話。

⑥ **OTHER MEANINGS** 其他意思

17 in other words used to introduce a simpler explanation or version of something you have said 換句話說, 也就是說〔用於較簡單地解釋剛才說的話〕: *In other words, the objective is to avoid losing.* 也就是說, 宗旨要避免失敗。| *The woman has stopped going through her monthly cycle, in other words she is pregnant.* 這位婦女已經不來月經, 換句話說, 她懷孕了。

18 in a word used to introduce a very simple answer or explanation 總之; 一句話; 簡言之〔用於引出十分簡單的答案或解釋〕: *"Did you enjoy the film?" "In a word – no."* "你喜歡這部電影嗎?" "一句話, 不喜歡。"

19 in as many words/not in so many words in a clear direct way or not in a clear direct way 明確地/不直截了當地: *"Did Kathy say she liked him?" "Not in so many words."* "凱西說過喜歡他嗎?" "沒有直說過。" | *Aunt Fay was angry and said so in as many words.* 費伊姑媽很氣憤, 並且明確地這樣說。

20 word for word a) in exactly the same words 逐字逐句: *The newspaper printed his speech more or less word for word.* 報紙幾乎逐字逐句刊登了他的講話。**b)** also 又作 **word by word** if you translate a piece of writing from a foreign language word for word, you translate the meaning of each single word rather than the meaning of a whole phrase or sentence 逐字〔翻譯〕, 一字對一字〔地翻譯〕

21 take the words (right) out of sb's mouth *spoken* if someone takes the words out of your mouth, they have just said what you were going to say【口】先說出某人想說的話

22 put words into sb's mouth *spoken* to suggest falsely that someone has said a particular thing【口】硬說某人說過某話〔事實上並沒說過〕: *Will you stop putting words into my mouth – I never said I disliked the job.* 你不要信口開河── 我從未說過不喜歡這工作。

23 too silly/ridiculous/stupid etc for words *spoken* very silly, ridiculous etc【口】傻/荒謬/笨得難以言傳

24 put in a (good) word for sb to praise someone or suggest them for a particular job 為某人說好話〔稱讚某人或推薦他做某工作〕: *Can you put in a good word for me with the Marketing Manager?* 你能替我跟市場經理美言幾句嗎?

25 words fail me *spoken* used to say that you are so surprised, angry, or shocked that you do not know what to say【口】〔因驚訝、生氣或震驚〕說不出話來; 不知說甚麼好: *I... words fail me.* 我...不知說甚麼好。

26 (Upon) my word! *old-fashioned spoken* used to say you are very surprised because something unusual has happened【過時, 口】哎呀!〔表示吃驚, 因發生不尋常的事〕

27 tired/angry/pleased isn't the word for it *spoken* used to say you are extremely tired or angry etc【口】疲勞/生氣/高興得難以言表

28 the last word in comfort/luxury/elegance etc the most comfortable or luxurious etc thing of its type〔在同類型中〕最舒適/最奢華/最雅致等: *a kitchen that is the last word in luxury* 最奢華的廚房

29 by word of mouth if information or news comes to you by word of mouth, someone tells you instead of you reading about it or seeing an advertisement〔消息或新聞〕口傳的; 口頭的

30 never have a good word to say for sb *spoken* if you never have a good word to say for someone, you never praise them even if they do something well【口】從不說某人好話〔儘管他做得好〕

31 get a word in edgeways also 又作 **edgewise** *AmE*【美】*informal* to get a chance to speak【非正式】找到說話的機會, 插嘴: *Once Terry starts talking it's difficult to get a word in edgeways.* 泰里一說起話來, 別人很難插嘴。

32 the Word (of God) the religious teachings in the Bible〔基督教〕《聖經》的教義

33 from the word go *spoken* from the beginning【口】從一開始: *Lena was against me from the word go.* 莉娜從一開始就跟我作對。—see also 另見 **eat your words** (EAT (8)), FOUR-LETTER WORD, **mark my words** (MARK[1] (9)), **not mince your words** (MINCE[1] (3)), **play on words** (PLAY[2] (8)), **say the word** (SAY[1] (28))

word² *v* [T] to use words that are carefully chosen in order to express something 用言語表達: *The final version was worded in general terms.* 最終版本採用概括的詞語表達。

word blind·ness /ˈ· ˌ··/ *n* [U] DYSLEXIA 閱讀困難症

word·ed /ˈwɝdɪd; ˈwɜːdɪ̣d/ *adj* **carefully/clearly strongly etc worded** using words that express an idea carefully or clearly 措辭嚴謹/清晰/激烈等: *a carefully worded question* 一個措辭嚴謹的問題

W

word·ing /ˈwɝdɪŋ; ˈwɜːdɪŋ/ *n* [U] the words and phrases used to express something 用詞; 措辭: *the exact wording of the contract* 合同裡的確切字眼

word·less /ˈwɝdlɪs; ˈwɜːdləs/ *adj* without words; silent 無話的; 默默無言的: *a wordless prayer* 默禱

word-per·fect /ˌ· ˈ··/ *adj BrE* able to remember and say every word of something correctly【英】背得一字不錯: *She rehearsed her speech until she was word-perfect.* 她反覆練習, 直到把講稿背得滾瓜爛熟。

word-play /ˈ· ·/ *n* [U] making jokes by using words in a clever way 文字遊戲; 俏皮話; 雙關語

word pro·cess·or /ˈ· ˌ···/ *n* [C] a small computer used especially for writing letters or storing information 文字處理機〔一種小型電腦〕—**word processing** *n* [U] —see picture on page A14 參見 A14 頁圖

word·y /ˈwɝdɪ; ˈwɜːdi/ *adj* using too many formal words 話太多的; 冗長的: *a wordy explanation* 冗長累贅的解釋 —**wordily** *adv* —**wordiness** *n* [U]

wore /wɔr; wɔː/ the past tense of WEAR[1]

S1 W1

work¹ /wɝk; wɜːk/ *v*

① DO A JOB 做工
② USE YOUR TIME AND ENERGY TO DO STH 花時間及精力做某事
③ MATERIAL/SUBSTANCE 材料/物質
④ MACHINE 機器
⑤ PRODUCE RESULTS/BE SUCCESSFUL 產生結果/成功
⑥ MOVE 活動
⑦ OTHER MEANINGS 其他意思

① **DO A JOB** 做工

1 [I] to do a job that you are paid for 做工作, 勞動: *Harry is 78, and still working.* 哈里 78 歲了, 仍在工作。| **[+for]** *David works for the BBC.* 大衛為英國廣播公司工作。|

work as a secretary/builder etc *She works as a management consultant for a design company.* 她為一家設計公司當管理顧問。| **work long hours/nights etc** *There's no way I'm working Sundays.* 星期天我決不會上班。

2 [I,T] to do the activities and duties that are part of your job 工作; 從事職業: *Sally isn't working tomorrow.* 莎莉明天不工作。| *I'm tired of working ten-hour days.* 我討厭每天工作十個小時。

3 ▶HELP 幫助◀ [I+with] if you work with someone or a group of people, your job involves trying to help them 與〔某人或羣體〕一起工作〔職責包括幫助他們〕: *Jane works with deaf children.* 簡幫助失聰兒童。

4 ▶AREA 地區◀ [T] to travel around a particular area as part of your job, especially in order to sell something 在〔某地區〕從事活動〔尤指兜售貨品〕: *Markowitz works the Tri-State area.* 馬克庫維茨在三州地區工作。

② USE YOUR TIME AND ENERGY TO DO STH 花時間及精力做某事

5 [I] to do an activity which needs time and effort, especially one that you want to do or that needs to be done 做事; 勞動〔尤指你想做或需要做的事〕: *Dad's been working all day in the garden.* 爸爸一整天都在花園裡做事。| *We had to work non-stop to get everything ready for the party.* 為使聚會一切準備就緒, 我們不得不馬不停蹄地幹。| **[+on]** *Whenever I get the time we go out to the camp and work on it.* 只要我有時間, 我們就去營房工作。| **[+at]** *Juan's English isn't very good, but he works at it.* 胡安的英語不很好, 但他很用功學習。

6 ▶STUDY 學習◀ [I] *BrE* to study a subject by reading books, doing exercises etc, especially in order to pass an exam【英】〔尤為通過考試而〕學習; 做作業: *You'll have to work really hard if you want to pass your exams.* 你如果想通過考試, 就必須非常刻苦地學習。

7 work sb hard [T] to make someone use a lot of time or effort when doing a job or activity 使某人努力工作[做某活動]: *The coach has been working us really hard this week.* 教練這星期使我們訓練得很辛苦。

8 [I] to try continuously and patiently to achieve a particular thing 〔持久堅定地〕努力: **[+for]** *a life spent working for peace and justice* 為和平與正義而奉獻的一生 | **work to do sth** *We worked hard to persuade the French to attend the meeting.* 我們竭力說服法國參加會議。| **work tirelessly** (=work hard) 孜孜不倦地工作 *an organization that works tirelessly on behalf of the poor* 為窮人孜孜不倦工作的組織 | **work your passage** (=to work instead of paying for a journey) 做工以代船費

③ MATERIAL/SUBSTANCE 材料/物質

9 [T] if you work a material such as metal, leather, or clay you cut, SEW, or shape it in order to make something 把〔金屬、皮革、黏土等〕加工成〔某物〕; 切割; 縫合; 製成...

10 [I] to use a particular material or substance in order to make something such as a picture, design, jewellery etc 〔用特定材料、物質〕製作〔畫、設計、珠寶飾物等〕: **[+in/with]** *a sculptor who works in steel* 用鋼創作的雕刻家 | *a jeweller who works with silver* 打製銀器的寶石匠

11 ▶LAND/SOIL 田地/土壤◀ [T] if you work the land or the soil, you do all the work necessary to grow crops on it 耕種

12 ▶MINE 礦◀ [T] if you work a mine you remove a substance such as coal, gold, or oil from it 開採〔煤、金、石油等〕

④ MACHINE 機器

13 a) [I] if a machine or piece of equipment works, it does what it is supposed to do 運轉; 活動: *The remote control doesn't work.* 遙控器失靈。| *Damn! The TV's not working again.* 該死!這台電視又壞了。**b)** [T] to make a complicated machine or piece of equipment do what it is supposed to do 操作〔複雜的機器〕; 使用: *Does anyone know how to work the microwave?* 有誰知道如何使用這微波爐?

⑤ PRODUCE RESULTS/BE SUCCESSFUL 產生結果/成功

14 [I] if a method, plan, or system works, it produces the results you want 〔方法、計劃或體制〕產生〔預想的〕效果: *What do you think of Jill's suggestion? Will it work?* 你覺得吉爾的建議怎麼樣? 可行嗎? | *The recipe works just as well if you use margarine instead of butter.* 食譜中用人造黃油代替天然黃油, 效果一樣。| *I told Mum I was too sick to go to school, but it didn't work.* 我對媽媽說我病得不能上學, 但卻不管用。

15 work like magic/like a charm if a plan, method, or trick works like magic or like a charm, it happens in exactly the way you planned it to happen 〔計劃、方法或把戲〕非常靈驗/非常有效

16 ▶ART/LITERATURE 藝術/文學◀ if a painting, film, piece of writing etc works, it is successful artistically because it has the effect on you that its maker intended 〔繪畫、電影、作品等〕奏效:*I don't think the scene where the family is seated around the table really works, do you?* 我覺得全家圍坐在桌子旁的場面不會真的產生效果, 你說呢?

17 ▶MEDICINE/TREATMENT 藥物/治療◀ [I] if a medicine or medical treatment works, it has the physical effect you want it to have 起作用; 有效: *The antibiotics will only work if you take them every day for ten days.* 這種抗生素只有連服十天才會產生療效。

18 ▶HAVE AN EFFECT 有效果◀ [I always+adv/prep] if something such as a fact, situation, or system works in particular way, it has a particular effect on someone or something 〔事實、情況或系統等對某人或事〕有特效: **work in sb's favour** (=help someone) 幫助某人; 對某人有利 *The fact that you went to the same school should work in your favour.* 你上同一所學校, 這個事實應該對你有利。| **work against sb** (=harm someone or cause them problems) 對某人不利 *Tax laws tend to work against small organizations.* 稅法往往不利於小機構。

⑥ MOVE 活動

19 [I always+adv/prep,T always+adv/prep] to move into a particular state or position very gradually, either in a series of small movements or after a long time 〔通過一連串小動作或長時間而〕逐步達到〔某情況或位置〕: *Slowly he worked the screwdriver into the crack.* 他慢慢地把螺絲刀插進縫隙。| **work (its way) loose** *One of the screws must have worked loose.* 其中一顆螺絲肯定已經鬆了。

20 [I,T] if a part of your body works or you work it, it moves (使)〔身體某部分〕活動起來: **work sth** *He tried to work his face into a smile.* 他盡力裝出笑臉。

21 work your way if you work your way somewhere, you go there slowly and with great effort 緩慢而費力地到達某處: *Although exhausted, he managed to work his way up the last few feet of rock.* 雖然疲憊不堪, 他還是爬上最後幾英尺的山岩。

⑦ OTHER MEANINGS 其他意思

22 ▶MIND/BRAIN 智力/頭腦◀ [I] if your mind or brain is working, you are thinking or trying to solve a problem 思考, 〔用頭腦或智力〕解決〔問題〕

23 work yourself into a state/rage/frenzy etc to make yourself become very excited, upset or angry 使自己非常激動/憤怒/發狂等: *You could tell he was working himself into a panic about it.* 可見他正在為此驚惶失措。

24 work wonders to be surprisingly effective in dealing with a difficult problem or situation 〔處理困難或困

境〕創奇跡; 取得驚人效果: *Try rubbing salt on it. It can work wonders with stains.* 試着在污垢上用鹽搓, 這種方法可以十分有效。

25 work it/things *spoken* to make arrangements for something to happen, especially by acting in a clever or skilful way【口】〔尤指巧妙地安排〕使某事發生: *We should try and work it so that we can all go together.* 我們應該設法作出安排, 讓大家都可以一起去。

26 work your fingers to the bone *informal* to work very hard【非正式】拚命幹活; 努力工作

27 ►BEER/WINE 啤酒/葡萄酒◄ [I] *technical* to FERMENT[1]【術語】發酵

28 ►CALCULATE 計算◄ [T] *AmE formal* to calculate the answer to a mathematical problem【美, 正式】計算〔數學問題的答案〕; 算出

29 work to rule *BrE* to protest about a situation at work by doing your job slowly with the excuse that you must obey all the rules exactly【英】故意死扣規章而少幹活; 按章工作

work sth ↔ **in** *phr v* [T] **1** to add one substance to another and mix them together in a very thorough way〔在一種物質中加進另一種後〕攙和, 混合: **work sth into sth** *Work the butter into the flour with your fingers.* 用手指把黃油摻到麵粉裡。**2** to include something you want to say or do while you are doing or saying something else〔說某話、做某事時〕插入〔某事〕: *Do you think you can work in a reference to our project?* 你覺得能順帶提一下我們的計劃嗎? | **work sth into sth** *The minister will try and work a visit to hospital into his schedule.* 部長會設法在他的日程安排中加進參觀醫院一項。

work sth ↔ **off** *phr v* [T] to try to get rid of a feeling such as anger, disappointment, or embarrassment, especially by being unpleasant to other people or behaving violently〔尤指通過無禮地對待他人或行為粗暴來〕發泄〔怒氣、沮喪、窘迫之情〕: *I'm sorry about all the yelling, it was Terry trying to work off his frustration.* 我為泰里喊叫表示歉意, 他是在發泄他的不滿。

work on *phr v* [T] **1 [work on** sth**]** to spend time making or fixing something 致力於: *Ken was working on some sets for an opera at the Met.* 肯恩正忙於為在大都會歌劇院演出的一部歌劇製作幾台佈景。| *I worked all night on that article.* 我通宵在寫那篇文章。**2** to try continuously to influence someone or persuade them to do something 努力影響[說服]〔某人做某事〕: **work on sb to do sth** *My parents spent the weekend working on me to go on holiday with them.* 爸媽用了一個週末來說服我和他們一起度假去。

work out *phr v*

1 ►CALCULATE 計算◄ [T **work** sth ↔ **out**] to calculate an answer, amount, price, or value 計算出〔答案、數量、價格、價值〕: *You can work out the answer by adding all the numbers.* 你把所有數加在一起就能算出答案了。| *See if you can work this bill out.* 看看你能不能把這份賬單算出來。| **work out how much/how many etc** *We'll have to work out how much food we'll need for the party.* 我們必須算出這次聚會需要多少食物。

2 ►UNDERSTAND 理解◄ *especially BrE*【尤英】[T **work** sth ↔ **out**] to think about something and manage to understand it 設法弄懂: *The plot is very complicated, it'll take you a while to work it out.* 情節極其複雜, 你要花一些時間才能弄明白。| **work sth out for yourself** *I'm not telling you the answer – work it out for yourself.* 我不告訴你答案 —— 你自己去弄明白。

3 [I, linking verb 連繫動詞+adj] if something works out at a particular amount, you calculate that it costs that amount 總計為〔某一費用〕: **work out at/to £10/$500 etc** *The bill works out at £15 each.* 賬單算下來是每人15英鎊。| **work out expensive/costly/cheap etc** (=be expensive or cheap) 算下來貴/費錢/便宜等 *If we go by taxi, it's going to work out very expensive.* 要是我們坐計程車去, 就要花不少錢。

4 ►PLAN 計劃◄ [T **work** sth ↔ **out**] to think carefully about how you are going to do something and plan a good way of doing it 精心制訂出: *UN negotiators have worked out a set of compromise proposal.* 聯合國談判人員制訂出一套折衷方案。| **work out what/ where/ how etc** *I haven't worked out who's going to look after the kids tonight.* 我還沒有計劃好讓誰今晚去照料小孩。| **have it all worked out** (=have completely planned how you are going to do something) 計劃周全 *Listen, I've got it all worked out. Here's what we should do.* 聽着, 我已經計劃好了。我們應該這麼辦。

5 ►GET BETTER 好起來◄ [I,T] if a problem or complicated situation works out, it gradually gets better or gets solved〔問題〕逐漸解決; 〔複雜情況〕逐漸化解: *Ken and Ella had loads of problems when they first got married, but things worked out in the end.* 肯恩和艾拉最初結婚時遇到大量問題, 但最終好了起來。| *I hope it all works out between Gina and Andy.* 我希望吉娜和安迪之間一切問題均會得到解決。| **work itself out** *I know you're not happy with things right now, but I'm sure everything will work itself out.* 我知道你現在諸事不如意, 但我相信一切問題都會自行解決。

6 ►HAPPEN 發生◄ if a situation works out in a particular way, it happens in that way 按某種方式發生: **work out well/badly** *Financially, things have worked out very well for us.* 我們的經濟情況很好。

7 I can't work sb out *spoken* an expression meaning you cannot understand someone's behaviour【口】我弄不懂某人〔指不理解某人的行為〕: *I can't work Geoff out, one day he's friendly the next day he ignores me completely.* 我對傑夫真是搞不明白, 他忽而對我友好, 忽而對我視同路人。

8 ►EXERCISE 鍛鍊◄ [I] to make your body fit and strong, especially by doing a programme of exercises regularly〔尤指定期〕鍛鍊; 健身: *He works out with weights twice a week.* 他每星期兩天練習舉重健身。

9 be worked out if a mine is worked out, all the coal, gold etc has been removed from it〔煤礦等〕採掘完

work sb **over** *phr v* [T] *informal* to hit someone hard and repeatedly all over their body【非正式】毆打; 狠狠地揍〔某人〕

work sb/sth ↔ **up** *phr v* **1 work up enthusiasm/ interest/courage etc** to become enthusiastic or interested etc 產生熱情/興趣/勇氣等: *I'm trying to work up enough courage to go to the dentist.* 我努力鼓起勇氣去看牙醫。**2 work up an appetite/thirst** to make yourself hungry or THIRSTY, especially by doing physical exercise or waiting a long time before you eat or drink〔尤指做運動或長時間沒飲食〕激起食慾/渴感: *You can work up a really big thirst playing tennis.* 打網球會令你十分口渴。**3** to make someone very angry, excited, or upset about something 使某人〔為某事〕感到氣憤[激動; 不安]: **work yourself up** *Paula has worked herself up into a complete state about the exam.* 波拉將自己調整到最佳狀態去迎接考試。**4** to develop and improve a skill or a piece of writing 逐步培養〔技能〕; 逐步完善〔文章、作品〕: *Jack took notes which he would work up into a report later.* 傑克記下筆記, 稍後將整理成一份報告。

work up to sth *phr v* [T] to prepare yourself to do something that you do not want to do by gradually making yourself more and more determined to do it 逐漸下決心〔去做不想做的事〕: *I haven't told Carmela I don't want to go, I'm still working up to it.* 我還沒有告訴卡梅拉我不想去, 我還在做心理準備。

work² *n*

1 [U] a job you are paid to do or an activity that you do regularly to earn money 工作; 職業: *My father started work when he was 14.* 我父親14歲就開始工作了。| *The work is interesting and well paid.* 工作有趣, 報酬優厚。| *There isn't a lot of work at this time of the year.* 每年這

個時候工作機會不多。| **be in work/out of work** (=have or not have a job) 有／沒有工作 | **look for work/find work** *Anne left college a year ago and she's still looking for work.* 安妮一年前大學畢業, 但她仍在找工作。| *He eventually found work on a construction site.* 他最終找到了一份在建築工地的工作。| **return to work** (=start work again after a long period of time)〔經過長時間後〕重新工作 *Dawn didn't return to work until the kids had started school.* 直到孩子開始上學, 唐才重新出去工作。| **after/before work** (=after or before you start work each day) 每天工作之後／工作之前 | **sb's line of work** (=the kind of work someone does) 某人從事的行業 *In my line of work we use a lot of heavy equipment – back-hoes, things like that.* 在我從事的行當中, 我們使用大量重型設備── 反鏟挖土機和諸如此類的機械。—see 見 JOB (USAGE)

2 ►PLACE 地點◄ [U] a place where you do your job, which is not your home 工作地點; 辦公室: *He left work at the usual time.* 他按平常時間離開辦公室。| *I'll see you at work tomorrow.* 明天上班見。| **be at work** (=be working at your job at a place which is not your home) 在工作的地方, 在工作 *My Dad's at work.* 我爸爸上班去了。

3 ►DUTIES 責任◄ [U] the duties and activities that are part of your job 差事; 職務: *What kind of work are you looking for?* 你要找甚麼樣的工作?| *A large part of the work we do involves using computers.* 我們一大部分工作要使用電腦。| **secretarial/legal/bar etc work** *I've been working in the field for 6 years, and would like a chance at some museum work.* 我從事野外考察6年, 我希望有機會去博物館工作。| **voluntary work** (=work that you do not get paid for) 義務工作

4 ►RESULT 成果◄ [U] something that you produce as a result of doing your job or doing an activity 工作成果; 產品: *Send a résumé and example of your work.* 請寄一份履歷及你所做的樣品。| **piece of work** *This report really is an excellent piece of work.* 這份報告真是一件傑出的作品。

5 ►USEFUL ACTIVITY 有用的活動◄ [U] the act of doing something that needs to be done or that you want to do, or the time and effort needed to do it 做〔需要做; 希望做〕的事; 做事花的時間和力量: *Ted's done a lot of work on the car.* 泰德在這輛汽車上花了很多功夫。| *The house must have taken a lot of work.* 在這房子上一定花了很多功夫。| *Come on – hard work never hurt anyone.* 加油── 吃苦沒壞處。| **get down to work** (=start doing work) 着手幹, 開始幹 *We decided to watch TV for a while before getting down to work.* 着手工作前我們決定先看一會兒電視。

6 ►STUDY 學習◄ [U] study or RESEARCH, especially for a particular purpose〔尤指為某一目的進行的〕學習, 研究: *He did his postgraduate work in Sociology.* 他研究生時學的是社會學。| *Limited work was carried out on subjects between the ages of 16 and 20.* 對16至20歲的對象所做的研究有限。

7 at work a) doing your job or a particular activity 在工作, 在幹活: *Danger – men at work.* 危險 ── 正在施工。**b)** having a particular influence or effect 有特別影響; 起特殊作用: *Listen to her voice, you can hear her operatic training at work.* 留意她的嗓音, 你就能聽出她的歌劇訓練在起作用。

8 ►BOOK/PAINTING/MUSIC 書/畫/音樂◄ [C] something such as a book, play, painting, or piece of music produced by a writer, painter, or musician 著作;〔藝術〕作品: *the Collected Works of Shakespeare* 莎士比亞全集 | *Thirty-five Old Master works will be on loan from the Met.* 三十五幅古典名畫家的作品將從大都會美術館借來展出。

9 the (whole) works *spoken* everything【口】所有的東西, 全部: *"What would you like – eggs, bacon, sausages, fries?" "The works."* "你喜歡吃甚麼?── 有雞蛋、鹹豬肉、香腸、炸馬鈴薯條。" "我全都吃。"

10 nice work/quick work *spoken* used to praise someone for doing something well or quickly【口】幹得好／幹得快〔用於稱讚某人〕: *The last image flickered on the screen and I turned to Herb and said 'Nice work!'* 最後一個畫面在屏幕上晃動的時候, 我回過頭去對赫布說: "幹得好!"

11 works a) *old-fashioned* a building or group of buildings in which goods are produced in large quantities or an industrial process happens【過時】工廠: **ironworks/gasworks/cement works** *The brick works closed last year.* 磚廠去年關閉了。**b)** the activity involved in building something on a large scale〔大規模的建築〕工程: **engineering works/irrigation works/roadworks** *the official in charge of the engineering works* 負責工程的官員

12 it's all in a day's work *spoken* used to say that you do not mind doing something even though it will give you more work than usual【口】這是習以為常[家常便飯]〔用於表示不介意做某事, 雖然這樣會增加工作〕

13 sb will have his/her work cut out *informal* it will be very difficult for someone to do something【非正式】某人會面臨艱巨的任務: *Dad and Sam will have their work cut out for them trying to calm her down.* 爸爸和森要讓她安靜下來, 並不是容易的事。

14 the works the moving parts of a machine〔機器的〕活動機件; 運轉機構

15 [U] *technical* force multiplied by distance【術語】功〔力乘以距離〕—see also 另見 CLERK OF WORKS, **do sb's dirty work** (DIRTY[1] (7)), **make short work of** (SHORT[1] (8)), PUBLIC WORKS

wor·ka·ble /ˈwɝkəbḷ; ˈwɜːkəbəl/ *adj* **1** a workable system, idea etc can be used in a practical and efficient way〔系統、思想等〕可行的: *a workable timetable* 可行的時間表 **2** a substance that is workable can be shaped with your hands〔物質〕可〔用手〕成形的; 可塑的: *workable clay for making pots* 製作盆罐的可塑黏土

work·a·day /ˈwɝkəˌde; ˈwɜːkədeɪ/ *adj* [only before noun 僅用於名詞前] ordinary and not interesting 平凡的; 乏味的: *The views from the plateau are in stark contrast to the workaday cottages below.* 從高原極目眺望的景色與坡下面平淡無奇的村舍形成了鮮明的對比。

work·a·hol·ic /ˌwɝkəˈhɔlɪk; ˌwɜːkəˈhɒlɪk/ *n* [C] *informal* someone who cannot stop working, and does not have time for anything else【非正式】醉心於工作的人, 工作狂

work·bas·ket /ˈwɝkˌbæskɪt; ˈwɜːkˌbɑːskɪt/ *n* [C] a container for SEWING equipment 針線籃[筐]

work·bench /ˈwɝkˌbɛntʃ; ˈwɜːkbentʃ/ *n* [C] a strong table with a hard surface for working on with tools 工作枱

work·book /ˈwɝkˌbuk; ˈwɜːkbʊk/ *n* [C] a school book containing questions and exercises〔包含問題與練習的〕作業本; 練習本

work·day /ˈwɝkˌde; ˈwɜːkdeɪ/ *n* the amount of time that you spend working in a day 工作日〔一天的工作時數〕: *a 10 hour workday* 十小時工作日

worked up /ˌ· ˈ·/ *adj* [not before noun 不用於名詞前] *informal* very upset or excited about something【非正式】〔對某事〕非常不安的; 激動的: **[+about]** *Don't get worked up about it! It was only a suggestion.* 別為此事激動!這只是個建議。—see also 另見 **work up** (WORK[1])

work·er /ˈwɝkɚ; ˈwɜːkə/ *n* [C] **1** one of the people who work for an organization, business etc and are below the level of a manager〔級別比管理人員低的〕工人; 雇員: **factory/farm/office etc worker** *new health and safety regulations for factory workers* 關於工廠工人健康和安全的新條例 | **skilled/ unskilled worker** (=someone who has or does not have special skills) 技術熟練的工人／非熟練工人 | **manual worker** (=someone who does physical work) 體力勞動者 **2 research/rescue etc worker** someone who works to achieve a particular purpose 研究／救援等人員: *Rescue workers worked all*

night to free the victims. 救援人員整夜都在解救災民。**3** someone who works very well or quickly 幹練[勤快]的人: *Mavis is a real worker – she gets twice as much done as everyone else.* 梅維斯是個能幹的人——她做的工作總是比別人多一倍。| **good/hard/quick etc worker** *Mike's always been a hard worker.* 邁克一直是個努力工作的人。**4 the workers** the members of the WORKING CLASS 工人階級的成員: *the workers' revolution* 工人階級革命 —see also 另見 SOCIAL WORKER

work eth·ic /ˈ· ˌ··/ *n* [singular, U] a belief in the moral value of work 職業道德: *the Protestant work ethic* 新教徒的職業道德

work ex·pe·ri·ence /ˈ· ·ˌ···/ *n* **1** the experience you have had of working in a particular type of job〔某類工作的〕工作經驗: *She's well qualified but has no relevant work experience.* 她資格完全夠, 但沒有相關的工作經驗。**2** *BrE* a period of time that a young person spends working in a particular place, as a form of training【英】實習〔年輕人在某地工作一段時間作為培訓的一部分〕

work·fare /ˈwɝkfɛr; ˈwɜːkfeə/ *n* [U] a system that requires unemployed people to work before they are given money for food, rent etc by the government 工作福利制〔要求失業者先從事某種工作, 然後才能領取政府提供的救濟金的制度〕

work·force /ˈwɝkˌfɔrs; ˈwɜːkfɔːs/ *n* [singular] all the people who work in a particular country, industry, or factory〔國家、行業或工廠〕全體從業人員, 勞動力: *a workforce of 3500 employees* 3500 名雇員

work·horse /ˈwɝkˌhɔrs; ˈwɜːkhɔːs/ *n* [C] **1** someone who does most of the work, especially when it is hard or boring 吃苦耐勞的人 **2** a machine or vehicle that can be used to do a lot of work 重負荷機器[運輸工具]: *a software program that is rapidly becoming the architect's workhorse* 很快成為建築師挑大梁的軟件程式

work·house /ˈwɝkˌhaus; ˈwɜːkhaus/ *n* [C] a building in Britain in the past where poor people lived〔英國昔日的〕濟貧院, 救貧院

work·ing¹ /ˈwɝkɪŋ; ˈwɜːkɪŋ/ *adj* [only before noun 僅用於名詞前]

1 ►HAVING A JOB 有工作◄ a) having a job that you are paid for 有工作的; 有職業的: a *working mother* 在職母親 **b)** having a job that requires physical rather than intellectual skill 從事體力勞動的: *an ordinary working man* 普通勞動者

2 ►CLOTHES 服裝◄ working clothes are designed for people to work in rather than to look attractive 穿來工作的; 工作上用的

3 ►CONDITIONS/PRACTICES 環境/常規◄ working conditions or practices are the ones you have in your job 工作的〔環境或常規〕: *recent improvements in working conditions* 工作環境近來的改善

4 ►HOURS 小時◄ your working hours are the period of time during the day when you are doing your job 上班時間的; 工作時間的

5 have a working knowledge of to have enough knowledge of a system, foreign language etc to be able to use it, although your knowledge is limited〔對某系統、外語等〕知識足夠的: *Gita has a working knowledge of Spanish and French.* 吉塔的西班牙語和法語還過得去。

6 ►RELATIONSHIP 關係◄ a working relationship is the kind of relationship that two people have who work well together〔兩人〕工作關係良好的: *The working relationship between Hodges and Bradley began to deteriorate.* 霍奇斯與布拉德利的工作關係開始惡化。

7 ►MODEL 模型◄ a working model is one that has parts that move〔模型〕部件能運轉的

8 ►PARTS OF A MACHINE 機器部件◄ the working parts of a machine are the parts that move and operate the machine〔機器部件〕能運轉的; 用於操作的

9 be in working order to be working properly and not broken 正常地運轉: **be in good/perfect working order** *The car was old, but the engine was still in good working order.* 汽車雖舊, 但引擎仍能良好地運轉。—see graph at 參見 ORDER¹ 圖表

10 ►THEORY/DEFINITION 理論/釋義◄ a working theory or definition is not complete in every detail, but is good enough for you to use as a basis for studying something or doing a job〔研究某事或做事時〕可作為基礎的

11 working breakfast/lunch/dinner a breakfast, lunch etc which is also a business meeting 工作早餐/午餐/晚餐

working² *n* **1** [singular] also 又作 **workings** the way something such as a system, piece of equipment, or organization works〔系統、設備、組織等的〕工作方式; 運行方式: **[+of]** *the inside workings of the Reagan presidency* 列根擔任總統期間政府內的工作方式 | *I shall never understand the workings of his mind.* 我永遠搞不懂他在想甚麼。**2** [C usually plural 一般用複數] a mine or part of a mine where soil has been dug out in order to remove metals or stone 礦坑; (礦內) 工作區: *the workings of a long-disused quarry* 廢棄已久的採石場的工作區

working cap·i·tal /ˌ·· ˈ···/ *n* [U] the money that is available to be used for the costs of a business 運營資金[資本] —see also 另見 VENTURE CAPITAL

working class /ˌ·· ˈ·◄/ *n* [singular] *especially BrE* the group of people in society who traditionally do physical work and do not have much money or power【尤英】工人[勞工]階級 —compare 比較 LOWER CLASS, MIDDLE CLASS, UPPER CLASS —**working class** *adj*

working day /ˌ·· ˈ·◄/ *n* [C] **1** the amount of time that you spend working in a day 一天的工作時間 **2** a day when you have to work 工作日

working girl /ˈ·· ·/ *n* [C] *old-fashioned*【過時】**1** a word for a woman who has sex for money, used when you want to avoid saying this directly 娼妓〔委婉語〕**2** a young woman who has a paid job 年輕職業女性

working group /ˈ·· ·/ *n* [C] a committee that is established to examine a particular situation or problem and suggest ways of dealing with it 專題調查委員會, 特別工作組

working life /ˌ·· ˈ·/ *n* [C] the part of your adult life when you work 工作生涯: *Geoff spent all his working life in the same company.* 傑夫在同一家公司幹了一輩子。

working ma·jor·i·ty /ˌ·· ·ˈ···/ *n* [singular] *BrE* enough support in parliament for a government to continue making laws and ruling a country【英】〔議會中支持政府的〕有效的多數

working or·der /ˈ·· ˌ··/ *n* [U] **in working order** a system, machine etc that is in working order is working well, with no problems〔系統、機器等〕良好的工作狀態; 正常的運轉狀態

working pa·pers /ˈ·· ˌ··/ *n* [plural] an official document that you need in the US in order to get a job if you are young or were born in a different country〔美國未成年或在外國出生的居民受雇時必須持有的〕工作許可證

working par·ty /ˈ·· ˌ··/ *n* [C] *BrE* a WORKING GROUP【英】專題調查委員會

working prac·tices /ˈ·· ˌ···/ *n* [plural] the way in which things are usually done in your job 工作常規: *The changes in working practices are designed to increase efficiency.* 改變工作常規是為了提高效率。

work·ings /ˈwɝkɪŋz; ˈwɜːkɪŋz/ *n* [plural] **1** the way in which something works〔某事的〕工作方式: *I shall never understand the workings of his mind.* 我永遠搞不懂他在想甚麼。**2** the parts of a mine that have been dug out 礦坑

working week /ˌ·· ˈ·/ *n* [C] the days when you do your job, usually between Monday and Friday 工作週, 一週的工作日〔通常指星期一至五〕

W

work·load /ˈwɝk͵lod; ˈwɜːkləʊd/ *n* [C] the amount of work that a person or machine is expected to do〔人或機器的〕工作量; 工作負荷: *Paul has a heavy workload at the moment.* 保羅目前的工作負荷很重。

work·man /ˈwɝkmən; ˈwɜːkmən/ *n* [C] someone who does physical work such as building, repairing things etc〔建築、維修等的〕工匠, 工人

work·man·like /ˈwɝkmən͵laɪk; ˈwɜːkmənlaɪk/ *adj* a workmanlike piece of work has been done well and looks good 能工巧匠的; 精巧細緻的

work·man·ship /ˈwɝkmən͵ʃɪp; ˈwɜːkmənʃɪp/ *n* [U] *formal* skill in making things, especially in a way that makes them look good【正式】〔尤指精細的〕工藝, 手藝

work·mate /ˈwɝk͵met; ˈwɜːkmeɪt/ *n* [C] someone you work with 同事, 一起工作的人

work of art /͵· · ˈ·/ *n plural* **works of art** [C] **1** a painting, SCULPTURE etc of very high quality〔繪畫、雕刻等〕藝術精品 **2** *often humorous* something that is very attractive and skilfully made【常幽默】精緻的東西: *That cake's a real work of art!* 那蛋糕簡直是藝術品!

workout 訓練

work·out /ˈwɝk͵aʊt; ˈwɜːkaʊt/ *n* [C] a period of physical exercise, especially as training for a sport〔尤指運動的〕鍛鍊, 訓練 —see also 另見 **work out** (WORK[1])

work per·mit /ˈ· ͵··/ *n* [C] an official document that you need if you want to work in a foreign country〔在外國工作時所需的〕工作許可證

work·place /ˈwɝk͵ples; ˈwɜːkpleɪs/ *n* [C] the room, building etc where you work 工作場所

work·room /ˈwɝk͵rum; ˈwɜːkrʊm/ *n* [C] a room that you work in 工作間, 作業室

work·sheet /ˈwɝk͵ʃit; ˈwɜːkʃiːt/ *n* [C] a piece of paper with questions, exercises etc for students〔印有問題、練習等的〕學生作業紙, 活頁練習題

3 3 **work·shop** /ˈwɝk͵ʃap; ˈwɜːkʃɒp/ *n* [C] **1** a room or building where tools and machines are used for making or repairing things 車間, 工場 **2** a meeting at which people try to improve their skills by discussing their experiences and doing practical exercises〔目的在提高技巧的〕研討會, 研習班

work-shy /ˈ· ·/ *adj* someone who is work-shy tries to avoid working because they do not like it 不願勞動的, 怕工作的

work·sta·tion /ˈwɝk͵steʃən; ˈwɜːk͵steɪʃən/ *n* [C] the part of an office where you work, where your desk, computer etc are〔辦公室中設有辦公桌、電腦等的〕工作區; 操作崗位 —see picture on page A14 參見A14頁圖

work-sur·face /ˈ· ͵··/ also 又作 **work·top** /ˈwɝktap; ˈwɜːktɒp/ *n* [C] *especially BrE* a flat surface for working on, especially in a kitchen【尤英】〔尤指廚房的〕工作枱; 操作枱; COUNTER[1] (4) *AmE*【美】—see picture on page A10 參見A10頁圖

work-to-rule /͵· · ˈ·/ *n* [singular] a situation in which people in a particular job refuse to do any additional work as a protest〔死扣規章制度, 拒絕做額外工作的〕怠工, 按章工作 —see also 另見 **work to rule** (WORK[1] (29))

work·week /ˈwɝk͵wik; ˈwɜːkwiːk/ *n* [C] *AmE* the total amount of time that you spend working during a week【美】工作週, 一週的工作時間: *a 40 hour workweek* 40小時工作週

world[1] /wɝld; wɜːld/ *n* S1 W1

1 ►OUR PLANET/EVERYONE ON IT 地球/全人類◄ **the world** the planet we live on, and all the people, cities, and countries on it; the Earth 世界; 地球: *the world's tallest building* 世界上最高的建築 | *Tuberculosis is still common in some parts of the world.* (肺)結核病在世界上某些地區仍很普遍。| *At that time China was the most powerful country in the world.* 在那時中國是世界上最強大的國家。| *The Press Association flashed the news to the world.* 英國新聞通訊社把消息迅速發往全世界。| **all over the world** (=everywhere in the world) 世界各地 *Delegates from all over the world will be at the conference.* 世界各地的代表都將參加這次會議。

2 in the world used to emphasize a statement you are making 究竟; 到底〔用於加強語氣〕: **the happiest/most exciting etc ... in the world** *If she asked me to marry her I'd be the happiest man in the world.* 她如果讓我娶她, 我便是世上最幸福的人。| **not have a care in the world** (=not be worried at all about anything) 無憂無慮 | **nothing in the world** (=nothing at all) 沒有甚麼 *Nothing in the world can save them now.* 現在甚麼也救不了他們。| **have all the time in the world** (=have a lot of time so that you do not have to hurry) 有的是時間 *Don't worry, we've got all the time in the world.* 別急, 我們有的是時間。| **What/Who/Where/How etc in the world...?** (=used after what or who etc to emphasize a question in order to show that you are very surprised, annoyed, or angry) 究竟是甚麼/是誰/在哪兒/怎麼樣等〔用於問句, 表示驚訝、煩惱或生氣〕*What in the world are you doing here at seven in the morning?* 早上七點你究竟在這兒幹甚麼?

3 the outside world the people who live outside a particular place, country etc; especially when the people living in that place or country cannot meet them or talk to them〔在某地方、國家等以外的〕外面世界: *a jungle tribe who have no contact with the outside world* 和外面的世界沒有接觸的一個叢林部落

4 ►THE SOCIETY WE LIVE IN 我們生活的社會◄ the society that we live in and the kind of life we have 社會; 生活: *The world is being transformed by information technology.* 資訊科技正在改變社會。| *Parents want a better world for their children.* 父母想給孩子更好的生活。—see 見 LAND[1] (USAGE)

5 ►GROUP OF COUNTRIES 國家集團◄ **the Western World/the industrialized world/the developing world etc** a particular group of countries 西方世界/工業化國家/發展中國家等: *The British are among the biggest sugar consumers in the developed world.* 在發達國家中, 英國是食糖消費最多的國家之一。—see also 另見 THIRD WORLD

6 ►PERIOD IN HISTORY 歷史上的時期◄ **the Roman world/the Medieval world etc** a particular period in history and the society and people of that time 古羅馬時代/中世紀等: *the artistic, literary, and intellectual culture of the Roman World* 古羅馬時代的藝術、文學及知識文化

7 ►AREA OF ACTIVITY/WORK 活動/工作的領域◄ [C usually singular 一般用單數] a particular area of activity or work, and the people who are involved in it〔人們活動或工作的〕領域; 界: *the world of politics* 政界 | *an influential figure in the business world* 在商界有影響力的人物 | *The show-business world was out in force at the Oscar ceremony.* 奥斯卡頒獎典禮上娛樂界人士雲集。

8 ►SB'S LIFE 某人的生活◄ [C] the life a particular person or group of people lives, especially the things they do and the people they know〔某人或一羣人的〕生活〔尤指他們做的事和認識的人〕; 生活經歷: *the world*

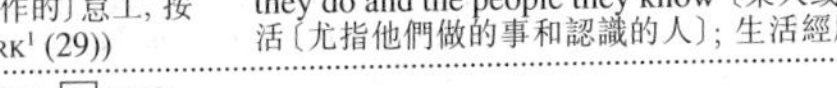

of children 孩子的世界 | *Dean's world was filled with music and laughter.* 迪安的生活充滿了音樂和笑聲。

9 in a world of your own *informal* if someone lives in a world of their own, they do not seem to notice what is happening around them and are more concerned with their own thoughts【非正式】活在自己的世界裡: *I can't get through to that girl – she seems to be in a world of her own.* 我無法使那女孩聽懂——她似乎活在自己的世界裡。

10 ►KIND OF PLACE/SITUATION 某類地方/情況◄ a particular kind of place or situation, especially one that someone describes or which you imagine〔尤指某人描述或想像的〕地方; 情景: *the nightmare world of Orwell's novel 1984* 奧威爾小說《一九八四》中的夢魘世界 | *Italy's mountains and lakes are a stunning world of peace and tranquillity.* 意大利的山脈和湖泊, 環境非常寧靜。

11 the animal/plant/insect world animals etc considered as a group of living things with their own particular way of living or behaving 動物/植物/昆蟲(世)界

12 ►PLACE LIKE THE EARTH 天體◄ [C] a place like the Earth in another part of the universe where other things may live〔可能有生物的〕天體, 星球: *strange creatures from another world* 從另一個星球來的奇異生物

13 be out of this world *informal* something that is out of this world is so good, enjoyable etc, it is unlike anything else you have ever experienced【非正式】好得不得了: *Tracy's new apartment is just out of this world.* 翠西的新公寓好得不得了。

14 do sb a world of good *informal* if something does someone a world of good, it makes them feel much better【非正式】〔某事〕對某人有好處: *Why don't you go for a walk, it'll do you a world of good.* 你為甚麼不去散步, 那會對你大有好處。

15 be/feel on top of the world *informal* to feel extremely happy【非正式】快活之極

16 be/mean all the world to to be more important to you than anyone or anything else〔某人或某物〕對…最重要, 最可寶貴: *I'd hate to lose her – she means all the world to me.* 我不願失去她——她就是我的一切。

17 think the world of sb to love and respect someone very much 非常喜歡某人; 對某人很尊重: *Lee thinks the world of you – you know that.* 李非常喜歡你——你是知道的。

18 see the world to travel to many different countries so that you can get a lot of different experiences 到各國旅遊豐富閱歷

19 the world over in every country or area of the world; everywhere 全世界, 世界各地: *It's the same the world over.* 天下皆同。| *Her books have delighted adults and children the world over.* 她的書受到全世界大人、小孩的喜愛。

20 move up/go up in the world to move into a higher social class 升到更高的社會地位; 發跡: *He's gone up in the world now – he's far too posh to talk to me.* 他發跡了——派頭大得不屑跟我說話。

21 go down/come down in the world to move down to a lower social class 落魄, 潦倒

22 there's a world of difference between used when saying that two things or situations are completely different and people should not expect them to be the same〔兩物或兩種情況〕有天淵之別: *There's a world of difference between enjoying cooking and doing it for a living.* 喜歡烹飪與為生計而烹飪有天壤之別。

23 be worlds apart/be a world apart people, beliefs, or ideas that are worlds apart are so completely different that there is almost nothing about them that is similar〔人、信念或想法〕完全不同: *Their political views are just worlds apart.* 他們的政治觀點截然不同。

24 for all the world as if/like *literary* exactly as if or exactly like【文】活像; 完全像: *She sat reading her paper, looking for all the world as if nothing had happened.* 她坐着看報, 就像甚麼事都沒有發生過一樣。

25 not for the world if someone would not do a particular thing for the world, they would never do it whatever happened 決不, 無論如何也不: *I wouldn't hurt her for the world.* 我決不傷害她。

26 be a man/woman of the world to be someone who has had many experiences and is not easily shocked 閱歷豐富的人, 老於世故的人: *Victor is a man of the world – I'm sure he'll understand.* 維克托閱歷豐富——我敢肯定他懂。

27 set the world on fire/alight *spoken* an expression meaning to have a big effect or be very successful, often used when you think someone or something has failed to do this【口】驚人之舉; 非常成功〔常用於否定〕: *His last film didn't exactly set the world on fire.* 他的最後一部電影全然沒有引起轟動。

28 set/put the world to rights to discuss or say how the world should be changed to make people's lives better 暢談如何改善世界, 指點江山: *We were having a few beers and generally putting the world to rights.* 我們一邊喝着啤酒, 一邊大談如何濟時匡時。

29 the next world/the world to come *literary* the place where people's souls are believed to go after they die【文】陰間; 冥府

30 not be long for this world to not be going to live much longer 不久於人世, 行將謝世

31 this world *literary* the state of being alive【文】人生, 今世: **depart/leave this world** (=die) 去世, 離開人世

32 bring a child into the world *formal*【正式】**a)** if a woman brings a child into the world she gives birth to it 生小孩 **b)** if a doctor brings a child into the world he helps the mother give birth〔醫生〕接生

33 come into the world *literary* to be born【文】降生, 出世

34 the Michael Jacksons/Paul Smiths etc of this world *spoken* used when making a general comment about a particular kind of person【口】米高·積遜/保羅·史密斯等一類人〔用於對某一類人作一般評論時〕: *The Frank Clarkes of this world are only interested in furthering their own careers.* 弗蘭克·克拉克這類人只顧成就自己的事業。

35 the world is your oyster used to tell someone that there is no limit to the opportunities that they have 你前途無量, 前程似錦: *"If you've got a good education, the world is your oyster," my father used to say.* 父親常說: "只要你有良好的教育, 在這個世界你就大有可為。"

36 workers/women etc of the world used when addressing all workers, women etc in a speech, book etc 工友們/各位女性朋友等〔發言、書中等稱呼〕

37 ►NOT RELIGIOUS 不是宗教的◄ the world the way of life most people live rather than a spiritual way of life 塵世, 世俗: *monks who renounce the world* 厭棄塵世的修道士們 —see also 另見 **best of both worlds** (BEST³ (5)), **dead to the world** (DEAD¹ (9)), NEW WORLD, OLD WORLD

world² *adj* [only before noun 僅用於名詞前] **1** existing in or affecting the whole world 遍及[影響]全世界的: *The prospects for world peace are improving.* 世界和平的前景正在改善。| *the world recession of the early nineties* 90 年代初的世界經濟衰退 | **world champion/record etc** (=the best in the world, especially in a sport) 世界冠軍/紀錄等 *Hawthorn became Britain's first world champion.* 霍桑成為英國第一個世界冠軍得主。**2** important or powerful enough to influence or affect the whole world 重要[強大]得足以影響世界的: *Britain's attempts to remain a world power* 英國保持世界強國地位的企圖 | *a world figure on the international stage* 國際舞台上舉足輕重的人物

world-beat·er /ˈ· ˌ··/ *n* [C] someone or something that is the best at a particular activity 舉世無雙的人[物]; 天

下無敵的人[物] —**world-beating** *adj*

world-class /ˌ· ˈ·◂/ *adj* among the best in the world 世界第一流水平的: *a world-class tennis champion* 世界一流的網球冠軍

world-fa·mous /ˌ· ˈ··◂/ *adj* known about by people all over the world 世界著名的, 舉世聞名的: *a world-famous singer* 世界著名的歌唱家

world·ly /ˈwɜldlɪ; ˈwɜːldli/ *adj* [only before noun 僅用於名詞前] **1 worldly goods** everything you own 財產 **2** having a lot of experience and knowledge about people and life 生活經驗豐富的; 老成練達的: *Crystal was worldly but willing to take a risk.* 克莉絲多爾老成練達, 但願意冒險。—opposite 反義詞 UNWORLDLY **3** connected with ordinary daily life rather than spiritual or religious ideas; MUNDANE 塵世的, 世俗的 —**worldliness** *n* [U]

worldly-wise /ˌ·· ˈ·◂/ *adj* having a lot of experience and knowledge about life so that you are not easily shocked or deceived 老於世故的; 會處世的

world pow·er /ˌ· ˈ··/ *n* [C] a country that has a lot of power and influence in many parts of the world 世界強國

world-shak·ing /ˈ· ˌ··/ *adj* extremely important and having a great effect 非常重要的; 震驚世界的: *a world-shaking announcement* 震驚世界的宣告

world-wear·y /ˌ· ˈ··◂/ *adj* no longer finding life interesting or exciting 厭世的 —**world-weariness** *n* [U]

world·wide /ˈwɜldˈwaɪd; ˌwɜːldˈwaɪd◂/ *adj, adv* everywhere in the world 遍及全世界的[地]; 在全世界: *cars with a worldwide reputation for reliability* 以性能可靠享譽世界的汽車

World Wide Web /ˌ· · ˈ·◂/ *n* [singular] the net work of computers that forms the Internet 萬維網

worm¹ /wɜm; wɜːm/ *n* [C] **1** a long thin creature with no bones and no legs that lives in soil 蠕蟲 **2** someone who you do not like or respect 討厭的人; 可鄙的人 **3 have worms** to have PARASITES (=small creature that eats your food or your blood) in your body 患有寄生蟲 **4 the worm turns** *literary* used to say that someone who is normally quiet and obedient will change if they really need to【文】沉默規矩的人(被逼)也反抗 —see also 另見 **can of worms** (CAN² (4))

worm² *v* [T] **1 worm your way into/through etc** to move through a small place or a crowd slowly, carefully, or with difficulty (在小的地方或人羣中)緩慢[小心, 艱難]地前行: *They wormed their way through the crowd.* 他們好不容易慢慢地擠出人羣。**2 worm your way into sb's affections/heart/confidence etc** to gradually make someone love or trust you, especially by being dishonest (尤指通過欺詐手段)漸漸獲得某人的感情/歡心/信任 **3 worm sth out of sb** to get information from someone who does not want to give it 從某人處套出消息 **4 worm your way out of (doing) sth** to avoid doing something that you have been asked to do by making an excuse that is dishonest but clever (不誠實但巧妙地)逃避做某事: *Steve has managed to worm his way out of going to the meeting.* 史蒂夫設法巧妙地逃避了參加會議。**5** to give an animal medicine in order to remove PARASITES (1) that live inside them 給(動物用藥)驅寄生蟲

worm-eat·en /ˈ· ˌ··/ *adj* **1** worm-eaten wood or fruit has holes in it because it has been eaten by worms (木材或水果)蟲蛀的; 多蛀孔的 **2** old and damaged 陳舊的; 破損的 —see picture on page A18 參見A18頁圖

worm·hole /ˈwɜmˌhol; ˈwɜːmhəʊl/ *n* [C] a hole in a piece of wood etc made by a type of WORM¹ (1) (木材等上的)蛀洞, 蟲孔

worm·wood /ˈwɜmˌwʊd; ˈwɜːmwʊd/ *n* [U] a plant with a bitter taste (一種植物)苦艾

worm·y /ˈwɜmɪ; ˈwɜːmi/ *adj* full of worms (WORM¹ (1)) 滿是蟲的

worn¹ /wɔrn; wɔːn/ the past participle of WEAR¹

worn² *adj* **1** a worn object is old and damaged (物品)陳舊的, 損壞的: *a worn patch on the carpet* 地毯上一小塊磨破的地方 **2** someone who looks worn seems tired 疲倦的; 精疲力盡的

worn out /ˌ· ˈ·◂/ *adj* **1** very tired because you have been working hard (因工作賣力而)精疲力竭的: *You look worn-out!* 你看來精疲力竭! **2** too old or damaged to be used 破舊的; 不能再用的: *a pair of old worn out walking boots* 一雙穿破了的舊步行靴

wor·ried /ˈwɜɪd; ˈwʌrid/ *adj* **1** unhappy because you keep thinking about a problem, or are anxious about something 擔心的, 焦慮的: *Don't look so worried – we'll find him.* 不要愁眉不展——我們會找到他的。| **[+about]** *She's so worried about her exams.* 她很擔心考試。| **worried that** *I was worried that we wouldn't have enough money.* 我擔心我們的錢不夠。| **get worried** *I got really worried when I saw a police car outside our house.* 看到警車停在我們屋外, 我真的膽戰心驚。| **worried expression/look/frown etc** *Jim looked up with a slightly worried expression.* 吉姆略帶愁容地抬頭看。| **worried sick** *spoken* (=extremely worried)【口】非常擔心 *Where on earth have you been? I was worried sick!* 你究竟到哪兒去了?我都急壞了! —see 見 NERVOUS (USAGE) **2 you had me worried** *spoken* used to say that someone made you feel confused or anxious because you did not properly understand what they said, or did not realize that it was a joke【口】你讓我擔心(因為誤解對方的話或不知道那是玩笑): *You had me worried there for a minute – I thought the house really had burnt down!* 你讓我擔心了一會——我以為房子真的燒毀了! **3 I'm not worried** *spoken* used to say that you do not mind what happens【口】我無所謂(用於表示你不在乎發生何事): *"Shall we go out or stay in?" "Oh, I'm not worried – whichever you want."* "我們是出去還是留在家裡?" "噢, 我無所謂——隨你喜歡。" —**worriedly** *adv*

wor·ri·er /ˈwɜɪɚ; ˈwʌriə/ *n* [C] someone who often worries about things 經常擔心的人, 經常發愁的人: *Her mother was a born worrier.* 她母親天生杞人憂天。

wor·ri·some /ˈwɜɪsəm; ˈwʌrisəm/ *adj formal* making you anxious【正式】令人焦慮的: *a worrisome problem* 一個令人擔心的問題

wor·ry¹ /ˈwɜɪ; ˈwʌri/ *v*

1 ►BE ANXIOUS 擔憂◄ [I] to be anxious or unhappy about something so that you think about it a lot 擔心; 為…發愁: **[+about]** *You've really got no need to worry about your weight.* 你真的不必擔心你的體重。| **worry that** *He's worried that he might lose his job.* 他擔心他會失業。| **[+over]** *Dad worries over the slightest thing.* 爸爸會為一點點小事發愁。

2 don't worry *spoken*【口】**a)** used when you are trying to make someone feel less anxious 別擔心(用於安慰別人): *Don't worry, darling, Daddy's here.* 小寶貝, 別怕, 爸爸在這兒。**b)** used to tell someone that they do not need to do something 不用費心(用於告訴某人不用做某事): *Don't worry about sorting them out – I'll do it later.* 不用把它整理出來——過一會我會做的。**c)** used to tell someone that you will definitely do something 別擔心(用於告訴某人你肯定會做某事): *Oh don't worry, I'll get my own back on him somehow!* 噢, 別擔心, 我總會想辦法向他報復的!

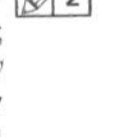

3 ►MAKE SB ANXIOUS 使某人擔憂◄ [T] to make someone feel anxious about something 使某人(為某事而)憂慮: *The recent changes in the Earth's climate are beginning to worry scientists.* 近來地球的氣候變化使科學家開始擔憂。| **worry sb that** *Doesn't it worry you that Sarah spends so much time away from home?* 莎拉整天往外跑你不擔心嗎? | **worry yourself** (=feel anxious, especially when there is no need to) (尤指不必要的)擔心; 發愁

4 not to worry *BrE spoken* used to say that something is not important【英口】沒關係(用於指某事不重要): *Not to worry, we can always go another time.* 沒關係, 我們總能找別的時間去。

5 nothing to worry about *spoken* used to tell some-

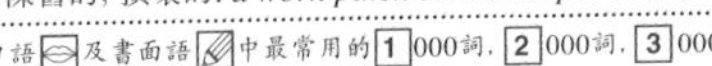

one that something is not as serious or difficult as they think【口】沒甚麼可擔心的: *It's just a routine check-up – nothing to worry about.* 這只是例行檢查 —— 沒甚麼可擔心的。

6 have enough to worry about *spoken* used to say that someone already has a lot of problems or is very busy【口】已經夠煩的: *I don't think we should tell Mum about this – she's got enough to worry about as it is.* 我不認為要把這事告訴媽媽 —— 事實上她已經夠煩的了。

7 ►ANNOY 煩惱◄ [T] to annoy someone 使〔某人〕惱怒: **worry sb with sth** *Stop worrying your grandfather with all those questions.* 不要再問這問那煩你爺爺了。

8 ►ANIMAL 動物◄ [T] if a dog worries sheep, it tries to bite or kill them〔狗〕追咬[殺]〔羊〕

worry at sth/sb *phr v* [T] **1** if an animal worries at a bone or piece of meat, it bites and shakes it〔動物〕撕咬〔骨頭或肉塊〕**2** if you worry at a problem, you think about it a lot in order to try and find a solution 設法解決〔問題〕: *Jez was never happy unless he was worrying at some problem.* 如果不在竭力思索解決某個問題的辦法, 傑斯就會不高興。

S3 **worry²** *n* **1** [C] a problem that you are anxious about or are not sure how to deal with 令人憂心[不知如何處理]的問題: *My main worry is how the divorce will affect the kids.* 我主要擔心的是離婚會對孩子產生甚麼影響。| *financial worries* 財務上的煩惱事 | **[+about]** *We've got no more worries about the schedule at the moment.* 我們現在不再為日程安排而擔心了。| **be a worry to/for sb** *Money was always a big worry for us.* 金錢總是我們的一大煩惱。**2** [U] the feeling of being anxious about something 擔心; 憂慮: *The missing child's parents were frantic with worry.* 失蹤孩子的父母急得發瘋。**3 no worries** *spoken* used to agree to what someone wants and to say that it will be no problem【口】沒問題〔用於應允別人的要求〕: *Can you deliver on Thursday? Yeah, no worries, mate.* 星期四你能送去嗎? 噢, 沒有問題, 老兄。

worry beads /'·· ·/ *n* [plural] small stones or wooden balls on a string that you move and turn in order to keep yourself calm 安神念珠, 解愁數珠

S3 **wor·ry·ing** /ˈwɜːrɪŋ; ˈwʌri-ɪŋ/ *adj* **1** making you feel anxious 令人擔心的; 使人發愁的: *a worrying development* 叫人憂慮的事態發展 **2 worrying time/week/year etc** a time etc when you have many problems 多煩惱的時刻/星期/年頭等: *It's been a worrying few weeks for us all.* 這幾個星期大家都憂心忡忡。—**worryingly** *adv*: *a worryingly high level of pollutants in the atmosphere* 令人擔憂的大氣中高含量的污染物

wor·ry·wart /ˈwɜːiˌwɔrt; ˈwʌriwɔːt/ *n* [C] *AmE informal* someone who worries about unimportant things【美, 非正式】〔為瑣事〕自尋煩惱的人

worse¹ /wɜ·s; wɜːs/ *adj* **1** [the comparative of *bad* bad 的比較級] not as good as someone or something else, or more unpleasant or of a lower standard 更壞的; 更糟的; 更差的: *The meal couldn't have been much worse.* 這飯菜糟糕透了。| **worse than** *The weather was worse than last year.* 天氣比去年更糟。| **there's nothing worse than** *spoken*【口】*There's nothing worse than being angry about something and knowing it's your own fault.* 為自己惹的禍生氣, 沒有比這更糟的了。| **a lot/much worse** *The traffic is much worse after five.* 五點之後交通情況會糟得多。| **get worse** *I didn't like the noise when I first came and it's got worse since then.* 初來時我就不喜歡這種噪聲, 那以後變得越來越討厭了。| **worse and worse** *Paul's manners seem to get worse and worse.* 保羅似乎越來越無禮了。| **make matters/things/it worse** (=make a bad or difficult situation even worse) 使情況更困難[更差] *I tried to help but I think I made things worse.* 我試圖去幫忙, 但我覺得自己使事情變得更糟。**2** [comparative of *ill* ill 的比較級] more ill than before 病情更重的: *If she's worse in the morning, I'll call the doctor.* 她如果早上病情惡化的話, 我要去請醫生來。| **get worse** *After the operation he got worse instead of better.* 手術後他不是越來越好, 而是越來越糟。**3 be none the worse for** to not have been harmed, or not be worse because of something 沒有因〔某事物〕受傷害[變得更差]: *The children were out in the rain all afternoon, but seem none the worse for it.* 孩子們整個下午都在淋雨, 但是看來並沒有怎麼樣。**4 worse luck** *spoken* used to say that you are disappointed or annoyed by something【口】真不幸〔因某事而感到沮喪或生氣時用〕: *When we got there the car had already been sold, worse luck!* 我們到那裡時汽車已經賣掉了, 真倒霉! **5 sb can/could do worse than do sth** *spoken* used to say that you think it is a good idea if someone does a particular thing【口】做某事是好主意: *You could do worse than buy a few bottles of the local wine.* 你買幾瓶當地的葡萄酒是個好主意。**6 it could have been worse** *spoken* used to say that a bad situation has something good about it【口】可能會更糟〔用於指實際情況並不那麼糟糕〕**7 take a change/turn for the worse** to change and become worse 惡化 **8 the worse for wear** *informal* in poor condition, or very tired【非正式】破舊不堪的; 精疲力竭的: *The living room carpet is looking the worse for wear.* 起居室的地毯看起來破舊不堪。—compare 比較 BETTER¹ —see also 另見 **go from bad to worse** (BAD¹ (13))

USAGE NOTE 用法說明: WORSE

GRAMMAR 語法

More and **most** are not used together with **worse** or **worst**. more 和 most 不與 worse 與 worst 連用: *Math is my worst subject* (NOT 不用 *my most worse/most worst subject*). 數學是我最差的科目。| *The situation is much worse than it was last week* (NOT 不用 *much more worse*). 形勢比上週更糟。

Some people think that **worse** should not be used as an adverb meaning 'in a worse way'. 有人認為 worse 不應用作副詞表示"更差", But in spoken English you will often hear 但在英語口語裡卻經常聽到: *Because we're so short of time we're doing it worse than we should.* 因為時間太少, 我們做得比預期的還要差。You can avoid this problem by saying for example 為避免此類問題, 可以說: *...we're not doing it as well as we should.* ...我們沒有做得像預期的那樣好。

Things *go/get bad*, but they *get worse*. 可以說事情 go bad 或 get bad (變壞), 但只可說事情 get worse (變得越來越壞)。

SPELLING 拼法

Remember the spellings: *even worse* is spelt with an 'e'; *the worst* with a 't'. 注意拼法: even worse 結尾是 e; 而 the worst 的結尾是 t。

worse² *n* [U] something worse 更差[壞]的事物: *We thought the situation was bad, but worse was to follow.* 我們以為形勢不好, 但更糟的事還在後頭。| **a change for the worse** (=a bad change) 變得更差[更壞] —compare 比較 BETTER³

worse³ *adv* [comparative of *badly* badly 的比較級] **1** in a more severe or serious way than before 更猛烈地; 更厲害地: *My head aches much worse than before.* 我頭痛得比以前更厲害了。**2** to a lower standard or quality or less successfully 更差地; 更糟地; 更不成功地: *Dick scored worse than you in the test.* 迪克在測驗中得的分數比你還差。

wors·en /ˈwɝsn̩; ˈwɜːsən/ *v* [I,T] to become worse or make something worse (使) 變得更差; (使) 惡化: *a worsening political situation* 日趨惡化的政治形勢

worse off /,· '·◄/ *adj* [not before noun 不用於名詞前] **1** having less money than before or than someone else; poorer 比以前[別人]錢較少 (的); 更貧窮: *The tax increases will leave us worse off.* 稅收增加後我們賺的錢會更少。**2** in a worse situation than before or than someone else 形勢比以前或別人〕更糟的: *The factories on the east bank of the river were even worse off as they had* *no direct link to the motorway.* 因為河東岸的工廠不直接與公路相連，所以處境就更糟。

wor·ship[1] /ˈwɝʃəp; ˈwɜːʃɪp/ *v* **worshipped, worshipping** also 又作 **worshiped, worshiping** *AmE*【美】**1** [I, T] to show respect and love for a god, especially by praying in a church, TEMPLE etc 敬奉（神）〔尤指在教堂、廟宇等禱告〕**2** [T] to admire and love someone very much 景仰；十分喜愛：*She absolutely worships those children.* 她十分喜愛那些孩子。**3 worship the ground sb walks on** to admire or love someone so much that you cannot see their faults 拜倒在某人腳下〔以致看不到他的缺點〕—**worshipper** *n* [C] *She was a regular worshipper at the Parish Church.* 她經常在教區的教堂做禮拜。

worship[2] *n* [U] **1** a strong feeling of respect and love for a god〔對神的〕崇敬；崇拜：*They bowed their heads in worship.* 他們低下頭以示崇敬。**2** the activity of praying in a church, TEMPLE etc in order to show respect and love for a god〔在教堂、廟宇等祈禱以示對神的〕崇拜；敬仰：**act of worship** (=religious service) 敬神儀式；禮拜｜**house/place of worship** (=a church, temple etc)〔教堂、廟宇等〕崇拜的場所 **3** a strong feeling of love or admiration for someone or something, especially so that you cannot see their faults〔對某人或物的〕強烈崇拜〔尤指看不見其錯誤〕；仰慕 —see also 另見 HERO WORSHIP **4 Your/His Worship** *BrE formal* used to address or talk about a public official such as a MAYOR or MAGISTRATE【英，正式】閣下〔對市長或地方法官等公務人員的稱呼〕

wor·ship·ful /ˈwɝʃəpfʊl; ˈwɜːʃɪpfəl/ *adj formal* showing respect or admiration for someone or something【正式】尊敬的；敬愛的

worst[1] /wɝst; wɜːst/ *adj* [the superlative of *bad* bad 的最高級] **1** [only before noun 僅用於名詞前] worse than anything else of the same kind or worse than at any time before〔同類中或與以前比較〕最壞的；最差的；最糟的：*Ken is easily the worst player in the team.* 肯恩無疑是隊裡最差的運動員。｜*What's the worst thing that could happen?* 最糟會發生甚麼事？｜**by far the worst** *This is by far the worst book she's written.* 這無疑是她寫的書中最差的一本。**2 be your own worst enemy** to continue to behave in a stupid or thoughtless way that harms you or stops you from becoming successful 自討苦吃；自己害自己 **3 come off worst** to lose a fight or argument〔在打架或爭論中〕被擊敗

worst[2] *n* **1 the worst** the person, thing, situation, state, part etc that is worse than all others of the same kind or worse than at any time before〔同類中或與以前比較〕最壞的人[事，形勢，國家，部分等]：*None of them can play well, but Jane is the worst.* 他們中沒有一個人打得好，然而簡打得最差。｜**the worst of it** (=the worst part of something) …中最糟的 *I think we've done the worst of it.* 我覺得我們做得最不像樣。｜*The worst of it is, I can't let her know what's happening.* 最糟糕的是，我不能讓她知道發生了甚麼事。｜**get/have the worst of it** *spoken* (=lose a fight or argument)【口】〔在打架或爭論中〕遭到失敗｜**expect/fear the worst** (=expect the situation to have the worst possible result) 作最壞打算 *England play Brazil next week and I fear the worst.* 下星期英格蘭隊對巴西隊，我已作了最壞打算。｜**at his/its etc worst** (=as bad as he or it can be) 在其最糟糕的時候 *You saw the garden at its worst, I'm afraid.* 恐怕你看到了花園最蕭條的情景。**2 at (the) worst** if things are as bad as they can be 在最壞的情況下：*Choosing the right software can be time-consuming at best and confusing or frustrating at worst.* 挑選合適的軟件起碼耗費時間，最糟糕的情況是使人感到混亂和沮喪。**3 sb/sth can do their worst** used to say that you are not worried by the power of someone or something to harm you 某人/某物有甚麼手段儘管使出來〔用於表示不擔心某人或物的力量對自己造成傷害〕：*All the wheat has been harvested, so the storm can do its worst.* 小麥都已收割完畢，暴風雨愛怎麼樣就怎麼樣吧。**4 if the worst comes to the worst** if the situation develops in the worst possible way 如果最壞的事情發生：*If the worst comes to the worst, we'll have to sell the car.* 如果遇上最壞的情況，我們只得把汽車賣掉。

worst[3] *adv* [the superlative of *badly* badly 的最高級] most badly 最壞地；最糟地；最差地：*Aid is being sent to the worst affected areas.* 援助物資正在送往受影響最嚴重的地區。｜*the worst-dressed man in the office* 辦公室裡衣着最差的男人

worst[4] *v* [T usually passive 一般用被動態] *old-fashioned* to defeat someone in a fight, competition, or argument【過時】〔打架、比賽或爭論中〕打敗；勝過〔某人〕

wor·sted /ˈwʊstɪd; ˈwʊstʒd/ *n* [U] a type of cloth made from wool 毛料

worth[1] /wɝθ; wɜːθ/ *prep* **1 be worth** to have a value in money 值…錢：*How much is the ring worth?* 這個戒指值多少錢？｜**be worth £10/ $500 etc** *The picture is worth about two thousand pounds.* 這幅畫約值兩千英鎊。｜**be worth a lot** *informal* (=be worth a lot of money)【非正式】值許多錢｜**be worth nothing/not be worth anything** *I don't think my stereo is worth anything* 我覺得我的立體聲唱機不值甚麼錢。｜**be worth a fortune** *informal* (=be extremely valuable)【非正式】非常有價值 *Now they've found oil the land must be worth a fortune.* 他們既然發現了石油，土地肯定是價值連城。**2 be worth millions/a fortune** *informal* to be extremely rich【非正式】極富有/極有錢：*The man who founded CNN must be worth a fortune.* 創辦美國有線新聞網的那個人肯定極有錢。**3 be worth doing/reading/finding etc** to be something that will be useful and helpful if you do it or read it etc 值得做/閱讀/尋找等：*a film worth seeing* 值得看的電影｜*It may be worth putting an advertisement in the local paper.* 也許值得在地方報紙上登廣告。｜**be worth it** *I didn't write to Louise, because I didn't think it was worth it.* 我沒有給路易斯寫信，因為我覺得沒有必要。**4 it's worth doing sth** used to say that someone should give the time or money needed to do something, because they will gain something useful 值得做某事：*It's worth taking your time when you visit the cathedral.* 值得花充分時間參觀這座大教堂。｜**it's worth the time/effort** *It's worth all the hard work you put in when you see so many happy children.* 你在看到那麼多幸福的孩子時，你會覺得那麼辛勞是值得的。｜**it's worth it** *Have a medical every year, it's worth it.* 一年做一次體格檢查，是上算的。｜**it's not worth it** *Don't get angry, it's not worth it.* 別生氣了，不值得。｜**it's well worth doing sth/it** *It's well worth getting there an hour early, if you want a good seat.* 你如果想佔一個好座位，很值得提前一個小時到那兒。**5 it's worth your/sb's while** *spoken* used to say that someone should give the time or money needed to do something, because they will gain something useful【口】值得某人花時間[錢]一幹：**it's worth your/sb's while to do sth** *It would be worth your while to talk to the editor.* 與那位編輯交談會獲益匪淺。｜*I don't sell French books, it's not worth my while.* (=I would not make any money) 我不賣法文書，划不來。**6 make it worth sb's while** *spoken* to offer someone money if they agree to do something for you, especially something dishonest【口】酬謝某人〔尤因他為你幹了不誠實的事〕，給某人報酬：*Look, if you forget about the whole thing I'll make it worth your while.* 瞧，要是你把所有事全忘了，我會酬謝你的。**7 what's it worth?** *spoken humorous* used to ask someone how they will reward you if you do something for them【口，幽默】會有甚麼好處？〔用於替別人做事時，問對方會怎樣酬謝自己〕**8 for what it's worth** *spoken* used to say that you are not sure of the value or usefulness of what you are saying【口】不管價值如何〔用於表示自己的見解不一定對〕；不管有沒有用：*My suggestion – for what it's worth – is that we buy a bigger car.* 我的意見不一定對，但我建議我們買一輛大點的汽車。**9 for all you are/he is etc worth** with as much effort as possible 竭盡全力：*Tom kept pulling away at the rope for all he was worth.* 湯姆

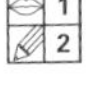

W

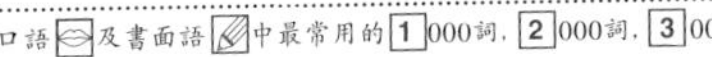

不斷地拚命扯繩子。**10 worth his/her salt** doing their job well or deserving respect 勝任的; 應受尊敬的: *No translator worth his salt would rely on a bilingual dictionary.* 沒有哪一位稱職的翻譯只靠一本雙語辭典。**11 worth its/his/her weight in gold** very useful or valuable 非常有用[有價值]的

USAGE NOTE 用法說明: WORTH
WORD CHOICE 詞語辨析: **worth, value**
Worth is common only after the verb **to be** and after words for amounts of something. worth 通常只用於 to be 及數量詞之後, as in 如: *$100 worth of damage* 損失價值 100 美元 | *a week's worth of newspapers* 一個星期的報紙。As a noun it means the same as **value** but is a little old-fashioned and literary 作名詞用時, worth 與 value 意思相同, 但略顯過時及文氣: *the value of life* (NOT 不用 the worth) 生命的價值。In an old story you might read 在舊故事中你可以讀到: *a pearl of great worth* 一顆極有價值的珍珠
GRAMMAR 語法
be worth is often followed by the *-ing* form of a verb. be worth 後常跟動詞的 -ing 形式: *Is it worth running such a risk?* (NOT 不用 *...worth to run...*)冒這險值得嗎? | *Niagara Falls is worth seeing* (NOT 不用 *...to be seen*). 尼亞加拉大瀑布值得一看。
be worth while may also be followed by the *-ing* form of a verb, or the infinitive. be worth while 也可以後接動詞的 -ing 形式及不定式: *It'll be well worth while you coming/for you to come* (NOT 不用 *...worth while you come*). 你來是很值得的。

3 **worth²** *n* **1** [U] value and importance, or value in money 價值; 用處: *Eliot's poems are of more lasting worth than the plays.* 艾略特的詩比他的劇本更有持久的價值。| *The balance sheet will not show the current worth of the company.* 資產負債表說明不了公司的當前資產價值。| **ten pounds'/$500 etc worth of sth** (=an amount of something worth ten pounds or $500) 值十英鎊/500美元的東西 *Dick cashed about a thousand pounds' worth of travellers cheques.* 迪克把約一千英鎊的旅行支票兌換成了現金。| *$4,000 worth of camera equipment* 價值4,000 美元的照相器材 **2 ten minutes'/a week's etc worth of sth** something that takes ten minutes or a week to happen, do, or use 可維持[使用]十分鐘/一星期的某物; 需要十分鐘/一星期等來完成的某物: *a quarter of an hour's worth of music* 持續十五分鐘的音樂 | *There's about a week's worth of work left.* 還剩下約一個星期的工作。

worth·less /ˈwɝθlɪs; ˈwɜːθləs/ *adj* **1** having no value, importance, or use 無價值的; 沒用處的: *a completely worthless exercise* 徒勞無功 **2** a worthless person has no good qualities or useful skills〔人〕一無是處的; 不中用的 —**worthlessly** *adv* —**worthlessness** *n* [U]

3 **worth·while** /ˌwɝθˈhwaɪl; ˌwɜːθˈwaɪl◂/ *adj* something worthwhile deserves the time, effort, or money you give to it 值得花時間[努力; 金錢]的: *I'd rather the money went to a worthwhile cause.* 我寧願把錢花在有價值的事情上。

wor·thy¹ /ˈwɝðɪ; ˈwɜːði/ *adj* **1** a worthy person, plan etc deserves respect or admiration because they have good qualities〔人因品行好而〕值得尊敬的; 值得讚賞的: *a worthy opponent* 值得欽佩的對手 **2 be worthy of** to deserve to be thought about or treated in a particular way 值得考慮的; 應用特殊方式對待的: [+of] *The plan is only worthy of our contempt.* 這計劃一文不值。**3** having many good qualities but not very interesting or exciting 品質優良但乏味的

worthy² *n* [C] *formal* someone who is important and should be respected【正式】知名人士, 傑出人物: *Victorian worthies such as Ruskin* 維多利亞時代的重要人物, 如拉斯金

wot¹ /wɑt; wɒt/ *BrE* an informal spelling of WHAT【英】what 的非正式拼法

wot² *v* [I] *old use* to know【舊】知道; 了解

wotch·a /ˈwɑtʃə; ˈwɒtʃə/ *interjection BrE slang* hello【英俚】喂, 你好

would /wud; wʊd/ *v* [modal verb 情態動詞] **1** used instead of 'will' to describe what someone has said, asked etc 將, 將會〔代替will, 轉述他人已說或問的事〕: *They said they would meet us at 10:30 at the station.* 他們說他們會在 10 點 30 分在車站接我們。**2** used instead of 'will' with a past tense verb or to show what is likely or possible 將會〔用於動詞過去式中代替 will 或表示可能〕: *What would you do if you won a million pounds?* 如果你贏了一百萬英鎊, 你會做甚麼呢? | *He said there had been a serious accident, but wouldn't give any details.* 他說曾經發生一宗嚴重的事故, 但不肯透露細節。**3** used to describe what someone used to do a lot or what used to happen a lot 老是, 總是〔用於表示經常做或發生的事〕: *When we worked in the same office, we would often have coffee together.* 我們過去在同一個辦公室工作的時候, 經常一起喝咖啡。**4** used to show disapproval when talking about someone's annoying habits or behaviour 會〔談論別人的討厭的習慣或行為時, 表示不同意〕: *You would go and spoil it, wouldn't you!* 你這樣下去會把它弄壞的, 不是嗎! **5 would rather** used to say that you would prefer to do or have one thing rather than another thing 寧願, 寧可: *Which would you rather do, go to the cinema or go for a meal?* 你寧願去看電影還是去吃飯? **6 would you...? a)** used to express a polite request 請…好嗎?〔表示客氣的請求〕: *Would you shut the window please?* 請把窗戶關上, 好嗎? **b)** used to express a polite offer or invitation …好嗎?〔表示客氣的提議或邀請〕: *Would you like to have a meal with us tomorrow evening?* 明晚你和我們一起吃飯好嗎? **7 I would...** *spoken* used to tell someone what you think they should do in a particular situation【口】我會〔用於告訴他人在某情況下應如何做〕: *I would ring Joe and explain that you can't see him tomorrow.* 要是我就會給喬打電話, 解釋明天不能去看他的理由。**8** used before verbs that express what you think, feel, or suppose, to make your opinion or feeling less definite〔用在表示意見、感受或推測的動詞前, 使意思婉轉〕: *I would imagine that the kids will stay with their grandparents.* 我猜想這些小孩子會與他們的祖父母在一起。**9 would that...** *literary* used to express a strong wish or desire【文】但願…; 要是…多好〔表示強烈的願望〕: *Would that we had seen her before she died.* 要是在她去世之前, 我們能見到她一面該有多好。

would-be /ˈ· ·/ *adj* **would-be actor/murderer etc** someone who hopes to have a particular job or intends to do a particular thing 想當演員的人/謀殺未遂的人

would·n't /ˈwudn̩t; ˈwʊdnt/ the short form of 縮略式= would not

wouldst /wudst; wʊdst/ *old use* the second person singular of 'would'【舊】would的第二人稱單數

would've /ˈwudəv; ˈwʊdəv/ the short form of 縮略式= would have

wound¹ /waund; waʊnd/ the past tense and past participle of WIND²

wound² /wund; wuːnd/ *n* [C] **1** an injury, especially a cut or hole made in your skin by a weapon such as a knife or a bullet 傷, 傷口, 創傷〔尤指刀傷、槍傷等〕: *A nurse cleaned and bandaged the wound.* 護士把傷口清洗包紮好。| *gunshot wounds* 槍傷 | **flesh wound** (=slight injury caused by a bullet touching your skin)〔子彈擦過而造成的〕輕傷, 皮肉之傷 **2** a feeling of emotional or mental pain that you get when someone says or does something unpleasant to you〔感情、心靈上的〕傷痛, 傷害: *the mental wounds caused by parental abuse* 父母虐待而引致的心靈傷害 | *a wound to my pride* 對我自尊心的傷害 **3 open old wounds** to remind someone of unpleasant things that happened in the past 揭舊瘡疤 — see also 另見 **lick your wounds** (LICK¹ (6)), **rub salt into the wounds** (RUB¹ (7))

wound³ *v* [T] **1** to injure someone, especially by making a cut or hole in their skin using a knife, gun etc〔尤指用刀或槍等〕傷害〔某人〕: *Gunmen killed two people and wounded six others in an attack today.* 在今天的襲擊中, 槍手打死了二人打傷了六人。**2** to make someone feel unhappy or upset 使〔某人〕不高興[煩惱]: *a wounding remark* 傷人的話語

wound·ed /ˋwundɪd; ˈwuːndɪ̠d/ *adj* **1** injured by a weapon such as a gun or knife 受〔刀、槍等〕傷害的, 負傷的: *a wounded soldier* 受傷的士兵 | **mortally wounded** (=injured so badly that you will die) 受致命傷害的 **2** very upset because of something that someone has said or done 受〔言語或行為〕傷害的; 受損害的: *wounded pride* 受到傷害的自尊心 **3 the wounded** people who have been injured, especially in a war〔尤指戰爭中的〕受傷者

wound up /ˋwaund ˌʌp; ˌwaʊnd ˈʌp/ *adj* [not before noun 不用於名詞前] anxious, worried, or excited 緊張[擔憂; 激動]的: *I was too wound up to sleep.* 我焦慮不安得無法入睡。

wove /wov; wəʊv/ the past tense of WEAVE¹

wov·en /ˋwovən; ˈwəʊvən/ the past participle of WEAVE¹

wow¹ /waʊ; waʊ/ *interjection informal* used when you think something is impressive or surprising【非正式】呀!哇!〔表示讚嘆或驚奇〕: *"Wow! Look at that car!"* "哇!看那輛車呀!"

wow² *v* [T] *informal* to make people admire you very much【非正式】使〔人們〕稱讚: *Her performance wowed the critics.* 她的表演得到評論家的讚賞。

wow³ *n* [singular] *informal* a great success【非正式】極大的成功

wow·ser, wowzer /ˋwauzɚ; ˈwaʊzə/ *n* [C] *AusE, NZE informal* someone who seems to stop you from having fun【澳, 新西蘭, 非正式】讓人掃興的人

WP /ˌdʌblju ˋpi; ˌdʌbəljuː ˈpiː/ the abbreviation of 縮寫= WORD PROCESSOR

WPC /ˌdʌblju pi ˋsi; ˌdʌbəljuː piː ˈsiː◂/ *n* [C] *BrE* Woman Police Constable; a female police officer【英】女警察

wpm /ˌdʌblju pi ˋɛm; ˌdʌbəljuː piː ˈem/ words per minute 每分鐘字數

wrack /ræk; ræk/ *n* [U] **1** a type of SEAWEED 海藻〔的一種〕**2** another spelling of RACK² rack²的另一種拼法

wraith /reθ; reɪθ/ *n* [C] *literary* a GHOST¹ (1) especially of someone who has just died【文】〔尤指剛去世者的〕陰魂, 幽靈; 新鬼

wran·gle¹ /ˋræŋgl; ˈræŋgəl/ *n* [C] a long and complicated argument〔長時間而複雜的〕爭辯: *a damaging legal wrangle* 具損害性的法律糾紛 | *a bitter wrangle over imports* 在進口問題上的激烈爭論

wrangle² *v* **1** [I] to argue with someone angrily for a long time〔長時間地〕吵架, 爭論 **2** [T] *AmE informal* to gather together cows or horses from a large area【美, 非正式】放牧, 看管〔牛、馬等〕

wran·gler /ˋræŋglɚ; ˈræŋglə/ *n* [C] *AmE informal* a COWBOY (1)【美, 非正式】牧人, 牛仔

3 **wrap¹** /ræp; ræp/ *v* [T] **1** to wind or fold cloth, paper etc around something〔用布、紙等〕包, 裹〔某物〕: *a present wrapped in shiny paper* 用閃光紙包着的一份禮物 | **wrap sth around sth/sb** *Ella wrapped a thick coat around her shoulders.* 艾拉在肩上圍了一件厚外套。| **wrap sth/sb in sth** *Wrap the cake in tinfoil.* 用錫紙把蛋糕包起來。**2** if you wrap your arms, legs, fingers etc around something, you use them to hold it 用〔手臂、腳、手指等〕包住〔某物〕: *Chloe sat with her arms wrapped round her knees.* 克洛伊坐下來用雙臂摟住膝蓋。—see also 另見 **wrap sb in cotton wool** (COTTON WOOL (2))

wrap 包, 裹

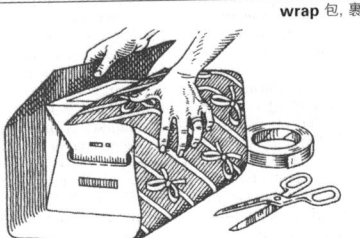

She wrapped the box in patterned paper.
她用有圖案的紙把盒子包起來。

wrap up *phr v* **1** [T **wrap** sth ↔ **up**] to completely cover something by folding paper, cloth etc around it〔用紙、布等〕包, 裹〔某物〕: *I haven't even wrapped my presents up yet!* 我甚至還沒有把禮物包好呢! **2** [I] to put on warm clothes 穿得暖和: **wrap up warm/well** *Make sure you wrap up warm – it's freezing outside.* 你務必要穿暖和點 — 外面冷極了。**3** [T **wrap** sth ↔ **up**] to finish or complete a job, meeting etc 完成; 結束〔工作、會議等〕: *The police will soon be wrapping up the investigation.* 警方將很快結束調查。**4 be wrapped up in your children/work etc** to give so much of your attention to your children, your work etc that you do not have time for anything else 全部精力放在小孩身上/工作等中 —see also 另見 **twist/ wrap sb around your little finger** (FINGER¹ (13))

wrap² *n* **1** [C] a piece of thick cloth that you wear around your shoulders〔厚〕披肩, 圍巾 **2** [U] *AmE* plastic used to cover food【美】〔食物的〕保鮮塑料薄膜 **3 keep sth under wraps** to keep something secret 保密; 隱藏 **4** [singular] the end of a day's filming〔一天的拍攝〕完成, 停機: *OK everybody, it's a wrap!* 好了, 各位, 今天就拍到這兒!

wrap-a·round /ˈ· ·ˌ·/ *adj* a wrap-around skirt is wound around your body with a double layer of cloth at the front〔裙子〕裹身的〔前面的部分交疊一起〕

wrap·per /ˋræpɚ; ˈræpə/ *n* [C] the piece of paper or plastic that covers something when it is sold〔貨物的〕包裝紙[塑料]: *a candy wrapper* 糖果包裝紙

wrap·ping /ˋræpɪŋ; ˈræpɪŋ/ also 又作 **wrappings** *n* [C, U] cloth, paper, or plastic that is wrapped around something to protect it〔起保護作用的〕包裝布; 包裝紙; 包裝塑料: *Torn Christmas wrapping littered the floor.* 撕破了的聖誕禮物包裝紙扔得滿地都是。

wrapping pa·per /ˈ·· ˌ··/ *n* [U] coloured paper that you use for wrapping presents〔禮物的〕彩色包裝紙

wrap-up /ˈ· ·/ *n* [C] *AmE informal* a short report at the end of something, giving the main points again【美, 非正式】結論; 總結說明: *And finally here's a wrap-up of the six o'clock news.* 最後是六點新聞的摘要。

wrath /ræθ; rɒθ/ *n* [U] *formal* extreme anger【正式】憤怒, 狂怒: *fearing the wrath of God* 害怕上帝的震怒 — **wrathful** *adj* —**wrathfully** *adv*

wreak /rik; riːk/ *v past tense and past participle* **wreaked** also 又作 **wrought** /rɔt; rɔːt/ **wreak havoc/revenge** to cause a lot of damage, problems, and suffering 造成巨大破壞/施行報復: *A major power failure wreaked havoc in New York last night.* 昨晚紐約大停電引起了一片混亂。

wreath /riθ; riːθ/ *n* [C] **1** a circle made from leaves or flowers that you put on a grave or hang on the door at Christmas〔放在墓前或聖誕期間掛在門上的〕花圈; 花環 **2** a circle made from leaves that was given to someone in past times as an honour 花冠〔舊時榮譽的象徵〕: *a laurel wreath* 桂冠

wreathe /rið; riːð/ *v literary*【文】**1 be wreathed in sth** to be surrounded by or covered in something 被…環繞[遮蓋]: *The mountains were wreathed in mist.* 羣山籠罩在霧中。**2 wreathed in smiles** looking very happy 笑容滿面

wreck¹ /rɛk; rek/ *v* [T] **1** to completely spoil or destroy something such as a plan, relationship, or opportunity

破壞，糟蹋〔計劃、關係、機遇等〕：*I just hope the weather doesn't wreck our plans!* 我真希望天氣不要破壞我們的計劃！**2** to damage something such as a building, vehicle etc so badly that it cannot be repaired 使〔建築、車輛等〕嚴重毀壞〔無法維修〕：*Hundreds of old buildings were wrecked by the earthquake.* 幾百棟舊建築在地震中遭到破壞。**3** [usually passive 一般用被動態] to destroy a ship, especially by hitting rocks in a storm〔尤指船隻在風暴中觸礁〕失事：*The ship was wrecked off the coast of Africa.* 那艘船在非洲海岸外失事了。

wreck² *n* [C] **1** a ship that has sunk or is so badly damaged that it cannot sail 沉船；失事船：*the wreck of an old Spanish galleon* 古代西班牙大帆船的殘骸 **2** something such as a car or plane that has been damaged very badly, especially in an accident〔尤指失事後汽車、飛機的〕殘骸：*a plane wreck off the coast* 海岸外的飛機殘骸 **3** [usually singular 一般用單數] *informal* someone who is very nervous, tired, or unhealthy【非正式】十分緊張[疲累；不健康]的人：*Look at me – I'm a complete wreck!* 看看我——我元氣大傷了！| **nervous wreck** *Dean hated flying, and by the time we reached the airport he was a nervous wreck.* 迪安討厭坐飛機，在我們到達機場時，他的神經快要崩潰了。**4** *AmE* an accident involving cars or other vehicles【美】〔涉及多輛車的〕交通事故：*The wreck caused a traffic jam three miles long.* 撞車事故使交通堵塞達三英里長。**5** *informal* something, especially a car, that is in a very bad condition【非正式】殘破的東西〔尤指汽車〕：*Jo drives an old wreck of a Ford.* 喬開着一輛殘破不堪的福特汽車。

wreck·age /ˈrɛkɪdʒ; ˈrekɪdʒ/ *n* [singular, U] **1** the parts of something such as a plane, ship, or building that are left after it has been destroyed in an accident〔飛機、船、建築物被毀後的〕殘骸：*sifting through the wreckage for survivors* 仔細地在殘骸中尋找倖存者 **2** the destruction of someone's relationships, hopes, plans etc〔關係、希望、計劃等的〕破壞，毀壞

wrecked /rɛkt; rekt/ *adj* [not before noun 不用於名詞前] *informal*【非正式】**1** *BrE* very drunk【英】喝醉的，醉醺醺的 **2** extremely tired 疲憊不堪的

wreck·er /ˈrɛkɚ; ˈrekə/ *n* [C] **1** someone who destroys a relationship, plan, opportunity etc〔關係、計劃、機遇等的〕破壞者：*a home wrecker* 破壞家庭的人 **2** *AmE* a vehicle used to move damaged cars or other vehicles【美】〔把損毀了的汽車拖走的〕拖吊車，救險車 **3** someone in past times who deliberately made ships hit rocks so that they could steal goods from them〔昔日〕毀船打劫者 **4** someone whose job is to save goods from ships that have been damaged〔工作〕打撈失事船貨物的人

wren /rɛn; ren/ *n* [C] a very small brown bird 鷦鷯〔一種褐色小鳥〕

wrench¹ /rɛntʃ; rentʃ/ *v* **1** [T always+adv/prep] to twist and pull something from its position using force 猛扭〔某物〕，猛擰，猛拉：**wrench sth away/free/off etc** *I managed to wrench the knife away from him.* 我設法從他那裡把刀奪過來。**2** [T always+adv/prep] to use your strength to pull yourself away from someone who is holding you 掙脫〔某人〕：**wrench yourself away/free etc** *Tim struggled to wrench himself free from her grasp.* 蒂姆奮力掙脫她的摟抱。**3** [T] to twist a joint in your body suddenly and painfully 扭傷〔關節〕：*I wrenched my knee playing soccer.* 踢足球時，我扭傷了膝蓋。

wrench² *n* **1** [singular] a strong feeling of sadness that you get when you leave a person or place that you love〔離別心愛的人或地方時的〕悲痛；離愁別緒：*Leaving Arizona for New York had been a terrible wrench.* 離開亞利桑那州到紐約痛苦不已。**2** [C usually singular 一般用單數] a twisting movement that pulls something violently 猛擰，猛扭，猛拉：*With one almighty wrench, the door opened.* 用力一拉，門開了。**3** [C] **a)** *AmE* a metal tool with a round end that fits over and turns nuts (NUT¹ (2))【美】扳手，扳鉗；SPANNER *BrE*【英】**b)** *especially AmE* also 又作 **monkey wrench** a tool that you can use to hold or turn nuts (NUT¹ (2) that are different sizes【尤美】活動扳手；adjustable spanner *BrE*【英】—see picture at 參見 TOOL¹ 圖

wrest /rɛst; rest/ *v* [T always+adv/prep] *formal*【正式】**1** to take power or influence away from someone, especially when this is difficult 費力取走〔某人或權力或影響〕**2** to pull something away from someone violently 猛拉，搶奪：*I wrested the photograph from his grasp.* 我從他緊握着的手中把照片奪了過來。

wres·tle /ˈrɛsl; ˈresəl/ *v* **1** [I,T] to fight someone by holding onto them and pulling or pushing them 與〔某人〕摔跤；扭打：[+with] *The kids were wrestling with each other in the yard.* 孩子們在院子裡扭打成一團。| **wrestle sb to the ground** (=make someone fall down by holding onto them and pushing them) 把某人摔倒在地上 **2** [I,T] to have difficulty controlling or holding something that is very large, heavy, or difficult to use 奮力控制[握住]〔很大、很重或很難使用的東西〕：[+with] Daisy *was wrestling with one of the larger boxes.* 黛西正努力搬動其中一個大箱子。**3** [I] to try to deal with or find a solution to a difficult problem 努力解決；絞盡腦汁：[+with] *I spent two hours wrestling with my maths homework.* 我花了兩個小時絞盡腦汁地做數學作業。

wres·tler /ˈrɛslɚ; ˈreslə/ *n* [C] someone who wrestles as a sport 摔跤運動員，摔跤手

wres·tling /ˈrɛslɪŋ; ˈreslɪŋ/ *n* [U] a sport in which two people fight by holding onto each other and trying to make each other fall to the ground 摔跤（運動）

wretch /rɛtʃ; retʃ/ *n* [C] **1** someone that you feel sorry for 可憐的人：*The poor wretch had really suffered.* 那個可憐蟲真吃足了苦頭。**2** *often humorous* someone you are annoyed with【常幽默】淘氣鬼；傢伙：*You wretch! You've soaked my dress!* 你這傢伙！把我的裙子弄得濕透了！**3** *literary* an evil person【文】惡棍，壞蛋

wretch·ed /ˈrɛtʃɪd; ˈretʃɨd/ *adj* **1** very unhappy or ill 極不愉快的；極不幸的：*I lay in bed feeling thoroughly wretched.* 我躺在牀上，心情壞透了。**2** [only before noun 僅用於名詞前] making you feel annoyed or angry 令人討厭的；使人憤怒的：*What does the wretched woman want this time?* 這討厭的女人，這次想要甚麼？**3** *literary* extremely bad or of very poor quality【文】惡劣的；質量低劣的：*wretched living conditions* 惡劣的生活條件 —**wretchedly** *adv* —**wretchedness** *n* [U]

wrig·gle¹ /ˈrɪgl; ˈrɪgəl/ *v* **1** [I] to twist from side to side with small quick movements 扭動；蠕動：*Stop wriggling and let me put your T-shirt on.* 別扭來扭去的，讓我把T恤給你穿上。| [+under/through/into] *The hole was just deep enough for the dog to wriggle under the fence.* 籬笆下面的洞剛夠深，狗扭動着身子就鑽了出去。**2** [T] to make a part of your body move in this way 使〔身體某一部分〕扭動 —**wriggly** *adj*

wriggle out of sth *phr v* [T] to avoid doing something by using clever excuses 用計逃脫〔做某事〕；擺脫

wriggle² *n* [C] a wriggling movement 扭動；蠕動

-wright /raɪt; raɪt/ *suffix* [in nouns 構成名詞] a maker of things of a particular kind〔某物的〕製作者：*wheelwright* (=someone who makes wheels) 車輪製造工匠 | *a playwright* (=someone who writes plays) 劇作家

wring /rɪŋ; rɪŋ/ *v past tense and past participle* **wrung** /rʌŋ; rʌŋ/ [T] **1** [always+adv/prep] to succeed in getting money, information, an agreement etc from someone, but only after a lot of effort〔經過很大努力從某人處〕逼取〔錢財、信息、協議等〕：**wring sth from sb/out of sb** *We finally succeeded in wringing a confession out of him.* 我們大費周折，終於使他招供。**2** also 又作 **wring out** to tightly twist a wet cloth or wet clothes in order to force out the water 把〔濕布或濕衣服〕擰乾；絞出〔水〕**3 wring your hands** to rub and twist your hands together because you are worried and upset〔因焦慮不安而〕絞緊雙手 **4 wring sth's neck** to kill something such as a chicken by twisting its neck 擰脖子以殺死某動物〈如小雞〉**5 I'll wring sb's neck** *spoken* used when someone has made you angry【口】〔生氣時說〕我要擰斷某人的脖子: *If you say that again I'll wring your neck!* 如果你再那樣說, 我會把你的脖子擰斷! **6 wringing wet** extremely wet 濕得能擰出水來的; 濕淋淋的 **7 wring sb's hand** to shake hands very firmly with someone 用力地握某人的手 **8 wring your heart/soul** *literary* to make you feel very sorry for someone【文】〔為某人〕非常傷心

wring·er /ˈrɪŋɚ; ˈrɪŋə/ *n* [C] **1** a machine with two rollers (ROLLER (1)) that press the water from washed clothes when you turn a handle 滾筒式衣服絞乾機 **2 go through the wringer** *AmE informal* to have an upsetting experience【美, 非正式】歷經千辛萬苦: *She's really been through the wringer since her husband died.* 丈夫去世之後, 她受盡煎熬。

wrin·kle¹ /ˈrɪŋkḷ; ˈrɪŋkəl/ *n* [C] **1** a line on your face or skin that you get when you are old〔因年老而在臉、皮膚上出現的〕皺紋: *wrinkles around the eyes* 眼角的魚尾紋 **2** a small untidy fold in a piece of clothing or paper〔布、紙上的〕皺褶 **3 iron out the wrinkles** to solve the small problems in something 解決小問題 —**wrinkly** *adj*

wrinkle² *v* **1** [I,T] if you wrinkle a piece of clothing or if it wrinkles, it gets small untidy folds in it (使) 起皺紋; (使) 皺起: *The trouble with linen is that it wrinkles so easily.* 亞麻布的毛病是太容易起褶。**2 wrinkle your nose/eyes/brow etc** to move part of your face so that there are wrinkles on or around it 皺起鼻子/眼睛/眉毛

wrin·kled /ˈrɪŋkḷd; ˈrɪŋkəld/ *adj* skin, cloth, or paper that is wrinkled has lines or small untidy folds in it〔皮膚、布、紙〕有皺紋的; 有皺褶的

wrin·kly /ˈrɪŋklɪ; ˈrɪŋkli/ *n plural* **wrinklies** [C] *BrE informal* an impolite expression meaning someone who is old【英, 非正式】老東西, 老傢伙〔不禮貌的表述〕

3 **wrist** /rɪst; rɪst/ *n* [C] the joint between your hand and the lower part of your arm 腕 (關節) —see picture at 參見 BODY 圖

wrist·band /ˈrɪstˌbænd; ˈrɪstbænd/ *n* [C] **1** a band worn especially by tennis players around their wrists to keep their hands dry〔尤指網球員戴的保持雙手乾爽的〕腕套 **2** a band worn around your wrist, for example in a hospital 腕帶〔例如在醫院裡用〕

wrist·watch /ˈrɪstˌwɑtʃ; ˈrɪstwɒtʃ/ *n* [C] a watch that you wear on your wrist 手錶

writ¹ /rɪt; rɪt/ *n* [C] a document from a court that orders someone to do or not to do something〔法院的〕令狀; 書面命令 —see also 另見 HOLY WRIT

writ² *adj* **writ large** *literary*【文】**a)** made clearer and easier to notice 顯而易見 **b)** in a clearer and stronger form 更明顯的; 更突出的: *The new evangelism is really old time religion writ large.* 新的福音派教義無非是舊教義的闡發。

write /raɪt; raɪt/ *v past tense* **wrote** /rot; rəʊt/ *past participle* **written** /ˈrɪtn̩; ˈrɪtn/

1 ►BOOK/ARTICLE ETC 書/文章等◄ a) [I,T] to produce a new book, poem song etc 寫〔新書、詩歌等〕; 寫作: *I can't come with you – I have an essay to write.* 我不能跟你一起去 — 我要寫一篇論文。| *a concerto written by Mozart* 莫札特作的協奏曲 | **write about** (=describe something) 描述 *The children are writing about their summer holidays.* 孩子在描述他們暑假的見聞。| **well/badly written** *The article's very well written.* 這篇文章寫得棒極了。| **write a program** (=produce it on a computer) 編寫〔電腦〕程式 *We're writing a program for a new spellchecker.* 我們正在編寫一個新的拼寫檢查程式。**b)** [I] to be a writer of books, plays, articles etc 寫作〔書、劇本、文章等〕, 創作: *"What do you do?" "I write."* "你是做甚麼的?" "我是作家。" | **[+for]** *Shaw started to write for the stage.* 蕭開始寫劇本。| **[+on]** *She writes on gardening for 'The Daily Telegraph'.* 她給《每日電訊報》撰寫園藝方面的文章。

2 ►LETTER 信◄ [I,T] to write a letter to someone 寫(信): **[+to]** *Have you written to John yet?* 你給約翰寫信了嗎? | **write sb a letter** *I wrote her several letters, but she didn't reply.* 我給她寫了幾封信, 可是她沒有回覆。| **write sb** *AmE*【美】: *Steve wrote me about the wedding.* 史蒂夫寫信告訴我婚禮的情況。| **write that** *The Ewings wrote that they might be able to visit us in the spring.* 尤因夫婦寫信來說, 他們也許能在春季來看望我們。

3 ►WORDS 字◄ a) [I,T] to form letters or numbers with a pen or pencil〔用鋼筆、鉛筆〕書寫; 寫字: *Kerry could read and write when he was five.* 克里五歲時就能讀書寫字了。| *The price is written on the label.* 價格寫在標籤上。**b)** [I] if a pen or pencil writes, it works properly〔筆〕好寫, 能寫(字): *What use is a pen that won't write?* 不能寫字的筆有甚麼用?

4 ►CHEQUE/DOCUMENT ETC 支票/文件等◄ [T] also 又作 **write** sth ↔ **out** to write information on a cheque, form etc 填寫〔支票、表格等〕: *Wouldn't it be easier if I just wrote a cheque for the lot?* 如果全部款項我用一張支票支付, 不是較方便的嗎?

5 have sth written all over your face to show very clearly what you are feeling or thinking 臉上明顯表露出〔感受或思想〕: *He had guilt written all over his face.* 他一臉內疚。

6 nothing to write home about *informal* not particularly good or special【非正式】平平常常的; 沒甚麼了不起的: *The hotel was good, but the food was nothing to write home about.* 酒店不錯, 但食物就不怎麼樣了。

7 sb wrote the book on it *spoken* used to say that someone knows a lot about a subject【口】某人熟悉某方面的事: *Ask Harry about shark fishing, he wrote the book on it!* 問哈里去, 他精通釣鯊魚之道!

write away for sth *phr v* [T] *AmE* to write to a company for something that has been advertised【美】寫信索取〔已刊登廣告的東西〕; 函購: *Write away for your free kitchen catalog today.* 請今天就來信索取免費廚房用具目錄。

write back *phr v* [I] to answer someone's letter by sending them a letter 回信: *I sent them a card once, but they never wrote back.* 我給他們寄去一張賀卡, 但他們根本沒有回信。

write sth ↔ **down** *phr v* [T] to write information, ideas etc on a piece of paper in order to remember them〔在紙上〕記下〔信息、想法等〕, 寫下: *I wrote down the address in the back of my diary.* 我在日記背後寫下地址。

write in *phr v* **1** [I] to write to an organization asking them for information or giving an opinion 給〔機構〕寫信索取〔資料〕; 提供書面意見: *Hundreds of viewers have written in wanting to know the name of our signature tune.* 成百上千的觀眾寫信來想知道我們節目主題曲的曲名。**2** [T **write** sb/sth ↔ **in**] *AmE*【美】**a)** to add someone's name to your BALLOT PAPER in order to vote for them 在選票上加進〔某人的名字, 以投他一票〕—see also 另見 WRITE-IN

write sth **into** sth *phr v* [T] to include something such as a rule or condition in a document, agreement etc 把〔規則、條件等〕寫進〔文件、協議等〕: *I have to attend regular training sessions – it's written into my contract.* 我必須參加定期培訓 — 這已寫入合同中。

write off *phr v* **1** [T **write** sb/sth ↔ **off**] to decide that someone or something is useless, unimportant, or a failure 認為〔某人[某事]〕不行[不重要; 失敗]: **[+as]** *We've written the project off as a non-starter.* 我們已經認為該計劃無望成功。**2** [T **write** sth ↔ **off**] to officially say that someone does not have to pay a debt〔正式〕勾銷, 注銷〔某人債款〕: *As part of the deal, all their debts were written off.* 作為交易的一部分, 他們的所有債務一筆勾銷。**3** [I] to write to a company asking them to send you information on one of their products 向〔公司〕寫信索取〔產品資料〕: **[+for]** *Are you going to write off for that free poster?* 你會寫信索取那免費海報嗎? **4** [T **write** sth ↔ **off**] *BrE* to damage a vehicle so badly that it can never be used again【英】使〔車輛〕報廢; 毀掉 —see also 另見 WRITE-OFF

write sb/sth ↔ **out** *phr v* [T] **1** to write a list, report etc including all the necessary details 全部寫出〔清單、報告等〕: *Write out exactly what happened and give it to your solicitor.* 如實寫出發生了甚麼, 然後把它交給你的律師。**2** to write information on a cheque or a form 填寫〔支票、表格〕: *She calmly wrote out a check for $500 and handed it to Will.* 她鎮定地開出一張 500 美元的支票, 然後交給威爾。**3** to write something again in a better or more complete way 謄寫, 抄寫: *I'll write my essay out neatly and give it in tomorrow.* 我要把文章抄寫整齊, 明天交上去。**4** to remove one of the characters from a regular radio or television programme 取消〔電台或電視長期節目中的角色〕

write sth ↔ **up** *phr v* [T] **1** to write a report, article etc using notes that you made earlier〔根據事前的筆記〕重新整理〔為報告、文章等〕: *I have to write up my report before the meeting.* 我必須在會議前把報告整理一下。**2** to write your opinion about a new book, play, or product for a newspaper, magazine etc〔替報刊等〕寫文章評論〔新書、戲劇、產品〕—see also 另見 WRITE-UP

write-in /'· ·/ *n* [C] *AmE* a vote you give to someone by writing their name on your BALLOT PAPER【美】選舉人對非原定候選人所投的票

write-off /'· ·/ *n* [C] **1** *BrE* a vehicle that has been so badly damaged that it can never be used again【英】報廢的車: *The car was a complete write-off.* 那輛汽車徹底報廢了。—see also 另見 **write off** (4) (WRITE) **2** an official agreement that someone does not have to pay a debt〔某人債款的〕注銷, 勾銷

writ·er /ˈraɪtə; ˈraɪtə/ *n* [C] someone who writes books, stories etc, especially as a job〔尤指職業〕作家; 作者: a *science-fiction writer* 科幻小說作家 | **[+on]** a *well-known writer on astrology* 著名的占星術作者 | **[+of]** a *writer of children's stories* 兒童故事撰稿人

writer's block /,·· '·/ *n* [U] the problem that a writer sometimes has of not being able to think of new ideas 作家一時文思不暢

writer's cramp /,·· '·/ *n* [U] a feeling of stiffness in your hand that you get after writing for a long time〔書寫時間過長而引起的〕書寫痙攣

write-up /'· ·/ *n* [C] a written opinion about a new book, play, or product in a newspaper, magazine etc〔報刊上對新書、新劇或新產品的〕評論文章: *The play got a really good write-up in the press.* 這部戲劇大受新聞界的好評。

writhe /raɪð; raɪð/ *v* [I] **1** to twist your body from side to side violently, especially because you are suffering pain〔尤指因痛苦〕劇烈地扭動身體: **writhe in pain/agony** *He lay on the floor writhing in pain.* 他痛苦地在地上打滾。**2 writhe with anger/hate/shame etc** *literary* to feel very violent emotions of anger etc【文】感到極度憤怒／憎惡／羞恥等

2 3 **writ·ing** /ˈraɪtɪŋ; ˈraɪtɪŋ/ *n* [U] **1** words that have been written or printed〔書寫、印刷的〕文字: *What does the writing on the back say?* 背面的文字講些甚麼? **2 in writing** if you get something in writing, it is official proof of an agreement, promise etc〔協議、諾言等〕書面形式: **put sth in writing** *Could you put that in writing please?* 請你把它寫下來好嗎? **3** books, poems etc in general, especially those by a particular writer or about a particular subject〔尤指某作者或主題的〕著作; 作品: *Some of his most powerful writing is based on his childhood experiences.* 他有些最震懾人心的作品是根據兒時的經歷寫成的。**4** the activity of writing books, stories etc 寫作; 著書: *In 1991 she retired from politics and took up writing as a career.* 1991 年她退出政界, 開始寫作。**5** the particular way that someone writes with a pen or pencil; HANDWRITING 字跡, 筆跡: *Your writing is very neat.* 你的筆跡很整齊。**6 writings** *plural* the books, stories etc that a particular person writes〔某人的〕著作〔書, 小說等〕: *Darwin's scientific writings* 達爾文的科學著作 **7 the writing is on the wall** used to say that it seems very likely that something will not exist much longer or someone will fail 厄運臨頭的預兆已經顯露〔指某事物很可能即將消失或某人將失敗〕: *The writing is on the wall for the old manufacturing industries.* 舊式製造業分明已經日薄西山, 江河日下了。

writing desk /'·· ·/ *n* [C] a desk with special places for pens, paper etc 書桌, 寫字枱

writing pa·per /'·· ,··/ *n* [U] good quality paper that you use for writing letters〔優質〕信紙

writ·ten¹ /ˈrɪtn; ˈrɪtn/ the past participle of WRITE

written² *adj* [only before noun 僅用於名詞前] **1** recorded in writing 書面的: **written agreement/reply etc** *You'll get a written report of my conclusions within ten days.* 十天之內你會收到我的結論的書面報告。**2 written test/exam** a test etc in which you have to write the answers 筆試 **3 the written word** *formal* writing as a way of expressing ideas, emotions etc【正式】〔表達思想、感情等的〕文字

wrong¹ /rɔŋ; rɒŋ/ *adj*

1 ▶NOT CORRECT 不正確◀ saying, believing, or depending on something that is not correct 不正確的; 錯誤的: *Your calculations must be wrong.* 你肯定算錯了。| **be wrong to think/say** *I'm sorry; I was wrong to assume that you wanted to go.* 對不起, 我誤以為你想去。| **prove sb wrong** *I wish you'd stop trying to prove me wrong all the time.* 我希望你不要總是想證明是我的錯。

2 ▶NOT THE RIGHT ONE 不是正確的那個◀ not the one that you intended or the one that you should use 不對的, 弄錯了的: *The letter was delivered to the wrong address.* 信寄錯地址了。| *driving on the wrong side of the road* 在馬路上開車逆行

3 ▶TELEPHONE 電話◀ wrong number used when you have telephoned the wrong person by mistake 撥錯〔電話〕號碼: *There's no-one called Julia here – I think you must have the wrong number.* 這兒沒有叫朱莉亞的——我想你肯定撥錯號碼了。

4 ▶NOT MORAL 不道德◀ not morally right or acceptable 不道德的; 不能接受的: **it is wrong to do sth** *You must have known it was wrong to take the money.* 你肯定知道偷錢是不對的。| **it is wrong that** *It's wrong that people should have to sleep on the streets.* 有人要露宿街頭是無法接受的。—opposite 反義詞 RIGHT¹ (6)

5 ▶NOT SUITABLE 不適合◀ not suitable for a particular purpose, situation, or person〔對某目的、情況或人〕不適合的: *It's the wrong time of year to be planning a holiday.* 計劃一年中的這個時間去休假是不合適的。| **[+for]** *This is the wrong climate for growing grapes.* 這種氣候不適合生長葡萄。

6 be the wrong way round/around a) to be in the wrong order〔次序〕顛倒, 相反: *These two paragraphs are the wrong way round.* 這兩個段落順序倒了。**b)** to be pointing in the wrong direction 方向不對: *You've got your T-shirt on the wrong way around.* 你的 T 恤穿反了。

7 be in the wrong place at the wrong time *spoken* to get involved in trouble without intending to【口】在錯誤的時間來到錯誤的地方〔指無意中落入困境〕

8 get on the wrong side of sb to do something that gives someone a bad opinion of you, so that they do not like or respect you in the future〔做某事〕冒犯某人, 招惹某人討厭

9 get on the wrong side of the law to get into trouble with the police 與警方發生麻煩; 犯事

10 get off on the wrong foot to start a job, relationship etc badly by making a mistake that annoys people〔工作、關係等〕一開始就不順利〔因犯錯而使別人討厭〕

11 take sth the wrong way to be offended by a remark because you have understood it wrongly 誤解某句話〔因而感到不快〕

12 get the wrong end of the stick *informal* to understand a situation in completely the wrong way【非正式】完全誤解形勢
13 be on the wrong track/tack to have the wrong idea about a situation so that you are unlikely to get the result you want〔思考的〕方向錯誤/路子不對頭
14 be from the wrong side of the tracks *AmE* to be from a poor part of a town or a poor part of society【美】來自貧民區, 來自下層社會
15 be on the wrong side of thirty/forty etc *informal* to be older than thirty etc【非正式】已過三十/四十歲 —see also 另見 **get out of bed on the wrong side** (BED[1] (9))

Frequencies of the adjective **wrong** in spoken and written English 形容詞 wrong 在英語口語和書面語中的使用頻率

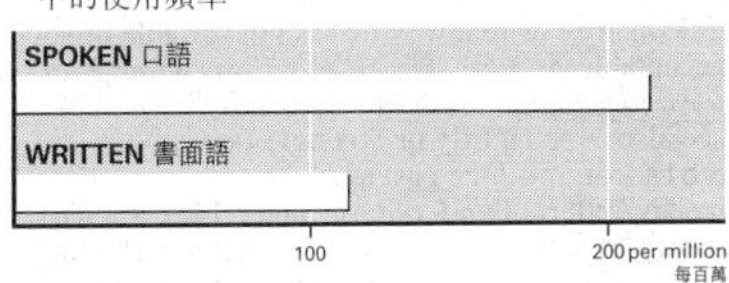

Based on the British National Corpus and the Longman Lancaster Corpus
據英國國家語料庫和朗文蘭卡斯特語料庫

This graph shows that the adjective **wrong** is much more common in spoken English than in written English. This is because it is used in some common spoken phrases. 本圖表顯示, 形容詞 wrong 在英語口語中的使用頻率遠遠高於書面語, 因為口語中一些常用片語是由 wrong 構成的。

wrong (*adj*) **SPOKEN PHRASES**
含 wrong 的口語片語

16 what's wrong? a) used to ask someone what problem they have, why they are unhappy etc 怎麼啦?〔用於問別人有甚麼問題、為何不開心等〕: *"What's wrong?" "Oh, I'm just a bit worried about tomorrow."* "怎麼啦?" "噢, 我對明天有點擔心。" **b)** used to ask why something doesn't work 出了甚麼毛病?〔用於問為甚麼某物不運轉〕: **[+with]** *What's wrong with this clock?* 這鐘出甚麼毛病了? **c)** used to say that you think something is good, fair etc, and you do not understand why other people think it is not 有甚麼不可以?〔用於表示你認為某物很好、不錯等, 但不明白為何別人的意見不同〕: **[+with]** *What's wrong with eating meat? I think it's natural.* 吃肉有甚麼不妥? 我覺得很正常。
17 there's something wrong used to say that there is a fault or problem with something〔用於表示某物〕有些毛病[問題]: *There's something wrong. The car won't start.* 有毛病了, 汽車發動不起來。| **[+with]** *There's something wrong with the phone, the line's dead.* 電話有毛病了, 線路不通。| **have sth wrong with** *She had to go home early – she's got something wrong with her back.* 她不得不早點回家 —— 她的背部覺得不太舒服。
18 there's nothing wrong a) used to say that something has not got any faults or problems 沒問題〔用於表示某物沒毛病〕: *It's O.K. don't worry, there's nothing wrong.* 好了, 別擔心, 沒問題了。| **[+with]** *There's nothing wrong with the TV, it just wasn't plugged in.* 電視機沒毛病, 只是沒有插上插頭。**b)** used to say that you do not think that something is bad or immoral 沒有甚麼不對〔認為某事並非不好或不道德〕: **[+with]** *There's nothing wrong with drinking, as long as you know when to stop.* 只要適可而止, 喝酒並不是壞事。
19 correct me if I'm wrong used as a polite way of saying that you think what you are going to say is correct 如果錯了請予糾正〔禮貌地表示自問將要說的話是正確的〕: *Correct me if I'm wrong, but didn't you say you were going to do it?* 如果我錯了, 請糾正, 你不是說過你準備做這事嗎?
20 you're not wrong used to agree with someone 你沒有錯〔表示同意〕: *"This government is ruining the country!" "You're not wrong!"* "本屆政府正把國家毀掉!" "說得一點都不錯!"

wrong² *adv* **1** not in the correct way 錯誤地; 不正確地: *You've spelt my name wrong.* 你把我的名字拼寫錯了。| **do sth all wrong** (=in completely the wrong way) 事情完全做錯了 *I asked him to sort those files, but he's done it all wrong.* 我讓他整理這些文件, 可是他全部做錯了。**2 go wrong a)** to stop working properly 出毛病; 出故障: *The television's gone wrong again.* 電視機又出毛病了。| **[+with]** *Something's gone wrong with my watch.* 我的手錶出故障了。**b)** to make a mistake during a process so that you do not get the right result〔在過程中〕出錯, 弄錯: **you can't go wrong** (=you are sure to succeed) 你不會出錯 *Follow these instructions and you can't go wrong.* 按照操作指南去做, 你就不會出錯。**c)** to do something that makes a plan, relationship etc fail〔計劃、關係等〕出現問題: *Thinking back on the marriage, I just don't know where we went wrong.* 回想起這段婚姻, 我真不知道問題出在哪裡。**3 get sth wrong** to make a mistake in the way you write, judge, or understand something 寫錯[誤解; 誤會]某事: *This isn't it. We must have got the address wrong.* 不是這裡, 我們肯定把地址搞錯了。| **get/have it all wrong** (=understand a situation in completely the wrong way) 完全誤解[曲解] *No, no – you've got it all wrong! We're just friends!* 不, 不 —— 你完全搞錯了! 我們只是朋友! **4 don't get me wrong** *spoken* used when you think someone may understand your remarks wrongly, or be offended by them【口】別誤會: *Don't get me wrong – I like Jenny.* 別誤會 —— 我喜歡珍妮。**5 you can't go wrong (with sth)** *spoken* used to say that a particular object will always be suitable, satisfactory or work well【口】〔某物〕不會出問題〔總是合適、令人滿意或運作良好〕: *You can't go wrong with a little black dress, can you?* 你穿短的黑色連衣裙不會錯, 是不是? 2

USAGE NOTE 用法說明: WRONG
COLLOCATION/GRAMMAR 搭配/語法
Many meanings of **wrong** only belong in particular phrases or structures that cannot be changed. wrong 的許多釋義只用在特定的不能改變的短語或結構中。For example, if someone's health is bad, you can say something **is wrong with** them but not: *They are wrong* (which means not correct). 如某人身體欠佳, 可以說 something is wrong with them, 但不可以說 They are wrong (這是他們沒做對的意思)。
You can **do something wrong** (=not in the correct way) but not **do a wrong thing** (though you can **do the wrong thing**). 犯錯是 do something wrong 而不是 do a wrong thing (但可以說 do the wrong thing)。If you **do something wrong**, that does not mean there is something **wrong with you**. you do something wrong (犯錯) 和 there is something wrong with you (身體欠佳) 不同: *He was angry with me but I hadn't done anything wrong.* 他生我的氣了, 但我沒做甚麼錯事。Note 注意 ...**there was nothing wrong with me** (=I was not sick 我沒生病)。
Wrong used before a noun usually means 'not correct', 'not correctly chosen' or 'not suitable'. wrong 用在名詞前通常表示"不正確", "選得不對"或"不合適": *the wrong answer/key/furniture* 不正確的答案/鑰匙/家具不合適。You would also say:

I can't find what is wrong/has gone wrong (NOT *I can't find the wrong thing*) if you mean that something is not working 表示某物不運轉時可以說: I can't find what is wrong/has gone wrong 我找不出哪裡有問題。(不用 I can't find the wrong thing). **Wrong** also means 'morally wrong', and is used in this way. wrong 也表示"不道德"並用於: *What you did was completely wrong* (NOT 不用 *You did wrong things/action*). 你做的事完全不道德。

Sometimes **bad** is a better word to use. You would call a day when everything **goes wrong** a *bad day* (NOT *a wrong day*). 有時選用單詞 bad 較好。事事不順利 (everything goes wrong) 的一天可以稱作 a bad day (而不說 a wrong day)。If you **get things wrong** you make a lot of mistakes, and may get a *bad record* but not a *wrong record* (which means not correct). 如果做了很多錯事 (get things wrong), 也許會有不良的記錄 (a bad record, 但不說 a wrong record — 這是錯誤的記錄的意思)。

wrong³ *n* **1** [U] behaviour that is not morally right 壞事; 邪惡: *He's too young to know right from wrong.* 他太年輕了, 還不能辨別是非。| **sb can do no wrong** (=they are perfect) 某人不會做錯事 *That man seems to think he can do no wrong.* 那個男人似乎認為自己不會做錯事。**2** [C] an action, judgement, or situation that is unfair〔行為、判決、情形〕不公正: *The black population suffered countless wrongs at the hands of a racist regime.* 在種族主義政權統治, 黑人遭受了無盡的冤屈。| **right a wrong** (=bring justice to an unfair situation) 糾正錯誤; 平反冤屈 **3 be in the wrong** to make a mistake or deserve the blame for something 犯錯誤; 應負責任: *Which driver was in the wrong?* 是哪個司機出的錯? **4 do sb wrong** *humorous* to treat someone badly and unfairly【幽默】冤枉某人; 不公平地對待某人 **5 two wrongs don't make a right** *spoken* used to say that punishing someone will not make a bad situation right or fair【口】負負不能得正〔用於表示懲罰某人不能使壞情況變好或公平〕

wrong⁴ *v* [T] *formal* to treat or judge someone unfairly【正式】不公正地對待〔某人〕, 冤枉: *I felt I had been grievously wronged.* 我感覺受到了極大的委屈。

wrong·do·ing /ˈrɔŋˋduɪŋ; ˈrɒŋˌduːɪŋ/ *n* [C,U] *formal* illegal or immoral behaviour【正式】不法行為; 不道德行為; 壞事 —**wrongdoer** *n*

wrong·foot /ˌrɔŋˋfut; ˌrɒŋˈfʊt/ *v* [T] to surprise and embarrass someone, especially by asking a question they did not expect 使大吃一驚; 使倉皇失措〔尤指提出意想不到的問題〕

wrong·ful /ˈrɔŋfəl; ˈrɒŋfəl/ *adj* **wrongful arrest/conviction/dismissal etc** a wrongful arrest etc is unfair or illegal because you have done nothing wrong 不公正的逮捕/判決/解雇: *She's threatening to sue her employers for wrongful dismissal.* 她揚言要控告雇主非法解雇。—**wrongfully** *adv*

wrong·head·ed /ˌrɔŋˋhɛdɪd; ˌrɒŋˈhedɪ̈d◂/ *adj* based on or influenced by wrong ideas that you are not willing to change 堅持錯誤的; 執迷不悟的 —**wrongheadedly** *adv*

wrong·ly /ˈrɔŋli; ˈrɒŋli/ *adv* **1** incorrectly or in a way that is not based on facts 不正確地; 錯誤地: *You're holding the racket wrongly.* 你球拍握得不對。| *Matthew was wrongly diagnosed as having a brain tumour.* 馬修被誤診患有腦瘤。**2** in a way that is unfair or immoral 不公正地; 不道德地: **wrongly convicted/imprisoned/accused/blamed** *Human rights organizations maintain that the men have been wrongly convicted.* 人權組織堅稱這些人被錯判了。**3** in a way that is not suitable or socially acceptable 不合適; 普遍不接受: *I was wrongly dressed for a formal dinner.* 我的衣着不適合出席正式宴會。— see also 另見 **rightly or wrongly** (RIGHTLY)

wrote /rot; rəʊt/ the past tense of WRITE

wroth /rɔθ; rəʊθ/ *adj old use* angry【舊】發怒的

wrought i·ron /ˌrɔt ˋaɪɚn; ˌrɔːt ˈaɪən◂/ *n* [U] long thin pieces of iron formed into shapes to make gates, fences etc〔製作閘門、柵欄等的〕鍛鐵, 熟鐵

wrought-up /ˌ· ˈ·◂/ *adj* very nervous and excited 非常緊張的; 極激動的

wrung /rʌŋ; rʌŋ/ the past tense and past participle of WRING

wry /raɪ; raɪ/ *adj* [only before noun 僅用於名詞前] showing a mixture of amusement and displeasure or disbelief 露出怪相的; 苦笑的〔表示不悅或不相信〕: *He took a gulp of his Scotch and gave a wry smile at the injustices of the world.* 他喝了一大口蘇格蘭威士忌酒, 對這個世界的不公平苦笑了一下。

wt the written abbreviation of 縮寫= WEIGHT

wun·der·kind /ˈwʌndɚkɪnd; ˈwʌndəkɪnd/ *n* [C] *German* a young person who is very successful【德】神童; 非常成功的年輕人

wuss /wʊs; wʌs/ *n* [C] *AmE slang* someone who you think is weak because they are afraid to do something difficult or unpleasant【美俚】軟弱無能的人

WYSIWYG /ˈwɪzɪˌwɪg; ˈwɪziwɪg/ *n* [U] What You See Is What You Get; a word used in computing meaning what you see on the screen is exactly what will be printed 所見即所得〔電腦用語, 指在屏幕上看見的與打印本絲毫不差〕

wy·vern /ˈwaɪvɚn; ˈwaɪvən/ *n* [C] an imaginary animal that has two legs and wings and looks like a DRAGON (1)〔想像中的〕雙足飛龍

X,x

X, x[1] /ɛks; eks/ *plural* **X's, x's** *n* [C] **1** the 24th letter of the English alphabet 英語字母表的第二十四個字母 **2** the number 10 in the system of ROMAN NUMERALS〔羅馬數字〕10 **3** *technical* a letter used in mathematics to represent an unknown quantity or value【術語】〔數學中的〕未知數[量]: *if 3x=6, x=2.* 假設3x=6, 則 x=2。**4** a mark used to show that a written answer is wrong〔表示書面答案錯誤的符號〕**5** a mark used to show that you have chosen something on an official piece of paper, for example when voting〔表示選中的符號, 如選舉時〕**6** a mark used instead of a signature by someone who cannot write〔不會寫字的人用以代替簽名的符號〕**7** a mark used to show a kiss, especially at the end of a letter〔表示親吻的符號, 尤用於信末〕**8** a letter used to show that a film is not suitable for people under 18 X級〔電影的級別, 表示未滿18歲者不宜觀看〕**9** a letter used instead of someone or something's real name because you want to keep it secret or you do not know it〔用以代替不宜公開或不知其名的人或事物的名稱〕: *At the trial, Ms X said that she had known the defendant for three years.* 在庭審中, X女士說她認識被告已有三年了。**10 X number of** used to say that there are a certain number of people or things when the exact number is not important X個〔用於說明有一些人或物, 而準確的數字並不重要〕**11 X marks the spot** used on maps in adventure stories to show that something is buried in a particular place〔地圖上〕標有X的地點〔在探險故事中指埋有某物的地方〕

X[2] *v*

X out sth *phr v* [T] *AmE* to mark or remove a mistake in a piece of writing using an X【美】〔在一篇文章中〕用X符號標出[刪去]〔錯誤〕; **cross out** (CROSS[1])

X-cer·tif·i·cate /ˋɛks sɚˌtɪfɪkət; ˈeks səˌtɪfɪkət/ *adj* an X-certificate film is one that people under 18 are not allowed to see in Britain because it includes sex or violence〔電影〕X級的〔含有性或暴力內容, 在英國18歲以下者禁看〕—compare 比較 PG, R[2] (4), U (1)

X chro·mo·some /ˋɛks ˏkroməˏsom; ˈeks ˌkrəʊməsəʊm/ *n* [C] a type of CHROMOSOME that exists in pairs in female cells, and with a Y CHROMOSOME in male cells X染色體

xen·on /ˋzinɑn; ˈzenɒn/ *n* [U] a rare gas that is one of the chemical elements (ELEMENT (1)) 氙

xen·o·pho·bi·a /ˏzɛnəˋfobɪə; ˌzenəˈfəʊbiə/ *n* [U] extreme fear or dislike of people from other countries 對外國人的極度畏懼[憎恨], 恐外症 —**xenophobic** *adj*

Xe·rox /ˋzirɑks; ˈzɪərɒks/ *n* [C] *trademark* a copy of a piece of paper with writing or printing on it, made using a special machine; a kind of PHOTOCOPY[1]【商標】〔用靜電複印法的〕複印本, 影印本 —**Xerox** *v* [T]

Xerox ma·chine /ˈ·· ·ˌ·/ *n* [C] *trademark* a special electric machine used for making copies of written or printed material; a kind of PHOTOCOPIER【商標】(靜電) 複印機 —see picture on page A14 參見A14頁圖

X·mas /ˋkrɪsməs; ˈkrɪsməs/ *n* [C,U] *informal* a word that means Christmas, often written on signs or cards【非正式】聖誕節〔常寫於標誌或賀卡上〕

X-rated /ˋɛks ˏretɪd; ˈeks ˌreɪtɪ̈d/ *adj* an X-rated film is one that people under 18 are not allowed to see because it includes sex or violence〔電影〕X級的〔X級電影含有性或暴力內容, 18歲以下者禁看〕

X-ray[1] /ˋɛks ˋre; ˈeks reɪ/ *n* [C] **1** a beam of RADIATION (1) that can go through solid objects and is used for photographing the inside of the body X射線, X光 **2** a photograph of part of the body, taken in this way to see if anything is wrong X光片: *The X-ray showed that her leg was not broken.* X光片顯示她的腿沒有骨折。| *a chest X-ray* 胸部X光片, 胸透片 **3** a medical examination made using X-rays X光檢查: *I had to go to hospital for an X-ray.* 我得去醫院作X光檢查。

X-ray[2] *v* [T] to photograph the inside of someone's body using X-rays 用X光拍照, 給…照X光: *The problem was only discovered when her lungs were X-rayed.* 她的肺部照了X光後才發現有問題。

xy·lo·phone /ˋzaɪləˏfon; ˈzaɪləfəʊn/ *n* [C] a musical instrument which consists of metal or wooden bars that you hit with a special stick to make sounds 木琴

Y, y

Y, y /waɪ; waɪ/ *plural* **Y's, y's 1** the 25th letter of the English alphabet 英語字母表的第二十五個字母 **2 the Y** *AmE informal* the YMCA or the YWCA【美, 非正式】基督教青年會; 基督教女青年會

-y¹, -ey /ɪ; i/ *suffix* [in adjectives 構成形容詞] **1** full of or covered with something 充滿…的; 被…覆蓋的: *dirty hands* (=covered with dirt) 髒手 | *a hairy chest* 多毛的胸膛 **2** tending to do something, or doing something 有…傾向的: *curly hair* (=hair that curls) 鬈髮 | *feeling sleepy* 感到睏倦〔欲睡〕的 **3** like or typical of something 似…的: *a cold wintry day* (=typical of winter) 寒冷的冬日 | *his long, horsy face* (=he looks like a horse) 他那長長的馬臉 **4** fond of or interested in something 熱衷於…的, 愛好…的: *a horsy woman* (=who likes riding horses) 喜歡騎馬的女人 **—-ily** [in adverbs 構成副詞] **—-iness** [in nouns 構成名詞]

-y² *suffix* [in nouns 構成名詞] **1** also 又作 **-ie** used, especially when speaking to children, to make a word or name less formal, and often to show fondness〔尤用於對兒童說話時, 表示親暱或喜愛〕: *Where's little Johnny?* (=John) 小約翰哪兒去了? | *my daddy* (=father) 我的爸爸 | *What a nice doggy!* (=dog) 多可愛的小狗啊! | *wellies* (=WELLINGTONs) 威靈頓長統靴 **2** the action of doing something …動作; …行為: *the expiry date* (=date when something EXPIREs) 到期日

yacht 大型帆船; 大遊艇

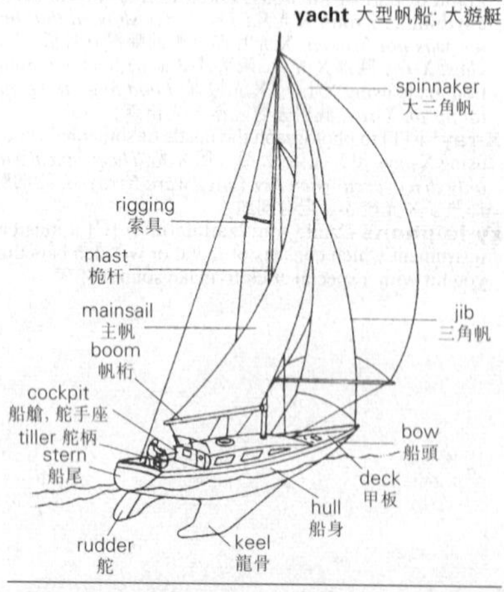

yacht /jɑt; jɒt/ *n* [C] a large sailing boat, especially one that you can sleep on〔尤指可在上面睡覺的〕大型帆船; 大遊艇 —compare 比較 SAILING BOAT, SAIL BOAT

yacht·ing /ˈjɑtɪŋ; ˈjɒtɪŋ/ *n* [U] *especially BrE* sailing, travelling, or racing in a yacht【尤英】駕駛帆船[遊艇]; 駕艇旅遊; 帆船比賽 —compare 比較 SAILING

yachts·man /ˈjɑtsmən; ˈjɒtsmən/ *n* [C] someone who owns or sails a yacht 遊艇主; 駕駛帆船[遊艇]的人

yachts·wom·an /ˈjɑts,wʊmən; ˈjɒtswʊmən/ *n* [C] a woman who owns or sails a yacht 女遊艇主; 駕駛帆船[遊艇]的女子

ya·hoo /ˈjɑˋhu; jɑːˈhuː/ *n* [C] *old-fashioned* someone who is rough, noisy, or bad-mannered【過時】粗人, 吵鬧粗魯的人

Yah·weh /ˈjɑwe; ˈjɑːweɪ/ *n* [singular] a Hebrew name for God 耶和華, 上帝〔希伯萊語〕

yak¹ /jæk; jæk/ *n* [C] an animal of central Asia that looks like a cow with long hair 牦牛〔產於中亞, 似牛但毛長〕

yak² *v* **yakked, yakking** [I] *informal* to talk continuously about things that are not very serious; CHATTER¹ (1)【非正式】喋喋不休地講, 嘮叨; 瞎扯

y'all /jɔl; jɔːl/ *pron AmE informal* a word meaning 'all of you', used mainly in the southern US states when speaking to more than one person【美, 非正式】你們大夥, 你們全部〔主要流行於美國南部〕: *Are y'all coming over for lunch?* 你們大夥都來吃午飯嗎?

yam /jæm; jæm/ *n* [C] **1** a tropical climbing plant grown for its root, which is eaten as a vegetable 薯蕷, 山藥 —see picture on page A9 參見 A9 頁圖 **2** *AmE* a type of SWEET POTATO【美】甘薯, 番薯

yam·mer /ˈjæmɚ; ˈjæmə/ also 又作 **yammer on** *v* [I] *BrE informal* to talk noisily and continuously【英, 非正式】〔不停地〕哇啦哇啦地大聲說話: *a crowd of yammering aunts and cousins* 一羣哇啦哇啦說個不停的姑嬸和堂姐妹

yang /jæŋ; jæŋ/ *n* [U] the male principle in Chinese PHILOSOPHY which is active, light, positive and which combines with YIN (=the female principle) to influence everything in the world〔中國哲學概念中的〕陽

Yank /jæŋk; jæŋk/ *n* [C] *informal*【非正式】**1** a word meaning someone from the US, sometimes used in an insulting way by someone who is not American 美國人, 美國佬〔有時為侮辱性說法〕**2** also 又作 **Yankee** *AmE* someone born or living in the northern, especially the northeastern, states of the US【美】美國北部各州的人, 北方佬

yank *v* [I,T] *informal* to suddenly pull something quickly and forcefully【非正式】猛拉, 使勁拉: **yank (on) sth** *John keeps yanking on my ponytail!* 約翰不停地拽我的馬尾辮! | **yank sth out/back/open etc** *Keith yanked Robert out of his chair.* 基思一把將羅伯特從椅子裡拉了出來。

Yan·kee /ˈjæŋkɪ; ˈjæŋki/ *n* [C] *informal*【非正式】**1** *AmE* someone born or living in the northern, especially the northeastern, states of the US【美】美國北部各州的人, 北方佬 **2** *especially BrE* someone from the US【尤英】美國人, 美國佬

yap¹ /jæp; jæp/ *v* **yapped, yapping** [I] **1** if a small dog yaps, it BARKs (=makes short loud sounds) in an excited way〔小狗〕狂吠, 汪汪亂叫 **2** to talk noisily without saying anything very important or serious 哇啦哇啦地說個不停; 瞎扯: *Don't start yapping again.* 別再瞎扯了。

yap² *n* [C] the sound a small dog makes when it yaps〔小狗的〕狂吠聲

yard /jɑrd; jɑːd/ *n* [C]

1 ►ENCLOSED AREA 封閉地區◄ an enclosed area next to a building or group of buildings, used for a special purpose, activity, or business〔作專門用途、活動、交易的〕場所; 圍欄; 工地: *a cattle yard* 牛[牲畜]欄 | *Their house is next to a builder's yard.* 他們的房子挨着一個建築工地。

2 ►MEASURE 尺度◄ written abbreviation 縮寫為 **yd** a unit for measuring length, equal to 3 feet or .9144 metres 碼〔長度單度, 等於 3 英尺或 0.9144 米〕—see table on page C3 參見 C3 頁附錄

3 ►GARDEN 園子◄ *AmE* the ground around a house, usually covered with grass【美】〔房子周圍通常種滿草的〕庭院; GARDEN¹ (1) *BrE*【英】: *backyard* 後院 | *Their*

front yard was full of kids playing tag. 他們的前院有很多孩子在玩捉人遊戲。—see also 另見 BACKYARD

4 prison/school yard an area outside a prison or school where prisoners or students go to do activities outdoors 監獄放風場/學校操場

5 ▶BACK OF HOUSE 宅子後部◀ *BrE* an enclosed area without grass at the back of a small house【英】後院

6 ▶SAILING 航行◀ *technical* a long pole that supports a square sail【術語】帆桁 —see also 另見 CHURCHYARD, FARMYARD, SHIPYARD

yard·age /ˈjɑrdɪdʒ; ˈjɑːdɪdʒ/ *n technical*【術語】**1** [C, U] the size of something measured in yards or square yards 碼數; 平方碼數: *a large yardage of sail* 碼數很大的帆 **2** [U] the number of yards that a team or player moves forward in a game of American football〔美式足球中〕將球向前推進的(總)碼數

yard·arm /ˈjɑrdˌɑrm; ˈjɑːd-ɑːm/ *n* [C] one of the ends of the pole that supports a square sail 帆桁的一端, 桁端

yard·bird /ˈjɑrdˌbɝd; ˈjɑːdbɜːd/ *n* [C] *AmE slang*【美俚】**1** someone who is in prison, especially for a long time (老)囚犯, 犯人 **2** someone who has just joined the army and has outdoor duties〔擔當戶外值勤等任務的〕入伍新兵

yard sale /ˈ· ·/ *n* [C] *AmE* a sale of used things from someone's house that takes place in their YARD (3)【美】〔在自家院子進行的〕舊貨出售 —compare 比較 GARAGE SALE

yard·stick /ˈjɑrdˌstɪk; ˈjɑːdˌstɪk/ *n* [C] **1** something that you compare another thing with, in order to judge how good or successful they are 衡量標準, 評判尺度: **[+of/against]** *Is profit the only yardstick of success?* 利潤是成功的唯一標準嗎? **2** a special stick for measuring things that is exactly one YARD (2) long 碼尺

yar·mul·ke /ˈjɑrməlkə; ˈjɑːmʊlkə/ *n* [C] a small circular cap worn by Jewish men 亞莫克便帽〔猶太男子戴的小圓帽〕

yarn /jɑrn; jɑːn/ *n* **1** [U] *especially AmE* long thick thread, made of cotton or wool used to KNIT or make cloth【尤美】紗; 線; 毛線 **2** [C] *informal* a story of adventures, travels etc, usually made more exciting and interesting by adding things that never really happened【非正式】〔探險、旅行中的〕故事, 奇談: **spin a yarn** (=tell a long and often not completely true story)〔添油加醋地〕講故事, 胡謅 *The old captain would often spin us a yarn about life aboard ship.* 老船長經常給我們講一些船上生活的奇聞軼事。

yash·mak /jæʃˈmæk; ˈjæʃmæk/ *n* [C] a piece of cloth that Muslim women wear across their faces〔穆斯林婦女所戴的〕面紗

yaw /jɔ; jɔː/ *v* [I] *technical* if a ship, aircraft etc yaws it makes a turn away from its proper course【術語】〔船、飛機等〕偏航 —compare 比較 PITCH[1] (4), ROLL[1] (9) —**yaw** *n* [C,U]

yawl /jɔl; jɔːl/ *n* [C] **1** a sailing boat with a main MAST (=pole) and sails and another small mast and sail close to the back 雙桅帆船 **2** a small boat carried on a ship 船載小艇

yawn¹ /jɔn; jɔːn/ *v* [I] **1** to open your mouth wide and breathe in deeply, usually because you are tired, or bored 打呵欠: *The boy stretched and yawned.* 那男孩伸懶腰打了個呵欠。**2** to be or become wide open 張得很大, 張開: *a yawning hole* 口子很大的洞 | **[+open]** *The pit yawned open in front of them.* 深坑在他們面前裂開。| **yawning gap/gulf** *the yawning gap between training needs and training resources* 培訓需求與培訓資源之間的巨大差距

yawn 打呵欠

yawn² *n* **1** [C] an act of yawning 呵欠: **stifle a yawn** (=try to stop yawning) 忍住呵欠 *Kay shook her head and stifled a yawn.* 凱晃了晃腦袋, 把呵欠壓了回去。**2** [singular] *informal* someone or something that is boring【非正式】乏味的人[事物]: *The party was a big yawn.* 這次聚會乏味透了。

yaws /jɔz; jɔːz/ *n* [U] a tropical skin disease 雅司病〔一種熱帶皮膚病〕

Y chro·mo·some /ˈwaɪ ˌkroməˌsom; ˈwaɪ ˌkrəʊməsəʊm/ *n* [C] the part of a GENE that makes someone a male instead of a female Y 染色體 —see also 另見 X CHROMOSOME

yd the written abbreviation of 縮寫= YARD (2) or yards

ye¹ /ji; jiː/ *pron old use* a word meaning 'you', used especially when speaking to more than one person【舊】汝等, 爾輩, 你們

ye² *determiner* **1** a word meaning 'the', used especially in the names of shops and PUBs to make them seem old〔相當於 the, 尤用於商號或酒吧名稱中, 以示其歷史悠久〕: *The sign said 'Ye Olde Dog and Duck'.* 招牌上寫着"老狗與老鴨"。**2 ye gods** *spoken* used to show that you are very surprised, or shocked, by something【口】哎喲〔表示驚訝〕: *Ye gods! I can't believe this.* 哎喲!真不敢相信。

yea¹ /je; jeɪ/ *adv old use* yes【舊】是, 對 —opposite 反義詞 NAY[1] (2) —see also 另見 AYE[2]

yea² *n* [C] a vote or voter that supports an idea, plan, law etc 贊成票; 投贊成票者 —opposite 反義詞 NAY[2] —see also 另見 AYE[1] (1)

yeah /jɛə; jeə/ *adv spoken* yes【口】是, 對 S1

year /jɪr; jɪə/ *n* [C] S1 W1

1 ▶12 MONTHS 12個月◀ a period of about 365 days or 12 months, measured from any particular time 年; 年度; 歲: *I arrived here two years ago.* 我兩年前來到這裡。| *We've known each other for over a year.* 我們彼此認識已逾一年。| *15 years old* 15歲 | *a three-year development* 三年的發展 | *a four-year-old child* 四歲的孩子 | **tax/fiscal/financial year** *The tax year begins in April.* 稅收年度從四月份開始。| **school year** (=period during a year when students are in school, university etc) 學年

2 ▶JANUARY TO DECEMBER 一月至十二月◀ also 又作 **calendar year** a period of 365 or 366 days divided into 12 months beginning on January 1st and ending on December 31st 曆年: *the year that Martin Luther King died* 馬丁·路德·金遇害那年 | *Their lease expires at the end of the year.* 他們的租約到年底滿期。| *1995 was a profitable year.* 1995年是個贏利年。| *the year 2000* 2000年 | **all (the) year round** (=during the whole year) 一年四季, 一年到頭

3 ▶MEASURE OF TIME 時間長度◀ *technical* a measure of time equal to 365 1/4 days, which is the amount of time it takes for the Earth to travel once around the sun【術語】年〔地球環繞太陽一周的時間〕

4 childhood/war/retirement etc years a particular period of time in someone's life or in history 童年/戰爭/退休等歲月: *He started writing poetry during his Harvard years.* 他是在唸哈佛期間開始寫詩的。| *the boom years of the 1980's* 20世紀80年代的迅速發展時期

5 years a) *informal* many years【非正式】多年, 長久: **in/for years** *I haven't been there for years.* 我多年沒去那裡了。| *It's years since I rode a bike.* 我多年沒騎腳踏車了。**b)** age, especially old age 年紀, 歲數〔尤指高齡〕: *Gramps is very active for a man of his years.* 從他的年齡來說, 格蘭普斯算是很活躍了。| **getting on in years** (=no longer young) 年事漸高, 不再年輕 | **be 12/21 etc years of age** (=12/21 etc years old) 12/21歲等

6 year by year as each year passes 年年, 每年: *Year by year their business grew.* 他們的業務年年增長。

7 year after year continuously for many years 一年又一年, 年復一年: *It's always the same, year after year.* 一如既往, 年年如此。

8 never/not in a million years *spoken* used to say strongly that you will never do something【口】決不, 永不〔幹某事〕: *I won't forgive him – never in a million years.* 我不原諒他——永遠也不。

9 first/second etc year *BrE* someone who is in their first etc year at school or university【英】〔中學或大學裡的〕一年級/二年級等

10 put years on sb/take years off sb to make someone look or feel older or younger 使某人顯得蒼老/年輕: *Theresa's divorce has put years on her.* 特麗莎離婚後顯老了。—see also 另見 **donkey's years** (DONKEY (3)), YEARLY

11 the year dot *BrE informal* a very long time ago【英, 非正式】很久以前: *Scientists have been involved in war since the year dot.* 很久以前, 科學家就捲入了戰爭。

year·book /ˈjɪrˌbʊk; ˈjɪəbʊk/ *n* [C] *AmE* a book printed once a year, especially by a school or college, with information and pictures about what happened there in the year just past【美】年鑑, 年刊

year·ling /ˈjɪrlɪŋ; ˈjɪəlɪŋ/ *n* [C] an animal, especially a young horse, between one and two years old〔一周歲至兩周歲之間的〕小動物;〔尤指〕小馬駒

year·long /ˈjɪrˋlɔŋ; ˌjɪəˈlɒŋ◂/ *adj* [only before noun 僅用於名詞前] lasting for a year or all through the year 持續一年的, 整整一年的: *We store the apples so we have a yearlong supply.* 我們把蘋果保存起來, 這樣就全年不缺了。

year·ly /ˈjɪrlɪ; ˈjɪəli/ *adj* happening or appearing every year or once a year 每年(發生或出現)的; 一年一次[度]的: *a yearly pay award* 每年一次的獎金 | **3-yearly/5-yearly etc** (=every three years etc) 三年/五年等一次的 *a check-up at five-yearly intervals* 每隔五年一次的檢查 —**yearly** *adv*: *We pay the fee yearly.* 我們按年付費。

yearn /jɝn; jɜːn/ *v* [I] *literary* to have a strong desire for something, especially something that is difficult or impossible to get【文】嚮往; 渴望: **yearn for sth** *Hannah yearned for a child.* 漢娜渴望有個孩子。| **yearn to do sth** *yearning to go home* 渴望回家

yearn·ing /ˈjɝnɪŋ; ˈjɜːnɪŋ/ *n* [C,U] a strong desire or feeling of wanting something 思慕, 嚮往: **[+for]** *an actor with a yearning for recognition* 渴望得到認同的演員 | **a yearning to do sth** *a yearning to travel* 渴望旅遊

yeast /jist; jiːst/ *n* [U] a substance used for producing alcohol in beer and wine and for making bread rise 酵母; 發酵物 —**yeasty** *adj*: *a yeasty taste* 發酵的味道

yeast ex·tract /ˈ· ˌ··/ *n* [U] a food made from yeast, used to make things taste better 酵母精

yeast in·fec·tion /ˈ· ·ˌ··/ *n* [C] an infectious condition that affects the VAGINA in adult women; THRUSH (2)〔成年婦女患的〕酵母菌[念珠菌]陰道炎

yecch /jʌk; jʌk/ *interjection AmE slang* used to say that you think something is very unpleasant; YUCK【美俚】呸, 討厭〔用於對某事表示強烈的厭惡〕

yell¹ /jɛl; jel/ *v* [I,T] **1** also 又作 **yell out** to shout or say something very loudly, especially because you are frightened, angry, or excited〔尤因恐懼、憤怒或激動而〕叫喊, 大嚷大叫: *The spectators yelled and cheered.* 觀眾又是喊叫又是歡呼。| **[+at]** *Don't you yell at me like that!* 別這樣對我大喊大叫的! | *"Go, go!" he yelled out.* "走, 走!"他大聲說。| **yell at sb to do sth** *They yelled at him to stop.* 他們朝他喊, 讓他停下。**2** *spoken, especially AmE* to ask for help【口, 尤美】大聲呼救: *If you need me just yell.* 需要我時就喊一聲。

yell² *n* [C] **1** a loud shout 叫喊: **let out a yell** *Frank let out a yell and jumped away.* 弗蘭克大叫一聲跳開了。| **a yell of delight/triumph/warning etc** *He gave a yell of delight as the election results came in.* 選舉結果出來後, 他高興得大喊了一聲。**2** *AmE* words or phrases that students and CHEERLEADERS shout to show support for their school, college etc【美】啦啦隊的叫喊聲

yel·low¹ /ˈjɛlo; ˈjeləʊ/ *adj* **1** having the colour of butter, gold, or the middle part of an egg 黃(色)的 —see picture on page A5 參見 A5 頁圖 **2** an offensive way of describing the skin colour of people from parts of Asia〔部分亞洲民族〕黃皮膚的〔冒犯說法〕**3** also 又作 **yellow-bellied** *informal* not brave; COWARDLY【非正式】膽小的, 卑怯的, 懦弱的 —**yellow** *n* [U]

yellow² *v* [I,T] to become yellow or make something become yellow (使)變黃, (使)發黃: *The paper was yellowed with age.* 這紙因年久而變黃了。

yellow card /ˌ·· ˈ·/ *n* [C] a yellow card held up by a football REFEREE¹ (1) to show that a player has done something wrong〔足球裁判對被罰球員出示的〕黃牌

yellow fe·ver /ˌ·· ˈ··/ *n* [C] a dangerous tropical disease in which your skin turns slightly yellow 黃熱病

yel·low·ham·mer /ˈjɛloˌhæmɚ; ˈjeləʊˌhæmə/ *n* [C] a small European bird with a yellow head 黃鵐〔歐洲的一種小鳥, 頭部呈黃色〕

yellow line /ˌ·· ˈ·/ *n* [C] a line of yellow paint along the edge of a street in Britain which means you can only park your car for a short time or at particular times 黃線〔英國街道邊的黃色標線, 表示在某一時段內不得在此停車〕: **double yellow line** (=two lines of paint that mean you cannot park there) 雙黃線〔表示禁止在此停車〕

Yellow Pag·es /ˌ·· ˈ··/ *n* [singular] *trademark* the name of a book that contains the telephone numbers of businesses and organizations in an area, arranged according to the type of business they do【商標】黃頁〔電話號碼簿〕—compare 比較 WHITE PAGES

yel·low·y /ˈjɛloɪ; ˈjeləʊi/ *adj* having a slight yellow colour 略帶黃色的, 淡黃色的: *The cream was thick and yellowy.* 奶油很稠, 略帶黃色。

yelp /jɛlp; jelp/ *v* [I] to make a short sharp high cry because of excitement, pain etc〔因興奮、痛苦等而〕尖叫, 叫喊: *The dog ran up and down, yelping.* 狗跳上跳下地叫個不停。| *He yelped as his bare foot hit the box.* 他光腳踢在箱子上, 痛得大叫起來。—**yelp** *n* [C]: *Rose gave a yelp of dismay.* 羅絲沮喪地叫了一聲。

yen /jɛn; jen/ *n plural* **yen 1** [C] the standard unit of money in Japan 日圓 **2** [singular] a strong desire 渴望, 熱望: **[+to/for]** *a yen to travel* 對旅遊的渴望

yeo·man /ˈjomən; ˈjəʊmən/ *n plural* **yeomen** /-mən; -mən/ [C] **1** *BrE especially literary or old use* a farmer who owned and worked on his own land in former times【英, 尤文或舊】自耕農 **2** an officer in the US navy who often has secretarial duties〔美國海軍〕文書軍官

yeo·man·ry /ˈjomənrɪ; ˈjəʊmənri/ *n* **the yeomanry** *BrE literary* the people who owned and farmed their own land in the past【英, 文】〔過去的〕自耕農〔總稱〕

yeoman ser·vice /ˌ·· ˈ··/ *n* [U] *BrE formal* long and loyal service, help and support【英, 正式】長期忠誠的服務[幫助、支持]

yer /jɚ; jə/ *determiner* used in writing as an informal way of saying 'your' 你的; 你們的〔書面語中 your 的非正式說法〕

yes¹ /jɛs; jes/ *adv spoken*【口】**1** used as an answer to say that something is true, that you agree, that you want something, or that you are willing to do something 是, 是的〔表示同意或願意〕: *"Is that real gold?" "Yes, it is."* "那是真金嗎?" "是的。" | *"It was a great film." "Yes, it was."* "這是部很棒的電影。" "是的。" | *"Would you like a sandwich?" "Yes, please."* "來個三明治吧?" "好的。" | *"Can you help us on Saturday?" "Yes I think so."* "星期六能幫我們一下嗎?" "行, 我想可以。" —opposite 反義詞 NO **2** used as an answer to give permission 可以〔表示允許〕: *"Can I have a glass of water?" "Yes, of course."* "我可以喝杯水嗎?" "當然可以。" | **say yes to (doing) sth** *I hope my parents will say yes to the party.* 我希望我父母會同意舉行這個聚會。**3** used to politely show that you do not agree with all or some of what someone has said 是的, 不錯〔禮貌地表示只部分同意〕: **yes but** *"We need a new car." "Yes, but where will we get the money?"* "我們需要一輛新車。" "是的, 可是從哪

兒弄到錢呢?" **4** used to show that you have heard a request, call, command etc 好的; 甚麼〔用於表示聽到請求、叫喚、命令等〕: *"Can you close the door, please?" "Yes, in a minute."* "請關上門好嗎?" "好的, 馬上就關。" | *"Michael!" "Yes?"* "邁克爾!" "甚麼事?" **5** used to ask someone what they want〔用於詢問別人的需求〕: *Yes? Can I help you find something, madam?* 我能幫你找甚麼嗎, 女士? **6 yes, yes** used to show annoyance when someone is talking to you and you do not want to listen 好的, 好的〔表示不耐煩〕: *"And don't forget to lock the door!" "Yes, yes ok."* "還有, 別忘了鎖門!" "好的, 好的, 可以。" **7 yes and no** used to show that there is not one clear answer to a question 既是又不是〔表示難以明確答覆〕: *"Did you have a good time?" "Well, yes and no. The lake was beautiful, but Craig and Jen fought the whole time."* "玩得好嗎?" "嗨, 一言難盡。湖確實很美, 可是克雷格和珍整天吵架。" **8 yes/no question** a question to which you only answer yes or no 只用是或否回答的問題 —see also 另見 YEAH

yes² *n* [C] a vote, voter, or reply that agrees with an idea, plan, law etc 贊成票; 贊成者; 贊成: *five yeses and three nos* 五張贊成票, 三張反對票 —**yes** *adj*: *a yes vote* 一張贊成票

ye·shi·va, ye·shi·vah /jəˋʃivə; jəˈʃiːvə/ *n* a school for Jewish students, where they can train to become RABBIS (=religious leaders)〔培養拉比的〕猶太神學院; 猶太高等學校

yes-man /ˋjɛs ˏmæn; ˈjes mæn/ *n plural* **yes-men** /-ˏmɛn; -men/ [C] someone who always agrees with and obeys their employer, leader, etc in order to gain some advantage 唯唯諾諾的人, 遵命先生

1 1 **yes·ter·day** /ˋjɛstɚdɪ; ˈjestədi/ *n* **1** [U] the day before today 昨天, 昨日: *What did you do yesterday?* 昨天你幹甚麼了? | *The day before yesterday was Monday.* 前天是星期一。| *He left yesterday afternoon.* 他昨天下午離開的。| *I'm looking for yesterday's paper.* 我在找昨天的報紙。—see picture at 參見 DAY 圖 **2** [C] the recent past 近來, 最近: **yesterday's news** (=not new or modern and therefore no longer of any interest) 昨日新聞, 舊聞 *The voters won't care about the scandal – that's yesterday's news.* 選民才不會計較這種醜事呢 —— 那已是舊聞啦。**3 I wasn't born yesterday** used to say that you cannot be easily deceived 我不是小孩子, 我不會輕易上當受騙: *Don't lie to me! Do you think I was born yesterday?* 別跟我撒謊! 你以為我是小孩子嗎?

yes·ter·year /ˋjɛstɚˏjɪr; ˈjestəjɪə/ *n* **of yesteryear** *literary* from a time in the past【文】往昔的: *the familiar songs of yesteryear* 熟悉的老歌

1 1 **yet¹** /jɛt; jet/ *adv* **1** [in questions or negatives 用於疑問句或否定句] until now or until a particular time (現在) 還; 至此, 迄今; 已經: *Has Edmund arrived yet?* 埃德蒙來了嗎? | *The potatoes aren't quite ready yet.* 馬鈴薯還沒做好呢。—see 見 JUST (USAGE) **2 as yet** an expression meaning until this moment, used in questions and negatives 到目前為止〔用於疑問句和否定句〕: *We've had no luck as yet.* 到目前為止, 我們運氣還不太好。| *As yet, there's been no news.* 目前還沒有消息。**3 not yet** an expression meaning not at the present time, used especially in the answer to questions 尚未, 仍未〔尤用於回答問題〕: *"Are you ready to leave?" "Not just yet."* "你準備走了嗎?" "還沒呢。" **4** but or in spite of something 但是, 而, 然而; 儘管: *a simple yet effective system* 簡單而有效的系統 **5 months/weeks/ages yet** used to emphasize how long it will be before something happens or how long a situation will last〔用於強調〕還早[遠]着呢: *"When's your holiday?" "Oh, not for ages yet."* "甚麼時候去休假?" "噢, 不知何年何月呢。" **6** in the future, in spite of the way that things seem now 將來, 遲早: *We may win yet.* 我們遲早會贏的。| *The plan could yet succeed.* 這計劃遲早會成功的。**7** even or still 更; 仍, 還: *yet another reason to be cautious* 再一個要謹慎的理由 | *a yet worse mistake* 一個更糟糕的錯誤 | **yet again** (=one more time after many others) 再一次 *I'm sorry to disturb you yet again.* 很抱歉再一次打擾你。**8** *formal* still【正式】仍然, 仍舊: *I have yet to hear Ray's version of what happened* (=I still have not heard it). 雷仍未告訴我所發生的事。

USAGE NOTE 用法説明: YET

FORMALITY 正式程度

Yet often comes either immediately after a negative word or at the end of a clause, but there is a difference of style. In a formal meeting you might hear yet 常用在否定詞後或子句末尾, 但兩者在文體上有差別。在正式會議中, 你或許會聽到: *We do not yet know the answer.* 我們還不知道答案呢。In informal conversation you might say 在非正式對話中, 你可以說: *I don't know the answer yet* (NOT 不用 *I don't know yet the answer*). 我還不知道答案呢。

Yet may also be placed immediately after the verb where a clause follows. yet 也可直接用在動詞與賓語從句之間: *I don't know yet whether she'll come or not.* 我還不知道她是否會來。

yet² *conjunction* used to introduce a statement that is surprising after what you have just said 但是, 可是, 然而〔連接句子, 表示含驚訝之意的轉折〕: *It's only a little shop and yet it always has such lovely decorations.* 這只是一家小店鋪, 然而它總是裝飾得那麼可愛。| *She's a funny girl, yet you can't help liking her.* 她是個古怪的姑娘, 然而你總禁不住會喜歡她。

yet·i /ˋjɛtɪ; ˈjeti/ *n* [C] a large hairy animal like a human which is supposed to live in the Himalayan mountains but many people do not believe exists 雪人〔傳説生活在喜瑪拉雅山上多毛的、形如人類的動物〕

yew /ju; juː/ *n* [C,U] a tree with dark green leaves and red berries, or the wood of this tree 紫杉樹; 紫杉木

y-fronts /ˋwaɪ frʌnts; ˈwaɪ frʌnts/ *n* [plural] *BrE* men's underwear which has a part at the front shaped like an upside down Y【英】〔男用〕倒 Y 形內褲, 三角短褲

yid /jɪd; jɪd/ *n* [C] *taboo* an extremely offensive word for a Jewish person【諱】猶太人〔極冒犯用語〕

Yid·dish /ˋjɪdɪʃ; ˈjɪdɪʃ/ *n* [U] a language based on German used by Jewish people, especially those who are from eastern Europe 依地語, 意第緒語〔尤指東歐的猶太人使用的一種語言〕

yield¹ /jild; jiːld/ *v*

1 ▶CROPS/PROFITS 莊稼/利潤◀ [T] to produce crops, profits etc 出產; 產生: *The land yielded a good wheat crop.* 這塊地盛產小麥。| *Mining shares often yield a high level of return.* 礦業股常有很高的回報率。

2 ▶RESULT 結果◀ [T] to produce a result, answer, or a piece of information 得出〔結果等〕: *Careful analysis yielded the following conclusions.* 經仔細分析得出以下結論。

3 ▶AGREE 同意◀ [I,T] to agree to do something you do not want to do because you have been forced or persuaded to 服從, 被迫同意: **[+to]** *The hijackers refuse to yield to demands to release the passengers.* 劫機者拒不答應釋放乘客的要求。

4 yield to your emotions/feelings to finally decide to do something because you cannot control your feelings any longer 屈從自己的感情/感覺

5 ▶TRAFFIC 交通◀ [I] *AmE* to allow other traffic on a bigger road to go first【美】讓〔其他車或人〕先行, 讓路; give way (WAY¹ (34)) *BrE*【英】

6 ▶GIVE UP FIGHTING 放棄戰鬥◀ [I] *literary* to stop fighting and accept defeat【文】投降, 屈服

7 ▶MOVE/BEND/BREAK 移動/彎曲/斷裂◀ [I] to move, bend, or break because of physical force or pressure〔因外在力量或壓力而〕移動; 彎曲; 斷裂: *The door wouldn't yield despite all our efforts to move it.* 雖然我們竭盡全力, 這門就是挪不動。

8 ▶CHANGE 變換◀ [I] *formal* if one thing yields to

another thing, this other thing replaces it【正式】讓與: [+to] *Open spaces around town are yielding to huge hyper-stores.* 該鎮周圍的空地都讓超級大商店給佔了。

yield sth ↔ **up** *phr v* [T] *literary* to show or give someone something that has been hidden for a long time or is very difficult to obtain【文】泄露, 揭示: *Little by little, the universe yields up its many secrets.* 宇宙一點一點地顯露出許多祕密。

yield² *n* [C] the amount of profits, crops etc that you get 產量; 收益: *investments with high yields* 高收益的投資

yield·ing /ˈjildɪŋ; ˈjiːldɪŋ/ *adj* **1** a surface that is yielding is soft and will move or bend when you press it〔物體表面〕易變形的, 易彎曲的 **2** willing to agree with other people's wishes and letting them decide instead of you 柔順的, 依從的: *She is too yielding when clients make demands on her time.* 她過於柔弱, 以致客戶們能隨意佔用她的時間。**3 high/low yielding** producing a large or small amount of something such as crops 高/低產的

yin /jɪn; jɪn/ *n* [U] the female principle in Chinese PHILOSOPHY which is inactive, dark and negative, and which combines with YANG (=the male principle) to influence everything in the world〔中國哲學概念中的〕陰

yin and yang /ˌ· · ˈ·/ *n* [U] the ancient Chinese PHILOSOPHY which is based on the idea that everything in the Universe is formed and influenced by the combination of two forces called YIN and YANG〔中國古代哲學概念中的〕陰和陽

yip·pee /ˈjɪpi; jɪˈpiː/ *interjection* used when you are very pleased or excited about something 好啊〔表示歡欣的歡呼聲〕

YMCA /ˌwaɪ ɛm si ˈe; ˌwaɪ em siː ˈeɪ/ *n* [singular] Young Men's Christian Association; an organization in many countries that provides places to stay and sports activities for young people 基督教青年會

yo /jo; jəʊ/ *interjection slang, especially AmE* used to greet someone or get their attention【俚, 尤美】唷〔用於招呼或喚起注意〕: *Yo dude! How's it goin'?* 唷, 老兄! 日子過得怎樣?

yob /jab; jɒb/ also 又作 **yob·bo** /ˈjabo; ˈjɒbəʊ/ *n* [C] *BrE*【英】**1** a rude, noisy, sometimes violent, young man 野小子, 粗魯吵鬧的年輕人 **2 yob culture/uniform/element etc** behaviour, clothes etc connected with yobs 野小子習氣/服裝/環境等 —**yobbery** *n* [U]

yo·del¹ /ˈjodəl; ˈjəʊdl/ *v* **yodelled, yodelling** *BrE*【英】, **yodeled, yodeling** *AmE*【美】[I,T] to sing while changing between your natural voice and a very high voice, traditionally done in the mountains of countries such as Switzerland and Austria 用岳得爾調唱(歌)〔瑞士和奧地利山區人用真假嗓音互換的唱法〕—**yodeller** *n* [C]

yodel² *n* [C] a song or sound made by yodelling〔用真假嗓音互換唱法的〕岳得爾唱法; 岳得爾曲; 岳得爾調

yo·ga /ˈjogə; ˈjəʊgə/ *n* [U] **1** a Hindu PHILOSOPHY in which you learn exercises to control your mind and body in order to try to achieve a union with God〔古印度哲學中的〕瑜伽 **2** a system of these exercises that helps you relax 瑜伽功

 3 **yog·hurt, yogurt** /ˈjogət; ˈjɒgət/ *n* [C,U] a thick liquid food that tastes slightly sour and is made from milk, or an amount of this 酸奶; 酸乳酪

yo·gi /ˈjogɪ; ˈjəʊgi/ *n* [C] someone who is very skilled at and has a lot of knowledge about yoga and who often teaches it to other people 瑜伽師, 教瑜伽者

yog·urt /ˈjogət; ˈjɒgət/ *n* [C,U] another spelling of yoghurt yoghurt 的另一種拼法

yoke¹ /jok; jəʊk/ *n* [C] **1** a wooden bar used for joining two animals, especially cattle, together in order to pull heavy loads 牛軛 **2** a frame fitted across someone's shoulders so that they can carry two equal loads〔挑東西用的〕軛狀扁擔 **3 the yoke of sth** *literary* something that restricts your freedom, making life hard or unpleasant【文】某事物的束縛[羈絆]: *the yoke of tradition* 傳統的束縛 **4** a part of a skirt or shirt just below the waist or collar, from which the main piece of material hangs in folds〔女服的〕上衣抵肩; 裙腰

yoke² *v* [T+together/to] **1** to join two animals with a yoke〔用軛〕把〔牲口〕套在一起 **2** *literary* to bring two ideas or people together so that they work well with each other【文】使結合; 使匹配: *The poet's choice of metaphor cleverly yokes together two dissimilar things.* 詩人的比喻把兩個不同的事物巧妙地連結在一起。

yo·kel /ˈjokḷ; ˈjəʊkəl/ *n* [C] *humorous* someone who comes from the countryside, seems to be a little stupid, and does not know much about modern life, ideas etc【幽默】鄉下佬, 土包子

yolk /jok; jəʊk/ *n* [C,U] the yellow part in the centre of an egg 蛋黃

Yom Kip·pur /ˌjom ˈkɪpɚ; ˌjɒm ˈkɪpə/ *n* [singular] the religious holiday when Jewish people do not eat, but pray to be forgiven for the things they have done wrong 贖罪日〔猶太教節日, 於此日禁食及作懺悔祈禱〕

yon·der /ˈjandɚ; ˈjɒndə/ also 又作 **yon** *adj, adv, determiner old use* used for telling someone which place or direction you mean【舊】那邊(的); 在遠處(的): *the fresh blooms on yonder tree* 那邊樹上新開的花

yonks /jaŋks; jɒŋks/ *n* [U] *BrE spoken* a long time【英口】好久, 很長一段時間: *It's yonks since we had a good night out.* 我們好久沒出去玩通宵了。| **not do sth for yonks** *We haven't seen Tom and Jean for yonks.* 我們很久沒看見湯姆和吉恩了。| **yonks ago** *We went to Blackpool once, yonks ago.* 我們很久以前到過布萊克浦一次。

yoo-hoo /ˌju ˈhu; ˌjuː ˈhuː/ *interjection informal* used to attract someone's attention when they are a long way from you【非正式】喂〔用於引起相距較遠之人的注意〕

yore /jɔr; jɔː/ *n* **of yore** *literary* of a long time ago【文】從前, 往昔, 很久以前

York·shire pud·ding /ˈjɔrkʃɚ ˈpʊdɪŋ; ˌjɔːkʃə ˈpʊdɪŋ/ *n* [C,U] a food made from flour, eggs and milk, eaten with meat in Britain〔英國的〕約克郡布丁

Yorkshire ter·ri·er /ˈjɔrkʃɚ ˈtɛrɪr; jɔːkʃə ˈteriə/ *n* [C] a type of dog that is very small with long brown hair 約克郡㹴犬〔一種小狗, 長着棕色的長毛〕

you /ju; jə; *strong* 強讀 ju; juː/ *pron* [used as a subject or an object 用作主詞或受詞] **1** the person or people someone is speaking or writing to 你; 你們: *You look nice, Sally.* 你看起來很好, 莎莉。| *You must all listen carefully.* 你們必須仔細聽着。| *I can see you.* 我能看見你。| *Did Robin give the money to you?* 羅賓把錢給你了嗎? | *I told you this would happen.* 我告訴過你會發生這種事的。| *Only you can make this decision.* 只有你能做出這種決定。**2** people in general〔泛指〕任何人: *You have to be careful with people you don't know.* 對陌生人要小心。| *You can't learn to ride a horse by reading books about it.* 光看書誰也學不會騎馬。**3** used with nouns or phrases when you are talking to or calling someone 你(這個), 你們(這些)〔與名詞或片語連用, 與某人談話或稱呼某人時用〕: *You boys have got to learn to behave yourselves.* 你們這些男孩得學規矩點兒。| *You twit!* 你這個傻瓜! | *Hey, you over there! Get out of the way!* 喂, 那邊的人! 走開!

you'd /jud; jəd; *strong* 強讀 jud; juːd/ **1** the short form of 縮略式= 'you had' **2** the short form of 縮略式= 'you would'

you'll /jul; jəl; *strong* 強讀 jul; juːl/ **1** the short form of 縮略式= 'you will' **2** the short form of 縮略式= 'you shall'

young¹ /jʌŋ; jʌŋ/ *adj* **1** not having lived for very long 年輕的; 幼小的: *a young child* 幼兒 | *young seedlings* 幼苗 | *You're too young to learn to drive.* 你太小了, 不能學開車。| **in your younger days** (=when you were young) 年輕時 *John was a great footballer in his younger days.* 約翰年輕時是個很棒的足球員。**2** not having existed for a long time 新建立的: *a young country* 新興的

國家 **3 young for your age** looking or behaving in a way that makes you seem as if you are younger than you really are 比實際年齡年輕 **4 young at heart** *approving* thinking and behaving as if you are young even though you are old【褒】(人老) 心不老: *Arthur's 96, but he's still young at heart.* 亞瑟96歲了, 但他心不老。**5** seeming or looking younger than you are; YOUTHFUL 有青春活力的, 朝氣蓬勃的: *Rosie has a very young face.* 羅西有一張很青春的面孔。**6** designed or meant for young people 專為年輕人設計的: *That hat is too young for you.* 那種帽子是年輕人戴的, 不適合你。

young[2] *n* **1 the young** young people considered as a group 年輕人〔總稱〕 **2** [plural] a group of young animals that belong to a particular mother or type of animal 幼小動物, 崽, 雛: *The lioness fought to protect her young.* 那頭母獅為保護幼獅而搏鬥。

young·er /ˈjʌŋgɚ; ˈjʌŋgə/ *adj* **sb the younger** *old-fashioned* someone who has the same name as their mother or father【過時】小…〔與父或母同名者〕: *William Pitt the younger* 小威廉·皮特 —compare 比較 ELDER[1] (2b)

young la·dy /ˌ· ˈ··/ *n* [C] *old-fashioned*【過時】**1** a way of speaking to a young girl when you are angry 小姐〔生氣時用語〕: *Now, listen to me, young lady!* 好了, 聽我說, 小姐! **2** someone's GIRLFRIEND〔某人的〕女朋友

young man /ˌ· ˈ·/ *n* [C] *old-fashioned*【過時】**1** a way of speaking to a young boy when you are angry 年輕人〔生氣時用語〕: *You'd better do as I tell you, young man.* 你最好照我說的做, 年輕人。**2** someone's BOYFRIEND〔某人的〕男朋友

young mar·rieds /ˌ· ˈ··/ *n* [plural] *especially AmE* young people who have recently got married【尤美】新婚的年輕人

young of·fend·er /ˌ· ·ˈ··/ *n* [C] a criminal in Britain who is not an adult according to the law〔英國的〕青少年罪犯

young·ster /ˈjʌŋstɚ; ˈjʌŋstə/ *n* [C] *old-fashioned* a young person【過時】年輕人

1 **your** /jur; jɚ; *strong* 強讀 jur; jɔː/ *determiner* **1** belong-
1 ing to or connected with the person or people someone is speaking to 你的; 你們的: *Could you move your car?* 你能把你的車挪一下嗎? | *That's your problem.* 那是你的問題。| *You must all come – and bring your husbands.* 你們都得來 — 還要帶上你們的丈夫。| *It's your own fault if you've lost them.* 你如果丢了它們, 就是你自己的錯。**2** belonging to any person 任何人的: *If you are facing north, east is on your right.* 假如你面向北, 你的右邊就是東。**3** *informal* used when mentioning something that is a good example of a particular type of thing or quality【非正式】〔用於提及典型的某物或某種品質〕: *Your typical 60s pop group had 3 guitarists and a drummer.* 60年代典型的流行樂隊有三個結他手和一個鼓手。| *Where are your Georgie Bests in today's game?* 今天的比賽中, 你們那喬治·貝斯特到哪裡去了?

you're /jur; jɚ; *strong* 強讀 jur; jɔː/ the short form of 縮略式= 'you are'

1 **yours** /jurz; jɔːz/ *pron* **1** belonging to or connected with
3 the person or people someone is speaking to 你的 (東西); 你們的 (東西): *This is our room, and yours* (=your room) *is just opposite.* 這是我們的房間, 你們的在對面。| *My eyes are blue and yours are green.* 我的眼睛是藍色的, 你的是綠色的。| *Is Maria a friend of yours?* 瑪麗亞是你的朋友嗎? **2 be yours for the taking/asking** if something important, desirable etc is yours for the taking, you can easily obtain or achieve it 探囊可取, 唾手可得: *If you want the job, it's yours for the taking.* 如果你想要這份工作, 那容易得很。**3 Yours faithfully/truly** used to end a formal letter that begins 'Dear Sir' or 'Dear Madam' 您忠誠的/您真誠的〔用於正式信函的結尾〕 **4 Yours sincerely/Yours** used to end a less formal letter that begins 'Dear Mr. Graves', 'Dear Miss Hope' etc 你的真摯的〔用於不太正式的信函的結尾〕 **5 yours truly** *informal* used to mean 'I', 'me', or 'myself'【非正式】我, 我自己: *They all went out, leaving yours truly to clear up the mess.* 他們都出去了, 留下我來收拾殘局。

your·self /jurˈsɛlf; jəˈself/ *pron plural* **yourselves** 1
/-ˈsɛlvz; -ˈselvz/ **1** the REFLEXIVE form of 'you' 你自己 2
〔you 的反身代詞〕: *Mind you don't hurt yourself with those scissors.* 注意, 別讓剪刀傷了你自己。| *Go and buy yourself an ice-cream.* 去給你自己買個冰淇淋吧。**2** used as a stronger form of "you"〔用以加強語氣〕你親自, 你本人: *You yourself said he was a dead loss.* 是你自己說他輸定了的。| *If you don't trust me you'd better go yourself.* 你如果不相信我, 最好自己去。**3 not be/feel yourself** *informal* to be slightly ill, tired, or upset【非正式】有點不適[疲憊、煩惱]: *Of course I'll forgive you; I know you weren't yourself yesterday.* 我當然不會跟你計較, 我知道你昨天有點兒煩。| *Are you all right? You don't seem yourself this morning.* 你沒事吧?今天早上你好像不太舒服。**4 (all) by yourself a)** without anyone helping you 獨力地, 全靠你自己: *Can you put your shoes on all by yourself, Ben?* 你能自己穿上鞋嗎, 本? **b)** with no other people with you 獨自地: *You can't go home by yourself in the dark.* 天黑你不能獨自回家。—see 見 ALONE[1] (USAGE) **5 to yourself** if you have a room, time etc to yourself, it is your own and you do not have to share it with anyone 獨自享有〔房間、時間等〕: *If you got there early you had the whole beach to yourself.* 你如果早點到達那裡, 整個沙灘都是你一人的天下了。| *It's nice to have an evening to yourself now and then.* 偶爾獨自呆一晚上也很愜意。—see also 另見 DO-IT-YOURSELF, **keep sth to yourself** (KEEP[1])

youth /juθ; juːθ/ *n plural* **youths** /juðz; juːðz/ **1** [U] the 2
period of time when someone is young, especially the 2
period between being a child and being fully grown 青少年時期: *Youth is a time when many people rebel against their parents.* 在青少年時期, 許多人都會違抗自己的父母。| **in sb's youth** (=when they were young) 在某人年輕時 *In his youth, Jimmy was an idealist and a rebel.* 吉米年輕時是個理想主義者和叛逆者。**2** [C] a word meaning boy or young man, especially a TEENAGER, used especially when you disapprove of them〔尤用於貶義〕(毛頭) 小伙子: *gangs of youths hanging about on street corners* 在街角閒蕩的一羣羣小伙子 —see 見 CHILD (USAGE) **3** [also+plural verb *BrE* 英] young people considered as a group 青年人〔總稱〕: *the courage of youth* 青年人的勇氣 | **the youth of** *The youth of the country are being ignored by politicians.* 這個國家的年輕人不受政治家的重視。**4** [singular,U] the quality or state of being young 青春 (活力), 朝氣: *a product that claims to restore youth and vitality to your skin* 一種聲稱可恢復肌膚青春活力的產品

youth club /ˈ· ·/ *n* [C] a meeting place for young people where they can drink coffee, play games etc 青年俱樂部

youth cul·ture /ˈ· ˌ··/ *n* [U] the interests and activities of young people, especially the music, films etc they enjoy 青年文化〔尤指年輕人感興趣的音樂、電影等〕

youth·ful /ˈjuθfəl; ˈjuːθfəl/ *adj* **1** typical of or having qualities typical of youth 富於青春活力的; 朝氣蓬勃的: *youthful enthusiasm* 年輕人特有的熱情 | *She's over 50, but has a youthful complexion.* 她五十多歲了, 但面容依然姣好。**2** young 年輕的; 青年的: *youthful soldiers* 年輕的士兵 —**youthfully** *adv* —**youthfulness** *n* [U]

youth hos·tel /ˈ· ˌ··/ *n* [C] a place where people, especially young people who are travelling, can stay very cheaply for a short time 青年旅舍

youth hos·tel·ling /ˈ· ˌ···/ *n* [U] *BrE* the activity of staying in youth hostels and walking or cycling between them【英】青年旅舍寄宿活動: **go youth hostelling** *I went youth hostelling in the Peak District.* 我到皮克區參加青年旅舍寄宿活動了。

you've /juv; jəv; *strong* 強讀 juv; juːv/ the short form of 縮略式= 'you have'

yowl /jaul; jaʊl/ *v* [I] to make a long loud cry, especially because you are sad or in pain〔尤指悲痛或疼痛時〕嚎

Y

叫; 惨叫: *A tomcat was yowling out on the lawn.* 一隻公貓在草坪上哀叫。—**yowl** *n* [C]

yo-yo /ˈjo jo; ˈjəʊ jəʊ/ *n* [C] a toy you hold in your hand made of two circular parts joined together that go up and down a string as you lift your hand up and down 搖搖, 悠悠, 溜溜球〔一種圓形玩具, 可用繩索拉上拉下〕

yr *plural* yrs the written abbreviation of 縮寫 = YEAR

yu·an /jʊˋɑn; jʊˈɑːn/ *n* [C] the standard unit of money in China 元〔中國貨幣單位〕

yuc·ca /ˋjʌkə; ˈjʌkə/ *n* [C] a desert plant with long pointed leaves on a thick straight stem 絲蘭〔屬植物〕

yuck, yuk /jʌk; jʌk/ *interjection informal* used to show that you think something is very unpleasant【非正式】呸! 啐! 討厭!〔表示強烈的厭惡〕

yuck·y /ˋjʌkɪ; ˈjʌki/ *adj informal* extremely unpleasant【非正式】令人極度厭惡的: *a yucky colour* 非常難看的顏色 | *The food was yucky.* 這食物令人厭惡。

yuk /jʌk; jʌk/ *interjection* another spelling of yuck yuck 的另一種拼法

Yule /jul; juːl/ *n old use* Christmas【舊】聖誕節

yule log /ˈ· ·/ *n* [C] **1** a LOG of wood traditionally burnt on the evening before Christmas 聖誕柴〔聖誕前夜焚燒的大塊木頭〕 **2** a chocolate cake shaped like a LOG and eaten at Christmas 形狀像聖誕柴的巧克力蛋糕

Yule·tide /ˋjulˌtaɪd; ˈjuːltaɪd/ *n* [U] *poetical* Christmas【詩】聖誕節

yum·my /ˋjʌmɪ; ˈjʌmi/ *adj informal* food that is yummy tastes very good【非正式】〔食物〕美味的, 可口的

yup·pie, yuppy /ˋjʌpɪ; ˈjʌpi/ *n* [C] a young person who seems to be only concerned with their job, making a lot of money, and spending it on expensive things 雅皮士, 優皮士〔只關心工作、有高收入並愛買高檔物品的職業青年〕: *The Docklands area has been converted into smart flats for yuppies.* 船塢區已成了雅皮士聚居的時髦公寓區。

YWCA /ˌwaɪ dʌbḷju si ˋe; ˌwaɪ dʌbəljuː siː ˈeɪ/ *n* [singular] Young Women's Christian Association; an organization in many countries that provides places to stay and sports activities for young people 基督教女青年會

Y

Z,z

Z, z /zi; zed/ *plural* **Z's, z's** or **Zs, zs** **1** the last letter of the English alphabet 英語字母表的最後一個字母 **2 Z's** *AmE informal* sleep【美, 非正式】睡覺: **catch/get some Z's** (=to sleep) 抓緊睡一會兒 *I think I'll go catch some Z's.* 我想我得抓緊睡一會兒去。

za·ny /ˋzenɪ; ˈzeɪni/ *adj* crazy or unusual in a way that is amusing 滑稽的, 可笑的: *zany comedian Lenny Henry* 滑稽可笑的喜劇演員倫尼·亨利

zap¹ /zæp; zæp/ *v* **zapped, zapping** *informal*【非正式】**1** [T] to quickly attack or destroy something, especially in a computer game〔尤指在電子遊戲中〕快速攻擊, 摧毀: *You get 100 points for each plane you zap.* 每擊落一架飛機你就能得 100 分。**2** [T always+adv/prep, I always+adv/prep] to do something very quickly or go somewhere very quickly 迅速做〔某事〕; 迅速到達〔某地〕: **zap sth in/into** *He zapped the car into fourth gear and screeched off.* 他迅速把車掛上四擋, 然後呼嘯而去。| **[+past/through/along etc]** *I'll have to zap through the work to make the deadline.* 我得趕在限期之前把這工作幹完。**3** [T] *AmE informal* to cook something in a MICROWAVE¹ (1)【美, 非正式】用微波爐烹製〔食物〕

zap² *n* [U] *BrE informal* interest and excitement; ENERGY (1)【英, 非正式】趣味; 活力; 精力: *The advert needs a bit more zap.* 這廣告需要再活潑一些。

zap·per /ˋzæpɚ; ˈzæpə/ *n* [C] *AmE informal*【美, 非正式】**1** a thing you use for changing channels (CHANNEL¹ (1)) on a television from a distance; REMOTE CONTROL (1)〔電視〕遙控器 **2** a piece of electrical equipment that attracts and kills insects 滅蟲器

zap·py /ˋzæpɪ; ˈzæpi/ *adj BrE informal* interesting and exciting【英, 非正式】活潑有趣的, 生動的: *a zappy poster* 活潑有趣的海報

zeal /zil; ziːl/ *n* [U] eagerness to do something, especially to achieve a particular religious or political aim〔尤指實現宗教或政治目標的〕熱情, 熱忱: *revolutionary zeal* 革命熱情

zeal·ot /ˋzɛlət; ˈzelət/ *n* [C] someone who has extremely strong beliefs, especially religious or political beliefs, and is too eager to make other people share them〔尤指政治或宗教信仰方面的〕熱心者; 狂熱者: *religious zealots* 宗教狂熱分子 —**zealotry** *n* [U]

zeal·ous /ˋzɛləs; ˈzeləs/ *adj* extremely enthusiastic about something that you believe in very strongly and behaving in a way that shows this 熱心[熱情]的; 狂熱的: *a zealous preacher* 熱心的傳教士 —**zealously** *adv* —**zealousness** *n* [U]

ze·bra /ˋzibrə; ˈziːbrə/ *n* [C] an animal that looks like a horse but has black and white lines all over its body 斑馬

zebra cross·ing /,.. ˈ../ *n* [C] *BrE* a place marked with black and white lines where people who are walking can cross a road safely【英】斑馬線; CROSSWALK *AmE*【美】—compare 比較 PELICAN CROSSING

zed /zɛd; zed/ *BrE*【英】, **zee** *AmE*【美】*n* [C] a way of writing the letter 'z' that shows how you pronounce it 字母 Z〔讀音的拼寫形式〕

zeit·geist /ˋzaɪt,gaɪst; ˈzaɪtgaɪst/ *n* [singular] *German* the general spirit or feeling of a period in history, as shown by people's ideas and beliefs at the time【德】時代精神[思潮]

Zen /zɛn; zen/ *n* [U] a kind of Buddhism that is popular in Japan 禪宗〔日本佛教的一大宗派〕

zen·ith /ˋzinɪθ; ˈzenɪθ/ *n* [C usually singular 一般用單數] **1** the most successful point in the development of something〔事物發展的〕頂點, 頂峯: **reach its zenith/be at its zenith** *Opera reached its zenith at the turn of the century.* 歌劇在世紀之交達到了巔峯。**2** the highest point that is reached by the sun or the moon in the sky 天頂〔太陽或月亮在天空中達到的最高點〕

zeph·yr /ˋzɛfɚ; ˈzefə/ *n* [C] *poetical* a soft gentle wind【詩】和風, 微風

zep·pe·lin /ˋzɛpəlɪn; ˈzepəlɪn/ *n* [C] a German AIRSHIP used in World War I 齊柏林飛艇〔第一次世界大戰時的德國飛艇〕

ze·ro¹ /ˋzɪro; ˈzɪərəʊ/ *n plural* **zeros** or **zeroes** *number*

1 ►NUMBER 數字◄ 0, 零

2 ►MEASUREMENT 計量◄ the point between + and - on a scale for measuring something, or the lowest point on a scale that shows how much there is left of something〔刻度上的〕零點, 零位: *The petrol gauge was already at zero.* 汽油表已指示零位。

3 ►TEMPERATURE 溫度◄ the point on the Celsius scale at which water freezes〔攝氏溫度表上的〕零度: *It was five degrees below zero last night.* 昨晚零下五度。| *sub-zero temperatures* 零下的溫度 —see also 另見 ABSOLUTE ZERO

4 ►NOTHING 全無◄ *informal* the lowest possible amount or level of something【非正式】〔某事物的〕最低點; 無, 沒有: *'Today?' I said, my spirits sinking to zero.* "今天?" 我說, 我的情緒降到了最低點。| *The kids showed zero interest in what I was saying.* 小孩子們對我說的話一點都不感興趣。

5 zero growth/inflation/gravity no growth, INFLATION (1) etc at all 零增長/通貨膨脹/重力: *The country is aiming at zero growth in its population by the year 2010.* 該國力爭到 2010 年使其人口達到零增長。

zero² *v*

zero in on sb/sth *phr v* [T] **1** to direct all your attention towards a particular person or thing 全神貫注於…: *Hayley zeroed in on the toys, the minute she saw them.* 海莉一看見玩具就心無旁騖了。**2** to aim a gun towards something or someone 把〔槍砲等〕瞄準…

zero hour /ˈ.. ,./ *n* [singular] the time when a military operation or an important event is planned to begin〔軍事行動或重要事件的〕開始時刻; 進攻時間

zero-sum game /,.. ˈ. ,./ *n* [singular] *AmE* a situation in which you receive as much money or advantages as you give away【美】得益與損失平衡的局面, 零和局面[遊戲]: *Diplomatic negotiations often aim at a zero-sum game.* 外交談判常常以得失平衡的局面為目標。

zest /zɛst; zest/ *n* **1** [U] eager interest and enjoyment 熱心, 熱情; 快樂: *zest for life* 對生活的熱情 **2** [singular, U] the quality of being exciting and interesting 趣味性; 刺激性: *The danger of being caught added a certain zest to the affair.* 有被捉的危險為這件事增添了一些刺激性。**3** [U] the outer skin of an orange or LEMON (1), used in cooking〔烹調中用作香料的〕橙皮; 檸檬皮 —**zestful** *adj* —**zestfully** *adv*

zig·zag¹ /ˋzɪgzæg; ˈzɪgzæg/ *n* [C] a pattern that looks like a line of z's joined together 之字形, Z 字形: *a zigzag path along the cliff* 沿懸崖而下的之字形小路—see picture on page A16 參見 A16 頁圖

zigzag² *v* **zigzagged, zigzagging** [I] to move forward in sharp angles, first to the left and then to the right etc 作之字形行進, 曲折移動: *The path zigzagged down the hillside.* 小路沿着山坡彎彎曲曲而下。

zilch /zɪltʃ; zɪltʃ/ *n* [U] *informal* nothing at all【非正式】

無, 烏有; 零: *"How much money is left?" "Zilch."* "還剩多少錢?" "一分也沒有了"。

zil·lion /ˈzɪljən; ˈzɪljən/ *n* [C] *informal* an extremely large number of something【非正式】極大的數目: **[+of]** *zillions of mosquitoes* 無數的蚊子

zim·mer frame /ˈzɪmɚ frem; ˈzɪmə freɪm/ *n* [C] *BrE trademark* a metal frame that old or ill people use to help them walk【英, 商標】〔老人或病人用的〕齊默助行架; WALKER (3) *AmE*【美】

zinc /zɪŋk; zɪŋk/ *n* [U] a bluish-white metal, used to make BRASS and to cover and protect objects made of iron 鋅

zing[1] /zɪŋ; zɪŋ/ *n* [U] *informal* the quality of being full of energy or taste【非正式】精力, 活力; 味道: *Lemon juice adds zing to drinks and sorbets.* 檸檬汁為飲料和果汁冰水增添了風味。—**zingy** *adj*

zing[2] *v* [I always+adv/prep] *informal* to move quickly, making a whistling noise【非正式】颼颼地掠過: **[+past/off]** *The shots went zinging off the rocks.* 子彈颼颼地擦過岩石彈開。

Zi·on·is·m /ˈzaɪən,ɪzəm; ˈzaɪənɪzəm/ *n* [U] support for the establishment and development of a state for the Jews in Israel 猶太復國主義 —**Zionist** *n* [C]

zip[1] /zɪp; zɪp/ *n* **1** [C] *BrE* two lines of small metal or plastic pieces that slide together to fasten a piece of clothing【英】拉鏈; ZIPPER *especially AmE*【尤美】: *The zip on my skirt had broken.* 我裙子上的拉鏈壞了。| **do up/undo your zip** (=close or open a piece of clothing using a zip) 拉上/拉開拉鏈 *Your zip's undone at the back.* 你背後的拉鏈開了。—see picture at 參見 FASTENER 圖 **2** [U] *informal* if someone or something has zip, they can do something quickly and with a lot of energy【非正式】精力, 活力: *This car goes with a bit more zip than my last one.* 這輛車的速度比我上一輛要快些。**3** [singular] *AmE informal* nothing at all or zero【美, 非正式】全無, 烏有; 零: *We beat them 10 to zip.* 我們以 10 比 0 贏了他們。| *"How much money have you got left?" "Zip!"* "你還剩多少錢?" "一分都不剩。"

zip[2] *v* **zipped, zipping 1** [T always+adv/prep] to open or shut something using a zip 用拉鏈拉開[拉上]: **[+in/inside]** *The money was safely zipped inside my jacket.* 錢在我的上衣內袋裡, 有拉鏈安全保護。| **zip sth shut/open** *Olsen zipped the bag shut.* 奧爾森把袋子的拉鏈拉上。**2** [I always+adv/prep] *informal* to do something or go somewhere very quickly【非正式】快速地做某事[到某地]: **[+through/past/along etc]** *We zipped through customs in no time.* 我們很快通過了海關。**3 zip your lip** *AmE spoken* used to tell someone not to say anything about something, or to tell them to be quiet【美口】別開口: *You'd better zip your lip or you'll be in trouble!* 你最好別開口, 不然會有麻煩的!

zip up *phr v* [T] **1 [zip** sth ↔ **up]** to fasten a piece of clothing using a zip 用拉鏈拉上〔衣服〕: *Zip your jacket up – you'll get cold.* 把夾克的拉鏈拉上——你會着涼的。—opposite 反義詞 UNZIP **2 [zip sb up]** to close the zip on a piece of clothing that someone else is wearing 拉上〔某人衣服〕的拉鏈: *"Could you zip me up please? I can't reach."* "幫我把拉鏈拉上好嗎? 我夠不着。"

zip code /ˈ· ·/ *n* [C] *AmE* a number that you put below the address on an envelope to help the post office deliver the mail more quickly【美】郵政編碼; POSTCODE *BrE*【英】

zip·per /ˈzɪpɚ; ˈzɪpə/ *n* [C] *especially AmE* two lines of small metal or plastic pieces that slide together to fasten a piece of clothing【尤美】拉鏈; ZIP[1] (1) *BrE*【英】—see picture at 參見 FASTENER 圖

zip·po /ˈzɪpo; ˈzɪpəʊ/ *n* [singular] *AmE informal* nothing at all or zero【美, 非正式】全無; 零

zit /zɪt; zɪt/ *n* [C] *informal* a spot on someone's skin; PIMPLE【非正式】丘疹

zith·er /ˈzɪðɚ; ˈzɪðə/ *n* [C] a musical instrument from Eastern Europe, played by pulling its wire strings with your fingers 齊特琴〔東歐的一種用手指彈撥的弦樂器〕

zo·di·ac /ˈzodɪ,æk; ˈzəʊdiæk/ *n* **the zodiac** an imaginary area through which the sun, moon, and PLANETS appear to travel, which some people believe influences our lives 黃道帶〔指太陽、月亮及行星所構成的假想帶〕: **sign of the zodiac** (=one of the twelve parts that this area is divided into) 黃道十二宮[星座]之一 *"Which sign of the zodiac were you born under?" "Leo."* "你的生辰屬於哪個星座?" "獅子座。" —see also 另見 HOROSCOPE —**zodiacal** /zoˈdaɪəkl; zəʊˈdaɪəkəl/ *adj*

zom·bie /ˈzɑmbɪ; ˈzɒmbi/ *n* [C] **1** *informal* someone who moves very slowly and does not seem to be thinking about what they are doing, especially because they are very tired【非正式】〔尤指因極度疲勞而〕行動呆板的人, 無精打采的人 **2** a dead person whose body is made to move by magic, according to some African and Caribbean religions〔非洲和加勒比海地區一些部族宗教信仰中的〕還魂屍, 殭屍, 行屍〔被巫術驅動的死屍〕

zon·al /ˈzonḷ; ˈzəʊnl/ *adj technical* connected with or arranged in zones【術語】區域性的; 分成區的; 劃好範圍的 —**zonally** *adv*

zone /zon; zəʊn/ *n* [C] a large area that is different from other areas around it in some way〔與周圍地區有所不同的〕地區; 地帶; 區域: *This is a no-parking zone.* 這是禁止泊車區。| *a nuclear-free zone* 無核區 | **danger zone** (=an area where it is dangerous to go) 危險地帶 | **war/battle/combat zone** *The south side of the city has virtually become a war zone.* 該城的南邊實際上已成為戰區。| **pedestrian zone** (=an area where no cars are allowed) 步行區 | **residential/industrial/commercial etc zone** (=an area of a city that is used for a particular purpose, such as houses or shops) 居民/工業/商業區等 —see also 另見 **buffer zone** (BUFFER[1] (3)), EROGENOUS ZONE, **exclusion zone** (EXCLUSION (3)), TIME ZONE

zoned /zond; zəʊnd/ also 又作 **zoned out** *adj* [not before noun 不用於名詞前] *AmE informal* unable to think clearly and quickly, especially because you are tired or ill【美, 非正式】〔尤因疲勞或患病而〕思維麻木的; 反應遲鈍的

zon·ing /ˈzonɪŋ; ˈzəʊnɪŋ/ *n* [U] a system of choosing areas to be developed for particular purposes, such as houses or shops, when planning a town 分區制; 分區佈局

zonked /zɑŋkt; zɒŋkt/ also 又作 **zonked out** *adj* [not before noun 不用於名詞前] *informal* extremely tired; EXHAUSTED (1)【非正式】筋疲力盡的: *Paul was zonked after the conference in Amsterdam.* 保羅在阿姆斯特丹的會議後累得疲憊不堪。

zoo /zu; zuː/ *n* [C] a place, usually in a city, where animals of many kinds are kept so that people can go to look at them 動物園

zoo-keep·er /ˈ· ,··/ *n* [C] someone who looks after animals in a zoo 動物園飼養員

zo·ol·o·gist /zoˈɑlədʒɪst; zuːˈɒlədʒɪst/ *n* [C] a scientist who studies animals and their behaviour 動物學家

zo·ol·o·gy /zoˈɑlədʒɪ; zuːˈɒlədʒi/ *n* [U] the scientific study of animals and their behaviour 動物學 —**zoological** /,zoəˈlɑdʒɪkḷ; ,zuːəˈlɒdʒɪkəl◂/ *adj* —**zoologically** /-kḷɪ; -kli/*adv*

zoom[1] /zum; zuːm/ *v* [I] *informal*【非正式】**1** [always+adv/prep] to go somewhere or do something very quickly 疾行; 快速做〔某事〕: **[+past/through/off etc]** *Brenda zoomed past on her Honda.* 布倫達騎着她的本田摩托車疾馳而過。| *The work was really easy and I was able to zoom through it in a couple of hours.* 這工作一點不難, 我用了兩三個小時就幹完了。**2** to increase suddenly and quickly 陡升, 激增: **[+to]** *Interest rates zoomed up to 20% in the late 80s.* 80 年代後期, 利率急升至 20%。

zoom in/out *phr v* [I] if a camera zooms in or out, it moves quickly between a picture that is close and detailed and one that is distant〔鏡頭〕拉近/推遠: **zoom in on sth/sb** *The camera zoomed in on the child's face.* 攝影機向孩子的臉部推近。

Z

zoom² *n* [singular] *informal* a sound made by a vehicle that is travelling fast【非正式】〔車輛快速行駛時發出的〕隆隆聲

zoom lens /ˈ· ˌ·/ *n* [C] a camera LENS (2) that can change from a distant to a close view 可變焦距透鏡, 變焦鏡頭 —see picture at 參見 CAMERA 圖

zoot suit /ˈzut ˌsut; ˈzuːt suːt/ *n* [C] a suit that consists of wide trousers and a JACKET with wide shoulders, worn especially in the 1940s and 1950s 祖特裝〔由寬肩夾克和寬大褲子組合的服裝, 尤流行於20世紀40和50年代〕

zuc·chi·ni /zuˈkini; zʊˈkiːni/ *n* [C] *AmE* a small vegetable with a dark green skin, shaped like a short stick【美】小胡瓜, 綠皮密生西葫蘆; COURGETTE *BrE*【英】—see picture on page A9 參見 A9 頁圖

Zu·lu /ˈzulu; ˈzuːluː/ *n* **1 the Zulu** a large tribe of people who live in South Africa〔南非的〕祖魯族 **2** [C] a member of this tribe 祖魯人 —**Zulu** *adj*

zwie·back /ˈzwaɪbæk; ˈzwiːbæk/ *n* [U] *AmE* a kind of hard dry bread, often given to babies【美】〔常給嬰兒食用的一種〕烤麵包乾 —compare 比較 RUSK *BrE*【英】

zy·de·co /ˈzaɪdəko; ˈzaɪdəkəʊ/ *n* [U] a kind of Cajun music 柴迪科舞曲

zy·gote /ˈzaɪgot; ˈzaɪgəʊt/ *n* [C] a cell that is formed when an egg is fertilized (FERTILIZE (1)) 受精卵

Position and Direction 位置和方向

The prepositions below refer to the picture opposite.

下面的介詞請參見右圖。

"Good Afternoon Ladies and Gentlemen. Welcome to the 6th national cycle race.

女士們，先生們，下午好！歡迎觀看第六屆全國腳踏車大賽。

It's turning into quite a day! **All about/around** me people are leaning **over**① the barriers to get a good view of the race. Local residents are hanging **out**② of their windows, and **beyond** the spectators, traffic is **at**③ a standstill.

今天是個相當熱鬧的日子。我周圍的人俯身探出柵欄外，以便看清楚這場比賽。當地的居民也都探身窗外。在觀眾那邊，交通都停頓了。

The police are out in full force. There's a police motorbike **next to/beside/alongside**④ the cyclists, a policewoman leaning **on**⑤ the barriers, and a helicopter **overhead**⑥.

警察全體出動。一輛警用摩托車跟在選手旁邊，一位女警察倚欄站立，一架直升機在賽場上空盤旋着。

Not far **from** me, **in/among** the crowd I can see last year's champion with his daughter **on**⑦ his shoulders. And **off** to the right, there are a number of fans pushing their way **through**⑧ the crowd **to/towards** the front.

離我不遠的人羣中，我看見去年的冠軍，他的肩上騎着他的女兒。在右邊的柵欄外，一羣賽車迷正從人羣中往前擠。

Across⑨ the finishing line **in** first place comes number thirty four. Directly **in front**⑩ of me photographers are trying to get shots of the winner, and just **below/beneath/underneath**⑪ me jubilant fans are cheering.

首先衝過終點線的是三十四號選手。在我的正前方，攝影師們正在搶拍冠軍的照片；就在我的下方，興高采烈的賽車迷正在雀躍歡呼。

On/to⑫ the left of the new champion, cycling **past** the photographers is number sixty one. Then, **behind**⑬ the leaders, **in** a red helmet is De Kosten **from** Belgium who is racing **towards/in the direction of** the finishing line. Chasing **after**⑭ him are numbers ninety two and a hundred and five, and at this very moment a small group of cyclists have just come **round**⑮ the corner **into** view.

在新冠軍的左側，六十一號選手騎着車在攝影師前掠過。緊跟着這兩位領先者後面的是戴着紅頭盔的比利時選手德·柯斯汀，他正向着終點線衝去。在他後面追趕的是九十二號和壹零五號選手。就在此刻，一小羣選手剛拐過那個街角，進入人們的視線。"

POLICE
6
3
15
2
Jupiter
4
14
13
11
1
12
61
34
FINISH
10
9
8
7
5

Car 汽車

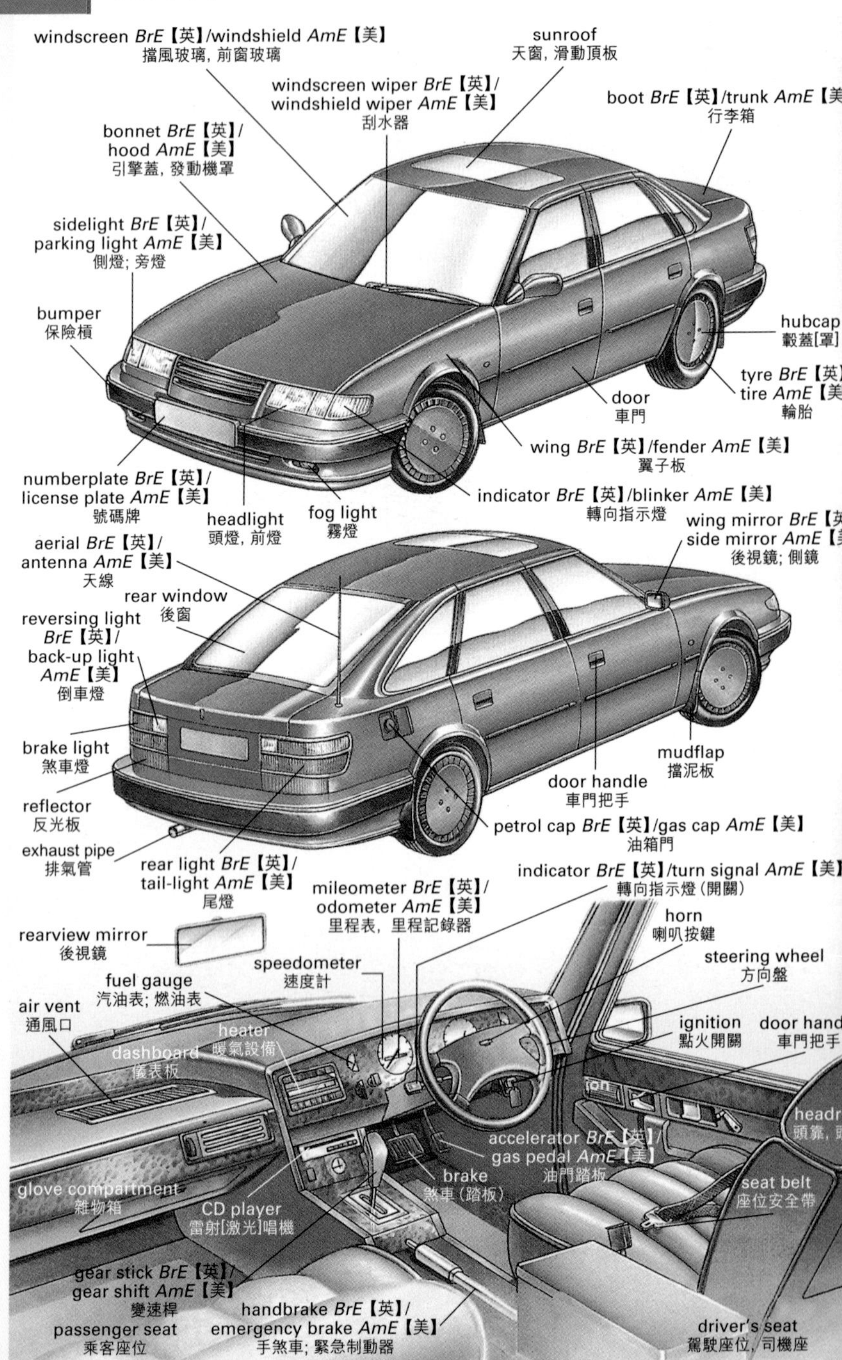
windscreen BrE【英】/windshield AmE【美】
擋風玻璃, 前窗玻璃
sunroof
天窗, 滑動頂板
windscreen wiper BrE【英】/
windshield wiper AmE【美】
刮水器
boot BrE【英】/trunk AmE【美
行李箱
bonnet BrE【英】/
hood AmE【美】
引擎蓋, 發動機罩
sidelight BrE【英】/
parking light AmE【美】
側燈; 旁燈
bumper
保險槓
hubcap
轂蓋[罩]
tyre BrE【英
tire AmE【美
輪胎
door
車門
wing BrE【英】/fender AmE【美】
翼子板
numberplate BrE【英】/
license plate AmE【美】
號碼牌
headlight
頭燈, 前燈
fog light
霧燈
indicator BrE【英】/blinker AmE【美】
轉向指示燈
wing mirror BrE【英
side mirror AmE【美
後視鏡; 側鏡
aerial BrE【英】/
antenna AmE【美】
天線
rear window
後窗
reversing light
BrE【英】/
back-up light
AmE【美】
倒車燈
brake light
煞車燈
reflector
反光板
exhaust pipe
排氣管
mudflap
擋泥板
door handle
車門把手
petrol cap BrE【英】/gas cap AmE【美】
油箱門
rear light BrE【英】/
tail-light AmE【美】
尾燈
indicator BrE【英】/turn signal AmE【美】
轉向指示燈(開關)
mileometer BrE【英】/
odometer AmE【美】
里程表, 里程記錄器
horn
喇叭按鍵
rearview mirror
後視鏡
speedometer
速度計
steering wheel
方向盤
fuel gauge
汽油表; 燃油表
air vent
通風口
heater
暖氣設備
dashboard
儀表板
ignition
點火開關
door hand
車門把手
headr
頭靠,
accelerator BrE【英】/
gas pedal AmE【美】
油門踏板
brake
煞車(踏板)
seat belt
座位安全帶
glove compartment
雜物箱
CD player
雷射[激光]唱機
gear stick BrE【英】/
gear shift AmE【美】
變速桿
handbrake BrE【英】/
emergency brake AmE【美】
手煞車; 緊急制動器
passenger seat
乘客座位
driver's seat
駕駛座位, 司機座

rse down the drive BrE【英】/
down the driveway AmE【美】
倒着駛出車道

drive BrE【英】/
driveway AmE【美】
私家車道
pavement BrE【英】/
sidewalk AmE【美】
人行道
back out into the street
倒車到街上

change up BrE【英】/
shift AmE【美】 into second gear
換到第二擋

30
maximum
speed sign
限速標誌
slow down
減速

signal/indicate left
指示向左轉

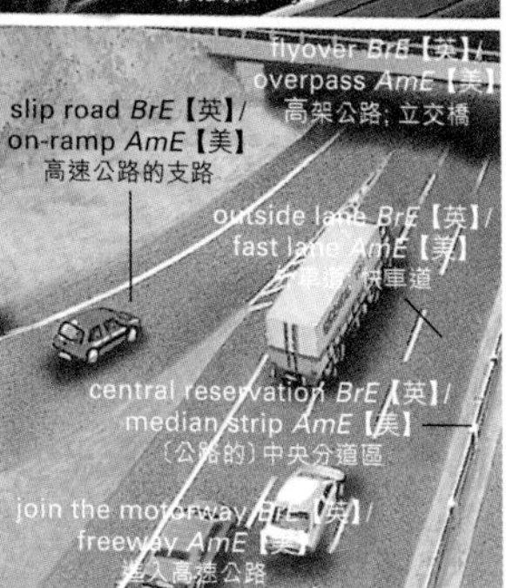
flyover BrE【英】/
overpass AmE【美】
高架公路; 立交橋
slip road BrE【英】/
on-ramp AmE【美】
高速公路的支路
outside lane BrE【英】/
fast lane AmE【美】
外車道; 快車道
central reservation BrE【英】/
median strip AmE【美】
(公路的)中央分道區
join the motorway BrE【英】/
freeway AmE【美】
進入高速公路

shoulder BrE【英】/
oulder AmE【美】
路肩
de lane BrE【英】/
w lane AmE【美】
內車道; 慢車道
ull out and overtake BrE【英】/
pass AmE【美】
趕上並超車

middle lane BrE【英】/
center lane AmE【美】
中央車道
change lanes
換線

pedestrian
行人
swerve to avoid a pedestrian
突然轉向以避免撞着行人

pull out into traffic
進入車流之中
cycle path BrE【英】/
bicycle route AmE【美】
腳踏[自行]車道

park the car
停車, 泊車
parking meter
停車計時收費器

put on the handbrake BrE【英】/
emergency brake AmE【美】
使用手煞車[緊急制動器]

House 房屋

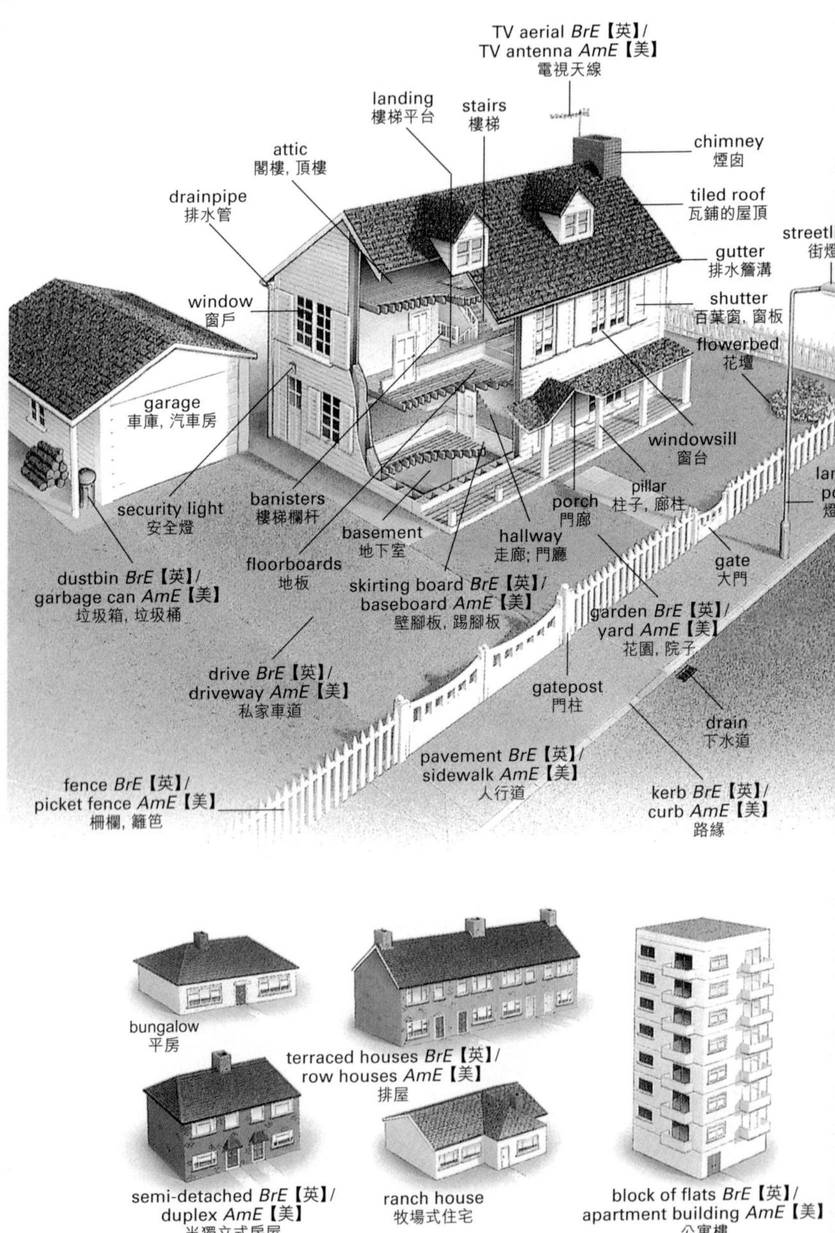
TV aerial *BrE*【英】/
TV antenna *AmE*【美】
電視天線
landing
樓梯平台
stairs
樓梯
chimney
煙囱
attic
閣樓, 頂樓
tiled roof
瓦鋪的屋頂
drainpipe
排水管
streetlig
街燈
gutter
排水簷溝
window
窗戶
shutter
百葉窗, 窗板
flowerbed
花壇
garage
車庫, 汽車房
windowsill
窗台
pillar
柱子, 廊柱
security light
安全燈
banisters
樓梯欄杆
porch
門廊
basement
地下室
hallway
走廊; 門廳
gate
大門
floorboards
地板
dustbin *BrE*【英】/
garbage can *AmE*【美】
垃圾箱, 垃圾桶
skirting board *BrE*【英】/
baseboard *AmE*【美】
壁腳板, 踢腳板
garden *BrE*【英】/
yard *AmE*【美】
花園, 院子
drive *BrE*【英】/
driveway *AmE*【美】
私家車道
gatepost
門柱
drain
下水道
pavement *BrE*【英】/
sidewalk *AmE*【美】
人行道
fence *BrE*【英】/
picket fence *AmE*【美】
柵欄, 籬笆
kerb *BrE*【英】/
curb *AmE*【美】
路緣
bungalow
平房
terraced houses *BrE*【英】/
row houses *AmE*【美】
排屋
semi-detached *BrE*【英】/
duplex *AmE*【美】
半獨立式房屋
ranch house
牧場式住宅
block of flats *BrE*【英】/
apartment building *AmE*【美】
公寓樓

sky-blue
天藍
lime
暗黃綠色
olive
橄欖(綠)色
jade
綠玉色，翡翠綠
beige
米黃色
violet
紫羅蘭色，藍紫色
poppy
罌粟花色，深橘紅色
scarlet
猩紅色，鮮紅色
tan
棕黃色，棕褐色
golden
金黃色
navy blue
海軍藍，深藍色
khaki
土黃色，黃褐色
bottle green
深綠色
russet
赤褐色
cream
乳白色，淡黃色
mustard
芥末黃；深黃色
turquoise
青綠色
royal blue
品藍色
emerald
綠寶石色；翡翠綠
maroon
褐紅色
peach
桃(紅)色
lemon
檸檬黃
burgundy
深(紫)紅色
rose
玫瑰紅色
magenta
洋紅色，紫紅色
tangerine
橘紅色
mauve
淡紫色
apricot
杏黃色
green
綠色
pink
粉紅色
lilac
丁香紫，淡紫色
coffee
咖啡色
purple
紫色
buff
暗黃色
blue
藍色
black
黑色
white
白色
grey
灰色
orange
橙色；橘黃色
brown
褐色，棕色
yellow
黃色
aquamarine
海藍色

Describing People 描寫人物

Emma has long wavy gingery-brown hair, with a centre parting *BrE* / center part *AmE*. She has freckles, hazel eyes and wears her hair pushed back behind her ears.
埃瑪梳着薑棕色的波浪形長髮，中間分縫。她臉上長有雀斑，眼睛是淺褐色的。她把頭髮撥到耳後。

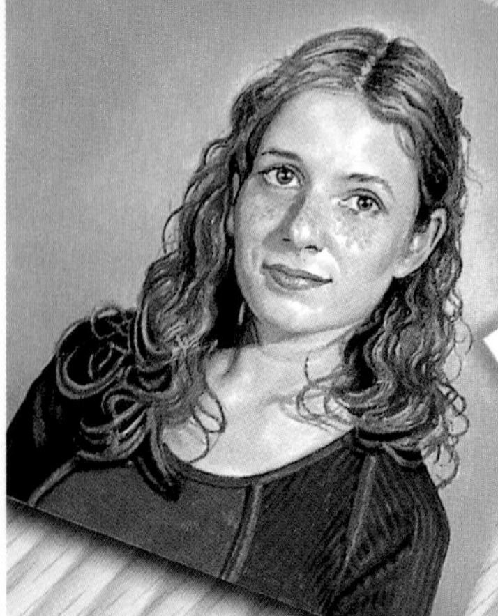

Roald has short spiky fair hair. He's got thick bushy eyebrows, a five o'clock shadow and sideburns.
勞爾德有一頭短而直豎的金髮。他的眉毛又粗又濃密，滿臉鬍子茬。他還留了鬢髮。

Kaori has straight shoulder-length hair, a side parting *BrE* /side part *AmE* and a short fringe *BrE* / short bangs *AmE*. She has dark brown eyes and high cheekbones.
考麗梳着齊肩的長直髮，側分縫，額前有短短的劉海。她的眼睛是深褐色的，顴骨很高。

Eduardo is clean-shaven with greying hair and a receding hairline. He has a small scar on his jaw and a dimple in his chin.
His wife, Nadia, has long straggly dark hair.
埃杜阿多鬍子剃得乾乾淨淨，他的頭髮有些灰白，而且已漸漸往後禿了。他的下頜處有一道小疤痕，下巴上有個小窩。他的妻子納迪亞梳着散亂的長黑髮。

Sue has blonde hair with a wispy fringe. She has a beauty spot on her cheek and a pointed chin.
蘇的頭髮是金黃色的，稍留了一小綹劉海。她的臉頰上有一個美人斑，下巴尖尖的。

John is slightly tanned with wavy ginger hair and a roman nose. He has stubble, a double chin and wears half moon spectacles *BrE* / reading glasses *AmE*. Nick has lank auburn hair, a pale complexion, and is growing a goatee beard.
約翰曬得有些黑，鬈曲的頭髮是薑黃色的。他長着高鼻梁鷹鉤鼻，蓄鬍子茬，雙下巴。他戴着半月形眼鏡。尼克的頭髮又軟又直，是紅褐色的。他面色蒼白，正在留起山羊鬍子。

Adjectival Word Order 形容詞詞序

Quality 特徵，特點	Size/Age/Shape 大小/年齡/形狀	Colour 顏色	Origin 起源；來源	Made of 由甚麼製成的	Type/Usage 類型/用法	Noun 名詞
beautiful 漂亮	long 長	brown 棕色的				hair 頭髮
	old 舊的		French 法國的			car 汽車
				metal 金屬的	half moon 半月形的	spectacles 眼鏡

bar of chocolate
一塊巧克力
bar of soap
一塊肥皂
hunk of cheese
一塊乾酪
chunk of rock
一塊岩石
rasher of bacon *BrE*【英】
一片熏豬肉
block of ice
一大塊冰
cube of sugar
一塊方糖
wad of banknotes *BrE*【英】/
bills *AmE*【美】一疊鈔票
slab of concrete
一塊混凝土
od of earth
土塊, 泥塊
slice of bread
一片麵包
slice of cake
一塊蛋糕
lump of butter
一塊黃油
dollop of jam
一匙果醬
sheet of newspaper
一張報紙
pane of glass
一塊玻璃
segment of orange
一瓣橙子
blob of paint
一滴油漆
trickle of rain
流淌下來的雨水
square of chocolate
一方塊巧克力
pinch of salt
一撮鹽
squirt of liquid
(噴出的)少量液體
ueeze of lemon
出的)少許檸檬汁
crumb of cake
蛋糕屑
speck of dirt
一點污漬
grain of sand
沙粒
flake of paint
(剝落的)一片油漆
dash of sauce
少許醬汁
shred of cloth
一小片碎布
chip of china
一塊碎瓷片
op of sauce
一滴醬汁
splinter of wood
一片尖木片
sliver of glass
一片碎玻璃
scrap of paper
一小片碎紙
isp of smoke
一縷煙
puff of perfume
(噴出的)少許香水

Fruit 水果

1 strawberries 草莓
2 cranberries 越橘
3 blackberries 黑莓
4 raspberries 山莓, 覆盆子
5 gooseberries 醋栗
6 grapes 葡萄
7 blueberries 藍莓
8 loganberries 羅甘莓
9 oranges 柑橘, 橙
10 grapefruit 西柚, 葡萄柚
11 limes 酸橙
12 lemon 檸檬
13 clementines 克萊門氏小柑橘
14 cantaloup *BrE*【英】/cantaloupe *AmE*【美】羅馬甜瓜, 皺皮香瓜
15 watermelon 西瓜
16 honeydew melon 白甜瓜, 蜜瓜
17 pineapple 菠蘿
18 mango 芒果
19 coconuts 椰子
20 plantains 大蕉
21 bananas 香蕉
22 papaya 木瓜
23 lychee 荔枝
24 passion fruit 西番蓮果實
25 starfruit 楊桃
26 persimmons 柿子
27 quinces 榲桲
28 figs 無花果
29 peaches 桃子
30 nectarines 油桃, 蜜桃
31 pears 梨
32 plums 李子
33 kiwi fruit 獼猴桃, 奇異果
34 cherries 櫻桃
35 apricots 杏子
36 apples 蘋果

garlic 蒜
leeks 韭葱
spring onions *BrE* 【英】/green onions *AmE*【美】大葱
onions 洋葱
yam 甘薯; 薯蕷
sweet potato 紅薯, 甘薯
potatoes 馬鈴薯
Jerusalem artichoke 菊芋, 洋薑
cucumbers 黃瓜
0 marrow *BrE*【英】/ squash *AmE*【美】 西葫蘆
1 courgettes *BrE*【英】/ zucchini *AmE*【美】 小胡瓜
12 pumpkin 南瓜
13 butter beans 利馬豆
14 green beans 青菜豆, 嫩菜豆
15 broad beans 蠶豆
16 aduki beans 赤豆
17 peas 豌豆
18 kidney beans 菜豆, 四季豆
19 runner beans 紅花菜豆
20 beansprouts 豆芽
21 swede *BrE*【英】/ rutabaga *AmE*【美】 蕪菁甘藍
22 beetroot *BrE*【英】/ beet *AmE*【美】 甜菜（根）
23 white radish 白蘿蔔
24 ginger 薑
25 radishes 小蘿蔔
26 carrots 胡蘿蔔
27 parsnips 歐洲防風根, 歐洲蘿蔔
28 turnips 蕪菁
29 cabbage 捲心菜, 洋白菜
30 corn cobs 玉米（棒子）
31 chinese leaves *BrE* 【英】/bok choy *AmE* 【美】白菜
32 celery 芹菜
33 artichoke 洋薊
34 okra 秋葵
35 asparagus 蘆筍
36 cauliflower 花椰菜
37 lettuce 生菜
38 spinach 菠菜
39 red pepper 紅辣椒
40 green pepper 青（甜）椒
41 broccoli 西蘭花; 花莖甘藍
42 aubergine *BrE*【英】/ egg plant *AmE*【美】 茄子
43 mushrooms 蘑菇
44 tomatoes 番茄, 西紅柿
45 brussels sprouts 球芽甘藍（菜）, 抱子甘藍

Kitchen 廚房

tap BrE【英】/ faucet AmE【美】
水龍頭
breadbin BrE【英
breadbox AmE【
麵包箱
fire extinguisher
滅火器
cupboard
碗櫥
washing-up liquid
BrE【英】/
dishwashing liquid
AmE【美】
洗滌液
microwave
微波爐
fridge
電冰箱
cooker BrE【英】/
stove AmE【美】
爐灶
scouring pad
百潔布
sink
洗滌槽
draining
board
滴水板
funnel
漏斗
FRY
煎炸
(electric) ring BrE【英】/
burner AmE【美】
環狀（電）爐頭
oven glove
烤爐用的手套
BAKE
烘，焙
freezer
冷藏箱
ROAST
烤
dishwasher
洗碗碟機
washin
machin
洗衣機
oven
烤爐
kettle
（電）水壺
floor
地板
baking tray BrE
【英】/ cookie
sheet AmE【美】
烘烤盤
scales BrE【英】/ scale AmE【美】
磅秤
measuring jug
量壺
BURN
烤焦
fish slice BrE【英】/
spatula AmE【美】
（煎魚）鏟；鍋鏟
measuring
spoons
量匙
toaster
烤麵包機
cake tin BrE【英】/
muffin tin AmE【美】
蛋糕烤盤；鬆餅烤盤
cloth
（桌）布
cutlery BrE【英】/
silverware AmE【美】
（西餐）餐具；銀餐具
corkscrew
開瓶的螺絲起子，瓶塞鑽
tin opener BrE【英】/
can opener AmE【美】
開罐頭器
food processor
食品加工器
drawer
抽屜
worktop BrE【英】/
counter AmE【美】
工作枱
bin BrE【英】/
wastebasket AmE【美】
垃圾桶
breadboard
切麵包板
napkin
餐巾
tea towel BrE【英】/
dishcloth AmE【美】
茶巾；抹布

Verbs in the Kitchen 廚房中常用的動詞

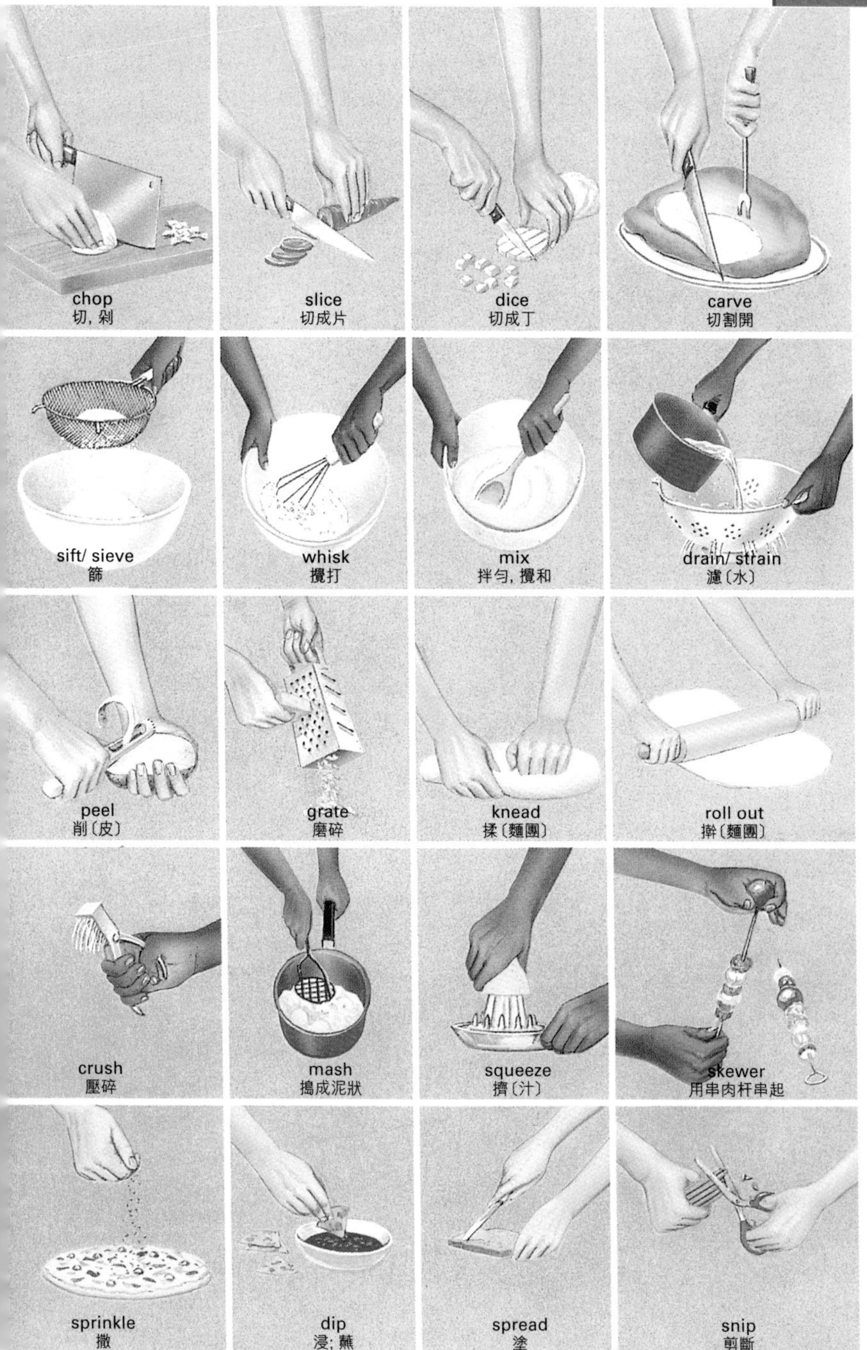

A12 Landscapes 風景地貌

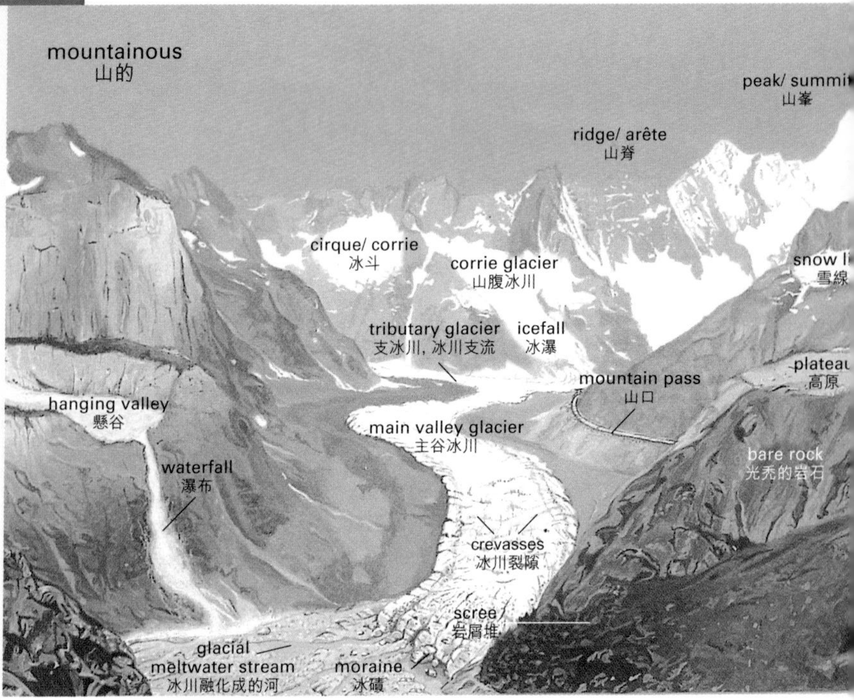

mountainous
山的

peak/ summi
山峯

ridge/ arête
山脊

cirque/ corrie
冰斗

corrie glacier
山腹冰川

snow li
雪線

tributary glacier
支冰川, 冰川支流

icefall
冰瀑

plateau
高原

mountain pass
山口

hanging valley
懸谷

main valley glacier
主谷冰川

bare rock
光禿的岩石

waterfall
瀑布

crevasses
冰川裂隙

scree
岩屑堆

glacial meltwater stream
冰川融化成的河

moraine
冰磧

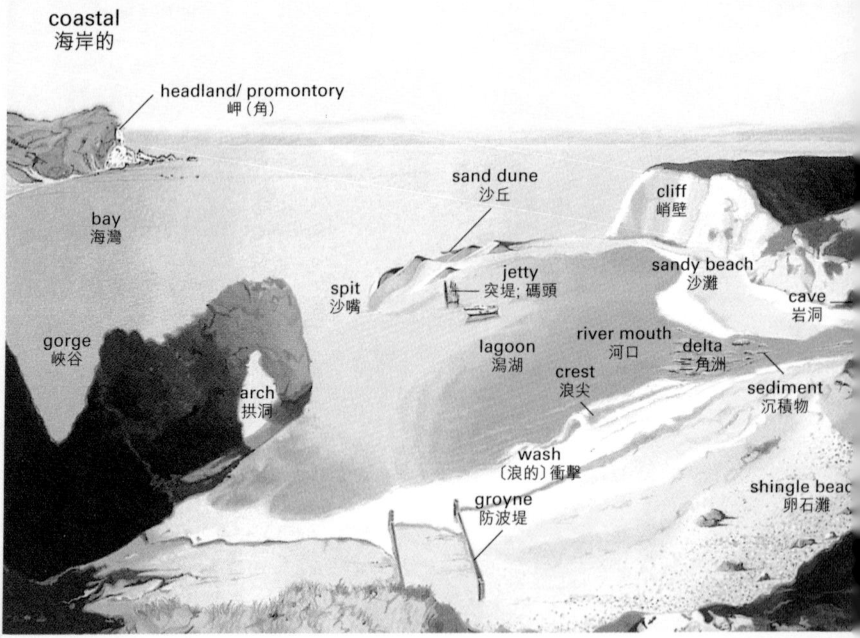

coastal
海岸的

headland/ promontory
岬（角）

sand dune
沙丘

cliff
峭壁

bay
海灣

jetty
突堤; 碼頭

spit
沙嘴

sandy beach
沙灘

cave
岩洞

gorge
峽谷

lagoon
瀉湖

river mouth
河口

delta
三角洲

crest
浪尖

arch
拱洞

sediment
沉積物

wash
〔浪的〕衝擊

shingle beac
卵石灘

groyne
防波堤

The car was stuck in a blizzard.
汽車被困在暴風雪中開不動了。

2 The sky was overcast and it had begun to sleet.
天空陰沉沉的，開始下起了雨夾雪。

3 We saw forked lightning as the storm got closer.
隨着暴風雨臨近，我們看到了叉狀的閃電。

The tree was blown down in a gale.
一陣大風把樹吹倒了。

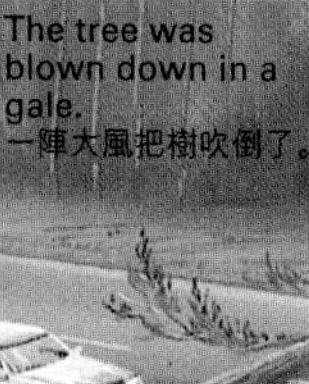

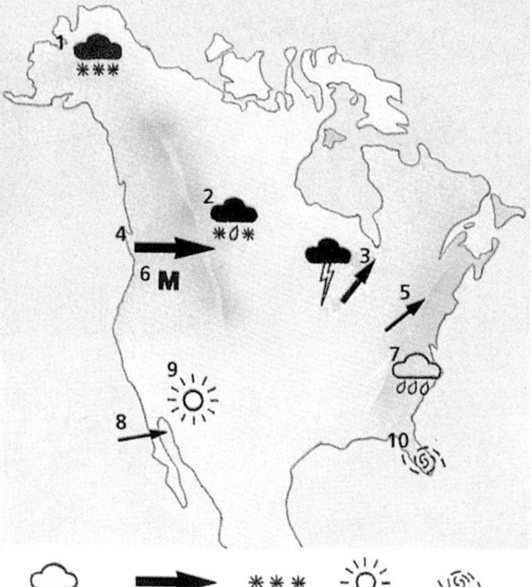

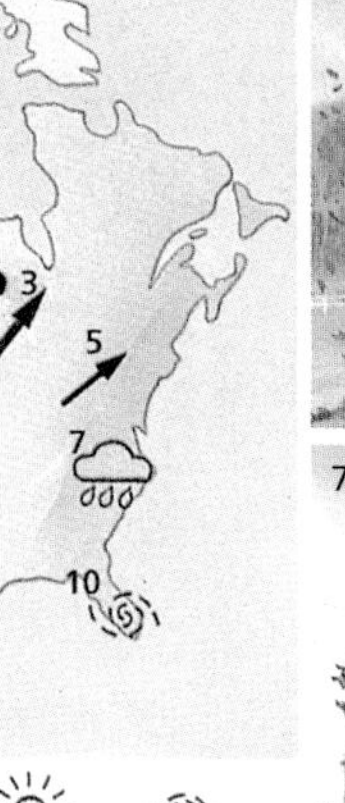

5 The wind was so blustery that leaves were blown from the trees.
狂風大作，樹葉紛紛從樹上吹落。

The mountains were veiled in mist.
羣山被薄霧籠罩。

cloud 雲 · wind 風 · snow 雪 · sun 太陽 · hurricane 颶風

storm cloud 暴風雲 · rain 雨 · mist 霧 · lightning 閃電

7 The downpour had caused a flood.
傾盆大雨引發了一場洪水。

Palm trees swayed in the breeze.
棕櫚樹在微風中搖曳。

9 Sun had baked the parched soil.
烈日把土壤曬得乾裂。

10 The hurricane tore the roofs off the houses.
颶風捲走了屋頂。

Office 辦公室

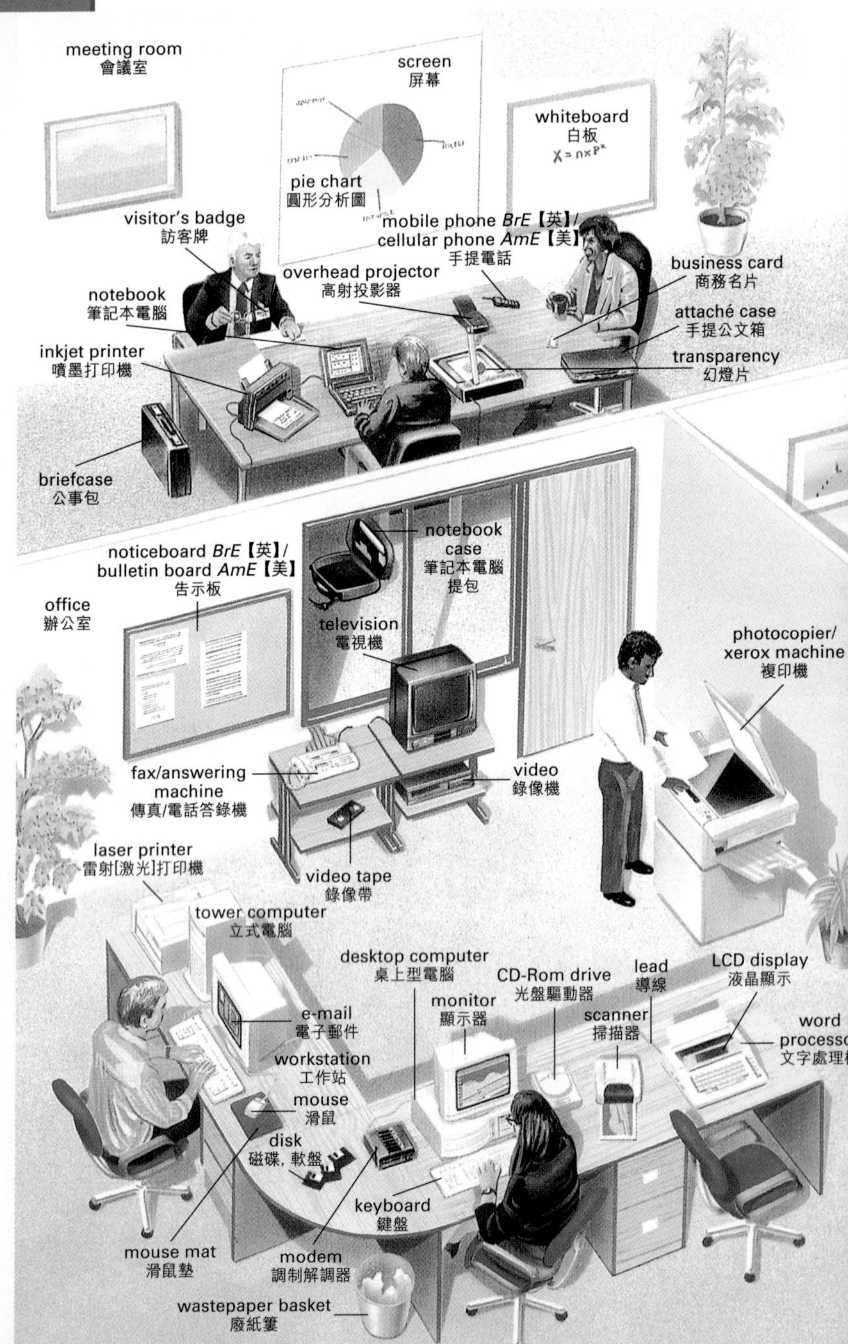
meeting room
會議室
screen
屏幕
whiteboard
白板
pie chart
圓形分析圖
visitor's badge
訪客牌
mobile phone *BrE*【英】/
cellular phone *AmE*【美】
手提電話
business card
商務名片
overhead projector
高射投影器
notebook
筆記本電腦
attaché case
手提公文箱
inkjet printer
噴墨打印機
transparency
幻燈片
briefcase
公事包
notebook
case
筆記本電腦
提包
noticeboard *BrE*【英】/
bulletin board *AmE*【美】
告示板
office
辦公室
television
電視機
photocopier/
xerox machine
複印機
fax/answering
machine
傳真/電話答錄機
video
錄像機
laser printer
雷射[激光]打印機
video tape
錄像帶
tower computer
立式電腦
desktop computer
桌上型電腦
CD-Rom drive
光盤驅動器
lead
導線
LCD display
液晶顯示
monitor
顯示器
e-mail
電子郵件
scanner
掃描器
word
processo
文字處理
workstation
工作站
mouse
滑鼠
disk
磁碟, 軟盤
keyboard
鍵盤
mouse mat
滑鼠墊
modem
調制解調器
wastepaper basket
廢紙簍

hat stand BrE【英】/coat stand AmE【美】
衣帽架
board
白板
coat rack
掛衣架
SPECIALS
Rainbow
Trout.
customer
顧客
POUR
倒 (酒)
waiter
侍應生
swing door
雙開式彈簧門
corkscrew
瓶塞鑽
UNCORK
開酒瓶塞
maitre d'/
head waiter
侍應生領班
SERVE
佈菜
bow tie
蝶形領結
napkin/
serviette BrE【英】
餐巾
chef
廚師
FLAMBÉ
澆酒點燃後食用的菜
ashtray
煙灰缸
RESERVED
RESERVED
已訂座
waitress
女侍應生
tablecloth
枱布
espresso cup
蒸餾咖啡杯
dessert trolley BrE【英】/
dessert cart AmE【美】
甜點推車
TAKE THE
ORDER
記下 (客人)
要點的菜
apron
圍裙
crudités
生拌涼菜
menu
菜單
TIP
付小費
cheeseboard
乾酪板
table mat
桌墊
dip
調味醬
bill BrE【英】/
check AmE【美】
賬單
cutlery/silverware AmE【美】
西餐具; 銀餐具

Patterns and Fabrics 圖案和布料

denim
斜紋粗棉布; 牛仔布
herringbone
人字紋布料
embroidered
刺繡的
lace
網眼
towelling *BrE*【英】/
terrycloth *AmE*【美】
毛巾布
leather
皮革
pinstripe
細條紋布料
suede
軟皮革, 絨面革
tweed
粗花呢
mohair
馬海毛(織物)
speckled
斑點花紋的
gingham
方格棉布
graph check
方眼格子紋
woollen *BrE*【英】/
woolen *AmE*【美】
羊毛(織物)
zigzag
之字形(圖案)
checkered
有不同顏色方格
圖案的
paisley
佩茲利渦旋紋
圖案
floral
花卉圖案的
check *BrE*【英】/
plaid *AmE*【美】
格子圖案布料; 格子花呢
plain
單色[無花紋]的
corduroy
燈芯絨
crushed
velvet
壓紋絲絨
tartan
batik
蠟染
patchwork
拼綴圖案
striped
有條紋的
tie-dye
紮染
dotted *BrE*【英】/
polka-dot *AmE*【美】
小圓點圖案的
spotted *BrE*【英】/
polka-dot *AmE*【美】
斑點[圓點]圖案的

utton-down collar
有鈕扣）可扣住的衣領
single cuff
單式袖口
drawstring waistline
拉繩式腰圍線
crew neck
圓領
polo neck BrE【英】/
turtle neck AmE【美】
高圓領
double cuff
複式袖口
collarless/
granddad collar
無領領型
collar
領子
bow tie
蝶形領結
waistband
裙帶
scooped neck
湯匙領
buttonhole
鈕扣眼
seam
接縫
sleeve
袖子
neck
領口
open-necked shirt
開領襯衫
top pocket
上口袋
turtle neck BrE【英】/
mock turtle AmE【美】
半高領口
shirt
襯衫
cuff
袖口
v-neck
V字形領口
jacket
上衣
uble-breasted jacket
雙排扣西裝
belt
皮帶
waistcoat
西裝背心
cufflinks
袖口鏈扣
trousers
BrE【英】/
pants AmE
【美】
褲子
pleated skirt
百褶裙
pencil skirt
直筒長裙，筆桿裙
ngle-breasted jacket
單排扣西裝
straight skirt
直筒裙
hem
褶邊
laces
鞋帶
tights
褲襪
capped sleeves
罩肩袖
straight trousers
BrE【英】/ pants
AmE【美】
直筒褲
wrap-over skirt
裹疊式裙
espadrille
帆布便鞋
long sleeves
長袖
flat shoe
平底鞋
high-heeled shoe
高跟鞋
flared trousers BrE【英】/
pants AmE【美】
喇叭褲
turn-ups BrE【英】/
cuffed pants AmE【美】
捲邊褲
short sleeves
短袖
thick-soled shoe
厚底鞋

Adjectives 形容詞: Broken 破的；損壞了的

cracked plaster
裂了的灰泥層
broken windowpane
破裂的窗玻璃
rusty window frame
生鏽的窗框
frayed cushions
邊緣已磨破的靠墊
tattered curtains
破舊的窗簾
peeling paintwork
剝落的漆面
leaky pipe
漏水的管子
wilted flowers
凋謝的花
faded sofa
褪色的沙發
dusty table top
佈滿灰塵的桌面
torn spine
撕破的書脊
dog-eared pages
邊角摺捲的書頁
ripped cover
劃破的沙發套
chipped cup
有缺口的茶杯
worm-eaten table
蟲蛀的桌子
rickety chair
快要散架的椅子
threadbare rug
磨薄的小地毯
crumpled paper
揉成一團的紙
stained carpet
有污漬的地毯

buzz
嗡嗡聲
clink
叮噹聲
crack
劈啪聲
crackle
噼啪聲
crash
碰撞聲，砰的一聲
crunch
嘎吱作響
fizz
嘶嘶聲
hiss
嘶嘶聲
honk
〔汽車的〕喇叭聲
jingle
叮噹聲
pop
啪［砰，噗］的一聲
ring
鈴聲
rustle
沙沙作響
sizzle
嗞嗞聲
snap
劈啪折斷聲
splash
濺潑聲，噗通一聲
quelch BrE【英】/
quish AmE【美】
咯吱咯吱聲
tick
滴答聲
tinkle
叮咚聲，叮噹聲
whirr
呼呼聲，嗡嗡聲

Physical Contact 身體接觸 1

nudge
〔用肘〕輕推[輕碰]

elbow
用肘推[擠]

pat
輕拍

stroke
撫摸, 捋

hug
擁抱

cuddle
摟抱

feel
〔觸〕摸

frisk
搜身

pull/drag
拖, 拉

prod/poke
戳

push/shove
推

chop
砍, 劈

Sports 體育運動 1

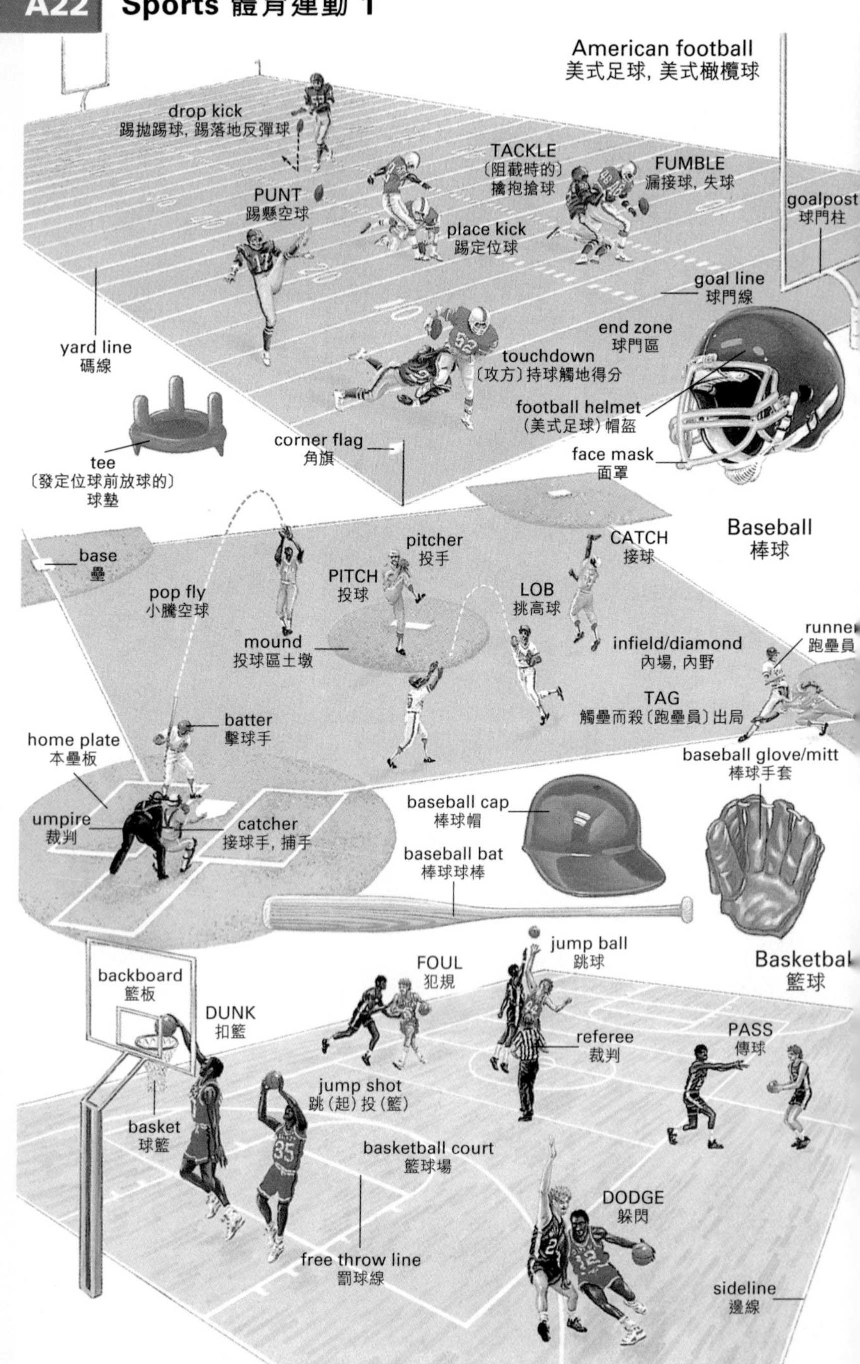

American football
美式足球, 美式橄欖球
drop kick
踢拋踢球, 踢落地反彈球
TACKLE
〔阻截時的〕擒抱搶球
FUMBLE
漏接球, 失球
PUNT
踢懸空球
place kick
踢定位球
goalpost
球門柱
goal line
球門線
yard line
碼線
end zone
球門區
touchdown
〔攻方〕持球觸地得分
football helmet
(美式足球) 帽盔
face mask
面罩
corner flag
角旗
tee
〔發定位球前放球的〕球墊
Baseball
棒球
base
壘
pitcher
投手
CATCH
接球
pop fly
小騰空球
PITCH
投球
LOB
挑高球
runner
跑壘員
mound
投球區土墩
infield/diamond
內場, 內野
TAG
觸壘而殺〔跑壘員〕出局
batter
擊球手
home plate
本壘板
baseball glove/mitt
棒球手套
baseball cap
棒球帽
umpire
裁判
catcher
接球手, 捕手
baseball bat
棒球球棒
Basketball
籃球
jump ball
跳球
FOUL
犯規
backboard
籃板
DUNK
扣籃
referee
裁判
PASS
傳球
jump shot
跳(起)投(籃)
basket
球籃
basketball court
籃球場
DODGE
躲閃
free throw line
罰球線
sideline
邊線

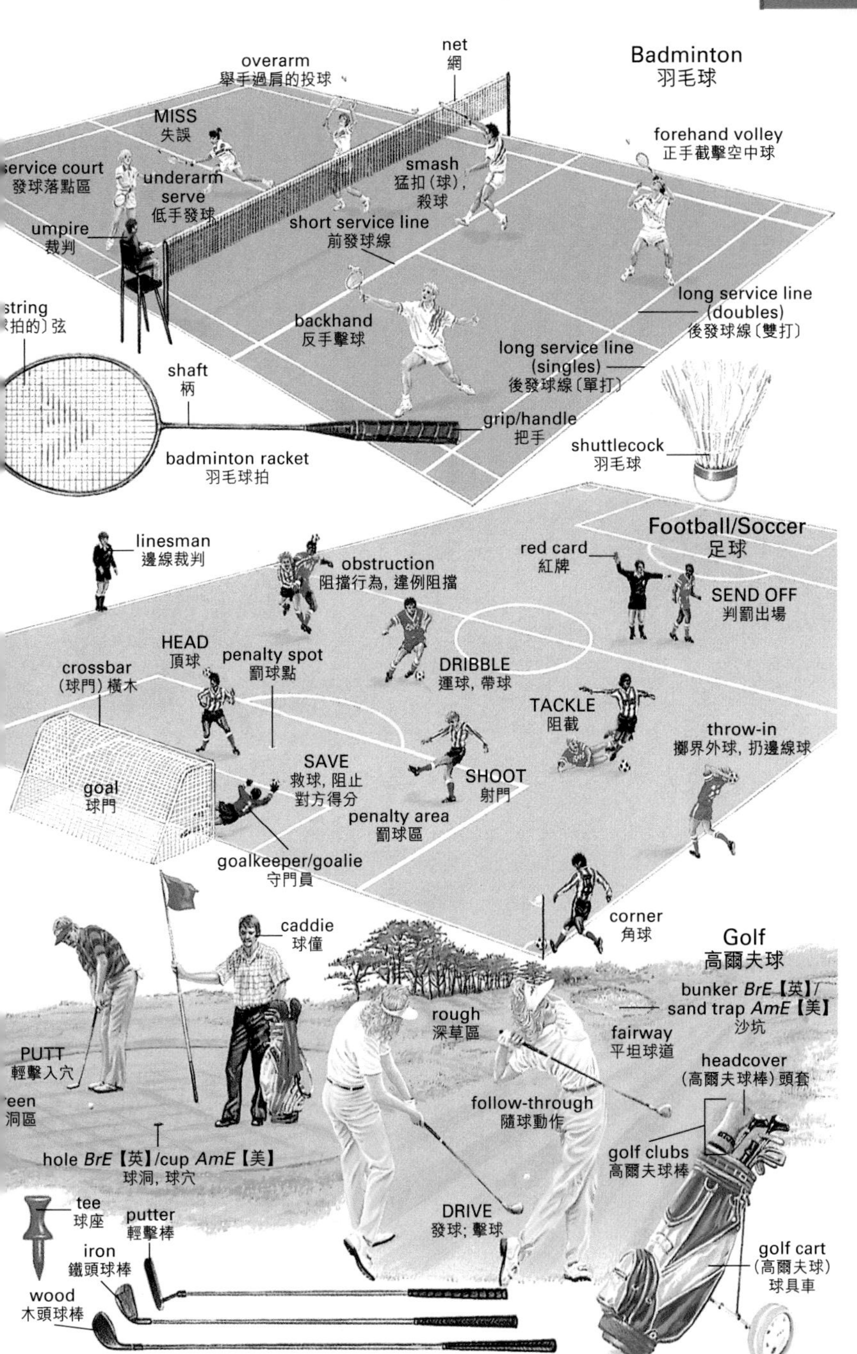
Badminton
羽毛球
overarm
舉手過肩的投球
net
網
MISS
失誤
service court
發球落點區
underarm serve
低手發球
smash
猛扣（球），殺球
forehand volley
正手截擊空中球
umpire
裁判
short service line
前發球線
string
弦
backhand
反手擊球
long service line (doubles)
後發球線〔雙打〕
long service line (singles)
後發球線〔單打〕
shaft
柄
grip/handle
把手
badminton racket
羽毛球拍
shuttlecock
羽毛球
Football/Soccer
足球
linesman
邊線裁判
obstruction
阻擋行為，違例阻擋
red card
紅牌
SEND OFF
判罰出場
HEAD
頂球
penalty spot
罰球點
DRIBBLE
運球，帶球
crossbar
（球門）橫木
TACKLE
阻截
throw-in
擲界外球，扔邊線球
SAVE
救球，阻止對方得分
SHOOT
射門
goal
球門
penalty area
罰球區
goalkeeper/goalie
守門員
corner
角球
caddie
球僮
Golf
高爾夫球
bunker BrE【英】/ sand trap AmE【美】
沙坑
rough
深草區
fairway
平坦球道
PUTT
輕擊入穴
headcover
（高爾夫球棒）頭套
follow-through
隨球動作
golf clubs
高爾夫球棒
hole BrE【英】/cup AmE【美】
球洞，球穴
tee
球座
putter
輕擊棒
DRIVE
發球；擊球
iron
鐵頭球棒
golf cart
（高爾夫球）球具車
wood
木頭球棒

A24 Types of Walk 各種步姿

Liz **crept** upstairs trying not to wake her parents.
莉茲躡手躡腳地上樓，以免把父母吵醒。

She **tiptoed** along the landing.
她踮起腳尖，沿着樓梯平台走去。

Bob **edged** aw
from the guar
鮑勃側身從守衛後
悄悄走了過去。

Garcia **limped** off in agony.
加西亞十分痛苦地一瘸一拐地走開。

Granny **shuffled** across the room.
老奶奶拖着緩慢的步伐走過房間。

She **trudged** home with the shopping.
她提着買來的東西，步履艱難地走回家。

Sue **paddled** *BrE*【英】/ **waded** *AmE*【美】in the sea.
蘇在海裡涉水玩。

The fisherman **waded** across the river.
那個釣魚者蹚着水過河。

He **paced** up and down waiting for news.
他來回踱步等消息。

The baby stood and **tottered** forwards.
小寶寶站了起來，搖搖晃晃地往前走。

He **staggered** under the weight of the box.
他在箱子的重壓下步履蹣跚。

We took a **stroll** in the park.
我們在公園漫步。

Language Notes

Language Note: Addressing People 語言提示: 稱呼

How do you address people (What do you call them) when you want to talk to them? 當你想要同人說話時, 應當怎樣稱呼他們呢?

■ Talking to strangers 同陌生人說話

When talking to strangers there is often no special form of address in English. Usually, if you want to attract the attention of a stranger it is necessary to use phrases such as **Excuse me** 同陌生人說話, 英語中沒有甚麼特定的稱呼。在通常情況下, 如果想吸引陌生人的注意, 就要用 **Excuse me** (對不起) 一類的片語:

> **Excuse me!** *Can you tell me how to get to Oxford Street?*
> 對不起, 請問到牛津街怎麼走?
>
> **Say!** (*AmE infml*) *Is it far to the subway from here?*
> 【美, 非正式】請問, 從這兒到地鐵站遠嗎?

In British English **Sir** and **Madam** are too formal for most situations. They are used mostly to customers in shops, restaurants, etc. 在英式英語中, **Sir** (先生) 和 **Madam** (太太) 都太正式, 在大多數場合是不用的, 這兩個詞通常是商店、餐館中店員對顧客的稱呼:

> *Would you like your coffee now,* **Madam/Sir***?*
> 太太 [先生], 現在上咖啡好嗎?
>
> *Shall I wrap it for you,* **Madam/Sir***?*
> 太太 [先生], 我替你把它包起來好嗎?

In American English **Sir** and **Ma'am** are not as formal and are commonly used in conversations with strangers, especially with older people whose names you do not know 在美式英語中, **Sir** 和 **Ma'am** 並不那麼正式, 經常用於同陌生人, 特別是同不知道其姓名的年長者的談話中:

> *Pleased to meet you,* **Ma'am**. 幸會, 太太。
>
> *Excuse me.* **Sir**. *Could you tell me the way to the nearest subway?*
> 對不起先生, 請問到最近的地鐵車站怎麼走?

Names of occupations 職業名稱

Doctor and **nurse** can be used as forms of address. **Doctor** 和 **nurse** 可用作稱呼:

> *Can I have a word with you,* **doctor***?*
> 醫生, 跟您說句話行嗎?
>
> **Nurse***, could I have a glass of water?*
> 護士小姐, 請給我一杯水。

The names of a few other occupations such as **porter** and **waiter** are sometimes used as forms of address, though some people consider that this is impolite. However, most names of occupations cannot be used in this way. (Note, especially, that **teacher** is not used as a form of address.) **porter** (搬運員) 和 **waiter** (侍應生) 等一些其他職業名稱有時也用於稱呼, 不過有些人認為這樣叫不禮貌。但大多數職

Language Note: Addressing People 語言提示: 稱呼

業名稱是不能用作稱呼的。(特別要注意的是, **teacher** 不能用作稱呼。)

Special forms of address 特殊的稱呼

There are some special forms of address that show respect to people, especially if they are in positions of authority. These are used in formal situations 為了對某些人, 特別是對那些處於權威職位的人表示尊敬, 可以用一些特殊的稱呼。這些稱呼都用於正式的場合:

Ladies and gentlemen (a formal opening of a speech)
女士們, 先生們〔講話的正式開頭〕

Your Excellency (to an ambassador) 閣下〔稱呼大使〕

Your Highness (for a prince or princess)
殿下〔稱呼王子或公主〕

Mr/Madam President 總統閣下

Prime Minister 總理閣下

Talking to people you know 同認識的人說話

When you know people you can use their names. People's names can be used to attract their attention or to show that you are talking particularly to them. If you are friends, use their first name; if your relationship is more formal, use **Ms/Mr Smith** etc. 對於認識的人, 可以叫他們的姓名。叫姓名可用以引起對方注意, 或者表示是特地同他們說話。如果是朋友, 可以用名字, 如果關係是公務上的, 可用 **Ms/Mr Smith** (史密斯女士 [先生] 等:

Mary, *could you help me with this box?*
瑪麗, 幫我抬一下這箱子好嗎?

What's your opinion, **Eric**? 埃里克, 你有甚麼意見?

Dr Davis, *could you tell us what the committee have decided?*
戴維斯博士, 你能告訴我們委員會作出了甚麼決定嗎?

Sign here please, **Ms Burton**. 伯頓女士, 請把名字簽在這裡。

Note that **Ms**, **Miss**, **Mrs**, and **Mr** are not usually used alone in speech or writing but are followed by the family name 請註意, 在口語或書寫中, **Ms**, **Miss**, **Mrs** 和 **Mr** 通常都不單獨使用, 而是用在姓氏的前面, 如: **Ms Green** (格林女士), **Mrs Brown** (布朗太太), etc.等

Talking to family or friends 同家人或朋友說話

Within a family or between friends there are many possible forms of address. "Family" words are most commonly used by children talking to parents: **dad/daddy** (*BrE*) | **mum/mom** (*AmE*) | **mummy** (*BrE*). **Father** and **mother** are also used, but they are more formal. **Aunt** (*fml*)/**auntie** and **uncle** are sometimes used alone as a form of address, but the name is often added: **auntie May** | **uncle Tom**. 在家人或朋友之間有許多種不同的稱呼方式。孩子們稱呼父母時, 最常用的是"親暱"詞語: **dad/daddy** (*BrE* 英)| **mum/mom** (*AmE* 美)| **mummy** (*BrE* 英). **Father** 和 **mother** 也可使用, 但是比較正式。**Aunt** (*fml* 正式)/**auntie** 和 **uncle** 有時單獨用作稱呼, 但常常要在後面加上名字: **auntie May** | **uncle Tom** 等。

Language Note: Addressing People 語言提示: 稱呼

Many words can be used informally to express friendship or love, 許多詞語可以作為非正式用語被用來表示友誼或愛情, such as 如 **darling/dear/honey** (*AmE* 美)/**(my) love/sweetheart**, etc. 等: *Hurry up,* **darling**, *or we'll be late.* (快點, 親愛的, 否則我們就要晚了。)

▶ Be careful! 注意!

There are many other forms of address which can be used between friends or strangers. However, many of these are limited in use. For example, **pal** and **mate** (*BrE*) can be used between strangers, but are usually only used by men talking to other men. 朋友之間或陌生人之間還有許多稱呼, 但其中有不少在使用上是有限制的。如 **pal** (老朋友) 和 **mate** (夥伴) (*BrE* 英) 可以用於陌生人之間, 但通常只在男人之間使用。

You will also hear such words as **darling**, **dear**, **honey**, and **love** used between strangers. In this case they do not, of course, express love, but are being used as informal forms of address. The use of these words is not general but depends on such things as the variety of English being spoken, the sex of speaker and hearer, and the social position of speaker and hearer. For example, in Britain a waiter or waitress might address a customer as **love**, but only in an informal restaurant or cafe, and never in an expensive restaurant. 你也會聽到 **darling, dear, honey** 和 **love** (親愛的) 這類詞用於陌生人之間。在這種情況下, 這些詞當然不表示愛情, 而只是作為一種非正式用語的稱呼。這些詞的使用並不普遍, 而且要取決於某些情況, 如所說的某一種類的英語、說話人和聽話人的性別以及他們的社會地位等。例如在英國, 一個侍應生可以稱呼顧客 **love**, 但只限於在非正規的餐館或咖啡館, 而從不會在上等餐館中使用。

See also 另見 MISS[2], SIR

Language Note: Apologies 語言提示: 道歉語

Apologies can be very short and direct, or longer and more complex. When deciding which expressions are suitable for which situations, it is useful to ask certain questions. 道歉語可以非常簡短而直截了當，也可以長一些、複雜一些。要決定哪些用語適合哪種情況，先問一些問題是有用的。

Considerations affecting choice of expression 影響選擇不同用語的幾種情況

— How bad is the thing which has happened? If it is very bad, the apology will be stronger. 已經發生的事情壞到甚麼程度？如果非常壞，道歉的語氣就應該重些。

— What is the relationship between the person who is apologizing (the speaker) and the person they are speaking to (the hearer)? If the hearer is in a position of authority, the apology may be stronger. 表示道歉的人（講話人）和接受道歉的人（聽話人）是甚麼關係？如果聽話的人處於有權威的地位，道歉的語氣可以重些。

— How responsible is the speaker for what has happened? If the speaker is really at fault, the apology will be stronger. 講話人對已發生的事所負責任的程度如何？如果講話人確有過錯，道歉的語氣要重些。

— Will the hearer immediately know the reason for the apology? If not, the speaker must make this clear. 聽話人是否會當即明白道歉的原因？如果不明白，講話人必須說清楚。

■ Quick apologies 簡捷的道歉語

For something small (such as accidentally bumping into someone on a bus) 為一些小事情（如在公共汽車上偶然碰撞了某人）：

apologies 道歉語	**aresponses** 答語
(I'm) sorry. 對不起。	*It's/That's all right.* 沒關係。
Excuse me. (*AmE* 美) 對不起。	*It's/That's OK.* (*infml* 非正式) 沒甚麼。
Pardon me. (*AmE* 美) 請原諒。	*Don't worry.* (*infml* 非正式)/*It's all right.* (*infml* 非正式) 沒事（兒）；沒關係。
I beg your pardon. (*fml* 正式) 請你原諒。	

For something bigger (such as spilling coffee all over someone's new clothes), it is usual to add a comment 為了大一些的事情（如把咖啡撒在某人的新衣服上），通常要多說一些客氣話：

(Oh!) I'm sorry.
（噢！）對不起

- *I didn't see you sitting there.* (explanation/excuse) 我沒看見您坐在那兒。〔解釋，辯白〕
- *Are you all right?* (expression of concern) 您沒事兒吧？〔表示關心〕
- *I'll fetch a cloth.* (offer of help) 我去拿塊布來。〔主動提出幫忙〕
- *That was really clumsy of me.* (self-criticism) 都是我笨手笨腳。〔自我批評，自責〕

Language Note: Apologies 語言提示: 道歉語

It is also possible to add words to make the apology stronger 也可以增加一些詞語以加重道歉的語氣:

> *I 'm* **really/awfully/so/terribly** (*BrE* 英) *sorry.* 我確實 [非常、很、極為] 抱歉。
>
> *I* **do** *beg your pardon.* (*BrE fml* 英, 正式) 請多多原諒。

■ Explaining an apology 説清楚道歉的緣由

When apologizing for something which the hearer does not yet know about or may not remember, the speaker needs to explain what has happened, or remind the hearer of the situation. It is usual to add an explanation, excuse, offer of help, etc. 對於所道歉的事, 如果聽話的人並不清楚, 或者可能已不記得, 説話的人就需要説明是甚麼事, 或讓聽話的人回想起當時的情況。常見的做法是作進一步的解釋、説明緣由或主動提出給予幫助等:

> *John, about the meeting. I'm sorry I was late — I missed the bus.* 約翰, 對不起, 這個會我來遲了— 我沒趕上公共汽車。
>
> *I really must apologize for my behaviour last night* (*fml* 正式). *I'm afraid I was in rather a bad mood.* 昨天晚上我太不對了, 實在對不起。當時我情緒不太好。
>
> *I've got something awful to tell you. I lost that book you lent me. I'm really sorry. I'll buy you another.* 有件糟糕的事要告訴你, 我把你借給我的書弄丟了, 真對不起。我會買一本還你的。
>
> *I feel dreadful about what I said on the phone. I didn't really mean it, you know.* 我覺得很不好受, 我在電話裡説了那些話, 其實我並不是真的那麼想的。

Note that, as in the last example, it is not always necessary to use any direct words of apology. 注意: 正像以上最後一例, 並非總是要使用直接的道歉語的。

■ Written and formal apologies 書面的和正式的道歉語

Formal apologies, especially in written form, are often marked by the use of the word **apology** or **apologize** 正式的, 特別是書面的道歉常以使用 **apology** 或 **apologize** 為標誌:

> *I am writing to apologize for my absence from last week's meeting. I was unexpectedly held up at work and was not able to contact you.* (*fml* 正式) 我未能參加上週的會議, 謹此致歉。我因突然有公事而無法脱身, 故未能同你們聯絡。
>
> *British Rail wishes to/would like to apologize for the late running of this train.* (*fml* 正式) (announcement at a station or on a train) 本列車晚點, 英國鐵路公司謹此表示歉意。〔火車站或列車上的通告〕
>
> *Please accept our (sincere) apologies for any inconvenience caused by the delay in delivery of your order. The goods have now been shipped to you.* (*fml* 正式) 您訂購的貨物我們未能按時交貨, 對因此而造成的不便, 我們謹表示 (誠摯的) 歉意, 該批貨物現已裝運發給貴方。

See 參見 EXCUSE[1] (USAGE)

Language Note: Articles 語言提示: 冠詞

In English, it is often necessary to use an article in front of a noun. There are two kinds of article: the definite article **the**, and the indefinite article **a** or **an**. In order to speak or write English well, it is important to know how articles are used. When deciding whether or not to use an article and which kind of article to use, you should ask the following questions 在英語中, 名詞之前往往需要加冠詞。冠詞有兩種: 定冠詞 **the** 和不定冠詞 **a** 或 **an**。為了説好英語和寫好英語, 正確掌握冠詞的用法具有重要意義。是否需要用冠詞, 是用定冠詞還是用不定冠詞, 應考慮以下幾個問題:

■ Is the noun countable or uncountable? 這個名詞是可數名詞還是不可數名詞?

Singular countable nouns always need an article or another determiner like **my**, **this**, etc. Other nouns can sometimes be used alone. The chart below tells you which articles can be used with which type of noun 單數的可數名詞前面總是需要有冠詞或其他限定詞如 **my**, **this** 等, 其他一些名詞有時可以不加冠詞。下表説明, 哪種類型的名詞可以用哪種冠詞:

the	+	singular countable nouns 單數的可數名詞	the bag, the apple
		plural countable nouns 複數的可數名詞	the bags, the apples
		uncountable nouns 不可數名詞	the water, the information
a/an	+	singular countable nouns 單數的可數名詞	a bag, an apple
no article or **some** 不用冠詞或用 **some**	+	plural countable nouns 複數的可數名詞	(some) bags, (some) apples
		uncountable nouns 不可數名詞	(some) water, (some) information

The dictionary shows you when nouns are countable [C] or uncountable [U]. (The nouns which have no letter after them are countable in all their meanings.) The examples below show how articles can be used with countable and uncountable nouns. 本辭典中的名詞標明何時是可數名詞 [C], 何時是不可數名詞 [U]。(名詞後面沒有標明字母的, 表示所有義項都是可數名詞。) 下面的例句表明可數名詞和不可數名詞前冠詞的用法:

countable/uncountable noun 可數 [不可數] 名詞	**examples** 例句
butterfly [C] 蝴蝶	**The butterfly** *is an insect.* 蝴蝶是一種昆蟲。 **The butterflies** *on that bush are very rare.* 灌木叢上那幾隻蝴蝶是非常罕見的。 *She caught* **a butterfly** *in her net.* 她用網捉到一隻蝴蝶。 *There were* **some butterflies** *in the tree.* 樹上有幾隻蝴蝶。 *The garden was full of* **butterflies**. 花園裡到處都是蝴蝶。
egg[1] [C] 雞蛋	**The egg** *I found in the fridge was bad.* 我在冰箱裡找到的雞蛋已經壞了。 **The eggs** *you bought last week have all been eaten.* 你上星期買的雞蛋都吃光了。 *I'd like* **an egg** *for tea.* 我在用茶點時想吃隻雞蛋。 *Can you buy* **some eggs** *on your way home?* 你在回家的路上買些雞蛋好嗎? *He hates* **eggs**. 他討厭吃雞蛋。
egg[2] [C] 〔煮熟後供食用的〕蛋	*He wiped* **the egg** *from round his mouth.* 他擦去嘴邊的蛋。 *Would you like* **some** *scrambled* **egg** *with your toast?* 你要不要來點炒蛋和烤麵包一起吃? *The baby had* **egg** *all over her face.* 小寶寶吃得滿臉都是蛋。
information [U] 信息	**The information** *they gave us was wrong.* 他們給我們的信息是錯誤的。 *We'd like* **some information**, *please.* 請給我們一些資料。 *What we really need is* **information**. 我們真正需要的是信息。

Language Note: Articles 語言提示: 冠詞

Note that most proper nouns, like **Susan**, **London**, and **Canada**, do not usually have an article: **Susan**'*s coming through* **London** *next week, on her way to* **Canada**. However, **the** is usually used with rivers (**the Thames**), seas (**the Pacific**), groups of mountains (**the Andes**), deserts (**the Gobi Desert**), cinemas and theatres (**the Playhouse**), and hotels (**the Ritz hotel**). It is also used with a few countries, especially those whose names contain a common countable noun, such as **the People's Republic of China**. 注意: 大多數專有名詞如 **Susan** (蘇珊), **London** (倫敦) 和 **Canada** (加拿大) 等通常都不用冠詞: **Susan's** *coming through* **London** *next week, on her way to* **Canada**. (蘇珊去加拿大的途中, 下星期將經過倫敦。) 可是, 在表示下列事物的專有名詞前通常要加 **the**: 河流 (**the Thames** 泰晤士河), 海洋 (**the Pacific** 太平洋), 山脈 (**the Andes** 安第斯山), 沙漠 (**the Gobi Desert** 戈壁沙漠), 電影院和戲院 (**the Playhouse** 普萊豪斯劇院), 旅館 (**the Ritz Hotel** 里兹飯店)。一些國家的名稱, 特別是其名稱中含有普通可數名詞的國家名稱也要加 **the**, 如 **the People's Republic of China** (中華人民共和國)。

■ Are you talking about things and people in general? 所述及的事物和人是籠統的嗎?

When nouns appear in general statements, they can be used with different articles, depending on whether they are countable or uncountable. 在籠統陳述中出現的名詞可以使用不同的冠詞, 視其為可數名詞或不可數名詞而定。

In general statements, countable nouns can be used 在籠統的陳述中可數名詞可以下列形式出現:

in the plural without an article 複數不加冠詞:

> *Elephants have tusks.* 大象有象牙。| *I like elephants.* 我喜歡大象。

in the singular with **the** 單數用 **the**:

> *The elephant is a magnificent animal.* 大象是一種巨獸。| *He is studying the elephant in its natural habitat.* 他正在研究生活在大自然棲息地的大象。

in the singular with **a/an** 單數用 **a/an**:

> *An elephant can live for a very long time.* 大象可以活很久。

Note that **a/an** can only be used in this way if the noun is the grammatical subject of the sentence. 注意: 如果名詞是句子中的主詞 [主語], **a/an** 只能這樣用。

In general statements, uncountable nouns are always used 在籠統的陳述中, 不可數名詞總是在以下情況中出現:

without an article 不用冠詞:

> *Photography is a popular hobby.* 攝影是一種很流行的業餘愛好。| *She's interested in photography.* 她對攝影很有興趣。| *Water is essential to life.* 水是生命所必不可少的。

■ Are you talking about things and people in particular? 所述及的事物和人是特定的嗎?

Nouns are more often used with a particular meaning. Particular meanings can be **definite** or **indefinite**, and they need different articles accordingly. 名詞的使用, 更多的情況是帶有特定的含義, 特定含義可以是限定的或不限定的, 因此便相應地要使用不同的冠詞。

Language Note: Articles 語言提示: 冠詞

Definite 限定的

Both countable and uncountable nouns are definite in meaning when the speaker and the hearer know exactly which people or things are being referred to. For example, the definite article **the** is used 當說話人和聽話人都明確地知道所說的人或事物何所指時, 可數名詞或不可數名詞在含義上都是限定的, 例如, 下列情況就需要使用定冠詞 **the**:

when the noun has already been mentioned 當該名詞已經被提到過:

I saw a man and a woman in the street. **The man** *looked very cold.* 我在街上看見一個男人和一個女人, 那個男人看起來很冷。| *I took her some paper and a pencil, but she said she didn't need* **the paper**. 我拿給她一些紙和一枝鉛筆, 但是她說她不需要那些紙。

when it is clear from the situation which noun you mean 當在具體情景中已經清楚你所指的名詞是甚麼:

Can you pass me **the salt** *please?* (=the salt on the table) 請把鹽〔指餐桌上的鹽瓶〕遞給我。| *I'm going to* **the market** *for some fruit.* (=the market I always go to) 我去市場〔指我常去的那個市場〕買些水果。

when the words following the noun explain exactly which noun you mean 當名詞後面的詞語確切地說明該名詞指的是甚麼:

I've just spoken to **the man from next door**. (=not just any man) 我剛剛同隔壁那個人〔非任何人〕說話。| **The information that you gave me** *was wrong.* (=not just any information) 你給我的信息〔非任何信息〕是錯誤的。

when the person or thing is the only one that exists 當所說的人或事物是唯一存在的:

I'm going to travel round **the world**. (there is only one world) 我要遊遍全世界。〔世界只有一個〕

indefinite 非限定的

Nouns can also be used with a particular meaning without being definite. For example, in the sentence *I met* **a man** *in the street*, the speaker is talking about one particular man (not all men in general) but we do not know exactly which man. 名詞還可以具體有所指而並不表示限定。例如, 在"我在街上遇到一個人"這個句子裡, 說話人說的是一個特定的人(不是一般概念上所有的人), 但是我們並不確切了解是哪一個人。

Singular countable nouns with an indefinite meaning are used with the indefinite article **a/an** 具有非限定意義的單數可數名詞用不定冠詞 **a/an**:

Would you like **a cup** *of coffee?* 喝一杯咖啡好嗎?
She's **an engineer**. 她是一位工程師。

When their meaning is indefinite, plural countable nouns and uncountable nouns are used with **some** or **any**, or sometimes with no article 當不可數名詞和複數的可數名詞具有非限定意義時則用 **some** 或 **any**, 或者有時不加冠詞:

I think you owe me **some money**. 我看你還欠我錢。
Have you got **any money** *on you?* 你身上帶着錢嗎?
We need **some matches**. 我們需要些火柴。
We haven't got **any biscuits**. 我們沒有餅乾。
Would you like **some coffee**? 你想喝咖啡嗎?
Would you like **coffee**, **tea**, *or* **orange juice**? 你想喝咖啡、茶、還是橙汁?

Language Note: Articles 語言提示: 冠詞

■ Does the noun follow a special rule for the use of articles? 名詞前面冠詞的用法有專門的規律可循嗎?

The dictionary will tell you if a noun is always used with a particular article. For example 本辭典會告訴你, 一個名詞是否總是與一個特定的冠詞相連用, 例如:

Nouns describing people or things which are considered to be the only ones of their kind are used with **the**. 表示人或事物的名詞如果被認為是其同類中唯一的一個時用 **the**。

private sec·tor /ˌ.. ˈ..◂/ *n* **the private sector** the industries and services in a country that are owned and run by private companies, and not by the state or government 私營企業: *pay increases in the private sector* 私營企業的工資增長 | *private sector employers* 私營企業的雇主 —compare 比較 PUBLIC SECTOR

Some nouns are used with different articles when they have different meanings. (The entry tells you that **French** in its third meaning is always used with **the** and is followed by a plural verb.) 某些名詞隨意義的不同而使用不同的冠詞。(右側詞條表示, **French** 的第三義項總是用 **the**, 後接的動詞為複數。)

French[1] /frɛntʃ; frentʃ/ *n* **1** the language of France, and some other countries 法語: *How do you ask for directions in French?* 你怎樣用法語問路? **2** the language and literature of France as a subject of study 法國語言文學: *She's studying French at London University.* 她在倫敦大學學習法國語言文學。**3 the French** the people of France 法國人: *The French celebrate 14th July.* 法國人慶祝 7 月 14 日國慶節。

Some nouns are never used with **the** 某些名詞從來不與 **the** 連用。

par·lia·ment /ˈpɑrləmənt; ˈpɑːləmənt/ *n* [C] **1** the group of people who are elected to make a country's laws and discuss important national affairs 議會, 國會 **2 Parliament** the main law-making institution in the United Kingdom, which consists of the HOUSE OF COMMONS and the HOUSE OF LORDS 英國議會〔由上議院和下議院組成〕: **enter Parliament/get into Parliament** (=be elected as a member of Parliament) 被選為議員

Nouns in some common expressions such as **do the housework** etc., use **the** 在諸如 **do the housework** (做家務) 等慣用語中, 名詞前加 **the**。

house·work /ˈhausˌwɝk; ˈhaʊswɜːk/ *n* [U] work that you do to take care of a house such as washing, cleaning etc 家務 (勞動): *I spent all morning doing the housework.* 我整個上午都在做家務。

In some common expressions with prepositions such as **on foot**, **go home**, **go to hospital** (*BrE*), **go to school**, **by plane**, **at noon**, the nouns do not use an article. (Note that the entry tells you if the use of the article is different in American and British English.) 某些帶前置詞 [介詞] 的常見用語, 如 **on foot** (步行), **go home** (回家), **go to hospital** (去醫院治病), **go to school** (上學), **by plane** (乘飛機), **at noon** (中午) 等, 其中的名詞不加冠詞。(注意: 如果美國英語和英國英語中冠詞用法不同, 有關詞條中會有所標注。)

hos·pi·tal /ˈhɑspɪtl; ˈhɒspɪtl/ *n* [C,U] a large building where sick or injured people are looked after and receive medical treatment 醫院: **in/to/from hospital** *BrE*【英】: *He's in hospital, recovering from an operation.* 他手術後正在醫院裡康復。| **in/to/from the hospital** *AmE*【美】*After the accident Jane was rushed to the hospital.* 事故發生後簡被緊急送往醫院。| **be admitted to (the) hospital** (=be brought into a hospital for treatment) 被收進醫院 *A man has been admitted to hospital with gunshot wounds.* 一個受槍傷的男人被收進了醫院。| **hospital bed** (=a place in a hospital for a sick person) 病牀

When you look up a word in this dictionary, check the entry and read the examples to see whether there is any special information about the use of the article. 查閱本辭典時請注意詞條及其例證中是否提供了關於冠詞的特別資料。

See also 另見 A, AN, ANY, SOME; see 參見 THE (USAGE)

Language Note: Collocations 語言提示: 詞語搭配

A collocation is a grouping of words which "naturally" go together through common usage. Unlike idioms, their meaning can usually be understood from the individual words. In order to speak natural English, you need to be familiar with collocations. You need to know, for example, that you say "a heavy smoker" because **heavy** (NOT **big**) collocates with **smoker**, and that you say "free of charge" because **free of** collocates with **charge** (NOT **cost**, **payment**, etc.). If you do not choose the right collocation, you will probably be understood but you will not sound natural. This dictionary will help you with the most common collocations.
詞語搭配是指在日常應用中"自然地"組合在一起的一羣詞語。它們和成語有所不同, 其含義一般可通過個別的詞反映出來。如果想學會運用地道的英語, 就必須熟悉詞語搭配。例如你應當知道英語說 *a heavy smoker*(抽煙抽得很多的人), 而不能說 a big smoker, 因為 **heavy** 和 **smoker** 搭配; 又如英語說 *free of charge*(免費的), 而不說 free of cost 或 free of payment 等, 因為 **free of** 和 **charge** 搭配。你使用英語時如用錯了搭配, 人家也許可以理解你的意思, 但你的英語就顯得很不地道, 聽起來很不自然。本辭典向你指出最常見的詞語搭配。

Common fixed collocations 常見的固定詞語搭配

When you look up a word, read the examples carefully. Common collocations are shown in blue:
你在辭典中查閱一個詞語時, 應仔細閱讀其例語或例句。常見的詞語搭配都用藍字印刷:

These entries show you that 右欄的詞目中顯示 **freak of nature** (畸形生物), **bring sth to a halt** (使停頓), **call a halt (to)** (停止), **keep the peace** (維護治安), and 和 **peace of mind** (安心) are all common collocations 都是常見的詞語搭配。Note that you cannot change the word order in these phrases and that you cannot use other words even if they have similar meanings. 請注意, 這些詞語搭配中的詞語次序是不能隨便改動的; 此外, 詞語搭配中的詞不能用其他詞取代, 即使其意義相同。We say 我們可以說 **call a halt** (NOT **stop**) **to**, **a freak** (NOT **monster**) **of nature** etc., 而不能說 call a stop to, 也不能說 a monster of nature 等。

Note that other examples in the entries show natural patterns of language. For example, 請注意右欄詞目中有些例子不是固定的詞語搭配, 例如 *a lasting peace* (持久的和平), and 和 *inner peace* (內心的平靜) are all very common uses of the word peace, although they are not such strong collocations as those shown in blue. 這些都是 **peace** 一詞的通常用法, 但因不是固定搭配, 故未用藍字印刷。

freak[1] /frik; fri:k/ *n* [C] **1 bike/fitness/film etc freak** *informal* someone who is so interested in bikes, fitness etc that other people think they are strange or unusual【非正式】腳踏車迷/健美迷/電影迷等: *Carrot juice is a favourite with health-food freaks.* 胡蘿蔔汁是健康食品迷最愛喝的。**2** someone who looks very strange or behaves in a very unusual way 怪異的人: *Women who were good at physics used to be considered freaks.* 擅長物理學的女性過去常被看作怪人。**3** something in nature, such as a strangely-shaped plant or animal, that is very unusual 畸形生物: *One of the lambs was a freak – it had two tails.* 其中一頭羔羊是畸形的 —— 牠有兩條尾巴。| **a freak of nature** (=something physically strange or unusual) 畸形物; 怪異的事物 *By some freak of nature there was a snowstorm in June.* 天公作怪, 六月份竟然有暴風雪。**4 control freak** someone who always wants to control situations and other people 支配慾極強的人

halt[1] /hɔlt; hɔ:lt/ *n* [singular] a stop or pause 停止, 停住; 暫停: **bring sth to a halt** (=make something stop moving or continuing) 使…停頓; 使…中止 *Heavy snowfalls brought traffic to a halt on the Brenner Pass.* 大雪使得布倫納山口的交通陷於停頓。| *fuel shortages that have brought the industry to a grinding halt* 使該工業慢慢地停止生產的燃料短缺 … | **call a halt (to)** (=officially stop an activity from continuing)〔正式〕中止, 停止 *The IRA leadership has called a halt to its campaign of violence.* 愛爾蘭共和軍的領導層已經停止其暴力活動。

peace /pis; pi:s/ *n*
1 ►NO WAR 沒有戰爭◄ a) [U] a situation in which there is no war between countries or in a country 和平: **world peace** *a dangerous situation that threatens world peace* 威脅世界和平的危險局面 | **peace agreement/treaty etc** *the Geneva peace talks* 日內瓦和談 | **be at peace with** *Germany has been at peace with France for fifty years.* 德國已與法國和平相處了五十年。**b)** [singular] a period of time in which there is no war 和平時期: *a lasting peace* 持久和平

Language Note: Collocations 語言提示: 詞語搭配

c) peace movement/campaign etc organized efforts to prevent war 和平運動

⋮ ⋮ ⋮

4 ▶CALMNESS 平靜, 安寧◀ [U] a feeling of calmness and lack of worry and problems 平靜, 安寧: *the search for inner peace* 尋求內心的平靜 | **peace of mind** (=to stop you from worrying) 心境的平靜, 安心 *Ann had to check the baby every few minutes for her own peace of mind.* 為使自己安心, 安不得不每隔幾分鐘就查看一下嬰兒。| **at peace with yourself** (=calm and happy) 平靜而快樂 *Lynn never seems to be at peace with herself.* 林恩好像永不會平靜下來似的。**5** [U] a situation in which there is no quarrelling between people who live or work together 和睦〔相處〕: *peace and stability in industrial relations* 勞資關係的和睦穩定 | **keep the peace** (=stop people from quarrelling, fighting, or causing trouble) 維持治安

■ Collocating prepositions 與介詞連用的搭配

When you look up a word, the entry will show you if there is a particular preposition which collocates with it. 你在本辭典中查閱一個詞時, 如果該詞需與某一介詞搭配, 條目中會告訴你。

These entries show that you say
右欄各條目告訴你:

graduate (from)〔graduate 與 from 連用〕:
Jerry graduated from high school last year.
(傑里去年中學畢業。)

graduate[3] *v* **1** [I] to obtain a degree, especially a first degree, from a college or university〔尤指以學士學位〕大學畢業: **[+from]** *Mitch graduated from Stanford with a degree in Law.* 米奇畢業於史丹福大學, 獲法學學位。**2** [I] *AmE* to complete your education at HIGH SCHOOL【美】中學畢業: **[+from]** *Jerry graduated from high school last year.* 傑里去年中學畢業。**3 graduate (from sth) to** to start doing something that is bigger, better or more important〔從某處〕升級到: *Bob played college baseball but never graduated to the Majors.* 鮑勃在大學是棒球隊隊員, 但從來沒有升級加入職業棒球隊。**4** [T] *especially AmE* to give a degree or DIPLOMA to someone who has completed a course【尤美】向〔畢業生〕授予學位[文憑]

gratitude (for)〔gratitude與 for 連用〕:
I didn't get a single word of gratitude for all my trouble.
(我沒有聽到一句對我的辛勞表示感謝的話。)

grat·i·tude /ˈgrætəˌtjud; ˈgrætɪ̣tjuːd/ *n* [U] the feeling of being grateful 感激(之情): *Tears of gratitude filled her eyes.* 她的眼裡充滿感激的淚水。| *I couldn't adequately express my gratitude to Francis.* 我對弗朗西斯的感激之情難以言盡。| **[+for]** *I didn't get a single word of gratitude for all my trouble.* 我沒有聽到一句對我的辛勞表示感謝的話。| **deepest gratitude** (=very great gratitude) 萬分的感激 —opposite 反義詞 INGRATITUDE —see also 另見 **owe a debt of gratitude to sb** (DEBT (4))

harmful (to)〔harmful 與 to 連用〕:
chemicals that are harmful to the environment
(對環境有害的化學品)

harm·ful /ˈhɑrmfəl; ˈhɑːmfəl/ *adj* causing or likely to cause harm 有害的; 致傷的: *the harmful effects of smoking* 吸煙的害處 | **[+to]** *chemicals that are harmful to the environment* 對環境有害的化學品 —**harmfully** *adv* —**harmfulness** *n* [U]

See 參見 LANGUAGE NOTES: **Idioms**, **Intensifying Adjectives**, **Make and Do**

Language Note: Criticism and Praise
語言提示: 批評和讚揚

■ Making criticisms 提出批評

Criticisms can be very short and direct, or they can be longer and more indirect. When deciding which expressions are suitable for which situations it is useful to ask certain questions. 批評可以很短而且直截了當, 也可以較長而且迂迴曲折。在決定何種場合採取何種批評方式時, 先來考慮一些問題是有益的。

Considerations affecting choice of expression 在選擇批評方式時的幾種考慮

— How bad is the thing or action which is being criticized? How important is it to the speaker? 要批評的事情或行為, 其嚴重程度如何? 對説話人來説, 其重要程度如何?

— What is the relationship between the person who is making the criticism (the speaker) and the person who is being criticized (the hearer)? The more direct expressions, for example, are mostly used between friends or when the speaker is in a position of authority. 批評者和被批評者之間的關係如何? 舉例來説, 直截了當的批評方式大多用於朋友之間或者批評者居於權威的地位。

— Is the attitude of the speaker friendly or unfriendly? 批評者所持的態度是友善的還是尖刻的?

Indirect criticism 迂迴的批評

Indirect expressions are commonly used in order to be polite. These expressions usually avoid very strong words such as **bad**, **failure**, **dreadful**, etc., and often use negative forms such as, **not quite right** and **not very good**. They also use other ways of softening what is being said. 為了表示客氣, 通常使用迂迴的批評方式。迂迴的批評方式常常避免使用像 **bad** (壞的, 拙劣的, 錯誤的)、**failure** (失敗) 和 **dreadful** (糟透了的) 之類感情色彩強烈的詞語, 而是代之以諸如 **not quite right** (不很對) 和 **not very good** (不很好) 之類的否定式, 或是使語氣緩和的其他形式。(see 參見 LANGUAGE NOTE: **Tentativeness**):

That **doesn't look quite right** *to me, you know. Maybe you should try again.* (Friend to friend) 我覺得這樣不很對, 或許你應該再試一試。〔朋友對朋友〕

I'm afraid your last essay was **not quite** *up to standard.* (Teacher to pupil) 我看你最近寫的一篇文章不大規範。〔老師對學生〕

Very often, speakers begin by saying something good about the person or thing they are going to criticize. 批評者往往對所要批評的人會事先説一些好話:

I love the colour, *but I wonder if the style is right for you.* (Friend to friend) 我喜歡這顏色, 但是我説不準這式樣是不是適合你。〔朋友對朋友〕

The band's great, *but I'm not so sure about the singer.* (Friend criticizing a friend's choice of music) 樂隊挺不錯, 但歌手就不好説了。〔批評朋友對音樂的選擇〕

Your written work has really improved, *but you still have a bit of a problem with your spelling.* (Teacher to pupil) 你的書面作業確有進步, 但你在拼寫方面還有些問題。〔教師對小學生〕

Language Note: Criticism and Praise
語言提示: 批評和讚揚

Direct criticism 直截了當的批評

Direct expressions are sometimes used informally between members of the same family or between good friends. 一家人或好朋友之間有時可在非正式場合進行直截了當的批評:

> *You can't possibly wear that tie. It looks awful.* (Wife to husband) 你無論如何也不能繫那條領帶, 難看極了。〔妻子對丈夫〕
>
> *Your room's an absolute mess; when are you going to clear it up?* (Mother to daughter) 你的房間亂得不成樣子, 你打算甚麼時候才清理房間?〔母親對女兒〕

Direct expressions are also used when the speaker is in a position of authority. Here, the effect is usually unfriendly, especially if the language is formal. 如果批評者居於權威的地位, 也可採用直截了當的批評方式。它給人的感覺常常是尖刻的, 尤其是在使用正式語言的情況之下:

> *Your uniform's filthy.* (Sergeant to soldier) 你的制服太髒。〔班長對兵士〕
>
> *There are a lot of typing errors in this report.* (Boss to secretary) 這份報告有許多打字錯誤。〔經理對祕書〕
>
> *The exam results this year are appalling.* (Teacher to class) 今年的考試成績簡直可怕。〔教師對全班學生〕

Giving praise 讚揚

Speakers usually feel that praise will be acceptable to the hearer, so praise can be given in a direct way. The hearer usually responds to the praise by thanking the speaker and often adds a comment. When responding, some people like to appear to disagree with the praise but this is not necessary in order to be polite. 說話人覺得讚揚的話通常都是人所愛聽的, 因此也就有甚麼說甚麼, 不必拐彎抹角。受讚揚的人的應答通常是除向對方表示感謝外, 還要再說點甚麼。有的人喜歡表示一下似乎不同意所受到的讚揚, 但是這並不是表示客氣所必需的:

praise 讚揚	**response 應答**
Well done!/That was great. 很不錯! 好極了。	*Thank you./Thanks.* 謝謝你。/謝謝。
I love that dress. Is it new? 我喜歡這件衣服, 是新的嗎?	*(Oh,) thank you. No, it's quite old, but I've always liked it.* (喔,) 謝謝你。不, 這衣服相當舊了, 但我一直都喜歡穿它。
That was a wonderful meal. 這頓飯好極了。	*Thank you. I'm glad you enjoyed it.* 謝謝你, 我很高興你喜歡吃。
You're a great cook. 你真是個了不起的廚師。	*Well, I don't know about that but I enjoy cooking/I do my best.* 嗯, 我看還談不上吧, 不過我喜歡做菜 [盡力而為]。
You've made a lot of progress this year. I'm very pleased with your performance. 你今年有不少進步, 我為你的表現感到十分高興。	*Thank you.* 謝謝你。

Language Note: Criticism and Praise
語言提示: 批評和讚揚

▶ Be careful! 注意!

In informal English, expressions of praise are sometimes used sarcastically as a form of criticism. The situation or the speaker's tone of voice usually makes the meaning clear. Between friends, this kind of sarcasm is usually used in a friendly way, often as a joke. 在非正式英語中, 一些讚揚的言辭有時被用作挖苦話來批評人。說話當時的具體情況和說話人的聲調通常能表達這種用意。在朋友之間通常是很善意地使用這種挖苦, 而且時常是作為一種玩笑:

> *You're a regular Albert Einstein, Tom.* (Tom has done or said something stupid.) 你倒是個十足的愛因斯坦, 湯姆。〔湯姆做了甚麼傻事或說了甚麼傻話。〕
>
> *Well, that's what I call a miracle of organization!* (The speaker is complaining about bad organization.) 喲, 這組織工作做得真是頂呱呱!〔講話者對組織工作太差表示不滿。〕

In other situations, it usually shows that the speaker has a very unfriendly attitude. 在其他情況下, 通常表現說話人的態度很不友善。

> *Another brilliant performance, Mr Smith!* (The speaker is furious about Mr Smith's failure.) 你又幹了件好事, 史密斯先生!〔說話人對史密斯先生的怠忽職守非常惱火。〕

See 參見 LANGUAGE NOTE : **Tentativeness**

Language Note: Gradable and Non-gradable Adjectives 可分等級和不可分等級的形容詞

■ Gradable adjectives 可分等級的形容詞

Most English adjectives are gradable. That is, their meaning can have different possible degrees of strength. They can therefore be used with adverbs which express these different degrees. Gradable adjectives can be divided into two kinds: scale adjectives and limit adjectives. 大多數英語形容詞都是可分等級的。就是說它們的含義可以有不同程度的強度, 這些形容詞因而可與副詞連用來表達這些不同的程度。可分等級的形容詞又可分成兩類: 程度形容詞和極限形容詞。

Scale adjectives 程度形容詞

These are adjectives like **small**, **cold**, **expensive**, which can have many different degrees. They make up the biggest group of adjectives in English. 這類形容詞, 如 **small**, **cold**, **expensive** 等是可以有不同程度的, 它們是英語形容詞中最大的一類。

Scale adjectives can be used in comparative and superlative forms 程度形容詞可有比較級和最高級形式:

He's happier than he used to be.
(他比過去更快樂。)

She's the strongest girl in the class.
(她是全班最有勁的女生。)

Scale adjectives can also be used with the following adverbs to express a high, medium, or small degree 程度形容詞也可與下列副詞連用來表達高、中或低級程度:

To express a high degree 表示高級程度

very, **extremely**, **incredibly**, etc. 等 **quite** (*AmE* 美)

That's a **very nice** *sweater you're wearing.*
(你穿的這件毛衣非常好看。)

New York's **extremely hot** *in July.*
(紐約在七月份非常熱。)

To express a medium degree 表示中級程度

fairly, **pretty** (*infml* 非正式), **quite**, **rather**

You don't need a coat. It's **quite warm** *outside.*
(你不需要穿外套, 外面相當暖和。)

She's **rather a famous** *poet.*
(她是一名比較有名的詩人。)

To express a small degree (when you want to reduce the effect of the adjective)
表示低級程度〔當你想減弱某個形容詞的效果時〕

slightly, **a little**, **a bit** (*infml* 非正式)

I'm afraid the milk is **slightly sour**.
(我看牛奶有點發酸了。)

He was **a bit upset** *when you mentioned the accident.*
(你提起那次事故時, 他有點不安。)

Language Note: Gradable and Non-gradable Adjectives 可分等級和不可分等級的形容詞

Note that in American English **quite** can be used with scale adjectives to express a high degree. In British English it is used with scale adjectives to express only a medium degree. An American person, for example, would be pleased to be told that a new shirt was **quite nice**; but a British person might think that the speaker did not really like it very much. 請注意, 在美國英語中 **quite** 與程度形容詞連用可表示高級程度。但在英國英語中, 它與程度形容詞連用只表示中級程度。例如, 如果你説某人的新襯衫 **quite nice**, 美國人就會很高興; 但若他是英國人, 就會覺得你其實不是很喜歡這件衣服。

(For a comparison of **fairly**, **quite**, and **rather**, see Usage Note at RATHER. 對 **fairly**, **quite** 和 **rather** 的比較, 請參見 RATHER 的用法説明。)

Limit adjective 極限形容詞

These are adjectives like **perfect**, **unique**, **impossible**, **worthless**, whose meaning already contains the idea of an absolute degree. These words are not usually used in comparative and superlative forms. Limit adjectives can be used with the following adverbs to express the "highest" or "close to the highest" degree 這類形容詞, 如 **perfect**, **unique**, **impossible**, **worthless** 等, 其含義已包括了極度的意思, 因此一般沒有比較級和最高級形式。極限形容詞可與以下副詞連用來表達"最高的"或"接近最高的"程度:

To express the highest degree (the meaning is used to its limit)
表示最高程度〔詞的含義已表達極限〕

absolutely, **completely**, **quite**, **totally**, **utterly**

That's **quite** *impossible.*
(那是完全不可能的。)

We were **absolutely** *speechless.*
(我們簡直連一句話都説不出來。)

To express closeness to the highest degree
表示接近最高程度

almost, **nearly**, **practically**, **virtually**

The waiting room was **virtually empty**.
(候診室裡已幾乎空無一人。)

It's **almost impossible** *to say.*
(要説幾乎是不可能的。)

Some adjectives which have extreme meanings, such as **disgusting**, **amazed**, **terrified**, are usually used with "highest degree" adverbs 有些有極端含義的形容詞, 如 **disgusting**, **amazed**, **terrified** 等, 一般都和"最高級"的副詞連用, 如: **absolutely disgusting** (討厭之極) | **utterly amazed** (非常吃驚) | **completely terrified** (徹底受驚)。

Note, however, that they are not usually used with "closeness to the highest degree" adverbs, such as **almost** or **nearly**. 但請注意, 這類形容詞一般不和表示"接近最高級程度"的副詞, 如 **almost** 或 **nearly** 連用。

You can often express a meaning more strongly by using a limit adjective rather than a scale adjective. The choice of adverb depends on which type of adjective you use. 用極限形容詞常常可以比程度形容詞表達更強烈的意思。選用哪個副詞完全要看你用的是哪一類的形容詞。Compare 請比較:

Language Note: Gradable and Non-gradable Adjectives 可分等級和不可分等級的形容詞

very good (很好)
incredibly tired (非常疲倦)
a bit difficult (有點困難)

absolutely marvellous (簡直美妙之極)
totally exhausted (完全筋疲力竭)
practically impossible (幾乎不可能)

Note that some adjectives, like **empty**, **full**, **new**, can be treated as both scale and limit adjectives 請注意, 有些形容詞, 如 **empty, full, new** 等, 既可作程度形容詞, 也可作極限形容詞: *Watch you don't spill that glass. It's* **very full**. (注意別撒了杯子裡的東西。杯子裝得很滿。) | *There are no more seats — the theatre's* **completely full**. (沒有座位了 — 劇場完全滿座了。)

▶ Be careful! 注意!

Sometimes adjectives like **unique**, **perfect**, **identical**, whose meaning contains the idea of an absolute degree, are treated as scale adjectives 有些形容詞, 如 **unique**, **perfect**, **identical** 雖然意思包含極度, 但使用時仍按程度形容詞處理: *It was* **rather a unique** *experience.* (那是一次比較獨特的經歷。) However, some people consider this use to be incorrect. 但也有人認為這種用法是不正確的。

■ Non-gradable adjectives 不可分等級的形容詞

Adjectives are non-gradable if their meaning cannot have different degrees. For example, the adjective **atomic** is non-gradable because things (bombs, reactions, science, etc.) are either atomic or not atomic; there are no degrees in between. 形容詞的意思如無不同程度之分當然就是不可分等級的形容詞了。例如形容詞 **atomic** (原子的) 就是不可分等級的, 因為事物 (如炸彈、反應、科學等) 不是原子的, 就是非原子的, 它們之間不存在不同的程度。

Non-gradable adjectives are not usually used in comparative and superlative forms, and are not usually used with adverbs of degree. 不可分等級形容詞一般無比較級和最高級, 通常也不和表示程度的副詞連用。

Here are some more examples of non-gradable adjectives 下面再舉一些不可分等級形容詞的例子:

American/British (and all nationality adjectives 以及一切表示國籍的形容詞) (美國的; 英國的)
biological (warfare etc.) (生物學的) 〈如細菌戰等〉
electric (oven, fire, etc.) (電氣的) 〈如電烤爐; 電熱爐等〉
medical (醫學的)
monthly (每月的) (of newspapers etc. 指報紙等)
painted (着了色的)
polar (bear, region, etc.) (地極的) 〈如北極態; 南、北極地區等〉
previous (先前的)
southern (南方的)
stainless (steel etc.) (無污點的) 〈如不鏽鋼等〉

▶ Be careful! 注意!

Note that some non-gradable adjectives can sometimes be used with a special meaning and may then be gradable. Adjectives of nationality, for example, may be used to refer to a person's way of behaving. *He's very French* means "he seems or behaves very much like a typical French person". 有些不可分等級的形容詞有時有特別的含義, 在這種情況下就有可能成為可分等級的形容詞。例如表示國籍的形容詞可用來形容某人的行為、舉止: *He's very French* 表示"他似乎是個典型的法國人"或"他的行為、舉止非常像法國人。"

See also 另見 NEARLY, UTTERLY, VIRTUALLY; see 參見 ALMOST (USAGE), RATHER (USAGE), and 以及 LANGUAGE NOTE: **Intensifying Adjectives**

Language Note: Idioms 語言提示: 習語

■ What is an idiom? 甚麼是習語?

An idiom is a fixed group of words with a special meaning which is different from the meanings of the individual words. 習語是一種具有特定含義的固定詞組, 其含義不同於組成固定詞組的每個單詞的含義。

Idioms are usually fixed 習語通常都是固定的

Although certain small changes can be made in idiomatic expressions (see below: **Using idioms**) you cannot usually change the words, the word order, or the grammatical forms in the same way as you can change a non-idiomatic expression. 習語雖然可作某些小的變動 (見下文: 習語的使用), 但通常不能像非習語詞語那樣改換其中的詞、詞序或語法形式。For example 如:

The answer's easy can be changed to *The answer's simple*. But in the expression *It's* **(as) easy as pie**, the word **simple** cannot be used. *The answer's easy* 可以改換成 *The answer's simple* (答案是容易的。) 但在 **It's (as) easy as pie** (容易之極) 中, 就不能改用 **simple**。

She likes cats and dogs can be changed to *She likes dogs and cats*. But in the expression *It's* **raining cats and dogs** (=raining hard), the word order is fixed. 句子 *She likes cats and dogs*. (她喜愛貓和狗) 可以改換成 *She likes dogs and cats*. (她喜愛狗和貓), 但在 **It's raining cats and dogs** (下傾盆大雨) 中, *cats and dogs* 的詞序則是固定不變的。

He always delivers the goods can be a literal expression meaning, for example, "he always brings the goods to his customer's house". In this case, **the goods** can be replaced by a pronoun: *He always delivers them*, or the verb can be used in the passive form: *The goods* **are** *always* **delivered** *on time*. However, *He always* **delivers the goods** can also be a fixed idiomatic expression meaning "he always produces the desired results". When this expression is used as an idiom, no word changes are possible. 句子 *He always delivers the goods* 可以按其字面意思來理解, 即 "他總是把貨物送到顧客家中"。在這種情況下 the goods 可以用代 (名) 詞代替: *He always delivers them*, 動詞也可以換用被動形式: *The goods are always* **delivered** *on time* (貨物總是準時送出)。但 *He always* **delivers the goods** 也可以是習語, 意思是 "他總是不負所望", 此時其中的詞便不能改換。

Idioms have a special meaning 習語有特定的含義

Sometimes the meaning of an idiom can be guessed from the meaning of one of the words 有時習語的含義可以從其中的一個詞猜測到:

to **rack your brains** (=to think hard; something to do with **brains**) (苦思冥想) 〔與 **brains** 有關〕

to live **in the lap of luxury** (=to live in a very luxurious way; something to do with **luxury**) (過奢侈生活) 〔與 **luxury** 有關〕

Usually, however, the meaning of an idiom is completely different from any of the separate words 然而, 通常習語的含義同構成詞語的個別單詞的含義全然不同:

She was **over the moon** *about her new job*. (=she was extremely happy) (她對她的新工作感到極為滿意。)

The exam was a **piece of cake**. (=the exam was very easy) (考試非常容易。)

Sometimes an expression can have two meanings, one literal and one idiomatic. This happens most often when the idiomatic expression is based on a physical image 有時一個詞語可以有兩個含義。一個是字面意義, 另一個是習語含義。這通常出現在人體形象的詞語中:

Language Note: Idioms 語言提示: 習語

a slap in the face (=a physical blow to the face 一記耳光; an insult or action which seems to be aimed directly at somebody 侮辱; 打擊)

to **keep your head above water** (=to prevent yourself sinking into the water 不要被水淹沒; to be just able to live on your income; to be just able to go on with life, work, etc. 收入僅夠糊口; 湊合着生活、工作等)

Recognizing idioms 習語的分辨

How do you recognize an idiom? It is sometimes difficult to know whether an expression is literal or idiomatic, so it is useful to remember some of the most common types of idioms. 怎樣才能辨認出習語? 一個詞語是表達字面意義或是習語含義, 有時很難分辨。因此記住某些最常見的習語類型就很有用了。

Pairs of words 成對詞

touch-and-go 無把握的; 不確定的
high and dry (船) 擱淺; 陷入困境
stuff and nonsense 胡說八道
the birds and the bees 〔可告訴兒童的〕兩性關係的基本常識

(Note that the word order in these pairs is fixed 注意成對詞中的詞序是固定的。)

Similes 明喻

(as) blind as a bat 眼睛完全看不見東西的
(as) large as life 與實物一般大小; 確確實實
(as) mad as a hatter 瘋瘋癲癲的
(as) old as the hills 非常古老的

Phrasal verbs 片語 [短語] 動詞

chicken out of (sthg.) 因害怕而退出〔某事〕
come across (sthg. or sbdy.) 偶然碰上〔某人〕; 無意中發現〔某物〕
nod off 打瞌睡, 睡著
put up with (sthg. or sbdy.) 忍受〔某事或某人〕

Actions which represent feelings 說明感情的動作

look down your nose (in scorn or dislike) 輕視, 瞧不起; 不喜歡

raise your eyebrows (in surprise, doubt, displeasure, or disapproval) 驚奇, 疑惑; 不悅; 不同意

These idioms can be used by themselves to express feelings even when the feeling is not stated. 上列習語本身就可用來表示一種感情, 即使這種感情沒有明說出來。

For example 例如: *There were a lot of raised eyebrows at the news of the minister's dismissal* (大家對部長被免職的消息都非常驚訝) just means "everyone was very surprised". 這個例句中的習語就是表示"大家都很驚訝"。

Sayings 諺語

Many sayings are complete sentences. Remember, however, that sayings are not always given in full 許多諺語都是完整的句子。但請記住, 諺語在使用時有時是不完整的:

Language Note: Idioms 語言提示: 習語

Well, **two's company** *I always say. What do you think, Mary?* (The speaker wants to be alone with someone and is asking the third person, Mary, to go away.) (嗯, 我總是覺得"二人結伴", 瑪麗, 你覺得怎麼樣?)〔講話的人想要單獨與某人在一起, 因此要求第三者的瑪麗走開。〕The full saying is 這句諺語的完整說法是: **Two's company, three's a crowd.** (二人結伴, 三人不歡。)

Ring up the dentist and make an appointment now. **A stitch in time**, *you know.* (The speaker wants the hearer to go to the dentist immediately, before she gets bad toothache.) (現在就給牙醫打電話約個門診時間, 你要知道"小洞不補"可不行呵。)〔講話的人要對方在牙痛惡化之前立即去看牙醫〕The full saying is 這句諺語的完整說法是: **A stitch in time saves nine.** (小洞不補, 大洞吃苦; 一針不補十針難縫。)

It's a bit of a **swings and roundabouts** *situation, I'm afraid.* (The speaker is discussing two possibilities which have equal advantages and disadvantages.) (我倒覺得現在的形勢有點利弊各半。)〔講話的人在討論兩種利弊參半的可能性〕The full saying is 這句諺語的完整說法是: **What you gain on the swings you lose on the roundabouts.** (失之東隅, 收之桑榆。)

Using idioms 習語的使用

Before using an idiom, ask yourself the following questions 使用習語時應注意以下問題:

How fixed is the expression? 詞語的固定程度如何?

Sometimes certain parts of an idiom can be changed. 有時習語的某些部分是可以更換的。

Verbs, for example, can often be used in different forms. (Note, however, that they are rarely used in the passive form.) 例如動詞可以用不同的形式 (注意: 很少用被動形式)。

He **caught** *her eye.* (他吸引住她的視線。) | *Something***'s just caught** *my eye.* (有件東西正引起我的注意。) | **Catching** *the waiter's eye, he asked for the bill.* (他招呼侍應生, 要求結賬。)

In many expressions, it is possible to change the **subject pronoun** 許多詞語的主格代 (名) 詞可以更換:

He *swallowed his pride.* (他暫時忍氣吞聲。) | **They** *swallowed their pride.* (他們暫時忍氣吞聲。) | **Janet** *swallowed her pride.* (珍妮特暫時忍氣吞聲。)

Someone can usually be replaced by other nouns or pronouns. **someone** 通常可以代之以其他名詞或代 (名) 詞:

jog **someone's** *memory* (喚起某人的回憶) | *She jogged* **my** *memory.* (她喚起我的回憶。) | *This photograph might jog* **your** *memory.* (這張照片可能會喚起你的回憶。)

Remember, however, that most idioms are far more fixed than literal expressions, and many cannot be changed at all. 不過請記住, 大多數習語較之一般按字面意思理解的詞語更為固定, 而且有許多是不能更換的。

Language Note: Idioms 語言提示: 習語

Is the style right for the situation? 文體與語境是否一致?

Many idiomatic expressions are informal or slang, and are only used in informal (usually spoken) language. 許多習語性詞語是非正式文體或者俚語, 只用於非正式語體 (通常是口語) 中。Compare 比較:

He said the wrong thing (他說了錯話。) and 和 *He* **put his foot in it**. (*infml* 非正式) (他把事情弄砸了。)

They all felt rather depressed (他們都很消沉。) and 和 *They were all* **down in the dumps**. (*infml* 非正式) (他們全都灰溜溜的。)

Some expressions are pompous, literary, or old-fashioned, and are not often used in everyday language except, perhaps, as a joke 某些習語文體浮華, 純屬書面語或用法過時, 因而除了作為開玩笑之外, 不常用於日常語言中:

Gird up your loins! *It's time to go home.* (humorous use of a literary idiom) (做好準備!該回家了。)〔文雅習語的幽默用法〕

You will find all the common English idioms in this dictionary. Look them up at the entry for the first main word in the idiom. Idioms are shown in blue at the end of an entry, and each idiom has its own number. 本辭典收錄了全部常用英語習語。習語置於以其第一個中心詞為詞目的詞條的末尾, 用藍字標出, 有自己的義項序碼。

See 參見 LANGUAGE NOTES: **Collocations**, **Phrasal Verbs**

Language Note: Intensifying Adjectives
語言提示: 強語勢形容詞

You can use many different adjectives to talk about large physical size: **big**, **large**, **enormous**, **huge**, **tall**, etc. But which adjectives can you use to intensify a noun (to express the idea of great degree or strength) when you are talking about something which is not physical? 有許多不同的形容詞如 **big**, **large**, **enormous**, **huge**, **tall** 等可用來表示物體之大, 但是哪些形容詞可用來表示非物體之大呢 (例如程度或力量之大)?

Below are some of the most common intensifying adjectives. Note that nouns can have different intensifying adjectives without really changing their meaning 下面是一些最常用的強語勢形容詞。請注意, 一些名詞儘管換了不同的強語勢形容詞, 整個語意卻是一樣的:

> *a* **great/large** *quantity* (大量); *a* **big/bitter/great** *disappointment* (非常失望); *a* **big/definite/distinct/marked** *improvement* (顯著的改進)

However, the choice of adjective depends on the noun; different nouns need different adjectives to intensify them. Below you will find some of the most common examples. 不過, 形容詞的選擇取決於名詞, 不同的名詞要由不同的形容詞來加強語勢, 以下是一些最常見的例子。

■ Great 重大的, 強烈的, 極大的

Great is used in front of uncountable nouns which express feelings or qualities 形容詞 **great** 用於表示感情或性質的不可數名詞的前面: *She takes* **great pride** *in her work.* (她對自己的工作感到很自豪。) | *His handling of the problem showed* **great sensitivity**. (他對這個問題的處理表明他非常敏銳。)

With uncountable nouns, **great** can be replaced by **a lot of** which is more informal, but very common. 當 **great** 與不可數名詞連用時, 可以由更為非正式但又很通用的 **a lot of** 取代: *I have* **a lot of admiration** *for her.* (我對她極為欽佩。) | *It takes* **a lot of skill** *to pilot a plane.* (駕駛飛機需要有很嫻熟的技能。)

When used with countable nouns, **great** is more formal than **big**. 當 **great** 與可數名詞連用時, 它比 **big** 要正式得多: *a* **big/great surprise** (非常驚訝)

Great can often be replaced by stronger adjectives, such as **enormous**, **terrific** (*infml* 非正式), and **tremendous**. 此外 **great** 常常可由更強烈的形容詞如 **enormous**, **terrific** 和 **tremendous** 取代: **enormous enjoyment** (極大的樂趣) | **tremendous admiration** (不勝欽佩)

Great is commonly used with these nouns 通常 **great** 可與下列名詞連用:

great admiration (非常欽佩)
great anger (大怒)
in great detail (很詳細地)
(a) great disappointment (極失望)
great enjoyment (巨大的樂趣)
great excitement (非常激動)
a great failure (重大失敗)
great fun (很好玩)
great happiness (非常的幸福)
great joy (大喜)
at great length (極為詳細地)
a great mistake (*esp. BrE* 尤英) (重大錯誤)
a great number (of) (大量的...)
great power (強國)
great pride (非常自豪)
a great quantity (of) (大量的...)
great sensitivity (非常敏銳)
great skill (很高的技術)
great strength (巨大的力量)
great understanding (非常理解)
great wealth 巨大的財富

Language Note: Intensifying Adjectives
語言提示: 強語勢形容詞

■ Absolute 純粹的, 完全的, 絕對的

Absolute, **complete**, **total**, and **utter** are used more frequently than **great** in front of words which express very strong feelings (such as **ecstasy** or **amazement**), or extreme situations, happenings, etc., especially bad ones (such as **chaos** or **disaster**). 形容詞 **absolute, complete, total** 和 **utter** 較 **great** 更經常用於表示強烈感情的詞(如 **ecstasy** 或 **amazement**) 或者極端的(尤指壞的)情況、事端的詞(如 **chaos** 或 **disaster**) 的前面:

She stared at him in **utter amazement**. (她極驚訝地盯着他看。) | *The expedition was* **a total disaster**. (這次探險是一次巨大的災難。)

In the examples below, **complete**, **total**, and **utter** could all be used in place of **absolute**. 在下列例句中, **absolute** 都可用 **complete**, **total** 和 **utter** 代替:

absolute agony (極大的痛苦)	absolute ecstasy (欣喜若狂)
absolute astonishment (非常驚訝)	absolute fury (狂怒)
absolute bliss (極大的幸福)	an absolute idiot (十足的白痴)
an absolute catastrophe (巨大的災難)	absolute loathing (極端的厭惡)
absolute despair (完全的絕望)	absolute madness (極端的瘋狂)

■ Big 大的, 重大的, 重要的

Big is mostly used when talking about physical size but it can also be used as an intensifying adjective. Note that it is not usually used with uncountable nouns. 形容詞 **big** 最常用於形容物體之大, 但也可用作強語勢形容詞。但要注意它通常不與不可數名詞連用:

a big decision (重大的決定)	a big improvement (重大的改善)
a big disappointment (巨大的失望)	a big mistake (嚴重的錯誤)
a big eater (=someone who eats a lot) (食量大的人)	a big surprise (巨大的驚喜)
	a big spender (=someone who spends a lot) (花錢大手大腳的人)

■ Large 大的, 巨大的

Large is mostly used to express physical size. It is also commonly used with nouns which are connected with numbers or measurements, as in the examples below. Note that it is not usually used with uncountable nouns. 形容詞 **large** 多數用來表示物體之大。它通常也同與數量或度量有關的名詞連用, 其用例如下。要注意它通常不與不可數名詞連用:

a large amount (大數額)	a large population (眾多的人口)	a large quantity (大量)
a large number (of) (大量的…)	a large proportion (一大份)	a large scale (大規模)

Language Note: Intensifying Adjectives
語言提示: 強語勢形容詞

■ Deep/heavy/high/strong 非常的, 極度的, 深厚的/大量的, 狂暴的, 嚴重的/高度的, 很大的/強烈的, 烈性的

Deep, **heavy**, **high**, and **strong** are also commonly used as intensifying adjectives, as in these examples
形容詞 **deep, heavy, high, strong** 通常也用作強語勢形容詞, 其用例如下:

deep

deep depression (極度的沮喪)	a deep feeling (=emotion) (深情)	in deep thought (在沉思中)
deep devotion (非常的忠誠)	(a) deep sleep (酣睡)	in deep trouble (陷入極困難的境地)

heavy

a heavy drinker (酒量大的人)	a heavy sleeper (不易醒來的人)	heavy snow (大雪)
heavy rain (大雨)	a heavy smoker (吸很多煙的人)	heavy traffic (交通繁忙)

high

high cost (高費用)	a high expectation (of) (對...的高期望)	high pressure (高壓)
high density (高密度)	a high level (of) (高水平的...)	a high price (高價)
high energy (高能量)	a high opinion (of someone or something) 〔對某人或某事的〕(高度評價)	high quality (高質量)
high esteem (高度尊敬)		high speed (高速)

strong

strong criticism (猛烈的批評)	a strong opinion (about something) 〔對某事的〕(堅定的看法)	a strong smell (濃烈的氣味)
a strong denial (強烈的否認)	a strong sense of (humour/fun etc.) (濃厚的〔幽默、風趣等〕感)	a strong taste (濃烈的味道)
a strong feeling (that) (=idea) 〔...的〕(強烈的想法)		

Language Note: Intensifying Adjectives
語言提示: 強語勢形容詞

■ Other intensifying adjectives 其他強語勢形容詞

The examples above show some of the most common intensifying adjectives, but many other adjectives are used to express the idea of great degree, size, or strength. When deciding which adjective to use, remember that it usually depends on the noun. Particular nouns need particular adjectives. 以上是一些最常用的強語勢形容詞, 但是還有很多其他的形容詞可用來表示程度、規模或者強度的巨大。在考慮用哪個形容詞時, 記住這通常都取決於被形容的名詞, 特定的名詞需要特定的形容詞:

a **fierce/heated argument** (激烈的爭論)　*a* **distinct/marked improvement** (顯著的改進)
a **close connection** (緊密的聯繫)　*a* **hard worker** (勤勞的工人)

Note that different adjectives are used with different senses of a noun. 還要注意, 一個名詞如有不同的意義, 與之連用的形容詞也不同:

He has a very **high opinion** *of her work.* (=he thinks it is very good) (他認為她工作得很好。) | *She has* **strong opinions** *about politics.* (她對政治有明確、堅定的看法。)

See 參見 LANGUAGE NOTES: **Collocations**, **Gradable and Non-gradable Adjectives**

Language Note: Invitations and Offers
語言提示: 邀請和提議

■ Politeness in invitations 邀請時的禮貌問題

It is possible to use both direct and indirect expressions when giving invitations. When deciding which expressions are suitable, it is important to ask the question: Can the speaker assume that the invitation will be acceptable to the hearer? 在表示邀請時, 可使用直接語氣的語句, 也可使用間接語氣的語句。究竟何者為宜, 重要的是邀請者有無把握知道被邀請者是否接受邀請。

When it is not clear whether an invitation will be acceptable (for example, when the speaker does not know the hearer very well), it is often safer to use an indirect expression. This makes it possible for the hearer to refuse without creating an uncomfortable situation. 當不清楚邀請是否會被接受 (例如邀請人對被邀請者不很瞭解) 時, 用間接語句比較穩妥。這樣, 被邀請者如果拒絕也不會出現任何不快:

Would you like some coffee? 您要喝點咖啡嗎?

We were wondering if you'd like to come to dinner. 不知你是否願來吃晚飯?

How about coming to the movies tonight? (*infml* 非正式) 今天晚上來看電影怎麼樣?

Why don't you come and eat with us? (*infml* 非正式) 何不過來和我們一起吃飯?

However, it is also polite to give invitations in a very direct way. This is possible whenever the speaker feels sure that the invitation will be to the hearer's advantage. 但是, 用很直接的方式提出邀請也是有禮貌的。當邀請者相信邀請是有利於對方時就可以用直接的方式:

Have a cup of tea. 請喝杯茶。

Help yourself. 請自 (己隨) 便 (吃) 。

Come and see us next time you're in town. 下次到城裡來時請來看看我們。

Try some of this cake. 嚐一點這種蛋糕吧。

■ Politeness in offers 提議時的禮貌問題

If the speaker does not know whether an offer will be acceptable, especially if the speaker and the hearer do not know each other very well, it is usual to use an indirect expression. 假使說話人不知道對方是否願意接受自己的提議, 特別是雙方彼此不甚瞭解時, 通常都使用間接方式:

May I give you a hand with the dishes? 我來幫你洗碗碟好嗎?

Would you like me to bring any food to the party? 我要不要帶些食品來參加聚會?

I was wondering whether you'd like me to check the figures with you. 我同你一起核對一下數字好嗎?

However, speakers often feel that an offer will be to the advantage of the hearer, and so offers can be made in a polite way by using a direct form. 但是, 說話人常常感到自己的提議有利於對方, 因此可以有禮貌地用直接方式提出:

Language Note: Invitations and Offers
語言提示: 邀請和提議

I'll get you a taxi. 我幫你叫輛計程車。

Leave the dishes to me. 碗碟留給我來洗。

Give me that heavy bag. 我來提這隻大袋子。

(You must) phone me if you need any help. 需要幫忙時(你就)給我打電話。

▶ Be careful! 注意!

In some cases an indirect form should not be used. For example *Would you like me to pay for this?* may suggest that the speaker does not really want to pay. In this situation it is much better to say *I'll pay for this* or *Let me pay for this.* 在某些情況下, 間接方式是不應該使用的, 例如: *Would you like me to pay for this?*(我來為這個東西付錢好嗎?) 可能表示説話的人並不真正想付錢。在這種情況下, 最好用以下兩種説法: *I'll pay for this.* (我來付錢。) 或者: *Let me pay for this.* (讓我來付錢吧。)

See also 另見 COULD, MAY; see 參見 LANGUAGE NOTES: **Politeness**, **Tentativeness**

Language Note: Make and Do 語言提示: Make 和 Do

Why do you **drive** a car but **ride** a bicycle, **do** your best but **make** a mistake, **give** a performance but **play** a part? There is often no real reason except that a particular noun needs a particular verb to express what is done to it. 為甚麼開汽車 (car) 的"開"用 **drive**, 而騎腳踏車 (bicycle) 的"騎"用 **ride**; 盡最大努力 (best) 的"盡"用 **do**, 而犯錯誤 (mistake) 的"犯"用 **make**; 作表演 (performance) 的"作"用 **give**, 而扮演角色 (part) 的"扮演"用 **play**? 除了特定的名詞需要特定的動詞來表示所施予的動作這個原因外, 往往沒有甚麼其他真正的理由。

In order to speak English well, it is important to know which nouns take **make** and which take **do**. There are some general rules to help you decide (see Usage Note at MAKE) but often it has to be learnt through practice. 為了說好英語, 懂得哪些名詞要與 **make** 連用, 哪些名詞要與 **do** 連用, 這是很重要的。有一些一般的規則可以幫助你作出選擇 (參見 MAKE 詞條的用法説明), 但往往還必須通過實踐才能學會。

■ Some typical uses of make and do
make 和 do 的一些典型搭配

You can **make** 可與 **make** 搭配的名詞		You can **do** 可與 **do** 搭配的名詞	
an accusation 提出控告	a meal (=prepare a meal) 做飯	your best 盡最大努力	the gardening 在園子裡侍弄花草
an arrangement 作安排	a mistake 犯錯誤	business (with someone) (與…) 做生意	(someone) a good turn 做一件有利於 (某人) 的事
an attempt 試圖	money 賺錢	the cleaning 打掃	harm 損害
a change 加以改變	a movement 動一動	a course (of study) 修讀課程	your homework 做你的家庭作業
a comment 加以評論	a noise 發出響聲	(some) damage 損壞	the housework 做家務
a deal (*AmE* 美) 做交易	an offer 提出幫助 [建議]	a dance 跳舞	the ironing 熨衣物
a decision 作出決定	progress 取得進步	a deal (*BrE* 英) 做交易	a job 做工作
a demand 提出要求	a promise 作出承諾	a degree (in engineering, etc.) 修讀 (工程等) 學位	research 進行研究
an effort 作出努力	a recommendation 加以推薦	the dishes/the washing-up (*BrE* 英) 洗碗碟	the shopping 購物
an estimate 作出估計	a remark 加以評論	your duty 盡你的責任	the washing/the wash (*AmE* 美) 洗衣服
a fuss 大驚小怪	a request 提出要求	(someone) a favour 給 (某人) 幫個忙	(some) work 做 (些) 工作
a gesture 作出姿態	a statement 發表聲明		
a guess (*BrE* 英) 猜測			
an impression (on someone) (給某人) 留下印象			

■ Other verbs commonly used with particular nouns
通常與特定名詞搭配的其它一些動詞

Language Note: Make and Do 語言提示: Make 和 Do

You can **give** 可與 **give** 搭配的名詞	You can **take** 可與 **take** 搭配的名詞	You can **have** 可與 **have** 搭配的名詞
(someone) a chance 給 (某人) 一個機會 a command 下指令 details 詳細敘述 evidence 作証 information 提供信息 a party (*esp. BrE* 尤英) 舉行聚會 a performance 舉行演出 permission 准許 an opinion 提出看法 an order 下命令 a talk/speech/lecture 發表談話; 作演講; 講課	action 採取行動 advantage (of something or someone) 利用 (某事或某人) a bath (*esp. AmE* 尤美) 洗澡 a guess (*AmE* 美) 猜測 a look 看一看 an exam 參加考試 medicine 服藥 notice (of something) 注意 (某事) a photo 拍照片 a pill 吃藥丸 responsibility (for) 承擔對…的責任 risks 冒險 a walk (*AmE* 美) 去散步	an accident 出了事故 a bath (*esp. BrE* 尤英) 洗澡 a fit 大發脾氣 a headache 頭痛 an idea 想出個主意 an illness (flu etc.) 生病[患流感等] an interview 進行訪談 a look 看一看 a meal (= eat a meal) 吃飯 an operation (if you are ill) 〔病人〕接受手術 a party 舉行聚會 a rest 休息 a thought 考慮

You can **play** 可與 **play** 搭配的名詞	You can **perform** 可與 **perform** 搭配的名詞
cards 打牌 a game 玩遊戲 a musical instrument 演奏樂器 (some) music 演奏 (某段) 樂曲 a part 扮演角色; 起作用 a record (cassette, tape, etc.) 放唱片[卡式錄音帶、磁帶等] a role 扮演角色; 起作用 a trick (on someone) 開 (某人) 玩笑 a tune 奏一曲	a duty 履行職責 a function 起某種功能 an operation (if you are a surgeon) 〔醫生〕施行手術 a piece of music 演奏一首樂曲 a play 演出戲劇 a task 執行任務

■ Using more than one verb with a noun 用不同的動詞與同一個名詞搭配

Using different verbs with a similar meaning 用不同的動詞表示相似的意義

Sometimes it is possible to use more than one verb with a noun to express a similar meaning, for example, you can **arrive at/come to/make/reach/take** a decision. Usually, however, the choice is limited. 有時, 用不同的動詞與同一個名詞搭配以表示相似的意義是可能的。例如, **arrive at** a decision, **come to** a decision, **make** a decision, **reach** a decision 和 **take** a decision 都表示“作出決定”的意思。但通常這種可供選擇的情況是有限的。

Language Note: Make and Do 語言提示: Make 和 Do

Using different verbs for different actions 用不同的動詞表示不同的動作

Of course there are usually several different things which can be done to a noun and different verbs are used to describe these actions. 當然，對於同一個名詞通常都可以施以不同的動作，因此就用不同的動詞來描述這些動作。

Compare 比較:

You **sit** (*BrE* 英)/**take** *an exam.* (if you are a student) 你參加考試。〔如果你是學生〕	*You* **drive** *a train.* (if you are the driver) 你開火車。〔如果你是司機〕
You **give/set** *an exam.* (if you are a teacher) 你主持考試[擬定試題]。〔如果你是教師〕	*You* **ride** (*AmE* 美)/ **take** *a train.* (to travel from A to B) 你乘火車。〔由 A 地往 B 地〕
You **pass** *an exam.* (if you are successful) 你考試及格。	*You* **catch** *a train.* (if you arrive on time) 你趕上某趟火車。
You **fail** *an exam.* (if you are not successful) 你考試不及格。	*You* **miss** *a train.* (if you are too late) 你未趕上某趟火車。

Using different verbs for different senses 用不同的動詞表示不同的意義

If a noun has more than one sense, different verbs may be used for the different senses. 如果一個名詞有若干語義，則可用不同的動詞與之搭配以表示這些不同的語義。

Compare 比較:

He **played** *a trick on his brother.* (trick=a joke) 他跟他的兄弟開了個玩笑。 *She* **performed/did** *some tricks at the party.* (tricks=card tricks or magic tricks) 她在聚會上表演了一些魔術。	*He* **placed** *an order for some new office furniture.* (order=a list of things to be bought) 他訂購了一些新的辦公室家具。 *The captain* **gave** *orders to advance.* (orders=military commands) 連長下令前進。

When you look up a word in this dictionary, remember to read the examples! They will often help you to choose a verb to go with the noun. 查閱本辭典中的某個詞時，記住要看一看例句！例句往往能幫助你選擇可同某個名詞搭配的動詞。

See 參見 LANGUAGE NOTE: **Collocations**

Language Note: Modals 語言提示: 情態動詞

Modal verbs are a small group of verbs which are used with other verbs to change their meaning in some way. The Tables below show you some of the many meanings which can be expressed by the modal verbs: **can**, **could**, **may**, **might**, **must**, **need**, **ought**, **shall**, **should**, **will**, and **would**. The examples show you some of the ways in which these verbs are commonly used.
情態動詞是指與其他動詞連用而在某些方面改變其語義的一小組動詞。下面幾個表告訴你可以用情態動詞 **can**, **could**, **may**, **might**, **must**, **need**, **ought**, **shall**, **should**, **will** 和 **would** 表示的某些語義。例句是告訴你這些情態動詞通常的用法:

prediction of future events 對未來事件的預料	*He'***ll** (= **will**) *forget his umbrella if you don't remind him.* 如果你不提醒他,他會忘記拿雨傘的。 *What* **will** *it be like, living in the 21st century?* 二十一世紀的生活會是甚麼樣子? *We'***ll** (= **will/shall**) *all be dead in a hundred years.* 一百年後我們全都死了。 *Stop crying! It* **won't** *make things any better, you know.* 別哭了! 哭是一點用處也沒有的, 你知道嗎?	**Shall** can be used with first person singular (**I**) and first person plural (**we**). However, it is less common than **will**, especially in American English. **shall** 可用於第一人稱單數 (**I**) 和第一人稱複數 (**we**), 但用得不如 **will** 多, 尤其是美國英語。

willingness, wish 意願,希望	**Will/would** *you help me with my homework?* (request) 你教我做作業好嗎?〔請求〕 *No, I* **won't**. (refusal) 不, 不行。〔拒絕〕 **I'll** (=**will**) *do it for you if you like.* (offer) 如果你願意, 我可以替你做。〔建議〕 **Shall I** *give you a hand with the dishes?* (*BrE* 英) (offer) 我幫你洗這些盤碟好嗎?〔建議〕 **Shall we** *buy her a present?* (*BrE* 英) (suggestion) 我們給她買件禮品吧?〔提議〕 *Did you ask him to the party?* **Will** *he come?* 你請了他來參加社交聚會嗎? 他願意來嗎?	In British English, first person questions expressing willingness or wish use **shall** (**Shall I/we?** = Do you wish me/us to...?) 英國英語中表示意願或希望的第一人稱疑問句用 **shall**。First person statements use **will (I/we will)** 第一人稱陳述句用 **will**。 Note that **shall** is not usually used in this way in American English. 請注意, 美國英語通常不這樣用 **shall**。

ability 能力	*I* **can** *speak Chinese, but I* **can't** *write it.* 我會説漢語, 但我不會寫。 *She* **could** *swim for miles when she was younger.* 她年輕時游泳能游好幾英里。	**Could** is used to talk about ability, NOT about particular events which actually happened in the past. Verbs like **manage to** or **be able to** are used instead. **could** 用於表示能力, 而不是表示過去實際發生的具體事情。表示後一種情況則用 **manage to** 或 **be able to** 等: *She finally* **managed to** *pass the exam.* (她終於設法通過了考試。)
	Can/Could *you close the window, please?* (request) 請你把窗子關上好嗎?〔請求〕	Polite requests are often made by appearing to ask about ability with **can** and **could**. 有禮貌的請求常常表現為用 **can** 和 **could** 詢問對方有無這樣做的能力。

Language Note: Modals 語言提示: 情態動詞

permission 允許	**Can/may** *I have another piece of cake, Dad?* (request) 爸爸, 我可以再吃一塊餅嗎?〔請求〕 *No, you* **can't**. *You'll make yourself sick.* 不可以, 你會吃壞肚子的。 *Do you think I* **could** *leave early tonight?* (request) 今天晚上我可以早些離開嗎?〔請求〕 *You* **can/may** *leave at 5.30 if you like.* 如果你願意, 你可以在五點半離開。 *I'm afraid you* **can't** *leave till you've finished that work.* 恐怕你要完成了那件工作才能走。 **Might** *I have a word with you?* (*BrE* 英) (formal request) 我同你説句話可以嗎?〔正式請求〕	**Can** is commonly used to ask for or give permission. **May** is more formal. 通常用 **can** 詢問是否允許或表示允許, **may** 則是較為正式的詞。 **Could** and **might** are used to ask for (NOT to give) permission. They are more tentative than **can**. **could** 和 **might** 用於詢問是否允許, 而不用於表示允許, 較之 **can** 更具試探性。
unreality, hypothesis 不真實, 假設	*I* **would** *love to travel round the world.* (if I had the chance) 我真願環遊全世界(如果我有這個機會的話)。 *What* **would** *you do if you won a lot of money?* 如果你贏了許多錢, 你會做甚麼呢? *I* **wouldn't have** *gone, if I'd known he was going to be there.* 如果我當初知道他也要到那裡去, 我就不會去的。 **Would** *you like some tea (if I made some)?* (invitation) (如果我沏茶) 你想喝點茶嗎?〔邀請〕 **Should** *he protest* (if he protested), *what would you say?* (fml) 如果他抗議, 你會説甚麼呢?〔正式〕	**Would** is commonly used in the main clause of conditional sentences to show that a situation is unreal or tentative. **would** 通常用於條件性句子的主句, 表示非真實或不確定的情況。 Because it can express tentativeness, **would** is also used in polite invitations, offers, and requests. 由於 **would** 可以表示不確定性, 因而也用於有禮貌的邀請、建議和請求。
possibility 可能性	*She* **may/might** *(not) go to Paris tomorrow.* 她明天可能(不)去巴黎。 *They* **may/might** *(not) be meeting her.* 他們可能(不)會見到她。 *Joe* **may have/might have** *missed the train.* 喬可能沒趕上火車。 *Where* **can/could** *they be?* 他們可能在甚麼地方呢? *You* **can't have** *forgotten my birthday!* 你不可能忘了我的生日吧! *Learning English* **can** *be fun.* (=is sometimes fun) 學習英語可以是很有趣的。 *Don't touch that wire. It* **could** *be dangerous.* 別碰那根電線, 可能有危險。 *They* **could have** *had an accident, I suppose.* 我猜想他們可能出了車禍。	**Could** suggests that something is less likely than **may** or **might**. **could** 所表示的可能性不及 **may** 或 **might** 大。 When it expresses possibility, **can** is most often used in question forms. **can** 在表示可能性時, 多半用於疑問句: *What* **can have** *happened?* (可能發生了甚麼事呢?) However it is also used to express general possibility in sentences where its meaning is similar to "sometimes". 但是, 如果 **can** 在句子中的語義近似 "sometimes" (有時), 則 **can** 也可用於表示一般的可能性: *His behaviour* **can** *make us laugh.* (=sometimes makes us laugh) (他的舉止有時會使我們發笑。) **Can't** and **can't have** are used to show that there is no possibility. (See **certainty** below) **can't** 和 **can't have** 用於表示沒有可能性。(參見下面的 **certainty**)

Language Note: Modals 語言提示: 情態動詞

certainty 肯定	*Joe* **must** *be at least 45.* (=I'm sure he's at least 45) 喬必定至少有四十五歲了。 *No, he* **can't** *be over 40.* (=I'm sure he isn't over 40) 不, 他一定不會超過四十歲。 *He* **must have** *graduated years ago.* (=I'm sure he graduated years ago) 他一定是多年以前畢業的。 *We* **can't have** *been at college together.* (=I'm sure we weren't at college together) 我們上大學不可能是同一個時候。 *They***'ll** *be back by now.* (=I'm sure they're back) 他們現在肯定已經回來了。 *No, they* **won't** *be there yet.* (=I'm sure they are not there yet) 不, 他們肯定還沒有到那裡。 *Mary* **will have** *arrived already.* (=I'm sure she's arrived already) 瑪麗肯定早已到了。 *No, she* **won't have** *left home yet.* (=I'm sure she hasn't left home yet) 不, 她肯定還沒有離開家。	**Must have** is the past form of **must** when it is used to express certainty. **must** 表示肯定時, 其過去式是 **must have**。 **Must** and **must have** express stronger certainty than **will** and **will have**. **must** 和 **must have** 所表示的肯定, 強於 **will** 和 **will have** 。 **Can't** and **can't have** express stronger certainty than **won't** and **won't have**. **can't** 和 **can't have** 所表示的肯定, 強於 **won't** 和 **won't have** 。
obligation, requirement 義務, 職責, 責任, 要求	*You* **must** *finish this job by tomorrow.* 你必須最遲在明天完成這一工作。 *I* **must** *phone my parents tonight.* 我今天晚上必須給我的父母打電話。 *He* **had to** *finish the job by the next day.* 他必須在不遲於第二天的時間之內完成這一工作。 *You* **don't have to/don't need to/needn't** (*BrE* 英) *do it until next week.* (=it is not necessary) 你現在不是一定要做那件事, 可以在下星期做。 *You* **must not** *smoke in the cinema.* (=it is forbidden) 你在電影院裡是不得吸煙的。 *I* **didn't need to/didn't have to** *get up early this morning.* (=**a** the speaker did not get up early, or **b** the speaker did, in fact, get up early) **a** 我今天早晨不必早起〔說話人沒有早起〕。或者 **b** 我今天早晨本來是沒必要早起的〔說話人事實上已早起了〕。 *You* **needn't have** *bought me a present.* (*BrE* 英) (=but you did buy a present) 你本來不必給我買禮物的〔實際上你已經買了〕。	**Had to** is the past form of **must** when it is used to express obligation. **must** 在表示"必須"時, 其過去式是 **had to**。 **Don't have to/don't need to/needn't** (*BrE* 英) are used to show that there is no obligation. **Must not** is used to show that there is an obligation not to do something. **don't have to/don't need to/needn't** 表示"不必"、"無義務"。**must not** 則表示"有義務不做某事"。 The contracted forms **needn't** and **mustn't** are common in British English but rarely used in American English. 縮略形式 **needn't** 和 **mustn't** 在英國英語中用得很多, 但很少用於美國英語。

Language Note: Modals 語言提示: 情態動詞

desirability 可取性, 應當, 應該	*You* **should/ought to** *give up smoking.* (advice) 你應當戒煙。〔忠告〕 *We* **should/ought to** *go to that new Japanese restaurant sometime.* (suggestion) 我們應當找個時間上那家新開的日本餐館。〔建議〕 *The farmers* **should have/ought to have** *been consulted.* (but they were not consulted) 本該找農場主們商量商量的〔但沒有商量〕。 *You* **shouldn't/ought not to** *work so hard, you know.* 你知道, 你是不應該工作得這樣辛苦的。	The contracted form **oughtn't** is common in British English but rarely used in American English. 縮略形式 **oughtn't** 在英國英語中用得很多, 但美國英語用得很少。
probability 或然性	*Their meeting* **should/ought to** *be over now.* (=I expect it is) 他們的會議現在該結束了〔我估計結束了〕。 *He* **should/ought to** *be home at 5 o'clock today.* (=I expect he will be) 他今天五點鐘該到家了〔我估計他會這樣的〕。 *They* **should have/ought to have** *received our letter by now.* (=I expect they have) 他們現在該已收到我們的信了〔我估計他們已收到了〕。	In this meaning **should** and **ought to** are not as strong as **will** and **must**. (See **certainty** above) **should** 和 **ought to** 在"或然性"的語義上較 **will** 和 **must** 弱。(參見上面的 **certainty**)
personal intention 個人的意向	**I'll** (= **will/shall**) *be back in a minute.* 我一會兒就回來。 *I* **won't/shan't** *ever speak to him again.* 我再也不(會)同他說話了。 *We* **will/shall** *overcome all difficulties.* 我們會克服一切困難。	**Shall** can be used with **I** and **we**, but is less common than **will**, especially in American English. **shall** 可用於 **I** 和 **we**, 但用得不如 **will** 多, 尤其是美國英語。

■ Grammatical behaviour of modal verbs 情態動詞在語法上的特點

Grammatically, modal verbs behave in a different way from ordinary verbs. 在語法上情態動詞與普通動詞是有區別的。

They have no **-s** in the third person singular. 情態動詞的第三人稱單數不加 **-s**。

Most modal verbs, except for **ought**, are followed by the infinitive of other verbs without **to**. 除了 **ought**，絕大多數情態動詞後接不帶 **to** 的其他動詞的不定式。

Modal verbs have no infinitive or **-ing** form. They can be replaced by other expressions if necessary. 情態動詞沒有不定式或 **-ing** 形式, 必要時可用其他詞語代替: *I* **must** *work hard.* (我必須苦幹。) | *I don't like* **having to** *work hard.* (我不喜歡非要苦幹不可。)

They make questions and negative forms without using **do/did**. 情態動詞不用 **do/did** 來構成疑問和否定形式: **May** *I see that?* (我可以看看那個東西嗎?) | *You* **mustn't** *shout.* (你不應該喊叫。)

Language Note: Modals 語言提示: 情態動詞

In British English **need** can be both a modal verb and an ordinary verb. As a modal, it is most often used in questions and negatives. (In American English it is not used as a modal.) 在英國英語中, **need** 可以是情態動詞也可以是普通動詞。作為情態動詞, 它大多用於疑問句和否定句。(在美國英語中 **need** 不用作情態動詞。)

Note that some modal verbs appear to have past tense forms (**could**, **should**, **might**), but these are not usually used with a past meaning. One exception is **could** which, when talking about ability, is used as a past form of **can**. 請注意, 某些情態動詞好像有過去式 (**could**, **should**, **might**), 但是它們通常並不具有"過去"的語義。**could** 是個例外, 在表示能力時, 用作 **can** 的過去形式: *I* **could** *run a long way when I was younger.* (我年輕時能跑很長一段距離。)

Most modal verbs can be used in some of their meanings with a perfect infinitive to talk about the past. 大多數情態動詞的某些語義可以與完成式不定式連用以表示過去的事情: *I* **may have seen** *him yesterday.* (我昨天可能見過他。) | *You* **should have told** *me last week.* (你本該上週告訴我的。) (See the Table for more examples. 參見表中的例子。)

In past indirect speech, the following modals usually change their form 下列情態動詞在過去式的間接引語中要改變時式:

can	*"You* **can't** *leave until tomorrow."* "你明天才能離開。" *They said she* **couldn't** *leave until the next day.* 他們說她要到第二天才能離開。
may	*"They* **may** *have missed the bus."* "他們或許沒有趕上公共汽車。" *He suggested that they* **might** *have missed the bus.* 他認為他們或許沒有趕上公共汽車。
shall	*"***Shall** *I post it?"* (*BrE* 英) "我把這封信寄出去好嗎?" *She asked if she* **should** *post the letter.* 她問她是否應把這封信寄出去。
will	*"I'***ll** *do that tomorrow."* "我明天做那件事。" *She said she* **would** *do it the next day.* 她說她第二天做那件事。

Other modals usually remain the same 其他情態動詞通常保持不變:

She said she **would** *like some coffee.* 她說她想喝點咖啡。| *She told me I* **ought to** *stop smoking.* 她對我說, 我應當停止吸煙。| *He told me I* **must/had to** *work harder.* 他對我說, 我應該更加努力工作。

See 參見 CAN (USAGE), and 和 LANGUAGE NOTES: **Invitations and Offers**, **Requests**, **Tentativeness**

Language Note: Phrasal Verbs
語言提示: 片語 [短語] 動詞

In this dictionary, a verb is considered to be a phrasal verb if it consists of two or more words. One of these words is always a verb; the other may be an adverb as in **throw away**, a preposition as in **look into**, or both an adverb and a preposition as in **put up with**. The meaning of a phrasal verb is often quite different from the meaning of the verb on its own. For example, **look into** (= investigate) and **look after** (= take care of) have quite separate meanings from **look**. In fact, many phrasal verbs are idiomatic.
在本辭典中, 一個動詞如果包含兩個或兩個以上的詞, 就被認為是片語 [短語] 動詞。片語 [短語] 動詞中有一個詞一定是動詞, 其餘的可以是副詞, 如 **throw away** 中的 **away**; 可以是介詞, 如 **look into** 中的 **into**; 也可以是一個副詞和一個介詞, 如 **put up with** 中的 **up** 和 **with**。片語 [短語] 動詞的詞義常常同其中的動詞本身的詞義很不相同。例如, **look into** (調查) 和 **look after** (照管) 同 **look** 的詞義就完全不一樣。實際上許多片語 [短語] 動詞都是習慣用語。(see 參見 Language Note: **Idioms**)

■ How are phrasal verbs listed? 片語 [短語] 動詞是如何排列的?

Phrasal verbs are listed in alphabetical order underneath the entry for the main verb. They are marked *phr v*. In this sample entry **polish off** and **polish up** are phrasal verbs listed after the entry for **polish**.
片語 [短語] 動詞放在主要動詞詞條之下, 按字母順序排列, 以 *phr v.* 表示。在本樣條中, **polish off** 和 **polish up** 都是片語 [短語] 動詞, 置於 **polish** 詞條之下。

pol·ish[1] /ˈpɑlɪʃ; ˈpɒlɪʃ/ *v* [T] to make something smooth, bright, and shiny by rubbing it 擦亮, 擦光: *The floor had been polished to a satiny sheen.* 地板已被擦得光亮如緞。| *It was my duty to polish the silver on Saturdays.* 我的職責是每星期六把銀器擦亮。—**polisher** *n* [C]: *an electric floor polisher* 電動地板磨光機[打蠟機] —**polishing** *n* [U] —see picture at 參見 CLEAN 圖

polish sth ↔ **off** *phr v* [T] *informal* to finish food, work etc, quickly or easily【非正式】快速[輕易]做完〔工作等〕; 很快吃完〔食物〕: *At lunch, Rowan polished off six sandwiches!* 吃午飯時, 羅旺一轉眼就吃掉了六份三文治!

polish sb ↔ **off** *phr v* [T] *AmE informal* to kill or defeat someone【美, 非正式】殺死〔某人〕; 擊敗〔某人〕: *Mather was polished off with a shotgun in another gangland killing.* 馬瑟在另一次黑社會仇殺中被人用獵槍打死了。

polish sth ↔ **up** *phr v* [T] **1** to improve a skill or an ability by practising it〔通過練習〕提高, 改善〔技術、能力〕: *I need to polish up my Spanish before we go on vacation.* 我們去度假前, 我需要練習一下我的西班牙語。**2** to polish something 擦亮, 擦光

Sometimes the main verb of a phrasal verb is not used alone. In these cases, the verb is shown as a headword but has no entry of its own. The phrasal verb is listed immediately underneath the headword. This sample entry tells you that the verb **gad** is not used alone but only as part of the phrasal verb **gad about /around**.
有時, 一個片語 [短語] 動詞中的主要動詞不單獨使用。在這種情況下, 本辭典中這類詞作為詞目出現, 但它本身不成其為詞條, 片語 [短語] 動詞緊列在該詞目之下。右列樣條顯示, **gad** 不單獨使用, 只用作片語 [短語] 動詞 **gad about /around** 的一部分。

gad /gæd; gæd/ *v* **gadded, gadding**

gad about/around *phr v* [I] *informal* to go out and enjoy yourself, going to many different places, especially when you should be doing something else【非正式】閒蕩, 外出尋樂〔尤指本應做點別的甚麼事〕: *While I'm at home cooking, he's gadding about with his friends.* 我在家做飯, 而他卻在跟他的朋友一起尋樂。

Language Note: Phrasal Verbs
語言提示: 片語 [短語] 動詞

Transitive or intransitive? 及物還是不及物?

Phrasal verbs, like all verbs, can be transitive or intransitive and are marked [T] or [I] accordingly. These sample entries show that **grow out of** is a transitive verb and **grow up** is an intransitive verb.
同所有動詞一樣, 片語 [短語] 動詞也有及物與不及物之分, 因而分別標以 [T] 和 [I]。右列樣條顯示 **grow out of** 是及物片語 [短語] 動詞, **grow up** 是不及物片語 [短語] 動詞。

grow out of sth *phr v* [T] **1** if a child grows out of clothes, they become too big to wear them〔小孩〕因長大而穿不進〔原來的衣服〕**2** if a child grows out of a habit, they stop doing it as they get older〔因年齡增長而〕戒除, 改掉〔原有的習慣〕: *She used to bite her nails but seems to have grown out of it.* 她過去經常咬指甲, 但現在似乎已經改掉了。**3** to develop from something small or simple into something bigger or more complicated 由〔小或簡單的事〕發展成〔大或複雜的事〕: *The dispute grew out of an argument between a worker and the foreman.* 這場爭執是從一名工人和工頭的爭論引發的。

grow up *phr v* [I] **1** develop from being a child to being an adult 長大成人: *What do you want to be when you grow up?* 你長大以後想當甚麼? | *I grew up on a farm.* 我是在農場裡長大的。**2 grow up!** *spoken* used to tell someone to behave more like an adult, especially when they have been behaving in a silly way【口】要像個大人樣!〔尤用於某人行為幼稚可笑之時〕**3** to start to exist and become bigger or more important 形成, 興起, 發展: *Trading settlements grew up along the river.* 河的兩岸形成了一些貿易區。

Position of the direct object 直接受詞 [賓語] 的位置

When a phrasal verb is transitive, it is important to know where to put the direct object. Sometimes it comes after the adverb or preposition. This entry tells you that the direct object, which can be a person or a thing, is always placed after the complete phrasal verb **pick on**.
對於及物片語 [短語] 動詞, 它的直接受詞 [賓語] 放在甚麼位置是很重要的。右列詞條顯示, 直接受詞 [賓語] 可以是人也可以是物, 而且永遠置於整個片語 [短語] 動詞 **pick on** 之後。

pick on sb/sth *phr v* [T] *spoken*【口】**1** to choose someone to do an unpleasant job or blame someone for something, especially unfairly 選中〔某人做不愉快的工作〕;〔尤指不公平地〕責備〔某人〕: *Why does the boss always pick on me?* 為甚麼老闆總是跟我過不去? | *You big bully – pick on someone your own size!* 你這個恃強凌弱的大壞蛋 —— 挑一個跟你個頭一樣大的人欺負呀! **2** to decide to choose someone or something 選中〔某人或某物〕: *First, pick on some daily task that you all share.* 首先, 挑選出某項你們都要分擔的日常工作。

Sometimes the direct object can appear in either position. This is shown by the use of the symbol ↔. This entry tells you that you can say **Hand in** *your papers* or **Hand** *your papers* **in**.
有時直接受詞 [賓語] 可放在整個片語 [短語] 動詞之後, 也可以放在主要動詞與介詞或副詞之間。符號 ↔ 就用於表示這種情況。右列詞條顯示, 既可以說 **Hand in** *your paper*, 也可以說 **Hand** *your paper* **in**.

hand sth ↔ **in** *phr v* [T] to give something to a person in authority 上交; 提交: *Hand your papers in at the end of the exam.* 考試結束後把試卷交上來。

Note, however, that with verbs of this type, when the direct object is a pronoun it MUST be put between the verb and the adverb or preposition.
但要注意, 如直接受詞 [賓語] 是代(名)詞, 則必須置於主要動詞與副詞或介詞之間。

Language Note: Phrasal Verbs
語言提示: 片語 [短語] 動詞

Hand in *your papers* but **Hand** *them* **in**.
可以說 **Hand in** your paper, 但必須說 **Hand** them **in**.

They **knocked down** *the building* but *They* **knocked** *it* **down**.
可以說 **They knocked down** the building, 但必須說 **They knocked** it **down**.

Some transitive phrasal verbs can have more than one object. The dictionary will help you decide where to put these objects. This entry tells you that **put down to** has two objects; the first always follows the verb and the second always follows **to**.
某些及物片語 [短語] 動詞可能有一個以上的受詞 [賓語]。本辭典可幫助讀者確定這些受詞 [賓語] 的位置。右列詞條表示 **put down to** 有兩個受詞 [賓語], 第一個總是放在動詞的後面, 第二個總是放在 **to** 的後面。

put sth **down to** sth *phr v* [T] **1** to explain the reason for something, especially when you are only guessing 把〔某事〕歸因於: *I put Jane's moodiness down to the stress she was under.* 我把簡的喜怒無常歸因於她所承受的壓力。**2 put it down to experience** used to tell someone not to feel too upset by failure, but to learn something useful from it 把它當作一次經驗教訓: *Everyone gets rejected from time to time; put it down to experience.* 每個人都偶爾會被拒絕, 把它當作一次經驗教訓吧。

Finally, note that some phrasal verbs can be both transitive and intransitive. This entry shows you that **join in** is one of these verbs. It also tells you that when it is transitive, the direct object comes after **in**.
最後請注意, 某些片語 [短語] 動詞可以是及物的, 又可以是不及物的。右列詞條表示 **join in** 就是這類動詞。同時表示, 作為及物的片語 [短語] 動詞, 其直接受詞 [賓語] 置於 **in** 的後面。

join in *phr v* [I,T] to take part in an activity as one of a group of people 參加〔活動〕; 加入進來: *Come on, Ian, join in! You can sing!* 伊恩, 你也來! 你會唱歌! | **join in the fun/party** *We couldn't wait to join in the fun.* 我們迫不及待地參加進去一起玩。

■ Passives 被動語態

In passive forms, phrasal verbs follow the usual pattern of word order with the subject coming in front of the main verb. 在被動形式中, 片語 [短語] 動詞按通常的詞序規律, 主詞 [主語] 置於主要動詞的前面。

When's this problem **going to be looked into**? 甚麼時候處理這個問題?

*He says he***'s** *always* **being picked on** *by the boss.* 他說, 老闆總是挑他的毛病。

Papers **must be handed in** *before the end of the week.* 作業必須在本週末以前交上來。

Her rudeness **was put down to** *her being so tired.* 她態度粗暴被解釋為是由於勞累過度。

See 參見 LANGUAGE NOTES: **Idioms**, **Prepositions**

Language Note: Politeness 語言提示: 禮貌

In most societies there are particular ways of behaving and speaking which are considered to be polite, but these are not the same in all societies. Forms of behaviour and language which are considered to be polite in one society can sometimes seem strange, insincere, or even rude in another. When learning a new language, it is often necessary to learn new ways of expressing politeness.
在大多數社會裡, 都有一些被認為是有禮貌的特定的行為方式和説話方式, 但這些禮貌言行並非在所有社會裡都是一樣的。有時候, 在某一個社會裡被認為是禮貌的言行在另一個社會裡, 卻會被看成是古怪的、虛偽的或者甚至是粗魯的。學習一種新語言時, 常常需要學習各種新的表達禮貌的方式。

Sometimes English expresses politeness in ways which are not commonly used in other languages 有時英語表示禮貌的方式在其他語言中並不普遍使用

For example, speakers of British English often use indirectness or tentativeness in order to be polite in situations where other languages are more direct. (Note also that speakers of American English tend to be more direct in similar situations.)
例如, 講英國英語的人常用間接的或猶疑的口吻來表示禮貌, 而其他語言在同樣情景下則用較為直接的方式表示 (請注意, 説美國英語的人在同樣情景下傾向於用較為直接的方式)。

(See 參見 LANGUAGE NOTES: **Criticism and Praise**, **Invitations and Offers**, **Requests**, **Tentativeness**)

Another example is the way in which speakers of British English tend to say *Thank you* for small or unimportant things in situations where speakers of other languages would not consider this to be necessary. (Often, for example, when a shop assistant is giving change to a customer, both people will say *Thank you*. Speakers of American English do not usually do this.) On the other hand, in some situations it is possible in British English to make no reply when somebody thanks you, but in American English, as in some other languages, it is necessary to respond, for example by saying *You're welcome*.
另一個例子是: 講英國英語的人一點點微不足道的小事也喜歡道一聲 *thank you* (謝謝你), 而講其他語言的人則往往會認為無此必要 (例如售貨員找給顧客零錢時, 雙方都會説一聲 *thank you*。講美國英語的人通常則沒有這種客套)。另一方面, 對於對方的道謝, 在某些情景下, 在英國英語中是不作甚麼表示的, 但講美國英語的人以及一些操其他語言的人則必須有所表示, 例如説一聲 *you're welcome* (不用謝)。

(See 參見 LANGUAGE NOTE: **Thanks**)

Sometimes English does not use forms of politeness which are common in other languages 有時英語不使用其他語言中普遍使用的禮貌形式

In some languages, for example, it is polite to respond to a compliment by refusing to accept it, and by saying something bad about yourself or the thing which has been complimented. In English, although it is possible to hesitate a little before accepting, it is usually considered impolite to reject a compliment too strongly.
例如, 在某些語言中, 對於對方的讚語或恭維都要用表示不同意來客氣一番, 對自己或對方所恭維的事説點貶低的話。在英語中, 儘管在接受讚語時可能要有一點猶豫, 但通常把太強烈的否認和拒絕看作是不禮貌的。

(See 參見 LANGUAGE NOTE: **Criticism and Praise**)

Language Note: Politeness 語言提示: 禮貌

To take another example, in some societies it is necessary to use different forms of language according to the social position (superior, inferior, or equal) of the person you are speaking to. Although English has some special forms of address which are used in particular situations, there are no strict rules of language which depend only on the social relationship of the speaker and the hearer.
另一個例子是: 在某些社會裡, 對不同社會地位 (上級、下級或同級) 的人説話, 使用不同的語言形式。英語雖然在特定的場合也有某些專門的稱呼, 但並沒有僅僅根據説者和聽者雙方社會關係而確定的嚴格的語言規則。

(See 参見 LANGUAGE NOTES: **Addressing People**, **Apologies**, **Criticism and Praise**, **Requests**)

Several of the Language Notes in this dictionary discuss ways of being polite in English. 本辭典有若干項語言提示都討論英語中表達禮貌的方式。

See 参見 LANGUAGE NOTES: **Addressing People**, **Apologies**, **Criticism and Praise**, **Invitations and Offers**, **Requests**, **Tentativeness**, **Thanks**

Language Note: Prepositions 語言提示: 介詞

A preposition is a word which is used to show the way in which other words are connected. Prepositions may be single words such as: **by**, **from**, **over**, **under**, or they may be more complex and composed of several words such as: **apart from**, **in front of**, **in spite of**, **instead of**. 介詞是用來表示詞與詞之間的連接方式的詞。介詞可以是單個的詞, 如 **by**, **from**, **over**, **under** 等, 也可以較為複雜, 由幾個詞組成, 如 **apart from**, **in front of**, **in spite of**, **instead of** 等。

Where are prepositions used? 介詞用在甚麼地方?

Prepositions are usually followed by a noun or pronoun, a verb with **-ing**, or a **wh-** clause. In the following sentences **in** is a preposition. 介詞通常後接名詞, 代(名)詞, 帶 **-ing** 的動詞, 或者 **wh-** 子句 [從句], 下列例句中的 **in** 就是介詞:

Write your name **in** *the book.* 在書本上寫上你的名字。

This tea's too sweet. There's too much sugar **in** *it.* 這茶太甜了, 放的糖太多了。

There's absolutely no point **in** *complaining.* 埋怨是毫無意義的。

I'm very interested **in** *what you've just said.* 我對你剛才說的很感興趣。

Note that prepositions are NOT used in front of infinitives or clauses beginning with **that**. 注意: 介詞不用在帶 to 的不定詞 [不定式] 或者以 **that** 開始的子句 [從句] 的前面:

I was astonished **at/by** *the news.* 這則新聞使我感到驚訝。

I was astonished to hear the news/to hear what she said. 我聽到這條新聞 [她所說的話] 感到驚訝。

*I was astonished (***by** *the fact) that she had left her job.* 她辭職了, (這件事) 使我感到驚訝。

What do prepositions mean? 介詞意味着甚麼?

Unlike some other languages, English makes frequent use of prepositions to express basic relationships between words. Relationships of time and place, for example, are usually expressed by the use of a preposition. 同某些其他語言不同, 英語經常用介詞來表示詞與詞之間的關係。例如時間關係和地點關係通常就是用介詞表示的:

I can see you **on Monday/in August/at 8 pm/for half an hour/during the holidays**, *etc.* 我可以在星期一見你 [在八月份見你; 在下午八點見你; 同你談半小時; 在假日見你等]。

I'll meet you **at school/in Rome/on the corner/outside the cinema/under the station clock**, *etc.* 我將在學校 [羅馬; 街角; 電影院外面; 火車站的鐘下面等] 同你會面。

Language Note: Prepositions 語言提示: 介詞

Prepositions are used to express many other different kinds of relationships, such as 介詞還用來表示其他許多種不同的關係, 如:

reason 原因	—	*I did it* **because of** *my father*/**for** *my mother*/**out of** *duty*. 我做這件事是因為我的父親 [為了我的母親; 出於責任心]。
manner 方式	—	*She spoke* **with** *a smile*/**in** *a soft voice*. 她微笑着 [柔聲地] 說話。
means 方法	—	*I came* **by** *bus*/**on** *foot*/**in** *a taxi, etc.* 我乘公共汽車 [步行; 乘計程車等] 來。
reaction 反應	—	*I was surprised* **at** *his attitude*/**by** *his refusal, etc.* 我對他的態度 [他的拒絕等] 感到驚訝。

Note that a particular preposition can often be used to express more than one kind of relationship. For example, **by** can be used for the following relationships 注意: 一個介詞常可用來表示不止一種關係。例如, **by** 可以表示以下各種不同的關係:

time 時間 — **by** *next week* 最遲到下星期

place 地點 — **by** *the window* 在窗子旁邊

means 方法 — **by** *working very hard* 通過非常努力地工作

The entries for prepositions in this dictionary will show you which relationships they can be used to express. 本辭典中的各個介詞詞條都會告訴你它們可用來表示甚麼樣的關係。

■ Prepositions in fixed phrases 固定片語 [短語] 中的介詞

Prepositions are often part of fixed phrases in phrasal verbs, collocations, and idioms. 介詞常常是片語 [短語] 動詞、搭配和習語等固定片語 [短語] 的一個組成部分。

Phrasal verbs 片語 [短語] 動詞

Sometimes a combination of a verb and a preposition has its own particular meaning: **call on**, **look after**, **send for**. In this dictionary, these combinations are treated as phrasal verbs. They are listed as separate entries after the entry for the main verb. 有時一個動詞和一個介詞結合在一起具有其自身的特定含義: **call on** (拜訪), **look after** (照顧), **send for** (派人去叫)。本辭典把這種片語 [短語] 作為片語 [短語] 動詞處理。它們作為另列的詞條排在主要動詞條目的後面。

Collocating prepositions 起搭配作用的介詞

Some nouns, verbs, and adjectives are often followed by particular prepositions: **example (of)**, **prohibit (from)**, **afraid (of)**. The prepositions which can be used with particular words are shown at the entries for these words. 某些名詞、動詞和形容詞常常後接特定的介詞, 如 **example (of)** (...的例子), **prohibit (from)** (禁止做...), **afraid (of)** (害怕...)。某個特定的詞應與哪個介詞連用, 在該特定詞的條目下都有明確的指示。

Language Note: Prepositions 語言提示: 介詞

Idioms and typical collocations 習語和典型搭配

Typical collocations (groups of words which "naturally" go together, through common usage) are shown in blue in the dictionary entries. These collocations often show a fixed use of prepositions. 典型搭配 (指通過慣常使用而"自然地"結合在一起的詞組) 在本辭典的詞條中以藍字標出, 這類搭配常常表示要固定使用某一介詞, 例如:

by the name of 名叫 | **beyond help** 無法挽救 | **be under an illusion** 存在幻想 | **in safe hands** 在穩妥可靠的人手中

■ Word order 詞序

In some situations it is possible for a preposition to come at the end of a clause or sentence. This happens especially with **wh-** questions, relative clauses, exclamations, passives, and some infinitive clauses. 在某些情況下, 介詞可能被放在子句 [從句] 或一句句子的末尾, 尤其是 **wh-** 問句、關係子句 [從句]、驚嘆句、被動形式以及某些不定式子句 [從句] 常有這種情況:

Who are you speaking **to**? 你在跟誰講話?

Is this the book you are interested **in**? 你感興趣的是這本書嗎?

What a mess we're **in**! 我們處於何等的混亂之中!

Don't worry. He's being looked **after**. 別擔心, 他有人照管。

She's really interesting to talk **to**. 同她談話確實很有趣。

This use is very common in everyday informal English. Some people feel that in formal English it is better to avoid putting the prepositions at the end, by using sentences like this 在日常非正式英語中, 這種用法很常見。有人認為在正式英語中最好避免把介詞放在末尾, 辦法是使用類似這樣的句子:

To whom *are you speaking?* 你在跟誰講話?

Is this the book **in which** *you are interested?* 你感興趣的是這本書嗎?

However, sentences such as these can sometimes sound too formal, especially in spoken English. 不過, 這樣的句子有時聽起來太正式, 尤其在英語口語中。

See 參見 LANGUAGE NOTES: **Collocations**, **Phrasal Verbs**, **Words Followed by Prepositions**

Language Note: Questions 語言提示: 問句

Why do people ask questions? 人們為何要發問?

People usually ask questions because they want to know something; they are asking for information. There are, however, many other possible reasons for asking questions. The question form is made to do a lot of work in the English language. Look, for example, at the following question:
人們通常因為想知道某事而發問, 他們要求得到信息。然而, 發問也還有許多其他原因。在英語中, 問句這種形式可以用來表達許多意思。例如, 請看下面這個問句:

How did you cook this fish? 你是怎麼燒這條魚的?

This may simply mean, "I'd like to have the recipe" (the speaker is asking for information). On the other hand, it may also mean, "It's delicious" (the speaker wants to compliment the cook). However it may also mean, "It tastes awful" (the speaker is criticizing or complaining). Usually, the situation and the way in which the words are spoken will tell the hearer which meaning is the right one, and the reply will depend on the way in which the hearer has understood the meaning. Here are some possible replies to the question above:
這句話的意思可以是"我想知道它的烹飪方法"〔要求得到信息〕。又可以是"味道好極了"〔想恭維廚師〕。但也可以是"難吃極了"〔提出批評或抱怨〕。通常, 說話時的情景以及說話的語氣和方式可以使人聽出確切的語意, 而答覆將取決於如何理解這問話的語意。以下是幾種可能的回答:

Well, first I did X and then I did Y... . (the cook is giving the recipe) 我先..., 然後...。〔廚師在說明烹飪方法〕

Oh! It's easy really. (the cook has recognized the compliment) 啊!做起來並不難。〔廚師接受恭維〕

Why? Don't you like it? (the cook has recognized possible criticism) 噢, 你不愛吃? 〔廚師聽出了對方的批評〕

Here is another question which can have several different meanings 下面的問句也有好幾種不同的含意:

Can you feel a draught from that window? 你感到有風從那窗戶吹過來嗎?

This may mean, "I think you are cold, and if you are, I'm going to close the window" (the speaker is offering to help). On the other hand, it may mean, "I'm feeling cold and I want you to close the window" (the speaker is asking the hearer to do something). It may also mean, "If you're as cold as I am, then, we should close the window, move to another room, etc." (the speaker is suggesting that they do something). It is, in fact, unlikely that this particular question is simply a request for information. Here are some possible replies:
這句話的含義可以是"我想你是覺得冷了, 如果是的話, 我就把窗戶關上"〔想幫對方做點事〕。又可以是"我覺得冷, 請你關一下窗戶"〔請對方做點事〕。也可以是"如果你同我一樣覺得冷, 那我們就把窗戶關起來, 或者移到別的房間去等"〔建議他們倆採取措施〕。事實上這一特定的詢問不會只是要求得到信息。以下是幾種可能的回答:

No, I'm fine thanks. (polite refusal of offer) 不, 我不冷, 謝謝。〔婉言謝絕幫助〕

Yes, it is a bit cold. (polite acceptance of offer) 是的, 是有點冷。〔有禮貌地接受對方的幫助〕

Oh, are you cold? I'll close the window. (response to request for action) 啊, 你覺得冷了? 我去把窗戶關起來。〔回應對方要採取行動的要求〕

Yes. Should we move to another room? (response to suggestion) 是的, 我們到別的房間去吧。〔回應對方的建議〕

Language Note: Questions 語言提示: 問句

Below are just a few examples of the ways in which questions can be used in English. Note that some of the questions are directly related to the speaker's meaning. Others, like the examples above, are more indirect, and their meaning depends on the situation in which they are used. 下面只是可以使用問句的情況的一些舉例。注意其中有些問句同説話人的用意是直接關聯的。有些如以上所舉各例子則較為間接, 其含意取決於使用時的情景。

■ Some ways in which questions can be used 可以使用問句的一些情況

when complaining or criticizing 表示不滿或批評:

Can't you drive more quickly? (you're too slow) 你不能開快點嗎?〔你開得太慢了〕

Have you washed your hands recently? (they look filthy) 你最近洗過手嗎?〔手看起來很髒〕

Why did you paint it red? (I don't like it) 你為甚麼把它漆成紅的?〔我不喜歡紅的〕

Where on earth did you get that hat? (it looks awful) 你從哪裡弄來這麼一頂帽子?〔帽子太難看了〕

when introducing people 介紹:

Have you met/Do you know Mr Jones? 你見過 [認識] 瓊斯先生嗎?

Do you two know each other? 你們兩位彼此相識嗎?

when inviting 邀請:

Are you doing anything tomorrow night? (used to introduce an invitation) 明天晚上你有空嗎?〔用於引出邀請〕

Would you like to come to a film on Friday? 你星期五想看場電影嗎?

Why don't you come dancing with us? 你何不來同我們一起跳舞?

when offering 提供幫助:

Won't you have some more coffee? 再來點咖啡好嗎?

Shall I give you a hand? 要我給你幫個忙嗎?

Would you like me to help you carry that? 我幫你提這個東西好嗎?

when ordering or instructing 指揮或指示:

Will you just roll up your sleeve? (doctor to patient) 請把袖子捲起來。〔醫生對病人〕

Close the window, will you/would you? (the speaker is in a position of authority) 請把窗子關上。〔當權者發話〕

Will you listen to me for a minute? (the speaker is probably angry) 你聽我說好不好?〔説話者可能生氣了〕

Language Note: Questions 語言提示：問句

when asking permission 請求同意:

Do you mind if I smoke? 你不介意我吸煙吧？

Can I come in? 我可以進來嗎？

when requesting 提出要求:

Could you pass me the newspaper? 請把報紙遞給我，行嗎？

Can you reach the salt? (please pass it to me) 你能拿到鹽嗎？〔請把它遞給我〕。

Have you got a minute? (I'd like to speak to you) 你現在有空嗎？〔我想同你說點事〕

when suggesting 提出建議:

Why don't we have lunch before we go? 我們何不吃了午飯再去？

Have you tried doing it this way? 你試過用這種方式做嗎？

How about asking Bill to the party? 請比爾參加聚會好不好？

when sympathizing 表示同情:

How are you feeling today? (after an illness) 你今天覺得怎麼樣？〔病後〕

Are you all right? (after a slight accident) 你沒有事兒吧？〔輕微事故之後〕

when threatening 威嚇:

Do you want a smack? (parent to naughty child) 你想挨巴掌嗎？〔父母對頑童〕

How would you like a punch on the nose? 給你鼻子上來一拳怎麼樣？

Note that even when a question is used in an indirect way it is still a question and so it usually needs an answer. For example, the question, *Do you know Mr Jones?* requires the answer, *Yes* or *No*. If the answer is "Yes", then it is not necessary to continue the introduction. Similarly, the answer to the question, *Are you doing anything tomorrow night?* may be *Yes* or *No*. The speaker will only go on to invite the hearer if the answer is "No". 注意，問句即使是以間接方式提問，仍然是個問句，因此通常需要回答。例如，問句 *Do you know Mr Jones?*（你認識瓊斯先生嗎？）就需要回答 *Yes* 或 *No*（"認識"或"不認識"）。如果回答是 *Yes*（認識），就沒有必要繼續介紹。同樣，問句 *Are you doing anything tomorrow night?*（你明天晚上有事嗎？）可以答 *Yes* 或 *No*（"有事"或"沒有事"）。如果對方答 *No*（"沒有事"），這時才可以提出邀請。

See 參見 LANGUAGE NOTES: **Apologies**, **Criticism and Praise**, **Invitations and Offers**, **Politeness**, **Requests**, **Tentativeness**, **Thanks**

Language Note: Requests 語言提示: 請求

Politeness in requests 提出請求時的禮貌問題

When you are asking someone to do something for you or trying to influence their actions, you can often show that you want to be polite by saying things in an indirect way. 在你請求別人為你做某事或者你企圖影響他們的行為時, 常常可以用間接的措詞來顯示你想表示出有禮貌:

direct 直接	*Help me lift this box (please).* (請) 幫我提一下這箱子。
↕	*(Please) will you help me lift this box?* (請) 幫我提一下這箱子好嗎?
	Could you help me lift this box (please)? (請) 幫我提一下這箱子行嗎?
	Do you think you could possibly help me lift this box? 想請您幫我提一下這箱子, 不知道可以嗎?
indirect 間接	*I was wondering if you could possibly help me lift this box.* 不知是否可以請您幫我提一下這箱子。

Generally speaking, the more indirect the expression you use, the more polite you will seem. If you are too direct you may be considered rude. However, the more indirect expressions can sound "too polite" or in some cases pompous if they are used in the wrong situations. When deciding which expressions are suitable for which situations it is useful to ask certain questions. 一般地說, 愈是間接的措詞愈是顯得有禮貌, 如果措詞太直接會被認為是粗魯。但是如果很間接的措詞用在不當的場合, 也會讓人聽起來"太客氣", 或者在某種情況下顯得"不實在"。在決定甚麼情況下使用甚麼措詞, 考慮以下一些問題是有裨益的。

Considerations affecting choice of expression 選擇措詞時的若干考慮

— What is the relationship between the person who is speaking (the speaker) and the person they are speaking to (the hearer)? The more direct expressions, for example, are mostly used between friends or when the speaker is in a position of authority. 說話人與聽話人之間是甚麼關係? 例如, 在朋友之間, 或者說話人處於當權的地位, 通常使用較為直接的措詞。

— How important is the action to the speaker? If the action is very important the speaker will probably use a more indirect expression. 請求對方做的行為對說話人的重要性如何?如果很重要, 說話人就可能使用較為間接的措詞。

— How much inconvenience will this action cause for the hearer? If, for example, the hearer is being asked to make a lot of effort or do something which they do not usually do, the speaker will probably use a more indirect expression. 該行為麻煩對方的程度如何?例如, 如果是使人家頗為費事或是做平常不做的事, 就可能使用較為間接的措詞。

Here are some examples from spoken English which show how these considerations can affect the choice of expression 以下是英語口語中顯示這類考慮如何影響措詞的選擇的一些例子:

polite indirectness 間接性措詞的禮貌程度		**request inconvenient or unusual** 所提的要求很麻煩或很不尋常	**speaker in authority** 說話人處於當權地位	**hearer in authority** 聽話人處於當權地位
	Put your plate in the kitchen when you've finished eating. (Father to child) 吃完了把盤子放到廚房裡去。〔父親對孩子〕		■	
	I want you to stop talking and listen to me. (Teacher to class) 別說話了, 聽我講。〔老師對全班學生〕		■	
	Give me a hand with this box, Joe. (Friend to friend) 喬, 幫我提一下這個箱子。〔朋友之間〕			

Language Note: Requests 語言提示: 請求

polite indirectness 間接性措詞的禮貌程度		**request inconvenient or unusual** 所提的要求很麻煩或很不尋常	**speaker in authority** 說話人處於當權地位	**hearer in authority** 聽話人處於當權地位
■	**Could you** *check these letters before I send them out Ms Wells?* (Employer to employee) 韋爾斯女士, 我發出這些信之前幫我檢查一下好嗎? 〔雇主對雇員〕		■	
■	**Could you** *buy some more milk on your way home from work?* (Friend to friend) 你下班回家時再買點牛奶好嗎? 〔朋友之間〕			
■■	**Could you possibly** *explain that point again?* (Student to Professor) 這個問題請您再解釋一下好嗎? 〔學生對教授〕			■
■■	**Do you think you could possibly** *stay late to type these letters?* (Employer to employee) 下班後您可否多呆些時候把這些信打出來? 〔雇主對雇員〕	■	■	
■■■	**Could you** *spare a moment?* **We were wondering whether you would be able to** *advise us on a small problem.* (Junior Manager to Managing Director) 耽誤您一點時間, 有個小問題要向您請示, 不知道是不是可以? 〔下級經理對董事總經理〕	■		■
■■■	**I was wondering if you could possibly** *lend me your car tomorrow.* (Friend to friend) 我想明天借用您的車子, 不知道行不行。〔朋友之間〕	■		

▶ Be careful! 注意!

Choosing to use polite expressions which seem to be "too polite" for the situation will usually be seen as sarcasm. In the following examples the requests are not inconvenient or unusual, but the speaker is using indirect expressions to emphasize a feeling of annoyance with the hearer. 使用"太客氣"的措詞通常被視為是有意諷刺挖苦。在以下數例中, 所要求的事並非很麻煩或不尋常, 但說話人使用間接措詞以強調對聽話人的反感:

I was wondering, Tom, whether it might be possible for you to help do the dishes occasionally? (Friend to friend)
湯姆, 我想請您偶爾幫幫忙洗一洗盤子, 不知道是否可以? 〔朋友之間〕

Mary, I wonder if I might ask you to turn your eyes in this direction? (Teacher to student)
瑪麗, 我不知道是否可以請你把眼睛轉向這邊? 〔老師對學生〕

Do you think it would be possible for you to refrain from smoking for five minutes? (Colleague to colleague)
不知道是否有可能請您停止吸煙五分鐘? 〔同事之間〕

See also 另見 COULD, MAY, POSSIBLY; see 參見 LANGUAGE NOTES: **Politeness**, **Tentativeness**

Language Note: Synonyms 語言提示: 同義詞

You will often find that several words share a similar general meaning. But be careful — their meanings are nearly always different in one way or another. When comparing two words in the dictionary, look at the definitions and examples and any Usage Notes. Then ask yourself these questions 有時幾個詞在總的含義上相似。但是要注意 — 它們的詞義幾乎經常不是在這方面就是在那方面多少有點不同。在對本辭典中的兩個詞進行比較時, 請注意看它們各自的釋義和例證以及可能有的用法說明, 然後向自己提出以下問題:

■ Is the meaning exactly the same? 詞義是否完全一樣?

Compare 比較:

injure/wound 傷害

Both words can mean "to damage part of someone's body" but **wound** is used to suggest that there is a hole or tear in the skin, especially if this has been done on purpose with a weapon. 這兩個詞都表示"傷害某人身體的一部分", 但 **wound** 用於表示在皮膚上造成傷口, 尤指是有意使用武器造成的:

> *He was badly* **injured** *in a car crash.* 他在車禍中受了重傷。| *Two people were killed and forty* **wounded** *when fighting broke out late last night.* 昨天深夜開戰, 有兩人被打死, 四十人受傷。

kill 殺死/**murder** 謀殺

To **murder** means "to **kill**" but always has the additional meaning of "unlawfully and on purpose". to **murder** 意為"殺死", 但又總是含有"非法地和有意地"之意:

> *She was sent to prison for* **killing/murdering** *her brother.* 她因殺死[謀殺] 她的兄弟被送入監獄。| *Fifty people were* **killed** (NOT **murdered**) *on the roads last weekend.* 上週末, 有五十人死於車禍〔不能用 **murdered**〕。

smell 氣味 *n*/**stink** 惡臭 *n*

A **smell** can be good or bad but a **stink** is always a bad smell,especially a very strong one. 名詞 **smell** 可以是好聞的氣味也可以是不好聞的氣味, 但 **stink** 就總是壞氣味, 尤其是惡臭:

> *a* **smell** *of roses/of stale cooking* 玫瑰的香味; 燒煮陳腐食物的氣味 | *a* **stink** *of burning rubber* 燃燒橡膠的難聞氣味

Sometimes the words are different in degree 有時各個詞在程度上是有區別的

adore is a stronger word than **love**	**adore** (很喜歡) 比 **love** (喜歡) 強烈
astonishment is a stronger word than **surprise**	**astonishment** (驚訝) 比 **surprise** (驚奇) 強烈
filthy is a stronger word than **dirty**	**filthy** (污穢的) 比 **dirty** (髒的) 強烈
furious is a stronger word than **angry**	**furious** (狂怒的) 比 **angry** (憤怒的) 強烈
soaked is a stronger word than **wet**	**soaked** (濕透的) 比 **wet** (濕的) 強烈
terror is a stronger word than **fear**	**terror** (恐怖) 比 **fear** (害怕) 強烈

Language Note: Synonyms 語言提示: 同義詞

Sometimes the words express a different attitude 有時各個詞表示不同的態度

You can say someone is **slim** if they are thin and you like the way they look. If you think they are too thin, you might say they are **skinny** or, if you really want to be rude, **scrawny**. 如果某人瘦, 而你又認為瘦得好看, 就可以用 **slim**（苗條的）, 但如果你認為某人太瘦, 則可用 **skinny**（瘦削的）, 或如你確實想説得粗魯一些, 則可用 **scrawny**（骨瘦如柴的）。

You say something is **newfangled** if you disapprove of it because it is too modern. If you do not feel disapproval you use words like **new** or **modern**. 如果你對某事物持否定態度, 認為它太新潮, 可用 **newfangled**（花樣翻新的）, 如不持否定態度, 則可用 **new** 或 **modern**（新式的）這一類詞。

■ Are the words used in the same situations? 各個詞用於同一語境嗎?

Words with a similar meaning are often used in quite different situations. 具有相似含義的詞往往用於相當不同的語境。

Sometimes the words have a different style 有時各個詞有不同的風格

In these pairs, one of the words has a particular style which means that it is not usually used in an ordinary situation. 在以下各對詞中, 其中的一個詞具有一種特殊的風格, 這意味着該詞通常不在一般的語境中使用。

Compare 比較:

brainy (*infml* 非正式) 伶俐的/**intelligent** 聰明的
comely (*lit* 文) 秀麗的/**beautiful** 美麗的
cop (*infml* 非正式) 差人/**policeman** 警察
fag (*BrE sl* 英俚) 煙捲兒/**cigarette** 香煙
kick the bucket (*humor sl* 幽俚) 翹辮子/**die** 死
pass away (*euph* 婉) 逝世, 作古/**die** 死
seek (*fml or lit* 正式或文) 尋覓/**look for** 尋找

Sometimes the words have a different register 有時候各個詞有不同的語域:

Some words are normally used by specialists, such as doctors or scientists. Other people will use another word for the same thing 某些詞是醫生或科學家等專業人員的術語。同樣一個事物, 其他人則用另外的詞來表達:

Compare 比較:

bequeath (*fml* 正式) 遺贈/**leave** (money etc. after death) 死後留下〔家產等〕
patella (*med* 醫) 髕/**kneecap** 膝蓋骨

Sometimes the words belong to a different variety of English 有時各詞分屬不同地方的英語

Compare 比較:

crook (*AustrE infml* 澳, 非正式)/**poorly** (*BrE infml* 英, 非正式) 健康狀況不佳的
elevator (*AmE* 美)/**lift** (*BrE* 英) 電梯
pavement (*BrE* 英)/**sidewalk** (*AmE* 美) 人行道

Language Note: Synonyms 語言提示: 同義詞

■ Do the words have the same grammar? 這些詞的語法搭配是一樣的嗎?

Sometimes words with a similar meaning are used in different grammatical patterns. 有時, 詞義相似的詞, 其語法搭配並不一樣。

Compare 比較:

rob 搶劫/**steal** 盜竊

You **rob** a bank or **rob** somebody (of something) 動詞 **rob** 可以後接機構 (to rob a bank 搶劫銀行) 或人 (to rob somebody 搶劫某人), 搶走的東西則要置於 **of** 的後面:

> *He* **robbed** *the old couple (of all their savings).* 他搶劫了這對老夫婦(的全部積蓄)。

You **steal** something (from somebody or from a place) 但 **steal** 後要接所盜竊的東西, 被盜竊的人或場所則要置於 **from** 的後面:

> *He* **stole** *a glass from the restaurant.* 他從這家餐館偷了一個玻璃杯。| *She* **stole** *some money from her sister.* 她從她姐姐那裡偷了一些錢。

answer *v*/**reply** *v* 回答

Answer can be both transitive and intransitive 動詞 **answer** 可以是及物的也可以是不及物的:

> *I called him but he didn't* **answer**. 我叫他了, 但他沒有回答。| *They never* **answer** *our letters.* 他們從來不回覆我們的信。

Reply is always intransitive 而 **reply** 則總是不及物的:

> *I wrote to her but she didn't* **reply**. 我給她寫了信, 但她沒有回覆。| *They never* **reply** *to our letters.* 他們從來不回覆我們的信。

advise 勸告/**recommend** 建議

Both verbs can mean "to tell someone what you think should be done" but are followed by different verb patterns 這兩個動詞的意思都表示"告訴某人你認為應該做甚麼", 但是後面接的動詞句型卻不一樣:

> *The doctor* **advised** *me to stay in bed.* 醫生要我臥牀。| *The doctor* **recommended** *that I (should) stay in bed.* 醫生建議我 (應該) 臥牀。

Notice that even when words appear to be synonyms they are rarely the same in all the ways discussed here. The entries in this dictionary will help you decide how they are different. 請注意, 當一些詞看來是同義詞時, 它們在以上所討論的各個方面卻極少是完全一致的, 本辭典的條目會幫助你認識它們的不一致之處。

See 參見 THIN (USAGE)

Language Note: Tentativeness 語言提示: 猶疑語氣

In English, speakers often show politeness by being indirect and tentative. This is especially true in situations where there is a risk of causing offence. 在英語中, 説話人常常通過間接方式和用猶疑的語氣來表示禮貌, 特別是在有可能引起對方反感的情況下尤其如此。

There are many different ways of expressing tentativeness. One way is to use words which "soften" what is being said, making it less forceful and direct. 表示猶疑有許多種不同的方法。一種方法是使用某些詞語使所説的話聽起來"柔和"一些, 使之不那麼強硬和直接。

Here are some common "softening words". 下面是一些常用的"柔和字眼"。

■ **Maybe** and **perhaps** are used **maybe** 和 **perhaps** 可用於以下場合:

— when making suggestions and recommendations 提出建議或忠告時:

Maybe *we should ask Liz for her opinion.* 也許我們應該徵求一下莉茲的意見。

Perhaps *you ought to talk to John about it.* 也許你該同約翰談談這件事。

— when making a request 提出要求時:

Could you **perhaps** *just say a few words about your new project?* 或許你可以就你的新項目説幾句話, 行嗎?

Maybe *you could phone me later this week.* 或許你可以在本週晚些時候給我打個電話。

Perhaps *you'd like to let me know when you've finished.* 你做完時或許可以通知我一下。

— when expressing criticism 表示批評時:

It's a beautiful pink, but it's **perhaps** *a little bright for my taste.* 這種粉紅色很漂亮, 不過從我的愛好來説, 似乎太鮮豔了一點。

■ **Possibly** is used **possibly** 可用於以下場合:

— mainly with can **and** could **in requests** 主要用於表示請求, 與 can 和 could 連用:

Could you **possibly** *write the report by tomorrow?* 您是否有可能至遲在明天寫好報告?

Do you think I could **possibly** *borrow your bike?* 我借用一下你的腳踏車你看可以嗎?

— but also when expressing criticism 但也可用於表示批評:

The food is wonderful but it's **possibly** *a little bit expensive.* 這食品味道好極了, 不過可能貴了一點。

Language Note: Tentativeness 語言提示: 猶疑語氣

■ **Wonder** is used **wonder** 可用於以下場合:

— when giving invitations 提出邀請時:

We were wondering *whether you'd like to come to dinner next week.* 我們正在想, 不知道你下週能不能過來吃晚飯。

— when making suggestions and recommendations 提出建議或忠告:

I wonder *if we should go by train.* 不知道我們是否該乘火車去?
I wonder *if you'd find it easier to do it this way.* 不知道這樣做你會不會覺得容易一些?

— when making requests 提出要求時:

I wonder *whether you could spare me a moment.* 不知道是不是可以打擾你一會兒?
We were wondering *if you could help us.* 不知道你能不能幫我們一下?

— when expressing criticism or disagreement 表示批評或不同意時:

It's a lovely dress but **I wonder** *if it's quite your colour.* 這衣服很漂亮, 可我不知道顏色是不是十分適合你。
I wonder *whether these figures are quite right.* 不知道這些數字是不是完全對。
Is that true, **I wonder**? 那是真的嗎?我可不敢説。

Notice that the use of past tense forms (**I wondered**, **I was wondering**, etc.) makes the suggestion, request, etc. even more tentative. 注意, 使用過去時式 (**I wondered**, **I was wondering** 等) 可以使建議、要求等更帶猶疑色彩。

■ **Quite** is used with negative forms **quite** 用於各種否定形式:

— when expressing disagreement or criticism 表示不同意或批評:

That's not **quite** *what I said, you know.* 恐怕我不完全是那樣説的, 你要知道。
Are you sure? That doesn't seem **quite** *right to me.* 你能肯定嗎?我似乎覺得那並不完全對頭。
I'm not **quite** *sure I agree with you there.* 我不敢完全肯定在那個問題上同你的看法一致。

Note that sometimes several softening words are used together, and this makes the suggestion, request, etc., even more tentative 注意, 有時若干柔和字眼可以連用, 從而更加強了建議、要求等的猶疑語氣:

I was wondering *whether I could* **possibly** *have the day off tomorrow.* 我在想, 不知我明天請一天假行不行。
I wonder *whether it isn't* **perhaps** *a little bit too bright.* 我不知道這是否太鮮亮了一點。
It's a lovely sweater but I think **maybe** *it's not* **quite** *the right size for me.* 這毛衣很漂亮, 但我看或許尺寸不怎麼合我的身材。

See also 另見 POSSIBLY, QUITE; see 參見 MAYBE (USAGE), and 和 LANGUAGE NOTE: **Politeness**

Language Note: Thanks 語言提示: 致謝

Expressions used to thank people can be very short and direct, or they can be longer and more complex. When deciding which expressions are suitable for which situations it is useful to ask certain questions. 用於對人表示感謝的詞語可以很短而且直接，也可以比較長而複雜。在考慮何種情況下使用何種詞語時，問幾個問題是很有用的。

Considerations affecting choice of expression 涉及選擇詞語的種種考慮

— How important is the thing or the action for which the speaker is thanking the hearer? If it is very important to the speaker, the expression of thanks will be stronger. 說話人對聽話人所要表示感謝的事物或行為，其重要性如何？如果對說話人很重要，感謝的詞語就要較為強烈。

— Is the action something which the hearer has to do or ought to do, or is it something unusual or special? If the hearer has done something unusual or special, the expression of thanks will be stronger. 這個行為是聽話人所必須或應該做的，抑或是一種不尋常的行為？如果是後者，感謝的詞語就要較為強烈。

— Will the hearer immediately know the reason for the thanks? If not, the speaker must make this clear. 聽話人是否會立即明白講話人感謝他的原因？如果不是這樣，講話人就必須說清楚。

■ Quick thanks 簡短的感謝語

When someone does something small for you which is part of normal polite behaviour, it is usual to say thank you. For instance, if a flight attendant brings you a meal, a friend holds the door open for you, a bank clerk gives you your money, or the person sitting next to you passes the salt, you should use a short expression of thanks. The examples below show the usual short forms of thanks and response. (Note that in British English it is not always necessary to respond.) 當有人為你做了一些屬於日常的有禮貌的事時，通常要表示感謝。例如，空中小姐送來飯菜，朋友為你開門，銀行職員把錢給你，或者鄰座的人遞給你鹽瓶，你都應用簡短的詞語表示感謝。以下所列為常用的簡短的感謝詞語以及答語（注意：在英國英語中，對於道謝並不是全都要回答的）：

thanks 感謝語	**responses** 答語
Thank you. 謝謝你。 *Thanks.* 謝謝	*You're welcome.* (*esp. AmE* 尤美) 別客氣。 *That's all right.* 不用謝。 *That's OK.* (*infml* 非正式) 沒甚麼。 *No problem.* (*AmE infml* 美，非正式) 沒問題。 *Not at all.* (*fml* 正式) 用不着客氣。

■ Stronger ways of thanking 較強烈的感謝方式

When someone gives you a present or does something special for you, it is usual to thank them in a stronger way. This can be done by making the expression stronger and adding a comment. (Note that the comment may come before or after the expression of thanks.) 當有人送給你禮物或者特地為你做了甚麼事情，通常都要用較為強烈的方式表示感謝。做法是使用較為強烈的詞語並加上說明。(注意，說明的話可以在感謝詞語之前，也可以在之後)：

Language Note: Thanks 語言提示: 致謝

stronger expressions 較強烈的詞語	**comments** 說明
Thank you **very much**. 非常感謝。 *(Oh great!) Thanks* **a lot**. (*rather infml* 較非正式) (嘀, 太好了!) 太感謝了。 **Many** *thanks*. (*rather fml* 較正式) 甚為感謝。	*It's wonderful/just what I wanted.* (comment on a present) 好極了 [正是我想要的]。〔稱讚禮物〕 *That's really kind of you.* 你真是太好了。| *You didn't have to, you know.* (comment on hearer's generosity) 你用不著這樣破費呀。〔稱讚對方的慷慨大方〕 *I don't know what I'd have done without you.* 我真不知道沒有你該怎麼辦。| *I'd never have managed on my own.* (when someone has helped you to do something) 我自己是怎麼也弄不成的。〔稱讚對方幫你做了某事〕

Explaining 解釋

When thanking someone for something which has already happened, the speaker needs to remind the hearer of the situation 為早已發生的某事感謝某人, 需要提醒一下對方當時的情況:

Thank you for all your hard work last week. I don't think we could have managed without you. 謝謝你上週的大力幫忙。我看要是沒有你, 我們是幹不成的。

My mother was thrilled to get those flowers on her birthday. Thanks a lot — it was really thoughtful of you. 我母親過生日那天收到那些花高興極了。太謝謝你了 — 你想得真周到。

It was very good of you to give Billy a lift home from school yesterday. Thank you. 你真好, 昨天比利放學時你讓他搭你的車回家。謝謝你了。

We're really grateful for all your help while Arthur was ill. Thank you very much. 亞瑟生病期間幸虧你多方幫助, 我們非常感謝。

(Note that **grateful** is most often used when the hearer has helped the speaker in some way. It is not usually used when saying thank you for a present. 注意, **grateful** 通常用於感謝聽者為說話人提供的某種幫忙, 一般不用於感謝對方贈送禮物。)

Written and formal thanks 書面的和正式的感謝語

Written and formal expressions of thanks often refer directly to the action of thanking 書面和正式的感謝用語常常是開門見山的:

I am writing to thank you for… 本人來信是為了特意感謝您…。

I am writing to say how grateful we are… 為向您表示我們感激之情, 本人現來函向您致意…

Please accept our (grateful) thanks… (*fml* 正式) 請接受我們衷心的感謝…

We would like to thank you for your contribution (*fml* 正式). 承蒙惠賜, 謹表謝忱。

We would like to express our gratitude for your cooperation. (*fml* 正式) 承蒙台端合作, 特此申謝。

The management would like to express its gratitude to the following people for their work in the fund-raising campaign… (*fml* 正式) 公司謹對在此次籌集資金活動中作出貢獻之下列人員表示感謝…

Language Note: Words Followed by Prepositions
語言提示: 後接介詞的詞語

In English many nouns, verbs, and adjectives are commonly followed by prepositions. If you do not know whether to use a preposition with a particular word or if you are not sure which preposition to use, look up the word in this dictionary. At each entry, you will be given the prepositions which are commonly used with that word. These are printed in dark type before the definition and the examples. After you have found the preposition, go on to look at the examples; these will often show you how the prepositions are used. 英語中許多名詞、動詞和形容詞通常都後接介詞。如果你不知道某一個詞是否與介詞連用或不能肯定用哪一個介詞, 請在本辭典中查閱該詞的詞條, 在每一個詞條中你都能找到通常與該詞連用的介詞, 這些介詞用黑體排在釋義和例證的前面, 找到這個介詞後再往下看例證, 了解其用法。

Below are some sample entries for nouns, verbs, and adjectives. 下面是一些名詞、動詞和形容詞的樣條。

■ Prepositions with nouns 介詞與名詞連用

This entry tells you that in its second meaning **insight** can be used with the preposition **into**. 這個詞條告訴你在第二個義項中 **insight** 可以與介詞 **into** 連用。

in·sight /ˈɪnˌsaɪt; ˈɪnsaɪt/ *n* **1** [U] the ability to understand and realize what people or situations are really like 洞察力, 眼光: *a woman of great insight* 一位極有眼光的婦女 **2** [C] a sudden clear understanding of something, especially something complicated〔尤指對複雜事情的〕頓悟, 猛省: **[+into]** *The article gives us a real insight into the causes of the present economic crisis.* 這篇文章分析目前經濟危機的原因, 發人深省。

This entry tells you that in its first meaning **intrusion** can be used with **into**, **on** or **upon**. The examples show you that the prepositions are used with the same meaning. 本詞條告訴你在第一個義項中 **intrusion** 可以與 **into**, **on** 或者 **upon** 連用。例證表示這幾個介詞用起來意思是一樣的。

in·tru·sion /ɪnˋtruʒən; ɪnˈtruːʒən/ *n* [C,U] **1** an unwanted event or person in a situation that is private〔討厭的事或人的〕干擾, 侵擾: *She considered Pam's presence in the kitchen an intrusion.* 她認為帕姆待在廚房是一種干擾。| **[+into/on/upon]** *I resented this intrusion into my domestic affairs.* 我討厭這種對我家事的干涉。**2** something that has an unwanted effect on a situation, on people's lives etc〔對某種情況、別人生活等的〕侵襲; 打擾: *the intrusion of Western values on a culture that has existed for centuries* 西方價值觀對一種已存在幾百年的文化的侵襲

This entry shows you that in its first meaning **preparation** can be used with either **for** or **of**. The choice of preposition will depend on the meaning of the sentence in which the word is used. 這個詞條向你顯示, 在第一個義項中 **preparation** 可以同 **for** 或者 **of** 連用。介詞的選擇取決於句子的語義。

prep·a·ra·tion /ˌprɛpəˋreʃən; ˌprepəˈreɪʃən/ *n* **1** [U] the act or process of preparing something 預備, 準備: **[+for]** *Business training is a good preparation for any career.* 商業培訓對任何職業都是良好的基礎。| **[+of]** *Richard's currently involved in the preparation of the budget.* 理查德當前在忙於編製預算。| **in preparation for** (=in order to prepare for something) 為…作準備 *Justin had opened several bottles of wine in preparation for the party.* 賈斯廷已開了好幾瓶葡萄酒為聚會作準備。| **be in preparation** (=being prepared) 在準備中 *Plans for the new school are now in preparation.* 建造新校舍的圖樣正在繪製之中。**2 preparations** [plural] arrangements for something that is going to happen 準備工作, 籌備工作: **[+for]** *preparations for the Queen's visit* 女王訪問的準備工作 | **make preparations** *The army is making preparations for a full-scale invasion.* 軍隊正在為全面侵略作準備。**3** [C] a medicine, COSMETIC etc 配製劑; 藥劑: *a new preparation for cleansing the skin* 清潔皮膚的新護膚劑

Language Note: Words Followed by Prepositions
語言提示: 後接介詞的詞語

Prepositions with verbs 介詞與動詞連用

This entry tells you that **compensate** is used with the preposition **for**. The example in its second meaning shows that you usually **compensate** somebody **for** something. 這個詞條告訴你 **compensate** 與介詞 **for** 連用。第二個義項中的例證說明用 **compensate** somebody **for** something 表示"為某事物賠償給某人"。

com·pen·sate /ˈkɑmpən,set; ˈkɒmpənseɪt/ *v* **1** [I] to replace or balance something good that has been lost or is lacking, by providing or doing something equally good 彌補, 補償: *Because my left eye is so weak, my right eye has to work harder to compensate.* 因為我左眼視力差, 右眼就要辛苦點來彌補一下。| [**+for**] *Her intelligence more than compensates for her lack of experience.* 她的才智過人, 因此雖然經驗不足, 也遊刃有餘。**2** [I,T] to pay someone money because they have suffered injury, loss or damage 賠償, 補償: **compensate sb for sth** *The firm agreed to compensate its workers for their loss of earnings.* 公司同意補償工人的收入損失。

This entry tells you that **joke** is used with the prepositions **about** and **with**. The first example shows that you joke **about** something. 這個詞條告訴你, **joke** 與介詞 **about** 和 **with** 連用。第一個例證說明 **joke about** something 用以表示"開有關某事的玩笑。"

joke² *v* [I] **1** to say things that are intended to be funny 開玩笑, 說笑話: [**+about/with**] *It's serious, Donny, don't joke about it!* 事情很嚴重, 唐尼, 別開玩笑了! **2 you're joking!/you must be joking!** *spoken* used to tell someone that what they are suggesting is so strange or silly that you cannot believe that they are serious【口】你(一定)是在開玩笑吧?〔用來表示某人說的話很奇怪或愚蠢, 你無法相信他們是認真的〕: *What! Buy a house on my salary? You must be joking!* 甚麼? 用我的薪水買房子?你一定是在開玩笑吧? **3 only joking** *BrE spoken* used to say that you did not really mean what you just said【英口】只是說着玩的; 開個玩笑而已〔用來表示剛才所說並不是認真的〕: *Only joking, darling – I love you really!* 親愛的, 只不過開個玩笑, 我真的很愛你! **4 joking apart/aside** *BrE* used before you say something serious after you have been joking【英】說正經的〔用來表示停止開玩笑, 開始說嚴肅的事〕: *Joking apart, she is a very talented painter.* 說正經的, 她真是一位很有才華的畫家。—**jokingly** *adv*

This entry tells you that **progress** is used with the preposition **to**. The example shows that the preposition can be followed by a verb in the **-ing** form. 這個詞條告訴你, **progress** 與 **to** 連用。例證說明 **to** 可以後接動詞的 **-ing** 形式。

progress² *v* [I] **1** to develop over a period of time and become something better or more complete 進步; 進展: *Work on the ship progressed quickly.* 輪船的建造進展迅速。| *I asked the nurse how my son was progressing.* 我向護士詢問我兒子身體恢復得如何。| [**+to**] *Cindy has progressed to reading on her own.* 辛迪進步了, 開始自己閱讀了。**2** if an activity or situation progresses, it continues to happen or develop gradually〔活動等〕繼續進行; 逐步發展: *As the meeting progressed, Nina grew more and more bored.* 隨着會議的進行, 妮娜越來越感到無聊。**3** to move forward slowly 緩慢行進: *Our taxi seemed to be progressing with agonizing slowness.* 我們的出租車彷彿以令人難以忍受的緩慢速度向前行駛。**4** to move on from doing one thing to doing another〔從做一件事〕轉向〔做另一件事〕: [**+to**] *We started with a bottle of wine, and then progressed to whisky.* 我們先喝了一瓶葡萄酒, 之後便喝起了威士忌。—compare 比較 REGRESS

Language Note: Words Followed by Prepositions
語言提示: 後接介詞的詞語

Prepositions with adjectives 介詞與形容詞連用

This entry tells you that **desirous** is followed by the preposition **of**. 這個詞條告訴你, **desirous** 後接介詞 **of**。

de·sir·ous /dɪˋzaɪrəs; dɪˈzaɪərəs/ *adj formal* wanting something very much【正式】希望的, 渴望的: **[+of]** *No one had ever been so openly desirous of my attention.* 從未有人如此公開地表示過渴望引起我的注意。

This entry tells you that in its second meaning **immune** is used with the preposition **to**, but in its third meaning it is used with the preposition **from**. 這個詞條告訴你, 在第二個義項中 **immune** 與介詞 **to** 連用, 而在第三個義項中與介詞 **from** 連用。

im·mune /ɪˋmjun; ɪˈmjuːn/ *adj* **1** someone who is immune to a particular disease cannot catch it〔對疾病〕有免疫力的**2** not affected by something such as criticism, bad treatment etc 不受〔批評、虐待等〕影響的: **[+to]** *They're always so rude that I've almost become immune to it.* 他們總是如此粗暴無禮, 我都幾乎習以為常了。**3** specially protected from something unpleasant 豁免的; 可免...的: **[+from]** *Peterson was told he would be immune from prosecution if he co-operated with the police.* 彼得森被告知, 如果他與警方合作, 就可免於起訴。

This entry tells you that when **impervious** means "not affected or influenced by something", it is used with the preposition **to**. Note that in its second meaning it is used without a preposition. 這個詞條告訴你, 當 **impervious** 作"不受影響的"解時, 與介詞 **to** 連用。請注意, 在第二個義項中 **impervious** 不與介詞連用。

im·per·vi·ous /ɪmˋpɝvɪəs; ɪmˈpɜːviəs/ *adj* **1** not affected or influenced by something and seeming not to notice it 不受影響的; 無動於衷的: **[+to]** *Janet carried on reading, impervious to the row going on around her.* 珍妮特不受周圍的嘈雜聲影響, 繼續看書。| *He seems to be impervious to criticism.* 他好像對批評毫不在乎。**2** not allowing anything to enter or pass through〔任何東西都〕不能進入的; 不能穿過的: *impervious volcanic rock* 不透水不透氣的火山岩

Summary 總結

Some words can be followed by different prepositions without changing their meaning. 某些詞可以後接不同的介詞而含義不變。(see 參見 **intrusion**)

Some words are followed by different prepositions according to their different meanings. 某些詞按不同的含義後接不同的介詞。(see 參見 **immune**)

Some words can be followed by more than one prepositon, but these are used in different ways. 某些詞可以後接一個以上的介詞, 但是用法是各不相同的。(see 參見 **joke**, **preparation**)

Some words can be used either with or without a prepositon. 某些詞可以與介詞連用, 也可以不與介詞連用。(see 參見 **prepared**)

Prepositions can be followed by verbs in the **-ing** form. They cannot be followed by infinitives. 介詞可以後接 **-ing** 形式的動詞, 但不可以後接不定詞。(see 參見 **progress**)

Phrasal verbs 片語 [短語] 動詞

The examples in this Language Note show words which can be used with a preposition but have a complete meaning in themselves. There are also many verbs where a word which looks like a preposition makes up part of the meaning, for example **come across** (=discover), **look into** (=investigate), etc. These are considered to be phrasal verbs and are listed in this dictionary as separate headwords in alphabetical order under the main verb. 本語言提示中所舉的例證展示了可以和介詞連用但本身具有完整語義的詞。此外, 也有許多動詞, 它們的構成中有像是介詞的詞, 這些詞組成了部分語義, 如 **come across**（發現）, **look into**（調查）等, 這些動詞稱作片語 [短語] 動詞, 本辭典把它們作為單獨詞條按字母順序列在主要動詞的下面。

See 參見 LANGUAGE NOTES: **Collocations**, **Phrasal Verbs**

Appendices

附錄

Table 1 附錄 1

Numbers 數字

How numbers are spoken 數字讀法

Numbers over 20 20以上的數字

21	twenty-one
22	twenty-two
32	thirty-two
99	ninety-nine

Numbers over 100 100以上的數字

101	a/one hundred (and) one
121	a/one hundred (and) twenty-one
200	two hundred
232	two hundred (and) thirty-two
999	nine hundred (and) ninety-nine

Note: In British English the "and" is always used 註：在英國英語中總是用 and: *two hundred and thirty-two.* But in American English it is often left out 但在美國英語中 and 往往略去: *two hundred thirty-two.*

Numbers over 1000 1000以上的數字

1001	a/one thousand (and) one
1121	one thousand one hundred (and) twenty-one
2000	two thousand
2232	two thousand two hundred (and) thirty-two
9999	nine thousand nine hundred (and) ninety-nine

Ordinal numbers 序數

20th	twentieth
21st	twenty-first
25th	twenty-fifth
90th	ninetieth
99th	ninety-ninth
100th	hundredth
101st	hundred and first
225th	two hundred (and) twenty-fifth

Dates 日期

1066	ten sixty-six
1624	sixteen twenty-four
1900	nineteen hundred
1903	nineteen-oh-three
1987	nineteen eighty-seven
2000	the year two thousand
2001	two thousand (and) one
6 January, 1990	the sixth of January nineteen ninety
January 6, 1990	January (the) sixth nineteen ninety

Numbers and grammar 數字和語法

Numbers can be used as 數字可用作:

Determiners 限定詞 *Five people were hurt in the accident.* 事故中有五人受了傷。| *the three largest companies in the US* 美國最大的三家公司 | *several hundred cars* 幾百輛小汽車

Pronouns 代（名）詞 *We invited a lot of people but only twelve came/only twelve of them came.* 我們邀請了許多人，但是（他們中）只來了十二個人。| *Do exercise five on page nine.* 做第九頁上的練習五。

Nouns 名詞 *Six can be divided by two and three.* 六可以被三和二整除[除盡]。| *Three twos make six.* 三乘二等於六。

What numbers represent 數字表示甚麼

Numbers are often used on their own to show:
不加任何量詞等的數字本身常用來表示:

Price 價格	*It costs eight seventy-five* (= 8 pounds 75 pence or 8 dollars 75 cents: £8.75 or $8.75). 這值8鎊75便士 [8美元75美分]。
Time 時間	*We left at two twenty-five* (= 25 minutes after 2 o'clock). 我們在2點25分離開。
Age 年齡	*She's forty-six* (= 46 years old). 她46歲。| *He's in his sixties* (= between 60 and 69 years old). 他60多歲。
Size 尺寸	*This shirt is a thirty-eight* (= size 38). 這件襯衣是38號的。
Temperature 溫度	*The temperature fell to minus fourteen* (= –14°). 溫度降至零下14度。| *The temperature was in the mid-thirties* (= about 34–36°). 溫度在35度上下。
The score in a game 比賽得分	*Becker won the first set six-three* (= by six games to three: 6–3). 貝克爾以6比3贏了第一盤。
Something marked with the stated number 標有某個數字的事物	*She played two nines and an eight* (= playing cards marked with these numbers). 她打出兩張9和一張8。
A set or group of the stated number 組 [枝等]	*The teacher divided us into fours* (= groups of 4). 老師把我們分成四人一組。| *You can buy cigarettes in tens or twenties* (= in packets containing 10 or 20). 你可以買10枝或20枝包裝的香煙。

Roman numerals 羅馬數字

I *(i)* = 1
II *(ii)* = 2
III *(iii)* = 3
IV *(iv)* = 4
V *(v)* = 5
VI *(vi)* = 6
IX *(ix)* = 9
X *(x)* = 10
XI *(xi)* = 11
XV *(xv)* = 15
XIX *(xix)* = 19
XX *(xx)* = 20
XL *(xl)* = 40
L *(l)* = 50
XC *(xc)* = 90
XCIX *(xcix)* = 99
C *(c)* = 100
D *(d)* = 500
CM *(cm)* = 900
M *(m)* = 1000

MCMXCIX = 1999
MDCCCI = 1801
MM = 2000

$\bar{X}$ = 10 × 1,000 = 10,000
$\bar{C}$ = 100 × 1,000 = 100,000
$\bar{M}$ = 1,000 × 1,000 = 1,000,000

Table 2 附錄 2

Weights and measures 度量衡單位

The words in **dark type** are the ones that are most commonly used in general speech.
排黑體字母的為口語中最常用的單位。

METRIC 公制

Units of length 長度單位

	1 **millimetre** (毫米[公厘])	= 0.03937 inch (英寸[吋])
10 mm	= 1 **centimetre** (厘米[公分])	= 0.3937 inch (英寸[吋])
10 cm	= 1 decimetre (分米[公寸])	= 3.937 inches (英寸[吋])
10 dm	= 1 **metre** (米[公尺])	= 39.37 inches (英寸[吋])
10 m	= 1 decametre (十米[公丈])	= 10.94 yards (碼)
10 dam	= 1 hectometre (百米[公引])	= 109.4 yards (碼)
10 hm	= 1 **kilometre** (千米[公里])	= 0.6214 mile (英里[哩])

Units of weight 重量單位

	1 **milligram** (毫克[公絲])	= 0.015 grain (格令[喱])
10 mg	= 1 centigram (厘克[公毫])	= 0.154 grain (格令[喱])
10 cg	= 1 decigram (分克[公銖])	= 1.543 grains (格令[喱])
10 dg	= 1 **gram** (克[公克])	= 15.43 grains (格令[喱]) = 0.035 ounce (盎司)
10 g	= 1 decagram (十克[公錢])	= 0.353 ounce (盎司)
10 dag	= 1 hectogram (百克[公兩])	= 3.527 ounces (盎司)
10 hg	= 1 **kilogram** (千克[公斤])	= 2.205 pounds (磅)
1000 kg	= 1 **tonne** (噸) (metric ton (公噸))	= 0.984 (long) ton (長噸)
		= 2204.62 pounds (磅)

Units of capacity 容量單位

	1 millilitre (毫升[公撮])	= 0.00176 pint (品脱)
10 ml	= 1 centilitre (厘升[公勺])	= 0.0176 pint (品脱)
10 cl	= 1 decilitre (分升[公合])	= 0.176 pint (品脱)
10 dl	= 1 **litre** (升[公升])	= 1.76 pints (品脱) = 0.22 UK gallon (加侖)
10 l	= 1 decalitre (十升[公斗])	= 2.20 gallons (加侖)
10 dal	= 1 hectolitre (百升[公石])	= 22.0 gallons (加侖)
10 hl	= 1 kilolitre (千升[公秉])	= 220.0 gallons (加侖)

Square measure 面積單位

	1 square millimetre (平方毫米[平方公厘])	= 0.00155 square inch (平方英寸)
100 mm²	= 1 square centimetre (平方厘米[平方公分])	= 0.1550 square inch (平方英寸)
100 cm²	= 0.01 square metre (平方米[平方公尺])	= 0.01196 square yard (平方碼)
100 m²	= 1 are (公畝)	= 119.6 square yards (平方碼)
100 ares	= 1 **hectare** (公頃)	= 2.471 acres (英畝)
100 ha	= 1 square kilometre (平方公里)	= 247.1 acres (英畝)

Cubic measure 體積單位

		1 cubic centimetre (立方厘米[立方公分])	= 0.06102 cubic inch (立方英寸)
1000 cm^3	=	1 cubic decimetre (立方分米[立方公寸])	= 0.03532 cubic foot (立方英尺)
1000 dm^3	=	1 cubic metre (立方米[立方公尺])	= 1.308 cubic yards (立方碼)

Circular measure 圓弧單位

	1 microradian (微弧度)	= 0.206 seconds (秒)
1000 μrad	= 1 milliradian (毫弧度)	= 3.437 minutes (分)
1000 mrad	= 1 radian (弧度)	= 57.296 degrees (度) = 180/π degrees (度)

Metric prefixes 公制詞首

	Abbreviation 縮寫	*Factor* 階乘, 因子		*Abbreviation* 縮寫	*Factor* 階乘, 因子
tera- 太拉, 百億	T	10^{12}	centi- 厘	c	10^{-2}
giga- 吉, 十億	G	10^{9}	milli- 毫	m	10^{-3}
mega-百萬	M	10^{6}	micro- 微	μ	10^{-6}
kilo- 千	k	10^{3}	nano- 納 (諾)	n	10^{-9}
hecto- 百	h	10^{2}	pico- 皮 (可)	p	10^{-12}
deca- 十	da	10^{1}	femto- 飛 (母托)	f	10^{-15}
deci- 分	d	10^{-1}	atto- 阿 (托)	a	10^{-18}

BRITISH AND AMERICAN 英、美制

Units of length 長度單位

	1 **inch** (英寸[吋])	= 2.54 cm
12 inches (英寸[吋])	= 1 **foot** (英尺[呎])	= 0.3048 m
3 feet (英尺[呎])	= 1 **yard** (碼)	= 0.9144 m
$5^1/_2$ yards (碼)	= 1 rod, pole, or perch (桿)	= 5.029 m
22 yards (碼)	= 1 chain (鏈)	= 20.12 m
10 chains (鏈)	= 1 furlong (浪)	= 0.2012 km
8 furlongs (浪)	= 1 **mile** (英里[哩])	= 1.609 km
6076.12 feet (英尺[呎])	= 1 nautical mile (海里[海哩])	= 1852 m

Units of weight 重量單位

	1 grain (格令[喱])	= 64.8 mg
	1 dram (打蘭[英錢])	= 1.772 g
16 drams (打蘭[英錢])	= 1 **ounce** (盎司)	= 28.35 g
16 ounces (盎司)	= 1 **pound** (磅)	= 0.4536 kg
14 pounds (磅)	= 1 stone (英石[呫])	= 6.350 kg
2 stones (英石[呫])	= 1 quarter (夸特)	= 12.70 kg
4 quarters (夸特)	= 1 (long) **hundredweight** (長擔)	= 50.80 kg
20 hundredweight (英擔)	= 1 (long) **ton** (長噸)	= 1.016 tonnes
100 pounds (磅)	= 1 (short) **hundredweight** (短擔)	= 45.36 kg
2000 pounds (磅)	= 1 (short) **ton** (短噸)	= 0.9072 tonnes

The short hundredweight and ton are more common in the US.
美國多用短擔和短噸。

Units of capacity 容量單位

	1 fluid ounce (液盎司)	= 28.41 cm³
5 fluid ounces (液盎司)	= 1 gill (吉耳)	= 0.1421 dm³
4 gills (吉耳)	= 1 **pint** (品脫)	= 0.5683 dm³
2 pints (品脫)	= 1 **quart** (夸脫)	= 1.137 dm³
4 quarts (夸脫)	= 1 (UK) **gallon** (英加侖)	= 4.546 dm³
231 cubic inches (立方英寸)	= 1 (US) **gallon** (美加侖)	= 3.785 dm³
8 gallons (加侖)	= 1 bushel (蒲式耳)	= 36.369 dm³

Square measure 面積量度單位

	1 square inch (平方英寸)	= 645.16 mm²
144 square inches (平方英寸)	= 1 square foot (平方英尺)	= 0.0929 m²
9 square feet (平方英尺)	= 1 square yard (平方碼)	= 0.8361 m²
4840 square yards (平方碼)	= 1 acre (英畝)	= 4047 m²
640 acres (英畝)	= 1 square mile (平方英里)	= 259 ha

Cubic measure 體積量度單位

	1 cubic inch (立方英寸)	= 16.39 cm³
1728 cubic inches (立方英寸)	= 1 cubic foot (立方英尺)	= 0.02832 m³
		= 28.32 dm³
27 cubic feet (立方英尺)	= 1 cubic yard (立方碼)	= 0.7646 m³
		= 764.6 dm³

Circular measure 圓弧單位

	1 second (秒)	= 4.860 μrad
60 seconds (秒)	= 1 minute (分)	= 0.2909 μrad
60 minutes (分)	= 1 degree (度)	= 17.45 μrad
		= π /180 rad
45 degrees (度)	= 1 oxtant (八分之一圓)	= π /4 rad
60 degrees (度)	= 1 sextant (六分之一圓)	= π /3 rad
90 degrees (度)	= 1 quadrant or (象限) 或 1 right angle (直角)	= π /2 rad
360 degrees (度)	= 1 circle or 1 circumference (圓周)	= 2π rad
1 grade or gon (百分度)	= 1/100th of a right angle (百分之一直角)	= π /200 rad

US dry measure 美制乾量單位

1 pint (品脫)	= 0.9689 UK pint (英品脫)	= 0.5506 dm³
1 bushel (蒲式耳)	= 0.9689 UK bushel (英蒲式耳)	= 35.238 dm³

US liquid measure 美制液量單位

1 fluid ounce (液盎司)	= 1.0408 UK fluid ounces (英液盎司)
	= 0.0296 dm³
16 fluid ounces (液盎司)	= 1 pint (品脫) = 0.8327 UK pint (英品脫)
	= 0.4732 dm³
8 pints (品脫)	= 1 gallon (加侖) = 0.8327 UK gallon (英加侖)
	= 3.7853 dm³

Temperature 溫度

°*Fahrenheit* (華氏) $= \left(\frac{9}{5} \times X°C\right) + 32$ °*Celsius* (攝氏) $= \frac{5}{9} \times \left(X°F - 32\right)$

Table 3 附錄 3

Military ranks 軍銜

Royal Navy 皇家海軍	US Navy 美國海軍	British Army 英國陸軍	US Army 美國陸軍
Admiral of the Fleet 海軍元帥	Fleet Admiral 海軍五星上將	Field-Marshal 陸軍元帥	General of the Army 陸軍五星上將
Admiral 上將	Admiral 上將	General 上將	General 上將
Vice-Admiral 中將	Vice Admiral 中將	Lieutenant-General 中將	Lieutenant General 中將
Rear-Admiral 少將	Rear Admiral 少將	Major-General 少將	Major General 少將
Commodore 准將	Commodore 准將	Brigadier 准將	Brigadier General 准將
Captain 上校	Captain 上校	Colonel 上校	Colonel 上校
Commander 中校	Commander 中校	Lieutenant-Colonel 中校	Lieutenant Colonel 中校
Lieutenant-Commander 少校	Lieutenant Commander 少校	Major 少校	Major 少校
Lieutenant 上尉	Lieutenant 上尉	Captain 上尉	Captain 上尉
Sub-Lieutenant 中尉	Lieutenant Junior Grade 中尉	Lieutenant 中尉	1st Lieutenant 中尉
Midshipman 候補少尉	Ensign 少尉	2nd Lieutenant 少尉	2nd Lieutenant 少尉
–	Chief Warrant Officer 一級准尉	–	Chief Warrant Officer 一級准尉
Fleet Chief Petty Officer 海軍總上士	Warrant Officer 二級准尉	Warrant Officer 1st Class 一級准尉	Warrant Officer 二級准尉
–	Master Chief Petty Officer 一級軍士長	Warrant Officer 2nd Class 二級准尉	–
–	Senior Chief Petty Officer 二級軍士長	Staff Sergeant 上士	Sergeant Major 軍士長
Chief Petty Officer 上士	Chief Petty Officer 三級軍士長	Sergeant 中士	Master Sergeant 一級軍士長
Petty Officer 軍士	Petty Officer 1st Class 上士	–	1st Sergeant 二級軍士長
–	Petty Officer 2nd Class 中士	–	Sergeant 1st Class 三級軍士長
Leading Seaman 上等水兵	Petty Officer 3rd Class 下士	–	Staff Sergeant 上士
Able Seaman 一等水兵	Seaman 一等兵	–	Sergeant 中士
Ordinary Seaman 二等水兵	Seaman Apprentice 二等兵	Corporal 下士	Corporal 下士
Junior Seaman 水兵	Seaman Recruit 三等兵	Lance Corporal 一等兵	Private 1st Class 一等兵
		Private 二等兵	Private 士兵

RAF 皇家空軍	USAF 美國空軍	Royal Marines 皇家海軍陸戰隊	US Marine Corps 美國海軍陸戰隊
Marshal of the Royal Air Force 空軍元帥	General of the Airforce 空軍五星上將	General 上將	General 上將
Air Chief Marshal 上將	General 上將	Lieutenant-General 中將	Lieutenant General 中將
Air Marshal 中將	Lieutenant General 中將	Major-General 少將	Major General 少將
Air Vice Marshal 少將	Major General 少將	Brigadier 准將	Brigadier General 准將
Air Commodore 准將	Brigadier General 准將	Colonel 上校	Colonel 上校
Group Captain 上校	Colonel 上校	Lieutenant-Colonel 中校	Lieutenant Colonel 中校
Wing Commander 中校	Lieutenant Colonel 中校	Major 少校	Major 少校
Squadron Leader 少校	Major 少校	Captain 上尉	Captain 上尉
Flight Lieutenant 上尉	Captain 上尉	Lieutenant 中尉	1st Lieutenant 中尉
Flying Officer 中尉	First Lieutenant 中尉	2nd Lieutenant 少尉	2nd Lieutenant 少尉
Pilot Officer 少尉	Second Lieutenant 少尉	–	Chief Warrant Officer 一級准尉
–	Chief Warrant Officer 准尉	Warrant Officer 1st Class 一級准尉	Warrant Officer 二級准尉
Warrant Officer 准尉	Chief Master Sergeant 一級軍士長	Warrant Officer 2nd Class 二級准尉	–
–	Senior Master Sergeant 二級軍士長	Colour Sergeant 上士	Sergeant Major 軍士長
Flight Sergeant 上士	Master Sergeant 三級軍士長	–	Master Gunnery Sergeant 一級軍士長
Chief Technician 總技術軍士	Technical Sergeant 上士		
Sergeant 中士	Staff Sergeant 中士	Sergeant 中士	Master Sergeant 二級軍士長
Corporal 下士	Airman 1st Class 一等兵	–	1st Sergeant 三級軍士長
Junior Technician 初級技術軍士	–	–	Gunnery Sergeant 槍砲軍士
Senior Aircraftman 一等兵	Airman 2nd Class 二等兵	–	Staff Sergeant 上士
Leading Aircraftman 二等兵	Airman 3rd Class 三等兵	–	Sergeant 中士
Aircraftman 新兵	Airman Basic 空軍士兵	Corporal 下士	Corporal 下士
		–	Lance Corporal 准下士
		Lance Corporal 一等兵	Private 1st Class 一等兵
		Marine 士兵	Private 二等兵

Table 4 附錄 4

Word formation 構詞法

In English there are many word beginnings (prefixes) and word endings (suffixes) that can be added to a word to change its meaning or its word class. The most common ones are shown here, with examples of how they are used in the process of word formation. Many more are listed in the dictionary. 在英語中有許多詞頭 [前綴] 和詞尾 [後綴] 可加在一個詞的前面或後面以改變其意義或詞性。此處列出最常見的一些, 並附有它們在構詞過程中如何使用的例證。更多的則列在本辭典的正文之中。

Verb formation 動詞的構成

The endings **-ize** and **-ify** can be added to many nouns and adjectives to form vebs, like this 詞尾 -ize 和 -ify 可加在許多名詞和形容詞之後構成動詞, 如:

American legal modern popular	**-ize**	Americanize legalize modernize popularize

They want to make the factory more **modern**. *They want to* **modernize** *the factory.* 他們要把該工廠現代化。

beauty liquid pure simple	**-ify**	beautify liquefy purify simplify

These tablets make the water **pure**. *They* **purify** *the water.* 這些藥片可以把水淨化。

Adverb formation 副詞的構成

The ending **-ly** can be added to most adjectives to form adverbs, like this 詞尾 -ly 可加在大多數形容詞之後構成副詞, 如:

easy main quick stupid	**-ly**	easily mainly quickly stupidly

His behaviour was **stupid**. *He behaved* **stupidly**. 他表現得很愚蠢。

Noun formation 名詞的構成

The endings **-er**, **-ment**, and **-ation** can be added to many verbs to form nouns, like this 詞尾 -er, -ment 和 -ation 可加在許多動詞之後構成名詞, 如:

drive fasten open teach	**-er**	driver fastener opener teacher

John **drives** *a bus. He is a bus* **driver**. 約翰駕駛公共汽車。他是公共汽車司機。
A can **opener** *is a tool for* **opening** *cans.* 開罐器是開罐頭的工具。

amaze develop pay retire	**-ment**	amazement development payment retirement

Children **develop** *very quickly. Their* **development** *is very quick.* 兒童發育得很快。

admire associate examine organize	**-ation**	admiration association examination organization

The doctor **examined** *me carefully. He gave me a careful* **examination**. 醫生仔細地給我作了檢查。

The endings **-ity** and **-ness** can be added to many adjectives to form nouns, like this 詞尾 -ity 和 -ness 可加在許多形容詞之後構成名詞, 如:

cruel odd pure stupid	**-ity** **-ty**	cruelty oddity purity stupidity

Don't be so **cruel**. *I hate* **cruelty**. 不要這麼殘忍。我討厭殘忍。

dark deaf happy kind	**-ness**	darkness deafness happiness kindness

It was very **dark**. *The* **darkness** *made it impossible to see.* 天色很黑。因天黑甚麼也看不見。

Adjective formation 形容詞的構成

The endings **-y**, **-ic**, **-ical**, **-ful**, and **-less** can be added to many nouns to form adjectives, like this 詞尾 -y, -ic, -ical, -ful 和 -less 可加在許多名詞之後構成形容詞, 如:

bush dirt hair smell	**-y**	bushy dirty hairy smelly

There was an awful **smell** *in the room. The room was very* **smelly**. 房間裡有一股難聞的氣味。

atom biology grammar poetry	**-ic** **-ical**	atomic biological grammatical poetic

This book contains exercises on **grammar**. *It contains* **grammatical** *exercises.* 這本書裡有一些語法練習。

pain hope care	**-ful**	painful hopeful careful

His broken leg caused him a lot of **pain**. *It was very* **painful**. 他的腿摔斷了, 很疼。

pain hope care	**-less**	painless hopeless careless

The operation didn't cause her any **pain**. *It was* **painless**. 手術沒有使她感到疼痛。手術不疼。

The ending **-able** can be added to many verbs to form adjectives, like this 詞尾 -able 可加在許多動詞之後構成形容詞, 如:

wash love debate break	**-able**	washable lovable debatable breakable

You can **wash** *this coat. It's* **washable**. 你可以洗洗這件外套。它是可以洗的。

Opposites 反義詞

The following prefixes can be used in front of many words to produce an opposite meaning. Note, however, that the words formed in this way are not always EXACT opposites and may have a slightly different meaning. 下列的詞頭可加在許多詞之前以產生反義。然而要注意這樣構成的詞並不總是恰好反義的, 而可能有稍稍不同的含義。

un-	happy fortunate wind block	unhappy unfortunate unwind unblock

I'm not very **happy**. *In fact I'm very* **unhappy**. 我不太高興。事實上我很不高興。

in- **im-** **il-** **ir-**	efficient possible literate regular	inefficient impossible illiterate irregular

It's just not **possible** *to do that. It's* **impossible**. 不可能那樣做。這是不可能的。

dis-	agree approve honest	disagree disapprove dishonest

I don't **agree** *with everything you said. I* **disagree** *with the last part.* 我並不完全同意你的話。我不同意你說的最後一部分。

de-	centralize increase ascend inflate	decentralize decrease descend deflate

Increase *means to make or become larger in amount or number.* **Decrease** *means to make or become smaller in amount or number.* increase 意為 (使) 數量變大。decrease 意為 (使) 數量變小。

non-	sense payment resident conformist	nonsense nonpayment nonresident nonconformist

The hotel serves meals to **residents** (= people who are staying in the hotel) *only.* **Nonresidents** *are not allowed in.* 這家旅館只為住宿的客人提供膳食。非住宿者不得入內。

Table 5 附錄 5

The verb "be" 動詞 be

present 現在式

		questions 疑問式	*negatives* 否定式
I	I am, I'm	am I?	I am not, I'm not, aren't I?
you	you are, you're	are you?	you are not, you're not, you aren't
she/he/it	she is, he's	is she/he/it?	it is not, he's not, she isn't
we/they	we are, they're	are we/they?	we are not, they're not, we aren't

present participle 現在分詞: being

past 過去式

		questions 疑問式	*negatives* 否定式
I	I was	was I?	I was not, I wasn't
you	you were	were you?	you were not, you weren't
she/he/it	she was	was she/he/it?	she was not, it wasn't
we/they	we were	were we/they?	they were not, we weren't

past participle 過去分詞: been

Table 6 附錄 6

Irregular verbs 不規則動詞

verb 動詞	past tense 過去式	past participle 過去分詞
abide	abided, abode	abided
arise	arose	arisen
awake	awoke	awoken
be	*see Table 5* 見附錄 5	
bear	bore	borne
beat	beat	beaten
become	became	become
befall	befell	befallen
beget	begot (also 又作 begat *bibl*【聖經】)	begotten
begin	began	begun
behold	beheld	beheld
bend	bent	bent
bereave	bereft, bereaved	bereft, bereaved
beseech	besought, beseeched	besought, beseeched
beset	beset	beset
bestride	bestrode	bestridden
bet	bet, betted	bet, betted
betake	betook	betaken
bethink	bethought	bethought
bid	bade, bid	bid, bidden
bind	bound	bound
bite	bit	bitten
bleed	bled	bled
bless	blessed, blest	blessed, blest
blow	blew	blown
break	broke	broken
breed	bred	bred
bring	brought	brought
broadcast	broadcast	broadcast
browbeat	browbeat	browbeaten
build	built	built
burn	burned, burnt	burned, burnt
burst	burst	burst
bust	(*BrE*【英】) bust, (esp *AmE*【尤美】) busted	(*BrE*【英】) bust, (esp *AmE*【尤美】) busted
buy	bought	bought
can	*see dictionary entry* 見詞典內該條目	
cast	cast	cast
catch	caught	caught
chide	chided, chid	chided, chid, chidden
choose	chose	chosen
cleave	cleaved, cleft, clove	cleaved, cleft, cloven
cling	clung	clung
come	came	come
cost ①	cost	cost
could	*see dictionary entry* 見詞典內該條目	
creep	crept	crept
cut	cut	cut
deal	dealt /dɛlt; delt/	dealt

verb 動詞	**past tense** 過去式	**past participle** 過去分詞
dig	dug	dug
dive	dived, (*AmE*【美】) dove	dived
do	did	done
draw	drew	drawn
dream	dreamed, dreamt	dreamed, dreamt
drink	drank	drunk
drive	drove	driven
dwell	dwelt, dwelled	dwelt, dwelled
eat	ate	eaten
fall ②	fell	fallen
feed	fed	fed
feel	felt	felt
fight	fought	fought
find	found	found
flee	fled	fled
fling	flung	flung
fly	flew	flown
forbear	forbore	forborne
forbid	forbade	forbidden
forecast	forecast	forecast
foresee	foresaw	foreseen
foretell	foretold	foretold
forget	forgot	forgotten
forgive	forgave	forgiven
forego	forewent	foregone
forsake	forsook	forsaken
forswear	forswore	forsworn
freeze	froze	frozen
gainsay	gainsaid	gainsaid
get	got	got (also 又作 gotten *AmE*【美】)
gird	girded, girt	girded, girt
give	gave	given
go	went	gone
grind	ground	ground
grow	grew	grown
hamstring	hamstrung	hamstrung
hang	hung	hung
have	had	had
hear	heard	heard
heave	heaved, hove	heaved, hove
hew	hewed	hewn, hewed
hide	hid	hidden
hit	hit	hit
hold	held	held
hurt	hurt	hurt
input	inputted, input	inputted, input
inset	inset, insetted	inset, insetted
interbreed	interbred	interbred
interweave	interwove	interwoven
keep	kept	kept
kneel	knelt, (esp *AmE*【尤美】) kneeled	knelt, (esp *AmE*【尤美】) kneeled
knit	knitted, knit	knitted, knit
know	knew	known
lay ③	laid	laid
lead	led	led
lean	leaned (also 又作 leant esp	leaned (also 又作 leant esp

verb 動詞	past tense 過去式	past participle 過去分詞
	BrE【尤英】)	*BrE*【尤英】)
leap	leapt, (esp *AmE*【尤美】) leaped	leapt, (esp *AmE*【尤美】) leaped
learn	learned, learnt	learned, learnt
leave	left	left
lend	lent	lent
let	let	let
lie ④	lay	lain
light	lit, lighted	lit, lighted
lose	lost	lost
make	made	made
may	*see dictionary entry* 見詞典內該條目	
mean	meant	meant
meet	met	met
might	*see dictionary entry* 見詞典內該條目	
miscast	miscast	miscast
mishear	misheard	misheard
mislay	mislaid	mislaid
mislead	misled	misled
misread	misread	misread
misspell	misspelt, misspelled	misspelt, misspelled
misspend	misspent	misspent
mistake	mistook	mistaken
misunderstand	misunderstood	misunderstood
mow	mowed	mown, mowed
outbid	outbid	outbid
outdo	outdid	outdone
outgrow	outgrew	outgrown
outride	outrode	outridden
outrun	outran	outrun
outsell	outsold	outsold
outshine	outshone	outshone
overbear	overbore	overborne
overcast	overcast	overcast
overcome	overcame	overcome
overdo	overdid	overdone
overdraw	overdrew	overdrawn
overeat	overate	overeaten
overhang	overhung	overhung
overhear	overheard	overheard
overlay	overlaid	overlaid
overload	overloaded	overloaded, overladen
overpay	overpaid	overpaid
override	overrode	overridden
overrun	overran	overrun
oversee	oversaw	overseen
oversell	oversold	oversold
overshoot	overshot	overshot
oversleep	overslept	overslept
overtake	overtook	overtaken
overthrow	overthrew	overthrown
partake	partook	partaken
pay	paid	paid
plead	pleaded, (esp *AmE*【尤美】) pled	pleaded, (esp *AmE*【尤美】) pled
pre-set	pre-set	pre-set
proofread	proofread	proofread
prove	proved	proved (also 又作 proven *AmE*【美】)

verb 動詞	past tense 過去式	past participle 過去分詞
put	put	put
quit	quit (also 又作 quitted *BrE*【英】)	quit (also 又作 quitted *BrE*【英】)
read	read /rɛd; red/	read /rɛd; red/
rebind	rebound	rebound
rebuild	rebuilt	rebuilt
recast	recast	recast
redo	redid	redone
relay	relaid	relaid
remake	remade	remade
rend	rent	rent
repay	repaid	repaid
rerun	reran	rerun
resell	resold	resold
reset	reset	reset
resit	resat	resat
retell	retold	retold
rethink	rethought	rethought
rewind	rewound	rewound
rewrite	rewrote	rewritten
rid	rid, ridded	rid
ride	rode	ridden
ring	rang	rung
rise	rose	risen
run	ran	run
saw	sawed	(esp *BrE*【尤英】) sawn, (esp *AmE*【尤美】) sawed
say	said	said
see ⑤	saw	seen
seek	sought	sought
sell	sold	sold
send	sent	sent
set	set	set
sew	sewed	sewn (also 又作 sewed *AmE*【美】)
shake	shook	shaken
shall	*see dictionary entry* 見詞典內該條目	
shear	sheared	shorn, sheared
shed	shed	shed
shine	shone	shone
shit	shit, shat	shit, shat
shoe	shod	shod
shoot	shot	shot
should	*see dictionary entry* 見詞典內該條目	
show	showed	shown
shrink	shrank	shrunk
shut	shut	shut
sing	sang	sung
sink	sank, sunk	sunk
sit	sat	sat
slay	slew	slain
sleep	slept	slept
slide	slid	slid
sling	slung	slung
slink	slunk	slunk
slit	slit	slit
smell	(esp *BrE*【尤英】) smelt, (esp *AmE*【尤美】) smelled	(esp *BrE*【尤英】) smelt, (esp *AmE*【尤美】) smelled

verb 動詞	past tense 過去式	past participle 過去分詞
smite	smote	smitten
sneak	sneaked (also 又作 snuck *AmE*【美】)	sneaked (also 又作 snuck *AmE*【美】)
sow	sowed	sown, sowed
speak	spoke	spoken
speed	sped, speeded	sped, speeded
spell	(esp *BrE*【尤英】) spelt, (esp *AmE*【尤美】) spelled	(esp *BrE*【尤英】) spelt, (esp *AmE*【尤美】) spelled
spend	spent	spent
spill	(esp *BrE*【尤英】) spilt, (esp *AmE*【尤美】) spilled	(esp *BrE*【尤英】) spilt, (esp *AmE*【尤美】) spilled
spin	spun	spun
spit	spat (also 又作 spit *AmE*【美】)	spat (also 又作 spit *AmE*【美】)
split	split	split
spoil	spoiled, spoilt	spoiled, spoilt
spoon-feed	spoon-fed	spoon-fed
spotlight	spotlighted, spotlit	spotlighted, spotlit
spread	spread	spread
spring	sprang (also 又作 sprung *AmE*【美】)	sprung
stand	stood	stood
steal	stole	stolen
stick	stuck	stuck
sting	stung	stung
stink	stank	stunk
strew	strewed	strewn, strewed
stride	strode	stridden
strike	struck	struck
string	strung	strung
strive	strove	striven
swear	swore	sworn
sweep	swept	swept
swell	swelled	swollen
swim	swam	swum
swing	swung	swung
take	took	taken
teach	taught	taught
tear	tore	torn
tell	told	told
think	thought	thought
thrive	thrived, throve	thrived
throw	threw	thrown
thrust	thrust	thrust
tread	trod	trodden
unbend	unbent	unbent
unbind	unbound	unbound
undergo	underwent	undergone
underlie	underlay	underlaid
undersell	undersold	undersold
understand	understood	understood
undertake	undertook	undertaken
underwrite	underwrote	underwritten
undo	undid	undone
unwind	unwound	unwound
uphold	upheld	upheld
upset	upset	upset
wake	woke (also 又作 waked *AmE*【美】)	woken (also 又作 waked *AmE*【美】)
waylay	waylaid	waylaid

wear	wore	worn
weave	wove	woven
wed	wedded, wed	wedded, wed
weep	wept	wept
wet	wetted, wet	wetted, wet
will	*see dictionary entry* 見詞典內該條目	
win	won	won
wind ⑥ /waɪnd; waɪnd/	wound	wound
withdraw	withdrew	withdrawn
withhold	withheld	withheld
withstand	withstood	withstood
would	*see dictionary entry* 見詞典內該條目	
wreak	wreaked, wrought	wreaked, wrought
wring	wrung	wrung
write	wrote	written

註: ① 注意與規則動詞 cost（估價）的不同: I've costed the work.（我已對工程估了價。）
② 注意與規則動詞 fell（砍伐）的不同: They've felled that tree.（他們已砍倒了那棵樹。）
③ 注意現在式 lay (laid, laid) 不要與 lie (lay, lain) 的過去式混淆。
④ 注意與規則動詞 lie（說謊）(lied, lied) 的不同: He lied to me.（他對我撒謊。）
⑤ 比較 see（看見）(saw, seen) 和 saw（鋸）(sawed, sawn/sawed)。
⑥ 注意與規則動詞 wind（使氣急）的不同: I was winded by the blow.（我被那拳打得喘不過氣來。）

Table 7 附錄 7

Geographical names 地名

This list of geographical names is included to help advanced students in their reading of contemporary newspapers and magazines. 此地名表供高年級學生閱讀當代報紙雜誌使用。

Name 地名		**Adjective** 形容詞
Afghanistan /æf`gænəˌstæn; æf'gænɪ̥stɑːn/	阿富汗	Afghan /'æfgən; 'æfgæn/ *person* 人: Afghanistani /æf`gænəˌstænɪ; æfˌgænɪ̥'stɑːni/, Afghan
Africa /`æfrɪkə; 'æfrɪkə/	非洲	African /`æfrɪkən; 'æfrɪkən/
Alaska /ə`læskə; ə'læskə/	阿拉斯加	Alaskan /ə`læskən; ə'læskən/
Albania /æl`benɪə; æl'beɪniə/	阿爾巴尼亞	Albanian /æl`benɪən; æl'beɪniən/
Algeria /æl`dʒɪrɪə; æl'dʒɪəriə/	阿爾及利亞	Algerian /æl`dʒɪrɪən; æl'dʒɪəriən/
America /ə`mɛrɪkə; ə'merɪ̥kə/	美洲; 美國	American /ə`mɛrɪkən; ə'merɪ̥kən/
Andorra /æn`dɔrə; æn'dɔːrə/	安道爾	Andorran /æn`dɔrən; æn'dɔːrən/
Angola /æŋ`golə; æŋ'gəʊlə/	安哥拉	Angolan /æŋ`golən; æŋ'gəʊlən/
Antarctic /ænt`ɑrktɪk; æn'tɑːktɪk/	南極（地區）	Antarctic
Antigua /æn`tigə; æn'tiːgə/	安提瓜島	Antiguan /æn`tigən; æn'tiːgən/
Arctic /`ɑrktɪk; 'ɑːktɪk/	北極（地區）	Arctic
Argentina /ˌɑrdʒən`tinə; ˌɑːdʒən'tiːnə/	阿根廷	Argentinian /ˌɑrdʒən`tɪnɪən; ˌɑːdʒən'tɪniən/
Armenia /ɑr`minɪə; ɑː'miːniə/	亞美尼亞	Armenian /ɑr`minɪən; ɑː'miːniən/
Asia /`eʃə, `eʒə; 'eɪʃə, -ʒə/	亞洲	Asian /`eʃən, `eʒən; 'eɪʃən, 'eɪʒən/
Atlantic /ət`læntɪk; ət'læntɪk/	大西洋	Atlantic
Australia /ɔ`streljə; ɒ'streɪliə/	澳大利亞, 澳洲	Australian /ɔ`streljən; ɒ'streɪliən/
Austria /`ɔstrɪə; 'ɒstriə/	奧地利	Austrian /`ɔstrɪən; 'ɒstriən/
Azerbaijan /ˌɑzɚbaɪ`dʒɑn; ˌæzəbaɪ'dʒɑːn/	阿塞拜疆	Azerbaijani /ˌɑzɚbaɪ`dʒɑnɪ; ˌæzəbaɪ'dʒɑːni◂/
Bahamas /bə`hɑməz; bə'hɑːməz/	巴哈馬	Bahamian /bə`hemɪən; bə'heɪmiən/
Bahrain /bɑ`ren; bɑː'reɪn/	巴林	Bahraini /bɑ`renɪ; bɑː'reɪni/
Baltic /`bɔltɪk; 'bɔːltɪk/	波羅的海	Baltic
Bangladesh /`bæŋgləˌdɛʃ; ˌbæŋglə'deʃ/	孟加拉國	Bangladeshi *person* 人: Bangladeshi /`bæŋgləˌdɛʃɪ; ˌbæŋglə'deʃi/
Barbados /bɑr`bedoz; bɑː'beɪdɒs/	巴巴多斯, 巴貝多	Barbadian /bɑr`bedɪən; bɑː'beɪdiən/
Belarus /ˌbjɛlə`rus; ˌbelə'ruːs/ (Belorussia) /ˌbɛlo`rʌʃə; ˌbeləʊ'rʌʃə/	白俄羅斯	Belorussian /ˌbɛlo`rʌʃən; ˌbeləʊ'rʌʃən/
Belgium /`bɛldʒɪəm; 'beldʒəm/	比利時	Belgian /`bɛldʒən; 'beldʒən/
Belize /bɛ`liz; bə'liːz/	伯利茲	Belizean /bɛ`lizɪən; bə'liːziən/
Benin /bə`nɪn; be'niːn/	貝寧	Beninese /ˌbɑnɪ`niz; ˌbenɪ'niːz◂/
Bermuda /bɚ`mjudə; bə'mjuːdə/	百慕大, 百慕達	Bermudan /bɚ`mjudn; bə'mjuːdn/
Bhutan /bu`tɑn; buː'tɑːn/	不丹	Bhutanese /ˌbutə`niz; ˌbuːtə'niːz◂/
Bolivia /bə`lɪvɪə; bə'lɪviə/	玻利維亞	Bolivian /bə`lɪvɪən; bə'lɪviən/
Bosnia and Herzegovina /`bɑznɪə ənd ˌhɝtsəgo`vinə; ˌbɒzniə ənd ˌhɜːtsəgəʊ'viːnə/	波斯尼亞－黑塞哥維那	Bosnian /`bɑznɪən; 'bɒzniən/
Botswana /bɑts`wɑnɑ; bɒt'swɑːnə/	博茨瓦納, 波札那	Tswana /`tswɑnə; 'tswɑːnə, 'swɑː-/ *person* 人: *sing.* 單數= Motswana /mɑt`swɑnə; mɒt'swɑːnə/ *pl.* 複數= Batswana /bæt`swɑnə; bæt'swɑːnə/

Name 地名		**Adjective** 形容詞
Brazil /brə`zɪl; brə'zɪl/	巴西	Brazilian /brə`zɪljən; brə'zɪliən/
Brunei /brʊ`naɪ; 'bru:naɪ/	文萊	Bruneian /brʊ`naɪən; bru:'naɪən/
Bulgaria /bʌl`gɛrɪə; bʌl'geəriə/	保加利亞	Bulgarian /bʌl`gɛrɪən; bʌl'geəriən/
Burkina Faso /bur͵kinə `fæso; bɜ:͵ki:nə 'fæsəʊ/	布基納法索	Burkina *person* 人: Burkinabe /͵burkinæ`be; ͵bɜ:ki:næ'beɪ/
Burma /`bɝmə; 'bɜ:mə/ former name of Myanmar	緬甸 〔Myanmar 的舊稱〕	
Burundi /bə`rʌndɪ; bʊ'rʊndi/	布隆迪, 蒲隆地	Burundian /bə`rʌndɪən; bʊ'rʊndiən/
Cambodia /kæm`bodɪə; kæm'bəʊdiə/	柬埔寨	Cambodian /kæm`bodɪən; kæm'bəʊdiən/
Cameroon /͵kæmə`run; ͵kæmə'ru:n/	喀麥隆	Cameroonian /͵kæmə`runɪən; ͵kæmə'ru:niən◂/
Canada /`kænədə; 'kænədə/	加拿大	Canadian /kə`nedɪən; kə'neɪdiən/
Cape Verde /͵kep `vɝd; keɪp 'vɜ:d/	佛得角	Cape Verdean /͵kep`vɝdɪən; keɪp 'vɜ:diən/
Caribbean /͵kærə`biən; ͵kærɪ'bi:ən◂/	加勒比	Caribbean
Cayman Islands /`kemən `aɪləndz; 'keɪmən ͵aɪləndz/	開曼羣島	Cayman Island /͵kemən `aɪlənd; ͵keɪmən 'aɪlənd◂/ *person* 人: Cayman Islander /͵kemən `aɪləndɚ; ͵keɪmən 'aɪləndə/
Central African Republic /͵sɛntrəl ͵æfrɪkən rɪ`pʌblɪk; ͵sentrəl ͵æfrɪkən rɪ'pʌblɪk/	中非共和國	
Chad /tʃæd; tʃæd/	乍得	Chadian /`tʃædɪən; 'tʃædiən/
Chile /`tʃɪlɪ; 'tʃɪli/	智利	Chilean /`tʃɪlɪən; 'tʃɪliən/
China /`tʃaɪnə; 'tʃaɪnə/	中國	Chinese /tʃaɪ`niz; ͵tʃaɪ'ni:z◂/
Colombia /kə`lʌmbɪə; kə'lʌmbiə/	哥倫比亞	Colombian /kə`lʌmbɪən; kə'lʌmbiən/
Congo /`kɑŋgo; 'kɒŋgəʊ/	剛果	Congolese /͵kɑŋgo`liz; ͵kɒŋgə'li:z◂/
Costa Rica /`kɑstə `rikə; ͵kɒstə 'ri:kə/	哥斯達黎加, 哥斯大黎加	Costa Rican /`kɑstə `rikn̩; ͵kɒstə 'ri:kən◂/
Croatia /kro`eʃə; krəʊ'eɪʃə/	克羅地亞	Croatian /kro`eʃən; krəʊ'eɪʃən/
Cuba /`kjubə; 'kju:bə/	古巴	Cuban /`kjubən; 'kju:bən/
Cyprus /`saɪprəs; 'saɪprəs/	塞浦路斯	Cypriot /`sɪprɪət; 'sɪpriət/
Czech Republic /͵tʃɛk rɪ`pʌblɪk; ͵tʃek rɪ'pʌblɪk/	捷克（共和國）	Czech /tʃɛk; tʃek/
Denmark /`dɛnmɑrk; 'denmɑ:k/	丹麥	Danish /`denɪʃ; 'deɪnɪʃ/ *person* 人: Dane /den; deɪn/
Djibouti /dʒɪ`butɪ; dʒɪ̵'bu:ti/	吉布提	Djiboutian /dʒə`butɪən; dʒɪ̵'bu:tiən/
Dominica /də`mɪnɪkə; ͵dɒmɪ̵'ni:kə/	多米尼加, 多明尼加	Dominican /də`mɪnɪkən; ͵dɒmɪ̵'ni:kən◂/
Dominican Republic /də`mɪnɪkən rɪ`pʌblɪk; də͵mɪnɪkən rɪ'pʌblɪk/	多米尼加共和國, 多明尼加共和國	Dominican /də`mɪnɪkən; də'mɪnɪkən/
Ecuador /`ɛkwə͵dɔr; 'ekwədɔ:/	厄瓜多爾	Ecuadorian /͵ɛkwə`dorɪən; ͵ekwə'dɔ:riən◂/
Egypt /`idʒəpt; 'i:dʒɪpt/	埃及	Egyptian /ɪ`dʒɪpʃən; ɪ'dʒɪpʃən/
El Salvador /ɛl`sælvə͵dɔr; el 'sælvə͵dɔ:/	薩爾瓦多	Salvadorian /͵sælvə`dorɪən; ͵sælvə'dɔ:riən◂/
Equatorial Guinea /͵ikwə`torɪəl `gɪnɪ; ͵ekwətɔ:riəl 'gɪni/	赤道幾內亞	Equatorial Guinean /͵ikwə`torɪəl 'gɪnɪən; ͵ekwətɔ:riəl 'gɪniən/
Eritrea /͵ɛrɪ`triə; ͵erɪ'treɪə/	厄立特里亞	Eritrean /͵ɛrɪ`treɪən; ͵erɪ'treɪən◂/
Estonia /ɛ`stonɪə; e'stəʊniə/	愛沙尼亞	Estonian /ɛ`stonɪən; e'stəʊniən/
Ethiopia /͵iθɪ`opɪə; ͵i:θi'əʊpiə/	埃塞俄比亞, 衣索比亞	Ethiopian /͵iθɪ`opɪən; ͵i:θi'əʊpiən◂/
Europe /`jʊrəp; 'jʊərəp/	歐洲	European /͵jʊrə`piən; ͵jʊərə'pi:ən◂/
Fiji /`fidʒi; 'fi:dʒi:/	斐濟	Fijian /fi`dʒiən; fi:'dʒi:ən/
Finland /`fɪnlənd; 'fɪnlənd/	芬蘭	Finnish /`fɪnɪʃ; 'fɪnɪʃ/ *person* 人: Finn /fɪn; fɪn/
France /fræns; frɑ:ns/	法國	French /frɛntʃ; frentʃ/ *person* 人: *sing.* 單數 = Frenchman /`frɛntʃmən; 'frentʃmən/

Name 地名		Adjective 形容詞
		(*fem.* 女性 -woman) /-ˏwʊmən; -ˌwʊmən/ *pl.* 複數= Frenchmen /ˋfrɛntʃmən; ˈfrentʃmən/ *people* 人民: French
Gabon /gaˋbõ; gæˈbɒn/	加蓬, 加彭	Gabonese /ˏgæbəˋniz; ˌgæbəˈniːz◂/
Gambia /ˋgæmbɪə; ˈgæmbiə/	岡比亞, 甘比亞	Gambian /ˋgæmbɪən; ˈgæmbiən/
Georgia /ˋdʒɔrdʒə; ˈdʒɔːdʒə/	格魯吉亞	Georgian /ˋdʒɔrdʒən; ˈdʒɔːdʒən/
Germany /ˋdʒɝmənɪ; ˈdʒɜːməni/	德國	German /ˋdʒɝmən; ˈdʒɜːmən◂/
Ghana /ˋgɑnə; ˈgɑːnə/	加納, 迦納	Ghanaian /gɑˋneɪən; gɑːˈneɪən/
Gibraltar /dʒɪˋbrɔltɚ; dʒɪˈbrɔːltə/	直布羅陀	Gibraltarian /dʒɪbrɔlˋtɛrɪən; ˌdʒɪbrɔːlˈteəriən/
Greece /gris; griːs/	希臘	Greek /grik; griːk/
Greenland /ˋgrinlənd; ˈgriːnlənd, -lænd/	格陵蘭 (島)	Greenlandic /grinˋlændɪk; griːnˈlændɪk/ *person* 人: Greenlander /ˋgrinləndɚ; ˈgriːnləndə/
Grenada /grɪˋnedə; grəˈneɪdə/	格林納達	Grenadian /grɪˋnedɪən; grəˈneɪdiən/
Guatemala /ˏgwɑtəˋmɑlə; ˌgwɑːtəˈmɑːlə/	危地馬拉, 瓜地瑪拉	Guatemalan /ˏgwɑtəˋmɑlən; ˌgwɑːtəˈmɑːlən◂/
Guiana /gɪˋɑnə; giˈɑːnə/	圭亞那 (高原)	Guianan /gɪˋɑnən; giˈɑːnən/
Guinea /ˋgɪnɪ; ˈgɪni/	幾內亞	Guinean /ˋgɪnɪən; ˈgɪniən/
Guinea-Bissau /ˏgɪnɪ bɪˋsaʊ; ˌgɪni bɪˈsaʊ/	幾內亞比紹	Guinea-Bissauan /ˏgɪnɪ bɪˋsaʊən; ˌgɪni bɪˈsaʊən/
Guyana /gaɪˋænə; gaɪˈænə/	圭亞那	Guyanese /gaɪæˋniz; ˌgaɪəˈniːz◂/
Haiti /ˋhetɪ; ˈheɪti/	海地	Haitian /ˋhetɪən; ˈheɪʃən/
Holland /ˋhɑlənd; ˈhɒlənd/ another name for 又作 The Netherlands	荷蘭	Dutch /dʌtʃ; dʌtʃ/
Honduras /hɑnˋdurəs; hɒnˈdjʊərəs/	洪都拉斯, 宏都拉斯	Honduran /hɑnˋdurən; hɒnˈdjʊərən/
Hong Kong /ˋhɑŋ ˋkɑŋ; ˌhɒŋ ˈkɒŋ/	香港	
Hungary /ˋhʌŋgrɪ; ˈhʌŋgəri/	匈牙利	Hungarian /hʌŋˋgɛrɪən; hʌŋˈgeəriən/
Iceland /ˋaɪslənd; ˈaɪslənd/	冰島	Icelandic /aɪsˋlændɪk; aɪsˈlændɪk/ *person* 人: Icelander /ˋaɪsˏlændɚ; ˈaɪsləndə/
India /ˋɪndɪə; ˈɪndiə/	印度	Indian /ˋɪndɪən; ˈɪndiən/
Indonesia /ˏɪndoˋniʃə, -ʒə; ˌɪndəˈniːʒə, -ziə/	印度尼西亞, 印尼	Indonesian /ˏɪndoˋniʃən, -zɪən; ˌɪndəˈniːʒən◂, -ziən◂/
Iran /ɪˋræn, iˋrɑn; ɪˈrɑːn, -æn/	伊朗	Iranian /ɪˋrenɪən; ɪˈreɪniən/
Iraq /ɪˋrɑk, ɪˋræk; ɪˈrɑːk, -æk/	伊拉克	Iraqi /ɪˋrɑkɪ; ɪˈrɑːki, -æki/
Irish Republic /ˏaɪrɪʃ rɪˋpʌblɪk; ˌaɪərɪʃ rɪˈpʌblɪk/	愛爾蘭共和國	Irish /ˋaɪrɪʃ; ˈaɪərɪʃ/ *person* 人: *sing.* 單數= Irishman /ˋaɪrɪʃmən; ˈaɪərɪʃmən/ (*fem.* 女性 -woman) /-ˏwʊmən; -ˌwʊmən/ *pl.* 複數= Irishmen /ˋaɪrɪʃmən; ˈaɪərɪʃmən/ *people* 人民 : Irish
Israel /ˋɪzrɪəl; ˈɪzreɪl/	以色列	Israeli /ɪzˋrelɪ; ɪzˈreɪli/
Italy /ˋɪtl̩ɪ; ˈɪtəli/	意大利, 義大利	Italian /ɪˋtæljən; ɪˈtæliən/
Ivory Coast /ˋaɪvərɪ kost; ˌaɪvəri ˈkəʊst/	象牙海岸	Ivorian /ˏaɪˋvorɪən; aɪˈvɔːriən/
Jamaica /dʒəˋmekə; dʒəˈmeɪkə/	牙買加	Jamaican /dʒəˋmekən; dʒəˈmeɪkən/
Japan /dʒəˋpæn; dʒəˈpæn/	日本	Japanese /ˏdʒæpəˋniz; ˌdʒæpəˈniːz◂/
Jordan /ˋdʒɔrdn̩; ˈdʒɔːdn/	約旦	Jordanian /dʒɔrˋdenɪən; dʒɔːˈdeɪniən/
Kazakhstan /ˏkɑzɑkˋstɑn; ˌkæzækˈstɑːn/	哈薩克	Kazakh /kəˋzæk; kəˈzæk, -ˈzɑːk/
Kenya /ˋkɛnjə, ˋkinjə; ˈkenjə, ˈkiː-/	肯尼亞	Kenyan /ˋkɛnjən, ˋkinjən; ˈkenjən, ˈkiː-/
Korea, North /ˏnɔrθ kəˋriə; ˌnɔːθ kəˈrɪə/	北韓	North Korean /ˏnɔrθ kəˋriən; ˌnɔːθ kəˈrɪən/
Korea, South /ˏsaʊθ kəˋriə; ˌsaʊθ kəˈrɪə/	南韓	South Korean /ˏsaʊθ kəˋriən; ˌsaʊθ kəˈrɪən/
Kuwait /kʊˋwaɪt; kʊˈweɪt/	科威特	Kuwaiti /kʊˋwetɪ; kʊˈweɪti/
Laos /laʊz; ˈlɑːɒs, laʊs/	老撾, 寮國	Laotian /leˋoʃən; ˈlaʊʃən/
Latvia /ˋlætvɪə; ˈlætviə/	拉脫維亞	Latvian /ˋlætvɪən; ˈlætviən/
Lebanon /ˋlɛbənən; ˈlebənən/	黎巴嫩	Lebanese /ˏlɛbəˋniz; ˌlebəˈniːz◂/

Name 地名		**Adjective** 形容詞
Lesotho /lə`sutu; lə'suːtuː/	萊索托	Sotho /`soto; 'suːtuː/ *person* 人: *sing.* 單數= Mosotho /mə`sutu; mə'suːtuː/ *pl.* 複數= Basotho /bə`sutu; bə'suːtuː/
Liberia /laɪ`bɪrɪə; laɪ'bɪəriə/	利比里亞, 賴比瑞亞	Liberian /laɪ`bɪrɪən; laɪ'bɪəriən/
Libya /`lɪbɪə; 'lɪbiə/	利比亞	Libyan /`lɪbɪən; 'lɪbiən/
Liechtenstein /`lɪktən,staɪn; 'lɪktənstaɪn/	列支敦士登, 列支敦斯登	Liechtenstein *person* 人: Liechtensteiner /`lɪktən,staɪnɚ; 'lɪktənstaɪnə/
Lithuania /,lɪθju`enɪə; ˌlɪθju'eɪniə/	立陶宛	Lithuanian /,lɪθju`enɪən; ˌlɪθju'eɪniən◂/
Luxemburg /`lʌksəm,bɝg; 'lʌksəmbɜːg/	盧森堡	Luxemburg *person* 人: Luxemburger /`lʌksəm,bɝgɚ; 'lʌksəmbɜːgə/
Macedonia /,mæsə`donɪə; ˌmæsɨ'dəʊniə/	馬其頓	Macedonian /,mæsə`donɪən; ˌmæsə'dəʊniən◂/
Madagascar /,mædə`gæskɚ; ˌmædə'gæskə/	馬達加斯加	Malagasy /,mælə`gæsɪ; ˌmælə'gæsi◂/
Malawi /mɑ`lɑwi; mə'lɑːwi/	馬拉維, 馬拉威	Malawian /mɑ`lɑwɪən; mə'lɑːwiən/
Malaysia /mə`leʒə; mə'leɪziə/	馬來西亞	Malaysian /mə`leʃən, -ʒən; mə'leɪziən/
Maldives /`mɔldivz; 'mɔːldiːvz/	馬爾代夫	Maldivian /mɔl`dɪvɪən; mɔːl'dɪviən/
Mali /`mɑlɪ; 'mɑːli/	馬里, 馬利	Malian /`mɑlɪən; 'mɑːliən/
Malta /`mɔltə; 'mɔːltə/	馬耳他, 馬爾他	Maltese /mɔl`tiz; ˌmɔːl'tiːz◂/
Marshall Islands /`mɑrʃəl ,aɪləndz; 'mɑːʃəl ˌaɪləndz/	馬紹爾羣島	Marshall Islander /`mɑrʃəl ,aɪləndɚ; ˌmɑːʃəl 'aɪləndə/
Mauritania /,mɔrɪ`tenɪə; ˌmɒrɨ'teɪniə/	毛里塔尼亞, 茅利塔尼亞	Mauritanian /,mɔrɪ`tenɪən; ˌmɒrɨ'teɪniən◂/
Mauritius /mɔ`rɪʃɪəs; mə'rɪʃəs, mɔː-/	毛里求斯, 模里西斯	Mauritian /mɔ`rɪʃɪən; mə'rɪʃən, mɔː-/
Mediterranean /,mɛdətə`renɪən; ˌmedɨtə'reɪniən◂/	地中海	Mediterranean
Melanesia /,mɛlə`niʒə; ˌmelə'niːziə/	美拉尼西亞	Melanesian /,mɛlə`niʒən; ˌmelə'niːziən◂/
Mexico /`mɛksɪ,ko; 'meksɪkəʊ/	墨西哥	Mexican /`mɛksɪkən; 'meksɪkən/
Micronesia /,maɪkro`niʒə; ˌmaɪkrəʊ'niːziə/	密克羅尼西亞	Micronesian /,maɪkrə`niʒən; ˌmaɪkrəʊ'niːziən, -ʒən/
Moldova /mɑl`dovə; mɒl'dəʊvə/	摩爾多瓦	Moldovian /mɑl`dovɪən; mɒl'dəʊviən/
Monaco /`mɑnə,ko; 'mɒnəkəʊ/	摩納哥	Monegasque /mɑnɪ`gæsk; ˌmɒnɪ'gæsk◂/
Mongolia /mɑŋ`goljə; mɒŋ'gəʊliə/	蒙古	Mongolian /mɑŋ`golɪən; mɒŋ'gəʊliən/ *person* 人: Mongolian or 或 Mongol /`mɑŋgəl; 'mɒŋgɒl, -gəl/
Montserrat /,mɑntsə`ræt; ˌmɒntse'ræt/	蒙特塞拉特島	Montserratian /,mɑntsə`reʃən; ˌmɒntse'reɪʃən◂/
Morocco /mə`rɑko; mə'rɒkəʊ/	摩洛哥	Moroccan /mə`rɑkən; mə'rɒkən/
Mozambique /,mozəm`bik; ˌməʊzəm'biːk/	莫桑比克	Mozambican /,mozəm`bikən; ˌməʊzəm'biːkən◂/
Myanmar /`mjænmɑr; 'mjænmɑː/	緬甸	Burmese /bɝ`miz; ˌbɜː'miːz◂/
Namibia /nə`mɪbɪə; nə'mɪbiə/	納米比亞	Namibian /nə`mɪbɪən; nə'mɪbiən/
Nauru /nɑ`uru, nɑ`ru; nɑː'uːruː, nɑː'ruː/	瑙魯, 諾魯	Nauruan /,neɪə`ruən; nɑː'uːruən, nɑː'ruːən/
Nepal /nɪ`pɔl; nɪ'pɔːl/	尼泊爾	Nepalese /,nɛpə`liz; ˌnepə'liːz◂/
The Netherlands /ðə `nɛðələndz; ðə 'neðələndz/	荷蘭	Dutch /dʌtʃ; dʌtʃ/ *person* 人: *sing.* 單數= Dutchman /`dʌtʃmən; 'dʌtʃmən/ (*fem.* 女性 -woman) /-,wʊmən; -ˌwʊmən/ *pl.* 複數= Dutchmen /`dʌtʃmən; 'dʌtʃmən/ *people* 人民 : Dutch
New Zealand /nju`zilənd; njuː'ziːlənd/	新西蘭, 紐西蘭	New Zealand, Maori /`maurɪ; 'maʊri/

Name 地名		Adjective 形容詞
		person 人: New Zealander /nju `zilǝndǝ˞; nju: 'zi:lǝndǝ/
Nicaragua /ˌnɪkǝ`rɑgwǝ; ˌnɪkǝ'ræɡjuǝ/	尼加拉瓜	Nicaraguan /ˌnɪkǝ`rɑgwǝn; ˌnɪkǝ'ræɡjuǝn◂/
Niger /`naɪdʒǝ˞, ni`ʒɛǝ; 'naɪdʒǝ, ni:'ʒeǝ/	尼日爾, 尼日	Nigerien /ni`ʒɛǝrɪǝn; ni:'ʒeǝriǝn/
Nigeria /naɪ`dʒɪrɪǝ; naɪ'dʒɪǝriǝ/	尼日利亞, 奈及利亞	Nigerian /naɪ`dʒɪrɪǝn; naɪ'dʒɪǝriǝn/
Norway /`nɔrwe; 'nɔ:weɪ/	挪威	Norwegian /nɔr`widʒǝn; nɔ:'wi:dʒǝn/
Oman /o`mæn; ǝʊ'mɑ:n/	阿曼	Omani /o`mænɪ; ǝʊ'mɑ:ni/
Pacific /pǝ`sɪfɪk; pǝ'sɪfɪk/	太平洋	Pacific
Pakistan /ˌpɑkɪ`stɑn, ˌpækɪ`stæn; ˌpɑ:kɪ'stɑ:n, ˌpækɪ'stæn/	巴基斯坦	Pakistani /ˌpɑkɪ`stɑnɪ, ˌpækɪ`stɑnɪ; ˌpɑ:kɪ'stɑ:ni◂, ˌpæk-/
Palestine /`pælǝsˌtaɪn; 'pælǝstaɪn/	巴勒斯坦	Palestinian /ˌpælǝs`tɪnɪǝn; ˌpælǝ'stɪniǝn/
Panama /ˌpænǝ`mɑ, `pænǝˌmɑ; ˌpænǝ'mɑ:◂/	巴拿馬	Panamanian /ˌpænǝ`menɪǝn; ˌpænǝ'meɪniǝn/
Papua New Guinea /ˌpæpjuǝ nju `gɪnɪ; ˌpæpuǝ nju: 'gɪni/	巴布亞新幾內亞	Papuan /`pæpjuǝn; 'pæpuǝn/
Paraguay /`pærǝˌgwe; 'pærǝgwaɪ/	巴拉圭	Paraguayan /ˌpærǝ`gweǝn; ˌpærǝ'gwaɪǝn◂/
Persia /`pɝʒǝ; 'pɜ:ʃǝ, -ʒǝ/ former name of Iran	波斯〔伊朗的舊稱〕	
Peru /pǝ`ru; pǝ'ru:/	祕魯	Peruvian /pǝ`ruvɪǝn; pǝ'ru:viǝn/
Philippines /`fɪlǝˌpinz; 'fɪlǝpi:nz/	菲律賓	Philippine /`fɪlǝˌpin; 'fɪlǝpi:n/ *person* 人: Filipino /ˌfɪlǝ`pino; ˌfɪlǝ'pi:nǝʊ/
Poland /`polǝnd; 'pǝʊlǝnd/	波蘭	Polish /`polɪʃ; 'pǝʊlɪʃ/ *person* 人: Pole /pol; pǝʊl/
Polynesia /ˌpɑlǝ`niʒǝ; ˌpɒlɪ'ni:ziǝ/	波利尼西亞	Polynesian /ˌpɑlǝ`niʒǝn; ˌpɒlɪ'ni:ziǝn◂/
Portugal /`portʃǝgl; 'pɔ:tʃʊgǝl/	葡萄牙	Portuguese /`portʃǝˌgiz; ˌpɔ:tʃʊ'gi:z◂/
Puerto Rico /ˌpwɛrtǝ`riko; ˌpwɜ:tǝʊ'ri:kǝʊ/	波多黎各	Puerto Rican /ˌpwɛrtǝ`rikǝn; ˌpwɜ:tǝʊ'ri:kǝn/
Qatar /`kɑtɑr; kʌ'tɑ:/	卡塔爾, 卡達	Qatari /`kɑtɑrɪ; kʌ'tɑ:ri/
Quebec /kwɪ`bɛk; kwɪ'bek/	魁北克	Quebecois /kwɪ`bɛkǝ; ˌkebe'kwɑ:/
Romania /ro`menjǝ; ru:'meɪniǝ/	羅馬尼亞	Romanian /ro`menɪǝn; ru:'meɪniǝn/
Russia /`rʌʃǝ; 'rʌʃǝ/	俄羅斯	Russian /`rʌʃǝn; 'rʌʃǝn/
Rwanda /ru`ɑndǝ; ru'ændǝ/	盧旺達, 盧安達	Rwandan /ru`ɑndǝn; ru'ændǝn/
Saint Kitts & Nevis /sent ˌkɪts ǝnd `nivǝs; sǝnt ˌkɪts ǝnd 'ni:vǝs/	聖基茨和尼維斯	Kittitian /kǝ`tɪʃǝn; kǝ'tɪʃǝn/ Nevisian /nǝ`vɪʒǝn; nǝ'vɪziǝn/
Saint Lucia /sent `luʃǝ; sǝnt 'lu:ʃǝ/	聖盧西亞, 聖露西亞	Saint Lucian /sent `luʃǝn; sǝnt 'lu:ʃǝn/
Samoa /sǝ`moǝ; sǝ'mǝʊǝ/	薩摩亞	Samoan /sǝ`moǝn; sǝ'mǝʊǝn/
San Marino /sæn mǝ`rino; sæn mǝ'ri:nǝʊ/	聖馬利諾	Sanmarinese /ˌsænˌmærǝ`niz; ˌsænmærǝ'ni:z/
São Tomé & Principe /saʊn tǝˌme ǝnd `prɪnsǝpǝ; ˌsaʊn tǝˌmeɪ ǝnd 'prɪnsǝpeɪ/	聖多美和普林西比	São Toméan /ˌsaʊn tǝ`meǝn; ˌsaʊn tǝ'meɪǝn/
Saudi Arabia /sǝ`udɪ ǝ`rebɪǝ; ˌsaʊdi ǝ'reɪbiǝ/	沙特阿拉伯, 沙烏地阿拉伯	Saudi Arabian /sǝ`udɪ ǝ`rebɪǝn; ˌsaʊdi ǝ'reɪbiǝn/ *person* 人: Saudi or 或 Saudi Arabian
Senegal /ˌsɛnɪ`gɔl; ˌsenɪ'gɔ:l/	塞內加爾	Senegalese /ˌsɛnɪgǝ`liz; ˌsenɪgǝ'li:z◂/
Seychelles /se`ʃɛlz; seɪ'ʃelz/	塞舌爾	Seychellois /seʃɛl`wɑ; ˌseɪʃel'wɑ:◂/
Sierra Leone /sɪ`ɛrǝ lɪ`onɪ; siˌerǝ li'ǝʊn/	塞拉利昂, 獅子山	Sierra Leonean /sɪ`ɛrǝ lɪ`onɪǝn; siˌerǝ li'ǝʊniǝn/
Singapore /`sɪŋgǝˌpor; ˌsɪŋǝ'pɔ:/	新加坡	Singaporean /ˌsɪŋgǝ`porɪǝn; ˌsɪŋǝ'pɔ:riǝn◂/
Slovak Republic /ˌslovɑk rɪ`pʌblɪk; ˌslǝʊvæk rɪ'pʌblɪk/	斯洛伐克共和國	Slovak /`slovæk; 'slǝʊvæk/
Slovenia /slo`vinɪǝ; slǝʊ'vi:niǝ/	斯洛文尼亞	Slovene /slo`vin; 'slǝʊvi:n/ *person* 人: Slovenian /slo`vinɪǝn; slǝʊ'vi:niǝn/
Solomon Islands /`sɑlǝmǝn ˌaɪlǝndz; 'sɒlǝmǝn ˌaɪlǝndz/	所羅門羣島	Solomon Islander /ˌsɑlǝmǝn `aɪlǝndǝ˞; ˌsɒlǝmǝn 'aɪlǝndǝ/

Name 地名		**Adjective** 形容詞
Somalia /səˋmɑlɪə; səʊˈmɑːliə/	索馬里, 索馬利亞	Somali /soˋmɑlɪ; səʊˈmɑːli/
South Africa /saʊθ ˋæfrɪkə; saʊθ ˈæfrɪkə/	南非	South African /saʊθ ˋæfrɪkən; saʊθ ˈæfrɪkən/
Spain /spen; speɪn/	西班牙	Spanish /ˋspænɪʃ; ˈspænɪʃ/ *person* 人: Spaniard /ˋspænjɚd; ˈspænjəd/
Sri Lanka /ˌsrɪˋlæŋkə; sriː ˈlæŋkə/	斯里蘭卡	Sri Lankan /ˌsrɪ ˋlæŋkən; sriː ˈlæŋkən/
Sudan /suˋdæn; sʊˈdæn, -ˈdɑːn/	蘇丹	Sudanese /ˌsudəˋniz; ˌsuːdəˈniːz◂/
Surinam /ˌsurɪˋnɑm; ˌsʊərɪ̮ˈnæm/	蘇里南, 蘇利南	Surinamese /ˌsurɪnɑˋmis; ˌsʊərɪ̮nəˈmiːz◂/ *person* 人: Surinamer /ˋsurɪˌnæmɚ; ˌsʊərɪ̮ˈnɑːmə/
Swaziland /ˋswɑzɪˌlænd; ˈswɑːzilænd/	斯威斯蘭, 史瓦濟蘭	Swazi /ˋswɑzɪ; ˈswɑːzi/
Sweden /ˋswidn̩; ˈswiːdn/	瑞典	Swedish /ˋswidɪʃ; ˈswiːdɪʃ/ *person* 人: Swede /swid; swiːd/
Switzerland /ˋswɪtsɚlənd; ˈswɪtsələnd/	瑞士	Swiss /swɪs; swɪs/
Syria /ˋsɪrɪə; ˈsɪriə/	敍利亞	Syrian /ˋsɪrɪən; ˈsɪriən/
Tahiti /tɑˋhitɪ; təˈhiːti/	塔希提島, 大溪地	Tahitian /tɑˋhitɪən; təˈhiːʃən/
Taiwan /ˋtaɪˋwɑn; ˌtaɪˈwɑːn/	台灣	Taiwanese /ˌtaɪwɑˋniz; ˌtaɪwəˈniːz◂/
Tajikistan /tɑˌdʒikɪˋstɑn; tɑːˌdʒiːkɪˈstɑːn/	塔吉克 (斯坦)	Tajik /tɑˋdʒik; tɑːˈdʒiːk/
Tanzania /ˌtænzəˋniə; ˌtænzəˈnɪə/	坦桑尼亞	Tanzanian /ˌtænzəˋniən; ˌtænzəˈnɪən◂/
Thailand /ˋtaɪlənd; ˈtaɪlænd, -lənd/	泰國	Thai /taɪ; taɪ/
Tibet /tɪˋbɛt; tɪˈbet/	西藏	Tibetan /tɪˋbɛtn̩; tɪˈbetn/
Timor, East /ˌist ˋtimɔr; ˌiːst ˈtiːmɔː/	東帝汶	Timorese /ˌtimɔˋrɪz; ˌtiːmɔːˈriːz◂/
Togo /ˋtogo; ˈtəʊgəʊ/	多哥	Togolese /ˌtogoˋliz; təʊgəˈliːz◂/
Tonga /ˋtɑŋgə; ˈtɒŋgə/	湯加, 東加	Tongan /ˋtɑŋgən; ˈtɒŋgən/
Trinidad & Tobago /ˋtrɪnəˌdæd ənd təˋbego; ˌtrɪnɪdæd ən təˈbeɪgəʊ/	特立尼達和多巴哥, 千里達－托貝哥	Trinidadian /ˋtrɪnəˌdædɪən; ˌtrɪnɪ̮ˈdædiən◂/ Tobagonian /ˌtobəˋgonɪən; ˌtəʊbəˈgəʊniən/
Tunisia /tjuˋnɪʃə; tjuːˈnɪziə/	突尼斯	Tunisian /tjuˋnɪʃɪən; tjuːˈnɪziən/
Turkey /ˋtɝkɪ; ˈtɜːki/	土耳其	Turkish /ˋtɝkɪʃ; ˈtɜːkɪʃ/ *person* 人: Turk /tɝk; tɜːk/
Turkmenistan /ˌtɝkmɛnɪˋstæn; ˌtɜːkmenɪ̮ˈstɑːn/	土庫曼 (斯坦)	Turkmen /ˋtɝkmɛn; ˈtɜːkmən/
Uganda /juˋgændə; juːˈgændə/	烏干達	Ugandan /juˋgændən; juːˈgændən/
Ukraine /ˋjukren, juˋkren; juːˈkreɪn/	烏克蘭	Ukranian /juˋkrenɪən; juːˈkreɪniən/
United Arab Emirates /juˋnaɪtɪd ˋærəb əˋmɪrɪts; juːˌnaɪtɪ̮d ˌærəb ˈemɪrɪ̮ts/	阿拉伯聯合酋長國	Emirian /əˋmɪrɪən; eˈmɪəriən/
United Kingdom of Great Britain and Northern Ireland /juˋnaɪtɪd ˋkɪŋdəm əf gret ˌbrɪtən ənd ˌnɔrðɚn ˋaɪrlənd; juːˌnaɪtɪ̮d ˈkɪŋdəm əv greɪt ˌbrɪtən ənd ˌnɔːðən ˈaɪələnd/	大不列顛及北愛爾蘭聯合王國, 英國	British /ˋbrɪtɪʃ; ˈbrɪtɪʃ/ *person* 人: Briton /ˋbrɪtən; ˈbrɪtən/, *AmE*【美】Britisher /ˋbrɪtɪʃɚ; ˈbrɪtɪʃə/ *people* 人民: British
England /ˋɪŋglənd; ˈɪŋglənd/	英格蘭; 英國	English /ˋɪŋglɪʃ; ˈɪŋglɪʃ/ *person* 人: *sing.* 單數= Englishman /ˋɪŋglɪʃmən; ˈɪŋglɪʃmən/ (*fem.* 女性 -woman) /-ˌwumən; -ˌwʊmən/; *pl.* 複數= Englishmen /ˋɪŋglɪʃmən; ˈɪŋglɪʃmən/ *people* 人民: English
Scotland /ˋskɑtlənd; ˈskɒtlənd/	蘇格蘭	Scottish /ˋskɑtɪʃ; ˈskɒtɪʃ/ or 或 Scots /skɑts; skɒts/ *person* 人: *sing.* 單數= Scot or 或 Scotsman /ˋskɑtsmən; ˈskɒtsmən/ (*fem.* 女性 -woman) /-ˌwumən; -ˌwʊmən/; *pl.* 複數= Scotsmen /ˋskɑtsmən; ˈskɒtsmən/ *people* 人民 : Scots

Name 地名		**Adjective** 形容詞
Wales /welz; weɪlz/	威爾斯	Welsh /wɛlʃ; welʃ/ *person* 人: *sing.* 單數= Welshman /ˋwɛlʃmən; ˈwelʃmən/ (*fem.* 女性 -woman) /-ˏwumən; -ˏwʊmən/; *pl.* 複數= Welshmen /ˋwɛlʃmən; ˈwelʃmən/ *people* 人民: Welsh
United States /juˋnaɪtɪd ˏstets; juːˌnaɪtɨd ˈsteɪts/	美利堅合眾國, 美國	American /əˋmɛrɪkən; əˈmerɨkən/ US, *person* 人: American /əˋmɛrɪkən; əˈmerɨkən/
Upper Volta /ˋʌpɚ ˋvɑltə; ˌʌpəˈvɒltə/ former name of Burkina Faso	上沃爾特, 上伏塔〔布基納法索的舊稱〕	
Uruguay /ˋjurəˏgwe; ˈjʊərəgwaɪ/	烏拉圭	Uruguayan /ˏjurəˋgweən; ˌjʊərəˈgwaɪən◂/
Uzbekistan /uzˏbɛkɪˋstæn; ˌʊzbekɨˈstɑːn/	烏茲別克	Uzbek /ˋuzbɛk; ˈʊzbek/
Vanuatu /ˏvænuˋɑtu; ˌvænuˈɑːtuː/	瓦努阿圖, 萬那杜	Vanuatuan /ˏvænuˋɑtuən; ˌvænuˈɑːtuən/
Venezuela /ˏvɛnəˋzwilə; ˌvenɨˈzweɪlə/	委內瑞拉	Venezuelan /ˏvɛnəˋzwilən; ˌvenɨˈzweɪlən◂/
Vietnam /ˏviɛtˋnɑm; ˌvjetˈnæm/	越南	Vietnamese /viˏɛtnɑˋmiz; ˌvjetnəˈmiːz◂/
West Samoa /wɛst səˋmoə; ˌwest səˈməʊə/	西薩摩亞	Samoan /səˋmoən; səˈməʊən/
Yemen /ˋjɛmən; ˈjemən/	也門	Yemeni /ˋjɛmənɪ; ˈjeməni/
Yugoslavia /ˏjugoˋslɑvɪə; ˌjuːgəʊˈslɑːviə/	南斯拉夫	Yugoslavian /ˏjugoˋslɑvɪən; ˌjuːgəʊˈslɑːviən◂/ *person* 人: Yugoslav /ˏjugoˋslɑv; ˈjuːgəʊslɑːv/
Zaire /zəˋɪr; zaɪˈɪə/	扎伊爾, 薩伊	Zairean /ˏzəˋɪrən; zaɪˈɪəriən/
Zambia /ˋzæmbɪə; ˈzæmbiə/	贊比亞, 尚比亞	Zambian /ˋzæmbɪən; ˈzæmbiən/
Zimbabwe /zɪmˋbɑbwe; zɪmˈbɑːbweɪ/	津巴布韋	Zimbabwean /zɪmˋbɑbweən; zɪmˈbɑːbweɪən/

Table 8 附錄 8

The Longman Defining Vocabulary 朗文釋義詞彙

The Longman Defining Vocabulary of around 2,000 common words has been used to write all the definitions in this dictionary. The words in the Defining Vocabulary have been carefully chosen to ensure that the definitions are clear and easy to understand, and that the words used in explanations are easier than the words being defined. Words in the Defining Vocabulary have been checked to make sure that they are frequent in the Longman Corpus Network, and that they are used correctly by learners in the Longman Learner's Corpus. Over 200 students took part in tests for this new dictionary, to check that they understood the definitions and could find the correct translation in their own language for words used. 本辭典採用大約2,000個常用詞的朗文釋義詞彙編寫所有釋義。這些詞語都經過精心挑選，以保證釋義淺顯易懂，釋義用詞比被解釋的詞容易。釋義詞彙中的詞都經過核對，以確保這些詞都是朗文語料庫網絡中使用頻率高的詞，而且是朗文學習語料庫中學習者正確使用的詞。有 200 多名學生參加了這部新辭典的測試，以檢查他們對釋義的理解，及他們能否把釋義詞彙正確地譯成母語。

We have also used a special computer program that checks every entry to make sure that words from outside the defining vocabulary have not been used. 我們還使用了專門的電腦程序核對每一個詞條，以確保沒有使用釋義詞彙以外的詞。

The words listed below are the main forms which are used in definitions. However, there are other limits on which word forms and meanings may be used 下表列出的詞是釋義中使用的主要形式。然而，在詞的形式和可能使用的意義方面還有其他的限制:

Word meanings 詞義

The definitions only use the most common and 'central' meanings of the words in the list. 釋義詞彙表中的詞在釋義時只取其最常用、最核心的詞義。

Word classes 詞類

For some words in the list, a word class label such as *n* or *adj* is shown. This means that this particular word is used in definitions only in the word class shown. So **anger**, for example, is used only as a noun and not as a verb. 釋義詞彙表中有些詞標註了詞類，如 *n, adj* 等，表示這個特定的詞只以標註的詞性用於釋義。例如 anger 只用作名詞，而不用作動詞。

Phrasal verbs 片語[短語]動詞

Phrasal verbs are not used in definitions, except for the ones included in the list. Other phrasal verbs which are common in English and could be formed from words in the Defining Vocabulary list (such as **put up with**) are not used. 除了釋義詞彙表中的片語[短語]動詞外，本辭典在釋義中不使用片語[短語]動詞。其他在英語中常見的而且能從釋義詞彙表中的詞構成的片語[短語]動詞（如 put up with）一律不採用。

Prefixes and suffixes 前綴和後綴

Some words on the list may have prefixes (like **un-**) or suffixes (like **-ly**) added to them to make different word forms in the definition. The list of these affixes is included at the end of the Defining Vocabulary list. The forms which are common, or which change their meaning when a prefix or suffix is added, (such as **acceptable** and **agreement**) are included in the full list. 部分釋義詞彙表中的詞可能會加上前綴（如 un-）或後綴（如 -ly）構成釋義中不同的詞形。這些詞綴列成表附在釋義詞彙表之後。那些常見的形式，或加上詞綴後意義有改變的詞（如 acceptable 和 agreement），則列於釋義詞彙表之中。

Proper names 專有名詞

The Defining Vocabulary does not include the names of actual places, nationalities, religions, and so on, which are occasionally mentioned in definitions. 釋義詞彙不包括實際地方、國籍、宗教等的名稱，儘管釋義中有時會提到這類詞。

Words not in the Defining Vocabulary 釋義詞彙以外的詞

It is sometimes necessary or helpful to use a word that is not in the Defining Vocabulary. These are shown in SMALL CAPITAL LETTERS, and sometimes followed by an explanation in brackets. 有時有必要使用釋義詞彙以外的詞，這些詞用小號大寫字母表示，有時並附有解釋（置於括號中）。

insider trad·ing /·,·· '··/ also 又作 **insider dealing** *n* [U] illegal buying and selling of a company's shares (SHARE[2] (5)) involving the use of secret information known only by people connected with the company〔股票的〕內幕交易，內線交易〔指利用祕密的內幕消息非法

買賣一家公司的股票〕

Sometimes a definition includes a word which has its own entry and definition very close by. This word is written in ordinary type, even if it is not in the defining vocabulary. For example 有時釋義中包含一個本身的詞條和釋義就在附近的詞, 這個詞用普通字體書寫, 即使它不在釋義詞彙之中。例如:

in·sin·u·a·tion /ɪn͵sɪnjʊˋeʃən; ɪn͵sɪnjuˈeɪʃən/ *n* **1** [C] something that someone insinuates 影射, 暗示: *the insinuation that they did not know how to run their own business* 關於他們經營無方的暗示 **2** [U] the act of insinuating something 暗示, 暗指

The word **insinuate** is not in the special list of defining words, but its own definition is only one entry away, so it can be found very easily. insinuate 這個詞不在這個專門的釋義詞彙表之中, 但它本身的釋義只有一個詞條之隔, 因此很容易就能查到。

Example sentences 例句

The example sentences in this dictionary are not written using only the Defining Vocabulary. They are based on corpus evidence, and show the ways in which a word or phrase is used in a natural, typical context. However, care has been taken to make sure that these examples are helpful to the student. Where necessary, changes have been made to sentences found on corpus, or new examples have been written, to show the uses found on corpus in a simpler form. 本辭典中的例句不限於使用釋義詞彙, 而是以語料庫中的證據為基礎, 說明詞或片語[短語]在自然、典型的語境中是如何使用的。然而我們注意確保這些例句對學生是有幫助的。必要時我們對語料庫中的句子進行了改寫, 或編寫了新的例句, 以較簡單的形式表示某詞在語料庫中的用法。

A
abbreviation
ability
able
about
above *adv, prep*
abroad
absence
absent *adj*
accept
acceptable
accident
accidental
according (to)
account *n*
achieve
achievement
acid
across
act
action
active
activity
actor, actress
actual
actually
add
addition
additional
address
adjective
admiration
admire
admit
adult
advanced
advantage
adventure *n*
adverb
advertise
advertisement
advice
advise
affair
affect
afford
afraid
after *adv, conj, prep*
afternoon
afterwards
again
against
age *n*
ago
agree
agreement
ahead
aim
air *n*
aircraft
airport
alcohol
alive
all *adv, pron, determiner, predeterminer*
allow
almost
alone
along
alphabet
already
also
although
always
among
amount *n*
amuse
amusement
amusing
an
ancient *adj*
and
anger *n*
angle *n*
angry
animal
announce
annoy
annoying
another
answer
anxiety
anxious
any
anyone
anything
anywhere
apart
apartment
appear
appearance
apple
approval
approve
area
argue
argument
arm *n*
army
around
arrange
arrangement
arrival
arrive
art
article
artificial
as
as opposed to
ashamed
ask
asleep
association
at
atom
attack
attempt
attend
attention
attitude
attract
attractive
authority
autumn
available
average *adj, n*
avoid
awake *adj*
away *adv*
awkward

B
baby
back *adj, adv, n*
background
backward(s) *adv*
bad
bag *n*
bake *v*
balance
ball *n*
band *n*
bank *n*
bar *n*
base *n, v*
basic
basket
bath *n*
battle *n*
be
beach *n*
beak
beam *n*
bean
bear
beat
beautiful
beauty
because
become
bed
beer
before
begin
beginning
behave
behaviour
behind *adv, prep*
belief
believe
bell
belong
below
belt *n*
bend
beneath
beside(s)
best
better *adj, adv*
between
beyond *adj, adv*
bicycle *n*
big *adj*
bill
bird
birth
bit
bite
bitter *adj*
black *adj, n*
blade
blame
blind *adj*
block
blood
blow
blue
board *n*
boat
body
boil
bomb
bone *n*
book *n*
boot *n*
border *n*
bored
boring
born
borrow
both
bottle *n*
bottom *n*
bowl *n*
box *n*
boy
brain *n*
branch *n*
brave *adj*
bread
break *v*
breakfast *n*
breast
breath
breathe
breed
brick
bridge *n*
bright
bring
broad *adj*
broadcast *v*
brother
brown *adj, n*
brush
build *v*
building
bullet
burn
burst *v*
bury
bus
bush
business
busy
but *conj*
butter *n*
button *n*
buy *v*
by *prep*

C
cake *n*
calculate
call *v*
calm *adj*
camera
camp *n,v*
can
cap
capital
car
card
care
careful
careless
carriage
carry
case *n*
castle
cat
catch *v*
cattle
cause
ceiling
celebrate
cell
central
centre *n*
century
ceremony
certain *adj, determiner*
chain *n*
chair *n*
chance *n*
change
character
charge
chase *v*
cheap
cheat *v*
check
cheek *n*
cheerful
cheese
chemical
chemistry
cheque
chest
chicken
chief
child
children
chin
chocolate
choice *n*
choose
church *n*
cigarette
cinema
circle *n*
circular *adj*
citizen
city
claim *v*
class *n*
clay
clean *adj, v*
clear *adj, v*
clever
cliff
climb *v*
clock *n*
close *adj, adv, v*
cloth
clothes
clothing
cloud *n*
club *n*
coal
coast *n*
coat *n*
coffee
coin *n*
cold *adj, n*
collar *n*
collect *v*
college
colour
comb
combination
combine *v*
come
comfort
comfortable
command
committee
common *adj*
communicate
communication
company
compare *v*
comparison
compete
competition
competitor
complain
complaint
complete
completely
complicated
compound *n*
computer
concern *v*
concerning
concert
condition *n*
confidence
confident
confuse
confusing
connect
connection
conscious
consider
consist
contain
container
continue
continuous
contract *n*
control
conversation
cook *n,v*
copy
corn
corner *n*
correct *adj, v*
cost
cotton
cough
could
council *n*
count *v*
country *n*
countryside
courage
course *n*
court *n*
cover
cow *n*
crack *n, v*
crash *n, v*
crazy
cream *n*
creature
crime
criminal
criticism
criticize
crop *n*
cross *n, v*
crowd
cruel
crush *v*
cry
cup *n*
cupboard
cure

curl
current *n*
curtain *n*
curve
custom *n*
customer
cut
cycle *v*

D

daily *adj, adv*
damage
dance
danger
dangerous
dark
date *n*
daughter
day
dead *adj*
deal *n*
deal with
death
debt
decay
deceive
decide
decision
decorate
decoration
decrease
deep *adj*
defeat
defence
defend
definite
definitely
degree
delay
deliberate *adj*
deliberately
delicate
deliver
demand
department
depend
dependent
depth
describe
description
desert *n*
deserve
design
desirable
desire
desk
destroy
destruction
detail *n*
determination
determined
develop
dictionary
die *v*
difference
different
difficult
difficulty
dig *v*
dinner
direct
direction
dirt
dirty *adj*
disappoint
disappointing
discover
discovery
discuss
discussion
disease *n*
dish *n*
dismiss
distance
distant
divide
do *v*
doctor *n*
document *n*
dog *n*
dollar
door
double *adj, v, predeterminer*
doubt
down *adv, prep*
draw *v*
drawer
dream
dress *n, v*
drink
drive *n, v*
drop
drug *n*
drum *n*
drunk *pastpart, adj*
dry
duck *n*
dull *adj*
during
dust *n*
duty

E

each
eager
ear
early
earn
earth *n*
east
eastern
easy *adj*
eat
economic
edge *n*
educate
educated
education
effect *n*
effective
effort
egg
eight
either
elbow
elect *v*
election
electric
electricity
electronic
else
embarrass
embarrassing
emotion
emphasize
employ *v*
employer
employment
empty *adj, v*
enclose
encourage
end
enemy
energy
engine
engineer *n*
enjoy
enjoyable
enjoyment
enough
enter
entertain
entertainment
entrance *n*
envelope
environment
equal *adj, n*
equipment
escape
especially
establish
even *adj, adv*
evening
event
ever
every
everyone
everything
everywhere
evil
exact *adj*
exactly
examination
examine
example
excellent
except *conj, prep*
exchange
excite
exciting
excuse
exercise
exist
existence
expect
expensive
experience
explain
explanation
explode
explosion
explosive
express *v*
expression
extreme *adj*
extremely
eye

F

face
fact
factory
fail *v*
failure
fair *adj*
fairly
faith
faithful *adj*
fall
false
familiar
family
famous
far
farm
farmer
fashion *n*
fashionable
fast *adj, adv*
fasten
fat
father *n*
fault *n*
favourable
favourite *adj*
fear *n*
feather *n*
feature *n*
feed *v*
feel *v*
feeling(s)
female
fence *n*
fever
few
field *n*
fifth
fight
figure *n*
fill *v*
film
final *adj*
finally
financial
find *v*
find out
fine *adj*
finger *n*
finish *v*
fire
firm *adj*
first *adj, determiner*
fish
fit *adj, v*
five
fix *v*
flag *n*
flame *n*
flash *n, v*
flat *adj*
flesh
flight
float *v*
flood
floor *n*
flour *n*
flow
flower *n*
fly *n, v*
fold
follow
fond
food
foot *n*
football
for *prep*
force
foreign
foreigner
forest *n*
forget
forgive
fork *n*
form
formal
former
fortunate
forward(s) *adv*
four(th)
frame *n*
free
freedom
freeze *v*
frequent *adj*
fresh
friend
friendly
frighten
frightening
from
front *adj, n*
fruit *n*
full *adj*
fun
funeral
funny
fur *n*
furniture
further *adj, adv*
future

G

gain *v*
game *n*
garage *n*
garden
gas *n*
gate
gather *v*
general *adj*
generally
generous
gentle
gentleman
get
gift
girl
give *v*
glad
glass *adj, n*
glue
go *v*
goat
god
gold
good
goodbye
goods
govern
government
graceful
gradual
grain
gram
grammar
grand *adj*
grandfather
grandmother
grandparent
grass *n*
grateful
grave *n*
great *adj*
green
greet
greeting
grey *adj, n*
ground *n*
group *n*
grow
growth
guard *v*
guess *v*
guest *n*
guide
guilty
gun *n*

H

habit
hair
half
hall
hammer *n*
hand *n*
handle
hang *v*
happen *v*
happy
hard
hardly
harm
harmful
hat
hate *v*
hatred
have
he
head *n*
health
healthy
hear
heart
heat
heaven
heavy *adj*
heel *n*
height
hello
help
helpful
her(s)
here
herself
hide *v*
high *adj, adv*
hill
him
himself
his
historical
history
hit
hold *v*
hole
holiday *n*
hollow *adj*
holy
home *adv, n*

honest
honour *n*
hook *n*
hope
hopeful
horn
horse *n*
hospital
hot *adj*
hotel
hour
house *n*
how *adv*
human
humorous
humour
hundred(th)
hungry
hunt *v*
hurry
hurt *v*
husband *n*

I

ice *n*
idea
if
ignore
ill *adj*
illegal
illness
image
imaginary
imagination
imagine
immediately
importance
important
impressive
improve
improvement
in *adv, prep*
include
including
income
increase
independent
indoor(s)
industrial
industry
infect
infection
infectious
influence *v*
inform
information
injure
injury
ink *n*
inner
insect
inside
instead
institution
instruction
instrument
insult *v*
insulting
insurance
insure
intelligence
intelligent
intend
intention
interest
interesting
international *adj*
interrupt
into
introduce
introduction
invent
invitation
invite *v*
involve
inwards
iron *adj, n*
island
it *pron*
its

J

jaw
jewel
jewellery
job
join
joint
joke
journey *n*
judge
judgement
juice
jump
just *adv*
justice

K

keen
keep *v*
key *n*
kick
kill *v*
kilo
kilogram
kilometre
kind
king
kiss
kitchen
knee *n*
kneel
knife *n*
knock *v*
knot
know *v*
knowledge

L

lack
lady
lake
lamb
lamp
land
language
large
last *adv, determiner*
late
lately
laugh
laughter
law
lawyer
lay *v*
layer *n*
lazy
lead *v*
leaf *n*
lean *v*
learn
least
leather
leave *v*
left
leg *n*
legal
lend
length *adv, pron, determiner*
less
lesson
let *v*
let go of
letter
level *adv, adj, n*
library
lid
lie
lie down
life
lift
light
like *prep, v*
likely
limit
line *n*
lion
lip
liquid
list *n*
listen *v*
literature
litre
little
live *v*
load
local *adj*
lock
lonely
long *adj, adv*
look
look after
look for
look sth up
loose *adj*
lord *n*
lose
loss
lot
loud
love
low *adj*
lower
loyal
loyalty
luck *n*
lucky
lung

M

machine *n*
machinery
magazine
magic
mail
main *adj*
make *v*
make into
make up *v*
male
man *n*
manage
manager
manner
many
map *n*
march *v*
mark
market *n*
marriage
married
marry
mass *n*
match
material *n*
mathematics
matter
may *v*
me
meal
mean *v*
meaning *n*
means
measure
measurement
meat
medical *adj*
medicine
meet *v*
meeting
melt
member
memory
mental
mention *v*
message
metal *n*
method
metre
middle
might *v*
mile
military *adj*
milk *n*
million(th)
mind
mine *n, pron*
mineral
minister *n*
minute *n*
mirror *n*
miss *v*
mist *n*
mistake *n*
mix *v*
mixture
model *n*
modern *adj*
moment
money
monkey *n*
month
moon *n*
moral *adj*
more
morning
most
mother *n*
motor *adj, n*
mountain
mouse
mouth *n*
move *v*
movement
much
mud
multiply
murder
muscle *n*
music
musician
must *v*
my
mysterious
mystery

N

nail
name
narrow *adj*
nasty
nation
national *adj*
natural *adj*
nature
navy
near *adj, adv, prep*
nearly
neat
necessary
neck
need
needle *n*
negative *adj*
neither
nerve *n*
nervous
net *n*
network *n*
never
new
news
newspaper
next *adj, adv*
nice
night
nine
ninth
no *adv, determiner*
noise *n*
none *pron*
nonsense
no one
nor
normal
north
northern
nose *n*
not
note *n*
nothing
notice
noticeable
noun
now
nowhere
number *n*
nurse
nut

O

obey
object *n*
obtain
occasion *n*
ocean
o'clock
of
off *adv, prep*
offence
offend
offensive *adj*
offer
office
officer
official
often
oil *n*
old
old-fashioned
on *adv, prep*
once *adv*
one
onion
only
only just
onto
open *adj, v*
operate
operation
opinion
opponent
opportunity
oppose
as opposed to
opposite
opposition
or
orange
order
ordinary
organ
organise
organization
origin
original
other
ought
our(s)
out *adj, adv*
outdoor(s)
outer
outside
over *adv, prep*
owe
own
owner
oxygen

P

pack *v*
package
page *n*
pain *n*
painful
paint
painting
pair *n*

pale *adj*
pan *n*
paper *n*
parallel *adj, n*
parent
park
parliament
part *n*
participle
particular *adj*
partly
partner *n*
party *n*
pass *v*
passage
passenger
past
path
patient *adj*
pattern *n*
pause
pay
payment
peace
peaceful
pen *n*
pence
pencil *n*
people *n*
pepper *n*
per cent
perfect *adj*
perform
performance
perhaps
period *n*
permanent
permission
person
personal
persuade
pet *n*
petrol
photograph
phrase *n*
physical *adj*
piano *n*
pick *v*
pick up
picture *n*
piece *n*
pig *n*
pile *n*
pilot *n*
pin
pink *adj, n*
pipe *n*
pity
place
plain *adj, n*
plan
plane *n*
plant
plastic
plate *n*
play
pleasant
please
pleased
pleasure *n*
plenty *pron*
plural
pocket *n*
poem
poet
poetry
point
pointed
poison
poisonous
pole *n*
police *n*
polish *v*
polite
political
politician
politics
pool *n*
poor
popular
population
port *n*
position *n*
positive
possess
possession
possible *adj*
possibly
possibility
post
pot *n*
potato
pound *n*
pour
powder *n*
power *n*
powerful
practical
practice
practise
praise
pray
prayer
prefer
preparation
prepare
present *adj, n*
preserve *v*
president
press *v*
pressure *n*
pretend
pretty *adj*
prevent
previous
price *n*
priest
prince
principle
print
prison
prisoner
private *adj*
prize *n*
probably *adv*
problem
process *n*
produce *v*
product
production
profession
profit *n*
programme
progress *n*
promise
pronounce
pronunciation
proof *n*
proper
property
proposal
protect
protection
protective
protest
proud
prove
provide
public
pull
pump
punish
punishment
pupil
pure
purple
purpose *n*
push
put

Q

quality
quantity
quarrel
quarter *n*
queen *n*
question
quick *adj*
quiet *adj, n*
quite

R

rabbit *n*
race
radio *n*
railway
rain
raise *v*
range *n*
rank *n*
rapid *adj*
rare
rat *n*
rate *n*
rather
raw
reach *v*
react
reaction
read *v*
ready *adj*
real
realize
really
reason
reasonable
receive
recent
recently
recognize
record *n, v*
red
reduce
reduction
refusal
refuse *v*
regard *v*
regular *adj*
related
relative
relation
relationship
relax
relaxing
religion
religious
remain
remark *n*
remember
remind
remove *v*
rent
repair
repeat *v*
replace
reply
report
represent
representative *n*
request *n*
respect
responsible
rest
restaurant
restrict
result
return *n, v*
reward
rice
rich
rid
ride
right *adj, adv, n*
ring *n*
rise
risk
river
road
rob
rock *n*
roll *v*
romantic *adj*
roof *n*
room *n*
root *n*
rope *n*
rose
rough *adj*
round *adj, adv, prep*
row
royal *adj*
rub *v*
rubber
rude
ruin *v*
rule
ruler
run
rush *v*

S

sad
safe *adj*
safety
sail
sale
salt *n*
same
sand *n*
satisfaction
satisfactory
satisfy
save *v*
say *v*
scale *n*
scatter *v*
scene
school *n*
science
scientific
scientist
scissors
screen *n*
screw
sea
search
season *n*
seat
second *adv, n, determiner*
secret
secretary
see *v*
seed *n*
seem
sell *v*
send
sense *n*
sensible
sensitive
sentence *n*
separate *adj, v*
series
serious
servant
serve
service *n*
set *n, v*
settle *v*
seven(th)
several
severe
sex *n*
sexual
shade
shadow *n*
shake
shall
shame *n*
shape
share
sharp *adj*
she
sheep
sheet
shelf
shell *n*
shelter
shine *v*
shiny
ship *n*
shirt
shock *n, v*
shocking
shoe *n*
shoot *v*
shop
shore *n*
short *adj*
shot *n*
should
shoulder *n*
shout
show *n, v*
shut
shy
sick *adj*
side *n*
sideways
sight *n*
sign
signal
silence *n*
silent
silk
silly
silver
similar
simple
since
sincere *adj*
sing
single *adj*
singular
sink *v*
sister
sit
situation
six(th)
size *n*
skilful
skill
skin *n*
skirt *n*
sky *n*
sleep
slide *v*
slight *adj*
slippery
slope
slow
small
smell
smile
smoke
smooth *adj*
snake *n*
snow
so
soap *n*
social *adj*
society
sock *n*
soft
soil *n*
soldier *n*
solid
solution
solve
some *pron, determiner*
somehow
someone
something
sometimes
somewhere
son
song
soon
sore *adj*
sorry

sort *n*
soul
sound *n, v*
soup
sour *adj*
south
southern
space *n*
speak
special *adj*
specific
speech
speed *n*
spell *v*
spend
spin *v*
spirit *n*
in spite of
split *v*
spoil *v*
spoon *n*
sport *n*
spot *n*
spread *v*
spring
square *adj, n*
stage *n*
stair
stamp
stand *v*
standard
star *n*
start
state
statement
station *n*
stay
steady *adj*
steal *v*
steam *n*
steel *n*
steep *adj*
stem *n*
step
stick
sticky
stiff *adj*
still *adj, adv*
sting
stitch
stomach *n*
stone *n*
stop
store
storm *n*
story
straight *adj, adv*
strange
stream *n*
street
strength
stretch *v*
strict
strike *v*

string *n*
strong
structure *n*
struggle
student
study
stupid
style *n*
subject *n*
substance
succeed
success
successful
such
suck *v*
sudden
suffer
sugar *n*
suggest
suit
suitable
sum *n*
summer
sun *n*
supply *n, v*
support *n, v*
suppose
sure *adj*
surface *n*
surprise
surprising
surround *v*
swallow *v*
swear
sweep *v*
sweet
swell *v*
swim
swing
sword
sympathetic
sympathy
system

T

table *n*
tail *n*
take *v*
talk
tall
taste
tax
taxi *n*
tea
teach
team *n*
tear
technical
telephone
television
tell
temper *n*
temperature
temporary

ten
tend
tendency
tennis
tense *n*
tent
terrible
test
than
thank
that *conj, pron, determiner*
the
theatre
their(s)
them
then *adv*
there
therefore
these
they
thick *adj*
thief
thin *adj*
thing
think *v*
third
this *pron, determiner*
thorough
those
though
thought
thousand(th)
thread *n*
threat
threaten
threatening
three
throat
through *adv, prep*
throw
thumb *n*
ticket *n*
tidy *adj, v*
tie
tight *adj*
time *n*
tired
tiring
title
to
tobacco
today
toe *n*
together
toilet
tomorrow
tongue
tonight
too
tool *n*
tooth
top *adj, n*

total *adj, n*
touch
tourist
towards
tower *n*
town
toy *n*
track *n*
trade *n*
traditional
traffic *n*
train
training
translate
transparent
trap
travel
treat *v*
treatment
tree
tribe
trick *n, v*
trip *n*
tropical
trouble
trousers
true *adj*
trust
truth
try *v*
tube
tune *n*
turn
twice
twist
two
type *n*
typical
tyre

U

ugly
under *prep*
understand
underwear
undo
unexpected
uniform *n*
union
unit
unite
universe
university
unless
until
unusual
up *adj, adv, prep*
upper
upright *adj, adv*
upset *v, adj*
upside down
upstairs *adj, adv*
urgent
us

use
useful
useless
usual

V

valley
valuable *adj*
value *n*
variety
various
vegetable
vehicle
verb
very *adv*
victory
view *n*
village
violence
violent
visit
voice *n*
vote
vowel

W

wages
waist
wait *v*
wake *v*
walk
wall *n*
want
war *n*
warm *adj, v*
warmth
warn
warning
wash
waste
watch
water
wave
way
we
weak
wealth
weapon
wear *v*
weather *n*
weave *v*
wedding
week
weekly *adj, adv*
weigh
weight *n*
welcome
well *adj, adv, n*
west
western *adj*
wet *adj*
what *predeterminer, determiner, pron*
whatever
wheat
wheel *n*
when *adv, conj*
whenever
where
whether
which
while *conj*
whip
whistle
white
who
whole
whose
why *adv, conj*
wide *adj, adv*
width
wife
wild *adj, adv*
will
willing
win *v*
wind
window
wine *n*
wing *n*
winter
wire *n*
wise *adj*
wish
with
within
without
woman
wood
wooden
wool
word *n*
work
world
worry
worse
worst
worth
would
wound
wrap *v*
wrist
write
wrong *adj, adv, n*

Y

year
yellow
yes
yet
you
young *adj*
your(s)

Z

zero

Prefixes and suffixes that can be used with words in the Defining Vocabulary
可以與釋義詞彙中的詞連用的前綴和後綴

-able
-al
-ance
-ation
dis-
-ed
-ence
-er
-ful
-ic
-ical
im-
in-
-ing
-ion
ir-
-ish
-ity
-ive
-ize
-less
-ly
-ment
-ness
non-
re-
self
-th
un-
-y

New Words

出版人的話

● 新詞是怎樣收進詞典內的?

我們經常被問及一個詞是如何收進詞典內的。這個問題尤其與新詞有關, 因為, 正如艾奇遜教授在她的結束語中所指出的, 並不是所有新詞都有用, 得以在語言中保存下來。《朗文當代英語辭典》新詞附錄的編輯方針是, 只有那些根據本辭典的編纂者和出版人的判斷, 認為極可能成為未來英語詞彙寶庫中一部分的新詞才收入。

要判斷是否收入某個詞有很大的難處, 但是, 我們主要的標準是: 收錄的新詞應在書面上至少使用過一次, 而在口語上應使用過數次, 而且其引文應至少出自三個不同的來源。但實際作出判斷時情況往往更為複雜, 假如詞典編纂者認為某一詞是新詞, 儘管只能 (在口語或書面材料) 找到一個出處, 也會遵循他們的語言學角度對其作出判斷。

● 新興的詞語

我們在"新詞附錄"中已收錄那些現有的, 但出於某些原因而開始得到更加廣泛使用的詞語。最明顯的例子是已在美國英語中用了一段時間, 然後又開始在英國英語和英語的其他變體中使用的一些詞語。例如, **farmer's market** (農產品集貿市場) 和 **conjoined twins** (連體兒) 已在美國英語中使用了一段時間, 但只是最近才開始用於英國英語。

類似的還有一些已在科學或其他專門領域通用的詞語, 然後突然在報刊文章中出現並逐漸成為英語中的一部分。

英語新詞不斷湧現

吉恩·艾奇遜

● 英語學習者為何需要掌握新詞

在英語中, 經常都會出現新詞。在報紙、電視、廣播及近來的萬維網上, 新的詞語不斷出現, 成為現有數以萬計詞語中的新成員。一個受過教育的、以英語為母語的人 (無論來自美國、英國、澳大利亞和其他以英語為主要交際語言的任何一個國家) 至少掌握5萬個英語單詞, 而這個數目僅為現有詞彙數量的一部分。母語為英語的人在13歲時就學會約2萬個單詞。[1] 最理想的是, 英語學習者能夠掌握這個數量的詞語才能書寫和談論他們可能涉及的各話題。

但是, 人們需要掌握哪些詞語呢? 隨着新的話題, 需要掌握的詞語亦時常有所不同, 新的詞項 (單詞、詞組或舊詞新義) 便會產生。英語學習者需要學習新加進英語中的這些詞語, 需學會它們的含義。達到這一目的最佳途徑之一是翻查一部如 Longman Web Dictionary (朗文網上詞典) http://www.longmanwebdict.com 那樣的線上 (online) 詞典, 因為這類詞典總收錄最新的詞彙。但是, 為了那些不上網的讀者,《朗文當代英語辭典》的編纂者和出版人編寫了這個新詞附錄以幫助學習者掌握這些新詞。

● 新詞進入英語的三個途徑

新詞語進入英語主要有三個途徑。第一, 是來自另一種語言、某地的方言、或英語的另一變體借來的外來詞。英語接受了來自多種不同語言的詞語。來自美國英語的詞語傳播到英語的其他變體已成為一種強烈的趨勢。《朗文當代英語辭典》的新詞部分收錄的詞語許多在美國英語中已是人盡皆知, 但對英國英語和世界其他地區的英語來説卻是新詞。

第二, 是通過構詞法生成新詞, 即用原有的詞語, 或原有詞語中的一部分, 合起來造出新詞 (例如, chat room (網上) 聊天室或 change management 變動管理) 。

第三, 新詞可以通過插入法生成, 即一個現存的詞語可以分解出不止一個詞義。這就會造成所謂的多義性 (一個詞具有幾個詞義) , 例如 campus 這個詞是指屬於某大公司的土地和全部建築的新用法 (〔大公司的〕園區) : Microsoft's campus in Redmond, Washington. 微軟公司在華盛頓州的雷德蒙德的園區。

以下將討論這三種途徑。英語的詞彙量一如既往地在不斷擴大, 這將會越來越明顯, 但由於英語已經成為全球貿易往來和新技術所使用的語言, 近年新詞增加的速度和數量都很驚人。

1　歷史上的外來詞

與其他一些語言不同, 英語從來沒有設法阻止外來詞語進入其詞彙。英語中的外來詞來自法語、拉丁語、希臘語、意大利語、西班牙語、漢語、日語、印地語, 以及許多其他語言。

這些外來的詞語往往已失去外來詞的色彩成為英語詞。

1066年, 征服者威廉從法國的諾曼底入侵英格蘭, 法語開始成為代表權力和威望的語言。這在格洛斯特的羅伯特約於1300年寫成的英格蘭史中就清楚地表明了這一點。他說(根據翻譯):

所以, 這塊土地上的貴族(征服英格蘭的法國人)的後裔始終堅持使用同一種語言(即法語)……因為一個人如果不通曉法語, 就幾乎不為人們所注意……但是, 下層人民一直使用英語。[2]

在那一時期, 大量法語詞進入英語, 尤其是與權力有關的詞語, 如duke(公爵)、duchess(公爵夫人或女公爵)、count(伯爵)、countess(伯爵夫人或女伯爵); 與官方有關的詞語, 如parliament(議會)、government(政府); 或與法律有關的詞語, 如accuse(控告)、attorney(律師)、crime(罪行)等。進入英語的另一些法語詞有的與服裝有關的, 如apparel(服飾)、dress(連衣裙); 與藝術有關的, 如music(音樂)、poem(詩歌); 有的與道德品質有關的, 如courtesy(謙恭有禮)、charity(仁慈、慈愛)等。

原有的英語詞語在當時並不一定消失, 它們會與新來的法語詞一起存在, 但用於更為普通的環境之中。例如, 說英語的下等階層仍然保留一些家畜的叫法, 如cow(母牛)、sheep(綿羊)、swine(豬)等(都來自古英語)。與此同時, 當指稱這些家畜作食用的肉時, 便採用它們的法語名稱, 如beef(牛肉)、mutton(羊肉)和pork(豬肉)等, 因為富裕家庭和貴族家庭才經常吃肉。

拉丁語, 作為教會的語言也扮演着重要的角色。在一些情況下, 表示類似意義而來源於英語、法語和拉丁語的詞並存, 如表示"幫助"的有help(源自英語)、aid(源自法語)和assistance(源自拉丁語), 表示"書本"的有book(源自英語)、volume(源自法語)和text(源自拉丁語)。

許多拉丁詞語是在16世紀和17世紀進入英語的。它們主要是書面語的一部分, 性質上往往涉及專門知識, 如species(物種)、specimen(標本)、tedium(冗長)、squalor(骯髒)和antenna(天線)等。有些拉丁詞, 如以上所舉的幾個例子直接以拉丁語形式進入英語, 另一些則採用了英語的拼寫方式, 如history(歷史, 拉丁語為historia)、maturity(成熟, 拉丁語為maturitas)、polite(禮貌的, 拉丁語為politus)和scripture(經文, 拉丁語為scriptura)。現在幾乎沒有人能看出如history或polite一類詞語是源於拉丁語的。

17世紀, 一些說英語的人開始對拉丁詞大量湧入英語感到擔心。伊莉莎白時代的劇作家本·瓊森在他的戲劇《冒牌詩人》(1601)中嘲弄了這一趨勢, 在該劇中的一個角色脫口說出一連串詞語, 其中許多只是開玩笑的空話:

barmy froth, chilblained, clumsy, clutched, conscious, damp, defunct, fatuate, furibund, glibbery, incubus, inflate, lubrical, magnificate, oblatrant, obstupefact, prorumpted, puffy, quaking custard, reciprocal, retrograde, snarling gusts, snotteries, spurious, strenuous, turgidous, ventositous.

但是, 其中也有一些詞是今天還在經常使用的, 例如clumsy(笨手笨腳的, 該詞在瓊森的時代居然是一個新詞)、conscious(神志清醒的)、damp(潮濕的)、defunct(已死去的)、puffy(膨脹的)、reciprocal(相互的)、retrograde(後退的)、spurious(假的)、strenuous(幹勁十足的）。

在17世紀，英語接觸到歐洲其他主要語言，這可從以下的外來詞反映出來，如借自法語的 colonel（上校）、machine（機器）、cartridge（彈藥）等，借自西班牙語的armada（艦隊）、banana（香蕉）、galleon（西班牙大帆船）等，借自意大利語的 ballot（選票）、carnival（狂歡節）、madrigal（牧歌）等。

2　來自其他語言的詞語 —“外來詞”

吸收外來詞語的這種趨勢仍然繼續。這種外來詞來自眾多不同的國家。但是，外來詞並不是新詞的主要來源。極大多數新詞來自新技術領域，如computers（電腦）、Internet（互聯網）、biotechnology（生物科技）、sport（運動）、entertainment（娛樂）、business（商業）、changes in society（社會變革）等。然而，你會發現現有的一些外來詞還有新的用法，如法語詞 beaucoup 的新用法：

beaucoup *quantifier French spoken informal*【法口，非正式】a lot of or many 許多，很多：*He makes beaucoup bucks* (=earns a lot of money) *in that job.* 他在那工作上掙了大把大把的錢。

來自印地語的：

bindi 吉祥痣（印度女子用在兩眉之間前額上的紅點）用帶色的化妝粉畫成或貼以小片飾物構成，使用吉祥痣出於宗教原因，婦女從前用之表示“已婚”，現在則只是為了裝飾。

許多來自其他語言的新詞是與食物有關的，如 **latte**（牛奶咖啡，源自意大利語），**taqueria**（墨西哥食品快餐店，源自墨西哥西班牙語），以及 **radicchio**（菊苣，源自意大利語）。

源自美國英語的詞語

美國英語的重要性與日俱增，這主要出於兩個原因，一是美國在世界經濟中所佔的優勢，這包括其作為電腦和互聯網軟件主要供應商的角色，二是美國通俗文化通過電影、電視和流行歌曲所起的影響。一些在美國已不是新詞、但已得到全世界認同和廣泛使用的詞語被視為新詞收錄在《朗文當代英語辭典》的新詞附錄中。例如，**majorly**（【俚】extremely 極其，非常）在美國並不是一個新詞，但已在全世界廣泛使用，因而被收進了新詞部分，並不標明為美國英語。

當然，美國英語中出現的一些新詞也收錄進來，因為《朗文當代英語辭典》除了收錄英國英語外，也收錄大量的美國英語，以及英語的其他變體。例如，新出現的 **somebody got game** 這個短語是美國英語口語中的一個習用語，用以表示某人做起某事來十分熟練，尤指體育運動。另一個新詞條為 **whassup**，這是一個美國俚語，源自‘What’s up?’（怎麼啦?），尤其作為和熟人之間打招呼時的用語。

採用了來自美國英語的詞，尤其來自工商業界、年輕一代和黑人文化、流行音樂、電腦和互聯網的詞彙成了英國英語發展的一個重要趨勢，這一點在新詞附錄中已有所反映。

但是，外來詞（從其他語言汲取的詞語）只是新詞的一個來源。另一個來源，也是主要的來源，便是構詞，接下來將討論這一點。

3 新詞語

德國哲學家和語言學家洪堡於1836年指出:“一種語言的詞彙決不能看作是無生命的完全整體……詞彙是會通過其構詞能力不斷地生成和再生成”。[3] 這種“構詞能力”可從兩種途徑進行探究。其一是探討產生新詞的生活領域。其二是研究構成新詞的語言手段。

通過新詞可以洞察某個時代所關注的事物。例如,在 20 世紀初期創造了許多與交通運輸有關的詞: 如汽車部件 accelerator (油門); 與航空運輸有關的詞, 如air line (航線)、airport (航空港)、air terminal (航線終點站) 等。此外, 還增加了一些與現代化家用電器有關的詞, 如central heating (中央供暖)、vacuum cleaner (吸塵器), 當然, 還有radio (收音機) 和 television (電視機)。

現在, 在21世紀之初, 與電腦和互聯網有關的新詞可能在數量上已超過所有其他來源的詞語, 例如:

cybersickness (電腦病) 因長時間使用電腦或呆在一間有許多電腦的房間裡面而產生的不適感覺

keypal (鍵盤友, 網友) 你經常與之交換電郵的人: If your daughter is interested in having a keypal next year, please have her get in touch. 你的女兒如果來年有意結交網友的話, 請讓她同我聯繫。

screenager【非正式】(屏幕青少年) 熱衷於使用電腦和互聯網的年輕人

金融領域也產生了許多的新詞, 如

dead cat bounce【術語, 非正式】(“死貓”式反彈, 指股票價格大跌之後出現的輕微回升, 有時這種回升出現在進一步下跌之前)

stealth tax【英, 非正式】隱形稅, 指購物所支付的, 而不是直接交給政府的稅, 人們對此不像對從自己收入中直接扣除的稅那麼在意。

有時, 可由金融和電腦兩個領域相結合產生新詞, 如**dot-com**【非正式】經營互聯網業務的, 指其業務與 (使用) 互聯網有關的個人或公司的: a dot-com company 經營互聯網業務的公司 | dot-com millionaires 經營互聯網業務的大富翁

e-cash 電子現金, 可用於網上購物, 但並不實際存在, 也不屬於某個特定的國家

新事物的出現需要新的詞語, 其中許多來自科學、技術和商務活動, 茲略舉數例——有來自電腦和互聯網的, 如 **on-line auction** (網上拍賣), **PDA** 或 **personal digital assistant** (個人數碼助理), **access provider** (網絡服務供應商), **animatronics** (電子動畫學), **cookie** (“甜餅”, 記錄網站訪問者的信息塊), **MP3** (動態影像專家壓縮標準音頻層面3文件); 有來自醫學和生物科學的, 如**biologically engineered** (生物工程的), **DNA profiling** (DNA基因圖測定), **genetically modified** (基因改造的, 轉基因的); 有來自商務活動方面的, 如 **benchmark** (基準測試), **best practice** (最佳舉措), **SOHO** (家庭辦公室) 等等。

4 構詞過程

新詞語並不都是全新的。其中大多數是由已有的一些成分構成的。同樣的構詞過程在全球各地都有發生, 儘管每一種語言各有其特有的慣用構詞方式。

首次引進的新詞, 通常置於引號(“ ”)之內, 例如, 在 The annual fee allows unlimited entry to district parks for your dog for a year and a case of 100 “pooper-scoopers”中, pooper-scooper(長柄糞鏟)是指鏟除狗糞的一種工具。某個詞被接受後, 其引號最終會被刪去。

i) 複合詞　在英語中, **複合構詞法**是整個20世紀最多產的構詞方式。複合構詞法包括簡單地把兩個詞語放在一起, 有時這仍然被視為分立的兩個詞語。最近的例子有 **airport fiction**(機場小說, 指在機場出售、供乘客在飛行途中閱讀的消閒小說)和 **hot desk**(共用辦公桌, 指供不同工作人員在不同日子裡輪着使用的同一張辦公桌)。

有時候, 兩個部分組拼成單一的一個新詞, 如 **jobseeker**(求職者)和 **webhead**(網絡迷, 指頻繁並熟練使用互聯網的人)。有時, 這兩個部分由連詞符連結, 如見於 **walk-in**(不用預約的), 這是新近出現的一個形容詞, 用以指某個地方毋需預約即可自行前往, 如用於 walk-in clinic(無需預約的診所)。

ii) 詞綴　加詞綴是構成新詞的另一常見方法。詞綴是一個詞的附加部分, 可加在其前面(前綴)或後面(後綴)。

在英語中, 在已有的詞加上一個結尾可產生許多新詞。例如, 往 brain(腦)一詞的結尾部加上後綴 -iac, 即生成最近出現的新詞 **brainiac**(【非正式, 幽默】怪才, 指整天思考高深問題, 但不善於與普通人交往、異常聰明的人): Electrical engineering is the perfect career for a brainiac like him. 電機工程是那些像他那樣的怪才的理想職業。這個詞也用作形容詞: The company is trying to change its brainiac image.(該公司試圖改變其智囊形象。)

許多新詞通過添加後綴 -ization 而成, 如 **dollarization**(美元化, 指美國以外的國家不想用本國貨幣而想使用美元的情況)或 **globalization**(全球化, 指世界各國的活動開始連成一體, 尤因一些大公司在不同國家內開展貿易活動所致)。這實際上是把兩個後綴連在一起, 如第一個為 **globalize** 中的 -ize(即 global+-ize), 然後再加上後綴 -ation。

另一個日常通用的後綴為 -land, 如見於 **adland**(廣告業, 指圍繞廣告進行的整個業務活動): Anything that grabs your attention is good in adland.(凡能吸引人們注意力的東西在廣告業中都是好的。)和 **cyberland**(網絡世界, 指涉及互聯網及其使用者的活動)。

前綴最近用得愈加廣泛。cyber- 就是一個很好的例子, 它已被用於構成一系列新詞(該前綴原意為“電腦”, 現在多含“使用互聯網”之意)。例如, **cybercafé**(網吧)、**cybercrime**(網絡犯罪)、**cyberforensics**(網絡犯罪學)、**cyberfraud**(網絡詐騙, 指為了獲取錢財和權力等利用網絡詐騙他人的不法行為)、**cyberland**(網絡世界)、**cyberporn**(網絡色情, 指顯示在互聯網上的色情圖像、影片等)。

還有很多關於尺寸大小的前綴構成的新詞, 如 micro-, super- 和 multi- 等, 如:

microbrewery(小啤酒廠, 指只生產少量啤酒的釀酒廠, 它們往往設有供應該啤酒的餐館)

microengineering(微型工程, 指設計極小的建構和機器)

micromanage(微觀管理, 指過分干預別人的工作): Professors warned that students will suffer if the state legislature tries to micromanage public education.(有教授提醒說, 如果州立法機關企圖對公眾教育實行微觀管理, 學生們將受害。)

supersize【美】巨無霸式的(指快餐店提供的飲料或餐點是超大份量的)

multi-tasking 1（電腦的）多重任務處理（能力）**2** 同時執行多項任務的能力

這些前綴大多意義清晰。後綴也有其意義。如 -ism 是近年來被賦予更具體含義的後綴，-ist 也是如此。-ism 的含義一度是相當"中性"的，如 pacifism（和平主義，指認為一切戰爭和一切暴力都是錯誤的）。但 -ism 逐漸帶上了貶義的色彩，如 ageism（歧視老人）指"人們因為年邁而受到的不公正的對待"，而持這種歧視態度的人就被稱為 ageist（歧視老人者）。同樣，**lookist**（adj. 以貌取人的）是指不公正地僅憑某人的外表如胖瘦和衣着等決定好惡，這樣的作風被稱為 **lookism**（以貌取人主義），而持這種態度的人就被稱作 **lookist**（以貌取人者）。

iii)（詞類）轉化　　這是一種構詞方式，有時會由此產生許多新詞或新的短語。詞類轉化是指某個詞從一個詞類轉變成另一詞類，這在今日英語中十分常見。對於沒有很多詞尾的語言，利用轉類過程很容易，如 **to bookmark**（將名詞用作動詞），其含義為"（往文檔中）標識"，指保存互聯網內的某個網頁，以便容易再找到它；**to ramp**（將名詞用作動詞）或 **to ramp something up** 的含義為"推高（公司股票價格）"，指想法子使人們相信某公司股票的價格超過其實際價值；又如 **to sample**（將名詞用作動詞）的含義為"將…取樣拼和"，指把取自激光唱盤或唱片中的小段樂曲用於新曲之中。

iv) 縮略詞和縮寫（詞）　　詞語的首字母縮略一直以來有其重要性，有些縮略詞已廣為人們所知和使用，如墓碑和悼詞用語 RIP（Rest in Peace 願他（或她）安息吧）或 asap（as soon as possible 盡快）等。有些縮略詞已被接受為完整的單詞，如 laser（light amplification by the stimulated emission of radiation 激光：受激輻射式光頻放大器），像一個單詞一樣讀作 /ˈleɪzə/。近來，使用縮略詞和縮寫（詞）日趨頻繁，至少在青少年和年輕人當中是這樣。這部分是因為手機雖然同樣能發送信息，但其屏幕空間卻非常有限。因此，縮寫（詞）構成的短信息愈來愈常見，如 **IMHO**（in my humble opinion 以鄙人之見）和 **CUL**（see you later 一會兒見），當然，使用這類詞要謹慎。有些縮寫（詞）容易引起混淆，可作不同解釋，如 **LOL** 既可表示 Lots of love（大量的愛），又可表示 Laughing out loud（放聲大笑）。

v) 混成詞　　兩個詞合成為一個詞稱為**混成詞**（此術語現在比舊有的 **portmanteau words** 常用得多，但後一術語有時仍用來描述這種現象）。

少數混成詞已被人們接受為英語的一部分，如 brunch（早午餐）是由 breakfast（早餐）和 lunch（午餐）兩詞混合而成，有些是故作幽默的，例如：

netizen（【俚】網民）該詞由 net（網）和 citizen（公民）混合而成：China and India will soon have far larger numbers of netizens than any Western nation. 中國和印度不久將會擁有大量網民，數量遠比任何一個西方國家多。

netiquette（【非正式】網規，指在網上與他人交流時應遵循的禮儀）：Netiquette says that you don't use all capital letters in an e-mail, because that shows you are angry. 網規說，你在電子郵件中不得全部用大寫字母，因為那樣做表示你在生氣。

由 imagination（想像）和 engineer（工程師）構成 **imagineer**（點子大王，意念工程師）一詞，指腦中有許多新的主意並能把這些主意實踐出來的人。

5 同層插入

然而新詞並非一定是新的語詞。一些現成的詞可藉着**同層插入**這一方式分出新的意義，如**client**（客戶機，指通過服務器在網上獲得信息的電腦）或**brother**兄弟（黑人之間的互稱）。同樣地，**lurk**（潛身漫遊者）現在不僅可指隱藏在矮樹林中的可疑分子，也可指潛入 **chat room**（網上聊天室）中只是讀取信息而不發表意見的潛身漫遊者。

同層插入的另一類型是語詞的含義“淡出”。事實上，如 devastated 增新的意義並未嚴重削弱原有的含義。The city was devastated（那座城市被徹底摧毀了）通常表示該城市遭到敵人或巨大的自然災害（如火山）的破壞。但在 Peggy was devastated when her new hat got wet（佩吉因為她的新帽被淋濕了而不高興）一句中，這裡指的純粹是一樁小事，所以只表示“佩吉不高興了”的意思。

● 結束語

可見，英語中不斷有新詞加入。那麼英語是不是變得越來越龐大？是的，是這樣。然而，詞語並不總是永遠存在下去的。當人們不使用某些詞語，這些詞語便會消亡。

那麼，一個人怎麼能學好所有這些詞語呢？辦法只有一個，就是購買一本最新的詞典。可幸的是，對於任何希望學好最新詞彙，以迎接21世紀的英語學習者，本版詞典已提供大量有用的詞彙，足以裝備好他們面對21世紀的需要。

....

吉恩·艾奇遜（Jean Aitchison）是牛津大學R·默多克講座語言和傳播學教授，著作頗豐，如《心裡想的詞語 —— 心智詞彙導論》第二版，牛津：布萊克韋爾，1994年；《語言的變革：進展還是衰亡？》第三版，劍橋：劍橋大學出版社，2001年

....

1. “論語詞的數目”，見吉恩·艾奇遜，《心裡想的詞語 —— 心智詞彙導論》第二版，牛津：布萊克韋爾，1994
2. 這段（英語）譯文引自傑弗里·休斯，《英語詞語的歷史》，牛津：布萊克韋爾 2000，第110頁
3. 洪堡，《論語言》(1836)。彼得·希思（英）譯，劍橋：劍橋大學出版社 1988，第93頁

A,a

abs /æbz; æbz/ *n* [plural]
informal the muscles on your ABDOMEN (=stomach)【非正式】腹肌: *exercises that improve your butt, legs, and abs* 改善臀部、腿部和腹部肌肉的鍛鍊

access pro·vid·er /ˈæksɛs prəˌvaɪdɚ; ˈækses prəˌvaɪdə/ *n* [C]
a company that provides the technical services that allow people to use the Internet, usually in exchange for a monthly payment; Internet Service Provider 網絡服務供應商, 互聯網服務供應商

acid jazz /ˌæsɪd ˋdʒæz; ˌæsɪ̈d ˈdʒæz/ *n* [U]
a type of popular music that combines features of many other kinds of music, especially JAZZ, HIP-HOP, and SOUL 迷幻爵士樂

acquaintance rape /əˋkwentəns ˌrep; əˈkweɪntəns ˌreɪp/ *n* [C,U]
a crime in which a person forces someone they know to have sex with them 熟人強姦: *The truth is acquaintance rape can occur at any time, no matter how long the two people have known each other.* 實際情況是任何時候都可發生熟人強姦, 不管這兩個人相互認識了多久。

ac·tu·als /ˈæktʃuəlz; ˈæktʃuəlz/ *n* [plural]
numbers that relate to something that has actually happened, rather than what was expected to happen, for example the sales of a particular product 實際數目: *Mobile phone operators had expected monthly usage of up to 250 minutes. Actuals are very different, at 100 minutes.* 流動電話經營者曾預計每個月通話量會達到250分鐘, 實際數字則相差甚遠, 只達到100分鐘。

add-on /ˈæd ˌɑn; ˈæd ˌɒn/ *n* [C]
NEW MEANING
1 something extra that is added to an existing plan, agreement, or law etc〔計劃、協議或法規等的〕附加內容: *The Senate's add-ons to the proposed budget are likely to cause controversy.* 參議院在預算案上添加的新內容看來會引起一番爭議。**2** a product that is designed to be used with another product〔旨在與其他產品配用的〕附件

ADHD /ˌe di etʃ ˋdi; ˌeɪ diː eɪtʃ ˈdiː/ *n* [U]
attention deficit hyperactivity disorder; a medical condition that especially affects children and causes them to be too active and unable to pay attention to anything for very long〔兒童〕注意力缺乏症, 多動症, 過度活躍症

ad·hoc·ra·cy /ædˋhɑkrəsɪ; ædˈhɒkrəsi/ *n* [C]
a company or organization that does not have a formal structure or many rules. This word is often used to talk about new companies that make computer SOFTWARE, which do not operate in a traditional way 沒有成規的公司[組織]〔常指不按傳統方式營運的電腦軟件公司〕, 變型蟲組織: *the emergence of adhocracies in the software engineering sector* 軟件工程業中出現一些不守成規的公司

ad·land /ˈædlænd; ˈædlænd/ *n* [U]
the activity or business of advertising, considered as a whole 廣告業: *Anything that grabs your attention is good in adland.* 凡能吸引人們注意力的東西在廣告業中都是好的。

adrenaline-charged /əˋdrɛnḷɪn ˌtʃɑrdʒd; əˈdrenəl-ɪ̈n ˌtʃɑːdʒd/ *adj*
a game, film, activity etc that is adrenaline-charged is very exciting and possibly frightening〔遊戲、影片、活動等〕非常刺激的; 驚心動魄的: *an adrenaline-charged movie starring Steven Seagal* 由史蒂文·西加爾主演的一部驚慄片

ADSL /ˌe di ɛs ˋɛl; ˌeɪ diː es ˈel/ *n* [U]
asymmetric digital subscriber line; a system that makes it possible for information, such as VIDEO images, to be sent to computers through telephone wires at a very high speed. The receiver is also able to send information back to the sender, but at a much slower speed. 非對稱數位用戶專線

ad·ver·to·ri·al /ˌædvɚˈtɔrɪəl; ˌædvəˈtɔːriəl/ *n* [C]
an advertisement in a newspaper or magazine that is made to look like a normal article. This word comes from a combination of the words 'ADVERT' and 'EDITORIAL'.〔報刊上的〕文章式廣告, 廣告特輯〔由advert和editorial縮合而成〕

aer·i·a·list /ˈɛrɪəlɪst; ˈeəriəlɪ̈st/ *n* [C]
someone who goes down a mountain on SKI*s* and performs complicated jumps and turns in the air 高空滑雪雜技演員

AFAIK, afaik
a written abbreviation of 縮寫= 'as far as I know', used in E-MAIL or TEXT MESSAGE*s* on MOBILE PHONE*s* 據我所知〔電子郵件或手機短信用語〕

affinity card /əˋfɪnətɪ ˌkɑrd; əˈfɪnɪ̈ti ˌkɑːd/ *n* [C]
a type of CREDIT CARD, where an amount of money is given by the credit card company to a CHARITY every time the card is used 慈善信用卡〔每次使用這卡, 信用卡公司便會捐一定數額的錢給慈善機構〕

af·flu·en·za /ˌæfluˋɛnzə; ˌæfluˈenzə/ *n* [U]
informal bad feelings such as shame or sadness that some people have when they suddenly become very rich. This word is a combination of the words 'AFFLUENCE' (=when you have a lot of money) and 'INFLUENZA' (=an illness which is like a very bad cold).【非正式】富貴病〔因暴富而產生羞恥或悲傷的情緒, 由affluence和influenza縮合而成〕

af·ter·mar·ket /ˈæftɚˌmarkɪt; ˈɑːftəˌmɑːkɪ̈t/ *n* [C] *BrE*
the market for the products that people buy after they have bought another related product, for example spare parts or additional pieces of equipment【英】配件[零件]市場: *There is a large aftermarket for replacement car parts.* 有一個巨大的汽車配件市場。

age·ist /ˈedʒɪst; ˈeɪdʒɪ̈st/ *adj*
treating old people unfairly because of a belief that they are less important than younger people 歧視老人的: *The article seemed somewhat insensitive and ageist to me.* 在我看來, 這篇文章有點麻木並帶有歧視老人的味道。—**ageist** *n* [C] *She actually accused me of being an ageist.* 事實上她指責我歧視老人。

aggressive-growth /əˌgrɛsɪv ˋgroθ; əˌgresɪv ˈgrəʊθ◂/ *adj*
aggressive-growth fund a group of STOCK*s* that earns a lot of money very quickly because the stock price keeps rising 高增長基金, 積極增長型基金: *A retired couple looking for stability and minimal risk should not choose an aggressive-growth fund.* 期待穩定和低風險的退休夫婦不應該選擇高增長基金。

a·git·pop /ˈædʒɪt ˌpɑp; ˈædʒɪ̈t ˌpɒp/ *n* [U] *BrE*
a type of popular music which has a political message and encourages people to get involved in political activities, such as improving working conditions for the poor and trying to stop big companies from being too powerful【英】鼓動音樂〔含有政治信息、鼓勵人們參加政治活動的一種流行音樂〕: *an agitpop band* 鼓動音樂樂隊

ag·ri·tour·ist /ˈægrɪˌturɪst; ˈægrɪˌtʊərɪ̈st/ *n* [C]
someone from a town or city who stays on a farm while they are on holiday 赴鄉村旅遊者: *Agritourists enjoy country vacations; rural bed and breakfasts such as the Fieldstone Inn near Regina are popular destinations too.* 喜歡去鄉下度假的人享受在鄉村度假的樂趣, 如加拿大里賈納附近的大卵石旅館一類提供住宿和早餐的小旅店也是受歡迎的目的地。—**agritourism** *n* [U]

air /ɛr; eə/ *n*
NEW MEANING
get/catch some air *slang* to jump high off the ground, especially when playing BASKETBALL, SKI*ing*, or riding

a SKATEBOARD【俚】〔尤指籃球、滑雪等運動中〕彈跳得極高

air kiss 噘唇示吻

air kiss /ˋɛr ˏkɪs; ˈeə ˌkɪs/ *n* [C]
humorous a way of greeting someone with a kiss that is near the side of their face, but that does not touch them【幽默】噘唇示吻〔一種問候方式, 嘴唇接近但不接觸對方的面頰〕 **—air-kiss** *v* [I,T]: *As soon as Alice appeared, Beth rushed over, and the two women air-kissed.* 艾麗斯一出現, 貝思便跑了過去, 兩個女人就噘唇示吻。

airport fic·tion /ˋɛrpɔrt ˏfɪkʃən; ˈeəpɔːt ˌfɪkʃən/ *n* [U]
books, especially ones that are not very serious, that people buy at airports to read while they are travelling on planes 機場小說〔在機場出售、供乘客在飛行途中閱讀的消閒小說〕

air quote /ˋɛr ˏkwot; ˈeə ˌkwəʊt/ *n* [C usually plural 一般用複數]
a movement that someone makes in the air with their fingers to show that what they are saying should be in QUOTATION MARK*s*, and that it should not be taken as their real opinion or their usual way of speaking 手示引號〔表示所說的話不是表達真正的意見或通常的說法〕: *Ryan used air quotes when he said the word 'band'.* 瑞安在說 band 一詞時用了手示引號。| *"It was a 'dinner party'", he said, waving his fingers to make air quotes in that annoying way he has.* "這是一次 dinner party (宴會)。" 他說着, 並揮動手指做了個令人討厭的引號動作。

air rage /ˋɛr ˏredʒ; ˈeə ˌreɪdʒ/ *n* [U]
violence and angry behaviour by a passenger on an aircraft towards other passengers or the people who work on the aircraft 坐飛機鬧事: *In another air rage incident, a flight to Spain was forced to land after a passenger threatened cabin staff when they refused to serve him more alcohol.* 在另一次空中鬧事事件中, 一名乘客由於機組人員拒絕再給他倒酒而作出恐嚇, 因此一架飛往西班牙的班機被迫降落。

airtime pro·vid·er /ˋɛrtaɪm prəˏvaɪdɚ; ˈeətaɪm prəˌvaɪdə/ *n* [C]
a company that provides the service that allows you to make and receive calls on a MOBILE PHONE 流動電話公司: *You may still receive invoices or statements from your airtime provider after you return the equipment.* 你在歸還設備之後, 仍可能會收到流動電話公司的發票或結算表。

al·co·pop /ˋælkoˏpɑp; ˈælkəʊˌpɒp/ *n* [C usually plural 一般用複數] *BrE*
a sweet drink with BUBBLE*s* which is sold in bottles and contains alcohol. Many people disapprove of these drinks because they think the makers want young people to buy them. This word comes from a combination of the words 'alcohol' and 'POP'【英】汽酒〔含有酒精、有泡的甜飲料, 由 alcohol 和 pop 縮合而成〕

A-list /ˋe lɪst; ˈeɪ lɪst/ *adj*
among the most popular or famous film stars, musicians etc 最受歡迎的; 最著名的, 一流的〔影星、音樂家等〕: *No doubt about it. A-list celebrities like Madonna really pull in the crowds to any music event.* 毫無疑問, 像麥當娜那樣的一流歌星在任何音樂演出中肯定會吸引許多的觀眾。

all /ɔl; ɔːl/ *adv*
NEW MEANING
1 sb was all... *AmE spoken* used to report what someone said or did, when telling a story【美口】某人所說[所做]的只是…: *He drove me somewhere once, and he was all, "I love this car – it's like a rocket!"* 他有一次開車把我帶到一個地方, 只是說了句"我喜歡這輛車, 它就像火箭一樣!" **2 sb/sth is not all that** *AmE slang* used to say that someone or something is not very attractive or desirable【美俚】某人/某物沒甚麼吸引[沒甚麼令人喜歡]: *I don't know why you keep chasing her around – she's not all that.* 我不明白你為甚麼一直追求她——她並沒有甚麼吸引。

all·fi·nanz /ɔlˋfaɪnæns; ɔːlˈfaɪnæns/ *n* [singular]
technical the combining of banking and insurance activities in one company【術語】銀行保險綜合業務, 全金融業務: *Colonial is attempting to turn itself from a life insurance company into an allfinanz group.* 康聯正設法由人壽保險公司轉變為合銀行、保險為一體的全金融業務機構。

al·lot·tee /əˏlɑˋti; əˌlɒˈtiː/ *n* [C]
technical a person or organization that is allowed to buy new SHARE*s* when they first become available【術語】可購買原始股者, 可認購新股的人[組織]

alpha geek /ˏælfə ˋgik; ˌælfə ˈgiːk/ *n* [C usually singular 一般用單數]
humorous the person who is the most skilful with computers in a group of people. This word comes from a combination of the words 'ALPHA MALE', which is a scientific word used about the most powerful male animal in a group, and 'GEEK', which means a person who is unfashionable and does not know how to behave in social situations【幽默】電腦高手[怪才]〔由 alpha male 和 geek 縮合而成〕: *Ask James – he's the alpha geek here.* 問詹姆斯吧, 他是這兒的電腦高手。

alpha male /ˏælfə ˋmel; ˌælfə ˈmeɪl/ *n* [C usually singular 一般用單數]
humorous the man who has the most power and influence and the highest social position in a particular group. This phrase was first used by scientists to talk about groups of animals, especially monkeys and CHIMPANZEE*s*.【幽默】大哥大〔指羣體中最有權勢者〕

alternative life·style /ɔlˏtɝnətɪv ˋlaɪfstaɪl; ɔːlˌtɜːnətɪv ˈlaɪfstaɪl/ *n* [C]
the way that someone lives their life, including things such as the type of food they eat, where they live, or the way that they educate their children, when this is not the usual way that other people live 另類生活方式, 非傳統生活方式: *Some people say schools need to protect gay and lesbian students and teach tolerance of alternative lifestyles.* 有人主張學校應該保護同性戀學生, 並教育學生對另類生活方式持寬容態度。

AM /ˏe ˋɛm; ˌeɪ ˈem/ *n* [C]
NEW MEANING
Assembly Member; a British politician who is one of the 60 members of the Welsh Assembly. The Welsh Assembly is the parliament for Wales. 〔英國威爾士議會的〕議員

am·bi·sex·u·al /ˏæmbɪˋsɛkʃuəl; ˌæmbɪˈsekʃuəl/ also 又作 **ambi** *adj*
informal【非正式】**1** BISEXUAL 具有雌雄兩性特徵的 **2** suitable for either sex 適於兩性的: *ambisexual fashion* 兩性都適合的時裝

ambulance chas·er /ˋæmbjələns ˏtʃesɚ; ˈæmbjələns ˌtʃeɪsə/ *n* [C]
a lawyer who uses a lot of pressure to persuade someone who has been hurt in an accident to SUE other people or companies. The lawyer's main reason for doing this is in order to get part of the money if they win. This word is used by people who disapprove of this behaviour and the lawyers who do it. 慫恿事故受害者興訟以從中

謀利的律師

amped /æmpt; æmpt/ *adj* [not before noun 不用於名詞前] *slang*【俚】
1 if you are amped about something, you are very excited about it 對…痴迷的[感興奮的]: *"Did you hear about Jenny's party?" "Yeah, I'm totally amped about it."* "你聽說過珍妮的晚會嗎?" "聽說了, 這次晚會太讓我興奮了!" 2 feeling extremely excited because you have taken an illegal drug〔在服食毒品後〕極度興奮的

an·dro·pause /ˈændroˌpɔz; ˈændrəʊˌpɔːz/ *n* [U]
the time when some men's bodies start producing less TESTOSTERONE (=a chemical substance produced in men's bodies) than before, and they have less energy and strength, usually around age 50 男性更年期〔通常在50歲左右〕: *Andropause is easy to treat and to prevent with proper medical supervision.* 在適當的醫療指導下, 男性更年期不難防治。—**andropausal** *adj*: *There's no way of predicting who will experience andropausal symptoms.* 誰會出現男性更年期症狀, 這是無法預料的。

an·i·ma·tron·ics /ˌænəməˈtrɑnɪks; ˌænɪməˈtrɒnɪks/ *n* [U]
the method or process of making or using moving models that look like real animals or people in films. This word comes from a combination of the words 'ANIMATE' and 'ELECTRONICS'. 電子動畫學〔由 animate 和 electronics 縮合而成〕

anorak /ˈænəˌræk; ˈænəræk/ *n* [C] *BrE*
NEW MEANING
a boring person who is very interested in the unimportant details of a particular subject【英】〔糾纏於細枝末節的〕愛鑽牛角尖的人: *1,200 anoraks have visited our website since 25th March.* 從3月25日以來, 已有1,200個愛鑽牛角尖的人進入了我們的網站。| **anorak brigade** (=a group of anoraks) 專摳小問題的人: *The anorak brigade certainly exist, but they tend to hide in the library for most of the year.* 的確有一批專摳小問題的人, 不過, 他們一年中大部分時間都往往躲在圖書館裡。

an·tic·i·point·ment /ænˌtɪsəˈpɔɪntmənt; ænˌtɪsɪˈpɔɪntmənt/ *n* [U]
humorous a feeling of disappointment that you have when you see or read something for the first time and realize that it is not as good as you expected it to be. This word comes from a combination of the words 'ANTICIPATION' and 'DISAPPOINTMENT'【幽默】期望落空, 大失所望〔由 anticipation 和 disappointment 縮合而成〕: *When you've heard too many good things about a film, it can become an anticipointment when you finally get to see it.* 你聽說某部影片大獲好評, 不過待你看過以後, 你可能會大失所望。

anti-dump·ing /ˌæntɪ ˈdʌmpɪŋ; ˌænti ˈdʌmpɪŋ/ *adj* [only before noun 僅用於名詞前]
anti-dumping taxes or laws prevent people or companies from bringing foreign goods into the country and selling them at a very low price 反傾銷的

an·ti·ox·i·dant /ˌæntɪˈɑksədənt; ˌæntiˈɒksɪdənt/ *n* [C]
a substance that helps to protect the body from CANCER by removing harmful substances from it 抗氧化劑: *Strawberries and spinach are full of antioxidants.* 草莓和菠菜含有豐富的抗氧化成分。| *antioxidant vitamins* 抗氧化的維生素

anti-spam /ˌæntɪ ˈspæm; ˌænti ˈspæm/ *adj*
anti-spam features/measures ways in which a computer PROGRAM finds and removes E-MAIL that someone does not want, for example advertisements sent by companies 清除網絡垃圾的性能/措施

anti-vi·rus soft·ware /ˌæntɪ ˈvaɪrəs ˌsɔftwɛr; ˌænti ˈvaɪərəs ˌsɒftweə/ also 又作 **anti-virus program** *n* [U]
a type of SOFTWARE that looks for and removes VIRUSes in programs and documents on your computer 抗病毒軟件: *You need to update your anti-virus software regularly.* 你(們)需要定期升級自己的抗病毒軟件。

ap·plet /ˈæplət; ˈæplət/ *n* [C]
technical a computer program that is part of a larger program, and which performs a particular task. Applets are used, for example, to find documents on the Internet, WEBSITES etc【術語】小(應用)程式: *Java-based miniprograms known as applets are beginning to make their presence felt on the Internet.* 以 Java 語言編寫的許多小程式開始在互聯網上引起人們注意。

application ser·vice pro·vid·er /ˌæpləkeʃən ˈsɝvɪs prəˌvaɪdɚ; ˌæplɪkeɪʃən ˈsɜːvɪs prəˌvaɪdə/ *n* [C]
a company that supplies organized sets of computer SOFTWARE to other companies so that they can do business on the Internet 應用軟件供應商

application soft·ware /æpləˈkeʃən ˌsɔftwɛr; æplɪˈkeɪʃən ˌsɒftweə/ *n* [U]
technical COMPUTER software that is designed for a particular use or user【術語】應用軟件: *We need to ensure that the application software on both the PC and the Macintosh produces compatible files.* 我們需要確保個人電腦和蘋果電腦的應用軟件能製造兼容的檔案。

appraisal /əˈprezl; əˈpreɪzəl/ also 又作 **performance appraisal** *n* [C] *BrE*【英】
NEW MEANING
a meeting between an employer and a worker to discuss the quality of the worker's work and how well they do their job 表現評估

aq·ua·e·ro·bics /ˌækwɛˌrobɪks; ˈækweəˌrəʊbɪks/ also 又作 **aqua-aerobics** /ˈækwə ɛˌrobɪks; ˈækwə eəˌrəʊbɪks/ *n* [U]
a type of physical exercise in which you stand in a SWIMMING POOL, usually with other people in a group, and move your arms and legs as music plays 水上韻律操, 韻律泳

arcade game /ɑrˈked ˌgem; ɑːˈkeɪd ˌgeɪm/ *n* [C]
a type of electronic game that was first popular in AMUSEMENT ARCADEs (=a place where you play games by putting coins in machines) in the early 1980s, but is now usually played on a computer 電子遊戲: *Play free classic arcade games right through your web browser!* 只需透過你的網上瀏覽器便可免費玩第一流的電子遊戲!

archive /ˈɑrkaɪv; ˈɑːkaɪv/ *v* [T]
technical to make a permanent copy of information held on a computer, or to store the original information so that it cannot be changed or lost【術語】將…存檔: *CleanSweep will monitor your system for programs you don't often use and recommend that you archive them.* "清掃"(程式)會監測你不常用的程式系統, 並建議你把它們存檔。—**archiving** *n* [U]: *electronic archiving systems* 電子儲存系統

arm can·dy /ˈɑrm ˌkændɪ; ˈɑːm ˌkændi/ *n* [U]
a disapproving word for a very beautiful man or woman who goes with someone else of the opposite sex to parties and other events, but who is not having a sexual relationship with them〔充當伴侶的〕美女, 俊男〔貶義詞〕: *Nora's acting as arm candy tonight.* 諾拉今晚充當女伴。

art ther·a·py /ˈɑrt ˌθɛrəpɪ; ˈɑːt ˌθerəpi/ *n* [U]
a treatment for mental or emotional problems in which you paint a picture, make a SCULPTURE etc and then examine the art you have made in order to understand your feelings and problems 藝(術)療(法) —**art therapist** *n* [C]

as /əz; əz; *strong* 強讀 æz; æz/ *conj*
NEW MEANING
as if! *slang* used as an answer to a suggestion that someone has made, to say that you think is untrue or wrong【俚】不對! 不是這樣!: *"You're not still interested in Brad, are you?" "As if!"* (=no, I am not) "你不會對布拉德還感興趣吧?" "才不會呢!"

ask /æsk; ɑːsk/ *n* [C]
1 a word meaning the lowest price that someone will

sell STOCKS, SHARES etc for, used especially by people whose job is buying and selling shares etc 最低出價〔股票市場術語〕: *When placing an ask, be sure to specify a price and a time limit.* 提出最低出價時, 一定要確切地說明價格和時限。**2 a big ask** a situation in a sports match when a team needs to get a lot of points in order to win〔體育比賽取勝所需的〕大比分: *Now they need to score twice in the last five minutes – it's a big ask.* 他們現在需要在最後5分鐘內兩次得分 —— 這可是個大比分。

ASP /ˌe ɛs ˋpi; ˌeɪ es ˈpiː/ *n* [C]
application service provider; a company that supplies organized sets of computer SOFTWARE to other companies so that they can do business on the Internet 應用系統服務供應商

assisted ar·e·a /əˌsɪstɪd ˋɛrɪə; əˌsɪstɪ̇d ˈeərɪə/ *n* [C]
in Britain, an area of the country that receives money from the government to help it develop, because many people in that area do not have jobs〔英國〕政府資助開發的地區

assisted-liv·ing fa·cil·i·ty /əˌsɪstɪd ˋlɪvɪŋ fəˌsɪlətɪ; əˌsɪstɪ̇d ˈlɪvɪŋ fəˌsɪlɪ̇ti/ *n* [C] *AmE*
a place where old or sick people can live, and where help and services such as medical care and social activities are provided【美】療養院, 護老院: *It's tough moving someone you love into an elder-care setting, such as a nursing home or an assisted-living facility.* 把你所愛的人遷入如私人療養院或療養所等老年保健機構中去, 是令人難受的事。

assisted re·pro·duc·tion /əˌsɪstɪd riprəˋdʌkʃən; əˌsɪstɪ̇d riːprəˈdʌkʃən/ *n* [U]
medical methods that are used to help a woman and her partner have a baby 助孕(方法)

asylum seek·er /əˋsaɪləm ˌsikɚ; əˈsaɪləm ˌsiːkə/ *n* [C]
someone who has left their home country because of war or political problems and has gone to another country which they think is safer; REFUGEE 避難者, (尋求)政治庇護者: *Police officers are trained to understand the customs and culture of the asylum seekers and the political situation from which they have fled.* 警員接受訓練以理解避難者的風俗習慣和文化背景, 以及他們出逃國的政治形勢。

ATM /ˌe ti ˋɛm; ˌeɪ tiː ˈem/ *n* [U]
NEW MEANING
technical asynchronous transfer mode; a way of sending writing, sound, or pictures very quickly over a computer network (=a system of computers that are connected to each other)【術語】異步傳輸[轉移]模式

ATP /ˌe ti ˋpi; ˌeɪ tiː ˈpiː/ *n* [U] *BrE*
automatic train protection; a system that can be put into railway trains to prevent accidents by warning the driver when the train is too near another train, or when it goes past a signal where it is meant to stop【英】火車預警系統〔一種防止火車意外的自動保護系統〕

attachment /əˋtætʃmənt; əˈtætʃmənt/ *n*
NEW MEANING
1 [C,U] *law* a situation in which part of the money someone earns or money that is owed to them is taken by a court of law and used to pay their debts【法律】扣押償債〔沒收所得收入以抵償欠他人之債〕**2** [C] a document, usually a file, that is sent with an E-MAIL message〔電子郵件的〕附件: *I'll send the spreadsheet as an attachment.* 我將把數據表以附件形式發送。**3** [C] *technical* a piece of paper fastened to a document such as an insurance agreement, which shows a special condition of the agreement【術語】〔保險契約等的〕附件, 附款

attention def·i·cit hy·per·ac·tiv·i·ty dis·or·der /əˌtɛnʃən ˌdɛfəsɪt haɪpəræk ˋtɪvətɪ dɪsˌɔrdɚ; əˌtenʃən ˌdefɪ̇sɪ̇t haɪpəræk ˈtɪvɪ̇ti dɪsˌɔːdə/ *abbreviation* 縮寫為 **ADHD** *n* [U]
a medical condition that especially affects children and causes them to be too active and unable to be quiet or pay attention to anything for very long〔兒童〕注意力缺乏症, 多動症, 過度活躍症

au·thor·ing /ˋɔθərɪŋ; ˈɔːθərɪŋ/ *n* [U]
the activity of writing and designing WEBSITES 網站設計: *Here are a few tips on authoring and site design.* 這是網站設計的一些提示。

aut·o·ma·gic·ally /ˌɔtəˋmædʒɪklɪ; ˌɔːtəˈmædʒɪkli/ *adv* *humorous* very quickly and without much effort, in a way that seems to be happening by magic. This word is often used about computer PROGRAMS that can perform complicated operations very quickly. It comes from a combination of the words 'AUTOMATICALLY' and 'MAGICALLY'【幽默】快捷、輕易地〔操作電腦〕〔由 automatically 和 magically 縮合而成〕: *If you press the return key, the date will be changed automagically.* 按一下返回鍵, 日期就會馬上給改正過來。

automated cred·it trans·fer /ˌɔtəmetɪd ˋkrɛdɪt ˌtrænsfɚ; ˌɔːtəmeɪtɪ̇d ˈkredɪ̇t ˌtrænsfɜː/ *n* [C,U] *BrE*
a way of moving money into someone's bank account by computer, especially at regular times【英】〔尤指定期的〕自動轉賬: *The Government's decision to pay benefits by automated credit transfer and to computerise the Post Office network is going to make a huge difference.* 政府決定通過自動轉賬發放津貼並使郵政網絡電腦化, 工作效率將大有改觀。

av·a·tar /ˋævətɑr; ˈævətɑː/ *n* [C]
technical a picture of a person or animal that represents you on a computer screen, for example in some CHAT ROOMS or when you are playing games over the Internet【術語】〔網絡〕虛擬化身, 圖形表達法: *Visitors to Alpha World can actually see each other, because each is given a virtual body or "avatar" that appears on screen.* 進入α世界的人可以相互見到, 因為每個人有一個虛擬身體或"圖形化身"出現在屏幕上。

AVC /ˌe vi ˋsi; ˌeɪ viː ˈsiː/ *n* [C] *BrE*
additional voluntary contribution; an additional amount of money that a worker can put into their PENSION PLAN to make the amount of money grow faster【英】〔退休金計劃中的〕自願追加款, 自願額外供款: *Can I transfer my benefits from another pension scheme into my AVC account?* 我能不能把我另一個退休金計劃中的金額轉到我的自願額外供款賬戶裡呢?

AZT /ˌe zi ˋti; ˌeɪ zed ˈtiː/ *n* [U]
a drug used by people with AIDS to slow down the progress of the disease 疊氮胸苷〔一種抗愛滋病藥〕

B,b

B2B /ˌbi tu ˋbi; ˌbiː tuː ˈbiː/
the abbreviation for 縮寫= BUSINESS TO BUSINESS

B2B2C /ˌbi tu ˌbi tu ˋsi; ˌbiː tuː ˌbiː tuː ˈsiː/
the written abbreviation of 縮寫= 'business to business to consumer'; the selling of a product or service from a company to a customer with the help of a second company, usually on the Internet 公司對公司對客戶〔透過另一家公司(通常在互聯網上)向顧客售賣貨品或提供服務〕

B2C /ˌbi tu ˋsi; ˌbiː tuː ˈsiː/
the written abbreviation of 縮寫= 'business to consumer'; the selling of a product or service from a company directly to a customer, usually on the Internet 公司對客戶〔直接(通常在互聯網上)向顧客售賣貨品或提供服務〕

B4
a written abbreviation of 縮寫= 'before', used in E-MAIL or TEXT MESSAGES on MOBILE PHONES〔電子郵件和手機短信用語〕

babes /bebz; beɪbz/ *n* [plural]
a friendly way of addressing someone, especially someone you love 可人兒, 小寶貝: *You're going to have to*

cheer up, babes, or we're both going to get depressed. 小寶貝，你必須振作起來，要不然我們兩個都會感到憂傷。

back /bæk; bæk/ *n* [C] *AmE*

NEW MEANING

spoken **I've got your back** an expression meaning that you are willing to protect or help someone who is going to be in a dangerous or difficult situation【美口】我會幫你一把的

back·burn·er, backburner /ˌbæk ˋbɝnɚ; ˌbæk ˈbɜːnə/ *v* [T]

informal to delay doing something, because it does not need your attention immediately or because it is not as important as other things that you need to do immediately【非正式】暫時擱置: *Allison back-burnered her prestigious law career when she had a baby.* 阿利森在生孩子時，把自己頗有聲望的律師生涯擱置了起來。| *The project has been back-burnered due to technical problems.* 這個項目由於技術問題被推遲了。—**back-burnering** *n* [U]

back·chan·nel /ˋbækˌtʃænḷ; ˈbækˌtʃænl/ *n* [C]

someone or something that passes information secretly or unofficially from one person to another 祕密（消息）渠道，非正規途徑: *He may have served as a backchannel between ministers because he can be trusted to carry sensitive information.* 他可能充當了部長之間的祕密渠道，因為在傳遞敏感信息的事上，他是可信任的。| *back-channel diplomacy* 非正規渠道的外交

back office /ˌbæk ˋɔfɪs; ˌbæk ˈɒfɪs◂/ *n* [C]

the department of a bank or other financial institution that manages or organizes the work of the institution, but that does not deal with customers〔銀行等〕內部辦公室，後勤部門 —**back-office** *adj* [only before noun 僅用於名詞前]: *back-office operations* 內部運作

back sto·ry /ˋbæk ˌstorɪ; ˈbæk ˌstɔːri/ *n* [C]

the things that happened to a character in a book or film before the beginning of the story being told in the book or film〔書籍、影片等中故事開始之前的〕背景介紹: *The back story of why she hates her father is a bit too contrived.* 關於她為甚麼憎恨自己的父親交待得有點牽強。

backup /ˋbækˌʌp; ˈbækʌp/ *n* [C usually singular 一般用單數]

a copy of a computer document, PROGRAM etc, which is made in case the original becomes lost or damaged 備份〔文件〕: *Don't forget to make a backup of any work you do.* 別忘了給自己做的所有工作留下拷貝。—**backup** *adj* [only before noun 僅用於名詞前] *We keep backup copies of all files on the network.* 我們在網絡上保留所有文件的備份。

back-up soft·ware /ˋbæk ʌp ˌsɔftwɛr; ˈbæk ʌp ˌsɒftweə/ *n* [U]

a type of computer SOFTWARE that makes copies of computer documents AUTOMATICALLY at regular times, to reduce the risk of losing documents that are stored on computers 自動備份軟件

bad /bæd; bæd/ *n*

NEW MEANING

my bad! *AmE slang* used to say that you have made a mistake or that something is your fault【美俚】我錯了！是我的錯！

bad-ass /ˋbæd ˌæs; ˈbæd ˌæs/ *adj* [only before noun 僅用於名詞前] *AmE slang*【美俚】

1 very good or impressive 頂刮刮的，印象深刻的: *This site is the best online magazine for bad-ass biker gear.* 這個網站是介紹頂級摩托車手裝備的最佳在線雜誌。**2** *approving* a bad-ass person is very determined and does not always obey rules【褒】意志堅決的，不盲從的: *Johnson plays this bad-ass cop named O'Riley.* 約翰遜扮演這個非常有個性的名叫奧賴利的警察。—**bad ass** *n* [C]: *Man, I think Steven Seagal rocks. The dude's just a total bad ass.* 老兄，我覺得史蒂文·西加爾真棒，這傢伙很有個性。

bag² /bæg; bæg/ *v* [T]

NEW MEANING

informal to end an arrangement or agreement【非正式】終止〔安排或協議〕: *If the cable service doesn't live up to your expectations, bag it.* 如果有線服務不合你（們）的期望，那就終止它吧。

bal·lis·tic /bəˋlɪstɪk; bəˈlɪstɪk/ *adj*

spoken【口】**go ballistic** to suddenly become very angry（突然）生氣，發怒: *I couldn't believe it! She went ballistic just because there were peas in her pasta.* 我不敢相信！她僅僅因為麵條中有豌豆而大發脾氣。

bal·sam·ic vin·e·gar /bɔlˌsæmɪk ˋvɪnɪgɚ; bɔːlˌsæmɪk ˈvɪnɪgə/ *n* [U]

a type of VINEGAR that is dark brown and has a strong taste 香油醋，香脂醋〔一種深棕色香醋〕

banc·as·sur·ance /ˋbæŋkəˌʃurəns; ˈbæŋkəˌʃʊərəns/ *n* [U]

the combining of banking and insurance activities in one organization 銀行保險業

ban·di·ni /bænˋdinɪ; bænˈdiːni/ *n* [C]

a type of BIKINI that has a wide band of material for its top part and no STRAPS over the shoulders 班迪尼〔比基尼泳裝的一種〕

band·width /ˋbændwɪdθ; ˈbændwɪdθ/ *n* [U]

technical the total amount of information that can be carried through a telephone wire, computer connection etc at one time【術語】〔標誌網絡傳輸速度的〕帶寬，頻寬: *Telecommunications equipment at the Milan office was replaced this year to increase capacity and bandwidth.* 米蘭辦事處的電信設備今年都更換過了，以增加容量和帶寬。

bank /bæŋk; bæŋk/ *v*

NEW MEANING

be makin' bank *slang* to earn a lot of money for the work that you do【俚】掙大錢: *Check out Omar's new car. The brother must be makin' bank.* 打聽一下奧馬爾的新車，這位老兄肯定賺了大錢。

bank·roll·er /ˋbæŋkˌrolɚ; ˈbæŋkˌrəʊlə/ *n* [C]

someone who provides the money that a person or organization needs in order to do something, especially start a new business 融資者，提供啟動資金者

banner ad /ˋbænɚ ˌæd; ˈbænər ˌæd/ *n* [C]

an advertisement that appears across the top of a page on the Internet 網頁標題廣告，網頁橫額廣告: *Part of the screen was taken up by a banner ad for NewsPage.* 屏幕上的一部分是新聞網頁的標題廣告。—**banner advertising** *n* [U]

bar-code hair·style /ˋbɑr kod ˌhɛrstaɪl; ˈbɑː kəʊd ˌheəstaɪl/ *n* [C]

humorous a hairstyle worn by some men who no longer have hair on the top of their head, in which they grow the hair on one side longer and COMB it over the top of their head. Some people believe that this style looks similar to a BAR CODE.【幽默】〔以遮掩地中海脱髮的〕條形碼式（男）髮型

BASE jump·ing, base jumping /ˋbes ˌdʒʌmpɪŋ; ˈbeɪs ˌdʒʌmpɪŋ/ *n* [U]

a sport in which people jump off tall objects such as buildings, bridges, or cliffs, using a PARACHUTE. BASE jumping is illegal in many countries. BASE is an abbreviation for Building, Antenna, Span, Earth 高處跳傘: *In BASE jumping, the parachute is opened anywhere between 1,000 and 200 feet above the ground.* 在高處跳傘運動中，降落傘在距離地面1,000英尺到200英尺之間打開。—**BASE jump** *n* [C] —**BASE jumper** *n* [C]

bcc /ˌbi si ˋsi; ˌbiː siː ˈsiː/

blind carbon copy; used in an E-MAIL to show that you are sending someone a copy of a message that you have also sent to someone else, and that this person does not know that other people will receive the message 暗抄，隱蔽副本，盲拷貝

BCNU
a written abbreviation of 縮寫= 'be seeing you', used in E-MAIL or TEXT MESSAGE*s* on MOBILE PHONE*s* 再見〔電子郵件或手機短信用語〕

b-day /ˋbi de; ˈbiː deɪ/ *n* [C]
slang a BIRTHDAY【俚】生日: *Kevin Richardson's 29th b-day* 凱文·理查森的 29 週歲生日

bean count·er /ˋbin ˌkauntɚ; ˈbiːn ˌkaʊntə/ *n* [C]
informal someone whose job is to examine the cost of doing something, and who is concerned only with making a profit【非正式】〔政府部門和企業的〕審計人員: *Since the bean counters took over the radio station, it's become a boring place to work.* 自從那些核數專家接管電台後, 在那個地方工作已變得枯燥乏味。

bear hug /ˋbɛr ˌhʌg; ˈbeə ˌhʌg/ *n* [C]
NEW MEANING
technical informal an offer to buy a company, in which more money is offered than the company is actually worth【術語, 非正式】超值收購〔某公司〕, 溢價收購

bear squeeze /ˋbɛr ˌskwiz; ˈbeə ˌskwiːz/ *n* [C]
technical a situation in which SHARE prices rise because people know that one group of people must buy the shares【術語】〔股票交易〕下家促漲, 空頭軋平, 挾淡倉

beau·coup /ˋboku; ˈbəʊkuː/ *quantifier French spoken informal* a lot of or many【法口, 非正式】許多, 很多: *He makes beaucoup bucks* (=earns a lot of money) *in that job.* 他在那工作上掙了大把大把的錢。

bed-and-break·fast·ing /ˌbɛd ən ˋbrɛkfəstɪŋ; ˌbed ən ˈbrekfəstɪŋ/ *n* [U] *BrE*
technical informal an illegal situation in which someone sells SHARE*s* one day and buys them back the next day, in order to reduce the amount of CAPITAL GAINS TAX that they have to pay【英, 術語, 非正式】〔股票交易〕暮售朝購, 以減少所需繳付之資產增值稅, 屬非行為

bed block·er /ˋbɛd ˌblɑkɚ; ˈbed blɒkə/ *n* [C] *BrE*
someone who has been ill but who is still in hospital because there is no one to look after them if they go home, and who is therefore using a bed that is needed for someone else who is more ill【英】〔病已好而〕賴着不肯出院者

Bee·mer /ˋbimɚ; ˈbiːmə/ *n* [C]
informal a car made by BMW【非正式】BMW製造的汽車

benchmark /ˋbɛntʃˌmɑrk; ˈbentʃmɑːk/ *v* [T]
to use a company's good performance as a standard by which to judge the performance of other companies of the same type〔企業管理上〕以…為基準進行評定: **benchmark sb/sth against sth** *British Steel is benchmarked against the best operations anywhere in the world.* 英國鋼鐵公司是以世界上最好的公司作為基準評定業績。—**bench-marking** *n* [U]

ben·to box /ˋbɛnto ˌbɑks; ˈbentəʊ ˌbɒks/ *n* [C]
a box containing SUSHI or other Japanese food, which you can take to eat wherever you want〔盛裝壽司等日式食品的〕便當盒

best /bɛst; best/ *adj BrE*
NEW MEANING
spoken informal favourite【英口, 非正式】最喜愛的: *What's your best band, or haven't you got a best at the moment?* 你最喜愛的是哪個樂隊?你現在有沒有一個自己最喜歡的樂隊呢?

best-ef·forts /ˌbɛst ˋɛfɚts; ˌbest ˈefəts/ *adj* [only before noun 僅用於名詞前]
technical a best-efforts arrangement is one in which a bank agrees to sell another company's new SHARE*s*, but will not have to buy the shares itself if it cannot sell them【術語】〔發售新股中〕不作包銷承諾的

best-of-breed, best of breed /ˌbɛst əv ˋbrid; ˌbest əv ˈbriːd/ *adj*
a best-of-breed computer system uses a combination of the best SOFTWARE from different companies rather than only using the software from one company 用最好的軟件拼裝的

best prac·tice /ˌbɛst ˋpræktɪs; ˌbest ˈpræktɪs/ *n* [C,U]
a description of the best way of performing a particular activity, especially in business, that can be used by other people or companies as a set of rules to follow 最佳舉措: *Management has proposed several steps to be adopted as best practice to bring the design and delivery processes closer together.* 管理層已把設計和生產過程緊密聯繫在一起的最佳措施作出若干建議。| *We are currently developing a number of best practices to help the Internet community enhance network security.* 目前我們正在研究若干最可行的方法, 以加強網絡社羣的保安系統。

beta car·o·tene /ˌbetə ˋkærətin; ˌbiːtə ˈkærətiːn/ *n* [U]
a type of CAROTENE (=a substance found in vegetables such as CARROT*s*, which is important for good health) β胡蘿蔔素: *Are you taking beta carotene supplements?* 你在服用β胡蘿蔔素補充劑嗎?

bev·vied up /ˌbɛvɪd ˋʌp; ˌbevid ˈʌp/ *adj* [not before noun 不用於名詞前] *BrE*
informal drunk. This phrase comes from 'BEVVY' which is an informal word meaning BEVERAGE.【英, 非正式】喝醉的: **be bevvied up** *After a couple of hours everyone was so bevvied up that they didn't know what they were doing.* 幾個小時後, 他們一個個都喝得醉醺醺的, 不知道自己在幹甚麼。| **get bevvied up** *We're all going out tonight to get bevvied up.* 今天晚上我們都去喝他個一醉方休。

bidding war /ˋbɪdɪŋ ˌwɔr; ˈbɪdɪŋ ˌwɔː/ *n* [C]
a situation in which two or more people or organizations compete to buy something, for example a house or a company 競價戰: *She said she had expected a bidding war for the 5,000-square-foot home on Vargas Road.* 她說她料到瓦爾加斯大道上那幢5,000平方英尺的住房會引起一場競價戰。

big /bɪg; bɪg/ *v*
big sth up *phr v* [T] *BrE spoken informal* to spend a lot of money and enjoy yourself in a social situation, in a way that other people will notice【英口, 非正式】擺闊, 充大方

big air 滑板滑雪

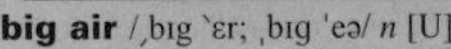

big air /ˌbɪg ˋɛr; ˌbɪg ˈeə/ *n* [U]
a type of SNOWBOARD*ing* in which people perform complicated jumps and turns in the air while going down a mountain 滑板滑雪: *After Saturday's big air competition, Christy says she's ready to come back next year.* 在星期六滑板滑雪賽之後, 克里斯蒂說她準備明年再來。

big·foot·ing /ˋbɪgˌfutɪŋ; ˈbɪgˌfʊtɪŋ/ *n* [U]
1 the practice of using your power or authority to take control of a situation from someone who is weaker than you 仗勢壓人 **2** a situation in which a large number of similar signals are sent at the same time from MOBILE PHONE*s* to a radio station so that it is difficult for the radio station to handle them〔對無線電通訊台的〕手機信息轟炸

big hair /ˌbɪg ˋhɛr; ˌbɪg ˈheə/ *n* [U]
informal a hair style in which someone's hair is high up above their head and wide at the sides, fashionable es-

pecially in the 1980s【非正式】蓬蓬頭〔尤指20世紀80年代流行的一種髮型〕: *Who's that woman with the big hair?* 那個留着蓬蓬頭的女人是誰?

big hit·ter /ˌbɪg ˋhɪtɚ; ˌbɪg ˈhɪtə/ *n* [C]
someone who is very important and successful and who has a lot of influence 要人, 大亨: *For many years, Kenneth Clarke was one of the big hitters in the Conservative Party.* 許多年來, 肯尼斯·克拉克一直是保守黨內的大佬之一。

bike /baɪk; baɪk/ *v* [T]
to take something to someone by motorbike in order to get it there quickly 用摩托車帶〔人或物〕: **bike sth over/round** *We're late for our deadline. Can you bike the photos over to us?* 我們要趕不上最後期限了, 你能用摩托車把那些照片捎過來嗎?

bin·di /ˋbɪndɪ; ˈbɪndi/ *n* [C]
a small amount of coloured powder or a piece of jewellery, usually in the shape of a round mark, that many Hindu people wear on their FOREHEADS between their EYEBROWS. Bindis are worn for religious reasons and by women to show they are married, but now many women wear them to make themselves more attractive or fashionable.〔印度女子加在兩眉之間前額上的〕吉祥痣〔以前用於表示已婚, 現在只是為了裝飾〕

bi·o·di·ver·si·ty /ˌbaɪodaɪˋvɝsətɪ; ˌbaɪəʊdaɪˈvɜːsɪ̇ti/ *n* [U]
technical the variety of plants and animals in a particular place【術語】〔某地的〕生物多樣性: *One of our goals will be to involve local communities in biodiversity conservation.* 我們的目標之一是要讓當地的社羣參加保護生物多樣性。

bi·o·eth·ics /ˌbaɪoˋɛθɪks; ˌbaɪəʊˈeθɪks/ *n* [U]
technical the study of whether some sciences, for example GENETIC ENGINEERING, are a good or bad thing for society【術語】生物倫理學

bi·o·in·for·ma·ti·cian /ˌbaɪoˌɪnfɚməˋtɪʃən; ˌbaɪəʊˌɪnfəməˈtɪʃən/ *n* [C]
someone who studies or works in BIOINFORMATICS 生物信息學〔研究〕者

bi·o·in·for·mat·ics /ˌbaɪoˌɪnfɔrˋmætɪks; ˌbaɪəʊˌɪnfɔːˈmætɪks/ *n* [U]
technical the use of computers to organize the large amounts of information produced in some kinds of science, for example GENETICS【術語】生物信息學

biologically en·gi·neered /baɪəˌlɑdʒɪkl̩ɪ ɛndʒəˋnɪrd; baɪəˌlɒdʒɪkli endʒɪ̇ˈnɪəd/ *adj*
another word for GENETICALLY MODIFIED genetically modified 的另一種説法

bi·o·nom·ics /ˌbaɪoˋnɑmɪks; ˌbaɪəʊˈnɒmɪks/ *n* [U]
technical a type of scientific study which compares economic systems to ECOSYSTEMS (=the living things in a particular area and how they relate to one another)【術語】生態經濟學

bi·o·phar·ma·ceu·ti·cal /ˌbaɪoˌfɑrməˋsjutɪkl̩; ˌbaɪəʊˌfɑːməˈsjuːtɪkəl/ *adj* [only before noun 僅用於名詞前]
technical relating to BIOTECHNOLOGY (=the use of living things to make drugs and chemicals) and PHARMACEUTICALS (= the development and production of drugs and medicines)【術語】生物製藥的: *Not all biopharmaceutical companies make drugs themselves.* 不是所有生物製藥公司都自製藥物。

bi·ra·cial /ˌbaɪˋreʃəl; ˌbaɪˈreɪʃəl◂/ *adj*
if someone is biracial, he or she has parents who come from different races 雙人種的, 雙族裔的: *biracial children* 混血兒

birth /bɝθ; bɜːθ/ *v* [T]
literary to be the origin of something new; ORIGINATE【文】開創: *McMillan's 1992 novel birthed a new genre of contemporary fiction.* 麥克米倫1992年的長篇小説開創了當代小説的一種新體裁。

biz·jet /ˋbɪzdʒɛt; ˈbɪzdʒet/ *n* [C]
informal an aircraft used especially by business people【非正式】商務人員專機

biz·zies /ˋbɪzɪz; ˈbɪziz/ *n* [plural] *BrE*
slang the police. This word is used especially in the city of Liverpool in north-west England【英俚】警察: *I just hid in the corner until the bizzies had gone.* 我躲在角落裡一直到警察離去。

black knight /ˌblæk ˋnaɪt; ˌblæk ˈnaɪt/ *n* [C]
a company that tries to take control of another company by offering to buy a lot of its SHARES "黑騎士"〔通過購買另一公司大量股票從而對它加以控制的公司〕

blad·dered /ˋblædɚd; ˈblædəd/ *adj* [not before noun 不用於名詞前] *BrE*
informal very drunk【英, 非正式】大醉的, 爛醉如泥的: **be bladdered** *Geoff was completely bladdered last night. He could hardly stand up.* 傑夫昨天夜裡醉得一塌糊塗, 幾乎站不起來。| **get bladdered** *He's down the pub getting bladdered.* 他去酒館裡買醉了。

blad·er /ˋbledɚ; ˈbleɪdə/ *n* [C]
informal someone who SKATES on ROLLERBLADES【非正式】滾軸溜冰者, 滑旱冰者

blag·ger /ˋblægɚ; ˈblægə/ *n* [C] *BrE*
informal someone who gets something they want by lying to people in a clever way【英, 非正式】騙徒

Blair·is·m /ˋblɛrɪzəm; ˈbleərɪzəm/ *n* [U] *BrE*
the political ideas of the British PRIME MINISTER, Tony Blair, and his government【英】〔英國首相〕布萊爾[貝理雅]主義〔布萊爾[貝理雅]及其政府所持的政治理念〕

Blair·ite /ˋblɛraɪt; ˈbleəraɪt/ *n* [C] *BrE*
someone who believes in the political ideas of the British PRIME MINISTER, Tony Blair, and his government【英】布萊爾[貝理雅]主義者 —**Blairite** *adj*

blame·storm·ing /ˋblemˌstɔrmɪŋ; ˈbleɪmˌstɔːmɪŋ/ *n* [U]
humorous the practice of sitting in a group and talking about why a particular job was not done properly, and deciding who was responsible for the failure. This word comes from a combination of the words 'BLAME' and 'BRAINSTORMING'.【幽默】〔為檢討某項目失敗原因等而舉行的〕責任追究會〔由 blame 和 brainstorming 縮合而成〕

bleeding edge /ˌblidɪŋ ˋɛdʒ; ˌbliːdɪŋ ˈedʒ/ *n* [singular]
the bleeding edge the most advanced stage or development of something. This expression developed from the phrase 'the cutting edge' and is used about things that are even newer, more advanced etc, especially related to computers 尖端技術水平: **on the bleeding edge of sth** *developments on the bleeding edge of information technology* 資訊科技尖端技術的發展 —**bleeding-edge** *adj* [only before noun 僅用於名詞前]: *bleeding-edge applications* 尖端技術的應用

blended fam·i·ly /ˌblɛndɪd ˋfæməlɪ; ˌblendɪ̇d ˈfæməli/ *n* [C]
a family in which one or both parents have children from previous marriages living with the family 混合型家庭〔由夫婦及其子女, 以及雙方或其中一方在過去婚姻中所生子女組成的家庭〕: *Some experts had estimated that by the year 2000 there would be more blended families than intact biological families.* 一些專家估計, 到2000年混合型家庭將多於純血緣的家庭。

bless /blɛs; bles/ *interjection BrE*
said to show that you think someone or something is very nice or loveable【英】棒極了!: *At that moment, a cute little dog came into the room. "Oh, bless," said Tamryn.* 就在那個時候, 一隻可愛的小狗走進了房間。"呵, 好酷, "塔姆林說。

blind call /ˌblaɪnd ˋkɔl; ˌblaɪnd ˈkɔːl/ *n* [C]
another word for COLD CALL cold call 的另一種説法

blissed out /ˌblɪst ˋaʊt; ˌblɪst ˈaʊt/ *adj BrE*
informal extremely happy and relaxed, especially as a result of using illegal drugs【英, 非正式】〔尤指吸食毒品後〕感到極度欣喜和放鬆的: *a bunch of blissed out partygoers* 一羣興高采烈的聚會者 | *He just stood with*

a blissed out look on his face and danced. 他帶着極其輕鬆愉快的表情站了起來，跳起了舞。| *I felt really blissed out.* 我真的感到極度的快樂和放鬆。—**bliss out** *v* [I]: *I blissed out on ecstasy.* 我服了"狂喜"迷幻藥後感到極度愉快和放鬆。

B-list /ˈbi ˌlɪst; ˈbiː ˌlɪst/ *adj*
among the group of film stars, musicians etc who are fairly famous or popular, but are not any of the most popular or famous〔影星、歌星等〕二流的: *The party was crowded by B-list personalities who could be relied on to turn up to any launch.* 這次晚會擠滿了二流角色，每逢有甚麼開張活動，他們準保都會到場。

bloat·ware /ˈblotˌwɛr; ˈbləʊtweə/ *n* [U]
informal【非正式】**1** computer SOFTWARE that has many features that are not needed〔包含許多無用性能的〕電腦軟件 **2** computer SOFTWARE that uses a large amount of the computer's MEMORY, and that is therefore not effective or useful〔因佔用大量記憶體而效率降低的〕膨脹軟件

blood /blʌd; blʌd/ *n*
NEW MEANING
blood on the carpet a situation where people have a very strong disagreement, with the result that something serious happens, such as someone losing his or her job 嚴重分歧

blood dop·ing /ˈblʌd ˌdopɪŋ; ˈblʌd ˌdəʊpɪŋ/ *n* [U]
the practice of removing red BLOOD CELLs from an ATHLETE's body, preserving them for a period of time, and then putting them back before he or she competes in a sports event. Blood doping improves an athlete's performance and is illegal in most sports 血攙，違規輸血〔從運動員體內抽出部分紅血球，參賽前再注回體內以提升運動員的表現〕

blow /blo; bləʊ/ *n* [U]
NEW MEANING
slang the illegal drug COCAINE【俚】雲霧〔指可卡因〕

blue·tooth /ˈblutuθ; ˈbluːtuːθ/ *n* [U]
trademark bluetooth technology allows electronic equipment to communicate by using radio, so that, for example, a computer and printer can work together without having a wire connecting them【商標】藍牙技術〔代替專用連接電纜的通用無線電鏈路〕

blunt /blʌnt; blʌnt/ *n* [C] *AmE*
slang a thick MARIJUANA cigarette that is made by taking the tobacco out of a CIGAR and filling the empty inner part with marijuana【美俚】大麻煙卷

BMP /ˌbi ɛm ˈpi; ˌbiː em ˈpiː/ *n* [C]
technical【術語】**1** basic multilingual plane 基本多文種平面 **2** bit mapped picture 位映像圖形

bo·de·ga /boˈdegə; bəʊˈdiːgə/ *n* [C] *Spanish*【西】
a small shop that sells food 小食品店

body warm·er /ˈbɑdɪ ˌwɔrmɚ; ˈbɒdi ˌwɔːmə/ *n* [C]
a piece of warm clothing without arms that you wear over a sweater or a shirt, especially when you are outside〔戶外穿的〕馬甲，背心: *a woolly fleece body warmer* 羊毛馬甲

boiler-room /ˈbɔɪlɚ ˌrum; ˈbɔɪlə ˌruːm/ also 又作 **boiler shop** *n* [C]
an organization that sells STOCKs, SHAREs etc by telephone, often using dishonest or illegal methods of selling "鍋爐房"〔以欺詐方式通過電話推銷股票等的非法組織〕: *boiler-room sales techniques* "鍋爐房"推銷術

bolt-on /ˈbolt ˌɑn; ˈbəʊlt ˌɒn/ *adj*
bolt-on part/component/extra *especially BrE* something that is connected to the outside of a machine after it has been made, and is then part of the machine【尤英】可用螺栓固定的部分/部件/附件

bomb /bɑm; bɒm/ *n*
NEW MEANING
be the bomb *AmE slang* to be very good or exciting【美俚】極好的，轟動的: *That new Puff Daddy CD is the bomb.* 那張新出的吹牛老爹雷射唱片非常轟動。

bone /bon; bəʊn/ *v* [T]
NEW MEANING
taboo to have sex with someone【諱】與某人性交

bonk·bust·er /ˈbɑŋkˌbʌstɚ; ˈbɒŋkˌbʌstə/ *n* [C] *BrE humorous* a book or film which contains a lot of sex and which is very popular and successful, but which is not considered to have serious value as art. This word comes from a combination of the words 'bonk', which is a British slang word meaning 'to have sex', and 'BLOCKBUSTER'【英，幽默】風靡一時的性愛小說[電影]〔由bonk和blockbuster縮合而成〕: *She spent her holiday lying by the pool, reading the latest bonkbuster.* 她躺在池邊，閱讀最新的性愛小說來消磨假日。—**bonkbuster** *adj*: *bonkbuster novels* 風靡一時的情慾小說

boob·ker·chief /ˈbubkɚˌtʃɪf; ˈbuːbkəˌtʃɪ̵f/ *n* [C] *BrE informal* a piece of clothing for women that is made from a TRIANGLE-shaped piece of cloth that is fastened at the back, so that the arms and shoulders are not covered. This word is a combination of the words 'boobs', which is an informal word for a woman's BREASTs, and 'HANDKERCHIEF'.【英，非正式】胸兜，兜肚〔由boobs和handkerchief縮合而成〕

boogie board /ˈbugɪ ˌbord; ˈbuːgi ˌbɔːd/ *n* [C]
an object that you lie on to ride on ocean waves, that is half the length of a SURFBOARD 臥式短衝浪板

bookmark¹ /ˈbukˌmark; ˈbʊkmɑːk/ *n* [C]
NEW MEANING
a way of saving the address of a page on the Internet, so that you can find it again easily〔網上〕書籤，鏈標記

bookmark² /ˈbukˌmark; ˈbʊkmɑːk/ *v* [T]
to save the address of a page on the Internet, so that you can find it again easily 標識〔網址，方便下次瀏覽〕

boom·er /ˈbumɚ; ˈbuːmə/ *n* [C]
a short form of 縮略式= BABY BOOMER

boot cut /ˈbut ˌkʌt; ˈbuːt ˌkʌt/ *adj*
boot cut trousers/jeans trousers or JEANS that are slightly wider at the bottom than at the knee so that you can wear boots with them 寬褲腳緊身褲/牛仔褲

bootstrap ac·qui·si·tion /ˈbutstræp ækwəˌzɪʃən; ˈbuːtstræp ækwɪ̵ˌzɪʃən/ *n* [C,U]
technical a way of buying a company over a period of time, in which you buy SHAREs that you then use to borrow money. You then use this money to buy more shares until you own the company.【術語】漸進式收購，抵押式收購〔在一段時間內收購一家公司，先是通過購買股票，然後以股票作抵押借錢，再用借來的款項購買更多股票，直到控制該公司為止〕

boss key /ˈbɔs ˌki; ˈbɒs ˌkiː/ *n* [C]
a key on a computer keyboard that changes what is displayed on a screen. Boss keys are used by workers who are, for example, playing games or looking at WEB PAGEs instead of working, when they hear their manager or BOSS coming close to them.〔電腦〕快速切換鍵

bot /bɑt; bɒt/ *n* [C]
technical a computer PROGRAM that performs the same operation many times in a row, for example, one that searches for information on the Internet as part of a SEARCH ENGINE【術語】網上機器人〔連續多次執行相同操作的電腦程序〕

Bo·tox¹ /ˈbotɑks; ˈbəʊtɒks/ *n* [U]
trademark a substance that makes muscles relax, which can be INJECTED into the skin around someone's eyes to make the lines disappear and the skin look younger and more attractive【商標】保妥適肉毒毒素，毒桿菌素: *Botox injections for wrinkles* 肉毒毒素注射劑用於去除皺紋

Botox² /ˈbotɑks; ˈbəʊtɒks/ *v* [T usually passive 一般用被動態]
trademark to use Botox to remove lines on your face【商標】使用保妥適去皺: *Getting Botoxed is pretty simple.* 使用保妥適去除臉上皺紋是很容易的。| *He Botoxed his forehead before the next film.* 他在演下一部影片前使用保妥適去掉前額的皺紋。

bottom fish·er /ˋbɑtəm ˌfɪʃɚ; ˈbɒtəm ˌfɪʃə/ *n* [C]
technical someone who buys companies, SHARES etc when their value is low, expecting the situation to improve later so that the companies etc increase in value【術語】趁低價時收購者

bounce /baʊns; baʊns/ *v* also 又作 **bounce back**
NEW MEANING
1 [I,T] if an E-MAIL message that you send bounces or is bounced, it is AUTOMATICALLY returned to you because of a technical problem〔電子郵件〕自動退回, 彈回: *I tried to send you a message about half an hour ago, but it bounced back.* 半個小時前我試着給你發去了一個信息, 但是被自動退了回來。**2** [T] *informal* to force someone to leave a place, job, or organization, especially because they have done something wrong【非正式】迫使〔尤指犯錯者〕去職, 把…從…中逐出: *That June, he bounced the other two leaders and named himself President.* 那年6月, 他迫使另外兩名領袖下台, 並任命自己為總統。| **bounce sb from sth** *Taylor was bounced from the team for six weeks for assaulting his ex-girlfriend.* 泰勒因為侵犯前女友而被停止隊籍六週。

boy band /ˋbɔɪ ˌbænd; ˈbɔɪ ˌbænd/ *n* [C]
a group of attractive young men who perform by singing and dancing, and who are especially popular with teenage girls 男孩樂隊: *Christy's favorite boy band is Boyzone.* 克里斯蒂最喜愛的男孩樂隊是"男孩地帶"。

bps, BPS /ˌbi pi ˋɛs; ˌbiː piː ˈes/ *n* [U]
technical bits per second; a measurement of how fast a computer or MODEM can send or receive information【術語】每秒位元數, 比特/秒: *a 28,800 bps modem* 28,800位/秒的調解器

brain·i·ac /ˋbrenɪˌæk; ˈbreɪniæk/ *n* [C]
informal humorous someone who spends a lot of time studying and thinking about complicated ideas, but who is often unable to communicate with people in ordinary social situations【非正式, 幽默】整天思考高深問題的人, 怪才: *Electrical engineering is the perfect career for a brainiac like him.* 電機工程是那些像他那樣整天愛琢磨的人的理想職業。—**brainiac** *adj*: *The company is trying to change its brainiac image.* 該公司試圖改變其學究形象。

branchless bank /ˌbræntʃlɪs ˋbæŋk; ˌbrɑːntʃləs ˈbæŋk/ *n* [C]
a bank that exists only on the Internet and which does not have a building that you can go to 網上銀行

brand·ing /ˋbrændɪŋ; ˈbrændɪŋ/ *n* [U]
technical a practice in which a company gives a group of their products the same BRAND NAME. This is done to help the brand name become well known and to encourage people to buy new or different products that have the same brand.【術語】創名牌, 品牌打造

BRB, brb
a written abbreviation of 縮寫= 'be right back', used by people communicating in CHAT ROOMS on the Internet 馬上回來〔網上聊天室用語〕

breadboard /ˋbrɛdˌbɔrd; ˈbredbɔːd/ *n* [C]
NEW MEANING
technical a model of a CIRCUIT BOARD (=a piece of electronic equipment) that is used in order to test the design before it is produced【術語】模擬試驗板

break·beat /ˋbrekˌbit; ˈbreɪkbiːt/ *n* [U] *BrE*
a type of dance music which is popular in Britain, has a fast beat, and uses SAMPLES (=a small part of a song from a CD or record that is used in a new song)【英】霹靂舞曲, 碎拍音樂

breeder /ˋbridɚ; ˈbriːdə/ *n* [C]
NEW MEANING
an offensive word meaning HETEROSEXUAL, used by HOMOSEXUALS, especially to talk about someone they do not like 配種人〔同性戀者稱異性戀者的冒犯語〕

breeze /briz; briːz/ *v* [T]
NEW MEANING
to do very well in a test, a piece of written work etc, with very little effort 輕易地通過: *Don't bother studying for the English exam – you'll breeze it.* 不要為應付英語考試而頭疼, 你會輕易通過的。

brilliant weap·on /ˋbrɪljənt ˌwɛpən; ˈbrɪljənt ˌwepən/ *n* [C]
a weapon that can find the object it is attacking without being guided by a computer 智能(化)武器

Brit·pop /ˋbrɪtpɑp; ˈbrɪtpɒp/ *n* [U]
a type of British popular music of the 1990s that often has tunes that are easy to remember, clever or interesting words, and is suitable for dancing. It is usually played by small bands with a drummer, one or two guitar players, and a singer. Well-known Britpop bands include Blur and Oasis.〔20世紀90年代流行的〕不列顛流行音樂〔一種曲調易記, 歌詞靈巧、有趣, 適合跳舞的音樂〕

broadband /ˋbrɔdˌbænd; ˈbrɔːdbænd/ *n* [U]
NEW MEANING
technical a system of connecting computers to the Internet and moving information, such as messages or pictures, at a very high speed【術語】寬〔頻〕帶 —**broadband** *adj* [only before noun 僅用於名詞前]: *broadband communications* 寬帶通訊

broad mon·ey /ˋbrɔd ˌmʌnɪ; ˈbrɔːd ˌmʌni/ *n* [U]
technical cash and all other forms of money that cannot easily be turned into cash【術語】廣義貨幣: *Broad money refers to money held both for transactions purposes and as a form of saving.* "廣義貨幣"指的是既可用於交易又可用於儲蓄的一種貨幣。

brother /ˋbrʌðɚ; ˈbrʌðə/ *n* [C]
NEW MEANING
slang a word meaning a black man, used especially by other black men【俚】〔黑人之間互稱〕兄弟

brown·field site /ˋbraʊnfild ˌsaɪt; ˈbraʊnfiːld ˌsaɪt/ *n* [C] *BrE*
a place, especially in a city, that is used for building homes, offices etc, where in the past there have already been buildings, industries etc【英】拆遷地, 重建區〔指城市中清除舊房後可用於建造新房的空地〕: *The government wants to raise the proportion of housing built on brownfield sites, rather than on unspoilt countryside.* 政府想提高在重建區而不是在未遭破壞的農村修建住房的比例。

brows·er /ˋbraʊzɚ; ˈbraʊzə/ *n* [C]
a computer program that finds information on the Internet and shows it on your computer screen 瀏覽器: *a Web browser* 網上瀏覽器

bruschetta 蓋澆吐司

bru·schet·ta /bruˋskɛtə; bruːˈsketə/ *n* [U]
bread that has been TOASTed and has OLIVE OIL and usually vegetables, cheese etc on top of it〔上面澆有橄欖油、蔬菜、乳酪等的〕蓋澆吐司, 意大利吐司

B-school /ˋbi ˌskul; ˈbiː ˌskuːl/ *n* [C]
a short form of 縮略式= BUSINESS SCHOOL

BTW, btw
a written abbreviation of 縮寫= 'by the way', often used in E-MAIL or TEXT MESSAGES on MOBILE PHONES 順便提一下〔電子郵件或手機短信用語〕

buffed /bʌft; bʌft/ *adj AmE spoken*【美口】**1 get buffed** if you get buffed, you lift weights regularly so that your muscles will get bigger 變得壯實: *This is a beginner's guide to getting buffed and maintaining a complete physique.* 這本初學者指南教導讀者如何鍛鍊肌肉和保持體形完美。**2** a buffed person has big strong muscles 肌肉發達的

buffer /ˋbʌfɚ; ˈbʌfə/ *v* [T]
if a computer buffers information, it holds it for a short while before using it. Computers buffer information when receiving VIDEO pictures over the Internet, for example, so that they have enough information to show the pictures smoothly and do not have to wait while more information arrives. 緩存〔信息〕

bug² /bʌg; bʌg/
bug sb out *phr v* [T] *informal* to annoy someone【非正式】使〔某人〕厭煩: *It really bugs me out how he's always talking about how much money he makes.* 他總在叨嘮自己能掙多少錢, 這真讓我煩透了。

bull bars /ˋbʊl ˌbɑrz; ˈbʊl ˌbɑːz/ *n* [plural] *BrE*
a set of metal bars fixed to the front of a large vehicle such as a Jeep or Land Rover in order to protect it from damage【英】〔機動車的〕保險槓: *They fitted their 4x4 with bull bars.* 他們給自己的四輪驅動車裝上了保險槓。—**bullbarred** *adj: bullbarred vehicles* 裝有保險槓的車輛

bum /bʌm; bʌm/ *n*
NEW MEANING
bums on seats *BrE humorous* the number of people who go to a concert, play, or other performance. This expression is often used by people who disapprove of performances that are intended to attract as many people as possible, but that may not have a lot of serious artistic value【英, 幽默】出席〔表演〕的人數〔常用於但求叫座不求高藝術價值的表演〕: *These managers just want to know what will put bums on seats.* 經理們只想知道如何能吸引人前來捧場。

bummed /bʌmd; bʌmd/ also 又作 **bummed out** *adj* [not before noun 不用於名詞前]
informal especially spoken feeling sad or disappointed【非正式, 尤口】悲傷的, 沮喪的: *I was really bummed that I missed the game.* 我錯過了這場比賽, 感到十分失望。

bump /bʌmp; bʌmp/ *v*
NEW MEANING
1 [T] *informal* to move someone or something into a different class or group, or to move them out of a class or group altogether【非正式】把〔某人或東西〕移到〔另一個級別或羣體〕, 把…攆走 [挪走]: *Jeff was bumped to first class by American Airlines when he told them why he was flying back to Arizona.* 傑夫告訴了美國航空公司他要飛回亞利桑那的原因後, 航空公司就安排他換到了頭等艙。| *The flight was overbooked, and as Dad hadn't reconfirmed he was the first one to be bumped.* 這個航班超員預訂, 爸爸因為沒有再確認機位, 就成了第一個被擠掉的人。| **bump sb up/out of/from etc** *The reforms bumped many families off the state-provided healthcare list.* 這連串改革把許多家庭擠出了公費醫療名單。**2** to move a radio or television programme to a different time〔將電台或電視節目〕改期播出: *The 'X Files' is moving from Friday to Sunday nights, and as a result, 'Married with Children' will be bumped from Sundays to Saturdays.*《X 檔案》由星期五改到星期天晚上播出, 因此,《寶貝家庭》將從星期天挪到星期六播出。

bun /bʌn; bʌn/ *n plural* **buns**
NEW MEANING
informal humorous the part of your body that you sit on【非正式, 幽默】屁股

bundle¹ /ˋbʌndl̩; ˈbʌndl/ *n* [C]
NEW MEANING
computer SOFTWARE and sometimes other equipment or services that are included with a new computer at little or no additional cost〔電腦〕捆綁式銷售, 附送: *Most computer makers include a bundle of useful software for you and the kids.* 許多電腦製造商隨電腦附送一些對你和孩子們有用的軟件。

bundle² /ˋbʌndl̩; ˈbʌndl/ *v* [T]
NEW MEANING
to include computer SOFTWARE or other services with a new computer at little or no extra cost〔銷售電腦時〕捆綁銷售, 附送: **bundle sth with sth** *Microsoft can bundle Windows NT at discounted prices with its popular desktop application programs.* 微軟打折銷售流行的桌面應用軟件時可附送視窗 NT。

burn¹ /bɝn; bɜːn/ *v* [T]
NEW MEANING
if you burn a CD, you record music, images, or other information onto it, using special computer equipment 刻錄, 燒錄〔盤片, 光碟〕

burn rate /ˋbɝn ˌret; ˈbɜːn ˌreɪt/ *n* [U]
the rate at which a new company spends money when it is just starting, especially used of new Internet companies〔新互聯網公司投入運作時〕花錢的速率

business-to-business /ˌbɪznɪs tə ˋbɪznɪs; ˌbɪznɪ̵s tə ˈbɪznɪ̵s/ *adj abbreviation* 縮寫為 **B2B**
business-to-business advertising/commerce/marketing/transactions etc advertising or other business activities between different businesses, rather than between a business and ordinary people who are customers 商家對商家的廣告/貿易/營銷/交易等: *We hope to offer full business-to-business transactions over the Internet by next year.* 我們希望來年能通過互聯網提供全面的商家對商家的交易。| *business-to-business credit information* 商家之間的信貸信息

bust /bʌst; bʌst/ *v*
NEW MEANING
bust a move *AmE slang* to make unusual and impressive movements while dancing【美俚】跳出不同尋常的舞步
bust sb not *phr v* [T] *AmE slang* to strongly criticize someone【美俚】對…嚴加指責: *I busted him out for forgetting to pay me back.* 他忘了還我錢, 我嚴責了他一頓。

bust·ed¹ /ˋbʌstɪd; ˈbʌstɪ̵d/ *adj* [not before noun 不用於名詞前] *AmE informal* caught doing something wrong and likely to be punished【美, 非正式】被逮個正着的: *You guys are so busted!* 這回你們這些傢伙可給逮個正着了!

busted² /ˋbʌstɪd; ˈbʌstɪ̵d/ *interjection AmE*
said when someone has been caught lying or doing something wrong【美】(這下) 可 (給) 逮住了!

bust-up ac·qui·si·tion /ˋbʌst ʌp ækwəˌzɪʃən; ˈbʌst ʌp ækwɪ̵ˌzɪʃən/ *n* [C,U]
technical a situation in which a company gets a loan to buy another company by promising that it will sell the things the second company owns if it cannot pay back the loan【術語】二手抵押借貸, 二手資產抵押

button-down /ˋbʌtn̩ ˌdaun; ˈbʌtn ˌdaʊn/ also 又作 **buttoned-down** *adj* [only before noun 僅用於名詞前]
a button-down company or style is formal and traditional 守舊的, 缺乏想像力的: *He didn't fit in with the button-down culture of his new boss.* 他不適應新老闆那套老式的做法。

buy² /baɪ; baɪ/ *n* [C usually singular 一般用單數, U]
NEW MEANING
an act of buying something, especially something illegal 購買, 進貨〔尤指私貨〕: *A couple of guys were sitting behind me discussing some kind of buy.* 坐在我後面的兩個傢伙正討論要進點私貨。

buy·back /ˋbaɪˌbæk; ˈbaɪbæk/ *n* [C,U]
an arrangement by which a person or company sells SHARES in a business and buys them back again later 回購〔股票〕: *Share buybacks are constrained by tight regulations.* 股票回購受到嚴格的條例規範。

buzzed-about /ˋbʌzd əˏbaut; ˈbʌzd əˌbaʊt/ *adj AmE informal* a buzzed-about film, book etc is one which a lot of people are talking about because it is new and interesting【美, 非正式】多人談論的: *It's one of the year's most buzzed-about movies.* 這是本年度最熱門的電影之一。

BWL, bwl
a written abbreviation of 縮寫= 'bursting with laughter', used in E-MAIL or TEXT MESSAGEs on MOBILE PHONEs 笑死人了〔電子郵件或手機短信用語〕

C,c

C++ /ˏsi plʌs ˋplʌs; ˌsiː plʌs ˈplʌs/ *n* [U]
a computer language that is popular because it is useful for developing complicated computer PROGRAMs〔電腦的〕C++ 語言

C2C /ˏsi tu ˋsi; ˌsiː tuː ˈsiː/
the written abbreviation of 縮寫= 'customer to customer'; the selling of a product or service from one customer to another, usually over the Internet, for example at an ONLINE AUCTION 客戶對客戶〔網上拍賣用語〕

ca·ble·cast /ˋkeblˏkæst; ˈkeɪbəlˌkɑːst/ *n* [C]
a show, film, sports event etc that is broadcast on a CABLE television station 有線電視廣播: *The MTV Video Awards cablecast is almost as popular as the Grammy Awards.* 透過有線電視廣播的音樂電視視頻獎幾乎和格林美獎一樣受歡迎。—**cablecast** *v* [T]

cable mo·dem /ˋkebl ˏmodɛm; ˈkeɪbəl ˌməʊdem/ *n* [C]
a MODEM (=a piece of equipment that allows information from one computer to be sent to another) that uses CABLE connections instead of telephone wires, and allows you to search the Internet very quickly 電纜調制解調器, 纜線數據機: *Millions of people use cable modems at home for faster online access.* 數以百萬計的人利用電纜調制解調器在家中以更快的速度上網。

cable-read·y /ˋkebl ˏrɛdɪ; ˈkeɪbəl ˌredi/ *adj*
a television that is cable-ready is able to receive CABLE TELEVISION signals directly without needing any special equipment〔電視〕能直接接收有線電視訊號的

cache¹ /kæʃ; kæʃ/ *n* [C]
NEW MEANING
technical a special section of MEMORY in a computer that helps it work faster by storing information for a short time【術語】高速緩衝存儲器, 快取記憶體: *Every time a user requests a Web page, the provider's machine checks whether a copy is already stored in the cache.* 每當用戶需要某個網頁時, 供應商的機器就會核查在高速緩衝存儲器中是否已留有副本。| *In practice, cache memory can improve a computer's performance dramatically.* 高速緩衝存儲器確能極大地改善電腦的性能。

cache² /kæʃ; kæʃ/ *v* [T]
NEW MEANING
technical to put information in a cache【術語】把資料存入快取記憶體

café, cafe /kæˋfe; ˈkæfeɪ/ *n* [C]
NEW MEANING
a part of a WEBSITE which has general information about the website, discussion groups, a place to read or leave messages for other users etc〔網站的〕聊天茶座: *Only registered users may log on to the site's cafe.* 只有註冊用戶才可進入該網站的聊天茶座。

CALL /kɔl; kɔːl/ *n* [U]
computer-assisted language learning; the use of computers to help people learn foreign languages 電腦輔助外語學習

call cen·tre /ˋkɔl ˏsɛntɚ; ˈkɔːl ˌsentə/ *n* [C] *BrE*
an office where people answer customers' questions, make sales etc over the telephone【英】電話服務中心

caller di·splay /ˋkɔlɚ dɪˏsple; ˈkɔːlə dɪˌspleɪ/ *BrE*【英】, **caller ID** /ˋkɔlɚ aɪ ˏdi; ˈkɔːlər aɪ ˌdiː/ *AmE*【美】 *n* [U]
a special service that uses a piece of equipment attached to your telephone to tell you the telephone number of the person who is calling 來電顯示

call screen·ing /ˋkɔl ˏskrinɪŋ; ˈkɔːl ˌskriːnɪŋ/ *n* [U]
1 a special service that prevents particular people from calling you because their telephone number is on a list of telephone numbers from which you do not wish to receive calls 電話篩選服務（裝置）**2** the practice of letting an ANSWERPHONE answer your telephone calls, and you then only talk to callers that you want to speak to 篩選式通話, 來電過濾

call sens·ing u·nit /ˋkɔl sɛnsɪŋ ˏjunɪt; ˈkɔːl sensɪŋ ˌjuːnɪ̈t/ *n* [C]
a piece of electronic equipment that tells Internet users when someone is trying to call them on the telephone〔上網時的〕來電提示裝置

call·time /ˋkɔlˏtaɪm; ˈkɔːltaɪm/ *n* [U]
the amount of time that is available for the user of a MOBILE PHONE to make calls 呼叫時間, 通話時間: *You get 20 minutes free calltime a day, but only after 7 p.m.* 每天你可以有20分鐘免費通話時間, 但這優惠只能在下午7點之後才生效。

cam·i·ki·ni /kæmɪˏkinɪ; ˈkæmɪˌkiːni/ *n* [C]
a type of BIKINI that has a top part that reaches down to the HIPs 卡米基尼〔比基尼的一種〕

campus /ˋkæmpəs; ˈkæmpəs/ *n* [C]
NEW MEANING
the land and buildings belonging to a large company〔大公司的〕園區〔包括土地和建築物〕: *Microsoft's campus in Redmond, Washington* 微軟公司的園區在華盛頓州的雷德蒙德

candy /ˋkændɪ; ˈkændi/ *n*
NEW MEANING
mind/brain candy *informal* something that is entertaining or pleasant to look at, but which you do not approve of because you think it is not serious【非正式】使心情/腦子輕鬆的東西: *Most video games are just brain candy.* 大多數視頻遊戲只不過是放鬆腦子的玩意兒。—see also 另見 EYE CANDY, ARM CANDY

cannibalize /ˋkænəblˏaɪz; ˈkænɪ̈bəlaɪz/ also 又作 **cannibalise** *BrE*【英】 *v* [T]
NEW MEANING
technical if one of a company's new products cannibalizes an older one, the older product stops selling because people buy the new product instead【術語】淘汰〔舊產品〕, 將…取而代之

canteen cul·ture /ˏkæntin ˋkʌltʃɚ; ˌkæntiːn ˈkʌltʃə/ *n* [U] *BrE*
old-fashioned and unfair behaviour and attitudes which some people think are typical of the police in Britain【英】〔警方的〕歧視性保守態度: *While the canteen culture flourishes, the police service will find it difficult to recruit and retain black officers.* 警察部門發現在歧視態度大行其道之時很難招募到和留住黑人警員。

can·yon·ing /ˋkænjənɪŋ; ˈkænjənɪŋ/ *n* [U]
a sport in which you walk and swim along a fast-moving river at the bottom of a CANYON (=a deep valley with very steep sides of rock) 溪降運動, 探谷運動〔沿溪谷步行和游泳〕: *Canyoning continues to grow in popularity, especially in the US.* 溪降運動日益受到歡迎, 尤其是在美國。| **go canyoning** *We're planning to go canyoning the weekend after next.* 我們計劃在下下個週末進行溪降活動。

cap·let /ˋkæplɪt; ˈkæplɪ̈t/ *n* [C]
a small smooth PILL (=solid piece of medicine) with a shape that is slightly longer and narrower than a TABLET (=a small round pill) 藥片〔較普通藥片稍長且窄〕

carbon sink /ˋkɑrbən ˏsɪŋk; ˈkɑːbən ˌsɪŋk/ *n* [C]
a large area of forest that is believed to help the environment by taking in CARBON from the air as a way of reducing the effects of GLOBAL WARMING〔相信可通過吸

收空氣中的碳能減緩地球變暖的〕森林帶，濾碳帶

carbs /kɑrbz; kɑːbz/ *n* [U]
spoken informal foods such as rice, bread, and potatoes that contain CARBOHYDRATE*s*【口，非正式】碳水化合物類食物: *Before a race, I make sure I eat plenty of carbs.* 賽跑之前，我一定要吃許多碳水化合物類的食物。

car·di·o /ˈkɑrdɪo; ˈkɑːdiəʊ/ *n* [U]
informal any type of exercise that makes the heart stronger and healthier, for example running【非正式】〔跑步等可使心臟強健的〕強心鍛鍊: *According to Max, the exhausting physical preparation – cardio, weight training, and kung fu – has changed him dramatically.* 按照馬克斯的說法，消耗體力的賽前身體訓練——強心鍛鍊、負重訓練和"功夫"——令他脫胎換骨。

care in the com·mu·ni·ty /ˌkɛr ɪn ðə kəˈmjunətɪ; ˌkeər ɪn ðə kəˈmjuːnəti/ *n* [U] *BrE*
the practice of helping and looking after people with mental problems in their homes, instead of making them stay in hospitals【英】社區護理（計劃）: *Many people have fears about care in the community, but mental patients pose a far greater threat to themselves than to the public.* 許多人對社區護理感到恐懼，但是精神病患者對自己造成的威脅遠大於對公眾構成的威脅。

care·ware /ˈkɛrˌwɛr; ˈkeəweə/ *n* [U]
computer SOFTWARE that is free, although the people who wrote it ask you to give them some money if you use it 愛心軟件〔一種共享的免費軟件〕

cargo pants /ˈkɑrgo ˌpænts; ˈkɑːgəʊ ˌpænts/ *n* [plural] also 又作 **cargoes**
big loose trousers with several large pockets 貨船褲，船員褲〔有多個大口袋的寬鬆褲〕

car·o·tene /ˈkærəˌtin; ˈkærətiːn/ *n* [C,U]
a chemical substance found in plants, such as CARROT*s*, that is important for good health and that might prevent CANCER 胡蘿蔔素: *Carotenes are found in orange and yellow vegetables.* 胡蘿蔔素存在於橙色和黃色蔬菜中。

carpetbagger /ˈkɑrpɪtˌbægɚ; ˈkɑːpətˌbægə/ *n* [C] *BrE*
NEW MEANING
someone who opens an account at a BUILDING SOCIETY because they think the building society will soon become a bank. When a building society becomes a bank, people who have accounts there receive money or SHARE*s* in the bank【英】在購房互助協會開立賬戶者

case /kes; keɪs/ *n*
NEW MEANING
be on the case *spoken* if someone says they are on the case, they are aware of a problem and are going to try to solve it【口】得悉問題並着手解決

cash ad·vance /ˈkæʃ ədˌvæns; ˈkæʃ ədˌvɑːns/ *n* [C]
money that you get from a bank, using a CREDIT CARD〔用信用卡〕取現金，透支: *It seems so easy to get a $100 cash advance every few days at a local ATM machine.* 每隔幾天在當地的自動取款機透支100美元似乎不費甚麼事。

cash·back /ˈkæʃˌbæk; ˈkæʃbæk/ *n* [U] *BrE*【英】
1 a way of getting money at a shop when you use a DEBIT CARD to pay for the things you are buying, in which the shop gives you money which it takes from your bank account 購物支錢〔顧客用借記卡在商店購物時可順便提取的現金〕: *I got £40 cashback.* 我購物時支取了40英鎊現金。**2** a way of reducing the price of a car, piece of furniture etc where the seller says what the price is and offers to give a certain amount of money back to the person who buys it 現金回贈〔打折銷售〕: *Price on the road – £8750. But on top of that, we'll give you £500 cashback.* 這輛車價格連稅項等是8750英鎊，但我們會回贈你500英鎊。

category kil·ler /ˈkætəgorɪ ˌkɪlɚ; ˈkætəgəri ˌkɪlə/ *n* [C]
technical a very large company that has many stores in many cities, and that is able to offer low prices and therefore makes smaller stores go out of business【術語】類別殺手〔專營某類產品的大型廉價連銷店〕

CBT /ˌsi bi ˈti; ˌsiː biː ˈtiː/ *n* [C]
1 an abbreviation for 縮寫= computer-based testing; a way of taking standard tests such as the GRE on a computer 用電腦測試 **2** computer based training 電腦輔助培訓: *OJ will provide full documentation and CBT software.* OJ會提供全套文本和電腦輔助培訓軟件。

CD burn·er /si ˈdi ˌbɝnɚ; siː ˈdiː ˌbɜːnə/ also 又作 **burner** *n* [C]
compact disc burner; a piece of computer equipment that records music, images, or other information onto a CD 光盤刻錄設備，燒碟機

CD-R /ˌsi di ˈɑr; ˌsiː diː ˈɑː/ *n* [C]
compact disc recordable; a type of CD that you can record music, images, or other information onto, using special equipment on your computer. It can be recorded onto only once. 可錄式光盤

CD-RW /ˌsi di ɑr ˈdʌbljụ; ˌsiː diː ɑː ˈdʌbəljuː/ *n* [C]
compact disc rewritable; a type of CD that you can record music, images, or other information onto, using special equipment on your computer. You can record onto it several times. 再寫式光盤，可擦寫光盤

cell /sɛl; sel/ *n* [C] *AmE*
NEW MEANING
a CELLULAR PHONE; a telephone that you can carry around with you, that works by using a network of radio stations to pass on signals【美】蜂窩電話，流動電話，手機; MOBILE *BrE*【英】: *Call me on my cell if you're running late.* 你要是晚了，就打我的手機。

cen·sor·ware /ˈsɛnsɚˌwɛr; ˈsensəˌweə/ *n* [U]
a type of computer PROGRAM that can be used to stop someone from seeing certain WEBSITE*s* on their computer. This word comes from a combination of the words 'CENSOR' and 'SOFTWARE' and is used by people who do not approve of limiting the information that people can see on the Internet. 〔阻止某人登陸某些網站的〕檢查性軟件〔由censor和software縮合而成〕

central /ˈsɛntrəl; ˈsentrəl/ *adj*
NEW MEANING
party/comedy etc central *informal* a place where something is happening a lot【非正式】經常聚會的地點: *Tim's house became party central for the band and their friends.* 蒂姆的房子成了樂隊和朋友經常聚會的場所。| *This bulletin board serves as communications central* (=a common place to leave a message for someone) *for the campus.* 這個佈告板成為校園內的聯絡中心。

ce·roc /sɪˈrɑk; səˈrɒk/ *n* [U]
a type of lively dance from France, similar to SALSA and JIVE 希洛克舞〔一種起源於法國，與薩爾薩舞和搖擺舞相似的輕快舞蹈〕

chad /tʃæd; tʃæd/ *n* [C,U]
small pieces of stiff paper that are produced when holes are made in cards, so that the cards can be ready by a computer or used in a machine〔卡片穿孔時產生的〕紙屑〔穿了孔的卡片可由電腦讀取或可在機器上使用〕

chak·ra /ˈtʃɑkrə; ˈtʃʌkrə/ *n* [C]
one of the seven particular areas of the body which, according to some Asian medical practices, are important to consider when curing illness or disease 權輪〔某些亞洲醫學認為對治療疾病是重要的人體特定部位〕

change man·age·ment /ˈtʃendʒ ˌmænɪdʒmənt; ˈtʃeɪndʒ ˌmænɪdʒmənt/ *n* [U]
the process of deciding which changes need to be made in a business or a computer system and how to make them 變動管理: *A team of consultants was commissioned to investigate and report on the best current thinking and practice regarding change management.* 顧問組受託調查和報告關於變動管理的最新思維和推行情況。

channel /ˈtʃænl; ˈtʃænl/ *n* [C]
NEW MEANING
an electronic connection between two computers or other electronic equipment such as MODEM*s*, that information can travel along. A channel can be a physical object such

as a CABLE or a particular radio FREQUENCY. 信道; 通路

chat /tʃæt; tʃæt/ *v* [I]
NEW MEANING
to communicate with several people in a chat room on the Internet（網上）聊天

chat room /ˈtʃæt ˌrum; ˈtʃæt ˌruːm/ *n* [C]
a place on the Internet where you can write messages to other people and receive messages back from them immediately, so that you can have a conversation while you are ONLINE（網上）聊天室: *As well as offering access to the Internet, we have our own information centers and chat rooms.* 除了提供上網服務之外, 我們還有自己的信息中心和聊天室。

cheat² /tʃit; tʃiːt/ *n* [C]
NEW MEANING
a set of instructions given to a computer that make it easier for someone who is playing a computer game to win〔玩電腦遊戲時使用的〕作弊碼

check card /ˈtʃɛk ˌkard; ˈtʃek ˌkɑːd/ *n* [C] *AmE*
a special plastic card, similar to a CREDIT CARD, that you can use to pay for things directly from your CHECKING ACCOUNT【美】支票卡

chill room /ˈtʃɪl ˌrum; ˈtʃɪl ˌruːm/ *n* [C]
1 a room in a bar, office etc where people go to play games, listen to music, watch television etc so that they can relax〔酒吧、辦公室等中的〕休閒室 **2** a WEBSITE or WEB PAGE that contains games, pictures, music etc and is designed for people who want to relax or have fun 休閒網站[頁]

chud·dies /ˈtʃʌdɪz; ˈtʃʌdiz/ *n* [plural] *BrE*
slang humorous【英俚, 幽默】**1** UNDERPANTS 襯褲, 內褲 **2 kiss my chuddies** a slightly insulting expression used to show that you do not respect someone or that you are angry with them. This expression was made popular in Britain by two characters on a television show who are TEENAGE boys and whose families originally came from South Asia. 親親我的內褲吧〔表示不尊重或惱怒對方, 稍帶侮辱性〕

churn /tʃɝn; tʃɜːn/ *v* [I]
to change from one service provider such as a bank or telephone company to another because the second one offers better conditions 更換（服務商）: *The arrival of free Internet Service Providers in Europe caused Internet users to churn between ISPs much faster than was expected.* 免費互聯網服務商抵達歐洲後, 互聯網用戶更換不同互聯網服務商的速度出乎意料的快。—**churn** *n* [U]: *The mobile phone industry has experienced a high churn rate – typically between 18% and 24% of subscribers.* 流動電話業的用戶流失率很高, 一般在18%至24%之間。

cin·e·phile /ˈsɪnɪˌfaɪl; ˈsɪnɪˌfaɪl/ *n* [C]
someone who likes films very much and considers them to be a form of art, not just entertainment 電影愛好者, 戲迷: *My last boyfriend was a complete cinephile.* 我的舊男友是個十足的戲迷。

CJD /ˌsi dʒe ˈdi; ˌsiː dʒeɪ ˈdiː/ *n* [U]
the abbreviation of 縮寫= CREUTZFELDT-JAKOB DISEASE

clam·dig·gers /ˈklæmˌdɪgɚz; ˈklæmˌdɪgəz/ *n* [plural]
a type of TROUSERS that fit closely and reach the middle of the lower leg 挖蛤褲,〔長及小腿肚的〕中長褲: *Shelly was wearing a pair of pink clamdiggers and a sleeveless blouse.* 謝利穿了一條粉紅色的中長褲和一件無袖襯衫。

click·a·ble /ˈklɪkəbl; ˈklɪkəbəl/ *adj*
if a word or picture that you can see on a computer screen is clickable, it will connect you to more information when you CLICK on it. You click on something by pressing a button on a computer MOUSE. 可（用滑鼠）點擊的

clicks and mor·tar /ˌklɪks ən ˈmɔrtɚ; ˌklɪks ən ˈmɔːtə/ *adj* [only before noun 僅用於名詞前]
relating to a business that has both a store and a WEBSITE that customers can buy things from. Customers can often look at or try items in the store before they buy them from the website, or they can buy things on the website and return them to the store if they do not like what they have bought 兩便的〔既有店鋪又提供網上銷售的〕: *Bellinger's new book shows how you can transform your company into a clicks-and-mortar business.* 貝林傑的新書會告訴你怎樣把你的公司變成一個既有店鋪又提供網上銷售的虛實兩便企業。—**clicks-and-mortar** *n* [C]

client /ˈklaɪənt; ˈklaɪənt/ *n* [C]
NEW MEANING
technical a computer on a network that receives information from a SERVER (=large powerful computer)【術語】客戶機

client-serv·er, client server /ˌklaɪənt ˈsɝvɚ; ˌklaɪənt ˈsɜːvə◂/ *adj*
client-server network/technology/system etc a computer system in which CLIENTs (=small computers) are connected to a SERVER (=large powerful computer) and receive information from it 主從式網絡/技術/系統等: *Client-server architecture usually links PCs to a database server, and most of the computing is done on the PC.* 主從式架構通常將個人電腦和數據伺服器連結起來, 大多數計算在個人電腦上進行。

clip art /ˈklɪp ˌart; ˈklɪp ˌɑːt/ *n* [U]
images, photographs, or pictures that are stored on particular WEBSITEs, which you can copy and use in your own computer documents. You can also buy collections of clip art on CD-ROM or FLOPPY DISK.〔網上的〕剪貼圖片集, 圖庫

clipboard /ˈklɪpˌbɔrd; ˈklɪpˌbɔːd/ *n* [C]
NEW MEANING
a part of a computer's MEMORY that stores information when you are moving it from one document to another 剪貼板

clipper chip /ˈklɪpɚ ˌtʃɪp; ˈklɪpə ˌtʃɪp/ *n* [C] *AmE*
a special computer CHIP that can be put into a computer, MOBILE PHONE etc, which allows an organization such as a government to listen to or read private conversations made using these machines【美】〔電腦、手機等〕解密集成芯片

C-list /ˈsi ˌlɪst; ˈsiː ˌlɪst/ *adj*
among the group of film stars or people who appear on TV, but who are not really very famous or popular〔影星等〕三流的: *You often see C-list, so-called celebrities, on the streets of London, just doing their shopping or going to a burger bar.* 倫敦的街上經常可以見到一些所謂名人的三流影星不是在店裡購物, 就是在漢堡包店裡進餐。

clock speed /ˈklɑk ˌspid; ˈklɒk ˌspiːd/ *n* [C usually singular 一般用單數]
technical a measurement of how quickly a computer's CPU (=main controlling part) can deal with instructions【術語】時鐘速度〔計算中央處理機的運算速度〕: *The system I tested uses a chip with a clock speed of 1 gigahertz.* 我測試過的那個系統使用時鐘速度為一千兆赫的芯片。

clone /klon; kləʊn/ *v* [T]
NEW MEANING
to copy the number of someone else's MOBILE PHONE onto a new CHIP and then use that number on a different telephone, so that the mobile phone's owner receives the telephone bill 燒機, 盜用他人手機號碼

closure /ˈkloʒɚ; ˈkləʊʒə/ *n* [U]
NEW MEANING
a word used especially by PSYCHOLOGISTs to describe the act of bringing an event or a period of time to an end, or the feeling that something has been completely dealt with〔尤為心理學家使用〕解脫: *Funerals help give people a sense of closure.* 葬禮讓人產生一種解脫的感覺。

club·land /ˈklʌbˌlænd; ˈklʌblænd/ *n* [U]
all the NIGHTCLUBs in an area, considered as a group and including the people who go to them and the performers that play in them 夜總會區, 夜總會〔總稱〕: *They are one*

of clubland's favorite bands. 他們是夜總會區最受歡迎的樂隊之一。

cluster home /ˋklʌstɚ ˏhom; ˈklʌstə ˌhəʊm/ *n* [C] *BrE* a house which is joined to other houses of the same kind to form a small group【英】密集型住宅，住宅羣

co-brand·ing /ˏko ˋbrændɪŋ; ˌkəʊ ˈbrændɪŋ/ *n* [U] a practice in which two companies help each other to do business or sell products by using both company names, for example, having a particular bank inside a particular store〔兩家公司〕商標合用[共享]

co·coon·ing /kəˋkunɪŋ; kəˈkuːnɪŋ/ *n* [U] *AmE* the practice of spending a lot of time in your own home because you feel comfortable and safe there【美】繭式生活，繭居: *They produce extra-wide armchairs for people with serious cocooning in mind.* 他們為熱衷於繭式生活者生產超寬扶手椅。

co·de·pend·en·cy /ˏkodɪˋpɛndənsɪ; ˌkəʊdɪˈpendənsi/ *n* [U] when two people exist in a very close relationship and cannot leave it, because one of them needs to be looked after and the other one needs to be needed 互賴性 —**codependent** *n, adj*

cod·er /ˋkodɚ; ˈkəʊdə/ *n* [C] *informal* a computer PROGRAMMER【非正式】程式設計員，電腦程序編製員: *a coders' convention* 程式設計員大會

code-shar·ing /ˋkod ˏʃɛrɪŋ; ˈkəʊd ˌʃeərɪŋ/ *n* [U] *technical* a practice in which two AIRLINE companies sell tickets together and use the same numbers for their flights【術語】共用班次，航班共享

coe·li·ac dis·ease *especially BrE*【尤英】, **celiac disease** *AmE*【美】/ˋsilɪæk dɪˏziz; ˈsiːliæk dɪˌziːz/ *n* [U] *technical* a disease caused by an ALLERGY to GLUTEN (=a substance in wheat flour)【術語】乳糜瀉〔一種疾病〕

co-fund /ˏko ˋfʌnd; ˌkəʊ ˈfʌnd/ *v* [T] if two organizations co-fund something, they pay for it together 為…共同提供資金: *The project is being co-funded by two California companies.* 這個項目由加州的兩家公司共同提供資金。

cold call /ˏkold ˋkɔl; ˌkəʊld ˈkɔːl/ *v* [T] to telephone someone you have never spoken to before and try to sell them a product or service〔推銷員〕冒昧地給…打電話

cold fu·sion /ˏkold ˋfjuʒən; ˌkəʊld ˈfjuːʒən/ *n* [U] a type of NUCLEAR FUSION (=the joining of the central parts of two atoms, which releases energy) that some scientists believe can occur at lower temperatures. Other scientists believe that nuclear fusion can only occur at temperatures of millions of degrees, and that cold fusion is not possible. 冷聚變

collateral /kəˋlætərəl; kəˈlætərəl/ *adj*

NEW MEANING

collateral damage a phrase meaning people who are hurt or property that is damaged as a result of war, although they are not the main TARGET. This phrase is used especially by the Army, Navy etc 附帶損害: *Hitting any non-military targets would risk 'collateral damage' – which the US military does not want.* 攻擊任何非軍事目標都會冒殃及池魚的風險，這是美國軍方所不願看到的。

color /ˋkʌlɚ; ˈkʌlə/ *v*

color me surprised/confused/embarrassed etc *AmE spoken informal* if you say color me surprised, confused etc, you mean that you are very surprised, confused etc by something【美口，非正式】我太驚訝/迷惑/窘迫了等: *"Color me amazed!" says prize winner Angela Harris.* 獲獎者安傑拉·哈里斯說: "我真是大吃一驚!"

com·bats /ˋkɑmbæts; ˈkɒmbæts/ *n* [plural] loose trousers, often with many pockets〔多口袋寬鬆式〕戰鬥褲: *She always wore combats, which were more fashionable than jeans.* 她老是穿着比牛仔褲更時髦的多口袋戰鬥褲。

commando /kəˋmændo; kəˈmɑːndəʊ/ *n*

NEW MEANING

go commando *AmE informal humorous* to not wear any underwear【美，非正式，幽默】沒有穿內衣

com·min·gle /kəˋmɪŋgḷ; kɒˈmɪŋgəl/ *v*

1 *formal* [I,T] to mix together, or to make different things do this【正式】(使) 混合，(使) 攙和: *Many towns allow recyclable items to be commingled for collection in a single container.* 許多城鎮允許將可循環再造的物品混放於一個容器內。**2** [T] if a bank, insurance company, or other financial organization commingles money, it mixes its own money with the money that belongs to one of its customers or to another part of the business, usually in an illegal way 挪用〔儲戶的錢款〕: *Southwest Securities faces charges that it commingled its own funds with customer funds.* 西南證券公司因把公司資金和顧客的錢款攙和在一起而面臨控告。

comms /kɑmz; kɒmz/ *n* [plural] *BrE informal* communications; used when talking about computer PROGRAMS that allow communication between different computers【英，非正式】通訊程式; communications software *AmE*【美】

community po·lic·ing /kəˏmjunətɪ pəˋlisɪŋ; kəˌmjuːnəti pəˈliːsɪŋ/ *n* [U] in Britain, a system in which the police and the people who live in an area work together to reduce crime 社區警政

comparison-shop /kəmˋpærəsṇ ˏʃɑp; kəmˈpærəsən ˌʃɒp/ *v* [I] to go to different shops in order to compare the prices of something, so that you can buy it at the cheapest possible price 貨比三家，比較價格進行購買 —**comparison shopping** *n* [U]

compassion fa·tigue /kəmˋpæʃən fəˏtig; kəmˈpæʃən fəˌtiːg/ *n* [U] the feeling some people have that stops them caring a lot or giving money to CHARITY because they have seen too many reports or television programmes about DISASTERS 同情心淡漠: *Several speakers will offer advice on overcoming compassion fatigue.* 幾名演講人將就如何克服同情心淡漠提出建議。

com·po·nent·ize also 又作 **-ise** *BrE*【英】/kəmˋponəntaɪz; kəmˈpəʊnəntaɪz/ *v* [I,T] to separate a system or machine into a number of smaller parts so that they can work together or work as part of another system or machine; used especially about computers and computer SOFTWARE 把…元件化〔把系統或機器分成較小的組件〕: *It is much easier to componentize your website before you design it.* 在設計之前把網站元件化要容易得多。

composed sal·ad /kəmˏpozd ˋsæləd; kəmˌpəʊzd ˈsæləd/ *n* [C] *AmE* a SALAD that is arranged carefully on a plate, rather than mixed together【美】〔精心配放的〕花式沙拉

compress /kəmˋprɛs; kəmˈpres/ *v* [I,T]

NEW MEANING

to make a computer FILE smaller by using a special computer PROGRAM, which makes the file easier to store or send 壓縮〔電腦文件〕

com·pu·ter·ate /kəmˋpjutərɪt; kəmˈpjuːtərɪ̇t/ *adj* able to use a computer well 通曉電腦的，擅長電腦操作的: *Students need to be computerate as well as literate.* 學生除了需要有讀寫能力外，還要具備熟練操作電腦的能力。

con·fe·renc·ing /ˋkɑnfərənsɪŋ; ˈkɒnfərənsɪŋ/ *n* **video/telephone conferencing** the use of VIDEO or telephone equipment that allows several people in different places to talk to each other at the same time 視像/電話會議

con·flic·ted /kənˋflɪktɪd; kənˈflɪktɪ̇d/ *adj AmE* **be/feel conflicted** to be confused about what choice to make, especially when the decision involves strong beliefs or opinions【美】思想掙扎，難於抉擇: *Neither Jane* *nor Neil feels conflicted about pursuing their careers while raising children.* 簡和尼爾對撫養孩子和追求事業成功從沒有感到難於抉擇。

congestion charg·ing /kənˋdʒɛstʃən ˏtʃardʒɪŋ; kənˈdʒestʃən ˌtʃɑːdʒɪŋ/ *n* [U]
a way of reducing traffic in city centres in Britain by charging drivers money to enter; ROAD PRICING 高峯期行車收費, 道路收費: *Plans to introduce congestion charging were dropped until after the election.* 高峯期行車收費的計劃已被擱置, 直至選舉過後。

conjoined twins /kənˏdʒɔɪnd ˋtwɪnz; kənˌdʒɔɪnd ˈtwɪnz/ *n* [plural]
two people who are born with their bodies joined to each other. This expression is used instead of SIAMESE TWINS, which some people consider to be offensive. 連體兒

con·nect·ed·ness /kəˋnɛktɪdnɪs; kəˈnektɪdnɪs/ *n* [U]
1 the feeling people have that they are members of a group in society and that they share particular qualities with other members of that group 歸屬感, 聯繫: *Human beings have a need for both independence and connectedness.* 人既需要保持獨立, 又需要與他人建立各種聯繫。 **2** the degree to which people are connected by electronic TECHNOLOGY such as the Internet and E-MAIL〔互聯網等構成的人際〕聯繫: **[+between/with]** *Communication technology has increased the connectedness between physicians and patients.* 通訊技術加強了醫師和病人之間的聯繫。

conspicuous /kənˋspɪkjuəs; kənˈspɪkjuəs/ *adj*
NEW MEANING
conspicuous consumption the act of buying a lot of things, especially expensive things that are not necessary, in order to IMPRESS other people and show them how rich you are 炫耀性消費: *Postwar Munich became rich, and flaunted it in expensive clothing and other forms of conspicuous consumption.* 戰後的慕尼黑富了起來, 並以昂貴的服飾和其他形式的炫耀性消費向世人顯示其財富。

content /ˋkantɛnt; ˈkɒntent/ *n* [U]
the information contained in a WEBSITE, considered separately from the software that makes the website work〔網站〕內容: *The graphics are brilliant. It's just a shame the content is so poor.* 圖像十分出色, 但內容如此貧乏, 實在可惜。

content pro·vid·er /ˋkantɛnt prəˏvaɪdɚ; ˈkɒntent prəˌvaɪdə/ *n* [C]
an organization or person that provides information on the Internet 網絡信息提供者

content site /ˋkantɛnt ˏsaɪt; ˈkɒntent ˌsaɪt/ *n* [C]
a WEBSITE that contains many pages of information on a particular subject 專題網站

contingent /kənˋtɪndʒənt; kənˈtɪndʒənt/ *adj AmE*【美】
NEW MEANING
1 contingent worker someone who is employed by a company for a fixed period of time, usually to do a particular piece of work 臨時員工, 短期員工 **2 contingent job** a job that is limited to a fixed period of time, usually because the company does not want to continue to employ the person who does that job after the end of that particular job 臨時工作

cookie /ˋkʊkɪ; ˈkʊki/ *n* [C]
NEW MEANING
technical information which a computer PROGRAM on the Internet leaves in your computer so that the program will recognize you when you use it again【術語】"甜餅", 魔塊〔記錄網站訪問者的信息塊, 以便下次使用時識別之〕

cookie bust·er /ˋkʊkɪ ˏbʌstɚ; ˈkʊki ˌbʌstə/ *n* [C]
a computer PROGRAM that prevents a cookie from being placed on your computer's HARD DISK (=the part that permanently stores information), or removes one that is already there "甜餅"屏障, 信息塊屏障

cool /kul; kuːl/ *adj*
NEW MEANING
be cool with sth *spoken informal* used to say that you agree with something or do not have a problem with it【口, 非正式】對…表示滿意, 對…不持異議: *"Do you want to come over to my house and watch a video tonight?" "I'm cool with that."* "你想不想今晚來我家看影視錄像?" "我很樂意。"

cop /kap; kɒp/ *v AmE*
NEW MEANING
slang【美俚】**1 cop an attitude** to behave in a way that is not nice, especially by showing that you think you are better or more intelligent than other people 擺架子 **2 cop a buzz** to feel the effects of taking illegal drugs or drinking alcohol〔吸毒或飲酒後〕產生快感

co-pay·ment, copayment /ˋko ˏpemənt; ˈkəʊ ˌpeɪmənt/ *n* [C]
a fairly small amount of money that you must pay a doctor in addition to the amount paid by your insurance company, if you have a particular type of health insurance〔病人在保險承擔的費用之外所要支付的〕共付醫療費

copy /ˋkapɪ; ˈkɒpi/ *v*
copy sb **in** *phr v* [T] to send someone a copy of an E-MAIL message you are sending to someone else 給〔某人〕抄送: **[+on]** *Can you copy me in on the memo you're sending to Chris?* 你發給克里斯的便箋, 能否給我也抄送一份?

cop·y·left /ˋkapɪˏlɛft; ˈkɒpileft/ *n* [U]
the right to use something such as computer SOFTWARE without paying for it, as long as you do not try to sell it or stop other people from using it. This word was formed by changing the last part of the word 'COPYRIGHT'. 複製權, 〔軟件〕通用許可證

core /kɔr; kɔː/ *adj*
core business/activity/product the business, activity etc that is the most important one for a company because it makes the most money〔某公司賺錢最多的〕核心業務/活動/產品: *The publishing company plans to sell its bookshops and concentrate on its core business.* 該出版公司打算把書店賣掉, 集中精力在核心業務上。

cor·po·rate·wear /ˋkɔrpərətˏwɛr; ˈkɔːpərətˌweə/ *n* [U]
clothes such as a SUIT and tie that are suitable for wearing to work in the offices of a large business 公司制服, 上班服

cos·me·ceu·ti·cal /ˏkazməˋsutɪkl; ˌkɒzməˈsjuːtɪkəl/ *n* [C]
a beauty product that contains special additional substances that are intended to improve the condition of your skin or health, almost like a medicine. This word comes from a combination of the words 'COSMETIC' and 'PHARMACEUTICAL'. 藥用化妝品〔由 cosmetic 和 pharmaceutical 縮合而成〕

couch hop·ping /ˋkaʊtʃ ˏhapɪŋ; ˈkaʊtʃ ˌhɒpɪŋ/ *n* [U]
humorous the activity of staying at different people's homes and sleeping on their SOFAS when you do not have anywhere to live【幽默】到處借宿: *Well, I spent the next couple of weeks couch hopping and eventually ended up at Max's place.* 哦, 後來的幾週我到處借宿, 最後住到馬克斯那裡。

counter[1] /ˋkaʊntɚ; ˈkaʊntə/ *n* [C]
NEW MEANING
a computer PROGRAM that counts the number of people that have used a WEBSITE〔統計進入網站人數的〕訪客計數器

course·ware /ˋkɔrsˏwɛr; ˈkɔːsˌweə/ *n* [U]
computer SOFTWARE that is designed to be used for education 課〔程軟〕件, 教學軟件

crack /kræk; kræk/ *v* [T]
NEW MEANING
informal to illegally copy computer SOFTWARE【非正式】非法複製〔電腦軟件〕: *You can find out how to crack any kind of software on the web.* 你可以在網上找到任何一類軟件的複製辦法。

crack into sth *phr v* [T] to secretly enter someone

else's computer system, especially in order to damage the system or steal the information stored on it 非法侵入〔電腦系統〕: *An Illinois teenager is accused of cracking into the company's network several times over the last several months.* 伊利諾伊州一名十幾歲的孩子被控在最近幾個月內幾次非法侵入公司的網絡。

crack onto sb *phr v* [T] *slang* to try to start a sexual relationship with someone【俚】試圖與某人發生性關係: *My best friend keeps trying to crack onto my boyfriend.* 我最要好的一個朋友一直在勾引我的男友。

crack ba·by /ˋkræk ˏbebɪ; ˈkræk ˌbeɪbi/ *n* [C] *plural* **crack babies**
a baby that is born with medical and mental problems because his or her mother regularly smoked the illegal drug CRACK before the baby was born 可卡因嬰兒

crack·er /ˋkrækɚ; ˈkrækə/ *n* [C]
NEW MEANING
someone who illegally breaks into a computer system in order to steal information or stop the system from working properly 非法侵入電腦系統者, 黑客: *Tough laws and security measures do little to deter computer crackers who steal company secrets or cause havoc by tapping into computer systems.* 嚴厲的法律和安全措施對阻止黑客非法入侵電腦系統竊取公司機密或製造混亂, 起不了多少作用。

crack·head /ˋkrækhɛd; ˈkrækhed/ *n* [C]
slang someone who uses the illegal drug CRACK【俚】吸食強效可卡因的人

crack house /ˋkræk ˏhaus; ˈkræk ˌhaʊs/ *n* [C]
a place where the illegal drug CRACK is sold, bought, and smoked 強效可卡因販賣點

crank /kræŋk; kræŋk/ *n* [U] *AmE*
NEW MEANING
slang METHAMPHETAMINE (=an illegal drug)【美俚】甲基安非他明毒品

crash /kræʃ; kræʃ/ *v*
NEW MEANING
informal **crash and burn** if a business or company crashes and burns, it fails completely【非正式】徹底失敗, 倒閉: *Dozens of Internet startups have crashed and burned in the last two years.* 許多新成立的網絡公司在最近兩年內都垮了。

cream puff /ˏkrim ˋpʌf; ˌkriːm ˈpʌf/ *adj*
having a quality that is pretty and decorative 花哨的, 裝門面的, 講排場的: *Cream puff weddings, with the bride in a fancy white dress and the groom in a tuxedo, are as popular as ever.* 現時講究排場的婚禮越來越流行, 新娘穿着別緻的白色婚紗, 新郎穿着無尾晚禮服。

cre·den·tialed /krɪˋdɛnʃəld; krɪˈdenʃəld/ *adj*
someone who is credentialed is legally allowed to do a particular job, because they have done the right type of training 具有認可資格的: *a newly credentialed teacher* 一名新近取得認可資格的教師 | *Ask if the experts you're consulting online are appropriately credentialed.* 問問你在網上諮詢的專家是否具有適當的認可資格。

Creutz·feldt-Jak·ob dis·ease /ˏkrɔɪtsfɛlt ˋjɑkob dɪˏziz; ˌkrɔɪtsfelt ˈjækɒb dɪˌziːz/ *n* [U] *abbreviation* 縮寫為 **CJD**
a very serious disease that kills people and that may be caused by eating BEEF that is affected by BSE 克羅伊茨費爾特－雅各布病, 克雅氏病〔可能與吃感染了瘋牛病的牛肉有關〕

crib /krɪb; krɪb/ *n* [C] *AmE*
NEW MEANING
slang the place where someone lives【美俚】住所, 窩: *I'm not at my crib, I'm at Jed's house.* 我不在自己的住所, 我在傑迪家裡。

crossover ve·hi·cle /ˋkrɔsovɚ ˏviɪkl; ˈkrɒsəʊvə ˌviːɪkəl/ *n* [C]
a vehicle that has some of the features of a car and some of the features of a larger vehicle such as a TRUCK 客貨兩用車

cross-sell·ing /ˏkrɔs ˋsɛlɪŋ; ˌkrɒs ˈselɪŋ/ *n* [U]
a situation in which one company helps to sell another company's products by, for example, advertising the second company's products at the same time as its own 代賣

cross-trad·ing /ˏkrɔs ˋtredɪŋ; ˌkrɒs ˈtreɪdɪŋ/ *n* [U]
a way of buying and selling different CURRENCIES (=the type of money a country uses, for example the pound) in which people in one country buy or sell the money of a second country in exchange for the money of a third country 炒匯, 交叉買賣外匯

cross-train·er /ˏkrɔs ˋtrenɚ; ˌkrɒs ˈtreɪnə/ *n* [C usually plural 一般用複數]
a type of shoe that can be worn for playing different types of sports 多用途運動鞋

cross-train·ing /ˏkrɔs ˋtrenɪŋ; ˌkrɒs ˈtreɪnɪŋ/ *n* [U]
1 the activity of training for more than one sport in the same period of time〔同時進行的〕多項運動訓練: *Reebok makes shoes designed for aerobics, cross-training, walking, and running.* 銳步公司生產的鞋子適用於有氧體操、多項運動訓練、散步和跑步。**2** the activity of learning different jobs in the same period of time〔同時進行的〕多項職業培訓: *Cross-training is a vital part of job rotation.* 多項職業培訓是職業輪換中關鍵的一環。
—**cross-train** *v* [I]

cruis·ing /ˋkruzɪŋ; ˈkruːzɪŋ/ *n* [U]
the activity of walking or driving slowly around public places, looking for sexual partners 獵豔〔在公共場所尋覓性伴侶〕: **go cruising** *If you're thinking, "I don't want to go cruising in the park for a date," there is an alternative.* 如果你在想: "我可不想在公園裡蹓躂找伴兒," 還有別的法子。

crush¹ /krʌʃ; krʌʃ/ *v* [T]
crush on sb *phr v* [T] *slang* to have a strong feeling of romantic love for someone that you are not already in a relationship with【俚】迷戀: *The guy I'd been crushing on for three years finally came into the diner where I work.* 我迷戀了三年的那個男子終於走進了我工作的餐館。

crush² /krʌʃ; krʌʃ/ *n* [C]
NEW MEANING
informal someone you have a CRUSH on (=have a strong feeling of romantic love for)【非正式】迷戀的對象: *"Who's that guy Elaine's talking to?" "Oh, he's just her latest crush."* "與伊萊恩交談的那個男子是誰?" "噢, 他正是她最近迷戀的對象。"

crusty /ˋkrʌstɪ; ˈkrʌsti/ *n* [C] *BrE*
informal a young person without a job or permanent home who is very dirty【英, 非正式】髒皮士, 硬殼族〔無固定職業或居所的青年人〕

CU, cu
a short way of writing 'see you', used in E-MAIL or TEXT MESSAGE*s* on MOBILE PHONE*s* 再見〔"see you" 的縮寫, 電子郵件和手機短信用語〕

cube farm /ˋkjub ˏfɑrm; ˈkjuːb ˌfɑːm/ *n* [C]
humorous a large office containing many rows of CUBICLE*s* (=small areas with low walls around three sides)【幽默】辦公農莊〔用矮身隔板分隔成許多小間的辦公室〕

cuckoo egg /ˋkuku ˏɛg; ˈkʊkuː ˌeg/ *n* [C]
a computer FILE which is designed to look like an MP3 music file but does not contain any music, and which is intended to confuse or annoy people who illegally trade COPYRIGHT*ed* music on the Internet using services that provide recordings for free 杜鵑蛋〔一種酷似MP3標準音樂盤但卻無音樂的反盜版電腦文件〕

cue² /kju; kjuː/ *v*
cue sth ↔ **up** *phr v* [T] to make a CASSETTE, VIDEO, or CD be exactly in the position you want it to be in, so that you can play something immediately when you are ready 將〔磁帶、錄像帶或光盤〕調到〔要播放的位置〕: *The videotape's cued up and ready to go!* 錄像帶調好, 可以播放了!

CUL, cul
a short way of writing 'see you later', used in E-MAIL or TEXT MESSAGES on MOBILE PHONES 一會兒見〔"see you later"的縮寫，電子郵件或手機短信用語〕

cus·tom·er-fac·ing /ˋkʌstəmɚ ˏfesɪŋ; ˈkʌstəmə ˌfeɪsɪŋ/ *adj*
in a company, the customer-facing workers are the people whose job involves them seeing and speaking to the customers 直接面對顧客的：*This course will prove invaluable for customer-facing staff and customer care personnel.* 這一課程將會對前線員工和客戶服務員有極大的價值。

cyber café 網吧

cy·ber·ca·fé, cyber cafe /ˋsaɪbɚkæˏfe; ˈsaɪbəˌkæfeɪ/ *n* [C]
a CAFÉ that has computers which are connected to the Internet for customers to use 網吧，網絡咖啡館

cy·ber·crime, cyber crime /ˋsaɪbɚˏkraɪm; ˈsaɪbəˌkraɪm/ *n* [C,U]
criminal activity that involves the use of computers or the Internet 網絡犯罪

cy·ber·fo·ren·sics /ˋsaɪbɚfəˏrɛnsɪks; ˈsaɪbəfəˌrensɪks/ *n* [U]
the study of how computer crimes happen, especially ones involving the computer systems of large companies or organizations 網絡犯罪學：*a new course to train law-enforcement officials in cyberforensics* 培訓執法官員熟悉網絡犯罪學的新教程

cy·ber·fraud /ˋsaɪbɚˏfrɔd; ˈsaɪbəˌfrɔːd/ *n* [U]
slang the illegal act of deceiving people on the Internet in order to gain money, power etc【俚】網絡詐騙

cy·ber·kid·nap·per /ˋsaɪbɚˏkɪdnæpɚ; ˈsaɪbəˌkɪdnæpə/ *n* [C]
someone who gets to know people on the Internet, makes plans to meet them, and then KIDNAPs them (=takes them away illegally, usually by force) 網上綁架者

cy·ber·land /ˋsaɪbəˏlænd; ˈsaɪbəˌlænd/ *n* [U]
activity that involves the Internet and the people who use it 網絡世界

cy·ber·porn /ˋsaɪbɚˏpɔrn; ˈsaɪbəˌpɔːn/ *n* [U]
slang sexual images, films etc shown on the Internet【俚】網絡色情

cy·ber·sick·ness /ˋsaɪbɚˏsɪknɪs; ˈsaɪbəˌsɪknǝs/ *n* [U]
a feeling of illness caused by using a computer for long periods of time or being in a room with a lot of computers〔長時間使用電腦引致的〕電腦病

cy·ber·squat·ter /ˋsaɪbɚˏskwɑtɚ; ˈsaɪbəˌskwɒtə/ *n* [C]
someone who officially records the names of companies that they do not own or work for as DOMAIN NAMEs on the Internet in order to try to sell these names to companies for profit〔網上〕搶註域名者，域名轉售者

cy·ber·squat·ting /ˋsaɪbɚˏskwɑtɪŋ; ˈsaɪbəˌskwɒtɪŋ/ *n* [U]
the practice of officially recording the names of companies that you do not own or work for as DOMAIN NAMEs on the Internet. People do this in order to try to sell the domain names at some time in the future for profit 搶註域名：*Many people think that cybersquatting should be made illegal.* 許多人認為應把搶註域名列為非法行為。

cy·ber·stalk·ing /ˋsaɪbɚˏstɔkɪŋ; ˈsaɪbəˌstɔːkɪŋ/ *n* [U]
the illegal use of the Internet, E-MAIL, or other electronic communication systems to follow someone or threaten them 網上騷擾：*The state's first cyberstalking laws went into effect a little over a year ago.* 這個州的第一部網上騷擾法生效才一年多。—**cyberstalker** *n* [C]

cy·ber·ter·ror·ism /ˌsaɪbɚˋtɛrərɪzəm; ˌsaɪbəˈterərɪzəm/ *n* [U]
using the Internet to damage computer systems, especially for political purposes 網絡恐怖主義：*I believe that cyberterrorism will emerge as one of the world's major post-Cold War security threats.* 我相信網絡恐怖主義將成為冷戰後對世界安全的主要威脅之一。

cy·ber·ter·ror·ist /ˌsaɪbɚˋtɛrərɪst; ˌsaɪbəˈterərǝst/ *n* [C]
someone who uses the Internet to damage computer systems, especially for political purposes 網絡恐怖分子：*Such a strategic attack, mounted by cyberterrorists, would shut down everything from power stations to air traffic control centres.* 網絡恐怖分子發動的這類戰略性攻擊，將導致發電站、空中交通管制中心等全部癱瘓。

cy·ber·wid·ow /ˋsaɪbɚˏwɪdo; ˈsaɪbəˌwɪdəʊ/ *n* [C]
informal the wife of a man who spends a lot of time working or playing on his computer【非正式】網上寡婦

cy·pher·punk /ˋsaɪfɚˏpʌŋk; ˈsaɪfəˌpʌŋk/ *n* [C]
NEW MEANING
someone who changes the information that they send from their computer into a form that can only be read by the people they send it to. Cypherpunks do this because they do not trust the government and people in authority and think that they will read this information. 網上朋客〔將資料加密傳送，以防止如政府等機構閱覽〕，網際浪人 —**cypherpunk** *adj* [only before a noun 僅用於名詞前]: *the cypherpunk subculture* 網上朋客次文化

D,d

dam·age con·trol /ˋdæmɪdʒ kənˏtrol; ˈdæmɪdʒ kənˌtrəʊl/ *n* [U]
an attempt to limit the bad effects of something 損害控制：*The call I received from Smith seemed to be an effort toward political damage control.* 史密斯給我打來電話，似乎是出於政治考慮，以防事件進一步惡化。| **do damage control** *Since the scandal broke, the Senator's staff have been busy doing damage control.* 自從這一醜聞傳開以後，參議員一班人馬一直忙於將該事件的不良影響控制在一定範圍。

dashboard din·ing /ˋdæʃbɔrd ˏdaɪnɪŋ; ˈdæʃbɔːd ˌdaɪnɪŋ/ *n* [U]
humorous the practice of eating a meal while driving a car【幽默】〔駕駛中〕在儀表板上進餐：*Dashboard dining has become the breakfast norm in many cities in America.* 邊開車邊吃早餐已成為美國許多城裡人的習慣。

data in·ter·change for·mat file /ˌdetə ˌɪntɚtʃendʒ ˋfɔrmæt ˏfaɪl; ˌdeɪtə ˌɪntətʃeɪndʒ ˈfɔːmæt ˌfaɪl/ *abbreviation* 縮寫為 **DIF** *n* [C]
a computer file that allows you to take information from one PROGRAM and move it to a different program 信息交換格式文件

data min·ing /ˋdetə ˏmaɪnɪŋ; ˈdeɪtə ˌmaɪnɪŋ/ *n* [U]
the process of using a computer to examine large amounts of information about customers, in order to discover things about them that are not easily seen or noticed 數據開採，數據剖析

dawg /dɔg; dɔːg/ *interjection*
slang used to emphasize how surprised, annoyed, or amused you are【俚】好傢伙，嗬〔表示驚訝、厭煩或開心等的感嘆語〕：*Dawg, I wish I'd gotten a chance to do that.* 嗬，我要是有機會那樣做該多美呀！

daytime run·ning light /ˌdetaɪm ˋrʌnɪŋ ˌlaɪt; ˌdeɪtaɪm ˈrʌnɪŋ ˌlaɪt/ *AmE*【美】, **daytime running lamp** *BrE*【英】*n* [C]
one of two HEADLIGHTs (=the large lights at the front of a vehicle) that turn on at low power during the day so that it is easier for the vehicle to be seen 白天開的汽車前燈

day trad·ing /ˋde ˌtredɪŋ; ˈdeɪ ˌtreɪdɪŋ/ *n* [U]
the activity of using a computer to buy and sell SHAREs on the Internet, often buying and selling very quickly to make a profit out of small price changes〔股票交易〕當天炒賣 —**day trader** *n* [C]

dead cat bounce /ˌdɛd kæt ˋbauns; ˌded kæt ˈbaʊns/ *n* [C]
technical informal a situation in which the price of SHAREs rises a small amount after a large fall, sometimes before falling further【術語, 非正式】"死貓"式反彈〔股票大跌後出現的輕微反彈〕

dead tree e·di·tion /ˌdɛd ˋtri ɪˌdɪʃən; ˌded ˈtriː ɪˌdɪʃən/ *n* [C]
humorous a paper copy of a magazine or newspaper that is also published on the Internet【幽默】〔與電子本同時出版的〕印刷本: *I was sitting at my desk reading the dead tree edition of the Times when Josh walked in.* 喬希進來時, 我正坐在桌前讀印刷版的《泰晤士報》。

de·bark /dɪˋbark; dɪˈbɑːk/ *v* [I]
to DISEMBARK 下船, 上岸: **[+from]** *I remember how glad I felt debarking from a ship in Bremerhaven after six days on the ocean.* 我記得那次在海上航行了六天之後, 在不梅港下船時我是多麼的高興。—**debarkation** *n* [U]

debt o·ver·hang /ˌdɛt ˋovəˌhæŋ; ˌdet ˈəʊvəhæŋ/ *n* [U]
technical a situation in which a business or government has so much debt that it cannot make new INVESTMENTs【術語】債台高築〔債務過多以致無法進行新的投資〕

decompress /ˌdikəmˋprɛs; ˌdiːkəmˈpres/ *v* [T]
NEW MEANING
technical to change the information in a computer document back into a form that can be easily read or used, when the information was stored on the computer in a special form that used less space on the computer's MEMORY【術語】解壓縮: *Most Macintosh computers can decompress files automatically.* 大多數蘋果電腦會自動為文件解壓縮。

de·crypt /diˋkrɪpt; diːˈkrɪpt/ *v* [T]
to change a message or information on a computer back into a form that can be read, when someone has sent it to you in a type of computer CODE 解密; 破譯: *Only certain employees will be able to decrypt sensitive documents.* 只有某些雇員可以對機密文件解密。

de·cryp·tion /diˋkrɪpʃən; diːˈkrɪpʃən/ *n* [U]
the process of changing a message or information on a computer back into a form that can be read when it was in a type of computer code 解密: *decryption software* 解密軟件

deep vein throm·bo·sis /ˌdip ven θrɑmˋbosɪs; ˌdiːp veɪn θrɒmˈbəʊsɪs/ *n, abbreviation* 縮寫為 **DVT**
a serious illness which happens when a small amount of blood becomes very thick and causes the heart to stop beating properly. People think it can sometimes happen on long plane journeys, and it is also called 'economy class syndrome' in British English 深靜脈血栓塞〔英國英語中亦稱"經濟艙綜合徵"〕: *Deaths from DVT in passengers on long-haul flights are estimated at 2,000 per year.* 長途飛機乘客因深靜脈血栓形成致死的估計每年有2,000人。

def /dɛf; def/ *adj*
slang fashionable and attractive【俚】棒極的, 呱呱叫的: *Hey, check out that def car.* 嗨, 好好看看那部靚車。

de·friz·zer /diˋfrɪzə; diːˈfrɪzə/ *n* [C,U]
informal a substance that you put in your hair to make it less tightly curled【非正式】鬈髮蓬鬆劑

de·gear·ing /diˋgɪrɪŋ; diːˈgɪərɪŋ/ *n* [U] *BrE*
DELEVERAGE【英】〔公司〕配股集資取代借貸

de·hir·ing /diˋhaɪrɪŋ; diːˈhaɪərɪŋ/ *n* [U] *AmE*
a situation in which a company stops employing people it no longer needs【美】解雇, 解聘

de·in·dus·tri·a·li·za·tion also 又作 **-isation** *BrE*【英】/ˌdiɪnˌdʌstrələˋzeʃən; ˌdiːɪnˌdʌstriəlaɪˈzeɪʃən/ *n* [U]
a situation in which there is less and less industry in an area or country 解除(某個地區或國家的)工業, 削減(某個地區或國家的)工業生產能力: *Britain's deindustrialization has meant more people are in service jobs.* 英國的工業式微意味着有更多人從事服務業工作。

de·lay·er·ing /diˋleərɪŋ; diːˈleɪərɪŋ/ *n* [U]
the act of reducing the levels of management in a company or organization 精簡(公司等的)管理架構

de·lev·er·age /diˋlɛvərɪdʒ; diːˈliːvərɪdʒ/ *n* [U]
technical a situation in which a company starts to get more of the money it needs by selling SHAREs, and less by borrowing【術語】〔公司〕配股集資取代借貸 —**deleverage** *v* [T]

demand man·age·ment /dɪˋmænd ˌmænɪdʒmənt; dɪˈmɑnd ˌmænɪdʒmənt/ *n* [U] *BrE*
a way of planning things such as new roads by trying to control the number of vehicles there will be, instead of always building new roads because the number of vehicles is always increasing【英】需求管理 —compare 比較 PREDICT AND PROVIDE

de·merge /diˋmɝdʒ; diːˈmɜːdʒ/ *v* [I,T]
technical to make one part of a large company into a separate company【術語】使分離, 拆分: *After the takeover, several subsidiary companies were demerged.* 收購之後, 幾個子公司被分拆出去。

demo¹ /ˋdɛmo; ˈdeməʊ/ *n* [C]
NEW MEANING
a computer PROGRAM that shows what a new piece of SOFTWARE will be able to do when it is ready to be sold〔軟件〕樣品: *Click here to download a demo of the new version of our personal finance software.* 點擊這裡下載我們個人理財軟件新文本的演示本。

demo² /ˋdɛmo; ˈdeməʊ/ *v* [T]
informal to show or explain how something works or is done, especially new computer equipment; DEMONSTRATE【非正式】示範, 演示: *They're going to demo some of the new software at this year's Mac convention.* 他們準備在今年的蘋果電腦大會上展示若干新軟件。

demolition job /ˌdɛməˋlɪʃən ˌdʒɑb; ˌdeməˈlɪʃən ˌdʒɒb/ *n* [C]
1 an act of criticizing someone severely or telling other people things about them which may be unfair or untrue, in order to harm them or to cause people to have a bad opinion of them 詆毀: **do a demolition job on sb** *He accused opposition leaders of doing a demolition job on the President.* 他指責反對黨領袖在詆毀總統。**2** an event, especially a sports event, in which one person or team is so strong that they defeat the opposition very severely〔體育比賽的〕大勝, 使慘敗: **[+against]** *Currie led the team with 55 points in the demolition job against Ireland.* 柯里率領該隊以55分大敗愛爾蘭隊。

dental dam /ˌdɛntl̩ ˋdæm; ˌdentl ˈdæm/ *n* [C]
a thin piece of rubber that a woman wears over her sex organs during ORAL SEX to protect herself or her partner from sexual diseases 牙障〔防止在口交中染上性病的橡皮牙套〕

de·or·bit /diˋɔrbɪt; diːˈɔːbɪt/ *v* [I,T]
technical to make a SATELLITE (=a machine that has been sent into space) come back to Earth in a controlled way when it is no longer needed in space【術語】(使)脫離軌道: *The Russian government decided not to deorbit Mir.* 俄羅斯政府決定不讓和平號返回地球。—**deorbit** *n* [C,U] *The crew is beginning final preparations for deorbit.* 全體人員開始作衛星脫離軌道返回地面的最後準備。

de·plane /diˋplen; diːˈpleɪn/ *v* [I]
to get off a plane 下飛機

depleted u·ra·ni·um /dɪˋplitɪd juˋrenɪəm; dɪ'pliːtᵻd jʊ'reɪniəm/ *abbreviation* 縮寫為 **DU** *n* [U]
a very hard, slightly RADIOACTIVE metal that is used on the outside of some bullets and shells (SHELL[1] (2)) 貧鈾

derm·a·ceu·ti·cal /ˌdɝməˋsutɪkḷ; ˌdɜːmə'sjuːtɪkəl/ *n* [C]
a substance that helps to improve the quality of someone's skin 護膚劑: *a privately owned company specializing in the development of dermaceutical products* 一家專門從事開發護膚產品的私營企業

de·sert·i·fi·ca·tion /dɪˌzɝtɪfɪˋkeʃən; dɪˌzɜːtᵻfᵻ'keɪʃən/ *n* [U]
a process in which useful land, especially farm land, gradually becomes dry and useless, especially because too many bushes or trees have been cut down, or because too many farm animals have used the land 沙（漠）化

desk·fast /ˋdɛskfəst; 'deskfəst/ *n* [C usually singular 一般用單數] *AmE*
humorous breakfast that is eaten at someone's desk in an office【美, 幽默】辦公桌早餐: *Hectic morning schedules mean that many families don't take time for breakfast. Some have a quick deskfast while others miss out altogether.* 忙亂的晨間安排意味着有許多家庭都抽不出時間用早餐, 一些人只得匆匆在辦公桌吃早餐, 另一些人乾脆不吃。

desk jock·ey /ˋdɛsk ˌdʒɑkɪ; 'desk ˌdʒɒki/ *n* [C]
informal someone who does all of their work at a desk or in an office【非正式】做文牘工作的人: *He's a desk jockey at a government agency in Detroit.* 他在底特律一個政府部門做文牘工作。

desktop charg·er /ˌdɛsktɑp ˋtʃɑrdʒɚ; ˌdesktɒp 'tʃɑːdʒə/ *n* [C]
a small piece of equipment that puts a new supply of electricity into the BATTERY of a MOBILE PHONE〔手機電池〕台式充電器

detail /ˋditel; 'diːteɪl/ *v* [T] *AmE*
NEW MEANING
to clean both the inside and outside of a car very thoroughly【美】全面清洗〔車輛〕—**detailing** *n* [U]

detox /ˋditɑks; 'diːtɒks/ *v* [I]
informal if someone detoxes, they are given special treatment at a hospital to help them stop drinking alcohol or taking drugs. This word is a short form of DETOXIFY.【非正式】戒除酒癮[毒癮]: *I detoxed in the hospital, and I've now been free of alcohol and drugs for 10 months – the longest I've ever been clean.* 我在醫院裡戒酒和戒毒, 現在我已 10 個月沒有喝酒和吸毒了 — 這是我戒酒、戒毒最長的一次。

development a·re·a /dɪˋvɛləpmənt ˌɛrɪə; dɪ'veləpmənt ˌeəriə/ *n* [C] *BrE*
an area of the country that the government tries to help by offering money, lower taxes etc to businesses that move to that area【英】(待) 開發區

dialogue box *BrE*【英】, **dialog box** *AmE*【美】/ˋdaɪəlɔg ˌbɑks; 'daɪəlɒg ˌbɒks/ *n* [C]
a box that appears on your computer screen when the PROGRAM you are using needs to ask you a question before it can continue to do something. You CLICK on one part of the box to give your answer. 對話框: *When the dialog box appears, click on 'OK.'* 出現對話框時, 就點擊"OK"。

dial-up /ˋdaɪəl ˌʌp; 'daɪəl ˌʌp/ *adj* [only before noun 僅用於名詞前]
relating to a telephone line that is used to send information from one computer to another 撥號上網的: *a dial-up connection* 撥號連結 —**dialup** *n* [C]

diamond lane /ˋdaɪəmənd ˌlen; 'daɪəmənd ˌleɪn/ *n* [C] *AmE*
a special LANE (=area that you drive in) on a road that is marked with a diamond shape and can be used only by buses, taxis, and sometimes cars with more than one passenger【美】鑽石形車道: *a bus-only diamond lane* 公共汽車專用的鑽石形車道 | *Diamond lanes are meant to encourage car-pooling.* 鑽石形車道旨在鼓勵合夥用車。

di·ge·rat·i /ˌdɪdʒəˋrɑtɪ; ˌdɪdʒə'rɑːti/ *n* [plural]
people who understand and use computers in a very skilful way. This word comes from a combination of the words 'DIGITAL' and 'LITERATI' (=people who know a lot about literature) 網上知識界, 電腦高手〔由 digital 和 literati 縮合而成〕: *the digerati who attended a software convention* 出席軟件會議的電腦高手

di·gi·cam /ˋdɪdʒɪkæm; 'dɪdʒɪkæm/ *n* [C]
a type of camera that can store pictures as DIGITAL FILES which can be put into a computer, rather than on film 數碼照相機

digital age /ˋdɪdʒətḷ ˌedʒ; 'dɪdʒᵻtl ˌeɪdʒ/ also 又作 **computer age** *n*
the Digital Age the time when computers become more common in a society and are used regularly in daily life to do ordinary activities. Most people believe the digital age has already begun. 數字[數碼]時代

digital sig·na·ture /ˌdɪdʒətḷ ˋsɪgnətʃɚ; ˌdɪdʒᵻtl 'sɪgnətʃə/ *n* [C]
information on an electronic message that proves who the person sending the message is 數字[數碼]式簽名, 數字[數碼]標記

digital vid·e·o /ˌdɪdʒətḷ ˋvɪdɪo; ˌdɪdʒᵻtl 'vɪdiəʊ/ *n* [U]
the process of recording pictures and sounds that are represented in the form of numbers, usually numbers in the BINARY system (=a system using the numbers 1 and 0), used especially in computing 數字視頻, 數字顯像, 數碼錄像

di·jo·naise /ˌdiʒəˋnez; ˌdiːʒɒ'neɪz/ *n* [U]
a mixture of a type of MAYONNAISE and MUSTARD that is eaten with some foods, especially meat or fish 第戎芥末蛋黃醬: *salmon with a dijonaise sauce* 用第戎芥末蛋黃醬調味的鮭魚

direct de·pos·it /dəˌrɛkt dɪˋpɑzɪt; dᵻˌrekt dɪ'pɒzᵻt/ *v* [T]
to pay the money someone earns directly into their bank account 直接存入〔銀行戶口〕: *My pay is direct deposited on the 27th of each month.* 我的薪金是每月 27 日直接存入戶口的。

direct-to-con·sum·er /dəˌrɛkt tə kənˋsumɚ; dᵻˌrekt tə kən'sjuːmə/ *adj* [only before noun 僅用於名詞前]
direct-to-consumer advertising is aimed at the customer who will buy the product, rather than at the shops that will sell them 直接面向消費者的: *Pharmaceutical advertising revenue is expected to soar 300%, reflecting a jump in direct-to-consumer advertising by drug companies.* 藥品廣告的收益可望上漲300%, 這反映了製藥公司在直接面向消費者的廣告支出有所激增。

director's cut /dəˋrɛktɚz ˌkʌt; dᵻ'rektəz ˌkʌt/ *n* [C]
a film that contains all the parts that the DIRECTOR wanted to include, when the film was originally shown in cinemas without those parts〔未經剪輯的〕足本影片: *The director's cut of The Godfather part III has nine minutes of film not included in the theatrical release.*《教父》第三集的足本有 9 分鐘的片段未有在劇院放映。

dirt-dish·er /ˋdɝt ˌdɪʃɚ; 'dɜːt ˌdɪʃə/ *n* [C] *AmE*
informal a DISHER【美, 非正式】熱衷於傳佈小道消息[內幕新聞]的人

dirty /ˋdɝtɪ; 'dɜːti/ *adj*
NEW MEANING
a dirty sports event is one in which people competing in the event have illegally used drugs to improve their performance〔指體育比賽〕不正當的, 使用違禁藥物的: *Many people think that the race has been a dirty event for years.* 許多人認為這項比賽多年來一直有人使用違禁藥物。

dis also 又作 **diss** /dɪs; dɪs/ *v* **dissed, dissing** [T]
slang another spelling of DISS; to make unfair and un-

kind remarks about someone 【俚】diss 的另一種拼法; 詆譭, 對…說無禮的話: *I feel bad for dissing him the way I did.* 我對自己曾經蔑視他的做法感到歉疚。| *Quit dissing me.* 別再貶低我了。

disco bis·cuit /ˋdɪsko ˏbɪskɪt; ˈdɪskəʊ ˌbɪskɪt/ *n* [C] *BrE*
slang the drug ECSTASY 【英俚】"狂喜"迷幻藥

dis·count·er /ˋdɪskaʊntɚ; ˈdɪskaʊntə/ *n* [C]
a person or business that sells goods or services at lower prices than normal 廉價零售商[店]

discretionary in·come /dɪˋskrɛʃənɛrɪ ˏɪnkʌm; dɪˈskreʃənəri ˌɪŋkʌm/ *n* [U]
the money remaining from your income after your bills have been paid, which can be spent on things such as entertainment or holidays〔賬款扣除後〕可隨意支配的收入

dish /dɪʃ; dɪʃ/ *v* [I,T]
NEW MEANING
informal to give a lot of information about something or someone, especially something that would usually be secret or private, or to give someone a lot of information 【非正式】傳播〔內幕新聞等〕, 炒作: **[+on]** *She's ready to dish on boys, beauty, and break-ups in her new column.* 她準備在她的新專欄中暢談男人、美容以及關係破裂等的話題。

dish·er /ˋdɪʃɚ; ˈdɪʃə/ also 又作 **dirt-disher** *n* [C] *AmE informal* someone who enjoys telling other people a lot of GOSSIP (=information about other people's behaviour and private lives) 【美, 非正式】熱衷於傳佈小道消息[內幕新聞]的人: *Women newspaper columnists have tended to play the role of the social commentator or the light-hearted Hollywood disher.* 報章專欄女作家往往扮演社會評論員或輕浮的好萊塢長舌婦的角色。

disrespect /ˏdɪsrɪˋspɛkt; ˌdɪsrɪˈspekt/ *v* [T]
to say or do things that show a lack of respect for someone 對…不敬: *Hicks accused Williams of disrespecting him at a record company party.* 希克斯指責威廉斯在一次唱片公司舉辦的聚會上對他不敬。

DLL /ˏdi ɛl ˋɛl; ˌdiː el ˈel/ *n*
dynamic link library; a collection of information in a computer file that is designed to be shared and used many times by many different programs 動態鏈接庫

DNA pro·fil·ing /ˏdi ɛn e ˋprofaɪlɪŋ; ˌdiː en eɪ ˈprəʊfaɪlɪŋ/ *n* [U]
the act of examining the DNA found where a crime has happened and the DNA of people who may have done the crime, in order to find out who is responsible 基因圖測定, 基因鑑證

do /du; duː/ *v*
NEW MEANING
do one! *BrE informal spoken* an impolite expression used to tell someone to go away 【英, 非正式, 口】滾! 滾蛋!

doc·u·soap, docusoap /ˋdɑkju ˏsop; ˈdɒkjʊ ˌsəʊp/ *n* [C] *BrE*
a television programme that shows what happens in the daily lives of real people. This word comes from a combination of 'DOCUMENTARY' and 'SOAP OPERA'. 【英】紀錄片式肥皂劇〔由 documentary 和 soap opera 縮合而成〕

dog /dɔg; dɒg/ *v*
NEW MEANING
dog it *AmE informal* to not try as hard as you should in order to do something 【美, 非正式】〔工作中〕偷懶: *Quit dogging it and do your work.* 別吊兒郎當, 好好幹你的活。

d'oh /do; dəʊ/ *interjection*
spoken humorous used when you have just realized that you have done or said something stupid 【口, 幽默】咳〔發現自己做了傻事或說了傻話後的感嘆〕

dol·lar·iza·tion /ˏdɑlərəˋzeʃən; ˌdɒləraɪˈzeɪʃən/ *n* [U]
technical a situation in which countries outside the US want to use the dollar rather than their own country's money 【術語】美元化〔不用本國貨幣而用美元〕

dolphin-safe /ˋdɑlfɪn ˏsef; ˈdɒlfɪn ˌseɪf/ *adj*
dolphin-safe fish is caught in a way that does not harm or kill DOLPHINS 不傷害海豚的: *I only buy dolphin-safe tuna.* 我只買那些在捕獲中不會殃及海豚的金槍魚。

domain name /dəˋmen ˏnem; dəˈmeɪn ˌneɪm/ *n* [C]
a company's or organization's address on the Internet. A domain name is followed by an abbreviation which shows its type, for example .com for company, or its country of origin, for example .uk for the United Kingdom. 域名

domestic part·ner /dəˏmɛstɪk ˋpɑrtnɚ; dəˌmestɪk ˈpɑːtnə/ *n* [C]
formal someone who you live with and have a sexual relationship with, but who you are not married to 【正式】家庭伴侶〔未婚而同居者〕: *The new law gave retirement and health benefits to the domestic partners of city employees.* 新的法律規定城市雇員的同居伴侶亦可享受退休津貼和醫療保健津貼。

done /dʌn; dʌn/ *adj*
NEW MEANING
be a done deal used to emphasize that something has been completed or that a final arrangement has been agreed (敲) 定了的: *Despite the developer's claims, the mayor says the proposed hotel is not a done deal.* 儘管發展商說得很肯定, 但是市長還是說計劃中的旅館並沒有定案。

dope /dop; dəʊp/ *adj AmE*
slang good or satisfactory 【美俚】很棒的: *If we could be friends, that'd be dope.* 我們要是能成為朋友, 那該有多棒啊。| *Eminem's dope new CD* 埃米內精彩的新雷射唱片

dot-com also 又作 **dot.com, dot com** /ˏdɑt ˋkɑm; ˌdɒt ˈkɒm/ *adj* [only before noun 僅用於名詞前]
informal relating to a person or company whose business is done using the Internet or involves the Internet 【非正式】經營互聯網業務的: *a dot-com company* 經營互聯網業務的公司 | *dot-com millionaires* 經營互聯網業務的大富翁 **—dot-com** *n* [C]: *Several of the leading dot.coms saw their share prices slide yesterday.* 幾家經營互聯網業務的大公司看到它們的股票價格在昨天下挫。**—dot-com** *v* [T]: *We'll have to decide whether to dot-com our business.* 我們得決定要不要把業務發展至互聯網上。

dot-com·mer also 又作 **dot.commer** /ˏdɑt ˋkɑmɚ; ˌdɒt ˈkɒmə/ *n* [C]
people who work for or own a company whose business involves the Internet, especially people who earn a lot of money 網絡公司工作人員[經營者]

doul·a /ˋdulə; ˈduːlə/ *n* [C]
a woman whose job is helping new parents care for their babies 嬰兒保姆〔幫助剛任父母親者照料嬰兒的婦女〕

down /daun; daʊn/ *adj*
NEW MEANING
be down with sb *slang spoken* to be friends with someone 【俚, 口】與某人關係密切

down·load /ˋdaunlod; ˈdaʊnləʊd/ *n* [C]
a computer FILE OR PROGRAM that has been moved from a large computer or the Internet to another computer 下載的電腦檔案或程式: *We've got reviews and downloads of the latest business software.* 我們有最新版本的商業軟件的評論和下載文件。

down·load·a·ble /ˏdaunˋlodəbl; ˌdaʊnˈləʊdəbəl/ *adj*
if a computer PROGRAM or FILE is downloadable, you are allowed to copy it from another computer onto your own computer 可下載的

downmarket /ˏdaunˋmɑrkɪt; ˌdaʊnˈmɑːkɪt/ *adv BrE* 【英】
NEW MEANING
1 go/move downmarket to start buying or selling cheaper goods or services 進入[面向]〔針對低收入消費者的〕下品市場, 低層次營銷 **2 take sth down-market**

to change a product or service, so that it is cheaper and more popular 使…進入下品市場, 使…轉為低層次營銷: *He was accused of taking the radio station downmarket in order to compete with commercial stations.* 他被指控為了與商營電台競爭而把該無線電台轉入低檔次市場。

down·scale[1] /ˋdaun͵skel; ˈdaʊnskeɪl/ *adj AmE*
downscale goods or services are cheap and not of very good quality【美】低檔的

downscale[2] /ˋdaun͵skel; ˈdaʊnskeɪl/ *v* [I,T] *AmE*
to sell or buy cheaper goods of lower quality【美】買賣低檔次貨品

down·shift /ˋdaun͵ʃɪft; ˈdaʊnʃɪft/ *v* [I]
if someone downshifts, they choose to do a less important or difficult job, so that they do not have to worry about their work and have more time to enjoy their life〔為過輕閒生活而改換次要或較容易的工作〕降格工作

down·time also 又作 **down time** /ˋdaun͵taɪm; ˈdaʊntaɪm/ *n* [U]
NEW MEANING
informal a period of time when you have finished what you were doing, and you can relax or do something that you had not originally planned to do【非正式】不幹活的時間, 空檔期: *Often, during semesters, you have down time when you can do some exercise.* 學期中間往往會有一段空閒時間讓你做一些運動。—**downtime** *adj*: *downtime activities for teachers* 教師的公餘活動

dreads /drɛdz; dredz/ *n* [plural]
a short form of the word DREADLOCKS "駭人"長髮辮〔dreadlocks 的縮略式〕: *He'd bounce into the room, his little dreads flying, and drop his enormous bag with a bang.* 他總是蹦蹦跳跳地走進房間, 一頭小巧的髮辮飛彈起來, 砰的一聲把大袋子扔下。

drip ad·ver·tis·ing /ˋdrɪp ͵ædvɚtaɪzɪŋ; ˈdrɪp ͵ædvətaɪzɪŋ/ *n* [U]
technical a situation in which advertisements for a product or service are shown repeatedly over a long period of time【術語】長期重複播放的廣告

drive-through de·liv·e·ry /͵draɪv θru dɪˋlɪvərɪ; ͵draɪv θruː dɪˈlɪvəri/ *n* [C] *AmE*
a system of delivering babies used in some hospitals in which a woman spends only a very short period of time at the hospital after giving birth to a child【美】快速留院分娩

drop dead date /͵drɑp ˋdɛd ͵det; ͵drɒp ˈded ͵deɪt/ *n* [C usually singular 一般用單數] *AmE*
NEW MEANING
informal a date by which you must have completed something, because after this date it is no longer worth doing【美, 非正式】最後期限

drum 'n' bass /͵drʌm ən ˋbes; ͵drʌm ən ˈbeɪs/ *n* [U]
a type of popular music with a strong low beat that started in Britain in the 1990s 鼓點低音, 鼓打貝斯〔20 世紀 90 年代在英國興起的一種強節奏的流行音樂〕

DSL /͵di ɛs ˋɛl; ͵diː es ˈel/ *n* [C]
digital subscriber line; a telephone line that has special equipment which allows it to receive information from the Internet, or send information at very high speeds 數字用戶線路, 數位用戶迴路, 數碼用戶專線: *the pros and cons of using a DSL connection to the Internet* 贊成和反對採用數字用戶線路上網的理由

DU /͵di ˋju; ͵diː ˈjuː/ *n* [U]
depleted uranium; a very hard slightly RADIO-ACTIVE metal that is used on the outside of some bullets and shells (SHELL[1] (2)) used by soldiers 貧鈾

dual-band /͵djuəl ˋbænd; ͵djuːəl ˈbænd/ *adj* [only before noun 僅用於名詞前]
a dual-band MOBILE PHONE is able to work in at least two different countries, because it can receive two different sorts of signal〔手提電話〕雙頻段的

dub·by /ˋdʌbɪ; ˈdʌbi/ *adj BrE*
if a piece of music is dubby, it has some features that are typical of DUB (=a style of music from the West Indies) in which sounds are repeated like an ECHO【英】達布式的〔達布是西印度羣島流行的一種節奏重複的音樂〕

dumb /dʌm; dʌm/ *v*
dumb sth ↔ **down** [I,T] to present something such as news or information in a simple and attractive way without many details so that everyone can understand it. People who use this expression show that they disapprove of making complicated information too simple 降低…的難度〔用於表示不同意把複雜的資料改得過分簡單〕, 使簡短易明: *Have history textbooks been dumbed down over the past decade?* 在過去 10 年期間, 歷史課本是否改得過分簡單? —**dumbing down** *n* [U]

duvet day /duˋve ͵de; ˈduːveɪ ͵deɪ/ *n* [C] *BrE*
a day when someone says that they are ill and does not go to work, even though they are not really ill【英】裝病請假日: *Some employers nowadays are even happy to reward their staff with an unscheduled duvet day from time to time.* 近來一些雇主甚至樂於讓雇員放不定期病假以作獎賞。

DVD /͵di vi ˋdi; ͵diː viː ˈdiː/ *n* [C]
digital versatile disk or digital video disk; a type of COMPACT DISC that can have information, sound, and pictures on it and that has enough space for a full-length film 數字激光視盤, 數字多功能光盤, 數碼光碟: *Every DVD player can also play standard audio CDs.* 所有數碼影碟播放機也可播放標準的激光唱片。| *The film is now out on video and DVD.* 這部影片現在有錄像帶和數碼影碟出售。

E,e

e-, E- /i; iː/ *prefix*
electronic; used before another word to mean something that is done on or involves the Internet 電子的, 網上的: *e-shopping* 網上購物 | *e-commerce* 電子商務

easter egg /ˋistɚ ͵ɛg; ˈiːstər ͵eg/ *n* [C]
NEW MEANING
a secret message that is hidden in a computer PROGRAM, usually containing a funny message or the names of the people who wrote the program 復活節彩蛋〔電腦程式的隱藏內容, 一般包括有趣的內容或程序製作者的名字〕

e-book /ˋi buk; ˈiː bʊk/ also 又作 **electronic book** *n* [C]
a book that you read on a computer screen or on a special small computer that you can hold in your hands, and that is not printed on paper 電子書

e-busi·ness /ˋi ͵bɪznɪs; ˈiː ͵bɪznɪ̇s/ *n* [U]
electronic business; the activity of buying and selling goods and services and doing other business activities using a computer and the Internet 電子商業, 電子貿易

e-cash /ˋi ͵kæʃ; ˈiː ͵kæʃ/ *n* [U]
money that can be used to buy things on the Internet, but that does not exist in a physical form or belong to any particular country 電子現金

e-comm /ˋi ͵kɑm; ˈiː ͵kɒm/ *n* [U]
informal【非正式】an abbreviation of 縮寫 = E-COMMERCE

e-com·merce /ˋi ͵kɑmɝs; ˈiː ͵kɒmɜːs/ *n* [U]
electronic commerce; the activity of buying and selling goods and services and doing other business activities using a computer and the Internet; E-BUSINESS 電子商務: *e-commerce applications such as online ticketing and reservations* 網上購票和網上預訂等電子商務應用系統

economy class syn·drome /ɪˋkɑnəmɪ klæs ͵sɪndrom; ɪˈkɒnəmi klɑːs ͵sɪndrəʊm/ *n* [U] *BrE*
a serious illness which happens when a small amount of blood becomes very thick and causes the heart to stop beating properly. People believe that travelling in ECONOMY CLASS (=the cheapest seats) on long journeys in planes can cause this because passengers sit for a very long time and cannot move around very easily. The

medical term is DEEP VEIN THROMBOSIS.【英】經濟艙綜合徵〔其醫學術語為“深靜脈血栓塞”〕

e·co·pol·i·tics /ˈiko,pɑlɪtɪks; ˈiːkəʊ,pɒlᵻtɪks/ *n* [U]
a type of political activity that is concerned with preserving and protecting the world's environment 生態政治學

e·co·tour·is·m /ˈiko,turɪzəm; ˈiːkəʊ,tʊərɪzəm/ *n* [U]
the business of providing services for tourists who come to see beautiful places that are in danger of being harmed, so that people can earn money from the tourists rather than from activities that harm the environment. This word comes from a combination of the words 'ECOLOGY' and 'TOURISM' 生態旅遊（業）〔由 ecology 和 tourism 縮合而成〕: *Ecotourism generated new wealth in the north of Chile.* 生態旅遊給智利北部創造了新的財富。

e-cur·ren·cy /ˈi ,kɝənsɪ; ˈiː ,kʌrənsi/ *n* [C]
one of the types of money that can be used only on the Internet 電子貨幣

edge city /ˈɛdʒ ,sɪtɪ; ˈedʒ ,sɪti/ *n* [C]
a SUBURB of a large city that has its own businesses, shops, offices etc, so that many of the people who used to live there while working in the large city now both live and work in the edge city〔興建於大城市市郊的〕邊緣城市

EDI /,i di ˈaɪ; ,iː diː ˈaɪ/
electronic data interchange; a way for companies and banks to send information to each other by computer. Documents are sent in an agreed FORMAT so that the company receiving them can easily read them on their computer and print them out on paper. 電子數據交換

e-fit /ˈi ,fɪt; ˈiː ,fɪt/ *n* [C] *BrE*
a picture, made by using a computer, of a person who the police think was responsible for a crime, which they show on television or the Internet in order to try and catch the person【英】〔嫌疑犯人的〕電腦模擬畫像

EFT /,i ɛf ˈti; ,iː ef ˈtiː/
electronic funds transfer; the process by which money is moved from one bank account, business etc to another using only computer systems 電子資金轉賬[匯兑]

ego-surf·ing /ˈigo ,sɝfɪŋ; ˈiːgəʊ ,sɜːfɪŋ/ *n* [U]
humorous the activity of searching for your name on the Internet in order to find out how many times it appears there【幽默】自我搜索，自我衝浪〔找尋自己的名字在互聯網上出現的次數〕

elder a·buse /ˈɛldɚ ə,bjuz; ˈeldər ə,bjuːz/ *n* [U] *especially AmE*
cruel actions or remarks to an old person that harm them mentally or hurt them physically【尤美】對老人的虐待[凌辱]: *an agency that assists victims of elder abuse* 幫助受虐待老人的機構

el·der·care /ˈɛldɚ,kɛr; ˈeldə ,keə/ also 又作 **elder care** *n* [U] *especially AmE*
the activity of looking after old people who cannot look after themselves properly, for example by making sure an old person gets good meals or medical care when they need it【尤美】老年保健: *More women than men have responsibility for elder care.* 婦女擔負照料老人者要比男性多。—**elder care** *adj*: *an eldercare program* 老人保健計劃 | *eldercare facilities* 老人保健設施

electronic bank·ing /,ɛlɪktrɑnɪk ˈbæŋkɪŋ; ,elɪktrɒnɪk ˈbæŋkɪŋ/ *n* [U]
a service provided by banks that allows people to pay money from one account to another, pay bills etc using the Internet 電子銀行業務

electronic cash /,ɛlɪktrɑnɪk ˈkæʃ; ,elɪktrɒnɪk ˈkæʃ/ *n* [U]
money that can be used to buy things on the Internet, but that does not exist in a physical form or belong to any particular country 電子貨幣

electronic da·ta in·ter·change /,ɛlɪktrɑnɪk ˈdetə ,ɪntɚtʃendʒ; ,elɪktrɒnɪk ˈdeɪtə ,ɪntətʃeɪndʒ/ *abbreviation* 縮寫為 **EDI** *n* [U]
a way for companies and banks to send information to each other by using a computer. The information is sent in an agreed FORMAT so that the company receiving the documents can easily read them on their computer and print them out on paper 電子數據交換: *software designed to facilitate Electronic Data Interchange* 旨在促進電子數據交換的軟件

electronic funds trans·fer /,ɛlɪktrɑnɪk ˈfʌndz ,trænsfɝ; ,elɪktrɒnɪk ˈfʌndz ,trænsfɜː/ *abbreviation* 縮寫為 **EFT** *n* [C,U]
the process by which money is moved from one bank account, business etc to another using only computer systems 電子資金轉賬[匯兑]

electronic mon·ey /,ɛlɪktrɑnɪk ˈmʌnɪ; ,elɪktrɒnɪk ˈmʌni/ *n* [U]
money that can be used to buy things on the Internet, but that does not exist in a physical form or belong to any particular country 電子貨幣

electronic or·ga·niz·er /,ɛlɪktrɑnɪk ˈɔrgənaɪzɚ; ,elɪktrɒnɪk ˈɔːgənaɪzə/ *n* [C]
a small piece of electronic equipment that you can use to record addresses, telephone numbers, dates of meetings etc 電子記事簿

electronic pay·ment sys·tem /,ɛlɪktrɑnɪk ˈpemənt ,sɪstəm; ,elɪktrɒnɪk ˈpeɪmənt ,sɪstᵻm/ *n* [C]
a system of paying or receiving money using the telephone or a computer and without using cash or cheques, for example DIRECT DEPOSIT 電子付款系統

electronic pub·lish·ing /,ɛlɪktrɑnɪk ˈpʌblɪʃɪŋ; ,elɪktrɒnɪk ˈpʌblɪʃɪŋ/ *n* [U]
the business of producing books, magazines, or newspapers that are designed to be read using a computer 電子出版（業）

electronic sig·na·ture /,ɛlɪktrɑnɪk ˈsɪgnətʃɚ; ,elɪktrɒnɪk ˈsɪgnətʃə/ *n*
—see 見 DIGITAL SIGNATURE

electronic tick·et·ing /,ɛlɪktrɑnɪk ˈtɪkɪtɪŋ; ,elɪktrɒnɪk ˈtɪkᵻtɪŋ/ *n* [U]
a service provided by airlines that allows people to buy their tickets on the Internet and usually does not give them tickets in the form of paper〔航空公司的〕網上購票（服務）

El Ni·ño /ɛl ˈninjo; el ˈniːnjəʊ/ *n* [singular, used without *the* 不與 the 連用]
a condition that occurs every 3 to 7 years in which the surface of the Pacific Ocean becomes warmer near the West coast of South America, affecting the weather in many parts of the world and killing fish and other sea animals in that area 厄爾尼諾（現象）

e-mail, email /ˈi ,mel; ˈiː ,meɪl/ *n* [C]
NEW MEANING
a message that is sent from one person to another electronically from one computer to another 電子郵件: *I'll send you an email when I know more about it.* 了解更多情況後我會給你發電子郵件。

e-mon·ey /ˈi ,mʌnɪ; ˈiː ,mʌni/ also 又作 **e-cash** *n* [U]
money that can be used to buy things on the Internet, but that does not exist in a physical form or belong to any particular country 電子貨幣

e·mo·ti·con /ɪˈmotɪkɑn; ɪˈməʊtɪkɒn/ *n* [C]
one of a set of special signs that is used to show an emotion in E-MAIL and on the Internet, often by making a picture. For example, the emoticon :-) looks like a smiling face when you look at it sideways and means that you have made a joke. This word comes from a combination of the words 'EMOTION' and 'ICON'.〔電子郵件或互聯網用符號表示的〕情感符〔由 emotion 和 icon 縮合而成〕

emotional in·tel·li·gence /ɪ,moʃənḷ ɪnˈtɛlədʒəns; ɪ,məʊʃənəl ɪnˈtelᵻdʒəns/ *n* [U]
the skills and qualities that make you good at understanding people and knowing how they feel about a situation, as well as being good at solving problems 情

感智力[商]: *Emotional intelligence is a quality that employers are now looking for.* 情感智力是雇主目前尋求的(雇員應有的)一種品質。| *The course will help you increase your emotional intelligence.* 這個課程會幫助你提高自己的情感智力。

EMU /ˋimju, ˌi ɛm ˋju; ˈiːmjuː, ˌiː em ˈjuː/ *n* [U]
economic and monetary union or European monetary union; the use by many European Union countries of the same money, the Euro 經濟與貨幣聯盟, 歐洲貨幣聯盟

-enabled /ɪnebl̩d; ɪneɪbəld/ *suffix* [in adjectives 構成形容詞]
Internet-enabled/Java-enabled etc a computer PROGRAM that is Internet-enabled, Java-enabled etc can be used with that program or includes it as one of its features 能上網的/能支援 Java 語言的等: *Find out more about our free Internet-enabled software.* 請進一步了解我們的免費可上網軟件。

en·a·bler /ɪˋnebl̩ɚ; ɪˈneɪblə/ *n* [C]
someone who thinks they are helping someone else when actually they are preventing that person from improving their bad behaviour, for example because they deal with that person's problems instead of letting them deal with the problems on their own 代庖者, 縱容者: *Fletcher became his daughter's enabler by continuing to lend her money.* 弗萊徹繼續借錢給女兒而成了她的縱容者。

en·crypt /ɪnˋkrɪpt; ɪnˈkrɪpt/ *v* [T]
to change information that has been written on a computer so that it is in a CODE, especially to prevent particular people from being able to read it 加密: *Users can click an on-screen button to encrypt an outgoing message.* 用戶可點擊屏幕鍵給要發送的信息加密。—**encryption** /ɪnˋkrɪpʃən; ɪnˈkrɪpʃən/ *n* [U] —**encrypted** *adj*

entry lev·el /ˋɛntrɪ ˌlɛvl̩; ˈentri ˌlevəl/ *adj* [only before noun 僅用於名詞前]
entry level product/model/computer etc a product etc that is most suitable for people who do not have much money to spend or who do not have experience using that kind of product 初級水平的產品/型號/電腦等

environmental im·pact as·sess·ment /ɪnˌvaɪrənmɛntl̩ ˋɪmpækt əˌsɛsmənt; ɪnˌvaɪərənmentl ˈɪmpækt əˌsesmənt/ *n* [C]
NEW MEANING
an examination of the possible effects of a new building development or new road on the environment 環境影響評估: *A full environmental impact assessment will be required before any development within 25 miles of the coast.* 距海岸25英里內的任何開發項目都先要進行全面的環境影響評估。

environmental im·pact state·ment /ɪnˌvaɪrənmɛntl̩ ˋɪmpækt ˌstetmənt; ɪnˌvaɪərənmɛntl ˈɪmpækt ˌsteɪtmənt/ *n* [C]
in the US, a report that explains what effects a new PROJECT, such as a building, will have on the environment. A company or organization must give this report to the government before the government will allow them to start the new project. 環境影響報告

EPROM /ˋipram; ˈiːprɒm/ *n* [C]
electrically programmable read-only memory; a type of computer CHIP where the contents of the chip can be replaced or changed only by a special machine 可刪可編程序唯讀記憶體

e-pub·lish·ing /ˋi ˌpʌblɪʃɪŋ; ˈiː ˌpʌblɪʃɪŋ/ *n* [U]
electronic publishing; the business of producing books, magazines, or newspapers that are designed to be read using a computer 電子出版(業): *"E-publishing is on the brink of acceptance but has to still fully develop into a common way to read," said Norris.* 諾里斯說:"電子出版差不多已得到認可, 但它還需要充分發展成為普及的閱讀方式才行。" —**e-publisher** *n* [C]

erectile dys·func·tion also 又作 **erectile disfunction** /ɪˌrɛktl̩ dɪsˋfʌŋkʃən; ɪˌrektaɪl dɪsˈfʌŋkʃən/ *n* [U]
if a man has erectile dysfunction, he is unable to have sex because he cannot get an ERECTION 勃起功能障礙, 不舉: *Regular exercise reduces a man's risk of erectile dysfunction.* 定期鍛鍊會減少男性患勃起功能障礙的風險。

e-res·u·me also 又作 **e-résumé** /ˋi ˌrɛzuˋme; ˈi ˌrezjʊmeɪ/ *n* [C]
an electronic written record of your education and previous jobs that you send to an employer over the Internet when you are looking for a new job 電子履歷

e-sig·na·ture /ˋi ˌsɪgnətʃɚ; ˈi ˌsɪgnətʃə/ also 又作 **electronic signature** *n* [C]
a sort of CODE that is used in an electronic document in order to prove who was responsible for writing the document, so that the person who receives it can be sure who it is from. Some companies use e-signatures in their legal documents instead of written SIGNATURES on paper. 電子簽名

e-tail·er /ˋi ˌtelɚ; ˈiː ˌteɪlə/ *n* [C]
electronic retailer; a business that sells products or services on the Internet, instead of in a shop 網上零售商: *Some e-tailers need to improve their customer services.* 一些網上零售商需要改進對顧客的服務。—**e-tail** *n* [U]

ethical au·dit /ˌɛθɪkl̩ ˋɔdɪt; ˌeθɪkəl ˈɔːdɪt/ also 又作 **social audit** *n* [C]
an official examination of how well a company behaves, for example how it treats its employees, the environment etc 道德審計〔檢查公司對雇員和環境的態度等〕

e-tick·et /ˋi ˌtɪkɪt; ˈiː ˌtɪkɪt/ *n* [C]
electronic ticket; a ticket, especially a ticket for a plane journey, that is stored in a computer and is not given to the customer in the form of paper 電子票證; 電子機票

euro /ˋjuro; ˈjʊərəʊ/ *n* [C]
NEW MEANING
a CURRENCY that can be used in some countries of the EU, and that will become the only currency that those countries will use 歐元, 歐羅

Eu·ro·land /ˋjurolænd; ˈjʊərəʊlænd/ *n*
the countries in Europe who have started to use the Euro as a legal CURRENCY 歐元[羅]區

Eu·ro·scep·tic also 又作 **eurosceptic** *BrE*【英】, **Euroskeptic** *AmE*【美】/ˋjuroˌskɛptɪk; ˈjʊərəʊˌskeptɪk/ *n* [C]
someone, especially a politician, who believes that Britain should not become closely connected to the European Union 對歐盟有懷疑的人〔尤指認為英國不應與歐盟太親密的政客〕—**eurosceptic** *adj*: *eurosceptic policies* 對歐盟持懷疑態度的政策

Eu·ro·trash /ˋjuroˌtræʃ; ˈjʊərəʊˌtræʃ/ *n* [U]
an insulting word for people from Europe who have a lot of money, wear fashionable clothes, and go to fashionable clubs and events, but who are considered lazy and too interested in their social lives "歐洲垃圾"〔對歐洲一些無所事事, 太着重社交生活的富人的蔑稱〕

Euro-zone /ˋjuro ˌzon; ˈjʊərəʊ ˌzəʊn/ *n* [singular]
the group of European countries that use the EURO as a standard unit of money 歐元區: *trade among the countries of the Euro-zone* 歐元區國家之間的貿易

eu·tha·nize /ˋjuθənaɪz; ˈjuːθənaɪz/ also 又作 **eu·tha·nase** /-nez; -neɪz/ *BrE*【英】*v* [T]
to kill an animal in a painless way, usually because it is very sick or old 對〔動物〕施行無痛致死術, 使〔動物〕安樂死: *The decision to euthanase a pet is one of the most heart-breaking anyone has to make.* 對寵物施行無痛致死術, 對任何人來說都是最令人心碎的決定之一。

EVP /ˌi vi ˋpi; ˌiː viː ˈpiː/ *n*
Executive Vice-President; a very important job at the top of a large company or organization 執行副總裁: *George Werner has been named EVP for corporate affairs, effective from January 1, 2001.* 喬治·沃納已被任命為處理公司事務的執行副總裁, 該任命從2001年1月1日起生效。

ex·ec·u·ta·ry /ɪg`zɛkjʊ,tɛrɪ; ɪg'zekjʊtəri/ *n* [C]
a secretary who works for an important person in a company, and who has more responsibility and a higher salary than secretaries usually have. This word comes from a combination of 'secretary' and 'EXECUTIVE'. 行政祕書〔由 secretary 和 executive 縮合而成〕: *An executary has to have the ability to make judgements and decisions when the executive is out of town.* 行政祕書必須具備主管不在時作出判斷和決定的能力。

expansion card /ɪk`spænʃən ,kɑrd; ɪk'spænʃən ,kɑːd/ *n* [C]
a CIRCUIT BOARD that fits into a computer and makes it possible for the computer to do more things, for example play sounds or VIDEO pictures, or use a telephone line〔電腦的〕擴充插件板[卡], 擴充卡

expansion slot /ɪk`spænʃən ,slɑt; ɪk'spænʃən ,slɒt/ *n* [C]
a place on a computer system CIRCUIT BOARD that can hold an EXPANSION CARD〔電腦的〕擴充槽

export /ɪks`pɔrt; ɪk'spɔːt/ *v* [T]
NEW MEANING
to arrange information or the space on a computer DISK so that the information can be understood and used by a different computer PROGRAM 導出〔資料〕, 輸出

ex·tra·net /`ɛkstrənɛt; 'ekstrənet/ *n* [C]
a computer system in a company that allows better communication between the company and its customers by combining Internet and INTRANET systems, so that some customers can view some of the company's private information that is not normally available on the Internet〔公司和客戶之間的〕外聯網

extreme /ɪk`strim; ɪk'striːm/ *adj*
NEW MEANING
1 [only before noun 僅用於名詞前] **extreme sports/surfing/skiing etc** an extreme sport is one that is done in a way that has much more risk and so is more dangerous than an ordinary form of the sport 極限運動/衝浪/滑雪等: *Far from being crazy, people who do extreme sports are usually very in control, but love the excitement.* 參加極限運動的人絕不瘋狂, 他們通常很有自制, 只是喜歡追求刺激而已。**2 extreme athlete/surfer/skier etc** someone who does extreme sports 極限運動員/衝浪者/滑雪手等: *Extreme surfers will ride waves that reach heights of more than fifty feet.* 極限衝浪者會在五十多英尺高的浪上滑行。

extreme fight·ing /ɪk,strim `faɪtɪŋ; ɪk,striːm 'faɪtɪŋ/ *n* [U]
a competition, similar to BOXING, in which two people are allowed to hit or kick each other and in which there are almost no rules. Extreme fighting is illegal in some countries, and in some parts of the US 極限打鬥: *Critics think extreme fighting should be banned completely.* 評論者認為極限打鬥應該完全禁止。

eye can·dy /`aɪ ,kændɪ; 'aɪ ,kændi/ *n* [U]
informal someone who is attractive, but who you do not approve of because you think they have been chosen for something because of their appearance rather than their intelligence【非正式】中看不中用的人

e-zine /`i ,zin; 'iː ,ziːn/ *n* [C]
a magazine that can be read on the Internet 電子雜誌

F,f

face /fes; feɪs/ *n*
NEW MEANING
1 get in sb's face *AmE spoken* to annoy someone and try to tell them what to do【美口】囉唆: *She's the coach – you don't get in her face.* 她是教練, 別當她的面囉唆個沒完。**2 get out of my face** *AmE spoken* used to tell someone in an impolite way to go away because they are annoying you【美口】滾開, 去你的 **3 in your face** *informal* behaviour, remarks etc that are in your face are very direct and often make people feel shocked or surprised【非正式】直截〔地〕; 突如其來〔地〕, 出乎意料〔地〕: *Bingham has a very 'in your face' writing style.* 賓厄姆的作品有一種大膽直接的風格。

face time /`fes ,taɪm; 'feɪs ,taɪm/ *n* [U] *AmE*
1 time that you spend at your job because you want other people, especially your manager, to see you there, whether or not you are actually doing good work【美】為考勤作門面功夫: *Here we reward performance, not face time.* 我們這兒獎勵的是工作表現, 而不是門面功夫。**2** time that you spend talking to someone when you are with them, rather than on the telephone 面對面交談的時間: *In return for his donation, he wanted face time with the President.* 他想與總統當面談談, 作為捐贈的回報。

fac·toid /`fæktɔɪd; 'fæktɔɪd/ *n* [C]
a small interesting piece of information that is often not important 瑣碎的新聞, 有趣的資料: *This is actually one of those rare football factoids that's useful to know.* 事實上這是那種難得聽到, 但很有用的關於足球的小新聞。

fa·ji·ta /fə`hitə; fə'hiːtə/ *n* [C usually plural 一般用複數]
a TEX-MEX dish made with onions, peppers, and chicken or meat that are put in a TORTILLA 墨西哥鐵板燒, 費雞特菜〔包含洋葱、辣椒以及雞肉或其他肉的玉米粉圓餅〕

fallen an·gel /,fɔlən `endʒəl; ,fɔːlən 'eɪndʒəl/ *n* [C]
informal something such as a STOCK that is not earning as much money as it did in the past【非正式】風光不再的東西〔如證券〕

FAQ, faq /fæk, ,ɛf e `kju; fæk, ,ef eɪ 'kjuː/ *n* [C usually plural 一般用複數]
frequently asked question(s); on WEBSITES, a list of questions that users often ask about the website, and answers to them〔網站上的〕常見問題〔附答案〕

farmer's mar·ket /,fɑrmɚz `mɑrkɪt; ,fɑːməz 'mɑːkɪt/ *n* [C]
a place where farmers bring their fruit and vegetables to sell directly to people in a town or city 農產品集貿市場, 農民自產自銷市場

fash·ion·ist·a /,fæʃən`istə; ,fæʃən'iːstə/ *n* [C]
informal someone who is very interested in fashion and who likes the very newest styles【非正式】超級時裝迷, 穿着非常時髦的人

fashion state·ment /`fæʃən ,stetmənt; 'fæʃən ,steɪtmənt/ *n* [C]
something that you own, do, or wear that is considered new, exciting, or different, and is intended to make other people notice you and give them an idea of the kind of person you are 時尚炫耀, 潮流象徵: *Camouflage – the latest fashion statement.* 迷彩服——最新的時尚服飾。| **make a fashion statement** *Mobile phones make a big fashion statement.* 手機現在成了熱門的潮流象徵。

fat /fæt; fæt/ *adj*
NEW MEANING
another spelling of PHAT; fashionable, attractive, or desirable phat 的另一種拼法; 時尚的, 精彩的, 極好的: **fat/phat beats** (=music that sounds good) 精彩的音樂 *Check out these fat beats.* 聽聽這些精彩的音樂。

fat camp /`fæt ,kæmp; 'fæt ,kæmp/ *n* [C]
a place where children go to lose weight and exercise, especially a place where they stay for several weeks〔兒童參加的〕減肥營

fat gram /`fæt ,græm; 'fæt ,græm/ *n* [C usually plural 一般用複數]
a gram of fat in food〔食物中的〕脂肪克數: *Is it more important to count fat grams or calories when losing weight?* 減肥時計算食物中的脂肪克數重要還是卡路里重要?

fault-tol·er·ant /`fɔlt ,tɑlərənt; 'fɔːlt ,tɒlərənt/ *adj*
fault-tolerant computer/machine a computer that

continues working even if it has a fault or when there is a fault in a PROGRAM 容錯電腦 / 機器

feel·bad fac·tor /ˋfilbæd ˏfæktɚ; ˈfiːlbæd ˏfæktə/ *n* [singular] *BrE*
an unfavourable economic situation in a country, which has a negative effect on people's attitudes. This expression developed from the phrase 'FEEL-GOOD FACTOR' and is used mainly in JOURNALISM.【英】令人擔心的經濟情況: *High house prices, low interest rates, and job insecurity all contribute to the feelbad factor.* 高房價、低利率和工作無保障都造成了令人擔心的經濟情況。

fence-mend·ing /ˋfɛns ˏmɛndɪŋ; ˈfens ˏmendɪŋ/ *adj* [only before noun 僅用於名詞前]
fence-mending measures/talks/trip etc fence-mending trips, talks etc are between countries who have a disagreement about something, and are meant to try to improve relations between them 修復(友好)關係的措施 / 會談 / 旅行等: *The Vice-President will be sent on a fence-mending trip throughout Latin America.* 副總統將被派往拉丁美洲作一次旨在修復關係的訪問。| *The British Foreign Secretary will begin fence-mending talks with his Chinese counterpart on Tuesday.* 英國外務大臣將在星期二和中國外交部長進行一次修復關係的會談。—**fence-mending** *n* [U]: *Behind the scenes, there are signs of a desire by Republicans and Democrats alike to engage in serious fence-mending.* 有跡象顯示, 共和黨和民主黨私下裡都有認真修復關係的願望。

feng shui[1] /ˏfʌŋ ˋʃwe; ˏfʌŋ ˈʃweɪ/ *n* [U]
a Chinese system of organizing the furniture and other things in a house or building in a way that people believe will bring good luck and happiness 風水

feng shui[2] *v* [T]
feng shui a room/house etc to place the furniture and other things in a room or house in a particular position so that it is arranged according to the feng shui position 將房間 / 房子裏的家具及物品按風水佈局擺放

fire·wall /ˋfaɪrwɔl; ˈfaɪəwɔːl/ *n* [C]
1 a system that stops people who do not have permission looking at particular information on a computer, especially information on the Internet〔電腦系統的〕防火牆: *British Aerospace uses a firewall between its corporate network and the outside world.* 英國航空航天工業公司使用"防火牆"分隔公司的電腦網絡和外界網絡。
2 a system that is used by large financial or law companies to stop secret information being passed from one department to another〔金融公司或律師事務所〕阻止泄密的防火牆

fit /fɪt; fɪt/ *v* **fitted, fitting** [I] *BrE*
NEW MEANING
to have a SEIZURE (=a sudden condition in which someone cannot control the movements of their body)【英】痙攣發作: *The patient was still fitting.* 病人仍處於痙攣狀態。—**fitting** *n* [U]: *Fitting continued for more than 5 minutes.* 痙攣持續了超過5分鐘。

flack /flæk; flæk/ *n* [C] *AmE*
NEW MEANING
informal someone whose job is to represent an organization and answer questions about it, especially when something bad has happened【美, 非正式】代言人

flake /flek; fleɪk/ *v*
NEW MEANING
flake out *phr v* [I] *AmE spoken* to do something strange or forgetful, or to not do what you said you would do【美口】靠不住, 反覆無常: **flake out on sb** *Kathy kind of flaked out on us today – said she couldn't take the stress.* 凱西今天臨陣脱逃 —— 她說她承受不了這種壓力。

flame /flem; fleɪm/ *v* [T]
NEW MEANING
informal to send someone an angry or insulting message in an E-MAIL or on a BULLETIN BOARD【非正式】發送言詞憤怒的電子郵件; 在電子公告板上發佈侮辱性信息: *I got flamed just for saying I thought Bruce Willis was cool!* 我只是說過我認為布斯·韋利士很酷便收到了語帶憤怒的電子郵件! —**flame** *n* [C]

flash cam·paign /ˋflæʃ kæmˏpen; ˈflæʃ kæmˏpeɪn/ *n* [C]
a sudden large amount of activity such as a protest which starts quickly because information can be sent to a lot of people almost instantly by using the Internet〔網上煽動的〕閃速行動

flat·line /ˋflætˏlaɪn; ˈflætlaɪn/ *v* [I]
be flatlining to be at a low level or standard that is neither increasing nor decreasing. This word comes from the field of medicine, where doctors use special equipment to measure the beating of people's hearts. If the equipment shows a flat line, it means that the person's heart is not beating and they are dead or nearly dead 呈現平線, 保持於低水平, 不升不降〔原為醫學用詞, 人在死亡或臨死時, 其心電圖等呈現平線〕: *The Tories have been flatlining in the polls for the last three months.* 保守黨在最近三個月的民意調查中的支持率一直處於低水平, 不升不跌。

flatpack 扁平組件

flat·pack /ˋflætˏpæk; ˈflætpæk/ *n* [C] *BrE*
a piece of furniture that is sold in pieces which are stored in a flat box so they are easy to carry. You put the piece of furniture together yourself at home【英】扁平(家具)組件: *flatpack furniture* 組合家具

fla·va /ˋflevʌ; ˈfleɪvʌ/ *n* [U]
slang flavour; an idea of what the typical qualities of something are【俚】特色

flex·ec·u·tive /flɛkˋsɛkjutɪv; flekˈsekjʊtɪv/ also 又作 **flex·ec** /ˋflɛksɛk; ˈfleksek/ *n* [C] *BrE*
a young, fashionable person who makes a lot of money, usually working in the computer or MEDIA industry, but who does not work in the usual way. For example, they often have more than one job, change jobs often, or spend a lot of time doing other things, such as travelling.【英】彈性行政人員〔通常為從事電腦或媒體行業的時尚青年, 他們收入甚豐, 而且工作方式靈活〕

float /flot; fləʊt/ *n* [C]
NEW MEANING
a time when you sit in a FLOTATION TANK in order to treat illness or injury, or to relax 浮桶鹽水浴療: *I experienced my first float last week and loved the total relaxation it provided.* 上週我第一次進行浮桶鹽水浴療, 就愛上了那種讓人完全放鬆的感覺。

floating /flotɪŋ; fləʊtɪŋ/ *n* [U]
the activity of sitting in a FLOTATION TANK in order to relax, or to treat illness or injury 浮桶鹽水浴療: *Floating helped my recovery.* 鹽水浴療幫助我康復。

flotation tank /floˋteʃən ˏtæŋk; fləʊˈteɪʃən ˏtæŋk/ *n* [C]
a large container full of warm salty water, often with a cover on it to make it dark inside, that you float in so that you can relax, or to treat illness or injury 鹽水浴療浮桶: *When I first stepped into the flotation tank, I found myself a bit anxious and unsure.* 我第一次步入鹽水浴療浮桶時, 感到有點擔心和不知所措。

fly /flaɪ; flaɪ/ *adj*

NEW MEANING
slang very fashionable and attractive【俚】非常時尚迷人的: *Put on your flyest skirt for your Friday date.* 穿上你最時髦的裙子去赴星期五的約會。

fly·er·ing /ˋflaɪərɪŋ; ˈflaɪərɪŋ/ *n* [U]
the activity of fixing printed notices onto trees and buildings in order to advertise something such as a concert 張貼小廣告

Flyover Coun·try /ˋflaɪovɚ ˏkʌntrɪ; ˈflaɪ-əʊvə ˌkʌntri/ *n* [U]
humorous the middle part of the US, which some people consider to be boring and which they only see when they are flying over it in a plane between the east and west coasts【幽默】飛越地區〔在飛機上看到的美國中部枯燥乏味的地區〕

food miles /ˋfud ˏmaɪlz; ˈfuːd ˌmaɪlz/ *n* [plural] *BrE*
an expression meaning the distance food has been moved by ship, plane, TRUCK, etc to get it to shops, used especially by people who think that it is better to eat food that has been produced near the area where you live rather than using a lot of energy to move it over long distances【英】〔食物運抵商店的〕食物運輸距離: *We wanted to support the rural economy by encouraging village shops to stock fresh local produce and to cut down on food miles.* 我們想通過鼓勵鄉村商店採購本地新鮮的農產品和減少食物運輸里程來支持農村的經濟。

footprint /ˋfʊtˏprɪnt; ˈfʊtˌprɪnt/ *n* [C]
NEW MEANING
the amount of space on a desk that a computer fills 電腦基座所佔面積: *These PCs have a 50% smaller footprint than older models.* 這些個人電腦的基座面積比舊款的小50%。

forklift up·grade /ˋfɔrklɪft ˏʌpgred; ˈfɔːklɪft ˌʌpgreɪd/ *n* [C]
an improvement to a computer system that involves buying a lot of expensive equipment rather than adding new SOFTWARE〔電腦的〕硬件升級: *This fix is convenient because it lets carriers add capacity or speed without going through a forklift upgrade.* 這次維修很方便, 因為它讓航空公司無需進行硬件升級便可提高容量和速度。

404 /ˏfɔr o ˋfɔr; ˌfɔːr əʊ ˈfɔː/ *adj* [not before noun 不用於名詞前]
humorous someone who is 404 is stupid and unable to use computers or other complicated electronic equipment. This word comes from the usual message which appears on the Internet when a particular page you are searching for cannot be found【幽默】電腦[電子設備]白痴〔源自無法找到網頁時出現的信息〕

four-one-one also 又作 **411** /ˏfɔr wʌn ˋwʌn; ˌfɔː wʌn ˈwʌn/ *n*
the 411 (on sb/sth) *AmE slang* information or facts about someone or something. This word comes from the telephone number of the service, often called 'information', that you can call in the US in order to find out what someone's telephone number is.【美俚】〔關於某人或某物的〕資料, 詳情〔411 原為查詢電話號碼的服務台〕: *Here's the 411 on all the hottest bands on tour.* 這裡有有關正在巡迴演出的所有當紅樂隊的資料。

frac·tal /ˋfræktḷ; ˈfræktəl/ *n* [C]
technical a pattern, usually produced by a computer, that is made by repeating the same shape many times at smaller and smaller sizes【術語】分形〔由一個圖形輾轉縮小、重複產生的圖形, 一般用電腦製作〕—**fractal** *adj* [only before noun 僅用於名詞前]: *fractal geometry* 分形幾何(學)

fran·ken·food /ˋfræŋkənˏfud; ˈfræŋkənˌfuːd/ also 又作 **Fran·ken·stein foods** /ˋfræŋkənstaɪn ˏfudz; ˈfræŋkənstaɪn ˌfuːdz/ *n* [C usually plural 一般用複數]
informal a word meaning a food that has been produced by plants that were GENETICALLY MODIFIED, used when you disapprove of this process. This word is a combination of 'Frankenstein' (=the scientist who created a monster in the story by Mary Shelley) and 'food'.【非正式】基因改造食品, 惡魔食品〔帶貶意, 由 Frankenstein（科學怪人——瑪麗·雪萊小說中一名製造怪物的科學家）和 food 縮合而成〕

free rad·icals /ˏfri ˋrædɪkḷz; ˌfriː ˈrædɪkəlz/ *n* [plural]
atoms or groups of atoms that have at least one ELECTRON that does not form a pair with another electron, so that the atom joins with other atoms, causing chemical changes 自由基, 游離基: *It is only recently that free radicals have been implicated in major diseases like cancer and heart disease.* 人們直到最近才知道自由基與癌症、心臟病等嚴重疾病有關。

freestyle¹ /ˋfriˏstaɪl; ˈfriːstaɪl/ *n* [C]
NEW MEANING
a RAP² (2) song in which the singer says words directly from their imagination, without planning or writing them first 即興的說唱歌曲

freestyle² /ˋfriˏstaɪl; ˈfriːstaɪl/ *v* [I,T]
to say the words of a RAP² (2) song directly from your imagination, without planning or writing them first 即興地說唱: *Anderson began by freestyling a rap about his baby son.* 安德森即興地說唱了一首關於他的小寶貝兒子的歌作序幕。

free-to-air /ˏfri tu ˋɛr; ˌfriː tʊ ˈeə/ *adj BrE*
free-to-air television or television programmes do not cost additional money to watch【英】〔電視節目〕不另外收費的: *The new channel will be free-to-air, funded by the licence fee.* 這個新設的頻道將是不收費的, 由牌照費提供資助。| *free-to-air television coverage of rugby league matches* 橄欖球聯賽的免費電視轉播

free·ware /ˋfriwɛr; ˈfriːweə/ *n* [U]
computer SOFTWARE that is given away free〔電腦的〕免費軟件

fro-yo /ˋfrojo; ˈfrəʊjəʊ/ *n* [C]
a frozen sweet food made from YOGHURT. This word comes from a combination of the words 'FROZEN' and 'YOGHURT' 冷凍酸奶〔由 frozen 和 yoghurt 縮合而成〕: *a strawberry fro-yo* 草莓冷凍酸奶

functional food /ˋfʌŋkʃənḷ ˏfud; ˈfʌŋkʃənəl ˌfuːd/ *n* [C,U]
food that contains special additional substances that are intended to have a good effect on your health 功能食品, 保健食品

func·tion·al·ity /ˏfʌŋkʃənˋælətɪ; ˌfʌŋkʃəˈnæləti/ *n* [U]
all of the operations that a computer is able to perform〔電腦的〕全部功能

fusion cui·sine /ˋfjuʒən kwɪˏzin; ˈfjuːʒən kwɪˌziːn/ also 又作 **fusion food** /ˋfjuʒən ˏfud; ˈfjuːʒən ˈfuːd/ *n* [U]
a style of cooking in which new dishes are developed which include foods from several different parts of the world, for example China and Mexico 融合烹飪法

future-o·ri·en·ted /ˏfjutʃɚ ˋɔrɪɛntɪd; ˌfjuːtʃər ˈɔːrientɪd/ *adj*
giving a lot of time, effort, or attention to what is going to happen or needs to be done in the future 面向未來的: *future-oriented technology* 面向未來的技術 | *"Bavaria is open-minded and future-oriented, and is now among the strongest economic states in Europe," says Schmidt.* 施密特說: "巴伐利亞州思想開放, 面向未來, 現在已成為歐洲經濟最強的地區之一。"

future-proof¹, futureproof /ˋfjutʃɚ ˏpruf; ˈfjuːtʃə ˌpruːf/ *v* [T]
to make or plan something in such a way that it will not become ineffective or unsuitable for use in the future 使〔某物〕不會過時: *Chairman Michael Cortese today announced dramatic plans to future-proof the company's network.* 邁克爾·科特西主席今天宣布了宏大的計劃, 該計劃將使公司的網絡能應付未來的需要。

future-proof² /ˋfjutʃɚ ˏpruf; ˈfjuːtʃə ˌpruːf/ *adj*
if something is future-proof, it will not become ineffective or unsuitable for use in the future 不會過時的, 不會失效的: *future-proof software* 不會過時的軟件 | *future-*

proof technology 經得起時間考驗的技術

FWIW, fwiw
the written abbreviation of 縮寫= 'for what it's worth', used in E-MAIL or TEXT MESSAGEs on MOBILE PHONEs, to mean that you are not sure of the value or usefulness of what you are saying 純屬個人意見, 不一定對〔電子郵件或手機短信用語〕

FYI, fyi
the written abbreviation of 縮寫= 'for your information', used especially in short business notes and E-MAILs, when you are telling someone something they need to know 供你參考〔尤作商業便箋和電子郵件用語〕

G,g

gag /gæg; gæg/ *v BrE*
NEW MEANING
slang【英俚】**1 be gagging to do sth/be gagging for sth** to be very eager to do or have something 急於幹某事/擁有某物: *They were gagging to sign the contract.* 他們急於簽訂這份合同。**2 be gagging for it** used by a man to say he thinks a woman wants to have sex〔男人用語, 指女人〕想幹那個

game /gem; geɪm/ *n*
NEW MEANING
sb got game *AmE spoken informal* used to say that someone is very skilful at doing something, especially playing a sport【美口, 非正式】某人幹起某事非常熟練〔尤指運動〕

gam·er /ˋgemɚ; ˈgeɪmə/ *n* [C]
1 *slang* someone who likes playing VIDEO GAMEs, or who likes to play games in which they pretend to be a particular character【俚】玩電腦遊戲者, 遊戲玩家: *40,000 gamers have logged on each day since the site began.* 自那個網站開張以來, 每天有4萬名電腦遊戲者登入。**2** *AmE informal* a person who is very good at a sport, and can help a team to win games【美, 非正式】〔幫助球隊贏得勝利的〕優秀運動員, 皇牌運動員

gaming /ˋgemɪŋ; ˈgeɪmɪŋ/ *n* [U]
NEW MEANING
the activity of playing VIDEO GAMEs 打電子遊戲, 打視頻遊戲: *Online gaming is becoming a huge business.* 網上視頻遊戲正成為一門龐大的生意。| *I've been involved in gaming for a long time.* 我迷上視頻遊戲有很長時間了。

gang·sta /ˋgæŋstʌ; ˈgæŋstʌ/ *n* [C] *AmE*
informal someone who is a member of a GANG【美, 非正式】幫派成員: *gangstas in South Central L.A.* 洛杉磯中南部的黑幫分子

gangsta rap /ˋgæŋstʌ ˌræp; ˈgæŋstʌ ˌræp/ *n* [U]
a type of RAP music with words about drugs, violence, and life in poor areas of cities〔以吸毒、暴力和貧民區生活為內容的〕岡斯特說唱樂 —**gangsta-rapper** *n* [C]

gap year /ˋgæp ˌjɪr; ˈgæp ˌjɪə/ *n* [C] *BrE*
a year between leaving school and going to university, which some young people use as an opportunity to travel, earn money, or get experience of working【英】休學年, 空檔年〔中學生畢業後上大學前旅遊、打工等的一段時間〕: *Some students choose to work in high-tech industries during their gap year.* 一些學生選擇在上大學前先去高技術產業工作一年。

garage /gəˋrɑʒ; ˈgærɑːʒ/ *n* [U]
NEW MEANING
a type of popular music played on electronic instruments, with a strong fast beat and singing 車庫樂〔一種由電子樂器伴奏的、快節奏的、帶吟詠的流行音樂〕: *a collection of the latest dance and garage hits* 最新流行的舞曲和車庫樂集錦

gas·tro·pub /ˋgæstroˌpʌb; ˈgæstrəʊˌpʌb/ *n* [C] *BrE*
a PUB that is fashionable inside and that has good and expensive food. The word 'gastropub' comes from a combination of the words 'GASTRONOMY' (preparing and enjoying good food) and 'PUB'【英】美食吧〔由 gastronomy 和 pub 縮合而成〕

gate[1] /get; geɪt/ *n*
NEW MEANING
right out of the gate immediately 立即: *The show bombed right out of the gate, and was canceled after two episodes.* 該節目一推出就砸鍋了, 播放了兩集之後就被停播了。

gatekeeper /ˋgetˌkipɚ; ˈgeɪtˌkiːpə/ *n* [C]
NEW MEANING
1 someone in an organization who has a lot of influence over what products the organization buys, who it buys them from etc〔機構中對買入甚麼產品、向誰購買等有巨大影響力的〕把關人 **2** someone in an organization who tells customers or people with questions which people in the organization should be able to help them 引導員〔機構中轉介顧客或查詢人至有關負責人〕

gay pride /ˌge ˋpraɪd; ˌgeɪ ˈpraɪd/ *n* [U]
a political and social movement that encourages HOMOSEXUAL people not to keep the fact that they are homosexual a secret, and to be proud of themselves 同性戀者尊嚴: *a gay pride march* 提倡同性戀者尊嚴的遊行

gay·dar /ˋgedɑr; ˈgeɪdɑː/ *n* [U] *AmE*
spoken humorous the ability to recognize that someone is HOMOSEXUAL. This word comes from a combination of the words 'GAY' and 'RADAR'.【美口, 幽默】同性戀雷達〔指識別某人為同性戀者的能力, 由 gay 和 radar 縮合而成〕

ga·zun·der /gəˋzʌndɚ; gəˈzʌndə/ *v* [T] *BrE*
be gazundered if you are gazundered, someone who has agreed to buy your house says that they will only buy it for less than the amount originally agreed【英】被壓價

gender a·ware·ness /ˋdʒɛndɚ əˌwɛrnɪs; ˈdʒendər əˌweənɪ̀s/ *n* [U]
if an employer or employee has gender awareness, they understand the differences between how men and women behave and are able to treat them both fairly and equally 性別意識〔能公平地對待不同性別〕

gender bi·as /ˋdʒɛndɚ ˌbaɪəs; ˈdʒendə ˌbaɪəs/ *n* [C,U]
if an employer or person has gender bias, they treat men and women differently in a way that is unfair 性別偏見〔歧視〕

Generation X /ˌdʒɛnəreʃən ˋɛks; ˌdʒenəreɪʃən ˈeks/ also 又作 **Gen-X** /dʒɛn ˋɛks; dʒen ˈeks/ *n* [U]
the group of people who are between about 20 and 35 years old 無名一代, X 世代〔指大約在 20 至 35 歲之間的一代人〕: *the needs and attitudes of Generation X* X 世代的需要和態度 —**Generation X-er** *n* [C] *Gen X-ers still attend more films than older age groups.* X 世代的人比起老一輩人看的影片多。

genetically mod·i·fied /dʒəˌnɛtɪklɪ ˋmɑdɪfaɪd; dʒəˌnetɪkli ˈmɒdɪ̀faɪd/ also 又作 **genetically en·gin·eered** /dʒəˌnɛtɪklɪ ɛndʒəˋnɪrd; dʒəˌnetɪkli endʒɪ̀ˈnɪəd/ *adj*
genetically modified food or plants have had their GENETIC structure changed, especially so that they are not affected by particular diseases or harmful insects 基因改造的, 轉基因的: *Consumers are worried by genetically modified products, and are becoming more interested in organic food.* 消費者對基因改造食品不甚放心, 而對有機食品越來越感興趣。—**genetic modification** *n* [U]

ge·no·mic /dʒɪˋnomɪk; dʒɪˈnəʊmɪk/ *adj*
technical relating to all the GENEs that are found in one type of living thing【術語】基因組的: *Researchers plan to use genomic information to develop drugs that specifically target the virus.* 研究人員計劃利用基因組信息開發專門針對該病毒的藥物。

gen·o·type /ˋdʒɛnoˌtaɪp; ˈdʒenəʊˌtaɪp/ *n* [C]
all the GENEs that are found in one type of living thing 基因型

GHB /ˌdʒi etʃ ˋbi; ˌdʒiː eɪtʃ ˈbiː/ *n* [U]
an illegal chemical substance that is taken as a drug by some people, especially at parties and dance clubs 丙種羥基丁酸鹽, 迷姦藥〔一種毒品〕

GIF /gɪf; gɪf/ *n* [C]
technical graphics interchange format; a type of computer FILE that contains images and is used on the Internet【術語】圖形文件交換格式, 圖像交換格式

gig /gɪg; gɪg/ *n* [C]
NEW MEANING
informal a GIGABYTE; one billion BYTEs of information【非正式】千兆字節〔即十億位元組的信息〕

gimme /ˋgɪmɪ; ˈgɪmi/ *n* [C usually singular 一般用單數]
informal something that is so easy to do or succeed at that you do not even have to try【非正式】輕而易舉的事, 輕易得到的東西: *The victory was a gimme for the New York Yankees.* 這場勝利對紐約洋基隊來說簡直輕而易舉。

girl /gɝl; gɜːl/ *n*
NEW MEANING
(you) go girl! *AmE slang* used to encourage a girl or woman, or to say that you agree with what she is saying【美俚】加油！說得對！〔鼓勵女孩或婦女, 或表示同意她說的話〕

girl pow·er /ˋgɝl ˌpauɚ; ˈgɜːl ˌpaʊə/ *n* [U]
1 the idea that women should take control over their own lives or situations 女性自主思想 **2** the social or political influence that women have 女性(在社會和政治上的)權力

give /gɪv; gɪv/ *v*
NEW MEANING
give up *phr v* [T] **give it up (for sb)** to APPLAUD (=hit your open hands together) to show that you approve of someone or what they have done (給某人)鼓掌: *Come on everybody, let's give it up for George!* 各位, 來, 我們為喬治鼓掌！

global e·con·o·my /ˌglobḷ ɪˋkɑnəmɪ; ˌgləʊbəl ɪˈkɒnəmi/ *n* [singular]
the economic activity of the world considered as a whole 全球經濟

glo·bal·i·za·tion also 又作 **-isation** *BrE*【英】/ˌglobḷəˋzeʃən; ˌgləʊbəlaɪˈzeɪʃən/ *n* [U]
the process by which countries all over the world become connected or similar, especially because large companies are doing business in many different countries 全球化: *the rapid globalization of the world economy* 世界經濟的迅速全球一體化

glo·bal·ize also 又作 **-ise** *BrE*【英】/ˋglobḷaɪz; ˈgləʊbəlaɪz/ *v* [I,T]
if a company, industry, or economy globalizes or is globalized, it has business activities all over the world, so that it is no longer dependent on the economic conditions in one country, but is affected by conditions all around the world 使全球化

glo·cal·i·za·tion /ˌglokḷəˋzeʃən; ˌgləʊkəlaɪˈzeɪʃən/ *n* [U]
the idea that companies should do business around the world, but use methods that are suitable for each particular country they work in 全球本地化〔指企業在全球做生意, 但在每個國家都應使用適合當地情況的方法〕

GM /ˌdʒi ˋɛm; ˌdʒiː ˈem/ *adj* [only before noun 僅用於名詞前] *especially BrE*
genetically modified; GM foods or plants have had their GENETIC structure changed, especially so that they are not affected by particular diseases or harmful insects【尤英】轉基因的, 基因改造的

GMO /ˌdʒi ɛm ˋo; ˌdʒiː em ˈəʊ/ *n* [C]
genetically modified organism; a plant or other living thing whose GENEs have been changed by scientists, especially in order to make it less likely to get diseases or be harmed by insects etc 轉基因生物(體), 基因改造生物(體) —**GMO** *adj* [only before noun 僅用於名詞前]: *GMO crops* 轉基因作物

go¹ /go; gəʊ/ *v*
NEW MEANING
don't (even) go there *spoken humorous* used to say that you do not want to talk or think about something【口, 幽默】打住, 別說了〔用於表示不想談或想某事〕: *"What if the two of you actually...?" "Don't even go there!"* "要是你們兩個人真的...?" "不要再提了！"
go down *phr v* [I] *slang* to happen【俚】發生: *People still don't know what went down that night.* 人們仍然不知道那天夜裡發生了甚麼。
go off on sb/sth *phr v* [T] *AmE* to show how angry you are at someone or about something by saying what you really think【美】直接表明生〔某人或某物〕的氣: *Lisa called him a geek, so Brett just went off on her.* 莉莎叫布雷特做怪人, 布雷特對她發火了。

go² /go; gəʊ/ *n*
NEW MEANING
sth is a go *AmE spoken* used to say that things are working correctly, or that you have permission to do something【美口】沒問題: *I just got word from the boss, and the trip to London is a go.* 老闆剛發了話, 倫敦之行沒問題。

God /gɑd; gɒd/ *n*
there is a God! *spoken humorous* said when someone is explaining that something really good happened to them at a time when they thought that their situation was very bad【口, 幽默】真是老天幫忙！這倒不錯！: *There was no-one interesting in the hotel, and then in walked four gorgeous, blond Swedish boys, and I thought "There is a God!"* 這飯店裡沒有一個讓人感興趣的人, 後來進來了四個衣着華麗、白膚金髮碧眼的瑞典小伙子, 我想: "這還不錯！"

go-go fund /ˋgo go ˌfʌnd; ˈgəʊ gəʊ ˌfʌnd/ *n* [C]
informal a company that makes INVESTMENTs that have a high risk, but also a chance of making large profits【非正式】以高風險博取高收益的投資公司

golden /ˋgoldn̩; ˈgəʊldən/ *adj*
NEW MEANING
sb is golden *AmE spoken informal* used to say that someone is in a very good situation【美口, 非正式】某人形勢大好了: *If the right editor looks at your article, you're golden.* 如果恰好那位編輯看到你的文章, 那你就形勢大好了。

golden hand·cuffs /ˌgoldn̩ ˋhændkʌfs; ˌgəʊldən ˈhændkʌfs/ *n* [plural]
informal things such as a large SALARY or a good PENSION that make important employees want to continue working for an organization, rather than leave to work for a competing organization【非正式】金手銬〔雇主為拴住骨幹職員而付給的高薪金或優厚的退休金〕

golden hel·lo /ˌgoldn̩ həˋlo; ˌgəʊldən həˈləʊ/ *n* [C] *especially BrE*
informal a large amount of money that is given to a new employee, in order to persuade them not to go to work for another organization【尤英, 非正式】〔公司給新員工的〕豐厚見面禮: *In Britain, new maths and science teachers are being given golden hellos.* 在英國, 新來的數學科和理科教員都會得到豐厚的見面禮。

Gol·di·locks e·con·o·my /ˋgoldɪlɑks ɪˌkɑnəmɪ; ˈgəʊldilɒks ɪˌkɒnəmi/ *n* [C] *BrE*
technical an economy that is not growing too slowly or too fast【英, 術語】〔增長速度適中的〕温和(型)經濟

good /gud; gʊd/ *adj*
NEW MEANING
it's all good *AmE spoken slang* used to say that a situation is good or acceptable, or that there is not a problem【美口, 俚】一切都沒有問題: *Don't worry about it, man – it's all good.* 別擔心, 老兄 —— 一切都挺好的。

gopher, GOPHER /ˋgofɚ; ˈgəʊfə/ *n* [U]
NEW MEANING

technical a computer PROGRAM that quickly collects information from many different places on the Internet. This word comes from 'GOFER' (=someone who carries messages or gets or takes things for their employer), which is a combination of the words 'go' and 'for'【術語】信息鼠〔互聯網上快速的信息查找程序，由 go 和 for 縮合而成〕: *Gopher uses a series of menus to lead you to things of interest.* 信息鼠使用一系列選單讓你找到感興趣的東西。

GPS /ˌdʒi pi ˋɛs; ˌdʒiː piː ˈes/ *n* [C]
Global Positioning System; a system that uses radio signals from SATELLITE*s* to show your exact position on the Earth on a special piece of equipment, often used by the military or in cars and boats 全球（衛星）定位系統

grandfather /ˋgrændˌfɑðɚ; ˈgrændˌfɑːðə/ *v* [T] *AmE* also 又作 **grandfather** sb/sth ↔ **in**
to give someone or something special permission to continue doing what they have been doing and not obey a new law or rule【美】使不受新法規約束: *Even though the new apartment owner banned pets, they grandfathered my cat so I could stay.* 儘管新的房東禁止養寵物，但是他們破例讓我養貓，我因而能夠住下來。

graphical us·er in·ter·face /ˌgræfɪkḷ ˋjuzɚ ˌɪntɚfes; ˌgræfɪkəl ˈjuːzər ˌɪntəfeɪs/ *abbreviation* 縮寫為 **GUI** *n* [C]
a way of showing and organizing information on a computer screen that is easy to use and understand 圖形用戶界面，視窗系統

graphics card /ˋgræfɪks ˌkɑrd; ˈgræfɪks ˌkɑːd/ also 又作 **graphics a·dapt·er** /ˋgræfɪks əˌdæptɚ; ˈgræfɪks əˌdæptə/, **video adapter** *n* [C]
a CIRCUIT BOARD that connects to a computer and allows the computer to show images, such as VIDEO images, on its screen〔電腦的〕圖形卡，圖像適配卡

graveyard mar·ket /ˋgrevjɑrd ˌmɑrkɪt; ˈgreɪvjɑːd ˌmɑːkɪ̵t/ *n* [singular]
technical a situation on the STOCK MARKET in which a lot of SHARE*s* are being sold and the prices are becoming lower, but people do not want to buy shares until the situation improves, so that the people who own shares are losing money【術語】"墓地"市場〔指股票經過大幅拋售後，股價下跌，但買方仍然觀望市場發展，不買進股票，因而對股票持有人造成損失〕

greed·head /ˋgridˌhɛd; ˈgriːdhed/ *n* [C]
slang someone who always wants more money, possessions etc【俚】財迷

green au·dit /ˌgrin ˋɔdɪt; ˌgriːn ˈɔːdɪt/ *n* [C]
an official examination of the effects of a company's activities on the environment 綠色審查〔即審查公司活動對環境的影響〕: *Businesses in York are being asked to carry out a green audit, and to report by the end of the year.* 約克的各家企業被要求進行一次環保審查，並在年底前交出報告。

green·ing /ˋgrinɪŋ; ˈgriːnɪŋ/ *n*
the greening of sth *informal* the process of making a person or organization be more concerned about environmental problems and what they can do to improve the environment【非正式】增強環保意識: *the greening of corporate America* 美國工商界環保意識的提升

green·mail /ˋgrinˌmel; ˈgriːnmeɪl/ *n* [U]
the practice of buying back SHARE*s* in your own company often for a very high price from someone who has bought them in order to try to take control of your company or the money paid to do this 綠票訛詐，購股勒索〔指以溢價收買吞併者手上自己公司的股票〕；付給綠票訛詐者的金錢: *He has a history of speculation in stocks and real estate and is known for his attempts at greenmail.* 他曾做過股票和房地產的投機買賣，以綠票訛詐著名。

green·shoe /ˋgrinˌʃu; ˈgriːnʃuː/ *n* [U]
technical a situation in which all the SHARE*s* in a company that are being offered are sold, and then more stocks are also sold【術語】〔股票的〕增售，綠鞋〔指發行的股票全部賣出後，出售額外的股票〕

green shoots /ˌgrin ˋʃuts; ˌgriːn ˈʃuːts/ *n* [plural] *BrE* NEW MEANING
an expression used to talk about the first signs of economic improvement during a RECESSION, used especially in newspapers【英】經濟復蘇的跡象〔尤用於報章上〕

greige /greʒ; greɪʒ/ *n* [U]
a colour that is a mixture of grey and BEIGE (=a light brown colour) 灰褐色: *The shoes are available in black or greige.* 鞋子備有黑色和灰褐色以供選擇。—**greige** *adj*

grey ec·on·o·my also 又作 **gray economy** *AmE*【美】/ˌgre ɪˋkɑnəmɪ; ˌgreɪ ɪˈkɒnəmi/ *n* [C]
business activity carried out by older people who have a lot of money because their children have left home and because they still work or they have a good PENSION 灰色經濟〔指老人的經濟活動〕

grey·ing usually 一般作 **graying** *AmE*【美】/ˋgre·ɪŋ; ˈgreɪ-ɪŋ/ *n*
the greying of sth the situation in which the average age of a population increases, so that there are more people who are old than there were in the past 老齡化，人口老化: *the graying of America* 美國的老齡化

grey mar·ket, gray market *AmE*【美】/ˋgre ˌmɑrkɪt; ˈgreɪ ˌmɑːkɪ̵t/ *n* [C,U]
a situation in which people are buying and selling SHARE*s* just before they are officially made available to be sold for the first time 灰市〔股票在正式上市前的暗盤交易〕

grey pound /ˌgre ˋpaund; ˌgreɪ ˈpaʊnd/ *n* [singular] *BrE*
the money that older people have available to spend, especially after their children have grown up and left home【英】灰鎊〔指老人的閒錢〕: *Although poverty amongst older people is a continuing concern, the power of the grey pound is growing as a proportion of the older community becomes increasingly affluent.* 雖然老年人的貧困現象一直讓人關注，但是隨着老人社羣日趨富裕，灰鎊的力量也日漸增大。

groov·er /ˋgruvɚ; ˈgruːvə/ *n* [C]
slang a musician, especially one who plays HOUSE music【俚】音樂家〔尤指豪斯音樂演奏者〕

ground·ed /ˋgraundɪd; ˈgraʊndɪ̵d/ *adj*
1 reasonable and in control of your emotions, even when this is difficult 沉得住氣的 **2 keep sb grounded** to prevent someone, especially someone you have known for a long time, from thinking they are more important than they really are by treating them in the way you always have. This is used especially about the friends and family of people who have become famous. 防止某人自視過高

group·think /ˋgrupˌθɪŋk; ˈgruːpθɪŋk/ *n* [U]
the process through which bad decisions are made because too many people are involved in trying to reach it〔因人多而作出錯誤決定的〕集體思考: *What approaches to decision-making were used by the Kennedy administration during the Cuban Missile Crisis to avoid groupthink?* 甘迺迪政府在古巴導彈危機期間要作出決定時，採取了哪些辦法避免人多口雜而作出錯誤決定？

GTG
a written abbreviation of 縮寫= 'got to go', used in E-MAIL or TEXT MESSAGE*s* on MOBILE PHONE*s* 該走了〔電子郵件和手機短信用語〕

GUI /ˌdʒi ju ˋaɪ, ˋguɪ; ˌdʒiː juː ˈaɪ, ˈguːi/ *n* [C]
graphical user interface; a way of showing and organizing information on a computer screen that is easy to use and understand 圖形用戶界面，視窗系統

guilt /gɪlt; gɪlt/ *v*
guilt sb **into** sth *phr v* [T] *AmE informal* to try to make someone feel guilty, especially so they will do what you want【美，非正式】設法使〔某人感到〕愧疚〔而做你希望他們做的事〕: **guilt sb into doing sth** *Her parents guilted*

her into not going to the concert. 她的父母親設法讓她感到內疚而不去聽音樂會。

guilt·ware /ˋgɪlt,wɛr; ˈgɪltweə/ *n* [U]
humorous a type of computer PROGRAM that is free but that contains a message describing how hard someone worked to write it, which is intended to make people feel that they should send some money to the person who wrote it. This word comes from a combination of the words 'GUILT' and 'SOFTWARE'.【幽默】負疚軟件〔一種免費軟件，但裡面附有描述編寫者如何辛苦地編寫它，使用戶感到內疚，認為應該付錢給編寫者，由 guilt 和 software 縮合而成〕

gurn·ing /ˋgɝnɪŋ; ˈgɜːnɪŋ/ *n* [U]
informal the extremely happy expression on someone's face that shows that they have taken the illegal drug ECSTASY【非正式】〔吸食搖頭丸"狂喜"者臉部呈現的〕陶醉感 —**gurn** *v* [I]

H,h

hack /hæk; hæk/ *v*
hack sb **off** *phr v* [T] *BrE* to make someone feel annoyed and angry【英】使生氣: *He hacks people off sometimes, but he's good at what he does.* 他有時真讓人生氣，但他做事情不錯。

haemorrhage /ˋhɛmərɪdʒ; ˈhemərɪdʒ/ *BrE*【英】, **hemorrhage** *AmE*【美】*v* [T]
NEW MEANING
to lose a lot of something over a short period of time, such as money or jobs〔短期內〕大量流失: *The once prosperous automobile town has hemorrhaged manufacturing jobs over the last 15 years.* 這個一度繁榮的汽車城鎮，在過去 15 年間流失了大量的生產職位。

Hail Mary /,hel ˋmɛrɪ; ,heɪl ˈmeəri/ *n* [C]
NEW MEANING
in American football, the act of throwing the ball as high and as far as you can, and hoping that a member of your team will catch it and gain some points〔美式足球的〕扔高遠球: *Bledsoe said he had thrown a dozen or so Hail Marys over his career.* 布萊索說，在他的職業生涯中扔出過約十多個高遠球。

half pipe /ˋhæf ,paɪp; ˈhɑːf ,paɪp/ *n* [C]
1 a CONCRETE structure which has a rounded bottom and sides and is used for SKATEBOARDING〔滑板運動的〕半圓形滑槽，U 型場地 **2** a structure which has a rounded bottom and sides, is made from snow, and is used for SNOWBOARDING〔滑雪板運動中的〕半圓形雪槽

halo ef·fect /ˋhelo ə,fɛkt; ˈheɪləʊ ɪ,fekt/ *n* [C]
technical a situation in which people think a company is good because it is owned by or related to another company that is famous and important【術語】光環效應

handover /ˋhænd,ovɚ; ˈhændəʊvə/ *n* [C,U]
the time when a MOBILE PHONE starts receiving signals from a different transmitter because the person using the phone has moved from one area to another〔流動電話〕交接，越區切換

hand·set /ˋhændsɛt; ˈhændset/ *n* [C]
the part of a MOBILE PHONE that you hold in your hand〔流動電話〕手持機: *There's a 20% discount when you buy five handsets or more.* 購買 5 部或以上手機可打八折。

hands·free /,hændzˋfri; ,hændzˈfriː/ *n* [C]
mobile phone equipment that allows you to speak to someone without having to hold the phone, either by having an EARPIECE or by having SPEAKERs in a car 免提流動電話裝置〔用耳機或車上的話筒〕: *For just £19.99 this innovative handsfree features a microphone built into the earpiece.* 這種新穎的免提電話裝置的特點是耳機內裝有話筒，售價僅為 19.99 英鎊。| *The A100 comes with a personal handsfree kit as well as slim and standard batteries.* A100 型號手機配有個人免提配套元件和標準薄電池。

handshake /ˋhænd,ʃek; ˈhænd,ʃeɪk/ *n* [C]
NEW MEANING
the sending of information from one computer to another computer, telling it that a connection has been made〔電腦之間〕聯絡，信號交換 —**handshaking** *n* [U]

ha·pa /ˋhɑpa; ˈhɑːpɑː/ *n* [C] *AmE*
informal an American who has some family members who originally came from Asia, and some family members who originally came from other places【美，非正式】有亞裔血統的美國人: *Members of our club have had experiences in their lives that only other hapas can relate to.* 本俱樂部成員的經歷只有有亞裔血統的美國人才能體會到。—**hapa** *adj*: *Kip explores issues related to hapa identity in his writing.* 基普的作品探討了有關有亞裔血統美國人的身分問題。

happy-clap·py /ˋhæpɪ ,klæpɪ; ˈhæpi ,klæpi/ *adj BrE*
informal related to a Christian church, where people sing, shout, show their emotions, and encourage other people to join their church. The word comes from a combination of 'happy' and 'CLAP'. It is sometimes used in a humorous way, and sometimes in a disapproving way【英，非正式】〔與基督教有關的〕熱情的〔有時用於幽默，有時帶貶義，由 happy 和 clap 縮合而成〕: *happy-clappy Christians* 熱情的基督徒 —**happy clappy** *n* [C]: *a retreat for travelling happy clappies* 給四處旅行的熱情基督徒的靜修所

hard-charg·ing /,hɑrd ˋtʃɑrdʒɪŋ; ,hɑːd ˈtʃɑːdʒɪŋ/ *adj*
someone who is hard-charging has a very strong desire to succeed, even if it is difficult 渴望成功的: *Elfman has developed from a cute little girl into a glamorous, hard-charging corporate hotshot.* 埃爾芙曼已從一個可愛的小女孩長大成為公司裡一個有魅力而事業心強的要人。

hard house /ˋhɑrd ,haus; ˈhɑːd ,haʊs/ *n* [U]
a type of HOUSE MUSIC that is fast and has a lot of energy 硬豪斯音樂

hard·wire /ˋhɑrd,waɪr; ˈhɑːdwaɪə/ *v* [T] *AmE*
to be influenced in a harmful way by looking at or listening to something that becomes fixed in your memory【美】〔指壞影響〕深深植入，根植: *Kids who listen to this kind of music are hardwiring garbage.* 聽這類音樂的孩子腦子裡灌滿了垃圾。

harsh /hɑrʃ; hɑːʃ/ *v*
harsh on sb *phr v* [T] *AmE slang* to criticize someone or say things to them that are not true【美俚】〔以不正確的事〕批評，指責: *Just quit harshing on me, will you?* 別老指責我了，行嗎?

harvesting strat·e·gy /ˋhɑrvɪstɪŋ ,strætədʒɪ; ˈhɑːvɪ̵stɪŋ ,strætɪ̵dʒi/ *n* [C,U]
a method for keeping as much profit as possible from a business or activity and spending as little as possible on it 開源節流策略

hate crime /ˋhet ,kraɪm; ˈheɪt ,kraɪm/ *n* [U]
a crime that is COMMITted against someone only because they belong to a particular race, religion etc〔因種族、宗教等的〕仇視性犯罪

HDL /,etʃ di ˋɛl; ,eɪtʃ diː ˈel/ *n* [U]
technical high-density lipoprotein; a type of CHOLESTEROL that is good for your health because it helps protect your body against heart disease by helping to get rid of fat in your arteries (=tubes that carry blood in your body)【術語】高密度脂蛋白: *People with high HDL ('good cholesterol') levels are less likely to have heart disease.* 高密度脂蛋白（好膽固醇）水平高的人通常不容易患上心臟病。—compare 比較 LDL

head game /ˋhɛd ,gem; ˈhed ,geɪm/ *n* [C usually plural 一般用複數] *AmE*
informal if you play head games with someone, you say or do things that you hope will make them show you what they really think or what their character is really like, in a way that confuses or annoys them【美，非正

式】〔使人顯示真實性格或思想的〕智力遊戲, 心理遊戲: *Guys hate it when women play head games with them.* 男人討厭女人跟他們玩心理遊戲。

help screen /ˋhɛlp ˏskrin; ˈhelp ˌskriːn/ *n* [C]
a screen that appears when you ask for help in using a computer program, showing extra information or advice 〔電腦的〕求助屏幕

hip /hɪp; hɪp/ *adj*
NEW MEANING
be hip to sth to understand and know about something, and not make mistakes about it 知曉某事, 靈通: *It's a part of the city that is hip to ever-changing retail and entertainment trends.* 對不斷變化的零售和娛樂趨勢瞭如指掌是城市生活的一部分。

hip-hop /ˋhɪp ˏhap; ˈhɪp ˌhɒp/ *n* [U]
NEW MEANING
a type of popular CULTURE among young people in big cities, especially African Americans, which includes RAP music, dancing, and GRAFFITI art 嬉蹦文化〔美國大城市裡黑人青年的流行文化, 包括説唱樂、舞蹈、牆上塗鴉等〕

his·sy fit /ˋhɪsɪ ˏfɪt; ˈhɪsi ˌfɪt/ *n* [C]
informal a sudden moment of unreasonable anger and annoyance; TANTRUM【非正式】無名火: **throw/have a hissy fit** *Williams threw a hissy fit when she decided her hotel room wasn't big enough.* 威廉斯認為旅館房間不夠大, 突然大發脾氣。

hit /hɪt; hɪt/ *n* [C]
NEW MEANING
1 an occasion when someone uses a WEBSITE〔訪問網站的〕點擊(數), 瀏覽次數: *Our site had 2,000 hits in the first month.* 我們的網站在第一個月的瀏覽次數是2,000次。**2** a result of a computer search that you do for something on the Internet, a DATABASE etc〔在互聯網、數據庫等的〕檢索結果: *You may get thousands of hits that are irrelevant to your question.* 你也許會得到數千條與你所提問題都不相干的檢索結果。

ho /ho; həʊ/ *n* [C] *AmE*
slang【美俚】**1** a PROSTITUTE 妓女 **2** an offensive word for a woman or girl who you do not respect because she is too willing to have sex with many different people 淫婦〔冒犯語〕

hold·out /ˋholdaut; ˈhəʊldaʊt/ *n* [C]
a person or organization that does not do what many other similar people or organizations are doing 不隨波逐流的人[公司]

home·girl /ˋhomˏgɝl; ˈhəʊmgɜːl/ *n* [C] *AmE*
informal a female HOMEY【美, 非正式】女老鄉

home health aide /ˏhom ˋhɛlθ ˏed; ˌhəʊm ˈhelθ ˌeɪd/ *n* [C] *AmE*
someone whose job is to help an old, sick, or DISABLED person in that person's home by cooking, cleaning, washing them, helping them get dressed etc, so that the person can continue to live in their own home rather than going to a hospital or NURSING HOME【美】〔照顧老弱病殘的〕家庭護理員

home of·fice /ˏhom ˋɔfɪs; ˌhəʊm ˈɒfɪs/ *n* [C]
a room in someone's home where that person works, which usually has equipment such as a computer, FAX MACHINE etc 家庭辦公室

home·page also 又作 **home page** /ˋhomˏpedʒ; ˈhəʊmpeɪdʒ/ *n* [C]
the part of an Internet WEBSITE that has all the basic information about a person or organization, which you look at first and from which you can get to other parts of the website〔網站〕主頁

home·stead·ing /ˋhomˏstɛdɪŋ; ˈhəʊmˌstedɪŋ/ *n* [U] *AmE*
a situation in which people are given money so that they can improve the condition of their homes, especially in poor areas【美】〔尤指貧困地區的〕房屋津貼

hon·o·ree /ˏanəˋri; ˌɒnəˈriː/ *n* [C]
someone who receives an honour or AWARD 獲獎者: *Guests clapped and cheered for the honorees.* 來賓為獲獎者鼓掌歡呼。

hood /hud; hʊd/ *n AmE*
NEW MEANING
slang a NEIGHBOURHOOD (=a small area of a town)【美俚】街坊, 鄰近地區

hook /huk; hʊk/ *v*
NEW MEANING
hook sb **up with** sth *phr v* [T] to help someone get something that they need or want 幫助〔某人〕獲得…: *Do you think you can hook me up with some tickets for the hockey game tonight?* 你看你能幫我拿到幾張今晚曲棍球賽的入場券嗎?

host² /host; həʊst/ *v* [T]
NEW MEANING
if an Internet company hosts a WEBSITE, it provides the computer equipment and technical knowledge needed to make the website work, but is not responsible for the information or ideas contained in it 主持, 託管〔網站〕: *The site is hosted by a small European access provider.* 網站是由歐洲一家小型網絡服務商託管的。—**hosting** *n* [U]

hot desk /ˋhat ˏdɛsk; ˈhɒt ˌdesk/ *n* [C] *BrE*
a desk which is used by different workers on different days, instead of by the same worker every day【英】共用辦公桌

hot-desk·ing /ˏhat ˋdɛskɪŋ; ˌhɒt ˈdeskɪŋ/ *n* [U] *BrE*
a situation in which people who work in an office do not have their own desks, but sit wherever a desk is not being used【英】辦公桌共用(制): *Hot-desking means that desks are never left unused when people are away from the office.* 辦公桌共用制意味着在有人離開辦公室時, 辦公桌從來也不會空着沒人用。—**hot desk** *v* [I]: *The part-timers here have to hot desk.* 這裡的兼職人員要共用辦公桌。

hot link /ˋhat ˏlɪŋk; ˈhɒt ˌlɪŋk/ *n* [C]
informal a HYPERTEXT LINK which allows you to move from one place in a computer document to another, or to a particular place in a different document, especially on the Internet【非正式】熱[超文本]鏈接

hot spot /ˋhat ˏspat; ˈhɒt ˌspɒt/ *n* [C]
a part of a computer screen that you can CLICK on to make other pictures, words etc appear 熱點〔用鼠標點擊可打開圖像、文字等〕

hotty, hottie /ˋhatɪ; ˈhɒti/ *n* [C]
slang someone who is sexually attractive【俚】性感者, 騷貨: *Jennifer's such a hotty.* 珍妮弗真是個性感女神。

house /haus; haʊs/ *n* [U]
NEW MEANING
house music, a type of dance music, usually with a fast beat, that is repeated in a very regular pattern. It is made using special electronic instruments, such as a SYNTHESIZER or by using a special computer PROGRAM. 豪斯音樂〔用電子合成器或電腦製成的快節拍舞曲〕

housing starts /ˋhauzɪŋ ˏstarts; ˈhaʊzɪŋ ˌstɑːts/ *n* [plural]
technical the number of new houses, apartments etc on which building work has started in a particular period of time【術語】〔某一時期的〕新屋動工數目

HOV lane /ˏetʃ o ˋvi len; ˌeɪtʃ əʊ ˈviː leɪn/ *n* [C]
high-occupancy vehicle lane; a LANE on main roads that can only be used by vehicles carrying three or more passengers during the time of day when there is a lot of traffic 高容量車道〔交通繁忙時, 只准載三人或以上的汽車使用的車道〕

HTH, hth
a written abbreviation of 縮寫= 'hope this helps', used in E-MAIL or TEXT MESSAGES on MOBILE PHONES when they have answered someone's question 希望能管用〔電子郵件或手機短信用語〕

HTML /ˏetʃ ti ɛm ˋɛl; ˌeɪtʃ tiː em ˈel/ *n* [U]
hypertext markup language; a computer language used

for producing pages of writing and pictures that can be put on the Internet 超文本標記語言: *There are three ways to produce HTML documents: write them yourself; use an HTML editor; or convert documents from other formats to HTML.* 有三種方式可製作超文本標記語言文件, 一是自己編寫, 二是使用超文本標記語言編輯裝置, 三是將文件從其他格式轉變成超文本標記語言格式。

http /ˌetʃ ti ti ˋpi; ˌeɪtʃ tiː tiː ˈpiː/ *n* [U]
hypertext transfer protocol; a set of standards that controls how computer documents that are written in HTML connect to each other 超文本傳輸協定

huge /hjudʒ; hjuːdʒ/ *adj*
informal very famous or successful【非正式】走紅: *Trust me – this band is going to be huge next year.* 相信我好了, 這樂隊明年準會走紅。

hype /haɪp; haɪp/ *v*
NEW MEANING
hype sb **up** *phr v* [T] to make someone feel excited 使〔某人〕興奮

hy·per·ki·ne·tic /ˌhaɪpɚkɪˋnɛtɪk; ˌhaɪpəkɪˈnetɪk/ *adj*
fast, exciting, and appearing to be uncontrolled 多動的; 令人亢奮的: *the director's hyperkinetic new film about American football* 該導演一部令人亢奮的新片是有關美式足球的

hy·per·link /ˋhaɪpɚˌlɪŋk; ˈhaɪpəˌlɪŋk/ *n* [C]
a word or picture in a WEBSITE or computer document that will take you to another page or document if you CLICK on it 超(文本)連結: *We should encourage hyperlinks to each others' webpages.* 我們應當鼓勵彼此網頁之間的超連結。

hy·per·text /ˋhaɪpɚˌtɛkst; ˈhaɪpəˌtekst/ *n* [U]
written information on a computer screen that has words marked in colour or with a line underneath them, in order to allow you to move from one document to another very quickly. You use the computer's MOUSE to CLICK on one of these words, and the information on the screen changes so that you see the new information〔電腦〕超(級)文本〔可以互訪的文本網絡〕: *Hypertext links take you directly from a listing of bestsellers on the home page to a particular book.* 超文本連結可以讓你直接從主頁的暢銷書目錄進入一本特定的書。

I,i

ice queen /ˋaɪs ˌkwin; ˈaɪs ˌkwiːn/ *n* [C]
a word used to talk about an attractive woman who you think is unfriendly and behaves as though she does not care about other people 冷美人

IIRC, iirc
a written abbreviation of 縮寫= 'if I remember correctly', used in E-MAIL or TEXT MESSAGES on MOBILE PHONES 如果我沒有記錯的話〔電子郵件或手機短信用語〕

ill /ɪl; ɪl/ *adj*
NEW MEANING
slang very good【俚】很棒的, 頂刮刮的: *Isn't Lucia Rijker the world's illest female boxer?* 露西亞·賴克不是世界上最棒的女拳擊手嗎?

IM /ˌaɪ ˋɛm; ˌaɪ ˈem/ *n* [U]
instant messaging; a type of service available on the Internet that allows you to quickly exchange written messages with people that you know 即時信息

image ad·ver·tis·ing /ˋɪmɪdʒ ˌædvɚtaɪzɪŋ; ˈɪmɪdʒ ˌædvətaɪzɪŋ/ *n* [U]
technical advertising that tries to make a connection between a particular product and a particular way of life, rather than telling you that the product is very good【術語】形象廣告

image host·ing /ˋɪmɪdʒ ˌhostɪŋ; ˈɪmɪdʒ ˌhəʊstɪŋ/ *n* [U]
the business of providing people with space on an Internet WEBPAGE, so that they can put pictures on this webpage to advertise products that they want to sell or exchange 圖像託管: *image hosting for online auctions* 用作網上拍賣的圖像託管 | *This image hosting service can be used to simply show off your collection.* 這個圖像託管服務可以讓你炫耀一下你的收藏品。

i·ma·gi·neer /ɪˌmædʒəˋnɪr; ɪˌmædʒɪˈnɪə/ *n* [C]
someone who has a lot of new ideas and who is able to use these ideas to do practical things. This word comes from a combination of the words 'imagination' and 'ENGINEER' 點子大王, 意念工程師〔由 imagination 和 engineer 縮合而成〕: *We're lucky to have great imagineers like Mr. Rose who are willing to apply their minds to the problem.* 我們幸好有羅斯先生那樣的點子大王, 他們樂意動腦子解決問題。—**imagineering** *n* [U]

im·a·ging /ˋɪmɪdʒɪŋ; ˈɪmɪdʒɪŋ/ *n* [U]
a technical process in which pictures of the inside of someone's body are produced, especially for medical reasons〔尤用於醫學目的的〕(體內器官) 成像: *New imaging technologies mean that doctors are better able to screen for breast cancer.* 新的成像技術意味着醫生能更容易檢查出乳腺癌。

IMHO, imho
a written abbreviation of 縮寫= 'in my humble opinion', used in E-MAIL or TEXT MESSAGES on MOBILE PHONES 以鄙人之見〔電子郵件或手機短信用語〕

im·mu·no·ther·a·py /ˌɪmjunoˋθɛrəpɪ; ˌɪmjʊnəʊˈθerəpi/ *n* [U]
a way of curing a disease by helping the body to produce the natural substances that protect it from the disease 免疫療法

IMO, imo
a written abbreviation of 縮寫= 'in my opinion', used in E-MAIL or TEXT MESSAGES on MOBILE PHONES 以本人之見〔電子郵件或手機短信用語〕

I-mode phone /ˋaɪ mod ˌfon; ˈaɪ məʊd ˌfəʊn/ *n* [C]
trademark a MOBILE PHONE (=a telephone that you can carry with you and use in any place) that has a small SCREEN which you can use for Internet and E-MAIL services【商標】流動互聯網制式電話〔可上網和發送電子郵件的一種流動電話〕

in·box /ˋɪnbɑks; ˈɪnbɒks/ *n* [C]
a place on a computer which stores the E-MAIL messages that you have received〔電子郵件的〕收件箱

incubator /ˋɪnkjəˌbetɚ; ˈɪŋkjʊbeɪtə/ *n* [C]
NEW MEANING
an organization which helps new businesses develop by giving them office space, services, and equipment, and providing them with business and technical advice〔企業〕培育基地: *a high-tech incubator on the East coast* 東海岸的高技術培育基地

index fund /ˋɪndɛks ˌfʌnd; ˈɪndeks ˌfʌnd/ also 又作 **tracker fund** *BrE*【英】*n* [C]
technical an INVESTMENT that includes a combination of SHARES that are in a particular SHARE INDEX, and that earns money depending on the value of the shares in that index【術語】指數基金

industrial-strength /ɪnˌdʌstrɪəl ˋstrɛŋθ; ɪnˌdʌstriəl ˈstreŋθ/ *adj*
humorous an industrial-strength liquid is very strong【幽默】〔液體〕濃度高的, 有效的: *They served us industrial-strength coffee.* 他們給我們端出了濃咖啡。

infected /ɪnˋfɛktɪd; ɪnˈfektɪd/ *adj*
NEW MEANING
if a computer or DISK is infected, the information in or on it has been changed or destroyed by a computer VIRUS〔受電腦病毒〕感染的

inflation-in·de·xed bond /ɪnˌfleʃən ɪndɛkst ˋbɑnd; ɪnˌfleɪʃən ɪndekst ˈbɒnd/ *n* [C]
technical a BOND sold by the government in which the amount paid in INTEREST goes up when the rate of INFLATION goes up【術語】通脹指數債券〔一種利率隨通脹率調節的債券〕

information o·ver·load /ˌɪnfɚmeʃən ˋovɚlod; ˌɪnfəmeɪʃən ˈəʊvələʊd/ *n* [U]
a situation in which someone gets too much information at one time, for example on the Internet, and becomes tired and unable to think very carefully about any of it 信息超載: *The greater the amount of data we have access to, the greater the risk of information overload.* 我們可以獲取的信息量越大，信息超載的風險也越大。| *a workshop to help you cope with information overload* 幫助處理信息超載的工作坊

ink /ɪŋk; ɪŋk/ *v* [T]
NEW MEANING
to make a document, agreement etc official and legal by writing your signature on it 簽署〔文件、合約等〕: *Motorola and IBM have inked a deal.* 摩托羅拉和國際商業機器公司已簽了合約。

in-line skate /ˌɪn laɪn ˋsket; ˌɪn laɪn ˈskeɪt/ *n* [C]
a special boot for ROLLER SKATING with a single row of wheels attached under it 滾軸溜冰鞋，單排輪溜冰鞋

inner /ˋɪnɚ; ˈɪnə/ *adj*
NEW MEANING
sb's inner child the part of someone's character that still feels like a child even though they are an adult 某人內心的孩童性格: *Through therapy she has got in touch with her inner child.* 通過治療，她得以認識自我內心的孩童性格。

in·nit /ˋɪnɪt; ˈɪnɪt/ *interjection BrE*
slang said at the end of a statement or in reply to a statement to mean 'isn't it?'. This word is often used by someone to emphasize what they have just said rather than to ask for someone else's opinion【英俚】可不是嘛！〔用於強調〕: *"Did you see the way Schumacher went past him?" "Innit."* "你看見舒馬赫超過他時的那個帥勁嗎?" "可不是嘛!"

instant mes·sag·ing /ˌɪnstənt ˋmɛsɪdʒɪŋ; ˌɪnstənt ˈmesɪdʒɪŋ/ *n* [U]
a type of service available on the Internet that allows you to quickly exchange written messages with people that you know 即時信息: *The Internet's two main instant messaging services are both owned and run by AOL.* 互聯網兩大即時信息服務是由美國在線公司擁有和經營的。

in·sti·net /ˋɪnstɪnɛt; ˈɪnstɪnet/ *n* [U]
trademark an electronic network that allows people to buy and sell SHARES using a computer when a STOCK EXCHANGE is closed. Instinet is owned by Reuters.【商標】〔隨時可進行股票買賣的〕瞬時網，即時電子交易網

institutionalized ra·cis·m /ˌɪnstətjuʃənl̩aɪzd ˋresɪzəm; ˌɪnstɪtjuːʃənəlaɪzd ˈreɪsɪzəm/ also 又作 **-ised** *BrE*【英】*n* [U]
racism that has become an established part of the normal behaviour and ideas of people in an organization 制度化的種族主義

interface /ˋɪntɚfes; ˈɪntəfeɪs/ *v* [I]
NEW MEANING
to have a conversation with someone, especially in a work-related situation or for example in a situation between a doctor and a PATIENT〔尤指工作場景下〕交談: [+with] *How often does your job require you to interface with people from other departments?* 你的工作需要你和其他部門互通情況有多頻繁？

in·ter·faith /ˌɪntɚˋfeθ; ˌɪntəˈfeɪθ◂/ *adj* [only before noun 僅用於名詞前]
between or involving people of different religions 不同宗教信仰者(間)的: *an interfaith Thanksgiving service* 跨宗教信仰的感恩(祈禱)儀式

in·ter·gen·e·ra·tion·al /ˌɪntɚdʒɛnəˋreʃənl̩; ˌɪntədʒenəˈreɪʃənəl/ *adj*
between or involving people from different age groups 兩代[多代]人之間的: *School officials say the intergenerational programs help both the children and the retired people.* 學校管理人員說，跨世代計劃對兒童和退休人員都有幫助。

in·ter·leu·kin /ˌɪntɚˋlukɪn; ˌɪntəˈluːkɪn/ *n* [C]
a type of PROTEIN (=a substance the body produces) that helps the body fight disease 白細胞介素

in·ter·mer·cial /ˌɪntɚˋmɝʃəl; ˌɪntəˈmɜːʃəl/ *n* [C]
advertisements that appear on the Internet. This word comes from a combination of the words 'Internet' and 'COMMERCIAL' (=a television advertisement). 網上(商業)廣告〔由 Internet 和 commercial 縮合而成〕

Internet ac·cess com·pa·ny /ˌɪntɚnɛt ˋæksɛs ˌkʌmpənɪ; ˌɪntənet ˋækses ˌkʌmpəni/ *n* [C]
a company whose business is providing a service that allows computer users to find information on the Internet 互聯網服務公司

Internet ac·count /ˋɪntɚnɛt əˌkaunt; ˈɪntənet əˌkaʊnt/ *n* [C]
an arrangement that you make with an ACCESS PROVIDER (=company that provides Internet services) that allows you to use the Internet from your computer, usually in exchange for a monthly payment 互聯網賬戶: *How do I set up an Internet account?* 我怎樣開一個互聯網賬戶呢？

Internet bank·ing /ˋɪntɚnɛt ˌbæŋkɪŋ; ˈɪntənet ˌbæŋkɪŋ/ also 又作 **online banking** *n* [U]
a service provided by banks so that people can find out information about their bank account, pay bills etc using the Internet 網上銀行

Internet pro·to·col /ˋɪntɚnɛt ˌprotəkɑl; ˈɪntənet ˌprəʊtəkɒl/ *abbreviation* 縮寫為 **IP** *n* [C]
technical a set of rules that describe how and in what form electronic information should be sent on the Internet【術語】網際協議，網絡協定

Internet store·front /ˌɪntɚnɛt ˋstorfrʌnt; ˌɪntənet ˈstɔːfrʌnt/ also 又作 **storefront** *n* [C]
a WEBSITE that is used to sell products or services to the public 銷售網站: *Now you can reach millions of potential customers with your own Internet storefront.* 你現在可通過自己的銷售網站接觸數以百萬計的潛在客戶。

in·ter·op·e·ra·bil·i·ty /ˌɪntɚˌɑpərəˋbɪlətɪ; ˌɪntərˌɒpərəˈbɪləti/ *n* [U]
technical the ability of different kinds of computer SOFTWARE or HARDWARE to work together or exchange information【術語】互操作性，協同性，通容性 —**interoperable** *adj* —**interoperate** *v* [I]

intolerance /ɪnˋtɑlərəns; ɪnˈtɒlərəns/ *n*
NEW MEANING
food/wheat/lactose etc intolerance if you have a food intolerance, you cannot DIGEST a type of food, or it makes you ill 食物/小麥/乳糖等的不耐(受): *People with a lactose* (=a substance in milk) *intolerance often find yogurt easier to digest.* 乳糖耐受不良者常發現酸乳酪較易消化。

in·tra·net /ˋɪntrənɛt; ˈɪntrənet/ *n* [C]
a computer network used for exchanging or seeing information within a company, which works in the same way as the Internet〔企業內部的〕內聯網: *Photographs of new employees appear on the company's intranet.* 新員工的相片出現在公司的內聯網上。

in·tra·pre·neur /ˌɪntrəprəˋnɝ; ˌɪntrəprəˈnɜː/ *n* [C]
someone who works for a large company and whose job is to develop new ideas or ways of doing business for that company. This word comes from a combination of 'INTRA-', which means 'within', and 'ENTREPRENEUR', which means 'a person who starts new businesses and takes risks in order to make money'. 內部企業家〔企業內進行創新性開發和營銷的部門經理，由 intra- 和 entrepreneur 縮合而成〕—**intrapreneuring** *n* [U]

investment club /ɪnˋvɛstmənt ˌklʌb; ɪnˈvestmənt ˌklʌb/ *n* [C]
a group of people who meet regularly to decide which INVESTMENTS to buy and sell together, with money that they all put into the group 投資俱樂部: *O'Hara belongs*

to an investment club in Detroit. 奧哈拉是底特律一家投資俱樂部的會員。

IPO /ˌaɪ pi ˋo; ˌaɪ piː ˈəʊ/ *n* [C usually singular 一般用單數]
technical initial public offering; an occasion when a company makes SHARES available for sale on the STOCK MARKET for the first time【術語】〔股票的〕首次公開發行，新股發行

ISA /ˋaɪsə; ˈaɪsə/ *n* [C] *BrE*
individual savings account; an arrangement in Britain by which you can save money in a bank without paying tax on it【英】個人儲蓄賬戶

ISDN /ˌaɪ ɛs di ˋɛn; ˌaɪ es diː ˈen/ *n* [U]
technical Integrated Services Digital Network; a special telephone network through which computers can send information much faster than usual【術語】綜合業務數字[位]網: *an ISDN line* 綜合業務數字網線路

ISP /ˌaɪ ɛs ˋpi; ˌaɪ es ˈpiː/ *n* [C]
technical Internet service provider; a business that connects people's computers to the Internet【術語】互聯網服務提供者

issue[1] /ˋɪʃu; ˈɪʃuː/ *n*
NEW MEANING
have issues (with sb/sth) *informal* if you have issues with someone or something, you do not agree with or approve of them【非正式】(與某人/對某事) 持不同看法: *I have a few issues with Marc.* 我與馬克在一些問題上有不同看法。

It girl /ˋɪt ˌgɝl; ˈɪt ˌgɜːl/ *n* [C]
informal especially BrE a young woman who is famous mainly because she is rich and beautiful, and whose photograph appears in a lot of magazines and newspapers【非正式，尤英】〔照片經常見報或雜誌的〕款姐，名媛

iTV /ˌaɪ ti ˋvi; ˌaɪ tiː ˈviː/ *n* [U]
interactive television; a type of television programme that allows people who are watching at home to answer questions or find out more information by using a computer or special electronic equipment 交互式電視，互動電視

J,j

jack /dʒæk; dʒæk/ *v* [T]
slang【俚】a short form of 縮略式= CARJACK

jam /dʒæm; dʒæm/ *n* [C]
NEW MEANING
informal【非正式】**1** a song or piece of music, especially one by a RAP or ROCK group 即興音樂〔一種搖滾樂〕: *a totally dope jam from Puff Daddy* 吹牛老爹一支勁道十足的即興樂曲 **2 kick out the jams** to play ROCK MUSIC loudly and with a lot of energy or emotion 賣勁地演奏即興音樂: *Make no mistake – these guys know how to kick out the jams.* 毫無疑問 —— 這幾個傢伙知道如何演奏即興音樂。

jam·cam /ˋdʒæmkæm; ˈdʒæmkæm/ *n* [C]
a camera that is connected to a WEBSITE that shows where the traffic is very bad〔與網站相連的〕交通堵塞情況攝錄裝置: *Remember you can always check out the jamcams on our website to avoid the worst of the traffic in the rush hour.* 記住，你可隨時查看我們網站上的交通堵塞情況，以避開繁忙時間最糟的交通擁堵。

Jaws of Life /ˌdʒɔz əv ˋlaɪf; ˌdʒɔːz əv ˈlaɪf/ *n* [plural]
the Jaws of Life *trademark* a tool used to make a hole in a car, TRUCK etc after an accident, so that the people inside can be taken out【商標】救生顎〔交通事故中在汽車開洞救人用的裝置〕

jelly /ˋdʒɛlɪ; ˈdʒeli/ *n*
NEW MEANING
1 jellies [plural] *BrE informal* amounts of a drug that makes you feel relaxed and sleepy, which some people use illegally【英，非正式】"果凍"〔一種鎮靜劑〕**2 jellies** [plural] shoes made of clear coloured plastic 透明彩色塑料鞋

jig·gy /ˋdʒɪgɪ; ˈdʒɪgi/ *adj*
get jiggy *AmE slang* to dance with a lot of energy to popular music【美俚】〔隨着流行音樂〕跳勁舞

JIT *adj*
the written abbreviation for 縮寫= JUST-IN-TIME

job lock /ˋdʒɑb ˌlɑk; ˈdʒɒb ˌlɒk/ *n* [C] *AmE*
informal a situation in which you are afraid to leave your job because you will lose your medical insurance【美，非正式】〔因擔心失去醫療保險而〕不願離開工作崗位

job·seek·er /ˋdʒɑbˌsikɚ; ˈdʒɒbˌsiːkə/ *n* [C] *BrE*
someone who is trying to find a job【英】求職者

job·seeker's al·low·ance /ˌdʒɑbsikɚz əˋlaʊəns; ˌdʒɒbsiːkəz əˈlaʊəns/ *n* [U]
in Britain, money that the government pays to people who do not have a job but who are trying to get one〔在英國給失業者的〕求職補貼

jock /dʒɑk; dʒɒk/ *n* [C]
NEW MEANING
informal a DISC JOCKEY【非正式】唱片騎師

joined-up /ˌdʒɔɪnd ˋʌp; ˌdʒɔɪnd ˈʌp◂/ *adj BrE*
joined-up systems, institutions etc combine many different groups, ideas, or parts in a way that works well【英】聯組的，聯合的: **joined-up thinking/government** *the need for joined-up thinking between departments* 需要各部門集思廣益 | *Partnerships are still not joined-up enough.* 合夥者之間還不夠羣策羣力。| *Joined-up government offers great opportunities to deliver better services.* 聯合政府締造很多機會以提供更好的服務。

joint /dʒɔɪnt; dʒɔɪnt/ *n* [C]
NEW MEANING
slang a record or film that someone has made【俚】唱片；影片: *Cypress Hill released their latest studio joint earlier this year.* "墓園三人組"今年早些時候發行了他們最新錄製的唱片。

jones /dʒonz; dʒəʊnz/ *n*
get your jones *slang* to get or do something that you want or need very much【俚】如願以償: *I'm a total sushi addict – I have to get my jones at least once a week.* 我對壽司特別上癮 —— 我每週至少要飽餐它一頓。

JPEG /ˋdʒe ˌpɛg; ˈdʒeɪ ˌpeg/ also 又作 **JPG** /ˌdʒe pi ˋdʒi; ˌdʒeɪ piː ˈdʒiː/ *n* [C]
technical Joint Photographic Experts Group; a type of computer FILE used on the Internet that contains pictures, photographs, or other images【術語】聯合圖像專家組，靜止圖像壓縮標準〔Joint Photographic Experts Group的縮寫〕

juice /dʒus; dʒuːs/ *n*
NEW MEANING
the juice information about people's private lives; GOSSIP 豔聞，逸聞: **[+about/on]** *Have you heard the juice about Maria and Tim?* 你聽到關於瑪麗亞和蒂姆的豔聞嗎?

juiced /dʒust; dʒuːst/ also 又作 **juiced up** *adj* [not before noun 不用於名詞前] *AmE*
NEW MEANING
informal excited【美，非正式】興奮的: *If I'm nervous and juiced up, I pitch better.* 我要是緊張興奮的話，我會把球投得更好。

jungle /ˋdʒʌŋgl; ˈdʒʌŋgəl/ *n* [U]
NEW MEANING
a type of popular British dance music that has a fast beat and uses SAMPLES (=small parts of a song from a CD or record that are copied and used in a new song) 叢林音樂〔英國的一種流行舞樂，節奏明快，使用取樣拼和〕: *Click here to download free jungle, drum and bass, and garage tracks.* 點擊這裡免費下載叢林音樂、鼓點低音和車庫樂。—**junglist** *n* [C]

just-in-time /ˌdʒʌst ɪn ˋtaɪm; ˌdʒʌst ɪn ˈtaɪm/ *abbreviation* 縮寫為 **JIT** *adj* [only before noun 僅用於名詞前]

technical if goods are produced or bought using a just-in-time system, they are produced or bought just before they are needed so that the company does not have to store things for a long time【術語】〔貨物〕適時製造的, 零庫存的: *The firm is worried that delays could cause problems with their just-in-time manufacturing methods.* 這家公司擔心那些延誤會影響他們的適時生產安排。

K,k

key·pal /ˈkipæl; ˈkiːpæl/ *n* [C]
someone with whom you regularly exchange E-MAIL 鍵盤友, 網友: *If your daughter is interested in having a keypal next year, please have her get in touch.* 你的女兒如果來年有意結交網友的話, 請讓她同我聯繫。

kick /kɪk; kɪk/ *v*
NEW MEANING
1 be kicking (it) *spoken* to be relaxing and having a good time【口】悠閒自得: *I was just kicking with my buddies.* 我正和朋友優哉游哉, 自得其樂。**2 be kicking it** *slang spoken* to be having a romantic relationship with someone【俚, 口】和…有一手〔有男女關係〕: *My sources say that Blige was kicking it with Thomas while she was on tour.* 我得到的消息說布萊奇在旅遊中和托馬斯有一手來着。

kiddie-cam /ˈkɪdɪ ˌkæm; ˈkɪdi ˌkæm/ *n* [C]
a camera that allows parents to see their child or children when the parents are somewhere else 觀察兒童攝像機: *She stays connected to her kids through e-mail and watching them on day-care kiddie-cam over the Internet.* 她通過電子郵件和自己的孩子保持聯繫, 並通過托兒園的互聯網攝像機觀察他們的情況。

kid·ult /ˈkɪdʌlt; ˈkɪdʌlt/ *n* [C]
an adult who likes to play games or buy things that most people consider more suitable for children. This word comes from a combination of the words 'KID' and 'adult' 喜歡兒童玩意的成人〔由 kid 和 adult 縮合而成〕: *What is amazing is the size of the kidult population and the money they are willing to spend on products.* 讓人感到驚訝的是竟有那麼多的"大孩子"願意花那麼多錢在一些兒童玩意兒上面。

killer app /ˈkɪlɚ ˌæp; ˈkɪlər ˌæp/ also 又作 **killer ap·pli·ca·tion** /ˈkɪlɚ æpləˌkeʃən; ˈkɪlər æplɪˌkeʃən/ *n* [C]
a piece of computer SOFTWARE that many people want to buy, especially one that works so well on a particular type of machine that people also want to buy the machine "殺手" 軟件〔許多人想買的軟件, 尤指在某類機器中運行良好, 使許多人想連帶買下機器的軟件〕

kite surf·ing /ˈkaɪt ˌsɝfɪŋ; ˈkaɪt ˌsɜːfɪŋ/ *n* [U]
the activity of moving across water on a SURFBOARD while holding a large KITE which is attached to strong strings 風箏衝浪

kluge /kludʒ; kluːdʒ/ *adj* [only before noun 僅用於名詞前] *AmE*
slang a kluge solution to a computer problem is not a good or intelligent solution【美俚】蹩腳的, 尚未整理完成的

knowledge-based soft·ware /ˌnɑlɪdʒ best ˈsɔftwɛr; ˌnɒlɪdʒ beɪst ˈsɒftweə/ *n* [U]
technical SOFTWARE that learns while it works and is able to use this knowledge to find more effective ways of doing a particular job【術語】知識軟件, 智能型軟件

L,l

lad mag /ˈlæd ˌmæg; ˈlæd ˌmæg/ *n* [C] *BrE*
a magazine for young men that includes articles about sports and fashion, pictures of women without many clothes on, and some writing about problems and experiences of young men【英】少男雜誌: *Sheena has been on the cover of almost all of the lad mags.* 希娜幾乎當過所有少男雜誌的封面女郎。

lad·dish /ˈlædɪʃ; ˈlædɪʃ/ *adj BrE*
a young man who is laddish likes spending time with other men, drinking alcohol and enjoying things like popular music and sport rather than being interested in CULTURE or intellectual things【英】有男子漢氣概的; 粗放的: *People expect us to be a bit laddish, like the characters we play in the series.* 人們以為我們比較粗放, 像我們在系列片中扮演的角色那樣。

lad·dis·m /ˈlædɪzəm; ˈlædɪzəm/ *n* [C] *BrE*
the attitudes and behaviour of some young men in Britain, who drink a lot of alcohol, are interested in sports, and think that women are less important than men【英】大男子漢作風, 大男子漢主義: *Experts in the U.K. blame the culture of laddism for boys' low test scores.* 英國的一些專家把男孩子測驗成績差歸咎於大男子主義的文化。

la·dette /læˈdɛt; læˈdet/ *n* [C] *BrE*
humorous a young woman who likes to do some things that young men typically do, such as drinking alcohol in pubs and talking about sex and sports【英, 幽默】野丫頭, 具男孩作風的女孩子

lai·ry /ˈlɛrɪ; ˈleəri/ *adj BrE*
slang behaving in a way that is very loud, or with too much confidence【英俚】喧鬧的, 大大咧咧的: *He's a bit lairy, your friend Mick.* 你的朋友米克多少有點大大咧咧的。

lap danc·ing /ˈlæp ˌdænsɪŋ; ˈlæp ˌdɑːnsɪŋ/ *n* [U]
dancing with sexy movements performed by a young woman who removes her clothes while sitting on a customer's LAP in a NIGHTCLUB 大腿豔舞 —**lapdancer** *n* [C]: *Carla, a single mother of two, says she can make more than three hundred dollars a night as a lap dancer.* 有兩個孩子的單身母親卡拉說, 她跳大腿舞, 一晚能掙三百多美元。—compare 比較 TABLE DANCING

large /lɑrdʒ; lɑːdʒ/ *v*
large it (up) *BrE slang* to enjoy yourself, especially in a way that involves drinking alcohol, dancing etc【英俚】自娛, 飲酒作樂: *Here's a picture of us larging it up in Brighton last summer.* 這是去年夏天我們在布賴頓歡宴的照片。

large-cap /ˈlɑrdʒ ˌkæp; ˈlɑːdʒ ˌkæp/ *n* [C]
a SHARE in a large company 大盤股, 高市值股票 —**large-cap** *adj*: *They put their money into some large-cap mutual funds.* 他們把錢投放在一些投資高市值股票的互惠基金上。—opposite 反義詞 SMALL-CAP

laser point·er /ˈlezɚ ˌpɔɪntɚ; ˈleɪzə ˌpɔɪntə/ *n* [C]
a small piece of equipment that produces a LASER BEAM (=powerful narrow beam of light) that you hold in your hand and use to point at things on a map, board etc so that other people will pay attention to them. Laser pointers are often used by teachers and people who are giving talks. 激光筆

lashed /læʃt; læʃt/ *adj* [not before noun 不用於名詞前] *BrE*
slang very drunk【英俚】醉醺醺的, 酩酊大醉的: **get lashed** *This might be my last chance to go out and get lashed with my mates.* 這可能是我和朋友們出去喝得酩酊大醉的最後一次機會。

lat·te /ˈlɑte; ˈlæteɪ/ *n* [C,U]
coffee with hot milk in it, or a cup of this type of coffee 牛奶咖啡, 那堤咖啡: *Jody was sipping a decaf latte.* 喬迪呷着脫咖啡因的牛奶咖啡。

launch /lɔntʃ; lɔːntʃ/ *v* [T]
NEW MEANING
to make a computer PROGRAM start 啟動〔電腦程式〕: *Double-click on an icon to launch an application.* 點擊圖標兩次啟動應用軟件。

LDL /ˌɛl di ˈɛl; ˌel diː ˈel/ *n* [C]

technical low-density lipoprotein; a type of CHOLESTEROL that is bad for your health because it helps fat stay on the inside of your heart and blood VESSEL*s*【術語】低密度脂蛋白: *Studies show that keeping your LDL ('bad cholesterol') levels below 160 can add years to your life.* 研究表明, 使低密度脂蛋白(壞膽固醇)水平保持在160以下可以延長壽命。—compare 比較 HDL

leap sec·ond /ˈlip ˌsɛkənd; ˈliːp ˌsekənd/ *n* [C]
a second that is sometimes officially added to the last minute of a day, occurring at the end of June or at the end of December, to make the very accurate clocks that scientists use more exact 閏秒

LEP /lɛp; lep/ *adj* [only before noun 僅用於名詞前] *AmE technical* limited English proficient; concerning someone whose first language is not English and who cannot communicate very well in English【美, 術語】英語不熟練的: **LEP students** *The number of LEP students in the district has risen since 1993.* 1993年以來, 該區英語不熟練的學生人數有所增加。

lep·tin /ˈlɛptɪn; ˈleptɪn/ *n* [U]
a HORMONE that controls how much you weigh, how hungry you are, and how much energy you have. Scientists think that taking leptin might help fat people lose weight. 瘦蛋白, 瘦身素

LETS /lɛts; lets/ *n* [C]
local exchange trading system; an arrangement among a group of people to exchange goods and services with each other instead of buying these things from a store 地區性交換式貿易系統: *the benefits of belonging to a LETS* 屬於地區性交換式貿易系統的好處

let·ter·box·ing /ˈlɛtɚˌbɑksɪŋ; ˈletəˌbɒksɪŋ/ *n* [U]
the practice of broadcasting a cinema film on television with black bands at the top and bottom of the television SCREEN so that the film will have the same DIMENSION*s* as it did on a cinema screen〔電視屏幕上下留一條黑邊的〕寬銀幕式

leverage /ˈlɛvərɪdʒ; ˈliːvərɪdʒ/ *v* [T]
NEW MEANING
to use borrowed money to buy a particular company or INVESTMENT 舉債投資: *They were extremely effective at capturing federal resources to leverage local development.* 他們極之懂得如何爭取聯邦貸款以投資當地經濟。

lifetime /ˈlaɪfˌtaɪm; ˈlaɪftaɪm/ *n*
NEW MEANING
not in this lifetime *spoken* not at all; never【口】這輩子不行: *"Would you go out with him after he dropped you?" "Not in this lifetime."* "他甩了你之後你還會跟他交往嗎?" "這輩子都不會。"

link /lɪŋk; lɪŋk/ *n* [C]
NEW MEANING
a special word or picture in an Internet document that you CLICK on to move quickly to another part of the same document or to another document 鏈接(點): *Click on the link below to return to the home page.* 點擊下面的鏈接點返回主頁。

lippy /ˈlɪpɪ; ˈlɪpi/ *n* [U] *BrE*
informal LIPSTICK【英, 非正式】口紅, 唇膏: *Wait a minute, I'll just put a bit of lippy on.* 等一會兒, 我塗一點口紅就好。

lipstick les·bi·an /ˈlɪpstɪk ˌlɛzbɪən; ˈlɪpstɪk ˌlezbiən/ *n* [C]
informal an offensive word for a LESBIAN who dresses in a typically female way and wears MAKE-UP, as opposed to one who dresses like a man【非正式】扮演女子角色的女同性戀者〔冒犯用語〕

list·serv /ˈlɪstˌsɝv; ˈlɪstˌsɜːv/ *n* [C]
a computer PROGRAM that allows a group of people to send and receive E-MAIL to and from each other about a particular subject〔電腦的〕專題通信程式

load fund /ˈlod ˌfʌnd; ˈləʊd ˌfʌnd/ *n* [C]
an amount of money that you give a company and pay them to INVEST for you 投資於抽佣基金的錢款

lo·gy /ˈlɑgɪ; ˈlɒgi/ *adj*
slang feeling as if you have no energy or no interest in doing anything; LETHARGIC【俚】懶洋洋的, 沒有勁的: *You seem a bit logy today.* 你今天似乎有點沒精打采。

LOL, lol
a written abbreviation of 縮寫= 'laughing out loud', used by people communicating in CHAT ROOM*s* on the Internet to say that they are laughing at something that someone else has written. LOL is also used at the end of informal letters, messages, meaning 'lots of love'. 放聲大笑〔用於網上聊天室中〕; 愛你〔'lots of love' 的縮寫, 用於非正式信件的結尾〕

look·ist /ˈlukɪst; ˈlʊkɪst/ *adj*
informal unfairly deciding to like or not like someone by considering only the way they look, their weight, their clothes etc【非正式】以貌取人的: *It's time for women to stop making lookist remarks about each other and to start feeling good about their own bodies.* 婦女是時候停止互相評頭品足, 而開始為各自的體態感到自豪了。—**lookist** *n* [C] —**lookism** *n* [U]

low-rent /ˌlo ˈrɛnt; ˌləʊ ˈrent/ *adj*
used to express disapproval of something that is not expensive or not good quality 質量低劣的, 廉價的〔有貶義〕

loyalty card /ˈlɔɪəltɪ ˌkɑrd; ˈlɔɪəlti ˌkɑːd/ *n* [C]
a card given by a shop, SUPERMARKET etc that gives regular customers lower prices, money back on goods they buy etc〔商店、超級市場等發的〕忠誠卡: *The loyalty card offers a 5% discount on the store's own-brand goods.* 用忠誠卡購買商店自己品牌的商品可得到九五折。

LPG /ˌɛl pi ˈdʒi; ˌel piː ˈdʒiː/ also 又作 **LP gas** /ˌɛl pi ˈgæs; ˌel piː ˈgæs/ *n* [U]
liquefied petroleum gas; a type of liquid FUEL that is burned to produce heat or power 液化石油氣

LRP /ˌɛl ɑr ˈpi; ˌel ɑː ˈpiː/ *n* [U] *BrE*
lead replacement petrol; a special type of PETROL that does not contain LEAD and is meant to be used in older cars which normally would require petrol containing lead【英】代鉛汽油

lurk /lɝk; lɜːk/ *v* [I]
NEW MEANING
if you lurk in a CHAT ROOM on the Internet, you read what other people are writing to each other, but you do not write any messages to them 旁觀〔閱讀網上留言, 但不發表意見〕, 潛身漫遊: [+in] *I think it's sort of creepy how people lurk in chat rooms.* 我認為人們在聊天室裡潛身漫遊有點令人毛骨悚然。—**lurker** *n* [C]

M,m

Maalox mo·ment /ˈmelɑks ˌmomənt; ˈmeɪlɒks ˌməʊmənt/ *n* [C usually singular 一般用單數] *AmE humorous* a short period when you suddenly become extremely anxious or nervous and have pains in your stomach. Maalox is a trademark for a type of stomach medicine sold in the US. In television advertisements for this product, several people in STRESSFUL situations said, "I'm having a Maalox moment!" which meant that they needed to take some of this medicine to make them feel better.【美, 幽默】梅洛克斯症〔因極度緊張或擔心而感到胃痛的一段時間, 此詞來自梅洛克斯公司的胃藥廣告〕

mad /mæd; mæd/ *adj*
NEW MEANING
1 be mad for sb/sth *informal* if you are mad for someone or something, you are extremely interested in or attracted to them【非正式】對某人/某物着迷: *All the girls at school are mad for him.* 學校裡的所有女孩都迷戀着他。**2 be mad for it** *BrE informal* if you are mad for it, you want to do something very much【英, 非正式】熱衷

[醉心]於

magnetic ink char·ac·ter rec·og·ni·tion /mæg,nɛtɪk ,ɪŋk ˋkærɪktɚ rɛkəg,nɪʃən; mæg,netɪk ,ɪŋk ˈkærɪktə rekəg,nɪʃən/ *abbreviation* 縮寫為 **MICR** *n* [U]
technical a system that recognizes printed letters of the alphabet, for example on a cheque or official document【術語】磁墨水字符識別

mail·bomb /ˋmel,bɑm; ˈmeɪlbɒm/ *n* [C]
a large number of E-MAIL messages sent to the same computer, with the result that the computer has too much DATA and cannot work properly any more 電子郵件炸彈〔把大量電子郵件傳送至某電腦, 使其因資料過多而無法正常運作〕

mailing list /ˋmelɪŋ ,lɪst; ˈmeɪlɪŋ ,lɪst/ *n* [C]
NEW MEANING
a list of names and E-MAIL addresses kept on a computer so that you can send the same message to a group of people at the same time〔電腦上的〕發函清單, 通訊名單

ma·jor·ly /ˋmedʒɚlɪ; ˈmeɪdʒəli/ *adv*
slang extremely【俚】極其, 非常: *It's majorly cool.* 酷極了。| *She got majorly depressed after they broke up.* 兩人分手之後, 她沮喪極了。

make·good /ˋmek,gud; ˈmeɪkgʊd/ *n* [C usually plural 一般用複數]
an occasion when a television company has to broadcast an advertisement without being paid to do so, because the advertisement was not seen by as many people as the television company promised when it was first shown〔電視台因觀眾未達到事先承諾的人數而〕免費播放廣告

makeover /ˋmek,ovɚ; ˈmeɪkəʊvə/ *n* [C]
NEW MEANING
a process of changing the way a place looks〔把地方〕改觀: *a kitchen makeover* 廚房改建

makeover TV /ˋmekovɚ ti ,vi; ˈmeɪkəʊvə tiː ,viː/ *n* [U]
television programmes in which skilled people help someone to improve the appearance of their house or garden 指導家居裝修的電視節目

mall·rat /ˋmɔlræt; ˈmɔːlræt/ *n* [C usually plural 一般用複數] *AmE*
informal a young person who goes to SHOPPING MALLS a lot in order to be with their friends, not to buy things【美, 非正式】商場逛客, 常在商場會友而不買東西的年輕人

man /mæn; mæn/ *n*
NEW MEANING
you the/da man! also 又作 **you're the man** *AmE slang* used to praise a man or boy for having done something well【美俚】做得好! 真棒!〔用以稱讚男性〕

managed care pro·vid·er /,mænɪdʒd ˋkɛr prə,vaɪdɚ; ,mænɪdʒd ˈkeə prə,vaɪdə/ *n* [C] *AmE*
a doctor or hospital that provides medical services for people who have a type of health insurance that limits the amount or type of medical care they can receive【美】提供管理式護理的醫生[醫院]〔他們的病人所接受的醫療服務在數量及種類上均有限制〕: *How can I change my managed care provider?* 我怎樣才能換一家提供管理式護理的醫院呢?

managed fund /,mænɪdʒd ˋfʌnd; ,mænɪdʒd ˈfʌnd/ *n* [C]
technical a FUND (=group of INVESTMENTS) in which some of the investments are bought and sold in order to try to increase the value of the fund【術語】管理基金

ma·no a ma·no /,mɑno ɑ ˋmɑno; ,mænəʊ ɑː ˈmænəʊ/ *adv*
with only two people involved; ONE-TO-ONE 一對一地: *Come on now – put your questions to the senator, mano a mano, by speaking to him online in real time.* 來吧, 把你的問題向參議員提出, 一對一地、實時地在網上跟他談。| *He finally faced up to his father, mano a mano, telling him he was going to leave college.* 他終於鼓起勇氣, 面對面告訴父親自己打算從大學輟學。

ma·qui·la·do·ra /mɑ,kiləˋdɔrə; mæ,kiːləˈdɔːrə/ *n* [C] *Spanish*
a factory in Mexico, especially one that is owned by a foreign company【西】〔尤指外資在墨西哥開設的〕保稅加工廠

mashed /mæʃt; mæʃt/ *adj* [not before noun 不用於名詞前] *BrE*
slang very drunk or strongly affected by drugs【英俚】爛醉的;〔吸毒後〕迷迷糊糊的: *We got completely mashed last night.* 我們昨夜醉得一塌糊塗。

massive¹ /ˋmæsɪv; ˈmæsɪv/ *n* [C] *BrE*
NEW MEANING
slang a group of friends from a particular place who share an interest in RAP, HIP-HOP, or HOUSE music, considered as a group【英俚】〔流行音樂迷〕組合: *the Staines massive* 斯坦斯組合

massive² /ˋmæsɪv; ˈmæsɪv/ *adj BrE*
NEW MEANING
slang extremely good【英俚】棒極的, 頂呱呱的: *Listen to this. It's a massive song.* 聽, 這歌棒極了。

mass vol·ume ver·ti·cal drink·ing /,mæs ,vɑljəm ,vɝtɪkḷ ˋdrɪŋkɪŋ; ,mæs ,vɑljuːm ,vɜːtɪkəl ˈdrɪŋkɪŋ/ *n* [U] *BrE*
technical an expression used by the British police to describe the way in which large numbers of young people drink large amounts of alcohol in bars that are so crowded that everyone is standing up【英, 術語】眾眾站着酗酒〔英國警方用語, 指很多年青人擠在酒吧裡站着喝酒〕

max /mæks; mæks/ *v*
NEW MEANING
max sth ↔ out *phr v* [T] *AmE informal* to use all of something such as money or supplies so that there is none left【美, 非正式】把〔金錢、供應品等〕用光, 一點不剩: *We maxed out the credit card last weekend at Oakland Mall.* 上週末我們在奧克蘭購物中心把信用卡的簽賬額用了個精光。

MBWA /,ɛm bi ,dʌbḷju ˋe; ,em biː ,dʌbəljuː ˈeɪ/ *n* [U]
management by walking around; a way of managing people in a company in which the manager often walks around and speaks to workers in order to find out what they are doing〔公司的〕巡查式管理

MC /,ɛm ˋsi; ,em ˈsiː/ *n* [C]
NEW MEANING
the person in a RAP group who holds the MICROPHONE and says the words to the songs 說唱樂隊中手持麥克風吟唱的人 —**MC** *v* [I]: *He was MC'ing in clubs in the evening.* 他晚上在夜總會演唱說唱樂曲。

m-com·merce /ˋɛm ,kɑmɝs; ˈem ,kɒmɜːs/ *n* [U]
mobile commerce; the buying or selling of goods and services using a radio connection to the Internet, for example using a LAPTOP or MOBILE PHONE〔通過便攜式電腦或手機進行的〕移動商務

meat·space /ˋmit,spes; ˈmiːtspeɪs/ *n* [U]
the real world of physical things and people, rather than CYBERSPACE〔相對於網絡的虛擬世界的〕現實(物質)世界: *I'm so pathetic that I'm updating my webpage at 8pm on a Friday night. I've apparently given up on having a life in meatspace.* 我太慘了, 星期五晚上八點鐘還在更新我的網頁。我顯然已經放棄了在物質世界的生活。

medal /ˋmɛdḷ; ˈmedl/ *v* **medalled, medalling** *BrE*【英】, **medaled, medaling** *AmE*【美】[I]
to win a MEDAL (=a prize) at the Olympic Games 贏得奧運獎牌: **[+in]** *Germany has the potential to medal at least four times in gymnastics this year.* 德國有潛力在本年度的奧運體操賽中取得至少四枚獎牌。

Med·i·gap /ˋmɛdɪ,gæp; ˈmedɪgæp/ *n* [U]
a system in the US by which people who have Medicaid pay money to a company so that they can receive additional medical care and services that they need〔美國的〕補充性醫療保險計劃: *My mom has to pay high pre-*

miums every month for Medigap to cover prescription drugs. 我媽媽每月得繳付高額的補充性醫療保險金以承擔處方藥物的費用。

meet-and-greet /ˌmit ən ˋgrit; ˌmiːt ən ˈgrit/ also 又作 **m and g** *n* [C]
1 an event that is organized for famous musicians, writers, artists etc to meet and talk to their FANS (=people who admire them)〔歌星、作家、藝術家等與他們的支持者的〕見面會: *There will be a meet-and-greet after the show.* 演出結束後將有一場觀眾招待會。**2** a service that sends people to greet and help a person or group when they arrive at an airport〔機場的〕接機（服務）**3** an event in which parents go to their children's school and meet the teachers and other people who work there〔家長與教師的〕見面會, 家長會

memory hog /ˋmɛmərɪ ˌhɑg; ˈmeməri ˌhɒg/ *n* [C] *informal*【非正式】
1 a computer program that uses a lot of memory 佔據大量記憶體的電腦程式 **2** someone who uses computer programs that use a lot of the power available, so that other people on the NETWORK have trouble using their programs〔電腦的〕高用量用戶〔他們使用佔據大量資源的程式, 為其他的網絡用戶帶來不便〕—**memory-hogging** *adj* [only before noun 僅用於名詞前]

mental health day /ˌmɛntl̩ ˋhɛlθ ˌde; ˌmentl ˈhelθ ˌdeɪ/ *n* [C] *AmE*
informal a day when you do not go to work, in order to rest【美, 非正式】歇工日, 休息日

menu bar /ˋmɛnju ˌbɑr; ˈmenjuː ˌbɑː/ *n* [C]
a bar across the top of a computer SCREEN that contains several PULL-DOWN MENUS, for example 'File', 'View', 'Help' etc〔電腦顯示屏上方的〕選項欄, 菜單條: *Some applications in LEO don't have a menu bar.* 一些低軌道衛星的應用程式沒有選項欄。

menu op·tion /ˋmɛnju ˌɑpʃən; ˈmenjuː ˌɒpʃən/ *n* [C]
one of the things you can choose in a PULL-DOWN MENU on a computer〔電腦的〕菜單選項

message[1] /ˋmɛsɪdʒ; ˈmesɪdʒ/ *n*
NEW MEANING
keep to the message an expression used especially by politicians which means that you should always emphasize your party's most important ideas when you are trying to gain people's support 堅持所屬政黨的政治思想, 不改初衷: *Don't confuse the voters. Keep to the message.* 別把投票的人搞糊塗了, 還是堅守政黨理念吧。—see also 另見 OFF-MESSAGE, ON-MESSAGE

message[2] /ˋmɛsɪdʒ; ˈmesɪdʒ/ *v* [T]
to send a message using electronic equipment, for example by E-MAIL〔用電子設備〕發信息〈如電子郵件〉: *I messaged the ship's owner to let him know that everything was going well.* 我給船主發信息, 讓他知道一切都很順利。

message board /ˋmɛsɪdʒ ˌbord; ˈmesɪdʒ ˌbɔːd/ *n* [C]
a place on a WEBSITE where you can read or leave messages; ELECTRONIC BULLETIN BOARD 電子公告板, 網上留言板: *Please read the healthnut.com message board guidelines before posting any messages.* 留言前請先閱讀 healthnut.com〔關心健康網站〕電子公告板上的說明。

mes·sag·ing /ˋmɛsɪdʒɪŋ; ˈmesɪdʒɪŋ/ *n* [U]
the system or process of sending messages using electronic equipment〔通過電子設備的〕信息發送: *automated messaging* 自動信息發送 | *new technology to protect the privacy of electronic messaging and online commerce* 保護電子信息發送和網上貿易的私隱的新技術

met·a·da·ta /ˋmɛtəˌdetə; ˈmetəˌdeɪtə/ *n* [U, plural]
information that describes what is contained in large computer DATABASES, for example who wrote the information, what it is for, and in what form it is stored 元數據, 詮釋資料

me-too /ˌmi ˋtu; ˌmiː ˈtuː/ *adj* [only before noun 僅用於名詞前]
informal a me-too product is one that a company begins to sell after it has seen that other companies are successful with the same type of product【非正式】〔產品〕仿效出售的

MICR /ˌɛm aɪ si ˋɑr; ˌem aɪ siː ˈɑː/ *n* [U]
magnetic ink character recognition; a system that recognizes printed letters of the alphabet, for example on a cheque or official document 磁墨水字符識別

mi·cro·brew /ˋmaɪkroˌbru; ˈmaɪkrəʊˌbruː/ *n* [C]
a type of beer that is produced by a company only in small quantities〔產量很少的〕微釀啤酒

mi·cro·brew·e·ry /ˋmaɪkroˌbruərɪ; ˈmaɪkrəʊˌbruːəri/ *n* [C]
a small company that makes only small quantities of beer, and often has a restaurant where its beer is served 小啤酒廠: *Hundreds of microbreweries across the country are making wonderful, full-flavoured beers.* 全國各地有數以百計的小啤酒廠在釀製可口味醇的啤酒。

mi·cro·en·gi·neer·ing /ˋmaɪkroɛndʒəˌnɪrɪŋ; ˈmaɪkrəʊendʒɪ̆ˌnɪərɪŋ/ *n* [U]
the activity of designing structures and machines that are extremely small 微（型）工程 —**microengineer** *n* [C]

mi·cro·fi·nance /ˋmaɪkrofəˌnæns; ˈmaɪkrəʊˌfaɪnæns/ *n* [U]
a system that allows people in poor countries to borrow small amounts of money to help them start a small business 小額創業貸款制: *Small loans schemes can raise living standards, but microfinance should not be the only tool for poverty reduction, says a new report from the World Bank.* 世界銀行的一份新報告指出, 小額創業貸款計劃能提高生活水平, 但是小額融資不應該是扶貧的唯一辦法。

mi·cro·loan /ˋmaɪkroˌlon; ˈmaɪkrəʊˌləʊn/ *n* [C]
a small amount of money that is lent by a government organization to people who want to start small businesses, especially in poor countries〔尤指在貧困國家由政府發放的〕小額創業貸款: *Write for a free brochure about the Microloan Program for Entrepreneurs.* 免費函索為創業者而設的小額貸款計劃的簡介。

mi·cro·man·age /ˋmaɪkroˌmænɪdʒ; ˈmaɪkrəʊˌmænɪdʒ/ *v* [T]
to organize and control all the details of other people's work in a way that they find annoying 微觀管理〔指過分干預別人的工作〕: *Professors warned that students will suffer if the state legislature tries to micromanage public education.* 有教授警告說, 如果州立法機關企圖對公費教育實行微觀管理, 學生們將受害。

MIDI /ˋmɪdɪ; ˈmɪdi/ *n* [U]
technical musical instrument digital interface; a system that allows computers to communicate with electronic musical instruments【術語】"迷笛"〔電子樂器數碼界面〕: *Unlike digital recordings, which can gobble up megabytes of disk space, MIDI files are relatively compact.* 有別於佔據大量磁盤空間的數碼唱片, 迷笛檔案比較緊致。| *With this special software, you can hook up a MIDI keyboard to your computer, play a song, and record it.* 借助這一專用軟件, 你可以把迷笛電子琴接到自己的電腦上, 彈奏一首歌曲並把它錄下來。

millennium bug /məˋlɛnɪəm ˌbʌg; mɪˈleniəm ˌbʌg/ *n* [singular]
the problem that some people believed would affect many computers which did not recognize the date when the year 2000 began 千年蟲

Millennium Man /məˋlɛnɪəm ˌmæn; mɪˈleniəm ˌmæn/ *n* [C]
a man whose personal qualities and behaviour are considered to be very modern〔性格特點和行為都十分新潮的〕千年[禧]男人: *Just answer these five simple questions to find out if your man's a true Millennium Man.* 回答這五個簡單的問題就可以知道你的男人是不是真正的"千禧男人"。

ming·ing /ˋmɪŋɪŋ; ˈmɪŋɪŋ/ *adj BrE*
informal very ugly or very dirty【英, 非正式】醜極的;

髒極的: *These toilets are minging.* 這些廁所髒透了。

mirror site /ˋmɪrɚ ˌsaɪt; ˈmɪrə ˌsaɪt/ *n* [C]
a WEBSITE that is an exact copy of another one, but which is in a different place on the Internet. Mirror sites make it possible for more people to find and use the information, especially if the original website is busy and slow to use. 鏡像網站〔其內容與另一網站完全相同〕

mission creep /ˋmɪʃən ˌkrip; ˈmɪʃən ˌkriːp/ *n* [U] *AmE*
a series of gradual unplanned changes in the purpose or aim of what someone or an organization is trying to do, with the result that they do something different from what they originally planned to do【美】任務蠕變〔任務的目的隨時間而逐漸變化〕: *The government has learned the lessons of the mission creep problem in Somalia, and would only expand the military's assignment in a careful, deliberate way.* 政府已從索馬里的任務蠕變問題中汲取了教訓, 並將仔細謹慎地擴大軍事任務範圍。

mission state·ment /ˋmɪʃən ˌstetmənt; ˈmɪʃən ˌsteɪtmənt/ *n*
personal mission statement a clear statement about what you want to achieve with your life 人生目標宣言, 個人的宗旨陳述: *Use a personal mission statement to chart your career course.* 利用人生目標宣言來制定你的事業進程。

mo' /mo; məʊ/ *quantifier AmE*
spoken informal a short form of 縮略式= MORE², used especially by people who listen to or perform RAP² (2) music【美口, 非正式】更多〔尤為聆聽或演奏說唱樂的人所使用〕: *It's just like Biggie says – mo' money means mo' problems.* 正如比吉所說, 鈔票越多, 問題也越多。

mock·ney /ˋmɑknɪ; ˈmɒkni/ *n* [U] *BrE*
a way of speaking English that is popular among fashionable people in London, England, which uses some sounds and words that are more typical of WORKING-CLASS speech. This word comes from a combination of the words 'MOCK', which means 'not real', and 'COCKNEY' which means a WORKING-CLASS person from the eastern part of London【英】模仿倫敦勞工階層人士的口音〔由 mock 和 cockney 縮合而成〕: *Jameson sings in this awful mockney accent.* 詹姆森用這種模仿倫敦鄉音的怪聲怪調唱歌。

mommy track /ˋmɑmɪ ˌtræk; ˈmɒmi ˌtræk/ *n* [singular] *AmE*
informal a situation in which women with children have less opportunity to make large amounts of money or become very successful in their jobs, for example because they are not able to work as many hours as other people【美, 非正式】媽咪軌道〔指母親為了照顧孩子而損失掙大錢和晉升等的機會〕: *The mommy track unfairly penalizes women, especially in the developed countries.* 媽咪軌道使婦女受到不公平的待遇, 這在發達國家尤為常見。

morph /mɔrf; mɔːf/ *v* [I,T]
to change, or to make something develop a new appearance or change into something else 變化, (使)變形: *The Sunnyvale computer animators morphed Woody Harrelson's face in the movie "Natural Born Killers."* 太陽谷電腦動畫製作師讓活地·夏里遜的臉在電影《天生殺人狂》中變了樣子。| [+ **into**] *The Consumnes River flooded its banks and morphed into a giant sea that swamped homes and ranches.* 孔蘇莫內斯河河水溢出河岸變成了一片汪洋, 淹沒了房屋和牧場。

mosh /mɑʃ; mɒʃ/ *v* [I]
slang to dance to ROCK music, especially at a concert, by jumping around and waving your arms in the air with a lot of energy【俚】〔隨着搖滾樂〕狂舞: *Few albums offer as much food for thought or music for moshing as "The Gray Race".* 很少有唱片集能像"灰色一族"那樣讓人思考, 讓人隨之狂舞。

mosh pit /ˋmɑʃ ˌpɪt; ˈmɒʃ ˌpɪt/ *n* [C]
slang an area in front of the stage at a ROCK concert where people dance with a lot of energy. People sometimes jump off the stage and are caught by people in the mosh pit.【俚】〔搖滾樂音樂會的舞台前的〕狂舞區: *bands who appeal to shirtless, sweaty boys in the mosh pit* 吸引那些不穿襯衣、滿身是汗地在舞台前狂舞的小伙子的樂隊

motor vot·er /ˋmotɚ ˌvotɚ; ˈməʊtə ˌvəʊtə/ *n* [U] *AmE*
a law which makes it easier for Americans to REGISTER to vote because they can do it at the same time and place where they get their DRIVER'S LICENSE*s*. The official name of this law is the National Voter Registration Act.【美】汽車選民登記法〔美國法律, 讓人可以在取駕駛執照時進行選舉登記〕

mountain board /ˋmaʊntn̩ ˌbɔrd; ˈmaʊntɪn ˌbɔːd/ also 又作 **all-terrain board** *n* [C]
a long wide board made of plastic or wood, with four rubber wheels, which people use to travel down the sides of mountains for sport 山地滑板 —**mountain boarding** *n* [U] —**mountain boarder** *n* [C]

mouse potato 電腦迷

mouse po·ta·to /ˋmaʊs pəˋteto; ˈmaʊs pəˈteɪtəʊ/ *n plural* **mouse potatoes** [C]
informal someone who spends a lot of time playing on a computer. This word developed from the words 'COUCH POTATO' which means someone who spends a lot of time watching television.【非正式】電腦迷〔老泡在電腦前的人, 由 couch potato (電視迷) 轉化而來〕

mover /ˋmuvɚ; ˈmuːvə/ *n* [C]
NEW MEANING
a company whose SHARE*s* are being bought and sold in large quantities〔其股票被大批買賣的〕公司

MP3 /ˌɛm pi ˋθri; ˌem piː ˈθriː/ *n* [C]
a type of computer FILE which contains music. MP3 files are COMPRESS*ed* (=made smaller) so that they can more easily be sent from computer to computer using the Internet. MP3 文件[檔案], 動態影像專家壓縮標準音頻層面 3 文件[檔案]〔一種壓縮的音樂檔案〕

MP3 play·er /ˌɛm pi ˋθri ˌpleɚ; ˌem piː ˈθriː ˌpleɪə/ *n* [C]
a piece of electronic equipment or computer SOFTWARE that allows you to play and listen to MP3 FILE*s* MP3 播放機[播放軟件]

MPEG /ˋɛm ˌpɛg; ˈem ˌpeg/ *n* [U]
Motion Picture Expert Group; a way in which sound and VIDEO material can be presented on the Internet 動態影像專家小組壓縮標準〔一種網上音頻及影像壓縮技術〕

MRI /ˌɛm ɑr ˋaɪ; ˌem ɑːr ˈaɪ/ *n* [C,U]
technical magnetic resonance imaging; a way of producing a picture of the inside of your body without cutting it open, by using radio waves and strong MAGNETIC FIELD*s*【術語】磁共振成像〔一種檢查人體內部器官的技術〕: *An MRI revealed a tear in the cartilage of his left knee.* 一張磁共振成像的片子顯示他左膝的軟骨撕裂了。

MSP /ˌɛm ɛs ˋpi; ˌem es ˈpiː/ *n* [C]
Member of the Scottish Parliament; a British politician who is a member of the Scottish Parliament 蘇格蘭議會議員

mullet /ˋmʌlɪt; ˈmʌlɪt/ *n* [C usually singular 一般用單數] *BrE*
NEW MEANING

a hairstyle for men in which the hair on the sides and top of the head is short and the hair on the back of the head is long. This style was quite common in the 1980s but is now considered unfashionable.【英】兩側短，後邊長的一種男子髮型〔20世紀80年代頗為流行〕

multi-eth·nic, multiethnic /ˌmʌltɪ ˋɛθnɪk; ˌmʌlti ˈeθnɪk/ *adj*
1 involving or including people of several different ETHNIC types 多種族的: *multi-ethnic Britain* 多種族的英國 **2 multiethnic people** *AmE* people who have parents from different races【美】混血兒〔雙親來自不同種族的人〕

multi-play·er gam·ing, multiplayer gaming /ˌmʌltɪ pleɚ ˋgemɪŋ; ˌmʌlti pleɪə ˈgemɪŋ/ *n* [U]
the playing of computer games on the Internet by more than one person at the same time, using different computers 網上多人參與的遊戲

mul·ti·plex·er /ˋmʌltɪˌplɛksɚ; ˈmʌltiˌpleksə/ *n* [C]
technical a piece of computer equipment that is used to send several electrical signals using only one connection, especially with a MODEM【術語】多路轉換器，多路復用器

mul·ti·plex·ing /ˋmʌltɪˌplɛksɪŋ; ˈmʌltiˌpleksɪŋ/ *n* [U]
technical a method used to send several electrical signals using only one connection, especially with a MODEM【術語】〔尤指通過調解器的〕多路傳輸: *Multiplexing is used to control such vehicle functions as lighting, automatic windows, and door locks.* 多路傳輸用於控制車輛的照明、自動窗和門鎖等功能。—**multiplex** *v* [I,T]

mul·ti·skill·ing /ˋmʌltɪˌskɪlɪŋ; ˈmʌltiˌskɪlɪŋ/ *n* [U]
the improvement of workers' skills so that they can do many different types of things 多技能化: *There are several training options for multiskilling in engineering firms.* 工程公司有幾套多技能化訓練方案可供選擇。

mul·ti·task, multi-task /ˋmʌltɪˌtæsk; ˈmʌltiˌtɑːsk/ *v* [I]
to do several things at the same time 同時執行多項任務: *The successful applicant for this job must be able to multitask.* 能同時執行多項任務的人才能成功申請到這個職位。—**multitasker** *n* [C]

multi-task·ing, multitasking /ˋmʌltɪ ˌtæskɪŋ; ˈmʌlti ˌtɑːskɪŋ/ *n* [U]
1 a computer's ability to do more than one job at a time〔電腦的〕多重任務處理(能力) **2** the ability to do different types of work at the same time 同時執行多項任務的能力

music des·ti·na·tion /ˋmjuzɪk dɛstəˋneʃən; ˈmjuːzɪk destɪ̵ˈneɪʃən/ *n* [C]
a type of WEBSITE on the Internet that has a lot of information about music and musicians, and through which you can buy music 音樂目的地〔介紹音樂知識並出售音樂產品的網站〕: *Clasica is the ultimate online music destination for classical music lovers.* Clasica 是古典音樂愛好者的最佳網上音樂目的地。

mu·so /ˋmjuzo; ˈmjuːzəʊ/ *n* [C] *BrE*
informal someone who plays popular music or knows a lot about it【英，非正式】流行樂師[樂迷]: *He's not just another actor turned muso.* 他並非一般轉做流行樂手的演員。| *To be a muso is a way of life.* 成為流行樂迷也是一種生活方式。

must /mʌst; mʌst/ *modal verb*
NEW MEANING
a must-see/must-do/must-read etc something that is so good, exciting, interesting etc that you think people should see it, do it, read it etc 必看／做／讀等的事物: *Rowling's latest Harry Potter book is a must-read for the kids.* 羅琳最近的一部《哈利·波特》是孩子們必讀的。

N,n

nag·ware /ˋnægˌwɛr; ˈnægweə/ *n* [U]
humorous a type of computer PROGRAM that is available free but that contains a message reminding people who use it to send their name, address, and other information to the person or company that created it so that they can use this information. This word comes from a combination of the words 'NAG' and 'SOFTWARE'.【幽默】提醒軟件〔可免費使用，但會提醒用戶給開發者發送其姓名、地址等信息的一種軟件。此詞由 nag 和 software 縮合而成〕

name /nem; neɪm/ *v*
name and shame *BrE* to publicly say that a person or a company has been responsible for something illegal or has not achieved a particular standard, so that a lot of people will know about it【英】使臭名昭著[遠揚] — **naming and shaming** *n* [U]: *The recent spate of naming and shaming of child-sex offenders has been severely criticized by the government.* 最近將大量對兒童進行性侵犯者的名字公諸於世的做法已經受到政府的嚴厲批評。

nanny cam /ˋnænɪ ˌkæm; ˈnæni ˌkæm/ *n* [C]
a small hidden VIDEO CAMERA which allows parents who are away from home to watch or record how their children are being treated by the person who is taking care of them. This word is a combination of 'NANNY', meaning a woman who takes care of children in their own home, and 'cam', which is a short form of 'camera'. 保姆攝像機〔父母在外出時用於觀察或攝錄孩子被照顧的情況，由 nanny 和 camera 的縮略形式 cam 縮合而成〕

nan·o·tech·nol·o·gy /ˋnænotɛkˌnɑlədʒɪ; ˈnænəʊtekˌnɒlədʒi/ *n* [U]
technical an area of science which involves developing and making extremely small structures【術語】納米技術

navigate /ˋnævəˌget; ˈnævɪ̵geɪt/ *v* [I,T]
NEW MEANING
to find your way around on a particular WEBSITE, or to move from one website to another 瀏覽，漫遊: *It's considered the most popular browser to navigate the Internet.* 這被認為是最受大眾歡迎的互聯網瀏覽器。| *The magazine's website is slick and easy to navigate.* 該雜誌的網站是第一流的，很容易瀏覽。

need-to-know /ˌnid tə ˋno; ˌniːd tə ˈnəʊ/ *adj*
on a need-to-know basis if information is given to people on a need-to-know basis, they are given only the details that they need at the time when they need them 在需知的基礎上: *Access to the manufacturing process is on a strictly need-to-know basis.* 得知生產工序的詳情絕對是點到即止。

negative eq·ui·ty /ˌnɛgətɪv ˋɛkwətɪ; ˌnegətɪv ˈekwɪ̵ti/ *n* [U] *BrE*
a situation in which someone's house is worth less than the amount of money they borrowed in order to buy it【英】〔抵押資產的〕負淨值，負資產

net·iquette /ˋnɛtɪkɛt; ˈnetɪket/ *n* [U]
informal the commonly accepted rules for polite behaviour when communicating with other people on the Internet【非正式】網規，網上禮儀: *Netiquette says that you don't use all capital letters in an e-mail, because that shows you are angry.* 網規說，你在電子郵件中不得全部用大寫字母，因為那樣做表示你在生氣。

net·i·zen /ˋnɛtɪzn̩; ˈnetɪzən/ *n* [C]
slang someone who uses the Internet, especially someone who uses it in a responsible way. This word comes from a combination of the words 'net', meaning 'the Internet', and 'citizen'.【俚】網民〔由 net 和 citizen 縮合而成〕: *China and India will soon have far larger numbers of netizens than any Western nation.* 中國和印度不久將會擁有大量網民，數量遠比任何一個西方國家多。

net·pre·neur /ˋnɛtprəˌnɝ; ˈnetprəˌnɜː/ also 又作 **net·re·pre·neur** /ˌnɛtrəprəˋnɝ; ˌnetrəprəˈnɜːr/ *n* [C]
informal someone who has started an Internet business. This word comes from a combination of the words 'net', meaning 'the Internet', and 'ENTREPRENEUR', which means

'a person who starts new businesses'.【非正式】網絡企業家〔由 net 和 entrepreneur 縮合而成〕

net·speak /ˋnɛtspik; 'netspi:k/ *n* [U]
the expressions, technical words, SLANG etc commonly used on the Internet 網絡用語: *a glossary of netspeak terms* 網絡術語匯編

neural com·pu·ter /ˌnjurəl kəm'pjutɚ; ˌnjʊərəl kəm'pju:tə/ *n* [C]
a computer that is designed to operate in a way similar to the human brain〔運作方式與人腦相似的〕神經電腦 —**neural computing** *n* [U]

neu·ro·in·for·mat·ics /ˋnjuroɪnfɚˌmætɪks; 'njʊərəʊɪnfəˌmætɪks/ *n* [U]
a scientific study which combines NEUROSCIENCE (=the study of the brain) and INFORMATION SCIENCE (=the collecting, storing, and arranging of information, especially using powerful computers) 神經信息學

new /nju; nju:/ *adj*
NEW MEANING
...is the new... *BrE* used to say that something is thought to be the new fashion that will replace an existing thing【英】時髦的: *Don't you know that vodka is the new water, my dear?* 我親愛的, 你難道不知道喝伏特加是最時髦的嗎? | *And grey is the new black! By which I mean – you can wear grey anywhere now and still be smart and fashionable.* 灰色取代黑色成了最時髦的顏色! 我的意思是現在你可以穿着灰色衣服到處走, 顯得那麼帥而入時。

New Age mu·sic /ˌnju ˋedʒ ˌmjuzɪk; ˌnju: 'eɪdʒ ˌmju:zɪk/ also 又作 **New Age** *n*
a type of music that is intended to help you relax and feel calm 新時代音樂

new·bie /ˋnjubɪ; 'nju:bi/ *n* [C]
informal someone who has just started doing something, especially using the Internet or computers【非正式】〔尤指互聯網或電腦的〕新手, 新用戶

new e·con·o·my /ˌnju ɪˋkɑnəmɪ; ˌnju: ɪ'kɒnəmi/ *n* [singular]
an economic system that is based on computers and modern TECHNOLOGY, and is therefore dependent on educated workers 新經濟: *As we move into a new economy, trade unions will have to reinvent themselves to stay relevant.* 我們進入了新經濟, 工會必須重新塑造自己的角色才能與時並進。| *a Washington conference on the New Economy* 討論新經濟的華盛頓會議 —**new economy** *adj: new economy methods* 新經濟的辦法

new lad /ˌnju ˋlæd; ˌnju: 'læd/ *n* [C] *BrE*
a young man whose attitudes and behaviour are a reaction to those of the NEW MAN. New lads do not feel embarrassed about enjoying traditionally male activities such as drinking too much alcohol, playing or watching sports, making rude jokes, and looking at pictures of attractive women.【英】新男青年, 新派小子

new school /ˋnju ˌskul; 'nju: ˌsku:l/ *adj* [only before noun 僅用於名詞前]
informal using new ideas in a type of music or art【非正式】新派的: *new school hip hop artists* 新派的嬉蹦族藝術家

news·group /ˋnjuzgrup; 'nju:zgru:p/ *n* [C]
a discussion group on the Internet, with a place where people with a shared interest can exchange messages〔網上的〕新聞組

new va·ri·ant CJD /ˌnju vɛrɪənt ˌsi dʒe ˋdi; ˌnju: veəriənt ˌsi: dʒeɪ 'di:/ *n* [U]
a deadly brain disease in humans that may be caused by eating BEEF that is affected by BSE 新變異型克雅病, 新變種克雅二氏病

NiCad /ˋnɪkæd; 'nɪkæd/ *n* [C]
the abbreviation of 縮寫= nickel-cadmium; a type of BATTERY that can be used in cameras and small electronic equipment. NiCad batteries can be RECHARGED. 鎳鎘電池

NIH syn·drome /ˌɛn aɪ ˋetʃ ˌsɪndrom; ˌen aɪ 'eɪtʃ ˌsɪndrəʊm/ *n*
the abbreviation of 縮寫= NOT-INVENTED-HERE SYNDROME

NiMH *n*
the abbreviation of 縮寫= nickel metal hydride; a type of BATTERY that can be used in cameras and small electronic equipment. Nickel metal hydride batteries can be RECHARGED. 鎳氫電池

no-brain·er /ˌno ˋbrenɚ; ˌnəʊ 'breɪnə/ *n* [singular]
a decision that is easy, and that you do not need to think about, used when you want to emphasize that it is really very easy 無需費腦的事: *Joining the savings plan is a no-brainer. Just do it.* 參加儲蓄計劃一點也不費神, 參加吧。

no-frills /ˌno ˋfrɪlz; ˌnəʊ 'frɪlz◂/ *adj* [only before noun 僅用於名詞前]
a no-frills product or service includes only basic features and is not of the highest possible quality 只提供必需品[服務]的, 無修飾的: *a no-frills airline* 只提供基本服務的航空公司 | *no-frills budget accommodation* 樸實無華的廉價膳宿

no-load fund /ˌno ˋlod ˌfʌnd; ˌnəʊ 'ləʊd ˌfʌnd/ *n* [C]
technical a FUND (=group of INVESTMENTS) that people can buy without having to pay any charges【術語】無負擔基金, 免佣金基金

non-tra·di·tion·al /ˌnɑn trəˋdɪʃənl; ˌnɒn trə'dɪʃənəl/ *adj* [only before noun 僅用於名詞前]
different from the way something happened or from what was considered typical in the past 非傳統的, 另類的: *older, non-traditional university students* 年歲較大的非傳統大學生 | *non-traditional workdays* 非傳統的工作日

north /nɔrθ; nɔ:θ/ *adv*
NEW MEANING
north of *AmE informal* if an amount is north of another amount, it is more than that amount【美, 非正式】比…大[多]: *To be a big player, a company must spend somewhere north of $500 million a year.* 一家公司若要成為行業裡的龍頭企業, 一年的支出肯定超過五億美元以上。

not-in·vent·ed-here syn·drome /ˌnɑt ɪnˌvɛntɪd ˋhɪr ˌsɪndrom; ˌnɒt ɪnˌventɪd 'hɪə ˌsɪndrəʊm/ *abbreviation* 縮寫為 **NIH syndrome** *n* [U]
a situation in which people in one department of a company consider new products or ideas from other departments as threats, rather than using them to make the whole company more successful 拒絕創新症候羣〔指某一部門的人視其他部門的新產品或意念為威脅, 而不加以採用, 使公司更成功〕

nu·tra·ceu·ti·cal /ˌnutrəˋsutɪkl; ˌnju:trə'sju:tɪkəl/ *n* [C]
a food or something added to food that is meant to have a good effect on health and that might help to prevent disease 保健食品, 營養食品: *a Canadian owned nutritional research company and manufacturer dedicated to setting new standards in the development of safe alternative nutraceuticals* 一家加拿大的營養研究和製造公司, 致力於為開發安全的替代性保健食品制定新標準

O,o

object /ˋɑbdʒɪkt; 'ɒbdʒɪkt/ *n* [C]
NEW MEANING
a combination of written information on a computer and instructions that act on the information, for example in the form of a document or a picture 信息單元: *object-oriented programming* 信息單元取向的程式設計 | *multimedia data objects* 多媒體數據信息單元

OCD /ˌo si ˋdi; ˌəʊ si: 'di:/ *n* [U]
obsessive compulsive disorder; a form of mental illness in which a person does the same thing again and again and cannot stop doing it, for example washing their hands many times a day 強迫症, 強迫性神經官能症〈例如潔癖〉

OCR /ˌo si ˋɑr; ˌəʊ siː ˈɑː/ *n* [U]
optical character recognition; computer software that recognizes letters of the alphabet, so that you can put paper documents onto a computer 光字符識別(軟件)

off-mes·sage /ˌɔf ˋmɛsɪdʒ; ˌɒf ˈmesɪdʒ◂/ *adj, adv*
a politician who is off-message says things that are different from the ideas and policies of the political party they belong to 與所屬政黨的思想[政策]不一致的: *I must be careful not to go off-message here!* 我必須小心不在這裡背離黨的政治策略!

OGM /ˌo dʒi ˋɛm; ˌəʊ dʒiː ˈem/ *n* [C]
outgoing message; the message that you record on your telephone and that people will hear if they telephone you and you do not answer the phone 表明已外出的電話留言

old e·con·o·my /ˋold ɪˌkɑnəmɪ; ˈəʊld ɪˌkɒnəmi/ *n* [singular]
an economic system that is based on older types of industry, such as steel, energy, and machinery 舊經濟〔以鋼鐵、能源、機械工業等為基礎的經濟體系〕: *The view that Australia has an old economy is wrong.* 認為澳大利亞擁有舊經濟的觀點是錯誤的。| *Is the Old Economy really dead?* 舊經濟真的壽終正寢了嗎? **—old economy** *adj*: *old economy practices* 舊經濟體系的慣例

old-growth /ˌold ˋgroθ; ˌəʊld ˈgrəʊθ◂/ *adj*
old-growth forest/trees/timber etc trees that have been growing in a place for a long time in an undisturbed way 原始林; 古樹; 陳年木材或木料

old-school /ˌold ˋskul; ˌəʊld ˈskuːl◂/ *adj*
old-fashioned, or relating to ideas from the past 舊式的, 老派的: *Wyclef Jean shows off some old-school dance moves in his latest video.* 威克萊夫·瓊在最近的錄像中賣弄了幾個老派的舞蹈動作。

O·les·tra /oˋlɛstrə; əʊˈlestrə/ *n* [U]
trademark an artificial substance that is similar to fat, but cannot be DIGEST*ed* by your body. It is sometimes used to make foods such as ICE CREAM.【商標】奧利斯特拉人造脂肪〔一種脂肪的代替物〕

online auc·tion /ˌɑnlaɪn ˋɔkʃən; ˌɒnlaɪn ˈɔːkʃən/ *n* [C]
a type of WEBSITE in which you can sell things to the person who offers you the highest price 網上拍賣: *We are the premier online auction site with more items and categories than any other.* 我們是首屈一指的網上拍賣站, 拍賣的物品最多, 種類也最多。

online bank·ing /ˌɑnlaɪn ˋbæŋkɪŋ; ˌɒnlaɪn ˈbæŋkɪŋ/ also 又作 **Internet banking** *n* [U]
a service provided by banks so that people can find out information about their bank account, pay bills etc using the Internet 網上銀行(業務): *the growth of online banking* 網上銀行業務的增長

on-mes·sage /ˌɑn ˋmɛsɪdʒ; ˌɒn ˈmesɪdʒ/ *adj, adv* [not before noun 不用於名詞前]
a politician who is on-message says things that are in agreement with the ideas of his or her political party 與所屬政黨的政策一致的: *She is a loyal supporter of the Government, and is always on-message.* 她是政府的忠實支持者, 言論總是與政府的政策保持一致。| *MPs were given every incentive to stay on-message.* 下議院議員得到各方鼓勵與所屬政黨的政策保持一致。

open /ˋopən; ˈəʊpən/ *v* [T]
NEW MEANING
to make a document or computer PROGRAM ready to use 打開, 啟動〔文件或電腦程式〕: *Click on this icon to open your File Manager.* 點擊這個圖標打開文件管理器。

open-jaw fare /ˋopən dʒɔ ˌfɛr; ˈəʊpən dʒɔː ˌfeə/ *n* [C]
the price you pay to travel on a plane, train etc when this includes travel to a place and travel back from a different place〔回程路線不同的〕雙程票價

optical char·ac·ter rec·og·ni·tion /ˌɑptɪkl̩ ˋkærɪktə rɛkəgˌnɪʃən; ˌɒptɪkəl ˈkærɪ̵ktə rekəgˌnɪʃən/ *abbreviation* 縮寫為 **OCR** *n* [U]
technical computer software that recognizes letters of the alphabet, so that you can put paper documents onto a computer【術語】光字符識別(軟件)

or·gan·o·gram /ɔrˋgænəˌgræm; ɔːˈgænəˌgræm/ *n* [C]
a chart that shows the different ranks of the people working in an organization 組織系統圖, 員工階級架構圖

OTE /ˌo ti ˋi; ˌəʊ tiː ˈiː/ *n* [U] *BrE*
on target earnings; used in advertisements for jobs to say that the person will receive the complete pay only if he or she succeeds in doing as much work or selling as many things as the employer wants them to, and will get less pay if he or she doesn't【英】〔隨工作業績浮動的〕績效收入

OTOH
a written abbreviation of 縮寫= 'on the other hand', used in E-MAIL or TEXT MESSAGE*s* on MOBILE PHONE*s* 另一方面〔電子郵件或手機短信用語〕

outlet mall /ˋaʊtlɛt ˌmɔl; ˈaʊtlet ˌmɔːl/ *n* [C] *AmE*
a large specially built area which is usually outside but still near to a town or city, where there are a lot of shops that sell popular products for less than the usual price. Outlet malls sometimes sell clothes that are no longer fashionable or products that are slightly damaged.【美】近郊購物中心, 特價商品購物中心

o·ver·class /ˋovəˌklæs; ˈəʊvəˌklɑːs/ *n* [C]
a word meaning a group of people who are powerful, or rich, or have a lot of influence 上層階層, 特權階層

oxygen bar /ˋɑksədʒən ˌbɑr; ˈɒksɪ̵dʒən ˌbɑː/ *n* [C]
a bar where you pay to breathe pure oxygen, or oxygen that has a pleasant smell, so that you can relax and have more energy 氧吧

P,p

packet /ˋpækɪt; ˈpækɪ̵t/ *n* [C]
NEW MEANING
technical a unit of electronic information sent over a computer network. When information is sent from one computer to another, it is often separated into pieces called packets in order to make it travel more quickly.【術語】數據包, 信息包

packet sniff·er /ˋpækɪt ˌsnɪfə; ˈpækɪ̵t ˌsnɪfə/ *n* [C]
technical a computer PROGRAM which helps a network to work well by checking PACKET*s* for problems【術語】數據[信息]包探測程式

page traf·fic /ˋpedʒ ˌtræfɪk; ˈpeɪdʒ ˌtræfɪk/ *n* [U]
technical the number of people who read a particular page in a magazine, newspaper etc【術語】頁面流量〔報紙、雜誌某頁的讀者人數〕

pain /pen; peɪn/ *n*
NEW MEANING
feel no pain *informal* to be drunk【非正式】喝醉了: *We saw her coming out of the club. I asked her how she was and she said, "Oh, you know, feeling no pain."* 我們看到她從夜總會出來, 我便問她身體怎麼樣, 她說, "哦, 你看, 我醉了。"

palm-sized /ˋpɑm ˌsaɪzd; ˈpɑːm ˌsaɪzd/ *adj*
palm-sized computer/PC/PDA a palm-sized computer, PC etc is small enough to fit in your hand 掌上電腦/個人電腦/個人數碼助手

pants /pænts; pænts/ *adj* [not before noun 不用於名詞前] *BrE*
slang extremely bad【英俚】極壞的, 糟透了的: *The film was pants.* 這部影片糟透了。

paradigm shift /ˋpærədaɪm ˌʃɪft; ˈpærədaɪm ˌʃɪft/ *n* [C]
an important change in which the usual way of thinking or doing something is replaced by another way of thinking or doing something 思考[做事]方式的重大改變, 根本變化

parallel da·ta que·ry /ˌpærəlɛl ˋdetə ˌkwɪrɪ; ˌpærəlel ˈdeɪtə ˌkwɪəri/ *n* [U] a system on a computer that can deal with several problems, tasks etc at the same time 並行數據查詢

parental leave /pə͵rɛntḷ ˋliv; pə͵rentl ˈliːv/ *n* [U] time that a parent is allowed to spend away from work with his or her baby 父母假，照顧子女假

pash·mi·na /pæʃˋminə; pæʃˈmiːnə/ *n* [C] a piece of soft cloth that is worn by women around their shoulders 羊絨軟披巾

pay-as-you-go /͵pe əz ju ˋgo; ͵peɪ əz jə ˈgəʊ/ *adj* [only before noun 僅用於名詞前] a pay-as-you-go MOBILE PHONE or Internet service is one that you must pay for before you can use it. You use the service until the moment when the time you have used has cost the same as the amount of money you paid. 預付多少用多少的，需先付費才能使用的〔流動電話、網上服務等〕

pay-per-view /͵pe pɚ ˋvju; ͵peɪ pə ˈvjuː/ *adj* [only before noun 僅用於名詞前] a pay-per-view television CHANNEL makes people pay for each programme they watch〔電視節目〕按次付費的 — **pay-per-view** *n* [U]: *The game is only being shown on pay-per-view.* 這場比賽只在按次付費節目中播出。

pay TV /ˋpe ti ͵vi; ˈpeɪ tiː ͵viː/ also 又作 **pay tel·e·vi·sion** /ˋpe ͵tɛləvɪʒən; ˈpeɪ ͵telɨvɪʒən/ *n* [U] television CHANNEL*s* that you must pay to watch 收費電視

PC Card /͵pi ˋsi ͵kɑrd; ͵piː ˈsiː ͵kɑːd/ *n* [C] *trademark* Personal Computer Card; a small flat object which stores information that can be added to some computers【商標】PC 卡，個人電腦界面卡

PCP /͵pi si ˋpi; ͵piː siː ˈpiː/ *n* [C] *AmE*

NEW MEANING

primary care physician; a doctor you go to when you are ill, who may treat you or advise you to see a SPECIALIST (=a doctor who deals with a particular part of the body)【美】初級保健醫師，普通科醫生

PCS /͵pi si ˋɛs; ͵piː siː ˈes/ *n* [U] personal communications service; a communication system that allows MOBILE PHONE*s* to communicate with each other 個人通訊服務

PDA /͵pi di ˋe; ͵piː diː ˈeɪ/ *n* [C] personal digital assistant; a very small, light computer that you can carry with you, and that you use to store information such as telephone numbers, addresses, and APPOINTMENT*s*. Some personal digital assistants can send and receive E-MAIL, and connect to the Internet. 個人數碼助手

PDF /͵pi di ˋɛf; ͵piː diː ˈef/ *n* [U] portable document format; a way of storing computer FILE*s* so that they can be easily read when they are moved from one computer to another 可攜式文件格式

pear-shaped /ˋpɛr ͵ʃept; ˈpeə ͵ʃeɪpt/ *adj*

NEW MEANING

go pear-shaped *BrE slang* if a situation goes pear-shaped, it fails completely or develops in a way that you do not want【英俚】一敗塗地，不如意: *I told him not to borrow so much money, but he wouldn't listen, and now it's all gone pear-shaped.* 我對他說過別借那麼多錢，可他就是不聽，現在甚麼都完了。

peep /pip; piːp/ *v* [T]

NEW MEANING

slang to look at something because it is interesting or attractive【俚】瞧，觀看: *On our website you can peep our video interview with R&B's newest supergroup.* 在我們的網站，你可以觀賞我們對節奏怨曲的最新超級樂隊所進行的採訪錄像。

peer-to-peer /͵pɪr tə ˋpɪr; ͵pɪə tə ˈpɪə/ also 又作 **P2P** /͵pi tə ˋpi; ͵piː tə ˈpiː/ *adj* [only before noun 僅用於名詞前] **peer-to-peer architecture/network/technology etc** a computer system etc in which all of the computers are connected to each other and they do not need a SERVER (=a main computer that controls all the others). Peer-to-peer networks are simpler and less expensive than CLIENT-SERVER NETWORKS, but they usually can only work well when a small number of computers are in the network〔電腦網絡上〕對等的架構/網絡/技術等: *Setting up a peer-to-peer network is not difficult.* 建立對等網絡並不困難。| *How will peer-to-peer technology be important to the average Internet user?* 對等技術對互聯網一般用戶有甚麼重要性?

performance en·han·cer /pɚˋfɔrməns ɪn͵hænsɚ; pəˈfɔːməns ɪn͵hɑːnsə/ also 又作 **enhancer** *n* [C] a drug used illegally by people competing in sports events to improve their performance 興奮劑: *Officials will be testing for the performance enhancer EPO at this year's Olympic Games.* 今年奧運會上官員們將對興奮劑 EPO〔紅細胞生成素〕進行檢測。—**performance-enhancing** *adj* [only before noun 僅用於名詞前]: *performance-enhancing drugs* 興奮劑類藥物

personal com·mu·ni·ca·tor /ˋpɝsṇḷ kəˋmjunəketɚ; ˈpɜːsənəl kəˈmjuːnɨkeɪtə/ *n* [C] a small computer that you can carry with you and use to send, store, and receive FAX*ed*, spoken, or written messages 個人通訊器

personal da·ta or·ga·niz·er /͵pɝsṇḷ ˋdetə ͵ɔrgənaɪzɚ; ͵pɜːsənəl ˈdeɪtə ͵ɔːgənaɪzə/ *n* [C] a personal digital assistant 個人信息整理器，個人數碼助理

personal di·gi·tal as·sis·tant /͵pɝsṇḷ ͵dɪdʒətḷ əˋsɪstənt; ͵pɜːsənəl ͵dɪdʒɨtl əˈsɪstənt/ *abbreviation* 縮寫為 **PDA** *n* [C] a very small light computer that you can carry with you, and that you use to store information such as telephone numbers, addresses, and APPOINTMENT*s*. Some personal digital assistants can send and receive E-MAIL, and connect to the Internet 個人數碼助理，電子記事簿: *This site will help you choose the right PDA.* 本網站會幫助你挑選合適的電子記事簿。

personal electronic devices
個人電子器材

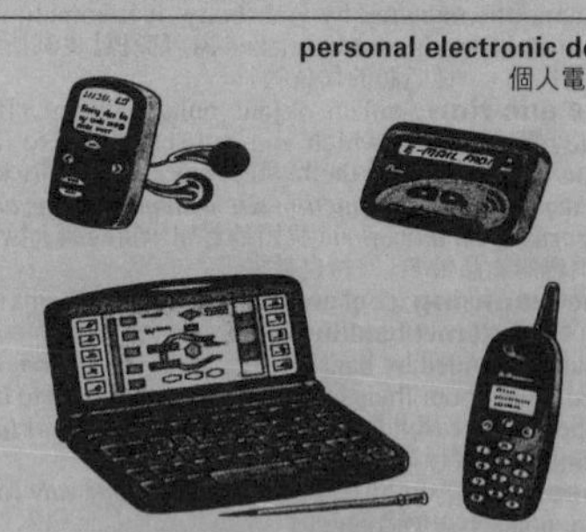

personal el·ec·tron·ic de·vice /͵pɝsṇḷ ɪlɛk͵trɑnɪk dɪˋvaɪs; ͵pɜːsənəl ɪlek͵trɒnɪk dɪˈvaɪs/ *n* [C] a piece of electronic equipment, such as a LAPTOP computer or a MOBILE PHONE, that is small and easy to carry 個人電子器材

personal shop·per /͵pɝsṇḷ ˋʃɑpɚ; ͵pɜːsənəl ˈʃɒpə/ *n* [C] someone whose job is to help people decide what to buy, or to go shopping for them 個人購物助理

personal train·er /͵pɝsṇḷ ˋtrenɚ; ͵pɜːsənəl ˈtreɪnə/ *n* [C] someone whose job is to help people decide what type of exercise is best for them and show them how to do it 個人健身教練: *He works out every day with his personal trainer.* 他每天和自己的健身教練一起鍛鍊。

pet·a·flop /ˋpɛtə͵flɑp; ˈpetə͵flɒp/ *n* [C usually plural 一般用複數] a unit that measures how fast a computer works. One petaflop is one million BILLION operations every second.

每秒 10[15] 次〔浮點運算〕

PET scan /ˋpɛt ˏskæn; ˈpet ˌskæn/ *n* [C]
technical positron emission tomography scan; a type of medical test that can produce a picture of areas in your body where cells are very active, for example the brain or where a TUMOUR is growing【術語】正子造影〔一種醫學掃描法〕: *Two people with different levels of intelligence were given PET scans to measure their brain activity while they worked on a difficult problem.* 兩個智力水平不同的人接受了正子造影，測定他們在解決一道難題時的大腦活動情況。

phantom pro·mo·tion /ˌfæntəm prəˋmoʃən; ˌfæntəm prəˈməʊʃən/ *n* [C]
a move to a new job in the same company that does not pay better or include more responsibility than the previous job, even though it appears to 假晉升

phat /fæt; fæt/ also 又作 **phat-ass** /ˋfæt ˏæs; ˈfæt ˌæs/ *adj AmE*
slang fashionable, attractive, or desirable【美俚】時髦的，酷的，稱心的: *a phat song* 流行的歌 | *These shoes are just so phat.* 這些鞋子真酷。

phe·nom /fɪˋnɑm; fɪˈnɒm/ *n* [C] *AmE*
informal someone who is unusual and impressive because they are very good or successful at something【美，非正式】傑出人才，奇才: *an 18-year-old tennis phenom* 一名 18 歲的網球奇才

phone sex /ˋfon ˏsɛks; ˈfəʊn ˌseks/ *n* [U]
the activity of talking with someone on the telephone about sex in order to become sexually excited 電話性愛: **have phone sex (with sb)** *She claimed the relationship consisted mainly of him calling her up to have phone sex.* 她聲稱同他的關係主要由他打電話來進行電話性愛。

phone tree /ˋfon ˏtri; ˈfəʊn ˌtriː/ *n* [C]
informal a list of all the telephone numbers of the people in an organization, the workers in a company etc, showing who should call whom if there is important information that everyone should know【非正式】電話樹，通訊錄

piece /pis; piːs/ *n* [C]
NEW MEANING
spoken humorous **sb's a (real) piece of work** used to say that someone behaves in an unusual or strange way, especially when this is annoying or difficult to deal with【口，幽默】某人真怪

piercing /ˋpɪrsɪŋ; ˈpɪəsɪŋ/ *n* [C,U]
the process of putting holes in different parts of your body, so that you can wear jewellery, or the holes produced in this way〔為懸掛珠寶飾物而在身體某個部位〕穿孔: *people with multiple piercings* 身上有多個穿孔的人

pik·ey /ˋpaɪkɪ; ˈpaɪki/ *n* [C] *BrE*
a disapproving word for someone who is uneducated and does not have much money【英】低教育及低收入人士〔含貶義〕

Pi·la·tes /pɪˋlɑtɪz; pɪˈlɑːtiz/ *n* [U]
a type of exercise that is based on YOGA and dance, that you do with special equipment, that makes you push, pull, and stretch, so that your body moves more easily and becomes stronger 佩拉梯茲操〔瑜伽式健身操〕: *The YMCA is offering Pilates classes.* 男青年會開辦佩拉梯茲操課程。| *Pilates is offered in health clubs and independent studios.* 健身俱樂部和獨立的排舞室都開設有佩拉梯茲操課程。

pink pound /ˌpɪŋk ˋpaʊnd; ˌpɪŋk ˈpaʊnd/ *n* [singular] *BrE*
the money that people who are HOMOSEXUAL have available to spend【英】〔代表同性戀者購買力的〕粉紅英鎊: *Companies are trying to attract the pink pound.* 各公司力圖吸引粉紅英鎊。

pink slip par·ty /ˌpɪŋk ˋslɪp ˏpɑrtɪ; ˌpɪŋk ˈslɪp ˌpɑːti/ *n* [C] *AmE*
a meeting in a bar where people who have recently lost their jobs get together to talk to each other and help each other find a new job【美】〔酒吧中的〕新失業者聚會: *Judging by the general flow of conversation, most of the pink slip party attendees want to stay in the dot-com world.* 根據交談中總的趨勢，參加新失業者聚會的大多數人仍然想留在科網圈裡。

pix·el·at·ed, pixellated /ˋpɪksəletɪd; ˈpɪksəleɪtɪd/ *adj*
consisting of PIXELS (=small spots that combine to form a picture on a computer SCREEN) 像素化的: *pixelated photographs* 像素化照片

plateau /plæˋto; ˈplætəʊ/ *v* [I]
if something plateaus, it reaches and then stays at a particular level 達到並保持一定的水平: *The athletic footwear market has not yet plateaued.* 運動鞋市場還沒有達到穩定的水平。

play /ple; pleɪ/ *v* [T]
NEW MEANING
to have a sexual relationship with someone and not tell them you are having other relationships at the same time 玩弄〔異性〕: *She went postal when she found out Jez has been playing her.* 她發現傑斯一直在玩弄自己之後真的發了火。

player /ˋpleɚ; ˈpleɪə/ *n* [C]
NEW MEANING
slang a man who is good at meeting women and persuading them to have sex with him【俚】玩弄女性者

pleath·er /ˋplɛðɚ; ˈpleðə/ *n* [U]
an artificial material that looks like leather and is used to make clothes 人造革: *a pleather jean jacket* 人造革牛仔夾克〔衫〕

PLS, pls
a written abbreviation of 縮寫= 'please', used in E-MAIL or TEXT MESSAGES on MOBILE PHONES 請〔電子郵件和手機短信用語〕

plug and play /ˌplʌg ən ˋple; ˌplʌg ən ˈpleɪ/ *abbreviation* 縮寫為 **PnP** *n* [U]
the ability of a computer and a new piece of equipment to be used together as soon as they are connected 即插即用

plug-in also 又作 **plugin** /ˋplʌg ɪn; ˈplʌg ɪn/ *n* [C]
a piece of computer SOFTWARE that can be used in addition to existing software in order to make particular PROGRAMS work properly 外加軟件

point /pɔɪnt; pɔɪnt/ *n*
NEW MEANING
be on point *slang spoken* used to say that someone is correct about something, or that you agree with what they have said【俚，口】說到點子上: *Your article in last month's issue about the rising cost of CDs was on point.* 你發表在上個月期刊上那篇關於雷射唱片漲價的文章真是說到點子上了。

poison pill /ˌpɔɪzn̩ ˋpɪl; ˌpɔɪzən ˈpɪl/ *n* [C]
technical informal something in a company's financial or legal structure that is intended to make it difficult for another company to take control of it【術語，非正式】"毒丸"〔指公司為避免被兼併而給對方設置的障礙〕

pop /pɑp; pɒp/ *n BrE*
informal **take a pop at** to criticize someone in public【英，非正式】當眾指責〔某人〕: *When you play for a Premier-ship football club, you expect people to take a pop at you now and again.* 當你為足球強隊效力，你要準備時不時會有人指責你。

pop psy·chol·o·gy /ˌpɑp saɪˋkɑlədʒɪ; ˌpɒp saɪˈkɒlədʒi/ *n* [U]
ways of dealing with personal problems that are made popular on television or in books, but are not considered serious or suitable for every situation 大眾心理學

port /port; pɔːt/ *v* [T]
to move SOFTWARE from one computer system to another 移植〔軟件〕: *Can Windows applications be ported to Unix?* 能否把視窗應用軟件移植到 Unix 上？

portable /ˋportəbl̩; ˈpɔːtəbəl/ *adj*
NEW MEANING

portable benefits health insurance, PENSION PLANS etc that workers can keep when they move from one job to another〔換工作時〕可轉移的福利〈如醫療保險、退休金計劃等〉

portal /ˋpɔrtl̩; ˈpɔːtl/ *n* [C]
NEW MEANING
a WEBSITE that helps you find other websites 入門網站, 網口

port·ing /ˋpɔrtɪŋ; ˈpɔːtɪŋ/ *n* [U]
the process of moving SOFTWARE or information from one computer system to another〔軟件、信息等的〕移植: *Call in at your local store where a consultant will organise the porting of your mobile phone number to your new network.* 請與本地商店聯繫, 那裡有顧問會安排把你的手機號碼移到你的新網絡去。

posse /ˋpɑsɪ; ˈpɒsi/ *n* [C]
slang a group of friends from a particular place who share an interest in RAP, HIP-HOP, or HOUSE music, considered as a group【俚】〔同一個地區説唱樂等愛好者組成的〕幫派, 哥兒們

post[1] /post; pəʊst/ also 又作 **posting** *n* [C]
NEW MEANING
a message sent to an Internet discussion group so that all members of these groups can read it〔在互聯網上討論區發布的〕信息, 留言: *It's amusing to read post after post criticizing the Prime Minister and his views.* 看到一則又一則批評首相及其觀點的留言, 實在有趣。| *In your last posting, you mentioned something about a new project.* 在上次的留言中, 你提到了一個新項目。

post[2] /post; pəʊst/ *v* [T]
NEW MEANING
1 to officially record and announce information about a company's financial situation or a country's economy 公布〔公司財政或國家經濟情況〕: *Golden West Financial Corp. posted a 25% gain in second-quarter net income.* 科爾登西部金融公司公布第二季度純收益增長了25%。| *Shares fell after the government posted worse than expected figures on inflation.* 在政府公布了比預期還糟的通脹數字後, 股票下跌了。**2** to put a message or computer document on the Internet so that other people can see it〔在互聯網上〕發布〔電子公告〕: *Chris has already asked Matt to post those new flyers on Vivid's website.* 克里斯已要求馬特在維維特的網站上發布那些新的廣告傳單。

postal /ˋpostl̩; ˈpəʊstl/ *adj*
NEW MEANING
go postal *AmE slang* to become very angry and behave in a violent way【美俚】怒不可遏

posting /ˋpostɪŋ; ˈpəʊstɪŋ/ also 又作 **post** *n* [C]
NEW MEANING
a message sent to an Internet discussion group so that all members of these groups can read it〔在互聯網上討論區發布的〕消息

post-mod·ern /ˌpost ˋmɑdən; ˌpəʊst ˈmɒdn◂/ *adj*
used to describe styles and attitudes that are IRONIC and that are not serious in the way they treat the ideas and beliefs that a lot of people have 後現代的: *They might be a bit young for post-modern, ironic stand-up comedy.* 要表演後現代諷刺滑稽説笑喜劇, 他們也許還有點嫩。

POTS /pɑts; pɒts/ *n* [singular]
informal plain old telephone service; the ordinary form of telephone services, rather than newer services such as the Internet【非正式】普通電話服務

power /ˋpauə; ˈpaʊə/ *v*
power sth ↔ **up** *phr v* [T] to make a machine start working 啟動, 開動: *Never move a computer while it is powered up.* 電腦在操作時不可搬動。

power-brok·ing /ˋpauə ˌbrokɪŋ; ˈpaʊə ˌbrəʊkɪŋ/ *n* [U]
the use of political power or influence, sometimes in an unfair way 政治權力運用: *an article about Washington power-broking in the 1990s* 一篇關於華盛頓在20世紀90年代政壇角力的文章 —**power broker** *n* [C]

power-nap /ˋpauə ˌnæp; ˈpaʊə ˌnæp/ *n* [C]
a short sleep in the middle of the day that helps you to have more energy, do your job better, and make better decisions〔恢復精力的〕午間小睡: *A power-nap lasts no longer than 20 minutes.* 午間小睡一般不超過20分鐘。—**power nap** *v* [I]: *Never power nap on your bed.* 不要在牀上打盹。

power-shar·ing /ˋpauə ˌʃɛrɪŋ; ˈpaʊə ˌʃeərɪŋ/ *n* [U]
a situation in which two or more people or groups run a government together 權力分享〔兩個或以上的人[組織]共同執政〕—**power-sharing** *adj* [only before noun 僅用於名詞前] *a power-sharing arrangement* 權力分享的安排

PPO /ˌpi pi ˋo; ˌpiː piː ˈəʊ/ *n* [U]
preferred provider organization; a type of health insurance in which people can go to any hospital or doctor, but the insurance company pays more to hospitals and doctors in their system than to those outside their system 優先提供者組織〔一種醫療保險〕

PPP /ˌpi pi ˋpi; ˌpiː piː ˈpiː/ *n*
1 *technical* point-to-point protocol; the information that your computer gives to an INTERNET SERVICE PROVIDER using the telephone line, so that you can connect your computer with them and use the Internet, send E-MAIL etc【術語】點對點協定 **2** [U] public-private partnership; a system of providing money for transport systems, hospitals, schools etc where the government pays some money and private INVESTORs provide the rest of the money 公私聯營

prairie-dog·ging /ˋprɛrɪ ˌdɔgɪŋ; ˈpreəri ˌdɒgɪŋ/ *n* [U]
humorous the activity of standing up in an office CUBICLE in order to look over the top of the short walls to see what is happening in the rest of the office. This word comes from PRAIRIE DOG (=a small American animal that lives in a hole in the ground) and describes a similarity to the way this animal comes out of its hole and stands up on its back legs to look for danger.【幽默】〔辦公室內〕隔着擋板站起來窺視

pre-but·tal /prɪˋbʌtl̩; prɪˈbʌtl/ *n* [C]
a statement that a politician makes saying that a criticism of them is false or unfair, before the criticism has been made〔針對政壇對手提出批評的〕預先駁斥: *Stark issued a prebuttal against his opponent's speech, even before the text was delivered to reporters.* 在對手連演講辭也未發放給記者前, 斯塔克已先發制人, 發表了反駁聲明。

predatory lend·ing /ˌprɛdətɔrɪ ˋlɛndɪŋ; ˌpredətərɪ ˈlendɪŋ/ *n* [U]
the use of unfair practices by banks, especially taking away people's homes, cars etc if they cannot pay back money they have borrowed 掠奪性貸款: *legislation designed to combat predatory lending* 針對掠奪性貸款的法規 —**predatory lender** *n* [C]

predict and pro·vide /prɪˌdɪkt ən prəˋvaɪd; prɪˌdɪkt ən prəˈvaɪd/ *n* [U] *BrE*
a way of planning things such as new roads by guessing the rate of increase in the number of vehicles using the roads, and building more roads to make sure there is enough space for all of them【英】超前規劃〔基於未來需求量而作出規劃〕—compare 比較 DEMAND MANAGEMENT

pre-loved /ˌpri ˋlʌvd; ˌpriː ˈlʌvd/ *adj*
a pre-loved house, pet etc has already been owned by someone else; used especially in advertisements to suggest the previous owner cared strongly about the object, animal etc〔尤用於廣告中, 表示某物、動物等〕曾被細心照料的: *The Animal Network helps place pre-loved pets with new pet guardians.* 動物網幫助失去關愛的寵物, 為牠們找新的保護人。

premium rate /ˌprimɪəm ˋret; ˌpriːmiəm ˈreɪt◂/ *n*
premium rate number/line/service a telephone connection to a particular service or company that costs a

lot more than the usual rate when you call it because the company you are calling takes some of the money that you pay for the call 高價電話號碼/線路/服務〔致電某公司需付出高昂電話費，因該公司從中圖利〕: *Companies who advertise misleading job vacancies using premium rate telephone lines are now facing a total ban.* 刊登不確招聘啟事的公司使用高價電話線路以從中圖利的做法現正面臨全面取締。

prenuptial a·gree·ment /pri`nʌpʃəl ə`grimənt; priːˌnʌpʃəl əˈgriːmənt/ also 又作 **prenup** /`prinʌp; ˈpriːnʌp/ *n* [C]
a legal document that is written before a man and a woman get married, in which they agree things such as how much money each will get if they DIVORCE 婚前協議

pre-owned /ˌpri `ond; ˌpriː ˈəʊnd◂/ *adj*
if something that is for sale is pre-owned, it has been owned and used by someone else before; SECOND-HAND. People use this word when they want to make something not sound old 二手(貨)的: *Pre-owned cars may still come with a warranty.* 二手車可能仍然有保單。

pre-pay /`pri ˌpe; ˈpriː ˌpeɪ/ *adj* [only before noun 僅用於名詞前]
pre-pay MOBILE PHONE systems make you pay before you use the service, rather than sending you a demand for money after you have been using the service〔流動電話〕預先付款的

pres·en·tee·ism /ˌprɛzən`tiɪzəm; ˌprezənˈtiːɪzəm/ *n* [U]
a situation when people spend a lot of time at work, even if they are ill or could take a holiday, because they want their employers to see that they are working very hard. This word developed from 'ABSENTEEISM', which means 'absences from work without a good reason'.〔為討好雇主而〕故意加班

pri·on /`praɪən; ˈpraɪɒn/ *n* [C]
a very small piece of PROTEIN that is thought to cause some infectious brain diseases such as BSE 朊病毒，普利航毒蛋白〔據認為引起瘋牛病等一些傳染性腦疾病的蛋白質〕

probs /prɑbz; prɒbz/ *n BrE*
spoken informal **no probs** used to say that you will be able to do something easily and with no problems【英口，非正式】沒問題: *Don't worry. We'll have it ready by six. No probs.* 別擔心，我們在六點之前就會準備好，不成問題的。

product place·ment /`prɑdəkt ˌplesmənt; ˈprɒdʌkt ˌpleɪsmənt/ *n* [U]
a form of advertising in which a company arranges for one or more of its products to appear in a television programme or a film 產品安插[在電視節目或電影中使產品出現的一種廣告形式]: *Does product placement have an effect on sales?* 產品安插對銷售起作用嗎？

pro·fil·ing /`profaɪlɪŋ; ˈprəʊfaɪlɪŋ/ *n* [U]
NEW MEANING
1 the way in which some police organizations stop people from particular races or other groups in society in order to ask them questions, search them etc, because they think that people in those groups are more likely to be involved in crimes or do bad things 種族[階級]定性〔有些警察因認為某類人較可能會犯罪或做壞事而截查他們〕 **2** the activity of collecting information about people that you wish to sell something to. Companies do this in order to make their ADVERTISING more effective. 顧客資料分析

prop² /prɑp; prɒp/ *n*
NEW MEANING
give props to sb also 又作 **give sb props** *AmE slang* to tell someone, or people in general, that someone has done something well or that you admire them【美俚】稱讚某人: *I just want to give all you girls props for going out and showing you can be just as good as us guys.* 姑娘們，你們出去並證明了你們和我們男孩一樣出色，我要向你們致敬。

proxy serv·er /`prɑksɪ ˌsɝvɚ; ˈprɒksi ˌsɜːvə/ *n* [C]
technical a powerful computer which helps a SERVER (=main computer on a network) operate a computer network【術語】代理伺服器

Pro·zac /`prozæk; ˈprəʊzæk/ *n* [U]
trademark a type of drug used for treating DEPRESSION (=when you feel very unhappy) and ANXIETY (=when you feel very worried). Prozac makes people feel happier, but some doctors worry that people may take it instead of trying to deal with their problems【商標】百憂解〔一種治療情緒抑鬱的藥〕: **be on Prozac** *Ben's been on Prozac for over a year.* 班服用百憂解有一年多了。

psychic in·come /ˌsaɪkɪk `ɪnkʌm; ˌsaɪkɪk ˈɪŋkʌm/ *n* [U]
the feeling of satisfaction, power, importance etc that you get from your job 精神收益〈如工作上得到的滿足感、權力等〉

pull·back /`pulbæk; ˈpʊlbæk/ *n* [C]
1 the act of moving soldiers away from the area where they were fighting 撤兵: **[+from]** *The government is planning to implement a second pullback from the area.* 政府正計劃從該地區第二次撤兵。 **2** a reduction in the value, amount or level of something 縮小，降低: *Don't be surprised if this spring or summer you see a significant pullback in the stock market.* 要是這個春季或夏季看到股票市場有明顯的資金撤走，不要感到驚訝。

pull-down men·u /`pul daun ˌmɛnju; ˈpʊl daʊn ˌmenjuː/ *n* [C]
a list of things a computer PROGRAM can do. You make a pull-down menu appear on the computer SCREEN by CLICKing on a special word with a MOUSE.〔電腦〕下拉式選單

pull strat·e·gy /`pul ˌstrætədʒɪ; ˈpʊl ˌstrætɪdʒi/ *n* [C,U]
a method of selling goods, in which a company uses advertising, letters etc to make people want the goods, so that people will ask for the goods at a store and the store will ask the company for the goods to be sold "拉顧客"促銷法，拉式策略〔一家公司利用廣告、信件等推銷商品，有人向店鋪查詢，店鋪就向該公司取貨售賣〕

pulse /pʌls; pʌls/ *v* [I,T]
NEW MEANING
to push a button on a FOOD PROCESSOR to make the machine go on and off regularly, rather than work continuously〔按動食品攪拌器上的按鈕〕使有規律地開機、停機: *Pulse several times until the mixture looks like oatmeal.* 將混合物用食品攪拌器有規律地攪拌幾次直到它看上去像燕麥糊那樣。

pump /pʌmp; pʌmp/ *v*
pump and dump the act of raising the price of STOCKs that are not worth very much money by buying a large amount of them when they are still cheap, and then selling them at a profit 先買後拋，低買高沽，推高出貨〔通過大量買進股票引起漲價後再拋出〕

pump-prim·ing /`pʌmp ˌpraɪmɪŋ; ˈpʌmp ˌpraɪmɪŋ/ *n* [U]
the process of trying to help a business, industry, or economy to develop by giving it money〔幫助企業、行業或經濟發展的〕注入性投資，資金扶植

push strat·e·gy /`puʃ ˌstrætədʒɪ; ˈpʊʃ ˌstrætɪdʒi/ *n* [C,U]
a method of selling goods in which a company tries to make stores want to have the goods, for example by selling them to the stores for a much lower price than usual〔公司吸引商店購買其商品的〕減價促銷法，推式策略

push tech·nol·o·gy /`puʃ tɛkˌnɑlədʒɪ; ˈpʊʃ tekˌnɒlədʒi/ *n* [U]
a system that allows information to be sent regularly over the Internet to people who have asked to receive it〔網上〕推送技術〔定期傳送信息給要求收到該信息的人〕

pussy-whipped /`pusɪ ˌhwɪpt; ˈpʊsi ˌwɪpt/ *adj* [not before noun 不用於名詞前] *AmE slang* an offensive word used to describe a man who does whatever his GIRLFRIEND or wife wants him to do. This expression is used to criticize someone for allowing himself to be treated like this.【美俚】〔冒犯語〕怕老婆的, 受女人支配的

Q,q

QALY /ˌkju e ɛl ˋwaɪ; ˌkjuː eɪ el ˈwaɪ/ *n* [C] *technical* quality adjusted life year; a way of measuring how much improvement in their health someone is likely to get as a result of having a particular type of medical treatment in the National Health Service in Britain【術語】〔英國國民保健制度中的〕療效檢查, 質量調整生命年

Q-rat·ing /ˋkju ˌretɪŋ; ˈkjuː ˌreɪtɪŋ/ *n* [C] *AmE* a way of describing how well known by the public someone is【美】受歡迎程度, 知名度: *His Q-rating increased after he landed a role in a sit-com.* 他在情景喜劇中擔任一個角色之後, 人氣指數有所上升。

quad bike /ˋkwɑd ˌbaɪk; ˈkwɒd ˌbaɪk/ *n* [C] *BrE* a small vehicle, similar to a MOTORCYCLE but with four wide wheels, usually ridden on rough paths or fields【英】四輪摩托車; FOUR WHEELER *AmE*【美】

queer·core /ˋkwɪrˌkɔr; ˈkwɪəˌkɔː/ *n* [U] *slang* a type of loud fast music performed by musicians who are HOMOSEXUAL【俚】同志朋克核心〔一種由同性戀者演奏的強勁的音樂〕

quotient /ˋkwoʃənt; ˈkwəʊʃənt/ *n* [C]
NEW MEANING
the amount or degree of a quality, feeling etc in a person, thing, or situation 商〈如智商、情緒商數等〉, 指數: *Is all this healthy food supposed to increase my happiness quotient?* 是不是所有這些保健食品都會增加我的幸福指數?

R,r

race-bait·ing /ˋres ˌbetɪŋ; ˈreɪs ˌbeɪtɪŋ/ *n* [U] the process of using pictures or words that make people afraid of or not trust people of another race, especially in order to gain a political advantage 種族挑撥: *The campaign has been marked by accusations of race-baiting.* 該次競選因被指責帶有種族挑撥成分而蒙上了污點。— **race-bait** *v* [I,T] —**race-baiter** *n* [C]

race card /ˋres ˌkɑrd; ˈreɪs ˌkɑːd/ *n*
NEW MEANING
play the race card if a politician plays the race card, he or she says or writes something which is unfair towards people from a different race, often to try and convince other people to vote for them 打種族牌: *But the leader of the opposition denied that he had been playing the race card, and insisted that his comments had been taken out of context.* 但反對黨的領導人否認他在打種族牌, 並堅稱他的評論被斷章取義了。

rad /ræd; ræd/ *adj* *slang* exciting or interesting【俚】頂呱呱的, 棒極的: *Have you guys seen Wendy's new place? It's so rad.* 你們幾個見過溫迪的新居沒有? 棒極了。

ra·dic·chi·o /rəˋdikɪo; rəˈdɪkiəʊ/ *n* [U] a type of plant used in SALADS that is red and has a bitter taste 菊苣〔做沙拉用的一種菜〕

-rage /redʒ; reɪdʒ/ *suffix* [in nouns 構成名詞] used to describe the particular situations in which people become extremely angry and violent. For example, road-rage is when someone becomes angry and violent because of something that happens while they are driving; air-rage happens when a passenger in a plane becomes angry and violent etc. 盛怒, 暴怒〔發作〕〈如 road-rage 路上駕車狂怒, air-rage 飛行途中狂怒等〉

rail trail /ˋrel ˌtrel; ˈreɪl ˌtreɪl/ *n* [C] *AmE* a path that used to be a railway track but has been covered with a hard-surface for people to walk, run, or ride bicycles on【美】〔鋪設硬路面因而讓人可以通行或騎車的〕鐵軌路

ramp /ræmp; ræmp/ *v*
ramp sth ↔ **up** *phr v* [T] **1** to try to persuade people that a company's SHARES are worth more than they really are 推高〔公司股票價格〕: *To ramp up a share price during a takeover bid is unacceptable.* 在出價收購期間推高股票的價格是不能接受的。**2** if a company ramps up an activity, it increases it 增加〔某種活動〕: *Producers can quickly ramp up production to prevent any shortages.* 製造商可以迅速增加生產以防止缺貨。

rat /ræt; ræt/ *v*
rat sb **out** [T] *AmE informal* to be disloyal to someone, especially by telling a person in authority about something wrong that he or she has done【美, 非正式】背信棄義: *You can't rat out your teammates.* 你不可以出賣你的隊友。

rat run /ˋræt ˌrʌn; ˈræt ˌrʌn/ *n* [C] a small road, often with houses along it, which is used by drivers as a quicker way of going somewhere, instead of using a larger road which has more traffic 住宅區小路, 捷徑

real /ˋriəl; rɪəl/ *adj*
NEW MEANING
keep it real *AmE spoken* used to tell someone to behave in an honest way and not pretend to be different from how they really are【美口】〔老實點〕別裝蒜

reality check /rɪˋælətɪ ˌtʃɛk; riˈælə̦ti ˌtʃek/ *n* [C usually singular 一般用單數] *informal* an occasion when you consider the facts of a situation, as opposed to what you would like or what you have imagined【非正式】面對現實: *It's time for a reality check. The Bears aren't as good a team as you think.* 該是面對現實的時候了, 熊隊不像你想像的那麼優秀。

reality soft·ware /rɪˋælətɪ ˌsɔftwɛr; riˈælə̦ti ˌsɒftweə/ *n* [U] *technical* computer PROGRAMS that allow you to show pictures on a screen that have height, depth, and length, so that you seem to see or be inside a real place【術語】現實仿真軟件

re-chip /ˌri ˋtʃɪp; ˌriː ˈtʃɪp/ *v* [T] to put a new computer CHIP into a piece of electronic equipment such as a MOBILE PHONE or a computer games CONSOLE so that you can use SOFTWARE that you are not supposed to use, or use a service that you have not paid for 給…裝上新的芯[晶]片

red goods /ˋrɛd ˌgudz; ˈred ˌgʊdz/ *n* [plural] goods such as food that people use quickly after buying them, and that do not make a lot of profit〔低利潤、消耗快的〕大路貨, 消耗品

red-line /ˌrɛd ˋlaɪn; ˌred ˈlaɪn◂/ *adj* **red-line issue** something that you want to do, or that you want to happen, and that you continue to want even when someone offers you something else instead; used especially when people are involved in political or business NEGOTIATIONS〔尤用於政治或商業談判中〕堅持不懈追求的目標, 堅定的方針: *Keeping the pound is a red-line issue as far as this party is concerned.* 就此黨而言, 繼續使用英鎊是其始終堅持的目標。

red-top /ˋrɛd ˌtɑp; ˈred ˌtɒp/ *n* [C] *BrE informal* a British newspaper that has its name in red at the top of the front page. Red tops have a lot of readers, but are not considered to be as serious as other newspapers.【英, 非正式】通俗小報〔因其頭版頂端的報紙名稱套紅刊印而得名〕

re·for·mat /riˋfɔrmæt; riːˈfɔːmæt/ **reformatted, reformatting** *v* [T] if you reformat a document, you change the way it is organized or arranged, for example the amount of space between lines 使〔文件〕重新格式化: *The books will be* *condensed and reformatted for electronic reading.* 這些書將被壓縮並重新格式化以供電子閱讀。

re·home /ri`hom; riː'həʊm/ *v* [T]
to arrange for a pet to have a new owner and home, especially a pet that has been looked after in a SHELTER 安排重新收養〔寵物〕，為〔寵物〕找尋新家：*The kittens have been rehomed.* 小貓已經被重新收養。| *We thought it would be difficult to rehome a maimed animal.* 我們以為為傷殘動物尋找新家會很困難。

rei·ki /`rekɪ; 'reɪki/ *n* [U]
a type of medicine of Japanese origin in which a person touches someone who has a mental or a physical illness in order to make them more healthy 靈氣〔源自日本的一種接觸療法〕：*I can't come on Thursday. That's the night I see my reiki healer.* 我星期四來不了，正好那天晚上我要看靈氣醫師。

re-look, relook /ri`lʊk; riː'lʊk/ *v* [I+at]
to consider something for a second time after you have already considered it 再考慮：*I think we should relook at John's proposal for car parking restrictions outside.* 我認為我們應重新考慮約翰提出的關於限制在戶外停車的建議。—**relook** /`rilʊk; 'riːlʊk/ *n* [C]: *The ministry ordered a relook at the contract.* 部長命令對該合約再作一次審查。

remote ac·cess /rɪˌmot `æksɛs; rɪˌməʊt 'ækses/ *n* [U]
a system that allows you to use information on a computer that is far away from your computer〔電腦的〕遙距存取

remote in·ter·ro·ga·tion /rɪˌmot ɪntɛrə`geʃən; rɪˌməʊt ɪnterə'geʃən/ *n* [U]
the process of calling your own telephone when you are away from your home or office so that you can listen to messages that people have left on your ANSWERPHONE 遠程電話留言查詢

remote work·ing /rɪˌmot `wɝkɪŋ; rɪˌməʊt 'wɜːkɪŋ/ *n* [U]
a situation in which people do their work at home, using a computer that is connected to the computer system in an office 遠程工作〔通過與辦公室的電腦聯網在家裡工作〕

rep /rɛp; rep/ *v*
slang【俚】**1** [T] to be someone's representative 代表〔某人〕：*It didn't take me long to realize that I wasn't very good with a camera, so I started repping other photographers.* 過不了多久我就意識到自己在攝影方面不太在行，於是我就當起了其他攝影師的代表。**2** [I] to be proud of your beliefs, your nationality, your race etc, and to make your feelings obvious to other people 自豪

re·plat·form /ri`plætfɔrm; riː'plætfɔːm/ *v* [T] *BrE*【英】
be replatformed when a train is replatformed, passengers have to go to a different part of the station than usual in order to get on it 換月台 —**replatformed** *adj*: *The replatformed 19:47 to Leeds will now leave from platform six.* 19 點 47 分開往利茲的火車將換到六號月台開車。

report /rɪ`port; rɪ'pɔːt/ *n* [C] *BrE*
NEW MEANING
someone who works for a particular manager【英】〔經理的〕下屬：*Only Gordon's direct reports are attending the training course.* 只有戈登的直系下屬會參加訓練班。

re·pur·pose /ri`pɝpəs; riː'pɜːpəs/ *v* [T]
if something such as equipment, a building, or a document is repurposed, it is used in a new way that is different from its original use, without having to be changed very much 改變用途：*We put a lot of material up on our website simply by repurposing our exising catalog and other content from our products.* 我們只是改變了一下現有的產品目錄和其他內容，就把大量的材料放上我們的網站。

rescue rem·e·dy /`rɛskju ˌrɛmədɪ; 'reskjuː ˌremədi/ *n* [C] *BrE*
an oil made from flowers that is used to make you feel calmer when you are not well or nervous【英】鎮靜藥

retail ther·a·py /ˌritel `θɛrəpɪ; ˌriːteɪl 'θerəpi/ *n* [U]
humorous the act of buying things that you do not need when you are unhappy because you think it will make you feel better【幽默】購物療法：*What you need is a bit of retail therapy!* 你需要接受一點購物治療！

re·tro·vi·rus /`rɛtroˌvaɪrəs; 'retrəʊˌvaɪərəs/ *n* [C]
a VIRUS of a type that includes some cancer viruses and the AIDS virus, but that also has a quality that makes it useful for GENETIC ENGINEERING 逆轉過濾性病毒

re-up /ri `ʌp; riː 'ʌp/ *v* [I]
informal to agree to work on something or for someone again, used especially about work in television, and film-making or sports【非正式】同意再次做…；同意為…繼續幹〔尤指電視、電影製作或運動方面〕：*Several of the actors have agreed to re-up for a sequel to the movie.* 有幾名演員已同意再為該部影片拍續集。

reverse en·gi·neering /rɪˌvɝs ɛndʒə`nɪrɪŋ; rɪˌvɜːs endʒə'nɪərɪŋ/ *n* [U]
technical a situation in which a product is examined to see how it is made, so that it can be copied【術語】倒序製造，反向工程 —**reverse engineer** *v* [T]

revolving door /rɪˌvɑlvɪŋ `dɔr; rɪˌvɒlvɪŋ 'dɔː/ *n* [singular]
NEW MEANING
1 used to say that the people involved in a situation, organization etc change often 人員流動頻繁：*The park director position has been a revolving door for seven appointees.* 公園經理這個職位已經接二連三地換了七個人。**2** used to say that people return to a situation, position etc often, but usually for a different reason 旋轉門〔指出於不同理由而屢次重返某場合或職位等〕：*This could mean that we end up with a revolving door Congress, in which former members return as lobbyists.* 這可能意味着我們的國會最後就成了一道旋轉門，一些前議員退下後又回來，搖身一變成了從事院外活動的說客。

right·size /`raɪtsaɪz; 'raɪtsaɪz/ *v* [I,T]
if a company or organization rightsizes, or if it rightsizes its operations, it reduces the number of people it employs in order to reduce costs. This word developed from 'DOWNSIZE', which has the same meaning, and is used to make the reduction in the number of workers sound good and sensible 縮小〔公司等的〕規模，精簡：*They have been given one year to rightsize their workforce.* 他們有一年時間精簡職工人數。—**rightsizing** *n* [U]: *Many aerospace workers lost their jobs as a result of rightsizing.* 航空航天部門的許多工人因裁員而失去了工作。

ring·tone /`rɪŋton; 'rɪŋtəʊn/ *n* [C]
the sound made by a telephone, especially a MOBILE PHONE, when someone is calling it〔電話，尤指手機的〕鈴聲：*Select a personal ringtone for your mobile from over 700 great tunes, including pop, rock, TV and movies.* 請從包括流行音樂、搖滾樂、電視和電影樂聲等超過 700 種樂曲中給你的手機挑選一種個人化的鈴聲。

riot grrl also 又作 **riot girl** /`raɪət ˌgɝl; 'raɪət ˌgɜːl/ *n* [C]
a young woman who believes that women should have the same rights and opportunities as men, especially one who uses music to express this belief in an angry and determined way 反叛女孩〔尤指通過用音樂等憤怒並堅決地表達其信仰的女權主義者〕

rip /rɪp; rɪp/ *v*
rip on sb/sth *phr v* [T] *AmE slang* to complain a lot about someone or something【美俚】抨擊，嚴厲批評：*Ginny's always ripping on her boss.* 金妮總是發老闆的牢騷。

ripped /rɪpt; rɪpt/ *adj*
slang having large strong-looking muscles【俚】肌肉發達的：*Fisher's sculpted, ripped physique* 費希爾雕塑一般健壯的體形 | *How can I get lean and ripped?* 我怎樣才能既清瘦又結實呢？

Rit·a·lin /ˋrɪtḷɪn; ˈrɪtəlɪn/ *n* [U]
trademark a drug that is used to treat ATTENTION DEFICIT HYPERACTIVITY DISORDER (=a condition that causes people, especially children, to be too active and not able to pay attention for very long)【商標】利他林〔一種用於治療兒童多動症的藥物〕: *Zack's parents don't want to put him on Ritalin.* 扎克的父母不想讓他服利他林。

road pric·ing /ˋrod ˌpraɪsɪŋ; ˈrəʊd ˌpraɪsɪŋ/ *n* [U]
a system in which drivers have to pay to use the roads at particular times 道路收費(制度)〔在某些時段收費以緩和交通擁堵〕: *Road pricing could fund pollution reduction projects.* 道路收費能為減輕污染項目提供資金。| *road pricing schemes for congested cities* 針對交通擁堵城市的道路收費計劃

road war·ri·or /ˋrod ˌwɔrɪɚ; ˈrəʊd ˌwɒriə/ *n* [C]
slang someone who uses computers, MOBILE PHONE*s*, PAGER*s* etc in a place other than their home or office【俚】馬路勇士〔指經常在路上奔波並使用便攜式電腦、手機、傳呼機等的人〕

roam·ing /ˋromɪŋ; ˈrəʊmɪŋ/ *n* [U]
the process that a MOBILE PHONE uses when it is in a different country or region from usual, and has to connect to a different NETWORK (手機)漫遊: *Our international roaming facility allows you to use 198 networks in 91 countries worldwide.* 我們的國際漫遊功能能讓你使用全球91個國家的198個網絡。

rock¹ /rɑk; rɒk/ *n* [U]
NEW MEANING
1 a very pure form of the illegal drug COCAINE, that some people smoke for pleasure 石毒〔結晶體可卡因〕 **2** [C] a small amount of this drug 少量石毒

rock² /rɑk; rɒk/ *v*
NEW MEANING
sb/sth rocks *slang* said to show that you strongly approve of someone or something【俚】某人/某物特別棒: *This band still rocks.* 這支樂隊仍然很棒。

rocket sci·en·tist /ˋrɑkɪt ˌsaɪəntɪst; ˈrɒkǀt ˌsaɪəntǀst/ *n* [C]
informal【非正式】**1 it doesn't take a rocket scientist** said to emphasize that something is easy to do or understand 這不需要有高深學問: *It doesn't take a rocket scientist to work out that doubling productivity will improve profits.* 生產率加倍會提高利潤, 這用不着學問高深的人也能想得到。**2** someone who is extremely clever and intelligent 特別聰明的人, 智力超常者: *Just cos my brother's a rocket scientist doesn't mean I know all the answers.* 我哥哥是天才並不等於我甚麼都懂。**3** someone working for a financial company who uses advanced mathematics to calculate what INVESTMENT*s* to make, to design new financial products etc 股市[投資]分析高手, 金融工程學家

rock 'n' roll /ˋrɑk ən ˋrol; ˌrɒk ən ˈrəʊl/ *n*
NEW MEANING
sth is the new rock 'n' roll *BrE* used to say that a particular activity has become very popular and fashionable and is being discussed a lot on television, in newspapers etc【英】非常流行和熱門的活動: *Hadn't Mark heard that cooking was the new rock 'n' roll?* 馬克難道沒有聽說烹飪是新的熱門活動嗎?

rogue trad·er /ˌrog ˋtredɚ; ˌrəʊg ˈtreɪdə/ *n* [C]
a STOCKBROKER who takes a lot of risks without permission from the company he or she works for, and who sometimes loses a lot of money and tries to hide this 無賴交易人〔未經公司授權進行風險投資而造成巨大損失的證券經紀人〕: *The Bank says a rogue trader in New York secretly racked up $1.1 billion in losses over 11 years.* 該銀行說紐約的一名違規交易人員在過去11年來私下累計造成了11億美元的虧損。

roll /rol; rəʊl/ *v*
NEW MEANING
roll sth ↔ **out** to make a new product available for people to buy or use 推出〔新產品〕: *L'Oreal rolled out a line of skin-care products called Plenitude.* 歐萊雅公司推出了一系列稱為"普蘭"的護膚新產品。

roof·ies /ˋrufɪz; ˈruːfiz/ *n* [plural] *AmE*
slang an illegal drug that is sometimes used to make someone unconscious so they can be RAPE*d*【美俚】魂飛, 迷姦藥〔一種令人失去知覺的違禁藥〕

ROTFL, rotfl
a written abbreviation of 縮寫= 'rolling on the floor laughing', used by people communicating in CHAT ROOM*s* on the Internet to say that they are laughing very hard at something that someone else has written 笑死人了〔網上聊天室用語〕

rout·er /ˋrutɚ; ˈruːtə/ *n* [C]
technical a piece of electronic equipment that makes sending messages between different computers or between different networks easier and faster【術語】路由器

RTF /ˌɑr ti ˋɛf; ˌɑː tiː ˈef/ *n* [U]
technical Rich Text Format; a system used to arrange and show the information in computer documents【術語】豐富文本格式〔電腦檔案的一種格式〕

RTM
the written abbreviation of 縮寫= 'read the manual', used by people whose job is to answer questions from customers who have problems with computer SOFTWARE or other equipment, when they think a customer's question is stupid and the customer could have easily found the answer by reading the instructions for using the product 請讀手冊〔用於回答顧客有關軟件等方面的問題〕

rur·ban /ˋrɝbən; ˈrɜːbən/ *adj*
happening or relating to areas on the edge of cities that are being developed and may soon become part of the city. This word is a combination of the words 'rural' meaning to do with the countryside, and 'urban' which means to do with towns. (發生在)城鄉結合地區的: *rurban areas north of London* 倫敦北部城鄉結合地區

S,s

SAD /ˌɛs e ˋdi, sæd; ˌes eɪ ˈdiː, sæd/ *n* [U]
seasonal affective disorder; a feeling of sadness and lack of energy that some people get in the winter because there is not enough light from the sun 季節性情感紊亂

safe /sef; seɪf/ *adj BrE*
NEW MEANING
slang used to say that something is fine and that there is no problem【英俚】不錯的, 挺好的: *"How's your new boss?" "She's safe."* "你的新老闆好嗎?" "她挺好的。"

sal·a·ry·man /ˋsælərɪˌmæn; ˈsælərimæn/ *n plural* **salarymen** /-ˌmɛn; -men/ [C]
a man who works in an office, often for many hours each day, and receives a salary as payment, especially in Japan〔尤指日本的〕白領階層人員

same-sex /ˌsem ˋsɛks; ˌseɪm ˈseks◂/ *adj*
same-sex marriage/relationship etc a marriage, relationship etc between two men or two women 同性婚姻/關係等

sample¹ /ˋsæmpḷ; ˈsɑːmpəl/ *n* [C]
NEW MEANING
a small part of a song from a CD or record that is used in a new song 經取樣拼和的樂曲: *Her latest album makes extensive use of samples from a wide range of acid jazz tracks.* 她最新的一張專輯廣泛採用了迷幻爵士樂的取樣拼和。

sample² /ˋsæmpḷ; ˈsɑːmpəl/ *v* [T]
NEW MEANING
to use a small part of a song from a CD or record in a new song 將…取樣拼和: *His songs have often been sampled by other people.* 他的歌曲經常被他人取樣拼和。

sampler /ˋsæmplɚ; ˈsɑːmplə/ *n* [C]

NEW MEANING
a machine that can record sounds or music so that you can change them and use them for a new piece of music 音樂取樣器

satellite /ˈsætḷˌaɪt; ˈsætḷlaɪt/ *v*
satellite sb **out** *phr v* to move a worker in a large company to an office or place of business that is smaller and separate from the company's main building 把〔大公司的職工〕派到分公司等: *They've decided to satellite Melrose out.* 他們已決定把梅爾羅斯調到分公司去。

sat·u·rate /ˈsætʃərɪt; ˈsætʃərḷt/ *n* [C,U]
a type of fat from meat or milk products that is thought to be less healthy than other kinds of fat from vegetables or fish; SATURATED FAT 飽和脂肪: *Choose a type of spread that's lower in saturates than butter.* 挑選一種飽和脂肪含量低於黃油的醬。

scal·a·bil·i·ty /ˌskeləˈbɪlətɪ; ˌskeɪləˈbɪlḷti/ *n* [U]
a computer system's scalability is the degree to which it is able to grow and become more powerful as the number of people using it increases〔電腦系統的〕可縮放性，可變比例性

SCART /skɑrt; skɑːt/ *n* [C]
a piece of equipment used in some countries to connect electrical equipment and transfer VIDEO and AUDIO signals from one piece of equipment to another, for example from a VIDEO RECORDER to a television〔連接錄像和音響等設備的〕21 針連接器: *a SCART cable* 21 針連接器電纜

school run /ˈskul ˌrʌn; ˈskuːl ˌrʌn/ *n* [C usually singular 一般用單數] *BrE*
a time when parents drive their children to school in the morning or home from school in the afternoon【英】父母開車接送孩子上下學: **do the school run** *We hope to increase the safety of children who walk to school and cut the number of cars doing the school run.* 我們希望能提高學童步行上學的安全，以減少接送的車輛。

schtick /ʃtɪk; ʃtɪk/ *n* [singular]
a typical quality or feature that someone, especially an entertainer, is famous for〔演員等的〕獨特風格: *Eminem's whole schtick is being outrageous, so he gets to do whatever he wants to do.* 埃米內的獨特風格就是肆無忌憚，所以他能做想做的任何事情。

scratch·card /ˈskrætʃˌkɑrd; ˈskrætʃkɑːd/ *n* [C] *BrE*
a small card you can buy which gives you a chance to win a prize. You rub off the surface of the card to find out whether you have won anything, for example by uncovering three SYMBOL*s* of the same type.【英】〔封蠟刮去後能顯示中獎與否的〕刮刮卡

scratch·ing /ˈskrætʃɪŋ; ˈskrætʃɪŋ/ *n* [U]
a special type of sound used in RAP MUSIC, which is produced by pushing a RECORD backwards and forwards on a TURNTABLE with your hands〔說唱樂中使用的〕擦音

scratch·pad /ˈskrætʃˌpæd; ˈskrætʃpæd/ *n* [C]
a small screen on a MOBILE PHONE that lets you write short notes and stores them for you〔流動電話的〕手寫屏幕

screen /skrin; skriːn/ *v*
NEW MEANING
screen (your) calls to find out who is calling you on the telephone, especially by using an ANSWER*ing* MACHINE, so that you do not have to speak to someone you do not want to speak to 篩選電話

screen·a·ger /ˈskrinedʒɚ; ˈskriːneɪdʒə/ *n* [C]
informal a young person who spends a lot of time using computers and the Internet【非正式】〔熱衷於使用電腦和互聯網的〕屏幕青少年

screen dump /ˈskrin ˌdʌmp; ˈskriːn ˌdʌmp/ *n* [C]
a picture of everything that appears on a computer screen at a particular time, which can be saved and put into a computer document, for example to show how to use a computer PROGRAM 屏幕轉儲

scrunch·y, scrunchie /ˈskrʌntʃɪ; ˈskrʌntʃi/ *n* [C]
a small circular piece of rubber that is covered with cloth, used for holding hair together in a PONYTAIL〔婦女紮頭髮的〕布包橡皮圈

SCSI /ˈskʌzɪ; ˈskʌzi/ *n* [U]
small computer systems interface; something that helps a small computer work with another piece of electronic equipment, such as a PRINTER, especially when they are connected by wires 小型電腦系統界面，SCSI 接口: *a SCSI port* SCSI 接口，SCSI 端口

scuz·zy /ˈskʌzɪ; ˈskʌzi/ *n* [C]
informal the usual pronunciation of SCSI. People sometimes also write 'scuzzy' to mean SCSI【非正式】SCSI 的通常發音〔有時也作為 SCSI 的書寫形式〕: *What's the biggest scuzzy hard drive you have?* 你最大的 SCSI 接口硬盤是甚麼？

search en·gine /ˈsɝtʃ ˌɛndʒən; ˈsɜːtʃ ˌendʒḷn/ *n* [C]
a computer PROGRAM that helps you find information on the Internet 搜索引擎: *You could try typing your query into another search engine.* 你可以試着把你的問題鍵入另一個搜索引擎。

seasonal af·fect·ive dis·or·der /ˌsiznəl əˌfɛktɪv dɪsˈɔrdɚ; ˌsiːzənəl əˌfektɪv dɪsˈɔːdə/ *abbreviation* 縮寫為 **SAD** *n* [U]
a feeling of sadness and lack of energy that some people get in the winter because there is not enough light from the sun 季節性情感紊亂

sector fund /ˈsɛktɚ ˌfʌnd; ˈsektə ˌfʌnd/ *n* [C]
technical a type of INVESTMENT in which the money buys many different STOCK*s* in a particular area of the ECONOMY, such as electronics, health care etc【術語】行業型基金〔購入某一經濟領域多種股票的投資方式〕

seed mon·ey /ˈsid ˌmʌnɪ; ˈsiːd ˌmʌni/ *n* [U]
the money needed to start a new business idea or project〔啟動一項新事業的〕種子基金，創業基金: *How much seed money will be needed to pay for the new factory?* 開辦這個新廠需要多少種子基金？

seismic /ˈsaɪzmɪk; ˈsaɪzmɪk/ *adj*
NEW MEANING
very great, serious, or important 十分重大的: *seismic changes in international relations* 國際關係方面的重大改變

self·build, self-build /ˌsɛlfˈbɪld; ˌselfˈbɪld◂/ *n* [U]
the activity of building your own house rather than paying professional builders to do it for you 自己建房: *a selfbuild kit* 自己建房的全套工具 —**self-builder** *n* [C]

self-di·rec·ted /ˌsɛlf dəˈrɛktɪd; ˌself dḷˈrektɪd◂/ *adj* [only before noun 僅用於名詞前] *AmE*
self-directed workers are responsible for organizing and judging their own work, rather than getting instructions from other people【美】自主的，無需他人指示的

senior mo·ment /ˈsinjɚ ˌmomənt; ˈsiːniə ˌməʊmənt/ *n* [C usually singular 一般用單數] *AmE*
informal humorous a short period of time when you are unable to remember a fact or piece of information that you are sure you know or should know. This expression is related to the phrase 'senior citizen' which is a polite way of talking about an old person【美，非正式，幽默】老痴瞬間〔短時間出現遺忘，由 senior citizen 衍生而來〕: **have a senior moment** *Oh, what's her name, the woman at the reception desk. Sorry, I'm having a senior moment.* 唉，接待處的那位女士叫甚麼名字？不好意思，我老糊塗了。

sensitivity train·ing /sɛnsəˈtɪvətɪ ˌtrenɪŋ; sensḷˈtɪvḷti ˌtreɪnɪŋ/ *n* [U]
training that teaches people to have more respect for people of different races, people who are DISABLED etc, especially as part of their job〔尊重其他種族的人、殘疾人等的〕敏感訓練

serial mo·nog·a·my /ˌsɪrɪəl məˈnɑgəmɪ; ˌsɪəriəl məˈnɒgəmi/ *n* [U]
the practice of having several romantic relationships in which you only have one sexual partner and do not see

anyone else 階段性單配偶生活 —**serial monogamist** *n* [C]

ser·o·to·nin /ˌsɛrə`tonɪn; ˌserəˈtəʊnɪn/ *n* [U] *technical* a chemical in the body that helps carry messages from the brain and is believed to make you feel happy【術語】血清素, 5-羥色胺

server /ˈsɝvɚ; ˈsɜːvə/ *n* [C]
NEW MEANING
someone whose job is to bring you your food in a restaurant〔餐館中的〕服務員, 侍者: *Our server told us about the day's specials.* 服務員給我們介紹了當天的特色菜。

server farm /ˈsɝvɚ ˌfɑrm; ˈsɜːvə ˌfɑːm/ *n* [C] an office which has a large amount of computer equipment holding all the SOFTWARE and DATA for WEBSITE*s* 服務器農場, 伺服器組羣〔具有大量電腦軟件和網址信息的電腦設備所在的辦公室〕: *Massive server farms are beginning to cause problems for local jurisdictions that have to deal with the sudden increase in demand for power.* 大規模的伺服器組羣開始為地區管轄帶來了問題, 管理當局不得不應付突然增加的電力需求。

set-a·side /ˈsɛt əˌsaɪd; ˈset əˌsaɪd/ *n* [C,U] **1** an amount of money that is kept so that it can be used for a special purpose; RESERVE 儲備金 **2** *BrE* an arrangement in which a government pays farmers to leave part of their fields empty, to avoid producing too much of a crop and to keep prices of those crops higher【英】〔政府提供津貼讓農戶減少農作物產量以保持高價位的〕農田閒置措施 **3** in the US, an arrangement in which a local government helps small businesses to develop by making loans and other financial help available to them〔美國地方政府提供給小企業的〕信貸支持措施: *In 1976, Connecticut established one of the nation's first setaside programs.* 1976 年, 康涅狄格州制定了小企業扶持計劃, 當時美國的同類計劃還很少。

set-top box /ˈsɛt tɑp ˌbɑks; ˈset tɒp ˌbɒks/ *n* [C] *BrE* a piece of electronic equipment that is connected to your television to make it able to receive a different form of BROADCASTING, especially DIGITAL signals【英】機頂盒〔連接在電視機上尤用於接收數碼信號的電子設備〕

sex tour·is·m /ˈsɛks ˌturɪzəm; ˈseks ˌtʊərɪzəm/ *n* [U] the activity of travelling to other countries in order to have sex, especially sexual activities that are illegal in your own country 性旅遊業, 色情旅遊業: *Sex tourism is closely connected with child prostitution throughout the world.* 世界各地的色情旅遊業都和童妓有着密切的聯繫。—**sex tourist** *n* [C]

sex work·er /ˈsɛks ˌwɝkɚ; ˈseks ˌwɜːkə/ *n* [C] *formal* a polite expression for a PROSTITUTE【正式】性工作者〔娼妓的婉稱〕

SGML /ˌɛs dʒi ɛm `ɛl; ˌes dʒiː em ˈel/ *n* [U] *technical* standard generalized markup language; a way of writing a document on a computer so that its structure is clear, and so that it can easily be read on a different computer system【術語】標準通用標記語言〔用這種電腦語言寫的文件結構清晰, 便於在其他電腦系統閱讀〕

shadow e·con·o·my /ˌʃædo ɪ`kɑnəmɪ; ˌʃædəʊ ɪˈkɒnəmi/ *n* [C] *technical* business activities that are difficult for the authorities to find out about, for example because they are illegal【術語】影子經濟, 地下經濟

shake /ʃek; ʃeɪk/ *v*
NEW MEANING
shake down *phr v* [I] if a new situation or arrangement shakes down, people start to get used to it and it becomes more effective〔新情況或安排〕逐漸為人們所適應: *The restructure has shaken down, and staff are showing a new sense of purpose.* 這次改組已經為人們所適應, 全體員工表現出一種新的幹勁。
NEW MEANING
shake out *phr v* **1** [I] if an organization or industry shakes out, it becomes calmer after a difficult period of time 恢復元氣: *He'll look for bargains in a year or two, after the real estate market shakes out.* 一兩年後, 等房地產市場恢復元氣後, 他將設法買便宜貨。**2** [T] **shake** sth ↔ **out** to change a situation by removing things from it that are not useful or that do not make a profit 淘汰, 剔除〔沒有用或不贏利的事物〕: *As the airline industry shakes out all but the very fittest, catering companies could face serious troubles.* 隨着航空業汰弱留強, 配餐公司有可能會面臨重大困難。

shake·down /ˈʃekdaun; ˈʃeɪkdaʊn/ *n* [C] **1** a period of time when people start to get used to a new arrangement and it becomes more effective 適應調整期 **2** a period of time when prices are falling on a financial market〔金融市場的〕疲軟時期

shark re·pel·lent /ˈʃɑrk rɪˌpɛlənt; ˈʃɑːk rɪˌpelənt/ *n* [C,U] *AmE* *informal* an action that a company takes to make it less likely that another company will try to control it【美, 非正式】驅鯊行動〔反收購措施〕: *How could the adoption of a shark repellent affect a firm's long-term performance?* 採取驅鯊行動會如何影響一家公司的長期業績呢?

shark watch·er /ˈʃɑrk ˌwɑtʃɚ; ˈʃɑːk ˌwɒtʃə/ *n* [C] *informal* a company whose business is to discover that someone may be trying to take control of other companies, for example by buying a lot of SHARE*s*, and to give advice about what those companies should do【非正式】反收購偵探公司, 鯊魚觀察員

sharp /ʃɑrp; ʃɑːp/ *adj*
NEW MEANING
not be the sharpest knife in the drawer *BrE humorous* to be stupid or slow to learn or understand things【英, 幽默】遲鈍的, 不機靈的: *Dave might not be the sharpest knife in the drawer, but he's a nice guy.* 戴夫也許不夠機靈, 可是個好人。

shed·load /ˈʃɛdlod; ˈʃedləʊd/ *n* **shedloads of sth** *BrE informal* a lot of something【英, 非正式】一大堆, 許許多多: *They've got shedloads of stuff for sale.* 他們有一大批東西要出售。

shock jock /ˈʃɑk ˌdʒɑk; ˈʃɒk ˌdʒɒk/ *n* [C] *especially AmE* someone on a radio show who plays music and talks about subjects that offend many people【尤美】驚世駭俗的電台音樂節目主持人

short sell·ing /ˌʃɔrt `sɛlɪŋ; ˌʃɔːt ˈselɪŋ/ *n* [U] the practice of selling SHARE*s*, currencies (CURRENCY) etc immediately after buying them, and then buying them back again later when the price has become lower, in order to make a profit 賣空: *Critics of short selling say it can cause huge falls in prices.* 賣空的批評者説這會造成價格的暴跌。

shorty /ˈʃɔrtɪ; ˈʃɔːti/ *n* [C]
NEW MEANING
slang【俚】**1** a word meaning a woman, used especially by people who play or listen to HIP-HOP music 娘兒們〔嘻蹦音樂家、愛好者尤常用〕: *I love it when a shorty can hang out with me when I drink.* 我喜歡在喝酒時有個娘兒們陪在身邊。**2** a word meaning a baby, used especially by people who play or listen to HIP-HOP music 娃娃〔嘻蹦音樂家、愛好者尤常用〕: *Shawna says she's gonna be having my shorty.* 肖娜説她懷了我的孩子。

shov·el·ware /ˈʃʌvl̩ˌwɛr; ˈʃʌvəlˌweə/ *n* [U] information that first appears in printed form, for example in a book or newspaper, and then is put onto the Internet or CD-ROM without any new or interesting ways to look at or use the information 鏟件〔指毫無新意的媒體產品, 內容只是照搬印刷品〕: *Many of the educational software titles are nothing but shovelware.* 許多教育軟件只是照搬書刊的內容而已。

shroud-wav·ing /ˈʃraud ˌwevɪŋ; ˈʃraʊd ˌweɪvɪŋ/ *n* [U] *BrE* the practice of making warnings in public, especially by doctors or politicians, about the poor quality of medical care in the British National Health Service, in order to make the government provide more money for it【英】國民保健制度狀況惡化警告: *Complaints about the NHS tend to focus on the problems of hospitals' waiting lists and shroud-waving in response to spending controls.* 對(英國)國民保健制度的抱怨往往集中在各醫院都有許多病人等待接受治療, 以及控制開支造成的醫療狀況惡化等問題上。

sick build·ing syn·drome /ˌsɪk ˋbɪldɪŋ ˌsɪndrom; ˌsɪk ˈbɪldɪŋ ˌsɪndrəʊm/ *n* [U]
a situation in which chemicals and GERMS stay in an office building and make the people who work there feel ill 病樓綜合徵〔指辦公樓內化學物質和病菌等積聚造成的不適〕: *Research has shown that a household fungus can contribute to sick building syndrome.* 研究表明室內真菌會引起病樓綜合徵。

side·bar /ˋsaɪdbɑr; ˈsaɪdbɑː/ *n* [C] *AmE*
law an occasion when the lawyers and the judge in a TRIAL discuss something without letting the JURY hear what they are saying【美, 法律】〔法庭中不讓陪審團聽到的〕法官與律師的討論

SIDS /sɪdz; sɪdz/ *n* [U] *AmE* SUDDEN INFANT DEATH SYNDROME【美】嬰兒猝死綜合徵

sim card /ˋsɪm ˌkɑrd; ˈsɪm ˌkɑːd/ *n* [C]
a plastic card in a MOBILE PHONE that stores your personal information and allows you to use the phone〔手機上的〕用戶識別卡, 用戶身分模塊

sin·gle·sit /ˋsɪŋglˌsɪt; ˈsɪŋgəlˌsɪt/ *n* [C] *BrE*
a house or apartment for a single person living on their own, rather than for a family【英】單身者住房[寓所]

sink /sɪŋk; sɪŋk/ *adj* [only before noun 僅用於名詞前]
sink estate/school *BrE* a sink estate or school is in a very bad condition and there is little hope of improvement【英】殘舊住宅區/學校: *Go to almost any city and you find sink estates where you get the feeling that the council hates the place and the people too.* 差不多到任何一個城市, 你都會發現有殘舊的住宅區, 讓你覺得那地方和那地方的人都遭市議會的嫌棄。

six-pack /ˋsɪks ˌpæk; ˈsɪks ˌpæk/ *n* [C]
humorous well-developed muscles that you can see on a man's stomach. This expression developed from the idea that these muscles look like a group of six CANs of beer or SOFT DRINK which are sold together, also called a six-pack【幽默】發達的腹肌: *Find out how to get a six-pack, or just a flat stomach, in six weeks.* 看看怎樣能在六週內收平肚子, 甚至鍛鍊出發達的肌肉。

skank /skæŋk; skæŋk/ *n* [C]
slang an offensive word for a woman who you have a bad opinion of, because she has sex with a lot of men【俚】騷婆娘〔冒犯用語〕—**skanky** *adj*

ski·jor·ing /ˋskiˌdʒɔrɪŋ; ˈskiːˌdʒɔːrɪŋ/ *n* [U]
a sport in which a SKIER is pulled over snow or ice by one or more dogs 狗拉滑雪: *long distance skijoring in Alaska* 在阿拉斯加的長途狗拉滑雪 —**skijor** *v* [I]

skin /skɪn; skɪn/ *n* [U]
NEW MEANING
the way particular information appears on a computer screen, especially when this can be changed quickly and easily〔軟件、網站等的〕介面, 面板, 外殼

skin art·ist /ˋskɪn ˌɑrtɪst; ˈskɪn ˌɑːtɪst/ also 又作 **skin de·sign·er** /ˋskɪn dɪˌzaɪnɚ; ˈskin dɪˌzaɪnə/ *n* [C]
someone who changes the way that a computer PROGRAM shows information on the screen to the user 軟件介面設計師

skunk works /ˋskʌŋk ˌwɝks; ˈskʌŋk ˌwɜːks/ *n* [singular]
informal a part of a large company where a small group of workers try to develop new products in secret, within a shorter period of time than usual. This phrase comes from 'Skonk Works', the name of a place in an old American COMIC STRIP. Alcohol was illegally made at the 'Skonk Works'【非正式】保密的開發部門〔本短語由舊時美國連環漫畫中製造私酒的地方 'Skonk Works' 衍生而來〕: *A few companies have a skunk works where secret projects are funded in the hope that they will lead to new products in a couple of years.* 一些公司設有保密的開發部門, 公司為那裡的祕密研究項目提供資金, 以期在兩三年內研製出新產品。

sky /skaɪ; skaɪ/ *v* [I]
to jump higher than everyone else when you are playing BASKETBALL〔籃球賽中〕高躍〔於其他人之上〕

slam·min /ˋslæmɪn; ˈslæmɪn/ *adj, adv AmE*
slang very good【美俚】頂棒的[地]: *Man, we had a slammin time last night.* 老兄, 我們昨天夜裡玩得真高興。

slap·head /ˋslæphɛd; ˈslæphed/ *n* [C] *BrE*
informal an impolite word for describing someone who is BALD (=has little or no hair on their head)【英, 非正式】禿頂, 光頭〔非禮貌用語〕

slaugh·tered /ˋslɔtɚd; ˈslɔːtəd/ *adj* [not before noun 不用於名詞前] *BrE*
informal very drunk【英, 非正式】爛醉(如泥)的: **get slaughtered** *We all got completely slaughtered last night.* 昨天夜裡我們全都喝得爛醉如泥。

smack /smæk; smæk/ *v* [T]
smack sb **up** *slang* to hit someone hard many times with your hand【俚】狠揍: *Don't make me come over there and smack you up.* 不要引我過來揍你。

small-cap /ˌsmɔl ˋkæp; ˌsmɔːl ˈkæp◂/ *n* [C]
a SHARE in a small company 小盤股, 細市值股票 — **small-cap** *adj*: *They poured their money into some small-cap mutual funds.* 他們把錢注入幾個專門投資小盤股的互助基金。—opposite 反義詞 LARGE-CAP

small of·fice/home of·fice /ˌsmɔl ˋɔfɪs ˋhom ˌɔfɪs; ˌsmɔːl ˈɒfɪs ˈhəʊm ˌɒfɪs/ *abbreviation* 縮寫為 **SOHO** *n* [C]
a room in someone's home with electronic equipment such as a computer and a FAX MACHINE, that is used as a place in which to work 家庭辦公室

smil·ey /ˋsmaɪlɪ; ˈsmaɪli/ *n* [C]
a sign that looks like a face when you look at it sideways, for example :-), used in E-MAIL messages to show that you are happy or pleased about something 笑容符〈如 :-), 用於電子郵件中〉

smoothie /ˋsmuðɪ; ˈsmuːði/ *n* [C]
NEW MEANING
a thick drink made of fruit and fruit juices, and sometimes YOGHURT, that have been mixed together until they are smooth 思樂冰, 沙冰〔一種由水果、果汁、酸奶等混合製成的飲料〕

SMS /ˌɛs ɛm ˋɛs; ˌes em ˈes/ *n*
short messaging system or short message service; a feature on a MOBILE PHONE that allows a user to send or receive written messages〔手機的〕短信息服務

snap /snæp; snæp/ *v*
snap on sb *phr v* [T] *slang* to suddenly stop being able to control your temper and attack someone physically or with words【俚】對〔某人〕發脾氣[大打出手, 大肆攻擊]: *I've seen him snap on people just for looking at him.* 我看見過他僅僅因為人家看了他一眼就對他們發脾氣。

snarf /snɑrf; snɑːf/ also 又作 **snarf down** *v* [T]
informal to eat something very quickly, often in an untidy or noisy way【非正式】很快(出聲)地吃: *Don't lie! I saw you snarfing down all those doughnuts!* 不要扯謊! 我看見你把所有的炸麵圈一下子全吃光了。

snar·ky /ˋsnɑrkɪ; ˈsnɑːki/ *adj*
saying unkind and unpleasant things about other people 尖刻的: *If she's bothering you and you say something snarky, she'll know she's getting to you.* 如果她不斷打擾你, 而你說了一些刻薄的話, 她就會知道她讓你感到煩透了。

snip·ing /ˋsnaɪpɪŋ; ˈsnaɪpɪŋ/ *n* [U]
the practice of waiting until the final moments of an ONLINE AUCTION and then offering the highest price for the thing being sold 狙擊〔網上拍賣中等到最後時刻出

最高價格〕—**sniper** *n* [C] —**snipe** *v* [I,T]

so /so; səʊ/ *adv*

NEW MEANING

1 *AmE spoken* a word used especially by TEENAGE girls, before noun phrases and verbs, to emphasize what they are saying【美口】簡直，確實〔表示強調，多為女孩用〕: **so not** *Orange is just so not the right color for Kari.* 橙色壓根兒和卡里不相配。| *I have so messed up!* 我真的把事情弄得一團糟！**2** *spoken* used to say that a particular action, attitude, type of behaviour etc is typical of someone ...型[式]的: *Jenna's hairstyle is so Lisa Bonet.* 詹納的髮型和莉薩·博內特一模一樣。

sobriety check·point /səˋbraɪətɪ ˌtʃɛkpɔɪnt; səˈbraɪəti ˌtʃekpɔɪnt/ *n* [C]

a place in the road where the police stop vehicles, so that police can test drivers to see if they have drunk too much alcohol or used illegal drugs 醉酒駕駛檢測站: *Officers will be conducting a sobriety checkpoint in the central Torrance area tomorrow.* 警察明天將在托蘭斯中部地區設一個醉酒駕駛檢測站。

soccer mom /ˋsakɚ ˌmam; ˈsɒkə ˌmɒm/ *n* [C] *AmE*

a mother who spends a lot of time driving her children to sports practice, music lessons etc, considered as a typical example of women from the middle to upper classes in US society【美】足球媽咪〔經常驅車帶領孩子參加體育活動、音樂課等的母親〕

social au·dit /ˌsoʃəl ˋɔdɪt; ˌsəʊʃəl ˈɔːdɪt/ also 又作 **ethical audit** *n* [C]

an official examination of how well a company behaves, for example how it treats its employees, the environment etc 社會[倫理]審計: *The social audit of Ben & Jerry's Ice Cream commends the company, which gives 7.5% of pre-tax profits to charity.* 對本－傑里冰淇淋的社會審查表揚了該公司，因為該公司將其稅前利潤的7.5%捐給了慈善事業。

social ex·clu·sion /ˌsoʃəl ɪkˋskluʒən; ˌsəʊʃəl ɪkˈskluːʒən/ *n* [U] *BrE*

the situation that results when people suffer the effects of a combination of problems such as unemployment, crime, and bad housing, and have very little chance of being able to improve their lives【英】為社會排斥〔指遭遇失業、犯罪、住房差等問題並無法改善生活〕: *A number of proposals have been submitted to combat poverty and social exclusion.* 已提出了許多消除貧窮和社會排斥的建議。

soft /sɔft; sɒft/ *adj*

NEW MEANING

1 soft loan/credit money that is lent at a lower INTEREST RATE than usual, because it will be used, for example, for creating a business in an area where many people do not have jobs 優惠貸款/信貸 **2 soft money** money that is given to political parties, rather than directly to particular CANDIDATES, by people, companies, or organizations. The amount of money that can be given to political parties in this way is not restricted. 軟性捐款〔指捐贈給競選人所屬政黨而非本人的款項〕

SOHO /ˋsoho; ˈsəʊhəʊ/

small office/home office; a room in someone's home with electronic equipment such as a computer and a FAX MACHINE, that is used as a place in which to work 家庭辦公室

solid /ˋsalɪd; ˈsɒlɪd/ *adj BrE*

NEW MEANING

slang【英俚】**1** used to say that something is good 了不起的 **2** used to say that something is very difficult 很難的: *I couldn't do any of the maths last night – it was solid.* 昨晚的數學題我一道也不會，太難了。

sort /sɔrt; sɔːt/ *v* [T] *BrE*

NEW MEANING

usually spoken to deal with a situation so that all the problems are solved and everything is organized as it should be【英，一般口】安排妥當: *Don't give me any more excuses. Just sort it!* 不要再找藉口了，把事情辦妥！

sort·ed /ˋsɔrtɪd; ˈsɔːtɪ̈d/ *adj* [not before noun 不用於名詞前] *BrE*

spoken informal【英口，非正式】**1** properly arranged or planned 安排有序的: *Good, that's your accommodation sorted.* 好，那就是給你安排的住所。**2** provided with the things that you want 滿足需要的: *"Can I get you anything?" "We're sorted, thanks."* "我要給你們拿甚麼東西來嗎?" "我們都不缺甚麼，謝謝。" | *"Did you manage to get a ticket for tonight?" "Sorted!"* "弄到今天晚上的票了嗎?" "弄到了。" | **be sorted for** *Are you sorted for booze and something to smoke?* 你有喝的酒和吸的煙嗎?

sound·card, sound card /ˋsaʊndˌkard; ˈsaʊndˌkɑːd/ *n* [C]

a CIRCUIT BOARD that can be added to a computer so that it is able to produce sound〔電腦的〕聲卡，音效卡

SPAD /spæd; spæd/ *n* [C] *BrE*

signal passed at danger; a signal near a railway track that has been passed by a train when it should not have passed. If a signal is passed in this way, it could cause an accident or a dangerous situation on the railway line.【英】超越〔鐵道〕危險信號

spam /spæm; spæm/ *n* [U]

E-MAIL messages that a computer user has not asked for and does not want to read, for example from someone who is advertising something 電子垃圾，〔網上的〕垃圾郵件: *You can filter out spam with special software.* 你可以用專門的軟件把電子垃圾濾除。

spam·mer /ˋspæmɚ; ˈspæmə/ *n* [C]

a person or company that sends the same computer message to many different people who do not want to receive it, usually as a way of advertising something 垃圾郵件發送者: *Some ISPs have cancelled contracts with spammers, but it's not easy.* 有些互聯網服務商中止了與垃圾郵件發送者的合同，但是這樣做並不容易。

species bar·ri·er /ˋspiʃɪz ˌbærɪɚ; ˈspiːʃiːz ˌbæriə/ *n* [singular]

a natural system which is believed to prevent diseases moving from one type of plant or animal to another. This expression is often used in relation to the cow disease BSE, which is believed to have crossed the species barrier and become the disease CJD in humans 物種屏障〔防止其他物種被傳染疾病的自然系統〕: **cross/jump the species barrier** *When and how the disease jumped the species barrier may never be known.* 這種疾病是在何時和以何種方式越過物種屏障，也許永遠不得而知。

speed dial /ˋspid ˌdaɪəl; ˈspiːd ˌdaɪəl/ also 又作 **speed dialing** *n* [U]

a special feature on a telephone that lets you DIAL someone's telephone number very quickly by pressing just one button〔電話的〕快速撥號: *Does this phone have speed dial?* 這部電話有快速撥號功能嗎? —**speed dial** *v* [I,T]

spider /ˋspaɪdɚ; ˈspaɪdə/ *n* [C]

NEW MEANING

a computer program that AUTOMATICALLY searches for WEB PAGES on the Internet（網上）蜘蛛〔互聯網上的網頁自動搜索程序〕

sport-u·til·i·ty ve·hi·cle /ˌspɔrt juˋtɪlətɪ ˌviɪkḷ; ˌspɔːt juːˈtɪlɪ̈ti ˌviːkəl/ *abbreviation* 縮寫為 **SUV** *n* [C] *AmE*

a type of vehicle that is bigger than a car and is made for travelling over rough ground【美】越野車，爬山車

spy·ware /ˋspaɪˌwɛr; ˈspaɪweə/ *n* [U]

computer SOFTWARE that secretly arrives onto someone's computer while they are using the Internet, which records information about which WEBSITES they visit. This information is then used by advertising companies, who try to sell them products 間諜軟件: *Most net surfers probably have spyware embedded in their computers.* 大多數網民的電腦都可能被埋置了間諜軟件。

squeegee merchants 耍賴擦車仔

squeegee mer·chant /ˋskwidʒi ˏmɝtʃənt; ˈskwiːdʒiː ˌmɜːtʃənt/ *n* [C] *BrE*
someone who uses water and a SQUEEGEE (=tool with a thin rubber blade and a short handle) to clean the front windows of cars that have stopped in traffic, and then asks the drivers for money, sometimes in a threatening way【英】耍賴擦車仔

stag /stæg; stæg/ *v past tense and past participle* **stagged** *present participle* **stagging** [T] *BrE*
stag an issue to buy SHARES in a company in order to sell them quickly and make a profit【英】炒賣股票〔迅速獲利〕

stakeholder /ˋstekˏholdɚ; ˈsteɪkˌhəʊldə/ *n* [C]
NEW MEANING
someone who is considered to be an important part of an organization or a society because they have responsibility in it and receive advantages from it 利益共享者〔組織中的重要部分, 因他們對組織有責任, 也從中得到好處〕: *How can we encourage students to become stakeholders in the classroom?* 我們怎樣才能激勵學生在課堂上一齊分擔責任, 共享成果呢?

stakeholder e·con·o·my /ˋstekholdɚ ɪˌkɑnəmɪ; ˈsteɪkhəʊldər ɪˌkɒnəmi/ *n* [C] *BrE*
an economic system in a society that citizens feel they receive advantages from and have responsibilities to【英】利益共享經濟: *The Prime Minister declared his intention to create a stakeholder economy involving all the people, not just a privileged few.* 首相宣布, 他打算建立的是全民的利益共享經濟, 而不是僅僅為少數特權者服務。

stand-a·lone /ˋstænd əˏlon; ˈstænd əˌləʊn/ *adj*
NEW MEANING
a stand-alone company or business is one that is not part of a larger company〔公司或企業〕獨立(經營)的

standby time /ˋstændbaɪ ˏtaɪm; ˈstændbaɪ ˌtaɪm/ *n* [U]
1 the time during which a person or a machine is available to work but is not able to work because they are waiting to be given a specific job to do〔人或機器的〕待命時間 **2** the period of time that passes while you wait for a computer to carry out a command or a request〔電腦運算時的〕等候時間

stand-up, standup /ˋstænd ˏʌp; ˈstænd ˌʌp/ *n* [C]
NEW MEANING
a COMEDIAN who does STAND-UP COMEDY (=tells jokes to an audience) 單人喜劇表演者, "棟篤笑"演員: *He's simply one of the best new standups around at the moment. Go see his show!* 他是目前最好的滑稽說笑新星之一, 去看他的演出吧!

start /stɑrt; stɑːt/ *n*
NEW MEANING
1 [C usually plural 一般用複數] a job that has just started, a business that has just been started, or someone who has just started a new job 新工作; 新商店; 新手: *The number of business starts plummeted 10.5% during the second half of the year.* 下半年開業的新店數目銳減了10.5%。| **new starts** *a training course for new starts* 新人培訓課程 **2 housing starts** the number of new houses, apartments etc on which building work has started in a particular period of time〔某段時間內的〕新屋動工數目: *The number of housing starts was lower than expected last quarter.* 上季度新屋動工數目比預期的少。

start-up /ˋstɑrt ˏʌp; ˈstɑːt ˌʌp/ *n* [C]
a small new company whose work usually involves computers or the Internet 新成立的小公司〔常與電腦或互聯網有關〕: *Jill works for an Internet start-up in San Jose.* 吉爾為聖何塞的一家新開的互聯網公司工作。

stay-at-home /ˋste ət ˏhom; ˈsteɪ ət ˌhəʊm/ *adj*
stay-at-home mother/father etc a stay-at-home mother or father stays at home, usually to take care of their children, rather than working in an office, factory etc〔不去工作, 在家照顧孩子的〕家庭媽媽/爸爸等: *The study found that stay-at-home moms are no longer the majority in America.* 研究發現家庭媽媽在美國已不再是大多數了。

stealth tax /ˋstɛlθ ˏtæks; ˈstelθ ˌtæks/ *n* [C] *BrE informal* a tax that you pay on something that you buy rather than tax you pay directly to the government, and which you are less aware of paying than, for example, direct tax on your income【英, 非正式】隱形稅, 銷售稅

steaming /ˋstimɪŋ; ˈstiːmɪŋ/ *n* [U]
a method of stealing in which a large group of young people go into a public place, surprise and scare the people there, and then rob them 眾眾[結幫]行劫: *The success of steaming depends on surprise.* 結幫行劫是否得逞取決於出其不意。—**steamer** *n* [C] *Steamers waited until a member of staff opened a security door.* 結幫行劫者等候到一個職員把防盜門打開才動手。—**steaming** *adj*: *The steaming gangs are often in their early teens.* 眾眾行劫的羣黨經常是一些十三四歲的青少年。

stellar /ˋstɛlɚ; ˈstelə/ *adj*
NEW MEANING
go stellar *BrE informal* if a pop band, TV actor, etc goes stellar, they become very popular and famous【英, 非正式】走紅, 受歡迎: *There's a stand-up comedian, and my sources tell me he is about to go stellar.* 有一個單人表演的喜劇演員, 根據我得到的消息, 他即將走紅。

stem cell /ˋstɛm ˏsɛl; ˈstem ˌsel/ *n* [C]
technical a special type of cell in the body that can divide in order to form other types of cells that have particular qualities or purposes【術語】幹細胞: *Research has now shown that stem cells are present in the adult brain and spinal cord.* 研究顯示幹細胞存在於成人的腦和脊髓中。

step aer·o·bics /ˋstɛp ɛˏrobɪks; ˈstep eəˌrəʊbɪks/ *n* [U]
a type of physical exercise in which you step on and off a small raised PLATFORM while doing movements with the upper part of your body 踏板健身操: *Which night is your step aerobics class?* 哪天晚上你上踏板健身操課?

sticky /ˋstɪkɪ; ˈstɪki/ *adj*
NEW MEANING
slang a WEBSITE that is sticky is interesting to the people looking at it and makes them want to look at it for a long period of time【俚】〔網站〕令人着迷的, 有魅力的 —**stickiness** *n* [U]

stif·fy /ˋstɪfɪ; ˈstɪfi/ *n* [C]
taboo an ERECTION (1)【諱】〔陰莖〕勃起

stock park·ing /ˋstɑk ˏpɑrkɪŋ; ˈstɒk ˌpɑːkɪŋ/ *n* [U]
a situation in which the owner of SHARES leaves them with another person or organization, usually in order to hide who really owns them 股票存託

stop-loss or·der /ˏstɑp ˋlɔs ˏɔrdɚ; ˌstɒp ˈlɒs ˌɔːdə/ *n* [C]
technical an arrangement in which the person who buys and sells your STOCKS for you agrees to buy or sell STOCKS when they reach a particular price【術語】〔指示經紀在股價漲或落到某價位時立即買進或賣出的〕限價買賣指令, 止蝕指令

straight-to-vid·e·o /ˏstret tə ˋvɪdɪo; ˌstreɪt tə ˈvɪdiəʊ/ *n* [C]
a film that is never shown in the cinema but that is avail-

able only on VIDEO 直接影像製品〔指未在電影院上映而直接製成錄像帶或光盤發行的影片〕

stream /strim; striːm/ *v* [T]
NEW MEANING
to play sound or VIDEO on your computer while it is being DOWNLOAD*ed* from the Internet, rather than saving it as a FILE and then playing it〔不下載直接從網上〕直流收看[收聽]: *Click here to stream video from the Olympic Games.* 點擊這裡直流收看奧運會的錄像。

stream·ing /ˋstrimɪŋ; ˈstriːmɪŋ/ *n* [U]
playing sound or VIDEO on your computer while it is being broadcast over the Internet instead of DOWNLOAD*ing* it and saving it into a FILE so that you can listen to it or watch it later〔從網上〕直流接收: **audio/video streaming** *Our service began with live audio streaming of radio programs.* 我們的服務以直流接收現場直播的電台節目開始。

stress /strɛs; stres/ *v* [T]
NEW MEANING
stress sb **out** *slang* to make someone so worried or nervous that they cannot relax【俚】使焦慮[緊張不安]: *Cathy's job really stresses her out.* 卡西的工作着實使她焦慮不安。

stuff /stʌf; stʌf/ *n*
NEW MEANING
and stuff *spoken informal* used to say that there are other things similar to what you have just mentioned, but you are not going to say what they are【口, 非正式】諸如此類的東西: *There's some very good music there, CD systems and stuff, and laser discs.* 那裡有一些極好的音樂、雷射唱片系統等東西, 還有雷射影碟。

style sheet /ˋstaɪl ˏʃit; ˈstaɪl ˌʃiːt/ *n* [C]
a set of instructions that specifies what the TYPEFACE and colours of an electronic document should be 樣式單, 格式頁: *When the electronic newspaper comes with style sheets, we will be able to specify that headings are in the right type-style, so it will look like the printed paper.* 電子報紙附有樣式頁時, 我們就能確定那標題的字體對不對, 那樣看起來會同印刷的報紙一樣。

styl·ing /ˋstaɪlɪŋ; ˈstaɪlɪŋ/ also 又作 **sty·lin'** /ˋstaɪlɪn; ˈstaɪlɪn/ *adj* [not before noun 不用於名詞前] *AmE slang* attractive and fashionable【美俚】時髦的, 引人注目的: *If I had a car like this, I'd be stylin'.* 我要是有這樣一輛車, 那才神氣呢。

STYS *especially BrE*
a written abbreviation of 縮寫= 'speak to you soon', used in E-MAIL or TEXT MESSAGE*s* on MOBILE PHONE*s*【尤英】很快與你通話〔電子郵件或手機短信用語〕

suck-up /ˋsʌk ˏʌp; ˈsʌk ˌʌp/ *n* [C] *AmE informal* someone who says or does nice things in order to make someone like them or get what they want【美, 非正式】馬屁精: *Nobody wants to seem like a suck-up.* 沒有人希望被人看作馬屁精。

Sudden In·fant Death Syn·drome /ˌsʌdn̩ ˏɪnfənt ˋdɛθ ˏsɪndrom; ˌsʌdn ˌɪnfənt ˈdeθ ˌsɪndrəʊm/ *abbreviation* 縮寫為 **SIDS** *n* [U]
a situation in which a baby stops breathing and dies while it is sleeping, for no known reason 嬰兒猝死綜合徵

suicide /ˋsuəˏsaɪd; ˈsuːǝsaɪd/ *n*
suicide by cop *humorous* an occasion in which someone who wants to kill himself or herself uses threatening behaviour towards a police officer so that the police officer kills the person in order to defend himself or herself【幽默】借警察之手自殺〔有人利用威脅警察的行為, 令警察在自衛的情況下把他/她殺死, 以達到自殺的目的〕

suit /sut; suːt/ *n* [C usually plural 一般用複數]
NEW MEANING
informal a man, especially a manager, who works in an office and who has to wear a suit when he is at work【非正式】〔上班時需穿套裝的〕高級管理人員: *I bought myself a mobile phone and joined the other suits on the train to the City.* 我給自己買了一部手機, 與其他穿得筆挺的高級職員一起上了進城的火車。

sunset in·dus·try /ˋsʌnsɛt ˏɪndəstrɪ; ˈsʌnset ˌɪndəstri/ *n* [C]
an industry that uses old equipment and methods, usually in an area that once had many industries like it, and that is becoming less successful 夕陽工業: *sunset industries such as steel* 諸如鋼鐵等的夕陽工業

su·per·cat /ˋsupɚˏkæt; ˈsuːpəˌkæt/ *n* [C] *especially BrE*
a word meaning someone who earns a very large amount of money for running a company, especially a company that was previously owned by the government, used in newspapers to show disapproval【尤英】超級貓〔利用原為政府辦的公司賺大錢的經營者, 為含貶義的報紙用語〕

su·per·size¹ /ˋsupɚˏsaɪz; ˈsuːpəˌsaɪz/ *adj* [only before noun 僅用於名詞前] *AmE*
a supersize drink or meal in a FAST-FOOD restaurant is the largest size that the restaurant serves【美】〔快餐店提供的食物或飲料〕巨無霸式的, 大份的: *Could I get a supersize fries with that?* 我能附帶得到大份的薯條嗎?

supersize² /ˋsupɚˏsaɪz; ˈsuːpəˌsaɪz/ *v* [T] *AmE*
to give someone a larger sized meal or drink in a FAST-FOOD restaurant【美】〔快餐店〕提供大份食物[飲料]: *Can I supersize that drink for you?* 那飲料我給你大份的好嗎?

surround-sound, surround sound /səˋraund ˏsaund; səˈraʊnd ˌsaʊnd/ *n* [U]
a system of four or more SPEAKER*s* (=pieces of equipment that sound comes out of) used with films and television so that the sounds from the film seem to come from all directions 環繞立體聲 —**surround-sound** *adj* [only before noun 僅用於名詞前]: *surround-sound speakers* 環繞立體聲揚聲器

SUV /ˏɛs ju ˋvi; ˌes juː ˈviː/ *n* [C] *AmE*
sport-utility vehicle; a type of vehicle that is bigger than a car and is made for travelling over rough ground【美】越野車, 爬山車

sweat eq·ui·ty /ˋswɛt ˏɛkwətɪ; ˈswet ˌekwǝti/ *n* [U] *AmE*
the amount of value that something gains as a result of a lot of work【美】血汗權益〔通過大量工作而獲得的增值部分〕: *The volunteer work that parents put into the school system was calculated to be worth $2.2 million in sweat equity.* 當局計算出家長投入學校系統的義務工作共值 220 萬美元。

sweet¹ /swit; swiːt/ *adj*
NEW MEANING
spoken **Sweet!** used to say that you think that something is very good【口】棒極了的: *"I got four tickets to the concert." "Sweet!"* "我弄到四張音樂會門票。" "太棒了!"

swipe card /ˋswaɪp ˏkɑrd; ˈswaɪp ˌkɑːd/ *n* [C]
a special plastic card that you slide through a machine in order to get into a building or open a door〔開門等的〕插卡

switch·ing /ˋswɪtʃɪŋ; ˈswɪtʃɪŋ/ *n* [U]
a system that allows information to be exchanged between different computer networks〔信息〕交換(系統), 轉接

SWOT /swɑt; swɒt/ *n*
strengths, weaknesses, opportunities, threats; a system for examining the way a company is run or the way someone works, to see what the good and bad points are 態勢〔公司或個人的情況分析, 包括強勢、弱勢、機會、威脅四個方面, 是 strengths, weaknesses, opportunities, threats 的首字母縮合〕

sync, synch /sɪŋk; sɪŋk/ *v*
sync up, synch up *phr v* [I,T] to arrange for two things to occur at the same time, or to occur at the same time, as arranged; SYNCHRONIZE 同步發生, 使...同步: *For some reason, I couldn't get the audio and video to synch up.* 由於某種原因, 我不能使音響和視頻同步。

T,t

table danc·ing /ˈtebḷ ˌdænsɪŋ; ˈteɪbəl ˌdɑːnsɪŋ/ *n* [U]
dancing with sexy movements that is performed close to a customer's table in a restaurant or NIGHTCLUB 桌上舞〔飯店或夜總會中在靠近客人的桌子的地方表演的一種色情舞蹈〕—compare 比較 LAP DANCING

T cell, T-cell /ˈti ˌsɛl; ˈtiː ˌsel/ *n* [C]
a type of WHITE BLOOD CELL that helps the body fight disease T〔淋巴〕細胞

Tae-Bo /ˌtaɪ ˋbo; ˌtaɪ ˈbəʊ/ *n* [U]
a type of exercise that combines dancing, kicking, and quick hand movements 太保操, 韻律搏擊〔包括跳舞踢打等動作〕

tag /tæg; tæg/ *n* [C] *AmE*
NEW MEANING
someone's name or NICKNAME that they have painted on a wall, train etc illegally【美】塗鴉簽名: *You can see the tags of young graffiti artists in railway yards in every major city of the world.* 全世界所有大城市的火車站裡都可以看到年輕的亂塗藝術家的塗鴉簽名。

tag·ging /ˈtægɪŋ; ˈtægɪŋ/ *n* [U] *AmE*
the crime of painting your name or NICKNAME (=a pretend name that you call yourself) on walls, trains etc【美】塗鴉簽名: *Tagging landed Torres in the Santa Clara County boys ranch for juvenile offenders for five months.* 托雷斯因為到處亂塗簽名而被關進聖克拉拉縣男少年勞教牧場五個月。| *These kids see the older boys going out and tagging, getting their names up, and they want to do it.* 這些小孩子見到那些大孩子出去把名字亂塗在牆上, 於是也想學樣。—**tagger** *n* [C]: *California's most prolific tagger is suspected of spray-painting the name 'Chaka' at 10,000 locations from Los Angeles to San Francisco.* 人們懷疑加利福尼亞最多產的塗鴉者在從洛杉磯到三藩市的一萬多處用油漆噴塗了"Chaka"這個名字。

talk /tɔk; tɔːk/ *v*
NEW MEANING
talk trash *AmE informal* to say impolite or offensive things to or about someone, especially to opponents in a sports competition【美, 非正式】〔尤指對運動比賽中的對手〕謾罵: *Both teams talk trash on the basketball court.* 兩隊在籃球場上對罵了起來。

talk time /ˈtɔk ˌtaɪm; ˈtɔːk ˌtaɪm/ *n* [U]
the time when a MOBILE PHONE is being used to make or receive calls or messages〔手機的〕通話時間: *The rechargeable battery allows approximately 135 minutes of talk time.* 充電式電池能維持大約 135 分鐘通話時間。

ta·mox·i·fen /təˋmɑksɪfɛn; təˈmɒksɪfen/ *n* [U]
trademark a drug that is used to treat breast cancer【商標】他莫昔芬, 三苯氧胺〔用於治療乳腺癌〕

tank /tæŋk; tæŋk/ *n*
NEW MEANING
in the tank *AmE informal* failing and losing money【美, 非正式】失敗賠錢: **be/go in the tank** *Sales can't keep going up, but that doesn't mean the industry is going in the tank.* 銷售額不能保持增長的勢頭, 但這並不意味該行業失敗賠錢。

tan·ki·ni /tæŋˋkini; tæŋˈkiːni/ *n* [C]
a type of BIKINI that has a small shirt with no SLEEVES as its top part 坦基尼〔比基尼的一種〕: *Julie was wearing a stylish tankini and sandals.* 朱莉穿着一件挺時髦的坦基尼和一雙涼鞋。

ta·que·ri·a /ˌtækəˋriə; ˌtækəˈriːə/ *n* [C] *Spanish*
an informal MEXICAN restaurant, especially in the southwest US【西】〔尤指美國西南部的〕墨西哥食品快餐店

tariff /ˈtærɪf; ˈtærɪ̵f/ *n* [C] *BrE*
NEW MEANING
a list or system of prices which MOBILE PHONE companies charge for the different services they provide【英】手機分項服務收費表

task /tæsk; tɑːsk/ *v* [T]
to give someone the responsibility for doing something 分配〔某人〕任務: **be tasked with sth** *We were tasked with completing the job by the end of 2004.* 我們被指派在 2004 年底完成該項工作。

TAXOL, taxol /ˈtæksɔl; ˈtæksɒl/ *n* [U]
a drug made from the outer surface of a particular tree, that is used to treat CANCER of the ovaries (OVARY) 泰素〔又譯紫杉酚, 是一種抗卵巢癌藥物〕

team play·er /ˈtim ˌpleɚ; ˈtiːm ˌpleɪə/ *n* [C]
someone who works well as a member of a team, especially in business〔尤指生意上的〕合作夥伴, 具有團隊精神的人: *He was a good businessman, but never a team player.* 他是一名出色的生意人, 但從來不是一個好的合夥人。

teaser ad /ˈtizɚ ˌæd; ˈtiːzər ˌæd/ *n* [C]
an advertisement that is used to make people interested in a product, but that does not give very much information about the product, so that people will pay attention to more advertisements later 吊胃口廣告〔這種廣告先引起人們對產品的興趣, 但不會給予很多資料, 藉此吸引人們注意其後推出的更多廣告〕

technical sup·port /ˌtɛknɪkḷ səˋpɔrt; ˌteknɪkəl səˈpɔːt/ also 又作 **tech support** /ˈtɛk səˌpɔrt; ˈtek səˌpɔːt/ *n* [U]
1 help or information that you receive to improve a computer program or system, make it continue working, or use it correctly〔軟硬件的〕技術支援 **2** the department of a company that provides this type of help 技術支援服務部: *Maybe you'd better try calling tech support.* 或許你最好打電話去技術支援服務部。

tel·e·con·fe·rence[1] /ˈtɛlɪˌkɑnfərəns; ˈtelɪˌkɒnfərəns/ *n* [C]
a business meeting in which people in different places communicate by telephone, television etc 電視[電話]會議 —**teleconferencing** [U]: *video teleconferencing equipment* 視像電話會議設備

teleconference[2] /ˈtɛlɪˌkɑnfərəns; ˈtelɪˌkɒnfərəns/ *v* [I]
to have a meeting with people who are not in the same place as you, and be able to see and talk to them by using special VIDEO equipment or computers and telephone lines 召開電視[電話]會議

telephone bank·ing /ˈtɛləfon ˌbæŋkɪŋ; ˈtelɪ̵fəʊn ˌbæŋkɪŋ/ *n* [U]
a service provided by banks so that people can find out information about their bank account, pay bills etc by telephone rather than by going to a bank 電話銀行服務

tel·e·port /ˈtɛlɪˌport; ˈtelɪˌpɔːt/ *v* [I,T]
a word used in SCIENCE FICTION meaning to move or move something from one place to another immediately by using special powers or a machine such as a computer〔科幻小說經常提到的〕心靈運輸: *If you slay the dragon, you will be teleported to the palace.* 你如果殺死這條龍, 你將會被心靈傳送到王宮。—**teleportation** /ˌtɛlɪporˋteʃən; ˌtelɪpɔːˈteɪʃən/ *n* [U]

tel·e·thon /ˈtɛlɪθɑn; ˈtelɪ̵θɒn/ *n* [C]
a special television programme, usually lasting many hours, in which famous people provide entertainment and ask people to give money to CHARITY〔為募捐等舉行的〕馬拉松式電視節目

tel·e·van·ge·list /ˌtɛlɪˋvændʒəlɪst; ˌtelɪ̵ˈvændʒɪ̵lɪ̵st/ *n* [C]
someone who appears regularly on television to try to persuade people to become Christians, and often also asks people to give them money. This word comes from a combination of the words 'TELEVISION' and 'EVANGELIST' 電視佈道者〔由 television 和 evangelist 縮合而成〕: *With mass media now available, televangelists are already at work in Eastern Europe.* 電視佈道者已經借助現有的大眾傳媒在東歐開展活動。—**televangelism** *n* [U]

ten-bag·ger /ˈtɛn ˌbægɚ; ˈten ˌbægə/ *n* [C]
informal a SHARE whose value becomes ten times as big as it was when you bought it【非正式】十倍股〔購進後

即增值十倍的股票〕

ter·a·byte /ˋtɛrəˏbaɪt; ˈterəˌbaɪt/ *n* [C]
a unit for measuring the amount of information a computer can store or use, equal to a TRILLION BYTE*s* 一兆位元組, 兆兆字節, 太拉字節

ter·a·flop /ˋtɛrəflɑp; ˈterəflɒp/ *n* [C usually plural 一般用複數]
a unit that measures how fast a computer works. One teraflop is one TRILLION operations every second. 每秒萬億次浮點運算: *Two weeks ago the machine hit an astonishing speed of 1.8 teraflops, easily outdistancing the previous record holder.* 兩週前這台機器達到了每秒1.8萬億次的驚人速度, 輕易就把原先的記錄保持者遠遠地拋在後面。

term /tɝm; tɜːm/ *v*
NEW MEANING
be termed out of office *AmE* to be forced to leave a political position because the law says that someone can be in that position for only a particular number of years 【美】任期到後即退, 屆滿即退: *Senator Jansen will be termed out of office next year.* 參議員詹森明年因任期已滿將不得不離任。

test·deck /ˋtɛstdɛk; ˈtestdek/ *n* [C]
technical a computer PROGRAM that is used to check a small amount of information, which is then compared to the same work done by a person, to make sure the computer is operating correctly 【術語】測試程式

tes·ti·ly·ing /ˋtɛstəˏlaɪ-ɪŋ; ˈtestḷˌlaɪ-ɪŋ/ *n* [U]
the activity of saying things that are not true in a court of law. Some people believe that police officers do this in order to make sure that people who they think are guilty of a crime will go to prison, even if there is not enough proof. This word comes from a combination of 'TESTIFYING' and 'LYING'. 〔警方在法庭審訊過程中〕弄虛作假〔由 testifying 和 lying 縮合而成〕

text /tɛkst; tekst/ *v*
—see 見 TEXT MESSAGE[2]

text mes·sage[1] /ˋtɛkst ˏmɛsɪdʒ; ˈtekst ˌmesɪdʒ/ *n* [C]
a written message that is sent or received on a MOBILE PHONE or PAGER 〔手機或傳呼機的〕短信(息)

text message[2] /ˋtɛkst ˏmɛsɪdʒ; ˈtekst ˌmesɪdʒ/ also 又作 **text** *v* [T]
to send someone a written message on a MOBILE PHONE or PAGER 〔用手機或傳呼機〕給…發送短信(息): *I'll text you as soon as I get the results.* 一有結果我就給你發短信。

them·self /ðəmˋsɛlf; ðəmˈself/ *pron*
spoken used when you are referring to one person, but you want to avoid saying 'himself' or 'herself' because you do not know the sex of the person. Many people think this use is incorrect 【口】其人〔指"他"或"她", 因不知其性別時用, 但許多人認為這種用法並不正確〕: *It makes me happy to help someone help themself.* 能幫助人自助讓我感到高興。

the·oph·yl·line /θɪˋɑfəlin; θiˈɒfḷliːn/ *n* [U]
a drug similar to CAFFEINE that is used to treat heart and breathing problems 茶鹼

ther·mo·bar·ic /ˏθɝmoˋbærɪk; ˌθɜːməʊˈbærɪk/ *adj*
thermobaric weapons make a lot of heat and pressure when they explode and kill people by damaging their lungs and other organs 〔武器〕熱壓的, 熱衝擊波的: *There's no doubt that US Marines will encounter thermobaric weapons on battlefields in the near future.* 毫無疑問, 美國海軍陸戰隊在不久的將來會在戰場上遭遇到熱壓武器。

third age, Third Age /ˏθɝd ˋedʒ; ˌθɜːd ˈeɪdʒ/ *n* [singular, U]
the part of your life when you are 55 or older. People sometimes say 'third age' instead of 'old age' to emphasize that in this time of life people can still be healthy and active. 〔生命的〕第三年齡段〔婉指 old age (老年)〕: *Bob reinvented himself during third age, enjoying a new and different career.* 到了第三年齡段, 鮑勃徹底改變自己, 高興地從事另一項新的事業。| *a magazine for people in the Third Age of life* 針對老年人的雜誌 —**third age** *adj* [only before noun 僅用於名詞前]: *third age professionals* 老年專業人員 —**third ager** *n* [C]: *university programmes for third agers* 為老年人而設的大學課程

thrash met·al /ˋθræʃ ˏmɛtḷ; ˈθræʃ ˌmetl/ *n* [U]
a type of loud fast music that combines features of PUNK and HEAVY METAL music 刺耳金屬搖滾樂

thread /θrɛd; θred/ *n* [C]
NEW MEANING
a series of electronic messages concerning the same subject, written by members of an Internet discussion group 〔網上討論區上涉及同一個題目的〕一連串電子留言: *I'd like to refer to something that was posted in an earlier thread.* 我想提一下早前的一連串電子留言中說到的一件事。

three-peat /ˋθri ˏpit; ˈθriː ˌpiːt/ *n* [C] *AmE informal* the act of winning a sports competition three times, one after the other. The word comes from a combination of the words 'three' and 'repeat' 【美, 非正式】三連冠〔由 three 和 repeat 縮合而成〕: **pull off a three-peat** *Laura Davies is trying to become the first player to pull off a three-peat since Sandra Haynie.* 勞拉·戴維斯正力爭成為繼桑德拉·海尼之後第一個贏得三連冠的運動員。

thumbnail /ˋθʌmˏnel; ˈθʌmneɪl/ *n* [C]
NEW MEANING
a small picture on a computer screen of a document, showing you what it will look like when you print it 縮略圖〔網頁上指甲大小的圖塊〕: *Click on the thumbnails to view a larger version of each image.* 點擊縮略圖, 看一下每個圖像的放大版本。

THX
a written abbreviation of 縮寫= 'thanks', used in E-MAIL or TEXT MESSAGE*s* on MOBILE PHONE*s* 謝謝〔電子郵件或手機短信用語〕

tick /tɪk; tɪk/ *v*
tick down *phr v* [I] *technical* if the price of a financial SHARE, BOND product etc ticks down, its value decreases 【術語】〔股票、債券等〕貶值: *Rates on 30-year mortgages ticked down last week.* 上週為期30年的抵押債券價格下跌。
tick up *phr v* [I] *technical* if the price of a financial SHARE, BOND product etc ticks up, its value increases 〔股票、債券等〕升值; 〔價格〕上揚: *Economists predict that oil prices will tick up again.* 經濟學家預言石油價格將再次上揚。

tick·et·ing /ˋtɪkɪtɪŋ; ˈtɪkḷtɪŋ/ *n* [U]
the process or system of selling or printing tickets for planes, trains, concerts etc 〔飛機、火車、音樂會等〕售票; 售票系統: *Most airlines are using electronic ticketing now.* 目前大多數航空公司都使用電子售票。

TIFF /tɪf; tɪf/ *n* [C]
technical Tag Image File Format; a type of computer FILE created by a SCANNER or DESKTOP PUBLISHING PROGRAM 【術語】〔掃描儀或桌面出版系統中的〕標記圖像檔案格式

time-poor /ˋtaɪm ˏpur; ˈtaɪm ˌpʊə/ *adj BrE*
someone who is time-poor does not have very much free time because they work all day and often work in the evenings too 【英】缺乏空閒時間的〔極為忙碌, 由早忙到晚〕: *These young men, exceedingly rich, are time-poor because of their demanding jobs on the Stock Exchange.* 這些年輕人雖然十分富裕但卻缺乏餘暇時間, 因為他們在證券交易所的工作十分忙碌。

tip·pee trad·ing /tɪˋpi ˏtredɪŋ; tɪˈpiː ˌtreɪdɪŋ/ *n* [U]
an illegal situation in which someone who receives secret information about a company, SHARE*s* etc tells another person about it, and then that person uses the information to gain a financial advantage 〔股票買賣等的〕內幕交易 —see also 另見 INSIDER TRADING

tip sheet /ˋtɪp ˏʃit; ˈtɪp ˌʃiːt/ *n* [C]

informal a newspaper that gives advice and information about which SHARES should be bought and sold【非正式】提供股市行情的報章: *a tip sheet for private investors* 面向私人投資者的股市行情報章

TLA /ˌti ɛl ˋe; ˌtiː el ˈeɪ/ *n* [C]
three-letter acronym; a combination of three letters, such as BTW or IMO, that are used as a short form of a phrase, especially on the Internet and in E-MAILS 三字母縮寫詞〔尤在互聯網和電子郵件中使用〕

to-die-for /tə ˋdaɪ ˌfɔr; tə ˈdaɪ ˌfɔː/ *adj*
informal humorous extremely good or desirable【非正式, 幽默】好得要命的, 極合意的: *Betty's strawberry cheesecake is simply to-die-for.* 貝蒂的草莓乾酪蛋糕美味極了！| *Their recently launched cosmetics line comes in to-die-for packaging of purple, orange, or red plastic.* 他們最近推出的化妝品系列採用了特酷的紫色、橙色和紅色塑料包裝。

toning ta·bles /ˋtonɪŋ ˌteblz; ˈtəʊnɪŋ ˌteɪbəlz/ *n* [plural]
a piece of equipment that you lie on and that moves your arms and legs up and down, which is supposed to make your muscles firmer 健身牀

top /tap; tɒp/ *adj, interjection BrE*
NEW MEANING
spoken informal very good【英口, 非正式】一流的: *I just love that man, he's a top guy.* 我就是愛那個男人, 他是個出色的人。| *D'you like onion on your pizza? —Oh, top!* 你想在意大利薄餅上放點洋葱嗎? —— 噢, 那可棒極了!

Total Qual·i·ty Man·age·ment /ˌtotl̩ ˋkwalətɪ ˌmænɪdʒmənt; ˌtəʊtl ˈkwɒlɪ̣ti ˌmænɪdʒmənt/ *abbreviation* 縮寫為 **TQM** *n* [U]
a system for making sure that each department in an organization works in the most effective way and that the goods or services it produces are of the best quality possible 全面質量管理

tot·ty, tottie /ˋtatɪ; ˈtɒti/ *n* [C,U] *BrE*
slang an offensive word used by men to describe women who they think are sexually attractive【英俚】騷貨〔男人形容女人的冒犯語〕

touch·y-feel·y /ˌtʌtʃɪ ˋfilɪ; ˌtʌtʃi ˈfiːli/ *adj*
informal expressing sympathy and care towards other people, often in a way that does not seem sincere, and using a lot of physical contact between people, such as HUG*ging*【非正式】〔常指通過擁抱等身體接觸, 不太真誠地〕表示關愛的: *a touchy-feely afternoon talk show* 一個流於表面關懷的午間清談節目 | *The whole atmosphere was getting a little too touchy-feely for me.* 整個氣氛對我來說有點肉麻。

TQM /ˌti kju ˋɛm; ˌtiː kjuː ˈem/
abbreviation of 縮寫= TOTAL QUALITY MANAGEMENT

tracker fund /ˋtrækɚ ˌfʌnd; ˈtrækə ˌfʌnd/ *n* [C] *BrE*
technical another name for an INDEX FUND: an INVESTMENT that includes a combination of SHARES that are in a particular SHARE INDEX, and that earns money depending on the value of the shares in that index【英, 術語】指數基金

trance /træns; trɑːns/ *n* [U]
NEW MEANING
a type of popular electronic dance music with a fast beat and long continuous notes played on a SYNTHESIZER〔用電子音響合成器演奏的〕電子舞曲

trans·gen·der /ˌtrænzˋdʒɛndɚ; ˌtrænzˈdʒendə/ also 又作 **transgendered** *adj* [only before noun 僅用於名詞前]
a transgender person wants to be or look like a member of the opposite sex, especially by having a medical operation〔尤指通過手術〕變換性別的 —**transgender** *n* [C] —**transgenderism** *n* [U]

trans·gen·ic /ˌtrænsˋdʒɛnɪk; ˌtrænzˈdʒenɪk/ *adj*
technical having one or more GENES from a different type of animal or plant【術語】轉基因的: *transgenic mice* 轉基因老鼠

trash /træʃ; træʃ/ *v* [T]
NEW MEANING
informal to criticize someone or something severely【非正式】抨擊: *Some of the people he trashed on the show are planning to sue.* 在電視節目中受到他抨擊的人中有幾個正打算向他提出訴訟。

trash talk·ing, trash-talking /ˋtræʃ ˌtɔkɪŋ; ˈtræʃ ˌtɔːkɪŋ/ *n* [U] *AmE*
rude or insulting language spoken by a member of a sports team to or about a member of another sports team, or the same kind of language spoken by sports FANS【美】〔運動員或運動迷〕用侮辱性語言罵人: *Coaches say they want to take trash talking out of high school football.* 教練們說他們想杜絕學校足球賽中的罵人現象。—**trash talker** *n* [C]

trash·talk /ˋtræʃˌtɔk; ˈtræʃtɔːk/ *n* [U] *AmE*
informal things you say about someone that are not nice【美, 非正式】侮辱性語言: *I'm not prepared to tolerate any trashtalk on court.* 我不會在法庭上容忍任何侮辱性語言。

trend-chas·ing, trend chasing /ˋtrɛnd ˌtʃezɪŋ; ˈtrend ˌtʃeɪzɪŋ/ *n* [U]
1 the act of copying what other people are doing or what is currently popular 趕時髦: *The music is complete, with no trend chasing or compromise.* 這首樂曲很完美, 沒有趕時髦或折中的傾向。**2** *technical* a way of INVESTING (=giving money to a company in order to get a profit) in which you watch how others are investing and copy them【術語】〔投資中的〕跟風: *trend-chasing among investors* 投資者中的跟風現象 —**trend-chaser** *n* [C]

trend·spot·ter /ˋtrɛndˌspatɚ; ˈtrendˌspɒtə/ *n* [C]
someone who notices and reports on new fashions, activities that people are starting to do, or the way a situation is developing 時尚觀察者

trey /tre; treɪ/ *n* [C] *AmE*
NEW MEANING
an action of throwing a basketball through the HOOP that is worth three points【美】〔籃球〕三分球

trial bal·loon /ˋtraɪəl bəˌlun; ˈtraɪəl bəˌluːn/ *n* [C]
something that you do or say in order to see whether other people will accept something or not 試探性言行: *Senator Lott is floating trial balloons to test public opinion on the bill.* 參議員洛特正試探公眾對該議案的看法。

tri-band /ˋtraɪ ˌbænd; ˈtraɪ ˌbænd/ *adj*
a tri-band MOBILE PHONE is one that will work in the US and Canada as well as in Britain〔手機〕三頻的〔可在美國、英國和加拿大使用〕

trickle[1] /ˋtrɪkl̩; ˈtrɪkəl/ *v* [I]
NEW MEANING
trickle up *phr v* [I] if money trickles up, it tends to move from the poorest people to the richest people in a society, or from the poorest countries to the richest countries 資金外流, 逆滴〔指金錢由窮人或窮國流向富人或富國〕

trip /trɪp; trɪp/ *v*
NEW MEANING
sb is tripping *AmE slang* used to say that you think someone is not thinking clearly or being reasonable【美俚】某人在犯糊塗: *Ken's tripping if he thinks I'm going to lend him $500.* 肯如果認為我會借給他500美元, 那是他腦子有病。

trol·leyed /ˋtralɪd; ˈtrɒlid/ *adj* [not before noun 不用於名詞前] *BrE*
slang very drunk or affected by drugs【英俚】大醉的; 吸毒後迷迷糊糊的: *I'm a totally different person when I'm trolleyed.* 喝醉了的時候, 我會變成完全另外的一個人。

trophy wife /ˋtrofɪ ˌwaɪf; ˈtrəʊfi ˌwaɪf/ *n* [C]
a young beautiful woman who is married to a rich and successful man〔嫁給大款的〕年輕貌美的妻子: *The resort was full of doctors and lawyers with their trophy wives.* 度假勝地到處皆見有嬌妻作伴的醫生和律師。

trouser /ˋtraʊzɚ; ˈtraʊzə/ *v* [T] *BrE*
informal to take and keep a large amount of money, usu-

ally dishonestly【英, 非正式】把〔錢〕佔為己有: *It's true that he trousered several hundred thousand pounds, but his dishonesty went far beyond that.* 不錯, 他是把幾十萬鎊的錢佔為己有, 但是, 他的不誠實行為遠不止此。

trust·a·fari·an /ˌtrʌstəˈfɛrɪən; ˌtrʌstəˈfeəriən/ *n* [C] *BrE informal* a young man or woman who has very rich parents and who usually lives in a rich area, but who dresses and acts like someone from a much poorer background【英, 非正式】〔衣着、舉止〕像窮人的富家子女

'tude /tud; tjuːd/ *n* [U] *AmE slang* an attitude, style, type of behaviour etc that shows you have the confidence to do unusual and exciting things without caring what other people think; attitude【美俚】自信, 神氣: **with 'tude** *Atlanta is definitely a city with 'tude.* 亞特蘭大確實是一座神氣十足的城市。

turn·ta·blist /ˈtɝnˌteblɪst; ˈtɜːnˌteɪblɪst/ *n* [C] *informal* a DEEJAY who plays recorded music at parties or dances, and who mixes together parts of different records to form new music【非正式】〔聚會或舞會上的〕混合音樂唱片騎師

TV-14 /ˌti vi fɔrˈtin; ˌtiː viː fɔːˈtiːn/ *adj* used in the US to show that a television programme is not suitable for children under the age of 14〔美國電視節目〕14歲以下兒童不宜的

TV-G /ˌti vi ˈdʒi; ˌtiː viː ˈdʒiː/ *adj* used in the US to show that a television programme is suitable for people of all ages, including children〔美國電視節目〕各年齡組皆宜的

TV-M /ˌti vi ˈɛm; ˌtiː viː ˈem/ *adj* used in the US to show that a television programme is not suitable for people under the age of 17〔美國電視節目〕適於17歲以上成人觀看的

TV-PG /ˌti vi pi ˈdʒi; ˌtiː viː piː ˈdʒiː/ *adj* used in the US to show that a television programme may include parts that are not suitable for young children to see〔美國電視節目〕含有部分兒童不宜的

TV-Y/ˌti vi ˈwaɪ; ˌtiː viː ˈwaɪ/ *adj* used in the US to show that a television programme is suitable for children〔美國電視節目〕適於兒童觀看的

TV-Y7 /ˌti vi waɪ ˈsɛvən; ˌtiː viː waɪ ˈsevən/ *adj* used in the US to show that a television programme is not suitable for children under the age of seven〔美國電視節目〕七歲以下兒童不宜的

tween /twin; twiːn/ also 又作 **tween·ag·er** /ˈtwinedʒɚ; ˈtwiːneɪdʒə/ *n* [C] children who are 11 or 12 years old; PRE-TEENS〔十一二歲的〕兒童: *The study found that tweens – not older teenagers – fight most often with their parents.* 研究顯示, 十一二歲的兒童〔而不是更大的少年〕和父母吵得最多。

24/7 /ˌtwɛntɪˌfɔr ˈsɛvən; ˌtwentifɔː ˈsevən/ *adv slang* twenty-four hours a day, seven days a week; all the time【俚】一天二十四小時, 一週七天; 每時每刻, 不間斷地: *I can't stop thinking about her 24/7.* 我忍不住時時都在想她。—**24/7** *adj*: *a 24/7 call center* 二十四小時運作的電話服務中心

twen·ty·some·thing /ˈtwɛntɪˌsʌmθɪŋ; ˈtwentiˌsʌmθɪŋ/ *n* [C] someone who is between the ages of 20 and 29 二十多歲的人: *A crowd of twentysomethings were gathered outside the club.* 俱樂部外面聚了一羣二十多歲的男女青年。

U,u

ultimate fight·ing /ˌʌltəmɪt ˈfaɪtɪŋ; ˌʌltɪmɪt ˈfaɪtɪŋ/ also 又作 **extreme fighting** *n* [U] a competition, similar to BOXING, in which two people are allowed to hit or kick each other and in which there are almost no rules. Ultimate fighting is not illegal in some countries, and in some parts of the US.〔類似拳擊的〕極限打鬥

un·plugged /ʌnˈplʌgd; ʌnˈplʌgd/ *adj, adv* if a group of musicians performs unplugged, they perform without electric instruments〔音樂演奏〕不用電子樂器的[地], 不插電的[地]

unzip /ʌnˈzɪp; ˌʌnˈzɪp/ *v* [T]
NEW MEANING
to change a computer FILE back to its normal size so that you can use it, after it has been made to take up less space 給〔電腦文檔〕解壓縮

up³ /ʌp; ʌp/ *adj*
NEW MEANING
be up for sth *spoken* to be willing to do something that someone invites you to do with them【口】心甘情願地做某事: *John wanted to see a movie last night, but I just wasn't up for it.* 約翰昨晚想去看電影, 可是我恰好沒有心思去。| **be up for doing sth** *I might be up for having a drink later.* 我也許晚些時候會樂意去喝上一杯。

up·draft /ˈʌpˌdræft; ˈʌpdrɑːft/ *n* [C] a situation in which prices, SHARES etc go up, or when business becomes better〔價格、股票等〕上揚;〔生意〕看好

up·load¹ /ˈʌpˌlod; ˈʌpləʊd/ *v* [I,T] if information, a computer PROGRAM etc uploads, or if you upload it, you move it from a small computer to a computer network so that many people can see it or use it 上傳, 上載〔由終端輸入中央電腦〕: *I was trying to upload something to an electronic bulletin board but crashed the system.* 我想上傳資料到電子告示牌上, 但卻把系統弄壞了。| *It might take a while for this to upload.* 把這些資料上傳也許需要一些時間。

upload² /ˈʌpˌlod; ˈʌpləʊd/ *n* [C] information, computer PROGRAMS etc that have been uploaded, or the process of uploading them 上傳的信息; 上傳的程式; 上傳: *You can receive regular e-mail updates of new uploads.* 你可以定期收到最新上傳內容的電子郵件。| *tips on handling file uploads* 上傳文檔的操作提示

up·skill·ing /ˈʌpˌskɪlɪŋ; ˈʌpˌskɪlɪŋ/ *n* [U] improving the skills of workers, usually through training, so that they will be better at their jobs 透過培訓提高工人的技能

up·tick /ˈʌpˌtɪk; ˈʌptɪk/ *n* [C] an increase or improvement in the level of something 提高, 上升: **[+in]** *We have had an uptick in sales this year.* 我們本年度的銷售額有所提高。

up·time /ˈʌpˌtaɪm; ˈʌptaɪm/ *n* [U] the period of time when a computer is working normally and is able to be used〔電腦的〕正常運行時間, 可使用時間: *Some customers need 99% or better uptime from their mainframe computers.* 一些顧客需要他們的主電腦能有99%或更長的正常運行時間。

URL /ˌju ɑr ˈɛl; ˌjuː ɑːr ˈel/ *n* [C] uniform resource locator; a description of where a particular computer FILE can be found, especially on the Internet. Internet URLs usually begin with http:// 統一信息源定位器

USB /ˌju ɛs ˈbi; ˌjuː es ˈbiː/ *n* [C] universal serial bus; a way of connecting equipment such as a MOUSE and printer to a computer using wires so that all the equipment can work together 通用串行總線, 通用序列埠: *Many USB devices come with their own built-in cable.* 許多帶通用序列埠接口的設備都有內置連線。

user fee /ˈjuzɚ ˌfi; ˈjuːzə ˌfiː/ *n* [C]
NEW MEANING
an amount of money someone pays for a service on the Internet〔上網〕用戶費

user name /ˈjuzɚ ˌnem; ˈjuːzə ˌneɪm/ also 又作 **user ID** /ˈjuzɚ aɪ ˌdi; ˈjuːzər aɪ ˌdiː/ *n* [C] a name or special word that proves who you are and allows you to enter a computer system or use the Internet. Usually, this name and PASSWORD must be entered into the computer before you are allowed to use the computer or the Internet 用戶名稱: *Please enter your user name and password and click 'OK'.* 請輸入你的用戶名稱和密碼, 然後點擊 'OK'。| *The computer keeps saying my user name is invalid.* 電腦反覆顯示我的用戶名稱無效。

USP /ˌju ɛs ˈpi; ˌjuː es ˈpiː/ *n* [C]
unique selling proposition; a feature of a product that makes it different from other similar products, and therefore more attractive to people who might buy it 商品特色, 賣點: *Your business needs to have a USP.* 你的生意需要有經營特色。

V,v

value-ad·ded re·sell·er /ˌvælju ædɪd rɪˈsɛlɚ; ˌvæljuː ædəd riˈselə/ *abbreviation* 縮寫為 **VAR** *n* [C]
a person or company who sells goods, especially computers, after combining them with other products or services, in order to increase their value〔尤指電腦的〕增值分銷商

vanilla /vəˈnɪlə; vəˈnɪlə/ also 又作 **plain vanilla** *adj*
NEW MEANING
very basic and having no special features 基本的, 普普通通的, 沒有特色的: *Their vanilla model is priced at just under five hundred dollars.* 他們的基本型號的價格僅在500美元以下。| *The company produces plain vanilla computer chips.* 該公司生產普通的電腦芯片。

va·pour·ware *BrE*【英】, **vaporware** *AmE*【美】/ˈvepɚˌwɛr; ˈveɪpəweə/ *n* [U]
humorous a new type of computer product that has been advertised but is not finished or available to buy yet. This word comes from a combination of the words 'VAPOUR', which means a mass of small drops of liquid floating in the air, and 'HARDWARE' or 'SOFTWARE'.【幽默】朦朧件, 霧件〔指已進行廣告宣傳但尚未上市的電腦新產品, 由 vapour 和 hardware 或 software 縮合而成〕

VAR /ˌvi e ˈɑr; ˌviː eɪ ˈɑː/ *n* [C]
abbreviation of 縮寫 = VALUE-ADDED RESELLER

V-chip /ˈvi ˌtʃɪp; ˈviː ˌtʃɪp/ *n* [C]
an electronic CHIP in a television that allows parents to prevent their children from watching programmes that are violent or have sex in them V芯[晶]片〔一種可裝入電視機內能阻斷暴力或色情節目的電子芯片〕

vCJD /ˌvi si dʒe ˈdi; ˌviː siː dʒeɪ ˈdiː/ *n* [U]
new variant Creutzfeldt-Jacob Disease; a human form of the deadly brain disease BSE 新變異型克雅病, 人類瘋牛症: *Early symptoms of vCJD may include memory loss and difficulty walking.* 變異克雅病的早期症狀包括喪失記憶和行走困難。

veg·e·ta·tive /ˈvɛdʒəˌtetɪv; ˈvedʒətətɪv/ *adj*
a vegetative state a condition in which you cannot think or move because your brain has been damaged in an accident 植物人狀態

vertical ex·pan·sion /ˌvɝtɪkl ɪkˈspænʃən; ˌvɜːtɪkəl ɪkˈspænʃən/ *n* [U]
technical a situation in which a company starts to do some of the business activities that were done in the past by companies that supplied it with goods or services, or by its customers【術語】縱向擴展, 搶行〔開始經營過去由供應商或客戶提供的業務〕

Vi·ag·ra /vaɪˈægrə; vaɪˈægrə/ *n* [U]
trademark a drug that helps men have an ERECTION (1)【商標】萬艾可, 偉哥〔一種男性春藥〕

vid·e·o·card /ˈvɪdɪoˌkɑrd; ˈvɪdiəʊˌkɑːd/ *n* [C]
a CIRCUIT BOARD (=piece of electronic equipment carrying electrical signals) that can be added to a computer so that it is able to show moving pictures〔電腦的〕視頻卡, 顯示卡

video on de·mand /ˌvɪdɪo ɑn dɪˈmænd; ˌvɪdiəʊ ɒn dɪˈmɑːnd/ *n* [U]
a service available on the Internet that allows you to choose and watch recordings of television programmes or films that have been stored as computer FILEs〔網上〕視頻點播(服務)

viral mar·ket·ing /ˌvaɪrəl ˈmɑrkɪtɪŋ; ˌvaɪərəl ˈmɑːkətɪŋ/ *n* [U]
a type of advertising used by Internet companies in which computer users receive and send out advertising messages or images through E-MAIL without being aware that they are doing this. This kind of marketing is named after the computer VIRUS, which spreads rapidly among computer users〔互聯網公司進行的〕病毒式行銷(手法): *You can reach more potential customers by using viral marketing techniques.* 利用病毒式行銷, 你可以接觸到更多潛在的客戶。

virgin /ˈvɝdʒɪn; ˈvɜːdʒən/ *n* [U]
NEW MEANING
spoken humorous someone who has never done a particular activity【口, 幽默】生手, 新手: *Even computer virgins should be able to quickly learn how to use this software.* 就連電腦新手也能很快地學會如何使用這軟件。

virtual /ˈvɝtʃuəl; ˈvɜːtʃuəl/ *adj* [only before noun 僅用於名詞前]
NEW MEANING
relating to something that is made, done, seen etc on a computer, rather than in the real world〔電腦〕虛擬的: *The website allows you to take a virtual tour of the campus.* 該網站能讓你對校園作一次虛擬遊覽。

virtual ad·ver·ti·sing /ˌvɝtʃuəl ˈædvɚtaɪzɪŋ; ˌvɜːtʃuəl ˈædvətaɪzɪŋ/ *n* [U]
advertising that is added to a television programme of a sports event, and which uses SPECIAL EFFECTS so that only the people who are watching the event on television can see it 虛擬廣告〔以特別效果放在電視播映的體育比賽節目中, 只有收看該節目的觀眾才看到〕

virtual cash /ˌvɝtʃuəl ˈkæʃ; ˌvɜːtʃuəl ˈkæʃ/ *n* [U]
money that is used to pay for something that you buy on the Internet, using a CREDIT CARD〔網上購物使用的〕虛擬現金

virtual com·mu·ni·ty /ˌvɝtʃuəl kəˈmjunətɪ; ˌvɜːtʃuəl kəˈmjuːnəti/ also 又作 **community** *n* [C]
a group of people who use the Internet to discuss things with each other and share ideas about a particular subject or common interest 虛擬社區〔指在網上討論共同題目的羣眾〕: *a list of online music communities* 在線音樂虛擬社區清單

virtually /ˈvɝtʃuəlɪ; ˈvɜːtʃuəli/ *adv*
NEW MEANING
on a computer, rather than in the real world〔電腦〕虛擬地: *Both articles were virtually published on the Internet before appearing in the magazine.* 兩篇文章都是先在網上發表, 然後才刊登在雜誌上的。

virtual of·fice /ˌvɝtʃuəl ˈɔfɪs; ˌvɜːtʃuəl ˈɒfəs/ *n* [C]
a situation in which a company's workers do not go to an office to work, but instead use computers that are connected to the Internet to work and communicate with each other from different places 虛擬辦公室: *Does the virtual office equal freedom or isolation?* 虛擬辦公室意味着自由還是隔絕呢?

virus /ˈvaɪrəs; ˈvaɪərəs/ *n* [C]
a PROGRAM that sends a large number of annoying messages to many people's MOBILE PHONEs in an uncontrolled way〔手提電話〕病毒

visit /ˈvɪzɪt; ˈvɪzət/ *v* [T]
NEW MEANING
to go to a WEBSITE on the Internet 訪問〔網站〕: *Over 1,000 people visit our site every week.* 每個星期有千餘人到訪我們的網站。—**visitor** *n* [C]

visitation /ˌvɪzəˈteʃən; ˌvɪzəˈteɪʃən/ *n* [C,U]
NEW MEANING
law in a situation where parents are DIVORCEd, an occasion when one parent is allowed to spend time with their children who are living with the other parent, or the right

to do this【法律】〔離婚夫婦對跟另一方生活的子女的〕探視: *visitation rights* 探視權

VOD /ˌvi o ˋdi; ˌviː əʊ ˈdiː/ *n* [U]
video on demand; a special service that lets television viewers pay to watch particular films at whatever time they choose to watch them 視頻點播（服務），自選電視（節目）

voice jail /ˋvɔɪs ˌdʒel; ˈvɔɪs ˌdʒeɪl/ *n* [U]
humorous a telephone system that contains recorded messages giving you information or instructions, and that requires you to make different choices by pressing buttons on your telephone. This expression comes from a combination of the words 'voice mail' and 'jail' because some people find it annoying not to be able to speak to a real person on these systems【幽默】電話語音提示系統〔由voice mail和jail縮合而成〕: *When the caller lost in voice jail is a potential customer, your company risks losing a sale.* 如果對電話語音提示搞不清楚的來電者是潛在的顧客，貴公司就有可能失去一次生意。

voice mail·box /ˋvɔɪs ˌmelbɑks; ˈvɔɪs ˌmeɪlbɒks/ *n* [C]
a system in which telephone messages are recorded onto a computer so that someone can listen to them later 語音信箱，留言信箱: *To access your voice mailbox, dial 3882.* 要進入你的語音信箱，請撥打3882。

voyeur TV /vwɑˋjɝ ti ˌvi; vwɑːˈjɜː tiː ˌviː/ *n* [U]
television programmes that show a group of ordinary people who have been chosen to be recorded while doing things in their daily lives, without a planned SCRIPT. Some people disapprove of this type of programme because they do not think it is right to watch other people's private lives 記實電視節目，窺視電視節目

VR /ˌvi ˋɑr; ˌviː ˈɑː/
the abbreviation of 縮寫= VIRTUAL REALITY

vulture cap·i·tal·ist /ˋvʌltʃɚ ˌkæpətl̩ɪst; ˈvʌltʃə ˌkæpɪ̈tlɪst/ *n* [C]
someone who INVESTS money in a new business but then takes control of the business, usually in an unfair way 禿鷹資本家，敵意收購資本家〔投資新企業，然後通常以不公正的手法取得控制權的人〕

vulture fund /ˋvʌltʃɚ ˌfʌnd; ˈvʌltʃə ˌfʌnd/ *n* [C]
technical informal a company that INVESTS in companies that are having difficulties, in order to gain control of them【術語，非正式】禿鷹基金，敵意收購基金〔為取得控制權而投入的資金〕

W,w

wack /wæk; wæk/ *adj*
slang very bad【俚】低劣的，極差的: *Man, that is just so wack.* 老兄，那真是太差勁了。

wack·o /ˋwæko; ˈwækəʊ/ *n* [C]
informal someone who is crazy or behaves in a strange way【非正式】瘋癲的人；古怪的人

wait·ron /ˋwetrən; ˈweɪtrən/ *n* [C]
humorous a WAITER or WAITRESS【幽默】侍者，服務員

wake /wek; weɪk/ *v*
NEW MEANING
wake up and smell the coffee *spoken* used to tell someone that they should realize what is really happening in a situation【口】面對現實

wake-up call /ˋwek ʌp ˌkɔl; ˈweɪk ʌp ˌkɔːl/ *n* [C usually singular 一般用單數]
an experience or event that shocks you and makes you realize that something bad is happening and that changes must be made 警鐘: *Maybe the results of his medical exam will give Dad the wake-up call he needs to start living a healthier lifestyle.* 爸爸的體檢結果也許會給他敲響警鐘，使他認識到需要展開一種較健康的方式生活。

walk-in /ˋwɔk ˌɪn; ˈwɔːk ˌɪn/ *adj* [only before noun 僅用於名詞前]
NEW MEANING
walk-in business/clinic/centre etc a business, doctor's office etc that you can use or go to without an APPOINTMENT (=an arrangement to be somewhere or meet someone at an agreed time or place)〔不用預約的〕即時業務/診所/中心等

walking bus /ˋwɔkɪŋ ˌbʌs; ˈwɔːkɪŋ ˌbʌs/ *n* [C] *BrE*
a group of children who walk to or from school together, with other children and their parents joining the group at different places along the way【英】步行巴士〔一起走路上學或放學的孩子和他們的父母〕

walk·through /ˋwɔkˌθru; ˈwɔːkθruː/ *n* [C]
written instructions that tell you all the details of how you should play a VIDEO GAME 電腦遊戲指南，通關方法，攻略本: [+for] *The site has a collection of hints, cheats and walkthroughs for PC games.* 網站上有一系列關於個人電腦遊戲的提示、作弊碼和通關方法。| *the official walkthrough for Tomb Raider*〔電腦遊戲〕《盜墓者羅拉》的正式攻略本

WAP /wæp; wæp/ *n* [U]
wireless application protocol; a system that uses radio waves to allow electronic equipment that is not physically attached to a computer, for example a MOBILE PHONE, to use the Internet 無線應用通訊協定〔一種通訊制式〕

WAP-en·a·bled /ˋwæp ɪnˌebl̩d; ˈwæp ɪnˌeɪbəld/ *adj*
a WAP-enabled MOBILE PHONE can receive written information from the Internet on a small screen that is part of the phone〔手機〕可支援無線（上網）的

war chest /ˋwɔr ˌtʃɛst; ˈwɔː ˌtʃest/ *n* [C]
the money that a government has available to solve a problem〔政府的〕應急基金: *The government's huge war chest could be used to improve transport in time for the election.* 政府龐大的應急基金在選舉前可及時用於改善交通狀況。

was·a·bi /ˋwɑsəbɪ; ˈwɒsəbi/ *n* [U]
a green strong-tasting Japanese food, which is added to SUSHI and other food in small amounts in order to make it taste hotter 辣根，綠芥末〔一種日本調味料〕

was·sup /wɑˋsʌp; wɒˈsʌp/ *interjection*
slang another spelling of WHASSUP【俚】whassup的另一種拼法

water cool·er /ˋwɔtɚ ˌkulɚ; ˈwɔːtə ˌkuːlə/ *n* [C]
1 a machine that you can get a cup of drinking water from 飲水器 **2 water cooler gossip** conversation about other people's behaviour or private lives that happens in offices when people meet each other by the water cooler〔人們在辦公室飲水器旁說的〕閒話

WAV /ˌdʌbl̩ju e ˋvi; ˌdʌbəljuː eɪ ˈviː/ *n* [U]
technical waveform audio; a type of computer FILE that contains sound【術語】波形音頻〔一種包含聲音的電腦文件〕

web brows·er /ˋwɛb ˌbrauzɚ; ˈweb ˌbraʊzə/ *n* [C]
a BROWSER; a computer PROGRAM that finds information on the Internet and shows it on your computer screen 網絡瀏覽器

web·cam /ˋwɛbˌkæm; ˈwebkæm/ *n* [C]
a special camera that films events and broadcasts them on a WEBSITE as they happen 網絡攝影機

web·cast¹ /ˋwɛbˌkæst; ˈwebkɑːst/ *n* [C]
a programme that is broadcast on the Internet 網絡播放節目: *Visitors to our website can download tomorrow night's webcast for free.* 進入我們網站的訪客可免費下載明晚的網絡播放節目。

webcast² /ˋwɛbˌkæst; ˈwebkɑːst/ *v* [I,T]
to broadcast an event on the Internet, at the time the event happens 網絡〔即時〕播放: *Various local news sites plan to webcast each of the mayoral debates.* 各個地區的新聞網站計劃通過網絡播放每場市長競選辯論。

web·cast·ing /ˋwɛbˌkæstɪŋ; ˈwebˌkɑːstɪŋ/ *n* [U]
the use of the Internet to send information, especially news or entertainment, to many people at the same time 網上播放〔尤指新聞和娛樂活動〕

web de·sign·er /ˈwɛb dɪˌzaɪnɚ; ˈweb dɪˌzaɪnə/ *n* [C]
someone who designs WEBSITE*s*, especially websites for businesses or organizations 網站設計師

web·head /ˈwɛbˌhɛd; ˈwebhed/ *n* [C]
informal someone who uses the Internet a lot, especially in a skilful way【非正式】〔尤指熟練使用互聯網的〕網民, 網絡迷

web·log /ˈwɛbˌlɔg; ˈweblɒg/ also 又作 **blog** *n* [C]
a WEBSITE that contains a list of LINK*s* (=connections) that allow you to go to other websites, and a short description of those sites〔可連結其他網站, 並有其簡介的〕網站資訊中心: *Jay's Picks remains one of the most popular weblogs on the Internet.* 傑伊精選一直是互聯網上最受歡迎的網站資訊中心之一。

web·mast·er /ˈwɛbˌmæstɚ; ˈwebˌmɑːstə/ *n* [C]
someone who organizes a WEBSITE and makes sure it keeps working properly 網站管理[維護]員

web·page /ˈwɛbˌpedʒ; ˈwebpeɪdʒ/ *n* [C]
all the information that you can see in one section of a website. You have to CLICK on a button to go to another webpage on the same website. 網頁

web ring /ˈwɛb ˌrɪŋ; ˈweb ˌrɪŋ/ *n* [C]
a group of similar WEBSITE*s* which are connected to each other by LINK*s* to make it easy for people to find a lot of information on a particular subject on the Internet 網站聯盟: *a classical music web ring* 古典音樂網站聯盟

web·site /ˈwɛbˌsaɪt; ˈwebsaɪt/ *n* [C]
a set of FILE*s* on a computer that people can read over the Internet using a BROWSER〔萬維〕網站; 網址: *Nearly all publishers have their own websites now.* 現在差不多所有出版社都有自己的網站。

web·zine /ˈwɛbˌzin; ˈwebziːn/ *n* [C]
a collection of articles, stories, and pictures that you can see and read on the Internet, but is not printed onto paper or sold in stores 網絡雜誌

wet sales /ˈwɛt ˌselz; ˈwet ˌseɪlz/ *n* [plural] *BrE*
technical the money that a restaurant, bar etc makes from the sale of alcoholic drinks【英, 術語】售酒精飲料所得: *Most of the pub's money is made in wet sales.* 酒吧的錢大多數是靠售賣酒精飲料賺來的。

whack /hwæk; wæk/ *v* [T] *AmE*
slang to murder someone, especially in connection with MAFIA activities【美俚】謀殺〔尤與黑手黨活動有關〕: *O'Neill learned that the New Yorkers were planning to whack him.* 奧尼爾得知"紐約幫"在計劃幹掉他。—**whack** *n* [C]

whas·sup /wɑˋsʌp; wɒˈsʌp/ *interjection*
slang a word meaning 'hello', used especially as a greeting to someone you know very well【俚】喂; 你好〔對熟人的一種問候語〕

what /hwɑt; wɒt/ *pron*
NEW MEANING
what's up with that? *AmE spoken* used to say that you do not understand a situation or think it is unreasonable【美口】那是怎麼回事?〔用於表示不明白某情形或認為那是不合理的〕: *The college is raising tuition by 20% – what's up with that?* 學院要把學費提高 20% —— 那是怎麼回事?

whip·saw /ˈhwɪpsɔ; ˈwɪpsɔː/ *v* [T]
technical informal【術語, 非正式】**be whipsawed** if money that people have used to buy SHARE*s*, or people who have bought shares are whipsawed, they are trapped in a STOCK MARKET where prices are falling and rising very quickly, and it is difficult to say what might happen〔股票買賣中〕被套牢

white flight /ˈhwaɪt ˌflaɪt; ˈwaɪt ˌflaɪt/ *n* [U] *AmE*
a situation in which white people move away from an area or send their children to private schools in order to avoid being near people who are not white【美】白人遷移〔以逃避非白種人〕

white hat hack·er /ˌhwaɪt hæt ˋhækɚ; ˌwaɪt hæt ˈhækə/ *n* [C]
a computer HACKER who has been hired by a company to help protect its computer system. This word comes from the tradition in old Western films for the good people to wear white hats, while the bad people wore black hats. Computer HACKER*s* are usually considered to do harmful things to computer systems, but white hat hackers use their skills to do helpful things. 白帽黑客〔公司雇用以保護自己的電腦系統的網絡高手〕—**white hat hacking** *n* [U]

white van man /ˈhwaɪt væn ˌmæn; ˈwaɪt væn ˌmæn/ *n* [C] *BrE*
informal humorous a word used to talk about a man who drives a white VAN, especially for delivering goods to places in towns or cities, in an AGGRESSIVE and dangerous way【英, 非正式, 幽默】白色飛車手〔指駕駛白色貨車、開車魯莽的司機〕

wig·ger /ˈwɪgɚ; ˈwɪgə/ *n* [C]
slang humorous a white person who speaks and acts like a black person who is interested in, for example, HIP HOP music and culture【俚, 幽默】〔談話舉止像黑人的〕白人嬉蹦族

windfall tax /ˈwɪndfɔl ˌtæks; ˈwɪndfɔːl ˌtæks/ *n* [C]
in Britain, an additional amount of tax that the government sometimes takes from a company that has suddenly earned a large amount of money that it did not expect to earn 意外利潤税〔英國政府對企業意外獲得的大額收入徵收的税項〕

win·ning·est /ˈwɪnɪŋɪst; ˈwɪnɪŋɪst/ *adj AmE*
slang **the winningest team/pitcher/coach etc (in sth)** used in news reports of sporting events to describe the team, player etc that has won the most games【美俚】〔贏得比賽最多的〕常勝球隊/投手/教練等〔新聞報道用語〕: *Smith became the winningest coach in college basketball history.* 史密斯成了大學籃球賽歷史上獲勝次數最多的球隊教練。

win-win /ˌwɪn ˋwɪn; ˌwɪn ˈwɪn◂/ *adj* [only before noun 僅用於名詞前]
a win-win situation, strategy, approach etc is one that will end well for everyone involved in it 雙贏的: *It's a win-win situation all around.* 這在各個方面都是一種雙贏局面。—**win-win** *n* [C]: *The agreement is a win-win for everyone.* 這項協議對大家來説都是雙贏。

WIP /ˌdʌbljuˌ aɪ ˋpi; ˌdʌbəljuː aɪ ˈpiː/ *n*
work in progress or work in process; work that is being done 進行中的工作, 正在辦的事

wireless com·mu·ni·ca·tions /ˌwaɪrlɪs kəmjunəˋkeʃənz; ˌwaɪələs kəmjuːnɪˈkeʃənz/ *n* [plural]
a system of sending and receiving electronic signals that does not use electrical or telephone wires, for example the system used by MOBILE PHONE*s* 無線通訊

word /wɝd; wɜːd/ *n*
NEW MEANING
word! *AmE slang* used to say that you understand or agree with what someone has just said【美俚】一句話!沒說的!〔表示明白或贊成某人剛才說的話〕

work·flow /ˈwɝkˌflo; ˈwɜːkfləʊ/ *n* [U]
the way that a particular PROJECT is organized by a company, including which part of a project someone is going to do, and when they are supposed to do it 工作流程

WORM /wɝm; wɜːm/ *n* [C]
write once, read many; a CD on which information can be stored only once, but seen or used many times 一寫多讀〔光盤〕

worthy /ˈwɝðɪ; ˈwɜːði/ *adj*
NEW MEANING
I'm/We're not worthy *spoken humorous* used to say that you consider it a great honour to be with someone because they are famous, or much more skilful at doing something than you are【口, 幽默】我/我們深感榮幸

wrap /ræp; ræp/ *n* [C]
NEW MEANING
a type of SANDWICH made with thin bread which is rolled

around meat, vegetables etc〔用薄麵包裹着肉、菜等的〕麵捲餅

wraparounds 貼面式太陽眼鏡

wrap·a·rounds /ˋræpə͵raundz; ˈræpə͵raʊndz/ *n* [plural] a type of SUNGLASSES curved in such a way that they fit close to your face, from one ear to the other 圍裹式墨鏡, 貼面式太陽眼鏡

wreckage /ˋrɛkɪdʒ; ˈrekɪdʒ/ *n* [U]
NEW MEANING
a word used in news reports meaning a business activity, company etc that has failed or is likely to fail〔生意、公司等的〕失敗, 破產〔新聞報道用語〕

WRT
a written abbreviation of 縮寫= 'with regard to', used in E-MAIL or by people communicating in CHAT ROOMs on the Internet 關於..., 就...而言〔電子郵件和網上聊天室用語〕

X,x

X /ɛks; eks/ *n* [U] *AmE*
NEW MEANING
slang the illegal drug ECSTACY【美俚】"狂喜"迷幻藥, 搖頭丸

xen·o·trans·plant /͵zɛnoˋtrænsplænt; ͵zenəʊˈtrænsplɑːnt/ *n*
1 [C,U] the operation of putting an organ, piece of skin etc from an animal into a person's body 異種器官移植術, 動物器官人體移植術: *Doctors in Mississippi performed the world's first heart xenotransplant.* 密西西比州的醫生完成了世界上第一例異種心臟移植。**2** [C] the organ that is moved in this type of operation 異種移植的器官 —**xenotransplant** *v* [T] —**xenotransplanted** *adj: xenotransplanted organs* 異種移植的器官

xen·o·trans·plan·ta·tion /͵zɛno͵trænsplænˋteʃən; ͵zenəʊ͵trænsplɑːnˈteɪʃən/ *n* [U]
the practice of putting organs or other body parts from animals into people's bodies 異種器官移植術: *health risks related to xenotransplantation* 異種器官移植給健康帶來的風險

XML /͵ɛks ɛm ˋɛl; ͵eks em ˈel/ *n* [U]
technical extensible markup language; a way of writing a document on a computer so that its structure is clear, and so that it can easily be read on a different computer system【術語】可擴展置標語言

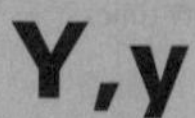

Y,y

Y2K /͵waɪ tu ˋke; ͵waɪ tuː ˈkeɪ/
the abbreviation of 縮寫= 'year two thousand', used especially to talk about problems that some people believed would affect many computers which did not recognize the date when the year 2000 began 公元2000年〔尤在談到千年蟲問題時使用〕: *Click here for a guide to the essential Y2K resources on the Internet.* 點擊此處可找到互聯網上2000年的重要資料的指南。

yad·a yad·a yad·a, yadda yadda yadda /͵jædə jædə ˋjædə; ͵jædə jædə ˈjædə/ *AmE*
spoken said when you do not want to give a lot of detailed information, because it is boring or because the person you are talking to already knows it【美口】如此這般〔不想提供詳細資料時用, 因為內容沉悶或聽者已經知道那事〕: *I started talking to her and – yada yada yada – it turns out she's from New York too.* 我開始跟她談話, 說了半天, 結果發現她也是紐約人。

Yard·ie /ˋjɑrdɪ; ˈjɑːdi/ *n* [C] *BrE*【英】
1 someone from the West Indies 西印度羣島人 **2** a member of an organized group of West Indian criminals 亞迪(幫成員)〔西印度羣島一個犯罪組織的成員〕

yoof /juf; juːf/ *adj* [only before noun 僅用於名詞前] *BrE humorous* relating to young people; YOUTH【英, 幽默】青年人的, 青年的: *a yoof magazine* 年輕人的雜誌 —**yoof** *n* [U] *today's yoof* 今日的年輕人

yup·pi·fy /ˋjʌpəfaɪ; ˈjʌpɪfaɪ/ *v* [T usually passive 一般用被動態]
humorous to improve the buildings in an area, or to open expensive restaurants, shops etc so that rich young people want to live in the buildings or use the restaurants etc. This word comes from the noun YUPPIE which is used to talk about young people in professional jobs with a high income that they enjoy spending.【幽默】〔建築物、昂貴的餐廳等〕使雅[優]皮士化〔源自名詞 yuppie 雅皮士, 指高收入、崇尚消費的專業人士〕: *The restaurant's yuppified interior was done in colors like teal and mauve.* 該飯館雅皮士化的內部裝修是以藍綠和淡紫等作為主色。

Z,z

zap /zæp; zæp/ *v* [I,T]
NEW MEANING
to change the CHANNEL on a television, using a remote control (=something that allows you to control a television without touching it)〔使用遙控器〕改換〔電視〕頻道: *Dave just sat there, zapping through all 70-plus channels.* 戴夫就坐在那裡, 用遙控器把70多個頻道全部掃視了一遍。

zero tol·e·rance /͵zɪro ˋtɑlərəns; ͵zɪərəʊ ˈtɒlərəns/ *n* [U]
a way of dealing with crime in which every person who breaks the law, even in a very small way, is punished as severely as possible 零容忍, 零寬容〔指對各種違法行為, 不論輕重, 一律嚴懲, 絕不容忍的做法〕: *The policy of zero tolerance has been proved effective in inner-city areas.* 零容忍政策證明在舊城區十分有效。

zine, 'zine /zin; ziːn/ *n* [C]
a small magazine, usually about things such as popular music, fashion etc, that is written and printed by people who are not professional writers〔由業餘人士編印的〕同好雜誌

zip file /ˋzɪp ͵faɪl; ˈzɪp ͵faɪl/ *n* [C]
technical a computer file in which the information is COMPRESSed (=made smaller) so that it uses less space【術語】壓縮文件[檔案]

IELTS Vocabulary

IELTS 常考詞彙

IELTS是International English Language Testing System的縮寫，即為國際英語水平測試，由英國文化協會聯同英國一些大學及澳洲教育機構等制訂，是國際認可的英語水平測試之一。由於其資格得到很多大學及企業的認可，近年吸引了不少人士投考。

IELTS的考試內容分四部分，包括聽力、會話、閱讀及寫作，考試時間共兩小時四十五分。每部分考試除有獨立分數外，亦有總分數。成績共分九級，考獲級數愈高，表示英語能力水平愈高。以考大學為例，一般要考獲第六級合格才有機會被大學錄取。目前已超過150個國家可提供IELTS考試。

詞彙在IELTS考試中佔有重要的位置。附錄所挑選的都是以往IELTS考卷中經常出現的詞彙。由於考試內容不斷更新變化，本附錄僅供各考生參考，不足之處，懇請原諒。

A, a

abandon[1] *v* **1** 拋棄，遺棄〔某人〕 **2** 離棄，逃離〔某地方或交通工具等〕 **3** 放棄，中止 **4** 放棄〔信仰或原則〕 **5 abandon yourself to** 沉湎於，放縱〔感情〕 **6 abandon ship** 〔由於船在下沉而〕棄船〔逃生〕 —**abandonment** *n*

abandon[2] *n* **with gay/wild abandon** 盡情；放縱

abnormal *adj* 不正常的，反常的；變態的

absorb *v* **1 ▶LIQUID 液體◀** 吸收〔液體〕 **2 ▶INFORMATION 信息◀** 理解，掌握 **3 ▶INTEREST 興趣◀** 吸引〔某人〕，使專心 **4 ▶BECOME PART OF 成為…的一部分◀** 併入；吞併 **5 ▶MONEY/TIME ETC 金錢/時間等◀** 消耗，花去 **6 ▶FORCE 力◀** 消減，緩衝 **7 ▶LIGHT/HEAT/ENERGY 光/熱/能◀** 吸收

abstract[1] *adj* **1** 純理論上的，純概念的 **2** 抽象的 **3** 〔藝術〕抽象派的

abstract[2] *n* **1 in the abstract** 抽象地，從理論上說 **2** 摘要，梗概 **3** 抽象派作品

abstract[3] *v* **1** 作摘要，節錄 **2** 轉移開

academic[1] *adj* **1** 學術的 **2** 學術上的；理論上的 **3** 不合實際的，理論的 **4** 學業〔成績〕優秀的 —**academically** *adv*

academic[2] *n* 大學教師

accelerate *v* **1** 加快，加速 **2** 〔使〕加快；〔使〕提前 —反義詞 DECELERATE

access[1] *n* **1** 入口；進入 **2** 途徑 **3** 進入權；使用權 **4 have access to** 有權接觸〔機密等〕 **5** 探視權 **6 have access to a phone/a computer etc** 附近有電話/電腦等可供使用 **7 gain/get access (to)** 到達〔某地〕；見到〔某人或某物〕

access[2] *v* 存取〔尤指電腦數據〕

accommodate *v* **1** 容納 **2** 為…提供住處[工作場所] **3** 迎合；遷就 **4** 〔使〕適應；〔使〕順應 **5** 寬限；通融

accompany *v* **1** 陪伴，陪同 **2** 為…伴奏 **3** 伴隨 **4** 附有，帶有，配有

accomplish *v* 完成〔任務等〕，取得〔成功〕

account[1] *n* **1 ▶DESCRIPTION 描述◀ a)** 報道，敍述，描寫 **b)** 詳盡的科學描述 **2 ▶AT A BANK 在銀行◀** 賬戶 **3 take account of sth/take sth into account** 把…考慮在內 **4 on account of** 因為，由於 **5 accounts a)** 賬目 **b)** 會計部 **6 on account** 賒賬 **7 ▶WITH A SHOP 與商店◀** 賒購賬 **8 ▶BILL 賬單◀** 賬單 **9 ▶ARRANGEMENT TO SELL GOODS 售貨安排◀** 客戶 **10 by/from all accounts** 根據各方面所說 **11 on my/his etc account** 為了我/他等的緣故 **12 on your own account** 靠自己；為自己 **13 on no account/not on any account** 決不 **14 by your own account** 據某人自己所說 **15 on that account/on this account** 考慮到那種/這種情況 **16 give a good/poor account of yourself** 表現好/表現差 **17 bring/call sb to account** 責令某人對…作出解釋 **18 put/turn sth to good account** 充分利用某物 **19 of no account/of little account** 不重要，沒關係 **20 of some account** 相當重要

account[2] *v*

account for sth *phr v* **1** 是…的原因 **2** 對…作出〔滿意的〕解釋 **3** 佔…〔比例〕 **4** 說明…在何處 **5 there's no accounting for taste** 人各有所好

accumulate *v* **1** 積累，積聚 **2** 大量聚積 —**accumulation** *n*

accurate *adj* **1** 〔資料、報道、描述等〕準確的 **2** 〔測量、計算、記錄等〕精確的，無差錯的 **3** 〔儀器〕精密的 **4** 〔射擊、投擲等〕準確的 —**accurately** *adv*

accustom *v* 使…習慣於

achieve *v* **1** 實現；取得；達到 **2** 獲得成功 —**achievable** *adj*

acknowledge *v* **1 ▶ADMIT 承認◀** 承認；供認 **2 be acknowledged as** 被公認為是… **3 ▶ACCEPT SB'S AUTHORITY 承認某人的權威◀** 承認〔政府、法庭、領袖等〕的合法性 **4 ▶LETTER/MESSAGE ETC 信/口信等◀** 確認〔收悉〕 **5 ▶SHOW THANKS FOR 表示感謝◀** 〔公開〕表示感謝 **6 ▶SHOW YOU NOTICE SB 表明注意到某人◀** 打招呼，理會

acquaintance *n* **1** 相識的人；泛泛之交 **2 make sb's acquaintance** 結識某人 **3 of your acquaintance** 你認識的〔人〕 **4** 所知；了解 **5 on further/closer acquaintance** 進一步了解

acquire *v* **1** 購得，得到〔尤指昂貴的或難以得到的東西〕 **2** 掌握，獲得〔知識、技能等〕 **3 acquire a taste for** 慢慢喜歡上 **4 be an acquired taste** 是

後來喜歡上的東西 **5** 以不正當的方式獲得[佔有]

adapt *v* **1** (使)適應, (使)適合 **2** 改造, 改裝 **3 be well adapted to** 特別適應 **4** 改編

address[1] *n* **1** 地址 **2** 講話, 演說 **3** 〔電腦的〕位址, 地址 **4 form/style/mode of address** 稱呼方式/風格/語氣

address[2] *v* **1** 在〔信封、包裹等〕上寫姓名和地址 **2** 向…講話 **3 address a meeting/crowd/conference etc** 在會上/對人羣/在大會上等發表演說 **4** 稱呼 **5** 探討〔如何處理問題〕

adequate *adj* **1** 適當的, 足夠的, 充分的 **2** 可以勝任的 **3** 差強人意的, 過得去的 —**adequately** *adv* —**adequacy** *n*

adjust *v* **1** 調整, 調節 **2** 適應; 使適合

administer *v* **1** 管理, 治理 **2** 執行, 實施 **3** 給予, 用〔藥等〕

admire *v* **1** 欽佩, 讚美, 羨慕 **2** 欣賞, 觀賞 **3 admire sb from afar** 暗自仰慕 —**admiring** *adj* —**admiringly** *adv*

admit *v* **1** 承認, 贊同 **2 admit to** 承認〔做錯了事, 犯了罪〕 **3** 允許…進入 **4** 允許加入, 接納 **5 be admitted to hospital** 被送進醫院 **6 admit defeat** 〔中途〕承認失敗, 認輸 **7 an admitted alcoholic/atheist etc** 自認的酒鬼/無神論者等

admit of sth *phr v* 容許有

adolescence *n* 青春期

adopt *v* **1** ►**CHILD** 孩子◄ 收養, 領養 **2 adopt an approach/strategy/policy**採用某方法/戰略/政策 **3** ►**STYLE/MANNER** 風格/方式◄ 採取, 採用 **4** ►**ACCEPT A SUGGESTION** 接受建議◄ 〔尤指通過表決〕正式批准; 認可; 接受 **5 adopt a name/country** 選定姓名/國家 **6** ►**ELECTION** 選舉◄ 提名…為候選人

adore *v* **1** 敬慕, 愛慕 **2** 非常喜歡

advance[1] *n* **1 in advance** 預先, 提前 **2** ►**DEVELOPMENT/IMPROVEMENT** 發展/改進◄ 進步, 進展 **3** ►**FORWARD MOVEMENT** 向前的移動◄ 前進 **4** ►**MONEY** 金錢◄ 預付款 **5 advances** 〔對異性的〕挑逗, 勾引 **6** ►**INCREASE** 增加◄ 上漲, 攀升

advance[2] *v* **1** ►**MOVE** 運動◄ 〔尤指緩慢而堅定地〕前進, 推進 **2** ►**DEVELOP** 發展◄ 進展 **3 advance a plan/idea/proposal etc** 提出計劃/看法/建議等 **4** ►**MONEY** 金錢◄ 預支 **5 advance a cause/your interests/your career etc** 拓展事業/興趣/職業生涯等 **6** ►**PRICE** 價格◄ 〔價格、價值〕上漲 **7** ►**CHANGE TIME** 改變時間◄ 提前 **8** ►**FILM/CLOCK** 電影/鐘錶◄ 進〔片〕;往前撥〔鐘錶〕

advance[3] *adj* **1 advance planning/warning/booking etc** 預先的計劃/警告/訂票[訂座]等 **2 advance party/team** 〔提前到某地為活動做準備的〕先行組

advantage *n* **1** ►**THAT HELPS YOU** 有利於你的◄ 有利條件, 優勢 **2 take advantage of sb** 〔不公正地〕利用某人, 佔某人的便宜 **3 take advantage of sth** 〔巧妙地〕利用某物 **4** ►**STH GOOD** 好事物◄ 好處, 優點, 利益 **5 to good advantage** 表現出優點地, 有利地 **6** ►**TENNIS** 網球◄ X佔先, X領先一分〔終局前平分後先得一分〕

adventure *n* 冒險〔經歷〕

advertise *v* **1** 〔為…〕做廣告〔宣傳〕 **2** 登廣告招聘; 做廣告宣傳〔某一活動等〕 **3** 宣揚〔不宜公開的事〕 —**advertiser** *n*

affect *v* **1** 影響 **2** [一般用被動態] 使某人產生強烈的感情, 使感動 **3** 故作姿態, 假裝

agenda *n* **1** 〔會議的〕議程 **2 be on the agenda** 〔事項的〕待辦; 待討論 **3** 話題, 議題

aid[1] *n* **1** 援助, 救助 **2** 幫助 **3** 輔助性工具 **4 what's this in aid of?** 這有甚麼用途? 這樣做是甚麼用意?

aid[2] *v* **1** 幫助, 援助 **2 aid and abet** 協助和教唆, 夥同…作案, 與…同謀

alarm[1] *n* **1** 驚恐, 驚慌 **2** 警報器 **3 sound/raise the alarm** 發出警報 **4** 鬧鐘

alarm[2] *v* 使恐慌[不安, 焦慮]

alcohol *n* **1** 含酒精的飲品, 酒 **2** 酒精, 乙醇

alien[1] *adj* **1** 外國的; 異族的 **2** 截然不同的; 非常怪異的 **3** 外星人的

alien[2] *n* **1** 外僑, 僑民 **2** 外星人

allowance *n* **1** 〔定期或出於特殊原因而給予的〕津貼, 補助 **2** 允許量, 限額 **3** 〔收入的〕免税額 **4** 零用錢 **5 make allowances** 體諒, 顧及 **6 make (an) allowance for** 考慮到

alter *v* **1** 使變化, 改變 **2** 使改動, 更改〔把衣服加長、加寬等〕 **3** 閹割〔貓或狗〕

amateur[1] *adj* **1** 業餘〔愛好〕的, 非職業的 **2** 外行的, 生手的

amateur[2] *n* 業餘愛好者

amaze *v* 使大為驚奇, 使驚愕

ambition *n* **1** 抱負, 雄心; 野心 **2** 願望, 志向

amend *v* 修改, 修訂〔法律或文件〕

ample *adj* **1** 充足的, 充裕的 **2 ample bosom/figure/torso etc** 寬闊的胸膛/豐滿的體形/魁梧的身材等 —**amply** *adv*

amuse *v* **1** 使開心, 逗笑 **2** 給…提供娛樂[消遣]

analyse【英】, **analyze**【美】 *v* **1** 分析 **2** 對…進行精神分析

ancestor *n* **1** 祖先, 祖宗 **2** 〔現代機器、車輛等的〕原型 —**ancestral** *adj*

ancient[1] *adj* **1** 古代的 **2** 古老的, 年代久遠的 **3** 老掉牙的, 老的

ancient[2] *n* **the ancients** 古人〔尤指古希臘及古羅馬人〕

announce *v* **1** 宣布, 通告, 公布於眾 **2** 大聲宣布 **3** 〔尤指在機場或火車站〕廣播 **4** 〔在電視或電台〕主持〔節目〕

annoy *v* 使煩惱, 煩擾, 打攪

annual[1] *adj* **1** 一年一度的, 每年的 **2** 按年度計算的 —**annually** *adv*

annual[2] *n* **1** 一年生植物; 一季生植物 **2** 年刊, 年報, 年鑑〔尤指兒童年冊〕

anticipation *n* 預期, 預料, 期望

anxiety *n* **1** 焦慮, 不安, 擔心 **2** 使人焦慮的事情 **3** 渴望

apologize *v* 道歉, 謝罪

apparatus *n* **1** 設備, 儀器, 裝置, 器械, 用具 **2** 機制

apparent *adj* **1** 顯而易見的; 明白的 **2** 顯得…的, 表面上的

appeal[1] *n* **1** 懇求; 呼籲 **2** 感染力, 吸引力 **3** 上訴

appeal² *v* **1** 懇請, 懇求; 呼籲 **2 appeal to sb** 吸引某人 **3** (提出)上訴 **4 appeal to sb's better nature/sense of honour/sense of justice etc** 呼喚某人的良知/榮譽感/正義感等

appearance *n* **1** ▶**WAY SB/STH LOOKS** 外貌◀ 外表; 外觀 **2** ▶**STH NEW** 新事物◀ 出現, 呈現 **3** ▶**ARRIVAL** 到達◀ 〔出其不意的〕到來, 出現 **4** ▶**PLAY/FILM/CONCERT ETC** 戲劇/電影/音樂會等◀ 登台, 表演 **5 keep up appearances** 維持面子; 裝門面 **6 for appearances' sake/for the sake of appearances** 為了面子關係 **7 put in an appearance/make an appearance** 露一下面 **8** ▶**LAW COURT/MEETING** 法庭/會議◀ 出庭; 出席

appetite *n* **1** 胃口, 食慾 **2** 慾望; 喜愛

applaud *v* **1** (為…)鼓掌 **2** 稱讚, 讚許

apply *v* **1** ▶**REQUEST PERMISSION/A JOB** 請求准許/求職◀ 申請 **2** ▶**USE STH** 使用某物◀ 使用, 應用, 運用 **3** ▶**AFFECT STH** 影響某事物◀ 適用於〔某人、某種情況〕; 有效 **4 apply yourself** 致力於, 專心於 **5** ▶**MAKE STH WORK** 使某物起作用◀ 使…起作用 **6** ▶**SPREAD PAINT/LIQUID ETC** 塗油漆/液體等◀ 塗, 敷 **7 apply force/pressure** 用力/施壓 **8** ▶**USE A WORD** 用某詞◀ 使用〔某個單詞或名稱〕

appointment *n* **1** 約定, 預約 **2** 任命, 委任 **3 by appointment** 按約定, 按事先確定的時間 **4** 委任的工作[職位] **5 by appointment to the Queen** 經女王御准〔可向王室出售商品或提供服務〕

appreciate *v* **1** 欣賞; 賞識; 鑑賞 **2** 感激 **3** 完全理解, 明白 **4** 增值 —反義詞 DEPRECIATE

approach¹ *v* **1** ▶**MOVE TOWARDS** 向…移動◀ 走近; 靠近; 接近 **2** ▶**ASK** 請求◀ 接洽, 交涉 **3** ▶**FUTURE EVENT** 未來事件◀ 臨近 **4** ▶**ALMOST REACH STH** 幾乎到…◀ 接近 **5** ▶**DEAL WITH** 對付◀ 對付, 處理

approach² *n* **1** 方法; 步驟 **2** 靠近; 接近; 臨近 **3** 通路, 入口 **4** 要求 **5 the approach of...** 的來臨[臨近]

appropriate¹ *adj* 恰當的; 合適的 —反義詞 INAPPROPRIATE —**appropriately** *adv* —**appropriateness** *n*

appropriate² *v* **1** 挪用; 佔用; 盜用 **2** 撥出〔款項〕

approve *v* **1** 批准; 認可 **2** 贊成, 同意

approximate¹ *adj* 大致的, 大約的, 大概的 —**approximately** *adv*

approximate² *v* **1** 接近 **2** 近似

arise *v* **1** 發生 **2** 由…引起 **3 when the need arises/should the need arise** 如果有必要 **4** 起牀; 起立; 起來 **5** 出現, 呈現 **6** 起來〔表示覺醒〕

arouse *v* **1 arouse interest/expectations etc** 引起興趣/期望等 **2 arouse anger/fear/dislike etc** 激起憤怒/恐懼/討厭等 **3** 激起…的性慾 **4** 喚醒

artificial *adj* **1** 人造的, 人工的 **2** 假的, 仿造的 **3** 虛假的, 不真摯的, 矯揉造作的 **4** 人為的 —**artificially** *adv* —**artificiality** *n*

ascend *v* **1** 上升, 升高 **2** 攀登, 爬 **3** 上升, 向上 **4 ascend the throne** 登上王位, 登基 **5 in ascending order** 按升序排列 —反義詞 DESCEND

aspect *n* **1** 方面 **2** 朝向, 方位 **3** 面貌, 外觀, 神態 **4** 〔動詞的〕體

assemble *v* **1** 集合, 聚集 **2** 收集; 召集 **3** 組裝, 裝配

assign *v* **1** 分配, 分派, 指派〔任務〕 **2** 訂出, 確定〔時間或期限〕 **3** 把〔財產、設備等〕轉讓與

assist¹ *v* **1** 幫助, 協助 **2** 使做…變得更容易

assist² *n* 〔體育項目中的〕助攻

associate¹ *v* **1 associate sb/sth with** 把某人/某事物與…聯繫起來 **2 be associated (with)** 與…有關, 與…有瓜葛 **3 associate with sb** 與〔他人不贊同的〕人交往[合夥, 結交]

associate² *n* **1** 同事; (生意)夥伴 **2** 準學位證書持有者

associate³ *adj* **associate member/director/head etc** 非正式會員/副主任/副主管等

assorted *adj* 各種各樣的

assume *v* **1** 假定, 假設 **2 assume control/power/responsibilities etc** 開始控制/掌權/承擔責任等 **3 assume a manner/air/expression etc** 裝出…的態度/樣子/表情等 **4** 呈現出, 出現為 **5** 以…為先決條件, 預先假定

assure *v* **1** 向…保證, 使確信, 讓…放心 **2 be assured of** 有信心, 有把握 **3** 確保, 提供保證

atmosphere *n* **1 the atmosphere** 大氣(層) **2** 〔室內的〕空氣 **3** 氣氛, 環境

atom *n* **1** 原子 **2** 一點兒

attach *v* **1** ▶**CONNECT** 連接◀ 繫; 綁; 貼; 固定; 連接; 附上 **2** ▶**LIKE** 喜歡◀ **be attached to** 喜歡, 依戀 **3 attach importance/significance etc** 重視, 認為…很重要 **4 attach blame** 與…有牽連 **5** ▶**FEELING/QUALITY** 感覺/質量◀ **be attached to** 與…聯繫起來 **6** ▶**ORGANIZATION/COMPANY** 組織/公司◀ **be attached to sth a)** 〔尤指短期地〕為…工作 **b)** 附屬於…, 屬於…的一個分支

attack¹ *n* **1** ▶**VIOLENCE AGAINST SB** 針對某人的暴力行為◀ 暴力事件, 打鬥 **2** ▶**IN A WAR** 在戰爭中◀ 進攻, 襲擊, 攻擊 **3** ▶**CRITICISM** 批評◀ 抨擊, 攻擊, 非難, 責罵 **4** ▶**ACTIONS TO STOP STH** 阻止某事的行動◀ 〔對體制、法律等的〕處理, 解決 **5** ▶**ILLNESS** 疾病◀ 突然發作 **6** ▶**SPORT** 體育◀ **a)** 進攻 **b)** 進攻隊員 **7 an attack of fear/panic/anxiety etc** 一陣恐懼/驚慌/焦慮等

attack² *v* **1** ▶**ATTACK SOMEONE** 攻擊某人◀ 襲擊, 毆打 **2** ▶**IN A WAR** 在戰爭中◀ 進攻, 攻擊, 襲擊 **3** ▶**CRITICIZE** 批評◀ 抨擊, 攻擊, 責難 **4** ▶**SPORT** 體育◀ 進攻 **5** ▶**BEGIN DOING** 開始做◀ 着手處理, 投入 **6** ▶**DISEASE** 疾病◀ 給…造成傷害; 侵襲, 侵蝕

attain *v* **1** 達到, 獲得, 贏得 **2** 達到, 漲到 —**attainable** *adj*

attempt¹ *n* **1** 努力, 嘗試, 企圖〔尤指較難的事情〕 **2 an attempt on sb's life** 企圖謀殺某人〔尤指名人或重要人物〕

attempt² *v* 試圖, 嘗試, 企圖

attend *v* **1** 參加, 出席, 到場 **2** 上〔學〕, 去〔教堂〕 **3** 陪伴, 伴隨…而至 **4** 看護, 照料

attend to sb/sth *phr v* **1** 處理, 料理〔生意或個人事務〕 **2** 〔在商店或飯店〕照顧, 接待〔顧客〕

attitude *n* **1** 態度, 心態; 感覺 **2** 姿態 **3** 我行我素的打扮

attract *v* **1** 吸引, 引起〔興趣、關注等〕 **2 be at-**

tracted to 喜愛, 為…所吸引 **3** 吸引; 引誘 **4** 招引; 吸引

audience *n* **1** 聽眾; 觀眾 **2**〔某節目的〕固定觀眾[聽眾]〔人數〕**3** 謁見, 覲見, 正式拜會

authority *n* **1** ►**POWER** 權力◄ 權力, 權威, 威信 **2 the authorities** 當局, 官方; 當權者 **3** ►**ORGANIZATION** 組織◄ 公共事業機構 **4 I have it on good authority** 我完全相信 **5** ►**EXPERT** 專家◄ 權威人士, 大師, 泰斗 **6** ►**PERMISSION** 允許◄〔正式的〕許可, 授權

automatic[1] *adj* **1** 自動的, 自動化的 **2** 必然發生的 **3** 不自覺的, 無意識的, 不假思索的

automatic[2] *n* **1** 自動武器 **2** 自動汽車, 有自動變速器的汽車

available *adj* **1** 可獲得的; 可用的 **2** 有暇的, 可接待客人的 **3** 未婚的; 未有伴侶的 —**availability** *n*

average[1] *adj* **1** 平均(數)的 **2** 中等的, 適中的 **3** 平常的, 普通的 **4** 不好不壞的, 一般的

average[2] *n* **1** 平均數 **2 on average** 平均來看 **3** 平均水平

average[3] *v* **1** 平均做; 平均是 **2** 算出…的平均數

average out *phr v* **1** 算出…的平均數 **2** 達到平均量

aware *adj* **1** 意識到的, 明白的, 知道的 **2** 意識到的, 注意到的, 察覺到的 **3** 有…意識的 **4 so/as far as I am aware** 就我所知

awkward *adj* **1** 尷尬的, 為難的 **2** 不方便的 **3** 笨拙的, 不靈活的; 彆扭的 **4** 難用的, 不好操作的 **5** 難相處的, 不好應付的 —**awkwardly** *adv* —**awkwardness** *n*

B, b

badge *n* **1** 徽章, 證章; 標記, 象徵 **2**〔佩戴在身上以顯示官職的〕徽章〈如警徽〉**3**〔給童子軍等的〕布製徽章 **4 badge of office** 職位標識物

balance[1] *n* **1** ►**STEADY** 穩定的◄ 平衡 **2** ►**EQUALITY** 均等◄ 均衡, 均勢, 平衡 — 反義詞 IMBALANCE **3 on balance** 全面考慮之後, 權衡利弊, 總的説來 **4 off balance a)** 沒站穩的, 失去平衡的 **b)** 吃驚的, 糊塗的 **5 the balance of evidence/probability etc** 從各方面的證據/可能性等來看 **6** ►**FOR WEIGHING** 用於稱重量◄ 天平, 秤 **7** ►**BANK** 銀行◄ 餘數, 餘額, 差額, 結餘 **8** ►**THE REST** 其餘的◄ 剩餘(部分) **9** ►**OPPOSITE FORCE** 相反的力◄ 平衡力; 制衡作用; 抵銷因素 **10 be/hang in the balance** 懸而未決 **11 tip/swing the balance** 影響事態的結果

balance[2] *v* **1** ►**KEEP STEADY** 保持穩定◄ (使)平穩, (使)保持平衡 **2** ►**BE EQUAL TO** 等於◄ (使)〔重量、數量、重要性等〕均衡, 相抵, 相等 **3** ►**GO WELL WITH** 與…相配◄ 使〔兩種相反的效果〕適中 **4** ►**KEEP STH EQUAL** 保持某物均衡◄ 平衡好, 處理好 **5** ►**THINK ABOUT** 思考◄ 權衡, 斟酌, 比較 **6 balance the books/budget** 使收支平衡

ban[1] *n* 禁止, 禁令

ban[2] *v* 禁止, 取締

band[1] *n* **1** ►**MUSIC** 音樂◄〔尤指演奏流行音樂的〕樂隊, 樂團 **2** ►**GROUP OF PEOPLE** 人羣◄ 一夥, 一羣, 一幫 **3** ►**PIECE OF MATERIAL** 材料◄ 繫物的帶子; 箍帶 **4** ►**PATTERN** 圖形◄ 條紋 **5 tax/income/age etc band** 税收/收入/年齡等範圍 **6** ►**RADIO** 無線電◄ 波段, 頻帶

band[2] *v* 給…加上條紋邊框, 給…鑲邊

band together *phr v* 團結起來, 聯手

bar[1] *n* **1** ►**PLACE TO DRINK IN** 飲酒場所◄ **a)** 酒吧 **b)** 酒吧間 **2** ►**PLACE TO BUY DRINK** 買飲料處◄ 出售酒的櫃台 **3 coffee/snack/salad etc bar** 咖啡店/小吃店/沙拉自助櫃台等 **4** ►**BLOCK OF STH** 一塊東西◄ 條, 棒, 根 **5** ►**PIECE OF METAL/WOOD** 金屬/木頭◄〔門, 窗等的〕門; 橫木; 阻礙物 **6** ►**MUSIC** 音樂◄〔樂曲中的〕一小節 **7 a bar to (doing) sth** 做某事的障礙 **8** ►**GROUP OF LAWYERS** 律師◄ **a) the bar**〔有資格出庭處理訴訟案件的〕大律師 **b)** 律師界, 律師業 **9 be called to the bar a)** 成為大律師 **b)** 成為律師 **10** ►**PILE OF SAND/STONES** 沙/石堆◄〔港口入口處的〕沙洲; 暗礁 **11** ►**COLOUR/LIGHT** 顏色/光◄ 線條, 條紋, 帶 **12** ►**UNIFORMS** 制服◄〔軍服上的〕軍階槓; 綬帶 **13** ►**HEATER** 加熱器◄〔電暖氣的〕電熱線[片] **14 behind bars** 在獄中

bar[2] *v* **1** 閂上, 閂住〔門、窗〕**2** 摒除, 排擠於…之外; 阻止 **3** 阻止通行; 阻擋, 阻攔

bar[3] *prep* **1** 除了…以外 **2 bar none** 無人可比

bare[1] *adj* **1** ►**WITHOUT CLOTHES** 未穿衣服◄ 赤裸的 **2** ►**LAND/TREES** 土地/樹木◄ 葉子全落的; 光禿禿的 **3** ►**ROOMS** 房間◄ 空的, 無裝飾的 **4 the bare facts/truth** 暴露無遺的事實/赤裸裸的真相 **5** ►**SMALLEST AMOUNT NECESSARY** 最少必需量◄ 僅有的, 勉強的, 最低限度的 **6 the bare bones** 梗概 **7 lay sth bare a)** 顯示出某事物, 使某事物暴露 **b)** 揭露, 揭發 **8 with your bare hands** 赤手空拳 —**bareness** *n*

bare[2] *v* **1** 使暴露, 使赤裸, 露出 **2 bare your soul** 敞開心扉, 剖白心事, 訴説真情, 披肝瀝膽

bargain[1] *n* **1** 便宜貨, 廉價貨 **2** 協議; 交易 **3 into the bargain** 此外, 外加, 而且 **4 make the best of a bad bargain** 困難時盡力而為; 善處逆境, 隨遇而安 —**bargainer** *n*

bargain[2] *v* 講價錢, 討價還價; 洽談(交易)條件

bargain for sth *phr v* 考慮到, 估計到, 預料到

bark[1] *v* **1**〔狗等動物〕吠, 叫 **2** 大聲嚷, 吼叫 **3 bark up the wrong tree** 打錯了主意; 認錯了目標 **4 bark at the moon** 狂犬吠月, 徒勞無功; 杞人憂天 **5** 擦破〔皮〕

bark[2] *n* **1** 狗叫聲 **2** 樹皮 **3** 響聲; 吼叫聲 **4 sb's bark is worse than their bite** 嘴巴兇, 心不狠 **5** 三桅[四桅, 五桅]帆船

barren *adj* **1** 貧瘠的, 荒蕪的 **2**〔婦女或雌性動物〕不孕的, 不生育的 **3** 不結果實的, 不結籽的 **4** 無用的; 無效果的

barrier *n* **1** 障礙物; 柵欄; 關卡 **2**〔阻止或妨礙人們做事的〕障礙 **3** 屏障 **4 the 10 second/40% etc barrier**〔難以超越的〕10秒/40% 等難關

battle[1] *n* **1** ►**BETWEEN ARMIES** 軍隊之間◄〔尤指大型戰爭中的局部〕戰鬥, 戰役 **2** ►**BETWEEN**

OPPONENTS 對手之間◀ 較量, 競爭, 爭奪 **3 ▶ATTEMPT** 試圖◀ 奮鬥, 抗爭 **4 be half the battle** 成功了一半, 勝利大有希望 **5 a battle of wits** 智慧的較量 **6 do battle (with)** 與…爭論[鬥爭] **7 the battle of the sexes** 男女之間權力的競爭

battle² *v* **1** 與…鬥爭, 與…搏鬥 **2 battle it out** 決出勝負 **3** 參戰; 與…作戰

beam¹ *n* **1 ▶LIGHT** 光◀ **a)** 光束, 光線 **b)** 束, 柱 **2 ▶WOOD/METAL** 木頭/金屬◀ 梁, 橫梁 **3 ▶SMILE** 微笑◀ 喜色, 笑容 **4 off (the) beam** 不正確的, 錯誤的, 不對頭的 **5 ▶SPORT** 體育◀〔體操〕平衡木 **6 ▶SHIP** 船◀ 船寬

beam² *v* **1** 笑, 眉開眼笑 **2** 向…發送〔電波〕 **3** 發光; 發熱, 發射

bear¹ *v* **1 can't bear a)** 忍受不了 **b)** 接受不了…的事實 **2 bear in mind (that)** 記住; 考慮到 **3 ▶BE BRAVE** 勇敢◀ 忍受, 忍耐, 經受住 **4 bear the costs/burden/expense etc** 承擔費用/負擔/開支等 **5 bear responsibility/the blame etc** 承擔責任/應受責備等 **6 ▶SUPPORT** 支持◀ 支撐〔重量〕 **7 doesn't bear thinking about** 不堪設想 **8 bear a resemblance/relation etc to** 與…相似/與…有關等 **9 bear the strain/pressure etc** 承受壓力等 **10 bear the brunt of** 首當其衝 **11 bear (sb) a grudge** 對〔某人〕懷恨在心 **12 bear fruit a)**〔尤指計劃、決定等長時間之後〕有了成果; 成功了 **b)**〔果樹〕結果 **13 ▶SHOW SIGNS OF** 顯出…的跡象◀ 顯示; 具有, 帶有〔標記或特徵〕 **14 not bear examination/inspection etc** 經受不住檢查/審查等 **15 bring influence/pressure etc to bear (on)**〔對…〕施加壓力; 敦促 **16 bear witness to** 證明, 作證 **17 bear right/left** 向右/左轉 **18 ▶BABY** 嬰兒◀ 生育 **19 bear yourself** 表現; 保持某種舉止 **20 ▶CARRY** 攜帶◀ 運送; 攜帶; 傳運 **21 ▶WIND/WATER** 風/水◀ 吹動; 傳送 **22 ▶SIGN/MARK** 記號/標記◀ 帶有〔標記〕 **23 ▶NAME/TITLE** 姓名/頭銜◀ 具有, 擁有〔名字或頭銜〕 **24 bear sb no malice/ill will etc** 對某人沒有惡意/敵意等

bear down *phr v* **1 bear down on** 向…逼近; 衝向 **2** 使勁推; 使勁壓下 **3** 壓倒; 征服; 打敗

bear on/upon sth *phr v* 與…有聯繫, 與…有關

bear sb/sth **out** *phr v* 為…作證, 證實, 支持〔某種説法〕

bear up *phr v* 支持住, 撐下去; 不氣餒

bear with sb/sth *phr v* **1 bear with me** 耐心等待; 別着急 **2** 容忍, 忍耐

bear² *n* **1** 熊 **2**〔股市或期貨〕看跌的人 **3** 粗暴魯莽的人, 脾氣暴躁的人 **4 be like a bear with a sore head** 脾氣暴躁

behaviour *n* **1** 舉止, 行為 **2 be on your best behaviour** 盡可能好地表現; 儘量行為檢點 **3** 性能; 特點; 活動 **—behavioural** *adj* **—behaviourally** *adv*

bend¹ *v* **1 ▶MOVE YOUR BODY** 挪動身體◀ 俯身; 彎腰 **2 ▶CURVE** 曲線◀ **a)** 使彎曲 **b)** 呈彎形; 變彎曲 **3 bend the rules** 放寬規則; 通融 **4 bend over backwards (to do sth)** 竭盡全力〔做某事〕 **5 bend sb's ear** 和某人談心〔尤指談令人煩惱的事〕 **6 on bended knee a)** 努力勸説; 懇求 **b)** 跪着 **7 bend your mind/efforts/thoughts etc to** 集中全力於…, 專心致志於…

bend² *n* **1**〔尤指道路或河流的〕彎曲處 **2**〔身體的〕彎曲〔動作〕 **3 the bends** 潛水夫病, 潛函病, 減壓病〔潛水員浮出水面過快引致的一種令人非常疼痛的病〕 **4 drive sb round the bend** 惹惱某人 **5 be/go round the bend** 發瘋

beneficial *adj* 有益的, 有利的, 有用的 **—beneficially** *adv*

bewilder *v* 使迷惑; 使昏亂

bind¹ *v* **1 ▶TIE/FASTEN** 束/縛◀ **a)** 捆, 綁 **b)**〔用布或帶子〕束緊; 捆紮 **2 ▶UNITE** 聯合◀ 把…緊緊聯繫在一起; 使關係密切 **3 ▶STICK TOGETHER** 黏起來◀〔使〕黏合;〔使〕凝結 **4 ▶RESTRICT** 限制◀ 約束; 使負有義務 **5 ▶STITCH** 縫◀ 給…加上飾邊; 給…鑲邊 **6 ▶BOOK** 書◀ 裝訂

bind² *n* **a bind** 窘境, 困境

bite¹ *v* **1 ▶WITH YOUR TEETH** 用牙◀ 咬 **2 ▶INSECT/SNAKE** 蟲/蛇◀〔昆蟲〕叮, 螫;〔蛇〕咬傷 **3 ▶FISH** 魚◀ 吞餌, 上鈎 **4 ▶NOT SLIP** 不滑◀ 抓緊; 卡緊; 咬住 **5 ▶HAVE AN EFFECT** 有效◀ 達到預期的〔壞〕效果 **6 bite your tongue** 強忍住不説 **7 bite the dust a)** 死亡; 失敗; 被擊敗 **b)** 完全不好用; 報廢 **8 bite the bullet** 咬緊牙關忍受痛苦, 勇敢地面對 **9 bite sb's head off** 發火; 蠻橫粗暴地説話[回答] **10 bite off more than you can chew** 試圖承擔力所不及的事 **11 he/she won't bite** 不必怕他/她〔尤指權威人士〕 **12 what's biting you/her etc?** 甚麼事煩擾着你/她等? 愁甚麼呢? **13 once bitten twice shy** 一次吃虧, 二次小心; 一朝被蛇咬, 十年怕井繩 **14 bite the hand that feeds you** 恩將仇報; 以怨報德 **15 be bitten by the bug/craze etc** 熱衷於, 迷上

bite back *phr v* **1** 強忍着不説出來 **2** 回嘴; 反唇相譏

bite into sth *phr v* 咬進; 陷進; 砍入

bite² *n* **1 ▶WITH YOUR TEETH** 用牙◀ 咬〔的動作〕 **2 ▶WOUND** 傷◀ 被咬[叮, 螫]的傷口 **3 a bite (to eat)** 量少的一餐 **4 ▶COLD** 冷◀ 冷意, 寒意 **5 ▶TASTE** 味道◀ 辛辣; 苦澀 **6 ▶EFFECTIVENESS** 效果◀〔演説或文章的〕犀利; 有説服力 **7 ▶FISH** 魚◀ 吞餌; 上鈎 **8 bite-size/bite-sized** 很小的, 一口大小的 **9 another bite/a second bite at the cherry** 第二次機會

blame¹ *v* **1** 責怪, 指摘; 把…歸咎於 **2 don't blame me** 不要怪我〔用於勸告某人不要做某事〕 **3 I don't blame you/them etc** 我理解某人的做法 **4 only have yourself to blame** 只能怪你自己 **5** 批評; 責難

blame² *n*〔對錯誤或壞事應負的〕責任

blank¹ *adj* **1** 無表情的; 漠然的; 不感興趣的 **2** 無字跡的; 空白的 **3 go blank a)** 腦子突然一片空白, 怎麼也想不起來 **b)**〔屏幕等〕一片空白 **—blankly** *adv* **—blankness** *n*

blank² *n* **1** 空白處 **2 my mind's a blank** 腦子裡一片空白, 怎麼也想不起來 **3**〔有火藥而無彈頭的〕空彈 **—blankness** *n*

blank³ *v* **1** 突然記不起, 腦子突然一片空白 **2** 不理睬

blank sth ↔ **out** *phr v* **1** 塗掉, 刪去 **2**〔尤指故意

地〕全部忘記

blaze¹ *v* **1** 熊熊燃燒 **2** 發光, 照亮 **3** 快速而連續地射擊 **4 blaze a trail** 做開路先鋒, 起先導作用 **5 be blazed across/all over** 使廣為人知地刊登

blaze² *n* **1 ►FIRE 火◄ a)** 火焰; 烈火 **b)** 危險的大火 **2 ►LIGHT/COLOUR 光/顏色◄** 〔光線、色彩等的〕光輝, 閃耀; 五彩繽紛 **3 ►GUNS 槍砲◄** 急促而連續的射擊 **4 a blaze of anger/hatred/passion etc** 突發的怒氣/仇恨/激情等 **5 in a blaze of glory/publicity etc** 在盛讚/公眾矚目之下等 **6 what the blazes/who the blazes etc** 到底在搞甚麼/是誰等〔用於加強問題的語氣, 表示厭煩〕 **7 like blazes** 盡可能地 **8 go to blazes** 滾開 **9 ►MARK 記號◄** 〔尤指馬鼻上的一條〕白斑

bless *v* **1 be blessed with** 有幸得到, 被賦予 **2** 祈求上帝祝福[保祐], 求神賜福於 **3** 使神聖; 視…為聖物; 讚頌 **4 bless you! a)** 長命百歲!〔別人打噴嚏時説〕 **b)** 謝謝〔某人〕 **5 bless him/her etc** 真不錯; 幹得好〔表示喜歡或滿意〕 **6 bless my soul/I'll be blessed!** 我的天哪!〔表示吃驚〕

block¹ *n* **1 ►SOLID MASS 固體◄** 一大塊〈如木、石等通常有直切邊的堅硬物體〉 **2 ►STREET/STREETS 街◄ a)** 街段 **b)** 街區 **3 ►LARGE BUILDING 大樓◄** 棟, 座, 幢 **4 ►QUANTITY OF THINGS 數量◄** 一組, 一批, 一套, 一疊 **5 block booking/voting** 成批購買/集體投票 **6 ►UNABLE TO THINK 不能思考◄** 阻滯 **7 ►STOPPING MOVEMENT 阻止行動◄** 障礙物, 堵塞物 **8 the block** 〔昔時的〕斷頭台 **9 lay/put your head on the block** 冒着敗壞自己名聲的危險 **10 ►SPORT 體育◄** 攔擋〔動作〕 **11 ►INFORMATION 信息◄** 信息組〔指磁帶或磁盤上儲存信息的物理單位〕 **12 ►PRINTING 印刷◄** 印版, 版墊, 襯版, 木印板 **13 ►LAND 土地◄** 一大片土地

block² *v* **1** 阻擋, 堵塞 **2** 阻止, 妨礙, 阻撓 **3** 擋住〔視線〕 **4 block sb's way** 擋住某人的去路 **5** 限制使用〔某國貨幣〕

block sth ↔ **in/out** *phr v* 草擬; 畫…的簡略圖

block sth ↔ **off** *phr v* 封閉, 封鎖〔道路〕

block sth ↔ **out 1** 擋〔光〕 **2** 不去想

bloom¹ *n* **1** 花 **2 in (full) bloom** 〔花朵〕盛開, 怒放 **3** 〔葡萄或李子等水果表面的一層〕粉霜, 粉衣 **4 the bloom of youth/love etc** 豆蔻年華; 全盛時期

bloom² *v* **1** 開花; 〔花〕盛開 **2** 精神煥發; 興旺

blot¹ *v* **1** 〔用軟紙或布等〕吸乾 **2 blot your copybook** 玷污自己的名聲

blot sth ↔ **out** *phr v* 把…遮住, 遮蓋; 塗去; 隱藏

blot sth ↔ **up** *phr v* 〔用軟布或紙張等〕擦乾, 吸乾

blot² *n* **1** 污點, 污漬 **2** 破壞了某地方景致的東西〈如樓房等〉 **3** 〔尤指名譽的〕污點, 瑕疵

blow¹ *v* **1 ►WIND MOVING 風移動◄** 〔風〕吹, 颳 **2 ►WIND MOVING STH 風吹動某物◄** 吹動; 颳走 **3 ►AIR FROM YOUR MOUTH 嘴裡呼出的空氣◄** 吹氣; 噴氣 **4 ►MAKE A NOISE 弄出聲響◄** 吹奏; (使)鳴響 **5 ►VIOLENCE 暴力◄** 炸毀, 摧毀 **6 ►LOSE MONEY 損失金錢◄** 亂花, 揮霍 **7 ►LOSE AN OPPORTUNITY 失去機會◄** 失掉, 斷送 **8 ►SURPRISE/ANNOYANCE 驚訝/煩惱◄ blow/blow me/blow that etc** 真沒料到; 糟糕〔表示驚訝、煩惱或決心〕 **9 ►MAKE A SHAPE 造成某形狀◄** 吹製 **10 blow sth (up) out of all proportion** 小題大作; 誇大 **11 ►LEAVE 離開◄ blow town** 匆忙離開 **12 ►ELECTRICITY STOPS 電力中斷◄** 〔保險絲〕燒斷 **13 ►TYRE 輪胎◄** 爆裂, (使)破裂 **14 ►MAKE A SECRET KNOWN 泄密◄** 泄露〔祕密〕 **15 blow hot and cold** 〔對…〕反覆無常, 忽冷忽熱, 搖擺不定 **16 blow sb a kiss** 給某人一個飛吻 **17 blow your mind** 使驚喜, 使吃驚 **18 blow your nose** 擤鼻涕 **19 blow sth sky-high a)** 粉碎; 使破滅 **b)** 把…炸得粉碎, 徹底摧毀 **20 blow your top/stack** 勃然大怒, 大發雷霆 **21 blow your own trumpet/horn** 自吹自擂, 自誇 **22 blow the whistle on** 〔向有關當局或公眾〕揭發〔錯事〕, 揭露 **23 blow a gasket/fuse** 大怒, 暴跳如雷

blow away *phr v* **1** 槍殺 **2** 〔尤指在比賽中〕徹底戰勝〔某人〕 **3** 〔尤指用某人羨慕的東西〕使大為驚訝

blow down *phr v* 吹倒, 颳倒

blow in *phr v* 突然到來

blow sb/sth **off** *phr v* 視〔某人或某事〕不重要, 不重視, 輕視

blow out *phr v* **1** 吹滅; 熄滅 **2** 〔車胎〕爆裂 **3 blow itself out** 〔風暴〕停止 **4 a)** 輕而易舉地戰勝 **b)** 失約; 失信於〔某人〕 **5** 〔油井或氣井〕井噴

blow over *phr v* **1** 颳倒 **2** 〔暴風雨等〕停止, 平息; 過去 **3** 〔重要性〕消失; 被遺忘

blow up *phr v* **1** 炸毀, (使)炸得粉碎 **2** 給…充氣, 打氣 **3** 放大〔照片〕 **4** 〔惡劣天氣〕來臨 **5** 〔形勢、爭論等〕變得嚴峻 **6** 大發雷霆

blow² *n* **1 ►HARD HIT 重擊◄** 重擊 **2 ►BAD EFFECT 壞效果◄** 〔對信心、成功的可能性等的〕打擊 **3 ►UNHAPPY EVENT 不幸事件◄** 突然的打擊; 不幸 **4 ►BLOWING 吹◄** 〔指動作〕吹 **5 come to blows** 打起來 **6 soften/cushion the blow** 緩和…的打擊 **7 ►WIND 風◄** 勁風; 風暴

blunt¹ *adj* **1** 鈍的, 不鋒利的, 不尖的 — 反義詞 SHARP **2** 〔説話〕不客氣的, 直言不諱的, 耿直的 — **bluntness** *n*

blunt² *v* **1** 減弱 **2** 把〔鉛筆尖或刀〕弄鈍

boast¹ *v* **1** 誇口, 誇耀, 吹噓 **2** 〔地方、物體或機構〕擁有〔好的事物或特徵〕 —**boaster** *n*

boast² *n* **1** 引以為豪的事物 **2 no idle boast** 決非吹牛

boil¹ *v* **1** 使達到沸點, 煮沸, 燒開 **2** (使)〔容器裡的液體〕沸騰 **3** 〔用開水〕煮〔食物〕 **4** 〔用高温水〕洗〔衣服〕

boil away *phr v* 煮乾, 汽化

boil down *phr v* **1** 煮稠, 濃縮 **2** 壓縮〔資料等〕

boil down to sth *phr v* 相當於, 歸結為

boil over *phr v* **1** 沸騰而溢出 **2** 〔局面或感情〕控制不住

boil up *phr v* **1** 發展到危險程度 **2** 把…加熱, 煮沸

boil² *n* **1 the boil** 煮沸; 沸騰 **2** 癤子, 疔 **3 go off the boil** 生疏了

bold *adj* **1 ►PERSON/ACTION 人/行動◄** 果敢的, 冒險的, 無畏的 **2 ►MANNER/APPEARANCE 舉止/外貌◄** 唐突的, 冒失的, 魯莽的, 放肆的 **3 ►COLOURS/SHAPES 顏色/形狀◄** 醒目的, 顯眼的, 輪廓清晰的 **4 ►LINES/WRITING 線條/書寫◄** 粗線條的;

粗大醒目的 **5 in bold (type)**〔印刷〕用黑體字排印的 **6 make so bold as to do sth** 冒昧, 膽敢 **7 if I may be so bold** 恕我冒昧地問 —**boldly** *adv* —**boldness** *n*

bond[1] *n* **1** ►**MONEY 錢**◄ 債券, 證券, 公債 **2** ►**UNITE 團結**◄〔因共同利益或感情而使人連繫起來的〕紐帶, 維繫, 連結物, 關係 **3 bonds a)** 枷鎖, 桎梏, 限制人自由的東西 **b)** 鐐銬, 繩索 **4** ►**GLUE 膠(水)**◄ 結合, 黏合 **5** ►**CHEMISTRY 化學**◄ 化學鍵 **6** 契約, 盟約 **7 my word is my bond** 我說的話(像契約一樣)可靠, 我一定會履行諾言 **8 in/out of bond**〔進口貨物〕存入關棧中以待完稅/已完稅出關

bond[2] *v* **1**〔尤指用膠水〕黏合 **2**〔與某人〕培養一種特殊的關係 **3**〔把貨物〕存入關棧[保稅倉庫]中

bonus *n* **1** 獎金; 紅利; 特別津貼 **2** 沒有預料到的好事 **3 no-claims bonus** 未索賠鼓勵金〔一種汽車保險優惠〕

boom[1] *n* **1** ►**INCREASE IN BUSINESS 業務增加**◄〔生意〕繁榮, 興旺, 景氣 **2** ►**WHEN STH IS POPULAR 某事物流行之時**◄ 流行時期 **3** ►**SOUND 聲音**◄ 隆隆聲 **4** ►**LONG POLE 長杆子**◄ **a)** 帆的下桁, 帆杆 **b)**〔裝卸貨物時用的〕吊杆, 起重臂 **c)**〔一端掛照相機或麥克風的〕活動支架, 吊杆 **5** ►**ON A RIVER 在河上**◄〔橫攔於河面以阻止物件漂走的〕擋柵, 水柵

boom[2] *v* **1 a)** 發低沉的聲音, 隆隆作響 **b)** 用洪亮而低沉的聲音說 **2**〔商業、貿易等〕繁榮;〔城鎮等〕興起; 迅速發展 —**booming** *adj*

boost[1] *v* **1** 增加, 提高, 促進 **2 boost sb's confidence/morale/ego** 增強某人的自信心/士氣/自尊 **3** 吹捧, 大肆宣傳 **4** 向上推起, 托一把

boost[2] *n* **1** 激勵, 鼓舞; 增加, 改進 **2**〔火箭、電器等的〕動力增強, 助推 **3 give sb a boost (up)** 推起, 托某人一把

border[1] *n* **1** 國界, 邊境, 邊界; 邊境地區 **2** 邊, 邊飾 **3** 草地的邊緣部分,〔花園等邊緣狹長的〕綠化帶

border[2] *v* **1** 形成…的邊界, 毗鄰 **2** 與…接壤

border on sth *phr v* 近似, 接近

bore[1] the past tense of BEAR[1]

bore[2] *v* **1**〔尤指以無聊的長話〕使〔人〕厭煩 **2** 鑽(孔), 開鑿, 挖(洞) **3**〔令人不安地〕盯住看

bore[3] *n* **1**〔尤指因過多談論自己而〕令人厭煩的人 **2** 令人厭煩的事 **3 12-bore/small bore etc**〔槍砲〕12毫米口徑/小口徑等 **4** 鑽孔, 井眼

bother[1] *v* **1** ►**MAKE AN EFFORT 作出努力**◄ 費心, 盡力(做某事), 因…操心 **2** ►**WORRY 擔心**◄ (使)擔心, (使)苦惱 **3** ►**ANNOY 使惱怒**◄ 打擾, 煩擾 **4 can't/couldn't be bothered** 不想費神[沒有心思]去做某事 **5 not bothered** 無所謂, 不在意 **6 sorry to bother you** 對不起打擾你一下 **7** ►**FRIGHTEN 嚇唬**◄ 騷擾; 恐嚇 **8 hot and bothered**〔尤指不必要地〕心急火燎的 **9 not bother yourself/not bother your head** 不為…操心[傷腦筋] **10 bother it/them etc** 真討厭〔表示厭煩〕

bother[2] *n* **1** 麻煩, 不便; 憂慮; 煩惱的事 **2** 難對付的事[人]

bother[3] *interjection* 真煩人! 真討厭!〔表示有些惱火〕

boundary *n* **1** ►**EDGE 邊**◄ 分界線, 邊界 **2** ►**WALL/FENCE 牆/籬笆**◄ 界限, 範圍 **3** ►**LIMIT 限制**◄ 限度, 界限 **4** ►**BETWEEN FEELINGS/QUALITIES ETC 感情/特質等之間**◄ 分野 **5 push back the boundaries (of)** 擴展…的領域 **6** ►**CRICKET 板球**◄ 球場邊界線; 擊球超過邊界線得分

bow[1] *v* **1** 鞠躬, 躬身行禮 **2** 躬身向前看〔尤指為靠近些看〕: **3 be bowed (under sth)**〔被背上重物〕壓得躬着身子 **4 bow and scrape**〔對人〕卑躬屈膝, 點頭哈腰

bow down *phr v* **1** 深度躬身致敬 **2 bow down to sb** 向某人屈服; 屈從於某人

bow out *phr v* **1** (從…)退出, 退場; 辭職 **2** 不守信用, 背信棄義

bow to sb/sth *phr v* 向…讓步, 屈服於

bow[2] *n* **1** 鞠躬 **2** 船頭 **3 take a bow**〔表演結束時〕謝幕

bow[3] *n* **1** 弓 **2** 蝴蝶結 **3**〔弦樂器的〕弓 **4 bow legs** 弓形腿, 羅圈腿

bow[4] *v* **1** 彎曲, 彎成弓形 **2** 用弓拉奏〔樂曲〕

brag *v* 自誇, 吹嘘

branch[1] *n* **1** ►**ON A TREE 樹上**◄ 樹枝 **2** ►**IN A LOCAL AREA 在當地**◄ 分行; 分支機構 **3** ►**OF AN ORGANIZATION 某機構的**◄〔政府或機構的〕部門 **4** ►**OF A SUBJECT 某學科的**◄ 分科 **5** ►**OF A FAMILY 某家族的**◄〔家族中的〕一支, 分支 **6** ►**SMALLER PART 較小的部分**◄ 分支; 支線; 支流

branch[2] *v* 分支; 分岔

branch off *phr v* **1** 分岔; 分支; 分道 **2** 離開主路[幹線], 走入岔道 **3** 岔開〔話題〕

branch out *phr v* 擴大〔興趣、活動〕範圍, 開闢新的領域

breed[1] *v* **1**〔動物〕繁殖, 下崽, 下蛋 **2** 育種, 飼養繁殖; 培植; 改良(品種) **3** 引起; 釀成, 招致〔一般指不良之事〕 **4 breed like rabbits** 生太多的孩子

breed[2] *n* **1**〔尤指人工培育的動植物〕品種 **2**〔人或物的〕某種類型

brief[1] *adj* **1** ►**TIME 時間**◄ 短時間的; 短暫的 **2 have a brief word** 說幾句話 **3 be brief** 長話短說 **4** ►**SPEECH/LETTER 演講/信**◄ 簡潔的, 簡明的 **5 in brief a)** 簡而言之; 簡單地說 **b)** 粗略地, 梗概地 **6** 唐突無禮的;〔說話〕草草的 **7** ►**CLOTHES 衣服**◄ 短的, 暴露的

brief[2] *n* **1** 簡短命令, 工作指示 **2** 案情摘要, 案情簡介 **3 briefs** 貼身短內褲, 三角褲

brief[3] *v* 作簡單的指示; 為…提供資訊

bruise[1] *n* **1** 青瘀, 傷痕, 擦傷 **2**〔水果的〕擦痕, 碰傷

bruise[2] *v* **1** (使)碰傷, 擦傷, (使)成瘀傷 **2** (使)〔水果〕碰傷, 擦傷 —**bruising** *n*

bud[1] *n* **1** 芽; 苞; 蓓蕾 **2** 老兄; 喂

bud[2] *v* 發芽, 長出花蕾, 含苞

bud·get[1] *n* **1** 預算 **2** 政府預算案

budget[2] *v* **1**〔精心地〕制定預算; 按預算來安排(開支) **2** (為…)作出安排

budget[3] *adj* 經濟的, 特價的, 便宜的

bump[1] *v* **1** 猛碰, 撞 **2**〔車輛〕顛簸而行

bump into sb *phr v* 巧遇, 邂逅, 碰見

bump sb ↔ **off** *phr v* 殺死〔某人〕

bump sth ↔ **up** *phr v* 突然大幅度提高, 增加

bump[2] *n* **1**〔撞擊造成的〕腫塊 **2** 隆起之處 **3**〔汽

車〕碰撞 **4** 砰然一聲; 撞擊聲

bunch¹ *n* **1 bunch of flowers/keys/grapes etc** 一束花/一串鑰匙/一串葡萄等 **2**〔人〕一羣, 一夥 **3 the pick of the bunch** 佼佼者 **4** 大量 **5 in bunches**〔把頭髮分在兩邊〕紮成兩簇 **6 thanks a bunch** 多謝了〔玩笑説法, 表示毫無感激之意〕

bunch² *v* **1** 聚成堆[羣] **2** 繃緊〔身體的一部分〕 **3** 將〔東西〕綁成一束 **4** 使起褶

burst¹ *v* **1** ►**BREAK OPEN** 裂開◄ (使)破裂; (使)爆裂; (使)脹破; (使)爆炸 **2 bursting with** 充滿 **3** ►**MOVE SUDDENLY** 突然移動◄ 衝, 闖, 突然出現 **4 burst open** 突然開了 **5 be bursting to do sth** 迫不及待要做某事 **6 be bursting with pride/confidence/energy etc** 充滿自豪/自信/精力等 **7 be bursting**〔大小便〕憋不住了 **8 full to bursting**〔吃得〕太飽 **9 bursting at the seams** 脹滿

burst in on/upon sb/sth *phr v* 突然闖入, 打擾; 突然插嘴

burst into sth *phr v* **1** 突然…起來〔尤指哭、笑、唱等〕 **2 burst into flames** 突然起火〔尤指火勢失去控制〕

burst out *phr v* **1 burst out laughing/crying etc** 突然大笑/大哭等 **2** 突然説出

burst² *n* **1** 破裂, 爆炸; 噴出; 裂口 **2 a burst of sth a)** 突然用力, 加速 **b)** 突發的響聲 **c)** 情感的突然爆發

C, c

calculate *v* **1** 計算, 核算 **2** 估算, 估計 **3 be calculated to do sth** 旨在, 用意在於; 打算; 適於(做)…

calculate on sth *phr v* 指望, 期望

candidate *n* **1** 候選人; 候補人 **2** 應考人, 投考者 **3** 極有可能有某結局的人[羣體、觀點等]

capacity *n* **1** 容量, 容積; 容納力 **2** 能力, 才能 **3** 職位; 地位; 身分; 職責 **4**〔工廠、公司、機器等的〕產量, 生產力

capital¹ *n* **1** ►**CITY** 城市◄ 首都; 首府; 省會 **2** ►**FINANCIAL** 金融的◄ 資本, 資金 **3** ►**LETTER** 字母◄ 大寫字母 **4** ►**CENTRE OF ACTIVITY** 活動中心◄〔工商業及其他活動的〕中心 **5 make capital out of** 利用…, 從…中撈一把[獲益] **6** ►**BUILDING** 建築物◄ 柱頭, 柱頂

capital² *adj* **1 capital letter** 大寫字母 **2 capital offence/crime** 可處死刑的罪 **3** 極好的

career¹ *n* **1** 職業, 事業 **2 career soldier/teacher etc** 職業士兵/教師等 **3** 生涯; (一段)工作經歷, 履歷

career² *v*〔常指失控地〕猛衝

carve *v* **1** 把〔熟肉〕切成小塊;〔從熟肉上〕割下薄片 **2** 雕, 刻; 把〔木、石等〕雕成〔某物〕 **3** 刻〔圖形或字母〕

carve sth ↔ **out** *phr v* **carve out a career/niche/reputation etc** 開創出事業/謀得合適的職位/贏得名聲

carve sb/sth ↔ **up** *phr v* **1** 瓜分, 分割 **2** 快速超車, 快速切入別人的行車線

category *n* 類別, 種類, 範疇

caution¹ *n* **1** 小心, 謹慎, 慎重 **2 word/note of caution** 警示, 警告〔某人小心〕 **3 throw/fling/cast caution to the winds** 不顧一切/魯莽行事 **4**〔給犯了輕罪的人的〕正式(口頭)警告, 訓誡 **5** 滑稽有趣的人

caution² *v* **1** 警告, 告誡, 提醒 **2** 給某人正式警告

cease¹ *v* 停止, 終止, 結束

cease² *n* **without cease** 不停地, 持續地

celebrate *v* **1** 慶祝 **2**〔口頭或書面〕讚揚, 讚美, 歌頌 **3** 主持〔宗教儀式, 尤指彌撒〕

ceremony *n* **1** 典禮, 儀式 **2** 禮儀, 禮節 **3 without ceremony** 隨意地; 無禮地

certainty *n* **1** 確定[確實]的事; 必然會發生的事 **2** 確實(性), 確信, 確知

certify *v* **1**〔尤指經過某種檢驗〕證明, 證實, 核證 **2** 給〔某人〕頒發(完成專業培訓的)合格證書[文憑] **3** 正式證明〔某人〕有精神病

chain¹ *n* **1** ►**JOINED RINGS** 連接在一起的環◄ 鏈子, 鏈條 **2 chain of events/circumstances etc** 一系列[一連串]的事件/情況等 **3** ►**SHOPS/HOTELS** 商店/旅館◄ 連鎖店, 連鎖集團 **4** ►**CONNECTED LINE** 連接線◄ 連成一行的人[山; 島嶼] **5** ►**PRISONER** 囚犯◄ **chains**〔鎖住囚犯四肢的〕鐐銬, 鎖鏈 **6** ►**BUYING A HOUSE** 購屋◄〔一些人先賣舊屋再買新屋的〕鏈式購屋法, 連環購房鏈 **7** ►**MEASURE** 度量◄ 鏈〔舊時的長度單位〕

chain² *v* **1**〔尤指為防逃跑或被盜而〕鎖在一起, 拴住, 束縛 **2 be chained to something** 受到〔責任〕的束縛

challenge¹ *n* **1** ►**STH DIFFICULT** 棘手的事◄ 挑戰, 具有挑戰性的事物, 考驗〔某人〕能力的事物 **2** ►**QUESTIONING OF RIGHTNESS** 對公正性的質疑◄〔對某事的正確性、合法性等的〕質疑 **3** ►**INVITATION TO COMPETE** 挑戰◄ 挑戰,〔比賽等的〕提議 **4** ►**A DEMAND TO STOP** 停止的命令◄ 喝停盤問 **5** ►**IN LAW** 法律方面◄〔開庭前律師〕反對某人任陪審團成員的聲明

challenge² *v* **1** 質疑〔某事的正確性、合法性等〕, 對…表示懷疑 **2** 向…挑戰; 邀請〔某人〕比賽 **3** 考驗…的技術[能力]; 激發; 激勵 **4** 喝停盤問〔某人的身分、意圖等〕 **5**〔開審前在選定陪審員時〕對(某候選陪審員)表示反對 —**challenger** *n*

chamber *n* **1**〔人體內或某些機器中的〕室; 腔 **2** 作特殊用途的房間〔尤指令人不快者〕 **3** 大會議室, 會議廳 **4**〔美國〕參[眾]議院;〔英國〕上[下]議院 **5** 私人房間, 寢室 **6 chambers**〔大律師或法官的〕辦公室; 事務所 **7** 槍膛, 砲膛

champion¹ *n* **1**〔尤指體育比賽中的〕冠軍, 第一名 **2 champion of**〔為某目標或原則如某羣人的權利而奮鬥的〕鬥士

champion² *v* 公開為〔某目標或原則〕而鬥爭; 維護

channel¹ *n* **1** ►**TELEVISION** 電視◄ 頻道 **2** ►**RADIO** 廣播◄〔發送和接收無線電信號的〕波道 **3** ►**SYSTEM OF INFORMATION** 信息系統◄ 又作 **channels**〔傳遞或獲得資料的〕途徑; 手段; 渠道 **4** ►**FOR WATER** 水◄ 管道; 水渠, 水溝 **5** ►**SEA/RIVER** 海洋/河流◄ **a)** 海峽 **b)** 航道 **6** ►**IN A SURFACE** 在表面◄〔在表面形成的〕槽, 溝 **7** ►**WAY TO EXPRESS YOURSELF** 表達方式◄〔表達思想、感情或發泄精力的〕方式, 渠道, 途徑

channel² *v* **1** 把〔錢或精力等〕導向〔某一特定目的〕; 引導 **2** 在〔某物上〕形成槽 **3** 〔透過管道〕輸送〔水等〕

character *n* **1** ►**ALL SB'S QUALITIES 某人所有的品質**◄ 〔某人的〕個性, 性格, 氣質 **2** ►**QUALITIES OF STH 某物的特徵**◄ 〔某物或某地的〕特色, 特點 **3** ►**INTERESTING QUALITY 有趣的特點**◄ 〔使某人或某物特別或有趣的〕特徵 **4** ►**MORAL STRENGTH 道德力量**◄ 人格, 好的品質, 品性 **5** ►**PERSON 人物**◄ **a)** 〔書、劇本、電影等中的〕人物, 角色 **b)** 人;〔尤指〕怪人 **c) be a character** 有趣的人; 不同尋常的人 **6** ►**REPUTATION 聲譽**◄ 名譽, 名聲, 聲譽 **7** ►**LETTER/SIGN 字母/符號**◄ 〔書寫、印刷或電腦的〕字; 字體; 符號

charge¹ *n* **1** ►**PRICE 價格**◄ 費用, 價錢 **2** ►**CONTROL 控制**◄ **a) be in charge (of)** 負責…, 掌管… **b) put sb in charge (of)** 讓…全權負責 **c) take charge (of)** 控制, 掌管〔局面、組織或人〕 **3** ►**RESPONSIBILITY/CARE FOR 責任/照料**◄ **a) be in/under sb's charge** 由…照料[照顧] **b)** 被照顧的人 **4** ►**THAT SB IS GUILTY 某人有罪**◄ 指控, 控告, 罪名 **5** ►**BLAME 責備**◄ 〔書面或口頭的〕指責, 批評, 責備 **6** ►**ATTACK 進攻**◄ 〔士兵或野生動物等〕猛烈的攻擊 **7** ►**ELECTRICAL FORCE 電力**◄ 電荷; 電量 **8** ►**EXPLOSIVE 爆炸物**◄ 〔一定量的〕炸藥 **9** ►**STRENGTH OF FEELINGS 感情的力量**◄ 〔感情的〕力量; 感染力 **10 get a charge out of sth** 從〔某事〕得到快樂[刺激、興奮] **11** ►**AN ORDER TO DO STH 命令**◄ 命令, 指示, 吩咐

charge² *v* **1** ►**MONEY 錢**◄ **a)** (向…) 收費; 開價 **b) charge sth to sb's account** 把某物記在某人的賬上 **c)** 用信用卡付賬 **2** ►**RUSH/ATTACK 衝擊/攻擊**◄ **a)** 進攻, 衝鋒; 衝向 **b)** 快步走向[跑向] **3** ►**WITH A CRIME 有罪**◄ 控告; 指控 **4** ►**BLAME SB 指責某人**◄ 〔公開〕指責, 責備 **5** ►**ELECTRICITY 電**◄ (使) 充電; **6** ►**ORDER SB 命令某人**◄ 吩咐, 命令 **7** ►**GUN 槍**◄ 給〔槍〕裝子彈 **8** ►**GLASS 杯子**◄ 斟滿〔杯〕

charity *n* **1** 救濟(金), 施捨(物) **2** 慈善機構, 慈善團體 **3** 寬容, 寬厚, 寬大 **4 charity begins at home** 慈善始於家庭, 施捨先及親友

charm¹ *n* **1** 魅力, 魔力, 吸引力; 可愛之處 **2** 魔法; 咒語 **3** 〔裝在手鏈、手鐲上表示吉祥的〕小裝飾品; 護身符 **4 work like a charm** 完全[迅速]地奏效

charm² *v* **1** 迷住, 吸引 **2** 向…施魔法, 用魔法控制 **3 have/lead a charmed life** 總是幸運的, 總能逢凶化吉的 —**charmed** *adj*

chart¹ *n* **1** 圖表, 圖 **2** 地圖; 〔尤指〕海圖, 航海圖 **3 the charts** 〔流行歌曲每週〕排行榜

chart² *v* **1** 給…製圖; 記述 **2** 繪製…的地圖[海圖]; 把〔途經路線〕繪入地圖[海圖]

chase¹ *v* **1** ►**FOLLOW 跟隨**◄ 追逐, 追趕; 追捕 **2** ►**HURRY 趕快**◄ 急忙趕往 **3** ►**TRY TO GET STH 試圖得到某物**◄ 努力贏得, 設法獲得 **4** ►**MAN/WOMAN 男人/女人**◄ 追求, 求愛 **5** ►**METAL 金屬**◄ 鏤刻, 雕鏤〔金屬製品〕 **6 chase the dragon** 吸食海洛因

chase sb/sth ↔ **up** *phr v* **1** 提醒某人〔實踐諾言〕 **2** 加速…的發生進程, 催促

chase² *n* **1** 追逐, 追趕; 追捕 **2 give chase** 追逐〔某人或某物〕

check¹ *v* **1** ►**FIND OUT 發現**◄ 檢查, 核對, 查驗 **2** ►**ASK SB 詢問某人**◄ 詢問; 徵求同意; 核實 **3** ►**NOT DO STH 不做某事**◄ 克制〔自己〕; 停止[阻止]〔自己〕做〔某事〕 **4** ►**STOP STH 停止某事**◄ 阻礙, 制止; 抑制 **5** ►**MAKE A MARK 作標記**◄ 給〔答案、清單的項目等〕打勾號 **6** ►**BAGS/CASES ETC 袋子/箱子等**◄ 托運〔行李〕; 接受托運〔行李〕

check in *phr v* **1** 〔在旅館〕登記辦理入住手續; 〔在機場〕辦理登機手續 **2** 〔到圖書館〕歸還〔圖書〕

check sth ↔ **off** *phr v* 在〔處理過或核對過的項目後〕打勾

check out *phr v* **1** ►**MAKE SURE 確定**◄ **a)** 調查, 檢查, 核實, 查證 **b)** 證實是對的, 得到證實, 查證無誤的 **2** ►**LOOK AT SB/STH 看某人/物**◄ 〔因某人或物有趣或吸引人而〕盯着看 **3** ►**GET INFORMATION 獲得資料**◄ 了解…的情況 **4** ►**TEST STH 檢測某物**◄ 檢測〔某物〕 **5** ►**HOTEL 旅館**◄ 辦理退房手續, 結賬退房 **6** ►**BOOKS 書籍**◄ 〔從圖書館〕借出〔書〕

check sth ↔ **over** *phr v* **1** 檢查; 查看 **2** 體檢, 健康檢查

check up on sb *phr v* 〔尤指祕密地〕調查, 查核〔某人〕

check on sb *phr v* 檢查; 查看〔某人是否安全等〕

check² *n* **1** ►**ON SAFETY/CORRECTNESS/TRUTH ETC 安全/正確/真實等**◄ 〔以確保某物安全、正確、真實等的〕檢查; 查核 **2 keep a check (on sb/sth)** 監視; 監聽 **3 run/do a check** 進行檢查[調查] **4** ►**A CONTROL ON STH 控制某事**◄ 制止(手段), 抑制(手段), 控制 **5** ►**PATTERN 圖案**◄ 〔尤指布料上的〕方格圖案 **6** ►**FROM YOUR BANK 從銀行**◄ 支票 **7** ►**IN A RESTAURANT 在餐館**◄ 賬單 **8** ►**FOR YOUR COAT/BAG 衣物/袋子**◄ **a) coat check/hat check** 〔餐館、劇院等的〕衣帽寄存處 **b)** 存放單, 寄存物品的憑證 **9** ►**MARK 記號**◄ 〔表示答案正確或某事項已處理的〕勾號 **10** ►**CHESS 國際象棋**◄ 〔國際象棋中〕被"將軍"的局面〔王棋處於被攻擊的位置上〕

cherish *v* [一般用被動態] **1** 珍愛, 珍惜, 鍾愛 **2** 視為珍貴[重要]

chill¹ *v* **1** (使) 冷卻, (使) 變冷 **2** [一般用被動態] 使〔某人〕感到很冷 **3** 〔尤指以殘忍和暴力的手段〕使…不寒而慄, 使…寒心 **4** 使失望; 使〔熱情〕冷卻

chill out *phr v* 完全放鬆, 不緊張

chill² *n* **1** 寒冷, 寒氣 **2** 害怕; 心寒 **3** 小感冒, 輕微發燒 **4** 不友好, 冷漠, 冷淡

chill³ *adj* 寒冷的, 寒氣襲人的

chop¹ *v* **1** ►**CUT STH 切某物**◄ 又作 **chop up** 將〔食物、木材等〕切碎; 劈開 **2** ►**REDUCE STH 減少某物**◄ 〔大幅度〕削減 **3** ►**SWING A TOOL 揮舞工具**◄ 〔用斧頭等〕砍, 劈 **4** ►**MAKE A PATH 開路**◄ 開路, 闢路 **5 chop and change** 不停改變主意; 變化無常 **6** ►**HIT STH 打中某物**◄ 〔用手向下〕砸

chop sth ↔ **down** *phr v* 〔用斧頭等利器〕砍倒, 伐倒

chop sth ↔ **off** *phr v* 〔用斧等〕砍掉, 砍斷

chop² *n* **1** ►**MEAT 肉**◄ 〔羊、豬等〕帶骨的肉塊 **2**

get the chop a) 被辭退, 被解雇 b) 被中止; 被削減 3 be for the chop 很可能停止[關閉] 4 ►WITH YOUR HAND 用手◄ 掌劈〔尤用掌側〕 5 ►WITH A TOOL 用工具◄〔用斧頭等利器〕砍, 劈 6 the chops 顎, 下巴

chore *n* 1 家庭雜務; 日常零星工作 2 令人厭煩的工作

circulate *v* 1 (使)循環 2 流傳; 傳播; 散佈 3 發送; 傳播 4〔在聚會上〕到處走動, 來回周旋 —**circulatory** *adj*

circumstance *n* 1 circumstances 情況, 情形 2 under/in no circumstances 決不, 無論如何都不 3 under/in the circumstances 在這種情況下, 情形既然如此 4 無法控制的因素; 環境; 境遇 5 live in reduced circumstances 財政狀況不佳, 經濟拮据 6 pomp and circumstance 盛大隆重的場面

cite *v* 1 引證, 援引 2 引用, 引述 3 傳召; 傳訊〔到法院〕 4 傳喚 5 嘉獎; 表揚, 表彰

civil *adj* 1 公民的; 民間的 2 普通公民的; 平民的; 民用的; 非軍事的 3 民事的 4 客氣的; 文明的; 有禮貌的

claim¹ *v* 1 聲稱; 斷言; 主張 2 索賠; 索取 3 認領; 要求; 索取〔應得的權利或財物〕 4 奪去, 奪走〔生命〕 5 值得; 需要〔花時間或精力〕

claim² *n* 1 ►MONEY 金錢◄ a)〔根據權利而提出的〕要求, 索款 b) 索賠金額 2 ►STATEMENT 聲明◄ 聲稱; 斷言; 主張 3 ►FOR PRAISE/RESPECT ETC 用於表揚/尊敬等◄ 應得的權利[資格] 4 ►TO OWN OR TAKE SOMETHING 擁有或拿某物◄ 所有權 5 lay claim to sth 聲稱對某物擁有所有權 6 stake your claim 聲稱對...擁有所有權〔尤指當別人也同時作出相同的聲明〕 7 claim to fame 出名的原因〔常為戲謔說法, 一般指實際上並不怎麼重要的東西〕 8 have a claim on sb 有權得到〔某人的〕注意; 有權佔用〔某人的〕時間 9 ►LAND 土地◄ 要求得到的東西〈如含有礦產的土地〉

clarify *v* 澄清, 講清楚, 闡明 —**clarification** *n*

classify *v* 1〔依據某系統〕將...分類 2 把...歸入一類[一個等級] —**classifiable** *adj*

climate *n* 1〔某一時期社會上的〕風氣; 思潮; 趨勢 2 氣候 3 氣候帶, 地帶

cling *v* 1〔尤指感覺不安全而〕緊緊抓住[抱住] 2 纏着; 黏着 3 挨近, 貼近; 依附

cling to sth *phr v* 堅持, 忠於

coarse *adj* 1 粗的, 粗糙的 2 粗線條構成的; 粗的 3 粗俗的; 猥褻的; 粗魯的 —**coarsely** *adv* —**coarseness** *n*

code¹ *n* 1 ►BEHAVIOUR 行為◄ 行為準則; 道德規範 2 ►RULES/LAWS 規章/法律◄ 法典, 法規 3 code of practice 行業規則 4 ►SECRET MESSAGE 祕密信息◄ 密碼; 代碼; 代號 5 ►SIGNS GIVING INFORMATION 信息符號◄ 編碼, 編號, 標記 6 ►TELEPHONES 電話◄ 又作 **dialling code, STD code** 長途電話區號 7 ►COMPUTERS 電腦◄〔電腦的〕編碼 8 ►SOUNDS/SIGNALS 聲音/信號◄〔電報等發出的〕電碼

code² *v* 1 把...編碼[編號] 2 把...編成密碼 3 colour code 顏色編碼 —**coded** *adj*

collective¹ *adj* 集體的; 共同的; 共有的

collective² *n* 1 集體企業[農莊]人員 2 集體經營的企業[農莊]

colossal *adj* 巨大的, 龐大的 —**colossally** *adv*

combine¹ *v* 1 (使)結合; (使)組合 2 (使)化合, (使)組合, 調和 3 同時做〔兩件完全不同的事〕 4 (使)聯合〔以達成某項目〕; 合併

combine² *n* 1 又作 **combine harvester** 聯合收割機 2〔為某一目的而組成的〕聯盟, 聯合(體)

comedy *n* 1 喜劇 2 喜劇性, 喜劇成分; 幽默

comfort¹ *n* 1 ►EMOTIONAL 情感的◄ 安慰, 慰藉 2 ►PHYSICAL 身體的◄ 舒適感, 滿足感 3 ►MONEY/POSSESSIONS 錢/財產◄ 舒適, 安逸 4 comforts 使生活舒適之物; 奢侈品 5 ►SB/STH THAT HELPS 有用的人/物◄ 安慰者; 慰藉物 6 too close/near etc for comfort〔因危險而〕使人憂慮[不快, 不適]的事情 7 cold/small comfort 不起作用的安慰 —**comfortless** *adj*

comfort² *v* 安慰, 慰問 —**comforting** *adj* —**comfortingly** *adv*

commemorate *v* 慶祝, 為...舉行紀念活動 —**commemorative** *adj*

comment¹ *n* 1 意見, 評論 2〔對某人所說或所做事情的〕批評; 議論 3 be a comment on 是〔反映事物不足之處的〕標誌, 特徵

comment² *v* 評論; 發表意見

commerce *n* 1 買賣, 貿易; 商務; 商業 2 聯繫; 交流

commit *v* 1 ►CRIME 罪行◄ 犯〔錯誤、罪行〕 2 ►SAY THAT SB WILL DO STH 保證某人會做某事◄ 使承擔義務, 作出保證 3 commit yourself 答應, 承諾 4 ►MONEY/TIME 金錢/時間◄ 撥出...供使用, 調撥 5 ►PRISON/HOSPITAL 監獄/醫院◄ 把...關進監獄[醫院], 監禁 6 commit sth to memory 牢記某事 7 commit sth to paper 寫下某事

commodity *n* 1 商品 2 有用的性質; 有用的東西

commonplace¹ *adj* 平常的; 平凡的; 不足為奇的

commonplace² *n* 1 平常的事, 司空見慣的事 2 the commonplace 一般, 沒有特色, 單調乏味

communicate *v* 1 ►EXPRESS 表達◄ 表達, 傳達〔思想、感情〕 2 ►EXCHANGE INFORMATION 交流信息◄〔用符號等〕與〔他人〕交流信息; 交談 3 ►CONTACT 聯繫◄〔尤指用電話、書信等〕與他人聯繫 4 ►UNDERSTAND 理解◄ 溝通〔思想、情感〕 5 ►ROOMS 房間◄〔不同房間或樓房的不同部分〕互通, 相連 6 ►DISEASE 疾病◄ [一般用被動態]〔疾病〕傳染

community *n* 1 ►PEOPLE 人們◄〔同住一地的人所構成的〕社區 2 ►PARTICULAR GROUP 特定團體◄ sense of community 社區歸屬感〔居住在同一地的人們所有的一種歸屬感〕 3〔由同國籍、同宗教等構成的〕羣體; 社區 4 the community 社會; 公眾 5 ►PLANTS/ANIMALS 植物/動物◄ 羣落〔生長或生活在同一環境中的植物或動物羣〕

compact¹ *adj* 1 小巧便攜的 2 小而緊湊的 3 緊密的; 密集的 4 矮小結實的, 壯實的 5 簡潔的 —**compactly** *adv* —**compactness** *n*

compact² *n* 1〔內有鏡子的〕女式化妝粉盒 2 小型汽車 3〔人與人、國與國之間的〕協定

compact[3] *v*〔將某柔軟或由小塊組成的物質〕壓緊, 壓實 —**compacted** *adj*

companion *n* **1** 同伴; 同行者 **2** 構成一對的兩件物品中的一件 **3** 伴侶〔尤指受雇陪一位老人一起生活或旅行的人, 尤為女子〕**4** 手冊, 指南〔用於書名〕

compare[1] *v* **1** ►**SIMILAR/DIFFERENT 類似的/不同的**◄ 比較 **2 compared to/with**〔尺寸、質量、數量〕與…相比 **3** ►**LIKE/EQUALLY GOOD 像/同樣好**◄〔表示某物、某人與另一物、另一人〕相像或一樣好, 一樣大等 **4 does not compare** 不能相比 **5** ►**BETTER/WORSE 較好/較糟**◄〔在某方面〕比〔某人/某物〕好[差] **6 compare notes**〔兩人對所做過的事〕交換意見

compare[2] *n* **beyond/without compare** 無可比擬; 無可匹配

compensate *v* **1** 彌補, 補償 **2** 賠償, 補償

complex[1] *adj* **1** 複雜的〔指由許多密切聯繫的部分或過程構成的〕**2** 難以理解的, 難處理的; 複雜的 **3**〔詞、句〕複合

complex[2] *n* **1** 綜合樓羣〔由眾多大樓或一座主樓和諸多輔樓組成〕**2** 情結, 誇大的情緒反應 **3 a complex of roads/regulations etc** 縱橫交織的道路網/紛繁蕪雜的條例等

complicated *adj* **1** 難懂的; 難處理的 **2** 結構複雜的

component *n*〔機器或系統的〕零件; 成分; 組成部分

compose *v* **1 be composed of** 由…組成 **2** 組成, 構成 **3** 作曲 **4 compose a letter/poem/speech etc** 寫信/詩/講稿等 **5 compose your thoughts/features** 鎮靜心情/使外表平靜 **6**〔為達到特殊效果而〕為〔繪畫、照片場景〕構圖

compound[1] *n* **1** 化合物 **2** 由兩件或更多事情, 兩種或更多情況結合造成的局勢 **3** 四周有籬笆或圍牆的建築羣 **4** 複合名詞; 複合形容詞

compound[2] *adj* **1 compound eye/leaf etc** 複眼/複葉等 **2 compound noun/adjective** 複合名詞/複合形容詞

compound[3] *v* **1** 使惡化, 加重 **2** 使混合; 使合成; 使化合 **3** 以複利計算支付〔利息〕

compute *v* 計算〔結果、答案、總數等〕

conceal *v* **1** 隱匿, 隱藏 **2** 隱藏真實感情; 隱瞞真相 —**concealment** *n*

concentrate[1] *v* **1** 專注, 專心; 集中注意力 **2 be concentrated on/in/around etc** 集中於; 匯集於 **3** 使…頭腦清醒 **4** 濃縮〔液體〕

concentrate sth ↔ **on** *phr v* 把注意力集中於, 全神貫注於

concentrate[2] *n* 濃縮物; 濃縮液

concern[1] *n* **1** ►**WORRY 擔憂**◄ **a)** 擔心的事, 關切的事 **b)** 憂慮; 擔心 **2 be of concern (to sb)** 令〔某人〕感到擔心的; 是〔某人〕所關心的 **3** 與某人有關的事, 對某人重要的事 **4** ►**FEELING FOR SB 對某人的情感**◄ 關心; 關懷 **5 sb's concern** 由某人負責的事 **6 not sb's concern/none of sb's concern** 某人不感興趣的事; 與某人無關的事 **7** ►**BUSINESS 企業**◄ 企業; 公司

concern[2] *v* **1**〔活動、情況、規則等〕對…有影響; 與…相關 **2** [不用被動態] 使憂慮, 使擔心 **3** [不用被動態]〔故事、書、報告等〕與…有關, 關於 **4 concern yourself with/about sth** 關心, 擔心 **5 to whom it may concern**〔寫在正式信函開頭的一句套話, 用於寫信人不知道收信人的姓名時〕

concise *adj* 簡潔的; 簡明的 —**concisely** *adv* —**conciseness** 又作 **concision** *n*

conclude *v* **1** 作出結論, 斷定 **2** 完成, 結束 **3**〔以做某事或講某話來〕結束〔會議或演說〕**4 conclude an agreement/treaty/contract etc** 達成協議/締結條約/簽訂合同等

concrete[1] *adj* **1** 混凝土的 **2** 有真憑實據的 **3** 具體的 —**concretely** *adv*

concrete[2] *n* 混凝土

concrete[3] *v* 用混凝土澆築[覆蓋]〔小路、牆等〕

conduct[1] *v* **1 conduct a survey/experiment/inquiry etc**〔尤指為獲取信息或證實某事時〕進行調查/實驗/調查研究等 **2** ►**MUSIC 音樂**◄ 指揮 **3** ►**ELECTRICITY/HEAT 電/熱**◄ 傳導 **4** ►**SHOW SB STH 帶某人參觀**◄ 帶領某人參觀某地 **5 conduct yourself** 行為, 表現〔尤指人們藉此作出評判〕

conduct[2] *n* **1**〔社會、職業等〕行為舉止 **2**〔某項生意、活動的〕組織安排; 管理; 經營

conference *n* **1** 會議〔指很多人參加討論重要事宜的大型會議, 尤指歷時數天的會議〕**2** 少數人參加的私下會議 **3**〔運動〕聯合會

confirm *v* **1** 證實, 證明 **2** 使〔想法、感覺〕鞏固, 更堅定, 加強 **3** 證實 **4** 肯定, 確認〔安排、日期等〕**5 be confirmed** 行堅信典禮〔從而正式成為基督教會成員〕

conflict[1] *n* **1**〔意見等〕衝突, 相左 **2**〔在對立的需要或影響之間選擇的〕矛盾, 衝突 **3** 戰鬥; 戰爭 **4** 矛盾心理 **5 conflict of interest/interests a)** 利益衝突 **b)**〔不同人之間的〕利益衝突

conflict[2] *v* 矛盾, 衝突, 抵觸

confront *v* **1** 以暴力相威脅 **2** 勇敢地面對; 正視 **3** [一般用被動態] 突然面臨 **4** 對質, 當面對證

confuse *v* **1** 使困惑; 把〔某人〕弄糊塗 **2**〔把人、物或想法〕混淆, 弄錯 **3 confuse the issue/matter/argument etc** 使問題/事情/爭論等更加難以弄清或處理

congratulate *v* **1** 祝賀, 向…道喜 **2 congratulate yourself (on)** 為自己高興, 感到自豪 —**congratulation** *n* —**congratulatory** *adj*

congress *n* **1** 代表大會 **2** 國會; 議會 **3 Congress**〔由參議院和眾議院組成的〕美國國會 —**congressional** *adj*

conquer *v* **1** 征服 **2** 擊敗, 戰勝 **3** 克服; 制伏 **4** 成功登上〔從未有人攀登過的山頂〕**5**〔在某地〕大獲成功 —**conqueror** *n* —**conquering** *adj*

conscious *adj* **1** 注意到的; 意識到的 **2** 清醒的 **3 a conscious effort/decision/attempt etc** 特意做出的努力/決定/嘗試等 **4 safety-conscious/fashion-conscious etc** 特別注意安全的/十分關注時尚的等 —反義詞 UNCONSCIOUS —**consciously** *adv*

consent[1] *n* **1** 許可, 允許 **2** 同意, 贊同 **3 with one consent** 全體一致同意

consent[2] *v* 同意, 允許

consequence *n* **1** 後果 **2 as a consequence (of sth)/in consequence (of sth)** 因為; 由於 **3 of little/**

no/any consequence 不重要的/無足輕重的

conservative¹ *adj* **1 Conservative**〔英國〕保守黨的 **2** 因循守舊的, 不喜變化的 **3**〔式樣、口味等〕不時興的, 傳統的 **4 a conservative estimate/guess** 保守的估計/猜測 **—conservatively** *adv*

conservative² *n* **1 Conservative** 英國保守黨的支持者; 保守黨黨員 **2** 因循守舊者, 保守者

considerable *adj* 相當大的〔尤指大到足以產生某種影響的程度〕

consist *v*

consist in sth *phr v* 在於, 決定於

consist of sth *phr v* 由…組成, 由…構成

constant¹ *adj* **1** 始終如一的, 恆久不變的 **2** 持續不斷的, 經常發生的 **3** 忠實的, 忠誠的

constant² *n* **1** 常數, 恒量 **2** 不變的事; 恆定的事物

consult *v* **1** 諮詢; 請教 **2** 取得〔某人〕的允許; 與〔某人〕商量共同決定 **3** 查閱

consume *v* **1** 消耗; 消費 **2 time-consuming** 耗費時間的 **3** 吃; 喝 **4 consumed with** 被〔某種情感〕所折磨 **5**〔大火〕(徹底)燒毀

contact¹ *n* **1 ►COMMUNICATION** 交流◄ 聯繫, 聯絡; 交往 **2 ►TOUCH** 觸摸◄ 接觸 **3 come into contact with sb** 會見某人 **4 ►PERSON WHO CAN HELP** 能提供幫助的人◄〔能提供幫助或建議的〕熟人 **5 ►SITUATION/PROBLEM** 局勢/問題◄〔處理某種局面或問題的〕經驗 **6 point of contact a)** 聯繫點; 聯繫人 **b)** 聯繫點; 接合點 **7 ►ELECTRICAL PART** 電路元件◄〔電路的〕觸點; 接頭 **8 ►EYES** 眼睛◄ 隱形眼鏡

contact² *v*〔寫信、打電話〕聯繫〔某人〕

contact³ *adj* **1** 可供聯繫的〔電話號碼或地址〕**2**〔炸藥或化學物質〕憑接觸起作用的

contain *v* **1** 包含; 容納; 裝盛 **2** 克制〔強烈的感情〕**3** 抑制, 控制 **4** 包圍〔區域或角〕

contemporary¹ *adj* **1** 當代的 **2** 發生[存在]於同一時代的

contemporary² *n* 同時代的人; 同輩

content¹ *n* **1 contents a)** 容納的東西 **b)**〔信、書等的〕內容 **2** 含量 **3**〔演講或文章的〕內容

content² *adj* **1** 滿意的, 滿足的 **2 not content with** 對…不滿足

content³ *n* **1** 滿意, 滿足 **2 do sth to your heart's content** 盡情[心滿意足]地做某事

content⁴ *v* **1 content yourself with sth** 使自己滿足[甘心]於某事 **2** 使滿意; 使滿足

contest¹ *n* **1** 比賽, 競賽 **2** 競爭, 爭奪, 角逐 **3 no contest** 輕易獲勝, 輕取

contest² *v* **1** 對…提出質疑; 抗辯 **2** 競爭, 爭奪, 角逐

contract¹ *n* **1** 契約; 合同 **2 subject to contract**〔達成協議但還〕須簽訂合約 **3** 刺殺協議

contract² *v* **1** 縮小; 收縮; 縮短 **2** 感染〔疾病〕, 患〔病〕**3 contract to do sth** 簽合同做… **4 contract a marriage/alliance etc** 訂立婚約/盟約等

contract in *phr v* 同意參與; 訂約加入

contract out *phr v* **1** 把〔工作等〕承包出去 **2** 同意不加入〔退休金計劃等〕

contrary¹ *n* **1 on the contrary** 正相反, 恰恰相反〔用於表示強烈不贊同別人剛說的話〕**2 to the contrary** 意思相反; 完全不同 **3 the contrary** 相反; 反面; 對立面

contrary² *adj* **1** 相反的, 相對的 **2** 故意作對的, 對抗的 **3 contrary to** 與…相反〔用於表示與別人觀點相反的事實〕**4**〔天氣〕不作美的, 不合人意的 **—contrariness** *n*

contrast¹ *n* **1** 差異, 差別 **2 in contrast/by contrast** 與…相反/相比之下 **3** 對照物, 明顯的對比物 **4**〔繪畫、照片中顏色、明暗的〕反差 **5**〔電視畫面的〕對比度, 襯度

contrast² *v* **1** 使成對比, 使成對照 **2** 形成對照; 對比之下現出區別

contribute *v* **1** 捐獻; 捐助; 出一分錢; 出一分力 **2 contribute to sth** 對某事起促成作用 **3**〔給報紙、雜誌等〕撰稿; 投稿

convenience *n* **1** 方便, 便利; 合宜 **2**〔個人的〕便利; 自在, 舒適 **3 at your earliest convenience** 儘快〔常用於書信〕**4** 便利措施; 帶來方便的裝置 **5** 又作 **public convenience** 公共廁所 **6 a marriage of convenience** 基於利害關係的婚姻

convey *v* **1** 傳達; 表達〔想法、感情〕**2** 傳遞〔信息〕; 傳送; 傳播 **3** 傳送〔物件〕; 輸送; 運送 **4** 把〔財產〕讓與; 轉讓

convince *v* **1** 使確信; 使信服 **2** 説服, 勸服

cooperate 又作 **co-operate** **1** 合作, 協作 **2** 配合; 協助

cope¹ *v* **1**〔成功地〕應付, 對付 **2**〔機器或系統〕能處理; 能應付

cope² *n*〔教士在特別日子穿的〕長袍, 法衣

core¹ *n* **1 ►FRUIT** 水果◄〔蘋果等的〕果心 **2 ►CENTRAL PART** 中心部分◄〔事物的〕核心, 最重要部分 **3 core values/beliefs/concerns** 最重要的標準/最重要的信仰/最關心的問題 **4 ►PEOPLE** 人們◄〔組織的〕核心成員 **5 to the core** 十分地; 徹底地 **6 ►PLANETS** 行星◄ 地心; 〔天體的〕核心 **7 ►NUCLEAR REACTOR** 核反應堆◄〔核反應堆的〕活性區

core² *v* 去掉〔水果的〕果心

corporation *n* **1** 大型公司; 大企業; 企業集團 **2** 市鎮當局; 市議會 **3 corporation tax** 公司(利潤)稅

correspond *v* **1** 符合; 相一致 **2** 相類似, 相當 **3** 通信

cosmetic *adj* **1** 裝門面的; 表面的 **2** 化妝的; 美容的

cosmopolitan¹ *adj* **1**〔某地的人〕來自世界各地的 **2**〔人〕見識廣的; 〔信仰、意見等〕兼容並包的

cosmopolitan² *n* 遊歷四方的人; 四海為家的人

costume *n* **1**〔代表某一特定地方或歷史時期的〕服裝 **2** 化裝服; 戲裝 **3** 游泳衣, 泳裝

counter¹ *n* **1 ►SHOP** 商店◄ 櫃台 **2 over the counter**〔買藥〕不用處方 **3 under the counter** 祕密地, 暗地裡〔通常違法地〕**4 ►KITCHEN** 廚房◄〔尤指廚房中的〕操作台面, 工作台 **5 ►GAME** 遊戲◄ 籌碼 **6 ►EQUIPMENT** 裝備◄ 計算器, 計數器 **7 ►ACTION AGAINST STH** 反對◄ 制止; 反駁

counter² *v* **1** 反駁, 反對 **2** 抵消; 對抗; 制止

counter³ *adv* 相反地 **—counter** *adj*

courteous *adj* 有禮貌的 —反義詞 DISCOURTEOUS

—courteously *adv* —courteousness *n*

coverage *n* **1** 新聞報道 **2** 保險範圍, 保險項目 **3** 課程內容; 一堂課的內容

crack¹ *v* **1** ►**BREAK 斷裂**◄ (使) 破裂; (使) 裂開 **2** ►**LOUD SOUND 響聲**◄ (使) 發爆裂聲 **3** ►**HIT STH 擊撞某物**◄ 重擊 **4** ►**HIT SB 擊打某人**◄ 重擊〔某人〕 **5** ►**LOSE CONTROL 失控**◄ 又作 **crack up**〔因受大壓力而〕失去控制; 崩潰 **6** ►**MENTALLY ILL 精神病**◄ 又作 **crack up** (使) 發瘋, (使) 神經錯亂 **7** ►**VOICE 聲音**◄〔聲音〕變嘶啞 **8** ►**NERVE 神經**◄ 失去勇氣 **9** ►**EGG/NUT 蛋/堅果**◄ 打開, 砸開〔雞蛋、堅果等的〕殼 **10** ►**STEAL 偷**◄ 非法地打開; 撬開〔保險櫃盜竊〕 **11** ►**SOLVE 解決**◄ 解決〔難題〕; 破解〔密碼〕 **12** ►**STOP CRIME/ENEMY 制止犯罪/敵人**◄ 消滅〔敵人〕; 制止〔敵人做的事〕 **13 crack it** 成功 **14 crack a deal**〔尤指費力地〕達成協議; 做成買賣 **15 crack a joke** 説笑話 **16 crack a smile** 轉怒為喜; 破涕為笑 **17 crack open a bottle** 打開一瓶酒 **18 not all/everything it's cracked up to be** 不如人們所説的那樣好; 名不副實 **19 get cracking** 抓緊時間 **20 crack the whip** 逼手下人努力工作

crack down *phr v*〔對…〕採取嚴厲措施; 制裁; 鎮壓

crack on *phr v* 繼續努力

crack up *phr v* **1** (使) 捧腹大笑 **2** 吃不消, 精神垮掉

crack² *n* **1** ►**THIN SPACE 狹窄的空間**◄ 裂縫, 縫隙 **2** ►**BREAK 斷裂**◄ 裂痕, 裂口 **3** ►**PROBLEM 問題**◄ 瑕疵, 缺點 **4** ►**SOUND 聲音**◄ 爆裂聲, 劈啪聲 **5** ►**JOKE/REMARK 玩笑/話語**◄ 俏皮話; 粗魯的話 **6** ►**CHANCE TO DO STH 機遇**◄ 試圖, 嘗試 **7 a crack on the head** 腦袋上挨了一下 **8 a crack in sb's voice**〔尤指因情緒激動而引起的〕嗓音的變化 **9 crack of dawn** 大清早, 黎明 **10** ►**DRUG 毒品**◄ 強效可卡因 **11 good crack** 一羣人友好的交談; 盡興的談話 **12 what's the crack?** 發生甚麼事了? 最近發生了甚麼事?

crack³ *adj* **1** 第一流的; 受過良好訓練的 **2 crack shot** 神槍手

cradle¹ *n* **1** ►**BED 牀**◄ 搖籃 **2 the cradle of** …的發源地; …的策源地 **3 from/in the cradle** 從/在嬰兒[幼年]時期 **4 from the cradle to the grave** 一輩子, 從生到死 **5**〔空中作業用的〕吊架, 吊籃 **6**〔電話的〕聽筒架, 叉簧

cradle² *v* 輕輕地抱着

craft¹ *n* **1 a)** 小船 **b)** 飛機, 飛行器, 航空器; 航天器 **2**〔尤指傳統的手工〕工藝; 手藝 **3** 行業, 職業 **4** 詭計, 手腕

craft² *v* [一般用被動態] 手工製作, 精製

crash¹ *v* **1** ►**CAR/PLANE ETC 汽車/飛機等**◄ (使)〔飛機、汽車等〕墜毀; 撞壞 **2** ►**HIT STH/SB HARD 重擊某物/某人**◄〔嘩啦啦地〕猛撞, 猛擊 **3** ►**MAKE A LOUD NOISE 發出巨響**◄ 發出巨響 **4** ►**SLEEP 睡覺**◄ 又作 **crash out a)**〔尤指由於很疲倦〕很快入睡 **b)**〔尤指事先沒有準備而留在別人家裡〕過夜 **5** ►**COMPUTER 電腦**◄〔電腦〕癱瘓 **6** ►**FINANCIAL 金融**◄〔股票〕狂跌 **7** ►**PARTY 聚會**◄ 不請自來〔參加聚會〕 **8 crashing bore** 令人厭煩的人

crash² *n* **1**〔汽車的〕撞車事故; 〔飛機的〕失事 **2** 突然發出的巨響; 〔東西倒下、打破等時發出的〕碰撞聲 **3**〔電腦或電腦系統的〕癱瘓, 失效, 死機 **4**〔股票的〕狂跌

create *v* **1** 創造; 創建 **2** 發明; 創作 **3 create sb/sth** 封爵; 任命; 授予 **4** 大喊大叫; 大發雷霆

credit¹ *n* **1** ►**DELAYED PAYMENT 推遲付款**◄ 賒購 **2** ►**PRAISE 讚揚**◄ 讚揚; 讚許 **3 be a credit to sb/sth** 又作 **do sb/sth credit** 為…增光 **4 have sth to your credit** 成功 **5 be in credit**〔銀行賬戶中〕有存款 **6** ►**FILM 電影**◄ **the credits**〔影片或電視節目的〕演員和攝製人員名單 **7 on the credit side** 好的方面; 正面 **8** ►**UNIVERSITY 大學**◄ 學分 **9** ►**TRUE/CORRECT 真的/正確的**◄ 信任

credit² *v* **1** 信任; 相信 **2** 把錢存入〔賬戶〕 **3 credit sb with sth** 相信某人有優點[做了好事] **4 be credited to** 歸功於…; …是某事發生的原因

creep¹ *v* **1** 悄悄地小心行進 **2** 爬行, 匍匐 **3** 漸漸侵入, 逐漸融進 **4**〔植物〕攀緣, 蔓生 **5**〔霧、雲等〕彌漫 **6** 卑躬屈膝, 巴結奉承 **7 sb/sth makes my flesh creep** 某人/某事物使我不舒服[恐懼]

creep up on sb/sth *phr v* **1** 躡手躡腳在後面走〔而嚇人一跳〕 **2**〔感情或觀點〕漸漸變強 **3** 不知不覺中到來

creep² *n* **1** 極討厭的人 **2** 獻媚者; 奴顏婢膝的人 **3 give sb the creeps**〔人或地方〕使某人毛骨悚然[緊張]

crime *n* **1** ►**CRIME IN GENERAL 犯罪**◄〔泛指〕違法犯罪活動 **2** ►**A PARTICULAR CRIME 罪行**◄ 罪, 罪行 **3 it's a crime**〔這麼做是〕不道德的 **4 crime against humanity** 違反人性的罪行 **5 crime of passion** 情殺罪; 桃色案件 **6 crime doesn't pay** 違法犯罪是沒有好處的

cripple¹ *n* **1** 跛子; 手臂殘廢者〔侮辱用語〕 **2 emotional cripple** 感情殘廢〔不能處理自己或他人的感情的人〕

cripple² *v* **1** 使〔手臂或腿〕受傷致殘 **2** 嚴重損壞[削弱] —crippled *adj* —crippling *adj*

crisis *n* **1**〔尤指政治、經濟等〕危機; 緊要關頭 **2**〔個人的〕危急之際 **3**〔重病的〕轉折點 **4 crisis management** 應付危機[困境]的技巧; 危機[困境]處理過程 **5 crisis of confidence** 信任危機

crude¹ *adj* **1** 粗俗的, 粗野的; 粗魯的 **2** 粗製的 **3**〔石油、橡膠等〕天然的, 未加提煉的 **4** 粗糙的; 未加修飾的; 簡陋的 **5 in crude terms** 簡單地説 —crudely *adv* —crudity 又作 crudeness *n*

crude² 又作 **crude oil** *n* 原油

crush¹ *v* **1** 壓碎, 壓壞, 壓扁 **2** 搗碎, 弄碎, 粉碎 **3 crush a rebellion/uprising/revolt etc** 平定叛亂/起義/反叛等 **4 crush sb's hopes/enthusiasm/confidence etc** 毀滅某人的希望/熱情/信心等 **5** 使非常傷心; 使震驚

crush up *phr v* 擠, 塞, 擠入

crush² *n* **1** 擁擠的人羣 **2**〔尤指對年齡比自己大者的〕迷戀 **3 orange/lemon etc crush** 橙汁/檸檬汁等

cure¹ *v* **1** 治癒〔病人〕 **2** 治癒, 治好〔疾病〕 **3** 解決〔問題〕; 改善〔困境〕 **4**〔用曬、熏、醃等方法〕保存〔食品、煙草等〕

cure² *n* **1** 藥, 藥劑; 療法 **2** 對策 **3** 治癒 **4 take the**

cure 進行礦泉治療

curious *adj* **1** 好奇的, 好打聽的 —反義詞 INCURIOUS **2** 稀奇古怪的 —**curiously** *adv*

curl¹ *n* **1** 鬈髮 **2** 捲曲物, 螺旋狀物 **3 a curl of your lip/mouth** 撇嘴〔表示不贊同〕

curl² *v* **1** 盤繞, 纏繞 **2**（使）彎曲 **3**〔表示反對〕撇〔嘴〕**4 make your hair curl**〔故事、經歷等〕使人毛骨悚然, 使…戰慄

curl up *phr v* **1** 蜷縮 **2** 捲曲 **3** 彎曲着上升, 螺旋着上升

current¹ *adj* 現時的, 當前的, 現行的 —**currently** *adv*

current² *n* **1** 流; 水流 **2** 電流

curse¹ *v* **1** 咒罵 **2**〔嘴上或心裡〕臭罵 **3** 詛咒

curse² *n* **1** 罵人話 **2** 詛咒, 咒語 **3** 禍因, 禍根 **4 the curse** 月經

cushion¹ *n* **1** 墊子 **2** 墊形物, 起墊子作用的東西; 緩衝物 **3**〔尤指金錢〕起緩解作用的東西; 防備不時之需的積蓄 **4**〔枱球桌的〕橡皮邊, 彈性襯邊

cushion² *v* **1** 緩衝 **2** 減輕〔令人不愉快的〕效果

custom *n* **1** 風俗, 習慣, 傳統 **2** 日常習慣 **3**〔經常性的〕惠顧, 光顧 **4 customs** 海關

cycle¹ *n* **1** 循環 **2** 自行車; 摩托車 **3** 週期 **4**〔表現同一重大事件的〕組歌, 組詩

cycle² *v* 騎自行車

D, d

damage¹ *n* **1 ►PHYSICAL HARM 對物體或身體的損害◄**〔對某物、某人造成的〕損害 **2 ►EMOTIONAL HARM 情感上受到的傷害◄**〔對一個人感情或心理造成的〕傷害 **3 ►BAD EFFECT 不好的影響◄** 壞影響 **4 ►MONEY 錢◄** 損害賠償金 **5 the damage is done** 已造成的傷害無法挽回 **6 what's the damage?** 要花多少錢? **7 damage limitation** 損失控制, 降低損失

damage² *v* **1** 損害, 損壞, 損傷〔某物或某人的身體部位〕**2**〔對某物或某人〕有不好的影響 —**damaging** *adj*

damp¹ *adj* **1** 潮濕的 **2 damp squib** 未達到預期效果而使人失望的事; 濕水爆竹 —**damply** *adv*

damp² *n* 潮濕的部分[地方]

damp³ *v* 減低〔聲響〕

damp sth ↔ **down** *phr v* **1**〔常指用蓋灰的方法〕封〔火〕, 減弱〔火勢〕**2** 抑制〔感情〕

dash¹ *v* **1** 猛衝 **2** 猛擊, 撞擊 **3 dash sb's hopes** 使某人的希望破滅, 讓某人失望 **4 (I) must dash/(I) have to dash**（我）得趕緊走了 **5 dash it (all)!**〔表示有些厭煩、生氣〕討厭! **6**〔波浪或大雨猛烈地〕撞擊, 沖擊

dash off *phr v* **1** 匆匆地離開 **2** 匆匆地寫[畫]〔某物〕

dash² *n*

1 ►LINE 線條◄ 破折號 **2 make a dash for** 猛衝, 飛奔 **3 ►SMALL AMOUNT 少量◄** 少許, 少量〔液體或其他物質〕**4 a mad dash** 急奔, 狂衝 **5 ►SOUND 聲音◄**〔用莫爾斯電碼發報時用的〕長音; 光的一長閃 **6 ►CAR 汽車◄**〔汽車的〕儀表板 **7 ►STYLE 風範◄**〔如士兵般的〕帥勁, 精力, 幹勁; 勇氣 **8 cut a dash**〔尤指穿着〕有氣派, 精神, 漂亮

date¹ *n* **1** 日期, 日子 **2** 日子〔特定的某一天〕**3 at a later date** 晚些時候〔將來的某個時間〕**4 to date** 迄今, 至今, 到目前為止 **5 a)**〔戀人之間的〕約會 **b)** 約會對象 **6 make a date** 約好時間 **7** 椰棗, 海棗

date² *v* **1**〔在某物上〕寫上[印上]日期 **2** 鑑定〔古書、古畫、古建築等的〕年代 **3**〔衣物、藝術等〕過時 **4**〔談戀愛〕與…約會 **5** 顯示〔某人〕老了

date from 又作 **date back to** *phr v* 自…存在至今, 追溯到…年代

dawn¹ *n* **1** 黎明, 破曉 **2 the dawn of civilization/time etc** 文明/時代等的開端 **3 a false down** 假曙光〔指虛幻的好跡象〕

dawn² *v* **1** 破曉, 天亮 **2** 開始 **3** 開始明白, 第一次想起〔某種感覺或想法〕

dawn on sb *phr v* [不用被動態] 開始明白〔某個事實〕, 醒悟

debate¹ *n* **1** 討論, 辯論 **2**〔就某一個話題進行的〕正式討論 **3 be open to debate** 又作 **be a matter for debate**〔某種觀點〕可以進行討論的 **4 under debate** 正在討論[辯論]中

debate² *v* **1**〔正式地〕討論, 辯論 **2**〔作出決定前〕反覆考慮, 斟酌 —**debater** *n*

decay¹ *v* **1**（使）腐爛;（使）變壞 **2**〔可以指建築物、結構或地區等的狀況〕變壞, 破敗 **3**〔傳統觀念、道德、標準等〕失去影響力, 衰敗, 衰落

decay² *n* **1** 腐爛, 朽爛 **2** 腐爛部分, 腐蝕部分 **3**〔觀念、信仰、社會組織或政治組織等的〕衰退, 衰敗 **4**〔經濟上的〕成功到貧窮的轉變, 衰退 **5**〔疏於管理而造成建築物和大樓的〕逐漸毀壞

deceive *v* **1** 欺騙 **2 deceive yourself** 自欺欺人 **3 are my eyes deceiving me?** 我是不是看錯了? 是不是我眼花了?〔表示非常驚訝〕—**deceiver** *n*

decent *adj* **1** 可接受的, 相當好的, 像樣的 **2**〔待人〕公平的; 和善的 **3** 正派的, 規矩的 **4** 穿着得體的, 不暴露太多的 —反義詞 INDECENT **5 a decent burial funeral** 體面的葬禮 —**decently** *adv*

declare *v* **1 ►STATE OFFICIALLY 正式宣布◄** 宣布, 聲明 **2 declare war (on sb) a)** 對〔某國〕宣戰 **b)** 向〔不好的事〕宣戰 **3 ►SAY WHAT YOU THINK/FEEL 說出所想/感覺到的◄** 聲稱, 宣稱 **4 ►MONEY/PROPERTY ETC 金錢/財產等◄** 申報〔收入、財產等〕**5 declare an interest** 宣布和…有關係 **6 declare bankruptcy** 宣告破產 **7 ►SURPRISE 驚奇◄ (Well) I declare!** 嘿! 真怪了!〔用於表示驚奇〕—**declarable** *adj*

declare against sb/sth *phr v* 聲明反對

declare for sb/sth *phr v* 聲明贊成

decline¹ *n* 減少, 削減

decline² *v* **1 ►BECOME LESS 變少◄** 減少, 下降, 衰退 **2 ►BECOME WORSE 變糟◄**〔質量〕越來越差 **3 ►SAY NO 說不◄** 拒絕, 謝絕 **4 ►REFUSE 拒絕◄** 拒絕〔做某事〕**5 sb's declining years** 某人的晚年, 殘生 **6 ►GRAMMAR 語法◄ a)**〔根據名詞、代名詞或形容詞在句中的作用, 作主詞、受詞或是其他成分〕變格, 詞形變化 **b)** 使〔名詞等〕詞形變化, 使變格

decorate *v* **1** 裝修 **2** 裝飾, 佈置, 美化 **3** 授予…勳

章[獎章] —**decorating** *n*

decrease¹ *v*（使）變小,（使）減少 — 反義詞 INCREASE —**decreasing** *adj*

decrease² *n* 減少; 減少的數量

dedicate *v* **1 a)** 把〔作品等〕獻給〔某人〕**b)** 用…命名〔建築物, 以表達崇敬之情〕**2 dedicate yourself/your life to sth** 獻身於/把一生獻給某事

defeat¹ *n* **1** 失敗 **2** 戰勝, 擊敗

defeat² *v* **1**〔在戰爭、競爭、比賽等中〕戰勝, 打敗 **2** 把〔某人〕難住 **3** 使…失敗

defect¹ *n* 缺陷, 瑕疵

defect² *v* 背叛, 叛變, 投敵, 變節 —**defector** *n* —**defection** *n*

defend *v* **1** 保護, 保衛 **2** 捍衛, 維護 **3** 為…辯護, 為…辯白, 為…辯解 **4**〔在比賽中〕防守, 防衛 **5 defend a title/championship**〔冠軍〕衛冕 **6**〔律師〕為〔被指控犯罪者〕辯護

define *v* **1** 闡明, 説明 **2** 給…下定義, 解釋 **3** 標明…界限, 顯出…輪廓 **4** 是…的特徵, 界定 —**definable** *adj*

delay¹ *n* **1** 延誤的時間, 耽擱的時間 **2** 延誤, 耽擱 **3** 推遲〔某事沒有按時發生或開始〕

delay² *v* **1** 推遲, 延期〔做某事〕**2** [常用被動態] 耽誤, 耽擱 —**delayed** *adj*

delegate¹ *n* 代表

delegate² *v* **1** 授權, 委託權限 **2** 委派〔某人〕做〔某項工作〕; 委任〔某人〕做代表

delete *v* 刪除, 刪掉

deliberate¹ *adj* **1** 故意的, 有意的, 蓄意的 **2**〔講話、思想或行動〕沉着的, 從容不迫的 —**deliberateness** *n*

deliberate² *v* 仔細考慮

delicate *adj*
1 ►EASILY DAMAGED 容易受損的◄ 易壞的, 易碎的, 脆弱的 **2 ►NEEDING SENSITIVITY 需要敏感性的◄** 微妙的, 需要謹慎處理的 **3 ►PERSON 人◄**〔人〕容易生病的; 嬌弱的 **4 ►PART OF THE BODY 身體的一部分◄** 優美的, 優雅的 **5 ►SKILFULLY MADE 製作精巧的◄** 精巧的, 精緻的, 精美的 **6 ►TASTE/SMELL/COLOUR 味道/氣味/顏色◄** 柔和的, 清淡的, 淡雅的 —**delicately** *adv*

delicious *adj* **1** 美味的, 可口的; 芳香的 **2** 宜人的, 令人愉快的

deliver *v* **1 ►TAKE STH SOMEWHERE 把某物帶到某處◄** 把〔貨物、信件等〕送往〔某處〕**2 deliver a speech/lecture/talk etc** 發言/授課/講話等 **3 ►DO STH YOU SHOULD DO 做應該做的事◄** 不負所望, 做該做的事 **4 ►BABY 嬰兒◄** 給…接生; 幫助〔產婦〕分娩 **5 deliver a blow/shock etc to** 給予〔某人〕打擊/使〔某人〕震驚等 **6 deliver a verdict/judgment/ruling etc** 作出裁決/判斷/裁定等 **7 ►PERSON 人◄** 把〔某人〕交出; 把〔某人〕送到…手中 **8 ►VOTES 投票◄**〔在競選中〕為…拉票 **9 ►MAKE SB FREE OF 解脱某人◄** 解救, 解脱〔某人〕—**deliverer** *n*

deliver sth **up** *phr v* [常用被動態] 把〔某物〕移交給〔某人〕

demand¹ *n* **1 ►FIRM REQUEST 堅決要求◄** 要求, 請求 **2 demands** 困難的[煩人的、累人的]事情 **3 ►GOODS/SERVICES 貨物/服務◄** 需求 **4 by popular demand** 應公眾要求 **5 on demand** 見票即付

demand² *v* **1**〔堅決〕要求〔尤其是別人不想給的東西〕**2** 詢問, 質問; 命令 **3** 需要〔時間、精力、技能等〕

demonstrate *v* **1** 證明, 論證, 證實 **2** 示範, 演示 **3**〔為公開抗議某事〕遊行示威 **4** 展示, 表露出〔某種技能、品質或能力〕

dense *adj* **1 ►CLOSE TOGETHER 挨在一起◄** 茂密的, 密集的, 稠密的 **2 ►SMOKE/MIST 煙/霧◄** 濃密的, 不易看透[呼吸]的 **3 ►STUPID 愚蠢的◄** 遲鈍的, 愚蠢的 **4 ►WRITING 寫作◄**〔寫的東西〕不易懂的 **5 ►SUBSTANCE 物質◄** 密度大的 —**densely** *adv* —**denseness** *n*

deny *v* **1 ►SAY STH IS UNTRUE 説某事不是事實◄** 否認, 否定 **2 ►NOT ALLOW 不允許◄** [常用被動態] 不允許〔某人擁有某物或做某事〕**3 there's no denying** 無可否認, 不容否認 **4 ►PRINCIPLES/BELIEFS 原則/信仰◄** 背棄, 拋棄 **5 ►FEELINGS 感情◄** 拒絕承認 **6 deny yourself**〔尤指出於道德或宗教原因〕克制自己, 自制

depart *v* **1** 離開〔尤指動身去旅行〕, 啟程, 上路 **2 depart this life** 去世, 故去, 離開人間

depart from sth *phr v* 背離, 違反, 不同於〔常規等〕

depend *v* **it/that depends** 那得看情況

depend on/upon *phr v* **1** 依靠, 依賴 **2** 信賴, 相信 **3** 取決於…, 視…而定

deposit¹ *n* **1 ►SUM OF MONEY 金額◄**〔購屋、買車、度假等的〕定金, 頭款, 首期 **2 ►RENT 租用◄**〔租用東西的〕押金, 保證金 **3 ►BANK 銀行◄** 存款 **4 ►SOIL/MINERALS 土壤/礦物質◄** 礦牀 **5 ►LAYER 層◄** 沉積物, 沉積層 **6 ►ELECTION 選舉◄** 選舉保證金〔在英國參加政治選舉的候選人付的保證金, 如果候選人得到足夠的選票, 保證金將發還給他〕

deposit² *v* **1** 把〔某物〕放在〔某地〕**2** 沉積 **3** 將〔錢等貴重物品〕存入〔銀行或其他安全的地方〕

depress *v* **1** 使憂愁, 使抑鬱 **2** 使不能正常運轉, 使不活躍, 使不景氣 **3** 按下, 壓下, 推下〔尤指機器的一部分〕**4** 減少, 降低〔價格或工資〕

deprive *v*

deprive sb **of** sth *phr v* [常用被動態] 剝奪

deputy *n* **1**〔經理的〕副手;〔經理不在時負責工作的〕代理人 **2**〔某些國家如法國的〕下議院議員 **3** 美國縣治安官的助理

descend *v* **1** 下來, 下降 —反義詞 ASCEND **2**〔黑暗、夜幕等〕降臨 **3 in descending order** 降序排列〔按照從大到小或從最重要的到最次要的順序排列〕

descend from sth *phr v* **1** 從〔過去的東西〕繼承下來, 傳下來 **2 be descended from sb** 為某人的後裔

descend on/upon sb/sth *phr v* **1** 使感覺到 **2** 突然造訪

descend to sth *phr v* 自降身分到…, 墮落到…

describe *v* **1** 描述, 描寫, 敍述, 形容 **2**〔用手在空中〕劃出〔某種形狀〕

desert¹ *n* **1** 沙漠, 荒漠 **2** 荒涼的地方

desert² *v* **1** 遺棄, 拋棄, 離棄 **2** 捨棄, 離開〔某地〕**3** 喪失, 失去〔感覺、品質〕**4** 擅自離開〔軍隊〕

deserve *v* **1** 應得, 應受到〔獎賞或懲罰〕**2 deserve consideration/attention etc**〔建議、觀點、計劃〕值得考慮/注意等 **3 deserve a medal** 該賞一枚勳章〔表示欣賞某人應付某種局面或處理某個問題的方式〕

design¹ *n* **1** ►**ARRANGEMENT OF PARTS** 各部分的安排◄ 設計〔包括其外觀及運作方式等〕**2** ►**PATTERN** 圖案◄ 裝飾圖案 **3** ►**DRAWING PLANS** 繪製圖表◄ 設計術, 製圖術 **4** ►**DRAWN PLAN** 繪製的圖紙◄ 設計圖, 圖樣, 圖紙 **5** ►**INTENTION** 意圖◄〔頭腦中的〕計劃 **6 have designs on sb** 對某人居心不良〔想和某人發生性關係〕**7 have designs on sth** 企圖將某物據為己有〔尤指可以帶來錢財的東西〕

design² *v* **1** 設計 **2** [一般用被動態]〔為某種特定目的〕計劃, 設計

desire¹ *v* **1** 想要, 希望 **2 leave a lot to be desired** 不夠好, 仍有許多有待提高之處〔表明某事做得不如期望的好〕**3** 想和〔某人〕發生性關係 —**desired** *adj*

desire² *n* **1** 渴望; 慾望 **2 sb's heart's desire** 某人內心的渴望 **3** 肉慾, 性慾

despair¹ *n* **1** 絕望 **2 the despair of sb** 令某人絕望的人[事]

despair² *v* 絕望, 感到無望

desperate *adj* **1**〔由於處在絕境而〕拚命的, 不顧一切的 **2** 非常需要的, 極其需要的 **3**〔局勢、情形等〕危急的, 嚴峻的 **4**〔在危急時刻〕孤注一擲的

destroy *v* **1** 破壞, 毀掉, 摧毀 **2** 殺死〔動物, 尤因其生病或產生危險〕**3 destroy sb** 毀掉某人

detach *v* **1** 拆下, 分開, 拆開, 卸下 **2 detach yourself** 使自己超然物外

detail¹ *n* **1** 細節, 詳情 **2 details** 詳細情況, 詳細資料 **3**〔軍隊中的〕特遣隊, 小分隊

detail² *v* **1** 詳述 **2 detail sb to do sth** 指派某人〔尤指士兵〕做某事

detect *v* 發現, 察覺〔尤指不易察覺到的事物〕—**detectable** *adj*

devote *v* **1 devote time/effort/money etc to** 為…付出時間/努力/金錢等 **2 devote yourself to** 獻身於…, 專心致力於…

diagnose *v* 判斷; 診斷

diagram *n* 圖解, 圖表, 示意圖 —**diagrammatic** *adj* —**diagrammatically** *adv*

dialect *n* 方言, 地方話, 土語

diameter *n* 直徑

dictate¹ *v* **1** 口授, 讓〔某人〕聽寫 **2** 命令, 強制規定, 指定 **3** 支配; 影響; 決定

dictate² *n* 命令, 規定, 指示

diet¹ *n* **1** ►**KIND OF FOOD** 食物種類◄ 日常飲食 **2** ►**TO GET THIN** 減肥◄ 節食 **3** ►**FOR HEALTH** 為了健康◄〔基於健康考慮的〕飲食限制, 規定飲食 **4 a diet of** 多得令人生厭的 **5** ►**MEETING** 會議◄〔討論政治或宗教問題的正式〕會議

diet² *v*〔為減肥而〕節食, 限食, 按規定進食

differ *v* **1**〔在質量、特徵等上〕不同於, 不一樣, 有區別 **2** 有異議,〔意見〕有分歧 **3 agree to differ** 承認意見分歧, 保留不同意見 **4 I beg to differ** 恕我不能同意, 恕我不能贊同

digest¹ *v* **1** 消化〔食物〕**2** 理解, 領悟, 消化〔尤指大量新資訊或難以理解的資訊〕

digest² *n* 摘要, 概要, 文摘

dignity *n* **1** 莊重, 尊貴, 尊嚴, 體面 **2** 莊嚴, 端莊 **3 be beneath your dignity** 有失身分, 有失體面 **4 stand on your dignity** 要求受到禮遇, 擺架子 **5** 高位, 顯職

diligent *adj* 勤奮的, 勤勉的 —**diligently** *adv* —**diligence** *n*

dim¹ *adj* **1** ►**DARK** 暗◄ 陰暗的, 昏暗的 **2** ►**SHAPE** 形狀◄ 朦朧的, 隱約的 **3** ►**EYES** 眼睛◄ 視力不好的, 弱視的 **4 dim recollection/awareness etc** 模糊的記憶/意識等 **5** ►**FUTURE CHANCES** 未來的機會◄〔未來成功的機會或可能〕暗淡的, 不樂觀的 **6 in the dim and distant past** 很久以前 **7 take a dim view of** 不贊成〔某事〕**8** ►**UNINTELLIGENT** 不聰明的◄ 愚笨的 —**dimly** *adv* —**dimness** *n*

dim² *v* **1**（使）變暗淡,（使）變得不亮 **2**〔感覺等〕變弱,〔質量等〕下降 **3 dim your headlights/lights**〔尤其當對面有車開來的時候〕使汽車前燈燈光變暗

dimension *n* **1**〔形勢的〕方面, 部分 **2**〔空間的〕量度, 維度〔如長度、高度等〕**3 dimensions a)** 大小, 尺寸, 規模〔尤指某物的長、寬、高〕**b)**〔問題的〕嚴重程度

diminish *v* **1**（使）減少,（使）減小 **2** 削弱, 貶低〔重要性、價值〕**3 diminishing returns** 收益遞減, 報酬遞減

dip¹ *v* **1** 蘸, 浸 **2** 下降, 下落 **3 dip your headlights/lights** 降低汽車前燈角度〔尤其當對面有車開來時〕**4** 讓〔動物〕洗藥浴〔滅蟲〕

dip into sth *phr v* **1** 翻閱, 瀏覽〔書或雜誌等〕**2** 動用〔存款〕**3** 把手伸進〔袋裡或盒子裡, 為了把裡面的東西掏出來〕

dip² *n* **1** ►**SWIM** 游泳◄〔為時較短的〕游泳 **2** ►**DECREASE** 下降◄〔某物數量上輕微的〕減少下降 **3** ►**IN A SURFACE** 在表面◄ 凹陷 **4** ►**FOOD** 食物◄〔用來蘸食物吃的〕調味醬汁 **5** ►**FOR ANIMALS** 動物用的◄〔給動物洗浴用的〕藥浴液〔以便殺蟲〕**6** ►**PERSON** 人◄ 傻瓜, 笨蛋

diplomatic *adj* **1** 外交的 **2** 世故的, 圓滑的 —**diplomatically** *adv*

disable *v* **1** [常用被動態] 使喪失能力, 使殘廢 **2** 故意毀壞〔機器設備〕, 使無法使用 —**disablement** *n*

disadvantage *n* 不利條件, 劣勢

disaster *n* **1** 災難, 災禍〈如水災、暴風雨、意外事故等〉**2** 徹底的失敗

discipline¹ *n* **1** 紀律, 紀律狀況 **2**〔思想或行為的〕訓練, 磨練 **3** 克制能力 **4** 處罰, 懲處, 處分 **5**〔大學裡學習的〕專業, 科目

discipline² *v* **1** 訓練, 管教 **2 discipline yourself (to do sth)** 嚴格要求自己, 約束自己〔去做某事〕**3** 懲處〔某人〕

disclose *v* **1**〔尤指在被隱瞞後〕透露, 揭露, 泄露; 公開〔某事〕**2**〔把蓋在某物上的東西去掉以〕顯露; 揭開

discourage *v* **1**（設法）阻止, 打消…的念頭 **2** 使灰心, 使泄氣 —反義詞 ENCOURAGE

discriminate *v* **1** 區別, 辨別 **2** 不公正地區別對待〔某人〕; 歧視

dismay¹ *n* 憂慮; 失望; 沮喪; 恐慌
dismay² *v* 使〔某人〕擔憂[失望、傷心]
dismiss *v* **1 ▶IDEA 觀點◀** 拒絕考慮〔某人的觀點、意見等〕 **2 ▶JOB 工作◀** 解雇, 開除 **3 ▶SEND AWAY 打發走◀** 把〔某人〕打發走; 讓〔某人〕離開; 解散 **4 ▶IN A COURT 在法庭上◀** 駁回, 不受理〔案子〕 **5 ▶SPORT 體育運動◀** 〔板球比賽中〕迫使〔對方擊球員或球隊〕退場
disorder *n* **1** 混亂; 凌亂; 雜亂; 無秩序 **2** 動亂; 暴亂; 騷亂 **3** 〔身體機能的〕失調; 功能紊亂
dispatch¹ 又作 **despatch**【英】*v* **1** 派遣; 發送 **2** 故意殺死〔人或動物〕 **3** 辦完〔全部事情〕
dispatch² 又作 **despatch**【英】*n* **1** 〔在軍官或政府官員之間傳遞的〕公文, 急件 **2** 〔由身在另一城市或國家的記者發給報刊的〕報道, 電訊 **3 with dispatch** 利落地, 迅速地 **4** 派遣, 發送
display¹ *n* **1 ▶ATTRACTIVE ARRANGEMENT 吸引人的佈置◀** 〔物品的〕展示, 陳列 **2 ▶PERFORMANCE 表演◀** 〔為了娛樂人們而進行的〕公開表演 **3 be on display** 被展示, 被陳列 **4 display of affection/temper/loyalty etc** 愛慕/脾氣/忠誠等的流露 **5 ▶EQUIPMENT 設備◀** 顯示器
display² *v* **1** 展示, 陳列 **2** 顯示, 顯露〔某種情感、態度、才能等〕 **3** 顯示〔信息等〕
dispose *v* 安排, 編排, 處理, 支配〔事物〕
dispose of sth *phr v* **1** 處置, 處理〔尤指難以處理的東西〕 **2** 成功地處理問題, 解決問題 **3** 戰勝, 打敗〔對手〕
dispose sb **to** sth *phr v* [一般用於被動態] 使〔某人〕較傾向於
dispute¹ *n* **1 ▶SERIOUS DISAGREEMENT 嚴重分歧◀** 爭吵; 爭端 **2 be beyond dispute** 無可爭辯; 確定無疑 **3 be in/under dispute** 處在爭論中; 有爭議 **4 be in dispute (with sb)** 〔與某人或某個羣體〕有分歧 **5 be open to dispute** 不確定的; 有爭議的
dispute² *v* **1** 對〔某事〕表示異議; 辯駁 **2** 與〔某人〕爭辯, 爭論, 爭執; 有分歧 **3** 〔與其他國家、羣體等〕爭奪〔土地〕
disregard¹ *v* 忽視; 輕視; 無視; 不顧
disregard² *n* 忽視; 輕視; 無視
dissolve *v* **1 ▶STH SOLID 固體物◀ a)** 〔固體〕溶解 **b)** 使〔固體〕溶解 **2 dissolve into laughter/tears** 開始哈哈大笑/淚流滿面 **3 ▶BECOME WEAKER 變弱◀** 變弱, 消失 **4 ▶PARLIAMENT 議會◀** 〔在大選前〕正式解散〔議會〕 **5 ▶MARRIAGE/BUSINESS/ORGANIZATION 婚姻/商務/組織◀** [一般用被動態] 解除〔婚姻關係〕; 取消〔商務安排〕; 解散〔組織〕
distinct *adj* **1** 明顯不同的; 不同種類的 **2 as distinct from** 與…有所區別〔用於表示強調你在談論的是某一事物〕 **3** 清晰的, 清楚的, 明顯的 **4** 〔指可能性、感覺、特徵等〕確實存在的; 確實重要的; 不容忽視的
distinguish *v* **1** 區別, 辨別 **2** 辨清〔某物的輪廓〕; 分清〔某種聲音〕 **3** 使有別於; 使有特色 **4 distinguish yourself** 表現突出
distort *v* **1** 歪曲〔事實、陳述、觀點等〕 **2** 使變形; 使失真; 使反常 **—distorted** *adj* **—distortion** *n*
distract *v* 分散〔某人的〕注意力; 使〔某人〕分心 **—distracting** *adj*
distress¹ *n* **1 ▶EXTREME WORRY 極度憂慮◀** 極度憂慮; 苦惱 **2 ▶PAIN 疼痛◀** 身體上的痛苦, 劇痛 **3 ▶LACK OF MONEY/FOOD 缺少錢/食物◀** 貧困; 困苦 **4 distress signal** 求救信號 **5 be in distress** 〔船隻、飛機等〕處於險境, 遇險
distress² *v* 使傷心, 使不安, 使憂慮
distribute *v* **1** 〔尤指有計劃地〕分發, 分配, 分送 **2** 提供, 配送〔貨物〕 **3** 分享〔財富或權力〕 **4** 散佈; 分佈; 撒; 播
district *n* **1** 地區; 區域 **2** 行政區
disturb *v* **1 ▶INTERRUPT 打擾◀** 干擾, 打擾, 使中斷 **2 ▶WORRY 憂慮◀** 使焦慮, 使驚訝 **3 ▶MOVE 移動◀** 挪動, 移動, 改變〔某物的〕位置 **4 do not disturb** 請勿打擾〔掛在門上的牌子〕 **5 disturb the peace** 擾亂治安
dizzy *adj* **1** 〔因旋轉或生病而〕頭暈目眩的 **2 the dizzy heights** 令人眩暈的高處〔指重要的職位〕 **3** 粗心大意的; 心不在焉的; 糊塗健忘的 **4 dizzy height/peak** 令人頭暈的高度/頂峯 **—dizzily** *adv* **—dizziness** *n*
document¹ *n* 文件; 公文
document² *v* 〔通過記述、拍電影或拍照片的方式來〕記載
domestic¹ *adj* **1 ▶WITHIN ONE COUNTRY 國內的◀** 國內的; 本國的 **2 ▶USED AT HOME 家用的◀** 家中使用的, 家用的 **3 ▶ABOUT FAMILY AND HOME 關於家庭的◀** 涉及家庭關係和生活的; 家事的 **4 ▶PERSON 人◀** 喜愛操持家務的, 善於烹飪、清潔等家務的 **5 ▶ANIMAL 動物◀** 馴養的; 家養的 **—domestically** *adv*
domestic² *n* 僕人, 傭人
donate *v* **1** 捐贈, 捐獻〔尤指錢〕 **2 donate blood** 捐血, 獻血
double¹ *adj* **1 ▶OF TWO PARTS 兩部分的◀** 成對的, 成雙的 **2 double l/s/9 etc** 兩個 l/s/9 等〔用在拼寫單詞或告訴某人某個數字時, 表示應該重複某個字母或數字〕 **3 ▶TWICE AS BIG 兩倍大◀** 雙倍的, 兩倍的 **4 ▶FOR TWO PEOPLE 雙人的◀** 供兩人使用的 **5 ▶WITH TWO DIFFERENT USES 雙重用途的◀** 有兩種用途的, 雙重的 **6 ▶DECEIVING 欺詐的◀** 兩面派的, 表裡不一的; 欺詐的 **7 ▶FLOWER 花◀** 雙瓣的; 重瓣的
double² *n* **1 ▶TWICE THE SIZE 兩倍◀** 兩倍, 雙倍(的量、數) **2 ▶SIMILAR PERSON 相似的人◀** 極為相似的人 **3 ▶IN FILMS 在電影中◀** 替身演員 **4 at the double**【英】, **on the double**【美】飛快地, 快步地 **5 ▶TENNIS 網球◀ doubles** 雙打 **6 double or nothing**【美】, **double or quits**【英】〔下注的一種方式〕要麼贏雙倍, 要麼輸得精光; 一賭決輸贏 **7 ▶IN RACING 在比賽中◀** 複式押注〔下注於兩場比賽, 第一場若贏將自動轉押到第二場上〕 **8 ▶A THROW 投擲◀** 〔投鏢遊戲中的〕投中加倍記分圈 **9 ▶A HIT 擊打◀** 〔棒球的〕二壘打
double³ *v* **1** (使)加倍 **2** 把某物對摺 **3** 〔棒球比賽中〕擊出二壘打 **4 double your fists** 握緊拳頭〔準備打鬥〕
double as sb/sth *phr v* 兼任, 兼作
double back *phr v* 原路折回

double up *phr v* **1**〔笑、痛得〕彎下腰; 使…直不起身 **2**〔尤指臥室的〕共用

double⁴ *adv* **1 see double**〔因眼睛有問題〕看到重影 **2 be bent double** 彎得很厲害 **3 fold sth double** 將某物對摺〔使其比以前厚一倍〕

double⁵ *predeterminer* 是…兩倍那麼多

doze *v* 小睡, 打瞌睡, 打盹兒 —**doze** *n*

doze off *phr v*〔尤指在無意的情況下〕打盹, 打瞌睡

draft¹ *n* **1** ►**UNFINISHED FORM** 未完成的形式◄ 草稿; 草圖; 草案 **2** ►**ARMY** 軍隊◄ **the draft a)** 徵兵, 徵募 **b)** 被徵入伍者 **3** ►**MONEY** 錢◄ 匯票 **4** ►**SPORTS** 體育運動◄〔美國一些職業球隊〕從大學選拔隊員的制度 **5** ►**COLD AIR/DRINKS** 冷空氣/飲料◄ draught 的美式拼法

draft² *v* **1** 起草, 草擬〔計劃、信件、報告等〕**2**〔戰時〕徵召〔某人〕入伍; 徵募

dramatic *adj* **1** 給人深刻印象的; 突然的; 驚人的 **2** 激動人心的 **3** 戲劇的 **4** 誇張的; 像演戲似的 —**dramatically** *adv*

drift¹ *v* **1** 飄移; 漂流 **2**〔毫無計劃或漫無目的地〕漂泊 **3 drift into sth** 不知不覺進入某種狀況 **4**〔指雪、沙等受風〕吹積 **5 let sth drift** 聽任某事發展下去, 聽之任之

drift apart *phr v*〔人們之間的關係逐漸地〕疏遠

drift off *phr v* 慢慢入睡

drift² *n* **1** ►**SNOW** 雪◄〔風吹積成的〕雪堆, 沙堆 **2** ►**SHIP** 船◄ 偏移, 偏離 **3** ►**GENERAL MEANING** 大意◄ **the drift**〔話語的〕大意, 要旨 **4** ►**CHANGE** 變化◄〔情形、意見等的〕漸變; 趨勢 **5** ►**MOVEMENT OF PEOPLE** 人口流動◄〔大量人口緩慢、無計劃的〕流動

drill¹ *n* **1** ►**TOOL** 工具◄ 鑽; 鑽牀; 鑽機 **2** ►**WAY OF LEARNING** 學習方法◄ 練習; 訓練 **3 fire/emergency drill** 消防/應急演習 **4** ►**MILITARY TRAINING** 軍事訓練◄ 軍事操練 **5** ►**CLOTH** 布◄ 粗斜紋布 **6 the drill** 正確的步驟; 程序 **7** ►**SEEDS** 種子◄ **a)** 條播機 **b)** 條播的一排種子

drill² *v* **1**〔用鑽〕鑽孔, 打眼 **2** 教〔某人〕反覆練習 **3** 訓練, 操練 **4** 條播〔種子〕

drill sth into sb *phr v* 向某人灌輸〔某事〕

drip¹ *v* **1** 滴水, 漏水 **2**（使）滴下; 瀝下 **3 be dripping with jewels/diamonds etc** 渾身戴滿了珠寶/鑽石等

drip² *n* **1** 滴水聲; 滴落 **2** 液滴 **3** 滴注器 **4** 怯懦無趣的人, 平庸乏味者

drown *v* **1**（使）淹死,（使）溺斃 **2** 又作 **drown out**〔用聲音〕淹沒 **3** 把〔某物〕浸泡在〔液體〕中 **4 drown your sorrows** 借酒澆愁

dual *adj* **dual nationality/controls/purpose etc** 雙重國籍/控制/目的等 —**duality** *n*

due¹ *adj* **1 be due** 預定, 預期 **2 due to** 由於, 因為 **3** ►**OWED** 欠下◄ 欠下的, 應給的 **4** ►**MONEY** 錢◄ 應付的, 到期的 **5 with (all) due respect** 恕我冒昧〔用以禮貌地反對某人或批評某人〕**6 in due course** 在適當[一定]的時候 **7** ►**PROPER** 適當的◄ 適當的, 適宜的

due² *n* **1 give sb his/her due** 給予某人應有的承認〔用於批評某人時〕**2 dues** 會（員）費 **3 your/his etc due** 某人應得的錢物[權益]

due³ *adv* **due north/south/east/west** 正北/正南/正東/正西

dull¹ *adj* **1** ►**BORING** 乏味的◄ 無趣的, 枯燥的; 沉悶的; 無聊的 **2 never a dull moment** 絕不會有沉悶無聊之時 **3** ►**COLOUR/LIGHT** 顏色/光◄ 暗淡的, 不鮮明的 **4** ►**SOUND** 聲音◄ 不清楚的, 沉悶的 **5** ►**PAIN** 疼痛◄ 隱約的, 不明顯的 **6** ►**WEATHER** 天氣◄ 陰沉的, 昏暗的 **7** ►**NOT INTELLIGENT** 不聰明的◄ 遲鈍的; 愚笨的 **8** ►**KNIFE/BLADE** 刀/刃◄ 不鋒利的, 鈍的 **9** ►**TRADE** 貿易◄ 蕭條的, 不景氣的 —**dully** *adv* **dullness** *n*

dull² *v* 使〔疼痛、感覺等〕不明顯, 使不清楚

dumb *adj* **1**〔指人〕啞巴的, 不能說話的〔有些人認為此詞具有冒犯性〕**2** 愚蠢的 **3**〔因憤怒、驚訝、震驚等而〕說不出話的 **4 dumb animals/beasts** 不會說話的動物, 啞巴牲口〔用於強調動物不會說話, 但人們常虐待它們〕—**dumbly** *adv* —**dumbness** *n*

dump¹ *v* **1** ►**PUT STH SOMEWHERE** 將某物放置某處◄ 亂放, 亂堆, 亂扔 **2** ►**GET RID OF** 丟棄◄ 拋棄〔某人〕; 丟棄, 扔掉〔某物〕**3** ►**SELL GOODS** 出售貨物◄〔向國外〕廉價傾銷〔貨物〕**4** ►**COPY INFORMATION** 複製資訊◄ 轉儲; 轉存; 轉出〔將存儲在電腦中的資料轉存到磁碟或磁帶中〕**5 dumping ground** 把想擺脫掉的人送往的地方; 垃圾傾倒場

dump on sb *phr v* **1**〔不公正地〕詆毀, 貶低 **2** 向〔某人〕傾訴〔所有的問題〕

dump² *n* **1** ►**WASTE** 廢品◄ 垃圾堆, 垃圾場, 廢品堆 **2** ►**WEAPONS** 武器◄ 軍需品存放處; 軍需品 **3** ►**UNPLEASANT PLACE** 討厭的地方◄ 髒亂的居住之地 **4 down in the dumps** 傷心的, 對生活失去興趣的 **5** ►**COMPUTER** 電腦◄ 轉儲, 轉存, 轉出

duplicate¹ *n* **1** 複製品 **2 in duplicate** 一式兩份 —**duplicate** *adj*

duplicate² *v* **1** 複製 **2**〔成功地〕重複 —**duplication** *n*

durable *adj* **1** 耐用的 **2** 持久的 —**durably** *adv* —**durability** *n*

dusk *n* 黃昏, 傍晚

duty *n* **1** ►**STH YOU HAVE TO DO** 應做的事情◄〔道德上或法律上的〕義務, 責任 **2** ►**PART OF YOUR JOB** 職責的一部分◄〔工作或社會方面的〕職責, 義務 **3 be on/off duty** 值班[勤]/下班[不值勤] **4** ►**TAX** 稅◄〔購物繳納的〕稅 **5 do duty as/for sth** 用以充當/代替某物

dwarf¹ *n* **1**〔虛構的人物〕小矮人 **2** 矮子, 侏儒〔一些人認為此詞對身材矮小者帶有侮辱性〕

dwarf² *adj*〔植物或動物等〕矮小的

dwarf³ *v* [一般用被動態]〔因自身巨大而〕使…顯得矮小; 使…相形見絀

dwell *v*〔在某一地方〕居住

dwell on/upon sth *phr v* 老是想着; 嘮叨〔令人不愉快的事情〕

E, e

edible *adj* 可以食用的

elegant *adj* **1** 高雅的, 優美的: **2**〔想法或計劃〕巧妙的, 簡潔的 —**elegantly** *adv* —**elegance** *n*
eligible *adj* **1** 合格的; 有資格的: **2**〔作為婚姻對象〕理想的, 合適的—**eligibility** *n*
eliminate *v* **1** 消除, 根除 **2** [一般用被動態] 淘汰 **3** 消滅; 鏟除
embark *v* 上船; 裝船; 使上船; 裝載 —反義詞 DISEMBARK —**embarkation** *n*
embark on/upon sth *phr v* 開始, 着手〔尤指新的、有難度且費時的事〕
embarrass *v* **1**〔尤指在社交場合〕使尷尬, 使窘迫 **2** 為〔政府、政治組織或政治人物〕出難題; 使...陷入困境
embrace[1] *v* **1** 抱, 擁抱 **2** 包括, 涉及 **3** 欣然接受, 採納 **4**〔開始〕信奉; 皈依
embrace[2] *n* 擁抱
emerge *v* **1** 浮現, 出現 **2** 顯露, 暴露 **3**〔從困境中〕擺脱出來, 出頭 **4** 開始被人所知; 興起 —**emergence** *n*
eminent *adj*〔指人〕傑出的, 顯赫的
emit *v* **1** 散發〔熱、光、氣等〕**2** 發出〔聲響〕
emphasize 又作 **-ise**【英】強調, 着重
employ[1] *v* **1** 雇用 **2** 使用, 運用 **3 be employed in doing sth** 花時間做某事; 忙於做某事
employ[2] *n* **in sb's employ** 受雇於某人, 為某人工作
enclose *v* **1** 隨信附上, 隨信裝入 **2** [常用被動態]〔用籬笆或圍牆〕圍起來
encounter[1] *v* **1** 遇到, 遭遇〔問題、困難、反對〕**2** 偶然碰到〔某人〕; 突然遇到〔某事〕
encounter[2] *n* **1** 相遇, 邂逅 **2** 遭遇戰; 衝突
encyclopedia 又作 **encyclopaedia**【英】*n* 百科全書;〔某一學科的〕專科全書, 大全
endanger *v* 使處於險境; 危及
endeavour[1]【英】**endeavor**【美】*v* 努力; 奮力
endeavour[2]【英】**endeavor**【美】*n* 嘗試; 努力
energetic *adj* 充滿活力的, 精力充沛的—**energetically** *adv*
enforce *v* **1** 執行〔法律〕, 實施 **2**〔強迫〕實行; 把...強加於 —**enforceable** *adj* —**enforcement** *n*
engage *v* **1** 吸引〔某人的興趣〕**2** 安排雇用, 聘請 **3**（使）〔機器〕齧合, 接合 —反義詞 DISENGAGE **4** 開始與〔敵人〕交戰
engage in *phr v* **1** 參加; 參與 **2 engage sb in conversation** 與某人攀談; 使某人加入談話中
enlighten *v* 指導, 教導; 啟迪 —**enlightening** *adj*
enormous *adj*〔尺寸、數量〕巨大的, 龐大的 —**enormously** *adv* —**enormousness** *n*
enrich *v* **1** 使豐富, 充實; 富集, 強化 **2** 使〔某人〕更富裕 —**enrichment** *n*
enrol【英】**enroll**【美】*v* 招（生）, 吸收（成員）; 註冊（學習）—**enrolment** *n*
ensure *v* 確保, 保證
enterprise *n* **1**〔尤指與人合作的〕大型而複雜的工作 **2** 創業能力, 開創能力 **3** 企業, 公司; 組織 **4** 創立和經營小企業（的行為）
entertain *v* **1** 招待, 款待, 請客 **2** 使〔某人〕快樂; 使〔某人〕有興趣 **3 entertain an idea/hope/doubt etc** 懷有想法/希望/疑惑等
enthusiasm *n* **1** 熱情, 熱忱 **2** 熱衷的活動; 熱愛的事物
entitle *v* **1** 給予〔某人獲得某物或做某事的〕權利 **2 be entitled sth** 給〔書、劇等〕命名, 起名 **3 be entitled to do something** 有權選擇做某些事情
environment *n* **1** 環境, 周圍狀況 **2 the environment** 自然環境
equip *v* **1** 裝備, 配備 **2** 使有準備, 使能夠〔做某事〕
equivalent[1] *adj* 等同的, 等價的, 相當的 —**equivalently** *adv* —**equivalence** *n*
equivalent[2] *n* 等同物; 等價物; 對應物
erase *v* **1** 刪除〔電腦文件〕; 抹去〔磁帶錄音〕**2** 擦掉; 抹去〔痕跡或文字〕**3** 消除, 消滅 **4 erase sth from your mind/memory** 忘卻〔壞事〕
erect[1] *adj* **1** 直立的, 垂直的 **2**〔陰莖〕勃起的;〔乳頭〕挺起的 —**erectly** *adv* —**erectness** *n*
erect[2] *v* **1** 建造, 建立 **2** 搭建, 豎起 **3** 創建, 確立〔體系或制度〕
essence *n* **1** 本質, 實質; 要素 **2** 香精, 精油 **3 in essence** 本質上, 實質上 **4 speed/time is of the essence** 速度/時間是至關重要的
establish *v* **1** 建立, 設立 **2** 證實, 確定 **3** 使被接受; 使得到承認 **4 establish links/contacts/trust etc** 建立關係/聯繫/信任等
esteem[1] *n* 尊敬, 敬重
esteem[2] *v* **1** 尊敬, 尊重 **2 esteem it an honour/favour/pleasure etc** 將某事物看作一種榮耀/恩惠/樂趣等 **3 esteem someone worthy/reliable etc** 認為某人值得信賴/可靠等
estimate[1] *n* **1** 估計, 估算 **2** 估價, 報價
estimate[2] *v* 估計, 估算 —**estimated** *adj* —**estimator** *n*
evaluate *v* 評估, 評價
evolve *v*（使）逐步發展;（使）逐漸演變
exceed *v* **1** 超過, 超出〔尤指超過一固定值〕**2** 超越〔政府或法律規定的範圍〕
excel *v* 優於, 擅長, 勝過他人
exclude *v* **1**〔故意〕不包括; 把...排除在外 **2** 不准...參與〔某事〕; 不准...進入 **3** 排斥〔某人〕; 不理睬〔某人〕**4** 認為...不可能; 排除...的可能性 — 反義詞 INCLUDE
execute *v* **1**〔尤指依法〕將...處死 **2** 實行; 執行; 履行 **3** 完成, 表演〔高難動作〕**4** 確保〔遺囑〕得到執行 **5** 創作〔繪畫等藝術作品〕
exhaust[1] *v* **1** 使精疲力竭 **2** 用完, 耗盡 **3 exhaust a subject/topic etc** 詳盡無遺地論述某主題/話題等
exhaust[2] *n* **1** 排氣管 **2**〔引擎排出的〕廢氣
expand *v* **1**（使）擴大; 增加 **2** 增加〔活動量〕; 擴展〔活動範圍〕**3** 擴展〔業務〕**4** 變得更自信[友善]
expand on/upon sth *phr v* 詳述, 進一步説明
expire *v* **1**〔正式文件等〕到期, 過期, 失效 **2**〔任期〕屆滿 **3** 死亡
explode *v* **1** ►**BURST 爆炸**◄（使）爆炸 **2** ►**GET ANGRY 發怒**◄ 勃然大怒; 變得危險 **3** ►**PROVE FALSE 證明錯誤**◄ 戳穿, 破除 **4** ►**GET BIGGER 變大**◄ 急劇增長, 激增 **5** ►**MAKE A LOUD NOISE 發出巨響**◄ 爆響, 發出巨大聲音 **6** ►**MOVE SUDDENLY 突然移動**◄ 迸發, 突發

explore *v* **1** 勘查，考察〔某地區〕**2** 檢查，探討

expose *v* **1** ►**SHOW** 顯示◄ 顯露，暴露 **2** ►**TO STH DANGEROUS** 遇到危險之物◄ 使暴露於〔險境〕，使置身於〔危險〕當中 **3** ►**TELL THE TRUTH** 講真話◄ 揭露，揭發 **4** ►**SEE/EXPERIENCE** 看/體驗◄ 使接觸〔學習新事物〕**5** ►**PHOTOGRAPH** 照片◄ 使曝光 **6** ►**FEELINGS** 感受◄ 顯露〔情感〕**7 expose yourself** 〔由於病態心理而在公共場所〕裸露性器官

extend *v* **1** ►**CONTINUE** 繼續◄ 延伸，伸展 **2** ►**MAKE STH BIGGER** 使某物增大◄ 擴大；延長〔建築或道路等〕**3** ►**HAPPEN/EXIST** 發生/存在◄ 延續，持續 **4** ►**TIME** 時間◄ 延長，推延〔期限〕**5** ►**CONTROL/INFLUENCE** 控制/影響◄ 延伸，擴大 **6** ►**OFFER HELP/THANKS** 提供幫助/表示感謝◄ 提供，給予，表示 **7** ►**ARMS/LEGS ETC** 手臂/腿等◄ 伸開，舒展 **8** ►**STRENGTH/INTELLIGENCE** 力量/智力◄ 使竭盡全力

exterminate *v* 滅絕，根除 —**exterminator** *n* —**extermination** *n*

external *adj* **1** 外面的；外部的 **2** 來自外部的，外來的 **3** 外國的 **4** 來自學校[大學]之外的，外來的 **5 external ear/gill/genitals etc** 〔動物長在身體〕外部的耳朵/鰓/生殖器等 — 反義詞 INTERNAL —**externally** *adv*

extinct *adj* **1** 滅絕的，絕種的 **2** 〔信仰或風俗〕已廢棄的 **3** 〔火山〕死的，不再活躍的

extinguish *v* **1** 熄滅〔火、光〕**2** 使〔想法或感情〕破滅；使消亡

extract[1] *v* **1** 取出，拔出 **2** 採掘；提煉 **3** 靈巧地取出，抽出 **4** 套出〔信息〕；逼問；索得〔錢財〕

extract[2] *n* **1** 摘錄；選段 **2** 提煉物，提取物

extravagant *adj* **1** 〔花錢〕浪費的，無必要的 **2 extravagant with sth** 大手大腳，過度使用[浪費]某物 **3** 豪華的；鋪張的 **4** 過度的；越軌的 —**extravagantly** *adv* —**extravagance** *n*

F, f

fabulous *adj* **1** 極好的；絕妙的 **2** 巨額的；巨大的 **3** 神話寓言中的，傳說中的

facilitate *v* 使容易，使便利；有助於 —**facilitation** *n*

faculty *n* **1** 天賦，能力 **2** 才能，技能 **3** 〔大學的〕系，部，院 **4 the faculty** 〔大學的〕全體教員

fade *v* **1** 逐漸消失 **2** （使）褪色；（使）失去光澤 **3** 又作 **fade away** 〔身體〕變得虛弱 **4** 〔運動隊〕水準下降

fade sth ↔ **in** *phr v* 使〔畫面〕淡出，漸顯；使〔聲音〕漸強 —**fade-in** *n*

fade sth ↔ **out** *phr v* 使〔畫面〕淡入，漸隱；使〔聲音〕漸弱 —**fade-out** *n*

faint[1] *adj* **1** 〔指看、聽、嗅等〕不清楚的，模糊的 **2 a faint hope/chance/feeling etc** 很小的希望/機會/感覺等 **3** 〔因生病、疲倦或飢餓而〕虛弱的 **4 not have the faintest idea** 〔對某事〕根本不知道，一無所知 —**faintly** *adv* —**faintness** *n*

faint[2] *v* **1** 暈倒，昏厥 **2 I nearly/almost fainted** 我差點昏過去〔表示很驚訝〕

faint[3] *n* 昏厥

faith *n* **1** ►**TRUST/BELIEF IN SB/STH** 信任/相信某人/某物◄ 信念；信任；信心 **2** ►**RELIGION** 宗教◄ **a)** 對上帝的信仰；宗教信仰 **b)** 宗教 **3 break faith with** 背棄；背信，不信守；脫離 **4 keep faith with** 恪守對…的信仰；信守；不背棄 **5 good faith** 真誠，誠意，誠信 **6 an act of faith** 信賴某人的行為[表示]

fake[1] *n* **1** 贋品，假貨 **2** 騙子，冒充者，假冒者

fake[2] *adj* **1** 偽造的，假的 **2** 冒充的，假冒的

fake[3] *v* **1** 仿造；捏造，偽造 **2** 假裝，偽裝 **3** 〔比賽中〕做（…的）假動作

fake sb **out** *phr v* 故意欺騙〔某人〕

familiar[1] *adj* **1** ►**EASY TO RECOGNIZE** 容易辨認的◄ 熟悉的 **2 be familiar with** 通曉，熟悉 **3** ►**PLACE/SITUATION** 地方/狀況◄ 熟悉的 **4** ►**COMMON** 普通的◄ 常見的，普通的 **5 be on familiar terms with** 和…交情很好，和…關係友好 **6** ►**TOO FRIENDLY** 過分友好的◄ 故作親密的，過分親暱的 **7** ►**INFORMAL STYLE** 非正式文體◄ 非正式的；隨和的

familiar[2] *n* **1** 〔與女巫共居的〕妖獸，妖精 **2 familiars** 密友，伴侶

fantastic *adj* **1** 極好的，吸引人的，有趣的 **2** 太好了 **3** 〔數量〕極大的 **4** 〔計劃、建議等〕不現實的，異想天開的 **5** 〔故事、生物或場所等〕奇異的，荒唐的，古怪的 —**fantastically** *adv*

fascinate *v* 迷住，吸引；使…着迷

fashion[1] *n* **1** 〔衣服、頭髮等的〕流行式樣；〔行為等的〕時髦；時尚 **2** 時裝；時尚 **3** 時裝業；時裝研究 **4 in a... fashion** 以…方式 **5 after a fashion** 不很好，馬馬虎虎，勉強湊合 **6 after the fashion of** 像〔某人〕的風格，模仿 **7 like it's going out of fashion** 大量地吃[喝，用] **8 fashion victim** 盲目趕時髦的人；穿戴只圖時髦而不管是否合適的人

fashion[2] *v* **1** 〔用手或幾件工具〕製作，把…做成〔…形狀〕**2** [一般用被動態] 影響；形成，塑造

fasten *v* **1** ►**CLOTHES/BAG ETC** 衣服/袋子等◄ 又作 **fasten up** —反義詞 UNFASTEN **a)** 扣牢；繫牢，縛緊；把拉鏈拉好 **b)** 扣牢；鉤住；繫牢；釘牢 **2** ►**WINDOW/GATE ETC** 窗子/大門等◄ **a)** 把〔窗、門等〕關住 —反義詞 UNFASTEN **b)** 扣牢，關緊 **3** ►**FIX STH TO STH** 將某物固定在某物上◄ 〔尤指用膠帶、別針等〕貼；固定；釘 **4 fasten your teeth/legs/arms etc** 用你的牙齒咬住/用你的腿夾住/用你的雙臂抱住等 **5 fasten your eyes on** 注視着，盯着 **6 fasten your attention on** 集中注意力於；認真地考慮 **7 fasten blame on** 責怪，指責，怪罪〔常為不公正地〕

fasten on/upon sth *phr v* 迅速決定〔採用某一主意或方法〕

fasten onto sb *phr v* 纏住，糾纏

fatal *adj* **1** 致命的 **2** 災難性的，毀滅性的

favourite[1]【英】，**favorite**【美】*adj* **1** 最喜歡的 **2 favourite son** 受家鄉人歡迎的政治家、運動員等

favourite[2]【英】，**favorite**【美】*n* **1** 最喜愛的東西 **2** 受寵的人，寵兒 **3** 最有希望獲勝的馬[選手等]；最被看好的競賽者

feasible *adj* 〔計劃、想法或方法〕可行的，可實行的，行得通的 —**feasibly** *adv* —**feasibility** *n*

feat *n* 業績, 功績, 壯舉
feature[1] *n* **1** 特點, 特徵, 特色 **2**〔報紙或雜誌上的〕特寫〔報道〕**3** 面貌的一部分〈如眼、鼻等〉; 面貌〔特徵〕; 五官 **4** 影片, 故事片, 正片
feature[2] *v* **1**〔在電影、雜誌、表演等中〕介紹, 特載; 特別推出; 以…為主要內容 **2** 是…的特色 **3** 以…為特色〔尤用於廣告〕**4** 展示〔某種產品〕, 為…做廣告 **5** 放映〔電影〕; 上演〔戲劇〕
fiction *n* **1** 小說 —反義詞 NON-FICTION **2** 虛構的事, 想像的事
fierce *adj* **1** 兇猛的; 兇狠的 **2**〔感情〕強烈的; 憤怒的 **3** 猛烈的; 激烈的 **4** 極度的, 極端的 **5 something fierce** 極其強烈, 很厲害 —**fiercely** *adv* —**fierceness** *n*
finite *adj* **1** 有限的; 有限制的 —反義詞 INFINITE **2** 限定的〔動詞的限定形式能顯示出具體的時態或主語, 例如 "am","was"和"are", 但 "being" 和 "been" 是動詞的非限定形式〕
flash[1] *v* **1 ▶SHINE 發光◀** 〔使〕閃光, 閃亮 **2 ▶MOVE QUICKLY 迅速移動◀** 飛馳, 掠過 **3 ▶SHOW STH QUICKLY 快速亮出某物◀** 亮出〔隨即收起〕**4 ▶MEMORIES/IMAGES 記憶/印象◀** 閃現 **5 ▶TIME 時間◀** 一閃而過, 飛逝 **6 ▶PICTURES 圖片◀**〔在電視或電影中〕閃現 **7 ▶EYES 眼睛◀**〔尤指由於突如其來的感情而〕閃耀, 發亮 **8 ▶NEWS/INFORMATION 新聞/消息◀**〔通過收音機、電腦或衛星〕迅速播出; 傳送 **9 flash a smile/glance/look etc at sb** 對某人一笑/一瞥/一看等 **10 ▶SEX ORGANS 性器官◀**〔男子〕當眾暴露性器官, 露陰 **11 your life flashes before your eyes**〔尤指處於極度危險或臨終時〕平生之事都閃現在眼前
  flash sth **around** *phr v* 炫耀〔金錢〕
flash[2] *n* **1 ▶LIGHT 光◀**〔一閃而後消失的〕閃光 **2 ▶CAMERA 照相機◀** 閃光燈 **3 in a flash/like a flash/quick as a flash** 一會兒, 馬上 **4 flash of brilliance/inspiration/intuition/anger** 才華/靈感/直覺/怒氣的閃現 **5 ▶BRIGHT COLOUR/STH SHINY 豔麗的顏色/閃亮的東西◀** 閃現物; 惹人注目的東西 **6 ▶LOOK 看◀** 一瞥 **7 ▶SIGNAL 信號◀**〔信號燈的〕閃亮 **8 a flash in the pan** 曇花一現 **9 ▶MILITARY 軍隊的◀**〔軍裝上的〕肩章
flash[3] *adj* **1** 閃現的, 突發的, 短暫的 **2** 奢華的, 華麗的 **3** 愛炫耀的
flatter *v* **1** 奉承, 討好, 向…諂媚 **2 be flattered**〔因被喜歡或看重而〕感到榮幸[高興] **3** 使形象勝過〔本人〕**4 flatter yourself** 自以為是, 自鳴得意
flavour[1]【英】**flavor**【美】*n* **1** 味, 味道 **2** 任何滋味, 味道 **3** 特色, 特點 **4** 特色; 情調; 風味 **5 flavour of the month** 當前最受歡迎的思想[人物、風格等]
flavour[2]【英】**flavor**【美】*v* 加味於…, 使更有…味道
flaw *n* **1** 瑕疵, 缺點 **2**〔論點、計劃或思想中的〕錯誤, 缺陷 **3**〔性格上的〕缺點
flee *v* 逃, 逃走
flexible *adj* **1** 靈活的, 可變通的 — 反義詞 INFLEXIBLE **2** 易彎曲的, 有彈性的 —**flexibly** *adv*
float[1] *v* **1 ▶ON WATER 在水上◀ a)** 浮; 漂 **b)** 使浮起 **2 ▶IN THE AIR 在空中◀** 飄浮 **3 ▶MUSIC/SOUNDS/SMELLS ETC 音樂/聲音/氣味等◀**〔聲音、氣味等〕飄 **4 ▶MONEY 貨幣◀**〔使〕浮動 **5 ▶SUGGEST 建議◀**〔尤指為了解人們的想法而〕提出〔建議或計劃〕**6 ▶COMPANY 公司◀** 首次發行〔股票〕**7 ▶CHEQUE 支票◀** 開〔空頭支票〕**8 ▶MOVE GRACEFULLY 優雅地走動◀** 飄然移動 **9 ▶NO DEFINITE PURPOSE 無明確目的◀** 不斷改變; 遊蕩 —**floater** *n*
float[2] *n* **1**〔遊行時用的〕彩車 **2** 浮有冰淇淋的飲料 **3**〔尤指釣魚用的〕漂浮物; 魚漂, 浮子 **4**〔游泳時用的〕救生衣; 救生圈 **5**〔商店的〕備用零錢
flock[1] *n* **1** 畜羣; 鳥羣 **2**〔同類型的〕一大羣人 **3**〔經常到某位牧師所屬教堂禮拜的〕全體教徒[會眾] **4**〔填充墊子的〕絮屑, 毛棉填料 **5** 又作 **flocking**〔供在牆紙、窗簾等表面製作圖案的〕植絨材料; 柔軟貼料
flock[2] *v* 成羣結隊; 蜂擁而至
flourish[1] *v* **1** 生長茂盛 **2** 繁榮, 興旺, 成功 **3**〔為引起注意〕揮動〔手中的東西〕
flourish[2] *n* **1 with a flourish** 用引人注意的動作, 揮舞 **2** 不必要的裝飾; 過分華麗的詞藻 **3**〔手寫花體字的〕花飾 **4**〔尤指重要人物進場時演奏的〕響亮的樂曲
flush[1] *n* **1**〔尤指因尷尬、生病或激動而引起的〕臉紅, 潮紅 **2 a flush of pride/embarrassment etc** 一陣自豪感/尷尬等 **3 the first flush of youth/success etc** 首次感到充滿青春活力的/首次感到成功的〔一陣〕喜悅 **4**〔紙牌戲中的〕同花牌 **5**〔馬桶裡的〕沖洗裝置 **6**〔用水〕沖洗, 沖水
flush[2] *v* **1**〔用水〕沖洗〔馬桶〕;〔馬桶〕被沖洗 **2** 臉紅,〔臉〕發紅 **3** 又作 **flush out**〔用水或其他液體〕沖洗, 沖出 **4** 使〔某人〕離開隱蔽之處
flush[3] *adj* **1** 在同一平面上的, 齊平的 **2** 突然很有錢的, 暴富的
flush[4] *adv* 齊平地
forbid *v* **1** 不許, 禁止 **2 God/Heaven forbid** 但願不會發生這樣的事 **3** 阻止; 妨礙, 使〔某人〕不可能做某事
forgive *v* **1** 原諒; 寬恕; 饒恕 **2 forgive me** 請原諒, 對不起 **3 sb could be forgiven for thinking/wondering/believing etc sth** 某人認為…/想知道…/相信…等, 那是可以理解的
foundation *n* **1 ▶BUILDING 建築物◀** 又作 **foundations** 地基, 基礎 **2 ▶BASIC IDEA 基本的思想◀** 基礎; 根據; 基本原理 **3 ▶ORGANIZATION 組織◀** 基金會 **4 ▶ESTABLISHMENT 建立◀** 建立; 創辦 **5 lay/provide the foundation(s) for** 為…打下基礎 **6 be without foundation/have no foundation** 沒有根據 **7 ▶SKIN 皮膚◀**〔與膚色相同的、化妝時打底用的〕粉底霜 **8 shake/rock sth to its foundations** 從根本上動搖某物; 動搖…的基礎
fraction *n* **1** 少量; 一點兒 **2**〔數學上的〕分數; 小數
framework *n* **1**〔建築物、車輛、物體的〕構架, 框架, 結構 **2** 體系, 體制; 參照標準; 準則 **3 social/political/legal etc framework** 社會/政治/法律等的結構[制度]
freeze[1] *v* **1 ▶LIQUID 液體◀**〔使〕結冰, 凝固 **2 ▶EARTH 土地◀**〔使〕凍硬;〔使〕封凍 **3 ▶MACHINE/ENGINE 機器/發動機◀** 又作 **freeze up**〔使〕凍住;〔使〕凍到不能正常運轉 **4 ▶FOOD 食品◀** 冷藏, 冷

凍; 適合冷藏 **5 it's freezing** 太冷了 **6 ►FEEL COLD** 感到寒冷◄ 感到很冷, 凍僵 **7 ►WAGES/PRICES** 工資/價格◄ (使) 凍結〔在某種水平上〕 **8 ►MONEY/PROPERTY** 錢/財產◄ 凍結〔存款、財產〕 **9 ►STOP MOVING** 停止移動◄ 突然停止; 呆住 **10 freeze to death** 冷死, 凍死

freeze sb **out** *phr v* 〔通過刁難或用冷淡的態度等〕不讓〔某人〕參加; 把〔某人〕排除在外

freeze over *phr v* 表面結冰, 封凍

freeze² *n* **1** 〔工資、價格等的〕凍結 **2** 〔活動〕停止 **3** 嚴寒期 **4** 〔尤指夜間的〕短時間的天寒地凍

freight¹ *n* **1** 〔船、火車或飛機運載的〕貨物; 貨運 **2** 貨運列車; 集裝箱列車

freight² *v* 〔用飛機、輪船或火車〕運送, 託運〔貨物〕

frustrate *v* **1** 使惱怒, 使灰心喪氣 **2** 挫敗; 阻撓

fundamental¹ *adj* **1** 根本的; 基本的; 基礎的 **2** 必不可少的; 十分重要的

fundamental² *n* 基本原理; 基本規則

furious *adj* **1** 狂怒的, 暴怒的 **2** 猛烈的, 強烈的, 激烈的 **—furiously** *adv*

furnish *v* **1** 為〔房屋或房間〕配備家具 **2** 供應, 提供 **—furnished** *adj*

G, g

gale *n* **1** 大風 **2 a gale/gales of laughter** 〔突發的〕一陣大笑聲/陣陣大笑聲

gamble¹ *v* **1** 賭博 **2** 投機, 冒險 **—gambler** *n*

gamble sth ↔ **away** *phr v* 賭輸掉

gamble² *n* 冒險, 碰運氣

gang¹ *n* **1** 〔常聚在一起鬧事打鬥的〕一幫年輕人 **2** 一羣合夥作案的罪犯 **3** 一羣朋友〔尤指年輕人〕 **4** 〔幹體力活的〕一羣工人, 一羣囚犯

gang² *v*

gang up on sb *phr v* 合夥打擊[反對]

gap *n* **1 ►A SPACE** 間隔◄ 缺口, 裂縫 **2 ►DIFFERENCE** 差別◄ 差距; 差額; 差別 **3 ►STH MISSING** 缺少的東西◄ 空白, 缺漏 **4 ►IN A MOUNTAIN** 在山裡◄ 山峽, 山口 **5 ►IN TIME** 在時間上◄ 間隙 **6 gap in the market** 市場空白〔開發銷售一種尚無人開發的產品的機會〕

garbage *n* **1** 垃圾 **2** 蠢話, 廢話, 愚蠢的看法 **3 garbage in, garbage out** 〔電腦運算中〕錯進, 錯出〔用來表示若將垃圾信息輸入電腦, 所輸出的也是垃圾〕

garment *n* 〔一件〕衣服

gather¹ *v* **1 ►COME TOGETHER** 聚集◄ 聚集, 集合 **2 ►KNOW/THINK** 了解/思考◄ 推斷, 推測, 知道, 認為 **3 ►COLLECT** 收集◄ **a)** 搜集, 採集 **b)** 收集〔信息、主意等〕 **4 gather speed/force** 加快速度/加大力量 **5 gather dust** 閒置 **6 gather momentum a)** 增加動量[速度] **b)** 勢頭日益增強 **7 ►CLOTH** 布◄ **a)** 給…打褶襉 **b)** 拉近 **8 gather yourself/gather your strength** 〔為某事, 尤指難事〕做好準備 **9 ►CLOUDS** 雲朵◄ 積聚 **10 the gathering darkness/dusk/shadows etc** 黃昏時分 **11 gather sb to you/gather sb up** 擁抱, 抱住

gather sth ↔ **in** *phr v* 收〔莊稼〕

gather sth ↔ **together/up** *phr v* 集攏, 拾攏

gather² *n* 褶襉

gay¹ *adj* **1** 同性戀的 **2** 鮮豔的 **3** 快樂的, 興奮的 **4 with gay abandon** 任意地, 縱情地, 放縱地 **—gayness** *n*

gay² *n* 〔尤指男〕同性戀者

gaze¹ *v* 〔尤指無意識地〕凝視, 盯着看

gaze² *n* 凝視, 注視

gem *n* **1** 寶石, 珠寶 **2** 精品 **3** 難能可貴的人, 非常有用的人

generalize 又作 **-ise**【英】*v* **1** 籠統地表達, 概括地論述 **2** 概括, 歸納 **3** 推廣, 擴大〔原則、論述或規律的〕應用範圍

generate *v* **1** 產生, 創造 **2 generate excitement/interest/ill-feeling** 〔在一大羣人之中〕引起興奮/興趣/敵意 **3** 產生〔熱能、電能或其他能量〕

genius *n* **1** 天才, 天賦 **2** 有天才的人, 天才 **3 have a genius for (doing) sth** 有(做)某事的天才 **4** 〔某一羣體的人、某個時期等的〕特徵

genuine *adj* **1** 〔感情、慾望等〕真誠的 **2** 〔物品〕真正的 **3** 真心實意的 **4 the genuine article** 〔某類型的人或物中〕真正的代表 **—genuinely** *adv* **—genuineness** *n*

gesture¹ *n* **1** 手勢, 姿勢 **2** 表示, 姿態 **—gestural** *adj*

gesture² *v* 用手勢示意

gigantic *adj* 巨大的, 龐大的 **—gigantically** *adv*

glance¹ *v* **1** 一瞥, 看一眼 **2** 快速閱讀 **3** 閃耀, 閃光

glance off *phr v* 擦過, 掠過

glance² *n* **1** 一瞥, 很快的一看 **2 at a glance** 看一眼便知道 **3 at first glance** 乍一看, 最初看到時

glare¹ *v* **1** 怒目而視 **2** 發出刺眼的強光

glare² *n* **1** 刺眼的強光 **2** 怒視 **3 the glare of publicity** 眾目睽睽

glide¹ *v* 滑行, 滑動

glide² *n* **1** 滑行, 滑動 **2** 滑音, 延音 **3** 滑音

global *adj* **1** 全球的, 世界的 **2** 全面的, 整體的 **—globally** *adv*

glorious *adj* **1** 輝煌的, 光榮的, 榮耀的 **2** 壯麗的, 吸引人的 **3** 極其愉快的, 極好的 **4 glorious day/summer/weather** 晴朗的一天/美好的夏季/宜人的天氣 **—gloriously** *adv*

glow¹ *n* **1** 〔尤指沒有火焰的燃燒物發出的〕光亮, 光輝 **2** 〔尤指紅色和橙色的〕鮮豔 **3** 〔運動後或興奮時臉部或身體發出的〕紅潤光澤 **4 a glow of pleasure/satisfaction/happiness etc** 強烈的愉快/滿足/幸福等

glow² *v* **1** 發出柔和穩定的光 **2** 〔無焰地〕發光生熱 **3** 〔由於運動或強烈情感〕面部[身體]發紅[發熱] **4 glow with pride/pleasure/triumph etc** 由於自豪/愉快/勝利等容光煥發

glue¹ *n* 膠, 膠水

glue² *v* **1** 膠合, 黏合, 黏貼 **2 be glued to** 盯着眼看, 審視 **3 glued to the spot** 〔由於驚恐或極感興趣而〕動彈不得的

goal *n* **1** 目標, 目的 **2** 〔足球、曲棍球等〕得分 **3** 球門

govern *v* **1** 管理, 統治〔國家〕 **2** 〔規則、原則等〕規定, 管制, 制約 **3** 〔語法中〕支配〔另一詞, 決定該詞應具有何種形式〕 **4** 抑制, 控制〔強烈或危險的感情〕

grab¹ *v* **1 ▶WITH YOUR HAND 用手◀** 攫取，抓住 **2 ▶FOOD/SLEEP 食品/睡◀** 〔因忙碌而〕趕緊，抓緊〔吃或睡〕**3 ▶GET STH FOR YOURSELF 為自己獲取某物◀** 〔尤指通過不公平手段〕霸佔，撈取，強奪 **4 how does sth grab you?** 你對某事是否有興趣? **5 grab a chance/opportunity** 抓住機會

grab at *phr v* **1** 〔迅速伸手〕抓住 **2** 抓住〔機會〕

grab² *n* **1 make a grab for/at** 〔猛然去〕抓 **2 be up for grabs** 〔工作、獎金、機會等〕人人都可以爭取得到的，供爭奪的 **3** 抓具，抓斗挖土機

graceful *adj* **1** 〔動作，線條〕優美的，雅緻的 **2** 優雅得體的，體面的 **—gracefully** *adv* **—gracefulness** *n*

gradual *adj* **1** 逐漸的，逐步的 **2** 〔坡〕緩的，不陡的 **—gradualness** *n*

graduate¹ *n* **1** 〔尤指完成學士學位課程的〕大學畢業生 **2** 畢業生

graduate² *adj* **1** 攻讀碩士[博士]研究生的 **2** 研究生〔課程〕

graduate³ *v* **1** 〔尤指以學士學位〕大學畢業 **2** 中學畢業 **3 graduate (from sth) to** 〔從某處〕升級到 **4** 向〔畢業生〕授予學位[文憑]

grant¹ *n* 〔政府發給的〕補助金

grant² *v* **1** 給予，准予〔尤指官方授權〕**2** 承認〔確有某事，但不影響自己的看法〕**3 take it for granted (that)** 想當然地認為 **4 take sb/sth for granted** 視某人/某事為當然〔因而對其從不特別關注或感謝〕

grasp¹ *v* **1** 抓牢，握緊 **2** 理解，領會〔尤指複雜的意思 **3 grasp a chance/opportunity** 〔急切地〕抓住機會 **4 grasp the nettle** 果斷地處理棘手問題

grasp at sth *phr v* **1** 急切嘗試利用〔一次機會〕**2** 企圖抓住

grasp² *n* **1** 抓，握 **2** 〔對複雜概念或棘手狀況的〕理解力 **3** 力所能及; 把握; 掌握 **4** 控制，權力

gratitude *n* 感激〔之情〕— 反義詞 INGRATITUDE

grave¹ *n* **1** 墳墓 **2 the grave** 死亡 **3 sb would turn/spin in their grave** 某人於九泉之下不得安寧〔表示某人在九泉之下也不會贊成〕

grave² *adj* **1** 嚴重的; 令人擔憂的 **2** 〔由於發生重大事情，表情或説話〕嚴肅的 **—gravely** *adv*

grave³ *adj* 有沉[抑]音符〔法語等語言中加在字母之上表示發音的符號〕的

greedy *adj* **1** 貪吃的，貪喝的 **2** 〔對金錢、財產等〕貪婪的，渴望的 **—greedily** *adv* **—greediness** *n*

greet *v* **1** 問候，迎接，招呼 **2** 對〔某事〕作出反應 **3** 最先映入〔某人的〕眼簾; 傳入〔某人的〕耳中

grief *n* **1** 極度悲傷〔尤指因所愛之人去世而感受的悲痛〕**2** 傷心事，不幸 **3 good grief!** 哎喲!〔用於略感驚訝或氣惱之時〕**4 come to grief** 失敗;〔在事故中〕受損; 被毀 **5 give sb grief** 數落[責備]某人

grind¹ *v* **1 ▶INTO SMALL PIECES 變成碎末◀ a)** 又作 **grind up** 把〔玉米、咖啡豆等〕碾碎，磨成粉末 **b)** 〔用機器將食物，尤指肉〕絞碎 **2 ▶SMOOTH/SHARP 光滑的/鋒利的◀** 磨光，磨利 **3 ▶PRESS STH DOWN 向下擠壓某物◀** 用力旋轉地擠壓 **4 grind your teeth** 把牙齒磨得嘎嘎響 **5 grind to a halt a)** 〔車輛〕慢慢停下來 **b)** 〔國家、組織或進程〕逐漸停頓，慢慢癱瘓 **6 grind the faces of the poor** 壓榨窮人

grind sb ↔ **down** *phr v* 長期欺壓某人〔使其達到絕望地步〕

grind on *phr v* 令人厭煩地長期持續

grind sth ↔ **out** *phr v* 大量撰寫，大量提供〔信息、文字或音樂作品等〕

grind² *n* **1** 令人疲勞[厭倦]的苦事 **2** 埋頭學習[死讀書]的學生

gross¹ *adj* **1 ▶TOTAL 總共的◀ a)** 〔扣去税或成本之前〕總的，毛的 **b)** 毛重的 **2 gross negligence/misconduct/injustice etc** 明顯的過失/行為不端/不公平等 **3 ▶RUDE 粗魯的◀** 〔行為〕極端粗魯的，完全不能接受的 **4 ▶NASTY 令人厭惡的◀** 看上去[想起來]令人厭惡的 **5 ▶FAT 胖的◀** 極胖而難看的 **—grossly** *adv* **—grossness** *n*

gross² *adv* **earn £20,000/$30,000 etc gross** 税前收入 20,000 英鎊/30,000 美元等

gross³ *v* 獲得…的總利潤[毛利，税前收入]

gross sb **out** *phr v* 但願某人沒看過[聽過]〔如此惡劣的事情〕

guarantee¹ *v* **1 ▶PROMISE STH WILL HAPPEN 許諾某事會發生◀** 擔保，保證 **2 ▶A PRODUCT 產品◀** 保修; 包換 **3 ▶LEGAL 法律上的◀** 保證付款 **4 ▶MAKE STH CERTAIN 確保某事◀** 保證〔某事必然發生〕**5 ▶CERTAIN TO DO STH 肯定做某事◀ be guaranteed to do sth** 肯定會以某種方式行事〔工作，發生〕**6 ▶PROTECT 保護◀ guarantee sth against** 〔為免受傷害或損毀〕提供完全的保護

guarantee² *n* **1** 保修單; 包換單 **2** 〔某事必將辦到或發生的〕正式而堅定的承諾 **3 a)** 擔保〔尤指為保證還債而作的擔保〕**b)** 〔尤指對債務的〕擔保物; 抵押品

guardian *n* **1** 監護人 **2** 〔尤指某種制度或道德準則的〕維護者，保衛者

guilt *n* **1** 內疚，自責 **2** 犯罪 **3** 責任，罪責 **4 guilt trip** 負疚感

gust¹ *n* **1** 一陣狂風 **2** 突發的一陣怒氣、興奮等

gust² *v* 〔狂風〕一陣陣勁吹

H, h

habitual *adj* **1** 已成習慣的 **2** 習慣〔性〕的，慣常的 **—habitually** *adv*

hail¹ *n* **1** 雹，冰雹 **2 a hail of bullets/stones** 一陣彈雨/一陣像雹子般襲來的石塊 **3 a hail of criticism/abuse** 連珠砲般的批評/辱罵

hail² *v* 呼喊; 大聲招呼

hail sb/sth **as** sth *phr v* [常用被動態] 把…稱作，把…譽為

hail from sth *phr v* [不用被動態] 出生地是，來自

halt¹ *n* 停止，停住; 暫停

halt² *v* **1** 停下，停止 **2 halt!** 〔口令〕站住! 立定! **3** 阻止

hamper¹ *v* 阻礙，妨礙; 牽制

hamper² *n* **1** 〔用於攜帶食品的〕有蓋籃子 **2** 〔放置待洗髒衣物的〕洗衣筐

handle¹ *v* **1 ▶DEAL WITH STH 處理某事◀ a)** 應付〔困難局面〕，處理〔難題〕**b)** 處理 **2 ▶DEAL WITH**

SB 應付某人◀ 對待, 應付〔某人〕 3 ▶HOLD 拿◀ 觸; 摸; 碰; 拿 4 ▶CONTROL WITH YOUR HANDS 用手操縱◀ a) 操縱, 操作〔車輛、工具等〕 b) handle well/ badly etc 容易/不易操縱 5 ▶IN CHARGE OF 負責◀ 負責 6 ▶MACHINES/SYSTEMS 機器/系統◀ 處理〔一定數量的工作、人員等〕 7 ▶BUY/SELL 買/賣◀ 經銷; 買賣; 處理

handle² *n* 1 把手 2 柄 3 **get a handle on** 開始理解, 了解〔某人、某形勢等〕 4 民用波段無線電用戶的呼號

harbour¹【英】, **harbor**【美】 *n* 港口, 港灣, 海港

harbour²【英】, **harbor**【美】 *v* 1 窩藏, 包庇〔罪犯〕 2 懷有〔不好的想法、恐懼等〕

harmony *n* 1〔音樂中的〕和聲 2 **be in harmony with** 〔思想、感情等的〕和睦, 一致, 融洽 3 **live/work in (perfect) harmony** 一起生活/工作得(十分)融洽 4 和諧, 協調

hatch¹ *v* 1 又作 **hatch out**〔蛋〕孵化 2 又作 **hatch out**〔幼禽等〕孵出, 破殼而出 3 **hatch a plot/plan/deal etc** 祕密策劃陰謀/計劃/交易等

hatch² *n* 1〔船、飛機上的〕艙口; 艙門 2 又作 **hatchway**〔牆、地板上的〕開口, 活板門 3 孵蛋

haul¹ *v* 1 拖, 拉 2 **haul sb over the coals** 狠狠責備, 訓斥 3〔用車輛〕運送〔貨物〕 4 **haul yourself up/out of etc a)** 提高〔社會地位〕; 取勝 **b)** 起來; 走出 5 **haul off and hit/punch sb** 重擊 6 **haul ass** 趕快

haul sb **up** *phr v* [一般用被動態] 傳訊, 把…拉上法庭

haul² *n* 1〔一大批〕贓物, 走私物品 2 **long/slow haul** 耗時費力的事 3 一網的捕魚量

haunt¹ *v* 1〔鬼魂〕經常出沒於… 2 纏擾, 煩擾; 縈繞在…心頭 3〔長期〕給〔某人〕帶來麻煩

haunt² *n*〔某人〕常去的地方

hazard¹ *n* 1 危險; 隱患; 會造成危害的事物 2〔不可避免的〕風險

hazard² *v* 1 斗膽提出; 大膽猜測 2 冒…的風險

heal *v* 1 又作 **heal up**〔傷口或折斷的骨〕長好, 癒合 2 醫治; 治癒 3 **heal the wounds/breach/divisions** 治癒創傷/彌補裂痕/消除分歧

heal over *phr v* 1〔傷口或破損的皮膚〕癒合, 痊癒 2 忘掉過去的爭吵, 重新和好

heap¹ *n* 1〔大而雜亂的〕堆 2 **heaps of** 大量, 許多 3 破舊的汽車 4 **fall/collapse in a heap** 癱倒/動彈不了 5 **be struck/knocked all of a heap** 被突然驚呆, 被弄得慌作一團

heap² *v* 1 又作 **heap up**〔雜亂地〕堆積, 堆放 2 **be heaped with**〔盤子〕堆滿〔食物〕 3 **heap praises/insults etc on** 極力稱讚/百般侮辱等

hearing *n* 1 聽覺 2 聽證會; 審訊; 聆訊 3 **give sb a (fair) hearing** 給某人一個(公平的)解釋機會 4 **in/within sb's hearing** 在某人聽力所及的範圍內

heighten *v* 加強, 增加

herd¹ *n* 1〔同一種類並一同棲息的〕獸羣 2 **the herd**〔易受人支配的〕民眾, 老百姓, 芸芸眾生

herd² *v* 1〔尤指粗暴地〕(使)集合在一起 2 放牧

hesitate *v* 1 猶豫, 躊躇, 遲疑(不決) 2 **hesitate to do sth** 不願做某事, 對…有顧慮 **—hesitatingly** *adv*

hesitation *n* 躊躇, 猶豫, 遲疑(不決)

hike¹ *n* 1〔在山區或鄉間〕徒步旅行, 遠足 2〔價格、工資、稅率等的〕大幅度上升 3 **take a hike** 滾開!

hike² *v* 1 徒步旅行, 遠足 2 又作 **hike** sth ↔ **up**〔大幅度〕提高〔價格、稅款、服務費等〕

hike sth ↔ **up** 1 提起, 拉起〔衣服〕 2 大幅度提高

hinder *v* 阻礙, 妨礙, 阻止

hint¹ *n* 1 暗示 2 (細微的)跡象; 少許, 微量 3 有益的建議[指點]

hint² *v* 暗示, 示意

historic *adj* 1 有重大歷史意義的, 歷史性的 2 有歷史記載的

hollow¹ *adj* 1 空(心)的, 中空的 2 **hollow face/eyes etc** 凹陷的臉頰/雙眼等 3〔聲音〕空洞的, 低沉的 4〔感情、語言〕虛假的, 無誠意的 5 **hollow laugh/voice etc** 乾巴巴的笑聲/聲音等 **—hollowly** *adv* **—hollowness** *n*

hollow² *n* 淺坑, 凹陷處

hollow³ *v*

hollow sth ↔ **out** *phr v* 把…挖空[掏空], 使成中空

holy *adj* 1 (有關)上帝[宗教]的, 神聖的 2 虔誠的 3 **holy cow/cats/shit/mackerel etc** 天啊! 上帝呀!〔表示驚訝、讚美或恐懼〕 4 **a holy terror** 搗蛋鬼, 頑皮的小孩

honest *adj* 1 ▶CHARACTER 人品◀ 誠實的, 正直的 2 ▶STATEMENT/ANSWER ETC 講話/回答等◀ 坦誠的, 直率的, 不隱瞞真相的 3 **to be honest** 說實話, 老實說 4 **honest!** 真的! 不騙你! 5 **honest to God** 確實, 千真萬確 6 ▶WORK 工作◀ 用正當手段的, 努力認真的 7 ▶ORDINARY/GOOD PEOPLE 普通的/好人◀ 誠實的; 規矩的 8 **make an honest woman (out) of** 因…已懷孕而娶她為妻

honesty *n* 1 誠實, 正直; 坦誠 2 **in all honesty** 說實話

hook¹ *n* 1 ▶FOR HANGING THINGS ON 用來掛東西◀ 掛鈎, 吊鈎 2 ▶FOR CATCHING FISH 用來釣魚◀ 魚鈎, 釣鈎 3 **by hook or by crook** 千方百計地, 下定決心地 4 **let/get sb off the hook** 讓/幫某人脫離困境 5 **leave/take the phone off the hook**〔因不想接聽電話而〕摘下電話聽筒 6 ▶WAY OF HITTING SB 拳擊方法◀〔拳擊中的〕鈎拳 7 **hook, line, and sinker** 完全地, 無保留地〔相信謊言〕 8 ▶A TUNE 曲調◀ 曲調中易記的部分

hook² *v* 1 ▶FISH 魚◀〔用鈎〕釣魚 2 ▶FASTEN 固定◀ 吊, 掛; 把…固定住 3 ▶BEND YOUR FINGER/ARM ETC 屈起手指/手臂等◀ 把〔手指、手臂或腿〕屈起〔以拉動或抱住某物〕 4 ▶ATTRACT 吸引◀ 勾引; 吸引

hook sth ↔ **up** *phr v*〔電器〕連接, 接通

hook up with *phr v* **a)** 跟…結交 **b)** 掛鈎〔指與某個組織合作〕

hop¹ *v* 1 ▶JUMP 跳躍◀〔人〕單足蹦跳 2〔鳥、昆蟲、小動物〕(快速小步)跳躍 3 跳上[跳下]〔車輛〕 4 **hop a plane/bus/train etc**〔尤指突然決定〕乘搭〔飛機、公共汽車、火車等〕 5 **hop it!** 走開! 滾開! 6 **hopping mad** 非常生氣, 暴跳如雷

hop² *n* 1 **keep sb on the hop** 讓某人十分忙碌 2 **catch sb on the hop** 使某人措手不及 3 ▶JUMP

跳躍◀〔小步〕跳躍, 蹦跳 **4 ▶PLANT 植物◀** 忽布, 啤酒花〔用來釀製啤酒〕**5 ▶FLIGHT 飛行◀** 短程飛行 **6 ▶DANCE 跳舞◀** 舞會

horizon *n* **1 the horizon** 地平線 **2 horizons**〔思想、知識、經驗的〕範圍, 界限; 眼界 **3 be on the horizon** 將要發生

horrible *adj* **1** 可怕的, 嚇人的, 令人恐懼的 **2** 糟糕的, 令人不快的, 極討厭的 **3** 粗魯的, 不友好的 — **horribly** *adv*

hospitality *n* 好客, 殷勤

host¹ *n* **1 ▶AT A PARTY 在聚會上◀** 東道主, 主人 **2 ▶ON TELEVISION 電視中◀** 節目主持人 **3 ▶COUNTRY/GOVERNMENT 國家/政府◀** 主辦者, 東道國 **4 a (whole) host of** 大量, 許多 **5 ▶IN CHURCH 在教堂裡◀ the Host**〔聖餐儀式中的〕聖餅 **6 ▶ANIMAL/PLANT 動物/植物◀** 寄主, 宿主〔寄生物所寄生的動物或植物〕**7 ▶ARMY 軍隊◀** 部隊 **8** 旅館老闆

host² *v* **1** 主辦, 作...的東道主 **2** 做〔廣播或電視的〕節目主持人

hostile *adj* **1** 懷有敵意的, 敵對的, 不友善的 **2** 強烈反對的 **3** 敵人的, 敵方的 **4 hostile environment** 逆境, 艱苦的條件

hover *v* **1**〔鳥、昆蟲〕盤旋;〔直升機〕懸停 **2**〔等待或拿不定主意時〕徘徊; 走來走去 **3** 不確定, 搖擺不定

hug¹ *v* **1** 熱烈地擁抱〔某人〕**2** 抱住〔某物〕**3** 靠近[緊挨]...走 **4 hug yourself with joy/delight etc** 沾沾自喜

hug² *n* 擁抱, 緊抱

humble¹ *adj* **1**〔地位〕卑微的, 低下的 **2** 謙虛的, 謙卑的 — 反義詞 PROUD **3 my humble apologies** 是我錯〔一種不太認真的口氣〕**4 in my humble opinion** 敝人以為, 依我愚見〔略帶幽默的説法〕**5** 簡單而實用的 **6 eat humble pie**〔低聲下氣地〕承認錯誤; 賠禮道歉 **7 your humble servant** 您卑微的僕人; 卑職; 愚〔舊時信末的自謙詞〕—**humbly** *adv*

humble² *v* **1 be humbled** 使謙卑, 使感到自慚 **2**〔輕易〕擊敗〔強敵〕**3 humble yourself** 作出謙恭的姿態; 不恥下問; 勇於認錯 —**humbling** *adj*

humidity *n* **1** 濕度; 濕氣 **2** 悶熱潮濕的空氣[天氣]

hygiene *n* **1** 衛生(學); 保健(學) **2** 個人衛生

I, i

ideal¹ *adj* **1** 理想的, 最好的 **2** 想像的; 理想中的〔世界、職業、制度等〕

ideal² *n* **1**〔希望實現的〕理想 **2** 完美典型〔想像中完美的事物〕

identical *adj* 完全相同的 —**identically** *adv*

identify *v* **1** 認出〔某人或某物〕, 識別 **2** 確定; 發現 **3** 表明[顯示]身分

identify with *phr v* **1** 與〔某人〕在感情上認同, 與〔某人〕有同感 **2 be identified with** 與〔政治派別等〕關係緊密 **3** 將〔某物〕等同於〔某物〕

idle¹ *adj* **1** 不工作的; 空閒的 **2** 懶惰的 **3** 不認真的; 漫無目的的 **4 the idle rich** 不用工作的富人

idle² *v* **1** 虛度時間, 閒混, 無所事事 **2**（使）〔發動機低速地〕空轉 **3**〔尤指暫時〕使〔工廠〕閒置; 使〔工人〕閒着

idle sth ↔ **away** *phr v* 虛度〔光陰〕, 消磨〔時間〕

ignorant *adj* **1** 無知的, 沒有學識的, 愚昧的 **2** 因無知而產生的 **3** 粗魯的, 不禮貌的

illusion *n* **1**〔尤指對自己的〕幻覺, 幻想 **2** 假象, 錯覺

illustrate *v* **1** 舉例説明〔某事物〕**2** 作為例證説明〔事實〕**3** [一般用被動態]〔給書籍、文章等〕作插圖

image *n* **1 ▶PUBLIC OPINION 公眾輿論◀**〔某人、組織、產品等的〕形象 **2 ▶IDEA IN MIND 腦海中的想法◀**〔腦海中對某人或某物的〕印象, 形象 **3 ▶PICTURE/WHAT YOU SEE 圖像/所見的東西◀ a)**〔鏡子或照相機鏡頭中的〕映像 **b)**〔電視機、電腦屏幕上或銀幕上的〕圖像 **c)**〔尤指用木頭或石頭雕刻成的人或物的形狀〕塑像, 雕像 **4 ▶DESCRIPTION 描繪◀**〔修辭中的〕比喻 **5 be the (very/living/spitting) image of** 酷似〔某人或某物〕**6 in the image of** 與...同形

imitate *v* **1**〔認為是好的而〕仿效〔某物〕**2** 模仿〔某人的行為、説話、動作等, 尤指引人發笑的模仿〕—**imitator** *n*

immense *adj* 巨大的

immigrate *v*〔為定居而從外國〕移入

impose *v* **1 impose a ban/tax/fine etc (on)**〔正式〕實施禁令/徵收稅款/懲收罰款等 **2 impose a burden/strain etc (on/upon)** 增加負擔/壓力等 **3**〔將想法、信仰〕強加於〔某人〕**4** 麻煩〔別人〕

impress¹ *v* **1** 令人稱羨, 使留下深刻印象 **2** 使〔某人〕了解〔某事的〕重要性 **3** 把〔某物〕壓入〔柔軟的平面〕; 壓印; 蓋〔印〕於

impress² *n* 印記; 壓痕

improve *v* **1** 改善, 改進 **2** 變得更好

improve on/upon sth *phr v* 改進, 做得比...更好, 超過

incident *n* **1**〔尤指不平常的〕事件 **2**〔導致爭論的〕嚴重[暴力]事件

inclination *n* **1 ▶DESIRE 慾望◀** 意向; 傾向 **2 ▶TENDENCY 趨勢◀**〔思想或行為的〕傾向 **3 inclination of the head** 點頭 **4 ▶SLOPE 斜面◀** 斜坡; 斜度

incorporate *v* 把〔某物〕併入, 包含; 吸收 —**incorporation** *n*

incur *v* **1**〔因自己的舉動而〕招致〔不愉快的事〕, 招惹, 遭受 **2 incur expenses** 招致花費

index¹ *n* **1**〔書後人名、題目等的〕索引 **2**〔用於圖書館等處的〕卡片索引 **3**〔用於判斷或量度水平的〕標誌 **4**〔用於比較今昔價格、費用等的〕指數

index² *v* **1** 為〔某物〕編索引 **2** 使〔工資、養老金等〕與物價指數掛鈎 —**indexation** *n*

indicate *v* **1 ▶FACTS 事實◀** 表明; 表示 **2 ▶POINT AT 指向◀** 指, 指着〔以引起注意〕**3 ▶YOUR WISHES/INTENTIONS 希望/意願◀**〔説或做某事〕表明〔意向等〕**4 ▶A SIGN FOR 為...的標誌◀** 標誌着; 代表 **5 ▶IN A CAR 在汽車裡◀**〔用指示車燈或手勢〕指示〔轉彎方向〕**6 ▶TREATMENT 治療◀ be indicated** 顯示有...的需要

individual¹ *adj* **1** 單獨的, 個別的 **2** 個人的, 供一個人的 **3**〔風格、做事方式等〕獨特的, 與眾不同的

individual² *n* **1** 個人, 個體 **2** 有自己的思想、感情和觀念的人 **3** 有某種特點的人〔尤指在某些方面與眾不同的人〕

induce *v* **1** 勸誘〔某人做某事, 尤指不好的事〕, 誘導 **2**〔用藥物〕為〔產婦〕引產 **3** 誘發〔某種身體反應〕

industrious *adj* 勤勞的, 勤奮的 **—industriously** *adv* **—industriousness** *n*

inevitable *adj* **1** 必然發生的, 難以避免的 **2 the inevitable** 不可避免的事情 **3** 照例必有的 **—inevitability** *n*

infant¹ *n* **1** 幼兒, 嬰兒 **2 infants**〔英國學校裡四至八歲的〕學童 **3 infant school/teacher/class etc**〔英國為四至八歲兒童設立的〕兒童學校/教師/班級等

infant² *adj*〔公司、組織等〕剛成立的, 初創的

infect *v* **1** 傳染〔疾病給人〕 **2**〔以病菌等〕污染〔食物、水、空氣等〕 **3**〔情緒等〕感染〔別人〕, 使〔人〕受影響

infer *v*〔根據其他資料〕推斷, 推定

inferior¹ *adj* **1**〔質量、價值、技能等〕差的, 次的 **2** 低級別的, 下級的 **—inferiority** *n*

inferior² *n* 下級, 下屬, 部下

inflation *n* **1** 物價上漲(率), 通貨膨脹(率) **2** 充氣

influence¹ *n* **1** 影響 **2** 有影響的人[物] **3 under the influence** 喝醉了

influence² *v* 影響, 起作用

informative *adj* 資料豐富的; 增進知識的 **—informatively** *adv* **—informativeness** *n*

inhabit *v*〔動物或人〕居住於〔某地〕 **—inhabitable** *adj*

inhabitant *n* 居民

inherit *v* **1** 繼承〔遺產〕 **2** 承擔〔他人過去錯誤造成的問題〕 **3** 遺傳得到〔父母的性格、外貌〕 **4** 接收〔別人不再需要的東西〕

inhibit *v* **1** 抑制, 約束 **2** 使羞於, 使怯於

initiate¹ *v* **1** 開始實施〔重要的事, 如官方程序或新計劃〕; 發起 **2** 向〔某人〕傳授專門知識[技巧] **3**〔通過特殊儀式〕使〔某人〕加入〔組織、俱樂部、社團等〕

initiate² *n* 被吸納加入某組織並授以訣竅的人

inject *v* **1**〔向體內〕注射〔液體, 尤指藥液〕 **2** 增加〔氣氛、興趣等〕 **3** 投入〔更多的資金、設備等〕

injury *n* **1**〔對身體的〕傷害, 損害 **2**〔因事故或攻擊造成的〕人身傷害 **3 do yourself an injury**〔意外地〕自我傷害

innocent¹ *adj* **1** 無罪的 **2 innocent victims/bystanders/ people etc**〔戰爭或犯罪行為〕無辜的受害者/旁觀者/人們等 **3** 不帶惡意的 **4** 天真無邪的, 閱世不深的 **—innocently** *adv*

innocent² *n* 涉世不深的人

innovation *n* **1** 新觀念, 新方法, 新發明 **2** 革新; 創新

innumerable *adj* 不可勝數的

inquire, enquire *v* **1** 詢問, 打聽 **2 inquire within** 詳情請入內查詢〔用於商店櫥窗內的告示, 意思是你若進入店內, 可得知更多情況〕 **—inquirer** *n*

inquire after sb/sth *phr v* 問候, 問好

inquire into sth *phr v* 查問, 查究, 調查

inquire sth **of** sb *phr v* 向〔某人〕詢問

insert¹ *v* **1** 插入, 放進 **2**〔在文件或文稿中〕加入, 加進

insert² *n* **1**〔夾在報刊中的〕插頁廣告 **2** 插入物

insist *v* **1** 堅持宣稱, 堅決認為 **2** 堅持主張, 堅決要求, 一定要 **3 if you insist** 如果你一定要這樣〔用來對你並不真正想做的事表示同意〕

insist on sth *phr v* **1** 認為〔某事〕非常重要〔並堅持得到它〕 **2** 堅持做〔尤指麻煩或令人討厭的事〕

inspect *v* **1** 仔細檢查; 檢驗 **2** 視察; 檢閱

inspire *v* **1** 鼓舞, 激勵 **2** 使〔某人〕產生〔某種感情或反應〕, 激起, 喚起 **3** 給〔某人〕創作靈感 **4** 吸氣

install, instal *v* **1** 安裝〔設備〕, 設置 **2**〔尤指通過特別儀式〕正式任命, 使正式就職 **3 install yourself in/at etc** 把自己安頓在〔某地逗留很長一段時間〕, 安置

instance¹ *n* **1 for instance** 例如 **2**〔特定情況的〕例子, 實例 **3 at sb's instance** 應某人的請求 **4 in the first instance**〔一連串行動的〕第一步, 首先

instance² *v* 舉...為例

instinct *n* 本能; 直覺; 天性

institute¹ *n* 學院; 研究院, 研究所

institute² *v* 制定〔制度、規則等〕; 提起〔訴訟〕

in·struct *v* **1** 命令; 指示 **2** 教授, 指導 **3** [一般用被動態] 通知 **4** 聘請〔律師〕出庭

instrument *n* **1 ►TOOL 工具◄**〔指用來進行細緻工作的〕器械, 器具 **2 ►MUSIC 音樂◄** 樂器 **3 ►FOR MEASURING 測量◄** 儀器, 儀表 **4 ►METHOD 方法◄** 制度; 方法; 法律 **5 ►DOCUMENT 文件◄** 法律文件 **6 instrument of fate/God** 受命運/上帝擺佈的人[物] **7 instrument of torture** 刑具

intellectual¹ *adj* **1** 智力的; 需用腦力的 **2** 有知識的, 受過良好教育的 **—intellectually** *adv* **—intellectualize** *v*

intellectual² *n* 知識分子

intelligence *n* **1 a)** 智力; 理解力 **b)** 聰穎; 聰明 **2 a)** 情報, 諜報 **b)** 情報機構; 諜報人員

intend *v* **1** 計劃, 打算, 想要 **2 be intended for sb/sth** 是為...而準備的; 專供...使用的 **3 intended target/victim/destination etc** 預期的目標/被害人/目的地等

intention *n* 意圖, 目的; 打算

interfere *v* 介入; 干涉; 干預

interfere with sth/sb *phr v* **1** 妨礙, 阻止 **2** 干擾〔廣播或電視播送〕 **3** 對〔兒童〕性侵犯

interior¹ *n* **1** 內部 —反義詞 EXTERIOR **2 the interior** 內地, 腹地 **3 Minister/Department of the Interior** 內政部長/內政部

interior² *adj* 內部的, 裡面的; 室內的 —反義詞 EXTERIOR

intermediate *adj* **1** 中間的, 居中的 **2** 中級程度的, 中等水平的

interpret *v* **1** 把〔某人的行為或某一事件〕理解為; 解釋為 **2** 口譯 **3** 解釋, 闡釋 **4**〔表演者根據自己對戲劇、音樂等的感受或理解來〕表演, 演繹; 體現

interrupt *v* **1** 打斷〔某人的〕講話; 中斷〔某人的〕行動; 打擾 **2** 使〔過程、活動〕暫時停止 **3** 中斷〔直線、平面、風景等的連續性〕 **—interruption** *n*

intersection *n* **1**〔尤指兩條道路的〕交叉口, 十字

路口;〔線的〕交點 **2** 橫斷; 交叉

interval *n* **1**〔兩件事情、兩種活動等之間的〕間隔, 間歇 **2 sunny/bright intervals**〔陰雨天中的〕短暫晴朗 **3 at weekly/20 minute etc intervals** 每週/每20分鐘等 **4 at regular intervals a)** 每隔一定時間 **b)**〔物件〕按相同間距〔擺放〕**5**〔戲劇、音樂會等〕幕間休息 **6** 音程

interview[1] *n* **1**〔求職、入學等的〕面試, 面談 **2**〔報紙、雜誌、電視的〕採訪; 訪談 **3**〔與提問者的〕正式晤談, 接見, 會見

interview[2] *v* **1** 對〔求職者、學校考生等〕進行面試 **2** 採訪〔名人〕**3** 向〔某人〕正式提問

intimate[1] *adj* **1 ▶FRIENDS 朋友◀** 親密的 **2 ▶PRIVATE 私人的◀** 隱私的, 個人的 **3 an intimate knowledge of sth**〔因細心研究或經驗豐富而〕精通某事 **4 ▶RESTAURANT/MEAL/PLACE 飯店/餐飲/地方◀** 幽靜親切的〔因此使人感覺舒服的〕**5 ▶CONNECTION 關聯◀ intimate link/connection etc**〔兩者間的〕密切聯繫 **6 ▶SEXUAL 性的◀ a)** 與性有關的 **b) be intimate with** 與…發生性關係 —**intimately** *adv*

intimate[2] *v* 暗示; 提示

intimate[3] *n* 知己, 密友, 至交

introduce *v* **1 ▶WHEN PEOPLE MEET 人們相遇時◀** 介紹, 引見; 使相互認識 **2 ▶MAKE STH HAPPEN/EXIST 使某事物發生/存在◀** 引進〔變革、計劃、制度等〕, 實施; 推行 **3 ▶BRING TO A PLACE 帶到某地◀** 首次引入〔某物〕, 使傳入 **4 ▶NEW EXPERIENCE 新經歷◀ introduce sb to sth** 使某人初次嘗試某物 **5 ▶TELEVISION/RADIO 電視/廣播◀**〔在電視或廣播節目開始時為節目〕作開場白 **6 ▶BE THE START OF 為…的開始◀**〔某事的發生〕作為[標誌着]〔一個時期或變化的〕開始 **7 ▶LAW 法律◀**〔尤指在英國議會, 將一項新法律〕提交討論 **8 ▶PUT STH INTO 把某物放入◀** 小心地把〔某物〕放入〔另一物裡〕

invaluable *adj* 極有價值的

invent *v* **1** 發明; 創造 **2** 捏造, 編造〔觀點、故事, 一般用來欺騙別人〕; 虛構

invest *v* **1** 投資; 入股 **2** 投入〔大量時間、精力等以成就某事〕

invest in sth *phr v* **1** 買進〔以便高價賣出賺錢〕**2** 買〔對自己有用的東西〕

invest sb/sth **with** sth *phr v* [常用被動態] **1** 授權給 **2** 使似乎具有〔某種特性或品質〕

investigate *v* **1** 查明〔犯罪、事故或科學問題等的真相〕; 調查; 審查 **2**〔由於可能牽涉犯罪而〕調查〔某人〕

invite[1] *v* **1** 邀請 **2**〔禮貌地〕請求〔某人做某事〕**3**〔尤指無意地〕招致〔麻煩或批評等不好的事〕; 引誘

invite sb **along** *phr v*〔去某地時〕邀請〔某人〕同往

invite sb **back** *phr v*〔在與某人一同外出之後〕再邀請他到自己的住處

invite sb **in** *phr v* 邀請〔某人〕進屋

invite sb **over** *phr v* 邀請〔某人〕來家裡〔通常是請他喝酒或吃飯〕

invite[2] *n*〔聚會、吃飯等的〕邀請

involve *v* **1** 包含〔必要的部分或結果〕, 包括, 需要 **2** 涉及; 影響 **3**〔邀請或允許某人〕參與 **4 involve yourself** 積極參與

isolate *v* **1** 孤立〔國家或政治團體等〕**2** 分離〔物質、疾病等以作研究〕**3** 分離〔觀點、單詞、問題等〕**4**〔在社會、團體中〕使〔某人〕孤立 **5** 使某地與其他地方隔離 **6** 把〔某人, 尤指病人〕與其他人隔離

issue[1] *n*
1 ▶SUBJECT/PROBLEM 話題/問題◀ 問題; 議題 **2 ▶MAGAZINE 雜誌◀**〔雜誌、報紙的〕期; 號 **3 at issue** 問題的焦點 **4 take issue with**〔向某人對某事〕提出異議 **5 make an issue (out) of sth** 挑起爭端〔尤指對方認為是小題大作〕**6 ▶SET OF THINGS FOR SALE 待售之物◀**〔新股票或郵票的〕發行 **7 ▶ACT OF GIVING STH 給予某物◀**〔正式〕發給; 分配 **8 die without issue** 死後無嗣

issue[2] *v* **1** 發表〔聲明〕; 頒布; 發出〔命令、警告等〕**2** 分給〔團體中每個成員〕; 配發 **3** 正式發行〔新郵票、硬幣、股票等〕

issue forth *phr v*〔從某處〕發出

issue from *phr v*〔尤指聲音或液體〕來自, 產生於

J, j

jam[1] *n* **1** 果醬 **2** 擁擠; 堵塞 **3 be in a jam** 處於困境 **4 jams**〔長及膝蓋以上的〕彩色短褲 **5 jam tomorrow** 許而不與的好東西〔指對耐心的人來說美好的事物總會到來〕

jam[2] *v* **1 ▶PUSH HARD 用力推◀** 用力推擠, 塞進〔將許多物件塞進一個小處所〕**2 ▶MACHINE 機器◀** 又作 **jam up**〔使〕卡住;〔使〕發生故障 **3 ▶BLOCK 堵塞◀** 又作 **jam up**〔人、車〕堵塞〔某地〕**4 ▶MUSIC 音樂◀** 未經練習的非正式演奏, 即興演奏 **5 jam on the brakes** 猛踩煞車 **6 jam the switchboard** 使電話線路堵塞 **7 ▶RADIO 無線電◀** 干擾〔無線電廣播或其他電子信號〕**8 sb is jamming** 某人幹得好

jar[1] *n* **1**〔用來盛果醬、蜂蜜等的玻璃〕廣口瓶 **2** 一廣口瓶所裝之量 **3**〔兩物碰撞引起的〕震動; 突然的痛楚 **4**〔過去用來盛食物或飲料、用黏土或石頭等製成的〕甕, 罐 **5** 一杯啤酒

jar[2] *v* **1** 撞傷〔身體的一部分 **2**〔使〕〔某物〕震動; 相撞 **3** 又作 **jar on** 令〔人〕略感不快[不舒服] **4** 不和諧, 不相配 —**jarring** *adj*

jealous *adj* **1** 嫉妒的, 妒忌的 **2** 吃醋的 **3 jealous of**〔因對某物引以自豪而〕珍惜的; 小心守護的—**jealously** *adv*

jog[1] *v* **1**〔尤指為鍛鍊身體而〕慢跑 **2**〔非故意〕輕碰, 輕推 **3 jog sb's memory** 使某人記起某事

jog along *phr v* 如常進行, 照舊繼續

jog[2] *n* **1**〔尤指為鍛鍊身體而進行的〕慢跑 **2**〔意外地〕輕碰, 輕推

joint[1] *adj* **1** 共享的; 共有的; 共同的 **2 joint effort** 共同努力 **3 joint venture** 合資經營項目; 合資企業 **4 joint resolution**〔由美國國會眾議院和參議院兩院同意並經總統簽署的〕共同決議 —**jointly** *adv*

joint[2] *n* **1** 骨關節 **2**〔供烹調的〕一大塊肉〔一般帶

有骨頭〕3〔兩個物體或部分的〕接合處; 匯合處 **4 out of joint a)**〔骨〕脱臼, 脱節 **b)**〔系統、組織〕混亂, 不協調 **5** 廉價酒館[俱樂部、餐廳] **6**〔含有大麻的〕香煙

joint³ *v* 把〔肉〕切成大塊

journal *n* **1**〔供專業人士或具有某種興趣的人讀的〕期刊, 雜誌 **2** 日記; 日誌

journey¹ *n* **1**〔尤指長途的〕旅行, 旅程 **2** 歷程, 過程

journey² *v* 旅行

judgment 又作 **judgement**【英】*n* **1** ►**OPINION** 看法◄〔認真思考後的〕意見; 看法; 評價 **2** ►**ABILITY TO DECIDE** 決斷力◄ 判斷力 **3** ►**LAW** 法律◄〔法官或法庭的〕審判, 判決 **4 against your better judgment**〔做某事〕違心的; 明知是不對的 **5 a judgment** 報應; 天譴 **6 sit in judgment over sb** 對某人的行為進行批評〔尤指不公正的批評〕 **7 judgment call** 裁判員的判決〔指由於沒有固定的規章可循而必須自行作出的決定〕

junction *n*〔公路、鐵軌等的〕聯接點, 匯合處, 交叉口

jungle *n* **1** 熱帶叢林 **2**〔堆滿東西的〕雜亂的地方 **3**〔尤因競爭者眾多〕難以成功的局面

junior¹ *adj* **1**〔在組織或行業中〕級別[職位]低的 —反義詞 SENIOR **2 be junior to sb**〔級別〕低於某人

junior² *n* **1 be two/five/ten etc years sb's junior** 比某人小兩歲/五歲/十歲等 **2** 低級職位的人 **3** 小學生 **4**〔四年制大學或高中的〕三年級學生 **5**〔指自己的〕兒子

junk¹ *n* **1** 廢舊雜物 **2** 中國平底帆船 **3** 毒品〔尤指海洛因〕 **4**〔多熱量、少營養的〕劣質[垃圾]食物

junk² *v* 丟掉〔廢舊物品〕

justice *n* **1** 正義; 公正; 合理 —反義詞 INJUSTICE **2** 司法制度; 審判; 法律制裁 **3 bring sb to justice** 將犯人緝拿歸案 **4 justice has been done/served** 正義得以伸張 **5 do justice to sb/sth** 又作 **do sb/sth justice** 公平對待某人/某物; 充分展現某人/某物的最佳素質 **6 do yourself justice**〔在考試等中〕充分發揮自己的能力 **7** 又作 **Justice a)** 法官 **b)**〔高等法院的〕法官的頭銜 **8** 正確; 公正

justify *v* **1** 證明〔別人認為不合理的事〕有道理; 為…辯護 **2 justify yourself (to sb)**（向某人）為自己辯護 **3** 是…的正當理由

juvenile *adj* **1** 少年的 **2** 幼稚的, 年幼無知的 —**juvenile** *n*

K, k

keen¹ *adj* **1** ►**INTERESTED/EAGER** 感興趣的/渴望的◄ 熱衷的, 渴望的, 熱切的 **2** ►**ATTRACTED** 着迷的◄ **be keen on sb** 對某人十分着迷 **3** ►**CLEVER** 聰明的◄ 頭腦敏捷的 **4** ►**COMPETITION** 競爭◄ **keen competition** 激烈的競爭 **5** ►**SIGHT/SMELL/HEARING** 視覺/嗅覺/聽覺◄ 靈敏的, 敏鋭的 **6** ►**SHARP** 鋒利的◄〔刀、刃〕鋒利的 **7** ►**WIND** 風◄〔風〕刺骨的 **8 keen as mustard a)** 極其渴望的 **b)** 非常聰穎的 —**keenly** *adj* —**keenness** *n*

keen² *v*〔為死者〕哀號, 哀歌, 唱輓歌

kneel 又作 **kneel down** *v* 跪着, 跪下

knit *v* **1** 又作 **knit up**〔用毛線和兩根編織針〕編織, 針織 **2** 織平針 **3** 使〔人、物或想法〕緊密結合 **4**〔折骨〕癒合 **5 knit your brows** 緊皺眉頭〔表示憂慮、思索等〕 —**knitter** *n*

knob *n* **1** 球形把手; 旋鈕 **2 a knob of** 一小塊 **3** 陰莖 **4 with (brass) knobs on**〔尤為小孩反唇相譏時用語〕更是那樣

knot¹ *n* **1** ►**TIED STRING** 綁好的繩◄〔繩索、布條、線等兩端打成的〕結 **2** ►**HAIR** 毛髮◄ **a)** 絞成一團的頭髮[線等] **b)** 髮髻, 圓髻 **3** ►**SHIP'S SPEED** 船速◄ 節〔即1,853米/小時, 船和飛機的速度單位〕 **4** ►**PEOPLE** 人◄〔站在一起的〕一小羣人 **5** ►**HARD MASS** 硬結◄ 硬結, 隆起（物） **6** ►**WOOD** 木頭◄〔木材上枝與幹分離處的〕節, 節疤 **7 a knot in your stomach/throat etc**〔恐懼或生氣等強烈情緒導致的〕心窩揪緊/喉嚨哽住等

knot² *v* **1** 使打結, 使纏結 **2 a)**（使）〔頭髮、線〕絞纏 **b) knot your hair** 把頭髮梳理成一個圓髻 **3**（使）〔肌肉〕暴突,（使）〔身體某部分〕緊揪

knowledgeable *adj* 有知識的; 博學的 —**knowledgeably** *adv*

L, l

label¹ *n* **1** 標籤, 標記 **2** 唱片公司名 **3**〔用以描述人、組織或事物的〕稱號, 外號, 綽號;〔以不公平或不正確的稱號將人扣上的〕帽子

label² *v* **1** 貼標籤於; 用標籤標明 **2**〔用稱號、外號、綽號〕描述〔某人或某物〕; 給…扣帽子

lame¹ *adj* **1** 瘸的, 跛的 **2**〔解釋或藉口〕無説服力的, 站不住腳的 **3 lame duck** 跛足鴨〔遭遇困難需要幫助的人或企業等〕 **4 lame duck president/administration etc** 任期即將結束的總統/政府等 —**lameness** *n*

lame² *v* [一般用被動態] 使〔人或動物〕跛[瘸]; 使殘廢

landscape¹ *n* **1**〔陸上的〕風景, 景致, 景色 **2** 風景照, 風景畫 **3** 風景繪畫, 山水繪畫 **4 the political/intellectual etc landscape** 政治/知識界的概貌 **5** 橫向格式

landscape² *v* [常用被動態] 用園藝美化〔公園、花園等〕

lane *n* **1**〔尤指鄉間〕小道; 小巷; 胡同; 里弄 **2** 車道, 行車線 **3** …巷〔用於路名〕 **4** 跑道; 泳道 **5**〔船舶或飛機的〕航線, 航道

launch¹ *v* **1** ►**START STH** 開始做某事◄ 發動, 發起, 開始進行 **2** ►**PRODUCT** 產品◄ 把〔新產品、新書等〕投放市場, 出版, 發行 **3** ►**BOAT** 船◄ 將〔船或艦〕下水 **4** ►**SKY/SPACE** 天空/太空◄ 發射〔武器或太空船〕 **5 launch yourself forwards/up/from etc**〔用力〕撲向前/躍起/從…撲過去等

launch into sth *phr v* 突然開始〔描述、敍述、抨擊〕

launch out *phr v* 開始, 着手〔新事情, 尤指有風險的事〕

launch[2] *n* **1**〔新產品的〕投放市場,〔新書的〕發行 **2** 遊艇, 汽艇

layer[1] *n* **1**〔覆蓋〕層 **2**〔物質〕層 **3**〔組織、系統、思想等的〕層次 **4 multi-layered/single-layered etc** 多/單層等的

layer[2] *v* **1** 鋪一層…; 把…堆成層 **2** 把〔頭髮〕分層剪短

leaflet[1] *n* 散頁印刷品; 傳單; 廣告單張

leaflet[2] *v* (向…) 散發傳單

leak[1] *v* **1** (使) 漏; (使) 滲 **2**〔氣體、液體〕漏出 **3** 泄露〔祕密給報紙、電視台等〕 **4 leak like a sieve** 漏得很厲害

leak out *phr v* 泄露

leak[2] *n* **1** 漏洞, 裂縫 **2 a gas/oil/water leak** 煤氣/油/水的泄漏 **3**〔向報紙、電視台等〕透露祕密 **4 take/have a leak** 小便, 撒尿

legal *adj* **1** 法律允許的, 合法的, 法定的 **2** (有關) 法律的 **3 take legal action/proceedings** 採取法律行動/提起法律訴訟 — 反義詞 ILLEGAL

legend *n* **1** 傳説, 傳奇 (故事) **2** 民間傳説 **3**〔某領域中的〕傳奇式人物 **4 a)**〔牌匾等上的〕鐫刻文字, 銘文 **b)**〔圖片、地圖等的〕文字説明, 圖例

liable *adj* **1 be liable to do sth** 易於〔做某事〕, 傾向於…的 **2** 有賠償責任的 **3** 易出問題的, 易得病的 **4** 可能受處罰的, 可能承擔有法律義務的

liberal[1] *adj* **1** 心胸寬闊的, 尊重別人想法[意見; 感情]的 **2** (思想) 開放的, 支持[主張]變革的 **3** 豐富的, 充足的 **4** 慷慨大方的 **5** 不拘一格的, 不拘泥字面的 **6 liberal education** 通才教育

liberal[2] *n* 開明人士

Liberal[3] *n*〔英國前〕自由黨支持者[黨員], 自由民主黨支持者[黨員] —**Liberal** *adj*

licence【英】, **license**【美】 *n* **1 ►DOCUMENT 文件◄** 許可證, 執照, 證書 **2 ►FREEDOM 自由◄ a)**〔行動、言論的〕自由, 不受拘束 **b)** 放縱, 淫蕩 **3 artistic/poetic licence** 藝術/詩的破格[奔放], 打破常規 **4 ►RIGHT TO DO STH 做某事的權利◄** 許可, 特許 **5 under licence** 獲許可〔出售、生產等〕

linguist *n* **1** 研究並通曉幾種外語的人 **2** 語言學家

link[1] *v* **1 be linked** 有聯繫, 有關聯 **2** 聯繫〔電腦、廣播系統等, 使電子信息能在它們之間傳遞〕, 連接 **3** 把〔兩個或以上的事物〕聯繫在一起 **4**〔某事或情況〕和…有聯繫; 由…引起 **5** 連接〔另一處〕 **6 link arms** 挽着手臂

link up *phr v* 連接; 聯繫

link[2] *n* **1**〔兩種事物或思想的因果〕關聯 **2**〔人、國家、組織等之間的〕聯繫, 關係 **3**〔鏈的〕一環 **4 rail/road/telephone link** 鐵路/公路/電話線連接 **5 link in the chain** 過程中的一環 **6 weak link**〔計劃中的〕薄弱環節;〔一隊中〕最弱的隊員

literacy *n* **1** 有讀寫能力, 有文化 **2 computer literacy** 使用電腦的能力

literature *n* **1** 文學 (作品) **2**〔作為學科研究的〕文學 **3**〔某一學科的〕著述, 文獻資料 **4**〔促銷商品或提供信息的〕印刷品; 宣傳品

litter[1] *n* **1**〔扔在公共場所的〕垃圾, 廢棄物 **2** 一窩〔小狗、小貓等〕 **3 cat/kitty litter** 貓沙〔特殊物質的顆粒, 放在容器中供貓便溺用〕 **4**〔家畜睡覺用的〕褥草 **5 a litter of** 雜亂的一堆 **6**〔舊時載重要人物的〕轎

litter[2] *v* **1** 又作 **litter up**〔在某處〕亂丟東西; 把〔某處〕弄亂 **2 be littered with** 充滿〔某物〕 **3**〔在公共場所〕亂扔〔廢棄物〕 **4**〔狗、貓等動物〕產仔

locality *n* 地區

locate *v* **1** 找出〔某物〕的準確位置 **2 be located in/by/near etc** 位於[坐落在]…/…邊上/…附近等 **3** 將〔公司等〕設立〔在某處〕

lodge[1] *v* **1 ►STAY SOMEWHERE 暫住在某處◄** 租住, 寄宿, 寄住 **2 lodge a complaint/protest/appeal etc** 提出控告/抗議/上訴等 **3 ►BE STUCK 卡住◄** [一般用被動態] (使) 卡住, (使) 固定在…裡 **4 ►PUT SB SOMEWHERE 安排某人住在某處◄** 供…寄住; 給…找寄住處〔通常要付錢〕 **5 ►IN A SAFE PLACE 在安全的地方◄** 把〔某物〕存放〔在正規的地方〕

lodge[2] *n* **1**〔鄉村大宅院中的〕小屋, 側屋 **2**〔建築物的〕門房, 管理員室 **3**〔鄉村或山間供獵人、滑雪者等使用的〕小屋, 小舍 **4 a)** 共濟會的分會 **b)** 共濟會分會集會處 **5**〔河狸的〕洞穴 **6** 山區旅館 **7**〔印第安人居住的〕棚屋

logic *n* **1** 邏輯學 **2** 推理方法 **3** 合乎邏輯的道理; 合理的想法 **4**〔電腦的〕邏輯

loyal *adj*〔對…〕忠貞的, 忠實的, 忠誠的 —**loyally** *adv*

luxurious *adj* 奢華的, 華麗的, 舒適的 —**luxuriously** *adv* —**luxuriousness** *n*

M, m

magnet *n* **1** 磁鐵; 磁石, 吸鐵石 **2** 有吸引力的人[地方]

magnify *v* **1** 放大 **2** 誇張, 誇大 **3** 使〔問題〕加重 **4** 讚美〔上帝〕 —**magnifier** *n*

maiden[1] *n* 少女; 姑娘

maiden[2] *adj* **1 maiden flight/voyage**〔飛機或船的〕首次飛行/航行 **2 maiden speech**〔在議會中的〕首次演説

maintain *v* **1 ►MAKE STH CONTINUE 使某事繼續◄** 保持; 維持 **2 ►LEVEL/RATE 水平/速度◄** 保持〔水平或速度〕 **3 ►MACHINE/BUILDING 機器/建築物◄** 維修; 保養〔機器、建築物等〕 **4 maintain your silence/opposition etc** 保持沉默/堅持反對意見等 **5 ►SAY 説◄** 斷言〔某事〕屬實; 堅持説… **6 ►MONEY/FOOD 金錢/食物◄** 供養; 贍養 **7 maintain life** 維持〔動植物等的〕生命

majesty *n* **1 Your/Her/His Majesty** 陛下〔對國王或女王的稱呼〕 **2** 雄偉, 壯麗; 莊嚴; 崇高

majority *n* **1** 多數, 大多數〔人或物〕 **2 be in the majority** 構成多數, 佔多數 **3** 超過的票數〔選舉中獲勝黨或個人所得票數與其他政黨或候選人所得票數之間的差額〕 **4** 成年; 法定年齡 — 反義詞 MINORITY

manifest[1] *v* **1** 顯示, 表明, 表露〔感情、態度等〕 **2 manifest itself** 顯現, 顯露

manifest[2] *adj* 顯而易見的, 明顯的 —**manifestly** *adv*

manual[1] *adj* **1** 手的; 手工的 **2** 用手操作的; 用手做

的; 靠人工的 —**manually** *adv*

manual² *n* **1**〔機器的〕説明書, 使用手冊 **2 on manual**〔機器〕手工操作的, 手動的

manufacture¹ *v* **1**〔用機器大量〕製造, 生產 **2**〔人體〕生成 **3** 編造〔虛假情況、藉口等〕

manufacture² *n* **1**〔大量的商品〕製造 **2 manufactures**〔用機器大批量製造的〕商品

manuscript *n* **1** 手稿; 底稿 **2** 手抄本, 手寫本

margin *n* **1** 頁邊的空白, 頁邊, 白邊 **2**〔選舉或競賽中勝方或負方在選票、時間或距離上的〕差數 **3**〔成本與售價間的〕差額, 利潤, 賺頭 **4 on the margin(s)** 處於〔社會、集團或活動〕的邊緣 **5 margin of error** 誤差幅度, 誤差值 **6**〔森林、島嶼或其他區域的〕邊緣

marine *adj* **1** 海洋的 **2** 船舶的; 海軍的

marvel¹ *v*〔尤指對某人的行為〕感到驚訝, 欽佩

marvel² *n* 十分有用[靈巧]的物[人]

massive *adj* **1** 大而重的, 厚重的 **2** 巨大的; 強大的, 強烈的; 極具破壞力的

material¹ *n* **1** 料子, 衣料, 布料 **2** 材料, 原料〈如木材、塑料、金屬等〉 **3** 又作 **materials** 材料 **4**〔用於書本、電影等中的〕素材 **5 officer material/executive material etc** 當軍官/管理人員等的材料

material² *adj* **1** 物質上的, 非精神上的 **2** 物質的, 實體的, 有形的 **3** 重要的, 需予以考慮的 **4** 重大並有顯著影響的

mature¹ *adj* **1 ►SENSIBLE 理智的◄**〔小孩或年輕人舉止〕成熟的, 理智的, 明白事理的 — 反義詞 IMMATURE **2 ►FULLY GROWN 成年的◄** 成年的; 成熟的 **3 ►WINE/CHEESE ETC 酒/乾酪等◄** 製成的; 已釀成的 **4 ►OLDER 較老的◄** 不再年輕的; 中年的〔禮貌或幽默的說法〕 **5 ►NOVEL/PAINTING ETC 小說/油畫等◄** 成熟的; 技巧嫻熟的; 老練的 **6 on mature reflection/consideration** 經過仔細考慮 **7 ►FINANCIAL 金融的◄**〔債券或保單〕到期應付的 —**maturely** *adv*

mature² *v* **matured, maturing 1** 變成熟; 完全長成 **2** 變理智;〔舉止〕變成熟 **3**(使)〔乾酪、葡萄酒、威士忌酒等〕製成, (使) 釀成; (使) 釀熟 **4**〔債券或保單〕到期

maximum¹ *adj* 最大量的, 最大限度的, 最大值的

maximum² *n*〔可能或可允許的〕最大量, 最大值

medium¹ *adj* **1**〔大小、高矮等〕中等的; 中號的 **2 medium brown/blue etc** 中等色調的褐色/藍色等

medium² *n* **1** 傳播媒介〈如報紙、電視等〉 **2**〔尤指作家或藝術家表達思想的〕方法, 手段; 藝術形式 **3 medium of instruction** 教學語言 **4 medium of exchange** 交換媒介〔指金錢或其他的支付方法〕 **5** 培養基 **6** 媒質, 媒介物; 傳導體

medium³ *n* 靈媒, 巫師, 招魂者

merchandise¹ *n* 商品〔尤指在商店陳列供出售的貨物〕

merchandise² *v*〔用廣告等方式〕推銷〔商品或服務〕

mercy *n* **1**〔對自己有權力支配的人所表示的〕仁慈, 寬容, 憐憫 **2 it's a mercy** 幸運的是, 幸虧〔用於表示更糟的情況得以避免總算是幸運〕 **3 at the mercy of** 任憑…的擺佈〔而無力保護自己〕 **4 leave sb to sb's (tender) mercies** 任憑某人受他人折磨[擺佈] **5 be thankful/grateful for small mercies** 慶幸一種壞的情況還沒有到更糟糕的地步 **6 mercy flight/mission etc** 救援飛行/任務等 **7 throw yourself on sb's mercy** 懇求某人幫忙[寬恕]

merit¹ *n* **1** 長處, 優點 — 反義詞 DEMERIT **2**〔使某物受讚揚或讚美的〕優秀品質 **3 judge sth on its (own) merits** 就某物自身的品質對其作出判斷〔不考慮其他因素〕

merit² *v* 應得到, 值得

microscope *n* **1** 顯微鏡 **2 put sth under the microscope** 認真仔細地檢查某物

might¹ *modal verb* **1** 也許, 可能, 大概 **2** 也許, 可能; 可以〔may 的過去式〕 **3** 可以〔用於提建議〕 **4 a)** 可以〔用於禮貌地請求允許做某事〕 **b) might I say/ask/add etc** 我可否說/問/補充等〔用於禮貌地提供更多信息、問問題、插話等〕 **5** 應該, 本該〔表示説話人因某人還沒做某事而生氣或驚奇〕 **6 I might have known/guessed etc** 我早該知道/猜到等〔表示對某種情況不感到吃驚〕 **7 might well** 很可能, 極有可能 **8 might (just) as well** 最好還是…, 還是…為好, 倒不如… **9 might...but...** 也許…但是…〔表示儘管某人所說是事實, 但與其似乎非常不同的事也真實〕 **10** 能, 會〔以表示原因〕 **11**〔用於客氣地詢問〕

might² *n* **1** 力量; 威力; 權力 **2 might is right**【英】, **might makes right**【美】強權就是公理

migrate *v* **1**〔鳥或獸〕遷徙, 移棲 **2**〔尤指為找工作〕移居; 遷移

mimic¹ *v* **1** 模仿〔某人的言行, 尤指為了逗樂〕, 學…的樣子 **2** 學…的樣子; 模擬 **3**〔動物為保護自己〕偽裝成〔另一事物〕—**mimicry** *n*

mimic² *n* **1**〔模仿名人言行的〕喜劇演員, 小丑 **2** 善於模仿的人[動物]

mimic³ *adj* **1** 擬態的 **2** 模仿的, 模擬的

minor¹ *adj* **1**〔尤指與其他事物相比〕小的; 不很重要的; 不很嚴重的 — 反義詞 MAJOR **2**〔音樂〕小調的; 小音階的

minor² *n* **1** 未成年人 **2**〔大學中的〕副修科目 **3 the minors**〔美國棒球的〕小聯盟; 小企業, 小公司; 小的機構[組織]

minor³ *v*

minor in sth *phr v*〔大學裡〕副修〔某課程〕— 反義詞 MAJOR³

minute¹ *n* **1 ►TIME 時間◄** 分, 分鐘 **2 at the last minute** 在最後一刻; 在緊要關頭 **3 by the minute** 又作 **every minute, minute by minute** 每過一分鐘; 越來越 **4 love/enjoy/hate etc every minute of** 特別喜歡/盡情享受/極其憎恨〔某物〕 **5 within minutes** 片刻後, 轉瞬間 **6 ►MEETING 會議◄ minutes** 會議記錄, 議事錄 **7 ►NOTE ON A REPORT 報告記錄◄** 簡短的批示; 備忘錄 **8 ►MATHEMATICS 數學◄** 分〔角的計量單位, 即六十分之一度〕 **9 a minute** 一會兒, 片刻 **10 in a minute** 很快, 立刻, 馬上 **11 wait a minute/just a minute/hold on a minute/hang on a minute a)** 稍等片刻 **b)** 且慢 **12 any minute now** 隨時, 馬上, 在任何時刻 **13 have you got a minute?**【英】, **do you have a minute?**【美】能耽誤你一點時間嗎? **14 one minute a)** 一會兒〔表示情況突然變化〕 **b)** 稍等一會兒 **15 the minute sb does sth** 某人一做某事就… **16 the next**

minute 馬上, 立刻, 緊接着 **17 not think/believe etc for one minute** 一點也不認為/相信等 **18 this minute** 立刻, 馬上〔用於叫人馬上做某事, 常帶有怒意〕

minute² *adj* **1** 極小的 **2** 非常仔細的, 極詳細的 —**minutely** *adv* —**minuteness** *n*

minute³ *v* 將…記入議事錄[會議記錄]

miracle *n* **1** 意外的奇事, 不可思議的事; 奇跡 **2**〔神創造的〕奇跡 **3 miracle cure/drug** 有奇效的療法/藥物 **4 work/perform miracles** 創造奇跡; 有奇效 **5 a miracle of engineering/design etc** 工程學/設計等上的奇跡

mirror¹ *n* **1** 鏡子 **2 a mirror of** 清楚地反映…的東西

mirror² *v* **1** 反映〔情況、事實、信念等〕 **2** 與…十分相似; 與…完全一樣

miserable *adj* **1** 極不愉快的, 痛苦的 **2** 總是不高興[不滿意]的; 總是抱怨的 **3** 令人不愉快的; 令人不舒服的, 使人難受的 **4** 質量極差的; 數量極少的 —**miserably** *adv*

mission *n* **1 ►AIRFORCE/ARMY ETC 空軍/陸軍等◄** 任務, 使命 **2 ►GOVERNMENT/GROUP 政府/團體◄** 代表團, 工作團; 外交使團 **3 ►JOB 工作◄**〔尤指給予被派遣人員的〕重要任務, 使命 **4 ►DUTY 職責◄** 職責, 天職; 使命 **5 ►RELIGION 宗教◄ a)**〔在國外進行基督教的〕傳教, 佈道 **b)** 佈道所用的建築物 **6 mission accomplished** 任務已完成

mock¹ *v* **1** 嘲笑, 譏笑, 嘲弄;〔以模仿〕取笑 **2** 使無效; 使失敗, 挫敗 —**mocker** *n* —**mockingly** *adv*

mock sth ↔ **up** *phr v*〔照原尺寸〕模仿, 仿製

mock² *adj* **1** 非真實的; 模擬的 **2 mock surprise/horror/indignation etc** 假裝的吃驚/害怕/憤怒等〔尤指開玩笑〕 **3 mock Tudor/Georgian** 仿都鐸/喬治王朝建築風格的

mock³ *n* **1 mocks** 模擬考試 **2 make mock of** 嘲笑; 嘲弄

mode *n* **1** 方式, 方法, 做法 **2**〔機器的〕運行方式; 狀態, 模式 **3 be in work mode/holiday mode etc** 思想上處於工作狀態/休假狀態等 **4 be the mode** 流行, 時髦 **5**〔音樂的〕調式

moderate¹ *adj* **1** 中等的, 適度的 **2** 不極端的, 溫和的; 穩健的 **3** 有節制的, 不過分的

moderate² *v* **1**（使）和緩;（使）減輕; 節制, 克制 **2** 做調解人; 做考試監督員; 做〔比賽等〕主持人

moderate³ *n* 持溫和觀點的人, 溫和派人士

modest *adj* **1** 謙虛的, 謙遜的, 謙恭的 **2** 不太大的; 不很貴的 **3** 羞怯的, 靦腆的; 忸怩的 **4**〔衣服〕莊重的 —**modestly** *adv*

modify *v* **1**〔略微地〕修改, 更改; 改進, 改造 **2**〔形容詞、副詞等〕修飾〔另一詞〕

moist *adj* 潮濕的, 微濕的, 濕潤的 —**moistness** *n*

monitor¹ *v* **1** 監視; 監測, 檢測; 監督 **2** 監聽

monitor² *n* **1** 監視器 **2**〔電腦的〕顯示器 **3**〔人體內部〕檢測監視儀, 監護儀 **4**〔學校的〕班長, 級長, 值勤生 **5**〔外國電台〕監聽員

monstrous *adj* **1** 極端錯誤的; 非常不道德的; 極不公正的 **2** 巨大而醜陋的 —**monstrously** *adv*

monument *n* **1** 紀念碑, 紀念塔, 紀念館 **2** 遺跡, 遺址, 名勝古跡 **3 be a monument to** 是…的例證[見證]

morality *n* **1** 道德; 道德觀 **2** 道德性; 道義性; 正當性 **3** 道德體系; 道德規範 — 反義詞 IMMORALITY

motion¹ *n* **1 ►MOVEMENT 移動◄** 動; 運動; 移動 **2 ►MOVING YOUR HEAD OR HAND 動頭或手◄**〔手或頭的〕示意動作; 手勢; 姿勢 **3 ►SUGGESTION AT A MEETING 會議上的建議◄** 提議, 動議 **4 in motion** 運動中的 **5 go through the motions** 裝樣子, 做姿態, 敷衍塞責地做 **6 set/put sth in motion** 使某事開始 **7 in slow motion** 以慢動作, 慢速地 **8 ►BOWELS 腸◄** 排便〔此詞尤為醫護人員所用〕

motion² *v* 用手勢示意

motivate *v* **1** 激發, 激勵, 促動 **2** [常用被動態] 為…的動機

motto *n* **1** 箴言, 格言, 座右銘 **2**〔聖誕彩包爆竹中印在紙片上的〕俏皮話, 妙語

mount¹ *v* **1 ►INCREASE 增加◄** 漸漸增加, 增長〔尤指朝着使情況更糟的方向〕 **2 mount a campaign/attack/exhibition etc** 發起戰役/發動進攻/舉辦展覽等 **3 ►HORSE/BICYCLE 馬/自行車◄** 騎上, 跨上 — 反義詞 DISMOUNT **4 ►CLIMB STAIRS 爬樓梯◄** 走上, 爬上, 登上 **5 be mounted to/on** 被固定在…上 **6 ►PICTURE 圖畫◄** 裱貼〔圖畫或照片〕 **7 ►SEX 性◄**〔雄性動物〕趴到〔雌性動物〕身上交配 **8 mount guard (over)** 擔任警衛; 站崗

mount up *phr v*〔規模或數量〕逐漸增加, 增長

mount² *n* **1 Mount** …山, …峯〔山名的一部分〕 **2** 被乘騎的馬, 坐騎 **3** 山, 山岳

muffle *v* [一般用被動態] **1** 使〔聲音〕減弱[低沉] **2** 又作 **muffle up**〔用保暖的衣物〕裹住

multiply *v* **1**（使）大大增加 **2** 乘, 乘以 **3** 繁殖

murmur¹ *v* **1** 小聲說, 咕噥 **2**〔向朋友和同事〕私下抱怨, 發牢騷 **3** 發出輕柔的聲音 —**murmuring** *n*

murmur² *n* **1** 輕輕的談話聲, 低語聲 **2**〔尤指向朋友和同事的〕私下的抱怨, 怨言, 咕噥 **3**〔溪流、風等發出的〕細聲, 輕柔的聲音 **4**〔心臟的〕雜音

muscular *adj* **1** 肌肉發達的; 強壯的 **2** 肌肉的; 影響肌肉的 —**muscularly** *adv* —**muscularity** *n*

mushroom¹ *n* 蘑菇

mushroom² *v* **1** 快速成長; 迅速發展 **2**〔在空中〕呈蘑菇狀擴散

mute¹ *adj* **1** 緘默的, 不說話的; 拒絕說話的 **2** 不會說話的, 啞的 **3**〔語音中〕不發音的 —**mutely** *adv* —**muteness** *n*

mute² *v* **1** 使〔聲音〕減弱 **2** 使〔樂器〕聽起來柔和些, 使〔樂器聲音〕弱化

mute³ *n* **1**〔樂器上的〕弱音器 **2** 啞巴

mutual *adj* **1 mutual respect/hatred/support** 相互尊重/仇恨/支持 **2 mutual friend/interest** 共同的朋友/興趣 **3 mutual admiration society** 相互吹捧 —**mutuality** *n*

myth *n* **1**〔許多人相信但不真實的〕荒誕傳說, 無根據的觀念 **2**〔古代的〕神話 **3** 神話故事

N, n

naive *adj* 無經驗的, 幼稚的, 天真的 —**naively** *adv* —**naivety** 又作 **naiveté** *n*

naked *adj* **1** 裸體的, 赤條條的 **2 with the naked eye** 憑肉眼 **3 naked sword/light/flame etc** 無鞘劍/無罩燈/沒有遮擋的火焰 **4 naked truth/self-interest/aggression etc** 明擺着的事實/明顯的私利/赤裸裸的侵略 —**nakedly** *adv* —**nakedness** *n*

narrate *v* 講〔故事〕; 敍述, 描述

naughty *adj* **1**〔孩子〕淘氣的, 頑皮的; 沒有規矩的; 不聽話的 **2**〔開玩笑地説成年人〕不聽話的; 不守規矩的 **3 naughty jokes/magazines/pictures etc** 黃色笑話/雜誌/圖片等 —**naughtily** *adv* —**naughtiness** *n*

navigable *adj*〔水域〕可通航的, 可航行的 —**navigability** *n*

navigation *n* **1** 航行學; 航海術; 航空術 **2** 航行; 航海; 航空 **3**〔船或飛機的〕航行 —**navigational** *adj*

neglect[1] *v* **1** 疏於照料; 疏忽 **2** 忽視; 忽略 **3 neglect to do sth** 沒有做某事

neglect[2] *n* **1** 忽視; 疏忽; 忽略 **2** 被忽略的狀況

negotiate *v* **1**〔尤指商業或政治〕談判, 協商 **2** 順利通過 —**negotiator** *n*

nerve[1] *n* **1 ►FEELINGS 情緒◄ nerves** 焦慮; 緊張 **2 get on sb's nerves** 煩擾某人, 使人心煩不安 **3 ►COURAGE 勇氣◄** 鎮定; 勇氣; 意志力 **4 have a nerve** 厚顏無恥; 放肆 **5 ►BODY PART 身體部分◄** 神經 **6 hit/touch a raw nerve**〔尤指無心地〕觸到敏感話題; 觸到痛處

nerve[2] *v* **nerve yourself** 鼓起勇氣

nightmare *n* **1** 惡夢, 夢魘 **2** 不愉快的[可怕的]經歷 **3** 可能發生的恐怖事件 —**nightmarish** *adj*

nobility *n* **1 the nobility** 貴族(階層) **2** 崇高, 高貴

notable *adj* 顯要的; 顯著的; 值得注意的

notify *v*〔正式地〕通知, 告知

notorious *adj* 臭名遠揚的, 聲名狼藉的 —**notoriously** *adv*

novelty *n* **1** 新奇的事物 **2** 新穎; 新奇性 **3** 新穎小巧而價廉的物品

novice *n* **1** 新手, 生手; 初學者 **2** 見習修道士; 見習修女

nuisance *n* **1** 討厭或麻煩的人[事物, 情況] **2** 妨害公共利益的行為 **3 nuisance value** 給對手造成麻煩的價值, 阻擾[騷擾]作用

numerous *adj* 許多的, 很多的

nutrition *n* 營養(作用); 滋養 —**nutritional** *adj* —**nutritionally** *adv*

O, o

obedient *adj* **1** 服從的, 順從的, 聽話的 **2 your obedient servant** 您恭順的僕人〔正式信尾用語〕— 反義詞 DISOBEDIENT —**obediently** *adv*

objection *n* **1** 反對, 不贊成; 異議 **2** 反對的原因

oblige *v* **1** [一般用被動態] 使〔某人〕非做…不可, 迫使; 責成 **2** 幫忙; 答應〔某人的〕請求 **3 I'd be obliged if** 多謝〔請別人幫忙時的客氣話〕 **4 (I'm) much obliged (to you)**(我)非常感謝(你)〔用於有禮貌地向某人致謝〕

obscure[1] *adj* **1** 無名的; 微賤的 **2** 難理解的, 晦澀的 —**obscurely** *adv*

obscure[2] *v* **1** 搞混, 使難理解 **2** 遮蔽, 使朦朧; 使聽不清

observe *v* **1** 看到, 注意到 **2** 觀察, 監視, 觀測 **3** 遵守, 奉行〔法律、協議或習俗〕 **4** 評述, 評論, 説 **5 closely observed**〔戲劇、人物等〕與現實生活非常相似的, 逼真的

obstacle *n* **1** 障礙, 阻礙, 妨礙 **2** 障礙物

obstruct *v* **1** 阻塞, 堵塞〔道路、通道等〕 **2** 阻撓, 妨礙, 阻止

obtain *v* **1**〔尤指通過自身的努力、技能或工作等〕獲得, 得到 **2**〔情況、系統、規則等〕繼續存在, 通用

occurrence *n* **1** 發生的事, 事件 **2**〔事件的〕發生, 出現

odour【英】, **odor**【美】*n* **1** 氣味;〔尤指〕臭氣 **2 be in bad odour (with)** 不得寵; 不受(…的)青睞[歡迎]

officious *adj* 愛發號施令的, 好管閒事的 —**officiously** *adv* —**officiousness** *n*

offspring *n* **1**〔某人的〕子女, 子孫, 後代 **2**〔動物的〕崽

omit *v* **1** 省去, 略去, 刪去; 遺漏 **2 omit to do sth** 忘記做某事; 故意不做某事

opponent *n* **1**〔競爭、比賽等的〕對手, 敵手 **2** 反對者

oppress *v* [常用被動態] **1** 壓迫, 壓制 **2** 使壓抑, 使煩惱

optimistic *adj* **1** 樂觀的; 樂觀主義的 **2**〔對未來〕(過於)有信心的, (過分)樂觀的 —**optimistically** *adv* — 反義詞 PESSIMISTIC

orbit[1] *v* 環繞…軌道運行

orbit[2] *n* **1**〔環繞地球或太陽等運行的〕軌道 **2** 勢力範圍

organism *n* **1** 生物, 有機體 **2** 有機組織[體系]

originate *v* **1** 發源; 開始; 起因 **2** 創始; 創造; 發起

ornament[1] *n* **1** 裝飾品, 點綴物, 飾物, 擺設 **2** 裝飾, 點綴 **3 be an ornament to** 給…增加光彩[重要性、美麗]

ornament[2] *v* **be ornamented with** 用…裝飾, 裝飾有…

outweigh *v* 比…更重要; 比…更有價值

oversee *v* 監管, 監察, 監督

P, p

pacific *adj* **1** 平靜的, 安寧的; 愛好和平的 **2** 求和的, 和解的; 息事寧人的 —**pacifically** *adv*

painstaking *adj* 小心的; 費盡心思的; 精心的 —**painstakingly** *adj*

panic[1] *n* **1** 惶恐, 驚恐, 驚慌 **2** 大恐慌 **3** 忙亂, 慌亂 **4 press/push the panic button** 驚慌失措, 在緊急情況下慌亂行事 **5 panic stations** 緊急慌亂的狀態, 驚慌

panic² *v* (使)恐慌, (使)驚慌失措
paraphrase¹ *v*〔把書面或口頭的文字以簡短、清晰的方式〕意譯, 釋義; 改述
paraphrase² *n*〔對一段口頭或書面文字的〕意譯, 釋義; 改述
partial *adj* **1** 部分的, 不完全的 **2 be partial to sth** 特別喜歡某物, 偏愛某物 **3** 偏向一方的, 偏袒的, 不公平的 — 反義詞 IMPARTIAL
participate *v* 參加, 參與
particle *n* **1** 微粒, 粒子 **2 not a particle of truth/evidence etc** 沒有一點真實性/證據等 **3**〔語法中的〕質詞, 小品詞, 虛詞〈如連詞、介詞〉
passion *n* **1** 強烈的情感, 激情〔尤指性愛、憤怒或對某種思想、原則的信念〕 **2** 對…的強烈愛好, 熱愛 **3 the Passion** 耶穌的受難 —**passionless** *adj*
passive¹ *adj* **1** 被動的; 消極的; 順從的 **2**〔動詞或句子〕被動的 —**passively** *adv* —**passiveness, passivity** *n*
passive² *n* **the passive**〔動詞的〕被動式; 被動語態〈如句子 'The ball was kicked by the boy.' 中的 'was kicked'〉
pastime *n* 消遣; 娛樂
peculiar *adj* **1** 奇怪的; 異常的; 乖僻的 **2 be peculiar to**〔某人、某地方或某情況所〕特有的 **3**〔行為〕怪癖的; 有點瘋狂的 **4 feel peculiar** 感到有點不舒服
penalty *n* **1**〔因違反法律、規則或合約而受到的〕懲罰, 處罰 **2**〔行為或處境所造成的〕不利結果; 苦惱 **3**〔體育運動中對犯規者的〕處罰 **4**〔足球中因一方犯規而給予對方的〕罰球
pension¹ *n* 養老金; 退休金; 撫恤金
pension² *v*
pension sb/sth ↔ **off 1**〔尤指由於年老或疾病而〕發給〔某人〕養老金使其(提早)退休 **2**〔因太舊或不再有用而〕丟棄某物
performance *n* **1 a)** 表演; 演出; 演奏 **b)**〔戲劇、音樂等的〕表演, 演出 **2 a)** 履行, 執行 **b)**〔工作或活動中的〕表現 **3**〔汽車或機器的〕性能 **4 a) a performance** 費時費力的事 **b)**〔帶有憤怒叫喊的〕糟糕的行為[舉止]
periodical *n* 期刊, 雜誌
permanent¹ *adj* 長久的; 永久的, 永恆的 —**permanently** *adv*
permanent² *n*〔用化學劑的〕燙髮
permissible *adj*〔根據法律或規定〕允許的, 許可的, 准許的 —**permissibly** *adv*
persevere *v* 堅忍不拔, 堅持不懈 —**persevering** *adj*
persist *v* **1** 堅持; 執意 **2** 繼續存在[發生]
personality *n* **1** 個性; 性格 **2**〔使某人有趣、友好、受人喜愛的〕品質; 個性 **3**〔因常出現在報紙、電視等上而知名的〕名人 **4 personalities** 人身攻擊, 誹謗 **5**〔地方或事物的〕特色
personnel *n* **1**〔公司、組織或軍隊等中的〕全體人員; 員工, 全體職員 **2** 人事部門
perspective *n* **1**〔思考問題的〕角度; 觀點; 想法 **2**〔對事物的〕合理判斷, 正確認識 **3** 透視(畫)法; 透視效果, 透視感 **4**〔尤指由近而遠的〕景, 遠景
persuade *v* **1** 説服; 勸服 **2** 使相信, 使信服
pessimistic *adj* 悲觀的; 悲觀主義的 — 反義詞 OPTIMISTIC —**pessimistically** *adv*
phenomenon *n* **1**〔尤指因不理解而加以研究的〕現象 **2** 非凡的人[事物]; 奇才; 奇跡
philosophy *n* **1** 哲學 **2**〔以哲學為基礎的〕思想體系; 哲學體系 **3** 人生哲學; 生活[工作]準則
picturesque *adj* **1**〔某個地方〕美麗的, 風景如畫的 **2**〔語言〕生動的, 形象化的, 繪聲繪色的 **3**〔人的外表或行為〕奇特的, 獨特的, 不同尋常的 —**picturesquely** *adv* —**picturesqueness** *n*
plateau *n* **1** 高原 **2** 平穩時期, 穩定狀態; 停滯時期
plea *n* **1** 懇求, 請求 **2**〔法庭上所作的〕答辯, 辯護, 抗辯 **3** 藉口, 託詞, 口實
plight¹ *n*〔壞的、嚴重的或悲傷的〕境況, 困境, 苦境
plight² *v* **plight your troth** 答應結婚, 訂婚
plunge¹ *v* **1** (使)突然向前倒下[跌落] **2**〔價格、價值等〕暴跌, 驟降 **3**〔船〕猛烈地顛簸
plunge in *phr v*〔迅速而自信地〕開始談論[做]〔某事〕
plunge into *phr v* **1 plunge sth into sth** 把某物投[插, 刺]入某物中 **2 plunge sb/sth into sth** 使某人/某物陷入[遭受]某種情況 **3 plunge into sth** 突然[倉促]地開始做某事
plunge² *n* **1 take the plunge**〔尤指經過拖延或躊躇之後〕最終決定做某事, 決定冒險一試 **2 ►DOWNWARD MOVEMENT 向下移動◄** 突降; 俯衝 **3 ►INTO WATER 進入水中◄** 跳水;〔短時間的〕游泳 **4 ►DECREASE 降低◄**〔財產、股票等價值的〕暴跌, 驟降
polish¹ *v* 擦亮, 擦光 —**polisher** *n* —**polishing** *n*
polish sth ↔ **off** *phr v* 快速[輕易]做完〔工作等〕; 很快吃完〔食物〕
polish sb ↔ **off** *phr v* 殺死〔某人〕; 擊敗〔某人〕
polish sth ↔ **up** *phr v* **1**〔通過練習〕提高, 改善〔技術、能力〕 **2** 擦亮, 擦光
polish² *n* **1** 上光劑; 擦光劑; 上光蠟; 鞋油; 亮漆 **2** 優美, 高雅, 精緻, 完善 **3**〔因摩擦而產生的〕光亮的表面 **4** 擦亮, 磨光
popularity *n* 流行, 普及, 受歡迎; 聲望
possession *n* **1 ►STH YOU OWN 個人擁有的東西◄** 所有物; 財產, 財物 **2 ►STATE OF HAVING STH 擁有某物的狀態◄** 擁有, 持有, 佔有〔尤指貴重物品、資料等〕 **3 take possession of sth** 擁有[佔有]某物, 拿到某物 **4 ►DRUGS/GUN 毒品/槍支◄**〔毒品或槍支的〕私藏, 持有, 管有 **5 ►COUNTRY 國家◄** 領地, 屬地, 殖民地 **6 ►BALL 球◄**〔一些體育運動中對球的〕控制 **7 ►AMERICAN FOOTBALL 美式足球◄**〔進攻一方球隊的〕控球時間 **8 ►EVIL SPIRITS 魔鬼◄** 鬼魂附體, 着魔 **9 in (full) possession of your faculties/senses** 神智[頭腦](非常)清醒 **10 possession is nine-tenths of the law** 現實佔有, 敗一勝九〔實際佔有者在財產訴訟中十有九勝〕
postpone *v* 使〔事件、行動等〕延期, 延遲, 推遲 —**postponement** *n*
potent *adj* **1** 有效力的, 效力大的; 有影響力的 **2** 強有力的, 有威力的; 有説服力的 —**potently** *adv*
potential¹ *adj* 潛在的, 可能的

potential² *n* **1** 可能性, 潛在性 **2** 潛力, 潛能 **3** 電勢, 電位, 電壓
precaution *n* 預防措施
precedent *n* **1**〔可援引的〕先例; 判例 **2** 先例, 前例 **3** 慣例
preference *n* **1**〔兩者之中〕較喜歡的東西; 偏愛, 偏好 **2**〔一組東西中〕最喜歡的東西, 偏愛的事物 **3 give/show preference to** 偏愛…; 給予…優先權; 流露出對…的偏愛 **4 in preference to** 優先於…
prejudice¹ *n* **1** 偏見, 成見; 歧視 **2 to the prejudice of** 對…不利; 有損於 **3 without prejudice**〔對…〕沒有不利; 無損〔於〕
prejudice² *v* **1** 使有偏見, 使有成見; 使不公正地偏向 **2** 損害, 不利於
preliminary¹ *adj* 初步的; 預備的
preliminary² *n* **1** 初步行動, 準備工作 **2 the preliminaries** 預賽, 預試
prescription *n* **1** 處方, 藥方 **2**〔醫生開的〕處方藥; 治療方法 **3 on prescription** 憑處方的, 根據藥方的 **4** 解救方法, 訣竅 **5** 開處方, 開藥; 指示療法
presence *n* **1** 出席; 到場; 存在 — 反義詞 ABSENCE **2 in sb's presence** 在某人面前, 當着某人的面 **3** 儀態, 風度; 風采 **4**〔某國在外國的〕勢力;〔部隊或警察的〕駐紮; 存在 **5**〔看不見的〕靈氣, 鬼怪 **6 make your presence felt** 使周圍的人感到你的重要
presentation *n* **1** ►**PROOF 證據**◄ 提出; 出示 **2** ►**APPEARANCE 外貌**◄ 講述, 描繪; 外觀, 外貌 **3** ►**PRESENT PRIZE 頒獎**◄ 授予, 頒發 **4** ►**TALK 講話**◄ 報告;〔新產品的〕介紹;〔觀點的〕陳述, 說明 **5** ►**PERFORMANCE 表演**◄ 表演, 演出 **6** ►**BABY 嬰兒**◄〔胎兒的〕先露位置, 產位 —**presentational** *adj*
preserve¹ *v* **1** 維護, 保護; 保存〔使免受破壞〕 **2** 醃製; 保存〔食物〕 **3** 保持, 維持 —**preservable** *adj*
preserve² *n* **1** 果醬 **2**〔某羣體〕獨有[專有]的活動 **3** 私人漁獵區
press¹ *n* **1** ►**NEWS 新聞**◄ **a)** 又作 **the press**〔報紙、電台、電視台的〕記者們; 新聞界 **b)**〔報紙、電台、電視台的〕新聞報道 **2 get/be given a bad press** 受到輿論界的批評 **3 get/be given a good press** 受到輿論界的好評 **4** ►**PRINTING 印刷**◄ **a)** 出版社 **b)** 又作 **printing press** 印刷機 **5 trouser/flower/wine press** 褲子熨燙機/壓花器/葡萄榨汁機 **6** ►**PUSH 推**◄ 按, 揿 **7 go to press** 付印, 開印 **8** ►**CROWD 人羣**◄ 擁擠的人羣
press² *v* **1** ►**AGAINST STH 靠着某物**◄ 按; 壓 **2** ►**BUTTON 按鈕**◄ 按, 揿 **3** ►**CLOTHES 衣服**◄ 熨平〔衣物〕 **4** ►**CROWD 人羣**◄ 擁擠着移動, 擠着走 **5** ►**PERSUADE 勸說**◄ 極力勸說, 敦促, 催促 **6** ►**FOR JUICE 為取得果汁**◄ 擠取, 榨取 **7** ►**MAKE STH FLAT 使某物平整**◄ 把…壓平[壓扁] **8** ►**HOLD SB/STH CLOSE 抱緊某人/某物**◄ 使緊貼; 緊抱, 緊握 **9 press sb's hand/arm** 緊握某人的手/手臂〔表示友好、同情等〕 **10 press charges** 提出訴訟 **11** ►**CLAIM/STATEMENT 聲稱/聲明**◄ 堅持, 竭力要求 **12 press sb/sth into service**〔因意外問題而〕將就使用[暫用]某人/某物 **13 press sth home a)** 把某物推入[壓入, 按入, 塞入]適當的位置 **b)** 重複[強調]某事物〔以使人們記住它〕 **14 press home your advantage** 盡量利用優勢大獲成功 **15 press the flesh** 與許多人握手 **16** ►**RECORD 唱片**◄ 壓製〔唱片〕

press (sb) **for** sth *phr v* 敦促, 催促; 迫切要求; 努力取得

press on *phr v* **1** 又作 **press ahead** 繼續堅定做某事〔尤指工作〕 **2** 硬給, 強迫〔某人〕接受〔某物〕

prestige *n* **1** 威望, 聲望, 威信 **2 prestige car/position/neighbourhood etc** 有氣派的汽車/令人羨慕的職位/有氣派的住宅區
presume *v* **1**〔沒有證據地〕相信, 認為; 推測 **2** 認定, 視為, 推定〔尤用於法律〕 **3** 冒昧做某事, 放肆, 擅作主張 **4** 意味着, 以…為先決條件

presume on/upon sth *phr v* 濫用, 不正當地利用〔某種關係、某人的好心〕

prevail *v* **1**〔信念、風俗等〕盛行, 流行 **2**〔某人或其觀點〕獲勝; 佔優勢, 佔上風

prevail on/upon sb *phr v* 勸說, 說服〔某人〕

primitive¹ *adj* **1** 原始的, 遠古的 **2**〔人類或動植物〕原始的; 早期的 **3** 簡陋的, 粗糙的, 簡單的 **4** 過時的, 老式的, 簡陋的, 不舒適的 —**primitively** *adv* —**primitiveness** *n*
primitive² *n* **1** 原始人 **2** 原始派畫家 **3** 文藝復興時期以前的畫家[雕塑家]
principal¹ *adj* 最重要的, 首要的; 主要的
principal² *n* **1** 本金; 資本 **2**〔中小學的〕校長 **3**〔大學、學院或中小學的〕校長 **4**〔戲劇、音樂等演出的〕主角, 主要演員 **5**〔代理關係中的〕委託人, 本人, 被代理人
principle *n* **1** ►**MORAL RULE 道德準則**◄ **a)** 道德, 操守, 準則, 為人之道 **b)**〔行為的〕準則, 規範 **2** ►**RULES OF A PROCESS 某個過程的規則**◄ **a)** 原理 **b) principles** 基本原理 **3** ►**BELIEF 信念**◄ 原則; 信念 **4 man/woman of principle** 正直的男人/女人, 是非分明的人 **5 in principle a)** 按道理, 在理論上 **b)** 原則上, 基本上, 大體上
privacy *n* **1** 隱居; 獨處; 清靜 **2** 隱私
privilege *n* **1**〔特定個人或羣體的〕特權 **2**〔某些有權有勢者的〕特權, 特別待遇 **3** 榮幸 **4** 言行自由權,〔尤指〕議員〔言行不受懲罰〕權
proceed *v* **1** 繼續進行, 繼續做 **2 proceed to do sth** 接着做某事〔尤指令人討厭或驚奇的事〕 **3**〔向某一方向〕前進, 移動

proceed against sb *phr v* 起訴〔某人〕, 對〔某人〕提起訴訟

proceed from sth *phr v* [不用被動態] 源於某物, 出自

productivity *n* 生產力; 生產率, 生產效率
professional¹ *adj* **1** ►**JOB 工作**◄ 職業的, 專業的 **2** ►**WELL TRAINED 受過良好訓練的**◄ 專業的, 內行的 **3** ►**PAID 有報酬的**◄ 職業性的; 專業的; 非業餘的 **4** ►**TEAM/EVENT 球隊/比賽項目**◄ 由職業人員參加的; 職業性的 **5 professional person/man/woman etc** 專業人員; 專家 **6 a professional liar/complainer etc** 撒謊過多的人/抱怨過多的人等 **7 professional foul**〔體育運動中的〕故意犯規
professional² *n* **1** 把〔別人通常作為消遣的活動〕作為職業的人, 專門職業者; 職業選手 **2** 專業人士, 專家 **3** 技術精湛經驗豐富的人, 內行 **4 tennis/golf/**

swimming etc professional〔私人俱樂部的〕網球/高爾夫球/游泳等教練
proficiency *n* 熟練; 精通
profound *adj* **1**〔感情〕強烈的; 深切的; 嚴肅的 **2**〔影響〕深刻的, 極大的 **3** 知識淵博的; 見解深刻的 **4** 深的; 深處的 **5** 完全的 —**profoundly** *adv*
prohibit *v* **1**〔以法令、規則等〕禁止 **2** 使不可能, 阻止
project[1] *n* **1** 項目; 工程; 計劃; 規劃 **2**〔學校的〕課題, 研究項目 **3** 又作 **the projects** 低收入人羣住宅區
project[2] *v* **1** ►CALCULATE 計算◄ 預計, 推斷 **2** ►STICK OUT 突出◄ 凸出, 突出 **3** ►FILM 電影◄ 放映; 投射 **4** ►YOURSELF 你自己◄ 使別人對自己有某種看法, 使〔自己的特點〕呈現, 表現〔自己〕 **5** ►FEELING 感情◄ 想像〔他人〕具有〔本人的思想感情〕; 把〔自己的感情〕投射給別人 **6** ►PLAN 計劃◄ **be projected** 計劃, 預定 **7** ►THROW 扔, 投◄ 投擲, 發射 **8** ►PICTURE 圖畫◄ **a)** 作〔立體物的〕投影圖 **b)** 用投影法製作地圖 **9 project yourself into the future/past etc** 設想自己身處將來/過去等 **10 project your voice** 放開聲音〔使大廳或大房間的每個人都能聽見〕
prolong *v* **1** 延長〔感覺、活動等〕, 拉長, 拖長 **2 prolong the agony** 延長痛苦〔拖延告訴某人他很想知道的事情〕
prominent *adj* **1** 著名的; 卓越的, 傑出的; 重要的 **2** 突出的, 凸出的 **3 a prominent place/position** 突出的[顯著的, 顯眼的]位置
promising *adj* 大有希望的, 很有前途的 —**promisingly** *adv*
promote *v* **1** 促進, 增進 **2** [一般用被動態] 擢升, 提升, 晉升〔某人〕 — 反義詞 DEMOTE **3** 促銷, 推銷〔貨物〕; 推廣〔產品〕 **4** 負責籌辦, 主辦〔大型活動〕〈如音樂會或體育比賽〉 **5** 倡議; 提倡 **6 be promoted**〔運動隊〕被升級 — 反義詞 RELEGATE
prompt[1] *v* **1** 促使; 激勵 **2** 引起, 激起〔某人説或做某事〕 **3** 為〔説話者〕提示 **4** 為〔演員〕提示台詞
prompt[2] *adj* **1** 迅速的; 立刻的; 及時的 **2** 準時的 —**promptly** *adv* —**promptness** *n*
prompt[3] *adv* 準時
prompt[4] *n* **1**〔給演員的〕提詞, 提白 **2**〔電腦屏幕上的〕提示〔顯示電腦已完成某項操作, 準備進入下一項〕
propel *v* 推動; 推進; 驅動
property *n* **1** 所有物; 資產, 財產 **2** 房產; 地產; 房地產 **3**〔尤指律師或房地產經紀人所指的〕房產, 建築, 房子; 地產, 房地產 **4** 特性, 性質; 屬性 **5** 所有權; 財產權
prophet *n* **1**〔基督教、猶太教、伊斯蘭教的〕先知 **2 the Prophet**〔伊斯蘭教的創始人〕穆罕默德 **3 the Prophets** 猶太教諸先知〔其著作構成《聖經·舊約》的一部分〕,《先知書》的作者們;《先知書》 **4 prophet of doom/disaster** 預言厄運/災難的人 **5**〔新觀念、新思想的〕提倡者, 首倡者, 倡導者
prospect[1] *n* **1**〔成功的〕可能性; 機會 **2** 可能的事情, 很可能發生的事情; 前景 **3 prospects** 將來成功的機會, 前途, 前程 **4** 有前途的人[工作, 計劃] **5**〔尤指從高處看到的〕景象, 開闊的景觀, 景色 **6 in prospect** 即將可能發生的
prospect[2] *v* 勘探, 勘察〔以尋找金、銀、石油等礦藏〕
prosper *v* **1** 成功; 興旺, 發達, 繁榮 **2** 健康成長, 順利發展, 蓬勃發展 **3** 使成功, 使繁榮
proverb *n* 諺語, 格言
provision[1] *n* **1** 供應, 供給, 提供 **2 make provision for** 為…作好準備, 為…預先採取措施 **3 provisions**〔尤指為旅行儲備的〕糧食, 食物 **4**〔協議或法律中的〕規定, 條款, 條件
provision[2] *v*〔尤指為旅行〕提供大量的食品和其他供應品
publicity *n* **1**〔報紙、電視等對某人或某物的〕關注 **2** 宣傳, 推廣
punctual *adj* 準時的, 守時的, 如期的 —**punctually** *adv* —**punctuality** *n*
purity *n* 純; 純潔; 潔淨; 純正; 純粹 — 反義詞 IMPURITY
pursuit *n* **1** 追求 **2** 追趕, 追蹤 **3** 花很多時間做的事情; 工作; 嗜好, 消遣; 追求

Q, q

qualification *n* **1** 合格證明 **2** 資歷, 資格; 技能條件 **3** 限制; 限定性條件 **4** 取得〔參賽或就業〕資格
queue[1] *n* **1**〔人或車輛為等候而排的〕隊, 行列 **2** 隊列〔電腦必須按一定順序處理的一系列工作〕
queue[2] *v* 又作 **queue up** 排隊〔等候〕
quiz[1] *n* **1** 問答比賽, 智力競賽 **2** 小測驗, 小考
quiz[2] *v* 查問, 盤問

R, r

radiate *v* **1** 輻射〔光或熱〕;〔向四面八方〕發射 **2** 流露, 顯示〔感情、態度等〕 **3** 從中心散開
radius *n* **1**〔圓的〕半徑 **2 within a 10 mile/200 metre etc radius** 在 10 英里/200 米等的半徑範圍內 **3** 半徑〔線〕 **4** 橈骨
rage[1] *n* **1** 盛怒, 狂怒 **2 be (all) the rage** 流行, 時髦 **3 a rage for** 最時髦的東西, 時新式樣, 時尚
rage[2] *v* **1**〔戰鬥、爭論〕激烈進行,〔風暴〕狂吹 **2** 大怒, 發脾氣
ragged *adj* **1** ►CLOTHES 衣服◄ 又作 **raggedy** 破舊的 **2** ►PEOPLE 人◄ 衣衫襤褸的 **3** ►UNEVEN 不平的◄ 又作 **raggedy**〔邊緣〕參差不齊的 **4** ►TIRED 疲倦的◄ 疲乏的 **5** ►PERFORMANCE 表演◄〔表演、呼喊聲等〕不協調的, 不齊的 **6 be on the ragged edge** 極度疲憊; 惴惴不安 —**raggedly** *adv* —**raggedness** *n*
raid[1] *n* **1** 突襲, 襲擊 **2**〔警察進行的〕突擊搜查 **3**〔對銀行等處的〕搶劫, 打劫 **4**〔某公司〕大量購買另一家公司的股票以獲得其控制權的企圖
raid[2] *v* **1**〔警察〕突然搜查 **2** 武裝突襲 **3** 搶劫, 洗劫 —**raider** *n*
random *adj* **1** 隨意的, 任意的, 隨機的 **2 at ran-**

dom 任意地, 隨便地 —**randomly** *adv* —**randomness** *n*

rash¹ *adj* 急躁的, 魯莽的, 草率的 —**rashly** *adv* —**rashness** *n*

rash² *n* **1** 皮疹 **2 a rash of** 大量的〔一下子出現的令人不快的事件、變化等〕

ratio *n*〔兩個數量之間的〕比, 比例, 比率

raw¹ *adj* **1** ►**FOOD** 食品◄ 生的, 未燒煮的 **2** ►**INFORMATION** 信息◄ **raw data/statistics etc** 原始數據/統計數字等 **3** ►**SKIN** 皮膚◄ 又紅又痛的, 刺痛的 **4** ►**MATERIALS** 材料◄〔棉、糖、羊毛等〕天然狀態的, 未經過處理加工的 **5** ►**NOT EXPERIENCED** 沒有經驗的◄ 沒有經驗的, 未經過充足訓練的 **6 touch/hit a raw nerve**〔說話〕觸及某人痛處 **7 get a raw deal** 受到不公正的待遇 **8** ►**WEATHER** 天氣◄ 濕冷的 **9** ►**EMOTIONS/QUALITIES** 情感/素質◄ 強烈的, 自然的〔但未經充分琢磨或約束的〕 **10** ►**LANGUAGE** 語言◄ 下流的, 粗俗的 **11** ►**DESCRIPTIONS** 描述◄ 不加掩飾的 —**rawness** *n*

raw² *n* **1 life/nature in the raw** 未開化的生活/原始的自然狀態 **2 in the raw** 裸體的 **3 catch/touch sb on the raw**〔說話或做事〕觸及某人的痛處

react *v* **1** 反應 **2** 產生化學反應 **3**〔因服某種藥品、食用某種食物而〕產生不良反應

react against sth *phr v* 反抗

realistic *adj* **1** 現實的, 實際的 — 反義詞 UNREALISTIC **2**〔圖畫、模型、戲劇等〕逼真的, 栩栩如生的

reap *v* **1** 收割 **2 reap the benefit/reward/profit (of)** 受益/得到回報/獲利 —**reaper** *n*

rear¹ *n* **1 the rear** 後部, 後面, 背部 **2** 臀部 **3 bring up the rear** 殿後

rear² *v* **1** 養育, 撫養; 飼養 **2** 又作 **rear up**〔動物〕用後腿站起 **3 be reared on**〔小時候〕總是吃〔某種食物〕; 看〔某類書〕; 玩〔某類遊戲〕 **4 rear its ugly head**〔問題、困境〕冒頭, 出現

rear³ *adj* 後部的, 後面的

reassure *v* 使安心, 使放心, 安慰

recall¹ *v* **1** ►**REMEMBER STH** 記起某事◄ 回憶, 回想 **2** ►**PERSON** 人◄ 召回 **3** ►**PRODUCT** 產品◄ 收回〔有問題的產品〕 **4** ►**ON A COMPUTER** 在電腦上◄〔在電腦屏幕上〕重新調出〔信息〕, 檢索 **5** ►**BE SIMILAR TO** 相似◄〔由於酷似而〕使回憶起 —**recallable** *adj*

recall² *n* **1** 記憶力 **2** 召回 **3 beyond/past recall** 無法回憶的, 記不起來的

recede *v* **1**〔景物、聲音〕逐漸遠去以至消失 **2**〔記憶〕變模糊;〔感情〕逐漸淡漠;〔可能性〕逐漸消失 **3**〔水〕退, 退去 **4**〔頭髮〕從前額開始向後脫落 **5 receding chin** 向後收縮的下巴

recipe *n* **1** 烹飪法; 食譜 **2 be a recipe for** 是…的祕訣[竅門]; 很可能是造成…的原因

recital *n* **1** 演奏會; 演唱會; 朗誦會〔一般由一個人表演〕 **2**〔一連串事件的〕敍述, 口頭描述

reckon *v* **1** 認為, 以為 **2** 估算, 估計 **3** 認為〔某人或物〕是… **4** 計算

reckon sth ↔ **in** *phr v* 把…計算在內

reckon on sth *phr v* 指望

reckon sth ↔ **up** *phr v* 把…加起來, 計算…的總數

reckon with sb/sth *phr v* **1 not reckon with** 沒有考慮到 **2 sb/sth to be reckoned with** 必須認真考慮[對待]的某人/某事 **3 have sb/sth to reckon with** 必須對付某人/某事

reckon without sb/sth *phr v* 沒有考慮到; 對…不加考慮

recognize 又作 **-ise**【英】*v* **1** 認出, 認識; 辨認出 **2** 正式承認, 認可 **3 be recognized as** 得到承認, 被公認為 **4**〔往往勉強地〕接受, 承認; 明白 **5** 表揚; 表彰; 嘉獎 —**recognizable** *adj* —**recognizably** *adv*

recollect *v* 記起; 想起

recommend *v* **1** 勸告; 建議 **2** 推薦, 介紹 **3 sth has much/little/nothing to recommend it** 某物有很多/少有/沒有可取之處

recreation *n* 娛樂, 消遣 —**recreational** *adj*

reel¹ *n* **1 a)** 卷軸, 卷筒; 卷盤; 繞線輪 **b)** 一卷〔之量〕 **2**〔一部影片的〕一盤 **3** 里爾舞〔一種輕快的蘇格蘭或愛爾蘭舞〕; 里爾舞曲

reel² *v* **1** 又作 **reel back**〔尤指遭受打擊或震驚而〕站立不穩 **2** 震驚; 迷惑 **3**〔感覺〕暈眩, 天旋地轉 **4** 捲, 繞 **5** 蹣跚

reel sth ↔ **off** *phr v* 滔滔不絕地重複

reference *n* **1** 提及, 談到 **2** 查閱, 查看 **3 with reference to** 關於〔尤用於公函〕 **4 a)** 推薦信, 介紹信 **b)** 推薦人, 介紹人 **5 a)** 出處; 參考書目 **b)**〔書籍或地圖等中的〕參照號, 參照符號

refine *v* **1**〔慢慢地、微小地〕改進; 完善 **2** 淨化; 提煉

reflect *v* **1** 反射〔光、熱、聲或影像等〕 **2** 顯示, 反映 **3** 仔細思考; 表達意見

reflect on/upon *phr v* 給某人對…的評價造成〔尤指不利的〕影響

reform¹ *v* **1** 改進, 改革 **2** 改過, 改造

reform² *n* 改進, 改革

refreshing *adj* **1** 消除疲勞的, 提神的; 清涼的 **2** 令人耳目一新的 —**refreshingly** *adv*

refund¹ *n* 退款

refund² *v* 退還; 償還〔尤指因對所購貨物或服務不滿意〕

refuse¹ *v* **1** 拒絕〔做某事〕 **2** 不接受, 謝絕〔別人給的東西〕 **3** 拒絕把…給…

refuse² *n* 廢料, 廢物

register¹ *n* **1** ►**OFFICIAL LIST** 正式名單◄ 名冊 **2** ►**OFFICIAL BOOK** 正式的簿/冊◄ 登記簿 **3** ►**MUSIC** 音樂◄〔人聲或樂器的〕音域 **4** ►**LANGUAGE STYLE** 語言風格◄ 語域 **5** ►**BUSINESS MACHINE** 商用機器◄ 現金出納機 **6** ►**HEATING CONTROL** 加熱控制裝置◄〔加熱或冷卻系統中控制氣流的〕調風器, 節氣門

register² *v* **1** ►**ON A LIST** 記入名單◄ **a)** 記錄, 登記 **b)**〔旅館入住〕登記;〔課程〕註冊 **2** ►**SHOW A FEELING** 表示感情◄ 流露[表達]感情 **3** ►**STATE YOUR OPINION** 發表意見◄ 正式表達, 說明 **4** ►**REALIZE** 意識到◄ 受到注意; 注意到, 意識到 **5** ►**MEASUREMENT** 度量◄〔儀器〕顯示, 記錄 **6** ►**MAIL** 郵件◄ 以掛號寄送

reinforce *v* **1** 加強〔信心、信念、感覺等〕 **2** 加強, 加固〔建築、結構、衣物等〕 **3** 增援, 加強…的力量〔尤

指軍隊〕

reject¹ *v* **1 ▶OFFER/SUGGESTION 提議/建議◀** 拒絕〔接受〕 **2 ▶NOT EMPLOY 不雇用◀** 拒絕〔雇用、錄取〕 **3 ▶PRODUCT 產品◀** 〔因質量不好而〕廢棄 **4 ▶BELIEF 信念◀** 摒棄 **5 ▶ORGAN 器官◀** 排斥〔移植器官〕 **6 ▶NOT LOVED 不受關愛的◀** 冷落 **—rejection** *n*

reject² *n* 次品, 廢品

relate *v* **1** 把…聯繫起來, 證明…有關聯; 有關聯 **2** 講述 **3** 認同, 理解〔別人的問題、處境等〕

relate to sb/sth *phr v* **1** 有關, 涉及 **2** 與…直接相關 **3** 和睦相處; 認同 **4** 認同, 產生共鳴

relax *v* **1 ▶REST 休息◀** 〔使〕放鬆, 〔使〕輕鬆 **2 ▶LOOSEN 放鬆◀** 使〔身體部位〕鬆弛, 放鬆 **3 relax your hold/grip a)** 鬆開手 **b)** 放寬 **4 relax rules/controls/regulations etc** 放寬規定/控制/管制等 **5 relax your vigilance/concentration etc** 放鬆警惕/使注意力鬆懈等

release¹ *v* **1 ▶LET SB FREE 釋放某人◀** 釋放, 放出 **2 ▶STOP HOLDING 鬆手◀** 鬆開, 放開〔某物〕 **3 ▶MAKE PUBLIC 公佈◀** 公開發表, 發佈 **4 ▶MACHINERY 機器◀** 放開, 鬆開 **5 ▶FEELINGS 感情◀** 表達; 發泄 **6 ▶FILM/RECORD 電影/唱片◀** 發行; 上映 **7 ▶CHEMICAL 化學品◀** 釋放 **8 ▶FROM A DUTY 從職務中◀** 解除〔職務或工作〕; 解脱 **9 ▶WEAPON 武器◀** 發射, 投〔彈〕

release² *n* **1 ▶FROM PRISON 從獄中◀** 釋放 **2 ▶FEELINGS 感情◀ a)** 流露, 表達 **b)** 解脱, 擺脱 **3 ▶RECORD/FILM 唱片/電影◀** 新唱片; 新電影 **4 on (general) release** 〔電影、唱片等〕已經上映[發行] **5 ▶OFFICIAL STATEMENT 正式聲明◀** 〔發布的〕正式聲明 **6 ▶CHEMICALS 化學品◀** 釋放 **7 ▶MAKING STH AVAILABLE 供應某物◀** 發布, 發行 **8 ▶ON A MACHINE 在機器上◀** 釋放裝置, 鬆脱裝置

relevant *adj* 有關的, 切題的 — 反義詞 IRRELEVANT **—relevance** 又作 **relevancy** *n* **—relevantly** *adv*

reliable *adj* 可信賴的, 可靠的 — 反義詞 UNRELIABLE **—reliably** *adv* **—reliability** *n*

relief *n* **1 ▶COMFORT 安慰◀** 〔因恐懼、憂慮或痛苦的解除而感到的〕安慰 **2 ▶REDUCTION OF PAIN 減少疼痛◀** 〔疼痛或不快的〕減輕; 緩解 **3 ▶HELP 幫助◀** 救濟品 **4 ▶MONEY 金錢◀** 救濟金 **5 ▶REPLACE SB 替換某人◀** 接班[替班]的人 **6 the relief of** …的解圍, …的解救 **7 ▶DECORATION 裝飾◀** 浮雕, 浮雕品 **8 ▶STICKING OUT 凸出◀ in relief** 凸出 **9 stand out in bold/stark/sharp relief** 與周圍形成鮮明的反差; 非常突出 **10 light/comic relief** 〔嚴肅的電影、書或情景中作為調劑的〕輕鬆/滑稽場面 **11 ▶MAP 地圖◀ in relief** 用地勢圖表示

religious *adj* **1** 宗教的 **2** 篤信宗教的; 虔誠的

reluctant *adj* 勉強的, 不願的 **—reluctance** *n* **—reluctantly** *adv*

remedy¹ *n* **1** 補救〔法〕 **2** 藥物; 治療物 **3 beyond/past/without remedy** 不可救藥的; 無法挽回的

remedy² *v* 補救; 糾正; 改善

remind *v* **1** 使想起; 提醒 **2** 使〔某人〕想起 **3 Don't remind me** 別跟我提這事〔某人提到使你尷尬或不快的事情時詼諧的説法〕 **4 let me remind you/may I remind you** 讓我提醒你〔用於加強警告或批評的語氣〕

remind sb **of** sb/sth *phr v* 使〔某人〕想起〔相似之人或物〕

remote¹ *adj* **1** 遙遠的 **2** 偏僻的, 偏遠的 **3** 很不相同的 **4 a remote chance/possibility** 渺茫的希望/微乎其微的可能性 **5** 不友善的, 冷淡的 **6 not have the remotest idea** 一無所知 **—remoteness** *n*

remote² *n* 遙控

renovate *v* 修復; 裝修; 整修 **—renovation** *n*

replace *v* **1** 取代, 接替 **2** 替換, 調換 **3** 更換 **4** 把…放回原處 **—replaceable** *adj*

represent *v* **1 ▶SPEAK FOR SB 代表某人説話◀ a)** 代表 **b)** 表達〔某團體的情感、意見等〕 **2 be represented** 〔某團體〕由〔某人〕代表出席 **3 represent an improvement/an obstacle/a challenge etc** 應視為進步/障礙/挑戰等〔用於表示某事有某些特質〕 **4 ▶GOVERNMENT 政府◀** 當〔某地區〕的議員[其他立法機構的成員] **5 ▶A SIGN 標誌◀** 〔尤指在地圖上或平面圖裡〕象徵, 表示 **6 ▶SHOW STH 展現某物◀** 用圖畫[雕塑]表示, 描繪, 雕出 **7 represent yourself as** 佯稱自己是… **8 represent sb as** 把某人描寫為

reproach¹ *n* **1** 責備, 指責, 責怪 **2** 責備的話 **3 a reproach to** 恥辱; 不名譽

reproach² *v* **1** 責備, 怪責〔表示失望但不含怒氣〕 **2 reproach yourself** 自責

reputation *n* **1** 名譽, 名望 **2 live up to your reputation** 名不虛傳, 不負盛名 **3 live up to its reputation** 〔行為〕與名聲相符

rescue¹ *v* 拯救, 解救; 救援 **—rescuer** *n*

rescue² *n* 救援, 營救

resemblance *n* 〔尤指樣子〕相似, 類似

reservoir *n* **1** 水庫, 蓄水池 **2** 儲藏, 積蓄 **3** 儲液器

reside *v* 居住

reside in sth/sb *phr v* [不用被動態] **1** 存在於 **2** 又作 **reside within** sth/sb 〔權力、權利等〕屬於

resignation *n* **1** 辭職; 辭呈 **2** 聽從, 順從

resist *v* **1** 抗拒, 對抗 **2** 反抗, 抵抗 **3** 忍住〔擁有某東西的慾望〕, 按捺 **4** 抵擋; 保持原狀; 不受…的損害 **5 resist arrest** 拒捕 **—resistable** *adj*

resolution *n* **1 ▶DECISION 決定◀** 決議, 決定 **2 ▶SOLUTION 解決◀** 解決 **3 ▶DETERMINATION 決心◀** 堅決, 堅定, 決心 **4 ▶PROMISE 諾言◀** 〔做事的〕決心 **5 ▶CLEARNESS 清晰◀** 〔電視、照相機、顯微鏡的〕清晰度, 分辨率

response *n* **1** 反應 **2** 回答 **3** 〔宗教儀式上會眾同牧師〕輪流應答[吟唱]的祈禱文

responsible *adj* **1 ▶GUILTY 有罪的◀** 〔對事故、錯誤、罪行等〕負有責任的, 應承擔責任的 **2 ▶IN CHARGE OF 負責◀** 〔對某人、某事〕負責的 **3 responsible job/position/post** 要職 **4 ▶SENSIBLE 明智的◀** 可信賴的, 可靠的 — 反義詞 IRRESPONSIBLE **5 be responsible to** 對〔某人〕負責 **6 ▶CAUSE 起因◀** 作為原由的

restore *v* **1 ▶FORMER SITUATION 以前的狀態◀** 恢復 **2 restore hope/confidence/calm etc** 恢復

希望/信心/鎮靜等 **3 restore order** 恢復秩序 **4 ►REPAIR 修理◄** 修復 **5 ►GIVE STH BACK 歸還某物◄** 歸還 **6 restore sb's sight/hearing etc** 恢復某人的視力/聽力等 **7 ►BRING BACK A LAW 恢復法律◄** 恢復, 重新採用〔法律、税收、權利等〕 **8 restore sb to power/the throne** 使某人重新掌權/恢復王位

restrain *v* **1** 阻止, 抑制〔某人做有害或愚蠢的事〕 **2** 控制, 限制〔趨於增長的東西〕

restrict *v* **1 ►SIZE/AMOUNT/RANGE 體積/數量/範圍◄** 限制; 控制 **2 ►MOVEMENT/ACTIVITY 運動/活動◄** 約束, 限制〔行動、活動〕 **3 restrict yourself to** 限制自己…

result[1] *n* **1 ►HAPPENING BECAUSE OF STH 因為某事而發生◄** 結果, 後果 **2 ►SPORTS/ELECTIONS 體育運動/選舉◄** 〔比賽〕成績, 比分; 〔選舉的〕結果 **3 ►SCIENTIFIC TESTS 科學測試◄** 〔科學研究、測試的〕結果 **4 ►EXAMINATIONS 考試◄** 成績 **5 ►SUCCESS 成功◄ results** 成效 **6 ►BUSINESS 生意◄ results** 〔年度〕業績 **7 get a result** 〔在體育比賽中〕贏, 取勝

result[2] *v* 〔因…〕產生, 發生; 〔由…而〕造成
result in sth *phr v* [不用被動態] 導致, 造成

resume[1] *v* **1** 〔中斷之後〕繼續 **2** 〔活動或過程〕重新開始 **3 resume your seat/place/position** 回到座位/原地/原職位

resume[2]**, résumé** *n* **1** 〔文章或講話等的〕梗概, 摘要 **2** 個人簡歷

retreat[1] *v* **1 ►MOVE BACK 後退◄ a)** 〔因恐懼或尷尬而〕後退, 退卻 **b)** 〔水、雪、土地〕範圍縮小 **2 ►OF AN ARMY 軍隊◄** 撤退 **3 ►CHANGE YOUR MIND 改變主意◄** 〔承諾、立場等〕撤回 **4 ►TO A QUIET PLACE 到僻靜處◄** 去寧靜、安全的地方 **5 retreat into yourself/your thoughts etc** 陷入沉思

retreat[2] *n* **1 ►MOVEMENT BACK 後退◄** 後退, 退卻, 躲避 **2 ►CHANGE OF INTENTION 改變意圖◄** 〔承諾的〕撤回, 〔立場的〕改變, 放棄 **3 ►OF AN ARMY 軍隊◄** 撤退 — 反義詞 ADVANCE **4 ►PLACE 地方◄** 靜養所, 靜居所 **5 ►THOUGHT AND PRAYER 冥想與祈禱◄** 〔宗教的〕靜修〔期〕

reveal *v* **1** 展現, 顯露 **2** 揭示, 揭露, 泄露

revenge[1] *n* **1** 報復, 報仇 **2 get your revenge** 雪恥〔指在比賽中戰勝曾擊敗自己的對手〕 **—revengeful** *adj*

revenge[2] *v* **revenge yourself on/be revenged on** 向…報仇

reverse[1] *v* **1 ►CHANGE STH 改變某事物◄** 推翻, 撤銷 **2 ►CAR 汽車◄** 倒車 **3 ►CHANGE THE ORDER 改變順序◄** 顛倒〔通常的次序〕 **4 ►TURN STH OVER 翻轉某物◄** 翻轉 **5 reverse the charges** 〔電話〕由受話方付款 **—reversible** *adj* **—reversibility** *n*

reverse[2] *n* **1 ►THE OPPOSITE 相反◄ the reverse** 正相反 **2 go into reverse** 逆轉 **3 ►IN A CAR 在汽車裡◄** 倒車擋 **4 ►A DEFEAT 失敗◄** 失敗; 挫折 **5 ►OTHER SIDE 另一面◄** 背面 **6 ►OF A COIN 硬幣◄** 背面

reverse[3] *adj* **1 reverse order/procedure/process etc** 相反的順序/程序/過程等 **2 the reverse side** 反面, 背面

ridiculous *adj* 愚蠢的; 荒唐的, 可笑的 **—ridiculously** *adv* **—ridiculousness** *n*

rim[1] *n* **1** 〔圓形物的〕外緣, 邊緣, 邊 **2 gold-rimmed/red-rimmed etc** 金框/紅框的等 **—rimless** *adj*

rim[2] *v* 環繞〔邊緣〕

ripe *adj* **1** 〔水果、莊稼〕成熟的 — 反義詞 UNRIPE **2 be ripe for** 適宜…, 〔尤指變革等〕條件成熟 **3 the time is ripe (for)** 〔…的〕時機已經成熟 **4 ripe old age** 很大年紀 **5** 〔乾酪〕熟透的 **6** 〔氣味〕濃烈難聞的 **7** 〔語言〕粗俗有趣的 **—ripeness** *n*

risk[1] *n* **1 ►POSSIBILITY OF BAD RESULT 不良後果的可能性◄** 危險性, 風險 **2 take a risk** 冒險 **3 at risk** 處境危險 **4 run a risk** 冒險 **5 at the risk of doing sth** 冒着…的危險 **6 at your own risk** 自擔風險, 責任自負 **7 ►CAUSE OF DANGER 危險的起因◄** 可能造成傷害[危險]的事[人] **8 ►INSURANCE/BUSINESS 保險/商業◄** 〔按其風險評估的〕保險對象; 貸款對象

risk[2] *v* **1** 使遭受〔失去、毀壞或傷害〕的危險 **2** 擔…風險, 冒…的危險 **3** 冒險做〔某事, 其結果是危險或令人討厭的〕

rival[1] *n* **1** 對手, 競爭者 **2** 匹敵者, 可相比的東西

rival[2] *v* 與…匹敵[媲美]

roar[1] *v* **1** 吼叫, 呼嘯 **2** 咆哮, 大聲喊叫 **3** 又作 **roar with laughter** 哄笑, 大笑, 狂笑 **4** 〔車輛〕轟鳴着疾駛

roar[2] *n* **1** 吼叫聲, 咆哮聲 **2** 〔機器〕轟鳴聲; 〔風〕呼嘯聲

robust *adj* **1** 強健的, 健壯的 **2** 〔東西〕結實的, 堅固的 **3** 〔系統、組織等〕健全的, 穩固的 **4** 〔行為或説話〕強硬的, 堅定的 **—robustly** *adj* **—robustness** *n*

romantic[1] *adj* **1 ►SHOWING LOVE 表現感情的◄** 多情的 **2 ►CONNECTED WITH LOVE 與愛情有關的◄** 浪漫的, 風流的 **3 ►BEAUTIFUL 美麗的◄** 富於浪漫色彩的; 充滿傳奇色彩的 **4 ►NOT PRACTICAL 不實際的◄** 不切實際的, 耽於幻想的, 空想的 **5 ►STORY/FILM 故事/電影◄** 關於愛情的, 浪漫的 **6 Romantic art/literature etc** 浪漫主義的藝術/文學等 **—romantically** *adv*

romantic[2] *n* **1** 富於浪漫氣息的人 **2** 愛幻想的人, 浪漫主義者 **3** 又作 **Romantic** 浪漫主義作家[畫家等]

rotate *v* **1** 〔使〕旋轉, 轉動 **2** 〔使〕輪流做…, 輪換 **3** 輪種, 輪作

rouse *v* **1 rouse sb (from their sleep/slumbers)** 〔艱難地把某人從熟睡中〕喚醒 **2** 激勵〔某人做某事, 尤其在他很疲倦或不願意做時〕, 使振奮 **3** 激起〔希望、恐懼等〕

route[1] *n* **1** 〔尤指經常使用, 可在地圖上顯示的〕路線 **2** 〔交通工具常用的〕路線 **3** 〔做事或達到特定結果的〕途徑, 方法 **4 Route 66, 54 etc** 〔美國〕66[54]號等公路

route[2] *v* 按特定路線發送〔東西或人〕

routine[1] *n* **1** 慣例, 常規 **2** 〔表演的〕一套固定舞步, 舞蹈動作 **3** 〔輸入電腦的〕程序 **—routinize** *v*

routine[2] *adj* **1 routine questions/examination/**

visit etc 例行問題/檢查/訪問等 2 一般的, 平淡的, 乏味的

row *n* 1 一排, 一行, 一列 2〔劇院或電影院裡的〕一排座位 3 **three/four etc times in a row** 連續三/四次等 4 **go for a row** 去划船

ruin[1] *v* 1〔完全地〕毀壞, 毀掉 2 使破產 —**ruined** *adj*

ruin[2] *n* 1 破產; 垮台; 身敗名裂 2 **be the ruin of** 使…破產[身體垮掉, 名譽掃地等] 3 又作 **ruins** 倒塌的建築物, 廢墟 4 **the ruins of**〔組織、體制或思想〕的殘餘部分 5 **be/lie in ruins a)**〔建築物〕傾塌了的, 破敗不堪的 **b)**〔人的生命、希望、計劃或組織有嚴重困難, 無法繼續而〕垮掉 6 **go to ruin** 又作 **fall into ruin**〔某物因缺乏照料而〕衰落, 敗落

rumour【英】, **rumor**【美】*n* 流言, 謠言, 謠傳

rural *adj* 1 農村的, 鄉村的, 田園的 2 像農村的; 使人想起農村的 — 反義詞 URBAN

rust[1] *n* 1 銹, 鐵銹 2〔植物的〕銹病

rust[2] *v*〔使〕生銹

rust away *phr v* 因生銹而慢慢爛掉

S, s

sacred *adj* 1 神的, 宗教〔性〕的 2 受崇敬的, 神聖的 3 極重要的〔尤指在他人看來有點愚蠢〕4 **is nothing sacred?** 怎麼能這樣呢?〔表示在貴重物品或重要事物受到損害時的驚訝〕—**sacredly** *adv* —**sacredness** *n*

sacrifice[1] *n* 1 犧牲 2 獻祭〔尤指從前在宗教儀式中把動物或人殺死作祭品〕3 祭品, 供品 4 **the final/supreme sacrifice** 犧牲自己的生命, 捐軀

sacrifice[2] *v* 1 犧牲, 獻出 2 獻祭; 以…作祭品

safeguard[1] *v* 保護, 保衛〔某物〕

safeguard[2] *n* 保障條款; 保護措施

salute[1] *v* 1〔向…〕行軍禮, 〔向…〕致敬 2〔尤指公開地〕讚揚, 頌揚 3〔以揮手等〕向〔某人〕打招呼, 致意

salute[2] *n* 1〔通常指士兵向軍官的〕敬禮, 致敬 2〔向要人致敬的〕鳴禮砲〔儀式〕3〔以揮手、點頭等動作表示的〕打招呼, 致意

sane *adj* 1 心智健全的, 神智正常的 — 反義詞 INSANE 2 明智的, 清醒的 3 **keep sb sane** 不讓某人擔憂 —**sanely** *adv*

sanitary *adj* 1 有關衛生的, 與健康有關的 2 清潔的; 於健康無害的 — 反義詞 INSANITARY

scan[1] *v* 1 細看, 審視, 查找 2 又作 **scan through** 粗略地看, 瀏覽, 快讀 3〔用電磁波等〕掃描 4〔用雷達或聲納〕搜索, 尋找, 探測 5 **a)**〔詩〕符合格律 **b)** 找出[標出]〔詩或詩句的〕格律

scan[2] *n* 1 細查, 審視 2 掃描〔檢查〕3〔胎兒的〕掃描影像

scar[1] *n* 1〔傷〕疤 2〔精神上的〕創傷 3 疤痕, 傷痕 4 懸崖, 峭壁, 陡岩坡

scar[2] *v* 1 **be scarred** 留下傷痕[疤痕] 2 使〔精神上〕受創傷 3 又作 **scar over** 結疤, 留下傷疤

scarce[1] *adj* 1 不足的, 缺乏的 2 **make yourself scarce**〔為避免麻煩等〕離開; 溜走

scarce[2] *adv* 幾乎不[沒有]; 僅僅

scatter *v* 1 撒 2〔使〕分散, 驅散, 〔使〕散開〔尤指為逃離危險〕3 **be scattered to the four winds** 東零西散

scene *n* 1 ►**PLAY/FILM** 戲劇/電影◄ **a)**〔戲劇中的〕一場 **b)**〔電影、書等中的〕場景, 場面 2 ►**VIEW/PICTURE** 風景/圖畫◄〔某地方或圖畫中的〕景色 3 ►**ACCIDENT/CRIME** 事故/罪行◄〔事故或罪行的〕發生地點, 現場 4 **the gay/fashion/political etc scene** 同性戀者天地/時裝界/政治領域 5 ►**ARGUMENT** 爭辯◄〔在公開場合的〕爭吵, 吵嘴 6 ►**SITUATION** 情景◄ 情景, 景象 7 **bad scene** 困境 8 **not your scene** 並非某人喜愛的事物, 不合口味的東西 9 **behind the scenes** 祕密地, 在幕後 10 **set the scene a)**〔為…〕提供條件 **b)**〔在講故事前〕敍述背景 11 **be/come on the scene** 出現, 到來; 參與, 捲進

scent[1] *n* 1 香味 2〔動物或人的〕臭氣, 臭跡 3 **throw/put sb off the scent**〔給某人錯誤信息〕使某人失去線索 4 香水

scent[2] *v* 1〔動物〕嗅出…的氣味 2 **scent fear/danger/victory etc** 覺察到恐怖/危險/勝利等的氣息

scheme[1] *n* 1 計劃, 規劃, 方案〔指正式計劃, 如教育、培訓等〕2 陰謀, 詭計 3〔用於組織資料等的〕系統, 體系, 組合 4 **be in the scheme of things** 按事物的一般規律, 在一般格局中

scheme[2] *v* 搞陰謀, 密謀, 策劃 —**schemer** *n*

scold[1] *v* 責罵, 斥責〔某人, 尤指小孩〕—**scolding** *n*

scold[2] *n* 愛埋怨指責的婦人

script *n* 1〔演講的〕原稿, 講稿; 戲劇[電影]劇本 2〔一種語言的〕全套字母, 字母表 3〔考生的〕筆試答卷, 考卷 4 筆跡, 手跡;〔尤指〕英語中字母連寫的手寫體

secondary *adj* 1 **secondary education/schooling/teaching etc** 中等教育/教學〔指對 11 歲至 16 歲孩子的教育〕2 第二的, 次要的 3 從屬的, 繼發〔性〕的 —**secondarily** *adv*

secure[1] *v* 1〔尤指經過努力而〕獲得, 永久得到〔某物〕2 使安全, 保護…〔免受攻擊、傷害或損失〕3 縛牢, 繫緊, 將〔某物〕固定 4 向〔債權人〕提供保證〔償還債務〕, 為〔借款〕作保

secure[2] *adj* 1 ►**PERMANENT/CERTAIN** 永久的/確定的◄ 穩固的, 可靠的, 穩定的 2 ►**SAFE PLACE** 安全的地方◄ **a)** 鎖牢的; 關緊的 **b)** 安全的, 受保護的 3 ►**SAFE FEELING** 安全感◄ 安心的, 無恐懼的, 感到安全的 4 ►**CONFIDENT** 有信心的◄ **a)**〔對自己和自己的能力〕有自信的 — 反義詞 INSECURE **b)** 有保障的, 沒有顧慮的 5 ►**FIRMLY FIXED** 牢固的◄ 固定住的, 繫牢的, 縛緊的

seize *v* 1〔突然猛烈地〕抓取, 攫取 2〔用武力〕奪取, 佔領, 搶去 3 沒收〔毒品、武器等非法物品〕, 收繳〔物品〕4 **seize a chance/opportunity (with both hands)** 抓住機會/機遇 5 **be seized with terror/desire etc** 突然感到恐懼/受到慾望支配等 6 抓獲, 捕獲

seize on/upon sth *phr v* 抓住, 利用〔藉口等〕

seize up *phr v* **a)**〔發動機或機器部件在運轉中因缺油等〕卡住, 停止運轉 **b)**〔背等身體部位〕突然僵痛

select¹ *v*〔經過認真思考〕挑選, 選擇, 選拔

select² *adj* **1** 挑選出的, 精選的 **2** 僅限於少數富人居住[參觀, 使用]的, 專用的, 高級的, 奢華的

senior¹ *adj* **1** 年長的 **2**〔地位或級別〕較高的

senior² *n* **1 be two/five/ten etc years sb's senior** 比某人大二歲/五歲/十歲 — 反義詞 JUNIOR **2**〔中學或大學〕最高年級的學生, 畢業班學生 **3** 老年人

sensible *adj* **1** 明智的, 合理的, 實際的 **2 sensible clothes/shoes** 實用的衣服/鞋子 **3 sensible of sth** 感知某事, 察覺到某事 **4** 可感覺到的, 明顯的 —**sensibly** *adv*

sensitive *adj* **1 ►UNDERSTANDING PEOPLE 理解別人◄** 能理解〔別人的感情和問題〕的 — 反義詞 INSENSITIVE **2 ►EASILY OFFENDED 容易生氣的◄**〔感情〕易受傷害的, 神經過敏的 **3 ►COLD/PAIN ETC 冷/疼痛等◄**〔尤對疼痛〕易感受的, 敏感的 **4 ►ART/MUSIC ETC 藝術/音樂等◄**〔對文學藝術〕感受力強的, 有表現能力的 **5 ►SITUATIONS/SUBJECTS 情況/問題◄**〔情況、問題等〕需小心處理的, 敏感的, 可能觸怒人的 **6 ►HEAT/LIGHT ETC 熱/光等◄**〔對光、熱等的變化〕能準確計量的, 靈敏度高的 —**sensitively** *adv* —**sensitivity** 又作 **sensitiveness** *n*

sequence *n* **1**〔通常導致某種結果的〕一連串相關事件[行動] **2**〔事件或行動發生的〕順序, 先後次序 **3**〔電影中描述同一主題或動作的〕連續鏡頭; 一段情節;〔故事的〕片段

series *n* **1** 連續發生的同類事件; 系列 **2**〔相互聯繫並有特定結果的〕系列〔事件〕 **3**〔電視、廣播等的〕系列片; 系列節目 **4**〔有計劃的〕系列活動 **5 in series**〔電器的〕串聯

session *n* **1** 會期;〔某團體從事某項活動的〕集會〔時間〕 **2** 正式會議;〔法院的〕〔一次〕開庭;〔議會的〕一次會議 **3 sessions a)** 簡易法庭 **b)** 季審法庭

severe *adj* **1 ►VERY BAD 非常糟◄** 嚴重的, 劇烈的 **2 ►WEATHER 天氣◄** 嚴酷的; 惡劣的; 極熱[冷, 乾]的 **3 ►STRICT 嚴格的◄**〔人〕嚴格的, 嚴厲的, 苛刻的 **4 ►EXTREME 極度的◄**〔批評、懲罰等〕極其嚴厲的 **5 ►UNFRIENDLY 不友好的◄** 不贊成的; 不友好的 **6 ►PLAIN 樸素的◄** 樸素的; 簡潔的; 不加裝飾的 —**severity** *n*

shallow¹ *adj* **1** 淺的, 不深的 **2**〔對問題的理解等〕膚淺的, 淺薄的 **3 shallow breathing** 淺呼吸〔吸入少量空氣〕 —**shallowly** *adv* —**shallowness** *n*

shallow² *v* 變淺

shed¹ *n* **1** 棚屋, 小屋, 小庫房〔通常為簡陋小木房, 尤用於存放雜物〕 **2**〔用作車間、停放大型車輛或存放機器等的〕棚式建築物

shed² *v* **1 ►LIGHT 光線◄**〔燈〕發出〔光線〕; 照亮, 照射 **2 ►DROP/FALL OFF 落下◄ a)** 落下, 使〔某物〕脫落 **b)**〔動物或植物〕使〔外皮、毛髮、葉子等〕蛻下, 脫落, 剝落 **3 ►GET RID OF 去掉◄** 去掉〔不需要或不想要的東西〕 **4 shed light on**〔通過提供新信息等〕使〔某事物〕清楚些[易於理解] **5 ►WATER 水◄**〔表面〕排掉, 不沾〔水〕 **6 shed blood** 流血〔尤指戰爭或打鬥中的殺戮或傷害〕 **7 shed tears** 流淚 **8 shed its load**〔車輛不經意〕掉落〔所載貨物〕

shift¹ *v* **1 ►MOVE 移動◄ a)**〔使〕移動〔地點、位置〕,〔使〕轉移 **b)** 移動; 搬動〔尤指提起來搬〕 **2 shift attention/emphasis/focus** 轉移注意力/重點/中心 **3 ►COSTS/SPENDING 費用/開支◄** 轉嫁, 轉給 **4 ►OPINIONS 意見◄** 改變〔意見、信仰, 尤指政治方面〕 **5 shift the blame/responsibility** 推卸責任 **6 ►DIRT/MARKS 污垢/痕跡◄** 除去〔表面或衣服上的污跡〕 **7 ►IN A CAR 在汽車中◄** 換擋, 調擋

shift² *n* **1**〔想法、做法等的〕改變 **2 a)**〔工作人員在工廠、醫院等輪值工作的〕當班時間 **b)** 輪班工人 **3 a)** 寬鬆直筒式家常女服 **b)** 裙式女內衣 **4**〔電腦、打字機上的〕大寫字母轉換鍵 **5** 手段, 計謀

shiver¹ *v*〔因寒冷或害怕而〕顫抖, 哆嗦, 發抖

shiver² *n* **1**〔因寒冷或恐懼引起身體的〕顫抖, 發抖 **2 give you the shivers** 使人打寒顫[害怕] **3 send shivers (up and) down your spine** 使人脊骨發涼, 令人毛骨悚然; 令人興奮 **4 shivers** 碎片, 破片

shower¹ *n* **1 ►FOR WASHING IN 洗澡用◄** 淋浴用的噴頭, 淋浴器 **2 ►ACT OF WASHING 洗澡◄** 淋浴 **3 ►RAIN 雨◄**〔短時間的〕降雨, 陣雨; 降雪 **4 ►THINGS IN THE AIR 空中的東西◄**〔許多細小而輕的東西〕大量灑落或出現 **5 ►PARTY 聚會◄**〔為將要結婚或分娩的女子舉行的〕送禮會 **6 ►PEOPLE 人◄** 一羣笨[懶]人

shower² *v* **1** 洗淋浴 **2**〔使〕〔大量細而輕的東西〕灑落 **3** 給〔某人〕大量東西

shrink¹ *v* **1**〔使〕縮小,〔使〕收縮 **2**〔數量、體積或價值〕變小, 減少, 縮小 **3**〔因恐懼而〕退縮, 畏縮

shrink from sth *phr v* 避免做, 不願做〔困難或不愉快的事〕

shrink² *n* 精神分析學家; 精神科醫生

sigh¹ *v* **1**〔尤指因厭煩、失望、疲倦等〕嘆氣, 嘆息 **2**〔風〕呼嘯, 嗚咽 **3 sigh for sth** 思念, 惋惜

sigh² *n* 嘆氣[嘆息]

significant *adj* **1** 重要的, 重大的, 影響深遠的 **2** 相當數量的, 影響明顯的 **3**〔眼神、微笑等〕表示某種意義的, 有特殊含義的

similarity *n* **1** 類似, 相似 **2** 類似之點, 相似之處

simplify *v* 使簡易, 使簡明, 簡化 —**simplified** *adj* —**simplification** *n*

sin¹ *n* **1**〔冒犯上帝或宗教法規的〕罪, 罪惡, 罪孽 **2** 過錯, 罪過 **3 live in sin**〔未婚男女〕同居, 姘居 **4 as miserable/ugly/guilty as sin** 非常不愉快/難看/內疚 **5 for my sins** 自作自受, 活該, 該死 —**sinless** *adj*

sin² *v* **1** 違反上帝的戒律, 違犯教規 **2 be more sinned against than sinning** 人負我甚於我負人; 受到超過應得的懲罰

sincere *adj* **1**〔感情等〕由衷的, 真誠的, 真心實意的 **2**〔人〕誠實的, 不虛偽的, 誠懇的 — 反義詞 INSINCERE

situated *adj* **1 be situated** 位於…的, 坐落在…的 **2 be well/badly situated** 境況良好/處境困難

skeleton *n* **1 ►BONES 骨◄ a)**〔人體或動物的〕全副骨骼 **b)**〔醫學研究用的〕骷髏, 骨架; 骨架模型 **2 ►MAIN PART 主要部分◄** 骨架, 框架; 梗概, 綱要 **3 ►THIN 瘦的◄** 骨瘦如柴的人[動物] **4 a skeleton in the cupboard/closet** 不可外揚的家醜, 隱私, 祕密 **5 skeleton staff/service** 最基本的人員/服務

sketch¹ *n* **1** 素描, 速寫; 草圖 **2**〔舞台、電視等上的〕滑稽短劇 **3** 短篇描寫, 隨筆; 簡介, 梗概

sketch[2] *v* （給…）寫生，（給…）畫素描
sketch in sth *phr v* 補充〔內容〕
sketch sth ↔ **out** *phr v* 概述；草擬
skim *v* **1** 從液體表面撇去〔漂浮的油脂或固體物質〕 **2**〔為掌握大意的〕略讀，瀏覽 **3** 飛快掠過，擦過 **4 skim stones/pebbles etc**〔用扁石在水面〕打水漂 **5**〔為逃税而〕瞞報〔收入〕；非法撈到〔錢〕
skim sb ↔ **off** *phr v* 挖走〔最優秀的人〕；選取〔精華〕；〔通過瞞報而〕撈走〔大部分的錢〕
skip[1] *v* **1 ►MOVEMENT 動◄** 蹦跳着走 **2 ►NOT DO STH 不做某事◄** 不做〔本來常做或應做的事〕 **3 ►NOT DEAL WITH 不處理◄** 略過，跳過，遺漏 **4 ►CHANGE SUBJECTS 換主題◄** 不按次序地改變話題，隨意跳動 **5** 又作 **skip rope** 跳繩 **6 skip town/skip the country** 逃出城/國境 **7 skip it!**〔生氣地説〕別再提這件事了！ **8 skip rocks/stones**〔用扁平小石〕打水漂 **9 skip a year/grade**〔在學校〕跳級 **10 sb's heart skips a beat** 心跳停一下〔用於表示非常興奮、驚訝或害怕〕
skip out 又作 **skip off** 偷偷離開，祕密逃走
skip[2] *n* **1** 輕跳，蹦跳 **2**〔用來清理磚、木等沉重廢料的〕廢料桶
slack[1] *adj* **1** 懶散的，懈怠的，馬虎的 **2**〔生意〕蕭條的，清淡的 **3**〔繩子等〕不（拉）緊的，鬆弛的 —**slackly** *adv* —**slackness** *n*
slack[2] *n* **1** 閒置的資源〈如不需要的資金、場地、人力等〉 **2 take up the slack a)** 把繩子拉緊 **b)** 接替別人停下的工作 **3**〔繩子、繩結等的〕鬆弛，不緊 **4 slacks** 寬鬆長褲，便褲 **5** 煤屑
slack[3] 又作 **slack off** *v* 放鬆，鬆勁，懈怠
slam[1] *v* **1 ►DOOR/GATE 門/大門◄**（使）砰地關上，使勁關閉 **2 ►PUT STH SOMEWHERE 放東西◄** 砰地放下，使勁放下 **3 slam on the brakes** 猛踩煞車 **4 ►CRITICIZE STH 批評某事◄** 猛烈抨擊〔報刊用語〕 **5 slam the door in sb's face a)** 用力關門不讓某人進入，讓某人吃閉門羹 **b)**〔粗魯地〕拒絕會見某人；拒絕與某人談話
slam into sth *phr v*〔駕駛等因速度太快而〕撞到…
slam[2] *n* 砰的關門聲；〔門〕砰的關上
slender *adj* **1** 細長而優美的，修長的；苗條的；纖細的 **2** 微少的，微薄的，不足的 —**slenderness** *n*
slice[1] *n* **1** 片，薄片，切片 **2**〔指好東西的〕份兒，部分 **3**〔用於分菜或鏟起食物的〕小鏟子，鍋鏟 **4 a)**〔網球、高爾夫球等的〕削球，斜切球，側旋球 **b)** 削球打法，斜切球打法 **5 a slice of life**〔電影、書等中〕如實地反映生活的一個側面，現實生活的片段
slice[2] *v* **1** 又作 **slice up** 把…切成薄片 **2**〔乾淨利落地〕切，割，切開，割破 **3**（使）輕鬆迅速地劃過〔水面等〕；（使）輕快地穿過〔空中等〕 **4**〔打網球、高爾夫球等時〕削〔球〕，斜切〔球〕，打〔側旋球〕 **5 any way you slice it** 無論你怎樣考慮這個問題
slice sth ↔ **off** *phr v*〔一刀〕切下，〔一刀〕割去
slide[1] *v* **1**（使）滑動 **2**（使）悄悄移動，偷偷溜走 **3**〔價格等〕下滑，降低 **4 let sth slide**〔對某事〕聽其自然，任其惡化，放任不管
slide[2] *n* **1 ►FOR CHILDREN 兒童用的◄**〔兒童遊戲用的〕滑梯 **2 ►FOR HAIR 用於頭髮◄** 小髮夾 **3 ►MOVEMENT 移動◄** 滑動，打滑 **4 ►PICTURE 圖片◄** 幻燈片 **5 ►PRICE/AMOUNT 價格/數量◄** 滑落，跌落，下降 **6 ►IN SCIENCE 在科學上◄**〔顯微鏡用的〕載（物）玻（璃）片 **7 ►MUSIC 音樂◄**〔機器或樂器的〕滑動部件〈如長號的 U 字形伸縮管〉 **8 ►EARTH/SNOW 土/雪◄**〔土、石、雪等的〕崩落，崩塌
slim[1] *adj* **1** 苗條的，修長的 **2 slim chance/hopes etc**〔機會、希望等〕微小的，渺茫的 **3** 非常薄[少]的
slim[2] *v* **1**〔通過節食、加強運動等〕減肥 **2** 又作 **slim down**（使）減少，縮小；裁減 —**slimmer** *n*
slippery *adj* **1**〔因濕或有油脂〕滑的，滑溜的 **2** 滑頭的，不可信賴的 **3 be on the slippery slope**〔惡習等〕無法克制以至後果嚴重 —**slipperiness** *n*
slogan *n* 口號，標語
smash[1] *v* **1** 打破，打碎，（使）粉碎 **2**（使）猛撞，猛擊，猛擲 **3** 擊潰，擊毀；消滅 **4**〔在網球等運動中〕殺〔球〕，猛扣〔球〕
smash sth ↔ **down** *phr v* 擊倒〔門、牆等〕
smash sth ↔ **in** *phr v* 將〔某物〕撞出窟窿
smash sth ↔ **up** *phr v*〔故意〕撞毀，打碎
smash[2] *n* **1** 撞碎聲，破碎聲 **2**〔網球等的〕殺球，扣球 **3** 嚴重的交通事故，車禍
snatch[1] *v* **1** 搶，強奪，攫取 **2** 抓住〔機會〕，抓緊〔時間〕 **3** 抓走，搶去，奪走
snatch at sth *phr v* 伸手試圖抓住[攫取]
snatch[2] *n* **1 a snatch of conversation/music/song etc** 談話/音樂/歌曲等的片段 **2 in snatches** 斷斷續續地 **3** 抓，搶，奪
soar *v* **1 ►AMOUNTS/PRICES ETC 數量/價格等◄** 猛增，驟升 **2 ►IN THE SKY 在天上◄ a)** 高飛，翱翔 **b)** 急速升高 **3 ►SPIRITS/HOPES 情緒/希望◄** 高漲，騰飛 **4 ►LOOK TALL 顯得很高◄** 聳立，屹立 —**soaring** *adj*
social[1] *adj* **1 ►SOCIETY 社會◄** 社會的，有關社會的 **2 ►RANK 地位◄** 社會地位[階層]的 **3 ►MEETING PEOPLE 與人交往◄** 社交的，交際的 **4 ►WITH FRIENDS 和朋友在一起◄** 交誼的，聯誼的 **5 ►ANIMALS 動物◄** 羣居的，合羣的 —**socially** *adv*
social[2] *n* 社交聚會；聯誼會；教友聯誼會
sophisticated *adj* **1** 老於世故的；有判斷力的；有鑑賞力的 **2**〔機器、系統、方法等〕複雜的，精密的，高級的，尖端的 **3** 富有經驗的，老練的；精通的 —**sophistication** *n*
sorrow[1] *n* **1** 悲傷，悲痛 **2** 引起悲傷的事，不幸 **3 more in sorrow than in anger**〔對某事〕悲哀多於憤怒
sorrow[2] *v* 感到[表示]悲傷
sound *adj* **1 ►WELL-JUDGED 判斷正確的◄** 明智的，合理的，正確的 —反義詞 UNSOUND **2 ►PERSON 人◄** 有判斷力的，見地高的 —反義詞 UNSOUND **3 ►THOROUGH 徹底的◄** 完全的，徹底的 **4 ►IN GOOD CONDITION 狀況良好的◄** 完好的，無損的 **5 ►HEALTHY 健康的◄**〔生理或心理上〕健康的 **6 ►SLEEP 睡覺◄** 酣的，深沉的，平靜的 **7 ►PUNISHMENT 懲罰◄** 嚴厲的，沉重的 —**soundness** *n*
souvenir *n* 紀念品，紀念物
spacious *adj* 寬敞的，廣闊的；廣大的 —**spa-**

ciously *adv* —**spaciousness** *n*

span¹ *n* 1〔注意力、生命等持續的〕時間 2〔兩個日期或兩件事之間的〕時距, 期間 3〔橋梁、拱門等的〕跨距; 墩距 4〔從一端到另一端的〕全長

span² *v* 1〔時間〕持續, 延伸 2〔空間、地域〕跨越, 包括 3〔橋梁〕跨越〔水面〕, 橫跨

specialize 又作 **-ise**【英】*v* 專門研究, 專門從事, 專攻 —**specialization** *n*

species *n*〔動植物的〕物種, 種

specimen *n* 1 樣品, 樣本, 標本 2 實例, 範例 3 某種類型的人, 傢伙

sphere *n* 1 球, 球形, 球體 2〔活動、工作、知識等的〕範圍, 領域 3 **sphere of influence** 勢力範圍, 影響所及的範圍

spill¹ *v* 1（使）溢出,（使）潑出,（使）灑落 2〔人羣〕湧出 3 **spill the beans** 泄露祕密, 走漏風聲 4 **spill your guts**〔尤指因心情不好〕把自己知道的一切和盤托出 5 **spill blood** 殺人; 傷人

spill over *phr v*〔問題或壞情況〕蔓延, 擴散

spill² *n* 1 灑出, 溢出; 灑出量, 溢出量 2〔用於點燈、生火等的〕木片; 紙捻 3〔從馬、自行車等上的〕摔下

spiritual¹ *adj* 1 精神(上)的, 心靈的 2 宗教(上)的 3 **spiritual home** 精神家園, 精神歸宿〔指一個自己能認同其思想和態度的地方〕—**spiritually** *adj*

spiritual² *n* 靈歌〔一種原為美國黑人唱的宗教歌曲〕

spoil *v* 1 ►**RUIN STH** 毀掉某物◄ 損壞, 糟蹋, 破壞 2 ►**FOOD** 食物◄〔開始〕變壞, 變質; 腐敗 3 ►**CHILD** 小孩◄ 寵壞, 慣壞, 溺愛〔小孩〕 4 ►**TREAT KINDLY** 體貼地對待◄ 無微不至地關心; 過分地照顧, 縱容 5 ►**VOTING PAPER** 選票◄〔因劃票不符規定〕使〔選票〕成廢票 6 **be spoiling for a fight/argument** 一心想打架/吵架

sponsor¹ *n* 1〔出資舉辦表演、廣播、體育比賽等以在其中做廣告的〕贊助者, 贊助商 2 慈善募捐活動的贊助者 3 擔保人, 保證人 4 提案人; 發起者, 倡議者 5 教父; 教母

sponsor² *v* 1 贊助, 資助〔體育比賽、演出等〕 2 贊助〔某人的慈善募捐活動〕 3 倡議〔法案〕; 支持〔法案〕

spot¹ *n* 1 ►**PLACE** 地方◄〔尤指休閒的〕地點, 場所 2 ►**AREA** 面積◄（圓）點, 斑點 3 ►**MARK** 痕跡◄ 污漬, 斑點 4 **on the spot** 立即, 馬上; 當場 5 **be on the spot** 在現場 6 ►**MARK ON SKIN** 皮膚上的斑點◄ **a)**〔皮膚上的〕紅斑 **b)**〔尤指臉上紅色的〕丘疹; 粉刺 7 ►**POSITION** 地位◄〔在比賽、電視節目等中的〕地位, 位置 8 **run/dance/hop etc on the spot** 原地跑步/跳舞/跳躍等 9 **weak spot a)** 弱點, 不足（之處） **b)**〔對某物的〕特別喜愛, 偏愛 10 **put sb on the spot**〔故意〕使某人處於難堪地位 11 **in a spot** 處於困難境地 12 **bright spot** 亮點, 困境中使人高興的事 13 **a spot of** 一點點 14 ►**ON CLOTH** 在布上面◄ **spots**〔指布上的〕圓點圖案, 斑點 15 **spots of rain** 幾滴雨 16 ►**LIGHT** 燈◄ 聚光燈 17 **five-spot/ten-spot etc** 一張五美元/十美元等鈔票 18 ►**ADVERTISEMENT** 廣告◄ 廣告插播〔尤指為政客作的廣播或電視短廣告〕

spot² *v* 1 ►**NOTICE** 注意到◄ 看出, 認出; 找出 2 ►**RECOGNIZE** 辨認出◄ 發現, 辨認出〔某人或某事的特性〕 3 **be spotted**〔表面〕有斑點, 有污漬 4 ►**GAME** 比賽◄〔在比賽中〕讓〔對手〕

spot³ *adj* 現貨的; 現付(款)的

spouse *n* 配偶〔指丈夫或妻子〕

spray¹ *v* 1 噴 2〔液體或碎屑〕飛濺出來 3 **spray (sb/sth with) bullets**〔向某人/某物〕開槍掃射

spray² *n* 1 ►**LIQUID** 液體◄ 噴霧液體 2 ►**A CAN** 一罐◄ 噴霧罐, 噴霧器 3 ►**FROM THE SEA** 海上來的◄ 浪花, 水花 4 ►**BRANCH** 樹枝◄〔裝飾用的〕小樹枝 5 ►**FLOWERS/JEWELS** 花朵/珠寶◄ 帶花[鑲有珠寶]的枝狀飾物 6 **a spray of bullets/dust etc** 一陣槍彈/灰塵等

spring¹ *n* 1 ►**SEASON** 季節◄ 春天, 春季 2 ►**BED/CARS ETC** 牀/汽車等◄ **a)** 彈簧; 發條 **b)** 彈性, 彈力 3 ►**WATER** 水◄ 泉, 泉源 4 **with a spring in your step** 步伐輕快 5 ►**SUDDEN JUMP** 突然一跳◄ 跳, 跳躍

spring² *v* 1 ►**MOVE SUDDENLY** 突然移動◄ 跳, 跳躍, 跳起 2 ►**EXPRESSION/TEARS** 表情/眼淚◄〔在臉上或眼中〕突然出現, 冒出 3 ►**MOVE BACK** 復原◄ 彈回原處, 反彈 4 **spring to mind** 馬上想到 5 **spring into action** 又作 **spring to life** 突然活躍起來 6 **spring into existence** 突然出現 7 **spring open/shut** 突然打開/合上 8 **spring a trap a)**〔動物〕觸發捕捉器〔而被捉〕 **b)** 誘使某人說出[幹]某事 9 **spring a leak**〔船或容器〕出現裂縫〔開始漏水〕 10 **spring to sb's defence** 迅速為某人辯護 11 **spring to attention**〔士兵〕霍然立正 12 **spring a surprise** 使突然發生, 使大吃一驚 13 ►**PRISON** 監獄◄ 幫助〔某人〕越獄

spring from *phr v* 1 由…引起 2 **where did you/she etc spring from?** 你/她等是從哪兒冒出來的?〔用於表示驚訝〕

spring sth **on** sb *phr v* 向〔某人〕突然說〔某事, 令人驚訝或震驚〕

spring up *phr v* 突然出現

squeeze¹ *v* 1 壓; 擠; 捏; 榨 2 壓出; 擠出; 榨出〔液體〕 3（使）擠進; 塞入 4 **squeeze sth out of sb** 強迫某人說出某事 5 **squeeze sb out (of sth)**〔通過吸引某人的顧客〕將某人擠出(某行業) 6〔在很忙的時候〕設法安排〔做某事〕 7 **squeeze in/into/through** 僥倖成功; 險勝; 勉強通過〔考試〕 8 緊縮〔公司或機構的〕資金; 使…經濟拮据

squeeze² *n* 1 **a (tight) squeeze** 擁擠; 密集 2 緊捏; 緊握; 擠壓 3 **a squeeze of lemon/lime etc** 擠出微量的檸檬汁/酸橙汁等 4 **a squeeze** 拮据; 緊縮 5 **put the squeeze on sb** 試圖說服某人 6 **your/her/his main squeeze** 你/她/他的男[女]朋友

stabilize 又作 **-ise**【英】*v*（使）穩固;（使）穩定 —**stabilization** *n*

stable¹ *adj* 1 穩定的; 安定的; 不變的 2 平靜的; 穩重的 3〔物質〕穩定的, 不易分解[變化]的 — 反義詞 UNSTABLE —**stably** *adv*

stable² *n* 1 馬廄, 馬房 2 牲口棚 3 **a)**〔一位馬主或馴馬師所擁有的〕一羣賽馬 **b)**〔在同一家公司工作或受同一教練訓練的〕一羣人 4 **shut/close the stable door after the horse has bolted** 亡羊補牢, 賊去關門

stable³ *v* 置〔馬〕於馬房

stage¹ *n* **1 ▶TIME/STATE 時間/狀態◀** 時期; 階段 **2 ▶THEATRE 戲院◀** 舞台 **3 ▶ACTING 表演◀ the stage** 舞台生涯; 戲劇表演 **4 take centre stage/be at the centre of the stage** 成為大家注意的中心; 非常重要 **5 ▶PLACE 地方◀** 〔重大事件發生的〕地點, 場所 **6 set the stage for** 為…做準備; 使…成為可能 **7 he's/she's going through a stage** 他/她正在經歷成長階段〔指某些年輕人過了這個階段後, 很快就會改變不良或者奇怪的行為〕

stage² *v* 舉辦; 舉行

stain¹ *v* **1** 染污, 沾污; 留下難以清除的污跡 **2** 給〔某物, 尤指木製品〕染色[着色] **3 stain sb's name/honour/reputation etc** 玷污某人的名譽

stain² *n* **1** 〔尤指液體做成的〕污跡, 污點 **2** 〔尤指木材的〕着色劑, 染色劑 **3 a stain on sb's character/reputation etc** 某人性格/名聲等上的污點

standard¹ *n* **1 ▶LEVEL OF QUALITY 質量水平◀** 水平; 水準; 標準 **2 ▶COMPARING 比較◀** 標準; 規範; 規格 **3 ▶MORAL RULE 道德準則◀** 道德標準; 道德準則 **4 ▶MEASUREMENT 計量, 測量◀** 〔重量、純度、價值等的〕標準, 基準 **5 ▶SONG 歌曲◀** 〔很多歌星演唱過的〕流行歌曲 **6 ▶FLAG 旗◀** 儀式用旗幟 **7 ▶MILITARY POLE 軍隊旗杆◀** 〔舊時軍隊的〕軍旗旗杆

standard² *adj* **1** 正常的; 普通的; 普遍接受的 **2** 〔形狀、大小、質量等〕規則的; 標準的 **3** 〔某一學科的書、作品、作者等〕公認為標準的; 有權威的 **4 standard English/spelling/pronunciation etc** 標準英語/拼法/發音等

stare¹ *v* **1** 凝視; 盯着看 **2 be staring sb in the face a)** 非常清楚而容易看見; 明顯的 **b)** 看來無法避免

stare sb **out** 【英】, **stare** sb **down** 【美】 *phr v* 盯得〔某人〕不敢再對視

stare² *n* 盯視; 凝視

stationary *adj* 不(移)動的; 靜止的

statue *n* 雕像; 塑像

status *n* **1** 〔人、組織、國家等的〕法律地位; 身分, 狀況 **2 a)** 社會地位; 專業資格; 職位 **b)** 重要地位; 重要身分 **3** 〔尤指爭論、討論等的〕狀態; 狀況

steer¹ *v* **1 ▶CAR/BOAT ETC 汽車/船等◀** 操縱〔車、船的行駛方向〕; 駕駛〔車、船等〕 **2 ▶CHANGE SB/STH 改變某人/某物◀** 引導, 指導, 帶領〔某人的行為〕 **3 ▶BE IN CHARGE OF 負責◀** 掌管, 控制; 〔尤指在困難時期〕帶領…度過 **4 ▶GUIDE SB TO A PLACE 引領某人到某處◀** 帶領, 引導〔尤指用手輕推某人的背或肩等〕 **5 steer clear (of)** 避開; 從…脫身 **6 steer a middle course** 選擇一條中間路線, 不走極端

steer² *n* 〔閹過的〕小公牛

stereotype¹ *n* 模式化的思想[形象]; 老一套; 舊框框 —**stereotypical** *adj*

stereotype² *v* [一般用被動態] 對…有老一套看法; 把…模式化 —**stereotyping** *n* —**stereotyped** *adj*

stir¹ *v* **1 ▶MIX 混合◀** 攪, 攪拌, 攪動 **2 ▶FEELINGS 感情◀ a)** 激發, 激起〔強烈的感情〕, 引起〔強烈的反應〕 **b)** 〔感情〕激起, 喚起, 挑起 **3 ▶MOVE SLIGHTLY 微動◀ a)** 〔睡覺時〕輕輕地移動[挪動] **b)** 微微地動 **4 ▶DO STH 做某事◀** 激發, 激勵〔某人做某事〕 **5 ▶CAUSE TROUBLE 導致麻煩◀** 〔通過散佈謠言〕搬弄是非, 挑撥 **6 ▶MAKE STH MOVE 使某物移動◀** 使輕輕地移動

stir sth ↔ **up** *phr v* **1** 惹起〔麻煩〕, 挑起〔爭吵〕 **2** 攪起, 攪動, 使揚起

stir² *n* **1** 攪拌, 攪動 **2** 激動[煩惱]的感覺

straightforward *adj* **1** 誠實的, 坦率的, 老實的 **2** 簡單的, 易懂的 **3** 無條件限制的, 明確的 —**straightforwardly** *adv* —**straightforwardness** *n*

strategy *n* **1** 〔戰爭中的〕戰略; 戰略學 **2** 〔為實現某目標, 尤指為戰勝對手而制定的〕行動計劃; 計謀, 策略 **3** 戰略, 策略

strengthen *v* **1 ▶FEELING/BELIEF/RELATIONSHIP 感情/信仰/關係◀** (使)變強, 加強; 使更堅固 **2 ▶TEAM/ARMY ETC 團隊/軍隊等◀** 增強〔某組織或軍隊等的〕實力 **3 ▶MONEY 錢◀** 〔貨幣〕增值; 增加〔貨幣的〕價值 **4 ▶FINANCIAL SITUATION 財政狀況◀** 增強, 改善〔某國或公司的財政狀況〕 **5 ▶STRUCTURE 結構◀** 加固 **6 ▶PROOF/REASON 證據/理由◀** 為…提供更有力的理由[證據] **7 ▶WIND/CURRENT 風/水流◀** 加強, 增大

stress¹ *n* **1** 壓力; 憂慮; 緊張 **2** 應力 **3** 強調; 重要性 **4** 重音, 重讀; 〔音樂中的〕加強

stress² *v* **1** 強調, 着重 **2** 重讀

stretch¹ *v* **1 ▶MAKE STH BIGGER/LOOSER 使某物更大/更鬆◀ a)** (使)變大; (使)變鬆; 拉長 **b)** 可伸展, 可延伸, 有彈性 **2 ▶ARM/BODY 手臂/身體◀** 伸開, 張開, 伸展〔肢體〕 **3 ▶MAKE STH TIGHT 使某物變緊◀** 拉緊, 拽緊 **4 ▶IN SPACE 在空間上◀** 延伸, 綿延 **5 ▶IN TIME 在時間上◀** 延續, 延伸 **6 ▶RULE/LIMIT 規則/限制◀** 放寬規則[限制] **7 stretch sb's patience/credulity etc** 使某人難以忍受/相信等 **8 ▶ABILITIES 能力◀** 使〔某人〕施展才華 **9 be stretched (to the limit)** 手頭拮据, 沒有足夠的錢[日用品] **10 stretch the truth** 誇大事實, 言過其實 **11 not stretch to sth** 買不起某物, 支付不起某物的費用 **12 stretch your legs** 〔尤指久坐後〕伸伸腿; 散散步 —**stretchable** *adj*

stretch out *phr v* **1** 躺下〔睡覺或休息〕 **2** 伸出, 伸開〔手、腳等〕

stretch² *n* **1 ▶LENGTH OF LAND/WATER 一片地域/水域◀** 〔尤指長而窄的〕一片地域; 一片水域 **2 ▶TIME 時間◀** 連續的一段時間 **3 ▶BODY 身體◀** 伸展動作; 〔肢體的〕伸展, 伸開, 張開 **4 ▶MATERIAL 材料◀** 伸展性, 彈性 **5 not by any stretch of the imagination** 無論怎樣想像都不〔表示某事怎麼想像或推想也不可能是真實的〕 **6 ▶JAIL 監獄◀** 服刑期, 徒刑 **7 at full stretch a)** 全力以赴, 竭盡所能 **b)** 身體[肢體]伸直

strict *adj* **1** 嚴格的, 嚴厲的 **2** 〔命令、規則〕必須嚴格遵守的 **3** 嚴謹的; 精確的, 確鑿的 **4 strict Muslim/vegetarian etc** 不折不扣的穆斯林/素食者等 —**strictness** *n*

stride¹ *v* 邁大步走, 大踏步走

stride² *n* **1 ▶WALKING 走, 步行◀** 大步, 闊步 **2 ▶PATTERN OF STEPS 步態◀** 步法, 步態 **3 ▶IMPROVEMENT 改進◀** 進步, 進展, 發展 **4 get**

into your stride【英】, hit your stride【美】〔做某工作〕開始上軌道, 駕輕就熟 5 take sth in your stride 從容地對付 6 put sb off their stride 使某人分心 7 (match sb) stride for stride〔設法與某人〕並駕齊驅 8 without breaking stride 不加停頓地; 心平氣和地 9 strides 褲子

striking *adj* 1 驚人的, 顯著的 2 吸引人的, 惹人注目的 —**strikingly** *adv*

strip[1] *v* 1 ►TAKE OFF CLOTHES 脱衣服◄ 又作 strip off 脱去〔…的〕衣服 2 ►REMOVE A LAYER 除去一層◄ 剝去, 除去 3 strip sb of sth〔作為懲罰〕剝奪某人的頭銜、財產或權力 4 ►ENGINES/EQUIPMENT 發動機/設備◄ 又作 strip down 拆卸〔發動機或設備以進行清理或檢修〕 5 ►BUILDING/SHIP 建築物/輪船◄ 搬走〔建築物、輪船、汽車等中的〕所有東西, 搬空

strip sth ↔ away *phr v* 逐漸擺脱〔習慣、風俗等〕

strip[2] *n* 1 條, 狹條狀物〔紙、布料等〕 2 狹長的一塊土地 3 do a strip 表演脱衣舞 4〔沿途有許多商店、餐館等的〕公路 5〔運動隊穿的某種顏色的〕運動服, 隊服 6 連環漫畫

strive *v*〔為獲得某物而〕努力, 奮鬥

stroke[1] *n* 1 ►ILLNESS 疾病◄ 卒中, 腦卒中; 中風 2 ►SWIMMING/ROWING 游泳/划船◄ a)〔游泳或划船的〕一次划水 b)〔游泳的〕游法;〔划船的〕划法 c)〔指揮划槳速度的〕尾槳手, 領槳手 3 a) at a/one stroke 一舉, 一下子 b) a bold stroke 勇敢的行動 4 ►A HIT 擊, 打◄ 一擊, 一抽 5 on the stroke of seven/nine etc 在七點正/九點正等 6 ►CLOCK/BELL 時鐘/鈴◄〔時鐘、鈴等報時的〕一次鳴響, 敲擊聲 7 a stroke of luck/fortune 一樁意外的幸事/運氣 8 a stroke of lightning〔尤指擊中某物的〕閃電的一擊 9 a stroke of genius/inspiration etc 聰明之舉/絕妙的主意等 10 ►SPORT 體育運動◄〔網球、高爾夫球、板球等的〕擊球; 一擊, 一抽 11 ►A MOVEMENT OF YOUR HAND 手的動作◄ 輕撫, 撫摸 12 ►PEN/BRUSH 鋼筆/毛筆◄ a)〔鋼筆或毛筆的〕一揮, 揮筆動作 b) 一筆, 一畫; 筆劃 13 with/at a stroke of the pen 大筆一揮〔簽字〕 14 not do a stroke (of work) 甚麼〔工作〕也不做 15 put sb off their stroke 使某人分心 16 ►IN NUMBERS 在數字中◄ 斜線〔號〕

stroke[2] *v* 1 輕撫, 撫摸 2 用手輕輕地移動〔某物〕

subjective *adj* 1 主觀的 — 反義詞 OBJECTIVE 2 主觀想像的, 只存在於想像之中的 3〔文法中〕主詞的, 主語的 —**subjectively** *adv* —**subjectivity** *n*

submit *v* 1 順從, 服從; 屈從 2 呈送, 提交, 呈遞〔計劃等〕 3 同意服從[遵守] 4 建議, 主張

subsequent *adj* 隨後的, 繼…之後的

substitute[1] *n* 1 代替者; 替補隊員[演員] 2 代替物, 替代品 3 be no substitute for sth 沒有…那樣好, 不如…稱心

substitute[2] *v* 1 用〔新的或不同的事物〕代替 2 替代, 頂替; 替換

subtract *v* 減去, 減掉

sufficient *adj* 足夠的, 充足的 — 反義詞 INSUFFICIENT

summary[1] *n* 總結, 摘要, 概要

summary[2] *adj* 立即的; 速決的〔未顧及慣常的程序、規定等〕 —**summarily** *adv*

summit *n* 1 山頂 2 首腦會議, 最高級會議, 峯會 3 the summit of …的頂峯, …的極點

superior[1] *adj* 1 職位[級別]更高的; 上級的 2 更好的; 更強的; 更有效的 3 質量上乘的, 優質的〔尤用於廣告〕 4 有優越感的, 高傲的, 傲慢的 5 上面的, 上部的 6 Mother Superior 女修道院院長

superior[2] *n* 上級, 上司, 長官

supervise *v* 監督; 管理; 指導 —**supervisor** *n* —**supervisory** *adj*

supplementary *adj* 補充的, 增補的, 附加的

suppose[1] *v* 1 be supposed to do sth a) 被期望做某事; 應該做某事 b) 本應, 本該〔用於表示某事本應發生而沒有發生〕 2 be supposed to be sth 被相信是…, 被認為… 3 認為, 料想, 猜想, 假定 4 假定, 預期; 以…為條件 5 I suppose a) 我想, 我認為〔用於認為某事真實, 但不敢肯定〕 b) 我想〔尤用於表示勉強同意某人做某事〕 c) 我猜想〔用於表示猜測〕 d) 我看〔用於生氣地表示預料某事真實〕 e) 恐怕〔用於表示某事很可能真實, 雖然自己希望並非如此〕 6 suppose/supposing 假設, 假定〔用於要某人設想如果某情況存在會發生甚麼事〕 7 I don't suppose (that) a)〔用於很禮貌地提出要求〕 b) 我以為不會〔用於表示某事不大可能發生〕 8 who/what etc do you suppose 你認為是誰/甚麼… 9 what's that supposed to mean? 這是甚麼意思?〔用於表示對某人剛說的話感到惱火〕

suppose[2] *conjunction* 1 假設, 假定〔用於假設某事發生後帶來的後果〕 2〔用於提出建議〕

supreme *adj* 1〔權力、地位、重要性或影響力〕最高的, 至高無上的 2〔程度〕最大的, 極度的 3 make the supreme sacrifice 為國捐軀;〔為原則等〕犧牲

surpass *v* 1 超過; 勝過 2 surpass yourself 超越自己〔表示比自己過去做得更好, 但常用於開玩笑, 表示做得很差〕

surplus[1] *n* 1 剩餘, 過剩; 剩餘額, 多餘的量 2 盈餘; 順差

surplus[2] *adj* 1 過剩的, 剩餘的, 多餘的 2 be surplus to requirements 不再需要

survey[1] *n* 1 調查 2〔尤指為購房者所做的〕房屋鑑定[查勘] 3〔繪製地圖前對某地的〕勘測, 測量, 測繪 4〔對某一專題或形勢的〕概論, 概述

survey[2] *v* 1 [常用被動態] 調查 2〔尤指為形成某種意見而〕審視, 仔細考慮 3〔尤指為購房者〕鑑定〔房屋〕 4 測量, 勘測, 勘定

survive *v* 1〔經歷事故、戰爭或疾病後〕活下來, 倖存; 倖免於難 2 經歷〔困難和危險後〕仍然存在; 保存下來 3 從〔困難中〕挺過來; 掙扎着過下去 4 survive on〔靠很少錢〕繼續維持生活 5 比〔尤指親人〕活得更長, 比〔某人〕長壽

suspect[1] *v* 1 猜想, 懷疑, 覺得〔尤指壞事〕可能是事實 2 懷疑〔某人〕有罪, 認為〔某人〕有嫌疑 3 不信任, 不相信; 懷疑…的真實性

suspect[2] *n*〔犯罪〕嫌疑人, 可疑分子

suspect[3] *adj* 1 可疑的; 不可信任的; 不可靠的 2〔包裹、貨物等〕可疑的

suspend *v* 1 暫停, 中止 2〔尤指因違反紀律〕使…暫時停學[停職] 3 懸, 掛, 吊 4 suspend judgment 暫不作出判斷 5 be suspended in 懸浮在

suspicious *adj* **1** 懷疑的, 猜疑的 **2** 可疑的, 引起懷疑的 **3** 感到懷疑的, 認為有問題的

swarm¹ *n* **1** 移動中的一羣昆蟲;〔尤指〕蜂羣 **2**〔迅速移動的〕人羣

swarm² *v* **1** 成羣結隊地移動, 蜂擁, 湧往 **2**〔蜜蜂〕成羣飛離蜂巢尋覓新巢

swarm with sb/sth *phr v* **be swarming with** 擠滿〔移動的人羣或動物〕

sway¹ *v* **1**（使）搖擺,（使）擺動,（使）搖晃 **2** [常用被動態] 影響〔某人〕; 使改變看法

sway² *n* **1** 搖擺, 擺動, 搖晃 **2** 影響力; 支配; 統治

swear *v* **1** ►**OFFENSIVE LANGUAGE 無禮的語言**◄〔尤指因生氣〕詛咒, 咒罵, 用粗話罵人 **2** ►**SERIOUS PROMISE 嚴肅的許諾**◄ 起誓保證 **3** ►**PUBLIC PROMISE 公開承諾**◄〔尤指在法庭上〕宣誓, 起誓 **4** ►**STATE THE TRUTH 説真話或實話**◄ 保證〔自己説的是真話〕, 鄭重説明 **5 swear sb to secrecy/silence** 使某人發誓保守祕密

swear by sth *phr v* 極其信賴

swear sb ↔ **in** *phr v* [一般用被動態] **1** 使〔某人〕宣誓就職 **2** 使〔某人〕在法庭宣誓

swear off sth *phr v* 承諾終止〔某種不良行為〕

swear to *phr v* **not swear to (doing) sth** 不能保證〔某事〕屬實

sweep¹ *v* **1** ►**CLEAN STH 把…弄乾淨**◄ 掃, 打掃, 清掃 **2** ►**PUSH STH SOMEWHERE 把某物推到某處**◄ **a)** 掃去, 拂去, 清除 **b)** 捲走; 沖走; 移去; 颳走 **3** ►**CROWD 人羣**◄ 迅速地移動; 衝過 **4** ►**PERSON 人**◄ 昂首闊步地走 **5** ►**WIND/WAVES ETC 風/浪等**◄〔風、浪、風暴等迅速猛烈地〕掃過, 掠過〔某地〕 **6** ►**IDEA/FEELING 思想/感情**◄ 風行;（在…）迅速傳播 **7 sweep sb along/away a)**〔人羣〕擁着某人向前 **b)**〔感情、思想〕令某人着迷; 使某人深受影響 **8 sweep to victory/power** 大獲全勝/一舉掌權 **9 sweep the board**〔尤指輕易地〕大獲全勝, 囊括全部獎項 **10** ►**FORM A CURVE 形成曲線**◄ 蜿蜒; 延伸 **11** ►**LOOK 看**◄〔目光等〕掃視 **12 sweep sb off their feet** 把某人一下子迷住, 使某人神魂顛倒 **13 sweep sth under the carpet** 又作 **sweep sth under the rug** 掩蓋某事〔尤指錯事〕

sweep sth ↔ **aside** *phr v* 拒不理會, 無視

sweep sth ↔ **away** *phr v* **1** 掃除; 消滅; 摧毀 **2 be swept away by** 深受…感染, 被…打動

sweep sth ↔ **back** *phr v* 把〔頭髮〕梳向後面, 向後掠〔頭髮〕

sweep up *phr v* **1** 打掃, 清掃 **2** 一下抱起〔某人〕 **3 sweep sb's hair up** 把某人的頭髮梳到後面

sweep² *n* **1** 揮動 **2** 打掃, 清掃 **3 the sweep of a)** 長而彎曲的一段〔土地〕; 連綿彎曲的地帶 **b)**〔思想、作品等的〕廣度, 範圍 **4**〔大面積的〕搜索, 搜查; 掃蕩 **5 sweeps** 賭金全贏制 **6** 煙囱清潔工

swell¹ *v* **1** ►**PART OF YOUR BODY 身體部位**◄ 又作 **swell up** 腫, 腫脹 **2** ►**PEOPLE 人**◄〔數量〕逐漸增加, 增多, 增大 **3** ►**SOUND 聲音**◄〔聲音〕增強, 變響亮 **4** ►**SHAPE 形狀**◄ 又作 **swell** (sth ↔) **out**（使）鼓起,（使）隆起 **5 swell with pride/anger etc** 揚揚得意/怒氣沖沖等 **6** ►**SEA 海**◄ 波濤洶湧

swell² *n* **1** 海面的起伏, 浪湧 **2**〔尤指音樂〕音量逐漸增強 **3** 膨脹; 鼓起; 隆起 **4** 時髦人物; 頭面人物, 要人

swell³ *adj* 極好的, 第一流的

swift¹ *adj* **1** 迅速的; 立刻的 **2**（能）迅速移動的; 速度非常快的 **3 be swift to do sth** 迅速做某事, 立刻做某事 —**swiftly** *adv* —**swiftness** *n*

swift² *n* 雨燕

switch¹ *v* **1**〔常指突然地〕轉換, 轉變, 改變 **2**〔祕密地〕換掉, 替換 **3**〔與同事〕調換上班時間, 調班 **4**〔用開關〕改變〔機器的運轉〕, 轉換

switch off *phr v* **1**〔用開關〕關掉, 關上 **2** 不聽; 對…不加理睬[注意]

switch on *phr v*〔用開關〕開, 打開

switch over *phr v* **1**〔方法、產品等〕完全改變, 完全轉變 **2** 轉換〔電台或電視頻道〕

switch² *n* **1**〔電燈、收音機、機器等的〕開關; 電閘 **2** 驟變, 突變 **3 make the switch**〔偷偷地〕調換, 掉包 **4** 細軟的枝條

symbolize 又作 **-ise**【英】*v* **1** 象徵, 是…的象徵 **2** 用符號代表, 用象徵物表示 —**symbolization** *n*

sympathetic *adj* **1** 同情的; 有同情心的 **2**〔對某目的或計劃〕贊成的, 支持的 **3** 合意的; 合適的 **4 sympathetic figure/character**〔書、戲劇等中〕令人喜愛的人物/角色 —**sympathetically** *adv*

symposium *n* **1** 專題研討會; 討論會 **2** 專題論文集

symptom *n* **1** 症狀 **2**〔嚴重問題存在的〕徵兆, 徵候

systematic *adj* 有系統的, 有條理的, 仔細周到的 —**systematically** *adv*

T, t

tailor¹ *n*〔為男顧客量體裁衣的〕裁縫

tailor² *v* **tailor sth to your needs/requirements** 根據特定需要製作…

talent *n* **1** 天資, 天賦; 才能 **2** 有才能的人, 天才, 才子 **3** 性感的人, 尤物

tame¹ *adj* **1** 平淡的; 枯燥乏味的; 令人失望的 **2**〔動物〕馴服的; 由人馴養的 —**tamely** *adv* —**tameness** *n*

tame² *v* **1** 制服, 控制; 駕馭 **2** 馴服〔野生動物〕, 使馴化

tap¹ *n* **1** ►**WATER/GAS 水/煤氣**◄〔水、煤氣等管道或容器的〕龍頭, 閥門 **2** ►**BARREL 桶**◄〔桶的〕塞子 **3** ►**A LIGHT HIT 輕輕的敲擊**◄〔尤指為了引起某人注意而對某物的〕輕輕敲擊, 輕叩, 輕拍 **4 on tap a)** 可隨時取用[使用]的 **b)**〔桶裝啤酒〕可隨時旋開旋塞供飲用的 **5** ►**DANCING 跳舞**◄ 又作 **tap dancing** 踢踏舞 **6** ►**TELEPHONE 電話**◄ 電話竊聽 **7** ►**TUNE 樂調**◄ **taps**〔軍營裡的〕熄燈號;〔軍隊的〕葬禮號

tap² *v* **1** ►**HAND OR FOOT 手或腳**◄〔用手或腳〕輕敲, 輕叩, 輕拍 **2** ►**ENERGY 能源**◄ 又作 **tap into** 發掘, 開發〔能源或電力〕 **3** ►**IDEAS 思想**◄ 又作 **tap into** 利用, 採用〔思想、經驗、知識等〕 **4** ►**TELEPHONE 電話**◄ 電話竊聽 **5** ►**TREE 樹木**◄ 在〔樹幹〕上鑿孔以取其液汁 **6 tap sb for sth** 從某人處弄

到錢

tap sth ↔ in *phr v* 把〔信息、數據等〕敲入[鍵入, 輸入]〔電腦、電話等〕

target¹ *n* **1 ▶OBJECT OF ATTACK 攻擊對象◀** 〔有意攻擊的〕目標; 攻擊對象 **2 ▶AN AIM 目標◀** 想要達到的結果〈如總數、時限等〉; 想要實現的目標; 指標 **3 ▶SHOOTING 射擊◀** 〔射擊的〕靶子 **4 target group/area/audience etc** 特別針對的羣體/領域/聽眾等 **5 be the target of criticism/complaints etc** 成為批評/抱怨等的對象

target² *v* **1** 對...瞄準, 把...當作靶子 **2** 以...為目標[對象] **3** 把...選作目標

technique *n* **1** 技巧; 手法 **2** 技術水平; 技能

tedious *adj* 枯燥乏味的; 冗長的 **—tediously** *adv* **—tediousness** *n*

temperate *adj* **1 temperate climate/region** 溫和的氣候; 溫帶地區 **2** 〔行為〕溫和的, 心平氣和的; 自我節制的

temporary *adj* **1** 暫時的, 臨時的 **2** 短期的, 短暫的 **—temporariness** *n* **—temporarily** *adv*

temptation *n* **1** 引誘, 誘惑 **2** 很有誘惑力的東西

tenant *n* 房客; 租戶

tendency *n* **1** 〔發育、思想、行為等的〕傾向 **2 artistic/alcoholic etc tendencies** 藝術的氣質/酗酒的危險 **3** 趨勢, 趨向 **4** 〔政黨內部觀點往往較為極端的〕激進派

tender¹ *adj* **1 ▶MEAT/VEGETABLES 肉食/蔬菜◀** 嫩的; 軟的; 易燉爛的〔尤指烹飪恰到好處〕— 反義詞 TOUGH **2 ▶PART OF YOUR BODY 身體的某一部分◀** 疼痛的, 一觸即痛的 **3 ▶GENTLE 溫柔的◀** 溫柔的; 體貼入微的; 慈愛的 **4 tender loving care** 體貼入微的關懷 **5 tender blossoms/plants etc** 嬌弱的花朵/幼嫩的植株 **6 tender age** 年幼時期; 未成熟時期 **—tenderly** *adv* **—tenderness** *n*

tender² *n* **1** 投標(書) **2** 〔來往於岸邊和大船之間運送人員或補給品的〕駁運船; 補給船; 交通艇 **3** 〔蒸汽火車的〕煤水車

tender³ *v* **1** 投標〔承辦某事〕 **2** 遞呈, 呈交; 提出 **3** 付款, 償還

tension *n* **1 ▶NERVOUS FEELING 緊張感覺◀** 緊張; 焦慮; 焦急 **2 ▶NO TRUST 不信任◀** 〔人與人、國家與國家之間的〕緊張關係, 緊張局勢 **3 ▶DIFFERENT INFLUENCES 不同的影響力◀** 〔需求、勢力或影響力間的〕衝突; 緊張狀況 **4 ▶TIGHTNESS 繃緊◀** 〔電線、繩子、肌肉等的〕拉緊, 繃緊 **5 ▶FORCE 力量◀** 張力, 拉力

term¹ *n* ① ONE WAY OF REGARDING SOMETHING 看待某事的一種方式 **1 in financial/artistic/psychological etc terms** 就金融/藝術/心理學等而言 **2 in terms of** 在...方面, 從...方面來說; 根據...來解釋 **3 in sb's terms** 在某人看來, 根據某人的觀點 **4 in real terms** 〔價格或費用的〕實際變化情況 ② WORDS/LANGUAGE 字詞/語言 **5 ▶WORD/EXPRESSION 字詞/詞組◀** 專門名詞; 術語 **6 a term of abuse/endearment etc** 罵人的詞/表示愛意的詞 **7 in glowing terms/in strong terms** 以十分讚許的口吻/以強烈的措辭 **8 in no uncertain terms** 〔通常帶着怒氣〕直截了當地 ③ PERIOD OF TIME 時段 **9 ▶SCHOOL/UNIVERSITY 中小學/大學◀** 學期〔一學年分為三學期〕 **10 in the long/short/medium term** 就長期/短期/中期而言 **11 ▶TIME IN A JOB 工作的時間◀** 〔當選重要政府職務的〕任期, 期限 **12 prison/jail term etc** 服刑期限 **13 ▶BUSINESS 商務◀** 〔合同等的〕有效期限 **14 ▶END OF BUSINESS AGREEMENT 商務協議的終止◀** 〔商務協議的〕終止期 **15 ▶HAVING A BABY 生孩子◀** 分娩期, 足月(分娩) ④ CONDITIONS/AGREEMENT 條件/協議 **16 ▶CONDITIONS 條件◀ terms a)** 〔協議、合同或法律文件的〕條款 **b)** 付款條件; 購買[出售]條件 **17 on your (own) terms** 按照自己的條件 **18 terms of reference** 〔對某一官方委員會或報告的〕授權範圍; 研究事項 ⑤ RELATIONSHIP 關係 **19 be on good/bad terms** 關係好/關係不好 **20 be on speaking terms** 〔尤指吵架後〕關係好, 友好地相互説話 ⑥ OTHER SENSES 其他意思 **21 come to terms with sth** 與...妥協, 對...讓步; 接受〔不愉快的事〕 **22 on equal terms/on the same terms** 在平等的條件下/在相同的條件下 **23 be thinking/talking in terms of** 正考慮做某事; 正打算做某事 **24 ▶NUMBER/SIGN 數字/符號◀** 〔數學運算中的〕項

term² *v* [一般用被動態] 把...稱為, 把...叫做

terminate *v* (使)結束, (使)終止

terrific *adj* **1** 極好的, 極棒的; 非常愉快的 **2** 〔尺寸或程度〕極其巨大的, 大得驚人的

territory *n* **1 ▶GOVERNMENT LAND 政府土地◀** 領土, 版圖, 領地 **2 ▶TYPE OF LAND 某一類土地◀** 〔某種特定的〕地區, 地方 **3 US Territory** 〔美國的〕屬地 **4 ▶EXPERIENCE 經驗◀** 〔經驗或知識的〕領域 **5 ▶ANIMAL 動物◀** 〔獸類、鳥類等的〕地盤, 領域 **6 ▶BUSINESS 商務◀** 〔商務活動、尤指商業銷售的〕地區 **7 come/go with the territory** 在某種工作、情況中難免碰到的事

testify *v* **1** 〔尤指在法庭上〕作證 **2** 證明, 證實 **3** 作見證〔指基督徒向人訴説上帝的恩典〕

theft *n* **1** 盜竊罪 **2** 偷竊, 偷盜

theme *n* **1** 主題 **2** 主調; 主旋律 **3** 〔為某一特定學科寫作的〕作文, 短論文 **4 theme music/song/tune** 主題音樂/主題歌/主調

theoretical 又作 **theoretic** *adj* **1** 〔科學〕理論的 **2** 理論上的; 推想的, 臆測的

thesis *n* **1** 論文〔指大學的高級學位論文, 如文學碩士論文或哲學博士論文〕 **2** 〔設法解釋某事的〕論點

thoughtful *adj* **1** 認真思考的, 沉思的; 若有所思的 **2** 想得周到的; 體貼的, 關心的 **—thoughtfully** *adv* **—thoughtfulness** *n*

threaten *v* **1** 威脅, 恐嚇〔某人〕 **2** 威脅到; 危害到 **3** 〔不利的事〕將要發生; 〔某事〕可能引起〔不利的後果〕

thrift *n* 節省, 節儉

timber *n* **1** 木材, 原木; 〔可作木材的〕樹木 **2** 〔尤指構成房屋主要結構的〕棟木, 大梁 **3 timber!** 倒啦! 避開! 〔用來警告人們所伐樹木快要倒下〕

timely *adj* 適時的, 及時的

toil¹ *v* **1** 又作 **toil away** 長時間地苦幹, 辛苦勞作 **2** 吃力地慢行, 跋涉

toil² *n* **1** 長時間的辛苦勞作 **2 the toils of** 困境; 困惑; 迷惑

tolerance *n* **1** 忍受, 容忍; 寬容 **2**〔痛苦、困難等的〕忍受程度, 忍耐力 **3**〔某物在大小、重量等方面的〕公差〔偏離公差則不能正常工作〕

toss[1] *v* **1** ▶**THROW** 扔◀ 扔, 擲, 拋〔尤指輕快地拋較輕的東西〕 **2** ▶**MOVE** 移動◀ (使) 動來動去; (使) 翻轉不停 **3** ▶**THROW A FLAT OBJECT** 拋扔扁平的物體◀ 把〔扁平的物體〕拋向空中使其翻轉落下 **4** ▶**A COIN** 硬幣◀ 又作 **toss up** 把〔硬幣〕拋向空中〔以決定某事〕 **5** ▶**IN COOKING** 烹調過程中◀〔在液體中〕搖晃, 攪拌〔食物〕 **6 toss your head** 把頭往後一仰〔表示氣憤〕 **7 toss your cookies** 嘔吐

toss off *phr v* **1** 輕而易舉地完成〔某事〕 **2** 將…一飲而盡 **3** 手淫

toss[2] *n* **1** 拋硬幣〔決定某事〕 **2** 猛一仰頭 **3 win/lose the toss**〔在比賽等開始時〕拋硬幣贏了/輸了 **4**〔輕輕的〕拋, 扔, 投 **5 not give a toss** 根本不在乎

tournament *n* **1 tennis/chess/badminton etc tournament** 網球/國際象棋/羽毛球等錦標賽 **2**〔中世紀的〕騎士比武大會

trace[1] *v* **1** ▶**FIND SB/STH** 發現某人/某物◀ 仔細找尋 **2** ▶**ORIGINS** 來源◀ 追溯; 追查 **3** ▶**HISTORY/DEVELOPMENT** 歷史/發展◀ 研究…的歷史; 探索…的發展; 追尋…的軌跡 **4** ▶**COPY** 謄寫◀〔用透明紙在圖上〕描摹, 描繪 **5** ▶**DRAW** 勾畫◀〔用手指或腳趾在物體表面〕畫〔線〕; 留下〔印跡〕 **6 trace a call**〔利用特殊的電子設備〕追查打電話的人 —**traceable** *adj*

trace[2] *n* **1** ▶**SIGN OF STH** 某物的跡象◀ 蹤跡, 痕跡, 跡象 **2** ▶**SMALL AMOUNT** 小量◀ 微量; 痕量 **3** ▶**TELEPHONE** 電話◀〔利用特殊電子設備對電話的〕追查, 追蹤 **4** ▶**INFORMATION RECORDED** 記錄的信息◀〔記錄電信號的機器在屏幕或紙上作的〕描記線 **5 kick over the traces** 掙脱羈絆, 擺脱約束 **6** ▶**CART/CARRIAGE** 大車/馬車◀〔大車或馬車上的〕挽繩

track[1] *n* **1** ▶**ROAD** 道路◀〔路面粗糙不平的、可行車的〕小道, 窄路 **2** ▶**PATH** 小徑◀〔尤指經常行走踩出來的〕小路, 小徑 **3** ▶**FOR RACING** 用於比賽◀ 跑道 **4** ▶**RAILWAY** 鐵路◀〔鐵路的〕軌道, 鐵路線 **5 tracks**〔人、獸等的〕足跡, 痕跡;〔車輛的〕軌跡, 車轍 **6 be on the right/wrong track** 思路正確/錯誤 **7** ▶**MUSIC/SONG** 音樂/歌曲◀〔唱片、錄音帶或CD上的〕一首歌; 一支曲子 **8 keep/lose track of** 掌握/失去…的線索; 了解/不了解…的動態 **9 stop (dead) in your tracks**〔尤指因驚嚇而〕突然停下 **10 cover/hide your tracks** 掩蓋/隱匿自己的行蹤[活動] **11 be on the track of** 追蹤, 追尋 **12** ▶**SPORT** 體育運動◀ **a)** 徑賽運動 **b)** 田徑運動 **13 I'd better make tracks** 我得馬上離開〔尤指自己並不想離開〕 **14** ▶**DIRECTION** 方向◀〔物體移動的〕方向; 行動路線 **15** ▶**ON A VEHICLE** 交通工具上◀〔車輛的〕履帶 **16** ▶**FOR RECORDING** 錄音用的◀〔錄音帶的〕音軌, 磁跡 **17 be on track** 有可能獲得〔想要的結果〕 **18 get off the track** 偏離正題, 離題

track[2] *v* **1** ▶**SEARCH** 搜尋◀ 追蹤, 跟蹤 **2** ▶**AIRCRAFT/SHIP** 飛行器/輪船◀〔用雷達〕跟蹤〔飛機或輪船〕 **3** ▶**CAMERA** 攝像機◀〔電影或電視攝像機〕跟蹤攝影, 移動攝影 **4** ▶**RECORD** 唱片◀〔唱針在唱片紋道中〕移動 **5** ▶**SCHOOL** 學校◀ 把〔學生〕按能力分組 **6** ▶**MARK** 印跡◀ 留下…的足印 —**tracker** *n*

track sb/sth ↔ down *phr v* 追蹤到; 追查到

tradition *n* **1 a)** 傳統 **b)** 傳統信仰; 傳統習俗 **2** 傳統方式, 慣例, 老規矩 **3 be in the tradition of** 沿襲…的傳統

tragedy *n* **1** 悲劇性事件, 慘劇, 慘案 **2**〔因浪費、失去或傷害而造成的〕不幸; 遺憾 **3 a)** 悲劇作品 **b)** 悲劇〔文學類別之一〕

trail[1] *v* **1** 拖, 拉; 拖在後面 **2** 又作 **trail along**〔尤指因疲倦或厭煩〕慢吞吞地走〔在後面〕 **3**〔體育比賽、競賽或選舉中〕落後於 **4** 跟蹤, 追蹤

trail away/off *phr v*〔説話的聲音〕逐漸變小, 減弱

trail[2] *n* **1 be on sb's trail** 跟蹤, 追蹤〔某人〕 **2 while the trail is still hot**〔某人〕剛離開〔就隨後追趕〕 **3**〔人或動物的〕足跡, 蹤跡; 嗅跡 **4** 小路, 小徑 **5 trail of blood/dust etc** 血跡/塵土等的痕跡 **6 a trail of broken hearts/unpaid bills etc**〔某人留下的〕一串破碎的心/一大摞未支付的賬單等

trait *n*〔人性格中的〕特性, 品質

tramp[1] *n* **1** 流浪者, 遊民 **2**〔長途〕跋涉 **3** 蕩婦 **4 the tramp of** …沉重的腳步聲

tramp[2] *v* 用重重的腳步走〔過〕

transfer[1] *v* **1** ▶**PERSON** 人◀ 轉移〔地方〕; 調動〔工作〕〔尤指在同一機構中〕 **2** ▶**THING/ACTIVITY** 東西/活動◀ 搬運; 遷移 **3** ▶**MONEY** 錢◀ 把〔錢〕轉到另一賬戶上 **4 transfer your affection/loyalty etc** 移情於別人/轉而支持別人 **5** ▶**PROPERTY** 財產◀ 把〔財產〕轉讓給另一人 **6 transfer power/responsibility/control (to)** 轉讓權力/責任/控制權〔給…〕 **7** ▶**PLANE** 飛機◀ 轉機; 轉乘, 改乘 **8** ▶**RECORDING** 錄音◀ 錄製, 轉錄〔信息、音樂等, 如從錄音帶轉換成光碟〕 —**transferable** *adj*

transfer[2] *n* **1 a)**〔地點的〕轉移;〔工作的〕調動 **b)** 已調動的人; 已轉移的東西 **2 transfer of power** 權力的轉讓[過渡] **3**〔可黏貼或印製的〕圖畫, 圖案 **4**〔公共汽車、火車等的〕轉乘票證

transform *v* 使改觀, 使變形; 使轉化 —**transformable** *adj*

translate *v* **1** 翻譯, 把〔話語或文字〕譯成〔另一種語言〕 **2**〔被〕翻譯 **3** 把…變成另一種形狀, 轉化為… —**translatable** *adj*

transmit *v* **1** 發送, 播送, 播放〔電子信號、信息等〕 **2** 傳送, 傳遞, 傳播 **3** 傳播〔聲音或光〕

transplant[1] *v* **1** 移植, 移栽〔植物〕 **2** 移植〔器官、皮膚等〕 **3** 搬運, 搬遷, 遷移 —**transplantation** *n*

transplant[2] *n* **1**〔器官、皮膚等〕移植〔手術〕 **2** 移植的器官, 移植物

transport[1] *n* **1**〔旅客或貨物的〕運輸, 運送 **2** 交通工具, 運輸途徑 **3** 運輸〔過程〕; 運輸〔業務〕 **4**〔運送士兵或供給品的〕運輸船; 運輸機 **5 be in a transport of delight/joy etc** 感到非常高興/快樂等

transport[2] *v* **1** 運輸, 運送〔貨物、人等〕 **2 be transported back/into etc**〔想像中〕被帶回到/被帶入〔另一地點或時間等〕 **3**〔舊時〕流放, 放逐〔犯人〕 **4 be transported with delight/joy etc** 欣喜若狂, 喜不自勝 —**transportable** *adj*

trap[1] *n* **1** ▶**FOR ANIMALS** 用於動物的◀〔捕捉動

物的〕夾子, 羅網, 陷阱 **2 ►BAD SITUATION** 惡劣的處境◄ 圈套; 困境 **3 ►CLEVER TRICK** 聰明的計策◄ 計謀, 策略; 陷阱 **4 fall into the trap of doing sth** 做〔某事〕不明智 **5 keep your trap shut** 不把...說出去, 不泄密 **6 shut your trap!** 閉上你的嘴! **7 ►VEHICLE 車輛◄** 雙輪輕便馬車 **8 ►SPORT 體育運動◄** 〔高爾夫球場的〕沙坑 **9 ►DOG RACE 賽狗◄** 〔賽狗開始時放狗出籠的〕圍欄

trap² *v* **1 ►IN A DANGEROUS PLACE** 在危險的地點◄ [一般用被動態] 困住, 關住; 使陷於危險中 **2 ►IN A BAD SITUATION** 在惡劣的處境中◄ **be trapped** 使陷於困境 **3 ►ANIMAL 動物◄** 用陷阱捕獵〔獸或鳥〕 **4 ►CATCH SB** 抓住某人◄ 把〔某人〕困住〔以便捕捉〕; 使陷入羅網 **5 ►TRICK SB** 欺騙某人◄ 誘騙, 誘使 **6 ►CRUSH 壓扁◄** 被夾住; 被壓扁 **7 ►GAS/WATER ETC 氣/水等◄** 把〔氣、水等〕儲存; 留存

treasure¹ *n* **1** 金銀財寶, 寶藏 **2** 珍寶, 珍品 **3** 很有用的人, 得力幫手

treasure² *v* 珍藏, 珍惜, 珍視

treatise *n* 專著, 專題論文

treatment *n* **1 ►MEDICAL 醫學的◄** 治療; 療法 **2 ►BEHAVIOUR TOWARDS SB 對待某人的行為◄** 對待(方式), 待遇 **3 ►OF A SUBJECT** 有關某一主題◄〔針對某一主題的〕討論, 論述 **4 ►CLEAN/PROTECT 清理/保護◄** 處理〔指清理、保護等的過程〕

treaty *n* **1** 〔國家或政府間的〕條約 **2** 〔尤指為了購房, 兩人之間簽訂的〕協議, 協定

tremble *v* **1** 〔尤指因難受或受到驚嚇而〕顫抖, 發抖, 戰慄 **2** 〔輕微地〕搖晃, 震顫 **3** 〔說話聲〕緊張, 發抖 **4** 焦慮, 擔憂; 擔驚受怕 —**tremble** *n* —**trembly** *adj*

tremendous *adj* **1** 巨大的; 極快的; 強有力的 **2** 極好的, 特棒的

trend *n* **1** 趨勢, 趨向, 傾向, 動向 **2 set the trend** 開創潮流

trial¹ *n* **1 ►COURT 法庭◄** 審判, 審理 **2 ►TEST 試驗◄ a)** 試驗, 試用 **b)** 試驗期, 試用期 **3 by trial and error** 反覆試驗〔以得出最佳效果〕 **4 ►WORRY/ANNOY 焦慮/厭煩◄ be a trial (to)** 〔令某人〕焦慮[厭煩] **5 trials and tribulations** 艱難困苦 **6 ►SPORTS 體育運動◄ trials** 預賽, 選拔賽

trial² *v* 〔全面徹底地〕測試, 試驗, 試用

trick¹ *n* **1 ►DECEIVING SB 欺騙某人◄** 騙局, 花招, 詭計 **2 dirty/rotten/mean trick** 下流的/無恥的/卑鄙的詭計 **3 ►JOKE 玩笑◄** 惡作劇 **4 do the trick** 奏效, 達到預期效果 **5 ►CLEVER METHOD 巧妙辦法◄** 訣竅; 技巧, 技法 **6 use every trick in the book** 使出各種絕招, 使出渾身解數 **7 sb can teach/show you a trick or two** 〔某人〕可以教你一兩招,〔某人〕比你懂得多 **8 be up to your (old) tricks** 耍〔老〕花招 **9 ►MAGIC 魔術◄** 戲法, 把戲 **10 a trick of the light** 燈光引起的錯覺 **11 ►CARDS 紙牌◄** 〔紙牌遊戲中出的或贏的〕一圈牌, 一墩牌 **12 ►HABIT 習慣◄ have a trick of doing sth** 有〔使用某句口頭禪或以特別的方式活動臉部或身體〕的習慣 **13 never miss a trick** 對所發生的事無所不曉; 了如指掌 **14 how's tricks?** 近來如何?〔寒暄語〕 **15 turn a trick** 賣淫

trick² *v* **1** 欺騙, 誘騙, 哄騙 **2 be tricked out with/in** 裝飾, 打扮

trick³ *adj* **1 trick photography** 特技攝影 **2 trick question** 看似容易其實困難的問題 **3 trick knee/ankle etc** 軟弱無力會突然撐不住的膝關節/腳踝骨等

trifle¹ *n* **1 a trifle** 有點兒, 稍稍 **2** 瑣碎事; 無價值的東西 **3** 蛋糕甜食〔一種由蛋糕、水果、果凍、牛奶蛋糊、奶油等層層構成的冷甜食〕

trifle² *v*

trifle with sb/sth *phr v* 輕視, 小看, 隨便對待

trivial *adj* **1** 微不足道的, 沒有甚麼價值的 **2** 普通的, 平常的 —**trivially** *adv*

trunk *n* **1** 樹幹 **2** 〔汽車後部的〕行李箱 **3** 象鼻 **4 trunks** 男式游泳褲 **5** 〔人體的〕軀幹 **6** 大箱子, 大旅行箱

trustworthy *adj* 值得信賴的, 可靠的 —**trustworthiness** *n*

tuition *n* **1** 〔尤指學生人數不多的〕教學, 講課 **2** 學費

twilight *n* **1** 暮色, 黃昏的天色 **2** 黃昏時分, 薄暮時分 **3** 〔人生的〕暮年時期 **4 twilight world** 朦朧世界; 陰暗世界

twin¹ *n* 雙胞胎中的一個

twin² *adj* **1 twin problems/goals etc** 兩個同時出現、密切相關的問題/目標等 **2 twin beds/engines etc** 成對的(單人)牀/雙引擎等

twin³ *v* [一般用被動態]〔不同國家的兩個類似城市〕結為姐妹城市

twinkle¹ *v* **1** 閃爍, 閃耀 **2** 〔眼睛〕閃閃發光 **3 in the twinkling of an eye** 轉眼間, 瞬間, 霎時

twinkle² *n* **1 a twinkle in your eye** 眼睛裡閃爍着愉悅的光芒 **2 when you were just a twinkle in your father's eye** 在你還未出世的時候 **3** 閃爍的光

typical *adj* **1** 典型的, 有代表性的 **2** 表現出個性的, 一向如此的 **3 typical!** 老是這樣!〔表示氣憤〕

U, u

undergo *v* [不用被動態] 經歷, 經受; 遭受

undertake *v* **1** 着手做; 承擔, 接受 **2 undertake to do sth** 答應做某事; 同意做某事

unfold *v* **1** 展開, 打開, 攤開〔捲着的東西〕 **2** 〔故事、計劃等〕逐漸明確; 逐漸呈現; 展示

uniform¹ *n* **1** 〔警察、軍人等穿的〕制服 **2 be in uniform a)** 穿着制服 **b)** 做一名軍人, 當兵

uniform² *adj* 全部相同的, 一致的 —**uniformly** *adv*

unify *v* **1** 統一〔國家、組織等〕, 使成一體 **2** 使相同, 使一致

unique *adj* **1** 獨一無二的; 獨特的 **2** 極好的; 難得的, 不同尋常的; 特別的 —**uniquely** *adv* —**uniqueness** *n*

universal *adj* **1** 全體(做)的, 一致的 **2** 普遍的, 一般的 **3** 通用的; 萬能的 —**universally** *adv* —**universality** *n*

update¹ *v* **1** 為...提供最新信息; 更新 **2** 使現代化

update² *n* 最新消息

uphold *v* **1** 支持, 維護〔法規、制度或原則〕 **2** 〔法

庭〕維持〔原判〕 —**upholder** *n*
urban *adj* 城市的, 都市的
urgent *adj* **1** 緊急的, 急迫的, 需迅速處理的 **2** 強求的; 急切的 —**urgency** *n* —**urgently** *adv*
utensil *n* 器皿, 用具〔尤指烹調用具〕
utmost[1] *adj* **the utmost importance/respect/care etc** 極度的重要/尊敬/關心等
utmost[2] *n* **1** 極度, 極限, 最大可能 **2 do your utmost** 竭盡全力
utterly *adv* 完全地, 十足地

V, v

vacant *adj* **1**〔座位、房屋等〕空的, 未被佔用的 **2**〔工作或職位〕空缺的 **3 vacant expression/smile/stare etc** 茫然的表情/微笑/凝視等 **4 situations vacant**〔報紙上的〕招聘欄 —**vacantly** *adv*
vacuum[1] *n* **1** 真空 **2** 失落感; 空虛(感) **3 in a vacuum** 在真空狀態中; 與外界隔絕 **4** 真空吸塵器
vacuum[2] *v* 用真空吸塵器打掃
vague *adj* **1** 含糊的, 不明確的, 不清楚的 **2 have a vague idea/feeling/recollection etc that** 隱約地想到/感到/憶起等 **3** 模糊不清的 —**vagueness** *n*
vain *adj* **1** 自負的, 自視過高的 **2 in vain** 徒勞, 無結果 **3 vain attempt/hope/effort etc** 徒勞的嘗試/希望/努力等 **4 vain threat/promise etc** 空洞的威脅/承諾等 **5 take sb's name in vain**〔趁其不在場而〕輕慢地談論某人 **6 take the Lord's name in vain** 褻瀆上帝之名 —**vainly** *adv*
vanish *v* **1** 突然不見, 消失〔尤指以一種不易解釋的方式〕 **2** 滅絕 **3 do a vanishing act** 突然消失〔尤指當有人在尋找你時〕
vapour【英】, **vapor**【美】*n* **1** 蒸汽, 水汽, 〔某種液體的〕蒸氣 **2 the vapours** 突然眩暈感 —**vaporous** *adj*
variation *n* **1**〔數量或形式的〕變化, 變動 **2**〔做事方式的〕變更 **3**〔音樂中的〕變奏(曲)
vast *adj* **1** 巨大的, 廣大的, 廣闊的 **2 the vast majority/bulk of** ...的絕大多數 —**vastness** *n*
vehicle *n* **1** 運載工具; 車輛 **2 vehicle for (doing) sth** 媒介(物); 用作...的工具
versatile *adj* **1** 多才多藝的 **2** 有多種用途的, 多功能的, 萬用的 —**versatility** *n*
version *n* **1**〔同一種物件稍有不同的〕樣式, 型號; 複製件, 變體 **2**〔某人對某一事件作出的〕描述; 說法, 講法 **3**〔依據書、音樂等稍作改編的戲劇、電影、音樂等的〕版本; 改編本 **4 an English/Japanese/Spanish version** 英文/日文/西班牙文譯本
vessel *n* **1** 船; 艦 **2**〔盛液體用的〕容器, 器皿 **3**〔人體的〕血管; 脈管; 〔植物的〕導管
victim *n* **1** 受害者; 犧牲者 **2**〔惡劣情況的〕受災者; 〔疾病的〕患者 **3** 犧牲品 **4 be a victim of its own success** 因成功而反受其害 **5 sacrificial victim** 獻祭用的人[牲畜], 犧牲品 **6 fashion/style victim** 盲目追求時尚者
victory *n* **1** 勝利, 成功, 贏 — 反義詞 DEFEAT **2 be a victory for common sense** 常理獲勝, 不偏不倚的裁決
vigorous *adj* **1** 強有力的; 積極的 **2 a vigorous opponent/defender etc** 頑強的反對者/捍衛者等 **3** 強健的, 精力旺盛的 —**vigorously** *adv*
violate *v* **1** 違背, 違反; 侵犯 **2**〔用暴力〕打開〔墳墓〕; 強行進入〔聖地〕; 褻瀆 **3 violate the peace/privacy of** 破壞...的和平/驚擾...的獨處 **4** 強姦 —**violator** *n*
virtue *n* **1** 善; 德 — 反義詞 VICE **2** 美德; 德行 **3** 優點, 長處 **4 by/in virtue of** 憑藉; 由於, 因為 **5 make a virtue of necessity** 爽爽快快[心甘情願]地做非做不可的事
visible *adj* **1** 看得見的; 可見的 **2**〔影響〕明顯的; 顯然的; 可察覺的 **3**〔經常在電視上、報紙上等〕露面的
vital *adj* **1** 極其重要的, 必不可少的 **2** 有生命力的; 充滿活力的, 生機勃勃的 **3** 維持生命所必需的
vivid *adj* **1**〔記憶、夢境、描述等〕生動的; 逼真的; 清晰的 **2 vivid imagination** 活躍的想像力 **3**〔色彩、圖案〕鮮豔的; 鮮明的 —**vividly** *adv* —**vividness** *n*
vocational *adj* **vocational training/guidance/course etc** 職業培訓/指導/課程等
voluntary[1] *adj* **1 voluntary work/service etc** 義務工作/服務等 **2 voluntary organization/society/institution etc** 志願組織/團體/機構等 **3 voluntary worker/helper/assistant etc** 志願人員/幫手/助手等 **4** 自願的, 志願的; 自發的 **5**〔身體活動〕自如的, 隨意的 — 反義詞 INVOLUNTARY —**voluntarily** *adv*
voluntary[2] *n*〔教堂中的〕(風琴) 演奏曲
voyage[1] *n*〔乘船的長途〕航行
voyage[2] *v* 航行, 航海

W, w

wander[1] *v* **1 ►MOVE WITHOUT A DIRECTION 無目的的行進◄**〔在某地方〕徘徊; 閒逛; 漫步 **2 ►MOVE AWAY 離開◄** 又作 **wander off**〔從應該逗留的地方〕離開 **3 ►CHANGE THE SUBJECT 改變話題◄** 離題 **4 ►MIND/THOUGHTS 精神/注意力◄**〔精神、注意力等因厭倦或焦慮而〕不集中, 走神 **5 sb's mind is wandering**〔尤因年老而〕頭腦糊塗 **6 ►ROAD/RIVER 道路/河流◄**〔河流、道路等〕蜿蜒曲折 —**wanderer** *n*
wander[2] *n* 漫步
ward[1] *n* **1**〔醫院內的〕病房, 病室 **2**〔城市的〕選區 **3** 受監護的人〔尤指兒童〕
ward[2] *v*
ward sth **off** *phr v* 防止〔疾病、危險、攻擊等〕, 抵擋
weave[1] *v* **1 ►CLOTH 布◄** 織; 織(布) **2 ►MAKE STH 製造某物◄** 編, 織 **3 ►STORY 故事◄** 編造〔故事或計劃〕 **4 get weaving** 趕快〔用於告訴某人趕快開始做某事〕 **5 ►MOVE 移動◄** 迂迴[穿插]行進
weave[2] *n* 織法; 編織式樣
weight[1] *n* **1 ►WHAT SB/STH WEIGHS 某人/某物的重量◄**〔某物的〕重量 **2 ►HOW FAT 有多胖◄**

〔某人的〕體重〔尤指肥胖〕 **3 ►HEAVINESS** 重◄ 重 **4 ►HEAVY THING** 重物◄ 重東西 **5 ►FOR MEASURING QUANTITIES** 測量分量◄ 砝碼, 秤砣 **6 ►FOR EXERCISE** 用於鍛鍊◄ 槓鈴 **7 ►SYSTEM** 制度◄ 重量單位制; 衡制 **8 ►RESPONSIBILITY/WORRY** 責任/憂慮◄ 重壓, 負擔 **9 a weight off your mind** 除去心理負擔 **10 ►IMPORTANCE** 重要性◄〔作出判斷或形成意見時某物的〕影響; 重要性 **11 throw your weight about/around** 指手畫腳; 濫用權勢 **12 throw your weight behind**〔用權力和影響力〕支持〔某人〕 **13 pull your weight** 做好分內事 **14 take the weight off your feet** 坐下 **15 weight of numbers**〔一個大羣體〕聯合起來的勢力[影響] **16 summer-weight/winter-weight** 夏服/冬裝〔用適合夏天或冬天穿的布料縫製〕 **17 ►SCIENCE** 科學◄〔作用在物體上的〕重力

weight² *v* 加重量於〔某物, 以使穩固不動〕, 使變重

wholesome *adj* **1** 對健康有益的 **2** 在道德上有益的 —**wholesomeness** *n*

wicked *adj* **1** 邪惡的; 缺德的 **2** 淘氣的; 惡作劇的 **3** 棒的; 極好的 —**wickedly** *adv* —**wickedness** *n*

wilderness *n* **1** 荒野, 不毛之地 **2** 杳無人煙的地方 **3 in the wilderness** 離開權力和活動的中心; 〔尤指政治上的〕在野狀態

wit *n* **1 ►AMUSING** 娛人的◄〔說話〕機智風趣 **2 ►AMUSING PERSON** 說話風趣的人◄ 說話風趣詼諧的人 **3 wits** 機智 **4 have the wit to do sth** 足夠明智, 作出正確決定〔做某事〕 **5 frighten/scare sb out of their wits** 嚇壞某人 **6 at your wits' end** 智窮計盡, 束手無策 **7 not beyond the wit of** 有做某事的才智 **8 to wit** 即, 就是 —**witless** *adj*

withdraw *v* **1 ►MONEY** 金錢◄ 提取〔銀行存款〕 **2 ►TAKE AWAY** 取走, 拿走◄〔常因正方決定而〕撤回, 撤銷, 收回 **3 withdraw a remark/accusation** 撤回評論/撤銷指控 **4 ►NOT TAKE PART** 不參加◄ **a)** 退出〔組織〕 **b)**〔使〕不參加〔活動、比賽等〕 **5 ►LEAVE** 離開◄ **a)** 離開〔尤指想獨處或悄悄地去某處〕 **b)**〔尤指軍隊避免戰敗而〕撤退 **6 ►STOP COMMUNICATING** 停止交流◄ 變得冷漠; 離羣索居

withstand *v* **1** 耐受, 承受〔酷熱、嚴寒、高壓等〕 **2** 抵擋; 頂住

witness¹ *n* **1**〔罪行或事故的〕目擊者 **2**〔法庭上的〕證人 **3 bear witness** 證明〔某事是事實〕, 證實〔過去的事〕 **4**〔正式文件的簽署的〕見證人, 連署人 **5 be witness to** 是…的目擊者 **6** 見證〔表示篤信基督教的公開聲明〕; 見證人〔作這種見證的人〕

witness² *v* **1** 目擊, 親眼看見〔尤指罪行或事故發生〕 **2 a)** 親自經歷〔重要事件或變遷〕 **b)** 是發生〔某事件〕的時間[地點] **3**〔在正式文件上〕連署; 在〔正式文件〕上簽署作證 **4 a)** 表明; 是〔某事〕的證明 **b)**〔用於給剛提及的事舉例〕作證 **5** 見證〔公開表示篤信基督教〕

witness to sth *phr v* 證實; 證明〔某事〕

worship¹ *v* **1** 敬奉〔神〕〔尤指在教堂、廟宇等禱告〕 **2** 景仰; 十分喜愛 **3 worship the ground sb walks on** 拜倒在某人腳下〔以致看不到他的缺點〕 —**worshipper** *n*

worship² *n* **1**〔對神的〕崇敬; 崇拜 **2**〔在教堂、廟宇等祈禱以示對神的〕崇拜; 敬仰 **3**〔對某人或物的〕強烈崇拜〔尤指看不見其錯誤〕; 仰慕 **4 Your/His Worship** 閣下〔對市長或地方法官等公務人員的稱呼〕

wreck¹ *v* **1** 破壞, 糟蹋〔計劃、關係、機遇等〕 **2** 使〔建築、車輛等〕嚴重毀壞〔無法維修〕 **3** [一般用被動態]〔尤指船隻在風暴中觸礁〕失事

wreck² *n* **1** 沉船; 失事船 **2**〔尤指失事後汽車、飛機的〕殘骸 **3** 十分緊張[疲累; 不健康]的人 **4**〔涉及多輛車的〕交通事故 **5** 殘破的東西〔尤指汽車〕

Y, y Z, z

yield¹ *v* **1 ►CROPS/PROFITS** 莊稼/利潤◄ 出產; 產生 **2 ►RESULT** 結果◄ 得出〔結果等〕 **3 ►AGREE** 同意◄ 服從, 被迫同意 **4 yield to your emotions/feelings** 屈從自己的感情/感覺 **5 ►TRAFFIC** 交通◄ 讓〔其他車或人〕先行, 讓路 **6 ►GIVE UP FIGHTING** 放棄戰鬥◄ 投降, 屈服 **7 ►MOVE/BEND/BREAK** 移動/彎曲/斷裂◄〔因外在力量或壓力而〕移動; 彎曲; 斷裂 **8 ►CHANGE** 變換◄ 讓與

yield sth ↔ **up** *phr v* 泄露, 揭示

yield² *n* 產量; 收益

zone *n*〔與周圍地區有所不同的〕地區; 地帶; 區域

Grammar Codes 語法代號表

[C] countable: a noun that can be counted and has a plural form 可數名詞, 即可以計數並有複數形式的名詞: *We planted an orange* **tree**. 我們種了一棵橘子樹。| *Children love to climb* **trees**. 小孩喜歡爬樹。

[U] uncountable: a noun that cannot be counted and has no plural form 不可數名詞, 即不可以計數, 也沒有複數形式的名詞: *the* **peace** *of the May afternoon* 五月下午的平靜 | *a blade of* **grass** 草的葉片

[I] intransitive: a verb that has no direct object 不及物動詞, 即沒有直接受詞[賓語]的動詞: *I'm sure I can* **cope**. 我肯定能應付。| *Our food supplies soon* **ran out**. 我們的食物補給很快就吃完了。

[T] transitive: a verb that is followed by a direct object, that can be either a noun phrase or a clause 及物動詞, 即後面跟直接受詞[賓語] (既可以是名詞片語[短語], 也可以是子句[從句]) 的動詞: *I* **like** *swimming, playing tennis, and things like that.* 我喜歡游泳、打網球等諸如此類的事情。| *I* **hope** *I'm not disturbing you.* 我希望沒有打擾你。| *We never* **found out** *her real name.* 我們始終沒有弄清楚她的真名。

[singular] a noun that is used only in the singular, and that has no plural form 單數名詞, 即只用單數形式, 沒有複數形式的名詞: *She gets in such a* **fuss** *before people come to dinner.* 有人來吃飯以前, 她總是如此小題大做。| *the distant* **hum** *of traffic* 遠處車輛的嘈雜聲

[plural] a noun that is used only with a plural verb or pronoun, and that has no singular form 複數名詞, 即只與複數動詞或代(名)詞連用的名詞, 沒有單數形式: *electrical* **goods** 電器商品 | *My* **spirits** *sank when I saw the mess.* 看到亂七八糟的情況, 我的情緒一下子低落了。

[linking verb] a verb that is followed by a noun or adjective complement, that refers to the subject of the verb 連繫動詞, 即後面跟說明動詞的主語的名詞或形容詞補語: *Her skin* **felt** *cold and rough.* 她的皮膚摸上去又冷又粗糙。| *We* **were** *hungry* 我們餓了。| *The weather* **became** *warmer.* 天氣變暖了。

[always + adv/prep] shows that a verb must be followed by an adverb or a prepositional phrase 這個代號表示某一動詞後面必須跟副詞或介詞片語[短語]: *The door suddenly* **flew** *open.* 門突然開了。| *Sandra* **flounced** *out of the room.* 桑德拉猛然從房間裡走出來。

[not in progressive] shows that a verb is not used in the progressive form, that is, the -ing form after be 這個代號表示某一動詞不能用於進行式, 即不能用 be + -ing 的形式: *I* **hate** *housework.* 我討厭做家務。(not 不能說 *I am hating housework*) | *Who* **knows** *the answer?* 誰知道答案?

[no comparative] shows that an adjective is not used in the comparative or superlative form, that is, not with -er and -est, or with more and most 這個代號表示某一形容詞不能用於比較級或最高級, 即不能與 -er [-est] 或 more [most] 連用: *She needs* **proper** *medical attention.* 她需要接受妥善治療。

[only before noun] shows that an adjective can only be used before a noun 這個代號表示某一形容詞只能用於名詞前: *the* **final** *episode of "Prime Suspect"*《頭號嫌疑犯》的最後一集 | *the* **main** *points of her speech* 她演講的要點

[not before noun] shows that an adjective cannot be used before a noun 這個代號表示某一形容詞不能用於名詞前: *Quiet! The baby is* **asleep**. 安靜點! 寶寶在睡覺。

[only after noun] shows that an adjective is only used immediately after a noun 這個代號表示某一形容詞只能用於名詞後: *There are bargains* **galore** *in the sales.* 大減價中有大量的特價商品出售。

[sentence adverb] shows that an adverb modifies a whole sentence 這個代號表示某一副詞修飾整個句子: **Apparently** *they've run out of tickets.* 顯然, 他們沒有票了。

[+ adj/adv] shows an adverb of degree 這個代號表示程度副詞: *She plays the violin* **remarkably** *well for a child of her age.* 就她這個年紀的孩子而言, 她拉小提琴拉得特別好。| *You look* **absolutely** *fantastic in that dress.* 你穿那件連衣裙絕對好看。

[also + plural verb *BrE*] shows that a group noun can take a plural verb in British English 這個代號表示某一集合名詞在英國英語中可以用複數動詞: *The* **committee** *have decided to raise membership fees for next year.* 委員會決定增加明年的會員費。

[+ **between**] [+ **about**] shows that a word is followed by a particular preposition 這種代號表示某個詞後面跟特定的介詞: *I'm trying to* **decide** *between the green and the blue. Now are you* **certain** *about that?* 我想在綠色與藍色之間作出抉擇。你現在對此肯定嗎?

Grammar Codes 語法代號表

decide that shows that a word can be followed by a clause beginning with that 這種形式表示某個詞後面可以跟以that引導的子句[從句]: *It* **was decided** *that four hospitals should be closed.* 決定要關閉四家醫院。

sure (that) shows that a word can be followed by a clause beginning with that, or the word 'that' can be left out 這種形式表示某個詞後面可以跟以 that 引導的子句[從句], 但 that 也可省略: *I'm* **sure** *there's a logical explanation for all this.* 我確信所有這一切都有一個合乎邏輯的解釋。

decide who/what/how etc shows that a word can be followed by a word beginning with wh- (such as where, why, or when) or by how 這種形式表示某個詞後面可以跟以 wh- 開頭的詞 (如 where, why, when 等) 或 how: *I can't* **decide** *what to do.* 我無法決定做甚麼。| *I'm not* **sure** *where James is.* 我不肯定詹姆斯在哪裡。

resolve to do sth shows that a word can be followed by an infinitive 這種形式表示某個詞後面可以跟不定式: *He* **resolved** *to apologise to her.* 他決心向她道歉。| *There's one boy who's* **certain** *to succeed!* 有一個男孩肯定能成功!

see sb/sth do sth shows that a verb can be followed by an infinitive verb without to 這種形式表示某一動詞後面可以跟不帶 to 的不定式: *Pat* **saw** *her drive off about an hour later.* 帕特看見她在大約一小時後驅車離開了。

see sb doing sth and **enjoy doing sth** show that a verb can be followed by a present participle or by a verbal noun with the same form 這種形式表示某一動詞後面可以跟現在分詞或相同形式的動名詞: *The suspect* **was seen** *entering the building.* 有人看見嫌疑犯進入大樓。| *Young children* **enjoy** *helping with household tasks.* 年幼的小孩喜歡幫忙做家務。

get lost/trapped/caught etc shows that a verb can be followed by a past participle 這種形式表示某一動詞後面可以跟過去分詞: *He's* **getting** *married in September.* 他打算九月結婚。

bring sb sth shows that a verb can be followed by an indirect object and then a direct object 這種形式表示某一動詞後面可以跟間接受詞[賓語], 然後再跟直接受詞[賓語]: *Could you* **bring** *me that chair?* 你可以把那把椅子搬過來給我嗎? | *Let me* **buy** *you a drink.* 讓我來給你買杯飲料。